The Norton Anthology
of World Masterpieces

EXPANDED EDITION
IN ONE VOLUME

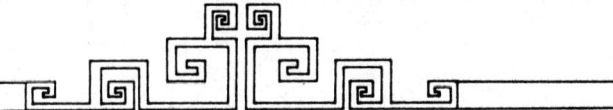

The Norton Anthology
of World Masterpieces

EXPANDED EDITION
IN ONE VOLUME

Maynard Mack, *General Editor*

STERLING PROFESSOR OF ENGLISH EMERITUS,
YALE UNIVERSITY

W • W • NORTON & COMPANY • *New York* • *London*

Copyright © 1997, 1995, 1992, 1985, 1979, 1973, 1965, 1956
by W. W. Norton & Company, Inc.
All rights reserved.
Printed in the United States of America.

The text of this book is composed in Electra, with the display set in Bernhard Modern.
Composition by Maple-Vail Composition Services.
Manufacturing by R. R. Donnelley & Sons
Book design by Antonina Krass.

Cover painting is *Shigeyuki Executing Calligraphy* (1783) by Torii Kiyonaga. Reproduced
by courtesy of the Philadelphia Museum of Art: Given by Mrs. John D. Rockefeller.

Library of Congress Cataloging-in-Publication Data
The Norton anthology of world masterpieces / Maynard Mack, general
editor.—Expanded ed. in one vol.
    p.   cm.
    Some material included in the 2 v. 1995 ed. has been excluded from
this ed.
    Includes bibliographical references and index.
    ISBN 0-393-97143-0 (pbk.)
    1. Literature—Collections.   I. Mack, Maynard, 1909–   .
PN6014.N67   1997
808.8—dc20   96-39009
                                                             CIP

W.W. Norton & Company, Inc., 500 Fifth Avenue, New York, N.Y.
10110
www.wwnorton.com

W.W. Norton & Company Ltd., Castle House, 75/76 Wells Street,
London W1T 3QT

Contents

PART I   BEGINNINGS TO A.D. 100

The Invention of Writing and the Earliest Literatures

Ancient Greece and the Formation of the Western Mind   87

Poetry and Thought in Early China   527

India's Heroic Age   567

The Roman Empire   627

PART II   100 TO 1500

From Roman Empire to Christian Europe   703

India's Classical Age   739

The Rise of Islam and Islamic Literature 861

The Formation of a Western Literature 951

The Golden Age of Japanese Culture 1275

PART III 1500 TO 1650

PART IV   1650 TO 1800

Vernacular Literature in China   1763

The Enlightenment in Europe   1889

The Rise of Popular Arts in Premodern Japan   2103

PART V   1800 TO 1900

Revolution and Romanticism in Europe and America 2137

Realism, Symbolism, and European Realities

PART VI

The Twentieth Century:
Self and Other in Global Context

Preface

In 1956, the first edition of this anthology brought to college and university courses in literature the option of a more spacious experience. More spacious in content because it was not confined to English or American literature but embraced the entire literature of the West and ranged in time from the Old Testament and Homer to Joyce, Brecht, Faulkner, Lorca, and Camus. More spacious likewise in purpose because its aim was not simply, as in older books, to place the individual work in its historical and authorial contexts but to penetrate and display as far as possible the inward complexity of structure and the outward reach into the realities of our common life that empower such works to inform and please through so many generations, even centuries.

Five further editions shaped on these principles have appeared in the years since, each more inclusive than the one before. In 1995 these gradual enlargements reached a logical conclusion in *The Norton Anthology of World Masterpieces*, Expanded Edition. The distinction of this edition is that while drawing almost as extensively as its predecessors on literatures in the Western tradition—European, British, and American—it simultaneously incorporates some two thousand pages of major works by major artists of Africa, the Arab countries of the Middle East, Israel, the Caribbean, China, Egypt, India, Japan, native America, and the Persia that became Iran. In its scope and presentation, the Expanded Edition is very much a new kind of book. It is this new kind of book that we offer you here, as many of you have requested, in a shortened form designed for programs in which the study of world literature occupies one semester. Though some retrenchments have been necessary, this one-volume Expanded Edition retains a range and variety of choice not possibly exhaustible in a year, let alone a semester.

It goes without saying that no anthology, however vast, can do full justice to the diversity and depth of the literatures of all places and all times. The basic principle of this anthology from its beginnings has been to offer works having recognized authority in their own languages and cultures, but also in the judgment of a larger world. We have sought to maintain that principle here, in the conviction that students of all dispositions and capacities retain more of value from an acquaintance of some depth with a few literatures than from a shrapnel burst of many.

Turning now specifically to this shorter version of the Expanded Edition, we want to clarify some important points about its structure and contents.

The volume consists of six parts. And since most of the terms customarily used in categorizing Western literatures—Middle Ages, Renaissance, Enlightenment, Romanticism, and the like—have little or no relevance when applied elsewhere, these parts are temporally determined. Parts I through III reach from the beginnings at around 2500 B.C. to A.D. 100, from 100 to 1500, and from 1500 to 1650; parts IV through VI, from 1650 to 1800, 1800 to 1900, and 1900 to the present. During some of these periods, it is important to add—notably the period that Western parlance assigns to "The Renaissance" and again during parts of the periods denoted by "The Enlightenment" and "Romanticism"—selections from the non-Western literatures diminish because in any culture the upwellings of creativity that produce works of great stature obey no time schedule.

Within the parts themselves we follow not a strict chronological sequence but rather an order that blends time's happenstance with pedagogical common sense. As you know from your experience in the classroom and we know from ours, it is folly to subject unsuspecting students (some of them already bewildered by the controversies surrounding "multiculturalism," others dug in to defend to the death some parochial point of view) to a strictly chronological succession of unrelated works from disparate and unfamiliar civilizations. It will remind them of nothing so much as the eating machine that force-feeds Charlie Chaplin in *Modern Times*, one strange dish slapped to his mouth to be replaced by another with such velocity that he all but strangles. The effect on Chaplin is acute indigestion; on students, intellectual nausea plus a hasty retreat from the subject and possibly from all future contacts with literature.

Mindful of this problem, and of the pedagogical difficulties involved in each part save the last, we have disposed our selections within "sweeps." These are continuities from a single cultural tradition enabling students to reach at least a modest familiarity with its characteristic forms of expression before moving on to the next. Admittedly, on some occasions this practice calls for difficult decisions. The placing of Petrarch, for instance. In strict chronology, he belongs with Boccaccio and Chaucer. Yet he speaks with a distinctly new voice and new concerns that give him more affinity with Machiavelli, Montaigne, and Shakespeare than with Chaucer. He can be read with his contemporaries as spokesman of a new era already forming, as new eras always do, in the heart of the old. Or he can be read with his successors—in our view more intelligibly—as precentor in a choir of voices for which his powerful individualism set the tone and mode. An equal difficulty arises with Rousseau. Should he be read in company with Voltaire, whose younger contemporary he was and who said of him wryly after their first and only meeting (anticipating much that was later to be called Romantic egoism): "That man has no talent for dialogue"? Or should he be read like Petrarch—and again, as we think, more intelligibly—in the vanguard of those whom his thought and example most inspired?

In this and all such instances, our first obligation is to the needs of the students. In that interest, we have supplied for each of our sweeps a map designed to facilitate understanding of the geographical settings of the several great civilizations whose master works these volumes offer. Likewise for each sweep, we have supplemented the map with a timeline clarifying the chronological relations of major works and events within the sweep. Informed use of these resources can generate fascinating classroom explorations of the impact of particular times, climes, and topographies on the characteristics of societies, individuals, and works of art.

You will also find here, prefacing most of our selections, brief glossaries for the pronunciation of unfamiliar words and names (a list of the phonetic equivalents we use is located on page xxxv). These make no attempt at linguistic exactitude, even if that were possible. Their much humbler aim is to supply useable English approximations—approximations that are necessarily governed sometimes by convention and long use (as, say, with *Ghent*, early naturalized in English to rhyme with *tent*); sometimes by arbitrary compromise between the actual or supposed sound of the original and the sounds available or recognizable in modern English speech. No one now alive can say with certainty exactly how the author of *Sir Gawain and the Green Knight* pronounced Uriel, the name he gives to Yvain's father at line 113. We can speak the name today only as it seems to us. Conversely, though we know for certain that he and his contemporaries pronounced his name *Bed-day*, few moderns would be able to identify from those sounds the author of the single most important source for the history of England in the Middle Ages, the Benedictine monk now known everywhere as the Venerable Bede. The finding of suitable English phonetic equivalents for foreign terms and names is as far from being an exact science as negotiating a mine field, and every step requires a judgment call involving risk. Nevertheless, if our efforts help even one student to feel more comfortable about speaking up in class or discussing a passage full of hard names with a classmate, the risk is worth it.

A final note on the sweeps. Though for the most part, as earlier stated, they bring you continuities from a single culture, we have allowed three exceptions, two minor and one major, again on practical grounds. The initial sweep of Part I intentionally presents works from three different cultural traditions—Babylonian, Egyptian, Judaic—each among the oldest works that have come down to us in written form, each in its origins reaching well back into a preliterate past, yet accessible and still provocative at the end of the twentieth century. They exemplify what we mean by "world-class," and they assure any student that, bizarre as some of the world's literary traditions may seem on first contact, there is always something in them that reflects our common human nature, our common hopes, lusts, ideals, and fears, our common vulnerability to time and change. This lesson must be learned early if any course drawing on unfamiliar cultures is to succeed.

A similar drawing together of two different cultures—Arabian and Persian—has been made in the fourth sweep of Part V, and for the same reasons. Both have a world-view in common and feed into each other with great effectiveness when contrasted and compared. The one *major* exception is made in Part VI. Here we meet almost uniformly with a modern sensibility that can be recognized as global, or quasi-global, no matter how variably colored it may be in the individual case by nationality, ethnicity, and history. At this point, having outlived their usefulness, sweeps disappear.

The considerations of classroom practicality that impel us to favor

sweeps over unmediated chronology have also impelled us to make the
next sweep after the introductory one a continuity of Greek literature featuring Homer, Sappho, and the Greek playwrights. Reading this sequence
early, parts of which many students know by hearsay and some by contact,
builds their confidence and can elicit lively comparisons between *Gilgamesh* and the Greek epics, Egyptian poetry and Sappho, and the Greek
and Judaic inheritances. Exploring these relationships lays a foundation
for further comparisons with the distinctive qualities of the Chinese and
Indian sweeps that immediately follow.

On similar grounds, we preserve in this shorter version of the Expanded
Edition as much as possible of the mainly Western literature found in *The
Norton Anthology of World Masterpieces*, Standard Edition. Whatever our
individual or ethnic associations may be, if we live in the United States it
is important to understand the moral and intellectual sources of the country that we inhabit and that in some inescapable sense (even more so when
we exercise our right to dissent from it) inhabits us. Though as a nation of
immigrants we are continually in the process of redefining our collective
life, that life for three centuries was defined primarily through ideas and
experiences brought here by immigrants from Britain and the countries of
western and eastern Europe. This tradition constitutes the American half
of such terms as African American, Asian American, German American,
Hispanic American, Irish American, Italian American, Polish American,
and the rest. So far as our collective life in this country has roots, these are
to be found in the Western tradition, whose influence in the fabric of
our everyday existence is best discovered by immersion in its recognized
masterpieces of drama, poetry, and fiction.

Still, our central objective in this volume is to encourage exploration of
other traditions as well. As in the forest world the effect of roots is the
production of spreading leaves and branches and the effect of spreading
leaves and branches is the invigoration of roots, so in our human world
the vigor of cultural traditions thrives rather from reaching out than from
closing in. All over the planet there flourish faiths, fears, arts, and aspirations; needs and markets, likes and dislikes; racial, gender, and ethnic
tensions—matters that our shrinking planet of airplanes, television, and
computer networks has made it materially important for us to know about
as well as intellectually and spiritually foolish to ignore. Hostilities at all
levels are usually first generated and then exacerbated by xenophobia
("fear of the stranger") and by the ease with which the unfamiliar book,
picture, person, food, custom, costume, or skin color can be demonized.
For this phobia the only cure is frequent and prolonged exposure to what
is different from ourselves until the unfamiliar becomes familiar, the unaccustomed perspective brings more generous ways of seeing, and we discover how much there is still to learn about ourselves.

With these thoughts in mind, we welcome you to the great menu from
multiple cuisines that awaits within. Here, complete, are fourteen of the
world's great plays, ranging in time and nature from Aeschylus's *Agamemnon* to Bertolt Brecht's *Mother Courage and Her Children*, with fascinating
excursions into Kālidāsa's *Śakuntalā and the Ring of Recollection*, best

loved and most influential of all Sanskrit plays, and Kanze Kojirō Nobumitsu's spectacular Nō play *Dōjōji*. Complete here also are twenty-one outstanding examples of short fiction, including two short novels that particularly invite literary and sociological comparisons: Voltaire's *Candide* and Chinua Achebe's *Things Fall Apart*.

If you would have your class visit those "long" novels and extended prose fictions that in some literatures run through several volumes, you will find in these pages substantial and eminently teachable selections from Japan's *Tale of Genji*, China's *Story of the Stone (Dream of the Red Chamber)*, Spain's *Don Quixote de la Mancha*, and France's *Remembrance of Things Past*—each a revelation of national character and characteristics in its own right, all four togther becoming immensely instructive in class when viewed in the light of customs, cultural backgrounds, cherished values, and differing literary structures and styles.

Likewise, for the long poem of action and developing nationhood produced by many societies in their epic or heroic phase, you will discover here rich options in the complete *Gilgamesh*, earliest of known epics, and in copious selections from the Greek *Odyssey* (we give twenty of its twenty-four books); the Indian *Rāmāyana*; the Roman *Aeneid*; the Persian *Shâhnâme*, or *Book of Kings* (excerpted here for the tragic story of Rostám, who unknowingly in battle kills his son Sohráb); the French *Song of Roland*; the Malian *Son-Jara*, and the Mayan *Popul Vuh*. Usefully contrasting definitions of "heroism"—definitions that for many centuries have contested the simpler, more martial conceptions—are also to be found here. For instance: in the hero's dedication in the *Rāmāyana* to the principle of *dharma*; in Arjuna's dilemma in reconciling to *dharma* the slaughters of warfare in the *Bhagavad-Gītā*; in the Old and New Testament struggle to locate God's will somewhere between justice and mercy; in the entire slant of early Chinese and Japanese literatures, centering in lyric rather than heroic individualism; and, of course, in numerous later Western works such as Dante's *Divine Comedy*, of which we print the *Inferno* complete, and Eliot's *The Waste Land*, also printed here complete.

As for narrative poetry that is not "heroic" in intention—as common in the Western tradition as it is uncommon elsewhere—we give you a selection of world-renowned tall tales from Ovid's *Metamorphoses*; the Prologue and two tales from Chaucer's *Canterbury Tales*; and the anonymous, ever-magical *Sir Gawain and the Green Knight* in a brilliant modernization by Marie Borroff.

Lyric poetry, including in that term not only the song to be sung but the relatively short, intensely personal reflection or meditation, has been even more central to some of the great non-Western literatures than to our own. Therefore, as counterpoint and challenge to classic Western practitioners such as Sappho, Catullus, Petrarch, Blake, Wordsworth, Baudelaire, Whitman, Dickinson, Rilke, Akhmatova, and Eliot, we bring you some of the great lyric treasures of three formidable civilizations of the East. Earliest of all, the Chinese, represented here in examples from the *Shi Jing*, or *Book of Songs* (a collection of 305 poems dating from 1000 to 600 B.C.) and from the poetry of T'ao Ch'ien. Next in time, the Japanese, whose *Man'yōshū*, or *Collection of 10,000 Leaves*, dates from the eighth century and contains, 4,516 short lyrics (eighteen of which are included in this volume), most of them in the *tanka* form, which at its breathtaking best can snare whole worlds of reflection and emotion in a net of five lines and thirty-one syllables.

Latest in time come the devotional lyrics of medieval India. Like mystical writings the world over, these give passionate voice to universal human impulses. In the religious dimension, the impulse is to escape the constrictions of everyday reality including those of one's own limited self in order to be assimilated to a higher level of perception or being. This is the experience that Dante records in his *Divine Comedy* as he progresses from *Inferno* to *Purgatorio* to *Paradiso*. In its social dimension, on the other hand, the impulse leads easily to devaluation of everyday reality and—as with these splendid examples from India—an eagerness to transgress its ties and obligations to facilitate union with the divine. It is perhaps not an accident that much of the great devotional poetry of both West and East has been composed by men and women living in a religious "Order" under "Rule" or by women struggling with an oppressive male society.

Other literary kinds are not neglected in this volume. From discursive prose, it offers Plato's *Apology of Socrates* (complete) and a portion of his *Phaedo* describing Socrates' death. Additionally, it offers several of the most characteristic chapters of the Old and New Testaments, of Augustine's *Confessions* and Rousseau's, of Machiavelli's *The Prince* and Montaigne's *Essays*. The brilliant reply-letter of Sor Juana Ines de la Cruz to her Episcopal superior the Bishop of Puebla is also here, perhaps most entertainingly read as rival as well as forerunner to Swift's *A Modest Proposal*.

These contributions from the Western literatures are flanked from the non-Western by portions of the *Bhagavad-Gītā* from India, aphorisms of Confucius and the meditations of Chuang Chou from China, some arresting chapters of the Koran from Islam—chapters that may shock students because they diverge so remarkably from Old and New Testament versions of these same stories—and, finally, from Japan, the shimmering nature-observations of the poet Matsuo, who took his quirky pen-name *Bashō* ("Banana") from a tree of that species planted in front of his austere cottage.

We cannot repeat too often that no anthology can replace the judgment of a teacher, who must appraise the makeup, ability, and possible areas of interest of the individual class together with the aims of the course and the time at her or his disposal. The opportunities in these pages for thought-provoking comparisons and contrasts of value systems, styles of living, habits of mind, lyric, narrative, and dramatic traditions and techniques are obvious and obviously inexhaustible. So are the opportunities for those fascinating but more speculative (and in the end never fully answerable) questions as to what aspects of a culture, ethnicity, race, or artistic tradition orient it toward some forms of self-expression and away from others. Why has the Chinese outlook and experience led to some of the world's finest songs and lyrics but never to an epic poem? What exactly was there in the world-view of ancient India and ancient Israel that left no room for the development of a tragic drama, yet created, in Israel, a religious literature that is among the wonders of the world and, in India, a sculpture and architecture that have few peers?

If the decision finally taken is to approach the least-known literatures through the somewhat more accessible and to allow each literature space enough and time to show its qualities before pressing on to the next, you will be well served by our sweeps. If the decision leans instead toward a program of topics, genres, themes, or parallel situations, you will discover in our Instructor's Guide many helpful considerations. As our arrangement of materials indicates, we ourselves tend to favor the former procedure, finding that it results in a surer grasp by students of temporal and geographical relationships and thus provides more frames of reference by which individual works are clarified and made memorable. We cheerfully agree, however, that any strategy that works is worth pursuing, since we all share the same objective: to widen our students' understanding along with our own, so that they and we may become the kind of human beings that Confucius's disciple Tzu-kung describes in describing Yen Hui—"when he is told one thing, he understands ten."

We want to remember in closing John C. McGalliard, gentleman, great scholar, and loyal friend, whose knowledge of medieval literature in all languages was profound and profoundly valuable to this anthology. The third of the founding editors to be taken from us, he died in the early summer of 1993. We pay tribute also to Barbara Stoler Miller, who, until her death in 1993, chaired the Department of Oriental Studies at Barnard College. A dedicated teacher, scholar, and translator, she is universally known for her masterly translations of Sanskrit poetry and drama, including *The Bhagavad-Gītā* and the plays of Kālidāsa. Her inspiration and great learning guided us in planning our selections from Indian literature, and we are deeply grateful for her wise and generous advice. We also remember here with greatest affection and admiration Barry K. Wade, former student of one of us, who quickly became a pillar of Norton publishing standards and the impresario of this anthology, most particularly the longer form of the Expanded Edition, which we have dedicated to his memory. He died too young, after a long illness, in the spring of 1993.

On a far happier note, we wish to take this occasion to welcome six new colleagues in the editorship of both forms of the Expanded Edition. John Bierhorst (B.A., Cornell) is a writer, editor, and translator specializing in native American literature; Jerome Wright Clinton (Ph.D., Michigan) is Professor of Near Eastern Studies at Princeton University; Robert Lyons Danly (Ph.D., Yale) is Professor of Asian Languages and Cultures at the University of Michigan; F. Abiola Irele (Ph.D., Sorbonne) is Professor of African, French, and Comparative Literatures at The Ohio State University; Stephen Owen (Ph.D., Yale) is Professor of Chinese and Comparative Literature at Harvard University; Indira Peterson (Ph.D., Harvard) is Professor of Asian Studies at Mount Holyoke College. Without them, this anthology would not be the flexible and innovative teaching instrument that it is.

The Editors

Acknowledgments

We would like to thank the following people who contributed to the planning of this one-volume version of *The Norton Anthology of World Masterpieces*, Expanded Edition: Ruth Albrecht (Lane Community College); Jan Anderson (Clackamas Community College); John S. Bak (Ball State University); Monika Brown (Pembroke State University); L. W. Brownley (University of Texas at Arlington); Michael J. Carson (University of Evansville); C. Lok Chua (California State University); Thomas L. Cooksey (Armstrong State University); Susan Dauer (University of Texas at Austin); J. F. R. Day (Troy State University); Nancy Dayton (Taylor University); Brian Doherty (University of Texas at Austin); Dawn D. Eidelman (University of Texas at Arlington); Randi Eldevik (Oklahoma State University); Harold Farwell (Western Carolina University); Patricia Gardner (Utah State University); James P. Gilroy (University of Denver); Stephen O. Glosecki (University of Alabama at Birmingham); Arthur Wayne Glowka (Georgia College); Daniel Gover (Kean College of New Jersey); Stephen W. Guy (Ball State University); Frances Hernández (University of Texas at El Paso); Dennis Hoilman (Ball State University); O. Glade Hunsaker (Brigham Young University); Theresa James (Xavier University of Louisiana); Edward Jayne (Western Michigan University); William T. Liston (Ball State University); Samuel E. Longmire (University of Evansville); Sandra W. Lott (University of Montevallo); Mary A. McCay (Loyola University); Marcia A. McDonald (Belmont University); James MacDougall (Ball State University); Donald N. Mager (Johnson C. Smith University); Barbara O. Mathieson (Southern Oregon State College); Louise C. Maynor (North Carolina Central University); Calin Mihailescu (University of Western Ontario); Louise Baughan Murdy (Winthrop University); James O'Neill (Umpqua Community College); Tomas N. Santos (University of Northern Colorado); Bill Siverly (Portland Community College); Barbara Stedman (Ball State University); Ward Swinson (Colorado State University); Katherine M. Thomas (Southeast Community College); David Upchurch (Ball State University); Janet Walker (Rutgers University); Rebecca A. Wall (Winston-Salem State University); Susan Weintrob (Ball State University); Sheila Willard (Middlesex Community College); John H. Wilson (Dakota Wesleyan University).

Among our many critics, advisers, and friends, the following were of special help in providing suggestions and corrections: Richard Adicks (University of Central Florida); Fawzia Afzal-Khan (Montclair State College); Sarah Bahous Allen (North Georgia College); Tommaso Astarita (Georgetown University); Murtha Baca (Getty Art History Information Program); Donald M. Bahr (Arizona State University); Michael Beard

(University of North Dakota); Paula Berggren (Bernard Baruch College—CUNY); Edith Blicksilver (Georgia Institute of Technology); Harold Boudreau (University of Massachusetts—Amherst); W. K. Buckley (Indiana University Northwest); Jerry Burns (Marian College); Victoria Carchidi (Massey University); Robert L. Casebeer (Southern Oregon State College); Thomas Cassidy (South Carolina State College); Robert W. Chambers (El Centro College); Roger Craik (Kent State University—Ashtabula); Jace Crouch (Michigan State University); Sara Cushing Smith (Piedmont Technical College); O. R. Dathorne (University of Kentucky); James Doan (Nova University); Caroline D. Eckhardt (Pennsylvania State University); Fidel Fajardo-Acosta (Creighton University); Joseph Fenley (St. Petersburg Junior College); Stephen D. Fox (Gallaudet University); Tidiane Gadio (Ohio State University); Bruce Golden (California State University—San Bernardino); Sharon L. Gravett (Valdosta State College); Cynthia A. Gravlee (University of Montevallo); Lynda Haas (Hillsborough Community College); Thomas Haberg (Northeastern Illinois University); Marjorie Hoskinson (Los Angeles Pierce College); Carolina Hospital (Miami-Dade Community College—Kendall Campus); Gail Houston (Brigham Young University); Richard Hull (New York University); William Hutchings (University of Alabama at Birmingham); Alan Jacobs (Wheaton College); Jane Anderson Jones (Manatee Community College—South Campus); Martha A. Kallstrom (Georgia Southern University); Alan Kaufman (Bergen Community College); Andrew Knoedler (University of Colorado); Margaret Kouidis (Auburn University); Charles S. Kraszewski (King's College); Victoria Lague (Miami Dade Community College—Kendall Campus); Bernard Levine (Wayne State University); Murray Levith (Skidmore College); Thomas E. Luddy (Salem State College); Philip Lutgendorf (University of Iowa); Antonia MacDonald (Ohio State University); Victor Manfredi (Boston University); Iely B. Mohamed (Jackson State University); Maggie P. Monteverde (Belmont University); Michael Palencia-Roth (University of Illinois at Urbana-Champaign); Philip Pfatteicher (East Stroudsburg University); Mary Sue Ply (Southeastern Louisiana University); Michael I. Prochilo (Salem State College); Joseph Roesch (Onondaga Community College); Roberta Rosenberg (Christopher Newport College); John Rosenwald (Beloit College); Treadwell Ruml (California State University—San Bernardino); John Paul Russo (University of Miami—Coral Gables); Francesca Santovetti (Georgetown University); Nina Scott (University of Massachusetts—Amherst); Lili Selden (University of Michigan); Jack Shreve (Allegany Community College); Jeanette Sordyl-Kibler (University of Michigan); Linda L. Strever (Pierce College); Robert H. Sykes (West Liberty State College); John S. Tanner (Brigham Young University); Dennis Tedlock (State University of New York—Buffalo); Cammy Thomas (Millsaps College); Diana E. Valdina (Cayuga County Community College); Sidney J. Vance (University of Montevallo); Benjamin R. Wiley (St. Petersburg Junior College—Clearwater Campus); Linda E. Yable (St. Petersburg Junior College—Clearwater Campus); Sape A. Zylstra (University of South Florida).

Phonetic Equivalents

for use with the Pronouncing Glossaries preceding
most selections in this volume

a as in *cat*
ah as in *father*
ai as in *light*
ay as in *day*
aw as in *raw*
e as in *pet*
ee as in *street*
ehr as in *air*
er as in *bird*
g as in *good*
i as in *sit*
j as in *joke*
nh as in *vin* (French)
o as in *pot*
oh as in *no*
oo as in *boot*
oy as in *toy*
or as in *bore*
ow as in *now*
s as in *mess*
ts as in *ants*
u as in *us*
zh as in *vision*

Part I

BEGINNINGS TO A.D. 100

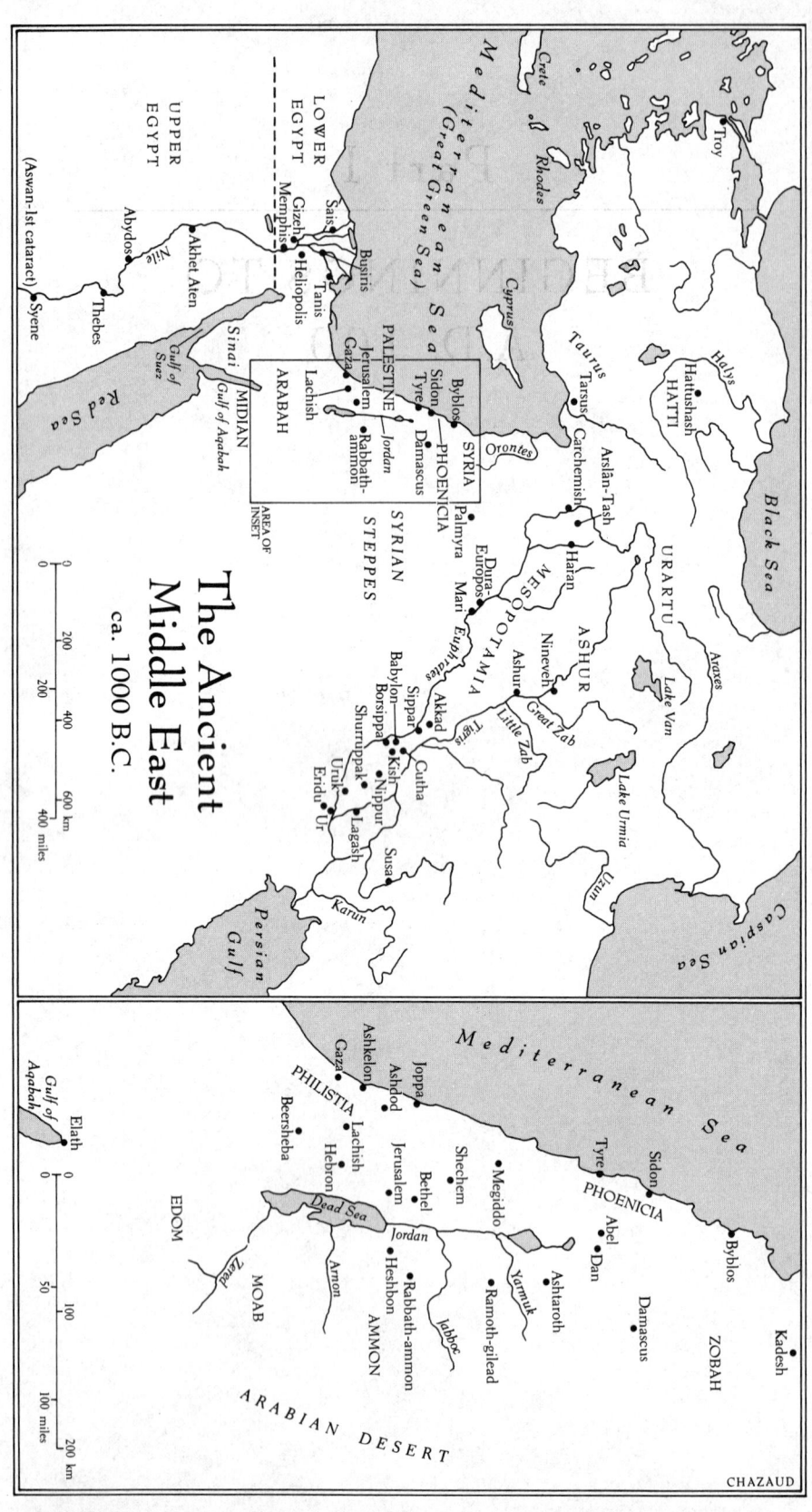

The Ancient
Middle East
ca. 1000 B.C.

CHAZAUD

We would also like to thank the following people who contributed to the Sixth Edition of *The Norton Anthology of World Masterpieces*, which served as the core for this text: Tamara Agha-Jaffar (Kansas City Community College); Kerry Ahearn (Oregon State University); David Anderson (Texas A & M University); Denise Baker (University of North Carolina—Greensboro); William F. Belcher (University of North Texas); L. Michael Bell (University of Colorado); Ernest Bernhardt (Indiana University); Craig Bernthal (Fresno State University); Gene Blanton (Jacksonville State University); Betsy Bowden (Rutgers University—Camden); Max Braffett (Southwest Texas State University); Edythe Briggs (Santa Rosa Junior College); Gary Brodsky (Northeastern Illinois University); Byron Brown (Valdosta State College); James L. Brown (Kansas City Kansas Community College); Corbin S. Carnell (University of Florida); Rose-Ann Cecere (Broward Community College); John Cech (University of Florida); Howard Clarke (University of California—Santa Barbara); Stephen Cooper (Troy State University); T. A. Copeland (Youngstown State University); Walter Coppedge (Virginia Commonwealth University); Bill Crider (Alvin Community College); George Crosland (California State University—Chico); Lennet Daigle (Georgia Southwestern College); Charles Daniel (Valdosta State College); Rosemary DePaolo (Augusta State College); Joseph DeRocco (Bridgewater State College); Ronald DiLorenzo (St. Louis University); Brooks Dodson (University of North Carolina—Wilmington); Patricia Doyle (Lynchburg College); Francis X. Duggan (Santa Clara University); Seth Ellis (University of North Carolina—Charlotte); Tom Ferte (Western Oregon State College); Joyce Field, Rowena Flanagan (Kansas City Community College); Marco Fraschella (San Joaquin Delta College); Ruth Fry (Auburn University); Michael Fukuchi (Atlantic Christian College); Robert Gariepy (Eastern Washington University); Robert Garrity (St. Joseph's College); Gerald Gordon (Kirkwood Community College); Richard Guzman (North Central College); Richard Hannaford (University of Idaho); Stephen Hemenway (Hope College); Beverly Heneghan (Northern Virginia Community College—Annandale); John Hennedy (Providence College); John Hiers (Valdosta State College); Robert Hogan (Rhode Island College); Rebecca Hogan (University of Wisconsin—Whitewater); Phil Holcomb (Angelo State University); Julia Bolton Holloway (University of Colorado); Wallace Hooker (Houston Baptist University); Richard Keithley (Georgia Southern College); Steven G. Kellman (University of Texas at San Antonio); Barbara Kemps (Union County College); Eric LaGuardia (University of Washington); Marthe LaVallee (Temple University); William Levison (Valdosta State College); Christiaan Lievestro (Santa Clara University); William Lutz (Rutgers University—Camden); Kathleen Lyons (Bellarmine College); Marianne Mayo (Valdosta State College); Barry McAndrew (Mercyhurst College); Glenn McCartney, James McKusick (University of Maryland—Baltimore College); David Middleton (Trinity University); Robert Miller (North Harris Community College, South); James Misenheimer (Indiana State University); David Neff (University of Alabama—Huntsville); Kurt Olsson (University of Idaho); Robert Oxley

(Embry-Riddle Aeronautical University); Richard Pacholski (Milliken University); Frank Palmeri (University of Miami); Elysee Peavy (Houston Baptist University); Larry H. Peer (Brigham Young University); John Pennington (Valdosta State College); K. J. Phillips (University of Hawaii); Ira Plybon (Marshall University); Willard Potts (Oregon State University); Victoria Poulakis (Northern Virginia Community College); Joseph Price (Northern Kentucky University); Richard Priebe (Virginia Commonwealth University); Otto Reinert (University of Washington); Janet Robinson (St. Petersburg Community College); James Rolleston (Duke University); John Rudy (Indiana University—Kokomo); Pamela Sheridan (Moorpark College); Judith P. Shoaf (University of Florida); Jack Shreve (Allegany Community College); Martha Simonsen (William Rainey Harper College); George Simson (University of Hawaii at Manoa); Melvin Storm (Emporia State University); Frank Stringfellow (University of Miami); Norman Stroh (Angelo State University); Nathaniel Teich (University of Oregon); Eric Thorn (Marshall University); Bruce Thornton (California State University—Fresno); Mason Tung (University of Idaho); Linnea Vacca (St. Mary's College); Robert Vuturo (Kansas City Community College); Sidney Wade (University of Florida); Martha Waller (Butler University); Roger Weaver (Oregon State University); Gibb Weber (Anderson University); Henry Weinfield (New Jersey Institute of Technology); Michael White (Odessa College); Gary Williams (University of Idaho); J. Wooliscroft (Edinboro University of Pennsylvania).

The Invention of Writing and the Earliest Literatures

Long before people learned to write, they made up and told stories; they composed and sang songs. Because people who have not learned to write must develop a retentive and accurate memory, such stories and songs could be preserved for generations in something like their original form or could be improved, expanded, or combined with other material to be passed on as, so to speak, another edition. But such oral traditional literature can be irrevocably lost if it is not transferred to a written medium; a sudden catastrophic break in the life of the community— foreign conquest, for example, which was always a present danger in the clash of ancient empires—might easily, through massacre, enslavement, and mass deportation, wipe out the memory of what had been a shared inheritance.

Writing, which has preserved some ancient literatures for us, was not invented for that purpose. The earliest written documents we have contain commercial, administrative, political, and legal information. They are the records of the first advanced, centralized civilizations, those that emerged in the area we know as the Middle East.

Ancient civilization was based on agriculture, and it flourished first in regions where the soil gave rich rewards: in the valley of the Nile, where annual floods left large tracts of land moist and fertile under the Egyptian sun, and in the valleys of the Euphrates and Tigris rivers, which flowed through the "Fertile Crescent," the land now known as Iraq and Iran. Great cities—Thebes and Memphis in Egypt and Babylon and Nineveh in the Fertile Crescent—came into being as centers for the complicated administration of the irrigated fields. Supported by the surplus the land produced, they became centers also for government, religion, and culture. Civilization begins with cities; the word itself is derived from a Latin word that means "citizen." As far back as 3000 B.C. the pharaohs of Egypt began to build their splendid temples and gigantic pyramids as well as to record their political acts and religious beliefs in hieroglyphic script. The Sumerians, Babylonians, and Assyrians began to build the palaces and temples of Babylon and record their laws in cuneiform script on clay tablets.

It was in the region of the Tigris and Euphrates rivers that writing was first developed; the earliest texts date from around 3300 to 2990 B.C. The characters were inscribed on tablets of wet clay with a pointed stick; the tablets were then left in the sun to bake to hardness. The characters are pictographic: the sign for *ox* looks like an ox head and so on. The bulk of the texts are economic—lists of foodstuffs, textiles, and cattle. But the script is too primitive to handle anything much more complicated than lists, and by 2800 B.C. scribes began to use the wedge-shaped end of the stick to make marks rather than the pointed end to draw pictures. The resulting script is known as cuneiform, from the Latin word *cuneus*, "a wedge." By 2500 B.C. the texts were no longer confined to lists; they record historical events and even material that could be regarded as literature.

This writing system was not, however, designed for a large reading public. The

3

wedge-shaped signs, grouped in various patterns, denote not letters of an alphabet but syllables—consonants plus a vowel—and this meant that the reader had to be familiar with a very large number of signs. Furthermore, the same sign often represents two or more different sounds, and the same sound can be represented by several different signs. It is a script that could be written and read only by experts, the scribes, who often proudly record their own names on the tablets.

It was, however, the most efficient system yet devised, and it stayed in use through all the historical vicissitudes of more than two millennia: the rise and fall of new dynasties and new conquerors, who became in their turn masters of the Fertile Crescent—Akkadians, Babylonians, Hittites, and Assyrians—until the area was incorporated in the Persian empire of Cyrus, who captured Babylon in 539 B.C. When in the fourth century B.C. the area became part of the Greek kingdom of one of the successors of Alexander the Great, the ancient script gradually fell out of use; the latest specimens to survive come from the first century A.D.

It was on clay tablets and in cuneiform script that the great Sumerian epic poem *Gilgamesh* was written down, in differing versions and in the different languages of the successive conquerors of the fertile river valleys, only to disappear in the ruins of the cities and be totally forgotten until modern excavators discovered the tablets and deciphered the enigmatic script that had preserved the poem through so many centuries.

The writing system invented by the Egyptians was even more esoteric than cuneiform. It is called hieroglyphic, an adjective formed from the Greek words for "sacred" and "carving." Although it appears on many different materials, its most conspicuous and continuous use was for inscriptions carved on the temple walls and public monuments. It was pictographic, like the earliest Sumerian script, but the pictures were more elaborate and artistic. Unlike the Sumerian pictographs, they were not replaced by a more efficient system; the pictures remained in use for the walls of temples and tombs, while more cursive versions of hieroglyphics— the hieratic and demotic scripts—were developed for faster writing. A writing system consisting of logograms (pictures standing for objects) is obviously incapable of communicating anything but the simplest of ideas, and at a very early stage the logograms were used to denote consonantal sounds. The Egyptian word for "house," for example, was *pr*, and its logogram was a rectangle with a gap in one of the long sides to indicate the door. The sign could still mean "house," but it could now also be used, in combination with other logograms indicating sounds, to denote simply the sound *pr*. This was only one of many complications that made even the modified versions of the script a difficult medium of communication for anyone not trained in its intricacies. The fact that only the consonantal sounds were represented (we do not know what vowel was sounded between the *p* and the *r* of *pr*) was one more barrier to easy interpretation. It is no wonder that one of the frequent figures to appear in Egyptian sculpture and painting is the professional scribe, his legs tucked underneath him, his writing material in his lap, and his brush in his hand.

Unlike the cuneiform tablets that remained buried, waiting for the trowel of the excavator, the Egyptian hieroglyphs were carved on the walls of ruined temples and remained open to view but defied interpretation. The key to the solution of the problem came in 1799, when some French soldiers of Napoleon's army, digging the foundation for a redoubt in Egypt, unearthed a large block of basalt, the Rosetta stone, on which was a text inscribed in three different versions. Two were Egyptian, one hieroglyphic and one demotic, and the other was in Greek, which had been the official language of Egypt ever since Ptolemy, one of Alexander's generals, had established himself as pharaoh in Egypt after Alexander died in 323 B.C.

There was one ancient writing system that, unlike cuneiform and hieroglyphic, was destined to survive, in modified forms, until the present day. It was a script developed by the Semitic peoples of the area, notably the enterprising Phoenicians, whose seaports on the Palestine coast, Tyre and Sidon, were bases for trading ventures and colonial expeditions to distant seas. The script consisted of twenty-two simple signs for consonantal sounds, an alphabet, to use the later Greek term, that could be easily learned. The Phoenicians have left us no literary texts, but the Hebrews, another Semitic people, used the system to record in a collection of books—part of which became what Christians call the Old Testament—their history; their sorrows and triumphs; and above all, their concept, unique in the polytheistic ancient world, of a single god.

Unlike the rulers of the Tigris-Euphrates and Nile valleys, the Hebrews, located in Palestine, did not control territory of economic or military importance; their record is not that of an imperial people. In their period of independence, from their beginnings as a pastoral tribe to their high point as a kingdom with a splendid capital in Jerusalem, they accomplished little of note in the political or military spheres. Their later history was a bitter and unsuccessful struggle for freedom against a series of foreign masters—Babylonian, Greek, and Roman.

After the period of expansion and prosperity under the great kings David and Solomon (1005–925 B.C.), the kingdom fell apart into warring factions, which called in outside powers. The melancholy end of a long period of internal and external struggle was the destruction of the cities and the deportation of the population to Babylon (586 B.C.). This period of exile (which ended in 539 B.C. when Cyrus, the Persian conqueror of Babylon, released the Hebrews from bondage) was a formative period for Hebrew religious thought, which was enriched and refined by the teachings of the prophet Ezekiel and the prophet known as the second Isaiah (pp. 51 and 84). The return to Palestine was crowned by the rebuilding of the Temple and the creation of the canonical version of the Pentateuch, or Torah—the first five books of the Bible. The religious legacy of the Hebrew people was now codified for future generations.

But the independent state of Israel was not destined to last long. By 300 B.C. the Macedonian successors of Alexander the Great had encroached on its borders and prerogatives; in spite of a heroic resistance, the territory eventually became part of a Hellenistic Greek-speaking kingdom and, finally, was absorbed by the Roman empire. A desperate revolt against Rome was crushed in A.D. 70 by the emperor Titus (on the arch of Titus in Rome a relief shows the legionaries carrying a seven-branched menorah, or candlestick, in Titus' triumph). A second revolt, against the emperor Hadrian (A.D. 131–134), resulted in the final extermination or removal from Palestine of the Hebrew people. Henceforward, they were the people of the Diaspora, the "scattering": religious communities in the great cities of the ancient world who maintained local cohesion and universal religious solidarity but who were stateless, as they were to be all through the centuries until the creation, in the mid-twentieth century, of the state of Israel.

The political history of the ancient Hebrews ended in a series of disasters. In the field of the arts they left behind them no painting or sculpture and little or no secular literature—no drama, for example, no epic poetry. What they did leave us is a religious literature, written down probably between the eighth and second centuries B.C., which is informed by an attitude different from that of any other nation of the ancient world. It is founded on the idea of one God, the Creator of all things, all-powerful and just—a conception of the divine essence and the government of the universe so simple that to those of us who have inherited it, it seems obvious. But in its time it was so revolutionary that it made the Hebrews a nation apart, sometimes laughed at, sometimes feared, but always alien.

The consonantal script in which their literary legacy was handed down to us was a great step forward from the hieroglyphic and cuneiform systems; writing now called for no artistic skills and reading for no long period of training. But it was still an unsatisfactory medium for mass communication; the absence of notation for the vowels made for ambiguity and possible misreading and, at times, may have called for inspired guesswork. We still do not know, for example, what the vowel sounds were in the sacred name of God, often called the Tetragrammaton, because it consists of four letters; in our alphabet the name is written as YHWH. The usual surmise is Jahweh *(ya'-way)*, but for a long time the traditional English-language version was Jehovah.

One thing was needed to make the script fully efficient: signs for the vowels. And this was the contribution of the Greeks, who, in the eighth or possibly the ninth century B.C., adopted the Phoenician script for their own language but used for the vowels some Phoenician signs that stood for consonantal combinations not native to Greek. They took over (but soon modified) the Phoenician letter shapes and also their names: *alpha*, a meaningless word in Greek, represents the original *aleph* ("ox"), and *beta* represents the original *beta* ("house"). The Greeks were frank to admit their indebtedness; Greek myths told the story of Cadmus, king of Tyre, who taught the Greeks how to write, and as the historian Herodotus tells us, the letters were called Phoenician. But in fact the Greek creation of signs for the vowels produced the first real alphabet, and the Romans, who adapted it for their own language, carved their inscriptions on stone in the same capital letters that we still use today.

FURTHER READING

Henri Frankfort et al., *Before Philosophy: The Intellectual Adventure of Ancient Man* (1949), is a brilliant evocation of the intellectual life of ancient cultures. For concise, informative, and up-to-date articles on three ancient literatures, see Miguel Civil, "Sumerian Poetry"; John L. Foster, "Egyptian Poetry"; and Erica Reiner, "Assyro-Babylonian Poetry," in *The New Princeton Encyclopedia of Poetry and Poetics* (1993). H. M. Orlinsky, *Ancient Israel* (1960), is a short but clearly written outline of the history of Israel up to the return from Babylonian exile.

THE INVENTION OF WRITING AND THE EARLIEST LITERATURES

TEXTS	CONTEXTS
	ca. 3000 B.C. Mesopotamia: Sumerian cuneiform writing on clay tablets • Egypt: writing in hieroglyphic script
	2700 Gilgamesh is king in Uruk
	ca. 2575–2130 Old Kingdom (Egypt) • Great Pyramids; Sphinx
	ca. 2130–1540 Middle Kingdom (Egypt)
2040–1651 B.C. *The Tale of the Shipwrecked Sailor* composed	
ca. 2000 Legends about King Gilgamesh appear on clay tablets	
	ca. 1900 Hebrew migration from Mesopotamia begins
	18th century Hammurabi's Code of Law written in Babylon
1600 The epic of **Gilgamesh** begins to take shape	
1500 Egyptian *Book of the Dead*	ca. 1539–1200 New Kingdom (Egypt)
1375–1358 Akhenaten's "*Hymn to the Sun*" composed	1375–1354 King Akhenaten dedicates his capital to Aten, the sun god
1300 The epic of **Gilgamesh** written down	
1300–1100 **Love songs** of the New Kingdom composed	
1238 **The Leiden Hymns** written down	
	ca. 1200 Moses leads the Jews in Exodus from Egypt to Palestine
1160 *Song of the Harper* inscribed on Inherkhawy's tomb	
1000 The Torah text assembled • Psalms	1005–925 David, then Solomon, king in Israel

TEXTS	CONTEXTS
6th century Aesop's *Fables*	
	586 Jerusalem captured by Babylonian king Nebuchadnezzar; many Jews taken to exile in Babylon
	539 The Persian shah, Cyrus the Great, conquers Babylon and allows the Jews to return to Israel. He founds the Iranian empire, which later envelops most of the Middle East and Central Asia
	525 Cambyses, king of Persia, conquers Egypt
ca. 450 Herodotus, *History*	
	331–330 Alexander the Great conquers Syria, Mesopotamia, and Iran; defeats the last Persian army at Sungamela and occupies Babylon and Persopolis
	330–323 Alexander conquers Central Asia and the Indus Valley, but dies in Babylon (323). His generals divide up the empire. Selenaus becomes king of the Mesopotamian area, Ptolemy of Egypt
	202–198 Palestine falls to Antiochus III, king of a land empire stretching east from Asia Minor • Rome defeats Antiochus III in 190 • Successful Jewish revolt against Antiochus IV between 173 and 167
	40–4 Herod is king of Judaea
	30 Rome conquers Egypt

GILGAMESH

ca. 2500–1300 B.C.

Gilgamesh is a poem of unparalleled antiquity, the first great heroic narrative of world literature. Its origins stretch back to the margins of prehistory, and its evolution spans millennia. When it was known, it was widely known. Tablets containing portions of *Gilgamesh* have been found at sites throughout the Middle East and in all the languages written in cuneiform characters, wedge-shaped characters incised in clay or stone. But then, at a time when the civilizations of the Hebrews, Greeks, and Romans had only just developed beyond their infancy, *Gilgamesh* vanished from memory. For reasons that scholars have not yet fathomed, the literature of the cuneiform languages was not translated into the new alphabets that replaced them. Some portions of this once-famous work survived in subsequent traditions, but they did so as scattered and anonymous fragments. They became a kind of invisible substratum that was buried under what was previously believed to be the earliest level of our common tradition. Until Utnapishtim's "Story of the Flood," a portion of *Gilgamesh*, was accidentally rediscovered and published in 1872, no one suspected that the biblical story of Noah and the Great Flood was neither original nor unique.

A great lost work like *Gilgamesh* poses particular problems of understanding beyond those posed by the discovery of a lost masterpiece by a known author or of a known time. The meaning of a work of literature is partly contextual—it is established by the culture that produced that work. Yet the whole context of *Gilgamesh* was lost along with the text. The names of the gods and humans who people the epic, the cities and lands in which they lived, and the whole of their history vanished for thousands of years from common memory. The story of Gilgamesh and his companion, Enkidu, speaks to contemporary readers with astonishing immediacy. Its moving depiction of the bonds of friendship, of the quest for worldly renown, and of the tragic attempt to escape that death which is the common fate of humanity has a timeless resonance and appeal. Yet despite this immediate recognition of something profoundly familiar there is, because of this millennial gap in the history of its transmission, a strangeness and remoteness about the work that strikes us in virtually every line. That strangeness has diminished each year as more tablets have been discovered and translated and as our understanding of the languages and cultures of the ancient Middle East has increased, but what we know is still relatively slight compared with what we know of the cultures that succeeded them. Today the names of Ulysses and Achilles and the gods and goddesses of Mount Olympus are familiar even to many who have not read Homer. The names of Gilgamesh, Enkidu, Utnapishtim, Enlil, and Ea are virtually unknown outside the poem itself.

Gilgamesh developed over a period of nearly a thousand years. The version discovered in the city of Nineveh amid the ruins of the great royal library of Assurbanipal, the last great king of the Assyrian empire—what modern scholars now call the Standard Version—circulated widely throughout the ancient Middle East for a millennium or more. While the history of the text is a long and complex one, and is still far from fully understood, it is possible to identify three principal stages in its development. The first begins in roughly 2700 B.C. when the historical Gilgamesh ruled in Uruk, a city in ancient Mesopotamia. Tales both mythical and legendary grew up around him and were repeated and copied for centuries. The stories that were later incorporated into the *Gilgamesh* epic existed in this literature, albeit in different form, as well as other material concerning the historical

Gilgamesh that was not included in the epic. The earliest written versions of these stories date from roughly 2000 B.C., but oral versions of the stories both preceded them and continued on, parallel with the written tradition. The language of these materials was Sumerian, the earliest written language in Mesopotamia and one that has little if any connection to any other known language.

The history of the epic itself begins sometime before 1600 B.C., some eight centuries before Homer, when a Babylonian author (Mesopotamian tradition identifies a priest-exorcist named Sîn-leqi-unninni) assembled free translations of the oral versions of some of these tales into a connected narrative. This new work was not simply a sequence of tales linked by the character of Gilgamesh but a conscious selection and recasting of the Sumerian materials into a new form. Some Gilgamesh tales were ignored, while elements from stories not associated with him in the Sumerian accounts were incorporated. This earliest version of the epic, which exists only in fragmentary form, continued to develop for the next few centuries. However, no comparable recasting of the poem was made. By the time of Assurbanipal (668–627 B.C.) the text was essentially stabilized.

Assurbanipal's synthetic version—the Standard Version—was also the first discovered. It was written on twelve hardened clay tablets in Akkadian, a Semitic language like Hebrew and Arabic and one of the principal languages of Babylonia and Assyria. The first eleven of these tablets make up the story as printed here. The twelfth tells another story of Gilgamesh, "Gilgamesh and the Underworld," and since it is unclear how it is to be incorporated into the preceding tablets, it is usually presented as a kind of appendix to the story.

The tablets of the Standard Version are poorly preserved at a number of points, most notably in the adventure in the Cedar Forest, and the translation relies heavily on the earlier, Old Babylonian version and fragments from a number of other versions.

The epic narrates the legendary deeds of Gilgamesh, king of Uruk, but it begins with a prologue that emphasizes not his adventures but the wisdom he acquired and the monuments he constructed at the end of his epic journey. It also tells us that Gilgamesh was endowed by his divine creators with extraordinary strength, courage, and beauty. He is more god than man. His father, however, is mortal, and that fact is decisive in shaping the narrative that follows. The prologue also suggests that Gilgamesh himself has written this account and left the tablets in the foundation of the city wall of Uruk for all to read.

In our first view of him, <u>Gilgamesh is the epitome of a bad ruler: arrogant, oppressive, and brutal. The people of Uruk complain of his oppression to the Sumerian gods</u>, and the gods' response is to create Enkidu as a foil or counterweight to Gilgamesh. Where the latter is a mixture of human and divine, Enkidu, who also appears godlike, is a blend of human and wild animal, with the animal predominating at first. He is raised by wild beasts, lives as they do (eating only uncooked food), and embodies the conflict between animal and human natures that is a recurrent theme in Mesopotamian literature and myth. When he becomes a kind of protector of the animals, breaking the hunters' traps and filling in their pits, Enkidu poses a threat to the human community. This threat is neutralized by civilizing him. First a prostitute seduces him across the line separating animal from human and educates him in the elements of human society. Then shepherds teach him to eat prepared food, wear clothing, and anoint himself as humans do. He is weakened somewhat by this transformation and estranged from his animal companions, but he is also glorified and made greater than he was. The prostitute leads him to Uruk and the confrontation with Gilgamesh for which the gods have created him. His coming has been announced to Gilgamesh in one of the many dreams that play such an important role in the poem. Although the two are bent on destroying each other at first, their encounter results, as it was meant to, in a deep bond of friendship. Each finds in the other the true companion he has sought. The consequence of their union is that their prodigious energies are directed outward toward heroic achievements.

Gilgamesh proposes the first of their adventures both to gain them universal renown and to refresh the spirit of Enkidu, who has been weakened and confused by civilization. He suggests that they go to the great Cedar Forest in the Country of the Living and there slay the terrible giant Humbaba. Enkidu is reluctant at first because he knows the danger in this adventure better than Gilgamesh. But the latter prevails, and with the blessing of the sun god Shamash they succeed. Their victory is not a simple, glorious triumph, however, and its meaning is unclear. Humbaba poses no apparent threat to Uruk and its people, and he curses them before he dies. Enlil, the god of wind and storm, is enraged by the slaying of his creature, curses the heroes, and gives to others the seven splendors that had been Humbaba's.

Their second adventure is not of their choosing and also leads to another ambiguous success. Gilgamesh's just but harsh rejection of Ishtar's advances provokes her to send the Bull of Heaven against the people of Uruk. The terrible destruction the Bull causes obliges Gilgamesh and Enkidu to destroy it, but that victory brings about the slow and painful death of Enkidu.

The death of his companion reveals to Gilgamesh the hollowness of mortal fame and leads him to undertake a solitary journey in search of immortality. This journey sets *Gilgamesh* apart from more straightforward heroic narratives and gives it a special appeal to modern readers. Gilgamesh's specific goal is to discover the secret of immortality from the one man, Utnapishtim, who has survived the Flood. His journey begins with a conventional challenge, the fierce lions who guard the mountain passes. But the challenges he faces subsequently—the dark tunnel that brings him to a prototypical garden of paradise, the puzzling and perilous voyage to Dilmun—have a different and more magical character. He is discouraged at every step, but Gilgamesh perseveres. Although he at last finds Utnapishtim and hears his story, his goal eludes him. He fails a simple test of his potential for immortality when he cannot remain awake for six days and seven nights. Moreover, he fails a second test as well when he first finds the plant that ensures eternal rejuvenation and then, in a moment of carelessness, loses it to the serpent. Discouraged and defeated, Gilgamesh returns at last to Uruk empty-handed. His consolation is the assurance that his worldly accomplishments will endure beyond his own lifetime.

In long, belated retrospect we can see that *Gilgamesh* explores many of the mysteries of the human condition for the first time in our literature—the complex and perilous relations between gods and mortals and between nature and civilization, the depths of friendship, and the immortality of art. It is both humbling and thrilling to hear so familiar a voice from so vast a distance.

The introduction to the present translation by N. K. Sandars in *The Epic of Gilgamesh* (1972) is readily available and contains a wealth of useful information. A. Leo Oppenheim gives a comprehensive interpretation of Mesopotamian civilization in *Ancient Mesopotamia* (1977), and Alexander Heidel addresses the importance of *Gilgamesh* for biblical studies in *The Gilgamesh Epic and Old Testament Parallels* (1963).

Gilgamesh[1]

PROLOGUE

Gilgamesh King in Uruk

I will proclaim to the world the deeds of Gilgamesh. This was the man to whom all things were known; this was the king who knew the countries of the world. He was wise, he saw mysteries and knew secret things, he brought us a tale of the days before the flood. He went on a long journey, was weary, worn-out with labour, returning he rested, he engraved on a stone the whole story.

When the gods created Gilgamesh they gave him a perfect body. Shamash[2] the glorious sun endowed him with beauty, Adad the god of the storm endowed him with courage, the great gods made his beauty perfect, surpassing all others, terrifying like a great wild bull. Two thirds they made him god and one third man.

In Uruk[3] he built walls, a great rampart, and the temple of blessed Eanna for the god of the firmament Anu,[4] and for Ishtar the goddess of love. Look at it still today: the outer wall where the cornice runs, it shines with the brilliance of copper; and the inner wall, it has no equal. Touch the threshold, it is ancient. Approach Eanna the dwelling of Ishtar, our lady of love and war, the like of which no latter-day king, no man alive can equal. Climb upon the wall of Uruk; walk along it, I say; regard the foundation terrace and examine the masonry: is it not burnt brick and good? The seven sages[5] laid the foundations.

1

The Coming of Enkidu

Gilgamesh went abroad in the world, but he met with none who could withstand his arms till he came to Uruk. But the men of Uruk muttered in their houses, "Gilgamesh sounds the tocsin for his amusement, his arrogance has no bounds by day or night. No son is left with his father, for Gilgamesh takes them all, even the children; yet the king should be a shepherd to his people. His lust leaves no virgin to her lover, neither the warrior's daughter nor the wife of the noble; yet this is the shepherd of the city, wise, comely, and resolute."

The gods heard their lament, the gods of heaven cried to the Lord of Uruk, to Anu the god of Uruk: "A goddess made him, strong as a savage bull, none can withstand his arms. No son is left with his father, for Gilgamesh takes them all; and is this the king, the shepherd of his people? His lust leaves no virgin to her lover, neither the warrior's daughter nor the wife of the nobel." When Anu had heard their lamentation the gods

---

1. Translated by N. K. Sandars.   2. Also judge and lawgiver, with some fertility attributes; he is the husband and brother of Ishtar, goddess of love, fertility, and war and queen of heaven.   3. City in southern Babylonia between Fara and Ur. Shown by excavation to have been an important city from very early times, with great temples to the gods Anu and Ishtar. After the Flood it was the seat of a dynasty of kings, among whom Gilgamesh was the fifth and most famous.   4. Also father of the gods; he had an important temple in Uruk. Eanna was the temple precinct in Uruk, sacred to Anu and Ishtar.   5. Wise men who brought civilization to the seven oldest cities of Mesopotamia.

cried to Aruru, the goddess of creation, "You made him, O Aruru, now create his equal; let it be as like him as his own reflection, his second self, stormy heart for stormy heart. Let them contend together and leave Uruk in quiet."

So the goddess conceived an image in her mind, and it was of the stuff of Anu of the firmament. She dipped her hands in water and pinched off clay, she let it fall in the wilderness, and noble Enkidu was created. There was virtue in him of the god of war, of Ninurta himself. His body was rough, he had long hair like a woman's; it waved like the hair of Nisaba, the goddess of corn. His body was covered with matted hair like Samuqan's, the god of cattle. He was innocent of mankind; he knew nothing of the cultivated land.

Enkidu ate grass in the hills with the gazelle and lurked with wild beasts at the water-holes; he had joy of the water with the herds of wild game. But there was a trapper who met him one day face to face at the drinking-hole, for the wild game had entered his territory. On three days he met him face to face, and the trapper was frozen with fear. He went back to his house with the game he had caught, and he was dumb, benumbed with terror. His face was altered like that of one who has made a long journey. With awe in his heart he spoke to his father: "Father, there is a man, unlike any other, who comes down from the hills. He is the strongest in the world, he is like an immortal from heaven. He ranges over the hills with wild beasts and eats grass; he ranges through your land and comes down to the wells. I am afraid and dare not go near him. He fills in the pits which I dig and tears up my traps set for the game; he helps the beasts to escape and now they slip through my fingers."

His father opened his mouth and said to the trapper, "My son, in Uruk lives Gilgamesh; no one has ever prevailed against him, he is strong as a star from heaven. Go to Uruk, find Gilgamesh, extol the strength of this wild man. Ask him to give you a harlot, a wanton from the temple of love; return with her, and let her woman's power overpower this man. When next he comes down to drink at the wells she will be there, stripped naked; and when he sees her beckoning he will embrace her, and then the wild beasts will reject him."

So the trapper set out on his journey to Uruk and addressed himself to Gilgamesh saying, "A man unlike any other is roaming now in the pastures; he is as strong as a star from heaven and I am afraid to approach him. He helps the wild game to escape; he fills in my pits and pulls up my traps." Gilgamesh said, "Trapper, go back, take with you a harlot, a child of pleasure. At the drinking-hole she will strip, and when he sees her beckoning he will embrace her and the game of the wilderness will surely reject him."

Now the trapper returned, taking the harlot with him. After a three days' journey they came to the drinking-hole, and there they sat down; the harlot and the trapper sat facing one another and waited for the game to come. For the first day and for the second day the two sat waiting, but on the third day the herds came; they came down to drink and Enkidu was with them. The small wild creatures of the plains were glad of the water, and Enkidu with them, who ate grass with the gazelle and was born in the hills; and she saw him, the savage man, come from far-off in the hills. The trapper spoke to her: "There he is. Now, woman, make your breasts bare, have no shame, do not delay but welcome his love. Let him see you naked, let him possess your body. When he comes near uncover yourself and lie with him; teach him, the savage man, your woman's art, for when he murmurs love to you the wild beasts that shared his life in the hills will reject him."

She was not ashamed to take him, she made herself naked and welcomed his eagerness; as he lay on her murmuring love she taught him the woman's art. For six days and seven nights they lay together, for Enkidu had forgotten his home in the hills; but when he was satisfied he went back to the wild beasts. Then, when the gazelle saw him, they bolted away; when the wild creatures saw him they fled. Enkidu would have followed, but his body was bound as though with a cord, his knees gave way when he started to run, his swiftness was gone. And now the wild creatures had all fled away; Enkidu was grown weak, for wisdom was in him, and the thoughts of a man were in his heart. So he returned and sat down at the woman's feet, and listened intently to what she said. "You are wise, Enkidu, and now you have become like a god. Why do you want to run wild with the beasts in the hills? Come with me. I will take you to strong-walled Uruk, to the blessed temple of Ishtar and of Anu, of love and of heaven: there Gilgamesh lives, who is very strong, and like a wild bull he lords it over men."

When she had spoken Enkidu was pleased; he longed for a comrade, for one who would understand his heart. "Come, woman, and take me to that holy temple, to the house of Anu and of Ishtar, and to the place where Gilgamesh lords it over the people. I will challenge him boldly, I will cry out aloud in Uruk, 'I am the strongest here, I have come to change the old order, I am he who was born in the hills, I am he who is strongest of all.' "

She said, "Let us go, and let him see your face. I know very well where Gilgamesh is in great Uruk. O Enkidu, there all the people are dressed in their gorgeous robes, every day is holiday, the young men and the girls are wonderful to see. How sweet they smell! All the great ones are roused from their beds. O Enkidu, you who love life, I will show you Gilgamesh, a man of many moods; you shall look at him well in his radiant manhood. His body is perfect in strength and maturity; he never rests by night or day. He is stronger than you, so leave your boasting. Shamash the glorious sun has given favours to Gilgamesh, and Anu of the heavens, and Enlil, and Ea the wise has given him deep understanding. I tell you, even before you have left the wilderness, Gilgamesh will know in his dreams that you are coming."

Now Gilgamesh got up to tell his dream to his mother, Ninsun, one of the wise gods. "Mother, last night I had a dream. I was full of joy, the young heroes were round me and I walked through the night under the stars of the firmament, and one, a meteor of the stuff of Anu, fell down from heaven. I tried to lift it but it proved too heavy. All the people of Uruk came round to see it, the common people jostled and the nobles thronged to kiss its feet; and to me its attraction was like the love of woman. They helped me, I braced my forehead and I raised it with thongs and brought it to you, and you yourself pronounced it my brother."

Then Ninsun, who is well-beloved and wise, said to Gilgamesh, "This star of heaven which descended like a meteor from the sky; which you tried to lift, but found too heavy, when you tried to move it it would not budge, and so you brought it to my feet; I made it for you, a goad and spur, and you were drawn as though to a woman. This is the strong comrade, the one who brings help to his friend in his need. He is the strongest of wild creatures, the stuff of Anu; born in the grass-lands and the wild hills reared him; when you see him you will be glad; you will love him as a woman and he will never forsake you. This is the meaning of the dream."

Gilgamesh said, "Mother, I dreamed a second dream. In the streets of strong-walled Uruk there lay an axe; the shape of it was strange and the people thronged round. I saw it and was glad. I bent down, deeply drawn towards it; I loved it like a woman and wore it at my side." Ninsun answered, "That axe, which you saw, which drew you so powerfully like love of a woman, that is the comrade whom I give you, and he will come in his strength like one of the host of heaven. He is the brave companion who rescues his friend in necessity." Gilgamesh said to his mother, "A friend, a counsellor has come to me from Enlil, and now I shall befriend and counsel him." So Gilgamesh told his dreams; and the harlot retold them to Enkidu.

And now she said to Enkidu, "When I look at you you have become like a god. Why do you yearn to run wild again with the beasts in the hills? Get up from the ground, the bed of a shepherd." He listened to her words with care. It was good advice that she gave. She divided her clothing in two and with the one half she clothed him and with the other herself; and holding his hand she led him like a child to the sheepfolds, into the shepherds' tents. There all the shepherds crowded round to see him, they put down bread in front of him, but Enkidu could only suck the milk of wild animals. He fumbled and gaped, at a loss what to do or how he should eat the bread and drink the strong wine. Then the woman said, "Enkidu, eat bread, it is the staff of life; drink the wine, it is the custom of the land." So he ate till he was full and drank strong wine, seven goblets. He became merry, his heart exulted and his face shone. He rubbed down the matted hair of his body and anointed himself with oil. Enkidu had become a man; but when he had put on man's clothing he appeared like a bride-groom. He took arms to hunt the lion so that the shepherds could rest at night. He caught wolves and lions and the herdsmen lay down in peace; for Enkidu was their watchman, that strong man who had no rival.

He was merry living with the shepherds, till one day lifting his eyes he saw a man approaching. He said to the harlot, "Woman, fetch that man here. Why has he come? I wish to know his name." She went and called the man saying, "Sir, where are you going on this weary journey?" The man answered, saying to Enkidu, "Gilgamesh has gone into the marriage-house and shut out the people. He does strange things in Uruk, the city of great streets. At the roll of the drum work begins for the men, and work for the women. Gilgamesh the king is about to celebrate marriage with the Queen of Love, and he still demands to be first with the bride, the king to be first and the husband to follow, for that was ordained by the gods from his birth, from the time the umbilical cord was cut. But now the drums roll for the choice of the bride and the city groans." At these words Enkidu turned white in the face. "I will go to the place where Gilgamesh lords it over the people, I will challenge him boldly, and I will cry aloud in Uruk, 'I have come to change the old order, for I am the strongest here.'"

Now Enkidu strode in front and the woman followed behind. He entered Uruk, that great market, and all the folk thronged round him where he stood in the street in strong-walled Uruk. The people jostled; speaking of him they said, "He is the spit of Gilgamesh." "He is shorter." "He is bigger of bone." "This is the one who was reared on the milk of wild beasts. His is the greatest strength." The men rejoiced: "Now Gilgamesh has met his match. This great one, this hero whose beauty is like a god, he is a match even for Gilgamesh."

In Uruk the bridal bed was made, fit for the goddess of love. The bride waited for the bridegroom, but in the night Gilgamesh got up and came to the house. Then Enkidu stepped out, he stood in the street and blocked the way. Mighty Gilgamesh came on and Enkidu met him at the gate. He put out his foot and prevented Gilgamesh from entering the house, so they grappled, holding each other like bulls. They broke the doorposts and the walls shook, they snorted like bulls locked together. They shattered the doorposts and the walls shook. Gilgamesh bent his knee with his foot planted on the ground and with a turn Enkidu was thrown. Then immediately his fury died. When Enkidu was thrown he said to Gilgamesh, "There is not another like you in the world. Ninsun, who is as strong as a wild ox in the byre, she was the mother who bore you, and now you are raised above all men, and Enlil has given you the kingship, for your strength surpasses the strength of men." So Enkidu and Gilgamesh embraced and their friendship was sealed.

2

The Forest Journey

Enlil of the mountain, the father of the gods,[6] had decreed the destiny of Gilgamesh. So Gilgamesh dreamed and Enkidu said, "The meaning of the dream is this. The father of the gods has given you kingship, such is your destiny, everlasting life is not your destiny. Because of this do not be sad at heart, do not be grieved or oppressed. He has given you power to bind and to loose, to be the darkness and the light of mankind. He has given you unexampled supremacy over the people, victory in battle from which no fugitive returns, in forays and assaults from which there is no going back. But do not abuse this power, deal justly with your servants in the palace, deal justly before Shamash."

The eyes of Enkidu were full of tears and his heart was sick. He sighed bitterly and Gilgamesh met his eye and said, "My friend, why do you sigh so bitterly?" But Enkidu opened his mouth and said, "I am weak, my arms

6. The breath and "word" of Anu; he is also god of earth, wind, and spirit.

have lost their strength, the cry of sorrow sticks in my throat, I am oppressed by idleness." It was then that the lord Gilgamesh turned his thoughts to the Country of the Living; on the Land of Cedars the lord Gilgamesh reflected. He said to his servant Enkidu, "I have not established my name stamped on bricks as my destiny decreed; therefore I will go to the country where the cedar is felled. I will set up my name in the place where the names of famous men are written, and where no man's name is written yet I will raise a monument to the gods. Because of the evil that is in the land, we will go to the forest and destroy the evil; for in the forest lives Humbaba whose name is 'Hugeness,' a ferocious giant." But Enkidu sighed bitterly and said, "When I went with the wild beasts ranging through the wilderness I discovered the forest; its length is ten thousand leagues in every direction. Enlil has appointed Humbaba to guard it and armed him in sevenfold terrors, terrible to all flesh is Humbaba. When he roars it is like the torrent of the storm, his breath is like fire, and his jaws are death itself. He guards the cedars so well that when the wild heifer stirs in the forest, though she is sixty leagues distant, he hears her. What man would willingly walk into that country and explore its depths? I tell you, weakness overpowers whoever goes near it: it is not an equal struggle when one fights with Humbaba; he is a great warrior, a battering-ram. Gilgamesh, the watchman of the forest never sleeps."

Gilgamesh replied: "Where is the man who can clamber to heaven? Only the gods live for ever with glorious Shamash, but as for us men, our days are numbered, our occupations are a breath of wind. How is this, already you are afraid! I will go first although I am your lord, and you may safely call out, 'Forward, there is nothing to fear!' Then if I fall I leave behind me a name that endures; men will say of me, 'Gilgamesh has fallen in fight with ferocious Humbaba.' Long after the child has been born in my house, they will say it, and remember." Enkidu spoke again to Gilgamesh, "O my lord, if you will enter that country, go first to the hero Shamash, tell the Sun God, for the land is his. The country where the cedar is cut belongs to Shamash."

Gilgamesh took up a kid, white without spot, and a brown one with it; he held them against his breast, and he carried them into the presence of the sun. He took in his hand his silver sceptre and he said to glorious Shamash, "I am going to that country, O Shamash, I am going; my hands supplicate, so let it be well with my soul and bring me back to the quay of Uruk. Grant, I beseech, your protection, and let the omen be good." Glorious Shamash answered, "Gilgamesh, you are strong, but what is the Country of the Living to you?"

"O Shamash, hear me, hear me, Shamash, let my voice be heard. Here in the city man dies oppressed at heart, man perishes with despair in his heart. I have looked over the wall and I see the bodies floating on the river, and that will be my lot also. Indeed I know it is so, for whoever is tallest among men cannot reach the heavens, and the greatest cannot encompass the earth. Therefore I would enter that country: because I have not established my name stamped on brick as my destiny decreed, I will go to the country where the cedar is cut. I will set up my name where the names of famous men are written; and where no man's name is written I will raise a monument to the gods." The tears ran down his face and he said, "Alas, it is a long journey that I must take to the Land of Humbaba. If this enterprise is not to be accomplished, why did you move me, Shamash, with the restless desire to perform it? How can I succeed if you will not succour me? If I die in that country I will die without rancour, but if I return I will make a glorious offering of gifts and of praise to Shamash."

So Shamash accepted the sacrifice of his tears; like the compassionate man he showed him mercy. He appointed strong allies for Gilgamesh, sons of one mother, and stationed them in the mountain caves. The great winds he appointed: the north wind, the whirlwind, the storm and the icy wind, the tempest and the scorching wind. Like vipers, like dragons, like a scorching fire, like a serpent that freezes the heart, a destroying flood and the lightning's fork, such were they and Gilgamesh rejoiced.

He went to the forge and said, "I will give orders to the armourers; they shall cast us our weapons while we watch them." So they gave orders to the armourers and the craftsmen sat down in conference. They went into the groves of the plain and cut willow and box-wood; they cast for them axes of nine score pounds, and great swords they cast with blades of six score pounds each one, with pommels and hilts of thirty pounds. They cast for Gilgamesh the axe "Might of Heroes" and the bow of Anshan;[7] and Gilgamesh was armed and Enkidu; and the weight of the arms they carried was thirty score pounds.

The people collected and the counsellors in the streets and in the market-place of Uruk; they came through the gate of seven bolts and Gilgamesh spoke to them in the market-place: "I, Gilgamesh, go to see that creature of whom such things are spoken, the rumour of whose name fills the world. I will conquer him in his cedar wood and show the strength of the sons of Uruk, all the world shall know of it. I am committed to this enterprise: to climb the mountain, to cut down the cedar, and leave behind me an enduring name." The counsellors of Uruk, the great market, answered him, "Gilgamesh, you are young, your courage carries you too far, you cannot know what this enterprise means which you plan. We have heard that Humbaba is not like men who die, his weapons are such that none can stand against them; the forest stretches for ten thousand leagues in every direction; who would willingly go down to explore its depths? As for Humbaba, when he roars it is like the torrent of the storm, his breath is like fire and his jaws are death itself. Why do you crave to do this thing, Gilgamesh? It is no equal struggle when one fights with Humbaba, that battering-ram."

When he heard these words of the counsellors Gilgamesh looked at his friend and laughed, "How shall I answer them; shall I say I am afraid of Humbaba, I will sit at home all the rest of my days?" Then Gilgamesh opened his mouth again and said to Enkidu, "My friend, let us go to the Great Palace, to Egalmah,[8] and stand before Ninsun the queen. Ninsun is wise with deep knowledge, she will give us counsel for the road we must go." They took each other by the hand as they went to Egalmah, and they

---

7. A district of Elam in southwest Persia; probably the source of supplies of wood for making bows.
8. Home of the goddess Ninsun.

went to Ninsun the great queen. Gilgamesh approached, he entered the palace and spoke to Ninsun. "Ninsun, will you listen to me; I have a long journey to go, to the Land of Humbaba, I must travel an unknown road and fight a strange battle. From the day I go until I return, till I reach the cedar forest and destroy the evil which Shamash abhors, pray for me to Shamash."

Ninsun went into her room, she put on a dress becoming to her body, she put on jewels to make her breast beautiful, she placed a tiara on her head and her skirts swept the ground. Then she went up to the altar of the Sun, standing upon the roof of the palace; she burnt incense and lifted her arms to Shamash as the smoke ascended: "O Shamash, why did you give this restless heart to Gilgamesh, my son; why did you give it? You have moved him and now he sets out on a long journey to the Land of Humbaba to travel an unknown road and fight a strange battle. Therefore from the day that he goes till the day he returns, until he reaches the cedar forest, until he kills Humbaba and destroys the evil thing which you, Shamash, abhor, do not forget him; but let the dawn, Aya, your dear bride, remind you always, and when day is done give him to the watchman of the night to keep him from harm." Then Ninsun the mother of Gilgamesh extinguished the incense, and she called to Enkidu with this exhortation: "Strong Enkidu, you are not the child of my body, but I will receive you as my adopted son; you are my other child like the foundlings they bring to the temple. Serve Gilgamesh as a foundling serves the temple and the priestess who reared him. In the presence of my women, my votaries and hierophants,[9] I declare it." Then she placed the amulet for a pledge round his neck, and she said to him, "I entrust my son to you; bring him back to me safely."

And now they brought to them the weapons, they put in their hands the great swords in their golden scabbards, and the bow and the quiver. Gilgamesh took the axe, he slung the quiver from his shoulder, and the bow of Anshan, and buckled the sword to his belt; and so they were armed and ready for the journey. Now all the people came and pressed on them and said, "When will you return to the city?" The counsellors blessed Gilgamesh and warned him, "Do not trust too much in your own strength, be watchful, restrain your blows at first. The one who goes in front protects his companion; the good guide who knows the way guards his friend. Let Enkidu lead the way, he knows the road to the forest, he has seen Humbaba and is experienced in battles; let him press first into the passes, let him be watchful and look to himself. Let Enkidu protect his friend, and guard his companion, and bring him safe through the pitfalls of the road. We, the counsellors of Uruk entrust our king to you, O Enkidu; bring him back safely to us." Again to Gilgamesh they said, "May Shamash give you your heart's desire, may he let you see with your eyes the thing accomplished which your lips have spoken; may he open a path for you where it is blocked, and a road for your feet to tread. May he open the mountains for your crossing, and may the nighttime bring you the blessings of night, and Lugulbanda, your guardian god, stand beside you for victory. May you

9. Priests.

have victory in the battle as though you fought with a child. Wash your feet in the river of Humbaba to which you are journeying; in the evening dig a well, and let there always be pure water in your water-skin. Offer cold water to Shamash and do not forget Lugulbanda."

Then Enkidu opened his mouth and said, "Forward, there is nothing to fear. Follow me, for I know the place where Humbaba lives and the paths where he walks. Let the counsellors go back. Here is no cause for fear." When the counsellors heard this they sped the hero on his way. "Go, Gilgamesh, may your guardian god protect you on the road and bring you safely back to the quay of Uruk."

After twenty leagues they broke their fast; after another thirty leagues they stopped for the night. Fifty leagues they walked in one day; in three days they had walked as much as a journey of a month and two weeks. They crossed seven mountains before they came to the gate of the forest. Then Enkidu called out to Gilgamesh, "Do not go down into the forest; when I opened the gate my hand lost its strength." Gilgamesh answered him, "Dear friend, do not speak like a coward. Have we got the better of so many dangers and travelled so far, to turn back at last? You, who are tried in wars and battles, hold close to me now and you will feel no fear of death; keep beside me and your weakness will pass, the trembling will leave your hand. Would my friend rather stay behind? No, we will go down together into the heart of the forest. Let your courage be roused by the battle to come; forget death and follow me, a man resolute in action, but one who is not foolhardy. When two go together each will protect himself and shield his companion, and if they fall they leave an enduring name."

Together they went down into the forest and they came to the green mountain. There they stood still, they were struck dumb; they stood still and gazed at the forest. They saw the height of the cedar, they saw the way into the forest and the track where Humbaba was used to walk. The way was broad and the going was good. They gazed at the mountain of cedars, the dwelling-place of the gods and the throne of Ishtar. The hugeness of the cedar rose in front of the mountain, its shade was beautiful, full of comfort; mountain and glade were green with brushwood.

There Gilgamesh dug a well before the setting sun. He went up the mountain and poured out fine meal on the ground and said, "O mountain, dwelling of the gods, bring me a favourable dream." Then they took each other by the hand and lay down to sleep; and sleep that flows from the night lapped over them. Gilgamesh dreamed, and at midnight sleep left him, and he told his dream to his friend. "Enkidu, what was it that woke me if you did not? My friend, I have dreamed a dream. Get up, look at the mountain precipice. The sleep that the gods sent me is broken. Ah, my friend, what a dream I have had! Terror and confusion; I seized hold of a wild bull in the wilderness. It bellowed and beat up the dust till the whole sky was dark, my arm was seized and my tongue bitten. I fell back on my knee; then someone refreshed me with water from his water-skin."

Enkidu said, "Dear friend, the god to whom we are travelling is no wild bull, though his form is mysterious. That wild bull which you saw is Shamash the Protector; in our moment of peril he will take our hands. The one who gave water from his water-skin, that is your own god who cares for your good name, your Lugulbanda.[1] United with him, together we will accomplish a work the fame of which will never die."

Gilgamesh said, "I dreamed again. We stood in a deep gorge of the mountain, and beside it we two were like the smallest of swamp flies; and suddenly the mountain fell, it struck me and caught my feet from under me. Then came an intolerable light blazing out, and in it was one whose grace and whose beauty were greater than the beauty of this world. He pulled me out from under the mountain, he gave me water to drink and my heart was comforted, and he set my feet on the ground."

Then Enkidu the child of the plains said, "Let us go down from the mountain and talk this thing over together." He said to Gilgamesh the young god, "Your dream is good, your dream is excellent, the mountain which you saw is Humbaba. Now, surely, we will seize and kill him, and throw his body down as the mountain fell on the plain."

The next day after twenty leagues they broke their fast, and after another thirty they stopped for the night. They dug a well before the sun had set and Gilgamesh ascended the mountain. He poured out fine meal on the ground and said, "O mountain, dwelling of the gods, send a dream for Enkidu, make him a favourable dream." The mountain fashioned a dream for Enkidu; it came, an ominous dream; a cold shower passed over him, it caused him to cower like the mountain barley under a storm of rain. But Gilgamesh sat with his chin on his knees till the sleep which flows over all mankind lapped over him. Then, at midnight, sleep left him; he got up and said to his friend, "Did you call me, or why did I wake? Did you touch me, or why am I terrified? Did not some god pass by, for my limbs are numb with fear? My friend, I saw a third dream and this dream was altogether frightful. The heavens roared and the earth roared again, daylight failed and darkness fell, lightning flashed, fire blazed out, the clouds lowered, they rained down death. Then the brightness departed, the fire went out, and all was turned to ashes fallen about us. Let us go down from the mountain and talk this over, and consider what we should do."

When they had come down from the mountain Gilgamesh seized the axe in his hand: he felled the cedar. When Humbaba heard the noise far off he was enraged; he cried out, "Who is this that has violated my woods and cut down my cedar?" But glorious Shamash called to them out of heaven, "Go forward, do not be afraid." But now Gilgamesh was overcome by weakness, for sleep had seized him suddenly, a profound sleep held him; he lay on the ground, stretched out speechless, as though in a dream. When Enkidu touched him he did not rise, when he spoke to him he did not reply. "O Gilgamesh, Lord of the plain of Kullab,[2] the world grows dark, the shadows have spread over it, now is the glimmer of dusk. Shamash has departed, his bright head is quenched in the bosom of his mother Ningal. O Gilgamesh, how long will you lie like this, asleep? Never let the mother who gave you birth be forced in mourning into the city square."

1. Hero of a cycle of Sumerian poems; protector of Gilgamesh.   2. In Uruk.

At length Gilgamesh heard him; he put on his breastplate, "The Voice of Heroes," of thirty shekels' weight; he put it on as though it had been a light garment that he carried, and it covered him altogether. He straddled the earth like a bull that snuffs the ground and his teeth were clenched. "By the life of my mother Ninsun who gave me birth, and by the life of my father, divine Lugulbanda, let me live to be the wonder of my mother, as when she nursed me on her lap." A second time he said to him, "By the life of Ninsun my mother who gave me birth, and by the life of my father, divine Lugulbanda, until we have fought this man, if man he is, this god, if god he is, the way that I took to the Country of the Living will not turn back to the city."

Then Enkidu, the faithful companion, pleaded, answering him, "O my lord, you do not know this monster and that is the reason you are not afraid. I who know him, I am terrified. His teeth are dragon's fangs, his countenance is like a lion, his charge is the rushing of the flood, with his look he crushes alike the trees of the forest and reeds in the swamp. O my Lord, you may go on if you choose into this land, but I will go back to the city. I will tell the lady your mother all your glorious deeds till she shouts for joy: and then I will tell the death that followed till she weeps for bitterness." But Gilgamesh said, "Immolation and sacrifice are not yet for me, the boat of the dead shall not go down, nor the three-ply cloth be cut for my shrouding. Not yet will my people be desolate, nor the pyre be lit in my house and my dwelling burnt on the fire. Today, give me your aid and you shall have mine: what then can go amiss with us two? All living creatures born of the flesh shall sit at last in the boat of the West, and when it sinks, when the boat of Magilum[3] sinks, they are gone; but we shall go forward and fix our eyes on this monster. If your heart is fearful throw away fear; if there is terror in it throw away terror. Take your axe in your hand and attack. He who leaves the fight unfinished is not at peace."

Humbaba came out from his strong house of cedar. Then Enkidu called out, "O Gilgamesh, remember now your boasts in Uruk. Forward, attack, son of Uruk, there is nothing to fear." When he heard these words his courage rallied; he answered, "Make haste, close in, if the watchman is there do not let him escape to the woods where he will vanish. He has put on the first of his seven splendours[4] but not yet the other six, let us trap him before he is armed." Like a raging wild bull he snuffed the ground; the watchman of the woods turned full of threatenings, he cried out. Humbaba came from his strong house of cedar. He nodded his head and shook it, menacing Gilgamesh; and on him he fastened his eye, the eye of death. Then Gilgamesh called to Shamash and his tears were flowing, "O glorious Shamash, I have followed the road you commanded but now if you send no succour how shall I escape?" Glorious Shamash heard his prayer and he summoned the great wind, the north wind, the whirlwind, the storm and the icy wind, the tempest and the scorching wind; they came like dragons, like a scorching fire, like a serpent that freezes the heart, a destroying flood and the lightning's fork. The eight winds rose up against Humbaba, they beat against his eyes; he was gripped, unable to go

3. Unclear; perhaps the boat of the dead.   4. Unclear; perhaps warlike attributes.

forward or back. Gilgamesh shouted, "By the life of Ninsun my mother and divine Lugulbanda my father, in the Country of the Living, in this Land I have discovered your dwelling; my weak arms and my small weapons I have brought to this Land against you, and now I will enter your house."

So he felled the first cedar and they cut the branches and laid them at the foot of the mountain. At the first stroke Humbaba blazed out, but still they advanced. They felled seven cedars and cut and bound the branches and laid them at the foot of the mountain, and seven times Humbaba loosed his glory on them. As the seventh blaze died out they reached his lair. He slapped his thigh in scorn. He approached like a noble wild bull roped on the mountain, a warrior whose elbows are bound together. The tears started to his eyes and he was pale, "Gilgamesh, let me speak. I have never known a mother, no, nor a father who reared me. I was born of the mountain, he reared me, and Enlil made me the keeper of this forest. Let me go free, Gilgamesh, and I will be your servant, you shall be my lord; all the trees of the forest that I tended on the mountain shall be yours. I will cut them down and build you a palace." He took him by the hand and led him to his house, so that the heart of Gilgamesh was moved with compassion. He swore by the heavenly life, by the earthly life, by the underworld itself: "O Enkidu, should not the snared bird return to its nest and the captive man return to his mother's arms?" Enkidu answered, "The strongest of men will fall to fate if he has no judgement. Namtar, the evil fate that knows no distinction between men, will devour him. If the snared bird returns to its nest, if the captive man returns to his mother's arms, then you my friend will never return to the city where the mother is waiting who gave you birth. He will bar the mountain road against you, and make the pathways impassable."

Humbaba said, "Enkidu, what you have spoken is evil: you, a hireling, dependent for your bread! In envy and for fear of a rival you have spoken evil words." Enkidu said, "Do not listen, Gilgamesh: this Humbaba must die. Kill Humbaba first and his servants after." But Gilgamesh said, "If we touch him the blaze and the glory of light will be put out in confusion, the glory and glamour will vanish, its rays will be quenched." Enkidu said to Gilgamesh, "Not so, my friend. First entrap the bird, and where shall the chicks run then? Afterwards we can search out the glory and the glamour, when the chicks run distracted through the grass."

Gilgamesh listened to the word of his companion, he took the axe in his hand, he drew the sword from his belt, and he struck Humbaba with a thrust of the sword to the neck, and Enkidu his comrade struck the second blow. At the third blow Humbaba fell. Then there followed confusion for this was the guardian of the forest whom they had felled to the ground. For as far as two leagues the cedars shivered when Enkidu felled the watcher of the forest, he at whose voice Hermon and Lebanon[5] used to tremble. Now the mountains were moved and all the hills, for the guardian of the forest was killed. They attacked the cedars, the seven splendours of Humbaba were extinguished. So they pressed on into the forest

5. Mountains in Lebanon.

bearing the sword of eight talents. They uncovered the sacred dwellings of the Anunnaki[6] and while Gilgamesh felled the first of the trees of the forest Enkidu cleared their roots as far as the banks of Euphrates. They set Humbaba before the gods, before Enlil; they kissed the ground and dropped the shroud and set the head before him. When he saw the head of Humbaba, Enlil raged at them. "Why did you do this thing? From henceforth may the fire be on your faces, may it eat the bread that you eat, may it drink where you drink." Then Enlil took again the blaze and the seven splendours that had been Humbaba's: he gave the first to the river, and he gave to the lion, to the stone of execration, to the mountain and to the dreaded daughter of the Queen of Hell.

O Gilgamesh, king and conqueror of the dreadful blaze; wild bull who plunders the mountain, who crosses the sea, glory to him, and from the brave the greater glory is Enki's![7]

3

Ishtar and Gilgamesh, and the Death of Enkidu

Gilgamesh washed out his long locks and cleaned his weapons; he flung back his hair from his shoulders; he threw off his stained clothes and changed them for new. He put on his royal robes and made them fast. When Gilgamesh had put on the crown, glorious Ishtar lifted her eyes, seeing the beauty of Gilgamesh. She said, "Come to me Gilgamesh, and be my bridegroom; grant me seed of your body, let me be your bride and you shall be my husband. I will harness for you a chariot of lapis lazuli and of gold, with wheels of gold and horns of copper; and you shall have mighty demons of the storm for draft-mules. When you enter our house in the fragrance of cedar-wood, threshold and throne will kiss your feet. Kings, rulers, and princes will bow down before you; they shall bring you tribute from the mountains and the plain. Your ewes shall drop twins and your goats triplets; your pack-ass shall outrun mules; your oxen shall have no rivals, and your chariot horses shall be famous far-off for their swiftness."

Gilgamesh opened his mouth and answered glorious Ishtar, "If I take you in marriage, what gifts can I give in return? What ointments and clothing for your body? I would gladly give you bread and all sorts of food fit for a god. I would give you wine to drink fit for a queen. I would pour out barley to stuff your granary; but as for making you my wife—that I will not. How would it go with me? Your lovers have found you like a brazier which smoulders in the cold, a backdoor which keeps out neither squall of wind nor storm, a castle which crushes the garrison, pitch that blackens the bearer, a water-skin that chafes the carrier, a stone which falls from the parapet, a battering-ram turned back from the enemy, a sandal that trips the wearer. Which of your lovers did you ever love for ever? What shepherd of yours has pleased you for all time? Listen to me while I tell the tale of your lovers. There was Tammuz,[8] the lover of your youth, for

---

6. Gods of the underworld, judges of the dead, and offspring of Anu.   7. Or Ea, god of the sweet waters and wisdom, a patron of arts, and one of the creators of humankind, toward whom he is usually well disposed.   8. The dying god of vegetation.

him you decreed wailing, year after year. You loved the many-coloured roller, but still you struck and broke his wing; now in the grove he sits and cries, "kappi, kappi, my wing, my wing." You have loved the lion tremendous in strength: seven pits you dug for him, and seven. You have loved the stallion magnificent in battle, and for him you decreed whip and spur and a thong, to gallop seven leagues by force and to muddy the water before he drinks; and for his mother Sinli[9] lamentations. You have loved the shepherd of the flock; he made meal-cake for you day after day, he killed kids for your sake. You struck and turned him into a wolf; now his own herd-boys chase him away, his own hounds worry his flanks. And did you not love Ishullanu, the gardener of your father's palm-grove? He brought you baskets filled with dates without end; every day he loaded your table. Then you turned your eyes on him and said, 'Dearest Ishullanu, come here to me, let us enjoy your manhood, come forward and take me, I am yours.' Ishullanu answered, 'What are you asking from me? My mother has baked and I have eaten; why should I come to such as you for food that is tainted and rotten? For when was a screen of rushes sufficient protection from frosts?' But when you had heard his answer you struck him. He was changed to a blind mole deep in the earth, one whose desire is always beyond his reach. And if you and I should be lovers, should not I be served in the same fashion as all these others whom you loved once?"

When Ishtar heard this she fell into a bitter rage, she went up to high heaven. Her tears poured down in front of her father Anu, and Antum her mother. She said, "My father, Gilgamesh has heaped insults on me, he has told over all my abominable behaviour, my foul and hideous acts." Anu opened his mouth and said, "Are you a father of gods? Did not you quarrel with Gilgamesh the king, so now he has related your abominable behaviour, your foul and hideous acts?"

Ishtar opened her mouth and said again, "My father, give me the Bull of Heaven to destroy Gilgamesh. Fill Gilgamesh, I say, with arrogance to his destruction; but if you refuse to give me the Bull of Heaven I will break in the doors of hell and smash the bolts; there will be confusion of people, those above with those from the lower depths. I shall bring up the dead to eat food like the living; and the hosts of dead will outnumber the living." Anu said to great Ishtar, "If I do what you desire there will be seven years of drought throughout Uruk when corn will be seedless husks. Have you saved grain enough for the people and grass for the cattle?" Ishtar replied, "I have saved grain for the people, grass for the cattle; for seven years of seedless husks there is grain and there is grass enough."

When Anu heard what Ishtar had said he gave her the Bull of Heaven to lead by the halter down to Uruk. When they reached the gates of Uruk the Bull went to the river; with his first snort cracks opened in the earth and a hundred young men fell down to death. With his second snort cracks opened and two hundred fell down to death. With his third snort cracks opened, Enkidu doubled over but instantly recovered, he dodged aside and leapt on the Bull and seized it by the horns. The Bull of Heaven

9. Perhaps a divine horse.

foamed in his face, it brushed him with the thick of its tail. Enkidu cried
to Gilgamesh, "My friend, we boasted that we would leave enduring
names behind us. Now thrust in your sword between the nape and the
horns." So Gilgamesh followed the Bull, he seized the thick of its tail, he
thrust the sword between the nape and the horns and slew the Bull. When
they had killed the Bull of Heaven they cut out its heart and gave it to
Shamash, and the brothers rested.

But Ishtar rose up and mounted the great wall of Uruk; she sprang on
to the tower and uttered a curse: "Woe to Gilgamesh, for he has scorned
me in killing the Bull of Heaven." When Enkidu heard these words he
tore out the Bull's right thigh and tossed it in her face saying, "If I could
lay my hands on you, it is this I should do to you, and lash the entrails to
your side." Then Ishtar called together her people, the dancing and singing girls, the prostitutes of the temple, the courtesans. Over the thigh of
the Bull of Heaven she set up lamentation.

But Gilgamesh called the smiths and the armourers, all of them
together. They admired the immensity of the horns. They were plated
with lapis lazuli two fingers thick. They were thirty pounds each in weight,
and their capacity in oil was six measures, which he gave to his guardian
god, Lugulbanda. But he carried the horns into the palace and hung them
on the wall. Then they washed their hands in Euphrates, they embraced
each other and went away. They drove through the streets of Uruk where
the heroes were gathered to see them, and Gilgamesh called to the singing
girls, "Who is most glorious of the heroes, who is most eminent among
men?" "Gilgamesh is the most glorious of heroes, Gilgamesh is most eminent among men." And now there was feasting, and celebrations and joy
in the palace, till the heroes lay down saying, "Now we will rest for the
night."

When the daylight came Enkidu got up and cried to Gilgamesh, "O
my brother, such a dream I had last night. Anu, Enlil, Ea and heavenly
Shamash took counsel together, and Anu said to Enlil, 'Because they have
killed the Bull of Heaven, and because they have killed Humbaba who
guarded the Cedar Mountain one of the two must die.' Then glorious
Shamash answered the hero Enlil, 'It was by your command they killed
the Bull of Heaven, and killed Humbaba, and must Enkidu die although
innocent?' Enlil flung round in rage at glorious Shamash, 'You dare to say
this, you who went about with them every day like one of themselves!' "

So Enkidu lay stretched out before Gilgamesh; his tears ran down in
streams and he said to Gilgamesh, "O my brother, so dear as you are to
me, brother, yet they will take me from you." Again he said, "I must sit
down on the threshold of the dead and never again will I see my dear
brother with my eyes."

While Enkidu lay alone in his sickness he cursed the gate as though it
was living flesh, "You there, wood of the gate, dull and insensible, witless,
I searched for you over twenty leagues until I saw the towering cedar.
There is no wood like you in our land. Seventy-two cubits high and
twenty-four wide, the pivot and the ferrule and the jambs are perfect. A
master craftsman from Nippur has made you; but O, if I had known the
conclusion! If I had known that this was all the good that would come of

it, I would have raised the axe and split you into little pieces and set up here a gate of wattle instead. Ah, if only some future king had brought you here, or some god had fashioned you. Let him obliterate my name and write his own, and the curse fall on him instead of on Enkidu."

With the first brightening of dawn Enkidu raised his head and wept before the Sun God, in the brilliance of the sunlight his tears streamed down. "Sun God, I beseech you, about that vile Trapper, that Trapper of nothing because of whom I was to catch less than my comrade; let him catch least, make his game scarce, make him feeble, taking the smaller of every share, let his quarry escape from his nets."

When he had cursed the Trapper to his heart's content he turned on the harlot. He was roused to curse her also. "As for you, woman, with a great curse I curse you! I will promise you a destiny to all eternity. My curse shall come on you soon and sudden. You shall be without a roof for your commerce, for you shall not keep house with other girls in the tavern, but do your business in places fouled by the vomit of the drunkard. Your hire will be potter's earth, your thievings will be flung into the hovel, you will sit at the cross-roads in the dust of the potter's quarter, you will make your bed on the dunghill at night, and by day take your stand in the wall's shadow. Brambles and thorns will tear your feet, the drunk and the dry will strike your cheek and your mouth will ache. Let you be stripped of your purple dyes, for I too once in the wilderness with my wife had all the treasure I wished."

When Shamash heard the words of Enkidu he called to him from heaven: "Enkidu, why are you cursing the woman, the mistress who taught you to eat bread fit for gods and drink wine of kings? She who put upon you a magnificent garment, did she not give you glorious Gilgamesh for your companion, and has not Gilgamesh, your own brother, made you rest on a royal bed and recline on a couch at his left hand? He has made the princes of the earth kiss your feet, and now all the people of Uruk lament and wail over you. When you are dead he will let his hair grow long for your sake, he will wear a lion's pelt and wander through the desert."

When Enkidu heard glorious Shamash his angry heart grew quiet, he called back the curse and said, "Woman, I promise you another destiny. The mouth which cursed you shall bless you! Kings, princes and nobles shall adore you. On your account a man though twelve miles off will clap his hand to his thigh and his hair will twitch. For you he will undo his belt and open his treasure and you shall have your desire; lapis lazuli, gold and carnelian from the heap in the treasury. A ring for your hand and a robe shall be yours. The priest will lead you into the presence of the gods. On your account a wife, a mother of seven, was forsaken."

As Enkidu slept alone in his sickness, in bitterness of spirit he poured out his heart to his friend. "It was I who cut down the cedar, I who levelled the forest, I who slew Humbaba and now see what has become of me. Listen, my friend, this is the dream I dreamed last night. The heavens roared, and earth rumbled back an answer; between them stood I before an awful being, the sombre-faced man-bird; he had directed on me his purpose. His was a vampire face, his foot was a lion's foot, his hand was an eagle's talon. He fell on me and his claws were in my hair, he held me fast and I smothered; then he transformed me so that my arms became wings covered with feathers. He turned his stare towards me, and he led me away to the palace of Irkalla, the Queen of Darkness,[1] to the house from which none who enters ever returns, down the road from which there is no coming back.

"There is the house whose people sit in darkness; dust is their food and clay their meat. They are clothed like birds with wings for covering, they see no light, they sit in darkness. I entered the house of dust and I saw the kings of the earth, their crowns put away for ever; rulers and princes, all those who once wore kingly crowns and ruled the world in the days of old. They who had stood in the place of the gods like Anu and Enlil, stood now like servants to fetch baked meats in the house of dust, to carry cooked meat and cold water from the water-skin. In the house of dust which I entered were high priests and acolytes, priests of the incantation and of ecstasy; there were servers of the temple, and there was Etana, that king of Kish whom the eagle carried to heaven in the days of old. I saw also Samuqan, god of cattle, and there was Ereshkigal the Queen of the Underworld; and Belit-Sheri squatted in front of her, she who is recorder of the gods and keeps the book of death. She held a tablet from which she read. She raised her head, she saw me and spoke: 'Who has brought this one here?' Then I awoke like a man drained of blood who wanders alone in a waste of rushes; like one whom the bailiff has seized and his heart pounds with terror."

Gilgamesh had peeled off his clothes, he listened to his words and wept quick tears, Gilgamesh listened and his tears flowed. He opened his mouth and spoke to Enkidu: "Who is there in strong-walled Uruk who has wisdom like this? Strange things have been spoken, why does your heart speak strangely? The dream was marvellous but the terror was great; we must treasure the dream whatever the terror; for the dream has shown that misery comes at last to the healthy man, the end of life is sorrow." And Gilgamesh lamented, "Now I will pray to the great gods, for my friend had an ominous dream."

This day on which Enkidu dreamed came to an end and he lay stricken with sickness. One whole day he lay on his bed and his suffering increased. He said to Gilgamesh, the friend on whose account he had left the wilderness, "Once I ran for you, for the water of life, and I now have nothing." A second day he lay on his bed and Gilgamesh watched over him but the sickness increased. A third day he lay on his bed, he called out to Gilgamesh, rousing him up. Now he was weak and his eyes were blind with weeping. Ten days he lay and his suffering increased, eleven and twelve days he lay on his bed of pain. Then he called to Gilgamesh, "My friend, the great goddess cursed me and I must die in shame. I shall not die like a man fallen in battle; I feared to fall, but happy is the man who falls in the battle, for I must die in shame." And Gilgamesh wept over Enkidu. With the first light of dawn he raised his voice and said to the counsellors of Uruk:

---

1. Also Ereshkigal, queen of the underworld.

Hear me, great ones of Uruk,
I weep for Enkidu, my friend,
Bitterly moaning like a woman mourning
I weep for my brother.
O Enkidu, my brother, 5
You were the axe at my side,
My hand's strength, the sword in my belt,
The shield before me,
A glorious robe, my fairest ornament;
An evil Fate has robbed me. 10
The wild ass and the gazelle
That were father and mother,
All long-tailed creatures that nourished you
Weep for you,
All the wild things of the plain and pastures; 15
The paths that you loved in the forest of cedars
Night and day murmur.
Let the great ones of strong-walled Uruk
Weep for you;
Let the finger of blessing 20
Be stretched out in mourning;
Enkidu, young brother. Hark,
There is an echo through all the country
Like a mother mourning.
Weep all the paths where we walked together; 25
And the beasts we hunted, the bear and hyena,
Tiger and panther, leopard and lion,
The stag and the ibex, the bull and the doe.
The river along whose banks we used to walk,
Weeps for you, 30
Ula of Elam and dear Euphrates
Where once we drew water for the water-skins.
The mountain we climbed where we slew the Watchman,
Weeps for you.
The warriors of strong-walled Uruk 35
Where the Bull of Heaven was killed,
Weep for you.
All the people of Eridu
Weep for you Enkidu.
Those who brought grain for your eating 40
Mourn for you now;
Who rubbed oil on your back
Mourn for you now;
Who poured beer for your drinking
Mourn for you now. 45
The harlot who anointed you with fragrant ointment
Laments for you now;
The women of the palace, who brought you a wife,
A chosen ring of good advice,
Lament for you now. 50
And the young men your brothers
As though they were women

Go long-haired in mourning.
What is this sleep which holds you now?
You are lost in the dark and cannot hear me.   55

He touched his heart but it did not beat, nor did he lift his eyes again. When Gilgamesh touched his heart it did not beat. So Gilgamesh laid a veil, as one veils the bride, over his friend. He began to rage like a lion, like a lioness robbed of her whelps. This way and that he paced round the bed, he tore out his hair and strewed it around. He dragged off his splendid robes and flung them down as though they were abominations.

In the first light of dawn Gilgamesh cried out, "I made you rest on a royal bed, you reclined on a couch at my left hand, the princes of the earth kissed your feet. I will cause all the people of Uruk to weep over you and raise the dirge of the dead. The joyful people will stoop with sorrow; and when you have gone to the earth I will let my hair grow long for your sake, I will wander through the wilderness in the skin of a lion." The next day also, in the first light, Gilgamesh lamented; seven days and seven nights he wept for Enkidu, until the worm fastened on him. Only then he gave him up to the earth, for the Anunnaki, the judges, had seized him.

Then Gilgamesh issued a proclamation through the land, he summoned them all, the coppersmiths, the goldsmiths, the stone-workers, and commanded them, "Make a statue of my friend." The statue was fashioned with a great weight of lapis lazuli for the breast and of gold for the body. A table of hard-wood was set out, and on it a bowl of carnelian filled with honey, and a bowl of lapis lazuli filled with butter. These he exposed and offered to the Sun; and weeping he went away.

4

The Search for Everlasting Life

Bitterly Gilgamesh wept for his friend Enkidu; he wandered over the wilderness as a hunter, he roamed over the plains; in his bitterness he cried, "How can I rest, how can I be at peace? Despair is in my heart. What my brother is now, that shall I be when I am dead. Because I am afraid of death I will go as best I can to find Utnapishtim[2] whom they call the Faraway, for he has entered the assembly of the gods." So Gilgamesh travelled over the wilderness, he wandered over the grasslands, a long journey, in search of Utnapishtim, whom the gods took after the deluge; and they set him to live in the land of Dilmun, in the garden of the sun; and to him alone of men they gave everlasting life.

At night when he came to the mountain passes Gilgamesh prayed: "In these mountain passes long ago I saw lions, I was afraid and I lifted my eyes to the moon; I prayed and my prayers went up to the gods, so now, O moon god Sin, protect me." When he had prayed he lay down to sleep, until he was woken from out of a dream. He saw the lions round him glorying in life; then he took his axe in his hand, he drew his sword from

2. A wise king and priest who, like the biblical Noah, survived the Flood along with his family and with "the seed of all living creatures." Afterward he was taken by the gods to live forever in Dilmun, the Sumerian paradise.

his belt, and he fell upon them like an arrow from the string, and struck and destroyed and scattered them.

So at length Gilgamesh came to Mashu, the great mountains about which he had heard many things, which guard the rising and the setting sun. Its twin peaks are as high as the wall of heaven and its paps reach down to the underworld. At its gate the Scorpions stand guard, half man and half dragon; their glory is terrifying, their stare strikes death into men, their shimmering halo sweeps the mountains that guard the rising sun. When Gilgamesh saw them he shielded his eyes for the length of a moment only; then he took courage and approached. When they saw him so undismayed the Man-Scorpion called to his mate, "This one who comes to us now is flesh of the gods." The mate of the Man-Scorpion answered, "Two thirds is god but one third is man."

Then he called to the man Gilgamesh, he called to the child of the gods: "Why have you come so great a journey; for what have you travelled so far, crossing the dangerous waters; tell me the reason for your coming?" Gilgamesh answered, "For Enkidu; I loved him dearly, together we endured all kinds of hardships; on his account I have come, for the common lot of man has taken him. I have wept for him day and night, I would not give up his body for burial, I thought my friend would come back because of my weeping. Since he went, my life is nothing; that is why I have travelled here in search of Utnapishtim my father; for men say he has entered the assembly of the gods, and has found everlasting life. I have a desire to question him concerning the living and the dead." The Man-Scorpion opened his mouth and said, speaking to Gilgamesh, "No man born of woman has done what you have asked, no mortal man has gone into the mountain; the length of it is twelve leagues of darkness; in it there is no light, but the heart is oppressed with darkness. From the rising of the sun to the setting of the sun there is no light." Gilgamesh said, "Although I should go in sorrow and in pain, with sighing and with weeping, still I must go. Open the gate of the mountain." And the Man-Scorpion said, "Go, Gilgamesh, I permit you to pass through the mountain of Mashu and through the high ranges; may your feet carry you safely home. The gate of the mountain is open."

When Gilgamesh heard this he did as the Man-Scorpion had said, he followed the sun's road to his rising, through the mountain. When he had gone one league the darkness became thick around him, for there was no light, he could see nothing ahead and nothing behind him. After two leagues the darkness was thick and there was no light, he could see nothing ahead and nothing behind him. After three leagues the darkness was thick, and there was no light, he could see nothing ahead and nothing behind him. After four leagues the darkness was thick and there was no light, he could see nothing ahead and nothing behind him. At the end of five leagues the darkness was thick and there was no light, he could see nothing ahead and nothing behind him. At the end of six leagues the darkness was thick and there was no light, he could see nothing ahead and nothing behind him. When he had gone seven leagues the darkness was thick and there was no light, he could see nothing ahead and nothing behind him. When he had gone eight leagues Gilgamesh gave a great cry, for the darkness was thick and he could see nothing ahead and nothing behind him. After nine leagues he felt the north wind on his face, but the darkness was thick and there was no light, he could see nothing ahead and nothing behind him. After ten leagues the end was near. After eleven leagues the dawn light appeared. At the end of twelve leagues the sun streamed out.

There was the garden of the gods; all round him stood bushes bearing gems. Seeing it he went down at once, for there was fruit of carnelian with the vine hanging from it, beautiful to look at; lapis lazuli leaves hung thick with fruit, sweet to see. For thorns and thistles there were haematite and rare stones, agate, and pearls from out of the sea. While Gilgamesh walked in the garden by the edge of the sea Shamash saw him, and he saw that he was dressed in the skins of animals and ate their flesh. He was distressed, and he spoke and said, "No mortal man has gone this way before, nor will, as long as the winds drive over the sea." And to Gilgamesh he said, "You will never find the life for which you are searching." Gilgamesh said to glorious Shamash, "Now that I have toiled and strayed so far over the wilderness, am I to sleep, and let the earth cover my head for ever? Let my eyes see the sun until they are dazzled with looking. Although I am no better than a dead man, still let me see the light of the sun."

Beside the sea she lives, the woman of the vine, the maker of wine; Siduri sits in the garden at the edge of the sea, with the golden bowl and the golden vats that the gods gave her. She is covered with a veil; and where she sits she sees Gilgamesh coming towards her, wearing skins, the flesh of the gods in his body, but despair in his heart, and his face like the face of one who has made a long journey. She looked, and as she scanned the distance she said in her own heart, "Surely this is some felon; where is he going now?" And she barred her gate against him with the cross-bar and shot home the bolt. But Gilgamesh, hearing the sound of the bolt, threw up his head and lodged his foot in the gate; he called to her, "Young woman, maker of wine, why do you bolt your door; what did you see that made you bar your gate? I will break in your door and burst in your gate, for I am Gilgamesh who seized and killed the Bull of Heaven, I killed the watchman of the cedar forest, I overthrew Humbaba who lived in the forest, and I killed the lions in the passes of the mountain."

Then Siduri said to him, "If you are that Gilgamesh who seized and killed the Bull of Heaven, who killed the watchman of the cedar forest, who overthrew Humbaba that lived in the forest, and killed the lions in the passes of the mountain, why are your cheeks so starved and why is your face so drawn? Why is despair in your heart and your face like the face of one who has made a long journey? Yes, why is your face burned from heat and cold, and why do you come here wandering over the pastures in search of the wind?"

Gilgamesh answered her, "And why should not my cheeks be starved and my face drawn? Despair is in my heart and my face is the face of one who has made a long journey, it was burned with heat and with cold. Why should I not wander over the pastures in search of the wind? My friend, my younger brother, he who hunted the wild ass of the wilderness and the panther of the plains, my friend, my younger brother who seized and killed the Bull of Heaven and overthrew Humbaba in the cedar forest, my friend who was very dear to me and who endured dangers beside me, Enkidu my brother, whom I loved, the end of mortality has overtaken him. I wept for him seven days and nights till the worm fastened on him. Because of my brother I am afraid of death, because of my brother I stray through the wilderness and cannot rest. But now, young woman, maker of wine, since I have seen your face do not let me see the face of death which I dread so much."

She answered, "Gilgamesh, where are you hurrying to? You will never find that life for which you are looking. When the gods created man they allotted to him death, but life they retained in their own keeping. As for you, Gilgamesh, fill your belly with good things; day and night, night and day, dance and be merry, feast and rejoice. Let your clothes be fresh, bathe yourself in water, cherish the little child that holds your hand, and make your wife happy in your embrace; for this too is the lot of man."

But Gilgamesh said to Siduri, the young woman, "How can I be silent, how can I rest, when Enkidu whom I love is dust, and I too shall die and be laid in the earth. You live by the sea-shore and look into the heart of it; young woman, tell me now, which is the way to Utnapishtim, the son of Ubara-Tutu? What directions are there for the passage; give me, oh, give me directions. I will cross the Ocean if it is possible; if it is not I will wander still farther in the wilderness." The wine-maker said to him, "Gilgamesh, there is no crossing the Ocean; whoever has come, since the days of old, has not been able to pass that sea. The Sun in his glory crosses the Ocean, but who beside Shamash has ever crossed it? The place and the passage are difficult, and the waters of death are deep which flow between. Gilgamesh, how will you cross the Ocean? When you come to the waters of death what will you do? But Gilgamesh, down in the woods you will find Urshanabi, the ferryman of Utnapishtim; with him are the holy things, the things of stone. He is fashioning the serpent prow of the boat. Look at him well, and if it is possible, perhaps you will cross the waters with him; but if it is not possible, then you must go back."

When Gilgamesh heard this he was seized with anger. He took his axe in his hand, and his dagger from his belt. He crept forward and he fell on them like a javelin. Then he went into the forest and sat down. Urshanabi saw the dagger flash and heard the axe, and he beat his head, for Gilgamesh had shattered the tackle of the boat in his rage. Urshanabi said to him, "Tell me, what is your name? I am Urshanabi, the ferryman of Utnapishtim the Faraway." He replied to him, "Gilgamesh is my name, I am from Uruk, from the house of Anu." Then Urshanabi said to him, "Why are your cheeks so starved and your face drawn? Why is despair in your heart and your face like the face of one who has made a long journey; yes, why is your face burned with heat and with cold, and why do you come here wandering over the pastures in search of the wind?"

Gilgamesh said to him, "Why should not my cheeks be starved and my face drawn? Despair is in my heart, and my face is the face of one who has made a long journey. I was burned with heat and with cold. Why should I not wander over the pastures? My friend, my younger brother who seized and killed the Bull of Heaven, and overthrew Humbaba in the cedar forest, my friend who was very dear to me, and who endured dangers beside me, Enkidu my brother whom I loved, the end of mortality has overtaken him. I wept for him seven days and nights till the worm fastened on him. Because of my brother I am afraid of death, because of my brother I stray through the wilderness. His fate lies heavy upon him. How can I be silent, how can I rest? He is dust and I too shall die and be laid in the earth for ever. I am afraid of death, therefore, Urshanabi, tell me which is the road to Utnapishtim? If it is possible I will cross the waters of death; if not I will wander still farther through the wilderness."

Urshanabi said to him, "Gilgamesh, your own hands have prevented you from crossing the Ocean; when you destroyed the tackle of the boat you destroyed its safety." Then the two of them talked it over and Gilgamesh said, "Why are you so angry with me, Urshanabi, for you yourself cross the sea by day and night, at all seasons you cross it." "Gilgamesh, those things you destroyed, their property is to carry me over the water, to prevent the waters of death from touching me. It was for this reason that I preserved them, but you have destroyed them, and the *urnu* snakes with them. But now, go into the forest, Gilgamesh; with your axe cut poles, one hundred and twenty, cut them sixty cubits long, paint them with bitumen, set on them ferrules and bring them back."

When Gilgamesh heard this he went into the forest, he cut poles one hundred and twenty; he cut them sixty cubits long, he painted them with bitumen, he set on them ferrules, and he brought them to Urshanabi. Then they boarded the boat, Gilgamesh and Urshanabi together, launching it out on the waves of Ocean. For three days they ran on as it were a journey of a month and fifteen days, and at last Urshanabi brought the boat to the waters of death. Then Urshanabi said to Gilgamesh, "Press on, take a pole and thrust it in, but do not let your hands touch the waters. Gilgamesh, take a second pole, take a third, take a fourth pole. Now, Gilgamesh, take a fifth, take a sixth and seventh pole. Gilgamesh, take an eighth, and ninth, a tenth pole. Gilgamesh, take an eleventh, take a twelfth pole." After one hundred and twenty thrusts Gilgamesh had used the last pole. Then he stripped himself, he held up his arms for a mast and his covering for a sail. So Urshanabi the ferryman brought Gilgamesh to Utnapishtim, whom they call the Faraway, who lives in Dilmun at the place of the sun's transit, eastward of the mountain. To him alone of men the gods had given everlasting life.

Now Utnapishtim, where he lay at ease, looked into the distance and he said in his heart, musing to himself, "Why does the boat sail here without tackle and mast; why are the sacred stones destroyed, and why does the master not sail the boat? That man who comes is none of mine; where I look I see a man whose body is covered with skins of beasts. Who is this who walks up the shore behind Urshanabi, for surely he is no man of mine?" So Utnapishtim looked at him and said, "What is your name, you who come here wearing the skins of beasts, with your cheeks starved and your face drawn? Where are you hurrying to now? For what reason have you made this great journey, crossing the seas whose passage is difficult? Tell me the reason for your coming."

He replied, "Gilgamesh is my name. I am from Uruk, from the house of Anu." Then Utnapishtim said to him, "If you are Gilgamesh, why are your cheeks so starved and your face drawn? Why is despair in your heart and your face like the face of one who has made a long journey? Yes, why is your face burned with heat and cold; and why do you come here, wandering over the wilderness in search of the wind?"

Gilgamesh said to him, "Why should not my cheeks be starved and my face drawn? Despair is in my heart and my face is the face of one who has made a long journey. It was burned with heat and with cold. Why should I not wander over the pastures? My friend, my younger brother who seized and killed the Bull of Heaven and overthrew Humbaba in the cedar forest, my friend who was very dear to me and endured dangers beside me, Enkidu, my brother whom I loved, the end of mortality has overtaken him. I wept for him seven days and nights till the worm fastened on him. Because of my brother I am afraid of death; because of my brother I stray through the wilderness. His fate lies heavy upon me. How can I be silent, how can I rest? He is dust and I shall die also and be laid in the earth for ever." Again Gilgamesh said, speaking to Utnapishtim, "It is to see Utnapishtim whom we call the Faraway that I have come this journey. For this I have wandered over the world, I have crossed many difficult ranges, I have crossed the seas, I have wearied myself with travelling; my joints are aching, and I have lost acquaintance with sleep which is sweet. My clothes were worn out before I came to the house of Siduri. I have killed the bear and hyena, the lion and panther, the tiger, the stag and the ibex, all sorts of wild game and the small creatures of the pastures. I ate their flesh and I wore their skins; and that was how I came to the gate of the young woman, the maker of wine, who barred her gate of pitch and bitumen against me. But from her I had news of the journey; so then I came to Urshanabi the ferryman, and with him I crossed over the waters of death. O, father Utnapishtim, you who have entered the assembly of the gods, I wish to question you concerning the living and the dead, how shall I find the life for which I am searching?"

Utnapishtim said, "There is no permanence. Do we build a house to stand for ever, do we seal a contract to hold for all time? Do brothers divide an inheritance to keep for ever, does the flood-time of rivers endure? It is only the nymph of the dragon-fly who sheds her larva and sees the sun in his glory. From the days of old there is no permanence. The sleeping and the dead, how alike they are, they are like a painted death. What is there between the master and the servant when both have fulfilled their doom? When the Anunnaki, the judges, come together, and Mammetun the mother of destinies, together they decree the fates of men. Life and death they allot but the day of death they do not disclose."

Then Gilgamesh said to Utnapishtim the Faraway, "I look at you now, Utnapishtim, and your appearance is no different from mine; there is nothing strange in your features. I thought I should find you like a hero prepared for battle, but you lie here taking your ease on your back. Tell me truly, how was it that you came to enter the company of the gods, and to possess everlasting life?" Utnapishtim said to Gilgamesh, "I will reveal to you a mystery, I will tell you a secret of the gods."

5

The Story of the Flood

"You know the city Shurrupak, it stands on the banks of Euphrates? That city grew old and the gods that were in it were old. There was Anu, lord of the firmament, their father, and warrior Enlil their counsellor, Ninurta the helper, and Ennugi watcher over canals; and with them also was Ea. In those days the world teemed, the people multiplied, the world bellowed like a wild bull, and the great god was aroused by the clamour. Enlil heard the clamour and he said to the gods in council, 'The uproar of mankind is intolerable and sleep is no longer possible by reason of the babel.' So the gods agreed to exterminate mankind. Enlil did this, but Ea because of his oath warned me in a dream. He whispered their words to my house of reeds, 'Reed-house, reed-house! Wall, O wall, hearken reed-house, wall reflect; O man of Shurrupak, son of Ubara-Tutu; tear down your house and build a boat, abandon possessions and look for life, despise worldly goods and save your soul alive. Tear down your house, I say, and build a boat. These are the measurements of the barque as you shall build her: let her beam equal her length, let her deck be roofed like the vault that covers the abyss; then take up into the boat the seed of all living creatures.'

"When I had understood I said to my lord, 'Behold what you have commanded I will honour and perform, but how shall I answer the people, the city, the elders?' Then Ea opened his mouth and said to me, his servant, 'Tell them this: I have learnt that Enlil is wrathful against me, I dare no longer walk in his land nor live in his city; I will go down to the Gulf to dwell with Ea my lord. But on you he will rain down abundance, rare fish and shy wild-fowl, a rich harvest-tide. In the evening the rider of the storm will bring you wheat in torrents.'

"In the first light of dawn all my household gathered round me, the children brought pitch and the men whatever was necessary. On the fifth day I laid the keel and the ribs, then I made fast the planking. The ground-space was one acre, each side of the deck measured one hundred and twenty cubits, making a square. I built six decks below, seven in all, I divided them into nine sections with bulkheads between. I drove in wedges where needed, I saw to the punt-poles, and laid in supplies. The carriers brought oil in baskets, I poured pitch into the furnace and asphalt and oil; more oil was consumed in caulking, and more again the master of the boat took into his stores. I slaughtered bullocks for the people and every day I killed sheep. I gave the shipwrights wine to drink as though it were river water, raw wine and red wine and oil and white wine. There was feasting then as there is at the time of the New Year's festival; I myself anointed my head. On the eleventh day the boat was complete.

"Then was the launching full of difficulty; there was shifting of ballast above and below till two thirds was submerged. I loaded into her all that I had of gold and of living things, my family, my kin, the beast of the field both wild and tame, and all the craftsmen. I sent them on board, for the time that Shamash had ordained was already fulfilled when he said, 'In the evening, when the rider of the storm sends down the destroying rain, enter the boat and batten her down.' The time was fulfilled, the evening came, the rider of the storm sent down the rain. I looked out at the weather and it was terrible, so I too boarded the boat and battened her down. All was now complete, the battening and the caulking; so I handed the tiller to Puzur-Amurri the steersman, with the navigation and the care of the whole boat.

"With the first light of dawn a black cloud came from the horizon; it thundered within where Adad, lord of the storm was riding. In front over hill and plain Shullat and Hanish, heralds of the storm, led on. Then the gods of the abyss rose up; Nergal pulled out the dams of the nether waters, Ninurta the war-lord threw down the dykes, and the seven judges of hell, the Annunaki, raised their torches, lighting the land with their livid flame. A stupor of despair went up to heaven when the god of the storm turned daylight to darkness, when he smashed the land like a cup. One whole day the tempest raged, gathering fury as it went, it poured over the people like the tides of battle; a man could not see his brother nor the people be seen from heaven. Even the gods were terrified at the flood, they fled to the highest heaven, the firmament of Anu; they crouched against the walls, cowering like curs. Then Ishtar the sweet-voiced Queen of Heaven cried out like a woman in travail: 'Alas the days of old are turned to dust because I commanded evil; why did I command this evil in the council of all the gods? I commanded wars to destroy the people, but are they not my people, for I brought them forth? Now like the spawn of fish they float in the ocean.' The great gods of heaven and of hell wept, they covered their mouths.

"For six days and six nights the winds blew, torrent and tempest and flood overwhelmed the world, tempest and flood raged together like warring hosts. When the seventh day dawned the storm from the south subsided, the sea grew calm, the flood was stilled; I looked at the face of the world and there was silence, all mankind was turned to clay. The surface of the sea stretched as flat as a roof-top; I opened a hatch and the light fell on my face. Then I bowed low, I sat down and I wept, the tears streamed down my face, for on every side was the waste of water. I looked for land in vain, for fourteen leagues distant there appeared a mountain, and there the boat grounded; on the mountain of Nisir the boat held fast, she held fast and did not budge. One day she held, and a second day on the mountain of Nisir she held fast and did not budge. A third day, and a fourth day she held fast on the mountain and did not budge; a fifth day and a sixth day she held fast on the mountain. When the seventh day dawned I loosed a dove and let her go. She flew away, but finding no resting-place she returned. Then I loosed a swallow, and she flew away but finding no resting-place she returned. I loosed a raven, she saw that the waters had retreated, she ate, she flew around, she cawed, and she did not come back. Then I threw everything open to the four winds, I made a sacrifice and poured out a libation on the mountain top. Seven and again seven cauldrons I set up on their stands, I heaped up wood and cane and cedar and myrtle. When the gods smelled the sweet savour, they gathered like flies over the sacrifice. Then, at last, Ishtar also came, she lifted her necklace with the jewels of heaven that once Anu had made to please her. 'O you gods here present, by the lapis lazuli round my neck I shall remember these days as I remember the jewels of my throat; these last days I shall not forget. Let all the gods gather round the sacrifice, except Enlil. He shall not approach this offering, for without reflection he brought the flood; he consigned my people to destruction."

"When Enlil had come, when he saw the boat, he was wrath and swelled with anger at the gods, the host of heaven, 'Has any of these mortals escaped? Not one was to have survived the destruction.' Then the god of the wells and canals Ninurta opened his mouth and said to the warrior Enlil, 'Who is there of the gods that can devise without Ea? It is Ea, alone who knows all things.' Then Ea opened his mouth and spoke to warrior Enlil, 'Wisest of gods, hero Enlil, how could you so senselessly bring down the flood?

> Lay upon the sinner his sin,
> Lay upon the transgressor his transgression,
> Punish him a little when he breaks loose,
> Do not drive him too hard or he perishes;
> Would that a lion had ravaged mankind   5
> Rather than the flood,
> Would that a wolf had ravaged mankind
> Rather than the flood,
> Would that famine had wasted the world
> Rather than the flood,   10
> Would that pestilence had wasted mankind
> Rather than the flood.

It was not I that revealed the secret of the gods; the wise man learned it in a dream. Now take your counsel what shall be done with him.'

"Then Enlil went up into the boat, he took me by the hand and my wife and made us enter the boat and kneel down on either side, he standing between us. He touched our foreheads to bless us saying, 'In time past Utnapishtim was a mortal man; henceforth he and his wife shall live in the distance at the mouth of the rivers.' Thus it was that the gods took me and placed me here to live in the distance, at the mouth of the rivers."

6

The Return

Utnapishtim said, "As for you, Gilgamesh, who will assemble the gods for your sake, so that you may find that life for which you are searching? But if you wish, come and put it to the test: only prevail against sleep for six days and seven nights." But while Gilgamesh sat there resting on his haunches, a mist of sleep like soft wool teased from the fleece drifted over him, and Utnapishtim said to his wife, "Look at him now, the strong man who would have everlasting life, even now the mists of sleep are drifting over him." His wife replied, "Touch the man to wake him, so that he may return to his own land in peace, going back through the gate by which he came." Utnapishtim said to his wife, "All men are deceivers, even you he will attempt to deceive; therefore bake loaves of bread, each day one loaf, and put it beside his head; and make a mark on the wall to number the days he has slept."

So she baked loaves of bread, each day one loaf, and put it beside his head, and she marked on the walls the days that he slept; and there came a day when the first loaf was hard, the second loaf was like leather, the third was soggy, the crust of the fourth had mould, the fifth was mildewed, the sixth was fresh, and the seventh was still on the embers. Then Utnapishtim touched him and he woke. Gilgamesh said to Utnapishtim the Faraway, "I hardly slept when you touched and roused me." But Utnapishtim said, "Count these loaves and learn how many days you slept, for your first is hard, your second like leather, your third is soggy, the crust of your fourth has mould, your fifth is mildewed, your sixth is fresh and your seventh was still over the glowing embers when I touched and woke you." Gilgamesh said, "What shall I do, O Utnapishtim, where shall I go? Already the thief in the night has hold of my limbs, death inhabits my room; wherever my foot rests, there I find death."

Then Utnapishtim spoke to Urshanabi the ferryman: "Woe to you Urshanabi, now and for ever more you have become hateful to this harbourage; it is not for you, nor for you are the crossings of this sea. Go now, banished from the shore. But this man before whom you walked, bringing him here, whose body is covered with foulness and the grace of whose limbs has been spoiled by wild skins, take him to the washing-place. There he shall wash his long hair clean as snow in the water, he shall throw off his skins and let the sea carry them away, and the beauty of his body shall be shown, the fillet on his forehead shall be renewed, and he shall be given clothes to cover his nakedness. Till he reaches his own city and his journey is accomplished, these clothes will show no sign of age, they will wear like a new garment." So Urshanabi took Gilgamesh and led him to the washing-place, he washed his long hair as clean as snow in the water, he threw off his skins, which the sea carried away, and showed the beauty of his body. He renewed the fillet on his forehead, and to cover his nakedness gave him clothes which would show no sign of age, but would wear like a new garment til he reached his own city, and his journey was accomplished.

Then Gilgamesh and Urshanabi launched the boat on to the water and boarded it, and they made ready to sail away; but the wife of Utnapishtim the Faraway said to him, "Gilgamesh came here wearied out, he is worn out; what will you give him to carry him back to his own country?" So Utnapishtim spoke, and Gilgamesh took a pole and brought the boat in to the bank. "Gilgamesh, you came here a man wearied out, you have worn yourself out; what shall I give you to carry you back to your own country? Gilgamesh, I shall reveal a secret thing, it is a mystery of the gods that I am telling you. There is a plant that grows under the water, it has a prickle like a thorn, like a rose; it will wound your hands, but if you succeed in taking it, then your hands will hold that which restores his lost youth to a man."

When Gilgamesh heard this he opened the sluices so that a sweet-water current might carry him out to the deepest channel; he tied heavy stones to his feet and they dragged him down to the water-bed. There he saw the plant growing; although it pricked him he took it in his hands; then he cut the heavy stones from his feet, and the sea carried him and threw him on to the shore. Gilgamesh said to Urshanabi the ferryman, "Come here, and see this marvellous plant. By its virtue a man may win back all his former strength. I will take it to Uruk of the strong walls; there I will give it to the old men to eat. Its name shall be 'The Old Men Are Young Again'; and at last I shall eat it myself and have back all my lost youth." So Gilgamesh returned by the gate through which he had come, Gilgamesh and Urshanabi went together. They travelled their twenty leagues and then they broke their fast; after thirty leagues they stopped for the night.

Gilgamesh saw a well of cool water and he went down and bathed; but deep in the pool there was lying a serpent, and the serpent sensed the sweetness of the flower. It rose out of the water and snatched it away, and immediately it sloughed its skin and returned to the well. Then Gilgamesh sat down and wept, the tears ran down his face, and he took the hand of Urshanabi; "O Urshanabi, was it for this that I toiled with my hands, is it for this I have wrung out my heart's blood? For myself I have gained nothing; not I, but the beast of the earth has joy of it now. Already the stream has carried it twenty leagues back to the channels where I found it. I found a sign and now I have lost it. Let us leave the boat on the bank and go."

After twenty leagues they broke their fast, after thirty leagues they stopped for the night; in three days they had walked as much as a journey of a month and fifteen days. When the journey was accomplished they arrived at Uruk, the strong-walled city. Gilgamesh spoke to him, to Urshanabi the ferryman, "Urshanabi, climb up on to the wall of Uruk, inspect its foundation terrace, and examine well the brickwork; see if it is not of burnt bricks; and did not the seven wise men lay these foundations? One third of the whole is city, one third is garden, and one third is field, with the precinct of the goddess Ishtar. These parts and the precinct are all Uruk."

This too was the work of Gilgamesh, the king, who knew the countries of the world. He was wise, he saw mysteries and knew secret things, he brought us a tale of the days before the flood. He went a long journey, was weary, worn out with labour, and returning engraved on a stone the whole story.

7

The Death of Gilgamesh

The destiny was fulfilled which the father of the gods, Enlil of the mountain, had decreed for Gilgamesh: "In nether-earth the darkness will show him a light: of mankind, all that are known, none will leave a monument for generations to come to compare with his. The heroes, the wise men, like the new moon have their waxing and waning. Men will say, 'Who has ever ruled with might and with power like him?' As in the dark month, the month of shadows, so without him there is no light. O Gilgamesh, this was the meaning of your dream. You were given the kingship, such was your destiny, everlasting life was not your destiny. Because of this do not be sad at heart, do not be grieved or oppressed; he has given you power to bind and to loose, to be the darkness and the light of mankind. He has given unexampled supremacy over the people, victory in battle from which no fugitive returns, in forays and assaults from which there is no going back. But do not abuse this power, deal justly with your servants in the palace, deal justly before the face of the Sun."

> The king has laid himself down and will not rise again,
> The Lord of Kullab will not rise again;
> He overcame evil, he will not come again;
> Though he was strong of arm he will not rise again;
>
> He had wisdom and a comely face, he will not come again;   5
> He is gone into the mountain, he will not come again;
> On the bed of fate he lies, he will not rise again,
> From the couch of many colours he will not come again.

The people of the city, great and small, are not silent; they lift up the lament, all men of flesh and blood lift up the lament. Fate has spoken; like a hooked fish he lies stretched on the bed, like a gazelle that is caught in a noose. Inhuman Namtar is heavy upon him, Namtar that has neither hand nor foot, that drinks no water and eats no meat.

For Gilgamesh, son of Ninsun, they weighed out their offerings; his dear wife, his son, his concubine, his musicians, his jester, and all his household; his servants, his stewards, all who lived in the palace weighed out their offerings for Gilgamesh the son of Ninsun, the heart of Uruk. They weighed out their offerings to Ereshkigal, the Queen of Death, and to all the gods of the dead. To Namtar, who is fate, they weighed out the offering. Bread for Neti the Keeper of the Gate, bread for Ningizzida the god of the serpent, the lord of the Tree of Life; for Dumuzi also, the young shepherd, for Enki and Ninki, for Endukugga and Nindukugga, for Enmul and Ninmul, all the ancestral gods, forbears of Enlil. A feast for Shulpae the god of feasting. For Samuqan, god of the herds, for the mother Ninhursag, and the gods of creation in the place of creation, for the host of heaven, priest and priestess weighed out the offering of the dead.

Gilgamesh, the son of Ninsun, lies in the tomb. At the place of offerings he weighed the bread-offering, at the place of libation he poured out the wine. In those days the lord Gilgamesh departed, the son of Ninsun, the king, peerless, without an equal among men, who did not neglect Enlil his master. O Gilgamesh, lord of Kullab, great is thy praise.

ANCIENT EGYPTIAN POETRY

ca. 1500–ca. 1200 B.C.

The architecture of the ancient Egyptians is well-known to us by reason of the vast tombs, temples, and pyramids they built for their pharaohs and gods. Their art is also available to us, both because they left many bas reliefs and paintings on the walls of these temples and tombs and because they filled the burial chambers of their noble and royal dead with a rich variety of objects that were to accompany the dead into the next world. The literature of ancient Egypt has survived to us only in scattered fragments, and because of the difficulty of the Egyptian language and writing system (a complex system of stylized pictographs called hieroglyphics), the literature is far less well known than either the art or the architecture. Yet even that small sample is enough to show that the ancient Egyptians possessed a poetry that was rich and varied in both its subjects and its forms. The largest and earliest group of poems comes from the pyramids that were constructed in the period of the Old Kingdom (ca. 2575–2130 B.C.). They include narratives, incantations, and invocations designed to help the pharaoh's soul on its journey to the other world. Despite their value in illuminating early Egyptian religious beliefs, the poems are prosaic and repetitive. Of far greater appeal are the lyrics, narratives, and devotional poems that were composed during the millenium that includes all the dynasties of the Middle and New Kingdoms (ca. 2130–1200 B.C.).

THE LEIDEN HYMNS

The Leiden Hymns cycle of poems appears on a papyrus dated to the fifty-second regnal year of Ramesses II (ca. 1238 B.C.) and so may be dated from this period or somewhat earlier. In *The Leiden Hymns* the poet evokes the image of the sun god—called Horus, Amun, and Amun-Re—as the one preeminent god, master of all creation, and the father of all other gods. Amun appears in a multitude of forms or incarnations, including those of the other gods: source of the Nile, inseminator of the earth, fashioner of day and night. The poem cycle is in large part built up by the repetition of titles such as these that are associated with individual gods. The effect, however, is to create the image of a god who is greater and more powerful than all individual gods. As the translator of these poems puts it, "He moves in unfathomable ways and takes many forms to human comprehension— as the various poems demonstrate; but though He is hidden from human sight, He is indeed the ultimate godhead, God alone." The poet-theologian who composed these poems uses all these metaphors to evoke the being who created all. One seems to hear in these poems echoes of the language of the Old and New Testaments, although, of course, these poems precede them. Like later Jewish and Christian poets, the author of *The Leiden Hymns* drew on the common stock of human experience to express the inexpressible.

LOVE SONGS

Love songs are the most immediately appealing of all ancient Egyptian poems and need the least explanation. In them one finds the entire range of love's possibilities. The moods and attitudes vary from chaste and idyllic to passionately erotic. Both males and females speak, and thus one sees both sides of love. These pieces all come from the Ramesside period (ca. 1300–1100 B.C.) and derive from small collections or anthologies on papyri, bits of smoothed limestone, and pottery (now in London, Turin, and Cairo). Reading these poems one feels that love has hardly altered at all over the intervening centuries.

The translations here are taken from John L. Foster, *Echoes of Egyptian Voices* (1992) and *Love Songs of Ancient Egypt* (1992). *Echoes* contains an extensive bibliography of works on ancient Egyptian culture in English. Among more general studies of ancient Egyptian culture, Cyril Aldred, *The Egyptians* (1984), is a useful general history by an art historian. B. G. Trigger et al., *Ancient Egypt: A Social*

History (1983), is, as its title promises, a work that gives more attention to Egyptian society.

The following list uses common English syllables and stress accents to provide rough equivalents of selected words whose pronunciation may be unfamiliar to the general reader.

Amun-Re: *ah-mun–ray'*

Ramesses: *ra'-me-seez*

THE LEIDEN HYMNS[1]

[How splendid you ferry the skyways]

How splendid you ferry the skyways,
       Horus of Twin Horizons,[2]
The needs of each new day
       firm in your timeless pattern,
Who fashion the years,   5
       weave months into order—
Days, nights, and the very hours
       move to the gait of your striding.

Refreshed by your diurnal shining, you quicken,
       bright above yesterday,   10
Making the zone of night sparkle
       although you belong to the light,
Sole one awake there
       —sleep is for mortals,
Who go to rest grateful: 15
       your eyes oversee.
And theirs by the millions you open
       when your face new-rises, beautiful;
Not a bypath escapes your affection
       during your season on earth.   20

Stepping swift over stars,
       riding the lightning flash,
You circle the earth in an instant,
       with a god's ease crossing heaven,
Treading dark paths of the underworld,   25
       yet, sun on each roadway,
You deign to walk daily with men.

       The faces of all are upturned to you,
As mankind and gods
       alike lift their morningsong: 30
"Lord of the daybreak,
       Welcome!"

---

1. All selections translated by John L. Foster.   2. Dawn and dusk. Horus is the hawk-headed sun god.

[God is a master craftsman]

God is a master craftsman;
        yet none can draw the lines of his Person.
Fair features first came into being
        in the hushed dark where he mused alone;
He forged his own figure there,   5
        hammered his likeness out of himself—
All powerful one (yet kindly,
        whose heart would lie open to men).

He mingled his heavenly god-seed
        with the inmost parts of his being.   10
Planting his image there
        in the unknown depths of his mystery.
He cared, and the sacred form
        took shape and contour, splendid at birth!
God, skilled in the intricate ways of the craftsman,   15
        first fashioned Himself to perfection.

[When Being began back in days of the genesis]

When Being began back in days of the genesis,
    it was Amun appeared first of all,
        unknown his mode of inflowing;
There was no god come before him,
    nor was other god with him there   5
        when he uttered himself into visible form;
There was no mother to him, that she might have borne him his name,
    there was no father to father the one
        who first spoke the words, "I Am!"
Who fashioned the seed of him all on his own,   10
    sacred first cause, whose birth lay in mystery,
        who crafted and carved his own splendor—
He is God the Creator, self-created, the Holy;
    all other gods came after;
        with Himself he began the world.   15

LOVE SONGS

[My love is one and only, without peer]

My love is one and only, without peer,
    lovely above all Egypt's lovely girls.
On the horizon of my seeing,
    see her, rising,
Glistening goddess of the sunrise star   5
    bright in the forehead of a lucky year.
So there she stands, epitome
    of shining, shedding light,
Her eyebrows, gleaming darkly, marking

eyes which dance and wander.   10
Sweet are those lips, which chatter
        (but never a word too much),
And the line of the long neck lovely, dropping
        (since song's notes slide that way)
To young breasts firm in the bouncing light   15
        which shimmers that blueshadowed sidefall of hair.
And slim are those arms, overtoned with gold,
        those fingers which touch like a brush of lotus.
And (ah) how the curve of her back slips gently
        by a whisper of waist to god's plenty below.   20
(Such thighs as hers pass knowledge
        of loveliness known in the old days.)
Dressed in the perfect flesh of woman
        (heart would run captive to such slim arms),
          she ladies it over the earth,   25
Schooling the neck of each schoolboy male
        to swing on a swivel to see her move.
(He who could hold that body tight
        would know at last
          perfection of delight—   30
Best of the bullyboys,
        first among lovers.)
Look you, all men, at that golden going,
        like Our Lady of Love,
          without peer.   35

[Love, how I'd love to slip down to the pond]

Love, how I'd love to slip down to the pond,
        bathe with you close by on the bank.
Just for you I'd wear my new Memphis swimsuit,
        made of sheer linen, fit for a queen—
Come see how it looks in the water!   5

Couldn't I coax you to wade in with me?
        Let the cool creep slowly around us?
Then I'd dive deep down
        and come up for you dripping,
Let you fill your eyes   10
        with the little red fish that I'd catch.

And I'd say, standing there tall in the shallows:
Look at my fish, love,
        how it lies in my hand,
How my fingers caress it,   15
        slip down its sides . . .

But then I'd say softer,
        eyes bright with your seeing:
          A gift, love. No words.
        Come closer and   20
          look, it's all me.

[Why, just now, must you question your heart?]

Why, just now, must you question your heart?
            Is it really the time for discussion?
To her, say I,
            take her tight in your arms!
For god's sake, sweet man,   5
            it's me coming at you,
My tunic
            loose at the shoulder!

[I was simply off to see Nefrus my friend]

I was simply off to see Nefrus my friend,
Just to sit and chat at her place
                        (about men),
When there, hot on his horses, comes Mehy
            (oh god, I said to myself, it's Mehy!)   5
Right over the crest of the road
            wheeling along with the boys.

Oh Mother Hathor, what shall I do?
            Don't let him see me!
                        Where can I hide?   10
Make me a small creeping thing
            to slip by his eye
                  (sharp as Horus')
                        unseen.

Oh, look at you, feet—   15
            (this road is a river!)
                  you walk me right out of my depth!
Someone, silly heart, is exceedingly ignorant here—
            aren't you a little too easy near Mehy?

If he sees that I see him, I know   20
            he will know how my heart flutters (Oh, Mehy!)
I know I will blurt out,
            "Please take me!"
                        (I mustn't!)

No, all he would do is brag out my name,   25
            just one of the many . . . (I know) . . .
Mehy would make me just one of the girls
            for all of the boys in the palace.
                        (Oh Mehy)

[I think I'll go home and lie very still]

I think I'll go home and lie very still,
    feigning terminal illness.
Then the neighbors will all troop over to stare,
    my love, perhaps, among them.
How she'll smile while the specialists   5
    snarl in their teeth!—
    she perfectly well knows what ails me.

THE BIBLE: THE OLD TESTAMENT

ca. 1000–300 B.C.

THE CREATION—THE FALL

The religious attitudes of the Hebrews appear in the story that they told of the creation of the world and of humankind. This creation is the work of one God, who is omnipotent and omniscient and who creates a perfect and harmonious order. The disorder that we see all around us, physical and moral, is not God's creation but Adam and Eve's; it is the consequence of humankind's disobedience. The story not only reconciles the undeniable existence of evil and disorder in the world with the conception of God's infinite justice but also attributes to humanity itself an independence of God, free will, which in this case had been used for evil. The Hebrew God is not limited in His power by other deities, who oppose His will (as in the Greek stories of Zeus and his undisciplined family); His power over inanimate nature is infinite. In all the range of His creation there is only one being able to resist Him—humankind.

Because God is all-powerful, even this resistance on Adam and Eve's part is in some mysterious way a manifestation of God's will. How this can be is not explained by the story, and we are left with the mystery that still eludes us, the coexistence of God's prescient power and humanity's unrestricted free will.

The story of the Fall ends with a situation in which Adam and Eve have earned for themselves and their descendants a short life of sorrow relieved only by death. It was the achievement of later Hebrew teachers to carry the story on and develop the concept of a God who is as merciful as He is just, who watches tenderly over the destinies of the creatures who have rebelled against Him, and who brings about the possibility of atonement and full reconciliation.

Adam and Eve's son Cain is the first person to shed human blood, but though God drives him out to be a wanderer on the face of the earth, He does not kill him. The brand on Cain's forehead, while it marks him as a murderer, also protects his life—no one is to touch him. Later when the descendants of Adam and Eve grow so wicked that God is sorry He has created the human race, He decides to destroy it by sending a universal flood. But He spares Noah and his family to beget a new human race, on which God pins His hopes. His rainbow in the sky reminds humankind of His promise that He will never again let loose the waters. But people do not learn their lesson: they start to build a tower high enough to reach to Heaven, and God is afraid that if they succeed they will then recognize no limit to their ambitions. Yet He does not destroy them; He merely frustrates their purpose by depriving them of their common language.

And yet humanity must eventually atone for Adam and Eve's act: human guilt must be wiped out by sacrifice. The development of this idea was extended over centuries of thought and suffering. For the Christians, it reached its culmination in the figure of Christ, the Son of God, who as a man pays the full measure due in human suffering and human death. But the idea of the one who suffers for all had long been a major theme in Hebrew religious literature. Not only did there emerge slowly a concept of the Hebrews as a chosen nation that suffers for the rest, but individual figures of Hebrew history and imagination embodied this theme in the form of the story of the suffering servant whose suffering brings relief to humanity and ultimate glory to himself. This is the idea behind the story of Joseph.

JOSEPH

Joseph, his father's favorite son, has a sense of his own great destiny, confirmed by his dreams, which represent him as the first of all his race. He is indeed to be the first, but to become so he must also be the last. He is sold into slavery by his brothers; the savior is rejected by those whom he is to save, as the Hebrews were rejected by their neighbors and as they rejected their own prophets.

With the loss of his liberty, Joseph's trials have only begun. In Egypt after making a new and successful life for himself, he is thrown into prison on a false accusation. He interprets the dream of Pharaoh's butler, who promises, if his interpretation is correct, to secure his release; the butler is restored to freedom and royal favor but, as is the way of the world, forgets his promise and leaves his comforter in jail. Joseph stays in prison two more years but finally obtains his freedom and becomes Pharaoh's most trusted adviser. When his brothers come from starving Palestine and bow down before him asking for help, he saves them; not only does he give them grain but he also provides a home for his people in Egypt. "I am Joseph your brother, whom ye sold into Egypt," he says to them when he reveals his identity. "God sent me before you to preserve you a posterity in the earth, and to save your lives by a great deliverance."

One of the essential points of this story, and the whole conception of the suffering servant, is the distinction that it emphasizes between an external, secular standard of good and a spiritual, religious standard. In the eyes of the average person, prosperity and righteousness are connected, if not identified, and the sufferer is felt to be one whose misfortune must be explained as a punishment for his or her wickedness. This feeling is strong in ancient (and especially in Greek) literature, but we should not be unduly complacent about our superiority to the ancients in this respect, for the attitude is still with us. It is in fact a basic assumption of a competitive society—the view, seldom expressed but strongly rooted, that the plight of the unfortunate is the result of their own laziness, the wealth of the rich the reward of superior virtue.

The writer of the Joseph story sees in the unfortunate sufferer the savior who is the instrument of God's will. It is because of what he suffers that the sun and the moon and the eleven stars will bow down to Joseph. Yet the story does not emphasize the sufferings of Joseph; he is pictured rather as the man of action who through native ability and divine protection turns the injuries done him into advantages. We are not made to feel the torment in his soul. When he weeps it is because of the memory of what he had suffered and his yearning for his youngest brother, and he is in full control of the situation. And his reward in the things of this world is great. Not only does he reveal himself as the savior of his nation but he becomes rich and powerful beyond his brothers' dreams, and in a great kingdom. The spiritual and secular standards are at the end of the story combined; Joseph's suffering is neatly balanced by his worldly reward.

JOB

Later Hebrew writers developed a sadder and profounder view. The greatest literary masterpiece of the Old Testament, the Book of Job, is also concerned with the inadequacy of worldly standards of happiness and righteousness; but the suffering of Job is so overwhelming and so magnificently expressed, that even with our knowledge of its purpose and its meaning it seems excessive. Joseph suffered slavery, exile, and imprisonment but turned them all to account. Job loses his family and wealth in a series of calamities, which strike one on the other like hammer blows, and is then plagued with a loathsome disease. Unlike Joseph, he is old; he cannot adapt himself and rise above adverse circumstances, and he no longer wishes to live. Except for one thing: he wishes to understand the reason for his suffering.

For his friends the explanation is simple. With the blindness of men who know no standards other than those of this world, they are sure that Job's misfortune must be the result of some wickedness on his part. But Job is confident in his righteousness; his torture is as much mental as physical. He cannot reconcile the fact of his innocence with the calamities that have come on him with all the decisive suddenness of the hand of God.

The full explanation is never given to him, but it is given to the reader in the two opening chapters of the book. This prologue to the dramatic section of the work gives us the knowledge that is hidden from the participants in the ensuing dialogue. The writer uses the method characteristic of Greek tragedy—irony, the deeper understanding of the dramatic spoken word that is based on the superior knowledge of the audience. The prologue explains God's motive in allowing Job to suffer. It is an important one: God intends to use Job as a demonstration to His skeptical subordinate Satan of the fact that a human being can retain faith in God's justice in the face of the greatest imaginable suffering. This motive, which Job does not know and which is never revealed to him, gives to the dialogue between Job and his friends its suspense and its importance. God has rested His case—that humanity is capable of keeping faith in divine justice, against all appearances to the contrary—on this one man.

The arguments of Job's friends are based on the worldly equation that success equals virtue. They attempt to undermine Job's faith, not in God, but in himself. "Who ever perished, being innocent?" asks Eliphaz, "or where were the righteous cut off?" Job's misfortune is a proof that he must have sinned; all he has to do is to admit his guilt and ask God for pardon, which he will surely receive. He refuses to accept this easy way out, and we know that he is right. In fact, we know from the prologue that he has been selected for misfortune not because he has sinned, but precisely because of his outstanding virtue. "There is none like him in the earth," God says, "a perfect and an upright man, one that feareth God, and escheweth evil." What Job must do is to persevere not only in his faith in God's justice but also in the conviction of his own innocence. He must believe the illogical, accept a paradox. His friends are offering him an easy way out, one that seems to be the way of humility and submission. But it is a false way. And God finally tells them so. "The Lord said to Eliphaz the Temanite, My wrath is kindled against thee, and against thy two friends: for ye have not spoken of me the thing that is right, as my servant Job hath."

Job's confidence in his own righteousness is not pride, but intellectual honesty. He sees that the problem is much harder than his friends imagine. To let them persuade him of his own guilt would lighten his mental burden by answering the question that tortures him, but his intelligence will not let him yield. Like Oedipus, he refuses to stop short of the truth. He even uses the same words: "let me alone, that I may speak, and let come on me what will." He finally expresses his understanding and acceptance of the paradox involved in the combination of his suffering with his innocence, but he does so with a human independence and dignity: "Though he slay me, yet will I trust in him: but I will maintain mine own ways before him." He sums up his case with a detailed account of the righteousness of his ways, and it is clear that this account is addressed not only to his three friends but also to God. "My desire is, that the Almighty would answer me," he says. His friends are silenced by the majesty and firmness of his statement. They "ceased to answer Job, because he was righteous in his own eyes," but God is moved to reply.

The magnificent poetry of that reply, the voice out of the whirlwind, still does not give Job the full explanation, God's motive in putting him to the torture. It is a triumphant proclamation of God's power and also of His justice, and it silences Job, who accepts it as a sufficient answer. That God does not reveal the key to the riddle even to the man who has victoriously stood the test and vindicated His faith in humanity is perhaps the most significant point in the story. It suggests that there is not and never will be an explanation of human suffering that humankind's intelligence can comprehend. Sufferers must, like Job, cling to their faith in themselves and in God; they must accept the inexplicable fact that their own undeserved suffering is the working of God's justice.

THE PROPHETS

In the last days of Israel's independence, before conquerors overran the land and transported the population to captivity in the East (an exile mourned in Psalm 137 — "By the rivers of Babylon . . ."), a series of prophets reproved the children of Israel for their transgressions and foretold the wrath to come, the end of the kingdom of Israel, and beyond that, the overthrow of the neighboring kingdoms. The prophet was a man who believed himself to be the spokesman of God, the messenger of a terrifying vision. The horror of the vision of destruction was often too heavy a load for the human mind, and the disbelief and mockery of his hearers tipped the precarious balance so that what might have been merely a strange urgency came often close to madness. The vision of things to come was expressed in magnificent but disconnected images, which to the workaday mind of the person in the street seemed only to confirm the suspicion that the prophet was deranged. Amos, Nahum, Jeremiah, and many others poured out their charged and clotted imagery of catastrophe to an unbelieving people.

The prophets were not always messengers of doom; it is in the words of an unnamed prophet (whose writings are included in the Book of Isaiah) that the theme of the one who suffers for others finds its most profound and moving expression. In the earlier versions the sufferer has it all made up to him in the end: Job, like Joseph, has his reward. Job's suffering is greater than Joseph's, and it is clear that the writer of the Book of Job shows, alike in the speeches and in the ironic framework of the whole, a profounder understanding of the nature and meaning of suffering than the narrator of the story of Joseph; but like Joseph, Job lives to see the end of his troubles and has his material reward. "The Lord gave Job twice as much as he had before. . . . After this lived Job an hundred and forty years, and saw his sons, and his sons' sons, even four generations."

But in the *Song of the Suffering Servant* there is no recompense in this life: the suffering ends in death. In this deeper vision there is no reconciliation between the standards of this world and the standards of the higher authority behind the suffering. The one who is to save Israel and the world is not well favored like Joseph: "he hath no form nor comeliness." Nor is he, like Job, "the greatest of all the men of the east"; he is "despised and rejected of men." He suffers for his fellow humans: "the Lord hath laid on him the iniquity of us all." His suffering knows no limit but death; he is oppressed and afflicted, imprisoned and executed. "He was cut off out of the land of the living" and "he made his grave with the wicked."

The circumstances described here are familiar from other cultures than the Hebrew; they are found in the primitive ritual of many peoples, and ceremonial relics of them still existed in civilized fifth-century Athens. In certain primitive societies, to rid the group of guilt a scapegoat was chosen, who was declared responsible for the misdeeds of all and who was then mocked, beaten, driven out of the community, and killed. The scapegoat was hated and despised as the embodiment of the guilt of the whole community; his death was the most ignominious imaginable. The memory of some such primitive ritual is unmistakable in the Hebrew song; but its meaning has been utterly changed. It is precisely in the figure of the hated and suffering scapegoat that the Hebrew prophet sees the savior of humankind—an innocent sufferer, "he had done no violence, neither was any deceit in his mouth"—and the prophet sees this without visible confirmation. There is no recognition by the brothers, no vindication by a voice out of the whirlwind. It is the highest expression of the Hebrew vision at its saddest and most profound, this portrayal of the savior who comes not in pomp and power but in suffering and meekness, who dies rejected and despised, and who atones for human sin and makes "intercession for the transgressors."

The student will find good background in R. R. Ackroyd and C. F. Evans, eds., *The Cambridge History of the Bible* (1970), vol. 1. R. H. Rowley, *The Growth of the Old Testament* (1950), concentrates on the Old Testament as a whole. For Job, see P. Sanders, ed., *Twentieth-Century Interpretations of the Book of Job* (1968). See also Robert Alter and Frank Kermode, eds., *The Literary Guide to the Bible* (1987), especially pages 283–303 (Job) and 244–61 (Psalms).

PRONOUNCING GLOSSARY

The following list uses common English syllables and stress accents to provide rough equivalents of selected words whose pronunciation may be unfamiliar to the general reader.

Canaan: *kay'-nuhn*

Euphrates: *yoo-fray'-teez*

Job: *johb*

THE BIBLE: THE OLD TESTAMENT[1]

Genesis 1–3

[The Creation—The Fall]

1. In the beginning God created the heaven and the earth. And the earth was without form, and void; and darkness was upon the face of the deep. And the Spirit of God moved upon the face of the waters.

And God said, Let there be light: and there was light. And God saw the light, that it was good: and God divided the light from the darkness. And God called the light Day, and the darkness he called Night. And the evening and the morning were the first day.

And God said, Let there be a firmament in the midst of the waters, and

---

1. The text of these selections is that of the King James, or Authorized, Version of 1611, so-called because it was the work of a team of fifty-four scholars named by King James I of England to produce a new translation "appointed to be read in churches." Since that time advances in biblical scholarship have corrected some of the translators' mistakes and substituted clearer versions where their prose is obscure. Yet the superiority of the Authorized Version as literature remains unquestioned; it is one of the greatest literary texts in the history of the English language. It was written at a time when English was at a creative peak—the age of William Shakespeare, Ben Jonson, and John Donne. It was written to be read aloud, as it was in churches and homes, and to be learned by heart, as it was in schools in the English-speaking world for centuries. The echoes of its magnificent rhythms and cadences can be heard in the verse of English poets from John Milton to T. S. Eliot, in the prose of John Bunyan and the speeches of Abraham Lincoln.

let it divide the waters from the waters. And God made the firmament, and divided the waters which were under the firmament from the waters which were above the firmament:[2] and it was so. And God called the firmament Heaven. And the evening and the morning were the second day.

And God said, Let the waters under the heaven be gathered together unto one place, and let the dry land appear: and it was so. And God called the dry land Earth; and the gathering together of the waters called he Seas: and God saw that it was good. And God said, Let the earth bring forth grass, the herb yielding seed, and the fruit tree yielding fruit after his kind, whose seed is in itself, upon the earth: and it was so. And the earth brought forth grass, and herb yielding seed after his kind, and the tree yielding fruit, whose seed was in itself, after his kind: and God saw that it was good. And the evening and the morning were the third day.

And God said, Let there be lights in the firmament of the heaven to divide the day from the night; and let them be for signs, and for seasons, and for days, and years: and let them be for lights in the firmament of the heaven to give light upon the earth: and it was so. And God made two great lights; the greater light to rule the day, and the lesser light to rule the night: he made the stars also. And God set them in the firmament of the heaven to give light upon the earth, and to rule over the day and over the night, and to divide the light from the darkness: and God saw that it was good. And the evening and the morning were the fourth day. And God said, Let the waters bring forth abundantly the moving creature that hath life, and fowl that may fly above the earth in the open firmament of heaven. And God created great whales, and every living creature that moveth, which the waters brought forth abundantly, after their kind, and every winged fowl after his kind: and God saw that it was good. And God blessed them, saying, Be fruitful, and multiply, and fill the waters in the seas, and let fowl multiply in the earth. And the evening and the morning were the fifth day.

And God said, Let the earth bring forth the living creature after his kind, cattle, and creeping thing, and beast of the earth after his kind: and it was so. And God made the beast of the earth after his kind, and cattle after their kind, and everything that creepeth upon the earth after his kind: and God saw that it was good.

And God said, Let us make man in our image, after our likeness: and let them have dominion over the fish of the sea, and over the fowl of the air, and over the cattle, and over all the earth, and over every creeping thing that creepeth upon the earth. So God created man in his own image, in the image of God created he him; male and female created he them. And God blessed them, and God said unto them, Be fruitful, and multiply, and replenish the earth, and subdue it: and have dominion over the fish of the sea, and over the fowl of the air, and over every living thing that moveth upon the earth.

And God said, Behold, I have given you every herb bearing seed, which

---

2. The sky, which seen from below has the appearance of a ceiling. The waters above are those that come down in the form of rain.

is upon the face of all the earth, and every tree, in which is the fruit of a tree yielding seed; to you it shall be for meat. And to every beast of the earth, and to every fowl of the air, and to every thing that creepeth upon the earth, wherein there is life, I have given every green herb for meat: and it was so. And God saw every thing that he had made, and, behold, it was very good. And the evening and the morning were the sixth day.

2. Thus the heavens and the earth were finished, and all the host of them. And on the seventh day God ended his work which he had made; and he rested on the seventh day from all his work which he had made. And God blessed the seventh day, and sanctified it: because that in it he had rested from all his work which God created and made.

These are the generations of the heavens and of the earth when they were created,[3] in the day that the Lord God made the earth and the heavens, and every plant of the field before it was in the earth, and every herb of the field before it grew: for the Lord God had not caused it to rain upon the earth, and there was not a man to till the ground. But there went up a mist from the earth, and watered the whole face of the ground. And the Lord God formed man of the dust of the ground, and breathed into his nostrils the breath of life; and man became a living soul.

And the Lord God planted a garden eastward in Eden; and there he put the man whom he had formed. And out of the ground made the Lord God to grow every tree that is pleasant to the sight, and good for food; the tree of life also in the midst of the garden, and the tree of knowledge of good and evil. And a river went out of Eden to water the garden; and from thence it was parted, and became into four heads. The name of the first is Pison: that is it which compasseth the whole land of Havilah, where there is gold; and the gold of that land is good: there is bdellium and the onyx stone. And the name of the second river is Gihon: the same is it that compasseth the whole land of Ethiopia. And the name of the third river is Hiddekel: that is it which goeth toward the east of Assyria. And the fourth river is Euphrates. And the Lord God took the man, and put him into the garden of Eden to dress it and to keep it. And the Lord God commanded the man, saying, Of every tree of the garden thou mayest freely eat: but of the tree of the knowledge of good and evil, thou shalt not eat of it: for in the day that thou eatest thereof thou shalt surely die.

And the Lord God said, It is not good that the man should be alone; I will make him an help meet for him. And out of the ground the Lord God formed every beast of the field, and every fowl of the air; and brought them unto Adam to see what he would call them: and whatsoever Adam called every living creature, that was the name thereof. And Adam gave names to all cattle, and to the fowl of the air, and to every beast of the field; but for Adam there was not found an help meet for him. And the Lord God caused a deep sleep to fall upon Adam, and he slept: and he took one of his ribs, and closed up the flesh instead thereof; and the rib, which the Lord God had taken from man, made he a woman, and brought her unto the man. And Adam said, This is now bone of my bones, and

3. This is the beginning of a different account of the Creation, which does not agree in all respects with the first.

flesh of my flesh: she shall be called Woman, because she was taken out of Man. Therefore shall a man leave his father and his mother, and shall cleave unto his wife: and they shall be one flesh. And they were both naked, the man and his wife, and were not ashamed.

3. Now the serpent was more subtil than any beast of the field which the Lord God had made. And he said unto the woman, Yea, hath God said, Ye shall not eat of every tree of the garden? And the woman said unto the serpent, We may eat of the fruit of the trees of the garden: but of the fruit of the tree which is in the midst of the garden, God hath said, Ye shall not eat of it, neither shall ye touch it, lest ye die. And the serpent said unto the woman, Ye shall not surely die: for God doth know that in the day ye eat thereof, then your eyes shall be opened, and ye shall be as gods, knowing good and evil. And when the woman saw that the tree was good for food, and that it was pleasant to the eyes, and a tree to be desired to make one wise, she took of the fruit thereof, and did eat, and gave also unto her husband with her; and he did eat. And the eyes of them both were opened, and they knew that they were naked; and they sewed fig leaves together, and made themselves aprons. And they heard the voice of the Lord God walking in the garden in the cool of the day: and Adam and his wife hid themselves from the presence of the Lord God amongst the trees of the garden. And the Lord God called unto Adam, and said unto him, Where art thou? And he said, I heard thy voice in the garden, and I was afraid, because I was naked; and I hid myself. And he said, Who told thee that thou wast naked? Hast thou eaten of the tree, whereof I commanded thee that thou shouldest not eat? And the man said, The woman whom thou gavest to be with me, she gave me of the tree, and I did eat. And the Lord God said unto the woman, What is this that thou hast done? And the woman said, The serpent beguiled me, and I did eat. And the Lord God said unto the serpent, Because thou hast done this, thou art cursed above all cattle, and above every beast of the field; upon thy belly shalt thou go, and dust shalt thou eat all the days of thy life: and I will put enmity between thee and the woman, and between thy seed and her seed; it shall bruise thy head, and thou shalt bruise his heel. Unto the woman he said, I will greatly multiply thy sorrow and thy conception; in sorrow thou shalt bring forth children; and thy desire shall be to thy husband, and he shall rule over thee. And unto Adam he said, Because thou hast hearkened unto the voice of thy wife, and hast eaten of the tree, of which I commanded thee, saying, Thou shalt not eat of it: cursed is the ground for thy sake; in sorrow shalt thou eat of it all the days of thy life; thorns also and thistles shall it bring forth to thee; and thou shalt eat the herb of the field; in the sweat of thy face shalt thou eat bread, till thou return unto the ground; for out of it wast thou taken: for dust thou art, and unto dust shalt thou return. And Adam called his wife's name Eve; because she was the mother of all living. Unto Adam also and to his wife did the Lord God make coats of skins, and clothed them.

And the Lord God said, Behold, the man is become as one of us, to know good and evil: and now, lest he put forth his hand, and take also of the tree of life, and eat, and live forever: therefore the Lord God sent him forth from the garden of Eden, to till the ground from whence he was taken. So he drove out the man; and he placed at the east of the garden of Eden Cherubims, and a flaming sword which turned every way, to keep the way of the tree of life.

Genesis 4

[The First Murder]

4. And Adam knew Eve his wife; and she conceived, and bare Cain, and said, I have gotten a man from the Lord. And she again bare his brother Abel. And Abel was a keeper of sheep, but Cain was a tiller of the ground. And in process of time it came to pass, that Cain brought of the fruit of the ground an offering unto the Lord. And Abel, he also brought of the firstlings of his flock and of the fat thereof. And the Lord had respect unto Abel and to his offering: but unto Cain and to his offering he had not respect. And Cain was very wroth, and his countenance fell. And the Lord said unto Cain, Why art thou wroth? and why is thy countenance fallen? If thou doest well, shalt thou not be accepted? and if thou doest not well, sin lieth at the door. And unto thee shall be his desire, and thou shall rule over him.[1] And Cain talked with Abel his brother: and it came to pass, when they were in the field, that Cain rose up against Abel his brother, and slew him.

And the Lord said unto Cain, Where is Abel thy brother? And he said, I know not: am I my brother's keeper? And he said, What hast thou done? the voice of thy brother's blood crieth unto me from the ground. And now art thou cursed from the earth, which hath opened her mouth to receive thy brother's blood from thy hand; when thou tillest the ground, it shall not henceforth yield unto thee her strength, a fugitive and a vagabond shalt thou be in the earth. And Cain said unto the Lord, My punishment is greater than I can bear. Behold, thou hast driven me out this day from the face of the earth; and from thy face shall I be hid; and I shall be a fugitive and a vagabond in the earth; and it shall come to pass, that every one that findeth me shall slay me. And the Lord said unto him, Therefore whosoever slayeth Cain, vengeance shall be taken on him sevenfold. And the Lord set a mark upon Cain, lest any finding him should kill him.

Genesis 6–9

[The Flood]

6. * * * And God saw that the wickedness of man was great in the earth, and that every imagination of the thoughts of his heart was only evil continually. And it repented the Lord that he had made man on the earth, and it grieved him at his heart. And the Lord said, I will destroy man

---

1. Obscure; it seems to mean something like: Sin shall be eager for you, but you must master it.

whom I have created from the face of the earth; both man, and beast, and the creeping thing, and the fowls of the air; for it repenteth me that I have made them. But Noah found grace in the eyes of the Lord.

These are the generations of Noah: Noah was a just man and perfect in his generations, and Noah walked with God. And Noah begat three sons, Shem, Ham, and Japheth.

The earth also was corrupt before God, and the earth was filled with violence. And God looked upon the earth, and, behold, it was corrupt; for all flesh had corrupted his way upon the earth. And God said unto Noah, The end of all flesh is come before me; for the earth is filled with violence through them; and, behold, I will destroy them with the earth. Make thee an ark of gopher wood;[1] rooms shalt thou make in the ark, and shalt pitch it within and without with pitch. And this is the fashion which thou shalt make it of: The length of the ark shall be three hundred cubits,[2] the breadth of it fifty cubits, and the height of it thirty cubits. A window[3] shalt thou make to the ark, and in a cubit shalt thou finish it above; and the door of the ark shalt thou set in the side thereof; with lower, second, and third stories shalt thou make it. And, behold, I, even I, do bring a flood of waters upon the earth, to destroy all flesh, wherein is the breath of life, from under heaven; and every thing that is in the earth shall die. But with thee will I establish my covenant; and thou shalt come into the ark, thou, and thy sons, and thy wife, and thy sons' wives with thee. And of every living thing of all flesh, two of every sort shalt thou bring into the ark, to keep them alive with thee; they shall be male and female. Of fowls after their kind, and of cattle after their kind, of every creeping thing of the earth after his kind, two of every sort shall come unto thee, to keep them alive. And take thou unto thee of all food that is eaten, and thou shalt gather it to thee; and it shall be for food for thee, and for them. Thus did Noah; according to all that God commanded him, so did he.

7. * * * And Noah was six hundred years old when the flood of waters was upon the earth. And Noah went in, and his sons, and his wife, and his sons' wives with him, into the ark, because of the waters of the flood. Of clean beasts, and of beasts that are not clean, and of fowls, and of every thing that creepeth upon the earth, There went in two and two unto Noah into the ark, the male and the female, as God had commanded Noah. And it came to pass after seven days, that the waters of the flood were upon the earth. In the six hundredth year of Noah's life, in the second month, the seventeenth day of the month, the same day were all the fountains of the great deep broken up, and the windows of heaven were opened. And the rain was upon the earth forty days and forty nights. In the selfsame day entered Noah, and Shem, and Ham, and Japheth, the sons of Noah, and Noah's wife, and the three wives of his sons with them, into the ark; they, and every beast after his kind, and all the cattle after their kind, and every creeping thing that creepeth upon the earth after his kind, and every fowl after his kind, every bird of every sort. And they went in unto Noah

1. Cypress. 2. A Hebrew measure of length, about one and a half feet. 3. Obscure; perhaps a skylight in the roof.

into the ark, two and two of all flesh, wherein is the breath of life. And they that went in, went in male and female of all flesh, as God had commanded him: and the Lord shut him in. And the flood was forty days upon the earth; and the waters increased, and bare up the ark, and it was lift up above the earth. And the waters prevailed, and were increased greatly upon the earth; and the ark went upon the face of the waters. And the waters prevailed exceedingly upon the earth; and all the high hills, that were under the whole heaven, were covered. Fifteen cubits upward did the waters prevail; and the mountains were covered. And all flesh died that moved upon the earth, both of fowl, and of cattle, and of beast, and of every creeping thing that creepeth upon the earth, and every man: all in whose nostrils was the breath of life, of all that was in the dry land, died. And every living substance was destroyed which was upon the face of the ground, both man, and cattle, and the creeping things, and the fowl of the heaven; and they were destroyed from the earth: and Noah only remained alive, and they that were with him in the ark. And the waters prevailed upon the earth an hundred and fifty days.

8. And God remembered Noah, and every living thing, and all the cattle that was with him in the ark: and God made a wind to pass over the earth, and the waters assuaged; The fountains also of the deep and the windows of heaven were stopped, and the rain from heaven was restrained; And the waters returned from off the earth continually: and after the end of the hundred and fifty days the waters were abated. And the ark rested in the seventh month, on the seventeenth day of the month, upon the mountains of Ararat. And the waters decreased continually until the tenth month: in the tenth month, on the first day of the month, were the tops of the mountains seen.

And it came to pass at the end of forty days, that Noah opened the window of the ark which he had made: and he sent forth a raven, which went forth to and fro, until the waters were dried up from off the earth. Also he sent forth a dove from him, to see if the waters were abated from off the face of the ground; but the dove found no rest for the sole of her foot, and she returned unto him into the ark, for the waters were on the face of the whole earth: then he put forth his hand, and took her, and pulled her in unto him into the ark. And he stayed yet another seven days; and again he sent forth the dove out of the ark; and the dove came in to him in the evening; and, lo, in her mouth was an olive leaf plucked off: so Noah knew that the waters were abated from off the earth. And he stayed yet other seven days; and sent forth the dove; which returned not again unto him any more.

And it came to pass in the six hundredth and first year, in the first month, the first day of the month, the waters were dried up from off the earth: and Noah removed the covering of the ark, and looked, and, behold, the face of the ground was dry. And in the second month, on the seven and twentieth day of the month, was the earth dried.

And God spake unto Noah, saying, Go forth of the ark, thou, and thy wife, and thy sons, and thy sons' wives with thee. Bring forth with thee every living thing that is with thee, of all flesh, both of fowl, and of cattle, and of every creeping thing that creepeth upon the earth; that they may breed abundantly in the earth, and be fruitful, and multiply upon the earth. And Noah went forth, and his sons, and his wife, and his sons' wives with him: every beast, every creeping thing, and every fowl, and whatsoever creepeth upon the earth, after their kinds, went forth out of the ark. And Noah builded an altar unto the Lord; and took of every clean beast, and of every clean fowl, and offered burnt offerings on the altar. And the Lord smelled a sweet savour; and the Lord said in his heart, I will not again curse the ground any more for man's sake; for the imagination of man's heart is evil from his youth; neither will I again smite any more every thing living, as I have done. While the earth remaineth, seedtime and harvest, and cold and heat, and summer and winter, and day and night shall not cease.

9. And God blessed Noah and his sons, and said unto them, Be fruitful, and multiply, and replenish the earth. And the fear of you and the dread of you shall be upon every beast of the earth, and upon every fowl of the air, upon all that moveth upon the earth, and upon all the fishes of the sea; into your hand are they delivered. Every moving thing that liveth shall be meat for you; even as the green herb have I given you all things. But flesh with the life thereof, which is the blood thereof, shall ye not eat.[4] And surely your blood of your lives will I require; at the hand of every beast will I require it, and at the hand of man; at the hand of every man's brother will I require the life of man. Whoso sheddeth man's blood, by man shall his blood be shed, for in the image of God made he man. And you, be ye fruitful, and multiply; bring forth abundantly in the earth, and multiply therein.

And God spake unto Noah, and to his sons with him, saying, And I, behold, I establish my covenant with you, and with your seed after you; And with every living creature that is with you, of the fowl, of the cattle, and of every beast of the earth with you; from all that go out of the ark, to every beast of the earth. And I will establish my covenant with you; neither shall all flesh be cut off any more by the waters of a flood; neither shall there any more be a flood to destroy the earth. And God said, This is the token of the covenant which I make between me and you and every living creature that is with you, for perpetual generations: I do set my bow in the cloud, and it shall be for a token of a covenant between me and the earth. And it shall come to pass, when I bring a cloud over the earth, that the bow shall be seen in the cloud: and I will remember my covenant, which is between me and you and every living creature of all flesh; and the waters shall no more become a flood to destroy all flesh. And the bow shall be in the cloud; and I will look upon it, that I may remember the everlasting covenant between God and every living creature of all flesh that is upon the earth. And God said unto Noah, This is the token of the covenant, which I have established between me and all flesh that is upon the earth.

---

4. A reference to the biblical dietary laws: blood was supposed to be drained from a slaughtered animal.

Genesis 11

[The Origin of Languages]

11. And the whole earth was of one language, and of one speech. And it came to pass, as they journeyed from the east, that they found a plain in the land of Shinar;[1] and they dwelt there. And they said one to another, Go to, let us make brick, and burn them throughly. And they had brick for stone, and slime[2] had they for mortar. And they said, Go to, let us build us a city and a tower,[3] whose top may reach unto heaven; and let us make us a name, lest we be scattered abroad upon the face of the whole earth. And the Lord came down to see the city and the tower, which the children of men builded. And the Lord said, Behold, the people is one, and they have all one language; and this they begin to do: and now nothing will be restrained from them, which they have imagined to do. Go to, let us go down, and there confound their language, that they may not understand one another's speech. So the Lord scattered them abroad from thence upon the face of all the earth: and they left off to build the city. Therefore is the name of it called Babel;[4] because the Lord did there confound the language of all the earth: and from thence did the Lord scatter them abroad upon the face of all the earth.

Genesis 37, 39–46

[The Story of Joseph]

37. * * * Joseph, being seventeen years old, was feeding the flock with his brethren; and the lad was with the sons of Bilhah, and with the sons of Zilpah, his father's wives: and Joseph brought unto his father their evil report.[1] Now Israel loved Joseph more than all his children, because he was the son of his old age: and he made him a coat of many colours. And when his brethren saw that their father loved him more than all his brethren, they hated him, and could not speak peaceably unto him.

And Joseph dreamed a dream, and he told it his brethren: and they hated him yet the more. And he said unto them, Hear, I pray you, this dream which I have dreamed: for, behold, we were binding sheaves in the field, and, lo, my sheaf arose, and also stood upright; and, behold, your sheaves stood round about, and made obeisance to my sheaf. And his brethren said to him, Shalt thou indeed reign over us? or shalt thou indeed have dominion over us? And they hated him yet the more for his dreams, and for his words.

And he dreamed yet another dream, and told it his brethren, and said, Behold, I have dreamed a dream more; and, behold, the sun and the moon and the eleven stars made obeisance to me. And he told it to his father, and to his brethren: and his father rebuked him, and said unto him, What is this dream that thou hast dreamed? Shall I and thy mother and

---

1. In Mesopotamia. *They:* humankind.   2. Bitumen.   3. This story is based on the Babylonian practice of building temples in the form of terraced pyramids (ziggurats).   4. Babylon.   1. Joseph reported their misdeeds. *Father:* Israel.

thy brethren indeed come to bow down ourselves to thee to the earth? And his brethren envied him; but his father observed the saying.

And his brethren went to feed their father's flock in Shechem. And Israel said unto Joseph, Do not thy brethren feed the flock in Shechem? come, and I will send thee unto them. And he said to him, Here am I. And he said to him, Go, I pray thee, see whether it be well with thy brethren, and well with the flocks; and bring me word again. So he sent him out of the vale of Hebron, and he came to Shechem.

And a certain man found him, and, behold, he was wandering in the field: and the man asked him, saying, What seekest thou? And he said, I seek my brethren: tell me, I pray thee, where they feed their flocks. And the man said, They are departed hence; for I heard them say, Let us go to Dothan. And Joseph went after his brethren, and found them in Dothan. And when they saw him afar off, even before he came near unto them, they conspired against him to slay him. And they said one to another, Behold, this dreamer cometh. Come now therefore, and let us slay him, and cast him into some pit, and we will say, Some evil beast hath devoured him: and we shall see what will become of his dreams. And Reuben heard it, and he delivered him out of their hands; and said, Let us not kill him. And Reuben said unto them, Shed no blood, but cast him into this pit that is in the wilderness, and lay no hand upon him; that he might rid him out of their hands, to deliver him to his father again.

And it came to pass, when Joseph was come unto his brethren, that they stripped Joseph out of his coat, his coat of many colours that was on him; and they took him, and cast him into a pit: and the pit was empty, there was no water in it. And they sat down to eat bread: and they lifted up their eyes and looked, and, behold, a company of Ishmeelites came from Gilead with their camels bearing spicery and balm and myrrh, going to carry it down to Egypt. And Judah said unto his brethren, What profit is it if we slay our brother, and conceal his blood? Come, and let us sell him to the Ishmeelites, and let not our hand be upon him; for he is our brother and our flesh. And his brethren were content. Then there passed by Midianites merchantmen; and they[2] drew and lifted up Joseph out of the pit, and sold Joseph to the Ishmeelites for twenty pieces of silver: and they[3] brought Joseph into Egypt.

And Reuben returned unto the pit; and, behold, Joseph was not in the pit; and he rent his clothes. And he returned unto his brethren, and said, The child is not; and I, whither shall I go? And they took Joseph's coat, and killed a kid of the goats, and dipped the coat in the blood; and they sent the coat of many colours, and they brought it to their father; and said, This have we found: know now whether it be thy son's coat or no. And he knew it, and said, It is my son's coat; an evil beast hath devoured him; Joseph is without doubt rent in pieces. And Jacob rent his clothes, and put sackcloth upon his loins, and mourned for his son many days. And all his sons and all his daughters rose up to comfort him; but he refused to be comforted; and he said, For I will go down into the grave unto my son mourning. Thus his father wept for him. * * *

2. The brothers. The confusion in this passage may be because the text we have is a composite of two different versions.   3. The Ishmeelites.

39. And Joseph was brought down to Egypt; and Potiphar, an officer of Pharaoh, captain of the guard, an Egyptian, bought him of the hands of the Ishmeelites, which had brought him down thither. And the Lord was with Joseph, and he was a prosperous man; and he was in the house of his master the Egyptian. And his master saw that the Lord was with him, and that the Lord made all he did to prosper in his hand. And Joseph found grace in his sight, and he served him: and he made him overseer over his house, and all that he had he put into his hand. And it came to pass from the time that he had made him overseer in his house, and over all that he had, that the Lord blessed the Egyptian's house for Joseph's sake; and the blessing of the Lord was upon all that he had in the house, and in the field. And he left all that he had in Joseph's hand; and he knew not ought he had, save the bread which he did eat. And Joseph was a goodly person, and well favoured.

And it came to pass after these things, that his master's wife cast her eyes upon Joseph; and she said, Lie with me. But he refused, and said unto his master's wife, Behold, my master wotteth not what is with me in the house, and he hath committed all that he hath to my hand; there is none greater in this house than I; neither hath he kept back any thing from me but thee, because thou art his wife: how then can I do this great wickedness, and sin against God? And it came to pass, as she spake to Joseph day by day, that he hearkened not unto her, to lie by her, or to be with her. And it came to pass about this time, that Joseph went into the house to do his business; and there was none of the men of the house there within. And she caught him by his garment, saying, Lie with me: and he left his garment in her hand, and fled, and got him out. And it came to pass, when she saw that he had left his garment in her hand, and was fled forth, that she called unto the men of her house, and spoke unto them, saying, See, he hath brought in an Hebrew unto us to mock us; he came in unto me to lie with me, and I cried with a loud voice: and it came to pass, when he heard that I lifted up my voice and cried, that he left his garment with me, and fled, and got him out. And she laid up his garment by her, until his lord came home. And she spake unto him according to these words, saying, The Hebrew servant, which thou hast brought unto us, came in unto me to mock me: and it came to pass, as I lifted up my voice and cried, that he left his garment with me, and fled out. And it came to pass, when his master heard the words of his wife, which she spake unto him, saying, After this manner did thy servant to me; that his wrath was kindled. And Joseph's master took him, and put him into the prison, a place where the king's prisoners were bound: and he was there in the prison.

But the Lord was with Joseph, and showed him mercy, and gave him favour in the sight of the keeper of the prison. And the keeper of the prison committed to Joseph's hand all the prisoners that were in the prison; and whatsoever they did there, he was the doer of it. The keeper of the prison looked not to any thing that was under his hand; because the Lord was with him, and that which he did, the Lord made it to prosper.

40. And it came to pass after these things that the butler of the king of Egypt and his baker had offended their lord the king of Egypt. And Pha-

raoh was wroth against two of his officers, against the chief of the butlers, and against the chief of the bakers. And he put them in ward in the house of the captain of the guard, into the prison, the place where Joseph was bound. And the captain of the guard charged Joseph with them, and he served them: and they continued a season in ward.

And they dreamed a dream both of them, each man his dream in one night, each man according to the interpretation of his dream, the butler and the baker of the king of Egypt, which were bound in the prison. And Joseph came in unto them in the morning, and looked upon them, and, behold, they were sad. And he asked Pharaoh's officers that were with him in the ward of his lord's house, saying, Wherefore look ye so sadly to day? And they said unto him, We have dreamed a dream, and there is no interpreter of it. And Joseph said unto them, Do not interpretations belong to God? tell me them, I pray you. And the chief butler told his dream to Joseph, and said to him, In my dream, behold, a vine was before me; and in the vine were three branches: and it was as though it budded, and her blossoms shot forth; and the clusters thereof brought forth ripe grapes: and Pharaoh's cup was in my hand: and I took the grapes, and pressed them into Pharaoh's cup, and I gave the cup into Pharaoh's hand. And Joseph said unto him, This is the interpretation of it: the three branches are three days: yet within three days shall Pharaoh lift up thine head, and restore thee unto thy place: and thou shalt deliver Pharaoh's cup into his hand, after the former manner when thou wast his butler. But think on me when it shall be well with thee, and shew kindness, I pray thee, unto me, and make mention of me unto Pharaoh, and bring me out of this house: for indeed I was stolen away out of the land of the Hebrews: and here also have I done nothing that they should put me into the dungeon. When the chief baker saw that the interpretation was good, he said unto Joseph, I also was in my dream, and, behold, I had three white baskets on my head: and in the uppermost basket there was of all manner of bakemeats for Pharaoh; and the birds did eat them out of the basket upon my head. And Joseph answered and said, This is the interpretation thereof: the three baskets are three days: yet within three days shall Pharaoh lift up thy head from off thee, and shall hang thee on a tree; and the birds shall eat thy flesh from off thee.

And it came to pass the third day, which was Pharaoh's birthday, that he made a feast unto all his servants: and he lifted up the head of the chief butler and of the chief baker among his servants. And he restored the chief butler unto his butlership again; and he gave the cup into Pharaoh's hand. But he hanged the chief baker: as Joseph had interpreted to them. Yet did not the chief butler remember Joseph, but forgat him.

41. And it came to pass at the end of two full years, that Pharaoh dreamed: and, behold, he stood by the river. And, behold, there came up out of the river seven well favoured kine[4] and fatfleshed; and they fed in a meadow. And, behold, seven other kine came up after them out of the river, ill favoured and leanfleshed; and stood by the other kine upon the brink of the river. And the ill favoured and leanfleshed kine did eat up the seven well favoured and fat kine. So Pharaoh awoke. And he slept

4. Cattle.

and dreamed the second time: and, behold, seven ears of corn came up upon one stalk, rank[5] and good. And, behold, seven thin ears and blasted with the east wind sprung up after them. And the seven thin ears devoured the seven rank and full ears. And Pharaoh awoke, and, behold, it was a dream. And it came to pass in the morning that his spirit was troubled; and he sent and called for all the magicians of Egypt, and all the wise men thereof: and Pharaoh told them his dream; but there was none that could interpret them unto Pharaoh.

Then spake the chief butler unto Pharaoh, saying, I do remember my faults this day: Pharaoh was wroth with his servants, and put me in ward in the captain of the guard's house, both me and the chief baker: and we dreamed a dream in one night, I and he; we dreamed each man according to the interpretation of his dream. And there was there with us a young man, an Hebrew, servant to the captain of the guard; and we told him, and he interpreted to us our dreams; to each man according to his dream he did interpret. And it came to pass, as he interpreted to us, so it was; me he restored unto mine office, and him he hanged.

Then Pharaoh sent and called Joseph, and they brought him hastily out of the dungeon: and he shaved himself, and changed his raiment, and came in unto Pharaoh. And Pharaoh said unto Joseph, I have dreamed a dream, and there is none that can interpret it: and I have heard say of thee that thou canst understand a dream to interpret it. And Joseph answered Pharaoh, saying, It is not in me: God shall give Pharaoh an answer of peace. And Pharaoh said unto Joseph, In my dream, behold, I stood upon the bank of the river; and, behold, there came up out of the river seven kine, fatfleshed and well favoured; and they fed in a meadow: and, behold, seven other kine came up after them, poor and very ill favoured and lean-fleshed, such as I never saw in all the land of Egypt for badness: and the lean and the ill favoured kine did eat up the first seven fat kine: and when they had eaten them up, it could not be known that they had eaten them; but they were still ill favoured, as at the beginning. So I awoke. And I saw in my dream, and, behold, seven ears came up in one stalk, full and good: and, behold, seven ears, withered, thin, and blasted with the east wind, sprung up after them: and the thin ears devoured the seven good ears: and I told this unto the magicians; but there was none that could declare it to me.

And Joseph said unto Pharaoh, The dream of Pharaoh is one: God hath shewed Pharaoh what he is about to do. The seven good kine are seven years; and the seven good ears are seven years: the dream is one. And the seven thin and ill favoured kine that came up after them are seven years; and the seven empty ears blasted with the east wind shall be seven years of famine. This is the thing which I have spoken unto Pharaoh: what God is about to do he sheweth unto Pharaoh. Behold, there come seven years of great plenty throughout all the land of Egypt: and there shall arise after them seven years of famine; and all the plenty shall be forgotten in the land of Egypt; and the famine shall consume the land; and the plenty shall not be known in the land by reason of that famine following; for it

5. Fat.

shall be very grievous. And for that the dream was doubled unto Pharaoh twice; it is because the thing is established by God, and God will shortly bring it to pass. Now therefore let Pharaoh look out a man discreet and wise, and set him over the land of Egypt. Let Pharaoh do this, and let him appoint officers over the land, and take up the fifth part of the land[6] of Egypt in the seven plenteous years. And let them gather all the food of those good years that come, and lay up corn under the hand of Pharaoh, and let them keep food in the cities. And that food shall be for store to the land against the seven years of famine, which shall be in the land of Egypt; that the land perish not through the famine.

And the thing was good in the eyes of Pharaoh, and in the eyes of all his servants. And Pharaoh said unto his servants, Can we find such a one as this is, a man in whom the Spirit of God is? And Pharaoh said unto Joseph, Forasmuch as God hath shewed thee all this, there is none so discreet and wise as thou art: thou shalt be over my house, and according unto thy word shall all my people be ruled: only in the throne will I be greater than thou. And Pharaoh said unto Joseph, See, I have set thee over all the land of Egypt. And Pharaoh took off his ring from his hand, and put it upon Joseph's hand, and arrayed him in vestures of fine linen, and put a gold chain about his neck; and he made him to ride in the second chariot which he had; and they cried before him, Bow the knee: and he made him ruler over all the land of Egypt. And Pharaoh said unto Joseph, I am Pharaoh, and without thee shall no man lift up his hand or foot in all the land of Egypt. And Pharaoh called Joseph's name Zaphnath-paaneah; and he gave him to wife Asenath, the daughter of Poti-pherah priest of On. And Joseph went out over all the land of Egypt.

And Joseph was thirty years old when he stood before Pharaoh king of Egypt. And Joseph went out from the presence of Pharaoh, and went throughout all the land of Egypt. And in the seven plenteous years the earth brought forth by handfuls. And he gathered up all the food of the seven years, which were in the land of Egypt, and laid up the food in the cities: the food of the field, which was round about every city, laid he up in the same. And Joseph gathered corn as the sand of the sea, very much, until he left numbering; for it was without number. And unto Joseph were born two sons before the years of famine came, which Asenath, the daughter of Poti-pherah priest of On, bare unto him. And Joseph called the name of the first born Manasseh:[7] For God, said he, hath made me forget all my toil, and all my father's house. And the name of the second called he Ephraim:[8] For God hath caused me to be fruitful in the land of my affliction.

And the seven years of plenteousness, that was in the land of Egypt, were ended. And the seven years of dearth began to come, according as Joseph had said: and the dearth was in all lands; but in all the land of Egypt there was bread. And when all the land of Egypt was famished, the people cried to Pharaoh for bread: and Pharaoh said unto all the Egyptians, Go unto Joseph; what he saith to you, do. And the famine was over all the face of the earth. And Joseph opened all the storehouses, and sold

---

6. Of the crop.   7. Which means "causing to forget."   8. Which means "fruitfulness."

double money in your hand: and the money that was brought again in the mouth of your sacks, carry it again in your hand; peradventure it was an oversight: take also your brother, and arise, go again unto the man: and God Almighty give you mercy before the man, that he may send away your other brother, and Benjamin. If I be bereaved of my children, I am bereaved.

And the men took that present, and they took double money in their hand, and Benjamin; and rose up, and went down to Egypt, and stood before Joseph. And when Joseph saw Benjamin with them, he said to the ruler of his house, Bring these men home, and slay,[9] and make ready; for these men shall dine with me at noon. And the man did as Joseph bade; and the man brought the men into Joseph's house. And the men were afraid, because they were brought into Joseph's house; and they said, Because of the money that was returned in our sacks at the first time are we brought in; that he may seek occasion against us, and fall upon us, and take us for bondmen, and our asses. And they came near to the steward of Joseph's house, and they communed with him at the door of the house, and said, O sir, we came indeed down at the first time to buy food; and it came to pass, when we came to the inn, that we opened our sacks, and behold, every man's money was in the mouth of his sack, our money in full weight: and we have brought it again in our hand. And other money have we brought down in our hands to buy food: we cannot tell who put our money in our sacks. And he said, Peace be to you, fear not: your God, and the God of your father, hath given you treasure in your sacks: I had your money. And he brought Simeon out unto them. And the man brought the men into Joseph's house, and gave them water, and they washed their feet; and he gave their asses provender. And they made ready the present against Joseph came at noon: for they heard that they should eat bread there.

And when Joseph came home, they brought him the present which was in their hand into the house, and bowed themselves to him to the earth. And he asked them of their welfare, and said, Is your father well, the old man of whom ye spake? Is he yet alive? And they answered, Thy servant our father is in good health, he is yet alive. And they bowed down their heads, and made obeisance. And he lifted up his eyes, and saw his brother Benjamin, his mother's son, and said, Is this your younger brother, of whom ye spake unto me? And he said, God be gracious unto thee, my son. And Joseph made haste; for his bowels did yearn upon his brother: and he sought where to weep; and he entered into his chamber, and wept there. And he washed his face, and went out, and refrained himself, and said, Set on bread. And they set on for him by himself, and for them by themselves, and for the Egyptians, which did eat with him, by themselves: because the Egyptians might not eat bread with the Hebrews; for that is an abomination unto the Egyptians. And they sat before him, the firstborn according to his birthright, and the youngest according to his youth: and the men marvelled one at another. And he took and sent messes[1] unto

9. Kill an animal for meat.   1. Portions.

them from before him: but Benjamin's mess was five times so much as any of theirs. And they drank, and were merry with him.

44. And he commanded the steward of his house, saying, Fill the men's sacks with food, as much as they can carry, and put every man's money in his sack's mouth. And put my cup, the silver cup, in the sack's mouth of the youngest, and his corn money. And he did according to the word that Joseph had spoken. As soon as the morning was light, the men were sent away, they and their asses. And when they were gone out of the city, and not yet far off, Joseph said unto his steward, Up, follow after the men; and when thou dost overtake them, say unto them, Wherefore have ye rewarded evil for good? Is not this it in which my lord drinketh, and whereby indeed he divineth?[2] ye have done evil in so doing.

And he overtook them, and he spake unto them these same words. And they said unto him, Wherefore saith my lord these words? God forbid that thy servants should do according to this thing: behold, the money, which we found in our sacks' mouths, we brought again unto thee out of the land of Canaan: how then should we steal out of thy lord's house silver or gold? With whomsoever of thy servants it be found, both let him die, and we also will be my lord's bondmen. And he said, Now also let it be according unto your words: he with whom it is found shall be my servant; and ye shall be blameless. Then they speedily took down every man his sack to the ground, and opened every man his sack. And he searched, and began at the eldest, and left at the youngest: and the cup was found in Benjamin's sack. Then they rent their clothes, and laded every man his ass, and returned to the city.

And Judah and his brethren came to Joseph's house; for he was yet there: and they fell before him on the ground. And Joseph said unto them, What deed is this that ye have done? wot ye not that such a man as I can certainly divine? And Judah said, What shall we say unto my lord? what shall we speak? or how shall we clear ourselves? God hath found out the iniquity of thy servants: behold, we are my lord's servants, both we, and he also with whom the cup is found. And he said, God forbid that I should do so: but the man in whose hand the cup is found, he shall be my servant; and as for you, get you up in peace unto your father.

Then Judah came near unto him, and said, Oh my lord, let thy servant, I pray thee, speak a word in my lord's ears, and let not thine anger burn against thy servant: for thou art even as Pharaoh. My lord asked his servants, saying, Have ye a father, or a brother? And we said unto my lord, We have a father, an old man, and a child of his old age, a little one; and his brother is dead, and he alone is left of his mother, and his father loveth him. And thou saidst unto thy servants, Bring him down unto me, that I may set mine eyes upon him. And we said unto my lord, The lad cannot leave his father: for if he should leave his father, his father would die. And thou saidst unto thy servants, Except your youngest brother come down with you, ye shall see my face no more. And it came to pass when we

---

2. Joseph's servant is to claim that this is the cup Joseph uses for clairvoyance; diviners stared into a cup of water and foretold the future.

came up unto thy servant my father, we told him the words of my lord. And our father said, Go again, and buy us a little food. And we said, We cannot go down: if our youngest brother be with us, then will we go down: for we may not see the man's face, except our youngest brother be with us. And thy servant my father said unto us, Ye know that my wife bare me two sons: and the one went out from me, and I said, Surely he is torn in pieces; and I saw him not since: and if ye take this also from me, and mischief befall him, ye shall bring down my gray hairs with sorrow to the grave. Now therefore when I come to thy servant my father, and the lad be not with us; seeing that his life is bound up in the lad's life; it shall come to pass, when he seeth that the lad is not with us, that he will die: and thy servants shall bring down the gray hairs of thy servant our father with sorrow to the grave. For thy servant became surety for the lad unto my father, saying, If I bring him not unto thee, then I shall bear the blame to my father for ever. Now therefore, I pray thee, let thy servant abide instead of the lad a bondman to my lord; and let the lad go up with his brethren. For how shall I go up to my father, and the lad be not with me? lest peradventure I see the evil that shall come on my father.

45. Then Joseph could not refrain himself before all them that stood by him; and he cried, Cause every man to go out from me. And there stood no man with him, while Joseph made himself known unto his brethren. And he wept aloud: and the Egyptians and the house of Pharaoh heard. And Joseph said unto his brethren, I am Joseph; doth my father yet live? And his brethren could not answer him; for they were troubled at his presence. And Joseph said unto his brethren, Come near to me, I pray you. And they came near. And he said, I am Joseph your brother, whom ye sold into Egypt. Now therefore be not grieved, nor angry with yourselves, that ye sold me hither: for God did send me before you to preserve life. For these two years hath the famine been in the land: and yet there are five years, in the which there shall neither be earing nor harvest. And God sent me before you to preserve you a posterity in the earth, and to save your lives by a great deliverance. So now it was not you that sent me hither, but God: and he hath made me a father to Pharaoh, and lord of all his house, and a ruler throughout all the land of Egypt. Haste ye, and go up to my father, and say unto him, Thus saith thy son Joseph, God hath made me lord of all Egypt: come down unto me, tarry not: and thou shalt dwell in the land of Goshen, and thou shalt be near unto me, thou, and thy children, and thy children's children, and thy flocks, and thy herds, and all that thou hast: and there will I nourish thee; for yet there are five years of famine; lest thou, and thy household, and all that thou hast, come to poverty. And, behold, your eyes see, and the eyes of my brother Benjamin, that it is my mouth that speaketh unto you. And ye shall tell my father of all my glory in Egypt, and of all that ye have seen; and ye shall haste and bring down my father hither. And he fell upon his brother Benjamin's neck, and wept; and Benjamin wept upon his neck. Moreover he kissed all his brethren, and wept upon them: and after that his brethren talked with him.

And the fame thereof was heard in Pharaoh's house, saying, Joseph's brethren are come: and it pleased Pharaoh well, and his servants. And Pharaoh said unto Joseph, Say unto thy brethren, This do ye; lade your beasts, and go, get you unto the land of Canaan; and take your father and your households, and come unto me: and I will give you the good of the land of Egypt, and ye shall eat the fat of the land. Now thou art commanded, this do ye; take you wagons out of the land of Egypt for your little ones, and for your wives, and bring your father, and come. Also regard not your stuff; for the good of all the land of Egypt is yours. And the children of Israel did so: and Joseph gave them wagons, according to the commandment of Pharaoh, and gave them provision for the way. To all of them he gave each man changes of raiment; but to Benjamin he gave three hundred pieces of silver, and five changes of raiment. And to his father he sent after this manner; ten asses laden with the good things of Egypt, and ten she-asses laden with corn and bread and meat for his father by the way. So he sent his brethren away, and they departed: and he said unto them, See that ye fall not out by the way.

And they went up out of Egypt, and came into the land of Canaan unto Jacob their father, and told him, saying, Joseph is yet alive, and he is governor over all the land of Egypt. And Jacob's heart fainted, for he believed them not. And they told him all the words of Joseph, which he had said unto them: and when he saw the wagons which Joseph had sent to carry him, the spirit of Jacob their father revived. And Israel said, It is enough; Joseph my son is yet alive: I will go and see him before I die.

46. And Israel took his journey with all that he had, and came to Beer-sheba, and offered sacrifices unto the God of his father Isaac. And God spake unto Israel in the visions of the night, and said, Jacob, Jacob. And he said, Here am I. And he said, I am God, the God of thy father: fear not to go down into Egypt; for I will there make of thee a great nation: I will go down with thee into Egypt; and I will also surely bring thee up again: and Joseph shall put his hand upon thine eyes. And Jacob rose up from Beer-sheba: and the sons of Israel carried Jacob their father, and their little ones, and their wives, in the wagons which Pharaoh had sent to carry him. And they took their cattle, and their goods, which they had gotten in the land of Canaan, and came into Egypt, Jacob, and all his seed with him: his sons, and his sons' sons with him, his daughters, and his sons' daughters, and all his seed brought he with him into Egypt.

From Job

1. There was a man in the land of Uz whose name was Job, and that man was perfect and upright, and one that feared God, and eschewed evil. And there were born unto him seven sons and three daughters. His substance also was seven thousand sheep, and three thousand camels, and five hundred yoke of oxen, and five hundred she asses, and a very great household; so that this man was the greatest of all the men of the east. And his sons went and feasted in their houses, every one his day;[1] and sent

1. In rotation at each son's house.

and called for their three sisters to eat and to drink with them. And it was so, when the days of their feasting were gone about, that Job sent and sanctified them, and rose up early in the morning, and offered burnt offerings according to the number of them all: for Job said, It may be that my sons have sinned, and cursed God in their hearts. Thus did Job continually.

Now there was a day when the sons of God came to present themselves before the Lord, and Satan came also among them. And the Lord said unto Satan, Whence comest thou? Then Satan answered the Lord, and said, From going to and fro in the earth, and from walking up and down in it. And the Lord said unto Satan, Hast thou considered my servant Job, that there is none like him in the earth, a perfect and an upright man, one that feareth God, and escheweth evil? Then Satan answered the Lord, and said, Doth Job fear God for nought? Hast not thou made an hedge about him, and about his house, and about all that he hath on every side? thou hast blessed the work of his hands, and his substance is increased in the land. But put forth thine hand now, and touch all that he hath, and he will curse thee to thy face. And the Lord said unto Satan, Behold, all that he hath is in thy power; only upon himself put not forth thine hand. So Satan went forth from the presence of the Lord.

And there was a day when his sons and his daughters were eating and drinking wine in their eldest brother's house: and there came a messenger unto Job, and said, The oxen were plowing, and the asses feeding beside them: and the Sabeans fell upon them, and took them away; yea, they have slain the servants with the edge of the sword; and I only am escaped alone to tell thee. While he was yet speaking, there came also another, and said, The fire of God is fallen from heaven, and hath burned up the sheep, and the servants, and consumed them; and I only am escaped alone to tell thee. While he was yet speaking, there came also another, and said, The Chaldeans made out three bands,[2] and fell upon the camels, and have carried them away, yea, and slain the servants with the edge of the sword; and I only am escaped alone to tell thee. While he was yet speaking, there came also another, and said, Thy sons and thy daughters were eating and drinking wine in their eldest brother's house: and, behold, there came a great wind from the wilderness, and smote the four corners of the house, and it fell upon the young men, and they are dead; and I only am escaped alone to tell thee.

Then Job arose and rent his mantle,[3] and shaved his head, and fell down upon the ground, and worshipped, and said, Naked came I out of my mother's womb, and naked shall I return thither: the Lord gave, and the Lord hath taken away; blessed be the name of the Lord. In all this Job sinned not, nor charged God foolishly.

2. Again there was a day when the sons of God came to present themselves before the Lord, and Satan came also among them to present himself before the Lord. And the Lord said unto Satan, From whence comest thou? And Satan answered the Lord, and said, From going to and fro in

---

2. That is, split up into three groups.   3. Tore his cloak.

the earth, and from walking up and down in it. And the Lord said unto Satan, Hast thou considered my servant Job, that there is none like him in the earth, a perfect and an upright man, one that feareth God, and escheweth evil? and still he holdeth fast his integrity, although thou movedst me against him, to destroy him without cause. And Satan answered the Lord, and said, Skin for skin, yea, all that a man hath will he give for his life. But put forth thine hand now, and touch his bone and his flesh, and he will curse thee to thy face. And the Lord said unto Satan, Behold, he is in thine hand; but save his life.

So went Satan forth from the presence of the Lord, and smote Job with sore boils from the sole of his foot unto his crown. And he took him a potsherd to scrape himself withal; and he sat down among the ashes.

Then said his wife unto him, Dost thou still retain thine integrity? curse God, and die. But he said unto her, Thou speakest as one of the foolish women speaketh. What? shall we receive good at the hand of God, and shall we not receive evil? In all this did not Job sin with his lips. * * *

3. After this opened Job his mouth, and cursed his day. And Job spake, and said, Let the day perish wherein I was born, and the night in which it was said, There is a man child conceived. Let that day be darkness; let not God regard it from above, neither let the light shine upon it. Let darkness and the shadow of death stain it; let a cloud dwell upon it; let the blackness of the day terrify it. As for that night, let darkness seize upon it; let it not be joined unto the days of the year, let it not come into the number of the months. Lo, let that night be solitary, let no joyful voice come therein. Let them curse it that curse the day, who are ready to raise up their mourning.[4] Let the stars of the twilight thereof be dark; let it look for light, but have none; neither let it see the dawning of the day: because it shut not up the doors of my mother's womb, nor hid sorrow from mine eyes. Why died I not from the womb? Why did I not give up the ghost when I came out of the belly? Why did the knees prevent[5] me? or why the breasts that I should suck? For now should I have lain still and been quiet, I should have slept: then had I been at rest, with kings and counsellors of the earth, which built desolate places for themselves; or with princes that had gold, who filled their houses with silver: or as an hidden untimely birth I had not been; as infants which never saw light. There the wicked cease from troubling; and there the weary be at rest. There the prisoners rest together; they hear not the voice of the oppressor. The small and great are there; and the servant is free from his master. Wherefore is light given to him that is in misery, and life unto the bitter in soul; which long for death, but it cometh not; and dig for it more than for hid treasures; which rejoice exceedingly, and are glad, when they can find the grave? Why is light given to a man whose way is hid, and whom God hath hedged in? For my sighing cometh before I eat, and my roarings are poured out like the waters. For the thing which I greatly feared is come upon me, and that which I was afraid of is come unto me. I was not in safety, neither had I rest, neither was I quiet; yet trouble came.

---

4. More literally: who are ready to rouse up leviathan, a dragon that was thought to produce darkness. *Them:* sorcerers, magicians. 5. Receive.

Summary   At this point three friends of Job come to comfort him. Their approach is to tell him that since God has punished him he must in some way have offended God; he must admit his guilt and ask forgiveness. But he refuses to do so.

12. And Job answered and said, No doubt but ye are the people, and wisdom shall die with you. But I have understanding as well as you; I am not inferior to you: yea, who knoweth not such things as these? I am as one mocked of his neighbour, who calleth upon God, and he answered him: the just upright man is laughed to scorn. He that is ready to slip with his feet is as a lamp despised in the thought of him that is at ease. The tabernacles of robbers prosper, and they that provoke God are secure; into whose hand God bringeth abundantly. But ask now the beasts, and they shall teach thee; and the fowls of the air, and they shall tell thee: or speak to the earth, and it shall teach thee: and the fishes of the sea shall declare unto thee. Who knoweth not in all these that the hand of the Lord hath wrought this? In whose hand is the soul of every living thing, and the breath of all mankind. Doth not the ear try words? and the mouth taste his meat? With the ancient is wisdom; and in length of days understanding. With him is wisdom and strength, he hath counsel and understanding. Behold, he breaketh down, and it cannot be built again: he shutteth up a man, and there can be no opening. Behold, he withholdeth the waters, and they dry up: also he sendeth them out, and they overturn the earth. With him is strength and wisdom: the deceived and the deceiver are his. He leadeth counsellors away spoiled, and maketh the judges fools. He looseth the bond of kings, and girdeth their loins with a girdle. He leadeth princes away spoiled, and overthroweth the mighty. He removeth away the speech of the trusty, and taketh away the understanding of the aged. He poureth contempt upon princes, and weakeneth the strength of the mighty. He discovereth deep things out of darkness, and bringeth out to light the shadow of death. He increaseth the nations, and destroyeth them: he enlargeth the nations, and straiteneth them again.[6] He taketh away the heart of the chief of the people of the earth, and causeth them to wander in a wilderness where there is no way. They grope in the dark without light, and he maketh them to stagger like a drunken man.

13. Lo, mine eye hath seen all this, mine ear hath heard and understood it. What ye know, the same do I know also: I am not inferior unto you. Surely I would speak to the Almighty, and I desire to reason with God. But ye are forgers of lies, ye are all physicians of no value. O that ye would altogether hold your peace! and it should be your wisdom. Hear now my reasoning, and hearken to the pleadings of my lips. Will ye speak wickedly for God? and talk deceitfully for him? Will ye accept[7] his person? Will ye contend for God? Is it good that he should search you out? or as one man mocketh another, do ye so mock him? He will surely reprove you, if ye do secretly accept persons.[8] Shall not his excellency make you afraid? and his dread fall upon you? Your remembrances[9] are like unto ashes, your bodies to bodies of clay. Hold your peace, let me alone, that I

6. Makes them small again.   7. Respect.   8. That is, if you back the winning side for personal reasons.   9. Memorable sayings.

may speak, and let come on me what will. Wherefore do I take my flesh in my teeth, and put my life in mine hand?[1] Though he slay me, yet will I trust in him: but I will maintain mine own ways before him. He also shall be my salvation: for an hypocrite shall not come before him. Hear diligently my speech, and my declaration with your ears. Behold now, I have ordered my cause; I know that I shall be justified. Who is he that will plead with me?[2] for now, if I hold my tongue, I shall give up the ghost. Only do not two things unto me: then will I not hide myself from thee.[3] Withdraw thine hand far from me: and let not thy dread make me afraid. Then call thou, and I will answer: or let me speak, and answer thou me. How many are mine iniquities and sins? Make me to know my transgression and my sin. Wherefore hidest thou thy face, and holdest me for thine enemy? Wilt thou break a leaf driven to and fro? and wilt thou pursue the dry stubble? For thou writest bitter things against me, and makest me to possess the iniquities of my youth. Thou puttest my feet also in the stocks, and lookest narrowly unto all my paths; thou settest a print upon the heels of my feet. And he, as a rotten thing, consumeth, as a garment that is moth eaten.

14. Man that is born of a woman is of few days, and full of trouble. He cometh forth like a flower, and is cut down: he fleeth also as a shadow, and continueth not. And dost thou open thine eyes upon such an one, and bringest me into judgment with thee? Who can bring a clean thing out of an unclean? not one. Seeing his days are determined, the number of his months are with thee, thou hast appointed his bounds that he cannot pass; turn from him, that he may rest, till he shall accomplish, as an hireling, his day. For there is hope of a tree, if it be cut down, that it will sprout again, and that the tender branch thereof will not cease. Though the root thereof wax old in the earth, and the stock thereof die in the ground; yet through the scent of water it will bud, and bring forth boughs like a plant. But man dieth, and wasteth away: yea, man giveth up the ghost, and where is he? As the waters fail from the sea, and the flood decayeth and drieth up: so man lieth down, and riseth not: till the heavens be no more, they shall not awake, nor be raised out of their sleep. O that thou wouldest hide me in the grave, that thou wouldest keep me secret, until thy wrath be past, that thou wouldest appoint me a set time, and remember me! If a man die, shall he live again? All the days of my appointed time will I wait, till my change[4] come. Thou shalt call, and I will answer thee: thou wilt have a desire to[5] the work of thine hands. For now thou numberest my steps: dost thou not watch over my sin? My transgression is sealed up in a bag, and thou sewest up mine iniquity. And surely the mountain falling cometh to nought, and the rock is removed out of his place. The waters wear the stones: thou washest away the things which grow out of the dust of the earth; and thou destroyest the hope of man. Thou prevailest for ever against him, and he passeth; thou changest his countenance, and sendest him away. His sons come to honour, and he knoweth it not; and they are brought low, but he perceiveth it not of

---

1. Like a wild beast at bay, defending its life with its teeth.   2. Accuse me.   3. He now addresses himself directly to God.   4. Release.   5. For.

them. But his flesh upon him shall have pain, and his soul within him shall mourn.

29. Moreover Job continued his parable, and said, Oh that I were as in months past, as in the days when God preserved me; when his candle shined upon my head, and when by his light I walked through darkness; as I was in the days of my youth, when the secret of God was upon my tabernacle; when the Almighty was yet with me, when my children were about me; when I washed my steps with butter and the rock poured me out rivers of oil; when I went out to the gate[6] through the city, when I prepared my seat in the street! The young men saw me, and hid themselves: and the aged arose, and stood up. The princes refrained talking, and laid their hand on their mouth. The nobles held their peace, and their tongue cleaved to the roof of their mouth. When the ear heard me, then it blessed me; and when the eye saw me, it gave witness to me: because I delivered the poor that cried, and the fatherless, and him that had none to help him. The blessing of him that was ready to perish came upon me: and I caused the widow's heart to sing for joy. I put on righteousness, and it clothed me: my judgment was as a robe and a diadem. I was eyes to the blind, and feet was I to the lame. I was a father to the poor: and the cause which I knew not I searched out. And I brake the jaws of the wicked, and plucked the spoil out of his teeth. Then I said, I shall die in my nest, and I shall multiply my days as the sand. My root was spread out by the waters, and the dew lay all night upon my branch. My glory was fresh in me, and my bow was renewed in my hand. Unto me men gave ear, and waited, and kept silence at my counsel. After my words they spake not again; and my speech dropped upon them. And they waited for me as for the rain; and they opened their mouth wide as for the latter rain. If I laughed on them, they believed it not; and the light of my countenance they cast not down. I chose out their way, and sat chief, and dwelt as a king in the army, as one that comforteth the mourners.

30. But now they that are younger than I have me in derision, whose fathers I would have disdained to have set with the dogs of my flock. Yea, whereto might the strength of their hands profit me, in whom old age was perished?[7] For want and famine they were solitary; fleeing into the wilderness in former time desolate and waste. Who cut up mallows by the bushes, and juniper roots for their meat. They were driven forth from among men, (they cried after them as after a thief;) to dwell in the cliffs of the valleys, in caves of the earth, and in the rocks. Among the bushes they brayed; under the nettles they were gathered together. They were children of fools, yea, children of base men: they were viler than the earth. And now am I their song, yea, I am their byword. They abhor me, they flee far from me, and spare not to spit in my face. Because he hath loosed my cord, and afflicted me, they have also let loose the bridle before me. Upon my right hand rise the youth; they push away my feet, and they raise up against me the ways of their destruction. They mar my path, they set forward my calamity, they have no helper. They came upon me as a wide

6. The town meeting place and law court was just inside the gate.   7. They were too old to work.

breaking in of waters: in the desolation they rolled themselves upon me. Terrors are turned upon me: they pursue my soul as the wind: and my welfare passeth away as a cloud. And now my soul is poured out upon[8] me; the days of affliction have taken hold upon me. My bones are pierced in me in the night season: and my sinews take no rest. By the great force of my disease is my garment changed: it bindeth me about as the collar of my coat. He hath cast me into the mire, and I am become like dust and ashes. I cry unto thee, and thou dost not hear me: I stand up, and thou regardest me not. Thou art become cruel to me: with thy strong hand thou opposest thyself against me. Thou liftest me up to the wind; thou causest me to ride upon it, and dissolvest my substance. For I know that thou wilt bring me to death, and to the house appointed for all living. Howbeit he will not stretch out his hand to the grave, though they cry in his destruction. Did not I weep for him that was in trouble? Was not my soul grieved for the poor? When I looked for good, then evil came unto me: and when I waited for light, there came darkness. My bowels boiled, and rested not: the days of affliction prevented me. I went mourning without the sun: I stood up, and I cried in the congregation. I am a brother to dragons, and a companion to owls. My skin is black upon me, and my bones are burned with heat. My harp also is turned to mourning, and my organ[9] into the voice of them that weep.

31. I made a covenant with mine eyes; why then should I think upon a maid? For what portion of God is there from above? and what inheritance of the Almighty from on high? Is not destruction to the wicked? and a strange punishment to the workers of iniquity? Doth not he see my ways, and count all my steps? If I have walked with vanity, or if my foot hath hasted to deceit; let me be weighed in an even balance, that God may know mine integrity. If my step hath turned out of the way, and mine heart walked after mine eyes, and if any blot hath cleaved to mine hands; then let me sow, and let another eat; yea, let my offspring be rooted out. If mine heart have been deceived by a woman, or if I have laid wait at my neighbour's door; then let my wife grind unto another, and let others bow down upon her. For this is an heinous crime; yea, it is an iniquity to be punished by the judges. For it is a fire that consumeth to destruction, and would root out all mine increase.

If I did despise the cause of my manservant or of my maidservant, when they contended with me; what then shall I do when God riseth up? and when he visiteth, what shall I answer him? Did not he that made me in the womb make him? and did not one fashion us in the womb? If I have withheld the poor from their desire, or have caused the eyes of the widow to fail; or have eaten my morsel myself alone, and the fatherless hath not eaten thereof; (For from my youth he was brought up with me, as with a father, and I have guided her from my mother's womb;) if I have seen any perish for want of clothing, or any poor without covering; if his loins have not blessed me, and if he were not warmed with the fleece of my sheep; if I have lifted up my hand against the fatherless, when I saw my help in the gate:[1] then let mine arm fall from my shoulder blade, and mine arm

---

8. Within.   9. Pipe.   1. That is, when I had influence in the court.

be broken from the bone. For destruction from God was a terror to me, and by reason of his highness I could not endure. If I have made gold my hope, or have said to the fine gold, Thou art my confidence; if I rejoiced because my wealth was great, and because mine hand had gotten much; if I beheld the sun when it shined, or the moon walking in brightness; and my heart hath been secretly enticed, or my mouth hath kissed my hand:[2] this also were an iniquity to be punished by the judge: for I should have denied the God that is above.

If I rejoiced at the destruction of him that hated me, or lifted up myself when evil found him: neither have I suffered my mouth to sin by wishing a curse to his soul. If the men of my tabernacle said not, Oh that we had of his flesh! We cannot be satisfied. The stranger did not lodge in the street: but I opened my doors to the traveller. If I covered my transgressions as Adam, by hiding mine iniquity in my bosom: did I fear a great multitude, or did the contempt of families terrify me, that I kept silence, and went not out of the door? Oh that one would hear me! Behold, my desire is, that the Almighty would answer me, and that mine adversary had written a book. Surely I would take it upon my shoulder, and bind it as a crown to me. I would declare unto him the number of my steps; as a prince would I go near unto him. If my land cry against me, or that the furrows likewise thereof complain; if I have eaten the fruits thereof without money, or have caused the owners thereof to lose their life: let thistles grow instead of wheat, and cockle instead of barley. The words of Job are ended.

38. Then the Lord answered Job out of the whirlwind, and said, Who is this that darkeneth counsel by words without knowledge? Gird up now thy loins like a man; for I will demand of thee, and answer thou me. Where wast thou when I laid the foundations of the earth? Declare, if thou hast understanding. Who hath laid the measures thereof, if thou knowest? or who hath stretched the line upon it? Whereupon are the foundations thereof fastened? or who laid the corner stone thereof; when the morning stars sang together, and all the sons of God shouted for joy? Or who shut up the sea with doors, when it brake forth, as if it had issued out of the womb? When I made the cloud the garment thereof, and thick darkness a swaddlingband for it, and brake up for it my decreed place,[3] and set bars and doors, and said, Hitherto shalt thou come, but no further: and here shall thy proud waves be stayed? Hast thou commanded the morning since thy days; and caused the dayspring[4] to know his place; that it might take hold of the ends of the earth, that the wicked might be shaken out of it? It is turned as clay to the seal; and they[5] stand as a garment. And from the wicked their light is withholden, and the high arm shall be broken. Hast thou entered into the springs of the sea? or hast thou walked in the search of the depth? Have the gates of death been opened unto thee? or hast thou seen the doors of the shadow of death? Hast thou perceived the breadth of the earth? Declare if thou knowest it all. Where

---

2. Idolatrous acts of worship of the sun and moon.　3. The broken coastline.　4. Dawn.　5. All things; God is describing the moment of the creation of the universe. *Turned as clay to the seal:* more literally, changed as clay under the seal.

is the way where light dwelleth? And as for darkness, where is the place thereof, that thou shouldest take it to the bound thereof, and that thou shouldest know the paths to the house thereof? Knowest thou it, because thou wast then born? or because the number of thy days is great? Hast thou entered into the treasures of the snow? or hast thou seen the treasures of the hail, which I have reserved against the time of trouble, against the day of battle and war? By what way is the light parted, which scattereth the east wind upon the earth? Who hath divided a watercourse for the overflowing of waters, or a way for the lightning of thunder; to cause it to rain on the earth, where no man is; on the wilderness, wherein there is no man; to satisfy the desolate and waste ground; and to cause the bud of the tender herb to spring forth? Hath the rain a father? or who hath begotten the drops of dew? Out of whose womb came the ice? And the hoary frost of heaven, who hath gendered it? The waters are hid as with a stone, and the face of the deep is frozen. Canst thou bind the sweet influences of Pleiades, or loose the bands of Orion? Canst thou bring forth Mazzaroth[6] in his season? or canst thou guide Arcturus with his sons? Knowest thou the ordinances of heaven? Canst thou set the dominion thereof in the earth? Canst thou lift up thy voice to the clouds, that abundance of waters may cover thee? Canst thou send lightnings, that they may go, and say unto thee, Here we are? Who hath put wisdom in the inward parts? or who hath given understanding to the heart? Who can number the clouds in wisdom? or who can stay the bottles of heaven, when the dust groweth into hardness, and the clods cleave fast together? Wilt thou hunt the prey for the lion? or fill the appetite of the young lions, when they couch in their dens, and abide in the covert to lie in wait? Who provideth for the raven his food? when his young ones cry unto God, they wander for lack of meat.

39. Knowest thou the time when the wild goats of the rock bring forth? or canst thou mark when the hinds do calve? Canst thou number the months that they fulfil? or knowest thou the time when they bring forth? They bow themselves, they bring forth their young ones, they cast out their sorrows. Their young ones are in good liking, they grow up with corn; they go forth, and return not unto them. Who hath sent out the wild ass free? or who hath loosed the bands of the wild ass? Whose house I have made the wilderness, and the barren land his dwellings. He scorneth the multitude of the city, neither regardeth he the crying of the driver. The range of the mountains is his pasture, and he searcheth after every green thing. Will the unicorn[7] be willing to serve thee, or abide by thy crib? Canst thou bind the unicorn with his band in the furrow? or will he harrow the valleys after thee? Wilt thou trust him, because his strength is great? or wilt thou leave thy labour to him? Wilt thou believe him, that he will bring home thy seed, and gather it into thy barn? Gavest thou the goodly wings unto the peacocks? or wings and feathers unto the ostrich? Which leaveth her eggs in the earth, and warmeth them in dust, and forgetteth that the foot may crush them, or that the wild beast may break

6. Meaning disputed; it may be a name for the signs of the zodiac or for some particular constellation.   7. The Hebrew has "wild ox."

them. She is hardened against her young ones, as though they were not hers: her labour is in vain without fear;[8] because God hath deprived her of wisdom, neither hath he imparted to her understanding. What time she lifteth up herself on high, she scorneth the horse and his rider. Hast thou given the horse strength? Hast thou clothed his neck with thunder? Canst thou make him afraid as a grasshopper? The glory of his nostrils is terrible. He paweth in the valley, and rejoiceth in his strength: he goeth on to meet the armed men. He mocketh at fear, and is not affrighted; neither turneth he back from the sword. The quiver rattleth against him, the glittering spear and the shield. He swalloweth the ground with fierceness and rage: neither believeth he that it is the sound of the trumpet. He saith among the trumpets, Ha, ha; and he smelleth the battle afar off, the thunder of the captains, and the shouting. Doth the hawk fly by thy wisdom, and stretch her wings toward the south? Doth the eagle mount up at thy command, and make her nest on high? She dwelleth and abideth on the rock, upon the crag of the rock, and the strong place. From thence she seeketh the prey, and her eyes behold afar off. Her young ones also suck up blood: and where the slain are, there is she.

40. Moreover the Lord answered Job, and said, Shall he that contendeth with the Almighty instruct him? He that reproveth God, let him answer it.

Then Job answered the Lord, and said, Behold, I am vile; what shall I answer thee? I will lay mine hand upon my mouth. Once have I spoken; but I will not answer: yea, twice; but I will proceed no further.

Then answered the Lord unto Job out of the whirlwind, and said, Gird up thy loins now like a man: I will demand of thee, and declare thou unto me. Wilt thou also disannul my judgment? Wilt thou condemn me, that thou mayest be righteous? Hast thou an arm like God: or canst thou thunder with a voice like him? Deck thyself now with majesty and excellency; and array thyself with glory and beauty. Cast abroad the rage of thy wrath: and behold every one that is proud, and abase him. Look on every one that is proud, and bring him low; and tread down the wicked in their place. Hide them in the dust together; and bind their faces in secret. Then will I also confess unto thee that thine own right hand can save thee.

Behold now behemoth,[9] which I made with thee; he eateth grass as an ox. Lo now, his strength is in his loins, and his force is in the navel of his belly. He moveth his tail like a cedar: the sinews of his stones[1] are wrapped together. His bones are as strong pieces of brass; his bones are like bars of iron. He is the chief of the ways of God: he that made him can make his sword to approach unto him. Surely the mountains bring him forth food, where all the beasts of the field play. He lieth under the shady trees, in the covert of the reed, and fens. The shady trees cover him with their shadow; the willows of the brook compass him about. Behold, he drinketh up a river, and hasteth not: he trusteth that he can draw up Jordan into his mouth. He taketh it with his eyes:[2] his nose pierceth through snares.

---

8. That is, although her labor is in vain, she is without fear.   9. Generally identified with the hippopotamus.   1. More literally: thighs.   2. Obscure; probably none can attack him in the eyes.

41. Canst thou draw out leviathan[3] with an hook? or his tongue with a cord which thou lettest down? Canst thou put an hook into his nose? or bore his jaw through with a thorn? Will he make many supplications unto thee? will he speak soft words unto thee? Will he make a covenant with thee? wilt thou take him for a servant for ever? Wilt thou play with him as with a bird? or wilt thou bind him for thy maidens? Shall the companions make a banquet of him? Shall they part him among the merchants? Canst thou fill his skin with barbed irons? or his head with fish spears? Lay thine hand upon him, remember the battle, do no more. Behold, the hope of him is in vain: shall not one be cast down even at the sight of him? None is so fierce that dare stir him up: who then is able to stand before me? Who hath prevented me,[4] that I should repay him? Whatsoever is under the whole heaven is mine. I will not conceal his parts, nor his power, nor his comely proportion. Who can discover the face of his garment?[5] or who can come to him with his double bridle? Who can open the doors of his face? His teeth are terrible round about. His scales are his pride, shut up together as with a close seal. One is so near to another, that no air can come between them. They are joined one to another, they stick together, that they cannot be sundered. By his neesings[6] a light doth shine, and his eyes are like the eyelids of the morning. Out of his mouth go burning lamps, and sparks of fire leap out. Out of his nostrils goeth smoke, as out of a seething pot or caldron. His breath kindleth coals, and a flame goeth out of his mouth. In his neck remaineth strength, and sorrow is turned into joy before him. The flakes of his flesh are joined together: they are firm in themselves; they cannot be moved. His heart is as firm as a stone; yea, as hard as a piece of the nether millstone. When he raiseth up himself, the mighty are afraid: by reason of breakings they purify themselves.[7] The sword of him that layeth at him cannot hold: the spear, the dart, nor the habergeon. He esteemeth iron as straw, and brass as rotten wood. The arrow cannot make him flee: slingstones are turned with him into stubble. Darts are counted as stubble: he laugheth at the shaking of a spear. Sharp stones are under him: he spreadeth sharp pointed things upon the mire. He maketh the deep to boil like a pot: he maketh the sea like a pot of ointment. He maketh a path to shine after him; one would think the deep to be hoary.[8] Upon earth there is not his like, who is made without fear. He beholdeth all high things: he is a king over all the children of pride.

42. Then Job answered the Lord, and said, I know that thou canst do every thing, and that no thought can be withholden from thee. Who is he that hideth counsel without knowledge? Therefore have I uttered that I understood not; things too wonderful for me, which I knew not. Hear, I beseech thee, and I will speak: I will demand of thee, and declare thou unto me. I have heard of thee by the hearing of the ear: but now mine eye seeth thee. Wherefore I abhor myself, and repent in dust and ashes.

And it was so, that after the Lord had spoken these words unto Job, the

---

3. Here probably the crocodile.   4. Given anything to me first.   5. His scales. *Discover:* strip off.   6. His breath (compare *sneeze*). The vapor exhaled by the crocodile appears luminous in the sunlight.   7. Corrupt text; probably in consternation they are beside themselves.   8. White (with foam).

Lord said to Eliphaz the Temanite, My wrath is kindled against thee, and against thy two friends: for ye have not spoken of me the thing that is right, as my servant Job hath. Therefore take unto you now seven bullocks and seven rams, and go to my servant Job, and offer up for yourselves a burnt offering; and my servant Job shall pray for you: for him will I accept: lest I deal with you after your folly, in that ye have not spoken of me the thing which is right, like my servant Job. So Eliphaz the Temanite and Bildad the Shuhite and Zophar the Naamathite went, and did according as the Lord commanded them: the Lord also accepted Job. And the Lord turned the captivity[9] of Job, when he prayed for his friends: also the Lord gave Job twice as much as he had before. Then came there unto him all his brethren, and all his sisters, and all they that had been of his acquaintance before, and did eat bread with him in his house: and they bemoaned him, and comforted him over all the evil that the Lord had brought upon him: every man also gave him a piece of money, and every one an earring of gold. So the Lord blessed the latter end of Job more than his beginning: for he had fourteen thousand sheep, and six thousand camels, and a thousand yoke of oxen, and a thousand she asses. He had also seven sons and three daughters. And he called the name of the first, Jemima; and the name of the second, Kezia; and the name of the third, Kerenhappuch. And in all the land were no women found so fair as the daughters of Job: and their father gave them inheritance among their brethren. After this lived Job an hundred and forty years, and saw his sons, and his sons' sons, even four generations. So Job died, being old and full of days.

Psalm 8

1. O Lord our Lord, how excellent is thy name in all the earth! who hast set thy glory above the heavens.

2. Out of the mouth of babes and sucklings hast thou ordained strength because of thine enemies, that thou mightest still the enemy and the avenger.

3. When I consider thy heavens, the work of thy fingers, the moon and the stars, which thou hast ordained;

4. What is man, that thou art mindful of him? and the son of man, that thou visitest him?

5. For thou hast made him a little lower than the angels, and hast crowned him with glory and honour.

6. Thou madest him to have dominion over the works of thy hands; thou hast put all things under his feet:

7. All sheep and oxen, yea, and the beasts of the field;

8. The fowl of the air, and the fish of the sea, and whatsoever passeth through the paths of the seas.

9. O Lord our Lord, how excellent is thy name in all the earth!

---

9. Put an end to the suffering.

Psalm 19

1. The heavens declare the glory of God; and the firmament sheweth his handywork.

2. Day unto day uttereth speech, and night unto night sheweth knowledge.

3. There is no speech nor language, where their voice is not heard.

4. Their line is gone out through all the earth, and their words to the end of the world. In them hath he set a tabernacle for the sun,

5. Which is as a bridegroom coming out of his chamber, and rejoiceth as a strong man to run a race.

6. His going forth is from the end of the heaven, and his circuit unto the ends of it: and there is nothing hid from the heat thereof.

7. The law of the Lord is perfect, converting the soul: the testimony of the Lord is sure, making wise the simple.

8. The statutes of the Lord are right, rejoicing the heart: the commandment of the Lord is pure, enlightening the eyes.

9. The fear of the Lord is clean, enduring for ever: the judgments of the Lord are true and righteous altogether.

10. More to be desired are they than gold, yea, than much fine gold: sweeter also than honey and the honeycomb.

11. Moreover by them is thy servant warned: and in keeping of them there is great reward.

12. Who can understand his errors? cleanse thou me from secret faults.

13. Keep back thy servant also from presumptuous sins; let them not have dominion over me: then shall I be upright, and I shall be innocent from the great transgression.

14. Let the words of my mouth, and the meditation of my heart, be acceptable in thy sight, O Lord, my strength, and my redeemer.

Psalm 23

1. The Lord is my shepherd; I shall not want.

2. He maketh me to lie down in green pastures: he leadeth me beside the still waters.

3. He restoreth my soul: he leadeth me in the paths of righteousness for his name's sake.

4. Yea, though I walk through the valley of the shadow of death, I will fear no evil: for thou art with me; thy rod and thy staff they comfort me.

5. Thou preparest a table before me in the presence of mine enemies: thou anointest my head with oil; my cup runneth over.

6. Surely goodness and mercy shall follow me all the days of my life: and I will dwell in the house of the Lord for ever.

Psalm 137

1. By the rivers of Babylon,[1] there we sat down, yea, we wept, when we remembered Zion.

2. We hanged our harps upon the willows in the midst thereof.

3. For there they that carried us away captive required of us a song; and they that wasted us required of us mirth, saying, Sing us one of the songs of Zion.

4. How shall we sing the Lord's song in a strange land?

5. If I forget thee, O Jerusalem, let my right hand forget her cunning.

6. If I do not remember thee, let my tongue cleave to the roof of my mouth; if I prefer not Jerusalem above my chief joy.

7. Remember, O Lord, the children of Edom[2] in the day of Jerusalem; who said, Rase it, rase it, even to the foundation thereof.

8. O daughter of Babylon, who art to be destroyed; happy shall he be, that rewardeth thee as thou hast served us.

9. Happy shall he be, that taketh and dasheth thy little ones against the stones.

Isaiah 52–53

[The Song of the Suffering Servant]

52. * * * Behold, my servant shall deal prudently, he shall be exalted and extolled, and be very high. As many were astonied at thee; his visage was so marred more than any man, and his form more than the sons of men: so shall he sprinkle many nations; the kings shall shut their mouths at him: for that which had not been told them shall they see; and that which they had not heard shall they consider.

53. Who hath believed our report? and to whom is the arm of the Lord revealed? For he shall grow up before him as a tender plant, and as a root out of a dry ground: he hath no form nor comeliness; and when we shall see him, there is no beauty that we should desire him. He is despised and rejected of men; a man of sorrows, and acquainted with grief: and we hid as it were our faces from him; he was despised, and we esteemed him not. Surely he hath borne our griefs, and carried our sorrows: yet we did esteem him stricken, smitten of God, and afflicted. But he was wounded for our transgressions, he was bruised for our iniquities: the chastisement of our peace was upon him; and with his stripes we are healed. All we like sheep have gone astray; we have turned every one to his own way; and the Lord hath laid on him the iniquity of us all. He was oppressed, and he was afflicted, yet he opened not his mouth: he is brought as a lamb to the slaughter, and as a sheep before her shearers is dumb, so he openeth not his mouth. He was taken from prison and from judgment: and who shall declare his generation? for he was cut off out of the land of the living: for

---

1. On the Euphrates River. Jerusalem was captured and sacked by the Babylonians in 586 B.C. The Hebrews were taken away into captivity in Babylon.   2. The Edomites helped the Babylonians to capture Jerusalem.

the transgression of my people was he stricken. And he made his grave with the wicked, and with the rich[1] in his death; because he had done no violence, neither was any deceit in his mouth. Yet it pleased the Lord to bruise him; he hath put him to grief: when thou shalt make his soul an offering for sin, he shall see his seed, he shall prolong his days, and the pleasure of the Lord shall prosper in his hand. He shall see of the travail of his soul, and shall be satisfied: by his knowledge shall my righteous servant justify many; for he shall bear their iniquities. Therefore will I divide him a portion with the great, and he shall divide the spoil with the strong; because he hath poured out his soul unto death: and he was numbered with the transgressors; and he bare the sin of many, and made intercession for the transgressors.

1. Some editors emend the Hebrew to "evildoers."

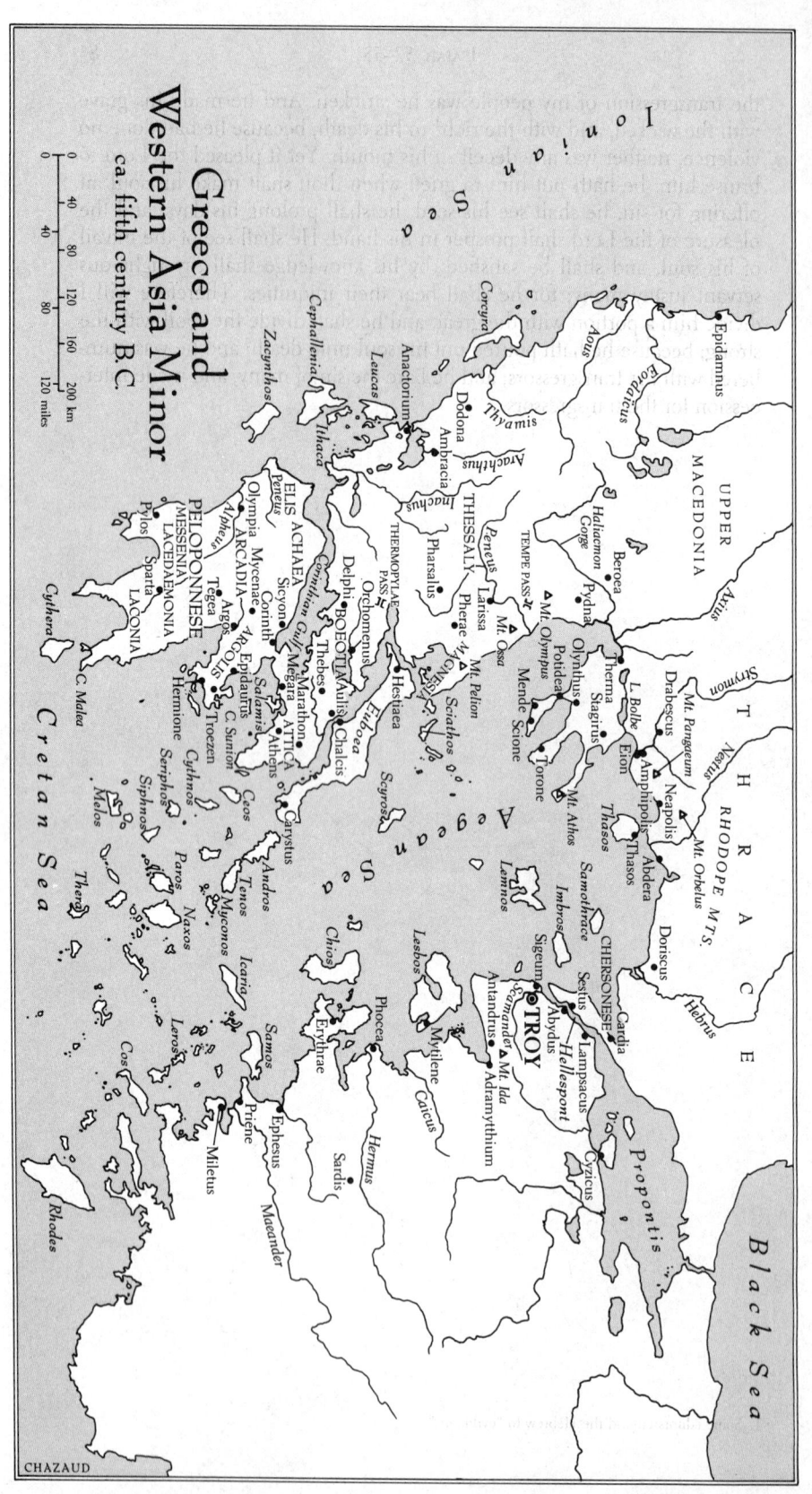

Greece and
Western Asia Minor
ca. fifth century B.C.

CHAZAUD

Ancient Greece and the
Formation of the Western Mind

The origin of the peoples who eventually produced the great literature of the eighth to the fourth centuries B.C. is still a mystery. The language they spoke clearly belongs to the great Indo-European family (which includes the Germanic, Celtic, Italic, and Sanskrit language groups), but many of the ancient Greek words and place names have terminations that are definitely not Indo-European—the word for sea, *thalassa*, for example. The Greeks of historic times were presumably a blend of the native tribes and the Indo-European invaders, en route from the European landmass.

In the last hundred years archaeology has given us a clearer picture than our forebears had of the level of civilization in early Greece. The second millennium B.C. saw a brilliant culture, called Minoan after the mythical king Minos, flourishing on the large island of Crete; and the citadel of Mycenae and the palace at Pylos show that mainland Greece, in that same period, had centers of wealth and power unsuspected before the excavators discovered the gold masks of the buried kings and the clay tablets covered with strange signs. The decipherment of these signs (published in 1953) revealed that the language of these Mycenaeans was an early form of Greek. It must have been the memory of these rich kingdoms that inspired Homer's vision of "Mycenae rich in gold" and the splendid armed hosts that assembled for the attack on Troy.

It was a blurred memory (Homer does not remember the writing, for example, or the detailed bureaucratic accounting recorded on the tablets), and this is easy to understand: some time in the last century of the millennium the great palaces were destroyed by fire. With them disappeared not only the arts and skills that had created Mycenaean wealth but even the system of writing. For the next few hundred poverty-stricken years the Greeks were illiterate and so no written evidence survives for what, in view of our ignorance about so many aspects of it, we call the Dark Age of Greece.

One thing we do know about it: it produced a body of oral epic poetry that was the raw material Homer shaped into two great poems: the *Iliad* and *Odyssey*. These Homeric poems seem from internal evidence to date from the eighth century B.C.—which is incidentally, or perhaps not incidentally, the century in which the Greeks learned how to write again. They played in the subsequent development of Greek civilization the same role that the Old Testament of the Bible writings had played in Palestine: they became the basis of an education and, therefore, of a whole culture. Not only did the great characters of the epic serve as models of conduct for later generations of Greeks but the figures of the Olympian gods retained, in the prayers, poems, and sculpture of the succeeding centuries, the shapes and attributes set down by Homer. The difference between the Greek and the Hebrew hero, between Achilles and Joseph, for example, is remarkable, but the difference between "the God of Abraham and of Isaac" and the Olympians who interfere capriciously in the lives of Hector and Achilles is an unbridgeable

87

chasm. The two conceptions of the power that governs the universe are irreconcilable, and in fact the struggle between them ended, not in synthesis, but in the complete victory of the one and the disappearance of the other. The Greek conception of the nature of the gods and of their relation to humanity is so alien to us that it is difficult for the modern reader to take it seriously. The Jewish basis of European religious thought has made it almost impossible for us to imagine a god who can be feared and laughed at, blamed and admired, and still sincerely worshiped. Yet all these are proper attitudes toward the gods on Olympus; they are all implicit in Homer's poems.

The Hebrew conception of God emphasizes those aspects of the universe that imply a harmonious order. The elements of disorder in the universe are, in the story of Creation, blamed on humans, and in all Hebrew literature the evidences of disorder are something the writer tries to reconcile with an a priori assumption of an all-powerful, just God; he never tampers with the fundamental datum. Just as clearly, the Greeks conceived their gods as an expression of the disorder of the world in which they lived. The Olympian gods, like the natural forces of sea and sky, follow their own will even to the extreme of conflict with each other, and always with a sublime disregard for the human beings who may be affected by the results of their actions. It is true that they are all subjects of a single more powerful god, Zeus. But his authority over them is based only on superior strength; though he cannot be openly resisted, he can be temporarily deceived by his fellow Olympians. And Zeus, although by virtue of his superior power his will is finally accomplished in the matter of Achilles' wrath, knows limits to his power too. He cannot save the life of his son, the Lycian hero Sarpedon. Behind Zeus stands the mysterious power of Fate, to which even he must bow.

Such gods as these, representing as they do the blind forces of the universe that people cannot control, are not thought of as connected with morality. Morality is a human creation, and though the gods may approve of it, they are not bound by it. And violent as they are, they cannot feel the ultimate consequence of violence: death is a human fear, just as the courage to face it is a human quality. There is a double standard, one for gods, one for humans, and the inevitable consequence is that our real admiration and sympathy are directed not toward the gods but toward humankind. With Hector, and even with Achilles at his worst, we can sympathize; but the gods, though they may excite terror or laughter, can never have our sympathy. We could as easily sympathize with a blizzard or the force of gravity. Homer imposed on Greek literature the anthropocentric emphasis that is its distinguishing mark and its great contribution to the Western mind. Though the gods are ever-present characters in the incidents of his poems, his true concern, first and last, is with men and women.

THE CITY-STATES OF GREECE

The stories told in the Homeric poems are set in the age of the Trojan War, which archaeologists (those, that is, who believe that it happened at all) date to the twelfth century B.C. Though the poems do perhaps preserve some faded memories of the Mycenaean age, there is no doubt that the poems as we have them are the creation of a later time, the tenth to the eighth centuries B.C., the so-called Dark Age that succeeded the collapse (or destruction) of Mycenaean civilization. This was the time of the final settlement of the Greek peoples, an age of invasion and migration that saw the foundation and growth of many small independent cities. The geography of Greece—a land of mountain barriers and scattered islands—encouraged this fragmentation. The Greek cities never lost sight of their common Hellenic heritage, but it was not enough to unite them—except in the face of unmistakable and overwhelming danger, and even then only partially and for a short time. They differed from each other in custom, political constitution, and even dialect; their relations with each other were those of rivals and fierce competitors.

In these cities, constantly at war in the pursuit of more productive land for growing populations, the kings of Homeric society gave way to aristocratic oligarchies, which maintained a stranglehold on the land and the economy of which it was the base. An important safety valve was colonization. In the eighth and seventh centuries B.C. landless families founded new cities (always near the sea and generally owing little or no allegiance to the home base) all over the Mediterranean coast—in Spain, southern France (Marseilles, Nice, and Antibes were all Greek cities), south Italy (Naples), Sicily (Syracuse), North Africa (Cyrene), all along the coast of Asia Minor (Smyrna, Miletus), and even on the Black Sea as far as Russian Crimea. Many of these new outposts of Greek civilization experienced a faster economic and cultural development than the older cities of the mainland. It was in the cities founded on the Asian coast that the Greeks adapted to their own language the Phoenician system of writing, adding signs for the vowels to create the first efficient alphabet. Its first use was probably for commercial records and transactions, but as literacy became a general condition all over the Greek world in the course of the seventh century B.C., treaties and political decrees were inscribed on stone and literary works written on rolls of paper made from the Egyptian papyrus plant.

ATHENS AND SPARTA

By the beginning of the fifth century B.C. the two most prominent city-states were Athens and Sparta. These two cities led the combined Greek resistance to the Persian invasion of Europe in 490–479 B.C. The defeat of the solid Persian power by the divided and insignificant Greek cities surprised the world and inspired in Greece, and particularly in Athens, a confidence that knew no bounds.

Athens was at this time a democracy, the first in Western history. It was a direct, not a representative, democracy, for the number of free citizens was small enough to permit the exercise of power by a meeting of the citizens as a body in assembly. (Athenean democracy had, of course, its limitations. Its political freedoms were the exclusive privilege of male full citizens; at the meetings of assembly there were no women, resident aliens, or slaves.) Athens' power lay in the fleet with which it had played its decisive part in the struggle against Persia, and with this fleet Athens rapidly became the leader of a naval alliance that included most of the islands of the Aegean Sea and many Greek cities on the coast of Asia Minor. Sparta, on the other hand, was a totalitarian state, rigidly conservative in government and policy, in which the individual citizen was reared and trained by the state for the state's business: war. The Spartan land army was consequently superior to any other in Greece, and the Spartans controlled, by direct rule or by alliance, a majority of the city-states of the Peloponnese.

These two cities, allies for the war of liberation against Persia, became enemies when the external danger was eliminated. The middle years of the fifth century B.C. were disturbed by indecisive hostilities between them and haunted by the probability of full-scale war to come. As the years went by, this war came to be accepted as "inevitable" by both sides, and in 431 B.C. it began. It was to end in 404 B.C. with the total defeat of Athens.

Before the beginning of this disastrous war Athenian democracy provided its citizens with a cultural and political environment that was without precedent in the ancient world. The institutions of Athens encouraged the maximum development of the individual's capacities and at the same time inspired the maximum devotion to the interests of the community. It was a moment in history of delicate and precarious balance between the freedom of the individual and the demands of the state. Its uniqueness was emphasized by the complete lack of balance in Sparta, where the necessities of the state annihilated the individual as a creative and independent being. It was the proud boast of the Athenians that without sacrificing the cultural amenities of civilized life they could yet, when called on, surpass in policy and war their adversary, whose citizen body was an army in constant training. The Athenians were, in this respect as in others, a nation of amateurs. "The individual Athenian," said Pericles, Athens' great statesman at this time, "in his own person seems to have the power of adapting himself to the most varied forms of action with the utmost versatility and grace." But the freedom of the individual did not, in Athens' great days, produce anarchy. "While we are . . . unconstrained in our private intercourse," Pericles had observed earlier in his speech, "a spirit of reverence pervades our public acts."

This balance of individual freedom and communal unity was not destined to outlast the century. It went down, with Athens, in the war. Under the mounting pressure of the long conflict, the Athenians lost the "spirit of reverence" that Pericles saw as the stabilizing factor in Athenian democracy. They subordinated all considerations to the immediate interest of the city and surpassed their enemy in the logical ferocity of their actions. They finally fell victim to leaders who carried the process one step further and subordinated all considerations to their own private interest. The war years saw the decay of that freedom in unity that is celebrated in Pericles' speech. By the end of the fifth century B.C. Athens was divided internally as well as defeated externally. The individual citizen no longer thought of himself and Athens as one and the same; the balance was gone forever.

One of the solvents of traditional values was an intellectual revolution that was taking place in the advanced Athenian democracy of the last half of the fifth century B.C., a critical reevaluation of accepted ideas in every sphere of thought and action. It stemmed from innovations in education. Democratic institutions had created a demand for an education that would prepare men for public life, especially by training them in the art of public speaking. The demand was met by the appearance of professional teachers, Sophists, as they were called, who taught, for a handsome fee, not only the techniques of public speaking but also the subjects that gave a man something to talk about—government, ethics, literary criticism, even astronomy. The curriculum of the Sophists, in fact, marks the first appearance in European civilization of the liberal education, just as they themselves were the first professors.

The Sophists were great teachers, but like most teachers they had little or no control over the results of their teaching. Their methods placed an inevitable emphasis on effective presentation of a point of view, to the detriment, and if necessary the exclusion, of anything that might make it less convincing. They produced a generation that had been trained to see both sides of any question and to argue the weaker side as effectively as the stronger, the false as effectively as the true. They taught how to argue inferentially from probability in the absence of concrete evidence, to appeal to the audience's sense of its own advantage rather than to accepted moral standards, and to justify individual defiance of general prejudice and even of law by making a distinction between "nature" and "convention." These methods dominated the thinking of the Athenians of the last half of the century. Emphasis on the technique of effective presentation of both sides of any case encouraged a relativistic point of view and finally produced a cynical mood that denied the existence of any absolute standards. The canon of probability (which implies an appeal to human reason as the supreme authority) became a critical weapon for an attack on myth and on traditional conceptions of the gods; though it had its constructive side, too, for it was the base for historical reconstruction of the unrecorded past and of the stages of human progress from savagery to civilization. The rhetorical appeal to the self-interest of the audience, to expediency, became the method of the political leaders of the wartime democracy and the fundamental doctrine of new theories of power politics. These theories served as cynical justification for the increasing severity of the measures Athens took to terrorize its rebellious subjects. Their distinction between nature and convention is the source of the doctrine of the superman, who breaks free of the conventional restraints of society and acts according to the law of his own nature. The new spirit in Athens has magnificent achievements to its credit, but it undermined old, solid moral convictions. At its roots was a supreme confidence in the human intelligence and a secular view of humanity's position in the universe that is best expressed in the statement of Protagoras, the most famous of the Sophists: "Man is the measure of all things."

THE DECLINE OF THE CITY-STATES

In the last half of the fifth century the whole traditional basis of individual conduct, which had been concern for the unity and cohesion of the city-state, was undermined—gradually at first by the critical approach of the Sophists and their pupils, and then rapidly, as the war accelerated the process of moral disintegration. "In peace and prosperity," says Thucydides, "both states and individuals are actuated by higher motives . . . but war, which takes away the comfortable provision of daily life, is a hard master, and tends to assimilate men's characters to their conditions." The war brought to Athens the rule of new politicians who were schooled in the doctrine of the new power politics and initiated savage reprisals against Athens' rebellious subject-allies, launching the city on an expansionist course that ended in disaster in Sicily (411 B.C.). Seven years later Athens, its last fleet gone, surrendered to the Spartans. A pro-Spartan antidemocratic regime, the Thirty Tyrants, was installed but was soon overthrown. Athens became a democracy again, but the confidence and unity of its great age were gone forever. Community and individual were no longer one, and the individual, cast on his own resources for guidance, found only conflicting attitudes which he could not refer to any absolute standards. The mood of postwar Athens oscillated between a fanatic, unthinking reassertion of traditional values and a weary cynicism that wanted only to be left alone. The only thing common to the two extremes was a distrust of intelligence.

In the disillusioned gloom of defeat, Athenians began to feel more and more exasperation with a voice they had been listening to for many years. This was the voice of Socrates, a stonemason who for most of his adult life had made it his business to discuss with his fellow citizens the great issues of which the Athenians were now so weary—the nature of justice, of truth, of piety. Unlike the Sophists, he did not lecture or charge a fee. His method was dialectic (a search for truth through questions and answers), and his dedication to his mission had kept him poor. But the initial results of his discussions were often infuriatingly like the results of Sophistic teaching. Through questions and answers he exposed the illogicality of his opponent's position but did not often provide a substitute for the belief he had destroyed. Yet it is clear that he did believe in absolute standards and, what is more, believed they could be discovered by a process of logical inquiry and supported by logical proof. His ethics rested on an intellectual basis. The resentment against him, which came to a head in 399 B.C., is partly explained by the fact that he satisfied neither extreme of the postwar mood. He questioned the old standards to establish new, and he refused to let the Athenians live in peace, for he preached that it was every man's duty to think his way through to the truth. In this last respect he was the prophet of the new age. For him, the city and the accepted code were no substitute for the task of self-examination, which each individual must set himself and carry through to a conclusion. The characteristic statement of the old Athens was public, in the assembly or the theater; Socrates proclaimed the right and duty of each individual to work out his own salvation and made clear his distrust of public life: "he who will fight for the right . . . must have a private station and not a public one."

The Athenians sentenced him to death on a charge of impiety. They hoped, no doubt, that he would go into exile to escape execution, but he remained, as he put it himself, at his post, and they were forced to have the sentence carried out. If they thought they were finished with him, they were sadly mistaken. In the next century Athens became the center for a large group of philosophical schools, all of them claiming to develop and interpret the ideas of Socrates.

The century that followed Socrates' death saw the exhaustion of the Greek city-states in constant internecine warfare. Politically and economically bankrupt, they fell under the power of Macedon in the north, whose king, Philip, combined a ferocious energy with a cynicism that enabled him to take full advantage of the corrupt governments of the city-states. Greek liberty ended at the battle of Chaeronea in 338 B.C., and Philip's son Alexander inherited a powerful army and the political control of all Greece. He led his Macedonian and Greek armies against Persia and in a few brilliant campaigns became master of an empire that extended into Egypt in the south and to the borders of India in the east. He died in Babylon in 323 B.C., and his empire broke up into a number of independent kingdoms, which were ruled by his generals, but the results of his fantastic achievements were more durable than might have been expected. Into the newly conquered territories came thousands of Greeks who wished to escape from the political futility and economic crisis of the homeland. Wherever they went, they took with them their language, their culture, and their typical buildings: the gymnasium and the theater. In Alexandria, Egypt, for example, a Greek library was formed to preserve the texts of Greek literature for the scholars who edited them, a school of Greek poetry flourished, and Greek mathematicians and geographers made new advances in science. The Middle East became, as far as the cities were concerned, a Greek-speaking area, and when, some two or three centuries later, the first accounts of the life and teaching of Jesus of Nazareth were written down, they were written in Greek, the language on which the cultural homogeneity of the whole area was based.

FURTHER READING

John Boardman, Jasper Griffin, and Oswyn Murray, eds., *The Oxford History of the Classical World* (1986), is an eminently readable (and profusely illustrated) history of the classical world that pays special attention to literature. For a more detailed survey of ancient Greek literature, see P. E. Easterling and B. M. W. Knox, eds., *The Cambridge History of Classical Literature, Volume I: Greek Literature* (1985). An excellent survey of the political history of Greece to the death of Alexander is J. B. Bury, *A History of Greece* (1975).

PRONOUNCING GLOSSARY

The following list uses common English syllables and stress accents to provide rough equivalents of selected words whose pronunciation may be unfamiliar to the general reader.

Achilles: *a-kil'-eez*

Chaeronea: *kai-ron-ee'-uh*

Mycenae: *mai-see'-nee*

Pericles: *pe'-ri-kleez*

Thucydides: *thyoo-si'-di-deez*

ANCIENT GREECE AND THE FORMATION OF THE WESTERN MIND

TEXTS	CONTEXTS
	2200–1450 Minoan civilization flourishes on Crete
	ca. 1450 Mycenaeans from mainland Greece occupy Crete
	ca. 1150 Troy destroyed by the Achaeans
	776 Olympic Games founded in Greece
late 8th century B.C. Greek alphabetic scripts	
ca. 700 Homer, *The Iliad, The Odyssey*	
600 Sappho writing her **lyrics** on the island of Lesbos	
	594 Solon reforms laws at Athens, which becomes the world's first democracy (508), and defeats a Persian invasion at Marathon (490)
	480–479 Greece turns back a massive Persian invasion by sea at Salamis and by land at Plataea
458 Aeschylus's dramatic trilogy, ***The Oresteia***, produced in Athens	
ca. 441 Sophocles, *Antigone*	
431 Euripides, ***Medea***	**431–404** Peloponnesian War between Athens and Sparta; Athens surrenders (404)
429–347 Plato, author of ***The Apology of Socrates*** and *Phaedo*	
426? Sophocles, ***Oedipus the King***	
411 Aristophanes, ***Lysistrata***	
	399 Trial and execution of Socrates
384–322 Aristotle, author of ***Poetics***	
	ca. 385? Plato founds the Academy

TEXTS	CONTEXTS
	ca. 350 Beginnings of Indian epic, *Mahābhārata* • Shuang-tse founds monist religious philosophy in China • Greek amphitheater built at Epidauros
	338 United Greeks defeated by Philip II of Macedon at Chaeronea
	335 Aristotle founds Peripatetic school of philosophy and lectures in the Lyceum
	334 Alexander of Macedon, Philip's son, conquers Persian empire
	323 Euclid writes *Elements*, the first work of geometry
	307 Library and museum established at Alexandria, Egypt
	148 Macedonia becomes a Roman province
	31 At Actium, Octavian Augustus Caesar defeats Antony and Cleopatra
	ca. 6 Birth of Jesus
	A.D. 26–36 Pontius Pilate, Roman governor
	ca. 33 Crucifixion of Jesus
	ca. 35 Conversion of Paul
	47–58 Paul's missionary journeys
	66–70 Jewish revolt against Roman rule; Roman emperor Titus captures Jerusalem
ca. A.D. 75 Luke, Gospels and Acts of the Apostles	
ca. 80 Matthew, Gospels	

HOMER

eighth century B.C.

Greek literature begins with two masterpieces, the *Iliad* and *Odyssey*, which cannot be accurately dated (the conjectural dates range over three centuries) and which are attributed to the poet Homer, about whom nothing is known except his name. The Greeks believed that he was blind, perhaps because the bard Demodokos in the *Odyssey* was blind (see p. 127), and seven different cities put forward claims to be his birthplace. They are all in what the Greeks called Ionia, the western coast of Asia Minor, which was heavily settled by Greek colonists. It does seem likely that he came from this area; the *Iliad* contains several accurate descriptions of natural features of the Ionian landscape, but his grasp of the geography of mainland, especially western, Greece is unsure. But even this is a guess, and all the other stories the Greeks told about him are obvious inventions.

The two great epics that have made his name supreme among poets may have been fixed in something like their present form before the art of writing was in general use in Greece; it is certain that they were intended not for reading but for oral recitation. The earliest stages of their composition date from long before the beginnings of Greek literacy—the late eighth century B.C. The poems exhibit the unmistakable characteristics of oral composition.

The oral poet had at his disposal not reading and writing but a vast and intricate system of metrical formulas—phrases that would fit in at different places in the line—and a repertoire of standard scenes (the arming of the warrior, the battle of two champions) as well as the known outline of the story. Of course he could and did invent new phrases and scenes as he recited—but his base was the immense poetic reserve created by many generations of singers who lived before him. When he told again for his hearers the old story of Achilles and his wrath, he was recreating a traditional story that had been recited, with variations, additions, and improvements, by a long line of predecessors. The poem was not, in the modern sense, the poet's creation, still less an expression of his personality. Consequently, there is no trace of individual identity to be found in it; the poet remains as hidden behind the action and speech of his characters as if he were a dramatist.

The *Iliad* and *Odyssey* as we have them, however, are unlike most of the oral literature we know from other times and places. The poetic organization of each of these two epics, the subtle interrelationship of the parts, which creates their structural and emotional unity, suggests that they owe their present form to the shaping hand of a single poet, the architect who selected from the enormous wealth of the oral tradition and fused what he took with original material to create, perhaps with the aid of the new medium of writing, the two magnificently ordered poems known as the *Iliad* and *Odyssey*.

THE ILIAD

Of the two poems the *Iliad* is perhaps the earlier. Its subject is war; its characters are men in battle and women whose fate depends on the outcome. The war is fought by the Achaeans* against the Trojans for the recovery of Helen, the wife of the Achaean chieftain Menelaus.

The *Iliad* describes the events of a few weeks in the ten-year siege of Troy. The particular subject of the poem, as its first line announces, is the anger of Achilles,

---

* Although the translation of *The Odyssey* included here transcribes Greek names in a manner closer to the Greek (Akhaians, Akhilleus), this headnote uses the traditional convention of spelling Greek names according to the form they were given in Latin—Achaeans, Achilles.

the bravest of the Achaean chieftains encamped outside the city. Achilles is a man who lives by and for violence, who is creative and alive only in violent action. He knows that he will be killed if he stays before Troy, but rather than decay, as he would decay, in peace, he accepts that certainty. In a dispute over the division of booty he is mortally insulted by Menelaus' brother Agamemnon, the commander in chief of the Achaean expedition. He withdraws from the fighting, and his mother, the goddess Thetis, persuades Zeus, the supreme Olympian god, to turn the tide of battle against the Achaeans. The Trojans, commanded by Hector, son of Priam, king of Troy, drive the Achaeans back on their beached ships. In an emergency meeting of the Achaean chieftains, Nestor, the oldest and wisest of them, proposes sending ambassadors to Achilles, to plead with him to help them; Agamemnon agrees and offers magnificent compensation for his insult to Achilles. Two of the ambassadors are Odysseus, the cleverest and most eloquent of the Achaeans, and Ajax, a warrior second only to Achilles in courage and tenacity in battle. But Achilles is not satisfied and sends them back empty-handed. The Achaean position grows more critical as some of their leading fighters, Odysseus among them, are wounded; finally, Patroclus, Achilles' closest friend, begs him to intervene. He refuses to fight in person but makes what turns out to be a fatal concession: he allows Patroclus to come to the aid of the Achaeans wearing the armor and wielding the spear of Achilles. Patroclus strikes terror into the Trojan ranks, but, disobeying Achilles' instructions, pursues them to the gates of Troy, where he is killed by Hector, who puts on Achilles' armor. Achilles thinks of nothing now but avenging his friend; he leads the Achaean onslaught and kills Hector, Troy's main defender. The fall of Troy is now assured, but so is Achilles' death in battle, which, as he very well knows, is fated to come soon after Hector's.

THE ODYSSEY

The other Homeric epic, the *Odyssey*, is concerned with the peace that followed the war and in particular with the return of the heroes who survived. Its subject is the long, drawn-out return of one of the heroes, Odysseus of Ithaca, who had come farther than most (all the way from western Greece) and who was destined to spend ten years wandering in unknown seas before he returned to his rocky kingdom. When Odysseus' wanderings began, Achilles had already received, at the hands of Apollo, the death that he had chosen, and that was the only appropriate end for his fatal and magnificent violence. Odysseus chose life, and his outstanding quality is a probing and versatile intelligence, which, combined with long experience, keeps him safe and alive through the trials and dangers of twenty years of war and seafaring. To stay alive he has to do things that Achilles would never have done and use an ingenuity and experience that Achilles did not possess, but his life is just as much a struggle. Troy has fallen, but "there is no discharge in the war." The way back is as perilous as the ten-year siege.

The opening lines of the poem state the theme:

> Sing in me, Muse, and through me tell the story
> of that man skilled in all ways of contending,
> the wanderer, harried for years on end,
> after he plundered the stronghold
> on the proud height of Troy.
>   He saw the townlands
> and learned the minds of many distant men,
> and weathered many bitter nights and days
> in his deep heart at sea, while he fought only
> to save his life. . . .

In this world it is a struggle even to stay alive, and it is a struggle for which Odysseus is naturally endowed. But his objective is not life at any price. Where honor demands, he can be soberly courageous in the face of death (as on Circe's island, where he goes alone and against his mate's advice to save his sailors), and he can even be led into foolhardiness by his insatiable curiosity (as in the expedition to see the island of the Cyclopes). Much as he clings to life, it must be life with honor; what he is trying to preserve is not just existence but a worldwide reputation. His name has become a byword for successful courage and intelligence, and he must not betray it. When he reveals his identity at the palace of the Phaeacians, he speaks of his fame in an objective manner, as if it were something apart from himself:

> I am Laertes' son, Odysseus.
>   Men hold me
> formidable for guile in peace and war:
> this fame has gone abroad to the sky's rim.

This is not boasting, but a calm recognition of the qualities and achievements for which he stands, and to which he must be true.

Ironically enough, to be true to his reputation, he is often forced to conceal his name. In the Cyclopes' cave, he calls himself "Nobody" to ensure his escape, and it is clear how hard he finds this denial of his reputation when, out of the cave and on board ship, he insists on telling Polyphemus his name. Not only does this reassertion of his identity bring himself, his ship, and his crew back within reach of Polyphemus' arm but it also enables the blinded giant to call down on his enemy the wrath of his father, Poseidon, who, from this point on, musters the full might of the sea against Odysseus' return. Warned by the consequences of this boastful revelation of his name, he conceals his identity even from the hospitable Phaeacians, until his emotional reaction to the singer's tale of Troy gives him away. And when he finally returns home, to a palace full of violent suitors for his wife's hand who think that he is dead and who have presumed so far that they will kill him if they now find out that he is alive, he has to become Nobody again. He disguises himself as an old dirty beggar, to flatter and fawn on his enemies for bread in his own house.

The trials of the voyage home are not just physical obstacles to his return, they are also temptations. Odysseus is tempted, time after time, to forget his identity, to secede from the life of struggle and constant vigilance for which his name stands. The lotus flower that makes people forget home and family is the most obvious form of temptation; it occurs early in the voyage and is easily resisted. But he is offered more attractive bait. Circe gives him a life of ease and self-indulgence on an enchanted island. His resistance has by this time been lowered, and he stays a full year before his sailors remonstrate with him and remind him of his home. At the Phaeacian palace where he tells the story of his voyages, he is offered the love of a young princess, Nausicaa; her hand in marriage by her father, Alkinoös; and a new life in a kingdom richer than his rocky Ithaca. The Sirens tempt him to live in the memory of the glorious past. "Come here, famous Odysseus," they sing, "great glory of the Achaeans, and hear our song. . . . For we know all that at broad Troy the Argives and the Trojans suffered by the will of the gods." If he had not been bound to the mast, he would have gone to hear and join the dead men whose bones rot on the Sirens' island. Calypso, the goddess with whom he spent seven years, longing all the time to escape, offers him the greatest temptation of all, immortality. If he will stay as her husband, he will live forever, a life of ease and tranquility, like that of the gods. Odysseus refuses this too; he prefers the human condition, with all its struggle, its disappointments, and its inevitable end. And the end, death, is an ever-present temptation. It is always near him; at the slightest slackening of effort, the smallest failure of intelligence, the first weakness of will, death will bring him release from his trials. But he hangs on tenaciously, and, toward the end of his ordeals, he is sent living to the world of the dead to see for himself what death means. It is dark and comfortless; Homer's land of the dead is, perhaps even more than Dante's *Inferno*, the most frightening picture of the afterlife in European literature. Odysseus talks to the dead, and any illusion he had about death as repose is shattered when he comforts the shade of Achilles with talk of his everlasting glory and hears him reply:

> Let me hear no smooth talk
> of death from you, Odysseus, light of councils.
> Better, I say, to break sod as a farm hand
> for some poor country man, on iron rations,
> than lord it over all the exhausted dead.

When he hears these words, Odysseus does not yet understand their full significance (that he, the living man, will taste the depths of degradation, not as a serf but as a despised beggar, mocked and mistreated in his own palace), but he is prepared now to face everything that may be necessary, to push on without another look behind.

In this scene Homer brings his two great prototypes face to face, and poses the tragic fury of Achilles against the mature intelligence of Odysseus. There can be little doubt where his sympathy lies. Against the dark background of Achilles' regret for life lost, the figure of Odysseus shines more warmly: a man dedicated to life, accepting its limitations and making full use of its possibilities, a man who is destined to endure to the end and be saved. He finds in the end the home and the peace he fought for, his wife faithful, a son worthy of his name ready to succeed him, and the knowledge that the death, which must come at last, will be gentle:

> Then a seaborne death
> soft as this hand of mist will come upon you
> when you are wearied out with rich old age,
> your country folk in blessed peace around you.

A very short but thoughtful discussion of the basic themes of the two poems is found in J. Griffin, *Homer* (1980); his *Homer on Life and Death* (1980) is a full and rewarding exploration of Homer's vision of the human condition and the nature of the gods. Mark W. Edwards, *Homer: Poet of the Iliad* (1987), attempts, in his words, "to combine the advantages of a general introduction to Homer and a commentary on the *Iliad*." The first part discusses traditional oral style and the ways in which Homer "used, adapted or ignored it for his own purposes," and the second is a detailed literary commentary on "the most important books of the poem." Jasper Griffin, *Homer: The Odyssey* (1987), is a short but comprehensive guide to the background and riches of the poem. George E. Dimock, *Unity of the Odyssey* (1989), is a brilliant reading, full of original insights and authoritative in its demonstration of the poem's thematic coherence. Sheila Murnaghan, *Disguise and Recognition in the Odyssey* (1987), is an enlightening guide through the intricacies of the second half of the poem.

PRONOUNCING GLOSSARY

The following list uses common English syllables and stress accents to provide rough equivalents of selected words whose pronunciation may be unfamiliar to the general reader.

Achaeans: *a-kee'-unz / a-kai'-uns*   Alkínoös: *al-kin-oh'-uhs / al-kin'-oh-us*

Achilles: *a-kil'-eez*   Circe: *ser'-see / keer'-kay*

Demodokos: *dee-mo'-do-kuhs*

Hêlios: *hee'-lee-os*

Hephaistos: *he-fess'-tus / hay-fais'-*
  tos

Hermês: *her'-meez*

Laertes/Laërtês: *lay-er'-teez*

Menelaus/Meneláos: *me-ne-lay'-us /*
  me-ne-lah'-os

Nausicaa: *naw-si'-kay-ah / now-si'-ka-ah*

Odysseus: *oh-dis'-yoos*

Phaeacians: *fee-ay'-shunz*

Polyphemus/Polyphêmos: *po-li-fee'-mus*

Priam: *prai'-am*

Scylla/Skylla: *si'-lah/skil'-ah*

Telémakhos: *te-le'-ma-kos*

Theseus: *thees'-yoos / thee'-syoos*

The Odyssey[1]

Summary   Odysseus, king of the island of Ithaka, leaves the ruins of Troy with twelve ships loaded with booty from the sack of the city. Nearing home, he is blown off course by a storm wind that takes him westward into unexplored seas full of marvels and dangers. He has many adventures—one of them an encounter with a one-eyed cannibal giant whom he blinds, so drawing on himself the wrath of the sea-god Poseidon, the giant's father—but in the end, ships and crews all lost at sea, he is stranded on the island of Ogygia, where the goddess Calypso keeps him for seven years as her unwilling lover while he yearns for his home, his wife Penelope, and his son Telémakhos. On Ithaka, where no news of Odysseus has been received in the twenty years since he left for the Trojan war, a gang of over one hundred young aristocratic suitors for Penelope's hand besiege Odysseus's palace, feast in his hall, consuming huge quantities of food and drink, all the while putting pressure on Penelope to choose one of them for her husband.

   Meanwhile, on Mt. Olympus, Athena, "grey-eyed" goddess of war, pleads with Zeus to allow Odysseus to leave Ogygia and return to Ithaka. Zeus agrees. Athena, disguised as a friend of Odysseus's family, visits Telémakhos in Ithaka, reassures him that Odysseus is not dead, and urges him to order the suitors to leave the palace. Telémakhos summons the suitors to a meeting but is jeered and dismissed as he pleads with them to stop pillaging Odysseus's household. In the meantime, Athena gathers a ship and crew for Telémakhos to search for news of his father.

   Telémakhos sets out the next morning, accompanied by a small crew of young Ithakans and by Athena disguised as Mentor, an Ithakan elder. He first visits Nestor, the oldest and wisest of the Achaean kings who fought at Troy. He has no news for Telémakhos, and instead advises him to visit Menelaus, the king of Sparta and husband of Helen, the cause of the Trojan War. Menelaus receives Telémakhos warmly, and tells him many tales about Odysseus's bravery and cunning, and about his own return home. Finally, he reveals the news that he was able to extract from the god Proteus during a violent struggle: Odysseus is alive but stranded on Calypso's island.

   Back in Ithaka, the suitors are enraged to find that Telémakhos has left the island in search of his father. Led by Antinoös, they set sail intending to intercept and kill Telémakhos upon his return. Book Five begins back on Mt. Olympus, where Athena reminds Zeus that he had promised to arrange for Odysseus's departure from Ogygia.

---

1. Translated by Robert Fitzgerald. Fitzgerald's translation provides its own pronunciation symbols. Thus ê is pronounced like *ee* and accented syllables are indicated.

BOOK V

[Sweet Nymph and Open Sea]

Dawn came up from the couch of her reclining,
leaving her lord Tithonos'[2] brilliant side
with fresh light in her arms for gods and men.
And the master of heaven and high thunder, Zeus,
went to his place among the gods assembled   5
hearing Athena tell Odysseus' woe.
For she, being vexed that he was still sojourning
in the sea chambers of Kalypso, said:

"O Father Zeus and gods in bliss forever,
let no man holding scepter as a king   10
think to be mild, or kind, or virtuous;
let him be cruel, and practice evil ways,
for those Odysseus ruled cannot remember
the fatherhood and mercy of his reign.
Meanwhile he lives and grieves upon that island   15
in thralldom to the nymph; he cannot stir,
cannot fare homeward, for no ship is left him,
fitted with oars—no crewmen or companions
to pull him on the broad back of the sea.
And now murder is hatched on the high sea   20
against his son, who sought news of his father
in the holy lands of Pylos and Lakedaimon."

To this the summoner of cloud replied:

"My child, what odd complaints you let escape you.
Have you not, you yourself, arranged this matter—   25
as we all know—so that Odysseus
will bring these men to book, on his return?
And are you not the one to give Telémakhos
a safe route for sailing? Let his enemies
encounter no one and row home again."   30

He turned then to his favorite son and said:

"Hermês, you have much practice on our missions,
go make it known to the softly-braided nymph
that we, whose will is not subject to error,
order Odysseus home; let him depart.   35
But let him have no company, gods or men,
only a raft that he must lash together,
and after twenty days, worn out at sea,
he shall make land upon the garden isle,
Skhería,[3] of our kinsmen, the Phaiákians.   40
Let these men take him to their hearts in honor
and berth him in a ship, and send him home,
with gifts of garments, gold, and bronze—
so much he had not counted on from Troy
could he have carried home his share of plunder.   45

2. A mortal man whom Eos, the dawn goddess, took for her husband.   3. Later Greeks identified it
as the island of Corcyra (modern Corfu) off the northwest coast of mainland Greece.

His destiny is to see his friends again
under his own roof, in his father's country."

No words were lost on Hermês the Wayfinder,
who bent to tie his beautiful sandals on,
ambrosial, golden, that carry him over water   50
or over endless land in a swish of the wind,
and took the wand with which he charms asleep—
or when he wills, awake—the eyes of men.
So wand in hand he paced into the air,
shot from Pieria[4] down, down to sea level,   55
and veered to skim the swell. A gull patrolling
between the wave crests of the desolate sea
will dip to catch a fish, and douse his wings;
no higher above the whitecaps Hermês flew
until the distant island lay ahead,   60
then rising shoreward from the violet ocean
he stepped up to the cave. Divine Kalypso,
the mistress of the isle, was now at home.
Upon her hearthstone a great fire blazing
scented the farthest shores with cedar smoke   65
and smoke of thyme, and singing high and low
in her sweet voice, before her loom a-weaving,
she passed her golden shuttle to and fro.
A deep wood grew outside, with summer leaves
of alder and black poplar, pungent cypress.   70
Ornate birds here rested their stretched wings—
horned owls, falcons, cormorants—long-tongued
beachcombing birds, and followers of the sea.
Around the smoothwalled cave a crooking vine
held purple clusters under ply of green;   75
and four springs, bubbling up near one another
shallow and clear, took channels here and there
through beds of violets and tender parsley.
Even a god who found this place
would gaze, and feel his heart beat with delight: 80
so Hermês did; but when he had gazed his fill
he entered the wide cave. Now face to face
the magical Kalypso recognized him,
as all immortal gods know one another
on sight—though seeming strangers, far from home.   85
But he saw nothing of the great Odysseus,
who sat apart, as a thousand times before,
and racked his own heart groaning, with eyes wet
scanning the bare horizon of the sea.
Kalypso, lovely nymph, seated her guest   90
in a bright chair all shimmering, and asked:

"O Hermês, ever with your golden wand,
what brings you to my island?
Your awesome visits in the past were few.
Now tell me what request you have in mind;   95
for I desire to do it, if I can,

4. The vicinity of Mount Olympus.

and if it is a proper thing to do.
But wait a while, and let me serve my friend."

She drew a table of ambrosia near him
and stirred a cup of ruby-colored nectar—   100
food and drink for the luminous Wayfinder,
who took both at his leisure, and replied:[5]

"Goddess to god, you greet me, questioning me?
Well, here is truth for you in courtesy.
Zeus made me come, and not my inclination;   105
who cares to cross that tract of desolation,
the bitter sea, all mortal towns behind
where gods have beef and honors from mankind?
But it is not to be thought of—and no use—
for any god to elude the will of Zeus.   110
He notes your friend, most ill-starred by renown
of all the peers who fought for Priam's town—
nine years of war they had, before great Troy was down.
Homing, they wronged the goddess with grey eyes,
who made a black wind blow and the seas rise,   115
in which his troops were lost, and all his gear,
while easterlies and current washed him here.
Now the command is: send him back in haste.
His life may not in exile go to waste.
His destiny, his homecoming, is at hand,   120
when he shall see his dearest, and walk on his own land."

That goddess most divinely made
shuddered before him, and her warm voice rose:

"Oh you vile gods, in jealousy supernal!
You hate it when we choose to lie with men—   125
immortal flesh by some dear mortal side.
So radiant Dawn once took to bed Orion
until you easeful gods grew peevish at it,
and holy Artemis, Artemis throned in gold,
hunted him down in Delos with her arrows.   130
Then Dêmêtêr[6] of the tasseled tresses yielded
to Iasion, mingling and making love
in a furrow three times plowed; but Zeus found out
and killed him with a white-hot thunderbolt.
So now you grudge me, too, my mortal friend.   135
But it was I who saved him—saw him straddle
his own keel board, the one man left afloat
when Zeus rent wide his ship with chain lightning
and overturned him in the winedark sea.
Then all his troops were lost, his good companions,   140
but wind and current washed him here to me.
I fed him, loved him, sang that he should not die
nor grow old, ever, in all the days to come.
But now there's no eluding Zeus's will.
If this thing be ordained by him, I say   145
so be it, let the man strike out alone

5. The translator put Hermês' speech into rhymed couplets; there is no rhyme in the original Greek.
6. Goddess associated with the growth of the crops, especially wheat.

on the vast water. Surely I cannot 'send' him.
I have no long-oared ships, no company
to pull him on the broad back of the sea.
My counsel he shall have, and nothing hidden,   150
to help him homeward without harm."

To this the Wayfinder made answer briefly:

"Thus you shall send him, then. And show more grace
in your obedience, or be chastised by Zeus."

The strong god glittering left her as he spoke,   155
and now her ladyship, having given heed
to Zeus's mandate, went to find Odysseus
in his stone seat to seaward—tear on tear
brimming his eyes. The sweet days of his life time
were running out in anguish over his exile,   160
for long ago the nymph had ceased to please.
Though he fought shy of her and her desire,
he lay with her each night, for she compelled him.
But when day came he sat on the rocky shore
and broke his own heart groaning, with eyes wet   165
scanning the bare horizon of the sea.
Now she stood near him in her beauty, saying:

"O forlorn man, be still.
Here you need grieve no more; you need not feel
your life consumed here; I have pondered it,   170
and I shall help you go.
Come and cut down high timber for a raft
or flatboat; make her broad-beamed, and decked over,
so you can ride her on the misty sea.
Stores I shall put aboard for you—bread, water,   175
and ruby-colored wine, to stay your hunger—
give you a seacloak and a following wind
to help you homeward without harm—provided
the gods who rule wide heaven wish it so.
Stronger than I they are, in mind and power."   180

For all he had endured, Odysseus shuddered.
But when he spoke, his words went to the mark:

"After these years, a helping hand? O goddess,
what guile is hidden here?
A raft, you say, to cross the Western Ocean,   185
rough water, and unknown? Seaworthy ships
that glory in god's wind will never cross it.
I take no raft you grudge me out to sea.
Or yield me first a great oath, if I do,
to work no more enchantment to my harm."   190

At this the beautiful nymph Kalypso smiled
and answered sweetly, laying her hand upon him:

"What a dog you are! And not for nothing learned,
having the wit to ask this thing of me!
My witness then be earth and sky   195

and dripping Styx[7] that I swear by—
the gay gods cannot swear more seriously—
I have no further spells to work against you.
But what I shall devise, and what I tell you,
will be the same as if your need were mine.   200
Fairness is all I think of. There are hearts
made of cold iron—but my heart is kind."

Swiftly she turned and led him to her cave,
and they went in, the mortal and immortal.
He took the chair left empty now by Hermês,   205
where the divine Kalypso placed before him
victuals and drink of men; then she sat down
facing Odysseus, while her serving maids
brought nectar and ambrosia to her side.
Then each one's hands went out on each one's feast   210
until they had had their pleasure; and she said:

"Son of Laërtês, versatile Odysseus,
after these years with me, you still desire
your old home? Even so, I wish you well.
If you could see it all, before you go—   215
all the adversity you face at sea—
you would stay here, and guard this house, and be
immortal—though you wanted her forever,
that bride for whom you pine each day.
Can I be less desirable than she is?   220
Less interesting? Less beautiful? Can mortals
compare with goddesses in grace and form?"

To this the strategist Odysseus answered:

"My lady goddess, here is no cause for anger.
My quiet Penélopê—how well I know—   225
would seem a shade before your majesty,
death and old age being unknown to you,
while she must die. Yet, it is true, each day
I long for home, long for the sight of home.
If any god has marked me out again   230
for shipwreck, my tough heart can undergo it.
What hardship have I not long since endured
at sea, in battle! Let the trial come."

Now as he spoke the sun set, dusk drew on,
and they retired, this pair, to the inner cave   235
to revel and rest softly, side by side.

When Dawn spread out her finger tips of rose
Odysseus pulled his tunic and his cloak on,
while the sea nymph dressed in a silvery gown
of subtle tissue, drew about her waist   240
a golden belt, and veiled her head, and then
took thought for the great-hearted hero's voyage.
A brazen axehead first she had to give him,

7. One of the rivers of the underworld.

two-bladed, and agreeable to the palm
with a smooth-fitting haft of olive wood;   245
next a well-polished adze; and then she led him
to the island's tip where bigger timber grew—
besides the alder and poplar, tall pine trees,
long dead and seasoned, that would float him high.
Showing him in that place her stand of timber   250
the loveliest of nymphs took her way home.
Now the man fell to chopping; when he paused
twenty tall trees were down. He lopped the branches,
split the trunks, and trimmed his puncheons true.
Meanwhile Kalypso brought him an auger tool   255
with which he drilled through all his planks, then drove
stout pins to bolt them, fitted side by side.
A master shipwright, building a cargo vessel,
lays down a broad and shallow hull; just so
Odysseus shaped the bottom of his craft.   260
He made his decking fast to close-set ribs
before he closed the side with longer planking,
then cut a mast pole, and a proper yard,
and shaped a steering oar to hold her steady.
He drove long strands of willow in all the seams   265
to keep out waves, and ballasted with logs.
As for a sail, the lovely nymph Kalypso
brought him a cloth so he could make that, too.
Then he ran up his rigging—halyards, braces—
and hauled the boat on rollers to the water.   270

This was the fourth day, when he had all ready;
on the fifth day, she sent him out to sea.
But first she bathed him, gave him a scented cloak,
and put on board a skin of dusky wine
with water in a bigger skin, and stores—   275
boiled meats and other victuals—in a bag.
Then she conjured a warm landbreeze to blowing—
joy for Odysseus when he shook out sail!
Now the great seaman, leaning on his oar,
steered all the night unsleeping, and his eyes   280
picked out the Pleiadês, the laggard Ploughman,[8]
and the Great Bear, that some have called the Wain,[9]
pivoting in the sky before Orion;
of all the night's pure figures, she alone
would never bathe or dip in the Ocean stream.[1]   285
These stars the beautiful Kalypso bade him
hold on his left hand as he crossed the main.
Seventeen nights and days in the open water
he sailed, before a dark shoreline appeared;
Skhería then came slowly into view   290
like a rough shield of bull's hide on the sea.

But now the god of earthquake,[2] storming home
over the mountains of Asia from the Sunburned land,

---

8. Another name for the constellation Boötes. Pleiadês is a cluster of stars in the constellation Tau-
rus.   9. The Big Dipper.   1. That is, it is visible all year long. Orion, the Hunter, also is a constellation.   2. Poseidon.

sighted him far away. The god grew sullen
and tossed his great head, muttering to himself: 295

"Here is a pretty cruise! While I was gone,
the gods have changed their minds about Odysseus.
Look at him now, just offshore of that island
that frees him from the bondage of his exile!
Still I can give him a rough ride in, and will."   300

Brewing high thunderheads, he churned the deep
with both hands on his trident—called up wind
from every quarter, and sent a wall of rain
to blot out land and sea in torrential night.
Hurricane winds now struck from the South and East   305
shifting North West in a great spume of seas,
on which Odysseus' knees grew slack, his heart
sickened, and he said within himself:

"Rag of man that I am, is this the end of me?
I fear the goddess told it all too well—   310
predicting great adversity at sea
and far from home. Now all things bear her out:
the whole rondure of heaven hooded so
by Zeus in woeful cloud, and the sea raging
under such winds. I am going down, that's sure.   315
How lucky those Danaans were who perished
on Troy's wide seaboard, serving the Atreidai!
Would God I, too, had died there—met my end
that time the Trojans made so many casts at me
when I stood by Akhilleus after death.   320
I should have had a soldier's burial
and praise from the Akhaians—not this choking
waiting for me at sea, unmarked and lonely."

A great wave drove at him with toppling crest
spinning him round, in one tremendous blow,   325
and he went plunging overboard, the oar-haft
wrenched from his grip. A gust that came on howling
at the same instant broke his mast in two,
hurling his yard and sail far out to leeward.
Now the big wave a long time kept him under,   330
helpless to surface, held by tons of water,
tangled, too, by the seacloak of Kalypso.
Long, long, until he came up spouting brine,
with streamlets gushing from his head and beard;
but still bethought him, half-drowned as he was,   335
to flounder for the boat and get a handhold
into the bilge—to crouch there, foiling death.
Across the foaming water, to and fro,
the boat careered like a ball of tumbleweed
blown on the autumn plains, but intact still.   340
So the winds drove this wreck over the deep,
East Wind and North Wind, then South Wind and West,
coursing each in turn to the brutal harry.

But Ino saw him—Ino, Kadmos' daughter,
slim-legged, lovely, once an earthling girl,   345

now in the seas a nereid, Leukothea.
Touched by Odysseus' painful buffeting
she broke the surface, like a diving bird,
to rest upon the tossing raft and say:

"O forlorn man, I wonder   350
why the Earthshaker, Lord Poseidon, holds
this fearful grudge—father of all your woes.
He will not drown you, though, despite his rage.
You seem clear-headed still; do what I tell you.
Shed that cloak, let the gale take your craft,   355
and swim for it—swim hard to get ashore
upon Skhería, yonder,
where it is fated that you find a shelter.
Here: make my veil your sash; it is not mortal;
you cannot, now, be drowned or suffer harm.   360
Only, the instant you lay hold of earth,
discard it, cast it far, far out from shore
in the winedark sea again, and turn away."

After she had bestowed her veil, the nereid
dove like a gull to windward   365
where a dark waveside closed over her whiteness.
But in perplexity Odysseus
said to himself, his great heart laboring:

"O damned confusion! Can this be a ruse
to trick me from the boat for some god's pleasure?   370
No I'll not swim; with my own eyes I saw
how far the land lies that she called my shelter.
Better to do the wise thing, as I see it.
While this poor planking holds, I stay aboard;
I may ride out the pounding of the storm,   375
or if she cracks up, take to the water then;
I cannot think it through a better way."

But even while he pondered and decided,
the god of earthquake heaved a wave against him
high as a rooftree and of awful gloom.   380
A gust of wind, hitting a pile of chaff,
will scatter all the parched stuff far and wide;
just so, when this gigantic billow struck
the boat's big timbers flew apart. Odysseus
clung to a single beam, like a jockey riding,   385
meanwhile stripping Kalypso's cloak away;
then he slung round his chest the veil of Ino
and plunged headfirst into the sea. His hands
went out to stroke, and he gave a swimmer's kick.

But the strong Earthshaker had him under his eye,   390
and nodded as he said:

            "Go on, go on;
wander the high seas this way, take your blows,
before you join that race[3] the gods have nurtured.

3. The Phaiákians, favored by the gods.

Nor will you grumble, even then, I think,
for want of trouble."

                    Whipping his glossy team   395
he rode off to his glorious home at Aigai.[4]
But Zeus's daughter Athena countered him:
she checked the course of all the winds but one,
commanding them, "Be quiet and go to sleep."
Then sent a long swell running under a norther   400
to bear the prince Odysseus, back from danger,
to join the Phaiákians, people of the sea.
Two nights, two days, in the solid deep-sea swell
he drifted, many times awaiting death,
until with shining ringlets in the East   405
the dawn confirmed a third day, breaking clear
over a high and windless sea; and mounting
a rolling wave he caught a glimpse of land.
What a dear welcome thing life seems to children
whose father, in the extremity, recovers   410
after some weakening and malignant illness:
his pangs are gone, the gods have delivered him.
So dear and welcome to Odysseus
the sight of land, of woodland, on that morning.
It made him swim again, to get a foothold   415
on solid ground. But when he came in earshot
he heard the trampling roar of sea on rock,
where combers, rising shoreward, thudded down
on the sucking ebb—all sheeted with salt foam.
Here were no coves or harborage or shelter,   420
only steep headlands, rockfallen reefs and crags.
Odysseus' knees grew slack, his heart faint,
a heaviness came over him, and he said:

"A cruel turn, this. Never had I thought
to see this land, but Zeus has let me see it—   425
and let me, too, traverse the Western Ocean—
only to find no exit from these breakers.
Here are sharp rocks off shore, and the sea a smother
rushing around them; rock face rising sheer
from deep water; nowhere could I stand up   430
on my two feet and fight free of the welter.
No matter how I try it, the surf may throw me
against the cliffside; no good fighting there.
If I swim down the coast, outside the breakers,
I may find shelving shore and quiet water—   435
but what if another gale comes on to blow?
Then I go cursing out to sea once more.
Or then again, some shark of Amphitrîtê's[5]
may hunt me, sent by the genius of the deep.
I know how he who makes earth tremble hates me."   440

During this meditation a heavy surge
was taking him, in fact, straight on the rocks.

4. Town on the coast of Euboia, where there was a temple of Poseidon.   5. A sea goddess.

He had been flayed there, and his bones broken,
had not grey-eyed Athena instructed him:
he gripped a rock-ledge with both hands in passing   445
and held on, groaning, as the surge went by,
to keep clear of its breaking. Then the backwash
hit him, ripping him under and far out.
An octopus, when you drag one from his chamber,
comes up with suckers full of tiny stones: 450
Odysseus left the skin of his great hands
torn on that rock-ledge as the wave submerged him.
And now at last Odysseus would have perished,
battered inhumanly, but he had the gift
of self-possession from grey-eyed Athena.   455
So, when the backwash spewed him up again,
he swam out and along, and scanned the coast
for some landspit that made a breakwater.
Lo and behold, the mouth of a calm river
at length came into view, with level shores   460
unbroken, free from rock, shielded from wind—
by far the best place he had found.
But as he felt the current flowing seaward
he prayed in his heart:

                "O hear me, lord of the stream:
how sorely I depend upon your mercy!   465
derelict as I am by the sea's anger.
Is he not sacred, even to the gods,
the wandering man who comes, as I have come,
in weariness before your knees, your waters?
Here is your servant; lord, have mercy on me."   470

Now even as he prayed the tide at ebb
had turned, and the river god made quiet water,
drawing him in to safety in the shallows.
His knees buckled, his arms gave way beneath him,
all vital force now conquered by the sea.   475
Swollen from head to foot he was, and seawater
gushed from his mouth and nostrils. There he lay,
scarce drawing breath, unstirring, deathly spent.
In time, as air came back into his lungs
and warmth around his heart, he loosed the veil,   480
letting it drift away on the estuary
downstream to where a white wave took it under
and Ino's hands received it. Then the man
crawled to the river bank among the reeds
where, face down, he could kiss the soil of earth,   485
in his exhaustion murmuring to himself:

"What more can this hulk suffer? What comes now?
In vigil through the night here by the river
how can I not succumb, being weak and sick,
to the night's damp and hoarfrost of the morning?   490
The air comes cold from rivers before dawn.
But if I climb the slope and fall asleep
in the dark forest's undergrowth—supposing

cold and fatigue will go, and sweet sleep come—
I fear I make the wild beasts easy prey."   495

But this seemed best to him, as he thought it over.
He made his way to a grove above the water
on open ground, and crept under twin bushes
grown from the same spot—olive and wild olive—
a thicket proof against the stinging wind   500
or Sun's blaze, fine soever the needling sunlight;
nor could a downpour wet it through, so dense
those plants were interwoven. Here Odysseus
tunnelled, and raked together with his hands
a wide bed—for a fall of leaves was there,   505
enough to save two men or maybe three
on a winter night, a night of bitter cold.
Odysseus' heart laughed when he saw his leaf-bed,
and down he lay, heaping more leaves above him.

A man in a distant field, no hearthfires near,   510
will hide a fresh brand in his bed of embers
to keep a spark alive for the next day;
so in the leaves Odysseus hid himself,
while over him Athena showered sleep
that his distress should end, and soon, soon.   515
In quiet sleep she sealed his cherished eyes.

BOOK VI

[The Princess at the River]

Far gone in weariness, in oblivion,
the noble and enduring man slept on;
but Athena in the night went down the land
of the Phaiákians, entering their city.
In days gone by, these men held Hypereia,[6]   5
a country of wide dancing grounds, but near them
were overbearing Kyklopês, whose power
could not be turned from pillage. So the Phaiákians
migrated thence under Nausíthoös
to settle a New World across the sea,   10
Skhería Island. That first captain walled
their promontory, built their homes and shrines,
and parcelled out the black land for the plow.
But he had gone down long ago to Death.
Alkínoös ruled, and Heaven gave him wisdom,   15
so on this night the goddess, grey-eyed Athena,
entered the palace of Alkínoös
to make sure of Odysseus' voyage home.
She took her way to a painted bedchamber
where a young girl lay fast asleep—so fine   20
in mould and feature that she seemed a goddess—
the daughter of Alkínoös, Nausikaa.

---

6. Probably an imaginary place; however, the migration under pressure and the founding of the new city (described below) suggest the atmosphere of the great age of Greek colonization (8th century B.C.).

On either side, as Graces[7] might have slept,
her maids were sleeping. The bright doors were shut,
but like a sudden stir of wind, Athena   25
moved to the bedside of the girl, and grew
visible as the shipman Dymas' daughter,
a girl the princess' age, and her dear friend.
In this form grey-eyed Athena said to her:

"How so remiss, and yet thy mother's daughter?   30
leaving thy clothes uncared for, Nausikaa,
when soon thou must have store of marriage linen,
and put thy minstrelsy in wedding dress!
Beauty, in these, will make the folk admire,
and bring thy father and gentle mother joy.   35
Let us go washing in the shine of morning!
Beside thee will I drub, so wedding chests
will brim by evening. Maidenhood must end!
Have not the noblest born Phaiákians
paid court to thee, whose birth none can excel?   40
Go beg thy sovereign father, even at dawn,
to have the mule cart and the mules brought round
to take thy body-linen, gowns and mantles.
Thou shouldst ride, for it becomes thee more,
the washing pools are found so far from home."   45

On this word she departed, grey-eyed Athena,
to where the gods have their eternal dwelling—
as men say—in the fastness of Olympos.
Never a tremor of wind, or a splash of rain,
no errant snowflake comes to stain that heaven,   50
so calm, so vaporless, the world of light.
Here, where the gay gods live their days of pleasure,
the grey-eyed one withdrew, leaving the princess.

And now Dawn took her own fair throne, awaking
the girl in the sweet gown, still charmed by dream.   55
Down through the rooms she went to tell her parents,
whom she found still at home: her mother seated
near the great hearth among her maids—and twirling
out of her distaff yarn dyed like the sea—;
her father at the door, bound for a council   60
of princes on petition of the gentry.
She went up close to him and softly said:

"My dear Papà, could you not send the mule cart
around for me—the gig with pretty wheels?
I must take all our things and get them washed   65
at the river pools; our linen is all soiled.
And you should wear fresh clothing, going to council
with counselors and first men of the realm.
Remember your five sons at home: though two
are married, we have still three bachelor sprigs;   70
they will have none but laundered clothes each time
they go to the dancing. See what I must think of!"

7. Goddesses (usually three) personifying charm and beauty.

She had no word to say of her own wedding,
though her keen father saw her blush. Said he:

"No mules would I deny you, child, nor anything.   75
Go along, now; the grooms will bring your gig
with pretty wheels and the cargo box upon it."

He spoke to the stableman, who soon brought round
the cart, low-wheeled and nimble;
harnessed the mules, and backed them in the traces.   80
Meanwhile the girl fetched all her soiled apparel
to bundle in the polished wagon box.
Her mother, for their luncheon, packed a hamper
with picnic fare, and filled a skin of wine,
and, when the princess had been handed up,   85
gave her a golden bottle of olive oil
for softening girls' bodies, after bathing.
Nausikaa took the reins and raised her whip,
lashing the mules. What jingling! What a clatter!
But off they went in a ground-covering trot,   90
with princess, maids, and laundry drawn behind.
By the lower river where the wagon came
were washing pools, with water all year flowing
in limpid spillways that no grime withstood.
The girls unhitched the mules, and sent them down   95
along the eddying stream to crop sweet grass.
Then sliding out the cart's tail board, they took
armloads of clothing to the dusky water,
and trod them in the pits, making a race of it.
All being drubbed, all blemish rinsed away,   100
they spread them, piece by piece, along the beach
whose pebbles had been laundered by the sea;
then took a dip themselves, and, all anointed
with golden oil, ate lunch beside the river
while the bright burning sun dried out their linen.   105
Princess and maids delighted in that feast;
then, putting off their veils,
they ran and passed a ball to a rhythmic beat,
Nausikaa flashing first with her white arms.

So Artemis goes flying after her arrows flown   110
down some tremendous valley-side—
                 Taÿgetos, Erymanthos[8]—
chasing the mountain goats or ghosting deer,
with nymphs of the wild places flanking her;
and Lêto's[9] heart delights to see them running,
for, taller by a head than nymphs can be,   115
the goddess shows more stately, all being beautiful.
So one could tell the princess from the maids.

Soon it was time, she knew, for riding homeward—
mules to be harnessed, linen folded smooth—

8. A mountain in Arcadia. Taÿgetos is the mountain range west of Sparta. Both places are rich in game.
9. Mother of Artemis and Apollo.

but the grey-eyed goddess Athena made her tarry,   120
so that Odysseus might behold her beauty
and win her guidance to the town.
                              It happened
when the king's daughter threw her ball off line
and missed, and put it in the whirling stream, —
at which they all gave such a shout, Odysseus   125
awoke and sat up, saying to himself:

"Now, by my life, mankind again! But who?
Savages, are they, strangers to courtesy?
Or gentle folk, who know and fear the gods?
That was a lusty cry of tall young girls—   130
most like the cry of nymphs, who haunt the peaks,
and springs of brooks, and inland grassy places.
Or am I amid people of human speech?
Up again, man; and let me see for myself."
He pushed aside the bushes, breaking off   135
with his great hand a single branch of olive,
whose leaves might shield him in his nakedness;
so came out rustling, like a mountain lion,
rain-drenched, wind-buffeted, but in his might at ease,
with burning eyes—who prowls among the herds   140
or flocks, or after game, his hungry belly
taking him near stout homesteads for his prey.
Odysseus had this look, in his rough skin
advancing on the girls with pretty braids;
and he was driven on by hunger, too.   145
Streaked with brine, and swollen, he terrified them,
so that they fled, this way and that. Only
Alkínoös' daughter stood her ground, being given
a bold heart by Athena, and steady knees.

She faced him, waiting. And Odysseus came,   150
debating inwardly what he should do:
embrace this beauty's knees in supplication?
or stand apart, and, using honeyed speech,
inquire the way to town, and beg some clothing?
In his swift reckoning, he thought it best   155
to trust in words to please her—and keep away;
he might anger the girl, touching her knees.
So he began, and let the soft words fall:

"Mistress: please: are you divine, or mortal?
If one of those who dwell in the wide heaven,   160
you are most near to Artemis, I should say—
great Zeus's daughter—in your grace and presence.
If you are one of earth's inhabitants,
how blest your father, and your gentle mother,
blest all your kin. I know what happiness   165
must send the warm tears to their eyes, each time
they see their wondrous child go to the dancing!
But one man's destiny is more than blest—
he who prevails, and takes you as his bride.

Never have I laid eyes on equal beauty   170
in man or woman. I am hushed indeed.
So fair, one time, I thought a young palm tree
at Delos[1] near the altar of Apollo—
I had troops under me when I was there
on the sea route that later brought me grief—   175
but that slim palm tree filled my heart with wonder:
never came shoot from earth so beautiful.
So now, my lady, I stand in awe so great
I cannot take your knees. And yet my case is desperate:
twenty days, yesterday, in the winedark sea,   180
on the ever-lunging swell, under gale winds,
getting away from the Island of Ogýgia.
And now the terror of Storm has left me stranded
upon this shore—with more blows yet to suffer,
I must believe, before the gods relent.   185
Mistress, do me a kindness!
After much weary toil, I come to you,
and you are the first soul I have seen—I know
no others here. Direct me to the town,
give me a rag that I can throw around me,   190
some cloth or wrapping that you brought along.
And may the gods accomplish your desire:
a home, a husband, and harmonious
converse with him—the best thing in the world
being a strong house held in serenity   195
where man and wife agree. Woe to their enemies,
joy to their friends! But all this they know best."

Then she of the white arms, Nausikaa, replied:

"Stranger, there is no quirk or evil in you
that I can see. You know Zeus metes out fortune   200
to good and bad men as it pleases him.
Hardship he sent to you, and you must bear it.
But now that you have taken refuge here
you shall not lack for clothing, or any other
comfort due to a poor man in distress.   205
The town lies this way, and the men are called
Phaiákians, who own the land and city.
I am daughter to the Prince Alkínoös,
by whom the power of our people stands."

Turning, she called out to her maids-in-waiting: 210

"Stay with me! Does the sight of a man scare you?
Or do you take this one for an enemy?
Why, there's no fool so brash, and never will be,
as to bring war or pillage to this coast,
for we are dear to the immortal gods,   215
living here, in the sea that rolls forever,
distant from other lands and other men.
No: this man is a castaway, poor fellow;
we must take care of him. Strangers and beggars

1. A small island in the middle of the Aegean Sea, the birthplace of Apollo and a center for his worship.

come from Zeus: a small gift, then, is friendly.   220
Give our new guest some food and drink, and take him
into the river, out of the wind, to bathe."

They stood up now, and called to one another
to go on back. Quite soon they led Odysseus
under the river bank, as they were bidden;   225
and there laid out a tunic, and a cloak,
and gave him olive oil in the golden flask.
"Here," they said, "go bathe in the flowing water."
But heard now from that kingly man, Odysseus:

"Maids," he said, "keep away a little; let me   230
wash the brine from my own back, and rub on
plenty of oil. It is long since my anointing.
I take no bath, however, where you can see me—
naked before young girls with pretty braids."

They left him, then, and went to tell the princess.   235
And now Odysseus, dousing in the river,
scrubbed the coat of brine from back and shoulders
and rinsed the clot of sea-spume from his hair;
got himself all rubbed down, from head to foot,
then he put on the clothes the princess gave him.   240
Athena lent a hand, making him seem
taller, and massive too, with crisping hair
in curls like petals of wild hyacinth,
but all red-golden. Think of gold infused
on silver by a craftsman, whose fine art   245
Hephaistos taught him, or Athena: one
whose work moves to delight: just so she lavished
beauty over Odysseus' head and shoulders.
Then he went down to sit on the sea beach
in his new splendor. There the girl regarded him,   250
and after a time she said to the maids beside her:

"My gentlewomen, I have a thing to tell you.
The Olympian gods cannot be all averse
to this man's coming here among our islanders.
Uncouth he seemed, I thought so, too, before;   255
but now he looks like one of heaven's people.
I wish my husband could be fine as he
and glad to stay forever on Skhería!

But have you given refreshment to our guest?"

At this the maids, all gravely listening, hastened   260
to set out bread and wine before Odysseus,
and ah! how ravenously that patient man
took food and drink, his long fast at an end.

The princess Nausikaa now turned aside
to fold her linens; in the pretty cart   265
she stowed them, put the mule team under harness,
mounted the driver's seat, and then looked down
to say with cheerful prompting to Odysseus:

"Up with you now, friend; back to town we go;
and I shall send you in before my father   270
who is wondrous wise; there in our house with him
you'll meet the noblest of the Phaiákians.
You have good sense, I think; here's how to do it:
while we go through the countryside and farmland
stay with my maids, behind the wagon, walking   275
briskly enough to follow where I lead.
But near the town—well, there's a wall with towers
around the Isle, and beautiful ship basins
right and left of the causeway of approach;
seagoing craft are beached beside the road   280
each on its launching ways. The agora,[2]
with fieldstone benches bedded in the earth,
lies either side Poseidon's shrine—for there
men are at work on pitch-black hulls and rigging,
cables and sails, and tapering of oars.   285
The archer's craft is not for the Phaiákians,
but ship designing, modes of oaring cutters
in which they love to cross the foaming sea.
From these fellows I will have no salty talk,
no gossip later. Plenty are insolent.   290
And some seadog might say, after we passed:
'Who is this handsome stranger trailing Nausikaa?
Where did she find him? Will he be her husband?
Or is she being hospitable to some rover
come off his ship from lands across the sea—   295
there being no lands nearer. A god, maybe?
a god from heaven, the answer to her prayer,
descending now—to make her his forever?
Better, if she's roamed and found a husband
somewhere else: none of our own will suit her,   300
though many come to court her, and those the best.'
This is the way they might make light of me.
And I myself should hold it shame
for any girl to flout her own dear parents,
taking up with a man, before her marriage.   305

Note well, now, what I say, friend, and your chances
are excellent for safe conduct from my father.
You'll find black poplars in a roadside park
around a meadow and fountain—all Athena's—
but Father has a garden in the place—   310
this within earshot of the city wall.
Go in there and sit down, giving us time
to pass through town and reach my father's house.
And when you can imagine we're at home,
then take the road into the city, asking   315
directions to the palace of Alkínoös.
You'll find it easily: any small boy
can take you there; no family has a mansion
half so grand as he does, being king.

2. Place of assembly.

As soon as you are safe inside, cross over   320
and go straight through into the mégaron[3]
to find my mother. She'll be there in firelight
before a column, with her maids in shadow,
spinning a wool dyed richly as the sea.
My father's great chair faces the fire, too;   325
there like a god he sits and takes his wine.
Go past him, cast yourself before my mother,
embrace her knees—and you may wake up soon
at home rejoicing, though your home be far.
On Mother's feeling much depends; if she   330
looks on you kindly, you shall see your friends
under your own roof in your father's country."

At this she raised her glistening whip, lashing
the team into a run; they left the river
cantering beautifully, then trotted smartly.   335
But then she reined them in, and spared the whip,
so that her maids could follow with Odysseus.
The sun was going down when they went by
Athena's grove. Here, then, Odysseus rested,
and lifted up his prayer to Zeus's daughter: 340

"Hear me, unwearied child of royal Zeus!
O listen to me now—thou so aloof
while the Earthshaker wrecked and battered me.
May I find love and mercy among these people."

He prayed for that, and Pallas Athena heard him—   345
although in deference to her father's brother
she would not show her true form to Odysseus,
at whom Poseidon smoldered on
until the kingly man came home to his own shore.

BOOK VII

[Gardens and Firelight]

As Lord Odysseus prayed there in the grove
the girl rode on, behind her strapping team,
and came late to the mansion of her father,
where she reined in at the courtyard gate. Her brothers
awaited her like tall gods in the court,   5
circling to lead the mules away and carry
the laundered things inside. But she withdrew
to her own bedroom, where a fire soon shone,
kindled by her old nurse, Eurymedousa.
Years ago, from a raid on the continent,   10
the rolling ships had brought this woman over
to be Alkínoös' share—fit spoil for him
whose realm hung on his word as on a god's.
And she had schooled the princess, Nausikaa,
whose fire she tended now, making her supper.   15

3. The great hall of the palace.

Odysseus, when the time had passed, arose
and turned into the city. But Athena
poured a sea fog around him as he went—
her love's expedient, that no jeering sailor
should halt the man or challenge him for luck.   20
Instead, as he set foot in the pleasant city,
the grey-eyed goddess came to him, in figure
a small girl child, hugging a water jug.

Confronted by her, Lord Odysseus asked:

"Little one, could you take me to the house   25
of that Alkínoös, king among these people?
You see, I am a poor old stranger here;
my home is far away; here there is no one
known to me, in countryside or city."

The grey-eyed goddess Athena replied to him: 30

"Oh yes, good grandfer, sir, I know, I'll show you
the house you mean; it is quite near my father's.
But come now, hush, like this, and follow me.
You must not stare at people, or be inquisitive.
They do not care for strangers in this neighborhood;   35
a foreign man will get no welcome here.
The only things they trust are the racing ships
Poseidon gave, to sail the deep blue sea
like white wings in the sky, or a flashing thought."

Pallas Athena turned like the wind, running   40
ahead of him, and he followed in her footsteps.
And no seafaring men of Phaiákia
perceived Odysseus passing through their town:
the awesome one in pigtails barred their sight
with folds of sacred mist. And yet Odysseus   45
gazed out marvelling at the ships and harbors,
public squares, and ramparts towering up
with pointed palisades along the top.
When they were near the mansion of the king,
grey-eyed Athena in the child cried out: 50

"Here it is, grandfer, sir—that mansion house
you asked to see. You'll find our king and queen
at supper, but you must not be dismayed;
go in to them. A cheerful man does best
in every enterprise—even a stranger.   55
You'll see our lady just inside the hall—
her name is Arêtê; her grandfather
was our good king Alkínoös' father—
Nausíthoös by name, son of Poseidon
and Periboia. That was a great beauty,   60
the daughter of Eurymedon, commander
of the Gigantês[4] in the olden days,
who led those wild things to their doom and his.

4. The Giants; an older race of gods who battled, unsuccessfully, against the Olympians.

Poseidon then made love to Periboia,
and she bore Nausíthoös, Phaiákia's lord,   65
whose sons in turn were Rhêxênor and Alkínoös.
Rhêxênor had no sons; even as a bridegroom
he fell before the silver bow of Apollo,
his only child a daughter, Arêtê.
When she grew up, Alkínoös married her   70
and holds her dear. No lady in the world,
no other mistress of a man's household,
is honored as our mistress is, and loved,
by her own children, by Alkínoös,
and by the people. When she walks the town   75
they murmur and gaze, as though she were a goddess.
No grace or wisdom fails in her; indeed
just men in quarrels come to her for equity.
Supposing, then, she looks upon you kindly,
the chances are that you shall see your friends   80
under your own roof, in your father's country."

At this the grey-eyed goddess Athena left him
and left that comely land, going over sea
to Marathon, to the wide roadways of Athens
and her retreat in the stronghold of Erekhtheus.[5]   85
Odysseus, now alone before the palace,
meditated a long time before crossing
the brazen threshold of the great courtyard.
High rooms he saw ahead, airy and luminous
as though with lusters of the sun and moon,   90
bronze-paneled walls, at several distances,
making a vista, with an azure molding
of lapis lazuli. The doors were golden
guardians of the great room. Shining bronze
plated the wide door sill; the posts and lintel   95
were silver upon silver; golden handles
curved on the doors, and golden, too, and silver
were sculptured hounds, flanking the entrance way,
cast by the skill and ardor of Hephaistos
to guard the prince Alkínoös' house —   100
undying dogs that never could grow old.
Through all the rooms, as far as he could see,
tall chairs were placed around the walls, and strewn
with fine embroidered stuff made by the women.
Here were enthroned the leaders of Phaiákia   105
drinking and dining, with abundant fare.
Here, too, were boys of gold on pedestals
holding aloft bright torches of pitch pine
to light the great rooms, and the night-time feasting.
And fifty maids-in-waiting of the household   110
sat by the round mill, grinding yellow corn,
or wove upon their looms, or twirled their distaffs,
flickering like the leaves of a poplar tree;

5. King of Athens. Marathon was a village north of Athens near the coast; later it was the site of the famous battle at which the Athenians repulsed a Persian invasion force (490 B.C.).

while drops of oil glistened on linen weft.
Skillful as were the men of Phaiákia   115
in ship handling at sea, so were these women
skilled at the loom, having this lovely craft
and artistry as talents from Athena.

To left and right, outside, he saw an orchard
closed by a pale—four spacious acres planted   120
with trees in bloom or weighted down for picking:
pear trees, pomegranates, brilliant apples,
luscious figs, and olives ripe and dark.
Fruit never failed upon these trees: winter
and summer time they bore, for through the year   125
the breathing Westwind ripened all in turn—
so one pear came to prime, and then another,
and so with apples, figs, and the vine's fruit
empurpled in the royal vineyard there.
Currants were dried at one end, on a platform   130
bare to the sun, beyond the vintage arbors
and vats the vintners trod; while near at hand
were new grapes barely formed as the green bloom fell,
or half-ripe clusters, faintly coloring.
After the vines came rows of vegetables   135
of all the kinds that flourish in every season,
and through the garden plots and orchard ran
channels from one clear fountain, while another
gushed through a pipe under the courtyard entrance
to serve the house and all who came for water.   140
These were the gifts of heaven to Alkínoös.

Odysseus, who had borne the barren sea,
stood in the gateway and surveyed this bounty.
He gazed his fill, then swiftly he went in.
The lords and nobles of Phaiákia   145
were tipping wine to the wakeful god, to Hermês—
a last libation before going to bed—
but down the hall Odysseus went unseen,
still in the cloud Athena cloaked him in,
until he reached Arêtê, and the king.   150
He threw his great hands round Arêtê's knees,
whereon the sacred mist curled back;
they saw him; and the diners hushed amazed
to see an unknown man inside the palace.
Under their eyes Odysseus made his plea: 155

"Arêtê, admirable Rhêxênor's daughter,
here is a man bruised by adversity, thrown
upon your mercy and the king your husband's,
begging indulgence of this company—
may the gods' blessing rest on them! May life   160
be kind to all! Let each one leave his children
every good thing this realm confers upon him!
But grant me passage to my father land.
My home and friends lie far. My life is pain."

He moved, then, toward the fire, and sat him down   165
amid the ashes.[6] No one stirred or spoke
until Ekhenêos broke the spell—an old man,
eldest of the Phaiákians, an oracle,
versed in the laws and manners of old time.
He rose among them now and spoke out kindly: 170

"Alkínoös, this will not pass for courtesy:
a guest abased in ashes at our hearth?
Everyone here awaits your word; so come, then,
lift the man up; give him a seat of honor,
a silver-studded chair. Then tell the stewards   175
we'll have another wine bowl for libation
to Zeus, lord of the lightning—advocate
of honorable petitioners. And supper
may be supplied our friend by the larder mistress."

Alkínoös, calm in power, heard him out,   180
then took the great adventurer by the hand
and led him from the fire. Nearest his throne
the son whom he loved best, Laódamas,
had long held place; now the king bade him rise
and gave his shining chair to Lord Odysseus.   185
A serving maid poured water for his hands
from a gold pitcher into a silver bowl,
and spread a polished table at his side;
the mistress of provisions came with bread
and other victuals, generous with her store.   190
So Lord Odysseus drank, and tasted supper.
Seeing this done, the king in majesty
said to his squire:

                    "A fresh bowl, Pontónoös;
we make libation to the lord of lightning,
who seconds honorable petitioners."   195

Mixing the honey-hearted wine, Pontónoös
went on his rounds and poured fresh cups for all,
whereof when all had spilt they drank their fill.
Alkínoös then spoke to the company:

"My lords and leaders of Phaiákia: 200
hear now, all that my heart would have me say.
Our banquet's ended, so you may retire;
but let our seniors gather in the morning
to give this guest a festal day, and make
fair offerings to the gods. In due course we   205
shall put our minds upon the means at hand
to take him safely, comfortably, well
and happily, with speed, to his own country,
distant though it may lie. And may no trouble
come to him here or on the way; his fate   210
he shall pay out at home, even as the Spinners[7]

_____

6. The fire, or hearth, was the sacred center of the home; the suppliant who sits there is, so to speak, on consecrated ground and cannot be forcibly removed.   7. The Fates, who spin the pattern of each individual destiny.

spun for him on the day his mother bore him.
If, as may be, he is some god, come down
from heaven's height, the gods are working strangely:
until now, they have shown themselves in glory   215
only after great hekatombs—those figures
banqueting at our side, throned like ourselves.
Or if some traveller met them when alone
they bore no least disguise; we are their kin; Gigantês,
Kyklopês, rank no nearer gods than we."   220

Odysseus' wits were ready, and he replied:

"Alkínoös, you may set your mind at rest.
Body and birth, a most unlikely god
am I, being all of earth and mortal nature.
I should say, rather, I am like those men   225
who suffer the worst trials that you know,
and miseries greater yet, as I might tell you—
hundreds; indeed the gods could send no more.
You will indulge me if I finish dinner—?
grieved though I am to say it. There's no part   230
of man more like a dog than brazen Belly,
crying to be remembered—and it must be—
when we are mortal weary and sick at heart;
and that is my condition. Yet my hunger
drives me to take this food, and think no more   235
of my afflictions. Belly must be filled.
Be equally impelled, my lords, tomorrow
to berth me in a ship and send me home!
Rough years I've had; now may I see once more
my hall, my lands, my people before I die!"   240

Now all who heard cried out assent to this:
the guest had spoken well; he must have passage.
Then tipping wine they drank their thirst away,
and one by one went homeward for the night.
So Lord Odysseus kept his place alone   245
with Arêtê and the king Alkínoös
beside him, while the maids went to and fro
clearing away the wine cups and the tables.
Presently the ivory-skinned lady
turned to him—for she knew his cloak and tunic   250
to be her own fine work, done with her maids—
and arrowy came her words upon the air:

"Friend, I, for one, have certain questions for you.
Who are you, and who has given you this clothing?
Did you not say you wandered here by sea?"   255

The great tactician carefully replied:

"Ah, majesty, what labor it would be
to go through the whole story! All my years
of misadventures, given by those on high!
But this you ask about is quickly told: 260
in mid-ocean lies Ogýgia, the island

haunt of Kalypso, Atlas' guileful daughter,
a lovely goddess and a dangerous one.
No one, no god or man, consorts with her;
but supernatural power brought me there   265
to be her solitary guest: for Zeus
let fly with his bright bolt and split my ship,
rolling me over in the winedark sea.
There all my shipmates, friends were drowned, while I
hung on the keelboard of the wreck and drifted   270
nine full days. Then in the dead of night
the gods brought me ashore upon Ogýgia
into her hands. The enchantress in her beauty
fed and caressed me, promised me I should be
immortal, youthful, all the days to come;   275
but in my heart I never gave consent
though seven years detained. Immortal clothing
I had from her, and kept it wet with tears.
Then came the eighth year on the wheel of heaven
and word to her from Zeus, or a change of heart,   280
so that she now commanded me to sail,
sending me out to sea on a craft I made
with timber and tools of hers. She gave me stores,
victuals and wine, a cloak divinely woven,
and made a warm land breeze come up astern.   285
Seventeen days I sailed in the open water
before I saw your country's shore, a shadow
upon the sea rim. Then my heart rejoiced—
pitiable as I am! For blows aplenty
awaited me from the god who shakes the earth.   290
Cross gales he blew, making me lose my bearings,
and heaved up seas beyond imagination—
huge and foundering seas. All I could do
was hold hard, groaning under every shock,
until my craft broke up in the hurricane.   295
I kept afloat and swam your sea, or drifted,
taken by wind and current to this coast
where I went in on big swells running landward.
But cliffs and rock shoals made that place forbidding,
so I turned back, swimming off shore, and came   300
in the end to a river, to auspicious water,
with smooth beach and a rise that broke the wind.
I lay there where I fell till strength returned.
Then sacred night came on, and I went inland
to high ground and a leaf bed in a thicket.   305
Heaven sent slumber in an endless tide
submerging my sad heart among the leaves.
That night and next day's dawn and noon I slept;
the sun went west; and then sweet sleep unbound me,
when I became aware of maids—your daughter's—   310
playing along the beach; the princess, too,
most beautiful. I prayed her to assist me,
and her good sense was perfect; one could hope
for no behavior like it from the young,
thoughtless as they most often are. But she   315

gave me good provender and good red wine,
a river bath, and finally this clothing.
There is the bitter tale. These are the facts."

But in reply Alkínoös observed:

"Friend, my child's good judgment failed in this—   320
not to have brought you in her company home.
Once you approached her, you became her charge."

To this Odysseus tactfully replied:

"Sir, as to that, you should not blame the princess.
She did tell me to follow with her maids,   325
but I would not. I felt abashed, and feared
the sight would somehow ruffle or offend you.
All of us on this earth are plagued by jealousy."

Alkínoös' answer was a declaration:

"Friend, I am not a man for trivial anger: 330
better a sense of measure in everything.
No anger here. I say that if it should please
our father Zeus, Athena, and Apollo—
seeing the man you are, seeing your thoughts
are my own thoughts—my daughter should be yours   335
and you my son-in-law, if you remained.
A home, lands, riches you should have from me
if you could be contented here. If not,
by Father Zeus, let none of our men hold you!
On the contrary, I can assure you now   340
of passage late tomorrow: while you sleep
my men will row you through the tranquil night
to your own land and home or where you please.
It may be, even, far beyond Euboia—
called most remote by seamen of our isle   345
who landed there, conveying Rhadamanthos
when he sought Títyos,[8] the son of Gaia.
They put about, with neither pause nor rest,
and entered their home port the selfsame day.
But this you, too, will see: what ships I have,   350
how my young oarsmen send the foam a-scudding!"

Now joy welled up in the patient Lord Odysseus
who said devoutly in the warmest tones:

"O Father Zeus, let all this be fulfilled
as spoken by Alkínoös! Earth of harvests   355
remember him! Return me to my homeland!"

In this manner they conversed with one another;
but the great lady called her maids, and sent them
to make a kingly bed, with purple rugs
piled up, and sheets outspread, and fleecy   360
coverlets, in an eastern colonnade.

---

8. A giant who tried to rape Lêto. In Book XI Odysseus sees him in the underworld, eternally punished for his crime. Why Rhadamanthos went to see Títyos we have no idea.

The girls went out with torches in their hands,
swift at their work of bedmaking; returning
they whispered at the lord Odysseus' shoulder:

"Sir, you may come; your bed has been prepared."   365

How welcome the word "bed" came to his ears!
Now, then, Odysseus laid him down and slept
in luxury under the Porch of Morning,
while in his inner chamber Alkínoös
retired to rest where his dear consort lay.   370

BOOK VIII

[The Songs of the Harper]

Under the opening fingers of the dawn
Alkínoös, the sacred prince, arose,
and then arose Odysseus, raider of cities.
As the king willed, they went down by the shipways
to the assembly ground of the Phaiákians.   5
Side by side the two men took their ease there
on smooth stone benches. Meanwhile Pallas Athena
roamed through the byways of the town, contriving
Odysseus' voyage home—in voice and feature
the crier of the king Alkínoös   10
who stopped and passed the word to every man:

"Phaiákian lords and counselors, this way!
Come to assembly: learn about the stranger,
the new guest at the palace of Alkínoös—
a man the sea drove, but a comely man;   15
the gods' own light is on him."

                              She aroused them,
and soon the assembly ground and seats were filled
with curious men, a throng who peered and saw
the master mind of war, Laërtês' son.
Athena now poured out her grace upon him,   20
head and shoulders, height and mass—a splendor
awesome to the eyes of the Phaiákians;
she put him in a fettle to win the day,
mastering every trial they set to test him.
When all the crowd sat marshalled, quieted,   25
Alkínoös addressed the full assembly:

"Hear me, lords and captains of the Phaiákians!
Hear what my heart would have me say!
Our guest and new friend—nameless to me still—
comes to my house after long wandering   30
in Dawn lands, or among the Sunset races.
Now he appeals to me for conveyance home.
As in the past, therefore, let us provide
passage, and quickly, for no guest of mine
languishes here for lack of it. Look to it: 35
get a black ship afloat on the noble sea,

and pick our fastest sailer; draft a crew
of two and fifty from our younger townsmen—
men who have made their names at sea. Loop oars
well to your tholepins, lads, then leave the ship,   40
come to our house, fall to, and take your supper:
we'll furnish out a feast for every crewman.
These are your orders. As for my older peers
and princes of the realm, let them foregather
in festival for our friend in my great hall;   45
and let no man refuse. Call in our minstrel,
Demódokos, whom God made lord of song,
heart-easing, sing upon what theme he will."

He turned, led the procession, and those princes
followed, while his herald sought the minstrel.   50
Young oarsmen from the assembly chose a crew
of two and fifty, as the king commanded,
and these filed off along the waterside
to where the ship lay, poised above open water.
They hauled the black hull down to ride the sea,   55
rigging a mast and spar in the black ship,
with oars at trail from corded rawhide, all
seamanly; then tried the white sail, hoisting,
and moored her off the beach. Then going ashore
the crew went up to the great house of Alkínoös.   60
Here the enclosures, entrance ways, and rooms
were filled with men, young men and old, for whom
Alkínoös had put twelve sheep to sacrifice,
eight tuskers and a pair of shambling oxen.
These, now, they flayed and dressed to make their banquet.   65
The crier soon came, leading that man of song
whom the Muse cherished; by her gift he knew
the good of life, and evil—
for she who lent him sweetness made him blind.
Pontónoös fixed a studded chair for him   70
hard by a pillar amid the banqueters,
hanging the taut harp from a peg above him,
and guided up his hands upon the strings;
placed a bread basket at his side, and poured
wine in a cup, that he might drink his fill.   75
Now each man's hand went out upon the banquet.

In time, when hunger and thirst were turned away,
the Muse brought to the minstrel's mind a song
of heroes whose great fame rang under heaven:
the clash between Odysseus and Akhilleus,   80
how one time they contended at the godfeast
raging, and the marshal, Agamémnon,
felt inward joy over his captains' quarrel;
for such had been foretold him by Apollo
at Pytho[9]—hallowed height—when the Akhaian   85
crossed that portal of rock to ask a sign—

9. The oracular shrine of Apollo at Delphi, high up on the mountainside.

in the old days when grim war lay ahead
for Trojans and Danaans, by God's will.
So ran the tale the minstrel sang. Odysseus
with massive hand drew his rich mantle down   90
over his brow, cloaking his face with it,
to make the Phaiákians miss the secret tears
that started to his eyes. How skillfully
he dried them when the song came to a pause!
threw back his mantle, spilt his gout of wine!   95
But soon the minstrel plucked his note once more
to please the Phaiákian lords, who loved the song;
then in his cloak Odysseus wept again.
His tears flowed in the mantle unperceived;
only Alkínoös, at his elbow, saw them,   100
and caught the low groan in the man's breathing.
At once he spoke to all the seafolk round him:

"Hear me, lords and captains of the Phaiákians.
Our meat is shared, our hearts are full of pleasure
from the clear harp tone that accords with feasting;   105
now for the field and track; we shall have trials
in the pentathlon. Let our guest go home
and tell his friends what champions we are
at boxing, wrestling, broadjump and foot racing."

On this he led the way and all went after.   110
The crier unslung and pegged the shining harp
and, taking Demódokos's hand,
led him along with all the rest—Phaiákian
peers, gay amateurs of the great games.
They gained the common, where a crowd was forming,   115
and many a young athlete now came forward
with seaside names like Tipmast, Tiderace, Sparwood,
Hullman, Sternman, Beacher and Pullerman,
Bluewater, Shearwater, Runningwake, Boardalee,
Seabelt, son of Grandfleet Shipwrightson;   120
Seareach stepped up, son of the Launching Master,
rugged as Arês,[1] bane of men: his build
excelled all but the Prince Laódamas;
and Laódamas made entry with his brothers,
Halios and Klytóneus, sons of the king.   125
The runners, first, must have their quarter mile.
All lined up tense; then Go! and down the track
they raised the dust in a flying bunch, strung out
longer and longer behind Prince Klytóneus.
By just so far as a mule team, breaking ground,   130
will distance oxen, he left all behind
and came up to the crowd, an easy winner.
Then they made room for wrestling—grinding bouts
that Seareach won, pinning the strongest men;
then the broadjump; first place went to Seabelt;   135
Sparwood gave the discus the mightiest fling,

1. The Greek war god.

and Prince Laódamas outboxed them all.
Now it was he, the son of Alkínoös,
who said when they had run through these diversions:

"Look here, friends, we ought to ask the stranger   140
if he competes in something. He's no cripple;
look at his leg muscles and his forearms.
Neck like a bollard; strong as a bull, he seems;
and not old, though he may have gone stale under
the rough times he had. Nothing like the sea   145
for wearing out the toughest man alive."

Then Seareach took him up at once, and said:

"Laódamas, you're right, by all the powers.
Go up to him, yourself, and put the question."

At this, Alkínoös' tall son advanced   150
to the center ground, and there addressed Odysseus:

"Friend, Excellency, come join our competition,
if you are practiced, as you seem to be.
While a man lives he wins no greater honor
than footwork and the skill of hands can bring him.   155
Enter our games, then; ease your heart of trouble.
Your journey home is not far off, remember;
the ship is launched, the crew all primed for sea."

Odysseus, canniest of men, replied:

"Laódamas, why do you young chaps challenge me?   160
I have more on my mind than track and field—
hard days, and many, have I seen, and suffered.
I sit here at your field meet, yes; but only
as one who begs your king to send him home."

Now Seareach put his word in, and contentiously: 165

"The reason being, as I see it, friend,
you never learned a sport, and have no skill
in any of the contests of fighting men.
You must have been the skipper of some tramp
that crawled from one port to the next, jam full   170
of chaffering hands: a tallier of cargoes,
itching for gold—not, by your looks, an athlete."

Odysseus frowned, and eyed him coldly, saying:

"That was uncalled for, friend, you talk like a fool.
The gods deal out no gift, this one or any—   175
birth, brains, or speech—to every man alike.
In looks a man may be a shade, a specter,
and yet be master of speech so crowned with beauty
that people gaze at him with pleasure. Courteous,
sure of himself, he can command assemblies,   180
and when he comes to town, the crowds gather.
A handsome man, contrariwise, may lack
grace and good sense in everything he says.

You now, for instance, with your fine physique—
a god's, indeed—you have an empty noddle.   185
I find my heart inside my ribs aroused
by your impertinence. I am no stranger
to contests, as you fancy. I rated well
when I could count on youth and my two hands.
Now pain has cramped me, and my years of combat   190
hacking through ranks in war, and the bitter sea.
Aye. Even so I'll give your games a trial.
You spoke heart-wounding words. You shall be answered."

He leapt out, cloaked as he was, and picked a discus,
a rounded stone, more ponderous than those   195
already used by the Phaiákian throwers,
and, whirling, let it fly from his great hand
with a low hum. The crowd went flat on the ground—
all those oar-pulling, seafaring Phaiákians—
under the rushing noise. The spinning disk   200
soared out, light as a bird, beyond all others.
Disguised now as a Phaiákian, Athena
staked it and called out:

                              "Even a blind man,
friend, could judge this, finding with his fingers
one discus, quite alone, beyond the cluster.   205
Congratulations; this event is yours;
not a man here can beat you or come near you."

That was a cheering hail, Odysseus thought,
seeing one friend there on the emulous field,
so, in relief, he turned among the Phaiákians   210
and said:

                       "Now come alongside that one, lads.
The next I'll send as far, I think, or farther.
Anyone else on edge for competition
try me now. By heaven, you angered me.
Racing, wrestling, boxing—I bar nothing   215
with any man except Laódamas,
for he's my host. Who quarrels with his host?
Only a madman—or no man at all—
would challenge his protector among strangers,
cutting the ground away under his feet.   220
Here are no others I will not engage,
none but I hope to know what he is made of.
Inept at combat, am I? Not entirely.
Give me a smooth bow; I can handle it,
and I might well be first to hit my man   225
amid a swarm of enemies, though archers
in company around me drew together.
Philoktêtês[2] alone, at Troy, when we
Akhaians took the bow, used to outshoot me.
Of men who now eat bread upon the earth   230

2. He inherited the bow of Herakles, which never missed its mark.

I hold myself the best hand with a bow—
conceding mastery to the men of old,
Heraklês, or Eurýtos of Oikhalía,[3]
heroes who vied with gods in bowmanship.
Eurýtos came to grief, it's true; old age   235
never crept over him in his long hall;
Apollo took his challenge ill, and killed him.
What then, the spear? I'll plant it like an arrow.
Only in sprinting, I'm afraid, I may
be passed by someone. Roll of the sea waves   240
wearied me, and the victuals in my ship
ran low; my legs are flabby."

> When he finished,
the rest were silent, but Alkínoös answered:

"Friend, we take your challenge in good part,
for this man angered and affronted you   245
here at our peaceful games. You'd have us note
the prowess that is in you, and so clearly,
no man of sense would ever cry it down!
Come, turn your mind, now, on a thing to tell
among your peers when you are home again,   250
dining in hall, beside your wife and children:
I mean our prowess, as you may remember it,
for we, too, have our skills, given by Zeus,
and practiced from our father's time to this—
not in the boxing ring nor the palestra[4]   255
conspicuous, but in racing, land or sea;
and all our days we set great store by feasting,
harpers, and the grace of dancing choirs,
changes of dress, warm baths, and downy beds.
O master dancers of the Phaiákians!   260
Perform now: let our guest on his return
tell his companions we excel the world
in dance and song, as in our ships and running.
Someone go find the gittern[5] harp in hall
and bring it quickly to Demódokos!"   265

At the serene king's word, a squire ran
to bring the polished harp out of the palace,
and place was given to nine referees—
peers of the realm, masters of ceremony—
who cleared a space and smoothed a dancing floor.   270
The squire brought down, and gave Demódokos,
the clear-toned harp; and centering on the minstrel
magical young dancers formed a circle
with a light beat, and stamp of feet. Beholding,
Odysseus marvelled at the flashing ring.   275

Now to his harp the blinded minstrel sang
of Arês' dalliance with Aphroditê:

---

3. Eurýtos of Oikhalía (in central Greece) challenged Apollo (also an archer) and was killed by the
god. Eurýtos' bow was given to Odysseus by his son Iphitos, and it is with that bow that Odysseus will
kill the suitors in Book XXII.   4. Wrestling ground.   5. Shaped like a guitar.

how hidden in Hephaistos' house they played
at love together, and the gifts of Arês,
dishonoring Hephaistos' bed—and how   280
the word that wounds the heart came to the master
from Hélios,[6] who had seen the two embrace;
and when he learned it, Lord Hephaistos went
with baleful calculation to his forge.
There mightily he armed his anvil block   285
and hammered out a chain whose tempered links
could not be sprung or bent; he meant that they should hold.
Those shackles fashioned, hot in wrath Hephaistos
climbed to the bower and the bed of love,
pooled all his net of chain around the bed posts   290
and swung it from the rafters overhead—
light as a cobweb even gods in bliss
could not perceive, so wonderful his cunning.
Seeing his bed now made a snare, he feigned
a journey to the trim stronghold of Lemnos,   295
the dearest of earth's towns to him.[7] And Arês?
Ah, golden Arês' watch had its reward
when he beheld the great smith leaving home.
How promptly to the famous door he came,
intent on pleasure with sweet Kythereia![8]   300
She, who had left her father's side but now,
sat in her chamber when her lover entered;
and tenderly he pressed her hand and said:

"Come and lie down, my darling, and be happy!
Hephaistos is no longer here, but gone   305
to see his grunting[9] Sintian friends on Lemnos."

As she, too, thought repose would be most welcome,
the pair went in to bed—into a shower
of clever chains, the netting of Hephaistos.
So trussed, they could not move apart, nor rise,   310
at last they knew there could be no escape,
they were to see the glorious cripple now—
for Hêlios had spied for him, and told him;
so he turned back this side of Lemnos Isle,
sick at heart, making his way homeward.   315
Now in the doorway of the room he stood
while deadly rage took hold of him; his voice,
hoarse and terrible, reached all the gods:

"O Father Zeus, O gods in bliss forever,
here is indecorous entertainment for you,   320
Aphroditê, Zeus's daughter,
caught in the act, cheating me, her cripple,
with Arês—devastating Arês.
Cleanlimbed beauty is her joy, not these
bandylegs I came into the world with: 325

---

6. The Sun, who sees everything.   7. When Zeus threw him off Olympus (*Iliad* I.711ff.), Hephaistos
landed on the island of Lemnos (off the coast of Asia Minor), where the inhabitants took care of
him.   8. A name for Aphrodite.   9. They do not speak Greek.

no one to blame but the two gods[1] who bred me!
Come see this pair entwining here
in my own bed! How hot it makes me burn!
I think they may not care to lie much longer,
pressing on one another, passionate lovers;					330
they'll have enough of bed together soon.
And yet the chain that bagged them holds them down
till Father sends me back my wedding gifts—
all that I poured out for his damned pigeon,
so lovely, and so wanton."

     All the others					335
were crowding in, now, to the brazen house—
Poseidon who embraces earth, and Hermês
the runner, and Apollo, lord of Distance.
The goddesses stayed home for shame; but these
munificences ranged there in the doorway,					340
and irrepressible among them all
arose the laughter of the happy gods.
Gazing hard at Hephaistos' handiwork
the gods in turn remarked among themselves:

"No dash in adultery now."

     "The tortoise tags the hare—					345
Hephaistos catches Arês—and Arês outran the wind."

"The lame god's craft has pinned him. Now shall he
pay what is due from gods taken in cuckoldry."

They made these improving remarks to one another,
but Apollo leaned aside to say to Hermês:					350

"Son of Zeus, beneficent Wayfinder,
would you accept a coverlet of chain, if only
you lay by Aphroditê's golden side?"

To this the Wayfinder replied, shining:

"Would I not, though, Apollo of distances!					355
Wrap me in chains three times the weight of these,
come goddesses and gods to see the fun;
only let me lie beside the pale-golden one!"

The gods gave way again to peals of laughter,
all but Poseidon, and he never smiled,					360
but urged Hephaistos to unpinion Arês,
saying emphatically, in a loud voice:

     "Free him;
you will be paid, I swear; ask what you will;
he pays up every jot the gods decree."

To this the Great Gamelegs replied:

     "Poseidon,					365
lord of the earth-surrounding sea, I should not

---

1. Zeus and Hera.

swear to a scoundrel's honor. What have I
as surety from you, if Arês leaves me
empty-handed, with my empty chain?"

The Earth-shaker for answer urged again: 370

"Hephaistos, let us grant he goes, and leaves
the fine unpaid; I swear, then, I shall pay it."

Then said the Great Gamelegs at last:

"No more;
you offer terms I cannot well refuse."

And down the strong god bent to set them free, 375
till disencumbered of their bond, the chain,
the lovers leapt away—he into Thrace,[2]
while Aphroditê, laughter's darling, fled
to Kypros[3] Isle and Paphos, to her meadow
and altar dim with incense. There the Graces 380
bathed and anointed her with golden oil—
a bloom that clings upon immortal flesh alone—
and let her folds of mantle fall in glory.

So ran the song the minstrel sang.

Odysseus,
listening, found sweet pleasure in the tale, 385
among the Phaiákian mariners and oarsmen.
And next Alkínoös called upon his sons,
Halios and Laódamas, to show
the dance no one could do as well as they—
handling a purple ball carven by Pólybos. 390
One made it shoot up under the shadowing clouds
as he leaned backward; bounding high in air
the other cut its flight far off the ground—
and neither missed a step as the ball soared.
The next turn was to keep it low, and shuttling 395
hard between them, while the ring of boys
gave them a steady stamping beat.
Odysseus now addressed Alkínoös:

"O majesty, model of all your folk,
your promise was to show me peerless dancers; 400
here is the promise kept. I am all wonder."

At this Alkínoös in his might rejoicing
said to the seafarers of Phaiákia:

"Attend me now, Phaiákian lords and captains:
our guest appears a clear-eyed man and wise. 405
Come, let him feel our bounty as he should.
Here are twelve princes of the kingdom—lords
paramount, and I who make thirteen;
let each one bring a laundered cloak and tunic,

2. Non-Greek territory to the north, which was supposed to be Arês' home.   3. Or Cyprus, where
Aphrodite had a famous shrine at Paphos.

and add one bar of honorable gold.   410
Heap all our gifts together; load his arms;
let him go joyous to our evening feast!
As for Seareach—why, man to man
he'll make amends, and handsomely; he blundered."

Now all as one acclaimed the king's good pleasure,   415
and each one sent a squire to bring his gifts.
Meanwhile Seareach found speech again, saying:

"My lord and model of us all, Alkínoös,
as you require of me, in satisfaction,
this broadsword of clear bronze goes to our guest.   420
Its hilt is silver, and the ringed sheath
of new-sawn ivory—a costly weapon."

He turned to give the broadsword to Odysseus,
facing him, saying blithely:

                                    "Sir, my best
wishes, my respects; if I offended,   425
I hope the seawinds blow it out of mind.
God send you see your lady and your homeland
soon again, after the pain of exile."

Odysseus, the great tactician, answered:

"My hand, friend; may the gods award you fortune.   430
I hope no pressing need comes on you ever
for this fine blade you give me in amends."

He slung it, glinting silver, from his shoulder,
as the light shone from sundown. Messengers
were bearing gifts and treasure to the palace,   435
where the king's sons received them all, and made
a glittering pile at their grave mother's side;
then, as Alkínoös took his throne of power,
each went to his own high-backed chair in turn,
and said Alkínoös to Arêtê: 440

"Lady, bring here a chest, the finest one;
a clean cloak and tunic; stow these things;
and warm a cauldron for him. Let him bathe,
when he has seen the gifts of the Phaiákians,
and so dine happily to a running song.   445
My own wine-cup of gold intaglio
I'll give him, too; through all the days to come,
tipping his wine to Zeus or other gods
in his great hall, he shall remember me."

Then said Arêtê to her maids:
                                    "The tripod: 450
stand the great tripod legs about the fire."

They swung the cauldron on the fire's heart,
poured water in, and fed the blaze beneath
until the basin simmered, cupped in flame.
The queen set out a rich chest from her chamber   455

and folded in the gifts—clothing and gold
given Odysseus by the Phaiákians;
then she put in the royal cloak and tunic,
briskly saying to her guest:

          "Now here, sir,
look to the lid yourself, and tie it down   460
against light fingers, if there be any,
on the black ship tonight while you are sleeping."

Noble Odysseus, expert in adversity,
battened the lid down with a lightning knot
learned, once, long ago, from the Lady Kirkê.[4]   465
And soon a call came from the Bathing Mistress
who led him to a hip-bath, warm and clear—
a happy sight, and rare in his immersions
after he left Kalypso's home—where, surely,
the luxuries of a god were ever his.   470
When the bath maids had washed him, rubbed him down,
put a fresh tunic and a cloak around him,
he left the bathing place to join the men
at wine in hall.

           The princess Nausikaa,
exquisite figure, as of heaven's shaping,   475
waited beside a pillar as he passed
and said swiftly, with wonder in her look:

"Fare well, stranger; in your land remember me
who met and saved you. It is worth your thought."

The man of all occasions now met this: 480

"Daughter of great Alkínoös, Nausikaa,
may Zeus the lord of thunder, Hera's consort,
grant me daybreak again in my own country!
But there and all my days until I die
may I invoke you as I would a goddess,   485
princess, to whom I owe my life."

             He left her
and went to take his place beside the king.

Now when the roasts were cut, the winebowls full,
a herald led the minstrel down the room
amid the deference of the crowd, and paused   490
to seat him near a pillar in the center—
whereupon that resourceful man, Odysseus,
carved out a quarter from his chine of pork,
crisp with fat, and called the blind man's guide:

"Herald! here, take this to Demódokos: 495
let him feast and be merry, with my compliments.
All men owe honor to the poets—honor

---

4. Or Circe, a divine sorceress on whose island Odysseus had spent some time during his travels (Book XII).

and awe, for they are dearest to the Muse
who puts upon their lips the ways of life."

Gentle Demódokos took the proffered gift   500
and inwardly rejoiced. When all were served,
every man's hand went out upon the banquet,
repelling hunger and thirst; until at length
Odysseus spoke again to the blind minstrel:

"Demódokos, accept my utmost praise.   505
The Muse, daughter of Zeus in radiance,
or else Apollo gave you skill to shape
with such great style your songs of the Akhaians—
their hard lot, how they fought and suffered war.
You shared it, one would say, or heard it all.   510
Now shift your theme, and sing that wooden horse
Epeios built, inspired by Athena—
the ambuscade Odysseus filled with fighters
and sent to take the inner town of Troy.
Sing only this for me, sing me this well,   515
and I shall say at once before the world
the grace of heaven has given us a song."

The minstrel stirred, murmuring to the god, and soon
clear words and notes came one by one, a vision
of the Akhaians in their graceful ships   520
drawing away from shore: the torches flung
and shelters flaring: Argive soldiers crouched
in the close dark around Odysseus: and
the horse, tall on the assembly ground of Troy.
For when the Trojans pulled it in, themselves,   525
up to the citadel, they sat nearby
with long-drawn-out and hapless argument—
favoring, in the end, one course of three:
either to stave the vault with brazen axes,
or haul it to a cliff and pitch it down,   530
or else to save it for the gods, a votive glory—
the plan that could not but prevail.
For Troy must perish, as ordained, that day
she harbored the great horse of timber; hidden
the flower of Akhaia lay, and bore   535
slaughter and death upon the men of Troy.
He sang, then, of the town sacked by Akhaians
pouring down from the horse's hollow cave,
this way and that way raping the steep city,
and how Odysseus came like Arês to   540
the door of Deïphobos, with Meneláos,
and braved the desperate fight there—
conquering once more by Athena's power.

The splendid minstrel sang it.

               And Odysseus
let the bright molten tears run down his cheeks,   545
weeping the way a wife mourns for her lord

on the lost field where he has gone down fighting
the day of wrath that came upon his children.
At sight of the man panting and dying there,
she slips down to enfold him, crying out;   550
then feels the spears, prodding her back and shoulders,
and goes bound into slavery and grief.
Piteous weeping wears away her cheeks:
but no more piteous than Odysseus' tears,
cloaked as they were, now, from the company.   555
Only Alkínoös, at his elbow, knew—
hearing the low sob in the man's breathing—
and when he knew, he spoke:

"Hear me, lords and captains of Phaiákia!
And let Demódokos touch his harp no more.   560
His theme has not been pleasing to all here.
During the feast, since our fine poet sang,
our guest has never left off weeping. Grief
seems fixed upon his heart. Break off the song!
Let everyone be easy, host and guest;   565
there's more decorum in a smiling banquet!
We had prepared here, on our friend's behalf,
safe conduct in a ship, and gifts to cheer him,
holding that any man with a grain of wit
will treat a decent suppliant like a brother.   570
Now by the same rule, friend, you must not be
secretive any longer! Come, in fairness,
tell me the name you bore in that far country;
how were you known to family, and neighbors?
No man is nameless—no man, good or bad,   575
but gets a name in his first infancy,
none being born, unless a mother bears him!
Tell me your native land, your coast and city—
sailing directions for the ships, you know—
for those Phaiákian ships of ours   580
that have no steersman, and no steering oar,
divining the crew's wishes, as they do,
and knowing, as they do, the ports of call
about the world. Hidden in mist or cloud
they scud the open sea, with never a thought   585
of being in distress or going down.
There is, however, something I once heard
Nausíthoös, my father, say: Poseidon
holds it against us that our deep sea ships
are sure conveyance for all passengers.   590
My father said, some day one of our cutters
homeward bound over the cloudy sea
would be wrecked by the god, and a range of hills
thrown round our city. So, in his age, he said,
and let it be, or not, as the god please.   595
But come, now, put it for me clearly, tell me
the sea ways that you wandered, and the shores
you touched; the cities, and the men therein,
uncivilized, if such there were, and hostile,

and those godfearing who had kindly manners.   600
Tell me why you should grieve so terribly
over the Argives and the fall of Troy.
That was all gods' work, weaving ruin there
so it should make a song for men to come!
Some kin of yours, then, died at Ilion,   605
some first rate man, by marriage near to you,
next your own blood most dear?
Or some companion of congenial mind
and valor? True it is, a wise friend
can take a brother's place in our affection."   610

BOOK IX

[New Coasts and Poseidon's Son]

Now this was the reply Odysseus made:

"Alkínoös, king and admiration of men,
how beautiful this is, to hear a minstrel
gifted as yours: a god he might be, singing!
There is no boon in life more sweet, I say,   5
then when a summer joy holds all the realm,
and banqueters sit listening to a harper
in a great hall, by rows of tables heaped
with bread and roast meat, while a steward goes
to dip up wine and brim your cups again.   10
Here is the flower of life, it seems to me!
But now you wish to know my cause for sorrow—
and thereby give me cause for more.
                             What shall I
say first? What shall I keep until the end?
The gods have tried me in a thousand ways.   15
But first my name: let that be known to you,
and if I pull away from pitiless death,
friendship will bind us, though my land lies far.

I am Laërtês' son, Odysseus.
                             Men hold me
formidable for guile in peace and war: 20
this fame has gone abroad to the sky's rim.
My home is on the peaked sea-mark of Ithaka
under Mount Neion's wind-blown robe of leaves,
in sight of other islands—Doulíkhion,
Samê, wooded Zakynthos—Ithaka   25
being most lofty in that coastal sea,
and northwest, while the rest lie east and south.
A rocky isle, but good for a boy's training;
I shall not see on earth a place more dear,
though I have been detained long by Kalypso,   30
loveliest among goddesses, who held me
in her smooth caves, to be her heart's delight,
as Kirkê of Aiaia, the enchantress,
desired me, and detained me in her hall.
But in my heart I never gave consent.   35

Where shall a man find sweetness to surpass
his own home and his parents? In far lands
he shall not, though he find a house of gold.

What of my sailing, then, from Troy?
                              What of those years
of rough adventure, weathered under Zeus?   40
The wind that carried west from Ilion
brought me to Ísmaros, on the far shore,
a strongpoint on the coast of the Kikonês.[5]
I stormed that place and killed the men who fought.
Plunder we took, and we enslaved the women,   45
to make division, equal shares to all—
but on the spot I told them: 'Back, and quickly!
Out to sea again!' My men were mutinous,
fools, on stores of wine. Sheep after sheep
they butchered by the surf, and shambling cattle, 50
feasting,—while fugitives went inland, running
to call to arms the main force of Kikonês.
This was an army, trained to fight on horseback
or, where the ground required, on foot. They came
with dawn over that terrain like the leaves   55
and blades of spring. So doom appeared to us,
dark word of Zeus for us, our evil days.
My men stood up and made a fight of it—
backed on the ships, with lances kept in play,
from bright morning through the blaze of noon   60
holding our beach, although so far outnumbered;
but when the sun passed toward unyoking time,
then the Akhaians, one by one, gave way.
Six benches were left empty in every ship
that evening when we pulled away from death.   65
And this new grief we bore with us to sea:
our precious lives we had, but not our friends.
No ship made sail next day until some shipmate
had raised a cry, three times, for each poor ghost
unfleshed by the Kikonês on that field.   70

Now Zeus the lord of cloud roused in the north
a storm against the ships, and driving veils
of squall moved down like night on land and sea.
The bows went plunging at the gust; sails
cracked and lashed out strips in the big wind.   75
We saw death in that fury, dropped the yards,
unshipped the oars, and pulled for the nearest lee:
then two long days and nights we lay offshore
worn out and sick at heart, tasting our grief,
until a third Dawn came with ringlets shining.   80
Then we put up our masts, hauled sail, and rested,
letting the steersmen and the breeze take over.

I might have made it safely home, that time,
but as I came round Malea the current

---

5. Allies of the Trojans, but Odysseus does not even mention this fact to excuse the piratical raid; he
did not think any excuse was needed.

took me out to sea, and from the north   85
a fresh gale drove me on, past Kythera.[6]
Nine days I drifted on the teeming sea
before dangerous high winds. Upon the tenth
we came to the coastline of the Lotos Eaters,[7]
who live upon that flower. We landed there   90
to take on water. All ships' companies
mustered alongside for the mid-day meal.
Then I sent out two picked men and a runner
to learn what race of men that land sustained.
They fell in, soon enough, with Lotos Eaters,   95
who showed no will to do us harm, only
offering the sweet Lotos to our friends—
but those who ate this honeyed plant, the Lotos,
never cared to report, nor to return:
they longed to stay forever, browsing on   100
that native bloom, forgetful of their homeland.
I drove them, all three wailing, to the ships,
tied them down under their rowing benches,
and called the rest: 'All hands aboard;
come, clear the beach and no one taste   105
the Lotos, or you lose your hope of home.'
Filing in to their places by the rowlocks
my oarsmen dipped their long oars in the surf,
and we moved out again on our sea faring.

In the next land we found were Kyklopês,[8]   110
giants, louts, without a law to bless them.
In ignorance leaving the fruitage of the earth in mystery
to the immortal gods, they neither plow
nor sow by hand, nor till the ground, though grain—
wild wheat and barley—grows untended, and   115
wine-grapes, in clusters, ripen in heaven's rain.
Kyklopês have no muster and no meeting,
no consultation or old tribal ways,
but each one dwells in his own mountain cave
dealing out rough justice to wife and child,   120
indifferent to what the others do.
                            Well, then:
across the wide bay from the mainland
there lies a desert island, not far out,
but still not close inshore. Wild goats in hundreds
breed there; and no human being comes   125
upon the isle to startle them—no hunter
of all who ever tracked with hounds through forests
or had rough going over mountain trails.
The isle, unplanted and untilled, a wilderness,
pastures goats alone. And this is why: 130
good ships like ours with cheekpaint at the bows[9]

---

6. A large island off Malea, the southeastern tip of the Peloponnese.   7. It is generally thought that
this story contains some memory of early Greek contact with North Africa. The north wind Odysseus
describes would have taken him to the area of Cyrenaica, or modern Libya. Identifications of the lotos
range from dates to hashish.   8. According to ancient tradition the Kyklopês lived in Sicily.   9. On
a Greek ship an emblem (often shown as a huge eye on vase paintings) was painted on the bows.

are far beyond the Kyklopês. No shipwright
toils among them, shaping and building up
symmetrical trim hulls to cross the sea
and visit all the seaboard towns, as men do   135
who go and come in commerce over water.
This isle—seagoing folk would have annexed it
and built their homesteads on it: all good land,
fertile for every crop in season: lush
well-watered meads along the shore, vines in profusion,   140
prairie, clear for the plow, where grain would grow
chin high by harvest time, and rich sub-soil.
The island cove is landlocked, so you need
no hawsers out astern, bow-stones[1] or mooring:
run in and ride there till the day your crews   145
chafe to be under sail, and a fair wind blows.
You'll find good water flowing from a cavern
through dusky poplars into the upper bay.
Here we made harbor. Some god guided us
that night, for we could barely see our bows   150
in the dense fog around us, and no moonlight
filtered through the overcast. No look-out,
nobody saw the island dead ahead,
nor even the great landward rolling billow
that took us in: we found ourselves in shallows,   155
keels grazing shore: so furled our sails
and disembarked where the low ripples broke.
There on the beach we lay, and slept till morning.

When Dawn spread out her finger tips of rose
we turned out marvelling, to tour the isle,   160
while Zeus's shy nymph daughters flushed wild goats
down from the heights—a breakfast for my men.
We ran to fetch our hunting bows and long-shanked
lances from the ships, and in three companies
we took our shots. Heaven gave us game a-plenty: 165
for every one of twelve ships in my squadron
nine goats fell to be shared; my lot was ten.
So there all day, until the sun went down,
we made our feast on meat galore, and wine—
wine from the ship, for our supply held out,   170
so many jars were filled at Ísmaros
from stores of the Kikonês that we plundered.
We gazed, too, at Kyklopês Land, so near,
we saw their smoke, heard bleating from their flocks.
But after sundown, in the gathering dusk,   175
we slept again above the wash of ripples.
When the young Dawn with finger tips of rose
came in the east, I called my men together
and made a speech to them:

                            'Old shipmates, friends,
the rest of you stand by; I'll make the crossing   180

---

1. A primitive anchor made up of a stone attached to a rope.

in my own ship, with my own company,
and find out what the mainland natives are—
for they may be wild savages, and lawless,
or hospitable and god-fearing men.'

At this I went aboard, and gave the word   185
to cast off by the stern. My oarsmen followed,
filing in to their benches by the rowlocks,
and all in line dipped oars in the grey sea.

As we rowed on, and nearer to the mainland,
at one end of the bay, we saw a cavern   190
yawning above the water, screened with laurel,
and many rams and goats about the place
inside a sheepfold—made from slabs of stone
earthfast between tall trunks of pine and rugged
towering oak trees.
             A prodigious man   195
slept in this cave alone, and took his flocks
to graze afield—remote from all companions,
knowing none but savage ways, a brute
so huge, he seemed no man at all of those
who eat good wheaten bread; but he seemed rather   200
a shaggy mountain reared in solitude.
We beached there, and I told the crew
to stand by and keep watch over the ship;
as for myself I took my twelve best fighters
and went ahead. I had a goatskin full   205
of that sweet liquor that Euanthês' son,
Maron, had given me. He kept Apollo's
holy grove at Ísmaros; for kindness
we showed him there, and showed his wife and child,
he gave me seven shining golden talents[2]   210
perfectly formed, a solid silver winebowl,
and then this liquor—twelve two-handled jars
of brandy, pure and fiery. Not a slave
in Maron's household knew this drink; only
he, his wife and the storeroom mistress knew;   215
and they would put one cupful—ruby-colored,
honey-smooth—in twenty more of water,
but still the sweet scent hovered like a fume
over the winebowl. No man turned away
when cups of this came round.
             A wineskin full   220
I brought along, and victuals in a bag,
for in my bones I knew some towering brute
would be upon us soon—all outward power,
a wild man, ignorant of civility.

We climbed, then, briskly to the cave. But Kyklops   225
had gone afield, to pasture his fat sheep,
so we looked round at everything inside:
a drying rack that sagged with cheeses, pens

2. Ingots of gold. The talent was a standard weight.

crowded with lambs and kids, each in its class:
firstlings apart from middlings, and the 'dewdrops,'   230
or newborn lambkins, penned apart from both.
And vessels full of whey were brimming there—
bowls of earthenware and pails of milking.
My men came pressing round me, pleading:

                                  'Why not
take these cheeses, get them stowed, come back,   235
throw open all the pens, and make a run for it?
We'll drive the kids and lambs aboard. We say
put out again on good salt water!'

                         Ah,
how sound that was! Yet I refused, I wished
to see the caveman, what he had to offer—   240
no pretty sight, it turned out, for my friends.
We lit a fire, burnt an offering,
and took some cheese to eat; then sat in silence
around the embers, waiting. When he came
he had a load of dry boughs on his shoulder   245
to stoke his fire at suppertime. He dumped it
with a great crash into that hollow cave,
and we all scattered fast to the far wall.
Then over the broad cavern floor he ushered
the ewes he meant to milk. He left his rams   250
and he-goats in the yard outside, and swung
high overhead a slab of solid rock
to close the cave. Two dozen four-wheeled wagons,
with heaving wagon teams, could not have stirred
the tonnage of that rock from where he wedged it   255
over the doorsill. Next he took his seat
and milked his bleating ewes. A practiced job
he made of it, giving each ewe her suckling;
thickened his milk, then, into curds and whey,
sieved out the curds to drip in withy baskets,   260
and poured the whey to stand in bowls
cooling until he drank it for his supper.
When all these chores were done, he poked the fire,
heaping on brushwood. In the glare he saw us.

'Strangers,' he said, 'who are you? And where from?   265
What brings you here by sea ways—a fair traffic?
Or are you wandering rogues, who cast your lives
like dice, and ravage other folk by sea?'

We felt a pressure on our hearts, in dread
of that deep rumble and that mighty man.   270
But all the same I spoke up in reply:

'We are from Troy, Akhaians, blown off course
by shifting gales on the Great South Sea;
homeward bound, but taking routes and ways
uncommon; so the will of Zeus would have it.   275
We served under Agamémnon, son of Atreus—
the whole world knows what city

he laid waste, what armies he destroyed.
It was our luck to come here; here we stand,
beholden for your help, or any gifts   280
you give—as custom is to honor strangers.[3]
We would entreat you, great Sir, have a care
for the gods' courtesy; Zeus will avenge
the unoffending guest.'

                  He answered this
from his brute chest, unmoved:

                        'You are a ninny,   285
or else you come from the other end of nowhere,
telling me, mind the gods! We Kyklopês
care not a whistle for your thundering Zeus
or all the gods in bliss; we have more force by far.
I would not let you go for fear of Zeus—   290
you or your friends—unless I had a whim to.
Tell me, where was it, now, you left your ship—
around the point, or down the shore, I wonder?'

He thought he'd find out, but I saw through this,
and answered with a ready lie:

                    'My ship?   295
Poseidon Lord, who sets the earth a-tremble,
broke it up on the rocks at your land's end.
A wind from seaward served him, drove us there.
We are survivors, these good men and I.'

Neither reply nor pity came from him,   300
but in one stride he clutched at my companions
and caught two in his hands like squirming puppies
to beat their brains out, spattering the floor.
Then he dismembered them and made his meal,
gaping and crunching like a mountain lion—   305
everything: innards, flesh, and marrow bones.
We cried aloud, lifting our hands to Zeus,
powerless, looking on at this, appalled;
but Kyklops went on filling up his belly
with manflesh and great gulps of whey,   310
then lay down like a mast among his sheep.
My heart beat high now at the chance of action,
and drawing the sharp sword from my hip I went
along his flank to stab him where the midriff
holds the liver. I had touched the spot   315
when sudden fear stayed me: if I killed him
we perished there as well, for we could never
move his ponderous doorway slab aside.
So we were left to groan and wait for morning.

When the young Dawn with finger tips of rose   320
lit up the world, the Kyklops built a fire

---

3. It is the mark of civilized people in the *Odyssey*, like Meneláos and Alkínoös, that they welcome
strangers and send them on their way with gifts.

and milked his handsome ewes, all in due order,
putting the sucklings to the mothers. Then,
his chores being all dispatched, he caught
another brace of men to make his breakfast,   325
and whisked away his great door slab
to let his sheep go through—but he, behind,
reset the stone as one would cap a quiver.
There was a din of whistling as the Kyklops
rounded his flock to higher ground, then stillness.   330
And now I pondered how to hurt him worst,
if but Athena granted what I prayed for.
Here are the means I thought would serve my turn:

a club, or staff, lay there along the fold—
an olive tree, felled green and left to season   335
for Kyklops' hand. And it was like a mast
a lugger of twenty oars, broad in the beam—
a deep-sea going craft—might carry:
so long, so big around, it seemed. Now I
chopped out a six foot section of this pole   340
and set it down before my men, who scraped it;
and when they had it smooth, I hewed again
to make a stake with pointed end. I held this
in the fire's heart and turned it, toughening it,
then hid it, well back in the cavern, under   345
one of the dung piles in profusion there.
Now came the time to toss for it: who ventured
along with me? whose hand could bear to thrust
and grind that spike in Kyklops' eye, when mild
sleep had mastered him? As luck would have it,   350
the men I would have chosen won the toss—
four strong men, and I made five as captain.

At evening came the shepherd with his flock,
his woolly flock. The rams as well, this time,
entered the cave: by some sheep-herding whim—   355
or a god's bidding—none were left outside.
He hefted his great boulder into place
and sat him down to milk the bleating ewes
in proper order, put the lambs to suck,
and swiftly ran through all his evening chores.   360
Then he caught two more men and feasted on them.
My moment was at hand, and I went forward
holding an ivy bowl of my dark drink,
looking up, saying:

                    'Kyklops, try some wine.
Here's liquor to wash down your scraps of men.   365
Taste it, and see the kind of drink we carried
under our planks. I meant it for an offering
if you would help us home. But you are mad,
unbearable, a bloody monster! After this,
will any other traveller come to see you?'   370

He seized and drained the bowl, and it went down
so fiery and smooth he called for more:

'Give me another, thank you kindly. Tell me,
how are you called? I'll make a gift will please you.
Even Kyklopês know the wine-grapes grow   375
out of grassland and loam in heaven's rain,
but here's a bit of nectar and ambrosia!'

Three bowls I brought him, and he poured them down.
I saw the fuddle and flush come over him,
then I sang out in cordial tones:

                              'Kyklops,   380
you ask my honorable name? Remember
the gift you promised me, and I shall tell you.
My name is Nohbdy: mother, father, and friends,
everyone calls me Nohbdy.'

                    And he said:

'Nohbdy's my meat, then, after I eat his friends.   385
Others come first. There's a noble gift, now.'

Even as he spoke, he reeled and tumbled backward,
his great head lolling to one side: and sleep
took him like any creature. Drunk, hiccuping,
he dribbled streams of liquor and bits of men.   390

Now, by the gods, I drove my big hand spike
deep in the embers, charring it again,
and cheered my men along with battle talk
to keep their courage up: no quitting now.
The pike of olive, green though it had been,   395
reddened and glowed as if about to catch.
I drew it from the coals and my four fellows
gave me a hand, lugging it near the Kyklops
as more than natural force nerved them; straight
forward they sprinted, lifted it, and rammed it   400
deep in his crater eye, and I leaned on it
turning it as a shipwright turns a drill
in planking, having men below to swing
the two-handled strap that spins it in the groove.
So with our brand we bored that great eye socket   405
while blood ran out around the red hot bar.
Eyelid and lash were seared; the pierced ball
hissed broiling, and the roots popped.

                              In a smithy
one sees a white-hot axehead or an adze
plunged and wrung in a cold tub, screeching steam—   410
the way they make soft iron hale and hard—:
just so that eyeball hissed around the spike.
The Kyklops bellowed and the rock roared round him,
and we fell back in fear. Clawing his face
he tugged the bloody spike out of his eye,   415
threw it away, and his wild hands went groping;
then he set up a howl for Kyklopês
who lived in caves on windy peaks nearby.

Some heard him; and they came by divers ways
to clump around outside and call:

       'What ails you,   420
Polyphêmos? Why do you cry so sore
in the starry night? You will not let us sleep.
Sure no man's driving off your flock? No man
has tricked you, ruined you?'

      Out of the cave
the mammoth Polyphêmos roared in answer: 425

'Nohbdy, Nohbdy's tricked me, Nohbdy's ruined me!'

To this rough shout they made a sage reply:

'Ah well, if nobody has played you foul
there in your lonely bed, we are no use in pain
given by great Zeus. Let it be your father,   430
Poseidon Lord, to whom you pray.'

       So saying
they trailed away. And I was filled with laughter
to see how like a charm the name deceived them.
Now Kyklops, wheezing as the pain came on him,
fumbled to wrench away the great doorstone   435
and squatted in the breach with arms thrown wide
for any silly beast or man who bolted—
hoping somehow I might be such a fool.
But I kept thinking how to win the game:
death sat there huge; how could we slip away?   440
I drew on all my wits, and ran through tactics,
reasoning as a man will for dear life,
until a trick came—and it pleased me well.
The Kyklops' rams were handsome, fat, with heavy
fleeces, a dark violet.

      Three abreast   445
I tied them silently together, twining
cords of willow from the ogre's bed;
then slung a man under each middle one
to ride there safely, shielded left and right.
So three sheep could convey each man. I took   450
the woolliest ram, the choicest of the flock,
and hung myself under his kinky belly,
pulled up tight, with fingers twisted deep
in sheepskin ringlets for an iron grip.
So, breathing hard, we waited until morning.   455

When Dawn spread out her finger tips of rose
the rams began to stir, moving for pasture,
and peals of bleating echoed round the pens
where dams with udders full called for a milking.
Blinded, and sick with pain from his head wound,   460
the master stroked each ram, then let it pass,
but my men riding on the pectoral fleece
the giant's blind hands blundering never found.

Last of them all my ram, the leader, came,
weighted by wool and me with my meditations.   465
The Kyklops patted him, and then he said:

'Sweet cousin ram, why lag behind the rest
in the night cave? You never linger so,
but graze before them all, and go afar
to crop sweet grass, and take your stately way   470
leading along the streams, until at evening
you run to be the first one in the fold.
Why, now, so far behind? Can you be grieving
over your Master's eye? That carrion rogue
and his accurst companions burnt it out   475
when he had conquered all my wits with wine.
Nohbdy will not get out alive, I swear.
Oh, had you brain and voice to tell
where he may be now, dodging all my fury!
Bashed by this hand and bashed on this rock wall   480
his brains would strew the floor, and I should have
rest from the outrage Nohbdy worked upon me.'

He sent us into the open, then. Close by,
I dropped and rolled clear of the ram's belly,
going this way and that to untie the men.   485
With many glances back, we rounded up
his fat, stiff-legged sheep to take aboard,
and drove them down to where the good ship lay.
We saw, as we came near, our fellows' faces
shining; then we saw them turn to grief   490
tallying those who had not fled from death.
I hushed them, jerking head and eyebrows up,
and in a low voice told them: 'Load this herd;
move fast, and put the ship's head toward the breakers.'
They all pitched in at loading, then embarked   495
and struck their oars into the sea. Far out,
as far off shore as shouted words would carry,
I sent a few back to the adversary:

'O Kyklops! Would you feast on my companions?
Puny, am I, in a Caveman's hands?   500
How do you like the beating that we gave you,
you damned cannibal? Eater of guests
under your roof! Zeus and the gods have paid you!'

The blind thing in his doubled fury broke
a hilltop in his hands and heaved it after us.   505
Ahead of our black prow it struck and sank
whelmed in a spuming geyser, a giant wave
that washed the ship stern foremost back to shore.
I got the longest boathook out and stood
fending us off, with furious nods to all   510
to put their backs into a racing stroke—
row, row, or perish. So the long oars bent
kicking the foam sternward, making head
until we drew away, and twice as far.

Now when I cupped my hands I heard the crew   515
in low voices protesting:

      'Godsake, Captain!
Why bait the beast again? Let him alone!'

'That tidal wave he made on the first throw
all but beached us.'

     'All but stove us in!'

'Give him our bearing with your trumpeting,   520
he'll get the range and lob a boulder.'

       'Aye
He'll smash our timbers and our heads together!'

I would not heed them in my glorying spirit,
but let my anger flare and yelled:

      'Kyklops,
if ever mortal man inquire   525
how you were put to shame and blinded, tell him
Odysseus, raider of cities, took your eye:
Laërtês' son, whose home's on Ithaka!'

At this he gave a mighty sob and rumbled: 530

'Now comes the weird[4] upon me, spoken of old.
A wizard, grand and wondrous, lived here—Télemos,
a son of Eurymos; great length of days
he had in wizardry among the Kyklopês,
and these things he foretold for time to come:
my great eye lost, and at Odysseus' hands.   535
Always I had in mind some giant, armed
in giant force, would come against me here.
But this, but you—small, pitiful and twiggy—
you put me down with wine, you blinded me.
Come back, Odysseus, and I'll treat you well,   540
praying the god of earthquake to befriend you—
his son I am, for he by his avowal
fathered me, and, if he will, he may
heal me of this black wound—he and no other
of all the happy gods or mortal men.'   545

Few words I shouted in reply to him:

'If I could take your life I would and take
your time away, and hurl you down to hell!
The god of earthquake could not heal you there!'

At this he stretched his hands out in his darkness   550
toward the sky of stars, and prayed Poseidon:

'O hear me, lord, blue girdler of the islands,
if I am thine indeed, and thou art father:
grant that Odysseus, raider of cities, never
see his home: Laërtês' son, I mean,   555

4. Fate, destiny.

who kept his hall on Ithaka. Should destiny
intend that he shall see his roof again
among his family in his father land,
far be that day, and dark the years between.
Let him lose all companions, and return   560
under strange sail to bitter days at home.'

In these words he prayed, and the god heard him.
Now he laid hands upon a bigger stone
and wheeled around, titanic for the cast,
to let it fly in the black-prowed vessel's track.   565
But it fell short, just aft the steering oar,
and whelming seas rose giant above the stone
to bear us onward toward the island.
                                   There
as we ran in we saw the squadron waiting,
the trim ships drawn up side by side, and all   570
our troubled friends who waited, looking seaward.
We beached her, grinding keel in the soft sand,
and waded in, ourselves, on the sandy beach.
Then we unloaded all the Kyklops' flock
to make division, share and share alike,   575
only my fighters voted that my ram,
the prize of all, should go to me. I slew him
by the sea side and burnt his long thighbones
to Zeus beyond the stormcloud, Kronos' son,
who rules the world. But Zeus disdained my offering;   580
destruction for my ships he had in store
and death for those who sailed them, my companions.
Now all day long until the sun went down
we made our feast on mutton and sweet wine,
till after sunset in the gathering dark   585
we went to sleep above the wash of ripples.

When the young Dawn with finger tips of rose
touched the world, I roused the men, gave orders
to man the ships, cast off the mooring lines;
and filing in to sit beside the rowlocks   590
oarsmen in line dipped oars in the grey sea.
So we moved out, sad in the vast offing,
having our precious lives, but not our friends.

BOOK X

[The Grace of the Witch]

We made our landfall on Aiolia Island,
domain of Aiolos[5] Hippotadês,
the wind king dear to the gods who never die —
an isle adrift upon the sea, ringed round

5. King of the winds (whose name in Greek means "shifting, changeable"). Aiolia was a moving island
that has been located by modern geographers in the Lipari Islands off the Sicilian coast. The great
ancient geographer Eratosthenes was not so confident. He once said that we would know exactly where
Odysseus wandered after we had traced the leatherworker who made the bag in which the winds were
contained.

with brazen ramparts on a sheer cliffside.   5
Twelve children had old Aiolos at home—
six daughters and six lusty sons—and he
gave girls to boys to be their gentle brides;
now those lords, in their parents' company,
sup every day in hall—a royal feast   10
with fumes of sacrifice and winds that pipe
'round hollow courts; and all the night they sleep
on beds of filigree beside their ladies.
Here we put in, lodged in the town and palace,
while Aiolos played host to me. He kept me   15
one full month to hear the tale of Troy,
the ships and the return of the Akhaians,
all which I told him point by point in order.
When in return I asked his leave to sail
and asked provisioning, he stinted nothing,   20
adding a bull's hide sewn from neck to tail
into a mighty bag, bottling storm winds;
for Zeus had long ago made Aiolos
warden of winds, to rouse or calm at will.
He wedged this bag under my afterdeck,   25
lashing the neck with shining silver wire
so not a breath got through; only the west wind
he lofted for me in a quartering breeze
to take my squadron spanking home.
                                No luck:
the fair wind failed us when our prudence failed.   30

Nine days and nights we sailed without event,
till on the tenth we raised our land. We neared it,
and saw men building fires along the shore;
but now, being weary to the bone, I fell
into deep slumber; I had worked the sheet   35
nine days alone, and given it to no one,
wishing to spill no wind on the homeward run.
But while I slept, the crew began to parley:
silver and gold, they guessed, were in that bag
bestowed on me by Aiolos' great heart;   40
and one would glance at his benchmate and say:
'It never fails. He's welcome everywhere:
hail to the captain when he goes ashore!
He brought along so many presents, plunder
out of Troy, that's it. How about ourselves—   45
his shipmates all the way. Nigh home we are
with empty hands. And who has gifts from Aiolos?
He has. I say we ought to crack that bag,
there's gold and silver, plenty, in that bag!'

Temptation had its way with my companions,   50
and they untied the bag.
                        Then every wind
roared into hurricane; the ships went pitching
west with many cries; our land was lost.
Roused up, despairing in that gloom, I thought:

'Should I go overside for a quick finish   55
or clench my teeth and stay among the living?'
Down in the bilge I lay, pulling my sea cloak
over my head, while the rough gale blew the ships
and rueful crews clear back to Aiolia.

We put ashore for water; then all hands   60
gathered alongside for a mid-day meal.
When we had taken bread and drink, I picked
one soldier, and one herald, to go with me
and called again on Aiolos. I found him
at meat with his young princes and his lady,   65
but there beside the pillars, in his portico,
we sat down silent at the open door.
The sight amazed them, and they all exclaimed:

'Why back again, Odysseus?'

                                      'What sea fiend
rose in your path?'

                              'Did we not launch you well   70
for home, or for whatever land you chose?'

Out of my melancholy I replied:

'Mischief aboard and nodding at the tiller—
a damned drowse—did for me. Make good my loss,
dear friends! You have the power!'

                              Gently I pleaded,   75
but they turned cold and still. Said Father Aiolos:

'Take yourself out of this island, creeping thing—
no law, no wisdom, lays it on me now
to help a man the blessed gods detest—
out! Your voyage here was cursed by heaven!'   80

He drove me from the place, groan as I would,
and comfortless we went again to sea,
days of it, till the men flagged at the oars—
no breeze, no help in sight, by our own folly—
six indistinguishable nights and days   85
before we raised the Laistrygonian height
and far stronghold of Lamos.[6] In that land
the daybreak follows dusk, and so the shepherd
homing calls to the cowherd setting out;
and he who never slept could earn two wages,   90
tending oxen, pasturing silvery flocks,
where the low night path of the sun is near
the sun's path by day.[7] Here, then, we found
a curious bay with mountain walls of stone
to left and right, and reaching far inland,—   95
a narrow entrance opening from the sea
where cliffs converged as though to touch and close.

6. Presumably the founder of the city of the Laistrygonians, a race of human-eating giants.   7. Generally thought to be a confused reference to the short summer nights of the far north.

All of my squadron sheltered here, inside
the cavern of this bay.
                    Black prow by prow
those hulls were made fast in a limpid calm   100
without a ripple stillness all around them.
My own black ship I chose to moor alone
on the sea side, using a rock for bollard;
and climbed a rocky point to get my bearings.
No farms, no cultivated land appeared,   105
but puffs of smoke rose in the wilderness;
so I sent out two picked men and a herald
to learn what race of men this land sustained.

My party found a track—a wagon road
for bringing wood down from the heights to town;   110
and near the settlement they met a daughter
of Antiphatês the Laistrygon—a stalwart
young girl taking her pail to Artakía,
the fountain where these people go for water.
My fellows hailed her, put their questions to her: 115
who might the king be? ruling over whom?
She waved her hand, showing her father's lodge,
so they approached it. In its gloom they saw
a woman like a mountain crag, the queen—
and loathed the sight of her. But she, for greeting,   120
called from the meeting ground her lord and master,
Antiphatês, who came to drink their blood.
He seized one man and tore him on the spot,
making a meal of him; the other two
leaped out of doors and ran to join the ships.   125
Behind, he raised the whole tribe howling, countless
Laistrygonês—and more than men they seemed,
gigantic when they gathered on the sky line
to shoot great boulders down from slings; and hell's own
crashing rose, and crying from the ships,   130
as planks and men were smashed to bits—poor gobbets
the wildmen speared like fish and bore away.
But long before it ended in the anchorage—
havoc and slaughter—I had drawn my sword
and cut my own ship's cable. 'Men,' I shouted,   135
'man the oars and pull till your hearts break
if you would put this butchery behind!'
The oarsmen rent the sea in mortal fear
and my ship spurted out of range, far out
from that deep canyon where the rest were lost.   140
So we fared onward and death fell behind,
and we took breath to grieve for our companions.

Our next landfall was on Aiaia, island
of Kirkê, dire beauty and divine,
sister of baleful Aiêtês, like him   145
fathered by Hêlios the light of mortals
on Persê, child of the Ocean stream.
                       We came

washed in our silent ship upon her shore,
and found a cove, a haven for the ship—
some god, invisible, conned us in. We landed,   150
to lie down in that place two days and nights,
worn out and sick at heart, tasting our grief.
But when Dawn set another day a-shining
I took my spear and broadsword and I climbed
a rocky point above the ship, for sight   155
or sound of human labor. Gazing out
from that high place over a land of thicket,
oaks and wide watercourses, I could see
a smoke wisp from the woodland hall of Kirkê.
So I took counsel with myself: should I   160
go inland scouting out that reddish smoke?
No: better not, I thought, but first return
to waterside and ship, and give the men
breakfast before I sent them to explore.
Now as I went down quite alone, and came   165
a bowshot from the ship, some god's compassion
set a big buck in motion to cross my path—
a stag with noble antlers, pacing down
from pasture in the woods to the riverside,
as long thirst and the power of sun constrained him.   170
He started from the bush and wheeled: I hit him
square in the spine midway along his back
and the bronze point broke through it. In the dust
he fell and whinnied as life bled away.
I set one foot against him, pulling hard   175
to wrench my weapon from the wound, then left it,
butt-end on the ground. I plucked some withies
and twined a double strand into a rope—
enough to tie the hocks of my huge trophy;
then pickaback I lugged him to the ship,   180
leaning on my long spearshaft; I could not
haul that mighty carcass on one shoulder.
Beside the ship I let him drop, and spoke
gently and low to each man standing near:

'Come, friends, though hard beset, we'll not go down   185
into the House of Death before our time.
As long as food and drink remain aboard
let us rely on it, not die of hunger.'

At this those faces, cloaked in desolation
upon the waste sea beach, were bared;   190
their eyes turned toward me and the mighty trophy,
lighting, foreseeing pleasure, one by one.
So hands were washed to take what heaven sent us.
And all that day until the sun went down
we had our fill of venison and wine,   195
till after sunset in the gathering dusk
we slept at last above the line of breakers.
When the young Dawn with finger tips of rose
made heaven bright, I called them round and said:

'Shipmates, companions in disastrous time,   200
O my dear friends, where Dawn lies, and the West,
and where the great Sun, light of men, may go
under the earth by night, and where he rises—
of these things we know nothing.[8] Do we know
any least thing to serve us now? I wonder.   205
All that I saw when I went up the rock
was one more island in the boundless main,
a low landscape, covered with woods and scrub,
and puffs of smoke ascending in mid-forest.'

They were all silent, but their hearts contracted,   210
remembering Antiphatês the Laistrygon
and that prodigious cannibal, the Kyklops.
They cried out, and the salt tears wet their eyes.
But seeing our time for action lost in weeping,
I mustered those Akhaians under arms,   215
counting them off in two platoons, myself
and my godlike Eurýlokhos commanding.
We shook lots in a soldier's dogskin cap
and his came bounding out—valiant Eurýlokhos!—
So off he went, with twenty-two companions   220
weeping, as mine wept, too, who stayed behind.

In the wild wood they found an open glade,
around a smooth stone house—the hall of Kirkê—
and wolves and mountain lions lay there, mild
in her soft spell, fed on her drug of evil.   225
None would attack—oh, it was strange, I tell you—
but switching their long tails they faced our men
like hounds, who look up when their master comes
with tidbits for them—as he will—from table.
Humbly those wolves and lions with mighty paws   230
fawned on our men—who met their yellow eyes
and feared them.
                        In the entrance way they stayed
to listen there: inside her quiet house
they heard the goddess Kirkê.
                        Low she sang
in her beguiling voice, while on her loom   235
she wove ambrosial fabric sheer and bright,
by that craft known to the goddesses of heaven.
No one would speak, until Politês—most
faithful and likable of my officers, said:

'Dear friends, no need for stealth: here's a young weaver   240
singing a pretty song to set the air
a-tingle on these lawns and paven courts.
Goddess she is, or lady. Shall we greet her?'

So reassured, they all cried out together,
and she came swiftly to the shining doors   245
to call them in. All but Eurýlokhos—

---

8. In view of the immediately preceding lines, this can hardly be taken literally. It is possibly a sailor's metaphorical way of saying, "We don't know where we are."

who feared a snare—the innocents went after her.
On thrones she seated them, and lounging chairs,
while she prepared a meal of cheese and barley
and amber honey mixed with Pramnian wine,[9]   250
adding her own vile pinch, to make them lose
desire or thought of our dear father land.
Scarce had they drunk when she flew after them
with her long stick and shut them in a pigsty—
bodies, voices, heads, and bristles, all   255
swinish now, though minds were still unchanged.
So, squealing, in they went. And Kirkê tossed them
acorns, mast, and cornel berries—fodder
for hogs who rut and slumber on the earth.

Down to the ship Eurýlokhos came running   260
to cry alarm, foul magic doomed his men!
But working with dry lips to speak a word
he could not, being so shaken; blinding tears
welled in his eyes; foreboding filled his heart.
When we were frantic questioning him, at last   265
we heard the tale: our friends were gone. Said he:

'We went up through the oak scrub where you sent us,
Odysseus, glory of commanders,
until we found a palace in a glade,
a marble house on open ground, and someone   270
singing before her loom a chill, sweet song—
goddess or girl, we could not tell. They hailed her,
and then she stepped through shining doors and said,
"Come, come in!" Like sheep they followed her,
but I saw cruel deceit, and stayed behind.   275
Then all our fellows vanished. Not a sound,
and nothing stirred, although I watched for hours.'

When I heard this I slung my silver-hilted
broadsword on, and shouldered my long bow,
and said, 'Come, take me back the way you came.'   280
But he put both his hands around my knees
in desperate woe, and said in supplication:

'Not back there, O my lord! Oh, leave me here!
You, even you, cannot return, I know it,
I know you cannot bring away our shipmates;   285
better make sail with these men, quickly too,
and save ourselves from horror while we may.'

But I replied:

                    'By heaven, Eurýlokhos,
rest here then; take food and wine;
stay in the black hull's shelter. Let me go,   290
as I see nothing for it but to go.'

I turned and left him, left the shore and ship,
and went up through the woodland hushed and shady

---

9. A harsh, dark wine.

to find the subtle witch in her long hall.
But Hermês met me, with his golden wand,   295
barring the way—a boy whose lip was downy
in the first bloom of manhood, so he seemed.
He took my hand and spoke as though he knew me:[1]

'Why take the inland path alone,
poor seafarer, by hill and dale   300
upon this island all unknown?
Your friends are locked in Kirkê's pale;
all are become like swine to see;
and if you go to set them free
you go to stay, and never more make sail   305
for your old home upon Thaki.[2]

But I can tell you what to do
to come unchanged from Kirkê's power
and disenthrall your fighting crew:
take with you to her bower   310
as amulet, this plant I know—
it will defeat her horrid show,
so pure and potent is the flower;
no mortal herb was ever so.

Your cup with numbing drops of night   315
and evil, stilled of all remorse,
she will infuse to charm your sight;
but this great herb with holy force
will keep your mind and senses clear:
when she turns cruel, coming near   320
with her long stick to whip you out of doors,
then let your cutting blade appear,

Let instant death upon it shine,
and she will cower and yield her bed—
a pleasure you must not decline,   325
so may her lust and fear bestead
you and your friends, and break her spell;
but make her swear by heaven and hell
no witches' tricks, or else, your harness shed,
you'll be unmanned by her as well.'   330

He bent down glittering for the magic plant
and pulled it up, black root and milky flower—
a *molü* in the language of the gods—
fatigue and pain for mortals to uproot;
but gods do this, and everything, with ease.   335

Then toward Olympos through the island trees
Hermês departed, and I sought out Kirkê,
my heart high with excitement, beating hard.
Before her mansion in the porch I stood
to call her, all being still. Quick as a cat   340
she opened her bright doors and sighed a welcome;

1. The four rhymed stanzas that follow are a translator's license; in the original there is no change of
meter and, of course, no rhyme.   2. Ithaka.

then I strode after her with heavy heart
down the long hall, and took the chair she gave me,
silver-studded, intricately carved,
made with a low footrest. The lady Kirkê   345
mixed me a golden cup of honeyed wine,
adding in mischief her unholy drug.
I drank, and the drink failed. But she came forward
aiming a stroke with her long stick, and whispered:

'Down in the sty and snore among the rest!'   350

Without a word, I drew my sharpened sword
and in one bound held it against her throat.
She cried out, then slid under to take my knees,
catching her breath to say, in her distress:

'What champion, of what country, can you be?   355
Where are your kinsmen and your city?
Are you not sluggish with my wine? Ah, wonder!
Never a mortal man that drank this cup
but when it passed his lips he had succumbed.
Hale must your heart be and your tempered will.   360
Odysseus then you are, O great contender,
of whom the glittering god with golden wand[3]
spoke to me ever, and foretold
the black swift ship would carry you from Troy.
Put up your weapon in the sheath. We two   365
shall mingle and make love upon our bed.
So mutual trust may come of play and love.'

To this I said:

            'Kirkê, am I a boy,
that you should make me soft and doting now?
Here in this house you turned my men to swine;   370
now it is I myself you hold, enticing
into your chamber, to your dangerous bed,
to take my manhood when you have me stripped.
I mount no bed of love with you upon it.
Or swear me first a great oath, if I do,   375
you'll work no more enchantment to my harm.'

She swore at once, outright, as I demanded,
and after she had sworn, and bound herself,
I entered Kirkê's flawless bed of love.

Presently in the hall her maids were busy,   380
the nymphs who waited upon Kirkê: four,
whose cradles were in fountains, under boughs,
or in the glassy seaward-gliding streams.
One came with richly colored rugs to throw
on seat and chairback, over linen covers;   385
a second pulled the tables out, all silver,
and loaded them with baskets all of gold;
a third mixed wine as tawny-mild as honey

3. Hermês.

in a bright bowl, and set out golden cups.
The fourth came bearing water, and lit a blaze   390
under a cauldron. By and by it bubbled,
and when the dazzling brazen vessel seethed
she filled a bathtub to my waist, and bathed me,
pouring a soothing blend on head and shoulders,
warming the soreness of my joints away.   395
When she had done, and smoothed me with sweet oil,
she put a tunic and a cloak around me
and took me to a silver-studded chair
with footrest, all elaborately carven.
Now came a maid to tip a golden jug   400
of water into a silver finger bowl,
and draw a polished table to my side.
The larder mistress brought her tray of loaves
with many savory slices, and she gave
the best, to tempt me. But no pleasure came;   405
I huddled with my mind elsewhere, oppressed.

Kirkê regarded me, as there I sat
disconsolate, and never touched a crust.
Then she stood over me and chided me:

'Why sit at table mute, Odysseus?   410
Are you mistrustful of my bread and drink?
Can it be treachery that you fear again,
after the gods' great oath I swore for you?'

I turned to her at once, and said:

                              'Kirkê,
where is the captain who could bear to touch   415
this banquet, in my place? A decent man
would see his company before him first.
Put heart in me to eat and drink—you may,
by freeing my companions. I must see them.'

But Kirkê had already turned away.   420
Her long staff in her hand, she left the hall
and opened up the sty, I saw her enter,
driving those men turned swine to stand before me.
She stroked them, each in turn, with some new chrism;
and then, behold! their bristles fell away,   425
the coarse pelt grown upon them by her drug
melted away, and they were men again,
younger, more handsome, taller than before.
Their eyes upon me, each one took my hands,
and wild regret and longing pierced them through,   430
so the room rang with sobs, and even Kirkê
pitied that transformation. Exquisite
the goddess looked as she stood near me, saying:

'Son of Laërtês and the gods of old,
Odysseus, master mariner and soldier,   435
go to the sea beach and sea-breasting ship;
drag it ashore, full length upon the land;

stow gear and stores in rock-holes under cover;
return; be quick; bring all your dear companions.'

Now, being a man, I could not help consenting.   440
So I went down to the sea beach and the ship,
where I found all my other men on board,
weeping, in despair along the benches.
Sometimes in farmyards when the cows return
well fed from pasture to the barn, one sees   445
the pens give way before the calves in tumult,
breaking through to cluster about mothers,
bumping together, bawling. Just that way
my crew poured round me when they saw me come—
their faces wet with tears as if they saw   450
their homeland, and the crags of Ithaka,
even the very town where they were born.
And weeping still they all cried out in greeting:

'Prince, what joy this is, your safe return!
Now Ithaka seems here, and we in Ithaka!   455
But tell us now, what death befell our friends?'

And, speaking gently, I replied:

'First we must get the ship high on the shingle,
and stow our gear and stores in clefts of rock
for cover. Then come follow me, to see   460
your shipmates in the magic house of Kirkê
eating and drinking, endlessly regaled.'

They turned back, as commanded, to this work;
only one lagged, and tried to hold the others;
Eurýlokhos it was, who blurted out: 465

'Where now, poor remnants? is it devil's work
you long for? Will you go to Kirkê's hall?
Swine, wolves, and lions she will make us all,
beasts of her courtyard, bound by her enchantment.
Remember those the Kyklops held, remember   470
shipmates who made that visit with Odysseus!
The daring man! They died for his foolishness!'

When I heard this I had a mind to draw
the blade that swung against my side and chop him,
bowling his head upon the ground—kinsman[4]   475
or no kinsman, close to me though he was.
But others came between, saying, to stop me,
'Prince, we can leave him, if you say the word;
let him stay here on guard. As for ourselves,
show us the way to Kirkê's magic hall.'   480

So all turned inland, leaving shore and ship,
and Eurýlokhos—he, too, came on behind,
fearing the rough edge of my tongue. Meanwhile
at Kirkê's hands the rest were gently bathed,

4. Eurýlokhos was related to Odysseus by marriage.

anointed with sweet oil, and dressed afresh   485
in tunics and new cloaks with fleecy linings.
We found them all at supper when we came.
But greeting their old friends once more, the crew
could not hold back their tears; and now again
the rooms rang with sobs. Then Kirkê, loveliest   490
of all immortals, came to counsel me:

'Son of Laërtês and the gods of old.
Odysseus, master mariner and soldier,
enough of weeping fits. I know—I, too—
what you endured upon the inhuman sea,   495
what odds you met on land from hostile men.
Remain with me, and share my meat and wine;
restore behind your ribs those gallant hearts
that served you in the old days, when you sailed
from stony Ithaka. Now parched and spent,   500
your cruel wandering is all you think of,
never of joy, after so many blows.'

As we were men we could not help consenting.
So day by day we lingered, feasting long
on roasts and wine, until a year grew fat.   505
But when the passing months and wheeling seasons
brought the long summery days, the pause of summer,
my shipmates one day summoned me and said:

'Captain, shake off this trance, and think of home—
if home indeed awaits us,
                            if we shall ever see   510
your own well-timbered hall on Ithaka.'

They made me feel a pang, and I agreed.
That day, and all day long, from dawn to sundown,
we feasted on roast meat and ruddy wine,
and after sunset when the dusk came on   515
my men slept in the shadowy hall, but I
went through the dark to Kirkê's flawless bed
and took the goddess' knees in supplication,
urging, as she bent to hear:

                            'O Kirkê,
now you must keep your promise; it is time.   520
Help me make sail for home. Day after day
my longing quickens, and my company
give me no peace, but wear my heart away
pleading when you are not at hand to hear.'

The loveliest of goddesses replied: 525

'Son of Laërtês and the gods of old,
Odysseus, master mariner and soldier,
you shall not stay here longer against your will;
but home you may not go

unless you take a strange way round and come   530
to the cold homes of Death and pale Perséphonê.[5]
You shall hear prophecy from the rapt shade
of blind Teirêsias of Thebes,[6] forever
charged with reason even among the dead;
to him alone, of all the flitting ghosts,   535
Perséphonê has given a mind undarkened.'

At this I felt a weight like stone within me,
and, moaning, pressed my length against the bed,
with no desire to see the daylight more.
But when I had wept and tossed and had my fill   540
of this despair, at last I answered her:

'Kirkê, who pilots me upon this journey?
No man has ever sailed to the land of Death.'

That loveliest of goddesses replied:

'Son of Laërtês and the gods of old,   545
Odysseus, master of land ways and sea ways,
feel no dismay because you lack a pilot;
only set up your mast and haul your canvas
to the fresh blowing North; sit down and steer,
and hold that wind, even to the bourne of Ocean,   550
Perséphonê's deserted stand and grove,
dusky with poplars and the drooping willow.
Run through the tide-rip, bring your ship to shore,
land there, and find the crumbling homes of Death.
Here, toward the Sorrowing Water, run the streams   555
of Wailing, out of Styx, and quenchless Burning[7]—
torrents that join in thunder at the Rock.
Here then, great soldier, setting foot obey me:
dig a well shaft a forearm square; pour out
libations round it to the unnumbered dead: 560
sweet milk and honey, then sweet wine, and last
clear water, scattering handfuls of white barley.
Pray now, with all your heart, to the faint dead;
swear you will sacrifice your finest heifer,
at home in Ithaka, and burn for them   565
her tenderest parts in sacrifice; and vow
to the lord Teirêsias, apart from all,
a black lamb, handsomest of all your flock—
thus to appease the nations of the dead.
Then slash a black ewe's throat, and a black ram,   570
facing the gloom of Erebos;[8] but turn
your head away toward Ocean. You shall see, now
souls of the buried dead in shadowy hosts,
and now you must call out to your companions
to flay those sheep the bronze knife has cut down,   575

5. Queen of the underworld.   6. A blind prophet who figures prominently in the legends of Thebes (he is a character in Sophocles' *Oedipus the King*).   7. Pyriphlegethon, a river of the underworld, as are the Sorrowing Water (Acheron), the stream of Wailing (Cocytus), and the Styx.   8. The darkest region of the underworld, usually imagined as below the underworld itself but here to the west.

for offerings, burnt flesh to those below,
to sovereign Death and pale Perséphonê.
Meanwhile draw sword from hip, crouch down, ward off
the surging phantoms from the bloody pit
until you know the presence of Teirêsias.   580
He will come soon, great captain; be it he
who gives you course and distance for your sailing
homeward across the cold fish-breeding sea.'

As the goddess ended, Dawn came stitched in gold.
Now Kirkê dressed me in my shirt and cloak,   585
put on a gown of subtle tissue, silvery,
then wound a golden belt about her waist
and veiled her head in linen,
while I went through the hall to rouse my crew.

I bent above each one, and gently said: 590

'Wake from your sleep; no more sweet slumber. Come,
we sail: the Lady Kirkê so ordains it.'

They were soon up, and ready at that word;
but I was not to take my men unharmed
from this place, even from this. Among them all   595
the youngest was Elpênor—
no mainstay in a fight nor very clever—
and this one, having climbed on Kirkê's roof[9]
to taste the cool night, fell asleep with wine.
Waked by our morning voices, and the tramp   600
of men below, he started up, but missed
his footing on the long steep backward ladder
and fell that height headlong. The blow smashed
the nape cord, and his ghost fled to the dark.
But I was outside, walking with the rest,   605
saying:

          'Homeward you think we must be sailing
to our own land; no, elsewhere is the voyage
Kirkê has laid upon me. We must go
to the cold homes of Death and pale Perséphonê
to hear Teirêsias tell of time to come.'   610

They felt so stricken, upon hearing this,
they sat down wailing loud, and tore their hair.
But nothing came of giving way to grief.
Down to the shore and ship at last we went,
bowed with anguish, cheeks all wet with tears,   615
to find that Kirkê had been there before us
and tied nearby a black ewe and a ram:
she had gone by like air.
For who could see the passage of a goddess
unless she wished his mortal eyes aware?   620

---

9. A flat roof and the coolest place to sleep.

BOOK XI

[A Gathering of Shades]

We bore down on the ship at the sea's edge
and launched her on the salt immortal sea,
stepping our mast and spar in the black ship;
embarked the ram and ewe and went aboard
in tears, with bitter and sore dread upon us.   5
But now a breeze came up for us astern—
a canvas-bellying landbreeze, hale shipmate
sent by the singing nymph with sun-bright hair;
so we made fast the braces, took our thwarts,
and let the wind and steersman work the ship   10
with full sail spread all day above our coursing,
till the sun dipped, and all the ways grew dark
upon the fathomless unresting sea.
                                   By night
our ship ran onward toward the Ocean's bourne,
the realm and region of the Men of Winter,[1]   15
hidden in mist and cloud. Never the flaming
eye of Hêlios lights on those men
at morning, when he climbs the sky of stars,
nor in descending earthward out of heaven;
ruinous night being rove[2] over those wretches.   20
We made the land, put ram and ewe ashore,
and took our way along the Ocean stream
to find the place foretold for us by Kirkê.
There Perimêdês and Eurýlokhos
pinioned the sacred beasts. With my drawn blade   25
I spaded up the votive pit, and poured
libations round it to the unnumbered dead:
sweet milk and honey, then sweet wine, and last
clear water; and I scattered barley down.
Then I addressed the blurred and breathless dead,   30
vowing to slaughter my best heifer for them
before she calved, at home in Ithaka,
and burn the choice bits on the altar fire;
as for Teirêsias, I swore to sacrifice
a black lamb, handsomest of all our flock.   35
Thus to assuage the nations of the dead
I pledged these rites, then slashed the lamb and ewe,
letting their black blood stream into the wellpit.
Now the souls gathered, stirring out of Erebos,
brides and young men, and men grown old in pain,   40
and tender girls whose hearts were new to grief;
many were there, too, torn by brazen lanceheads,
battle-slain, bearing still their bloody gear.
From every side they came and sought the pit
with rustling cries; and I grew sick with fear.   45
But presently I gave command to my officers
to flay those sheep the bronze cut down, and make

1. Although Homer usually places Hades below the earth, here he puts it across a great expanse of sea,
apparently in the far north.   2. Stretched or spread.

burnt offerings of flesh to the gods below—
to sovereign Death, to pale Perséphonê.
Meanwhile I crouched with my drawn sword to keep   50
the surging phantoms from the bloody pit
till I should know the presence of Teirêsias.

One shade came first—Elpênor, of our company,
who lay unburied still on the wide earth
as we had left him—dead in Kirkê's hall,   55
untouched, unmourned, when other cares compelled us.
Now when I saw him there I wept for pity
and called out to him:

                    'How is this, Elpênor,
how could you journey to the western gloom
swifter afoot than I in the black lugger?'   60

He sighed, and answered:

                    'Son of great Laërtês,
Odysseus, master mariner and soldier,
bad luck shadowed me, and no kindly power;
ignoble death I drank with so much wine.
I slept on Kirkê's roof, then could not see   65
the long steep backward ladder, coming down,
and fell that height. My neck bone, buckled under,
snapped, and my spirit found this well of dark.
Now hear the grace I pray for, in the name
of those back in the world, not here—your wife   70
and father, he who gave you bread in childhood,
and your own child, your only son, Telémakhos,
long ago left at home.
                    When you make sail
and put these lodgings of dim Death behind,
you will moor ship, I know, upon Aiaia Island;   75
there, O my lord, remember me, I pray,
do not abandon me unwept, unburied,
to tempt the gods' wrath, while you sail for home;
but fire my corpse, and all the gear I had,
and build a cairn for me above the breakers—   80
an unknown sailor's mark for men to come.
Heap up the mound there, and implant upon it
the oar I pulled in life with my companions.'

He ceased, and I replied:

                    'Unhappy spirit,
I promise you the barrow and the burial.'   85

So we conversed, and grimly, at a distance,
with my long sword between, guarding the blood,
while the faint image of the lad spoke on.
Now came the soul of Antikleía, dead,
my mother, daughter of Autólykos,   90
dead now, though living still when I took ship
for holy Troy. Seeing this ghost I grieved,

but held her off, through pang on pang of tears,
till I should know the presence of Teirêsias.
Soon from the dark that prince of Thebes came forward   95
bearing a golden staff; and he addressd me:

'Son of Laërtês and the gods of old,
Odysseus, master of land ways and sea ways,
why leave the blazing sun, O man of woe,
to see the cold dead and the joyless region?   100
Stand clear, put up your sword;
let me but taste of blood, I shall speak true.'

At this I stepped aside, and in the scabbard
let my long sword ring home to the pommel silver,
as he bent down to the sombre blood. Then spoke   105
the prince of those with gift of speech:[3]

                                        'Great captain,
a fair wind and the honey lights of home
are all you seek. But anguish lies ahead;
the god who thunders on the land prepares it,
not to be shaken from your track, implacable,   110
in rancor for the son whose eye you blinded.
One narrow strait may take you through his blows:
denial of yourself, restraint of shipmates.
When you make landfall on Thrinakia first
and quit the violet sea, dark on the land   115
you'll find the grazing herds of Hêlios
by whom all things are seen, all speech is known.
Avoid those kine, hold fast to your intent,
and hard seafaring brings you all to Ithaka.
But if you raid the beeves, I see destruction   120
for ship and crew. Though you survive alone,
bereft of all companions, lost for years,
under strange sail shall you come home, to find
your own house filled with trouble: insolent men
eating your livestock as they court your lady.   125
Aye, you shall make those men atone in blood!
But after you have dealt out death—in open
combat or by stealth—to all the suitors,
go overland on foot, and take an oar,
until one day you come where men have lived   130
with meat unsalted, never known the sea,
nor seen seagoing ships, with crimson bows
and oars that fledge light hulls for dipping flight.
The spot will soon be plain to you, and I
can tell you how: some passerby will say,   135
"What winnowing fan is that upon your shoulder?"
Halt, and implant your smooth oar in the turf
and make fair sacrifice to Lord Poseidon:
a ram, a bull, a great buck boar; turn back,

---

3. Tiresias here predicts the future of Odysseus. Like many Greek prophecies, it contains alternatives. The second (lines 120ff.) is what happens. The journey inland to find a people who have never seen the sea (and so mistake an oar for a winnowing fan, line 136) does not take place within the *Odyssey* itself.

and carry out pure hekatombs at home   140
to all wide heaven's lords, the undying gods,
to each in order. Then a seaborne death
soft as this hand of mist will come upon you
when you are wearied out with rich old age,
your country folk in blessed peace around you.   145
And all this shall be just as I foretell.'

When he had done, I said at once,

                    'Teirêsias,
my life runs on then as the gods have spun it.
But come, now, tell me this; make this thing clear:
I see my mother's ghost among the dead   150
sitting in silence near the blood. Not once
has she glanced this way toward her son, nor spoken.
Tell me, my lord,
may she in some way come to know my presence?'

To this he answered:

                 'I shall make it clear   155
in a few words and simply. Any dead man
whom you allow to enter where the blood is
will speak to you, and speak the truth; but those
deprived will grow remote again and fade.'

When he had prophesied, Teirêsias' shade   160
retired lordly to the halls of Death;
but I stood fast until my mother stirred,
moving to sip the black blood; then she knew me
and called out sorrowfully to me:

                 'Child,
how could you cross alive into this gloom   165
at the world's end?—No sight for living eyes;
great currents run between, desolate waters,
the Ocean first, where no man goes a journey
without ship's timber under him.
                Say, now,
is it from Troy, still wandering, after years,   170
that you come here with ship and company?
Have you not gone at all to Ithaka?
Have you not seen your lady in your hall?'

She put these questions, and I answered her:

'Mother, I came here, driven to the land of death   175
in want of prophecy from Teirêsias' shade;
nor have I yet coasted Akhaia's hills
nor touched my own land, but have had hard roving
since first I joined Lord Agamémnon's host
by sea for Ilion, the wild horse country,   180
to fight the men of Troy.
But come now, tell me this, and tell me clearly,
what was the bane that pinned you down in Death?
Some ravaging long illness, or mild arrows

a-flying down one day from Artemis?   185
Tell me of Father, tell me of the son
I left behind me; have they still my place,
my honors, or have other men assumed them?
Do they not say that I shall come no more?
And tell me of my wife: how runs her thought,   190
still with her child, still keeping our domains,
or bride again to the best of the Akhaians?'

To this my noble mother quickly answered:

'Still with her child indeed she is, poor heart,
still in your palace hall. Forlorn her nights   195
and days go by, her life used up in weeping.
But no man takes your honored place. Telémakhos
has care of all your garden plots and fields,
and holds the public honor of a magistrate,
feasting and being feasted. But your father   200
is country bound and comes to town no more.
He owns no bedding, rugs, or fleecy mantles,
but lies down, winter nights, among the slaves,
rolled in old cloaks for cover, near the embers.
Or when the heat comes at the end of summer,   205
the fallen leaves, all round his vineyard plot,
heaped into windrows, make his lowly bed.
He lies now even so, with aching heart,
and longs for your return, while age comes on him.
So I, too, pined away, so doom befell me,   210
not that the keen-eyed huntress[4] with her shafts
had marked me down and shot to kill me; not
that illness overtook me—no true illness
wasting the body to undo the spirit;
only my loneliness for you, Odysseus,   215
for your kind heart and counsel, gentle Odysseus,
took my own life away.'
                                    I bit my lip,
rising perplexed, with longing to embrace her,
and tried three times, putting my arms around her,
but she went sifting through my hands, impalpable   220
as shadows are, and wavering like a dream.
Now this embittered all the pain I bore,
and I cried in the darkness:
                            'O my mother,
will you not stay, be still, here in my arms,
may we not, in this place of Death, as well,   225
hold one another, touch with love, and taste
salt tears' relief, the twinge of welling tears?
Or is this all hallucination, sent
against me by the iron queen, Perséphonê,
to make me groan again?'

4. Artemis.

My noble mother   230
answered quickly:

'O my child—alas,
most sorely tried of men—great Zeus's daughter,
Perséphonê, knits no illusion for you.
All mortals meet this judgment when they die.
No flesh and bone are here, none bound by sinew,   235
since the bright-hearted pyre consumed them down—
the white bones long exanimate—to ash;
dreamlike the soul flies, insubstantial.

You must crave sunlight soon.
                              Note all things strange
seen here, to tell your lady in after days.'   240

So went our talk; then other shadows came,
ladies in company, sent by Perséphonê—
consorts or daughters of illustrious men—
crowding about the black blood.
                              I took thought
how best to separate and question them,   245
and saw no help for it, but drew once more
the long bright edge of broadsword from my hip,
that none should sip the blood in company
but one by one, in order; so it fell
that each declared her lineage and name.   250

Here was great loveliness of ghosts![5] I saw
before them all, that princess of great ladies,
Tyro,[6] Salmoneus' daughter, as she told me,
and queen to Krêtheus, a son of Aiolos.
She had gone daft for the river Enipeus,[7]   255
most graceful of all running streams, and ranged
all day by Enipeus' limpid side,
whose form the foaming girdler of the islands,
the god who makes earth tremble, took[8] and so
lay down with her where he went flooding seaward,   260
their bower a purple billow, arching round
to hide them in a sea-vale, god and lady.
Now when his pleasure was complete, the god
spoke to her softly, holding fast her hand:

'Dear mortal, go in joy! At the turn of seasons,   265
winter to summer, you shall bear me sons;
no lovemaking of gods can be in vain.
Nurse our sweet children tenderly, and rear them.
Home with you now, and hold your tongue, and tell
no one your lover's name—though I am yours,   270
Poseidon, lord of surf that makes earth tremble.'

He plunged away into the deep sea swell,
and she grew big with Pelias and Neleus,[9]

5. Here follows a list of famous and beautiful women of former times.   6. A queen of Thessaly.
7. Tyro had fallen in love with the river god of the Enipeus (a river in Thessaly).   8. Poiseidon
assumed his shape.   9. Father of Nestor of Pylos.

powerful vassals, in their time, of Zeus.
Pelias lived on broad Iolkos seaboard   275
rich in flocks, and Neleus at Pylos.
As for the sons borne by that queen of women
to Krêtheus, their names were Aison,[1] Pherês,
and Amytháon, expert charioteer.

Next after her I saw Antiopê,   280
daughter of Ásopos.[2] She too could boast
a god for lover, having lain with Zeus
and borne two sons to him: Amphion and
Zêthos, who founded Thebes, the upper city,
and built the ancient citadel. They sheltered   285
no life upon that plain, for all their power,
without a fortress wall.

                              And next I saw
Amphitrion's true wife, Alkmênê, mother,
as all men know, of lionish Heraklês,
conceived when she lay close in Zeus's arms;   290
and Megarê, high-hearted Kreon's daughter,
wife of Amphitrion's unwearying son.

I saw the mother of Oidipous, Epikastê,[3]
whose great unwitting deed it was
to marry her own son. He took that prize   295
from a slain father; presently the gods
brought all to light that made the famous story.
But by their fearsome wills he kept his throne
in dearest Thebes, all through his evil days,
while she descended to the place of Death,   300
god of the locked and iron door. Steep down
from a high rafter, throttled in her noose,
she swung, carried away by pain, and left him
endless agony from a mother's Furies.

And I saw Khloris, that most lovely lady,   305
whom for her beauty in the olden time
Neleus wooed with countless gifts, and married.
She was the youngest daughter of Amphion,
son of Iasos. In those days he[4] held
power at Orkhómenos, over the Minyai.   310
At Pylos then as queen she bore her children—
Nestor, Khromios, Periklýmenos,
and Pêro, too, who turned the heads of men
with her magnificence. A host of princes
from nearby lands came courting her; but Neleus   315
would hear of no one, not unless the suitor
could drive the steers of giant Iphiklos
from Phylakê—longhorns, broad in the brow,
so fierce that one man only, a diviner,[5]
offered to round them up. But bitter fate   320

1. Father of Jason, the Argonaut.   2. A river in Boeotia, the territory of Thebes.   3. Usually known
as Jocasta. *Oidipous*: Oedipus.   4. Amphion (not the same Amphion who founded Thebes, line
283).   5. Named Melampus.

saw him bound hand and foot by savage herdsmen.
Then days and months grew full and waned, the year
went wheeling round, the seasons came again,
before at last the power of Íphiklos,
relenting, freed the prisoner, who foretold 325
all things to him. So Zeus's will was done.

And I saw Lêda, wife of Tyndareus,
upon whom Tyndareus had sired twins
indomitable: Kastor, tamer of horses,
and Polydeukês, best in the boxing ring.[6] 330
Those two live still, though life-creating earth
embraces them: even in the underworld
honored as gods by Zeus, each day in turn[7]
one comes alive, the other dies again.

Then after Lêda to my vision came 335
the wife of Aloeus, Iphimedeia,
proud that she once had held the flowing sea[8]
and borne him sons, thunderers for a day,
the world-renowned Otos and Ephialtês.
Never were men on such a scale 340
bred on the plowlands and the grainlands, never
so magnificent any, after Orion.
At nine years old they towered nine fathoms tall,
nine cubits in the shoulders, and they promised
furor upon Olympos, heaven broken by battle cries, 345
the day they met the gods in arms.
     With Ossa's
mountain peak they meant to crown Olympos
and over Ossa Pelion's forest pile
for footholds up the sky. As giants grown
they might have done it, but the bright son of Zeus[9] 350
by Lêto of the smooth braid shot them down
while they were boys unbearded; no dark curls
clustered yet from temples to the chin.

Then I saw Phaidra, Prokris; and Ariadnê,
daughter of Minos,[1] the grim king. Theseus took her 355
aboard with him from Krete for the terraced land
of ancient Athens; but he had no joy of her.
Artemis killed her on the Isle of Dia
at a word from Dionysos.[2]
     Maira, then,
and Klymênê, and that detested queen, 360
Eríphylê,[3] who betrayed her lord for gold . . .

6. They also had a daughter, Clytemnestra, who was Agamémnon's wife.   7. They shared, as it were, one immortality between them.   8. Poseidon.   9. Apollo. Ossa and Pelion are mountains near Olympus in Thessaly.   1. King of Krete and father of Phaidra and Ariadnê. Phaidra was the wife of Theseus of Athens, who fell in love with her stepson Hippolytus. Prokris was the unfaithful wife of Cephalus, king of Athens. Ariadnê helped Theseus slay the Minotaur on Krete.   2. We have no other account of this version of the episode that explains why Dionysus wanted Ariadnê killed; the prevalent version of the story in later times is that Dionysus carried Ariadnê off to be his bride.   3. Bribed with a golden necklace by Polynices, son of Oedipus, she persuaded her husband, Amphiaraus, to take part in the attack on Thebes, where he was killed. Maira was a nymph of Artemis who broke her vow of chasity and was killed by the goddess. Some story must have been attached to the name Klymênê, but we do not know what it is.

but how name all the women I beheld there,
daughters and wives of kings? The starry night
wanes long before I close.
                              Here, or aboard ship,
amid the crew, the hour for sleep has come.   365
Our sailing is the gods' affair and yours."[4]

Then he fell silent. Down the shadowy hall
the enchanted banqueters were still. Only
the queen with ivory pale arms, Arêtê, spoke,
saying to all the silent men:

                              "Phaiákians,   370
how does he stand, now, in your eyes, this captain,
the look and bulk of him, the inward poise?
He is my guest, but each one shares that honor.
Be in no haste to send him on his way
or scant your bounty in his need. Remember   375
how rich, by heaven's will, your possessions are."

Then Ekhenêos, the old soldier, eldest
of all Phaiákians, added his word:

"Friends, here was nothing but our own thought spoken,
the mark hit square. Our duties to her majesty.   380
For what is to be said and done,
we wait upon Alkínoös' command."

At this the king's voice rang:

                              "I so command—
as sure as it is I who, while I live,
rule the sea rovers of Phaiákia. Our friend   385
longs to put out for home, but let him be
content to rest here one more day, until
I see all gifts bestowed. And every man
will take thought for his launching and his voyage,
I most of all, for I am master here."   390

Odysseus, the great tactician, answered:

"Alkínoös, king and admiration of men,
even a year's delay, if you should urge it,
in loading gifts and furnishing for sea—
I too could wish it; better far that I   395
return with some largesse of wealth about me—
I shall be thought more worthy of love and courtesy
by every man who greets me home in Ithaka."

The king said:

                              "As to that, one word, Odysseus:
from all we see, we take you for no swindler—   400
though the dark earth be patient of so many,
scattered everywhere, baiting their traps with lies

---

4. Odysseus breaks off the story of his wanderings, and we are transported back to the scene of the banqueting hall of the Phaiakians.

of old times and of places no one knows.
You speak with art, but your intent is honest.
The Argive troubles, and your own troubles,
you told as a poet would, a man who knows the world.   405
But now come tell me this: among the dead
did you meet any of your peers, companions
who sailed with you and met their doom at Troy?
Here's a long night—an endless night—before us,   410
and no time yet for sleep, not in this hall.
Recall the past deeds and the strange adventures.
I could stay up until the sacred Dawn
as long as you might wish to tell your story."

Odysseus the great tactician answered: 415

"Alkínoös, king and admiration of men,
there is a time for story telling; there is
also a time for sleep. But even so,
if, indeed, listening be still your pleasure,
I must not grudge my part. Other and sadder   420
tales there are to tell, of my companions,
of some who came through all the Trojan spears,
clangor and groan of war,
only to find a brutal death at home—
and a bad wife behind it.
                              After Perséphonê,   425
icy and pale, dispersed the shades of women,
the soul of Agamémnon, son of Atreus,
came before me, sombre in the gloom,
and others gathered round, all who were with him
when death and doom struck in Aegísthos' hall.   430
Sipping the black blood, the tall shade perceived me,
and cried out sharply, breaking into tears;
then tried to stretch his hands toward me, but could not,
being bereft of all the reach and power
he once felt in the great torque of his arms.   435
Gazing at him, and stirred, I wept for pity,
and spoke across to him:

                      'O son of Atreus,
illustrious Lord Marshal, Agamémnon,
what was the doom that brought you low in death?
Were you at sea, aboard ship, and Poseidon   440
blew up a wicked squall to send you under,
or were you cattle-raiding on the mainland
or in a fight for some strongpoint, or women,
when the foe hit you to your mortal hurt?'

But he replied at once:

                      'Son of Laërtês,   445
Odysseus, master of land ways and sea ways,
neither did I go down with some good ship
in any gale Poseidon blew, nor die
upon the mainland, hurt by foes in battle.
It was Aigísthos who designed my death,   450

he and my heartless wife, and killed me, after
feeding me, like an ox felled at the trough.
That was my miserable end—and with me
my fellows butchered, like so many swine
killed for some troop, or feast, or wedding banquet   455
in a great landholder's household. In your day
you have seen men, and hundreds, die in war,
in the bloody press, or downed in single combat,
but these were murders you would catch your breath at:
think of us fallen, all our throats cut, winebowl   460
brimming, tables laden on every side,
while blood ran smoking over the whole floor.
In my extremity I heard Kassandra,[5]
Priam's daughter, piteously crying
as the traitress Klytaimnéstra made to kill her   465
along with me. I heaved up from the ground
and got my hands around the blade, but she
eluded me, that whore. Nor would she close
my two eyes[6] as my soul swam to the underworld
or shut my lips. There is no being more fell,   470
more bestial than a wife in such an action,
and what an action that one planned!
The murder of her husband and her lord.
Great god, I thought my children and my slaves
at least would give me welcome. But that woman,   475
plotting a thing so low, defiled herself
and all her sex, all women yet to come,
even those few who may be virtuous.'

He paused then, and I answered:

                         'Foul and dreadful.
That was the way that Zeus who views the wide world   480
vented his hatred on the sons of Atreus—
intrigues of women, even from the start.
                         Myriads
died by Helen's fault, and Klytaimnéstra
plotted against you half the world away.'

And he at once said:

                         'Let it be a warning   485
even to you. Indulge a woman never,
and never tell her all you know. Some things
a man may tell, some he should cover up.
Not that I see a risk for you, Odysseus,
of death at your wife's hands. She is too wise,   490
too clear-eyed, sees alternatives too well,
Penélopê, Ikários' daughter—
that young bride whom we left behind—think of it!—
when we sailed off to war. The baby boy
still cradled at her breast—now he must be   495

5. She was part of Agamémnon's share of the booty at Troy.   6. She would not give me a proper
burial.

a grown man, and a lucky one. By heaven,
you'll see him yet, and he'll embrace his father
with old fashioned respect, and rightly.

                    My own
lady never let me glut my eyes
on my own son, but bled me to death first.   500
One thing I will advise, on second thought;
stow it away and ponder it.
                    Land your ship
in secret on your island; give no warning.
The day of faithful wives is gone forever.

But tell me, have you any word at all   505
about my son's life? Gone to Orkhómenos
or sandy Pylos, can he be? Or waiting
with Meneláos in the plain of Sparta?
Death on earth has not yet taken Orestês.'

But I could only answer:

                    'Son of Atreus,   510
why do you ask these questions of me? Neither
news of home have I, nor news of him,
alive or dead. And empty words are evil.'

So we exchanged our speech, in bitterness,
weighed down by grief, and tears welled in our eyes,   515
when there appeared the spirit of Akhilleus,
son of Peleus; then Patróklos' shade,
and then Antílokhos,[7] and then Aias,
first among all the Danaans in strength
and bodily beauty, next to prince Akhilleus.   520
Now that great runner, grandson of Aíakhos,[8]
recognized me and called across to me:

'Son of Laërtês and the gods of old,
Odysseus, master mariner and soldier,
old knife, what next? What greater feat remains   525
for you to put your mind on, after this?
How did you find your way down to the dark
where these dimwitted dead are camped forever,
the after images of used-up men?'

                    I answered:

'Akhilleus, Peleus' son, strongest of all   530
among the Akhaians, I had need of foresight
such as Teirêsias alone could give
to help me, homeward bound for the crags of Ithaka.
I have not yet coasted Akhaia, not yet
touched my land; my life is all adversity.   535
But was there ever a man more blest by fortune
than you, Akhilleus? Can there ever be?
We ranked you with immortals in your lifetime,

7. Son of Nestor.   8. Akhilleus.

we Argives did, and here your power is royal
among the dead men's shades. Think, then, Akhilleus: 540
you need not be so pained by death.'

                   To this
he answered swiftly:

                   'Let me hear no smooth talk
of death from you, Odysseus, light of councils.
Better, I say, to break sod as a farm hand
for some poor country man, on iron rations,   545
than lord it over all the exhausted dead.
Tell me, what news of the prince my son:[9] did he
come after me to make a name in battle
or could it be he did not? Do you know
if rank and honor still belong to Peleus   550
in the towns of the Myrmidons? Or now, may be,
Hellas and Phthia spurn him, seeing old age
fetters him, hand and foot. I cannot help him
under the sun's rays, cannot be that man
I was on Troy's wide seaboard, in those days   555
when I made bastion for the Argives
and put an army's best men in the dust.
Were I but whole again, could I go now
to my father's house, one hour would do to make
my passion and my hands no man could hold   560
hateful to any who shoulder him aside.'

Now when he paused I answered:

                   'Of all that—
of Peleus' life, that is—I know nothing;
but happily I can tell you the whole story
of Neoptólemos, as you require.   565
In my own ship I brought him out from Skyros[1]
to join the Akhaians under arms.

                   And I can tell you,
in every council before Troy thereafter
your son spoke first and always to the point;
no one but Nestor and I could out-debate him.   570
And when we formed against the Trojan line
he never hung back in the mass, but ranged
far forward of his troops—no man could touch him
for gallantry. Aye, scores went down before him
in hard fights man to man. I shall not tell   575
all about each, or name them all—the long
roster of enemies he put out of action,
taking the shock of charges on the Argives.
But what a champion his lance ran through
in Eurýpolos the son of Télephos! Keteians[2]   580
in throngs around that captain also died—
all because Priam's gifts had won his mother

---

9. Neoptólemos (the name means "new war").   1. The Greeks were told by a prophet that Troy
would fall only to the son of Akhilleus, who was living on the rocky island of Skyros.   2. Eurýpolos'
people (from Asia Minor) who came to the aid of the Trojans.

to send the lad to battle; and I thought
Memnon[3] alone in splendor ever outshone him.

But one fact more: while our picked Argive crew   585
still rode that hollow horse Epeios built,
and when the whole thing lay with me, to open
the trapdoor of the ambuscade or not,
at that point our Danaan lords and soldiers
wiped their eyes, and their knees began to quake,   590
all but Neoptólemos. I never saw
his tanned cheek change color or his hand
brush one tear away. Rather he prayed me,
hand on hilt, to sortie, and he gripped
his tough spear, bent on havoc for the Trojans.   595
And when we had pierced and sacked Priam's tall city
he loaded his choice plunder and embarked
with no scar on him; not a spear had grazed him
nor the sword's edge in close work—common wounds
one gets in war. Arês in his mad fits   600
knows no favorites.'

　　　　　　But I said no more,
for he had gone off striding the field of asphodel,
the ghost of our great runner, Akhilleus Aíákidês,[4]
glorying in what I told him of his son.

Now other souls of mournful dead stood by,   605
each with his troubled questioning, but one
remained alone, apart: the son of Télamon,
Aîas, it was—the great shade burning still
because I had won favor on the beachhead
in rivalry over Akhilleus' arms.[5]   610
The Lady Thetis, mother of Akhilleus,
laid out for us the dead man's battle gear,
and Trojan children, with Athena,
named the Danaan fittest to own them. Would
god I had not borne the palm that day!   615
For earth took Aîas then to hold forever,
the handsomest and, in all feats of war,
noblest of the Danaans after Akhilleus.
Gently therefore I called across to him:

'Aîas, dear son of royal Télamon,   620
you would not then forget, even in death,
your fury with me over those accurst
calamitous arms?—and so they were, a bane
sent by the gods upon the Argive host.
For when you died by your own hand we lost   625
a tower, formidable in war. All we Akhaians
mourn you forever, as we do Akhilleus;
and no one bears the blame but Zeus.
He fixed that doom for you because he frowned

---

3. Son of the dawn goddess, king of the Ethiopians, and a Trojan ally.　　4. Akhilleus was the son of
Peleus, whose father was Aiakos.　　5. In the *Iliad*, Aîas tried to kill Odysseus and then committed
suicide because the slain Akhilleus' armor was awarded to Odysseus.

on the whole expedition of our spearmen.   630
My lord, come nearer, listen to our story!
Conquer your indignation and your pride.'

But he gave no reply, and turned away,
following other ghosts toward Erebos.
Who knows if in that darkness he might still   635
have spoken, and I answered?
                                    But my heart
longed, after this, to see the dead elsewhere.
And now there came before my eyes Minos,
the son of Zeus, enthroned, holding a golden staff,
dealing out justice among ghostly pleaders   640
arrayed about the broad doorways of Death.

And then I glimpsed Orion,[6] the huge hunter,
gripping his club, studded with bronze, unbreakable,
with wild beasts he had overpowered in life
on lonely mountainsides, now brought to bay   645
on fields of asphodel.
                          And I saw Títyos,
the son of Gaia, lying
abandoned over nine square rods of plain.
Vultures, hunched above him, left and right,
rifling his belly, stabbed into the liver,   650
and he could never push them off.
                                    This hulk
had once committed rape of Zeus's mistress,
Léto, in her glory, when she crossed
the open grass of Panopeus toward Pytho.

Then I saw Tántalos[7] put to the torture: 655
in a cool pond he stood, lapped round by water
clear to the chin, and being athirst he burned
to slake his dry weasand with drink, though drink
he would not ever again. For when the old man
put his lips down to the sheet of water   660
it vanished round his feet, gulped underground,
and black mud baked there in a wind from hell.
Boughs, too, drooped low above him, big with fruit,
pear trees, pomegranates, brilliant apples,
luscious figs, and olives ripe and dark;   665
but if he stretched his hand for one, the wind
under the dark sky tossed the bough beyond him.

Then Sísyphos[8] in torment I beheld
being roustabout to a tremendous boulder.
Leaning with both arms braced and legs driving,   670
he heaved it toward a height, and almost over,
but then a Power spun him round and sent

---

6. According to later legend he was transformed into the constellation that bears his name; Homer, however, has him in the underworld after his death.   7. King of Lydia. He was the confidant of the gods and ate at their table, but he betrayed their secrets.   8. King of Corinth, the archetype of the liar and trickster; we do not know what misdeed he is being punished for in this passage.

the cruel boulder bounding again to the plain.
Whereon the man bent down again to toil,
dripping sweat, and the dust rose overhead. 675
Next I saw manifest the power of Heraklês—
a phantom, this, for he himself has gone
feasting amid the gods, reclining soft
with Hêbê of the ravishing pale ankles,
daughter of Zeus and Hêra, shod in gold. 680
But, in my vision, all the dead around him
cried like affrighted birds; like Night itself
he loomed with naked bow and nocked arrow
and glances terrible as continual archery.
My hackles rose at the gold swordbelt he wore 685
sweeping across him: gorgeous intaglio
of savage bears, boars, lions with wildfire eyes,
swordfights, battle, slaughter, and sudden death—
the smith who had that belt in him, I hope
he never made, and never will make, another. 690
The eyes of the vast figure rested on me,
and of a sudden he said in kindly tones:

'Son of Laërtês and the gods of old,
Odysseus, master mariner and soldier,
under a cloud, you too? Destined to grinding 695
labors like my own in the sunny world?[9]
Son of Kroníon Zeus or not, how many
days I sweated out, being bound in servitude
to a man far worse than I, a rough master!
He made me hunt this place one time 700
to get the watchdog of the dead: no more
perilous task, he thought, could be; but I
brought back that beast, up from the underworld;
Hermês and grey-eyed Athena showed the way.'

And Heraklês, down the vistas of the dead, 705
faded from sight; but I stood fast, awaiting
other great souls who perished in times past.
I should have met, then, god-begotten Theseus
and Peirithoös,[1] whom both I longed to see,
but first came shades in thousands, rustling 710
in a pandemonium of whispers, blown together,
and the horror took me that Perséphonê
had brought from darker hell some saurian death's head.
I whirled then, made for the ship, shouted to crewmen
to get aboard and cast off the stern hawsers, 715
an order soon obeyed. They took their thwarts,
and the ship went leaping toward the stream of Ocean
first under oars, then with a following wind.

---

9. Heraklês, son of Zeus, was made subject to the orders of Eurýstheus of Argos, who ordered him to perform the twelve famous labors.   1. After his adventures in Krete, Theseus went with his friend Perithoös to Hades to kidnap Perséphonê; the venture failed, and the two heroes, imprisoned in Hades, were rescued by Heraklês.

BOOK XII

[Sea Perils and Defeat]

The ship sailed on, out of the Ocean Stream,
riding a long swell on the open sea
for the Island of Aiaia.
                              Summering Dawn
has dancing grounds there, and the Sun his rising;[2]
but still by night we beached on a sand shelf   5
and waded in beyond the line of breakers
to fall asleep, awaiting the Day Star.

When the young Dawn with finger tips of rose
made heaven bright, I sent shipmates to bring
Elpênor's body from the house of Kirkê.   10
We others cut down timber on the foreland,
on a high point, and built his pyre of logs,
then stood by weeping while the flame burnt through
corse and equipment.
                          Then we heaped his barrow,
lifting a gravestone on the mound, and fixed   15
his light but unwarped oar against the sky.
These were our rites in memory of him. Soon, then,
knowing us back from the Dark Land, Kirkê came
freshly adorned for us, with handmaids bearing
loaves, roast meats, and ruby-colored wine.   20
She stood among us in immortal beauty
jesting:

         'Hearts of oak, did you go down
alive into the homes of Death? One visit
finishes all men but yourselves, twice mortal!
Come, here is meat and wine, enjoy your feasting   25
for one whole day; and in the dawn tomorrow
you shall put out to sea. Sailing directions,
landmarks, perils, I shall sketch for you, to keep you
from being caught by land or water
in some black sack of trouble.'

                          In high humor   30
and ready for carousal, we agreed;
so all that day until the sun went down
we feasted on roast meat and good red wine,
till after sunset, at the fall of night,
the men dropped off to sleep by the stern hawsers.   35
She took my hand then, silent in that hush,
drew me apart, made me sit down, and lay
beside me, softly questioning, as I told
all I had seen, from first to last.
                          Then said the Lady Kirkê:

'So: all those trials are over.

---

2. This places Kirkê's island in the east, whereas Odysseus' ship, when it was blown past Cape Malea, was headed west. It is one more indication that Odyssean geography is highly imaginative.

Listen with care   40
to this, now, and a god will arm your mind.
Square in your ship's path are Seirênês,[3] crying
beauty to bewitch men coasting by;
woe to the innocent who hears that sound!
He will not see his lady nor his children   45
in joy, crowding about him, home from sea;
the Seirênês will sing his mind away
on their sweet meadow lolling. There are bones
of dead men rotting in a pile beside them
and flayed skins shrivel around the spot.
                              Steer wide;   50
keep well to seaward; plug your oarsmen's ears
with beeswax kneaded soft; none of the rest
should hear that song.
                      But if you wish to listen,
let the men tie you in the lugger, hand
and foot, back to the mast, lashed to the mast,   55
so you may hear those harpies' thrilling voices;
shout as you will, begging to be untied,
your crew must only twist more line around you
and keep their stroke up, till the singers fade.
What then? One of two courses you may take,   60
and you yourself must weigh them. I shall not
plan the whole action for you now, but only
tell you of both.
                  Ahead are beetling rocks
and dark blue glancing Amphitritê, surging,
roars around them. Prowling Rocks,[4] or Drifters, 65
the gods in bliss have named them—named them well.
Not even birds can pass them by, not even
the timorous doves that bear ambrosia
to Father Zeus; caught by downdrafts, they die
on rockwall smooth as ice.
                          Each time, the Father   70
wafts a new courier to make up his crew.

Still less can ships get searoom of these Drifters,
whose boiling surf, under high fiery winds,
carries tossing wreckage of ships and men.
Only one ocean-going craft, the far-famed   75
Argo, made it, sailing from Aiêta;
but she, too, would have crashed on the big rocks
if Hêra had not pulled her through, for love
of Iêson, her captain.
                      A second course
lies between headlands. One is a sharp mountain   80
piercing the sky, with stormcloud round the peak
dissolving never, not in the brightest summer,
to show heaven's azure there, nor in the fall.

3. Or Sirens.   4. Homer does not precisely identify them with the Symplegades, the Clashing Rocks
that came together and crushed whatever tried to pass between them. They were thought to be located
at the entrance to the Black Sea. Homer's Prowling Rocks seem to be located, like Scylla and Charybdis,
near the straits between Sicily and Italy. *Amphitritê:* the sea.

No mortal man could scale it, nor so much
as land there, not with twenty hands and feet,   85
so sheer the cliffs are—as of polished stone.
Midway that height, a cavern full of mist
opens toward Erebos and evening.[5] Skirting
this in the lugger, great Odysseus,
your master bowman, shooting from the deck,   90
would come short of the cavemouth with his shaft;
but that is the den of Skylla, where she yaps
abominably, a newborn whelp's cry,
though she is huge and monstrous. God or man,
no one could look on her in joy. Her legs—   95
and there are twelve—are like great tentacles,
unjointed, and upon her serpent necks
are borne six heads like nightmares of ferocity,
with triple serried rows of fangs and deep
gullets of black death. Half her length, she sways   100
her heads in air, outside her horrid cleft,
hunting the sea around that promontory
for dolphins, dogfish, or what bigger game
thundering Amphitritê feeds in thousands.
And no ship's company can claim   105
to have passed her without loss and grief; she takes,
from every ship, one man for every gullet.
The opposite point seems more a tongue of land
you'd touch with a good bowshot, at the narrows.
A great wild fig, a shaggy mass of leaves,   110
grows on it, and Kharybdis lurks below
to swallow down the dark sea tide. Three times
from dawn to dusk she spews it up
and sucks it down again three times, a whirling
maelstrom; if you come upon her then   115
the god who makes earth tremble could not save you.
No, hug the cliff of Skylla, take your ship
through on a racing stroke. Better to mourn
six men than lose them all, and the ship, too.'

So her advice ran; but I faced her, saying: 120

'Only instruct me, goddess, if you will,
how, if possible, can I pass Kharybdis,
or fight off Skylla when she raids my crew?'

Swiftly that loveliest goddess answered me:

'Must you have battle in your heart forever?   125
The bloody toil of combat? Old contender,
will you not yield to the immortal gods?
That nightmare cannot die, being eternal
evil itself—horror, and pain, and chaos;
there is no fighting her, no power can fight her,   130
all that avails is flight.
                    Lose headway there
along that rockface while you break out arms,

5. That is, to the northwest.

and she'll swoop over you, I fear, once more,
taking one man again for every gullet.
No, no, put all your backs into it, row on;   135
invoke Blind Force, that bore this scourge of men,
to keep her from a second strike against you.

Then you will coast Thrinákia,[6] the island
where Hêlios' cattle graze, fine herds, and flocks
of goodly sheep. The herds and flocks are seven,   140
with fifty beasts in each.
                                No lambs are dropped,
or calves, and these fat cattle never die.
Immortal, too, their cowherds are—their shepherds—
Phaëthousa and Lampetía, sweetly braided
nymphs that divine Neaira bore   145
to the overlord of high noon, Hêlios.
These nymphs their gentle mother bred and placed
upon Thrinákia, the distant land,
in care of flocks and cattle for their father.

Now give those kine a wide berth, keep your thoughts   150
intent upon your course for home,
and hard seafaring brings you all to Ithaka.
But if you raid the beeves, I see destruction
for ship and crew.
                        Rough years then lie between
you and your homecoming, alone and old,   155
the one survivor, all companions lost.'

As Kirkê spoke, Dawn mounted her golden throne,
and on the first rays Kirkê left me, taking
her way like a great goddess up the island.
I made straight for the ship, roused up the men   160
to get aboard and cast off at the stern.
They scrambled to their places by the rowlocks
and all in line dipped oars in the grey sea.
But soon an off-shore breeze blew to our liking—
a canvas-bellying breeze, a lusty shipmate   165
sent by the singing nymph with sunbright hair.
So we made fast the braces, and we rested,
letting the wind and steersman work the ship.
The crew being now silent before me, I
addressed them, sore at heart:

                                'Dear friends,   170
more than one man, or two, should know those things
Kirkê foresaw for us and shared with me,
so let me tell her forecast: then we die
with our eyes open, if we are going to die,
or know what death we baffle if we can. Seirênês   175
weaving a haunting song over the sea
we are to shun, she said, and their green shore
all sweet with clover; yet she urged that I

6. Later Greeks identified this island as Sicily.

alone should listen to their song. Therefore
you are to tie me up, tight as a splint,   180
erect along the mast, lashed to the mast,
and if I shout and beg to be untied,
take more turns of the rope to muffle me.'

I rather dwelt on this part of the forecast,
while our good ship made time, bound outward down   185
the wind for the strange island of Seirênês.
Then all at once the wind fell, and a calm
came over all the sea, as though some power
lulled the swell.
          The crew were on their feet
briskly, to furl the sail, and stow it; then,   190
each in place, they poised the smooth oar blades
and sent the white foam scudding by. I carved
a massive cake of beeswax into bits
and rolled them in my hands until they softened—
no long task, for a burning heat came down   195
from Hêlios, lord of high noon. Going forward
I carried wax along the line, and laid it
thick on their ears. They tied me up, then, plumb
amidships, back to the mast, lashed to the mast,
and took themselves again to rowing. Soon,   200
as we came smartly within hailing distance,
the two Seirênês, noting our fast ship
off their point, made ready, and they sang:[7]

    This way, oh turn your bows,
      Akhaia's glory,   205
    As all the world allows—
      Moor and be merry.

    Sweet coupled airs we sing.
      No lonely seafarer
    Holds clear of entering   210
      Our green mirror.

    Pleased by each purling note
      Like honey twining
    From her throat and my throat,
      Who lies a-pining?   215

    Sea rovers here take joy
      Voyaging onward,
    As from our song of Troy
    Greybeard and rower-boy
    Goeth more learnèd.   220

---

7. The translator has turned the eight unrhymed lines of the original into a lyric poem. Here is a prose
version of the Greek: "Draw near, illustrious Odysseus, flower of Akhaian chivalry, and bring your ship
to rest so that you may hear our voices. No seaman ever sailed his black ship past this spot without
listening to the sweet tones that flow from our lips, and none that has listened has not been delighted
and gone on a wiser man. For we know all that the Argives and Trojans suffered on the broad plain of
Troy by the will of the gods, and we have foreknowledge of all that is going to happen on this fruitful
earth."

All feats on that great field
   In the long warfare,
Dark days the bright gods willed,
   Wounds you bore there,

Argos' old soldiery   225
   On Troy beach teeming,
Charmed out of time we see.
No life on earth can be
   Hid from our dreaming.

The lovely voices in ardor appealing over the water   230
made me crave to listen, and I tried to say
'Untie me!' to the crew, jerking my brows;
but they bent steady to the oars. Then Perimêdês
got to his feet, he and Eurýlokhos,
and passed more line about, to hold me still.   235
So all rowed on, until the Seirênês
dropped under the sea rim, and their singing
dwindled away.
           My faithful company
rested on their oars now, peeling off
the wax that I had laid thick on their ears;   240
then set me free.
           But scarcely had that island
faded in blue air than I saw smoke
and white water, with sound of waves in tumult—
a sound the men heard, and it terrified them.
Oars flew from their hands; the blades went knocking   245
wild alongside till the ship lost way,
with no oarblades to drive her through the water.

Well, I walked up and down from bow to stern,
trying to put heart into them, standing over
every oarsman, saying gently,
                   'Friends,   250
have we never been in danger before this?
More fearsome, is it now, than when the Kyklops
penned us in his cave? What power he had!
Did I not keep my nerve, and use my wits
to find a way out for us?
               Now I say   255
by hook or crook this peril too shall be
something that we remember.
              Heads up, lads!
We must obey the orders as I give them.
Get the oarshafts in your hands, and lay back
hard on your benches; hit these breaking seas.   260
Zeus help us pull away before we founder.
You at the tiller, listen, and take in
all that I say—the rudders are your duty;
keep her out of the combers and the smoke;
steer for that headland; watch the drift, or we   265
fetch up in the smother, and you drown us.'

That was all, and it brought them round to action.
But as I sent them on toward Skylla, I
told them nothing, as they could do nothing.
They would have dropped their oars again, in panic,   270
to roll for cover under the decking. Kirkê's
bidding against arms had slipped my mind,
so I tied on my cuirass and took up
two heavy spears, then made my way along
to the foredeck—thinking to see her first from there,   275
the monster of the grey rock, harboring
torment for my friends. I strained my eyes
upon that cliffside veiled in cloud, but nowhere
could I catch sight of her.

                And all this time,
in travail, sobbing, gaining on the current,   280
we rowed into the strait—Skylla to port
and on our starboard beam Kharybdis, dire
gorge of the salt sea tide. By heaven! when she
vomited, all the sea was like a cauldron
seething over intense fire, when the mixture   285
suddenly heaves and rises.

                The shot spume
soared to the landside heights, and fell like rain.

But when she swallowed the sea water down
we saw the funnel of the maelstrom, heard
the rock bellowing all around, and dark   290
sand raged on the bottom far below.
My men all blanched against the gloom, our eyes
were fixed upon that yawning mouth in fear
of being devoured.

                Then Skylla made her strike,
whisking six of my best men from the ship.   295
I happened to glance aft at ship and oarsmen
and caught sight of their arms and legs, dangling
high overhead. Voices came down to me
in anguish, calling my name for the last time.

A man surfcasting on a point of rock   300
for bass or mackerel, whipping his long rod
to drop the sinker and the bait far out,
will hook a fish and rip it from the surface
to dangle wriggling through the air:

                      so these
were borne aloft in spasms toward the cliff.   305

She ate them as they shrieked there, in her den,
in the dire grapple, reaching still for me—
and deathly pity ran me through
at that sight—far the worst I ever suffered,
questing the passes of the strange sea.

                    We rowed on.   310
The Rocks were now behind; Kharybdis, too,
and Skylla dropped astern.

                Then we were coasting

the noble island of the god, where grazed
those cattle with wide brows, and bounteous flocks
of Hêlios, lord of noon, who rides high heaven.   315

From the black ship, far still at sea, I heard
the lowing of the cattle winding home
and sheep bleating; and heard, too, in my heart
the words of blind Teirêsias of Thebes
and Kirkê of Aiaia: both forbade me   320
the island of the world's delight, the Sun.
So I spoke out in gloom to my companions:

'Shipmates, grieving and weary though you are,
listen: I had forewarning from Teirêsias
and Kirkê, too; both told me I must shun   325
this island of the Sun, the world's delight.
Nothing but fatal trouble shall we find here.
Pull away, then, and put the land astern.'

That strained them to the breaking point, and, cursing,
Eurýlokhos cried out in bitterness: 330

'Are you flesh and blood, Odysseus, to endure
more than a man can? Do you never tire?
God, look at you, iron is what you're made of.
Here we all are, half dead with weariness,
falling asleep over the oars, and you   335
say "No landing"—no firm island earth
where we could make a quiet supper. No:
pull out to sea, you say, with night upon us—
just as before, but wandering now, and lost.
Sudden storms can rise at night and swamp   340
ships without a trace.
                          Where is your shelter
if some stiff gale blows up from south or west—
the winds that break up shipping every time
when seamen flout the lord gods' will? I say
do as the hour demands and go ashore   345
before black night comes down.
                          We'll make our supper
alongside, and at dawn put out to sea.'

Now when the rest said 'Aye' to this, I saw
the power of destiny devising ill.
Sharply I answered, without hesitation: 350

'Eurýlokhos, they are with you to a man.
I am alone, outmatched.
                          Let this whole company
swear me a great oath: Any herd of cattle
or flock of sheep here found shall go unharmed;
no one shall slaughter out of wantonness   355
ram or heifer; all shall be content
with what the goddess Kirkê put aboard.'

They fell at once to swearing as I ordered,
and when the round of oaths had ceased, we found

a halfmoon bay to beach and moor the ship in,   360
with a fresh spring nearby. All hands ashore
went about skillfully getting up a meal.
Then, after thirst and hunger, those besiegers,
were turned away, they mourned for their companions
plucked from the ship by Skylla and devoured,   365
and sleep came soft upon them as they mourned.

In the small hours of the third watch, when stars
that shone out in the first dusk of evening
had gone down to their setting, a giant wind
blew from heaven, and clouds driven by Zeus   370
shrouded land and sea in a night of storm;
so, just as Dawn with finger tips of rose
touched the windy world, we dragged our ship
to cover in a grotto, a sea cave
where nymphs had chairs of rock and sanded floors.   375
I mustered all the crew and said:

        'Old shipmates,
our stores are in the ship's hold, food and drink;
the cattle here are not for our provision,
or we pay dearly for it.
        Fierce the god is
who cherishes these heifers and these sheep: 380
Hêlios; and no man avoids his eye.'

To this my fighters nodded. Yes. But now
we had a month of onshore gales, blowing
day in, day out—south winds, or south by east.
As long as bread and good red wine remained   385
to keep the men up, and appease their craving,
they would not touch the cattle. But in the end,
when all the barley in the ship was gone,
hunger drove them to scour the wild shore
with angling hooks, for fishes and sea fowl,   390
whatever fell into their hands; and lean days
wore their bellies thin.

        The storms continued.
So one day I withdrew to the interior
to pray the gods in solitude, for hope
that one might show me some way of salvation.   395
Slipping away, I struck across the island
to a sheltered spot, out of the driving gale.
I washed my hands there, and made supplication
to the gods who own Olympos, all the gods—
but they, for answer, only closed my eyes   400
under slow drops of sleep.
        Now on the shore Eurýlokhos
made his insidious plea:

        'Comrades,' he said,
'You've gone through everything; listen to what I say.
All deaths are hateful to us, mortal wretches,

but famine is the most pitiful, the worst   405
end that a man can come to.
                            Will you fight it?
Come, we'll cut out the noblest of these cattle
for sacrifice to the gods who own the sky;
and once at home, in the old country of Ithaka,
if ever that day comes—   410
we'll build a costly temple and adorn it
with every beauty for the Lord of Noon.
But if he flares up over his heifers lost,
wishing our ship destroyed, and if the gods
make cause with him, why, then I say: Better   415
open your lungs to a big sea once for all
than waste to skin and bones on a lonely island!'

Thus Eurýlokhos; and they murmured 'Aye!'
trooping away at once to round up heifers.
Now, that day tranquil cattle with broad brows   420
were grazing near, and soon the men drew up
around their chosen beasts in ceremony.
They plucked the leaves that shone on a tall oak—
having no barley meal—to strew the victims,
performed the prayers and ritual, knifed the kine   425
and flayed each carcass, cutting thighbones free
to wrap in double folds of fat. These offerings,
with strips of meat, were laid upon the fire.
Then, as they had no wine, they made libation
with clear spring water, broiling the entrails first;   430
and when the bones were burnt and tripes shared,
they spitted the carved meat.
                            Just then my slumber
left me in a rush, my eyes opened,
and I went down the seaward path. No sooner
had I caught sight of our black hull, than savory   435
odors of burnt fat eddied around me;
grief took hold of me, and I cried aloud:

'O Father Zeus and gods in bliss forever,
you made me sleep away this day of mischief!
O cruel drowsing, in the evil hour!   440
Here they sat, and a great work they contrived.'

Lampetía in her long gown meanwhile
had borne swift word to the Overlord of Noon:

'They have killed your kine.'

                            And the Lord Hêlios
burst into angry speech amid the immortals: 445

'O Father Zeus and gods in bliss forever,
punish Odysseus' men! So overweening,
now they have killed my peaceful kine, my joy
at morning when I climbed the sky of stars,
and evening, when I bore westward from heaven.   450
Restitution or penalty they shall pay—

and pay in full—or I go down forever
to light the dead men in the underworld.'

Then Zeus who drives the stormcloud made reply:

'Peace, Hêlios: shine on among the gods,   455
shine over mortals in the fields of grain.
Let me throw down one white-hot bolt, and make
splinters of their ship in the winedark sea.'

—Kalypso later told me of this exchange,
as she declared that Hermês had told her.   460
Well, when I reached the sea cave and the ship,
I faced each man, and had it out; but where
could any remedy be found? There was none.
The silken beeves of Hêlios were dead.
The gods, moreover, made queer signs appear: 465
cowhides began to crawl, and beef, both raw
and roasted, lowed like kine upon the spits.

Now six full days my gallant crew could feast
upon the prime beef they had marked for slaughter
from Hêlios' herd; and Zeus, the son of Kronos,   470
added one fine morning.
                          All the gales
had ceased, blown out, and with an offshore breeze
we launched again, stepping the mast and sail,
to make for the open sea. Astern of us
the island coastline faded, and no land   475
showed anywhere, but only sea and heaven,
when Zeus Kroníon piled a thunderhead
above the ship, while gloom spread on the ocean.
We held our course, but briefly. Then the squall
struck whining from the west, with gale force, breaking   480
both forestays, and the mast came toppling aft
along the ship's length, so the running rigging
showered into the bilge.
                          On the after deck
the mast had hit the steersman a slant blow
bashing the skull in, knocking him overside,   485
as the brave soul fled the body, like a diver.
With crack on crack of thunder, Zeus let fly
a bolt against the ship, a direct hit,
so that she bucked, in reeking fumes of sulphur,
and all the men were flung into the sea.   490
They came up 'round the wreck, bobbing a while
like petrels on the waves.
                          No more seafaring
homeward for these, no sweet day of return;
the god had turned his face from them.
                                    I clambered
fore and aft my hulk until a comber   495
split her, keel from ribs, and the big timber
floated free; the mast, too, broke away.
A backstay floated dangling from it, stout

rawhide rope, and I used this for lashing
mast and keel together. These I straddled,   500
riding the frightful storm.
                    Nor had I yet
seen the worst of it: for now the west wind
dropped, and a southeast gale came on—one more
twist of the knife—taking me north again,
straight for Kharybdis. All that night I drifted,   505
and in the sunrise, sure enough, I lay
off Skylla mountain and Kharybdis deep.
There, as the whirlpool drank the tide, a billow
tossed me, and I sprang for the great fig tree,
catching on like a bat under a bough.   510
Nowhere had I to stand, no way of climbing,
the root and bole being far below, and far
above my head the branches and their leaves,
massed, overshadowing Kharybdis' pool.
But I clung grimly, thinking my mast and keel   515
would come back to the surface when she spouted.
And ah! how long, with what desire, I waited!
till, at the twilight hour, when one who hears
and judges pleas in the marketplace all day
between contentious men, goes home to supper,   520
the long poles at last reared from the sea.

Now I let go with hands and feet, plunging
straight into the foam beside the timbers,
pulled astride, and rowed hard with my hands
to pass by Skylla. Never could I have passed her   525
had not the Father of gods and men, this time,
kept me from her eyes. Once through the strait,
nine days I drifted in the open sea
before I made shore, buoyed up by the gods,
upon Ogýgia Isle. The dangerous nymph   530
Kalypso lives and sings there, in her beauty,
and she received me, loved me.

                    But why tell
the same tale that I told last night in hall
to you and to your lady? Those adventures
made a long evening, and I do not hold   535
with tiresome repetition of a story."

BOOK XIII

[One More Strange Island]

He ended it, and no one stirred or sighed
in the shadowy hall, spellbound as they all were,
until Alkínoös answered:

                    "When you came
here to my strong home, Odysseus, under
my tall roof, headwinds were left behind you.   5
Clear sailing shall you have now, homeward now,
however painful all the past.

in his deep heart, breaking through ranks in war
and waves on the bitter sea.
                              This night at last
he slept serene, his long-tried mind at rest.   105

When on the East the sheer bright star arose
that tells of coming Dawn, the ship made landfall
and came up islandward in the dim of night.
Phorkys, the old sea baron, has a cove
here in the realm of Ithaka; two points   110
of high rock, breaking sharply, hunch around it,
making a haven from the plunging surf
that gales at sea roll shoreward. Deep inside,
at mooring range, good ships can ride unmoored.
There, on the inmost shore, an olive tree   115
throws wide its boughs over the bay; nearby
a cave of dusky light is hidden
for those immortal girls, the Naiadês.[8]
Within are winebowls hollowed in the rock
and amphorai; bees bring their honey here;   120
and there are looms of stone, great looms, whereon
the weaving nymphs make tissues, richly dyed
as the deep sea is; and clear springs in the cavern
flow forever. Of two entrances,
one on the north allows descent of mortals,   125
but beings out of light alone, the undying,
can pass by the south slit; no men come there.

This cove the sailors knew. Here they drew in,
and the ship ran half her keel's length up the shore,
she had such way on her from those great oarsmen.   130
Then from their benches forward on dry ground
they disembarked. They hoisted up Odysseus
unruffled on his bed, under his cover,
handing him overside still fast asleep,
to lay him on the sand; and they unloaded   135
all those gifts the princes of Phaiákia
gave him, when by Athena's heart and will
he won his passage home. They bore this treasure
off the beach, and piled it close around
the roots of the olive tree, that no one passing   140
should steal Odysseus' gear before he woke.
That done, they pulled away on the homeward track.

But now the god that shakes the islands, brooding
over old threats of his against Odysseus,
approached Lord Zeus to learn his will. Said he: 145

"Father of gods, will the bright immortals ever
pay me respect again, if mortals do not?—
Phaiákians, too, my own blood kin?
                              I thought
Odysseus should in time regain his homeland;

---

8. Nymphs of lake, river, and stream.

I had no mind to rob him of that day— 150
no, no; you promised it, being so inclined;
only I thought he should be made to suffer
all the way.
            But now these islanders
have shipped him homeward, sleeping soft, and put him
on Ithaka, with gifts untold 155
of bronze and gold, and fine cloth to his shoulder.
Never from Troy had he borne off such booty
if he had got home safe with all his share."

Then Zeus who drives the stormcloud answered, sighing:

"God of horizons, making earth's underbeam 160
tremble, why do you grumble so?
The immortal gods show you no less esteem,
and the rough consequence would make them slow
to let barbs fly at their eldest and most noble.
But if some mortal captain, overcome 165
by his own pride of strength, cuts or defies you,
are you not always free to take reprisal?
Act as your wrath requires and as you will."

Now said Poseidon, god of earthquake:

                                    "Aye,
god of the stormy sky, I should have taken 170
vengeance, as you say, and on my own;
but I respect, and would avoid, your anger.
The sleek Phaiákian cutter, even now,
has carried out her mission and glides home
over the misty sea. Let me impale her, 175
end her voyage, and end all ocean-crossing
with passengers, then heave a mass of mountain
in a ring around the city."

Now Zeus who drives the stormcloud said benignly:

"Here is how I should do it, little brother: 180
when all who watch upon the wall have caught
sight of the ship, let her be turned to stone—
an island like a ship, just off the bay.
Mortals may gape at that for generations!
But throw no mountain round[9] the sea port city." 185

When he heard this, Poseidon, god of earthquake,
departed for Skhería, where the Phaiákians
are born and dwell. Their ocean-going ship
he saw already near, heading for harbor;
so up behind her swam the island-shaker 190
and struck her into stone, rooted in stone, at one
blow of his palm,

---

9. This translates a correction of the text made in antiquity by the Alexandrian scholar Aristophanes of
Byzantium. But another great Alexandrian scholar, Aristarchus, defended the original text, which means
"and throw a big mountain round." Zeus, in other words, approved of Poseidon's intention to cut the
Phaiákians off from the sea altogether and adds the proposal to turn the ship into a rock. It is a difficult
question to decide, because Homer does not tell us what happened to the Phaiákians in the end.

        then took to the open sea.
Those famous ship handlers, the Phaiákians,
gazed at each other, murmuring in wonder;
you could have heard one say:

                  "Now who in thunder   195
has anchored, moored that ship in the seaway,
when everyone could see her making harbor?"

The god had wrought a charm beyond their thought.
But soon Alkínoös made them hush, and told them:

"This present doom upon the ship—on me—   200
my father prophesied in the olden time.
If we gave safe conveyance to all passengers
we should incur Poseidon's wrath, he said,
whereby one day a fair ship, manned by Phaiákians,
would come to grief at the god's hands; and great   205
mountains would hide our city from the sea.
So my old father forecast.
           Use your eyes:
these things are even now being brought to pass.
Let all here abide by my decree:
             We make
an end henceforth of taking, in our ships,   210
castaways who may land upon Skhería;
and twelve choice bulls we dedicate at once
to Lord Poseidon, praying him of his mercy
not to heave up a mountain round our city."

In fearful awe they led the bulls to sacrifice   215
and stood about the altar stone, those captains,
peers of Phaiákia, led by their king in prayer
to Lord Poseidon.

           Meanwhile, on his island,
his father's shore, that kingly man, Odysseus,
awoke, but could not tell what land it was   220
after so many years away; moreover,
Pallas Athena, Zeus's daughter, poured
a grey mist all around him, hiding him
from common sight—for she had things to tell him
and wished no one to know him, wife or townsmen,   225
before the suitors paid up for their crimes.

The landscape then looked strange, unearthly strange
to the Lord Odysseus: paths by hill and shore,
glimpses of harbors, cliffs, and summer trees.
He stood up, rubbed his eyes, gazed at his homeland,   230
and swore, slapping his thighs with both his palms,
then cried aloud:

           "What am I in for now?
Whose country have I come to this time? Rough
savages and outlaws, are they, or
godfearing people, friendly to castaways?   235

Where shall I take these things? Where take myself,
with no guide, no directions? These should be
still in Phaiákian hands, and I uncumbered,
free to find some other openhearted
prince who might be kind and give me passage.   240
I have no notion where to store this treasure;
first-comer's trove it is, if I leave it here.

My lords and captains of Phaiákia
were not those decent men they seemed, not honorable,
landing me in this unknown country—no,   245
by god, they swore to take me home to Ithaka
and did not! Zeus attend to their reward,
Zeus, patron of petitioners, who holds
all other mortals under his eye; he takes
payment from betrayers!
                     I'll be busy.   250
I can look through my gear. I shouldn't wonder
if they pulled out with part of it on board."

He made a tally of his shining pile—
tripods, cauldrons, cloaks, and gold—and found
he lacked nothing at all.
                     And then he wept,   255
despairing, for his own land, trudging down
beside the endless wash of the wide, wide sea,
weary and desolate as the sea. But soon
Athena came to him from the nearby air,
putting a young man's figure on—a shepherd,   260
like a king's son, all delicately made.
She wore a cloak, in two folds off her shoulders,
and sandals bound upon her shining feet.
A hunting lance lay in her hands.
                     At sight of her
Odysseus took heart, and he went forward   265
to greet the lad, speaking out fair and clear:

"Friend, you are the first man I've laid eyes on
here in this cove. Greetings. Do not feel
alarmed or hostile, coming across me; only
receive me into safety with my stores.   270
Touching your knees I ask it, as I might
ask grace of a god.
                     O sir, advise me,
what is this land and realm, who are the people?
Is it an island all distinct, or part
of the fertile mainland, sloping to the sea?"   275

To this grey-eyed Athena answered:

                     "Stranger,
you must come from the other end of nowhere,
else you are a great booby, having to ask
what place this is. It is no nameless country.
Why, everyone has heard of it, the nations   280
over on the dawn side, toward the sun,

and westerners in cloudy lands of evening.
No one would use this ground for training horses,
it is too broken, has no breadth of meadow;
but there is nothing meager about the soil,   285
the yield of grain is wondrous, and wine, too,
with drenching rains and dewfall.
                                There's good pasture
for oxen and for goats, all kinds of timber,
and water all year long in the cattle ponds.
For these blessings, friend, the name of Ithaka   290
has made its way even as far as Troy—
and they say Troy lies far beyond Akhaia."

Now Lord Odysseus, the long-enduring,
laughed in his heart, hearing his land described
by Pallas Athena, daughter of Zeus who rules   295
the veering stormwind; and he answered her
with ready speech—not that he told the truth,
but, just as she did, held back what he knew,
weighing within himself at every step
what he made up to serve his turn.

                                Said he: 300

"Far away in Krete I learned of Ithaka—
in that broad island over the great ocean.
And here I am now, come myself to Ithaka!
Here is my fortune with me. I left my sons
an equal part, when I shipped out. I killed   305
Orsílokhos, the courier, son of Idómeneus.
This man could beat the best cross country runners
in Krete, but he desired to take away
my Trojan plunder, all I had fought and bled for,
cutting through ranks in war and the cruel sea.   310
Confiscation is what he planned; he knew
I had not cared to win his father's favor
as a staff officer in the field at Troy,
but led my own command.

                                I acted: I
hit him with a spearcast from a roadside   315
as he came down from the open country. Murky
night shrouded all heaven and the stars.
I made that ambush with one man at arms.
We were unseen. I took his life in secret,
finished him off with my sharp sword. That night   320
I found asylum on a ship off shore
skippered by gentlemen of Phoinikia;[1] I gave
all they could wish, out of my store of plunder,
for passage, and for landing me at Pylos
or Elis Town, where the Epeioi[2] are in power.   325
Contrary winds carried them willy-nilly
past that coast; they had no wish to cheat me,
but we were blown off course.

---

1. Phoenicia.   2. The people of Elis Town, in the western Peloponnese.

                                    Here, then, by night
we came, and made this haven by hard rowing.
All famished, but too tired to think of food,   330
each man dropped in his tracks after the landing,
and I slept hard, being wearied out. Before
I woke today, they put my things ashore
on the sand here beside me where I lay,
then reimbarked for Sidon, that great city.   335
Now they are far at sea, while I am left
forsaken here."

                    At this the grey-eyed goddess
Athena smiled, and gave him a caress,
her looks being changed now, so she seemed a woman,
tall and beautiful and no doubt skilled   340
at weaving splendid things. She answered briskly:

"Whoever gets around you must be sharp
and guileful as a snake; even a god
might bow to you in ways of dissimulation.
You! You chameleon!   345
Bottomless bag of tricks! Here in your own country
would you not give your stratagems a rest
or stop spellbinding for an instant?

You play a part as if it were your own tough skin.

No more of this, though. Two of a kind, we are,   350
contrivers, both. Of all men now alive
you are the best in plots and story telling.
My own fame is for wisdom among the gods—
deceptions, too.
                    Would even you have guessed
that I am Pallas Athena, daughter of Zeus,   355
I that am always with you in times of trial,
a shield to you in battle, I who made
the Phaiákians befriend you, to a man?
Now I am here again to counsel with you—
but first to put away those gifts the Phaiákians   360
gave you at departure—I planned it so.
Then I can tell you of the gall and wormwood
it is your lot to drink in your own hall.
Patience, iron patience, you must show;
so give it out to neither man nor woman   365
that you are back from wandering. Be silent
under all injuries, even blows from men."

His mind ranging far, Odysseus answered:

"Can mortal man be sure of you on sight,
even a sage, O mistress of disguises?   370
Once you were fond of me—I am sure of that—
years ago, when we Akhaians made
war, in our generation, upon Troy.
But after we had sacked the shrines of Priam

and put to sea, God scattered the Akhaians;   375
I never saw you after that, never
knew you aboard with me, to act as shield
in grievous times—not till you gave me comfort
in the rich hinterland of the Phaiákians
and were yourself my guide into that city.   380

Hear me now in your father's name, for I
cannot believe that I have come to Ithaka.
It is some other land. You made that speech
only to mock me, and to take me in.
Have I come back in truth to my home island?"   385

To this the grey-eyed goddess Athena answered:

"Always the same detachment! That is why
I cannot fail you, in your evil fortune,
coolheaded, quick, well-spoken as you are!
Would not another wandering man, in joy,   390
make haste home to his wife and children? Not
you, not yet. Before you hear their story
you will have proof about your wife.
                              I tell you,
she still sits where you left her, and her days
and nights go by forlorn, in lonely weeping.   395
For my part, never had I despaired; I felt
sure of your coming home, though all your men
should perish; but I never cared to fight
Poseidon, Father's brother, in his baleful
rage with you for taking his son's eye.   400

Now I shall make you see the shape of Ithaka.
Here is the cove the sea lord Phorkys owns,
there is the olive spreading out her leaves
over the inner bay, and there the cavern
dusky and lovely, hallowed by the feet   405
of those immortal girls, the Naiadês—
the same wide cave under whose vault you came
to honor them with hekatombs—and there
Mount Neion, with his forest on his back!"

She had dispelled the mist, so all the island   410
stood out clearly. Then indeed Odysseus'
heart stirred with joy. He kissed the earth,
and lifting up his hands prayed to the nymphs:

"O slim shy Naiadês, young maids of Zeus,
I had not thought to see you ever again!
                              O listen smiling   415
to my gentle prayers, and we'll make offering
plentiful as in the old time, granted I
live, granted my son grows tall, by favor
of great Athena, Zeus's daughter,
who gives the winning fighter his reward!"   420

The grey-eyed goddess said directly:

"Courage;
and let the future trouble you no more.
We go to make a cache now, in the cave,
to keep your treasure hid. Then we'll consider
how best the present action may unfold."   425

The goddess turned and entered the dim cave,
exploring it for crannies, while Odysseus
carried up all the gold, the fire-hard bronze,
and well-made clothing the Phaiákians gave him.
Pallas Athena, daughter of Zeus the storm king,   430
placed them, and shut the cave mouth with a stone,
and under the old grey olive tree those two
sat down to work the suitors death and woe.
Grey-eyed Athena was the first to speak, saying:

"Son of Laërtês and the gods of old,   435
Odysseus, master of land ways and sea ways,
put your mind on a way to reach and strike
a crowd of brazen upstarts.
                    Three long years
they have played master in your house: three years
trying to win your lovely lady, making   440
gifts as though betrothed. And she? Forever
grieving for you, missing your return,
she has allowed them all to hope, and sent
messengers with promises to each—
though her true thoughts are fixed elsewhere."

                                    At this   445
the man of ranging mind, Odysseus, cried:

"So hard beset! An end like Agamémnon's
might very likely have been mine, a bad end,
bleeding to death in my own hall. You forestalled it,
goddess, by telling me how the land lies.   450
Weave me a way to pay them back! And you, too,
take your place with me, breathe valor in me
the way you did that night when we Akhaians
unbound the bright veil from the brow of Troy!
O grey-eyed one, fire my heart and brace me!   455
I'll take on fighting men three hundred strong
if you fight at my back, immortal lady!"

The grey-eyed goddess Athena answered him:

"No fear but I shall be there; you'll go forward
under my arm when the crux comes at last.   460
And I foresee your vast floor stained with blood,
spattered with brains of this or that tall suitor
who fed upon your cattle.
                    Now, for a while,
I shall transform you; not a soul will know you,
the clear skin of your arms and legs shriveled,   465
your chestnut hair all gone, your body dressed

in sacking that a man would gag to see,
and the two eyes, that were so brilliant, dirtied—
contemptible, you shall seem to your enemies,
as to the wife and son you left behind.   470

But join the swineherd first—the overseer
of all your swine, a good soul now as ever,
devoted to Penélopê and your son.
He will be found near Raven's Rock and the well
of Arethousa, where the swine are pastured,   475
rooting for acorns to their hearts' content,
drinking the dark still water. Boarflesh grows
pink and fat on that fresh diet. There
stay with him and question him, while I
am off to the great beauty's land of Sparta,   480
to call your son Telémakhos home again—
for you should know, he went to the wide land
of Lakedaimon, Meneláos' country,
to learn if there were news of you abroad."

Odysseus answered:

                    "Why not tell him, knowing   485
my whole history, as you do? Must he
traverse the barren sea, he too, and live
in pain, while others feed on what is his?"

At this the grey-eyed goddess Athena said:

"No need for anguish on that lad's account.   490
I sent him off myself, to make his name
in foreign parts—no hardship in the bargain,
taking his ease in Meneláos' mansion,
lapped in gold.
                    The young bucks here, I know,
lie in wait for him in a cutter, bent   495
on murdering him before he reaches home.
I rather doubt they will. Cold earth instead
will take in her embrace a man or two
of those who fed so long on what is his."

Speaking no more, she touched him with her wand,   500
shriveled the clear skin of his arms and legs,
made all his hair fall out, cast over him
the wrinkled hide of an old man, and bleared
both his eyes, that were so bright. Then she
clapped an old tunic, a foul cloak, upon him,   505
tattered, filthy, stained by greasy smoke,
and over that a mangy big buck skin.
A staff she gave him, and a leaky knapsack
with no strap but a loop of string.
                    Now then,
their colloquy at an end, they went their ways—   510
Athena toward illustrious Lakedaimon
far over sea, to join Odysseus' son.

BOOK XIV

[*Hospitality in the Forest*]

He went up from the cove through wooded ground,
taking a stony trail into the high hills, where
the swineherd lived, according to Athena.
Of all Odysseus' field hands in the old days
this forester cared most for the estate;   5
and now Odysseus found him
in a remote clearing, sitting inside the gate
of a stockade he built to keep the swine
while his great lord was gone.
                                              Working alone,
far from Penélopê and old Laërtês,   10
he had put up a fieldstone hut and timbered it
with wild pear wood. Dark hearts of oak he split
and trimmed for a high palisade around it,
and built twelve sties adjoining in this yard
to hold the livestock. Fifty sows with farrows   15
were penned in each, bedded upon the earth,
while the boars lay outside—fewer by far,
as those well-fatted were for the suitors' table,
fine pork, sent by the swineherd every day.
Three hundred sixty now lay there at night,   20
guarded by dogs—four dogs like wolves, one each
for the four lads the swineherd reared and kept
as under-herdsmen.
                                When Odysseus came,
the good servant sat shaping to his feet
oxhide for sandals, cutting the well-cured leather.   25
Three of his young men were afield, pasturing
herds in other woods; one he had sent
with a fat boar for tribute into town,
the boy to serve while the suitors got their fill.

The watch dogs, when they caught sight of Odysseus,   30
faced him, a snarling troop, and pelted out
viciously after him. Like a tricky beggar
he sat down plump, and dropped his stick. No use.
They would have rolled him in the dust and torn him
there by his own steading if the swineherd   35
had not sprung up and flung his leather down,
making a beeline for the open. Shouting,
throwing stone after stone,
he made them scatter; then turned to his lord
and said:

                "You might have got a ripping, man!   40
Two shakes more and a pretty mess for me
you could have called it, if you had the breath.
As though I had not trouble enough already,
given me by the gods, my master gone,
true king that he was. I hang on here,   45
still mourning for him, raising pigs of his

to feed foreigners, and who knows where the man is,
in some far country among strangers! Aye—
if he is living still, if he still sees the light of day.

Come to the cabin. You're a wanderer too.   50
You must eat something, drink some wine, and tell me
where you are from and the hard times you've seen."

The forester now led him to his hut
and made a couch for him, with tips of fir
piled for a mattress under a wild goat skin,   55
shaggy and thick, his own bed covering.
                                               Odysseus,
in pleasure at this courtesy, gently said:

"May Zeus and all the gods give you your heart's desire
for taking me in so kindly, friend."

                                  Eumaios—
O my swineherd![3]—answered him:

                                      "Tush, friend,   60
rudeness to a stranger is not decency,
poor though he may be, poorer than you.
                                      All wanderers
and beggars come from Zeus. What we can give
is slight but well-meant—all we dare. You know
that is the way of slaves, who live in dread   65
of masters—new ones like our own.
                                      I told you
the gods, long ago, hindered our lord's return.
He had a fondness for me, would have pensioned me
with acres of my own, a house, a wife
that other men admired and courted; all   70
gifts good-hearted kings bestow for service,
for a life work the bounty of god has prospered—
for it does prosper here, this work I do.
Had he grown old in his own house, my master
would have rewarded me. But the man's gone.   75
God curse the race of Helen and cut it down,
that wrung the strength out of the knees of many!
And he went, too—for the honor of Agamémnon
he took ship overseas for the wild horse country
of Troy, to fight the Trojans."

                            This being told,   80
he tucked his long shirt up inside his belt
and strode into the pens for two young porkers.
He slaughtered them and singed them at the fire,
flayed and quartered them, and skewered the meat
to broil it all; then gave it to Odysseus   85

---

3. This direct address by the poet to one of his characters is confined to Eumaios; it occurs frequently
in connection with his name in Books XIV–XVII. A medieval commentator suggested that it showed a
special affection for Eumaios on Homer's part, but because in the *Iliad* a similar form of address is used
for five different characters (among them the god Apollo and the obscure Melanippos) this seems
unlikely. In the case of Eumaios it may have been a formula devised to avoid hiatus (clashing vowels).

hot on the spits. He shook out barley meal,
took a winebowl of ivy wood and filled it,
and sat down facing him, with a gesture, saying:

"There is your dinner, friend, the pork of slaves.
Our fat shoats are all eaten by the suitors,   90
cold-hearted men, who never spare a thought
for how they stand in the sight of Zeus. The gods
living in bliss are fond of no wrongdoing,
but honor discipline and right behavior.
Even the outcasts of the earth, who bring   95
piracy from the sea, and bear off plunder
given by Zeus in shiploads—even those men
deep in their hearts tremble for heaven's eye.
But the suitors, now, have heard some word, some oracle
of my lord's death, being so unconcerned   100
to pay court properly or to go about their business.
All they want is to prey on his estate,
proud dogs: they stop at nothing. Not a day
goes by, and not a night comes under Zeus,
but they make butchery of our beeves and swine—   105
not one or two beasts at a time, either.
As for swilling down wine, they drink us dry.
Only a great domain like his could stand it—
greater than any on the dusky mainland
or here in Ithaka. Not twenty heroes   110
in the whole world were as rich as he. I know:
I could count it all up: twelve herds in Elis,
as many flocks, as many herds of swine,
and twelve wide ranging herds of goats, as well,
attended by his own men or by others—   115
out at the end of the island, eleven herds
are scattered now, with good men looking after them,
and every herdsman, every day, picks out
a prize ram to hand over to those fellows.
I too as overseer, keeper of swine,   120
must go through all my boars and send the best."

While he ran on, Odysseus with zeal
applied himself to the meat and wine, but inwardly
his thought shaped woe and ruin for the suitors.
When he had eaten all that he desired   125
and the cup he drank from had been filled again
with wine—a welcome sight—,
he spoke, and the words came light upon the air:

"Who is this lord who once acquired you,
so rich, so powerful, as you describe him?   130
You think he died for Agamémnon's honor.
Tell me his name: I may have met someone
of that description in my time. Who knows?
Perhaps only the immortal gods could say
if I should claim to have seen him: I have roamed   135
about the world so long."

The swineherd answered
as one who held a place of trust:

"Well, man,
his lady and his son will put no stock
in any news of him brought by a rover.
Wandering men tell lies for a night's lodging,   140
for fresh clothing; truth doesn't interest them.
Every time some traveller comes ashore
he has to tell my mistress his pretty tale,
and she receives him kindly, questions him,
remembering her prince, while the tears run   145
down her cheeks—and that is as it should be
when a woman's husband has been lost abroad.
I suppose you, too, can work your story up
at a moment's notice, given a shirt or cloak.
No: long ago wild dogs and carrion   150
birds, most like, laid bare his ribs on land
where life had left him. Or it may be, quick fishes
picked him clean in the deep sea, and his bones
lie mounded over in sand upon some shore.
One way or another, far from home he died,   155
a bitter loss, and pain, for everyone,
certainly for me. Never again shall I
have for my lot a master mild as he was
anywhere—not even with my parents
at home, where I was born and bred. I miss them   160
less than I do him—though a longing comes
to set my eyes on them in the old country.
No, it is the lost man I ache to think of—
Odysseus. And I speak the name respectfully,
even if he is not here. He loved me, cared for me.   165
I call him dear my lord, far though he be."

Now royal Odysseus, who had borne the long war,
spoke again:

"Friend, as you are so dead sure
he will not come—and so mistrustful, too—
let me not merely talk, as others talk,   170
but swear to it: your lord is now at hand.
And I expect a gift for this good news
when he enters his own hall. Till then I would not
take a rag, no matter what my need.
I hate as I hate Hell's own gate that weakness   175
that makes a poor man into a flatterer.
Zeus be my witness, and the table garnished
for true friends, and Odysseus' own hearth—
by heaven, all I say will come to pass!
He will return, and he will be avenged   180
on any who dishonor his wife and son."

Eumaios—O my swineherd!—answered him:

"I take you at your word, then: you shall have
no good news gift from me. Nor will Odysseus

enter his hall. But peace! drink up your wine. 185
Let us talk now of other things. No more
imaginings. It makes me heavy-hearted
when someone brings my master back to mind—
my own true master.
               No, by heaven,
let us have no oaths! But if Odysseus 190
can come again god send he may! My wish
is that of Penélopê and old Laërtês
and Prince Telémakhos.
                Ah, he's another
to be distressed about—Odysseus' child,
Telémakhos! By the gods' grace he grew 195
like a tough sapling, and I thought he'd be
no less a man than his great father—strong
and admirably made; but then someone,
god or man, upset him, made him rash,
so that he sailed away to sandy Pylos 200
to hear news of his father. Now the suitors
lie in ambush on his homeward track,
ready to cut away the last shoot of Arkêsios'
line, the royal stock of Ithaka.
              No good
dwelling on it. Either he'll be caught 205
or else Kroníon's[4] hand will take him through.

Tell me, now, of your own trials and troubles.
And tell me truly first, for I should know,
who are you, where do you hail from, where's your home
and family? What kind of ship was yours, 210
and what course brought you here? Who are your sailors?
I don't suppose you walked here on the sea."

To this the master of improvisation answered:

"I'll tell you all that, clearly as I may.
If we could sit here long enough, with meat 215
and good sweet wine, warm here, in peace and quiet
within doors, while the work of the world goes on—
I might take all this year to tell my story
and never end the tale of misadventures
that wore my heart out, by the gods' will. 220

My native land is the wide seaboard of Krete
where I grew up. I had a wealthy father,
and many other sons were born to him
of his true lady. My mother was a slave,
his concubine; but Kastor Hylákidês, 225
my father, treated me as a true born son.
High honor came to him in that part of Krete
for wealth and ease, and sons born for renown,
before the death-bearing Kêrês drew him down
to the underworld. His avid sons thereafter 230

4. Zeus, son of Kronos.

dividing up the property by lot
gave me a wretched portion, a poor house.
But my ability won me a wife
of rich family. Fool I was never called,
nor turn-tail in a fight.

        My strength's all gone,   235
but from the husk you may divine the ear
that stood tall in the old days. Misery owns me
now, but then great Arês and Athena
gave me valor and man-breaking power,
whenever I made choice of men-at-arms   240
to set a trap with me for my enemies.
Never, as I am a man, did I fear Death
ahead, but went in foremost in the charge,
putting a spear through any man whose legs
were not as fast as mine. That was my element,   245
war and battle. Farming I never cared for,
nor life at home, nor fathering fair children.
I reveled in long ships with oars; I loved
polished lances, arrows in the skirmish,
the shapes of doom that others shake to see.   250
Carnage suited me; heaven put those things
in me somehow. Each to his own pleasure!
Before we young Akhaians shipped for Troy
I led men on nine cruises in corsairs
to raid strange coasts, and had great luck, taking   255
rich spoils on the spot, and even more
in the division. So my house grew prosperous,
my standing therefore high among the Kretans.
Then came the day when Zeus who views the wide world
drew men's eyes upon that way accurst   260
that wrung the manhood from the knees of many!
Everyone pressed me, pressed King Idómeneus
to take command of ships for Ilion.
No way out; the country rang with talk of it.
So we Akhaians had nine years of war.   265
In the tenth year we sacked the inner city,
Priam's town, and sailed for home; but heaven
dispersed the Akhaians. Evil days for me
were stored up in the hidden mind of Zeus.
One month, no more, I stayed at home in joy   270
with children, wife, and treasure. Lust for action
drove me to go to sea then, in command
of ships and gallant seamen bound for Egypt.
Nine ships I fitted out; my men signed on
and came to feast with me, as good shipmates,   275
for six full days. Many a beast I slaughtered
in the gods' honor, for my friends to eat.
Embarking on the seventh, we hauled sail
and filled away from Krete on a fresh north wind
effortlessly, as boats will glide down stream.   280
All rigging whole and all hands well, we rested,
letting the wind and steersmen work the ships,

for five days; on the fifth we made the delta.[5]
I brought my squadron in to the river bank
with one turn of the sweeps. There, heaven knows,   285
I told the men to wait and guard the ships
while I sent out patrols to rising ground.
But reckless greed carried them all away
to plunder the rich bottomlands; they bore off
wives and children, killed what men they found.   290

When this news reached the city, all who heard it
came at dawn. On foot they came, and horsemen,
filling the river plain with dazzle of bronze;
and Zeus lord of lightning
threw my men into blind panic: no one dared   295
stand against that host closing around us.
Their scything weapons left our dead in piles,
but some they took alive, into forced labor.
And I—ah, how I wish that I had died
in Egypt, on that field! So many blows   300
awaited me!— Well, Zeus himself inspired me;
I wrenched my dogskin helmet off my head,
dropped my spear, dodged out of my long shield,
ran for the king's chariot and swung on
to embrace and kiss his knees. He pulled me up,   305
took pity on me, placed me on the footboards,
and drove home with me crouching there in tears.
Aye—for the troops, in battle fury still,
made one pass at me after another, pricking me
with spears, hoping to kill me. But he saved me,   310
for fear of the great wrath of Zeus that comes
when men who ask asylum are given death.

Seven years, then, my sojourn lasted there,
and I amassed a fortune, going about
among the openhanded Egyptians.   315
But when the eighth came round, a certain
Phoinikian adventurer came too,
a plausible rat, who had already done
plenty of devilry in the world.

                    This fellow
took me in completely with his schemes,   320
and led me with him to Phoinikia,
where he had land and houses. One full year
I stayed there with him, to the month and day,
and when fair weather came around again
he took me in a deepsea ship for Libya,   325
pretending I could help in the cargo trade;
he meant, in fact, to trade me off, and get
a high price for me. I could guess the game
but had to follow him aboard. One day
on course due west, off central Krete, the ship   330
caught a fresh norther, and we ran southward

5. Of the Nile.

before the wind while Zeus piled ruin ahead.
When Krete was out of sight astern, no land
anywhere to be seen, but sky and ocean,
Kroníon put a dark cloud in the zenith   335
over the ship, and gloom spread on the sea.
With crack on crack of thunder, he let fly
a bolt against the ship, a direct hit,
so that she bucked, in sacred fumes of sulphur,
and all the men were flung into the water.   340
They came up round the wreck, bobbing a while
like petrels on the waves. No homecoming
for these, from whom the god had turned his face!
Stunned in the smother as I was, yet Zeus
put into my hands the great mast of the ship—   345
a way to keep from drowning. So I twined
my arms and legs around it in the gale
and stayed afloat nine days. On the tenth night,
a big surf cast me up in Thesprotia.[6]
Pheidon the king there gave me refuge, nobly,   350
with no talk of reward. His son discovered me
exhausted and half dead with cold, and gave me
a hand to bear me up till he reached home
where he could clothe me in a shirt and cloak.
In that king's house I heard news of Odysseus,   355
who lately was a guest there, passing by
on his way home, the king said; and he showed me
the treasure that Odysseus had brought:
bronze, gold, and iron wrought with heavy labor—
in that great room I saw enough to last   360
Odysseus' heirs for ten long generations.
The man himself had gone up to Dodona[7]
to ask the spelling leaves of the old oak
the will of God: how to return, that is,
to the rich realm of Ithaka, after so long   365
an absence—openly, or on the quiet.
And, tipping wine out, Pheidon swore to me
the ship was launched, the seamen standing by
to take Odysseus to his land at last.
But he had passage first for me: Thesprotians   370
were sailing, as luck had it, for Doulíkhion,[8]
the grain-growing island; there, he said,
they were to bring me to the king, Akastos.
Instead, that company saw fit to plot
foul play against me; in my wretched life   375
there was to be more suffering.
                              At sea, then,
when land lay far astern, they sprang their trap.
They'd make a slave of me that day, stripping
cloak and tunic off me, throwing around me
the dirty rags you see before you now.   380

6. On the west coast of the Greek mainland, north of Ithaka.   7. An oracle of Zeus. The message of
the god was supposed to come from the sacred oak, perhaps from the rushing of the leaves in the
wind.   8. An island off the west coast of Greece.

At evening, off the fields of Ithaka,
they bound me, lashed me down under the decking
with stout ship's rope, while they all went ashore
in haste to make their supper on the beach.
The gods helped me to pry the lashing loose   385
until it fell away. I wound my rags
in a bundle round my head and eased myself
down the smooth lading plank into the water,
up to the chin, then swam an easy breast stroke
out and around, putting that crew behind,   390
and went ashore in underbrush, a thicket,
where I lay still, making myself small.
They raised a bitter yelling, and passed by
several times. When further groping seemed
useless to them, back to the ship they went   395
and out to sea again. The gods were with me,
keeping me hid; and with me when they brought me
here to the door of one who knows the world.
My destiny is yet to live awhile."

The swineherd bowed and said:

                    "Ah well, poor drifter,   400
you've made me sad for you, going back over it,
all your hard life and wandering. That tale
about Odysseus, though, you might have spared me;
you will not make me believe that.
Why must you lie, being the man you are,   405
and all for nothing?
                    I can see so well
what happened to my master, sailing home!
Surely the gods turned on him, to refuse him
death in the field, or in his friends' arms
after he wound up the great war at Troy.   410
They would have made a tomb for him, the Akhaians,
and paid all honor to his son thereafter. No,
stormwinds made off with him. No glory came to him.

I moved here to the mountain with my swine.
Never, now, do I go down to town   415
unless I am sent for by Penélopê
when news of some sort comes. But those who sit
around her go on asking the old questions—
a few who miss their master still,
and those who eat his house up, and go free.   420
For my part, I have had no heart for inquiry
since one year an Aitolian[9] made a fool of me.
Exiled from land to land after some killing,
he turned up at my door; I took him in.
My master he had seen in Krete, he said,   425
lodged with Idómeneus, while the long ships,
leaky from gales, were laid up for repairs.
But they were all to sail, he said, that summer,

---

9. Aitolia is on the mainland, east of Ithaka.

or the first days of fall—hulls laden deep
with treasure, manned by crews of heroes.
                          This time   430
you are the derelict the Powers bring.
Well, give up trying to win me with false news
or flattery. If I receive and shelter you,
it is not for your tales but for your trouble,
and with an eye to Zeus, who guards a guest."   435

Then said that sly and guileful man, Odysseus:

"A black suspicious heart beats in you surely;
the man you are, not even an oath could change you.
Come then, we'll make a compact; let the gods
witness it from Olympos, where they dwell.   440
Upon your lord's homecoming, if he comes
here to this very hut, and soon—
then give me a new outfit, shirt and cloak,
and ship me to Doulíkhion—I thought it
a pleasant island. But if Odysseus   445
fails to appear as I predict, then Swish!
let the slaves pitch me down from some high rock,
so the next poor man who comes will watch his tongue."

The forester gave a snort and answered:
                              "Friend,
if I agreed to that, a great name   450
I should acquire in the world for goodness—
at one stroke and forever: your kind host
who gave you shelter and the hand of friendship,
only to take your life next day!
How confidently, after that, should I   455
address my prayers to Zeus, the son of Kronos!

It is time now for supper. My young herdsmen
should be arriving soon to set about it.
We'll make a quiet feast here at our hearth."

At this point in their talk the swine had come   460
up to the clearing, and the drovers followed
to pen them for the night—the porkers squealing
to high heaven, milling around the yard.
The swineherd then gave orders to his men:

"Bring in our best pig for a stranger's dinner.   465
A feast will do our hearts good, too; we know
grief and pain, hard scrabbling with our swine,
while the outsiders live on our labor."

                            Bronze
axe in hand, he turned to split up kindling,
while they drove in a tall boar, prime and fat,   470
planting him square before the fire. The gods,
as ever, had their due in the swineherd's thought,
for he it was who tossed the forehead bristles
as a first offering on the flames, calling

upon the immortal gods to let Odysseus   475
reach his home once more.
                            Then he stood up
and brained the boar with split oak from the woodpile.
Life ebbed from the beast; they slaughtered him,
singed the carcass, and cut out the joints.
Eumaios, taking flesh from every quarter,   480
put lean strips on the fat of sacrifice,
floured each one with barley meal, and cast it
into the blaze. The rest they sliced and skewered,
roasted with care, then took it off the fire
and heaped it up on platters. Now their chief,   485
who knew best the amenities, rose to serve,
dividing all that meat in seven portions—
one to be set aside, with proper prayers,
for the wood nymphs and Hermês, Maia's son;
the others for the company. Odysseus   490
he honored with long slices from the chine—
warming the master's heart. Odysseus looked at him
and said:

              "May you be dear to Zeus
as you are dear to me for this, Eumaios,
favoring with choice cuts a man like me."   495

And—O my swineherd!—you replied, Eumaios:

"Bless you, stranger, fall to and enjoy it
for what it is. Zeus grants us this or that,
or else refrains from granting, as he wills;
all things are in his power."

                            He cut and burnt   500
a morsel for the gods who are young forever,
tipped out some wine, then put it in the hands
of Odysseus, the old soldier, raider of cities,
who sat at ease now with his meat before him.
As for the loaves, Mesaúlios dealt them out,   505
a yard boy, bought by the swineherd on his own,
unaided by his mistress or Laërtês,
from Taphians, while Odysseus was away.
Now all hands reached for that array of supper,
until, when hunger and thirst were turned away   510
Mesaúlios removed the bread and, heavy
with food and drink, they settled back to rest.

Now night had come on, rough, with no moon,
but a nightlong downpour setting in, the rainwind
blowing hard from the west. Odysseus   515
began to talk, to test the swineherd, trying
to put it in his head to take his cloak off
and lend it, or else urge the others to.
He knew the man's compassion.
                            "Listen," he said,
"Eumaios, and you others, here's a wishful   520
tale that I shall tell. The wine's behind it,

vaporing wine, that makes a serious man
break down and sing, kick up his heels and clown,
or tell some story that were best untold.
But now I'm launched, I can't stop now.
                      Would god I felt   525
the hot blood in me that I had at Troy!
Laying an ambush near the walls one time,
Odysseus and Meneláos were commanders
and I ranked third. I went at their request.
We worked in toward the bluffs and battlements   530
and, circling the town, got into canebreaks,
thick and high, a marsh where we took cover,
hunched under arms.
               The northwind dropped, and night
came black and wintry. A fine sleet descending
whitened the cane like hoarfrost, and clear ice   535
grew dense upon our shields. The other men,
all wrapt in blanket cloaks as well as tunics,
rested well, in shields up to their shoulder,
but I had left my cloak with friends in camp,
foolhardy as I was. No chance of freezing hard,   540
I thought, so I wore kilts and a shield only.
But in the small hours of the third watch, when stars
that rise at evening go down to their setting,
I nudged Odysseus, who lay close beside me;
he was alert then, listening, and I said: 545

'Son of Laërtês and the gods of old,
Odysseus, master mariner and soldier,
I cannot hold on long among the living.
The cold is making a corpse of me. Some god
inveigled me to come without a cloak.   550
No help for it now; too late.'
               Next thing I knew
he had a scheme all ready in his mind—
and what a man he was for schemes and battles!
Speaking under his breath to me, he murmured:

'Quiet; none of the rest should hear you.'
                    Then,   555
propping his head on his forearm, he said:

'Listen, lads, I had an ominous dream,
the point being how far forward from our ships
and lines we've come. Someone should volunteer
to tell the corps commander, Agamémnon;   560
he may reinforce us from the base.'
               At this,
Thoas jumped up, the young son of Andraimon,
put down his crimson cloak and headed off,
running shoreward.
             Wrapped in that man's cloak
how gratefully I lay in the bitter dark   565

until the dawn came stitched in gold! I wish
I had that sap and fiber in me now!"

Then—O my swineherd!—you replied, Eumaios:

"That was a fine story, and well told,
not a word out of place, not a pointless word.   570
No, you'll not sleep cold for lack of cover,
or any other comfort one should give
to a needy guest. However, in the morning,
you must go flapping in the same old clothes.
Shirts and cloaks are few here; every man   575
has one change only. When our prince arrives,
the son of Odysseus, he will make you gifts—
cloak, tunic, everything—and grant you passage
wherever you care to go."

                                On this he rose
and placed the bed of balsam near the fire,   580
strewing sheepskins on top, and skins of goats.
Odysseus lay down. His host threw over him
a heavy blanket cloak, his own reserve
against the winter wind when it came wild.
So there Odysseus dropped off to sleep,   585
while herdsmen slept nearby. But not the swineherd:
not in the hut could he lie down in peace,
but now equipped himself for the night outside;
and this rejoiced Odysseus' heart, to see him
care for the herd so, while his lord was gone.   590
He hung a sharp sword from his shoulder, gathered
a great cloak round him, close, to break the wind,
and pulled a shaggy goatskin on his head.
Then, to keep at a distance dogs or men,
he took a sharpened lance, and went to rest   595
under a hollow rock where swine were sleeping
out of the wind and rain.

                        BOOK XV

                [How They Came to Ithaka]

                        South into Lakedaimon
into the land where greens are wide for dancing
Athena went, to put in mind of home
her great-hearted hero's honored son,
rousing him to return.
                        And there she found him   5
with Nestor's lad in the late night at rest
under the portico of Meneláos,
the famous king. Stilled by the power of slumber
the son of Nestor lay, but honeyed sleep
had not yet taken in her arms Telémakhos.   10
All through the starlit night, with open eyes,
he pondered what he had heard about his father,
until at his bedside grey-eyed Athena
towered and said:

"The brave thing now, Telémakhos,
would be to end this journey far from home.   15
All that you own you left behind
with men so lost to honor in your house
they may devour it all, shared out among them.
How will your journey save you then?
        Go quickly
to the lord of the great war cry, Meneláos;   20
press him to send you back. You may yet find
the queen your mother in her rooms alone.
It seems her father and her kinsmen say
Eurýmakhos is the man for her to marry.
He has outdone the suitors, all the rest,   25
in gifts to her, and made his pledges double.
Check him, or he will have your lands and chattels[1]
in spite of you.
     You know a woman's pride
at bringing riches to the man she marries.
As to her girlhood husband, her first children,   30
he is forgotten, being dead—and they
no longer worry her.
      So act alone.
Go back; entrust your riches to the servant
worthiest in your eyes, until the gods
make known what beauty you yourself shall marry.   35

This too I have to tell you: now take heed:
the suitors' ringleaders are hot for murder,
waiting in the channel between Ithaka
and Samê's rocky side; they mean to kill you
before you can set foot ashore. I doubt   40
they'll bring it off. Dark earth instead
may take to her cold bed a few brave suitors
who preyed upon your cattle.
       Bear well out
in your good ship, to eastward of the islands,
and sail again by night. Someone immortal   45
who cares for you will make a fair wind blow.
Touch at the first beach, go ashore, and send
your ship and crew around to port by sea,
while you go inland to the forester,
your old friend, loyal keeper of the swine.   50
Remain that night with him; send him to town
to tell your watchful mother Penélopê
that you are back from Pylos safe and sound."

With this Athena left him for Olympos.
He swung his foot across and gave a kick   55
and said to the son of Nestor:

---

1. The Greek could also mean "be careful she [Penélopê] doesn't carry off, against your will, some of
your property," i.e., for her new husband. This would explain why Athena tells Telémakhos (lines 33–
34) to turn the property over to the servant he has most confidence in. The suggestion that Penélopê is
planning to marry Eurýmakhos and take Telémakhos' property with her is not to be taken seriously;
Athena uses it to get Telémakhos moving.

"Open your eyes,
Peisístratos. Get our team into harness.
We have a long day's journey."

                   Nestor's son
turned over and answered him:

                      "It is still night,
and no moon. Can we drive now? We can not,   60
itch as we may for the road home. Dawn is near.
Allow the captain of spearmen, Meneláos,
time to pack our car with gifts and time
to speak a gracious word, sending us off.
A guest remembers all his days   65
that host who makes provision for him kindly."

The Dawn soon took her throne of gold, and Lord
Meneláos, clarion in battle,
rose from where he lay beside the beauty
of Helen with her shining hair. He strode   70
into the hall nearby.
             Hearing him come,
Odysseus' son pulled on his snowy tunic
over the skin, gathered his long cape
about his breadth of shoulder like a captain,
the heir of King Odysseus. At the door   75
he stood and said:

             "Lord Marshal, Meneláos,
send me home now to my own dear country:
longing has come upon me to go home."

The lord of the great war cry said at once:

"If you are longing to go home, Telémakhos,   80
I would not keep you for the world, not I.
I'd think myself or any other host
as ill-mannered for over-friendliness
as for hostility.
          Measure is best in everything.
To send a guest packing, or cling to him   85
when he's in haste—one sin equals the other.
'Good entertaining ends with no detaining.'
Only let me load your car with gifts
and fine ones, you shall see.
              I'll bid the women
set out breakfast from the larder stores;   90
honor and appetite—we'll attend to both
before a long day's journey overland.
Or would you care to try the Argive midlands
and Hellas, in my company? I'll harness
my own team, and take you through the towns.   95
Guests like ourselves no lord will turn away;
each one will make one gift, at least,
to carry home with us: tripod or cauldron
wrought in bronze, mule team, or golden cup."

Clearheaded Telémakhos replied:

"Lord Marshal   100
Meneláos, royal son of Atreus,
I must return to my own hearth. I left
no one behind as guardian of my property.
This going abroad for news of a great father—
heaven forbid it be my own undoing,   105
or any precious thing be lost at home."

At this the tall king, clarion in battle,
called to his lady and her waiting women
to give them breakfast from the larder stores.
Eteóneus, the son of Boethoös, came   110
straight from bed, from where he lodged nearby,
and Meneláos ordered a fire lit
for broiling mutton. The king's man obeyed.
Then down to the cedar chamber Meneláos
walked with Helen and Prince Megapénthês.   115
Amid the gold he had in that place lying
the son of Atreus picked a wine cup, wrought
with handles left and right, and told his son
to take a silver winebowl.
                    Helen lingered
near the deep coffers filled with gowns, her own   120
handiwork.
                    Tall goddess among women,
she lifted out one robe of state so royal,
adorned and brilliant with embroidery,
deep in the chest it shimmered like a star.
Now all three turned back to the door to greet   125
Telémakhos. And red-haired Meneláos
cried out to him:

                    "O prince Telémakhos,
may Hêra's Lord of Thunder see you home
and bring you to the welcome you desire!
Here are your gifts—perfect and precious things   130
I wish to make your own, out of my treasure."

And gently the great captain, son of Atreus,
handed him the goblet. Megapénthês
carried the winebowl glinting silvery
to set before him, and the Lady Helen   135
drew near, so that he saw her cheek's pure line.
She held the gown and murmured:

                    "I, too,
bring you a gift, dear child, and here it is;
remember Helen's hands by this; keep it
for your own bride, your joyful wedding day;   140
let your dear mother guard it in her chamber.
My blessing: may you come soon to your island,
home to your timbered hall."

So she bestowed it,
and happily he took it. These fine things
Peisístratos packed well in the wicker carrier,   145
admiring every one. Then Meneláos
led the two guests in to take their seats
on thrones and easy chairs in the great hall.
Now came a maid to tip a golden jug
of water over a silver finger bowl,   150
and drew the polished tables up beside them;
the larder mistress brought her tray of loaves,
with many savories to lavish on them;
viands were served by Eteóneus, and wine
by Meneláos' son. Then every hand   155
reached out upon good meat and drink to take them,
driving away hunger and thirst. At last,
Telémakhos and Nestor's son led out
their team to harness, mounted their bright car,
and drove down under the echoing entrance way,   160
while red-haired Meneláos, Atreus' son,
walked alongside with a golden cup—
wine for the wayfarers to spill at parting.
Then by the tugging team he stood, and spoke
over the horses' heads:

"Farewell, my lads.   165
Homage to Nestor, the benevolent king;
in my time he was fatherly to me,
when the flower of Akhaia warred on Troy."

Telémakhos made this reply:

"No fear
but we shall bear at least as far as Nestor   170
your messages, great king. How I could wish
to bring them home to Ithaka! If only
Odysseus were there, if he could hear me tell
of all the courtesy I have had from you,
returning with your finery and your treasure."   175

Even as he spoke, a beat of wings went skyward
off to the right—a mountain eagle, grappling
a white goose in his talons, heavy prey
hooked from a farmyard. Women and men-at-arms
made hubbub, running up, as he flew over,   180
but then he wheeled hard right before the horses—
a sight that made the whole crowd cheer, with hearts
lifting in joy. Peisístratos called out:

"Read us the sign, O Meneláos, Lord
Marshal of armies! Was the god revealing   185
something thus to you, or to ourselves?"

At this the old friend of the god of battle
groped in his mind for the right thing to say,
but regal Helen put in quickly:

"Listen:
I can tell you—tell what the omen means,   190
as light is given me, and as I see it
point by point fulfilled. The beaked eagle
flew from the wild mountain of his fathers
to take for prey the tame house bird. Just so,
Odysseus, back from his hard trials and wandering,   195
will soon come down in fury on his house.
He may be there today, and a black hour
he brings upon the suitors."

                    Telémakhos
gazed and said:

            "May Zeus, the lord of Hêra,
make it so! In far-off Ithaka, all my life,   200
I shall invoke you as a goddess, lady."

He let the whip fall, and the restive mares
broke forward at a canter through the town
into the open country.
                    All that day
they kept their harness shaking, side by side,   205
until at sundown when the roads grew dim
they made a halt at Pherai. There Dióklês
son of Ortílokhos whom Alpheios fathered,
welcomed the young men, and they slept the night.
Up when the young Dawn's finger tips of rose   210
opened in the east, they hitched the team
once more to the painted car
and steered out westward through the echoing gate,
whipping their fresh horses into a run.
Approaching Pylos Height at that day's end,   215
Telémakhos appealed to the son of Nestor:

"Could you, I wonder, do a thing I'll tell you,
supposing you agree?
We take ourselves to be true friends—in age
alike, and bound by ties between our fathers,   220
and now by partnership in this adventure.
Prince, do not take me roundabout,
but leave me at the ship, else the old king
your father will detain me overnight
for love of guests, when I should be at sea."   225

The son of Nestor nodded, thinking swiftly
how best he could oblige his friend.
Here was his choice: to pull the team hard over
along the beach till he could rein them in
beside the ship. Unloading Meneláos'   230
royal keepsakes into the stern sheets,
he sang out:

            "Now for action! Get aboard,
and call your men, before I break the news
at home in hall to father. Who knows better

the old man's heart than I? If you delay,   235
he will not let you go, but he'll descend on you
 in person and imperious; no turning
back with empty hands for him, believe me,
once his blood is up."

                         He shook the reins
to the lovely mares with long manes in the wind,   240
guiding them full tilt toward his father's hall.
Telémakhos called in the crew, and told them:

"Get everything shipshape aboard this craft;
we pull out now, and put sea miles behind us."

The listening men obeyed him, climbing in   245
to settle on their benches by the rowlocks,
while he stood watchful by the stern. He poured out
offerings there, and prayers to Athena.

Now a strange man came up to him, an easterner
fresh from spilling blood in distant Argos,   250
a hunted man. Gifted in prophecy,
he had as forebear that Melampous, wizard
who lived of old in Pylos, mother city
of western flocks.[2]
                     Melampous, a rich lord,
had owned a house unmatched among the Pylians,   255
until the day came when king Neleus, noblest
in that age, drove him from his native land.
And Neleus for a year's term sequestered
Melampous' fields and flocks, while he lay bound
hand and foot in the keep of Phylakos.   260
Beauty of Neleus' daughter put him there
and sombre folly the inbreaking Fury
thrust upon him. But he gave the slip
to death, and drove the bellowing herd of Iphiklos
from Phylakê to Pylos, there to claim   265
the bride that ordeal won him from the king.
He led her to his brother's house, and went on
eastward into another land, the bluegrass
plain of Argos. Destiny held for him
rule over many Argives. Here he married,   270
built a great manor house, fathered Antíphatês
and Mantios, commanders both, of whom
Antíphatês begot Oikleiês

2. The complicated story that follows (obscure in some of its details) gives us the genealogical background of the young man who comes up to Telémakhos. His name, as we learn only at the end of the
genealogy, is Theoklýmenos, and he has an important role to play in the last part of the *Odyssey*. His
gift for prophecy is hereditary; his ancestor Melampous had it. Melampous' brother (who lived in Pylos
under King Neleus, Nestor's father) asked for the hand of Neleus' daughter. Neleus demanded as bride-
price the herds of cattle of a neighboring lord, Phylakos. Melampous tried to steal the cattle for his
brother, was caught, and was imprisoned. In prison he heard the worms in the roof beams announce
that the wood was almost eaten through, and he predicted the collapse of the roof. Phylakos, impressed,
released him, with the cattle; his brother was given the bride. Melampous then left for Argos where he
settled and prospered. One of his great-grandsons was the prophet Amphiaraos who foresaw that if he
joined the champions who went to besiege Thebes (The Seven against Thebes) he would lose his life.
Melampous' son Mantios had a son named Polypheidês, and it is his son Theoklymenos who now begs
Telémakhos for a place in his ship.

and Oikleiês the firebrand Amphiaraos.
This champion the lord of stormcloud, Zeus,   275
and strong Apollo loved; nor had he ever
to cross the doorsill into dim old age.
A woman, bought by trinkets, gave him over
to be cut down in the assault on Thebes.
His sons were Alkmáon and Amphílokhos.   280
In the meantime Lord Mantios begot
Polypheidês, the prophet, and
Kleitos—famous name! For Dawn in silks
of gold carried off Kleitos for his beauty
to live among the gods. But Polypheidês,   285
high-hearted and exalted by Apollo
above all men for prophecy, withdrew
to Hyperesia[3] when his father angered him.
He lived on there, foretelling to the world
the shape of things to come.

       His son it was,   290
Theoklýmenos, who came upon Telémakhos
as he poured out the red wine in the sand
near his trim ship, with prayer to Athena;
and he called out, approaching:

       "Friend, well met
here at libation before going to sea.   295
I pray you by the wine you spend, and by
your god, your own life, and your company;
enlighten me, and let the truth be known.
Who are you? Of what city and what parents?"

Telémakhos turned to him and replied: 300

"Stranger, as truly as may be, I'll tell you.
I am from Ithaka, where I was born;
my father is, or he once was, Odysseus.
But he's a long time gone, and dead, may be;
and that is what I took ship with my friends   305
to find out—for he left long years ago."

Said Theoklýmenos in reply:

       "I too
have had to leave my home. I killed a cousin.
In the wide grazing lands of Argos live
many kinsmen of his and friends in power,   310
great among the Akhaians. These I fled.
Death and vengeance at my back, as Fate
has turned now, I came wandering overland.
Give me a plank aboard your ship, I beg,
or they will kill me. They are on my track."   315

Telémakhos made answer:

       "No two ways
about it. Will I pry you from our gunnel

3. Near Argos.

when you are desperate to get to sea?
Come aboard; share what we have, and welcome."

He took the bronze-shod lance from the man's hand   320
and laid it down full-length on deck; then swung
his own weight after it aboard the cutter,
taking position aft, making a place
for Theoklýmenos near him. The stern lines
were slacked off, and Telémakhos commanded: 325

"Rig the mast; make sail!" Nimbly they ran
to push the fir pole high and step it firm
amidships in the box, make fast the forestays,
and hoist aloft the white sail on its halyards.
A following wind came down from grey-eyed Athena,   330
blowing brisk through heaven, and so steady
the cutter lapped up miles of salt blue sea,
passing Krounoi abeam and Khalkis estuary[4]
at sundown when the sea ways all grew dark.
Then, by Athena's wind borne on, the ship   335
rounded Pheai by night and coasted Elis,
the green domain of the Epeioi; thence
he put her head north toward the running pack
of islets, wondering if by sailing wide
he sheered off Death, or would be caught.

                           That night   340
Odysseus and the swineherd supped again
with herdsmen in their mountain hut. At ease
when appetite and thirst were turned away,
Odysseus, while he talked, observed the swineherd
to see if he were hospitable still—   345
if yet again the man would make him stay
under his roof, or send him off to town.

"Listen," he said, "Eumaios; listen, lads.
At daybreak I must go and try my luck
around the port. I burden you too long.   350
Direct me, put me on the road with someone.
Nothing else for it but to play the beggar
in populous parts. I'll get a cup or loaf,
maybe, from some householder. If I go
as far as the great hall of King Odysseus   355
I might tell Queen Penélopê my news.
Or I can drift inside among the suitors
to see what alms they give, rich as they are.
If they have whims, I'm deft in ways of service—
that I can say, and you may know for sure.   360
By grace of Hermês the Wayfinder, patron
of mortal tasks, the god who honors toil,
no man can do a chore better than I can.
Set me to build a fire, or chop wood,

---

4. The precise location of these places is disputed but the mention of Elis in line 336 shows that they
are all on the west coast of the Peloponnese, south of the Gulf of Corinth. The Olympic Games were
held in Elis.

cook or carve, mix wine and serve—or anything   365
inferior men attend to for the gentry."

Now you were furious at this, Eumaios,
and answered—O my swineherd!—

              "Friend, friend,
how could this fantasy take hold of you?
You dally with your life, and nothing less,   370
if you feel drawn to mingle in that company—
reckless, violent, and famous for it
out to the rim of heaven. Slaves
they have, but not like you. No—theirs are boys
in fresh cloaks and tunics, with pomade   375
ever on their sleek heads, and pretty faces.
These are their minions, while their tables gleam
and groan under big roasts, with loaves and wine.
Stay with us here. No one is burdened by you,
neither myself nor any of my hands.   380
Wait here until Odysseus' son returns.
You shall have clothing from him, cloak and tunic,
and passage where your heart desires to go."

The noble and enduring man replied:

"May you be dear to Zeus for this, Eumaios,   385
even as you are to me. Respite from pain
you give me—and from homelessness. In life
there's nothing worse than knocking about the world,
no bitterness we vagabonds are spared
when the curst belly rages! Well, you master it   390
and me, making me wait for the king's son.
But now, come, tell me:
what of Odysseus' mother, and his father
whom he took leave of on the sill of age?
Are they under the sun's rays, living still,   395
or gone down long ago to lodge with Death?"

To this the rugged herdsman answered:

              "Aye,
that I can tell you; it is briefly told.
Laërtês lives, but daily in his hall
prays for the end of life and soul's delivery,   400
heartbroken as he is for a son long gone
and for his lady. Sorrow, when she died,
aged and enfeebled him like a green tree stricken;
but pining for her son, her brilliant son,
wore out her life.

             Would god no death so sad   405
might come to benefactors dear as she!
I loved always to ask and hear about her
while she lived, although she lived in sorrow.
For she had brought me up with her own daughter,
Princess Ktimenê, her youngest child.   410
We were alike in age and nursed as equals

nearly, till in the flower of our years
they gave her, married her, to a Samian prince,[5]
taking his many gifts. For my own portion
her mother gave new clothing, cloak and sandals,   415
and sent me to the woodland. Well she loved me.
Ah, how I miss that family! It is true
the blissful gods prosper my work; I have
meat and drink to spare for those I prize;
but so removed I am, I have no speech   420
with my sweet mistress, now that evil days
and overbearing men darken her house.
Tenants all hanker for good talk and gossip
around their lady, and a snack in hall,
a cup or two before they take the road   425
to their home acres, each one bearing home
some gift to cheer his heart."

                      The great tactician
answered:

        "You were still a child, I see,
when exiled somehow from your parents' land.
Tell me, had it been sacked in war, the city   430
of spacious ways in which they made their home,
your father and your gentle mother? Or
were you kidnapped alone, brought here by sea
huddled with sheep in some foul pirate squadron,
to this landowner's hall? He paid your ransom?"   435

The master of the woodland answered:

                      "Friend,
now that you show an interest in that matter,
attend me quietly, be at your ease,
and drink your wine. These autumn nights are long,
ample for story-telling and for sleep.   440
You need not go to bed before the hour;
sleeping from dusk to dawn's a dull affair.
Let any other here who wishes, though,
retire to rest. At daybreak let him breakfast
and take the king's own swine into the wilderness.   445
Here's a tight roof; we'll drink on, you and I,
and ease our hearts of hardships we remember,
sharing old times. In later days a man
can find a charm in old adversity,
exile and pain. As to your question, now: 450

A certain island, Syriê by name—
you may have heard the name—lies off Ortýgia[6]
due west, and holds the sunsets of the year.
Not very populous, but good for grazing
sheep and kine; rich too in wine and grain.   455

5. From Same, a nearby island or town.   6. Another name for Delos, the central island of the
Cyclades, but also the name of the central island of the city of Syracuse in Sicily. However, the fact that
on Syriê there is no disease and that everyone there dies painlessly suggests that it is not located in this
world at all—like Phaiákia, it is in fairyland.

No dearth is ever known there, no disease
wars on the folk, of ills that plague mankind;
but when the townsmen reach old age, Apollo
with his longbow of silver comes, and Artemis,
showering arrows of mild death.
                              Two towns   460
divide the farmlands of that whole domain,
and both were ruled by Ktêsios, my father,
Orménos' heir, and a great godlike man.

Now one day some of those renowned seafaring
men, sea-dogs, Phoinikians, came ashore   465
with bags of gauds for trading. Father had
in our household a woman of Phoinikia,
a handsome one, and highly skilled. Well, she
gave in to the seductions of those rovers.
One of them found her washing near the mooring   470
and lay with her, making such love to her
as women in their frailty are confused by,
even the best of them.
                         In due course, then,
he asked her who she was and where she hailed from:
and nodding toward my father's roof, she said: 475

'I am of Sidon town, smithy of bronze
for all the East. Arubas Pasha's daughter.
Taphian pirates caught me in a byway
and sold me into slavery overseas
in this man's home. He could afford my ransom.'   480

The sailor who had lain with her replied:

'Why not ship out with us on the run homeward,
and see your father's high-roofed hall again,
your father and your mother? Still in Sidon
and still rich, they are said to be.'

                              She answered: 485

'It could be done, that, if you sailors take
oath I'll be given passage home unharmed.'

Well, soon she had them swearing it all pat
as she desired, repeating every syllable,
whereupon she warned them:

                              'Not a word   490
about our meeting here! Never call out to me
when any of you see me in the lane
or at the well. Some visitor might bear
tales to the old man. If he guessed the truth,
I'd be chained up, your lives would be in peril.   495
No: keep it secret. Hurry with your peddling,
and when your hold is filled with livestock, send
a message to me at the manor hall.
Gold I'll bring, whatever comes to hand,
and something else, too, as my passage fee —   500

the master's child, my charge: a boy so high,
bright for his age; he runs with me on errands.
I'd take him with me happily; his price
would be I know not what in sale abroad.'

Her bargain made, she went back to the manor.   505
But they were on the island all that year,
getting by trade a cargo of our cattle;
until, the ship at length being laden full,
ready for sea, they sent a messenger
to the Phoinikian woman. Shrewd he was,   510
this fellow who came round my father's hall,
showing a golden chain all strung with amber,
a necklace. Maids in waiting and my mother
passed it from hand to hand, admiring it,
engaging they would buy it. But that dodger,   515
as soon as he had caught the woman's eye
and nodded, slipped away to join the ship.
She took my hand and led me through the court
into the portico. There by luck she found
winecups and tables still in place—for Father's   520
attendant counselors had dined just now
before they went to the assembly. Quickly
she hid three goblets in her bellying dress
to carry with her while I tagged along
in my bewilderment. The sun went down   525
and all the lanes grew dark as we descended,
skirting the harbor in our haste to where
those traders of Phoinikia held their ship.
All went aboard at once and put to sea,
taking the two of us. A favoring wind   530
blew from the power of heaven. We sailed on
six nights and days without event. Then Zeus
the son of Kronos added one more noon—and sudden
arrows from Artemis pierced the woman's heart.
Stone-dead she dropped   535
into the sloshing bilge the way a tern
plummets; and the sailors heaved her over
as tender pickings for the seals and fish.
Now I was left in dread, alone, while wind
and current bore them on to Ithaka.   540
Laërtês purchased me. That was the way
I first laid eyes upon this land."

                          Odysseus,
the kingly man, replied:

                          "You rouse my pity,
telling what you endured when you were young.
But surely Zeus put good alongside ill: 545
torn from your own far home, you had the luck
to come into a kind man's service, generous
with food and drink. And a good life you lead,
unlike my own, all spent in barren roaming
from one country to the next, till now."   550

So the two men talked on, into the night,
leaving few hours for sleep before the Dawn
stepped up to her bright chair.
                                    The ship now drifting
under the island lee, Telémakhos'
companions took in sail and mast, unshipped   555
the oars and rowed ashore. They moored her stern
by the stout hawser lines, tossed out the bow stones,
and waded in beyond the wash of ripples
to mix their wine and cook their morning meal.
When they had turned back hunger and thirst, Telémakhos   560
arose to give the order of the day.

"Pull for the town," he said, "and berth our ship,
while I go inland across country. Later,
this evening, after looking at my farms,
I'll join you in the city. When day comes   565
I hope to celebrate our crossing, feasting
everyone on good red meat and wine."

His noble passenger, Theoklýmenos,
now asked:

              "What as to me, my dear young fellow,
where shall I go? Will I find lodging here   570
with some one of the lords of stony Ithaka?
Or go straight to your mother's hall and yours?"

Telémakhos turned round to him and said:

"I should myself invite you to our hall
if things were otherwise; there'd be no lack   575
of entertainment for you. As it stands,
no place could be more wretched for a guest
while I'm away. Mother will never see you;
she almost never shows herself at home
to the suitors there, but stays in her high chamber   580
weaving upon her loom. No, let me name
another man for you to go to visit:
Eurýmakhos, the honored son of Pólybos.
In Ithaka they are dazzled by him now—
the strongest of their princes, bent on making   585
mother and all Odysseus' wealth his own.
Zeus on Olympos only knows
if some dark hour for them will intervene."

The words were barely spoken, when a hawk,
Apollo's courier, flew up on the right,   590
clutching a dove and plucking her—so feathers
floated down to the ground between Telémakhos
and the moored cutter. Theoklýmenos
called him apart and gripped his hand, whispering:

"A god spoke in this bird-sign on the right.   595
I knew it when I saw the hawk fly over us.
There is no kinglier house than yours, Telémakhos,

here in the realm of Ithaka. Your family
will be in power forever."

                    The young prince,
clear in spirit, answered:

                    "Be it so,   600
friend, as you say. And may you know as well
the friendship of my house, and many gifts
from me, so everyone may call you fortunate."

He called a trusted crewman named Peiraios,
and said to him:

                    "Peiraios, son of Klýtios,   605
can I rely on you again as ever, most
of all the friends who sailed with me to Pylos?
Take this man home with you, take care of him,
treat him with honor, till I come."

                    To this
Peiraios the good spearman answered:

                                        "Aye,   610
stay in the wild country while you will,
I shall be looking after him, Telémakhos.
He will not lack good lodging."
                    Down to the ship
he turned, and boarded her, and called the others
to cast off the stern lines and come aboard.   615
So the men climbed in to sit beside the rowlocks.
Telémakhos now tied his sandals on
and lifted his tough spear from the ship's deck;
hawsers were taken in, and they shoved off
to reach the town by way of the open sea   620
as he commanded them—royal Odysseus'
own dear son, Telémakhos.
                    On foot
and swiftly he went up toward the stockade
where swine were penned in hundreds, and at night
the guardian of the swine, the forester,   625
slept under arms on duty for his masters.

BOOK XVI

[Father and Son]

But there were two men in the mountain hut—
Odysseus and the swineherd. At first light
blowing their fire up, they cooked their breakfast
and sent their lads out, driving herds to root
in the tall timber.
                    When Telémakhos came,   5
the wolvish troop of watchdogs only fawned on him
as he advanced. Odysseus heard them go
and heard the light crunch of a man's footfall—
at which he turned quickly to say:

"Eumaios,
here is one of your crew come back, or maybe   10
another friend: the dogs are out there snuffling
belly down; not one has even growled.
I can hear footsteps—"

But before he finished
his tall son stood at the door.
The swineherd
rose in surprise, letting a bowl and jug   15
tumble from his fingers. Going forward,
he kissed the young man's head, his shining eyes
and both hands, while his own tears brimmed and fell.
Think of a man whose dear and only son,
born to him in exile, reared with labor,   20
has lived ten years abroad and now returns:
how would that man embrace his son! Just so
the herdsman clapped his arms around Telémakhos
and covered him with kisses—for he knew
the lad had got away from death. He said: 25

"Light of my days, Telémakhos,
you made it back! When you took ship for Pylos
I never thought to see you here again.
Come in, dear child, and let me feast my eyes;
here you are, home from the distant places!   30
How rarely anyway, you visit us,
your own men, and your own woods and pastures!
Always in the town, a man would think
you loved the suitors' company, those dogs!"

Telémakhos with his clear candor said: 35

"I am with you, Uncle. See now, I have come
because I wanted to see you first, to hear from you
if Mother stayed at home—or is she married
off to someone and Odysseus' bed
left empty for some gloomy spider's weaving?"   40

Gently the forester replied to this:

"At home indeed your mother is, poor lady,
still in the women's hall. Her nights and days
are wearied out with grieving."

Stepping back
he took the bronze-shod lance, and the young prince   45
entered the cabin over the worn door stone.
Odysseus moved aside, yielding his couch,
but from across the room Telémakhos checked him:

"Friend, sit down; we'll find another chair
in our own hut. Here is the man to make one!"   50

The swineherd, when the quiet man sank down,
built a new pile of evergreens and fleeces—
a couch for the dear son of great Odysseus—

then gave them trenchers of good meat, left over
from the roast pork of yesterday, and heaped up   55
willow baskets full of bread, and mixed
an ivy bowl of honey-hearted wine.
Then he in turn sat down, facing Odysseus,
their hands went out upon the meat and drink
as they fell to, ridding themselves of hunger,   60
until Telémakhos paused and said:

            "Oh, Uncle,
what's your friend's home port? How did he come?
Who were the sailors brought him here to Ithaka?
I doubt if he came walking on the sea."

And you replied, Eumaios—O my swineherd—   65

"Son, the truth about him is soon told.
His home land, and a broad land, too, is Krete,
but he has knocked about the world, he says,
for years, as the Powers wove his life. Just now
he broke away from a shipload of Thesprotians   70
to reach my hut. I place him in your hands.
Act as you will. He wishes your protection."

The young man said:

            "Eumaios, my protection!
The notion cuts me to the heart. How can I
receive your friend at home? I am not old enough   75
or trained in arms. Could I defend myself
if someone picked a fight with me?

                 Besides,
mother is in a quandary, whether to stay with me
as mistress of our household, honoring
her lord's bed, and opinion in the town,   80
or take the best Akhaian who comes her way—
the one who offers most.

              I'll undertake,
at all events, to clothe your friend for winter,
now he is with you. Tunic and cloak of wool,
a good broadsword, and sandals—these are his.   85
I can arrange to send him where he likes
or you may keep him in your cabin here.
I shall have bread and wine sent up; you need not
feel any pinch on his behalf.

              Impossible
to let him stay in hall, among the suitors.   90
They are drunk, drunk on impudence, they might
injure my guest—and how could I bear that?
How could a single man take on those odds?
Not even a hero could.

            The suitors are too strong."

At this the noble and enduring man, Odysseus,   95
addressed his son:

"Kind prince, it may be fitting
for me to speak a word. All that you say
gives me an inward wound as I sit listening.
I mean this wanton game they play, these fellows,
riding roughshod over you in your own house, 100
admirable as you are. But tell me,
are you resigned to being bled? The townsmen,
stirred up against you, are they, by some oracle?
Your brothers—can you say your brothers fail you?
A man should feel his kin, at least, behind him 105
in any clash, when a real fight is coming.
If my heart were as young as yours, if I were
son of Odysseus, or the man himself,
I'd rather have my head cut from my shoulders
by some slashing adversary, if I 110
brought no hurt upon that crew! Suppose
I went down, being alone, before the lot,
better, I say, to die at home in battle
than see these insupportable things, day after
day the stranger cuffed, the women slaves 115
dragged here and there, shame in the lovely rooms,
the wine drunk up in rivers, sheer waste
of pointless feasting, never at an end!"

Telémakhos replied:

"Friend, I'll explain to you.
There is no rancor in the town against me, 120
no fault of brothers, whom a man should feel
behind him when a fight is in the making;
no, no—in our family the First Born
of Heaven, Zeus, made single sons the rule.
Arkeísios had but one, Laërtês; he 125
in his turn fathered only one, Odysseus,
who left me in his hall alone, too young
to be of any use to him.
And so you see why enemies fill our house
in these days: all the princes of the islands, 130
Doulíkhion, Samê, wooded Zakýnthos,
Ithaka, too—lords of our island rock—
eating our house up as they court my mother.
She cannot put an end to it; she dare not
bar the marriage that she hates; and they 135
devour all my substance and my cattle,
and who knows when they'll slaughter me as well?
It rests upon the gods' great knees.
                              Uncle,
go down at once and tell the Lady Penélopê
that I am back from Pylos, safe and sound. 140
I stay here meanwhile. You will give your message
and then return. Let none of the Akhaians
hear it; they have a mind to do me harm."

To this, Eumaios, you replied:

"I know.
But make this clear, now—should I not likewise   145
call on Laërtês with your news? Hard hit
by sorrow though he was, mourning Odysseus,
he used to keep an eye upon his farm.
He had what meals he pleased, with his own folk.
But now no more, not since you sailed for Pylos;   150
he has not taken food or drink, I hear,
sitting all day, blind to the work of harvest,
groaning, while the skin shrinks on his bones."

Telémakhos answered:

                              "One more misery,
but we had better leave it so.   155
If men could choose, and have their choice, in everything,
we'd have my father home.
                              Turn back
when you have done your errand, as you must,
not to be caught alone in the countryside.[7]
But wait—you may tell Mother   160
to send our old housekeeper on the quiet
and quickly; she can tell the news to Grandfather."

The swineherd, roused, reached out to get his sandals,
tied them on, and took the road.

                              Who else
beheld this but Athena? From the air   165
she walked, taking the form of a tall woman,
handsome and clever at her craft, and stood
beyond the gate in plain sight of Odysseus,
unseen, though, by Telémakhos, unguessed,
for not to everyone will gods appear.   170
Odysseus noticed her; so did the dogs,
who cowered whimpering away from her. She only
nodded, signing to him with her brows,
a sign he recognized. Crossing the yard,
he passed out through the gate in the stockade   175
to face the goddess. There she said to him:

"Son of Laërtês and the gods of old,
Odysseus, master of land ways and sea ways,
dissemble to your son no longer now.
The time has come: tell him how you together   180
will bring doom on the suitors in the town.
I shall not be far distant then, for I
myself desire battle."

                              Saying no more,
she tipped her golden wand upon the man,
making his cloak pure white, and the knit tunic   185
fresh around him. Lithe and young she made him,

---

7. The Greek says something more like "and don't go wandering round the countryside after him
[Laërtês]."

ruddy with sun, his jawline clean, the beard
no longer grey upon his chin. And she
withdrew when she had done.
                                   Then Lord Odysseus
reappeared—and his son was thunderstruck.   190
Fear in his eyes, he looked down and away
as though it were a god, and whispered:

                                   "Stranger,
you are no longer what you were just now!
Your cloak is new; even your skin! You are
one of the gods who rule the sweep of heaven!   195
Be kind to us, we'll make you fair oblation
and gifts of hammered gold. Have mercy on us!"

The noble and enduring man replied:

"No god. Why take me for a god? No, no.
I am that father whom your boyhood lacked   200
and suffered pain for lack of. I am he."

Held back too long, the tears ran down his cheeks
as he embraced his son.
                                   Only Telémakhos,
uncomprehending, wild
with incredulity, cried out:

                                   "You cannot   205
be my father Odysseus! Meddling spirits
conceived this trick to twist the knife in me!
No man of woman born could work these wonders
by his own craft, unless a god came into it
with ease to turn him young or old at will.   210
I swear you were in rags and old,
and here you stand like one of the immortals!"

Odysseus brought his ranging mind to bear
and said:

                                   "This is not princely, to be swept
away by wonder at your father's presence.   215
No other Odysseus will ever come,
for he and I are one, the same; his bitter
fortune and his wanderings are mine.
Twenty years gone, and I am back again
on my own island.
                                   As for my change of skin,   220
that is a charm Athena, Hope of Soldiers,[8]
uses as she will; she has the knack
to make me seem a beggar man sometimes
and sometimes young, with finer clothes about me.
It is no hard thing for the gods of heaven   225
to glorify a man or bring him low."

8. Athena was a warrior goddess.

When he had spoken, down he sat.
                                  Then, throwing
his arms around this marvel of a father
Telémakhos began to weep. Salt tears
rose from the wells of longing in both men,   230
and cries burst from both as keen and fluttering
as those of the great taloned hawk,
whose nestlings farmers take before they fly.
So helplessly they cried, pouring out tears,
and might have gone on weeping so till sundown,   235
had not Telémakhos said:

                        "Dear father! Tell me
what kind of vessel put you here ashore
on Ithaka? Your sailors, who were they?
I doubt you made it, walking on the sea!"

Then said Odysseus, who had borne the barren sea: 240

"Only plain truth shall I tell you, child.
Great seafarers, the Phaiákians, gave me passage
as they give other wanderers. By night
over the open ocean, while I slept,
they brought me in their cutter, set me down   245
on Ithaka, with gifts of bronze and gold
and stores of woven things. By the gods' will
these lie all hidden in a cave. I came
to this wild place, directed by Athena,
so that we might lay plans to kill our enemies.   250
Count up the suitors for me, let me know
what men at arms are there, how many men.
I must put all my mind to it, to see
if we two by ourselves can take them on
or if we should look round for help."

                                  Telémakhos   255
replied:

            "O Father, all my life your fame
as a fighting man has echoed in my ears—
your skill with weapons and the tricks of war—
but what you speak of is a staggering thing,
beyond imagining, for me. How can two men   260
do battle with a houseful in their prime?
For I must tell you this is no affair
of ten or even twice ten men, but scores,
throngs of them. You shall see, here and now.
The number from Doulíkhion alone   265
is fifty-two picked men, with armorers,
a half dozen; twenty-four came from Samê,
twenty from Zakýnthos; our own island
accounts for twelve, high-ranked, and their retainers,
Medôn the crier, and the Master Harper,   270
besides a pair of handymen at feasts.
If we go in against all these
I fear we pay in salt blood for your vengeance.

You must think hard if you would conjure up
the fighting strength to take us through."

                           Odysseus   275
who had endured the long war and the sea
answered:

        "I'll tell you now.
Suppose Athena's arm is over us, and Zeus
her father's, must I rack my brains for more?"

Clearheaded Telémakhos looked hard and said: 280

"Those two are great defenders, no one doubts it,
but throned in the serene clouds overhead;
other affairs of men and gods they have
to rule over."

       And the hero answered:

"Before long they will stand to right and left of us   285
in combat, in the shouting, when the test comes—
our nerve against the suitors' in my hall.
Here is your part: at break of day tomorrow
home with you, go mingle with our princes.
The swineherd later on will take me down   290
the port-side trail—a beggar, by my looks,
hangdog and old. If they make fun of me
in my own courtyard, let your ribs cage up
your springing heart, no matter what I suffer,
no matter if they pull me by the heels   295
or practice shots at me, to drive me out.
Look on, hold down your anger. You may even
plead with them, by heaven! in gentle terms
to quit their horseplay—not that they will heed you,
rash as they are, facing their day of wrath.   300
Now fix the next step in your mind.
                        Athena,
counseling me, will give me word, and I
shall signal to you, nodding: at that point
round up all armor, lances, gear of war
left in our hall, and stow the lot away   305
back in the vaulted store room. When the suitors
miss those arms and question you, be soft
in what you say: answer:

                    'I thought I'd move them
out of the smoke. They seemed no longer those
bright arms Odysseus left us years ago   310
when he went off to Troy. Here where the fire's
hot breath came, they had grown black and drear.
One better reason, too, I had from Zeus:
Suppose a brawl starts up when you are drunk,
you might be crazed and bloody one another,   315
and that would stain your feast, your courtship. Tempered
iron can magnetize a man.'

Say that.
But put aside two broadswords and two spears
for our own use, two oxhide shields nearby
when we go into action. Pallas Athena   320
and Zeus All Provident will see you through,
bemusing our young friends.
                        Now one thing more.
If son of mine you are and blood of mine,
let no one hear Odysseus is about.
Neither Laërtês, nor the swineherd here,   325
nor any slave, nor even Penélopê.
But you and I alone must learn how far
the women are corrupted; we should know
how to locate good men among our hands,
the loyal and respectful, and the shirkers   330
who take you lightly, as alone and young."

His admirable son replied:

                        "Ah, Father,
even when danger comes I think you'll find
courage in me. I am not scatterbrained.
But as to checking on the field hands now,   335
I see no gain for us in that. Reflect,
you make a long toil, that way, if you care
to look men in the eye at every farm,
while these gay devils in our hall at ease
eat up our flocks and herds, leaving us nothing.   340

As for the maids I say, Yes: make distinction
between good girls and those who shame your house;
all that I shy away from is a scrutiny
of cottagers just now. The time for that
comes later—if in truth you have a sign   345
from Zeus the Stormking."

                        So their talk ran on,
while down the coast, and round toward Ithaka,
hove the good ship that had gone out to Pylos
bearing Telémakhos and his companions.
Into the wide bay waters, on to the dark land,   350
they drove her, hauled her up, took out the oars
and canvas for light-hearted squires to carry
homeward—as they carried, too, the gifts
of Meneláos round to Klýtios'[9] house.
But first they sped a runner to Penélopê.   355
They knew that quiet lady must be told
the prince her son had come ashore, and sent
his good ship round to port; not one soft tear
should their sweet queen let fall.
                        Both messengers,
crewman and swineherd—reached the outer gate   360
in the same instant, bearing the same news,

9. The father of Peiraios (XV.604), the man to whom Telémakhos entrusted Theoklýmenos.

and went in side by side to the king's hall.
He of the ship burst out among the maids:

"Your son's ashore this morning, O my Queen!"

But the swineherd calmly stood near Penélopê   365
whispering what her son had bade him tell
and what he had enjoined on her. No more.
When he had done, he left the place and turned
back to his steading in the hills.

                                   By now,
sullen confusion weighed upon the suitors.   370
Out of the house, out of the court they went,
beyond the wall and gate, to sit in council.
Eurýmakhos, the son of Pólybos,
opened discussion:

                    "Friends, face up to it;
that young pup, Telémakhos, has done it;   375
he made the round trip, though we said he could not.
Well—now to get the best craft we can find
afloat, with oarsmen who can drench her bows,
and tell those on the island to come home."

He was yet speaking when Amphínomos,   380
craning seaward, spotted the picket ship
already in the roadstead under oars
with canvas brailed up; and this fresh arrival
made him chuckle. Then he told his friends:

"Too late for messages. Look, here they come   385
along the bay. Some god has brought them news,
or else they saw the cutter pass—and could not
overtake her."

                    On their feet at once,
the suitors took the road to the sea beach,
where, meeting the black ship, they hauled her in.   390
Oars and gear they left for their light-hearted
squires to carry, and all in company
made off for the assembly ground. All others,
young and old alike, they barred from sitting.
Eupeithês' son, Antínoös, made the speech: 395

"How the gods let our man escape a boarding,
that is the wonder.
                    We had lookouts posted
up on the heights all day in the sea wind,
and every hour a fresh pair of eyes;
at night we never slept ashore   400
but after sundown cruised the open water
to the southeast, patrolling until Dawn.
We were prepared to cut him off and catch him,
squelch him for good and all. The power of heaven
steered him the long way home.   405

Well, let this company plan his destruction,
and leave him no way out, this time. I see
our business here unfinished while he lives.
He knows, now, and he's no fool. Besides,
his people are all tired of playing up to us.   410
I say, act now, before he brings the whole
body of Akhaians to assembly—
and he would leave no word unsaid, in righteous
anger speaking out before them all
of how we plotted murder, and then missed him.   415
Will they commend us for that pretty work?
Take action now, or we are in for trouble;
we might be exiled, driven off our lands.
Let the first blow be ours.
If we move first, and get our hands on him   420
far from the city's eye, on path or field,
then stores and livestock will be ours to share;
the house we may confer upon his mother—
and on the man who marries her. Decide
otherwise you may—but if, my friends,   425
you want that boy to live and have his patrimony,
then we should eat no more of his good mutton,
come to this place no more.
                                    Let each from his own hall
court her with dower gifts. And let her marry
the destined one, the one who offers most."   430

He ended, and no sound was heard among them,
sitting all hushed, until at last the son
of Nísos Aretíadês arose—
Amphínomos.
                          He led the group of suitors
who came from grainlands on Doulíkhion,   435
and he had lightness in his talk that pleased
Penélopê, for he meant no ill.
Now, in concern for them, he spoke:
                                                          "O Friends
I should not like to kill Telémakhos.
It is a shivery thing to kill a prince   440
of royal blood.
                          We should consult the gods.
If Zeus hands down a ruling for that act,
then I shall say, 'Come one, come all,' and go
cut him down with my own hand—
but I say Halt, if gods are contrary."   445

Now this proposal won them, and it carried.
Breaking their session up, away they went
to take their smooth chairs in Odysseus' house.
Meanwhile Penélopê the Wise,
decided, for her part, to make appearance   450
before the valiant young men.
                                        She knew now
they plotted her child's death in her own hall,

for once more Medôn, who had heard them, told her.
Into the hall that lovely lady came,
with maids attending, and approached the suitors,   455
till near a pillar of the well-wrought roof
she paused, her shining veil across her cheeks,
and spoke directly to Antínoös:

                              "Infatuate,
steeped in evil! Yet in Ithaka they say
you were the best one of your generation   460
in mind and speech. Not so, you never were.
Madman, why do you keep forever knitting
death for Telémakhos? Have you no pity
toward men dependent on another's mercy?
Before Lord Zeus, no sanction can be found   465
for one such man to plot against another!
Or are you not aware that your own father
fled to us when the realm was up in arms
against him? He had joined the Taphian pirates
in ravaging Thesprotian folk, our friends.   470
Our people would have raided *him*, then—breached
his heart, butchered his herds to feast upon—
only Odysseus took him in, and held
the furious townsmen off. It is Odysseus'
house you now consume, his wife you court,   475
his son you kill, or try to kill. And me
you ravage now, and grieve. I call upon you
to make an end of it!—and your friends too!"

The son of Pólybos it was, Eurýmakhos,
who answered her with ready speech:

                              "My lady   480
Penélopê, wise daughter of Ikários,
you must shake off these ugly thoughts. I say
that man does not exist, nor will, who dares
lay hands upon your son Telémakhos,
while I live, walk the earth, and use my eyes.   485
The man's life blood, I swear,
will spurt and run out black around my lancehead!
For it is true of me, too, that Odysseus,
raider of cities, took me on his knees
and fed me often—tidbits and red wine.   490
Should not Telémakhos, therefore, be dear to me
above the rest of men? I tell the lad
he must not tremble for his life, at least
alone in the suitors' company. Heaven
deals death no man avoids."

                              Blasphemous lies   495
in earnest tones he told—the one who planned
the lad's destruction!

                 Silently the lady
made her way to her glowing upper chamber,
there to weep for her dear lord, Odysseus,

until grey-eyed Athena   500
cast sweet sleep upon her eyes.

                                    At fall of dusk
Odysseus and his son heard the approach
of the good forester. They had been standing
over the fire with a spitted pig,
a yearling. And Athena coming near   505
with one rap of her wand made of Odysseus
an old old man again, with rags about him—
for if the swineherd knew his lord were there
he could not hold the news; Penélopê
would hear it from him.
                              Now Telémakhos   510
greeted him first:

                    "Eumaios, back again!
What was the talk in town? Are the tall suitors
home again, by this time, from their ambush,
or are they still on watch for my return?"

And you replied, Eumaios—O my swineherd: 515

"There was no time to ask or talk of that;
I hurried through the town. Even while I spoke
my message, I felt driven to return.
A runner from your friends turned up, a crier,
who gave the news first to your mother. Ah!   520
One thing I do know; with my own two eyes
I saw it. As I climbed above the town
to where the sky is cut by Hermês' ridge,
I saw a ship bound in for our own bay
with many oarsmen in it, laden down   525
with sea provisioning and two-edged spears,
and I surmised those were the men.
                                    Who knows?"

Telémakhos, now strong with magic, smiled
across at his own father—but avoided
the swineherd's eye.
                      So when the pig was done,   530
the spit no longer to be turned, the table
garnished, everyone sat down to feast
on all the savory flesh he craved. And when
they had put off desire for meat and drink,
they turned to bed and took the gift of sleep.   535

BOOK XVII

[The Beggar at the Manor]

When the young Dawn came bright into the East
spreading her finger tips of rose, Telémakhos
the king's son, tied on his rawhide sandals
and took the lance that bore his handgrip. Burning

to be away, and on the path to town,   5
he told the swineherd:

        "Uncle, the truth is
I must go down myself into the city.
Mother must see me there, with her own eyes,
or she will weep and feel forsaken still,
and will not set her mind at rest. Your job   10
will be to lead this poor man down to beg.
Some householder may want to dole him out
a loaf and pint. I have my own troubles.
Am I to care for every last man who comes?
And if he takes it badly—well, so much   15
the worse for him. Plain truth is what I favor."

At once Odysseus the great tactician
spoke up briskly:

        "Neither would I myself
care to be kept here, lad. A beggar man
fares better in the town. Let it be said   20
I am not yet so old I must lay up
indoors and mumble, 'Aye, Aye' to a master.
Go on, then. As you say, my friend can lead me
as soon as I have had a bit of fire
and when the sun grows warmer. These old rags   25
could be my death, outside on a frosty morning,
and the town is distant, so they say."

        Telémakhos
with no more words went out, and through the fence,
and down hill, going fast on the steep footing,
nursing woe for the suitors in his heart.   30
Before the manor hall, he leaned his lance
against a great porch pillar and stepped in
across the door stone.
        Old Eurýkleia
saw him first, for that day she was covering
handsome chairs nearby with clean fleeces.   35
She ran to him at once, tears in her eyes;
and other maidservants of the old soldier
Odysseus gathered round to greet their prince,
kissing his head and shoulders.
        Quickly, then,
Penélopê the Wise, tall in her beauty   40
as Artemis or pale-gold Aphroditê,
appeared from her high chamber and came down
to throw her arms around her son. In tears
she kissed his head, kissed both his shining eyes,
then cried out, and her words flew:

        "Back with me!   45
Telémakhos, more sweet to me than sunlight!
I thought I should not see you again, ever,
after you took the ship that night to Pylos—
against my will, with not a word! you went

for news of your dear father. Tell me now   50
of everything you saw!"

But he made answer:

"Mother, not now. You make me weep. My heart
already aches—I came near death at sea.
You must bathe, first of all, and change your dress,
and take your maids to the highest room to pray.   55
Pray, and burn offerings to the gods of heaven,
that Zeus may put his hand to our revenge.

I am off now to bring home from the square
a guest, a passenger I had. I sent him
yesterday with all my crew to town.   60
Peiraios was to care for him, I said,
and keep him well, with honor, till I came."

She caught back the swift words upon her tongue.
Then softly she withdrew
to bathe and dress her body in fresh linen,   65
and make her offerings to the gods of heaven,
praying Almighty Zeus
to put his hand to their revenge.

                          Telémakhos
had left the hall, taken his lance, and gone
with two quick hounds at heel into the town,   70
Athena's grace in his long stride
making the people gaze as he came near.
And suitors gathered, primed with friendly words,
despite the deadly plotting in their hearts—
but these, and all their crowd, he kept away from.   75
Next he saw sitting some way off, apart,
Mentor, with Antiphos and Halithersês,
friends of his father's house in years gone by.
Near these men he sat down, and told his tale
under their questioning.
                          His crewman, young Peiraios,   80
guided through town, meanwhile, into the Square,
the Argive exile, Theoklýmenos.
Telémakhos lost no time in moving toward him;
but first Peiraios had his say:

                          "Telémakhos,
you must send maids to me, at once, and let me   85
turn over to you those gifts from Meneláos!"

The prince had pondered it, and said:

                          "Peiraios,
none of us knows how this affair will end.
Say one day our fine suitors, without warning,
draw upon me, kill me in our hall,   90
and parcel out my patrimony—I wish
you, and no one of them, to have those things.
But if my hour comes, if I can bring down

bloody death on all that crew,
you will rejoice to send my gifts to me—   95
and so will I rejoice!"

                    Then he departed,
leading his guest, the lonely stranger, home.

Over chair-backs in hall they dropped their mantles
and passed in to the polished tubs, where maids
poured out warm baths for them, anointed them,   100
and pulled fresh tunics, fleecy cloaks around them.
Soon they were seated at their ease in hall.
A maid came by to tip a golden jug
over their fingers into a silver bowl
and draw a gleaming table up beside them.   105
The larder mistress brought her tray of loaves
and savories, dispensing each.
                              In silence
across the hall, beside a pillar, propped
in a long chair, Telémakhos' mother
spun a fine wool yarn.
                    The young men's hands   110
went out upon the good things placed before them,
and only when their hunger and thirst were gone
did she look up and say:

                    "Telémakhos,
what am I to do now? Return alone
and lie again on my forsaken bed—   115
sodden how often with my weeping
since that day when Odysseus put to sea
to join the Atreidai[1] before Troy?
                    Could you not
tell me, before the suitors fill our house,
what news you have of his return?"

                    He answered: 120

"Now that you ask a second time, dear Mother,
here is the truth.
                    We went ashore at Pylos
to Nestor, lord and guardian of the West,
who gave me welcome in his towering hall.
So kind he was, he might have been my father   125
and I his long-lost son—so truly kind,
taking me in with his own honored sons.
But as to Odysseus' bitter fate,
living or dead, he had no news at all
from anyone on earth, he said. He sent me   130
overland in a strong chariot
to Atreus' son, the captain, Meneláos.
And I saw Helen there, for whom the Argives
fought, and the Trojans fought, as the gods willed.
Then Meneláos of the great war cry   135

---

1. The sons of Atreus: Agamémnon and Meneláos.

asked me my errand in that ancient land
of Lakedaimon. So I told our story,
and in reply he burst out:

'Intolerable!
That feeble men, unfit as those men are,
should think to lie in that great captain's bed,   140
fawns in the lion's lair! As if a doe
put down her litter of sucklings there, while she
sniffed at the glen or grazed a grassy hollow.
Ha! Then the lord returns to his own bed
and deals out wretched doom on both alike.   145

So will Odysseus deal out doom on these.
O Father Zeus, Athena, and Apollo!
I pray he comes as once he was, in Lesbos,
when he stood up to wrestle Philomeleidês—
champion and Island King—   150
and smashed him down. How the Akhaians cheered!
If that Odysseus could meet the suitors,
they'd have a quick reply, a stunning dowry!
Now for your questions, let me come to the point.
I would not misreport it for you; let me   155
tell you what the Ancient of the Sea,
that infallible seer, told me.

On an island
your father lies and grieves. The Ancient saw him
held by a nymph, Kalypso, in her hall;
no means of sailing home remained to him,   160
no ship with oars, and no ship's company
to pull him on the broad back of the sea.'

I had this from the lord marshal, Meneláos,
and when my errand in that place was done
I left for home. A fair breeze from the gods   165
brought me swiftly back to our dear island."

The boy's tale made her heart stir in her breast,
but this was not all. Mother and son now heard
Theoklýmenos, the diviner, say:

"He does not see it clear—
O gentle lady,   170
wife of Odysseus Laërtiadês,
listen to me, I can reveal this thing.
Zeus be my witness, and the table set
for strangers and the hearth to which I've come—
the lord Odysseus, I tell you,   175
is present now, already, on this island!
Quartered somewhere, or going about, he knows
what evil is afoot. He has it in him
to bring a black hour on the suitors. Yesterday,
still at the ship, I saw this in a portent.   180
I read the sign aloud, I told Telémakhos!"

The prudent queen, for her part, said:

        "Stranger,
if only this came true—
our love would go to you, with many gifts;
aye, every man who passed would call you happy!"   185

So ran the talk between these three.
        Meanwhile,
swaggering before Odysseus' hall,
the suitors were competing at the discus throw
and javelin, on the level measured field.
But when the dinner hour drew on, and beasts   190
were being driven from the fields to slaughter—
as beasts were, every day—Medôn spoke out:
Medôn, the crier, whom the suitors liked;
he took his meat beside them.

       "Men," he said,
"each one has had his work-out and his pleasure,   195
come in to Hall now; time to make our feast.
Are discus throws more admirable than a roast
when the proper hour comes?"

       At this reminder
they all broke up their games, and trailed away
into the gracious, timbered hall. There, first,   200
they dropped their cloaks on chairs; then came their ritual:
putting great rams and fat goats to the knife—
pigs and a cow, too.
      So they made their feast.

During these hours, Odysseus and the swineherd
were on their way out of the hills to town.   205
The forester had got them started, saying:

"Friend, you have hopes, I know, of your adventure
into the heart of town today. My lord
wishes it so, not I. No, I should rather
you stood by here as guardian of our steading.   210
But I owe reverence to my prince, and fear
he'll make my ears burn later if I fail.
A master's tongue has a rough edge. Off we go.
Part of the day is past; nightfall will be
early, and colder, too."

      Odysseus,   215
who had it all timed in his head, replied:

"I know, as well as you do. Let's move on.
You lead the way—the whole way. Have you got
a staff, a lopped stick, you could let me use
to put my weight on when I slip? This path   220
is hard going, they said."

      Over his shoulders
he slung his patched-up knapsack, an old bundle
tied with twine. Eumaios found a stick for him,
the kind he wanted, and the two set out,

leaving the boys and dogs to guard the place.   225
In this way good Eumaios led his lord
down to the city.
            And it seemed to him
he led an old outcast, a beggar man,
leaning most painfully upon a stick,
his poor cloak, all in tatters, looped about him.   230

Down by the stony trail they made their way
as far as Clearwater, not far from town—
a spring house where the people filled their jars.
Ithakos, Nêritos, and Polýktor[2] built it,
and round it on the humid ground a grove,   235
a circular wood of poplars grew. Ice cold
in runnels from a high rock ran the spring,
and over it there stood an altar stone
to the cool nymphs, where all men going by
laid offerings.
            Well, here the son of Dólios   240
crossed their path—Melánthios.
                    He was driving
a string of choice goats for the evening meal,
with two goatherds beside him; and no sooner
had he laid eyes upon the wayfarers
than he began to growl and taunt them both   245
so grossly that Odysseus' heart grew hot:

"Here comes one scurvy type leading another!
God pairs them off together, every time.
Swineherd, where are you taking your new pig,
that stinking beggar there, licker of pots?   250
How many doorposts has he rubbed his back on
whining for garbage, where a noble guest
would rate a cauldron or a sword?
                   Hand him
over to me, I'll make a farmhand of him,
a stall scraper, a fodder carrier! Whey   255
for drink will put good muscle on his shank!
No chance: he learned his dodges long ago—
no honest sweat. He'd rather tramp the country
begging, to keep his hoggish belly full.
Well, I can tell you this for sure: 260
in King Odysseus' hall, if he goes there,
footstools will fly around his head—good shots
from strong hands. Back and side, his ribs will catch it
on the way out!"

            And like a drunken fool
he kicked at Odysseus' hip as he passed by.   265
Not even jogged off stride, or off the trail,
the Lord Odysseus walked along, debating

---

2. Presumably the first rulers of Ithaka. Ithakos gave the island its name. Nêritos' name was given to the mountain on Íthaka (IX.23). Polýktor's name may possibly mean "having great possessions."

inwardly whether to whirl and beat
the life out of this fellow with his stick,
or toss him, brain him on the stony ground.   270
Then he controlled himself, and bore it quietly.
Not so the swineherd.
     Seeing the man before him,
he raised his arms and cried:

      "Nymphs of the spring,
daughters of Zeus, if ever Odysseus
burnt you a thighbone in rich fat—a ram's   275
or kid's thighbone, hear me, grant my prayer:
let our true lord come back, let heaven bring him
to rid the earth of these fine courtly ways
Melánthios picks up around the town—
all wine and wind! Bad shepherds ruin flocks!"   280

Melánthios the goatherd answered:

      "Bless me!
The dog can snap: how he goes on! Some day
I'll take him in a slave ship overseas
and trade him for a herd!
     Old Silverbow
Apollo, if he shot clean through Telémakhos   285
in hall today, what luck! Or let the suitors
cut him down!
    Odysseus died at sea;
no coming home for him."

      He flung this out
and left the two behind to come on slowly,
while he went hurrying to the king's hall.   290
There he slipped in, and sat among the suitors,
beside the one he doted on—Eurýmakhos.
Then working servants helped him to his meat
and the mistress of the larder gave him bread.

Reaching the gate, Odysseus and the forester   295
halted and stood outside, for harp notes came
around them ripping on the air
as Phêmios picked out a song. Odysseus
caught his companion's arm and said:

      "My friend,
here is the beautiful place—who could mistake it?   300
Here is Odysseus' hall: no hall like this!
See how one chamber grows out of another;
see how the court is tight with wall and coping;
no man at arms could break this gateway down!
Your banqueting young lords are here in force,   305
I gather, from the fumes of mutton roasting
and strum of harping—harping, which the gods
appoint sweet friend of feasts!"

    And—O my swineherd!

you replied:

> "That was quick recognition;
> but you are no numbskull—in this or anything.
> Now we must plan this action. Will you take
> leave of me here, and go ahead alone
> to make your entrance now among the suitors?
> Or do you choose to wait?—Let me go forward
> and go in first.   310
>   Do not delay too long;   315
> someone might find you skulking here outside
> and take a club to you, or heave a lance.
> Bear this in mind, I say."

                    The patient hero
Odysseus answered:

>   "Just what I was thinking.
> You go in first, and leave me here a little.   320
> But as for blows and missiles,
> I am no tyro at these things. I learned
> to keep my head in hardship—years of war
> and years at sea. Let this new trial come.
> The cruel belly, can you hide its ache?   325
> How many bitter days it brings! Long ships
> with good stout planks athwart—would fighters rig them
> to ride the barren sea, except for hunger?
> Seawolves—woe to their enemies!"

                        While he spoke
an old hound, lying near, pricked up his ears   330
and lifted up his muzzle. This was Argos,
trained as a puppy by Odysseus,
but never taken on a hunt before
his master sailed for Troy. The young men, afterward,
hunted wild goats with him, and hare, and deer,   335
but he had grown old in his master's absence.
Treated as rubbish now, he lay at last
upon a mass of dung before the gates—
manure of mules and cows, piled there until
fieldhands could spread it on the king's estate.   340
Abandoned there, and half destroyed with flies,
old Argos lay.
           But when he knew he heard
Odysseus' voice nearby, he did his best
to wag his tail, nose down, with flattened ears,
having no strength to move nearer his master.   345
And the man looked away,
wiping a salt tear from his cheek; but he
hid this from Eumaios. Then he said:

> "I marvel that they leave this hound to lie
> here on the dung pile;   350
> he would have been a fine dog, from the look of him,
> though I can't say as to his power and speed
> when he was young. You find the same good build

in house dogs, table dogs landowners keep
all for style."

And you replied, Eumaios: 355

"A hunter owned him—but the man is dead
in some far place. If this old hound could show
the form he had when Lord Odysseus left him,
going to Troy, you'd see him swift and strong.
He never shrank from any savage thing   360
he'd brought to bay in the deep woods; on the scent
no other dog kept up with him. Now misery
has him in leash. His owner died abroad,
and here the women slaves will take no care of him.
You know how servants are: without a master   365
they have no will to labor, or excel.
For Zeus who views the wide world takes away
half the manhood of a man, that day
he goes into captivity and slavery."

Eumaios crossed the court and went straight forward   370
into the mégaron among the suitors;
but death and darkness in that instant closed
the eyes of Argos, who had seen his master,
Odysseus, after twenty years.

                              Long before anyone else
Telémakhos caught sight of the grey woodsman   375
coming from the door, and called him over
with a quick jerk of his head. Eumaios'
narrowed eyes made out an empty bench
beside the one the carver used—that servant
who had no respite, carving for the suitors.   380
This bench he took possession of, and placed it
across the table from Telémakhos
for his own use. Then the two men were served
cuts from a roast and bread from a bread basket.

At no long interval, Odysseus came   385
through his own doorway as a mendicant,
humped like a bundle of rags over his stick.
He settled on the inner ash wood sill,
leaning against the door jamb—cypress timber
the skilled carpenter planed years ago   390
and set up with a plumbline.

                              Now Telémakhos
took an entire loaf and a double handful
of roast meat; then he said to the forester:

"Give these to the stranger there. But tell him
to go among the suitors, on his own;   395
he may beg all he wants. This hanging back
is no asset to a hungry man."

The swineherd rose at once, crossed to the door,
and halted by Odysseus.

"Friend," he said,
"Telémakhos is pleased to give you these,   400
but he commands you to approach the suitors;
you may ask all you want from them. He adds,
your shyness is no asset to a beggar."

The great tactician, lifting up his eyes,
cried:

        "Zeus aloft! A blessing on Telémakhos!   405
Let all things come to pass as he desires!"

Palms held out, in the beggar's gesture, he
received the bread and meat and put it down
before him on his knapsack—lowly table!—
then he fell to, devouring it. Meanwhile   410
the harper in the great room sang a song.
Not till the man was fed did the sweet harper
end his singing—whereupon the company
made the walls ring again with talk.

                                     Unseen,
Athena took her place beside Odysseus   415
whispering in his ear:

                 "Yes, try the suitors.
You may collect a few more loaves, and learn
who are the decent lads, and who are vicious—
although not one can be excused from death!"

So he appealed to them, one after another,   420
going from left to right, with open palm,
as though his life time had been spent in beggary.
And they gave bread, for pity—wondering, though,
at the strange man. Who could this beggar be,
where did he come from? each would ask his neighbor;   425
till in their midst the goatherd, Melánthios,
raised his voice:

                 "Hear just a word from me,
my lords who court our illustrious queen!
                                     This man,
this foreigner, I saw him on the road;
the swineherd, here was leading him this way;   430
who, what, or whence he claims to be, I could not
say for sure."

                 At this, Antínoös
turned on the swineherd brutally, saying:

                                     "You famous
breeder of pigs, why bring this fellow here?
Are we not plagued enough with beggars,   435
foragers and such rats?
                 You find the company
too slow at eating up your lord's estate—
is that it? So you call this scarecrow in?"

The forester replied:

"Antínoös,
well born you are, but that was not well said.   440
Who would call in a foreigner?—unless
an artisan with skill to serve the realm,
a healer, or a prophet, or a builder,
or one whose harp and song might give us joy.
All these are sought for on the endless earth,   445
but when have beggars come by invitation?
Who puts a field mouse in his granary? My lord,
you are a hard man, and you always were,
more so than others of this company—hard
on all Odysseus' people and on me.   450
But this I can forget
as long as Penélopê lives on, the wise and tender
mistress of this hall; as long
as Prince Telémakhos—"

But he broke off
at a look from Telémakhos, who said:

"Be still.   455
Spare me a long-drawn answer to this gentleman.
With his unpleasantness, he will forever make
strife where he can—and goad the others on."

He turned and spoke out clearly to Antínoös:

"What fatherly concern you show me! Frighten   460
this unknown fellow, would you, from my hall
with words that promise blows—may God forbid it!
Give him a loaf. Am I a niggard? No,
I call on you to give. And spare your qualms
as to my mother's loss, or anyone's—   465
not that in truth you have such care at heart:
your heart is all in feeding, not in giving."

Antínoös replied:

"What high and mighty
talk, Telémakhos! No holding you!
If every suitor gave what I may give him,   470
he could be kept for months—kept out of sight!"

He reached under the table for the footstool
his shining feet had rested on—and this
he held up so that all could see his gift.

But all the rest gave alms,   475
enough to fill the beggar's pack with bread
and roast meat.
So it looked as though Odysseus
had had his taste of what these men were like
and could return scot free to his own doorway—
but halting now before Antínoös   480
he made a little speech to him. Said he:

"Give a mite, friend. I would not say, myself,
you are the worst man of the young Akhaians.
The noblest, rather; kingly, by your look;
therefore you'll give more bread than others do.   485
Let me speak well of you as I pass on
over the boundless earth!

                            I, too, you know,
had fortune once, lived well, stood well with men,
and gave alms, often, to poor wanderers
like this one that you see—aye, to all sorts,   490
no matter in what dire want. I owned
servants—many, god knows—and all the rest
that goes with being prosperous, as they say.
But Zeus the son of Kronos brought me down.

                                        No telling
why he would have it, but he made me go   495
to Egypt with a company of rovers—
a long sail to the south—for my undoing.
Up the broad Nile and in to the river bank
I brought my dipping squadron. There, indeed,
I told the men to stand guard at the ships;   500
I sent patrols out—out to rising ground;
but reckless greed carried my crews away
to plunder the Egyptian farms; they bore off
wives and children, killed what men they found.
The news ran on the wind to the city, a night cry,   505
and sunrise brought both infantry and horsemen,
filling the river plain with dazzle of bronze;
then Zeus lord of lightning
threw my men into a blind panic; no one dared
stand against that host closing around us.   510
Their scything weapons left our dead in piles,
but some they took alive, into forced labor,
myself among them. And they gave me, then,
to one Dmêtor, a traveller, son of Iasos,
who ruled at Kypros.[3] He conveyed me there.   515
From that place, working northward, miserably—"

But here Antínoös broke in, shouting:

                                        "God!
What evil wind blew in this pest?
                            Get over,
stand in the passage! Nudge my table, will you?
Egyptian whips are sweet   520
to what you'll come to here, you nosing rat,
making your pitch to everyone!
These men have bread to throw away on you
because it is not theirs. Who cares? Who spares
another's food, when he has more than plenty?"   525

With guile Odysseus drew away, then said:

3. Or Cyprus.

"A pity that you have more looks than heart.
You'd grudge a pinch of salt from your own larder
to your own handy man. You sit here, fat
on others' meat, and cannot bring yourself   530
to rummage out a crust of bread for me!"

Then anger made Antínoös' heart beat hard,
and, glowering under his brows, he answered:

                                        "Now!
You think you'll shuffle off and get away
after that impudence? Oh, no you don't!"   535

The stool he let fly hit the man's right shoulder
on the packed muscle under the shoulder blade—
like solid rock, for all the effect one saw.
Odysseus only shook his head, containing
thoughts of bloody work, as he walked on,   540
then sat, and dropped his loaded bag again
upon the door sill. Facing the whole crowd
he said, and eyed them all:
                              "One word only,
my lords, and suitors of the famous queen.
One thing I have to say.   545
There is no pain, no burden for the heart
when blows come to a man, and he defending
his own cattle—his own cows and lambs.
Here it was otherwise. Antínoös
hit me for being driven on by hunger—   550
how many bitter seas men cross for hunger!
If beggars interest the gods, if there are Furies
pent in the dark to avenge a poor man's wrong, then may
Antínoös meet his death before his wedding day!"

Then said Eupeithês' son, Antínoös:

                                  "Enough.   555
Eat and be quiet where you are, or shamble elsewhere,
unless you want these lads to stop your mouth
pulling you by the heels, or hands and feet,
over the whole floor, till your back is peeled!"

But now the rest were mortified, and someone   560
spoke from the crowd of young bucks to rebuke him:

"A poor show, that—hitting this famished tramp—
bad business, if he happened to be a god.
You know they go in foreign guise, the gods do,
looking like strangers, turning up   565
in towns and settlements to keep an eye
on manners, good or bad."

                      But at this notion
Antínoös only shrugged.
                        Telémakhos,
after the blow his father bore, sat still

without a tear, though his heart felt the blow.   570
Slowly he shook his head from side to side,
containing murderous thoughts.
                    Penélopê
on the higher level of her room had heard
the blow, and knew who gave it. Now she murmured:

"Would god you could be hit yourself, Antínoös—   575
hit by Apollo's bowshot!"

                    And Eurýnomê
her housekeeper, put in:

                    "He and no other?
If all we pray for came to pass, not one
would live till dawn!"

                    Her gentle mistress said:

"Oh, Nan, they are a bad lot; they intend   580
ruin for all of us; but Antínoös
appears a blacker-hearted hound than any.
Here is a poor man come, a wanderer,
driven by want to beg his bread, and everyone
in hall gave bits, to cram his bag—only   585
Antínoös threw a stool, and banged his shoulder!"

So she described it, sitting in her chamber
among her maids—while her true lord was eating.
Then she called in the forester and said:

"Go to that man on my behalf, Eumaios,   590
and send him here, so I can greet and question him.
Abroad in the great world, he may have heard
rumors about Odysseus—may have known him!"

Then you replied—O swineherd!

                    "Ah, my queen,
if these Akhaian sprigs would hush their babble   595
the man could tell you tales to charm your heart.
Three days and nights I kept him in my hut;
he came straight off a ship, you know, to me.
There was no end to what he made me hear
of his hard roving and I listened, eyes   600
upon him, as a man drinks in a tale
a minstrel sings—a minstrel taught by heaven
to touch the hearts of men. At such a song
the listener becomes rapt and still. Just so
I found myself enchanted by this man.   605
He claims an old tie with Odysseus, too—
in his home country, the Minoan land
of Krete. From Krete he came, a rolling stone
washed by the gales of life this way and that
to our own beach.
                    If he can be believed   610
he has news of Odysseus near at hand

alive, in the rich country of Thesprotia,
bringing a mass of treasure home."

Then wise Penélopê said again:

"Go call him, let him come here, let him tell   615
that tale again for my own ears.
                        Our friends
can drink their cups outside or stay in hall,
being so carefree. And why not? Their stores
lie intact in their homes, both food and drink,
with only servants left to take a little.   620
But these men spend their days around our house
killing our beeves, our fat goats and our sheep,
carousing, drinking up our good dark wine;
sparing nothing, squandering everything.
No champion like Odysseus takes our part.   625
Ah, if he comes again, no falcon ever
struck more suddenly than he will, with his son,
to avenge this outrage!"
                        The great hall below
at this point rang with a tremendous sneeze—
"kchaou!" from Telémakhos—like an acclamation.   630
And laughter seized Penélopê.
                        Then quickly,
lucidly she went on:

                        "Go call the stranger
straight to me. Did you hear that, Eumaios?
My son's thundering sneeze at what I said!
May death come of a sudden so; may death   635
relieve us, clean as that, of all the suitors!
Let me add one thing—do not overlook it—
if I can see this man has told the truth,
I promise him a warm new cloak and tunic."

With all this in his head, the forester   640
went down the hall, and halted near the beggar,
saying aloud:

                        "Good father, you are called
by the wise mother of Telémakhos,
Penélopê. The queen, despite her troubles,
is moved by a desire to hear your tales   645
about her lord—and if she finds them true,
she'll see you clothed in what you need, a cloak
and a fresh tunic.
                        You may have your belly
full each day you go about this realm
begging. For all may give, and all they wish."   650

Now said Odysseus, the old soldier:

                        "Friend,
I wish this instant I could tell my facts
to the wise daughter of Ikários, Penélopê—

and I have much to tell about her husband;
we went through much together.
                                    But just now   655
this hard crowd worries me. They are, you said
infamous to the very rim of heaven
for violent acts: and here, just now, this fellow
gave me a bruise. What had I done to him?
But who would lift a hand for me? Telémakhos?   660
Anyone else?
                No; bid the queen be patient.
Let her remain till sundown in her room,
and then—if she will seat me near the fire—
inquire tonight about her lord's return.
My rags are sorry cover; you know that;   665
I showed my sad condition first to you."

The woodsman heard him out, and then returned;
but the queen met him on her threshold, crying:

"Have you not brought him? Why? What is he thinking?
Has he some fear of overstepping? Shy   670
about these inner rooms? A hangdog beggar?"

To this you answered, friend Eumaios:

                                    "No:
he reasons as another might, and well,
not to tempt any swordplay from these drunkards.
Be patient, wait—he says—till darkness falls.   675
And, O my queen, for you too that is better:
better to be alone with him, and question him,
and hear him out."

                Penélopê replied:

"He is no fool; he sees how it could be.
Never were mortal men like these   680
for bullying and brainless arrogance!"

Thus she accepted what had been proposed,
so he went back into the crowd. He joined
Telémakhos, and said at once in whispers—
his head bent, so that no one else might hear: 685

"Dear prince, I must go home to keep good watch
on hut and swine, and look to my own affairs.
Everything here is in your hands. Consider
your own safety before the rest; take care
not to get hurt. Many are dangerous here.   690
May Zeus destroy them first, before we suffer!"

Telémakhos said:

                "Your wish is mine, Uncle.
Go when your meal is finished. Then come back
at dawn, and bring good victims for a slaughter.
Everything here is in my hands indeed—   695
and in the disposition of the gods."

Taking his seat on the smooth bench again,
Eumaios ate and drank his fill, then rose
to climb the mountain trail back to his swine,
leaving the mégaron and court behind him   700
crowded with banqueters.
     These had their joy
of dance and song, as day waned into evening.

BOOK XVIII

[Blows and a Queen's Beauty]

Now a true scavenger came in—a public tramp
who begged around the town of Ithaka,
a by-word for his insatiable swag-belly,
feeding and drinking, dawn to dark. No pith
was in him, and no nerve, huge as he looked.   5
Arnaios, as his gentle mother called him,
he had been nicknamed "Iros" by the young
for being ready to take messages.[4]
      This fellow
thought he would rout Odysseus from his doorway,
growling at him:

     "Clear out, grandfather,   10
or else be hauled out by the ankle bone.
See them all giving me the wink? That means,
'Go on and drag him out!' I hate to do it.
Up with you! Or would you like a fist fight?"

Odysseus only frowned and looked him over,   15
taking account of everything, then said:

"Master, I am no trouble to you here.
I offer no remarks. I grudge you nothing.
Take all you get, and welcome. Here is room
for two on this doorslab—or do you own it?   20
You are a tramp, I think, like me. Patience:
a windfall from the gods will come. But drop
that talk of using fists; it could annoy me.
Old as I am, I might just crack a rib
or split a lip for you. My life would go   25
even more peacefully, after tomorrow,
looking for no more visits here from you."

Iros the tramp grew red and hooted:

        "Ho,
listen to him! The swine can talk your arm off,
like an old oven woman! With two punches   30
I'd knock him snoring, if I had a mind to—
and not a tooth left in his head, the same
as an old sow caught in the corn! Belt up!

---

4. The goddess Iris often served as messenger for the gods.

And let this company see the way I do it
when we square off. Can you fight a fresher man?"   35

Under the lofty doorway, on the door sill
of wide smooth ash, they held this rough exchange.
And the tall full-blooded suitor, Antínoös,
overhearing, broke into happy laughter.
Then he said to the others:

                              "Oh, my friends,   40
no luck like this ever turned up before!
What a farce heaven has brought this house!
                                        The stranger
and Iros have had words, they brag of boxing!
Into the ring they go, and no more talk!"

All the young men got on their feet now, laughing,   45
to crowd around the ragged pair. Antínoös
called out:

                  "Gentlemen, quiet! One more thing:
here are goat stomachs ready on the fire
to stuff with blood and fat, good supper pudding.
The man who wins this gallant bout   50
may step up here and take the one he likes.
And let him feast with us from this day on:
no other beggar will be admitted here
when we are at our wine."

                              This pleased them all.
But now that wily man, Odysseus, muttered: 55

"An old man, an old hulk, has no business
fighting a young man, but my belly nags me;
nothing will do but I must take a beating.
Well, then, let every man here swear an oath
not to step in for Iros. No one throw   60
a punch for luck. I could be whipped that way."

So much the suitors were content to swear,
but after they reeled off their oaths, Telémakhos
put in a word to clinch it, saying:
                                        "Friend,
if you will stand and fight, as pride requires,   65
don't worry about a foul blow from behind.
Whoever hits you will take on the crowd.
You have my word as host; you have the word
of these two kings, Antínoös and Eurýmakhos—
a pair of thinking men."

                              All shouted, "Aye!"   70
So now Odysseus made his shirt a belt
and roped his rags around his loins, baring
his hurdler's thighs and boxer's breadth of shoulder,
the dense rib-sheath and upper arms. Athena

stood nearby to give him bulk and power,   75
while the young suitors watched with narrowed eyes—
and comments went around:

"By god, old Iros now retires."

                         "Aye,
he asked for it, he'll get it—bloody, too."

"The build this fellow had, under his rags!"   80

Panic made Iros' heart jump, but the yard-boys
hustled and got him belted by main force,
though all his blubber quivered now with dread.
Antínoös' angry voice rang in his ears:

"You sack of guts, you might as well be dead,   85
might as well never have seen the light of day,
if this man makes you tremble! Chicken-heart,
afraid of an old wreck, far gone in misery!
Well, here is what I say—and what I'll do.
If this ragpicker can outfight you, whip you,   90
I'll ship you out to that king in Epeíros,
Ékhetos⁵—he skins everyone alive.
Let him just cut your nose off and your ears
and pull your privy parts out by the roots
to feed raw to his hunting dogs!"

                        Poor Iros   95
felt a new fit of shaking take his knees.
But the yard-boys pushed him out. Now both contenders
put their hands up. Royal Odysseus
pondered if he should hit him with all he had
and drop the man dead on the spot, or only   100
spar, with force enough to knock him down.
Better that way, he thought—a gentle blow,
else he might give himself away.
                     The two
were at close quarters now, and Iros lunged
hitting the shoulder. Then Odysseus hooked him   105
under the ear and shattered his jaw bone,
so bright red blood came bubbling from his mouth,
as down he pitched into the dust, bleating,
kicking against the ground, his teeth stove in.
The suitors whooped and swung their arms, half dead   110
with pangs of laughter.
                  Then, by the ankle bone,
Odysseus hauled the fallen one outside,
crossing the courtyard to the gate, and piled him
against the wall. In his right hand he stuck
his begging staff, and said:

                    "Here, take your post.   115
Sit here to keep the dogs and pigs away.
You can give up your habit of command

---

5. All we know of him is what Homer tells us here. Epeíros (Epirus) is north of Ithaka.

over poor waifs and beggarmen—you swab.
Another time you may not know what hit you."

When he had slung his rucksack by the string   120
over his shoulder, like a wad of rags,
he sat down on the broad door sill again,
as laughing suitors came to flock inside;
and each young buck in passing gave him greeting,
saying, maybe,

        "Zeus fill your pouch for this!   125
May the gods grant your heart's desire!"

                "Well done
to put that walking famine out of business."

"We'll ship him out to that king in Epeíros,
Ékhetos—he skins everyone alive."

Odysseus found grim cheer in their good wishes—   130
his work had started well.
        Now from the fire
his fat blood pudding came, deposited
before him by Antínoös—then, to boot,
two brown loaves from the basket, and some wine
in a fine cup of gold. These gifts Amphínomos   135
gave him. Then he said:

        "Here's luck, grandfather;
a new day; may the worst be over now."

Odysseus answered, and his mind ranged far:

"Amphínomos, your head is clear, I'd say;
so was your father's—or at least I've heard   140
good things of Nísos the Doulíkhion,
whose son you are, they tell me—an easy man.
And you seem gently bred.
        In view of that,
I have a word to say to you, so listen.

Of mortal creatures, all that breathe and move,   145
earth bears none frailer than mankind. What man
believes in woe to come, so long as valor
and tough knees are supplied him by the gods?
But when the gods in bliss bring miseries on,
then willy-nilly, blindly, he endures.   150
Our minds are as the days are, dark or bright,
blown over by the father of gods and men.

So I, too, in my time thought to be happy;
but far and rash I ventured, counting on
my own right arm, my father, and my kin;   155
behold me now.
        No man should flout the law,
but keep in peace what gifts the gods may give.

I see you young blades living dangerously,
a household eaten up, a wife dishonored—

and yet the master will return, I tell you,   160
to his own place, and soon; for he is near.
So may some power take you out of this,
homeward, and softly, not to face that man
the hour he sets foot on his native ground.
Between him and the suitors I foretell   165
no quittance, no way out, unless by blood,
once he shall stand beneath his own roof-beam."

Gravely, when he had done, he made libation
and took a sip of honey-hearted wine,
giving the cup, then, back into the hands   170
of the young nobleman. Amphínomos, for his part,
shaking his head, with chill and burdened breast,
turned in the great hall.
                Now his heart foreknew
the wrath to come, but he could not take flight,
being by Athena bound there.
                Death would have him   175
broken by a spear thrown by Telémakhos.
So he sat down where he had sat before.

And now heart-prompting from the grey-eyed goddess
came to the quiet queen, Penélopê:
a wish to show herself before the suitors;   180
for thus by fanning their desire again
Athena meant to set her beauty high
before her husband's eyes, before her son.
Knowing no reason, laughing confusedly,
she said:
        "Eurýnomê, I have a craving   185
I never had at all—I would be seen
among those ruffians, hateful as they are.
I might well say a word, then, to my son,
for his own good—tell him to shun that crowd;
for all their gay talk, they are bent on evil."   190

Mistress Eurýnomê replied:
              "Well said, child,
now is the time. Go down, and make it clear,
hold nothing back from him.
               But you must bathe
and put a shine upon your cheeks—not this way,
streaked under your eyes and stained with tears.   195
You make it worse, being forever sad,
and now your boy's a bearded man! Remember
you prayed the gods to let you see him so."

Penélopê replied:
        "Eurýnomê,
it is a kind thought, but I will not hear it—   200
to bathe and sleek with perfumed oil. No, no,
the gods forever took my sheen away

when my lord sailed for Troy in the decked ships.
Only tell my Autonoë to come,
and Hippodameía; they should be attending me   205
in hall, if I appear there. I could not
enter alone into that crowd of men."

At this the good old woman left the chamber
to tell the maids her bidding. But now too
the grey-eyed goddess had her own designs.   210
Upon the quiet daughter of Ikários
she let clear drops of slumber fall, until
the queen lay back asleep, her limbs unstrung,
in her long chair. And while she slept the goddess
endowed her with immortal grace to hold   215
the eyes of the Akhaians. With ambrosia
she bathed her cheeks and throat and smoothed her brow—
ambrosia, used by flower-crowned Kythereia[6]
when she would join the rose-lipped Graces dancing.
Grandeur she gave her, too, in height and form,   220
and made her whiter than carved ivory.
Touching her so, the perfect one was gone.
Now came the maids, bare-armed and lovely, voices
breaking into the room. The queen awoke
and as she rubbed her cheek she sighed:

                              "Ah, soft   225
that drowse I lay embraced in, pain forgot!
If only Artemis the Pure would give me
death as mild, and soon! No heart-ache more,
no wearing out my lifetime with desire
and sorrow, mindful of my lord, good man   230
in all ways that he was, best of the Akhaians!"

She rose and left her glowing upper room,
and down the stairs, with her two maids in train,
this beautiful lady went before the suitors.
Then by a pillar of the solid roof   235
she paused, her shining veil across her cheek,
the two girls close to her and still;
and in that instant weakness took those men
in the knee joints, their hearts grew faint with lust;
not one but swore to god to lie beside her.   240
But speaking for her dear son's ears alone
she said:

          "Telémakhos, what has come over you?
Lightminded you were not, in all your boyhood.
Now you are full grown, come of age; a man
from foreign parts might take you for the son   245
of royalty, to go by your good looks;
and have you no more thoughtfulness or manners?
How could it happen in our hall that you
permit the stranger to be so abused?

6. Aphrodite.

Here, in our house, a guest, can any man   250
suffer indignity, come by such injury?
What can this be for you but public shame?"

Telémakhos looked in her eyes and answered,
with his clear head and his discretion:

                              "Mother,
I cannot take it ill that you are angry.   255
I know the meaning of these actions now,
both good and bad. I had been young and blind.
How can I always keep to what is fair
while these sit here to put fear in me?—princes
from near and far whose interest is my ruin;   260
are any on my side?
                    But you should know
the suitors did not have their way, matching
the stranger here and Iros—for the stranger
beat him to the ground.
                    O Father Zeus!
Athena and Apollo! could I see   265
the suitors whipped like that! Courtyard and hall
strewn with our friends, too weak-kneed to get up,
chapfallen to their collarbones, the way
old Iros rolls his head there by the gate
as though he were pig-drunk! No energy   270
to stagger on his homeward path; no fight
left in his numb legs!"

                    Thus Penélopê
reproached her son, and he replied. Now, interrupting,
Eurýmakhos called out to her:

                         "Penélopê,
deep-minded queen, daughter of Ikários,   275
if all Akhaians in the land of Argos
only saw you now! What hundreds more
would join your suitors here to feast tomorrow!
Beauty like yours no woman had before,
or majesty, or mastery."

                    She answered: 280

"Eurýmakhos, my qualities—I know—
my face, my figure, all were lost or blighted
when the Akhaians crossed the sea to Troy,
Odysseus my lord among the rest.
If he returned, if he were here to care for me,   285
I might be happily renowned!
But grief instead heaven sent me—years of pain.
Can I forget?—the day he left this island,
enfolding my right hand and wrist in his,
he said:

                    'My lady, the Akhaian troops   290
will not easily make it home again

full strength, unhurt, from Troy. They say the Trojans
are fighters too; good lances and good bowmen,
horsemen, charioteers—and those can be
decisive when a battle hangs in doubt.   295
So whether God will send me back, or whether
I'll be a captive there, I cannot tell.
Here, then, you must attend to everything.
My parents in our house will be a care for you
as they are now, or more, while I am gone.   300
Wait for the beard to darken our boy's cheek;
then marry whom you will, and move away.'

The years he spoke of are now past; the night
comes when a bitter marriage overtakes me,
desolate as I am, deprived by Zeus   305
of all the sweets of life.
                        How galling, too,
to see newfangled manners in my suitors!
Others who go to court a gentlewoman,
daughter of a rich house, if they are rivals,
bring their own beeves and sheep along; her friends   310
ought to be feasted, gifts are due to her;
would any dare to live at her expense?"

Odysseus' heart laughed when he heard all this—
her sweet tones charming gifts out of the suitors
with talk of marriage, though she intended none.   315
Eupeithês' son, Antínoös, now addressed her:

"Ikários' daughter, O deep-minded queen!
If someone cares to make you gifts, accept them!
It is no courtesy to turn gifts away.
But we go neither to our homes nor elsewhere   320
until of all Akhaians here you take
the best man for your lord."

                        Pleased at this answer,
every man sent a squire to fetch a gift—
Antínoös, a wide resplendent robe,
embroidered fine, and fastened with twelve brooches,   325
pins pressed into sheathing tubes of gold;
Eurýmakhos, a necklace, wrought in gold,
with sunray pieces of clear glinting amber.
Eurýdamas' men came back with pendants,
ear-drops in triple clusters of warm lights;   330
and from the hoard of Lord Polýktor's son,
Peisándros, came a band for her white throat,
jewelled adornment. Other wondrous things
were brought as gifts from the Akhaian princes.
Penélopê then mounted the stair again,   335
her maids behind, with treasure in their arms.

And now the suitors gave themselves to dancing,
to harp and haunting song, as night drew on;
black night indeed came on them at their pleasure.
But three torch fires were placed in the long hall   340

to give them light. On hand were stores of fuel,
dry seasoned chips of resinous wood, split up
by the bronze hatchet blade—these were mixed in
among the flames to keep them flaring bright;
each housemaid of Odysseus took her turn.   345

Now he himself, the shrewd and kingly man,
approached and told them:

     "Housemaids of Odysseus,
your master so long absent in the world,
go to the women's chambers, to your queen.
Attend her, make the distaff whirl, divert her,   350
stay in her room, comb wool for her.
        I stand here
ready to tend these flares and offer light
to everyone. They cannot tire me out,
even if they wish to drink till Dawn.
I am a patient man."

      But the women giggled,   355
glancing back and forth—laughed in his face;
and one smooth girl, Melántho, spoke to him
most impudently. She was Dólios' daughter,
taken as ward in childhood by Penélopê
who gave her playthings to her heart's content   360
and raised her as her own. Yet the girl felt
nothing for her mistress, no compunction,
but slept and made love with Eurýmakhos.
Her bold voice rang now in Odysseus' ears:

"You must be crazy, punch drunk, you old goat.   365
Instead of going out to find a smithy
to sleep warm in—or a tavern bench—you stay
putting your oar in, amid all our men.
Numbskull, not to be scared! The wine you drank
has clogged your brain, or are you always this way,   370
boasting like a fool? Or have you lost
your mind because you beat that tramp, that Iros?
Look out, or someone better may get up
and give you a good knocking about the ears
to send you out all bloody."

      But Odysseus   375
glared at her under his brows and said:

        "One minute:
let me tell Telémakhos how you talk
in hall, you slut; he'll cut your arms and legs off!"

This hard shot took the women's breath away
and drove them quaking to their rooms, as though   380
knives were behind: they felt he spoke the truth.
So there he stood and kept the firelight high
and looked the suitors over, while his mind
roamed far ahead to what must be accomplished.

They, for their part, could not now be still   385
or drop their mockery—for Athena wished
Odysseus mortified still more.
                              Eurýmakhos,
the son of Pólybos, took up the baiting,
angling for a laugh among his friends.

"Suitors of our distinguished queen," he said,   390
"hear what my heart would have me say.
                              This man
comes with a certain aura of divinity
into Odysseus' hall. He shines.
                              He shines
around the noggin, like a flashing light,
having no hair at all to dim his lustre."   395

Then turning to Odysseus, raider of cities,
he went on:

                "Friend, you have a mind to work,
do you? Could I hire you to clear stones
from wasteland for me—you'll be paid enough—
collecting boundary walls and planting trees?   400
I'd give you a bread ration every day,
a cloak to wrap in, sandals for your feet.
Oh no: you learned your dodges long ago—
no honest sweat. You'd rather tramp the country
begging, to keep your hoggish belly full."   405

The master of many crafts replied:

                              "Eurýmakhos,
we two might try our hands against each other
in early summer when the days are long,
in meadow grass, with one good scythe for me
and one as good for you: we'd cut our way   410
down a deep hayfield, fasting to late evening.
Or we could try our hands behind a plow,
driving the best of oxen—fat, well-fed,
well-matched for age and pulling power, and say
four strips apiece of loam the share could break: 415
you'd see then if I cleft you a straight furrow.
Competition in arms? If Zeus Kroníon
roused up a scuffle now, give me a shield,
two spears, a dogskin cap with plates of bronze
to fit my temples, and you'd see me go   420
where the first rank of fighters lock in battle.
There would be no more jeers about my belly.
You thick-skinned menace to all courtesy!
You think you are a great man and a champion,
but up against few men, poor stuff, at that.   425
Just let Odysseus return, those doors
wide open as they are, you'd find too narrow
to suit you on your sudden journey out."

Now fury mounted in Eurýmakhos,
who scowled and shot back:

               "Bundle of rags and lice!   430
By god, I'll make you suffer for your gall,
your insolent gabble before all our men."

He had his foot-stool out: but now Odysseus
took to his haunches by Amphínomos' knees,
fearing Eurýmakhos' missile, as it flew.   435
It clipped a wine steward on the serving hand,
so that his pitcher dropped with a loud clang
while he fell backward, cursing, in the dust.
In the shadowy hall a low sound rose — of suitors
murmuring to one another.

             "Ai!" they said,   440
"This vagabond would have done well to perish
somewhere else, and make us no such rumpus.
Here we are, quarreling over tramps; good meat
and wine forgotten; good sense gone by the board."

Telémakhos, his young heart high, put in: 445

"Bright souls, alight with wine, you can no longer
hide the cups you've taken.[7] Aye, some god
is goading you. Why not go home to bed? —
I mean when you are moved to. No one jumps
at my command."

          Struck by his blithe manner,   450
the young men's teeth grew fixed in their under lips,
but now the son of Nísos, Lord Amphínomos
of Aretíadês, addressed them all:

"O friends, no ruffling replies are called for;
that was fair counsel.
           Hands off the stranger, now,   455
and hands off any other servant here
in the great house of King Odysseus. Come,
let my own herald wet our cups once more,
we'll make an offering, and then to bed.
The stranger can be left behind in hall;   460
Telémakhos may care for him; he came
to Telémakhos' door, not ours."

               This won them over.
The soldier Moulios, Doulíkhion herald,
comrade in arms of Lord Amphínomos,
mixed the wine and served them all. They tipped out   465
drops for the blissful gods, and drank the rest,
and when they had drunk their thirst away
they trailed off homeward drowsily to bed.

7. That is, you cannot hide the fact that you are drunk.

BOOK XIX

[Recognitions and a Dream]

Now by Athena's side in the quiet hall
studying the ground for slaughter, Lord Odysseus
turned to Telémakhos.

                           "The arms," he said.
"Harness and weapons must be out of sight
in the inner room. And if the suitors miss them,   5
be mild; just say 'I had a mind to move them
out of the smoke. They seemed no longer
the bright arms that Odysseus left at home
when he went off to Troy. Here where the fire's
hot breath came, they had grown black and drear.   10
One better reason struck me, too:
suppose a brawl starts up when you've been drinking—
you might in madness let each other's blood,
and that would stain your feast, your courtship.
                                         Iron
itself can draw men's hands.' "

                           Then he fell silent,   15
and Telémakhos obeyed his father's word.
He called Eurýkleia, the nurse, and told her:

"Nurse, go shut the women in their quarters
while I shift Father's armor back
to the inner rooms—these beautiful arms unburnished,   20
caked with black soot in his years abroad.
I was a child then. Well, I am not now.
I want them shielded from the draught and smoke."

And the old woman answered:

                           "It is time, child,
you took an interest in such things. I wish   25
you'd put your mind on all your house and chattels.
But who will go along to hold a light?
You said no maids, no torch-bearers."

                                         Telémakhos
looked at her and replied:

                           "Our friend here.
A man who shares my meat can bear a hand,   30
no matter how far he is from home."

                           He spoke so soldierly
her own speech halted on her tongue. Straight back
she went to lock the doors of the women's hall.
And now the two men sprang to work—father
and princely son, loaded with round helms   35
and studded bucklers, lifting the long spears,
while in their path Pallas Athena
held up a golden lamp of purest light.
Telémakhos at last burst out:

"Oh, Father,
here is a marvel! All around I see   40
the walls and roof beams, pedestals and pillars,
lighted as though by white fire blazing near.
One of the gods of heaven is in this place!"

Then said Odysseus, the great tactician,

"Be still: keep still about it: just remember it.   45
The gods who rule Olympos make this light.
You may go off to bed now. Here I stay
to test your mother and her maids again.
Out of her long grief she will question me."

Telémakhos went across the hall and out   50
under the light of torches—crossed the court
to the tower chamber where he had always slept.
Here now again he lay, waiting for dawn,
while in the great hall by Athena's side
Odysseus waited with his mind on slaughter.   55

Presently Penélopê from her chamber
stepped in her thoughtful beauty.
                            So might Artemis
or golden Aphroditê have descended;
and maids drew to the hearth her own smooth chair
inlaid with silver whorls and ivory. The artisan   60
Ikmálios had made it, long before,
with a footrest in a single piece, and soft
upon the seat a heavy fleece was thrown.
Here by the fire the queen sat down. Her maids,
leaving their quarters, came with white arms bare   65
to clear the wine cups and the bread, and move
the trestle boards where men had lingered drinking.
Fiery ashes out of the pine-chip flares
they tossed, and piled on fuel for light and heat.
And now a second time Melántho's voice   70
rang brazen in Odysseus' ears:

                         "Ah, stranger,
are you still here, so creepy, late at night
hanging about, looking the women over?
You old goat, go outside, cuddle your supper;
get out, or a torch may kindle you behind!"   75

At this Odysseus glared under his brows
and said:

          "Little devil, why pitch into me again?
Because I go unwashed and wear these rags,
and make the rounds? But so I must, being needy;
that is the way a vagabond must live.   80
And do not overlook this: in my time
I too had luck, lived well, stood well with men,
and gave alms, often, to poor wanderers
like him you see before you—aye, to all sorts,
no matter in what dire want. I owned   85

servants—many, I say—and all the rest
that goes with what men call prosperity.
But Zeus the son of Kronos brought me down.
Mistress, mend your ways, or you may lose
all this vivacity of yours. What if her ladyship   90
were stirred to anger? What if Odysseus came?—
and I can tell you, there is hope of that—
or if the man is done for, still his son
lives to be reckoned with, by Apollo's will.
None of you can go wantoning on the sly   95
and fool him now. He is too old for that."

Penélopê, being near enough to hear him,
spoke out sharply to her maid:

                              "Oh, shameless,
through and through! And do you think me blind,
blind to your conquest? It will cost your life.   100
You knew I waited—for you heard me say it—
waited to see this man in hall and question him
about my lord; I am so hard beset."

She turned away and said to the housekeeper:

"Eurýnomê, a bench, a spread of sheepskin,   105
to put my guest at ease. Now he shall talk
and listen, and be questioned."

                              Willing hands
brought a smooth bench, and dropped a fleece upon it.
Here the adventurer and king sat down;
then carefully Penélopê began: 110

"Friend, let me ask you first of all:
who are you, where do you come from, of what nation
and parents were you born?"

                         And he replied:

"My lady, never a man in the wide world
should have a fault to find with you. Your name   115
has gone out under heaven like the sweet
honor of some god-fearing king, who rules
in equity over the strong: his black lands bear
both wheat and barley, fruit trees laden bright,
new lambs at lambing time—and the deep sea   120
gives great hauls of fish by his good strategy,
so that his folk fare well.
                              O my dear lady,
this being so, let it suffice to ask me
of other matters—not my blood, my homeland.
Do not enforce me to recall my pain.   125
My heart is sore; but I must not be found
sitting in tears here, in another's house:
it is not well forever to be grieving.
One of the maids might say—or you might think—
I had got maudlin over cups of wine."   130

And Penélopê replied:

"Stranger, my looks,
my face, my carriage, were soon lost or faded
when the Akhaians crossed the sea to Troy,
Odysseus my lord among the rest.
If he returned, if he were here to care for me,   135
I might be happily renowned!
But grief instead heaven sent me—years of pain.
Sons of the noblest families on the islands,
Doulíkhion, Samê, wooded Zakýnthos,
with native Ithakans, are here to court me,   140
against my wish; and they consume this house.
Can I give proper heed to guest or suppliant
or herald on the realm's affairs?
                              How could I?
wasted with longing for Odysseus, while here
they press for marriage.
                              Ruses served my turn   145
to draw the time out—first a close-grained web
I had the happy thought to set up weaving
on my big loom in hall. I said, that day:
'Young men—my suitors, now my lord is dead,
let me finish my weaving before I marry,   150
or else my thread will have been spun in vain.
It is a shroud I weave for Lord Laërtês
when cold Death comes to lay him on his bier.
The country wives would hold me in dishonor
if he, with all his fortune, lay unshrouded.'   155
I reached their hearts that way, and they agreed.
So every day I wove on the great loom,
but every night by torchlight I unwove it;
and so for three years I deceived the Akhaians.
But when the seasons brought a fourth year on,   160
as long months waned, and the long days were spent,
through impudent folly in the slinking maids
they caught me—clamored up to me at night;
I had no choice then but to finish it.
And now, as matters stand at last,   165
I have no strength left to evade a marriage,
cannot find any further way; my parents
urge it upon me, and my son
will not stand by while they eat up his property.
He comprehends it, being a man full grown,   170
able to oversee the kind of house
Zeus would endow with honor.
                              But you too
confide in me, tell me your ancestry.
You were not born of mythic oak or stone."

And the great master of invention answered: 175

"O honorable wife of Lord Odysseus,
must you go on asking about my family?
Then I will tell you, though my pain

be doubled by it: and whose pain would not
if he had been away as long as I have   180
and had hard roving in the world of men?
But I will tell you even so, my lady.

One of the great islands of the world
in midsea, in the winedark sea, is Krete:
spacious and rich and populous, with ninety   185
cities and a mingling of tongues.
Akhaians there are found, along with Kretan
hillmen of the old stock, and Kydonians,
Dorians in three blood-lines, Pelasgians—
and one among their ninety towns is Knossos.[8]   190
Here lived King Minos whom great Zeus received
every ninth year in private council—Minos,
the father of my father, Deukálion.
Two sons Deukálion had: Idómeneus,
who went to join the Atreidai before Troy   195
in the beaked ships of war; and then myself,
Aithôn by name—a stripling next my brother.
But I saw with my own eyes at Knossos once
Odysseus.
            Gales had caught him off Cape Malea,
driven him southward on the coast of Krete,   200
when he was bound for Troy. At Ámnisos,
hard by the holy cave of Eileithuía,[9]
he lay to, and dropped anchor, in that open
and rough roadstead riding out the blow.
Meanwhile he came ashore, came inland, asking   205
after Idómeneus: dear friends he said they were;
but now ten mornings had already passed,
ten or eleven, since my brother sailed.
So I played host and took Odysseus home,
saw him well lodged and fed, for we had plenty;   210
then I made requisitions—barley, wine,
and beeves for sacrifice—to give his company
abundant fare along with him.
                                    Twelve days
they stayed with us, the Akhaians, while that wind
out of the north shut everyone inside—   215
even on land you could not keep your feet,
such fury was abroad. On the thirteenth,
when the gale dropped, they put to sea."

Now all these lies he made appear so truthful
she wept as she sat listening. The skin   220
of her pale face grew moist the way pure snow
softens and glistens on the mountains, thawed

---

8. The site of the great palace discovered by Evans, who called the civilization that produced it Minoan.
It is impossible to extract historical fact from this confused account of the population of Krete. Kydonians may be the inhabitants of the western end of the island. Dorians were the people who, according
to Greek belief, invaded Greece and destroyed the Mycenaean palace-civilizations (but Homer does
not mention them elsewhere). Pelasgians were the pre-Greek inhabitants of the area.   9. Goddess of
childbirth. Ámnisos is on the coast near Knossos.

by Southwind after powdering from the West,
and, as the snow melts, mountain streams run full:
so her white cheeks were wetted by these tears   225
shed for her lord—and he close by her side.
Imagine how his heart ached for his lady,
his wife in tears; and yet he never blinked;
his eyes might have been made of horn or iron
for all that she could see. He had this trick—   230
wept, if he willed to, inwardly.
                                   Well, then,
as soon as her relieving tears were shed
she spoke once more:

          "I think that I shall say, friend,
give me some proof, if it is really true
that you were host in that place to my husband   235
with his brave men, as you declare. Come, tell me
the quality of his clothing, how he looked,
and some particular of his company."

Odysseus answered, and his mind ranged far:

"Lady, so long a time now lies between,   240
it is hard to speak of it. Here is the twentieth year
since that man left the island of my father.
But I shall tell what memory calls to mind.
A purple cloak, and fleecy, he had on—
a double thick one. Then, he wore a brooch   245
made of pure gold with twin tubes for the prongs,
and on the face a work of art: a hunting dog
pinning a spotted fawn in agony
between his forepaws—wonderful to see
how being gold, and nothing more, he bit   250
the golden deer convulsed, with wild hooves flying.
Odysseus' shirt I noticed, too—a fine
closefitting tunic like dry onion skin,
so soft it was, and shiny.
                                   Women there,
many of them, would cast their eyes on it.   255
But I might add, for your consideration,
whether he brought these things from home, or whether
a shipmate gave them to him, coming aboard,
I have no notion: some regardful host
in another port perhaps it was. Affection   260
followed him—there were few Akhaians like him.
And I too made him gifts: a good bronze blade,
a cloak with lining and a broidered shirt,
and sent him off in his trim ship with honor.
A herald, somewhat older than himself,   265
he kept beside him; I'll describe this man:
round-shouldered, dusky, woolly-headed;
Eurýbatês, his name was—and Odysseus
gave him preferment over the officers.
He had a shrewd head, like the captain's own."   270

Now hearing these details—minutely true—
she felt more strangely moved, and tears flowed
until she had tasted her salt grief again.
Then she found words to answer:

                 "Before this
you won my sympathy, but now indeed   275
you shall be our respected guest and friend.
With my own hands I put that cloak and tunic
upon him—took them folded from their place—
and the bright brooch for ornament.
                           Gone now,
I will not meet the man again   280
returning to his own home fields. Unkind
the fate that sent him young in the long ship
to see that misery at Ilion, unspeakable!"

And the master improviser answered:

                 "Honorable
wife of Odysseus Laërtiadês,   285
you need not stain your beauty with these tears,
nor wear yourself out grieving for your husband.
Not that I can blame you. Any wife
grieves for the man she married in her girlhood,
lay with in love, bore children to—though he   290
may be no prince like this Odysseus,
whom they compare even to the gods. But listen:
weep no more, and listen:
I have a thing to tell you, something true.
I heard but lately of your lord's return,   295
heard that he is alive, not far away,
among Thesprótians in their green land
amassing fortune to bring home. His company
went down in shipwreck in the winedark sea
off the coast of Thrinákia. Zeus and Hêlios   300
held it against him that his men had killed
the kine of Hêlios. The crew drowned for this.
He rode the ship's keel. Big seas cast him up
on the island of Phaiákians, godlike men
who took him to their hearts. They honored him   305
with many gifts and a safe passage home,
or so they wished. Long since he should have been here,
but he thought better to restore his fortune
playing the vagabond about the world;
and no adventurer could beat Odysseus   310
at living by his wits—no man alive.
I had this from King Phaidôn of Thesprótia;
and, tipping wine out, Phaidôn swore to me
the ship was launched, the seamen standing by
to bring Odysseus to his land at last,   315
but I got out to sea ahead of him
by the king's order—as it chanced a freighter
left port for the grain bins of Doulíkhion.
Phaidôn, however, showed me Odysseus' treasure.

Ten generations of his heirs or more   320
could live on what lay piled in that great room.
The man himself had gone up to Dodona
to ask the spelling leaves of the old oak
what Zeus would have him do—how to return to Ithaka
after so many years—by stealth or openly.   325
You see, then, he is alive and well, and headed
homeward now, no more to be abroad
far from his island, his dear wife and son.
Here is my sworn word for it. Witness this,
god of the zenith, noblest of the gods,   330
and Lord Odysseus' hearthfire, now before me:
I swear these things shall turn out as I say.
Between this present dark and one day's ebb,
after the wane, before the crescent moon,
Odysseus will come."

                  Penélopê,   335
the attentive queen, replied to him:

                          "Ah, stranger,
if what you say could ever happen!
You would soon know our love! Our bounty, too:
men would turn after you to call you blessed.
But my heart tells me what must be.   340
Odysseus will not come to me; no ship
will be prepared for you. We have no master
quick to receive and furnish out a guest
as Lord Odysseus was.
                   Or did I dream him?

Maids, maids: come wash him, make a bed for him,   345
bedstead and colored rugs and coverlets
to let him lie warm into the gold of Dawn.
In morning light you'll bathe him and anoint him
so that he'll take his place beside Telémakhos
feasting in hall. If there be one man there   350
to bully or annoy him, that man wins
no further triumph here, burn though he may.
How will you understand me, friend, how find in me,
more than in common women, any courage
or gentleness, if you are kept in rags   355
and filthy at our feast? Men's lives are short.
The hard man and his cruelties will be
cursed behind his back, and mocked in death.
But one whose heart and ways are kind—of him
strangers will bear report to the wide world,   360
and distant men will praise him."

                   Warily
Odysseus answered:

                "Honorable lady,
wife of Odysseus Laërtiadês,
a weight of rugs and cover? Not for me.

I've had none since the day I saw the mountains   365
of Krete, white with snow, low on the sea line
fading behind me as the long oars drove me north.
Let me lie down tonight as I've lain often,
many a night unsleeping, many a time
afield on hard ground waiting for pure Dawn.   370
No: and I have no longing for a footbath
either; none of these maids will touch my feet,
unless there is an old one, old and wise,
one who has lived through suffering as I have:
I would not mind letting my feet be touched   375
by that old servant."

                    And Penélopê said:

          "Dear guest, no foreign man so sympathetic
ever came to my house, no guest more likeable,
so wry and humble are the things you say.
I have an old maidservant ripe with years,   380
one who in her time nursed my lord. She took him
into her arms the hour his mother bore him.
Let her, then, wash your feet, though she is frail.
Come here, stand by me, faithful Eurýkleia,
and bathe—bathe your master, I almost said,   385
for they are of an age, and now Odysseus'
feet and hands would be enseamed like his.
Men grow old soon in hardship."

                    Hearing this,
the old nurse hid her face between her hands
and wept hot tears, and murmured:

                              "Oh, my child!   390
I can do nothing for you! How Zeus hated you,
no other man so much! No use, great heart,
O faithful heart, the rich thighbones you burnt
to Zeus who plays in lightning—and no man
ever gave more to Zeus—with all your prayers   395
for a green age, a tall son reared to manhood.
There is no day of homecoming for you.
Stranger, some women in some far off place
perhaps have mocked my lord when he'd be home
as now these strumpets mock you here. No wonder   400
you would keep clear of all their whorishness
and have no bath. But here am I. The queen
Penélopê, Ikários' daughter, bids me;
so let me bathe your feet to serve my lady—
to serve you, too.

                    My heart within me stirs,   405
mindful of something. Listen to what I say:
strangers have come here, many through the years,
but no one ever came, I swear, who seemed
so like Odysseus—body, voice and limbs—
as you do."

Ready for this, Odysseus answered: 410

"Old woman, that is what they say. All who have seen
the two of us remark how like we are,
as you yourself have said, and rightly, too."

Then he kept still, while the old nurse filled up
her basin glittering in firelight; she poured   415
cold water in, then hot.
                              But Lord Odysseus
whirled suddenly from the fire to face the dark.
The scar: he had forgotten that. She must not
handle his scarred thigh, or the game was up.
But when she bared her lord's leg, bending near,   420
she knew the groove at once.
                              An old wound
a boar's white tusk inflicted, on Parnassos[1]
years ago. He had gone hunting there
in company with his uncles and Autólykos,
his mother's father—a great thief and swindler   425
by Hermês'[2] favor, for Autólykos pleased him
with burnt offerings of sheep and kids. The god
acted as his accomplice. Well, Autólykos
on a trip to Ithaka
arrived just after his daughter's boy was born.   430
In fact, he had no sooner finished supper
than Nurse Eurýkleia put the baby down
in his own lap and said:
                              "It is for you, now,
to choose a name for him, your child's dear baby;
the answer to her prayers."

                              Autólykos replied: 435

"My son-in-law, my daughter, call the boy
by the name I tell you. Well you know, my hand
has been against the world of men and women;
odium[3] and distrust I've won. Odysseus
should be his given name. When he grows up,   440
when he comes visiting his mother's home
under Parnassos, where my treasures are,
I'll make him gifts and send him back rejoicing."

Odysseus in due course went for the gifts,
and old Autólykos and his sons embraced him   445
with welcoming sweet words; and Amphithéa,
his mother's mother, held him tight and kissed him,
kissed his head and his fine eyes.
                              The father
called on his noble sons to make a feast,

---

1. The mountain range above Apollo's oracular shrine at Delphi.   2. Not only the messenger of the gods and the god who guided the dead down to the lower world but also the god of the marketplace and so of trickery and swindling.   3. The translator is reproducing a pun in the original Greek: Autólykos speaks of himself as *odyssamenos*, one who is angry and gives cause for anger.

and going about it briskly they led in   450
an ox of five years, whom they killed and flayed
and cut in bits for roasting on the skewers
with skilled hands, with care; then shared it out.
So all the day until the sun went down
they feasted to their hearts' content. At evening,   455
after the sun was down and dusk had come,
they turned to bed and took the gift of sleep.

When the young Dawn spread in the eastern sky
her finger tips of rose, the men and dogs
went hunting, taking Odysseus. They climbed   460
Parnassos' rugged flank mantled in forest,
entering amid high windy folds at noon
when Hêlios beat upon the valley floor
and on the winding Ocean whence he came.
With hounds questing ahead, in open order,   465
the sons of Autólykos went down a glen,
Odysseus in the lead, behind the dogs,
pointing his long-shadowing spear.
                                    Before them
a great boar lay hid in undergrowth,
in a green thicket proof against the wind   470
or sun's blaze, fine soever the needling sunlight,
impervious too to any rain, so dense
that cover was, heaped up with fallen leaves.
Patter of hounds' feet, men's feet, woke the boar
as they came up—and from his woody ambush   475
with razor back bristling and raging eyes
he trotted and stood at bay. Odysseus,
being on top of him, had the first shot,
lunging to stick him; but the boar
had already charged under the long spear.   480
He hooked aslant with one white tusk and ripped out
flesh above the knee, but missed the bone.
Odysseus' second thrust went home by luck,
his bright spear passing through the shoulder joint;
and the beast fell, moaning as life pulsed away.   485
Autólykos' tall sons took up the wounded,
working skillfully over the Prince Odysseus
to bind his gash, and with a rune[4] they stanched
the dark flow of blood. Then downhill swiftly
they all repaired to the father's house, and there   490
tended him well—so well they soon could send him,
with Grandfather Autólykos' magnificent gifts,
rejoicing, over sea to Ithaka.
His father and the Lady Antikleía
welcomed him, and wanted all the news   495
of how he got his wound; so he spun out
his tale, recalling how the boar's white tusk
caught him when he was hunting on Parnassos.

---

4. An incantation; magic to stop the flow of blood.

This was the scar the old nurse recognized;
she traced it under her spread hands, then let go,   500
and into the basin fell the lower leg
making the bronze clang, sloshing the water out.
Then joy and anguish seized her heart; her eyes
filled up with tears; her throat closed, and she whispered,
with hand held out to touch his chin:

                     "Oh yes!   505
You are Odysseus! Ah, dear child! I could not
see you until now—not till I knew
my master's very body with my hands!"

Her eyes turned to Penélopê with desire
to make her lord, her husband, known—in vain,   510
because Athena had bemused the queen,
so that she took no notice, paid no heed.
At the same time Odysseus' right hand
gripped the old throat; his left hand pulled her near,
and in her ear he said:

                   "Will you destroy me,   515
nurse, who gave me milk at your own breast?
Now with a hard lifetime behind I've come
in the twentieth year home to my father's island.
You found me out, as the chance was given you.
Be quiet; keep it from the others, else   520
I warn you, and I mean it, too,
if by my hand god brings the suitors down
I'll kill you, nurse or not, when the time comes—
when the time comes to kill the other women."

Eurýkleia kept her wits and answered him: 525

"Oh, what mad words are these you let escape you!
Child, you know my blood, my bones are yours;
no one could whip this out of me. I'll be
a woman turned to stone, iron I'll be.
And let me tell you too—mind now—if god   530
cuts down the arrogant suitors by your hand,
I can report to you on all the maids,
those who dishonor you, and the innocent."

But in response the great tactician said:

"Nurse, no need to tell me tales of these.   535
I will have seen them, each one, for myself.
Trust in the gods, be quiet, hold your peace."

Silent, the old nurse went to fetch more water,
her basin being all spilt.
               When she had washed
and rubbed his feet with golden oil, he turned,   540
dragging his bench again to the fire side
for warmth, and hid the scar under his rags.
Penélopê broke the silence, saying:

"Friend,
allow me one brief question more. You know,
the time for bed, sweet rest, is coming soon,   545
if only that warm luxury of slumber
would come to enfold us, in our trouble. But for me
my fate at night is anguish and no rest.
By day being busy, seeing to my work,
I find relief sometimes from loss and sorrow;   550
but when night comes and all the world's abed
I lie in mine alone, my heart thudding,
while bitter thoughts and fears crowd on my grief.
Think how Pandáreos' daughter, pale forever,
sings as the nightingale[5] in the new leaves   555
through those long quiet hours of night,
on some thick-flowering orchard bough in spring;
how she rills out and tilts her note, high now, now low,
mourning for Itylos whom she killed in madness—
her child, and her lord Zêthos' only child.   560
My forlorn thought flows variable as her song,
wondering: shall I stay beside my son
and guard my own things here, my maids, my hall,
to honor my lord's bed and the common talk?
Or had I best join fortunes with a suitor,   565
the noblest one, most lavish in his gifts?
Is it now time for that?
My son being still a callow boy forbade
marriage, or absence from my lord's domain;
but now the child is grown, grown up, a man,   570
he, too, begins to pray for my departure,
aghast at all the suitors gorge on.

                    Listen:
interpret me this dream: From a water's edge
twenty fat geese have come to feed on grain
beside my house. And I delight to see them.   575
But now a mountain eagle with great wings
and crooked beak storms in to break their necks
and strew their bodies here. Away he soars
into the bright sky; and I cry aloud—
all this in dream—I wail and round me gather   580
softly braided Akhaian women mourning
because the eagle killed my geese.
                    Then down
out of the sky he drops to a cornice beam
with mortal voice telling me not to weep.
'Be glad,' says he, 'renowned Ikários' daughter: 585
here is no dream but something real as day,
something about to happen. All those geese
were suitors, and the bird was I. See now,

---

5. The reference is to one of the many Greek legends that explain the song of the nightingale. In this one the daughter of Pandáreos, a Cretan king, was married to Zêthos, king of Thebes. She had only one son; her sister-in-law Niobe had many. In a fit of jealousy she tried to kill Niobe's eldest son but by mistake (in the dark) killed her own son, Itylos, instead. Zeus changed her into a nightingale, and she sings in mourning for Itylos.

I am no eagle but your lord come back
to bring inglorious death upon them all!'   590
As he said this, my honeyed slumber left me.
Peering through half-shut eyes, I saw the geese
in hall, still feeding at the self-same trough."

The master of subtle ways and straight replied:

"My dear, how can you choose to read the dream   595
differently? Has not Odysseus himself
shown you what is to come? Death to the suitors,
sure death, too. Not one escapes his doom."

Penélopê shook her head and answered:

                                   "Friend,
many and many a dream is mere confusion,   600
a cobweb of no consequence at all.
Two gates for ghostly dreams there are: one gateway
of honest horn, and one of ivory.
Issuing by the ivory gate are dreams
of glimmering illusion, fantasies,   605
but those that come through solid polished horn
may be borne out, if mortals only know them.
I doubt it came by horn, my fearful dream—
too good to be true, that, for my son and me.
But one thing more I wish to tell you: listen   610
carefully. It is a black day, this that comes.
Odysseus' house and I are to be parted.
I shall decree a contest for the day.
We have twelve axe heads. In his time, my lord
could line them up, all twelve, at intervals   615
like a ship's ribbing; then he'd back away
a long way off and whip an arrow through.[6]
Now I'll impose this trial on the suitors.
The one who easily handles and strings the bow
and shoots through all twelve axes I shall marry,   620
whoever he may be—then look my last
on this my first love's beautiful brimming house.
But I'll remember, though I dream it only."

Odysseus said:

                        "Dear honorable lady,
wife of Odysseus Laërtiadês,   625
let there be no postponement of the trial.
Odysseus, who knows the shifts of combat,
will be here: aye, he'll be here long before
one of these lads can stretch or string that bow
or shoot to thread the iron!"

6. The nature of this archery contest is a puzzle that has never been satisfactorily solved. The axes were
probably double-headed; the aperture through which the arrow passed must have been the socket in
which the wood handle fit. If the twelve ax heads were lined up, fixed in the ground (Telémakhos later
digs a trench for them) so that the empty sockets were in a straight line, an archer might be able to
shoot through them. When Odysseus finally does so, he is sitting down (XXI.441).

                                   Grave and wise,   630
Penélopê replied:

                          "If you were willing
to sit with me and comfort me, my friend,
no tide of sleep would ever close my eyes.
But mortals cannot go forever sleepless.
This the undying gods decree for all   635
who live and die on earth, kind furrowed earth.
Upstairs I go, then, to my single bed,
my sighing bed, wet with so many tears
after my Lord Odysseus took ship
to see that misery at Ilion, unspeakable.   640
Let me rest there, you here. You can stretch out
on the bare floor, or else command a bed."

So she went up to her chamber softly lit,
accompanied by her maids. Once there, she wept
for Odysseus, her husband, till Athena   645
cast sweet sleep upon her eyes.

                             BOOK XX

                        [*Signs and a Vision*]

Outside in the entry way he made his bed—
raw oxhide spread on level ground, and heaped up
fleeces, left from sheep the Akhaians killed.
And when he had lain down, Eurýnomê
flung out a robe to cover him. Unsleeping   5
the Lord Odysseus lay, and roved in thought
to the undoing of his enemies.
                           Now came a covey of women
laughing as they slipped out, arm in arm,
as many a night before, to the suitors' beds;
and anger took him like a wave to leap   10
into their midst and kill them, every one—
or should he let them all go hot to bed
one final night? His heart cried out within him
the way a brach[7] with whelps between her legs
would howl and bristle at a stranger—so   15
the hackles of his heart rose at that laughter.
Knocking his breast he muttered to himself:

"Down; be steady. You've seen worse, that time
the Kyklops like a rockslide ate your men
while you looked on. Nobody, only guile,   20
got you out of that cave alive."

                            His rage,
held hard in leash, submitted to his mind,
while he himself rocked, rolling from side to side,
as a cook turns a sausage, big with blood

---

7. Bitch (obsolete).

and fat, at a scorching blaze, without a pause,   25
to broil it quick: so he rolled left and right,
casting about to see how he, alone,
against the false outrageous crowd of suitors
could press the fight.

                  And out of the night sky
Athena came to him; out of the nearby dark   30
in body like a woman; came and stood
over his head to chide him:

                      "Why so wakeful,
most forlorn of men? Here is your home,
there lies your lady; and your son is here,
as fine as one could wish a son to be."   35

Odysseus looked up and answered:

                        "Aye,
goddess, that much is true; but still
I have some cause to fret in this affair.
I am one man; how can I whip those dogs?
They are always here in force. Neither   40
is that the end of it, there's more to come.
If by the will of Zeus and by your will
I killed them all, where could I go for safety?
Tell me that!"

              And the grey-eyed goddess said:

"Your touching faith! Another man would trust   45
some villainous mortal, with no brains — and what
am I? Your goddess-guardian to the end
in all your trials. Let it be plain as day:
if fifty bands of men surrounded us
and every sword sang for your blood,   50
you could make off still with their cows and sheep.
Now you, too, go to sleep. This all night vigil
wearies the flesh. You'll come out soon enough
on the other side of trouble."

                    Raining soft
sleep on his eyes, the beautiful one was gone   55
back to Olympos. Now at peace, the man
slumbered and lay still, but not his lady.
Wakeful again with all her cares, reclining
in the soft bed, she wept and cried aloud
until she had had her fill of tears, then spoke   60
in prayer first to Artemis:

                   "O gracious
divine lady Artemis, daughter of Zeus,
if you could only make an end now quickly,
let the arrow fly, stop my heart,
or if some wind could take me by the hair   65
up into running cloud, to plunge in tides of Ocean,

as hurricane winds took Pandareos' daughters[8]
when they were left at home alone. The gods
had sapped their parents' lives. But Aphroditê
fed those children honey, cheese, and wine,   70
and Hêra gave them looks and wit, and Artemis,
pure Artemis, gave lovely height, and wise
Athena made them practised in her arts—
till Aphroditê in glory walked on Olympos,
begging for each a happy wedding day   75
from Zeus, the lightning's joyous king, who knows
all fate of mortals, fair and foul—
but even at that hour the cyclone winds
had ravished them away
to serve the loathsome Furies.
                                        Let me be   80
blown out by the Olympians! Shot by Artemis,
I still might go and see amid the shades
Odysseus in the rot of underworld.
No coward's eye should light by my consenting!
Evil may be endured when our days pass   85
in mourning, heavy-hearted, hard beset,
if only sleep reign over nighttime, blanketing
the world's good and evil from our eyes.
But not for me: dreams too my demon sends me.
Tonight the image of my lord came by   90
as I remember him with troops. O strange
exultation! I thought him real, and not a dream."

Now as the Dawn appeared all stitched in gold,
the queen's cry reached Odysseus at his waking,
so that he wondered, half asleep: it seemed   95
she knew him, and stood near him! Then he woke
and picked his bedding up to stow away
on a chair in the mégaron. The oxhide pad
he took outdoors. There, spreading wide his arms,
he prayed:

            "O Father Zeus, if over land and water,   100
after adversity, you willed to bring me home,
let someone in the waking house give me good augury,
and a sign be shown, too, in the outer world."

He prayed thus, and the mind of Zeus in heaven
heard him. He thundered out of bright Olympos   105
down from above the cloudlands in reply—
a rousing peal for Odysseus. Then a token
came to him from a woman grinding flour
in the court nearby. His own handmills were there,
and twelve maids had the job of grinding out   110
whole grain and barley meal, the pith of men.

8. The fate of these daughters was different from the one who married Zêthos and became a nightingale
(see n. 5, p. 282). They paid for the sin of their father, who stole a golden image from the temple of
Hephaistos. Though the gods showered gifts on them, in the end they were swept away to their deaths
by the stormwinds.

Now all the rest, their bushels ground, were sleeping;
one only, frail and slow, kept at it still.
She stopped, stayed her hand, and her lord heard
the omen from her lips:

             "Ah, Father Zeus   115
almighty over gods and men!
A great bang of thunder that was, surely,
out of the starry sky, and not a cloud in sight.
It is your nod to someone. Hear me, then,
make what I say come true: 120
let this day be the last the suitors feed
so dainty in Odysseus' hall!
They've made me work my heart out till I drop,
grinding barley. May they feast no more!"

The servant's prayer, after the cloudless thunder   125
of Zeus, Odysseus heard with lifting heart,
sure in his bones that vengeance was at hand.
Then other servants, wakening, came down
to build and light a fresh fire at the hearth.
Telémakhos, clear-eyed as a god, awoke,   130
put on his shirt and belted on his sword,
bound rawhide sandals under his smooth feet,
and took his bronze-shod lance. He came and stood
on the broad sill of the doorway, calling Eurýkleia:

"Nurse, dear Nurse, how did you treat our guest?   135
Had he a supper and a good bed? Has he lain
uncared for still? My mother is like that,
perverse for all her cleverness:
she'd entertain some riff-raff, and turn out
a solid man."

            The old nurse answered him: 140

"I would not be so quick to accuse her, child.
He sat and drank here while he had a mind to;
food he no longer hungered for, he said—
for she did ask him. When he thought of sleeping,
she ordered them to make a bed. Poor soul!   145
Poor gentleman! So humble and so miserable,
he would accept no bed with rugs to lie on,
but slept on sheepskins and a raw oxhide
in the entry way. We covered him ourselves."

Telémakhos left the hall, hefting his lance,   150
with two swift flickering hounds for company,
to face the island Akhaians in the square;
and gently born Eurýkleia the daughter
of Ops Peisenóridês, called to the maids:

"Bestir yourselves! you have your brooms, go sprinkle   155
the rooms and sweep them, robe the chairs in red,
sponge off the tables till they shine.
Wash out the winebowls and two-handled cups.

You others go fetch water from the spring;
no loitering; come straight back. Our company   160
will be here soon; morning is sure to bring them;
everyone has a holiday today."

The women ran to obey her—twenty girls
off to the spring with jars for dusky water,
the rest at work inside. Then tall woodcutters   165
entered to split up logs for the hearth fire,
the water carriers returned; and on their heels
arrived the swineherd, driving three fat pigs,
chosen among his pens. In the wide court
he let them feed, and said to Odysseus kindly: 170

"Friend, are they more respectful of you now,
or still insulting you?"

                    Replied Odysseus:

"The young men, yes. And may the gods requite
those insolent puppies for the game they play
in a home not their own. They have no decency."   175

During this talk, Melánthios the goatherd
came in, driving goats for the suitors' feast,
with his two herdsmen. Under the portico
they tied the animals, and Melánthios
looked at Odysseus with a sneer. Said he:

                              "Stranger,   180
I see you mean to stay and turn our stomachs
begging in this hall. Clear out, why don't you?
Or will you have to taste a bloody beating
before you see the point? Your begging ways
nauseate everyone. There are feasts elsewhere."   185

Odysseus answered not a word, but grimly
shook his head over his murderous heart.
A third man came up now: Philoítios
the cattle foreman, with an ox behind him
and fat goats for the suitors. Ferrymen   190
had brought these from the mainland, as they bring
travellers, too—whoever comes along.
Philoítios tied the beasts under the portico
and joined the swineherd.

                    "Who is this," he said,
"Who is the new arrival at the manor?   195
Akhaian? or what else does he claim to be?
Where are his family and fields of home?
Down on his luck, all right: carries himself like a captain.
How the immortal gods can change and drag us down
once they begin to spin dark days for us!—   200
Kings and commanders, too."

                    Then he stepped over
and took Odysseus by the right hand, saying:

"Welcome, Sir. May good luck lie ahead
at the next turn. Hard times you're having, surely.
O Zeus! no god is more berserk in heaven   205
if gentle folk, whom you yourself begot,
you plunge in grief and hardship without mercy!
Sir, I began to sweat when I first saw you,
and tears came to my eyes, remembering
Odysseus: rags like these he may be wearing   210
somewhere on his wanderings now—
I mean, if he's alive still under the sun.
But if he's dead and in the house of Death,
I mourn Odysseus. He entrusted cows to me
in Kephallênia, when I was knee high,   215
and now his herds are numberless, no man else
ever had cattle multiply like grain.
But new men tell me I must bring my beeves
to feed them, who care nothing for our prince,
fear nothing from the watchful gods. They crave   220
partition of our lost king's land and wealth.
My own feelings keep going round and round
upon this tether: can I desert the boy
by moving, herds and all, to another country,
a new life among strangers? Yet it's worse   225
to stay here, in my old post, herding cattle
for upstarts.
               I'd have gone long since,
gone, taken service with another king; this shame
is no more to be borne; but I keep thinking
my own lord, poor devil, still might come   230
and make a rout of suitors in his hall."

Odysseus, with his mind on action, answered:

"Herdsman, I make you out to be no coward
and no fool: I can see that for myself.
So let me tell you this. I swear by Zeus   235
all highest, by the table set for friends,
and by your king's hearthstone to which I've come,
Odysseus will return. You'll be on hand
to see, if you care to see it,
how those who lord it here will be cut down."   240

The cowman said:

               "Would god it all came true!
You'd see the fight that's in me!"

               Then Eumaios
echoed him, and invoked the gods, and prayed
that his great-minded master should return.
While these three talked, the suitors in the field   245
had come together plotting—what but death
for Telémakhos?—when from the left an eagle
crossed high with a rockdove in his claws.

Amphínomos got up. Said he, cutting them short:

"Friends, no luck lies in that plan for us,   250
no luck, knifing the lad. Let's think of feasting."

A grateful thought, they felt, and walking on
entered the great hall of the hero Odysseus,
where they all dropped their cloaks on chairs or couches
and made a ritual slaughter, knifing sheep,   255
fat goats and pigs, knifing the grass-fed steer.
Then tripes were broiled and eaten. Mixing bowls
were filled with wine. The swineherd passed out cups,
Philoítios, chief cowherd, dealt the loaves
into the panniers, Melánthios poured wine,   260
and all their hands went out upon the feast.

Telémakhos placed his father to advantage
just at the door sill of the pillared hall,
setting a stool there and a sawed-off table,
gave him a share of tripes, poured out his wine   265
in a golden cup, and said:

                    "Stay here, sit down
to drink with our young friends. I stand between you
and any cutting word or cuffing hand
from any suitor. Here is no public house
but the old home of Odysseus, my inheritance.   270
Hold your tongues then, gentlemen, and your blows,
and let no wrangling start, no scuffle either."

The others, disconcerted, bit their lips
at the ring in the young man's voice. Antínoös,
Eupeithês' son, turned round to them and said: 275

"It goes against the grain, my lords, but still
I say we take this hectoring by Telémakhos.
You know Zeus balked at it, or else
we might have shut his mouth a long time past,
the silvery speaker."

                    But Telémakhos   280
paid no heed to what Antínoös said.

Now public heralds wound through Ithaka
leading a file of beasts for sacrifice, and islanders
gathered under the shade trees of Apollo,
in the precinct of the Archer[9]—while in hall   285
the suitors roasted mutton and fat beef
on skewers, pulling off the fragrant cuts;
and those who did the roasting served Odysseus
a portion equal to their own, for so
Telémakhos commanded.
                    But Athena   290
had no desire now to let the suitors
restrain themselves from wounding words and acts.

9. An epithet of Apollo. The trees are in his open-air precinct.

Laërtês' son again must be offended.
There was a scapegrace fellow in the crowd
named Ktésippos, a Samian, rich beyond   295
all measure, arrogant with riches, early
and late a bidder for Odysseus' queen.
Now this one called attention to himself:

"Hear me, my lords, I have a thing to say.
Our friend has had his fair share from the start   300
and that's polite; it would be most improper
if we were cold to guests of Telémakhos—
no matter what tramp turns up. Well then, look here,
let me throw in my own small contribution.
He must have prizes to confer, himself,   305
on some brave bathman or another slave
here in Odysseus' house."

His hand went backward
and, fishing out a cow's foot from the basket,
he let it fly.
Odysseus rolled his head
to one side softly, ducking the blow, and smiled   310
a crooked smile with teeth clenched. On the wall
the cow's foot struck and fell. Telémakhos
blazed up:

"Ktésippos, lucky for you, by heaven,
not to have hit him! He took care of himself,
else you'd have had my lance-head in your belly;   315
no marriage, but a grave instead on Ithaka
for your father's pains.
You others, let me see
no more contemptible conduct in my house!
I've been awake to it for a long time—by now
I know what is honorable and what is not.   320
Before, I was a child. I can endure it
while sheep are slaughtered, wine drunk up, and bread—
can one man check the greed of a hundred men?—
but I will suffer no more viciousness.
Granted you mean at last to cut me down: 325
I welcome that—better to die than have
humiliation always before my eyes,
the stranger buffeted, and the serving women
dragged about, abused in a noble house."

They quieted, grew still, under his lashing,   330
and after a long silence, Ageláos,
Damástor's son, spoke to them all:

"Friends, friends,
I hope no one will answer like a fishwife.
What has been said is true. Hands off this stranger,
he is no target, neither is any servant   335
here in the hall of King Odysseus.
Let me say a word, though, to Telémakhos

and to his mother, if it please them both:
as long as hope remained in you to see
Odysseus, that great gifted man, again,   340
you could not be reproached for obstinacy,
tying the suitors down here; better so,
if still your father fared the great sea homeward.
How plain it is, though, now, he'll come no more!
Go sit then by your mother, reason with her,   345
tell her to take the best man, highest bidder,
and you can have and hold your patrimony,
feed on it, drink it all, while she
adorns another's house."

                          Keeping his head,
Telémakhos replied:

                       "By Zeus Almighty,   350
Ageláos, and by my father's sufferings,
far from Ithaka, whether he's dead or lost,
I make no impediment to Mother's marriage.
'Take whom you wish,' I say, 'I'll add my dowry.'
But can I pack her off against her will   355
from her own home? Heaven forbid!"

                              At this,
Pallas Athena touched off in the suitors
a fit of laughter, uncontrollable.
She drove them into nightmare, till they wheezed
and neighed as though with jaws no longer theirs,   360
while blood defiled their meat, and blurring tears
flooded their eyes, heart-sore with woe to come.
Then said the visionary, Theoklýmenos:

"O lost sad men, what terror is this you suffer?
Night shrouds you to the knees, your heads, your faces;   365
dry retch of death runs round like fire in sticks;
your cheeks are streaming; these fair walls and pedestals
are dripping crimson blood. And thick with shades
is the entry way, the courtyard thick with shades
passing athirst toward Érebos, into the dark,   370
the sun is quenched in heaven, foul mist hems us in . . ."

The young men greeted this with shouts of laughter,
and Eurýmakhos, the son of Pólybos, crowed:

"The mind of our new guest has gone astray.
Hustle him out of doors, lads, into the sunlight;   375
he finds it dark as night inside!"

The man of vision looked at him and said:

"When I need help, I'll ask for it, Eurýmakhos.
I have my eyes and ears, a pair of legs,
and a straight mind, still with me. These will do   380
to take me out. Damnation and black night
I see arriving for yourselves: no shelter,

no defence for any in this crowd —
fools and vipers in the king's own hall."

With this he left that handsome room and went   385
home to Peiraios, who received him kindly.
The suitors made wide eyes at one another
and set to work provoking Telémakhos
with jokes about his friends. One said, for instance:

"Telémakhos, no man is a luckier host   390
when it comes to what the cat dragged in. What burning
eyes your beggar had for bread and wine!
But not for labor, not for a single heave —
he'd be a deadweight on a field. Then comes
this other, with his mumbo-jumbo. Boy,   395
for your own good, I tell you, toss them both
into a slave ship for the Sikels.[1] That would pay you."

Telémakhos ignored the suitors' talk.
He kept his eyes in silence on his father,
awaiting the first blow. Meanwhile   400
the daughter of Ikários, Penélopê,
had placed her chair to look across and down
on father and son at bay; she heard the crowd,
and how they laughed as they resumed their dinner,
a fragrant feast, for many beasts were slain —   405
but as for supper, men supped never colder
than these, on what the goddess and the warrior
were even then preparing for the suitors,
whose treachery had filled that house with pain.

BOOK XXI

[*The Test of the Bow*]

Upon Penélopê, most worn in love and thought,
Athena cast a glance like a grey sea
lifting her. Now to bring the tough bow out and bring
the iron blades. Now try those dogs at archery
to usher bloody slaughter in.
                                    So moving stairward   5
the queen took up a fine doorhook of bronze,
ivory-hafted, smooth in her clenched hand,
and led her maids down to a distant room,
a storeroom where the master's treasure lay:
bronze, bar gold, black iron forged and wrought.   10
In this place hung the double-torsion bow
and arrows in a quiver, a great sheaf —
quills of groaning.
                          In the old time in Lakedaimon
her lord had got these arms from Íphitos,[2]
Eurýtos' son. The two met in Messenia   15

1. The ancient (pre-Greek) inhabitants of Sicily.   2. Son of Eurýtos, king of Oekhalia in Thessaly.

at Ortílokhos'[3] table, on the day
Odysseus claimed a debt owed by that realm —
sheep stolen by Messenians out of Ithaka
in their long ships, three hundred head, and herdsmen.
Seniors of Ithaka and his father sent him   20
on that far embassy when he was young.
But Íphitos had come there tracking strays,
twelve shy mares, with mule colts yet unweaned.
And a fatal chase they led him over prairies
into the hands of Heraklês. That massive   25
son of toil and mortal son of Zeus
murdered his guest[4] at wine in his own house —
inhuman, shameless in the sight of heaven —
to keep the mares and colts in his own grange.
Now Íphitos, when he knew Odysseus, gave him   30
the master bowman's arm; for old Eurýtos
had left it on his deathbed to his son.
In fellowship Odysseus gave a lance
and a sharp sword. But Heraklês killed Íphitos
before one friend could play host to the other.   35
And Lord Odysseus would not take the bow
in the black ships to the great war at Troy.
As a keepsake he put it by:
it served him well at home in Ithaka.

Now the queen reached the storeroom door and halted.   40
Here was an oaken sill, cut long ago
and sanded clean and bedded true. Foursquare
the doorjambs and the shining doors were set
by the careful builder. Penélopê untied the strap
around the curving handle, pushed her hook   45
into the slit, aimed at the bolts inside
and shot them back. Then came a rasping sound
as those bright doors the key had sprung gave way —
a bellow like a bull's vaunt in a meadow —
followed by her light footfall entering   50
over the plank floor. Herb-scented robes
lay there in chests, but the lady's milkwhite arms
went up to lift the bow down from a peg
in its own polished bowcase.
                              Now Penélopê
sank down, holding the weapon on her knees,   55
and drew her husband's great bow out, and sobbed
and bit her lip and let the salt tears flow.
Then back she went to face the crowded hall,
tremendous bow in hand, and on her shoulder hung
the quiver spiked with coughing death. Behind her   60
maids bore a basket full of axeheads, bronze
and iron implements for the master's game.
Thus in her beauty she approached the suitors,
and near a pillar of the solid roof
she paused, her shining veil across her cheeks,   65

3. King of Pherai in Thessaly (see III.528).   4. Íphitos.

her maids on either hand and still,
then spoke to the banqueters:

        "My lords, hear me:
suitors indeed, you commandeered this house
to feast and drink in, day and night, my husband
being long gone, long out of mind. You found   70
no justification for yourselves—none
except your lust to marry me. Stand up, then:
we now declare a contest for that prize.
Here is my lord Odysseus' hunting bow.
Bend and string it if you can. Who sends an arrow   75
through iron axe-helve sockets, twelve in line?
I join my life with his, and leave this place, my home,
my rich and beautiful bridal house, forever
to be remembered, though I dream it only."

Then to Eumaios:

        "Carry the bow forward.   80
Carry the blades."

        Tears came to the swineherd's eyes
as he reached out for the big bow. He laid it
down at the suitors' feet. Across the room
the cowherd sobbed, knowing the master's weapon.
Antínoös growled, with a glance at both:

        "Clods.   85
They go to pieces over nothing.
        You two, there,
why are you sniveling? To upset the woman
even more? Has she not pain enough
over her lost husband? *Sit down.*
Get on with dinner quietly, or cry about it   90
outside, if you must. Leave us the bow.
A clean-cut game, it looks to me.
Nobody bends that bowstave easily
in this company. Is there a man here
made like Odysseus? I remember him   95
from childhood: I can see him even now."

That was the way he played it, hoping inwardly
to span the great horn bow with corded gut
and drill the iron with his shot—he, Antínoös,
destined to be the first of all to savor   100
blood from a biting arrow at his throat,
a shaft drawn by the fingers of Odysseus
whom he had mocked and plundered, leading on
the rest, his boon companions. Now they heard
a gay snort of laughter from Telémakhos,   105
who said then brilliantly:

        "A queer thing, that!
Has Zeus almighty made me a half-wit?
For all her spirit, Mother has given in,

promised to go off with someone—and
is that amusing? What am I cackling for?   110
Step up, my lords, contend now for your prize.
There is no woman like her in Akhaia,
not in old Argos, Pylos, or Mykênê,
neither in Ithaka nor on the mainland,
and you all know it without praise of mine.   115
Come on, no hanging back, no more delay
in getting the bow bent. Who's the winner?
I myself should like to try that bow.
Suppose I bend it and bring off the shot,
my heart will be less heavy, seeing the queen my mother   120
go for the last time from this house and hall,
if I who stay can do my father's feat."

He moved out quickly, dropping his crimson cloak,
and lifted sword and sword belt from his shoulders.
His preparation was to dig a trench,   125
heaping the earth in a long ridge beside it
to hold the blades half-bedded. A taut cord
aligned the socket rings. And no one there
but looked on wondering at his workmanship,
for the boy had never seen it done.
                    He took his stand then   130
on the broad door sill to attempt the bow.
Three times he put his back into it and sprang it,
three times he had to slack off. Still he meant
to string that bow and pull for the needle shot.
A fourth try and he had it all but strung—   135
when a stiffening in Odysseus made him check.
Abruptly then he stopped and turned and said:

"Blast and damn it, must I be a milksop
all my life? Half-grown, all thumbs,
no strength or knack at arms, to defend myself   140
if someone picks a fight with me.
                    Take over,
O my elders and betters, try the bow,
run off the contest."

                    And he stood the weapon
upright against the massy-timbered door
with one arrow across the horn aslant,   145
then went back to his chair. Antínoös
gave the word:

               "Now one man at a time
rise and go forward. Round the room in order;
left to right from where they dip the wine."

As this seemed fair enough, up stood Leódês   150
the son of Oinops. This man used to find
visions for them in the smoke of sacrifice.
He kept his chair well back, retired by the winebowl,
for he alone could not abide their manners

but sat in shame for all the rest. Now it was he   155
who had first to confront the bow,
standing up on the broad door sill. He failed.
The bow unbending made his thin hands yield,
no muscle in them. He gave up and said:

"Friends, I cannot. Let the next man handle it.   160
Here is a bow to break the heart and spirit
of many strong men. Aye. And death is less
bitter than to live on and never have
the beauty that we came here laying siege to
so many days. Resolute, are you still,   165
to win Odysseus' lady Penélopê?
Pit yourselves against the bow, and look
among Akhaians for another's daughter.
Gifts will be enough to court and take her.
Let the best offer win."

    With this Leódês   170
thrust the bow away from him, and left it
upright against the massy-timbered door,
with one arrow aslant across the horn.
As he went down to his chair he heard Antínoös'
voice rising:

    "What is that you say?   175
It makes me burn. You cannot string the weapon,
so 'Here is a bow to break the heart and spirit
of many strong men.' Crushing thought!
You were not born—you never had it in you—
to pull that bow or let an arrow fly.   180
But here are men who can and will."

He called out to the goatherd, Melánthios:

"Kindle a fire there, be quick about it,
draw up a big bench with a sheepskin on it,
and bring a cake of lard out of the stores.   185
Contenders from now on will heat and grease the bow.
We'll try it limber, and bring off the shot."

Melánthios darted out to light a blaze,
drew up a bench, threw a big sheepskin over it,
and brought a cake of lard. So one by one   190
the young men warmed and greased the bow for bending,
but not a man could string it. They were whipped.
Antínoös held off; so did Eurýmakhos,
suitors in chief, by far the ablest there.
Two men had meanwhile left the hall: 195
swineherd and cowherd, in companionship,
one downcast as the other. But Odysseus
followed them outdoors, outside the court,
and coming up said gently:

    "You, herdsman,
and you, too, swineherd, I could say a thing to you,   200
or should I keep it dark?

                          No, no; speak,
my heart tells me. Would you be men enough
to stand by Odysseus if he came back?
Suppose he dropped out of a clear sky, as I did?
Suppose some god should bring him?   205
Would you bear arms for him, or for the suitors?"

The cowherd said:

                    "Ah, let the master come!
Father Zeus, grant our old wish! Some courier
guide him back! Then judge what stuff is in me
and how I manage arms!"

                         Likewise Eumaios   210
fell to praying all heaven for his return,
so that Odysseus, sure at least of these,
told them:

                    "I am at home, for I am he.
I bore adversities, but in the twentieth year
I am ashore in my own land. I find   215
the two of you, alone among my people,
longed for my coming. Prayers I never heard
except your own that I might come again.
So now what is in store for you I'll tell you:
If Zeus brings down the suitors by my hand   220
I promise marriages to both, and cattle,
and houses built near mine. And you shall be
brothers-in-arms of my Telémakhos.
Here, let me show you something else, a sign
that I am he, that you can trust me, look: 225
this old scar from the tusk wound that I got
boar hunting on Parnassos—
Autólykos' sons and I."

                         Shifting his rags
he bared the long gash. Both men looked, and knew,
and threw their arms around the old soldier, weeping,   230
kissing his head and shoulders. He as well
took each man's head and hands to kiss, then said—
to cut it short, else they might weep till dark—

"Break off, no more of this.
Anyone at the door could see and tell them.   235
Drift back in, but separately at intervals
after me.
           Now listen to your orders:
when the time comes, those gentlemen, to a man,
will be dead against giving me bow or quiver.
Defy them. Eumaios, bring the bow   240
and put it in my hands there at the door.
Tell the women to lock their own door tight.
Tell them if someone hears the shock of arms
or groans of men, in hall or court, not one
must show her face, but keep still at her weaving.   245

Philoítios, run to the outer gate and lock it.
Throw the cross bar and lash it."

                              He turned back
into the courtyard and the beautiful house
and took the stool he had before. They followed
one by one, the two hands loyal to him.   250

Eurýmakhos had now picked up the bow.
He turned it round, and turned it round
before the licking flame to warm it up,
but could not, even so, put stress upon it
to jam the loop over the tip
                    though his heart groaned to bursting.   255
Then he said grimly:

              "Curse this day.
What gloom I feel, not for myself alone,
and not only because we lose that bride.
Women are not lacking in Akhaia,
in other towns, or on Ithaka. No, the worst   260
is humiliation—to be shown up for children
measured against Odysseus—we who cannot
even hitch the string over his bow.
What shame to be repeated of us, after us!"

Antínoös said:

              "Come to yourself. You know   265
that is not the way this business ends.
Today the islanders held holiday, a holy day,
no day to sweat over a bowstring.
                        Keep your head.
Postpone the bow. I say we leave the axes
planted where they are. No one will take them.   270
No one comes to Odysseus' hall tonight.
Break out good wine and brim our cups again,
we'll keep the crooked bow safe overnight,
order the fattest goats Melánthios has
brought down tomorrow noon, and offer thighbones burning   275
to Apollo, god of archers,
while we try out the bow and make the shot."

As this appealed to everyone, heralds came
pouring fresh water for their hands, and boys
filled up the winebowls. Joints of meat went round,   280
fresh cuts for all, while each man made his offering,
tilting the red wine to the gods, and drank his fill.
Then spoke Odysseus, all craft and gall:

"My lords, contenders for the queen, permit me:
a passion in me moves me to speak out.   285
I put it to Eurýmakhos above all
and to that brilliant prince, Antínoös. Just now
how wise his counsel was, to leave the trial
and turn your thoughts to the immortal gods! Apollo

will give power tomorrow to whom he wills.   290
But let me try my hand at the smooth bow!
Let me test my fingers and my pull
to see if any of the oldtime kick is there,
or if thin fare and roving took it out of me."

Now irritation beyond reason swept them all,   295
since they were nagged by fear that he could string it.
Antínoös answered, coldly and at length:

"You bleary vagabond, no rag of sense is left you.
Are you not coddled here enough, at table
taking meat with gentlemen, your betters,   300
denied nothing, and listening to our talk?
When have we let a tramp hear all our talk?
The sweet goad of wine has made you rave!
Here is the evil wine can do
to those who swig it down. Even the centaur[5]   305
Eurýtion, in Peiríthoös' hall
among the Lapíthai, came to a bloody end
because of wine; wine ruined him: it crazed him,
drove him wild for rape in that great house.
The princes cornered him in fury, leaping on him   310
to drag him out and crop his ears and nose.
Drink had destroyed his mind, and so he ended
in that mutilation—fool that he was.
Centaurs and men made war for this,
but the drunkard first brought hurt upon himself.   315

The tale applies to you: I promise you
great trouble if you touch that bow. You'll come by
no indulgence in our house; kicked down
into a ship's bilge, out to sea you go,
and nothing saves you. Drink, but hold your tongue.   320
Make no contention here with younger men."
At this the watchful queen Penélopê
interposed:

                "Antínoös, discourtesy
to a guest of Telémakhos—whatever guest—
that is not handsome. What are you afraid of?   325
Suppose this exile put his back into it
and drew the great bow of Odysseus—
could he then take me home to be his bride?
You know he does not imagine that! No one
need let that prospect weigh upon his dinner!   330
How very, very improbable it seems."

It was Eurýmakhos who answered her:

"Penélopê, O daughter of Ikários,
most subtle queen, we are not given to fantasy.

5. Half-horse, half-man. At a wedding in the house of the Lapíthai, their human neighbors, the centaurs got drunk and tried to rape the women; a fight ensued. The great pediment at Olympia presents this scene, and individual contests of Lapith and centaur are portrayed on the Parthenon at Athens.

No, but our ears burn at what men might say   335
and women, too. We hear some jackal whispering:
'How far inferior to the great husband
her suitors are! Can't even budge his bow!
Think of it; and a beggar, out of nowhere,
strung it quick and made the needle shot!'   340
That kind of disrepute we would not care for."

Penélopê replied, steadfast and wary:

"Eurýmakhos, you have no good repute
in this realm, nor the faintest hope of it—
men who abused a prince's house for years,   345
consumed his wine and cattle. Shame enough.
Why hang your heads over a trifle now?
The stranger is a big man, well-compacted,
and claims to be of noble blood.
                                Ai!
Give him the bow, and let us have it out!   350
What I can promise him I will:
if by the kindness of Apollo he prevails
he shall be clothed well and equipped.
A fine shirt and a cloak I promise him;
a lance for keeping dogs at bay, or men;   355
a broadsword; sandals to protect his feet;
escort, and freedom to go where he will."

Telémakhos now faced her and said sharply:

"Mother, as to the bow and who may handle it
or not handle it, no man here   360
has more authority than I do—not one lord
of our own stony Íthaka nor the islands lying
east toward Elis: no one stops me if I choose
to give these weapons outright to my guest.
Return to your own hall. Tend your spindle.   365
Tend your loom. Direct your maids at work.
This question of the bow will be for men to settle,
most of all for me. I am master here."

She gazed in wonder, turned, and so withdrew,
her son's clearheaded bravery in her heart.   370
But when she had mounted to her rooms again
with all her women, then she fell to weeping
for Odysseus, her husband. Grey-eyed Athena
presently cast a sweet sleep on her eyes.

The swineherd had the horned bow in his hands   375
moving toward Odysseus, when the crowd
in the banquet hall broke into an ugly din,
shouts rising from the flushed young men:

                                        "Ho! Where
do you think you are taking that, you smutty slave?"

"What is this dithering?"

"We'll toss you back alone   380
among the pigs, for your own dogs to eat,
if bright Apollo nods and the gods are kind!"
He faltered, all at once put down the bow, and stood
in panic, buffeted by waves of cries,
hearing Telémakhos from another quarter   385
shout:

"Go on, take him the bow!
              Do you obey this pack?
You will be stoned back to your hills! Young as I am
my power is over you! I wish to God
I had as much the upper hand of these!   390
There would be suitors pitched like dead rats
through our gate, for the evil plotted here!"

Telémakhos' frenzy struck someone as funny,
and soon the whole room roared with laughter at him,
so that all tension passed. Eumaios picked up   395
bow and quiver, making for the door,
and there he placed them in Odysseus' hands.
Calling Eurýkleia to his side he said:

                              "Telémakhos
trusts you to take care of the women's doorway.
Lock it tight. If anyone inside   400
should hear the shock of arms or groans of men
in hall or court, not one must show her face,
but go on with her weaving."

                    The old woman
nodded and kept still. She disappeared
into the women's hall, bolting the door behind her.   405
Philoítios left the house now at one bound,
catlike, running to bolt the courtyard gate.
A coil of deck-rope of papyrus[6] fiber
lay in the gateway; this he used for lashing,
and ran back to the same stool as before,   410
fastening his eyes upon Odysseus.

                    And Odysseus took his time,
turning the bow, tapping it, every inch,
for borings that termites might have made
while the master of the weapon was abroad.
The suitors were now watching him, and some   415
jested among themselves:

                    "A bow lover!"

"Dealer in old bows!"

                    "Maybe he has one like it
at home!"

        "Or has an itch to make one for himself."

"See how he handles it, the sly old buzzard!"

6. A plant grown in Egypt. Its fibers were used here for rope; they were also made into paper.

And one disdainful suitor added this: 420

"May his fortune grow an inch for every inch he bends it!"

But the man skilled in all ways of contending,
satisfied by the great bow's look and heft,
like a musician, like a harper, when
with quiet hand upon his instrument   425
he draws between his thumb and forefinger
a sweet new string upon a peg: so effortlessly
Odysseus in one motion strung the bow.
Then slid his right hand down the cord and plucked it,
so the taut gut vibrating hummed and sang   430
a swallow's note.
              In the hushed hall it smote the suitors
and all their faces changed. Then Zeus thundered
overhead, one loud crack for a sign.
And Odysseus laughed within him that the son
of crooked-minded Kronos had flung that omen down.   435
He picked one ready arrow from his table
where it lay bare: the rest were waiting still
in the quiver for the young men's turn to come.
He nocked it, let it rest across the handgrip,
and drew the string and grooved butt of the arrow,   440
aiming from where he sat upon the stool.
                   Now flashed
arrow from twanging bow clean as a whistle
through every socket ring, and grazed not one,
to thud with heavy brazen head beyond.
                 Then quietly
Odysseus said:

             "Telémakhos, the stranger   445
you welcomed in your hall has not disgraced you.
I did not miss, neither did I take all day
stringing the bow. My hand and eye are sound,
not so contemptible as the young men say.
The hour has come to cook their lordships' mutton—   450
supper by daylight. Other amusements later,
with song and harping that adorn a feast."

He dropped his eyes and nodded, and the prince
Telémakhos, true son of King Odysseus,
belted his sword on, clapped hand to his spear,   455
and with a clink and glitter of keen bronze
stood by his chair, in the forefront near his father.

BOOK XXII

[Death in the Great Hall]

Now shrugging off his rags the wiliest fighter of the islands[7]
leapt and stood on the broad door sill, his own bow in his hand.

---

7. In the account of the battle in the hall the translator occasionally, as here, uses a longer line than usual. There is no such variation of length in the original.

He poured out at his feet a rain of arrows from the quiver
and spoke to the crowd:

                    "So much for that. Your clean-cut game is over.
Now watch me hit a target that no man has hit before,   5
if I can make this shot. Help me, Apollo."

He drew to his fist the cruel head of an arrow for Antínoös
just as the young man leaned to lift his beautiful drinking cup,
embossed, two-handled, golden: the cup was in his fingers:
the wine was even at his lips: and did he dream of death?   10
How could he? In that revelry amid his throng of friends
who would imagine a single foe—though a strong foe indeed—
could dare to bring death's pain on him and darkness on his eyes?
Odysseus' arrow hit him under the chin
and punched up to the feathers through his throat.   15

Backward and down he went, letting the winecup fall
from his shocked hand. Like pipes his nostrils jetted
crimson runnels, a river of mortal red,
and one last kick upset his table
knocking the bread and meat to soak in dusty blood.   20
Now as they craned to see their champion where he lay
the suitors jostled in uproar down the hall,
everyone on his feet. Wildly they turned and scanned
the walls in the long room for arms; but not a shield,
not a good ashen spear was there for a man to take and throw.   25
All they could do was yell in outrage at Odysseus:

"Foul! to shoot at a man! That was your last shot!"

"Your own throat will be slit for this!"

                        "Our finest lad is down!
You killed the best on Ithaka."

                  "Buzzards will tear your eyes out!"

For they imagined as they wished—that it was a wild shot,   30
an unintended killing—fools, not to comprehend
they were already in the grip of death.
But glaring under his brows Odysseus answered:

"You yellow dogs, you thought I'd never make it
home from the land of Troy. You took my house to plunder,   35
twisted my maids to serve your beds. You dared
bid for my wife while I was still alive.
Contempt was all you had for the gods who rule wide heaven,
contempt for what men say of you hereafter.
Your last hour has come. You die in blood."   40

As they all took this in, sickly green fear
pulled at their entrails, and their eyes flickered
looking for some hatch or hideaway from death.
Eurýmakhos alone could speak. He said:

"If you are Odysseus of Ithaka come back,   45
all that you say these men have done is true.

Rash actions, many here, more in the countryside.
But here he lies, the man who caused them all.
Antínoös was the ringleader; he whipped us on
to do these things. He cared less for a marriage   50
than for the power Kroníon has denied him
as king of Ithaka. For that
he tried to trap your son and would have killed him.
He is dead now and has his portion. Spare
your own people. As for ourselves, we'll make   55
restitution of wine and meat consumed,
and add, each one, a tithe of twenty oxen
with gifts of bronze and gold to warm your heart.
Meanwhile we cannot blame you for your anger."

Odysseus glowered under his black brows   60
and said:

     "Not for the whole treasure of your fathers,
all you enjoy, lands, flocks, or any gold
put up by others, would I hold my hand.
There will be killing till the score is paid.
You forced yourselves upon this house. Fight your way out,   65
or run for it, if you think you'll escape death.
I doubt one man of you skins by."

They felt their knees fail, and their hearts—but heard
Eurýmakhos for the last time rallying them.

"Friends," he said, "the man is implacable.   70
Now that he's got his hands on bow and quiver
he'll shoot from the big door stone there
until he kills us to the last man.
                Fight, I say,
let's remember the joy of it. Swords out!
Hold up your tables to deflect his arrows.   75
After me, everyone: rush him where he stands.
If we can budge him from the door, if we can pass
into the town, we'll call out men to chase him.
This fellow with his bow will shoot no more."

He drew his own sword as he spoke, a broadsword of fine bronze,   80
honed like a razor on either edge. Then crying hoarse and loud
he hurled himself at Odysseus. But the kingly man let fly
an arrow at that instant, and the quivering feathered butt
sprang to the nipple of his breast as the barb stuck in his liver.
The bright broadsword clanged down. He lurched and fell aside,   85
pitching across his table. His cup, his bread and meat,
were spilt and scattered far and wide, and his head slammed on the
    ground.
Revulsion, anguish in his heart, with both feet kicking out,
he downed his chair, while the shrouding wave of mist closed on his eyes.

Amphínomos now came running at Odysseus,   90
broadsword naked in his hand. He thought to make
the great soldier give way at the door.
But with a spear throw from behind Telémakhos hit him

between the shoulders, and the lancehead drove
clear through his chest. He left his feet and fell   95
forward, thudding, forehead against the ground.
Telémakhos swerved around him, leaving the long dark spear
planted in Amphínomos. If he paused to yank it out
someone might jump him from behind or cut him down with a sword
at the moment he bent over. So he ran—ran from the tables   100
to his father's side and halted, panting, saying:

"Father let me bring you a shield and spear,
a pair of spears, a helmet.
I can arm on the run myself; I'll give
outfits to Eumaios and this cowherd.   105
Better to have equipment."

                    Said Odysseus:

"Run then, while I hold them off with arrows
as long as the arrows last. When all are gone
if I'm alone they can dislodge me."

                                        Quick
upon his father's word Telémakhos   110
ran to the room where spears and armor lay.
He caught up four light shields, four pairs of spears,
four helms of war high-plumed with flowing manes,
and ran back, loaded down, to his father's side.
He was the first to pull a helmet on   115
and slide his bare arm in a buckler strap.
The servants armed themselves, and all three took their stand
beside the master of battle.
                              While he had arrows
he aimed and shot, and every shot brought down
one of his huddling enemies.   120
But when all barbs had flown from the bowman's fist,
he leaned his bow in the bright entry way
beside the door, and armed: a four-ply shield
hard on his shoulder, and a crested helm,
horsetailed, nodding stormy upon his head,   125
then took his tough and bronze-shod spears.
                                          The suitors
who held their feet, no longer under bowshot,
could see a window high in a recess of the wall,
a vent, lighting the passage to the storeroom.
This passage had one entry, with a door,   130
at the edge of the great hall's threshold, just outside.

Odysseus told the swineherd to stand over
and guard this door and passage. As he did so,
a suitor named Ageláos asked the others:

"Who will get a leg up on that window   135
and run to alarm the town? One sharp attack
and this fellow will never shoot again."

                              His answer
came from the goatherd, Melánthios:

                    "No chance, my lord.
The exit into the courtyard is too near them,
too narrow. One good man could hold that portal   140
against a crowd. No: let me scale the wall
and bring you arms out of the storage chamber.
Odysseus and his son put them indoors,
I'm sure of it; not outside."

                The goatish goatherd
clambered up the wall, toes in the chinks,   145
and slipped through to the storeroom. Twelve light shields,
twelve spears he took, and twelve thick-crested helms,
and handed all down quickly to the suitors.
Odysseus, when he saw his adversaries
girded and capped and long spears in their hands   150
shaken at him, felt his knees go slack,
his heart sink, for the fight was turning grim.
He spoke rapidly to his son:

"Telémakhos, one of the serving women
is tipping the scales against us in this fight,   155
or maybe Melánthios."

              But sharp and clear
Telémakhos said:

             "It is my own fault, Father,
mine alone. The storeroom door—I left it
wide open. They were more alert than I.
Eumaios, go and lock that door,   160
and bring back word if a woman is doing this
or Melánthios, Dólios' son. More likely he."

Even as they conferred, Melánthios
entered the storeroom for a second load,
and the swineherd at the passage entry saw him.   165
He cried out to his lord:

           "Son of Laërtês,
Odysseus, master mariner and soldier,
there he goes, the monkey, as we thought,
there he goes into the storeroom.
             Let me hear your will:
put a spear through him—I hope I am the stronger—   170
or drag him here to pay for his foul tricks
against your house?"

           Odysseus said:

             "Telémakhos and I
will keep these gentlemen in hall, for all their urge to leave.
You two go throw him into the storeroom, wrench his arms
and legs behind him, lash his hands and feet   175
to a plank, and hoist him up to the roof beams.
Let him live on there suffering at his leisure."

The two men heard him with appreciation
and ducked into the passage. Melánthios,
rummaging in the chamber, could not hear them   180
as they came up; nor could he see them freeze
like posts on either side the door.
He turned back with a handsome crested helmet
in one hand, in the other an old shield
coated with dust—a shield Laërtês bore   185
soldiering in his youth. It had lain there for years,
and the seams on strap and grip had rotted away.
As Melánthios came out the two men sprang,
jerked him backward by the hair, and threw him.
Hands and feet they tied with a cutting cord   190
behind him, so his bones ground in their sockets,
just as Laërtês' royal son commanded.
Then with a whip of rope they hoisted him
in agony up a pillar to the beams,
and—O my swineherd—you were the one to say: 195

"Watch through the night up there, Melánthios.
An airy bed is what you need.
You'll be awake to see the primrose Dawn
when she goes glowing from the streams of Ocean
to mount her golden throne.
                              No oversleeping   200
the hour for driving goats to feed the suitors."

They stopped for helm and shield and left him there
contorted, in his brutal sling,
and shut the doors, and went to join Odysseus,
whose mind moved through the combat now to come.   205
Breathing deep, and snorting hard, they stood
four at the entry, facing two score men.
But now into the gracious doorway stepped
Zeus's daughter Athena. She wore the guise of Mentor,
and Odysseus appealed to her in joy: 210

"O Mentor, join me in this fight! Remember
how all my life I've been devoted to you,
friend of my youth!"

                       For he guessed it was Athena,
Hope of Soldiers. Cries came from the suitors,
and Ageláos, Damástor's son, called out: 215

"Mentor, don't let Odysseus lead you astray
to fight against us on his side.
Think twice: we are resolved—and we will do it—
after we kill them, father and son,
you too will have your throat slit for your pains   220
if you make trouble for us here. It means your life.
Your life—and cutting throats will not be all.
Whatever wealth you have, at home, or elsewhere,
we'll mingle with Odysseus' wealth. Your sons
will be turned out, your wife and daughters   225
banished from the town of Ithaka."

Athena's anger grew like a storm wind as he spoke
until she flashed out at Odysseus:

                              "Ah, what a falling off!
Where is your valor, where is the iron hand
that fought at Troy for Helen, pearl of kings,   230
no respite and nine years of war? How many foes
your hand brought down in bloody play of spears?
What stratagem but yours took Priam's town?
How is it now that on your own door sill,
before the harriers of your wife, you curse your luck   235
not to be stronger?
                        Come here, cousin, stand by me,
and you'll see action! In the enemies' teeth
learn how Mentor, son of Álkimos,
repays fair dealing!"

                        For all her fighting words
she gave no overpowering aid—not yet;   240
father and son must prove their mettle still.
Into the smoky air under the roof
the goddess merely darted to perch on a blackened beam—
no figure to be seen now but a swallow.

Command of the suitors had fallen to Ageláos.   245
With him were Eurýnomos, Amphímedon,
Demoptólemos, Peisándros, Pólybos,
the best of the lot who stood to fight for their lives
after the streaking arrows downed the rest.
Ageláos rallied them with his plan of battle: 250

"Friends, our killer has come to the end of his rope,
and much good Mentor did him, that blowhard, dropping in.
Look, only four are left to fight, in the light there at the door.
No scattering of shots, men, no throwing away good spears;
we six will aim a volley at Odysseus alone,   255
and may Zeus grant us the glory of a hit.
If he goes down, the others are no problem."

At his command, then, "Ho!" they all let fly
as one man. But Athena spoiled their shots.
One hit the doorpost of the hall, another   260
stuck in the door's thick timbering, still others
rang on the stone wall, shivering hafts of ash.
Seeing his men unscathed, royal Odysseus
gave the word for action.

                        "Now I say, friends,
the time is overdue to let them have it.   265
Battlespoil they want from our dead bodies
to add to all they plundered here before."

Taking aim over the steadied lanceheads
they all let fly together. Odysseus killed
Demoptólemos; Telémakhos   270
killed Eurýadês; the swineherd, Élatos;
and Peisándros went down before the cowherd.

As these lay dying, biting the central floor,
their friends gave way and broke for the inner wall.
The four attackers followed up with a rush   275
to take spears from the fallen men.

        Re-forming,
the suitors threw again with all their strength,
but Athena turned their shots, or all but two.
One hit a doorpost in the hall, another
stuck in the door's thick timbering, still others   280
rang on the stone wall, shivering hafts of ash.
Amphímedon's point bloodied Telémakhos'
wrist, a superficial wound, and Ktésippos'
long spear passing over Eumaios' shield
grazed his shoulder, hurtled on and fell.   285
No matter: with Odysseus the great soldier
the wounded threw again. And Odysseus raider of cities
struck Eurýdamas down. Telémakhos
hit Amphímedon, and the swineherd's shot
killed Pólybos. But Ktésippos, who had last evening thrown   290
a cow's hoof at Odysseus, got the cowherd's heavy cast
full in the chest—and dying heard him say:

"You arrogant joking bastard!
Clown, will you, like a fool, and parade your wit?
Leave jesting to the gods who do it better.   295
This will repay your cow's-foot courtesy
to a great wanderer come home."

        The master
of the black herds had answered Ktésippos.
Odysseus, lunging at close quarters, put a spear
through Ageláos, Damastor's son. Telémakhos   300
hit Leókritos from behind and pierced him,
kidney to diaphragm. Speared off his feet,
he fell face downward on the ground.

At this moment that unmanning thunder cloud,
the aegis,[8] Athena's shield,   305
took form aloft in the great hall.
        And the suitors mad with fear
at her great sign stampeded like stung cattle by a river
when the dread shimmering gadfly strikes in summer,
in the flowering season, in the long-drawn days.
After them the attackers wheeled, as terrible as falcons   310
from eyries in the mountains veering over and diving down
with talons wide unsheathed on flights of birds,
who cower down the sky in chutes and bursts along the valley—
but the pouncing falcons grip their prey, no frantic wing avails,
and farmers love to watch those beakèd hunters.   315
So these now fell upon the suitors in that hall,
turning, turning to strike and strike again,

---

8. A magical shield (or breastplate) used by Athena and Zeus; it created a panic when displayed.

while torn men moaned at death, and blood ran smoking
over the whole floor.
                    Now there was one
who turned and threw himself at Odysseus' knees—   320
Leódês, begging for his life:

                    "Mercy,
mercy on a suppliant, Odysseus!
Never by word or act of mine, I swear,
was any woman troubled here. I told the rest
to put an end to it. They would not listen,   325
would not keep their hands from brutishness,
and now they are all dying like dogs for it.
I had no part in what they did: my part
was visionary—reading the smoke of sacrifice.
Scruples go unrewarded if I die."   330

The shrewd fighter frowned over him and said:

"You were diviner to this crowd? How often
you must have prayed my sweet day of return
would never come, or not for years!—and prayed
to have my dear wife, and beget children on her.   335
No plea like yours could save you
from this hard bed of death. Death it shall be!"

He picked up Ageláos' broadsword
from where it lay, flung by the slain man,
and gave Leódês' neck a lopping blow   340
so that his head went down to mouth in dust.

One more who had avoided furious death
was the son of Terpis, Phêmios, the minstrel,
singer by compulsion to the suitors.
He stood now with his harp, holy and clear,   345
in the wall's recess, under the window, wondering
if he should flee that way to the courtyard altar,
sanctuary of Zeus, the Enclosure God.[9]
Thighbones in hundreds had been offered there
by Laërtês and Odysseus. No, he thought;   350
the more direct way would be best—to go
humbly to his lord. But first to save
his murmuring instrument he laid it down
carefully between the winebowl and a chair,
then he betook himself to Lord Odysseus,   355
clung hard to his knees, and said:

                    "Mercy,
mercy on a suppliant, Odysseus!
My gift is song for men and for the gods undying.
My death will be remorse for you hereafter.
No one taught me: deep in my mind a god   360
shaped all the various ways of life in song.
And I am fit to make verse in your company

---

9. Zeus Herkeios, guardian of the inner space of the home.

as in the god's. Put aside lust for blood.
Your own dear son Telémakhos can tell you,
never by my own will or for love   365
did I feast here or sing amid the suitors.
They were too strong, too many; they compelled me."

Telémakhos in the elation of battle
heard him. He at once called to his father:

"Wait: that one is innocent: don't hurt him.   370
And we should let our herald live—Medôn;
he cared for me from boyhood. Where is *he?*
Has he been killed already by Philoítios
or by the swineherd? Else he got an arrow
in that first gale of bowshots down the room."   375

Now this came to the ears of prudent Medôn
under the chair where he had gone to earth,
pulling a new-flayed bull's hide over him.
Quiet he lay while blinding death passed by.
Now heaving out from under   380
he scrambled for Telémakhos' knees and said:

"Here I am, dear prince; but rest your spear!
Tell your great father not to see in me
a suitor for the sword's edge—one of those
who laughed at you and ruined his property!"   385

The lord of all the tricks of war surveyed
this fugitive and smiled. He said:

"Courage: my son has dug you out and saved you.
Take it to heart, and pass the word along:
fair dealing brings more profit in the end.   390
Now leave this room. Go and sit down outdoors
where there's no carnage, in the court,
you and the poet with his many voices,
while I attend to certain chores inside."

At this the two men stirred and picked their way   395
to the door and out, and sat down at the altar,
looking around with wincing eyes
as though the sword's edge hovered still.
And Odysseus looked around him, narrow-eyed,
for any others who had lain hidden   400
while death's black fury passed.
                              In blood and dust
he saw that crowd all fallen, many and many slain.

Think of a catch that fishermen haul in to a halfmoon bay
in a fine-meshed net from the white-caps of the sea:
how all are poured out on the sand, in throes for the salt sea,   405
twitching their cold lives away in Hêlios' fiery air:
so lay the suitors heaped on one another.

Odysseus at length said to his son:

"Go tell old Nurse I'll have a word with her.
What's to be done now weighs on my mind."   410

Telémakhos knocked at the women's door and called:

"Eurýkleia, come out here! Move, old woman.
You kept your eye on all our servant girls.
Jump, my father is here and wants to see you."

His call brought no reply, only the doors   415
were opened, and she came. Telémakhos
led her forward. In the shadowy hall
full of dead men she found his father
spattered and caked with blood like a mountain lion
when he has gorged upon an ox, his kill—   420
with hot blood glistening over his whole chest,
smeared on his jaws, baleful and terrifying—
even so encrimsoned was Odysseus
up to his thighs and armpits. As she gazed
from all the corpses to the bloody man   425
she raised her head to cry over his triumph,
but felt his grip upon her, checking her.
Said the great soldier then:

                    "Rejoice
inwardly. No crowing aloud, old woman.
To glory over slain men is no piety.   430
Destiny and the gods' will vanquished these,
and their own hardness. They respected no one,
good or bad, who came their way.
For this, and folly, a bad end befell them.
Your part is now to tell me of the women,   435
those who dishonored me, and the innocent."

His own old nurse Eurýkleia said:

                    "I will, then.
Child, you know you'll have the truth from me.
Fifty all told they are, your female slaves,
trained by your lady and myself in service,   440
wool carding and the rest of it, and taught
to be submissive. Twelve went bad,
flouting me, flouting Penélopê, too.
Telémakhos being barely grown, his mother
would never let him rule the serving women—   445
but you must let me go to her lighted rooms
and tell her. Some god sent her a drift of sleep."

But in reply the great tactician said:

"Not yet. Do not awake her. Tell those women
who were the suitors' harlots to come here."   450

She went back on this mission through his hall.
Then he called Telémakhos to his side
and the two herdsmen. Sharply Odysseus said:

"These dead must be disposed of first of all.
Direct the women. Tables and chairs will be   455
scrubbed with sponges, rinsed and rinsed again.
When our great room is fresh and put in order,
take them outside, these women,
between the roundhouse and the palisade,
and hack them with your swordblades till you cut   460
the life out of them, and every thought of sweet
Aphroditê under the rutting suitors,
when they lay down in secret."

                          As he spoke
here came the women in a bunch, all wailing,
soft tears on their cheeks. They fell to work   465
to lug the corpses out into the courtyard
under the gateway, propping one
against another as Odysseus ordered,
for he himself stood over them. In fear
these women bore the cold weight of the dead.   470
The next thing was to scrub off chairs and tables
and rinse them down. Telémakhos and the herdsman
scraped the packed earth floor with hoes, but made
the women carry out all blood and mire.
When the great room was cleaned up once again,   475
at swordpoint they forced them out, between
the roundhouse and the palisade, pell-mell
to huddle in that dead end without exit.
Telémakhos, who knew his mind, said curtly:

"I would not give the clean death of a beast[1]   480
to trulls who made a mockery of my mother
and of me too—you sluts, who lay with suitors."

He tied one end of a hawser to a pillar
and passed the other about the roundhouse top,
taking the slack up, so that no one's toes   485
could touch the ground. They would be hung like doves
or larks in springès triggered in a thicket,
where the birds think to rest—a cruel nesting.
So now in turn each woman thrust her head
into a noose and swung, yanked high in air,   490
to perish there most piteously.
Their feet danced for a little, but not long.

From storeroom to the court they brought Melánthios,
chopped with swords to cut his nose and ears off,
pulled off his genitals to feed the dogs   495
and raging hacked his hands and feet away.
As their own hands and feet called for a washing,
they went indoors to Odysseus again.
Their work was done. He told Eurýkleia:

                          "Bring me

---

1. That is, by sword or spear. Hanging was considered an ignominious way to die.

brimstone and a brazier—medicinal   500
fumes to purify my hall. Then tell
Penélopê to come, and bring her maids.
All servants round the house must be called in."

His own old nurse Eurýkleia replied:

"Aye, surely that is well said, child. But let me   505
find you a good clean shirt and cloak and dress you.
You must not wrap your shoulders' breadth again
in rags in your own hall. That would be shameful."

Odysseus answered:

                    "Let me have the fire.
The first thing is to purify this place."   510

With no more chat Eurýkleia obeyed
and fetched out fire and brimstone. Cleansing fumes
he sent through court and hall and storage chamber.
Then the old woman hurried off again
to the women's quarters to announce her news,   515
and all the servants came now, bearing torches
in twilight, crowding to embrace Odysseus,
taking his hands to kiss, his head and shoulders,
while he stood there, nodding to every one,
and overcome by longing and by tears.   520

BOOK XXIII

[*The Trunk of the Olive Tree*]

The old nurse went upstairs exulting,
with knees toiling, and patter of slapping feet,
to tell the mistress of her lord's return,
and cried out by the lady's pillow:

                    "Wake,
wake up, dear child! Penélopê, come down,   5
see with your own eyes what all these years you longed for!
Odysseus is here! Oh, in the end, he came!
And he has killed your suitors, killed them all
who made his house a bordel and ate his cattle
and raised their hands against his son!"

                              Penélopê said: 10

"Dear nurse . . . the gods have touched you.
They can put chaos into the clearest head
or bring a lunatic down to earth. Good sense
you always had. They've touched you. What is this
mockery you wake me up to tell me,   15
breaking in on my sweet spell of sleep?
I had not dozed away so tranquilly
since my lord went to war, on that ill wind
to Ilion.
              Oh, leave me! Back down stairs!
If any other of my women came in babbling   20

things like these to startle me, I'd see her
flogged out of the house! Your old age spares you that."

Eurýkleia said:

"Would I play such a trick on you, dear child?
It is true, true, as I tell you, he has come!   25
That stranger they were baiting was Odysseus.
Telémakhos knew it days ago—
cool head, never to give his father away,
till he paid off those swollen dogs!"

The lady in her heart's joy now sprang up   30
with sudden dazzling tears, and hugged the old one,
crying out:

      "But try to make it clear!
If he came home in secret, as you say,
could he engage them singlehanded? How?
They were all down there, still in the same crowd."   35

To this Eurýkleia said:

      "I did not see it,
I knew nothing; only I heard the groans
of men dying. We sat still in the inner rooms
holding our breath, and marvelling, shut in,
until Telémakhos came to the door and called me—   40
your own dear son, sent this time by his father!
So I went out, and found Odysseus
erect, with dead men littering the floor
this way and that. If you had only seen him!
It would have made your heart glow hot!—a lion   45
splashed with mire and blood.
      But now the cold
corpses are all gathered at the gate,
and he has cleansed his hall with fire and brimstone,
a great blaze. Then he sent me here to you.
Come with me: you may both embark this time   50
for happiness together, after pain,
after long years. Here is your prayer, your passion,
granted: your own lord lives, he is at home,
he found you safe, he found his son. The suitors
abused his house, but he has brought them down."   55

The attentive lady said:

      "Do not lose yourself
in this rejoicing: wait: you know
how splendid that return would be for us,
how dear to me, dear to his son and mine;
but no, it is not possible, your notion   60
must be wrong.
      Some god has killed the suitors,
a god, sick of their arrogance and brutal
malice—for they honored no one living,
good or bad, who ever came their way.

Blind young fools, they've tasted death for it.   65
But the true person of Odysseus?
He lost his home, he died far from Akhaia."

The old nurse sighed:

                              "How queer, the way you talk!
Here he is, large as life, by his own fire,
and you deny he ever will get home!   70
Child, you always were mistrustful!
But there is one sure mark that I can tell you:
that scar left by the boar's tusk long ago.
I recognized it when I bathed his feet
and would have told you, but he stopped my mouth,   75
forbade me, in his craftiness.
                              Come down,
I stake my life on it, he's here!
Let me die in agony if I lie!"

                         Penélopê said:

"Nurse dear, though you have your wits about you,
still it is hard not to be taken in   80
by the immortals. Let us join my son, though,
and see the dead and that strange one who killed them."

She turned then to descend the stair, her heart
in tumult. Had she better keep her distance
and question him, her husband? Should she run   85
up to him, take his hands, kiss him now?
Crossing the door sill she sat down at once
in firelight, against the nearest wall,
across the room from the lord Odysseus.
                              There
leaning against a pillar, sat the man   90
and never lifted up his eyes, but only waited
for what his wife would say when she had seen him.
And she, for a long time, sat deathly still
in wonderment—for sometimes as she gazed
she found him—yes, clearly—like her husband,   95
but sometimes blood and rags were all she saw.
Telémakhos' voice came to her ears:

                         "Mother,
cruel mother, do you feel nothing,
drawing yourself apart this way from Father?
Will you not sit with him and talk and question him?   100
What other woman could remain so cold?
Who shuns her lord, and he come back to her
from wars and wandering, after twenty years?
Your heart is hard as flint and never changes!"

Penélopê answered:

                         "I am stunned, child.   105
I cannot speak to him. I cannot question him.
I cannot keep my eyes upon his face.

If really he is Odysseus, truly home,
beyond all doubt we two shall know each other
better than you or anyone. There are   110
secret signs we know, we two."

                                   A smile
came now to the lips of the patient hero, Odysseus,
who turned to Telémakhos and said:

"Peace: let your mother test me at her leisure.
Before long she will see and know me best.   115
These tatters, dirt—all that I'm caked with now—
make her look hard at me and doubt me still.
As to this massacre, we must see the end.
Whoever kills one citizen, you know,
and has no force of armed men at his back,   120
had better take himself abroad by night
and leave his kin. Well, we cut down the flower of Ithaka,
the mainstay of the town. Consider that."

Telémakhos replied respectfully:

                                   "Dear Father,
enough that you yourself study the danger,   125
foresighted in combat as you are,
they say you have no rival.
                        We three stand
ready to follow you and fight. I say
for what our strength avails, we have the courage."

And the great tactician, Odysseus, answered:

                                          "Good.   130
Here is our best maneuver, as I see it:
bathe, you three, and put fresh clothing on,
order the women to adorn themselves,
and let our admirable harper choose a tune
for dancing, some lighthearted air, and strum it.   135
Anyone going by, or any neighbor,
will think it is a wedding feast he hears.
These deaths must not be cried about the town
till we can slip away to our own woods. We'll see
what weapon, then, Zeus puts into our hands."   140

They listened attentively, and did his bidding,
bathed and dressed afresh; and all the maids
adorned themselves. Then Phêmios the harper
took his polished shell and plucked the strings,
moving the company to desire   145
for singing, for the sway and beat of dancing,
until they made the manor hall resound
with gaiety of men and grace of women.
Anyone passing on the road would say:

"Married at last, I see—the queen so many courted.   150
Sly, cattish wife! She would not keep—not she!—
the lord's estate until he came."

So travellers'
thoughts might run—but no one guessed the truth.
Greathearted Odysseus, home at last,
was being bathed now by Eurýnomê   155
and rubbed with golden oil, and clothed again
in a fresh tunic and a cloak. Athena
lent him beauty, head to foot. She made him
taller, and massive, too, with crisping hair
in curls like petals of wild hyacinth   160
but all red-golden. Think of gold infused
on silver by a craftsman, whose fine art
Hephaistos taught him, or Athena: one
whose work moves to delight: just so she lavished
beauty over Odysseus' head and shoulders.   165
He sat then in the same chair by the pillar,
facing his silent wife, and said:

                    "Strange woman,
the immortals of Olympos made you hard,
harder than any. Who else in the world
would keep aloof as you do from her husband   170
if he returned to her from years of trouble,
cast on his own land in the twentieth year?

Nurse, make up a bed for me to sleep on.
Her heart is iron in her breast."

                    Penélopê
spoke to Odysseus now. She said:

                              "Strange man,   175
if man you are . . . This is no pride on my part
nor scorn for you—not even wonder, merely.
I know so well how you—how he—appeared
boarding the ship for Troy. But all the same . . .

Make up his bed for him, Eurýkleia.   180
Place it outside the bedchamber my lord
built with his own hands. Pile the big bed
with fleeces, rugs, and sheets of purest linen."

With this she tried him to the breaking point,
and he turned on her in a flash raging: 185

"Woman, by heaven you've stung me now!
Who dared to move my bed?
No builder had the skill for that—unless
a god came down to turn the trick. No mortal
in his best days could budge it with a crowbar.   190
There is our pact and pledge, our secret sign,
built into that bed—my handiwork
and no one else's!
                    An old trunk of olive
grew like a pillar on the building plot,
and I laid out our bedroom round that tree,   195
lined up the stone walls, built the walls and roof,

gave it a doorway and smooth-fitting doors.
Then I lopped off the silvery leaves and branches,
hewed and shaped that stump from the roots up
into a bedpost, drilled it, let it serve   200
as model for the rest. I planed them all,
inlaid them all with silver, gold and ivory,
and stretched a bed between—a pliant web
of oxhide thongs dyed crimson.
                              There's our sign!
I know no more. Could someone's else's hand   205
have sawn that trunk and dragged the frame away?"

Their secret! as she heard it told, her knees
grew tremulous and weak, her heart failed her.
With eyes brimming tears she ran to him,
throwing her arms around his neck, and kissed him,   210
murmuring:

              "Do not rage at me, Odysseus!
No one ever matched your caution! Think
what difficulty the gods gave: they denied us
life together in our prime and flowering years,
kept us from crossing into age together.   215
Forgive me, don't be angry. I could not
welcome you with love on sight! I armed myself
long ago against the frauds of men,
impostors who might come—and all those many
whose underhanded ways bring evil on!   220
Helen of Argos, daughter of Zeus and Leda,
would she have joined the stranger, lain with him,
if she had known her destiny? known the Akhaians
in arms would bring her back to her own country?
Surely a goddess moved her to adultery,   225
her blood unchilled by war and evil coming,
the years, the desolation; ours, too.
But here and now, what sign could be so clear
as this of our own bed?
No other man has ever laid eyes on it—   230
only my own slave, Aktoris, that my father
sent with me as a gift—she kept our door.
You make my stiff heart know that I am yours."

Now from his breast into his eyes the ache
of longing mounted, and he wept at last,   235
his dear wife, clear and faithful, in his arms,
longed for
          as the sunwarmed earth is longed for by a swimmer
spent in rough water where his ship went down
under Poseidon's blows, gale winds and tons of sea.
Few men can keep alive through a big surf   240
to crawl, clotted with brine, on kindly beaches
in joy, in joy, knowing the abyss behind:
and so she too rejoiced, her gaze upon her husband,
her white arms round him pressed as though forever.
The rose Dawn might have found them weeping still   245

had not grey-eyed Athena slowed the night
when night was most profound, and held the Dawn
under the Ocean of the East. That glossy team,
Firebright and Daybright, the Dawn's horses
that draw her heavenward for men—Athena   250
stayed their harnessing.

                Then said Odysseus:

"My dear, we have not won through to the end.
One trial—I do not know how long—is left for me
to see fulfilled. Teirêsias' ghost forewarned me
the night I stood upon the shore of Death, asking   255
about my friends' homecoming and my own.

But now the hour grows late, it is bed time,
rest will be sweet for us; let us lie down."

To this Penélopê replied:

                "That bed,
that rest is yours whenever desire moves you,   260
now the kind powers have brought you home at last.
But as your thought has dwelt upon it, tell me:
what is the trial you face? I must know soon;
what does it matter if I learn tonight?"

The teller of many stories said:

                    "My strange one,   265
must you again, and even now,
urge me to talk? Here is a plodding tale;
no charm in it, no relish in the telling.
Teirêsias told me I must take an oar
and trudge the mainland, going from town to town,   270
until I discover men who have never known
the salt blue sea, nor flavor of salt meat—
strangers to painted prows, to watercraft
and oars like wings, dipping across the water.
The moment of revelation he foretold   275
was this, for you may share the prophecy:
some traveller falling in with me will say:
'A winnowing fan, that on your shoulder, sir?'
There I must plant my oar, on the very spot,
with burnt offerings to Poseidon of the Waters: 280
a ram, a bull, a great buck boar. Thereafter
when I come home again, I am to slay
full hekatombs to the gods who own broad heaven,
one by one.
              Then death will drift upon me
from seaward, mild as air, mild as your hand,   285
in my well-tended weariness of age,
contented folk around me on our island.
He said all this must come."

                Penélopê said:

"If by the gods' grace age at least is kind,
we have that promise—trials will end in peace."   290

So he confided in her, and she answered.
Meanwhile Eurýnomê and the nurse together
laid soft coverlets on the master's bed,
working in haste by torchlight. Eurýkleia
retired to her quarters for the night,   295
and then Eurýnomê, as maid-in-waiting,
lighted her lord and lady to their chamber
with bright brands.
                    She vanished.
                              So they came
into that bed so steadfast, loved of old,
opening glad arms to one another.[2]   300
Telémakhos by now had hushed the dancing,
hushed the women. In the darkened hall
he and the cowherd and the swineherd slept.

The royal pair mingled in love again
and afterward lay revelling in stories: 305
hers of the siege her beauty stood at home
from arrogant suitors, crowding on her sight,
and how they fed their courtship on his cattle,
oxen and fat sheep, and drank up rivers
of wine out of the vats.
                    Odysseus told   310
of what hard blows he had dealt out to others
and of what blows he had taken—all that story.
She could not close her eyes till all was told.

His raid on the Kikonês, first of all,
then how he visited the Lotos Eaters,   315
and what the Kyklops did, and how those shipmates,
pitilessly devoured, were avenged.
Then of his touching Aiolos's isle
and how that king refitted him for sailing
to Ithaka; all vain: gales blew him back   320
groaning over the fishcold sea. Then how
he reached the Laistrygonians' distant bay
and how they smashed his ships and his companions.
Kirkê, then: of her deceits and magic,
then of his voyage to the wide underworld   325
of dark, the house of Death, and questioning
Teirêsias, Theban spirit.
                    Dead companions,
many, he saw there, and his mother, too.
Of this he told his wife, and told how later
he heard the choir of maddening Seirênês,   330

2. Two great Alexandrian critics said that this line was the "end" of the *Odyssey* (though one of the
words they are said to have used could mean simply "culmination"). Modern critics are divided; some
find the rest of the poem banal, unartistic, full of linguistic anomalies, and so on. But if the poem stops
here we are left in suspense about many important themes that have been developed and demand a
sequel—the question of reprisals for the slaughter in the hall, to mention only one.

coasted the Wandering Rocks, Kharybdis' pool
and the fiend Skylla who takes toll of men.
Then how his shipmates killed Lord Hêlios' cattle
and how Zeus thundering in towering heaven
split their fast ship with his fuming bolt,   335
so all hands perished.
                              He alone survived,
cast away on Kalypso's isle, Ogýgia.
He told, then, how that nymph detained him there
in her smooth caves, craving him for her husband,
and how in her devoted lust she swore   340
he should not die nor grow old, all his days,
but he held out against her.
                              Last of all
what sea-toil brought him to the Phaiákians;
their welcome; how they took him to their hearts
and gave him passage to his own dear island   345
with gifts of garments, gold and bronze . . .
                              Remembering,
he drowsed over the story's end. Sweet sleep
relaxed his limbs and his care-burdened breast.

Other affairs were in Athena's keeping.
Waiting until Odysseus had his pleasure   350
of love and sleep, the grey-eyed one bestirred
the fresh Dawn from her bed of paling Ocean
to bring up daylight to her golden chair,
and from his fleecy bed Odysseus
arose. He said to Penélopê: 355
                              "My lady,
what ordeals have we not endured! Here, waiting
you had your grief, while my return dragged out—
my hard adventures, pitting myself against
the gods' will, and Zeus, who pinned me down
far from home. But now our life resumes: 360
we've come together to our longed-for bed.
Take care of what is left me in our house;
as to the flocks that pack of wolves laid waste
they'll be replenished: scores I'll get on raids
and other scores our island friends will give me   365
till all the folds are full again.
                              This day
I'm off up country to the orchards. I must see
my noble father, for he missed me sorely.
And here is my command for you—a strict one,
though you may need none, clever as you are.   370
Word will get about as the sun goes higher
of how I killed those lads. Go to your rooms
on the upper floor, and take your women. Stay there
with never a glance outside or a word to anyone."

Fitting cuirass and swordbelt to his shoulders,   375
he woke his herdsmen, woke Telémakhos,
ordering all in arms. They dressed quickly,

and all in war gear sallied from the gate,
led by Odysseus.
                    Now it was broad day
but these three men Athena hid in darkness,   380
going before them swiftly from the town.

BOOK XXIV

[Warriors, Farewell]

Meanwhile the suitors' ghosts were called away
by Hermês of Kyllênê,[3] bearing the golden wand
with which he charms the eyes of men or wakens
whom he wills.
                    He waved them on, all squeaking
as bats will in a cavern's underworld,   5
all flitting, flitting criss-cross in the dark
if one falls and the rock-hung chain is broken.
So with faint cries the shades trailed after Hermês,
pure Deliverer.
                    He led them down dank ways,
over grey Ocean tides, the Snowy Rock,   10
past shores of Dream and narrows of the sunset,
in swift flight to where the Dead inhabit
wastes of asphodel at the world's end.

Crossing the plain they met Akhilleus' ghost,
Patróklos and Antílokhos, then Aias,   15
noblest of Danaans after Akhilleus
in strength and beauty. Here the newly dead
drifted together, whispering. Then came
the soul of Agamémnon, son of Atreus,
in black pain forever, surrounded by men-at-arms   20
who perished with him in Aigísthos' hall.

Akhilleus greeted him:
                    "My lord Atreidês,
we held that Zeus who loves the play of lightning
would give you length of glory, you were king
over so great a host of soldiery   25
before Troy, where we suffered, we Akhaians.
But in the morning of your life
you met that doom that no man born avoids.
It should have found you in your day of victory,
marshal of the army, in Troy country;   30
then all Akhaia would have heaped your tomb
and saved your honor for your son. Instead
piteous death awaited you at home."

And Atreus' son replied:
                    "Fortunate hero,
son of Pêleus, godlike and glorious,   35
at Troy you died, across the sea from Argos,

---

3. A mountain in Arcadia, Hermês' birthplace.

and round you Trojan and Akhaian peers
fought for your corpse and died. A dustcloud wrought
by a whirlwind hid the greatness of you slain,
minding no more the mastery of horses.   40
All that day we might have toiled in battle
had not a storm from Zeus broken it off.
We carried you out of the field of war
down to the ships and bathed your comely body
with warm water and scented oil. We laid you   45
upon your long bed, and our officers
wept hot tears like rain and cropped their hair.
Then hearing of it in the sea, your mother, Thetis,
came with nereids of the grey wave crying
unearthly lamentation over the water,   50
and trembling gripped the Akhaians to the bone.
They would have boarded ship that night and fled
except for one man's wisdom—venerable
Nestor, proven counselor in the past.
He stood and spoke to allay their fear: 'Hold fast,   55
sons of the Akhaians, lads of Argos.
His mother it must be, with nymphs her sisters,
come from the sea to mourn her son in death.'

Veteran hearts at this contained their dread
while at your side the daughters of the ancient   60
seagod wailed and wrapped ambrosial shrouding
around you.
            Then we heard the Muses sing
a threnody in nine immortal voices.
No Argive there but wept, such keening rose
from that one Muse who led the song.
                              Now seven   65
days and ten, seven nights and ten, we mourned you,
we mortal men, with nymphs who know no death,
before we gave you to the flame, slaughtering
longhorned steers and fat sheep on your pyre.

Dressed by the nereids and embalmed with honey,   70
honey and unguent in the seething blaze,
you turned to ash. And past the pyre Akhaia's
captains paraded in review, in arms,
clattering chariot teams and infantry.
Like a forest fire the flame roared on, and burned   75
your flesh away. Next day at dawn, Akhilleus,
we picked your pale bones from the char to keep
in wine and oil. A golden amphora
your mother gave for this—Hephaistos' work,
a gift from Dionysos.[4] In that vase,   80
Akhilleus, hero, lie your pale bones mixed
with mild Patróklos' bones, who died before you,
and nearby lie the bones of Antílokhos,

---

4. A god of the countryside especially associated with wine. Rarely mentioned in Homer, he later
presides, at the Athenian festivals, over tragedy and comedy.

the one you cared for most of all companions
after Patróklos.
                    We of the Old Army,   85
we who were spearmen, heaped a tomb for these
upon a foreland over Hellê's waters,[5]
to be a mark against the sky for voyagers
in this generation and those to come.
Your mother sought from the gods magnificent trophies   90
and set them down midfield for our champions. Often
at funeral games after the death of kings
when you yourself contended, you've seen athletes
cinch their belts when trophies went on view.
But these things would have made you stare—the treasures   95
Thetis on her silver-slippered feet
brought to your games—for the gods held you dear.
You perished, but your name will never die.
It lives to keep all men in mind of honor
forever, Akhilleus.
                    As for myself, what joy   100
is this, to have brought off the war? Foul death
Zeus held in store for me at my coming home;
Aigísthos and my vixen cut me down."

While they conversed, the Wayfinder came near,
leading the shades of suitors overthrown   105
by Lord Odysseus. The two souls of heroes
advanced together, scrutinizing these.
Then Agamémnon recognized Amphímedon,
son of Meláneus—friends of his on Ithaka—
and called out to him:

                    "Amphímedon,   110
what ruin brought you into this undergloom?
All in a body, picked men, and so young?
One could not better choose the kingdom's pride.
Were you at sea, aboard ship, and Poseidon
blew up a dire wind and foundering waves,   115
or cattle-raiding, were you, on the mainland,
or in a fight for some stronghold, or women,
when the foe hit you to your mortal hurt?
Tell me, answer my question. Guest and friend
I say I am of yours—or do you not remember   120
I visited your family there? I came
with Prince Meneláos, urging Odysseus
to join us in the great sea raid on Troy.
One solid month we beat our way, breasting
south sea and west, resolved to bring him round,   125
the wily raider of cities."

                    The new shade said:

"O glory of commanders, Agamémnon,
all that you bring to mind I remember well.

5. The Hellespont, the strait separating Asia Minor from Europe, visible from Troy.

As for the sudden manner of our death
I'll tell you of it clearly, first to last.   130
After Odysseus had been gone for years
we were all suitors of his queen. She never
quite refused, nor went through with a marriage,
hating it, ever bent on our defeat.
Here is one of her tricks: she placed her loom,   135
her big loom, out for weaving in her hall,
and the fine warp of some vast fabric on it.
We were attending her, and she said to us:
'Young men, my suitors, now my lord is dead,
let me finish my weaving before I marry,   140
or else my thread will have been spun in vain.
This is a shroud I weave for Lord Laërtês
when cold Death comes to lay him on his bier.
The country wives would hold me in dishonor
if he, with all his fortune, lay unshrouded.'   145
We had men's hearts; she touched them; we agreed.
So every day she wove on the great loom—
but every night by torchlight she unwove it,
and so for three years she deceived the Akhaians.
But when the seasons brought the fourth around,   150
as long months waned, and the slow days were spent,
one of her maids, who knew the secret, told us.
We found her unraveling the splendid shroud,
and then she had to finish, willy nilly—
finish, and show the big loom woven tight   155
from beam to beam with cloth. She washed the shrouding
clean as sun or moonlight.
                          Then, heaven knows
from what quarter of the world, fatality
brought in Odysseus to the swineherd's wood
far up the island. There his son went too   160
when the black ship put him ashore from Pylos.
The two together planned our death-trap. Down
they came to the famous town—Telémakhos
long in advance: we had to wait for Odysseus.
The swineherd led him to the manor later   165
in rags like a foul beggar, old and broken,
propped on a stick. These tatters that he wore
hid him so well that none of us could know him
when he turned up, not even the older men.
We jeered at him, took potshots at him, cursed him.   170
Daylight and evening in his own great hall
he bore it, patient as a stone. That night
the mind of Zeus beyond the stormcloud stirred him
with Telémakhos at hand to shift his arms
from mégaron to storage room and lock it.   175
Then he assigned his wife her part: next day
she brought his bow and iron axeheads out
to make a contest. Contest there was none;
that move doomed us to slaughter. Not a man
could bend the stiff bow to his will or string it,   180
until it reached Odysseus. We shouted,

'Keep the royal bow from the beggar's hands
no matter how he begs!' Only Telémakhos
would not be denied.
                         So the great soldier
took his bow and bent it for the bowstring   185
effortlessly. He drilled the axeheads clean,
sprang, and decanted arrows on the door sill,
glared, and drew again. This time he killed
Antínoös.
             There facing us he crouched
and shot his bolts of groaning at us, brought us   190
down like sheep. Then some god, his familiar,
went into action with him round the hall,
after us in a massacre. Men lay groaning,
mortally wounded, and the floor smoked with blood.

That was the way our death came, Agamémnon.   195
Now in Odysseus' hall untended still
our bodies lie, unknown to friends or kinsmen
who should have laid us out and washed our wounds
free of the clotted blood, and mourned our passing.
So much is due the dead."

                         But Agamémnon's   200
tall shade when he heard this cried aloud:

"O fortunate Odysseus, master mariner
and soldier, blessed son of old Laërtês!
The girl you brought home made a valiant wife!
True to her husband's honor and her own,   205
Penélopê, Ikários' faithful daughter!
The very gods themselves will sing her story
for men on earth—mistress of her own heart,
                                        Penélopê!
Tyndáreus' daughter waited, too—how differently!
Klytaimnéstra, the adulteress,   210
waited to stab her lord and king. That song
will be forever hateful. A bad name
she gave to womankind, even the best."

These were the things they said to one another
under the rim of earth where Death is lord.   215

Leaving the town, Odysseus and his men
that morning reached Laërtês garden lands,
long since won by his toil from wilderness—
his homestead, and the row of huts around it
where fieldhands rested, ate and slept. Indoors   220
he had an old slave woman, a Sikel, keeping
house for him in his secluded age.

Odysseus here took leave of his companions.

"Go make yourselves at home inside," he said.
"Roast the best porker and prepare a meal.   225
I'll go to try my father. Will he know me?
Can he imagine it, after twenty years?"

He handed spear and shield to the two herdsmen,
and in they went, Telémakhos too. Alone
Odysseus walked the orchard rows and vines.   230
He found no trace of Dólios and his sons
 nor the other slaves—all being gone that day
to clear a distant field, and drag the stones
for a boundary wall.
            But on a well-banked plot
Odysseus found his father in solitude   235
spading the earth around a young fruit tree.

He wore a tunic, patched and soiled, and leggings—
oxhide patches, bound below his knees
against the brambles; gauntlets on his hands
and on his head a goatskin cowl of sorrow.   240
This was the figure Prince Odysseus found—
wasted by years, racked, bowed under grief.
The son paused by a tall pear tree and wept,
then inwardly debated: should he run
forward and kiss his father, and pour out   245
his tale of war, adventure, and return,
or should he first interrogate him, test him?
Better that way, he thought—
first draw him out with sharp words, trouble him.
His mind made up, he walked ahead. Laërtês   250
went on digging, head down, by the sapling,
stamping the spade in. At his elbow then
his son spoke out:
            "Old man, the orchard keeper
you work for is no townsman. A good eye
for growing things he has; there's not a nurseling,   255
fig tree, vine stock, olive tree or pear tree
or garden bed uncared for on this farm.
But I might add—don't take offense—your own
appearance could be tidier. Old age
yes—but why the squalor, and rags to boot?   260
It would not be for sloth, now, that your master
leaves you in this condition; neither at all
because there's any baseness in your self.
No, by your features, by the frame you have,
a man might call you kingly,   265
one who should bathe warm, sup well, and rest easy
in age's privilege. But tell me:
who are your masters? whose fruit trees are these
you tend here? Tell me if it's true this island
is Ithaka, as that fellow I fell in with   270
told me on the road just now? He had
a peg loose, that one: couldn't say a word
or listen when I asked about my friend,
my Ithakan friend. I asked if he were alive
or gone long since into the underworld.   275
I can describe him if you care to hear it:
I entertained the man in my own land

when he turned up there on a journey; never
had I a guest more welcome in my house.
He claimed his stock was Ithakan: Laërtês   280
Arkeísiadês, he said his father was.
I took him home, treated him well, grew fond of him—
though we had many guests—and gave him
gifts in keeping with his quality: seven
bars of measured gold, a silver winebowl   285
filigreed with flowers, twelve light cloaks,
twelve rugs, robes and tunics—not to mention
his own choice of women trained in service,
the four well-favored ones he wished to take."

His father's eyes had filled with tears. He said: 290

"You've come to that man's island, right enough,
but dangerous men and fools hold power now.
You gave your gifts in vain. If you could find him
here in Ithaka alive, he'd make
return of gifts and hospitality,   295
as custom is, when someone has been generous.
But tell me accurately—how many years
have now gone by since that man was your guest?
your guest, my son—if he indeed existed—
born to ill fortune as he was. Ah, far   300
from those who loved him, far from his native land,
in some sea-dingle fish have picked his bones,
or else he made the vultures and wild beasts
a trove ashore! His mother at his bier
never bewailed him, nor did I, his father,   305
nor did his admirable wife, Penélopê,
who should have closed her husband's eyes in death
and cried aloud upon him as he lay.
So much is due the dead.
                         But speak out, tell me further:
who are you, of what city and family?   310
where have you moored the ship that brought you here,
where is your admirable crew? Are you a peddler
put ashore by the foreign ship you came on?"

Again Odysseus had a fable ready.

"Yes," he said, "I can tell you all those things.   315
I come from Rover's Passage where my home is,
and I'm King Allwoes' only son. My name
is Quarrelman.
               Heaven's power in the westwind
drove me this way from Sikania,[6]
off my course. My ship lies in a barren   320
cove beyond the town there. As for Odysseus,
now is the fifth year since he put to sea
and left my homeland—bound for death, you say.
Yet landbirds flying from starboard crossed his bow—

6. Another name for Sicily.

a lucky augury. So we parted joyously,   325
in hope of friendly days and gifts to come."

A cloud of pain had fallen on Laërtês.
Scooping up handfuls of the sunburnt dust
he sifted it over his grey head, and groaned,
and the groan went to the son's heart. A twinge   330
prickling up through his nostrils warned Odysseus
he could not watch this any longer.
He leaped and threw his arms around his father,
kissed him, and said:

                    "Oh, Father, I am he!
Twenty years gone, and here I've come again   335
to my own land!
                    Hold back your tears! No grieving!
I bring good news—though still we cannot rest.
I killed the suitors to the last man!
Outrage and injury have been avenged!"

Laërtês turned and found his voice to murmur: 340

"If you are Odysseus, my son, come back,
give me some proof, a sign to make me sure."

His son replied:

                    "The scar then, first of all.
Look, here the wild boar's flashing tusk
wounded me on Parnassos; do you see it?   345
You and my mother made me go, that time,
to visit Lord Autólykos, her father,
for gifts he promised years before on Ithaka.
Again—more proof—let's say the trees you gave me
on this revetted plot of orchard once.   350
I was a small boy at your heels, wheedling
amid the young trees, while you named each one.
You gave me thirteen pear, ten apple trees,
and forty fig trees. Fifty rows of vines
were promised too, each one to bear in turn   355
Bunches of every hue would hang there ripening,
weighed down by the god of summer days."

The old man's knees failed him, his heart grew faint,
recalling all that Odysseus calmly told.
He clutched his son. Odysseus held him swooning   360
until he got his breath back and his spirit
and spoke again:

                    "Zeus, Father! Gods above!—
you still hold pure Olympos, if the suitors
paid for their crimes indeed, and paid in blood!
But now the fear is in me that all Ithaka   365
will be upon us. They'll send messengers
to stir up every city of the islands."

Odysseus the great tactician answered:

"Courage, and leave the worrying to me.
We'll turn back to your homestead by the orchard.   370
I sent the cowherd, swineherd, and Telémakhos
ahead to make our noonday meal."

                    Conversing
in this vein they went home, the two together,
into the stone farmhouse. There Telémakhos
and the two herdsmen were already carving   375
roast young pork, and mixing amber wine.
During these preparations the Sikel woman
bathed Laërtês and anointed him,
and dressed him in a new cloak. Then Athena,
standing by, filled out his limbs again,   380
gave girth and stature to the old field captain
fresh from the bathing place. His son looked on
in wonder at the godlike bloom upon him,
and called out happily:

                    "Oh, Father,
surely one of the gods who are young forever   385
has made you magnificent before my eyes!"

Clearheaded Laërtês faced him, saying:

"By Father Zeus, Athena and Apollo,
I wish I could be now as once I was,
commander of Kephallenians, when I took   390
the walled town, Nérikos,[7] on the promontory!
Would god I had been young again last night
with armor on me, standing in our hall
to fight the suitors at your side! How many
knees I could have crumpled, to your joy!"   395

While son and father spoke, cowherd and swineherd
attended, waiting, for the meal was ready.
Soon they were all seated, and their hands
picked up the meat and bread.

                    But now old Dólios
appeared in the bright doorway with his sons,   400
work-stained from the field. Laërtês' housekeeper,
who reared the boys and tended Dólios
in his bent age, had gone to fetch them in.
When it came over them who the stranger was
they halted in astonishment. Odysseus   405
hit an easy tone with them. Said he:

"Sit down and help yourselves. Shake off your wonder.
Here we've been waiting for you all this time,
and our mouths watering for good roast pig!"

But Dólios came forward, arms outstretched,   410
and kissed Odysseus' hand at the wrist bone,
crying out:

---

7. On the mainland; its exact location is unknown.

"Dear master, you returned!
You came to us again! How we had missed you!
We thought you lost. The gods themselves have brought you!
Welcome, welcome; health and blessings on you!   415
And tell me, now, just one thing more: Penélopê,
does she know yet that you are on the island?
or should we send a messenger?"

Odysseus gruffly said,
                    "Old man, she knows.
Is it for you to think of her?"

                    So Dólios   420
quietly took a smooth bench at the table
and in their turn his sons welcomed Odysseus,
kissing his hands; then each went to his chair
beside his father. Thus our friends
were occupied in Laërtês' house at noon.   425

Meanwhile to the four quarters of the town
the news ran: bloody death had caught the suitors;
and men and women in a murmuring crowd
gathered before Odysseus' hall. They gave
burial to the piteous dead, or bore   430
the bodies of young men from other islands
down to the port, thence to be ferried home.
Then all the men went grieving to assembly
and being seated, rank by rank, grew still,
as old Eupeithês rose to address them. Pain   435
lay in him like a brand for Antínoös,
the first man that Odysseus brought down,
and tears flowed for his son as he began:

"Heroic feats that fellow did for us
Akhaians, friends! Good spearmen by the shipload   440
he led to war and lost—lost ships and men,
and once ashore again killed these, who were
the islands' pride.
                    Up with you! After him!—
before he can take flight to Pylos town
or hide at Elis, under Epeian law!   445
We'd be disgraced forever! Mocked for generations
if we cannot avenge our sons' blood, and our brothers'!
Life would turn to ashes—at least for me;
rather be dead and join the dead!
                    I say
we ought to follow now, or they'll gain time   450
and make the crossing."
                    His appeal, his tears,
moved all the gentry listening there;
but now they saw the crier and the minstrel
come from Odysseus' hall, where they had slept.
The two men stood before the curious crowd,   455
and Medôn said:

"Now hear me, men of Ithaka.
When these hard deeds were done by Lord Odysseus
the immortal gods were not far off. I saw
with my own eyes someone divine who fought
beside him, in the shape and dress of Mentor;   460
it was a god who shone before Odysseus,
a god who swept the suitors down the hall
dying in droves."
        At this pale fear assailed them,
and next they heard again the old forecaster,
Halithérsês Mastóridês. Alone   465
he saw the field of time, past and to come.
In his anxiety for them he said:

"Ithakans, now listen to what I say.
Friends, by your own fault these deaths came to pass.
You would not heed me nor the captain, Mentor;   470
would not put down the riot of your sons.
Heroic feats they did!—all wantonly
raiding a great man's flocks, dishonoring
his queen, because they thought he'd come no more.
Let matters rest; do as I urge; no chase,   475
or he who wants a bloody end will find it."

The greater number stood up shouting "Aye!"
But many held fast, sitting all together
in no mind to agree with him. Eupeithês
had won them to his side. They ran for arms,   480
clapped on their bronze, and mustered
under Eupeithês at the town gate
for his mad foray.
        Vengeance would be his,
he thought, for his son's murder; but that day
held bloody death for him and no return.   485

At this point, querying Zeus, Athena said:

"O Father of us all and king of kings,
enlighten me. What is your secret will?
War and battle, worse and more of it,
or can you not impose a pact on both?"   490

The summoner of cloud replied:

        "My child,
why this formality of inquiry?
Did you not plan that action by yourself—
see to it that Odysseus, on his homecoming,
should have their blood?
        Conclude it as you will.   495
There is one proper way, if I may say so:
Odysseus' honor being satisfied,
let him be king by a sworn pact forever,
and we, for our part, will blot out the memory
of sons and brothers slain. As in the old time   500

let men of Ithaka henceforth be friends;
prosperity enough, and peace attend them."

Athena needed no command, but down
in one spring she descended from Olympos
just as the company of Odysseus finished   505
wheat crust and honeyed wine, and heard him say:

"Go out, someone, and see if they are coming."

One of the boys went to the door as ordered
and saw the townsmen in the lane. He turned
swiftly to Odysseus.

        "Here they come,"   510
he said, "best arm ourselves, and quickly."

All up at once, the men took helm and shield—
four fighting men, counting Odysseus,
with Dólios' half dozen sons. Laërtês
armed as well, and so did Dólios—   515
greybeards, they could be fighters in a pinch.
Fitting their plated helmets on their heads
they sallied out, Odysseus in the lead.
Now from the air Athena, Zeus's daughter,
appeared in Mentor's guise, with Mentor's voice,   520
making Odysseus' heart grow light. He said
to put cheer in his son:

        "Telémakhos,
you are going into battle against pikemen
where hearts of men are tried. I count on you
to bring no shame upon your forefathers.   525
In fighting power we have excelled this lot
in every generation."

        Said his son:

"If you are curious, Father, watch and see
the stuff that's in me. No more talk of shame."

And old Laërtês cried aloud: 530

"Ah, what a day for me, dear gods!
to see my son and grandson vie in courage!"

Athena halted near him, and her eyes
shone like the sea. She said:

        "Arkeísiadês,
dearest of all my old brothers-in-arms,   535
invoke the grey-eyed one and Zeus her father,
heft your spear and make your throw."

Power flowed into him from Pallas Athena,
whom he invoked as Zeus's virgin child,
and he let fly his heavy spear.

        It struck   540
Eupeithês on the cheek plate of his helmet,

and undeflected the bronze head punched through.
He toppled, and his armor clanged upon him.
Odysseus and his son now furiously
closed, laying on with broadswords, hand to hand,   545
and pikes: they would have cut the enemy down
to the last man, leaving not one survivor,
had not Athena raised a shout
that stopped all fighters in their tracks.

                              "Now hold!"
she cried, "Break off this bitter skirmish;   550
end your bloodshed, Ithakans, and make peace."

Their faces paled with dread before Athena,
and swords dropped from their hands unnerved, to lie
strewing the ground, at the great voice of the goddess.
Those from the town turned fleeing for their lives.   555
But with a cry to freeze their hearts
and ruffling like an eagle on the pounce,
the lord Odysseus reared himself to follow—
at which the son of Kronos dropped a thunderbolt
smoking at his daughter's feet.
                              Athena   560
cast a grey glance at her friend and said:

"Son of Laërtês and the gods of old,
Odysseus, master of land ways and sea ways,
command yourself. Call off this battle now,
or Zeus who views the wide world may be angry."   565

He yielded to her, and his heart was glad.
Both parties later swore to terms of peace
set by their arbiter, Athena, daughter
of Zeus who bears the stormcloud as a shield—
though still she kept the form and voice of Mentor.   570

SAPPHO OF LESBOS
born ca. 630 B.C.

About Sappho's life we know very little: she was born about 630 B.C. on the fertile
island of Lesbos off the coast of Asia Minor and spent most of her life there; she
was married and had a daughter. Her lyric poems (poems sung to the accompaniment of the lyre) were so admired in the ancient world that a later poet called her
the tenth Muse. In the third century B.C. scholars at the great library in Alexandria
arranged her poems in nine books, of which the first contained more than a thousand lines. But what we have now is a pitiful remnant: one (or possibly two) complete short poems, and a collection of quotations from her work by ancient writers,
supplemented by bits and pieces written on ancient scraps of papyrus found in
excavations in Egypt. Yet these remnants fully justify the enthusiasm of the ancient
critics; Sappho's poems (insofar as we can guess at their nature from the fragments)
give us the most vivid evocation of the joys and sorrows of love in all Greek literature.

Her themes are those of a Greek woman's world—girlhood, marriage, and love, especially the love of young women for each other and the poignancy of their parting as they leave to assume the responsibilities of a wife. About the social context of these songs we can only guess; all that can be said is that they reflect a world in which women, at least women of the aristocracy, lived an intense communal life of their own, one of female occasions, functions, and festivities, in which their young passionate natures were fully engaged with each other; to most of them, presumably, this was a stage preliminary to their later career in that world as wife and mother.

The first two poems printed here were quoted in their entirety by ancient critics (though it is possible that there was another stanza at the end of the second); their text is not a problem. But the important recent additions to our knowledge of Sappho's poetry, the pieces of ancient books found in Egypt, are difficult to read and usually full of gaps. Our third selection, in fact, comes from the municipal rubbish heap of the Egyptian village Oxyrhyncos. Most of the gaps in the text are due to holes or tears in the papyrus and can easily be filled in from our knowledge of Sappho's dialect and the strict meter in which she wrote, but the end of the third stanza and the whole of the fourth are imaginative reconstructions by the translator. The papyrus, for instance, tells us only that someone or something led Helen astray; Lattimore's "Queen of Cyprus" (the love goddess Aphrodite) may well be right but is not certain. In the next stanza all that we have is part of a word that means something like "flexible" (Lattimore's "hearts that can be persuaded"); an adverb, *lightly*; and "remembering Anaktoria who is not here." As a matter of fact we don't have that all-important *not*, but the sense demands it. Fortunately, the final stanza, with its telling echo of the opening theme, is almost intact.

The most recent short survey of Sappho's poetry (by David A. Campbell) is in *The Cambridge History of Classical Literature* (1985). For a fuller treatment see C. M. Bowra, *Greek Lyric Poetry* (1961). Worth consulting also is A. Lesky, *A History of Greek Literature* (1966).

[Throned in splendor, deathless, O Aphrodite][1]

Throned in splendor, deathless, O Aphrodite,[2]
child of Zeus, charm-fashioner, I entreat you
not with griefs and bitternesses to break my
    spirit, O goddess:

standing by me rather, if once before now   5
far away you heard, when I called upon you,
left your father's dwelling place and descended,
    yoking the golden

chariot to sparrows,[3] who fairly drew you
down in speed aslant the black world, the bright air   10
trembling at the heart to the pulse of countless
    fluttering wingbeats.

Swiftly then they came, and you, blessed lady,
smiling on me out of immortal beauty,

---

1. All selections translated by Richmond Lattimore.   2. A prayer to the goddess of love, Aphrodite. The translator has skillfully reproduced the metrical form of the Greek, the "Sapphic" stanza.   3. Aphrodite's sacred birds.

asked me what affliction was on me, why I   15
    called thus upon you,

what beyond all else I would have befall my
tortured heart: "Whom then would you have Persuasion
force to serve desire in your heart? Who is it,
    Sappho, that hurt you?   20

Though she now escape, she soon will follow;
though she take not gifts from you, she will give them:
though she love not, yet she will surely love you
    even unwilling."

In such guise come even again and set me   25
free from doubt and sorrow; accomplish all those
things my heart desires to be done; appear and
    stand at my shoulder.

[Like the very gods in my sight is he]

Like the very gods in my sight is he who
sits where he can look in your eyes, who listens
close to you, to hear the soft voice, its sweetness
    murmur in love and

laughter, all for him. But it breaks my spirit;   5
underneath my breast all the heart is shaken.
Let me only glance where you are, the voice dies,
    I can say nothing,

but my lips are stricken to silence, under-
neath my skin the tenuous flame suffuses;   10
nothing shows in front of my eyes, my ears are
    muted in thunder.

And the sweat breaks running upon me, fever
shakes my body, paler I turn than grass is;
I can feel that I have been changed, I feel that   15
    death has come near me.

[Some there are who say that the fairest thing seen]

Some there are who say that the fairest thing seen
on the black earth is an array of horsemen;
some, men marching; some would say ships; but I say
    she whom one loves best

is the loveliest. Light were the work to make this   5
plain to all, since she, who surpassed in beauty
all mortality, Helen, once forsaking
    her lordly husband,

fled away to Troy—land across the water.
Not the thought of child nor beloved parents   10

was remembered, after the Queen of Cyprus[1]
   won her at first sight.

Since young brides have hearts that can be persuaded
easily, light things, palpitant to passion
as am I, remembering Anaktória   15
   who has gone from me

and whose lovely walk and the shining pallor
of her face I would rather see before my
eyes than Lydia's chariots in all their glory
   armored for battle.   20

1. Aphrodite.

AESCHYLUS
524?–456 B.C.

The earliest documents in the history of the Western theater are the seven plays
of Aeschylus that have come down to us through the more than two thousand
years since his death. When he produced his first play in the opening years of the
fifth century B.C., the performance that we know as drama was still less than half
a century old, still open to innovation—and Aeschylus, in fact, made such significant contributions to its development that he has been called "the creator of
tragedy."

The origins of the theatrical contests in Athens are obscure; they were a puzzle
even for Aristotle who in the fourth century B.C. wrote a famous treatise on tragedy.
All that we know for certain is that the drama began as a religious celebration that
took the form of song and dance.

Such ceremonies are of course to be found in the communal life of many early
cultures, but it was in Athens, and in Athens alone, that the ceremony gave rise to
what we know as tragedy and comedy and produced dramatic masterpieces that
are still admired, read, and performed.

At some time in the late sixth century B.C. the Athenians converted what seems
to have been a rural celebration of Dionysus, a vegetation deity especially associated with the vine, into an annual city festival at which dancing choruses, competing for prizes, sang hymns of praise to the god. It was from this choral performance
that tragedy and comedy developed. Some unknown innovator (his name was
probably Thespis) combined the choral song with the speech of a masked actor,
who, playing a god or hero, engaged the chorus in dialogue. It was Aeschylus who
added a second actor and so created the possibility of conflict and the prototype of
the drama as we know it.

After the defeat of the Persian invaders (480–479 B.C.), as Athens with its fleets
and empire moved toward supremacy in the Greek world, this spring festival
became a splendid occasion. The Dionysia, as it was now called, lasted for four
days, during which public business (except in emergencies) was suspended and
prisoners were released on bail for the duration of the festival. In an open-air
theater that could seat seventeen thousand spectators, tragic and comic poets competed for the prizes offered by the city. Three poets in each genre had been
selected by the magistrates for the year. After an opening day devoted to the tradi-

tional choral hymns, a tragic poet with three plays and a comic poet with one provided the program for each of the three remaining days.

The three tragedies could deal with quite separate stories or, as in the case of Aeschylus' *Oresteia*, with the successive stages of one extended action. By the time this trilogy was produced (458 B.C.) the number of actors had been raised to three; the spoken part of the performance became steadily more important. In the *Oresteia* an equilibrium between the two elements of the performance has been established. The actors, with their speeches, create the dramatic situation and its movement, the plot; the chorus, while contributing to dramatic suspense and illusion, ranges free of the immediate situation in its odes, which extend and amplify the significance of the action.

In 458 B.C. Aeschylus was at the end of a great career; he died two years later in the Greek city Gela, in Sicily. He had begun his career as a dramatist before the Persian Wars, in the first days of the new Athenian democracy. He fought against the Persians at Marathon (where his brother was killed) and almost certainly also in the great sea fight at Salamis in 480 B.C. (his play the *Persians*, produced in 472 B.C., contains what sounds like an eyewitness account of that battle). Only seven of his plays survive (we know that he produced ninety); besides the *Persians* and the three plays of the *Oresteia*, we have the text of *Suppliants* (sometime in the 460s), *The Seven against Thebes* (467), and the famous and influential play *Prometheus Bound* (date unknown).

The *Oresteia* is a trilogy. The first play, *Agamemnon*, was followed at its performance by two more plays, *The Libation Bearers* and *The Eumenides*, which carried on its story and theme to a conclusion. The theme of the trilogy is justice, and its story, like that of almost all Greek tragedies, is a legend that was already well known to the audience that saw the first performance of the play. This particular legend, the story of the house of Atreus, is rich in dramatic potential, for it deals with a series of retributive murders that stained the hands of three generations of a royal family, and it has also a larger significance, social and historical, of which Aeschylus took full advantage. The legend preserves the memory of an important historical process through which the Greeks had passed: the transition from tribal institutions of justice to communal justice, from a tradition that demanded that a murdered person's next of kin avenge the death to a system requiring settlement of the private quarrel by a court of law (the typical institution of the city-state, which replaced the primitive tribe). When Agamemnon returns victorious from Troy, he is killed by his wife, Clytemnestra, and her lover, Aegisthus, who is Agamemnon's cousin. Clytemnestra kills her husband to avenge her daughter Iphigenia, whom Agamemnon sacrificed to the goddess Artemis when he had to choose between his daughter's life and his ambition to conquer Troy. Aegisthus avenges the crime of a previous generation, the hideous murder of his brothers by Agamemnon's father, Atreus. The killing of Agamemnon is, by the standards of the old system, justice; but it is the nature of this justice that the process can never be arrested, that one act of violence must give rise to another. Agamemnon's murder must be avenged too, as it is in the second play of the trilogy by Orestes, his son, who kills both Aegisthus and Clytemnestra, his own mother. Orestes has acted justly according to the code of tribal society based on blood relationship, but in doing so he has violated the most sacred blood relationship of all, the bond between mother and son. The old system of justice has produced an insoluble dilemma.

At the end of *The Libation Bearers*, Orestes sees a vision of the Furies. They are serpent-haired female hunters, the avengers of blood. Agamemnon had a son to avenge him, but for Clytemnestra there was no one to exact payment. This task is taken up by the Furies, who are the guardians of the ancient tribal sanctities; they enforce the old dispensation when no earthly agent is at hand to do so. Female themselves, they assert the claim of the mother against the son who killed her to avenge his father. At the end of the second play they are only a vision in Orestes' mind—"You can't see them," he says to the chorus. "I can; they drive me on. I must move on." But in the final play we see them too; they are the chorus, and they have pursued Orestes to the great shrine of Apollo at Delphi where he has come to seek refuge.

Apollo can save him from immediate destruction at the Furies' hands, but he cannot resolve the dilemma. Orestes must go to Athens, where Athena, the patron goddess of the city, will set up the first court of law to try his case. At Athens, before the ancient court of the Areopagus, the Furies argue eloquently, but Apollo himself arrives to testify that he ordered Orestes to act. Athena instructs the judges in Orestes' favor, and Orestes, acquitted, goes home to Argos. The Furies threaten to turn their dreadful wrath against Athens itself, but the goddess persuades them to accept a home deep in Athenian earth, to act as protectors of the court and of the land.

More important than the arguments employed in the trial and the decision reached by the judges is the fact of the court's establishment. This is the end of an old era and the beginning of a new. The existence of the court is a guarantee that the tragic series of events that drove Orestes to the murder of his mother will never be repeated. The system of communal justice, which allows consideration of circumstance and motive and which punishes impersonally, has at last replaced the inconclusive anarchy of individual revenge.

But the play is concerned with much more than the history of human institutions—with more even than the general problem of violence between individual and individual for which the particular instances of the trilogy stand. It is also a religious statement. The whole sequence of events, stretching over many generations, is presented as the working out of the will of Zeus. The tragic action of the *Iliad* was also the expression of the will of Zeus (though it is characteristic of Homer that Achilles was at least equally responsible), but for Aeschylus the will of Zeus means something new. In this trilogy the working out of Zeus' will proceeds intricately through three generations of bloodshed to the creation of a human institution that will prevent any repetition of the cycle of murder that produced it. Agamemnon dies, and Clytemnestra dies in her turn, and Orestes is hounded over land and sea to his trial, but out of all this suffering comes an important advance in human understanding and civilization. The chorus of *Agamemnon*, celebrating the power of Zeus, tells us that he

> . . . has led us on to know,
> that Helmsman lays it down as law
> that we must suffer, suffer into truth.

From the suffering comes knowledge of the truth, whereas in the *Iliad* nothing at all comes out of the suffering, except the certainty of more. "Far from the land of my fathers," says Achilles to Priam, "I sit here in Troy, and bring nothing but sorrow to you and your children." But his last words to Priam are a reminder that this interval of sympathy is only temporary. After Hector's burial the war will go on as before. This is Zeus' will; Homer does not attempt to explain it. But the Aeschylean trilogy is nothing less than an attempt to "justify the ways of God to men." The suffering is shown to us as the fulfillment of a purpose we can understand, a purpose beneficent to humanity.

The full scope of Zeus' will is apparent only to the audience, which follows the pattern of its execution through the three plays of the trilogy. As in the Book of

Job, the characters who act and suffer are in the dark. They claim a knowledge of Zeus' will and boast that their actions are its fulfillment (it is in these terms that Agamemnon speaks of the sack of Troy, and Clytemnestra of Agamemnon's murder), and they are, of course, in one sense, right. But their knowledge is limited; Agamemnon does not realize that Zeus' will includes his death at the hands of Clytemnestra, nor Clytemnestra that it demands her death at the hands of her son. The chorus has, at times, a deeper understanding. In its opening ode it announces the law of Zeus, that we must learn by suffering, and at the end it recognizes the responsibility of Zeus in the death of Agamemnon—"all through the will of Zeus, the cause of all, the one who works it all." But the chorus cannot interpret the event in any way it can accept, for it can see no further than the immediate present. Its knowledge of Zeus' law is an abstraction that it cannot relate to the terrible fact.

In this murky atmosphere (made all the more terrible by the beacon fire of the opening lines, which brings not light but deeper darkness), one human being sees clear; she possesses the concrete vision of the future, which complements the chorus's abstract knowledge of the law. This is the prophet Cassandra, Priam's daughter, brought from Troy as Agamemnon's share of the spoils. She has been given the power of true prophecy by the god Apollo, but the gift is nullified by the condition that her prophecies will never be believed. Like the Hebrew prophets, she sees reality—past, present, and future—so clearly that she is cut off from ordinary human beings by the clarity of her vision and the terrible burden of her knowledge. Like them she expresses herself in poetic figures, and like them she is rejected by her hearers. To the everyday world, represented by the chorus, she appears to be mad, the fate of prophets in all ages. And it is only as she goes into the palace to the death she foresees that the old men of the chorus begin to accept, fearfully and hesitantly, the truth that she has been telling them.

The great scene in which she mouths her hysterical prophecies at them delays the action for which everything has been prepared—the death of Agamemnon. Before we hear his famous cry offstage, Cassandra presents us with a mysterious vision in which she combines cause, effect, and result: the murders that have led to this terrible moment, the death of Agamemnon (which will not take place until she leaves the stage), and the murders that will follow. We do not see Agamemnon's death—we see much more. The past, present, and future of Clytemnestra's action and Agamemnon's suffering are fused into a timeless unity in Cassandra's great lines, an unearthly unity that is dissolved only when Agamemnon, in the real world of time and space, screams in mortal agony.

The tremendous statement of the trilogy is made in a style that for magnificence and richness of suggestion can be compared only with the style of Shakespeare at the height of his poetic power, the Shakespeare of *King Lear* and *Antony and Cleopatra*. The language of the *Oresteia* is an Oriental carpet of imagery in which combinations of metaphor, which at first seem bombastic in their violence, take their place in the ordered pattern of the poem as a whole. An image, once introduced, recurs and reappears again, to run its course verbally and visually through the whole length of the trilogy, richer in meaning with each fresh appearance. In the second choral ode, for example, the chorus, welcoming the news of Agamemnon's victory at Troy, sings of the net that Zeus and Night threw over the city, trapping the inhabitants like animals. The net is here an image of Zeus' justice, a retributive justice, since Troy is paying for the crime of taking Helen, and the image identifies Zeus' justice with Agamemnon's action in sacking the city. This image occurs again, with a different emphasis, in the hypocritical speech of welcome that Clytemnestra makes to her husband on his return. She tells how she feared for his safety at Troy, how she trembled at the rumors of his death:

and the rumors spread and fester,
a runner comes with something dreadful,
close on his heels the next and his news worse,
and they shout it out and the whole house can hear;
and wounds—if he took one wound for each report
to penetrate these walls, he's gashed like a dragnet.

This vision of Agamemnon dead she speaks of as her fear, but we know that it represents her deepest desire and, more, the purpose that she is now preparing to execute. When, later, she stands in triumph over her husband's corpse, she uses the same image to describe the robe that she threw over his limbs to blind and baffle him before she stabbed him—"Inextricable like a net for fishes / I cast about him a vicious wealth of raiment"—and this time the image materializes into an object visible on stage. We can see the net, the gashed robe still folded round Agamemnon's body. We shall see it again, for in the second play Orestes, standing over his mother's body as she now stands over his father's, will display the robe before us, with its holes and bloodstains, as a justification for what he has just done. Elsewhere in *Agamemnon* the chorus compares Cassandra to a wild animal caught in the net, and later Aegisthus exults to see Agamemnon's body lying "in the nets of Justice." For each speaker the image has a different meaning, but not one realizes the terrible sense in which it applies to them all. They are all caught in the net, the system of justice by vengeance that only binds tighter the more its captives struggle to free themselves. Clytemnestra attempts to escape, to arrest the process of the chain of murders and the working out of the will of Zeus. "But I will swear a pact with the spirit born within us," she says, but Agamemnon's body and the net she threw over him are there on the stage to remind us that her appeal will not be heard; one more generation must act and suffer before the net will vanish, never to be seen again.

Richmond Lattimore, *Aeschylus, Oresteia* (1953), contains a valuable introduction aimed at the general reader. D. J. Conacher, *Aeschylus' Oresteia: A Literary Commentary* (1987), is a scene-by-scene (and sometimes line-by-line) commentary that combines literary analysis and philological discussion; it is addressed as much to Greekless readers as to classical scholars. James Hogan, *A Commentary on the Complete Greek Tragedies: Aeschylus* (1987), contains a line-by-line commentary on Richmond Lattimore's translation of the *Oresteia*. Hugh Lloyd-Jones's three volumes—*Agamemnon, The Libation Bearers,* and *The Eumenides* (1970)—provide helpful introductions, a precise prose translation, and a valuable running commentary at the bottom of the page. John Herington, *Aeschylus* (1986), deals with the political and religious background of the tragedies and provides a perceptive discussion of the plays (*Oresteia*, pp. 111–56).

PRONOUNCING GLOSSARY

The following list uses common English syllables and stress accents to provide rough equivalents of selected words whose pronunciation may be unfamiliar to the general reader.

Aegisthus: *ee-jis'-thus / ai-gis'-thus*	Hermes: *her'-meez*
Aeschylus: *ess'-kel-us / ees'-kel-us*	Iphigeneia: *i-fe-jen-ai'-uh*
Calchas: *kal'-kahs*	Menelaus: *me-ne-lay'-us*
Clytaemnestra: *klai-tem-nes'-truh*	Oresteia: *o-res-tai'-uh*
Dionysus: *dai-oh-nai'-sus*	Orestes: *o-res'-teez*
Eumenides: *yoo-me'-ni-deez*	Thyestes: *thai-es'-teez*

THE ORESTEIA[1]

Agamemnon

CHARACTERS

WATCHMAN

CLYTAEMNESTRA

HERALD

AGAMEMNON

CASSANDRA

AEGISTHUS

CHORUS, *the Old Men of Argos and
their* LEADER

*Attendants of Clytaemnestra and of
Agamemnon, bodyguard of
Aegisthus*

[TIME AND SCENE: *A night in the tenth and final autumn of the Trojan
war. The house of Atreus in Argos. Before it, an altar stands unlit; a* WATCH-
MAN *on the high roofs fights to stay awake.*]

WATCHMAN: Dear gods, set me free from all the pain,
    the long watch I keep, one whole year awake . . .
    propped on my arms, crouched on the roofs of Atreus
    like a dog.
           I know the stars by heart,
    the armies of the night, and there in the lead   5
    the ones that bring us snow or the crops of summer,
    bring us all we have—
    our great blazing kings of the sky,
    I know them, when they rise and when they fall . . .
    and now I watch for the light, the signal-fire[2]   10
    breaking out of Troy, shouting Troy is taken.
    So she commands, full of her high hopes.
    That woman[3]—she maneuvers like a man.

    And when I keep to my bed, soaked in dew,
    and the thoughts go groping through the night   15
    and the good dreams that used to guard my sleep . . .
    not here, it's the old comrade, terror, at my neck.
    I mustn't sleep, no—
        [*Shaking himself awake.*]
                Look alive, sentry.
    And I try to pick out tunes, I hum a little,
    a good cure for sleep, and the tears start,   20
    I cry for the hard times come to the house,
    no longer run like the great place of old.

    Oh for a blessed end to all our pain,
    some godsend burning through the dark—
        [*Light appears slowly in the east; he struggles to his feet and scans it.*]
                I salute you!

---

1. Translated by Robert Fagles.   2. That is, the bonfire nearest to Argos, the last in a chain extending
all the way to Troy, each one visible, when fired at night, from the next.   3. Clytaemnestra.

You dawn of the darkness, you turn night to day— 25
I see the light at last.
They'll be dancing in the streets of Argos[4]
thanks to you, thanks to this new stroke of—
                              Aieeeeee!
There's your signal clear and true, my queen!
Rise up from bed—hurry, lift a cry of triumph 30
through the house, praise the gods for the beacon,
if they've taken Troy . . .
                    But there it burns,
fire all the way. I'm for the morning dances.
Master's luck is mine. A throw of the torch
has brought us triple-sixes[5]—we have won! 35
My move now—
    [Beginning to dance, then breaking off, lost in thought.]
                    Just bring him home. My king,
I'll take your loving hand in mine and then . . .
the rest is silence. The ox is on my tongue.[6]
Aye, but the house and these old stones,
give them a voice and what a tale they'd tell. 40
And so would I, gladly . . .
I speak to those who know; to those who don't
my mind's a blank. I never say a word.
    [He climbs down from the roof and disappears into the palace
    through a side entrance. A CHORUS, the old men of Argos who have
    not learned the news of victory, enters and marches round the altar.]
CHORUS: Ten years gone, ten to the day
our great avenger went for Priam— 45
    Menelaus[7] and lord Agamemnon,
two kings with the power of Zeus,
the twin throne, twin sceptre,
Atreus' sturdy yoke of sons
launched Greece in a thousand ships, 50
armadas cutting loose from the land,
armies massed for the cause, the rescue—
    [From within the palace CLYTAEMNESTRA raises a cry of triumph.]
the heart within them screamed for all-out war!
Like vultures robbed of their young,
    the agony sends them frenzied, 55
soaring high from the nest, round and
round they wheel, they row their wings,

4. In Homer, Agamemnon, son of Atreus, is king of Mycenae. Later Greek poets, however, referred to
his kingdom as Argos or Mycenae, perhaps because the Achaeans in Homer are sometimes called
Argives. In 463 B.C., just five years before the production of the play, Argos had defeated Mycenae in
battle and put an end to the city, displacing the inhabitants or selling them into slavery. Soon after,
Argos and Athens entered into an alliance, aimed, of course, at Sparta. Since this alliance will be
alluded to in the last play of the trilogy, it is important for Aeschylus to establish the un-Homeric
location of the action right at the beginning.   5. The highest throw in the ancient Greek dice game.
6. A proverbial phrase for enforced silence.   7. Another son of Atreus, also a king of Argos and commander of the Greek expedition against Troy. Priam was the king of Troy. His son Paris abducted (or
seduced) Menelaus' wife, Helen.

stroke upon churning thrashing stroke,
but all the labor, the bed of pain,
   the young are lost forever.   60
Yet someone hears on high—Apollo,
Pan or Zeus[8]—the piercing wail
these guests of heaven raise,
and drives at the outlaws, late
but true to revenge, a stabbing Fury![9]   65
   [CLYTAEMNESTRA *appears at the doors and pauses with her entou-*
   rage.][1]
So towering Zeus the god of guests[2]
drives Atreus' sons at Paris,
all for a woman manned by many
the generations wrestle, knees
grinding the dust, the manhood drains,   70
the spear snaps in the first blood rites
   that marry Greece and Troy.
And now it goes as it goes
and where it ends is Fate.
And neither by singeing flesh   75
nor tipping cups of wine[3]
nor shedding burning tears can you
enchant away the rigid Fury.
   [CLYTAEMNESTRA *lights the altar-fires.*]
We are the old, dishonoured ones,[4]
the broken husks of men.   80
Even then they cast us off,
the rescue mission left us here
to prop a child's strength upon a stick.
What if the new sap rises in his chest?
He has no soldiery in him,   85
   no more than we,
and we are aged past aging,
gloss of the leaf shriveled,
three legs[5] at a time we falter on.
Old men are children once again,   90
   a dream that sways and wavers
into the hard light of day.
               But you,
daughter of Leda, queen Clytaemnestra,

8. The movements of birds are regarded as prophetic signs; Apollo perhaps as a prophetic god; Pan as
a god of the wild places; Zeus because eagles and vultures were symbolic of his power.   9. This is the
first mention of one of these avenging spirits who will actually appear on stage as the chorus of the final
play. Furies are called Erinyes in Greek.   1. There are no stage directions on the manuscript copies
of the plays that have come down to us. Here the translator has the queen enter so that she will be
visible on stage when the chorus addresses her by name in line 93. Other scholars, pointing out that in
Greek tragedy characters who are offstage are often addressed, disagree, and bring Clytaemnestra on
stage only at line 256.   2. Zeus was thought to be particularly interested in punishing those who
violated the code of hospitality. Paris had been a guest in Menelaus' house.   3. Neither by burnt
sacrifice nor by pouring libations.   4. The general sense of the passage is that only two classes of the
male population are left in Argos: those who are too young to fight and those who, like the chorus, are
too old.   5. Because they use a stick, or cane, to support them when they walk.

what now, what news, what message
drives you through the citadel   95
    burning victims?[6] Look,
the city gods, the gods of Olympus,
gods of the earth and public markets—
all the altars blazing with your gifts!
    Argos blazes! Torches   100
race the sunrise up her skies—
drugged by the lulling holy oils,
    unadulterated,
run from the dark vaults of kings.
    Tell us the news!   105
What you can, what is right—
Heal us, soothe our fears!
Now the darkness comes to the fore,
now the hope glows through your victims,
beating back this raw, relentless anguish   110
    gnawing at the heart.
    [CLYTAEMNESTRA *ignores them and pursues her rituals; they assemble*
    for the opening chorus.]
O but I still have power to sound the god's command at the roads
that launched the kings. The gods breathe power through my song,
    my fighting strength, Persuasion grows with the years—
I sing how the flight of fury hurled the twin command,   115
            one will that hurled young Greece
and winged the spear of vengeance straight for Troy!
The kings of birds to kings of the beaking prows, one black,
    one with a blaze of silver
        skimmed the palace spearhand right   120
            and swooping lower, all could see,
                plunged their claws in a hare, a mother
    bursting with unborn young—the babies spilling,
quick spurts of blood—cut off the race just dashing into life!
Cry, cry for death, but good win out in glory in the end.   125
But the loyal seer of the armies studied Atreus' sons,
two sons with warring hearts—he saw two eagle-kings
    devour the hare and spoke the things to come,[7]
"Years pass, and the long hunt nets the city of Priam,
            the flocks beyond the walls,   130
a kingdom's life and soul—Fate stamps them out.
Just let no curse of the gods lour on us first,
    shatter our giant armor
        forged to strangle Troy. I see
            pure Artemis bristle in pity—   135

---

6. Clytaemnestra is sacrificing in thanksgiving for the news of Troy's fall; the chorus does not know that
the news has come via the signal fires.   7. The seer Calchas identified the two eagles (*kings of birds*)
as symbolic of the two kings and their action as a symbolic prophecy of the destruction of Troy. The
two eagles seized and tore a pregnant hare, which meant that the two kings would destroy Troy, thus
killing not only the living Trojans but the Trojan generations yet unborn.

yes, the flying hounds of the Father
  slaughter for armies . . . their own victim . . . a woman
trembling young, all born to die—She[8] loathes the eagles' feast!"
Cry, cry for death, but good win out in glory in the end.
  "Artemis, lovely Artemis, so kind   140
to the ravening lion's tender, helpless cubs,
the suckling young of beasts that stalk the wilds—
  bring this sign for all its fortune,
    all its brutal torment home to birth!
I beg you, Healing Apollo, soothe her before   145
her crosswinds hold us down and moor the ships too long,[9]
pressing us on to another victim . . .
  nothing sacred, no
    no feast to be eaten[1]
      the architect of vengeance   150
[*Turning to the palace.*]
    growing strong in the house
with no fear of the husband
here she waits
the terror raging back and back in the future
  the stealth, the law of the hearth, the mother—   155
    Memory womb of Fury child-avenging Fury!"
So as the eagles wheeled at the crossroads,
Calchas clashed out the great good blessings mixed with doom
  for the halls of kings, and singing with our fate
we cry, cry for death, but good win out in glory in the end.   160

          Zeus, great nameless all in all,
          if that name will gain his favor,
            I will call him Zeus.[2]
          I have no words to do him justice,
            weighing all in the balance,   165
            all I have is Zeus, Zeus—
        lift this weight, this torment from my spirit,
            cast it once for all.

---

8. Artemis, a virgin goddess, patron of hunting, and the protectress of wildlife, is angry that the eagles (*the flying hounds*) have destroyed a pregnant animal. The prophet fears that she may turn her wrath against the kings whom the eagles represent. A *woman trembling young:* just as the eagles kill the hare, the kings will kill Agamemnon's daughter Iphigenia. The Greek text refers only to the hare, but the translator has made the allusion clear.   9. Calchas foresees the future. Artemis will send unfavorable winds to prevent the sailing of the Greek expedition from Aulis, the port of embarkation. She will demand the sacrifice of Agamemnon's daughter Iphigenia as the price of the fleet's release. He prays that in spite of its bad aspects, the omen will be truly prophetic—that is, that the Achaeans will capture Troy. He goes on to anticipate and try to avert some of the evils it portends.   1. At an ordinary sacrifice the celebrants gave the gods their due portion and then feasted on the animal's flesh. The word *sacrifice* comes to have the connotation of "feast." There will be no feast at this sacrifice, since the victim will be a human being. The ominous phrase reminds us of a feast of human flesh that has already taken place, Thyestes' feasting on his own children.   2. It was important, in prayer, to address the divinity by his or her right name: here the chorus uses an inclusive formula—they call on Zeus by whatever name pleases him.

He who was so mighty once,[3]
   storming for the wars of heaven,
     he has had his day. 170
And then his son[4] who came to power
   met his match in the third fall
   and he is gone. Zeus, Zeus—
raise your cries and sing him Zeus the Victor! 175
   You will reach the truth:

Zeus has led us on to know,
   the Helmsman lays it down as law
   that we must suffer, suffer into truth.
We cannot sleep, and drop by drop at the heart 180
   the pain of pain remembered comes again,
   and we resist, but ripeness comes as well.
From the gods enthroned on the awesome rowing-bench[5]
   there comes a violent love.

     So it was that day the king, 185
   the steersman at the helm of Greece,
would never blame a word the prophet said—
   swept away by the wrenching winds of fortune
he conspired! Weatherbound we could not sail,
   our stores exhausted, fighting strength hard-pressed, 190
and the squadrons rode in the shallows off Chalkis[6]
   where the riptide crashes, drags,

and winds from the north pinned down our hulls at Aulis,
   port of anguish . . . head winds starving,
sheets and the cables snapped 195
   and the men's minds strayed,
     the pride, the bloom of Greece
   was raked as time ground on,
ground down, and then the cure for the storm
   and it was harsher—Calchas cried, 200
"My captains, Artemis must have blood!"—
   so harsh the sons of Atreus
     dashed their scepters on the rocks,
   could not hold back the tears,

and I still can hear the older warlord saying, 205
"Obey, obey, or a heavy doom will crush me!—
Oh but doom *will* crush me
   once I rend my child,
     the glory of my house—
a father's hands are stained, 210
blood of a young girl streaks the altar.
Pain both ways and what is worse?

3. Uranus, father of Kronos, grandfather of Zeus, the first lord of heaven. This whole passage refers to a primitive legend that told how Uranus was violently supplanted by his son, Kronos, who was in his turn overthrown by his son, Zeus. This legend is made to bear new meaning by Aeschylus, for he suggests that it is not a meaningless series of acts of violence but a progression to the rule of Zeus, who stands for order and justice. Thus the law of human life that Zeus proclaims and administers—that wisdom comes through suffering—has its counterpart in the history of the establishment of the divine rule.   4. Kronos.   5. The bench of the ship where the helmsman sat.   6. The unruly water of the narrows between Aulis on the mainland and Chalkis on the island of Euboea.

Desert the fleets, fail the alliance?
  No, but stop the winds with a virgin's blood,
    feed their lust, their fury?—feed their fury!—   215
Law is law!—
            Let all go well."

And once he slipped his neck in the strap of Fate,
his spirit veering black, impure, unholy,
once he turned he stopped at nothing,
    seized with the frenzy   220
        blinding driving to outrage—
wretched frenzy, cause of all our grief!
Yes, he had the heart
    to sacrifice his daughter!—
to bless the war that avenged a woman's loss,   225
    a bridal rite that sped the men-of-war.

"My father, father!"—she might pray to the winds;
no innocence moves her judges mad for war.
Her father called his henchmen on,
    on with a prayer,   230
        "Hoist her over the altar
like a yearling, give it all your strength!
She's fainting—lift her,
    sweep her robes around her,
but slip this strap in her gentle curving lips . . .   235
    here, gag her hard, a sound will curse the house"—

and the bridle chokes her voice . . . her saffron robes
pouring over the sand
                    her glance like arrows showering
wounding every murderer through with pity
    clear as a picture, live,   240
she strains to call their names . . .
I remember often the days with father's guests
when over the feast her voice unbroken,
    pure as the hymn her loving father
bearing third libations,[7] sang to Saving Zeus—   245
transfixed with joy, Atreus' offspring
    throbbing out their love.

What comes next? I cannot see it, cannot say.
The strong techniques of Calchas do their work.[8]
But Justice turns the balance scales,   250
    sees that we suffer
and we suffer and we learn.
And we will know the future when it comes.
Greet it too early, weep too soon.
    It all comes clear in the light of day.   255
Let all go well today, well as she could want,
    [*Turning to* CLYTAEMNESTRA.]

---

7. Offerings of wine. At a banquet three libations were poured, the third and last to Zeus the savior;
the last libation was accompanied by a hymn of praise.   8. This seems to refer to the sacrifice of
Iphigenia. Some scholars take the Greek words to refer to the fulfillment of Calchas' prophecies.

our midnight watch, our lone defender,
   single-minded queen.
LEADER: We've come,
Clytaemnestra. We respect your power.
Right it is to honor the warlord's woman   260
once he leaves the throne.
                       But why these fires?
Good news, or more good hopes? We're loyal,
we want to hear, but never blame your silence.
CLYTAEMNESTRA: Let the new day shine, as the proverb says,
   glorious from the womb of Mother Night.   265
   [*Lost in prayer, then turning to the* CHORUS.]
You will hear a joy beyond your hopes.
Priam's citadel—the Greeks have taken Troy!
LEADER: No, what do you mean? I can't believe it.
CLYTAEMNESTRA: Troy is ours. Is that clear enough?
LEADER: The joy of it,
   stealing over me, calling up my tears—   270
CLYTAEMNESTRA: Yes, your eyes expose your loyal hearts.
LEADER: And you have proof?
CLYTAEMNESTRA: I do,
   I must. Unless the god is lying.
LEADER: That,
   or a phantom spirit sends you into raptures.
CLYTAEMNESTRA: No one takes me in with visions—senseless dreams.   275
LEADER: Or giddy rumor, you haven't indulged yourself—
CLYTAEMNESTRA: You treat me like a child, you mock me?
LEADER: Then when did they storm the city?
CLYTAEMNESTRA: Last night, I say, the mother of this morning.
LEADER: And who on earth could run the news so fast?   280
CLYTAEMNESTRA: The god of fire—rushing fire from Ida![9]
   And beacon to beacon rushed it on to me,
   my couriers riding home the torch.
                       From Troy
   to the bare rock of Lemnos, Hermes' Spur,[1]
   and the Escort winged the great light west   285
   to the Saving Father's face, Mount Athos[2] hurled it
   third in the chain and leaping Ocean's back
   the blaze went dancing on to ecstasy—pitch-pine
   streaming gold like a new-born sun—and brought
   the word in flame to Mount Makistos'[3] brow.   290
   No time to waste, straining, fighting sleep,
   that lookout heaved a torch glowing over
   the murderous straits of Euripos to reach
   Messapion's[4] watchmen craning for the signal.

9. The mountain range near Troy. The names that follow in this speech designate the places where
beacon fires flashed the message of Troy's fall to Argos. The chain began at Ida.   1. Hermes' cliff is
on the island of Lemnos (off the coast of Asia Minor).   2. On a rocky peninsula in north Greece.
3. On the island of Euboea off the coast of central Greece.   4. A mountain on the mainland.

Fire for word of fire! tense with the heather   295
withered gray, they stack it, set it ablaze—
the hot force of the beacon never flags,
it springs the Plain of Asôpos, rears
like a harvest moon to hit Kithairon's[5] crest
and drives new men to drive the fire on.   300
That relay pants for the far-flung torch,
they swell its strength outstripping my commands
and the light inflames the marsh, the Gorgon's Eye,[6]
it strikes the peak where the wild goats range[7]—
my laws, my fire whips that camp!   305
They spare nothing, eager to build its heat,
and a huge beard of flame overcomes the headland
beetling down the Saronic Gulf,[8] and flaring south
it brings the dawn to the Black Widow's[9] face—
the watch that looms above your heads—and now   310
the true son of the burning flanks of Ida
crashes on the roofs of Atreus' sons!
And I ordained it all.
Torch to torch, running for their lives,
one long succession racing home my fire.

                                            One,   315
first in the laps and last,[1] wins out in triumph.
There you have my proof, *my* burning sign, I tell you—
the power my lord passed on from Troy to me![2]
LEADER: We'll thank the gods, my lady—first this story,
let me lose myself in the wonder of it all!   320
Tell it start to finish, tell us all.
CLYTAEMNESTRA: The city's ours—in our hands this very day!
I can hear the cries in crossfire rock the walls.
Pour oil and wine in the same bowl,
what have you, friendship? A struggle to the end.   325
So with the victors and the victims—outcries,
you can hear them clashing like their fates.

They are kneeling by the bodies of the dead,
embracing men and brothers, infants over

---

5. A mountain near Thebes.   6. Lake Gorgopis.   7. Mount Aegiplanctus on the Isthmus of Corinth.   8. The sea.   9. Mount Arachnaeus ("spider") in Argive territory. This is the fire seen by the
watchman at the beginning of the play.   1. The chain of beacons is compared to a relay race in
which the runners carry torches; the last runner (who runs the final lap) comes in first to win.   2. This
speech has often been criticized as discursive, but it has great poetic importance. The image of the light
that will dispel the darkness, first introduced by the watchman, is one of the dominant images of the
trilogy and is here developed with magnificent ambiguous effect. For the watchman the light means the
safe return of Agamemnon and the restoration of order in the house; for Clytaemnestra it means the
return of Agamemnon to his death at her hands. Each swift jump of the racing light is one step nearer
home and death for Agamemnon. The light the watchman longs for brings only greater darkness, but
eventually it brings darkness for Clytaemnestra too. The final emergence of the true light comes in the
glare of the torchlight procession that ends the last play of the trilogy, a procession that symbolizes
perfect reconciliation on both the human and the divine levels and the working out of the will of Zeus
in the substitution of justice for vengeance. The conception of the beacons as a chain of descendants
(compare line 311) is also important; the fire at Argos that announces Agamemnon's imminent death is
a direct descendant of the fire on Ida that announces the sack of Troy and Agamemnon's sacrilegious
conduct there. The metaphor thus reminds us of the sequence of crimes from generation to generation
that is the history of the house of Pelops.

the aged loins that gave them life, and sobbing,   330
as the yoke constricts their last free breath,
for every dear one lost.
                          And the others,
there, plunging breakneck through the night—
the labor of battle sets them down, ravenous;
to breakfast on the last remains of Troy.   335
Not by rank but the lots of chance they draw,
they lodge in the houses captured by the spear,
settling in so soon, released from the open sky,
the frost and dew. Lucky men, off guard at last,
they sleep away their first good night in years.   340

If only they are revering the city's gods,
the shrines of the gods who love the conquered land,
no plunderer will be plundered in return.
Just let no lust, no mad desire seize the armies[3]   345
to ravish what they must not touch—
overwhelmed by all they've won!
                                  The run for home
and safety waits, the swerve at the post,[4]
the final lap of the gruelling two-lap race.
And even if the men come back with no offense
to the gods, the avenging dead may never rest—   350
Oh let no new disaster strike! And here
you have it, what a woman has to say.
Let the best win out, clear to see.
A small desire but all that I could want.
LEADER: Spoken like a man, my lady, loyal,   355
full of self-command. I've heard your sign
and now your vision.
        [*Reaching towards her as she turns and re-enters the palace.*]
                          Now to praise the gods.
The joy is worth the labor.
CHORUS: O Zeus my king and Night, dear Night,[5]
queen of the house who covers us with glories,[6]   360
you slung your net on the towers of Troy,
neither young nor strong could leap
the giant dredge net of slavery,
        all-embracing ruin.
I adore you, iron Zeus of the guests   365
and your revenge—you drew your longbow
year by year to a taut full draw
till one bolt, not falling short
or arching over the stars,
        could split the mark of Paris!   370

3. She, of course, hopes for the opposite of what she prays for here. The audience was familiar with
the traditional account, according to which Agamemnon and his army failed signally to respect the gods
and temples of Troy.   4. Greek runners turned at a post and came back on a parallel track.   5. Troy
fell to a night attack.   6. Probably the moon and stars; an obscure expression in the original.

The sky stroke of god!—it is all Troy's to tell,
but even I can trace it to its cause:
god does as god decrees.
    And still some say
that heaven would never stoop to punish men   375
who trample the lovely grace of things
untouchable. How wrong they are!
    A curse burns bright on crime—
        full-blown, the father's crimes will blossom,
            burst into the son's.[7]   380
Let there be less suffering . . .
give us the sense to live on what we need.

          Bastions of wealth
          are no defense for the man
          who treads the grand altar of Justice   385
            down and out of sight.

Persuasion, maddening child of Ruin
overpowers him—Ruin plans it all.
And the wound will smolder on,
    there is no cure,   390
a terrible brilliance kindles on the night.
He is bad bronze scraped on a touchstone:
put to the test, the man goes black.[8]
    Like the boy who chases
        a bird on the wing, brands his city,   395
           brings it down and prays,
but the gods are deaf
to the one who turns to crime, they tear him down.

          So Paris learned:
          he came to Atreus' house   400
          and shamed the tables spread for guests,
            he stole away the queen.

And she left her land *chaos,* clanging shields,
companions tramping, bronze prows, men in bronze,
    and she came to Troy with a dowry, death,   405
strode through the gates
    defiant in every stride,
as prophets of the house[9] looked on and wept,
"Oh the halls and the lords of war,
    the bed and the fresh prints of love.   410
I *see* him, unavenging, unavenged,
the stun of his desolation is so clear—

---

7. The language throughout this passage is significantly general. The chorus refers to Paris, but everything it says is equally applicable to Agamemnon, who sacrificed his daughter for his ambitions. The
original Greek is corrupt (that is, has been garbled in the handwritten tradition) but seems to proclaim
the doctrine that the sins of the fathers are visited on the children. So Paris (and Agamemnon) pay for
the misdeeds of their ancestors (as well as their own).   8. Inferior bronze, adulterated with lead, turns
black with use.   9. Menelaus'.

he longs for the one who lies across the sea
until her phantom seems to sway the house.

> Her curving images,   415
> her beauty hurts her lord,
> the eyes starve and the touch
> of love is gone,

and radiant dreams are passing in the night,
the memories throb with sorrow, joy with pain . . .   420
   it is pain to dream and see desires
slip through the arms,
     a vision lost forever
winging down the moving drifts of sleep."
So he grieves at the royal hearth   425
   yet others' grief is worse, far worse.
All through Greece for those who flocked to war
they are holding back the anguish now,
   you can feel it rising now in every house;
I tell you there is much to tear the heart.   430

> They knew the men they sent,
> but now in place of men
> ashes and urns come back
> to every hearth.[1]

War, War, the great gold-broker of corpses   435
holds the balance of the battle on his spear!
Home from the pyres he sends them,
   home from Troy to the loved ones,
weighted with tears, the urns brimmed full,
   the heroes return in gold-dust,[2]   440
dear, light ash for men; and they weep,
they praise them, "He had skill in the swordplay,"
  "He went down so tall in the onslaught,"
"All for another's woman." So they mutter
in secret and the rancor steals   445
toward our staunch defenders, Atreus' sons.

> And there they ring the walls, the young,
> the lithe, the handsome hold the graves
> they won in Troy; the enemy earth
> rides over those who conquered.   450

The people's voice is heavy with hatred,
now the curses of the people must be paid,
and now I wait, I listen . . .
   there—there is something breathing
under the night's shroud. God takes aim   455

---

1. This strikes a contemporary note. In Homer the fallen Achaeans are buried at Troy, but in Aeschylus'
Athens the dead were cremated on the battlefield, and their ashes were brought home for burial.
2. That is, in ashes. The war god is a broker who gives, in exchange for bodies, gold dust (the word
used for "bodies" could mean living bodies or corpses).

at the ones who murder many;
the swarthy Furies stalk the man
gone rich beyond all rights—with a twist
    of fortune grind him down, dissolve him
into the blurring dead—there is no help.   460
The reach for power can recoil,
the bolt of god can strike you at a glance.

                Make me rich with no man's envy,
                neither a raider of cities, no,
                nor slave come face to face with life   465
                overpowered by another.
[*Speaking singly.*]
—Fire comes and the news is good,
    it races through the streets
but is it true? Who knows?
Or just another lie from heaven?[3]   470

—Show us the man so childish, wonderstruck,
    he's fired up with the first torch,
then when the message shifts
he's sick at heart.

                —Just like a woman
to fill with thanks before the truth is clear.   475

—So gullible. Their stories spread like wildfire,
    they fly fast and die faster;
rumors voiced by women come to nothing.
LEADER: Soon we'll know her fires for what they are,
her relay race of torches hand-to-hand—   480
know if they're real or just a dream,
the hope of a morning here to take our senses.
I see a herald running from the beach
and a victor's spray of olive shades his eyes
and the dust he kicks, twin to the mud of Troy,   485
shows he has a voice—no kindling timber
on the cliffs, no signal-fires for him.
He can shout the news and give us joy,
or else . . . please, not that.
                Bring it on,
good fuel to build the first good fires.   490
And if anyone calls down the worst on Argos
let him reap the rotten harvest of his mind.
[*The* HERALD *rushes in and kneels on the ground.*]
HERALD: Good Greek earth, the soil of my fathers!
Ten years out, and a morning brings me back.

---

3. Later we will see Agamemnon come on stage with Cassandra (his Trojan captive) and the spoils of
Troy. The chorus, which started out to sing a hymn of praise for the fall of Troy (line 359), ends in fear
and despondency. It now questions the truth of Clytaemnestra's announcement; perhaps Troy has not
fallen after all (line 469).

All hopes snapped but one—I'm home at last.   495
Never dreamed I'd die in Greece, assigned
the narrow plot I love the best.
                              And now
I salute the land, the light of the sun,
our high lord Zeus and the king of Pytho[4]—
no more arrows, master, raining on our heads!   500
At Scamander's banks we took our share,
your longbow brought us down like plague.[5]
Now come, deliver us, heal us—lord Apollo!
Gods of the market, here, take my salute.
And you, my Hermes,[6] Escort,   505
loving Herald, the herald's shield and prayer!—
And the shining dead[7] of the land who launched the armies,
warm us home . . . we're all the spear has left.
You halls of the kings, you roofs I cherish,
sacred seats—you gods that catch the sun,   510
if your glances ever shone on him in the old days,
greet him well—so many years are lost.
He comes, he brings us light in the darkness,
free for every comrade, Agamemnon lord of men.

Give him the royal welcome he deserves!   515
He hoisted the pickax of Zeus who brings revenge,
he dug Troy down, he worked her soil down,
the shrines of her gods and the high altars, gone!—
and the seed of her wide earth he ground to bits.
That's the yoke he claps on Troy. The king,   520
the son of Atreus comes. The man is blest,
the one man alive to merit such rewards.

Neither Paris nor Troy, partners to the end,
can say their work outweighs their wages now.
Convicted of rapine, stripped of all his spoils,   525
and his father's house and the land that gave it life—
he's scythed them to the roots. The sons of Priam
pay the price twice over.
LEADER: Welcome home
from the wars, herald, long live your joy.
HERALD: Our joy—
now I could die gladly. Say the word, dear gods.   530
LEADER: Longing for your country left you raw?
HERALD: The tears fill my eyes, for joy.
LEADER: You too,
down the sweet disease that kills a man
with kindness . . .
HERALD: Go on, I don't see what you—

4. Apollo.   5. In the opening scene of the *Iliad* I, Apollo punishes the Greeks with his arrows (a metaphor for plague).   6. The gods' messenger and patron deity of heralds.   7. The heroes of the past, who are buried in Argos and worshiped.

LEADER: Love
for the ones who love you—that's what took you.
HERALD: You mean   535
the land and the armies hungered for each other?
LEADER: There were times I thought I'd faint with longing.
HERALD: So anxious for the armies, why?
LEADER: For years now,
only my silence kept me free from harm.
HERALD: What,
with the kings gone did someone threaten you?
LEADER: So much . . .[8]   540
now as you say, it would be good to die.
HERALD: True, we *have* done well.
Think back in the years and what have you?
A few runs of luck, a lot that's bad.
Who but a god can go through life unmarked?   545

A long, hard pull we had, if I would tell it all.
The iron rations, penned in the gangways
hock by jowl like sheep. Whatever miseries
break a man, our quota, every sunstarved day.

Then on the beaches it was worse. Dug in   550
under the enemy ramparts—deadly going.
Out of the sky, out of the marshy flats
the dews soaked us, turned the ruts we fought from
into gullies, made our gear, our scalps
crawl with lice.
                 And talk of the cold,   555
the sleet to freeze the gulls, and the big snows
come avalanching down from Ida. Oh but the heat,
the sea and the windless noons, the swells asleep,
dropped to a dead calm . . .

But why weep now?   560
It's over for us, over for them.
The dead can rest and never rise again;
no need to call their muster. We're alive,
do we have to go on raking up old wounds?
Good-by to all that. Glad I am to say it.   565

For us, the remains of the Greek contingents,
the good wins out, no pain can tip the scales,
not now. So shout this boast to the bright sun—
fitting it is—wing it over the seas and rolling earth:

"Once when an Argive expedition captured Troy   570
they hauled these spoils back to the gods of Greece,

---

8. Throughout this dialogue the chorus has been gearing itself up to warn the herald that there may be danger for Agamemnon at home; at this point its nerve fails and it abandons the attempt.

they bolted them high across the temple doors,
the glory of the past!"
                              And hearing that,
men will applaud our city and our chiefs,
and Zeus will have the hero's share of fame—   575
he did the work.
                    That's all I have to say.
LEADER: I'm convinced, glad that I was wrong.
Never too old to learn; it keeps me young.
   [CLYTAEMNESTRA enters with her women.]
First the house and the queen, it's their affair,
but I can taste the riches.
CLYTAEMNESTRA: I cried out long ago!⁹—   580
for joy, when the first herald came burning
through the night and told the city's fall.
And there were some who smiled and said,
"A few fires persuade you Troy's in ashes.
Women, women, elated over nothing."   585

You made me seem deranged.
For all that I sacrificed—a woman's way,
you'll say—station to station on the walls
we lifted cries of triumph that resounded
in the temples of the gods. We lulled and blessed   590
the fires with myrrh and they consumed our victims.
   [Turning to the HERALD.]
But enough. Why prolong the story?
From the king himself I'll gather all I need.
Now for the best way to welcome home
my lord, my good lord . . .
                              No time to lose!   595
What dawn can feast a woman's eyes like this?
I can see the light, the husband plucked from war
by the Saving God and open wide the gates.

Tell him that, and have him come with speed,
the people's darling—how they long for him.   600
And for his wife,
may he return and find her true at hall,
just as the day he left her, faithful to the last.
A watchdog gentle to him alone,
   [Glancing towards the palace.]
                              savage
to those who cross his path. I have not changed.   605
The strains of time can never break our seal.
In love with a new lord, in ill repute I am
as practiced as I am in dyeing bronze.¹

_____

9. As the watchman had told her to (line 30).   1. She claims she is no more capable of adultery than
she is of dyeing bronze; but she will later kill Agamemnon with a bronze weapon.

That is my boast, teeming with the truth.
I am proud, a woman of my nobility—   610
I'd hurl it from the roofs!
   [*She turns sharply, enters the palace.*]
LEADER: She speaks well, but it takes no seer to know
  she only says what's right.
   [*The* HERALD *attempts to leave; the* LEADER *takes him by the arm.*]
                  Wait, one thing.
Menelaus, is he home too, safe with the men?[2]
The power of the land—dear king.   615
HERALD: I doubt that lies will help my friends,
  in the lean months to come.
LEADER: Help us somehow, tell the truth as well.
  But when the two conflict it's hard to hide—
  out with it.
HERALD: He's lost, gone from the fleets![3]   620
He and his ship, it's true.
LEADER: After you watched him
  pull away from Troy? Or did some storm
  attack you all and tear him off the line?
HERALD: There,
  like a marksman, the whole disaster cut to a word.
LEADER: How do the escorts give him out—dead or alive?   625
HERALD: No clear report. No one knows . . .
  only the wheeling sun that heats the earth to life.
LEADER: But then the storm—how did it reach the ships?
  How did it end? Were the angry gods on hand?
HERALD: This blessed day, ruin it with *them?*   630
  Better to keep their trophies far apart.

When a runner comes, his face in tears,
saddled with what his city dreaded most,[4]
the armies routed, two wounds in one,
one to the city, one to hearth and home . . .   635
our best men, droves of them, victims
herded from every house by the two-barb whip
that Ares[5] likes to crack,
               that charioteer
who packs destruction shaft by shaft,
careening on with his brace of bloody mares—   640
When he comes in, I tell you, dragging that much pain,
wail your battle-hymn to the Furies, and high time!
But when he brings salvation home to a city
singing out her heart—
how can I mix the good with so much bad   645

---

2. The relevance of this question and the following speeches lies in the fact that Menelaus' absence makes Agamemnon's murder easier (his presence might have made it impossible) and in the fact that Menelaus is bringing Helen home.   3. For what happened to Menelaus see the *Odyssey* IV.
4. The herald creates a vivid picture of a messenger bringing news of disaster to his city—a role he wishes to avoid.   5. The war god.

and blurt out this?—
                    "Storms swept the Greeks,
and not without the anger of the gods!"

Those enemies for ages, fire[6] and water,
sealed a pact and showed it to the world—
they crushed our wretched squadrons.
                                Night looming,   650
breakers lunging in for the kill
and the black gales come brawling out of the north—
ships ramming, prow into hooking prow, gored
by the rush-and-buck of hurricane pounding rain
by the cloudburst—
                    ships stampeding into the darkness,   655
lashed and spun by the savage shepherd's hand![7]

But when the sun comes up to light the skies
I see the Aegean heaving into a great bloom
of corpses . . . Greeks, the pick of a generation
scattered through the wrecks and broken spars.   660

But not us, not our ship, our hull untouched.
Someone stole us away or begged us off.
No mortal—a god, death grip on the tiller,
or lady luck herself, perched on the helm,
she pulled us through, she saved us. Aye,   665
we'll never battle the heavy surf at anchor,
never shipwreck up some rocky coast.

But once we cleared that sea-hell, not even
trusting luck in the cold light of day,
we battened on our troubles, they were fresh—   670
the armada punished, bludgeoned into nothing.

And now if one of them still has the breath
he's saying we are lost. Why not?
We say the same of him. Well,
here's to the best.
                    And Menelaus?   675
Look to it, he's come back, and yet . . .
if a shaft of the sun can track him down,
alive, and his eyes full of the old fire—
thanks to the strategies of Zeus, Zeus
would never tear the house out by the roots—   680
then there's hope our man will make it home.

You've heard it all. Now you have the truth.
    [*Rushing out.*]

---

6. Lightning.   7. The ships were scattered like sheep dispersed by a cruel shepherd.

CHORUS: Who—what power named the name[8] that drove your fate?—
what hidden brain could divine your future,
steer that word to the mark,   685
to the bride of spears,
    the whirlpool churning armies,
        Oh for all the world a Helen!
Hell at the prows, hell at the gates
hell on the men-of-war,   690
from her lair's sheer veils she drifted
    launched by the giant western wind,
        and the long tall waves of men in armor,
huntsmen[9] trailing the oar-blades' dying spoor
slipped into her moorings,   695
    Simois'[1] mouth that chokes with foliage,
        bayed for bloody strife,
for Troy's Blood Wedding Day—she drives her word,
her burning will to the birth, the Fury
late but true to the cause,   700
to the tables shamed
    and Zeus who guards the hearth[2]—
        the Fury makes the Trojans pay!
Shouting their hymns, hymns for the bride
hymns for the kinsmen doomed   705
to the wedding march of Fate.
    Troy changed her tune in her late age,
        and I think I hear the dirges mourning
"Paris, born and groomed for the bed of Fate!"
They mourn with their life breath,   710
    they sing their last, the sons of Priam
        born for bloody slaughter.

    So a man once reared
a lion cub at hall, snatched
from the breast, still craving milk   715
    in the first flush of life.
A captivating pet for the young,
and the old men adored it, pampered it
    in their arms, day in, day out,
like an infant just born.   720
Its eyes on fire, little beggar,
fawning for its belly, slave to food.

    But it came of age
and the parent strain broke out
and it paid its breeders back.   725
    Grateful it was, it went

---

8. Helen. The name contains the Greek root *hele*, which means "destroy." The chorus is so obsessed
with Helen's guilt that it fails to recognize the true responsibility for the war and the imminence of
disaster.   9. The Achaean army, which came after her.   1. A river in Troy.   2. That is, protects
the host and guest.

through the flock to prepare a feast,
an illicit orgy—the house swam with blood,
   none could resist that agony—
      massacre vast and raw!   730
From god there came a priest of ruin,
adopted by the house to lend it warmth.

And the first sensation Helen brought to Troy . . .
call it a spirit
    shimmer of winds dying   735
      glory light as gold
   shaft of the eyes dissolving, open bloom
   that wounds the heart with love.
But veering wild in mid-flight
she whirled her wedding on to a stabbing end,   740
slashed at the sons of Priam—hearthmate, friend to the death,
   sped by Zeus who speeds the guest,
a bride of tears, a Fury.

There's an ancient saying, old as man himself:
men's prosperity   745
   never will die childless,
     once full-grown it breeds.
    Sprung from the great good fortune in the race
comes bloom on bloom of pain—
insatiable wealth. But not I,   750
I alone say this. Only the reckless act
can breed impiety, multiplying crime on crime,
   while the house kept straight and just
is blessed with radiant children.[3]

      But ancient Violence longs to breed,   755
        new Violence comes
    when its fatal hour comes, the demon comes
    to take her toll—no war, no force, no prayer
      can hinder the midnight Fury stamped
    with parent Fury moving through the house.   760

      But Justice shines in sooty hovels,[4]
        loves the decent life.
   From proud halls crusted with gilt by filthy hands
    she turns her eyes to find the pure in spirit—
  spurning the wealth stamped counterfeit with praise,   765
   she steers all things toward their destined end.[5]

[AGAMEMNON *enters in his chariot, his plunder borne before him by
his entourage; behind him, half hidden, stands* CASSANDRA. *The old
men press toward him.*]
Come, my king, the scourge of Troy,

---

3. These lines begin with the traditional Greek view that immoderate good fortune (or excellence of
any kind beyond the average) is itself the cause of disaster. The chorus, however, rejects this view and
states that only an act of evil produces evil consequences.   4. The homes of the poor.   5. Here the
chorus admits, by implication, that the poor are less likely to commit evil acts.

the true son of Atreus—
How to salute you, how to praise you
neither too high nor low, but hit   770
the note of praise that suits the hour?
So many prize some brave display,
they prefer some flaunt of honor
    once they break the bounds.
When a man fails they share his grief,   775
but the pain can never cut them to the quick.
When a man succeeds they share his glory,
torturing their faces into smiles.
But the good shepherd knows his flock.
When the eyes seem to brim with love   780
    and it is only unction,
he will know, better than we can know.
That day you marshaled the armies
all for Helen—no hiding it now—
I drew you in my mind in black;   785
you seemed a menace at the helm,
    sending men to the grave
to bring her home, that hell on earth.
But now from the depths of trust and love
I say Well fought, well won—   790
    the end is worth the labor!
Search, my king, and learn at last
who stayed at home and kept their faith
    and who betrayed the city.[6]

AGAMEMNON: First,
with justice I salute my Argos and my gods,   795
my accomplices who brought me home and won
my rights from Priam's Troy—the just gods.
No need to hear our pleas. Once for all
they consigned their lots to the urn of blood,[7]
they pitched on death for men, annihilation   800
for the city. Hope's hand, hovering
over the urn of mercy, left it empty.
Look for the smoke—it is the city's seamark,
building even now.
                        The storms of ruin live!
Her last dying breath, rising up from the ashes   805
sends us gales of incense rich in gold.

For that we must thank the gods with a sacrifice
our sons will long remember. For their mad outrage
of a queen we raped their city—we were right.
The beast of Argos, foals of the wild mare,[8]   810
thousands massed in armor rose on the night
the Pleiades went down,[9] and crashing through

---

6. The chorus tries to warn Agamemnon against flatterers and dissemblers, but he misses its drift.
7. In an Athenian law court there were two urns—one for acquittal, one for condemnation—into which
the jurors dropped their pebbles. (The audience will see them on stage in the final play of the trilogy.)
8. The wooden horse, the stratagem with which the Greeks captured the city.   9. The setting of the
constellation Pleiades, late in the fall.

their walls our bloody lion lapped its fill,
gorging on the blood of kings.
                    Our thanks to the gods,
long drawn out, but it is just the prelude.   815
   [CLYTAEMNESTRA *approaches with her women; they are carrying dark
   red tapestries.* AGAMEMNON *turns to the* LEADER.]
And your concern, old man, is on my mind.
I hear you and agree, I will support you.
How rare, men with the character to praise
a friend's success without a trace of envy,
poison to the heart—it deals a double blow.   820
Your own losses weigh you down but then,
look at your neighbor's fortune and you weep.
Well I know. I understand society,
the fawning mirror of the proud.
                    My comrades . . .
they're shadows, I tell you, ghosts of men   825
who swore they'd die for me. Only Odysseus:
I dragged that man to the wars[1] but once in harness
he was a trace-horse, he gave his all for me.
Dead or alive, no matter, I can praise him.

And now this cause involving men and gods.   830
We must summon the city for a trial,
found a national tribunal. Whatever's healthy,
shore it up with law and help it flourish.
Wherever something calls for drastic cures
we make our noblest effort: amputate or wield   835
the healing iron, burn the cancer at the roots.

Now I go to my father's house—
I give the gods my right hand, my first salute.
The ones who sent me forth have brought me home.
   [*He starts down from the chariot, looks at* CLYTAEMNESTRA, *stops, and
   offers up a prayer.*]
Victory, you have sped my way before,   840
now speed me to the last.
   [CLYTAEMNESTRA *turns from the king to the* CHORUS.]
CLYTAEMNESTRA: Old nobility of Argos
gathered here, I am not ashamed to tell you
how I love the man. I am older,
and the fear dies away . . . I am human.
Nothing I say was learned from others.   845
This is my life, my ordeal, long as the siege
he laid at Troy and more demanding.
                    First,
when a woman sits at home and the man is gone,

---

1. Feigning madness to escape going to Troy, Odysseus was tricked into demonstrating his sanity. Agamemnon's remark shows that the truth is far from his mind; he has no thought that his danger comes
from a woman.

the loneliness is terrible,
unconscionable . . .   850
and the rumors spread and fester,
a runner comes with something dreadful,
close on his heels the next and his news worse,
and they shout it out and the whole house can hear;
and wounds—if he took one wound for each report   855
to penetrate these walls, he's gashed like a dragnet,
more, if he had only died . . .
for each death that swelled his record, he could boast
like a triple-bodied Geryon[2] risen from the grave,
"Three shrouds I dug from the earth, one for every body   860
that went down!"
                    The rumors broke like fever,
broke and then rose higher. There were times
they cut me down and eased my throat from the noose.
I wavered between the living and the dead.
        [*Turning to* AGAMEMNON.]
                                        And so
our child is gone, not standing by our side,   865
the bond of our dearest pledges, mine and yours;
by all rights our child should be here . . .
Orestes. You seem startled.
You needn't be. Our loyal brother-in-arms
will take good care of him, Strophios[3] the Phocian.   870
He warned from the start we court two griefs in one.
You risk all on the wars—and what if the people
rise up howling for the king, and anarchy
should dash our plans?
                        Men, it is their nature,
trampling on the fighter once he's down.   875
Our child is gone. That is my self-defense
and it is true.
                For me, the tears that welled
like springs are dry. I have no tears to spare.
I'd watch till late at night, my eyes still burn,
I sobbed by the torch I lit for you alone.   880
        [*Glancing towards the palace.*]
I never let it die . . . but in my dreams
the high thin wail of a gnat would rouse me,
piercing like a trumpet—I could see you
suffer more than all
the hours that slept with me could ever bear.   885

I endured it all. And now, free of grief,
I would salute that man the watchdog of the fold,

---

2. A monster (eventually killed by Heracles) who had three bodies and three heads. 3. King of
Phocis, a mountainous region near Delphi. His son, Pylades, accompanies Orestes when he returns to
avenge Agamemnon's death.

the mainroyal,[4] saving stay of the vessel,
rooted oak that thrusts the roof sky-high,
the father's one true heir.   890
Land at dawn to the shipwrecked past all hope,
light of the morning burning off the night of storm,
the cold clear spring to the parched horseman—
O the ecstasy, to flee the yoke of Fate!

It is right to use the titles he deserves.   895
Let envy keep her distance. We have suffered
long enough.
          [*Reaching toward* AGAMEMNON.]
                    Come to me now, my dearest,
down from the car of war, but never set the foot
that stamped out Troy on earth again, my great one.

Women, why delay? You have your orders.   900
Pave his way with tapestries.[5]
          [*They begin to spread the crimson tapestries between the king and
          the palace doors.*]
                              Quickly.
Let the red stream flow and bear him home
to the home he never hoped to see—Justice,
lead him in!
                    Leave all the rest to me.
The spirit within me never yields to sleep.   905
We will set things right, with the god's help.
We will do whatever Fate requires.
AGAMEMNON: There
is Leda's daughter,[6] the keeper of my house.
And the speech to suit my absence, much too long.
But the praise that does us justice,   910
let it come from others, then we prize it.
                              This—
You treat me like a woman. Groveling, gaping up at me!
What am I, some barbarian[7] peacocking out of Asia?
Never cross my path with robes and draw the lightning.
Never—only the gods deserve the pomps of honor   915
and the stiff brocades of fame. To walk on them . . .
I am human, and it makes my pulses stir
with dread.
                    Give me the tributes of a man
and not a god, a little earth to walk on,
not this gorgeous work.   920

---

4. Upper section of the mainmast.   5. To walk on those tapestries, wall hangings dyed with the expensive crimson, would be an act of extravagant pride. Pride is the keynote of Agamemnon's character, and
it suits Clytaemnestra's sense of fitness that he should go into his death in godlike state, *trampling
royal crimson* (line 957), the color of blood.   6. Clytaemnestra. Helen is also a daughter of Leda.
7. Foreigner, especially Asiatic. Aeschylus is thinking of the pomp and servility of the contemporary
Persian court.

There is no need to sound my reputation.
I have a sense of right and wrong, what's more —
heaven's proudest gift. Call no man blest
until he ends his life in peace, fulfilled.
If I can live by what I say, I have no fear.   925
CLYTAEMNESTRA: One thing more. Be true to your ideals and tell me —
AGAMEMNON: True to my ideals? Once I violate them I am lost.
CLYTAEMNESTRA: Would you have sworn this act to god in a time of terror?
AGAMEMNON: Yes, if a prophet called for a last, drastic rite.
CLYTAEMNESTRA: But Priam — can you see him if he had your success?   930
AGAMEMNON: Striding on the tapestries of God, I see him now.
CLYTAEMNESTRA: And *you* fear the reproach of common men?
AGAMEMNON: The voice of the people — aye, they have enormous power.
CLYTAEMNESTRA: Perhaps, but where's the glory without a little gall?
AGAMEMNON: And where's the woman in all this lust for glory?   935
CLYTAEMNESTRA: But the great victor — it becomes him to give way.
AGAMEMNON: Victory in this . . . war of ours, it means so much to you?
CLYTAEMNESTRA: O give way! The power is yours if you surrender
all of your own free will to me.
AGAMEMNON: Enough.
If you are so determined —   940
[*Turning to the women, pointing to his boots.*]
Let someone help me off with these at least.
Old slaves, they've stood me well.
                                            Hurry,
and while I tread his splendors dyed red in the sea,[8]
may no god watch and strike me down with envy
from on high. I feel such shame —   945
to tread the life of the house, a kingdom's worth
of silver in the weaving.
[*He steps down from the chariot to the tapestries and reveals* CASSAN-
DRA, *dressed in the sacred regalia, the fillets, robes and scepter of
Apollo.*]
                                            Done is done.
Escort this stranger[9] in, be gentle.
Conquer with compassion. Then the gods
shine down upon you, gently. No one chooses   950
the yoke of slavery, not of one's free will —
and she least of all. The gift of the armies,
flower and pride of all the wealth we won,
she follows me from Troy.
                                            And now,
since you have brought me down with your insistence,   955
just this once I enter my father's house,
trampling royal crimson as I go.

8. The dye was made from shellfish.   9. Cassandra, daughter of Priam, Agamemnon's share of the
human booty of the sack of Troy. She was loved by Apollo, who gave her the gift of prophecy, but when
she refused her love to the god, he saw to it that her prophecies, though true, would never be believed
until it was too late.

[*He takes his first steps and pauses.*]
CLYTAEMNESTRA: There is the sea
and who will drain it dry? Precious as silver,
inexhaustible, ever-new, it breeds the more we reap it—
tides on tides of crimson dye our robes blood-red.   960
Our lives are based on wealth, my king,
the gods have seen to that.
Destitution, our house has never heard the word.
I would have sworn to tread on legacies of robes,
at one command from an oracle, deplete the house—   965
suffer the worst to bring that dear life back!
    [*Encouraged,* AGAMEMNON *strides to the entrance.*]
When the root lives on, the new leaves come back,
spreading a dense shroud of shade across the house
to thwart the Dog Star's[1] fury. So you return
to the father's hearth, you bring us warmth in winter   970
like the sun—
                    And you are Zeus when Zeus
tramples the bitter virgin grape for new wine
and the welcome chill steals through the halls, at last
the master moves among the shadows of his house, fulfilled.
    [AGAMEMNON *goes over the threshold; the women gather up the tap-
    estries while* CLYTAEMNESTRA *prays.*]
Zeus, Zeus, master of all fullfillment, now fulfill our prayers—   975
speed our rites to their fulfillment once for all!
    [*She enters the palace, the doors close, the old men huddle in terror.*]
CHORUS: Why, why does it rock me, never stops,
this terror beating down my heart,
    this seer that sees it all—
it beats its wings, uncalled unpaid   980
thrust on the lungs
the mercenary song beats on and on
singing a prophet's strain—
    and I can't throw it off
like dreams that make no sense,   985
and the strength drains
that filled the mind with trust,
and the years drift by and the driven sand
        has buried the mooring lines
that churned when the armored squadrons cut for Troy . . .   990
and now I believe it, I can prove he's home,
        my own clear eyes for witness—
                            Agamemnon!
Still it's chanting, beating deep so deep in the heart
this dirge of the Furies, oh dear god,
not fit for the lyre,[2] its own master   995

---

1. Sirius; its appearance in the summer sky marked the beginning of the hot season (the "dog days" of summer).   2. A stringed instrument played on joyful occasions (hence "lyric" poetry).

it kills our spirit
kills our hopes
and it's real, true, no fantasy—
    stark terror whirls the brain
      and the end is coming   1000
        Justice comes to birth—
I pray my fears prove false and fall
and die and never come to birth!
Even exultant health, well we know,
    exceeds its limits,[3] comes so near disease   1005
it can breach the wall between them.

Even a man's fate, held true on course,
    in a blinding flash rams some hidden reef;
but if caution only casts the pick of the cargo—
one well-balanced cast—   1010
the house will not go down, not outright;[4]
laboring under its wealth of grief
the ship of state rides on.

Yes, and the great green bounty of god,
sown in the furrows year by year and reaped each fall   1015
can end the plague of famine.

But a man's lifeblood
    is dark and mortal.
Once it wets the earth
what song can sing it back?   1020
Not even the master-healer[5]
    who brought the dead to life—
Zeus stopped the man before he did more harm.

Oh, if only the gods had never forged
the chain that curbs our excess,   1025
    one man's fate curbing the next man's fate,
my heart would outrace my song, I'd pour out all I feel—
      but no, I choke with anguish,
        mutter through the nights.
Never to ravel out a hope in time   1030
and the brain is swarming, burning—
    [CLYTAEMNESTRA *emerges from the palace and goes to* CASSANDRA,
    impassive in the chariot.]
CLYTAEMNESTRA: Won't you come inside? I mean you, Cassandra.
Zeus in all his mercy wants you to share
some victory libations with the house.
The slaves are flocking. Come, lead them   1035

---

3. Excess, even in blessings like health, is always dangerous. The chorus fears that Agamemnon's triumphant success may threaten his safety.   4. These lines refer to a traditional Greek belief that the fortunate person could avert the envy of heaven by deliberately getting rid of some precious possession.   5. Asclepius, the great physician who was so skilled that he finally succeeded in restoring a dead man to life. Zeus struck him with a thunderbolt for going too far.

up to the altar of the god who guards
our dearest treasures.
                    Down from the chariot,
no time for pride. Why even Heracles,[6]
they say, was sold into bondage long ago,
he had to endure the bitter bread of slaves.   1040
But if the yoke descends on you, be grateful
for a master born and reared in ancient wealth.
Those who reap a harvest past their hopes
are merciless to their slaves.
                    From us
you will receive what custom says is right.   1045
    [CASSANDRA *remains impassive.*]
LEADER: It's *you* she is speaking to, it's all too clear.
    You're caught in the nets of doom—obey
    if you can obey, unless you cannot bear to.
CLYTAEMNESTRA: Unless she's like a swallow, possessed
    of her own barbaric song,[7] strange, dark.   1050
    I speak directly as I can—she must obey.
LEADER: Go with her. Make the best of it, she's right.
    Step down from the seat, obey her.
CLYTAEMNESTRA: Do it *now*—
    I have no time to spend outside. Already
    the victims crowd the hearth, the Navelstone,[8]   1055
    to bless this day of joy I never hoped to see!—
    our victims waiting for the fire and the knife,
    and you,
    if you want to taste our mystic rites, come now.
    If my words can't reach you—
        [*Turning to the* LEADER.]
                    Give her a sign,   1060
    one of her exotic handsigns.
LEADER: I think
    the stranger needs an interpreter, someone clear.
    She's like a wild creature, fresh caught.
CLYTAEMNESTRA: She's mad,
    her evil genius murmuring in her ears.
    She comes from a *city* fresh caught.   1065
    She must learn to take the cutting bridle
    before she foams her spirit off in blood—
    and that's the last I waste on her contempt!
        [*Wheeling, re-entering the palace. The* LEADER *turns to* CASSANDRA,
        who remains transfixed.]
LEADER: Not I, I pity her. I will be gentle.
    Come, poor thing. Leave the empty chariot—   1070

6. The Greek hero, famous for his twelve labors that rid the earth of monsters, was at one time forced
to be the slave to Omphale, an Eastern queen.   7. The comparison of foreign speech to the twittering
of a swallow was a Greek commonplace.   8. An altar of Zeus Herkeios, guardian of the hearth, which
was the religious center of the home.

Of your own free will try on the yoke of Fate.
CASSANDRA: Aieeeeee! Earth—Mother—
　　Curse of the Earth—Apollo Apollo!
LEADER: Why cry to Apollo?
　　He's not the god to call with sounds of mourning.   1075
CASSANDRA: Aieeeeee! Earth—Mother—
　　Rape of the Earth—Apollo Apollo!
LEADER: Again, it's a bad omen.
　　She cries for the god who wants no part of grief.[9]
　　[CASSANDRA *steps from the chariot, looks slowly towards the rooftops*
　　of the palace.]
CASSANDRA: God of the long road,   1080
　　Apollo *Apollo* my destroyer—
you destroy me once,[1] destroy me twice—
LEADER: She's about to sense her own ordeal, I think.
　　Slave that she is, the god lives on inside her.
CASSANDRA: God of the iron marches,   1085
　　Apollo *Apollo* my destroyer—
where, where have you led[2] me now? what house—
LEADER: The house of Atreus and his sons. Really—
　　don't you know? It's true, see for yourself.
CASSANDRA: No . . . the house that hates god,   1090
　　an echoing womb of guilt, kinsmen
　　　　torturing kinsmen, severed heads,
　　slaughterhouse of heroes, soil streaming blood—
LEADER: A keen hound, this stranger.
　　Trailing murder, and murder she will find.   1095
CASSANDRA: See, my witnesses—
　　I trust to them, to the babies
　　　　wailing, skewered on the sword,
　　their flesh charred, the father gorging on their parts[3]—
LEADER: We'd heard your fame as a seer,   1100
　　but no one looks for seers in Argos.
CASSANDRA: Oh no, what horror, what new plot,[4]
　　new agony this?—
it's growing, massing, deep in the house,
　　a plot, a monstrous—*thing*   1105
　　　　to crush the loved ones, no,
　　there is no cure, and rescue's far away[5] and—
LEADER: I can't read these signs; I knew the first,
　　the city rings with them.
CASSANDRA: You, you godforsaken—you'd do *this?*   1110
　　The lord of your bed,

9. Apollo (and the Olympian gods in general) was not invoked in mourning or lamentation.　　1. The
name *Apollo* suggests the Greek word *apollumi*, "destroy." He destroyed her the first time when he saw
to it that no one would believe her prophecies. *God of the long road:* Apollo Agyieus. This statue, a
conical pillar, was set up outside the door of the house; no doubt there was one on stage.　　2. The
Greek word (a form of the verb *ago*) suggests the god's title Agyieus.　　3. The feast of Thyestes.　　4. Clytaemnestra's murder of Agamemnon.　　5. A reference to Menelaus (distant in space) and Orestes (distant in time).

you bathe him . . . his body glistens, then—
   how to tell the climax?—
      comes so quickly, see,
  hand over hand shoots out, hauling ropes—
                      then lunge!   1115
LEADER: Still lost. Her riddles, her dark words of god—
  I'm groping, helpless.
CASSANDRA: No no, look *there!*—
  what's that? some net flung out of hell—
   No, *she* is the snare,
  the bedmate, deathmate, murder's strong right arm!   1120
    Let the insatiate discord in the race
  rear up and shriek "Avenge the victim—stone them dead!"
LEADER: What Fury is this? Why rouse it, lift its wailing
  through the house? I hear you and lose hope.
CHORUS: Drop by drop at the heart, the gold of life ebbs out.   1125
    We are the old soldiers . . . wounds will come
  with the crushing sunset of our lives.
  Death is close, and quick.
CASSANDRA: Look out! *look out!*—
  Ai, drag the great bull from the mate!—
    a thrash of robes, she traps him—   1130
  writhing—
     black horn glints, twists—
                 she gores him through!
    And now he buckles, look, the bath swirls red—
There's stealth and murder in the cauldron, do you hear?
LEADER: I'm no judge, I've little skill with the oracles,   1135
  but even I know danger when I hear it.
CHORUS: What good are the oracles to men? Words, more words,
  and the hurt comes on us, endless words
  and a seer's techniques have brought us
  terror and the truth.   1140
CASSANDRA: The agony—O I am breaking!—Fate's so hard,
  and the pain that floods my voice is mine alone.
  Why have you brought me here, tormented as I am?
  Why, unless to die with him, why else?
LEADER AND CHORUS: Mad with the rapture—god speeds you on   1145
  to the song, the deathsong,
like the nightingale[6] that broods on sorrow,
  mourns her son, her son,
her life inspired with grief for him,
  she lilts and shrills, dark bird that lives for night.   1150
CASSANDRA: The nightingale—O for a song, a fate like hers!
    The gods gave her a life of ease, swathed her in wings,
  no tears, no wailing. The knife waits for me.

---

6. Philomela was raped by Tereus, the husband of her sister Procne. The two sisters avenged themselves by killing Tereus' son, Itys, and serving up his flesh to Tereus to eat. Procne was changed into a nightingale mourning for Itys (the name is an imitation of the sound of the nightingale's song).

They'll splay me on the iron's double edge.
LEADER AND CHORUS: Why?—what god hurls you on, stroke on stroke   1155
    to the long dying fall?
Why the horror clashing through your music,
    terror struck to song?—
why the anguish, the wild dance?
Where do your words of god and grief begin?   1160
CASSANDRA: Ai, the wedding, wedding of Paris,
death to the loved ones. Oh Scamander,[7]
you nursed my father . . . once at your banks
    I nursed and grew, and now at the banks
of Acheron[8] the stream that carries sorrow,   1165
it seems I'll chant my prophecies too soon.
LEADER AND CHORUS: What are you saying? Wait, it's clear,
a child could see the truth, it wounds within,
      like a bloody fang it tears—
    I hear your destiny—breaking sobs,   1170
    cries that stab the ears.
CASSANDRA: Oh the grief, the grief of the city
ripped to oblivion. Oh the victims,
the flocks my father burned at the wall,
    rich herds in flames . . . no cure for the doom   1175
that took the city after all, and I,
her last ember, I go down with her.
LEADER AND CHORUS: You cannot stop, your song goes on—
some spirit drops from the heights and treads you down
      and the brutal strain grows—   1180
    your death-throes come and come and
      I cannot see the end!
CASSANDRA: Then off with the veils that hid the fresh young
    bride[9]—
we will see the truth.   1185
Flare up once more, my oracle! Clear and sharp
as the wind that blows toward the rising sun,
I can feel a deeper swell now, gathering head
to break at last and bring the dawn of grief.

No more riddles. I will teach you.   1190
Come, bear witness, run and hunt with me.
We trail the old barbaric works of slaughter.

These roofs—look up—there is a dancing troupe
that never leaves. And they have their harmony
but it is harsh, their words are harsh, they drink   1195
beyond the limit. Flushed on the blood of men
their spirit grows and none can turn away
their revel breeding in the veins—the Furies!

---

7. A Trojan river.   8. One of the rivers of the underworld.   9. At this point, as the meter indicates,
Cassandra changes from lyric song, the medium of emotion, to spoken iambic lines, the medium of
rational discourse.

They cling to the house for life. They sing,
sing of the frenzy that began it all,   1200
strain rising on strain, showering curses
on the man who tramples on his brother's bed.[1]

There. Have I hit the mark or not? Am I a fraud,
a fortune-teller babbling lies from door to door?
Swear how well I know the ancient crimes   1205
that live within this house.

LEADER: And if I did?
Would an oath bind the wounds and heal us?
But you amaze me. Bred across the sea,
your language strange, and still you sense the truth
as if you had been here.

CASSANDRA: Apollo the Prophet   1210
introduced me to his gift.

LEADER: A *god*—and moved with love?

CASSANDRA: I was ashamed to tell this once,
but now . . .

LEADER: We spoil ourselves with scruples,
long as things go well.

CASSANDRA: He came like a wrestler,   1215
magnificent, took me down and breathed his fire
through me and—

LEADER: You bore him a child?

CASSANDRA: I yielded,
then at the climax I recoiled—I deceived Apollo!

LEADER: But the god's skills—they seized you even then?

CASSANDRA: Even then I told my people all the grief to come.   1220

LEADER: And Apollo's anger never touched you?—is it possible?

CASSANDRA: Once I betrayed him I could never be believed.

LEADER: We believe you. Your visions seem so true.

CASSANDRA: Aieeeee!—
the pain, the terror! the birth-pang of the seer
who tells the truth—
                        it whirls me, oh,   1225
the storm comes again, the crashing chords!
Look, you see them nestling at the threshold?
Young, young in the darkness like a dream,
like children really, yes, and their loved ones
brought them down . . .
                        their hands, they fill their hands   1230
with their own flesh, they are serving it like food,
holding out their entrails . . . now it's clear,
I can see the armfuls of compassion, see the father
reach to taste and—
                        For so much suffering,
I tell you, someone plots revenge.   1235

---

1. Thyestes, who seduced the wife of his brother, Atreus.

A lion[2] who lacks a lion's heart,
he sprawled at home in the royal lair
and set a trap for the lord on his return.
My lord . . . I must wear his yoke, I am his slave.
The lord of the men-of-war, he obliterated Troy—   1240
he is so blind, so lost to that detestable hellhound
who pricks her ears and fawns and her tongue draws out
her glittering words of welcome—
                          No, he cannot see
the stroke that Fury's hiding, stealth, murder.
What outrage—the woman kills the man!
                              What to call   1245
that . . . monster of Greece, and bring my quarry down?
Viper coiling back and forth?
                          Some sea-witch?—
Scylla[3] crouched in her rocky nest—nightmare of sailors?
Raging mother of death, storming deathless war against
the ones she loves!
                          And how she howled in triumph,   1250
boundless outrage. Just as the tide of battle
broke her way, she seems to rejoice that he
is safe at home from war, saved for her.
Believe me if you will. What will it matter
if you won't? It comes when it comes,   1255
and soon you'll see it face to face
and say the seer was all too true.
You will be moved with pity.
LEADER: Thyestes' feast,
the children's flesh—that I know,
and the fear shudders through me. It's true,   1260
real, no dark signs about it. I hear the rest
but it throws me off the scent.
CASSANDRA: Agamemnon.
You will see him dead.
LEADER: Peace, poor girl!
Put those words to sleep.
CASSANDRA: No use,
the Healer[4] has no hand in this affair.   1265
LEADER: Not if it's true—but god forbid it is!
CASSANDRA: You pray, and they close in to kill!
LEADER: What man prepares this, this dreadful—
CASSANDRA: Man?
You *are* lost, to every word I've said.
LEADER: Yes—
I don't see who can bring the evil off.   1270
CASSANDRA: And yet I know my Greek, too well.

---

2. Aegisthus.   3. A human-eating sea monster (see *Odyssey* XII, p. 183).   4. Apollo.

LEADER: So does the Delphic oracle,[5]
  but he's hard to understand.
CASSANDRA: His *fire!*—
sears me, sweeps me again—the torture!
Apollo Lord of the Light, you burn,   1275
you blind me—
                Agony!
                      She is the lioness,
she rears on her hind legs, she beds with the wolf
when her lion king goes ranging—
                              she will kill me—
Ai, the torture!
              She is mixing her drugs,
adding a measure more of hate for me.   1280
She gloats as she whets the sword for him.
He brought me home and we will pay in carnage.

Why mock yourself with these—trappings, the rod,
the god's wreath, his yoke around my throat?
Before I die I'll tread you—
  [*Ripping off her regalia, stamping it into the ground.*]
                              Down, out,   1285
die die die!
Now you're down. I've paid you back.
Look for another victim—I am free at last—
make her rich in all your curse and doom.
  [*Staggering backwards as if wrestling with a spirit tearing at her
  robes.*]
                                    See,
Apollo himself, his fiery hands—I feel him again,   1290
he's stripping off my robes, the Seer's robes!
And after he looked down and saw me mocked,
even in these, his glories, mortified by friends
I loved, and they hated me, they were so blind
to their own demise—
                    I went from door to door,   1295
I was wild with the god, I heard them call me
"Beggar! Wretch! Starve for bread in hell!"

And I endured it all, and now he will
extort me as his due. A seer for the Seer.
He brings me here to die like this,   1300
not to serve at my father's altar. No,
the block is waiting. The cleaver steams
with my life blood, the first blood drawn
for the king's last rites.
  [*Regaining her composure and moving to the altar.*]

---

5. Its replies were celebrated for their obscurity and ambiguity.

We will die,
but not without some honor from the gods.   1305
There will come another[6] to avenge us,
born to kill his mother, born
his father's champion. A wanderer, a fugitive
driven off his native land, he will come home
to cope the stones of hate that menace all he loves.   1310
The gods have sworn a monumental oath: as his father lies
upon the ground he draws him home with power like a prayer.

Then why so pitiful, why so many tears?
I have seen my city faring as she fared,
and those who took her, judged by the gods,   1315
faring as they fare. I must be brave.
It is my turn to die.
     [Approaching the doors.]
I address you as the Gates of Death.
I pray it comes with one clear stroke,
no convulsions, the pulses ebbing out   1320
in gentle death. I'll close my eyes and sleep.
LEADER: So much pain, poor girl, and so much truth,
     you've told so much. But if you *see* it coming,
     clearly—how can you go to your own death,
     like a beast to the altar driven on by god,   1325
     and hold your head so high?
CASSANDRA: No escape, my friends,
     not now.
LEADER: But the last hour should be savored.
CASSANDRA: My time has come. Little to gain from flight.
LEADER: You're brave, believe me, full of gallant heart.
CASSANDRA: Only the wretched go with praise like that.
LEADER: But to go nobly lends a man some grace.   1330
CASSANDRA: My noble father—you and your noble children.
     [She nears the threshold and recoils, groaning in revulsion.]
LEADER: What now? what terror flings you back?
     Why? Unless some horror in the brain—
CASSANDRA: Murder.
     The house breathes with murder—bloody shambles![7]   1335
LEADER: No, no, only the victims at the hearth.
CASSANDRA: I know that odor. I smell the open grave.
LEADER: But the Syrian myrrh,[8] it fills the halls with splendor,
     can't you sense it?
CASSANDRA: Well, I must go in now,
     mourning Agamemnon's death and mine.   1340
     Enough of life!
     [Approaching the doors again and crying out.]

6. Orestes.   7. A slaughterhouse.   8. Incense burned at the sacrifice. Another interpretation of this
line runs, "What you speak of (that is, the smell of the open grave) is no Syrian incense, giving splendor
to the palace."

Friends—I cried out,
not from fear like a bird fresh caught,
but that you will testify to *how* I died.
When the queen, woman for woman, dies for me,
and a man falls for the man who married grief.   1345
That's all I ask, my friends. A stranger's gift
for one about to die.
LEADER: Poor creature, you
and the end you see so clearly. I pity you.
CASSANDRA: I'd like a few words more, a kind of dirge,
it is my own. I pray to the sun,   1350
the last light I'll see,
that when the avengers cut the assassins down
they will avenge me too, a slave who died,
an easy conquest.
                    Oh men, your destiny.
When all is well a shadow can overturn it.   1355
When trouble comes a stroke of the wet sponge,
and the picture's blotted out. And that,
I think that breaks the heart.

[*She goes through the doors.*]

CHORUS: But the lust for power never dies—
men cannot have enough.   1360
No one will lift a hand to send it
from his door, to give it warning,
"Power, never come again!"
Take this man: the gods in glory
gave him Priam's city to plunder,   1365
brought him home in splendor like a god.
But now if he must pay for the blood
his fathers shed, and die for the deaths
he brought to pass, and bring more death
to avenge his dying, show us one   1370
who boasts himself born free
of the raging angel, once he hears—

[*Cries break out within the palace.*]

AGAMEMNON: Aagh!
Struck deep—the death-blow, deep—
LEADER: Quiet. Cries,
but who? Someone's stabbed—
AGAMEMNON: Aaagh, again . . .
second blow—struck home.
LEADER: The work is done,   1375
you can feel it. The king, and the great cries—
Close ranks now, find the right way out.

[*But the old men scatter, each speaks singly.*]

CHORUS:—I say send out heralds, muster the guard,
they'll save the house.

—And I say rush in now,
catch them red-handed—butchery running on their blades.   1380

—Right with you, do something—now or never!

—Look at them, beating the drum for insurrection.

—Yes,
we're wasting time. They rape the name of caution,
their hands will never sleep.

—Not a plan in sight.
Let men of action do the planning, too.   1385

—I'm helpless. Who can raise the dead with words?

—What, drag out our lives? bow down to the tyrants,
the ruin of the house?

—Never, better to die
on your feet than live on your knees.

—Wait,
do we take the cries for signs, prophesy like seers   1390
and give him up for dead?

—No more suspicions,
not another word till we have proof.

—Confusion
on all sides—one thing to do. See how it stands
with Agamemnon, once and for all we'll see—
[*He rushes at the doors. They open and reveal a silver cauldron that
holds the body of* AGAMEMNON *shrouded in bloody robes, with the
body of* CASSANDRA *to his left and* CLYTAEMNESTRA *standing to his
right, sword in hand. She strides towards the* CHORUS.]
CLYTAEMNESTRA: Words, endless words I've said to serve the moment— 1395
Now it makes me proud to tell the truth.
How else to prepare a death for deadly men
who seem to love you? How to rig the nets
of pain so high no man can overleap them?
I brooded on this trial, this ancient blood feud   1400
year by year. At last my hour came.
Here I stand and here I struck
and here my work is done.
I did it all. I don't deny it, no.
He had no way to flee or fight his destiny—   1405
[*Unwinding the robes from* AGAMEMNON'*s body, spreading them
before the altar where the old men cluster around them, unified as a
chorus once again.*]
our never-ending, all embracing net, I cast it
wide for the royal haul, I coil him round and round
in the wealth, the robes of doom, and then I strike him
once, twice, and at each stroke he cries in agony—

he buckles at the knees and crashes here! 1410
And when he's down I add the third, last blow,
to the Zeus who saves the dead beneath the ground
I send that third blow home in homage like a prayer.[9]

So he goes down, and the life is bursting out of him—
great sprays of blood, and the murderous shower 1415
wounds me, dyes me black and I, I revel
like the Earth when the spring rains come down,
the blessed gifts of god, and the new green spear
splits the sheath and rips to birth in glory!

So it stands, elders of Argos gathered here. 1420
Rejoice if you can rejoice—I glory.
And if I'd pour upon his body the libation
it deserves, what wine could match my words?
It is right and more than right. He flooded
the vessel of our proud house with misery, 1425
with the vintage of the curse and now
he drains the dregs. My lord is home at last.
LEADER: You appall me, you, your brazen words—
exulting over your fallen king.
CLYTAEMNESTRA: And you,
you try me like some desperate woman. 1430
My heart is steel, well you know. Praise me,
blame me as you choose. It's all one.
Here is Agamemnon, my husband made a corpse
by this right hand—a masterpiece of Justice.
Done is done.
CHORUS: Woman!—what poison cropped from the soil 1435
or strained from the heaving sea, what nursed you,
drove you insane? You brave the curse of Greece.
     You have cut away and flung away and now
the people cast you off to exile,
broken with our hate.
CLYTAEMNESTRA: And now you sentence me?— 1440
you banish *me* from the city, curses breathing
down my neck? But *he*—
name one charge you brought against him then.
He thought no more of it than killing a beast,
and his flocks were rich, teeming in their fleece, 1445
but he sacrificed his own child, our daughter,
the agony I labored into love,
to charm away the savage winds of Thrace.[1]

Didn't the law demand you banish him?—
hunt him from the land for all his guilt? 1450
But now you witness what I've done
and you are ruthless judges.

9. Like the third libation to Zeus (see n. 7, p. 350).   1. Winds from the North (at Aulis).

Threaten away!
I'll meet you blow for blow. And if I fall
the throne is yours. If god decrees the reverse,
late as it is, old men, you'll learn your place.   1455
CHORUS: Mad with ambition,
        shrilling pride!—some Fury
crazed with the carnage rages through your brain—
    I can see the flecks of blood inflame your eyes!
But vengeance comes—you'll lose your loved ones,   1460
stroke for painful stroke.
CLYTAEMNESTRA: Then learn this, too, the power of my oaths.
By the child's Rights I brought to birth,
by Ruin, by Fury—the three gods to whom
I sacrificed this man—I swear my hopes   1465
will never walk the halls of fear so long
as Aegisthus lights the fire on my hearth.
Loyal to me as always, no small shield
to buttress my defiance.
                    Here he lies.
He brutalized me. The darling of all   1470
the golden girls[2] who spread the gates of Troy.
And here his spearprize . . . what wonders she beheld!—
the seer of Apollo shared my husband's bed,
his faithful mate who knelt at the rowing-benches,
worked by every hand.
                    They have their rewards.   1475
He as you know. And she, the swan of the gods
who lived to sing her latest, dying song—
his lover lies beside him.
She brings a fresh, voluptuous relish to my bed!
CHORUS: Oh quickly, let me die—   1480
no bed of labor, no, no wasting illness . . .
bear me off in the sleep that never ends,
    now that he has fallen,
now that our dearest shield lies battered—
    Woman made him suffer,   1485
    woman struck him down.

        Helen the wild, maddening Helen,
        one for the many, the thousand lives
        you murdered under Troy. Now you are crowned
        with this consummate wreath, the blood   1490
        that lives in memory, glistens age to age.
        Once in the halls she walked and she was war,
        angel of war, angel of agony, lighting men to death

CLYTAEMNESTRA: Pray no more for death, broken
as you are. And never turn   1495

2. In Greek *chryseidon*, which recalls the girl in the first book of the *Iliad*, Chryseis, whom Agamemnon
said he preferred to Clytaemnestra.

your wrath on her, call her
the scourge of men, the one alone
who destroyed a myriad Greek lives—
Helen the grief that never heals.
CHORUS: The *spirit!*—you who tread   1500
the house and the twinborn sons of Tantalus[3]—
you empower the sisters, Fury's twins
    whose power tears the heart!
Perched on the corpse your carrion raven
    glories in her hymn,   1505
       her screaming hymn of pride.
CLYTAEMNESTRA: Now you set your judgment straight,
  you summon *him!* Three generations
    feed the spirit in the race.
Deep in the veins he feeds our bloodlust—   1510
aye, before the old wound dies
it ripens in another flow of blood.
CHORUS: The great curse of the house, the spirit,
    dead weight wrath—and you can praise it!
Praise the insatiate doom that feeds   1515
relentless on our future and our sons.
Oh all through the will of Zeus,
the cause of all, the one who works it all.
    What comes to birth that is not Zeus?
Our lives are pain, what part not come from god?   1520

    Oh, my king, my captain,
    how to salute you, how to mourn you?
    What can I say with all my warmth and love?
    Here in the black widow's web you lie,
    gasping out your life   1525
    in a sacrilegious death, dear god,
    reduced to a slave's bed,
    my king of men, yoked by stealth and Fate,
    by the wife's hand that thrust the two-edged sword.

CLYTAEMNESTRA: You claim the work is mine, call me   1530
Agamemnon's wife—you are so wrong.
Fleshed in the wife of this dead man,
    the spirit lives within me,
  our savage ancient spirit of revenge.
In return for Atreus' brutal feast   1535
he kills his perfect son—for every
murdered child, a crowning sacrifice.
CHORUS: And *you,* innocent of his murder?
    And who could swear to that? and how? . . .
and still an avenger could arise,   1540
bred by the fathers' crimes, and lend a hand.
He wades in the blood of brothers,

---

3. Father of Pelops, grandfather of Atreus. *Sons:* descendants—that is, Agamemnon and Menelaus.

stream on mounting stream—black war erupts
  and where he strides revenge will stride,
clots will mass for the young who were devoured.   1545

  Oh my king, my captain,
  how to salute you, how to mourn you?
  What can I say with all my warmth and love?
  Here in the black widow's web you lie,
  gasping out your life   1550
  in a sacrilegious death, dear god,
  reduced to a slave's bed,
  my king of men, yoked by stealth and Fate,
  by the wife's hand that thrust the two-edged sword.

CLYTAEMNESTRA: No slave's death, I think—   1555
no stealthier than the death he dealt
our house and the offspring of our loins,
  Iphigeneia, girl of tears.
Act for act, wound for wound!
Never exult in Hades, swordsman,   1560
here you are repaid. By the sword
you did your work and by the sword you die.

CHORUS: The mind reels—where to turn?
              All plans dashed, all hope! I cannot think . . .
        the roofs are toppling, I dread the drumbeat thunder   1565
            the heavy rains of blood will crush the house
                the first light rains are over—
              Justice brings new acts of agony, yes,
    on new grindstones Fate is grinding sharp the sword of Justice.
Earth, dear Earth,   1570
if only you'd drawn me under
long before I saw him huddled
in the beaten silver bath.
Who will bury him, lift his dirge?
  [*Turning to* CLYTAEMNESTRA.]
You, can you dare *this?*   1575
To kill your lord with your own hand
then mourn his soul with tributes, terrible tributes—
do his enormous works a great dishonor.
This godlike man, this hero. Who at the grave
will sing his praises, pour the wine of tears?   1580
Who will labor there with truth of heart?
CLYTAEMNESTRA: This is no concern of yours.
The hand that bore and cut him down
will hand him down to Mother Earth.
This house will never mourn for him.   1585
  Only our daughter Iphigeneia,
by all rights, will rush to meet him
first at the churning straits,[4]

---

4. The river of the underworld over which the dead were ferried.

the ferry over tears—
she'll fling her arms around her father,   1590
pierce him with her love.

CHORUS: Each charge meets counter-charge.
                    None can judge between them. Justice.
          The plunderer plundered, the killer pays the price.
          The truth still holds while Zeus still holds the throne: 1595
                    the one who acts must suffer—
               that is law. Who, who can tear from the veins
            the bad seed, the curse? The race is welded to its ruin.

CLYTAEMNESTRA: At last you see the future and the truth!
     But I will swear a pact with the spirit   1600
     born within us. I embrace his works,
     cruel as they are but done at last,
          if he will leave our house
     in the future, bleed another line
     with kinsmen murdering kinsmen.   1605
     Whatever he may ask. A few things
     are all I need, once I have purged
     our fury to destroy each other—
          purged it from our halls.
     [AEGISTHUS *has emerged from the palace with his bodyguard and*
     stands triumphant over the body of AGAMEMNON.]
AEGISTHUS: O what a brilliant day
     it is for vengeance! Now I can say once more   1610
     there are gods in heaven avenging men,
     blazing down on all the crimes of earth.
     Now at last I see this man brought down
     in the Furies' tangling robes. It feasts my eyes—
     he pays for the plot his father's hand contrived.   1615

     Atreus, this man's father, was king of Argos.
     My father, Thyestes—let me make this clear—
     Atreus' brother challenged him for the crown,
     and Atreus drove him out of house and home
     then lured him back, and home Thyestes came,   1620
     poor man, a suppliant to his own hearth,
     to pray that Fate might save him.
                              So it did.
     There was no dying, no staining our native ground
     with *his* blood. Thyestes was the guest,
     and this man's godless father—   1625
          [*Pointing to* AGAMEMNON.]
     the zeal of the host outstripping a brother's love,
     made my father a feast that seemed a feast for gods,
     a love feast of his children's flesh.

He cuts
the extremities, feet and delicate hands
into small pieces, scatters them over the dish   1630
and serves it to Thyestes throned on high.
He picks at the flesh he cannot recognize,
the soul of innocence eating the food of ruin—
look,
    [*Pointing to the bodies at his feet.*]
    that feeds upon the house! And then,
when he sees the monstrous thing he's done, he shrieks,   1635
he reels back head first and vomits up that butchery,
tramples the feast—brings down the curse of Justice:
"Crash to ruin, all the race of Pleisthenes,[5] crash down!"

So you see him, down. And I, the weaver of Justice,
plotted out the kill. Atreus drove us into exile,   1640
my struggling father and I, a babe-in-arms,
his last son, but I became a man
and Justice brought me home. I was abroad
but I reached out and seized my man,
link by link I clamped the fatal scheme   1645
together. Now I could die gladly, even I—
now I see this monster in the nets of Justice.
LEADER: Aegisthus, you revel in pain—you sicken me.
    You say you killed the king in cold blood,
singlehanded planned his pitiful death?   1650
I say there's no escape. In the hour of judgment,
trust to this, your head will meet the people's
rocks and curses.
AEGISTHUS: You say! you slaves at the oars—
while the master of the benches cracks the whip?
You'll learn, in your late age, how much it hurts   1655
to teach old bones their place. We have techniques—
chains and the pangs of hunger,
two effective teachers, excellent healers.
They can even cure old men of pride and gall.
Look—can't you see? The more you kick   1660
against the pricks, the more you suffer.
LEADER: You, pathetic—
    the king had just returned from battle.
You waited out the war and fouled his lair,
you planned my great commander's fall.
AEGISTHUS: Talk on—   1665
you'll scream for every word, my little Orpheus.[6]
We'll see if the world comes dancing to your song,
your absurd barking—snarl your breath away!
I'll make you dance, I'll bring you all to heel.

---

5. A name sometimes inserted into the genealogy of the house of Tantalus.   6. A mythical singer
who charmed all nature with his music.

LEADER: *You* rule Argos? You who schemed his death   1670
    but cringed to cut him down with your own hand?
AEGISTHUS: The treachery was the woman's work, clearly.
    I was a marked man, his enemy for ages.
    But I will use his riches, stop at nothing
    to civilize his people. All but the rebel: 1675
    him I'll yoke and break—
    no cornfed colt, running free in the traces.
    Hunger, ruthless mate of the dark torture-chamber,
    trains her eyes upon him till he drops!
LEADER: Coward, why not kill the man yourself?   1680
    Why did the woman, the corruption of Greece
    and the gods of Greece, have to bring him down?
    Orestes—If he still sees the light of day,
    bring him home, good Fates, home to kill
    this pair at last. Our champion in slaughter!   1685
AEGISTHUS: Bent on insolence? Well, you'll learn, quickly.
    At them, men—you have your work at hand!
        [*His men draw swords; the old men take up their sticks.*]
LEADER: At them, fist at the hilt, to the last man—
AEGISTHUS: Fist at the hilt, I'm not afraid to die.
LEADER: It's death you want and death you'll have—   1690
    we'll make that word your last.
        [CLYTAEMNESTRA *moves between them, restraining* AEGISTHUS.]
CLYTAEMNESTRA: No more, my dearest,
    no more grief. We have too much to reap
    right here, our mighty harvest of despair.
    Our lives are based on pain. No bloodshed now.

    Fathers of Argos, turn for home before you act   1695
    and suffer for it. What we did was destiny.
    If we could end the suffering, how we would rejoice.
    The spirit's brutal hoof has struck our heart.
    And that is what a woman has to say.
    Can you accept the truth?
        [CLYTAEMNESTRA *turns to leave.*]
AEGISTHUS: But these . . . mouths   1700
    that bloom in filth—spitting insults in my teeth.
    You tempt your fates, you insubordinate dogs—
    to hurl abuse at me, your master!
LEADER: No Greek
    worth his salt would grovel at your feet.
AEGISTHUS: I—I'll stalk you all your days!   1705
LEADER: Not if the spirit brings Orestes home.
AEGISTHUS: Exiles feed on hope—well I know.
LEADER: More,
    gorge yourself to bursting—soil justice, while you can.
AEGISTHUS: I promise you, you'll pay, old fools—in good time, too!
LEADER: Strut on your own dunghill, you cock beside your mate.   1710

CLYTAEMNESTRA: Let them howl—they're impotent. You and I have
power now.
We will set the house in order once for all.
[*They enter the palace; the great doors close behind them; the old
men disband and wander off.*]

SOPHOCLES
ca. 496–406 B.C.

Aeschylus belonged to the generation that fought at Marathon; his manhood and
his old age were passed in the heroic period of the Persian defeat on Greek soil
and the war that Athens fought to liberate its kin in the islands of the Aegean and
on the Asiatic coast. Sophocles, his younger contemporary, lived to see an Athens
that had advanced in power and prosperity far beyond the city that Aeschylus
knew. The league of free Greek cities against Persia that Athens had led to victory
in the Aegean had become an empire, in which Athens taxed and coerced the
subject cities that had once been its free allies. Sophocles, born around 496 B.C.,
played his part—a prominent one—in the city's affairs. In 443 B.C. he served as
one of the treasurers of the imperial league and, with Pericles, as one of the ten
generals elected for the war against the island of Samos, which tried to secede
from the Athenian league a few years later. When the Athenian expedition to
Sicily ended in disaster, Sophocles was appointed to a special committee set up in
411 B.C. to deal with the emergency. He died two years before Athens surrendered
to Sparta.

His career as a brilliantly successful dramatist began in 468; in that year he won
first prize at the Dionysia, competing against Aeschylus. Over the next sixty-two
years he produced more than 120 plays. He won first prize no fewer than twenty-
four times, and when he was not first, he came in second, never third.

Aeschylus had been an actor as well as a playwright and director, but Sophocles,
early in his career, gave up acting. It was he who added a third actor to the team;
the early Aeschylean plays (*Persians*, *Seven Against Thebes*, and *Suppliants*) can
be played by two actors (who of course can change masks to extend the range of
dramatis personae). In the *Oresteia*, Aeschylus has taken advantage of the Sophoclean third actor; this makes possible the role of Cassandra. But Sophocles used
his third actor to create complex triangular scenes like the dialogue between Oedipus and the Corinthian messenger, which reveals to a listening Jocasta the ghastly
truth that Oedipus will not discover until the next scene.

We have only seven of his plays, and not many of them can be accurately dated.
Ajax (which deals with the suicide of the hero whose shade turns silently away
from Odysseus in the *Odyssey*) and *Trachiniae* (the story of the death of Heracles)
are both generally thought to be early productions. *Antigone* is fairly securely fixed
in the late 440s, and *Oedipus the King* was probably staged during the early years
of the Peloponnesian War (431–404 B.C.). For *Electra* we have no date, but it is
probably later than *Oedipus the King*. *Philoctetes*, a tale of the Trojan War, was
staged in 409 B.C. and *Oedipus at Colonus*, which presents Oedipus' strangely
triumphant death on Athenian soil, was produced after Sophocles' death.

Most of these plays date from the last half of the fifth century B.C.; they were written in and for an Athens that, since the days of Aeschylus, had undergone an intellectual revolution. It was in a time of critical reevaluation of accepted standards and traditions (see p. 91) that Sophocles produced his masterpiece, *Oedipus the King*, and the problems of the time are reflected in the play.

OEDIPUS THE KING

This tragedy, which deals with a man of high principles and probing intelligence who follows the prompting of that intelligence to the final consequence of true self-knowledge—which makes him put out his eyes—was as full of significance for Sophocles' contemporaries as it is for us. Unlike a modern dramatist, Sophocles used for his tragedy a story well known to the audience and as old as their own history, a legend told by parent to child, handed down from generation to generation because of its implicit wealth of meaning, learned in childhood, and rooted deep in the consciousness of every member of the community. Such a story the Greeks called a myth, and the use of it presented Sophocles, as it did Aeschylus in his trilogy, with material that, apart from its great inherent dramatic potential, already possessed the significance and authority that modern dramatists must create for themselves. It had the authority of history, for the history of ages that leave no records is myth—that is to say, the significant event of the past, stripped of irrelevancies and imaginatively shaped by the oral tradition. It had a religious authority, for the Oedipus story, like the story of the house of Atreus, is concerned with the relation between humanity and gods. Last, and this is especially true of the Oedipus myth, it had the power, because of its subject matter, to arouse the irrational hopes and fears that lie deep and secret in the human consciousness.

The use of the familiar myth enabled the dramatist to draw on all its wealth of unformulated meaning, but it did not prevent him from striking a contemporary note. Oedipus, in Sophocles' play, is at one and the same time the mysterious figure of the past who broke the most fundamental human taboos and a typical fifth-century Athenian. His character contains all the virtues for which the Athenians were famous and the vices for which they were notorious. The best commentary on Oedipus' character is the speech that Thucydides, the contemporary historian of the Peloponnesian War, attributed to a Corinthian spokesman at Sparta; it is a hostile but admiring assessment of the Athenian genius. "Athenians . . . [are] equally quick in the conception and in the execution of every new plan"—so Oedipus has already sent to Delphi when the priest advises him to do so and has already sent for Tiresias when the chorus suggests this course of action. "They are bold beyond their strength; they run risks which prudence would condemn"—as Oedipus risked his life to answer the riddle of the Sphinx and later, in spite of the oracle about his marriage, accepted the hand of the queen. "In the midst of misfortune they are full of hope"—so Oedipus, when he is told that he is not the son of Polybus and Merope, and Jocasta has already realized whose son he is, claims that he is the "child of Fortune." "When they do not carry out an intention that they have formed, they seem to have sustained a personal bereavement"—so Oedipus, shamed by Jocasta and the chorus into sparing Creon's life, yields sullenly and petulantly.

The Athenian devotion to the city, which received the main emphasis in Pericles' praise of Athens, is strong in Oedipus; his answer to the priest at the beginning of the play shows that he is a conscientious and patriotic ruler. His sudden unreasoning rage is the characteristic fault of Athenian democracy, which in 406 B.C., to give only one instance, condemned and executed the generals who had failed, in the stress of weather and battle, to pick up the drowned bodies of their own men killed in the naval engagement at Arginusae. Oedipus is like the fifth-century Athenian most of all in his confidence in the human intelligence, especially his own. This confidence takes him in the play through the whole cycle of the critical, rationalist movement of the century, from the piety and orthodoxy he displays in the opening scene, through his taunts at oracles when he hears that Polybus is dead, to the despairing courage with which he accepts the consequences when he sees the abyss opening at his feet. "I'm right at the edge, the horrible truth—I've got to say it!" says the herdsman from whom he is dragging the truth. "And I'm right at the edge of hearing horrors, yes," Oedipus replies, "but I must hear!" And hear he does. He learns that the oracle he had first fought against and then laughed at has been fulfilled, that every step his intelligence prompted was one step nearer to disaster, that his knowledge was ignorance and his clear vision blindness. Faced with the reality that his determined probing finally reveals, he puts out his eyes.

The relation of Oedipus' character to the development of the action is the basis of the most famous attempt to define the nature of the tragic process. Aristotle, in his *Poetics* written in the next century, developed the theory that pity and terror are aroused most effectively by the spectacle of a man who is "not pre-eminent in virtue and justice, and yet on the other hand does not fall into misfortune through vice or depravity, but falls because of some mistake, one among the number of the highly renowned and prosperous, such as Oedipus." Other references by Aristotle to this play make it clear that this influential doctrine of the fall of the tragic hero was based particularly on Sophocles' masterpiece, and it has been universally applied to the play. But the great influence (and validity) of the Aristotelian theory should not be allowed to obscure the fact that Sophocles' *Oedipus the King* is more highly organized and economical than Aristotle implies. The fact that the critics have differed about the nature of Oedipus' mistake or frailty (his errors are many, and his frailties include anger, impiety, and self-confidence) is a clue to the real situation. Oedipus falls not through "some vicious mole of nature" or some "particular fault" (to use Hamlet's terms) but because he is the man he is, because of all aspects of his character, good and bad alike; and the development of the action right through to the catastrophe shows us every aspect of his character at work in the process of self-revelation and self-destruction. His first decision in the play, to hear Creon's message from Delphi in public rather than, as Creon suggests, in private, is evidence of his kingly solicitude for his people and his trust in them, but it makes certain the full publication of the truth. His impetuous proclamation of a curse on the murderer of Laius, an unnecessary step prompted by his civic zeal, makes his final situation worse than it need have been. His anger at Tiresias forces a revelation that drives him on to accuse Creon, this in turn provokes Jocasta's revelations. And throughout the play his confidence in the efficacy of his own action, his hopefulness as the situation darkens, and his passion for discovering the truth guide the steps of the investigation that is to reveal the detective as the criminal. All aspects of his character, good and bad alike, are equally involved; it is no frailty or error that leads him to the terrible truth, but his total personality.

The character of Oedipus as revealed in the play does something more than explain the present action; it also explains his past. In Oedipus' speeches and actions on stage we can see the man who, given the circumstances in which Oedipus was involved, would inevitably do just what Oedipus has done. Each action on stage shows us the mood in which he committed some action in the past; his angry death sentence on Creon reveals the man who killed Laius because of an insult on the highway; his impulsive proclamation of total excommunication for the unknown murderer shows us the man who, without forethought, accepted the hand of Jocasta; his intelligent, persistent search for the truth shows us the brain and the courage that solved the riddle of the Sphinx. The revelation of his character in the play is at once a re-creation of his past and an interpretation of the oracle that predicted his future.

This organization of the material is what makes it possible for us to accept the story as tragedy at all, for it emphasizes Oedipus' independence of the oracle. When we first see Oedipus, he has already committed the actions for which he is to suffer—actions prophesied, before his birth, by Apollo. But the dramatist's emphasis on Oedipus' character suggests that although Apollo has predicted what Oedipus will do, he does not determine it; Oedipus determines his own conduct, by being the man he is. Milton's explanation of a similar situation, Adam's fall and God's foreknowledge of it, may be applied to Oedipus; foreknowledge had no influence on his fault. The relationship between Apollo's prophecy and Oedipus' actions is not that of cause and effect. It is the relationship of two independent entities that are equated.

This correspondence between his character and his fate removes the obstacle to our full acceptance of the play that an external fate governing his action would set up. Nevertheless, we feel that he suffers more than he deserves. He has served as an example of the inadequacy of the human intellect and a warning that there is a power in the universe that humanity cannot control or even fully understand, but Oedipus the man still has our sympathy. Sophocles felt this too, and in his last play, *Oedipus at Colonus*, he dealt with the reward that finally balanced Oedipus' suffering. In *Oedipus the King* itself there is a foreshadowing of this final development; the last scene shows us a man already beginning to recover from the shock of the catastrophe and reasserting a natural superiority.

"I am going—you know on what condition?" he says to Creon when ordered back into the house, and a few lines later Creon has to say bluntly to him: "Still the king, the master of all things? / No more: here your power ends." This renewed imperiousness is the first expression of a feeling on his part that he is not entirely guilty, a beginning of the reconstitution of the magnificent man of the opening scenes; it reaches its fulfillment in the final Oedipus play, *Oedipus at Colonus*, in which he is a titanic figure, confident of his innocence and more masterful than he has ever been.

C. H. Whitman, *Sophocles, A Study in Heroic Humanism* (1951), is a brilliant study that explores an approach very different from that proposed here. For a short, general survey of Sophoclean drama, see P. E. Easterling in *The Cambridge History of Classical Literature* (1985), pp. 295–316. B. M. W. Knox, *Oedipus at Thebes* (1957), is a detailed examination of the play in the context of its age; Knox's *The Heroic Temper* (1964) concentrates on the characters of Oedipus, Antigone, Electra, and Philoctetes. Sophocles, *The Three Theban Plays* (1982), contains a substantial introduction to *Oedipus the King*. See also R. P. Winnington-Ingram, *Sophocles: An Interpretation* (1980), pp. 150–204; and Charles Segal, *An Interpretation of Sophocles* (1981), pp. 207–48.

PRONOUNCING GLOSSARY

The following list uses common English syllables and stress accents to provide rough equivalents of selected words whose pronunciation may be unfamiliar to the general reader.

Antigone: *an-ti'-go-nee*

Oedipus: *ee'-di-pus*

Tiresias: *tai-ree'-see-uhs* / *ti-ray'-see-uhs*

Oedipus the King[1]

CHARACTERS

OEDIPUS, *king of Thebes*

A PRIEST *of Zeus*

CREON, *brother of Jocasta*

A CHORUS *of Theban citizens and*
       their LEADER

TIRESIAS, *a blind prophet*

JOCASTA, *the queen, wife of*
       Oedipus

A MESSENGER *from Corinth*

A SHEPHERD

A MESSENGER *from inside the*
       palace

ANTIGONE, ISMENE, *daughters of*
       Oedipus and Jocasta

GUARDS *and attendants*

PRIESTS *of Thebes*

[TIME AND SCENE: *The royal house of Thebes. Double doors dominate the façade; a stone altar stands at the center of the stage.*

Many years have passed since OEDIPUS *solved the riddle of the Sphinx and ascended the throne of Thebes, and now a plague has struck the city. A procession of priests enters; suppliants, broken and despondent, they carry branches wound in wool and lay them on the altar.*

The doors open. Guards assemble. OEDIPUS *comes forward, majestic but for a telltale limp, and slowly views the condition of his people.*]

OEDIPUS: Oh my children, the new blood of ancient Thebes,
   why are you here? Huddling at my altar,
   praying before me, your branches wound in wool.[2]
   Our city reeks with the smoke of burning incense,
   rings with cries for the Healer[3] and wailing for the dead.   5
   I thought it wrong, my children, to hear the truth
   from others, messengers. Here I am myself—
   you all know me, the world knows my fame:
   I am Oedipus.
      [*Helping a* PRIEST *to his feet.*]
                     Speak up, old man. Your years,
   your dignity—you should speak for the others.   10
   Why here and kneeling, what preys upon you so?
   Some sudden fear? some strong desire?
   You can trust me. I am ready to help,
   I'll do anything. I would be blind to misery
   not to pity my people kneeling at my feet.   15
PRIEST: Oh Oedipus, king of the land, our greatest power!
   You see us before you now, men of all ages
   clinging to your altars. Here are boys,
   still too weak to fly from the nest,
   and here the old, bowed down with the years,   20
   the holy ones—a priest of Zeus myself—and here
   the picked, unmarried men, the young hope of Thebes.
   And all the rest, your great family gathers now,

---

1. Translated by Robert Fagles.   2. The insignia of suppliants, laid on the altar and left there until the suppliant's request was granted. At the end of the scene, when Oedipus promises action, he will tell them to take the branches away.   3. Apollo.

branches wreathed, massing in the squares,
kneeling before the two temples of queen Athena   25
or the river-shrine where the embers glow and die
and Apollo sees the future in the ashes.[4]
                                        Our city—
look around you, see with your own eyes—
our ship pitches wildly, cannot lift her head
from the depths, the red waves of death . . .   30
Thebes is dying. A blight on the fresh crops
and the rich pastures, cattle sicken and die,
and the women die in labor, children stillborn,
and the plague, the fiery god of fever hurls down
on the city, his lightning slashing through us—   35
raging plague in all its vengeance, devastating
the house of Cadmus![5] And black Death luxuriates
in the raw, wailing miseries of Thebes.
Now we pray to you. You cannot equal the gods,
your children know that, bending at your altar.   40
But we do rate you first of men,
both in the common crises of our lives
and face-to-face encounters with the gods.
You freed us from the Sphinx, you came to Thebes
and cut us loose from the bloody tribute we had paid   45
that harsh, brutal singer.[6] We taught you nothing,
no skill, no extra knowledge, still you triumphed.
A god was with you, so they say, and we believe it—
you lifted up our lives.
                          So now again,
Oedipus, king, we bend to you, your power—   50
we implore you, all of us on our knees:
find us strength, rescue! Perhaps you've heard
the voice of a god or something from other men,
Oedipus . . . what do you know?
The man of experience—you see it every day—   55
his plans will work in a crisis, his first of all.

Act now—we beg you, best of men, raise up our city!
Act, defend yourself, your former glory!
Your country calls you savior now
for your zeal, your action years ago.   60
Never let us remember of your reign:
you helped us stand, only to fall once more.
Oh raise up our city, set us on our feet.
The omens were good that day you brought us joy—

---

4. At a temple of Apollo in Thebes the priests foretold the future according to patterns they saw in the ashes of the burned flesh of sacrificial victims.   5. Mythical founder of Thebes and its first king. 6. The sphinx was the winged female monster that terrorized the city of Thebes until her riddle was finally answered by Oedipus. The riddle was "What is it that walks on four feet and two feet and three feet and has only one voice; when it walks on most feet, it is weakest?" Oedipus's answer was "Man." (We have four feet as children crawling on all fours and three feet in old age when we walk with the aid of a stick.) Many young men of Thebes had tried to answer the riddle, failed, and been killed.

be the same man today!   65
Rule our land, you know you have the power,
but rule a land of the living, not a wasteland.
Ship and towered city are nothing, stripped of men
alive within it, living all as one.
OEDIPUS: My children,
I pity you. I see—how could I fail to see   70
what longings bring you here? Well I know
you are sick to death, all of you,
but sick as you are, not one is sick as I.
Your pain strikes each of you alone, each
in the confines of himself, no other. But my spirit   75
grieves for the city, for myself and all of you.
I wasn't asleep, dreaming. You haven't wakened me—
I've wept through the nights, you must know that,
groping, laboring over many paths of thought.
After a painful search I found one cure: 80
I acted at once. I sent Creon,
my wife's own brother, to Delphi—
Apollo the Prophet's oracle[7]—to learn
what I might do or say to save our city.

Today's the day. When I count the days gone by   85
it torments me . . . what is he doing?
Strange, he's late, he's gone too long.
But once he returns, then, then I'll be a traitor
if I do not do all the god makes clear.
PRIEST: Timely words. The men over there   90
are signaling—Creon's just arriving.
OEDIPUS: [*Sighting* CREON, *then turning to the altar.*]
                              Lord Apollo,
let him come with a lucky word of rescue,
shining like his eyes!
PRIEST: Welcome news, I think—he's crowned, look,
and the laurel wreath is bright with berries.[8]   95
OEDIPUS: We'll soon see. He's close enough to hear—
    [*Enter* CREON *from the side; his face is shaded with a wreath.*]
Creon, prince, my kinsman, what do you bring us?
What message from the god?
CREON: Good news.
I tell you even the hardest things to bear,
if they should turn out well, all would be well.   100
OEDIPUS: Of course, but what were the god's *words?* There's no hope
and nothing to fear in what you've said so far.
CREON: If you want my report in the presence of these . . .
    [*Pointing to the priests while drawing* OEDIPUS *toward the palace.*]
I'm ready now, or we might go inside.

7. Below Mount Parnassus in central Greece.   8. Creon is wearing a crown of laurel as a sign that
he brings good news.

OEDIPUS: Speak out,
   speak to us all. I grieve for these, my people,   105
   far more than I fear for my own life.
CREON: Very well,
   I will tell you what I heard from the god.
   Apollo commands us—he was quite clear—
   "Drive the corruption from the land,
   don't harbor it any longer, past all cure,   110
   don't nurse it in your soil—root it out!"
OEDIPUS: How can we cleanse ourselves—what rites?
   What's the source of the trouble?
CREON: Banish the man, or pay back blood with blood.
   Murder sets the plague-storm on the city.
OEDIPUS: Whose murder?   115
   Whose fate does Apollo bring to light?
CREON: Our leader,
   my lord, was once a man named Laius,
   before you came and put us straight on course.
OEDIPUS: I know—
   or so I've heard. I never saw the man myself.
CREON: Well, he was killed, and Apollo commands us now—   120
   he could not be more clear,
   "Pay the killers back—whoever is responsible."
OEDIPUS: Where on earth are they? Where to find it now,
   the trail of the ancient guilt so hard to trace?
CREON: "Here in Thebes," he said.   125
   Whatever is sought for can be caught, you know,
   whatever is neglected slips away.
OEDIPUS: But where,
   in the palace, the fields or foreign soil,
   where did Laius meet his bloody death?
CREON: He went to consult an oracle, Apollo said,   130
   and he set out and never came home again.
OEDIPUS: No messenger, no fellow-traveler saw what happened?
   Someone to cross-examine?
CREON: No,
   they were all killed but one. He escaped,
   terrified, he could tell us nothing clearly,   135
   nothing of what he saw—just one thing.
OEDIPUS: What's that?
   one thing could hold the key to it all,
   a small beginning give us grounds for hope.
CREON: He said thieves attacked them—a whole band,
   not single-handed, cut King Laius down.
OEDIPUS: A thief,   140
   so daring, so wild, he'd kill a king? Impossible,
   unless conspirators paid him off in Thebes.
CREON: We suspected as much. But with Laius dead
   no leader appeared to help us in our troubles.

OEDIPUS: Trouble? Your *king* was murdered—royal blood!   145
  What stopped you from tracking down the killer
  then and there?
CREON: The singing, riddling Sphinx.
  She . . . persuaded us to let the mystery go
  and concentrate on what lay at our feet.
OEDIPUS: No,
  I'll start again—I'll bring it all to light myself!   150
  Apollo is right, and so are you, Creon,
  to turn our attention back to the murdered man.
  Now you have *me* to fight for you, you'll see:
  I am the land's avenger by all rights,
  and Apollo's champion too.   155
  But not to assist some distant kinsman, no,
  for my own sake I'll rid us of this corruption.
  Whoever killed the king may decide to kill me too,
  with the same violent hand—by avenging Laius
  I defend myself.
      [*To the priests.*]
                          Quickly, my children.   160
  Up from the steps, take up your branches now.
      [*To the guards.*]
  One of you summon the city[9] here before us,
  tell them I'll do everything. God help us,
  we will see our triumph—or our fall.
      [OEDIPUS *and* CREON *enter the palace, followed by the guards.*]
PRIEST: Rise, my sons. The kindness we came for   165
  Oedipus volunteers himself.
  Apollo has sent his word, his oracle—
  Come down, Apollo, save us, stop the plague.
      [*The priests rise, remove their branches and exit to the side. Enter a*
      CHORUS, *the citizens of Thebes, who have not heard the news that*
      CREON *brings. They march around the altar, chanting.*]
CHORUS: Zeus!
  Great welcome voice of Zeus,[1] what do you bring?
  What word from the gold vaults of Delphi   170
  comes to brilliant Thebes? Racked with terror—
      terror shakes my heart
  and I cry your wild cries, Apollo, Healer of Delos[2]
  I worship you in dread . . . what now, what is your price?
  some new sacrifice? some ancient rite from the past   175
  come round again each spring?—
      what will you bring to birth?
  Tell me, child of golden Hope
      warm voice that never dies!

9. Represented by the chorus, which comes on to the circular dancing floor immediately after this
scene.   1. Apollo was his son, and spoke for him.   2. A sacred island, Apollo's birthplace.

You are the first I call, daughter of Zeus   180
deathless Athena—I call your sister Artemis,[3]
heart of the market place enthroned in glory,
     guardian of our earth—
I call Apollo, Archer astride the thunderheads of heaven—
O triple shield against death, shine before me now!   185
If ever, once in the past, you stopped some ruin
launched against our walls
    you hurled the flame of pain
far, far from Thebes—you gods
   come now, come down once more!
                      No, no   190
the miseries numberless, grief on grief, no end—
too much to bear, we are all dying
O my people . . .
   Thebes like a great army dying
and there is no sword of thought to save us, no   195
and the fruits of our famous earth, they will not ripen
no and the women cannot scream their pangs to birth—
screams for the Healer, children dead in the womb
   and life on life goes down
     you can watch them go   200
  like seabirds winging west, outracing the day's fire
down the horizon, irresistibly
   streaking on to the shores of Evening
                    Death
so many deaths, numberless deaths on deaths, no end—
Thebes is dying, look, her children   205
stripped of pity . . .
   generations strewn on the ground
unburied, unwept, the dead spreading death
and the young wives and gray-haired mothers with them
cling to the altars, trailing in from all over the city—   210
Thebes, city of death, one long cortege
   and the suffering rises
     wails for mercy rise
and the wild hymn for the Healer blazes out
clashing with our sobs our cries of mourning—   215
O golden daughter of god,[4] send rescue
radiant as the kindness in your eyes!

Drive him back!—the fever, the god of death
   that raging god of war
not armored in bronze, not shielded now, he burns me,[5]   220
battle cries in the onslaught burning on—

---

3. Apollo's sister, a goddess associated with hunting and also a protector of women in childbirth.
4. Athena, daughter of Zeus.   5. The plague is identified with Ares, the war god, though he comes now without armor and shield. Ares is not elsewhere connected with plague; this passage may be an allusion to the early years of the Peloponnesian War, when Spartan troops threatened the city from outside and the plague raged inside the walls.

O rout him from our borders!
Sail him, blast him out to the Sea-queen's chamber
      the black Atlantic gulfs
   or the northern harbor, death to all   225
where the Thracian[6] surf comes crashing.
Now what the night spares he comes by day and kills—
the god of death.

                  O lord of the stormcloud,
you who twirl the lightning, Zeus, Father,
thunder Death to nothing!   230

Apollo, lord of the light, I beg you—
      whip your longbow's golden cord
showering arrows on our enemies—shafts of power
champions strong before us rushing on!

Artemis, Huntress,   235
torches flaring over the eastern ridges—
      ride Death down in pain!

God of the headdress gleaming gold, I cry to you—
your name and ours are one, Dionysus—
      come with your face aflame with wine   240
            your raving women's[7] cries
      your army on the march! Come with the lightning
come with torches blazing, eyes ablaze with glory!
Burn that god of death that all gods hate!
      [OEDIPUS *enters from the palace to address the* CHORUS, *as if*
      addressing the entire city of Thebes.]
OEDIPUS: You pray to the gods? Let me grant your prayers.   245
   Come, listen to me—do what the plague demands:
   you'll find relief and lift your head from the depths.
   I will speak out now as a stranger to the story,
   a stranger to the crime. If I'd been present then,
   there would have been no mystery, no long hunt   250
   without a clue in hand. So now, counted
   a native Theban years after the murder,
   to all of Thebes I make this proclamation:
   if any one of you knows who murdered Laius,
   the son of Labdacus, I order him to reveal   255
   the whole truth to me. Nothing to fear,
   even if he must denounce himself,
   let him speak up
   and so escape the brunt of the charge—
   he will suffer no unbearable punishment,   260
   nothing worse than exile, totally unharmed.
      [OEDIPUS *pauses, waiting for a reply.*]

6. Ares was thought to be at home among the savages of Thrace, to the northeast of Greece proper.
7. The Bacchanals, nymphs or human female votaries of the god Dionysus (Bacchus) who celebrated
him with wild dancing rites.

                                        Next,
if anyone knows the murderer is a stranger,
a man from alien soil, come, speak up.
I will give him a handsome reward, and lay up
gratitude in my heart for him besides.   265
    [*Silence again, no reply.*]
But if you keep silent, if anyone panicking,
trying to shield himself or friend or kin,
rejects my offer, then hear what I will do.
I order you, every citizen of the state
where I hold throne and power: banish this man —   270
whoever he may be — never shelter him, never
speak a word to him, never make him partner
to your prayers, your victims burned to the gods.
Never let the holy water touch his hands
Drive him out, each of you, from every home.   275
He is the plague, the heart of our corruption,
as Apollo's oracle has just revealed to me.
So I honor my obligations:
I fight for the god and for the murdered man.

Now my curse on the murderer. Whoever he is,   280
a lone man unknown in his crime
or one among many, let that man drag out
his life in agony, step by painful step —
I curse myself as well . . . if by any chance
he proves to be an intimate of our house,   285
here at my hearth, with my full knowledge,
may the curse I just called down on him strike me!

These are your orders: perform them to the last.
I command you, for my sake, for Apollo's, for this country
blasted root and branch by the angry heavens.   290
Even if god had never urged you on to act,
how could you leave the crime uncleansed so long?
A man so noble — your king, brought down in blood —
you should have searched. But I am the king now,
I hold the throne that he held then, possess his bed   295
and a wife who shares our seed . . . why, our seed
might be the same, children born of the same mother
might have created blood-bonds between us
if his hope of offspring hadn't met disaster —
but fate swooped at his head and cut him short.   300
So I will fight for him as if he were my father,
stop at nothing, search the world
to lay my hands on the man who shed his blood,
the son of Labdacus descended of Polydorus,
Cadmus of old and Agenor, founder of the line: 305
their power and mine are one.

                                                Oh dear gods,
my curse on those who disobey these orders!
Let no crops grow out of the earth for them—
shrivel their women, kill their sons,
burn them to nothing in this plague   310
that hits us now, or something even worse.
But you, loyal men of Thebes who approve my actions,
may our champion, Justice, may all the gods
be with us, fight beside us to the end!

LEADER: In the grip of your curse, my king, I swear   315
I'm not the murderer, I cannot point him out.
As for the search, Apollo pressed it on us—
he should name the killer.

OEDIPUS: Quite right,
but to force the gods to act against their will—
no man has the power.

LEADER: Then if I might mention   320
the next best thing . . .

OEDIPUS: The third best too—
don't hold back, say it.

LEADER: I still believe . . .
Lord Tiresias[8] sees with the eyes of Lord Apollo.
Anyone searching for the truth, my king,
might learn it from the prophet, clear as day.   325

OEDIPUS: I've not been slow with that. On Creon's cue
I sent the escorts, twice, within the hour.
I'm surprised he isn't here.

LEADER: We need him—
without him we have nothing but old, useless rumors.

OEDIPUS: Which rumors? I'll search out every word.   330

LEADER: Laius was killed, they say, by certain travelers.

OEDIPUS: I know—but no one can find the murderer.

LEADER: If the man has a trace of fear in him
he won't stay silent long,
not with your curses ringing in his ears.   335

OEDIPUS: He didn't flinch at murder,
he'll never flinch at words.

        [Enter TIRESIAS, *the blind prophet, led by a boy with escorts in atten-*
        dance. He remains at a distance.]

LEADER: Here is the one who will convict him, look,
they bring him on at last, the seer, the man of god.
The truth lives inside him, him alone.

OEDIPUS: O Tiresias,   340
master of all the mysteries of our life,
all you teach and all you dare not tell,
signs in the heavens, signs that walk the earth!
Blind as you are, you can feel all the more

---

8. The blind prophet of Thebes (whose ghost Odysseus goes to consult in Hades in *Odyssey* XI).

what sickness haunts our city. You, my lord,   345
are the one shield, the one savior we can find.

We asked Apollo—perhaps the messengers
haven't told you—he sent his answer back:
"Relief from the plague can only come one way.
Uncover the murderers of Laius,   350
put them to death or drive them into exile."
So I beg you, grudge us nothing now, no voice,
no message plucked from the birds, the embers
or the other mantic ways within your grasp.
Rescue yourself, your city, rescue me—   355
rescue everything infected by the dead.
We are in your hands. For a man to help others
with all his gifts and native strength:
that is the noblest work.
TIRESIAS: How terrible—to see the truth
    when the truth is only pain to him who sees!   360
    I knew it well, but I put it from my mind,
    else I never would have come.
OEDIPUS: What's this? Why so grim, so dire?
TIRESIAS: Just send me home. You bear your burdens,
    I'll bear mine. It's better that way,   365
    please believe me.
OEDIPUS: Strange response . . . unlawful,
    unfriendly too to the state that bred and reared you—
    you withhold the word of god.
TIRESIAS: I fail to see
    that your own words are so well-timed.
    I'd rather not have the same thing said of me . . .   370
OEDIPUS: For the love of god, don't turn away,
    not if you know something. We beg you,
    all of us on our knees.
TIRESIAS: None of you knows—
    and I will never reveal my dreadful secrets,
    not to say your own.   375
OEDIPUS: What? You know and you won't tell?
    You're bent on betraying us, destroying Thebes?
TIRESIAS: I'd rather not cause pain for you or me.
    So why this . . . useless interrogation?
    You'll get nothing from me.
OEDIPUS: Nothing! You,   380
    you scum of the earth, you'd enrage a heart of stone!
    You won't talk? Nothing moves you?
    Out with it, once and for all!
TIRESIAS: You criticize my temper . . . unaware
    of the one[9] *you* live with, you revile me.   385

---

9. In the Greek the veiled reference to Jocasta is more forceful, because the word translated "the one"
has a feminine ending (agreeing with the feminine noun *orgê,* "temper").

OEDIPUS: Who could restrain his anger hearing you?
  What outrage—you spurn the city!
TIRESIAS: What will come will come.
  Even if I shroud it all in silence.
OEDIPUS: What will come? You're bound to *tell* me that.   390
TIRESIAS: I'll say no more. Do as you like, build your anger
  to whatever pitch you please, rage your worst—
OEDIPUS: Oh I'll let loose, I have such fury in me—
  now I see it all. You helped hatch the plot,
  you did the work, yes, short of killing him   395
  with your own hands—and given eyes I'd say
  you did the killing single-handed!
TIRESIAS: Is that so!
  I charge you, then, submit to that decree
  you just laid down: from this day onward
  speak to no one, not these citizens, not myself.   400
  You are the curse, the corruption of the land!
OEDIPUS: You, shameless—
  aren't you appalled to start up such a story?
  You think you can get away with this?
TIRESIAS: I have already.
  The truth with all its power lives inside me.   405
OEDIPUS: Who primed you for this? Not your prophet's trade.
TIRESIAS: You did, you forced me, twisted it out of me.
OEDIPUS: What? Say it again—I'll understand it better.
TIRESIAS: Didn't you understand, just now?
  Or are you tempting me to talk?   410
OEDIPUS: No, I can't say I grasped your meaning.
  Out with it, again!
TIRESIAS: I say you are the murderer you hunt.
OEDIPUS: That obscenity, twice—by god, you'll pay.
TIRESIAS: Shall I say more, so you can really rage?   415
OEDIPUS: Much as you want. Your words are nothing—futile.
TIRESIAS: You cannot imagine . . . I tell you,
  you and your loved ones live together in infamy,
  you cannot see how far you've gone in guilt.
OEDIPUS: You think you can keep this up and never suffer?   420
TIRESIAS: Indeed, if the truth has any power.
OEDIPUS: It does
  but not for you, old man. You've lost your power,
  stone-blind, stone-deaf—senses, eyes blind as stone!
TIRESIAS: I pity you, flinging at me the very insults
  each man here will fling at you so soon.
OEDIPUS: Blind,   425
  lost in the night, endless night that cursed you!
  You can't hurt me or anyone else who sees the light—
  you can never touch me.
TIRESIAS: True, it is not your fate
  to fall at my hands. Apollo is quite enough,

and he will take some pains to work this out.   430
OEDIPUS: Creon! Is this conspiracy his or yours?
TIRESIAS: Creon is not your downfall, no, you are your own.
OEDIPUS: O power—
    wealth and empire, skill outstripping skill
    in the heady rivalries of life,
    what envy lurks inside you! Just for this,   435
    the crown the city gave me—I never sought it,
    they laid it in my hands—for this alone, Creon,
    the soul of trust, my loyal friend from the start
    steals against me . . . so hungry to overthrow me
    he sets this wizard on me, this scheming quack,   440
    this fortune-teller peddling lies, eyes peeled
    for his own profit—seer blind in his craft!

    Come here, you pious fraud. Tell me,
    when did you ever prove yourself a prophet?
    When the Sphinx, that chanting Fury kept her deathwatch here,   445
    why silent then, not a word to set our people free?
    There was a riddle, not for some passer-by to solve—
    it cried out for a prophet. Where were you?
    Did you rise to the crisis? Not a word,
    you and your birds, your gods—nothing.   450
    No, but I came by, Oedipus the ignorant,
    I stopped the Sphinx! With no help from the birds,
    the flight of my own intelligence hit the mark.

    And this is the man you'd try to overthrow?
    You think you'll stand by Creon when he's king?   455
    You and the great mastermind—
    you'll pay in tears, I promise you, for this,
    this witch-hunt. If you didn't look so senile
    the lash would teach you what your scheming means!
LEADER: I would suggest his words were spoken in anger,   460
    Oedipus . . . yours too, and it isn't what we need.
    The best solution to the oracle, the riddle
    posed by god—we should look for that.
TIRESIAS: You are the king no doubt, but in one respect,
    at least, I am your equal: the right to reply.   465
    I claim that privilege too.
    I am not your slave. I serve Apollo.
    I don't need Creon to speak for me in public.
                      So,
    you mock my blindness? Let me tell you this.
    You with your precious eyes,   470
    you're blind to the corruption of your life,
    to the house you live in, those you live with—
    who *are* your parents? Do you know? All unknowing
    you are the scourge of your own flesh and blood,
    the dead below the earth and the living here above,   475

and the double lash of your mother and your father's curse
will whip you from this land one day, their footfall
treading you down in terror, darkness shrouding
your eyes that now can see the light!

                         Soon, soon
you'll scream aloud—what haven won't reverberate?   480
What rock of Cithaeron[1] won't scream back in echo?
That day you learn the truth about your marriage,
the wedding-march that sang you into your halls,
the lusty voyage home to the fatal harbor!
And a crowd of other horrors you'd never dream   485
will level you with yourself and all your children.

There. Now smear us with insults—Creon, myself,
and every word I've said. No man will ever
be rooted from the earth as brutally as you.
OEDIPUS: Enough! Such filth from him? Insufferable—   490
what, still alive? Get out—
faster, back where you came from—vanish!
TIRESIAS: I would never have come if you hadn't called me here.
OEDIPUS: If I thought you would blurt out such absurdities,
you'd have died waiting before I'd had you summoned.   495
TIRESIAS: Absurd, am I! To you, not to your parents:
the ones who bore you found me sane enough.
OEDIPUS: Parents—who? Wait . . . who is my father?
TIRESIAS: This day will bring your birth and your destruction.
OEDIPUS: Riddles—all you can say are riddles, murk and darkness.   500
TIRESIAS: Ah, but aren't you the best man alive at solving riddles?
OEDIPUS: Mock me for that, go on, and you'll reveal my greatness.
TIRESIAS: Your great good fortune, true, it was your ruin.
OEDIPUS: Not if I saved the city—what do I care?
TIRESIAS: Well then, I'll be going.
    [*To his attendant.*]
                         Take me home, boy.   505
OEDIPUS: Yes, take him away. You're a nuisance here.
Out of the way, the irritation's gone.
    [*Turning his back on* TIRESIAS, *moving toward the palace.*][2]
TIRESIAS: I will go,
once I have said what I came here to say.
I'll never shrink from the anger in your eyes—
you can't destroy me. Listen to me closely: 510
the man you've sought so long, proclaiming,
cursing up and down, the murderer of Laius—
he is here. A stranger,
you may think, who lives among you,
he soon will be revealed a native Theban   515

1. The mountain range near Thebes, on which Oedipus was left to die when an infant.   2. There
are no stage directions in the texts. It is suggested here that Oedipus moves off stage and does not hear
the critical section of Tiresias's speech (lines 520ff.), which he could hardly fail to connect with the
prophecy made to him by Apollo many years ago.

but he will take no joy in the revelation.
Blind who now has eyes, beggar who now is rich,
he will grope his way toward a foreign soil,
a stick tapping before him step by step.
   [OEDIPUS *enters the palace.*]
Revealed at last, brother and father both   520
to the children he embraces, to his mother
son and husband both—he sowed the loins
his father sowed, he spilled his father's blood!

Go in and reflect on that, solve that.
And if you find I've lied   525
from this day onward call the prophet blind.
   [TIRESIAS *and the boy exit to the side.*]
CHORUS: Who—
  who is the man the voice of god denounces
resounding out of the rocky gorge of Delphi?
    The horror too dark to tell,
whose ruthless bloody hands have done the work?   530
His time has come to fly
    to outrace the stallions of the storm
       his feet a streak of speed—
Cased in armor, Apollo son of the Father
lunges on him, lightning-bolts afire!   535
And the grim unerring Furies[3]
     closing for the kill.
           Look,
the word of god has just come blazing
flashing off Parnassus' snowy heights!
    That man who left no trace—   540
after him, hunt him down with all our strength!
Now under bristling timber
    up through rocks and caves he stalks
      like the wild mountain bull—
cut off from men, each step an agony, frenzied, racing blind   545
but he cannot outrace the dread voices of Delphi
ringing out of the heart of Earth,
    the dark wings beating around him shrieking doom
      the doom that never dies, the terror—
The skilled prophet scans the birds and shatters me with terror!   550
I can't accept him, can't deny him, don't know what to say,
I'm lost, and the wings of dark foreboding beating—
I cannot see what's come, what's still to come . . .
and what could breed a blood feud between
    Laius' house and the son of Polybus?[4]   555
I know of nothing, not in the past and not now,
no charge to bring against our king, no cause

---

3. Avenging spirits who pursued a murderer when no earthly avenger was at hand.   **4.** King of Corinth and, so far as anyone except Tiresias knows, the father of Oedipus.

to attack his fame that rings throughout Thebes—
  not without proof—not for the ghost of Laius,
  not to avenge a murder gone without a trace.   560

Zeus and Apollo know, they know, the great masters
    of all the dark and depth of human life.
But whether a mere man can know the truth,
  whether a seer can fathom more than I—
there is no test, no certain proof   565
    though matching skill for skill
a man can outstrip a rival. No, not till I see
  these charges proved will I side with his accusers.
We saw him then, when the she-hawk[5] swept against him,
  saw with our own eyes his skill, his brilliant triumph—   570
    there was the test—he was the joy of Thebes!
    Never will I convict my king, never in my heart.
    [*Enter* CREON *from the side.*]
CREON: My fellow-citizens, I hear King Oedipus
  levels terrible charges at me. I had to come.
I resent it deeply. If, in the present crisis   575
he thinks he suffers any abuse from me,
  anything I've done or said that offers him
  the slightest injury, why, I've no desire
to linger out this life, my reputation in ruins.
The damage I'd face from such an accusation   580
is nothing simple. No, there's nothing worse:
branded a traitor in the city, a traitor
to all of you and my good friends.
LEADER: True,
  but a slur might have been forced out of him,
  by anger perhaps, not any firm conviction.   585
CREON: The charge was made in public, wasn't it?
  I put the prophet up to spreading lies?
LEADER: Such things were said . . .
  I don't know with what intent, if any.
CREON: Was his glance steady, his mind right   590
  when the charge was brought against me?
LEADER: I really couldn't say. I never look
  to judge the ones in power.
    [*The doors open.* OEDIPUS *enters.*]
                Wait,
here's Oedipus now.
OEDIPUS: You—here? You have the gall
  to show your face before the palace gates?   595
You, plotting to kill me, kill the king—
I see it all, the marauding thief himself
scheming to steal my crown and power!
              Tell me,

5. The Sphinx.

in god's name, what did you take me for,
coward or fool, when you spun out your plot?   600
Your treachery—you think I'd never detect it
creeping against me in the dark? Or sensing it,
not defend myself? Aren't you the fool,
you and your high adventure. Lacking numbers,
powerful friends, out for the big game of empire—   605
you need riches, armies to bring that quarry down!
CREON: Are you quite finished? It's your turn to listen
for just as long as you've . . . instructed me.
Hear me out, then judge me on the facts.
OEDIPUS: You've a wicked way with words, Creon,   610
but I'll be slow to learn—from you.
I find you a menace, a great burden to me.
CREON: Just one thing, hear me out in this.
OEDIPUS: Just one thing,
don't tell *me* you're not the enemy, the traitor.
CREON: Look, if you think crude, mindless stubbornness   615
such a gift, you've lost your sense of balance.
OEDIPUS: If you think you can abuse a kinsman,
then escape the penalty, you're insane.
CREON: Fair enough, I grant you. But this injury
you say I've done you, what is it?   620
OEDIPUS: Did you induce me, yes or no,
to send for that sanctimonious prophet?
CREON: I did. And I'd do the same again.
OEDIPUS: All right then, tell me, how long is it now
since Laius . . .
CREON: Laius—what did *he* do?
OEDIPUS: Vanished,   625
swept from sight, murdered in his tracks.
CREON: The count of the years would run you far back . . .
OEDIPUS: And that far back, was the prophet at his trade?
CREON: Skilled as he is today, and just as honored.
OEDIPUS: Did he ever refer to me then, at that time?
CREON: No,   630
never, at least, when I was in his presence.
OEDIPUS: But you did investigate the murder, didn't you?
CREON: We did our best, of course, discovered nothing.
OEDIPUS: But the great seer never accused me then—why not?
CREON: I don't know. And when I don't, *I* keep quiet.   635
OEDIPUS: You do know this, you'd tell it too—
if you had a shred of decency.
CREON: What?
If I know, I won't hold back.
OEDIPUS: Simply this:
if the two of you had never put heads together,
we would never have heard about *my* killing Laius.   640
CREON: If that's what he says . . . well, you know best.

But now I have a right to learn from you
as you just learned from me.
OEDIPUS: Learn your fill,
you never will convict me of the murder.
CREON: Tell me, you're married to my sister, aren't you?   645
OEDIPUS: A genuine discovery—there's no denying that.
CREON: And you rule the land with her, with equal power?
OEDIPUS: She receives from me whatever she desires.
CREON: And I am the third, all of us are equals?
OEDIPUS: Yes, and it's there you show your stripes—   650
you betray a kinsman.
CREON: Not at all.
Not if you see things calmly, rationally,
as I do. Look at it this way first:
who in his right mind would rather rule
and live in anxiety than sleep in peace?   655
Particularly if he enjoys the same authority.
Not I, I'm not the man to yearn for kingship,
not with a king's power in my hands. Who would?
No one with any sense of self-control.
Now, as it is, you offer me all I need,   660
not a fear in the world. But if I wore the crown . . .
there'd be many painful duties to perform,
hardly to my taste.
                         How could kingship
please me more than influence, power
without a qualm? I'm not that deluded yet,   665
to reach for anything but privilege outright,
profit free and clear.
Now all men sing my praises, all salute me,
now all who request your favors curry mine.
I am their best hope: success rests in me.   670
Why give up that, I ask you, and borrow trouble?
A man of sense, someone who sees things clearly
would never resort to treason.
No, I've no lust for conspiracy in me,
nor could I ever suffer one who does.   675

Do you want proof? Go to Delphi yourself,
examine the oracle and see if I've reported
the message word-for-word. This too:
if you detect that I and the clairvoyant
have plotted anything in common, arrest me,   680
execute me. Not on the strength of one vote,
two in this case, mine as well as yours.
But don't convict me on sheer unverified surmise.
How wrong it is to take the good for bad,
purely at random, or take the bad for good.   685
But reject a friend, a kinsman? I would as soon

tear out the life within us, priceless life itself.
You'll learn this well, without fail, in time.
Time alone can bring the just man to light—
the criminal you can spot in one short day.

LEADER: Good advice, 690
my lord, for anyone who wants to avoid disaster.
Those who jump to conclusions may go wrong.

OEDIPUS: When my enemy moves against me quickly,
plots in secret, I move quickly too, I must,
I plot and pay him back. Relax my guard a moment, 695
waiting his next move—he wins his objective,
I lose mine.

CREON: What do you want?
You want me banished?

OEDIPUS: No, I want you dead.

CREON: Just to show how ugly a grudge can . . .

OEDIPUS: So,
still stubborn? you don't think I'm serious? 700

CREON: I think you're insane.

OEDIPUS: Quite sane—in my behalf.

CREON: Not just as much in mine?

OEDIPUS: You—my mortal enemy?

CREON: What if you're wholly wrong?

OEDIPUS: No matter—I must rule.

CREON: Not if you rule unjustly.

OEDIPUS: Hear him, Thebes, my city!

CREON: My city too, not yours alone! 705

LEADER: Please, my lords.

[Enter JOCASTA from the palace.]
Look, Jocasta's coming,
and just in time too. With her help
you must put this fighting of yours to rest.

JOCASTA: Have you no sense? Poor misguided men,
such shouting—why this public outburst? 710
Aren't you ashamed, with the land so sick,
to stir up private quarrels?

[To OEDIPUS.]
Into the palace now. And Creon, you go home.
Why make such a furor over nothing?

CREON: My sister, it's dreadful . . . Oedipus, your husband, 715
he's bent on a choice of punishments for me,
banishment from the fatherland or death.

OEDIPUS: Precisely. I caught him in the act, Jocasta,
plotting, about to stab me in the back.

CREON: Never—curse me, let me die and be damned 720
if I've done you any wrong you charge me with.

JOCASTA: Oh god, believe it, Oedipus,
honor the solemn oath he swears to heaven.
Do it for me, for the sake of all your people.

[*The* CHORUS *begins to chant.*]

CHORUS: Believe it, be sensible   725
  give way, my king, I beg you!

OEDIPUS: What do you want from me, concessions?

CHORUS: Respect him—he's been no fool in the past
  and now he's strong with the oath he swears to god.

OEDIPUS: You know what you're asking?

CHORUS: I do.

OEDIPUS: Then out with it!   730

CHORUS: The man's your friend, your kin, he's under oath—
  don't cast him out, disgraced
  branded with guilt on the strength of hearsay only.

OEDIPUS: Know full well, if that is what you want
  you want me dead or banished from the land.

CHORUS: Never—   735
  no, by the blazing Sun, first god of the heavens!
    Stripped of the gods, stripped of loved ones,
  let me die by inches if that ever crossed my mind.
  But the heart inside me sickens, dies as the land dies
  and now on top of the old griefs you pile this,   740
  your fury—both of you!

OEDIPUS: Then let him go,
  even if it does lead to my ruin, my death
  or my disgrace, driven from Thebes for life.
  It's you, not him I pity—your words move me.
  He, wherever he goes, my hate goes with him.   745

CREON: Look at you, sullen in yielding, brutal in your rage—
  you'll go too far. It's perfect justice:
  natures like yours are hardest on themselves.

OEDIPUS: Then leave me alone—get out!

CREON: I'm going.
  You're wrong, so wrong. These men know I'm right.   750

  [*Exit to the side. The* CHORUS *turns to* JOCASTA.]

CHORUS: Why do you hesitate, my lady
  why not help him in?

JOCASTA: Tell me what's happened first.

CHORUS: Loose, ignorant talk started dark suspicions
  and a sense of injustice cut deeply too.   755

JOCASTA: On both sides?

CHORUS: Oh yes.

JOCASTA: What did they say?

CHORUS: Enough, please, enough! The land's so racked already
  or so it seems to me . . .
  End the trouble here, just where they left it.

OEDIPUS: You see what comes of your good intentions now?   760
  And all because you tried to blunt my anger.

CHORUS: My king,
  I've said it once, I'll say it time and again—
    I'd be insane, you know it,

senseless, ever to turn my back on you.
You who set our beloved land—storm-tossed, shattered— 765
straight on course. Now again, good helmsman,
steer us through the storm!

[*The* CHORUS *draws away, leaving* OEDIPUS *and* JOCASTA *side by side.*]
JOCASTA: For the love of god,
Oedipus, tell me too, what is it?
Why this rage? You're so unbending.
OEDIPUS: I will tell you. I respect you, Jocasta, 770
much more than these . . .

[*Glancing at the* CHORUS.]
Creon's to blame, Creon schemes against me.
JOCASTA: Tell me clearly, how did the quarrel start?
OEDIPUS: He says *I* murdered Laius—I am guilty.
JOCASTA: How does he know? Some secret knowledge 775
or simple hearsay?
OEDIPUS: Oh, he sent his prophet in
to do his dirty work. You know Creon,
Creon keeps his own lips clean.
JOCASTA: A prophet?
Well then, free yourself of every charge!
Listen to me and learn some peace of mind: 780
no skill in the world,
nothing human can penetrate the future.
Here is proof, quick and to the point.

An oracle came to Laius one fine day
(I won't say from Apollo himself 785
but his underlings, his priests) and it said
that doom would strike him down at the hands of a son,
our son, to be born of our own flesh and blood. But Laius,
so the report goes at least, was killed by strangers,
thieves, at a place where three roads meet . . . my son— 790
he wasn't three days old and the boy's father
fastened his ankles, had a henchman fling him away
on a barren, trackless mountain.
                    There, you see?
Apollo brought neither thing to pass. My baby
no more murdered his father than Laius suffered— 795
his wildest fear—death at his own son's hands.
That's how the seers and all their revelations
mapped out the future. Brush them from your mind.
Whatever the god needs and seeks
he'll bring to light himself, with ease.
OEDIPUS: Strange, 800
hearing you just now . . . my mind wandered,
my thoughts racing back and forth.
JOCASTA: What do you mean? Why so anxious, startled?
OEDIPUS: I thought I heard you say that Laius

was cut down at a place where three roads meet.   805
JOCASTA: That was the story. It hasn't died out yet.
OEDIPUS: Where did this thing happen? Be precise.
JOCASTA: A place called Phocis, where two branching roads,
   one from Daulia, one from Delphi,
   come together—a crossroads.   810
OEDIPUS: When? How long ago?
JOCASTA: The heralds no sooner reported Laius dead
   than you appeared and they hailed you king of Thebes.
OEDIPUS: My god, my god—what have you planned to do to me?
JOCASTA: What, Oedipus? What haunts you so?
OEDIPUS: Not yet.   815
   Laius—how did he look? Describe him.
   Had he reached his prime?
JOCASTA: He was swarthy,
   and the gray had just begun to streak his temples,
   and his build . . . wasn't far from yours.
OEDIPUS: Oh no no,
   I think I've just called down a dreadful curse   820
   upon myself—I simply didn't know!
JOCASTA: What are you saying? I shudder to look at you.
OEDIPUS: I have a terrible fear the blind seer can see.
   I'll know in a moment. One thing more—
JOCASTA: Anything,
   afraid as I am—ask, I'll answer, all I can.   825
OEDIPUS: Did he go with a light or heavy escort,
   several men-at-arms, like a lord, a king?
JOCASTA: There were five in the party, a herald among them,
   and a single wagon carrying Laius.
OEDIPUS: Ai—
   now I can see it all, clear as day.   830
   Who told you all this at the time, Jocasta?
JOCASTA: A servant who reached home, the lone survivor.
OEDIPUS: So, could he still be in the palace—even now?
JOCASTA: No indeed. Soon as he returned from the scene
   and saw you on the throne with Laius dead and gone,   835
   he knelt and clutched my hand, pleading with me
   to send him into the hinterlands, to pasture,
   far as possible, out of sight of Thebes.
   I sent him away. Slave though he was,
   he'd earned that favor—and much more.   840
OEDIPUS: Can we bring him back, quickly?
JOCASTA: Easily. Why do you want him so?
OEDIPUS: I'm afraid,
   Jocasta, I have said too much already.
   That man—I've got to see him.
JOCASTA: Then he'll come.
   But even I have a right, I'd like to think,   845
   to know what's torturing you, my lord.

OEDIPUS: And so you shall—I can hold nothing back from you,
now I've reached this pitch of dark foreboding.
Who means more to me than you? Tell me,
whom would I turn toward but you   850
as I go through all this?

My father was Polybus, king of Corinth.
My mother, a Dorian, Merope. And I was held
the prince of the realm among the people there,
till something struck me out of nowhere,   855
something strange . . . worth remarking perhaps,
hardly worth the anxiety I gave it.
Some man at a banquet who had drunk too much
shouted out—he was far gone, mind you—
that I am not my father's son. Fighting words!   860
I barely restrained myself that day
but early the next I went to mother and father,
questioned them closely, and they were enraged
at the accusation and the fool who let it fly.
So as for my parents I was satisfied,   865
but still this thing kept gnawing at me,
the slander spread—I had to make my move.
                                              And so,
unknown to mother and father I set out for Delphi,
and the god Apollo spurned me, sent me away
denied the facts I came for,   870
but first he flashed before my eyes a future
great with pain, terror, disaster—I can hear him cry,
"You are fated to couple with your mother, you will bring
a breed of children into the light no man can bear to see—
you will kill your father, the one who gave you life!"   875
I heard all that and ran. I abandoned Corinth,
from that day on I gauged its landfall only
by the stars, running, always running
toward some place where I would never see
the shame of all those oracles come true.   880
And as I fled I reached that very spot
where the great king, you say, met his death.

Now, Jocasta, I will tell you all.
Making my way toward this triple crossroad
I began to see a herald, then a brace of colts   885
drawing a wagon, and mounted on the bench . . . a man,
just as you've described him, coming face-to-face,
and the one in the lead and the old man himself
were about to thrust me off the road—brute force—
and the one shouldering me aside, the driver,   890
I strike him in anger!—and the old man, watching me
coming up along his wheels—he brings down
his prod, two prongs straight at my head!

I paid him back with interest!
Short work, by god—with one blow of the staff   895
in this right hand I knock him out of his high seat,
roll him out of the wagon, sprawling headlong—
I killed them all—every mother's son!

Oh, but if there is any blood-tie
between Laius and this stranger . . .   900
what man alive more miserable than I?
More hated by the gods? *I* am the man
no alien, no citizen welcomes to his house,
law forbids it—not a word to me in public,
driven out of every hearth and home.   905
And all these curses I—no one but I
brought down these piling curses on myself!
And you, his wife, I've touched your body with these,
the hands that killed your husband cover you with blood.

Wasn't I born for torment? Look me in the eyes!   910
I am abomination—heart and soul!
I must be exiled, and even in exile
never see my parents, never set foot
on native ground again. Else I am doomed
to couple with my mother and cut my father down . . .   915
Polybus who reared me, gave me life.
                                        But why, why?
Wouldn't a man of judgment say—and wouldn't he be right—
some savage power has brought this down upon my head?

Oh no, not that, you pure and awesome gods,
never let me see that day! Let me slip   920
from the world of men, vanish without a trace
before I see myself stained with such corruption,
stained to the heart.
LEADER: My lord, you fill our hearts with fear.
    But at least until you question the witness,   925
    do take hope.
OEDIPUS: Exactly. He is my last hope—
    I am waiting for the shepherd. He is crucial.
JOCASTA: And once he appears, what then? Why so urgent?
OEDIPUS: I will tell you. If it turns out that his story
    matches yours, I've escaped the worst.   930
JOCASTA: What did I say? What struck you so?
OEDIPUS: You said *thieves*—
    he told you a whole band of them murdered Laius.
    So, if he still holds to the same number,
    I cannot be the killer. One can't equal many.
    But if he refers to one man, one alone,   935
    clearly the scales come down on me:
    I am guilty.

JOCASTA: Impossible. Trust me,
  I told you precisely what he said,
  and he can't retract it now;
  the whole city heard it, not just I.   940
  And even if he should vary his first report
  by one man more or less, still, my lord,
  he could never make the murder of Laius
  truly fit the prophecy. Apollo was explicit:
  my son was doomed to kill my husband . . . my son,   945
  poor defenseless thing, he never had a chance
  to kill his father. They destroyed him first.

  So much for prophecy. It's neither here nor there.
  From this day on, I wouldn't look right or left.
OEDIPUS: True, true. Still, that shepherd,   950
  someone fetch him—now!
JOCASTA: I'll send at once. But do let's go inside.
  I'd never displease you, least of all in this.
     [OEDIPUS and JOCASTA *enter the palace.*]
CHORUS: Destiny guide me always
  Destiny find me filled with reverence   955
    pure in word and deed.
  Great laws tower above us, reared on high
  born for the brilliant vault of heaven—
    Olympian Sky their only father,
  nothing mortal, no man gave them birth,   960
  their memory deathless, never lost in sleep:
  within them lives a mighty god, the god does not grow old.

  Pride breeds the tyrant
  violent pride, gorging, crammed to bursting
    with all that is overripe and rich with ruin—   965
  clawing up to the heights, headlong pride
  crashes down the abyss—sheer doom!
    No footing helps, all foothold lost and gone.
  But the healthy strife that makes the city strong—
  I pray that god will never end that wrestling: 970
  god, my champion, I will never let you go.

  But if any man comes striding, high and mighty
    in all he says and does,
  no fear of justice, no reverence
  for the temples of the gods—   975
    let a rough doom tear him down,
  repay his pride, breakneck, ruinous pride!
  If he cannot reap his profits fairly
    cannot restrain himself from outrage—
  mad, laying hands on the holy things untouchable!   980

    Can such a man, so desperate, still boast
    he can save his life from the flashing bolts of god?

If all such violence goes with honor now
  why join the sacred dance?

Never again will I go reverent to Delphi,   985
  the inviolate heart of Earth
or Apollo's ancient oracle at Abae
or Olympia[6] of the fires—
  unless these prophecies all come true
for all mankind to point toward in wonder.   990
King of kings, if you deserve your titles
  Zeus, remember, never forget!
You and your deathless, everlasting reign.

They are dying, the old oracles sent to Laius,
  now our masters strike them off the rolls.   995
    Nowhere Apollo's golden glory now—
      the gods, the gods go down.

[*Enter* JOCASTA *from the palace, carrying a suppliant's branch wound
in wool.*]

JOCASTA: Lords of the realm,[7] it occurred to me,
  just now, to visit the temples of the gods,
so I have my branch in hand and incense too.   1000

Oedipus is beside himself. Racked with anguish,
  no longer a man of sense, he won't admit
the latest prophecies are hollow as the old—
  he's at the mercy of every passing voice
if the voice tells of terror.   1005
I urge him gently, nothing seems to help,
so I turn to you, Apollo, you are nearest.

[*Placing her branch on the altar, while an old herdsman enters from
the side, not the one just summoned by the King but an unexpected*
MESSENGER *from Corinth.*]

I come with prayers and offerings . . . I beg you,
cleanse us, set us free of defilement!
Look at us, passengers in the grip of fear,   1010
watching the pilot of the vessel go to pieces.

MESSENGER: [*Approaching* JOCASTA *and the* CHORUS.]
  Strangers, please, I wonder if you could lead us
to the palace of the king . . . I think it's Oedipus.
Better, the man himself—you know where he is?

LEADER: This is his palace, stranger. He's inside.   1015
  But here is his queen, his wife and mother
of his children.

MESSENGER: Blessings on you, noble queen,
  queen of Oedipus crowned with all your family—
blessings on you always!

JOCASTA: And the same to you, stranger, you deserve it . . . 1020

---

6. In the western Peloponnese, a site of an oracle of Zeus. Abae is a city in central Greece.   7. The
chorus.

such a greeting. But what have you come for?
Have you brought us news?
MESSENGER: Wonderful news—
  for the house, my lady, for your husband too.
JOCASTA: Really, what? Who sent you?
MESSENGER: Corinth.
  I'll give you the message in a moment.   1025
  You'll be glad of it—how could you help it?—
  though it costs a little sorrow in the bargain.
JOCASTA: What can it be, with such a double edge?
MESSENGER: The people there, they want to make your Oedipus
  king of Corinth, so they're saying now.   1030
JOCASTA: Why? Isn't old Polybus still in power?
MESSENGER: No more. Death has got him in the tomb.
JOCASTA: What are you saying? Polybus, dead?—dead?
MESSENGER: If not,
  if I'm not telling the truth, strike me dead too.
JOCASTA: [To a servant.] Quickly, go to your master, tell him this!   1035
  You prophecies of the gods, where are you now?
  This is the man that Oedipus feared for years,
  he fled him, not to kill him—and now he's dead,
  quite by chance, a normal, natural death,
  not murdered by his son.
OEDIPUS: [Emerging from the palace.]
                                    Dearest,   1040
  what now? Why call me from the palace?
JOCASTA: [Bringing the MESSENGER closer.]
  Listen to him, see for yourself what all
  those awful prophecies of god have come to.
OEDIPUS: And who is he? What can he have for me?
JOCASTA: He's from Corinth, he's come to tell you   1045
  your father is no more—Polybus—he's dead!
OEDIPUS: [Wheeling on the MESSENGER.]
  What? Let me have it from your lips.
MESSENGER: Well,
  if that's what you want first, then here it is:
  make no mistake, Polybus is dead and gone.
OEDIPUS: How—murder? sickness?—what? what killed him?   1050
MESSENGER: A light tip of the scales can put old bones to rest.
OEDIPUS: Sickness then—poor man, it wore him down.
MESSENGER: That,
  and the long count of years he'd measured out.
OEDIPUS: So!
  Jocasta, why, why look to the Prophet's hearth,
  the fires of the future? Why scan the birds   1055
  that scream above our heads? They winged me on
  to the murder of my father, did they? That was my doom?
  Well look, he's dead and buried, hidden under the earth,
  and here I am in Thebes, I never put hand to sword—

unless some longing for me wasted him away, 1060
then in a sense you'd say I caused his death.
But now, all those prophecies I feared—Polybus
packs them off to sleep with him in hell!
They're nothing, worthless.

JOCASTA: There.
    Didn't I tell you from the start? 1065

OEDIPUS: So you did. I was lost in fear.

JOCASTA: No more, sweep it from your mind forever.

OEDIPUS: But my mother's bed, surely I must fear—

JOCASTA: Fear?
    What should a man fear? It's all chance,
    chance rules our lives. Not a man on earth 1070
    can see a day ahead, groping through the dark.
    Better to live at random, best we can.
    And as for this marriage with your mother—
    have no fear. Many a man before you,
    in his dreams, has shared his mother's bed. 1075
    Take such things for shadows, nothing at all—
    Live, Oedipus,
    as if there's no tomorrow!

OEDIPUS: Brave words,
    and you'd persuade me if mother weren't alive.
    But mother lives, so for all your reassurances 1080
    I live in fear, I must.

JOCASTA: But your father's death,
    that, at least, is a great blessing, joy to the eyes!

OEDIPUS: Great, I know . . . but I fear her—she's still alive.

MESSENGER: Wait, who is this woman, makes you so afraid?

OEDIPUS: Merope, old man. The wife of Polybus. 1085

MESSENGER: The queen? What's there to fear in her?

OEDIPUS: A dreadful prophecy, stranger, sent by the gods.

MESSENGER: Tell me, could you? Unless it's forbidden
    other ears to hear.

OEDIPUS: Not at all.
    Apollo told me once—it is my fate— 1090
    I must make love with my own mother,
    shed my father's blood with my own hands.
    So for years I've given Corinth a wide berth,
    and it's been my good fortune too. But still,
    to see one's parents and look into their eyes 1095
    is the greatest joy I know.

MESSENGER: You're afraid of that?
    That kept you out of Corinth?

OEDIPUS: My *father*, old man—
    so I wouldn't kill my father.

MESSENGER: So that's it.
    Well then, seeing I came with such good will, my king,
    why don't I rid you of that old worry now? 1100

OEDIPUS: What a rich reward you'd have for that!
MESSENGER: What do you think I came for, majesty?
　So you'd come home and I'd be better off.
OEDIPUS: Never, I will never go near my parents.
MESSENGER: My boy, it's clear, you don't know what you're doing.　　1105
OEDIPUS: What do you mean, old man? For god's sake, explain.
MESSENGER: If you ran from *them*, always dodging home . . .
OEDIPUS: Always, terrified Apollo's oracle might come true—
MESSENGER: And you'd be covered with guilt, from both your parents.
OEDIPUS: That's right, old man, that fear is always with me.　　1110
MESSENGER: Don't you know? You've really nothing to fear.
OEDIPUS: But why? If I'm their son—Merope, Polybus?
MESSENGER: Polybus was nothing to you, that's why, not in blood.
OEDIPUS: What are you saying—Polybus was not my father?
MESSENGER: No more than I am. He and I are equals.
OEDIPUS: My father—　　1115
　how can my father equal nothing? You're nothing to me!
MESSENGER: Neither was he, no more your father than I am.
OEDIPUS: Then why did he call me his son?
MESSENGER: You were a gift,
　years ago—know for a fact he took you
　from my hands.
OEDIPUS: No, from another's hands?　　1120
　Then how could he love me so? He loved me, deeply . . .
MESSENGER: True, and his early years without a child
　made him love you all the more.
OEDIPUS: And you, did you . . .
　buy me? find me by accident?
MESSENGER: I stumbled on you,
　down the woody flanks of Mount Cithaeron.
OEDIPUS: So close,　　1125
　what were you doing here, just passing through?
MESSENGER: Watching over my flocks, grazing them on the slopes.
OEDIPUS: A herdsman, were you? A vagabond, scraping for wages?
MESSENGER: Your savior too, my son, in your worst hour.
OEDIPUS: Oh—
　when you picked me up, was I in pain? What exactly?　　1130
MESSENGER: Your ankles . . . they tell the story. Look at them.
OEDIPUS: Why remind me of that, that old affliction?
MESSENGER: Your ankles were pinned together. I set you free.
OEDIPUS: That dreadful mark—I've had it from the cradle.
MESSENGER: And you got your name[8] from that misfortune too,　　1135
　the name's still with you.
OEDIPUS: Dear god, who did it?—
　mother? father? Tell me.
MESSENGER: I don't know.
　The one who gave you to me, he'd know more.

---

8. In Greek the name *Oidipous* suggests "swollen foot."

OEDIPUS: What? You took me from someone else?
  You didn't find me yourself?
MESSENGER: No sir,   1140
  another shepherd passed you on to me.
OEDIPUS: Who? Do you know? Describe him.
MESSENGER: He called himself a servant of . . .
  if I remember rightly—Laius.
    [JOCASTA *turns sharply.*]
OEDIPUS: The king of the land who ruled here long ago?   1145
MESSENGER: That's the one. That herdsman was *his* man.
OEDIPUS: Is he still alive? Can I see him?
MESSENGER: They'd know best, the people of these parts.
    [OEDIPUS *and the* MESSENGER *turn to the* CHORUS.]
OEDIPUS: Does anyone know that herdsman,
  the one he mentioned? Anyone seen him   1150
  in the fields, in the city? Out with it!
  The time has come to reveal this once for all.
LEADER: I think he's the very shepherd you wanted to see,
  a moment ago. But the queen, Jocasta,
  she's the one to say.
OEDIPUS: Jocasta,   1155
  you remember the man we just sent for?
  Is *that* the one he means?
JOCASTA: That man . . .
  why ask? Old shepherd, talk, empty nonsense,
  don't give it another thought, don't even think—
OEDIPUS: What—give up now, with a clue like this?   1160
  Fail to solve the mystery of my birth?
  Not for all the world!
JOCASTA: Stop—in the name of god,
  if you love your own life, call off this search!
  My suffering is enough.
OEDIPUS: Courage!
  Even if my mother turns out to be a slave,   1165
  and I a slave, three generations back,
  you would not seem common.
JOCASTA: Oh no,
  listen to me, I beg you, don't do this.
OEDIPUS: Listen to you? No more. I must know it all,
  must see the truth at last.
JOCASTA: No, please—   1170
  for your sake—I want the best for you!
OEDIPUS: Your best is more than I can bear.
JOCASTA: You're doomed—
  may you never fathom who you are!
OEDIPUS: [*To a servant.*] Hurry, fetch me the herdsman, now!
  Leave her to glory in her royal birth.   1175
JOCASTA: Aieeeeee—
        man of agony—

that is the only name I have for you,
that, no other—ever, ever, ever!
  [*Flinging through the palace doors. A long, tense silence follows.*]
LEADER: Where's she gone, Oedipus?
  Rushing off, such wild grief . . .   1180
  I'm afraid that from this silence
  something monstrous may come bursting forth.
OEDIPUS: Let it burst! Whatever will, whatever must!
  I must know my birth, no matter how common
  it may be—I must see my origins face-to-face.   1185
  She perhaps, she with her woman's pride
  may well be mortified by my birth,
  but I, I count myself the son of Chance,
  the great goddess, giver of all good things—
  I'll never see myself disgraced. She is my mother!   1190
  And the moons have marked me out, my blood-brothers,
  one moon on the wane, the next moon great with power.
  That is my blood, my nature—I will never betray it,
  never fail to search and learn my birth!
CHORUS: Yes—if I am a true prophet   1195
    if I can grasp the truth,
    by the boundless skies of Olympus,
  at the full moon of tomorrow, Mount Cithaeron
  you will know how Oedipus glories in you—
  you, his birthplace, nurse, his mountain-mother!   1200
  And we will sing you, dancing out your praise—
  you lift our monarch's heart!
    Apollo, Apollo, god of the wild cry
      may our dancing please you!
                              Oedipus—
      son, dear child, who bore you?   1205
  Who of the nymphs who seem to live forever[9]
  mated with Pan,[1] the mountain-striding Father?
  Who was your mother? who, some bride of Apollo
  the god who loves the pastures spreading toward the sun?
    Or was it Hermes, king of the lightning ridges?   1210
  Or Dionysus,[2] lord of frenzy, lord of the barren peaks—
  did he seize you in his hands, dearest of all his lucky finds?—
    found by the nymphs, their warm eyes dancing, gift
  to the lord who loves them dancing out his joy!
    [OEDIPUS *strains to see a figure coming from the distance. Attended
    by palace guards, an old* SHEPHERD *enters slowly, reluctant to
    approach the king.*]
OEDIPUS: I never met the man, my friends . . . still,   1215
  if I had to guess, I'd say that's the shepherd,

---

9. Nymphs were not immortal, like the gods, but lived much longer than mortals.   1. A woodland
god, patron of shepherds and flocks.   2. Dionysus, like Pan and Hermes, haunted the wild country,
woods, and mountains. Hermes was born on Mount Kyllene in Arcadia.

the very one we've looked for all along.
Brothers in old age, two of a kind,
he and our guest here. At any rate
the ones who bring him in are my own men,   1220
I recognize them.
        [*Turning to the* LEADER.]
                        But you know more than I,
you should, you've seen the man before.
LEADER: I know him, definitely. One of Laius' men,
    a trusty shepherd, if there ever was one.
OEDIPUS: You, I ask you first, stranger,   1225
    you from Corinth—is this the one you mean?
MESSENGER: You're looking at him. He's your man.
OEDIPUS: [*To the* SHEPHERD.]
    You, old man, come over here—
    look at me. Answer all my questions.
    Did you ever serve King Laius?
SHEPHERD: So I did . . .   1230
    a slave, not bought on the block though,
    born and reared in the palace.
OEDIPUS: Your duties, your kind of work?
SHEPHERD: Herding the flocks, the better part of my life.
OEDIPUS: Where, mostly? Where did you do your grazing?
SHEPHERD: Well,   1235
    Cithaeron sometimes, or the foothills round about.
OEDIPUS: This man—you know him? ever see him there?
SHEPHERD: [*Confused, glancing from the* MESSENGER *to the King.*]
    Doing what?—what man do you mean?
OEDIPUS: [*Pointing to the* MESSENGER.]
    This one here—ever have dealings with him?
SHEPHERD: Not so I could say, but give me a chance,   1240
    my memory's bad . . .
MESSENGER: No wonder he doesn't know me, master.
    But let me refresh his memory for him.
    I'm sure he recalls old times we had
    on the slopes of Mount Cithaeron;   1245
    he and I, grazing our flocks, he with two
    and I with one—we both struck up together,
    three whole seasons, six months at a stretch
    from spring to the rising of Arcturus[3] in the fall,
    then with winter coming on I'd drive my herds   1250
    to my own pens, and back he'd go with his
    to Laius' folds.
        [*To the* SHEPHERD.]
                    Now that's how it was,
    wasn't it—yes or no?

---

3. The principal star in the constellation Boötes; its appearance in the sky (*rising*) just before dawn in
September signals the end of summer.

SHEPHERD: Yes, I suppose . . .
  it's all so long ago.
MESSENGER: Come, tell me,
  you gave me a child back then, a boy, remember? 1255
  A little fellow to rear, my very own.
SHEPHERD: What? Why rake up that again?
MESSENGER: Look, here he is, my fine old friend—
  the same man who was just a baby then.
SHEPHERD: Damn you, shut your mouth—quiet! 1260
OEDIPUS: Don't lash out at him, old man—
  you need lashing more than he does.
SHEPHERD: Why,
  master, majesty—what have I done wrong?
OEDIPUS: You won't answer his question about the boy.
SHEPHERD: He's talking nonsense, wasting his breath. 1265
OEDIPUS: So, you won't talk willingly—
  then you'll talk with pain.
    [*The guards seize the* SHEPHERD.]
SHEPHERD: No, dear god, don't torture an old man!
OEDIPUS: Twist his arms back, quickly!
SHEPHERD: God help us, why?—
  what more do you need to know? 1270
OEDIPUS: Did you give him that child? He's asking.
SHEPHERD: I did . . . I wish to god I'd died that day.
OEDIPUS: You've got your wish if you don't tell the truth.
SHEPHERD: The more I tell, the worse the death I'll die.
OEDIPUS: Our friend here wants to stretch things out, does he? 1275
    [*Motioning to his men for torture.*]
SHEPHERD: No, no, I gave it to him—I just said so.
OEDIPUS: Where did you get it? Your house? Someone else's?
SHEPHERD: It wasn't mine, no, I got it from . . . someone.
OEDIPUS: Which one of them?
    [*Looking at the citizens.*]
                  Whose house?
SHEPHERD: No—
  god's sake, master, no more questions! 1280
OEDIPUS: You're a dead man if I have to ask again.
SHEPHERD: Then—the child came from the house . . . of Laius.
OEDIPUS: A slave? or born of his own blood?
SHEPHERD: Oh no,
  I'm right at the edge, the horrible truth—I've got to say it!
OEDIPUS: And I'm at the edge of hearing horrors, yes, but I must hear! 1285
SHEPHERD: All right! His son, they said it was—his son!
  But the one inside, your wife,
  she'd tell it best.
OEDIPUS: My wife—
  she gave it to you?
SHEPHERD: Yes, yes, my king. 1290
OEDIPUS: Why, what for?

SHEPHERD: To kill it.

OEDIPUS: Her own child,
how could she?   1295

SHEPHERD: She was afraid—
frightening prophecies.

OEDIPUS: What?

SHEPHERD: They said—
he'd kill his parents.   1300

OEDIPUS: But you gave him to this old man—why?

SHEPHERD: I pitied the little baby, master,
hoped he'd take him off to his own country,
far away, but he saved him for this, this fate.
If you are the man he says you are, believe me,   1305
you were born for pain.

OEDIPUS: O god—
all come true, all burst to light!
O light—now let me look my last on you!
I stand revealed at last—
cursed in my birth, cursed in marriage,   1310
cursed in the lives I cut down with these hands!

    [*Rushing through the doors with a great cry. The Corinthian* MESSEN-
    GER, *the* SHEPHERD *and attendants exit slowly to the side.*]

CHORUS: O the generations of men
the dying generations—adding the total
of all your lives I find they come to nothing . . .
       does there exist, is there a man on earth   1315
who seizes more joy than just a dream, a vision?
And the vision no sooner dawns than dies
blazing into oblivion.

You are my great example, you, your life
your destiny, Oedipus, man of misery—   1320
I count no man blest.

           You outranged all men!
   Bending your bow to the breaking-point
you captured priceless glory, O dear god,
and the Sphinx came crashing down,
       the virgin, claws hooked   1325
like a bird of omen singing, shrieking death—
like a fortress reared in the face of death
you rose and saved our land.

From that day on we called you king
we crowned you with honors, Oedipus, towering over all—   1330
mighty king of the seven gates of Thebes.

But now to hear your story—is there a man more agonized?
More wed to pain and frenzy? Not a man on earth,
the joy of your life ground down to nothing
O Oedipus, name for the ages—   1335

one and the same wide harbor served you
    son and father both
son and father came to rest in the same bridal chamber.
How, how could the furrows your father plowed
bear you, your agony, harrowing on   1340
in silence O so long?

                But now for all your power
Time, all-seeing Time has dragged you to the light,
judged your marriage monstrous from the start—
the son and the father tangling, both one—
O child of Laius, would to god   1345
    I'd never seen you, never never!
      Now I weep like a man who wails the dead
and the dirge comes pouring forth with all my heart!
I tell you the truth, you gave me life
my breath leapt up in you   1350
and now you bring down night upon my eyes.
    [*Enter a* MESSENGER *from the palace.*]
MESSENGER: Men of Thebes, always first in honor,
what horrors you will hear, what you will see,
what a heavy weight of sorrow you will shoulder . . .
if you are true to your birth, if you still have   1355
some feeling for the royal house of Thebes.
I tell you neither the waters of the Danube
nor the Nile[4] can wash this palace clean.
Such things it hides, it soon will bring to light—
terrible things, and none done blindly now,   1360
all done with a will. The pains
we inflict upon ourselves hurt most of all.
LEADER: God knows we have pains enough already.
    What can you add to them?
MESSENGER: The queen is dead.
LEADER: Poor lady—how?   1365
MESSENGER: By her own hand. But you are spared the worst,
you never had to watch . . . I saw it all,
and with all the memory that's in me
you will learn what that poor woman suffered.

Once she'd broken in through the gates,   1370
dashing past us, frantic, whipped to fury,
ripping her hair out with both hands—
straight to her rooms she rushed, flinging herself
across the bridal-bed, doors slamming behind her—
once inside, she wailed for Laius, dead so long,   1375
remembering how she bore his child long ago,
    the life that rose up to destroy him, leaving

---

4. The Greek reads "Phasis," a river in Asia Minor. The translator has substituted a big river more
familiar to modern readers.

its mother to mother living creatures
with the very son she'd borne.
Oh how she wept, mourning the marriage-bed   1380
where she let loose that double brood—monsters—
husband by her husband, children by her child.
                                        And then—
but how she died is more than I can say. Suddenly
Oedipus burst in, screaming, he stunned us so
we couldn't watch her agony to the end,   1385
our eyes were fixed on him. Circling
like a maddened beast, stalking, here, there,
crying out to us—
                    Give him a sword!⁵ His wife,
no wife, his mother, where can he find the mother earth
that cropped two crops at once, himself and all his children?   1390
He was raging—one of the dark powers pointing the way,
none of us mortals crowding around him, no,
with a great shattering cry—someone, something leading him on—
he hurled at the twin doors and bending the bolts back
out of their sockets, crashed through the chamber.   1395
And there we saw the woman hanging by the neck,
cradled high in a woven noose, spinning,
swinging back and forth. And when he saw her,
giving a low, wrenching sob that broke our hearts,
slipping the halter from her throat, he eased her down,   1400
in a slow embrace he laid her down, poor thing . . .
then, what came next, what horror we beheld!

He rips off her brooches, the long gold pins
holding her robes—and lifting them high,
looking straight up into the points,   1405
he digs them down the sockets of his eyes, crying, "You,
you'll see no more the pain I suffered, all the pain I caused!
Too long you looked on the ones you never should have seen,
blind to the ones you longed to see, to know! Blind
from this hour on! Blind in the darkness—blind!"   1410
His voice like a dirge, rising, over and over
raising the pins, raking them down his eyes.
And at each stroke blood spurts from the roots,
splashing his beard, a swirl of it, nerves and clots—
black hail of blood pulsing, gushing down.   1415

These are the griefs that burst upon them both,
coupling man and woman. The joy they had so lately,
the fortune of their old ancestral house
was deep joy indeed. Now, in this one day,
wailing, madness and doom, death, disgrace   1420

---

5. Presumably so that he could kill himself.

all the griefs in the world that you can name,
all are theirs forever.
LEADER: Oh poor man, the misery—
has he any rest from pain now?
[*A voice within, in torment.*]
MESSENGER: He's shouting,
"Loose the bolts, someone, show me to all of Thebes!
My father's murderer, my mother's—"   1425
No, I can't repeat it, it's unholy.
Now he'll tear himself from his native earth,
not linger, curse the house with his own curse.
But he needs strength, and a guide to lead him on.
This is sickness more than he can bear.
[*The palace doors open.*]
                              Look,   1430
he'll show you himself. The great doors are opening—
you are about to see a sight, a horror
even his mortal enemy would pity.
[*Enter* OEDIPUS, *blinded, led by a boy. He stands at the palace steps,
as if surveying his people once again.*]
CHORUS: O the terror—
the suffering, for all the world to see,
the worst terror that ever met my eyes.   1435
What madness swept over you? What god,
what dark power leapt beyond all bounds,
beyond belief, to crush your wretched life?—
godforsaken, cursed by the gods!
I pity you but I can't bear to look.   1440
I've much to ask, so much to learn,
so much fascinates my eyes,
but you . . . I shudder at the sight.
OEDIPUS: Oh, Ohh—
the agony! I am agony—
where am I going? where on earth?   1445
        where does all this agony hurl me?
where's my voice?—
        winging, swept away on a dark tide—
My destiny, my dark power, what a leap you made!
CHORUS: To the depths of terror, too dark to hear, to see.   1450
OEDIPUS: Dark, horror of darkness
    my darkness, drowning, swirling around me
    crashing wave on wave—unspeakable, irresistible
        headwind, fatal harbor! Oh again,
    the misery, all at once, over and over   1455
    the stabbing daggers, stab of memory
raking me insane.
CHORUS: No wonder you suffer
    twice over, the pain of your wounds,
    the lasting grief of pain.

OEDIPUS: Dear friend, still here?
   Standing by me, still with a care for me,   1460
   the blind man? Such compassion,
     loyal to the last. Oh it's you,
   I know you're here, dark as it is
   I'd know you anywhere, your voice—
   it's yours, clearly yours.
CHORUS: Dreadful, what you've done . . .   1465
   how could you bear it, gouging out your eyes?
   What superhuman power drove you on?
OEDIPUS: Apollo, friends, Apollo—
   he ordained my agonies—these, my pains on pains!
   But the hand that struck my eyes was mine,   1470
   mine alone—no one else—
     I did it all myself!
   What good were eyes to me?
   Nothing I could see could bring me joy.
CHORUS: No, no, exactly as you say.
OEDIPUS: What can I ever see?   1475
   What love, what call of the heart
   can touch my ears with joy? Nothing, friends.
     Take me away, far, far from Thebes,
      quickly, cast me away, my friends—
   this great murderous ruin, this man cursed to heaven,   1480
   the man the deathless gods hate most of all!
CHORUS: Pitiful, you suffer so, you understand so much . . .
   I wish you'd never known.
OEDIPUS: Die, die—
   whoever he was that day in the wilds
   who cut my ankles free of the ruthless pins,   1485
   he pulled me clear of death, he saved my life
   for this, this kindness—
     Curse him, kill him!
   If I'd died then, I'd never have dragged myself,
   my loved ones through such hell.   1490
CHORUS: Oh if only . . . would to god.
OEDIPUS: I'd never have come to this,
   my father's murderer—never been branded
   mother's husband, all men see me now! Now,
     loathed by the gods, son of the mother I defiled
      coupling in my father's bed, spawning lives in the loins   1495
   that spawned my wretched life. What grief can crown this grief?
     It's mine alone, my destiny—I am Oedipus!
CHORUS: How can I say you've chosen for the best?
   Better to die than be alive and blind.
OEDIPUS: What I did was best—don't lecture me,   1500
   no more advice. I, with *my* eyes,
   how could I look my father in the eyes
   when I go down to death? Or mother, so abused . . .

I have done such things to the two of them,
crimes too huge for hanging.
                              Worse yet,   1505
the sight of my children, born as they were born,
how could I long to look into their eyes?
No, not with these eyes of mine, never.
Not this city either, her high towers,
the sacred glittering images of her gods—   1510
I am misery! I, her best son, reared
as no other son of Thebes was ever reared,
I've stripped myself, I gave the command myself.
All men must cast away the great blasphemer,
the curse now brought to light by the gods,   1515
the son of Laius—I, my father's son!

Now I've exposed my guilt, horrendous guilt,
could I train a level glance on you, my countrymen?
Impossible! No, if I could just block off my ears,
the springs of hearing, I would stop at nothing—   1520
I'd wall up my loathsome body like a prison,
blind to the sound of life, not just the sight.
Oblivion—what a blessing . . .
for the mind to dwell a world away from pain.

O Cithaeron, why did you give me shelter?   1525
Why didn't you take me, crush my life out on the spot?
I'd never have revealed my birth to all mankind.

O Polybus, Corinth, the old house of my fathers,
so I believed—what a handsome prince you raised—
under the skin, what sickness to the core.   1530
Look at me! Born of outrage, outrage to the core.
O triple roads—it all comes back, the secret,
dark ravine, and the oaks closing in
where the three roads join . . .
You drank my father's blood, my own blood   1535
spilled by my own hands—you still remember me?
What things you saw me do? Then I came here
and did them all once more!
                              Marriages! O marriage,
you gave me birth, and once you brought me into the world
you brought my sperm rising back, springing to light   1540
fathers, brothers, sons—one murderous breed—
brides, wives, mothers. The blackest things
a man can do, I have done them all!
                              No more—
it's wrong to name what's wrong to do. Quickly,
for the love of god, hide me somewhere,   1545
kill me, hurl me into the sea
where you can never look on me again.

[*Beckoning to the* CHORUS *as they shrink away.*]
                            Closer,
  it's all right. Touch the man of grief.
  Do. Don't be afraid. My troubles are mine
  and I am the only man alive who can sustain them.   1550
  [*Enter* CREON *from the palace, attended by palace guards.*]
LEADER: Put your requests to Creon. Here he is,
  just when we need him. He'll have a plan, he'll act.
  Now that he's the sole defense of the country
  in your place.
OEDIPUS: Oh no, what can I say to him?
  How can I ever hope to win his trust?   1555
  I wronged him so, just now, in every way.
  You must see that—I was so wrong, so wrong.
CREON: I haven't come to mock you, Oedipus,
  or to criticize your former failings.
  [*Turning to the guards.*]
                          You there,
  have you lost all respect for human feelings?   1560
  At least revere the Sun, the holy fire
  that keeps us all alive. Never expose a thing
  of guilt and holy dread so great it appalls
  the earth, the rain from heaven, the light of day!
  Get him into the halls—quickly as you can.   1565
  Piety demands no less. Kindred alone
  should see a kinsman's shame. This is obscene.
OEDIPUS: Please, in god's name . . . you wipe my fears away,
  coming so generously to me, the worst of men.
  Do one thing more, for your sake, not mine.   1570
CREON: What do you want? Why so insistent?
OEDIPUS: Drive me out of the land at once, far from sight,
  where I can never hear a human voice.
CREON: I'd have done that already, I promise you.
  First I wanted the god to clarify my duties.   1575
OEDIPUS: The god? His command was clear, every word:
  death for the father-killer, the curse—
  he said destroy me!
CREON: So he did. Still, in such a crisis
  it's better to ask precisely what to do.
OEDIPUS: So miserable—   1580
  you'd consult the god about a man like me?
CREON: By all means. And this time, I assume,
  even you will obey the god's decrees.
OEDIPUS: I will,
  I will. And you, I command you—I beg you . . .
  the woman inside, bury her as you see fit.   1585
  It's the only decent thing,
  to give your own the last rites. As for me,
  never condemn the city of my fathers

to house my body, not while I'm alive, no,
let me live on the mountains, on Cithaeron,   1590
my favorite haunt, I have made it famous.
Mother and father marked out that rock
to be my everlasting tomb—buried alive.
Let me die there, where they tried to kill me.

Oh but this I know: no sickness can destroy me,   1595
nothing can. I would never have been saved
from death—I have been saved
for something great and terrible, something strange.
Well let my destiny come and take me on its way!
About my children, Creon, the boys at least,   1600
don't burden yourself. They're men,
wherever they go, they'll find the means to live.
But my two daughters, my poor helpless girls,
clustering at our table, never without me
hovering near them . . . whatever I touched,   1605
they always had their share. Take care of them,
I beg you. Wait, better—permit me, would you?
Just to touch them with my hands and take
our fill of tears. Please . . . my king.
Grant it, with all your noble heart.   1610
If I could hold them, just once, I'd think
I had them with me, like the early days
when I could see their eyes.
> [ANTIGONE *and* ISMENE, *two small children, are led in from the palace by a nurse.*]
                              What's that
O god! Do I really hear you sobbing?—
my two children. Creon, you've pitied me?   1615
Sent me my darling girls, my own flesh and blood!
Am I right?

CREON: Yes, it's my doing.
I know the joy they gave you all these years,
the joy you must feel now.

OEDIPUS: Bless you, Creon!
May god watch over you for this kindness,   1620
better than he ever guarded me.
                              Children, where are you?
Here, come quickly—
> [*Groping for* ANTIGONE *and* ISMENE, *who approach their father cautiously, then embrace him.*]
                              Come to these hands of mine,
your brother's hands, your own father's hands
that served his once bright eyes so well—
that made them blind. Seeing nothing, children,   1625
knowing nothing, I became your father,
I fathered you in the soil that gave me life.

How I weep for you—I cannot see you now . . .
just thinking of all your days to come, the bitterness,
the life that rough mankind will thrust upon you.   1630
Where are the public gatherings you can join,
the banquets of the clans? Home you'll come,
in tears, cut off from the sight of it all,
the brilliant rites unfinished.
And when you reach perfection, ripe for marriage,   1635
who will he be, my dear ones? Risking all
to shoulder the curse that weighs down my parents,
yes and you too—that wounds us all together.
What more misery could you want?
Your father killed his father, sowed his mother,   1640
one, one and the selfsame womb sprang you—
he cropped the very roots of his existence.

Such disgrace, and you must bear it all!
Who will marry you then? Not a man on earth.
Your doom is clear: you'll wither away to nothing,   1645
single, without a child.
    [*Turning to* CREON.]
               Oh Creon,
you are the only father they have now . . .
we who brought them into the world
are gone, both gone at a stroke—
Don't let them go begging, abandoned,   1650
women without men. Your own flesh and blood!
Never bring them down to the level of my pains.
Pity them. Look at them, so young, so vulnerable,
shorn of everything—you're their only hope.
Promise me, noble Creon, touch my hand!   1655
    [*Reaching toward* CREON, *who draws back.*]
You, little ones, if you were old enough
to understand, there is much I'd tell you.
Now, as it is, I'd have you say a prayer.
Pray for life, my children,
live where you are free to grow and season.   1660
Pray god you find a better life than mine,
the father who begot you.
CREON: Enough.
You've wept enough. Into the palace now.
OEDIPUS: I must, but I find it very hard.
CREON: Time is the great healer, you will see.   1665
OEDIPUS: I am going—you know on what condition?
CREON: Tell me. I'm listening.
OEDIPUS: Drive me out of Thebes, in exile.
CREON: Not I. Only the gods can give you that.
OEDIPUS: Surely the gods hate me so much—   1670
CREON: You'll get your wish at once.

OEDIPUS: You consent?
CREON: I try to say what I mean; it's my habit.
OEDIPUS: Then take me away. It's time.
CREON: Come along, let go of the children.
OEDIPUS: No—
   don't take them away from me, not now! No no no!   1675
     [*Clutching his daughters as the guards wrench them loose and take*
     them through the palace doors.]
CREON: Still the king, the master of all things?
   No more: here your power ends.
   None of your power follows you through life.
     [*Exit* OEDIPUS *and* CREON *to the palace. The* CHORUS *comes forward*
     to address the audience directly.]
CHORUS: People of Thebes, my countrymen, look on Oedipus.
   He solved the famous riddle with his brilliance,   1680
   he rose to power, a man beyond all power.
   Who could behold his greatness without envy?
   Now what a black sea of terror has overwhelmed him.
   Now as we keep our watch and wait the final day,
   count no man happy till he dies, free of pain at last.   1685
     [*Exit in procession.*]

EURIPIDES
480–406 B.C.

Euripides' *Medea*, produced in 431 B.C., the year that brought the beginning of
the Peloponnesian War, appeared earlier than Sophocles' *Oedipus the King*, but
it has a bitterness that is more in keeping with the spirit of a later age. If *Oedipus*
is, in one sense, a warning to a generation that has embarked on an intellectual
revolution, *Medea* is the ironic expression of the disillusion that comes after the
shipwreck. In this play we are conscious for the first time of an attitude characteristic of modern literature, the artist's feeling of separation from the audience, the
isolation of the poet. "Often previously," says Medea to the king,

> Through being considered clever I have suffered much. . . .
> If you put new ideas before the eyes of fools
> They'll think you foolish and worthless into the bargain;
> And if you are thought superior to those who have
> Some reputation for learning, you will become hated.

The common background of audience and poet is disappearing, the old certainties
are being undermined, the city divided. Euripides is the first Greek poet to suffer
the fate of so many of the great modern writers: rejected by most of his contemporaries (he rarely won first prize and was the favorite target for the scurrilous humor
of the comic poets), he was universally admired and revered by the Greeks of the
centuries that followed his death.

   It is significant that what little biographical information we have for Euripides
makes no mention of military service or political office; unlike Aeschylus, who
fought in the ranks at Marathon, and Sophocles, who took an active part in public

affairs from youth to advanced old age, Euripides seems to have lived a private, an intellectual life. Younger than Sophocles (though they died in the same year), he was more receptive to the critical theories and the rhetorical techniques offered by the Sophist teachers; his plays often subject received ideas to fundamental questioning, expressed in vivid dramatic debate. His *Medea* is typical of his iconoclastic approach; his choice of subject and central characters is in itself a challenge to established canons. He still dramatizes myth, but the myth he chooses is exotic and disturbing, and the protagonist is not a man but a woman. Medea is both woman and foreigner—that is, in terms of the audience's prejudice and practice she is a representative of the two free-born groups in Athenian society that had almost no rights at all (though the male foreign resident had more rights than the native woman). The tragic hero is no longer a king, "one who is highly renowned and prosperous such as Oedipus," but a woman who, because she finds no redress for her wrongs in society, is driven by her passion to violate that society's most sacred laws in a rebellion against its typical representative, Jason, her husband. She is not just a woman and a foreigner, she is also a person of great intellectual power. Compared with her the credulous king and her complacent husband are children, and once her mind is made up, she moves them like pawns to their proper places in her barbaric game. The myth is used for new purposes, to shock the members of the audience, attack their deepest prejudices, and shake them out of their complacent pride in the superiority of Greek masculinity.

But the play is more compelling than that. Before it is over, our sympathies have come full circle; the contempt with which we regard the Jason of the opening scenes turns to pity as we feel the measure of his loss and the ferocity of Medea's revenge. Medea's passion has carried her too far; the death of Kreon (Creon) and his daughter we might have accepted, but the murder of the children is too much. It was, of course, meant to be. Euripides' theme, like Homer's, is violence, but this is the unspeakable violence of the oppressed, which is greater than the violence of the oppressor and which, because it has been long pent up, cannot be controlled.

In this, as in the other Greek plays, the gods have their place. In *Oresteia* the will of Zeus is manifested in every action and implied in every word; in *Oedipus the King* the gods bide their time and watch Oedipus fulfill the truth of their prophecy, but in *Medea*, the divine will, which is revealed at the end, is enigmatic and, far from bringing harmony, concludes the play with a terrifying discord. All through *Medea* the human beings involved call on the gods; two especially are singled out for attention: Earth and Sun. It is by these two gods that Medea makes Aegeus swear to give her refuge in Athens, the chorus invokes them to prevent Medea's violence against her sons, and Jason wonders how Medea can look on Earth and Sun after she has killed her own children. These emphatic appeals clearly raise the question of the attitude of the gods, and the answer to the question is a shock. We are not told what Earth does, but Sun sends the magic chariot on which Medea makes her escape. His reason, too, is stated: it is not any concern for justice but the fact that Medea is his granddaughter. Euripides is here using the letter of the myth for his own purposes. This jarring detail emphasizes the significance of the whole. The play creates a world in which there is no relation whatsoever between the powers that rule the universe and the fundamental laws of human morality. It dramatizes disorder, not just the disorder of the family of Jason and Medea but the disorder of the universe as a whole. It is the nightmare in which the dream of the fifth century B.C. was to end, the senseless fury and degradation of permanent violence. "Flow backward to your sources, sacred rivers," the chorus sings, "And let the world's great order be reversed."

For a short, general survey of Euripidean drama, see B. M. W. Knox in *The Cambridge History of Classical Literature* (1985), pp. 316–39. Perceptive analyses of *Medea* can be found in Emily A. McDermott, *Euripides' Medea: The Incarna-*

tion of Disorder (1989), and E. Segal, ed., *Euripides, A Collection of Critical Essays* (1968). Knox, "The *Medea* of Euripides," and P. E. Easterling, "The Infanticide in Euripides' *Medea*," both in *Yale Classical Studies* 24 (1977), will also be helpful to students.

PRONOUNCING GLOSSARY

The following list uses common English syllables and stress accents to provide rough equivalents of selected words whose pronunciation may be unfamiliar to the general reader.

Aigeus: *ai'-jioos*   Medea: *me-dee'-uh*

Aphrodite: *a-froh-dai'-tee*   Pelias: *pee'-lee-as*

Hecate: *he'-kah-tee*   Pieria: *pai-ee'-ree-uh / pee-ehr'-ee-uh*

Iolcus: *yol'-kuhs / ee-ol'-kuhs*

Medea[1]

CHARACTERS

MEDEA, *princess of Colchis and wife of Jason*	AIGEUS, *king of Athens*
	NURSE *to Medea*
JASON, *son of Aeson, king of Iolcos*	TUTOR *to Medea's children*
Two CHILDREN *of Medea and Jason*	MESSENGER
KREON, *king of Corinth*	CHORUS OF CORINTHIAN WOMEN

[SCENE—*In front of* MEDEA'*s house in Corinth. Enter from the house* MEDEA'*s* NURSE.]

NURSE: How I wish the Argo[2] never had reached the land
Of Colchis, skimming through the blue Symplegades,
Nor ever had fallen in the glades of Pelion[3]
The smitten fir-tree to furnish oars for the hands
Of heroes who in Pelias'[4] name attempted   5
The Golden Fleece! For then my mistress Medea[5]
Would not have sailed for the towers of the land of Iolcos,
Her heart on fire with passionate love for Jason;
Nor would she have persuaded the daughters of Pelias
To kill their father,[6] and now be living here   10
In Corinth[7] with her husband and children. She gave
Pleasure to the people of her land of exile,

---

1. Translated by Rex Warner.   2. The ship in which Jason and his companions sailed on the quest for the Golden Fleece.   3. A mountain in northern Greece near Iolcos, the place from which Jason sailed. The Symplegades were clashing rocks that crushed ships endeavoring to pass between them. They were supposed to be located at the Hellespont, the passage between the Mediterranean and Black seas.   4. He seized the kingdom of Iolcos, expelling Aeson, Jason's father. When Jason came to claim his rights, Pelias sent him to get the Golden Fleece.   5. Daughter of the king of Colchis who fell in love with Jason and helped him take the Golden Fleece away from her own country.   6. After Jason and Medea returned to Iolcos, Medea (who had a reputation as a sorceress) persuaded Pelias' daughters to cut Pelias up and boil the pieces, which would restore him to youth. The experiment was, of course, unsuccessful, and Pelias' son banished Jason and Medea from the kingdom.   7. On the isthmus between the Peloponnese and Attica, where they took refuge. In Euripides' time it was a wealthy trading city, a commercial rival of Athens.

And she herself helped Jason in every way.
This is indeed the greatest salvation of all, —
For the wife not to stand apart from the husband.   15
But now there's hatred everywhere. Love is diseased.
For, deserting his own children and my mistress,
Jason has taken a royal wife to his bed,
The daughter of the ruler of this land, Kreon.
And poor Medea is slighted, and cries aloud on the   20
Vows they made to each other, the right hands clasped
In eternal promise. She calls upon the gods to witness
What sort of return Jason has made to her love.
She lies without food and gives herself up to suffering,
Wasting away every moment of the day in tears.   25
So it has gone since she knew herself slighted by him.
Not stirring an eye, not moving her face from the ground,
No more than either a rock or surging sea water
She listens when she is given friendly advice.
Except that sometimes she twists back her white neck and   30
Moans to herself, calling out on her father's name,
And her land, and her home betrayed when she came away with
A man who now is determined to dishonor her.
Poor creature, she has discovered by her sufferings
What it means to one not to have lost one's own country.   35
She has turned from the children and does not like to see them.
I am afraid she may think of some dreadful thing,
For her heart is violent. She will never put up with
The treatment she is getting. I know and fear her
Lest she may sharpen a sword and thrust to the heart,   40
Stealing into the palace where the bed is made,
Or even kill the king and the new-wedded groom,
And thus bring a greater misfortune on herself.
She's a strange woman. I know it won't be easy
To make an enemy of her and come off best.   45
But here the children come. They have finished playing.
They have no thought at all of their mother's trouble.
Indeed it is not usual for the young to grieve.

    [*Enter from the right the slave who is the* TUTOR *to* MEDEA*'s two small*
    CHILDREN. *The* CHILDREN *follow him.*]

TUTOR: You old retainer of my mistress's household,
    Why are you standing here all alone in front of the   50
    Gates and moaning to yourself over your misfortune?
    Medea could not wish you to leave her alone.
NURSE: Old man, and guardian of the children of Jason,
    If one is a good servant, it's a terrible thing
    When one's master's luck is out; it goes to one's heart.   55
    So I myself have got into such a state of grief
    That a longing stole over me to come outside here
    And tell the earth and air of my mistress's sorrows.
TUTOR: Has the poor lady not yet given up her crying?

NURSE: Given up? She's at the start, not halfway through her tears.   60
TUTOR: Poor fool,—if I may call my mistress such a name,—
  How ignorant she is of trouble more to come.
NURSE: What do you mean, old man? You needn't fear to speak.
TUTOR: Nothing. I take back the words which I used just now.
NURSE: Don't, by your beard, hide this from me, your fellow-servant.   65
  If need be, I'll keep quiet about what you tell me.
TUTOR: I heard a person saying, while I myself seemed
  Not to be paying attention, when I was at the place
  Where the old draught-players[8] sit, by the holy fountain,
  That Kreon, ruler of the land, intends to drive   70
  These children and their mother in exile from Corinth.
  But whether what he said is really true or not
  I do not know. I pray that it may not be true.
NURSE: And will Jason put up with it that his children
  Should suffer so, though he's no friend to their mother?   75
TUTOR: Old ties give place to new ones. As for Jason, he
  No longer has a feeling for this house of ours.
NURSE: It's black indeed for us, when we add new to old
  Sorrows before even the present sky has cleared.
TUTOR: But you be silent, and keep all this to yourself.   80
  It is not the right time to tell our mistress of it.
NURSE: Do you hear, children, what a father he is to you?
  I wish he were dead,—but no, he is still my master.
  Yet certainly he has proved unkind to his dear ones.
TUTOR: What's strange in that? Have you only just discovered   85
  That everyone loves himself more than his neighbor?
  Some have good reason, others get something out of it.
  So Jason neglects his children for the new bride.
NURSE: Go indoors, children. That will be the best thing.
  And you, keep them to themselves as much as possible.   90
  Don't bring them near their mother in her angry mood.
  For I've seen her already blazing her eyes at them
  As though she meant some mischief and I am sure that
  She'll not stop raging until she has struck at someone.
  May it be an enemy and not a friend she hurts!   95
    [MEDEA *is heard inside the house.*]
MEDEA: Ah, wretch! Ah, lost in my sufferings,
  I wish, I wish I might die.
NURSE: What did I say, dear children? Your mother
  Frets her heart and frets it to anger.
  Run away quickly into the house,   100
  And keep well out of her sight.
  Don't go anywhere near, but be careful
  Of the wildness and bitter nature
  Of that proud mind.
  Go now! Run quickly indoors.   105

8. Checker players.

It is clear that she soon will put lightning
In that cloud of her cries that is rising
With a passion increasing. Oh, what will she do,
Proud-hearted and not to be checked on her course,
A soul bitten into with wrong?   110

[*The* TUTOR *takes the* CHILDREN *into the house.*]

MEDEA: Ah, I have suffered
  What should be wept for bitterly. I hate you,
  Children of a hateful mother. I curse you
  And your father. Let the whole house crash.

NURSE: Ah, I pity you, you poor creature.   115
  How can your children share in their father's
  Wickedness? Why do you hate them? Oh children,
  How much I fear that something may happen!
  Great people's tempers are terrible, always
  Having their own way, seldom checked,   120
  Dangerous they shift from mood to mood.
  How much better to have been accustomed
  To live on equal terms with one's neighbors.
  I would like to be safe and grow old in a
  Humble way. What is moderate sounds best,   125
  Also in practice *is* best for everyone.
  Greatness brings no profit to people.
  God indeed, when in anger, brings
  Greater ruin to great men's houses.

[*Enter, on the right, a* CHORUS OF CORINTHIAN WOMEN. *They have
come to inquire about* MEDEA *and to attempt to console her.*]

CHORUS: I heard the voice, I heard the cry   130
  Of Colchis' wretched daughter.
  Tell me, mother, is she not yet
  At rest? Within the double gates
  Of the court I heard her cry. I am sorry
  For the sorrow of this home. O, say, what has happened?   135

NURSE: There is no home. It's over and done with.
  Her husband holds fast to his royal wedding,
  While she, my mistress, cries out her eyes
  There in her room, and takes no warmth from
  Any word of any friend.   140

MEDEA: Oh, I wish
  That lightning from heaven would split my head open.
  Oh, what use have I now for life?
  I would find my release in death
  And leave hateful existence behind me.   145

CHORUS: O God and Earth and Heaven!
  Did you hear what a cry was that
  Which the sad wife sings?
  Poor foolish one, why should you long
  For that appalling rest?   150
  The final end of death comes fast.

No need to pray for that.
Suppose your man gives honor
To another woman's bed.
It often happens. Don't be hurt.   155
God will be your friend in this.
You must not waste away
Grieving too much for him who shared your bed.
MEDEA: Great Themis, lady Artemis,[9] behold
The things I suffer, though I made him promise,   160
My hateful husband. I pray that I may see him,
Him and his bride and all their palace shattered
For the wrong they dare to do me without cause.
Oh, my father! Oh, my country! In what dishonor
I left you, killing my own brother for it.[1]   165
NURSE: Do you hear what she says, and how she cries
On Themis, the goddess of Promises, and on Zeus,
Whom we believe to be the Keeper of Oaths?
Of this I am sure, that no small thing
Will appease my mistress's anger.   170
CHORUS: Will she come into our presence?
Will she listen when we are speaking
To the words we say?
I wish she might relax her rage
And temper of her heart.   175
My willingness to help will never
Be wanting to my friends.
But go inside and bring her
Out of the house to us,
And speak kindly to her: hurry,   180
Before she wrongs her own.
This passion of hers moves to something great.
NURSE: I will, but I doubt if I'll manage
To win my mistress over.
But still I'll attempt it to please you.   185
Such a look she will flash on her servants
If any comes near with a message,
Like a lioness guarding her cubs.
It is right, I think, to consider
Both stupid and lacking in foresight   190
Those poets of old who wrote songs
For revels and dinners and banquets,
Pleasant sounds for men living at ease;
But none of them all has discovered
How to put an end with their singing   195
Or musical instruments grief,
Bitter grief, from which death and disaster

9. The protector of women in pain and distress. Themis, a Titan, was justice personified.   1. Medea killed him to delay the pursuit when she escaped with Jason.

Cheat the hopes of a house. Yet how good
If music could cure men of this! But why raise
To no purpose the voice at a banquet? For *there* is   200
Already abundance of pleasure for men
With a joy of its own.
   [*The* NURSE *goes into the house.*]
CHORUS: I heard a shriek that is laden with sorrow.
  Shrilling out her hard grief she cries out
  Upon him who betrayed both her bed and her marriage.   205
  Wronged, she calls on the gods,
  On the justice of Zeus, the oath sworn,
  Which brought her away
  To the opposite shore of the Greeks
  Through the gloomy salt straits to the gateway   210
  Of the salty unlimited sea.
   [MEDEA, *attended by servants, comes out of the house.*]
MEDEA: Women of Corinth, I have come outside to you
Lest you should be indignant with me; for I know
That many people are overproud, some when alone,
And others when in company. And those who live   215
Quietly, as I do, get a bad reputation.
For a just judgment is not evident in the eyes
When a man at first sight hates another, before
Learning his character, being in no way injured;
And a foreigner[2] especially must adapt himself.   220
I'd not approve of even a fellow-countryman
Who by pride and want of manners offends his neighbors.
But on me this thing has fallen so unexpectedly,
It has broken my heart. I am finished. I let go
All my life's joy. My friends, I only want to die.   225
It was everything to me to think well of one man,
And he, my own husband, has turned out wholly vile.
Of all things which are living and can form a judgment
We women are the most unfortunate creatures.[3]
Firstly, with an excess of wealth it is required   230
For us to buy a husband and take for our bodies
A master; for not to take one is even worse.
And now the question is serious whether we take
A good or bad one; for there is no easy escape
For a woman, nor can she say no to her marriage.   235
She arrives among new modes of behavior and manners,
And needs prophetic power, unless she has learnt at home,
How best to manage him who shares the bed with her.
And if we work out all this well and carefully,
And the husband lives with us and lightly bears his yoke,   240

---

2. Foreign residents were encouraged to come to Athens but were rarely admitted to the rights of full citizenship, which was a jealously guarded privilege.   3. Athenian rights and institutions were made for men; the women had few privileges and almost no legal rights. Lines 230–31 refer to the dowry that had to be provided for the bride.

Then life is enviable. If not, I'd rather die.
A man, when he's tired of the company in his home,
Goes out of the house and puts an end to his boredom
And turns to a friend or companion of his own age.
But we are forced to keep our eyes on one alone.   245
What they say of us is that we have a peaceful time
Living at home, while they do the fighting in war.
How wrong they are! I would very much rather stand
Three times in the front of battle than bear one child.
Yet what applies to me does not apply to you.   250
You have a country. Your family home is here.
You enjoy life and the company of your friends.
But I am deserted, a refugee, thought nothing of
By my husband,—something he won in a foreign land.
I have no mother or brother, nor any relation   255
With whom I can take refuge in this sea of woe.
This much then is the service I would beg from you:
If I can find the means or devise any scheme
To pay my husband back for what he has done to me,—
Him and his father-in-law and the girl who married him,— 260
Just to keep silent. For in other ways a woman
Is full of fear, defenseless, dreads the sight of cold
Steel; but, when once she is wronged in the matter of love,
No other soul can hold so many thoughts of blood.
CHORUS: This I will promise. You are in the right, Medea,   265
In paying your husband back. I am not surprised at you
For being sad. But look! I see our king Kreon
Approaching. He will tell us of some new plan.
     [*Enter, from the right,* KREON, *with attendants.*]
KREON: You, with that angry look, so set against your husband,
Medea, I order you to leave my territories   270
An exile, and take along with you your two children,
And not to waste time doing it. It is my decree,
And I will see it done. I will not return home
Until you are cast from the boundaries of my land.
MEDEA: Oh, this is the end for me. I am utterly lost.   275
Now I am in the full force of the storm of hate
And have no harbor from ruin to reach easily.
Yet still, in spite of it all, I'll ask the question:
What is your reason, Kreon, for banishing me?
KREON: I am afraid of you,—why should I dissemble it?—   280
Afraid that you may injure my daughter mortally.
Many things accumulate to support my feeling.
You are a clever woman, versed in evil arts,
And are angry at having lost your husband's love.
I hear that you are threatening, so they tell me,   285
To do something against my daughter and Jason
And me, too. I shall take my precautions first.
I tell you, I prefer to earn your hatred now

Than to be soft-hearted and afterwards regret it.
MEDEA: This is not the first time, Kreon. Often previously   290
Through being considered clever I have suffered much.
A person of sense ought never to have his children
Brought up to be more clever than the average.
For, apart from cleverness bringing them no profit,
It will make them objects of envy and ill-will.   295
If you put new ideas before the eyes of fools
They'll think you foolish and worthless into the bargain;
And if you are thought superior to those who have
Some reputation for learning, you will become hated.
I have some knowledge myself of how this happens;   300
For being clever, I find that some will envy me,
Others object to me. Yet all my cleverness
Is not so much. Well, then, are you frightened, Kreon,
That I should harm you? There is no need. It is not
My way to transgress the authority of a king.   305
How have you injured me? You gave your daughter away
To the man you wanted. O, certainly I hate
My husband, but you, I think, have acted wisely;
Nor do I grudge it you that your affairs go well.
May the marriage be a lucky one! Only let me   310
Live in this land. For even though I have been wronged,
I will not raise my voice, but submit to my betters.
KREON: What you say sounds gentle enough. Still in my heart
I greatly dread that you are plotting some evil,
And therefore I trust you even less than before.   315
A sharp-tempered woman, or for that matter a man,
Is easier to deal with than the clever type
Who holds her tongue. No. You must go. No need for more
Speeches. The thing is fixed. By no manner of means
Shall you, an enemy of mine, stay in my country.   320
MEDEA: I beg you. By your knees, by your new-wedded girl.
KREON: Your words are wasted. You will never persuade me.
MEDEA: Will you drive me out, and give no heed to my prayers?
KREON: I will, for I love my family more than you.
MEDEA: O my country! How bitterly now I remember you!   325
KREON: I love my country too,—next after my children.
MEDEA: O what an evil to men is passionate love!
KREON: That would depend on the luck that goes along with it.
MEDEA: O God, do not forget who is the cause of this!
KREON: Go. It is no use. Spare me the pain of forcing you.   330
MEDEA: I'm spared no pain. I lack no pain to be spared me.
KREON: Then you'll be removed by force by one of my men.
MEDEA: No, Kreon, not that! But do listen, I beg you.
KREON: Woman, you seem to want to create a disturbance.
MEDEA: I *will* go into exile. *This* is not what I beg for.   335
KREON: Why then this violence and clinging to my hand?
MEDEA: Allow me to remain here just for this one day,

So I may consider where to live in my exile,
And look for support for my children, since their father
Chooses to make no kind of provision for them. 340
Have pity on them! You have children of your own.
It is natural for you to look kindly on them.
For myself I do not mind if I go into exile.
It is the children being in trouble that I mind.
KREON: There is nothing tyrannical about my nature, 345
And by showing mercy I have often been the loser.
Even now I know that I am making a mistake.
All the same you shall have your will. But this I tell you,
That if the light of heaven tomorrow shall see you,
You and your children in the confines of my land, 350
You die. This word I have spoken is firmly fixed.
But now, if you must stay, stay for this day alone.
For in it you can do none of the things I fear.
  [*Exit* KREON *with his attendants.*]
CHORUS: Oh, unfortunate one! Oh, cruel!
Where will you turn? Who will help you? 355
What house or what land to preserve you
From ill can you find?
Medea, a god has thrown suffering
Upon you in waves of despair.
MEDEA: Things have gone badly every way. No doubt of that. 360
But not these things this far, and don't imagine so.
There are still trials to come for the new-wedded pair,
And for their relations pain that will mean something.
Do you think that I would ever have fawned on that man
Unless I had some end to gain or profit in it? 365
I would not even have spoken or touched him with my hands.
But he has got to such a pitch of foolishness
That, though he could have made nothing of all my plans
By exiling me, he has given me this one day
To stay here, and in this I will make dead bodies 370
Of three of my enemies,—father, the girl and my husband.
I have many ways of death which I might suit to them,
And do not know, friends, which one to take in hand;
Whether to set fire underneath their bridal mansion,
Or sharpen a sword and thrust it to the heart, 375
Stealing into the palace where the bed is made.
There is just one obstacle to this. If I am caught
Breaking into the house and scheming against it,
I shall die, and give my enemies cause for laughter.
It is best to go by the straight road, the one in which 380
I am most skilled, and make away with them by poison.
So be it then.
And now suppose them dead. What town will receive me?
What friend will offer me a refuge in his land,
Or the guarantee of his house and save my own life? 385

There is none. So I must wait a little time yet,
And if some sure defense should then appear for me,
In craft and silence I will set about this murder.
But if my fate should drive me on without help,
Even though death is certain, I will take the sword   390
Myself and kill, and steadfastly advance to crime.
It shall not be,—I swear it by her, my mistress,
Whom most I honor and have chosen as partner,
Hecate,[4] who dwells in the recesses of my hearth,—
That any man shall be glad to have injured me.   395
Bitter I will make their marriage for them and mournful,
Bitter the alliance and the driving me out of the land.
Ah, come, Medea, in your plotting and scheming
Leave nothing untried of all those things which you know.
Go forward to the dreadful act. The test has come   400
For resolution. You see how you are treated. Never
Shall you be mocked by Jason's Corinthian wedding,
Whose father was noble, whose grandfather Helios.[5]
You have the skill. What is more, you were born a woman,
And women, though most helpless in doing good deeds,   405
Are of every evil the cleverest of contrivers.
CHORUS: Flow backward to your sources, sacred rivers,
And let the world's great order be reversed.
It is the thoughts of *men* that are deceitful,
Their pledges that are loose.   410
Story shall now turn my condition to a fair one,
Women are paid their due.
No more shall evil-sounding fame be theirs.

Cease now, you muses of the ancient singers,
To tell the tale of my unfaithfulness;   415
For not on us did Phoebus,[6] lord of music,
Bestow the lyre's divine
Power, for otherwise I should have sung an answer
To the other sex. Long time
Has much to tell of us, and much of them.   420

You sailed away from your father's home,
With a heart on fire you passed
The double rocks of the sea.
And now in a foreign country
You have lost your rest in a widowed bed,   425
And are driven forth, a refugee
In dishonor from the land.

Good faith has gone, and no more remains
In great Greece a sense of shame.
It has flown away to the sky.   430

4. The patron of witchcraft, sometimes identified with Artemis; Medea has a statue and shrine of her in the house.   5. The sun, father of Medea's father, Aeëtes.   6. Apollo.

No father's house for a haven
Is at hand for you now, and another queen
Of your bed has dispossessed you and
Is mistress of your home.
    [*Enter* JASON, *with attendants.*]
JASON: This is not the first occasion that I have noticed   435
How hopeless it is to deal with a stubborn temper.
For, with reasonable submission to our ruler's will,
You might have lived in this land and kept your home.
As it is you are going to be exiled for your loose speaking.
Not that I mind myself. You are free to continue   440
Telling everyone that Jason is a worthless man.
But as to your talk about the king, consider
Yourself most lucky that exile is your punishment.
I, for my part, have always tried to calm down
The anger of the king, and wished you to remain.   445
But you will not give up your folly, continually
Speaking ill of him, and so you are going to be banished.
All the same, and in spite of your conduct, I'll not desert
My friends, but have come to make some provision for you,
So that you and the children may not be penniless   450
Or in need of anything in exile. Certainly
Exile brings many troubles with it. And even
If you hate me, I cannot think badly of you.
MEDEA: O coward in every way,—that is what I call you,
With bitterest reproach for your lack of manliness,   455
You have come, you, my worst enemy, have come to me!
It is not an example of over-confidence
Or of boldness thus to look your friends in the face,
Friends you have injured,—no, it is the worst of all
Human diseases, shamelessness. But you did well   460
To come, for I can speak ill of you and lighten
My heart, and you will suffer while you are listening.
And first I will begin from what happened first.
I saved your life, and every Greek knows I saved it
Who was a ship-mate of yours aboard the Argo,   465
When you were sent to control the bulls that breathed fire
And yoke them, and when you would sow that deadly field.
Also that snake, who encircled with his many folds
The Golden Fleece and guarded it and never slept,[7]
I killed, and so gave you the safety of the light.   470
And I myself betrayed my father and my home,
And came with you to Pelias' land of Iolcos.
And then, showing more willingness to help than wisdom,
I killed him, Pelias, with a most dreadful death
At his own daughters' hands, and took away your fear.   475

7. These lines refer to ordeals through which Jason had to pass to win the fleece and in which Medea
helped him. He had to yoke a team of fire-breathing bulls, then sow a field that immediately sprouted
armed warriors, and then deal with the snake that guarded the fleece.

This is how I behaved to you, you wretched man,
And you forsook me, took another bride to bed
Though you had children; for, if that had not been,
You would have had an excuse for another wedding.
Faith in your word has gone. Indeed I cannot tell   480
Whether you think the gods whose names you swore by then
Have ceased to rule and that new standards are set up,
Since you must know you have broken your word to me.
O my right hand, and the knees which you often clasped
In supplication, how senselessly I am treated   485
By this bad man, and how my hopes have missed their mark!
Come, I will share my thoughts as though you were a friend,—
You! Can I think that you would ever treat me well?
But I will do it, and these questions will make you
Appear the baser. Where am I to go? To my father's?   490
Him I betrayed and his land when I came with you.
To Pelias' wretched daughters? What a fine welcome
They would prepare for me who murdered their father!
For this is my position,—hated by my friends
At home, I have, in kindness to you, made enemies   495
Of others whom there was no need to have injured.
And how happy among Greek women you have made me
On your side for all this! A distinguished husband
I have,—for breaking promises. When in misery
I am cast out of the land and go into exile,   500
Quite without friends and all alone with my children,
That will be a fine shame for the new-wedded groom,
For his children to wander as beggars and she who saved him.
O God, you have given to mortals a sure method
Of telling the gold that is pure from the counterfeit;   505
Why is there no mark engraved upon men's bodies,
By which we could know the true ones from the false ones?
CHORUS: It is a strange form of anger, difficult to cure
    When two friends turn upon each other in hatred.
JASON: As for me, it seems I must be no bad speaker.   510
    But, like a man who has a good grip of the tiller,
    Reef up his sail, and so run away from under
    This mouthing tempest, woman, of your bitter tongue.
    Since you insist on building up your kindness to me,
    My view is that Cypris[8] was alone responsible   515
    Of men and gods for the preserving of my life.
    You are clever enough,—but really I need not enter
    Into the story of how it was love's inescapable
    Power that compelled you to keep my person safe.
    On this I will not go into too much detail.   520
    In so far as you helped me, you did well enough.
    But on this question of saving me, I can prove

8. Aphrodite, goddess of love.

You have certainly got from me more than you gave.
Firstly, instead of living among barbarians,
You inhabit a Greek land and understand our ways, 525
How to live by law instead of the sweet will of force.
And all the Greeks considered you a clever woman.
You were honored for it; while, if you were living at
The ends of the earth, nobody would have heard of you.
For my part, rather than stores of gold in my house 530
Or power to sing even sweeter songs than Orpheus,
I'd choose the fate that made me a distinguished man.
There is my reply to your story of my labors.
Remember it was you who started the argument.
Next for your attack on my wedding with the princess: 535
Here I will prove that, first, it was a clever move,
Secondly, a wise one, and, finally, that I made it
In your best interests and the children's. Please keep calm.
When I arrived here from the land of Iolcos,
Involved, as I was, in every kind of difficulty, 540
What luckier chance could I have come across than this,
An exile to marry the daughter of the king?
It was not,—the point that seems to upset you—that I
Grew tired of your bed and felt the need of a new bride;
Nor with any wish to outdo your number of children. 545
We have enough already. I am quite content.
But,—this was the main reason—that we might live well,
And not be short of anything. I know that all
A man's friends leave him stone-cold if he becomes poor.
Also that I might bring my children up worthy 550
Of my position, and, by producing more of them
To be brothers of yours, we would draw the families
Together and all be happy. You need no children.
And it pays me to do good to those I have now
By having others. Do you think this a bad plan? 555
You wouldn't if the love question hadn't upset you.
But you women have got into such a state of mind
That, if your life at night is good, you think you have
Everything; but, if in that quarter things go wrong,
You will consider your best and truest interests 560
Most hateful. It would have been better far for men
To have got their children in some other way, and women
Not to have existed. Then life would have been good.
CHORUS: Jason, though you have made this speech of yours look well,
Still I think, even though others do not agree, 565
You have betrayed your wife and are acting badly.
MEDEA: Surely in many ways I hold different views
From others, for I think that the plausible speaker
Who is a villain deserves the greatest punishment.
Confident in his tongue's power to adorn evil, 570
He stops at nothing. Yet he is not really wise.

As in your case. There is no need to put on the airs
Of a clever speaker, for one word will lay you flat.
If you were not a coward, you would not have married
Behind my back, but discussed it with me first.   575
JASON: And you, no doubt, would have furthered the proposal,
  If I had told you of it, you who even now
  Are incapable of controlling your bitter temper.
MEDEA: It was not that. No, you thought it was not respectable
  As you got on in years to have a foreign wife.   580
JASON: Make sure of this: it was not because of a woman
  I made the royal alliance in which I now live,
  But, as I said before, I wished to preserve you
  And breed a royal progeny to be brothers
  To the children I have now, a sure defense to us.   585
MEDEA: Let me have no happy fortune that brings pain with it,
  Or prosperity which is upsetting to the mind!
JASON: Change your ideas of what you want, and show more sense.
  Do not consider painful what is good for you,
  Nor, when you are lucky, think yourself unfortunate.   590
MEDEA: You can insult me. You have somewhere to turn to.
  But I shall go from this land into exile, friendless.
JASON: It was what you chose yourself. Don't blame others for it.
MEDEA: And how did I choose it? Did I betray my husband?
JASON: You called down wicked curses on the king's family.   595
MEDEA: A curse, that is what I am become to your house too.
JASON: I do not propose to go into all the rest of it;
  But, if you wish for the children or for yourself
  In exile to have some of my money to help you,
  Say so, for I am prepared to give with open hand,   600
  Or to provide you with introductions to my friends
  Who will treat you well. You are a fool if you do not
  Accept this. Cease your anger and you will profit.
MEDEA: I shall never accept the favors of friends of yours,
  Nor take a thing from you, so you need not offer it.   605
  There is no benefit in the gifts of a bad man.
JASON: Then, in any case, I call the gods to witness that
  I wish to help you and the children in every way,
  But you refuse what is good for you. Obstinately
  You push away your friends. You are sure to suffer for it.   610
MEDEA: Go! No doubt you hanker for your virginal bride,
  And are guilty of lingering too long out of her house.
  Enjoy your wedding. But perhaps,—with the help of God—
  You will make the kind of marriage that you will regret.
      [JASON *goes out with his attendants.*]
CHORUS: When love is in excess   615
  It brings a man no honor
  Nor any worthiness.
  But if in moderation Cypris comes,
  There is no other power at all so gracious.

O goddess, never on me let loose the unerring   620
Shaft of your bow in the poison of desire.

Let my heart be wise.
It is the gods' best gift.
On me let mighty Cypris
Inflict no wordy wars or restless anger   625
To urge my passion to a different love.
But with discernment may she guide women's weddings,
Honoring most what is peaceful in the bed.

O country and home,
Never, never may I be without you,   630
Living the hopeless life,
Hard to pass through and painful,
Most pitiable of all.
Let death first lay me low and death
Free me from this daylight.   635
There is no sorrow above
The loss of a native land.

I have seen it myself,
Do not tell of a secondhand story.
Neither city nor friend   640
Pitied you when you suffered
The worst of sufferings.
O let him die ungraced whose heart
Will not reward his friends,
Who cannot open an honest mind   645
No friend will he be of mine.

[*Enter* AIGEUS, *king of Athens, an old friend of* MEDEA.]
AIGEUS: Medea, greeting! This is the best introduction
  Of which men know for conversation between friends.
MEDEA: Greeting to you too, Aigeus, son of King Pandion,
  Where have you come from to visit this country's soil?   650
AIGEUS: I have just left the ancient oracle of Phoebus.
MEDEA: And why did you go to earth's prophetic center?
AIGEUS: I went to inquire how children might be born to me.
MEDEA: Is it so? Your life still up to this point childless?
AIGEUS: Yes. By the fate of some power we have no children.   655
MEDEA: Have you a wife, or is there none to share your bed?
AIGEUS: There is. Yes, I am joined to my wife in marriage.
MEDEA: And what did Phoebus say to you about children?
AIGEUS: Words too wise for a mere man to guess their meaning.
MEDEA: Is it proper for me to be told the God's reply?   660
AIGEUS: It is. For sure what is needed is cleverness.
MEDEA: Then what was his message? Tell me, if I may hear.
AIGEUS: I am not to loosen the hanging foot of the wine-skin[9] . . .
MEDEA: Until you have done something, or reached some country?

---

9. Cryptic; probably not to have intercourse.

AIGEUS: Until I return again to my hearth and house.   665
MEDEA: And for what purpose have you journeyed to this land?
AIGEUS: There is a man called Pittheus, king of Troezen.[1]
MEDEA: A son of Pelops, they say, a most righteous man.
AIGEUS: With him I wish to discuss the reply of the god.
MEDEA: Yes. He is wise and experienced in such matters.   670
AIGEUS. And to me also the dearest of all my spear-friends.[2]
MEDEA: Well, I hope you have good luck, and achieve your will.
AIGEUS: But why this downcast eye of yours, and this pale cheek?
MEDEA: O Aigeus, my husband has been the worst of all to me.
AIGEUS: What do you mean? Say clearly what has caused this grief.   675
MEDEA: Jason wrongs me, though I have never injured him.
AIGEUS: What has he done? Tell me about it in clearer words.
MEDEA: He has taken a wife to his house, supplanting me.
AIGEUS: Surely he would not dare to do a thing like that.
MEDEA: Be sure he has. Once dear, I now am slighted by him.   680
AIGEUS: Did he fall in love? Or is he tired of your love?
MEDEA: He was greatly in love, this traitor to his friends.
AIGEUS: Then let him go, if, as you say, he is so bad.
MEDEA: A passionate love,—for an alliance with the king.
AIGEUS: And who gave him his wife? Tell me the rest of it.   685
MEDEA: It was Kreon, he who rules this land of Corinth.
AIGEUS: Indeed, Medea, your grief was understandable.
MEDEA: I am ruined. And there is more to come: I am banished.
AIGEUS: Banished? By whom? Here you tell me of a new wrong.
MEDEA: Kreon drives me an exile from the land of Corinth.   690
AIGEUS: Does Jason consent? I cannot approve of this.
MEDEA: He pretends not to, but he will put up with it.
   Ah, Aigeus, I beg and beseech you, by your beard
   And by your knees I am making myself your suppliant,
   Have pity on me, have pity on your poor friend,   695
   And do not let me go into exile desolate,
   But receive me in your land and at your very hearth.
   So may your love, with God's help, lead to the bearing
   Of children, and so may you yourself die happy.
   You do not know what a chance you have come on here.   700
   I will end your childlessness, and I will make you able
   To beget children. The drugs I know can do this.
AIGEUS: For many reasons, woman, I am anxious to do
   This favor for you. First, for the sake of the gods,
   And then for the birth of children which you promise,   705
   For in that respect I am entirely at my wits' end.
   But this is my position: if you reach my land,
   I, being in my rights, will try to befriend you.
   But this much I must warn you of beforehand:
   I shall not agree to take you out of this country;   710

---

1. In the Peloponnese. Pittheus was Aigeus' father-in-law. Corinth was on the way from Delphi to
Troezen.   2. Allies in war, companions in fighting.

But if you by yourself can reach my house, then you
Shall stay there safely. To none will I give you up.
But from this land you must make your escape yourself,
For I do not wish to incur blame from my friends.
MEDEA: It shall be so. But, if I might have a pledge from you   715
For this, then I would have from you all I desire.
AIGEUS: Do you not trust me? What is it rankles with you?
MEDEA: I trust you, yes. But the house of Pelias hates me,
And so does Kreon. If you are bound by this oath,
When they try to drag me from your land, you will not   720
Abandon me; but if our pact is only words,
With no oath to the gods, you will be lightly armed,
Unable to resist their summons. I am weak,
While they have wealth to help them and a royal house.
AIGEUS: You show much foresight for such negotiations.   725
Well, if you will have it so, I will not refuse.
For, both on my side this will be the safest way
To have some excuse to put forward to your enemies,
And for you it is more certain. You may name the gods.
MEDEA: Swear by the plain of Earth, and Helios, father   730
Of my father, and name together all the gods. . . .
AIGEUS: That I will act or not act in what way? Speak.
MEDEA: That you yourself will never cast me from your land,
Nor, if any of my enemies should demand me,
Will you, in your life, willingly hand me over.   735
AIGEUS: I swear by the Earth, by the holy light of Helios,
By all the gods, I will abide by this you say.
MEDEA: Enough. And, if you fail, what shall happen to you?
AIGEUS: What comes to those who have no regard for heaven.
MEDEA: Go on your way. Farewell. For I am satisfied,   740
And I will reach your city as soon as I can,
Having done the deed I have to do and gained my end.
    [AIGEUS *goes out.*]
CHORUS: May Hermes, god of travelers,
Escort you, Aigeus, to your home!
And may you have the things you wish   745
So eagerly; for you
Appear to me to be a generous man.
MEDEA: God, and God's daughter, justice, and light of Helios!
Now, friends, has come the time of my triumph over
My enemies, and now my foot is on the road.   750
Now I am confident they will pay the penalty.
For this man, Aigeus, has been like a harbor to me
In all my plans just where I was most distressed.
To him I can fasten the cable of my safety
When I have reached the town and fortress of Pallas.[3]   755
And now I shall tell to you the whole of my plan.

3. Athens, city of Pallas Athene.

Listen to these words that are not spoken idly.
I shall send one of my servants to find Jason
And request him to come once more into my sight.
And when he comes, the words I'll say will be soft ones.   760
I'll say that I agree with him, that I approve
The royal wedding he has made, betraying me.
I'll say it was profitable, an excellent idea.
But I shall beg that my children may remain here:
Not that I would leave in a country that hates me   765
Children of mine to feel their enemies' insults,
But that by a trick I may kill the king's daughter.
For I will send the children with gifts in their hands
To carry to the bride, so as not to be banished, —
A finely woven dress and a golden diadem.   770
And if she takes them and wears them upon her skin
She and all who touch the girl will die in agony;
Such poison will I lay upon the gifts I send.
But there, however, I must leave that account paid.
I weep to think of what a deed I have to do   775
Next after that; for I shall kill my own children.
My children, there is none who can give them safety.
And when I have ruined the whole of Jason's house,
I shall leave the land and flee from the murder of my
Dear children, and I shall have done a dreadful deed.   780
For it is not bearable to be mocked by enemies.
So it must happen. What profit have I in life?
I have no land, no home, no refuge from my pain.
My mistake was made the time I left behind me
My father's house, and trusted the words of a Greek,   785
Who, with heaven's help, will pay me the price for that.
For those children he had from me he will never
See alive again, nor will he on his new bride
Beget another child, for she is to be forced
To die a most terrible death by these my poisons.   790
Let no one think me a weak one, feeble-spirited,
A stay-at-home, but rather just the opposite,
One who can hurt my enemies and help my friends;
For the lives of such persons are most remembered.
CHORUS: Since you have shared the knowledge of your plan with us,   795
  I both wish to help you and support the normal
  Ways of mankind, and tell you not to do this thing.
MEDEA: I can do no other thing. It is understandable
  For you to speak thus. You have not suffered as I have.
CHORUS: But can you have the heart to kill your flesh and blood?   800
MEDEA: Yes, for this is the best way to wound my husband.
CHORUS: And you too. Of women you will be most unhappy.
MEDEA: So it must be. No compromise is possible.
  [*She turns to the* NURSE.]
  Go, you, at once, and tell Jason to come to me.

You I employ on all affairs of greatest trust.   805
Say nothing of these decisions which I have made,
If you love your mistress, if you were born a woman.
CHORUS: From of old the children of Erechtheus[4] are
Splendid, the sons of blessed gods. They dwell
In Athens' holy and unconquered land,[5]   810
Where famous Wisdom feeds them and they pass gaily
Always through that most brilliant air where once, they say,
That golden Harmony gave birth to the nine
Pure Muses of Pieria.[6]

And beside the sweet flow of Cephisos' stream,   815
Where Cypris[7] sailed, they say, to draw the water,
And mild soft breezes breathed along her path,
And on her hair were flung the sweet-smelling garlands
Of flowers of roses by the Lovers, the companions
Of Wisdom, her escort, the helpers of men   820
In every kind of excellence.

How then can these holy rivers
Or this holy land love you,
Or the city find you a home,
You, who will kill your children,   825
You, not pure with the rest?
O think of the blow at your children
And think of the blood that you shed.
O, over and over I beg you,
By your knees I beg you do not   830
Be the murderess of your babes!

O where will you find the courage
Or the skill of hand and heart,
When you set yourself to attempt
A deed so dreadful to do?   835
How, when you look upon them,
Can you tearlessly hold the decision
For murder? You will not be able,
When your children fall down and implore you,
You will not be able to dip   840
Steadfast your hand in their blood.
    [*Enter* JASON *with attendants.*]
JASON: I have come at your request. Indeed, although you are
Bitter against me, this you shall have: I will listen
To what new thing you want, woman, to get from me.
MEDEA: Jason, I beg you to be forgiving towards me   845

---

4. An early king of Athens, a son of Hephaestus.   5. It was the Athenians' boast that their descent
from the original settlers was uninterrupted by an invasion. There is a topical reference here, for the
play was produced in 431 B.C., in a time of imminent war.   6. A fountain in Boeotia where the Muses
were supposed to live. The sentence means that the fortunate balance (*Harmony*) of the elements and
the genius of the people produced the cultivation of the arts (*the nine Pure Muses*).   7. The goddess
of love and, therefore, of the principle of fertility. Cephisos is an Athenian river.

For what I said. It is natural for you to bear with
My temper, since we have had much love together.
I have talked with myself about this and I have
Reproached myself. "Fool" I said, "why am I so mad?
Why am I set against those who have planned wisely?   850
Why make myself an enemy of the authorities
And of my husband, who does the best thing for me
By marrying royalty and having children who
Will be as brothers to my own? What is wrong with me?
Let me give up anger, for the gods are kind to me.   855
Have I not children, and do I not know that we
In exile from our country must be short of friends?"
When I considered this I saw that I had shown
Great lack of sense, and that my anger was foolish.
Now I agree with you. I think that you are wise   860
In having this other wife as well as me, and I
Was mad. I should have helped you in these plans of yours,
Have joined in the wedding, stood by the marriage bed,
Have taken pleasure in attendance on your bride.
But we women are what we are,—perhaps a little   865
Worthless; and you men must not be like us in this,
Nor be foolish in return when we are foolish.
Now I give in, and admit that then I was wrong.
I have come to a better understanding now.
    [*She turns towards the house.*]
Children, come here, my children, come outdoors to us!   870
Welcome your father with me, and say goodbye to him,
And with your mother, who just now was his enemy,
Join again in making friends with him who loves us.
    [*Enter the* CHILDREN, *attended by the* TUTOR.]
We have made peace, and all our anger is over.
Take hold of his right hand,—O God, I am thinking   875
Of something which may happen in the secret future.
O children, will you just so, after a long life,
Hold out your loving arms at the grave? O children,
How ready to cry I am, how full of foreboding!
I am ending at last this quarrel with your father,   880
And, look, my soft eyes have suddenly filled with tears.
CHORUS: And the pale tears have started also in my eyes.
    O may the trouble not grow worse than now it is!
JASON: I approve of what you say. And I cannot blame you
    Even for what you said before. It is natural   885
For a woman to be wild with her husband when he
Goes in for secret love. But now your mind has turned
To better reasoning. In the end you have come to
The right decision, like the clever woman you are.
And of you, children, your father is taking care.   890
He has made, with God's help, ample provision for you.
For I think that a time will come when you will be

The leading people in Corinth with your brothers.
You must grow up. As to the future, your father
And those of the gods who love him will deal with that.   895
I want to see you, when you have become young men,
Healthy and strong, better men than my enemies.
Medea, why are your eyes all wet with pale tears?
Why is your cheek so white and turned away from me?
Are not these words of mine pleasing for you to hear?   900
MEDEA: It is nothing. I was thinking about these children.
JASON: You must be cheerful. I shall look after them well.
MEDEA: I will be. It is not that I distrust your words,
    But a woman is a frail thing, prone to crying.
JASON: But why then should you grieve so much for these children?   905
MEDEA: I am their mother. When you prayed that they might live
    I felt unhappy to think that these things will be.
    But come, I have said something of the things I meant
    To say to you, and now I will tell you the rest.
    Since it is the king's will to banish me from here,—   910
    And for me too I know that this is the best thing,
    Not to be in your way by living here or in
    The king's way, since they think me ill-disposed to them,—
    I then am going into exile from this land;
    But do you, so that you may have the care of them,   915
    Beg Kreon that the children may not be banished.
JASON: I doubt if I'll succeed, but still I'll attempt it.
MEDEA: Then you must tell your wife to beg from her father
    That the children may be reprieved from banishment.
JASON: I will, and with her I shall certainly succeed.   920
MEDEA: If she is like the rest of us women, you will.
    And I too will take a hand with you in this business,
    For I will send her some gifts which are far fairer,
    I am sure of it, than those which now are in fashion,
    A finely-woven dress and a golden diadem,   925
    And the children shall present them. Quick, let one of you
    Servants bring here to me that beautiful dress.
        [*One of her attendants goes into the house.*]
    She will be happy not in one way, but in a hundred,
    Having so fine a man as you to share her bed,
    And with this beautiful dress which Helios of old,   930
    My father's father, bestowed on his descendants.
        [*Enter attendant carrying the poisoned dress and diadem.*]
    There, children, take these wedding presents in your hands.
    Take them to the royal princess, the happy bride,
    And give them to her. She will not think little of them.
JASON: No, don't be foolish, and empty your hands of these.   935
    Do you think the palace is short of dresses to wear?
    Do you think there is no gold there? Keep them, don't give them
    Away. If my wife considers me of any value,
    She will think more of me than money, I am sure of it.

MEDEA: No, let me have my way. They say the gods themselves   940
   Are moved by gifts, and gold does more with men than words.
   Hers is the luck, her fortune that which god blesses;
   She is young and a princess; but for my children's reprieve
   I would give my very life, and not gold only.
   Go children, go together to that rich palace,   945
   Be suppliants to the new wife of your father,
   My lady, beg her not to let you be banished.
   And give her the dress,—for this is of great importance,
   That she should take the gift into her hand from yours.
   Go, quick as you can. And bring your mother good news   950
   By your success of those things which she longs to gain.
     [JASON *goes out with his attendants, followed by the* TUTOR *and the*
     CHILDREN *carrying the poisoned gifts.*]
CHORUS: Now there is no hope left for the children's lives.
   Now there is none. They are walking already to murder.
   The bride, poor bride, will accept the curse of the gold,
   Will accept the bright diadem.   955
   Around her yellow hair she will set that dress
   Of death with her own hands.
   The grace and the perfume and glow of the golden robe
   Will charm her to put them upon her and wear the wreath,
   And now her wedding will be with the dead below,   960
   Into such a trap she will fall,
   Poor thing, into such a fate of death and never
   Escape from under that curse.
   You too, O wretched bridegroom, making your match with kings,
   You do not see that you bring   965
   Destruction on your children and on her,
   Your wife, a fearful death.
   Poor soul, what a fall is yours!

   In your grief too I weep, mother of little children,
   You who will murder your own,   970
   In vengeance for the loss of married love
   Which Jason has betrayed
   As he lives with another wife.
     [*Enter the* TUTOR *with the* CHILDREN.]
TUTOR: Mistress, I tell you that these children are reprieved,
   And the royal bride has been pleased to take in her hands   975
   Your gifts. In that quarter the children are secure.
   But come,
   Why do you stand confused when you are fortunate?
   Why have you turned round with your cheek away from me?
   Are not these words of mine pleasing for you to hear?   980
MEDEA: Oh! I am lost!
TUTOR: That word is not in harmony with my tidings.
MEDEA: I am lost, I am lost!
TUTOR: Am I in ignorance telling you

Of some disaster, and not the good news I thought?
MEDEA: You have told what you have told. I do not blame you.   985
TUTOR: Why then this downcast eye, and this weeping of tears?
MEDEA: Oh, I am forced to weep, old man. The gods and I,
    I in a kind of madness have contrived all this.
TUTOR: Courage! You too will be brought home by your children.
MEDEA: Ah, before that happens I shall bring others home.   990
TUTOR: Others before you have been parted from their children.
    Mortals must bear in resignation their ill luck.
MEDEA: That is what I shall do. But go inside the house,
    And do for the children your usual daily work.
    [*The* TUTOR *goes into the house.* MEDEA *turns to her* CHILDREN.]
    O children, O my children, you have a city,   995
    You have a home, and you can leave me behind you,
    And without your mother you may live there for ever.
    But I am going in exile to another land
    Before I have seen you happy and taken pleasure in you,
    Before I have dressed your brides and made your marriage beds   1000
    And held up the torch at the ceremony of wedding.
    Oh, what a wretch I am in this my self-willed thought!
    What was the purpose, children, for which I reared you?
    For all my travail and wearing myself away?
    They were sterile, those pains I had in the bearing of you.   1005
    O surely once the hopes in you I had, poor me,
    Were high ones: you would look after me in old age,
    And when I died would deck me well with your own hands;
    A thing which all would have done. O but now it is gone,
    That lovely thought. For, once I am left without you,   1010
    Sad will be the life I'll lead and sorrowful for me.
    And you will never see your mother again with
    Your dear eyes, gone to another mode of living.
    Why, children, do you look upon me with your eyes?
    Why do you smile so sweetly that last smile of all?   1015
    Oh, Oh, what can I do? My spirit has gone from me,
    Friends, when I saw that bright look in the children's eyes.
    I cannot bear to do it. I renounce my plans
    I had before. I'll take my children away from
    This land. Why should I hurt their father with the pain   1020
    They feel, and suffer twice as much of pain myself?
    No, no, I will not do it. I renounce my plans.
    Ah, what is wrong with me? Do I want to let go
    My enemies unhurt and be laughed at for it?
    I must face this thing. Oh, but what a weak woman   1025
    Even to admit to my mind these soft arguments.
    Children, go into the house. And he whom law forbids
    To stand in attendance at my sacrifices,
    Let him see to it. I shall not mar my handiwork.
    Oh! Oh!   1030
    Do not, O my heart, you must not do these things!

Poor heart, let them go, have pity upon the children.
If they live with you in Athens they will cheer you.
No! By Hell's avenging furies it shall not be,—
This shall never be, that I should suffer my children   1035
To be the prey of my enemies' insolence.
Every way is it fixed. The bride will not escape.
No, the diadem is now upon her head, and she,
The royal princess, is dying in the dress, I know it.
But,—for it is the most dreadful of roads for me   1040
To tread, and them I shall send on a more dreadful still—
I wish to speak to the children.
     [*She calls the* CHILDREN *to her.*]
                         Come, children, give
Me your hands, give your mother your hands to kiss them.
O the dear hands, and O how dear are these lips to me,
And the generous eyes and the bearing of my children!   1045
I wish you happiness, but not here in this world.
What is here your father took. O how good to hold you!
How delicate the skin, how sweet the breath of children!
Go, go! I am no longer able, no longer
To look upon you. I am overcome by sorrow.   1050
     [*The* CHILDREN *go into the house.*]
I know indeed what evil I intend to do,
But stronger than all my afterthoughts is my fury,
Fury that brings upon mortals the greatest evils.
     [*She goes out to the right, towards the royal palace.*]
CHORUS: Often before
I have gone through more subtle reasons,   1055
And have come upon questionings greater
Than a woman should strive to search out.
But we too have a goddess to help us
And accompany us into wisdom.
Not all of us. Still you will find   1060
Among many women a few,
And our sex is not without learning.
This I say, that those who have never
Had children, who know nothing of it,
In happiness have the advantage   1065
Over those who are parents.
The childless, who never discover
Whether children turn out as a good thing
Or as something to cause pain, are spared
Many troubles in lacking this knowledge.   1070
And those who have in their homes
The sweet presence of children, I see that their lives
Are all wasted away by their worries.
First they must think how to bring them up well and
How to leave them something to live on.   1075
And then after this whether all their toil

Is for those who will turn out good or bad,
Is still an unanswered question.
And of one more trouble, the last of all,
That is common to mortals I tell.   1080
For suppose you have found them enough for their living,
Suppose that the children have grown into youth
And have turned out good, still, if God so wills it,
Death will away with your children's bodies,
And carry them off into Hades.   1085
What is our profit, then, that for the sake of
Children the gods should pile upon mortals
After all else
This most terrible grief of all?
   [*Enter* MEDEA, *from the spectators' right.*]
MEDEA: Friends, I can tell you that for long I have waited   1090
   For the event. I stare towards the place from where
   The news will come. And now, see one of Jason's servants
   Is on his way here, and that labored breath of his
   Shows he has tidings for us, and evil tidings.
   [*Enter, also from the right, the* MESSENGER.]
MESSENGER: Medea, you who have done such a dreadful thing,   1095
   So outrageous, run for your life, take what you can,
   A ship to bear you hence or chariot on land.
MEDEA: And what is the reason deserves such flight as this?
MESSENGER: She is dead, only just now, the royal princess,
   And Kreon dead too, her father, by your poisons.   1100
MEDEA: The finest words you have spoken. Now and hereafter
   I shall count you among my benefactors and friends.
MESSENGER: What! Are you right in the mind? Are you not mad,
   Woman? The house of the king is outraged by you.
   Do you enjoy it? Not afraid of such doings?   1105
MEDEA: To what you say I on my side have something too
   To say in answer. Do not be in a hurry, friend,
   But speak. How did they die? You will delight me twice
   As much again if you say they died in agony.
MESSENGER: When those two children, born of you, had entered in,   1110
   Their father with them, and passed into the bride's house,
   We were pleased, we slaves who were distressed by your wrongs.
   All through the house we were talking of but one thing,
   How you and your husband had made up your quarrel.
   Some kissed the children's hands and some their yellow hair,   1115
   And I myself was so full of my joy that I
   Followed the children into the women's quarters.
   Our mistress, whom we honor now instead of you,
   Before she noticed that your two children were there,
   Was keeping her eye fixed eagerly on Jason.   1120
   Afterwards however she covered up her eyes,
   Her cheek paled and she turned herself away from him,
   So disgusted was she at the children's coming there.

But your husband tried to end the girl's bad temper,
And said "You must not look unkindly on your friends.   1125
Cease to be angry. Turn your head to me again.
Have as your friends the same ones as your husband has.
And take these gifts, and beg your father to reprieve
These children from their exile. Do it for my sake."
She, when she saw the dress, could not restrain herself.   1130
She agreed with all her husband said, and before
He and the children had gone far from the palace,
She took the gorgeous robe and dressed herself in it,
And put the golden crown around her curly locks,
And arranged the set of the hair in a shining mirror,   1135
And smiled at the lifeless image of herself in it.
Then she rose from her chair and walked about the room,
With her gleaming feet stepping most soft and delicate,
All overjoyed with the present. Often and often
She would stretch her foot out straight and look along it.   1140
But after that it was a fearful thing to see.
The color of her face changed, and she staggered back,
She ran, and her legs trembled, and she only just
Managed to reach a chair without falling flat down.
An aged woman servant who, I take it, thought   1145
This was some seizure of Pan[8] or another god,
Cried out "God bless us," but that was before she saw
The white foam breaking through her lips and her rolling
The pupils of her eyes and her face all bloodless.
Then she raised a different cry from that "God bless us,"   1150
A huge shriek, and the women ran, one to the king,
One to the newly wedded husband to tell him
What had happened to his bride; and with frequent sound
The whole of the palace rang as they went running.
One walking quickly round the course of a race-track   1155
Would now have turned the bend and be close to the goal,
When she, poor girl, opened her shut and speechless eye,
And with a terrible groan she came to herself.
For a two-fold pain was moving up against her.
The wreath of gold that was resting around her head   1160
Let forth a fearful stream of all-devouring fire,
And the finely-woven dress your children gave to her,
Was fastening on the unhappy girl's fine flesh.
She leapt up from the chair, and all on fire she ran,
Shaking her hair now this way and now that, trying   1165
To hurl the diadem away; but fixedly
The gold preserved its grip, and, when she shook her hair,
Then more and twice as fiercely the fire blazed out.
Till, beaten by her fate, she fell down to the ground,

---

8. As the god of wild nature he was supposed to be the source of the sudden, apparently causeless terror
that solitude in wild surroundings may produce and hence of all kinds of sudden madness (compare
the English word *panic*).

Hard to be recognized except by a parent.   1170
Neither the setting of her eyes was plain to see,
Nor the shapeliness of her face. From the top of
Her head there oozed out blood and fire mixed together.
Like the drops on pine-bark, so the flesh from her bones
Dropped away, torn by the hidden fang of the poison.   1175
It was a fearful sight; and terror held us all
From touching the corpse. We had learned from what had happened.
But her wretched father, knowing nothing of the event,
Came suddenly to the house, and fell upon the corpse,
And at once cried out and folded his arms about her,   1180
And kissed her and spoke to her, saying, "O my poor child,
What heavenly power has so shamefully destroyed you?
And who has set me here like an ancient sepulchre,
Deprived of you? O let me die with you, my child!"
And when he had made an end of his wailing and crying,   1185
Then the old man wished to raise himself to his feet;
But, as the ivy clings to the twigs of the laurel,
So he stuck to the fine dress, and he struggled fearfully.
For he was trying to lift himself to his knee,
And she was pulling him down, and when he tugged hard   1190
He would be ripping his aged flesh from his bones.
At last his life was quenched and the unhappy man
Gave up the ghost, no longer could hold up his head.
There they lie close, the daughter and the old father,
Dead bodies, an event he prayed for in his tears.   1195
As for your interests, I will say nothing of them,
For you will find your own escape from punishment.
Our human life I think and have thought a shadow,
And I do not fear to say that those who are held
Wise amongst men and who search the reasons of things   1200
Are those who bring the most sorrow on themselves.
For of mortals there is no one who is happy.
If wealth flows in upon one, one may be perhaps
Luckier than one's neighbor, but still not happy.
    [Exit.]
CHORUS: Heaven, it seems, on this day has fastened many   1205
    Evils on Jason, and Jason has deserved them.
    Poor girl, the daughter of Kreon, how I pity you
    And your misfortunes, you who have gone quite away
    To the house of Hades because of marrying Jason.
MEDEA: Women, my task is fixed: as quickly as I may   1210
    To kill my children, and start away from this land,
    And not, by wasting time, to suffer my children
    To be slain by another hand less kindly to them.
    Force every way will have it they must die, and since
    This must be so, then I, their mother, shall kill them.   1215
    O arm yourself in steel, my heart! Do not hang back
    From doing this fearful and necessary wrong.

O come, my hand, poor wretched hand, and take the sword,
Take it, step forward to this bitter starting point,
And do not be a coward, do not think of them,   1220
How sweet they are, and how you are their mother. Just for
This one short day be forgetful of your children,
Afterwards weep; for even though you will kill them,
They were very dear,— O, I am an unhappy woman!
    [*With a cry she rushes into the house.*]
CHORUS: O Earth, and the far shining   1225
    Ray of the sun, look down, look down upon
    This poor lost woman, look, before she raises
    The hand of murder against her flesh and blood.
    Yours was the golden birth from which
    She sprang, and now I fear divine   1230
    Blood may be shed by men.
    O heavenly light, hold back her hand,
    Check her, and drive from out the house
    The bloody Fury raised by fiends of Hell.

    Vain waste, your care of children;   1235
    Was it in vain you bore the babes you loved,
    After you passed the inhospitable strait
    Between the dark blue rocks, Symplegades?
    O wretched one, how has it come,
    This heavy anger on your heart,   1240
    This cruel bloody mind?
    For God from mortals asks a stern
    Price for the stain of kindred blood
    In like disaster falling on their homes.
        [*A cry from one of the* CHILDREN *is heard.*]
CHORUS: Do you hear the cry, do you hear the children's cry?   1245
    O you hard heart, O woman fated for evil!
ONE OF THE CHILDREN: [*From within.*]
    What can I do and how escape my mother's hands?
ONE OF THE CHILDREN: [*From within.*] O my dear brother, I cannot tell.
    We are lost.
CHORUS: Shall I enter the house? O surely I should   1250
    Defend the children from murder.
A CHILD: [*From within.*]
    O help us, in God's name, for now we need your help.
    Now, now we are close to it. We are trapped by the sword.
CHORUS: O your heart must have been made of rock or steel,
    You who can kill   1255
    With your own hand the fruit of your own womb.
    Of one alone I have heard, one woman alone
    Of those of old who laid her hands on her children,
    Ino, sent mad by heaven when the wife of Zeus
    Drove her out from her home and made her wander;   1260
    And because of the wicked shedding of blood

Of her own children she threw
Herself, poor wretch, into the sea and stepped away
Over the sea-cliff to die with her two children.
What horror more can be? O women's love,   1265
So full of trouble,
How many evils have you caused already!
   [*Enter* JASON, *with attendants.*]
JASON: You women, standing close in front of this dwelling,
  Is she, Medea, she who did this dreadful deed,
  Still in the house, or has she run away in flight?   1270
  For she will have to hide herself beneath the earth,
  Or raise herself on wings into the height of air,
  If she wishes to escape the royal vengeance.
  Does she imagine that, having killed our rulers,
  She will herself escape uninjured from this house?   1275
  But I am thinking not so much of her as for
  The children,—her the king's friends will make to suffer
  For what she did. So I have come to save the lives
  Of my boys, in case the royal house should harm them
  While taking vengeance for their mother's wicked deed.   1280
CHORUS: O Jason, if you but knew how deeply you are
  Involved in sorrow, you would not have spoken so.
JASON: What is it? That she is planning to kill me also?
CHORUS: Your children are dead, and by their own mother's hand.
JASON: What! This is it? O woman, you have destroyed me.   1285
CHORUS: You must make up your mind your children are no more.
JASON: Where did she kill them? Was it here or in the house?
CHORUS: Open the gates and there you will see them murdered.
JASON: Quick as you can unlock the doors, men, and undo
  The fastenings and let me see this double evil,   1290
  My children dead and her,—O her I will repay.
   [*His attendants rush to the door.* MEDEA *appears above the house in
   a chariot drawn by dragons. She has the dead bodies of the* CHILDREN
   with her.*]
MEDEA: Why do you batter these gates and try to unbar them,
  Seeking the corpses and for me who did the deed?
  You may cease your trouble, and, if you have need of me,
  Speak, if you wish. You will never touch me with your hand,   1295
  Such a chariot has Helios, my father's father,
  Given me to defend me from my enemies.
JASON: You hateful thing, you woman most utterly loathed
  By the gods and me and by all the race of mankind,
  You who have had the heart to raise a sword against   1300
  Your children, you, their mother, and left me childless,—
  You have done this, and do you still look at the sun
  And at the earth, after these most fearful doings?
  I wish you dead. Now I see it plain, though at that time
  I did not, when I took you from your foreign home   1305
  And brought you to a Greek house, you, an evil thing,

A traitress to your father and your native land.
The gods hurled the avenging curse of yours on me.
For your own brother you slew at your own hearthside,
And then came aboard that beautiful ship, the Argo.   1310
And that was your beginning. When you were married
To me, your husband, and had borne children to me,
For the sake of pleasure in the bed you killed them.
There is no Greek woman who would have dared such deeds,
Out of all those whom I passed over and chose you   1315
To marry instead, a bitter destructive match,
A monster not a woman, having a nature
Wilder than that of Scylla⁹ in the Tuscan sea.
Ah! no, not if I had ten thousand words of shame
Could I sting you. You are naturally so brazen.   1320
Go, worker in evil, stained with your children's blood.
For me remains to cry aloud upon my fate,
Who will get no pleasure from my newly-wedded love,
And the boys whom I begot and brought up, never
Shall I speak to them alive. Oh, my life is over!   1325
MEDEA: Long would be the answer which I might have made to
These words of yours, if Zeus the father did not know
How I have treated you and what you did to me.
No, it was not to be that you should scorn my love,
And pleasantly live your life through, laughing at me;   1330
Nor would the princess, nor he who offered the match,
Kreon, drive me away without paying for it.
So now you may call me a monster, if you wish,
Or Scylla housed in the caves of the Tuscan sea
I too, as I had to, have taken hold of your heart.   1335
JASON: You feel the pain yourself. You share in my sorrow.
MEDEA: Yes, and my grief is gain when you cannot mock it.
JASON: O children, what a wicked mother she was to you!
MEDEA: They died from a disease they caught from their father.
JASON: I tell you it was not my hand that destroyed them.   1340
MEDEA: But it was your insolence, and your virgin wedding.
JASON: And just for the sake of that you chose to kill them.
MEDEA: Is love so small a pain, do you think, for a woman?
JASON: For a wise one, certainly. But you are wholly evil.
MEDEA: The children are dead. I say this to make you suffer.   1345
JASON: The children, I think, will bring down curses on you.
MEDEA: The gods know who was the author of this sorrow.
JASON: Yes, the gods know indeed, they know your loathsome heart.
MEDEA: Hate me. But I tire of your barking bitterness.
JASON: And I of yours. It is easier to leave you.   1350
MEDEA: How then? What shall I do? I long to leave you too.
JASON: Give me the bodies to bury and to mourn them.

---

9. A monster located in the straits between Italy and Sicily, who snatched sailors off passing ships and
devoured them.

MEDEA: No, that I will not. I will bury them myself,
　Bearing them to Hera's temple on the promontory;
　So that no enemy may evilly treat them　　　　　　1355
　By tearing up their grave. In this land of Corinth
　I shall establish a holy feast and sacrifice[1]
　Each year for ever to atone for the blood guilt.
　And I myself go to the land of Erechtheus
　To dwell in Aigeus' house, the son of Pandion.　　1360
　While you, as is right, will die without distinction,
　Struck on the head by a piece of the Argo's timber,
　And you will have seen the bitter end of my love.
JASON: May a Fury for the children's sake destroy you,
　And justice, requitor of blood.　　　　　　　　　1365
MEDEA: What heavenly power lends an ear
　To a breaker of oaths, a deceiver?
JASON: O, I hate you, murderess of children.
MEDEA: Go to your palace. Bury your bride.
JASON: I go, with two children to mourn for.　　　　1370
MEDEA: Not yet do you feel it. Wait for the future.
JASON: Oh, children I loved!
MEDEA:　　　　　　　　　I loved them, you did not.
JASON: You loved them, and killed them.
MEDEA:　　　　　　　　　　To make you feel pain
JASON: Oh, wretch that I am, how I long
　To kiss the dear lips of my children!　　　　　　1375
MEDEA: Now you would speak to them, now you would kiss them.
　Then you rejected them.
JASON:　　　　　　　　Let me, I beg you,
　Touch my boys' delicate flesh.
MEDEA: I will not. Your words are all wasted.
JASON: O God, do you hear it, this persecution,　　1380
　These my sufferings from this hateful
　Woman, this monster, murderess of children?
　Still what I can do that I will do:
　I will lament and cry upon heaven,
　Calling the gods to bear me witness　　　　　　　1385
　How you have killed my boys and prevent me from
　Touching their bodies or giving them burial.
　I wish I had never begot them to see them
　Afterwards slaughtered by you.
CHORUS: Zeus in Olympus is the overseer　　　　　　1390
　Of many doings. Many things the gods
　Achieve beyond our judgment. What we thought
　Is not confirmed and what we thought not god
　Contrives. And so it happens in this story.

---

1. Some such ceremony was still performed at Corinth in Euripides' time.

ARISTOPHANES
450?–385? B.C.

By the fifth century B.C. both tragedy and comedy were regularly produced at the winter festivals of the god Dionysus in Athens. Comedy, like tragedy, employed a chorus, that is to say, a group of dancers (who also sang) and actors, who wore masks; its tone was burlesque and parodic, though there was often a serious theme emphasized by the crude clowning and the free play of wit. The only comic poet of the fifth century whose work has survived is Aristophanes; in his thirteen extant comedies, produced over the years 425–388 B.C., the institutions and personalities of his time are caricatured and criticized in a brilliant combination of poetry and obscenity, of farce and wit that has no parallel in European literature. It can be described only in terms of itself, by the adjective *Aristophanic.*

He was born sometime in the middle of the fifth century and died in the next, around 385 B.C. The earliest of his plays to survive, *The Acharnians*, was produced in 425 B.C., and the bulk of his extant work dates from the years of the Peloponnesian War (431–404 B.C.). The war, in fact, is one of his comic targets; in *The Acharnians*, an Athenian citizen, fed up with the privations caused by the Spartan invasions that shut the Athenians inside their walls, makes a separate peace for himself and his family, defends his decision against an irate chorus of patriots (the Acharnians of the title), and proceeds to enjoy all the benefits of peace while his fellow citizens suffer as before. In *Peace* (421 B.C.) another Athenian flies up to heaven on a gigantic dung beetle (a parody of a Euripidean play in which a hero flew up on a winged horse); once arrived, he petitions Zeus to stop the war. Euripides is another favorite target and was held up to ridicule in play after play; and Socrates was the "hero" of a play, *Clouds* (423 B.C.), that held him up to ridicule as a Sophistic charlatan. (Socrates refers to this play in his speech in court, p. 501). In *Birds* (414 B.C.) two Athenians, tired of the war and taxes, go off to found a new city; they organize the birds, who cut off the smoke of sacrifice that the gods live on, and force Zeus to surrender the government of the universe to the birds. These plays are all excellent fooling; they are also sexually and scatologically explicit. But coarse humor and exquisite wit combine with lyric poetry of a high quality and comic plots of startling audacity to produce a mixture unlike anything that went before or has come after it.

Lysistrata, which is outstanding among the Aristophanic comedies in its coherence of structure and underlying seriousness of theme, was first produced in 411 B.C. In 413 the news of the total destruction of the Athenian fleet in Sicily had reached Athens, and though heroic efforts to carry on the war were under way, the confidence in victory with which Athens had begun the war had disappeared forever. It is a recurring feature of Aristophanic comedy that the comic hero upsets the status quo to produce a series of extraordinary results that are exploited to the full for their comic potential. In this play the Athenian women, who have no political rights, seize the Acropolis and leave the men without women. At the same time similar revolutions take place in all the Greek cities according to a coordinated plan. The men are eventually "starved" into submission, and the Spartans come to Athens to end the war.

Aristophanes does not miss a trick in his exploitation of the possibilities for ribald humor inherent in this situation, a female sex-strike against war; Myrrhine's teasing game with her husband, Cinesias, for example, is rare fooling, and the final appearance of the uncomfortably rigid Spartan ambassadors and their equally tense Athenian hosts is a visual and verbal climax of astonishing brilliance. But underneath all the fooling, real issues are pursued, and they come to the surface with telling effect in the argument between Lysistrata and the magistrate who has been sent to suppress the revolt. Reversing the words of Hector to Andromache, which had become proverbial, Lysistrata claims that "war shall be the concern of Women!"—it is too important a matter to be left to men, for women are its real victims. And when asked what the women will do, she explains that they will treat politics just as they do wool in their household tasks: "when it's confused and snarled . . . draw out a thread here and a thread there . . . we'll unsnarl this war."

We do not know how the Athenians welcomed the play. All we know is that they were not impressed by its serious undertone; the war continued for seven more exhausting years, until Athens's last fleet was defeated, the city laid open to the enemy, the empire lost.

K. J. Dover, *Aristophanic Comedy* (1972), is a general survey of the whole range of Aristophanic comedy. Jeffrey Henderson, *Aristophanes' Lysistrata* (1987), pp. xv–xli, is a helpful introduction to the play. See also Kenneth J. Rockford, *Aristophanes' Old-and-New Comedy* (1987), pp. 301–11.

PRONOUNCING GLOSSARY

The following list uses common English syllables and stress accents to provide rough equivalents of selected words whose pronunciation may be unfamiliar to the general reader.

Andromache: *an-dro'-ma-kee*   Lysistrata: *lai-sis'-trah-tuh / li-sis-trah'-tuh*

Aristophanes: *a-ri-sto'-fa-neez*   Myrrhine: *meer-ree'-nee*

Calonice: *ka-lo-nee'-see*

Lysistrata[1]

Characters[2]

LYSISTRATA		THREE ATHENIAN WOMEN
CALONICE	*Athenian women*	CINESIAS, *an Athenian, husband of*
MYRRHINE		*Myrrhine*
LAMPITO, *a Spartan woman*		SPARTAN HERALD
LEADER *of the Chorus of Old Men*		SPARTAN AMBASSADORS
CHORUS *of Old Men*		ATHENIAN AMBASSADORS
LEADER *of the Chorus of Old*		TWO ATHENIAN CITIZENS
Women		CHORUS *of Athenians*
CHORUS *of Old Women*		CHORUS *of Spartans*
ATHENIAN MAGISTRATE		

[SCENE: *In Athens, beneath the Acropolis. In the center of the stage is the Propylaea, or gate-way to the Acropolis; to one side is a small grotto, sacred to Pan. The Orchestra represents a slope leading up to the gate-way.*

It is early in the morning. LYSISTRATA *is pacing impatiently up and down.*]

---

1. Translated by Charles T. Murphy.   2. As is usual in ancient comedy, the leading characters have significant names. *Lysistrata* is "she who disbands the armies." *Lampito* is a celebrated Spartan name. *Cinesias*, although a real name in Athens, was chosen to suggest the Greek verb *kinein*, "to move," then "to make love" or "to have intercourse." *Paionidai* suggests the verb *paiein*, which has about the same significance.

LYSISTRATA: If they'd been summoned to worship the God of Wine, or Pan, or to visit the Queen of Love, why, you couldn't have pushed your way through the streets for all the timbrels.[3] But now there's not a single woman here—except my neighbor; here she comes.

[*Enter* CALONICE.]

Good day to you, Calonice.

CALONICE: And to you, Lysistrata. [*Noticing* LYSISTRATA's *impatient air.*] But what ails you? Don't scowl, my dear; it's not becoming to you to knit your brows like that.

LYSISTRATA: [*Sadly.*] Ah, Calonice, my heart aches; I'm so annoyed at us women. For among men we have a reputation for sly trickery—

CALONICE: And rightly too, on my word!

LYSISTRATA: —but when they were told to meet here to consider a matter of no small importance, they lie abed and don't come.

CALONICE: Oh, they'll come all right, my dear. It's not easy for a woman to get out, you know. One is working on her husband, another is getting up the maid, another has to put the baby to bed, or wash and feed it.

LYSISTRATA: But after all, there are other matters more important than all that.

CALONICE: My dear Lysistrata, just what is this matter you've summoned us women to consider? What's up? Something big?

LYSISTRATA: Very big.

CALONICE: [*Interested.*] Is it stout, too?

LYSISTRATA: [*Smiling.*] Yes indeed—both big and stout.

CALONICE: What? And the women still haven't come?

LYSISTRATA: It's not what you suppose; they'd have come soon enough for *that.* But I've worked up something, and for many a sleepless night I've turned it this way and that.

CALONICE: [*In mock disappointment.*] Oh, I guess it's pretty fine and slender, if you've turned it this way and that.

LYSISTRATA: So fine that the safety of the whole of Greece lies in us women.

CALONICE: In us women? It depends on a very slender reed then.

LYSISTRATA: Our country's fortunes are in our hands; and whether the Spartans shall perish—

CALONICE: Good! Let them perish, by all means.

LYSISTRATA: —and the Boeotians shall be completely annihilated.

CALONICE: Not completely! Please spare the eels.[4]

LYSISTRATA: As for Athens, I won't use any such unpleasant words. But you understand what I mean. But if the women will meet here— the Spartans, the Boeotians, and we Athenians—then all together we will save Greece.

CALONICE: But what could women do that's clever or distinguished? We just sit around all dolled up in silk robes, looking pretty in our sheer gowns and evening slippers.

---

3. Musical instruments used in most orgiastic cults, especially in the worship of Dionysus, the *God of Wine.* 4. A favorite Athenian delicacy from the Boeotian lakes, eels were then very rare in Athens because of the war.

LYSISTRATA: These are just the things I hope will save us: these silk robes, perfumes, evening slippers, rouge, and our chiffon blouses.

CALONICE: How so?

LYSISTRATA: So never a man alive will lift a spear against the foe—

CALONICE: I'll get a silk gown at once. 50

LYSISTRATA: —or take up his shield—

CALONICE: I'll put on my sheerest gown!

LYSISTRATA: —or sword.

CALONICE: I'll buy a pair of evening slippers.

LYSISTRATA: Well then, shouldn't the women have come? 55

CALONICE: Come? Why, they should have *flown* here.

LYSISTRATA: Well, my dear, just watch: they'll act in true Athenian fashion—everything too late! And now there's not a woman here from the shore or from Salamis.[5]

CALONICE: They're coming, I'm sure; at daybreak they were laying— 60 to their oars to cross the straits.

LYSISTRATA: And those I expected would be the first to come—the women of Acharnae[6]—they haven't arrived.

CALONICE: Yet the wife of Theagenes[7] means to come: she consulted Hecate about it. [*Seeing a group of women approaching.*] But look! 65 Here come a few. And there are some more over here. Hurrah! Where do they come from?

LYSISTRATA: From Anagyra.[8]

CALONICE: Yes indeed! We've raised up quite a stink from Anagyra anyway. 70

[*Enter* MYRRHINE *in haste, followed by several other women.*]

MYRRHINE: [*Breathlessly.*] Have we come in time, Lysistrata? What do you say? Why so quiet?

LYSISTRATA: I can't say much for you, Myrrhine, coming at this hour on such important business.

MYRRHINE: Why, I had trouble finding my girdle in the dark. But if 75 it's so important, we're here now; tell us.

LYSISTRATA: No. Let's wait a little for the women from Boeotia and the Peloponnesus.

MYRRHINE: That's a much better suggestion. Look! Here comes Lampito now. 80

[*Enter* LAMPITO *with two other women.*]

LYSISTRATA: Greetings, my dear Spartan friend. How pretty you look, my dear. What a smooth complexion and well-developed figure! You could throttle an ox.

LAMPITO: Faith, yes, I think I could. I take exercises and kick my heels against my bum. [*She demonstrates with a few steps of the Spartan* 85 *"bottom-kicking" dance.*]

LYSISTRATA: And what splendid breasts you have.

LAMPITO: La! You handle me like a prize steer.

---

5. Just across the bay from Piraeus, the port of Athens.   6. A large village a few miles northwest of Athens.   7. A very superstitious Athenian (perhaps he was sitting in the audience) who never went out without consulting the shrine of Hecate at his doorstep.   8. A district south of Athens. It was also the name of a bad-smelling shrub, and the phrase *to stir up the anagyra* was proverbially used to describe people who brought trouble on themselves by interfering.

LYSISTRATA: And who is this young lady with you?

LAMPITO: Faith, she's an Ambassadress from Boeotia.

LYSISTRATA: Oh yes, a Boeotian, and blooming like a garden too. 90

CALONICE: [Lifting up her skirt.] My word! How neatly her garden's weeded!

LYSISTRATA: And who is the other girl?

LAMPITO: Oh, she's a Corinthian swell.

MYRRHINE: [After a rapid examination.] Yes indeed. She swells very 95 nicely [Pointing.] here and here.

LAMPITO: Who has gathered together this company of women?

LYSISTRATA: I have.

LAMPITO: Speak up, then. What do you want?

MYRRHINE: Yes, my dear, tell us what this important matter is. 100

LYSISTRATA: Very well, I'll tell you. But before I speak, let me ask you a little question.

MYRRHINE: Anything you like.

LYSISTRATA: [Earnestly.] Tell me: don't you yearn for the fathers of your children, who are away at the wars? I know you all have hus- 105 bands abroad.

CALONICE: Why, yes; mercy me! my husband's been away for five months in Thrace keeping guard on — Eucrates.⁹

MYRRHINE: And mine for seven whole months in Pylos.¹

LAMPITO: And mine, as soon as ever he returns from the fray, readjusts 110 his shield and flies out of the house again.

LYSISTRATA: And as for lovers, there's not even a ghost of one left. Since the Milesians revolted from us, I've not even seen an eight-inch dingus to be a leather consolation for us widows.² Are you willing, if I can find a way, to help me end the war? 115

MYRRHINE: Goodness, yes! I'd do it, even if I had to pawn my dress and — get drunk on the spot!

CALONICE: And I, even if I had to let myself be split in two like a flounder.

LAMPITO: I'd climb up Mt. Taygetus³ if I could catch a glimpse of 120 peace.

LYSISTRATA: I'll tell you, then, in plain and simple words. My friends, if we are going to force our men to make peace, we must do without—

MYRRHINE: Without what? Tell us. 125

LYSISTRATA: Will you do it?

MYRRHINE: We'll do it, if it kills us.

LYSISTRATA: Well, then we must do without sex altogether. [General consternation.] Why do you turn away? Where go you? Why turn so pale? Why those tears? Will you do it or not? What means this 130 hesitation?

MYRRHINE: I won't do it! Let the war go on.

9. We have no details on this campaign in Thrace.   1. A point on the west coast of the Peloponnese held by an Athenian garrison.   2. The city of Miletus, an Athenian ally ever since the Persian War, had deserted the Athenian cause in the previous year. The object Lysistrata speaks of was supposed to be manufactured there.   3. The mountain that towers over Sparta.

CALONICE: Nor I! Let the war go on.

LYSISTRATA: So, my little flounder? Didn't you say just now you'd split yourself in half? 135

CALONICE: Anything else you like. I'm willing, even if I have to walk through fire. Anything rather than sex. There's nothing like it, my dear.

LYSISTRATA: [*To* MYRRHINE.] What about you?

MYRRHINE: [*Sullenly.*] I'm willing to walk through fire, too. 140

LYSISTRATA: Oh vile and cursed breed! No wonder they make trage-dies about us: we're naught but "love-affairs and bassinets."[4] But you, my dear Spartan friend, if you alone are with me, our enter-prise might yet succeed. Will you vote with me?

LAMPITO: 'Tis cruel hard, by my faith, for a woman to sleep alone 145 without her nooky; but for all that, we certainly do need peace.

LYSISTRATA: O my dearest friend! You're the only real woman here.

CALONICE: [*Wavering.*] Well, if we do refrain from—[*Shuddering.*] what you say (God forbid!), would that bring peace?

LYSISTRATA: My goodness, yes! If we sit at home all rouged and pow- 150 dered, dressed in our sheerest gowns, and neatly depilated, our men will get excited and want to take us; but if you don't come to them and keep away, they'll soon make a truce.

LAMPITO: Aye; Menelaus caught sight of Helen's naked breast and dropped his sword, they say. 155

CALONICE: What if the men give us up?

LYSISTRATA: "Flay a skinned dog," as Pherecrates[5] says.

CALONICE: Rubbish! These make-shifts are no good. But suppose they grab us and drag us into the bedroom?

LYSISTRATA: Hold on to the door. 160

CALONICE: And if they beat us?

LYSISTRATA: Give in with a bad grace. There's no pleasure in it for them when they have to use violence. And you must torment them in every possible way. They'll give up soon enough; a man gets no joy if he doesn't get along with his wife. 165

MYRRHINE: If this is your opinion, we agree.

LAMPITO: As for our own men, we can persuade them to make a just and fair peace; but what about the Athenian rabble? Who will per-suade them not to start any more monkey-shines?

LYSISTRATA: Don't worry. We guarantee to convince them. 170

LAMPITO: Not while their ships are rigged so well and they have that mighty treasure in the temple of Athene.

LYSISTRATA: We've taken good care for that too: we shall seize the Acropolis today. The older women have orders to do this, and while we are making our arrangements, they are to pretend to make a 175 sacrifice and occupy the Acropolis.

LAMPITO: All will be well then. That's a very fine idea.

LYSISTRATA: Let's ratify this, Lampito, with the most solemn oath.

---

4. In Sophocles' *Tyro*, which had recently been produced, the heroine had borne twin sons to the god Poseidon and left them exposed in a bassinet. 5. A 5th-century B.C. comic poet. *Flay a skinned dog:* a proverb for a useless activity.

LAMPITO: Tell us what oath we shall swear.

LYSISTRATA: Well said. Where's our Policewoman? [*To a Scythian* 180 *slave.*] What are you gaping at? Set a shield upside-down here in front of me, and give me the sacred meats.

CALONICE: Lysistrata, what sort of an oath are we to take?

LYSISTRATA: What oath? I'm going to slaughter a sheep over the shield, as they do in Aeschylus.[6] 185

CALONICE: Don't, Lysistrata! No oaths about peace over a shield.

LYSISTRATA: What shall the oath be, then?

CALONICE: How about getting a white horse somewhere and cutting out its entrails for the sacrifice?

LYSISTRATA: White horse indeed! 190

CALONICE: Well then, how shall we swear?

MYRRHINE: I'll tell you: let's place a large black bowl upside-down and then slaughter—a flask of Thasian wine.[7] And then let's swear— not to pour in a single drop of water.

LAMPITO: Lord! How I like that oath! 195

LYSISTRATA: Someone bring out a bowl and a flask.
[*A slave brings the utensils for the sacrifice.*]

CALONICE: Look, my friends! What a big jar! Here's a cup that 'twould give me joy to handle. [*She picks up the bowl.*]

LYSISTRATA: Set it down and put your hands on our victim. [*As* CALO- NICE *places her hands on the flask.*] O Lady of Persuasion and dear 200 Loving Cup, graciously vouchsafe to receive this sacrifice from us women. [*She pours the wine into the bowl.*]

CALONICE: The blood has a good color and spurts out nicely.

LAMPITO: Faith, it has a pleasant smell, too.

MYRRHINE: Oh, let me be the first to swear, ladies! 205

CALONICE: No, by our Lady! Not unless you're allotted the first turn.

LYSISTRATA: Place all your hands on the cup, and one of you repeat on behalf of all what I say. Then all will swear and ratify the oath.
I will suffer no man, be he husband or lover,

CALONICE: *I will suffer no man, be he husband or lover,* 210

LYSISTRATA: *To approach me all hot and horny.* [*As* CALONICE *hesi- tates.*] Say it!

CALONICE: [*Slowly and painfully.*] *To approach me all hot and horny.* O Lysistrata, I feel so weak in the knees!

LYSISTRATA: *I will remain at home unmated,* 215

CALONICE: *I will remain at home unmated,*

LYSISTRATA: *Wearing my sheerest gown and carefully adorned,*

CALONICE: *Wearing my sheerest gown and carefully adorned,*

LYSISTRATA: *That my husband may burn with desire for me.*

CALONICE: *That my husband may burn with desire for me.* 220

LYSISTRATA: *And if he takes me by force against my will,*

CALONICE: *And if he takes me by force against my will,*

---

6. In Aeschylus' *Seven against Thebes*, the enemy champions are described as swearing loyalty to each other and slaughtering a bull so that the blood flowed into the hollow of a shield.   7. Strong wine from the island of Thasos in the northern Aegean. In Athens the wife was in charge of the household supplies, and it is a frequent Aristophanic joke to present her as addicted to the bottle.

LYSISTRATA: *I shall do it badly and keep from moving.*
CALONICE: *I shall do it badly and keep from moving.*
LYSISTRATA: *I will not stretch my slippers toward the ceiling,* 225
CALONICE: *I will not stretch my slippers toward the ceiling,*
LYSISTRATA: *Nor will I take the posture of the lioness on the knife-handle.*
CALONICE: *Nor will I take the posture of the lioness on the knife-handle.*
LYSISTRATA: *If I keep this oath, may I be permitted to drink from this* 230
cup,
CALONICE: *If I keep this oath, may I be permitted to drink from this*
cup,
LYSISTRATA: *But if I break it, may the cup be filled with water.*
CALONICE: *But if I break it, may the cup be filled with water.* 235
LYSISTRATA: Do you all swear to this?
ALL: I do, so help me!
LYSISTRATA: Come then, I'll just consummate this offering. [*She takes a long drink from the cup.*]
CALONICE: [*Snatching the cup away.*] Shares, my dear! Let's drink to our continued friendship. 240
[*A shout is heard from off-stage.*]
LAMPITO: What's that shouting?
LYSISTRATA: That's what I was telling you: the women have just seized the Acropolis. Now, Lampito, go home and arrange matters in Sparta; and leave these two ladies here as hostages. We'll enter the Acropolis to join our friends and help them lock the gates. 245
CALONICE: Don't you suppose the men will come to attack us?
LYSISTRATA: Don't worry about them. Neither threats nor fire will suffice to open the gates, except on the terms we've stated.
CALONICE: I should say not! Else we'd belie our reputation as unmanageable pests. 250
[LAMPITO *leaves the stage. The other women retire and enter the Acropolis through the Propylaea.*]
[*Enter the* CHORUS OF OLD MEN, *carrying fire-pots and a load of heavy sticks.*]
LEADER OF MEN: Onward, Draces, step by step, though your shoulder's aching.
Cursèd logs of olive-wood, what a load you're making!
FIRST SEMI-CHORUS OF OLD MEN: [*Singing.*] Aye, many surprises await a man who lives to a ripe old age; 255
For who could suppose, Strymodorus my lad, that the women we've nourished (alas!),
 Who sat at home to vex our days,
 Would seize the holy image here
 And occupy this sacred shrine, 260
 With bolts and bars, with fell design,
 To lock the Propylaea?
LEADER OF MEN: Come with speed, Philourgus, come! to the temple hast'ning.
There we'll heap these logs about in a circle round them, 265

> And whoever has conspired, raising this rebellion,
> Shall be roasted, scorched, and burnt, all without exception,
> Doomed by one unanimous vote—but first the wife of Lycon.[8]

SECOND SEMI-CHORUS: [*Singing.*] No, no! by Demeter, while I'm
  alive, no woman shall mock at me.   270
Not even the Spartan Cleomenes,[9] our citadel first to seize,
  Got off unscathed; for all his pride
  And haughty Spartan arrogance,
  He left his arms and sneaked away,
  Stripped to his shirt, unkempt, unshav'd,   275
  With six years' filth still on him.

LEADER OF MEN: I besieged that hero bold, sleeping at my station,
  Marshalled at these holy gates sixteen deep against him.
  Shall I not these cursèd pests punish for their daring,
  Burning these Euripides-and-God-detested women?[1]   280
  Aye! or else may Marathon overturn my trophy.[2]

FIRST SEMI-CHORUS: [*Singing.*] There remains of my road
  Just this brow of the hill;
  There I speed on my way.
Drag the logs up the hill, though we're got no ass to help.   285
  (God! my shoulder's bruised and sore!)
  Onward still must we go
  Blow the fire! Don't let it go out
  Now we're near the end of our road.

ALL: [*Blowing on the fire-pots.*] Whew! Whew! Drat the smoke!   290

SECOND SEMI-CHORUS: [*Singing.*] Lord, what smoke rushing forth
  From the pot, like a dog
  Running mad, bites my eyes!
This must be Lemnos[3]-fire. What a sharp and stinging smoke!
  Rushing onward to the shrine   295
  Aid the gods. Once for all
  Show your mettle, Laches my boy!
  To the rescue hastening all!

ALL: [*Blowing on the fire-pots.*] Whew! Whew! Drat the smoke!
  [*The* CHORUS *has now reached the edge of the Orchestra nearest the
  stage, in front of the Propylaea. They begin laying their logs and fire-
  pots on the ground.*]

LEADER OF MEN: Thank heaven, this fire is still alive. Now let's first   300
  put down these logs here and place our torches in the pots to catch;
  then let's make a rush for the gates with a battering-ram. If the

---

8. The ancient commentaries tell us that she was called Rhodia and was not too careful about her
reputation.   9. In 508 B.C., the Athenians expelled the tyrant Hippias and were about to install a
democratic regime under the leadership of Cleisthenes when the oligarchic party appealed to Sparta for
help. The Spartan king Cleomenes invaded Attica, seized the city, and began a purge of the democrats.
A popular uprising, however, forced him into the Acropolis, where he was besieged; after two days he
was allowed to withdraw with his troops, and Cleisthenes began the reforms that established the democracy.   1. Euripides is always presented in Aristophanic comedy as a misogynist and hence hated by
women in return. There does not seem to be any foundation for Aristophanes' view, though Euripides'
realistic (if sympathetic) presentation of women may possibly have enraged Athenian society ladies.
2. If the chorus really fought at Marathon, they are very old men. The trophy was on a high mound
that covered the Athenian dead and is still in place.   3. A volcanic island in the Aegean.

women don't unbar the gate at our summons, we'll have to smoke
them out.

Let me put down my load. Ouch! That hurts! [*To the audience.*] 305
Would any of the generals in Samos[4] like to lend a hand with this
log? [*Throwing down a log.*] Well, *that* won't break my back any
more, at any rate. [*Turning to his fire-pot.*] Your job, my little pot,
is to keep those coals alive and furnish me shortly with a red-hot
torch. 310

O mistress Victory, be my ally and grant me to rout these audacious women in the Acropolis.

[*While the men are busy with their logs and fires, the* CHORUS OF
OLD WOMEN *enters, carrying pitchers of water.*]

LEADER OF WOMEN: What's this I see? Smoke and flames? Is that a fire
ablazing?

Let's rush upon them. Hurry up! They'll find us women ready. 315

FIRST SEMI-CHORUS OF OLD WOMEN: [*Singing.*] With wingèd foot
onward I fly,
Ere the flames consume Neodice;
Lest Critylla be overwhelmed
By a lawless, accurst herd of old men. 320
I shudder with fear. Am I too late to aid them?
At break of the day filled we our jars with water
Fresh from the spring, pushing our way straight through the
crowds.
Oh, what a din! 325
Mid crockery crashing, jostled by slave-girls,
Sped we to save them, aiding our neighbors,
Bearing this water to put out the flames.

SECOND SEMI-CHORUS OF OLD WOMEN: [*Singing.*]
Such news I've heard: doddering fools
Come with logs, like furnace-attendants, 330
Loaded down with three hundred pounds,
Breathing many a vain, blustering threat,
That all these abhorred sluts will be burnt to charcoal.
O goddess, I pray never may they be kindled;
Grant them to save Greece and our men; madness and war help 335
them to end.
With this as our purpose, golden-plumed Maiden,
Guardian of Athens, seized we thy precinct.
Be my ally, Warrior-maiden,
'Gainst these old men, bearing water with me. 340

[*The women have now reached their position in the Orchestra, and
their* LEADER *advances toward the* LEADER OF THE MEN.*]

LEADER OF WOMEN: Hold on there! What's this, you utter scoundrels?
No decent, God-fearing citizens would act like this.

LEADER OF MEN: Oho! Here's something unexpected: a swarm of
women have come out to attack us.

---

4. At this time, the headquarters of the Athenian fleet.

LEADER OF WOMEN: What, do we frighten you? Surely you don't think   345
we're too many for you. And yet there are ten thousand times more
of us whom you haven't even seen.

LEADER OF MEN: What say, Phaedria?[5] Shall we let these women wag
their tongues? Shan't we take our sticks and break them over their
backs?   350

LEADER OF WOMEN: Let's set our pitchers on the ground; then if anyone lays a hand on us, they won't get in our way.

LEADER OF MEN: By God! If someone gave them two or three smacks
on the jaw, like Bupalus,[6] they wouldn't talk so much!

LEADER OF WOMEN: Go on, hit me, somebody! Here's my jaw! But no   355
other bitch will bite a piece out of you before me.

LEADER OF MEN: Silence! or I'll knock out your—senility!

LEADER OF WOMEN: Just lay one finger on Stratyllis, I dare you!

LEADER OF MEN: Suppose I dust you off with this fist? What will you
do?   360

LEADER OF WOMEN: I'll tear the living guts out of you with my teeth.

LEADER OF MEN: No poet is more clever than Euripides: "There is no
beast so shameless as a woman."

LEADER OF WOMEN: Let's pick up our jars of water, Rhodippe.

LEADER OF MEN: Why have you come here with water, you detestable   365
slut?

LEADER OF WOMEN: And why have you come with fire, you funeral
vault? To cremate yourself?

LEADER OF MEN: To light a fire and singe your friends.

LEADER OF WOMEN: And I've brought water to put out your fire.   370

LEADER OF MEN: What? You'll put out my fire?

LEADER OF WOMEN: Just try and see!

LEADER OF MEN: I wonder: shall I scorch you with this torch of mine?

LEADER OF WOMEN: If you've got any soap, I'll give you a bath.

LEADER OF MEN: Give *me* a bath, you stinking hag?   375

LEADER OF WOMEN: Yes—a bridal bath!

LEADER OF MEN: Just listen to her! What crust!

LEADER OF WOMEN: Well, I'm a free citizen.

LEADER OF MEN: I'll put an end to your bawling.

    [*The men pick up their torches.*]

LEADER OF WOMEN: You'll never do jury-duty[7] again.   380

    [*The women pick up their pitchers.*]

LEADER OF MEN: Singe her hair for her!

LEADER OF WOMEN: Do your duty, water!

    [*The women empty their pitchers on the men.*]

LEADER OF MEN: Ow! Ow! For heaven's sake!

LEADER OF WOMEN: Is it too hot?

LEADER OF MEN: What do you mean "hot"? Stop! What are you doing?   385

LEADER OF WOMEN: I'm watering you, so you'll be fresh and green.

---

5. A man's name; the remark is addressed to another member of the male chorus.   6. A 6th-century
sculptor, the target of the poet Hipponax's satirical attacks.   7. Paid attendance at the courts, the usual
source of income for older Athenians.

LEADER OF MEN: But I'm all withered up with shaking.

LEADER OF WOMEN: Well, you've got a fire; why don't you dry yourself?

[*Enter an Athenian* MAGISTRATE, *accompanied by four Scythian
policemen.*[8]]

MAGISTRATE: Have these wanton women flared up again with their   390
timbrels and their continual worship of Sabazius?[9] Is this another
Adonis-dirge[1] upon the roof-tops—which we heard not long ago in
the Assembly? That confounded Demostratus was urging us to sail
to Sicily, and the whirling women shouted, "Woe for Adonis!" And
then Demostratus said we'd best enroll the infantry from Zacyn-   395
thus, and a tipsy woman on the roof shrieked, "Beat your breasts
for Adonis!" And that vile and filthy lunatic forced his measure
through. Such license do our women take.

LEADER OF MEN: What if you heard of the insolence of these women
here? Besides their other violent acts, they threw water all over us,   400
and we have to shake out our clothes just as if we'd leaked in them.

MAGISTRATE: And rightly, too, by God! For we ourselves lead the
women astray and teach them to play the wanton; from these roots
such notions blossom forth. A man goes into the jeweler's shop and
says, "About that necklace you made for my wife, goldsmith: last   405
night, while she was dancing, the fastening-bolt slipped out of the
hole. I have to sail over to Salamis today; if you're free, do come
around tonight and fit in a new bolt for her." Another goes to the
shoe-maker, a strapping young fellow with manly parts, and says,
"See here, cobbler, the sandal-strap chafes my wife's little—toe; it's   410
so tender. Come around during the siesta and stretch it a little, so
she'll be more comfortable." Now we see the results of such treatment: here I'm a special Councilor and need money to procure
oars for the galleys; and I'm locked out of the Treasury by these
women.   415

But this is no time to stand around. Bring up crow-bars there! I'll
put an end to their insolence. [*To one of the policemen.*] What are
you gaping at, you wretch? What are you staring at? Got an eye out
for a tavern, eh? Set your crow-bars here to the gates and force them
open. [*Retiring to safe distance.*] I'll help from over here.   420

[*The gates are thrown open and* LYSISTRATA *comes out followed by
several other women.*]

LYSISTRATA: Don't force the gates; I'm coming out of my own accord.
We don't need crow-bars here; what we need is good sound com-
mon-sense.

MAGISTRATE: Is that so, you strumpet? Where's my policeman? Officer, arrest her and tie her arms behind her back.   425

---

8. The regular police of Athens; they carried bows and arrows.   9. The cult of the Oriental deity
Sabazius had been recently introduced in Athens. It was considered somewhat disorderly and immoral
by religious conservatives.   1. The lament of the women for Adonis (Tammuz), another Oriental cult.
When the great expedition to Sicily set sail, the women were mourning the death of Adonis—a bad
omen that proved all too true. Demostratus was one of the supporters of the expedition (the most
prominent was Alcibiades), and he proposed to enlist heavy armed infantry from the island of Zacynthus,
off the west coast of Greece, on the way to Sicily.

LYSISTRATA: By Artemis, if he lays a finger on me, he'll pay for it, even if he is a public servant.

[*The policeman retires in terror.*]

MAGISTRATE: You there, are you afraid? Seize her round the waist— and you, too. Tie her up, both of you!

FIRST WOMAN: [*As the second policeman approaches* LYSISTRATA.] By   430 Pandrosus,[2] if you but touch her with your hand, I'll kick the stuffings out of you.

[*The second policeman retires in terror.*]

MAGISTRATE: Just listen to that: "kick the stuffings out." Where's another policeman? Tie *her* up first, for her chatter.

SECOND WOMAN: By the Goddess of the Light, if you lay the tip of   435 your finger on her, you'll soon need a doctor.

[*The third policeman retires in terror.*]

MAGISTRATE: What's this? Where's my policeman? Seize *her* too. I'll soon stop your sallies.

THIRD WOMAN: By the Goddess of Tauros,[3] if you go near her, I'll tear out your hair until it shrieks with pain.   440

[*The fourth policeman retires in terror.*]

MAGISTRATE: Oh, damn it all! I've run out of policemen. But women must never defeat us. Officers, let's charge them all together. Close up your ranks!

[*The policemen rally for a mass attack.*]

LYSISTRATA: By heaven, you'll soon find out that we have four compa- nies of warrior-women, all fully equipped within!   445

MAGISTRATE: [*Advancing.*] Twist their arms off, men!

LYSISTRATA: [*Shouting.*] To the rescue, my valiant women!

O sellers-of-barley-green-stuffs-and-eggs,

O sellers-of-garlic, ye keepers-of-taverns, and vendors-of-bread,

Grapple! Smite! Smash!   450

Won't you heap filth on them? Give them a tongue-lashing!

[*The women beat off the policemen.*]

Halt! Withdraw! No looting on the field.

MAGISTRATE: Damn it! My police-force has put up a very poor show.

LYSISTRATA: What did you expect? Did you think you were attacking slaves? Didn't you know that women are filled with passion?   455

MAGISTRATE: Aye, passion enough—for a good strong drink!

LEADER OF MEN: O chief and leader of this land, why spend your words in vain?

Don't argue with these shameless beasts. You know not how we've fared: 460

A soapless bath they've given us; our clothes are soundly soaked.

LEADER OF WOMEN: Poor fool! You never should attack or strike a peaceful girl.

But if you do, your eyes must swell. For I am quite content

To sit unmoved, like modest maids, in peace and cause no pain;   465

2. A mythical Athenian princess.   3. Artemis.

But let a man stir up my hive, he'll find me like a wasp.

CHORUS OF MEN: [*Singing.*]

O God, whatever shall we do with creatures like Womankind?
This can't be endured by any man alive. Question them!
  Let us try to find out what this means.
  To what end have they seized on this shrine,   470
    This steep and rugged, high and holy,
      Undefiled Acropolis?

LEADER OF MEN: Come, put your questions; don't give in, and probe
  her every statement.
  For base and shameful it would be to leave this plot untested.   475

MAGISTRATE: Well then, first of all I wish to ask her this: for what
  purpose have you barred us from the Acropolis?

LYSISTRATA: To keep the treasure safe, so you won't make war on
  account of it.

MAGISTRATE: What? Do we make war on account of the treasure?   480

LYSISTRATA: Yes, and you cause all our other troubles for it, too. Pei-
  sander[4] and those greedy office-seekers keep things stirred up so
  they can find occasions to steal. Now let them do what they like:
  they'll never again make off with any of this money.

MAGISTRATE: What will you do?   485

LYSISTRATA: What a question! We'll administer it ourselves.

MAGISTRATE: *You* will administer the treasure?

LYSISTRATA: What's so strange in that? Don't we administer the household money for you?

MAGISTRATE: That's different.   490

LYSISTRATA: How is it different?

MAGISTRATE: We've got to make war with this money.

LYSISTRATA: But that's the very first thing: you mustn't make war.

MAGISTRATE: How else can we be saved?

LYSISTRATA: We'll save you.   495

MAGISTRATE: *You?*

LYSISTRATA: Yes, we!

MAGISTRATE: God forbid!

LYSISTRATA: We'll save you, whether you want it or not.

MAGISTRATE: Oh! This is terrible!   500

LYSISTRATA: You don't like it, but we're going to do it none the less.

MAGISTRATE: Good God! it's illegal!

LYSISTRATA: We *will* save you, my little man!

MAGISTRATE: Suppose I don't want you to?

LYSISTRATA: That's all the more reason.   505

MAGISTRATE: What business have you with war and peace?

LYSISTRATA: I'll explain.

MAGISTRATE: [*Shaking his fist.*] Speak up, or you'll smart for it.

LYSISTRATA: Just listen, and try to keep your hands still.

MAGISTRATE: I can't. I'm so mad I can't stop them.   510

---

4. A leader of the war party.

FIRST WOMAN: Then you'll be the one to smart for it.

MAGISTRATE: Croak to yourself, old hag! [*To* LYSISTRATA.] Now then, speak up.

LYSISTRATA: Very well. Formerly we endured the war for a good long time with our usual restraint, no matter what you men did. You 515 wouldn't let us say "boo," although nothing you did suited us. But we watched you well, and though we stayed at home we'd often hear of some terribly stupid measure you'd proposed. Then, though grieving at heart, we'd smile sweetly and say, "What was passed in the Assembly today about writing on the treaty-stone?"[5] "What's 520 that to you?" my husband would say. "Hold your tongue!" And I held my tongue.

FIRST WOMAN: But I wouldn't have—not I!

MAGISTRATE: You'd have been soundly smacked, if you hadn't kept still. 525

LYSISTRATA: So I kept still at home. Then we'd hear of some plan still worse than the first; we'd say, "Husband, how could you pass such a stupid proposal?" He'd scowl at me and say, "If you don't mind your spinning, your head will be sore for weeks. *War shall be the concern of Men.*"[6] 530

MAGISTRATE: And he was right, upon my word!

LYSISTRATA: Why right, you confounded fool, when your proposals were so stupid and we weren't allowed to make suggestions?
"There's not a *man* left in the country," says one. "No, not one," says another. Therefore all we women have decided in council to 535 make a common effort to save Greece. How long should we have waited? Now, if you're willing to listen to our excellent proposals and keep silence for us in your turn, we still may save you.

MAGISTRATE: We men keep silence for you? That's terrible; I won't endure it! 540

LYSISTRATA: Silence!

MAGISTRATE: Silence for *you*, you wench, when you're wearing a snood? I'd rather die!

LYSISTRATA: Well, if that's all that bothers you—here! take my snood and tie it round your head. [*During the following words the women* 545 *dress up the* MAGISTRATE *in women's garments.*] And *now* keep quiet! Here, take this spinning-basket, too, and card your wool with robes tucked up, munching on beans. *War shall be the concern of Women!*

LEADER OF WOMEN: Arise and leave your pitchers, girls; no time is this 550 to falter.
We too must aid our loyal friends; our turn has come for action.

CHORUS OF WOMEN: [*Singing.*]
I'll never tire of aiding them with song and dance; never may
Faintness keep my legs from moving to and fro endlessly.
For I yearn to do all for my friends; 555

---

5. The text of a treaty was inscribed on a stone, which was set up in a public place. 6. Hector to Andromache (*Iliad* VI.528).

They have charm, they have wit, they have grace,
  With courage, brains, and best of virtues —
    Patriotic sapience.
LEADER OF WOMEN: Come, child of manliest ancient dames, offspring
  of stinging nettles.   560
Advance with rage unsoftened; for fair breezes speed you onward.
LYSISTRATA: If only sweet Eros and the Cyprian Queen of Love shed
  charm over our breasts and limbs and inspire our men with amo-
  rous longing and priapic spasms, I think we may soon be called
  Peacemakers among the Greeks.   565
MAGISTRATE: What will you do?
LYSISTRATA: First of all, we'll stop those fellows who run madly about
  the Marketplace in arms.
FIRST WOMAN: Indeed we shall, by the Queen of Paphos.[7]
LYSISTRATA: For now they roam about the market, amid the pots and   570
  greenstuffs, armed to the teeth like Corybantes.[8]
MAGISTRATE: That's what manly fellows ought to do!
LYSISTRATA: But it's so silly: a chap with a Gorgon-emblazoned shield
  buying pickled herring.
FIRST WOMAN: Why, just the other day I saw one of those long-haired   575
  dandies who command our cavalry ride up on horseback and pour
  into his bronze helmet the egg-broth he'd bought from an old
  dame. And there was a Thracian slinger too, shaking his lance like
  Tereus;[9] he'd scared the life out of the poor fig-peddler and was
  gulping down all her ripest fruit.   580
MAGISTRATE: How can you stop all the confusion in the various states
  and bring them together?
LYSISTRATA: Very easily.
MAGISTRATE: Tell me how.
LYSISTRATA: Just like a ball of wool, when it's confused and snarled: we 585
  take it thus, and draw out a thread here and a thread there with our
  spindles; thus we'll unsnarl this war, if no one prevents us, and draw
  together the various states with embassies here and embassies there.
MAGISTRATE: Do you suppose you can stop this dreadful business with
  balls of wool and spindles, you nit-wits?   590
LYSISTRATA: Why, if *you* had any wits, you'd manage all affairs of state
  like our wool-working.
MAGISTRATE: How so?
LYSISTRATA: First you ought to treat the city as we do when we wash
  the dirt out of a fleece: stretch it out and pluck and thrash out of   595
  the city all those prickly scoundrels; aye, and card out those who
  conspire and stick together to gain office, pulling off their heads.
  Then card the wool, all of it, into one fair basket of goodwill, mingling in the aliens residing here, any loyal foreigners, and anyone
  who's in debt to the Treasury; and consider that all our colonies lie   600
  scattered round about like remnants; from all of these collect the

---

7. Aphrodite.   8. The armed priests of the goddess Cybele.   9. A mythical king of Thrace. Thracian mercenaries served in the Athenian ranks during the war.

wool and gather it together here, wind up a great ball, and then
weave a good stout cloak for the democracy.

MAGISTRATE: Dreadful! Talking about thrashing and winding balls of
wool, when you haven't the slightest share in the war!   605

LYSISTRATA: Why, you dirty scoundrel, we bear more than twice as
much as you. First, we bear children and send off our sons as soldiers.

MAGISTRATE: Hush! Let bygones be bygones!

LYSISTRATA: Then, when we ought to be happy and enjoy our youth,   610
we sleep alone because of your expeditions abroad. But never mind
us married women: I grieve most for the maids who grow old at
home unwed.

MAGISTRATE: Don't men grow old, too?

LYSISTRATA: For heaven's sake! That's not the same thing. When a   615
man comes home, no matter how grey he is, he soon finds a girl to
marry. But woman's bloom is short and fleeting; if she doesn't grasp
her chance, no man is willing to marry her and she sits at home a
prey to every fortune-teller.

MAGISTRATE: [*Coarsely.*] But if a man can still get it up—   620

LYSISTRATA: See here, you: what's the matter? Aren't you dead yet?
There's plenty of room for you. Buy yourself a shroud and I'll bake
you a honey-cake. [*Handing him a copper coin for his passage
across the Styx.*][1] Here's your fare! Now get yourself a wreath.

[*During the following dialogue the women dress up the* MAGISTRATE
as a corpse.]

FIRST WOMAN: Here, take these fillets.   625

SECOND WOMAN: Here, take this wreath.

LYSISTRATA: What do you want? What's lacking? Get moving; off to
the ferry! Charon is calling you; don't keep him from sailing.

MAGISTRATE: Am I to endure these insults? By God! I'm going straight
to the magistrates to show them how I've been treated.   630

LYSISTRATA: Are you grumbling that you haven't been properly laid
out? Well, the day after tomorrow we'll send around all the usual
offerings early in the morning.

[*The* MAGISTRATE *goes out still wearing his funeral decorations.*
LYSISTRATA *and the women retire into the Acropolis.*]

LEADER OF MEN: Wake, ye sons of freedom, wake! 'Tis no time for
sleeping. Up and at them, like a man! Let us strip for action.   635

[*The* CHORUS OF MEN *remove their outer cloaks.*]

CHORUS OF MEN: [*Singing.*]
Surely there is something here greater than meets the eye;
For without a doubt I smell Hippias'[2] tyranny.
Dreadful fear assails me lest certain bands of Spartan men,
Meeting here with Cleisthenes,[3] have inspired through treachery

---

1. The coin was used to pay Charon, who ferried the dead over the river Styx. The dead were provided
with a honey cake to throw to Cerberus, the three-headed dog that guarded the entry to the underworld.
2. The last tyrant of Athens, driven out in 510 B.C. with the help of Spartan soldiers.   3. Not the
great reformer (see n. 9, p. 474) but a contemporary of Aristophanes, notorious for his effeminacy and,
therefore, suspected of conspiring with the women.

All these god-detested women secretly to seize 640
Athens' treasure in the temple, and to stop that pay
   Whence I live at my ease.
LEADER OF MEN: Now isn't it terrible for them to advise the state and
chatter about shields, being mere women?
   And they think to reconcile us with the Spartans—men who hold 645
nothing sacred any more than hungry wolves. Surely this is a web
of deceit, my friends, to conceal an attempt at tyranny. But they'll
never lord it over me; I'll be on my guard and from now on,
     "The blade I bear   A myrtle spray shall wear."
I'll occupy the market under arms and stand next to Aristogeiton.[4] 650
   Thus I'll stand beside him. [*He strikes the pose of the famous
statue of the tyrannicides, with one arm raised.*] And here's my
chance to take this accurst old hag and—[*Striking the* LEADER OF
WOMEN.] smack her on the jaw!
LEADER OF WOMEN: You'll go home in such a state your Ma won't 655
recognize you!
   Ladies all, upon the ground let us place these garments.
   [*The* CHORUS OF WOMEN *remove their outer garments.*]
CHORUS OF WOMEN: [*Singing.*]
   Citizens of Athens, hear useful words for the state.
   Rightly; for it nurtured me in my youth royally.
   As a child of seven years carried I the sacred box; 660
   Then I was a Miller-maid, grinding at Athene's shrine;
   Next I wore the saffron robe and played Brauronia's Bear;
   And I walked as Basket-bearer, wearing chains of figs,
     As a sweet maiden fair.[5]
LEADER OF WOMEN: Therefore, am I not bound to give good advice to 665
the city? Don't take it ill that I was born a woman, if I contribute
something better than our present troubles. I pay my share; for I
contribute.
MEN: But you miserable old fools contribute nothing, and after squan-
dering our ancestral treasure, the fruit of the Persian Wars, you 670
make no contribution in return. And now, all on account of you,
we're facing ruin.
LEADER OF WOMEN: What, muttering, are you? If you annoy me, I'll
take this hard, rough slipper and—[*Striking the* LEADER OF MEN.]
smack you on the jaw! 675
CHORUS OF MEN: [*Singing.*]
   This is outright insolence! Things go from bad to worse.
   If you're men with any guts, prepare to meet the foe.
   Let us strip our tunics off! We need the smell of male
   Vigor. And we cannot fight all swaddled up in clothes.

4. One of the two heroes of the democracy who assassinated Hipparchus, the brother of the tyrant Hippias. A drinking song that was frequently heard at Athenian banquets ran: "In a branch of myrtle, I'll hide my sword, like Harmodius and Aristogeiton, who killed the tyrant, and made Athens free." 5. These lines describe the religious duties of a well-born Athenian girl. The sacred box contained religious objects connected with the worship of Athena in the Erechtheum. The miller maids ground flour for sacred cakes. At Brauron, in Attica, young girls who represented themselves as bears (the saffron robe was a substitute for a more primitive bearskin) worshiped Artemis. In the Panathenaic procession certain selected girls carried baskets on their heads.

[*They strip off their tunics.*]
Come then, my comrades, on to the battle, ye who once to Leipsy-   680
drion[6] came;
Then ye were men. Now call back your youthful vigor.
    With light, wingèd footstep advance,
    Shaking old age from your frame.

LEADER OF MEN: If any of us give these wenches the slightest hold,   685
they'll stop at nothing: such is their cunning.
    They will even build ships and sail against us, like Artemisia.[7]
Or if they turn to mounting, I count our Knights as done for: a
woman's such a tricky jockey when she gets astraddle, with a good
firm seat for trotting. Just look at those Amazons that Micon[8]   690
painted, fighting on horseback against men!
    But we must throw them all in the pillory— [*Seizing and choking
the* LEADER OF WOMEN.] grabbing hold of yonder neck!

CHORUS OF WOMEN: [*Singing.*]
'Ware my anger! Like a boar 'twill rush upon you men.
Soon you'll bawl aloud for help, you'll be so soundly trimmed!   695
Come, my friends, let's strip with speed, and lay aside these robes;
Catch the scent of women's rage. Attack with tooth and nail!
[*They strip off their tunics.*]
Now then, come near me, you miserable man! you'll never eat
garlic or black beans again.
And if you utter a single hard word, in rage I will "nurse" you as   700
once
    The beetle[9] requited her foe.

LEADER OF WOMEN: For you don't worry me; no, not so long as my
Lampito lives and our Theban friend, the noble Ismenia.
    You can't do anything, not even if you pass a dozen—decrees!   705
You miserable fool, all our neighbours hate you. Why, just the
other day when I was holding a festival for Hecate, I invited as
playmate from our neighbours the Boeotians a charming, well-bred
Copaic—eel. But they refused to send me one on account of your
decrees.   710
    And you'll never stop passing decrees until I grab your foot and—
[*Tripping up the* LEADER OF MEN.] toss you down and break your
neck!
    [*Here an interval of five days is supposed to elapse.* LYSISTRATA *comes
out from the Acropolis.*]

LEADER OF WOMEN: [*Dramatically.*] Empress of this great emprise and
undertaking,   715
Why come you forth, I pray, with frowning brow?[1]

LYSISTRATA: Ah, these cursèd women! Their deeds and female notions
make me pace up and down in utter despair.

---

6. The base of the aristocratic family of the Almaeonidae (the family of Pericles) in their first attempt
to overthrow Hippias.   7. Queen of Halicarnassus in Asia Minor. She played a prominent part in
Xerxes' invasion of Greece, and her ships fought at Salamis.   8. A painter who had lately decorated
several public buildings with frescoes. The battles of the Greeks and Amazons were favorite subjects of
sculptors and painters all through the 5th century.   9. In an Aesop's fable the beetle revenges itself
on the eagle by breaking its eggs.   1. The tone of this passage is mock-tragic.

LEADER OF WOMEN: Ah, what sayest thou?

LYSISTRATA: The truth, alas! the truth.   720

LEADER OF WOMEN: What dreadful tale hast thou to tell thy friends?

LYSISTRATA: 'Tis shame to speak, and not to speak is hard.

LEADER OF WOMEN: Hide not from me whatever woes we suffer.

LYSISTRATA: Well then, to put it briefly, we want—laying!

LEADER OF WOMEN: O Zeus, Zeus!   725

LYSISTRATA: Why call on Zeus? That's the way things are. I can no
  longer keep them away from the men, and they're all deserting. I
  caught one wriggling through a hole near the grotto of Pan, another
  sliding down a rope, another deserting her post; and yesterday I
  found one getting on a sparrow's back to fly off to Orsilochus,[2] and   730
  had to pull her back by the hair. They're digging up all sorts of
  excuses to get home. Look, here comes one of them now. [A
  woman comes hastily out of the Acropolis.] Here you! Where are
  you off to in such a hurry?

FIRST WOMAN: I want to go home. My very best wool is being devoured   735
  by moths.

LYSISTRATA: Moths? Nonsense! Go back inside.

FIRST WOMAN: I'll come right back; I swear it. I just want to lay it out
  on the bed.

LYSISTRATA: Well, you won't lay it out, and you won't go home, either.   740

FIRST WOMAN: Shall I let my wool be ruined?

LYSISTRATA: If necessary, yes. [Another woman comes out.]

SECOND WOMAN: Oh dear! Oh dear! My precious flax! I left it at home
  all unpeeled.

LYSISTRATA: Here's another one, going home for her "flax." Come   745
  back here!

SECOND WOMAN: But I just want to work it up a little and then I'll be
  right back.

LYSISTRATA: No indeed! If you start this, all the other women will want
  to do the same. [A third woman comes out.]   750

THIRD WOMAN: O Eilithyia, goddess of travail, stop my labor till I come
  to a lawful spot![3]

LYSISTRATA: What's this nonsense?

THIRD WOMAN: I'm going to have a baby—right now!

LYSISTRATA: But you weren't even pregnant yesterday.   755

THIRD WOMAN: Well, I am today. O Lysistrata, do send me home to
  see a midwife, right away.

LYSISTRATA: What are you talking about? [Putting her hand on her
  stomach.] What's this hard lump here?

THIRD WOMAN: A little boy.   760

LYSISTRATA: My goodness, what have you got there? It seems hollow;
  I'll just find out. [Pulling aside her robe.] Why, you silly goose,
  you've got Athene's sacred helmet there. And you said you were
  having a baby!

---

2. He ran a house of ill repute. The sparrow was Aphrodite's bird and pulled her chariot.   3. The
Acropolis was holy ground, and would be polluted by either birth or death.

THIRD WOMAN: Well, I *am* having one, I swear!   765
LYSISTRATA: Then what's this helmet for?
THIRD WOMAN: If the baby starts coming while I'm still in the Acropo-
  lis, I'll creep into this like a pigeon and give birth to it there.
LYSISTRATA: Stuff and nonsense! It's plain enough what you're up to.
  You just wait here for the christening of this—helmet.   770
THIRD WOMAN: But I can't sleep in the Acropolis since I saw the sacred
  snake.[4]
FIRST WOMAN: And I'm dying for lack of sleep: the hooting of the owls[5]
  keeps me awake.
LYSISTRATA: Enough of these shams, you wretched creatures. You   775
  want your husbands, I suppose. Well, don't you think they want us?
  I'm sure they're spending miserable nights. Hold out, my friends,
  and endure for just a little while. There's an oracle that we shall
  conquer, if we don't split up. [*Producing a roll of paper.*] Here it is.
FIRST WOMAN: Tell us what it says.   780
LYSISTRATA: Listen.
  "When in the length of time the Swallows shall gather together,
  Fleeing the Hoopoe's amorous flight and the Cockatoo shunning,
  Then shall your woes be ended and Zeus who thunders in heaven
  Set what's below on top—"   785
FIRST WOMAN: What? Are we going to be on top?
LYSISTRATA: "But if the Swallows rebel and flutter away from the
  temple,
  Never a bird in the world shall seem more wanton and worthless."
FIRST WOMAN: That's clear enough, upon my word!   790
LYSISTRATA: By all that's holy, let's not give up the struggle now. Let's
  go back inside. It would be a shame, my dear friends, to disobey
  the oracle.
  [*The women all retire to the Acropolis again.*]
CHORUS OF MEN: [*Singing.*] I have a tale to tell,
      Which I know full well.   795
        It was told me
        In the nursery.

      Once there was a likely lad,
        Melanion they name him;
      The thought of marriage made him mad,   800
        For which I cannot blame him.

      So off he went to mountains fair;
        (No women to upbraid him!)
      A mighty hunter of the hare,
        He had a dog to aid him.   805

      He never came back home to see
        Detested women's faces.

---

4. A snake was kept in the Erechtheum.   5. The sacred bird of Athene.

He showed a shrewd mentality.
  With him I'd fain change places!⁶
ONE OF THE MEN: [*To one of the women.*] Come here, old dame, give   810
  me a kiss.
WOMAN: You'll ne'er eat garlic, if you dare!
MAN: I want to kick you—just like this!
WOMAN: Oh, there's a leg with bushy hair!
MAN: Myronides and Phormio⁷   815
  Were hairy—and they thrashed the foe.
CHORUS OF WOMEN: [*Singing.*] I have another tale,
    With which to assail
      Your contention
      'Bout Melanion.   820

    Once upon a time a man
      Named Timon⁸ left our city,
    To live in some deserted land.
      (We thought him rather witty.)

He dwelt alone amidst the thorn;   825
  In solitude he brooded.
From some grim Fury he was born:
  Such hatred he exuded.

He cursed you men, as scoundrels through
  And through, till life he ended.   830
He couldn't stand the sight of YOU!
  But women he befriended.⁹
WOMAN: [*To one of the men.*] I'll smash your face in, if you like.
MAN: Oh no, please don't! You frighten me.
WOMAN: I'll lift my foot—and thus I'll strike.   835
MAN: Aha! Look there! What's that I see?
WOMAN: Whate'er you see, you cannot say
  That I'm not neatly trimmed today.
  [LYSISTRATA *appears on the wall of the Acropolis.*]
LYSISTRATA: Hello! Hello! Girls, come here quick!
  [*Several women appear beside her.*]
WOMAN: What is it? Why are you calling?   840
LYSISTRATA: I see a man coming: he's in a dreadful state. He's mad
  with passion. O Queen of Cyprus, Cythera, and Paphos, just keep
  on this way!
WOMAN: Where is the fellow?
LYSISTRATA: There, beside the shrine of Demeter.   845
WOMAN: Oh yes, so he is. Who is he?

---

6. The chorus of men here recasts a well-known myth for its own purposes. In the myth it was Atalanta who avoided marriage, challenging her suitors to a foot race that she always won. Melanion threw a golden apple in front of her; when she stopped to pick it up, she lost the race to him.   7. Successful Athenian generals.   8. The famous misanthrope, the subject of Shakespeare's play.   9. There is no evidence of this; his hatred seems to have been directed at the whole human race.

LYSISTRATA: Let's see. Do any of you know him?

MYRRHINE: Yes indeed. That's my husband, Cinesias.

LYSISTRATA: It's up to you, now: roast him, rack him, fool him, love him—and leave him! Do everything, except what our oath forbids. 850

MYRRHINE: Don't worry; I'll do it.

LYSISTRATA: I'll stay here to tease him and warm him up a bit. Off with you.

[*The other women retire from the wall. Enter* CINESIAS *followed by a slave carrying a baby.* CINESIAS *is obviously in great pain and distress.*]

CINESIAS: [*Groaning.*] Oh-h! Oh-h-h! This is killing me! O God, what tortures I'm suffering! 855

LYSISTRATA: [*From the wall.*] Who's that within our lines?

CINESIAS: Me.

LYSISTRATA: A *man?*

CINESIAS: [*Pointing.*] A *man*, indeed!

LYSISTRATA: Well, go away! 860

CINESIAS: Who are you to send me away?

LYSISTRATA: The captain of the guard.

CINESIAS: Oh, for heaven's sake, call out Myrrhine for me.

LYSISTRATA: Call Myrrhine? Nonsense! Who are you?

CINESIAS: Her husband, Cinesias of Paionidai. 865

LYSISTRATA: [*Appearing much impressed.*] Oh, greetings, friend. Your name is not without honor here among us. Your wife is always talking about you, and whenever she takes an egg or an apple, she says, "Here's to my dear Cinesias!"

CINESIAS: [*Quivering with excitement.*] Oh, ye gods in heaven! 870

LYSISTRATA: Indeed she does! And whenever our conversations turn to men, your wife immediately says, "All others are mere rubbish compared with Cinesias."

CINESIAS: [*Groaning.*] Oh! Do call her for me.

LYSISTRATA: Why should I? What will you give me? 875

CINESIAS: Whatever you want. All I have is yours—and you see what I've got.

LYSISTRATA: Well then, I'll go down and call her. [*She descends.*]

CINESIAS: And hurry up! I've had no joy of life ever since she left home. When I go in the house, I feel awful: everything seems so 880 empty and I can't enjoy my dinner. I'm in such state all the time!

MYRRHINE: [*From behind the wall.*] I *do* love him so. But he won't let me love him. No, no! Don't ask me to see him!

CINESIAS: O my darling, O Myrrhine honey, why do you do this to me? [MYRRHINE *appears on the wall.*] Come down here! 885

MYRRHINE: No, I won't come down.

CINESIAS: Won't you come, Myrrhine, when *I* call you?

MYRRHINE: No; you don't want me.

CINESIAS: *Don't want you?* I'm in agony!

MYRRHINE: I'm going now. 890

CINESIAS: Please don't! At least, listen to your baby. [*To the baby.*] Here you, call your mamma! [*Pinching the baby.*]

BABY: Ma-ma! Ma-ma! Ma-ma!

CINESIAS: [*To* MYRRHINE.] What's the matter with you? Have you no
 pity for your child, who hasn't been washed or fed for five whole   895
 days?
MYRRHINE: Oh, poor child; your father pays no attention to you.
CINESIAS: Come down then, you heartless wretch, for the baby's sake.
MYRRHINE: Oh, what it is to be a mother! I've got to come down, I
 suppose. [*She leaves the wall and shortly reappears at the gate.*]   900
CINESIAS: [*To himself.*] She seems much younger, and she has such
 a sweet look about her. Oh, the way she teases me! And her pretty,
 provoking ways make me burn with longing.
MYRRHINE: [*Coming out of the gate and taking the baby.*] O my sweet
 little angel. Naughty papa! Here, let Mummy kiss you, Mamma's   905
 little sweetheart! [*She fondles the baby lovingly.*]
CINESIAS: [*In despair.*] You heartless creature, why do you do this?
 Why follow these other women and make both of us suffer so? [*He
 tries to embrace her.*]
MYRRHINE: Don't touch me!
CINESIAS: You're letting all our things at home go to wrack and ruin.   910
MYRRHINE: I don't care.
CINESIAS: You don't care that your wool is being plucked to pieces by
 the chickens?
MYRRHINE: Not in the least.
CINESIAS: And you haven't celebrated the rites of Aphrodite for ever   915
 so long. Won't you come home?
MYRRHINE: Not on your life, unless you men make a truce and stop
 the war.
CINESIAS: Well then, if that pleases you, we'll do it.
MYRRHINE: Well then, if that pleases *you*, I'll come home—afterwards!   920
 Right now I'm on oath not to.
CINESIAS: Then just lie down here with me for a moment.
MYRRHINE: No—[*In a teasing voice.*] and yet, I won't say I don't love
 you.
CINESIAS: You love me? Oh, do lie down here, Myrrhine dear!   925
MYRRHINE: What, you silly fool! in front of the baby?
CINESIAS: [*Hastily thrusting the baby at the slave.*] Of course not.
 Here—home! Take him, Manes! [*The slave goes off with the baby.*]
 See, the baby's out of the way. Now won't you lie down?
MYRRHINE: But where, my dear?   930
CINESIAS: Where? The grotto of Pan's a lovely spot.
MYRRHINE: How could I purify myself before returning to the shrine?
CINESIAS: Easily: just wash here in the Clepsydra.[1]
MYRRHINE: And then, shall I go back on my oath?
CINESIAS: On my head be it! Don't worry about the oath.   935
MYRRHINE: All right, then. Just let me bring out a bed.
CINESIAS: No, don't. The ground's all right.
MYRRHINE: Heavens, no! Bad as you are, I won't let you lie on the
 bare ground. [*She goes into the Acropolis.*]

1. A spring on the Acropolis.

CINESIAS: Why, she really loves me; it's plain to see.   940

MYRRHINE: [*Returning with a bed.*] There! Now hurry up and lie down. I'll just slip off this dress. But—let's see: oh yes, I must fetch a mattress.

CINESIAS: Nonsense! No mattress for me.

MYRRHINE: Yes indeed! It's not nice on the bare springs.   945

CINESIAS: Give me a kiss.

MYRRHINE: [*Giving him a hasty kiss.*] There! [*She goes.*]

CINESIAS: [*In mingled distress and delight.*] Oh-h! Hurry back!

MYRRHINE: [*Returning with a mattress.*] Here's the mattress; lie down on it. I'm taking my things off now—but—let's see: you have no   950 pillow.

CINESIAS: I don't *want* a pillow!

MYRRHINE: But I do. [*She goes.*]

CINESIAS: Cheated again, just like Heracles and his dinner![2]

MYRRHINE: [*Returning with a pillow.*] Here, lift your head. [*To her-*   955 *self, wondering how else to tease him.*] Is that all?

CINESIAS: Surely that's all! Do come here, precious!

MYRRHINE: I'm taking off my girdle. But remember: don't go back on your promise about the truce.

CINESIAS: Hope to die, if I do.   960

MYRRHINE: You don't have a blanket.

CINESIAS: [*Shouting in exasperation.*] *I don't want one!* I want to—

MYRRHINE: Sh-h! There, there, I'll be back in a minute. [*She goes.*]

CINESIAS: She'll be the death of me with these bed-clothes.

MYRRHINE: [*Returning with a blanket.*] Here, get up.   965

CINESIAS: I've got *this* up!

MYRRHINE: Would you like some perfume?

CINESIAS: Good heavens, no! I won't have it!

MYRRHINE: Yes, you shall, whether you want it or not. [*She goes.*]

CINESIAS: O lord! Confound all perfumes anyway!   970

MYRRHINE: [*Returning with a flask.*] Stretch out your hand and put some on.

CINESIAS: [*Suspiciously.*] By God, I don't much like this perfume. It smells of shilly-shallying, and has no scent of the marriage-bed.

MYRRHINE: Oh dear! This is Rhodian perfume I've brought.   975

CINESIAS: It's quite all right dear. Never mind.

MYRRHINE: Don't be silly! [*She goes out with the flask.*]

CINESIAS: Damn the man who first concocted perfumes!

MYRRHINE: [*Returning with another flask.*] Here, try this flask.

CINESIAS: I've got another one all ready for you. Come, you wretch,   980 lie down and stop bringing me things.

MYRRHINE: All right; I'm taking off my shoes. But, my dear, see that you vote for peace.

CINESIAS: [*Absently.*] I'll consider it. [MYRRHINE *runs away to the Acropolis.*] I'm ruined! The wretch has skinned me and run away!   985

---

2. The point of this proverb seems to be that the hero is such a glutton that his hosts are never quick enough with their entertainment.

[*Chanting, in tragic style.*] Alas! Alas! Deceived, deserted by this fairest of women, whom shall I—lay? Ah, my poor little child, how shall I nurture thee? Where's Cynalopex?[3] I needs must hire a nurse!

LEADER OF MEN: [*Chanting.*] Ah, wretched man, in dreadful wise 990 beguiled, bewrayed, thy soul is sore distressed. I pity thee, alas! alas! What soul, what loins, what liver could stand this strain? How firm and unyielding he stands, with naught to aid him of a morning.

CINESIAS: O lord! O Zeus! What tortures I endure!

LEADER OF MEN: This is the way she's treated you, that vile and cursèd 995 wanton.

LEADER OF WOMEN: Nay, not vile and cursèd, but sweet and dear.

LEADER OF MEN: Sweet, you say? Nay, hateful, hateful!

CINESIAS: Hateful indeed! O Zeus, Zeus!
Seize her and snatch her away,   1000
Like a handful of dust, in a mighty,
Fiery tempest! Whirl her aloft, then let her drop
Down to the earth, with a crash, as she falls—
On the point of this waiting
Thingummybob! [*He goes out.*]   1005
   [*Enter a Spartan* HERALD, *in an obvious state of excitement, which he is doing his best to conceal.*]

HERALD: Where can I find the Senate or the Prytanes?[4] I've got an important message.
   [*The Athenian* MAGISTRATE *enters.*]

MAGISTRATE: Say there, are you a man or Priapus?[5]

HERALD: [*In annoyance.*] I'm a herald, you lout! I've come from Sparta about the truce.   1010

MAGISTRATE: Is that a spear you've got under your cloak?

HERALD: No, of course not!

MAGISTRATE: Why do you twist and turn so? Why hold your cloak in front of you? Did you rupture yourself on the trip?

HERALD: By gum, the fellow's an old fool.   1015

MAGISTRATE: [*Pointing.*] Why, you dirty rascal, you're all excited.

HERALD: Not at all. Stop this tom-foolery.

MAGISTRATE: Well, what's that I see?

HERALD: A Spartan message-staff.[6]

MAGISTRATE: Oh, certainly! That's just the kind of message-staff I've 1020 got. But tell me the honest truth: How are things going in Sparta?

HERALD: All the land of Sparta is up in arms—and our allies are up, too. We need Pellene.[7]

MAGISTRATE: What brought this trouble on you? A sudden Panic?

HERALD: No, Lampito started it and then all the other women in 1025 Sparta with one account chased their husbands out of their beds.

MAGISTRATE: How do you feel?

3. A local brothel keeper.   4. The permanent committee of the council (senate).   5. A god whose grossly phallic statue was set to guard orchards and gardens.   6. An encoding device; the papyrus was wrapped around the staff on a spiral, and the message could be read only when the papyrus was wound around an exactly similar staff.   7. A city held by the Athenians and claimed by the Spartans; also the name of a famous Athenian prostitute.

HERALD: Terrible. We walk around the city bent over like men lighting matches in a wind. For our women won't let us touch them
until we all agree and make peace throughout Greece.   1030
MAGISTRATE: This is a general conspiracy of the women; I see it now.
Well, hurry back and tell the Spartans to send ambassadors here
with full powers to arrange a truce. And I'll go tell the Council to
choose ambassadors from here; I've got a little something here that
will soon persuade them!   1035
HERALD: I'll fly there; for you've made an excellent suggestion.
     [*The* HERALD *and the* MAGISTRATE *depart on opposite sides of the
     stage.*]
LEADER OF MEN: No beast or fire is harder than womankind to tame.
     Nor is the spotted leopard so devoid of shame.
LEADER OF WOMEN: Knowing this, you dare provoke us to attack?
     I'd be your steady friend, if you'd but take us back.   1040
LEADER OF MEN: I'll never cease my hatred keen of womankind.
LEADER OF WOMEN: Just as you will. But now just let me help you find
     That cloak you threw aside. You look so silly there
     Without your clothes. Here, put it on and don't go bare.
LEADER OF MEN: That's very kind, and shows you're not entirely bad.   1045
     But I threw off my things when I was good and mad.
LEADER OF WOMEN: At last you seem a man, and won't be mocked,
     my lad.
     If you'd been nice to me, I'd take this little gnat
     That's in your eye and pluck it out for you, like that.   1050
LEADER OF MEN: So that's what's bothered me and bit my eye so long!
     Please dig it out for me. I own that I've been wrong.
LEADER OF WOMEN: I'll do so, though you've been a most ill-natured
     brat.
     Ye gods! See here! A huge and monstrous little gnat!   1055
LEADER OF MEN: Oh, how that helps! For it was digging wells in me.
     And now it's out, my tears can roll down hard and free.
LEADER OF WOMEN: Here, let me wipe them off, although you're such
     a knave,
     And kiss me.   1060
LEADER OF MEN: No!
LEADER OF WOMEN: Whate'er you say, a kiss I'll have. [*She kisses him.*]
LEADER OF MEN: Oh, confound these women! They've a coaxing way
     about them.
     He was wise and never spoke a truer word, who said,   1065
     "We can't live with women, but we cannot live without them."
     Now I'll make a truce with you. We'll fight no more: instead,
     I will not injure you if you do me no wrong.
     And now let's join our ranks and then begin a song.
COMBINED CHORUS: [*Singing.*] Athenians, we're not prepared,   1070
     To say a single ugly word
     About our fellow-citizens.
     Quite the contrary: we desire but to say and to do
     Naught but good. Quite enough are the ills now on hand.

Men and women, be advised: 1075
  If anyone requires
Money—minae two or three—
  We've got what he desires.

My purse is yours, on easy terms:
  When Peace shall reappear,
Whate'er you've borrowed will be due.   1080
  So speak up without fear.

You needn't pay me back, you see,
  If you can get a cent from me!

We're about to entertain   1085
  Some foreign gentlemen;
We've soup and tender, fresh-killed pork.
  Come round to dine at ten.

Come early; wash and dress with care,
  And bring the children, too.   1090
Then step right in, no "by your leave."
  We'll be expecting you.

Walk in as if you owned the place.
  You'll find the door—shut in your face!

[*Enter a group of* SPARTAN AMBASSADORS; *they are in the same desperate condition as the* HERALD *in the previous scene.*]

LEADER OF CHORUS: Here come the envoys from Sparta, sprouting 1095
long beards and looking for all the world as if they were carrying
pig-pens in front of them.
    Greetings, gentlemen of Sparta. Tell me, in what state have you
come?

SPARTAN: Why waste words? You can plainly see what state we're come 1100
in!

LEADER OF CHORUS: Wow! You're in a pretty high-strung condition,
and it seems to be getting worse.

SPARTAN: It's indescribable. Won't someone please arrange a peace for
us—in any way you like.   1105

LEADER OF CHORUS: Here come our own, native ambassadors, crouching like wrestlers and holding their clothes in front of them; this
seems an athletic kind of malady.

[*Enter several* ATHENIAN AMBASSADORS.]

ATHENIAN: Can anyone tell us where Lysistrata is? You see our condition.   1110

LEADER OF CHORUS: Here's another case of the same complaint. Tell
me, are the attacks worse in the morning?

ATHENIAN: No, we're always afflicted this way. If someone doesn't
soon arrange this truce, you'd better not let me get my hands on—
Cleisthenes!   1115

LEADER OF CHORUS: If you're smart, you'll arrange your cloaks so none of the fellows who smashed the Hermae[8] can see you.

SPARTAN: Right you are; a very good suggestion.

ATHENIAN: Greetings, Spartan. We've suffered dreadful things.

SPARTAN: My dear fellow, we'd have suffered still worse if one of those   1120
fellows had seen us in this condition.

ATHENIAN: Well, gentlemen, we must get down to business. What's
your errand here?

SPARTAN: We're ambassadors about peace.

ATHENIAN: Excellent; so are we. Only Lysistrata can arrange things for   1125
us; shall we summon her?

SPARTAN: Aye, and Lysistratus too, if you like.

LEADER OF CHORUS: No need to summon her, it seems. She's coming
out of her own accord.

[*Enter* LYSISTRATA *accompanied by a statue of a nude female figure,
which represents Reconciliation.*]

Hail, noblest of women; now must thou be   1130
A judge shrewd and subtle, mild and severe,
Be sweet yet majestic: all manners employ.
The leaders of Hellas, caught by thy love-charms
Have come to thy judgment, their charges submitting.

LYSISTRATA: This is no difficult task, if one catch them still in amorous   1135
passion, before they've resorted to each other. But I'll soon find out.
Where's Reconciliation? Go, first bring the Spartans here, and
don't seize them rudely and violently, as our tactless husbands used
to do, but as befits a woman, like an old, familiar friend; if they
won't give you their hands, take them however you can. Then go   1140
fetch these Athenians here, taking hold of whatever they offer you.
Now then, men of Sparta, stand here beside me, and you Athenians
on the other side, and listen to my words.

I am a woman, it is true, but I have a mind; I'm not badly off in
native wit, and by listening to my father and my elders, I've had a   1145
decent schooling.

Now I intend to give you a scolding which you both deserve.
With one common font you worship at the same altars, just like
brothers, at Olympia, at Thermopylae, at Delphi—how many more
might I name, if time permitted;—and the Barbarians stand by   1150
waiting with their armies; yet you are destroying the men and towns
of Greece.

ATHENIAN: Oh, this tension is killing me!

LYSISTRATA: And now, men of Sparta,—to turn to you—don't you
remember how the Spartan Pericleidas came here once as a suppli-   1155
ant, and sitting at our altar, all pale with fear in his crimson cloak,
begged us for an army?[9] For all Messene had attacked you and the
god sent an earthquake too? Then Cimon went forth with four
thousand hoplites and saved all Lacedaemon. Such was the aid you

8. Small statues of the god Hermes equipped with phalluses that stood at the door of most Athenian houses. Just before the great expedition left for Sicily, rioters (probably oligarchic conspirators opposed to the expedition) smashed many of these statues.   9. After a disastrous earthquake the Spartans were in great danger as a result of a rebellion of their serfs, the Helots. In 464 B.C. the Athenians under Cimon sent a large force of soldiers to help them.

received from Athens, and now you lay waste the country which 1160
once treated you so well.

ATHENIAN: [*Hotly.*] They're in the wrong, Lysistrata, upon my word,
they are!

SPARTAN: [*Absently, looking at the statue of Reconciliation.*] We're in
the wrong. What hips! How lovely they are! 1165

LYSISTRATA: Don't think I'm going to let you Athenians off. Don't you
remember how the Spartans came in arms when you were wearing
the rough, sheepskin cloak of slaves and slew the host of Thessali-
ans, the comrades and allies of Hippias? Fighting with you on that
day, alone of all the Greeks, they set you free and instead of a 1170
sheepskin gave your folk a handsome robe to wear.[1]

SPARTAN: [*Looking at* LYSISTRATA.] I've never seen a more distinguished woman.

ATHENIAN: [*Looking at Reconciliation.*] I've never seen a more voluptuous body! 1175

LYSISTRATA: Why then, with these many noble deeds to think of, do
you fight each other? Why don't you stop this villainy? Why not
make peace? Tell me, what prevents it?

SPARTAN: [*Waving vaguely at Reconciliation.*] We're willing, if you're
willing to give up your position on yonder flank. 1180

LYSISTRATA: What position, my good man?

SPARTAN: Pylos; we've been panting for it for ever so long.

ATHENIAN: No, by God! You shan't have it!

LYSISTRATA: Let them have it, my friend.

ATHENIAN: Then, what shall we have to rouse things up? 1185

LYSISTRATA: Ask for another place in exchange.

ATHENIAN: Well, let's see: first of all [*Pointing to various parts of Reconciliation's anatomy.*] give us Echinus here, this Maliac Inlet in
back there, and these two Megarian legs.[2]

SPARTAN: No, by heavens! You can't have *everything*, you crazy fool! 1190

LYSISTRATA: Let it go. Don't fight over a pair of legs.

ATHENIAN: [*Taking off his cloak.*] I think I'll strip and do a little planting now.

SPARTAN: [*Following suit.*] And I'll just do a little fertilizing, by gosh!

LYSISTRATA: Wait until the truce is concluded. Now if you've decided 1195
on this course, hold a conference and discuss the matter with your
allies.

ATHENIAN: Allies? Don't be ridiculous! They're in the same state we
are. Won't all our allies want the same thing we do—to jump in
bed with their women? 1200

SPARTAN: Ours will, I know.

ATHENIAN: Especially the Carystians,[3] by God!

LYSISTRATA: Very well. Now purify yourselves, that your wives may

---

1. Hippias had allowed exiled democrats to return to Attica, but they had to stay outside the city and
wear sheepskins so that they could readily be identified (see n. 2, p. 482).   2. Like Pylos (on the
"flank" of the Peloponnese), these names are all double-barreled references to territories in dispute in
the war and salient portions of the anatomy of Reconciliation.   3. The people of Carystus on the
island of Euboea were supposed to be of pre-Hellenic stock and, therefore, primitive and savage.

feast and entertain you in the Acropolis; we've provisions by the
basketful. Exchange your oaths and pledges there, and then each 1205
of you may take his wife and go home.

ATHENIAN: Let's go at once.

SPARTAN: Come on, where you will.

ATHENIAN: For God's sake, let's hurry!

[They all go into the Acropolis.]

CHORUS: [Singing.] Whate'er I have of coverlets 1210
  And robes of varied hue
  And golden trinkets,—without stint
    I offer them to you.

  Take what you will and bear it home,
    Your children to delight, 1215
  Or if your girl's a Basket-maid;
    Just choose whate'er's in sight.

  There's naught within so well secured
    You cannot break the seal
  And bear it off; just help yourselves; 1220
    No hesitation feel.

  But you'll see nothing, though you try,
    Unless you've sharper eyes than I!

  If anyone needs bread to feed
    A growing family, 1225
  I've lots of wheat and full-grown loaves;
    So just apply to me.

  Let every poor man who desires
    Come round and bring a sack
  To fetch the grain; my slave is there 1230
    To load it on his back.

  But don't come near my door, I say.
    Beware the dog, and stay away!

[An ATHENIAN enters carrying a torch; he knocks at the gate.]

ATHENIAN: Open the door! [To the CHORUS, which is clustered around
  the gate.] Make way, won't you! What are you hanging around for? 1235
  Want me to singe you with this torch? [To himself.] No; it's a stale
  trick, I won't do it! [To the audience.] Still, if I've got to do it to
  please you, I suppose I'll have to take the trouble.

    [A SECOND ATHENIAN comes out of the gate.]

SECOND ATHENIAN: And I'll help you.

FIRST ATHENIAN: [Waving his torch at the CHORUS.] Get out! Go bawl 1240
  your heads off! Move on there, so the Spartans can leave in peace
  when the banquet's over.

    [They brandish their torches until the CHORUS leaves the Orchestra.]

SECOND ATHENIAN: I've never seen such a pleasant banquet: the Spartans are charming fellows, indeed they are! And we Athenians are
  very witty in our cups. 1245

FIRST ATHENIAN: Naturally: for when we're sober we're never at our best. If the Athenians would listen to me, we'd always get a little tipsy on our embassies. As things are now, we go to Sparta when we're sober and look around to stir up trouble. And then we don't hear what they say—and as for what they *don't* say, we have all sorts 1250 of suspicions. And then we bring back varying reports about the mission. But this time everything is pleasant; even if a man should sing the Telamon-song when he ought to sing "Cleitagoras,"[4] we'd praise him and swear it was excellent.

[*The two* CHORUSES *return, as a* CHORUS OF ATHENIANS *and a* CHORUS OF SPARTANS.]

Here they come back again. Go to the devil, you scoundrels!   1255

SECOND ATHENIAN: Get out, I say! They're coming out from the feast.

[*Enter the Spartan and Athenian envoys, followed by* LYSISTRATA *and all the women.*]

SPARTAN: [*To one of his fellow-envoys.*] My good fellow, take up your pipes; I want to do a fancy two-step and sing a jolly song for the Athenians.

ATHENIAN: Yes, do take your pipes, by all means. I'd love to see 1260 you dance.

SPARTAN: [*Singing and dancing with the* CHORUS OF SPARTANS.]
  These youths inspire
 To song and dance, O Memory;
 Stir up my Muse, to tell how we
 And Athens' men, in our galleys clashing   1265
 At Artemisium, 'gainst foemen dashing
  In godlike ire,
 Conquered the Persian and set Greece free.

  Leonidas[5]
 Led on his valiant warriors   1270
 Whetting their teeth like angry boars.
 Abundant foam on their lips was flow'ring,
 A stream of sweat from their limbs was show'ring.
  The Persian was
 Numberless as the sand on the shores.   1275

 O Huntress[6] who slayest the beasts in the glade,
 O Virgin divine, hither come to our truce,
 Unite us in bonds which all time will not loose.
 Grant us to find in this treaty, we pray,
 An unfailing source of true friendship today,   1280
 And all of our days, helping us to refrain
 From weaseling tricks which bring war in their train.
  Then hither, come hither! O huntress maid.

LYSISTRATA: Come then, since all is fairly done, men of Sparta, lead away your wives, and you, Athenians, take yours. Let every man 1285

---

4. At an Athenian banquet each guest in turn, when the time came to sing, was supposed to cap the singer before him by choosing an appropriate drinking song.   5. He held the pass at Thermopylae. Artemisium was an indecisive naval battle that occurred at the same time.   6. Artemis.

stand beside his wife, and every wife beside her man, and then, to
celebrate our fortune, let's dance. And in the future, let's take care
to avoid these misunderstandings.

CHORUS OF ATHENIANS: [*Singing and dancing.*]
    Lead on the dances, your graces revealing.
    Call Artemis hither, call Artemis' twin,   1290
    Leader of dances, Apollo the Healing,
    Kindly God—hither! let's summon him in!

        Nysian Bacchus call,
    Who with his Maenads, his eyes flashing fire,
        Dances, and last of all   1295
    Zeus of the thunderbolt flaming, the Sire.
        And Hera in majesty,
        Queen of prosperity.

        Come, ye Powers who dwell above
        Unforgetting, our witnesses be   1300
    Of Peace with bonds of harmonious love—
    The Peace which Cypris[7] has wrought for me.
        Alleluia! Io Paean!
        Leap in joy—hurrah! hurrah!
        'Tis victory—hurrah! hurrah!   1305
        Euoi! Euoi! Euai! Euai!

LYSISTRATA: [*To the Spartans.*] Come now, sing a new song to cap
ours.

CHORUS OF SPARTANS: [*Singing and dancing.*]
    Leaving Taygetus fair and renown'd,
    Muse of Laconia, hither come: 1310
    Amyclae's god in hymns resound,
    Athene of the Brazen Home,
    And Castor and Pollux, Tyndareus' sons,
    Who sport where Eurotas[8] murmuring runs.

        On with the dance! Heia! Ho!   1315
            All leaping along,
        Mantles a-swinging as we go!
            Of Sparta our song.

    There the holy chorus ever gladdens,
    There the beat of stamping feet,   1320
    As our winsome fillies, lovely maidens,
    Dance, beside Eurotas' banks a-skipping,—
        Nimbly go to and fro
    Hast'ning, leaping feet in measures tripping,
    Like the Bacchae's revels, hair a-streaming.   1325
    Leda's child,[9] divine and mild,
    Leads the holy dance, her fair face beaming.

---

7. Aphrodite.   8. The river of Sparta. Laconia is the Spartan region. Amyclae is part of Sparta. *Brazen
Home:* the bronze-plated temple of Athena in Sparta.   9. Helen (of Troy).

On with the dance! as your hand
    Presses the hair
Streaming away unconfined.   1330
    Leap in the air
Light as the deer; footsteps resound
Aiding our dance, beating the ground.

Praise Athene, Maid divine, unrivalled in her might,   1335
Dweller in the Brazen Home, unconquered in the fight.
[*All go out singing and dancing.*]

PLATO

429–347 B.C.

Socrates himself (see pp. 91–92) wrote nothing; we know what we do about him mainly from the writings of his pupil Plato, a philosophical and literary genius of the first rank. It is very difficult to distinguish between what Socrates actually said and what Plato put into his mouth, but there is general agreement that the *Apology*, which Plato wrote as a representation of what Socrates said at his trial, is the clearest picture we have of the historical Socrates. He is on trial for impiety and "corrupting the youth." He deals with these charges, but he also takes the opportunity to present a defense and explanation of the mission to which his life has been devoted.

The *Apology* is a defiant speech; Socrates rides roughshod over legal forms and seems to neglect no opportunity of outraging his listeners. But this defiance is not stupidity (as he hints himself, he could, if he had wished, have made a speech to please the court), nor is it a deliberate courting of martyrdom. It is the only course possible for him in the circumstances if he is not to betray his life's work, for Socrates knows as well as his accusers that what the Athenians really want is to silence him without having to take his life. What Socrates is making clear is that there is no such easy way out; he will have no part of any compromise that would restrict his freedom of speech or undermine his moral position. The speech is a sample of what the Athenians will have to put up with if they allow him to live; he will continue to be the gadfly that stings the sluggish horse. He will go on persuading them not to be concerned for their persons or their property but first and chiefly to care about the improvement of the soul. He has spent his life denying the validity of worldly standards, and he will not accept them now.

He was declared guilty and condemned to death. Though influential friends offered means of escape (and there is reason to think the Athenians would have been glad to see him go), Socrates refused to disobey the laws; in any case he had already, in his court speech, rejected the possibility of living in some foreign city. The sentence was duly carried out.

The form of the *Apology* is dramatic: Plato re-creates the personality of his beloved teacher by presenting him as speaking directly to the reader. In most of the many books that he wrote in the course of a long life, Plato continued to feature Socrates as the principal speaker in philosophical dialogues that explored the ethical and political problems of the age. These dialogues (the *Republic* the most famous) were preserved in their entirety and have exerted an enormous influence on Western thought ever since. Plato also founded a philosophical school, the Academy, in 385 B.C., and it remained active as a center of philosophi-

cal training and research until it was suppressed by the Roman emperor Justinian in A.D. 529. Plato came from an aristocratic Athenian family and as a young man thought of a political career; the execution of Socrates by the courts of democratic Athens disgusted him with politics and prompted his famous remark that there was no hope for the cities until the rulers became philosophers or the philosophers, rulers. His attempts, however, to influence real rulers—the tyrant Dionysius of Syracuse in Sicily and, later, his son—ended in failure.

A. E. Taylor, *Plato, The Man and His Work* (1927), is a detailed analysis of the whole corpus of Platonic dialogues. G. M. A. Grube, *Plato's Thought* (1935), studies six principal themes of Platonic philosophy. R. S. Brumbaugh, *Plato for the Modern Age* (1962), presents a general introduction with stress on the historical background and an emphasis on the scientific and mathematical aspects of Plato's thought. On the importance of Socrates, see W. K. C. Guthrie, *A History of Greek Philosophy*, vol. 3 (1969), pp. 378–567.

PRONOUNCING GLOSSARY

The following list uses common English syllables and stress accents to provide rough equivalents of selected words whose pronunciation may be unfamiliar to the general reader.

Adeimantus: *ad-ee-mant'-us*	Gorgias: *gor'-jee-as*
Aeacus: *ea'-ak-us*	Leontium: *lay-on'-tee-um*
Acantodorus: *ak-ant-o-dor'-us*	Lysanias: *lai-san'-ee-as*
Aeschines: *es'-kin-eez / ais'-kin-eez*	Meletus: *mee-lee'-tus*
Amphipolis: *am-fip'-o-lis*	Minos: *mai'-nos*
Anytus: *an'-i-tuhs*	Musaeus: *myoo-zee'-us / moo-sai'-us*
Arginusae: *ar-gin-yoo'-sai*	Nicostratus: *ni-kos'-tra-tus*
Asclepius: *as-klee'-pee-us*	Palamedes: *pal-am-ee'-deez*
Ceos: *ke'-os*	Potidaea: *pot-i-dee'-ah*
Cephisus: *see'-fi-sus*	Prodicus: *proh'-di-kus*
Chaerephon: *kai'-re-fon*	Prytanes: *pri'-tan-eez*
Crito: *crai'-toh*	Prytaneum: *pri-tan-ee'-um / pri-tan-ai'-um*
Critobulus: *cri-to'-boo-luhs*	Rhadamanthus: *rad-am-anth'-us*
Demodocus: *dee-mod'-o-kus*	Theages: *thee-ay'-jeez / thee-ah'-geez*
Epigenes: *e-pij'-en-eez*	Theosdotides: *thee-oh-zot'-id-eez*
Evenus: *ee-vee'-nus*	Triptolemus: *trip-to'-le-muhs*

The Apology of Socrates[1]

How you, O Athenians, have been affected by my accusers, I cannot tell; but I know that they almost made me forget who I was—so persuasively did they speak; and yet they have hardly uttered a word of truth. But of the many falsehoods told by them, there was one which quite amazed

---

1. Translated by Benjamin Jowett. *Apology* here means "defense."

me;—I mean when they said that you should be upon your guard and not allow yourselves to be deceived by the force of my eloquence. To say this, when they were certain to be detected as soon as I opened my lips and proved myself to be anything but a great speaker, did indeed appear to me most shameless—unless by the force of eloquence they mean the force of truth; for if such is their meaning, I admit that I am eloquent. But in how different a way from theirs! Well, as I was saying, they have scarcely spoken the truth at all; but from me you shall hear the whole truth: not, however, delivered after their manner in a set oration duly ornamented with words and phrases. No, by heaven! but I shall use the words and arguments which occur to me at the moment; for I am confident in the justice of my cause: at my time of life I ought not to be appearing before you, O men of Athens, in the character of a juvenile orator—let no one expect it of me. And I must beg of you to grant me a favor:—If I defend myself in my accustomed manner, and you hear me using the words which I have been in the habit of using in the agora,[2] at the tables of the money-changers, or anywhere else, I would ask you not to be surprised, and not to interrupt me on this account. For I am more than seventy years of age, and appearing now for the first time in a court of law, I am quite a stranger to the language of the place; and therefore I would have you regard me as if I were really a stranger, whom you would excuse if he spoke in his native tongue, and after the fashion of his country:—Am I making an unfair request of you? Never mind the manner, which may or may not be good; but think only of the truth of my words, and give heed to that: let the speaker speak truly and the judge decide justly.

And first, I have to reply to the older charges and to my first accusers, and then I will go on to the later ones.[3] For of old I have had many accusers, who have accused me falsely to you during many years; and I am more afraid of them than of Anytus and his associates, who are dangerous, too, in their own way. But far more dangerous are the others, who began when you were children, and took possession of your minds with their falsehoods, telling of one Socrates, a wise man, who speculated about the heaven above, and searched into the earth beneath, and made the worse appear the better cause.[4] The disseminators of this tale are the accusers whom I dread; for their hearers are apt to fancy that such enquirers do not believe in the existence of the gods. And they are many, and their charges against me are of ancient date, and they were made by them in the days when you were more impressible than you are now—in childhood, or it may have been in youth—and the cause when heard went by default, for there was none to answer. And hardest of all, I do not know and cannot tell the names of my accusers; unless in the chance case of a Comic poet.[5] All who from envy and malice have persuaded you—some

2. The marketplace.   3. Socrates had been the object of much criticism and satire for many years before the trial. He here disregards legal forms and announces that he will deal first with the prejudices that lie behind the formal charge that has been brought against him.   4. He was accused by some of his enemies of being a materialist philosopher who speculated about the physical nature of the universe and by others of being one of the Sophists, professional teachers of rhetoric and other subjects, many of whom taught methods that were more effective than honest.   5. He is referring to the poet Aristophanes, whose play *Clouds* (produced in 423 B.C.) is a broad satire on Socrates and his associates and a good example of the prejudice Socrates is dealing with, for it presents him propounding fantastic theories about matter and religion and teaching students how to avoid payment of debts.

of them having first convinced themselves—all this class of men are most difficult to deal with; for I cannot have them up here, and cross-examine them, and therefore I must simply fight with shadows in my own defence, and argue when there is no one who answers. I will ask you then to assume with me, as I was saying, that my opponents are of two kinds; one recent, the other ancient: and I hope that you will see the propriety[6] of my answering the latter first, for these accusations you heard long before the others, and much oftener.

Well, then, I must make my defence, and endeavor to clear away, in a short time, a slander which has lasted a long time. May I succeed, if to succeed be for my good and yours, or likely to avail me in my cause! The task is not an easy one; I quite understand the nature of it. And so leaving the event with God, in obedience to the law I will now make my defence.

I will begin at the beginning, and ask what is the accusation which has given rise to the slander of me, and in fact has encouraged Meletus to prefer this charge against me. Well, what do the slanderers say? They shall be my prosecutors, and I will sum up their words in an affidavit: 'Socrates is an evil-doer, and a curious person, who searches into things under the earth, and in heaven, and he makes the worse appear the better cause; and he teaches the aforesaid doctrines to others.' Such is the nature of the accusation: it is just what you have yourselves seen in the comedy of Aristophanes, who has introduced a man whom he calls Socrates, going about and saying that he walks in air, and talking a deal of nonsense concerning matters of which I do not pretend to know either much or little— not that I mean to speak disparagingly of any one who is a student of natural philosophy.[7] I should be very sorry if Meletus could bring so grave a charge against me. But the simple truth is, O Athenians, that I have nothing to do with physical speculations. Very many of those here present are witnesses to the truth of this, and to them I appeal. Speak then, you who have heard me, and tell your neighbors whether any of you have ever known me hold forth in few words or in many upon such matters. . . . You hear their answer. And from what they say of this part of the charge you will be able to judge of the truth of the rest.

As little foundation is there for the report that I am a teacher, and take money;[8] this accusation has no more truth in it than the other. Although, if a man were really able to instruct mankind, to receive money for giving instruction would, in my opinion, be an honor to him. There is Gorgias of Leontium, and Prodicus of Ceos, and Hippias of Elis,[9] who go the round of the cities, and are able to persuade the young men to leave their own citizens by whom they might be taught for nothing, and come to

6. He says this tongue in cheek, for he is actually paying no attention to legal propriety. This becomes clearer below, where he goes so far as to paraphrase the actual terms of the indictment and put into the mouths of his accusers the prejudice he claims is the basis of their action. 7. In Aristophanes' comedy Socrates first appears suspended in a basket; when asked what he is doing, he replies, "I walk in air and contemplate the sun." He explains that only by suspending his intelligence can he investigate celestial matters. 8. Unlike Socrates, who beggared himself in the quest for truth, the professional teachers made great fortunes. The wealth of Protagoras, the first of the Sophists who demanded fees, was proverbial. 9. In the Peloponnese. Hippias claimed to be able to teach any and all subjects, including handicrafts. Gorgias was famous as the originator of an antithetical, ornate prose style that had great influence. Leontium is in Sicily. Prodicus taught rhetoric and was well known for his pioneering grammatical studies. Ceos is an island in the Aegean.

them whom they not only pay, but are thankful if they may be allowed to pay them. There is at this time a Parian[1] philosopher residing in Athens, of whom I have heard; and I came to hear of him in this way:—I came across a man who has spent a world of money on the Sophists, Callias, the son of Hipponicus, and knowing that he had sons, I asked him: 'Callias,' I said, 'if your two sons were foals or calves, there would be no difficulty in finding some one to put over them; we should hire a trainer of horses, or a farmer probably, who would improve and perfect them in their own proper virtue and excellence; but as they are human beings, whom are you thinking of placing over them? Is there any one who understands human and political virtue? You must have thought about the matter, for you have sons; is there any one?' 'There is,' he said. 'Who is he?' said I; 'and of what country? and what does he charge?' 'Evenus the Parian,' he replied; 'he is the man, and his charge is five minae.'[2] Happy is Evenus, I said to myself; if he really has this wisdom, and teaches at such a moderate charge. Had I the same, I should have been very proud and conceited; but the truth is that I have no knowledge of the kind.

I dare say, Athenians, that some one among you will reply, 'Yes, Socrates, but what is the origin of these accusations which are brought against you; there must have been something strange which you have been doing? All these rumors and this talk about you would never have arisen if you had been like other men: tell us, then, what is the cause of them, for we should be sorry to judge hastily of you.' Now I regard this as a fair challenge, and I will endeavor to explain to you the reason why I am called wise and have such an evil fame. Please to attend then. And although some of you may think that I am joking, I declare that I will tell you the entire truth. Men of Athens, this reputation of mine has come of a certain sort of wisdom which I possess. If you ask me what kind of wisdom, I reply, wisdom such as may perhaps be attained by man, for to that extent I am inclined to believe that I am wise; whereas the persons of whom I was speaking have a superhuman wisdom, which I may fail to describe, because I have it not myself; and he who says that I have, speaks falsely, and is taking away my character. And here, O men of Athens, I must beg you not to interrupt me, even if I seem to say something extravagant. For the word which I will speak is not mine. I will refer you to a witness who is worthy of credit; that witness shall be the God of Delphi[3]—he will tell you about my wisdom, if I have any, and of what sort it is. You must have known Chaerephon;[4] he was early a friend of mine, and also a friend of yours, for he shared in the recent exile of the people,[5] and returned with you. Well, Chaerephon, as you know, was very impetuous in all his doings, and he went to Delphi and boldly asked the oracle to tell him whether—as I was saying, I must beg you not to interrupt—he asked the oracle to tell him whether any one was wiser than I was, and the Pythian prophetess answered, that there was no man wiser. Chaerephon is dead

1. From Paros, a small island in the Aegean.   2. A relatively moderate sum; Protagoras is said to have charged one hundred minae for a course of instruction.   3. Apollo.   4. One of Socrates' closest associates (he appears in Aristophanes' comedy); he was an enthusiastic enough partisan of the democratic regime to have to go into exile in 404 B.C. when the Thirty Tyrants carried on an oligarchic reign of terror.   5. This refers to the exile into which all known champions of democracy were forced until the democracy was restored.

himself; but his brother, who is in court, will confirm the truth of what I am saying.

Why do I mention this? Because I am going to explain to you why I have such an evil name. When I heard the answer, I said to myself, What can the god mean? and what is the interpretation of his riddle? for I know that I have no wisdom, small or great. What then can he mean when he says that I am the wisest of men? And yet he is a god, and cannot lie; that would be against his nature. After long consideration, I thought of a method of trying the question. I reflected that if I could only find a man wiser than myself, then I might go to the god with a refutation in my hand. I should say to him, 'Here is a man who is wiser than I am; but you said that I was the wisest.' Accordingly I went to one who had the reputation of wisdom, and observed him—his name I need not mention; he was a politician whom I selected for examination—and the result was as follows: When I began to talk with him, I could not help thinking that he was not really wise, although he was thought wise by many, and still wiser by himself; and thereupon I tried to explain to him that he thought himself wise, but was not really wise; and the consequence was that he hated me, and his enmity was shared by several who were present and heard me. So I left him, saying to myself, as I went away: Well, although I do not suppose that either of us knows anything really beautiful and good, I am better off than he is,—for he knows nothing, and thinks that he knows; I neither know nor think that I know. In this latter particular, then, I seem to have slightly the advantage of him. Then I went to another who had still higher pretensions to wisdom, and my conclusion was exactly the same. Whereupon I made another enemy of him, and of many others besides him.

Then I went to one man after another, being not unconscious of the enmity which I provoked, and I lamented and feared this: But necessity was laid upon me,—the word of God, I thought, ought to be considered first. And I said to myself, Go I must to all who appear to know, and find out the meaning of the oracle. And I swear to you, Athenians, by the dog I swear![6]—for I must tell you the truth—the result of my mission was just this: I found that the men most in repute were all but the most foolish; and that others less esteemed were really wiser and better. I will tell you the tale of my wanderings and of the 'Herculean' labors, as I may call them, which I endured only to find at last the oracle irrefutable. After the politicians, I went to the poets; tragic, dithyrambic,[7] and all sorts. And there, I said to myself, you will be instantly detected; now you will find out that you are more ignorant than they are. Accordingly, I took them some of the most elaborate passages in their own writings, and asked what was the meaning of them—thinking that they would teach me something. Will you believe me? I am almost ashamed to confess the truth, but I must say that there is hardly a person present who would not have talked better about their poetry than they did themselves. Then I knew that not by wisdom do poets write poetry, but by a sort of genius and inspiration; they are like diviners or soothsayers who also say many fine things, but do not

---

6. A euphemistic oath (compare "by George").   7. The dithyramb was a short performance by a chorus, produced, like tragedy, at state expense and at a public festival.

understand the meaning of them.[8] The poets appeared to me to be much in the same case; and I further observed that upon the strength of their poetry they believed themselves to be the wisest of men in other things in which they were not wise. So I departed, conceiving myself to be superior to them for the same reason that I was superior to the politicians.

At last I went to the artisans, for I was conscious that I knew nothing at all, as I may say, and I was sure that they knew many fine things; and here I was not mistaken, for they did know many things of which I was ignorant, and in this they certainly were wiser than I was. But I observed that even the good artisans fell into the same error as the poets;—because they were good workmen they thought that they also knew all sorts of high matters, and this defect in them overshadowed their wisdom; and therefore I asked myself on behalf of the oracle, whether I would like to be as I was, neither having their knowledge nor their ignorance, or like them in both; and I made answer to myself and to the oracle that I was better off as I was.

This inquisition has led to my having many enemies of the worst and most dangerous kind, and has given occasion also to many calumnies. And I am called wise, for my hearers always imagine that I myself possess the wisdom which I find wanting in others: but the truth is, O men of Athens, that God only is wise; and by his answer he intends to show that the wisdom of men is worth little or nothing; he is not speaking of Socrates, he is only using my name by way of illustration, as if he said, He, O men, is the wisest, who, like Socrates, knows that his wisdom is in truth worth nothing. And so I go about the world, obedient to the god, and search and make enquiry into the wisdom of any one, whether citizen or stranger, who appears to be wise; and if he is not wise, then in vindication of the oracle I show him that he is not wise; and my occupation quite absorbs me, and I have no time to give either to any public matter of interest or to any concern of my own, but I am in utter poverty by reason of my devotion to the god.

There is another thing:—young men of the richer classes, who have not much to do, come about me of their own accord; they like to hear the pretenders examined, and they often imitate me, and proceed to examine others; there are plenty of persons, as they quickly discover, who think that they know something, but really know little or nothing; and then those who are examined by them instead of being angry with themselves are angry with me: This confounded Socrates, they say; this villainous mis-leader of youth!—and then if somebody asks them, Why, what evil does he practice or teach? they do not know, and cannot tell; but in order that they may not appear to be at a loss, they repeat the ready-made charges which are used against all philosophers about teaching things up in the clouds and under the earth, and having no gods, and making the worse appear the better cause; for they do not like to confess that their pretence of knowledge has been detected—which is the truth; and as they are numerous and ambitious and energetic, and are drawn up in battle array and have persuasive tongues, they have filled your ears with their loud and inveterate calumnies. And this is the reason why my three accusers, Mele-

---

8. For a fuller exposition of this famous theory of poetic inspiration see Plato's *Ion.*

tus and Anytus and Lycon, have set upon me; Meletus, who has a quarrel
with me on behalf of the poets; Anytus, on behalf of the craftsmen and
politicians; Lycon, on behalf of the rhetoricians:[9] and as I said at the beginning, I cannot expect to get rid of such a mass of calumny all in a moment.
And this, O men of Athens, is the truth and the whole truth; I have concealed nothing, I have dissembled nothing. And yet, I know that my plain-
ness of speech makes them hate me, and what is their hatred but a proof
that I am speaking the truth?—Hence has arisen the prejudice against me;
and this is the reason of it, as you will find out either in this or in any
future enquiry.

I have said enough in my defence against the first class of my accusers;
I turn to the second class. They are headed by Meletus, that good man
and true lover of his country, as he calls himself. Against these, too, I must
try to make a defence:—Let their affidavit be read: it contains something
of this kind: It says that Socrates is a doer of evil, who corrupts the youth;
and who does not believe in the gods of the state, but has other new
divinities of his own.[1] Such is the charge; and now let us examine the
particular counts. He says that I am a doer of evil, and corrupt the youth;
but I say, O men of Athens, that Meletus is a doer of evil, in that he
pretends to be in earnest when he is only in jest, and is so eager to bring
men to trial from a pretended zeal and interest about matters in which he
really never had the smallest interest. And the truth of this I will endeavor
to prove to you.

Come hither, Meletus, and let me ask a question of you.[2] You think a
great deal about the improvement of youth?

Yes, I do.

Tell the judges, then, who is their improver; for you must know, as you
have taken the pains to discover their corrupter, and are citing and accusing me before them. Speak, then, and tell the judges who their improver
is.—Observe, Meletus, that you are silent, and have nothing to say. But is
not this rather disgraceful, and a very considerable proof of what I was
saying, that you have no interest in the matter? Speak up, friend, and tell
us who their improver is.

The laws.

But that, my good sir, is not my meaning. I want to know who the
person is, who, in the first place, knows the laws.

The judges,[3] Socrates, who are present in court.

9. The connection of Meletus with poetry and of Lycon with rhetoric is known only from this passage.
1. The precise meaning of the charge is not clear. As this translation indicates, the Greek words may
mean "new divinities," with a reference to Socrates' famous inner voice, which from time to time
warned him against action on which he had decided. Or the words may mean "practicing strange rites,"
though this charge is difficult to understand. In any case, the importance of the phrase is that it implies
religious belief of some sort and can later be used against Meletus when he loses his head and accuses
Socrates of atheism.   2. Socrates avails himself of his right to interrogate the accuser. He is, of course,
a master in this type of examination, for he has spent his life in the practice of puncturing inflated
pretensions and exposing logical contradictions in the arguments of his adversaries. He is here fulfilling
his earlier promise to defend himself in the manner to which he has been accustomed and use the
words that he has been in the habit of using in the agora (p. 501).   3. The jury; there was no judge
in the Athenian law court. The Athenian jury was large; in this trial it probably consisted of five hundred
citizens. In the following questions Socrates forces Meletus to extend the capacity to improve the youth
to successively greater numbers, until it appears that the entire citizen body is a good influence and
Socrates the only bad one. Meletus is caught in the trap of his own demagogic appeal.

What, do you mean to say, Meletus, that they are able to instruct and improve youth?

Certainly they are.

What, all of them, or some only and not others?

All of them.

By the goddess Here,[4] that is good news! There are plenty of improvers, then. And what do you say of the audience,—do they improve them?

Yes, they do.

And the senators?[5]

Yes, the senators improve them.

But perhaps the members of the assembly[6] corrupt them?— or do they too improve them?

They improve them.

Then every Athenian improves and elevates them; all with the exception of myself; and I alone am their corrupter? Is that what you affirm?

That is what I stoutly affirm.

I am very unfortunate if you are right. But suppose I ask you a question: How about horses?[7] Does one man do them harm and all the world good? Is not the exact opposite the truth? One man is able to do them good, or at least not many;—the trainer of horses, that is to say, does them good, and others who have to do with them rather injure them? Is not that true, Meletus, of horses, or any other animals? Most assuredly it is; whether you and Anytus say yes or no. Happy indeed would be the condition of youth if they had one corrupter only, and all the rest of the world were their improvers. But you, Meletus, have sufficiently shown that you never had a thought about the young: your carelessness is seen in your not caring about the very things which you bring against me.

And now, Meletus, I will ask you another question—by Zeus I will: Which is better, to live among bad citizens, or among good ones? Answer, friend, I say; the question is one which may be easily answered. Do not the good do their neighbors good, and the bad do them evil?

Certainly.

And is there any one who would rather be injured than benefited by those who live with him? Answer, my good friend, the law requires you to answer—does any one like to be injured?

Certainly not.

And when you accuse me of corrupting and deteriorating the youth, do you allege that I corrupt them intentionally or unintentionally?

Intentionally, I say.

But you have just admitted that the good do their neighbors good, and evil do them evil. Now, is that a truth which your superior wisdom has recognized thus early in life, and am I, at my age, in such darkness and ignorance as not to know that if a man with whom I have to live is corrupted by me, I am very likely to be harmed by him; and yet I corrupt him, and intentionally, too—so you say, although neither I nor any other

4. Hera.   5. The five hundred members of the standing council of the assembly.   6. The sovereign body in the Athenian constitution, theoretically an assembly of the whole citizen body.   7. This simple analogy is typical of the Socratic method; he is still defending himself in his accustomed manner.

human being is ever likely to be convinced by you. But either I do not corrupt them, or I corrupt them unintentionally; and on either view of the case you lie. If my offence is unintentional, the law has no cognizance of unintentional offences: you ought to have taken me privately, and warned and admonished me; for if I had been better advised, I should have left off doing what I only did unintentionally—no doubt I should; but you would have nothing to say to me and refused to teach me. And now you bring me up in this court, which is not a place of instruction, but of punishment.

It will be very clear to you, Athenians, as I was saying, that Meletus has no care at all, great or small, about the matter. But still I should like to know, Meletus, in what I am affirmed to corrupt the young. I suppose you mean, as I infer from your indictment, that I teach them not to acknowledge the gods which the state acknowledges, but some other new divinities or spiritual agencies in their stead. These are the lessons by which I corrupt the youth, as you say.

Yes, that I say emphatically.

Then, by the gods, Meletus, of whom we are speaking, tell me and the court, in somewhat plainer terms, what you mean! for I do not as yet understand whether you affirm that I teach other men to acknowledge some gods, and therefore that I do believe in gods, and am not an entire atheist—this you do not lay to my charge,—but only you say that they are not the same gods which the city recognizes—the charge is that they are different gods. Or, do you mean that I am an atheist simply, and a teacher of atheism?

I mean the latter—that you are a complete atheist.[8]

What an extraordinary statement! Why do you think so, Meletus? Do you mean that I do not believe in the godhead of the sun or moon, like other men?

I assure you, judges, that he does not: for he says that the sun is stone, and the moon earth.[9]

Friend Meletus, you think that you are accusing Anaxagoras: and you have but a bad opinion of the judges, if you fancy them illiterate to such a degree as not to know that these doctrines are found in the books of Anaxagoras the Clazomenian,[1] which are full of them. And so, forsooth, the youth are said to be taught them by Socrates, when [they can buy the book in the theater district for one drachma at most][2] and laugh at Socrates if he pretends to father these extraordinary views. And so, Meletus, you really think that I do not believe in any god?

I swear by Zeus that you believe absolutely in none at all.

Nobody will believe you, Meletus, and I am pretty sure that you do not believe yourself. I cannot help thinking, men of Athens, that Meletus is

---

8. Meletus jumps at the most damaging charge, and falls into the trap (see n. 1, p. 506).   9. Meletus falls back on the old prejudices that Socrates claims are the real indictment against him.   1. Clazomenae is in Asia Minor. Anaxagoras was a 5th-century philosopher and an intimate friend of Pericles, but this did not save him from indictment for impiety. He was condemned and forced to leave Athens. He is famous for his doctrine that matter was set in motion and ordered by Intelligence (Nous), which, however, did not create it. He also declared that the sun was a mass of red-hot metal larger than the Peloponnese and that there were hills and ravines on the moon.   2. The translator took this to mean that the doctrines of Anaxagoras were reflected in the works of the tragic poets; the bracketed passage reflects what is now the generally accepted interpretation.

reckless and impudent, and that he has written this indictment in a spirit of mere wantonness and youthful bravado. Has he not compounded a riddle, thinking to try me? He said to himself:—I shall see whether the wise Socrates will discover my facetious contradiction, or whether I shall be able to deceive him and the rest of them. For he certainly does appear to me to contradict himself in the indictment as much as if he said that Socrates is guilty of not believing in the gods, and yet of believing in them—but this is not like a person who is in earnest.

I should like you, O men of Athens, to join me in examining what I conceive to be his inconsistency; and do you, Meletus, answer. And I must remind the audience of my request that they would not make a disturbance[3] if I speak in my accustomed manner:

Did ever man, Meletus, believe in the existence of human things, and not of human beings? . . . I wish, men of Athens, that he would answer, and not be always trying to get up an interruption. Did ever any man believe in horsemanship, and not in horses? or in flute-playing, and not in flute-players? No, my friend; I will answer to you and to the court, as you refuse to answer for yourself. There is no man who ever did. But now please to answer the next question: Can a man believe in spiritual and divine agencies, and not in spirits or demigods?

He cannot.

How lucky I am to have extracted that answer, by the assistance of the court! But then you swear in the indictment that I teach and believe in divine or spiritual agencies (new or old, no matter for that); at any rate, I believe in spiritual agencies,—so you say and swear in the affidavit; and yet if I believe in divine beings, how can I help believing in spirits or demigods;—must I not? To be sure I must; and therefore I may assume that your silence gives consent. Now what are spirits or demigods? are they not either gods or the sons of gods?

Certainly they are.

But this is what I call the facetious riddle invented by you: the demigods or spirits are gods, and you say first that I do not believe in gods, and then again that I do believe in gods; that is, if I believe in demigods. For if the demigods are the illegitimate sons of gods, whether by the nymphs or by any other mothers, of whom they are said to be the sons—what human being will ever believe that there are no gods if they are the sons of gods? You might as well affirm the existence of mules, and deny that of horses and asses. Such nonsense, Meletus, could only have been intended by you to make trial of me. You have put this into the indictment because you had nothing real of which to accuse me. But no one who has a particle of understanding will ever be convinced by you that the same men can believe in divine and superhuman things, and yet not believe that there are gods and demigods and heroes.

I have said enough in answer to the charge of Meletus: any elaborate defence is unnecessary; but I know only too well how many are the enmities which I have incurred, and this is what will be my destruction if I am

---

3. Presumably due to the frustration of the enemies of Socrates, who see him assuming complete control of the proceedings and turning them into a street-corner argument of the type in which he is invincible.

destroyed;—not Meletus, nor yet Anytus, but the envy and detraction of the world, which has been the death of many good men, and will probably be the death of many more; there is no danger of my being the last of them.

Some one will say: And are you not ashamed, Socrates, of a course of life which is likely to bring you to an untimely end? To him I may fairly answer: There you are mistaken: a man who is good for anything ought not to calculate the chance of living or dying; he ought only to consider whether in doing anything he is doing right or wrong—acting the part of a good man or of a bad. Whereas, upon your view, the heroes who fell at Troy were not good for much, and the son of Thetis[4] above all, who altogether despised danger in comparison with disgrace; and when he was so eager to slay Hector, his goddess mother said to him, that if he avenged his companion Patroclus, and slew Hector, he would die himself—'Fate,' she said, in these or the like words, 'waits for you next after Hector'; he, receiving this warning, utterly despised danger and death, and instead of fearing them, feared rather to live in dishonor, and not to avenge his friend. 'Let me die forthwith,' he replies, 'and be avenged of my enemy, rather than abide here by the beaked ships, a laughing-stock and a burden of the earth.' Had Achilles any thought of death and danger? For wherever a man's place is, whether the place which he has chosen or that in which he has been placed by a commander, there he ought to remain in hour of danger; he should not think of death or of anything but of disgrace. And this, O men of Athens, is a true saying.

Strange, indeed, would be my conduct, O men of Athens, if I who, when I was ordered by the generals whom you chose to command me at Potidaea and Amphipolis and Delium,[5] remained where they placed me, like any other man, facing death—if now, when, as I conceive and imagine, God orders me to fulfil the philosopher's mission of searching into myself and other men, I were to desert my post through fear of death, or any other fear; that would indeed be strange, and I might justly be arraigned in court for denying the existence of the gods, if I disobeyed the oracle because I was afraid of death, fancying that I was wise when I was not wise. For the fear of death is indeed the pretence of wisdom, and not real wisdom, being a pretence of knowing the unknown; and no one knows whether death, which men in their fear apprehend to be the greatest evil, may not be the greatest good. Is not this ignorance of a disgraceful sort, the ignorance which is the conceit that man knows what he does not know? And in this respect only I believe myself to differ from men in general, and may perhaps claim to be wiser than they are:—that whereas I know but little of the world below,[6] I do not suppose that I know: but I do know that injustice and disobedience to a better, whether God or man, is evil and dishonorable, and I will never fear or avoid a possible good

---

4. Achilles.   **5.** Three battles of the Peloponnesian War in which Socrates had fought as an infantryman. The battle at Potidaea (in northern Greece) occurred in 432 B.C. (for a fuller account of Socrates' conduct there see Plato's *Symposium*). The date of the battle at Amphipolis (in northern Greece) is uncertain. The battle at Delium (in central Greece) took place in 424 B.C.   **6.** The next world (that is, the underworld); the dead were supposed to carry on a sort of existence below the earth.

rather than a certain evil. And therefore if you let me go now, and are not
convinced by Anytus, who said that since I had been prosecuted I must be
put to death (or if not that I ought never to have been prosecuted at all);
and that if I escape now, your sons will all be utterly ruined by listening
to my words—if you say to me, Socrates, this time we will not mind Anytus, and you shall be let off, but upon one condition, that you are not to
enquire and speculate in this way any more, and that if you are caught
doing so again you shall die:—if this was the condition on which you let
me go, I should reply: Men of Athens, I honor and love you; but I shall
obey God rather than you, and while I have life and strength I shall never
cease from the practice and teaching of philosophy, exhorting any one
whom I meet and saying to him after my manner: You, my friend,—a
citizen of the great and mighty and wise city of Athens,—are you not
ashamed of heaping up the greatest amount of money and honor and
reputation, and caring so little about wisdom and truth and the greatest
improvement of the soul, which you never regard or heed at all? And if
the person with whom I am arguing, says: Yes, but I do care; then I do not
leave him or let him go at once; but I proceed to interrogate and examine
and cross-examine him, and if I think that he has no virtue in him, but
only says that he has, I reproach him with undervaluing the greater, and
overvaluing the less. And I shall repeat the same words to every one whom
I meet, young and old, citizen and alien, but especially to the citizens,
inasmuch as they are my brethren. For know that this is the command of
God; and I believe that no greater good has ever happened in the state
than my service to the God. For I do nothing but go about persuading you
all, old and young alike, not to take thought for your persons or your
properties, but first and chiefly to care about the greatest improvement of
the soul. I tell you that virtue is not given by money, but that from virtue
comes money and every other good of man, public as well as private. This
is my teaching, and if this is the doctrine which corrupts the youth, I am
a mischievous person. But if any one says that this is not my teaching, he
is speaking an untruth. Wherefore, O men of Athens, I say to you, do as
Anytus bids or not as Anytus bids, and either acquit me or not; but whichever you do, understand that I shall never alter my ways, not even if I have
to die many times.

Men of Athens, do not interrupt,[7] but hear me; there was an understanding between us that you should hear me to the end: I have something
more to say, at which you may be inclined to cry out; but I believe that to
hear me will be good for you, and therefore I beg that you will not cry out.
I would have you know, that if you kill such an one as I am, you will
injure yourselves more than you will injure me. Nothing will injure me,
not Meletus nor yet Anytus—they cannot, for a bad man is not permitted
to injure a better than himself. I do not deny that Anytus may, perhaps,
kill him, or drive him into exile, or deprive him of civil rights; and he may
imagine, and others may imagine, that he is inflicting a great injury upon

---

7. The disturbance this time is presumably more general, for Socrates is defying the court and the
people.

him: but there I do not agree. For the evil of doing as he is doing—the evil of unjustly taking away the life of another—is greater far.

And now, Athenians, I am not going to argue for my own sake, as you may think, but for yours, that you may not sin against the God by condemning me, who am his gift to you. For if you kill me you will not easily find a successor to me, who, if I may use such a ludicrous figure of speech, am a sort of gadfly, given to the state by God; and the state is a great and noble steed who is tardy in his motions owing to his very size, and requires to be stirred into life. I am that gadfly which God has attached to the state, and all day long and in all places am always fastening upon you, arousing and persuading and reproaching you. You will not easily find another like me, and therefore I would advise you to spare me. I dare say that you may feel out of temper (like a person who is suddenly awakened from sleep), and you think that you might easily strike me dead as Anytus advises, and then you would sleep on for the remainder of your lives, unless God in his care of you sent you another gadfly. When I say that I am given to you by God, the proof of my mission is this:—if I had been like other men, I should not have neglected all my own concerns or patiently seen the neglect of them during all these years, and have been doing yours, coming to you individually like a father or elder brother, exhorting you to regard virtue; such conduct, I say, would be unlike human nature. If I had gained anything, or if my exhortations had been paid, there would have been some sense in my doing so; but now, as you will perceive, not even the impudence of my accusers dares to say that I have ever exacted or sought pay of any one; of that they have no witness. And I have a sufficient witness to the truth of what I say—my poverty.

Some one may wonder why I go about in private giving advice and busying myself with the concerns of others, but do not venture to come forward in public and advise the state. I will tell you why. You have heard me speak at sundry times and in divers places of an oracle or sign which comes to me, and is the divinity which Meletus ridicules in the indictment. This sign, which is a kind of voice, first began to come to me when I was a child; it always forbids but never commands me to do anything which I am going to do. This is what deters me from being a politician. And rightly, as I think. For I am certain, O men of Athens, that if I had engaged in politics, I should have perished long ago, and done no good either to you or to myself. And do not be offended at my telling you the truth: for the truth is, that no man who goes to war with you or any other multitude, honestly striving against the many lawless and unrighteous deeds which are done in a state, will save his life; he who will fight for the right, if he would live even for a brief space, must have a private station and not a public one.

I can give you convincing evidence of what I say, not words only, but what you value far more—actions. Let me relate to you a passage of my own life which will prove to you that I should never have yielded to injustice from any fear of death, and that 'as I should have refused to yield' I must have died at once. I will tell you a tale of the courts, not very interesting perhaps, but nevertheless true. The only office of state which I ever

held, O men of Athens, was that of senator: the tribe Antiochis,[8] which is my tribe, had the presidency at the trial of the generals who had not taken up the bodies of the slain after the battle of Arginusae;[9] and you proposed to try them in a body, contrary to law, as you all thought afterwards; but at the time I was the only one of the Prytanes who was opposed to the illegality, and I gave my vote against you; and when the orators threatened to impeach and arrest me, and you called and shouted, I made up my mind that I would run the risk, having law and justice with me, rather than take part in your injustice because I feared imprisonment and death. This happened in the days of the democracy. But when the oligarchy of the Thirty was in power,[1] they sent for me and four others into the rotunda, and bade us bring Leon the Salaminian from Salamis,[2] as they wanted to put him to death. This was a specimen of the sort of commands which they were always giving with the view of implicating as many as possible in their crimes; and then I showed, not in word only but in deed, that, if I may be allowed to use such an expression, I cared not a straw for death, and that my great and only care was lest I should do an unrighteous or unholy thing. For the strong arm of that oppressive power did not frighten me into doing wrong; and when we came out of the rotunda the other four went to Salamis and fetched Leon, but I went quietly home. For which I might have lost my life, had not the power of the Thirty shortly afterwards come to an end. And many will witness to my words.

Now do you really imagine that I could have survived all these years, if I had led a public life, supposing that like a good man I had always maintained the right and had made justice, as I ought, the first thing? No indeed, men of Athens, neither I nor any other man. But I have been always the same in all my actions, public as well as private, and never have I yielded any base compliance to those who are slanderously termed my disciples, or to any other. Not that I have any regular disciples. But if any one likes to come and hear me while I am pursuing my mission, whether he be young or old, he is not excluded. Nor do I converse only with those who pay; but any one, whether he be rich or poor, may ask and answer me and listen to my words; and whether he turns out to be a bad man or a good one, neither result can be justly imputed to me; for I never taught or professed to teach him anything. And if any one says that he has ever

---

8. The Council of the Five Hundred consisted of fifty members of each of the ten tribes into which the population was divided. Socrates' tribe, like the other nine, was named after a mythical hero, in this case Antiochus. Each tribal delegation acted as a standing committee of the whole body for a part of the year. The members of this standing committee were called Prytanes. In acting as a member of the council Socrates was not "engaging in politics" but simply fulfilling his duty as a citizen when called on.   9. An Athenian naval victory over Sparta, in 406 B.C. The Athenian commanders failed to pick up the bodies of a large number of Athenians whose ships had been destroyed. Whether they were prevented from doing so by the wind or simply neglected this duty in the excitement of victory is not known; in any case, the Athenian population suspected the worst and put all ten generals on trial, not in a court of law but before the assembly. The generals were tried not individually, but in a group, and condemned to death. The six who had returned to Athens were executed, among them a son of Pericles. 1. Socrates gives two instances of his political actions, one under the democracy and one under the Thirty Tyrants. In both cases, he was in opposition to the government. In 404 B.C., with Spartan backing, the Thirty Tyrants (as they were known to their enemies) ruled for eight months over a defeated Athens. Prominent among them was Critias, who had been one of the rich young men who listened eagerly to Socrates.   2. Athenian territory, an island off Piraeus, the port of Athens. *Rotunda*: the circular building in which the Prytanes held their meetings.

learned or heard anything from me in private which all the world has not heard, let me tell you that he is lying.

But I shall be asked, Why do people delight in continually conversing with you? I have told you already, Athenians, the whole truth about this matter: they like to hear the cross-examination of the pretenders to wisdom; there is amusement in it. Now this duty of cross-examining other men has been imposed upon me by God; and has been signified to me by oracles, visions, and in every way in which the will of divine power was ever intimated to any one. This is true, O Athenians; or, if not true, would be soon refuted. If I am or have been corrupting the youth, those of them who are now grown up and become sensible that I gave them bad advice in the days of their youth should come forward as accusers, and take their revenge; or if they do not like to come themselves, some of their relatives, fathers, brothers, or other kinsmen, should say what evil their families have suffered at my hands. Now is their time. Many of them I see in the court. There is Crito, who is of the same age and of the same deme[3] with myself, and there is Critobulus his son, whom I also see. Then again there is Lysanias of Sphettus, who is the father of Aeschines—he is present; and also there is Antiphon of Cephisus, who is the father of Epigenes; and there are the brothers of several who have associated with me. There is Nicostratus the son of Theosdotides, and the brother of Theodotus (now Theodotus himself is dead, and therefore he, at any rate, will not seek to stop him); and there is Paralus the son of Demodocus, who had a brother Theages; and Adeimantus the son of Ariston, whose brother Plato[4] is present; and Aeantodorus, who is the brother of Apollodorus, whom I also see. I might mention a great many others, some of whom Meletus should have produced as witnesses in the course of his speech; and let him still produce them, if he has forgotten—I will make way for him. And let him say, if he has any testimony of the sort which he can produce. Nay, Athenians, the very opposite is the truth. For all these are ready to witness on behalf of the corrupter, of the injurer of their kindred, as Meletus and Anytus call me; not the corrupted youth only—there might have been a motive for that—but their uncorrupted elder relatives. Why should they too support me with their testimony? Why, indeed, except for the sake of truth and justice, and because they know that I am speaking the truth, and that Meletus is a liar.

Well, Athenians, this and the like of this is all the defence which I have to offer. Yet a word more. Perhaps there may be some one who is offended at me, when he calls to mind how he himself on a similar, or even a less serious occasion, prayed and entreated the judges with many tears, and how he produced his children in court, which was a moving spectacle, together with a host of relations and friends; whereas I, who am probably in danger of my life, will do none of these things. The contrast may occur to his mind, and he may be set against me, and vote in anger because he is displeased at me on this account.[5] Now if there be such a person among

---

3. Precinct; the local unit of Athenian administration. Crito was a friend of Socrates who later tried to persuade him to escape from prison.   4. The writer of the *Apology*.   5. The accepted ending of the speech for the defense was an unrestrained appeal to the pity of the jury. Socrates' refusal to make it is another shock for the prejudices of the audience.

you,—mind, I do not say that there is,—to him I may fairly reply: My friend, I am a man, and like other men, a creature of flesh and blood, and not 'of wood or stone,' as Homer says;[6] and I have a family, yes, and sons, O Athenians, three in number, one almost a man, and two others who are still young; and yet I will not bring any of them hither in order to petition you for an acquittal. And why not? Not from any self-assertion or want of respect for you. Whether I am or am not afraid of death is another question, of which I will not now speak. But, having regard to public opinion, I feel that such conduct would be discreditable to myself, and to you, and to the whole state. One who has reached my years, and who has a name for wisdom, ought not to demean himself. Whether this opinion of me be deserved or not, at any rate the world has decided that Socrates is in some way superior to other men. And if those among you who are said to be superior in wisdom and courage, and any other virtue, demean themselves in this way, how shameful is their conduct! I have seen men of reputation, when they have been condemned, behaving in the strangest manner: they seemed to fancy that they were going to suffer something dreadful if they died, and that they could be immortal if you only allowed them to live; and I think that such are a dishonor to the state, and that any stranger coming in would have said of them that the most eminent men of Athens, to whom the Athenians themselves give honor and command, are no better than women. And I say that these things ought not to be done by those of us who have a reputation; and if they are done, you ought not to permit them; you ought rather to show that you are far more disposed to condemn the man who gets up a doleful scene and makes the city ridiculous, than him who holds his peace.

But, setting aside the question of public opinion, there seems to be something wrong in asking a favor of a judge, and thus procuring an acquittal, instead of informing and convincing him. For his duty is, not to make a present of justice, but to give judgment; and he has sworn that he will judge according to the laws, and not according to his own good pleasure; and we ought not to encourage you, nor should you allow yourself to be encouraged, in this habit of perjury—there can be no piety in that. Do not then require me to do what I consider dishonorable and impious and wrong, especially now, when I am being tried for impiety on the indictment of Meletus. For if, O men of Athens, by force of persuasion and entreaty I could overpower your oaths, then I should be teaching you to believe that there are no gods, and in defending should simply convict myself of the charge of not believing in them. But that is not so—far otherwise. For I do believe that there are gods, and in a sense higher than that in which any of my accusers believe in them. And to you and to God I commit my cause, to be determined by you as is best for you and me.[7]

6. In the *Odyssey* (XIX.173–74) Penelope says to her husband, Odysseus (who is disguised as a beggar), "Tell me of your family and where you come from. For you did not spring from an oak or a rock, as the old saying goes."   7. The jury reaches a verdict of guilty. It appears from what Socrates says later that the jury was split: 280 for this verdict and 220 against it. The penalty is to be settled by the jury's choice between the penalty proposed by the prosecution and that offered by the defense. The jury itself cannot propose a penalty. Meletus demands death. Socrates must propose the lightest sentence he thinks he can get away with, but one heavy enough to satisfy the majority of the jury who voted him guilty. The prosecution probably expects him to propose exile from Athens, but Socrates surprises them.

There are many reasons why I am not grieved, O men of Athens, at the vote of condemnation. I expected it, and am only surprised that the votes are so nearly equal; for I had thought that the majority against me would have been far larger; but now, had thirty votes gone over to the other side, I should have been acquitted. And I may say, I think, that I have escaped Meletus. I may say more; for without the assistance of Anytus and Lycon, any one may see that he would not have had a fifth part of the votes,[8] as the law requires, in which case he would have incurred a fine of a thousand drachmae.

And so he proposes death as the penalty. And what shall I propose on my part, O men of Athens? Clearly that which is my due. And what is my due? What return shall be made to the man who has never had the wit to be idle during his whole life; but has been careless of what the many care for—wealth, and family interests, and military offices, and speaking in the assembly, and magistracies, and plots, and parties. Reflecting that I was really too honest a man to be a politician and live, I did not go where I could do no good to you or to myself; but where I could do the greatest good privately to every one of you, thither I went, and sought to persuade every man among you that he must look to himself, and seek virtue and wisdom before he looks to his private interests, and look to the state before he looks to the interests of the state; and that this should be the order which he observes in all his actions. What shall be done to such an one? Doubtless some good thing, O men of Athens, if he has his reward; and the good should be of a kind suitable to him. What would be a reward suitable to a poor man who is your benefactor, and who desires leisure that he may instruct you? There can be no reward so fitting as maintenance in the Prytaneum,[9] O men of Athens, a reward which he deserves far more than the citizen who has won the prize at Olympia in the horse or chariot race, whether the chariots were drawn by two horses or by many. For I am in want, and he has enough; and he only gives you the appearance of happiness, and I give you the reality. And if I am to estimate the penalty fairly, I should say that maintenance in the Prytaneum is the just return.

Perhaps you think that I am braving you in what I am saying now, as in what I said before about the tears and prayers. But this is not so. I speak rather because I am convinced that I never intentionally wronged any one, although I cannot convince you—the time has been too short; if there were a law at Athens, as there is in other cities, that a capital cause should not be decided in one day,[1] then I believe that I should have convinced you. But I cannot in a moment refute great slander; and, as I am convinced that I never wronged another, I will assuredly not wrong myself. I will not say of myself that I deserve any evil, or propose any penalty. Why should I? Because I am afraid of the penalty of death which Meletus proposes? When I do not know whether death is a good or an evil, why should I propose a penalty which would certainly be an evil? Shall I say imprisonment? And why should I live in prison, and be the slave of the magistrates

8. Socrates jokingly divides the votes against him into three parts, one for each of his three accusers, and points out that Meletus' votes fall below the minimum necessary to justify the trial.   9. The place in which the Prytanes, as representatives of the city, entertained distinguished visitors and winners at the athletic contests at Olympia.   1. There was such a law in Sparta.

of the year—of the Eleven?[2] Or shall the penalty be a fine, and imprisonment until the fine is paid? There is the same objection. I should have to
lie in prison, for money I have none, and cannot pay. And if I say exile
(and this may possibly be the penalty which you will affix), I must indeed
be blinded by the love of life, if I am so irrational as to expect that when
you, who are my own citizens, cannot endure my discourses and words,
and have found them so grievous and odious that you will have no more
of them, others are likely to endure me. No indeed, men of Athens, that
is not very likely. And what a life should I lead, at my age, wandering from
city to city, ever changing my place of exile, and always being driven out!
For I am quite sure that wherever I go, there, as here, the young men will
flock to me; and if I drive them away, their elders will drive me out at
their request; and if I let them come, their fathers and friends will drive
me out for their sakes.

Some one will say: Yes, Socrates, but cannot you hold your tongue, and
then you may go into a foreign city, and no one will interfere with you?
Now I have great difficulty in making you understand my answer to this.
For if I tell you that to do as you say would be a disobedience to the God,
and therefore that I cannot hold my tongue, you will not believe that I am
serious; and if I say again that daily to discourse about virtue, and of those
other things about which you hear me examining myself and others, is the
greatest good of man, and that the unexamined life is not worth living,
you are still less likely to believe me. Yet I say what is true, although a
thing of which it is hard for me to persuade you. Also, I have never been
accustomed to think that I deserve to suffer any harm. Had I money I
might have estimated the offence at what I was able to pay, and not have
been much the worse. But I have none, and therefore I must ask you to
proportion the fine to my means. Well, perhaps I could afford a mina,[3]
and therefore I propose that penalty: Plato, Crito, Critobulus, and Apollodorus, my friends here, bid me say thirty minae, and they will be the
sureties. Let thirty minae be the penalty; for which sum they will be ample
security to you.[4]

Not much time will be gained, O Athenians, in return for the evil name
which you will get from the detractors of the city, who will say that you
killed Socrates, a wise man; for they will call me wise, even although I am
not wise, when they want to reproach you. If you had waited a little while,
your desire would have been fulfilled in the course of nature. For I am far
advanced in years, as you may perceive, and not far from death. I am
speaking now not to all of you, but only to those who have condemned
me to death. And I have another thing to say to them: You think that I was
convicted because I had no words of the sort which would have procured
my acquittal—I mean, if I had thought fit to leave nothing undone or
unsaid. Not so; the deficiency which led to my conviction was not of

2. A committee that had charge of prisons and public executions.   3. It is almost impossible to
express the value of ancient money in modern terms. A mina was a considerable sum; in Aristotle's time
(4th century B.C.) one mina was recognized as a fair ransom for a prisoner of war.   4. The jury
decides for death (according to a much later source, the vote this time was three hundred to two
hundred). The decision is not surprising in view of Socrates' intransigence. Socrates now makes a final
statement to the court.

words—certainly not. But I had not the boldness or impudence or inclination to address you as you would have liked me to do, weeping and wailing and lamenting, and saying and doing many things which you have been accustomed to hear from others, and which, as I maintain, are unworthy of me. I thought at the time that I ought not to do anything common or mean when in danger: nor do I now repent of the style of my defence; I would rather die having spoken after my manner, than speak in your manner and live. For neither in war nor yet at law ought I or any man to use every way of escaping death. Often in battle there can be no doubt that if a man will throw away his arms, and fall on his knees before his pursuers, he may escape death; and in other dangers there are other ways of escaping death, if a man is willing to say and do anything. The difficulty, my friends, is not to avoid death, but to avoid unrighteousness; for that runs faster than death. I am old and move slowly, and the slower runner has overtaken me, and my accusers are keen and quick, and the faster runner, who is unrighteousness, has overtaken them. And now I depart hence condemned by you to suffer the penalty of death,—they too go their ways condemned by the truth to suffer the penalty of villainy and wrong; and I must abide by my award—let them abide by theirs. I suppose that these things may be regarded as fated,—and I think that they are well.

And now, O men who have condemned me, I would fain prophesy to you; for I am about to die, and in the hour of death men are gifted with prophetic power.[5] And I prophesy to you who are my murderers, that immediately after my departure punishment far heavier than you have inflicted on me will surely await you. Me you have killed because you wanted to escape the accuser, and not to give an account of your lives. But that will not be as you suppose: far otherwise. For I say that there will be more accusers of you than there are now; accusers whom hitherto I have restrained:[6] and as they are younger they will be more inconsiderate with you, and you will be more offended at them. If you think that by killing men you can prevent some one from censuring your evil lives, you are mistaken; that is not a way of escape which is either possible or honorable; the easiest and the noblest way is not to be disabling others, but to be improving yourselves. This is the prophecy which I utter before my departure to the judges who have condemned me.

Friends, who would have acquitted me, I would like also to talk with you about the thing which has come to pass, while the magistrates are busy, and before I go to the place at which I must die. Stay then a little, for we may as well talk with one another while there is time. You are my friends, and I should like to show you the meaning of this event which has happened to me. O my judges—for you I may truly call judges—I should like to tell you of a wonderful circumstance. Hitherto the divine faculty of which the internal oracle is the source has constantly been in the habit of opposing me even about trifles, if I was going to make a slip or error in any matter; and now as you see there has come upon me that which may be thought, and is generally believed to be, the last and worst

---

5. As the dying Hector foretells the death of Achilles in the *Iliad*.   6. Socrates' prophecy was fulfilled, for all of the many different philosophical schools of the early 4th century B.C. claimed descent from Socrates and developed one or another aspect of his teachings.

evil. But the oracle made no sign of opposition, either when I was leaving my house in the morning, or when I was on my way to the court, or while I was speaking, at anything which I was going to say; and yet I have often been stopped in the middle of a speech, but now in nothing I either said or did touching the matter in hand has the oracle opposed me. What do I take to be the explanation of this silence? I will tell you. It is an intimation that what has happened to me is a good, and that those of us who think that death is an evil are in error. For the customary sign would surely have opposed me had I been going to evil and not to good.

Let us reflect in another way, and we shall see that there is great reason to hope that death is a good; for one of two things—either death is a state of nothingness and utter unconsciousness, or, as men say, there is a change and migration of the soul from this world to another. Now if you suppose that there is no consciousness, but a sleep like the sleep of him who is undisturbed even by dreams, death will be an unspeakable gain. For if a person were to select the night in which his sleep was undisturbed even by dreams, and were to compare with this the other days and nights of his life, and then were to tell us how many days and nights he had passed in the course of his life better and more pleasantly than this one, I think that any man, I will not say a private man, but even the great king will not find many such days or nights, when compared with the others. Now if death be of such a nature, I say that to die is gain; for eternity is then only a single night. But if death is the journey to another place, and there, as men say, all the dead abide, what good, O my friends and judges, can be greater than this? If indeed when the pilgrim arrives in the world below, he is delivered from the professors of justice in this world, and finds the true judges who are said to give judgment there, Minos and Rhadamanthus and Aeacus and Triptolemus,[7] and other sons of God who were righteous in their own life, that pilgrimage will be worth making. What would not a man give if he might converse with Orpheus and Musaeus and Hesiod[8] and Homer? Nay, if this be true, let me die again and again. I myself, too, shall have a wonderful interest in there meeting and conversing with Palamedes, and Ajax the son of Telamon,[9] and any other ancient hero who has suffered death through an unjust judgment; and there will be no small pleasure, as I think, in comparing my own sufferings with theirs. Above all, I shall then be able to continue my search into true and false knowledge; as in this world, so also in the next and I shall find out who is wise, and who pretends to be wise, and is not. What would not a man give, O judges, to be able to examine the leader of the great Trojan expedition; or Odysseus or Sisyphus,[1] or numberless others, men and women too! What infinite delight would there be in conversing

7. The mythical inventor of agriculture who is associated with judgment in the next world only in this passage. Minos appears as a judge of the dead in Homer's *Odyssey* XI; Rhadamanthus and Aeacus, like Minos, were models of just judges in life and after death. The first three named by Socrates are sons of Zeus.   8. Greek poet (8th century B.C.?) who wrote *The Works and Days*, a didactic poem containing precepts for the farmer. Orpheus and Musaeus are legendary poets and religious teachers.   9. Both victims of unjust trials. Palamedes, one of the Greek chieftains at Troy, was unjustly executed for treason on the false evidence of Odysseus. Ajax committed suicide after the arms of the dead Achilles were adjudged to Odysseus as the bravest warrior on the Greek side.   1. Famous for his unscrupulousness and cunning. Odysseus was the most cunning of the Greek chieftains at Troy and the hero of Homer's *Odyssey*. Each is presumably an example of the man who "pretends to be wise and is not."

with them and asking them questions! In another world they do not put a man to death for asking questions: assuredly not. For besides being happier than we are, they will be immortal, if what is said is true.

Wherefore, O judges, be of good cheer about death, and know of a certainty, that no evil can happen to a good man, either in life or after death. He and his are not neglected by the gods; nor has my own approaching end happened by mere chance. But I see clearly that the time had arrived when it was better for me to die and be released from trouble; wherefore the oracle gave no sign. For which reason, also, I am not angry with my condemners, or with my accusers; they have done me no harm, although they did not mean to do me any good; and for this I may gently blame them.

Still I have a favor to ask of them. When my sons are grown up, I would ask you, O my friends, to punish them; and I would have you trouble them, as I have troubled you, if they seem to care about riches, or anything more than about virtue; or if they pretend to be something when they are really nothing,—then reprove them, as I have reproved you, for not caring about that for which they ought to care, and thinking that they are something when they are really nothing. And if you do this, both I and my sons will have received justice at your hands.

The hour of departure has arrived, and we go our ways—I to die, and you to live. Which is better God only knows.

ARISTOTLE
384–322 B.C.

One member of Plato's Academy, Aristotle, was to become as celebrated and influential as his teacher. He was not, like Plato, a native Athenian; he was born in northern Greece, at Stagira, close to the kingdom of Macedonia, which was eventually to become the dominant power in the Greek world. Aristotle entered the Academy at the age of seventeen but left it when Plato died (347 B.C.). He carried on his researches (he was especially interested in zoology) at various places on the Aegean; served as tutor to the young Alexander, son of Philip II of Macedon; and returned to Athens in 355, to found his own philosophical school, the Lyceum, where he established the world's first research library. At the Lyceum he and his pupils carried on research in zoology, botany, biology, physics, political science, ethics, logic, music, and mathematics. He left Athens when Alexander died in Babylon (323 B.C.) and the Athenians, for a while, were able to demonstrate their hatred of Macedon and everything connected with it; he died a year later.

The scope of his written work, philosophical and scientific, is immense; he is represented here by some excerpts from the *Poetics*, the first systematic work of literary criticism in our tradition.

Aristotle's Poetics, translated by james Hutton (1982), is the best source for the student.

From Poetics[1]

* * * Thus, Tragedy is an imitation of an action that is serious, complete, and possessing magnitude; in embellished language, each kind of which is used separately in the different parts; in the mode of action and not narrated; and effecting through pity and fear [what we call] the *catharsis*[2] of such emotions. By "embellished language" I mean language having rhythm and melody, and by "separately in different parts" I mean that some parts of a play are carried on solely in metrical speech while others again are sung.

The constituent parts of tragedy. Since the imitation is carried out in the dramatic mode by the personages themselves, it necessarily follows, first, that the arrangement of Spectacle will be a part of tragedy, and next, that Melody and Language will be parts, since these are the media in which they effect the imitation. By "language" I mean precisely the composition of the verses, by "melody" only that which is perfectly obvious. And since tragedy is the imitation of an action and is enacted by men in action, these persons must necessarily possess certain qualities of Character and Thought, since these are the basis for our ascribing qualities to the actions themselves—character and thought are two natural causes of actions— and it is in their actions that men universally meet with success or failure. The imitation of the action is the Plot. By plot I here mean the combination of the events; Character is that in virtue of which we say that the personages are of such and such a quality; and Thought is present in everything in their utterances that aims to prove a point or that expresses an opinion. Necessarily, therefore, there are in tragedy as a whole, considered as a special form, six constituent elements, viz. Plot, Character, Language, Thought, Spectacle, and Melody. Of these elements, two [Language and Melody] are the *media* in which they effect the imitation, one [Spectacle] is the *manner*, and three [Plot, Character, Thought] are the *objects* they imitate; and besides these there are no other parts. So then they employ these six forms, not just some of them so to speak; for every drama has spectacle, character, plot, language, melody, and thought in the same sense, but the most important of them is the organization of the events [the plot].

Plot and character. For tragedy is not an imitation of men but of actions and of life. It is in action that happiness and unhappiness are found, and the end[3] we aim at is a kind of activity, not a quality; in accordance with their characters men are of such and such a quality, in accordance with their actions they are fortunate or the reverse. Consequently, it is not for the purpose of presenting their characters that the agents engage in action,

---

1. Translated by James Hutton. Bracketed text has been added for clarity.   2. This is probably the most disputed passage in the Western critical tradition. There are two main schools of interpretation, which differ in their understanding of the metaphor implied in the word *catharsis*. Some critics take the word to mean "purification," implying a metaphor from the religious process of purification from guilt; the passions are "purified" by the tragic performance because the excitement of these passions by the performance weakens them and reduces them to just proportions in the individual. This theory was supported by the German critic Lessing. Others take the metaphor to be medical, reading the word as "purging" and interpreting the phrase to mean that the tragic performance excites the emotions only to allay them, thus ridding the spectator of the disquieting emotions from which he or she suffers in everyday life. Tragedy thus has a therapeutic effect.   3. Purpose.

but rather it is for the sake of their actions that they take on the characters they have. Thus, what happens—that is, the plot—is the end for which a tragedy exists, and the end or purpose is the most important thing of all. What is more, without action there could not be a tragedy, but there could be without characterization. * * *

Now that the parts are established, let us next discuss what qualities the plot should have, since plot is the primary and most important part of tragedy. I have posited that tragedy is an imitation of an action that is a whole and complete in itself and of a certain magnitude—for a thing may be a whole, and yet have no magnitude to speak of. Now a thing is a whole if it has a beginning, a middle, and an end. A beginning is that which does not come necessarily after something else, but after which it is natural for another thing to exist or come to be. An end, on the contrary, is that which naturally comes after something else, either as its necessary sequel or as its usual [and hence probable] sequel, but itself has nothing after it. A middle is that which both comes after something else and has another thing following it. A well-constructed plot, therefore, will neither begin at some chance point nor end at some chance point, but will observe the principles here stated. * * *

Contrary to what some people think, a plot is not ipso facto a unity if it revolves about one man. Many things, indeed an endless number of things, happen to any one man some of which do not go together to form a unity, and similarly among the actions one man performs there are many that do not go together to produce a single unified action. Those poets seem all to have erred, therefore, who have composed a *Heracleid*, a *Theseid*, and other such poems, it being their idea evidently that since Heracles was one man, their plot was bound to be unified. * * *

From what has already been said, it will be evident that the poet's function is not to report things that have happened, but rather to tell of such things as might happen, things that are possibilities by virtue of being in themselves inevitable or probable. Thus the difference between the historian and the poet is not that the historian employs prose and the poet verse—the work of Herodotus[4] could be put into verse, and it would be no less a history with verses than without them; rather the difference is that the one tells of things that have been and the other of such things as might be. Poetry, therefore, is a more philosophical and a higher thing than history, in that poetry tends rather to express the universal, history rather the particular fact. A universal is: The sort of thing that (in the circumstances) a certain kind of person will say or do either probably or necessarily, which in fact is the universal that poetry aims for (with the addition of names for the persons); a particular, on the other hand is: What Alcibiades[5] did or had done to him. * * *

Among plots and actions of the simple type, the episodic form is the worst. I call episodic a plot in which the episodes follow one another in no probable or inevitable sequence. Plots of this kind are constructed by bad poets on their own account, and by good poets on account of the

---

4. Historian of the Persian Wars, a contemporary of Sophocles.   5. A brilliant but unscrupulous Athenian statesman (5th century B.C.).

actors; since they are composing entries for a competitive exhibition, they stretch the plot beyond what it can bear and are often compelled, therefore, to dislocate the natural order. * * *

Some plots are simple, others complex; indeed the actions of which the plots are imitation are at once so differentiated to begin with. Assuming the action to be continuous and unified, as already defined, I call that action simple in which the change of fortune takes place without a reversal or recognition, and that action complex in which the change of fortune involves a recognition or a reversal or both. These events [recognitions and reversals] ought to be so rooted in the very structure of the plot that they follow from the preceding events as their inevitable or probable outcome; for there is a vast difference between following from and merely following after. * * *

Reversal (Peripety) is, as aforesaid, a change from one state of affairs to its exact opposite, and this, too, as I say, should be in conformance with probability or necessity. For example, in *Oedipus*, the messenger[6] comes to cheer Oedipus by relieving him of fear with regard to his mother, but by revealing his true identity, does just the opposite of this. * * *

Recognition, as the word itself indicates, is a change from ignorance to knowledge, leading either to friendship or to hostility on the part of those persons who are marked for good fortune or bad. The best form of recognition is that which is accompanied by a reversal, as in the example from *Oedipus*. * * *

Next in order after the points I have just dealt with, it would seem necessary to specify what one should aim at and what avoid in the construction of plots, and what it is that will produce the effect proper to tragedy.

Now since in the finest kind of tragedy the structure should be complex and not simple, and since it should also be a representation of terrible and piteous events (that being the special mark of this type of imitation), in the first place, it is evident that good men ought not to be shown passing from prosperity to misfortune, for this does not inspire either pity or fear, but only revulsion; nor evil men rising from ill fortune to prosperity, for this is the most untragic plot of all—it lacks every requirement, in that it neither elicits human sympathy nor stirs pity or fear. And again, neither should an extremely wicked man be seen falling from prosperity into misfortune, for a plot so constructed might indeed call forth human sympathy, but would not excite pity or fear, since the first is felt for a person whose misfortune is undeserved and the second for someone like ourselves—pity for the man suffering undeservedly, fear for the man like ourselves—and hence neither pity nor fear would be aroused in this case. We are left with the man whose place is between these extremes. Such is the man who on the one hand is not pre-eminent in virtue and justice, and yet on the other hand does not fall into misfortune through vice or depravity, but falls because of some mistake;[7] one among the number of the highly

6. The Corinthian herdsman.   7. The Greek word is *hamartia*. It has sometimes been translated as "flaw" (hence the expression "tragic flaw") and thought of as a moral defect, but comparison with Aristotle's use of the word in other contexts suggests strongly that he means by it "mistake" or "error" (of judgment).

renowned and prosperous, such as Oedipus and Thyestes and other famous men from families like theirs.

It follows that the plot which achieves excellence will necessarily be single in outcome and not, as some contend, double, and will consist in a change of fortune, not from misfortune to prosperity, but the opposite from prosperity to misfortune, occasioned not by depravity, but by some great mistake on the part of one who is either such as I have described or better than this rather than worse. (What actually has taken place confirms this; for though at first the poets accepted whatever myths came to hand, today the finest tragedies are founded upon the stories of only a few houses, being concerned, for example, with Alcmeon, Oedipus, Orestes, Meleager, Thyestes, Telephus, and such others as have chanced to suffer terrible things or to do them.) So, then, tragedy having this construction is the finest kind of tragedy from an artistic point of view. And conse-quently, those persons fall into the same error who bring it as a charge against Euripides that this is what he does in his tragedies and that most of his plays have unhappy endings. For this is in fact the right procedure, as I have said; and the best proof is that on the stage and in the dramatic contests, plays of this kind seem the most tragic, provided they are success-fully worked out, and Euripides, even if in everything else his manage-ment is faulty, seems at any rate the most tragic of the poets. * * *

In the characters and the plot construction alike, one must strive for that which is either necessary or probable, so that whatever a character of any kind says or does may be the sort of thing such a character will inevita-bly or probably say or do and the events of the plot may follow one after another either inevitably or with probability. (Obviously, then, the denouement of the plot should arise from the plot itself and not be brought about "from the machine," as it is in *Medea* and in the embarka-tion scene in the *Iliad*.[8] The machine is to be used for matters lying out-side the drama, either antecedents of the action which a human being cannot know, or things subsequent to the action that have to be prophe-sied and announced; for we accept it that the gods see everything. Within the events of the plot itself, however, there should be nothing unreason-able, or if there is, it should be kept outside the play proper, as is done in the *Oedipus* of Sophocles.) * * *

The chorus in tragedy. The chorus ought to be regarded as one of the actors, and as being part of the whole and integrated into performance, not in Euripides' way but in that of Sophocles. In the other poets, the choral songs have no more relevance to the plot than if they belonged to some other play. And so nowadays, following the practice introduced by Agathon,[9] the chorus merely sings interludes. But what difference is there between the singing of interludes and taking a speech or even an entire episode from one play and inserting it into another?

8. The reference is to an incident in the second book of the *Iliad*: an attempt of the Greek rank and file to return home and abandon the siege is arrested by the intervention of Athena. If it were a drama she would appear *on the machine*, literally the machine that was employed in the theater to show the gods flying in space. It has come to mean any implausible way of solving complications of the plot. Medea escapes from Corinth "on the machine" in her magic chariot.   9. A younger contemporary of Euripides; most of his plays were produced in the 4th century B.C.

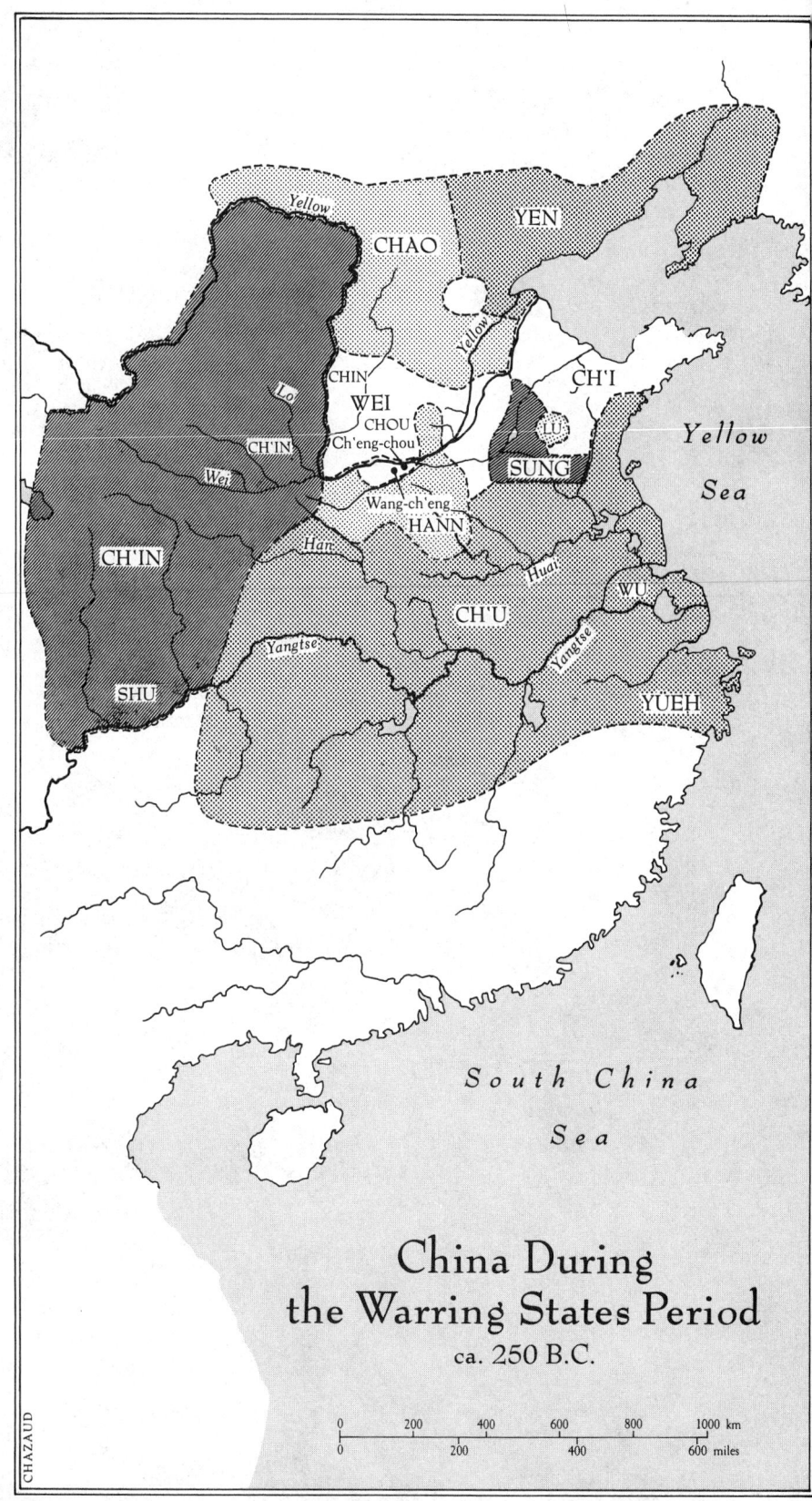

China During
the Warring States Period
ca. 250 B.C.

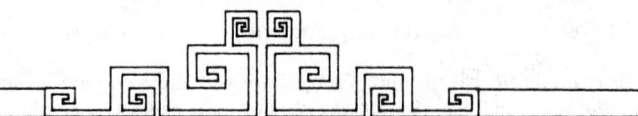

Poetry and Thought in Early China

Many great civilizations have perished without consequence; they have left vast ruins in deserts and jungles. What we know of them comes from the imaginative reconstructions of scholars, from inscriptions, and from the accounts of early travelers. Other civilizations, like those of ancient Egypt and Mesopotamia, left extensive written records only to be at last swallowed up by other civilizations; the very names by which we refer to them—*Egypt* and *Mesopotamia*—are Greek.

Still other ancient civilizations began long histories that continue to the present; they set patterns and posed questions that shaped the actions and values of their descendants for thousands of years. The writings they produced—continuously read and reinterpreted—served as the binding that gave these civilizations a sense of their unity and continuity. Early in the third century A.D. Ts'ao P'i, the first emperor of the short Wei Dynasty, observed that literary works were "the greatest legacy in governing the kingdom." A writer himself, Ts'ao P'i understood the transience of power, even power well exercised, and he understood that the image of the period preserved in literary works would eventually become—far more than his substantial accomplishments—the "reality" of his age for the future.

In many ways, then, "China" is a literary fiction of cultural and historical unity that eventually became reality by being generally accepted as true. Ancient China covered a vast territory that was inhabited by a diverse people, who spoke a language divided by widely divergent dialects, as well as by many tribes, who spoke their own languages. It might easily have been fragmented, like Europe, by regional interests and linguistic differences. By accepting the writings of ancient China as their own, peoples on the expanding margins of the ancient heartland became "Chinese." Rome was truly an empire, a political center that ruled over many peoples, each with its own sense of distinct identity as a people. Although traditional China is called an empire, regional identity gave way to a belief in cultural unity, a cultural unity that has always sought expression in political unity.

ARCHAIC CHINA

Chinese civilization developed independently from that of the West in the Yellow River basin. Although scholars have noted the possibility of contact with central Asia in the development of its early civilization, China was geographically separated from the earlier Mesopotamian and Indus valley city civilizations and followed its own course. The first historical dynasty was the Shang (ca. 1750–1020 B.C.). Although traditional Chinese historians have treated it as a dynasty in the later sense, the Shang seems to have been a loose confederation of city-states ruled by princes who had (or claimed) a common ancestry, one of whom was acknowledged as king. It was during the Shang Dynasty that Chinese writing first developed, and from this period we have inscriptions on tortoiseshells that were used in divination. Throughout its history China retained the use of "characters," rather than changing to an alphabet or syllabary. Some written characters are pictograms

(for example *jih* 日, meaning "sun," from ☉) and some are ideograms (for example, *shang* 上, signifying "above"), but most characters combine an element that indicates the sound and an element, called a "radical," that indicates a conceptual category (for example, *chao* 昭, "shining," consists of the sound element 召 and the radical 日, for "sun"). The fact that written characters remained the same, though they were pronounced differently at different times and in different regions, contributed significantly to the coherence of Chinese civilization.

The end of the second millennium B.C. saw the migration of the Chou peoples from the west into the Yellow River heartland and their conquest of the Shang. The Chou were an agrarian people, who traced their descent from Hou Chi, or Lord Millet. The Chou's justification of its conquest set the model for a Chinese polity that was to last for three thousand years. The last rulers of the Shang Dynasty were accused of misrule, of causing such hardship that Heaven grew angry and transferred its "mandate" to the Chou king Wen, whose son, King Wu, completed the overthrow. Such at least were the stories told in the courts of the Chou princes, who were given feudal domains throughout the territory that had once belonged to the Shang Dynasty. They ruled as stewards, responsible to the Chou king, who was in turn only a steward for Heaven.

The idea of Heaven changed through the centuries, and it was never a clearly defined deity: sometimes it was an anthropomorphic divinity, sometimes a natural and moral force, and in this early period, sometimes a collective of ancestral spirits. Power depended on virtuous rule, which in large measure meant holding to the statutes and models of the former kings. These models were preserved in a body of unwritten ritual practice and in a group of early texts: the *Book of Documents,* a collection of royal statements and proclamations from the early Chou; the *Book of Changes,* used for divination; and the *Book of Songs,* containing, among other things, hymns to the Chou ancestors and ballads recounting the history of the Chou people. These works, which became the core of the Confucian classics, were attributed to various ancient sages; most modern scholars take them as anonymous.

The belief that virtuous government would ensure continuous power proved tenacious even in the face of political realities that undermined it. After a few prosperous reigns, the Chou Dynasty grew increasingly weak. In 770 B.C., under pressure from new warlike tribes pressing in from the north and west, the capital was shifted east, marking the beginning of the period known as the Eastern Chou. A half century later saw the beginning of a court chronicle, called the *Spring and Autumn Annals,* from the feudal state of Lu in east China. The period it covers, from 722 to 466 B.C., is thus known as the Spring and Autumn Annals Period.

THE SPRING AND AUTUMN ANNALS AND WARRING STATES PERIODS

The Chou Dynasty proved far more influential in its dissolution than at the height of its dominion. Politically, it was reduced to a tiny sphere surrounded by vigorous states that were still, nominally, its feudal domains. The princes of these states plotted and warred with one another, struggling to reconcile political realities with a nostalgic sense of ceremony and custom. Meanwhile, on the southern and western borders of the old Chou domain, powerful new kingdoms were rising: Ch'u, Wu, and Yüeh in the south and Ch'in in the west. Although many of these new kingdoms developed from autonomous traditions, they gradually absorbed Chou culture, and their rulers often sought to trace their descent either from the Chou royal house or from more ancient north Chinese ancestors (much as European royal families in the Middle Ages and Renaissance often claimed Greek or Trojan ancestry).

The state that most saw itself as the preserver of Chou traditions was the eastern

duchy of Lu, the home of Confucius (551–479 B.C.). In his collected sayings, the *Analects (Lun-yü)*, Confucius created a remarkable fusion of ethics and idealized Chou traditions. Although later Confucians credited him with the editorship of the Confucian classics, modern scholars doubt this. Rather he was a teacher of traditional learning, around whom gathered a large group of disciples; the lineages of those disciples preserved through the difficult centuries that followed a version of Chou traditions that lasted until the Han Dynasty, when they were institutionalized.

Although the philosophers that followed Confucius offered compelling alternatives, his union of idealized history and social thought finally won out in the Chinese tradition. The small details of ceremony and decorum were accepted as outer forms of a social order in which respect for others came naturally. In the context of the times, it was a heroic position: it promised a dignity in one's actions that could stubbornly resist a world in which expediency increasingly ruled. One story tells of a disciple of Confucius who, about to be executed, asked the archers to wait a moment so that he could straighten his cap.

The early wars between the feudal domains were ceremonious affairs. The nobility rode in chariots and engaged in single combat. Battles seem to have involved more display than bloodshed, and often one side, recognizing the superior force of the enemy, would simply withdraw. As technology improved and allegiance to Chou traditions declined, wars among the domains became increasingly destructive. Early in the Spring and Autumn Annals Period small regions were ruled by aristocratic families, and their officers were chosen from lesser clans. By the fifth century B.C. these domains were evolving into centralized states, with bureaucracies whose primary loyalty was not to their families but to the prince. Chinese historians have called this period the Warring States.

Political upheaval precipitated intellectual upheaval. Various rival schools of thought appeared, most offering a political program meant to appeal to competing princes. The followers of the philosopher Mo-tzu (second half of the fifth century B.C.) preached an austere utilitarianism. Seeing that warfare, like Confucian ceremony, was wasteful, they became inventive technicians, developing means of defense against military aggression.

The overriding Confucian concern with government and social life inevitably produced extreme reactions. Some schools were interested more in the individual than in the polity. The most remarkable figure among such thinkers was Chuang Chou (fourth century B.C.), who was concerned almost exclusively with the life of the mind, and his writings return to the theme of the relativity of perception and value. Chuang Chou is often grouped with the shadowy figure Lao-tzu as an ancestor of Taoism. Lao-tzu's name is attached to a collection of poems from the late Warring States Period that advocate passivity and following the Way, the natural course of things.

In that same century the Confucian tradition was eloquently represented by Mencius. He held (like Rousseau and others later on) that the innate goodness of human nature was warped only by circumstance and that good government would permit the natural goodness of men and women to show itself once again. But the age clearly favored those who believed not in moral influence and self-cultivation but in increasing outward control. Arguing against Mencius, Hsün-tzu (third century B.C.) chose to view learning and Confucian ethics as a means to govern the human creature, otherwise driven by passions and appetites.

Hsün-tzu's vision of human nature and his fascination with control influenced the writings of Han Fei (died 233 B.C.). Han Fei, who belonged to a long Chinese tradition of writers on statecraft, composed treatises outlining a policy of rigid state control to strengthen his own tiny state of Han. The treatises did little for his own realm but found particular favor in the western kingdom of Ch'in, which already

had a long tradition of authoritarian control. Those who followed the teachings of Han Fei's school came to be known as Legalists for their belief that the state depended on its subjects' absolute adherence to its laws and policies. Among the other states, Ch'in had a reputation for ruthlessness and untrustworthiness, but Ch'in's armies—well disciplined, well equipped, and well supplied—had steadily increased the size of the kingdom and, by the middle of the third century B.C., were driving west and south, overwhelming all rivals.

CH'IN AND HAN

As the ancient Mediterranean world is brought to a symbolic close by the fall of Rome, ancient China may be said to end in 221 B.C., with the establishment of a unified empire under Emperor Ch'in Shih-huang. Ch'in Shih-huang's draconian megalomania became legendary in later Chinese history, exerting as much fascination as horror. Though much of his statecraft was subtle, many of his most famous policies had a chilling simplicity. Some, such as unifying the currency and the script, deserve credit. But his solution to intellectual disagreement was to burn the books of all schools but those of the Legalists, whom he favored, and his solution to regional loyalties toward the old states was massive deportation. The final victory of Confucian traditionalism in the Han Dynasty was, in no small part, a reaction against Ch'in Shih-huang's disregard for all traditions and norms of humane behavior.

Ch'in's greatest enemy had been the large southern state of Ch'u. Like Ch'in, it had been steadily expanding at the expense of its neighbors and had spread along both sides of the Yangtse River. Though long within the north Chinese cultural sphere, Ch'u had rather different traditions from its neighbors, and it also had the strongest regional consciousness of any of the states. After its conquest by Ch'in, a folk rhyme circulated in Ch'u: "Though only three households be left in Ch'u, / The destroyer of Ch'in will surely be Ch'u." After Ch'in Shih-huang's death, rebellions broke out everywhere, and the Ch'u rebel Hsiang Yü defeated the major Ch'in armies. The last decade of the third century B.C. saw not only the destruction of Ch'in but also Hsiang Yü's struggle with a rival Ch'u army led by Liu Pang. Ultimately, Liu Pang was victorious and founded a new dynasty, the Han.

Ch'in survived less than twenty years; the Han Dynasty lasted more than four hundred. The imperial house of Liu (in Chinese the surname comes first), having inherited a unified empire and benefited from Ch'in's destruction of the old aristocracy, learned the lesson of flexibility. Some emperors tightened central control and others loosened it, but none attempted the absolute exercise of imperial will that Ch'in Shih-huang had assumed. The Liu patronized Taoism, shamanistic cults, and Confucianism, freely mixing adherence to traditions with policies that served state interest. With an eye to the reigning emperor and to the example of Ch'in, the Confucians liked to invoke the model of Chou, of rule that depends on the goodwill of those ruled. The Western term *China* names the civilization after Ch'in, but ever thereafter the Chinese have referred to themselves as the "people of Han."

FURTHER READING

A good general introduction to writing in this period can be found in Burton Watson, *Early Chinese Literature* (1962). Henri Maspero, *China in Antiquity* (first published 1927, English translation 1978), is an older, but still useful survey of early Chinese history and culture. Wang Ching-hsien, *From Ritual to Allegory: Seven Essays in Early Chinese Poetry* (1988), is a study of the *Book of Songs* and the *Chu-tz'u*. The best study of early Chinese philosophers is A. C. Graham, *Disputers of the Tao: Philosophical Argument in Ancient China* (1989). Early Chinese

reflection on and interpretation of the ancient classics, using the case of the *Book of Songs,* are studied in Steven Van Zoeren, *Poetry and Personality* (1991).

The following list uses common English syllables to provide rough equivalents of selected words whose pronunciation may be unfamiliar to the general reader.

Ch'in: *chin*

Ch'in Shih-huang: *chin sherr–h-ang*

Chou: *joh*

Ch'u: *choo*

Chuang Chou: *jwahng joh*

Han Fei: *hahn fay*

Hou Chi: *hoh jee*

Hsiang Yü: *shyang yoo*

Hsün-tzu: *shyun–dzuh*

Lao-tzu: *lau–dzuh*

Liu Pang: *lyoo bahng*

Lun-yü: *lwun–yoo*

Mo-tzu: *mwo–dzuh*

Ts'ao P'i: *tsaw pee*

Wei: *way*

Wen: *wun*

Yüeh: *yoo-eh*

TEXTS	CONTEXTS
ca. 1700–1020 B.C. Writing used on tortoiseshells for divination and in inscriptions on bronze vessels	ca. 1700–1020 B.C. Shang Dynasty 1020 Chou Dynasty overthrows the Shang Dynasty
ca. 1000 Earliest portions of *The Book of Songs.* • Earliest parts of the *Book of Changes*, the *Yi Ching*	
	ca. 820 Reign of King Hsüan and the expansion of the Chou kingdom south toward the Yangtse River 770–256 Steady decline of the power of the Chou royal house and the rise of feudal states 722 Beginning of the Spring and Autumn Annals period
ca. 600 *The Book of Songs* reaches its final form 551–479 Confucius and the *Analects*	
	403 "Warring States" period begins 400–250 Period of the "hundred schools" of Chinese thought ca. 390–305 Confucian philosopher Mencius, who taught the inherent goodness of human nature
ca. 369–286 Taoist philosopher Chuang Chou and the early chapters of the *Chuang Tzu*	
	350–221 Rise of the state of Ch'in in western China under the influence of a totalitarian political philosophy known as Legalism
340?–278 Ch'ü Yüan, poet of the southern state of Ch'u, to whom was attributed the composition of *The Nine Songs*	
	256 Ch'in dethrones the last Chou ruler

TEXTS	CONTEXTS
	221–206 Under influence of Ch'in Legalism, Confucianism and other schools of thought suppressed
	221 Ch'in Dynasty unifies China under Ch'in Shih-huang, the "First Emperor" • Great Wall extended
	206 Fall of Ch'in and the founding of the Han Dynasty; Han sponsors Confucianism
179–117 Ssu-ma Hsiang-ju, the greatest court poet of the Han and master of a form of long verse known as *fu* or "rhapsody"	**140–86** Reign of Emperor Wu of the Han, with Chinese military conquests in Central Asia
	120 The Han court establishes a "Music Bureau," one of whose functions is to collect popular songs. Some of these lyrics survive
97 Ssu-ma Ch'ien completes the *Shih-chi*, the "Historian's Records," a comprehensive history of China up to the reign of Emperor Wu	
	A.D. 57 Japan sends envoys to the Han court
A.D. 32–92 Pan Ku, author of the *Han History* and of many rhapsodies	**ca. 100** Earliest introduction of Buddhism into China
	105 Earliest paper made
100–200 The rise of anonymous poetry in the five-character line, which would be the most common poetic form for the rest of the premodern period	**196–220** The breakup of the Han into competing regions dominated by warlords • Ts'ao Ts'ao (155–220) is warlord of north China (200–220) and gathers the most eminent writers of the day to his court

BOOK OF SONGS

ca. 1000–600 B.C.

In contrast to other ancient literary cultures, which begin with epics, prose legends, or hymns to the gods, the Chinese tradition begins with lyric poetry. The *Book of Songs* is a collection of 305 songs representing the heritage of the Chou people. The earliest in the collection are believed to date from around 1000 B.C. and the latest from around 600 B.C., at which time it seems to have reached something like its present form.

Although the collection circulated among the Chou aristocracy, it obviously drew from a wide variety of sources, and its diversity represents many levels of Chou society. There are temple hymns to the ancestors of the Chou ruling house, narrative ballads on the foundation and history of the dynasty, royal laments, songs of soldiers glorifying war and deploring war, love songs, marriage songs, hunting songs, songs of women whose husbands had deserted them, banquet songs, poems of mourning, and others. Many seem to have originated as folk songs, but these are mixed together with poems from the Chou aristocracy.

Down through the fifth century B.C. the *Book of Songs* served as the basic educational text of the Chou upper class. As the various Chou domains gradually evolved into independent states, the *Book of Songs* represented their common Chou heritage. The philosopher Confucius (551–479 B.C.) advised his disciples:

> By the *Book of Songs* you can stir people and you can observe things through them; you can express your resentment in them and you can show sociable feelings. Close to home you can use them to serve your father, and on a larger scale you can use them to serve your ruler. Moreover, you can learn to recognize many names of birds, beasts, plants, and trees.*

By *observe* Confucius meant something like discovering universal precepts in the *Songs*. But that was not the only way in which the *Songs* were used. The power of the *Book of Songs* to "stir people" probably refers to their frequent use in conversation and diplomacy. Citation of one of the poems was often used to clinch a point in an argument or, more subtly, to express an opinion that one would rather not say openly. As with Homer's epics in early Greece, knowledge of the *Book of Songs* was considered an essential part of cultural education in early China.

Gradually, the transmission of the *Book of Songs* passed into the hands of the Confucian school, and by the fourth century B.C. it had become one of the texts in the canon of Confucian classics. Confucius was presumed to have been the editor of the collection, choosing and arranging these particular poems to show implicitly the glory and decline of Chou society. As a Confucian classic, the *Book of Songs* remained an essential part of Chinese education up to the twentieth century.

The great epics of early civilizations hold up an image of the values of those civilizations. The heroic values of the Homeric epics and their transformation in the *Aeneid* (p. 639) tell us much about how those civilizations wished to see themselves. Ancient China produced no epic; it left instead the *Book of Songs*. In place of the relatively homogeneous point of view of the ancient epics, the *Book of Songs* is a collection of many voices; there are the voices of kings, aristocrats, peasants, soldiers, men, and women. The Chou Dynasty's sense of its own authority depended on Heaven's charge to rule, which was contingent on ruling well and

---

*Translated by Stephen Owen.

receiving the support of the common people. As the ballad that tells of Chou's rise to power says, "Heaven cannot be trusted; / Kingship is easily lost." This same law, by which the Chou Dynasty destroyed the Shang Dynasty, applied no less to the Chou itself. Because the dynasty depended on the common people, their concerns were considered an essential part of the polity. Voices of protest are mingled with voices of celebration. And the great influence of the *Book of Songs* in later ages was as a continual reminder that society contains many legitimate voices.

Confucius is said to have once told his son that if he did not learn the *Book of Songs* he would have no way to speak. The *Songs* gave words to feelings that would otherwise be hard or uncomfortable to articulate. One famous story of a slightly later period tells of a ruler who, on discovering that his people were criticizing him, sent out spies to inform on anyone who spoke against him. His adviser was horrified and warned the ruler strongly against taking such an action, but the ruler ignored his advice. Eventually, the people became frightened and kept their silence, with the result that the ruler was finally overthrown. Traditional Chinese interpretations of the *Book of Songs* have always stressed the role of the *Songs* as vehicles for political and social protest. But in a broader sense, the diversity of the *Songs* acknowledged that the contrary forces in individual hearts could still, when given utterance, contribute to a society that would ultimately prove more durable than one dominated by social authority and ideology. The immense cultural authority of the *Book of Songs* made it a means to say what one truly thought, rather than silently submitting to social authority. This principle is often found as a theme within the *Songs* themselves, as in these lines of a young woman being pressed to marry against her will: "My heart is not a mirror / To reflect what others will."

Even the most pious Confucian moralists always stressed that the voices in the *Book of Songs* came naturally and spontaneously from human feeling. The way in which students were taught to read the *Book of Songs* had a profound influence on the future development of Chinese literature. It encouraged poets and readers alike to assume that a poem revealed the state of mind of the writer, the writer's nature, and the writer's circumstances. And this led to a notion of literature, particularly poetry, as a form of interior history, revealing in an intensely direct way both the person and the age.

However simple the poems of the *Book of Songs* may appear on the surface, they embody the central values (if not the realities) of early Chinese civilization. Again and again the poems return to a fascination with timely action, to the need to speak out, to balances and exchanges, and to acts of explanation. These are the values of an antiheroic world, in which domination and absolute superiority threaten the social fabric. Its gods, the collective ancestors or Heaven, function as numinous mechanisms, holy enforcers of the natural and moral order; unlike the Greek or Mesopotamian gods, they almost never have favorites or act on whim. These values of natural balance can appear in the humblest forms. A young woman tosses a man a piece of fruit as a love gift, and the young man answers with an exchange:

> She threw a quince to me;
> In requital I gave a bright girdle-gem.
> No, not just as requital;
> But meaning I would love her for ever.

The exchange is economically unequal, a jewel returned for fruit. But the young man acts at once to restore the exchange to balance, explaining that the jewel was not given as an object of value, but as a token and message, just as the fruit she threw had been a message.

The poem itself can be an exchange of sorts. In poem 24, when the lover Chung Tzu shows his rashly masculine daring by breaking into the girl's homestead, the poem serves to block his advances; it is a force of words to counterbalance his physical force. Through the words she can tell him that she loves him but also remind him of her family and others in the village, whose opinions should be taken into consideration and weighed against his desires.

A basic introduction to the *Book of Songs* can be found in Wang Ching-hsien, *From Ritual to Allegory: Seven Essays in Early Chinese Poetry* (1988). Pauline Yu, *The Reading of Imagery in the Chinese Tradition* (1987), has an excellent chapter on the traditional understanding of imagery in the *Book of Songs*.

PRONOUNCING GLOSSARY

The following list uses common English syllables to provide rough equivalents of selected words whose pronunciation may be unfamiliar to the general reader.

Chiang Yüan: *jyahng yoo-en*   Hsia: *shyah*

Ch'ien-hu: *chyen–hoo*   Hsien-yün: *shyen–yoon*

Chung Tzu: *jong dzuh*

Book of Songs[1]

17

Plop fall the plums; but there are still seven.
Let those gentlemen that would court me
Come while it is lucky!

Plop fall the plums; there are still three.
Let any gentleman that would court me   5
Come before it is too late!

Plop fall the plums; in shallow baskets we lay them.
Any gentleman who could court me
Had better speak while there is time.

18

She threw a quince to me;
In requital I gave a bright girdle-gem.[2]
No, not just as requital;
But meaning I would love her for ever.

She threw a tree-peach to me;   5
As requital I gave her a bright greenstone.

---

1. Translated by Arthur Waley.   2. In ancient China men and women wore complex assemblies of cut jade and gemstones hanging from their sashes. Individual pieces could be given to express esteem or love.

No, not just as requital;
But meaning I would love her for ever.

She threw a tree-plum to me;
In requital I gave her a bright jet-stone.   10
No, not just as requital,
But meaning I would love her for ever.

22

Of fair girls the loveliest
Was to meet me at the corner of the Wall.
But she hides and will not show herself;
I scratch my head, pace up and down.

Of fair girls the prettiest   5
Gave me a red flute.
The flush of that red flute
Is pleasure at the girl's beauty.

She has been in the pastures and brought for me rush-wool,
Very beautiful and rare.   10
It is not you that are beautiful;
But you were given by a lovely girl.

24

I beg of you, Chung Tzu,
Do not climb into our homestead,
Do not break the willows we have planted.
Not that I mind about the willows,
But I am afraid of my father and mother.   5
Chung Tzu I dearly love;
But of what my father and mother say
Indeed I am afraid.

I beg of you, Chung Tzu,
Do not climb over our wall,   10
Do not break the mulberry-trees we have planted.
Not that I mind about the mulberry-trees,
But I am afraid of my brothers.
Chung Tzu I dearly love;
But of what my brothers say   15
Indeed I am afraid.

I beg of you, Chung Tzu,
Do not climb into our garden,
Do not break the hard-wood we have planted.
Not that I mind about the hard-wood,   20
But I am afraid of what people will say.
Chung Tzu I dearly love;
But of all that people will say
Indeed I am afraid.

25

The lady says: "The cock has crowed";
The knight says: "Day has not dawned."
"Rise, then, and look at the night;
The morning star is shining.
You must be out and abroad,   5
Must shoot the wild-duck and wild-geese.

When you have shot them, you must bring them home
And I will dress them for you,
And when I have dressed them we will drink wine
And I will be yours till we are old.   10
I will set your zithers before you;
All shall be peaceful and good.

Did I but know those who come to you,
I have girdle-stones of many sorts to give them;
Did I but know those that have followed you,   15
I have girdle-stones of many sorts as presents for them.
Did I know those that love you,
I have girdle-stones of many sorts to requite them."

28

Cold blows the northern wind,
Thick falls the snow.
Be kind to me, love me,
Take my hand and go with me.
Yet she lingers, yet she havers![1]   5
There is no time to lose.

The north wind whistles,
Whirls the falling snow.
Be kind to me, love me,
Take my hand and go home with me.   10
Yet she lingers, yet she havers!
There is no time to lose.

Nothing is redder than the fox,
Nothing blacker than the crow.
Be kind to me, love me,   15
Take my hand and ride with me.
Yet she lingers, yet she havers!
There is no time to lose.

54

HE: The gourd has bitter leaves;
       The ford is deep to wade.

1. Hesitates.

SHE: If a ford is deep, there are stepping-stones;
     If it is shallow, you can tuck up your skirts.

HE: The ford is in full flood,   5
    And baleful is the pheasant's cry.
SHE: The ford is not deep enough to wet your axles;
     The pheasant cried to find her mate.

On one note the wild-geese cry,
A cloudless dawn begins to break.   10
A knight that brings home his bride
Must do so before the ice melts.

The boatman beckons and beckons.
Others cross, not I;
Others cross, not I.   15
"I am waiting for my friend."

56

If along the highroad
I caught hold of your sleeve,
Do not hate me;
Old ways take time to overcome.

If along the highroad   5
I caught hold of your hand,
Do not be angry with me;
Friendship takes time to overcome.

57

By the willows of the Eastern Gate,
Whose leaves are so thick,
At dusk we were to meet;
And now the morning star is bright.

By the willows of the Eastern Gate,   5
Whose leaves are so close,
At dusk we were to meet;
And now the morning star is pale.

63

In the wilds there is a dead doe;
With white rushes we cover her.
There was a lady longing for the spring;
A fair knight seduced her.

In the wood there is a clump of oaks,   5
And in the wilds a dead deer
With white rushes well bound;
There was a lady fair as jade.

"Heigh, not so hasty, not so rough;
Heigh, do not touch my handkerchief.[1]   10
Take care, or the dog will bark."

75

Tossed is that cypress boat,
Wave-tossed it floats.
My heart is in turmoil, I cannot sleep.
But secret is my grief.
Wine I have, all things needful   5
For play, for sport.

My heart is not a mirror,
To reflect what others will.
Brothers too I have;
I cannot be snatched away.   10
But lo, when I told them of my plight
I found that they were angry with me.

My heart is not a stone;
It cannot be rolled.
My heart is not a mat;   15
It cannot be folded away.
I have borne myself correctly
In rites more than can be numbered.

My sad heard is consumed, I am harassed
By a host of small men.   20
I have borne vexations very many,
Received insults not few.
In the still of night I brood upon it;
In the waking hours I rend my breast.

O sun, ah, moon,   25
Why are you changed and dim?
Sorrow clings to me
Like an unwashed dress.
In the still of night I brood upon it,
Long to take wing and fly away.   30

131

We plucked the bracken, plucked the bracken
While the young shoots were springing up.
Oh, to go back, go back!
The year is ending.
We have no house, no home   5
Because of the Hsien-yün.[2]
We cannot rest or bide
Because of the Hsien-yün.

1. A piece of cloth worn at the waist like an apron.   2. A non-Chinese people who frequently raided the Chou domains.

We plucked the bracken, plucked the bracken
While the shoots were soft.   10
Oh, to go back, go back!
Our hearts are sad,
Our sad hearts burn,
We are hungry and thirsty,
But our campaign is not over,   15
Nor is any of us sent home with news.

We plucked the bracken, plucked the bracken;
But the shoots were hard.
Oh, to go back, go back!
The year is running out.   20
But the king's business never ends;
We cannot rest or bide.
Our sad hearts are very bitter;
We went, but do not come.

What splendid thing is that?   25
It is the flower of the cherry-tree.
What great carriage is that?
It is our lord's chariot,
His war-chariot ready yoked,
With its four steeds so eager.   30
How should we dare stop or tarry?
In one month we have had three alarms.

We yoke the teams of four,
Those steeds so strong,
That our lord rides behind,   35
That lesser men protect.
The four steeds so grand,
The ivory bow-ends, the fish-skin quiver.
Yes, we must be always on our guard;
The Hsien-yün are very swift.   40

Long ago, when we started,
The willows spread their shade.
Now that we turn back
The snowflakes fly.
The march before us is long,   45
We are thirsty and hungry,
Our hearts are stricken with sorrow,
But no one listens to our plaint.

157

They clear away the grass, the trees;
Their ploughs open up the ground.
In a thousand pairs they tug at weeds and roots,
Along the low grounds, along the ridges.
There is the master and his eldest son,   5
There the headman and overseer.
They mark out, they plough.

Deep the food-baskets that are brought;
Dainty are the wives,
The men press close to them.   10
And now with shares so sharp
They set to work upon the southern acre.
They sow the many sorts of grain,
The seeds that hold moist life.
How the blade shoots up,   15
How sleek, the grown plant;
Very sleek, the young grain!
Band on band, the weeders ply their task.
Now they reap, all in due order;
Close-packed are their stooks—   20
Myriads, many myriads and millions,
To make wine, make sweet liquor,
As offering to ancestor and ancestress,
For fulfilment of all the rites.
"When sweet the fragrance of offering,   25
Glory shall come to the fatherland.
When pungent the scent,
The blessed elders are at rest."
Not only here is it like this,
Not only now is it so.   30
From long ago it has been thus.

238

She who in the beginning gave birth to the people,
This was Chiang Yüan.
How did she give birth to the people?
Well she sacrificed and prayed
That she might no longer be childless.   5
She trod on the big toe of God's footprint,
Was accepted and got what she desired.
Then in reverence, then in awe
She gave birth, she nurtured;
And this was Hou Chi.[1]   10

Indeed, she had fulfilled her months,
And her first-born came like a lamb
With no bursting or rending,
With no hurt or harm.
To make manifest His magic power   15
God on high gave her ease.
So blessed were her sacrifice and prayer
That easily she bore her child.

Indeed, they[2] put it in a narrow lane;
But oxen and sheep tenderly cherished it.   20
Indeed, they put it in a far-off wood;

---

1. Lord Millet, the legendary ancestor of the Chou people.   2. The ballad does not tell us who exposed the child. According to one version it was the mother herself; according to another, her husband [Translator's note].

But it chanced that woodcutters came to this wood.
Indeed, they put it on the cold ice;
But the birds covered it with their wings.
But birds at last went away,   25
And Hou Chi began to wail.

Truly far and wide
His voice was very loud.
Then sure enough he began to crawl;
Well he straddled, well he reared,   30
To reach food for his mouth.
He planted large beans;
His beans grew fat and tall.
His paddy-lines were close set,
His hemp and wheat grew thick,   35
His young gourds teemed.

Truly Hou Chi's husbandry
Followed the way that had been shown.
He cleared away the thick grass,
He planted the yellow crop.   40
It failed nowhere, it grew thick,
It was heavy, it was tall,
It sprouted, it eared,
It was firm and good,
It nodded, it hung—   45
He made house and home in T'ai.

Indeed, the lucky grains were sent down to us,
The black millet, the double-kernelled,
Millet pink-sprouted and white.
Far and wide the black and the double-kernelled   50
He reaped and acred;
Far and wide the millet pink and white
He carried in his arms, he bore on his back,
Brought them home, and created the sacrifice.

Indeed, what are they, our sacrifices?   55
We pound the grain, we bale it out,
We sift, we tread,
We wash it—soak, soak;
We boil it all steamy.
Then with due care, due thought   60
We gather southernwood, make offering of fat,
Take lambs for the rite of expiation,
We roast, we broil,
To give a start to the coming year.

High we load the stands,   65
The stands of wood and of earthenware.
As soon as the smell rises
God on high is very pleased:
"What smell is this, so strong and good?"
Hou Chi founded the sacrifices,   70
And without blemish or flaw
They have gone on till now.

276

Big rat, big rat,
Do not gobble our millet!
Three years we have slaved for you,
Yet you take no notice of us.
At last we are going to leave you　　　　5
And go to that happy land;
Happy land, happy land,
Where we shall have our place.

Big rat, big rat,
Do not gobble our corn!　　　　10
Three years we have slaved for you,
Yet you give us no credit.
At last we are going to leave you
And go to that happy kingdom;
Happy kingdom, happy kingdom,　　　　15
Where we shall get our due.

Big rat, big rat,
Do not eat our rice-shoots!
Three years we have slaved for you.
Yet you did nothing to reward us.　　　　20
At last we are going to leave you
And go to those happy borders;
Happy borders, happy borders
Where no sad songs are sung.

278 [1]

"Kio" sings the oriole
As it lights on the thorn-bush.
Who went with Duke Mu to the grave?
Yen-hsi of the clan Tzǔ-chü.
Now this Yen-hsi　　　　5
Was the pick of all our men;
But as he drew near the tomb-hole
His limbs shook with dread.
That blue one, Heaven,
Takes all our good men.　　　　10
Could we but ransom him
There are a hundred would give their lives.

"Kio" sings the oriole
As it lights on the mulberry-tree.
Who went with Duke Mu to the grave?　　　　15
Chung-hang of the clan Tzǔ-chü.
Now this Chung-hang
Was the sturdiest of all our men;
But as he drew near the tomb-hole

1. This poem is dated to 621 B.C., the year that Duke Mu of Ch'in died. The poem reflects the archaic funeral practice of killing some of a lord's retainers to accompany him to the next world.

His limbs shook with dread. 20
That blue one, Heaven,
Takes all our good men.
Could we but ransom him
There are a hundred would give their lives.

"Kio" sings the oriole 25
As it lights on the brambles.
Who went with Duke Mu to the grave?
Ch'ien-hu of the clan Tzǔ-chü.
Now this Ch'ien-hu
Was the strongest of all our men. 30
But as he drew near the tomb-hole
His limbs shook with dread.
That blue one, Heaven,
Takes all our good men.
Could we but ransom him 35
There are a hundred would give their lives.

CONFUCIUS

551–479 B.C.

The *Analects* of Confucius (a title more lucidly translated as "Sayings") is the only work that we can confidently connect with the teacher Confucius, who gives his name to the secular social philosophy known as Confucianism. Confucius lived in a period when the unified Chou kingdom had split into a number of feudal states, most supposedly ruled by descendants of the Chou royal house. The period saw even that fragmented vestige of Chou legitimacy threatened by the rise of powerful families within the states.

Confucius himself was a native of Lu in eastern China, a state that prided itself on the preservation of Chou royal traditions but whose dukes were often at the mercy of the powerful Chi clan. Apparently because of a political conflict, Confucius left Lu in 497 B.C. and spent the next thirteen years wandering from regional court to regional court, gaining disciples and unsuccessfully seeking a prince who would try to implement his vision of traditional Chou values. At last he returned to Lu and lived out the rest of his life as a teacher, gathering a considerable following.

The *Analects* represents the memory of Confucius's teachings on the part of his disciples and was probably not written down until many centuries after his death. In its present form the *Analects* consists of twenty "books" or chapters, of which modern scholars consider the first fifteen to be authentic (we include passages from two of the last five books, because they were considered just as authoritative as the first fifteen well into modern times). Although we can occasionally detect groupings of sayings, in general passages in the *Analects* are put together randomly.

To be a Confucian (the Chinese term is *Ju*, meaning roughly "traditionalist scholar") has meant many things during the nearly twenty-five hundred years since Confucius's death. These various meanings shifted and overlapped from age to age. For some scholars Confucianism was the study of ancient texts that embodied rituals and norms of behavior, for others it was a political philosophy, a social philosophy of the family, or the moral order of nature.

In the centuries that followed Confucius's death his teachings were absorbed

into a growing interest in statecraft, and during the Han Dynasty, Confucian values became interwoven with the ideology of the imperial state. In later periods Chinese emperors may have supported Buddhism or religious Taoism out of personal devotion or political expediency, but Confucian learning and values were the very basis of the imperial state, by which the emperor held his office.

Confucius's reverence for antiquity centered on received texts and bodies of learning; these were the *Book of Songs*, the *Book of Documents* (*Shang shu*), the *Book of Changes* (*Yi ching*), the rituals (later written down in different texts), and a body of musical practice that accompanied the rituals and the *Book of Songs* (the music was lost after Confucius's time). In the third century B.C. these texts and traditions, along with a chronicle known as the *Ch'un-ch'iu*, became the core of what would be known as the Confucian classics. Other works came to be added to this core, including the *Analects* itself in the ninth century.

Before commenting on some of the central concerns of the *Analects*, we should consider its peculiar form and the significance of that form. In contrast to the imaginative sweep of works that founded other religious and philosophical traditions (and to the imaginative range of the *Chuang-tzu* within the Chinese tradition), the *Analects* is a collection of terse and sometimes apparently innocuous sayings as well as a few longer anecdotes. The unity of the *Analects* resides not in an argument or a unified philosophy but rather in a person, Confucius. Instead of writing a treatise explaining his thoughts, the Confucius of the *Analects* responds to people and situations. The words are never thought of as the final and adequate statement of doctrine but as the circumstantial evidence of deeper wisdom. Confucianism is a philosophy of the relations between human beings, and its persuasive force rests not on a claim of transcendental truth but on the wisdom embodied in a person. Thus Confucius's terseness is read as a pregnant terseness, the utterances of someone who knew more and might have said more. The ideal here is captured in the disciple Tzu-kung's praise of Yen Hui, the most brilliant of Confucius's disciples: "When he is told one thing he understands ten." Throughout the *Analects* the reader is reminded that wisdom comes in fragments and fractions; the burden of full understanding is placed on the reader.

The moral philosophy of the *Analects* presupposes an idealized vision of the Chou past and its norms of behavior, which Confucius felt had been lost in his own age. The historically specific aspects of Confucius's values, such as his devotion to ancient rituals, make those values seem alien to a modern age; and indeed the modern reader may wonder why Confucianism remained so persuasive as a social philosophy, revived even in modern times.

The answer lies in looking beneath what is historically specific in the *Analects* to the hope of a perfect unity of social norm and natural behavior. This is succinctly expressed in Confucius's account of his spiritual development, culminating in the following: "At seventy I followed my heart's desire without overstepping the line." By study and self-cultivation, individuals can join their instinctive being and their social being. The hope is for a society whose members behave with a natural decency toward one another, respecting age and hierarchy and adapting to their changing roles. If the Confucianism of the *Analects* has a repugnance for anarchy and struggle, it has an equal repugnance for order achieved by coercion.

In one of the few extended passages in the *Analects*, Confucius asks a group of his disciples about their ambitions. Tzu-lu begins with a grand vision of restoring a state to power and morality. Sensing the master's disapproval, each of the subsequent disciples restricts his ambitions to an ever-narrower scope. At last the master comes to Tseng Hsi, who speaks of the joy in returning home from a festival with a group of friends. "The Master sighed and said, 'I am all in favour of Tien [Tseng Hsi].' " This is a touchstone text of Confucianism: what moves Confucius is the immediacy of Tseng Hsi's prospective joy in ritual and moral action. As

Confucius says elsewhere, to delight in the Way is better than merely to understand it.

Confucius generally confined his interests to the human world and, as the *Analects* itself observes, did not speak about Heaven or the supernatural. This was not disbelief in transcendent being, but a remarkable desire to keep it out of human affairs, an ancient separation of church and state: "To keep one's distance from the gods and spirits while showing them reverence can be called wisdom."

The Confucian Way was one of social roles. These usually involved hierarchies of relations, but to Confucius social hierarchy was valid only if it came naturally and spontaneously. The only hierarchical relation that was above judgment was the relation between parent and child, and that natural relation of mutual but differing qualities of affection was the model to which all other social relations aspired.

No contemporary account of Confucianism can be complete without acknowledging the deep hostility it often inspires in modern China and Taiwan. Later, Confucianism became a tool of social coercion, and its demand that social norms of behavior be experienced as "natural" was an invitation to hypocrisy. But as with all religions and cultural philosophies, its historical failures do not entirely discredit the vision and hopes that first made it compelling.

Like other Chinese philosophers, Confucius speaks of the "Way." Each of the ancient Chinese philosophical schools used the term and interpreted the attributes of the Way differently. One should not grant too much value to the term itself; its importance lies in conceptualizing values and truth as process, a natural course of events and a natural course of action.

D. C. Lau's translation of the *Analects* (1979) has a long introduction that offers a lucid exposition of key concepts used in the work. The philosopher Herbert Fingarette, *Confucius—The Secular as Sacred* (1972), remains one of the most persuasive accounts of the appeal of the *Analects*.

PRONOUNCING GLOSSARY

The following list uses common English syllables to provide rough equivalents of selected words whose pronunciation may be unfamiliar to the general reader.

Ch'ang Chü: *chahng-joo*	Jan Ch'iu: *rahn chyoh*
Chi: *jee*	Jan Yu: *rahn yoh*
Ch'i: *chee*	K'uang: *kwahng*
Chieh Ni: *jyeh nee*	K'ung: *koong*
Ch'ih: *cherr*	Kung-hsi Hua: *goong–shee hwah*
Chi K'ang Tzu: *jee kahng dzuh*	Meng Ching Tzu: *mung jing dzuh*
Chi-lu: *jee–loo*	Shang shu: *shahng shoo*
Ching: *jing*	Shih Yü: *sherr yoo*
Ch'iu: *chyoh*	Shun: *shoo-un*
Chi Wen Tzu: *jee wun dzuh*	Tien: *dyen*
Ch'ü: *choo*	Tsai Yü: *dzai yoo*
Ch'un-ch'iu: *choo-en–chyoh*	Tseng Hsi: *dzung shee*
Chung-kung: *jong–goong*	Tseng Tzu: *dzung dzuh*
Ch'u Po-yu: *choo bwoh–yoo*	Tzu-chang: *dzuh–jahng*
Fan Ch'ih: *fahn cherr*	Tzu-kung: *dzuh–goong*

Tzu-lu: *dzuh–loo*   Yen Yüan: *yen yoo-en*
Wu Ch'eng: *woo chung*   Yi ching: *ee jing*
Yen Hui: *yen hway*

From Analects [1]

BOOK I

1. The Master said, "Is it not a pleasure, having learned something, to try it out at due intervals? Is it not a joy to have friends come from afar? Is it not gentlemanly not to take offence when others fail to appreciate your abilities?"

BOOK II

1. The Master said, "The rule of virtue can be compared to the Pole Star which commands the homage of the multitude of stars without leaving its place."

3. The Master said, "Guide them by edicts, keep them in line with punishments, and the common people will stay out of trouble but will have no sense of shame. Guide them by virtue, keep them in line with the rites, and they will, besides having a sense of shame, reform themselves."

4. The Master said, "At fifteen I set my heart on learning; at thirty I took my stand; at forty I came to be free from doubts; at fifty I understood the Decree of Heaven; at sixty my ear was atuned; at seventy I followed my heart's desire without overstepping the line."

19. Duke Ai asked "What must I do before the common people will look up to me?"
Confucius answered, "Raise the straight and set them over the crooked and the common people will look up to you. Raise the crooked and set them over the straight and the common people will not look up to you."

BOOK III

8. The Master said, "He has not lived in vain who dies the day he is told about the Way."

9. The Master said to Tzu-kung, "Who is the better man, you or Hui?"
"How dare I compare myself with Hui? When he is told one thing he understands ten. When I am told one thing I understand only two."
The Master said, "You are not as good as he is. Neither of us is as good as he is."

10. Tsai Yü was in bed in the daytime. The Master said, "A piece of rotten wood cannot be carved, nor can a wall of dried dung be trowelled. As far as Yü is concerned what is the use of condemning him?" The Master added, "I used to take on trust a man's deeds after having listened to

1. Translated by D. C. Lau.

his words. Now having listened to a man's words I go on to observe his deeds. It was on account of Yü that I have changed in this respect."

20. Chi Wen Tzu always thought three times before taking action. When the Master was told of this, he commented, "Twice is quite enough."

26. Yen Yüan and Chi-lu were in attendance. The Master said, "I suggest you each tell me what it is you have set your hearts on."

Tzu-lu said, "I should like to share my carriage and horses, clothes and furs with my friends, and to have no regrets even if they become worn."

Yen Yüan said, "I should like never to boast of my own goodness and never to impose onerous tasks upon others."

Tzu-lu said, "I should like to hear what you have set your heart on."

The Master said, "To bring peace to the old, to have trust in my friends, and to cherish the young."

BOOK VI

12. Jan Ch'iu said, "It is not that I am not pleased with your way, but rather that my strength gives out." The Master said, "A man whose strength gives out collapses along the course. In your case you set the limits beforehand."

20. The Master said, "To be fond of something is better than merely to know it, and to find joy in it is better than merely to be fond of it."

22. Fan Ch'ih asked about wisdom. The Master said, "To work for the things the common people have a right to and to keep one's distance from the gods and spirits while showing them reverence can be called wisdom."

Fan Ch'ih asked about benevolence. The Master said, "The benevolent man reaps the benefit only after overcoming difficulties. That can be called benevolence."

23. The Master said, "The wise find joy in water; the benevolent find joy in mountains. The wise are active; the benevolent are still. The wise are joyful; the benevolent are long-lived."

BOOK VII

3. The Master said, "It is these things that cause me concern: failure to cultivate virtue, failure to go more deeply into what I have learned, inability, when I am told what is right, to move to where it is, and inability to reform myself when I have defects."

5. The Master said, "How I have gone downhill! It has been such a long time since I dreamt of the Duke of Chou."

16. The Master said, "In the eating of coarse rice and the drinking of water, the using of one's elbow for a pillow, joy is to be found. Wealth and rank attained through immoral means have as much to do with me as passing clouds."

27. The Master used a fishing line but not a cable; he used a corded arrow but not to shoot at roosting birds.

4. Tseng Tzu was seriously ill. When Meng Ching Tzu visited him, this was what Tseng Tzu said,

> "Sad is the cry of a dying bird;
> Good are the words of a dying man.

These are three things which the gentleman values most in the Way: to stay clear of violence by putting on a serious countenance, to come close to being trusted by setting a proper expression on his face, and to avoid being boorish and unreasonable by speaking in proper tones. As for the business of sacrificial vessels, there are officials responsible for that."

5. Tseng Tzu said, "To be able yet to ask the advice of those who are not able. To have many talents yet to ask the advice of those who have few. To have yet to appear to want. To be full yet to appear empty. To be transgressed against yet not to mind. It was towards this end that my friend used to direct his efforts."

13. The Master said, "Have the firm faith to devote yourself to learning, and abide to the death in the good way. Enter not a state that is in peril; stay not in a state that is in danger. Show yourself when the Way prevails in the Empire, but hide yourself when it does not. It is a shameful matter to be poor and humble when the Way prevails in the state. Equally, it is a shameful matter to be rich and noble when the Way falls into disuse in the state."

17. The Master said, "Even with a man who urges himself on in his studies as though he was losing ground, my fear is still that he may not make it in time."

BOOK IX

5. When under siege in K'uang, the Master said, "With King Wen[2] dead, is not culture (wen) invested here in me? If Heaven intends culture to be destroyed, those who come after me will not be able to have any part of it. If Heaven does not intend this culture to be destroyed, then what can the men of K'uang do to me?"

12. The Master was seriously ill. Tzu-lu told his disciples to act as retainers. During a period when his condition had improved, the Master said, "Yu has long been practising deception. In pretending that I had retainers when I had none, who would we be deceiving? Would we be deceiving Heaven? Moreover, would I not rather die in your hands, my friends, than in the hands of retainers? And even if I were not given an elaborate funeral, it is not as if I was dying by the wayside."

13. Tzu-kung said, "If you had a piece of beautiful jade here, would you put it away safely in a box or would you try to sell it for a good price?" The Master said, "Of course I would sell it. Of course I would sell it. All I am waiting for is the right offer."

---

2. First ruler of the Chou Dynasty.

14. The Master wanted to settle amongst the Nine Barbarian Tribes of the east. Someone said, "But could you put up with their uncouth ways?" The Master said, "Once a gentleman settles amongst them, what uncouthness will there be?"

22. The Master said, "There are, are there not, young plants that fail to produce blossoms, and blossoms that fail to produce fruit?"

23. The Master said, "It is fitting that we should hold the young in awe. How do we know that the generations to come will not be the equal of the present? Only when a man reaches the age of forty or fifty without distinguishing himself in any way can one say, I suppose, that he does not deserve to be held in awe."

28. The Master said, "Only when the cold season comes is the point brought home that the pine and the cypress are the last to lose their leaves."

BOOK XI

10. When Yen Yüan died, in weeping for him, the Master showed undue sorrow. His followers said, "You are showing undue sorrow." "Am I? Yet if not for him, for whom should I show undue sorrow?"

26. When Tzu-lu, Tseng Hsi, Jan Yu and Kung-hsi Hua were seated in attendance, the Master said, "Do not feel constrained simply because I am a little older than you are. Now you are in the habit of saying, 'My abilities are not appreciated,' but if someone did appreciate your abilities, do tell me how you would go about things."
Tzu-lu promptly answered, "If I were to administer a state of a thousand chariots, situated between powerful neighbours, troubled by armed invasions and by repeated famines, I could, within three years, give the people courage and a sense of direction."
The Master smiled at him.
"Ch'iu, what about you?"
"If I were to administer an area measuring sixty or seventy li^3 square, or even fifty or sixty li square, I could, within three years, bring the size of the population up to an adequate level. As to the rites and music, I would leave that to abler gentlemen."
"Ch'ih, how about you?"
"I do not say that I already have the ability, but I am ready to learn. On ceremonial occasions in the ancestral temple or in diplomatic gatherings, I should like to assist as a minor official in charge of protocol, properly dressed in my ceremonial cap and robes."
"Tien, how about you?"
After a few dying notes came the final chord, and then he stood up from his lute. "I differ from the other three in my choice."
The Master said, "What harm is there in that? After all each man is stating what he has set his heart upon."

---

3. A unit of distance, about one-quarter of a mile.

"In late spring, after the spring clothes have been newly made, I should like, together with five or six adults and six or seven boys, to go bathing in the River Yi and enjoy the breeze on the Rain Altar, and then to go home chanting poetry."

The Master sighed and said, "I am all in favour of Tien."

When the three left, Tseng Hsi stayed behind. He said, "What do you think of what the other three said?"

"They were only stating what they had set their hearts upon."

"Why did you smile at Yu?"

"It is by the rites that a state is administered, but in the way he spoke Yu showed a lack of modesty. That is why I smiled at him."

"In the case of Ch'iu, was he not concerned with a state?"

"What can justify one in saying that sixty or seventy *li* square or indeed fifty or sixty *li* square do not deserve the name of 'state'?"

"In the case of Ch'ih, was he not concerned with a state?"

"What are ceremonial occasions in the ancestral temple and diplomatic gatherings if not matters which concern rulers of feudal states? If Ch'iu plays only a minor part, who would be able to play a major role?"

BOOK XII

2. Chung-kung asked about benevolence. The Master said, "When abroad behave as though you were receiving an important guest. When employing the services of the common people behave as though you were officiating at an important sacrifice. Do not impose on others what you yourself do not desire. In this way you will be free from ill will whether in a state or in a noble family."

Chung-kung said, "Though I am not quick, I shall direct my efforts towards what you have said."

7. Tzu-kung asked about government. The Master said, "Give them enough food, give them enough arms, and the common people will have trust in you."

Tzu-kung said, "If one had to give up one of these three, which should one give up first?"

"Give up arms."

Tzu-kung said, "If one had to give up one of the remaining two, which should one give up first?"

"Give up food. Death has always been with us since the beginning of time, but when there is no trust, the common people will have nothing to stand on."

10. Tzu-chang asked about the exaltation of virtue and the recognition of misguided judgment. The Master said, "Make it your guiding principle to do your best for others and to be trustworthy in what you say, and move yourself to where rightness is, then you will be exalting virtue. When you love a man you want him to live and when you hate him you want him to die. If, having wanted him to live, you then want him to die, this is misguided judgement.

If you did not do so for the sake of riches,
You must have done so for the sake of novelty."[4]

11. Duke Ching of Ch'i asked Confucius about government. Confucius answered, "Let the ruler be a ruler, the subject a subject, the father a father, the son a son." The Duke said, "Splendid! Truly, if the ruler be not a ruler, the subject not a subject, the father not a father, the son not a son, then even if there be grain, would I get to eat it?"

18. The prevalence of thieves was a source of trouble to Chi K'ang Tzu who asked the advice of Confucius. Confucius answered, "If you yourself were not a man of desires,[5] no one would steal even if stealing carried a reward."

19. Chi K'ang Tzu asked Confucius about government, saying, "What would you think if, in order to move closer to those who possess the Way, I were to kill those who do not follow the Way?"
Confucius answered, "In administering your government, what need is there for you to kill? Just desire the good yourself and the common people will be good. The virtue of the gentleman is like in straitened circumstances for a long time, he may be said to be a complete man."

BOOK XIII

1. Tzu-lu asked about government. The Master said, "Encourage the people to work hard by setting an example yourself." Tzu-lu asked for more. The Master said, "Do not allow your efforts to slacken."

10. The Master said, "If anyone were to employ me, in a year's time I would have brought things to a satisfactory state, and after three years I should have results to show for it."

11. The Master said, "How true is the saying that after a state has been ruled for a hundred years by good men it is possible to get the better of cruelty and to do away with killing."

12. The Master said, "Even with a true king it is bound to take a generation for benevolence to become a reality."

20. Tzu-kung asked, "What must a man be like before he can be said truly to be a Gentleman?" The Master said, "A man who has a sense of shame in the way he conducts himself and, when sent abroad, does not disgrace the commission of his lord can be said to be a Gentleman."
"May I ask about the grade below?"
"Someone praised for being a good son in his clan and for being a respectful young man in the village."
"And the next?"
"A man who insists on keeping his word and seeing his actions through to the end can, perhaps, qualify to come next, even though he shows a stubborn petty-mindedness."

4. The quotation seems to have no bearing on the subject under discussion and may not in fact belong here.   5. That is, if you were not a thief yourself.

"What about men who are in public life in the present day?"

The Master said, "Oh, they are of such limited capacity that they hardly count."

BOOK XIV

35. The Master said, "There is no one who understands me." Tzu-kung said, "How is it that there is no one who understands you?" The Master said, "I do not complain against Heaven, nor do I blame Man. In my studies, I start from below and get through to what is up above. If I am understood at all, it is, perhaps, by Heaven."

38. Tzu-lu put up for the night at the Stone Gate. The gatekeeper said, "Where have you come from?" Tzu-lu said, "From the K'ung family." "Is that the K'ung who keeps working towards a goal the realization of which he knows to be hopeless?"

BOOK XV

3. The Master said, "Ssu, do you think that I am the kind of man who learns widely and retains what he has learned in his mind?"

"Yes, I do. Is it not so?"

"No. I have a single thread binding it all together."

5. The Master said, "If there was a ruler who achieved order without taking any action, it was, perhaps, Shun. There was nothing for him to do but to hold himself in a respectful posture and to face due south."[6]

7. The Master said, "How straight Shih Yü is! When the Way prevails in the state he is as straight as an arrow, yet when the Way falls into disuse in the state he is still as straight as an arrow.

"How gentlemanly Ch'ü Po-yü is! When the Way prevails in the state he takes office, but when the Way falls into disuse in the state he allows himself to be furled and put away safely."

31. The Master said, "I once spent all day thinking without taking food and all night thinking without going to bed, but I found that I gained nothing from it. It would have been better for me to have spent the time in learning.

BOOK XVII

4. The Master went to Wu Ch'eng. There he heard the sound of stringed instruments and singing. The Master broke into a smile and said, "Surely you don't need to use an ox-knife to kill a chicken."

Tzu-yu answered, "Some time ago I heard it from you, Master, that the gentleman instructed in the Way loves his fellow men and that the small man instructed in the Way is easy to command."

The Master said, "My friends, what Yen says is right. My remark a moment ago was only made in jest."

---

6. The direction the emperor's seat faces.

9. The Master said, "Why is it none of you, my young friends, study the *Odes*? An apt quotation from the *Odes* may serve to stimulate the imagination, to show one's breeding, to smooth over difficulties in a group and to give expression to complaints.

"Inside the family there is the serving of one's father; outside, there is the serving of one's lord; there is also the acquiring of a wide knowledge of the names of birds and beasts, plants and trees."

BOOK XVIII

5. Chieh Yü, the Madman of Ch'u, went past Confucius, singing,

> Phoenix, oh phoenix!
> How thy virtue has declined!
> What is past is beyond help,
> What is to come is not yet lost.
> Give up, give up!
> Perilous is the lot of those in office today.

Confucius got down from his carriage with the intention of speaking with him, but the Madman avoided him by hurrying off, and in the end Confucius was unable to speak with him.

6. Ch'ang Chü and Chieh Ni were ploughing together yoked as a team. Confucius went past them and sent Tzu-lu to ask them where the ford was. Ch'ang Chü said, "Who is that taking charge of the carriage?" Tzu-lu said, "It is K'ung Ch'iu." "Then, he must be the K'ung Ch'iu of Lu." "He is," "Then, he doesn't have to ask where the ford is."

Tzu-lu asked Chieh Ni. Chieh Ni said, "Who are you?" "I am Chung Yu." "Then, you must be the disciple of K'ung Ch'iu of Lu?" Tzu-lu answered, "I am." "Throughout the Empire men are all the same. Who is there for you to change places with? Moreoever, for your own sake, would it not be better if, instead of following a Gentleman who keeps running away from men, you followed one who runs away from the world altogether?" All this while he carried on harrowing without interruption.

Tzu-lu went and reported what was said to Confucius.

The Master was lost in thought for a while and said, "One cannot associate with birds and beasts. Am I not a member of this human race? Who, then, is there for me to associate with? While the Way is to be found in the Empire, I will not change places with him."

CHUANG CHOU
ca. 369–286 B.C.

The period known as the Warring States, from 403 B.C. until the unification of China by the kingdom of Ch'in in 221 B.C., saw an intellectual diversity and vigor of philosophical debate unparalleled in later Chinese history. As the old Chou domains were gradually transforming themselves into contentious independent states, so the map of Chinese thought contained numerous schools and philosoph-

ical positions, and these also waged wars for hegemony. The relation between the political and philosophical maps was more than metaphorical; many of the philosophical schools dealt entirely or largely with political philosophy, and thinkers would travel from state to state, arguing with one another and competing for the patronage of princes.

There were, however, some philosophers who sought neither disciples nor patronage, who founded no school, and who were content to write. Such was the fourth-century philosopher Chuang Chou, to whom is attributed the first seven chapters of a work now called the *Chuang Tzu* (Master Chuang). Apart from the evidence of the *Chuang Tzu* itself, we know little about Chuang Chou as a historical person. Yet the first chapters of the *Chuang Tzu* show a remarkable mind at work.

The *Chuang Tzu* is often linked with the *Lao Tzu* as constituting the two primary texts of philosophical Taoism. The two works are quite different, both in style of writing and in style of thought. The *Lao Tzu* is largely in verse and repeats its pithy paradoxes over and over again. The *Chuang Tzu* is in a prose of constantly changing styles, with embedded verse passages. It moves from wise jokes and funny parables to moments of passionate seriousness, to tight philosophical arguments that turn imperceptibly into parodies of tight philosophical arguments. The structure of the first seven chapters is intricate: what seems at first to be a discontinuous series of parables gradually reveals itself as an echoing interplay of themes, sometimes taking the train of thought off in another direction, sometimes standing an earlier argument on its head.

Chuang Chou uses rapid shifts in scale and perspective to remind his readers that proportions, like values, are relative to a particular viewpoint. In *Free and Easy Wandering* he begins with a monstrous sea creature, whose name is K'un (Fish Eggs). The K'un is transformed into the P'eng bird, which is so large that its wings hang over the sky to both horizons. The P'eng flies so high that when it looks down all it sees is blue. All of a sudden the passage shifts to a hollow in a floor that, if filled with water, floats scraps. On a tiny scale this becomes the analogy of the huge P'eng requiring an amplitude of air to bear up its mighty wings. In dizzying sequence Chuang Chou constantly shifts scales, exercising the reader's imagination to break down his or her habitual perspective, which is based on human magnitude.

As he shifts physical perspective, Chuang Chou also shifts his own standpoint, undermining the authority of what he has previously written. Readers are often uncertain whether he is serious or putting them on, or serious in his putting them on. In Chapter 2 he moves into a logical argument on the relativity of the concepts "this" and "that" as well as "right" and "wrong." The argument is intricate and stylized, and at some point readers begin to suspect that they are reading the parody of an argument, a suspicion confirmed when Chuang Chou reaches his grand summation in a joke. But then readers realize that this was the only proper conclusion for an argument against the absolute validity of arguments.

In the present version of the *Chuang Tzu*, twenty-six additional chapters follow the first seven. These are a miscellaneous gathering of Taoist works and works from related schools. Although none can match the first seven chapters as unified wholes, they contain many smaller sections as good as anything found earlier. Here we find an endless parade of crazy sages, wise peasants, and craftsmen, with all the commonplaces of habitual authority and conventional morality held up for ridicule.

The *Chuang Tzu* is the most inventive and diverse writing in early China, yet throughout the book we find doubts about the capacity of language, and particularly of written language, to convey truth. We read of a duke reading; his wheelwright comes in and asks him what he is reading. When the duke says that he is

reading the words of the sages, the wheelwright asks if they are dead. And when the duke says that they are indeed, the wheelwright tells him that he is reading only the "chaff and dregs," that what they really knew could not be passed on by words. Yet the *Chuang Tzu* rarely loses sight of the fact that it too is words, and it solves the problem by laughing at itself, stepping out from behind its own statements with a wink. This happens in the following famous passage from the later chapters, put in the mouth of Chuang Chou:

> The fish trap exists because of the fish; once you've gotten the fish, you can forget the trap. The rabbit snare exists because of the rabbit; once you've gotten the rabbit, you can forget the snare. Words exist because of the meaning; once you've gotten the meaning, you can forget the words. Where can I find a man who has forgotten the words so I can have a word with him?

The term *Tao* ("Way") was used by the Confucians and other thinkers as well as by the Taoists. The Way is simply the natural course of things. For the Confucians the Way is moral and potentially to be realized within society; in the *Chuang Tzu* the Way is amoral and escapes conventional human categories. Oppositions such as "up and down," "right and wrong," "this and that" all presume a limited perspective from which such distinctions can occur. The Way, in contrast, is everywhere and has no perspective whatsoever. Knowing that the words used to speak of such a Way are precisely the categories he is trying to get beyond, Chuang Chou can only use language against itself.

For another translation of the *Chuang Tzu* by one of the most distinguished scholars of Chinese philosophy, see A. C. Graham, *Chuang Tzu: The Inner Chapters* (1981). Graham also includes an excellent discussion of the *Chuang Tzu* in the context of other early thinkers in *Disputers of the Tao: Philosophical Argument in Ancient China* (1989).

PRONOUNCING GLOSSARY

The following list uses common English syllables to provide rough equivalents of selected words whose pronunciation may be unfamiliar to the general reader.

Chang Wu-tzu: *jang woo–dzuh*   Mao-ch'iang: *mow–jyahng*

Chao: *jow*   Nieh Ch'üeh: *nyeh choo-eh*

Chü Ch'üeh-tzu: *joo choo-eh–dzuh*   P'eng-tsu: *puhng–dzuh*

Hsi-shih: *shee–sher*   Tzu-ch'i: *dzuh–chee*

Hui Tzu: *hway dzuh*

Chuang Tzu[1]

CHAPTER 2

Discussion on Making All Things Equal

Tzu-ch'i of south wall sat leaning on his armrest, staring up at the sky and breathing—vacant and far away, as though he'd lost his companion.[2] Yen Ch'eng Tzu-yu, who was standing by his side in attendance, said, "What is this? Can you really make the body like a withered tree and the

---

1. Translated by Burton Watson.   2. The word "companion" is interpreted variously to mean his associates, his wife, or his own body [Translator's note].

mind like dead ashes? The man leaning on the armrest now is not the one who leaned on it before!"

Tzu-ch'i said, "You do well to ask the question, Yen. Now I have lost myself. Do you understand that? You hear the piping of men, but you haven't heard the piping of earth. Or if you've heard the piping of earth, you haven't heard the piping of Heaven!"

Tzu-yu said, "May I venture to ask what this means?"

Tzu-ch'i said, "The Great Clod[3] belches out breath and its name is wind. So long as it doesn't come forth, nothing happens. But when it does, then ten thousand hollows begin crying wildly. Can't you hear them, long drawn out? In the mountain forests that lash and sway, there are huge trees a hundred spans around with hollows and openings like noses, like mouths, like ears, like jugs, like cups, like mortars, like rifts, like ruts. They roar like waves, whistle like arrows, screech, gasp, cry, wail, moan, and howl, those in the lead calling out *yeee!*, those behind calling out *yuuu!* In a gentle breeze they answer faintly, but in a full gale the chorus is gigantic. And when the fierce wind has passed on, then all the hollows are empty again. Have you never seen the tossing and trembling that goes on?"

Tzu-yu said, "By the piping of earth, then, you mean simply [the sound of] these hollows, and by the piping of man [the sound of] flutes and whistles. But may I ask about the piping of Heaven?"

Tzu-ch'i said, "Blowing on the ten thousand things in a different way, so that each can be itself—all take what they want for themselves, but who does the sounding?"

Great understanding is broad and unhurried; little understanding is cramped and busy. Great words are clear and limpid; little words are shrill and quarrelsome. In sleep, men's spirits go visiting; in waking hours, their bodies hustle. With everything they meet they become entangled. Day after day they use their minds in strife, sometimes grandiose, sometimes sly, sometimes petty. Their little fears are mean and trembly; their great fears are stunned and overwhelming. They bound off like an arrow or a crossbow pellet, certain that they are the arbiters of right and wrong. They cling to their position as though they had sworn before the gods, sure that they are holding on to victory. They fade like fall and winter—such is the way they dwindle day by day. They drown in what they do—you cannot make them turn back. They grow dark, as though sealed with seals—such are the excesses of their old age. And when their minds draw near to death, nothing can restore them to the light.

Joy, anger, grief, delight, worry, regret, fickleness, inflexibility, modesty, willfulness, candor, insolence—music from empty holes, mushrooms springing up in dampness, day and night replacing each other before us, and no one knows where they sprout from. Let it be! Let it be! [It is enough that] morning and evening we have them, and they are the means by which we live. Without them we would not exist; without us they would have nothing to take hold of. This comes close to the matter. But I do not know what makes them the way they are. It would seem as though they

3. The earth.

have some True Master, and yet I find no trace of him. He can act—that is certain. Yet I cannot see his form. He has identity but no form.

The hundred joints, the nine openings, the six organs, all come together and exist here [as my body]. But which part should I feel closest to? I should delight in all parts, you say? But there must be one I ought to favor more. If not, are they all of them mere servants? But if they are all servants, then how can they keep order among themselves? Or do they take turns being lord and servant? It would seem as though there must be some True Lord among them. But whether I succeed in discovering his identity or not, it neither adds to nor detracts from his Truth.

Once a man receives this fixed bodily form, he holds on to it, waiting for the end. Sometimes clashing with things, sometimes bending before them, he runs his course like a galloping steed, and nothing can stop him. Is he not pathetic? Sweating and laboring to the end of his days and never seeing his accomplishment, utterly exhausting himself and never knowing where to look for rest—can you help pitying him? I'm not dead yet! he says, but what good is that? His body decays, his mind follows it—can you deny that this is a great sorrow? Man's life has always been a muddle like this. How could I be the only muddled one, and other men not muddled?

If a man follows the mind given him and makes it his teacher, then who can be without a teacher? Why must you comprehend the process of change and form your mind on that basis before you can have a teacher? Even an idiot has his teacher. But to fail to abide by this mind and still insist upon your rights and wrongs—this is like saying that you set off for Yüeh today and got there yesterday.[4] This is to claim that what doesn't exist exists. If you claim that what doesn't exist exists, then even the holy sage Yü couldn't understand you, much less a person like me!

Words are not just wind. Words have something to say. But if what they have to say is not fixed, then do they really say something? Or do they say nothing? People suppose that words are different from the peeps of baby birds, but is there any difference, or isn't there? What does the Way rely upon, that we have true and false? What do words rely upon, that we have right and wrong? How can the Way go away and not exist? How can words exist and not be acceptable? When the Way relies on little accomplishments and words rely on vain show, then we have the rights and wrongs of the Confucians and the Mo-ists.[5] What one calls right the other calls wrong; what one calls wrong the other calls right. But if we want to right their wrongs and wrong their rights, then the best thing to use is clarity.

Everything has its "that," everything has its "this." From the point of view of "that" you cannot see it, but through understanding you can know it. So I say, "that" comes out of "this" and "this" depends on "that"— which is to say that "this" and "that" give birth to each other. But where there is birth there must be death; where there is death there must be birth. Where there is acceptability there must be unacceptability; where there is unacceptability there must be acceptability. Where there is recognition of right there must be recognition of wrong; where there is recogni-

---

4. This was one of the paradoxes of the logician Hui Tzu [Translator's note].   5. Followers of a utilitarian philosophical school who opposed the traditional ceremonies that the Confucians saw as essential to a good society.

tion of wrong there must be recognition of right. Therefore the sage does not proceed in such a way, but illuminates all in the light of Heaven.[6] He too recognizes a "this," but a "this" which is also "that," a "that" which is also "this." His "that" has both a right and a wrong in it; his "this" too has both a right and a wrong in it. So, in fact, does he still have a "this" and "that"? Or does he in fact no longer have a "this" and "that"? A state in which "this" and "that" no longer find their opposites is called the hinge of the Way. When the hinge is fitted into the socket, it can respond endlessly. Its right then is a single endlessness and its wrong too is a single endlessness. So, I say, the best thing to use is clarity.

To use an attribute to show that attributes are not attributes is not as good as using a nonattribute to show that attributes are not attributes. To use a horse to show that a horse is not a horse is not as good as using a non-horse to show that a horse is not a horse.[7] Heaven and earth are one attribute; the ten thousand things are one horse.

What is acceptable we call acceptable; what is unacceptable we call unacceptable. A road is made by people walking on it; things are so because they are called so. What makes them so? Making them so makes them so. What makes them not so? Making them not so makes them not so. Things all must have that which is so; things all must have that which is acceptable. There is nothing that is not so, nothing that is not acceptable.

For this reason, whether you point to a little stalk or a great pillar, a leper or the beautiful Hsi-shih, things ribald and shady or things grotesque and strange, the Way makes them all into one. Their dividedness is their completeness; their completeness is their impairment. No thing is either complete or impaired, but all are made into one again. Only the man of far-reaching vision knows how to make them into one. So he has no use [for categories], but relegates all to the constant. The constant is the useful; the useful is the passable; the passable is the successful; and with success, all is accomplished. He relies upon this alone, relies upon it and does not know he is doing so. This is called the Way.

But to wear out your brain trying to make things into one without realizing that they are all the same—this is called "three in the morning." What do I mean by "three in the morning"? When the monkey trainer was handing out acorns, he said, "You get three in the morning and four at night." This made all the monkeys furious. "Well, then," he said, "you get four in the morning and three at night." The monkeys were all delighted. There was no change in the reality behind the words, and yet the monkeys responded with joy and anger. Let them, if they want to. So the sage harmonizes with both right and wrong and rests in Heaven the Equalizer. This is called walking two roads.

The understanding of the men of ancient times went a long way. How far did it go? To the point where some of them believed that things have never existed—so far, to the end, where nothing can be added. Those at the next stage thought that things exist but recognized no boundaries among them. Those at the next stage thought there were boundaries but

---

6. Nature or the Way.　　7. A reference to the statements of the logician Kung-sun Lung, "A white horse is not a horse" and "Attributes are not attributes in and of themselves" [Translator's note].

recognized no right and wrong. Because right and wrong appeared, the Way was injured, and because the Way was injured, love became complete. But do such things as completion and injury really exist, or do they not?

There is such a thing as completion and injury—Mr. Chao playing the lute is an example. There is such a thing as no completion and no injury—Mr. Chao not playing the lute is an example.[8] Chao Wen played the lute; Music Master K'uang waved his baton; Hui Tzu leaned on his desk. The knowledge of these three was close to perfection. All were masters, and therefore their names have been handed down to later ages. Only in their likes they were different from him [the true sage]. What they liked, they tried to make clear. What he is not clear about, they tried to make clear, and so they ended in the foolishness of "hard" and "white."[9] Their sons, too, devoted all their lives to their fathers' theories, but till their death never reached any completion. Can these men be said to have attained completion? If so, then so have all the rest of us. Or can they not be said to have attained completion? If so, then neither we nor anything else have ever attained it.

The torch of chaos and doubt—this is what the sage steers by. So he does not use things but relegates all to the constant. This is what it means to use clarity.

Now I am going to make a statement here. I don't know whether it fits into the category of other people's statements or not. But whether it fits into their category or whether it doesn't, it obviously fits into some category. So in that respect it is no different from their statements. However, let me try making my statement.

There is a beginning. There is not yet beginning to be a beginning. There is a not yet beginning to be a not yet beginning to be a beginning. There is being. There is nonbeing. There is a not yet beginning to be nonbeing. There is a not yet beginning to be a not yet beginning to be nonbeing. Suddenly there is nonbeing. But I do not know, when it comes to nonbeing, which is really being and which is nonbeing. Now I have just said something. But I don't know whether what I have said has really said something or whether it hasn't said something.

There is nothing in the world bigger than the tip of an autumn hair,[1] and Mount T'ai is tiny. No one has lived longer than a dead child, and P'eng-tsu died young. Heaven and earth were born at the same time I was, and the ten thousand things are one with me.

We have already become one, so how can I say anything? But I have just *said* that we are one, so how can I not be saying something? The one and what I said about it make two, and two and the original one make three. If we go on this way, then even the cleverest mathematician can't

---

8. Chao Wen was a famous lute (*ch'in*) player. But the best music he could play (i.e., complete) was only a pale and partial reflection of the ideal music, which was thereby injured and impaired, just as the unity of the Way was injured by the appearance of love—i.e., man's likes and dislikes. Hence, when Mr. Chao refrained from playing the lute, there was neither completion nor injury [Translator's note]. 9. The logicians Hui Tzu and Kung-sun Lung spent much time discussing the relationship between attributes such as "hard" and "white" and the thing to which they pertain [Translator's note]. 1. The strands of animal fur were believed to grow particularly fine in autumn; hence "the tip of an autumn hair" is a cliché for something extremely tiny [Translator's note].

tell where we'll end, much less an ordinary man. If by moving from non-being to being we get to three, how far will we get if we move from being to being? Better not to move, but to let things be!

The Way has never known boundaries; speech has no constancy. But because of [the recognition of a] "this," there came to be boundaries. Let me tell you what the boundaries are. There is left, there is right, there are theories, there are debates, there are divisions, there are discriminations, there are emulations, and there are contentions. These are called the Eight Virtues. As to what is beyond the Six Realms,[2] the sage admits its existence but does not theorize. As to what is within the Six Realms, he theorizes but does not debate. In the case of the *Spring and Autumn*,[3] the record of the former kings of past ages, the sage debates but does not discriminate. So [I say,] those who divide fail to divide; those who discriminate fail to discriminate. What does this mean, you ask? The sage embraces things. Ordinary men discriminate among them and parade their discriminations before others. So I say, those who discriminate fail to see.

The Great Way is not named; Great Discriminations are not spoken; Great Benevolence is not benevolent; Great Modesty is not humble; Great Daring does not attack. If the Way is made clear, it is not the Way. If discriminations are put into words, they do not suffice. If benevolence has a constant object, it cannot be universal. If modesty is fastidious, it cannot be trusted. If daring attacks, it cannot be complete. These five are all round, but they tend toward the square.[4]

Therefore understanding that rests in what it does not understand is the finest. Who can understand discriminations that are not spoken, the Way that is not a way? If he can understand this, he may be called the Reservoir of Heaven. Pour into it and it is never full, dip from it and it never runs dry, and yet it does not know where the supply comes from. This is called the Shaded Light.

So it is that long ago Yao said to Shun, "I want to attack the rulers of Tsung, K'uai, and Hsü-ao. Even as I sit on my throne, this thought nags at me. Why is this?"

Shun replied, "These three rulers are only little dwellers in the weeds and brush. Why this nagging desire? Long ago, ten suns came out all at once and the ten thousand things were all lighted up. And how much greater is virtue than these suns!"[5]

Nieh Ch'üeh asked Wang Ni, "Do you know what all things agree in calling right?"

"How would I know that?" said Wang Ni.

"Do you know that you don't know it?"

"How would I know that?"

---

2. Heaven, earth, and the four directions, i.e., the universe [Translator's note].   3. Perhaps a reference to the *Spring and Autumn Annals*, a history of the state of Lu said to have been compiled by Confucius. But it may be a generic term referring to the chronicles of the various feudal states [Translator's note].   4. All are originally perfect, but may become "squared," i.e., impaired by the misuses mentioned [Translator's note].   5. Here virtue is to be understood in a good sense, as the power of the Way [Translator's note].

"Then do things know nothing?"

"How would I know that? However, suppose I try saying something. What way do I have of knowing that if I say I know something I don't really not know it? Or what way do I have of knowing that if I say I don't know something I don't really in fact know it? Now let me ask *you* some questions. If a man sleeps in a damp place, his back aches and he ends up half paralyzed, but is this true of a loach? If he lives in a tree, he is terrified and shakes with fright, but is this true of a monkey? Of these three creatures, then, which one knows the proper place to live? Men eat the flesh of grass-fed and grain-fed animals, deer eat grass, centipedes find snakes tasty, and hawks and falcons relish mice. Of these four, which knows how food ought to taste? Monkeys pair with monkeys, deer go out with deer, and fish play around with fish. Men claim that Mao-ch'iang and Lady Li were beautiful, but if fish saw them they would dive to the bottom of the stream, if birds saw them they would fly away, and if deer saw them they would break into a run. Of these four, which knows how to fix the standard of beauty for the world? The way I see it, the rules of benevolence and righteousness and the paths of right and wrong are all hopelessly snarled and jumbled. How could I know anything about such discriminations?"

Nieh Ch'üeh said, "If you don't know what is profitable or harmful, then does the Perfect Man likewise know nothing of such things?"

Wang Ni replied, "The Perfect Man is godlike. Though the great swamps blaze, they cannot burn him; though the great rivers freeze, they cannot chill him; though swift lightning splits the hills and howling gales shake the sea, they cannot frighten him. A man like this rides the clouds and mist, straddles the sun and moon, and wanders beyond the four seas. Even life and death have no effect on him, much less the rules of profit and loss!"

Chü Ch'üeh-tzu said to Chang Wu-tzu, "I have heard Confucius say that the sage does not work at anything, does not pursue profit, does not dodge harm, does not enjoy being sought after, does not follow the Way, says nothing yet says something, says something yet says nothing, and wanders beyond the dust and grime. Confucius himself regarded these as wild and flippant words, though I believe they describe the working of the mysterious Way. What do you think of them?"

Chang Wu-tzu said, "Even the Yellow Emperor would be confused if he heard such words, so how could you expect Confucius to understand them? What's more, you're too hasty in your own appraisal. You see an egg and demand a crowing cock, see a crossbow pellet and demand a roast dove. I'm going to try speaking some reckless words and I want you to listen to them recklessly. How will that be? The sage leans on the sun and moon, tucks the universe under his arm, merges himself with things, leaves the confusion and muddle as it is, and looks on slaves as exalted. Ordinary men strain and struggle; the sage is stupid and blockish. He takes part in ten thousand ages and achieves simplicity in oneness. For him, all the ten thousand things are what they are, and thus they enfold each other.

"How do I know that loving life is not a delusion? How do I know that

in hating death I am not like a man who, having left home in his youth, has forgotten the way back?

"Lady Li was the daughter of the border guard of Ai.[6] When she was first taken captive and brought to the state of Chin, she wept until her tears drenched the collar of her robe. But later, when she went to live in the palace of the ruler, shared his couch with him, and ate the delicious meats of his table, she wondered why she had ever wept. How do I know that the dead do not wonder why they ever longed for life?

"He who dreams of drinking wine may weep when morning comes; he who dreams of weeping may in the morning go off to hunt. While he is dreaming he does not know it is a dream, and in his dream he may even try to interpret a dream. Only after he wakes does he know it was a dream. And someday there will be a great awakening when we know that this is all a great dream. Yet the stupid believe they are awake, busily and brightly assuming they understand things, calling this man ruler, that one herds- man—how dense! Confucius and you are both dreaming! And when I say you are dreaming, I am dreaming, too. Words like these will be labeled the Supreme Swindle. Yet, after ten thousand generations, a great sage may appear who will know their meaning, and it will still be as though he appeared with astonishing speed.

"Suppose you and I have had an argument. If you have beaten me instead of my beating you, then are you necessarily right and am I neces- sarily wrong? If I have beaten you instead of your beating me, then am I necessarily right and are you necessarily wrong? Is one of us right and the other wrong? Are both of us right or are both of us wrong? If you and I don't know the answer, then other people are bound to be even more in the dark. Whom shall we get to decide what is right? Shall we get someone who agrees with you to decide? But if he already agrees with you, how can he decide fairly? Shall we get someone who agrees with me? But if he already agrees with me, how can he decide? Shall we get someone who disagrees with both of us? But if he already disagrees with both of us, how can he decide? Obviously, then, neither you nor I nor anyone else can decide for each other. Shall we wait for still another person?

"But waiting for one shifting voice [to pass judgment on] another is the same as waiting for none of them. Harmonize them all with the Heavenly Equality, leave them to their endless changes, and so live out your years. What do I mean by harmonizing them with the Heavenly Equality? Right is not right; so is not so. If right were really right, it would differ so clearly from not right that there would be no need for argument. If so were really so, it would differ so clearly from not so that there would be no need for argument. Forget the years; forget distinctions. Leap into the boundless and make it your home!"

Penumbra said to Shadow, "A little while ago you were walking and now you're standing still; a little while ago you were sitting and now you're standing up. Why this lack of independent action?"

Shadow said, "Do I have to wait for something before I can be like this?

---

6. She was taken captive by Duke Hsien of Chin in 671 B.C., and later became his consort [Translator's note].

Does what I wait for also have to wait for something before it can be like this? Am I waiting for the scales of a snake or the wings of a cicada? How do I know why it is so? How do I know why it isn't so?"

Once Chuang Chou dreamt he was a butterfly, a butterfly flitting and fluttering around, happy with himself and doing as he pleased. He didn't know he was Chuang Chou. Suddenly he woke up and there he was, solid and unmistakable Chuang Chou. But he didn't know if he was Chuang Chou who had dreamt he was a butterfly, or a butterfly dreaming he was Chuang Chou. Between Chuang Chou and a butterfly there must be *some* distinction! This is called the Transformation of Things.

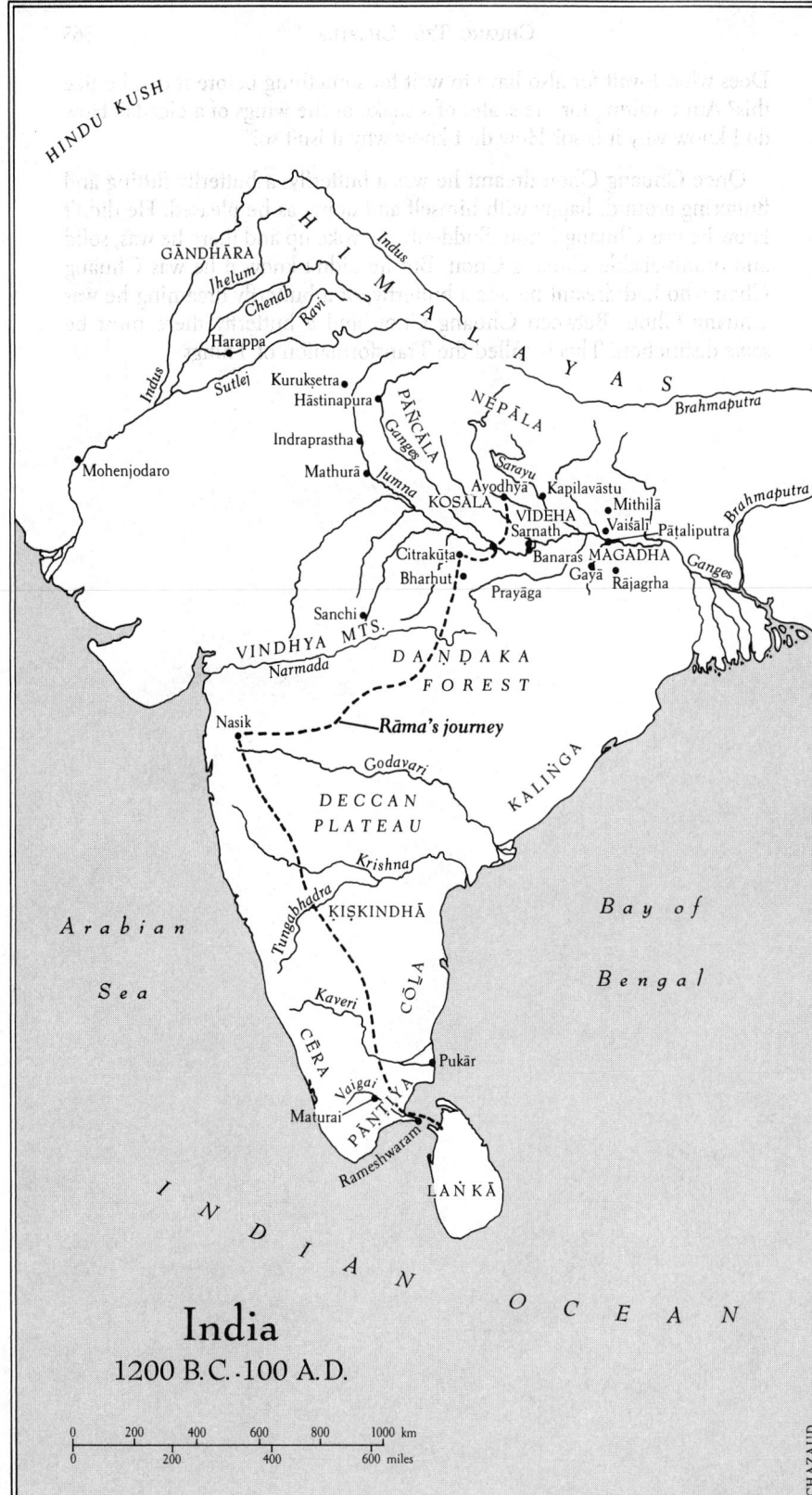

India

1200 B.C.-100 A.D.

India's Heroic Age

Modern India, with a population of eight hundred million, has remained remarkably in touch with its ancient roots in the face of centuries of change. The dominant pattern of Indian cultural history is a many-layered pluralism in which numerous subcultures defined by ethnic, religious, and linguistic differences coexist and relate with each other in complex yet coherent ways. This pluralism pervades and colors the vast body of oral and written literature that India has produced over thirty-five hundred years, in more than twenty languages and innumerable local dialects.

The Aryans, a group of nomadic tribes who apparently originated in central Asia and entered India around 1500 B.C., brought with them an early form of Sanskrit, a language that, along with nearly all the major languages of Europe and many in Asia, belongs to the Indo-European family. In India, Sanskrit became the principal language of classical literature, administration, and all forms of intellectual endeavor, maintaining this role almost up to the nineteenth century. Sanskrit's primary cultural association is with Hinduism, India's dominant religious tradition, a direct descendant of the Vedic religion of the Aryans. Gautama Buddha (563–483 B.C.) and Mahāvīra (died 468 B.C.), noblemen of Aryan clans who founded the Buddhist and Jain religious paths as radical alternatives to the Vedic religion, preached their messages in Pali and Prakrit, popular dialects related to Sanskrit. Hindi and the other modern languages of north India descended from the various Prakrit dialects. Sanskrit and its related languages and dialects are known as the Indo-Aryan languages.

Classical Tamil, the language of the ancient literature (first through third centuries A.D.) of south India, is the oldest example of Dravidian, a family of languages to which all the modern languages in south India belong. In later times, the literatures and cultures of both north and south India developed through continuous and fruitful interchange. From the twelfth century onward, various conquering Muslim dynasties—the Mughals (or Moguls) were the latest of these—brought to Indian literature and civilization not only the sensibility of Islam but also the heritage of the Arabic and Persian languages and literatures. Beginning in the seventeenth century, the activities of the British East India Company laid the foundation for British colonial rule and led to the establishment of Western-style education. Though British rule lasted only until India's independence in 1947, the English language and Western ideas have become a permanent piece of India's cultural mosaic.

THE LEGACY OF THE *VEDAS* AND *UPANIṢADS*

As in China, Egypt, and the Near East, civilization in India appears to have begun in a river valley. Of the Indus Valley civilization that flourished in great cities such as Mohenjo Daro and Harappa (ca. 3000–1500 B.C.) in northwestern India (now largely in Pakistan) we have only archaeological remains, which include writing in a script that has not yet been deciphered. Thus it is with the Aryans that the continuous history of Indian civilization and religion begins together with the history of Indian literature. Cattle breeders who eventually developed an agricul-

ture, the Aryans settled in the Indus Valley and left as their legacy the *Vedas*, four books of sacred hymns that accompanied the worship of gods who were personifications of nature and the powers of the cosmos. The following verses—from a hymn in the *Rig Veda* to Sūrya, the sun god—epitomize the spirit and imagery of Vedic myth and poetry:

> His brilliant banners draw upwards the god who knows all
> creatures, so that everyone may see the sun.
> The constellations, along with the nights, steal away like
> thieves, making way for the sun who gazes on everyone . . .
> He is the eye with which, O Purifying Varuna [god of law], you
> look upon the busy one among men.
> You cross heaven and the vast realm of space, O sun, measuring
> days by nights, looking upon the generations.
> Seven bay mares carry you in the chariot, O sun god with hair of
> flame, gazing from afar.
> We have come up out of darkness, seeing the higher light
> around us, going to the sun, the god among the gods, the highest
> light.*

Preserved in what appears to be an unbroken oral tradition of memorization and recitation, the *Vedas* are Hinduism's primary scripture. For thousands of years priests have chanted Vedic hymns at the major sacramental rites of naming, initiation, marriage, and death; and Hindu rituals are modeled on the Vedic fire sacrifice. Hindus regard the hymns as divine revelation: poet-seers called *ṛṣi* "saw" the verses in their mind's eye and spontaneously recited them in the form of sacred utterance (*mantra*). Tracing their ancestry to the ancient *ṛṣi*, the brahmans, priestly transmitters of the Vedic hymns and rites, have traditionally commanded the highest status in the Hindu class hierarchy.

The last hymns of the *Rig Veda* (ca. 1000 B.C.), reflect a change in the Aryan worldview. The concluding verses of the creation hymn called *Nāsadīya* (The hymn of nonexistence) capture the skeptical spirit that signaled the end of the Vedic age and the beginning of an age of spiritual quest and philosophical speculation:

> Who really knows? Who will here proclaim it? Whence was it
> produced? Whence is this creation? The gods came afterwards,
> with the creation of this universe. Who then knows whence it
> has arisen?
> Whence this creation has arisen—perhaps it formed itself, or
> perhaps it did not—the one who looks down on it, in the
> highest heaven, only he knows—or perhaps he does not know.*

The *Vedas* were followed by the *Upaniṣads* (Mystic doctrines), a genre of philosophical texts containing the mystical and philosophical speculations of thinkers who rejected the ritualistic religion of the *Vedas* in favor of a quest for ultimate wisdom. The prose dialogues of the oldest of these works, the *Bṛhadāraṇyaka Upaniṣad* (The great mystic doctrine of the forest) and *Chāndogya Upaniṣad* (The mystic doctrine of the *Sāma Veda*), written around 900 to 800 B.C., take place between eager pupils—men and women from diverse social classes—and wise teachers, among whom are warriors and artisans as well as brahmans and hermits. The sages of the early *Upaniṣads* teach that a single divine essence (Brahman, different from brahman, the priestly class) pervades the universe, that the human

---

*Translated by Wendy Doniger O'Flaherty.

soul is a manifestation of this divine essence, and that spiritual emancipation consists in mystically knowing the essential unity between self and universe. The teachings of the sages did not in effect undermine the authority of the *Vedas*, nor did they result in significant social upheaval. On the other hand, the concepts of the personal spiritual quest, the wise teacher (*guru*), and the transforming power of knowledge remain enduring motifs in Indian civilization.

THOUGHT AND LITERATURE OF THE HEROIC AGE

The literature of India's heroic age, produced between 550 B.C. and A.D. 100, reflects the spread of Aryan civilization over much of north India. It records the development of the Buddhist and Hindu religions from the Vedic civilization and provides a window into the non-Aryan civilization of the Tamil-speaking peoples of south India. The Sanskrit poems *Rāmāyaṇa* (ca. 550 B.C.) and *Mahābhārata* (the main portions of which date back in their present form at least to the fourth century B.C.) are India's earliest epics and express seminal Hindu values in the making.

Composed and edited over a period of nine hundred years (roughly 550 B.C.–A.D. 400), the epics are heroic narratives of an earlier time, originally recited by bards on the battlefield and at royal rituals, preserved in a fluid oral tradition, and finally reworked (like much of the Old Testament of the Bible) by priestly elites. Although the poems contain much mythic and legendary material and each is attributed to a legendary author who, like the Vedic poets, is called a seer (*ṛṣi*), there is reason to believe that they are grounded in actual events that took place between the ninth and seventh centuries B.C., when carriers of the Vedic culture spread eastward in north India. The *Mahābhārata*, attributed to Vyāsa, tells the story of a great civil war among Aryan clans, while the *Rāmāyaṇa* of Vālmīki narrates the exile and adventures of prince Rāma of Kosala. Together the two epics present a poetic history of the north Indian royal houses and the foundations of Aryan rule in the valley of the river Ganges. Hence their traditional Indian classification as *itihāsa* ("historical narrative," literally "thus it was").

Despite similarities with the *Iliad* and *Odyssey* (which suggest a kinship that might well go back to common Indo-European roots), the flavor of the *Rāmāyaṇa* and *Mahābhārata* is unmistakably Indian, and Hindus have valued the epics above all as sacred narratives that embody religious and ethical teachings. Included among the Hindu scriptures (in a class of texts known as "tradition"), the two epics have served, and continue to serve, as living cultural forces with deep personal meaning for Hindus from all walks of life. The Sanskrit versions of Vālmīki and Vyāsa have given rise to innumerable subsequent retellings in the major Indian languages, while the epic narratives have provided the themes for much of Indian art and literature over the last two thousand years. And their universal dimensions have allowed the Indianized cultures of Southeast Asia—Java, Thailand, and Malaysia, for instance—to "translate" them into their own cultural idioms and so to embrace them as beloved epics of their own.

Not only Hindus but most Indians grow up hearing the *Rāmāyaṇa* and *Mahābhārata*, as told by members of the family or professional storytellers, and seeing them enacted in diverse forms of theater and dance. And it is here that young Hindus first encounter *dharma*, held to be the guiding principle of proper human conduct, and the doctrine of *karma*. In traditional Hindu thought *dharma* (literally, "that which holds") is the force that supports the universe, that is, "holds" it together. It is the underlying principle of the social, moral, and cosmic orders, which are described and classified in hierarchically ordered, interlinked sets of four categories. There are four cyclic ages of the cosmos (*yuga*). There are four "classes" (*varna*) in society: the learned or priestly brahman, the kṣatriya (warrior

and administrator), the *vaiśya* (merchant, farmer, or other member of the productive community), and the *śūdra* (laborer). Likewise, there are four stages of life: celibate student, householder, forest dweller, and wandering ascetic. Although the progression of *yugas* from one to four records a process of decay (somewhat analogous to the decline from golden to iron ages in traditional Western thought) and the four classes are organized from high to low, the stages of life reverse the progression, moving from lower to higher on the spiritual plane.

The dynamic center of all these schemes is the scheme of the four spheres, or goals, that should, ideally, govern life. This set of categories begins with *dharma* (here used in a second, somewhat narrower, sense to mean the sphere of sacred duty, righteousness, and moral law); followed by *artha*, the sphere of worldly profit, wealth, and political power; *kāma*, the sphere of pleasure and love; and *mokṣa*, the ultimate goal of life, the sphere in which one seeks liberation from the constraints of worldly existence. The traditional system as a whole excludes women and *śūdras*, the lowest of the four social classes, from the ultimate goal of religion. All men, including *śūdras*, are bound by a prescribed program of sacred duty (*dharma*) that is appropriate to their class (*varṇa*), but only men of the three upper classes, known as the "twice-born" classes (initiation into the rites and texts of the Veda is considered to be a second birth), may work their way through the stages of life toward *mokṣa*. Women form a class in themselves, for a woman's *dharma* is defined as that of a wife, allowing women no identities or aspirations apart from their allegience to their husbands.

The four classes are concerned only with determining one's place in the cosmic scheme of things. The Hindu man's actual status is determined by his being born into one of the innumerable castes (*jāti*, literally, "birth"), which, defined by occupation, kinship, marriage practices, and other factors, make up a minutely stratified society with rigid divisions among groups and individuals. Although the epics and later Hindu texts reflect a constantly shifting balance of power among the brahman, warrior, and merchant classes, the religious basis of the caste system guarantees the subordination of a large number of "service" castes to a small number of elite groups. Furthermore, the idea of sacred duty combines with the doctrine of *karma* to form a powerful rationale for the perpetuation of social hierarchy.

Karma is the premise on which all three ancient religions of India build their doctrines of the ultimate goal of religion. According to the theory of *karma*, all creatures are ultimately responsible for their own existential conditions, and existence is invariably bound up with suffering. To exist is to be perpetually engaged in action (the basic meaning of the word *karma* is "a deed, that which is done"). All deeds, good and bad, have inevitable results, which must be borne by the doer in an existential state, so that the soul is trapped in an endless cycle of birth and death (known as *samsara*, "going round and round").

The earliest descriptions of the theory of *karma*, implying the entire sequence described above, are found in the *Upaniṣads*, whose authors were engaged in contemplating ways to transcend the limitations of the human condition. The thinkers of the *Upaniṣads* put forward the theory that the soul or self is a pure and immutable entity, untouched by *karma*, and that liberation from the cycle of rebirth can be achieved by identifying oneself with this pure self. Gautama Buddha rejected the concept of an immortal soul, concentrating instead on the suffering that was thought to result from *karma* and on the urgent need of all creatures to be freed from this burden of suffering. In the form of animal fables and popular tales, the *Jātaka* stories illustrate the Buddha's teaching regarding the path to liberation from rebirth, a unique combination of radical detachment from desire, the root cause of *karma*, and an ethic of action directed only toward the welfare of one's fellow creatures. Every person, regardless of caste, gender, or social status, could follow

the Buddha's path (the *Dharma*) with the ultimate aim of becoming liberated from *karma* rebirth by becoming a *buddha*, or "an enlightened one."

Buddhism arose from social and political contexts that were very different from those of the Hindu epics. Gautama Buddha was a prince of the Śākyas, an Aryan republican tribe on the Nepal border in the Himalayas. It was among the many tribal oligarchies and republics that flourished in northeastern India in the sixth century that he found his largest following, constituted especially of merchants, artisans, women, and others to whom the ritual religion and social hierarchies of early Hinduism had little to offer. Buddhist literature vividly reflects the cosmopolitan atmosphere and urban, mercantile civilization of the Mauryan empire (322–186 B.C.), India's first major empire, established by kings of an eastern Indian dynasty who, in the wake of Alexander of Macedon's invasion (326 B.C.), conquered most of India. A Buddhist canonical text records the conversion of Menander, a Greek king of northwestern India; and under the enthusiastic patronage of Aśoka (269–232 B.C.)—the greatest of the Mauryan emperors—Buddhism spread as far south as the island of Sri Lanka and traveled, along with textiles and spices, to lands to the north and west of India.

The populist, egalitarian religions preached by Gautama Buddha and his near-contemporary Mahāvīra presented a formidable challenge to the elaborate socio-religious system engineered by the Hindu elites. The god Kṛṣṇa's teachings to the hero Arjuna in the *Bhagavad-Gītā* represent, among other things, a synthesis of the attempts of Hindu thinkers to come to grips with the need of all Hindus, men and women alike, for a nonhierarchical and more personal path to the distant goal of liberation from *karma* rebirth. The eventual triumph of the Hindu religion in India is based, however, not on the greater appeal of its philosophical tenets over those of the rival religions but on its ability to synthesize and absorb features from those very rivals and, above all, on its molding of the cults of charismatic popular gods such as Kṛṣṇa (or Krishna) into a religion of salvation and grace, which attracted even the Greco-Bactrians, Sakas, and others who ruled in north India from the dissolution of the Mauryan Empire to the fourth century A.D.

For Hindus the terror of rebirth is mitigated by belief in a triad of great gods who are the highest manifestations of the divine principle underlying the universe. Brahmā, Viṣṇu, and Śiva respectively create, preserve, and destroy the universe and all creatures through the *yuga* cycles of cosmic time. Although there are many gods, Viṣṇu, the preserver, and Śiva, the destroyer, stand out as supreme deities, for Hindus worship one or the other as God, whose grace will help deliver them from the bonds of *karma* rebirth. Kṛṣṇa, the teacher of the *Bhagavad-Gītā*, is an incarnation of Viṣṇu, and his revelation of his divine identity to his devotee Arjuna constitutes the supreme mystery of this mystical text. For the heroes of the epics the belief in God and gods offers an alternative to the mechanistic view of *karma* and suffering. In explaining actions and events, they refer as often to the deeds of the gods and to fate (by which they mean the collective will of the gods as opposed to the will of the individual) as to *karma*.

Although ancient Tamil poems reveal an intimate knowledge of Aryan civilization and religion, everything about them—from the society they portray to the metaphors they employ—is permeated with a Tamil warrior ethos that is completely different from the values embodied in the texts in the north Indian languages. These poems, which give supreme value to love and war and to the lives of men and women in this world, perhaps come closest to Western ideals of the literature of a "heroic age." For most Hindus, however, Rāma and Arjuna are heroes precisely because they are able to temper the inherent violence of the warrior's way of life with compassion and ascetic self-control, thereby lifting their acts to a higher moral plane. In the Buddhist tradition, Gautama Buddha is a

superhuman hero-king, one who was destined to become a "world conqueror" (*cakravartin*) with his teaching of spiritual perfection, and a little more than two hundred years after the Buddha's death, Emperor Aśoka affirmed the power of this heroic ideal by laying down his weapons and proclaiming, by public edicts carved on rock, his preference for the "conquest of righteousness" to conquest by the sword.

FURTHER READING

Arthur Llewellyn Basham, *The Wonder That Was India* (1954), is the best general introduction to Indian civilization up to 1565. William Theodore De Bary, ed., *Sources of Indian Tradition* (1958), is a comprehensive volume of the textual sources of Indian thought from the beginnings to the present, with concise, accessible introductory notes. Thomas J. Hopkin, *The Hindu Religious Tradition* (1971), and R. C. Zaehner, *Hinduism* (1900), are more detailed introductions to Hinduism, while similar treatments of Buddhism may be found in Edward Conze, *Buddhism: Its Essence and Development* (1900), and Richard Robinson and Willard Johnson, *The Buddhist Religion* (1900). Edward C. Dimock et al., eds., *The Literatures of India: An Introduction* (1974), is an excellent introduction to Indian literature. For Indian mythology and the Hindu gods, consult Veronica Ions, *Indian Mythology* (1967), as well as A. K. Coomaraswamy and Sister Nivedita, *Myths of the Hindus and Buddhists* (1967).

PRONOUNCING GLOSSARY

The following list uses common English syllables and stress accents to provide rough equivalents of selected words whose pronunciation may be unfamiliar to the general reader.

Arjuna: *uhr'-joo-nuh*

artha: *uhr'-tuh*

Aśoka: *uh-shoh'-kuh*

Bhagavad-Gītā: *buh'-guh-vuhd–gee'-tah*

Bṛhadāraṇyaka Upaniṣad: *bree-huhd-ah'-ruhn-yuh-kuh oo-puh'-nee-shuhd*

cakravartin: *chuh'-kruh-vuhr-ten*

kāma: *kah'-muh*

Kṛṣṇa: *krish'-nuh*

kṣatriya: *kshuh-tree-yuh*

Mahābhārata: *muh-hah-bah'-ruh-tah*

mokṣa: *mohk'-shuh*

Rāmāyana: *rah-mah'-yuh-nuh*

ṛṣi: *ri'-shee*

Śākya: *shahk'-yuh*

saṃsāra: *suhm-sah'-ruh*

Śiva: *shee'-vuh*

śūdra: *shoo'-druh*

Sūrya: *soor'-yuh*

Upaniṣad: *oo-puhn'-ee-shuhd*

vaiśya: *vai'-shyuh*

Viṣṇu: *vish'-noo*

Vyāsa: *vee-yah'-suh*

yuga: *yoo'-guh*

TEXTS	CONTEXTS
	ca. 3000–1500 **B.C.** Indus Valley civilization flourishes in urban centers • Writing in use
ca. 1500–1200 **B.C.** Composition of the *Rig Veda*, oldest of the four Vedas, texts of hymns and chants in an archaic form of the Sanskrit language, for the fire sacrifice of the Aryan Vedic religion	ca. 1500 Aryan tribes speaking Sanskrit, an Indo-European language, enter India via the northwest and settle in the Indus Valley
ca. 900 The Sanskrit *Upaniṣads*, dialogues and meditations of philosophers on the nature of existence, the soul, and the universe	
ca. 700 Homer's *Iliad* and *Odyssey*	ca. 700 Emergence of kingdoms and republics in northern India
	563–483 Gautama Buddha, founder of Buddhism, preaches in Pāli, a dialect related to Sanskrit. He establishes an order of monks and nuns and spreads his new religion in the Ganges River Valley in north India • Mahāvīra, Buddha's contemporary, founds Jainism, a religion emphasizing nonviolence and asceticism
ca. 550 Vālmīki's Sanskrit poem *The Rāmāyaṇa*, a heroic epic recounting the deeds of the north Indian prince Rāma	
480–400 Aeschylus, Sophocles, and Euripides	
ca. 400 **B.C.**–400 **A.D.** The Sanskrit epic *The Mahābhārata*, the narrative of a great war among north Indian clansmen, takes shape	
ca. 400 **B.C.** Pāṇini writes the *Aṣṭādhyāyī* (Eight chapters), the authoritative grammar of the Sanskrit language and a model for modern linguistic science	

TEXTS	CONTEXTS
4th century B.C. Early version of *The Jātaka*, a collection of stories about the Buddha in the spoken dialect known as Pali	**ca. 326** Alexander of Macedon invades India
	269–232 Aśoka Maurya, emperor of India, spreads Buddhism in Sri Lanka, patronizes Buddhist art, and issues royal edicts in praise of Buddhist ethics in Prakrit, spoken dialects related to Sanskrit
200–100 The Sanskrit text *Saddharma-puṇḍarīka* (The lotus of the good law), expounding the doctrines of Mahayana (later) Buddhism, is written	**ca. 200** Beginning of Buddhist cave sanctuaries and art at Ajanta in western India, and of the Hindu Bhagavata cult of devotion to a personal God
100 B.C.–A.D. 250 Under the patronage of South Indian kings, anthologies of lyric poems of love and war are produced in Tamil, a language unrelated to Sanskrit and the north Indian languages	
1st century B.C. *The Bhagavad-Gītā,* the mystical teaching of the god Krishna to the hero Arjuna, is added to *The Mahābhārata*	**ca. 90** The Śakas, a Scythian tribe from Bactria (to the northwest of modern Afghanistan), invade India
	50 B.C.–A.D. 250 The Sātavāhana kings of central India patronize lyric poetry and narrative literature in Prakrit dialects
ca. A.D. 100 Aśvaghoṣa writes *Buddhacarita* (Acts of the Buddha), a Sanskrit epic poem in the courtly style, on the life of the Buddha • The early Buddhist canonical texts in the Pali language, including the *Jātaka* stories, are written down in Sri Lanka	**1st–2nd centuries** Buddhism spreads to China
100–200 The *Dharma Śāstra* of Manu (The laws of Manu), the authoritative treatise on laws and codes of conduct according to the Hindu religion, is completed	

THE RĀMĀYAṆA OF VĀLMĪKI

ca. 550 B.C.

The Sanskrit epic poem *Rāmāyaṇa* (The way of Rāma) by Vālmīki is the oldest literary version of the tale of the exile and adventures of Prince Rāma, a story that was known to Indian folk traditions as early as the seventh century B.C. Because ancient tradition the world over placed little value on the identity of authors or artists, all we know about Vālmīki is gleaned from legends about the circumstances that led him to compose the *Rāmāyaṇa*, a work of twenty-four thousand verses, divided into seven "books," called *kāṇḍa*. It is probable that like Homer he gathered and shaped the scattered material of many oral traditions into the poetic whole that we read today.

Vālmīki's *Rāmāyaṇa* became the source for a multitude of versions composed in all the major Indian languages over several centuries. The story has also been preserved in oral traditions by storytellers and continues to be enacted in countless regional folk theaters in India. It would be no exaggeration to say that the Rāma story is *the* great story of Indian civilization, the one narrative that all Indians have known and loved through the ages and whose popularity remains undiminished to this day.

In the Indian tradition Vālmīki is celebrated as the "first poet," and his *Rāmāyaṇa* as the "original poem." The poem itself begins with the tale of the sage Vālmīki's invention of metrical verse. Responding to Vālmīki's question about who in the world is a perfect man, the sage Nārada outlines the story of the hero Rāma, whose wife was abducted by a demon king. Brooding on the sad tale, Vālmīki goes for a walk along the banks of the Tamasā River, where he sees a pair of mating herons. Suddenly, a hunter shoots the male bird, and the female cries in anguish as she sees her mate's body writhing on the ground. Moved to intense compassion by her grief, Vālmīki utters inspired words in lyric verse, in the form of a couplet. Thus was born, Vālmīki tells us, the *śloka*, the meter of the epics and of many other works in Sanskrit. The legend reflects the classical Indian ideal of the poet as one who transforms the raw emotion and chaos of real life into an ordered work of art. In point of fact, Vālmīki's style is only a crude forerunner of the later *kāvya* style of classical Sanskrit poetry, which abounds in complex meters, figures of speech, and descriptions. On the other hand, the epic retains many of the formulaic devices of oral poetry that we have already met in Homer, such as ready-made epithets that can slip easily into convenient slots in the metrical line, for instance, the formula "Rāma, champion of righteousness," which in Sanskrit occupies exactly one quarter of the *śloka* verse.

The *Rāmāyaṇa* blends historical saga, nature myth, morality tale, and religious mythology. Rāma is associated with the line of Ikṣvāku kings who ruled the kingdom of Kosala in the Ganges Valley of north India from their capital in Ayodhyā in the sixth and fifth centuries B.C. Legends surrounding the Ikṣvāku royal house and the adventures of Rāma form the core of the epic, Books 2 to 6. Books 1, *Bāla* (Childhood), and 7, *Uttara* (The last book), generally agreed to be additions to the original Vālmīki text, form a frame for the central narrative, introducing and completing the story of Rāma as a divine incarnation, or *avatāra*.

In the core story, Rāvana, a powerful king of the *rakṣasas*—evil demons who continually threaten social and moral order, or *dharma*, in the world—has obtained a boon (gift) of invulnerability to gods and other superhuman beings who combat him. The gods persuade Viṣṇu, the great god whose function it is to pre-

serve *dharma* in the universe, to incarnate himself as a man to destroy Rāvaṇa. Viṣṇu is thus born as Rāma, the son of Daśaratha, king of Kosala, and his senior queen Kausalyā. Sons born at the same time to Daśaratha's two younger queens— Kaikeyī bore Bharata and Sumitrā bore the twins Lakṣmaṇa and Śatrughna—share in Viṣṇu's divine essence. All four princes are noble heroes, but Rāma is a paragon of princely virtues. As youths, Rāma and Lakṣmaṇa go to the forest retreat of the hermit Viśvāmitra to guard his sacrificial rites from hostile demons. They then travel to Mithilā, the capital of Videha in eastern India, where Rāma wins the princess Sītā by besting other suitors in a contest to bend a magical bow, a motif we have already seen in Homer's *Odyssey*. Sītā, whose name means "furrow," is in reality the daughter of goddess Earth, but she has been been brought up by King Janaka.

Book 2, *Ayodhyā*, of which a substantial portion is printed here, centers on Prince Rāma's disinheritance. When King Daśaratha proclaims Rāma as his heir-apparent, the whole capital city of Ayodhyā rejoices. Queen Kaikeyī, her jealousy roused by the counsel of a hunchback maidservant, decides to place her own son, Bharata, on the throne. She demands that Rāma be exiled to a life of hardship in the forest for fourteen years and that Bharata—who is absent from the court at this time—be made heir to the kingdom, reminding the king that, according to a promise he had made her in the past, he owes her two favors of her choice. Bound by his word, Daśaratha has no alternative but to comply. Rāma accepts his exile, and Sītā and Lakṣmaṇa voluntarily join him. When the three have departed, Ayodhyā is left desolate and the king dies of a broken heart. Upon his return, Bharata is horrified at the events that have taken place in his name. He chastises Kaikeyī and tries to hand over the kingdom to Rāma, but Rāma, wishing to honor his father's word, chooses to serve out his exile, and Bharata agrees to rule as regent until his return.

A very different atmosphere dominates Books 3 to 6—*Araṇya* (The forest), *Kiṣkindhā* (The kingdom of the monkeys), *Sundara* (The beautiful), and *Yuddha* (The war). Book 3 narrates the adventures of Rāma, Sītā, and Lakṣmaṇa in the wilderness of central and western India. In several episodes Rāma puts to rout the *rākṣasa* demons who infest the forest, and Rāvaṇa, their ten-headed king, vows revenge. Using a magic deer to lure Rāma and Lakṣmaṇa away from their forest home, he kidnaps Sītā in his flying chariot. Rāma and Lakṣmaṇa set out in search of Sītā. Their southward journey brings them to Kiṣkindhā, kingdom of the monkeys, and Rāma strikes up an alliance with the monkey chief Sugrīva. In return for Rāma's help in killing his powerful brother Vāli, who has unfairly seized his kingdom, Sugrīva sends out a horde of monkeys to locate Sītā.

In the south, the powerful ape Hanumān, whose father is the wind god, leaps the ocean in a single bound and searches for Rāma's wife in the *rākṣasas'* fabulous island kingdom of Laṅkā (identified with modern Sri Lanka). He finds Sītā to be a prisoner in Rāvaṇa's pleasure grove, still rejecting his suit (like Penelope in the *Odyssey*) and despairing of Rāma's ever coming to rescue her. Hanumān consoles her, wreaks havoc in Laṅkā, and returns to report to Rāma. The monkeys build a fabulous bridge and Rāma leads a monkey army to attack Rāvaṇa's rich city. The demons are routed, Rāma kills the *rākṣasa* king and liberates Sītā. After Sītā proves her chastity in an ordeal by fire, the hero returns with her and Lakṣmaṇa to Ayodhyā, where he is crowned.

Tragedy pervades Book 7, *Uttara* (The last book). Public scandal concerning Sītā's chastity during her captivity in Rāvaṇa's palace forces King Rāma to abandon her to a life in the forest. She takes refuge in the hermitage of the poet-sage Vālmīki on a bank of the Ganges River and there gives birth to Rāma's twin sons. From Vālmīki the twins, Lava and Kuśa, learn the saga of Rāma, which they later

sing in their father's court. On hearing the story, Rāma asks Sītā to come back to him, but Sītā declares that the purpose of her life has been fulfilled and cries out to her mother, the goddess Earth, who opens up to receive her. Rāma continues his rule until it is time for him to end his incarnation as a mortal.

As noted in "Thought and Literature of the Heroic Age" (p. 569), the *Rāmāyaṇa* and its later adaptations have been enjoyed by Indian audiences in forms as vastly different as religious plays, bedtime stories, and most recently, a comic book version and a television serial. Every year, all over India, millions of readers, listeners, and viewers weep at Rāma's exile and the death of Daśaratha, cheer as the monkey Hanumān leaps the sea to Laṅkā, share in Sītā's anguish as she climbs the pyre for her trial by fire, and rejoice at the death of Rāvaṇa. For them, the poem's mythic, political, and social dimensions are of a piece, and the deeds of a warrior-prince of ancient Kosala seem as relevant today as in India's heroic age. The story's enduring appeal for Indians, especially as Vālmīki presents it, lies in the affinities they continue to feel with its moral and psychological world.

Character and situation particularly occupy the book *Ayodhyā*, perhaps the most dramatic of the epic's books. Rāma's character remains the focal point throughout, as he responds to the arguments of various members of his family at a time of personal crisis. At stake are issues of political importance, like succession to the throne, but also the complex relationships within a large patriarchal family. Through the drama of *Ayodhyā*, Rāma teaches the ways of right action according to *dharma*, or sacred duty, the principle on which the hierarchical relationships of the Indian family and society are based.

Faced with disinheritance, Rāma sees clearly that a son's highest duty is to honor his father's word, even if this means giving up the kingdom. His position does not go unchallenged. His mother protests against the exile, his brother is angered and recommends rising against the unjust king, the helpless Daśaratha himself begs Rāma to foil his wicked stepmother and take power. Rāma rejects all these arguments, considering them tainted by self-interest, whereas the actions of the ideal man and perfect king are governed by *dharma*, conceived to be the transcendent ethical basis of the entire social order. In accepting his exile, Rāma points out, he is not merely obeying his father's command but upholding the integrity of the king's word. The prince's deference to father and king is not simple filial subservience, or "duty" in any narrow sense, but an act honoring *dharma* and, therefore, of cosmic significance and requiring the highest moral courage. It is precisely Rāma's act of renunciation that makes him fit for kingship. On the other hand, where injustice unambiguously demands aggressive action, as when Sītā is abducted, he acts in the manner of the conventional warrior-king, though even here he is guided by his sense of a cosmic rather than merely personal responsibility.

For Indians Rāma's heroism lies in his attitude as well as in his acts. He gives up the kingdom with a generous spirit, cheerfully undertakes the exile imposed on him, treats with kindness and courtesy even those who would harm him, and faces adversity with stoic courage. A slayer of demons, he is equally able to subordinate all personal interest to the universally applicable value of *dharma*. In this he differs from the heroes of the Homeric epics and Greek tragedies, whose nobility centers in the passionate intensity with which they illuminate particular heroic virtues. Virgil's "virtuous Aeneas" perhaps comes closest to Vālmīki's Rāma in his dedication to founding Rome, a mandate for the sake of which he gives up his love for Dido; but Rāma embodies a unique blend of virtues, one not expressed even in the characters of the heroes of the *Mahābhārata*, the other great Indian epic. In the broader context of Indian civilization only Rāma's heroism combines the strong sense of duty and dedication to social responsibility demanded of the ideal

king and the ideal member of the structured Hindu social order with the ascetic qualities of such figures as the Buddha, who renounce the world to seek perfection on the spiritual plane. It was this combination of qualities that moved Mahatma Gandhi to admire Rāma as his personal hero and the image of the ideal man.

In Vālmīki the portraits of Rāma and Sītā as models of behavior for Indian men and women take on depth and color through contrast with other figures, who act in less-than-perfect ways. Rāma's brothers Bharata and Lakṣmaṇa are clearly idealized in their unswerving devotion to their elder brother; yet both are capable of rebelling at the unjust behavior of their elders. Daśaratha is portrayed as a venial old man, Rāvaṇa's intelligence is clouded by lust. If Rāma is both the ideal man and king, Sītā's role as the exemplar for women is focused solely on her conduct as a wife; not only does she voluntarily accompany her husband in exile but also obeys and honors him during the public trial that he makes her undergo. Measured against this paragon of wifely devotion both Kaikeyī and Rāma's mother, the benign Kausalyā, emerge as flawed women. If Kaikeyī's selfishness leads her to inflict great suffering on her husband, Kausalyā needs to be reminded by her son, Rāma, that it is her duty to stand by her husband in adversity.

Not perfect conduct alone but the capacity to suffer deeply endears Rāma and Sītā to traditional Indian audiences. Although he is an incarnation, throughout the epic Rāma is painfully aware of his own—and others'—suffering, and his awareness of the absolute, transcendent nature of *dharma* in no way prevents him from being compassionate to those who are less perfect than he. The hero's compassion, coupled with the solitude of his burden of duty and knowledge, renders him a lonely yet sympathetic figure. As the eternally self-sacrificing wife, Sītā, on the other hand, embodies the suffering of the Hindu Everywoman. These very qualities have been passionately criticized by some modern Indian readers, who see in the idealization of Rāma and Sītā the perpetuation of patriarchal and hierarchical values that go against the spirit of modern India's striving toward an egalitarian society.

But even critics of the epic's social implications acknowledge the emotional power of Vālmīki's treatment of the story of Rāma. Despite its stress on absolute standards of morality and despite the fairy tale–like quality of the hero's conflict with demons, the *Rāmāyaṇa* is sensitive to the complexity of human character. Although the moral standards of Ayodhyā are superior to those of the monkey kingdom and Rāvaṇa's kingdom, even these lesser realms are redeemed by inhabitants who perform acts of goodness, piety, and love. The hunchback Mantharā and the weak-willed Kaikeyī are able to generate evil in Ayodhyā itself, while in Laṅkā Rāvaṇa's wife Maṇḍodarī is as devoted to him as Sītā is to Rāma. The greatest appeal of the ape Hanumān, perhaps the most beloved and popular character in the *Rāmāyaṇa*, lies in his childlike innocence and his supreme devotion to Rāma, which moves him to risk his life for his lord. Rāvaṇa himself exhibits humanity in his love for his sister, brothers, and sons, while his two *rākṣasa* brothers follow contrasting codes, both virtuous; Kumbhakarṇa remains loyal to his elder brother Rāvaṇa to the end, while the pious Vibhīṣaṇa, measuring *dharma* by a more abstract standard than simple loyalty, abandons the evil Rāvaṇa for Rāma. Much as it is a poem about *dharma*, *Rāmāyaṇa* is also about human emotion and the redemptive power of love.

Noteworthy among the many popular retellings of the main story of Vālmīki's *Rāmāyaṇa* are A. K. Coomaraswamy and Sister Nivedita's version in *Myths of the Hindus and Buddhists* (1967), and C. Rajagopalachari's in *Rāmāyaṇa* (1951). Swami Venkatasananda, *The Concise Rāmāyaṇa* (1988), is an abridged prose translation. Hari Prasad Shastri's complete prose translation in three volumes (*The Rāmāyaṇa of Vālmīki*, 1957) will be superseded by a readable, liberally annotated

translation, with good introductory essays, by a number of scholars headed by Robert Goldman, *The Rāmāyaṇa of Vālmīki: An Epic of Ancient India* (1984), when all seven volumes are complete. (Four of the seven volumes have appeared so far.) Readers interested in the social background of Vālmīki's epic should refer to J. L. Brockington, *Righteous Rāma: The Evolution of an Epic* (1984). For later versions of the Rāma story in relation to Vālmīki, see Paula Richman, ed., *Many Rāmāyaṇas: The Diversity of a Narrative Tradition in South Asia* (1991).

PRONOUNCING GLOSSARY

The following list uses common English syllables and stress accents to provide rough equivalents of selected words whose pronunciation may be unfamiliar to the general reader.

Araṇya: *uh-ruhn'-yuh*

Aśvin: *uhsh'-veen*

avatāra: *uh-vuh-tah'-ruh*

Ayodhyā: *uh-yo'-dee-yah*

Bharata: *buh'-ruh-tuh*

Bṛhaspati: *bree-huhs'-puh-tee*

Daśaratha: *dah'-shuh-ruh'-tha*

Dhātṛ: *dah'-tree*

Hanumān: *huh-noo'-mahn*

Ikṣvāku: *iksh-vah'-koo*

Janaka: *jah'-nah-kah*

Kaikeyī: *kai'-kay-eeh*

Kausalyā: *kow'-suhl-yah*

Kekaya: *kay'-kuh-yuh*

Kiṣkindhā: *keesh-keen'-dah*

Kumbhakarṇa: *koom-buh-kuhr'-nuh*

kuśa: *koo'-shuh*

Lakṣmaṇa: *luhk'-shmuh-nuh*

Mahābhārata: *muh-hah-bah'-ruh-tuh*

Mandodarī: *muhn-doh'-duh-ree*

Mārīca Kāśyapa: *mah-ree'-chuh kah'-shyuh-puh*

Mithilā: *mee'-tee-lah*

Nahuṣa: *nuh'-hoo-shuh*

Puṣya: *poosh'-yuh*

rākṣasa: *rahk'-shuh-suh*

Rāma: *rah'-muh*

Rāmāyaṇa: *rah-mah'-yuh-nuh*

Śacī: *shuh'-see*

Śaibya: *shai'-bee-yuh*

Śakra: *shuh'-kruh*

Śatrughna: *shuh-troog'-nuh*

Śiva: *shee'-vah*

śrī: *shree*

Sugrīva: *soo-gree'-vuh*

Sumitrā: *soo-mee'-trah*

Sundara: *soon'-duh-ruh*

Suyajña: *soo-yuhg'-nuh*

Uttara: *oo'-tuh-ruh*

Vaiśravaṇa: *vai-shrah'-vuh-nuh*

Vālmīki: *vahl-mee'-kee*

Vibhīṣaṇa: *vee-bee'-shuh-nuh*

Videha: *vee-day'-huh*

Vidhātṛ: *vee-dah'-tree*

Viṣṇu: *veesh'-noo*

Vísvāmitra: *veesh-vah'-mee-truh*

Vṛtra: *vree'-truh*

Yuddha: *yood'-duh*

Yudhājit: *yoo-dah'-jeet*

The Rāmāyaṇa[1]

From *Book 2*

Rāma Exiled

SARGA[2] 1

Time passed and then one day King Daśaratha, the delight of the Raghus, spoke to Bharata, his son by Kaikeyī:[3]

"My mighty son, your mother's brother Yudhājit, the son of the king of Kekaya, has come and is waiting to take you back home with him."

When he had heard what Daśaratha told him, Kaikeyī's son Bharata prepared to depart with Śatrughna.[4]

Taking leave of his father, of tireless Rāma, and of his mothers, the hero, the best of men, went off with Śatrughna.

Delighted to have Bharata and Śatrughna with him, mighty Yudhājit returned to his native city, to the great satisfaction of his father.

There Bharata lived with his brother, enjoying the warm hospitality of his uncle Aśvapati, who showered him with all the affection one shows a son.

And yet, as the mighty brothers stayed on, their every desire satisfied, they often thought with longing of aged King Daśaratha.

The great king likewise often thought of his two absent sons, Bharata and Śatrughna, the equals of great Indra and Varuṇa.[5]

For he cherished every one of the four bulls among men, as if they were four arms extending from his body.[6]

But still, of all of them, it was mighty Rāma who brought his father the greatest joy. For he surpassed his brothers in virtue just as the self-existent Brahmā[7] surpasses all other beings.

In Bharata's absence Rāma and powerful Lakṣmaṇa showed reverence to their godlike father.

Following his father's orders, righteous Rāma did all that was required to please and benefit the people of the city.

He scrupulously did all that his mothers required of him and attended to his gurus' requirements with strict punctuality.

Thus Daśaratha was pleased with Rāma's conduct and character, as were the brahmans,[8] the merchants, and all who lived in the realm.

Rāma was always even-tempered and kind-spoken. Even if he were to be harshly addressed, he would not answer back.

He would be satisfied with a single act of kindness, whatever its motive, and would ignore a hundred injuries, so great was his self-control.

With good men—men advanced in years, virtue, and wisdom—he

---

1. Translated by Sheldon I. Pollock.   2. Chapter.   3. Princess of Kekaya and second queen of Daśaratha. Raghus are descendants of King Raghu, the eponymous ancestor of Daśaratha's clan.   4. Son of Daśaratha and Queen Sumitrā and twin of Lakṣmaṇa.   5. Great gods of the Hindu pantheon. From the epics onward Indra is the king of the celestial gods and serves as the model for human kings. He is the hero god of the *Rig Veda* (see p. 568).   6. Daśaratha is implicitly compared with the four-armed Viṣṇu, the preserver god in the Hindu triad, whose sacred power human kings are said to embody. *Bulls among men*: a standard metaphor for mighty warriors in ancient texts. The bull is admired for its virility and strength. Indra is compared with a bull.   7. The creator god of the Hindu triad; he is *self-existent* because, being the creator, he was not created by any other being.   8. The highest of the four classes in Hinduism.

would converse at every opportunity, even during breaks in his weapons practice.

He was of noble descent on both sides of his family, he was upright and cheerful, truthful, and honest. Aged brahmans had seen to his training, men who were wise in the ways of righteousness and statecraft.

And thus he understood the true nature of righteousness, statecraft, and personal pleasure.[9] He was retentive and insightful, knowledgeable and adept in the social proprieties.

He was learned in the sciences and skilled in the practice of them as well. He was an excellent judge of men and could tell when it was appropriate to show his favor or withhold it.

He knew the right means for collecting revenue and the accepted way of regulating expenditure. He had achieved preeminence in the sum total of the sciences, even the most complex.

Only after satisfying the claims of righteousness and statecraft would he give himself up to pleasure, and then never immoderately. He was a connoisseur of the fine arts and understood all aspects of political life.

He was proficient in training and riding horses and elephants, eminently knowledgeable in the science of weapons, and esteemed throughout the world as a master chariot fighter.

He could head a charge and give battle and lead an army skillfully. He was invincible in combat, even if the gods and asuras[1] themselves were to unite in anger against him.

He was never spiteful, haughty, or envious, and he had mastered his anger. He would never look down on any creature nor bow to the will of time.

By his eminent virtues the prince won the esteem of people throughout all the three worlds,[2] for he was patient as the earth, wise as Bṛhaspati, and mighty as Indra, Śacī's[3] lord.

Rāma's virtues were prized by all the people, a source of joy to his father, and lent the prince himself such splendor as the sun derives from its shining beams.

His conduct and invincible valor made him so like one of the gods who guard the world that Earth herself desired to have him as her master.

Now, as King Daśaratha, slayer of enemies, observed the many incomparable virtues of his son, he fell to thinking.

In his heart he cherished this single joyous thought: "When shall I see my dear son consecrated?

"His one desire is that the world should prosper, he shows compassion to all creatures and is loved in the world even more than I, like a cloud laden with rain.

"He is as mighty as Yama or Śakra,[4] wise as Bṛhaspati, steady as a mountain, and far richer in virtues than I.

---

9. A reference to *dharma* ("righteousness") and *artha* ("wealth and politics"), the first two of the set of four goals of life in the Hindu tradition.   1. Demonic beings with whom the gods share a common origin, yet engage with in eternal struggle.   2. That is, earth, air (or the underworld), and heaven, the three regions inhabited by humans; the heavens of the immortal gods are situated above these. 3. Indra's wife. Bṛhaspati is the wise *guru* (preceptor) of the gods.   4. Or Indra. Yama is the god of death and the worlds attained by souls after death.

"O that at my age I might go to heaven seeing my son holding sway over this entire land."

Recognizing that his son was endowed with these consummate virtues, the great king consulted with his advisers and chose him to be prince regent.

✼   ✼   ✼

SARGA 4

After the townsmen had gone the king held further consultation with his counsellors. When he learned what they had determined the lord declared with determination,

"Tomorrow is Puṣya,[5] so tomorrow my son Rāma, his eyes as coppery as lotuses,[6] shall be consecrated as prince regent."

Retiring then to his private chamber, King Daśaratha instructed the charioteer Sumantra to fetch Rāma again.

Upon receiving his orders the charioteer set out at once for Rāma's abode to fetch him.

The guards informed Rāma that Sumantra had returned, and as soon as he learned of his arrival he felt uneasy.

Rāma had him shown in at once. "Tell me the reason for your returning," he said, "and omit nothing."

The charioteer replied, "The king wishes to see you. Such is the message, but you of course must be the judge of your comings and goings."

Such were the charioteer's words, and, upon hearing them, Rāma hurried out and went to the palace to see the lord of men once more.

When word was brought that Rāma had arrived, King Daśaratha had him shown into his chamber, anxious to pass on the important news.

As majestic Rāghava entered the residence he caught sight of his father, and at a distance prostrated himself, cupping his hands in reverence.

He bowed low until the protector of the earth bade him rise and embraced him. Then, directing him to a splendid seat, the king once again addressed him:

"Rāma, I am old, my life has been long. I have enjoyed all the pleasures I desired. I have performed hundreds of sacrifices rich in food, with lavish priestly stipends.[7]

"The child I wanted—and you are he—was born to me, a son who has no peer on earth today, the very best of men. I have given alms, offered sacrifices, and studied the scriptures.

"I have experienced every pleasure, everything I wanted—and thus, my mighty son, I have discharged all my debts, to the gods, the seers, my ancestors, the brahmans, and to myself.

"There is nothing further required of me except your consecration. Therefore you must do for me what I am about to tell you.

---

5. A constellation consisting of three stars in Cancer, which is part of the zodiac. In India important events are still arranged according to the good or evil conjunction of planets and constellations. Belief in cosmic networks of *karma* undergirds the Indian view that planetary and stellar events influence human events.   6. In ancient India reddish eyes were considered to be a sign of health and beauty. 7. These acts contribute to the king's prestige.

"All the subjects today expressed their wish to have you for their king, and so, my dear son, I will consecrate you as prince regent.

"But there is more, Rāma: I have had dreams lately, inauspicious, ominous dreams. Great meteors and lightning bolts out of a clear sky have been falling nearby with a terrible crash.

"The astrologers also inform me, Rāma, that my birth star is obstructed by hostile planets, Aṅgāraka, Rāhu,[8] and the sun.

"When such portents as these appear it usually means a king is about to die or meet with some dreadful misfortune.

"You must therefore have yourself consecrated, Rāghava, before my resolve fails me. For the minds of men are changeable.

"Today the moon has reached Punarvasu,[9] just to the east of Puṣya; tomorrow, the astrologers predict, its conjunction with Puṣya is certain.

"On this very Puṣya day you must have yourself consecrated—I feel a sense of great urgency. Tomorrow, slayer of enemies, I will consecrate you as prince regent.

"Therefore today you and your wife must take a vow to remain chaste this night, to fast and sleep upon a bed of *darbha* grass.[1]

"Have your friends guard you warily today at every turn, for there are many impediments to affairs of this sort.

"I believe the best time for your consecration is precisely while Bharata is absent from the city.

"Granted your brother keeps to the ways of the good, defers to his elder brother, and is righteous, compassionate, and self-disciplined.

"Still, Rāghava, it is my firm belief that the mind of man is inconstant, even the mind of a good man constant in righteousness. Even such a man is best presented with an accomplished fact."

Once told his consecration was set for the next day, Rāma was given leave to go, and after doing obeisance to his father, he went home.

In keeping with the king's instructions regarding the consecration, he entered his house but then left immediately and went to his mother's apartment.

There in the shrine-room he saw her, clothed in linen, solemnly and silently praying for his royal fortune.

Sumitrā and Lakṣmaṇa had already come, and Sītā had been sent for as soon as they heard the news of Rāma's consecration.

At that moment Kausalyā stood with her eyes closed, while Sumitrā, Sītā, and Lakṣmaṇa were seated behind her.

From the moment she received word that her son was to be consecrated as prince regent on Puṣya day, she had been controlling her breathing and meditating on the Primal Being, Janārdana.[2]

While she was engaged in these observances Rāma approached her and did obeisance. Then to her delight he said:

"Mother, my father has appointed me to the task of protecting the people. On father's instructions my consecration will take place tomorrow.

---

8. In myth, the eclipse demon. *Aṅgāraka*: Mars.   9. A constellation consisting of two stars in Gemini, which is part of the zodiac.   1. Sacred grass used in Hindu rituals.   2. That is, Viṣṇu, the preserver god; although he is known as the *Primal Being*, he is different from Brahma, who performs the actual creation.

"And as Father, with his priests and preceptors, directs, Sītā and I both are to fast tonight.

"Please see that any auspicious rites appropriate for my consecration tomorrow are performed today on behalf of Vaidehī[3] and me."

Hearing him say what she had so long desired, Kausalyā spoke to Rāma in words muffled with sobs of joy:

"Rāma, my child, long may you live. May all who block your way be vanquished. And when you are invested with sovereignty may you bring joy to my kinsmen and Sumitrā's.

"Truly it was under a lucky star I bore you, my dear son, since by your virtues you have won the favor of your father, Daśaratha.

"Truly the vows of self-denial I made to the lotus-eyed Primal Being were not in vain, since the royal fortune of the Ikṣvākus will pass to you, my son."

So his mother spoke, and Rāma then turned to his brother. He smiled as he looked at him sitting diffidently nearby, hands cupped in reverence, and he said:

"Come, Lakṣmaṇa, rule this land with me. Sovereignty falls to your share, too, for you are my second self.

"You too shall enjoy every pleasure you desire, Saumitri, and all the fruits of kingship, for the kingship, and life itself, I covet only for your sake."

So Rāma spoke to Lakṣmaṇa, and then doing obeisance to his mothers and bidding Sītā to take leave of them, he returned home.

The end of the fourth *sarga* of the *Ayodhyākāṇḍa* of the *Śrī*[4] *Rāmāyaṇa*.

SARGA 6

When the family priest had gone Rāma bathed and then, restraining his desire, he worshiped Nārāyaṇa[5] in the company of his large-eyed wife.

With bowed head he held out the oblation vessel. Then, in accordance with the ritual precepts, he offered the clarified butter in a blazing fire[6] to the great divinity.

He consumed the remains of the oblation and earnestly made his wish. Meditating on the god Nārāyaṇa, maintaining silence and restraining his desire, the prince lay down to sleep with Vaidehī on a thick-spread bed of *kuśa* grass[7] in the majestic sanctuary of Viṣṇu.

With one watch of the night remaining, he awoke and saw to the decorating of the entire house.

This done and hearing the pleasant voices of the bards, genealogists, and panegyrists, he began to intone his prayers in deep concentration, performing the morning worship.

Dressed in spotless linen, his head bowed low, he glorified Viṣṇu, crusher of Madhu,[8] and had the brahmans pronounce their blessings.

The deep sweet sound of their benedictions was echoed by the sound of pipes and pervaded all Ayodhyā.

---

3. Princess of Videha, or Sītā.   4. Sacred. *Ayodhyākāṇḍa*: The book of Ayodhyā, which is the capital of Kosala.   5. Viṣṇu.   6. This act, accompanied by chants, constituted the basic ritual act in most Vedic rites.   7. Sacred grass.   8. A demon.

All the people who lived in Ayodhyā were elated to hear that Rāghava and Vaidehī had undertaken their fast.

All of the people of the town heard about Rāma's consecration, and so when they saw night brighten into dawn they began to adorn the city.

On sanctuaries that looked like mountain peaks wreathed in white clouds, at crossroads and thoroughfares, on shrines and watchtowers, on the shops of merchants rich in their many kinds of wares, on the majestic, rich dwellings of householders, on all the assembly halls, and on prominent trees colorful banners and pennants were run up high.

There were troupes of actors and dancers, there were minstrels singing and their voices could be heard everywhere, so pleasing to the ear and heart.

In public squares and private houses people spoke with one another in praise of Rāma, now that his consecration was at hand.

Even children playing in groups at their front doors talked together in praise of Rāma.

The townsmen beautified the royal highway, too, for Rāma's consecration, placing offerings of flowers there and perfuming it with fragrant incense.

And anticipating that night would fall, they set up lantern-trees for illumination everywhere along the thoroughfares.

Thus the residents decorated their city. Afterwards, eagerly waiting for Rāma's consecration as prince regent, they grouped together in public squares and in assembly halls. And there in conversation with each other they sang the praises of the lord of the people:

"Ah, what a great man our king is, the delight of the House of the Ikṣvākus, to recognize that he is old and to be ready to consecrate Rāma as king. * * *

SARGA 7

Now, Kaikeyī's family servant, who had lived with her from the time of her birth, had happened to ascend to the rooftop terrace that shone like the moon.

From the terrace Mantharā could see all Ayodhyā—the king's way newly sprinkled, the lotuses and waterlilies strewn about, the costly ornamental pennants and banners, the sprinkling of sandalwood water, and the crowds of freshly bathed people.

Seeing a nursemaid standing nearby, Mantharā asked, "Why is Rāma's mother so delighted and giving away money to people, when she has always been so miserly? Tell me, why are the people displaying such boundless delight? Has something happened to delight the lord of earth? What is he planning to do?"

Bursting with delight and out of sheer gladness the nursemaid told the hunchback Mantharā about the greater majesty in store for Rāghava:

"Tomorrow on Puṣya day King Daśaratha is going to consecrate Rāma Rāghava as prince regent, the blameless prince who has mastered his anger."

When she heard what the nursemaid said, the hunchback was furious and descended straightway from the terrace that was like the peak of Mount Kailāsa.

Consumed with rage, the malevolent Mantharā approached Kaikeyī as she lay upon her couch, and she said:

"Get up, you foolish woman! How can you lie there when danger is threatening you? Don't you realize that a flood of misery is about to overwhelm you?

"Your beautiful face has lost its charm. You boast of the power of your beauty, but it has proved to be as fleeting as a river's current in the hot season."

So she spoke, and Kaikeyī was deeply distraught at the bitter words of the angry, malevolent hunchback.

"Mantharā," she replied, "is something wrong? I can tell by the distress in your face how sorely troubled you are."

Hearing Kaikeyī's gentle words the wrathful Mantharā spoke—and a very clever speaker she was.

The hunchback grew even more distraught, and with Kaikeyī's best interests at heart, spoke out, trying to sharpen her distress and turn her against Rāghava:

"Something is very seriously wrong, my lady, something that threatens to ruin you. For King Daśaratha is going to consecrate Rāma as prince regent.

"I felt myself sinking down into unfathomable danger, stricken with grief and sorrow, burning as if on fire. And so I have come here, with your best interests at heart.

"When you are sorrowful, Kaikeyī, I am too, and even more, and, when you prosper, so do I. There is not the slightest doubt of this.

"You were born into a family of kings, you are a queen of the lord of earth. My lady, how can you fail to know that the ways of kings are ruthless?

"Your husband talks of righteousness, but he is deceiving you; his words are gentle but he is cruel. You are too innocent to understand, and so he has utterly defrauded you like this.

"When expedient, your husband reassures you, but it is all worthless. Now that there is something of real worth he is ready to bestow it upon Kausalyā.

"Having got Bharata out of the way by sending him off to your family, the wicked man shall tomorrow establish Rāma in unchallenged kingship.

"He is an enemy pretending to be your husband. He is like a viper, child, whom you have taken to your bosom and lovingly mothered.

"For what an enemy or a snake would do if one ignored them, King Daśaratha is now doing to you and your son.

"The man is evil, his assurances false, and, by establishing Rāma in the kingship, dear child who has always known comfort, he will bring ruin upon you and your family.

"Kaikeyī, the time has come to act, and you must act swiftly, for your own good. You must save your son, yourself, and me, my enchanting beauty."

After listening to Mantharā's speech, the lovely woman rose from the couch and presented the hunchback with a lovely piece of jewelry.

And, when she had given the hunchback the jewelry, Kaikeyī, most beautiful of women, said in delight to Mantharā,

"What you have reported to me is the most wonderful news. How else may I reward you, Mantharā, for reporting such good news to me?

"I draw no distinction between Rāma and Bharata, and so I am perfectly content that the king should consecrate Rāma as king.

"You could not possibly tell me better news than this, or speak more welcome words, my well-deserving woman. For what you have told me I will give you yet another boon, something you might like more—just choose it!"

The end of the seventh *sarga* of the *Ayodhyākāṇḍa* of the *Śrī Rāmāyaṇa*.

SARGA 8

But Mantharā was beside herself with rage and sorrow. She threw the jewelry away and said spitefully:

"You foolish woman, how can you be delighted at such a moment? Are you not aware that you stand in the midst of a sea of grief?

"It is Kausalyā who is fortunate; it is her son the eminent brahmans will consecrate as the powerful prince regent tomorrow, on Puṣya day.

"Once Kausalyā secures this great object of joy, she will cheerfully eliminate her enemies. And you will have to wait on her with hands cupped in reverence, like a serving woman.

"Delight is truly in store for Rāma's exalted women, and all that is in store for your daughters-in-law is misery, at Bharata's downfall."

Seeing how deeply distressed Mantharā was as she spoke, Queen Kaikeyī began to extol Rāma's virtues:

"Rāma knows what is right, his gurus have taught him self-restraint. He is grateful, truthful, and honest, and as the king's eldest son, he deserves to be prince regent.

"He will protect his brothers and his dependents like a father; and long may he live! How can you be upset, hunchback, at learning of Rāma's consecration?

"Surely Bharata as well, the bull among men, will obtain the kingship of his fathers and forefathers after Rāma's one hundred years.

"Why should you be upset, Mantharā, when we have prospered in the past, and prosper now, and shall have good fortune in the future? For he obeys me even more scrupulously than he does Kausalyā."

When she heard what Kaikeyī said, Mantharā was still more sorely troubled. She heaved a long and hot sigh and then replied:

"You are too simple-minded to see what is good for you and what is not. You are not aware that you are sinking in an ocean of sorrow fraught with disaster and grief.

"Rāghava will be king, Kaikeyī, and then the son of Rāghava, while Bharata will be debarred from the royal succession altogether.

"For not all the sons of a king stand in line for the kingship, my lovely. Were all of them to be so placed, grave misfortune would ensue.

"That is why kings place the powers of kingship in the hands of the eldest, faultless Kaikeyī, however worthy the others.

"Like a helpless boy that son of yours, the object of all your motherly love, will be totally excluded from the royal succession and from its pleasures as well.

"Here I am, come on your behalf, but you pay me no heed. Instead, you want to reward me in token of your rival's good luck!

"Surely once Rāma secures unchallenged kingship he will have Bharata sent off to some other country—if not to the other world!

"And you had to send Bharata, a mere boy, off to your brother's, though knowing full well that proximity breeds affection, even in insentient things.

"Now, Rāghava will protect Lakṣmaṇa, just as Saumitri will protect Rāma, for their brotherly love is as celebrated as that of the Aśvins.[9]

"And so Rāma will do no harm to Lakṣmaṇa, but he will to Bharata without question.

"So let your son go straight from Rājagṛha to the forest.[1] That is the course I favor, and it is very much in your own best interests.

"For in this way good fortune may still befall your side of the family—if, that is, Bharata secures, as by rights he should, the kingship of his forefathers.

"Your child has known only comfort, and, at the same time, he is Rāma's natural enemy. How could the one, with his fortunes lost, live under the sway of the other, whose fortunes are thriving?

"Like the leader of an elephant herd attacked by a lion in the forest, your son is about to be set upon by Rāma, and you must save him.

"Then, too, because of your beauty's power you used to spurn your co-wife, Rāma's mother, so proudly. How could she fail to repay that enmity?

"When Rāma secures control of the land, Bharata will be lost for certain. You must therefore devise some way of making your son the king and banishing his enemy this very day."

The end of the eighth *sarga* of the *Ayodhyākāṇḍa* of the Śrī Rāmāyaṇa.

SARGA 9

So Mantharā spoke, and Kaikeyī, her face glowing with rage, heaved a long and burning sigh and said to her:

"Today, at once, I will have Rāma banished to the forest, and at once have Bharata consecrated as prince regent.

"But now, Mantharā, think: In what way can Bharata, and not Rāma, secure the kingship?"

So Queen Kaikeyī spoke, and the malevolent Mantharā answered her, to the ruin of Rāma's fortunes:

"Well then, I shall tell you, Kaikeyī—and pay close attention—how your son Bharata may secure sovereign kingship."

9. Gods of the *Rig Veda*, known as the twin horsemen and famed for their beauty. Although Lakṣmaṇa's real twin is Śatrughna, he and Rāma are compared with the Aśvins because they are inseparable.
1. That is, to go into exile and the ascetic life of fasting, penance, and hardship. Rājagṛha is the capital of Kekaya, where Bharata is staying with his maternal uncle.

Hearing Manthara's words, Kaikeyī half rose from her sumptuous couch and exclaimed:

"Tell me the way, Mantharā! How can Bharata, and not Rāma, secure the kingship?"

So the queen spoke, and the malevolent hunchback answered her, to the ruin of Rāma's fortunes:

"When the gods and *asuras* were at war, your husband went with the royal seers to lend assistance to the king of the gods, and he took you along. He set off toward the south, Kaikeyī, to the Daṇḍakas and the city called Vaijayanta. It was there that Timidhvaja ruled, the same who is called Śambara,[2] a great *asura* of a hundred magic powers. He had given battle to Śakra, and the host of gods could not conquer him.

"In the great battle that followed, King Daśaratha was struck unconscious, and you, my lady, conveyed him out of battle. But there, too, your husband was wounded by weapons, and once again you saved him, my lovely. And so in his gratitude he granted you two boons.[3]

"Then, my lady, you said to your husband, 'I shall choose my two boons when I want them,' and the great king consented. I myself was unaware of this, my lady, until you yourself told me, long ago.

"You must now demand these two boons of your husband: the consecration of Bharata and the banishment of Rāma for fourteen years.

"Now go into your private chamber, daughter of Aśvapati, as if in a fit of rage. Put on a dirty garment, lie down on the bare ground, and don't speak to him, don't even look at him.

"Your husband has always adored you, I haven't any doubt of it. For your sake the great king would even go through fire.

"The king could not bring himself to anger you, nor even bear to look at you when you are angry. He would give up his own life to please you.

"The lord of the land is powerless to refuse your demand. Dull-witted girl, recognize the power of your beauty.

"King Daśaratha will offer gems, pearls, gold, a whole array of precious gifts—but pay no mind to them.

"Just keep reminding Daśaratha of those two boons he granted at the battle of the gods and *asuras*. Illustrious lady, you must not let this opportunity pass you by.

"When the great king Rāghava helps you up himself and offers you a boon, then you must ask him for this one, first making sure he swears to it: 'Banish Rāma to the forest for nine years and five, and make Bharata king of the land, the bull among kings.'

"In this way Rāma will be banished and cease to be 'the pleasing prince,' and your Bharata, his rival eliminated, will be king.

"And by the time Rāma returns from the forest, your steadfast son and his supporters will have struck deep roots and won over the populace.

"I think it high time you overcame your timidity. You must forcibly prevent the king from carrying out Rāma's consecration."

---

2. A demon, who is known from the *Rig Veda* onward as an enemy of Indra (Śakra). Rāma spends most of his exile in the Daṇḍaka forest.   3. Favors.

And so Mantharā induced her to accept such evil by disguising it as good, and Kaikeyī, now cheered and delighted, replied:

"Hunchback, I never recognized your excellence, nor how excellent your advice. Of all the hunchbacks in the land there is none better at devising plans.

"You are the only one who has always sought my advantage and had my interests at heart. I might never have known, hunchback, what the king intended to do.

"There are hunchbacks who are misshapen, crooked and hideously ugly—but not you, you are lovely, you are bent no more than a lotus in the breeze.

"Your chest is arched, raised as high as your shoulders, and down below your waist, with its lovely navel, seems as if it had grown thin in envy of it.

"Your girdle-belt beautifies your hips and sets them jingling. Your legs are set strong under you, while your feet are long.

"With your wide buttocks, Mantharā, and your garment of white linen, you are as resplendent as a wild goose when you go before me.

"And this huge hump of yours, wide as the hub of a chariot wheel— your clever ideas must be stored in it, your political wisdom and magic powers.

"And there, hunchback, is where I will drape you with a garland made of gold, once Bharata is consecrated and Rāghava has gone to the forest.

"When I have accomplished my purpose, my lovely, when I am satis- fied, I will anoint your hump with precious liquid gold.

"And for your face I will have them fashion an elaborate and beautiful forehead mark of gold and exquisite jewelry for you, hunchback.

"Dressed in a pair of lovely garments you shall go about like a goddess; with that face of yours that challenges the moon, peerless in visage; and you shall strut holding your head high before the people who hate me.

"You too shall have hunchbacks, adorned with every sort of ornament, to humbly serve you, hunchback, just as you always serve me."

Being flattered in this fashion, she replied to Kaikeyī, who still lay on her luxurious couch like a flame of fire on an altar:

"One does not build a dike, my precious, after the water is gone. Get up, apprise the king, and see to your own welfare!"

Thus incited, the large-eyed queen went with Mantharā to her private chamber, puffed up with the intoxicating power of her beauty.

There the lovely lady removed her pearl necklace, worth many hundred thousands, and her other costly and beautiful jewelry.

And then, under the spell of the hunchback Mantharā's words, the golden Kaikeyī got down upon the floor and said to her:

"Hunchback, go inform the king that I will surely die right here unless Bharata receives as his portion the land and Rāghava, as his, the forest."

And uttering these ruthless words, the lady put all her jewelry aside and lay down upon the ground bare of any spread, like a fallen *kimnara* woman.[4]

---

4. Demigoddess with the face of a horse and the body of a human.

Her face enveloped in the darkness of her swollen rage, her fine garlands and ornaments stripped off, the wife of the lord of men grew distraught and took on the appearance of a darkened sky, when all the stars
have set.

The end of the ninth *sarga* of the *Ayodhyākāṇḍa* of the *Śrī Rāmāyaṇa*.

SARGA 10

Now, when the great king had given orders for Rāghava's consecration,
he gladly entered the inner chamber to tell his beloved wife the good
news.

But when the lord of the world saw her fallen on the ground and lying
there in a posture so ill-befitting her, he was consumed with sorrow.

The guileless old man saw her on the floor, that guileful young wife of
his, who meant more to him than life itself.

He began to caress her affectionately, as a great bull elephant in the
wilderness might caress his cow wounded by the poisoned arrow of a
hunter lurking in the forest.

And, as he caressed his lotus-eyed wife with his hands, sick with worry
and desire, he said to her:

"I do not understand, my lady, why you should be angry. Has someone
offended you, or shown you disrespect, that you should lie here in the
dust, my precious, and cause me such sorrow? What reason have you to
lie upon the floor as if possessed by a spirit, driving me to distraction,
when you are so precious to me?

"I have skilled physicians, who have been gratified in every way. They
will make you well again. Tell me what hurts you, my lovely.

"Is there someone to whom you would have favor shown, or has someone aroused your disfavor? The one shall find favor at once, the other
incur my lasting disfavor.

"Is there some guilty man who should be freed, or some innocent man
I should execute? What poor man should I enrich, what rich man impoverish?

"I and my people, we all bow to your will. I could not bring myself to
thwart any wish of yours, not if it cost me my life. Tell me what your heart
desires, for all the earth belongs to me, as far as the wheel of my power
reaches."

So he spoke, and now encouraged she resolved to tell her hateful plan.
She then commenced to cause her husband still greater pain.

"No one has mistreated me, my lord, or shown me disrespect. But there
is one wish I have that I should like you to fulfill.

"You must first give me your promise that you are willing to do it. Then
I shall reveal what it is I desire."

So his beloved Kaikeyī spoke, and the mighty king, hopelessly under
the woman's power, said to her with some surprise:

"Do you not yet know, proud lady, that except for Rāma, tiger among
men, there is not a single person I love as much as you?

"Take hold of my heart, rip it out, and examine it closely, my lovely
Kaikeyī; then tell me if you do not find it true.

"Seeing that I have the power, you ought not to doubt me. I will do what will make you happy, I swear to you by all my acquired merit."

His words filled her with delight, and she made ready to reveal her dreadful wish, which was like a visitation of death:

"Let the three and thirty gods,[5] with Indra at their head, hear how you in due order swear an oath and grant me a boon.

"Let the sun and moon, the sky, the planets, night and day, the quarters of space, heaven and earth, let all the *gandharvas* and *rākṣasas*,[6] the spirits that stalk the night, the household gods in every house, and all the other spirits take heed of what you have said.

"This mighty king, who is true to his word and knows the ways of righteousness, in full awareness grants me a boon—let the deities give ear to this for me."

Thus the queen ensnared the great archer and called upon witnesses. She then addressed the king, who in his mad passion had granted her a boon.

"I will now claim the two boons you once granted me, my lord. Hear my words, your Majesty.

"Let my son Bharata be consecrated with the very rite of consecration you have prepared for Rāghava.

"Let Rāma withdraw to Daṇḍaka wilderness and for nine years and five live the life of an ascetic, wearing hides and barkcloth garments and matted hair.

"Let Bharata today become the uncontested prince regent, and let me see Rāghava depart this very day for the forest."

When the great king heard Kaikeyī's ruthless demands, he was shaken and unnerved, like a stag at the sight of a tigress.

The lord of men gasped as he sank down upon the bare floor. "Oh damn you!" he cried in uncontrollable fury before he fell into a stupor, his heart crushed by grief.

Gradually the king regained his senses and then, in bitter sorrow and anger, he spoke to Kaikeyī, with fire in his eyes:

"Malicious, wicked woman, bent on destroying this House! Evil woman, what evil did Rāma or I ever do to you?

"Rāghava has always treated you just like his own mother. What reason can you have for trying to wreck his fortunes, of all people?

"It was sheer suicide to bring you into my home. I did it unwittingly, thinking you a princess—and not a deadly poisonous viper.

"When praise for Rāma's virtues is on the lips of every living soul, what crime could I adduce as pretext for renouncing my favorite son?

"I would sooner renounce Kausalyā, or Sumitrā, or sovereignty, or life itself, than Rāma, who so cherishes his father.

"The greatest joy I know is seeing my first-born son. If I cannot see Rāma, I shall lose my mind.

"The world might endure without the sun, or crops without water, but without Rāma life could not endure within my body.

---

5. Sometimes the number of gods is thirty-three hundred or thirty-three thousand.   6. Ogre-like demons; Rāvaṇa, Rāma's enemy, is a rākṣasa.

"Enough then, give up this scheme, you evil-scheming woman. I beg you! Must I get down and bow my head to your feet?"

His heart in the grip of a woman who knew no bounds, the guardian of the earth began helplessly to cry, and as the queen extended her feet he tried in vain to touch them, and collapsed like a man on the point of death.

The end of the tenth *sarga* of the *Ayodhyākāņda* of the *Śrī Rāmāyaņa*.

SARGA 11

The king lay there, in so unaccustomed a posture, so ill-befitting his dignity, like Yayāti himself, his merit exhausted, fallen from the world of the gods.[7] But the woman was unafraid, for all the fear she awoke. She was misfortune incarnate and had yet to secure her fortunes. Once more she tried to force him to fulfill the boon.

"You are vaunted, great king, as a man true to his word and firm in his vows. How then can you be prepared to withhold my boon?"

So Kaikeyī spoke, and King Daśaratha, faltering for a moment, angrily replied:

"Vile woman, mortal enemy! Will you not be happy, will you not be satisfied until you see me dead, and Rāma, the bull among men, gone to the forest?

"To satisfy Kaikeyī Rāma must be banished to the forest, but if I keep my word in this, then I must be guilty of another lie. My infamy will be unequaled in the eyes of the people and my disgrace inevitable."

While he was lamenting like this, his mind in a whirl, the sun set and evening came on.

To the anguished king lost in lamentation, the night, adorned with the circlet of the moon, no longer seemed to last a mere three watches.

Heaving burning sighs, aged King Daśaratha sorrowfully lamented in his anguish, his eyes fixed upon the sky.

"I do not want you to bring the dawn—here, I cup my hands in supplication. But no, pass as quickly as you can, so that I no longer have to see this heartless, malicious Kaikeyī, the cause of this great calamity."

But with this, the king cupped his hands before Kaikeyī and once more, begging her mercy, he spoke:

"Please, I am an old man, my life is nearly over. I am desolate, I place myself in your hands. Dear lady, have mercy on me for, after all, I am king.

"Truly it was thoughtless of me, my fair-hipped lady, to have said those things just now. Have mercy on me, please, my child. I know you have a heart."

So the pure-hearted king lamented, frantically and piteously, his eyes reddened and dimmed by tears, but the malicious, black-hearted woman only listened and made no reply.

And as the king stared at the woman he loved but could not appease, whose demand was so perverse—for the exile of his own son—he once

---

7. Yayāti had reached the heaven of the gods by the power of his self-control; Indra ejected him when the effects of his good *karma* (*merit*) were used up.

again was taken faint, overcome with grief, and dropped unconscious to the floor.

The end of the eleventh *sarga* of the *Ayodhyākāṇḍa* of the *Śrī Rāmāyaṇa*.

SARGA 12

The evil woman watched as Aikṣvāka lay writhing unconscious on the ground where he had fallen, tortured with grief for his son. Then she spoke:

"How can you collapse like this and lie upon the floor, as though you deemed it a sin to fulfill the promise you made me? You must stand by your obligation.

"For people who understand the meaning of righteousness hold truth to be its essence. Now, I am simply appealing to truth and exhorting you to do what is right.

"Śaibya, the lord of the world, once promised his very own body to a hawk,[8] and he actually gave it to the bird, your majesty, thereby attaining the highest goal.

"The same was true of mighty Alarka. When a brahman versed in the *vedas* begged him for his eyes, he plucked them out, his own two eyes, and gave them unflinchingly.[9]

"The ocean, lord of rivers, respects the truth, keeping his narrow limits, and in accordance with the truth does not transgress the shore he pledged to keep.

"If you do not make good this pledge to me, my noble husband, then right before your eyes I will abandon my life, as you have abandoned me."

So the shameless Kaikeyī pressed the king, and he could no more free himself from her snare than Bali could from Indra's.[1]

His heart began to beat wildly, his face was drained of color, he was like an ox struggling between the yoke and wheels.

His eyes so clouded he could hardly see, barely steadying himself by an act of will, the lord of earth said to Kaikeyī:

"Once, in accordance with the sacred hymn, I took and held your hand in mine before the marriage fire. I now repudiate you, evil woman, as well as the son I fathered on you."

Blind with rage, the wicked Kaikeyī again addressed the king in the harshest words at her command.

"What are these venomous and cutting words you are speaking? Just have your son Rāma brought here without delay.

"Not until you have placed my son on the throne, sent Rāma to live in the forest, and rid me of all my rivals, will you have met your obligations."

Subjected to this constant pressure, like a noble horse prodded by a sharp goad, the king finally said:

"I am bound by the bond of righteousness. My mind is failing me! I want to see righteous Rāma, my beloved eldest son."

---

8. King Śaibya promised to protect a dove that had come to him for refuge and so gave his own flesh as compensation to the hawk. This story has many Buddhist and Hindu versions and appears in both the *Mahābhārata* and *Jātaka*.　9. A similar story appears in the *Jātaka*, where the deed is attributed to King Śaibya.　1. In a Vedic myth Indra tricks the demon Bali and binds him.

When Kaikeyī heard the king's words she immediately said to the charioteer on her own initiative, "Go! Bring Rāma."

Then the righteous and majestic king, utterly joyless on account of his
son, looked up at the charioteer through eyes red with grief and tried to
speak to him.

Hearing the pitiful sound and seeing the king's desolate expression,
Sumantra cupped his hands in reverence and withdrew some steps from
his presence.

When in his desolation the lord of earth proved incapable of speaking,
Kaikeyī, who well knew her counsels, addressed Sumantra herself:

"Sumantra, I will see Rāma. Bring the handsome prince at once."
Thinking this meant all was well, he rejoiced with all his heart.

For as she pressed him to hurry Sumantra reflected, "Clearly the righteous king has exhausted himself in preparing Rāma's consecration."

This is what the mighty charioteer thought, and he departed in great
delight, eager to see Rāghava.

*   *   *

SARGA 16

Rāma saw his father, with a wretched look and his mouth all parched,
slumped upon his lovely couch, Kaikeyī at his side.

First he made an obeisance with all deference at his father's feet and
then did homage most scrupulously at the feet of Kaikeyī.

"Rāma!" cried the wretched king, his eyes brimming with tears, but he
was unable to say anything more or to look at him.

As if his foot had grazed a snake, Rāma was seized with terror to see the
expression on the king's face, one more terrifying than he had ever seen
before.

For the great king lay heaving sighs, racked with grief and remorse, all
his senses numb with anguish, his mind stunned and confused.

It was as if the imperturbable, wave-wreathed ocean had suddenly been
shaken with perturbation, as if the sun had been eclipsed, or a seer had
told a lie.

His father's grief was incomprehensible to him, and the more he pondered it, the more his agitation grew, like that of the ocean under a full
moon.

With his father's welfare at heart, Rāma struggled to comprehend, "Why
does the king not greet me, today of all days?

"On other occasions, when Father might be angry, the sight of me
would calm him. Why then, when he looked at me just now, did he
instead become so troubled?

"He seems desolate and grief-stricken, and his face has lost its glow."
Doing obeisance to Kaikeyī, Rāma spoke these words:

"I have not unknowingly committed some offense, have I, to anger my
father? Tell me, and make him forgive me.

"His face is drained of color, he is desolate and does not speak to me. It
cannot be, can it, that some physical illness or mental distress afflicts him?
But it is true, well-being is not something one can always keep.

"Some misfortune has not befallen the handsome prince Bharata, has it, or courageous Śatrughna, or one of my mothers?

"I should not wish to live an instant if his majesty, the great king, my father, were angered by my failure to satisfy him or do his bidding.

"How could a man not treat him as a deity incarnate, in whom he must recognize the very source of his existence in this world?

"Can it be that in anger you presumed to use harsh words with my father, and so threw his mind into such turmoil?

"Answer my questions truthfully, my lady: What has happened to cause this unprecedented change in the lord of men?

"At the bidding of the king, if enjoined by him, my guru, father, king, and benefactor, I would hurl myself into fire, drink deadly poison, or drown myself in the sea.

"Tell me then, my lady, what the king would have me do. I will do it, I promise. Rāma need not say so twice."

The ignoble Kaikeyī then addressed these ruthless words to Rāma, the upright and truthful prince:

"Long ago, Rāghava, in the war of the gods and *asuras*, your father bestowed two boons on me, for protecting him when he was wounded in a great battle.

"By means of these I have demanded of the king that Bharata be consecrated and that you, Rāghava, be sent at once to Daṇḍaka wilderness.

"If you wish to ensure that your father be true to his word, and you to your own, best of men, then listen to what I have to say.

"Abide by your father's guarantee, exactly as he promised it, and enter the forest for nine years and five.

"Forgo the consecration and withdraw to Daṇḍaka wilderness, live there seven years and seven, wearing matted hair and barkcloth garments.

"Let Bharata rule this land from the city of the Kosalans, with all the treasures it contains, all its horses, chariots, elephants."

When Rāma, slayer of enemies, heard Kaikeyī's hateful words, like death itself, he was not the least disconcerted, but only replied,

"So be it. I shall go away to live in the forest, wearing matted hair and barkcloth garments, to safeguard the promise of the king.

"But I want to know why the lord of earth, the invincible tamer of foes, does not greet me as he used to?

"You need not worry, my lady. I say it to your face: I shall go to the forest—rest assured—wearing barkcloth and matted hair.

"Enjoined by my father, my benefactor, guru, and king, a man who knows what is right to do, what would I hesitate to do in order to please him?

"But there is still one thing troubling my mind and eating away at my heart: that the king does not tell me himself that Bharata is to be consecrated.

"For my wealth, the kingship, Sītā, and my own dear life I would gladly give up to my brother Bharata on my own, without any urging.

"How much more readily if urged by my father himself, the lord of men, in order to fulfill your fond desire and safeguard his promise?

"So you must reassure him. Why should the lord of earth keep his eyes fixed upon the ground and fitfully shed these tears?

"This very day let messengers depart on swift horses by order of the king to fetch Bharata from his uncle's house.

"As for me, I shall leave here in all haste for Daṇḍaka wilderness, without questioning my father's word, to live there fourteen years."

Kaikeyī was delighted to hear these words of Rāma's, and trusting them implicitly, she pressed Rāghava to set out at once.

"So be it. Men shall go as messengers on swift horses to bring home Bharata from his uncle's house.

"But since you are now so eager, Rāma, I do not think it wise to linger. You should therefore proceed directly from here to the forest.

"That the king is ashamed and does not address you himself, that is nothing, best of men, you needn't worry about that.

"But so long as you have not hastened from the city and gone to the forest, Rāma, your father shall neither bathe nor eat."

"Oh curse you!" the king gasped, overwhelmed with grief, and upon the gilt couch he fell back in a faint.

Rāma raised up the king, pressed though he was by Kaikeyī—like a horse whipped with a crop—to make haste and depart for the forest.

Listening to the ignoble Kaikeyī's hateful words, so dreadful in their consequences, Rāma remained unperturbed and only said to her,

"My lady, it is not in the hopes of gain that I suffer living in this world. You should know that, like the seers, I have but one concern and that is righteousness.

"Whatever I can do to please this honored man I will do at any cost, even if it means giving up my life.

"For there is no greater act of righteousness than this: obedience to one's father and doing as he bids.

"Even unbidden by this honored man, at your bidding alone I shall live for fourteen years in the desolate forest.

"Indeed, Kaikeyī, you must ascribe no virtue to me at all if you had to appeal to the king, when you yourself are so venerable in my eyes.

"Let me only take leave of my mother, and settle matters with Sītā. Then I shall go, this very day, to the vast forest of the Daṇḍakas.

"You must see to it that Bharata obeys Father and guards the kingdom, for that is the eternal way of righteousness."

When his father heard Rāma's words, he was stricken with such deep sorrow that he could not hold back his sobs in his grief and broke out in loud weeping.

Splendid Rāma did homage at the feet of his unconscious father and at the feet of that ignoble woman, Kaikeyī; then he turned to leave.

Reverently Rāma circled his father and Kaikeyī,[2] and, withdrawing from the inner chamber, he saw his group of friends.

Lakṣmaṇa, the delight of Sumitrā, fell in behind him, his eyes brimming with tears, in a towering rage.

---

2. A gesture of honor. Even in modern Hinduism individuals honor their elders, gods, sacred objects, and holy ones by walking around them in reverence.

Reverently circling the equipment for the consecration, but careful not to gaze at it,[3] Rāma slowly went away.

The loss of the kingship diminished his great majesty as little as night diminishes the loveliness of the cool-rayed moon, beloved of the world.

Though he was on the point of leaving his native land and going to the forest, he was no more discomposed than one who has passed beyond all things of this world.

Holding back his sorrow within his mind, keeping his every sense in check, and fully self-possessed he made his way to his mother's residence to tell her the sad news.

As Rāma entered her residence, where joy still reigned supreme, as he reflected on the sudden wreck of all his fortunes, even then he showed no sign of discomposure, for fear it might endanger the lives of those he loved.

The end of the sixteenth *sarga* of the *Ayodhyākāṇḍa* of the *Śrī Rāmāyaṇa*.

SARGA 17

Sorely troubled, heaving sighs like an elephant, Rāma of his own accord went with his brother to his mother's inner chamber.[4]

He observed the venerable elder seated there at the door of the house and many other people standing about.

Passing through the first courtyard, he saw the brahmans in the second, old men expert in the *vedas* and held in honor by the king.

Rāma bowed to the old men and passed into the third courtyard, where he saw women old and young vigilantly standing guard at the door.

In delight the women congratulated him and then rushed into the house to pass on the news to Rāma's mother.

Queen Kausalyā had spent the night in meditation, and now in the early morning was worshiping Viṣṇu to secure the welfare of her son.

Dressed in linen, intent upon her vow and with deep delight, she was then pouring an oblation into the fire in accordance with the vedic verses and pronouncing benedictions.

Entering her lovely private chamber, Rāma saw his mother as she was pouring the oblation into the fire.

When she saw that her son, his mother's one joy, had finally come, she approached him in delight, as a mare might her colt.

In her deep maternal affection for her son, the invincible Rāghava, Kausalyā addressed him with these kind and beneficial words:

"May you attain the life-span of the great and aged royal seers[5] who keep to the ways of righteousness. May you attain their fame and the righteousness that benefits a ruling house.

"See, Rāghava, your father is as good as his word. This very day the righteous king will consecrate you as prince regent."

Extending a little the hands he held cupped in reverence, Rāghava

---

3. So as not to cast the evil eye on the items, which would jeopardize Bharata's welfare and his rule.
4. This contradicts the description of Rāma at the end of *Sarga* 16, pointing perhaps to the inconsistencies that have been retained in Vālmīki's editing and recasting of the ancient tale.   5. An epithet conferred on kings who lead by their self-control and pious championship of *dharma*.

bowed low out of natural courtesy and profound respect. Then he said to his mother,

"My lady, I see you do not know of the great danger at hand. It will bring sadness to you, Vaidehī, and Lakṣmaṇa.

"For fourteen years I must dwell in the desolate forest, living on honey, fruit, and roots, giving up meat like a sage.

"The great king is awarding Bharata the office of prince regent and banishing me to Daṇḍaka wilderness and a life of asceticism."

A sorrow such as she had never known swept over her, and Rāma saw his mother fall down in a faint, like a broken plantain tree. He came to her side and helped her up, and as she stood there in her desolation, like a mare forced to draw a heavy load, he brushed away the dust that covered her whole body.

Tortured by such unhappiness as she had never known before, she spoke to Rāghava, tiger among men, as he attended on her, with Lakṣmaṇa listening:

"Rāghava, my son, had you never been born to bring me such grief, had I been childless, I would have been spared any further sorrow.

"A barren woman's grief is only of the mind and only a single grief— the painful thought, 'I have no child'; she never comes to feel another, my son.

"But the joy and comfort I had not found to be within my husband's power to give me, Rāma, I cherished hopes I perhaps might find in a son.

"How their words will break my heart, the many, painful words I shall hear from those junior co-wives, being their senior as I am. And what could bring a woman greater sorrow?

"Even with you present this is how I am spurned. What will it be like when you are gone, my child? Surely nothing is left me but to die.

"For anyone who used to serve me or respect my wishes will look anxiously toward Kaikeyī's son without so much as a word for me.

"The ten years and seven since you were born,[6] Rāghava, I have passed yearning to put an end to my sorrow.

"It was so difficult to raise you in my wretched state, and it was all in vain,[7] the meditation and the fasts, and all the pains I took.

"How hard this heart of mine must be that it does not crumble, as the bank of a great river crumbles in the rains when the fresh waters wash over it.

"It must be that I can never die, or that no room is left for me in the house of Yama, if even now Death will not carry me off, as brutally as a lion carries off a whimpering doe.

"My heart must be made of iron that it does not split and shatter upon the ground, and my body, too, under this crushing sorrow. How true it is that no one can die before his fated hour.

"What a sorrowful thing that my vows, my gifts of alms, and acts of self-denial have all been to no avail, that the austerities I practiced for my child's sake have proved to be as barren as seed sown in a desert.

6. More probably since his initiation, which would have taken place when he was about eight, making him about twenty-five.   7. Her own status in the royal household would have risen if Rāma had been consecrated.

"For if a person broken by heavy sorrow could die before his fated hour, of his own free will, then left without you as I am, like a cow without her calf, I would go this very instant to the congregation of the dead."

When she looked at Rāghava and contemplated the great calamity to come, her unhappiness was too much for her to bear, and she broke out in lamentation, as a cow will do at the sight of her calf being bound and dragged away.

The end of the seventeenth *sarga* of the *Ayodhyākāṇḍa* of the *Śrī Rāmāyaṇa*.

SARGA 18

Lakṣmaṇa grew desolate while Rāma's mother Kausalyā made this lamentation and then, in the heat of the moment, he addressed her:

"I do not approve of it either, my lady, that Rāghava should abdicate the majesty of kingship and go off to the forest, bowing to the demands of a woman.

"The king is perverse, old, and debauched by pleasures. What would he not say under pressure, mad with passion as he is?

"I know of no crime on Rāghava's part nor any fault that could justify his banishment from the kingdom to a life in the forest.

"I do not know of a single man in this world, not an adversary, nor even an outcast, who would assert such a fault, even behind our backs.

"Who that has any regard for what is right could renounce, without any provocation, a son so godlike, upright, and self-restrained, who cherishes even his enemies?

"What son, mindful of the conduct of kings, would take to heart the words of a king who has become a child again?

"Before anyone learns of this matter, let me help you seize control of the government.

"With me at your side, bow in hand to protect you, who could prevail against you, Rāghava, when you take your stand like Death itself?

"With my sharp arrows, bull among men, I will empty Ayodhyā of men if it stands in opposition.

"I will slaughter everyone who sides with Bharata or champions his cause. Leniency always ends in defeat.

"Now that the king has provoked our implacable enmity, yours and mine, chastiser of foes, what power can he summon to bestow sovereignty on Bharata?

"Truly, my lady, the loyalty I feel to my brother comes from the bottom of my heart. I swear it to you by my truth and my bow, by my gifts of alms and sacrifices.

"Should Rāma enter the forest, or a blazing fire, my lady, rest assured that I shall have entered first.

"I will drive your sorrow away with all the power of the rising sun that drives away the dark. Let the queen behold my power! Let Rāghava behold it!"

When she heard great Lakṣmaṇa's words, Kausalyā, weeping and sick with grief, said to Rāma,

"My son, you have heard your brother Lakṣmaṇa speak. Whatever is best to do next you must do, as you see fit.

"But you must not, heeding the unrighteous words spoken by my co-wife, go away and leave me stricken with grief.

"You know what is right and if you would do it, my most righteous son, obey me. Stay here and do your supreme duty.

"Kāśyapa obeyed his mother, my son, and lived a life of self-discipline at home. In this way he acquired ultimate ascetic power and reached the highest heaven.

"In no way am I less deserving than the king of the respect you owe a guru. I will not give you permission, you may not go away to the forest.

"Parted from you what use have I for a life of comfort? Better for me to be with you and eat the grass of the fields.

"If you go to the forest leaving me sick with grief, I will fast to death right here, for I could not bear to go on living.

"And you will then be guilty of a crime held in infamy in the world, like the ocean, lord of rivers, who through unrighteous conduct incurred the guilt of brahman-murder."

So his desolate mother Kausalyā lamented, and righteous Rāma replied to her in a manner consistent with righteousness:

"It is not within my power to defy my father's bidding. I bow my head in supplication; I wish to go to the forest.

"Even the wise seer Kaṇḍu, a man strict in his observances, slew a cow at the bidding of his father,[8] for he knew that it was right.

"And in our own family long ago the sons of Sagara at their father's command dug up the earth and thereby met with wholesale slaughter.[9]

"Rāma Jāmadagnya, at his father's bidding, took an ax and by his own hand butchered his mother Reṇukā[1] in the forest.

"So you see, it is not I alone who acts as his father instructs. I am only following the path sanctioned and taken by those men of old.

"It is this that is my duty on earth, and I cannot shirk it. Besides, no one who does his father's bidding ever comes to grief."

So he spoke to his mother, and then he turned to Lakṣmaṇa and said, "I well know, Lakṣmaṇa, the profound affection you bear me. But you fail to understand the real meaning of truth and self-restraint.

"Righteousness[2] is paramount in the world and on righteousness is truth founded. This command of Father's is based on righteousness and is absolute.

"Having once heard a father's command, a mother's, or a brahman's, one must not disregard it, my mighty brother, if one would hold to what is right.

"I cannot disobey my father's injunction, mighty brother, and it is at Father's bidding that Kaikeyī has coerced me.

"So give up this ignoble notion that is based on the code of the kshatri-

---

8. The legends of the brahman murder and Kaṇḍu have not been preserved.   9. This tale of Rāma's ancestors is related in Book 1: Sagara and his thousand sons followed a sacrificial horse into the underworld, where they were burned to ashes by an angry sage.   1. Her husband suspected her of infidelity.   2. Dharma.

yas; be of like mind with me and base your actions on righteousness, not violence." [3]

So Lakṣmaṇa's eldest brother spoke affectionately to his brother. Then, with head bowed and hands cupped in reverence, he once more addressed Kausalyā:

"Give me your permission, my lady, to go away to the forest. By my very life I adjure you, bestow your blessings on my journey. Once I have fulfilled the promise, I will return to the city from the forest.

"I cannot for the sake of mere kingship turn my back on glory, whose reward is great; nor, since life is so short, my lady, would I choose today this paltry land against all that is right."

The bull among men earnestly pleaded with his mother—he wanted only to go to the Daṇḍakas—and firmly taught his younger brother the proper view of things. Then, in his heart, he reverently circled the woman who gave him birth.

The end of the eighteenth *sarga* of the *Ayodhyākāṇḍa* of the *Śrī Rāmāyaṇa*.

Summary   Rāma convinces Lakṣmaṇa and Queen Kausalyā that he should not oppose his father's decision.

SARGA 23

So Kausalyā bade him farewell and Rāma did obeisance to her, ready to depart for the forest, keeping to the path of righteousness.

Along the royal highway crowded with men, the prince went illuminating it and melting the hearts of the people, it seemed, with all his virtues.

Poor Vaidehī had heard nothing of all this; she still believed he was being consecrated as prince regent.

She knew the rites for the gods and had performed them in deep delight. Thus she waited for the prince, knowing the kingly attributes to expect.

As Rāma entered his residence—still decorated and thronged with delighted people—he lowered his head a little, in shame.

Sītā started up and began to tremble as she looked at her husband consumed with grief, his senses numb with anxious care.

When she saw how his face was drained of color, how he sweated and chafed, she was consumed with sorrow. "What is the meaning of this, my lord?" she asked.

"Today was surely the day for which the learned brahmans had forecast the conjunction of Puṣya, the majestic constellation ruled by Bṛhaspati. Why are you so sad, Rāghava?

"The hundred-ribbed parasol with its hue of white-capped water is not throwing its shade upon your handsome face.

3. Rāma rejects the *dharma* of the *kshatriya* (warrior class) and chooses to follow a more universal ethical code.

"Your face, with eyes like the hundred-petaled lotus, is not fanned by the pair of splendid flywhisks,[4] the color of the moon or the wild goose.

"And I see no eloquent panegyrists, bull among men, singing your praises in delight, no bards or genealogists with their auspicious recitation.

"Nor have the brahmans, masters of the *vedas*, sprinkled your head and poured honey and curds upon it, as custom requires.

"No one wishes to follow in your train, not the officials, nor the heads of guilds in their finery, nor the people of the city and provinces.

"How is it the splendid Puṣya chariot[5] does not precede you, with its team of four swift horses with trappings of gold?

"I see no sign of the royal elephant, revered for its auspicious marks and resembling a mountain black with clouds. It is not leading your procession, my mighty husband.

"Nor do I see your escort, my handsome and mighty husband, proceeding with the gold-wrought throne held before them.

"What can all this mean, when your consecration is already under way? Never before has your face had such color, and I see no sign of delight."

Such were her anxious words, and the delight of the Raghus replied to her: "Sītā, my honored father is banishing me to the forest.

"O Jānakī, you are the daughter of a great house, you know what is right and always practice it. Listen to the course of events that has brought this upon me.

"Once, long ago, when Kaikeyī had found favor with him, my father King Daśaratha, a man true to his promise, granted her two great boons.

"Today, when my consecration was already under way at the instigation of the king, she pressed him for them. Since he had made an agreement, he was compelled by righteousness.

"For fourteen years I must live in Daṇḍaka, while my father will appoint Bharata prince regent. I have come to see you before I leave for the desolate forest.

"You are never to boast of me in the presence of Bharata. Men in power cannot bear to hear others praised, and so you must never boast of my virtues in front of Bharata.

"You must not ever expect to receive any special treatment from him. Life with him will be possible only by constant acquiescence.

"I will safeguard my guru's promise and leave this very day for the forest. Be strong, my sensible wife.

"When I have gone to the forest where sages make their home, my precious, blameless wife, you must earnestly undertake vows and fasts.

"You must rise early and worship the gods according to custom and then pay homage to my father Daśaratha, lord of men.

"And my aged mother Kausalyā, who is tormented by misery, deserves your respect as well, for she has subordinated all to righteousness.

"The rest of my mothers, too, must always receive your homage. My mothers are all equal in my eyes for their love, affection, and care.

"And what is most important, you must look on Bharata and Śatrughna as your brother and your son, for they are dearer to me than life itself.

---

4. The yak-tail fans.   5. A ceremonial—not war—chariot.

"You must never show opposition to Bharata, for he is now both king of the country and master of our House.

"Kings show their favor when they are pleased with good conduct and sedulously attended to—and if they are not, they grow angry.

"Lords of men will repudiate their sons, their own flesh and blood, if they serve them ill, and will adopt even strangers, should they prove capable.

"My beloved, I am going to the great forest, and you must stay here. You must do as I tell you, my lovely, and not give offense to anyone."

The end of the twenty-third *sarga* of the *Ayodhyākāṇḍa* of the *Śrī Rāmāyaṇa*.

SARGA 24

So Rāma spoke, and Vaidehī, who always spoke kindly to her husband and deserved kindness from him, grew angry just because she loved him, and said,

"My lord, a man's father, his mother, brother, son, or daughter-in-law all experience the effects of their own past deeds and suffer an individual fate.[6]

"But a wife, and she alone, bull among men, must share her husband's fate. Therefore I, too, have been ordered to live in the forest.

"It is not her father or mother, not her son or friends or herself, but her husband, and he alone, who gives a woman permanent refuge in this world and after death.

"If you must leave this very day for the trackless forest, Rāghava, I will go in front of you, softening the thorns and sharp *kuśa* grass.

"Cast out your anger and resentment, like so much water left after drinking one's fill. Do not be reluctant to take me, my mighty husband. There is no evil in me.

"The shadow of a husband's feet in any circumstances surpasses the finest mansions, an aerial chariot, or even flying through the sky.

"My mother and father instructed me in all these different questions. I do not have to be told now the proper way to behave.[7]

"I shall live as happily in the forest as if it were my father's house, caring for nothing in the three worlds but to be faithful to my husband.

"I will obey you always and practice self-discipline and chastity.[8] What pleasures I shall share with you, my mighty husband, in the honey-scented forests!

"O Rāma, bestower of honor, you have the power to protect any other person in the forest. Why then not me?

"You need not doubt that I can survive on nothing but fruit and roots; I shall not cause you any trouble by living with you.

"I want to see the streams and mountains, the ponds and forests, and nowhere shall I be afraid with my wise husband to defend me.

"I want to see the lotus ponds in full bloom, blanketed with geese and ducks, happy in your company, my mighty husband.

---

6. Here from *bhāgya*, the condition that results from the sum total of one's deeds done over successive births.   7. That is, she understands the wife's *dharma*.   8. If she were to accompany Rāma to the forest, she would also be bound to follow the ascetic life.

"What pleasures I shall share with you, my large-eyed husband, what bliss for me to be with you like this, were it for a hundred thousand years!

"If I were to be offered a place to live in heaven itself, Rāghava, tiger among men, I would refuse it if you were not there.

"I will go to the trackless forest teeming with deer, monkeys, and elephants, and live there as if in my father's house, clinging to your feet alone, in strict self-discipline.

"I love no one else; my heart is so attached to you that were we to be parted I am resolved to die. Take me, oh please grant my request. I shall not be a burden to you."

Despite what Sītā said, the best of men, who so cherished righteousness, was still unwilling to take her, and in order to dissuade her, he began to describe how painful life in the forest is.

The end of the twenty-fourth *sarga* of the *Ayodhyākāṇḍa* of the *Śrī Rāmāyaṇa*.

SARGA 25

When Sītā finished speaking, the righteous prince, who knew what was right and cherished it, attempted to dissuade her.

"Sītā, you are the daughter of a great house and have always been earnest in doing what is right. You must stay here and do your duty, not what your heart desires.

"My frail Sītā, you must do as I say. There are so many hardships in the forest. Listen to me and I shall tell you.

"Sītā, give up this notion of living in the forest. The name 'forest' is given only to wild regions where hardships abound.

"It is, in fact, with your welfare at heart that I am saying this. The forest is never a place of pleasure—I know—but only of pain.

"There are lions that live in mountain caves; their roars are redoubled by mountain torrents and are a painful thing to hear—the forest is a place of pain.[9]

"At night, worn with fatigue, one must sleep upon the ground on a bed of leaves, broken off of themselves—the forest is a place of utter pain.

"And one has to fast, Maithilī, to the limit of one's endurance, wear clothes of barkcloth and bear the burden of matted hair.

"The wind is so intense there and the darkness, too. One is always hungry and the dangers are so great—the forest is a place of utter pain.

"There are many creeping creatures, of every size and shape, my lovely, ranging aggressively over the ground—the forest is a place of utter pain.

"There are snakes, too, that live in the rivers, moving as sinuously as rivers, and they are always there obstructing one's way—the forest is a place of utter pain.

"Moths, scorpions, worms, gnats, and flies continually harass one, my frail Sītā—the forest is wholly a place of pain.

"There are thorn trees, *kuśa*, and *kāśa* grass, my lovely, and the forest is a tangle of their branches and blades—the forest is a place of utter pain.

9. A characteristic refrain of Indian archaic epics and oral and folk poetry in general.

"So no more of your going to the forest, you could not bear it. The more I think about it the more I see how many hardships the forest holds."

When great Rāma had thus made up his mind not to take her to the forest, Sītā did not reply to him at once, but then in bitter sorrow she spoke.

The end of the twenty-fifth *sarga* of the *Ayodhyākāṇḍa* of the *Śrī Rāmāyaṇa*.

SARGA 26

Sītā was overcome with sorrow when she heard what Rāma said. With tears trickling down her face, she answered him in a faint voice.

"Do you not know that what you call the hardships of life in the forest would all be luxuries if your love accompanied them?

"By the order of our elders I must go with you, Rāma. I would die here and now if parted from you.

"But if I were by your side, Rāghava, not even Śakra, lord of the gods, could harm me for all his might.

"A woman whose husband has left her cannot go on living, regardless of what advice you give me, Rāma.

"Besides, my wise husband, long ago in my father's house I heard the brahmans prophesy that some day I should have to live in the forest.

"The twice-born[1] could read the marks on a person's body, my powerful husband, and from that moment at home, when I heard what they foretold, I have constantly yearned to live in the forest.

"The prediction that I should have to live in the forest must some day be fulfilled. And it is with you that I would go there, my love, not otherwise.

"I will go with you and carry out the prediction. The moment has arrived; let the prophecy of the twice-born come true.

"I know that in living in the forest there is indeed much pain, my mighty husband, but it is only those who are unprepared that suffer from it.

"When I was a girl in my father's house I happened to hear, in the presence of my mother, all about forest life from a holy mendicant woman.[2]

"And, in fact, I have begged you many times before to let us go and live together in the forest, my lord, so much do I desire it.

"Please, Rāghava, I have been waiting for the chance to go. I want nothing more than to serve my hero as he lives in the forest.

"If from feelings of love I follow you, my pure-hearted husband, I shall have no sin to answer for, because my husband is my deity.

"My union with you is sacred and shall last even beyond death. There is a holy scripture, my high-minded husband, which glorious brahmans recite: 'When in this world, in accordance with their own customs and by means of the ritual waters, a woman's father gives her to a man, she remains his even in death.'

---

1. Here the brahman; more generally, a member of the brahman, warrior, or merchant class.   2. A woman who presumably lived the life of an ascetic. Aristocratic women in Indian epics are constantly faced with the need to explain how they acquired a seemingly extensive knowledge of the outside world.

"What then is the reason you are set against taking me away from here, your own wife, a woman of good conduct and faithful to her husband?

"I am devoted and faithful to my husband. I have always shared your joy and sorrow, and now I am so desolate. You must take me, Kākutstha: your joy has always been mine to share, and your sorrow.

"If you refuse to take me to the forest despite the sorrow that I feel, I shall have no recourse but to end my life by poison, fire, or water."

Though she pleaded with him in this and every other way to be allowed to go, great-armed Rāma would not consent to taking her to the desolate forest.

And when he told her as much, Maithilī[3] fell to brooding, and drenched the ground, it seemed, with the hot tears that fell from her eyes.

And as Vaidehī brooded, wondering how to change his mind, anger took hold of her. But Kākutstha did not lose his self-composure and tried his best to appease her.

The end of the twenty-sixth *sarga* of the *Ayodhyākāṇḍa* of the *Śrī Rāmāyaṇa*.

SARGA 27

Rāma tried to appease her, but Maithilī, daughter of Janaka, addressed her husband once more in the hopes of living in the forest.

Sītā was deeply distraught, and out of love and indignation she began to revile broad-chested Rāghava.

"What could my father Vaideha, the lord of Mithilā, have had in mind when he took you for a son-in-law, Rāma, a woman with the body of a man?[4]

"How the people lie in their ignorance. Rāma's 'great power' is not at all like the power of the blazing sun that brings the day.

"On what grounds are you so reluctant, what are you afraid of that you are ready to desert me, who has no other refuge?

"Do you not know, my mighty husband, that I bow to your will, that I am as faithful to you as Sāvitrī was to Satyavant,[5] Dyumatsena's son?

"Were I to go with you, blameless Rāghava, I would not even think of looking at any man but you, unlike some women who disgrace their family.

"But like a procurer, Rāma, you are willing of your own accord to hand me over to others—your wife, who came to you a virgin and who has been a good woman all the long while she has lived with you.

"You must not leave for the forest without taking me. Let it be austerities, or the wilderness, or heaven, but let it be with you.

"As I follow behind you I shall no more tire on the path than on our pleasure beds.

"The *kuśa* and *kāśa* grass, the reeds, the rushes, and thorn trees will feel just like cotton or a pelt to me on the road with you.

---

3. Sītā, who is princess of Mithilā, capital of Videha.   4. In desperation Sītā taunts Rāma in an uncharacteristic manner. Vaideha is another name for Janaka.   5. A reference to the ancient narrative of how Sāvitrī, famous as the faithful wife, recovered the life of her husband, Satyavant, from the god Yama. This legend appears in the *Mahābhārata*, but this reference is probably to a different, perhaps oral, version.

"The dust raised by heavy winds that will settle on me, my love, I shall look upon as the costliest sandalwood cream.

"As I roam through the deep forest there will be meadows for me to rest in, and to rest on couches spread with blankets could not give more pleasure.

"The leaves and roots and fruit you gather with your own hands and give me, however much or little there is, will taste like nectar to me.

"There will be fruits and flowers in their seasons to enjoy, and I shall not think with longing of my mother or father or home.

"And when you are there you will not know any grief or displeasure on my account. I shall not be a burden.

"To be with you is heaven, to be without you hell. Knowing how deep my love is, Rāma, you must take me when you go.

"But if you will not let me go to the forest when I am so set on it, I will take poison this very day, sooner than come under the sway of those who hate us.

"Afterwards I could not live anyway, my lord, for the sorrow of being deserted by you. Better to die that very instant.

"I could not bear the grief of it even for a moment, much less ten years of sorrow, and three, and one."

Consumed with grief, she lamented long and piteously. Crying out in anguish, she shrieked and embraced her husband with all her might.

His many words had wounded her, the way poison arrows wound a cow elephant. And the tears she had held in so long burst forth like a flame from a kindling stick.

Water clear as crystal, springing from her torment, came gushing from all around her eyes, like water from two lotuses.

She was nearly insensible with sorrow when Rāma took her in his arms and comforted her with these words:

"If its price were your sorrow, my lady, I would refuse heaven itself. No, I am not afraid of anything, any more than is the Self-existent Brahmā.

"But without knowing your true feelings, my lovely, I could not consent to your living in the wilderness, though I am perfectly capable of protecting you.

"Since you are determined to live with me in the forest, Maithilī, I could no sooner abandon you than a self-respecting man his reputation.

"But it is righteousness, my smooth-limbed wife, the righteousness good men in the past have practiced, that I am set on following today, as its radiance follows the sun.

"And righteousness is this, my fair-hipped wife: submission to one's mother and father. I could not bear to live were I to disobey their command.

"My father keeps to the path of righteousness and truth, and I wish to act just as he instructs me. That is the eternal way of righteousness. Follow me, my timid one, be my companion in righteousness.[6]

"Go now and bestow precious objects on the brahmans, give food to the mendicants and all who ask for it. Hurry, there is not time to waste."

6. Rāma yields to Sītā's plea but cites righteousness as his chief reason for doing so. *Timid one:* a stereotyped form of address for a woman, even when incongruous, as here.

Finding that her husband had acquiesced in her going, the lady was elated and set out at once to make the donations.

Glorious Sītā was delighted, her every wish fulfilled by what her husband said, and in high spirits the woman set off to give money and precious objects to all who upheld righteousness.

The end of the twenty-seventh *sarga* of the *Ayodhyākāṇḍa* of the *Śrī Rāmāyaṇa.*

SARGA 28

Mighty Rāma then turned to Lakṣmaṇa, who came and stood before him, hands cupped in reverence, begging that he might be allowed to go, in the very lead.

"Saumitri, were you to go with me now to the forest, who would support Kausalyā and glorious Sumitrā?

"The mighty lord of the land, who used to shower them with all they desired, as a raincloud showers the earth, is now caught up in the snare of desire.

"And once the daughter of King Aśvapati[7] gains control of the kingdom, she will not show any good will to her co-wives in their sorrow."

So Rāma eloquently spoke, and Lakṣmaṇa in a gentle voice replied to him with equal eloquence:

"Your own power, my mighty brother, will no doubt ensure that Bharata scrupulously honors Kausalyā and Sumitrā.

"The noble Kausalyā could support a thousand men like me, for she has acquired a thousand villages as her living.[8]

"I will take my bow and arrows and bear the spade and basket. I will go in front of you, leading the way.

"I will always be there to bring you roots and fruit and such other produce of the forest as is proper fare for ascetics.

"You shall take your pleasure with Vaidehī on the mountain slopes while I do everything for you, when you are awake and when you sleep."

His words pleased Rāma, and he replied, "Go, Saumitri, and take leave of all your friends.

"And those two divine, awesome-looking bows that great Varuṇa[9] himself bestowed on Janaka at the grand sacrifice; the two suits of divine, impenetrable armor; the two quivers with inexhaustible arrows and the two swords bright as the sun and plated with gold—all was deposited in perfect order in our preceptor's residence. Collect the arms, Lakṣmaṇa, and come back at once."

So, resolved to live in the forest, he bade farewell to his friends and to the guru of the Ikṣvākus, and gathered up the all-powerful arms.

Saumitri, tiger of the Raghus, displayed to Rāma all the divine arms, in perfect order still and adorned with garlands.

When Lakṣmaṇa had come back, Rāma joyfully and with full self-possession, said to him, "You have come, dear Lakṣmaṇa, at the very moment I desired.

---

7. King of Kekaya and father of Kaikeyī.   8. An indication of her high status and economic power; it is not clear whether she *acquired* this wealth from her own family, from her dowry, or from Daśaratha (perhaps as compensation for his favoring Kaikeyī).   9. A major god.

"I want your help, slayer of enemies, in giving away whatever wealth I possess to the poor brahmans,[1] to the best of the twice-born who live here in firm devotion to my gurus, and in particular to all my dependents.

"Fetch at once the foremost of the twice-born, noble Suyajña, Vasiṣṭha's son. I will leave for the forest after paying homage to him and all the other twice-born men of learning."

The end of the twenty-eighth *sarga* of the *Ayodhyākāṇḍa* of the *Śrī Rāmāyaṇa*.

SARGA 30

Now, after the two Rāghavas and Vaidehī had bestowed vast wealth upon the brahmans, they went to see their father.

How brilliant they looked when they took up their formidable weapons, which Sītā had ornamented and hung with flower garlands.

The wealthy townspeople went up to the roofs of their palaces and mansions and to the tops of many-storied buildings and watched despondently.

The streets were so thronged with people as to be impassable, and so they went up to the roofs of their palaces and in desolation gazed down at Rāghava.

When the people saw Rāma going on foot and without the royal parasol, their hearts were crushed with grief, and they said many different things:

"The prince, whom a vast army of four divisions[2] used to follow as he went forth, is all alone now, with only Lakṣmaṇa and Sītā to follow behind."

"Though he has known the taste of kingly power and has always met the needs of the needy, in his veneration for righteousness he refuses to let his father break his word."

"People on the royal highway can now look at Sītā, a woman whom even creatures of the sky have never had a glimpse of before."

"Sītā is used to cosmetics and partial to red sandalwood cream, but the rain and the heat and the cold will soon ruin her complexion."

"Surely it is some spirit that has possessed Daśaratha and spoken today, for the king could never bring himself to exile his beloved son."

"How could a man force his own son into exile, even an unvirtuous son, let alone one who has vanquished the world simply by his good conduct?"

"Benevolence, compassion, learning, good character, restraint, and equanimity—these are the six virtues that adorn Rāghava, the best of men."

"And so the people are sorely hurt by any injury to him, like water creatures when the water dries up in the summertime."

"When the lord of the world is hurt so is all the world, as the fruit and flowers of a tree are hurt by an injury to its root."

"Let us at once take our wives and kinsmen, and like Lakṣmaṇa follow Rāghava as he goes forth, wherever he may go."

---

1. Before undertaking the ascetic life, even temporarily, one must give away all of his or her possessions. Giving gifts to the brahmans is an act of piety; the priesthood depended on the munificence of the warrior and merchant classes. Rāma and Lakṣmaṇa are allowed to keep their weapons, which will be used for hunting and protection.   2. That is, of foot soldiers, cavalry, elephants, and chariots.

"Let us abandon our gardens, our fields and homes, and follow righteous Rāma, to share his sorrow and joy."

"Let us unearth our buried treasure, remove our stores of grain and our wealth, and take all our valuables. And when the household gods have abandoned them, and their courtyards are falling into disrepair and the dust settling thick upon them, let Kaikeyī take possession of the dwellings we have left."

"Let the wilderness where Rāghava goes become our city, and the city we abandon turn into a wilderness."

"Let all the animals leave their haunts, the snakes their lairs, the birds and beasts their mountain slopes, and take possession of what we have left."

Such were the kinds of remarks people were making one after the other, and Rāma heard them, but for all that he heard his mind remained unmoved.

And even when Rāma looked at the people in their anguish, not the least anguish touched him—he was smiling instead as he walked on, eager to see his father, eager to carry out his father's order to the letter. * * *

THE BHAGAVAD-GĪTĀ

first century B.C.

The Sanskrit poem *Bhagavad-Gītā* (Song of the Lord) has been for centuries the great scripture of the Hindus and the Indian text most familiar to the West. The American writer Henry David Thoreau (1817–1862) took the *Gītā* with him to his retreat on Walden Pond, and the *Gītā* was the inspiring force in the life and thought of the eminent modern Indian leader Mahatma Gandhi (1869–1948). The enduring and seemingly universal appeal of this philosophical poem written in India two thousand years ago derives from the powerful, immediate way in which it addresses fundamental human concerns.

The *Bhagavad-Gītā* is a poem in eighteen chapters (and seven hundred verses), forming part of the sixth book of the Sanskrit epic the *Mahābhārata*, which narrates the story of a great war between the virtuous Pāṇḍavas and their evil cousins, the Kauravas, sons of King Dhṛtarāṣṭra of Hāstinapura. The *Gītā* opens at a dramatic moment in the epic narrative, with the blind Kaurava king asking the bard Sanjaya to describe to him what his sons and their enemies did after gathering at the battlefield of Kurukṣetra. The bard reports the reactions of Arjuna, champion among the Pāṇḍava heroes, and the ensuing dialogue between him and his charioteer Krishna (or Kṛṣṇa). Arriving at the battlefield, Arjuna sees cousins, teachers, uncles, and kinsmen standing ready to fight against each other. Horrified at the prospect of killing his kin and overcome by dejection, he lays down his weapons and refuses to fight. But Krishna, who is in reality an incarnation of Viṣṇu (the preserver god), tells Arjuna that his sacred duty (*dharma*) requires him to fight and explains to him how, far from miring him in the dreaded cycle of *karma* and rebirth, action performed in the spirit of sacred duty will advance him on the path to emancipation of the spirit, the Hindu's ultimate religious goal. Krishna's discourse, punctuated by Arjuna's questions, becomes *The Song of the Lord* (*Bhagavad-Gītā*).

There is reason to believe that the *Gītā*, originally an independent philosophical dialogue similar to earlier and contemporary texts such as the *Upaniṣads* and the Buddhist scriptures, was deliberately placed in the popular *Mahābhārata* epic at the beginning of the tale of the great war to give dramatic force to its teachings and underscore its relevance to the lives of common people. Although also an exalted hero, at this point in the narrative Arjuna is a vulnerable human being caught in a very human dilemma. Krishna, on the other hand, is no ordinary teacher, but God, come to instruct his human friend. This new configuration of elements fortified a view that was at once revolutionary for its time (ca. A.D. first century) and designed to preserve the Hindu social hierarchy.

By the end of the first century B.C. the Buddhist and Jain religions had gained a considerable following among the Indian masses and among kings and merchants as well. Focusing on the problem of *karma* — the belief that all actions involve consequences that must be suffered through many lives — Buddhism in particular offered men and women from all walks of life a religious path on which ethical action could be combined with contemplative spiritual practices, eventually leading to liberation from the burden of *karma*. In the Hindu social order, on the other hand, rigid and hierarchical correlations between birth and occupation locked people into existential situations that held no such prospect of ultimate freedom.

Arjuna's dilemma is a dramatic illustration of the problem: how can a Hindu warrior (*kṣatriya*), whose sacred duty (*dharma*) involves the taking of life (which, by an absolute standard, would entail evil *karma*) ever be liberated from rebirth, which is the ultimate goal of the religious person? The *Gītā* appears to have been the response of brahman thinkers who stood to lose the most from the potential disintegration of the Hindu social system. Through Krishna's teachings, the anonymous author of the *Gītā* articulates a new doctrine that will justify the hierarchies of class and social duty (he uses the word *lokasaṃgraha*, "social solidarity") at the same time that it offers universal access to the ultimate goal of the emancipation of the soul from suffering and rebirth, thus answering the personal spiritual needs of Hindus from resistant and disenfranchised groups.

The *Gītā* owes its success to the attractive and ingenious way in which it harmonizes widely differing strands of ancient Indian religious thought and practice. The text synthesizes the contemplative vision of the Buddhists and the sages of the *Upaniṣads* with a philosophy of active engagement in worldly life. Krishna's teachings allow each Hindu to venture on a personal spiritual quest without abandoning social responsibility and its attendant security. Drawing on all of the older religious sects and schools of philosophy, the *Gītā* has accommodated radically different interpretations through the centuries. But the author's stroke of genius is without question his integration of a new teaching of salvation through divine grace, linked to the cult of a popular god, with the older theory of *karma*.

The *Gītā* is a complex text, weaving together ancient, often contradictory ideas regarding existential questions that have preoccupied Indians for centuries. The poet uses the rhetorical device of Arjuna's doubts to repeat and consolidate previous arguments or to reject them as no longer useful, in what is essentially a technique of progressive illumination. In response to Arjuna's anguish at being unable to reconcile the conflict between sacred duty and the personal desire for liberation, Krishna explains to him the real nature of the soul and of action in the universe. He tells the hero that the soul (*ātman*, "the individual self") is not simply the ego but is in reality identical with Brahman, the immortal spirit underlying the entire universe. The knowledge of the soul's immortality, says Krishna, will dispel Arjuna's fear that he is personally responsible for particular actions. For the philosopher-teachers of the *Upaniṣads*, who propounded the theory of an immortal soul, this knowledge (*jñāna*) is the highest end of religious life, but for Krishna it is only a discipline (*yoga*), the first step toward liberation from birth and death.

If the soul is immortal, then Arjuna wants to know why it is involved in action, which inevitably causes rebirth. Adapting aspects of the doctrine of the Sāṃkhya philosophy, Krishna explains the riddle of an immortal soul's engagement in worldly action and a material universe. The perpetual action of all things with and on each other that constitutes the world process is an aspect of the union between God, who is the supreme embodiment of the immortal soul, and material nature, which is the substance of the universe. Action or change is an inescapable reality of living in the world; although the soul is immortal, in its embodied condition it is inevitably involved in deeds. God is himself engaged in the perpetual process of the world on which depend the cosmic, moral, and social orders, constituting *dharma* in its broadest sense. To withdraw from action, says Krishna, is thus an act of self-delusion and the abdication of moral and social responsibility.

This explanation only increases Arjuna's perplexity. If action is inevitable, how can the soul ever cease to be embodied (reborn)? Here Krishna turns to the Yoga philosophy, which propounds the doctrine of *yoga* ("a yoking"), the disciplining of the senses and the mind as the soul's path to transcendence over matter. Moving beyond the thought of traditional Yoga philosophers, he offers the new teaching of *karma yoga* (the "discipline of action") as the solution to Arjuna's problem. It is not action itself but desire for the fruit (profit or reward) of action that results in rebirth. If a person were to discipline his (the *Gītā*'s descriptions are all in the masculine gender) senses and mind to act with no desire whatsoever for the gains that will result, *karma* would not affect his soul. A person who acts in this disciplined way is the perfected *yogi* ("man of discipline"), and his soul is certain to be liberated from birth and death.

But how then does one know right action from wrong? The Hindu social order of *dharma*, based on cosmic and moral principles, relieves individuals of the responsibility of determining the content of action: right, or good, action is simply the sacred duty that has been prescribed for one's class, caste, and stage of life. In short, social and moral law takes care of the content of action, but the individual has control over the spirit in which he performs action and, therefore, over how his deeds will affect his soul. When acting in the world is transformed into *yoga*, a key concept in the *Gītā*, it becomes the very means for the soul's liberation from worldly existence.

Intriguing as Krishna's teachings are, they are still philosophical discourses whose greatest appeal is to the intellect. What drives the doctrine home for the majority of Hindus is the emotional power of Arjuna's vision of Krishna's omnipotent form as God, the theophany with which the teaching is clinched. At Arjuna's request, Krishna reveals to him his infinite form, showing himself as the source and refuge of all creatures and the entire universe and, as "time grown old," their destroyer as well. Profoundly moved, Arjuna sings a hymn to Krishna, but he is eventually overcome by terror and awe and begs Krishna to resume his familiar, gentle form once more.

In Chapter 11, and elsewhere, the *Gītā* draws on the theology of the Bhagavatas—a group who worshiped Krishna as God and an incarnation of Viṣṇu—and develops the doctrine of *bhakti yoga*, the discipline of devotion. Recognizing God's grace and love in Krishna's earlier discourse as much as in the cosmic vision, Arjuna is at last ready to accept this final teaching, according to which the best way to overcome worldly desire is to make of all one's deeds a loving sacrifice to God. Krishna asserts that love of God will annul the power of desire and, therefore, of *karma*, but what is equally important is that the discipline of sacred duty will become a joyous, transfiguring experience. In his revelation of himself as God, Krishna declares, "If they rely on me, Arjuna, / women, commoners, men of low rank, / even men born in the womb of evil, / reach the highest way." And as if to

illustrate this transition from duty to joy, the author of the *Bhagavad-Gītā* gives his auditors and readers not a dry philosophical tract but a poem in which the simple epic stanzas—in the *śloka* and *triṣṭubh* meters—acquire an elegant, epigrammatic quality rendered memorable by vivid metaphors such as the one of the yogi who "does not waver, / like a lamp sheltered from the wind" and the likening of the brilliance of Krishna's divine epiphany to "the light of a thousand suns" rising in the sky at once.

Thoreau is only one among many Western thinkers who have found the *Gītā* ideal of the man of spiritual discipline (*yogi*) attractive. For Indian intellectuals in the late nineteenth century the work had an additional dimension. It was in response to Western education and Western critiques of Hinduism and Indian civilization under British colonial rule that Indian leaders from a wide range of philosophies—from Swami Vivekananda (1863–1902) to Mahatma Gandhi—found the ideal text for India and the twentieth century in the *Bhagavad-Gītā*.

Much Western writing of the nineteenth century depicts Indians as a passive people with no social consciousness, attributing these shortcomings in part to the lack of a universal scripture and ethical code in Hinduism. Modern Indian leaders have found in the moral teaching of the *Gītā* and its spirit of pluralism and synthesis their greatest inspiration for political and social activism, for service to the Indian people, and for the creation of a modern democratic nation. Most have interpreted the text's spiritual egalitarianism in social terms, arguing that the *Gītā* teachings support, indeed demand, the abolition of traditional social hierarchies such as caste. For Swami Vivekananda, the twentieth-century Indian philosopher Sarvepalli Radhakrishnan (1888–1975), and others, the *Gītā* represents not a scripture for Hindus alone but a universal ethic for the modern world. In our own time, its vision of Krishna as God has flowered anew in the International Krishna Consciousness movement initiated by Swami A. C. Bhaktivedanta (1896–1977). The most remarkable reading of the *Gītā's* teachings, however, is the one offered by Mahatma Gandhi, who argued that absolute nonviolence is the only logical culmination of Krishna's doctrine of "desireless action." That this ancient text continues to capture the imagination of so many modern thinkers is eloquent testimony to its vitality.

Among the scriptures of the world, the *Bhagavad-Gītā* is second only to the Bible in the number of times it has been translated. Barbara Stoler Miller, *The Bhagavad-Gītā: Krishna's Counsel in Time of War* (1986), is the most accessible modern translation of the work, enhanced by a lucid introductory essay and a glossary of key words. Among older translations and interpretations, readers might find it useful to consult Eliot Deutsch for a good explanation of key philosophical ideas, and S. Radhakrishnan for the parallel Sanskrit text (in transliteration), accompanied by a commentary from the point of view of an eminent modern Indian philosopher. On Indian interpreters of the *Gītā*, see Robert Minor, *Modern Interpreters of the Bhagavadgītā* (1986). For the *Gītā's* career in the West, consult Eric Sharpe, *The Universal Gītā: Western Images of the Bhagavad Gītā; A Bicentennial Survey* (1985).

PRONOUNCING GLOSSARY

The following list uses common English syllables and stress accents to provide rough equivalents of selected words whose pronunciation may be unfamiliar to the general reader.

Bhagavad-Gītā: *buh'-guh-vuhd–gee'-tah*

Bhagavān: *buh'-guh-vahn*

Dhṛtarāṣṭra: *dree'-tuh-rahsh-truh*

Jñāna: *gyah'-nuh*

Krishna (Kṛṣṇa): *krish'-nuh*

kṣatriya: *kshuh'-tree-yuh*

Kurukṣetra: *koo-roo-kshay'-truh*

lokasaṃgraha: *loh'-kuh-suhn'-gruh-huh*

Mahābhārata: *muh-hah-bah'-ruh-tuh*

Sāṃkhya: *sahn'-kyuh*

śloka: *shloh'-kuh*

triṣṭubh: *tree'-shtoobh*

Upaniṣad: *oo-puhn'-ee-shuhd*

The Bhagavad-Gītā[1]

FROM THE SECOND TEACHING

Philosophy and Spiritual Discipline

LORD KRISHNA:

11 You grieve for those beyond grief,
and you speak words of insight;
but learned men do not grieve
for the dead or the living.

12 Never have I not existed,
nor you, nor these kings;
and never in the future
shall we cease to exist.

13 Just as the embodied self
enters childhood, youth, and old age,
so does it enter another body;
this does not confound a steadfast man.[2]

14 Contacts with matter make us feel
heat and cold, pleasure and pain.
Arjuna, you must learn to endure
fleeting things—they come and go!

15 When these cannot torment a man,
when suffering and joy are equal
for him and he has courage,
he is fit for immortality.

16 Nothing of nonbeing comes to be,
nor does being cease to exist;
the boundary between these two
is seen by men who see reality.

17 Indestructible is the presence
that pervades all this;
no one can destroy
this unchanging reality.

---

1. Translated by Barbara Stoler Miller. Verse numbers run to the left of the text.   2. Here Krishna begins to explain the implications of reincarnation, emphasizing the identity of the seemingly finite embodied soul with the infinite and imperishable universal spirit (Brahman).

18   Our bodies are known to end,
but the embodied self is enduring,
indestructible, and immeasurable;
therefore, Arjuna, fight the battle!

19   He who thinks this self a killer
and he who thinks it killed,
both fail to understand;
it does not kill, nor is it killed.

20   It is not born,
it does not die;
having been,
it will never not be;
unborn, enduring,
constant, and primordial,
it is not killed
when the body is killed.

21   Arjuna, when a man knows the self
to be indestructible, enduring, unborn,
unchanging, how does he kill
or cause anyone to kill?

22   As a man discards
worn-out clothes
to put on new
and different ones,
so the embodied self
discards
its worn-out bodies
to take on other new ones.

23   Weapons do not cut it,
fire does not burn it,
waters do not wet it,
wind does not wither it.

24   It cannot be cut or burned;
it cannot be wet or withered;
it is enduring, all-pervasive,
fixed, immovable, and timeless.

25   It is called unmanifest,
inconceivable, and immutable;
since you know that to be so,
you should not grieve!

26   If you think of its birth
and death as ever-recurring,
then too, Great Warrior,
you have no cause to grieve!

27   Death is certain for anyone born,
and birth is certain for the dead;
since the cycle is inevitable,
you have no cause to grieve!

28   Creatures are unmanifest in origin,
     manifest in the midst of life,
     and unmanifest again in the end.
     Since this is so, why do you lament?

29   Rarely someone
     sees it,
     rarely another
     speaks it,
     rarely anyone
     hears it—
     even hearing it,
     no one really knows it.

30   The self embodied in the body
     of every being is indestructible;
     you have no cause to grieve
     for all these creatures, Arjuna!

31   Look to your own duty;[3]
     do not tremble before it;
     nothing is better for a warrior
     than a battle of sacred duty.

32   The doors of heaven open
     for warriors who rejoice
     to have a battle like this
     thrust on them by chance.

33   If you fail to wage this war
     of sacred duty,
     you will abandon your own duty
     and fame only to gain evil.

34   People will tell
     of your undying shame,
     and for a man of honor
     shame is worse than death.

               ✳   ✳   ✳

47   Be intent on action,
     not on the fruits of action;
     avoid attraction to the fruits
     and attachment to inaction!

48   Perform actions, firm in discipline,
     relinquishing attachment;
     be impartial to failure and success—
     this equanimity is called discipline.

49   Arjuna, action is far inferior
     to the discipline of understanding;[4]
     so seek refuge in understanding—pitiful
     are men drawn by fruits of action.

---

3. *Dharma*, which for Arjuna is that of his class (warrior) and stage of life (householder).   **4.** The rational facilities, including intuitive intelligence, in contrast to the mind, or discursive intellect.

50 Disciplined by understanding,
    one abandons both good and evil deeds;
    so arm yourself for discipline—
    discipline is skill in actions.

51 Wise men disciplined by understanding
    relinquish the fruit born of action;
    freed from these bonds of rebirth,
    they reach a place beyond decay.

52 When your understanding passes beyond
    the swamp of delusion,
    you will be indifferent to all
    that is heard in sacred lore.[5]

53 When your understanding turns
    from sacred lore to stand fixed,
    immovable in contemplation,
    then you will reach discipline.[6]

54 ARJUNA:
    Krishna, what defines a man
    deep in contemplation whose insight
    and thought are sure? How would he speak?
    How would he sit? How would he move?

55 LORD KRISHNA:
    When he gives up desires in his mind,
    is content with the self within himself,[7]
    then he is said to be a man
    whose insight is sure, Arjuna.

56 When suffering does not disturb his mind,
    when his craving for pleasures has vanished,
    when attraction, fear, and anger are gone,
    he is called a sage whose thought is sure.

57 When he shows no preference
    in fortune or misfortune
    and neither exults nor hates,
    his insight is sure.

58 When, like a tortoise retracting
    its limbs, he withdraws his senses
    completely from sensuous objects,
    his insight is sure.

FROM THE THIRD TEACHING

Discipline of Action

ARJUNA:
1 If you think understanding
    is more powerful than action,

5. The *Vedas* and their ritualistic doctrine. Krishna says that the older ritualistic learning is useless for the emancipation of the soul from *karma*.   6. Used in its broadest sense.   7. A play on the word *ātman*, which means both "the self" (soul) and "oneself." Only one who has realized the true (immutable) nature of the self can be *content with the self within himself.* Krishna now begins to describe the techniques and effects of withdrawing one's senses from the outside and focusing them on the interior self, the infinite soul.

why, Krishna, do you urge me
to this horrific act?

2 You confuse my understanding
with a maze of words;
speak one certain truth
so I may achieve what is good.

LORD KRISHNA:

3 Earlier I taught the twofold
basis of good in this world —
for philosophers, disciplined knowledge;
for men of discipline, action.

4 A man cannot escape the force
of action by abstaining from actions;
he does not attain success
just by renunciation.

5 No one exists for even an instant
without performing action;
however unwilling, every being is forced
to act by the qualities of nature.[8]

6 When his senses are controlled
but he keeps recalling
sense objects with his mind,
he is a self-deluded hypocrite.

7 When he controls his senses
with his mind and engages in the discipline
of action with his faculties of action,
detachment sets him apart.

8 Perform necessary action;
it is more powerful than inaction;
without action you even fail
to sustain your own body.

9 Action imprisons the world
unless it is done as sacrifice;
freed from attachment, Arjuna,
perform action as sacrifice!

*   *   *

19 Always perform with detachment
any action you must do;
performing action with detachment,
one achieves supreme good.

20 Janaka[9] and other ancient kings
attained perfection by action alone;
seeing the way to preserve
the world, you should act.

8. That is, sublimity, dynamism (passion), and inertia.   9. Celebrated character in the dialogues of the *Bṛhadāraṇyaka Upaniṣad*; an exemplar of the warrior-king who is also a man of discipline (a *yogi*).

21 Whatever a leader does,
the ordinary people also do.
He sets the standard
for the world to follow.

22 In the three worlds,[1]
there is nothing I must do,
nothing unattained to be attained,
yet I engage in action.

23 What if I did not engage
relentlessly in action?
Men retrace my path
at every turn, Arjuna.

24 These worlds would collapse
if I did not perform action;
I would create disorder in society,
living beings would be destroyed.

25 As the ignorant act with attachment
to actions, Arjuna,
so wise men should act with detachment
to preserve the world.

*   *   *

FROM THE SIXTH TEACHING

The Man of Discipline[2]

10 A man of discipline should always
discipline himself, remain in seclusion,
isolated, his thought and self well controlled,
without possessions or hope.

11 He should fix for himself
a firm seat in a pure place,
neither too high nor too low,
covered in cloth, deerskin, or grass.

12 He should focus his mind and restrain
the activity of his thought and senses;
sitting on that seat, he should practice
discipline for the purification of the self.

13 He should keep his body, head,
and neck aligned, immobile, steady;
he should gaze at the tip of his nose
and not let his glance wander.

14 The self tranquil, his fear dispelled,
firm in his vow of celibacy, his mind restrained,
let him sit with discipline,
his thought fixed on me, intent on me.

---

1. Heaven, earth, and the underworld.   2. The *yogi*. This teaching has much in common with the
descriptions of the psychological and physical techniques of *yoga* presented by Yoga philosophers.

15 Disciplining himself,
his mind controlled,
a man of discipline finds peace,
the pure calm that exists in me.

16 Gluttons have no discipline,
nor the man who starves himself,
nor he who sleeps excessively
or suffers wakefulness.

17 When a man disciplines his diet
and diversions, his physical actions,
his sleeping and waking,
discipline destroys his sorrow.

18 When his controlled thought
rests within the self alone,
without craving objects of desire,
he is said to be disciplined.

19 "He does not waver, like a lamp sheltered
from the wind" is the simile recalled
for a man of discipline, restrained in thought
and practicing self-discipline.

20 When his thought ceases,
checked by the exercise of discipline,
he is content within the self,
seeing the self through himself.

21 Absolute joy beyond the senses
can only be grasped by understanding;
when one knows it, he abides there
and never wanders from this reality.

22 Obtaining it, he thinks
there is no greater gain;
abiding there, he is unmoved,
even by deep suffering.

23 Since he knows that discipline
means unbinding the bonds of suffering,
he should practice discipline resolutely,
without despair dulling his reason.

24 He should entirely relinquish
desires aroused by willful intent;
he should entirely control
his senses with his mind.

25 He should gradually become tranquil,
firmly controlling his understanding;
focusing his mind on the self,
he should think nothing.

26 Wherever his faltering mind
unsteadily wanders,
he should restrain it
and bring it under self-control.

27 When his mind is tranquil, perfect joy
comes to the man of discipline;
his passion is calmed, he is without sin,
being one with the infinite spirit.

28 Constantly disciplining himself,
free from sin, the man of discipline
easily achieves perfect joy
in harmony with the infinite spirit.

29 Arming himself with discipline,
seeing everything with an equal eye,
he sees the self in all creatures
and all creatures in the self.

30 He who sees me everywhere
and sees everything in me
will not be lost to me,
and I will not be lost to him.

31 I exist in all creatures,
so the disciplined man devoted to me
grasps the oneness of life;
wherever he is, he is in me.

32 When he sees identity in everything,
whether joy or suffering,
through analogy with the self,
he is deemed a man of pure discipline.

Summary   In the Seventh to Tenth Teachings Krishna explains diverse aspects
of the nature of the infinite spirit, gradually unveiling the mystery of his own
identity as the highest manifestation of that universal spirit and thus leading up to
the revelation of his cosmic form in the Eleventh Teaching.

FROM THE ELEVENTH TEACHING

The Vision of Krishna's Totality

ARJUNA:

1 To favor me you revealed
the deepest mystery of the self,
and by your words
my delusion is dispelled.

2 I heard from you in detail
how creatures come to be and die,
Krishna, and about the self
in its immutable greatness.

3 Just as you have described
yourself, I wish to see your form
in all its majesty,
Krishna, Supreme among Men.

4 If you think I can see it,
reveal to me

your immutable self.
Krishna, Lord of Discipline.

LORD KRISHNA:
5   Arjuna, see my forms
in hundreds and thousands;
diverse, divine,
of many colors and shapes.

6   See the sun gods, gods of light,
howling storm gods, twin gods of dawn,
and gods of wind, Arjuna,
wondrous forms not seen before.

7   Arjuna, see all the universe,
animate and inanimate,
and whatever else you wish to see;
all stands here as one in my body.

8   But you cannot see me
with your own eye;
I will give you a divine eye to see
the majesty of my discipline.

SANJAYA:[3]
9   O King, saying this, Krishna,
the great lord of discipline,
revealed to Arjuna
the true majesty of his form.

10   It was a multiform, wondrous vision,
with countless mouths and eyes[4]
and celestial ornaments,
brandishing many divine weapons.

11   Everywhere was boundless divinity
containing all astonishing things,
wearing divine garlands and garments,
anointed with divine perfume.

12   If the light of a thousand suns
were to rise in the sky at once,
it would be like the light
of that great spirit.

13   Arjuna saw all the universe
in its many ways and parts,
standing as one in the body
of the god of gods.

*   *   *

3. The bard who is retelling the events of the battle to King Dhṛtarāṣṭra.   4. Standard elements of icons of the Hindu gods, which are worshiped as manifestations of the gods themselves. In most icons, the Hindu gods have four or more arms.

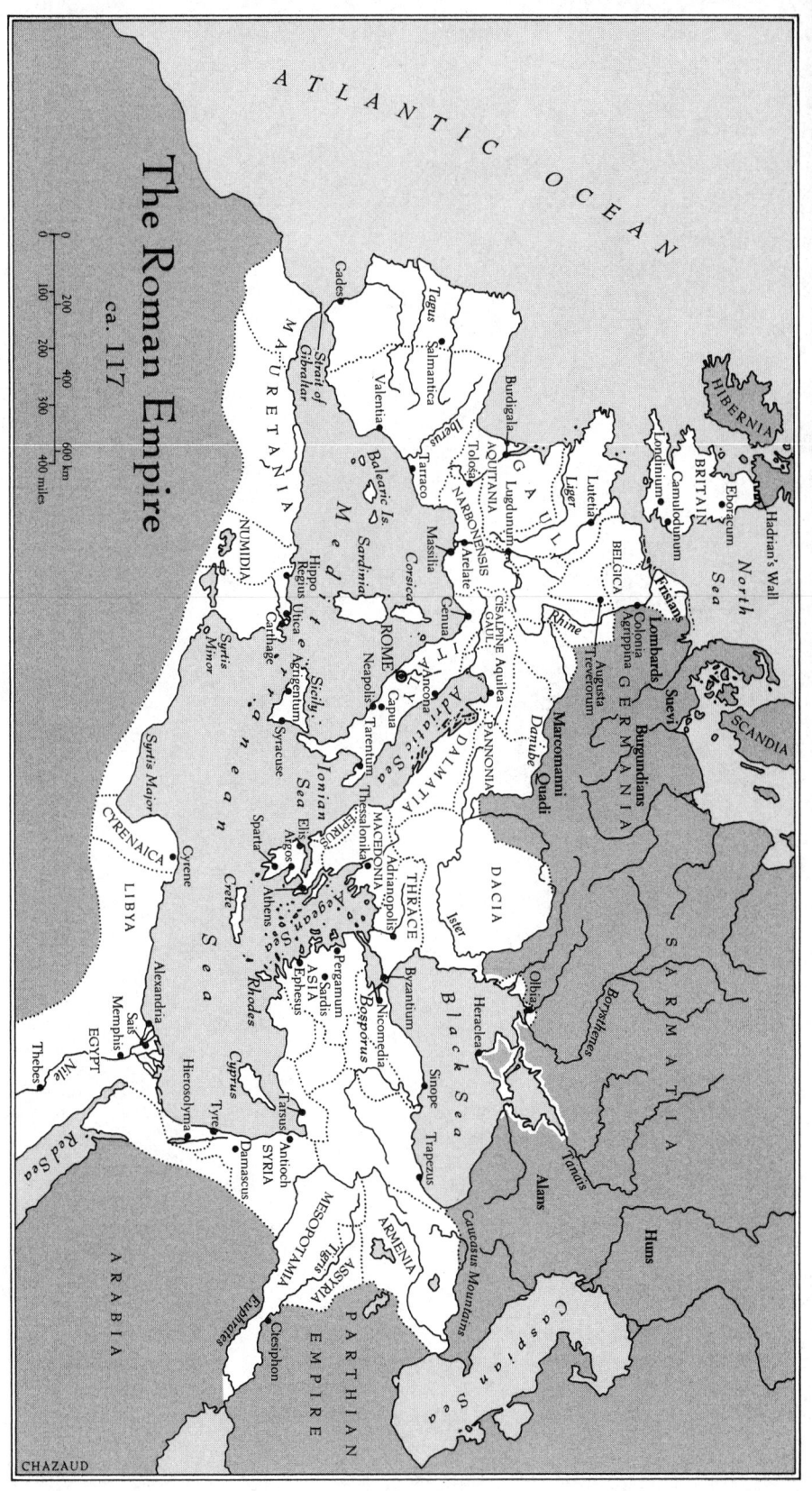

The Roman Empire
ca. 117

0 100 200 300 400 km
0 200 400 600 400 miles

ATLANTIC OCEAN

HIBERNIA

BRITAIN
Eboracum
Hadrian's Wall
Camulodunum
Londinium
Frisians
North Sea

SCANDIA

Gades
Strait of Gibraltar
Tagus
Salmantica
Valentia
Balearic Is.
Iberus
Tarraco
Burdigala
Tolosa
AQUITANIA
Lugdunum
GAUL
Liger
Lutetia
BELGICA
Colonia Agrippina
Augusta Treverorum
GERMANIA
Lombards
Burgundians
Suevi
Longinium

MAURETANIA
NUMIDIA
Hippo Regius
Utica
Carthage
Agrippina
Syrtis Minor

Sardinia
Corsica
Massilia
Arelate
NARBONENSIS
CISALPINE GAUL
Aquileia
Genua
ROME
Neapolis
Capua
Tarentum
ITALY
Ancona
Adriatic Sea
DALMATIA
PANNONIA
Rhine
Danube
Marcomanni
Quadi

Sicily
Agrigentum
Syracuse
Ionian Sea
Elis
EPIRUS
Thessalonica
MACEDONIA
Adrianopolis
THRACE
Byzantium
DACIA
Ister

CYRENAICA
Cyrene
LIBYA
Crete
Sparta
Argos
Athens
Rhodes
Aegean Sea
ASIA
Pergamum
Sardis
Ephesus
Nicomedia
Bosporus
Heraclea
Sinope
Trapezus
Black Sea

SARMATIA
Borysthenes
Olbia
Tanais
Alans
Huns

Alexandria
Sais
Memphis
Thebes
Nile
EGYPT
Hierosolyma
Tyre
Tarsus
Antioch
Damascus
SYRIA
MESOPOTAMIA
Tigris
ASSYRIA
ARMENIA
Caucasus Mountains
Caspian Sea

Red Sea
ARABIA
Euphrates
Ctesiphon
PARTHIAN EMPIRE

Mediterranean Sea
Syrtis Major

CHAZAUD

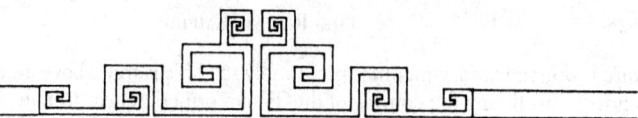

The Roman Empire

When Alexander died at Babylon in 323 B.C., the Italian city of Rome, situated on the Tiber in the western coastal plain, was engaged in a struggle for the control of central Italy. Less than a hundred years later (269 B.C.) Rome, in control of the whole Italian peninsula, was drawn into a hundred-year war against the Phoenician city of Carthage, on the North African coast, from which it emerged master of the western Mediterranean. At the end of the first century B.C., in spite of a series of civil wars fought with savage vindictiveness and on a continental scale, Rome was the capital of an empire that stretched from the Strait of Gibraltar to the frontiers of Palestine. This empire gave peace and orderly government to the Mediterranean area for the next two centuries, and for two centuries after that maintained a desperate but losing battle against the invading savage peoples moving in from the north and east. When it finally went down, it left behind it the ideal of the world-state, an ideal that was to be reconstituted as a reality by the medieval church, which ruled from the same center, Rome, and with a spiritual authority as great as the secular authority it replaced.

The achievements of the Romans, not only their conquests but also their success in consolidating the conquests and organizing the conquered, are best understood in the light of the Roman character. Unlike the Greeks, Romans were above all a practical people. They might have had no aptitude for pure mathematics, but they could build an aqueduct that lasted two thousand years. Though they were not notable as political theorists, they organized a complicated yet stable federation that held Italy loyal to them in the presence of invading armies. Romans were conservative to the core; their strongest authority was *mos maiorum*, the custom of predecessors. A monument of this conservatism, the great body of Roman law is one of their greatest contributions to Western civilization. The quality Romans most admired was *gravitas*, seriousness of attitude and purpose, and their highest words of commendation were *manliness*, *industry*, and *discipline*. Pericles, in his funeral speech, praised Athenians for their adaptability, versatility, and grace. This would have seemed strange praise to a Roman, whose idea of personal and civic virtue was different. "By her ancient customs and her men the Roman state stands," says Ennius the Roman poet, in a line that by its metrical heaviness emphasizes the stability implied in the key word *stands: moribus antiquis res stat Romana virisque.*

Greek history begins, not with a king, a battle, or the founding of a city but with an epic poem; the literary achievement preceded the political by many centuries. The Romans, on the other hand, had conquered half the world before they began to write. The stimulus to the creation of Latin literature was the Greek literature that the Romans discovered when, in the second century B.C., they assumed political responsibility for Greece and the Near East. Latin literature began with a translation of the *Odyssey*, made by a Greek prisoner of war, and with the exception of satire, until Latin literature became Christian, the model was always Greek. The Latin writer (especially the poet) borrowed wholesale from the Greek original, not furtively, but openly and proudly, as a tribute to the master. But this frank acknowledgment of indebtedness should not blind us to the fact that Latin litera-

ture is original, and sometimes profoundly so. This is true above all of Virgil, who chose as his theme the coming of the Trojan prince Aeneas to Italy, where he was to found a city from which, in the fullness of time, would come "the Latin race, . . . and the walls of lofty Rome."

When Virgil was born in 70 B.C. the Roman republic, which had conquered and now governed the Mediterranean world, had barely recovered from one civil war and was drifting inexorably toward another. The institutions of the city-state proved inadequate for world government. The civil conflict that had disrupted the republic for more than one hundred years ended finally in the establishment of a powerful executive. Although the Senate, which had been the controlling body of the republic, retained an impressive share of the power, the new arrangement developed inevitably toward autocracy, the rule of the executive, the emperor, as he was called once the system was stabilized. The first of the long line of Roman emperors who gave stable government to the Roman world during the first two centuries A.D. was Octavius, known generally by his title, Augustus. He had made his way cautiously through the intrigues and bloodshed that followed the murder of his uncle Julius Caesar in 44 B.C. until by 31 B.C. he controlled the western half of the empire. In that year he fought a decisive battle with the ruler of the eastern half of the empire, Mark Antony, who was supported by Cleopatra, queen of Egypt. Octavius's victory at Actium united the empire under one authority and ushered in an age of peace and reconstruction.

For the next two hundred years the successors of Augustus, the Roman emperors, ruled the ancient world with only occasional disturbances, most of them confined to Rome, where emperors who flagrantly abused their immense power— Nero, for example—were overthrown by force. The second half of this period was described by Gibbon, the great historian of imperial Rome, as the period "in the history of the world during which the condition of the human race was most happy and prosperous." The years A.D. 96–180, those of the "five good emperors," were in fact remarkable; this was the longest period of peace that has ever been enjoyed by the inhabitants of an area that included Britain, France, all southern Europe, the Middle East, and the whole of North Africa. Trade and agriculture flourished, and the cities with their public baths, theaters, and libraries offered all the amenities of civilized life. Yet there was apparent, especially in the literature of the second century, a spiritual emptiness. Petronius's *Satyricon* paints a sardonic portrait of the vulgar display and intellectual poverty of the newly rich who can think only in terms of money and possessions. The old religion offered no comfort to those who looked beyond mere material ends; it had been too closely knit into the fabric of the independent city-state and was inadequate for a time in which individuals were citizens of the world. New religions arose or were imported from the East, universal religions that made their appeal to all nations and classes: the worship of the Egyptian goddess Isis; of the Persian god Mithras, who offered bliss in the life to come; and of the Hebrew prophet Jesus, crucified in Jerusalem and believed risen from the dead. This was the religion that, working underground and often suppressed (there was a persecution of the Christians under Nero in the first century, another under the last of the "good emperors" Marcus Aurelius in the second), finally triumphed and became the official and later the exclusive religion of the Roman world. As the empire in the third and fourth centuries disintegrated under the never-ending invasions by barbarian tribes from the north, the church, with its center and spiritual head in Rome, converted the new inhabitants and so made possible the preservation of much of the Latin and Greek literature that was to serve the European Middle Ages and, later, the Renaissance as a model and a basis for their own great achievements in the arts and letters.

FURTHER READING

John Boardman, Jasper Griffin, and Oswyn Murray, eds., *The Oxford History of the Classical World* (1986), is a superb survey, by many different specialists, of the whole sweep of classical culture—social, political, literary, artistic, and religious. For a detailed survey of Roman literature, see E. J. Kenney and W. V. Clausen, eds., *The Cambridge History of Classical Literature, Volume 2: Latin Literature* (1982). Michael Grant, *History of Rome* (1978), presents a well-illustrated, eminently readable overview.

TEXTS	CONTEXTS
	753 B.C. Traditional date of the foundation of Rome
	ca. 750 Foundation of Carthage (North Africa)
	735 Greek colony at Syracuse (Sicily)
	7th century Greek colonies at Marseilles (France) and Cyrene (North Africa)
	509 Expulsion of the king; Rome becomes a republic
	451 Roman law codified—the Twelve Tablets
	264 Rome controls Italy south of the River Po; defeats Carthage at sea
	227 Sicily becomes the first Roman province
	218–202 Hannibal of Carthage invades Italy, fails to capture Rome, defeated at Zama near Carthage in 202
	197 Spain becomes a Roman province
	91–89 Social war in Italy; Italians gain Roman citizenship
	87–81 Civil war ending in dictatorship of Sulla
ca. 84–54 B.C. Catullus	
	74 Cyrene becomes a Roman province
70–19 Virgil, author of *The Aeneid*	
	58–50 Julius Caesar conquers Gaul
	47 Julius Caesar dictator; murdered in 44
43–ca. A.D. 17 Ovid, author of *Metamorphoses*	

TEXTS	CONTEXTS
	27–23 Octavian (now Augustus) establishes imperial regime
	1. 6 Birth of Jesus
ca. A.D. 10–65 Petronius, author of *The Satyricon*	
	A.D. 14–37 Tiberius emperor
	37–41 Caligula emperor
	41–54 Claudius emperor
	54–68 Nero emperor
	64 Persecution of Christians under Nero

CATULLUS
84?–54? B.C.

Gaius Valerius Catullus, born in the north Italian city of Verona around 84 B.C., lived out his short life in the last violent century of the Roman republic—a time of political upheaval that broke out more than once into civil war and culminated in the establishment of imperial authority by Augustus (see the introduction, "The Roman Empire," p. 627). The 116 of his poems that have come down to us present a rich variety: imitations of Greek poets (including a brilliant translation of one of Sappho's most passionate lyrics), long poems on Greek mythological themes, scurrilous personal attacks on contemporary politicians and private individuals, lighthearted verses designed to amuse his friends, and a magnificent marriage hymn. He also wrote a series of poems that deal with his love affair—at first ecstatically happy, then despairing—with a Roman woman he calls Lesbia but who was probably Clodia, the enchanting but viciously corrupt sister of one of Rome's most cynical and violent aristocrats turned political gangster. These poems present all the phases of the liaison, from the unalloyed happiness of the first encounters through doubt and hesitation to despair and virulent accusation, ending in heartbroken resignation to the bitter fact. They express both the joy of passionate love requited and the torment of betrayal in language so direct and simple, so charged with ecstasy and fury, that they have been the despair of translators ever since.

For a sensitive appreciation of Catullus's poetry see E. A. Havelock, *The Lyric Genius of Catullus* (1967). For a brief but masterly assessment see J. W. Mackail, *Latin Literature* (1962).

5[1]

Come, Lesbia, let us live and love,
nor give a damn what sour old men say.
The sun that sets may rise again
but when our light has sunk into the earth,
it is gone forever.   5
    Give me a thousand kisses,
then a hundred, another thousand,
another hundred
    and in one breath
still kiss another thousand,   10
another hundred.
    O then with lips and bodies joined
many deep thousands;
    confuse
their number,   15
    so that poor fools and cuckolds (envious
even now) shall never
learn our wealth and curse us
with their
evil eyes.   20

---

1. All selections translated by Horace Gregory.

87

No woman, if she is honest, can say that she's
been blessed with greater love, my Lesbia,
than I have given you;
nor has any man held to a contract made
with more fidelity   5
than I have shown, my dear,
in loving you.

107

When at last after long despair, our hopes ring true again
and long-starved desire eats, O then the mind leaps in the sunlight—
    Lesbia
so it was with me when you returned. Here was a treasure
more valuable than gold; you, whom I love beyond hope, giving yourself
to me again. That hour, a year of holidays, radiant,   5
where is the man more fortunate than I,
where can he find anything in life more glorious
than the sight of all his wealth restored?

109

My life, my love, you say our love will last forever;
O gods remember
  her pledge, convert the words of her avowal into a prophecy.
Now let her blood speak, let sincerity govern each syllable fallen
from her lips, so that the long years of our lives shall be   5
a contract of true love inviolate
against time itself, a symbol of eternity.

83

Lesbia speaks evil of me with her husband near and he (damned idiot)
    loves to hear her.
Chuckling, the fool is happy, seeing nothing, understanding nothing.
If she forgetting me fell silent, her heart would be his alone, content and
    peaceful;
but she raves, spitting hatred upon me, all of which carries this meaning:
I am never out of her mind, and what is more, she rises in fury against
    me   5
with words that make her burn, her blood passionate for me.

70

My woman says that she would rather wear the wedding-veil for me
than anyone: even if Jupiter[2] himself came storming after her;

2. Jupiter (sometimes called Jove) was the supreme god of the Roman pantheon, corresponding to the
Greek Zeus.

that's what she says, but when a woman talks to a hungry,
ravenous lover, her words should be written upon the wind
and engraved in rapid waters.   5

72

There was a time, O Lesbia, when you said Catullus was the only man
    on earth who could understand you,
who could twine his arms round you, even Jove himself less welcome.
And when I thought of you, my dear, you were not the mere flesh and
the means by which a lover finds momentary rapture.
My love was half paternal, as a father greets his son or   5
smiles at his daughter's husband.

Although I know you well (too well), my love now turns to fire
and you are small and shallow.
Is this a miracle? Your wounds in love's own battle
have made me your companion, perhaps, a greater lover,   10
but O, my dear, I'll never be
the modest boy who saw you as a lady, delicate and sweet,
a paragon of virtue.

85

I hate and love.
    And if you ask me why,
I have no answer, but I discern,
    can feel, my senses rooted in eternal torture.

8

Poor damned Catullus, here's no time for nonsense,
open your eyes, O idiot, innocent boy, look at what has happened:
once there were sunlit days when you followed after
where ever a girl would go, she loved with greater
love than any woman knew.   5
Then you took your pleasure
and the girl was not unwilling. Those were the bright days, gone;
now she's no longer yielding; you must be, poor idiot,
more like a man! not running after
her your mind all tears; stand firm, insensitive.   10
Say with a smile, voice steady, "Good-bye, my girl," Catullus
strong and manly no longer follows you, nor comes when you are
    calling
him at night and you shall need him.
You whore! Where's your man to cling to, who will praise your
    beauty,
where's the man that you love and who will call you his,   15
and when you fall to kissing, whose lips will you devour?
But always, your Catullus will be as firm as rock is.

11

Furius, Aurelius,[3] bound to Catullus
though he marches piercing farthest India
where echoing waves of the Eastern Oceans
    break up the shores:

Under Caspian seas, to mild Arabia,   5
east of Parthia, dark with savage bowmen,
or where the Nile, sevenfold and uprising,
    stains its leveled sands,—

Even though he marches over Alps to gaze on
great Caesar's monuments: the Gallic Rhine and   10
Britons[4] who live beyond torn seas, remotest
    men of distant lands—

Friends who defy with me all things, whatever
gods may send us, go now, friends, deliver
these words to my lady, nor sweet—flattering,   15
    nor kind nor gentle:

Live well and sleep with adulterous lovers,
three hundred men between your thighs, embracing
all love turned false, again, again, and breaking
    their strength, now sterile.   15

She will not find my love (once hers) returning;
she it was who caused love, this lonely flower,
tossed aside, to fall by the plough dividing
    blossoming meadows.

76

If man can find rich consolation, remembering his good deeds and all he
    has done,
if he remembers his loyalty to others, nor abuses his religion by heartless
    betrayal
of friends to the anger of powerful gods,
then, my Catullus, the long years before you shall not sink in darkness
    with all hope gone,
wandering, dismayed, through the ruins of love.
All the devotion that man gives to man, you have given, Catullus,   5
your heart and your brain flowed into a love that was desolate, wasted, nor
    can it return.
But why, why do you crucify love and yourself through the years?
Take what the gods have to offer and standing serene, rise forth as a rock
    against darkening skies;
and yet you do nothing but grieve, sunken deep in your sorrow,
    Catullus,   10
for it is hard, hard to throw aside years lived in poisonous love that has
    tainted your brain
and must end.

---

3. Friends of Catullus.   4. Julius Caesar (100–44 B.C.) began the conquest of Gaul in 58 B.C. and in
55 B.C. made an expedition to Britain.

If this seems impossible now, you must rise
to salvation. O gods of pity and mercy, descend and witness my sorrow, if
    ever
you have looked upon man in his hour of death, see me now in despair.   15
Tear this loathsome disease from my brain. Look, a subtle corruption has
    entered my bones,
no longer shall happiness flow through my veins like a river.
    No longer I pray
that she love me again, that her body be chaste, mine forever.
Cleanse my soul of this sickness of love, give me power to rise, resurrected,
    to thrust love aside,   20
I have given my heart to the gods, O hear me, omnipotent heaven,
and ease me of love and its pain.

VIRGIL

70–19 B.C.

Publius Virgilius Maro was born in northern Italy, and very little is known about his life. The earliest work which is certainly his is the *Bucolics*, a collection of poems in the pastoral genre that have had enormous influence. These were followed by the *Georgics*, a didactic poem on farming, in four books, which many critics consider his finest work. The *Aeneid*, the Roman epic, was left unfinished at his death.

Like all the Latin poets, Virgil built on the solid foundations of his Greek predecessors. The story of Aeneas, the Trojan prince who came to Italy and whose descendants founded Rome, combines the themes of the *Odyssey* (the wanderer in search of home) and the *Iliad* (the hero in battle). Virgil borrows Homeric turns of phrase, similes, sentiments, and whole incidents; his Aeneas, like Achilles, sacrifices prisoners to the shade of a friend and, like Odysseus, descends alive to the world of the dead. But unlike Achilles, Aeneas does not satisfy the great passion of his life, nor, like Odysseus, does he find a home and peace. The personal objectives of both of Homer's heroes are sacrificed by Aeneas for a greater objective. There is something greater than himself. His mission, imposed on him by the gods, is to found a city, from which, in the fullness of time, will spring the Roman state.

Homer presents us in the *Iliad* with the tragic pattern of the individual will, Achilles' wrath. But Aeneas is more than an individual. He is the prototype of the ideal Roman ruler; his qualities are the devotion to duty and the seriousness of purpose that were to give the Mediterranean world two centuries of ordered government. Aeneas's mission begins in disorder in the burning city of Troy, but he leaves it, carrying his father on his shoulders and leading his little son by the hand. This famous picture emphasizes the fact that, unlike Achilles, he is securely set in a continuity of generations, the immortality of the family group, just as his mission to found a city, a home for the gods of Troy whose statues he carries with him, places him in a political and religious continuity. Achilles has no future. When he mentions his father and son, neither of whom he will see again, he emphasizes for us the loneliness of his short career; the brilliance of his life is that of a meteor that burns itself out to darkness. Odysseus has a father, wife, and son, and his heroic efforts are directed toward reestablishing himself in his proper context, that home in which he will be no longer a man in a world of magic and terror but a

man in an organized and continuous community. But he fights for himself.
Aeneas, on the other hand, suffers and fights, not for himself but for the future;
his own life is unhappy, and his death miserable. Yet he can console himself with
the glory of his sons to come, the pageant of Roman achievement that he is shown
by his father in the world below and that he carries on his shield. Aeneas's future
is Virgil's present; the consolidation of the Roman peace under Augustus is the
reward of Aeneas's unhappy life of effort and suffering.

Summarized like this, the *Aeneid* sounds like propaganda, which, in one sense
of the word, it is. What saves it from the besetting fault of even the best propaganda—the partial concealment of the truth—is the fact that Virgil maintains an
independence of the power that he is celebrating and sees his hero in the round.
He knows that the Roman ideal of devotion to duty has another side, the suppression of many aspects of the personality, and that the man who wins and uses power
must sacrifice much of himself, must live a life that, compared with that of Achilles
or Odysseus, is constricted. In Virgil's poem Aeneas betrays the great passion of
his life, his love for Dido, queen of Carthage. He does it reluctantly, but nevertheless he leaves her, and the full realization of what he has lost comes to him only
when he meets her ghost in the world below. He weeps (as he did not at Carthage)
and he pleads, in stronger terms than he did then, the overriding power that forced
him to depart: "I left your land against my will, my queen." She leaves him without
a word, her silence as impervious to pleas and tears as his was once at Carthage,
and he follows her weeping as she goes back to join her first love, her husband,
Sychaeus. Aeneas has sacrificed his love to something greater, but this does not
insulate him from unhappiness. The limitations on the dedicated individual are
emphasized by the contrasting figure of Dido, who follows her own impulse
always, even in death. By her death, Virgil tells us expressly, she forestalls fate,
breaks loose from the pattern in which Aeneas remains to the bitter end.

The angry reactions that this part of the poem has produced in many critics are
the true measure of Virgil's success. Aeneas does act in such a way that he forfeits
much of our sympathy, but this is surely exactly what Virgil intended. The Dido
episode is not, as many critics have supposed, a flaw in the great design, a case of
Virgil's sympathy outrunning his admiration for Aeneas; it is Virgil's emphatic
statement of the sacrifice that the Roman ideal of duty demands. Aeneas's sacrifice
is so great that few of us could make it ourselves, and none of us can contemplate
it in another without a feeling of loss. It is an expression of the famous Virgilian
sadness that informs every line of the *Aeneid* and that makes a poem that was in its
historical context a command performance into the great epic that has dominated
Western literature ever since.

VIRGIL IN LATIN

Conticuere omnes intentique ora tenebant;
inde toro pater Aeneas sic orsus ab alto:
    Infandum, regina, iubes renovare dolorem,
Troianas ut opes et lamentabile regnum
eruerint Danai, quaeque ipse miserrima uidi   5
et quorum pars magna fui. quis talia fando
Myrmidonum Dolopomue aut duri miles Ulixi
temperet a lacrimis? et iam nox umida caelo
praecipitat suadentque cadentia sidera somnos.
sed si tantus amor casus cognoscere nostros   10
et breviter Troiae supremum audire laborem,
quamquam animus meminisse horret luctuque refugit,
incipiam.

This is the beginning of Book II of the *Aeneid*; Aeneas, at the banquet in Carthage, tells the story of the fall of Troy. The long lines do not employ rhyme but they have a regular rhythmic pattern based not on stress, as in English verse, but on length of syllable—that is, the time taken to pronounce it. Some vowels are naturally long, and others naturally short, but a short vowel may be made long by position (if it is followed by two consonants, it takes just as much time to pronounce as if it were naturally long). The line consists of six feet, either dactyl ($-\smile\smile$) or spondee ($--$). In the first four feet various combinations are employed, but the last two feet, except in cases where a special effect is sought, are always dactyl plus spondee.

This hexameter (six-foot) line is capable of great variety, contained always in the formal pattern. Unfortunately, attempts to reproduce its disciplined variety in English stressed verse (Longfellow's "This is the forest primeval," for example) have not proved successful, and the translator has used a modern adaptation of the basic English line, the iambic pentameter of Shakespeare and Milton.

The subtle variation of the rhythm is not the only problem faced by translators; they must also try to compensate for the loss of effects that depend on the flexibility of Latin word order. In English, syntactical relationship is determined by that order: "man bites dog" means the opposite of "dog bites man." In Latin, because the terminations of the nouns show who does what to whom, "man bites dog" is *vir mordet canem*, and "dog bites man" *canis mordet virum*. Consequently, the words can be arranged in any order with no change of meaning. *Virum canis mordet, canis virum mordet,* and any other combination of these three elements all mean the same thing: "dog bites man." But the word order is not without its force; it can indicate emphasis. Normal order—subject, object, verb (for the Latin verb tends toward the end of the sentence)—would be *canis virum mordet*. But putting *virum*, the object, first—*virum canis mordet*—would draw attention to that word: "it was a *man* the dog bit."

This is a simple example; much more complicated effects are available to a poet in extended sentences. Line 3 of the passage quoted above, for example, uses the flexibility of word order not only for emphasis but also for exploring the possibilities of ambiguity and surprise offered by a highly inflected language. *Infandum* ("unspeakable, something that cannot be said") is the first word, and we do not know from its termination whether it is subject or object or whether it is to be understood as a noun ("an unspeakable thing") or an adjective for which a noun will be supplied later. *Regina* ("queen") could, according to its termination, be the subject of the sentence, but the context, Aeneas's reply to the queen's request for his story, suggests strongly that it is a form of address: "Unspeakable, oh Queen." The subject comes with the next word, the verb *iubes*; its termination shows that this is the second person, the "you" form—"you command." She has commanded something unspeakable. Is the reader being prepared for a refusal on the part of Aeneas to tell his story? *Renovare* defines the queen's order—"to renew"—and *dolorem* tells us what he is to renew—"sorrow." And the termination of this word suggests that the first word of the line, *infandum*, is in fact an adjective defining *dolorem*. The line, when one reaches this last word, re-forms itself into an unexpected pattern: "Unspeakable, oh Queen, is the sorrow you command me to renew." The line is enclosed between the two most important words in Aeneas's statement, *infandum* and *dolorem*; its last word imposes on us a slight change in our understanding of its first and so redirects attention to that solemn opening word of Aeneas's evocation of the fall of Troy, three long syllables heavy with grief for the lost splendor of a city that is now ash and rubble.

W. A. Camps, *An Introduction to Virgil's Aeneid* (1969), is a short and simply written discussion of all aspects of the poem. Steele Commager, ed., *Virgil: A Collection of Critical Essays* (1966), contains essays by various authors, ten of them

on the *Aeneid*. Jasper Griffin, *Virgil* (1986), is a splendid introduction to the world and work of the poet. See also R. D. Williams, "The *Aeneid*," *The Cambridge History of Classical Literature*, vol. 2 (1982), pp. 333–69.

PRONOUNCING GLOSSARY

The following list uses common English syllables and stress accents to provide rough equivalents of selected words whose pronunciation may be unfamiliar to the general reader.

Aeneas: *i-nee'-uhs*

Aeneid: *i-nee'-id*

Anchisës: *an-kai'-seez*

Andromachë: *an-dro'-ma-kee*

Automedon: *aw-to'-me-don / ow-to'-me-don*

Charon: *kah'-ron*

Cyllenë: *si-lee'-nee*

Chimaera: *kai-meer'-uh / ki-mai'-ruh*

Cytherëa: *si-the-ree'-uh / si-ther-ai'-uh*

Danaans: *da'-nay-unz / dan'-a-ans*

Dido: *dai'-doh*

Dionysus: *dai-oh-nai'-sus*

Eumenidës: *yoo-me'-ni-deez*

Peneleus: *pee-nee'-lyoos*

Phrygian: *fri'-jun*

Scaean: *see'-an / skai'-an*

Teucer: *tyoo'-ser*

Thymoetes: *thai-mee'-teez*

Xanthus: *zan'-thus / ksan'-thus*

The Aeneid[1]

FROM BOOK I

[Prologue]

I sing of warfare and a man at war.[2]
From the sea-coast of Troy in early days
He came to Italy by destiny,
To our Lavinian[3] western shore,
A fugitive, this captain, buffeted   5
Cruelly on land as on the sea
By blows from powers of the air—behind them
Baleful Juno[4] in her sleepless rage.
And cruel losses were his lot in war,
Till he could found a city and bring home   10
His gods to Latium, land of the Latin race,
The Alban[5] lords, and the high walls of Rome.
Tell me the causes now, O Muse, how galled
In her divine pride, and how sore at heart
From her old wound, the queen of gods compelled him—   15
A man apart, devoted to his mission—

1. Translated by Robert Fitzgerald.   2. Aeneas, a Trojan champion in the fight for Troy, son of Venus (or Aphrodite, the goddess of love) and Anchisës, and a member of the royal house of Troy.   3. Near Rome, named after the city of Lavinium. After the fall of Troy, Aeneas went in search of a new home, eventually settling here.   4. Wife of the ruler of the gods (Hera in Greek). As in the *Iliad*, she is a bitter enemy of the Trojans.   5. The city of Alba Longa was founded by Aeneas's son Ascanius. Romulus and Remus, the builders of Rome, were also from Alba. Latium is the coastal plain on which Rome is situated.

To undergo so many perilous days
And enter on so many trials. Can anger
Black as this prey on the minds of heaven?
Tyrian[6] settlers in that ancient time   20
Held Carthage,[7] on the far shore of the sea,
Set against Italy and Tiber's[8] mouth,
A rich new town, warlike and trained for war.
And Juno, we are told, cared more for Carthage
Than for any walled city of the earth,   25
More than for Samos,[9] even. There her armor
And chariot were kept, and, fate permitting,
Carthage would be the ruler of the world.
So she intended, and so nursed that power.
But she had heard long since   30
That generations born of Trojan blood
Would one day overthrow her Tyrian walls,
And from that blood a race would come in time
With ample kingdoms, arrogant in war,
For Libya's ruin: so the Parcae[1] spun.   35
In fear of this, and holding in memory
The old war she had carried on at Troy
For Argos'[2] sake (the origins of that anger,
That suffering, still rankled: deep within her,
Hidden away, the judgment Paris[3] gave,   40
Snubbing her loveliness; the race she hated;
The honors given ravished Ganymede),
Saturnian Juno,[4] burning for it all,
Buffeted on the waste of sea those Trojans
Left by the Greeks and pitiless Achilles,   45
Keeping them far from Latium. For years
They wandered as their destiny drove them on
From one sea to the next: so hard and huge
A task it was to found the Roman people.

[Aeneas Arrives in Carthage]

Summary   The story opens with a storm, provoked by Juno's agency, which scatters Aeneas's fleet off Sicily and separates him from his companions. He lands on the African coast near Carthage. Setting out with his friend Achatës to explore the country, he meets his mother, Venus (Aphrodite), who tells him that the rest

6. From Tyre, on the coast of Palestine, the principal city of the Phoenicians, a seafaring people. 7. On the coast of North Africa, opposite Sicily. Originally a Tyrian colony, it became a rich commercial center, controlling traffic in the western Mediterranean.   8. The river that flows through Rome. 9. A large island off the coast of Asia Minor, famous for its cult of Hera (Juno).   1. The Fates, who were imagined as female divinities who spun human destinies. Rome captured and destroyed Carthage in 146 B.C. Libya is used as an inclusive name for the North African coast.   2. Home city of the Achaean (Greek) kings Agamemnon and Menelaus. Juno was on their side when they went to Troy to retrieve Helen, Menelaus' wife.   3. Son of King Priam of Troy. He was asked to judge which goddess—Venus, Juno, or Minerva (Athena)—was most beautiful. All three offered bribes, but Venus's promise (of Helen's love) prevailed, and Paris awarded her the prize.   4. Her father was Saturn, a Titan. Ganymede was a Trojan boy of extreme beauty who was taken up into heaven by Jupiter (Zeus), ruler of the gods.

of his ships are safe and directs him to the city just founded by Dido, the queen of
Carthage. Venus surrounds Aeneas and Achatës with a cloud so that they can see
without being seen.

                              Meanwhile
The two men pressed on where the pathway led,
Soon climbing a long ridge that gave a view
Down over the city and facing towers.
Aeneas found, where lately huts had been,   5
Marvelous buildings, gateways, cobbled ways,
And din of wagons. There the Tyrians[5]
Were hard at work: laying courses for walls,
Rolling up stones to build the citadel,
While others picked out building sites and plowed   10
A boundary furrow. Laws were being enacted,
Magistrates and a sacred senate chosen.
Here men were dredging harbors, there they laid
The deep foundation of a theater,
And quarried massive pillars to enhance   15
The future stage—as bees in early summer
In sunlight in the flowering fields
Hum at their work, and bring along the young
Full-grown to beehood; as they cram their combs
With honey, brimming all the cells with nectar,   20
Or take newcomers' plunder, or like troops
Alerted, drive away the lazy drones,
And labor thrives and sweet thyme scents the honey.
Aeneas said: "How fortunate these are
Whose city walls are rising here and now!"   25

He looked up at the roofs, for he had entered,
Swathed in cloud—strange to relate—among them,
Mingling with men, yet visible to none.
In mid-town stood a grove that cast sweet shade
Where the Phoenicians, shaken by wind and sea,   30
Had first dug up that symbol Juno showed them,
A proud warhorse's head: this meant for Carthage
Prowess in war and ease of life[6] through ages.
Here being built by the Sidonian[7] queen
Was a great temple planned in Juno's honor,   35
Rich in offerings and the godhead there.
Steps led up to a sill of bronze, with brazen
Lintel, and bronze doors on groaning pins.
Here in this grove new things that met his eyes
Calmed Aeneas' fear for the first time.   40
Here for the first time he took heart to hope

5. See p. 640, n. 6.   6. Because they would have a land fertile enough to support horses.   7. From
Sidon, a Phoenician city.

For safety, and to trust his destiny more
Even in affliction. It was while he walked
From one to another wall of the great temple
And waited for the queen, staring amazed　　　　　　　　　　45
At Carthaginian promise, at the handiwork
Of artificers and the toil they spent upon it:
He found before his eyes the Trojan battles
In the old war, now known throughout the world—
The great Atridae, Priam, and Achilles,　　　　　　　　　　50
Fierce in his rage at both sides.[8] Here Aeneas
Halted, and tears came.
　　　　　　　　　　"What spot on earth,"
He said, "what region of the earth, Achatës,
Is not full of the story of our sorrow?
Look, here is Priam. Even so far away　　　　　　　　　　55
Great valor has due honor; they weep here
For how the world goes, and our life that passes
Touches their hearts. Throw off your fear. This fame
Insures some kind of refuge."
　　　　　　　　　　He broke off
To feast his eyes and mind on a mere image,　　　　　　　　　　60
Sighing often, cheeks grown wet with tears,
To see again how, fighting around Troy,
The Greeks broke here, and ran before the Trojans,
And there the Phrygians[9] ran, as plumed Achilles
Harried them in his warcar. Nearby, then,　　　　　　　　　　65
He recognized the snowy canvas tents
Of Rhesus,[1] and more tears came: these, betrayed
In first sleep, Diomedes devastated,
Swording many, till he reeked with blood,
Then turned the mettlesome horses toward the beachhead　　　　70
Before they tasted Trojan grass or drank
At Xanthus ford.[2]
　　　　　　　　　　And on another panel
Troilus,[3] without his armor, luckless boy,
No match for his antagonist, Achilles,
Appeared pulled onward by his team: he clung　　　　　　　　　　75
To his warcar, though fallen backward, hanging
On to the reins still, head dragged on the ground,
His javelin scribbling S's in the dust.
Meanwhile to hostile Pallas'[4] shrine
The Trojan women walked with hair unbound,　　　　　　　　　　80
Bearing the robe of offering, in sorrow,

---

8. Because Achilles, the greatest warrior on the Achaean side, quarreled with Agamemnon. *Atridae:*
sons of Atreus: Agamemnon and Menelaus.　　9. Trojans.　　1. King of Thrace, who came to the aid
of Troy just before the end of the war.　　2. An oracle proclaimed that if Rhesus's horses ate Trojan
grass and drank the water of the river Xanthus, Troy would not fall. Odysseus and Diomedes went into
the Trojan lines at night, killed the king, and stole the horses.　　3. A young son of Priam.　　4. Athena
(*Iliad* VI.297ff.).

Entreating her, beating their breasts. But she,
Her face averted, would not raise her eyes.
And there was Hector, dragged around Troy walls
Three times, and there for gold Achilles sold him,   85
Bloodless and lifeless. Now indeed Aeneas
Heaved a mighty sigh from deep within him,
Seeing the spoils, the chariot, and the corpse
Of his great friend, and Priam, all unarmed,
Stretching his hands out.
                                        He himself he saw   90
In combat with the first of the Achaeans,
And saw the ranks of Dawn, black Memnon's[5] arms;
Then, leading the battalion of Amazons
With half-moon shields, he saw Penthesilëa[6]
Fiery amid her host, buckling a golden   95
Girdle beneath her bare and arrogant breast,
A girl who dared fight men, a warrior queen.
Now, while these wonders were being surveyed
By Aeneas of Dardania,[7] while he stood
Enthralled, devouring all in one long gaze,   100
The queen paced toward the temple in her beauty,
Dido, with a throng of men behind.

As on Eurotas bank or Cynthus ridge
Diana[8] trains her dancers, and behind her
On every hand the mountain nymphs appear,   105
A myriad converging; with her quiver
Slung on her shoulders, in her stride she seems
The tallest, taller by a head than any,
And joy pervades Latona's[9] quiet heart:
So Dido seemed, in such delight she moved   110
Amid her people, cheering on the toil
Of a kingdom in the making. At the door
Of the goddess' shrine, under the temple dome,
All hedged about with guards on her high throne,
She took her seat. Then she began to give them   115
Judgments and rulings, to apportion work
With fairness, or assign some tasks by lot,
When suddenly Aeneas saw approaching,
Accompanied by a crowd, Antheus and Sergestus
And brave Cloanthus,[1] with a few companions,   120
Whom the black hurricane had driven far
Over the sea and brought to other coasts.
He was astounded, and Achatës too
Felt thrilled by joy and fear: both of them longed

---

5. King of the Ethiopians, who fought on the Trojan side.   6. Queen of the Amazons, killed by
Achilles.   7. The kingdom of Troy.   8. Virgin goddess of the hunt (Artemis in Greek). Eurotas is a
river near Sparta where Diana was worshiped. Cynthus is a mountain on the island of Delos, Diana's
birthplace.   9. Diana's mother (Leto in Greek).   1. Ship captains of Aeneas's fleet from whom he
had been separated in the storm.

To take their friends' hands, but uncertainty   125
Hampered them. So, in their cloudy mantle,
They hid their eagerness, waiting to learn
What luck these men had had, where on the coast
They left their ships, and why they came. It seemed
Spokesmen for all the ships were now arriving,   130
Entering the hall, calling for leave to speak.
When all were in, and full permission given
To make their plea before the queen, their eldest,
Ilioneus, with composure said:
                              "Your majesty,
Granted by great Jupiter freedom to found   135
Your new town here and govern fighting tribes
With justice—we poor Trojans, worn by winds
On every sea, entreat you: keep away
Calamity of fire from our ships!
Let a godfearing people live, and look   140
More closely at our troubles. Not to ravage
Libyan hearths or turn with plunder seaward
Have we come; that force and that audacity
Are not for beaten men.
                              There is a country
Called by the Greeks Hesperia, very old,   145
Potent in warfare and in wealth of earth;
Oenotrians farmed it; younger settlers now,
The tale goes, call it by their chief's[2] name, Italy.
We laid our course for this.
But stormy Orion[3] and a high sea rising   150
Deflected us on shoals and drove us far,
With winds against us, into whelming waters,
Unchanneled reefs. We kept afloat, we few,
To reach your coast. What race of men is this?
What primitive state could sanction this behavior?   155
Even on beaches we are denied a landing,
Harried by outcry and attack, forbidden
To set foot on the outskirts of your country.
If you care nothing for humanity
And merely mortal arms, respect the gods   160
Who are mindful of good actions and of evil!

We had a king, Aeneas—none more just,
More zealous, greater in warfare and in arms.
If fate preserves him, if he does not yet
Lie spent amid the insensible shades but still   165
Takes nourishment of air, we need fear nothing;
Neither need you repent of being first
In courtesy, to outdo us. Sicily too

---

2. Italus. *Hesperia:* the western country. The Oenotrians were the original inhabitants of Italy.
3. The setting of this constellation in November signaled the onset of stormy weather at sea.

Has towns and plowlands and a famous king
Of Trojan blood, Acestës.[4] May we be   170
Permitted here to beach our damaged ships,
Hew timbers in your forest, cut new oars,
And either sail again for Latium, happily,
If we recover shipmates and our king,
Or else, if that security is lost,   175
If Libyan waters hold you, Lord Aeneas,
Best of Trojans, hope of Iulus[5] gone,
We may at least cross over to Sicily
From which we came, to homesteads ready there,
And take Acestës for our king."
                            Ilioneus   180
Finished, and all the sons of Dardanus[6]
Murmured assent. Dido with eyes downcast
Replied in a brief speech:
                            "Cast off your fear,
You Teucrians, put anxiety aside.
Severe conditions and the kingdom's youth   185
Constrain me to these measures, to protect
Our long frontiers with guards.
                            Who has not heard
Of the people of Aeneas, of Troy city,
Her valors and her heroes, and the fires
Of the great war? We are not so oblivious,   190
We Phoenicians. The sun yokes his team
Within our range[7] at Carthage. Whether you choose
Hesperia Magna and the land of Saturn
Or Eryx[8] in the west and King Acestës,
I shall dispatch you safely with an escort,   195
Provisioned from my stores. Or would you care
To join us in this realm on equal terms?
The city I build is yours; haul up your ships;
Trojan and Tyrian will be all one to me.
If only he were here, your king himself,   200
Caught by the same easterly, Aeneas!
Indeed, let me send out trustworthy men
Along the coast, with orders to comb it all
From one end of Libya to the other,
In case the sea cast the man up and now   205
He wanders lost, in town or wilderness."

Elated at Dido's words, both staunch Achatës
And father Aeneas had by this time longed
To break out of the cloud. Achatës spoke
With urgency:

4. His mother was Trojan; he had offered Aeneas and his people a home in his dominions.   5. Ascanius, Aeneas's son.   6. Ancestor of the Trojans.   7. That is, we are not outside the circuit of the sun;
we are part of the civilized world and hear the news.   8. On the west coast of Sicily. *Land of Saturn:*
an old legend connected Italy with Saturn, the father of Jupiter.

"My lord, born to the goddess,   210
What do you feel, what is your judgment now?
You see all safe, our ships and friends recovered.
One is lost;[9] we saw that one go down
Ourselves, amid the waves. Everything else
Bears out your mother's own account of it."   215

He barely finished when the cloud around them
Parted suddenly and thinned away
Into transparent air. Princely Aeneas
Stood and shone in the bright light, head and shoulders
Noble as a god's. For she who bore him[1]   220
Breathed upon him beauty of hair and bloom
Of youth and kindled brilliance in his eyes,
As an artist's hand gives style to ivory,
Or sets pure silver, or white stone of Paros,[2]
In framing yellow gold. Then to the queen   225
He spoke as suddenly as, to them all,
He had just appeared:
                    "Before your eyes I stand,
Aeneas the Trojan, that same one you look for,
Saved from the sea off Libya.
                              You alone,
Moved by the untold ordeals of old Troy,   230
Seeing us few whom the Greeks left alive,
Worn out by faring ill on land and sea,
Needy of everything—you'd give these few
A home and city, allied with yourselves.
Fit thanks for this are not within our power,   235
Not to be had from Trojans anywhere
Dispersed in the great world.
                              May the gods—
And surely there are powers that care for goodness,
Surely somewhere justice counts—may they
And your own consciousness of acting well   240
Reward you as they should. What age so happy
Brought you to birth? How splendid were your parents
To have conceived a being like yourself!
So long as brooks flow seaward, and the shadows
Play over mountain slopes, and highest heaven   245
Feeds the stars, your name and your distinction
Go with me, whatever lands may call me."

With this he gave his right hand to his friend
Ilioneus, greeting Serestus with his left,
Then took the hands of those brave men, Cloanthus,   250
Gyas, and the rest.

9. One ship, captained by Orontes, sank in the storm.   1. Venus.   2. The marble of the island of
Paros was famous.

Sidonian Dido
Stood in astonishment, first at the sight
Of such a captain, then at his misfortune,
Presently saying:
                    "Born of an immortal
Mother though you are, what adverse destiny   255
Dogs you through these many kinds of danger?
What rough power brings you from sea to land
In savage places? Are you truly he,
Aeneas, whom kind Venus bore
To the Dardanian, the young Anchisës,   260
Near to the stream of Phrygian Simoïs?
I remember the Greek, Teucer,[3] came to Sidon,
Exiled, and in search of a new kingdom.
Belus, my father, helped him. In those days
Belus campaigned with fire and sword on Cyprus   265
And won that island's wealth. Since then, the fall
Of Troy, your name, and the Pelasgian kings
Have been familiar to me. Teucer, your enemy,
Spoke often with admiration of the Tyrians
And traced his own descent from Tyrian stock.   270
Come, then, soldiers, be our guests. My life
Was one of hardship and forced wandering
Like your own, till in this land at length
Fortune would have me rest. Through pain I've learned
To comfort suffering men."
                    She led Aeneas   275
Into the royal house, but not before
Declaring a festal day in the gods' temples.
As for the ships' companies, she sent
Twenty bulls to the shore, a hundred swine,
Huge ones, with bristling backs, and fatted lambs,   280
A hundred of them, and their mother ewes—
All gifts for happy feasting on that day.

Now the queen's household made her great hall glow
As they prepared a banquet in the kitchens.
Embroidered table cloths, proud crimson-dyed,   285
Were spread, and set with massive silver plate,
Or gold, engraved with brave deeds of her fathers,
A sequence carried down through many captains
In a long line from the founding of the race.

Summary   At the banquet, Aeneas, at Dido's request, tells the story of the fall of Troy and of his wanderings in search of a new home. By the end of the evening, Dido, who began to fall in love with him before the banquet (through the intervention of Venus and Juno, who both promote the affair, each for different reasons), now feels the full force of her passion for Aeneas.

3. A warrior who fought at Troy and was later exiled from his home. He founded a city on the island of Cyprus. He is not the Trojan king Teucer.

BOOK IV

[The Passion of the Queen]

The queen, for her part, all that evening ached
With longing that her heart's blood fed, a wound
Or inward fire eating her away.
The manhood of the man, his pride of birth,
Came home to her time and again; his looks,   5
His words remained with her to haunt her mind,
And desire for him gave her no rest.
                  When Dawn
Swept earth with Phoebus' torch and burned away
Night-gloom and damp, this queen, far gone and ill,
Confided to the sister of her heart: 10
"My sister Anna, quandaries and dreams
Have come to frighten me—such dreams!
                      Think what a stranger
Yesterday found lodging in our house:
How princely, how courageous, what a soldier.
I can believe him in the line of gods,   15
And this is no delusion. Tell-tale fear
Betrays inferior souls. What scenes of war
Fought to the bitter end he pictured for us!
What buffetings awaited him at sea!
Had I not set my face against remarriage   20
After my first love died and failed me, left me
Barren and bereaved—and sick to death
At the mere thought of torch and bridal bed—
I could perhaps give way in this one case
To frailty. I shall say it: since that time   25
Sychaeus, my poor husband, met his fate,
And blood my brother[4] shed stained our hearth gods,
This man alone has wrought upon me so
And moved my soul to yield. I recognize
The signs of the old flame, of old desire.   30
But O chaste life, before I break your laws,
I pray that Earth may open, gape for me
Down to its depth, or the omnipotent
With one stroke blast me to the shades, pale shades
Of Erebus[5] and the deep world of night!   35
That man who took me to himself in youth
Has taken all my love; may that man keep it,
Hold it forever with him in the tomb."

At this she wept and wet her breast with tears.
But Anna answered:
                 "Dearer to your sister   40
Than daylight is, will you wear out your life,
Young as you are, in solitary mourning,
Never to know sweet children, or the crown
Of joy that Venus brings? Do you believe

---

4. Pygmalion, king of Tyre who killed Sychaeus, Dido's *first love* (line 21). Sychaeus's ghost warned her in a dream to leave Tyre and seek a new home.   5. The lower depths of Hades, the underworld.

This matters to the dust, to ghosts in tombs?   45
Granted no suitors up to now have moved you,
Neither in Libya nor before, in Tyre—
Iarbas[6] you rejected, and the others,
Chieftains bred by the land of Africa
Their triumphs have enriched—will you contend   50
Even against a welcome love? Have you
Considered in whose lands you settled here?
On one frontier the Gaetulans, their cities,
People invincible in war—with wild
Numidian horsemen, and the offshore banks,   55
The Syrtës; on the other, desert sands,
Bone-dry, where fierce Barcaean[7] nomads range.
Or need I speak of future wars brought on
From Tyre, and the menace of your brother?
Surely by dispensation of the gods   60
And backed by Juno's will, the ships from Ilium
Held their course this way on the wind.
                                        Sister,
What a great city you'll see rising here,
And what a kingdom, from this royal match!
With Trojan soldiers as companions in arms   65
By what exploits will Punic[8] glory grow!
Only ask the indulgence of the gods,
Win them with offerings, give your guests ease,
And contrive reasons for delay, while winter
Gales rage, drenched Orion storms at sea,   70
And their ships, damaged still, face iron skies."

This counsel fanned the flame, already kindled,
Giving her hesitant sister hope, and set her
Free of scruple. Visiting the shrines
They begged for grace at every altar first,   75
Then put choice rams and ewes to ritual death
For Ceres Giver of Laws, Father Lyaeus,
Phoebus, and for Juno most of all
Who has the bonds of marriage in her keeping.[9]
Dido herself, splendidly beautiful,   80
Holding a shallow cup, tips out the wine
On a white shining heifer, between the horns,
Or gravely in the shadow of the gods
Approaches opulent altars. Through the day
She brings new gifts, and when the breasts are opened   85
Pores over organs, living still, for signs.[1]
Alas, what darkened minds have soothsayers!

6. The most prominent of Dido's African suitors.   7. African groups that lived near Carthage. The Gaetulans, a savage people, lived to the southwest. The Numidians were the most powerful group. The Syrtes lived on the coast to the west. The Barcaeans lived to the east.   8. Carthaginian.   9. Ceres, the goddess who guarantees the growth of crops; Lyaeus (Dionysus or Bacchus), the wine god; and Phoebus (Apollo) are selected as deities especially connected with the founding of cities. One of Apollo's titles is "founder," and Ceres and Lyaeus control the essential crops that will enable the colonists to live. Dido prays to these gods at the moment when she is about to abandon her responsibilities as founder of a city. A similar irony is present in her prayer to Juno, who oversees the marriage bond, at the moment when she is about to break her long fidelity to the memory of Sychaeus.   1. An Etruscan and Roman practice was to inspect the entrails of the sacrificial victim and interpret irregular or unusual features as signs of the future.

What good are shrines and vows to maddened lovers?
The inward fire eats the soft marrow away,
And the internal wound bleeds on in silence.   90

Unlucky Dido, burning, in her madness
Roamed through all the city, like a doe
Hit by an arrow shot from far away
By a shepherd hunting in the Cretan woods—
Hit by surprise, nor could the hunter see   95
His flying steel had fixed itself in her;
But though she runs for life through copse and glade
The fatal shaft clings to her side.
                              Now Dido
Took Aeneas with her among her buildings,
Showed her Sidonian wealth, her walls prepared,   100
And tried to speak, but in mid-speech grew still.
When the day waned she wanted to repeat
The banquet as before, to hear once more
In her wild need the throes of Ilium,
And once more hung on the narrator's words.   105
Afterward, when all the guests were gone,
And the dim moon in turn had quenched her light,
And setting stars weighed weariness to sleep,
Alone she mourned in the great empty hall
And pressed her body on the couch he left: 110
She heard him still, though absent—heard and saw him.
Or she would hold Ascanius in her lap,
Enthralled by him, the image of his father,
As though by this ruse to appease a love
Beyond all telling.
                         Towers, half-built, rose   115
No farther; men no longer trained in arms
Or toiled to make harbors and battlements
Impregnable. Projects were broken off,
Laid over, and the menacing huge walls
With cranes unmoving stood against the sky.   120

As soon as Jove's[2] dear consort saw the lady
Prey to such illness, and her reputation
Standing no longer in the way of passion,
Saturn's daughter said to Venus:
                              "Wondrous!
Covered yourself with glory, have you not,   125
You and your boy, and won such prizes, too.
Divine power is something to remember
If by collusion of two gods one mortal
Woman is brought low.
                         I am not blind.
Your fear of our new walls has not escaped me,   130
Fear and mistrust of Carthage at her height.
But how far will it go? What do you hope for,
Being so contentious? Why do we not

---

2. Jupiter's.

Arrange eternal peace and formal marriage?
You have your heart's desire: Dido in love,   135
Dido consumed with passion to her core.
Why not, then, rule this people side by side
With equal authority? And let the queen
Wait on her Phrygian lord, let her consign
Into your hand her Tyrians as a dowry."   140

Now Venus knew this talk was all pretence,
All to divert the future power from Italy
To Libya; and she answered:
                              "Who would be
So mad, so foolish as to shun that prospect
Or prefer war with you? That is, provided   145
Fortune is on the side of your proposal.
The fates here are perplexing: would one city
Satisfy Jupiter's will for Tyrians
And Trojan exiles? Does he approve
A union and a mingling of these races?   150
You are his consort: you have every right
To sound him out. Go on, and I'll come, too."

But regal Juno pointedly replied:
"That task will rest with me. Just now, as to
The need of the moment and the way to meet it,   155
Listen, and I'll explain in a few words.
Aeneas and Dido in her misery
Plan hunting in the forest, when the Titan
Sun comes up with rays to light the world.
While beaters in excitement ring the glens   160
My gift will be a black raincloud, and hail,
A downpour, and I'll shake heaven with thunder.
The company will scatter, lost in gloom,
As Dido and the Trojan captain come
To one same cavern. I shall be on hand,   165
And if I can be certain you are willing,
There I shall marry them and call her his.
A wedding, this will be."
                              Then Cytherëa,[3]
Not disinclined, nodded to Juno's plea,
And smiled at the stratagem now given away.   170

Dawn came up meanwhile from the Ocean stream,
And in the early sunshine from the gates
Picked huntsmen issued: wide-meshed nets and snares,
Broad spearheads for big game, Massylian[4] horsemen
Trooping with hounds in packs keen on the scent.   175
But Dido lingered in her hall, as Punic
Nobles waited, and her mettlesome hunter
Stood nearby, cavorting in gold and scarlet,
Champing his foam-flecked bridle. At long last
The queen appeared with courtiers in a crowd,   180
A short Sidonian cloak edged in embroidery

---

3. Venus.   4. After Massilia (Marseilles), in southern France.

Caught about her, at her back a quiver
Sheathed in gold, her hair tied up in gold,
And a brooch of gold pinning her scarlet dress.
Phrygians came in her company as well,   185
And Iulus, joyous at the scene. Resplendent
Above the rest, Aeneas walked to meet her,
To join his retinue with hers. He seemed —
Think of the lord Apollo in the spring
When he leaves wintering in Lycia   190
By Xanthus torrent, for his mother's isle
Of Delos, to renew the festival;
Around his altars Cretans, Dryopës,
And painted Agathyrsans' raise a shout,
But the god walks the Cynthian ridge alone   195
And smooths his hair, binds it in fronded laurel,
Braids it in gold; and shafts ring on his shoulders.
So elated and swift, Aeneas walked
With sunlit grace upon him.
                            Soon the hunters,
Riding in company to high pathless hills,   200
Saw mountain goats shoot down from a rocky peak
And scamper on the ridges; toward the plain
Deer left the slopes, herding in clouds of dust
In flight across the open lands. Alone,
The boy Ascanius, delightedly riding   205
His eager horse amid the lowland vales,
Outran both goats and deer. Could he only meet
Amid the harmless game some foaming boar,
Or a tawny lion down from the mountainside!

Meanwhile in heaven began a rolling thunder,   210
And soon the storm broke, pouring rain and hail.
Then Tyrians and Trojans in alarm —
With Venus' Dardan grandson[6] — ran for cover
Here and there in the wilderness, as freshets
Coursed from the high hills.
                            Now to the self-same cave   215
Came Dido and the captain of the Trojans.
Primal Earth herself and Nuptial Juno
Opened the ritual, torches of lightning blazed,
High Heaven became witness to the marriage,
And nymphs cried out wild hymns from a mountain top.   220
        That day was the first cause of death, and first
Of sorrow. Dido had no further qualms
As to impressions given and set abroad;
She thought no longer of a secret love
But called it marriage. Thus, under that name,   225
She hid her fault.
                    Now in no time at all
Through all the African cities Rumor goes —
Nimble as quicksilver among evils. Rumor
Thrives on motion, stronger for the running,

5. Pilgrims from various regions.   6. Ascanius.

Lowly at first through fear, then rearing high,   230
She treads the land and hides her head in cloud.
As people fable it, the Earth, her mother,
Furious against the gods, bore a late sister
To the giants Coeus and Enceladus,
Giving her speed on foot and on the wing: 235
Monstrous, deformed, titanic. Pinioned, with
An eye beneath for every body feather,
And, strange to say, as many tongues and buzzing
Mouths as eyes, as many pricked-up ears,
By night she flies between the earth and heaven   240
Shrieking through darkness, and she never turns
Her eye-lids down to sleep. By day she broods,
On the alert, on rooftops or on towers,
Bringing great cities fear, harping on lies
And slander evenhandedly with truth.   245
In those days Rumor took an evil joy
At filling countrysides with whispers, whispers,
Gossip of what was done, and never done:
How this Aeneas landed, Trojan born,
How Dido in her beauty graced his company,   250
Then how they reveled all the winter long
Unmindful of the realm, prisoners of lust.

These tales the scabrous goddess put about
On men's lips everywhere. Her twisting course
Took her to King Iarbas, whom she set   255
Ablaze with anger piled on top of anger.
Son of Jupiter Hammon by a nymph,
A ravished Garamantean, this prince
Had built the god a hundred giant shrines,
A hundred altars, each with holy fires.   260
Alight by night and day, sentries on watch,
The ground enriched by victims' blood, the doors
Festooned with flowering wreaths. Before his altars
King Iarbas, crazed by the raw story,
Stood, they say, amid the Presences,   265
With supplicating hands, pouring out prayer:

"All powerful Jove, to whom the feasting Moors
At ease on colored couches tip their wine,
Do you see this? Are we then fools to fear you
Throwing down your bolts? Those dazzling fires   270
Of lightning, are they aimless in the clouds
And rumbling thunder meaningless? This woman
Who turned up in our country and laid down
A tiny city at a price, to whom
I gave a beach to plow—and on my terms—   275
After refusing to marry me has taken
Aeneas to be master in her realm.
And now Sir Paris with his men, half-men,
His chin and perfumed hair tied up
In a Maeonian bonnet, takes possession.   280
As for ourselves, here we are bringing gifts

Into these shrines—supposedly your shrines—
Hugging that empty fable."
                                    Pleas like this
From the man clinging to his altars reached
The ears of the Almighty. Now he turned   285
His eyes upon the queen's town and the lovers
Careless of their good name; then spoke to Mercury,[7]
Assigning him a mission:
                                    "Son, bestir yourself,
Call up the Zephyrs,[8] take to your wings and glide.
Approach the Dardan captain where he tarries   290
Rapt in Tyrian Carthage, losing sight
Of future towns the fates ordain. Correct him,
Carry my speech to him on the running winds:
No son like this did his enchanting mother
Promise to us, nor such did she deliver   295
Twice from peril at the hands of Greeks.
He was to be the ruler of Italy,
Potential empire, armorer of war;
To father men from Teucer's[9] noble blood
And bring the whole world under law's dominion.   300
If glories to be won by deeds like these
Cannot arouse him, if he will not strive
For his own honor, does he begrudge his son,
Ascanius, the high strongholds of Rome?
What has he in mind? What hope, to make him stay   305
Amid a hostile race, and lose from view
Ausonian progeny, Lavinian lands?[1]
The man should sail: that is the whole point.
Let this be what you tell him, as from me."

He finished and fell silent. Mercury   310
Made ready to obey the great command
Of his great father, and he first tied on
The golden sandals, winged, that high in air
Transport him over seas or over land
Abreast of gale winds; then he took the wand   315
With which he summons pale souls out of Orcus
And ushers others to the undergloom,
Lulls men to slumber or awakens them,
And opens dead men's eyes. This wand in hand,
He can drive winds before him, swimming down   320
Along the stormcloud. Now aloft, he saw
The craggy flanks and crown of patient Atlas,
Giant Atlas, balancing the sky
Upon his peak[2]—his pine-forested head
In vapor cowled, beaten by wind and rain.   325
Snow lay upon his shoulders, rills cascaded
Down his ancient chin and beard a-bristle,

7. The messenger god; Hermes in Greek.   8. The west winds.   9. The first Trojan king.   1. The
dowry of Lavinia, daughter of Latinus, whom Aeneas marries. *Ausonian:* Italian.   2. The Atlas Mountains are in western North Africa; the reference here is also to the Titan Atlas, who, as punishment for
his part in the revolt against Jupiter, must hold up the heavens on his shoulders.

Caked with ice. Here Mercury of Cyllenë[3]
Hovered first on even wings, then down
He plummeted to sea-level and flew on   330
Like a low-flying gull that skims the shallows
And rocky coasts where fish ply close inshore.
So, like a gull between the earth and sky,
The progeny of Cyllenë, on the wing
From his maternal grandsire, split the winds   335
To the sand bars of Libya.
                            Alighting tiptoe
On the first hutments, there he found Aeneas
Laying foundations for new towers and homes.
He noted well the swordhilt the man wore,
Adorned with yellow jasper; and the cloak   340
Aglow with Tyrian dye upon his shoulders—
Gifts of the wealthy queen, who had inwoven
Gold thread in the fabric. Mercury
Took him to task at once:
                            "Is it for you
To lay the stones for Carthage's high walls,   345
Tame husband that you are, and build their city?
Oblivious of your own world, your own kingdom!
From bright Olympus he that rules the gods
And turns the earth and heaven by his power—
He and no other sent me to you, told me   350
To bring this message on the running winds:
What have you in mind? What hope, wasting your days
In Libya? If future history's glories
Do not affect you, if you will not strive
For your own honor, think of Ascanius,   355
Think of the expectations of your heir,
Iulus, to whom the Italian realm, the land
Of Rome, are due."
                            And Mercury, as he spoke,
Departed from the visual field of mortals
To a great distance, ebbed in subtle air.   360
Amazed, and shocked to the bottom of his soul
By what his eyes had seen, Aeneas felt
His hackles rise, his voice choke in his throat.
As the sharp admonition and command
From heaven had shaken him awake, he now   365
Burned only to be gone, to leave that land
Of the sweet life behind. What can he do? How tell
The impassioned queen and hope to win her over?
What opening shall he choose? This way and that
He let his mind dart, testing alternatives,   370
Running through every one. And as he pondered
This seemed the better tactic: he called in
Mnestheus, Sergestus and stalwart Serestus,
Telling them:
                    "Get the fleet ready for sea,

---

3. A mountain in Arcadia and Mercury's birthplace.

But quietly, and collect the men on shore.   375
Lay in ship stores and gear."
                                As to the cause
For a change of plan, they were to keep it secret,
Seeing the excellent Dido had no notion,
No warning that such love could be cut short;
He would himself look for the right occasion,   380
The easiest time to speak, the way to do it.
The Trojans to a man gladly obeyed.

The queen, for her part, felt some plot afoot
Quite soon—for who deceives a woman in love?
She caught wind of a change, being in fear   385
Of what had seemed her safety. Evil Rumor,
Shameless as before,[4] brought word to her
In her distracted state of ships being rigged
In trim for sailing. Furious, at her wits' end,
She traversed the whole city, all aflame   390
With rage, like a Bacchanté[5] driven wild
By emblems shaken, when the mountain revels
Of the odd year possess her, when the cry
Of Bacchus rises and Cithaeron[6] calls
All through the shouting night. Thus it turned out   395
She was the first to speak and charge Aeneas:

"You even hoped to keep me in the dark
As to this outrage, did you, two-faced man,
And slip away in silence? Can our love
Not hold you, can the pledge we gave not hold you,   400
Can Dido not, now sure to die in pain?
Even in winter weather must you toil
With ships, and fret to launch against high winds
For the open sea? Oh, heartless!
                                Tell me now,
If you were not in search of alien lands   405
And new strange homes, if ancient Troy remained,
Would ships put out for Troy on these big seas?
Do you go to get away from me? I beg you,
By these tears, by your own right hand,[7] since I
Have left my wretched self nothing but that—   410
Yes, by the marriage that we entered on,
If ever I did well and you were grateful
Or found some sweetness in a gift from me,
Have pity now on a declining house!
Put this plan by, I beg you, if a prayer   415
Is not yet out of place.
Because of you, Libyans and nomad kings
Detest me, my own Tyrians are hostile;
Because of you, I lost my integrity

---

4. Earlier, Rumor (a semidivine being) had spread the report of Dido's "marriage," which had incited
Iarbas to make his indignant prayer to Jupiter.   5. A female devotee of the god Bacchus, in an ecstatic
trance at the festival held every other year in the god's honor.   6. Mountain near Thebes, sacred to
Bacchus.   7. The handclasp with which he pledged his love and that Dido took as an earnest of
marriage.

And that admired name by which alone   420
I made my way once toward the stars.
                      To whom
Do you abandon me, a dying woman,
Guest that you are—the only name now left
From that of husband? Why do I live on?
Shall I, until my brother Pygmalion comes   425
To pull my walls down? Or the Gaetulan
Iarbas leads me captive? If at least
There were a child by you for me to care for,
A little one to play in my courtyard
And give me back Aeneas, in spite of all,   430
I should not feel so utterly defeated,
Utterly bereft."
             She ended there.
The man by Jove's command held fast his eyes
And fought down the emotion in his heart.
At length he answered:
                 "As for myself, be sure   435
I never shall deny all you can say,
Your majesty, of what you meant to me.
Never will the memory of Elissa[8]
Stale for me, while I can still remember
My own life, and the spirit rules my body.   440
As to the event, a few words. Do not think
I meant to be deceitful and slip away.
I never held the torches of a bridegroom,
Never entered upon the pact of marriage.
If Fate permitted me to spend my days   445
By my own lights, and make the best of things
According to my wishes, first of all
I should look after Troy and the loved relics
Left me of my people. Priam's great hall
Should stand again; I should have restored the tower   450
Of Pergamum for Trojans in defeat.
But now it is the rich Italian land
Apollo tells me I must make for: Italy,
Named by his oracles. There is my love;
There is my country. If, as a Phoenician,   455
You are so given to the charms of Carthage,
Libyan city that it is, then tell me,
Why begrudge the Teucrian new lands
For homesteads in Ausonia? Are we not
Entitled, too, to look for realms abroad?   460
Night never veils the earth in damp and darkness,
Fiery stars never ascend the east,
But in my dreams my father's troubled ghost[9]
Admonishes and frightens me. Then, too,
Each night thoughts come of young Ascanius,   465
My dear boy wronged, defrauded of his kingdom,
Hesperian lands of destiny. And now

8. Dido.   9. Anchisēs had died in Sicily just before Aeneas, leaving for Italy, was blown by the storm winds to Carthage.

The gods' interpreter, sent by Jove himself—
I swear it by your head and mine—has brought
Commands down through the racing winds! I say   470
With my own eyes in full daylight I saw him
Entering the building! With my very ears
I drank his message in! So please, no more
Of these appeals that set us both afire.
I sail for Italy not of my own free will."   475

During all this she had been watching him
With face averted, looking him up and down
In silence, and she burst out raging now:

"No goddess was your mother. Dardanus
Was not the founder of your family.   480
Liar and cheat! Some rough Caucasian cliff
Begot you on flint. Hyrcanian[1] tigresses
Tendered their teats to you. Why should I palter?
Why still hold back for more indignity?
Sigh, did he, while I wept? Or look at me?   485
Or yield a tear, or pity her who loved him?
What shall I say first, with so much to say?
The time is past when either supreme Juno
Or the Saturnian father[2] viewed these things
With justice. Faith can never be secure.   490
I took the man in, thrown up on this coast
In dire need, and in my madness then
Contrived a place for him in my domain,
Rescued his lost fleet, saved his shipmates' lives.
Oh, I am swept away burning by furies!   495
Now the prophet Apollo, now his oracles,
Now the gods' interpreter, if you please,
Sent down by Jove himself, brings through the air
His formidable commands! What fit employment
For heaven's high powers! What anxieties   500
To plague serene immortals![3] I shall not
Detain you or dispute your story. Go,
Go after Italy on the sailing winds,
Look for your kingdom, cross the deepsea swell!
If divine justice counts for anything,   505
I hope and pray that on some grinding reef
Midway at sea you'll drink your punishment
And call and call on Dido's name!
From far away I shall come after you
With my black fires, and when cold death has parted   510
Body from soul I shall be everywhere
A shade to haunt you! You will pay for this,
Unconscionable! I shall hear! The news will reach me
Even among the lowest of the dead!"

---

1. Near the Caspian Sea. *Caucasian*: after Caucasus Mountains also near the Caspian Sea. The adjective connoted outlandishness and cruelty.   2. Jupiter.   3. A reference to the Epicurean idea that the gods are unaffected by human events.

At this abruptly she broke off and ran   515
In sickness from his sight and the light of day,
Leaving him at a loss, alarmed, and mute
With all he meant to say. The maids in waiting
Caught her as she swooned and carried her
To bed in her marble chamber.
                      Duty-bound,   520
Aeneas, though he struggled with desire
To calm and comfort her in all her pain,
To speak to her and turn her mind from grief,
And though he sighed his heart out, shaken still
With love of her, yet took the course heaven gave him   525
And went back to the fleet. Then with a will
The Teucrians fell to work and launched ships
Along the whole shore: slick with tar each hull
Took to the water. Eager to get away,
The sailors brought oar-boughs out of the woods   530
With leaves still on, and oaken logs unhewn.
Now you could see them issuing from the town
To the water's edge in streams, as when, aware
Of winter, ants will pillage a mound of spelt
To store it in their granary; over fields   535
The black battalion moves, and through the grass
On a narrow trail they carry off the spoil;
Some put their shoulders to the enormous weight
Of a trundled grain, while some pull stragglers in
And castigate delay; their to-and-fro   540
Of labor makes the whole track come alive.
At that sight, what were your emotions, Dido?
Sighing how deeply, looking out and down
From your high tower on the seething shore
Where all the harbor filled before your eyes   545
With bustle and shouts! Unconscionable Love,
To what extremes will you not drive our hearts!
She now felt driven to weep again, again
To move him, if she could, by supplication,
Humbling her pride before her love— to leave   550
Nothing untried, not to die needlessly.

"Anna, you see the arc of waterfront
All in commotion: they come crowding in
From everywhere. Spread canvas calls for wind,
The happy crews have garlanded the sterns.   555
If I could brace myself for this great sorrow,
Sister, I can endure it, too. One favor,
Even so, you may perform for me.
Since that deserter chose you for his friend
And trusted you, even with private thoughts,   560
Since you alone know when he may be reached,
Go, intercede with our proud enemy.
Remind him that I took no oath at Aulis[4]
With Danaans to destroy the Trojan race;

4. Alluding to Agamemnon's oath when departing from Aulis for Troy.

I sent no ship to Pergamum. Never did I   565
Profane his father Anchisës' dust and shade.
Why will he not allow my prayers to fall
On his unpitying ears? Where is he racing?
Let him bestow one last gift on his mistress:
This, to await fair winds and easier flight.   570
Now I no longer plead the bond he broke
Of our old marriage, nor do I ask that he
Should live without his dear love, Latium,
Or yield his kingdom. Time is all I beg,
Mere time, a respite and a breathing space   575
For madness to subside in, while my fortune
Teaches me how to take defeat and grieve.
Pity your sister. This is the end, this favor—
To be repaid with interest when I die."

She pleaded in such terms, and such, in tears,   580
Her sorrowing sister brought him, time and again.
But no tears moved him, no one's voice would he
Attend to tractably. The fates opposed it;
God's will blocked the man's once kindly ears.
And just as when the north winds from the Alps   585
This way and that contend among themselves
To tear away an oaktree hale with age,
The wind and tree cry, and the buffeted trunk
Showers high foliage to earth, but holds
On bedrock, for the roots go down as far   590
Into the underworld as cresting boughs
Go up in heaven's air: just so this captain,
Buffeted by a gale of pleas
This way and that way, dinned all the day long,
Felt their moving power in his great heart,   595
And yet his will stood fast; tears fell in vain.

On Dido in her desolation now
Terror grew at her fate. She prayed for death,
Being heartsick at the mere sight of heaven.
That she more surely would perform the act   600
And leave the daylight, now she saw before her
A thing one shudders to recall: on altars
Fuming with incense where she placed her gifts,
The holy water blackened, the spilt wine
Turned into blood and mire. Of this she spoke   605
To no one, not to her sister even. Then, too,
Within the palace was a marble shrine
Devoted to her onetime lord, a place
She held in wondrous honor, all festooned
With snowy fleeces and green festive boughs.   610
From this she now thought voices could be heard
And words could be made out, her husband's words,
Calling her, when midnight hushed the earth;
And lonely on the rooftops the night owl
Seemed to lament, in melancholy notes,   615
Prolonged to a doleful cry. And then, besides,

The riddling words of seers in ancient days,
Foreboding sayings, made her thrill with fear.
In nightmare, fevered, she was hunted down
By pitiless Aeneas, and she seemed   620
Deserted always, uncompanioned always,
On a long journey, looking for her Tyrians
In desolate landscapes—
                              as Pentheus gone mad
Sees the oncoming Eumenidës[5] and sees
A double sun and double Thebes appear,   625
Or as when, hounded on the stage, Orestës[6]
Runs from a mother armed with burning brands,
With serpents hellish black,
And in the doorway squat the Avenging Ones.

So broken in mind by suffering, Dido caught   630
Her fatal madness and resolved to die.
She pondered time and means, then visiting
Her mournful sister, covered up her plan
With a calm look, a clear and hopeful brow.

"Sister, be glad for me! I've found a way   635
To bring him back or free me of desire.
Near to the Ocean boundary, near sundown,
The Aethiops' farthest territory lies,
Where giant Atlas turns the sphere of heaven
Studded with burning stars. From there   640
A priestess of Massylian[7] stock has come;
She had been pointed out to me: custodian
Of that shrine named for daughters of the west,
Hesperidës;[8] and it is she who fed
The dragon, guarding well the holy boughs   645
With honey dripping slow and drowsy poppy.
Chanting her spells she undertakes to free
What hearts she wills, but to inflict on others
Duress of sad desires; to arrest
The flow of rivers, make the stars move backward,   650
Call up the spirits of deep Night. You'll see
Earth shift and rumble underfoot and ash trees
Walk down mountainsides. Dearest, I swear
Before the gods and by your own sweet self,
It is against my will that I resort   655
For weaponry to magic powers. In secret
Build up a pyre in the inner court
Under the open sky, and place upon it
The arms that faithless man left in my chamber,
All his clothing, and the marriage bed   660

---

5. Pentheus was King of Thebes, who persecuted the worshipers of Bacchus and imprisoned the god himself. He was later mocked by the god, who inspired him with the Dionysiac spirit (and perhaps with wine) so that he saw double. In this state he was led off to his death on Cithaeron. These events are dramatized in Euripides' play The Bacchanals (Bacchae) but the Eumenidës (Furies) are not mentioned there. Perhaps Virgil is using them simply as a symbol for madness.   6. Another reference to Greek tragedy; in Aeschylus's Choephoroe (The libation bearers), Orestës kills his mother, Clytemnestra, and is pursued by the Furies. In other tragic contexts he is represented as pursued by the ghost of his mother. 7. From the African tribe.   8. The daughters of Hesperus, who lived in a garden that contained golden apples, guarded by a dragon.

On which I came to grief—solace for me
To annihilate all vestige of the man,
Vile as he is: my priestess shows me this."

While she was speaking, cheek and brow grew pale.
But Anna could not think her sister cloaked   665
A suicide in these unheard-of rites;
She failed to see how great her madness was
And feared no consequence more grave
Than at Sychaeus' death. So, as commanded,
She made the preparations. For her part,   670
The queen, seeing the pyre in her inmost court
Erected huge with pitch-pine and sawn ilex,
Hung all the place under the sky with wreaths
And crowned it with funereal cypress boughs.
On the pyre's top she put a sword he left   675
With clothing, and an effigy on a couch,
Her mind fixed now ahead on what would come.
Around the pyre stood altars, and the priestess,
Hair unbound, called in a voice of thunder
Upon three hundred gods, on Erebus,   680
On Chaos, and on triple Hecatë,[9]
Three-faced Diana. Then she sprinkled drops
Purportedly from the fountain of Avernus.[1]
Rare herbs were brought out, reaped at the new moon
By scythes of bronze, and juicy with a milk   685
Of dusky venom; then the rare love-charm
Or caul torn from the brow of a birthing foal
And snatched away before the mother found it.
Dido herself with consecrated grain
In her pure hands, as she went near the altars,   690
Freed one foot from sandal straps, let fall
Her dress ungirdled, and, now sworn to death,
Called on the gods and stars that knew her fate.
She prayed then to whatever power may care
In comprehending justice for the grief   695
Of lovers bound unequally by love.

The night had come, and weary in every land
Men's bodies took the boon of peaceful sleep.
The woods and the wild seas had quieted
At that hour when the stars are in mid-course   700
And every field is still; cattle and birds
With vivid wings that haunt the limpid lakes
Or nest in thickets in the country places
All were asleep under the silent night.
Not, though, the agonized Phoenician queen: 705
She never slackened into sleep and never
Allowed the tranquil night to rest
Upon her eyelids or within her heart.
Her pain redoubled; love came on again,

---

9. Diana as goddess of sorcery and the moon. *Erebus:* the lowest depth of the underworld. *Chaos:* the
Greek personification of the disorder that preceded the creation of the universe.   1. A lake in southern
Italy that was supposed to be the entrance to the lower world.

Devouring her, and on her bed she tossed   710
In a great surge of anger.
                              So awake,
She pressed these questions, musing to herself:

"Look now, what can I do? Turn once again
To the old suitors, only to be laughed at—
Begging a marriage with Numidians   715
Whom I disdained so often? Then what? Trail
The Ilian ships and follow like a slave
Commands of Trojans? Seeing them so agreeable,
In view of past assistance and relief,
So thoughtful their unshaken gratitude?   720
Suppose I wished it, who permits or takes
Aboard their proud ships one they so dislike?
Poor lost soul, do you not yet grasp or feel
The treachery of the line of Laömedon?[2]
What then? Am I to go alone, companion   725
Of the exultant sailors in their flight?
Or shall I set out in their wake, with Tyrians,
With all my crew close at my side, and send
The men I barely tore away from Tyre
To sea again, making them hoist their sails   730
To more sea-winds? No: die as you deserve,
Give pain quietus with a steel blade.
                              Sister,
You are the one who gave way to my tears
In the beginning, burdened a mad queen
With sufferings, and thrust me on my enemy.   735
It was not given me to lead my life
Without new passion, innocently, the way
Wild creatures live, and not to touch these depths.
The vow I took to the ashes of Sychaeus
Was not kept."
                              So she broke out afresh   740
In bitter mourning. On his high stern deck
Aeneas, now quite certain of departure,
Everything ready, took the boon of sleep.
In dream the figure of the god returned
With looks reproachful as before: he seemed   745
Again to warn him, being like Mercury
In every way, in voice, in golden hair,
And in the bloom of youth.
                              "Son of the goddess,
Sleep away this crisis, can you still?
Do you not see the dangers growing round you,   750
Madman, from now on? Can you not hear
The offshore westwind blow? The woman hatches
Plots and drastic actions in her heart,
Resolved on death now, whipping herself on
To heights of anger. Will you not be gone   755
In flight, while flight is still within your power?

2. A king of Troy who twice broke his promise, once to Heracles and once to Apollo and Poseidon.

Soon you will see the offing boil with ships
And glare with torches; soon again
The waterfront will be alive with fires,
If Dawn comes while you linger in this country.   760
Ha! Come, break the spell! Woman's a thing
Forever fitful and forever changing."

At this he merged into the darkness. Then
As the abrupt phantom filled him with fear,
Aeneas broke from sleep and roused his crewmen: 765
"Up, turn out now! Oarsmen, take your thwarts!
Shake out sail! Look here, for the second time
A god from heaven's high air is goading me
To hasten our break away, to cut the cables.
Holy one, whatever god you are,   770
We go with you, we act on your command
Most happily! Be near, graciously help us,
Make the stars in heaven propitious ones!"

He pulled his sword aflash out of its sheath
And struck at the stern hawser. All the men   775
Were gripped by his excitement to be gone,
And hauled and hustled. Ships cast off their moorings,
And an array of hulls hid inshore water
As oarsmen churned up foam and swept to sea.

Soon early Dawn, quitting the saffron bed   780
Of old Tithonus,[3] cast new light on earth,
And as air grew transparent, from her tower
The queen caught sight of ships on the seaward reach
With sails full and the wind astern. She knew
The waterfront now empty, bare of oarsmen.   785
Beating her lovely breast three times, four times,
And tearing her golden hair,
                          "O Jupiter,"
She said, "will this man go, will he have mocked
My kingdom, stranger that he was and is?
Will they not snatch up arms and follow him   790
From every quarter of the town? and dockhands
Tear our ships from moorings? On! Be quick
With torches! Give out arms! Unship the oars!
What am I saying? Where am I? What madness
Takes me out of myself? Dido, poor soul,   795
Your evil doing has come home to you.
Then was the right time, when you offered him
A royal scepter. See the good faith and honor
Of one they say bears with him everywhere
The hearthgods of his country! One who bore   800
His father, spent with age, upon his shoulders!
Could I not then have torn him limb from limb
And flung the pieces on the sea? His company,
Even Ascanius could I not have minced

3. Human consort of Aurora (Eos in Greek), the dawn goddess. He is old because, although she made
him immortal when she took him to her bed, she forgot to obtain for him the gift of eternal youth.

And served up to his father at a feast?   805
The luck of battle might have been in doubt—
So let it have been! Whom had I to fear,
Being sure to die? I could have carried torches
Into his camp, filled passage ways with flame,
Annihilated father and son and followers   810
And given my own life on top of all!
O Sun, scanning with flame all works of earth,
And thou, O Juno, witness and go-between
Of my long miseries; and Hecatë,
Screeched for at night at crossroads in the cities;   815
And thou, avenging Furies, and all gods
On whom Elissa dying may call: take notice,
Overshadow this hell with your high power,
As I deserve, and hear my prayer!
If by necessity that impious wretch   820
Must find his haven and come safe to land,
If so Jove's destinies require, and this,
His end in view, must stand, yet all the same
When hard beset in war by a brave people,
Forced to go outside his boundaries   825
And torn from Iulus, let him beg assistance,
Let him see the unmerited deaths of those
Around and with him, and accepting peace
On unjust terms, let him not, even so,
Enjoy his kingdom or the life he longs for,   830
But fall in battle before his time and lie
Unburied on the sand![4] This I implore,
This is my last cry, as my last blood flows.
Then, O my Tyrians, besiege with hate
His progeny and all his race to come: 835
Make this your offering to my dust. No love,
No pact must be between our peoples; No,
But rise up from my bones, avenging spirit!
Harry with fire and sword the Dardan countrymen
Now, or hereafter, at whatever time   840
The strength will be afforded. Coast with coast
In conflict, I implore, and sea with sea,
And arms with arms: may they contend in war,
Themselves and all the children of their children!"[5]

Now she took thought of one way or another,   845
At the first chance, to end her hated life,
And briefly spoke to Barcë, who had been
Sychaeus' nurse; her own an urn of ash
Long held in her ancient fatherland.
                              "Dear nurse,
Tell Sister Anna to come here, and have her   850

---

4. Dido's prophecy-wish does come true. Aeneas meets resistance in Italy, and at one point in the war
he must leave Ascanius behind and beg aid from King Evander. One of the conditions of peace is that
his people call themselves Latins (not Trojans). He is eventually drowned in an Italian river, never to
see the glory of his descendants.   5. These prophecies also come true. The Romans and Carthaginians
fought three wars (the Punic Wars); Rome won them all, razing Carthage after the third. In the 3rd
century B.C. Hannibal invaded Italy, winning many battles, although he failed to take Rome.

Quickly bedew herself with running water
Before she brings out victims for atonement.
Let her come that way. And you, too, put on
Pure wool around your brows. I have a mind
To carry out that rite to Stygian[6] Jove   855
That I have readied here, and put an end
To my distress, committing to the flames
The pyre of that miserable Dardan."

At this with an old woman's eagerness
Barcë hurried away. And Dido's heart   860
Beat wildly at the enormous thing afoot.
She rolled her bloodshot eyes, her quivering cheeks
Were flecked with red as her sick pallor grew
Before her coming death. Into the court
She burst her way, then at her passion's height   865
She climbed the pyre and bared the Dardan sword—
A gift desired once, for no such need.
Her eyes now on the Trojan clothing there
And the familiar bed, she paused a little,
Weeping a little, mindful, then lay down   870
And spoke her last words:
                              "Remnants dear to me
While god and fate allowed it, take this breath
And give me respite from these agonies.
I lived my life out to the very end
And passed the stages Fortune had appointed.   875
Now my tall shade goes to the under world.
I built a famous town, saw my great walls,
Avenged my husband, made my hostile brother
Pay for his crime. Happy, alas, too happy,
If only the Dardanian keels had never   880
Beached on our coast." And here she kissed the bed.
"I die unavenged," she said, "but let me die.
This way, this way,[7] a blessed relief to go
Into the undergloom. Let the cold Trojan,
Far at sea, drink in this conflagration   885
And take with him the omen of my death!"

Amid these words her household people saw her
Crumpled over the steel blade, and the blade
Aflush with red blood, drenched her hands. A scream
Pierced the high chambers. Now through the shocked city   890
Rumor went rioting, as wails and sobs
With women's outcry echoed in the palace
And heaven's high air gave back the beating din,
As though all Carthage or old Tyre fell
To storming enemies, and, out of hand,   895
Flames billowed on the roofs of men and gods.
Her sister heard the trembling, faint with terror,
Lacerating her face, beating her breast,
Ran through the crowd to call the dying queen:

6. After the river Styx, which flowed in the underworld.   7. In Latin *sic, sic;* the repetition represents
two thrusts of the sword.

"It came to this, then, sister? You deceived me?   900
The pyre meant this, altars and fires meant this?
What shall I mourn first, being abandoned? Did you
Scorn your sister's company in death?
You should have called me out to the same fate!
The same blade's edge and hurt, at the same hour,   905
Should have taken us off. With my own hands
Had I to build this pyre, and had I to call
Upon our country's gods, that in the end
With you placed on it there, O heartless one,
I should be absent? You have put to death   910
Yourself and me, the people and the fathers
Bred in Sidon, and your own new city.
Give me fresh water, let me bathe her wound
And catch upon my lips any last breath
Hovering over hers."

                  Now she had climbed   915
The topmost steps and took her dying sister
Into her arms to cherish, with a sob,
Using her dress to stanch the dark blood flow.
But Dido trying to lift her heavy eyes
Fainted again. Her chest-wound whistled air.   920
Three times she struggled up on one elbow
And each time fell back on the bed. Her gaze
Went wavering as she looked for heaven's light
And groaned at finding it. Almighty Juno,
Filled with pity for this long ordeal   925
And difficult passage, now sent Iris[8] down
Out of Olympus to set free
The wrestling spirit from the body's hold.
For since she died, not at her fated span
Nor as she merited, but before her time   930
Enflamed and driven mad, Proserpina
Had not yet plucked from her the golden hair,[9]
Delivering her to Orcus of the Styx.
So humid Iris through bright heaven flew
On saffron-yellow wings, and in her train   935
A thousand hues shimmered before the sun.
At Dido's head she came to rest.

                    "This token
Sacred to Dis[1] I bear away as bidden
And free you from your body."

                    Saying this,
She cut a lock of hair. Along with it   940
Her body's warmth fell into dissolution,
And out into the winds her life withdrew.

Summary   After his hurried departure from Carthage, Aeneas goes to Sicily, to the kingdom of his friend Acestës. There he organizes funeral games in honor of

8. As in Homer, a divine messenger; sometimes identified with the rainbow.   9. Queen of the underworld. Before a human died she was thought to cut a lock of his or her hair as an offering to Dis, god of the underworld. Dido (by suicide) dies unexpectedly; thus Juno sends Iris to cut the lock.   1. Hades in Greek.

his father, Anchises (who had died in Sicily on their first visit there), and leaves behind those of his following who are unwilling to go on to the uncertainty of a settlement in Italy. Once on Italian soil, Aeneas, obeying instructions from his dead father, who had appeared to him in a dream, consults the Sibyl, who guides him down to the world of the dead. There he is to see his father and the vision of his race, which is to be his only reward, for he will die before his people are settled in their new home.

FROM BOOK VI

[Aeneas in the Underworld]

Gods who rule the ghosts; all silent shades;
And Chaos and infernal Fiery Stream,[2]
And regions of wide night without a sound,
May it be right to tell what I have heard,
May it be right, and fitting, by your will,   5
That I describe the deep world sunk in darkness
Under the earth.
          Now dim to one another
In desolate night they[3] walked on through the gloom,
Through Dis's homes all void, and empty realms,
As one goes through a wood by a faint moon's   10
Treacherous light, when Jupiter veils the sky
And black night blots the colors of the world.
Before the entrance, in the jaws of Orcus,
Grief and avenging Cares have made their beds,
And pale Diseases and sad Age are there,   15
And Dread, and Hunger that sways men to crime,
And sordid Want—in shapes to affright the eyes—
And Death and Toil and Death's own brother, Sleep,
And the mind's evil joys; on the door sill
Death-bringing War, and iron cubicles   20
Of the Eumenidës, and raving Discord,
Viperish hair bound up in gory bands.
In the courtyard a shadowy giant elm
Spreads ancient boughs, her ancient arms where dreams,
False dreams, the old tale goes, beneath each leaf   25
Cling and are numberless. There, too,
About the doorway forms of monsters crowd—
Centaurs, twiformed Scyllas, hundred-armed
Briareus, and the Lernaean hydra
Hissing horribly, and the Chimaera   30
Breathing dangerous flames, and Gorgons, Harpies,[4]
Huge Geryon, triple-bodied ghost.
Here, swept by sudden fear, drawing his sword,
Aeneas stood on guard with naked edge
Against them as they came. If his companion,   35

---

2. A translation of *Phlegethon*, the name of one of the underworld rivers.   3. Aeneas and the Sibyl.
4. All mythical creatures. Centaurs were half human and half horse. Scyllas have many heads. Briareus had fifty heads. The Hydra had nine heads; but if one were cut off, two would grow in its place. The Chimaera was one-third lion, one-third goat, and one-third snake. Here the Harpies are spirits of the storm wind that carry souls to Hades.

Knowing the truth, had not admonished him
How faint these lives were—empty images
Hovering bodiless—he had attacked
And cut his way through phantoms, empty air.

The path goes on from that place to the waves   40
Of Tartarus's Acheron. Thick with mud,
A whirlpool out of a vast abyss
Boils up and belches all the silt it carries
Into Cocytus.[5] Here the ferryman,
A figure of fright, keeper of waters and streams,   45
Is Charon, foul and terrible, his beard
Grown wild and hoar, his staring eyes all flame,
His sordid cloak hung from a shoulder knot.
Alone he poles his craft and trims the sails
And in his rusty hull ferries the dead,   50
Old now—but old age in the gods is green.[6]

Here a whole crowd came streaming to the banks,
Mothers and men, the forms with all life spent
Of heroes great in valor, boys and girls
Unmarried, and young sons laid on the pyre   55
Before their parents' eyes—as many souls
As leaves that yield their hold on boughs and fall
Through forests in the early frost of autumn,
Or as migrating birds from the open sea
That darken heaven when the cold season comes   60
And drives them overseas to sunlit lands.
There all stood begging to be first across
And reached out longing hands to the far shore.

But the grim boatman now took these aboard,
Now those, waving the rest back from the strand.   65
In wonder at this and touched by the commotion,
Aeneas said:
              "Tell me, Sister, what this means,
The crowd at the stream. Where are the souls bound?
How are they tested, so that these turn back,
While those take oars to cross the dead-black water?"   70

Briefly the ancient priestess answered him:

"Cocytus is the deep pool that you see,
The swamp of Styx beyond, infernal power
By which the gods take oath and fear to break it.
All in the nearby crowd you notice here   75
Are pauper souls, the souls of the unburied.
Charon's the boatman. Those the water bears
Are souls of buried men. He may not take them
Shore to dread shore on the hoarse currents there
Until their bones rest in the grave, or till   80
They flutter and roam this side a hundred years;

5. A river of the underworld; the name suggests "mourning" or "lamentation." Tartarus is in the lower
depths of the underworld. Acheron is another river.   6. That is, age in gods does not affect their
vitality or strength. Thus Charon, although old, is still able to ferry the souls of the dead over the river
Styx.

They may have passage then, and may return
To cross the deeps they long for."
                              Anchisës' son
Had halted, pondering on so much, and stood
In pity for the souls' hard lot. Among them   85
He saw two sad ones of unhonored death,
Leucaspis and the Lycian fleet's commander,
Orontës,[7] who had sailed the windy sea
From Troy together, till the Southern gale
Had swamped and whirled them down, both ship and men.   90
Of a sudden he saw his helmsman, Palinurus,
Going by, who but a few nights before
On course from Libya, as he watched the stars,
Had been pitched overboard astern. As soon
As he made sure of the disconsolate one   95
In all the gloom, Aeneas called:
                              "Which god
Took you away from us and put you under,
Palinurus? Tell me. In this one prophecy
Apollo, who had never played me false,
Falsely foretold you'd be unharmed at sea   100
And would arrive at the Ausonian coast.
Is the promise kept?"
                    But the shade said:
                    "Phoebus' caldron[8]
Told you no lie, my captain, and no god
Drowned me at sea. The helm that I hung on to,
Duty bound to keep our ship on course,   105
By some great shock chanced to be torn away,
And I went with it overboard. I swear
By the rough sea, I feared less for myself
Than for your ship: with rudder gone and steersman
Knocked overboard, it might well come to grief   110
In big seas running. Three nights, heavy weather
Out of the South on the vast water tossed me.
On the fourth dawn, I sighted Italy
Dimly ahead, as a wave-crest lifted me.
By turns I swam and rested, swam again   115
And got my footing on the beach, but savages
Attacked me as I clutched at a cliff-top,
Weighted down by my wet clothes. Poor fools,
They took me for a prize and ran me through.
Surf has me now, and sea winds, washing me   120
Close inshore.
              By heaven's happy light
And the sweet air, I beg you, by your father,
And by your hopes of Iulus' rising star,
Deliver me from this captivity,
Unconquered friend! Throw earth on me—you can—   125
Put in to Velia[9] port! Or if there be

---

7. Trojans lost at sea in the storm that took Aeneas to Carthage.   8. The Pythia, priestess of Apollo
at Delphi, delivered the god's prophecies seated on a tripod, a three-legged shallow caldron.   9. South
of the Bay of Naples, near Cape Palinuro (named after Aeneas's pilot).

Some way to do it, if your goddess mother
Shows a way—and I feel sure you pass
These streams and Stygian marsh by heaven's will—
Give this poor soul your hand, take me across,   130
Let me at least in death find quiet haven."
When he had made his plea, the Sibyl said:
"From what source comes this craving, Palinurus?
Would you though still unburied see the Styx
And the grim river of the Eumenidës,   135
Or even the river bank, without a summons?
Abandon hope by prayer to make the gods
Change their decrees. Hold fast to what I say
To comfort your hard lot: neighboring folk
In cities up and down the coast will be   140
Induced by portents to appease your bones,
Building a tomb and making offerings there
On a cape forever named for Palinurus."

The Sibyl's words relieved him, and the pain
Was for a while dispelled from his sad heart,   145
Pleased at the place-name. So the two walked on
Down to the stream. Now from the Stygian water
The boatman, seeing them in the silent wood
And headed for the bank, cried out to them
A rough uncalled-for challenge:
                                "Who are you   150
In armor, visiting our rivers? Speak
From where you are, stop there, say why you come.
This is the region of the Shades, and Sleep,
And drowsy Night. It breaks eternal law
For the Stygian craft to carry living bodies.   155
Never did I rejoice, I tell you, letting
Alcidës cross, or Theseus and Pirithous,[1]
Demigods by paternity though they were,
Invincible in power. One forced in chains
From the king's own seat the watchdog of the dead   160
And dragged him away trembling. The other two
Were bent on carrying our lady off
From Dis's chamber."
                        This the prophetess
And servant of Amphrysian Apollo[2]
Briefly answered:
                    "Here are no such plots,   165
So fret no more. These weapons threaten nothing.
Let the great watchdog at the door howl on
Forever terrifying the bloodless shades.
Let chaste Proserpina remain at home
In her uncle's house. The man of Troy, Aeneas,   170
Remarkable for loyalty, great in arms,

1. They came to kidnap Proserpina, failed, and were imprisoned. *Alcidës:* Heracles, who, as one of his labors, was to bring Cerberus, the watchdog of Hades, up from the lower world. He also managed to rescue Theseus.   2. An elaborate learned allusion; Apollo had once served as herdsman to King Admetus on the banks of the river Amphrysus in Thessaly.

Goes through the deepest shades of Erebus
To see his father.
                    If the very image
Of so much goodness moves you not at all,
Here is a bough"[3]—at this she showed the bough   175
That had been hidden, held beneath her dress—
"You'll recognize it."
                    Then his heart, puffed up
With rage, subsided. They had no more words.
His eyes fixed on the ancient gift, the bough,
The destined gift, so long unseen, now seen,   180
He turned his dusky craft and made for shore.
There from the long thwarts where they sat he cleared
The other souls and made the gangway wide,
Letting the massive man step in the bilge.
The leaky coracle groaned at the weight   185
And took a flood of swampy water in.
At length, on the other side, he put ashore
The prophetess and hero in the mire,
A formless ooze amid the grey-green sedge.
Great Cerberus barking with his triple throat   190
Makes all that shoreline ring, as he lies huge
In a facing cave. Seeing his neck begin
To come alive with snakes, the prophetess
Tossed him a lump of honey and drugged meal
To make him drowse. Three ravenous gullets gaped   195
And he snapped up the sop. Then his great bulk
Subsided and lay down through all the cave.
Now seeing the watchdog deep in sleep, Aeneas
Took the opening: swiftly he turned away
From the river over which no soul returns.   200

Now voices crying loud were heard at once—
The souls of infants wailing. At the door
Of the sweet life they were to have no part in,
Torn from the breast, a black day took them off
And drowned them all in bitter death. Near these   205
Were souls falsely accused, condemned to die.
But not without a judge, or jurymen,
Had these souls got their places: Minos reigned
As the presiding judge, moving the urn,
And called a jury of the silent ones[4]   210
To learn of lives and accusations. Next
Were those sad souls, benighted, who contrived
Their own destruction, and as they hated daylight,
Cast their lives away. How they would wish
In the upper air now to endure the pain   215
Of poverty and toil! But iron law
Stands in the way, since the drear hateful swamp
Has pinned them down here, and the Styx that winds
Nine times around exerts imprisoning power.

3. The golden bough that Aeneas had been ordered to take as tribute to Proserpina.   **4.** The dead.
Minos was a king of Crete, who is now judge of the dead. The magistrate of a Roman court decided
the order in which cases were heard by drawing lots from an urn.

Not far away, spreading on every side,   220
The Fields of Mourning came in view, so called
Since here are those whom pitiless love consumed
With cruel wasting, hidden on paths apart
By myrtle woodland growing overhead.
In death itself, pain will not let them be.   225
He saw here Phaedra, Procris, Eriphylë
Sadly showing the wounds her hard son gave;
Evadnë and Pasiphaë, at whose side
Laodamia walked, and Caeneus,[5]
A young man once, a woman now, and turned   230
Again by fate into the older form.
Among them, with her fatal wound still fresh,
Phoenician Dido wandered the deep wood.
The Trojan captain paused nearby and knew
Her dim form in the dark, as one who sees,   235
Early in the month, or thinks to have seen, the moon
Rising through cloud, all dim. He wept and spoke
Tenderly to her:
                    "Dido, so forlorn,
The story then that came to me was true,
That you were out of life, had met your end   240
By your own hand. Was I, was I the cause?
I swear by heaven's stars, by the high gods,
By any certainty below the earth,
I left your land against my will, my queen.
The gods' commands drove me to do their will,   245
As now they drive me through this world of shades,
These mouldy waste lands and these depths of night.
And I could not believe that I would hurt you
So terribly by going. Wait a little.
Do not leave my sight.   250
Am I someone to flee from? The last word
Destiny lets me say to you is this."

Aeneas with such pleas tried to placate
The burning soul, savagely glaring back,
And tears came to his eyes. But she had turned   255
With gaze fixed on the ground as he spoke on,
Her face no more affected than if she were
Immobile granite or Marpesian[6] stone.
At length she flung away from him and fled,
His enemy still, into the shadowy grove   260
Where he whose bride she once had been, Sychaeus,

---

5. Virgil's words in the original are ambiguous (perhaps to reflect the ambiguity of the sex of Caeneus). The usual explanation of the passage is that Caenis (a woman) was changed by Neptune into a man (Caeneus) but returned to her original sex after death. Because the name occurs here in a list of women, this seems the most likely explanation. Phaedra was the wife of Theseus, king of Athens, who fell in love with Hippolytus, her husband's son by another woman; the result was her death by suicide and Hippolytus's death through his father's curse. Procris was killed by her husband in an accident that was brought about by her own jealousy. Eriphylë betrayed her husband for gold and was killed by her own son. Evadnë threw herself on the pyre of her husband, who was killed by Jupiter for impiety. Pasiphaë was the wife of Minos; she was made to fall in love with a bull, and their union produced the Minotaur. Laodamia begged to be allowed to talk with her dead husband; the request was granted by the gods, and when his time came to return she went with him to the underworld.   6. From the island of Paros.

Joined in her sorrows and returned her love.
Aeneas still gazed after her in tears,
Shaken by her ill fate and pitying her.

Summary   After being shown a pageant of the great Romans who will make
Rome mistress of the world, Aeneas returns to the upper air and begins his settlement in Italy. He is offered the hand of the princess Lavinia by her father Latinus,
but this provokes a war against the Trojans, led by King Turnus of Laurentum, in
the course of which Aeneas is wounded and stops by a stream to rest. At this
point his mother, Venus, comes to him with the armor made for him by Vulcan
(Hephaestus in Greek), her husband and guardian of fire. On the shield is carved
a representation of the future glories of Rome.

FROM BOOK VIII

[The Shield of Aeneas]

Venus the gleaming goddess,
Bearing her gifts, came down amid high clouds
And far away still, in a vale apart,
Sighted her son beside the ice-cold stream.
Then making her appearance as she willed   5
She said to him:
                 "Here are the gifts I promised,
Forged to perfection by my husband's craft,
So that you need not hesitate to challenge
Arrogant Laurentines or savage Turnus,
However soon, in battle."
                          As she spoke   10
Cytherëa[7] swept to her son's embrace
And placed the shining arms before his eyes
Under an oak tree. Now the man in joy
At a goddess' gifts, at being so greatly honored,
Could not be satisfied, but scanned each piece   15
In wonder and turned over in his hands
The helmet with its terrifying plumes
And gushing flames, the sword-blade edged with fate,
The cuirass of hard bronze, blood-red and huge—
Like a dark cloud burning with sunset light   20
That sends a glow for miles—the polished greaves[8]
Of gold and silver alloy, the great spear,
And finally the fabric of the shield
Beyond description.
                    There the Lord of Fire,
Knowing the prophets, knowing the age to come,   25
Had wrought the future story of Italy,
The triumphs of the Romans: there one found
The generations of Ascanius' heirs,
The wars they fought, each one. Vulcan had made
The mother wolf, lying in Mars' green grotto;   30

---

7. So-called because she was born from the sea foam off the Greek island Cythera.   8. Leg pieces.

Made the twin boys at play about her teats,[9]
Nursing the mother without fear, while she
Bent round her smooth neck fondling them in turn
And shaped their bodies with her tongue.
                                        Nearby,
Rome had been added by the artisan,   35
And Sabine women roughly carried off
Out of the audience at the Circus games;
Then suddenly a new war coming on
To pit the sons of Romulus against
Old Tatius[1] and his austere town of Curës.   40
Later the same kings, warfare laid aside,
In arms before Jove's altar stood and held
Libation dishes as they made a pact
With offering of wine. Not far from this
Two four-horse war-cars, whipped on, back to back,   45
Had torn Mettus apart (still, man of Alba,
You should have kept your word) and Roman Tullus[2]
Dragged the liar's rags of flesh away
Through woods where brambles dripped a bloody dew.
There, too, Porsenna stood, ordering Rome   50
To take the exiled Tarquin back,[3] then bringing
The whole city under massive siege.
There for their liberty Aeneas' sons
Threw themselves forward on the enemy spears.
You might have seen Porsenna imaged there   55
To the life, a menacing man, a man in anger
At Roman daring: Cocles who downed the bridge,
Cloelia[4] who broke her bonds and swam the river.

On the shield's upper quarter Manlius,
Guard of the Tarpeian Rock, stood fast   60
Before the temple and held the Capitol,[5]
Where Romulus' house[6] was newly thatched and rough.
Here fluttering through gilded porticos
At night, the silvery goose warned of the Gauls
Approaching: under cover of the darkness   65
Gauls amid the bushes had crept near
And now lay hold upon the citadel.
Golden locks they had and golden dress,
Glimmering with striped cloaks, their milky necks
Entwined with gold. They hefted Alpine spears,   70

---

9. The twins who were to build Rome, Romulus and Remus, sons of Mars the war god, were cast out
into the woods and there suckled by a she-wolf.   1. A Sabine king. Because the new city of Rome
consisted mostly of men, the Romans decided to steal women from the Sabines. The Romans invited
them to an athletic festival, and at a given signal every Roman carried off a Sabine bride. The war that
followed ended in the amalgamation of the Roman and Sabine peoples.   2. The king who punished
Mettus for breaking an agreement made during the early wars of Rome. Mettus was torn apart by two
chariots moving in opposite directions.   3. The Etruscan king Porsenna attempted to restore Tarquin,
the last of the Roman kings, to the throne from which he had been expelled.   4. A Roman hostage
held by Porsenna. Horatius Cocles, with two companions, defended the bridge across the Tiber to give
the Romans time to destroy it.   5. In 392 B.C. Manlius was in charge of the citadel (*Tarpeian Rock*)
at a time when the Gauls from the north held all the rest of the city. They made a night attack on the
citadel, but Manlius, awakened by the cackling of the sacred geese, beat it off, and saved Rome.   6. In
Virgil's time there was still preserved at Rome a rustic building that was supposed to have been the
dwelling place of Romulus.

Two each, and had long body shields for cover.
Vulcan had fashioned naked Luperci
And Salii[7] leaping there with woolen caps
And fallen-from-heaven shields, and put chaste ladies
Riding in cushioned carriages through Rome   75
With sacred images. At a distance then
He pictured the deep hell of Tartarus,
Dis's high gate, crime's punishments, and, yes,
You, Catiline,[8] on a precarious cliff
Hanging and trembling at the Furies' glare.   80
Then, far away from this, were virtuous souls
And Cato[9] giving laws to them. Mid-shield,
The pictured sea flowed surging, all of gold,
As whitecaps foamed on the blue waves, and dolphins
Shining in silver round and round the scene   85
Propelled themselves with flukes and cut through billows.
Vivid in the center were the bronze-beaked
Ships and the fight at sea off Actium.
Here you could see Leucata[1] all alive
With ships maneuvering, sea glowing gold,   90
Augustus Caesar leading into battle
Italians, with both senators and people,
Household gods and great gods: there he stood
High on the stern, and from his blessed brow
Twin flames gushed upward, while his crest revealed   95
His father's star. Apart from him, Agrippa,[2]
Favored by winds and gods, led ships in column,
A towering figure, wearing on his brows
The coronet adorned with warships' beaks,
Highest distinction for command at sea.   100
Then came Antonius with barbaric wealth
And a diversity of arms, victorious
From races of the Dawnlands and Red Sea,
Leading the power of the East, of Egypt,
Even of distant Bactra[3] of the steppes.   105
And in his wake the Egyptian consort came
So shamefully. The ships all kept together
Racing ahead, the water torn by oar-strokes,
Torn by the triple beaks, in spume and foam.
All made for the open sea. You might believe   110
The Cyclades[4] uprooted were afloat
Or mountains running against mountain heights
When seamen in those hulks pressed the attack

---

7. The twelve priests of Mars, who danced in his honor carrying shields that had fallen from heaven. *Luperci*: priests of Lupercus, a Roman god corresponding to the Greek Pan.   8. Leader of a conspiracy to overthrow the republic; it was halted mainly through the efforts of Cicero, consul in 63 B.C. Catiline connotes the type of discord, represented by the civil war that almost destroyed the Roman state, to which Augustus later put an end.   9. The noblest of the republicans who had fought Julius Caesar; he stood for honesty and the seriousness that the Romans most admired. He committed suicide in 47 B.C. after Caesar's victory in Africa. Before taking his life he read through Plato's *Phaedo*, a dialogue concerned with the immortality of the soul, which ends with an account of the death of Socrates. 1. A promontory near Actium, on the west coast of Greece, which had a temple of Apollo on it. The naval battle fought here in 31 B.C. was the decisive engagement of the civil war. Augustus, the master of the western half of the empire, defeated Antony, who held the eastern half and was supported by Cleopatra, queen of Egypt.   2. Augustus's admiral at Actium.   3. On the borders of India.   4. The islands of the southern Aegean Sea.

Upon the other turreted ships. They hurled
Broadsides of burning flax on flying steel,   115
And fresh blood reddened Neptune's fields. The queen
Amidst the battle called her flotilla on
With a sistrum's[5] beat, a frenzy out of Egypt,
Never turning her head as yet to see
Twin snakes of death behind, while monster forms   120
Of gods of every race, and the dog-god
Anubis[6] barking, held their weapons up
Against our Neptune, Venus, and Minerva.
Mars, engraved in steel, raged in the fight
As from high air the dire Furies came   125
With Discord, taking joy in a torn robe,
And on her heels, with bloody scourge, Bellona.[7]

Overlooking it all, Actian[8] Apollo
Began to pull his bow. Wild at this sight,
All Egypt, Indians, Arabians, all   130
Sabaeans[9] put about in flight, and she,
The queen, appeared crying for winds to shift
Just as she hauled up sail and slackened sheets.
The Lord of Fire had portrayed her there,
Amid the slaughter, pallid with death to come,   135
Then borne by waves and wind from the northwest,
While the great length of mourning Nile awaited her
With open bays, calling the conquered home
To his blue bosom and his hidden streams.
But Caesar then in triple triumph[1] rode   140
Within the walls of Rome, making immortal
Offerings to the gods of Italy—
Three hundred princely shrines throughout the city.
There were the streets, humming with festal joy
And games and cheers, an altar to every shrine,   145
To every one a mothers' choir, and bullocks
Knifed before the altars strewed the ground.
The man himself, enthroned before the snow-white
Threshold of sunny Phoebus, viewed the gifts
The nations of the earth made, and he fitted them   150
To the tall portals. Conquered races passed
In long procession, varied in languages
As in their dress and arms. Here Mulciber,[2]
Divine smith, had portrayed the Nomad tribes
And Afri with ungirdled flowing robes,   155
Here Leleges and Carians, and here
Gelonians[3] with quivers. Here Euphrates,
Milder in his floods now, there Morini,[4]
Northernmost of men; here bull-horned Rhine,
And there the still unconquered Scythian Dahae;   160
Here, vexed at being bridged, the rough Araxes.[5]

5. An Oriental rattle, used in the worship of Isis.   6. The Egyptian death god, depicted with the head
of a jackal.   7. A Roman war goddess.   8. So-called because of his temple at Actium; the temple
(and its cult statue) overlooked the sea battle.   9. Arabs from the Yemen.   1. For victories in Dalmatia and at Actium and Alexandria.   2. Vulcan.   3. Peoples from Scythia (in the Balkans). The
Leleges and Carians were from Asia Minor.   4. A Belgian tribe.   5. A turbulent river in Armenia.
Augustus built a new bridge over it.

All these images on Vulcan's shield,
His mother's gift, were wonders to Aeneas.
Knowing nothing of the events themselves,
He felt joy in their pictures, taking up   165
Upon his shoulder all the destined acts
And fame of his descendants.

Summary   In the course of the desperate battles that follow, the young Pallas,
entrusted to Aeneas's care by his father, is killed by the Italian champion Turnus,
who takes and wears the belt of Pallas as the spoil of victory. The fortunes of the
war later change in favor of the Trojans, and Aeneas kills the Etruscan king Mez-
entius, Turnus's ally. Eventually, as the Italians prepare to accept the generous
peace terms offered by Aeneas, Turnus forestalls them by accepting Aeneas's challenge to single combat to decide the issue. But this solution is frustrated by the
intervention of Juno, who foresees Aeneas's victory. She prompts Turnus's sister,
the river nymph Juturna, to intervene in an attempt to save Turnus's life. Juturna
stirs up the Italians, who are watching the champions prepare for the duel; the
truce is broken, and in the subsequent fighting Aeneas is wounded by an arrow.
Healed by Venus, he returns to the fight, and the Italians are driven back. Turnus
finally faces his adversary. His sword breaks on the armor forged by Vulcan, and
he runs from Aeneas. He is saved by Juturna, who, assuming the shape of his
charioteer, hands him a fresh sword. At this point Jupiter intervenes to stop the
vain attempts of Juno and Juturna to save Turnus.

FROM BOOK XII

[The Death of Turnus]

Omnipotent Olympus' king meanwhile
Had words for Juno, as she watched the combat
Out of a golden cloud. He said:
                    "My consort,
What will the end be? What is left for you?
You yourself know, and say you know, Aeneas   5
Born for heaven, tutelary of this land,
By fate to be translated to the stars.[6]
What do you plan? What are you hoping for,
Keeping your seat apart in the cold clouds?
Fitting, was it, that a mortal archer   10
Wound an immortal? That a blade let slip
Should be restored to Turnus, and new force
Accrue to a beaten man? Without your help
What could Juturna do? Come now, at last
Have done, and heed our pleading, and give way.   15
Let yourself no longer be consumed
Without relief by all that inward burning;
Let care and trouble not forever come to me
From your sweet lips. The finish is at hand.
You had the power to harry men of Troy   20
By land and sea, to light the fires of war
Beyond belief, to scar a family

---

6. Aeneas is destined for immortality, because after his death he will be worshiped as a local god.

With mourning before marriage.[7] I forbid
Your going further."
           So spoke Jupiter,
And with a downcast look Juno replied: 25

"Because I know that is your will indeed,
Great Jupiter, I left the earth below,
Though sore at heart, and left the side of Turnus.
Were it not so, you would not see me here
Suffering all that passes, here alone,   30
Resting on air. I should be armed in flames
At the very battle-line, dragging the Trojans
Into a deadly action. I persuaded
Juturna—I confess—to help her brother
In his hard lot, and I approved her daring   35
Greater difficulties to save his life,
But not that she should fight with bow and arrow.
This I swear by Styx' great fountainhead
Inexorable, which high gods hold in awe.
I yield now and for all my hatred leave   40
This battlefield. But one thing not retained
By fate I beg for Latium, for the future
Greatness of your kin: when presently
They crown peace with a happy wedding day—
So let it be—and merge their laws and treaties,   45
Never command the land's own Latin folk
To change their old name, to become new Trojans,
Known as Teucrians; never make them alter
Dialect or dress. Let Latium be.
Let there be Alban kings for generations,   50
And let Italian valor be the strength
Of Rome in after times. Once and for all
Troy fell, and with her name let her lie fallen."

The author of men and of the world replied
With a half-smile:
           "Sister of Jupiter[8]   55
Indeed you are, and Saturn's other child,
To feel such anger, stormy in your breast.
But come, no need; put down this fit of rage.
I grant your wish. I yield, I am won over
Willingly. Ausonian folk will keep   60
Their fathers' language and their way of life,
And, that being so, their name. The Teucrians
Will mingle and be submerged, incorporated.
Rituals and observances of theirs
I'll add, but make them Latin, one in speech.   65
The race to come, mixed with Ausonian blood,
Will outdo men and gods in its devotion,

---

7. A reference not only to the Italian losses but also to the suicide of Amata, wife of King Latinus, who hanged herself when the Trojans assaulted the city just before the duel between Aeneas and Turnus began.   8. Jupiter and Juno (like the Greek Zeus and Hera) are brother and sister as well as husband and wife.

You shall see—and no nation on earth
Will honor and worship you so faithfully."

To all this Juno nodded in assent   70
And, gladdened by his promise, changed her mind.
Then she withdrew from sky and cloud.
                                    That done,
The Father set about a second plan—
To take Juturna from her warring brother.
Stories are told of twin fiends, called the Dirae,   75
Whom, with Hell's Megaera,[9] deep Night bore
In one birth. She entwined their heads with coils
Of snakes and gave them wings to race the wind.
Before Jove's throne, a step from the cruel king,
These twins attend him and give piercing fear   80
To ill mankind, when he who rules the gods
Deals out appalling death and pestilence,
Or war to terrify our wicked cities.
Jove now dispatched one of these, swift from heaven,
Bidding her be an omen to Juturna.   85
Down she flew, in a whirlwind borne to earth,
Just like an arrow driven through a cloud
From a taut string, an arrow armed with gall
Of deadly poison, shot by a Parthian[1]—
A Parthian or a Cretan[2]—for a wound   90
Immedicable; whizzing unforeseen
It goes through racing shadows: so the spawn
Of Night went diving downward to the earth.

On seeing Trojan troops drawn up in face
Of Turnus' army, she took on at once   95
The shape of that small bird[3] that perches late
At night on tombs or desolate roof-tops
And troubles darkness with a gruesome song.
Shrunk to that form, the fiend in Turnus' face
Went screeching, flitting, flitting to and fro   100
And beating with her wings against his shield.
Unstrung by numbness, faint and strange, he felt
His hackles rise, his voice choke in his throat.
As for Juturna, when she knew the wings,
The shriek to be the fiend's, she tore her hair,   105
Despairing, then she fell upon her cheeks
With nails, upon her breast with clenched hands.

"Turnus, how can your sister help you now?
What action is still open to me, soldierly
Though I have been? Can I by any skill   110
Hold daylight for you? Can I meet and turn
This deathliness away? Now I withdraw,
Now leave this war. Indecent birds, I fear you;
Spare me your terror. Whip-lash of your wings

---

9. One of the Dirae, literally "dreadful ones."   1. Parthia was the most dangerous neighbor of the
Roman Empire in the east.   2. Parthian mounted archers were famous, as were Cretan archers.
3. The owl.

I recognize, that ghastly sound, and guess 115
Great-hearted Jupiter's high cruel commands.
Returns for my virginity, are they?
He gave me life eternal[4]—to what end?
Why has mortality been taken from me?
Now beyond question I could put a term 120
To all my pain, and go with my poor brother
Into the darkness, his companion there.
Never to die? Will any brook of mine
Without you, brother, still be sweet to me?
If only earth's abyss were wide enough 125
To take me downward, goddess though I am,
To join the shades below!"
                So she lamented,
Then with a long sigh, covering up her head
In her grey mantle, sank to the river's depth.

Aeneas moved against his enemy 130
And shook his heavy pine-tree spear. He called
From his hot heart:
            "Rearmed now, why so slow?
Why, even now, fall back? The contest here
Is not a race, but fighting to the death
With spear and sword. Take on all shapes there are, 135
Summon up all your nerve and skill, choose any
Footing, fly among the stars, or hide
In caverned earth—"
           The other shook his head,
Saying:
      "I do not fear your taunting fury,
Arrogant prince. It is the gods I fear 140
And Jove my enemy."
             He said no more,
But looked around him. Then he saw a stone,
Enormous, ancient, set up there to prevent
Landowners' quarrels. Even a dozen picked men
Such as the earth produces in our day 145
Could barely lift and shoulder it. He swooped
And wrenched it free, in one hand, then rose up
To his heroic height, ran a few steps,
And tried to hurl the stone against his foe—
But as he bent and as he ran 150
And as he hefted and propelled the weight
He did not know himself. His knees gave way,
His blood ran cold and froze. The stone itself,
Tumbling through space, fell short and had no impact.

Just as in dreams when the night-swoon of sleep 155
Weighs on our eyes, it seems we try in vain
To keep on running, try with all our might,
But in the midst of effort faint and fail;
Our tongue is powerless, familiar strength

4. Jupiter had been the lover of Juturna and had rewarded her with immortality.

Will not hold up our body, not a sound   160
Or word will come: just so with Turnus now:
However bravely he made shift to fight
The immortal fiend blocked and frustrated him.
Flurrying images passed through his mind.
He gazed at the Rutulians,[5] and beyond them,   165
Gazed at the city, hesitant, in dread.
He trembled now before the poised spear-shaft
And saw no way to escape; he had no force
With which to close, or reach his foe, no chariot
And no sign of the charioteer, his sister.   170
At a dead loss he stood. Aeneas made
His deadly spear flash in the sun and aimed it,
Narrowing his eyes for a lucky hit.
Then, distant still, he put his body's might
Into the cast. Never a stone that soared   175
From a wall-battering catapult went humming
Loud as this, nor with so great a crack
Burst ever a bolt of lightning. It flew on
Like a black whirlwind bringing devastation,
Pierced with a crash the rim of sevenfold shield,   180
Cleared the cuirass' edge, and passed clean through
The middle of Turnus' thigh. Force of the blow
Brought the huge man to earth, his knees buckling,
And a groan swept the Rutulians as they rose,
A groan heard echoing on all sides from all   185
The mountain ra.ige, and echoed by the forests.
The man brought down, brought low, lifted his eyes
And held his right hand out to make his plea:

"Clearly I earned this, and I ask no quarter.
Make the most of your good fortune here.   190
If you can feel a father's grief—and you, too,
Had such a father in Anchises—then
Let me bespeak your mercy for old age
In Daunus,[6] and return me, or my body,
Stripped, if you will, of life, to my own kin.   195
You have defeated me. The Ausonians
Have seen me in defeat, spreading my hands.
Lavinia is your bride. But go no further
Out of hatred."
                    Fierce under arms, Aeneas
Looked to and fro, and towered, and stayed his hand   200
Upon the sword-hilt. Moment by moment now
What Turnus said began to bring him round
From indecision. Then to his glance appeared
The accurst swordbelt surmounting Turnus' shoulder,
Shining with its familiar studs—the strap   205
Young Pallas wore when Turnus wounded him
And left him dead upon the field; now Turnus
Bore that enemy token on his shoulder—
Enemy still. For when the sight came home to him,

5. The Italian troops watching the combat between Turnus and Aeneas.   6. Father of Turnus.

Aeneas raged at the relic of his anguish 210
Worn by this man as trophy. Blazing up
And terrible in his anger, he called out:

"You in your plunder, torn from one of mine,
Shall I be robbed of you? This wound will come
From Pallas: Pallas makes this offering 215
And from your criminal blood exacts his due."

He sank his blade in fury in Turnus' chest.
Then all the body slackened in death's chill,
And with a groan for that indignity
His spirit fled into the gloom below. 220

OVID

43 B.C.–A.D. 17

Virgil had grown to manhood in the years of civil war, when no one's property, or even life, was safe. He knew all too well the horrors that would inevitably recur if Augustus's attempt to establish stable government should fail; like all his generation, he knew how precarious the newfound peace was and felt himself deeply engaged in the Augustan program. But a new generation of poets, who had not known the time of troubles, took much of what had been achieved for granted and turned to new themes. The most brilliant of them, Ovid, was a boy of eleven when Octavius (later Augustus) defeated Antony at Actium. The early years of his manhood, far from being dominated by fear of chaos come again, were marked by rapid literary and social success in the brilliant society of a capital intent on enjoying the peace and prosperity that had been restored with so much effort.

Ovid was a versifier of genius. "Whatever I tried to say," he wrote, "came out in verse," and Pope adapted the line for his own case: "I lisped in numbers for the numbers came." Elegance, wit, and precision remained the hallmarks of Ovid's poetry throughout his long and productive career; though his themes are often frivolous, the technical perfection of the medium carries the dazzled reader along. The *Amores*, unabashed chronicles of a Roman Don Juan, was his first publication; it was soon followed by the *Art of Love*, a handbook of seduction (originally circulated as Books I and II, for men — Book III, for women, was added by popular request).

In A.D. 8 Ovid was banished by imperial decree to the town of Tomi, in what is now Rumania; it was outside the frontiers of the empire. He remained there until his death, sending back to Rome poetic epistles, the *Sorrows*, that asked for pardon but to no effect. The reason for his banishment is not known; involvement in some scandal concerning Augustus's daughter Julia is a possibility, but the cynical love poetry may have been a contributing factor. Augustus was trying hard, by propaganda and legislation, to revive old Roman standards of morality and Ovid's *Art of Love* was not exactly helpful. His most influential work, the *Metamorphoses*, is a treasure house of Greek and Roman mythological stories brilliantly combined in a long narrative and retold with such wit, charm, and surpassing beauty that poets ever since — Chaucer, Shakespeare, and Milton among them — have used it as a source.

It consists of fifteen books. Beginning with the creation of the world, the trans-

formation of matter into living bodies, Ovid regales his readers with tales of human beings changed into animals, flowers, and trees. He proceeds through Greek myth to stories of early Rome and so to his own day, including the ascension of the murdered Julius Caesar to the heavens in the form of a star and the divine promise that Augustus too, on some day far in the future, will become a god.

H. Fraenkel, *Ovid: A Poet Between Two Worlds* (1945), looks at Ovid as a poet in his historical context. G. K. Galinsky, *Ovid's Metamorphoses: An Introduction to the Basic Aspects* (1975), is a useful guide. Sara Mack, *Ovid* (1988), is an introduction to all the poems of Ovid intended for the general reader. It is especially illuminating on Ovid's narrative technique. See also Brooks Otis, *Ovid as an Epic Poet* (1970), and E. J. Kenney in *The Cambridge History of Classical Literature*, vol. 2 (1982), pp. 430–41.

PRONOUNCING GLOSSARY

The following list uses common English syllables and stress accents to provide rough equivalents of selected words whose pronunciation may be unfamiliar to the general reader.

Aeolus: *ee'-o-lus*	Lycaon: *lai-kay'-on*
Cyllene: *si-lee'-nee*	Zephyrus: *ze'-fer-us*

Metamorphoses[1]

FROM BOOK I

My intention is to tell of bodies changed
To different forms; the gods, who made the changes,
Will help me—or I hope so—with a poem
That runs from the world's beginning to our own days.[2]

[The Creation]

Before the ocean was, or earth, or heaven,   5
Nature was all alike, a shapelessness,
Chaos, so-called, all rude and lumpy matter,
Nothing but bulk, inert, in whose confusion
Discordant atoms warred: there was no sun
To light the universe; there was no moon   10
With slender silver crescents filling slowly;
No earth hung balanced in surrounding air;
No sea reached far along the fringe of shore.
Land, to be sure, there was, and air, and ocean,
But land on which no man could stand, and water   15
No man could swim in, air no man could breathe,
Air without light, substance forever changing,
Forever at war: within a single body
Heat fought with cold, wet fought with dry, the hard
Fought with the soft, things having weight contended   20
With weightless things.

---

1. Translated by Rolfe Humphries.   2. In fact the last metamorphosis in the poem is that of the soul of the murdered dictator Julius Caesar, who is turned into a star. Caesar was murdered in 44 B.C.; Ovid was born in the next year.

Till God, or kindlier Nature,
Settled all argument, and separated
Heaven from earth, water from land, our air
From the high stratosphere, a liberation
So things evolved, and out of blind confusion   25
Found each its place, bound in eternal order.
The force of fire, that weightless element,
Leaped up and claimed the highest place[3] in heaven;
Below it, air; and under them the earth
Sank with its grosser portions; and the water,   30
Lowest of all, held up, held in, the land.

Whatever god it was, who out of chaos
Brought order to the universe, and gave it
Division, subdivision, he molded earth,
In the beginning, into a great globe,   35
Even on every side, and bade the waters
To spread and rise, under the rushing winds,
Surrounding earth; he added ponds and marshes,
He banked the river-channels, and the waters
Feed earth or run to sea, and that great flood   40
Washes on shores, not banks. He made the plains
Spread wide, the valleys settle, and the forest
Be dressed in leaves; he made the rocky mountains
Rise to full height, and as the vault of Heaven
Has two zones, left and right,[4] and one between them   45
Hotter than these, the Lord of all Creation
Marked on the earth the same design and pattern.
The torrid zone too hot for men to live in,
The north and south too cold, but in the middle
Varying climate, temperature and season.   50
Above all things the air, lighter than earth,
Lighter than water, heavier than fire,
Towers and spreads; there mist and cloud assemble,
And fearful thunder and lightning and cold winds,
But these, by the Creator's order, held   55
No general dominion; even as it is,
These brothers brawl and quarrel; though each one
Has his own quarter, still, they come near tearing
The universe apart. Eurus is monarch
Of the lands of dawn,[5] the realms of Araby,   60
The Persian ridges under the rays of morning.
Zephyrus holds the west that glows at sunset,
Boreas, who makes men shiver, holds the north,
Warm Auster governs in the misty southland,
And over them all presides the weightless ether,   65
Pure without taint of earth.
                              These boundaries given,
Behold, the stars, long hidden under darkness,
Broke through and shone, all over the spangled heaven,

---

3. The upper atmosphere, the *aether* as the Greeks called it, was thought of as a fiery element.
4. That is, two zones to the north (*right*) and two to the south (*left*).   5. The sunrise, the east. Eurus
is the east wind.

Their home forever, and the gods lived there,
And shining fish were given the waves for dwelling   70
And beasts the earth, and birds the moving air.

But something else was needed, a finer being,
More capable of mind, a sage, a ruler,
So Man was born, it may be, in God's image,
Or Earth, perhaps, so newly separated   75
From the old fire of Heaven, still retained
Some seed of the celestial force which fashioned
Gods out of living clay and running water.
All other animals look downward; Man,
Alone, erect, can raise his face toward Heaven.   80

[The Four Ages[6]]

The Golden Age was first, a time that cherished
Of its own will, justice and right; no law,
No punishment, was called for; fearfulness
Was quite unknown, and the bronze tablets held
No legal threatening; no suppliant throng   85
Studied a judge's face; there were no judges,
There did not need to be. Trees had not yet
Been cut and hollowed, to visit other shores.
Men were content at home, and had no towns
With moats and walls around them; and no trumpets   90
Blared out alarums; things like swords and helmets
Had not been heard of. No one needed soldiers.
People were unaggressive, and unanxious;
The years went by in peace. And Earth, untroubled,
Unharried by hoe or plowshare, brought forth all   95
That men had need for, and those men were happy,
Gathering berries from the mountain sides,
Cherries, or blackcaps, and the edible acorns.
Spring was forever, with a west wind blowing
Softly across the flowers no man had planted,   100
And Earth, unplowed, brought forth rich grain; the field,
Unfallowed, whitened with wheat, and there were rivers
Of milk, and rivers of honey, and golden nectar
Dripped from the dark-green oak-trees.
                                              After Saturn
Was driven to the shadowy land of death,   105
And the world was under Jove,[7] the Age of Silver
Came in, lower than gold, better than bronze.
Jove made the springtime shorter, added winter,
Summer, and autumn, the seasons as we know them.
That was the first time when the burnt air glowed   110
White-hot, or icicles hung down in winter.
And men built houses for themselves; the caverns,
The woodland thickets, and the bark-bound shelters
No longer served; and the seeds of grain were planted

6. In this myth of the four ages Ovid is following the account of the archaic Greek poet Hesiod (who, however, counted five ages; he interposed the age of the heroes—the wars of Thebes and Troy—between the Bronze and Iron ages).   7. Or Jupiter, who (like Zeus) overthrew his father's, Saturn's, regime.

In the long furrows, and the oxen struggled   115
Groaning and laboring under the heavy yoke.

Then came the Age of Bronze, and dispositions
Took on aggressive instincts, quick to arm,
Yet not entirely evil. And last of all
The Iron Age succeeded, whose base vein   120
Let loose all evil: modesty and truth
And righteousness fled earth, and in their place
Came trickery and slyness, plotting, swindling,
Violence and the damned desire of having.
Men spread their sails to winds unknown to sailors,   125
The pines came down their mountain-sides, to revel
And leap in the deep waters,[8] and the ground,
Free, once, to everyone, like air and sunshine,
Was stepped off by surveyors. The rich earth,
Good giver of all the bounty of the harvest,   130
Was asked for more; they dug into her vitals,
Pried out the wealth a kinder lord had hidden
In Stygian[9] shadow, all that precious metal,
The root of evil. They found the guilt of iron,
And gold, more guilty still. And War came forth   135
That uses both to fight with; bloody hands
Brandished the clashing weapons. Men lived on plunder.
Guest was not safe from host, nor brother from brother,
A man would kill his wife, a wife her husband,
Stepmothers, dire and dreadful, stirred their brews   140
With poisonous aconite, and sons would hustle
Fathers to death, and Piety lay vanquished,
And the maiden Justice, last of all immortals,
Fled from the bloody earth.
                           Heaven was no safer.
Giants attacked the very throne of Heaven,   145
Piled Pelion on Ossa,[1] mountain on mountain
Up to the very stars. Jove struck them down
With thunderbolts, and the bulk of those huge bodies
Lay on the earth, and bled, and Mother Earth,
Made pregnant by that blood, brought forth new bodies,   150
And gave them, to recall her older offspring,
The forms of men. And this new stock was also
Contemptuous of gods, and murder-hungry
And violent. You would know they were sons of blood.

[Jove's Intervention]

And Jove was witness from his lofty throne   155
Of all this evil, and groaned as he remembered
The wicked revels of Lycaon's[2] table,
The latest guilt, a story still unknown
To the high gods. In awful indignation
He summoned them to council. No one dawdled.   160

---

8. That is, after the wood was made into ships.   9. From the river Styx in the underworld.   1. Two
mountains in central Greece, south of Olympus.   2. King of Arcadia, in the Peloponnese.

Easily seen when the night skies are clear,
The Milky Way shines white. Along this road
The gods move toward the palace of the Thunderer,
His royal halls, and, right and left, the dwellings
Of other gods are open, and guests come thronging.   165
The lesser gods live in a meaner section,
An area not reserved, as this one is,
For the illustrious Great Wheels of Heaven.
(Their Palatine Hill,[3] if I might call it so.)

They took their places in the marble chamber   170
Where high above them all their king was seated,
Holding his ivory sceptre, shaking out
Thrice, and again, his awful locks, the sign
That made the earth and stars and ocean tremble,
And then he spoke, in outrage: "I was troubled   175
Less for the sovereignty of all the world
In that old time when the snake-footed giants
Laid each his hundred hands on captive Heaven.
Monstrous they were, and hostile, but their warfare
Sprung from one source, one body. Now, wherever   180
The sea-gods roar around the earth, a race
Must be destroyed, the race of men. I swear it!
I swear by all the Stygian rivers gliding
Under the world, I have tried all other measures.
The knife must cut the cancer out, infection   185
Averted while it can be, from our numbers.
Those demigods, those rustic presences,
Nymphs, fauns, and satyrs, wood and mountain dwellers,
We have not yet honored with a place in Heaven,
But they should have some decent place to dwell in,   190
In peace and safety. Safety? Do you reckon
They will be safe, when I, who wield the thunder,
Who rule you all as subjects, am subjected
To the plottings of the barbarous Lycaon?"

They burned, they trembled. Who was this Lycaon,   195
Guilty of such rank infamy? They shuddered
In horror, with a fear of sudden ruin,
As the whole world did later, when assassins
Struck Julius Caesar down, and Prince Augustus
Found satisfaction in the great devotion   200
That cried for vengeance, even as Jove took pleasure,
Then, in the gods' response. By word and gesture
He calmed them down, awed them again to silence,
And spoke once more:

[The Story of Lycaon]

"He has indeed been punished.
On that score have no worry. But what he did,   205
And how he paid, are things that I must tell you.
I had heard the age was desperately wicked,

3. Where the emperor Augustus lived (in Rome).

I had heard, or so I hoped, a lie, a falsehood,
So I came down, as man, from high Olympus,
Wandered about the world. It would take too long   210
To tell you how widespread was all that evil.
All I had heard was grievous understatement!
I had crossed Maenala, a country bristling
With dens of animals, and crossed Cyllene,
And cold Lycaeus'[4] pine woods. Then I came   215
At evening, with the shadows growing longer,
To an Arcadian palace, where the tyrant
Was anything but royal in his welcome.
I gave a sign that a god had come, and people
Began to worship, and Lycaon mocked them,   220
Laughed at their prayers, and said: 'Watch me find out
Whether this fellow is a god or mortal,
I can tell quickly, and no doubt about it.'
He planned, that night, to kill me while I slumbered;
That was his way to test the truth. Moreover,   225
And not content with that, he took a hostage,
One sent by the Molossians,[5] cut his throat,
Boiled pieces of his flesh, still warm with life,
Broiled others, and set them before me on the table.
That was enough. I struck, and the bolt of lightning   230
Blasted the household of that guilty monarch.
He fled in terror, reached the silent fields,
And howled,[6] and tried to speak. No use at all!
Foam dripped from his mouth; bloodthirsty still, he turned
Against the sheep, delighting still in slaughter,   235
And his arms were legs, and his robes were shaggy hair,
Yet he is still Lycaon, the same grayness,
The same fierce face, the same red eyes, a picture
Of bestial savagery. One house has fallen,
But more than one deserves to. Fury reigns   240
Over all the fields of Earth. They are sworn to evil,
Believe it. Let them pay for it, and quickly!
So stands my purpose."
                         Part of them approved
With words and added fuel to his anger,
And part approved with silence, and yet all   245
Were grieving at the loss of humankind,
Were asking what the world would be, bereft
Of mortals: who would bring their altars incense?
Would earth be given the beasts, to spoil and ravage?
Jove told them not to worry; he would give them   250
Another race, unlike the first, created
Out of a miracle; he would see to it.

He was about to hurl his thunderbolts
At the whole world, but halted, fearing Heaven
Would burn from fire so vast, and pole to pole   255

4. Maenala, Cyllene, and Lycaeus are mountains in Arcadia.   5. Peoples from Epirus, the northern-
most extremity of Greece.   6. The beginning of the first metamorphosis—Lycaon (the first part of
whose name is the Greek for "wolf") becomes a wolf.

Break out in flame and smoke, and he remembered
The fates had said that some day land and ocean,
The vault of Heaven, the whole world's mighty fortress,
Besieged by fire, would perish. He put aside
The bolts made in Cyclopean[7] workshops; better,   260
He thought, to drown the world by flooding water.

[The Flood]

So, in the cave of Aeolus,[8] he prisoned
The North-wind, and the West-wind, and such others
As ever banish cloud, and he turned loose
The South-wind, and the South-wind came out streaming   265
With dripping wings, and pitch-black darkness veiling
His terrible countenance. His beard is heavy
With rain-cloud, and his hoary locks a torrent,
Mists are his chaplet, and his wings and garments
Run with the rain. His broad hands squeeze together   270
Low-hanging clouds, and crash and rumble follow
Before the cloudburst, and the rainbow, Iris,
Draws water from the teeming earth, and feeds it
Into the clouds again. The crops are ruined,
The farmers' prayers all wasted, all the labor   275
Of a long year, comes to nothing.
                              And Jove's anger,
Unbounded by his own domain, was given
Help by his dark-blue brother. Neptune[9] called
His rivers all, and told them, very briefly,
To loose their violence, open their houses,   280
Pour over embankments, let the river horses
Run wild as ever they would. And they obeyed him.
His trident struck the shuddering earth; it opened
Way for the rush of waters. The leaping rivers
Flood over the great plains. Not only orchards   285
Are swept away, not only grain and cattle,
Not only men and houses, but altars, temples,
And shrines with holy fires. If any building
Stands firm, the waves keep rising over its roof-top,
Its towers are under water, and land and ocean   290
Are all alike, and everything is ocean,
An ocean with no shore-line.
                              Some poor fellow
Seizes a hill-top; another, in a dinghy,
Rows where he used to plough, and one goes sailing
Over his fields of grain or over the chimney   295
Of what was once his cottage. Someone catches
Fish in the top of an elmtree, or an anchor
Drags in green meadow-land, or the curved keel brushes
Grape-arbors under water. Ugly sea-cows
Float where the slender she-goats used to nibble   300
The tender grass, and the Nereids[1] come swimming

7. Made by the Cyclopes, one-eyed giants like Polyphemus in *Odyssey* IX. But unlike Polyphemus and his pastoral relatives, these Cyclopes are metalworkers who forge the thunderbolts of Jupiter.   8. King of the winds (see *Odyssey* X).   9. The sea god (Poseidon in Greek).   1. Sea nymphs.

With curious wonder, looking, under water,
At houses, cities, parks, and groves. The dolphins
Invade the woods and brush against the oak-trees;
The wolf swims with the lamb; lion and tiger   305
Are borne along together; the wild boar
Finds all his strength is useless, and the deer
Cannot outspeed that torrent; wandering birds
Look long, in vain, for landing-place, and tumble,
Exhausted, into the sea. The deep's great license   310
Has buried all the hills and new waves thunder
Against the mountain-tops. The flood has taken
All things, or nearly all, and those whom water,
By chance, has spared, starvation slowly conquers.

[Deucalion and Pyrrha]

Phocis, a fertile land, while there was land,   315
Marked off Oetean from Boeotian[2] fields.
It was ocean now, a plain of sudden waters.
There Mount Parnassus lifts its twin peaks skyward,
High, steep, cloud-piercing. And Deucalion came there
Rowing his wife. There was no other land,   320
The sea had drowned it all. And here they worshipped
First the Corycian nymphs and native powers,
Then Themis,[3] oracle and fate-revealer.
There was no better man than this Deucalion,
No one more fond of right; there was no woman   325
More scrupulously reverent than Pyrrha.
So, when Jove saw the world was one great ocean,
Only one woman left of all those thousands,
And only one man left of all those thousands,
Both innocent and worshipful, he parted   330
The clouds, turned loose the North-wind, swept them off,
Showed earth to heaven again, and sky to land,
And the sea's anger dwindled, and King Neptune
Put down his trident, calmed the waves, and Triton,
Summoned from far down under, with his shoulders   335
Barnacle-strewn, loomed up above the waters,
The blue-green sea-god, whose resounding horn
Is heard from shore to shore. Wet-bearded, Triton
Set lip to that great shell, as Neptune ordered,
Sounding retreat, and all the lands and waters   340
Heard and obeyed. The sea has shores; the rivers,
Still running high, have channels; the floods dwindle,
Hill-tops are seen again; the trees, long buried,
Rise with their leaves still muddy. The world returns.

Deucalion saw that world, all desolation,   345
All emptiness, all silence, and his tears
Rose as he spoke to Pyrrha: "O my wife,
The only woman, now, on all this earth,

---

2. On the Theban plain. Phocis is a district in central Greece, north of the gulf of Corinth. *Oetean*:
from Mount Oeta, in southern Thessaly.   3. One of the predecessors of Apollo at Delphi; her name
means "tradition" (Greek). The Corycian cave is high above Delphi, on the upper slopes of Parnassus.

My consort and my cousin and my partner
In these immediate dangers, look! Of all the lands   350
To East or West, we two, we two alone,
Are all the population. Ocean holds
Everything else; our foothold, our assurance,
Are small as they can be, the clouds still frightful.
Poor woman—well, we are not all alone—   355
Suppose you had been, how would you bear your fear?
Who would console your grief? My wife, believe me,
Had the sea taken you, I would have followed.
If only I had the power, I would restore
The nations as my father[4] did, bring clay   360
To life with breathing. As it is, we two
Are all the human race, so Heaven has willed it,
Samples of men, mere specimens."
                          They wept,
and prayed together, and having wept and prayed,
Resolved to make petition to the goddess   365
To seek her aid through oracles. Together
They went to the river-water, the stream Cephisus,
Still far from clear, but flowing down its channel,
And they took river-water, sprinkled foreheads,
Sprinkled their garments, and they turned their steps   370
To the temple of the goddess, where the altars
Stood with the fires gone dead, and ugly moss
Stained pediment and column. At the stairs
They both fell prone, kissed the chill stone in prayer:
"If the gods' anger ever listens   375
To righteous prayers, O Themis, we implore you,
Tell us by what device our wreck and ruin
May be repaired. Bring aid, most gentle goddess,
To sunken circumstance."
                         And Themis heard them,
And gave this oracle: "Go from the temple,   380
Cover your heads, loosen your robes, and throw
Your mother's bones behind you!" Dumb, they stood
In blank amazement, a long silence, broken
By Pyrrha, finally: she would not do it!
With trembling lips she prays whatever pardon   385
Her disobedience might merit, but this outrage
She dare not risk, insult her mother's spirit
By throwing her bones around. In utter darkness
They voice the cryptic saying over and over,
What can it mean? They wonder. At last Deucalion   390
Finds the way out: "I might be wrong, but surely
The holy oracles would never counsel
A guilty act. The earth is our great mother,
And I suppose those bones the goddess mentions
Are the stones of earth; the order means to throw them,   395
The stones, behind us."
                        She was still uncertain,

4. Prometheus, who, according to a Greek legend, made the first human beings out of clay.

And he by no means sure, and both distrustful
Of that command from Heaven; but what damage,
What harm, would there be in trying? They descended,
Covered their heads, loosened their garments, threw   400
The stones behind them as the goddess ordered.
The stones—who would believe it, had we not
The unimpeachable witness of Tradition?—
Began to lose their hardness, to soften, slowly,
To take on form, to grow in size, a little,   405
Become less rough, to look like human beings,
Or anyway as much like human beings
As statues do, when the sculptor is only starting,
Images half blocked out. The earthy portion,
Damp with some moisture, turned to flesh, the solid   410
Was bone, the veins were as they always had been.
The stones the man had thrown turned into men,
The stones the woman threw turned into women,
Such being the will of God. Hence we derive
The hardness that we have, and our endurance   415
Gives proof of what we have come from.
                                        Other forms
Of life came into being, generated
Out of the earth: the sun burnt off the dampness,
Heat made the slimy marshes swell; as seed
Swells in a mother's womb to shape and substance,   420
So new forms came to life. When the Nile river
Floods and recedes and the mud is warmed by sunshine,
Men, turning over the earth, find living things,
And some not living, but nearly so, imperfect,
On the verge of life,[5] and often the same substance   425
Is part alive, part only clay. When moisture
Unites with heat, life is conceived; all things
Come from this union. Fire may fight with water,
But heat and moisture generate all things,
Their discord being productive. So when earth,   430
After that flood, still muddy, took the heat,
Felt the warm fire of sunlight, she conceived,
Brought forth, after their fashion, all the creatures,
Some old, some strange and monstrous.
                                        One, for instance,
She bore unwanted, a gigantic serpent,[6]   435
Python by name, whom the new people dreaded,
A huge bulk on the mountain-side. Apollo,
God of the glittering bow, took a long time
To bring him down, with arrow after arrow
He had never used before except in hunting   440
Deer and the skipping goats. Out of the quiver
Sped arrows by the thousand, till the monster,
Dying, poured poisonous blood on those black wounds.
In memory of this, the sacred games,
Called Pythian, were established, and Apollo   445

5. This strange doctrine, the spontaneous generation of living species in warm river mud, stems from Greek philosophical speculation about the origins of life.   6. Pytho.

Ordained for all young winners in the races,
On foot or chariot, for victorious fighters,
The crown of oak. That was before the laurel,
That was before Apollo wreathed his forehead
With garlands from that tree, or any other.[7]   450

[Apollo and Daphne]

Now the first girl Apollo loved was Daphne,
Whose father was the river-god Peneus,[8]
And this was no blind chance, but Cupid's malice.
Apollo, with pride and glory still upon him
Over the Python slain, saw Cupid bending   455
His tight-strung little bow. "O silly youngster,"
He said, "What are you doing with such weapons?
Those are for grown-ups! The bow is for my shoulders;
I never fail in wounding beast or mortal,
And not so long ago I slew the Python   460
With countless darts; his bloated body covered
Acre on endless acre, and I slew him!
The torch, my boy, is enough for you to play with,
To get the love-fires burning. Do not meddle
With honors that are mine!" And Cupid answered: 465
"Your bow shoots everything, Apollo—maybe—
But mine will fix you! You are far above
All creatures living, and by just that distance
Your glory less than mine." He shook his wings,
Soared high, came down to the shadows of Parnassus,   470
Drew from his quiver different kinds of arrows,
One causing love, golden and sharp and gleaming,
The other blunt, and tipped with lead, and serving
To drive all love away, and this blunt arrow
He used on Daphne, but he fired the other,   475
The sharp and golden shaft, piercing Apollo
Through bones, through marrow, and at once he loved
And she at once fled from the name of lover,
Rejoicing in the woodland hiding places
And spoils of beasts which she had taken captive,   480
A rival of Diana,[9] virgin goddess.
She had many suitors, but she scorned them all;
Wanting no part of any man, she traveled
The pathless groves, and had no care whatever
For husband, love, or marriage. Her father often   485
Said, "Daughter, give me a son-in-law!" and "Daughter,
Give me some grandsons!" But the marriage torches
Were something hateful, criminal, to Daphne,
So she would blush, and put her arms around him,
And coax him: "Let me be a virgin always;   490

---

7. These lines are a good example of Ovid's witty and skillful transitions from one story to another. He varies them like a virtuoso in the course of the fifteen books. From the spontaneous birth of animals in the Nile mud he singles out one, Pytho, killed by Apollo, who instituted games in commemoration of the feat and decreed for the winner a crown of oak. As every one of Ovid's readers knew, the crown at the Pythian games was of laurel, but, says Ovid, the laurel did not then exist; this launches him on the story of its origin, the transformation of Daphne (whose name means "laurel").   8. The main river of Thessaly.   9. A hunting goddess, daughter of Jupiter (Artemis in Greek).

Diana's father said she might. Dear father!
Dear father—please!" He yielded, but her beauty
Kept arguing against her prayer. Apollo
Loves at first sight; he wants to marry Daphne,
He hopes for what he wants—all wishful thinking!—   495
Is fooled by his own oracles. As stubble
Burns when the grain is harvested, as hedges
Catch fire from torches that a passer-by
Has brought too near, or left behind in the morning,
So the god burned, with all his heart, and burning   500
Nourished that futile love of his by hoping.
He sees the long hair hanging down her neck
Uncared for, says, "But what if it were combed?"
He gazes at her eyes—they shine like stars!
He gazes at her lips, and knows that gazing   505
Is not enough. He marvels at her fingers,
Her hands, her wrists, her arms, bare to the shoulder,
And what he does not see he thinks is better.
But still she flees him, swifter than the wind,
And when he calls she does not even listen: 510
"Don't run away, dear nymph! Daughter of Peneus,
Don't run away! I am no enemy,
Only your follower: don't run away!
The lamb flees from the wolf, the deer the lion,
The dove, on trembling wing, flees from the eagle.   515
All creatures flee their foes. But I, who follow,
Am not a foe at all. Love makes me follow,
Unhappy fellow that I am, and fearful
You may fall down, perhaps, or have the briars
Make scratches on those lovely legs, unworthy   520
To be hurt so, and I would be the reason.
The ground is rough here. Run a little slower,
And I will run, I promise, a little slower.
Or wait a minute: be a little curious
Just who it is you charm. I am no shepherd,   525
No mountain-dweller, I am not a ploughboy,
Uncouth and stinking of cattle. You foolish girl,
You don't know who it is you run away from,
That must be why you run. I am lord of Delphi
And Tenedos and Claros and Patara.[1]   530
Jove is my father. I am the revealer
Of present, past and future; through my power
The lyre and song make harmony; my arrow
Is sure in aim—there is only one arrow surer,
The one that wounds my heart. The power of healing   535
Is my discovery; I am called the Healer
Through all the world: all herbs are subject to me.
Alas for me, love is incurable
With any herb; the arts which cure the others
Do me, their lord, no good!"
                                    He would have said   540
Much more than this, but Daphne, frightened, left him

---

1. All famous oracular shrines of Apollo.

With many words unsaid, and she was lovely
Even in flight, her limbs bare in the wind,
Her garments fluttering, and her soft hair streaming,
More beautiful than ever. But Apollo,   545
Too young a god to waste his time in coaxing,
Came following fast. When a hound starts a rabbit
In an open field, one runs for game, one safety,
He has her, or thinks he has, and she is doubtful
Whether she's caught or not, so close the margin,   550
So ran the god and girl, one swift in hope,
The other in terror, but he ran more swiftly,
Borne on the wings of love, gave her no rest,
Shadowed her shoulder, breathed on her streaming hair.
Her strength was gone, worn out by the long effort   555
Of the long flight; she was deathly pale, and seeing
The river of her father, cried "O help me,
If there is any power in the rivers,
Change and destroy the body which has given
Too much delight!" And hardly had she finished,   560
When her limbs grew numb and heavy, her soft breasts
Were closed with delicate bark, her hair was leaves,
Her arms were branches, and her speedy feet
Rooted and held, and her head became a tree top,
Everything gone except her grace, her shining.   565
Apollo loved her still. He placed his hand
Where he had hoped and felt the heart still beating
Under the bark; and he embraced the branches
As if they still were limbs, and kissed the wood,
And the wood shrank from his kisses, and the god   570
Exclaimed: "Since you can never be my bride,
My tree at least you shall be! Let the laurel
Adorn, henceforth, my hair, my lyre, my quiver:
Let Roman victors, in the long procession,
Wear laurel wreaths for triumph and ovation.   575
Beside Augustus' portals let the laurel
Guard and watch over the oak, and as my head
Is always youthful, let the laurel always
Be green and shining!" He said no more. The laurel,
Stirring, seemed to consent, to be saying Yes.   580

FROM BOOK IV

[*Pyramus and Thisbe*]

Next door to each other, in the brick-walled city[2]
Built by Semiramis, lived a boy and girl,
Pyramus, a most handsome fellow, Thisbe,
Loveliest of all those Eastern girls. Their nearness
Made them acquainted, and love grew, in time,   5
So that they would have married, but their parents
Forbade it. But their parents could not keep them

---

2. Babylon, built, according to legend, by Semiramis, the queen of Aesyria.

From being in love: their nods and gestures showed it—
You know how fire suppressed burns all the fiercer.
There was a chink in the wall between the houses,   10
A flaw the careless builder had never noticed,
Nor anyone else, for many years, detected,
But the lovers found it—love is a finder, always—
Used it to talk through, and the loving whispers
Went back and forth in safety. They would stand   15
One on each side, listening for each other,
Happy if each could hear the other's breathing,
And then they would scold the wall: "You envious barrier,
Why get in our way? Would it be too much to ask you
To open wide for an embrace, or even   20
Permit us room to kiss in? Still, we are grateful,
We owe you something, we admit; at least
You let us talk together." But their talking
Was futile, rather; and when evening came
They would say *Good-night!* and give the good-night kisses   25
That never reached the other.
                    The next morning
Came, and the fires of night burnt out, and sunshine
Dried the night frost, and Pyramus and Thisbe
Met at the usual place, and first, in whispers,
Complained, and came—high time!—to a decision.   30
That night, when all was quiet, they would fool
Their guardians, or try to, come outdoors,
Run away from home, and even leave the city.
And, not to miss each other, as they wandered
In the wide fields, where should they meet? At Ninus'   35
Tomb, they supposed, was best; there was a tree there,
A mulberry-tree, loaded with snow-white berries,
Near a cool spring. The plan was good, the daylight
Was very slow in going, but at last
The sun went down into the waves, as always,   40
And the night rose, as always, from those waters.

And Thisbe opened her door, so sly, so cunning,
There was no creaking of the hinge, and no one
Saw her go through the darkness, and she came,
Veiled, to the tomb of Ninus, sat there waiting   45
Under the shadow of the mulberry-tree.
Love made her bold. But suddenly, here came something!—
A lioness, her jaws a crimson froth
With the blood of cows, fresh-slain, came there for water,
And far off through the moonlight Thisbe saw her   50
And ran, all scared, to hide herself in a cave,
And dropped her veil as she ran. The lioness,
Having quenched her thirst, came back to the woods, and saw
The girl's light veil, and mangled it and mouthed it
With bloody jaws. Pyramus, coming there   55
Too late, saw tracks in the dust, turned pale, and paler
Seeing the bloody veil. "One night," he cried,
"Will kill two lovers, and one of them, most surely,
Deserved a longer life. It is all my fault,

I am the murderer, poor girl; I told you   60
To come here in the night, to all this terror,
And was not here before you, to protect you.
Come, tear my flesh, devour my guilty body,
Come, lions, all of you, whose lairs lie hidden
Under this rock! I am acting like a coward,   65
Praying for death." He lifts the veil and takes it
Into the shadow of their tree; he kisses
The veil he knows so well, his tears run down
Into its folds: "Drink my blood too!" he cries,
And draws his sword, and plunges it into his body,   70
And, dying, draws it out, warm from the wound.
As he lay there on the ground, the spouting blood
Leaped high, just as a pipe sends water spurting
Through a small hissing opening, when broken
With a flaw in the lead, and all the air is sprinkled.   75
The fruit of the tree, from that red spray, turned crimson,
And the roots, soaked with the blood, dyed all the berries
The same dark hue.
                        Thisbe came out of hiding,
Still frightened, but a little fearful, also,
To disappoint her lover. She kept looking   80
Not only with her eyes, but all her heart,
Eager to tell him of those terrible dangers,
About her own escape. She recognized
The place, the shape of the tree, but there was something
Strange or peculiar in the berries' color.   85
Could this be right? And then she saw a quiver
Of limbs on bloody ground, and started backward,
Paler than boxwood, shivering, as water
Stirs when a little breeze ruffles the surface.
It was not long before she knew her lover,   90
And tore her hair, and beat her innocent bosom
With her little fists, embraced the well-loved body,
Filling the wounds with tears, and kissed the lips
Cold in his dying. "O my Pyramus,"
She wept, "What evil fortune takes you from me?   95
Pyramus, answer me! Your dearest Thisbe
Is calling you. Pyramus, listen! Lift your head!"
He heard the name of Thisbe, and he lifted
His eyes, with the weight of death heavy upon them,
And saw her face, and closed his eyes.
                                        And Thisbe   100
Saw her own veil, and saw the ivory scabbard
With no sword in it, and understood. "Poor boy,"
She said, "So, it was your own hand,
Your love, that took your life away. I too
Have a brave hand for this one thing, I too   105
Have love enough, and this will give me strength
For the last wound. I will follow you in death,
Be called the cause and comrade of your dying.
Death was the only one could keep you from me,
Death shall not keep you from me. Wretched parents   110

Of Pyramus and Thisbe, listen to us,
Listen to both our prayers, do not begrudge us,
Whom death has joined, lying at last together
In the same tomb. And you, O tree, now shading
The body of one, and very soon to shadow   115
The bodies of two, keep in remembrance always
The sign of our death, the dark and mournful color."
She spoke, and fitting the sword-point at her breast,
Fell forward on the blade, still warm and reeking
With her lover's blood. Her prayers touched the gods,   120
And touched her parents, for the mulberry fruit
Still reddens at its ripeness, and the ashes
Rest in a common urn.

Part II

---

100 TO 1500

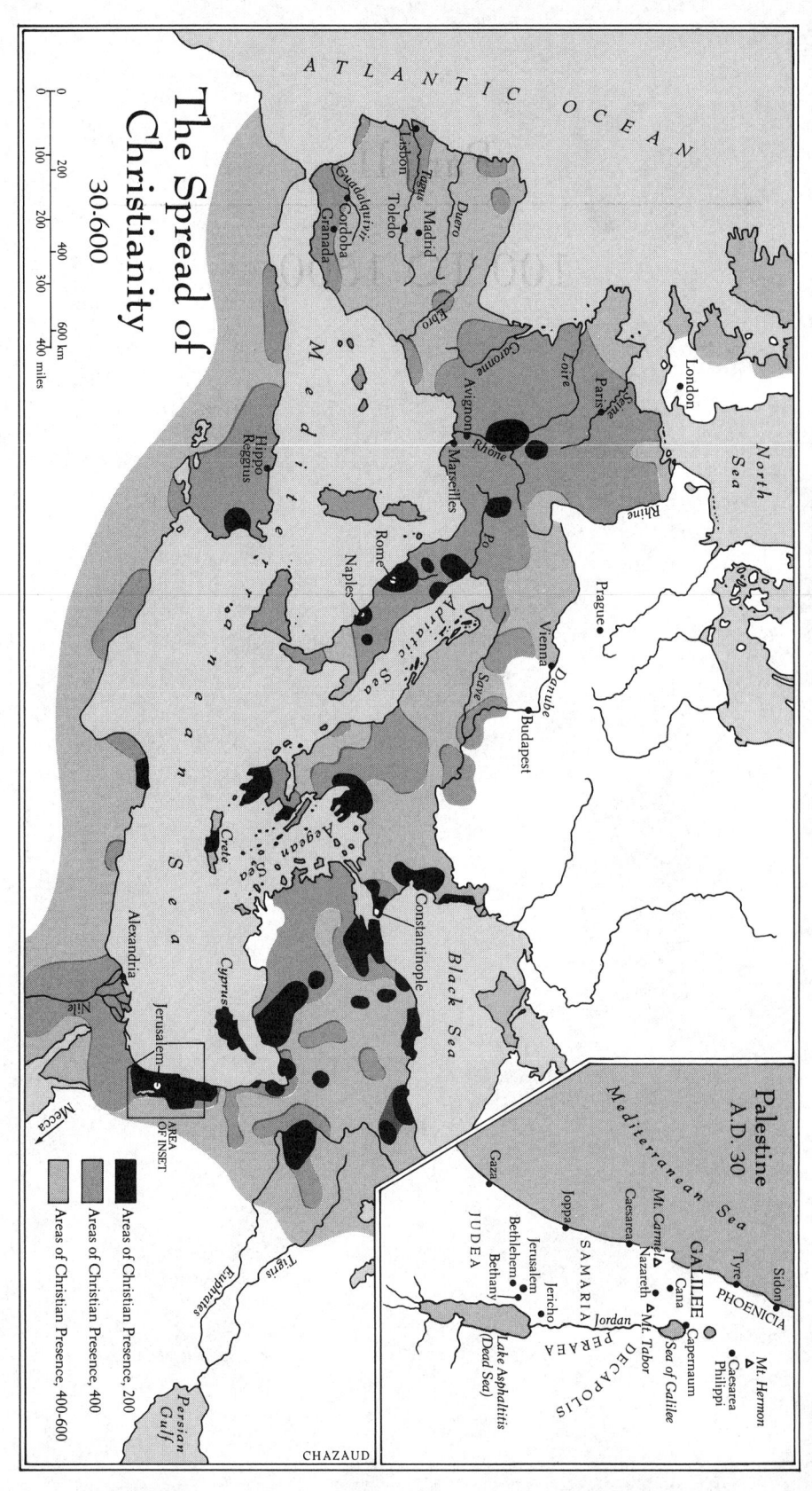

The Spread of Christianity
30·600

Areas of Christian Presence, 200

Areas of Christian Presence, 400

Areas of Christian Presence, 400-600

AREA OF INSET

ATLANTIC OCEAN

North Sea

Lisbon
Madrid
Toledo
Córdoba
Granada
Guadalquivir
Tagus
Duero
Ebro

Garonne
Loire
Seine
Paris
London

Rhine
Rhône
Avignon
Marseilles

Hippo Regius

Rome
Naples
Po
Save
Danube
Vienna
Budapest
Prague

Adriatic Sea

Mediterranean Sea

Crete
Aegean Sea
Constantinople
Cyprus
Black Sea

Alexandria
Nile
Jerusalem
Mecca

Euphrates
Tigris
Persian Gulf

0   100   200   300   400 miles
0   200   400   600 km

Palestine
A.D. 30

Mediterranean Sea

Sidon
Tyre
PHOENICIA
Mt. Hermon
Caesarea Philippi
Cana
Nazareth
Mt. Carmel
Mt. Tabor
Capernaum
Sea of Galilee
GALILEE
Caesarea
DECAPOLIS
Joppa
SAMARIA
Jericho
Jerusalem
Bethlehem
Bethany
Jordan
PERAEA
JUDEA
Gaza
Lake Asphaltitis
(Dead Sea)

CHAZAUD

From Roman Empire to Christian Europe

In the last years of Augustus's life, in the Roman province of Judea, there was born to Joseph, a carpenter of Nazareth, and his wife, Mary, a son who was in the tradition of the Hebrew prophets but was also the bearer of a message that was to transform the world. His life on earth was short; it ended in the agony of crucifixion in about his thirty-third year. This event is a point of intersection of three of the main lines of development of the ancient world—Hebrew, Greek, and Latin— for this Hebrew prophet was executed by a Roman governor, and his life and teachings were written down in the Greek language. These documents became the sacred texts of a church that, at first persecuted by and then triumphantly associated with Roman imperial power, outlasted the destruction of the empire and ruled over a spiritual empire that still exists.

The teaching of Jesus was revolutionary not only in terms of Greek and Roman feeling but also in terms of the Hebrew religious tradition. The Hebrew idea of a personal God who is yet not anthropomorphic, who is omnipotent, omniscient, and infinitely just was now broadened to include among His attributes an infinite mercy that tempered the justice. Greek and Roman religion was outward and visible, the formal practice of ritual acts in a social context; Christianity was inward and spiritual, the important relationship was that between the individual soul and God. All human beings were on an equal plane in the eyes of their Creator. This idea ran counter to the theory and practice of an institution basic to the economy of the ancient world, slavery. Like the earlier Hebrew prophets, Jesus was rejected by His own people, as prophets have always been, and His death on the Cross and resurrection provided his followers and future converts with an unforgettable symbol of a new dispensation, the son of God in human form suffering to atone for the sins of humanity, the supreme expression of divine mercy. This conception is the basis of the teaching of Paul, the apostle to the Gentiles, who in the middle years of the first century A.D. changed Christianity from a Jewish sect to a worldwide movement with flourishing churches all over Asia Minor and Greece—and even in Rome. The burden of his teaching was the frailty and corruption of this life and world and the certainty of resurrection. "For this corruptible must put on incorruption, and this mortal must put on immortality." To those who had accepted this vision, the secular materialism that was the dominant view in the new era of peace and progress guaranteed by the stabilization of Roman rule was no longer tenable.

In any case, the stability of Roman rule did not outlast the reign of the philosopher emperor Marcus Aurelius, who died in A.D. 180. His son and successor, Commodus, was assassinated in 192, and for years rival military commanders fought for mastery of the empire. In the years between 218 and 268 there were more than fifty claimants to the imperial power; one short-lived emperor after another was killed by his own troops, while new and formidable enemies—the Goths to the north and the Persians to the east—invaded and plundered the Bal-

kan and eastern provinces. The empire seemed to be on the brink of collapse, but a succession of soldier emperors reestablished central power and secured the frontiers. This success was won at tremendous cost, however; the economic resources of the empire were drained to pay and equip the armies, and inflation caused by government debasement of the gold and silver currency undermined the economic system. Under Diocletian (ruled 284–305) there was an ineffectual attempt to fix the maximum price of all goods and a successful consolidation of the emperor's powers as the rule of a semidivine despotic monarch.

Through all the years of turmoil the Christian church, often persecuted by the imperial authorities—by Nero in the first century, by Marcus Aurelius and, more severely, by Diocletian in the third—was growing in numbers and influence, its network of religious communities organized by bishops. After Diocletian's retirement from power in 305 a new civil war began; the victor, Constantine, declared himself a Christian and enlisted the support of the Church in his reorganization of the empire.

In the course of the long series of defensive wars on the frontiers it had become clear that Rome could no longer serve as the strategic center of the empire; it was too far away from the endangered areas on the northern and eastern frontiers. It had also become clear that the western and eastern halves of the empire needed separate administrative and military organization, and under Diocletian such a system was established. The two halves of the empire were in any case distinct cultural and linguistic entities: Latin and Greek. This was also true of the Christian church. Constantine established a new capital for his reign on the site of the Greek city Byzantium and renamed it Constantinople. By the time one of his successors, Theodosius, made Christianity the official religion of the Roman Empire in 391, the two halves of the empire were to all intents and purposes separate states.

They were to have separate destinies. In the east the imperial power based on the capital founded by Constantine maintained a Greek-speaking Christian empire for many centuries, until after fighting a long losing battle against the advance of Islam, the city fell to the Ottoman Turks in 1453. But in the west, collapse came much sooner. In 410 Rome fell to Alaric at the head of an army of Visigoths; many of the western provinces had already been overrun by new peoples moving south. But the Church survived, to convert the conquerors to the Christian religion and establish the cultural and religious foundations of the European Middle Ages.

FURTHER READING

Jaroslav Pelikan, *The Excellent Empire: The Fall of Rome and the Triumph of the Church* (1987), is a collection of brilliant essays by a famous historian of the Christian church on Gibbon's *Decline and Fall*, the early centuries of the Church, and St. Augustine. For a critical assessment of Constantine by a noted historian of Rome, see Ramsay MacMullen, *Constantine* (1969); Michael Grant, *Constantine the Great* (1994), is also recommended. Averil Cameron, *The Later Roman Empire* (1993), is a basic source for the study of "late antiquity" (Diocletian to Constantine) by a well-known specialist on the period. F. W. Walbank, *The Awful Revolution: The Decline of the Roman Empire in the West* (1969), provides a detailed but lucid analysis of the crisis and collapse of Roman imperial power—Gibbon's "awful Revolution."

FROM ROMAN EMPIRE TO CHRISTIAN EUROPE

TEXTS	CONTEXTS
100 The four **Gospels** of the life and sayings of Jesus and the Acts of the Apostles are complete	
	117–138 Hadrian emperor
	131–134 Jewish revolt against Roman rule; Jews expelled from Palestine in 134
	138–161 Antoninus Pius emperor
	161–180 Marcus Aurelius emperor
	ca. 200–300 Systematic effort by the Roman Empire to destroy Christianity fails
	284–305 Diocletian emperor
	303–311 Last persecution of Christians
	312–337 Constantine I emperor
	313 Constantine issues Edict of Milan, declaring toleration of all religions
	330 Constantine moves capital of the Roman Empire to Byzantium, renaming the city Constantinople
367 Final canon of the New Testament of the Bible is established	
387 Augustine baptized as a Christian	
	391 Christianity becomes official religion of the Roman Empire; pagan religions outlawed
ca. 393–405 Jerome translates the Bible into Latin	
	395 The Roman Empire is permanently divided into the Eastern Empire, based in Constantinople, and the Western Empire, based in Rome

TEXTS	CONTEXTS
397 Augustine begins *Confessions*	
	410 Rome sacked by Alaric and the Visigoths
	455 Rome invaded by Vandals
	476 Last emperor of the Western Empire is deposed by Odoacer, king of Heruli

THE BIBLE: THE NEW TESTAMENT
ca. first century

When Jesus was born in the Roman province of Judea, there were four languages spoken in the area, a consequence of its complicated history. Classical Hebrew, the language of the sacred books of the Jews, was understood by educated people, especially the priestly caste, but the general population spoke Aramaic. This was a Semitic language close to classical Hebrew—the relationship has been compared with that between Portuguese and Spanish—but different enough to necessitate an Aramaic paraphrase of the sacred texts for use in the synagogue. Aramaic was the language in which Jesus preached to crowds and conversed with his disciples; the last words he spoke in agony on the cross were Aramaic: *Eli, eli, lama sabach-thani?* ("My God, my God, why hast thou forsaken me?").

But Judea, like all of the territory conquered by Alexander the Great, had come under Macedonian-Greek rule by the beginning of the second century B.C., and many Jews, especially those of the upper and educated classes, had learned Greek, an entry to the new administrative, commercial, and cultural milieux of the Hellenistic empires. Finally, in the last half of the first century B.C. Judea became a Roman province, and Latin (the language of the Roman governor and the military establishment) became the language of government. Most cultured Romans, however, knew Greek, and Greek remained the lingua franca of the educated classes all over the huge territory now called the Middle East.

If the disciples of Jesus were to obey his command—"Go into all the world and preach the good news to all creation"—they would have to use Greek outside the Aramaic-speaking world. And it is in Greek that the four Gospels (the word is an Old English translation of the Greek for "good news") were written, probably some forty to sixty years after Jesus' death. They must have been based on the oral teaching of the original disciples, and the first three (selections from which are printed here) were clearly designed with an eye to different readerships. The Gospel according to Matthew, for example, has a Jewish public in mind; one of its main concerns is to convince its readers not only that Jesus was the legitimate heir to the throne of the royal house of David but also that Jesus was the king, the Messiah, announced by the Hebrew prophets. Mark, on the other hand, is clearly written with a Gentile audience in mind and pays particular attention to the needs of the Roman reader, translating Aramaic words and even explaining that the courtyard into which the Roman soldiers took Jesus after he was condemned was the place the Romans called the *praetorium*. And the Gospel according to Luke is obviously addressed to cultured Greek readers; it makes very few references to the Hebrew prophecies and is in fact dedicated to a Greek called Theophilos.

These three Gospels contain a central core of identical material that must come from an earlier source now lost (it is known as the Q document). The fourth Gospel, that of John, draws on different sources and also has greater theological density than the other three. The collection known to Christians as the New Testament was formed by combining the four Gospels with another book by Luke, The Acts of the Apostles, which is an account of Paul's missionary journeys to the cities of Greece and Asia Minor. Added to this were letters of Paul and others to the Christian communities in such cities as Corinth, Thessalonica, and Rome and the book called Revelation, a vision of the end of the world and the second coming of Jesus.

There were, of course, many other documents that gave accounts of the life and teaching of Jesus, but this particular collection contained those judged most reli-

able by the Church authorities and was declared canonical some time in the third
century. Latin translations of the Greek texts were made for the use of the
Churches of the Western Roman Empire, but there was no official version until
in 382 Pope Damasus commissioned a scholar called Jerome to produce a correct
translation. It soon became known as the Vulgate—the "common" or "popular"
version. This was the text used and quoted by Augustine, and with some revisions
over the centuries, the one that remained in use in the Christian churches of the
west through the Middle Ages.

Recommended reading is Bruce M. Metzger, *The New Testament, Its Background, Growth, and Content* (1965). For a translation in modern English, with
commentary, see *The New Oxford Annotated Bible* (1975), edited by Herbert E.
May and Bruce Metzger.

THE BIBLE: THE NEW TESTAMENT[1]

Luke 2

[The Birth and Youth of Jesus]

2. And it came to pass in those days, that there went out a decree from
Cæsar Augustus, that all the world[2] should be taxed. (And this taxing was
first made when Cyrenius was governor of Syria.) And all went to be taxed,
every one unto his own city. And Joseph also went up from Galilee, out
of the city of Nazareth, into Judæa, unto the city of David, which is called
Bethlehem; (because he was of the house and lineage of David:) to be
taxed with Mary his espoused wife, being great with child. And so it was,
that, while they were there, the days were accomplished that she should
be delivered. And she brought forth her firstborn son, and wrapped him
in swaddling clothes, and laid him in a manger; because there was no
room for them in the inn. And there were in the same country shepherds
abiding in the field, keeping watch over their flock by night. And, lo, the
angel of the Lord came upon them, and the glory of the Lord shone round
about them: and they were sore afraid. And the angel said unto them, Fear
not: for, behold, I bring you good tidings of great joy, which shall be to all
people. For unto you is born this day in the city of David a Saviour, which
is Christ[3] the Lord. And this shall be a sign unto you; ye shall find the
babe wrapped in swaddling clothes, lying in a manger. And suddenly there
was with the angel a multitude of the heavenly host praising God, and
saying, Glory to God in the highest, and on earth peace, good will toward
men. And it came to pass, as the angels were gone away from them into
heaven, the shepherds said one to another, Let us now go even unto Bethlehem, and see this thing which is come to pass, which the Lord hath
made known unto us. And they came with haste, and found Mary, and
Joseph, and the babe lying in a manger. And when they had seen it, they
made known abroad the saying which was told them concerning this
child. And all they that heard it wondered at those things which were told

1. The King James Version.   2. The Roman Empire.   3. Anointed (Greek); used of kings, priests,
and the deliverer promised by the prophets.

them by the shepherds. But Mary kept all these things, and pondered them in her heart. And the shepherds returned, glorifying and praising God for all the things that they had heard and seen, as it was told unto them. And when eight days were accomplished for the circumcising of the child, his name was called JESUS, which was so named of the angel[4] before he was conceived in the womb. And when the days of her purification according to the law of Moses were accomplished, they brought him to Jerusalem, to present him to the Lord; (as it is written in the law of the Lord, Every male that openeth the womb[5] shall be called holy to the Lord;) and to offer a sacrifice according to that which is said in the law of the Lord, A pair of turtledoves, or two young pigeons. And, behold, there was a man in Jerusalem, whose name was Simeon; and the same man was just and devout, waiting for the consolation of Israel: and the Holy Ghost was upon him. And it was revealed unto him by the Holy Ghost, that he should not see death, before he had seen the Lord's Christ. And he came by the Spirit into the temple: and when the parents brought in the child Jesus, to do for him after the custom of the law, then took he him up in his arms, and blessed God, and said, Lord, now lettest thou thy servant depart in peace, according to thy word: for mine eyes have seen thy salvation, which thou hast prepared before the face of all people; a light to lighten the Gentiles,[6] and the glory of thy people Israel. And Joseph and his mother marvelled at those things which were spoken of him. And Simeon blessed them, and said unto Mary his mother, Behold, this child is set for the fall and rising again[7] of many in Israel; and for a sign which shall be spoken against; (yea, a sword shall pierce through thy own soul also,) that the thoughts of many hearts may be revealed. And there was one Anna, a prophetess, the daughter of Phanuel, of the tribe of Aser: she was of a great age, and had lived with an husband seven years from her virginity; and she was a widow of about fourscore and four years, which departed not from the temple, but served God with fastings and prayers night and day. And she coming in that instant gave thanks likewise unto the Lord, and spoke of him to all them that looked for redemption in Jerusalem. And when they had performed all things according to the law of the Lord, they returned into Galilee, to their own city Nazareth. And the child grew, and waxed strong in spirit, filled with wisdom: and the grace of God was upon him. Now his parents went to Jerusalem every year at the feast of the passover. And when he was twelve years old, they went up to Jerusalem after the custom of the feast. And when they had fulfilled the days, as they returned, the child Jesus tarried behind in Jerusalem; and Joseph and his mother knew not of it. But they, supposing him to have been in the company, went a day's journey; and they sought him among their kinsfolk and acquaintance. And when they found him not, they turned back again to Jerusalem, seeking him. And it came to pass that after three days they found him in the temple, sitting in the midst of the doctors,[8] both hearing them, and asking them questions. And all that

---

4. In the Annunciation to Mary (Luke 1:31). *Jesus* is a form of the name Joshua, which means "he shall save."   5. The firstborn son is believed to belong to God (Exodus 13:2). The purification laws are given in Leviticus 12.   6. Non-Jews.   7. The Greek word is the one always used for the resurrection of the dead.   8. Teachers, rabbis.

heard him were astonished at his understanding and answers. And when they saw him, they were amazed: and his mother said unto him, Son, why hast thou thus dealt with us? behold, thy father and I have sought thee sorrowing. And he said unto them, How is it that ye sought me? wist ye not that I must be about my Father's business? And they understood not the saying which he spake unto them. And he went down with them, and came to Nazareth, and was subject unto them: but his mother kept all these sayings in her heart. And Jesus increased in wisdom and stature, and in favour with God and man.

Matthew 5–7

[The Teaching of Jesus: The Sermon on the Mount]

5. And seeing the multitudes, he went up into a mountain: and when he was set, his disciples came unto him: and he opened his mouth, and taught them, saying, Blessed are the poor in spirit: for theirs is the kingdom of heaven. Blessed are they that mourn: for they shall be comforted. Blessed are the meek: for they shall inherit the earth. Blessed are they which do hunger and thirst after righteousness: for they shall be filled. Blessed are the merciful: for they shall obtain mercy. Blessed are the pure in heart: for they shall see God. Blessed are the peacemakers: for they shall be called the children of God. Blessed are they which are persecuted for righteousness' sake: for theirs is the kingdom of heaven. Blessed are ye, when men shall revile you, and persecute you, and shall say all manner of evil against you falsely, for my sake. Rejoice, and be exceeding glad: for great is your reward in heaven: for so persecuted they the prophets which were before you.

Ye are the salt of the earth: but if the salt have lost his savour, wherewith shall it be salted?[1] it is thenceforth good for nothing, but to be cast out, and to be trodden under foot of men. Ye are the light of the world. A city that is set on a hill cannot be hid. Neither do men light a candle, and put it under a bushel,[2] but on a candlestick; and it giveth light unto all that are in the house. Let your light so shine before men, that they may see your good works, and glorify your Father which is in heaven.

Think not that I am come to destroy the law, or the prophets: I am not come to destroy, but to fulfil. For verily I say unto you, Till heaven and earth pass, one jot or one tittle shall in no wise pass from the law, till all be fulfilled. Whosoever therefore shall break one of these least commandments, and shall teach men so, he shall be called the least in the kingdom of heaven: but whosoever shall do and teach them, the same shall be called great in the kingdom of heaven. For I say unto you, That except your righteousness shall exceed the righteousness of the scribes and Pharisees,[3] ye shall in no case enter into the kingdom of heaven.

Ye have heard that it was said by them of old time, Thou shalt not kill; and whosoever shall kill shall be in danger of the judgment: but I say unto

---

1. How can it regain its savor?   2. A household vessel with the capacity of a bushel.   3. A sect that insisted on strict observance of the Mosaic law. *Scribes:* the official interpreters of the sacred Scriptures.

you, That whosoever is angry with his brother without a cause shall be in danger of the judgment: and whosoever shall say to his brother, Raca,[4] shall be in danger of the council: but whosoever shall say, Thou fool, shall be in danger of hell fire.[5] Therefore if thou bring thy gift to the altar, and there rememberest that thy brother hath ought against thee; leave there thy gift before the altar, and go thy way; first be reconciled to thy brother, and then come and offer thy gift. Agree with thine adversary quickly, whiles thou art in the way with him; lest at any time the adversary deliver thee to the judge, and the judge deliver thee to the officer, and thou be cast into prison. Verily I say unto thee, Thou shalt by no means come out thence, till thou hast paid the uttermost farthing.

Ye have heard that it was said by them of old time, Thou shalt not commit adultery: but I say unto you, That whosoever looketh on a woman to lust after her hath committed adultery with her already in his heart. And if thy right eye offend thee, pluck it out, and cast it from thee: for it is profitable for thee that one of thy members should perish, and not that thy whole body should be cast into hell. And if thy right hand offend thee, cut it off, and cast it from thee: for it is profitable for thee that one of thy members should perish, and not that thy whole body should be cast into hell. It hath been said, Whosoever shall put away his wife, let him give her a writing of divorcement: but I say unto you, That whosoever shall put away his wife, saving for the cause of fornication, causeth her to commit adultery: and whosoever shall marry her that is divorced committeth adultery.

Again, ye have heard that it hath been said by them of old time, Thou shalt not forswear thyself, but shalt perform unto the Lord thine oaths: but I say unto you, Swear not at all; neither by heaven; for it is God's throne: nor by the earth; for it is his footstool: neither by Jerusalem; for it is the city of the great King. Neither shalt thou swear by thy head, because thou canst not make one hair white or black. But let your communication be, Yea, yea; Nay, nay: for whatsoever is more than these cometh of evil.

Ye have heard that it hath been said, An eye for an eye, and a tooth for a tooth: but I say unto you, That ye resist not evil: but whosoever shall smite thee on thy right cheek, turn to him the other also. And if any man will sue thee at the law, and take away thy coat, let him have thy cloak also. And whosoever shall compel thee to go a mile, go with him twain. Give to him that asketh thee, and from him that would borrow of thee turn not thou away.

Ye have heard that it hath been said, Thou shalt love thy neighbour, and hate thine enemy. But I say unto you, Love your enemies, bless them that curse you, do good to them that hate you, and pray for them which despitefully use you, and persecute you; that ye may be the children of your Father which is in heaven: for he maketh his sun to rise on the evil and on the good, and sendeth rain on the just and on the unjust. For if ye

---

4. Empty (Aramaic?).   5. The reference is to Jewish legal institutions. The penalties that might be inflicted for murder were death by the sword (a sentence of a local court, *the judgment*), death by stoning (the sentence of a higher court, *the council*), and the burning of the criminal's body in the place where refuse was thrown, Gehenna, which is hence used as a name for hell. Jesus compares the different degrees of punishment (administered by God) for the new sins, which he here lists, with the degrees of punishment recognized by Jewish law.

love them which love you, what reward have ye? do not even the publicans[6] the same? And if ye salute your brethren only, what do ye more than others? do not even the publicans so? Be ye therefore perfect, even as your Father which is in heaven is perfect.

6. Take heed that ye do not your alms before men, to be seen of them: otherwise ye have no reward of your Father which is in heaven. Therefore when thou doest thine alms, do not sound a trumpet before thee, as the hypocrites do in the synagogues and in the streets, that they may have glory of men. Verily I say unto you, They have their reward. But when thou doest alms, let not thy left hand know what thy right hand doeth: that thine alms may be in secret: and thy Father which seeth in secret himself shall reward thee openly.

And when thou prayest, thou shalt not be as the hypocrites are: for they love to pray standing in the synagogues and in the corners of the streets, that they may be seen of men. Verily I say unto you, They have their reward. But thou, when thou prayest, enter into thy closet, and when thou hast shut thy door, pray to thy Father which is in secret; and thy Father which seeth in secret shall reward thee openly. But when ye pray, use not vain repetitions, as the heathen do; for they think that they shall be heard for their much speaking. Be not ye therefore like unto them: for your Father knoweth what things ye have need of, before ye ask him. After this manner therefore pray ye: Our Father which art in heaven, Hallowed be thy name. Thy kingdom come. Thy will be done in earth, as it is in heaven. Give us this day our daily bread. And forgive us our debts, as we forgive our debtors. And lead us not into temptation, but deliver us from evil: For thine is the kingdom, and the power, and the glory, for ever. Amen. For if ye forgive men their trespasses, your heavenly Father will also forgive you: but if ye forgive not men their trespasses, neither will your Father forgive your trespasses.

Moreover when ye fast, be not, as the hypocrites, of a sad countenance: for they disfigure their faces, that they may appear unto men to fast. Verily I say unto you, They have their reward. But thou, when thou fastest, anoint thine head, and wash thy face; that thou appear not unto men to fast, but unto thy Father which is in secret: and thy Father, which seeth in secret shall reward thee openly.

Lay not up for yourselves treasures upon earth, where moth and rust doth corrupt, and where thieves break through and steal: but lay up for yourselves treasures in heaven, where neither moth nor rust doth corrupt, and where thieves do not break through nor steal: for where your treasure is, there will your heart be also. The light of the body is the eye: if therefore thine eye be single,[7] thy whole body shall be full of light. But if thine eye be evil, thy whole body shall be full of darkness. If therefore the light that is in thee be darkness, how great is that darkness!

No man can serve two masters: for either he will hate the one, and love the other; or else he will hold to the one, and despise the other. Ye cannot serve God and Mammon. Therefore I say unto you, Take no thought for

6. The men who collected the taxes for the Roman tax-farming corporations; they were, naturally, universally despised and hated.   7. Clear.

your life, what ye shall eat, or what ye shall drink; nor yet for your body, what ye shall put on. Is not the life more than meat, and the body than raiment? Behold the fowls of the air: for they sow not, neither do they reap, nor gather into barns; yet your heavenly Father feedeth them. Are ye not much better than they? Which of you by taking thought can add one cubit unto his stature? And why take ye thought for raiment? Consider the lilies of the field, how they grow; they toil not, neither do they spin. And yet I say unto you, That even Solomon in all his glory was not arrayed like one of these. Wherefore, if God so clothe the grass of the field, which to-day is, and tomorrow is cast into the oven, shall he not much more clothe you, O ye of little faith? Therefore take no thought, saying, What shall we eat? or, What shall we drink? or, Wherewithal shall we be clothed? (For after all these things do the Gentiles seek:) for your heavenly Father knoweth that ye have need of all these things. But seek ye first the kingdom of God, and his righteousness; and all these things shall be added unto you. Take therefore no thought for the morrow: for the morrow shall take thought for the things of itself. Sufficient unto the day is the evil thereof.

7. Judge not, that ye be not judged. For with what judgment ye judged, ye shall be judged: and with what measure ye mete, it shall be measured to you again. And why beholdest thou the mote that is in thy brother's eye, but considerest not the beam[8] that is in thine own eye? Or how wilt thou say to thy brother, Let me pull out the mote out of thine eye; and, behold, a beam is in thine own eye? Thou hypocrite, first cast out the beam out of thine own eye; and then shalt thou see clearly to cast out the mote out of thy brother's eye.

Give not that which is holy unto the dogs, neither cast ye your pearls before swine, lest they trample them under their feet, and turn again and rend you.

Ask, and it shall be given you; seek, and ye shall find; knock, and it shall be opened unto you: for every one that asketh receiveth; and he that seeketh findeth; and to him that knocketh it shall be opened. Or what man is there of you, whom if his son ask bread, will he give him a stone? Or if he ask a fish, will he give him a serpent? If ye then, being evil, know how to give good gifts unto your children, how much more shall your Father which is in heaven give good things to them that ask him? Therefore all things whatsoever ye would that men should do to you, do ye even so to them: for this is the law and the prophets.

Enter ye in at the strait gate: for wide is the gate, and broad is the way, that leadeth to destruction, and many there be which go in thereat: because strait is the gate, and narrow is the way, which leadeth unto life, and few there be that find it.

Beware of false prophets, which come to you in sheep's clothing, but inwardly they are ravening wolves. Ye shall know them by their fruits. Do men gather grapes of thorns, or figs of thistles? Even so every good tree bringeth forth good fruit; but a corrupt tree bringeth forth evil fruit. A good tree cannot bring forth evil fruit, neither can a corrupt tree bring

---

8. A long piece of heavy timber, in contrast to a *mote*, a particle or speck.

forth good fruit. Every tree that bringeth not forth good fruit is hewn down, and cast into the fire. Wherefore by their fruits ye shall know them.

Not every one that saith unto me, Lord, Lord, shall enter into the kingdom of heaven; but he that doeth the will of my Father which is in heaven. Many will say to me in that day, Lord, Lord, have we not prophesied in thy name? and in thy name have cast out devils? and in thy name done many wonderful works? And then will I profess unto them, I never knew you: depart from me, ye that work iniquity.

Therefore whosoever heareth these sayings of mine, and doeth them, I will liken him unto a wise man, which built his house upon a rock; and the rain descended, and the floods came and the winds blew, and beat upon that house; and it fell not: for it was founded upon a rock. And every one that heareth these sayings of mine, and doeth them not, shall be likened unto a foolish man, which built his house upon the sand: and the rain descended, and the floods came, and the winds blew, and beat upon that house; and it fell: and great was the fall of it. And it came to pass, when Jesus had ended these sayings, the people were astonished at his doctrine: for he taught them as one having authority, and not as the scribes.

Luke 15

[The Teaching of Jesus: Parables]

15. Then drew near unto him all the publicans and sinners for to hear him. And the Pharisees and scribes murmured, saying, This man receiveth sinners, and eateth with them.

And he spoke this parable unto them, saying, What man of you, having a hundred sheep, if he lose one of them, doth not leave the ninety and nine in the wilderness, and go after that which is lost, until he find it? And when he hath found it, he layeth it on his shoulders, rejoicing. And when he cometh home, he calleth together his friends and neighbours, saying unto them, Rejoice with me; for I have found my sheep which was lost. I say unto you that likewise joy shall be in heaven over one sinner that repenteth, more than over ninety and nine just persons, which need no repentance.

Either what woman having ten pieces of silver, if she lose one piece, doth not light a candle, and sweep the house, and seek diligently till she find it? And when she hath found it, she calleth her friends and her neighbours together, saying, Rejoice with me; for I have found the piece which I had lost. Likewise, I say unto you, there is joy in the presence of the angels of God over one sinner that repenteth.

And he said, A certain man had two sons: and the younger of them said to his father, Father, give me the portion of goods that falleth to me. And he divided unto them his living. And not many days after the younger son gathered all together, and took his journey into a far country, and there wasted his substance with riotous living. And when he had spent all, there arose a mighty famine in that land; and he began to be in want. And he

went and joined himself to a citizen of that country; and he sent him into his fields to feed swine. And he would fain have filled his belly with the husks that the swine did eat: and no man gave unto him. And when he came to himself, he said, How many hired servants of my father's have bread enough and to spare, and I perish with hunger! I will arise and go to my father, and will say unto him, Father, I have sinned against heaven, and before thee, and am no more worthy to be called thy son: make me as one of thy hired servants. And he arose, and came to his father. But when he was yet a great way off, his father saw him, and had compassion, and ran, and fell on his neck, and kissed him. And the son said unto him, Father, I have sinned against heaven, and in thy sight, and am no more worthy to be called thy son. But the father said to his servants, Bring forth the best robe, and put it on him; and put a ring on his hand, and shoes on his feet: and bring hither the fatted calf, and kill it; and let us eat, and be merry: for this my son was dead, and is alive again; he was lost, and is found. And they began to be merry. Now his elder son was in the field: and as he came and drew nigh to the house, he heard musick and dancing. And he called one of the servants, and asked what these things meant. And he said unto him, Thy brother is come; and thy father hath killed the fatted calf, because he hath received him safe and sound. And he was angry, and would not go in: therefore came his father out, and intreated him. And he answering said to his father, Lo, these many years do I serve thee, neither transgressed I at any time thy commandment: and yet thou never gavest me a kid, that I might make merry with my friends: but as soon as this thy son was come, which hath devoured thy living with harlots, thou hast killed for him the fatted calf. And he said unto him, Son, thou art ever with me, and all that I have is thine. It was meet that we should make merry, and be glad: for this thy brother was dead, and is alive again; and was lost, and is found.

Matthew 26[1]

[The Betrayal of Jesus]

26. * * * Then one of the twelve, called Judas Iscariot, went unto the chief priests, and said unto them, What will ye give me, and I will deliver him unto you? And they covenanted with him for thirty pieces of silver. And from that time he sought opportunity to betray him.

Now the first day of the feast of unleavened bread[2] the disciples came to Jesus, saying unto him, Where wilt thou that we prepare for thee to eat the passover? And he said, Go into the city to such a man, and say unto him, The Master saith, My time is at hand; I will keep the passover at thy house with my disciples. And the disciples did as Jesus had appointed them; and they made ready the passover. Now when the even was come, he sat down with the twelve. And as they did eat, he said, Verily I say unto

1. Verses 14–75.   2. Passover, held in remembrance of the delivery of the Jews from captivity in Egypt (Exodus 12).

you, that one of you shall betray me. And they were exceeding sorrowful, and began every one of them to say unto him, Lord, is it I? And he answered and said, He that dippeth his hand with me in the dish, the same shall betray me. The Son of man goeth as it is written of him: but woe unto that man by whom the Son of man is betrayed! it had been good for that man if he had not been born. Then Judas, which betrayed him, answered and said, Master, is it I? He said unto him, Thou hast said.

And as they were eating, Jesus took bread, and blessed it, and brake it, and gave it to the disciples, and said, Take, eat; this is my body. And he took the cup, and gave thanks, and gave it to them, saying, Drink ye all of it; for this is my blood of the new testament,[3] which is shed for many for the remission of sins. But I say unto you, I will not drink henceforth of this fruit of the vine, until that day when I drink it new with you in my Father's kingdom. And when they had sung an hymn, they went out into the mount of Olives. Then saith Jesus unto them, All ye shall be offended because of me this night: for it is written,[4] I will smite the shepherd, and the sheep of the flock shall be scattered abroad. But after I am risen again, I will go before you into Galilee. Peter answered and said unto him, Though all men shall be offended because of thee, yet will I never be offended. Jesus said unto him, Verily I say unto thee, That this night, before the cock crow, thou shalt deny me thrice. Peter said unto him, Though I should die with thee, yet will I not deny thee. Likewise also said all the disciples.

Then cometh Jesus with them unto a place called Gethsemane, and saith unto the disciples, Sit ye here, while I go and pray yonder. And he took with him Peter and the two sons of Zebedee,[5] and began to be sorrowful and very heavy. Then saith he unto them, My soul is exceeding sorrowful, even unto death: tarry ye here, and watch[6] with me. And he went a little farther, and fell on his face, and prayed, saying, O my Father, if it be possible, let this cup pass from me: nevertheless, not as I will, but as thou wilt. And he cometh unto the disciples, and findeth them asleep, and saith unto Peter, What, could ye not watch with me one hour? Watch and pray, that ye enter not into temptation: the spirit indeed is willing, but the flesh is weak. He went away again the second time, and prayed, saying, O my Father, if this cup may not pass away from me, except I drink it, thy will be done. And he came and found them asleep again: for their eyes were heavy. And he left them, and went away again, and prayed the third time, saying the same words. Then cometh he to his disciples, and saith unto them, Sleep on now, and take your rest: behold, the hour is at hand, and the Son of man is betrayed into the hands of sinners. Rise, let us be going: behold, he is at hand that doth betray me.

And while he yet spake, lo, Judas, one of the twelve, came, and with him a great multitude with swords and staves, from the chief priests and elders of the people. Now he that betrayed him gave them a sign, saying, Whomsoever I shall kiss, that same is he: hold him fast. And forthwith he came to Jesus and said, Hail, master; and kissed him. And Jesus said unto

3. That is, of the new covenant, or agreement. Jesus compares himself to the lamb that was killed at the Passover as a sign of the covenant between God and the Jews.   4. In Zechariah 13:7. *Be offended*: be made to stumble (literal trans. of the Greek).   5. James and John.   6. Stay awake.

him, Friend, wherefore art thou come? Then came they and laid hands on Jesus, and took him. And behold, one of them[7] which were with Jesus stretched out his hand, and drew his sword, and struck a servant of the high priest's, and smote off his ear. Then said Jesus unto him, Put up again thy sword into his place: for all they that take the sword shall perish with the sword. Thinkest thou that I cannot now pray to my Father, and he shall presently give me more than twelve legions[8] of angels? But how then shall the scriptures be fulfilled, that thus it must be? In that same hour said Jesus to the multitudes, Are ye come out as against a thief with swords and staves for to take me? I sat daily with you teaching in the temple, and ye laid no hold on me. But all this was done that the scriptures of the prophets might be fulfilled. Then all the disciples forsook him, and fled.

And they that had laid hold on Jesus led him away to Caiaphas the high priest, where the scribes and the elders were assembled. But Peter followed him afar off unto the high priest's palace, and went in, and sat with the servants, to see the end. Now the chief priests, and elders, and all the council, sought false witness against Jesus, to put him to death; but found none: yea, though many false witnesses came, yet found they none. At the last came two false witnesses, and said, This fellow said, I am able to destroy the temple of God, and to build it in three days. And the high priest arose, and said unto him, Answerest thou nothing? What is it which these witness against thee? But Jesus held his peace. And the high priest answered and said unto him, I adjure thee by the living God, that thou tell us whether thou be the Christ, the Son of God. Jesus saith unto him, Thou hast said: nevertheless I say unto you, Hereafter shall ye see the Son of man sitting on the right hand of power, and coming in the clouds of heaven. Then the high priest rent his clothes, saying, He hath spoken blasphemy; what further need have we of witnesses? behold, now ye have heard his blasphemy. What think ye? They answered and said, He is guilty of death.[9] Then did they spit in his face, and buffeted him; and others smote him with the palms of their hands, saying, Prophesy unto us, thou Christ, Who is he that smote thee?

Now Peter sat without in the palace: and a damsel came unto him, saying, Thou also wast with Jesus of Galilee. But he denied before them all, saying, I know not what thou sayest. And when he was gone out into the porch, another maid saw him and said unto them that were there, This fellow was also with Jesus of Nazareth. And again he denied with an oath, I do not know the man. And after a while came unto him they that stood by, and said to Peter, Surely thou also art one of them; for thy speech betrayeth thee.[1] Then began he to curse and to swear, saying, I know not the man. And immediately the cock crew. And Peter remembered the word of Jesus, which said unto him, Before the cock crow thou shalt deny me thrice. And he went out, and wept bitterly.

---

7. Peter.   8. A legion was a Roman military formation; its full complement was six thousand men.
9. Liable to the death penalty.   1. In other words, Peter's speech revealed his Galilean origin.

Matthew 27

[The Trial and Crucifixion of Jesus]

27. When the morning was come, all the chief priests and elders of the people took counsel against Jesus to put him to death: and when they had bound him, they led him away, and delivered him to Pontius Pilate the governor.[1]

Then Judas, which had betrayed him, when he saw that he was condemned, repented himself, and brought again the thirty pieces of silver to the chief priests and elders, saying, I have sinned in that I have betrayed the innocent blood. And they said, What is that to us? see thou to that. And he cast down the pieces of silver in the temple, and departed, and went and hanged himself. And the chief priests took the silver pieces, and said, It is not lawful for to put them into the treasury, because it is the price of blood. And they took counsel, and bought with them the potter's field,[2] to bury strangers in. Wherefore that field was called, The field of blood, unto this day. Then was fulfilled that which was spoken by Jeremy the prophet,[3] saying, And they took the thirty pieces of silver, the price of him that was valued, whom they of the children of Israel did value; and gave them for the potter's field, as the Lord appointed me.[4] And Jesus stood before the governor: and the governor asked him, saying, Art thou the King of the Jews? And Jesus said unto him, Thou sayest.

And when he was accused of the chief priests and elders, he answered nothing. Then said Pilate unto him, Hearest thou not how many things they witness against thee? And he answered him to never a word; insomuch that the governor marvelled greatly. Now at that feast the governor was wont to release unto the people a prisoner, whom they would. And they had then a notable prisoner, called Barabbas.[5] Therefore when they were gathered together, Pilate said unto them, Whom will ye that I release unto you? Barabbas, or Jesus which is called Christ? For he knew that for envy they had delivered him.[6]

When he was set down on the judgment seat, his wife sent unto him, saying, Have thou nothing to do with that just man: for I have suffered many things this day in a dream because of him. But the chief priests and elders persuaded the multitude that they should ask Barabbas, and destroy Jesus. The governor answered and said unto them, Whether of the twain will ye that I release unto you? They said, Barabbas. Pilate saith unto them, What shall I do then with Jesus which is called Christ? They all say unto him, Let him be crucified.[7] And the governor said, Why, what evil hath he done? But they cried out the more, saying, Let him be crucified.

When Pilate saw that he could prevail nothing, but that rather a tumult was made, he took water, and washed his hands before the multitude, saying, I am innocent of the blood of this just person: see ye to it. Then

---

1. His official title was procurator of the province of Judea. Roman policy was to allow the Jews as much independence as possible (especially in religious matters), but only the Roman authorities could impose a death sentence. 2. A field that had been dug for potter's clay and thus was not worth very much as land. 3. Jeremiah. 4. Compare Zechariah 11:13: "And the Lord said unto me, Cast it unto the potter: a goodly price that I was prised at of them." 5. Under sentence of death for sedition and murder. 6. Delivered him to the Roman authorities. 7. The regular Roman punishment for sedition.

answered all the people, and said, His blood be on us, and on our children.

Then released he Barabbas unto them: and when he had scourged[8] Jesus, he delivered him to be crucified. Then the soldiers of the governor took Jesus into the common hall, and gathered unto him the whole band of soldiers. And they stripped him, and put on him a scarlet robe.

And when they had platted a crown of thorns, they put it upon his head, and a reed[9] in his right hand: and they bowed the knee before him, and mocked him, saying, Hail, King of the Jews! And they spit upon him, and took the reed, and smote him on the head. And after that they had mocked him, they took the robe off from him, and put his own raiment on him, and led him away to crucify him. And as they came out, they found a man of Cyrene,[1] Simon by name: him they compelled to bear his cross. And when they were come unto a place called Golgotha, that is to say, a place of a skull,

They gave him vinegar to drink mingled with gall:[2] and when he had tasted thereof, he would not drink. And they crucified him, and parted his garments, casting lots: that it might be fulfilled which was spoken by the prophet, They parted my garments among them, and upon my vesture did they cast lots.[3] And sitting down they watched him there; and set up over his head his accusation written, THIS IS JESUS THE KING OF THE JEWS. Then were there two thieves crucified with him, one on the right hand, and another on the left.

And they that passed by reviled him, wagging their heads, and saying, Thou that destroyest the temple, and buildest it in three days, save thyself. If thou be the Son of God, come down from the cross. Likewise also the chief priests mocking him, with the scribes and elders, said, He saved others; himself he cannot save. If he be the King of Israel, let him now come down from the cross, and we will believe him. He trusted in God; let him deliver him now, if he will have him: for he said, I am the Son of God. The thieves also, which were crucified with him, cast the same in his teeth. Now from the sixth hour there was darkness over all the land unto the ninth hour. And about the ninth hour Jesus cried with a loud voice, saying, Eli, Eli, lama sabachthani? that is to say, My God, my God, why hast thou forsaken me?[4] Some of them that stood there, when they heard that, said, This man calleth for Elias.[5] And straightway one of them ran, and took a sponge, and filled it with vinegar, and put it on a reed, and gave him to drink. The rest said, Let be, let us see whether Elias will come to save him.

Jesus, when he had cried again with a loud voice, yielded up the ghost. And, behold, the veil of the temple[6] was rent in twain from the top to the bottom; and the earth did quake, and the rocks rent; and the graves were opened; and many bodies of the saints which slept arose, and came out of the graves after his resurrection, and went into the holy city, and appeared

---

8. Whipped, a routine part of the punishment.   9. To represent the king's scepter.   1. On the coast of North Africa.   2. The Greek word translated *vinegar* describes a sour wine that was the regular drink of the Roman soldiery; the addition of bitter gall is further mockery.   3. It is generally agreed that this sentence is a late addition to the text.   4. The opening words of Psalm 22. Jesus spoke Aramaic, a language closely related to Hebrew.   5. The prophet Elijah.   6. The curtain that screened off the holy of holies.

unto many. Now when the centurion,[7] and they that were with him, watching Jesus, saw the earthquake, and those things that were done, they feared greatly, saying, Truly this was the Son of God. And many women were there beholding afar off, which followed Jesus from Galilee, ministering unto him: among which was Mary Magdalene, and Mary the mother of James and Joseph, and the mother of Zebedee's children. When the even was come, there came a rich man of Arimathæa, named Joseph, who also himself was Jesus' disciple. He went to Pilate, and begged the body of Jesus. Then Pilate commanded the body to be delivered. And when Joseph had taken the body, he wrapped it in clean linen cloth, and laid it in his own new tomb, which he had hewn out in the rock: and he rolled a great stone to the door of the sepulchre, and departed. And there was Mary Magdalene, and the other Mary, sitting over against the sepulchre.

Now the next day, that followed the day of the preparation, the chief priests and Pharisees came together unto Pilate, saying, Sir, we remember that that deceiver said, while he was yet alive, After three days I will rise again. Command therefore that the sepulchre be made sure[8] until the third day, lest his disciples come by night, and steal him away, and say unto the people, He is risen from the dead: so the last error shall be worse than the first. Pilate said unto them, Ye have a watch:[9] go your way, make it as sure as ye can. So they went, and made the sepulchre sure, sealing the stone, and setting a watch.

Matthew 28

[The Resurrection]

28. In the end of the sabbath, as it began to dawn toward the first day of the week, came Mary Magdalene and the other Mary to see the sepulchre. And, behold, there was a great earthquake: for the angel of the Lord descended from heaven, and came and rolled back the stone from the door, and sat upon it. His countenance was like lightning, and his raiment white as snow: and for fear of him the keepers did shake, and became as dead men. And the angel answered and said unto the women, Fear not ye: for I know that ye seek Jesus, which was crucified. He is not here: for he is risen, as he said. Come, see the place where the Lord lay. And go quickly, and tell his disciples that he is risen from the dead; and, behold, he goeth before you into Galilee; there shall ye see him: lo, I have told you. And they departed quickly from the sepulchre with fear and great joy; and did run to bring his disciples word.

And as they went to tell his disciples, behold, Jesus met them, saying, All hail! And they came and held him by the feet, and worshipped him. Then said Jesus unto them, Be not afraid: go tell my brethren that they go into Galilee, and there shall they see me.

Now when they were going, behold, some of the watch came into the city, and shewed unto the chief priests all the things that were done. And when they were assembled with the elders, and had taken counsel, they

7. The Roman officer in charge of the execution.   8. Guarded.   9. Police force.

gave large money unto the soldiers, saying, Say ye, His disciples came by night, and stole him away while we slept. And if this come to the governor's ears, we will persuade him, and secure you. So they took the money, and did as they were taught: and this saying is commonly reported among the Jews until this day.

Then the eleven disciples went away into Galilee, unto a mountain where Jesus had appointed them. And when they saw him, they worshipped him: but some doubted. And Jesus came and spake unto them, saying, All power is given unto me in heaven and in earth.

Go ye therefore, and teach all nations, baptizing them in the name of the Father, and of the Son, and of the Holy Ghost: teaching them to observe all things whatsoever I have commanded you: and, lo, I am with you always, even unto the end of the world. Amen.

AUGUSTINE

354–430

Aurelius Augustinus was born in 354 in Tagaste, in North Africa. He was baptized as a Christian in 387 and ordained bishop of Hippo, in North Africa, in 395. When he died there in 430, the city was besieged by Gothic invaders. Besides the *Confessions* (begun in 397) he wrote *The City of God* (finished in 426) and many polemical works against schismatics and heretics.

He was born into a world that no longer enjoyed the "Roman peace." Invading barbarians had pierced the empire's defenses and were increasing their pressure every year. The economic basis of the empire was cracking under the strain of the enormous taxation needed to support the army; the land was exhausted. The empire was Christian, but the Church was split, beset by heresies and organized heretical sects. The empire was on the verge of ruin, and there was every prospect that the Church would go down with it.

Augustine, one of the men responsible for the consolidation of the Church in the West, especially for the systematization of its doctrine and policy, did not convert to Christianity until he had reached middle life. "Late have I loved Thee, O Beauty so ancient and so new," he says in his *Confessions*, written long after his conversion. The lateness of his conversion and his regret for his wasted youth were among the sources of the energy that drove him to assume the intellectual leadership of the Western church and to guarantee, by combating heresy on the one hand and laying new ideological foundations for Christianity on the other, the Church's survival through the dark centuries to come. Augustine had been brought up in the literary and philosophical tradition of the classical world, and it is partly because of his assimilation of classical literature and method to Christian training and teaching that the literature of the ancient world survived at all when Roman power collapsed in a welter of bloodshed and destruction that lasted for generations.

In his *Confessions* he set down, for the benefit of others, the story of his early life and his conversion to Christianity. This is, as far as we know, the first authentic ancient autobiography, and that fact itself is a significant expression of the Christian spirit, which proclaims the value of the individual soul and the importance of its relation with God. Throughout the *Confessions* Augustine talks directly to God,

in humility, yet conscious that God is concerned for him personally. At the same time he comes to an understanding of his own feelings and development as a human being which marks his *Confessions* as one of the great literary documents of the Western world. His description of his childhood is the only detailed account of the childhood of a great man that antiquity has left us, and his accurate observation and keen perception are informed by the Hebrew and Christian idea of the sense of sin. "So small a boy and so great a sinner"—from the beginning of his narrative to the end Augustine sees individuals not as the Greeks at their most optimistic tended to see humanity, the center and potential masters of the universe, but as children, wandering in ignorance, capable of reclamation only through the divine mercy that waits eternally for them to turn to it.

In Augustine are combined the intellectual tradition of the ancient world and the religious feeling that was characteristic of the Middle Ages. The transition from the old world to the new can be seen in his pages; his analytical intellect pursues its odyssey through strange and scattered islands—the mysticism of the Manichees, the skepticism of the academic philosophers, the fatalism of the astrologers—until he finds his home in the Church, to which he was to render such great service. His account of his conversion in the garden at Milan records the true moment of transition from the ancient to the medieval world. The innumerable defeats and victories, the burning towns and ravaged farms, the bloodshed, dates, and statistics of the end of an era are all illuminated and ordered by this moment in the history of the human spirit. Here is the point of change itself.

For criticism and biography see P. Brown, *Augustine of Hippo* (1967), an authoritative and engrossing account of his whole career.

From Confessions[1]

FROM BOOK I

[Childhood]

What have I to say to Thee, God, save that I know not where I came from, when I came into this life-in-death—or should I call it death-in-life? I do not know. I only know that the gifts Your mercy had provided sustained me from the first moment: not that I remember it but so I have heard from the parents of my flesh, the father from whom, and the mother in whom, You fashioned me in time.

Thus for my sustenance and my delight I had woman's milk: yet it was not my mother or my nurses who stored their breasts for me: it was Yourself, using them to give me the food of my infancy, according to Your ordinance and the riches set by You at every level of creation. It was by Your gift that I desired what You gave and no more, by Your gift that those who suckled me willed to give me what You had given them: for it was by the love implanted in them by You that they gave so willingly that milk which by Your gift flowed in the breasts. It was a good for them that I received good from them, though I received it not *from* them but only through them: since all good things are from You, O God, and *from God is all my health*.[2] But this I have learnt since: You have made it abundantly

---

1. Translated by F. J. Sheed.   2. Throughout the *Confessions* Augustine quotes liberally from the Bible; the quotations are set off in italics. When a quotation bears on Augustine's situation, it is annotated.

clear by all that I have seen You give, within me and about me. For at that time I knew how to suck, to lie quiet when I was content, to cry when I was in pain: and that was all I knew.

Later I added smiling to the things I could do, first in sleep, then awake. This again I have on the word of others, for naturally I do not remember; in any event, I believe it, for I have seen other infants do the same. And gradually I began to notice where I was, and the will grew in me to make my wants known to those who might satisfy them; but I could not, for my wants were within me and those others were outside: nor had they any faculty enabling them to enter into my mind. So I would fling my arms and legs about and utter sounds, making the few gestures in my power— these being as apt to express my wishes as I could make them: but they were not very apt. And when I did not get what I wanted, either because my wishes were not clear or the things not good for me, I was in a rage— with my parents as though I had a right to their submission, with free human beings as though they had been bound to serve me; and I took my revenge in screams. That infants are like this, I have learnt from watching other infants; and that I was like it myself I have learnt more clearly from these other infants, who did not know me, than from my nurses who did.

*   *   *

From infancy I came to boyhood, or rather it came to me, taking the place of infancy. Yet infancy did not go: for where was it to go to? Simply it was no longer there. For now I was not an infant, without speech, but a boy, speaking. This I remember; and I have since discovered by observation how I learned to speak. I did not learn by elders teaching me words in any systematic way, as I was soon after taught to read and write. But of my own motion, using the mind which You, my God, gave me, I strove with cries and various sounds and much moving of my limbs to utter the feelings of my heart—all this in order to get my own way. Now I did not always manage to express the right meanings to the right people. So I began to reflect [I observed that]³ my elders would make some particular sound, and as they made it would point at or move towards some particular thing: and from this I came to realize that the thing was called by the sound they made when they wished to draw my attention to it. That they intended this was clear from the motions of their body, by a kind of natural language common to all races which consists in facial expressions, glances of the eye, gestures, and the tones by which the voice expresses the mind's state—for example whether things are to be sought, kept, thrown away, or avoided. So, as I heard the same words again and again properly used in different phrases, I came gradually to grasp what things they signified; and forcing my mouth to the same sounds, I began to use them to express my own wishes. Thus I learnt to convey what I meant to those about me; and so took another long step along the stormy way of human life in society, while I was still subject to the authority of my parents and at the beck and call of my elders.

O God, my God, what emptiness and mockeries did I now experience:

---

3. Words in brackets are the translator's.

for it was impressed upon me as right and proper in a boy to obey those who taught me, that I might get on in the world and excel in the handling of words[4] to gain honor among men and deceitful riches. I, poor wretch, could not see the use of the things I was sent to school to learn; but if I proved idle in learning, I was soundly beaten. For this procedure seemed wise to our ancestors: and many, passing the same way in days past, had built a sorrowful road by which we too must go, with multiplication of grief and toil upon the sons of Adam.

Yet, Lord, I observed men praying to You: and I learnt to do likewise, thinking of You (to the best of my understanding) as some great being who, though unseen, could hear and help me. As a boy I fell into the way of calling upon You, my Help and my Refuge; and in those prayers I broke the strings of my tongue—praying to You, small as I was but with no small energy, that I might not be beaten at school.[5] And when You did not hear me *(not as giving me over to folly)*, my elders and even my parents, who certainly wished me no harm, treated my stripes as a huge joke, which they were very far from being to me. Surely, Lord, there is no one so steeled in mind or cleaving to You so close—or even so insensitive, for that might have the same effect—as to make light of the racks and hooks and other torture instruments[6] (from which in all lands men pray so fervently to be saved) while truly loving those who are in such bitter fear of them. Yet my parents seemed to be amused at the torments inflicted upon me as a boy by my masters, though I was no less afraid of my punishments or zealous in my prayers to You for deliverance. But in spite of my terrors I still did wrong, by writing or reading or studying less than my set tasks. It was not, Lord, that I lacked mind or memory, for You had given me as much of these as my age required; but the one thing I revelled in was play; and for this I was punished by men who after all were doing exactly the same things themselves. But the idling of men is called business; the idling of boys, though exactly like, is punished by those same men: and no one pities either boys or men. Perhaps an unbiased observer would hold that I was rightly punished as a boy for playing with a ball: because this hindered my progress in studies—studies which would give me the opportunity as a man to play at things more degraded. And what difference was there between me and the master who flogged me? For if on some trifling point he had the worst of the argument with some fellow-master, he was more torn with angry vanity than I when I was beaten in a game of ball.

* * *

But to continue with my boyhood, which was in less peril of sin than my adolescence. I disliked learning and hated to be forced to it. But I *was* forced to it, so that good was done to me though it was not my doing. Short of being driven to it, I certainly would not have learned. But no one does well against his will, even if the thing he does is a good thing to do.

---

4. The study of rhetoric, which was the passport to eminence in public life.   5. Augustine recognizes the necessity of this rigorous training; that he never forgot its harshness is clear from his remark in the *City of God* (XXI.14): "If a choice were given him between suffering death and living his early years over again, who would not shudder and choose death?"   6. The instruments of public execution.

Nor did those who forced me do well: it was by You, O God, that well was done. Those others had no deeper vision of the use to which I might put all they forced me to learn, but to sate the insatiable desire of man for wealth that is but penury and glory that is but shame. But You, Lord, *by Whom the very hairs of our head are numbered*,[7] used for my good the error of those who urged me to study; but my own error, in that I had no will to learn, you used for my punishment—a punishment richly deserved by one so small a boy and so great a sinner. Thus, You brought good for me out of those who did ill, and justly punished me for the ill I did myself. So You have ordained and so it is: that every disorder of the soul is its own punishment.

To this day I do not quite see why I so hated the Greek tongue[8] that I was made to learn as a small boy. For I really liked Latin—not the rudiments that we got from our first teachers but the literature that we came to be taught later. For the rudiments—reading and writing and figuring—I found as hard and hateful as Greek. Yet this too could come only from sin and the vanity of life, because *I was flesh, and a wind that goes away and returns not*. For those first lessons were the surer. I acquired the power I still have to read what I find written and to write what I want to express; whereas in the studies that came later I was forced to memorize the wanderings of Aeneas[9]—whoever *he* was—while forgetting my own wanderings; and to weep for the death of Dido who killed herself for love,[1] while bearing dry-eyed my own pitiful state, in that among these studies I was becoming dead to You, O God, my life.

Nothing could be more pitiful than a pitiable creature who does not see to pity himself, and weeps for the death that Dido suffered through love of Aeneas and not for the death he suffers himself through not loving You, O God, Light of my heart, Bread of my soul, Power wedded to my mind and the depths of my thought. I did not love You and I went away from You in fornication:[2] and all around me in my fornication echoed applauding cries "Well done! Well done!" *For the friendship of this world is fornication against Thee*: and the world cries "Well done" so loudly that one is ashamed of unmanliness not to do it. And for this I did not grieve; but I grieved for Dido, slain as she sought by the sword an end to her woe, while I too followed after the lowest of Your creatures, forsaking You, earth going unto earth. And if I were kept from reading, I grieved at not reading the tales that caused me such grief. This sort of folly is held nobler and richer than the studies by which we learn to read and write!

But now let my God cry aloud in my soul, and let Your truth assure me that it is not so: the earlier study is the better. I would more willingly forget the wanderings of Aeneas and all such things than how to write and read. Over the entrance of these grammar schools hangs a curtain:[3] but this should be seen not as lending honor to the mysteries, but as a cloak to the errors taught within. Let not those masters—who have now lost their ter-

---

7. Who knows and attends to the smallest detail of each life (compare Matthew 10:30).   8. Important not only for gaining knowledge of Greek literature but also because it was the official language of the Eastern Roman Empire. Augustine never really mastered Greek, though his remark elsewhere that he had acquired so little Greek that it amounted to practically none is overmodest.   9. Virgil's *Aeneid* III.   1. *Aeneid* IV.   2. Here, metaphorically.   3. School was often held in a building open on one side and curtained off from the street.

rors for me—cry out against me, because I confess to You, my God, the desire of my soul, and find soul's rest in blaming my evil ways that I may love Your holy ways. Let not the buyers or sellers of book-learning cry out against me. If I ask them whether it is true, as the poet says, that Aeneas ever went to Carthage, the more ignorant will have to answer that they do not know, the more scholarly that he certainly did not. But if I ask with what letters the name Aeneas is spelt, all whose schooling has gone so far will answer correctly, according to the convention men have agreed upon for the use of letters. Or again, were I to ask which loss would be more damaging to human life—the loss from men's memory of reading and writing or the loss of these poetic imaginings—there can be no question what anyone would answer who had not lost his own memory. Therefore as a boy I did wrong in liking the empty studies more than the useful—or rather in loving the empty and hating the useful. For one and one make two, two and two make four, I found a loathsome refrain; but such empty unrealities as the Wooden Horse with its armed men, and Troy on fire, and Creusa's Ghost, were sheer delight.[4]

Give me leave, O my God, to speak of my mind, Your gift, and of the follies in which I wasted it. It chanced that a task was set me, a task which I did not like but had to do. There was the promise of glory if I won, the fear of ignominy, and a flogging as well, if I lost. It was to declaim the words uttered by Juno in her rage and grief when she could not keep the Trojan prince from coming to Italy.[5] I had learnt that Juno had never said these words, but we were compelled to err in the footsteps of the poet who had invented them: and it was our duty to paraphrase in prose what he had said in verse. In this exercise that boy won most applause in whom the passions of grief and rage were expressed most powerfully and in the language most adequate to the majesty of the personage represented.

What could all this mean to me, O My true Life, My God? Why was there more applause for the performance I gave than for so many classmates of my own age? Was not the whole business so much smoke and wind? Surely some other matter could have been found to exercise mind and tongue. Thy praises, Lord, might have upheld the fresh young shoot of my heart, so that it might not have been whirled away by empty trifles, defiled, a prey to the spirits of the air. For there is more than one way of sacrificing to the fallen angels. * * *

FROM BOOK II

[The Pear Tree]

I propose now to set down my past wickedness and the carnal corruptions of my soul, not for love of them but that I may love Thee, O my God. I do it for love of Thy love, passing again in the bitterness of remembrance over my most evil ways that Thou mayest thereby grow ever lovelier

4. *Aeneid* II.   5. Augustine was assigned the task of delivering a prose paraphrase of Juno's angry speech in *Aeneid* I. In it she complains that her enemies, the Trojans under Aeneas, are on their way to their destined goal in Italy in spite of her resolution to prevent them. Rhetorical exercises such as this were common in the schools, because they served the double purpose of teaching both literature and rhetorical composition.

to me, O Loveliness that dost not deceive, Loveliness happy and abiding:
and I collect my self out of that broken state in which my very being was
torn asunder because I was turned away from Thee, the One, and wasted
myself upon the many.

Arrived now at adolescence I burned for all the satisfactions of hell, and
I sank to the animal in a succession of dark lusts: *my beauty consumed
away*, and I stank in Thine eyes, yet was pleasing in my own and anxious
to please the eyes of men.

My one delight was to love and to be loved. But in this I did not keep
the measure of mind to mind, which is the luminous line of friendship;
but from the muddy concupiscence of the flesh and the hot imagination
of puberty mists steamed up to becloud and darken my heart so that I
could not distinguish the white light of love from the fog of lust. Both love
and lust boiled within me, and swept my youthful immaturity over the
precipice of evil desires to leave me half drowned in a whirlpool of abominable sins. Your wrath had grown mighty against me and I knew it not. I
had grown deaf from the clanking of the chain of my mortality, the punishment for the pride of my soul: and I departed further from You, and
You left me to myself: and I was tossed about and wasted and poured out
and boiling over in my fornications: and You were silent, O my late-won
Joy. You were silent, and I, arrogant and depressed, weary and restless,
wandered further and further from You into more and more sins which
could bear no fruit save sorrows.

☼   ☼   ☼

Where then was I, and how far from the delights of Your house, in that
sixteenth year of my life in this world, when the madness of lust—needing
no licence from human shamelessness, receiving no licence from Your
laws—took complete control of me, and I surrendered wholly to it? My
family took no care to save me from this moral destruction by marriage:
their only concern was that I should learn to make as fine and persuasive
speeches as possible.

☼   ☼   ☼

Your law, O Lord, punishes theft; and this law is so written in the hearts
of men that not even the breaking of it blots it out: for no thief bears
calmly being stolen from—not even if he is rich and the other steals
through want. Yet I chose to steal, and not because want drove me to it—
unless a want of justice and contempt for it and an excess for iniquity. For
I stole things which I already had in plenty and of better quality. Nor had
I any desire to enjoy the things I stole, but only the stealing of them and
the sin. There was a pear tree near our vineyard, heavy with fruit, but fruit
that was not particularly tempting either to look at or to taste. A group of
young blackguards, and I among them, went out to knock down the pears
and carry them off late one night, for it was our bad habit to carry on our
games in the streets till very late. We carried off an immense load of pears,
not to eat—for we barely tasted them before throwing them to the hogs.
Our only pleasure in doing it was that it was forbidden. Such was my
heart, O God, such was my heart: yet in the depth of the abyss You had

pity on it. Let that heart now tell You what it sought when I was thus evil for no object, having no cause for wrongdoing save my wrongness. The malice of the act was base and I loved it—that is to say I loved my own undoing, I loved the evil in me—not the thing for which I did the evil, simply the evil: my soul was depraved, and hurled itself down from security in You into utter destruction, seeking no profit from wickedness but only to be wicked. * * *

FROM BOOK III

[Student at Carthage]

I came to Carthage[6] where a cauldron of illicit loves leapt and boiled about me. I was not yet in love, but I was in love with love, and from the very depth of my need hated myself for not more keenly feeling the need. I sought some object to love, since I was thus in love with loving; and I hated security and a life with no snares for my feet. For within I was hungry, all for the want of that spiritual food which is Thyself, my God; yet [though I was hungry for want of it] I did not hunger for it: I had no desire whatever for incorruptible food, not because I had it in abundance but the emptier I was, the more I hated the thought of it. Because of all this my soul was sick, and broke out in sores, whose itch I agonized to scratch with the rub of carnal things—carnal, yet if there were no soul in them, they would not be objects of love. My longing then was to love and to be loved, but most when I obtained the enjoyment of the body of the person who loved me.

Thus I polluted the stream of friendship with the filth of unclean desire and sullied its limpidity with the hell of lust. And vile and unclean as I was, so great was my vanity that I was bent upon passing for clean and courtly. And I did fall in love, simply from wanting to. O my God, my Mercy, with how much bitterness didst Thou in Thy goodness sprinkle the delights of that time! I was loved, and our love came to the bond of consummation: I wore my chains with bliss but with torment too, for I was scourged with the red hot rods of jealousy, with suspicions and fears and tempers and quarrels.

I developed a passion for stage plays, with the mirror they held up to my own miseries and the fuel they poured on my flame. How is it that a man wants to be made sad by the sight of tragic sufferings that he could not bear in his own person? Yet the spectator does want to feel sorrow, and it is actually his feeling of sorrow that he enjoys. Surely this is the most wretched lunacy? For the more a man feels such sufferings in himself, the more he is moved by the sight of them on the stage. Now when a man suffers himself, it is called misery; when he suffers in the suffering of another, it is called pity. But how can the unreal sufferings of the stage possibly move pity? The spectator is not moved to aid the sufferer but merely to be sorry for him; and the more the author of these fictions makes the audience grieve, the better they like him. If the tragic sorrows of the

---

6. The capital city of the province, where Augustine went to study rhetoric.

characters—whether historical or entirely fictitious—be so poorly represented that the spectator is not moved to tears, he leaves the theatre unsatisfied and full of complaints; if he *is* moved to tears, he stays to the end,
fascinated and revelling in it.

*   *   *

Those of my occupations at that time which were held as reputable[7] were
directed towards the study of the law, in which I meant to excel—and the
less honest I was, the more famous I should be. The very limit of human
blindness is to glory in being blind. By this time I was a leader in the
School of Rhetoric and I enjoyed this high station and was arrogant and
swollen with importance: though You know, O Lord, that I was far quieter
in my behavior and had no share in the riotousness of the *eversores*—the
Overturners[8]—for this blackguardly diabolical name they wore as the very
badge of sophistication. Yet I was much in their company and much
ashamed of the sense of shame that kept me from being like them. I was
with them and I did for the most part enjoy their companionship, though
I abominated the acts that were their specialty—as when they made a butt
of some hapless newcomer, assailing him with really cruel mockery for no
reason whatever, save the malicious pleasure they got from it. There was
something very like the action of devils in their behavior. They were
rightly called Overturners, since they had themselves been first overturned
and perverted, tricked by those same devils who were secretly mocking
them in the very acts by which they amused themselves in mocking and
making fools of others.

With these men as companions of my immaturity, I was studying the
books of eloquence; for in eloquence it was my ambition to shine, all from
a damnable vaingloriousness and for the satisfaction of human vanity. Following the normal order of study I had come to a book of one Cicero,
whose tongue[9] practically everyone admires, though not his heart. That
particular book is called *Hortensius*[1] and contains an exhortation to philosophy. Quite definitely it changed the direction of my mind, altered my
prayers to You, O Lord, and gave me a new purpose and ambition. Suddenly all the vanity I had hoped in I saw as worthless, and with an incredible intensity of desire I longed after immortal wisdom. I had begun that
journey upwards by which I was to return to You. My father was now dead
two years; I was eighteen and was receiving money from my mother for
the continuance of my study of eloquence. But I used that book not for
the sharpening of my tongue; what won me in it was what it said, not the
excellence of its phrasing.

*   *   *

So I resolved to make some study of the Sacred Scriptures and find what
kind of books they were. But what I came upon was something not grasped
by the proud, not revealed either to children, something utterly humble

---

7. That is, his rhetorical studies.   8. *Eversores* is the Latin word that means "overturners": a group of
students who prided themselves on their wild actions and lack of discipline.   9. Style.   1. Only
fragments of this dialogue remain. In it Cicero replies to an opponent of philosophy with an impassioned
defense of the intellectual life.

in the hearing but sublime in the doing, and shrouded deep in mystery. And I was not of the nature to enter into it or bend my neck to follow it. When I first read those Scriptures, I did not feel in the least what I have just said; they seemed to me unworthy to be compared with the majesty of Cicero. My conceit was repelled by their simplicity, and I had not the mind to penetrate into their depths. They were indeed of a nature to grow in Your little ones.[2] But I could not bear to be a little one; I was only swollen with pride, but to myself I seemed a very big man. * * *

FROM BOOK VI

[*Worldly Ambitions*]

By this time my mother had come to me, following me over sea and land with the courage of piety and relying upon You in all perils. For they were in danger from a storm, and she reassured even the sailors—by whom travelers newly ventured upon the deep are ordinarily reassured—promising them safe arrival because thus You had promised her in a vision. She found me in a perilous state through my deep despair of ever discovering the truth. But even when I told her that if I was not yet a Catholic Christian, I was no longer a Manichean,[3] she was not greatly exultant as at some unlooked-for good news, because she had already received assurance upon that part of my misery; she bewailed me as one dead certainly, but certainly to be raised again by You, offering me in her mind as one stretched out dead, that You might say to the widow's son: "*Young man, I say to thee arise*":[4] and he should sit up and begin to speak and You should give him to his mother.

* * *

Nor did I then groan in prayer for Your help. My mind was intent upon inquiry and unquiet for argumentation. I regarded Ambrose[5] as a lucky man by worldly standards to be held in honor by such important people: only his celibacy seemed to me a heavy burden. I had no means of guessing, and no experience of my own to learn from, what hope he bore within him, what struggles he might have against the temptations that went with his high place, what was his consolation in adversity, and on what joys of Your bread the hidden mouth of his heart fed. Nor did he know how I was inflamed nor the depth of my peril. I could not ask of him what I wished as I wished, for I was kept from any face to face conversation with him by the throng of men with their own troubles, whose infirmities he served. The very little time he was not with these he was refreshing either his body with necessary food or his mind with reading. When he read, his eyes traveled across the page and his heart sought into the sense, but voice

---

2. Refers not only to the rhetorical simplicity of Jesus' teachings but also to his interest in teaching children; compare Matthew 19:14: "For of such is the kingdom of heaven."   3. Augustine had for nine years been a member of this religious sect, which followed the teaching of the Babylonian mystic Mani (216–277). The Manicheans believed that the world was a battleground for the forces of good and evil; redemption in a future life would come to the elect, who renounced worldly occupations and possessions and practiced a severe asceticism (including abstention from meat). Augustine's mother, Monica, was a Christian, and lamented her son's Manichean beliefs.   4. Luke 7:14, recounting one of Christ's miracles.   5. The leading personality among the Christians of the West; not many years after this he defied the power of Emperor Theodosius and forced him to beg for God's pardon in the church at Milan for having put the inhabitants of Thessalonica to the sword.

and tongue were silent. No one was forbidden to approach him nor was it his custom to require that visitors should be announced: but when we came into him we often saw him reading and always to himself; and after we had sat long in silence, unwilling to interrupt a work on which he was so intent, we would depart again. We guessed that in the small time he could find for the refreshment of his mind, he would wish to be free from the distraction of other men's affairs and not called away from what he was doing. Perhaps he was on his guard lest [if he read aloud] someone listening should be troubled and want an explanation if the author he was reading expressed some idea over-obscurely, and it might be necessary to expound or discuss some of the more difficult questions. And if he had to spend time on this, he would get through less reading than he wished. Or it may be that his real reason for reading to himself was to preserve his voice, which did in fact readily grow tired. But whatever his reason for doing it, that man certainly had a good reason.

*   *   *

I was all hot for honors, money, marriage: and You made mock of my hotness. In my pursuit of these, I suffered most bitter disappointments, but in this You were good to me since I was thus prevented from taking delight in anything not Yourself. Look now into my heart, Lord, by whose will I remember all this and confess it to You. Let my soul cleave to You now that You have freed it from the tenacious hold of death. At that time my soul was in misery, and You pricked the soreness of its wound, that leaving all things it might turn to You, who are over all and without whom all would return to nothing, that it might turn to You and be healed. I was in utter misery and there was one day especially on which You acted to bring home to me the realization of my misery. I was preparing an oration in praise of the Emperor[6] in which I was to utter any number of lies to win the applause of people who knew they were lies. My heart was much wrought upon by the shame of this and inflamed with the fever of the thoughts that consumed it. I was passing along a certain street in Milan when I noticed a beggar. He was jesting and laughing and I imagine more than a little drunk. I fell into gloom and spoke to the friends who were with me about the endless sorrows that our own insanity brings us: for here was I striving away, dragging the load of my unhappiness under the spurring of my desires, and making it worse by dragging it: and with all our striving, our one aim was to arrive at some sort of happiness without care: the beggar had reached the same goal before us, and we might quite well never reach it at all. The very thing that he had attained by means of a few pennies begged from passers-by—namely the pleasure of a temporary happiness—I was plotting for with so many a weary twist and turn.

Certainly his joy was no true joy; but the joy I sought in my ambition was emptier still. In any event he was cheerful and I worried, he had no cares and I nothing but cares. Now if anyone had asked me whether I would rather be cheerful or fearful, I would answer: "Cheerful"; but if he had gone on to ask whether I would rather be like that beggar or as I

---

6. Probably the young Valentinian, whose court was at Milan.

actually was, I would certainly have chosen my own state though so troubled and anxious. Now this was surely absurd. It could not be for any true reason. I ought not to have preferred my own state rather than his merely because I was the more learned, since I got no joy from my learning, but sought only to please men by it—not even to teach them, only to please them. Therefore did You break my bones with the rod of Your discipline.

*   *   *

Great effort was made to get me married. I proposed, the girl was promised me. My mother played a great part in the matter for she wanted to have me married and then cleansed with the saving waters of baptism,[7] rejoicing to see me grow every day more fitted for baptism and feeling that her prayers and Your promises were to be fulfilled in my faith. By my request and her own desire she begged You daily with the uttermost intensity of her heart to show her in a vision something of my future marriage, but You would never do it. She did indeed see certain vain fantasies, under the pressure of her mind's preoccupation with the matter; and she told them to me, not, however, with the confidence she always had when You had shown things to her, but as if she set small store by them; for she said that there was a certain unanalyzable savor, not to be expressed in words, by which she could distinguish between what You revealed and the dreams of her own spirit. Still she pushed on with the matter of my marriage, and the girl was asked for. She was still two years short of the age for marriage[8] but I liked her and agreed to wait.

There was a group of us friends who had much serious discussion together, concerning the cares and troubles of human life which we found so hard to endure. We had almost decided to seek a life of peace, away from the throng of men. This peace we hoped to attain by putting together whatever we could manage to get, and making one common household for all of us: so that in the clear trust of friendship, things should not belong to this or that individual, but one thing should be made of all our possessions, and belong wholly to each one of us, and everybody own everything. It seemed that there might be perhaps ten men in this fellowship. Among us there were some very rich men, especially Romanianus, our fellow townsman, who had been a close friend of mine from childhood and had been brought to the court in Milan by the press of some very urgent business. He was strongest of all for the idea and he had considerable influence in persuasion because his wealth was much greater than anyone else's. We agreed that two officers should be chosen every year to handle the details of our life together, leaving the rest undisturbed. But then we began to wonder whether our wives would agree, for some of us already had wives and I meant to have one. So the whole plan, which we had built up so neatly, fell to pieces in our hands and was simply dropped. We returned to our old sighing and groaning and treading of this world's broad and beaten ways:[9] for many thoughts were in our hearts, but

---

7. He could not be baptized while living in sin with his mistress, a liaison that resulted in the birth of a son, Adeodatus, who later accompanied Augustine to Italy.   8. The legal age was twelve years; Augustine was in his early thirties.   9. Compare Matthew 7:13: "Broad is the way that leadeth to destruction," that is, to damnation.

Thy counsel standeth forever. And out of Thy counsel didst Thou deride ours and didst prepare Thine own things for us, meaning to *give us meat in due season and to open Thy hands and fill our souls with Thy blessing.*

Meanwhile my sins were multiplied. She with whom I had lived so long was torn from my side as a hindrance to my forthcoming marriage. My heart which had held her very dear was broken and wounded and shed blood. She went back to Africa, swearing that she would never know another man, and left with me the natural son I had had of her. But I in my unhappiness could not, for all my manhood, imitate her resolve. I was unable to bear the delay of two years which must pass before I was to get the girl I had asked for in marriage. In fact it was not really marriage that I wanted. I was simply a slave to lust. So I took another woman, not of course as a wife; and thus my soul's disease was nourished and kept alive as vigorously as ever, indeed worse than ever, that it might reach the realm of matrimony in the company of its ancient habit. Nor was the wound healed that had been made by the cutting off of my former mistress. For there was first burning and bitter grief; and after that it festered, and as the pain grew duller it only grew more hopeless. * * *

FROM BOOK VIII

[Conversion]

* * * Thus I was sick at heart and in torment, accusing myself with a new intensity of bitterness, twisting and turning in my chain in the hope that it might be utterly broken, for what held me was so small a thing! But it still held me. And You stood in the secret places of my soul, O Lord, in the harshness of Your mercy redoubling the scourges of fear and shame lest I should give way again and that small slight tie which remained should not be broken but should grow again to full strength and bind me closer even than before. For I kept saying within myself: "Let it be now, let it be now," and by the mere words I had begun to move toward the resolution. I almost made it, yet I did not quite make it. But I did not fall back into my original state, but as it were stood near to get my breath. And I tried again and I was almost there, and now I could all but touch it and hold it: yet I was not quite there, I did not touch it or hold it. I still shrank from dying unto death and living unto life. The lower condition which had grown habitual was more powerful than the better condition which I had not tried. The nearer the point of time came in which I was to become different, the more it struck me with horror; but it did not force me utterly back nor turn me utterly away, but held me there between the two.

Those trifles of all trifles, and vanities of vanities, my one-time mistresses, held me back, plucking at my garment of flesh and murmuring softly: "Are you sending us away?" And "From this moment shall we not be with you, now or forever?" And "From this moment shall this or that not be allowed you, now or forever?" What were they suggesting to me in the phrase I have written "this or that," what were they suggesting to me, O my God? Do you in your mercy keep from the soul of Your servant the vileness and uncleanness they were suggesting. And now I began to hear them not half so loud; they no longer stood against me face to face, but

were softly muttering behind my back and, as I tried to depart, plucking stealthily at me to make me look behind. Yet even that was enough, so hesitating was I, to keep me from snatching myself free, from shaking them off and leaping upwards on the way I was called: for the strong force of habit said to me: "Do you think you can live without them?"

But by this time its voice was growing fainter. In the direction toward which I had turned my face and was quivering in fear of going, I could see the austere beauty of Continence, serene and indeed joyous but not evilly, honorably soliciting me to come to her and not linger, stretching forth loving hands to receive and embrace me, hands full of multitudes of good examples. With her I saw such hosts of young men and maidens, a multitude of youth and of every age, gray widows and women grown old in virginity, and in them all Continence herself, not barren but the fruitful mother of children, her joys, by You, Lord, her Spouse. And she smiled upon me and her smile gave courage as if she were saying: "Can you not do what these men have done, what these women have done? Or could men or women have done such in themselves, and not in the Lord their God? The Lord their God gave me to them. Why do you stand upon yourself and so not stand at all? Cast yourself upon Him and be not afraid; He will not draw away and let you fall. Cast yourself without fear, He will receive you and heal you."

Yet I was still ashamed, for I could still hear the murmuring of those vanities, and I still hung hesitant. And again it was as if she said: "Stop your ears against your unclean members, that they may be mortified. They tell you of delights, but not of such delights as the law of the Lord your God tells." This was the controversy raging in my heart, a controversy about myself against myself. And Alypius[1] stayed by my side and awaited in silence the issue of such agitation as he had never seen in me.

When my most searching scrutiny had drawn up all my vileness from the secret depths of my soul and heaped it in my heart's sight, a mighty storm arose in me, bringing a mighty rain of tears. That I might give way to my tears and lamentations, I rose from Alypius: for it struck me that solitude was more suited to the business of weeping. I went far enough from him to prevent his presence from being an embarrassment to me. So I felt, and he realized it. I suppose I had said something and the sound of my voice was heavy with tears. I arose, but he remained where we had been sitting, still in utter amazement. I flung myself down somehow under a certain fig tree and no longer tried to check my tears, which poured forth from my eyes in a flood, *an acceptable sacrifice to Thee*. And much I said not in these words but to this effect: "*And Thou, O Lord, how long? How long, Lord; wilt Thou be angry forever? Remember not our former iniq-uities.*"[2] For I felt that I was still bound by them. And I continued my miserable complaining: "How long, how long shall I go on saying tomor-row and again tomorrow? Why not now, why not have an end to my uncleanness this very hour?"

1. A student of Augustine's at Carthage; he had joined the Manichees with Augustine, followed him to Rome and Milan, and now shared his desires and doubts. Alypius finally became a bishop in North Africa.   2. Compare Psalm 79:5–8; Augustine compares his spiritual despair with that of captive and subjected Israel.

Such things I said, weeping in the most bitter sorrow of my heart. And suddenly I heard a voice from some nearby house, a boy's voice or a girl's voice, I do not know: but it was a sort of singsong, repeated again and again. "Take and read, take and read." I ceased weeping and immediately began to search my mind most carefully as to whether children were accustomed to chant these words in any kind of game, and I could not remember that I had ever heard any such thing. Damming back the flood of my tears I arose, interpreting the incident as quite certainly a divine command to open my book of Scripture and read the passage at which I should open. For it was part of what I had been told about Anthony,[3] that from the Gospel which he happened to be reading he had felt that he was being admonished as though what he read was spoken directly to himself: *Go, sell what thou hast and give to the poor and thou shalt have treasure in heaven; and come follow Me.*[4] By this experience he had been in that instant converted to You. So I was moved to return to the place where Alypius was sitting, for I had put down the Apostle's[5] book there when I arose. I snatched it up, opened it and in silence read the passage upon which my eyes first fell: *Not in rioting and drunkenness, not in chambering and impurities, not in contention and envy, but put ye on the Lord Jesus Christ and make not provision for the flesh in its concupiscences.* [Romans 13.13.] I had no wish to read further, and no need. For in that instant, with the very ending of the sentence, it was as though a light of utter confidence shone in all my heart, and all the darkness of uncertainty vanished away. Then leaving my finger in the place or marking it by some other sign, I closed the book and in complete calm told the whole thing to Alypius and he similarly told me what had been going on in himself, of which I knew nothing. He asked to see what I had read. I showed him, and he looked further than I had read. I had not known what followed. And this is what followed: *"Now him that is weak in faith, take unto you."* He applied this to himself and told me so. And he was confirmed by this message, and with no troubled wavering gave himself to God's goodwill and purpose—a purpose indeed most suited to his character, for in these matters he had been immeasurably better than I.

Then we went in to my mother and told her, to her great joy. We related how it had come about: she was filled with triumphant exultation, and praised You who are mighty beyond what we ask or conceive: for she saw that You had given her more than with all her pitiful weeping she had ever asked. For You converted me to Yourself so that I no longer sought a wife nor any of this world's promises, but stood upon that same rule of faith in which You had shown me to her so many years before.[6] Thus You changed her mourning into joy, a joy far richer than she had thought to wish, a joy much dearer and purer than she had thought to find in grandchildren of my flesh.

---

3. The Egyptian saint whose abstinence and self-control are still proverbial; he was one of the founders of the system of monastic life.　4. Luke 18:22.　5. Paul.　6. At Carthage, when Augustine was still a Manichee, Monica had dreamed that she was standing on a wooden ruler weeping for her son and then saw that he was standing on the same ruler as herself.

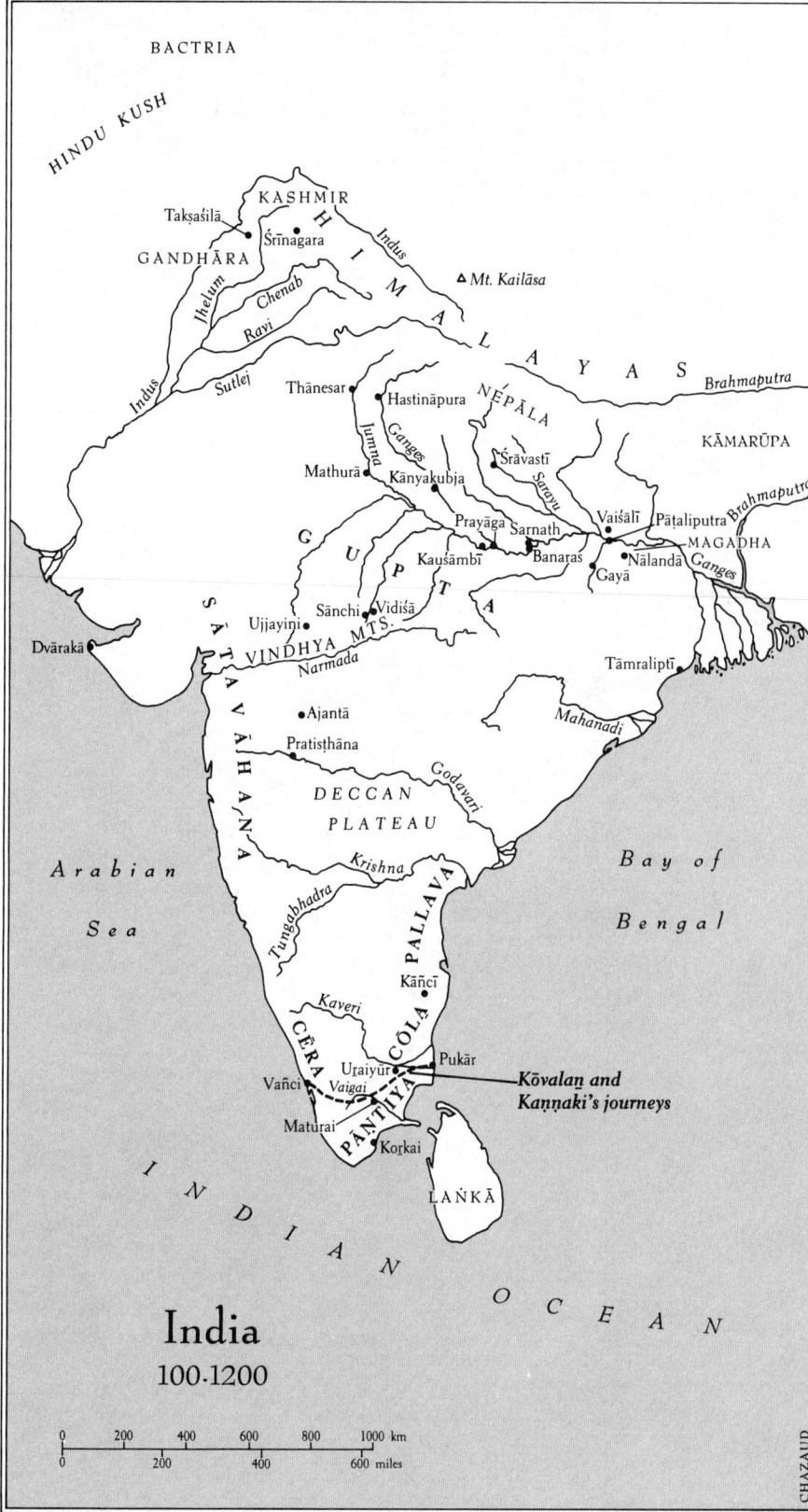

BACTRIA

HINDU KUSH

KASHMIR
Takṣaśilā
GANDHĀRA
Śrīnagara

HIMALAYAS

Indus

△ Mt. Kailāsa

Jhelum
Chenab
Ravi

Indus
Sutlej

Thānesar
Hastināpura
NEPĀLA
Brahmaputra
KĀMARŪPA

Mathurā
Kānyakubja
Śrāvastī
Jumna
Ganges
Sarayu

G
U
P
T
A

Prayāga Sarnath
Kauśāmbī
Banaras
Vaiśālī Pāṭaliputra
Brahmaputra
Nālandā MAGADHA
Gayā Ganges

SĀTAVĀHANA

Ujjayinī
Sānchi Vidiśā

Dvārakā

VINDHYA MTS.
Narmadā

Tāmraliptī

Ajantā
Pratiṣṭhāna

Mahānadi

DECCAN
PLATEAU

Godavari

Arabian

Sea

Krishna

Bay of

Bengal

Tungabhadra

PALLAVA

CĒRA
Kaveri
Kāñcī

CŌLA
Uṟaiyūr Pukār
Vañci Vaigai
Maturai PĀṆṬIYA
Korkai

Kōvalaṉ and
Kaṇṇaki's journeys

INDIAN

LAṄKĀ

OCEAN

India
100-1200

| 0 | 200 | 400 | 600 | 800 | 1000 km |
| 0 | | 200 | 400 | | 600 miles |

CHAZAUD

India's Classical Age

The classical literature of India had its great flowering under the Guptas, who ruled over much of India from their north Indian capitals in Pāṭaliputra (modern Patna) and Ujjayinī (modern Ujjain) between 335 and 470. During the Gupta era Ujjayinī in the west and the seaport Tāmraliptī in the east were centers of a flourishing trade with Rome, China, and Southeast Asia. While Indian merchants voyaged on the seas to Java and other islands in the Indonesian archipelago, Chinese pilgrims traveled to the holy sites of Buddhism in the land of its birth. Ancient India's greatest achievements in mathematics, logic, and astronomy as well as in literature and the fine arts were made in this prosperous, cosmopolitan milieu, and the classical ideals expressed in the masterworks of the Gupta period continued to be influential well into the twelfth century and later.

Gupta classicism was closely connected with the development of Sanskrit as a literary language. Saṃskṛta, the very name of the language, means "perfected, classified, refined." Already by the end of the Heroic Age the veneration of the Vedic hymns had led to the ideal of Sanskrit as "correct speech," a speech that was fully codified and frozen in the Aṣṭādhyāyī (The book of eight chapters [of the rules of grammar]) of Pāṇini, a pioneer in the science of linguistics. In the Indian view, Sanskrit's nature as a code and construct made it the ideal language for the classics, in contrast to the Prakrit (prākṛta, meaning "original" or "natural") dialects that were allowed to change and develop in the manner of "natural," spoken languages.

The Prakrit literature that developed around the second century was soon absorbed into the Sanskrit classical tradition. Until the development of the south Indian regional languages in the tenth and eleventh centuries, Tamil alone continued to nourish a classical tradition that was distinct from that of Sanskrit, in spite of the many features absorbed into Tamil civilization from centuries of interaction with Indo-Aryan culture and literature. The fifth-century Cilappatikāram (The poem of the anklet) is the oldest extant epic in Tamil. This classical poem, written at the court of a Cēra king, bears no resemblance whatsoever to the Indo-Aryan epics, although its author, Iḷaṅkōvaṭikaḷ, was a Jaina monk and the Tamil folk narrative on which the epic is based is heavily overlaid with Jaina doctrine.

Classical Sanskrit literature is permeated with the culture of the courts of ancient India. Learned poets (kavi) wrote poetry under the patronage of kings and recited their works at court for audiences of connoisseurs, known as sahṛdaya ("with-heart," or responsive) or rasika ("enjoyer of aesthetic mood"). Whatever their specific subject matter, only works whose primary aim was to evoke an aesthetic response were admitted into the classical literary canon, and such works were called kāvya, "poetry" in the broadest sense of the word, that is, literature as art. Kāvya literature is governed by meticulously formulated norms and conventions that circumscribe the poet's freedom, at the same time putting at his or her disposal a rich array of traditional poetic means, along with the opportunity to refine on the achievements of the past.

The court epic, drama, short lyric, and narrative are the major genres of kāvya. The first of these, the mahākāvya ("great poem," or court epic), grew out of the

older epics and bardic praise poems and treats the martial exploits of kings, warriors, and gods. Unlike the older narrative epics, however, the *kāvya* epics are made up of lyric stanzas, with elaborate figures of speech and a descriptive emphasis. The drama, or *nāṭya* (exemplified in plays: *rūpaka*, "representation"), is a more heterogeneous genre, employing prose and verse, in Sanskrit and Prakrit, and a somewhat wider range of characters than the court epic. In classical plays the warrior-king is portrayed as a romantic hero, and here, too, lyrical description dominates over dramatic action.

The short lyric poem (*muktaka*, "detached verse") is the quintessential genre of classical Sanskrit poetry. Sanskrit poets achieved their finest and most characteristic effects in poems of a single stanza divided into "quarters" (*pāda*), normally of equal length. The brevity of the form (the longest *kāvya* meter has only twenty-one syllables per verse quarter) combined with the complexities of the Sanskrit language and the rules of *kāvya* poetry results in miniature poems that are at once complex and extraordinarily compact, similar in effect to the miniature paintings produced at Indian courts in the seventeenth and eighteenth centuries. The *muktaka* genre encompasses the trenchant epigrams of Bhartṛhari, and Kālidāsa's idyllic verses on nature and love as well as the erotic vignettes of Amaru. Designated *subhāṣita* ("well-wrought verse"), the best stanzas of the classical poets—both men and women—were anthologized in such collections as the eleventh-century *Subhāṣitaratnakoṣa* (A treasury of well-wrought verse), to be memorized, recited, and savored by connoisseurs. Such poets as Bhartṛhari and Amaru, who specialized in particular themes, earned their own anthologies, organized into "centuries [of stanzas]," or *śataka*, perhaps on the model of earlier anthologies of Tamil and Prakrit lyric poetry.

From the earliest times India has been a vast storehouse of tales, many of which have traveled all over the world. Among the most widely known works in the narrative genre known as *kathā* or *ākhyāyikā* ("story") is the *Pañcatantra*, a Gupta-period collection of animal fables. The most popular of the later *kāvya* tale collections, however, is the Kashmirian poet Somadeva's eleventh-century *Kathāsaritsāgara* (Ocean to the rivers of story), a compendium in narrative verse of picaresque tales, tales of the marvelous, and romances. With its gentle but pointed satire of ancient Indian society and manners and its array of vivid, earthy characters, Sanskrit story literature presents a marked contrast to the sober elegance of the other *kāvya* genres.

The practice of *kāvya* literature seems always to have been correlated with an influential body of works on poetics. The first major work devoted solely to poetic theory is the seventh-century *Kāvyādarśa* (Mirror for poetry), in which the south Indian writer on poetic theory Daṇḍin systematically discusses the figures of speech (*alaṃkāra*, literally "ornament") that differentiate poetry from ordinary discourse. An earlier concept, *rasa* or "aesthetic mood," remained the dominant theoretical framework for the aesthetics of drama and also influenced the criticism of the other *kāvya* genres. Finally, in the ninth century, the master-critic Ānandavardhana expounded in his *Dhvanyāloka* (Light of suggestion) the aesthetic ideal of *dhvani* ("poetic suggestion"; literally, "resonance") as the measure of the best kind of poetry in all the forms of *kāvya*. Besides poetic theory *kāvya* texts are keyed to technical treatises (*śāstra* or *sūtra*) in every branch of classical learning, ranging from Pāṇini's grammar and Vātsyāyana's *Kāmasūtra* (Treatise on erotics) to the *Dharmaśāstra* of Manu (Manu's treatise on the religious law) and the *Arthaśāstra*, Kauṭilya's influential text on politics.

Reflecting the conservative values of courtly and learned elites, the masterworks of *kāvya* carry forward the idealization of *dharma* (religious duty), the first of the four aims of human endeavor enjoined for Hindu men and a seminal theme in the major texts of the Heroic Age, such as the *Rāmāyaṇa* and the *Bhagavad-Gītā*.

In the classical texts, however, the concern with religious duty is offset by a more direct preoccupation with *artha* (wealth, politics, public life) and *kāma* (the realm of erotic pleasure and the emotions), the second and third aims, and their vision is of a life in which all four goals of action are harmoniously balanced. Like earlier epic heroes such as Arjuna and Rāma, the exemplary warriors and kings of the courtly literature combine sagelike self-control with more active, worldly, heroic traits, for in Hindu belief austerity is an essential means by which a person may attain the ultimate goal of life—liberation (*mokṣa*) from the chain of birth and death in which souls are trapped because of the results of good and bad action (*karma*).

The philosophy of *karma*-rebirth implies fluid relationships among the human, animal, and divine worlds. In a universe where a king might be a divine incarnation, a god come down to earth (*avatāra*: "descent"), sages and holy people, who have amassed superhuman powers by exercising extraordinary self-control, represent the possibility of the ascent of human beings to godlike states; hence the great respect given to these gods-on-earth. As keepers of both sacred and secular learning, members of the brahman class, the highest of the four classes of Hindu society, and the class to which most of the classical poets belonged, are naturally portrayed in a most favorable light in the works of the classical era. Certain genres, however, were allowed the privilege of satire and critique. The "Fool" of the Sanskrit drama is a dull-witted, gluttonous brahman; the story literature is full of corrupt monks and less than perfect religious figures; and the animal fables of the *Pañcatantra* offer an unvarnished picture of courtly intrigue.

Śakuntalā, the heroine of Kālidāsa's celebrated play *Śakuntala* (fourth century), a representative *kāvya* classic, reinforces the image of the ideal Hindu wife, a role already exemplified in the personality of the long-suffering Sītā in the *Rāmāyaṇa*. The indispensability of marriage for women in Hindu society, and their near-total dependence on the will of their husbands, dominates even this work with its explicit focus on the erotic aspect of gender relations. In the course of the play, Śakuntalā matures from a naive girl into the ideal wife: chaste, loyal, submissive, and willing to bear suffering patiently. However, the classical literature offers very different images of women as well. The Tamil epic *Cilappatikāram* portrays Kaṇṇaki as a woman whose chastity endows her with independent agency and superhuman power. Chaste though they may be, there is nothing submissive about the women of the Sanskrit story literature, a literature of the merchant-class milieu. Women are as often likely to be the protagonists of these stories as men, and they surpass men—very often, their own husbands—in wit, wisdom, resourcefulness, and the ability to act.

The hierarchy of gender roles is often reversed in the Sanskrit erotic lyrics, which also challenge the normative emphasis on female chastity by their sympathetic treatment of extramarital love. In the spectrum of female figures in classical literature, the courtesan, whose skill in the arts enables her to earn her own living and dispense with marriage, stands at the opposite end from the chaste wife. The courtesans of Sanskrit and Tamil literature are beautiful, intelligent, ruthless and rapacious women; but there are also sympathetic potraits, such as that of the *Cilappatikāram*'s Mātavi, who combines the talents of a courtesan with the loyalty of a chaste wife. Finally, in such characters as the female hermit Gautamī in *Śakuntala*, and the Jaina nun Kavunti Aṭikaḷ in the Tamil epic, we have exemplars of women who, as religious contemplatives, are figures of authority and free agents on a par with their male counterparts.

The lives of many *kāvya* poets are shrouded in myth and legend. This is true even of Kālidāsa, the greatest poet, not only of the age of the Guptas but also of the entire *kāvya* tradition. Likewise, the identities of the royal patrons of early *kāvya*, except in the odd case, remain a matter for speculation. *Kāvya* is a poetry

of universals and ideals, and its heroes and heroines are, by and large, types, not individuals. The early epic poetry, too, idealized and universalized its heroes. Whether the hero is a king, merchant, or brahman, and regardless of his distinctive virtues, the ideal personage of the classical literature must possess—to a greater or lesser degree—the generalized qualities of a *nāgaraka*, "citizen" or "courtier," the cultivated person of the courtly civilization. So, too, must the ideal *kāvya* heroine—whether she is a courtesan or a chaste wife—be beautiful and refined in the courtly manner.

Vātsyāyana devotes the opening section of the *Kāmasūtra* to the qualifications of the *nāgaraka* and his female counterpart. The gentleman is enjoined to equip his house (a pleasant villa surrounded by a garden) with the requisites of a cultivated life. These include "a box containing ornaments, and also a lute hanging from a peg made of the tooth of an elephant, a board for drawing, a pot containing perfume, and some garlands of yellow amaranth flowers." All women, not just professional courtesans, are encouraged to learn the sixty-four arts, among which are enumerated several kinds of verse making and "writing and drawing, and spreading and arranging beds or couches of flowers, and scenic representation and stage playing." Life itself is an art, and the ideal person is a *rasika*, or a *sahṛdaya*— one whose sensibility has been cultivated to celebrate and respond to life as art. This aesthetic ideal, more than any other trait, characterizes the literature of India's classical age.

FURTHER READING

The Literatures of India (1974), edited by Edward C. Dimock et al., contains good introductions to the various genres of classical Sanskrit literature, and Daniel H. H. Ingalls, *Sanskrit Poetry from Vidyākara's Treasury* (1968), offers an outstanding introduction to *kāvya* poetry and its aesthetic. A. L. Basham, *The Wonder That Was India* (1956), is the best study of India's classical civilization. For a history of Sanskrit literature, see A. B. Keith, *History of Classical Sanskrit Literature*. The *Kāmasūtra* may be consulted in Richard Burton's translation, *The Kama Sutra of Vatsyayana* (1923). On women in classical civilization, see A. S. Altekar, *The Position of Women in Hindu Civilization* (1938), and J. J. Meyer, *Sexual Life in Ancient India* (1930).

PRONOUNCING GLOSSARY

The following list uses common English syllables and stress accents to provide rough equivalents of selected words whose pronunciation may be unfamiliar to the general reader.

ākhyāyikā: *ah-khyah'-yee-kah*

alaṃkāra: *uh'-luhng-kah-ruh*

Amaru: *uh'-muh-roo*

Ānandavardhana: *ah-nuhn-duh-vuhrd'-huh-nuh*

artha: *uhrt'-huh*

Arthaśāstra: *uhrt-huh-shahs'-truh*

Aṣṭādhyāyī: *uhsh'-tahdh-yah'-yee*

Bhagavad Gītā: *buh'-guh-vuhd gee'-taa*

Bharata: *buh'-ruh-tuh*

Bhartṛhari: *buhr'-tree-huh'-ree*

Cēra: *say'-ruh*

Cilappatikāram: *see-luhp'-puh-dee-kah-ruhm*

Daṇḍin: *duhn'-din*

Dharma-śāstra: *duhr'-muh-shahs'-truh*

dhvani: *dvuh'-nee*

Dhvanyāloka: *d-vuhn'-yah-loh'-kuh*

Gupta: *goop'-tuh*

Iḷaṅkōvaṭikaḷ: *ee-luhn'-goh-vuh-dee-guhl*

Jaina: *jai'-nuh*

Kālidāsa: *kah-lee-dah'-suh*

kāma: *kah'-muh*

Kāmasūtra: *kah-muh-soot'-ruh*

karma: *kuhr'-muh*

kathā: *kuht'-hah*

Kathāsaritsāgara: *kuht-hah'-suh-reet-sah'-guh-ruh*

Kauṭilya: *kow-teel'-yuh*

kavi: *kuh'-vee*

kāvya: *kahv'-yuh*

Kāvyādarśa: *kahv-yah-duhr'-shuh*

mahākāvya: *muh-hah-kahv'-yuh*

Manu: *muh'-noo*

Mātavi: *mah'-duh-vee*

mokṣa: *mohk'-shuh*

muktaka: *mook-tuh'-kuh*

nāgaraka: *nah'-guh-ruh-kuh*

nāṭya: *naht'-yuh*

Nāṭyaśāstra: *naht'-yuh-shahs'-truh*

pāda: *pah'-duh*

Pañcatantra: *puhn'-chuh-tuhn'-truh*

Pāṇini: *pah'-nee-nee*

Pāṭaliputra: *pah'-tuh-lee-poo'-truh*

prākṛta: *prah'-kri-tuh*

Rāmāyana: *rah-mah'-yuh-nuh*

rasa: *ruh'-suh*

rasika: *ruh'-see-kuh*

rūpaka: *roo'-puh-kuh*

sahṛdaya: *suh-hree'-duh-yuh*

Śākuntala: *shah-koon'-tuh-luh*

saṃskṛta: *suhms'-kree-tuh*

śāstra: *shah'-struh*

śataka: *shuh'-tuh-kuh*

śloka: *shloh'-kuh*

Somadeva: *soh'-muh-day'-vuh*

subhāṣita: *soob-hah'-shee-tuh*

Subhāṣitaratnakoṣa: *soob-hah'-shee-tuh-ruht'-nuh-koh'-shuh*

sūtra: *soo'-truh*

Tāmraliptī: *tahm'-ruh-lip'-tee*

Ujjayinī: *ooj'-juh-yee-nee*

Vātsyāyana: *vahts-yah'-yuh-nuh*

TEXTS	CONTEXTS
ca. 2nd century The Sanskrit *Nāṭyaśās-tra* of Bharata, the authoritative work on drama, poetry, and aesthetics, is completed	
2nd or 3rd century Viṣṇuśarman completes the Sanskrit animal tale collection *Pañcatantra*	
	ca. 335–470 The reign of the Gupta emperors in north India, an age of great achievement in arts, letters, science, international trade, and conquest • Indian civilization spreads to Southeast Asia
ca. 375–425 Kālidāsa, preeminent poet of the Gupta age, writes the play *Śakuntala* and other works in Sanskrit	
5th century The Sanskrit epigrams of Bhartṛhari are collected in the *Śatakatrayam* (The anthology of three centuries)	
ca. 400–500 Tiruvaḷḷuvar composes the Tamil *Tirukkuṛaḷ*, a collection of ethical aphorisms • Vātsyāyana writes the Sanskrit *Kāmasūtra*, the authoritative treatise on the science of erotics	**ca. 400–500** A great Buddhist monastery and university are founded in Nalanda in eastern India
	454 The Huns invade India
late 5th century The Jaina monk Iḷaṅkō Aṭikaḷ writes the *Cilappati-kāram* (The epic of the anklet), an epic poem in Tamil concerning the heroic deeds and apotheosis of the chaste wife Kaṇṇaki	
7th century *Amaruśataka*	
600–700 The poet-leaders of the South Indian devotional *(bhakti)* movements dedicated to the god Śiva compose Tamil hymns praising the god	**ca. 600–800** Pallava rulers of Kanchipuram in South India patronize populist religious movements and poetry in the Tamil language
	629–645 Chinese Buddhist pilgrim Hsuan-tsang visits India

TEXTS	CONTEXTS
	ca. 711–715 Arabs conquer the province of Sind in western India, bringing Islam to the region
ca. 800 Hindu philosopher Śaṅkara writes commentaries on the *Upaniṣads* and the ***Bhagavad-Gītā***	
900–1000 Māṇikkavācakar, preeminent devotional poet of South India, writes the *Tiruvācakam* ("sacred utterance"), a sequence of hymns to the Hindu god Śiva, in Tamil • The *Bhāgavata Purāṇa*, the Sanskrit sacred narrative *(purāṇa)* of the life and deeds of the god Krishna, is completed	
11th century Somadeva writes the Sanskrit compendium of stories called *Kathāsaritsāgara* (Ocean to the rivers of story) for Queen Sūryamatī of Kashmir	**1000** The Cōḷa king Rajaraja I builds a great temple for the Hindu god Siva at Tanjore in south India
12th century Kampaṉ authors the *Irāmāvatāram*, a version of the ***Rāmāyaṇa*** epic in Tamil • The Buddhist monk Vidyākara of Bengal (in eastern India) compiles the *Subhāṣitaratnakoṣa* (Treasury of well-turned verse), an anthology of Sanskrit lyric poems • Cēkkilār completes the *Periyapurāṇam* (The great sacred history), a long poem on the lives of the Tamil saints who are devotees of Śiva • Jayadeva composes the Sanskrit lyric-dramatic poem *Gītagovinda* in Bengal, on Krishna's love for the herdswoman Rādhā, the central theme of later poetry about Krishna	**ca. 1100–1200** Buddhist monuments are built at Angkor Wat in Cambodia **ca. 1193** Turkish warrior Qutb-ud-din Aibak captures the city of Delhi, initiating a period of several centuries of rule in north India by Delhi-based Muslim kings

KĀLIDĀSA
fourth century

Kālidāsa, the author of the Sanskrit play *Abhijñānaśākuntala* (Śakuntalā and the ring of recollection, commonly referred to as *Śakuntala*), is India's preeminent classical poet. As with other great writers of the classical era, his life is clothed in popular legend, but royal inscriptions and other sources indicate that he flourished during the Gupta period, between ca. 335 and 470, possibly in Ujjayinī (Ujjain), the Gupta capital in north India, where he may have served at the court of the greatest of the Gupta kings, Candragupta II (375–415), called Vikramāditya (Like the Sun in Valor).

Śakuntala is the most beloved of Indian plays. Sir William Jones's English translation (1789) created a sensation in Europe, especially in Germany, where it had a powerful impact on Goethe and the writers of the German Romantic movement. Rooted in the values of India's classical civilization, and at the same time articulating a profoundly human vision, this play about lovers parted and reunited transcends cultural particularities.

The plot, adapted from an older epic tale, is simplicity itself. On seeing the lovely maiden Śakuntalā in the enchanting setting of the woodland hermitage presided over by the sage Kaṇva, Duṣyanta (model king and romantic hero) inevitably falls in love with her. The young woman, daughter of a celestial nymph and a child of nature, returns his passion. Circumstances cause the lovers to part. A sage's curse and the loss of the king's signet ring result in the king's forgetting his liaison with Śakuntalā, and plunge her into further suffering, far away from her lover. The recovery of the ring jogs the king's memory, and now it is his turn to suffer, not knowing where to find his beloved. With the intervention of gods and sages, the lovers are reunited, together with their young son.

In Sanskrit dramaturgy, *Śakuntala* is a heroic romance (*nāṭaka*), a play about love between a noble hero and a beautiful woman. The *nāṭaka* is the most important of the ten types of plays (*rūpaka*, "representation") described in the classical texts on dramaturgy. While in some respects the play resembles the romantic comedies of the Western tradition, such as Euripides' *Alcestis* or Shakespeare's *Winter's Tale*, its cultural premises and aesthetic goals are entirely different from those of Greek or Shakespearean drama, following instead the canons of Bharata's *Nāṭyaśāstra* (ca. second century), the authoritative text on aesthetics and dramatic theory.

Some Sanskrit critics consider drama (*nāṭya*) to be the best of the *kāvya* genres, because it is most inclusive, or complete. Although rhythmic speech is the only expressive medium available to lyric poetry, with the occasional addition of music, drama has at its command both prose and lyric verse as well as an entire range of nonverbal expression. Hence it is also called, from the perspective of the audience, "poetry to be seen" (*dṛśyakāvya*), as opposed to other kinds of *kāvya* texts, which are "poetry to be heard" (*śravyakāvya*). From stage directions in the texts themselves and from ancient accounts and treatises on dramatic theory, we know that extensive use was made of stylized gesture, facial expression, eye movement, music, and dance in enacting the poetic text. Meaning was to be conveyed to the audience through *abhinaya*, acting conceived as a symphony of "languages," the verbal text being only one of them. The *Nāṭyaśāstra* treats dance, music, and poetry as aspects of dramatic action in the unified aesthetic of *rasa*, preserved in the major traditions of classical dance in India today.

In classical aesthetic theory, *rasa* signifies "sentiment" or "mood," the aesthetic experience evoked by the artistic depiction of human emotion. Sanskrit poetic theory distinguishes eight fundamental emotions (*bhāva*), expressed in eight major *rasas*, ranging from the erotic to the horrific. (Later tradition added "the calm" as a ninth.) According to Bharata, both text and performance are aimed at such emotional states, stimulating in readers and viewers their aesthetic flavor. This is not *actual* emotion but rather its universalized counterpart, to be conveyed through the stylized interplay of text, character, and the nuances of affect and response produced by the actors. Where real emotion limits by its particularity, *rasa* liberates the individual from the limitations of the everyday world, propelling him or her toward a higher apprehension of beauty, an experience of extraordinary universality.

Like all Sanskrit plays, *Śakuntala* ends in happiness and harmony because it must do so. The absence of tragedy sharply differentiates Sanskrit drama from Greek drama, its ancient counterpart in the Western tradition. Tragedy is impossible in the Hindu and Buddhist conceptual universes, in which time and life function as open-ended cycles and human beings are linked with nature and the cosmos through *karma*—impersonal networks of volition, action, and response. The characters of the Sanskrit drama, especially the hero and heroine, are types, not individuals. The universalization of emotion in aesthetic terms depends on the predictability of character and behavior; kings, sages, and beautiful women are defined by their social roles and dramatic personae and must look, speak, and behave in entirely recognizable ways. The individual will and personal destiny, which are essential to the notion of tragedy, have no place in this vision.

Performed at seasonal festivals and auspicious occasions such as weddings, the ancient dramas were regarded as rites of renewal and order. The goal of Sanskrit drama is to reestablish emotional harmony in the spectators by showing underlying correspondences that reconcile the apparent conflicts of existence. In *Śakuntala*, the realization of the play's dominant mood, the erotic *rasa*, turns on the tension between duty (*dharma*) and desire (*kāma*), traced through the relationship between the king and Śakuntalā. At first each acts impulsively, moved purely by passion. In the end, each is refined by duty and chastened by suffering. The king needs Śakuntalā, as she needs him, for both the reclusive life of the hermitage and the outwardly vital life of the court are, in reality, incomplete and sterile. The ideal life is the life of the golden mean, of mutually tempered duty and desire, of vitality shaped by self-control, of nature celebrated as culture's foundation and its complement. At the end of *Śakuntala*, through the intense, transporting savoring of *rasa*, we are to reach a state of integrity with ourselves and our world.

The curse and the loss and recovery of the ring, the "chance" events that guide the course of the plot, are Kālidāsa's invention, necessitated precisely by an ideal of plot that is not "action" in the Aristotelian sense but a chart of emotional interactions. We trace not the progression of external events but the finely calibrated play of suggested emotional states, through individual moments and "scenes" such as the one in which we observe the king watching Śakuntalā from his hidden vantage point, while the frightened young woman wards off an annoying bee. We must also remember that the full effect of the text is to be realized in performance, with the actors suggesting the transitory emotions of eagerness, fear, and nascent attraction, through dance, mime, gesture, the language of the eyes, and in the king's case, lyric verse. The verses and songs in *Śakuntala* embody moments of concentrated emotion in the progression of the plot.

The effectiveness of a Sanskrit play depends to a great extent on canonically required contrasts and complementarities among its diverse elements. The contrasts in Kālidāsa's play—between lyric verse and prose dialogue; the erotic and

the heroic moods; the gluttonous buffoon and the disciplined king; the Sanskrit spoken by noblemen and the Prakrit dialects assigned to women, children, and male characters of the lower castes (including the buffoon who, although he is a high-caste brahman, normally speaks Prakrit)—are staples of Sanskrit dramatic theory. The play's plot, too, is analyzable according to the precisely delineated stages and junctures of the ideal dramatic plot according to Bharata. The contrasts in Śakuntala, however, transcend these traditional requirements. Court and hermitage, the active and the contemplative life, are pitted against each other, as are the domestic and public worlds and the emotional universes of women and men. The women's rites in Act IV contrast with the king's court of Act V; Duṣyanta moves freely between earthly and celestial hermitages, Indra's court in heaven, and his own on earth, paralleling the audience's movement, through the prologue, from the real world into the world of the theater.

Among the many excellences impossible to convey in translation are the limpid clarity and sweetness of Kālidāsa's language and the powerful imagery and formal perfection of his lyric verse. His genius shines equally in his deep feeling for nature and the delicate and personal sensibility he brings to the stereotyped characters and situations of his play. The comparison between women and nature is a commonplace of Sanskrit poetry, rooted in the notion of the relatedness of all life, but Śakuntalā's personal kinship with nature makes her unforgettable. Born of a nymph and a sage but reared by the *śakunta* birds of the forest, Kālidāsa's heroine expresses a touching love of the plants, birds, and deer of her adoptive father's hermitage. Act IV, in which the animals and plants bid farewell to the heroine as one of their own, is in the original a passage of haunting, lyrical beauty and affective power.

In contrast to the heroine, and similar to the other kings of Kālidāsa's poems and plays, Duṣyanta is an establishment figure, in whose persona the poet gathers up the conservative values of *dharma* and the royal ethic of action and protection. It is clear from the focus of the psychological plot, however, that the king's heroic persona is equally grounded in his vulnerability to the awakening of love and its permeation into the depths of his being. In Indian thought, with its framework of *karma* and rebirth, all learning is recognition or recollection, a recovery or retrieval, through memory, of lost knowledge and lost sensibilities. Memory can carry us back not only into the past in this life but to the pasts of all our previous lives. In this sense then, love is a union with our deepest selves. In the symbolic acts of recollection in the play, and in the very symbol after which the play is named, "the ring of recollection or recognition," Kālidāsa has given profound artistic expression to the Indian belief that memory and love have the power of making human lives whole.

Barbara Stoler Miller, ed., *Theater of Memory: The Plays of Kālidāsa* (1984), contains the best translations of Kālidāsa's three plays, along with an excellent introduction to Sanskrit drama and dramaturgy. A selection of the major Sanskrit plays is available in (adapted) translation in P. Lal, *Great Sanskrit Plays* (1964). In *Two Plays of Ancient India* (1968) J. A. B. van Buitenen has translated Śūdraka's *Mṛcchakaṭikā* (The little clay cart) and Viśākhadatta's *Mudrārākṣasa* (Rākṣasa's signet ring), major plays of the Gupta period, both very different from *Śākuntala*. For a comparative perspective, see Henry W. Wells, *The Classical Drama of India* (1963). Readers interested in Kālidāsa's lyric poems should consult the beautiful translations of the court epic *Kumārasambhava* in Hank Heifetz, *The Origin of the Young God* (1985), and of the minor lyric poem *Meghadūta* in Leonard Nathan, *The Transport of Love* (1976).

PRONOUNCING GLOSSARY

The following list uses common English syllables and stress accents to provide rough equivalents of selected words whose pronunciation may be unfamiliar to the general reader.

Abhijñānaśākuntala: *uhb-hee-gnyah'-nuh-shah'-koon-tuh-luh*

Anasūyā: *uh-nuh-soo'-yah*

Aparājitā: *uh-puh-rah'-jee-tah*

aśoka: *uh-shoh'-kuh*

Ayodhyā: *uh-yodh'-yah*

Bhāratavarṣa: *bah'-ruh-tuh-vuhr-shuh*

cakravāka: *chuhk-ruh-vah'-kuh*

cakravartin: *chuhk'-ruh-vuhr-teen*

Candragupta: *chuhn'-druh-goop-tuh*

Caturikā: *chuh-too'-ree-kah*

Dakṣa: *duhk'-shuh*

Dhanamitra: *duh'-nuh-meet-ruh*

dṛśyakāvya: *dreesh'-yuh-kahv'-yuh*

Durvāsas: *door-vah'-suhs*

Duṣyanta: *doosh-yuhn'-tuh*

Haṃsapadikā: *huhm'-sah-puh-dee-kah*

Hastināpura: *huhs'-tee-nah-poo-ruh*

Jayanta: *juh-yuhn'-tuh*

Kālanemi: *kah'-luh-nay-mee*

Karabhaka: *kuh-ruh'-buh-kuh*

kṣatriya: *kshuh'-tree-yuh*

Mādhavya: *mahd'-huhv-yuh*

Madhukarikā: *muhd'-hoo-kuh-ree-kah*

Mārīca: *mah-ree'-chuh*

Marīci: *muh-ree'-chee*

Mitrāvasu: *meet-rah'-vuh-soo*

mokṣa: *mohk'-shuh*

Nāṭyaśāstra: *naht-yuh-shahs'-truh*

Parabhṛtikā: *puh'-ruh-bree-tee-kah*

Parivaha: *puh-ree'-vuh-huh*

Paulomī: *pow'-loh-mee*

Priyaṃvadā: *pree-yuhm'-vuh-dah*

Puru: *poo'-roo*

Raivataka: *rai'-vuh-tuh-kuh*

śakunta: *shuh-koon'-tuh*

Śākuntala: *shah-koon'-tuh-luh*

Śakuntalā: *shuh-koon'-tuh-lah*

śamī: *shuh'-mee*

Sānumatī: *sah'-noo-muh-tee*

Śāradvata: *shah'-ruhd-vuh-tuh*

Śarṅgarava: *shahrn'-guh-ruh-vuh*

Sarvadamana: *suhr'-vuh-duh-muh-nuh*

śirīṣa: *shee-ree'-shuh*

Somarāta: *soh-muh-rah'-tuh*

Somatīrtha: *soh-muh-teert'-huh*

śravyakāvya: *shruhv'-yuh-kahv'-yuh*

sṛṅgāra: *shreen-gah'-ruh*

Sūcaka: *soo'-chuh-kuh*

svabhāvokti: *svuh-bah'-vok-tee*

svarga: *svuhr'-guh*

svayaṃvara: *svuh-yuhm'-vuh-ruh*

Taralikā: *tuh-ruh'-lee-kah*

Triśaṅku: *tree-shuhn'-koo*

Triṣṭubh: *treesh'-toob*

Vasumatī: *vuh-soo'-muh-tee*

Vātāyana: *vah-tah'-yuh-nuh*

Vetravatī: *vay'-truh-vuh-tee*

viduṣaka: *vee-doo'-shuh-kuh*

Viṣṇu: *vish'-noo*

Viśvāmitra: *veesh-vah'-meet-ruh*

yakṣī: *yuhk'-shee*

Śakuntalā and the Ring of Recollection[1]

CHARACTERS

Players in the prologue:
DIRECTOR: Director of the players and manager of the theater.
ACTRESS: The lead actress.

Principal roles:
KING: Duṣyanta, the hero; ruler of Hastināpura; a royal sage of the lunar
    dynasty of Puru.
ŚAKUNTALĀ: The heroine; daughter of the royal sage Viśvāmitra and the
    celestial nymph Menakā; adoptive daughter of the ascetic Kaṇva.
BUFFOON: Māḍhavya, the king's comical brahman companion.

Members of Kaṇva's hermitage:
ANASŪYĀ and PRIYAṀVADĀ: Two young female ascetics; friends of Śakun-
    talā.
KAṆVA: Foster father of Śakuntalā and master of the hermitage; a sage
    belonging to the lineage of the divine creator Marīci, and thus related
    to Mārīca.
GAUTAMĪ: The senior female ascetic.
ŚĀRṄGARAVA and ŚĀRADVATA: Kaṇva's disciples.
Various inhabitants of the hermitage: a monk with his two pupils, two boy
    ascetics (named Gautama and Nārada), a young disciple of Kaṇva, a
    trio of female ascetics.

Members of the king's forest retinue:
CHARIOTEER: Driver of the king's chariot.
GUARD: Raivataka, guardian of the entrance to the king's quarters.
GENERAL: Commander of the king's army.
KARABHAKA: Royal messenger.
Various attendants, including Greco-Bactrian bow-bearers.

Members of the king's palace retinue:
CHAMBERLAIN: Vātāyana, chief officer of the king's household.
PRIEST: Somarāta, the king's religious preceptor and household priest.
DOORKEEPER: Vetravatī, the female attendant who ushers in visitors and
    presents messages.
PARABHṚTIKĀ and MADHUKARIKĀ: Two maids assigned to the king's garden.
CATURIKĀ: A maidservant.

City dwellers:
MAGISTRATE: The king's low-caste brother-in-law; chief of the city's
    policemen.

---

1. Translated by Barbara Stoler Miller.

POLICEMEN: Sūcaka and Jānuka.
FISHERMAN: An outcaste.

Celestials:
MĀRĪCA: A divine sage; master of the celestial hermitage in which Śakun-
   talā gives birth to her son; father of Indra, king of the gods, whose
   armies Duṣyanta leads.
ADITI: Wife of Mārīca.
MĀTALI: Indra's charioteer.
SĀNUMATĪ: A nymph; friend of Śakuntalā's mother Menakā.
Various members of Mārīca's hermitage: two female ascetics, Mārīca's
disciple Gālava.
BOY: Sarvadamana, son of Śakuntalā and Duṣyanta; later known as
   Bharata.

Offstage voices:
VOICES OFFSTAGE: From the backstage area or dressing room; behind the
   curtain, out of view of the audience. The voice belongs to various
   players before they enter the stage, such as the monk, Śakuntalā's
   friends, the buffoon, Mātali; also to figures who never enter the stage,
   such as the angry sage Durvāsas, the two bards who chant royal pan-
   egyrics (*vaitālikau*).
VOICE IN THE AIR: A voice chanting in the air from somewhere offstage:
   the bodiless voice of Speech quoted in Sanskrit by Priyaṁvadā; the
   voice of a cuckoo who represents the trees of the forest blessing
   Śakuntalā in Sanskrit; the voice of Haṁsapadikā singing a Prakrit
   love song.

The setting of the play shifts from the forest hermitage (Acts I–IV) to
the palace (Acts V–VI) to the celestial hermitage (Act VII). The season is early summer when the play begins and spring during the sixth
act; the passage of time is otherwise indicated by the birth and boyhood of Śakuntalā's son.

Act I

The water that was first created,
the sacrifice-bearing fire, the priest,
the time-setting sun and moon,
audible space that fills the universe,
what men call nature,[2] the source of all seeds,   5
the air that living creatures breathe—
through his eight embodied forms,
may Lord Śiva come to bless you![3]

2. Here, earth.   3. This verse is a *nāndī* ("benedictory verse") recited at the beginning of a Sanskrit
play, immediately after the preparatory rituals performed before a dramatic performance in ancient
India. The benedictory verses of Sanskrit plays usually invoke the blessings of Śiva, dancer of the cosmic
dance of creation and destruction as well as patron god of the drama. In this verse, Kālidāsa praises Śiva
as the cosmic divinity pervading the universe in his eight manifest forms—the five elements (ether, air,
fire, water, and earth), the sun and moon, and the sacrificing priest.

Prologue

DIRECTOR: [*Looking backstage.*] If you are in costume now, madam,
 please come on stage!   10
ACTRESS: I'm here, sir.[4]
DIRECTOR: Our audience is learned. We shall play Kālidāsa's new
 drama called *Śakuntalā and the Ring of Recollection*. Let the play-
 ers take their parts to heart!
ACTRESS: With you directing, sir, nothing will be lost.   15
DIRECTOR: Madam, the truth is:

> I find no performance perfect
> until the critics are pleased;
> the better trained we are
> the more we doubt ourselves.   20

ACTRESS: So true . . . now tell me what to do first!
DIRECTOR: What captures an audience better than a song?
 Sing about the new summer season and its pleasures:

> To plunge in fresh waters
> swept by scented forest winds   25
> and dream in soft shadows
> of the day's ripened charms.

ACTRESS: [*Singing.*]

> Sensuous women
> in summer love
> weave   30
> flower earrings
> from fragile petals
> of mimosa
> while wild bees
> kiss them gently.[5]   35

DIRECTOR: Well sung, madam! Your melody enchants the audience.
 The silent theater is like a painting. What drama should we play to
 please it?
ACTRESS: But didn't you just direct us to perform a new play called
 Śakuntalā and the Ring of Recollection?   40
DIRECTOR: Madam, I'm conscious again! For a moment I forgot.

> The mood of your song's melody
> carried me off by force,
> just as the swift dark antelope
> enchanted King Duṣyanta.   45

[*They both exit; the prologue ends. Then the* KING *enters with his*
CHARIOTEER, *in a chariot, a bow and arrow in his hand, hunting an
antelope.*]

---

4. The prologues to many plays present the actress as the director's wife.   5. Such verses are sung by
women in Prakrit and set to a melody, whereas the Sanskrit *kāvya* verses of the play are recited or sung
to a simple tune that follows the rhythmic pattern of the verse quarter. The women's songs generally
feature nature descriptions or the nuances of love in natural settings.

CHARIOTEER: [*Watching the* KING *and the antelope.*]

> I see this black buck move
> as you draw your bow
> and I see the wild bowman Śiva,
> hunting the dark antelope.[6]

KING: Driver, this antelope has drawn us far into the forest. There he   50
is again:

> The graceful turn of his neck
> as he glances back at our speeding car,
> the haunches folded into his chest
> in fear of my speeding arrow,   55
> the open mouth dropping
> half-chewed grass on our path—
> watch how he leaps, bounding on air,
> barely touching the earth.

[*He shows surprise.*]
Why is it so hard to keep him in sight?   60
CHARIOTEER: Sir, the ground was rough. I tightened the reins to slow
the chariot and the buck raced ahead. Now that the path is smooth,
he won't be hard to catch.
KING: Slacken the reins!
CHARIOTEER: As you command, sir. [*He mimes the speeding chariot.*]   65
Look!

> Their legs extend as I slacken the reins,
> plumes and manes set in the wind, ears angle back;
> our horses outrun their own clouds of dust,
> straining to match the antelope's speed.   70

KING: These horses would outrace the steeds of the sun.[7]

> What is small suddenly looms large,
> split forms seem to reunite,
> bent shapes straighten before my eyes—
> from the chariot's speed   75
> nothing ever stays distant or near.

CHARIOTEER: The antelope is an easy target now. [*He mimes the fix-
ing of an arrow.*]
VOICE OFFSTAGE: Stop! Stop, king! This antelope belongs to our her-
mitage! Don't kill him!
CHARIOTEER: [*Listening and watching.*] Sir, two ascetics are pro-   80
tecting the black buck from your arrow's deadly aim.
KING: [*Showing confusion.*] Rein in the horses!
CHARIOTEER: It is done!

[*He mimes the chariot's halt. Then a* MONK *enters with* TWO PUPILS,
his hand raised.]

---

6. The comparison is based on an ancient myth of Śiva's pursuit of the creator god Prajāpati, who had
taken the form of an antelope. The verse flatters the king.   7. The seven horses that draw the sun
god's chariot.

MONK: King, this antelope belongs to our hermitage.
Withdraw your well-aimed arrow! Your weapon should rescue vic-   85
tims, not destroy the innocent!
KING: I withdraw it. [*He does as he says.*]
MONK: An act worthy of the Puru dynasty's shining light!

> Your birth honors
> the dynasty of the moon![8]   90
> May you beget a son
> to turn the wheel of your empire![9]

THE TWO PUPILS: [*Raising their arms.*] May you beget a son to turn
the wheel of your empire!
KING: [*Bowing.*] I welcome your blessing.   95
MONK: King, we were going to gather firewood.[1] From here you can
see the hermitage[2] of our master Kaṇva on the bank of the Mālinī
river. If your work permits, enter and accept our hospitality.

> When you see the peaceful rites of devoted ascetics,
> you will know how well your scarred arm protects us.[3]   100

KING: Is the master of the community there now?
MONK: He went to Somatīrtha,[4] the holy shrine of the moon, and put
his daughter Śakuntalā in charge of receiving guests. Some evil
threatens her, it seems.
KING: Then I shall see her. She will know my devotion and commend   105
me to the great sage.
MONK: We shall leave you now.
[*He exits with his pupils.*]
KING: Driver, urge the horses on! The sight of this holy hermitage will
purify us.
CHARIOTEER: As you command, sir. [*He mimes the chariot's speed.*]   110
KING: [*Looking around.*] Without being told one can see that this is a
grove where ascetics live.
CHARIOTEER: How?
KING: Don't you see—

> Wild rice grains under trees   115
> where parrots nest in hollow trunks,
> stones stained by the dark oil
> of crushed iṅgudī nuts,[5]
> trusting deer who hear human voices
> yet don't break their gait,   120
> and paths from ponds streaked
> by water from wet bark cloth.[6]

CHARIOTEER: It is perfect.

---

8. Known as the "lunar dynasty," because it traces its descent to the moon god.   9. Any ancient
Indian emperor is a *cakravartin*, a turner of the wheel of empire.   1. For the fire rituals and Vedic
sacrifices performed at the hermitage.   2. It includes men and women and is organized like an
extended family.   3. One of a king's chief duties is to protect hermits and ascetics.   4. A place of
pilgrimage in western India.   5. These nuts are pressed by forest dwellers for oil.   6. Forest dwellers
wear a cloth made of tree bark.

KING: [*Having gone a little inside.*] We should not disturb the grove! Stop the chariot and let me get down!   125

CHARIOTEER: I'm holding the reins. You can dismount now, sir.

KING: [*Dismounting.*] One should not enter an ascetics' grove in hunting gear. Take these! [*He gives up his ornaments and his bow.*] Driver, rub down the horses while I pay my respects to the residents of the hermitage!   130

CHARIOTEER: Yes, sir! [*He exits.*]

KING: This gateway marks the sacred ground. I will enter.
   [*He enters, indicating he feels an omen.*]

> The hermitage is a tranquil place,
> yet my arm is quivering . . .
> do I feel a false omen of love   135
> or does fate have doors everywhere?

VOICE OFFSTAGE: This way, friends!

KING: [*Straining to listen.*] I think I hear voices to the right of the grove. I'll find out.
   [*Walking around and looking.*]
Young female ascetics with watering pots cradled on their hips are   140
coming to water the saplings. [*He mimes it in precise detail.*] This view of them is sweet.

> These forest women have beauty
> rarely seen inside royal palaces—
> the wild forest vines far surpass   145
> creepers in my pleasure garden.

I'll hide in the shadows and wait.
   [ŚAKUNTALĀ *and her two friends enter, acting as described.*]

ŚAKUNTALÁ: This way, friends!

ANASŪYĀ: I think Father Kaṇva cares more about the trees in the hermitage than he cares about you. You're as delicate as a jasmine, yet   150
he orders you to water the trees.

ŚAKUNTALĀ: Anasūyā, it's more than Father Kaṇva's order. I feel a sister's love for them. [*She mimes the watering of trees.*]

KING: [*To himself.*] Is this Kaṇva's daughter? The sage does show poor judgment in imposing the rules of the hermitage on her.   155

> The sage who hopes to subdue
> her sensuous body by penances
> is trying to cut firewood
> with a blade of blue-lotus leaf.

Let it be! I can watch her closely from here in the trees.   160
   [*He does so.*]

ŚAKUNTALĀ: Anasūyā, I can't breathe! Our friend Priyaṁvadā tied my bark dress too tightly! Loosen it a bit!

ANASŪYĀ: As you say. [*She loosens it.*]

PRIYAṀVADĀ: [*Laughing.*] Blame your youth for swelling your breasts. Why blame me?   165

KING: This bark dress fits her body badly, but it ornaments her
   beauty . . .

> A tangle of duckweed adorns a lotus,
> a dark spot heightens the moon's glow,
> the bark dress increases her charm—   170
> beauty finds its ornaments anywhere.

ŚAKUNTALĀ: [*Looking in front of her.*] The new branches on this
   mimosa tree are like fingers moving in the wind, calling to me. I
   must go to it! [*Saying this, she walks around.*]
PRIYAMVADĀ: Wait, Śakuntalā! Stay there a minute! When you stand   175
   by this mimosa tree, it seems to be guarding a creeper.
ŚAKUNTALĀ: That's why your name means "Sweet-talk."[7]
KING: "Sweet-talk" yes, but Priyamvadā speaks the truth about Śakuntalā:

> Her lips are fresh red buds,   180
> her arms are tendrils,
> impatient youth is poised
> to blossom in her limbs.

ANASŪYĀ: Śakuntalā, this is the jasmine creeper who chose the mango
   tree in marriage,[8] the one you named "Forestlight." Have you for-   185
   gotten her?
ŚAKUNTALĀ: I would be forgetting myself? [*She approaches the creeper
   and examines it.*] The creeper and the tree are twined together in
   perfect harmony. Forestlight has just flowered and the new mango
   shoots are made for her pleasure.   190
PRIYAMVADĀ: [*Smiling.*] Anasūyā, don't you know why Śakuntalā looks
   so lovingly at Forestlight?
ANASŪYĀ: I can't guess.
PRIYAMVADĀ: The marriage of Forestlight to her tree makes her long
   to have a husband too.   195
ŚAKUNTALĀ: You're just speaking your own secret wish. [*Saying this,
   she pours water from the jar.*]
KING: Could her social class be different from her father's?[9] There's
   no doubt!

> She was born to be a warrior's bride,
> for my noble heart desires her—   200
> when good men face doubt,
> inner feelings are truth's only measure.

Still, I must learn everything about her.
ŚAKUNTALĀ: [*Flustered.*] The splashing water has alarmed a bee. He is

---

7. The characters of the two friends correspond to their names: Anasūyā (Without Envy) is a serious,
straightforward, decisive young woman, while Priyamvadā (Sweet Talker) loves to tease and laugh and
has a way with words. As noted above, the women speak Prakrit, whereas the king and other upper-class
male characters speak Sanskrit.   8. In calling the jasmine creeper *svayaṃvara-vadhū* ("bride by her
own choice"), Anasūyā refers to the public ceremony called *svayaṃvara* ("choosing one's own bridegroom") in which women of the warrior class chose their own husbands, thus foreshadowing Śakuntalā's
own action later in the play.   9. Marrying outside one's class in the fourfold Hindu scheme of classes
(*varṇa*) is forbidden. As the sage Kaṇva's daughter, Śakuntalā would be a brahman, and the king, being
of the *kṣatriya* (warrior) class, would not be allowed to marry her.

flying from the jasmine to my face. [*She dances to show the bee's* 205
attack.]

KING: [*Looking longingly.*]

> Bee, you touch the quivering
> corners of her frightened eyes,
> you hover softly near
> to whisper secrets in her ear;
> a hand brushes you away,   210
> but you drink her lips' treasure—
> while the truth we seek defeats us,
> you are truly blessed.

ŚAKUNTALĀ: This dreadful bee won't stop. I must escape. [*She steps to
one side, glancing about.*] Oh! He's pursuing me.... Save me! 215
Please save me! This mad bee is chasing me!

BOTH FRIENDS: [*Laughing.*] How can we save you? Call King Duṣyanta. The grove is under his protection.

KING: Here's my chance. Have no fear ... [*With this half-spoken, he
stops and speaks to himself.*] Then she will know that I am the king. 220
... Still, I shall speak.

ŚAKUNTALĀ: [*Stopping after a few steps.*] Why is he still following me?

KING: [*Approaching quickly.*]

> While a Puru king rules the earth
> to punish evildoers,
> who dares to molest   225
> these innocent young ascetics?

[*Seeing the* KING, *all act flustered.*]

ANASŪYĀ: Sir, there's no real danger. Our friend was frightened when
a bee attacked her. [*She points to* ŚAKUNTALĀ.]

KING: [*Approaching* ŚAKUNTALĀ.] Does your ascetic practice go well?
[ŚAKUNTALĀ *stands speechless.*]

ANASŪYĀ: It does now that we have a special guest. Śakuntalā, go to 230
our hut and bring the ripe fruits. We'll use this water to bathe his
feet.[1]

KING: Your kind speech is hospitality enough.

PRIYAMVADĀ: Please sit in the cool shadows of this shade tree and rest,
sir.   235

KING: You must also be tired from your work.

ANASŪYĀ: Śakuntalā, we should respect our guest. Let's sit down. [*All
sit.*]

ŚAKUNTALĀ: [*To herself.*] When I see him, why do I feel an emotion
that the forest seems to forbid?

KING: [*Looking at each of the girls.*] Youth and beauty complement 240
your friendship.

PRIYAMVADĀ: [*In a stage whisper.*] Anasūyā, who is he? He's so polite,
fine looking, and pleasing to hear. He has the marks of royalty.

---

1. A traditionally mandated rite of hospitality.

ANASŪYĀ: I'm curious too, friend. I'll just ask him. [*Aloud.*] Sir, your kind speech inspires trust. What family of royal sages do you adorn? What country mourns your absence? Why does a man of refinement subject himself to the discomfort of visiting an ascetics' grove?[2]

ŚAKUNTALĀ: [*To herself.*] Heart, don't faint! Anasūyā speaks your thoughts.

KING: [*To himself.*] Should I reveal myself now or conceal who I am? I'll say it this way: [*Aloud.*] Lady, I have been appointed by the Puru king as the officer in charge of religious matters. I have come to this sacred forest to assure that your holy rites proceed unhindered.

ANASŪYĀ: Our religious life has a guardian now.

[ŚAKUNTALĀ *mimes the embarrassment of erotic emotion.*]

BOTH FRIENDS: [*Observing the behavior of* ŚAKUNTALĀ *and the* KING; *in a stage whisper.*] Śakuntalā, if only your father were here now!

ŚAKUNTALĀ: [*Angrily.*] What if he were?

BOTH FRIENDS: He would honor this distinguished guest with what he values most in life.

ŚAKUNTALĀ: Quiet! Such words hint at your hearts' conspiracy. I won't listen.

KING: Ladies, I want to ask about your friend.

BOTH FRIENDS: Your request honors us, sir.

KING: Sage Kaṇva has always been celibate, but you call your friend his daughter. How can this be?

ANASŪYĀ: Please listen, sir. There was a powerful royal sage[3] of the Kauśika clan . . .

KING: I am listening.

ANASŪYĀ: He begot our friend, but Kaṇva is her father because he cared for her when she was abandoned.

KING: "Abandoned"? The word makes me curious. I want to hear her story from the beginning.

ANASŪYĀ: Please listen, sir. Once when this great sage was practicing terrible austerities on the bank of the Gautamī river, he became so powerful that the jealous gods sent a nymph named Menakā to break his self-control.[4]

KING: The gods dread men who meditate.

ANASŪYĀ: When springtime came to the forest with all its charm, the sage saw her intoxicating beauty . . .

KING: I understand what happened then. She is the nymph's daughter.

ANASŪYĀ: Yes.

KING: It had to be!

> No mortal woman could give birth to such beauty—
> lightning does not flash out of the earth.

---

2. Anasūyā uses the formal, florid style of courtly conversation.   3. Viśvāmitra, who was born in the warrior class but acquired the spiritual powers of a brahman sage.   4. A standard theme in classical Indian mythology, appearing in the narratives of the life of the Buddha as well. The gods feel threatened by the supernatural powers that ascetics amass through self-denial.

[ŚAKUNTALĀ *stands with her face bowed. The* KING *continues speaking to himself.*]

My desire is not hopeless. Yet, when I hear her friends teasing her   285
about a bridegroom, a new fear divides my heart.

PRIYAṂVADĀ: [*Smiling, looking at* ŚAKUNTALĀ, *then turning to the* KING.] Sir, you seem to want to say more.

[ŚAKUNTALĀ *makes a threatening gesture with her finger.*]

KING: You judge correctly. In my eagerness to learn more about your
pious lives, I have another question.

PRIYAṂVADĀ: Don't hesitate! Ascetics can be questioned frankly.   290

KING: I want to know this about your friend:

> Will she keep the vow of hermit life
> only until she marries . . .
> or will she always exchange
> loving looks with deer in the forest?   295

PRIYAṂVADĀ: Sir, even in her religious life, she is subject to her father,
but he does intend to give her to a suitable husband.

KING: [*To himself.*] His wish is not hard to fulfill.

> Heart, indulge your desire—
> now that doubt is dispelled,   300
> the fire you feared to touch
> is a jewel in your hands.

ŚAKUNTALĀ: [*Showing anger.*] Anasūyā, I'm leaving!

ANASŪYĀ: Why?

ŚAKUNTALĀ: I'm going to tell Mother Gautamī that Priyaṃvadā is talk-   305
ing nonsense.

ANASŪYĀ: Friend, it's wrong to neglect a distinguished guest and leave
as you like.[5]

[ŚAKUNTALĀ *starts to go without answering.*]

KING: [*Wanting to seize her, but holding back, he speaks to himself.*]
A lover dare not act on his impulsive thoughts!

> I wanted to follow the sage's daughter,   310
> but decorum abruptly pulled me back;
> I set out and returned again
> without moving my feet from this spot.

PRIYAṂVADĀ: [*Stopping* ŚAKUNTALĀ.] It's wrong of you to go!

ŚAKUNTALĀ: [*Bending her brow into a frown.*] Give me a reason why!   315

PRIYAṂVADĀ: You promised to water two trees for me. Come here and
pay your debt before you go! [*She stops her by force.*]

KING: But she seems exhausted from watering the trees:

> Her shoulders droop, her palms
> are red from the watering pot—   320
> even now, breathless sighs
> make her breasts shake;

5. Śakuntalā's failure here foreshadows her neglect of this duty and its consequences later in the play.

beads of sweat on her face
wilt the flower at her ear;
her hand holds back   325
disheveled locks of hair.

Here, I'll pay her debt!
[*He offers his ring. Both friends recite the syllables of the name on
the seal and stare at each other.*][6]
Don't mistake me for what I am not! This is a gift from the king to
identify me as his royal official.

PRIYAMVADĀ: Then the ring should never leave your finger. Your word   330
has already paid her debt. [*She laughs a little.*] Śakuntalā, you are
freed by this kind man . . . or perhaps by the king. Go now!

ŚAKUNTALĀ: [*To herself.*] If I am able to . . . [*Aloud.*] Who are you to
keep me or release me?

KING: [*Watching* ŚAKUNTALĀ.] Can she feel toward me what I feel   335
toward her? Or is my desire fulfilled?

She won't respond directly to my words,
but she listens when I speak;
she won't turn to look at me,
but her eyes can't rest anywhere else.   340

VOICE OFFSTAGE: Ascetics, be prepared to protect the creatures of our
forest grove! King Duṣyanta is hunting nearby!

Dust raised by his horses' hooves
falls like a cloud of locusts swarming
at sunset over branches of trees   345
where wet bark garments hang.

In terror of the chariots, an elephant
charged into the hermitage
and scattered the herd of black antelope,
like a demon foe of our penances—   350
his tusks garlanded with branches
from a tree crushed by his weight,
his feet tangled in vines
that tether him like chains.

[*Hearing this, all the girls are agitated.*]

KING: [*To himself.*] Oh! My palace men are searching for me and   355
wrecking the grove. I'll have to go back.

BOTH FRIENDS: Sir, we're all upset by this news. Please let us go to our
hut.

KING: [*Showing confusion.*] Go, please. We will try to protect the
hermitage.   360

[*They all stand to go.*]

BOTH FRIENDS: Sir, we're ashamed that our bad hospitality is our only
excuse to invite you back.

KING: Not at all. I am honored to have seen you.

---

6. A clear indication that women were part of the literate courtly culture of classical India.

[ŚAKUNTALĀ *exits with her two friends, looking back at the* KING, *lingering artfully.*]
I have little desire to return to the city. I'll join my men and have
them camp near the grove. I can't control my feelings for Śakun-   365
talā.

> My body turns to go,
> my heart pulls me back,
> like a silk banner
> buffeted by the wind.   370

[*All exit.*]

Act II

[*The* BUFFOON *enters, despondent.*]
BUFFOON: [*Sighing.*] My bad luck! I'm tired of playing sidekick to a
king who's hooked on hunting.[7] "There's a deer!" "There's a boar!"
"There's a tiger!" Even in the summer midday heat we chase from
jungle to jungle on paths where trees give barely any shade. We
drink stinking water from mountain streams foul with rusty leaves.   5
At odd hours we eat nasty meals of spit-roasted meat. Even at night
I can't sleep. My joints ache from galloping on that horse. Then at
the crack of dawn, I'm woken rudely by a noise piercing the forest.
Those sons of bitches hunt their birds then. The torture doesn't
end—now I have sores on top of my bruises. Yesterday, we lagged   10
behind. The king chased a buck into the hermitage. As luck would
have it, an ascetic's daughter called Śakuntalā caught his eye. Now
he isn't even thinking of going back to the city. This very dawn I
found him wide-eyed, mooning about her. What a fate! I must see
him after his bath. [*He walks around, looking.*] Here comes my   15
friend now, wearing garlands of wild flowers. Greek women carry
his bow in their hands.[8] Good! I'll stand here pretending my arms
and legs are broken. Maybe then I'll get some rest.
[*He stands leaning on his staff. The* KING *enters with his retinue, as
described.*]
KING: [*To himself.*]

> My beloved will not be easy to win,
> but signs of emotion revealed her heart—   20
> even when love seems hopeless,
> mutual longing keeps passion alive.

[*He smiles.*] A suitor who measures his beloved's state of mind by
his own desire is a fool.

---

7. The brahman *vidūṣaka* (buffoon), though the king's constant companion, differs from him in every
respect, from his obsession with creature comforts and his cowardice to his coarse language. A caricature
of the learned brahman and Sanskrit scholar, the buffoon speaks only Prakrit and is incapable of versi-
fying.   8. In Kālidāsa's plays the king's bow bearers are identified as *yavanī* ("Greek women"). North
Indian kings of the Gupta age and earlier employed Bactrian Greek women as bodyguards and bow
bearers.

> She threw tender glances   25
> though her eyes were cast down,
> her heavy hips swayed
> in slow seductive movements,
> she answered in anger
> when her friend said, "Don't go!"   30
> and I felt it was all for my sake . . .
> but a lover sees in his own way.

BUFFOON: [*Still in the same position.*] Dear friend, since my hands can't move to greet you, I have to salute you with my voice.

KING: How did you cripple your limbs?   35

BUFFOON: Why do you ask why I cry after throwing dust in my eyes yourself?

KING: I don't understand.

BUFFOON: Dear friend, when a straight reed is twisted into a crooked reed, is it by its own power, or is it the river current?[9]   40

KING: The river current is the cause.

BUFFOON: And so it is with me.

KING: How so?

BUFFOON: You neglect the business of being a king and live like a woodsman in this awful camp. Chasing after wild beasts every day   45 jolts my joints and muscles till I can't control my own limbs anymore. I beg you to let me rest for just one day!

KING: [*To himself.*] He says what I also feel. When I remember Kaṇva's daughter, the thought of hunting disgusts me.

> I can't draw my bowstring   50
> to shoot arrows at deer
> who live with my love
> and teach her tender glances.[1]

BUFFOON: Sir, you have something on your mind. I'm crying in a wilderness.[2]   55

KING: [*Smiling.*] Yes, it is wrong to ignore my friend's plea.

BUFFOON: Live long! [*He starts to go.*]

KING: Dear friend, stay! Hear what I have to say!

BUFFOON: At your command, sir!

KING: When you have rested, I need your help in some work that you   60 will enjoy.

BUFFOON: Is it eating sweets? I'm game!

KING: I shall tell you. Who stands guard?

GUARD: [*Entering.*] At your command, sir!

KING: Raivataka! Summon the general!   65

[*The* GUARD *exits and reenters with the* GENERAL.]

GUARD: The king is looking this way, waiting to give you his orders. Approach him, sir!

---

9. Like Shakespeare's fools, the buffoon likes to speak in riddles.   1. A comparison of women's eyes with the eyes of deer, conventional in Sanskrit poetry.   2. A paraphrase of the Sanskrit proverbial expression *araṇyaruditam* ("a cry in the wilderness"); this is an expression of his puzzlement at the king's behavior.

GENERAL: [*Looking at the* KING.] Hunting is said to be a vice,[3] but our
   king prospers.

> Drawing the bow only hardens his chest,   70
> he suffers the sun's scorching rays unburned,
> hard muscles mask his body's lean state—
> like a wild elephant, his energy sustains him.

[*He approaches the* KING.] Victory, my lord! We've already tracked
   some wild beasts. Why the delay?   75
KING: Mādhavya's[4] censure of hunting has dampened my spirit.
GENERAL: [*In a stage whisper, to the* BUFFOON.] Friend, you stick to
   your opposition! I'll try to restore our king's good sense. [*Aloud.*]
   This fool is talking nonsense. Here is the king as proof:

> A hunter's belly is taut and lean,   80
> his slender body craves exertion;
> he penetrates the spirit of creatures
> overcome by fear and rage;
> his bowmanship is proved
> by arrows striking a moving target—   85
> hunting is falsely called a vice.
> What sport can rival it?

BUFFOON: [*Angrily.*] The king has come to his senses. If you keep
   chasing from forest to forest, you'll fall into the jaws of an old bear
   hungry for a human nose . . .   90
KING: My noble general, we are near a hermitage; your words cannot
   please me now.

> Let horned buffaloes plunge into muddy pools!
> Let herds of deer huddle in the shade to eat grass!
> Let fearless wild boars crush fragrant swamp grass!   95
> Let my bowstring lie slack and my bow at rest!

GENERAL: Whatever gives the king pleasure.
KING: Withdraw the men who are in the forest now and forbid my
   soldiers to disturb the grove!

> Ascetics devoted to peace   100
> possess a fiery hidden power,
> like smooth crystal sunstones
> that reflect the sun's scorching rays.

GENERAL: Whatever you command, sir!
BUFFOON: Your arguments for keeping up the hunt fall on deaf ears!   105
   [*The* GENERAL *exits.*]
KING: [*Looking at his* RETINUE.] You women, take away my hunting
   gear! Raivataka, don't neglect your duty!
RETINUE: As the king commands!
   [*They exit.*]

---

3. The censure of hunting in Hindu law reflects the influence of the theory of *karma* rebirth and the
impact of nonviolent creeds.   4. The buffoon's.

BUFFOON: Sir, now that the flies are cleared out, sit on a stone bench under this shady canopy. Then I'll find a comfortable seat too. 110

KING: Go ahead!

BUFFOON: You first, sir!

[*Both walk about, then sit down.*]

KING: Mādhavya, you haven't really used your eyes because you haven't seen true beauty.

BUFFOON: But you're right in front of me, sir! 115

KING: Everyone is partial to what he knows well, but I'm speaking about Śakuntalā, the jewel of the hermitage.

BUFFOON: [*To himself.*] I won't give him a chance! [*Aloud.*] Dear friend, it seems that you're pursuing an ascetic's daughter.

KING: Friend, the heart of a Puru king wouldn't crave a forbidden 120
fruit . . .

> The sage's child is a nymph's daughter,
> rescued by him after she was abandoned,
> like a fragile jasmine blossom
> broken and caught on a sunflower pod. 125

BUFFOON: [*Laughing.*] You're like the man who loses his taste for dates and prefers sour tamarind![5] How can you abandon the gorgeous gems of your palace?

KING: You speak this way because you haven't seen her.

BUFFOON: She must be delectable if you're so enticed! 130

KING: Friend, what is the use of all this talk?

> The divine creator imagined perfection
> and shaped her ideal form in his mind—
> when I recall the beauty his power wrought,
> she shines like a gemstone among my jewels. 135

BUFFOON: So she's the reason you reject the other beauties!

KING: She stays in my mind:

> A flower no one has smelled,
> a bud no fingers have plucked,
> an uncut jewel, honey untasted, 140
> unbroken fruit of holy deeds—
> I don't know who is destined
> to enjoy her flawless beauty.

BUFFOON: Then you should rescue her quickly! Don't let her fall into the arms of some ascetic who greases his head with iṅgudī oil! 145

KING: She is someone else's ward and her guardian is away.

BUFFOON: What kind of passion did her eyes betray?

KING: Ascetics are timid by nature:

> Her eyes were cast down in my presence,
> but she found an excuse to smile— 150
> modesty barely contained the love
> she could neither reveal nor conceal.

---

5. A fruit, the extract of which is used to flavor Indian sauces.

BUFFOON: Did you expect her to climb into your lap when she'd barely seen you?

KING: When we parted her feelings for me showed despite her modesty. 155

> "A blade of kuśa grass[6]
> pricked my foot,"
> the girl said for no reason
> after walking a few steps away; 160
> then she pretended to free
> her bark dress from branches
> where it was not caught
> and shyly glanced at me.

BUFFOON: Stock up on food for a long trip! I can see you've turned 165
that ascetics' grove into a pleasure garden.

KING: Friend, some of the ascetics recognize me. What excuse can we find to return to the hermitage?

BUFFOON: What excuse? Aren't you the king? Collect a sixth of their wild rice as tax! 170

KING: Fool! These ascetics pay tribute that pleases me more than mounds of jewels.

> Tribute that kings collect
> from members of society decays,
> but the share of austerity 175
> that ascetics give lasts forever.[7]

VOICE OFFSTAGE: Good, we have succeeded!

KING: [Listening.] These are the steady, calm voices of ascetics.

GUARD: [Entering.] Victory, sir! Two boy ascetics are waiting near the gate. 180

KING: Let them enter without delay!

GUARD: I'll show them in. [He exits; reenters with the boys.] Here you are!

FIRST BOY: His majestic body inspires trust. It is natural when a king is virtually a sage.[8] 185

> His palace is a hermitage
> with its infinite pleasures,
> the discipline of protecting men
> imposes austerities every day—
> pairs of celestial bards praise 190
> his perfect self-control,
> adding the royal word "king"
> to "sage," his sacred title.

SECOND BOY: Gautama, is this Duṣyanta, the friend of Indra?[9]

FIRST BOY: Of course! 195

---

6. Used in Hindu sacred rites.   7. The king values the sacred power that the sages amass through self-denial.   8. While Duṣyanta may appear worldly to a modern audience, his sacred royal office, his respect for the sages, and his disciplined adherence to the standards of *dharma* make him, in the sages' eyes, a person of tremendous self-control.   9. His friendship with Indra underscores the king's status as the earthly counterpart of the king of the gods.

SECOND BOY:

> It is no surprise that this arm of iron
> rules the whole earth bounded by dark seas—
> when demons harass the gods, victory's hope
> rests on his bow and Indra's thunderbolt.

BOTH BOYS: [*Coming near.*] Victory to you, king!   200
KING: [*Rising from his seat.*] I salute you both!
BOTH BOYS: To your success, sir! [*They offer fruits.*]
KING: [*Accepting their offering.*] I am ready to listen.
BOTH BOYS: The ascetics know that you are camped nearby and send
  a petition to you.   205
KING: What do they request?
BOTH BOYS: Demons are taking advantage of Sage Kaṇva's absence
  to harass us.[1] You must come with your charioteer to protect the
  hermitage for a few days!
KING: I am honored to oblige.   210
BUFFOON: [*In a stage whisper.*] Your wish is fulfilled!
KING: [*Smiling.*] Raivataka, call my charioteer! Tell him to bring the
  chariot and my bow!
GUARD: As the king commands! [*He exits.*]
BOTH BOYS: [*Showing delight.*]

> Following your ancestral duties   215
> suits your noble form—
> the Puru kings are ordained
> to dispel their subjects' fear.

KING: [*Bowing.*] You two return! I shall follow.
BOTH BOYS: Be victorious! [*They exit.*]   220
KING: Mādhavya, are you curious to see Śakuntalā?
BUFFOON: At first there was a flood, but now with this news of demons,
  not a drop is left.
KING: Don't be afraid! Won't you be with me?
BUFFOON: Then I'll be safe from any demon . . .   225
GUARD: [*Entering.*] The chariot is ready to take you to victory . . . but
  Karabhaka has just come from the city with a message from the
  queen.
KING: Did my mother send him?
GUARD: She did.   230
KING: Have him enter then.
GUARD: Yes. [*He exits; reenters with* KARABHAKA.] Here is the king.
  Approach!
KARABHAKA: Victory, sir! Victory! The queen has ordered a ceremony
  four days from now to mark the end of her fast. Your Majesty will   235
  surely give us the honor of his presence.
KING: The ascetics' business keeps me here and my mother's com-
  mand calls me there. I must find a way to avoid neglecting either!

---

1. The motif of a royal hero slaying demons who destroy the sacred rituals of forest sages, as seen in
the *Rāmāyaṇa* (p. 576), is traditional.

BUFFOON: Hang yourself between them the way Triśaṅku[2] hung
between heaven and earth. 240

KING: I'm really confused . . .

> My mind is split in two
> by these conflicting duties,
> like a river current split
> by boulders in its course. 245

[*Thinking.*] Friend, my mother has treated you like a son. You must
go back and report that I've set my heart on fulfilling my duty to
the ascetics. You fulfill my filial duty to the queen.

BUFFOON: You don't really think I'm afraid of demons?

KING: [*Smiling.*] My brave brahman, how could you be? 250

BUFFOON: Then I can travel like the king's younger brother.

KING: We really should not disturb the grove! Take my whole entourage with you!

BUFFOON: Now I've turned into the crown prince!

KING: [*To himself.*] This fellow is absent-minded. At any time he may 255
tell the palace women about my passion. I'll tell him this: [*Taking
the* BUFFOON *by the hand, he speaks aloud.*] Dear friend, I'm going
to the hermitage out of reverence for the sages. I really feel no
desire for the young ascetic Śakuntalā.

> What do I share with a rustic girl 260
> reared among fawns, unskilled in love?
> Don't mistake what I muttered
> in jest for the real truth, friend!

[*All exit.*]

Act III

[*A disciple of* KAṆVA *enters, carrying kuśa grass for a sacrificial rite.*]
DISCIPLE: King Duṣyanta is certainly powerful. Since he entered the
hermitage, our rites have not been hindered.

> Why talk of fixing arrows?
> The mere twang of his bowstring
> clears away menacing demons 5
> as if his bow roared with death.

I'll gather some more grass for the priests to spread on the sacrificial
altar. [*Walking around and looking, he calls aloud.*] Priyaṁvadā,
for whom are you bringing the ointment of fragrant lotus root fibers
and leaves? [*Listening.*] What are you saying? Śakuntalā is suffering 10
from heat exhaustion? They're for rubbing on her body? Priyaṁvadā, take care of her! She is the breath of Father Kaṇva's life.
I'll give Gautamī this water from the sacrifice to use for soothing
her.

2. A mythic king who was left suspended between heaven and earth in a contest of power between the
sage Viśvāmitra and the gods.

[*He exits; the interlude ends. Then the* KING *enters, suffering from love, deep in thought, sighing.*]

KING:

> I know the power ascetics have
> and the rules that bind her,   15
> but I cannot abandon my heart
> now that she has taken it.

[*Showing the pain of love.*] Love, why do you and the moon both contrive to deceive lovers by first gaining our trust?

> Arrows of flowers and cool moon rays   20
> are both deadly for men like me —
> the moon shoots fire through icy rays
> and you hurl thunderbolts of flowers.

[*Walking around.*] Now that the rites are concluded and the priests have dismissed me, where can I rest from the weariness of this   25 work? [*Sighing.*] There is no refuge but the sight of my love. I must find her. [*Looking up at the sun.*] Śakuntalā usually spends the heat of the day with her friends in a bower of vines on the Mālinī riverbank. I shall go there. [*Walking around, miming the touch of breeze.*] This place is enchanted by the wind.   30

> A breeze fragrant with lotus pollen
> and moist from the Mālinī waves
> can be held in soothing embrace
> by my love-scorched arms.

[*Walking around and looking.*]

> I see fresh footprints   35
> on white sand in the clearing,
> deeply pressed at the heel
> by the sway of full hips.

I'll just look through the branches. [*Walking around, looking, he becomes joyous.*] My eyes have found bliss! The girl I desire is lying   40 on a stone couch strewn with flowers, attended by her two friends. I'll eavesdrop as they confide in one another. [*He stands watching.* ŚAKUNTALĀ *appears as described, with her two friends.*]

BOTH FRIENDS: [*Fanning her affectionately.*] Śakuntalā, does the breeze from this lotus leaf please you?

ŚAKUNTALĀ: Are you fanning me?   45

[*The friends trade looks, miming dismay.*]

KING: [*Deliberating.*] Śakuntalā seems to be in great physical pain. Is it the heat or is it what is in my own heart? [*Miming ardent desire.*] My doubts are unfounded!

> Her breasts are smeared with lotus balm,
> her lotus-fiber bracelet hangs limp,   50
> her beautiful body glows in pain —
> love burns young women like summer heat
> but its guilt makes them more charming.

PRIYAṂVADĀ: [*In a stage whisper.*] Anasūyā, Śakuntalā has been pining
since she first saw the king. Could he be the cause of her sickness?   55
ANASŪYĀ: She must be suffering from lovesickness. I'll ask her . . .
[*Aloud.*] Friend, I have something to ask you. Your pain seems so
deep . . .
ŚAKUNTALĀ: [*Raising herself halfway.*] What do you want to say?
ANASŪYĀ: Śakuntalā, though we don't know what it is to be in love,   60
your condition reminds us of lovers we have heard about in stories.
Can you tell us the cause of your pain? Unless we understand your
illness, we can't begin to find a cure.
KING: Anasūyā expresses my own thoughts.
ŚAKUNTALĀ: Even though I want to, suddenly I can't make myself tell   65
you.
PRIYAṂVADĀ: Śakuntalā, my friend Anasūyā means well. Don't you see
how sick you are? Your limbs are wasting away. Only the shadow
of your beauty remains . . .
KING: What Priyaṃvadā says is true: 70

> Her cheeks are deeply sunken,
> her breasts' full shape is gone,
> her waist is thin, her shoulders bent,
> and the color has left her skin—
> tormented by love,   75
> she is sad but beautiful to see,
> like a jasmine creeper
> when hot wind shrivels its leaves.

ŚAKUNTALĀ: Friends, who else can I tell? May I burden you?
BOTH FRIENDS: We insist! Sharing sorrow with loving friends makes it   80
bearable.
KING:

> Friends who share her joy and sorrow
> discover the love concealed in her heart—
> though she looked back longingly at me,
> now I am afraid to hear her response.   85

ŚAKUNTALĀ: Friend, since my eyes first saw the guardian of the hermits' retreat, I've felt such strong desire for him!
KING: I have heard what I want to hear.

> My tormentor, the god of love,
> has soothed my fever himself,   90
> like the heat of late summer
> allayed by early rain clouds.

ŚAKUNTALĀ: If you two think it's right, then help me to win the king's
pity. Otherwise, you'll soon pour sesame oil and water[3] on my
corpse . . .   95
KING: Her words destroy my doubt.

---

3. Offerings to the dead in Hindu funeral rites. Śakuntalā and her friends have learned of the king's
real identity, because the hermits have asked him to guard their hermitage from demons.

PRIYAMVADĀ: [*In a stage whisper.*] She's so dangerously in love that there's no time to lose. Since her heart is set on the ornament of the Puru dynasty, we should rejoice that she desires him.

ANASŪYĀ: What you say is true. 100

PRIYAMVADĀ: [*Aloud.*] Friend, by good fortune your desire is in harmony with nature. A great river can only descend to the ocean. A jasmine creeper can only twine around a mango tree.

KING: Why is this surprising when the twin stars of spring serve the crescent moon?[4] 105

ANASŪYĀ: What means do we have to fulfill our friend's desire secretly and quickly?

PRIYAMVADĀ: "Secretly" demands some effort. "Quickly" is easy.

ANASŪYĀ: How so?

PRIYAMVADĀ: The king was charmed by her loving look; he seems thin 110 these days from sleepless nights.

KING: It's true . . .

> This golden armlet
> slips to my wrist
> without touching the scars 115
> my bowstring has made;
> its gemstones are faded
> by tears of secret pain
> that every night wets my arm
> where I bury my face. 120

PRIYAMVADĀ: [*Thinking.*] Compose a love letter and I'll hide it in a flower. I'll deliver it to his hand on the pretext of bringing an offering to the deity.

ANASŪYĀ: This subtle plan pleases me. What does Śakuntalā say?

ŚAKUNTALĀ: I'll try my friend's plan. 125

PRIYAMVADĀ: Then compose a poem to declare your love!

ŚAKUNTALĀ: I'm thinking, but my heart trembles with fear that he'll reject me.

KING: [*Delighted.*]

> The man you fear will reject you
> waits longing to love you, timid girl— 130
> a suitor may lose or be lucky,
> but the goddess always wins.

BOTH FRIENDS: Why do you belittle your own virtues? Who would cover his body with a piece of cloth to keep off cool autumn moonlight? 135

ŚAKUNTALĀ: [*Smiling.*] I'm trying to follow your advice. [*She sits thinking.*]

KING: As I gaze at her, my eyes forget to blink.

> She arches an eyebrow,
> struggling to compose the verse—

---

4. The king refers metaphorically to the two friends attending Śakuntalā as stars attending a young moon that is waning.

the down rises on her cheek,   140
showing the passion she feels.[5]

ŚAKUNTALĀ: I've thought of a verse, but I have nothing to write it on.

PRIYAMVADĀ: Engrave the letters with your nail on this lotus leaf! It's
as delicate as a parrot's breast.

ŚAKUNTALĀ: [Miming what PRIYAMVADĀ described.] Listen and tell me   145
this makes sense!

BOTH FRIENDS: We're both paying attention.

ŚAKUNTALĀ: [Singing.]

I don't know
your heart,
but day and night   150
for wanting you,
love violently
tortures
my limbs,
cruel man.   155

KING: [Suddenly revealing himself.]

Love torments you, slender girl,
but he completely consumes me—
daylight spares the lotus pond
while it destroys the moon.

BOTH FRIENDS: [Looking, rising with delight.] Welcome to the swift   160
success of love's desire!

[ŚAKUNTALĀ tries to rise.]

KING: Don't exert yourself!

Limbs lying among crushed petals
like fragile lotus stalks
are too weakened by pain   165
to perform ceremonious acts.

ANASŪYĀ: Then let the king sit on this stone bench!

[The KING sits; ŚAKUNTALĀ rises in embarrassment.]

PRIYAMVADĀ: The passion of two young lovers is clear. My affection
for our friend makes me speak out again now.[6]

KING: Noble lady, don't hesitate! It is painful to keep silent when one   170
must speak.

PRIYAMVADĀ: We're told that it is the king's duty to ease the pain of
his suffering subjects.

KING: My duty, exactly!

PRIYAMVADĀ: Since she first saw you, our dear friend has been reduced   175
to this sad condition. You must protect her and save her life.

KING: Noble lady, our affection is shared and I am honored by all you
say.

---

5. "Thrilling" of the cheek is held to be a sign of inner emotion which the actress is supposed to be
able to represent.   6. Śakuntala's modesty and good breeding prevent her from making her own declaration of love.

ŚAKUNTALĀ: [*Looking at* PRIYAṀVADĀ.] Why are you keeping the king
here? He must be anxious to return to his palace.   180
KING:

> If you think that my lost heart
> could love anyone but you,
> a fatal blow strikes a man
> already wounded by love's arrows!

ANASŪYĀ: We've heard that kings have many loves. Will our dear   185
friend become a sorrow to her family after you've spent time with
her?
KING: Noble lady, enough of this!

> Despite my many wives,
> on two the royal line rests—   190
> sea-bound earth
> and your friend.[7]

BOTH FRIENDS: You reassure us.
PRIYAṀVADĀ: [*Casting a glance.*] Anasūyā, this fawn is looking for its
mother. Let's take it to her!   195
  [*They both begin to leave.*]
ŚAKUNTALĀ: Come back! Don't leave me unprotected!
BOTH FRIENDS: The protector of the earth is at your side.
ŚAKUNTALĀ: Why have they gone?
KING: Don't be alarmed! I am your servant.

> Shall I set moist winds in motion   200
> with lotus-leaf fans to cool your pain,
> or rest your soft red lotus feet[8]
> on my lap to stroke them, my love

ŚAKUNTALĀ: I cannot sin against those I respect!
  [*Standing as if she wants to leave.*]
KING: Beautiful Śakuntalā, the day is still hot.   205

> Why should your frail limbs
> leave this couch of flowers
> shielded by lotus leaves
> to wander in the heat?

[*Saying this, he forces her to turn around.*]
ŚAKUNTALĀ: Puru king, control yourself! Though I'm burning with   210
love, how can I give myself to you?
KING: Don't fear your elders! The father of your family knows the law.
When he finds out, he will not blame you.

> The daughters of royal sages often marry
> in secret[9] and then their fathers bless them.   215

---

7. Royal polygamy was common in ancient India; it served to make and cement political alliances.
Here the king speaks of the conventional ideal of a ruler's two "chief queens": the royal consort, whose
son will inherit the kingdom, and the earth, personified as the king's spouse.   8. A common metaphor
for feet in Indian verse.   9. The *gāndharva* form of marriage, a secret marriage of mutual consent,
was permitted for the warrior class. By the beginning of Act IV this has taken place.

ŚAKUNTALĀ: Release me! I must ask my friends' advice!
KING: Yes, I shall release you.
ŚAKUNTALĀ: When?
KING:

> Only let my thirsting mouth
> gently drink from your lips,   220
> the way a bee sips nectar
> from a fragile virgin blossom.

[*Saying this, he tries to raise her face.* ŚAKUNTALĀ *evades him with a dance.*]
VOICE OFFSTAGE: Red goose,[1] bid farewell to your gander! Night has arrived!
ŚAKUNTALĀ: [*Flustered.*] Puru king, Mother Gautamī is surely coming   225
to ask about my health. Hide behind this tree!
KING: Yes.
    [*He conceals himself and waits. Then* GAUTAMĪ *enters with a vessel in her hand, accompanied by* ŚAKUNTALĀ's *two friends.*]
BOTH FRIENDS: This way, Mother Gautamī!
GAUTAMĪ: [*Approaching* ŚAKUNTALĀ.] Child, does the fever in your limbs burn less?   230
ŚAKUNTALĀ: Madam, I do feel better.
GAUTAMĪ: Kuśa grass and water will soothe your body. [*She sprinkles* ŚAKUNTALĀ's *head.*] Child, the day is ended. Come, let's go back to our hut! [*She starts to go.*]
ŚAKUNTALĀ: [*To herself.*] My heart, even when your desire was within   235
reach, you were bound by fear. Now you'll suffer the torment of separation and regret. [*Stopping after a few steps, she speaks aloud.*] Bower of creepers, refuge from my torment, I say goodbye until our joy can be renewed ... [*Sorrowfully,* ŚAKUNTALĀ *exits with the other women.*]
KING: [*Coming out of hiding.*] Fulfillment of desire is fraught with obstacles.   240

> Why didn't I kiss her face
> as it bent near my shoulder,
> her fingers shielding lips
> that stammered lovely warning?

Should I go now? Or shall I stay here in this bower of creepers that   245
my love enjoyed and then left?

> I see the flowers her body pressed
> on this bench of stone,
> the letter her nails inscribed
> on the faded lotus leaf,   250
> the lotus-fiber bracelet
> that slipped from her wrist—
> my eyes are prisoners
> in this empty house of reeds.

1. Also known as the sheldrake (*cakravāka*). In Sanskrit poetry, separated lovers are symbolized by these birds, subject to a curse that separates them from their mates every night.

VOICE IN THE AIR: King!   255

> When the evening rituals begin,
> shadows of flesh-eating demons swarm
> like amber clouds of twilight,
> raising terror at the altar of fire.

KING: I am coming.   260
[*He exits.*]

Act IV

[*The two friends enter, miming the gathering of flowers.*]

ANASŪYĀ: Priyaṁvadā, I'm delighted that Śakuntalā chose a suitable husband for herself, but I still feel anxious.

PRIYAṀVADĀ: Why?

ANASŪYĀ: When the king finished the sacrifice, the sages thanked him and he left. Now that he has returned to his palace women in the   5
city, will he remember us here?

PRIYAṀVADĀ: Have faith! He's so handsome, he can't be evil. But I don't know what Father Kaṇva will think when he hears about what happened.

ANASŪYĀ: I predict that he'll give his approval.   10

PRIYAṀVADĀ: Why?

ANASŪYĀ: He's always planned to give his daughter to a worthy husband. If fate accomplished it so quickly, Father Kaṇva won't object.

PRIYAṀVADĀ: [*Looking at the basket of flowers.*] We've gathered enough flowers for the offering ceremony.   15

ANASŪYĀ: Shouldn't we worship the goddess who guards Śakuntalā?

PRIYAṀVADĀ: I have just begun. [*She begins the rite.*]

VOICE OFFSTAGE: I am here!

ANASŪYĀ: [*Listening.*] Friend, a guest is announcing himself.

PRIYAṀVADĀ: Śakuntalā is in her hut nearby, but her heart is far away.   20

ANASŪYĀ: You're right! Enough of these flowers!
[*They begin to leave.*]

VOICE OFFSTAGE: So . . . you slight a guest . . .

> Since you blindly ignore
> a great sage like me,
> the lover you worship   25
> with mindless devotion
> will not remember you,
> even when awakened—
> like a drunkard who forgets
> a story he just composed!   30

PRIYAṀVADĀ: Oh! What a terrible turn of events! Śakuntalā's distraction has offended someone she should have greeted. [*Looking ahead.*] Not just an ordinary person, but the angry sage Durvāsas himself cursed her and went away in a frenzy of quivering, mad gestures. What else but fire has such power to burn?   35

ANASŪYĀ: Go! Bow at his feet and make him return while I prepare the water for washing his feet!

PRIYAMVADĀ: As you say. [*She exits.*]

ANASŪYĀ: [*After a few steps, she mimes stumbling.*] Oh! The basket of flowers fell from my hand when I stumbled in my haste to go. [*She* 40 *mimes the gathering of flowers.*]

PRIYAMVADĀ: [*Entering.*] He's so terribly cruel! No one could pacify him! But I was able to soften him a little.

ANASŪYĀ: Even that is a great feat with him! Tell me more!

PRIYAMVADĀ: When he refused to return, I begged him to forgive a daughter's first offense, since she didn't understand the power of 45 his austerity.

ANASŪYĀ: Then? Then?

PRIYAMVADĀ: He refused to change his word, but he promised that when the king sees the ring of recollection, the curse will end. Then he vanished. 50

ANASŪYĀ: Now we can breathe again. When he left, the king himself gave her the ring engraved with his name. Śakuntalā will have her own means of ending the curse.

PRIYAMVADĀ: Come friend! We should finish the holy rite we're performing for her. 55

[*The two walk around, looking.*]

Anasūyā, look! With her face resting on her hand, our dear friend looks like a picture. She is thinking about her husband's leaving, with no thought for herself, much less for a guest.

ANASŪYĀ: Priyamvadā, we two must keep all this a secret between us. Our friend is fragile by nature; she needs our protection. 60

PRIYAMVADĀ: Who would sprinkle a jasmine with scalding water?

[*They both exit; the interlude ends. Then a* DISCIPLE *of* KAṆVA *enters, just awakened from sleep.*]

DISCIPLE: Father Kaṇva has just returned from his pilgrimage and wants to know the exact time. I'll go into a clearing to see what remains of the night. [*Walking around and looking.*] It is dawn.

> The moon sets over the western mountain 65
> as the sun rises in dawn's red trail—
> rising and setting, these two bright powers
> portend the rise and fall of men.

> When the moon disappears, night lotuses
> are but dull souvenirs of its beauty— 70
> when her lover disappears, the sorrow
> is too painful for a frail girl to bear.

ANASŪYĀ: [*Throwing aside the curtain and entering.*][2] Even a person withdrawn from worldly life knows that the king has treated Śakuntalā badly. 75

DISCIPLE: I'll inform Father Kaṇva that it's time for the fire oblation.

2. The *javanikā* ("impeller"), a curtain hung over two doors separating the backstage area from the stage of the ancient Indian playhouse. An agitated entrance was indicated when, as here, a character entered the stage by throwing aside the curtain.

[*He exits.*]

ANASŪYĀ: Even when I'm awake, I'm useless. My hands and feet don't do their work. Love must be pleased to have made our innocent friend put her trust in a liar ... but perhaps it was the curse of Durvāsas that changed him ... otherwise, how could the king have   80
made such promises and not sent even a message by now? Maybe we should send the ring to remind him. Which of these ascetics who practice austerities can we ask? Father Kaṇva has just returned from his pilgrimage. Since we feel that our friend was also at fault, we haven't told him that Śakuntalā is married to Duṣyanta and is   85
pregnant. The problem is serious. What should we do?

PRIYAMVADĀ: [*Entering, with delight.*] Friend, hurry! We're to celebrate the festival of Śakuntalā's departure for her husband's house.

ANASŪYĀ: What's happened, friend?

PRIYAMVADĀ: Listen! I went to ask Śakuntalā how she had slept. Father   90
Kaṇva embraced her and though her face was bowed in shame, he blessed her: "Though his eyes were filled with smoke, the priest's oblation luckily fell on the fire. My child, I shall not mourn for you ... like knowledge given to a good student I shall send you to your husband today with an escort of sages."   95

ANASŪYĀ: Who told Father Kaṇva what happened?

PRIYAMVADĀ: A bodiless voice was chanting when he entered the fire sanctuary. [*Quoting in Sanskrit.*]

> Priest, know that your daughter
> carries Duṣyanta's potent seed
> for the good of the earth —   100
> like fire in mimosa[3] wood.

ANASŪYĀ: I'm joyful, friend. But I know that Śakuntalā must leave us today and sorrow shadows my happiness.

PRIYAMVADĀ: Friend, we must chase away sorrow and make this hermit girl happy!   105

ANASŪYĀ: Friend, I've made a garland of mimosa flowers. It's in the coconut-shell box hanging on a branch of the mango tree. Get it for me! Meanwhile I'll prepare the special ointments of deer musk, sacred earth, and blades of dūrvā grass.[4]

PRIYAMVADĀ: Here it is!   110

[ANASŪYĀ *exits;* PRIYAMVADĀ *gracefully mimes taking down the box.*]

VOICE OFFSTAGE: Gautamī! Śārṅgarava and some others have been appointed to escort Śakuntalā.

PRIYAMVADĀ: [*Listening.*] Hurry! Hurry! The sages are being called to go to Hastināpura.

ANASŪYĀ: [*Reentering with pots of ointments in her hands.*] Come,   115
friend! Let's go!

PRIYAMVADĀ: [*Looking around.*] Śakuntalā stands at sunrise with freshly washed hair while the female ascetics bless her with hand-

---

3. Here, the *śamī* tree, which Indians consider the repository of fire.   4. Materials prepared by women for the ritual of farewell to a young woman moving from her father's to her husband's home.

fuls of wild rice and auspicious words of farewell. Let's go to her
together.   120

[*The two approach as* ŚAKUNTALĀ *enters with* GAUTAMĪ *and other
female ascetics, and strikes a posture as described. One after another,
the female ascetics address her.*]

FIRST FEMALE ASCETIC: Child, win the title "Chief Queen" as a sign
of your husband's high esteem!

SECOND FEMALE ASCETIC: Child, be a mother to heroes!

THIRD FEMALE ASCETIC: Child, be honored by your husband!

BOTH FRIENDS: This happy moment is no time for tears, friend.   125

[*Wiping away her tears, they calm her with dance gestures.*]

PRIYAMVADĀ: Your beauty deserves jewels, not these humble things
we've gathered in the hermitage.

[*Two boy ascetics enter with offerings in their hands.*]

BOTH BOYS: Here is an ornament for you!

[*Everyone looks amazed.*]

GAUTAMĪ: Nārada, my child, where did this come from?

FIRST BOY: From Father Kaṇva's power.   130

GAUTAMĪ: Was it his mind's magic?

SECOND BOY: Not at all! Listen! You ordered us to bring flowers from
the forest trees for Śakuntalā.

> One tree produced this white silk cloth,
> another poured resinous lac to redden her feet—   135
> the tree nymphs produced jewels in hands
> that stretched from branches like young shoots.[5]

PRIYAMVADĀ: [*Watching* ŚAKUNTALĀ.] This is a sign that royal fortune
will come to you in your husband's house.

[ŚAKUNTALĀ *mimes modesty.*]

FIRST BOY: Gautama, come quickly! Father Kaṇva is back from bath-   140
ing. We'll tell him how the trees honor her.

SECOND BOY: As you say.

[*The two exit.*]

BOTH FRIENDS: We've never worn them ourselves, but we'll put these
jewels on your limbs the way they look in pictures.

ŚAKUNTALĀ: I trust your skill.   145

[*Both friends mime ornamenting her. Then* KAṆVA *enters, fresh from
his bath.*]

KAṆVA:

> My heart is touched with sadness
> since Śakuntalā must go today,
> my throat is choked with sobs,
> my eyes are dulled by worry—
> if a disciplined ascetic   150
> suffers so deeply from love,

---

5. The verse suggests that Śakuntalā is a kinswoman of the tree goddesses (*yakṣīs*), worshiped in popular
cults. *Lac:* a substance secreted by a species of beetle, used by Indian women as a cosmetic dye for
coloring fingernails and toenails.

how do fathers bear the pain
of each daughter's parting?[6]

[*He walks around.*]

BOTH FRIENDS: Śakuntalā, your jewels are in place; now put on the
pair of silken cloths.   155

[*Standing,* ŚAKUNTALĀ *wraps them.*]

GAUTAMĪ: Child, your father has come. His eyes filled with tears of joy
embrace you. Greet him reverently!

ŚAKUNTALĀ: [*Modestly.*] Father, I welcome you.

KAṆVA: Child,

May your husband honor you   160
the way Yayāti honored Śarmiṣṭhā.
As she bore her son Puru,[7]
may you bear an imperial prince.

GAUTAMĪ: Sir, this is a blessing, not just a prayer.

KAṆVA: Child, walk around the sacrificial fires![8]   165

[*All walk around;* KAṆVA *intoning a prayer in Vedic meter.*[9]]

Perfectly placed around the main altar,
fed with fuel, strewn with holy grass,
destroying sin by incense from oblations,
may these sacred fires purify you!

You must leave now! [*Looking around.*] Where are Śārṅgarava and   170
the others?

DISCIPLE: [*Entering.*] Here we are, sir!

KAṆVA: You show your sister the way!

ŚĀRṄGARAVA: Come this way!

[*They walk around.*]

KAṆVA: Listen, you trees that grow in our grove!   175

Until you were well watered
she could not bear to drink;
she loved you too much
to pluck your flowers for her hair;
the first time your buds bloomed,   180
she blossomed with joy —
may you all bless Śakuntalā
as she leaves for her husband's house.

[*Miming that he hears a cuckoo's cry.*]

The trees of her forest family
have blessed Śakuntalā —   185
the cuckoo's melodious song
announces their response.

---

6. A celebrated passage, prized for its convincing portrait of an Indian father's sorrow at losing his
daughter to another household.   7. Yayāti and Puru are ancestors of Duṣyanta.   8. Holy objects,
persons, and places are honored by ritually walking around them.   9. The version of the Triṣṭubh
meter used in the Vedic hymns, the oldest scriptures of the Hindu tradition.

VOICE IN THE AIR:

> May lakes colored by lotuses mark her path!
> May trees shade her from the sun's burning rays!
> May the dust be as soft as lotus pollen!   190
> May fragrant breezes cool her way!

[*All listen astonished.*]

GAUTAMĪ: Child, the divinities of our grove love you like your family
and bless you. We bow to you all!

ŚAKUNTALĀ: [*Bowing and walking around; speaking in a stage whisper.*] Priyaṁvadā, though I long to see my husband, my feet move
with sorrow as I start to leave the hermitage.   195

PRIYAṀVADĀ: You are not the only one who grieves. The whole hermitage feels this way as your departure from our grove draws near.

> Grazing deer
> drop grass,
> peacocks   200
> stop dancing,
> vines loose
> pale leaves
> falling
> like tears.   205

ŚAKUNTALĀ: [*Remembering.*] Father, before I leave, I must see my
sister, the vine Forestlight.

KAṆVA: I know that you feel a sister's love for her. She is right here.

ŚAKUNTALĀ: Forestlight, though you love your mango tree, turn to
embrace me with your tendril arms! After today, I'll be so far   210
away . . .

KAṆVA:

> Your merits won you the husband
> I always hoped you would have
> and your jasmine has her mango tree—
> my worries for you both are over.   215

Start your journey here!

ŚAKUNTALĀ: [*Facing her two friends.*] I entrust her care to you.

BOTH FRIENDS: But who will care for us? [*They wipe away their tears.*]

KAṆVA: Anasūyā, enough crying! You should be giving Śakuntalā
courage!   220

[*All walk around.*]

ŚAKUNTALĀ: Father, when the pregnant doe who grazes near my hut
gives birth, please send someone to give me the good news.

KAṆVA: I shall not forget.

ŚAKUNTALĀ: [*Miming the interrupting of her gait.*] Who is clinging to
my skirt?   225

[*She turns around.*]

KAṆVA: Child,

> The buck whose mouth you healed with oil
> when it was pierced by a blade of kuśa grass

and whom you fed with grains of rice—
your adopted son will not leave the path.   230

ŚAKUNTALĀ: Child, don't follow when I'm abandoning those I love! I
raised you when you were orphaned soon after your birth, but now
I'm deserting you too. Father will look after you. Go back! [*Weeping, she starts to go.*]

KAṆVA: Be strong!

> Hold back the tears that blind   235
> your long-lashed eyes—
> you will stumble if you cannot see
> the uneven ground on the path.

ŚĀRṄGARAVA: Sir, the scriptures prescribe that loved ones be escorted
only to the water's edge. We are at the shore of the lake. Give us   240
your message and return!

ŚAKUNTALĀ: We shall rest in the shade of this fig tree.
[*All walk around and stop;* KAṆVA *speaks to himself.*]

KAṆVA: What would be the right message to send to King Duṣyanta?
[*He ponders.*]

ŚAKUNTALĀ: [*In a stage whisper.*] Look! The wild goose cries in
anguish when her mate is hidden by lotus leaves. What I'm suffer-   245
ing is much worse.

ANASŪYĀ: Friend, don't speak this way!.

> This goose spends
> every long night
> in sorrow   250
> without her mate,
> but hope lets her
> survive
> the deep pain
> of loneliness.   255

KAṆVA: Śārṅgarava, speak my words to the king after you present
Śakuntalā!

ŚĀRṄGARAVA: As you command, sir!

KAṆVA:

> Considering our discipline,
> the nobility of your birth   260
> and that she fell in love with you
> before her kinsmen could act,
> acknowledge her with equal rank
> among your wives—
> what more is destined for her,   265
> the bride's family will not ask.

ŚĀRṄGARAVA: I grasp your message.

KAṆVA: Child, now I must instruct you. We forest hermits know something about worldly matters.

ŚĀRṄGARAVA: Nothing is beyond the scope of wise men.   270

KAṆVA: When you enter your husband's family;

Obey your elders, be a friend to the other wives!
If your husband seems harsh, don't be impatient!
Be fair to your servants, humble in your happiness!
Women who act this way become noble wives; 275
sullen girls only bring their families disgrace.

But what does Gautamī think?

GAUTAMĪ: This is good advice for wives, child. Take it all to heart!

KAṆVA: Child, embrace me and your friends!

ŚAKUNTALĀ: Father, why must Priyaṁvadā and my other friends turn 280
back here?

KAṆVA: They will also be given in marriage. It is not proper for them
to go there now. Gautamī will go with you.

ŚAKUNTALĀ: [*Embracing her father.*] How can I go on living in a
strange place, torn from my father's side, like a vine torn from the 285
side of a sandalwood tree growing on a mountain slope?[1]

KAṆVA: Child, why are you so frightened?

> When you are your husband's honored wife,
> absorbed in royal duties and in your son,[2]
> born like the sun to the eastern dawn, 290
> the sorrow of separation will fade.

[ŚAKUNTALĀ *falls at her father's feet.*]
Let my hopes for you be fulfilled!

ŚAKUNTALĀ: [*Approaching her two friends.*] You two must embrace
me together!

BOTH FRIENDS: [*Embracing her.*] Friend, if the king seems slow to 295
recognize you, show him the ring engraved with his name!

ŚAKUNTALĀ: Your suspicions make me tremble!

BOTH FRIENDS: Don't be afraid! It's our love that fears evil.

ŚĀRṄGARAVA: The sun is high in the afternoon sky. Hurry, please!

ŚAKUNTALĀ: [*Facing the sanctuary.*] Father, will I ever see the grove 300
again?

KAṆVA:

> When you have lived for many years
> as a queen equal to the earth
> and raised Duṣyanta's son
> to be a matchless warrior, 305
> your husband will entrust him
> with the burdens of the kingdom
> and will return with you
> to the calm of this hermitage.[3]

GAUTAMĪ: Child, the time for our departure has passed. Let your father 310
turn back! It would be better, sir, if you turn back yourself. She'll
keep talking this way forever.

1. Śakuntalā's sorrow reflects the real world of every Indian bride as she permanently leaves the home
of her birth to join the extended family into which she has married. 2. The son, heir to the throne,
will ensure an honored place for Śakuntalā among the hitherto childless wives of King Duṣyanta.
3. It was a custom of Hindu kings (and commoners of the twice-born classes) to retire to the forest with
their wives to concentrate on the spiritual life.

KAṆVA: Child, my ascetic practice has been interrupted.

ŚAKUNTALĀ: My father's body is already tortured by ascetic practices. He must not grieve too much for me! 315

KAṆVA: [*Sighing.*]

> When I see the grains of rice
> sprout from offerings you made
> at the door of your hut,
> how shall I calm my sorrow!

[ŚAKUNTALĀ *exits with her escort.*]

BOTH FRIENDS: [*Watching* ŚAKUNTALĀ.] Śakuntalā is hidden by forest trees now. 320

KAṆVA: Anasūyā, your companion is following her duty. Restrain yourself and return with me!

BOTH FRIENDS: Father, the ascetics' grove seems empty without Śakuntalā. How can we enter? 325

KAṆVA: The strength of your love makes it seem so. [*Walking around in meditation.*] Good! Now that Śakuntalā is on her way to her husband's family, I feel calm.

> A daughter belongs to another man—
> by sending her to her husband today, 330
> I feel the satisfaction
> one has on repaying a loan.

[*All exit.*]

Act V

[*The* KING *and the* BUFFOON *enter; both sit down.*]

BUFFOON: Pay attention to the music room, friend, and you'll hear the notes of a song strung into a delicious melody ... the lady Haṁsapadikā is practicing her singing.

KING: Be quiet so I can hear her!

VOICE IN THE AIR: [*Singing.*]

> Craving sweet 5
> new nectar,
> you kissed
> a mango bud once—
> how could you
> forget her, bee, 10
> to bury your joy
> in a lotus

KING: The melody of the song is passionate.

BUFFOON: But did you get the meaning of the words?

KING: I once made love to her. Now she reproaches me for loving 15 Queen Vasumatī. Friend Mādhavya, tell Haṁsapadikā that her words rebuke me soundly.

BUFFOON: As you command! [*He rises.*] But if that woman grabs my

hair tuft, it will be like a heavenly nymph grabbing some ascetic
. . . there go my hopes of liberation![4]   20
KING: Go! Use your courtly charm to console her.
BUFFOON: What a fate!
    [*He exits.*]
KING: [*To himself.*] Why did hearing the song's words fill me with
such strong desire? I'm not parted from anyone I love . . .

> Seeing rare beauty,   25
> hearing lovely sounds,
> even a happy man
> becomes strangely uneasy . . .
> perhaps he remembers,
> without knowing why,   30
> loves of another life
> buried deep in his being.[5]

[*He stands bewildered. Then the* KING'S CHAMBERLAIN *enters.*]
CHAMBERLAIN: At my age, look at me!

> Since I took this ceremonial bamboo staff
> as my badge of office in the king's chambers   35
> many years have passed; now I use it
> as a crutch to support my faltering steps.

A king cannot neglect his duty. He has just risen from his seat of
justice and though I am loath to keep him longer, Sage Kaṇva's
pupils have just arrived. Authority to rule the world leaves no time   40
for rest.

> The sun's steeds were yoked before time began,
> the fragrant wind blows night and day,
> the cosmic serpent always bears earth's weight,[6]
> and a king who levies taxes has his duty.   45

Therefore, I must perform my office. [*Walking around and
looking.*]

> Weary from ruling them like children,
> he seeks solitude far from his subjects,
> like an elephant bull who seeks cool shade
> after gathering his herd at midday.   50

[*Approaching.*] Victory to you, king! Some ascetics who dwell in
the forest at the foothills of the Himālayas have come. They have
women with them and bring a message from Sage Kaṇva. Listen,
king, and judge!
KING: [*Respectfully.*] Are they Sage Kaṇva's messengers?   55
CHAMBERLAIN: They are.

---

4. The buffoon is referring, in his own inimitable way, to the seduction of the ascetic by the courtesan
and the thwarting of the former's quest for liberation from *karma* and rebirth. The buffoon's joke turns
on the word *mokṣa*, which means "release," in the physical sense as well as in the spiritual one of
liberation from *karma*.   5. Alludes to the power of art to revive buried memories of experiences from
former lives.   6. According to Hindu mythology the earth rests on Śeṣa, the cosmic serpent. *Sun's
steeds:* see n. 7, p. 753.

KING: Inform the teacher Somarāta that he should welcome the ascetics with the prescribed rites and then bring them to me himself. I'll wait in a place suitable for greeting them.

CHAMBERLAIN: As the king commands. [*He exits.*]   60

KING: [*Rising.*] Vetravatī, lead the way to the fire sanctuary.

DOORKEEPER: Come this way, king!

KING: [*Walking around, showing fatigue.*] Every other creature is happy when the object of his desire is won, but for kings success contains a core of suffering.   65

> High office only leads to greater greed;
> just perfecting its rewards is wearisome —
> a kingdom is more trouble than it's worth,
> like a royal umbrella one holds alone.

TWO BARDS OFFSTAGE: Victory to you, king!   70

FIRST BARD:

> You sacrifice your pleasures every day
> to labor for your subjects —
> as a tree endures burning heat
> to give shade from the summer sun.

SECOND BARD:

> You punish villains with your rod of justice,   75
> you reconcile disputes, you grant protection —
> most relatives are loyal only in hope of gain,
> but you treat all your subjects like kinsmen.

KING: My weary mind is revived. [*He walks around.*]

DOORKEEPER: The terrace of the fire sanctuary is freshly washed and   80
the cow is waiting to give milk for the oblation. Let the king ascend!

KING: Vetravatī, why has Father Kaṇva sent these sages to me?

> Does something hinder their ascetic life?
> Or threaten creatures in the sacred forest?
> Or do my sins stunt the flowering vines?   85
> My mind is filled with conflicting doubts.

DOORKEEPER: I would guess that these sages rejoice in your virtuous conduct and come to honor you.

[*The ascetics enter;* ŚAKUNTALĀ *is in front with* GAUTAMĪ; *the* CHAMBERLAIN *and the* KING'S PRIEST *are in front of her.*]

CHAMBERLAIN: Come this way, sirs!

ŚĀRṄGARAVA: Śāradvata, my friend: 90

> I know that this renowned king is righteous
> and none of the social classes follows evil ways,
> but my mind is so accustomed to seclusion
> that the palace feels like a house in flames.

ŚĀRADVATA: I've felt the same way ever since we entered the city.   95

> As if I were freshly bathed, seeing a filthy man,
> pure while he's defiled, awake while he's asleep,

as if I were a free man watching a prisoner,
I watch this city mired in pleasures.

ŚAKUNTALĀ: [*Indicating she feels an omen.*] Why is my right eye   100
twitching?

GAUTAMĪ: Child, your husband's family gods turn bad fortune into
blessings! [*They walk around.*]

PRIEST: [*Indicating the* KING.] Ascetics, the guardian of sacred order
has left the seat of justice and awaits you now. Behold him!   105

ŚĀRṄGARAVA: Great priest, he seems praiseworthy, but we expect no
less.

> Boughs bend, heavy with ripened fruit,
> clouds descend with fresh rain,
> noble men are gracious with wealth —   110
> this is the nature of bountiful things.

DOORKEEPER: King, their faces look calm. I'm sure that the sages have
confidence in what they're doing.

KING: [*Seeing* ŚAKUNTALĀ.]

> Who is she? Carefully veiled
> to barely reveal her body's beauty,   115
> surrounded by the ascetics
> like a bud among withered leaves.

DOORKEEPER: King, I feel curious and puzzled too. Surely her form
deserves closer inspection.

KING: Let her be! One should not stare at another man's wife!   120

ŚAKUNTALĀ: [*Placing her hand on her chest, she speaks to herself.*] My
heart, why are you quivering? Be quiet while I learn my noble
husband's feelings.

PRIEST: [*Going forward.*] These ascetics have been honored with due
ceremony. They have a message from their teacher. The king   125
should hear them!

KING: I am paying attention.

SAGES: [*Raising their hands in a gesture of greeting.*] May you be
victorious, king!

KING: I salute you all!   130

SAGES: May your desires be fulfilled!

KING: Do the sages perform austerities unhampered?

SAGES:

> Who would dare obstruct the rites
> of holy men whom you protect —
> how can darkness descend   135
> when the sun's rays shine?

KING: My title "king" is more meaningful now. Is the world blessed
by Father Kaṇva's health?

SAGES: Saints control their own health. He asks about your welfare
and sends this message . . .   140

KING: What does he command?

ŚĀRṄGARAVA: At the time you secretly met and married my daughter, affection made me pardon you both.

> We remember you to be a prince of honor;
> Śakuntalā is virtue incarnate—   145
> the creator cannot be condemned
> for mating the perfect bride and groom.

And now that she is pregnant, receive her and perform your sacred duty together.

GAUTAMĪ: Sir, I have something to say, though I wasn't appointed to   150
speak:

> She ignored her elders
> and you failed to ask her kinsmen—
> since you acted on your own,
> what can I say to you now?   155

ŚAKUNTALĀ: What does my noble husband say?

KING: What has been proposed?

ŚAKUNTALĀ: [To herself.] The proposal is as clear as fire.

ŚĀRṄGARAVA: What's this? Your Majesty certainly knows the ways of the world!   160

> People suspect a married woman who stays
> with her kinsmen, even if she is chaste—
> a young wife should live with her husband,
> no matter how he despises her.

KING: Did I ever marry you?   165

ŚAKUNTALĀ: [Visibly dejected, speaking to herself.] Now your fears are real, my heart!

ŚĀRṄGARAVA:

> Does one turn away from duty in contempt
> because his own actions repulse him?

KING: Why ask this insulting question?   170

ŚĀRṄGARAVA:

> Such transformations take shape
> when men are drunk with power.

KING: This censure is clearly directed at me.

GAUTAMĪ: Child, this is no time to be modest. I'll remove your veil.
Then your husband will recognize you.   175
[She does so.]

KING: [Staring at ŚAKUNTALĀ.]

> Must I judge whether I ever married
> the flawless beauty they offer me now?
> I cannot love her or leave her, like a bee
> near a jasmine filled with frost at dawn.

[He shows hesitation.]

DOORKEEPER: Our king has a strong sense of justice. Who else would   180
hesitate when beauty like this is handed to him?

ŚĀRṄGARAVA: King, why do you remain silent?

KING: Ascetics, even though I'm searching my mind, I don't remember marrying this lady. How can I accept a woman who is visibly pregnant when I doubt that I am the cause?   185

ŚAKUNTALĀ: [*In a stage whisper.*] My lord casts doubt on our marriage. Why were my hopes so high?

ŚĀRṄGARAVA: It can't be!

> Are you going to insult the sage
> who pardons the girl you seduced   190
> and bids you keep his stolen wealth,
> treating a thief like you with honor?

ŚĀRADVATA: Śārṅgarava, stop now! Śakuntalā, we have delivered our message and the king has responded. He must be shown some proof.   195

ŚAKUNTALĀ: [*In a stage whisper.*] When passion can turn to this, what's the use of reminding him? But, it's up to me to prove my honor now. [*Aloud.*] My noble husband . . . [*She breaks off when this is half-spoken.*] Since our marriage is in doubt, this is no way to address him. Puru king, you do wrong to reject a simple-hearted   200 person with such words after you deceived her in the hermitage.

KING: [*Covering his ears.*] Stop this shameful talk!

> Are you trying to stain my name
> and drag me to ruin —
> like a river eroding her own banks,   205
> soiling water and uprooting trees?

ŚAKUNTALĀ: Very well! If it's really true that fear of taking another man's wife turns you away, then this ring will revive your memory and remove your doubt.

KING: An excellent idea!   210

ŚAKUNTALĀ: [*Touching the place where the ring had been.*] I'm lost! The ring is gone from my finger. [*She looks despairingly at* GAUTAMĪ.]

GAUTAMĪ: The ring must have fallen off while you were bathing in the holy waters at the shrine of the goddess near Indra's grove.

KING: [*Smiling.*] And so they say the female sex is cunning.   215

ŚAKUNTALĀ: Fate has shown its power. Yet, I will tell you something else.

KING: I am still obliged to listen.

ŚAKUNTALĀ: One day, in a jasmine bower, you held a lotus-leaf cup full of water in your hand.   220

KING: We hear you.

ŚAKUNTALĀ: At that moment the buck I treated as my son approached. You coaxed it with the water, saying that it should drink first. But he didn't trust you and wouldn't drink from your hand. When I took the water, his trust returned. Then you jested, "Every creature   225 trusts what its senses know. You both belong to the forest."

KING: Thus do women further their own ends by attracting eager men with the honey of false words.

GAUTAMĪ: Great king, you are wrong to speak this way. This child   230
raised in an ascetics' grove doesn't know deceit.

KING: Old woman,

> When naive female beasts show cunning,
> what can we expect of women who reason?
> Don't cuckoos let other birds nurture
> their eggs and teach the chicks to fly?   235

ŚAKUNTALĀ: [*Angrily.*] Evil man! you see everything distorted by your
own ignoble heart. Who would want to imitate you now, hiding
behind your show of justice, like a well overgrown with weeds?

KING: [*To himself.*] Her anger does not seem feigned; it makes me
doubt myself.   240

> When the absence of love's memory
> made me deny a secret affair with her,
> this fire-eyed beauty bent her angry brows
> and seemed to break the bow of love.[7]

[*Aloud.*] Lady, Duṣyanta's conduct is renowned, so what you say is   245
groundless.

ŚAKUNTALĀ: All right! I may be a self-willed wanton woman! But it was
faith in the Puru dynasty that brought me into the power of a man
with honey in his words and poison in his heart. [*She covers her
face at the end of the speech and weeps.*]

ŚĀRṄGARAVA: A willful act unchecked always causes pain.   250

> One should be cautious
> in forming a secret union—
> unless a lover's heart is clear,
> affection turns to poison.

KING: But sir, why do you demean me with such warnings? Do you   255
trust the lady?

ŚĀRṄGARAVA: [*Scornfully.*] You have learned everything backwards.

> If you suspect the word of one
> whose nature knows no guile,
> then you can only trust   260
> people who practice deception.

KING: I presume you speak the truth. Let us assume so. But what could
I gain by deceiving this woman?

ŚĀRṄGARAVA: Ruin.

KING: Ruin? A Puru king has no reason to want his own ruin!   265

ŚĀRADVATA: Śārṅgarava, this talk is pointless. We have delivered our
master's message and should return.

> Since you married her, abandon her or take her—
> absolute is the power a husband has over his wife.

GAUTAMĪ: You go ahead.   270

[*They start to go.*]

---

7. Of the love god Kāma.

ŚAKUNTALĀ: What? Am I deceived by this cruel man and then abandoned by you? [*She tries to follow them.*]

GAUTAMĪ: [*Stopping.*] Śārṅgarava my son, Śakuntalā is following us,
crying pitifully. What will my child do now that her husband has
refused her?   275

ŚĀRṄGARAVA: [*Turning back angrily.*] Bold woman, do you still insist
on having your way?

   [ŚAKUNTALĀ *trembles in fear.*]

> If you are what the king says you are,
> you don't belong in Father Kaṇva's family —
> if you know that your marriage vow is pure,   280
> you can bear slavery in your husband's house.

Stay! We must go on!

KING: Ascetic, why do you disappoint the lady too?

> The moon only makes lotuses open,
> the sun's light awakens lilies —   285
> a king's discipline forbids him
> to touch another man's wife.

ŚĀRṄGARAVA: If you forget a past affair because of some present attachment, why do you fear injustice now?

KING: [*To the* PRIEST.] Sir I ask you to weigh the alternatives: 290

> Since it's unclear whether I'm deluded
> or she is speaking falsely —
> should I risk abandoning a wife
> or being tainted by another man's?

PRIEST: [*Deliberating.*] I recommend this . . .   295

KING: Instruct me! I'll do as you say.

PRIEST: Then let the lady stay in our house until her child is born. If
you ask why: the wise men predict that your first son will be born
with the marks of a king who turns the wheel of empire.[8] If the
child of the sage's daughter bears the marks, congratulate her and   300
welcome her into your palace chambers. Otherwise, send her back
to her father.

KING: Whatever the elders desire.

PRIEST: Child, follow me!

ŚAKUNTALĀ: Mother earth, open to receive me!   305

   [*Weeping,* ŚAKUNTALĀ *exits with the* PRIEST *and the hermits. The*
   KING, *his memory lost through the curse, thinks about her.*]

VOICE OFFSTAGE: Amazing! Amazing!

KING: [*Listening.*] What could this be?

PRIEST: [*Reentering, amazed.*] King, something marvelous has
occurred!

KING: What?   310

PRIEST: When Kaṇva's pupils had departed,

> The girl threw up her arms and wept,
> lamenting her misfortune . . . then . . .

8. See n. 9, p. 754.

KING: Then what?
PRIEST:

> Near the nymph's shrine a ray of light   315
> in the shape of a woman carried her away.

[*All mime amazement.*]
KING: We've already settled the matter. Why discuss it further?
PRIEST: [*Observing the* KING.] May you be victorious! [*He exits.*]
KING: Vetravatī, I am bewildered. Lead the way to my chamber!
DOORKEEPER: Come this way, my lord! [*She walks forward.*]   320
KING:

> I cannot remember marrying
> the sage's abandoned daughter,
> but the pain my heart feels
> makes me suspect that I did.

[*All exit.*]

Act VI

[*The* KING's *wife's brother, who is city* MAGISTRATE, *enters with two policemen leading a* MAN *whose hands are tied behind his back.*
BOTH POLICEMEN: [*Beating the* MAN.] Speak, thief? Where'd you steal this handsome ring with the king's name engraved in the jewel?
MAN: [*Showing fear.*] Peace, sirs! I wouldn't do a thing like that.
FIRST POLICEMAN: Don't tell us the king thought you were some   5
  famous priest and gave it to you as a gift!
MAN: Listen, I'm a humble fisherman who lives near Indra's grove.
SECOND POLICEMAN: Thief, did we ask you about your caste?
MAGISTRATE: Sūcaka, let him tell it all in order! Don't interrupt him!
BOTH POLICEMEN: Whatever you command, chief!
MAN: I feed my family by catching fish with nets and hooks.   10
MAGISTRATE: [*Mocking.*] What a pure profession![9]
MAN:

> The work I do
> may be vile
> but I won't deny
> my birthright—   15
> a priest
> doing his holy rites
> pities the animals
> he kills.

MAGISTRATE: Go on!   20
MAN: One day as I was cutting up a red carp, I saw the shining stone of this ring in its belly. When I tried to sell it, you grabbed me. Kill me or let me go! That's how I got it!
MAGISTRATE: Jānuka, I'm sure this ugly butcher's a fisherman by his

---

9. Because their profession involves taking animal life, fishermen rank low in the caste system.

stinking smell. We must investigate how he got the ring. We'll go   25
straight to the palace.

BOTH POLICEMEN: Okay. Go in front, you pickpocket!
    [*All walk around.*]

MAGISTRATE: Sūcaka, guard this villain at the palace gate! I'll report
    to the king how we found the ring, get his orders, and come back.

BOTH POLICEMEN: Chief, good luck with the king!   30
    [*The* MAGISTRATE *exits.*]

FIRST POLICEMAN: Jānuka, the chief's been gone a long time.

SECOND POLICEMAN: Well, there are fixed times for seeing kings.

FIRST POLICEMAN: Jānuka, my hands are itching to tie on his execu-
    tion garland.[1] [*He points to the* MAN.]

MAN: You shouldn't think about killing a man for no reason.   35

SECOND POLICEMAN: [*Looking.*] I see our chief coming with a letter
    in his hand. It's probably an order from the king. You'll be thrown
    to the vultures or you'll see the face of death's dog[2] again . . .

MAGISTRATE: [*Entering.*] Sūcaka, release this fisherman! I'll tell you
    how he got the ring.   40

FIRST POLICEMAN: Whatever you say, chief!

SECOND POLICEMAN: The villain entered the house of death and came
    out again. [*He unties the prisoner.*]

MAN: [*Bowing to the* MAGISTRATE.] Master, how will I make my living
    now?   45

MAGISTRATE: The king sends you a sum equal to the ring. [*He gives
    the money to the* MAN.]

MAN: [*Bowing as he grabs it.*] The king honors me.

FIRST POLICEMAN: This fellow's certainly honored. He was lowered
    from the execution stake and raised up on a royal elephant's back.

SECOND POLICEMAN: Chief, the reward tells me this ring was special   50
    to the king.

MAGISTRATE: I don't think the king valued the stone, but when he
    caught sight of the ring, he suddenly seemed to remember some-
    one he loved, and he became deeply disturbed.

FIRST POLICEMAN: You served him well, chief!   55

SECOND POLICEMAN: I think you better served this king of fish. [*Look-
    ing at the fisherman with jealousy.*]

MAN: My lords, half of this is yours for your good will.

FIRST POLICEMAN: It's only fair!

MAGISTRATE: Fisherman, now that you are my greatest and dearest
    friend, we should pledge our love over kadamba-blossom wine.   60
    Let's go to the wine shop!
    [*They all exit together; the interlude ends. Then a nymph named*
    SĀNUMATĪ *enters by the skyway.*]

SĀNUMATĪ: Now that I've performed my assigned duties at the nymph's
    shrine, I'll slip away to spy on King Duṣyanta while the worshipers
    are bathing. My friendship with Menakā makes me feel a bond

---

1. Condemned prisoners were taken to their executions dressed in robes and garlands, in the manner
of sacrificial victims.   2. In Hindu myth two four-eyed dogs guard the path of the dead.

with Śakuntalā. Besides, Menakā asked me to help her daughter.   65
[*Looking around.*] Why don't I see preparations for the spring festival in the king's palace? I can learn everything by using my mental
powers, but I must respect my friend's request. So be it! I'll make
myself invisible and spy on these two girls who are guarding the
pleasure garden.   70

> [SĀNUMATĪ *mimes descending and stands waiting. Then a* MAID *ser-
> vant named Parabhṛtikā, "Little Cuckoo," enters, looking at a mango
> bud. A* SECOND MAID, *named Madhukarikā, "Little Bee," is following
> her.*]

FIRST MAID:

> Your pale green stem
> tinged with pink
> is a true sign
> that spring has come—
> I see you,   75
> mango-blossom bud,
> and I pray
> for a season of joy.

SECOND MAID: What are you muttering to yourself?
FIRST MAID: A cuckoo goes mad when she sees a mango bud.   80
SECOND MAID: [*Joyfully rushing over.*] Has the sweet month of spring
   come?
FIRST MAID: Now's the time to sing your songs of love.
SECOND MAID: Hold me while I pluck a mango bud and worship the
   god of love.   85
FIRST MAID: Only if you'll give me half the fruit of your worship.
SECOND MAID: That goes without saying . . . our bodies may be separate, but our lives are one . . .[*Leaning on her friend, she stands
   and plucks a mango bud.*] The mango flower is still closed, but this
   broken stem is fragrant. [*She makes the dove gesture with her*   90
   hands.]

> Mango blossom bud,
> I offer you to Love
> as he lifts
> his bow of passion.
> Be the first   95
> of his flower arrows
> aimed at lonely girls
> with lovers far away!

[*She throws the mango bud.*]
MAGISTRATE: [*Angrily throwing aside the curtain and entering.*] Not
   now, stupid girl! When the king has banned the festival of spring,   100
   how dare you pluck a mango bud!
BOTH MAIDS: [*Frightened.*] Please forgive us, sir. We don't know what
   you mean.
CHAMBERLAIN: Did you not hear that even the spring trees and the
   nesting birds obey the king's order?   105

The mango flowers bloom without spreading pollen,
the red amaranth buds, but will not bloom,
cries of cuckoo cocks freeze though frost is past,
and out of fear, Love holds his arrow half-drawn.

BOTH MAIDS: There is no doubt about the king's great power!   110

FIRST MAID: Sir, several days ago we were sent to wait on the queen
by Mitrāvasu, the king's brother-in-law. We were assigned to guard
the pleasure garden. Since we're newcomers, we've heard no news.

CHAMBERLAIN: Let it be! But don't do it again!

BOTH MAIDS: Sir, we're curious. May we ask why the spring festival   115
was banned?

SĀNUMATĪ: Mortals are fond of festivals. The reason must be serious.

CHAMBERLAIN: It is public knowledge. Why should I not tell them?
Has the scandal of Śakuntalā's rejection not reached your ears?

BOTH MAIDS: We only heard from the king's brother-in-law that the   120
ring was found.

CHAMBERLAIN: [To himself.] There is little more to tell. [Aloud.]
When he saw the ring, the king remembered that he had married
Śakuntalā in secret and had rejected her in his delusion. Since then
the king has been tortured by remorse.   125

> Despising what he once enjoyed,
> he shuns his ministers every day
> and spends long sleepless nights
> tossing at the edge of his bed—
> when courtesy demands that   130
> he converse with palace women,
> he stumbles over their names,
> and then retreats in shame.

SĀNUMATĪ: This news delights me.

CHAMBERLAIN: The festival is banned because of the king's melan-   135
choly.

BOTH MAIDS: It's only right.

VOICE OFFSTAGE: This way, sir!

CHAMBERLAIN: [Listening.] The king is coming. Go about your business!   140

BOTH MAIDS: As you say.

[Both maids exit. Then the KING enters, costumed to show his grief,
accompanied by the BUFFOON and the DOORKEEPER.]

CHAMBERLAIN: [Observing the KING.] Extraordinary beauty is appealing under all conditions. Even in his lovesick state, the king is wonderful to see.

> Rejecting his regal jewels,   145
> he wears one golden bangle
> above his left wrist;
> his lips are pale with sighs,
> his eyes wan from brooding at night—
> like a gemstone ground in polishing,   150
> the fiery beauty of his body
> makes his wasted form seem strong.

SĀNUMATĪ: [*Seeing the* KING.] I see why Śakuntalā pines for him though he rejected and disgraced her.

KING: [*Walking around slowly, deep in thought.*]

> This cursed heart slept 155
> when my love came to wake it,
> and now it stays awake
> to suffer the pain of remorse.

SĀNUMATĪ: The girl shares his fate.

BUFFOON: [*In a stage whisper.*] He's having another attack of his 160
Śakuntalā disease. I doubt if there's any cure for that.

CHAMBERLAIN: [*Approaching.*] Victory to the king! I have inspected
the grounds of the pleasure garden. Let the king visit his favorite
spots and divert himself.

KING: Vetravatī, deliver a message to my noble minister Piśuna: "After 165
being awake all night, we cannot sit on the seat of justice today. Set
in writing what your judgment tells you the citizens require and
send it to us!"

DOORKEEPER: Whatever you command! [*She exits.*]

KING: Vātāyana, attend to the rest of your business! 170

CHAMBERLAIN: As the king commands! [*He exits.*]

BUFFOON: You've cleared out the flies. Now you can rest in some
pretty spot. The garden is pleasant now in this break between morning cold and noonday heat.

KING: Dear friend, the saying "Misfortunes rush through any crack" is 175
absolutely right:

> Barely freed by the dark force
> that made me forget Kaṇva's daughter,
> my mind is threatened by an arrow
> of mango buds fixed on Love's bow. 180

BUFFOON: Wait, I'll destroy the love god's arrow with my wooden
stick.[3] [*Raising his staff, he tries to strike a mango bud.*]

KING: [*Smiling.*] Let it be! I see the majesty of brahman bravery.
Friend, where may I sit to divert my eyes with vines that remind
me of my love? 185

BUFFOON: Didn't you tell your maid Caturikā, "I'll pass the time in
the jasmine bower. Bring me the drawing board on which I painted
a picture of Śakuntalā with my own hand!"

KING: Such a place may soothe my heart. Show me the way!

BUFFOON: Come this way! 190

[*Both walk around; the nymph* SĀNUMATĪ *follows.*]
The marble seat and flower offerings in this jasmine bower are certainly trying to make us feel welcome. Come in and sit down!

[*Both enter the bower and sit.*]

SĀNUMATĪ: I'll hide behind these creepers to see the picture he's drawn

---

3. It is clear in the original that the buffoon's staff parodies Indra's rod (a symbol of virility) and the
phallic arrows of the god of love.

of my friend. Then I'll report how great her husband's passion is.
[*She does as she says and stands waiting.*]

KING: Friend, now I remember everything. I told you about my first 195
meeting with Śakuntalā. You weren't with me when I rejected her,
but why didn't you say anything about her before? Did you suffer a
loss of memory too?

BUFFOON: I didn't forget. You did tell me all about it once, but then
you said, "It's all a joke without any truth." My wit is like a lump 200
of clay, so I took you at your word . . . or it could be that fate is
powerful . . .

SĀNUMATĪ: It is!

KING: Friend, help me!

BUFFOON: What's this? It doesn't become you! Noblemen never take 205
grief to heart. Even in storms, mountains don't tremble.

KING: Dear friend, I'm defenseless when I remember the pain of my
love's bewilderment when I rejected her.

> When I cast her away, she followed her kinsmen,
> but Kaṇva's disciple harshly shouted, "Stay!"   210
> The tearful look my cruelty provoked
> burns me like an arrow tipped with poison.

SĀNUMATĪ: The way he rehearses his actions makes me delight in his
pain.

BUFFOON: Sir, I guess that the lady was carried off by some celestial 215
creature or other.

KING: Who else would dare to touch a woman who worshiped her
husband? I was told that Menakā is her mother. My heart suspects
that her mother's companions carried her off.

SĀNUMATĪ: His delusion puzzled me, but not his reawakening.   220

BUFFOON: If that's the case, you'll meet her again in good time.

KING: How?

BUFFOON: No mother or father can bear to see a daughter parted from
her husband.

KING:

> Was it dream or illusion or mental confusion,   225
> or the last meager fruit of my former good deeds?
> It is gone now, and my heart's desires are
> like riverbanks crumbling of their own weight.

BUFFOON: Stop this! Isn't the ring evidence that an unexpected meeting is destined to take place?   230

KING: [*Looking at the ring.*] I only pity it for falling from such a place.

> Ring, your punishment is proof
> that your face is as flawed as mine—
> you were placed in her lovely fingers,
> glowing with crimson nails, and you fell.   235

SĀNUMATĪ: The real pity would have been if it had fallen into some
other hand.

BUFFOON: What prompted you to put the signet ring on her hand?

SĀNUMATĪ: I'm curious too.

KING: I did it when I left for the city. My love broke into tears and 240
asked, "How long will it be before my noble husband sends news
to me?"

BUFFOON: Then? What then?

KING: Then I placed the ring on her finger with this promise:

> One by one, day after day,   245
> count each syllable of my name!
> At the end, a messenger will come
> to bring you to my palace.

But in my cruel delusion, I never kept my word.

SĀNUMATĪ: Fate broke their charming agreement!   250

BUFFOON: How did it get into the belly of the carp the fisherman was
cutting up?

KING: While she was worshiping at the shrine of Indra's wife, it fell
from her hand into the Gaṅgā.[4]

BUFFOON: It's obvious now!   255

SĀNUMATĪ: And the king, doubtful of his marriage to Śakuntalā, a
female ascetic, was afraid to commit an act of injustice. But why
should such passionate love need a ring to be remembered?

KING: I must reproach the ring for what it's done.

BUFFOON: [To himself.] He's gone the way of all madmen . . .   260

KING:

> Why did you leave her delicate finger
> and sink into the deep river?

of course . . .

> A mindless ring can't recognize virtue,
> but why did I reject my love?   265

BUFFOON: [To himself again.] Why am I consumed by a craving for
food?

KING: Oh ring! Have pity on a man whose hate is tormented because
he abandoned his love without cause! Let him see her again!
[Throwing the curtain aside, the maid CATURIKĀ enters, with the
drawing board in her hand.]

CATURIKĀ: Here's the picture you painted of the lady. [She shows the 270
drawing board.]

BUFFOON: Dear friend, how well you've painted your feelings in this
sweet scene? My eyes almost stumble over the hollows and hills.

SĀNUMATĪ: What skill the king has! I feel as if my friend were before
me.

KING:

> The picture's imperfections are not hers,   275
> but this drawing does hint at her beauty.

4. The Ganges River.

SĀNUMATĪ: Such words reveal that suffering has increased his modesty as much as his love.

BUFFOON: Sir, I see three ladies now and they're all lovely to look at. Which is your Śakuntalā? 280

SĀNUMATĪ: Only a dim-witted fool like this wouldn't know such beauty!

KING: You guess which one!

BUFFOON: I guess Śakuntalā is the one you've drawn with flowers falling from her loosened locks of hair, with drops of sweat on her face, 285 with her arms hanging limp and tired as she stands at the side of a mango tree whose tender shoots are gleaming with the fresh water she poured. The other two are her friends.

KING: You are clever! Look at these signs of my passion!

> Smudges from my sweating fingers 290
> stain the edges of the picture
> and a tear fallen from my cheek
> has raised a wrinkle in the paint.

Caturikā, the scenery is only half-drawn. Go and bring my paints!

CATURIKĀ: Noble Mādhavya, hold the drawing board until I come 295 back!

KING: I'll hold it myself. [*He takes it, the maid exits.*]

> I rejected my love when she came to me,
> and how I worship her in a painted image—
> having passed by a river full of water, 300
> I'm longing now for an empty mirage.

BUFFOON: [*To himself.*] He's too far gone for a river now! He's looking for a mirage! [*Aloud.*] Sir, what else do you plan to draw here?

SĀNUMATĪ: He'll want to draw every place my friend loved.

KING:

> I'll draw the river Mālinī 305
> flowing through Himālaya's foothills
> where pairs of wild geese nest in the sand
> and deer recline on both riverbanks,
> where a doe is rubbing her left eye
> on the horn of a black buck antelope 310
> under a tree whose branches
> have bark dresses hanging to dry.

BUFFOON: [*To himself.*] Next he'll fill the drawing board with mobs of ascetics wearing long grassy beards.

KING: Dear friend, I've forgotten to draw an ornament that Śakuntalā 315 wore.

BUFFOON: What is it?

SĀNUMATĪ: It will suit her forest life and her tender beauty.

KING:

> I haven't drawn the mimosa flower on her ear,
> its filaments resting on her cheek, 320

or the necklace of tender lotus stalks,
lying on her breasts like autumn moonbeams.

BUFFOON: But why does the lady cover her face with her red lotus-
bud fingertips and stand trembling in fear? [*Looking closely.*] That
son-of-a-bee who steals nectar from flowers is attacking her face.   325
KING: Drive the impudent rogue away!
BUFFOON: You have the power to punish criminals. You drive him off!
KING: All right! Bee, favored guest of the flowering vines, why do you
frustrate yourself by flying here?[5]

A female bee waits on a flower,   330
thirsting for your love—
she refuses to drink
the sweet nectar without you.

SĀNUMATĪ: How gallantly he's driving him away!
BUFFOON: When you try to drive it away, this creature becomes   335
vicious.
KING: Why don't you stop when I command you?

Bee, if you touch the lips of my love
that lure you like a young tree's virgin buds,
lips I gently kissed in festivals of love,   340
I'll hold you captive in a lotus flower cage.

BUFFOON: Why isn't he afraid of your harsh punishment? [*Laughing,
he speaks to himself.*] He's gone crazy and I'll be the same if I go
on talking like this. [*Aloud.*] But sir, it's just a picture!
KING: A picture? How can that be?   345
SĀNUMATĪ: When I couldn't tell whether it was painted, how could he
realize he was looking at a picture?
KING: Dear friend, are you envious of me?

My heart's affection made me feel
the joy of seeing her—   350
but you reminded me again
that my love is only a picture.

[*He wipes away a tear.*]
SĀNUMATĪ: The effects of her absence make him quarrelsome.
KING: Dear friend, why do I suffer this endless pain?   355

Sleepless nights prevent our meeting in dreams;
her image in a picture is ruined by my tears.

SĀNUMATĪ: You have clearly atoned for the suffering your rejection
caused Śakuntalā.
CATURIKĀ: [*Entering.*] Victory my lord! I found the paint box and   360
started back right away ... but I met Queen Vasumatī with her
maid Taralikā on the path and she grabbed the box from my hand,
saying, "I'll bring it to the noble lord myself!"
BUFFOON: You were lucky to get away!

5. The king's preoccupation with the bee recalls the events of Act I.

CATURIKĀ: The queen's shawl got caught on a tree. While Taralikā was freeing it, I made my escape.

KING: Dear friend, the queen's pride can quickly turn to anger. Save this picture!

BUFFOON: You should say, "Save yourself!" [*Taking the picture, he stands up.*] If you escape the woman's deadly poison, then send   370
word to me in the Palace of the Clouds. [*He exits hastily.*]

SĀNUMATĪ: even though another woman has taken his heart and he feels indifferent to the queen, he treats her with respect.[6]

DOORKEEPER: [*Entering with a letter in her hand.*] Victory, king!

KING: Vetravatī, did you meet the queen on the way?   375

DOORKEEPER: I did, but when she saw the letter in my hand, she turned back.

KING: She knows that this is official and would not interrupt my work.

DOORKEEPER: King, the minister requests that you examine the con-   380
tents of this letter. He said that the enormous job of reckoning the revenue in this one citizen's case had taken all his time.

KING: Show me the letter! [*The girl hands it to him and he reads barely aloud.*] What is this? "A wealthy merchant sea captain named Dhanamitra has been lost in a shipwreck and the laws say that since the brave man was childless, his accumulated wealth all   385
goes to the king." It's terrible to be childless! A man of such wealth probably had several wives. We must find out if any one of his wives is pregnant!

DOORKEEPER: King, it's said that one of his wives, the daughter of a merchant of Ayodhyā, has performed the rite to ensure the birth of   390
a son.[7]

KING: The child in her womb surely deserves his parental wealth. Go! Report this to my minister!

DOORKEEPER: As the king commands! [*She starts to go.*]

KING: Come here a moment!   395

DOORKEEPER: I am here.

KING: Is it his offspring or not?

> When his subjects lose a kinsman,
> Duṣyanta will preserve the estates—
> unless there is some crime.   400
> Let this be proclaimed.

DOORKEEPER: It shall be proclaimed loudly. [*She exits; reenters.*] The king's order will be as welcome as rain in the right season.

KING: [*Sighing long and deeply.*] Families without offspring whose lines of succession are cut off lose their wealth to strangers when   405
the last male heir dies. When I die, this will happen to the wealth of the Puru dynasty.

DOORKEEPER: Heaven forbid such a fate!

KING: I curse myself for despising the treasure I was offered.

SĀNUMATĪ: He surely has my friend in mind when he blames himself.   410

---

6. Royal polygamy called for elaborate courtesies.   7. This rite (*puṃsavana*) is performed in the third month of pregnancy.

KING:

> I abandoned my lawful wife, the holy ground
> where I myself planted my family's glory,
> like earth sown with seed at the right time,
> ready to bear rich fruit in season.

SĀNUMATĪ: But your family's line will not be broken.   415

CATURIKĀ: [*In a stage whisper.*] The king is upset by the story of the merchant. Go and bring noble Mādhavya from the Palace of the Clouds to console him!

DOORKEEPER: A good idea! [*She exits.*]

KING: Duṣyanta's ancestors are imperiled.   420

> Our fathers drink the yearly libation
> mixed with my childless tears,
> knowing that there is no other son
> to offer the sacred funeral waters.

[*He falls into a faint.*]

CATURIKĀ: [*Looking at the bewildered* KING.] Calm yourself, my lord!   425

SĀNUMATĪ: Though a light shines, his separation from Śakuntalā keeps him in a state of dark depression. I could make him happy now, but I've heard Indra's consort consoling Śakuntalā with the news that the gods are hungry for their share of the ancestral oblations and will soon conspire to have her husband welcome his lawful   430 wife. I'll have to wait for the auspicious time, but meanwhile I'll cheer my friend by reporting his condition. [*She exits, flying into the air.*]

VOICE OFFSTAGE: Help! Brahman-murder![8]

KING: [*Regaining consciousness, listening.*] Is it Mādhavya's cry of pain? Who's there?   435

DOORKEEPER: King, your friend is in danger. Help him!

KING: Who dares to threaten him?

DOORKEEPER: Some invisible spirit seized him and dragged him to the roof of the Palace of the Clouds.

KING: [*Getting up.*] Not this! Even my house is haunted by spirits.   440

> When I don't even recognize
> the blunders I commit every day,
> how can I keep track
> of where my subjects stray?

VOICE OFFSTAGE: Dear friend! Help! Help!   445

KING: [*Breaking into a run.*] Friend, don't be afraid! I'm coming!

VOICE OFFSTAGE: [*Repeating the call for help.*] Why shouldn't I be afraid? Someone is trying to split my neck in three, like a stalk of sugar cane.

KING: [*Casting a glance.*] Quickly, my bow!   450

BOW-BEARER: [*Entering with a bow in hand.*] Here are your bow and quiver.

---

8. Murder of a brahman is among the most heinous sins.

[*The* KING *takes his bow and arrows.*]
VOICE OFFSTAGE:

> I'll kill you as a tiger kills struggling prey!
> I'll drink fresh blood from your tender neck!
> Take refuge now in the bow Duṣyanta lifts   455
> to calm the fears of the oppressed!

KING: [*Angrily.*] How dare you abuse my name? Stop, carrion-eater!
Or you will not live! [*He strings his bow.*] Vetravatī, lead the way
to the stairs!

DOORKEEPER: This way, king.   460
[*All move forward in haste.*]

KING: [*Searching around.*] There is no one here!

VOICE OFFSTAGE: Help! Help! I see you. Don't you see me? I'm like a
mouse caught by a cat! My life is hopeless!

KING: Don't count on your powers of invisibility! My magical arrows
will find you. I aim this arrow: 465

> It will strike its doomed target
> and spare the brahman it must save —
> a wild goose can extract the milk
> and leave the water untouched.[9]

[*He aims the arrow. Then Indra's charioteer* MĀTALI *enters, having
released the* BUFFOON.]

MĀTALI: King!   470

> Indra sets demons as your targets;
> draw your bow against them!
> Send friends gracious glances
> rather than deadly arrows!

KING: [*Withdrawing his arrow.*] Mātali, welcome to great Indra's char-   475
ioteer!

BUFFOON: [*Entering.*] He tried to slaughter me like a sacrificial beast
and this king is greeting him with honors!

MĀTALI: [*Smiling.*] Your Majesty, hear why Indra has sent me to you!

KING: I am all attention.   480

MĀTALI: There is an army of demons descended from one-hundred-
headed Kālanemi, known to be invincible . . .

KING: I have already heard it from Nārada, the gods' messenger.

MĀTALI:

> He is invulnerable to your friend Indra,
> so you are appointed to lead the charge —   485
> the moon dispels the darkness of night
> since the sun cannot drive it out.

Take your weapon, mount Indra's chariot, and prepare for victory!

KING: Indra favors me with this honor. But why did you attack Māḍhavya?   490

---

9. The *haṃsa*; in Sanskrit poetry this bird is said to have the ability to separate milk from the water
with which it has been diluted.

MĀTALI: I'll tell you! From the signs of anguish Your Majesty showed,
I knew that you were despondent. I attacked him to arouse your
anger.

> A fire blazes when fuel is added;
> a cobra provoked raises its hood—   495
> men can regain lost courage
> if their emotions are aroused.

KING: [*In a stage whisper.*] Dear friend, I cannot disobey a command
from the lord of heaven. Inform my minister Piśuna of this and tell
him this for me: 500

> Concentrate your mind on guarding my subjects!
> My bow is strung to accomplish other work.

BUFFOON: Whatever you command!
[*He exits.*]
MĀTALI: Mount the chariot, Your Majesty!
[*The* KING *mimes mounting the chariot; all exit.*]

Act VII

[*The* KING *enters with* MĀTALI *by the skyway, mounted on a chariot.*]
KING: Mātali, though I carried out his command, I feel unworthy of
the honors Indra gave me.
MĀTALI: [*Smiling.*] Your Majesty, neither of you seems satisfied.

> You belittle the aid you gave Indra
> in face of the honors he conferred,   5
> and he, amazed by your heroic acts,
> deems his hospitality too slight.

KING: No, not so! When I was taking leave, he honored me beyond
my heart's desire and shared his throne with me in the presence of
the gods: 10

> Indra gave me a garland of coral flowers[1]
> tinged with sandalpowder from his chest,
> while he smiled at his son Jayanta,
> who stood there barely hiding his envy.

MĀTALI: Don't you deserve whatever you want from Indra?   15

> Indra's heaven of pleasures has twice
> been saved by rooting out thorny demons—
> your smooth-jointed arrows have now done
> what Viṣṇu once did with his lion claws.[2]

KING: Here too Indra's might deserves the praise.   20

> When servants succeed in great tasks,
> they act in hope of their master's praise—

---

1. The coral trees of heaven bear never-fading flowers.   2. In his incarnation as half-man, half-lion, the god Viṣṇu slew a demon.

> would dawn scatter the darkness
> if he were not the sun's own charioteer?

MĀTALI: This attitude suits you well! [*He moves a little distance.*] Look 25
over there, Your Majesty! See how your own glorious fame has
reached the vault of heaven!

> Celestial artists are drawing your exploits
> on leaves of the wish-granting creeper[3]
> with colors of the nymphs' cosmetic paints, 30
> and bards are moved to sing of you in ballads.

KING: Mātali, in my desire to do battle with the demons, I did not
notice the path we took to heaven as we climbed through the sky
yesterday. Which course of the winds are we traveling?

MĀTALI:

> They call this path of the wind Parivaha— 35
> freed from darkness by Viṣṇu's second stride,
> it bears the Gaṅgā's three celestial streams[4]
> and turns stars in orbit, dividing their rays.

KING: Mātali, this is why my soul, my senses, and my heart feel calm.
[*He looks at the chariot wheels.*] We've descended to the level of 40
the clouds.

MĀTALI: How do you know?

KING:

> Crested cuckoos fly between the spokes,
> lightning flashes glint off the horses' coats,
> and a fine mist wets your chariot's wheels— 45
> all signs that we go over rain-filled clouds.

MĀTALI: In a moment you'll be back in your own domain, Your Majesty.

KING: [*Looking down.*] Our speeding chariot makes the mortal world
appear fantastic. Look! 50

> Mountain peaks emerge as the earth descends,
> branches spread up from a sea of leaves,
> fine lines become great rivers to behold—
> the world seems to hurtle toward me.

MĀTALI: You observe well! [*He looks with great reverence.*] The 55
beauty of earth is sublime.

KING: Mātali, what mountain do I see stretching into the eastern and
western seas, rippled with streams of liquid gold, like a gateway of
twilight clouds?

MĀTALI: Your Majesty, it is called the "Golden Peak," the mountain 60
of the demigods, a place where austerities are practiced to perfection.

---

3. The *kalpalatā* vine that grows in Indra's heaven.   4. In heaven the Ganges flows with three streams
before descending to earth. As the cosmic strider, Viṣṇu scattered the darkness from heaven.

Mārīca, the descendant of Brahmā,
a father of both demons and gods,
lives the life of an ascetic here
in the company of Aditi, his wife.   65

KING: One must not ignore good fortune! I shall perform the rite of
circumambulating the sage.
MĀTALI: An excellent idea!
  [*The two mime descending.*]
KING: [*Smiling.*]

The chariot wheels make no sound,
they raise no clouds of dust,   70
they touch the ground unhindered—
nothing marks the chariot's descent.

MĀTALI: It is because of the extraordinary power that you and Indra
both possess.
KING: Mātali, where is Mārīca's hermitage?   75
MĀTALI: [*Pointing with his hand.*]

Where the sage stands staring at the sun,
as immobile as the trunk of a tree,
his body half-buried in an ant hill,
with a snake skin on his chest,
his throat pricked by a necklace   80
of withered thorny vines,
wearing a coil of long matted hair
filled with nests of śakunta birds.

KING: I do homage to the sage for his severe austerity.
MĀTALI: [*Pulling hard on the chariot reins.*] Great king, let us enter   85
Mārīca's hermitage, where Aditi nurtures the celestial coral trees.
KING: This tranquil place surpasses heaven. I feel as if I'm bathing in
a lake of nectar.
MĀTALI: [*Stopping the chariot.*] Dismount, Your Majesty!
KING: [*Dismounting.*] Mātali, what about you?   90
MĀTALI: I have stopped the chariot. I'll dismount too. [*He does so.*]
This way, Your Majesty! [*He walks around.*] You can see the
grounds of the ascetics' grove ahead.
KING: I am amazed!

In this forest of wish-fulfilling trees   95
ascetics live on only the air they breathe
and perform their ritual ablutions
in water colored by golden lotus pollen.
They sit in trance on jeweled marble slabs
and stay chaste among celestial nymphs,   100
practicing austerities in the place
that other seek to win by penances.

MĀTALI: Great men always aspire to rare heights! [*He walks around,
calling aloud.*] O venerable Śākalya, what is the sage Mārīca doing
now? What do you say? In response to Aditi's question about the   105

duties of a devoted wife, he is talking in a gathering of great sages' wives.[5]

KING: [*Listening.*] We must wait our turn.

MĀTALI: [*Looking at the* KING.] Your Majesty, rest at the foot of this aśoka tree. Meanwhile, I'll look for a chance to announce you to 110 Indra's father.

KING: As you advise . . . [*He stops.*]

MĀTALI: Your Majesty, I'll attend to this. [*He exits.*]

KING: [*Indicating he feels an omen.*]

> I have no hope for my desire.
> Why does my arm throb in vain?   115
> Once good fortune is lost,
> it becomes constant pain.

VOICE OFFSTAGE: Don't be so wild! Why is his nature so stubborn?

KING: [*Listening.*] Unruly conduct is out of place here. Whom are they reprimanding? [*Looking toward the sound, surprised.*] Who is 120 this child, guarded by two female ascetics? A boy who acts more like a man.

> He has dragged this lion cub
> from its mother's half-full teat
> to play with it, and with his hand   125
> he violently tugs its mane.

[*The* BOY *enters as described, with two female ascetics.*]

BOY: Open your mouth, lion! I want to count your teeth!

FIRST ASCETIC: Nasty boy, why do you torture creatures we love like our children? You're getting too headstrong! The sages gave you the right name when they called you "Sarvadamana, Tamer-of-everything." 130

KING: Why is my heart drawn to this child, as if he were my own flesh? I don't have a son. That is why I feel tender toward him . . .

SECOND ASCETIC: The lioness will maul you if you don't let go of her cub!

BOY: [*Smiling.*] Oh, I'm scared to death! [*Pouting.*]

KING:

> This child appears to be   135
> the seed of hidden glory,
> like a spark of fire
> awaiting fuel to burn.

FIRST ASCETIC: Child, let go of the lion cub and I'll give you another toy!   140

BOY: Where is it? Give it to me! [*He reaches out his hand.*]

KING: Why does he bear the mark of a king who turns the wheel of empire?

> A hand with fine webs connecting the fingers
> opens as he reaches for the object greedily,   145

---

5. In Gupta society, the sages were teachers of *dharma* and of the norms of behavior for women of the upper classes.

like a single lotus with faint inner petals
spread open in the red glow of early dawn.

SECOND ASCETIC: Suvratā, you can't stop him with words! The sage
Mārkaṇḍeya's son left a brightly painted clay bird in my hut. Get it
for him!   150
FIRST ASCETIC: I will! [*She exits.*]
BOY: But until it comes I'll play with this cub.
KING: I am attracted to this pampered boy . . .

> Lucky are fathers whose laps give refuge
> to the muddy limbs of adoring little sons   155
> when childish smiles show budding teeth
> and jumbled sounds make charming words.

SECOND ASCETIC: Well, he ignores me. [*She looks back.*] Is one of the
sage's sons here? [*Looking at the* KING.] Sir, please come here!
Make him loosen his grip and let go of the lion cub! He's tor-   160
menting it in his cruel child's play.
KING: [*Approaching the* BOY, *smiling.*] Stop! You're a great sage's son!

> When self-control is your duty by birth,
> why do you violate the sanctuary laws
> and ruin the animals' peaceful life,   165
> like a young black snake in a sandal tree?

SECOND ASCETIC: Sir, he's not a sage's son.
KING: His actions and his looks confirm it. I based my false assumption
on his presence in this place. [*He does what she asked; responding
to the* BOY'*s touch, he speaks to himself.*]

> Even my limbs feel delighted   170
> from the touch of a stranger's son—
> the father at whose side he grew
> must feel pure joy in his heart.

SECOND ASCETIC: [*Examining them both.*] It's amazing! Amazing!
KING: What is it, madam?   175
SECOND ASCETIC: This boy looks surprisingly like you. He doesn't even
know you, and he's acting naturally.
KING: [*Fondling the child.*] If he's not the son of an ascetic, what
lineage does he belong to?
SECOND ASCETIC: The family of Puru.   180
KING: [*To himself.*] What? His ancestry is the same as mine . . . so this
lady thinks he resembles me. The family vow of Puru's descendants
is to spend their last days in the forest.

> As world protectors they first choose
> palaces filled with sensuous pleasures,   185
> but later, their homes are under trees
> and one wife shares the ascetic vows.

[*Aloud.*] But mortals cannot enter this realm on their own.
SECOND ASCETIC: You're right, sir. His mother is a nymph's child. She
gave birth to him here in the hermitage of Mārīca.   190

KING: [*In a stage whisper.*] Here is a second ground for hope! [*Aloud.*] What famed royal sage claims her as his wife?

SECOND ASCETIC: Who would even think of speaking the name of a man who rejected his lawful wife?

KING: [*To himself.*] Perhaps this story points to me. What if I ask the 195 name of the boy's mother? No, it is wrong to ask about another man's wife.

FIRST ASCETIC: [*Returning with a clay bird in her hand.*] Look, Sarvadamana, a śakunta! Look! Isn't it lovely?

BOY: Where's my mother? 200

BOTH ASCETICS: He's tricked by the similarity of names.[6] He wants his mother.

SECOND ASCETIC: Child, she told you to look at the lovely clay śakunta bird.

KING: [*To himself.*] What? Is his mother's name Śakuntalā? But 205 names can be the same. Even a name is a mirage . . . a false hope to herald despair.

BOY: I like this bird! [*He picks up the toy.*]

FIRST ASCETIC: [*Looking frantically.*] Oh, I don't see the amulet-box on his wrist! 210

KING: Don't be alarmed! It broke off while he was tussling with the lion cub. [*He goes to pick it up.*]

BOTH ASCETICS: Don't touch it! Oh, he's already picked it up! [*With their hands on their chests, they stare at each other in amazement.*]

KING: Why did you warn me against it?

FIRST ASCETIC: It contains the magical herb called Aparājitā,[7] honored 215 sir. Mārīca gave it to him at his birth ceremony. He said that if it fell to the ground no one but his parents or himself could pick it up.

KING: And if someone else does pick it up?

FIRST ASCETIC: Then it turns into a snake and strikes. 220

KING: Have you two seen it so transformed?

BOTH ASCETICS: Many times.

KING: [*To himself, joyfully.*] Why not rejoice in the fulfillment of my heart's desire? [*He embraces the child.*]

SECOND ASCETIC: Suvratā, come, let's tell Śakuntalā that her penances 225 are over.

[*Both ascetics exit.*]

BOY: Let me go! I want my mother!

KING: Son, you will greet your mother with me.

BOY: My father is Duṣyanta, not you!

KING: This contradiction confirms the truth. 230

[*ŚAKUNTALĀ enters, wearing the single braid of a woman in mourning.*]

---

6. Śakunta, one of the Sanskrit and Prakrit words for "bird," is etymologically related to Śakuntalā (Woman of the Birds), who was so named because she was found in the forest in the company of birds. Now her son, Bharata, mistakes śakunta for śakuntalā. Like the women, the child speaks Prakrit, the "natural" language, but once he has entered the social world of men he must speak Sanskrit.
7. Meaning "invincible" or "unvanquished."

ŚAKUNTALĀ: Even though Sarvadamana's amulet kept its natural form instead of changing into a snake, I can't hope that my destiny will be fulfilled. But maybe what my friend Sānumatī reports is right.

KING: [*Looking at* ŚAKUNTALĀ.] It is Śakuntalā!

> Wearing dusty gray garments,   235
> her face gaunt from penances,
> her bare braid[8] hanging down —
> she bears with perfect virtue
> the trial of long separation
> my cruelty forced on her.   240

ŚAKUNTALĀ: [*Seeing the* KING *pale with suffering.*] He doesn't resemble my noble husband. Whose touch defiles my son when the amulet is protecting him?

BOY: [*Going to his mother.*] Mother, who is this stranger who calls me "son"?   245

KING: My dear, I see that you recognize me now. Even my cruelty to you is transformed by your grace.

ŚAKUNTALĀ: [*To herself.*] Heart, be consoled! My cruel fate has finally taken pity on me. It is my noble husband!

KING:

> Memory chanced to break my dark delusion   250
> and you stand before me in beauty,
> like the moon's wife Rohiṇī
> as she rejoins her lord after an eclipse.

ŚAKUNTALĀ: Victory to my noble husband![9] Vic . . . [*She stops when the word is half-spoken, her throat choked with tears.*]

KING: Beautiful Śakuntalā,   255

> Even choked by your tears,
> the word "victory" is my triumph
> on your bare pouting lips,
> pale-red flowers of your face.

BOY: Mother, who is he?   260

ŚAKUNTALĀ: Child, ask the powers of fate!

KING: [*Falling at* ŚAKUNTALĀ*'s feet.*][1]

> May the pain of my rejection
> vanish from your heart;
> delusion clouded my weak mind
> and darkness obscured good fortune —   265
> a blind man tears off a garland,
> fearing the bite of a snake.

ŚAKUNTALĀ: Noble husband, rise! Some crime I had committed in a former life surely came to fruit and made my kind husband indifferent to me.   270

> [*The* KING *rises.*]

---

8. A woman separated from her lover neglected her looks and wore her hair in a single braid.   9. The traditional formula for greeting a royal husband.   1. In Sanskrit poetry, the repentant lover, regardless of his rank, must fall at the feet of his beloved, expressing his remorse and asking for her forgiveness.

But how did my noble husband come to remember this woman
who was doomed to pain?

KING: I shall tell you after I have removed the last barb of sorrow.

> In my delusion I once ignored
> a teardrop burning your lip—   275
> let me dry the tear on your lash
> to end the pain of remorse!

[*He does so.*]

ŚAKUNTALĀ: [*Seeing the signet ring.*] My noble husband, this is the
ring!

KING: I regained my memory when the ring was recovered.   280

ŚAKUNTALĀ: When it was lost, I tried in vain to convince my noble
husband who I was.

KING: Let the vine take back this flower as a sign of her union with
spring.

ŚAKUNTALĀ: I don't trust it. Let my noble husband wear it!   285

[MĀTALI *enters.*]

MĀTALI: Good fortune! This meeting with your lawful wife and the
sight of your son's face are reasons to rejoice.

KING: The sweet fruit of my desire! Mātali, didn't Indra know about
all this?

MĀTALI: What is unknown to the gods? Come Your Majesty! The sage   290
Mārīca grants you an audience.

KING: Śakuntalā, hold our son's hand! We shall go to see Mārīca
together.

ŚAKUNTALĀ: I feel shy about appearing before my elders in my husband's company.   295

KING: But it is customary at a joyous time like this. Come! Come!

[*They all walk around. Then* MĀRĪCA *enters with* ADITI; *they sit.*]

MĀRĪCA: [*Looking at the* KING.]

> Aditi, this is king Duṣyanta,
> who leads Indra's armies in battle;
> his bow lets your son's thunderbolt
> lie ready with its tip unblunted.   300

ADITI: He bears himself with dignity.

MĀTALI: Your Majesty, the parents of the gods look at you with
affection reserved for a son. Approach them!

KING: Mātali, the sages so describe this pair.

> Source of the sun's twelve potent forms,   305
> parents of Indra, who rules the triple world,
> birthplace of Viṣṇu's primordial form,
> sired by Brahmā's sons,[2] Marīci and Dakṣa.

MĀTALI: Correct!

KING: [*Bowing.*] Indra's servant, Duṣyanta, bows to you both.   310

MĀRĪCA: My son, live long and protect the earth!

---

2. These references establish Aditi and Marīca's status as primordial parents of the universe and of the
gods themselves.

ADITI: My son, be an invincible warrior!
ŚAKUNTALĀ: I worship at your feet with my son.
MĀRĪCA:

> Child, with a husband like Indra
> and a son like his son Jayanta,   315
> you need no other blessing.
> Be like Indra's wife Paulomī!

ADITI: Child, may your husband honor you and may your child live
long to give both families joy! Be seated!
[*All sit near* MĀRĪCA.]
MĀRĪCA: [*Pointing to each one.*]

> By the turn of fortune,   320
> virtuous Śakuntalā, her noble son,
> and the king are reunited—
> faith and wealth with order.

KING: Sir, first came the success of my hopes, then the sight of you.
Your kindness is unparalleled.   325

> First flowers appear, then fruits,
> first clouds rise, then rain falls,
> but here the chain of events is reversed—
> first came success, then your blessing.

MĀTALI: This is the way the creator gods give blessings.   330
KING: Sir, I married your charge by secret marriage rites. When her
relatives brought her to me after some time, my memory failed and
I sinned against the sage Kaṇva, your kinsman. When I saw the ring,
I remembered that I had married his daughter. This is all so strange!

> Like one who doubts the existence   335
> of an elephant who walks in front of him
> but feels convinced by seeing footprints,
> my mind has taken strange turns.

MĀRĪCA: My son, you need not take the blame. Even your delusion
has another cause. Listen!   340
KING: I am attentive.
MĀRĪCA: When Menakā took her bewildered daughter from the steps
of the nymph's shrine and brought her to my wife, I knew through
meditation that you had rejected this girl as your lawful wife
because of Durvāsas' curse, and that the curse would end when you   345
saw the ring.
KING: [*Sighing.*] So I am freed of blame.
ŚAKUNTALĀ: [*To herself.*] And I am happy to learn that I wasn't
rejected by my husband without cause. But I don't remember being
cursed. Maybe the empty heart of love's separation made me deaf   350
to the curse ... my friends did warn me to show the ring to my
husband ...
MĀRĪCA: My child, I have told you the truth. Don't be angry with your
husband!

> You were rejected when the curse   355
> that clouded memory made him cruel,
> but now darkness is lifted
> and your power is restored—
> a shadow has no shape
> in a badly tarnished mirror,   360
> but when the surface is clean
> it can easily be seen.

KING: Sir, here is the glory of my family! [*He takes the child by the hand.*]

MĀRĪCA: Know that he is destined to turn the wheel of your empire!

> His chariot will smoothly cross   365
> the ocean's rough waves
> and as a mighty warrior
> he will conquer the seven continents.
> Here he is called Sarvadamana,
> Tamer-of-everything;   370
> later when his burden is the world,
> men will call him Bharata, Sustainer.[3]

KING: Since you performed his birth ceremonies, we can hope for all this.

ADITI: Sir, let Kaṇva be told that his daughter's hopes have been ful-   375
filled. Menakā, who loves her daughter, is here in attendance.

ŚAKUNTALĀ: [*To herself.*] The lady expresses my own desire.

MĀRĪCA: He knows everything already through the power of his austerity.

KING: This is why the sage was not angry at me.   380

MĀRĪCA: Still, I want to hear his response to this joyful reunion. Who is there?

DISCIPLE: [*Entering.*] Sir, it is I.

MĀRĪCA: Gālava, fly through the sky and report the joyous reunion to Kaṇva in my own words: "The curse is ended. Śakuntalā and her   385 son are embraced by Duṣyanta now that his memory is restored."

DISCIPLE: As you command, sir! [*He exits.*]

MĀRĪCA: My son, mount your friend Indra's chariot with your wife and son and return to your royal capital!

KING: As you command, sir!   390

MĀRĪCA: My son, what other joy can I give you?

KING: There is no greater joy, but if you will:

> May the king serve nature's good!
> May priests honor the goddess of speech!
> And may Śiva's dazzling power   395
> destroy my cycle of rebirths![4]

[*All exit.*]

---

3. Bharata is to become the emperor after whom ancient India (*Bhāratavarṣa*) is named. *Seven continents:* those of the Hindu universe.   4. All Sanskrit plays end with a traditional verse called *bharatavākya* ("the utterance of [the sage] Bharata"), in which the play's protagonist invokes the blessings of the gods on himself and the universal order.

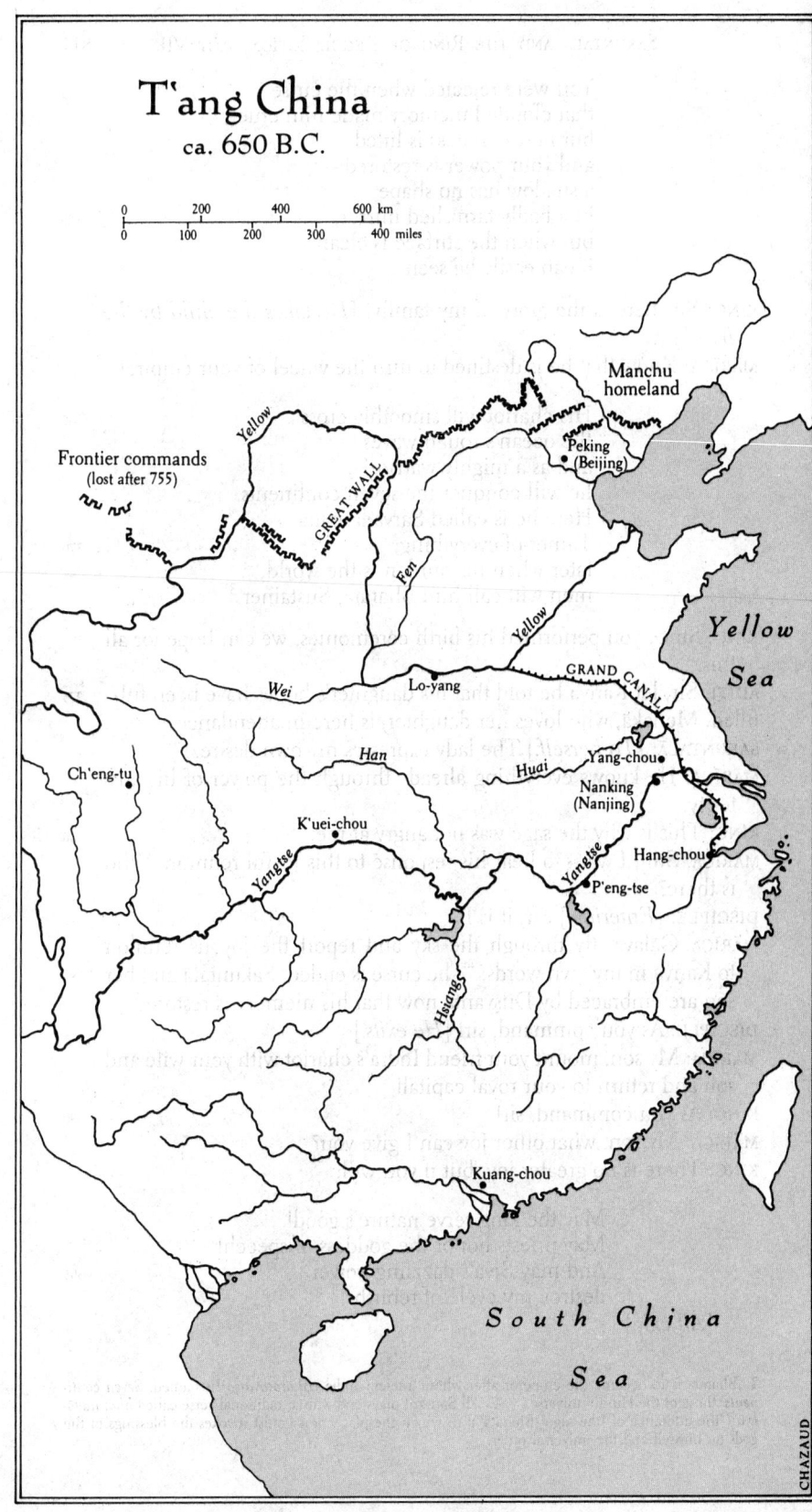

T'ang China
ca. 650 B.C.

0   200   400   600 km
0   100   200   300   400 miles

Manchu
homeland

Frontier commands
(lost after 755)

Peking
(Beijing)

Yellow

GREAT WALL

Fen

Yellow

Wei

Lo-yang

GRAND CANAL

Yellow
Sea

Han

Huai

Yang-chou

Ch'eng-tu

Nanking
(Nanjing)

K'uei-chou

Hang-chou

Yangtse

P'eng-tse

Yangtse

Huang

South China

Sea

Kuang-chou

CHAZAUD

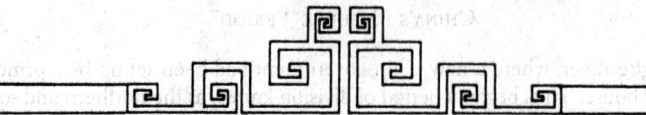

China's "Middle Period"

The "middle" in our Western concept of the Middle Ages signifies an "in between," the centuries between the collapse of the Roman Empire and the Renaissance. And though many cultural and literary historians have sought to correct the common image of these centuries as a period of intellectual and cultural stagnation, they remain a problematic phase in the story of Western civilization and its literature. In the case of China the situation is quite the reverse. If we use Western period terms, the *middle* of a Chinese "Middle Age" would mean "central." It is a period when Chinese thought and literature reached what many regard as their highest forms. And it is a period that later ages of Chinese history looked back to with awe. In the eleventh century Su Shih expressed a sense of intimidation by the past that was to continue through later centuries.

> Those with knowledge first fashion a thing; those with ability carry it through to fullness. It is not accomplished by one person alone. The superior man in his studies and all the various artisans in their skills reached a state of completion in the passage from the Three Dynasties of antiquity through the Han to the T'ang. When poetry reached Tu Fu, when prose reached Han Yü, when calligraphy reached Yen Chen-ch'ing, and when painting reached Wu Tao-tzu, all the variations of past and present and all the possibilities in the world were over.

Tu Fu, Han Yü, Yen Chen-ch'ing, and Wu Tao-tzu all lived during the T'ang Dynasty (618–907). Su Shih's own dynasty, the Sung (960–1279), might equally claim to have brought thought (and despite Su Shih's partiality for Wu Tao-tzu, painting as well) to a height that became a standard of achievement for the centuries that followed. Neither claim is true, of course. Chinese culture and literature continued to evolve after this splendid "Middle Age." They did not merely repeat the past any more than the European Renaissance merely recapitulated classical antiquity. Nevertheless, the great medieval dynasties of T'ang and Sung have loomed large in the national imagination.

In the second century the Han Empire was crumbling. Great families dominated the central government, regional warlords were carving out their own domains, and peasant uprisings weakened the central government's authority. In the face of a collapsing social order, writers and intellectuals began to show widespread disenchantment with the Confucian values of public service. By the turn of the third century, China had become divided into three regional states, known as the Three Kingdoms: Shu in the west; Wu in the south; and in the heartland in the state of the warlord Ts'ao Ts'ao, who used the last puppet emperor of the Han Empire to give him legitimacy.

After Ts'ao Ts'ao's death in A.D. 220, his successor declared the Han Empire ended and established a new dynasty, the Wei. This survived only a few generations before it was overthrown by another dynasty, the Chin, which managed briefly to reunify the old empire. The Chin Dynasty fell in 316 to non-Chinese invaders from the north, and many of the great families of the north fled south of

the Yangtse River, where a new Chin government had been set up by a prince of
the royal house. Thus began a period of division known as the northern and southern dynasties. The north was divided among various states, each with a non-
Chinese ruling and military class. The south was ruled by a succession of short-
lived Chinese dynasties.

During this period Confucianism ebbed dramatically. Taoist sects, concentrating on medical, alchemical, and magical arts, flourished and founded great temples in the south. Buddhism, which had been making minor inroads for many
centuries, became a major force. Buddhist missionaries from India and central
Asia came to China in increasing numbers, and working together with Chinese
monks, they began the immense task of translating the important Buddhist scriptures into Chinese. Both Taoism and Buddhism promised, each in its own way,
the means for personal salvation, which lay outside the purely social and ethical
interests of Confucianism.

Hence the private life of the individual apart from social role became an
important concern in literature after the Han Empire. Writers were fascinated by
the figure of the "recluse," whether a true hermit or simply someone who decided,
like T'ao Ch'ien, to live at home and not serve in government. This interest was
greatly encouraged by political instability and court factionalism, which led to the
execution of more than a few writers. But the concern for the individual was
deeper than a simple desire to escape the hazards of public life. Those who did
serve in the government often cultivated and approved a stylish self-conscious
eccentricity that was the very opposite of the self-effacing norms of behavior
enjoined by the Confucian tradition. Nature, rather than the polity, held their
attention, whether *nature* meant that of the individual or the magnificent and
solitary landscapes of south China.

Owing to the loss of north China to non-Chinese overlords, most literature of
the period comes from the southern dynasties, where the people saw themselves
as the inheritors of traditional Chinese culture. In an important moment for the
history of Chinese civilization, cultural legitimacy came to be defined not as occupation of a place (the north China plain, the ancient heartland) but as a portable
tradition. Most of our knowledge of early China reaches us through the filter of
the southern dynasties—their libraries, their literary histories, their criticism, and
their anthologies. Although the north tried desperately to assert itself as the legitimate heir of the Chinese past, it too felt the power of the southern dynasties'
appropriation of "tradition."

In the long run it was a northern dynasty, the Sui, that reunified China, to be
quickly supplanted by another northern dynasty, the T'ang. Drawn by the cultural
legacy of the south, the two dynasties slowly forged a new culture that combined
northern and southern traditions. The T'ang Dynasty was an age of cultural confidence and, initially at least, of expansion, with T'ang armies pushing at the frontiers on all sides. Particularly important was the expansion to the northwest and
control of the trade routes to the west. The upper class was attracted by the exotic
goods, music, and ideas that came in along the caravan routes. Taoism and Buddhism continued to be powerful, supported by the common people and the imperial government alike; and Confucianism, the basis of state organization, enjoyed
a resurgence.

Even today, a reader's first association with the T'ang period is likely to be its
poetry. The composition of poetry came to be used in the examination by which
intellectuals entered government service. It became an integral part of social life,
a medium of basic social exchange. Perhaps nowhere else in the world has lyric
poetry ever occupied such a central position, and from this context emerged a
number of major poets whose work made them familiar personalities throughout

the rest of Chinese history. A great poem might deal with large philosophical issues but just as easily with meeting an old friend. Poetry was seen as a way to record both individual personality and the historical moment. Through the poem the poet became alive for future readers, and in that person the philosophical idea or the moment became alive.

In the 750s, the confidence of the dynasty was broken by a major rebellion of the northeastern armies. The capital at Ch'ang-an was taken and the emperor was forced to flee. Although the rebellion was soon put down, the dynasty never quite regained its former authority. In 907 the T'ang Dynasty finally fell, and after a half-century interregnum of warring kingdoms, it was replaced in 960 by a new dynasty, the Sung.

The Sung Dynasty saw major social and intellectual changes. The old aristo-cratic families that dominated the T'ang Dynasty had lost their power, and the government was opened up to social groups that had previously been largely excluded from political participation. The lower Yangtse River region became a major population center, and southeasterners increasingly dominated Chinese intellectual life, as they would in later ages. In 1127 the Chin, a sinicized but non-Chinese state on the northeastern frontier, conquered north China, and the Sung Dynasty was reestablished in the south, with its capital in Hang-chou.

Although printing existed earlier, the eleventh century saw the rapid develop-ment of commercial printing, allowing literary works and scholarship a far wider audience than ever before. As in Europe, the dissemination of learning through the printed book had a significant impact on the civilization. A reexamination of the Confucian classics gave rise to a movement known as neo-Confucianism, which came to dominate intellectual life. Meanwhile Sung Dynasty classical liter-ature continued the forms of the T'ang period, but with a difference of tone—a less intense, more reflective manner that for later ages seemed to embody the personality of the dynasty. In the urban centers of the south in the twelfth and thirteenth centuries there also developed a new vernacular literature, recreating in writing the ambience of professional storytelling. Thus began a vernacular literary tradition that would evolve alongside classical literature up to the present.

FURTHER READING

A general study of Chinese poetry from the Han Dynasty through the T'ang can be found in Burton Watson, *Chinese Lyricism* (1971). For a general introduction to the forms of Chinese poetry there is James J. Y. Liu, *The Art of Chinese Poetry* (1962). A somewhat different approach can be found in Stephen Owen, *Traditional Chinese Poetry and Poetics: Omen of the World* (1985). A general study of poetry before the T'ang is Kang-i Sun Chang, *Six Dynasties Poetry* (1986); the eighth century is covered in Stephen Owen, *The Great Age of Chinese Poetry: The High T'ang* (1980). The Sung period is studied in Burton Watson's translation of Yoshikawa Kojiro, *An Introduction to Sung Poetry* (1967).

PRONOUNCING GLOSSARY

The following list uses common English syllables to provide rough equivalents of selected words whose pronunciation may be unfamiliar to the general reader.

Ch'ang-an: *chahng–ahn*

Hang-chou: *hahng–joe*

Sui: *sway*

Su Shih: *soo shir*

Tao Ch'ien: *tau chyen*

Wei: *way*

Wu Tao-tzu: *woo dau–dzuh*

Yen Chen-ch'ing: *yen juhn–ching*

CHINA'S "MIDDLE PERIOD"

TEXTS	CONTEXTS
	220–280 The Three Kingdoms period, when China is divided into three regional states
	280 China is briefly reunified under the Chin Dynasty
	316 North China falls into the hands of non-Chinese invaders and the court moves to the south; the following period is known as the northern and southern dynasties
	350–550 Flourishing of Buddhism and translation of Buddhist scriptures
365–427 T'ao Ch'ien, poet and farmer	
400–450 The flourishing of landscape poetry	
500–550 Development of literary criticism, literary history, and anthology-making in the south	
	589 A northern dynasty, the Sui, reunifies China
	618 The T'ang Dynasty supplants the Sui
	629 The journey of the Buddhist monk Tripitaka, the hero of *Monkey*
ca. 690 Composition of poetry included as part of the *chin-shih* examination, which young men take to qualify for the best posts in the government	
ca. 699–761 Wang Wei, poet	
701–762 Li Po, poet	
712–770 Tu Fu, poet	713–755 The "High T'ang" and the reign of Hsüan-tsung; the capital, Ch'ang-an, is a cosmopolitan center
	755 The rebellion of the northeastern armies under their general An Lu-shan drives the emperor from the capital

TEXTS	CONTEXTS
768–824 Han Yü, poet and prose writer, advocate of "old-style" prose	
772–846 Po Chü-yi, poet	
779–831 Yüan Chen, poet and author of *The Story of Ying-ying*	
791–817 Li Ho, poet	
803–852 Tu Mu, poet	**800** Revival of Confucianism under Han Yu
813–858 Li Shang-yin, poet	
	907 Final collapse of the T'ang into numerous regional kingdoms
	960 Founding of the Sung Dynasty and the reunification of China
981 Completion of the *Tai-p'ing kuang-chi*, a vast compendium in which is preserved almost all the prose fiction from the T'ang and earlier	
1000–1100 Rise in popularity of song lyrics or *tz'u*, sung at parties and by courtesans from the Entertainment Quarters • Rapid expansion od commercial and state-supported printing	**1000–1100** Development of Neo-Confucianism, which used the Confucian classics as a ground for philosophical reflection on human nature
1084–ca. 1151 Li Ch'ing-chao, lyricist and author of Afterword to *Records on Metal and Stone*	
1127–1279 Rise of drama and professional storytelling in vernacular Chinese, especially in Hang-chou, the capital of the Southern Sung	**1127** North China falls to non-Chinese invaders from the northeast; the dynasty is reestablished south of the Yangtse River. This period, lasting until the Mongol conquest, is known as the Southern Sung
	1279 Mongols conquer South China
	1299 Marco Polo's account of his visit to China

T'AO CH'IEN
365–427

In the second decade of the fourth century, non-Chinese invaders from the north conquered north China and took the reigning Chin emperor captive. In the ensuing turmoil many of the great families and their retainers emigrated to the region south of the Yangtse River, where one of the Chin imperial princes had established his own branch of the dynasty. This was an unprecedented situation, in which "China" became a purely cultural tradition, no longer tied to the traditional heartland.

The great families from the north considered themselves an aristocracy, as compared with the local population. Buddhism established itself as a major force and received lavish patronage from the court and aristocracy. Monasteries supported schools and housed non-Chinese monks, who joined their Chinese counterparts in translating the Buddhist scriptures into Chinese. The Taoist "church" (an organized religion to be distinguished from the philosophical Taoism of early China) grew in importance and attracted distinguished followers. While society since the Han Empire had always offered many alternatives to a Confucian dedication to political life, in the southern dynasties such alternatives became more and more prominent.

Individualism and eccentricity were much admired in this period, both within the aristocracy and by those who scorned social life altogether and went to live as recluses among the beautiful mountain regions south of the Yangtse. T'ao Ch'ien, who finally came to be seen as the outstanding writer of the age, was very much an individualist, and his courage of conviction was undoubtedly strengthened by the intellectual currents of the time. Despite a claim to at least one illustrious ancestor, T'ao's immediate family consisted of poor provincial gentry. He prided himself on bumbling naïveté rather than aristocratic sophistication, and instead of opulent leisure, he saw pleasure in the simple life of a rural community, offering contentment in the rhythms of farm labor.

An old strain in the Chinese tradition idealized and even sentimentalized the peasant farmer. T'ao Ch'ien stands out from earlier writers by choosing such a life as his own and finding contentment in it. Celebration of this decision and his subsequent life can be found throughout his poetry. T'ao Ch'ien's family background made him a good candidate for minor provincial posts or a place in the entourage of one of the powerful aristocrats who had usurped the political power of the eastern Chin ruler, and he did indeed serve in both capacities. Each time, however, something happened that led him to resign his post: sometimes a death in the family, sometimes sheer dissatisfaction with a career whose formalities and burdens he loathed. His final post was as magistrate of P'eng-tse, a county seat not far from his hometown. After only a little more than two months in office, he quit his post and went home, where he quietly spent the last twenty-two years of his life. It was on this occasion that he wrote his long poem *The Return*, in which he states the problem eloquently: "Whenever I have been in official life I was mortgaging myself to my mouth and belly."

In his own distinctive way, T'ao Ch'ien shared with other Chin intellectuals a fascination with freedom and the idea of leading a natural life. It was thought that what individuals felt was "natural" and was distinct from their will and bodily desires. Thus T'ao could will himself to serve, even wish to serve, and could satisfy his "mouth and belly," yet still be going against his nature. A joke of the same period clarifies the issue. A poor scholar once visited the house of a wealthy aristo-

crat. He had to use the toilet and came to a room so lavishly decorated that he thought he had stumbled into the women's quarters by mistake. He made a hasty retreat and apologized to the aristocrat, who told him that it had, indeed, been the toilet. So informed, he returned, but on trying to use the room as it was intended, he found that he could not relieve himself. He returned, said good-bye, and as the anecdote ends, "went to somebody else's toilet." Beneath the joke lies a recognition that we each have a nature in which we feel at ease; that nature can be compelled neither by will (the intention to use the opulent toilet) nor by the body's demands (which sent the scholar to the toilet in the first place). Happiness is possible only in circumstances in which one's nature is not violated.

Throughout his work T'ao returns again and again to defining what is natural to him as an individual, discovering how to live so that his nature will be content, and observing how few needs he actually has. When a fire burns down his house, he looks around and concludes that he still has enough, though the danger of hunger and want is always there, threatening to drive him forth into the world, as it does on several occasions.

The good society, then, is the small world of the farming community, supplying human needs adequately but without excess. The unpleasant alternative is the empire and its government, with its false hierarchies and continual threat of violence. His most famous image of the happy life is based on a legend then current about Peach Blossom Spring, a farming community hidden deep in the mountains, whose inhabitants were the descendants of people who had fled the Chinese heartland during wars some five centuries earlier. A fisherman, following a trail of peach blossoms in the water, stumbles on this village and gives the curious villagers a summary of the war-torn preceding half millennium of Chinese history. On leaving to go home, he pays careful attention to the route, but no one is ever able to find the place again.

In many ways the fisherman is the emblem of T'ao Ch'ien's poetry and prose. He moves from the public world to an enclosed private world, safely cut off from the outside. For the sake of the story he must go back to the public world to tell about Peach Blossom Spring, even though no one will ever be able to get there. In the same way T'ao Ch'ien's poetry and prose writings are sent out from his village to the larger world, to be read by the literate officials who serve in the imperial government. These poems tell them of a possibility of contentment that eludes them and will be hard to find even if they go looking for it.

There are two complete English translations of T'ao Ch'ien's poetry (and much of his prose), *The Poetry of T'ao Ch'ien* (1970), by James Robert Hightower, and *T'ao Yüan-ming* (1984), by A. R. Davis.

PRONOUNCING GLOSSARY

The following list uses common English syllables to provide rough equivalents of selected words whose pronunciation may be unfamiliar to the general reader.

Ch'ien-lou: *chyen–loh*

Han Hsin: *hahn shin*

Ko-t'ien: *guh–tyen*

Liu Pang: *lyoh bahng*

Liu Tzu-chi: *lyoh dzuh–jee*

P'eng-tse: *puhng–dzuh*

T'ai-yüan: *tay–yooan*

T'ao Ch'ien: *tau chyen*

The Peach Blossom Spring[1]

During the T'ai-yüan period[2] of the Chin dynasty a fisherman of Wu-ling once rowed upstream unmindful of the distance he had gone, when he suddenly came to a grove of peach trees in bloom. For several hundred paces on both banks of the stream there was no other kind of tree. The wild flowers growing under them were fresh and lovely, and fallen petals covered the ground—it made a great impression on the fisherman. He went on for a way with the idea of finding out how far the grove extended. It came to an end at the foot of a mountain whence issued the spring that supplied the stream. There was a small opening in the mountain and it seemed as though light was coming through it. The fisherman left his boat and entered the cave, which at first was extremely narrow, barely admitting his body; after a few dozen steps it suddenly opened out onto a broad and level plain where well-built houses were surrounded by rich fields and pretty ponds. Mulberry, bamboo and other trees and plants grew there, and criss-cross paths skirted the fields. The sounds of cocks crowing and dogs barking could be heard from one courtyard to the next. Men and women were coming and going about their work in the fields. The clothes they wore were like those of ordinary people. Old men and boys were carefree and happy.

When they caught sight of the fisherman, they asked in surprise how he had got there. The fisherman told the whole story, and was invited to go to their house, where he was served wine while they killed a chicken for a feast. When the other villagers heard about the fisherman's arrival they all came to pay him a visit. They told him that their ancestors had fled the disorders of Ch'in times[3] and, having taken refuge here with wives and children and neighbors, had never ventured out again; consequently they had lost all contact with the outside world. They asked what the present ruling dynasty was, for they had never heard of the Han, let alone the Wei and the Chin. They sighed unhappily as the fisherman enumerated the dynasties one by one and recounted the vicissitudes of each. The visitors all asked him to come to their houses in turn, and at every house he had wine and food. He stayed several days. As he was about to go away, the people said, 'There's no need to mention our existence to outsiders.'

After the fisherman had gone out and recovered his boat, he carefully marked the route. On reaching the city, he reported what he had found to the magistrate, who at once sent a man to follow him back to the place. They proceeded according to the marks he had made, but went astray and were unable to find the cave again.

A high-minded gentleman of Nan-yang named Liu Tzu-chi heard the story and happily made preparations to go there, but before he could leave he fell sick and died. Since then there has been no one interested in trying to find such a place.

---

1. All selections translated by James Robert Hightower except *Biography of Master Five Willows*, translated by Stephen Owen.   2. From 376 to 396.   3. From 221 to 207 B.C.

The Return

I was poor, and what I got from farming was not enough to support my family. The house was full of children, the rice-jar was empty, and I could not see any way to supply the necessities of life. Friends and relatives kept urging me to become a magistrate, and I had at last come to think I should do it, but there was no way for me to get such a position. At the time I happened to have business abroad and made a good impression on the grandees as a conciliatory and humane sort of person. Because of my poverty an uncle offered me a job in a small town, but the region was still unquiet and I trembled at the thought of going away from home. However, P'eng-tse was only thirty miles from my native place, and the yield of the fields assigned the magistrate was sufficient to keep me in wine, so I applied for the office. Before many days had passed, I longed to give it up and go back home. Why, you may ask. Because my instinct is all for freedom, and will not brook discipline or restraint. Hunger and cold may be sharp, but this going against myself really sickens me. Whenever I have been involved in official life I was mortgaging myself to my mouth and belly, and the realization of this greatly upset me. I was deeply ashamed that I had so compromised my principles, but I was still going to wait out the year, after which I might pack up my clothes and slip away at night. Then my sister who had married into the Ch'eng family died in Wu-ch'ang, and my only desire was to go there as quickly as possible. I gave up my office and left of my own accord. From mid-autumn to winter I was altogether some eighty days in office, when events made it possible for me to do what I wished. I have entitled my piece 'The Return'; my preface is dated the eleventh moon of the year *i-ssu*.[1]

To get out of this and go back home!
My fields and garden will be overgrown with weeds—I must go back.
It was my own doing that made my mind my body's slave
Why should I go on in melancholy and lonely grief?
I realize that there's no remedying the past   5
But I know that there's hope in the future.
After all I have not gone far on the wrong road
And I am aware that what I do today is right, yesterday wrong.
My boat rocks in the gentle breeze
Flap, flap, the wind blows my gown;   10
I ask a passerby about the road ahead,
Grudging the dimness of the light at dawn.
Then I catch sight of my cottage—
    Filled with joy I run.
The servant boy comes to welcome me   15
    My little son waits at the door.
The three paths are almost obliterated
    But pines and chrysanthemums are still here.
Leading the children by the hand I enter my house
    Where there is a bottle filled with wine.   20
I draw the bottle to me and pour myself a cup;

1. A cyclical date name. China used a lunar calendar in which the first month began in late January or early February. The eleventh moon or month was probably December.

Seeing the trees in the courtyard brings joy to my face.
I lean on the south window and let my pride expand,
I consider how easy it is to be content with a little space.
Every day I stroll in the garden for pleasure,   25
There is a gate there, but it is always shut.
Cane in hand I walk and rest
Occasionally raising my head to gaze into the distance.
The clouds aimlessly rise from the peaks,
The birds, weary of flying, know it is time to come home.   30
As the sun's rays grow dim and disappear from view
I walk around a lonely pine tree, stroking it.

Back home again!
May my friendships be broken off and my wanderings come to an end.
The world and I shall have nothing more to do with one another.   35
If I were again to go abroad, what should I seek?
Here I enjoy honest conversation with my family
And take pleasure in books and zither to dispel my worries.
The farmers tell me that now spring is here
There will be work to do in the west fields.   40
Sometimes I call for a covered cart
Sometimes I row a lonely boat
Following a deep gully through the still water
Or crossing the hill on a rugged path.
The trees put forth luxuriant foliage,   45
The spring begins to flow in a trickle.
I admire the seasonableness of nature
And am moved to think that my life will come to its close.
    It is all over—
So little time are we granted human form in the world!   50
Let us then follow the inclinations of the heart:
Where would we go that we are so agitated?
I have no desire for riches
And no expectation of Heaven.
Rather on some fine morning to walk alone   55
Now planting my staff to take up a hoe,
Or climbing the east hill and whistling long
Or composing verses beside the clear stream:
So I manage to accept my lot until the ultimate homecoming.
Rejoicing in Heaven's command, what is there to doubt?   60

Biography of Master Five Willows[1]

We don't know what age the master lived in, and we aren't certain about
his real name. Beside his cottage were five willow trees, so he took his
name from them. He lived in perfect peace, a man of few words, with no
desire for glory or gain. He liked to read but didn't try too hard to understand. Yet whenever there was something that caught his fancy, he would
be so happy he would forget to eat. He had a wine-loving nature, but his
household was so poor he couldn't always obtain wine. His friends, know-

---

1. Master Five Willows is T'ao Ch'ien's image of himself.

ing how he was, would invite him to drink. And whenever he drank, he
finished what he had right away, hoping to get very drunk. When drunk,
he would withdraw, not really caring whether he went or stayed. His dwelling was a shambles, providing no protection against wind and sun. His
coarse clothes were full of holes and patches; his plate and pitcher always
empty; he was at peace. He forgot all about gain and loss and in this way
lived out his life.

Ch'ien-lou's[2] wife once said, "Feel no anxiety about loss or low station;
don't be too eager for wealth and honor." When we reflect on her words,
we suspect that Five Willows may have been such a man—swigging wine
and writing poems to satisfy his inclinations. Was he a person of the age
of Lord No-Cares? Was he a person of the age of Ko-t'ien?[3]

Returning to the Farm to Dwell

I

From early days I have been at odds with the world;
My instinctive love is hills and mountains.
By mischance I fell into the dusty net
And was thirteen years away from home.
The migrant bird longs for its native grove.   5
The fish in the pond recalls the former depths.
Now I have cleared some land to the south of town,
Simplicity intact, I have returned to farm.
The land I own amounts to a couple of acres
The thatched-roof house has four or five rooms.   10
Elms and willows shade the eaves in back,
Peach and plum stretch out before the hall.
Distant villages are lost in haze,
Above the houses smoke hangs in the air.
A dog is barking somewhere in a hidden lane,   15
A cock crows from the top of a mulberry tree.
My home remains unsoiled by worldly dust
Within bare rooms I have my peace of mind.
For long I was a prisoner in a cage
And now I have my freedom back again.   20

II

Here in the country human contacts are few
On this narrow lane carriages seldom come.
In broad daylight I keep my rustic gate closed,
From the bare rooms all dusty thoughts are banned.
From time to time through the tall grass   5
Like me, village farmers come and go;
When we meet we talk of nothing else
Than how the hemp and mulberry are growing.

2. A figure of antiquity who preferred a life of poverty to serving in office.   3. Both are mythical
emperors of earliest antiquity, before there were troubles in the world.

Hemp and mulberry grow longer every day
Every day the fields I have plowed are wider;   10
My constant worry is that frost may come
And my crops will wither with the weeds.

Begging for Food

Hunger came and drove me out
To go I had no notion where.
I walked until I reached this town,
Knocked at a door and fumbled for words
The owner guessed what I was after   5
And gave it, but not just the gift alone.
We talked together all day long,
And drained our cups as the bottle passed.
Happy in our new acquaintance
We sang old songs and wrote new poems.   10
You are as kind as the washerwoman,
But to my shame I lack Han's talent.
I have no way to show my thanks[1]
And must repay you from the grave.[2]

On Moving House

I

For long I yearned to live in Southtown—
Not that a diviner told me to—
Where many simple-hearted people live
With whom I would rejoice to pass my days.
This I have had in mind for several years   5
And now at last have carried out my plan.
A modest cottage does not need be large
To give us shelter where we sit and sleep.
From time to time my neighbors come
And we discuss affairs of long ago.   10
A good poem excites our admiration
Together we expound the doubtful points.

II

In spring and fall are many perfect days
For climbing high to write new poetry.
As we pass the doors, we hail each other,
And anyone with wine will pour us some.
When the farm work is done, we all go home   5
And then have time to think of one another—
So thinking, we at once throw on a coat

1. When Han Hsin was a young man, he found himself in hard straits; a washerwoman pitied him and fed him. Later he became a general of Liu Pang, the founder of the Han Dynasty, and was made a nobleman, able to repay the kindness he had received long before.   2. This echoes a story of a ghost who, out of gratitude, tripped the enemy of Lord Huan of Wei at a crucial moment.

And visit, never tired of talk and jokes.
There is no better way of life than this,
No need to be in a hurry to go away. 10
Since food and clothing have to be provided,
If I do the plowing, it will not cheat me.

In the Sixth Month of 408, Fire

I built my thatched hut in a narrow lane,
Glad to renounce the carriages of the great.
In midsummer, while the wind blew long and sharp,
Of a sudden grove and house caught fire and burned.
In all the place not a roof was left to us 5
And we took shelter in the boat by the gate.

Space is vast this early autumn evening,
The moon, nearly full, rides high above.
The vegetables begin to grow again
But the frightened birds still have not returned. 10
Tonight I stand a long time lost in thought;
A glance encompasses the Nine Heavens.[1]
Since youth I've held my solitary course
Until all at once forty years have passed.
My outward form follows the way of change 15
But my heart remains untrammelled still.
Firm and true, it keeps its constant nature,
No jadestone is as strong, adamantine.
I think back to the time when East-Gate[2] ruled
When there was grain left out in the fields 20
And people, free of care, drummed full bellies,
Rising mornings and coming home to sleep.
Since I was not born in such a time,
Let me just go on watering my garden.

From Twenty Poems after Drinking Wine

Preface

Living in retirement here I have few pleasures, and now the nights are
growing longer; so, as I happen to have some excellent wine, not an evening passes without a drink. All alone with my shadow I empty a bottle
until suddenly I find myself drunk. And once I am drunk I write a few
verses for my own amusement. In the course of time the pages have
multiplied, but there is no particular sequence in what I have written. I
have had a friend make a copy, with no more in mind than to provide a
diversion.

1. Heaven was described as having nine levels; here, simply the whole sky. 2. One of the mythical
rulers of high antiquity when there was such plenty that no one bothered to steal.

V

I built my hut beside a traveled road
Yet here no noise of passing carts and horses.
You would like to know how it is done?
With the mind detached, one's place becomes remote.
Picking chrysanthemums by the eastern hedge   5
I catch sight of the distant southern hills:
The mountain air is lovely as the sun sets
And flocks of flying birds return together.
In these things is a fundamental truth
I would like to tell, but lack the words.   10

IX

I heard a knock this morning at my door
In haste I pulled my gown on wrongside out
And went to ask the caller, Who is there?
It was a well-intentioned farmer, come
With a jug of wine to pay a distant call.   5
Suspecting me to be at odds with the times:
'Dressed in rags beneath a roof of thatch
Is not the way a gentleman should live.
All the world agrees on what to do—
I hope that you will join the muddy game.'   10
'My sincere thanks for your advice, old man.
It's my nature keeps me out of tune.
Though one can learn of course to pull the reins,
To go against oneself is a real mistake.
So let's just have a drink of this together—   15
There's no turning back my carriage now.'[1]

X

Once I made a distant trip
Right to the shore of the Eastern Sea
The road I went was long and far,
The way beset by wind and waves.
Who was it made me take this trip?   5
It seems that I was forced by hunger.
I gave my all to eat my fill
When just a bit was more than enough.
Since this was not a famous plan
I stopped my cart and came back home.   10

From On Reading the Seas and Mountains Classic[2]

I

In early summer when the grasses grow
And trees surround my house with greenery,

---

1. That is, from following the course of life he has chosen.   2. A fabulous geography of the countries surrounding China, inhabited by strange creatures and oddly shaped human beings.

The birds rejoice to have a refuge there
And I too love my home.
The fields are plowed and the new seed planted   5
And now is time again to read my books.
This out-of-the-way lane has no deep-worn ruts
And tends to turn my friends' carts away.
With happy face I pour the spring-brewed wine
And in the garden pick some greens to cook.   10
A gentle shower approaches from the east
Accompanied by a temperate breeze.
I skim through the *Story of King Mu*[3]
And view the pictures in the *Seas and Mountains Classic*.
A glance encompasses the ends of the universe—   15
Where is there any joy, if not in these?

3. This is a travel narrative of the Chou king Mu's visits to fantastic places beyond China.

T'ANG POETRY

Lyric poetry has generally been considered China's most important traditional literary form, and in the two millennia during which classical poetry played a powerful role in the culture, no period ever quite seemed to equal the T'ang Dynasty (618–907). The role of lyric poetry in traditional China was very different from that of lyric poetry in the West. By the T'ang Dynasty lyric poems had come to be used in a wide range of situations in both private and social life—in letters to friends, as contributions to a party, or as commemorations of visits to famous places. An educated person visiting the home of a friend might leave a poem if the host was not at home. On returning the host might reply by sending a poem to express regret at having missed the visit. Officials traveling on imperial business would write poems about their journeys on the white plaster walls of government post houses, sometimes responding to other poems on the wall left by previous visitors. In addition to the wide range of social situations that called for or invited the composition of poetry, poems were also written for the more private occasions that are familiar subjects of Western poetry: finding words for the difficult moments of life, communicating love, and simply evoking imaginary scenes and old legends.

In such a world few people defined themselves exclusively as "poets." To write poetry with grace (or at least technical competence) was expected of an educated person. During much of the T'ang period, poetic composition made part of the *chin-shih* examination, by which a candidate qualified for a government appointment. Thus poetic skill touched career, social life, and private life. Although in later centuries women's circles engaged widely in poetic composition, in the T'ang period composition of poetry by women was most common at the top and on the margins of the social order. In certain periods women of the imperial court actively participated in poetry competitions and court occasions for composition. But poetry played an even larger role in the demimonde, as part of the commerce between courtesans, often trained in music and song, and their clients.

On one level, poetry was a craft that taught people how to pay attention to significant moments in their lives—to find something lovely in a scene, to express feelings about some painful or joyous event, and to find words for what would

otherwise be awkward or impossible to say. Among a much smaller group, that shared social craft achieved the status of great art. Of some fifty thousand T'ang poems that survive today, by more than twenty-two hundred individuals, the works of thirty or forty truly talented poets constitute about half. Yet there are a remarkable number of memorable poems by otherwise undistinguished writers, who, by some gift of circumstance and their shared poetic training, rose briefly to compose poems that would be read and memorized for the next thousand years.

Most Chinese poems of this period have lines of either five or seven syllables. Because Chinese words are of either one or two syllables, these rhythms came as easily as iambic pentameter comes to English. The couplet was the basic unit of verse, and the last syllable of the couplet rhymed with the last syllable of other couplets. There were many forms; the most common were the two-couplet quatrain (chüeh-chü) and the four-couplet regulated verse (lü-shih). Longer poems and stanzaic ballads were also common. Poems that had no metrical requirements other than line length and rhyme were called old-style verse. Poems requiring a balance of tones (Chinese being a tonal* language) and parallelism within the couplet were said to be in the recent style.

Parallelism, which involved matching words of similar categories in corresponding positions in the lines of a couplet, was not only a structuring device but also a way of looking at the world and seeing significant pattern in it. Hence a brilliant parallel couplet held the kind of aesthetic interest that a good metaphor has in English poetry. The following couplet is by Po Chü-i:

徑	滑	苔	粘	履
path	slippery	moss	stick to	shoes

潭	深	水	沒	篙
pool	deep	water	sinks	boat-pole

Or to paraphrase: "the path is glossy and slick, so that the moss sticks to the bottom of my shoes; where the stream deepens into a pool, the pole, by which the boat is pushed along, sinks under the water." The reader first notices the visual similarity between the shiny wet surface of the mossy path and the surface of the stream (the "pool" here is a deep and wide section of a river or stream). The word *hua* ("slippery" or "glossy") suggests the danger of losing one's footing. The couplet encourages us to imagine legs walking on this shiny, slippery surface, a foot sinking down into the moss, meeting solid ground, and coming up with moss stuck to the shoe. The second line shifts to a parallel motion, punting down a stream instead of walking down a path, with the boat pole taking the place of the walking legs. Coming to a deep pool, the pilot pushes the pole into the water but instead of hitting bottom, the pole unexpectedly sinks under the surface. With wit and a beautiful play of visual pattern, Po Chü-i says something about peril and pitfalls, both anticipated and unexpected.

The Chinese poetic language differs strongly from English or European poetic languages. Although in context a couplet like the one above would be only slightly more ambiguous than an English couplet, much depends on the reader's trained expectations. A situation established in the title will let a reader know that such a couplet is to be read with a first person subject and in the present tense, even though pronouns and tense markers are missing in the text. Furthermore, what seems impersonal and general in English glosses can be personal and even idiosyncratic in Chinese.

---

* All languages are "tonal," but in most languages, including English, the tones are associated with sentence patterns. Chinese differs in having the tones attached to individual words.

Because poetry was a sociable art exchanged among friends, readers who would never meet the poets whose work they read came to think of them as familiar characters. Even today T'ang period poets are often spoken of as acquaintances, each with a distinct, sometimes quirky personality. The best way to approach such poetry is as a cultural drama with a vivid cast of characters. Their real lives, mostly spent passing through the vagaries of government service, are finally less important than the personalities they created for themselves in their poetry.

A general survey of the poetry of the eighth century can be found in Stephen Owen, *The Great Age of Chinese Poetry: The High T'ang* (1980). A more general introduction to Chinese poetry can be found in James Liu, *The Art of Chinese Poetry* (1962), and in Stephen Owen, *Traditional Chinese Poetry and Poetics: An Omen of the World* (1985).

The pronouncing glossaries for the T'ang poetry use common English syllables to provide rough equivalents of selected words whose pronunciation may be unfamiliar to the general reader.

PRONOUNCING GLOSSARY

chin-shih: *jin–sherr*   lü-shih: *loo–shir*

chüeh-chü: *jooeh–joo*   Po Chü-i: *bwoh joo-ee*

hua: *hwa*

LI PO
701–762

Li Po was from western China, and some have suspected that his family was of Turkish origin. In an age that valued family background, he was a nobody. To make a place for himself in upper-class society, he had to "invent" himself as an eccentric personality and as poet, a task he undertook with gusto. Social success in T'ang period China depended either on family connections or on the civil service examination (the training for which depended in some measure on family). Li Po had neither. But the dynasty also patronized Taoist "wizards," and through his connection with one eminent wizard, Li Po gained entrance to the Han-lin Academy, an imperial establishment for entertainers, intellectuals who did not advance through the normal channels, and interesting eccentrics.

In the Han-lin Academy Li Po seems to have been something of a cross between court poet and jester. As legend has it, his much-admired eccentricity, aided by alcohol, passed over the delicate boundary into rudeness; he offended powerful figures in the court and was dismissed. He dignified this dismissal as an exile brought on by the slander of his enemies and a failure to recognize his exceptional worth. The emperor may have been no longer amused, but Li Po retained the admiration of many intellectuals, who saw his rare talent.

Much T'ang poetry tended to treat the world at hand; Li Po gave it an additional dimension of poetic fantasy, describing the worlds of the Taoist heavens, evoking moments of history and legend, and even transforming more everyday occasions into something wondrous and strange. For such flair and capacity to see the world with fresh eyes, his contemporaries called him the "banished immortal," one of

those ethereal beings who dwell in the heavens and who, for some extravagant misdemeanor, have been exiled to live out a lifetime in the world of mortals.

Arthur Waley, *The Genius of Li Po* (1950), is an excellent biography. There is a long chapter on Li Po's poetry in Stephen Owen, *The Great Age of Chinese Poetry: The High T'ang* (1980).

PRONOUNCING GLOSSARY

Ch'ang-an: *chahng–ahn*   P'ing-lo: *ping–luh*

Ching-t'ing: *jing–ting*   Tan-ch'iu: *dahn–chyoh*

Hsi-ho: *shee–huh*   Ts'ao Chih: *tsau jerr*

Jo-yeh: *rwoh–ye*   Ts'en: *tsuhn*

Li Po: *lee bwoh*   Yüeh: *yooeh*

Lu-yang: *loo–yahng*

The Sun Rises and Sets[1]

The sun comes up from its nook in the east,
Seems to rise from beneath the earth,
Passes on through Heaven,
    sets once again in the western sea,
And where, oh, where, can its team of six dragons   5
    ever find any rest?
Its daily beginnings and endings,
    since ancient times never resting.
And man is not made of its Primal Stuff—
    how can he linger beside it long?   10
Plants feel no thanks for their flowering in spring's wind,
Nor do trees hate losing their leaves
    under autumn skies:
Who wields the whip that drives along
    four seasons of changes—   15
The rise and the ending of all things
    is just the way things are.

Hsi-ho![2] Hsi-ho!
Why must you always drown yourself
    in those wild and reckless waves?   20
What power had Lu-yang[3]
That he halted your course by shaking his spear?
This perverts the Path of things,
    errs from Heaven's will—
So many lies and deceits!   25
I'll wrap this Mighty Mudball of a world
    all up in a bag
And be wild and free like Chaos itself!

---

1. All selections translated by Stephen Owen.   2. Goddess who drove the sun's carriage.   3. Reference to the legend that the lord of Lu-yang, engaged in combat, made the sun stop in its course so that the fight could continue.

Bring in the Wine

Look there!
  The waters of the Yellow River,
  coming down from Heaven,
  rush in their flow to the sea,
  never turn back again
Look there!
  Bright in the mirrors of mighty halls
  a grieving for white hair,
  this morning blue-black strands of silk,
  now turned to snow with evening.
For satisfaction in this life
  taste pleasure to the limit,
And never let a goblet of gold
  face the bright moon empty.
Heaven bred in me talents,
  and they must be put to use.
I toss away a thousand in gold,
  it comes right back to me.
So boil a sheep,
  butcher an ox,
    make merry for a while,
And when you sit yourself to drink, always
  down three hundred cups.
  Hey, Master Ts'en,
  Ho, Tan-ch'iu,[1]
  Bring in the wine!
  Keep the cups coming!
And I, I'll sing you a song,
You bend me your ears and listen—
The bells and the drums, the tastiest morsels,
  it's not these that I love—
All I want is to stay dead drunk
  and never sober up.
The sages and worthies of ancient days
  now lie silent forever,
And only the greatest drinkers
  have a fame that lingers on!
Once long ago
  the prince of Ch'en[2]
  held a party at P'ing-lo Lodge.[3]
A gallon of wine cost ten thousand cash,
  all the joy and laughter they pleased.
    So you, my host,
How can you tell me you're short on cash?
Go right out!
  Buy us some wine!
    And I'll do the pouring for you!
Then take my dappled horse,
  Take my furs worth a fortune,

5

10

15

20

25

30

35

40

45

1. Master Ts'en and Tan-ch'iu are Li Po's friends. 2. The poet Ts'ao Chih (192–232). 3. Reference to a party described in one of Ts'ao Chih's poems.

Just call the boy to get them,   50
     and trade them for lovely wine,
And here together we'll melt the sorrows
     of all eternity!

Yearning

Endless yearning
     Here in Ch'ang-an,[1]
Where the cricket spinners cry autumn
     by the rail of the golden well,
Where flecks of frost blow chill,   5
     and the bedmat's color, cold.
No light from the lonely lantern,
     the longing almost broken—
Then roll up the curtain, gaze on the moon,
     heave the sigh that does no good.   10
A lady lovely like the flowers,
     beyond that wall of clouds,
And above, the blue dark of heavens high,
And below, the waves of pale waters.
Endless the sky, far the journey,   15
     the fleet soul suffers in flight,
And in its dreams can't touch its goal
     through the fastness of barrier mountains—
     Then endless yearning
     Crushes a man's heart.   20

Ballad of Youth

A young man of Five Barrows suburb
     east of the Golden Market,[2]
Silver saddle and white horse
     cross through wind of spring.
When fallen flowers are trampled all under,   5
     where is it he will roam?
With a laugh he enters the tavern
     of a lovely Turkish wench.

The Girls of Yüeh

A girl picking lotus on Jo-yeh Creek[3]
Sees the boatman return, singing a rowing song.
With a giggle she hides in the lotus flowers
And, pretending shyness, won't come out.

1. The T'ang Dynasty's capital.   2. In Ch'ang-an.   3. In southeastern China in a region famous for its beautiful women.

Dialogue in the Mountains

You ask me why I lodge in these emerald hills;
I laugh, don't answer—my heart is at peace.
Peach blossoms and flowing waters
    go off to mysterious dark,
And there is another world,[1]   5
    not of mortal men.

Summer Day in the Mountains

Lazily waving a fan of white feathers,
Stripped naked here in the green woods,
I take off my headband, hang it on a cliff,
My bare head splattered by wind through pines.

My Feelings

Facing my wine, unaware of darkness growing,
Falling flowers cover my robes.
Drunk I rise, step on the moon in the creek—
Birds are turning back now,
    men too are growing fewer.   5

Drinking Alone by Moonlight

Here among flowers a single jug of wine,
No close friends here, I pour alone
And lift cup to bright moon, ask it to join me,
Then face my shadow and we become three.
The moon never has known how to drink,   5
All my shadow does is follow my body,
But with moon and shadow as companions a while,
This joy I find must catch spring while it's here.
I sing, the moon just lingers on,
I dance, and my shadow scatters wildly.   10
When still sober we share friendship and pleasure,
Then entirely drunk each goes his own way—
Let us join in travels beyond human feelings
And plan to meet far in the river of stars.

Sitting Alone by Ching-t'ing Mountain

The flocks of birds have flown high and away,
A solitary cloud goes off calmly alone.
We look at each other and never get bored—
Just me and Ching-t'ing Mountain.

---

1. The image suggests the Peach Blossom Spring described by T'ao Ch'ien, a place removed from the
troubles of this world.

TU FU

712–770

If Li Po was associated with Taoism and the free, uncaring immortals, Tu Fu has always been strongly associated with Confucian virtues, embodied in his political commitment, his social concerns, and his love of family. A consensus of readers considers Tu Fu to be China's greatest poet, with each successive age finding in Tu Fu's work its own sense of what constitutes greatness. That very ability to satisfy changing values is a tribute to the diversity of his work. Yet he was esteemed in every age of Chinese poetry but his own.

During his lifetime Tu Fu was eminently unsuccessful, both as political figure and as poet. The grandson of one of the most famous court poets of the early eighth century, the young Tu Fu sought political office with no success. When the great rebellion of 755 took the capital by surprise and the emperor fled west, Tu Fu was trapped behind enemy lines. Some of his finest early poems were written at this period, as he heard of the defeat of one imperial army after another. Eventually he slipped through the lines and made his way to the court of the new emperor, who was directing military operations against the rebels. There he briefly held one of those court posts he had so much desired, but following the recapture of the capital, he was exiled to a minor provincial post, a job he came to detest. He quit this post in disgust and took up a life of wandering, first to the northwest, then west to Ch'eng-tu, the capital of Szechwan, then down the Yangtse River, coming in his last year to the lakes region in central China. It was during these last years of his life that Tu Fu wrote most of his poetry.

Because Chinese poetry treats both the minor details and the major crises of a person's life, a poet's work as a whole can be seen as autobiography or even diary. The culture valued poetry as a key to the historical person. One reason for Tu Fu's appeal may be the way he documents his life, from the smallest details to the largest dimensions of social context. Traditional critics often refer to him as the poet historian, in whose work incidents from that important moment in Chinese history come alive. He was also a meticulous craftsman, constantly revising his poems. In that process, like Li Po, he created the personality later readers so admire. But unlike Li Po, he presents himself as a character who has suffered, endured much, and changed.

Particularly recommended is David Hawkes, A *Little Primer of Tu Fu* (1967), which gives the Chinese text and a word-by-word explanation of a small group of Tu Fu's poems. Another study is A. R. Davis, *Tu Fu* (1971).

PRONOUNCING GLOSSARY

An Lu-shan: *ahn loo–shahn*   Lu-tzu: *loo–dzuh*

Ch'ang-an: *chahng–ahn*   P'eng-ya: *puhng–yah*

Ch'eng-tu: *chuhng–doo*   Sun Tsai: *swun dzai*

Chiang: *jyahng*   T'ung-chia: *toohng–jyah*

Fu-chou: *foo–joe*

Song of P'eng-ya[1]

I remember when first we fled the rebellion,[2]
Hurrying north, we passed through hardship and danger.
The night was deep on the P'eng-ya Road,
And the moon was shining on Whitewater Mountain.
The whole family had been traveling long on foot—   5
Most whom we met seemed to have no shame.
Here and there birds of the valley sang,
We saw no travelers going the other way.
My baby girl gnawed at me in her hunger,
And I feared wild beasts would hear her cries: 10
I held her to my chest, covered her mouth,
But she twisted and turned crying louder in rage.
My little son did his best to take care of things,
With purpose went off and got sour plums to eat.
It had thundered and rained half the past week,   15
We clung together, pulling through mud and mire,
And having made no provision against the rain,
The paths were slippery, our clothes were cold.
At times we went through great agony
Making only a few miles in an entire day.   20
Fruits of the wilds served as our provisions,
Low-hanging branches became our roof.
Then early in mornings we went through the runoff,
To spend the evening at homestead smoke on horizon.
We stayed a while in T'ung-chia Swamp   25
And were about to go out Lu-tzu Pass,
When an old friend of mine, Sun Tsai by name—
His great goodness reached the tiers of cloud—
Welcomed us as night's blackness was falling,
Hung out lanterns, opened his many gates,   30
With warm water had us wash our feet,
Cut paper flags to summon our souls,
Then afterward brought in his wife and children,
Whose eyes, seeing us, streamed with tears.
As if unconscious, my brood was sleeping;   35
He woke them kindly and gave them plates of food.
And I make this vow to you,
That forever I will be your brother, your kin.
Then he emptied the hall where we sat,
I rested peacefully—he offered what gave me joy.   40
Who else would be willing in times of such trouble
To show his good heart so openly?
Since we have parted, a year has run its course,
And still the barbarian weaves his calamities.
When shall I ever have the wings   45
To fly off and alight before your eyes?

---

1. All selections translated by Stephen Owen.   2. That is, the time Tu Fu took his family out of the
path of An Lu-shan's rebel army.

Moonlit Night[1]

The moon tonight in Fu-chou
She[2] watches alone from her chamber,
While faraway I think lovingly on daughters and sons,
Who do not yet know how to remember Ch'ang-an.[3]
In scented fog, her cloudlike hairdo moist,   5
In its clear beams, her jade-white arms are cold.
When shall we lean in the empty window,
Moonlit together, its light drying traces of tears.

Chiang Village[1]

From west of the towering ochre clouds
the sun's rays descend to the level earth.

Birds raise a racket in the brushwood gate
as the traveler comes home from a thousand miles.

Wife and children are amazed I survived,   5
when surprise settles, they wipe away tears.

I was swept along in the turmoil of the times,
by chance I managed to make it back alive.

Our neighbors are filling the wall,[2]
so deeply moved they're sobbing too.   10

Toward night's end I take another candle,
and face you, as if it still is a dream.

Thousand League Pool

The blue creek fuses dark mystery within,
A holy creature, sometimes appearing, sometimes concealed—
A dragon resting in massed waters coiled,
His lair sunken under a thousand leagues.
Pace each step with care, pass over cliff rim,   5
Bent for balance go down into mist and haze,
Look out over a stretch of mighty waves,
Then stand back on a greatness of gray stone.
The mountain is steep, the one path here now ends
Where sheer banks form two facing walls: 10
Thus were they hewn, rooted in nothingness,
Their inverted reflections hung in shaking waters.
The black tells of the vortex's bottom,
The clear parts display a shattered sparkling.
Deep within it a lone cloud comes,   15
And the birds in flight are not outside.
High-hung vines for its battle tents,

1. Tu Fu is trapped behind rebel lines in the capital Ch'ang-an.   2. His wife.   3. That is, the person in the capital, Tu Fu himself.   1. Written after Tu Fu finally rejoined his wife after escaping through rebel lines.   2. In other words, all the neighbors are gathering to witness the reunion. Even modest houses had low walls around the yard.

The winter trees rank its legions' standards.
Streams from afar twist their flows to reach here,
Caves give subterranean vent to swift scouring.   20
I have come to a place hidden, a realm without men,
The response it stirs is all our own.
Now, asking my leave, unwillingness hangs strongly on,
As old age approaches, this visit, the finest.

Hiding himself away, he sleeps in long scales;   25
The mighty stone blocks his going and his coming—
Oh, when shall the blazing skies of summer pass,
That his will may exult in the meeting of wind and rain.

My Thatched Roof Is Ruined by the Autumn Wind

In the high autumn skies of September
   the wind cried out in rage,
Tearing off in whirls from my rooftop
   three plies of thatch.
The thatch flew across the river,   5
   was strewn on the floodplain,
The high stalks tangled in tips
   of tall forest trees,
The low ones swirled in gusts across ground
   and sank into mud puddles.   10
The children from the village to the south
   made a fool of me, impotent with age,
Without compunction plundered what was mine
   before my very eyes,
Brazenly took armfuls of thatch,   15
   ran off into the bamboo,
And I screamed lips dry and throat raw,
   but no use.
Then I made my way home, learning on staff,
   sighing to myself.   20
A moment later the wind calmed down,
   clouds turned dark as ink,
The autumn sky rolling and overcast,
   blacker towards sunset,
And our cotton quilts were years old   25
   and cold as iron,
My little boy slept poorly,
   kicked rips in them.
Above the bed the roof leaked,
   no place was dry,   30
And the raindrops ran down like strings,
   without a break.
I have lived through upheavals and ruin
   and have seldom slept very well,
But have no idea how I shall pass   35
   this night of soaking.
Oh, to own a mighty mansion
   of a hundred thousand rooms,

A great roof for the poorest gentlemen
   of all this world,
   a place to make them smile,   40
A building unshaken by wind or rain,
   as solid as a mountain,
Oh, when shall I see before my eyes
   a towering roof such as this?   45
Then I'd accept the ruin of my own little hut
   and death by freezing.

A Guest Comes

North of my cottage, south of my cottage,
   spring waters everywhere,
And all that I see are the flocks of gulls
   coming here day after day,
My path through the flowers has never yet   5
   been swept for a visitor,
But today this wicker gate of mine
   stands open just for you.
The market is far, so for dinner
   there'll be no wide range of tastes,   10
Our home is poor, and for wine
   we have only an older vintage.
Are you willing to sit here and drink
   with the old man who lives next door?
I'll call to him over the hedge,   15
   and we'll finish the last of the cups.

Spending the Night in a Tower by the River

A visible darkness grows up mountain paths,
I lodge by river gate high in a study,
Frail cloud on cliff edge passing the night,
The lonely moon topples amid the waves.
Steady, one after another, a line of cranes in flight;   5
Howling over the kill, wild dogs and wolves.
No sleep for me. I worry over battles.
I have no strength to right the universe.

Writing of My Feelings Traveling by Night

Slender grasses, breeze faint on the shore;
here, the looming mast, the lonely night boat.

Stars hang down on the breadth of the plain,
the moon gushes in the great river's current.

My name shall not be known from my writing,   5
sick, growing old, I must yield up my post.

Wind-tossed, fluttering—what is my likeness?
in Heaven and Earth, a single gull of the sands.

YÜAN CHEN
779–831

Long fiction was a relatively late development in China. Some elements of a tradition of historical saga survive from the ancient period, but early Chinese literature showed its considerable narrative genius primarily in the anecdote and parable. During the early middle period, between the third and seventh centuries, the anecdotal tradition was further developed in accounts of eccentric or exemplary behavior and witty dialogues. At the same time we begin to find collections of short tales about ghosts, fox spirits, and assorted demons, a genre that remained very popular up to the present century. During the T'ang period (618–907), writers began to expand on the skeletal narrative style of the earlier period.

There are two distinct groups of T'ang stories: one written in classical Chinese and the other in early vernacular Chinese. The vernacular narratives, elaborating known stories from the Buddhist tradition and Chinese history, were discovered early in the twentieth century in a sealed Buddhist repository at Tun-huang, an outpost of the caravan route in northwest China. Most of the tales in classical Chinese, a far larger corpus, were printed in a large collection in 981 and have been known throughout the tradition. The classical tales, known as *ch'uan-ch'i* ("accounts of remarkable things"), are still comparatively short by Western standards, but they show a true delight in the craft of telling—in atmosphere, characterization, and detail. Unlike the vernacular stories, these classical tales are all "original" material (even though most claim to have heard the story from someone else). Supernatural stories, particularly of erotic encounters between mortal men and supernatural women, are the most common; but the *ch'uan-ch'i* also incorporate tales of heroism and love.

T'ang love stories, whether between mortals or between mortals and supernatural beings, often turn on the question of faith kept or broken. The love was usually in some way illicit, and by the end of the eighth century we can see a fully developed idea of romantic love, which offers interesting comparisons with images of romantic love in the Western tradition. *The Story of Ying-ying* is the most famous but in many ways the most anomalous work in this tradition of love stories. The usual literary love affair involves a talented young scholar and a courtesan or a supernatural being in the guise of a mortal woman. *The Story of Ying-ying* describes an illicit affair between a young man and his distant cousin, a situation in which marriage is not only acceptable but the obvious solution. Yet the lovers, each in his or her own way, thwart the possibility of legitimate marriage to create a conventional tale of broken love. In a tradition of fiction so consistently concerned with the extraordinary, the treatment of the ordinary becomes itself extraordinary. So unexpected is this story in the context of T'ang tales of romantic love that Chinese critics have wished to see it as a thinly disguised account of the personal experiences of the author, the famous poet Yüan Chen. If it is indeed autobiographical, the author is portraying himself in a most unflattering way.

The plot of *The Story of Ying-ying* could not be more straightforward: a young man has an affair with his cousin, leaves her to go to the capital to take the civil service examination, loses interest in her, and breaks off the relationship. But within this simple plot *The Story of Ying-ying* mocks the T'ang love narrative. Both of the lovers are acting roles that never quite fit them. The young man, like any hero of a T'ang love story, at first disdains the usual erotic adventures of his peers, looking for the perfect woman; and as a lover should, he falls helplessly in love

with Ying-ying at their first meeting. When he falls out of love and it serves his interests, he changes his role and condemns Ying-ying with platitudes of conventional public morality. Yet this pose of rectitude does not keep him from wanting to see her again, after she is married, when he happens to be in the neighborhood.

Ying-ying herself is no less an actor. By a display of bad temper to her mother she blocks the first stage of an easy route to a socially acceptable marriage. Then she plays the role of the conventionally virtuous young woman, offended by the young man's advances. Next she is the romantic heroine, overcome with passion. Finally she plays the lover who keeps faith, cruelly abandoned by a heartless young man. Yet despite her vows of undying love and faith unto death, she soon marries someone else. Everywhere the story calls attention to the difference between real people and the roles they play, both literary and social. In the context of the narrative, even poetry is exposed as a glittering lie: Yüan Chen's poem transforms the rather mundane affair into one between a mortal and a goddess, and poetic convention transforms his desertion into the inevitable separation of the goddess and her mortal lover.

The context makes Ying-ying's letter to her lover Chang, written in the most florid and formal prose, an ambiguous piece of T'ang eloquence. It may be read either as a genuine expression of a young woman's pain or as a manipulative attempt to work on his sympathies and regain control of the situation. Irony, whether intentional or not, pervades the story. At the close of the letter she warns him, "Be circumspect [in what you say] and careful, and do not think too often of my unworthy person." The very next sentence is: "Chang showed her letter to his friends, and in this way word of the affair got around." Both Ying-ying and Chang try to make claims on the reader's sympathy and approval, but in the end it is hard to give full approval to either. None of the cherished values of T'ang society survive unquestioned—whether pious public values or the private values of passionate and faithful love. By the end of the story these all seem merely the convenient excuses of the fallible human beings who use them. Almost unique among contemporary works, the story is finally ambivalent; each of the main characters tries to assert that his or her viewpoint is correct, and neither succeeds.

Yüan Chen was a well-known poet and close friend of the poet Po Chü-i. Passing through the usual phases of exile and reinstatement in party politics, he eventually rose to a high position in the T'ang government. *The Story of Ying-ying* is his only tale.

The story became a popular one, and in the process of its popularization it went through some drastic transformations. The final and most famous version was the thirteenth-century play *Romance of the Western Chamber*. Here all the troubling aspects of the work are ironed smooth. The remarkably willful and tempestuous Ying-ying is transformed into an ordinary, docile heroine, and the lovers are at last reunited to live happily ever after.

PRONOUNCING GLOSSARY

The following list uses common English syllables to provide rough equivalents of selected words whose pronunciation may be unfamiliar to the general reader.

Chen-yüan: *juhn–yooahn*

Cho Wen-chün: *jwoh wuhn–joon*

ch'uan-ch'i: *chwahn–chee*

Hsiao shih: *shyao shir*

Hsieh K'un: *shyeh kwun*

Hsi wang-mu: *shee wahng–moo*

Huan-lang: *hwahn–lahng*

Hung-niang: *huhng–nyahng*

Li Kung-ch'ui: *lee guhng–chway*

Pao-ssu: *bao–suh*

Po Chü-i: *bwoh joo–ee*

P'u: *poo*

Ssu-ma Hsiang-ju: *szih–mah shyahng–roo*

Teng-tu tzu: *duhng–too dzuh*

Ting Wen-ya: *ding wun–yah*

Ts'ui: *tsway*

Tu Ch'üeh: *doo chooeh*

Tun-huang: *dwuhn–hwahng*

Yu: *yoh*

Yü: *yoo*

Yüan Chen: *yooahn juhn*

The Story of Ying-ying[1]

During the Chen-yüan period[2] there lived a young man named Chang. He was agreeable and refined, and good looking, but firm and self-contained, and capable of no improper act. When his companions included him in one of their parties, the others could all be brawling as though they would never get enough, but Chang would just watch tolerantly without ever taking part. In this way he had gotten to be twenty-three years old without ever having had relations with a woman. When asked by his friends, he explained, "Teng-t'u tzu[3] was no lover, but a lecher. I am the true lover—I just never happened to meet the right girl. How do I know that? It's because things of outstanding beauty never fail to make a permanent impression on me. That shows I am not without feelings." His friends took note of what he said.

Not long afterward Chang was traveling in P'u,[4] where he lodged some ten *li*[5] east of the city in a monastery called the Temple of Universal Salvation. It happened that a widowed Mrs. Ts'ui had also stopped there on her way back to Ch'ang-an. She had been born a Cheng; Chang's mother had been a Cheng, and when they worked out their common ancestry, this Mrs. Ts'ui turned out to be a rather distant cousin once removed on his mother's side.

This year Hun Chen[6] died in P'u, and the eunuch Ting Wen-ya proved unpopular with the troops, who took advantage of the mourning period to mutiny. They plundered the citizens of P'u, and Mrs. Ts'ui, in a strange place with all her wealth and servants, was terrified, having no one to turn to. Before the mutiny Chang had made friends with some of the officers in P'u, and now he requested a detachment of soldiers to protect the Ts'ui family. As a result all escaped harm. In about ten days the imperial commissioner of inquiry, Tu Ch'üeh, came with full power from the throne and restored order among the troops.

Out of gratitude to Chang for the favor he had done them, Mrs. Ts'ui invited him to a banquet in the central hall. She addressed him: "Your widowed aunt with her helpless children would never have been able to escape alive from these rioting soldiers. It is no ordinary favor you have

1. Translated by James Robert Hightower.   2. From 785 to 804.   3. An archetypal lecher.   4. A province northeast of Ch'ang-an.   5. A unit of measure equal to one-quarter of a mile.   6. The regional commander of Chiang-chow died in P'u-chou in 799 [Translator's note].

done us; it is rather as though you had given my son and daughter their lives, and I want to introduce them to you as their elder brother so that they can express their thanks." She summoned her son Huan-lang, a very attractive child of ten or so. Then she called her daughter: "Come out and pay your respects to your brother, who saved your life." There was a delay; then word was brought that she was indisposed and asked to be excused. Her mother exclaimed in anger, "Your brother Chang saved your life. You would have been abducted if it were not for him—how can you give yourself airs?"

After a while she appeared, wearing an everyday dress and no makeup on her smooth face, except for a remaining spot of rouge. Her hair coils straggled down to touch her eyebrows. Her beauty was extraordinary, so radiant it took the breath away. Startled, Chang made her a deep bow as she sat down beside her mother. Because she had been forced to come out against her will, she looked angrily straight ahead, as though unable to endure the company. Chang asked her age. Mrs. Ts'ui said, "From the seventh month of the fifth year of the reigning emperor to the present twenty-first year, it is just seventeen years."

Chang tried to make conversation with her, but she would not respond, and he had to leave after the meal was over. From this time on Chang was infatuated but had no way to make his feelings known to her. She had a maid named Hung-niang with whom Chang had managed to exchange greetings several times, and finally he took the occasion to tell her how he felt. Not surprisingly, the maid was alarmed and fled in embarrassment. Chang was sorry he had said anything, and when she returned the next day he made shamefaced apologies without repeating his request. The maid said, "Sir, what you said is something I would not dare repeat to my mistress or let anyone else know about. But you know very well who Miss Ts'ui's relatives are; why don't you ask for her hand in marriage, as you are entitled to do because of the favor you did them?"

"From my earliest years I have never been one to make any improper connections," Chang said. "Whenever I have found myself in the company of young women, I would not even look at them, and it never occurred to me that I would be trapped in any such way. But the other day at the dinner I was hardly able to control myself, and in the days since, I walk without knowing where I am going and eat without hunger—I am afraid I cannot last another day. If I were to go through a regular matchmaker, taking three months and more for the exchange of betrothal presents and names and birthdates[7]—you might just as well look for me among the dried fish in the shop.[8] Can't you tell me what to do?"

"Miss Ts'ui is so very strict that not even her elders could suggest anything improper to her," the maid replied. "It would be hard for someone in my position to say such a thing. But I have noticed she writes a lot. She is always reciting poetry to herself and is moved by it for a long time after.

---

7. To determine an astrologically suitable date for a wedding [Translator's note].   8. An allusion to the parable of help that comes too late in chapter 9 of pre-Ch'in philosophical work *Chuang-tzu* [Translator's note].

You might see if you can seduce her with a love poem. That is the only way I can think of."

Chang was delighted and on the spot composed two stanzas of spring verses which he handed over to her. That evening Hung-niang came back with a note on colored paper for him, saying, "By Miss Ts'ui's instructions."

The title of her poem was "Bright Moon on the Night of the Fifteenth":

> I await the moon in the western chamber
> Where the breeze comes through the half-opened door.
> Sweeping the wall the flower shadows move:
> I imagine it is my lover who comes.

Chang understood the message: that day was the fourteenth of the second month, and an apricot tree was next to the wall east of the Ts'uis' courtyard. It would be possible to climb it.

On the night of the fifteenth Chang used the tree as a ladder to get over the wall. When he came to the western chamber, the door was ajar. Inside, Hung-niang was asleep on a bed. He awakened her, and she asked, frightened, "How did you get here?"

"Miss Ts'ui's letter told me to come," he said, not quite accurately. "You go tell her I am here."

In a minute Hung-niang was back. "She's coming! She's coming!"

Chang was both happy and nervous, convinced that success was his. Then Miss Ts'ui appeared in formal dress, with a serious face, and began to upbraid him: "You did us a great kindness when you saved our lives, and that is why my mother entrusted my young brother and myself to you. Why then did you get my silly maid to bring me that filthy poem? You began by doing a good deed in preserving me from the hands of ravishers, and you end by seeking to ravish me. You substitute seduction for rape — is there any great difference? My first impulse was to keep quiet about it, but that would have been to condone your wrongdoing, and not right. If I told my mother, it would amount to ingratitude, and the consequences would be unfortunate. I thought of having a servant convey my disapproval, but feared she would not get it right. Then I thought of writing a short message to state my case, but was afraid it would only put you on your guard. So finally I composed those vulgar lines to make sure you would come here. It was an improper thing to do, and of course I feel ashamed. But I hope that you will keep within the bounds of decency and commit no outrage."

As she finished speaking, she turned on her heel and left him. For some time Chang stood, dumbfounded. Then he went back over the wall to his quarters, all hope gone.

A few nights later Chang was sleeping alone by the veranda when someone shook him awake. Startled, he rose up, to see Hung-niang standing there, a coverlet and pillow in her arms. She patted him and said, "She is coming! She is coming! Why are you sleeping?" And she spread the quilt and put the pillow beside his. As she left, Chang sat up straight and rubbed his eyes. For some time it seemed as though he were still dreaming, but nonetheless he waited dutifully. Then there was Hung-niang again, with

Miss Ts'ui leaning on her arm. She was shy and yielding, and appeared almost not to have the strength to move her limbs. The contrast with her stiff formality at their last encounter was complete.

This evening was the night of the eighteenth, and the slanting rays of the moon cast a soft light over half the bed. Chang felt a kind of floating lightness and wondered whether this was an immortal who visited him, not someone from the world of men. After a while the temple bell sounded. Daybreak was near. As Hung-niang urged her to leave, she wept softly and clung to him. Hung-niang helped her up, and they left. The whole time she had not spoken a single word. With the first light of dawn Chang got up, wondering, was it a dream? But the perfume still lingered, and as it got lighter he could see on his arm traces of her makeup and the teardrops sparkling still on the mat.

For some ten days afterward there was no word from her. Chang composed a poem of sixty lines on "An Encounter with an Immortal" which he had not yet completed when Hung-niang happened by, and he gave it to her for her mistress. After that she let him see her again, and for nearly a month he would join her in what her poem called the "western chamber," slipping out at dawn and returning stealthily at night. Chang once asked what her mother thought about the situation. She said, "She knows there is nothing she can do about it, and so she hopes you will regularize things."

Before long Chang was about to go to Ch'ang-an, and he let her know his intentions in a poem. Miss Ts'ui made no objections at all, but the look of pain on her face was very touching. On the eve of his departure he was unable to see her again. Then Chang went off to the west. A few months later he again made a trip to P'u and stayed several months with Miss Ts'ui.

She was a very good calligrapher and wrote poetry, but for all that he kept begging to see her work, she would never show it. Chang wrote poems for her, challenging her to match them, but she paid them little attention. The thing that made her unusual was that, while she excelled in the arts, she always acted as though she were ignorant, and although she was quick and clever in speaking, she would seldom indulge in repartee. She loved Chang very much, but would never say so in words. At the time she was subject to moods of profound melancholy, but she never let on. She seldom showed on her face the emotions she felt. On one occasion she was playing her zither alone at night. She did not know Chang was listening, and the music was full of sadness. As soon as he spoke, she stopped and would play no more. This made him all the more infatuated with her.

Some time later Chang had to go west again for the scheduled examinations. It was the eve of his departure, and though he had said nothing about what it involved, he sat sighing unhappily at her side. Miss Ts'ui had guessed that he was going to leave for good. Her manner was respectful, but she spoke deliberately and in a low voice. "To seduce someone and then abandon her is perfectly natural, and it would be presumptuous of me to resent it. It would be an act of charity on your part if, having first seduced me, you were to go through with it and fulfill your oath of lifelong

devotion. But in either case, what is there to be so upset about in this trip? However, I see you are not happy and I have no way to cheer you up. You have praised my zither playing, and in the past I have been embarrassed to play for you. Now that you are going away, I shall do what you so often requested."

She had them prepare her zither and started to play the prelude to the "Rainbow Robe and Feather Skirt." After a few notes, her playing grew wild with grief until the piece was no longer recognizable. Everyone was reduced to tears, and Miss Ts'ui abruptly stopped playing, put down the zither, and ran back to her mother's room with tears streaming down her face. She did not come back.

The next morning Chang went away. The following year he stayed on in the capital, having failed the examinations. He wrote a letter to Miss Ts'ui to reassure her, and her reply read roughly as follows:

> I have read your letter with its message of consolation, and it filled my childish heart with mingled grief and joy. In addition you sent me a box of ornaments to adorn my hair and a stick of pomade to make my lips smooth. It was most kind of you; but for whom as I to make myself attractive? As I look at these presents my breast is filled with sorrow.
>
> Your letter said that you will stay on in the capital to pursue your studies, and of course you need quiet and the facilities there to make progress. Still it is hard on the person left alone in this far-off place. But such is my fate, and I should not complain. Since last fall I have been listless and without hope. In company I can force myself to talk and smile, but come evening I always shed tears in the solitude of my own room. Even in my sleep I often sob, yearning for the absent one. Or I am in your arms for a moment as it used to be, but before the secret meeting is done I am awake and heartbroken. The bed seems still warm beside me, but the one I love is far away.
>
> Since you said good-bye the new year has come. Ch'ang-an is a city of pleasure with chances for love everywhere. I am truly fortunate that you have not forgotten me and that your affection is not worn out. Loving you as I do, I have no way of repaying you, except to be true to our vow of lifelong fidelity.
>
> Our first meeting was at the banquet, as cousins. Then you persuaded my maid to inform me of your love; and I was unable to keep my childish heart firm. You made advances, like that other poet, Ssuma Hsiang-ju.[9] I failed to repulse them as the girl did who threw her shuttle.[1] When I offered myself in your bed, you treated me with the greatest kindness, and I supposed, in my innocence, that I could always depend on you. How could I have foreseen that our encounter could not possibly lead to something definite, that having disgraced myself by coming to you, there was no further chance of serving you openly as a wife? To the end of my days this will be a lasting regret—I must hide my sighs and be silent. If you, out of kindness, would condescend to fulfill my selfish wish, though it came on my dying day it would seem to be a new lease on life. But if, as a man of the world, you curtail your feelings, sacrificing the lesser to the more important, and look on this connection as shameful, so that your solemn vow can be dispensed with, still my true love will not vanish though my bones decay and my frame dissolve; in wind and dew it will seek out the ground you walk on. My love in life and death is told in this. I weep as I write, for feelings I cannot express. Take care of yourself; a thousand times over, take care of your dear self.
>
> This bracelet of jade is something I wore as a child; I send it to serve as a

9. An allusion to the story of the Han poet, Ssu-ma Hsiang-ju (179–117 B.C.), who enticed the young widow Cho Wen-chün to elope by his zither playing [Translator's note].   1. A neighboring girl, named Kao, repulsed Hsieh K'un's (280–322) advances by throwing her shuttle in his face. He lost two teeth [Translator's note].

gentleman's belt pendant. Like jade may you be invariably firm and tender; like a bracelet may there be no break between what came before and what is to follow. Here are also a skein of multicolored thread and a tea roller of mottled bamboo. These things have no intrinsic value, but they are to signify that I want you to be true as jade, and your love to endure unbroken as a bracelet. The spots on the bamboo are like the marks of my tears,[2] and my unhappy thoughts are as tangled as the thread: these objects are symbols of my feelings and tokens for all time of my love. Our hearts are close, though our bodies are far apart and there is no time I can expect to see you. But where the hidden desires are strong enough, there will be a meeting of spirits. Take care of yourself, a thousand times over. The springtime wind is often chill; eat well for your health's sake. Be circumspect and careful, and do not think too often of my unworthy person.

Chang showed her letter to his friends, and in this way word of the affair got around. One of them, Yang Chü-yüan, a skillful poet, wrote a quatrain on "Young Miss Ts'ui":

> For clear purity jade cannot equal his complexion;
> On the iris in the inner court snow begins to melt.
> A romantic young man filled with thoughts of love.
> A letter from the Hsiao girl,[3] brokenhearted.

Yüan Chen[4] of Ho-nan wrote a continuation of Chang's poem "Encounter with an Immortal," also in thirty couplets:

> Faint moonbeams pierce the curtained window;
> Fireflies glimmer across the blue sky.
> The far horizon begins now to pale;
> Dwarf trees gradually turn darker green.
> A dragon song crosses the court bamboo;   5
> A phoenix air brushes the wellside tree.
> The silken robe trails through the thin mist;
> The pendant circles tinkle in the light breeze.
> The accredited envoy accompanies Hsi wang-mu;[5]
> From the cloud's center comes Jade Boy.[6]   10
> Late at night everyone is quiet;
> At daybreak the rain drizzles.
> Pearl radiance shines on her decorated sandals;
> Flower glow shows off the embroidered skirt.
> Jasper hairpin: a walking colored phoenix;   15
> Gauze shawl: embracing vermilion rainbow.
> She says she comes from Jasper Flower Bank
> And is going to pay court at Green Jade Palace.
> On an outing north of Lo-yang's[7] wall,
> By chance he came to the house east of Sung Yü's.[8]

2. Alluding to the legend of the two wives of the sage ruler Shun, who stained the bamboo with their tears [Translator's note]. 3. In T'ang times the term "Hsiao-niang" referred to young women in general. Here it means Ying-ying [Translator's note]. 4. Yüan Chen (775–831) was a key literary figure in the middle of the T'ang period [Translator's note]. 5. Hsi wang-mu, the Queen Mother of the West, is a mythological figure supposedly dwelling in the K'un-lun Mountains in China's far west. In early accounts she is sometimes described as part human and part beast, but since early post-Han times she has usually been described as a beautiful immortal. Her huge palace is inhabited by other immortals. Within its precincts grow the magic peach trees which bear the fruits of immortality once every three thousand years. This might be an allusion to Ying-ying's mother [Translator's note]. 6. The Jade Boy might allude to Ying-ying's brother [Translator's note]. 7. Possibly a reference to the goddess of the Lo River [Translator's note]. 8. In "The Lechery of Master Teng-t'u," Sung Yü tells about the beautiful girl next door to the east who climbed up on the wall to flirt with him [Translator's note].

His dalliance she rejects a bit at first,
But her yielding love already is disclosed.
Lowered locks put in motion cicada shadows;[9]
Returning steps raise jade dust.
Her face turns to let flow flower snow   25
As she climbs into bed, silk covers in her arms.
Love birds in a neck-entwining dance;
Kingfishers in a conjugal cage.
Eyebrows, out of shyness, contracted;
Lip rouge, from the warmth, melted.   30
Her breath is pure: fragrance of orchid buds;
Her skin is smooth: richness of jade flesh.
No strength, too limp to lift a wrist;
Many charms, she likes to draw herself together.
Sweat runs: pearls drop by drop;   35
Hair in disorder: black luxuriance.
Just as they rejoice in the meeting of a lifetime
They suddenly hear the night is over.
There is no time for lingering;
It is hard to give up the wish to embrace.   40
Her comely face shows the sorrow she feels;
With fragrant words they swear eternal love.
She gives him a bracelet to plight their troth;
He ties a lovers' knot as sign their hearts are one.
Tear-borne powder runs before the clear mirror;   45
Around the flickering lamp are nighttime insects.
Moonlight is still softly shining
As the rising sun gradually dawns.
Riding on a wild goose she returns to the Lo River.
Blowing a flute he ascends Mount Sung.[1]   50
His clothes are fragrant still with musk perfume;
The pillow is slippery yet with red traces.
Thick, thick, the grass grows on the dyke;
Floating, floating, the tumbleweed yearns for the isle.
Her plain zither plays the "Resentful Crane Song";   55
In the clear Milky Way she looks for the returning wild goose.[2]
The sea is broad and truly hard to cross;
The sky is high and not easy to traverse.
The moving cloud is nowhere to be found—
Hsiao Shih[3] *stays in his chamber.*   60

All of Chang's friends who heard of the affair marveled at it, but Chang had determined on his own course of action. Yüan Chen was especially close to him and so was in a position to ask him for an explanation. Chang said, "It is a general rule that those women endowed by Heaven with great beauty invariably either destroy themselves or destroy someone else. If this Ts'ui woman were to meet someone with wealth and position, she would use the favor her charms gain her to be cloud and rain or dragon or mon-

---

9. Referring to her hairdo in the cicada style [Translator's note].   1. This is also known as the Central Mountain.... Here the one ascending the mountain may refer to Chang [Translator's note]. 2. Which might be carrying a message [Translator's note].   3. Hsiao Shih was a well-known flute-playing immortal of the Spring and Autumn period [Translator's note].

ster—I can't imagine what she might turn into. Of old, King Hsin of the
Shang and King Yu of the Chou[4] were brought low by women, in spite of
the size of their kingdoms and the extent of their power; their armies were
scattered, their persons butchered, and down to the present day their
names are objects of ridicule. I have no inner strength to withstand this
evil influence. That is why I have resolutely suppressed my love."

At this statement everyone present sighed deeply.

Over a year later Ts'ui was married, and Chang for his part had taken a
wife. Happening to pass through the town where she was living, he asked
permission of her husband to see her, as a cousin. The husband spoke to
her, but Ts'ui refused to appear. Chang's feelings of hurt showed on his
face, and she was told about it. She secretly sent him a poem:

> Emaciated, I have lost my looks,
> Tossing and turning, too weary to leave my bed.
> It's not because of others I am ashamed to rise;
> For you I am haggard and before you ashamed.

She never did appear. Some days later when Chang was about to leave,
she sent another poem of farewell:

> Cast off and abandoned, what can I say now,
> Whom you loved so briefly long ago?
> Any love you had then for me
> Will do for the one you have now.

After this he never heard any more about her. His contemporaries for
the most part conceded that Chang had done well to rectify his mistake. I
have often mentioned this among friends so that, forewarned, they might
avoid doing such a thing, or if they did, that they might not be led astray
by it. In the ninth month of a year in the Chen-yüan period, when an
official, Li Kung-ch'ui, was passing the night in my house at the Pacification Quarter, the conversation touched on the subject. He found it most
extraordinary and composed a "Song of Ying-ying" to commemorate the
affair. Ts'ui's child-name was Ying-ying, and Kung-ch'ui used it for his
poem.

---

4. Hsin (Chou) was the familiar last ruler of the Shang Dynasty, whose misrule and fall are attributed
to the influence of his favorite Ta-chi. King Yu (ruled 781–771 B.C.), last ruler of the Western Chou,
was misled by his consort Pao-ssu. The behavior of both rulers is traditionally attributed to their infatuation with the wicked women they loved [Translator's note].

LI CH'ING-CHAO
1084–ca. 1151

There is no better introduction to Li Ch'ing-chao's life than her *Afterword* to her
husband's study of early inscriptions, the *Records on Metal and Stone*. Prefaces
and afterwords were usually stylized, scholarly, and relatively impersonal; but in
Li Ch'ing-chao's hands the form became the means to show the relation between

a work of scholarship and a pair of lives. The *Afterword* tells first of the idyllic early years of marriage while her husband Chao Te-fu was a student in the Imperial Academy and of their shared passion for books and learning. Their fate as a couple was somehow mirrored in the fate of their collection of books and antiques: begun for their joint pleasure, it increasingly grew into an obsession that dominated her husband's life, until at last both the collection and her husband's scholarly work came to reveal only the differences between them.

The fate of both the marriage and the collection are set within the larger context of the fate of the Sung Dynasty, which in 1126 and 1127 lost its capital, its emperor, and north China to the invading Chin Tartars. The captured Sung emperor, whose extravagance and inattention to political matters were blamed for the loss of the north, happened himself to be an obsessive connoisseur of artworks. As Li Ch'ing-chao hastily fled south, the huge collection was gradually scattered and lost. Soon after they escaped the north, her husband died. Thereafter the residue of the collection represented many things to Li Ch'ing-chao. At one point it seemed to be the means to purchase her husband's posthumous honor after he was falsely accused of treason; the books were also her companions in her constant flight from place to place, and the few pieces that finally remained became cherished mementos of her former life. Throughout this short work Li Ch'ing-chao returns again and again to the relation between people and their possessions, to their role in human relationships, and to the way in which such objects gain value and meaning.

Li Ch'ing-chao is considered one of the finest writers of traditional song lyric. There was a long and complex relation between poetry and song in traditional China. The works of poets were often set to music and were sometimes modified to answer musical needs. During the T'ang period, however, an entirely new kind of music became popular, stanzaic melodies with musical lines of unequal length. In a language where the pitch of a word (or "tone") is essential to understanding its meaning, Chinese song lyrics had to pay careful attention to the requirements of a particular melody to be comprehensible: the pitch of the word had to match the pitch of the music. T'ang poets began the practice of composing new lyrics for these popular irregular melodies, and this new poetic form came to be known as *tz'u*, best translated as "song lyrics." These often concerned love and were performed in the entertainment quarters of the great cities and at parties. By the early Sung Dynasty (960–1279) the song lyric had evolved into a verse form with a very different character from that of classical poetry. It was primarily associated with delicate sensibility, and it sought to evoke the mood of moments.

The relatively few of Li Ch'ing-chao's song lyrics that survive are among the finest examples of the form. In the lyrics to the melody "Every Note Slow" she takes up the essential concerns of the form and one of the oldest questions in the Chinese tradition, which is the capacity of language to express adequately what occurs in the mind and heart. The lyric attempts to evoke the mood of the moment and closes by comparing the emotion she has evoked to the simple word *sorrow*, which is true, yet too broad to convey what she feels. Li Ch'ing-chao had a genius for scenes that could evoke feeling, as in the lyrics to "Southern Song," in which she changes from her light summer clothes to a warmer autumn dress, decorated with scenes of a lotus pond. But the dress is old and its gilt lotus leaves are flaking off, making it look like the dying vegetation of a real lotus pond, which becomes both the physical evidence and the symbol of her own aging. It is at such moments that she solves in her own way the ancient problem of how words can express the feeling of the moment.

A discussion of the *Afterword* can be found in the Stephen Owen, *Remembrances: The Experience of the Past in Classical Chinese Literature* (1986). For a discussion of the development of the song lyric, see Kang-i (Sun) Chang, *The*

Evolution of Chinese Tz'u Poetry: From Late T'ang to Northern Sung (1980). For a complete and very free translation of Li Ch'ing-chao's song lyrics, see Kenneth Rexroth and Ling Chung, *Li Ch'ing-chao: Complete Poems* (1979).

PRONOUNCING GLOSSARY

The following list uses common English syllables to provide rough equivalents of selected words whose pronunciation may be unfamiliar to the general reader.

ch'ai-hu: *chai–hoo*

Chang Fei-ch'ing: *jahng fay–ching*

Chao Te-fu: *jau duh–foo*

Chiang-tu: *jyahng–doo*

Chien-chung: *jyen–juhng*

Ch'ih-yang: *chur–yahng*

Ch'ing-chou: *ching–joh*

chüan: *jooan*

Ch'u-chou: *choo–joh*

Chung Fu-hao: *juhng foo–hau*

Ch'ung-ning: *chuhng–ning*

Hsiang-kuo: *shyahng–gwoh*

Hsiao Yi: *shyau ee*

Hsü Hsi: *shoo shee*

Ko-t'ien: *guh–tyen*

Lai-chou: *lai–joh*

Li Ch'ing-chao: *lee ching–jau*

Liu Tsung-yüan: *lyoh dzuhng–yooan*

P'eng: *puhng*

Shao-hsing: *shau–shing*

Sui: *sway*

Tse-ch'uan: *dzuh–chooahn*

Tso-chuan: *dzwoh–jooahn*

tz'u: *tsuh*

Yüan Tsai: *yooan dzai*

Yüeh-chou: *yooeh–joh*

Afterword to Records on Metal and Stone[1]

What are the preceding chapters of *Records on Metal and Stone?*—the work of the governor, Chao Te-fu. In it he took inscriptions on bells, tripods, steamers, kettles, washbasins, ladles, goblets, and bowls from the Three Dynasties of high antiquity all the way down to the Five Dynasties (immediately preceding our Sung); here also he took the surviving traces of acts by eminent men and obscure scholars inscribed on large steles and stone disks. In all there were two thousand sections of what appeared on metal and stone. Through all these inscriptions, one might be able to correct historical errors, make historical judgements, and mete out praise and blame. It contains things which, on the highest level, correspond to the Way of the Sages, and on a lower level, supplement the omissions of historians. It is a great amount indeed. Yet catastrophe fell on Wang Ya and Yüan Tsai alike: what did it matter that the one hoarded books and paintings while the other merely hoarded pepper? Ch'ang-yu and Yüan-k'ai both had a disease—it made no difference that the disease of one was a passion for money, and of the other, a passion for transmission of knowledge and commentary. Although their reputations differed, they were the same in being deluded.

---

1. All selections translated by Stephen Owen.

In 1101, in the first year of the Chien-chung Reign, I came as a bride to the Chao household. At that time my father was a division head in the Ministry of Rites, and my father-in-law, later Grand Councilor, was an executive in the Ministry of Personnel. My husband was then twenty-one and a student in the Imperial Academy. In those days both families, the Chaos and the Lis, were not well-to-do and were always frugal. On the first and fifteenth day of every month, my husband would get a short vacation from the Academy: he would "pawn some clothes"[2] for five hundred cash and go to the market at Hsiang-kuo Temple, where he would buy fruit and rubbings of inscriptions. When he brought these home, we would sit facing one another, rolling them out before us, examining and munching. And we thought ourselves persons of the age of Ko-t'ien.[3]

When, two years later, he went to take up a post, we lived on rice and vegetables, dressed in common cloth; but he would search out the most remote spots and out-of-the-way places to fulfill his interest in the world's most ancient writings and unusual characters. When his father, the Grand Councilor, was in office, various friends and relations held positions in the Imperial Libraries; there one might find many ancient poems omitted from the *Book of Songs*, unofficial histories, and writings never before seen, works hidden in walls and recovered from tombs. He would work hard at copying such things, drawing ever more pleasure from the activity, until he was unable to stop himself. Later, if he happened to see a work of painting or calligraphy by some person of ancient or modern times, or unusual vessels of the Three Dynasties of high antiquity, he would still pawn our clothes to buy them. I recall that in the Ch'ung-ning Reign[4] a man came with a painting of peonies by Hsü Hsi and asked twenty thousand cash for it. In those days twenty thousand cash was a hard sum to raise, even for children of nobility. We kept it with us a few days, and having thought of no plan by which we could purchase it, we returned it. For several days afterward husband and wife faced one another in deep depression.

Later we lived privately at home for ten years, gathering what we could here and there to have enough for food and clothing. Afterward, my husband governed two provinces in succession, and he used up all his salary on "lead and wooden tablets" [for scholarly work]. Whenever he got a book, we would collate it with other editions and make corrections together, repair it, and label it with the correct title. When he got hold of a piece of calligraphy, a painting, a goblet, or a tripod, we would go over it at our leisure, pointing out faults and flaws, setting for our nightly limit the time it took one candle to burn down. Thus our collection came to surpass all others in fineness of paper and the perfection of the characters.

I happen to have an excellent memory, and every evening after we finished eating, we would sit in the hall called "Return Home" and make tea. Pointing to the heaps of books and histories, we would guess on which line of which page in which chapter of which book a certain passage could be found. Success in guessing determined who got to drink his or her tea

---

2. Refers to the allowance for students at the Imperial Academy.   3. A mythical emperor of earliest antiquity, when all the world was at peace.   4. From 1102 to 1106.

first. Whenever I got it right, I would raise the teacup, laughing so hard that the tea would spill in my lap, and I would get up, not having been able to drink anything at all. I would have been glad to grow old in such a world. Thus, even though we were living in anxiety, hardship, and poverty, our wills were not broken.

When the book collection was complete, we set up a library in "Return Home" hall, with huge bookcases where the books were catalogued in sequence. There we put the books. Whenever I wanted to read, I would ask for the key, make a note in the ledger, then take out the books. If one of them was a bit damaged or soiled, it would be our responsibility to repair the spot and copy it out in a neat hand. There was no longer the same ease and casualness as before. This was an attempt to gain convenience which led instead to nervousness and anxiety. I couldn't bear it. And I began to plan how to do away with more than one meat in our meals, how to do away with all finery in my dress; for my hair there were no ornaments of bright pearls or kingfisher feathers; the household had no implements for gilding or embroidery. Whenever we would come upon a history or the work of a major writer, if there was nothing wrong with the printing and no errors in the edition, we would buy it on the spot to have as a second copy. His family had always specialized in *The Book of Changes*[5] and the *Tso chuan*,[6] so the collection of works in those two traditions was most perfect and complete. Books lay ranged on tables and desks, scattered on top of one another on pillows and bedding. This was what took our fancy and what occupied our minds, what drew our eyes and what our spirits inclined to; and our joy was greater than the pleasure others had in dancing girls, dogs, and horses.

In 1126, the first year of the Ching-k'ang Reign, my husband was governing Tse-ch'uan when we heard that the Chin Tartars were moving against the capital. He was in a daze, realizing that all those full trunks and overflowing chests, which he regarded so lovingly and mournfully, would surely soon be his possessions no longer. In the third month of spring in 1127, the first year of the Chien-yen Reign, we hurried south for the funeral of his mother. Since we could not take the overabundance of our possessions with us, we first gave up the bulky printed volumes, the albums of paintings, and the most cumbersome of the vessels. Thus we reduced the size of the collection several times, and still we had fifteen cartloads of books. When we reached Tung-hai, it took a string of boats to ferry them all across the Huai, and again across the Yangtse to Chien-k'ang. In our old mansion in Ch'ing-chou we still had more than ten rooms of books and various items locked away, and we planned to have them all brought by boat the next year. But in the twelfth month Chin forces sacked Ch'ing-chou, and those ten or so rooms I spoke of were all reduced to ashes.

The next autumn, the ninth month of 1128, my husband took charge of Chien-k'ang Prefecture but relinquished the position in the spring of the following year. Again we put everything in boats and went up to Wu-

---

5. One of the Confucian classics teaching divination.   6. Another Confucian classic treating early history.

hu and Ku-shu, intending to take up lodging on the River Kan. That summer in the fifth month we had reached Ch'ih-yang. At that point an imperial decree arrived, ordering my husband to take charge of Hu-chou, and before he assumed that office, to proceed to an audience with the Emperor. Therefore he had the household stop at Ch'ih-yang from which he would go off alone to answer the summons. On the thirteenth day of the sixth month he set off to carry out his duty. He had the boats pulled up onto the shore, and he sat there on the bank, in summer clothes with his headband set high on his forehead, his spirit like a tiger's, his eyes gleaming as though they would shoot into a person, while he gazed toward the boats and took his leave. I was in a terrible state of mind. I shouted to him, "If I hear the city is in danger, what should I do?" He answered from afar, his hands on his hips: "Follow the crowd. If you can't do otherwise, abandon the household goods first, then the clothes, then the books and scrolls, then the old bronzes—but carry the sacrificial vessels for the ancestral temple yourself; live or die with them; don't give *them* up." With this he galloped off on his horse.

As he was hurrying on his journey, he suffered sunstroke from the intense heat, and by the time he reached imperial headquarters, he had contracted a malarial fever. At the end of the seventh month I received a letter that he was lying sick. I was much alarmed, considering my husband's excitable nature and how nothing had been able to prevent the illness deteriorating into fever; his temperature might rise even higher, and in that case he would have to take chilled medicines; then the sickness would really be something to be worried about. Thereupon I set out by boat and in one day and night traveled three hundred leagues. At the point when I arrived he was taking large doses of *ch'ai-hu* and yellow *ch'in*;[7] he had a recurring fever with dysentery, and the illness appeared terminal. I was weeping, and in such a desperate situation I could not bring myself to ask him what was to be done after his death. On the eighteenth day of the eighth month he could no longer get up; he took his brush and wrote a poem; when he finished, he passed away, with no thought at all for the future provision of his family.

When the funeral was over I had nowhere to go. His Majesty had already sent the palace ladies elsewhere, and I heard that crossings of the Yangtse were to be prohibited. At the time I still had twenty thousand *chüan* of books, two thousand copies of inscriptions on metal and stone with colophons,[8] table service and mats enough to entertain a hundred guests, along with other possessions equaling those already mentioned. I also grew very sick, to the point that my only vital sign was a rasping breath. The situation was getting more serious every day. I thought of my husband's brother-in-law, an executive in the Ministry of War on garrison duty in Hung-chou, and I dispatched two former employees of my husband to go ahead to my brother-in-law, taking the baggage. That winter in the twelfth month Chin invaders sacked Hung-chou and all was lost. Those books which, as I said, took a string of boats to ferry across the

---

7. Knowledge of herbal lore was expected of wives.   8. Short prose works giving the essential scholarly information on the inscriptions. These were Chao Te-fu's copies and rubbings of early inscriptions. *Chüan*: like a chapter and the measure used to count the size of a library.

Yangtse were scattered into clouds of smoke. What remained were a few light scrolls and calligraphy pieces; manuscript copies of the collections of Li Po, Tu Fu, Han Yü, and Liu Tsung-yüan;[9] a copy of *A New Account of Tales of the World*; a copy of *Discourses on Salt and Iron*; a few dozen rubbings of stone inscriptions from the Han and T'ang; ten or so ancient tripods and cauldrons; a few boxes of Southern T'ang manuscript editions—all of which I happened to have had removed to my chambers to pass the time during my illness—now a solitary pile of leftovers.

Since I could no longer go upriver, and since the movements of the invaders were unfathomable, I went to stay with my younger brother Li Hang, a reviser of edicts. By the time I reached T'ai-chou, the governor of the place had already fled. Proceeding on to Shan through Mu-chou, we left the clothing and linen behind. Hurrying to Yellow Cliff, we hired a boat to take us toward the sea, following the fleeing court. The court halted a while in Chang-an, then we followed the imperial barge on the sea route to Wen-chou and Yüeh-chou.[1] In the twelfth month of the fourth year of the Chien-yen Reign, early in 1131, all the officials of the government were released from their posts. We went to Ch'ü-chou, and then in the third month of spring, now the first year of the Shao-hsing Reign (1131), we returned to Yüeh-chou, and in 1132, back again to Hang-chou.

When my husband had been gravely ill, a certain academician, Chang Fei-ch'ing, had visited him with a jade pot—actually it wasn't really jade but *min*, a stone like jade. I have no idea who started the story, but there was a false rumor that they had been discussing presenting it to the Chin as a tribute gift. I also learned that someone had made formal charges in the matter. I was terrified and dared say nothing, but I took all the bronze vessels and such things in the household and was about to turn them over to the imperial court. But by the time I reached Yüeh-chou, the court had already gone on to Ssu-ming. I didn't dare keep these things in the household any longer, so I sent them along with the manuscript books to Shan. Later, when the imperial army was rounding up defeated enemy troops, I heard that these had all been taken into the household of General Li. That "solitary pile of leftovers" of which I spoke had now been reduced by about fifty or sixty percent. All that remained were six or so baskets of books, painting, ink, and inkstones that I hadn't been able to part with. I always kept these under my bed and opened them only with my own hands.

At K'uai-chi I chose lodging in a cottage belonging to a local named Chung. Suddenly one night someone made off with five of the baskets through a hole in the wall. I was terribly upset and offered a substantial reward to get them back. Two days later Chung Fu-hao next door produced eighteen of the scrolls and asked for a reward. By that I knew the thief was not far away.[2] I tried every means I could, but I still couldn't get hold of the rest. I have now found out that they were all purchased at a low price by the Circuit Fiscal Supervisor, Wu Yüeh. Now seventy or

9. T'ang poets and prose writers.   1. This itinerary follows the general flight the northerner took to the southeast toward the sea, escaping the threat of an invasion of south China by the Chin Tatars.   2. This suggests that her landlord, Chung Fu-hao, was involved in the theft.

eighty percent of that "solitary pile of leftovers" is gone. I still have a few volumes from three or so sets, none complete, and some very ordinary pieces of calligraphy, but I still treasure them as if I were protecting my own head—how foolish I am!

Nowadays, when I chance to look over these books, it's like meeting old friends. And I recall when my husband was in the hall called "Calm Governance" in Lai-chou: he had first finished binding the volumes, making title slips of rue leaves to keep out insects and tie-ribbons of pale blue silk, binding ten *chüan* into one volume. Every day in the evening when the office clerks would go home, he would do editorial collations on two *chüan* and write a colophon for one inscription. Of those two thousand items, colophons were written on five hundred and two. It is so sad—today the ink of his writing seems still fresh, yet the trees by his grave have grown to an armspan in girth.

Long ago when the city of Chiang-ling fell, Hsiao Yi, Emperor Yüan of the Liang, did not regret the fall of his kingdom, yet destroyed his books and printings [unwilling to see them fall into the hands of his conquerors]. When his capital Chiang-tu was sacked, Yang Kuang, Emperor Yang of the Sui, wasn't concerned with his own death, only with recovering his books [his spirit overturning the boat in which they were being transported so that he could have his library in the land of the dead]. It must be that the passions of human nature cannot be forgotten, even standing between life and death. Or maybe it is Heaven's will that beings as insignificant as ourselves are not fit to enjoy these superb things. Or it might be that the dead too have consciousness, and they still treasure such things, give them their devoted attention, unwilling to leave them in the world of the living. How hard they are to obtain and how easy to lose!

From the time I was eighteen until now at the age of fifty-two—a span of thirty years—how much calamity, how much gain and loss I have witnessed! When there is possession, there must be lack of possession; when there is a gathering together, there must be a dissolution—that is the constant principle of things. Someone loses a bow; someone else happens to find a bow—what's worth noticing in that? The reason why I have so minutely recorded this story from beginning to end is to serve as a warning for scholars and collectors in later generations.

Written this second year of the Shao-hsing Reign (1132), the eighth month, first day.

Li Ch'ing-chao

Song Lyrics

To "Southern Song"

Up in heaven the star-river turns,
    in man's world below
        curtains are drawn.
A chill comes to pallet and pillow,
    damp with tracks of tears.

I rise to take off my gossamer dress   5
and just happen to ask, "How late is it now?"

The tiny lotus pods,
    kingfisher feathers sewn on;
as the gilt flecks away
    the lotus leaves grow few.   10
Same weather as in times before,
    the same old dress—
only the feelings in the heart
are not as they were before.

To "Free-Spirited Fisherman"

Billowing clouds touch sky and reach
    the early morning fog,
the river of stars is ready to set,
    a thousand sails dance.
My dreaming soul moves in a daze   5
    to where the high god dwells—
I hear Heaven speak,
asking me with urgent concern
    where I am going now.

And I reply that my road is long,   10
    and, alas, twilight draws on;
I worked at my poems and for nothing have
    bold lines that cause surprise.
Into strong winds ninety thousand miles
    upward the P'eng[1] now flies.   15
Let that wind never stop,
let it blow this tiny boat away
    to the Three Immortal Isles.[2]

To "Like a Dream"

I will always recall that day at dusk,
    the pavilion by the creek,
and I was so drunk I couldn't tell
    the way home. My mood left me,
it was late when I turned back in my boat   5
and I strayed deep among lotuses—
how to get through?
how to get through?
and I startled to flight a whole shoal
    of egrets and gulls.   10

1. The P'eng was a huge mythical bird described in the *Chuang Tzu*. When it was ready to fly from the northern ocean to the southern ocean, it would rise up ninety thousand miles in a whirlwind. Here it is used as a figure whose greatness smaller creatures cannot comprehend.   **2.** In the eastern sea, believed to be inhabited by immortals.

To "Drunk in the Shadow of Flowering Trees"

Pale fog, then dense clouds—
    gloomy all day long;
in the animal-shaped censer
    incense burns away.
Once again it is that autumn holiday: 5
to my jade pillow behind the gauze screen
at midnight the cold first comes.

By the eastern hedge I took wine in hand
    after twilight fell.
A fragrance filled my sleeves unseen.   10
Don't tell me this does not break your heart—
the west wind blowing up the curtains
and the person,
    as gaunt as the chrysanthemums.

To "Spring in Wu-ling"

The wind dies down, the fragrance in dirt,
    the flowers now are gone;
late afternoon, too weary to comb my hair.
Everything in the world is right; I am wrong;
    all that will happen is done;   5
before I can say it, tears come.

Yet I've heard it said that at Double Creek
    the spring is lovely still,
and I think I'll go boating there.
But then I fear   10
    those little boats of Double Creek
won't budge if they are made to bear
    this much melancholy.

To "Note After Note"

Searching and searching, seeking and seeking,
so chill, so clear,
dreary,
    and dismal,
        and forlorn.   5
That time of year
    when it's suddenly warm,
        then cold again,
now it's hardest of all to take care.
Two or three cups of weak wine—
how can they resist the biting wind   10
    that comes with evening?
The wild geese pass by—
that's what hurts the most—
and yet they're old acquaintances.

In piles chrysanthemums fill the ground,   15
looking all wasted, damaged—
who could pick them, as they are now?
I stay by the window,
how can I wait alone until blackness comes?
The beech tree,
  on top of that   20
    the fine rain,
on until dusk,
the dripping drop after drop.
In a situation like this
how can that one word "sorrow" grasp it?   25

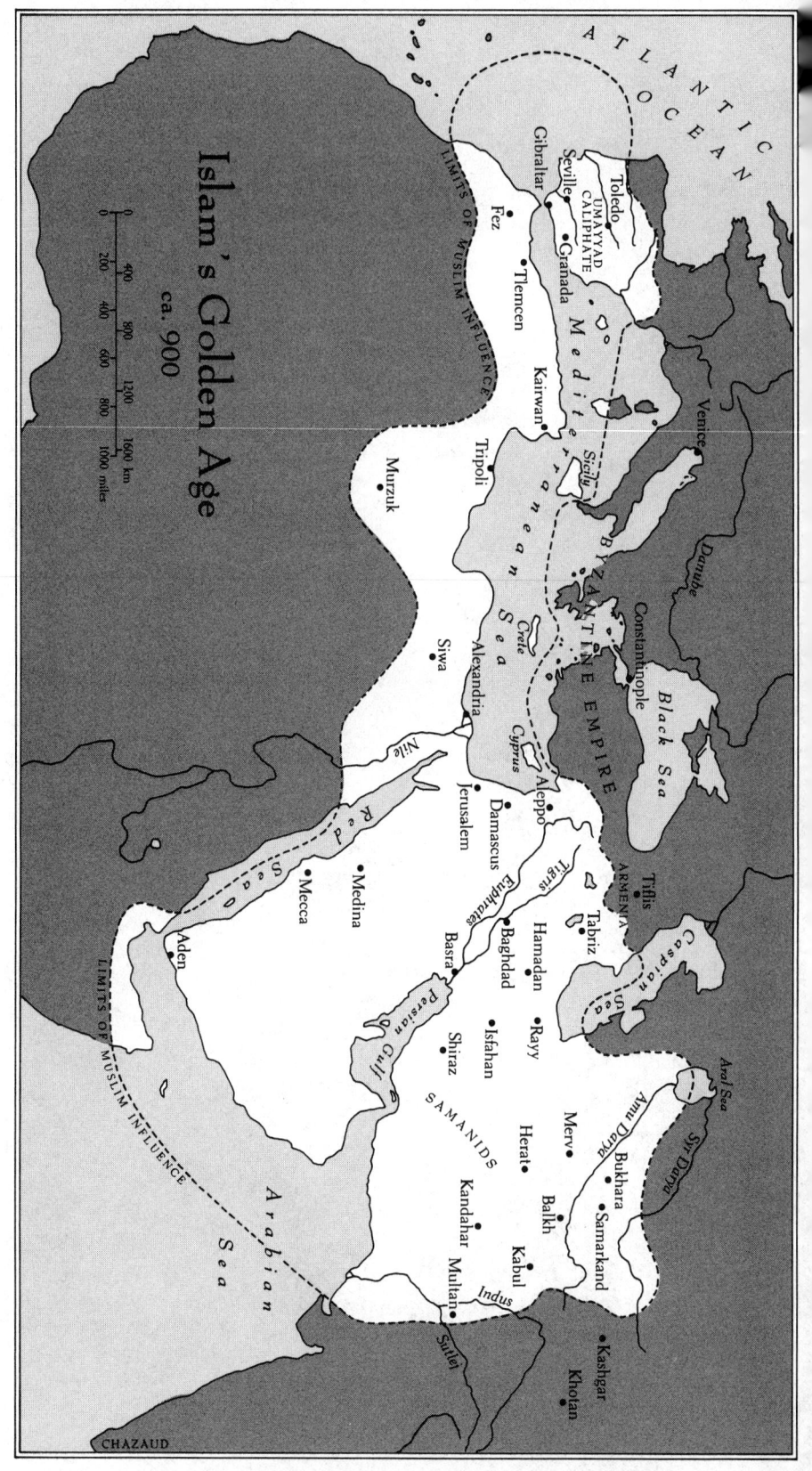

Islam's Golden Age
ca. 900

0 200 400 800 1200 1600 km
0 400 800 1000 miles

ATLANTIC OCEAN

UMAYYAD CALIPHATE

Gibraltar
Seville
Toledo
Granada
Fez
Tlemcen
Kairwan
Murzuk
Tripoli
Siwa
Alexandria

Mediterranean Sea

Sicily
Crete
Cyprus

BYZANTINE EMPIRE

Venice
Danube
Constantinople
Black Sea

ARMENIA
Tiflis
Tabriz
Aleppo
Jerusalem
Damascus
Euphrates
Tigris
Hamadan
Baghdad
Basra
Rayy
Isfahan
Shiraz

Nile
Red Sea
Mecca
Medina
Aden

Persian Gulf

Caspian Sea
Aral Sea

Amu Darya
Syr Darya

SAMANIDS

Merv
Herat
Bukhara
Samarkand
Balkh
Kabul
Kandahar
Mullan
Kashgar
Khotan
Indus
Sutlej

Arabian Sea

LIMITS OF MUSLIM INFLUENCE

CHAZAUD

The Rise of Islam and Islamic Literature

In the early seventh century the prophet Muhammad received revelations in the Arabic language that his followers gathered together after his death into a book known as the Koran. That book, together with his teachings, became the basis of a new religion and community that we know as Islam. Under Muhammad's leadership, the Muslim community quickly expanded until it included the whole of Arabia, uniting all its many tribes for the first time in their history. After Muhammad's death, these tribes, now united and inspired by the faith of Islam, swept out of Arabia to conquer the Persian and Byzantine empires to the east and west of them. In so doing they radically altered the history of the world.

Charles Martel defeated a Muslim invading force at Tours in 732, an event celebrated in *The Song of Roland*, and so checked the Muslim advance into western Europe; Byzantium also halted the invading armies in central Anatolia, but elsewhere the forces of Islam advanced with miraculous invincibility. Within a century the new empire stretched from southern Spain to northern India and from the Caucasus to the Indian Ocean. Iberia, North Africa, Arabia, Syria, eastern Anatolia and the Caucasus, Mesopotamia, Iran, central Asia and the Indus Valley were all governed by Muslims. This vast empire was ruled by a succession of caliphs (vicars) drawn from the prophet's family. They continued his political and religious leadership of the Islamic community but not his prophetic office. Factional strife, regional loyalties, and personal ambition combined to fragment and weaken the political integrity of the Islamic empire at times, but the primacy of the Islamic religion throughout the region remained constant, and the caliph retained great spiritual authority even when his political authority was challenged. The Islamic civilization that grew up in the wake of the great conquests was a synthesis of the religion and culture of Arabia with the great imperial traditions of the eastern Mediterranean and the Persian empire of the Sassanians. This synthesis molded the politics, science, literature, and arts of the diverse peoples who adopted Islam and, as the dominant culture of the region, had a shaping influence on such non-Islamic peoples as the Armenians in the Caucasus region and Jewish communities throughout the region. In every arena of human endeavor, Islamic norms prevailed.

Although the Koran explicitly prohibits forcible conversion to Islam, the spread of the Islamic faith was inevitably linked to the expansion of Islamic rule. Muslim rulers were tolerant of those religions whose faith was based on revelation, such as Judaism and Christianity, but strictly forbade them to increase their numbers by conversion. Islam checked the growth of these religions throughout its empire and within two centuries had virtually eliminated Zoroastrianism as a significant presence in Iran. After the period of the great conquests, the borders of Islam were extended into sub-Saharan Africa, southern India and Ceylon, and throughout Southeast Asia as far as the Philippine Islands. This further expansion was not the result of a single concerted effort but carried out over several centuries by merchants and traders as much as by military conquest.

The history of Islam in its early centuries was both turbulent and violent. The earliest dynasty of caliphs, the Umayyads, was overthrown in a long and violent revolution from which they retained only their hold over the western-most province of Islam, al-Andalus (Spain). Their successors, the Abbasids, ruled Islam for five centuries (750–1258) and presided over its fortunes at their height. They founded Islam's great imperial city, Baghdad, in the mid-eighth century; it became the center of a rich, cosmopolitan culture that was nourished by the ablest minds and greatest talents of every community within the empire. But after the first two centuries of their rule, the Abbasid caliphate's hold on the empire became increasingly tenuous as nominally subordinate dynasties in both the east and west came to exercise virtually independent rule.

Religious factionalism also threatened the caliphate itself in the tenth century. Muhammad had not designated a successor before his death, and the Muslim community quickly divided between those who believed that the caliphate should remain in the prophet's bloodlines (shi'ites) and those who insisted only that it remain within his clan, the Quraysh (sunnis). Shi'ites were instrumental in the overthrow of the Umayyads, but the Abbasids betrayed their shi'ite followers almost at once, and they became an enduring opposition. In the tenth century, a shi'ite dynasty (the Fatimids) conquered Egypt and established their own caliph there, and a second shi'ite dynasty, the Buyids, gained control of the orthodox sunni caliph in Baghdad. In the eleventh century, the Saljuqs, a Turkoman tribal federation that had only recently been converted to Islam, defeated the established rulers of central Asia and Iran and established themselves as the effective rulers of the lands between Damascus and Bukhara. Despite this turbulence, throughout the Abbasid caliphate Islam enjoyed a long period of relative prosperity and surprising cultural growth.

This long, sunny day of the Islamic empire was shattered in the east by an invasion from outside. In 1219–1220 the Mongol Chinghis Khan's armies, which had already subjugated all of China, swept through central Asia, northern Iran, and Iraq, leveling cities and annihilating whole populations as they advanced. This first incursion was essentially a long, punitive raid, and the Mongols did not establish effective rule over the region in the wake of their devastating conquest. In 1253 they began a new campaign under the leadership of Hulegu Khan, with the intention of adding the Middle East to their empire. They retook the cities of central Asia and northern Iran and extended their conquests into Iraq and Syria. No Muslim army could halt them until the Mamluk rulers of Egypt defeated the Mongols at Ayn Jalut in Palestine in 1260 and ended the myth of their invincibility. However, Hulegu had already dealt the Islamic empire a blow from which it never fully recovered. In 1258 he defeated the caliphal army defending Baghdad, abandoned the city to seven days of looting and burning, and had the caliph al-Musta'sim trampled to death. Hundreds of thousands were killed in the Mongol attack on Baghdad; libraries were burned and the riches that had accumulated there during five centuries of Abbasid rule were looted or destroyed. Successors to the Abbasid caliphate of Baghdad were established in Cairo by the Mamluks, who ruled in Egypt and Syria until 1517, and later in Istanbul, by the Ottomans who dominated the whole Mediterranean region from the fifteenth century to modern times. But these caliphs never became the independent political force that the original dynasty had been, and their spiritual leadership was diminished as well. Nor did Baghdad ever regain its eminence as the chief city of Islam.

The Mongol dynasties that succeeded to rule in the eastern Islamic world converted to Islam, and within a generation they accommodated themselves to Islamic norms of rule. In the fourteenth century Tamerlane (*Timur Lang*; 1336–1405), who claimed the descent from the Mongol great Khans, emulated their example and led his armies from his capital at Samarkand in central Asia in successive

campaigns of conquest into Iran, Turkey, and Russia. He died as he was planning further campaigns into China. The dynasty Tamerlane founded ruled in central Asia, Iran, and Iraq until the late fifteenth century, but his successors, happily, are remembered now principally for their patronage of the arts, letters, and architecture and for the promotion of Turkish as a literary language. The Timurids were the last powerful dynasty to originate in the steppes. After them, the world of Islam came to be divided between the Ottomans in the west, the Safavids in Iran, and the Moghuls in India. The Ottomans launched the last great movement of conquest, begun in the fourteenth century, when they expanded across the Bosphorus into the Balkans, eventually threatening Vienna itself (1683). The Ottomans and the Moghuls, who came to power as the impact of Columbus's discoveries was beginning to be felt, were also the first dynasties to confront the imperial ambitions of European colonial powers.

ISLAMIC LITERATURE

Before the advent of Islam, Arabia was a small state on the margin of the "civilized" world, and Arabic was the vehicle for a great but little known poetry. Islam established Arabic as the dominant language of religion, trade, and learning throughout a vast empire. The third Abbasid caliph, al-Ma'mun (died 813), established a center of translation in Baghdad in the early ninth century, and Greek science and philosophy, Indian mathematics, Chinese medicine, and Persian literature and natural history were all translated into Arabic, vastly enriching the language. By the latter half of the eighth century Arabic had ceased to be the exclusive property of the Arabs and had become instead the lingua franca of all the many communities that made up Islam, and Arabic literature had extended its horizons beyond tribal Arabia to reflect the international, cosmopolitan culture that Islam had become. Prose, which had next to no role in the pre-Islamic literature of Arabia, came to enjoy exceptional currency because it was a better vehicle than poetry both for the religious learning that was being generated by Islamic religious scholars and for the new secular and humanistic learning that was flooding into Islam from all sides. The literary aesthetic that developed in this period—a synthesis, again, of the language and poetics of pre-Islamic Arabian poetry—extended its shadows over all the literary languages of Islam that developed in subsequent centuries.

Though poetry enjoyed precedence over prose in the classical period, as it continued to do in all the languages of Islamic literature until virtually the present day, prose was the accepted vehicle for narrative. Given the Koranic intolerance of fiction, which it categorized as "lying," prose narratives were strongly didactic or informative—moralistic beast fables like those of Aesop (known as Luqman in Arabic), essays on natural history, collections of curious and wonderful information. Works of popular entertainment such as *The Thousand and One Nights* were not welcomed into the classical canon.

While Islamic literature began in Arabic, and Arabic remained the exclusive literary language of Islam for several centuries, some time in the early ninth century Islamic poetry and prose began to be written in Persian as well, and by the beginning of the eleventh century Persian had established itself as a second language of the Islamic literary tradition. Persian poetry adopted both the Arabic poetic style and the Arabic genres, but it also invented, or radically expanded, the use of new forms—the quatrain (*ruba'i*), the erotic lyric (*ghazal*), and the long narrative poem. Persian poets drew on the vast repertory of pre-Islamic Iranian stories from its national epic tradition and long tradition of court and popular poetry to create an extremely rich and varied literature in the eleventh through thirteenth centuries—generally regarded as its golden age. In the course of this golden age Persian poetry became increasingly infused with sufi mysticism, and

by the end of the period the sufi brotherhood provided a new and attractive focus for poetry to set in opposition to that of the court. Persian continued to be a significant vehicle for literary production down to the fifteenth century, after which it endured a long period of decline until the rise of modernism in the late nineteenth century.

Other languages followed Persian, and over these Persian exerted an influence as great or greater than Arabic, passing on to them the forms of the *ruba'i*, the *ghazal*, and long narrative; a vast repertory of themes and stories; and a deep devotion to sufism. The origins of Islamic literature in Turkish can be traced to the eleventh century, but only with the establishment of the Ottoman state in the thirteenth century did Turkish literature begin to gain parity with Persian and Arabic. Eventually, it emerged as the third major vehicle of Islamic literature. Islamic poetry began to be written in the regional languages of India—Kashmiri, Sindhi, Panjabi—from roughly the fourteenth century on. Of these, Urdu, which began to be used for poetry in about the sixteenth century, achieved exceptional preeminence at the courts of Delhi and Lahore. A number of the other languages of the far-flung Islamic communities of Africa, eastern Europe, and Asia also added themselves to the list of languages, and at present the number of languages that should be included under the rubric of Islamic literature roughly equals the number of communities included within Islam itself.

FURTHER READING

The best brief introduction to Arabic literature is still H. A. R. Gibb, *Arabic Literature* (1926). The articles "Arabic Poetics and Arabic Poetry" and "Arabic Prosody" by Roger M. A. Allen and David Semah, respectively, in *The New Princeton Encyclopedia of Poetry and Poetics* (1993) provide brief introductions to these topics as well as extensive bibliographies. For the Persian tradition, see Ehsan Yarshater, ed., *Persian Literature* (1988), and Julie Scott Meisami, *Medieval Persian Court Poetry* (1987). There are few good introductory studies of Ottoman poetry, but Walter G. Andrews, *An Introduction to Ottoman Poetry* (1976), is by far the best of these, and his study of the Ottoman lyric poetry, *Poetry's Voice, Society's Song* (1985), gives clear and illuminating insight into the relation of poetic production to the larger dynamics of an Islamic society. Marshall G. S. Hodgson, *The Venture of Islam: Volumes One to Three* (1974), is the best general history of the Islamic world and contains sections on the literary tradition. There are a number of anthologies of Arabic poetry. Charles Greville Tuetey, *Classical Arabic Poetry: 162 Poems from Imrulkais to Ma'arri* (1985), has the advantage of being comprehensive and highly readable. Tuetey also provides good historical and critical introductions to each poem.

PRONOUNCING GLOSSARY

The following list uses common English syllables and stress accents to provide rough equivalents of selected words whose pronunciation may be unfamiliar to the general reader.

Abbasids: *uh-bah'-sids*

al-Andalus: *al–an'-duh-loos*

al-Ma'mun: *al–ma-moon'*

al-Musta'sim: *al–moos-ta'-sim*

Ayn Jalut: *ayn juh-loot'*

Buyids: *boo'-yids*

Chinghis Khan: *ching'-iz kahn'*

Fatimids: *fat'-i-midz*

ghazal: *guh-zal'*

Hulegu Khan: *hoo'-luh-goo kahn'*

Kashmiri: *cash-mee'-ree*

Lahore: *luh-hore'*

Luqman: *luk-mahn'*

Mamluk: *mam-luke'*

Muhammad: *mu-ham'-mad*

Panjabi: *pun-jaw'-bee*

Quraysh: *koo-raysh'*

ruba'i: *roo-bah-ee'*

Safavids: *sa'-fuh-vids*

Saljuqs: *sal'-jooks*

Sassanians: *suh-say'-nee-unz*

shi'ite: *she'-ite*

Sindhi: *sin'-dee*

Timur Lang: *ti-moor' lang'*

Turkoman: *tur'-koh-man*

Umayyad: *oo-my'-yad*

Urdu: *oor'-due*

THE RISE OF ISLAM AND ISLAMIC LITERATURE

TEXTS	CONTEXTS
510–622 The great age of Arabic oral heroic poetry	
6th century The Sassanian court encourages the collection of heroic and legendary tales about Iran's kings and heroes	**570?** Birth of Muhammad into the Quraysh tribe of Mecca
	610–632 The period of Muhammad's prophesy from first revelation, through the growth of his following, his flight *(hijra)* to Medina, and his final pilgrimage to Mecca
622–750 Invention of the love lyric *(ghazal)*	
	633–656 Muslim armies conquer as far as India to the east and as far as Morocco to the west
653? The third caliph, 'Uthman, authorizes the collection and establishment of the official text of the **Koran**	
	711–720 Extension of Muslim conquests into al-Andalus (Spain), northwest India, and central Asia
750–1055 The Golden Age of Arabic letters	
750 Ibn Ishaq composes *The Biography of the Prophet*, the definitive biography of Muhammad	
	778 Defeat of Charlemagne in northern Spain by Muslim armies and the fall of Roland at Roncesvalles
	786–809 Caliphate of Haroun al-Rashid, who together with his vizier, Ja'far the Barmakid, appears in stories of **The Thousand and One Nights**
810–850 Heyday of Al-Jahiz, the greatest master of Arabic prose literature	
813–833 Caliphate of al-Ma'mun, who promotes the translation of Greek philosophy and science into Arabic • The tales of **The Thousand and One Nights** may have entered Arabic at about this time	
819–1005 The Samanid court encourages poets and writers in Persian and sponsors a new version of the **Shâhnâme**	**819–1005** The Samanids, the first Persian Muslim dynasty, become hereditary governors of eastern Iran and central Asia
912–961 The golden age of Islamic culture in Spain, which includes the	

TEXTS	CONTEXTS
establishment of the first major centers of learning in medieval Europe	950 The Turkish tribes of central Asia begin conversion to Islam
	998 Mahmud of Ghazna extends his rule over central Asia and northern India and establishes a dynasty that endures until shortly before the Mongol conquests
1010 Ferdowsi completes his poetic version of the *Shâhnâme*	
	1036–1055 The Seljuqs conquer as far as the Mediterranean, bringing with them the tales that will become *The Book of Dede Korkut*
	1096–1290 The European crusades to regain Christian control of the Holy Lands (little noted in the East)
1177 Attar completes *The Conference of the Birds.*	1171–1193 Saladin (Salâh al-Din), who expels the crusaders and denies European traders access to India through the Red Sea route
1218? Jalâloddin Rumi composes both his great lyric works and the *Spiritual Couplets* (1283)	1219–1260 The Mongols establish themselves as rulers of central Asia, Iran, Iraq, eastern Turkey, and parts of Syria and the Caucasus
	1236 In Spain, Muslim Cordoba capitulates to the Christian ruler, Ferdinand III
	1250–1517 The Turkish slave *(mamluk)* soldiers who served Saladin and his successors in Egypt found their own dynasty, known as the Mamluks
1257–1258 Sa'di composes the *Bustan* and *Golestan*	1256–1353 The Il-Khanids rule over the lands conquered by Hülegü
	1281–1924 In post-Mongol Turkey, the Ottoman rulers gradually establish the last great Islamic dynasty to rule in the Middle East. They dominate the region until World War II
1370–1405 Persian poetry enters a period of decline that continues to the early twentieth century	1370–1405 Timur the Lame, or Tamerlane, claiming descent from Jenghiz Khan, retakes most of the lands ruled by the Il-Khanids • Timur and his successors are generous patrons of poetry and painting and construct remarkable buildings

THE KORAN
610–632

For Muslims the Koran is something greater than prophetic revelation. It is an earthly duplicate of a divine Koran that exists in Paradise engraved in figures of gold on tablets of marble. Like God, it was not created but exists for all eternity— a complete and sufficient guide to our conduct on earth. It is God's final revelation to humanity and was sent by Him to complete and correct all prior revelations. In its divinity it is greater than any prophet or any prophecy. It stands to Muslims as Christ does to Christians. To the glory of Muhammad's community, God chose to make this, His final revelation, in Arabic and through an Arab prophet. Because the Koran is, literally, God's word and is, like Him, miraculous and eternal, it cannot be translated. Interpretive renderings into other languages have been made and used for teaching purposes since the earliest period of Islam, but Muslims do not accept them as the Koran in the sense that Christians accept the Bible in English, or any of the other languages into which it has been translated, as still the Bible.

The Koran's revelations were received by Muhammad, known to Muslims as the Prophet of God, during the last two decades of his life—from roughly 610, when the angel Gabriel first appeared to him, to his death on June 8, 632. During his lifetime these revelations were recorded by various of his followers, but they were only gathered together into a comprehensive volume after his death. The title given this collection is the Koran (al-qur'ân), or The Recitation, and as its title suggests, the Koran is a work to be heard and recited, an oral work with a music and rhythm of its own that does not appear to best advantage on the printed page. The text itself is far more dialogic than narrative. God speaks with Muhammad, or instructs him to give his community a particular message, or to "Recite!" Muhammad and other earlier prophets carry on frustrated dialogues with their doubting communities on the one hand and, on the other, with a demanding God. Only rarely does narrative replace the intermingling of voices in dialogue.

The revelations came to Muhammad in verses (âya) of varying length and number. These were gathered into larger divisions (Suras) that were organized roughly by subject. These gatherings often appear arbitrary, and there are abrupt transitions from subject in the longer Suras. Only the shortest are thematically unified and only Sura 12, Yusuf, tells a complete narrative. The Suras were then arranged by length, with the longer Suras preceding the shorter. Each Sura was given a name taken from some striking image or theme that appears in it. They are also identified as having been received in either Mecca or Medina, the two communities in which Muhammad lived. It is an article of faith with Muslims that the Koran we now have is a complete and accurate record of God's revelations to Muhammad and an exact copy of the divine Koran that exists in the seventh heaven.

Although the Koran was revealed over a relatively brief period, its style varies enormously. The earliest and shortest Suras sound like charms or incantations, evoking the wonder and glory of God:

> In the Name of God, the Compassionate, the Merciful
>   Say: "I seek refuge in the Lord of men, the King of men, the God of men, from the mischief of the slinking prompter who whispers in the hearts of men; from jinn and men" (Men [entire] 114:1–6).

The later and longer ones are filled with legal prescriptions:

Do not give the feeble-minded the property with which God has entrusted you for their support; but maintain and clothe them with its proceeds, and give them good advice (Women 4:6).

And many, perhaps most, of the Suras have the quality of sermons delivered in a highly charged and poetic language, often enriched by parables and brief narratives that exhort us to remember God and live pious lives. The earlier and longer Suras, like sermons, are mixtures of various styles—exhortation, evocation, legal prescription, and sage counsel.

The style of the individual Suras reflects in general terms the moments in Muhammad's life when they were revealed. In the early Meccan period of his mission, his concerns were those of an embattled prophet exhorting his community to believe in God and fear Him and defending himself against the hostility and skepticism of those who doubted both him and his God. The Suras from this period are filled with fierce and eloquent exhortations promising paradise to those who believe in God and eternal damnation to those who deny Him. These Suras are also marked by calls for social justice, expressed principally in concern for the plight of widows and orphans. It was in Mecca, too, that the accounts of earlier prophets from Noah (Nuh) to Jesus (Isâ)—who, like Muhammad, had to defend themselves against a hostile and unbelieving community—were revealed to him.

Eventually, Muhammad's success in creating a community of believers made him so unwelcome in his home that the Meccans forced him and his followers to emigrate to the nearby oasis of Medina. There he established his community among the tribes already settled around the oasis. While Muhammad continued to be the Prophet of Islam, the legal and political demands of his community now demanded most of his attention. He also had to cope with the growing number of believers who flocked to him and, eventually, to manage a war with the Meccans. The Suras revealed in Medina reflect these concerns in setting forth an extensive and detailed legal code that addresses the demands of the day-to-day life of the community as well as its spiritual needs.

These stylistic differences point out an obvious distinction between the Koran and the Bible. The essence of the Koran is admonition and guidance. No narrative thread runs through it, nor is it embedded in the history of a single people. The Koran's coherence is a product of the themes that are reiterated throughout its many Suras. For all the importance it gives to one language, Arabic, its message is a more general one. The many allusions to Moses (Musa), for example, stress that God may choose even an ordinary, flawed man to be His prophet, and as in the story of Joseph, say nothing of Moses' role as the leader of his people. The meaning of the Koran, as it often asserts, is for all humanity.

The Exordium, the opening Sura of the Koran, has an exceptional resonance in the life of Muslims. Muslims recite it at the beginning of every formal address and inscribe it at the head of every written document from works of scholarship to the stones that mark a grave. It begins every prayer.

Joseph (Sura 12) is, of course, not a prophet in Judaism or Christianity, but he is in Islam. He is also the only one whose tale is told continuously, and the only one to be mentioned exclusively in a single Sura. The Koranic version of this story includes most of the key events of Genesis 36–38 but excludes virtually everything that links Joseph to the Hebrew nation. In Genesis, Joseph is a divinely guided young man who is first tested severely and then becomes the leader of his nation, guiding them to prosperity in Egypt. In the Koran he is a divinely guided young man but not the leader of any nation. Although God tests Joseph, it is to prove that only those who follow divine guidance prosper. In the most famous scene, the temptation by his master's wife, he is not more righteous than she, but God gives him a sign that he should not succumb. Islam does not believe in original sin, and

is more accepting of human error than Genesis. Joseph's innocence in this encounter is also explicitly established in Sura 12, while in Genesis only we and God see that Joseph is blameless. His master's wife, identified as Zuleikha in the commentaries, is also treated in a more tolerant fashion than Potiphar's wife. In a remarkable scene she shows the women of the city that they, too, would have been seduced by Joseph's angelic beauty. In the Koran, in short, the story of Joseph has nothing of the epic dimensions it has in Genesis but focuses instead on the smaller and more general theme of the importance of trusting in God.

Sura 19 contains the only allusion to Mary in the Koran, although Jesus appears repeatedly. The miracles surrounding the birth of Jesus do occur here but in a very different form from that in the New Testament of the Bible. Islam does not accept that Jesus was the son of God. For Muslims such a mixture of divine and human attributes is unthinkable. Jesus they account a great prophet but no more, and, again, one who has no allegiance to a particular community. There is also nothing of the story of his conflicts with the Jews or his execution by the Romans. Muslims do not accept the martyrdom of Jesus but believe that at the crucial moment God placed a substitute in Jesus' place.

In the Koran, Noah (Sura 71) is the first of the major prophets, a step well above his position in the Bible. He establishes the pattern for the role of the prophet in his community. It is a disheartening one and probably reflects Muhammad's view of his relations with his fellow Meccans. The emphasis is on his prophetic role rather than on the details of the ark and the salvation of the animals. Like Muhammad he is a warner who comes to call his people to God and to threaten them with torment if they do not. His people revile and reject him for years. At last, when it is abundantly clear that their hearts are so hardened that they will never heed him, he calls down God's wrath on his tormentors. His story is alluded to in a great many Suras. One detail found only in the Koran (11:42–46) points out God's concern to give faith priority over blood. Noah has a son who refuses to enter the ark, effectively denying his father's prophecy. The rising waters kill him along with the rest of humanity. When Noah asks God why He has done this, because He promised that Noah's family would be spared, God replies, "Noah, he was no kinsman of yours: he had acted unjustly." That is, shared belief replaces blood as the strongest bond uniting people.

The most informative general introduction to the Koran is the revised edition of *Bell's Introduction to the Qur'ân* (1970). Michael Cook, *Muhammad* (1983), is an excellent brief biography of the Prophet of Islam. Fazlur Rahman, *Major Themes of the Qur'ân* (1980), is a lucid presentation by a Muslim scholar who has taught in the United States for many years of the principal beliefs of Islam as they appear in the Koran. Marilyn R. Waldman, "New Approaches to 'Biblical' Materials in the Qur'ân," *The Muslim World* 75, no. 1 (January 1985), 1–16, gives a good comparison of Joseph in the Koran and the Bible.

PRONOUNCING GLOSSARY

The following list uses common English syllables and stress accents to provide rough equivalents of selected words whose pronunciation may be unfamiliar to the general reader.

al-qur'ân: *al-ko-ran'*

âya: *eye'-yuh*

Idris: *ee-drees'*

Isâ: *ee'-suh*

Nuh: *nooh*

Potiphar: *poh'-tee-far*

Suwâ: *soo-wah'*

Ya'uq: *yah-ook'*

Yaghuth: *yah-gooth'*

Yusuf: *you'-suff*

Zuleikha: *zoo-lay'-kuh*

FROM THE KORAN[1]

1. The Exordium

[MECCA]

In the Name of God the Compassionate the Merciful[2]

Praise be to God, Lord of the Creation,
The Compassionate, the Merciful,
King of the Last Judgement!
You alone we worship, and to You alone
we pray for help.
Guide us to the straight path,
The path of those whom You have favoured,
Not of those who have incurred Your wrath,
Nor of those who have gone astray.

From 4. Women

[MEDINA]

In the Name of God, the Compassionate, the Merciful

Men, have fear of your Lord, who created you from a single soul. From that soul He created its mate, and through them He bestrewed the earth with countless men and women.

Fear God, in whose name you plead with one another, and honour the mothers who bore you. God is ever watching over you.

Give orphans[3] the property which belongs to them. Do not exchange their valuables for worthless things or cheat them of their possessions; for this would surely be a great sin. If you fear that you cannot treat orphans with fairness, then you may marry other women who seem good to you: two, three, or four of them. But if you fear that you cannot maintain equality among them, marry one only or any slavegirls you may own. This will make it easier for you to avoid injustice.

Give women their dowry as a free gift; but if they choose to make over to you a part of it, you may regard it as lawfully yours.

Do not give the feeble-minded the property with which God has entrusted you for their support; but maintain and clothe them with its proceeds, and give them good advice.

Put orphans to the test until they reach a marriageable age. If you find them capable of sound judgement, hand over to them their property, and do not deprive them of it by squandering it before they come of age.

Let not the rich guardian touch the property of his orphan ward; and let him who is poor use no more than a fair portion of it for his own advantage.

1. Translated by N. J. Dawood.   2. According to Islamic law, this phrase, spoken or written, must precede all written work; it is also used by Muslims at the beginning of most formal tasks.   3. Orphan girls.

When you hand over to them their property, call in some witnesses; sufficient is God's accounting of your actions.

Men shall have a share in what their parents and kinsmen leave; and women shall have a share in what their parents and kinsmen leave: whether it be little or much, they shall be legally entitled to their share.

If relatives, orphans, or needy men are present at the division of an inheritance, give them, too, a share of it, and speak to them kind words.

Let those who are solicitous about the welfare of their young children after their own death take care not to wrong orphans. Let them fear God and speak for justice.

Those that devour the property of orphans unjustly, swallow fire into their bellies; they shall burn in a mighty conflagration.

God has thus enjoined you concerning your children:

A male shall inherit twice as much as a female. If there be more than two girls, they shall have two-thirds of the inheritance; but if there be one only, she shall inherit the half. Parents shall inherit a sixth each, if the deceased have a child; but if he leave no child and his parents be his heirs, his mother shall have a third. If he have brothers, his mother shall have a sixth after payment of any legacy he may have bequeathed or any debt he may have owed.

You may wonder whether your parents or your children are more beneficial to you. But this is the law of God; God is all-knowing and wise.

You shall inherit the half of your wives' estate if they die childless. If they leave children, a quarter of their estate shall be yours after payment of any legacies they may have bequeathed or any debt they may have owed.

Your wives shall inherit one quarter of your estate if you die childless. If you leave children, they shall inherit one-eighth, after payment of any legacies you may have bequeathed or any debts you may have owed.

If a man or a woman leave neither children nor parents and have a brother or a sister, they shall each inherit one-sixth. If there be more, they shall equally share the third of the estate, after payment of any legacy that he may have bequeathed or any debt he may have owed, without prejudice to the rights of the heirs. That is a commandment from God. God is all-knowing and gracious.

Such are the bounds set by God. He that obeys God and His apostle shall dwell for ever in gardens watered by running streams. That is the supreme triumph. But he that defies God and His apostle and transgresses His bounds, shall be cast into a fire wherein he will abide for ever. A shameful punishment awaits him.

If any of your women commit fornication, call in four witnesses from among yourselves against them; if they testify to their guilt confine them to their houses till death overtakes them or till God finds another way for them.

If two men among you commit indecency punish them both. If they repent and mend their ways, let them be. God is forgiving and merciful.

God forgives those who commit evil in ignorance and then quickly turn to Him in repentance. God will pardon them. God is wise and all-knowing. But He will not forgive those who do evil and, when death comes to

them, say: 'Now we repent!' Nor those who die unbelievers: for them We have prepared a woeful scourge.

Believers, it is unlawful for you to inherit the women of your deceased kinsmen against their will, or to bar them from re-marrying, in order that you may force them to give up a part of what you have given them, unless they be guilty of a proven crime. Treat them with kindness; for even if you dislike them, it may well be that you may dislike a thing which God has meant for your own abundant good.

If you wish to (replace a wife with) another, do not take from her the dowry you have given her even if it be a talent of gold. That would be improper and grossly unjust; for how can you take it back when you have lain with each other and entered into a firm contract?

You shall not marry the women whom your fathers married. That was an evil practice, indecent and abominable.

Forbidden to you are your mothers, your daughters, your sisters, your paternal and maternal aunts, the daughters of your brothers and sisters, your foster-mothers, your foster sisters, the mothers of your wives, your step-daughters who are in your charge, born of the wives with whom you have lain (it is no offence for you to marry your step-daughters if you have not consummated your marriage with their mothers), and the wives of your own begotten sons. You are also forbidden to take in marriage two sisters at one and the same time: all previous such marriages excepted. God is forgiving and merciful.

Also married women, except those whom you own as slaves. Such is the decree of God. All women other than these are lawful to you, provided you seek them with your wealth in modest conduct, not in fornication. Give them their dowry for the enjoyment you have had of them as a duty; but it shall be no offence for you to make any other agreement among yourselves after you have fulfilled your duty. God is all-knowing and wise.

If any one of you cannot afford to marry a free believing woman, let him marry a slave-girl who is a believer (God best knows your faith: you are born one of another). Marry them with the permission of their masters and give them their dowry in all justice, provided they are honourable and chaste and have not entertained other men. If after marriage they commit adultery, they shall suffer half the penalty inflicted upon free adulteresses. Such is the law for those of you who fear to commit sin: but if you abstain, it will be better for you. God is forgiving and merciful.

God desires to make this known to you and to guide you along the paths of those who have gone before you, and to turn to you in mercy. God is all-knowing and wise.

God wishes to forgive you, but those who follow their own appetites wish to see you far astray. God wishes to lighten your burdens, for man was created weak.

Believers, do not consume your wealth among yourselves in vanity, but rather trade with it by mutual consent.

Do not destroy yourselves. God is merciful to you, but he that does that through wickedness and injustice shall be burned in fire. That is easy enough for God.

If you avoid the enormities you are forbidden, We shall pardon your misdeeds and usher you in with all honour. Do not covet the favours by which God has exalted some of you above others. Men shall be rewarded according to their deeds, and women shall be rewarded according to their deeds. Rather implore God to bestow on you His gifts. God has knowledge of all things.

To every parent and kinsman We have appointed heirs who will inherit from him. As for those with whom you have entered into agreements, let them, too, have their due. God bears witness to all things.

Men have authority over women because God has made the one superior to the other, and because they spend their wealth to maintain them. Good women are obedient. They guard their unseen parts because God has guarded them. As for those from whom you fear disobedience, admonish them and send them to beds apart and beat them. Then if they obey you, take no further action against them. God is high, supreme.

If you fear a breach between a man and his wife, appoint an arbiter from his people and another from hers. If they wish to be reconciled God will bring them together again. God is all-knowing and wise.

Serve God and associate none with Him. Show kindness to your parents and your kindred, to orphans and to the helpless, to near and distant neighbours, to those that keep company with you, to the traveller in need, and to the slaves whom you own. God does not love arrogant and boastful men, who are themselves niggardly and enjoin others to be niggardly; who conceal the riches which God of His bounty has bestowed upon them (We have prepared a shameful punishment for the unbelievers); and who spend their wealth for the sake of ostentation, believing neither in God nor in the Last Day. He that chooses Satan for his friend, an evil friend has he.

*　　　*　　　*

12. Joseph

[MECCA]

In the Name of God, the Compassionate, the Merciful

Alif lām rā. These are the verses of the Glorious Book. We have revealed the Koran in the Arabic tongue so that you may grow in understanding.

In revealing this Koran We will recount to you the best of narratives, though before it you were heedless.

Joseph said to his father: "Father, I dreamt of eleven stars and the sun and the moon; I saw them prostrate themselves before me."

"My son," he replied, "say nothing of this dream to your brothers, lest they plot evil against you: Satan is the sworn enemy of man. You shall be chosen by your Lord. He will teach you to interpret visions, and will perfect His favour to you and to the house of Jacob, as He perfected it to your forefathers Abraham and Isaac before you. Your Lord is wise and all-knowing."

Surely in Joseph and his brothers there are signs for doubting men.

They said to each other: "Joseph and his brother are dearer to our father than ourselves, though we are many. Truly, our father is much mistaken. Let us slay Joseph, or cast him away in some far-off land, so that we may have no rivals in our father's love, and after that be honourable men."

One of them said: "Do not slay Joseph; but if you must, rather cast him into a dark pit. Some caravan will take him up."

They said to their father: "Why do you not trust us with Joseph? Surely we wish him well. Send him with us tomorrow, that he may play and enjoy himself. We will take good care of him."

He replied: "It would much grieve me to let him go with you; for I fear lest the wolf should eat him when you are off your guard."

They said: "If the wolf could eat him despite our numbers, then we should surely be lost!"

And when they took Joseph with them, they decided to cast him into a dark pit. We revealed to him, saying: "You shall tell them of all this when they will not know you."

At nightfall they returned weeping to their father. They said: "We went off to compete together and left Joseph with our packs. The wolf devoured him. But you will not believe us, though we speak the truth." And they showed him their brother's shirt, stained with false blood.

"No!" he cried. "Your souls have tempted you to evil. Sweet patience! God alone can help me bear the loss you speak of."

And a caravan passed by, who sent their water-bearer to the pit. And when he had let down his pail, he cried: "Rejoice! A boy!"

They concealed him as part of their merchandise. But God knew what they did. They sold him for a trifling price, for a few pieces of silver. They cared nothing for him.

The Egyptian who bought him said to his wife:[4] "Be kind to him. He may prove useful to us, or we may adopt him as our son."

Thus We established Joseph in the land, and taught him to interpret dreams. God has power over all things, though most men may not know it. And when he reached maturity We bestowed on him wisdom and knowledge. Thus We reward the righteous.

His master's wife sought to seduce him. She bolted the doors and said: "Come!"

"God forbid!" he replied. "My lord has treated me with kindness. Wrongdoers never prosper."

She made for him, and he himself would have succumbed to her had he not been shown a sign from his Lord. Thus did We shield him from wantonness, for he was one of Our faithful servants.

They both rushed to the door. She tore his shirt from behind. And at the door they met her husband.

She cried: "Shall not the man who wished to violate your wife be thrown into prison or sternly punished?"

Joseph said: "It was she who attempted to seduce me."

"If his shirt is torn from the front," said one of her people, "she is speak-

4. Traditionally given the name Zuleikha.

ing the truth and he is lying. If it is torn from behind, then he is speaking the truth and she is lying."

And when her husband saw Joseph's shirt rent from behind, he said to her: "This is but one of your tricks. Your cunning is great indeed! Joseph, say no more about this. Woman, ask pardon for your sin. You have done wrong."

In the city women were saying: "The Prince's wife has sought to seduce her servant. She has conceived a passion for him. It is clear that she has gone astray."

When she heard of their intrigues, she invited them to a banquet at her house. To each she gave a knife, and ordered Joseph to present himself before them. When they saw him, they were amazed at him and cut their hands, exclaiming: "God preserve us! This is no mortal, but a gracious angel."

"This is the man," she said, "on whose account you blamed me. I sought to seduce him, but he was unyielding. If he declines to do my bidding, he shall be thrown into prison and shall be held in scorn."

"Lord," said Joseph, "sooner would I go to prison than give in to their advances. Shield me from their cunning, or I shall yield to them and lapse into folly."

His Lord heard his prayer and warded off their wiles from him. He hears all and knows all.

Yet for all the evidence they had seen, they thought it right to jail him for a time.

Two young men entered the prison with him. One of them said: "I dreamt that I was pressing grapes." And the other said: "I dreamt that I was carrying a loaf upon my head, and that the birds came and ate of it. Tell us the meaning of these dreams, for we can see you are a virtuous man."

Joseph replied: "I can interpret them long before they are fulfilled. Whatever food you are provided with, I can divine for you its meaning, even before it reaches you. This knowledge my Lord has given me, for I have left the faith of those that disbelieve in God and deny the life to come. I follow the faith of my forefathers, Abraham, Isaac, and Jacob. We will serve no idols besides God. Such is the grace which God has bestowed on us and on all mankind. Yet most men do not give thanks.

"Fellow-prisoners! Are sundry gods better than God, the One, the One who conquers all? Those you serve besides Him are nothing but names which you and your fathers have devised and for which God has revealed no sanction. Judgement rests only with God. He has commanded you to worship none but Him. That is the true faith: yet most men do not know it.

"Fellow-prisoners, one of you will serve his lord with wine. The other will be crucified, and the birds will peck at his head. This is the answer to your question."

And Joseph said to the prisoner who he knew would be freed: "Remember me in the presence of your lord."

But Satan made him forget to mention Joseph to his lord, so that he stayed in prison for several years.

The king said: "I saw seven fatted cows which seven lean ones devoured; also seven green ears of corn and seven others dry. Tell me the meaning of this vision, my nobles, if you can interpret visions."

They replied: "It is but a medley of dream; nor are we skilled in the interpretation of dreams."

Thereupon the man who had been freed remembered Joseph after all that time. He said: "I shall tell you what it means. Give me leave to go."

He said to Joseph: "Tell us, man of truth, of the seven fatted cows which seven lean ones devoured; also of the seven green ears of corn and the other seven which were dry: so that I may go back to my masters and inform them."

He replied: "You shall sow for seven consecutive years. Leave in the ear the corn you reap, except a little which you may eat. Then there shall follow seven hungry years which will consume all but little of what you have stored. Then there will come a year of abundant rain, in which the people will press the grape."

The king said: "Bring this man before me."

But when the envoy came to him, Joseph said: "Go back to your master and ask him about the women who cut their hands. My master knows their cunning."

The king questioned the women, saying: "What made you attempt to seduce Joseph?"

"God forbid!" they replied. "We know no evil of him."

"Now the truth must come to light," said the Prince's wife. "It was I who sought to seduce him. He has told the truth."

"From this," said Joseph, "my lord will know that I did not betray him in his absence, and that God does not guide the work of the treacherous. Not that I am free from sin: man's soul is prone to evil, except his to whom God has shown mercy. My Lord is forgiving and merciful."

The king said: "Bring him before me. I will choose him for my own."

And when he had spoken with him, the king said: "You shall henceforth dwell with us, honoured and trusted."

Joseph said: "Give me charge of the granaries of the realm. I shall husband them wisely."

Thus did We establish Joseph in the land, and he dwelt there as he pleased. We bestow Our mercy on whom We will, and never deny the righteous their reward. Better is the reward of the life to come for those who believe in God and keep from evil.

Joseph's brothers arrived and presented themselves before him. He recognized them, but they knew him not. And when he had given them their provisions, he said: "Bring me your other brother from your father. Do you not see that I give just measure and am the best of hosts? If you do not bring him, you shall have no corn, nor shall you come near me again."

They replied: "We will endeavour to fetch him from his father. This we will surely do."

Joseph said to his servants: "Put their money into their packs, so that they may find it when they return to their people. Perchance they will come back."

When they returned to their father, they said: "Father, corn is henceforth denied us. Send our brother with us and we shall have our measure. We will take good care of him."

He replied: "Am I to trust you with him as I once trusted you with his brother? But God is the best of guardians: and of all those that show mercy He is the most merciful."

When they opened their packs, they discovered that their money had been returned to them. "Father," they said, "what more can we desire? Here is our money paid back to us. We will buy provisions for our people and take good care of our brother. We shall receive an extra camel-load; a camel-load should be easy enough."

He replied: "I will not let him go with you until you promise in God's name to bring him back to me, unless the worst befall you."

And when they had given him their pledge, he said: "God is the witness of your oath. My sons, enter the town by different gates. If you do wrong, I cannot ward off from you the wrath of God: judgement is His alone. In Him I have put my trust. In Him alone let the faithful put their trust."

And when they entered as their father had bade them, his counsel availed them nothing against the decree of God. It was but a wish in Jacob's soul which he had thus fulfilled. He was possessed of knowledge which We had given him, though most men have no knowledge.

When they went in to Joseph, he embraced his brother, and said: "I am your brother. Do not grieve at what they did."

And when he had given them their provisions, he hid a drinking-cup in his brother's pack.

Then a crier called out after them: "Travellers, you are thieves!"

They turned back and asked: "What have you lost?"

"We miss the king's drinking-cup," he replied. "He that brings it shall have a camel-load of corn. I pledge my word for it."

"In God's name," they cried, "you know we did not come to do evil in this land. We are no thieves."

The Egyptians said: "What penalty shall be his who stole it, if you prove to be lying?"

They replied: "He in whose pack the cup is found shall be your bondsman. Thus we punish the wrongdoers."

Joseph searched their bags before his brother's, and then took out the cup from his brother's bag.

Thus We directed Joseph. By the king's law he had no right to seize his brother: but God willed otherwise. We exalt in knowledge whom We will: but above those that have knowledge there is One more knowing.

They said: "If he has stolen—know then that a brother of his has committed theft before him."[5]

But Joseph kept his secret and revealed nothing to them. He said: "Your deed was worse. God best knows the things you speak of."

They said: "Noble prince, this boy has an aged father. Take one of us, instead of him. We can see you are a generous man."

---

5. Commentators say that Joseph had stolen an idol of his maternal grandfather's and broken it, so that he might not worship it.

He replied: "God forbid that we should take any but the man with whom our property was found: for then we should be unjust."

When they despaired of him, they went aside to confer in private. The eldest said: "Have you forgotten that your father took from you a pledge in God's name, and that long ago you did your worst with Joseph. I will not stir from this land until my father gives me leave or God makes known to me His judgement: He is the best of judges. Return to your father and say to him: 'Father, your son has committed a theft. We testify only to what we know. How could we guard against the unforeseen? Inquire at the city where we lodged, and from the caravan with which we travelled. We speak the truth.'"

"No!" cried their father. "Your souls have tempted you to evil. But I will have sweet patience. God may bring them all to me. He alone is all-knowing and wise." And he turned away from them, crying: "Alas for Joseph!" His eyes went white with grief and he was oppressed with silent sorrow.

His sons exclaimed: "In God's name, will you not cease to think of Joseph until you ruin your health and die?"

He replied: "I complain to God of my sorrow and sadness. He has made known to me things that you know not. Go, my sons, and seek news of Joseph and his brother. Do not despair of God's spirit; none but unbelievers despair of God's spirit."

And when they went in to him, they said: "Noble prince, we and our people are scourged with famine. We have brought but little money. Give us some corn, and be charitable to us: God rewards the charitable."

"Do you know," he replied, "what you did to Joseph and his brother? You are surely unaware."

They cried: "Can you indeed be Joseph?"

"I am Joseph," he answered, "and this is my brother. God has been gracious to us. Those that keep from evil and endure with fortitude, God will not deny them their reward."

"By the Lord," they said, "God has exalted you above us all. We have indeed been guilty."

He replied: "None shall reproach you this day. May God forgive you: Of all those who show mercy, He is the most merciful. Take this shirt of mine and throw it over my father's face: he will recover his sight. Then return to me with all your people."

When the caravan departed their father said: "I feel the breath of Joseph, though you will not believe me."

"In God's name," said those who heard him, "it is but your old illusion."

And when the bearer of good news arrived, he threw Joseph's shirt over the old man's face, and he regained his sight. He said: "Did I not tell you that God has made known to me what you know not?"

His sons said: "Father, implore forgiveness for our sins. We have indeed done wrong."

He replied: "I shall implore my Lord to forgive you. He is forgiving and merciful."

And when they went in to Joseph, he embraced his parents and said: "Welcome to Egypt, safe, if God wills!"

He helped his parents to a couch, and they all fell on their knees and prostrated themselves before him.

"This," said Joseph to his father, "is the meaning of my old vision: my Lord has fulfilled it. He has been gracious to me. He has released me from prison and brought you out of the desert after Satan had stirred up strife between me and my brothers. My lord is gracious to whom He will. He alone is all-knowing and wise.

"Lord, You have given me authority and taught me to interpret dreams. Creator of the heavens and the earth, my Guardian in this world and in the hereafter. Allow me to die in submission, and admit me among the righteous."

That which We have now revealed to you[6] is a tale of the unknown. You were not present when Joseph's brothers conceived their plans and schemed against him. Yet strive as you may, most men will not believe.

You shall demand of them no recompense for this. It is an admonition to all mankind.

Many are the marvels of the heavens and the earth; yet they pass them by and pay no heed to them. The greater part of them believe in God only if they can worship other gods besides Him.

Are they confident that God's scourge will not fall upon them, or that the Hour of Doom will not overtake them unawares, without warning?

Say: "This is my path. With sure knowledge I call on you to have faith in God, I and all my followers. Glory be to God! I am no idolater."

Nor were the apostles whom We sent before you other than mortals inspired by Our will and chosen from among their people.

Have they not travelled in the land and seen what was the end of those who disbelieved before them? Better is the world to come for those that keep from evil. Can you not understand?

And when at length Our apostles despaired and thought they were denied, Our help came down to them, delivering whom We pleased. The evil-doers could not be saved from Our scourge. Their annals point to a moral to men of understanding.

This[7] is no invented tale, but a confirmation of previous scriptures, an explanation of all things, a guide and a blessing to true believers.

19. Mary

[MECCA]

In the Name of God, the Compassionate, the Merciful

Kaf hā' yā' 'ain sād. An account of your Lord's goodness to His servant Zacharias:

He invoked Him in secret, saying: "My bones are enfeebled, and my

6. Muhammad.   7. The Koran.

head grows silver with age. Yet never, Lord, have I prayed to You in vain. I now fear my kinsmen who will succeed me, for my wife is barren. Grant me a son who will be my heir and an heir to the house of Jacob, and who will find grace in Your sight."

"Rejoice, Zacharias," came the answer. "You shall be given a son, and he shall be called John; a name no man has borne before him."

"How shall I have a son, Lord," asked Zacharias, "when my wife is barren and I am well-advanced in years?"

He replied: "Such is the will of your Lord. It shall be no difficult task for Me, for I brought you into being when you were nothing before."

"Lord," said Zacharias, "give me a sign."

"Your sign is that for three days and three nights," He replied, "you shall be bereft of speech, though otherwise sound in body."

Then Zacharias came out from the Shrine and exhorted his people to give glory to their Lord morning and evening.

To John We said: "Observe the Scriptures with a firm resolve." We bestowed on him wisdom, grace, and purity while yet a child, and he grew up a righteous man; honouring his father and mother, and neither arrogant nor rebellious. Blessed was he on the day he was born and the day of his death; and may peace be on him when he is raised to life.

And you shall recount in the Book the story of Mary: how she left her people and betook herself to a solitary place to the east.

We sent to her Our spirit in the semblance of a full-grown man. And when she saw him she said: "May the Merciful defend me from you! If you fear the Lord, leave me and go your way."

"I am the messenger of your Lord," he replied, "and have come to give you a holy son."

"How shall I bear a child," she answered, "when I am a virgin, untouched by man?"

"Such is the will of your Lord," he replied. "That is no difficult thing for Him. 'He shall be a sign to mankind,' says the Lord, 'and a blessing from Ourself. This is Our decree.'"

Thereupon she conceived him, and retired to a far-off place. And when she felt the throes of childbirth she lay down by the trunk of a palm-tree crying: "Oh, would that I had died and passed into oblivion!"

But a voice from below cried out to her: "Do not despair. Your Lord has provided a brook that runs at your feet, and if you shake the trunk of this palm-tree it will drop fresh ripe dates in your lap. Therefore eat and drink and rejoice; and should you meet any mortal say to him: 'I have vowed a fast to the Merciful and will not speak with any man today.'"

Carrying the child, she came to her people, who said to her: "This is indeed a strange thing! Sister of Aaron,[8] your father was never a whoremonger, nor was your mother a harlot."

She made a sign to them, pointing to the child. But they replied: "How can we speak with a babe in the cradle?"

Whereupon he spoke and said: "I am the servant of God. He has given

---

8. Muslim commentators deny the charge that there is confusion here between Miriam, Aaron's sister, and Maryam (Mary), mother of Jesus. *Sister of Aaron*, they argue, simply means "virtuous woman" in this context.

me the Book and ordained me a prophet. His blessing is upon me wherever I go, and He has commanded me to be steadfast in prayer and to give alms to the poor as long as I shall live. He has exhorted me to honour my mother and has purged me of vanity and wickedness. I was blessed on the day I was born, and blessed I shall be on the day of my death; and may peace be upon me on the day when I shall be raised to life."

Such was Jesus, the son of Mary. That is the whole truth, which they still doubt. God forbid that He Himself should beget a son! When He decrees a thing He need only say: "Be," and it is.

God is my Lord and your Lord: therefore serve Him. That is the right path.

Yet the Sects are divided concerning Jesus. But when the fateful day arrives, woe to the unbelievers! Their sight and being shall be sharpened on the day when they appear before Us. Truly, the unbelievers are in the grossest error.

Forewarn them of that woeful day, when Our decrees shall be fulfilled whilst they heedlessly persist in unbelief. For We shall inherit the earth and all who dwell upon it. To Us they shall return.

You shall also recount in the Book the story of Abraham:

He was a saintly man and a prophet. He said to his father: "How can you serve a worthless idol, a thing that can neither see nor hear?

"Father, things you know nothing of have come to my knowledge: therefore follow me, that I may guide you along an even path.

"Father, do not worship Satan; for he has rebelled against the Lord of Mercy.

"Father, I fear that a scourge will fall upon you from the Merciful, and you will become one of Satan's minions."

He replied: "Do you dare renounce my gods, Abraham? Desist from this folly or I shall stone you. Begone from my house this instant!"

"Peace be with you," said Abraham. "I shall implore my Lord to forgive you: for to me He has been gracious. But I will not live with you or with your idols. I will call on my Lord, and trust that my prayers will not be ignored."

And when Abraham had cast off his people and the idols which they worshipped, We gave him Isaac and Jacob. Each of them We made a prophet, and We bestowed on them gracious gifts and high renown.

In the Book tell also of Moses, who was a chosen man, an apostle, and a prophet.

We called out to him from the right side of the Mountain, and when he came near We communed with him in secret. We gave him, of Our mercy, his brother Aaron, himself a prophet.

And in the Book you shall tell of Ishmael: he, too, was a man of his word, an apostle, and a prophet.

He enjoined prayer and almsgiving on his people, and his Lord was pleased with him.

And of Idris:[9] he, too, was a saint and a prophet, whom We honoured and exalted.

---

9. Enoch.

These are the men to whom God has been gracious: the prophets from among the descendants of Adam and of those whom We carried in the Ark with Noah; the descendants of Abraham, of Israel, and of those whom We have guided and chosen. For when the revelations of the Merciful were recited to them they fell down on their knees in tears and adoration.

But the generations who succeeded them neglected their prayers and succumbed to their desires. These shall assuredly be lost. But those that repent and embrace the Faith and do what is right shall be admitted to Paradise and shall in no way be wronged. They shall enter the gardens of Eden, which the Merciful has promised His servants in reward for their faith. His promise shall be fulfilled.

There they shall hear no idle talk, but only the voice of peace. And their sustenance shall be given them morning and evening. Such is the Paradise which We shall give the righteous to inherit.

We do not descend from Heaven save at the bidding of your Lord.[1] To Him belongs what is before us and behind us, and all that lies between.

Your Lord does not forget. He is the Lord of the heavens and the earth and all that is between them. Worship Him, then, and be patient in His service; for do you know any other worthy of His name?

"What!" says man. "When I am once dead, shall I be raised to life?"

Does man forget that We created him out of the void? By the Lord, We will call them to account in company with all the devils and set them on their knees around the fire of Hell: from every sect We will carry off its stoutest rebels against the Lord of Mercy. We know best who deserves most to be burnt therein.

There is not one of you who shall not pass through it: such is the absolute decree of your Lord. We will deliver those who fear Us, but the wrong-doers shall be left there on their knees.

When Our clear revelations are recited to them the unbelievers say to the faithful: "Which of us two will have a finer dwelling and better companions?"

How many generations have We destroyed before them, far greater in riches and in splendour!

Say: "The Merciful will bear long with those in error, until they witness the fulfilment of His threats: be it a worldly scourge or the Hour of Doom. Then shall they know whose is the worse plight and whose the smaller following."

God will add guidance to those that are rightly guided. Deeds of lasting merit shall earn you a better reward in His sight and a more auspicious end.

Mark the words of him who denies Our signs and who yet boasts: "I shall surely be given wealth and children!" he boasts.

Has the future been revealed to him? Or has the Merciful made him such a promise?

By no means! We will record his words and make his punishment long

---

1. Commentators say that these are the words of the angel Gabriel, in reply to Muhammad's complaint of long intervals elapsing between periods of revelation.

and terrible. All he speaks of he shall leave behind and come before us all alone.

They have chosen other gods to help them. But in the end they will renounce their worship and turn against them.

Know that We send down to the unbelievers devils who incite them to evil. Therefore have patience: their days are numbered. The day will surely come when We will gather the righteous in multitudes before the Lord of Mercy, and drive the sinful in great hordes into Hell. None has power to intercede for them save him who has received the sanction of the Merciful.

Those who say: "The Lord of Mercy has begotten a son," preach a monstrous falsehood, at which the very heavens might crack, the earth break asunder, and the mountains crumble to dust. That they should ascribe a son to the Merciful, when it does not become the Lord of Mercy to beget one!

There is none in the heavens or the earth but shall return to the Merciful in utter submission. He has kept strict count of all His creatures, and one by one they shall approach Him on the Day of Resurrection. He will cherish those who accepted the true faith and were charitable in their lifetime.

We have revealed to you the Koran in your own tongue that you may thereby proclaim good tidings to the upright and give warning to a contentious nation.

How many generations have We destroyed before them! Can you find one of them still alive, or hear so much as a whisper from them?

55. The Merciful[2]

[MECCA]

In the Name of God, the Compassionate, the Merciful

It is the Merciful who has taught the Koran.

He created man and taught him articulate speech. The sun and the moon pursue their ordered course. The plants and the trees bow down in adoration.

He raised the heaven on high and set the balance of all things, that you might not transgress that balance. Give just weight and full measure.

He laid the earth for His creatures, with all its fruits and blossom-bearing palm, chaff-covered grain and scented herbs. Which of your Lord's blessings would you deny?

He created man from potter's clay and the jinn[3] from smokeless fire. Which of your Lord's blessings would you deny?

The Lord of the two easts[4] is He, and the Lord of the two wests. Which of your Lord's blessings would you deny?

He has let loose the two oceans:[5] they meet one another. Yet between

---

2. Compare this Sura with Psalm 136.   3. A separate order of creation from humans. The question that follows is addressed to both beings.   4. The points at which the sun rises in summer and winter. 5. Saltwater and freshwater; more specifically, a reference to freshwater springs in the ocean floor.

them stands a barrier which they cannot overrun. Which of your Lord's blessings would you deny?

Pearls and corals come from both. Which of your Lord's blessings would you deny?

His are the ships that sail like mountains upon the ocean. Which of your Lord's blessings would you deny?

All that lives on earth is doomed to die. But the face of your Lord will abide for ever, in all its majesty and glory. Which of your Lord's blessings would you deny?

All who dwell in heaven and earth entreat Him. Each day some mighty task engages Him. Which of your Lord's blessings would you deny?

Mankind and jinn, We shall surely find the time to judge you! Which of your Lord's blessings would you deny?

Mankind and jinn, if you have power to penetrate the confines of heaven and earth, then penetrate them! But this you shall not do except with Our own authority. Which of your Lord's blessings would you deny?

Flames of fire shall be lashed at you, and molten brass. There shall be none to help you. Which of your Lord's blessings would you deny?

When the sky splits asunder and reddens like a rose or stainéd leather (which of your Lord's blessings would you deny?), on that day neither man nor jinnee shall be asked about his sins. Which of your Lord's blessings would you deny?

The wrongdoers shall be known by their looks; they shall be seized by their forelocks and their feet. Which of your Lord's blessings would you deny?

That is the Hell which the sinners deny. They shall wander between fire and water fiercely seething. Which of your Lord's blessings would you deny?

But for those that fear the majesty of their Lord there are two gardens (which of your Lord's blessings would you deny?) planted with shady trees. Which of your Lord's blessings would you deny?

Each is watered by a flowing spring. Which of your Lord's blessings would you deny?

Each bears every kind of fruit in pairs. Which of your Lord's blessings would you deny?

They shall recline on couches lined with thick brocade, and within their reach will hang the fruits of both gardens. Which of your Lord's blessings would you deny?

They shall dwell with bashful virgins whom neither man nor jinnee will have touched before. Which of your Lord's blessings would you deny?

Virgins as fair as corals and rubies. Which of your Lord's blessings would you deny?

Shall the reward of goodness be anything but good? Which of your Lord's blessings would you deny?

And beside these there shall be two other gardens (which of your Lord's blessings would you deny?) of darkest green. Which of your Lord's blessings would you deny?

A gushing fountain shall flow in each. Which of your Lord's blessings would you deny?

Each planted with fruit-trees, the palm and the pomegranate. Which of your Lord's blessings would you deny?

In each there shall be virgins chaste and fair. Which of your Lord's blessings would you deny?

Dark-eyed virgins sheltered in their tents (which of your Lord's blessings would you deny?) whom neither man nor jinnee will have touched before. Which of your Lord's blessings would you deny?

They shall recline on green cushions and rich carpets. Which of your Lord's blessings would you deny?

Blessed be the name of your Lord, the lord of majesty and glory!

62. Friday, or the Day of Congregation

[MEDINA]

In the Name of God, the Compassionate, the Merciful

All that is in heaven and earth gives glory to God, the Sovereign Lord, the Holy One, the Almighty, the Wise One.

It is He that has sent forth among the gentiles an apostle of their own to recite to them His revelations, to purify them, and to instruct them in the Book and in wisdom though they have hitherto been in gross error, together with others of their own kin who have not yet followed them. He is the Mighty, the Wise One.

Such is the grace of God: He bestows it on whom He will. His grace is infinite.

Those to whom the burden of the Torah was entrusted and yet refused to bear it are like a donkey laden with books. Wretched is the example of those who deny God's revelations. God does not guide the wrong-doers.

Say to the Jews: "If your claim be true that of all men you alone are God's friends, then you should wish for death, if what you say be true!" But, because of what their hands have done, they will never wish for death. God knows the wrongdoers.

Say: "The death from which you shrink is sure to overtake you. Then you shall be sent back to Him who knows the unknown and the manifest, and He will declare to you all that you have done."

Believers, when you are summoned to Friday prayers hasten to the remembrance of God and cease your trading. That would be best for you, if you but knew it. Then, when the prayers are ended, disperse and go in quest of God's bounty. Remember God always, so that you may prosper.

Yet no sooner do they see some commerce or merriment than they flock to it eagerly, leaving you standing all alone.

Say: "That which God has in store is far better than any commerce or merriment. God is the Most Munificent Giver."

71. Noah

In the Name of God, the Compassionate, the Merciful

We sent forth Noah to his people, saying: "Give warning to your people before a woeful scourge overtakes them."

He said: "My people, I come to warn you plainly. Serve God and fear Him, and obey me. He will forgive you your sins and give you respite for an appointed time. When God's time arrives, none shall put it back. Would that you understood this!"

"Lord," said Noah, "day and night I have pleaded with my people, but my pleas have only added to their aversion. Each time I call on them to seek Your pardon, they thrust their fingers in their ears and draw their cloaks over their heads, persisting in sin and bearing themselves with insolent pride. I called out loud to them, and appealed to them in public and in private. 'Seek forgiveness of your Lord,' I said. 'He is ever ready to forgive you. He sends down for you abundant rain from heaven and bestows upon you wealth and children. He has provided you with gardens and with running brooks. Why do you deny the greatness of God when He has made you in gradual stages? Can you not see how He created the seven heavens one above the other, placing in them the moon for a light and the sun for a lantern? God has brought you forth from the earth like a plant, and to the earth He will restore you. Then He will bring you back afresh. He has made the earth a vast expanse for you, so that you may roam in spacious paths.'"

And Noah said: "Lord, my people disobey me and follow those whose wealth and offspring will only hasten their perdition. They have devised an outrageous plot, and said to each other: 'Do not renounce your gods. Do not forsake Wadd or Suwā' or Yaghuth or Ya'uq or Nasr.'[6] They have led led numerous men astray. You surely drive the wrongdoers to further error."

And because of their sins they were overwhelmed by the Flood and cast into the Fire. They found none besides God to help them.

And Noah said: "Lord, do not leave a single unbeliever in the land. If you spare them they will mislead Your servants and beget none but sinners and unbelievers. Forgive me, Lord, and forgive my parents and every true believer who seeks refuge in my house. Forgive all the faithful, men and women, and hasten the destruction of the wrongdoers."

76. Man

In the Name of God, the Compassionate, the Merciful

Does there not pass over man a space of time when his life is a blank?[7] We have created man from the union of the two sexes so that We may

6. Names of idols that were worshiped in Mecca before Muhammad had them destroyed.   7. In the womb.

put him to the proof. We have endowed him with hearing and sight and, be he thankful or oblivious of Our favours, We have shown him the right path.

For the unbelievers We have prepared fetters and chains, and a blazing Fire. But the righteous shall drink of a cup tempered at the Camphor Fountain, a gushing spring at which the servants of God will refresh themselves: they who keep their vows and dread the far-spread terrors of Judgement-day; who, though they hold it dear, give sustenance to the poor man, the orphan, and the captive, saying: "We feed you for God's sake only; we seek of you neither recompense nor thanks: for we fear from God a day of anguish and of woe."

God will deliver them from the evil of that day and make their faces shine with joy. He will reward them for their steadfastness with robes of silk and the delights of Paradise. Reclining there upon soft couches, they shall feel neither the scorching heat nor the biting cold. Trees will spread their shade around them, and fruits will hang in clusters over them.

They shall be served with silver dishes, and beakers as large as goblets; silver goblets which they themselves shall measure: and cups brim-full with ginger-flavoured water from the Fount of Salsabīl. They shall be attended by boys graced with eternal youth, who to the beholder's eyes will seem like sprinkled pearls. When you gaze upon that scene you will behold a kingdom blissful and glorious.

They shall be arrayed in garments of fine green silk and rich brocade, and adorned with bracelets of silver. Their Lord will give them pure nectar to drink.

Thus you shall be rewarded; your high endeavours are gratifying to God.

We have made known to you the Koran by gradual revelation; therefore wait with patience the judgement of your Lord and do not yield to the wicked and the unbelieving. Remember the name of your Lord morning and evening; in the nighttime worship Him: praise Him all night long.

The unbelievers love this fleeting life too well, and thus prepare for themselves a heavy day of doom. We created them, and endowed their limbs and joints with strength; but if We please We can replace them by other men.

This is indeed an admonition. Let him that will, take the right path to his Lord. Yet you cannot will, except by the will of God. God is wise and all-knowing.

He is merciful to whom He will: but for the wrongdoers He has prepared a woeful punishment.

ABOLQASEM FERDOWSI

932–1025

Nothing in Western literature quite prepares us for the *Shâhnâme* (Book of kings) of Abolqasem Ferdowsi. We call it an epic because it is a long poem—some fifty

thousand couplets—and is filled with heroic tales that are drawn from Iran's history and mythology. *Epic* is the only descriptive term we have that seems to fit such a work. Yet for us *epic* really means Homer and the Homeric tradition—all those poems from Virgil's *Aeneid* to Milton's *Paradise Lost* that were written in conscious imitation of the *Odyssey* and the *Iliad*, or which, like *The Song of Roland* or *Beowulf*, were written to celebrate a particular historic moment or a "heroic" way of life. The *Shâhnâme* is a very different poem from any of these, and it developed independently from the Homeric tradition. It does not begin "in the midst of things," as does the *Iliad*, but with the creation of the world and the appearance of the first shah. It lacks the elaborate celestial machinery of gods and goddesses that one finds in other epic traditions, from the *Odyssey* and the *Iliad* to *Gilgamesh* in the ancient Near East and to the *Mahābhārata* and the *Rāmāyaṇa* in India. It is a monotheistic epic like *Paradise Lost*, but its focus on the life of the royal court makes it seem closer to the tales of King Arthur and the knights of the round table than to Milton's great poem. It contains not one story but many, not a single climactic event, but a multitude of them, and not one hero but a long sequence of heroes and heroic princes. Rostám, who is the last and greatest of a family of heroes from the Iranian province of Sistan, and who dominates several of its finest stories, is no more than an offstage presence in other tales. He also dies when the poem is only two-thirds finished. The events in *Gilgamesh*, Homer, and the European epics are tailored to the limits of a single human life, but the events of the *Shâhnâme* stretch across millennia and a single hero may live for centuries.

Some of the stories that make up the *Shâhnâme* can be traced back well before the coming of Islam to at least the time of Cyrus and Darius some twenty-five hundred years ago. Other stories from later times were added to these, and all were gathered together into comprehensive collections from time to time. Late in the reign of the Sassanians (third to seventh centuries), the last pre-Islamic Iranian dynasty to rule in Iran, a chronicle was compiled at the court and called the *khudáy nâmág* (Book of kings). The original of this work has been lost, but Arabic translations of portions of it survive in the work of early Arab historians. During the first two centuries of the Islamic period, Iran's rulers were Arab and interested only in Arabic culture. When an Iranian Muslim dynasty, the Samanids (819–1005), returned to power in central Asia, interest in the national epic of Iran revived as well. Once more the court ordered that the old stories be gathered into a single chronicle, in prose. When it was complete they sought a poet to turn this prose into verse. The first likely candidate, Daqiqi, was killed by one of his slaves after he had completed only two thousand verses (later incorporated into the finished work) and so the way was opened for Abolqasem Ferdowsi.

Ferdowsi deliberately set about making his poetic version a vehicle for preserving Iran's pre-Islamic heritage. He ends his tale by saying that he has given new life to stories that had begun to be forgotten. He also assumed that in giving poetic life to these tales he was ensuring the survival of his own name as well.

> And when this famous book shall reach its end,
> Throughout the land my praises will be heard.
> From this day on I shall not die, but live,
> For I'll have sown my words both far and wide.

In this he was successful beyond his wildest dreams. Since Ferdowsi completed the *Shâhnâme* it has remained a work of central importance in the Iranian cultural tradition.

No story in the *Shâhnâme* has more engaged the interest and sympathy of audiences in the West than that of the tragic encounter between Sohráb and his father, Rostám. It was translated into English and the languages of Europe repeatedly in

the nineteenth century and Matthew Arnold gave it a place in English literature by his brilliant retelling of it (*The Story of Sohráb and Rustúm*, 1853). It is easy to understand why it was so successful. The action is fast paced and engrossing. It includes a brief but wonderful romantic interlude and several compelling battles. Besides the principal characters there are dreadful villains and a woman warrior who is both courageous and seductive—and this in a work in which there are relatively few major roles for women. Finally, it has a death scene that would make a stone weep. Yet the story's most compelling attraction is surely the central event itself, the death of Sohráb at the unwitting hands of his father, Rostám.

The theme of filicide is a powerful and compelling one, especially when both father and son are figures of great appeal. Rostám is the greatest hero of the *Shâh-nâme*, the exemplar of heroism and loyalty, and Sohráb is clearly the son who was meant to succeed Rostám, as he has succeeded Zal and Sam and Narimán. Why should he, of all people, be obliged to kill him? Sohráb in turn is a young man who is devoted to his father and whose principal ambition is to find him. His death seems a ghastly reward for filial piety. Worst of all, those who benefit most by the death of Sohráb, Kay Kavús, and Afrasiyáb, hardly seem to deserve such a reward. Kay Kavús is a dreadful ruler, and Afrasiyáb, the shah of Turán, is Iran's greatest enemy. The death of Sohráb at his father's hands also violates what we accept as the normal order of things. Sons replace fathers as youth triumphs over age. The story of Sohráb fascinates us in part because it violates this natural order and adds a nightmarish element to a confrontation that is already freighted with meaning.

This sense of horror and outrage at the death of Sohráb is not something we impose on the text. The story concludes with the famous lines: "It is a tale that's filled with tears and grief. / The tender heart will rage against Rostám." Rostám himself recognizes the horror of his deed the moment after he has committed it, and laments the death of his son in some of the most beautiful and moving passages in the poem. The poem, in short, raises two compelling questions for us: why must Sohráb die, and why must Rostám be responsible for his death? The first answer is the easier to supply and leads to the second. As modern readers we are inclined to see Sohráb's desire to overthrow Afrasiyáb and Kay Kavús and replace them with the worthier figure of Rostám as commendable, as a protomodern anticipation of meritocratic rule. Yet in the world of the *Shâhnâme* only God has the authority to choose a monarch. His choice in this matter is as unchallengeable as it is unfathomable. What is more important, the underlying belief of the text is that Iran will endure only for so long as it is ruled by a line of divinely appointed shahs. To overthrow, or attempt to overthrow, one of God's chosen shahs, however great the provocation, is a crime against both God and the state. That God would choose so inept a ruler for Iran as Kay Kavús is indeed puzzling. But one has no right to question or dispute His choice. By his first bold decision to overthrow Kay Kavús and put his father on the throne, Sohráb ensures his own destruction. In the same way, Rostám's harsh and arrogant rejection of the shah's authority (When I'm enraged, who then is Shah Kavús? / Who's there to humble me? Who is this Tus?), however justified, provides the dramatic justification for his bearing the tragic responsibility of killing his own son. His lapse in loyalty and obedience is brief and the breach is soon healed, but the memory lingers. Kay Kavús later alludes to it in explaining his refusal to send Rostám the royal remedy that would save Sohráb.

> ". . . [Sohráb] will make his father yet more powerful.
> Rostám will slay me then, I have no doubt. . . .
> You heard him, how he said, 'Who is Kavús?
> If he's the shah, then who is Tus?' And with
> That chest and neck, that mighty arm and fist,

In this wide world who's there to equal him?
Will he stand humbly by my royal seat,
Or march beneath my banner's eagle wings?"

Rostám is in part to blame for Sohráb's assault on the Iranian shah. He was as casual as a god in siring his son and left him to grow up without the guidance that would have made him a loyal subject. However, Tahminé is equally to blame, because she hides the true nature of her son's heroic abilities from his father, fearing to lose him. But behind both of them stands the implacable and malignant fate that so often intrudes in the story to ensure that father and son will not recognize each other.

In the larger context of the *Shâhnâme*, the story of Sohráb underscores the primacy of the monarch and marks a transition from stories in which the conflict between hero and shah dominates to ones in which the conflict is between princely heir and royal father. Much of the tragedy of Sohráb turns on Rostám's crucial failure to raise his own son. In the story of Siyavash, which immediately follows that of Sohráb, Rostám takes the infant Siyavash, the son of Kay Kavús, to his castle in Sistan and raises him there as virtually his own child. By this act he allows his own heroic heritage to join that of the royal line. Rostám's role in the epic diminishes from this point on. He remains an important but essentially off-stage presence until, centuries later, he reappears to fight the last great battle of his life. It is as though the evolution of the *Shâhnâme* requires a shift in emphasis at this point from the conflict of shah and hero to that of shah and prince, and the sacrifice of Sohráb is the means whereby the energy of the Sistanian heroes is diverted into the royal line

The only complete translation of the *Shâhnâme* into English verse is that of Arthur George and Edmond Warner, *The Shâhnâma of Firdausi* (1905–1925). Unfortunately, it is available only in large research libraries. There is also a prose translation by Reuben Levy, *The Epic of the Kings* (1967) that summarizes many passages very briefly and skips others altogether. Besides the translation of *Sohráb* printed here, the only modern poetic version of one of the stories from the *Shâhnâme* is Dick Davis's fine verse translation, *The Legend of Seyavash* (1992). Davis has also written the best study of the *Shâhnâme* in English, *Epic and Sedition: The Case of the Shâhnâme* (1992). There is an extended discussion of Sohráb by Jerome W. Clinton in *The Tragedy of Sohráb* (1984), edited by Roger M. Savory and Dionisius A. Agius. Every literary history of Iran contains a chapter or so on Ferdowsi and the *Shâhnâme*, most recently, *Persian Literature* (1988), edited by Ehsan Yarshater.

PRONOUNCING GLOSSARY

The following list uses common English syllables and stress accents to provide rough equivalents of selected words whose pronunciation may be unfamiliar to the general reader.

Abolqasem Ferdowsi: *a'-bowl qah'-sem fair-doe-see'*	Kay Kavús: *kay kah-voos'*
Afrâsiyáb: *af-raw'-see-ahb'*	Kay Qobád: *kay qo-bahd'*
	Khuday Nâmag: *koo-dai' nah-mag'*
Ahriman: *ah-ree-man'*	nushdarú: *noosh-dah-roo'*
Daqiqi: *da-kee-kee'*	piltán: *peel-tan'*
Gordafaríd: *gor-dah'-fa-reed'*	Rostám: *ros-tam'*
Gudárz: *goo-darz'*	Rudabé: *roo-dah-bay'*
Human: *hoo-mahn'*	Shâhnâme: *shah-nah-may'*

Siyavash: *see-uh-vash'*   Yazdán: *yaz-dawn'*

Sohráb: *soh-rawb'*   Zavaré: *za-vah-ray'*

Tahminé: *tah-mee-nay'*   Zhende Razm: *zhén-day razm'*

From Shâhnâme[1]
The Tragedy of Sohráb and Rostám
The Beginning

*   *   *

In the stories of the *dehqáns'*[2] there is a tale,
To which I've added from old narratives.
The teller of tales begins to speak, and says—
Rostám one day just as the sun rose up,
Was sad at heart, and so prepared to hunt.   5
He armed himself, put arrows in their sheaf,
Then like a fearsome lion on the chase,
He galloped toward the borders of Turán.[3]
As he approached the Turkish borderlands,
He saw the plain was filled with onagers.[4]   10
The Giver of the Crown[5] glowed like a rose.
He laughed aloud and spurred Rakhsh[6] from his place.
With bow and arrow, and with mace and rope,
He brought down many onagers upon.
The plain. Then from dead branches, brush, and thorns,   15
Rostám built up a fiercely blazing fire.
And when the fire had spread, he wrenched a tree
Out of the ground to serve him as a spit.
He placed a heavy stallion on that tree,
That was a feather in his palm, no more.   20
When it was done he tore its limbs apart
And wolfed it down, the marrow bones and all.
Rostám then slept and rested from the hunt.
Nearby Rakhsh wandered, grazing in a meadow.
Turkish horsemen, some seven or eight, passed by   25
That plain and hunting ground, and as they did
They spied a horse's tracks and turned aside
To follow them along the river's bank.
When they saw Rakhsh grazing in the meadow,
They raced ahead to snare him with their ropes.   30
When he was caught, they bore him galloping
Toward the town; each eager for his share.

*   *   *

---

1. Translated by Jerome W. Clinton.   2. The Iranian provincial nobility of central Asia, principal repository of the pre-Islamic Iranian culture.   3. In the land of the Turks, the traditional enemy of Iran.   4. A species of wild ass native to the Iranian Plateau.   5. Rostám; he brought Kay Qobád (the first shah of the Kaianian dynasty) to the throne. Kay Kavús was Kay Qobád's successor.   6. Rostám's steed, who is hugely proportioned (as is Rostám) and the only horse able to bear his weight. He is Rostám's companion in all his adventures, sometimes taking an active role.

In Semengán

As he drew near to Semengán,[7] the shah
And nobles heard, "The Giver of the Crown
Approaches now on foot. While they were on
A hunt, the shining Rakhsh fled from his hand."
The shah and all his nobles greeted him,   5
All those who wore a crown upon their heads.
The shah of Semengán inquired of him,
"What can this mean? Who's dared to challenge you?
Within this city we are all your friends.
We stand beside your path, alert to serve.   10
You may command our persons as our wealth.
The worthy heads and hearts of all are yours."
Rostám considered well his words and saw
That he'd small cause for his distrust and doubt.
He answered him and said, "While in the field,   15
Rakhsh fled from me, with neither bit nor reins.
His tracks come to the city's edge; and on
The other side, there's only reeds and swamp.
Find him and you will have my thanks. In my
Reward I'll show you all my gratitude.   20
But if you don't, and he remains unfound,
Then many noble lords will lose their heads."
To him the shah replied, "Oh worthy man!
No one would dare to treat with you like that.
Don't act in haste, but be my welcome guest.   25
This matter will conclude as you desire.
Tonight let us rejoice our hearts with wine,
And keep them free of evil thoughts as well.
The tracks of shining Rakhsh, a steed who is
Well known to all, will not stay hidden long."   30
     Brave Tahamtán[8] rejoiced to hear his words.
His soul was freed of all disquietude.
It now seemed right to him to visit in
His home. This happy news made him his guest.
The ruler then gave him a place within   35
His castle keep, and waited by his side.
He summoned all the city's great, those who
Were worthy to be seated at the feast.
The bearer of the wine, the harper too,
And dark-eyed, rose-cheeked idols of Taráz,[9]   40
All joined with the musicians gathered there,
To see that great Rostám should not be sad.
When he grew drunk, and sleep came to his eyes,
He wished to leave the feast and seek his rest.
They led him to a place fit for a prince,   45
A quiet chamber sweet with scent and musk.

---

7. A city within the borders of Turán.   8. Rostám; it means "huge-bodied."   9. A city in central Asia famous for the beauty of its women.

Tahminé[1]

And when one watch had passed on that dark night,
And Sirius rose on the heaven's wheel.
The sound of secret voices could be heard.
The chamber door was opened quietly.
A single slave, a scented candle in   5
Her hand, came to the pillow of Rostám.
Behind the slave, a moon-faced[2] maid appeared,
Adorned and scented like the shining sun.
Her eyebrows bows, her tresses lassos coiled,
In stature like a slender cypress tree.   10
Her soul was wisdom and her body seemed
Of spirit pure, as though not made of earth.
Amazed, Rostám the fearless lion-heart,
Cried out unto the Maker of the World.
He questioned her, and asked, "What is your name?   15
Here in the dead of night, what do you seek?"
She answered him, "My name is Tahminé.
It seems my heart's been rent in two by grief.
The daughter of the shah of Semengán,
From lions and from tigers comes my seed.   20
In all the world no beauty is my match.
Few are my like beneath the azure wheel.[3]
Outside these walls, there's none who's looked on me.
Nor has my voice been heard by any ear.
From everyone have I heard tales of you—   25
So wonderful they seemed to me like myths.
They say you fear no leopard and no demon.
No crocodile or lion is so fierce.
At night alone, you journey to Turán,
And wander freely there, and even sleep.   30
You spit an onager with just one hand,
And with your sword you cause the air to weep.
When you approach them with your mace in hand,
The leopard rends his claws, the lion his heart.
The eagle when he sees your naked blade,   35
Dares not take wing and fly off to the hunt.
The tiger's skin is branded by your rope.
The clouds weep blood in fear of your sharp lance.
As I would listen to these tales of you,
I'd bite my lip in wonder, and yearn   40
To look upon those shoulders and that chest.
And then Izád[4] sent you to Semengán.
I'm yours now should you want me, and, if not,
None but the fish and birds will see my face.
It's first because I do so long for you,   45
That I've slain reason for my passion's sake.
And next, perhaps the Maker of the World
Will place a son from you within my womb.
Perhaps he'll be like you in manliness

1. Sohráb's mother and princess of Semengán.   2. In Persian poetry the round face and pale skin of
the moon are the models of feminine beauty.   3. The sky.   4. One of the names of God.

And strength, a child of Saturn and the Sun.   50
And third, that I may bring your horse to you,
I'll search throughout the whole of Semengán."
    Rostám, when he looked on her angel face,
And saw in her a share of every art,
And that she'd given him some news of Rakhsh,   55
He saw no end to this that was not good.
As she had wished, and with goodwill and joy,
Rostám sealed firm his bond with her that night.
And when in secret she'd become his mate,
The night that followed lasted late and long.   60
But then at last, from high above the world,
The radiant sun cast down his shining rope.
Upon his arm Rostám had placed a jewel,
A seal that was well known throughout the world.
He gave it to her as he said, "Keep this.   65
And if the times should bring a girl to you,
Then take this gem and plait it in her hair—
A world-illumining omen of good luck.
But if the star of fate should send a son,
Then bind this father's token to his arm.   70
He'll be as tall as Sam or Narimán,[5]
In strength and manliness a noble youth,
He'll bring the eagle from the clouds above.
The sun will not look harshly on this boy."
Rostám conversed the night with his new moon,   75
And spoke with her of all he'd known and seen.
    The radiant sun at last rose to the heights
And shed his glorious light upon the earth.
The worthy shah approached the chamber of
Rostám, to ask if he had rested well.   80
And this once said, he gave him news of Rakhsh.
The Giver of the Crown rejoiced at this.
He went and stroked his steed and saddled him,
Then thanked the shah, well pleased at his return.

The Birth of Sohráb

When nine months passed for Tahminé, she bore
A healthy boy whose face shone like the moon.
It seemed he was the pahlavan[6] Rostám,
Or that he was the lion Sam, or Narimán.
Because he laughed and had a cheerful face,   5
His mother called him by the name Sohráb.[7]
In but a single month he'd grown a year.
His chest was like Rostám's, the son of Zal.
At three he learned the game of polo, and
At five he mastered bow and javelin.   10
When he was ten, in all of Semengán

---

5. Rostám's ancestors. His line included heroes famed for generations. The likeness of Sohráb to his great-grandfather Sam is remarked on repeatedly in the course of the poem.   6. Hero, warrior.
7. "Rosy-hued," because his face flushed red when he laughed. In Persia red is the color of health and good cheer; yellow is the color of fear and ill health.

Not one would dare to meet him in the field.
Sohráb went to his mother, Tahminé,
To question her, "Tell me the truth," he said.
"I'm taller than the boys who nursed with me.   15
It seems my head can touch the very sky.
Whose seed am I, and of what family?
When asked, 'Who is your sire?' What shall I say?
If you should keep this answer from me now,
I will not leave you in this world alive."   20
His mother answered him, "Be not so harsh,
But hear my words and be rejoiced by them.
Your father is the pahlaván Rostám.
Your ancestors are Sam and Narimán.
And thus it is your head can touch the sky.   25
You are descended from that famous line.
Since first the World Creator made the earth,
There's been no other horseman like Rostám.
Nor one like Sam the son of Narimán.
The turning sphere does not dare brush his head."   30
And then she brought a letter from his sire,
Rostám, and showed it secretly to him.
Enclosed with it Rostám had sent as well,
Three shining emeralds in three golden seals.
"Afrasiyáb,[8] must never know of this,"   35
She said, "he must not hear a single word.
And if your father learns that you've become
A brave and noble warrior like this,
He'll call you to his side, I know.
And then your mother's heart will break."   40
The bold Sohráb replied, "In all the world
No man could keep a secret such as this.
From ancient times till now, those great in war
Recite for all the tales of brave Rostám.
When I have such a warlike lineage,   45
For me to keep it hidden can't be right.
Now from among the warlike Turks will I
Amass an army boundless as the sea
I'll drive Kavús from off his throne,
And from Irán I'll scour all trace of Tus.[9]   50
To brave Rostám I'll give throne, mace, and crown,
And seat him in the place of Shah Kavús.
Then from Irán will I attack Turán,
And here confront the shah, Afrasiyáb.
I'll rout his army and I'll seize his throne.   55
I'll thrust my lance's tip above the sun.
For when Rostám's the father, I the son,
Who else in all the world should wear a crown?
When sun and moon illuminate the sky,
What need is there for stars to flaunt their crowns?"   60
From every side an army flocked to him,
Who all were noble men, brave swordsmen too.

8. Shah of Turán.   9. Rostám's rival, a hero resident at the Iranian court.

The Campaign Begins

Summary   Shah Afrasiyáb hears of Sohráb's plan. He sends troops and his own generals, Humán and Barmán, ostensibly to aid Sohráb, but in fact, to assure that father and son meet in mortal combat.

Afrasiyáb addressed his generals thus,
"This secret must not ever come to light.
When these two face each other on the field,
The bold Rostám will surely try some ruse.   20
His father must the boy not recognize,
Or else his love will bind his heart to him.
Rather, that brave and ancient pahlaván
Must lose his life to this young lion-heart.
Then later on destroy the fierce Sohráb.   25
Bind him one night forever in his dreams."

                    *   *   *

Word of Humán, Barmán, and all their troops
Soon reached Sohráb from lookouts on the road.   50
He and his grandsire[1] went to greet this host.
He saw so vast an army and his heart rejoiced.
Humán, when he first saw his shoulders and
His massive chest, stood speechless there in awe.
He gave Sohráb the royal letter and   55
The horses, camels, and their precious loads.
When that ambitious youth had read the words,
He quickly led his army from their camp.
For none could stand against him in a fight,
Not even if a lion should attack.   60
There was a fortress which they called the White;
The hopes of all Irán were placed in it.
The battle-tried Hojír,[2] a man of strength
And bravery, was keeper of the fort.
For in that time, Gostáhm[3] was still a youth,   65
Although a youth of gold, heroic mien.
He had a warlike sister too, who was
Well known for her ferocity and strength.
The army of Sohráb approached the fort,
The brave Hojír observed the army there.   70
Swift as the wind he mounted on his steed,
And galloped out to battle from the fort.
When bold Sohráb saw that Hojír approached,
He flushed in rage and drew his vengeful sword,
And like a lion raced onto the field.   75
As he approached the battle-tried Hojír,
Sohráb the valiant called to him and said,
"Oh foolish man, to fight with me alone!
What is your name, and which your family?
Who is the mother that must weep for you?"   80
Hojír thus answered him, "In all Turán

---

1. The shah of Semengán.   2. Commander of the garrison at the White Fortress.   3. An Iranian hero, whose adventures come in later stories.

There can be few or none to equal me.
I am Hojír the brave, the army's chief.
I mean to tear your head from off your trunk
And send it to the world's shah, Kay Kavús.   85
Your body will I hide beneath the soil."
Sohráb just laughed when he had heard this boast,
And galloped forward to attack Hojír.
So swiftly did they hurl their weapons that
The eye could not distinguish lance from lance.   90
One lance Hojír thrust at Sohráb, the point
Of which slid off his waist and did not stick.
Sohráb then seized the lance, reversed its butt,
And struck his chest a fierce and telling blow
That lifted him right off his horse's back,   95
And stretched him stunned and gasping on the ground.
Sohráb sprang down and sat upon his chest,
Then drew his sword to sever head from trunk.
Hojír beneath him twisted to his right,
And begged Sohráb for mercy in his fear.   100
The youth released his grip and spared his life.
Pleased with himself, he counseled him instead.
The warrior quickly bound his hands with rope,
And sent him as a captive to Humán.
Within the fort, when all had heard the news,   105
"Hojír's been taken captive by the Turks,"
They cried aloud, and men and women wept,
"The brave Hojír has now been lost to us."

Gordafaríd[4]

The daughter of Gazhdáhm,[5] when she had heard
The leader of their company'd been lost;
And she was a woman who like a knight,
Had gained renown in war, and who was called
Gordafaríd—for in her time there was   5
No mother who had borne her like—she found
The conduct of Hojír so shameful that
The tulips in her cheeks turned black as pitch.
She wasted not a moment, but bound on
The coat of mail a horseman wears to fight.   10
She hid her hair beneath that coat of mail,
And knotted on her head a Roman casque.
Then lionlike she raced down from the fort,
Girded for battle, and seated on the wind.
She faced the army like a warrior,   15
And roared a challenge like a thunderbolt,
"Who are your heroes, who your pahlaváns,
And who your brave and battle-tested chiefs?"
Sohráb the lion-killer laughed when he
Saw her, and in amazement bit his lip.   20

4. The only woman hero in the *Shâhnâme*; her name means "created a warrior." She is Gostáhm's sister.   5. Gordafaríd's father.

"Another onager has rushed into
The trap set by the lord of mace and blade."
Swift as the wind he donned his armored shirt,
And bound a Chinese helmet on his head,
Then galloped out to meet Gordafaríd.   25
When that rope-hurling maid saw him approach,
She strung her heavy bow and drew a breath.
No bird escaped her arrows with its life.
She rained her darts upon Sohráb, and as
She rode, she dodged and feinted right and left.   30
Sohráb observed her charge and felt ashamed,
Then flushed with rage and galloped to the fray.
He lifted up his shield and charged his foe,
The blood of battle coursing in his veins.
Gordafaríd, when she could see Sohráb   35
Was racing toward her like a raging flame,
She drew the bow she'd strung upon her arm;
Her yellow steed reared up to paw the clouds.
She turned her lance's point toward Sohráb,
And then reined in her steed to face her foe.   40
Sohráb, as fierce as any leopard, had
Just like his foe, prepared himself to fight.
He turned the reins and brought his horse around,
Then set upon her like the God of Fire.
He snatched away her polished lance's point,   45
And closed upon her like a cloud of smoke.
He struck Gordafaríd upon the waist,
And one by one he split her armor's links.
Then like a mallet when it strikes the ball,
He drove her from her saddle with one blow.   50
Gordafaríd, as she was turning in
Her saddle, drew a sharp blade from her waist,
Struck at his lance, and parted it in two.
She fell back in her seat, and dust rose up.
    She saw she was no match for him in war,   55
And quickly turned away from him, and fled.
Sohráb then gave his dragon steed its head.
His anger robbed the world of all its light.
As he approached her roaring in his wrath,
She swiftly snatched the helmet from her head,   60
Her hair was freed then of its armored cloak;
Her face shone forth as radiant as the sun.
Sohráb now saw a maiden seated there,
Whose face was worthy of a royal crown.
He spoke in awe, "That from the army of   65
Irán a maid like this should come, and fight
With mounted warriors in the field of war,
And raise the dust of battle to the sky!"
He loosed his twisted lasso from its loop,
And threw it, catching her around the waist.   70
Sohráb thus spoke to her, "Don't seek to flee.
Oh beauteous moon, why do you wish to fight?
I've never caught an onager like you.

You'll not escape my grip. Don't even try."
Gordafaríd knew she was caught at last.   75
She could not free herself, save through some trick.
She turned her face to him and said, "Oh, brave
And peerless youth, so like a lion when
You face your foe, two armies watch our fight,
Our combat here of heavy mace and blade.   80
Should I reveal to them my face and hair,
Your army will be filled with murmuring.
'Sohráb in battle with a maiden foe,
Raised dust in clouds that rose up to the sky.'
To parley here in secret would be best.   85
A noble man must use his head as well.
Do not bring shame upon yourself before
These two ranked armies here because of me.
You now command the garrison and fort.
Why then should you make war instead of peace?   90
Once you accept this treaty which you wish,
The fort, its chief and treasure are all yours."
She turned her face and smiled upon Sohráb,
And showed him pearly teeth and ruby lips.
She seemed a garden fair as paradise.   95
No gardener's seen so tall a cypress tree.
Her eyes were like a deer's, her eyebrows bows.
She seemed a flower in the height of bloom.
    These words of hers perplexed Sohráb at heart.
His cheeks grew flaming hot, his thoughts confused.   100
He said to her, "Do not betray your word—
You've faced me on the field of battle once—
Nor fix your hopes on these high fortress walls.
They are not higher than the clouds above.
My mace's blows will bring them to the ground,   105
And there's no lance will ever pierce my chest."
Gordafaríd pulled at her horse's reins,
And turned her yellow steed toward the fort.
She rode along; Sohráb was at her side,
And Gazhdahám watched from the battlements.   110
    Gordafaríd swung wide the fortress gate,
And drew her bound and weary body through.
They sadly closed the gate behind her then.
Their hearts were filled with grief, their eyes with tears.
Her grievous wounds and those of brave Hojír,   115
Had saddened all within, both young and old.
"Oh brave and lion-hearted maid," they said,
"The hearts of all are mournful at your state.
You have fought well, and tried deceit and guile.
Your deeds have brought no shame upon your line."   120
Gordafaríd laughed loud and long, then climbed
The fortress wall to look upon their foes.
She saw Sohráb still seated on his mount,
And called, "Oh shah who leads the Chinese Turks,
Why strive so hard? Turn back from this attack,   125
And from all combat on the field of war."

She laughed aloud but spoke with kindliness,
"The Turks will find no brides within Irán;
That's how it is, you had no luck with me.
But don't distress yourself too much at that.   130
You're surely not descended from these Turks.
You must be born of some more noble race.
For with your strength of arm, your chest and neck,
None of these pahlaváns can equal you.
However when Shah Kay Kavús learns that   135
Some warrior's brought an army from Turán,
He'll tell Rostám to arm himself for war,
And he's a hero you can never match.
Of all your host he'll leave not one alive.
And I can't guess what evil you'll endure.   140
I'm saddened that a chest and neck like yours
Should disappear within some leopard's maw.
It's better if you heed my warning now,
And turn your noble face toward Turán.
Don't trust your arm alone. The foolish bull   145
Will only feed, and think not of the knife."
    Sohráb felt shame at what he heard. The fort
Had come so easily within his grasp.
Around the citadel there lay a settlement,
A town and fields, in which the fortress stood.   150
He razed the town and burned the fields,
And so prepared himself for evil deeds.
Sohráb then said, "The day's come to an end;
Our hands are stayed from battle now by night.
At dawn tomorrow I'll pull down these walls;   155
They too shall look upon defeat in war."

Gazhdahám's Letter to Kay Kavús[6]

And when Sohráb had gone, old Gazhdahám
Sent for a scribe and sat him by his side.
He then composed a letter to the shah,
And sent a courier swiftly on his way.

[The letter tells of Hojír's defeat, describes Sohráb, and warns Shah Kay Kavús to prepare for war.]

*   *   *

Kay Kavús

When this report was brought to Kay Kavús,
The words of Gazhdahám dismayed his heart.
He called the army's leaders to his side,
And spoke at length of his account with them.
The army's chiefs, both great and small, men like   5
Gudárz of Keshvád's house, like Tus and Giv,
Like Bahrám and Gorgín, and like Farhád,

6. Shah of Iran.

Sat down to take their counsel with the shah.
He read the letter for them all, and spoke
Of his distress and grave perplexity.   10
He said thus privately to all his chiefs,
"I fear this matter won't be settled soon.
Gazhdáhm's report of how this matter stands
Has overwhelmed my heart with woe.
What can we do, where lies the remedy?   15
In all Irán what warrior's his match?"
They all agreed that Giv should leave at once
To seek the martial chieftain of Zaból.[7]
    The shah sent for his minister at once;
This was a matter of great urgency.   20
When they'd conferred he ordered him to write
A letter to the world-renowned Rostám.
He praised the Maker of the World at first,
Him who created all, and shapes our Fate.
And then he praised the noble pahlaván.   25
Be vigilant of heart and of bright soul.
You are the spine and heart of all our chiefs—
A lion in ferocity and strength.
You freed the captives of Hamavarán,
You seized the region of Mazandarán.[8]   30
The sun itself weeps at your heavy mace.
Your bright blade singes Nahid's[9] *brow.*
No indigo's so dark as Rakhsh's dust.
No elephant's so fierce as you in war.
Your lasso binds the lion on the plain;   35
Your spear uproots the mountain from the earth.
You are the refuge of Irán from every ill.
You are the diadem in all our crowns.
An urgent, fearful threat confronts us now,
The very thought of which has pierced my heart.   40
The heroes of Irán have counseled me,
As we read Gazhdahám's account, and we've
Concluded thus, in all the world there's none
Save you who triumphs over every foe.
Since that's the case, our noble chieftains saw   45
That worthy Giv should hasten to your court.
When you have read these words, whether it be day
Or night, don't part your lips to speak of it,
Unless to raise the battle cry and lead
Your horsemen galloping from Zaból's gates.   50
As Gazhdahám describes Sohráb, you are
His only equal on the battlefield.
The shah then ordered Giv, "Now you must seize
Your horse's reins and gallop swift as smoke.
Proceed at once to brave Rostám, but in   55
Zaból don't pause to rest or think of sleep.

---

7. Capital city of Zabolestán, a province in southeastern Iran of which Rostám's family are the hereditary rulers.   8. Kavús flatters Rostám by alluding to the famous occasions when Rostám single-handedly rescued him and his army from defeat and captivity by the rebellious monarch of Hamavarán and
by the demon army of Mazandarán.   9. Venus, both the planet and the goddess.

If you arrive by night, return at dawn.
Tell him the battle presses at our door."
He took the letter from his hand and rode,
Swift as a stream, and neither paused nor slept. 60
As Giv approached Zabolestán, the cries
Of his patrols brought word of this to Zal.[1]
    Rostám rode out to greet him with his troops,
The leaders dressed in crowns and robes of state.
Then all dismounted from their steeds as one, 65
The nobles great and small, and Giv as well.
Rostám approached him then on foot, and asked
His news of both Irán and Shah Kavús.
They left the road to seek the royal court,
And rested there a while, and drew their breath. 70
Giv told him all he'd heard, spoke of
Sohráb, and gave Rostám the letter from
The shah. When he had heard and read these words,
He frowned, then laughed aloud in disbelief.
"A noble warrior has now appeared 75
Who is the equal of the hero Sam.
Were he Iranian this might be so.
Among the Turks it cannot be believed.
I have a son by princess Tahminé
Of Semengán, but he is still a child. 80
That precious infant's not yet learned a man
Must fight to keep his name and honor pure.
I sent a message to his mother once
From here, and many jewels, and gold as well.
She answered me, 'This precious boy is still 85
A child, although he'll soon be tall and strong.
He drinks his wine with lips that smell of milk,
Though doubtless he'll grow fierce and warlike soon.'
Let's stay one day, and so refresh ourselves.
Our lips are dry, let's moisten them with wine. 90
And after that, we'll hasten to the shah,
And lead the heroes of Irán to war.
It may be that our shining fortune's slept.
If so, such matters are not difficult.
For when the ocean rises up in waves, 95
The fiercest flame cannot resist it long.
My banner when he spies it from afar,
Will turn his victory feast into a wake.
I doubt that he'll be eager then to fight.
This is no threat to trouble hearts like ours." 100
    They called for wine, first toasted Kay Kavús
And then Dastán, then drank the whole day through,
The next day just at dawn, Rostám appeared,
Still dazed with drink, and called again for wine.
They drank away that second day as well, 105
Nor did they give a thought to their return.
And on the third, when they brought wine at dawn,
No thought of Kay Kavús came to his mind.

1. Rostám's father; also called Dastán.

But on the fourth, the noble Giv prepared
Himself to leave and spoke thus with Rostám,   110
"Kavús is quick of temper and not shrewd,
And this affair's a burden on his mind.
It's vexed his soul and sorely pained his heart.
He neither eats nor sleeps nor takes his ease.
Should we delay here longer in Zaból,   115
We'll draw this strife and turmoil to Irán."
Rostám replied, "Be easy in your mind.
There's none who dares to turn his wrath on me."
He had them saddle Rakhsh with greatest speed,
And ordered them to sound the brazen horns.   120
The horsemen of Zaból heard this alarm,
And swiftly left their homes with shields and arms.

Rostám at Court

They galloped toward the court of Shah Kavús,
With loyal thoughts and open hearts they came.
But when they entered and bowed low to him,
Kavús grew angry and he answered not
At all. At first he shouted once, at Giv,   5
Then washed his eyes quite free of shame.
"Who is Rostám to turn his back to me,
And give so little heed to my command?
Seize him, take him from here, and gibbet him
Alive. Then speak no more of him to me!"   10
Giv's heart was rent asunder by these words.
"Will you indeed mistreat Rostám like this?"
When he grew angry with Piltán[2] and Giv,
Those gathered in the court were thunderstruck.
The shah commanded Tus as he stood there.   15
"Go now and hang the both of them alive!"
The shah himself then rose up from his throne,
His anger flaring up like flames from reeds,
As Tus approached Rostám and seized his arm
The warriors there could scarce believe their eyes.   20
Did he intend to march him from the court?
Or did his brusqueness mask a shrewd deceit?
  Tahamtán in turn grew angry with the shah.
"Don't nurse so hot a fire within your breast.
Each thing you do shames that already done.   25
You are unworthy of both throne and rule.
You go and hang the brave Sohráb alive!
Take arms, set forth and humble him yourself!"
Rostám struck Tus's hand a single blow,
But like that of a raging elephant,   30
And sent that worthy sprawling on the ground.
Rostám passed by him then with rapid strides,
Went out the door and mounted Rakhsh. "I am,"
He said, "the lion-heart who gave this crown.

2. Rostám; it means "elephant body."

When I'm enraged, who then is Shah Kavús?   35
Who's there to humble me? Who is this Tus?
The earth's my servant and my throne is Rakhsh;
This mace my signet ring, this helm my crown.
My sword illuminates the darkest night,
And scatters heads upon the battlefield.   40
My comrades are this spear and shining blade;
My heart and these two arms my only shah.
How dare he order me! I'm not his slave.
I serve the World Creator, only Him.
If this Sohráb should now invade Irán,   45
There's none who will be spared, not great or small.
You all must seek some way to save your souls.
You all must bend your wisdom to that task.
You'll see Rostám no more within Irán.
You have the land, I fly on vultures' wings."[3]   50
    The hearts of all the notables were sad.
Their shepherd was Rostám, and they the flock.
They sought Gudárz, "This is a task for you.
What's broken will be mended in your hand.
The *sepahbód*[4] will hear no speech but yours,   55
Nor will our fortune slumber at your words.
Approach this crazed and foolish shah at once,
And speak with him anew of what's just passed.
If you speak shrewdly and at length, you may
Regain the smiling fortune we have lost."   60
The *sepahdár*[5] Gudárz, Keshvád's brave son,
Rode swiftly off to court, and to the shah.
He asked Kavús, "What can Rostám have done
That you would cast Irán into the dust?
When he is gone, an army will attack,   65
Led by that wolflike pahlaván, Sohráb.
Who's there to equal him upon the field
Of war. Who'll heap dark dust upon his head?
Your warriors, both great and small, are known
To Gazhdahám, he's seen and heard them all.   70
He says, 'I pray the day may never come
That one of us must challenge him.'
Whoever has a champion like Rostám,
And drives him from the court, has little sense."
When Kay Kavús had heard the counsel of   75
Gudárz, he realized he spoke the truth.
He was ashamed of everything he'd said.
His wits had been confused by fear and wrath.
"Your speech is to the point," he told Gudárz.
"Advice sits well upon an old man's lips.   80
A padisháh should be more wise of speech,
For anger and quick words bring no reward.
You must now hasten to the brave Rostám
And speak with him at length and counsel him.

---

3. That is, "I will leave here as swiftly as I can and not return."   4. Leader of the army; may be applied to chiefs such as Rostám and Tus as well as to Shah Kay Kavús.   5. Another word for leader of the army.

Make him forget this hastiness of mine.   85
Recall to him the thoughts of better times."
    Gudárz rose up and left the royal court,
Then galloped swiftly off toward Rostám.
The army's leaders joined him on the road,
And followed in the tracks of Tahamtán.   90
When they could see the dust that hero raised,
The lords and notables all gathered to
His side. They praised the pahlaván and said,
"Be of bright soul and live forever young.
May all the world be ever at your feet,   95
And may you sit forever on a throne.
You know Kavús, he has no brains at all.
He speaks too hastily, and that's not good.
He'll boil up in a flash, then be ashamed,
And meekly seek to mend his bonds anew.   100
If Tahamtán is angry with the shah,
The people of Irán have done no wrong.
The shah himself regrets his words and bites
The knuckles of his hand in rage and shame."
    The brave Rostám thus answered them in turn,   105
"I have no need of Kay Kavús, not I.
This saddle is my throne, this helm my crown.
Chainmail's my robe; my heart is set on death.
Why should I fear the anger of Kavús?
The shah's no more to me than is this dirt.   110
My head's grown weary, and my heart is full.
Besides Yazdán[6] the Pure, whom should I fear?"
When they had had their fill of his reply,
Gudárz spoke bluntly with Piltán and said,
"The shah, the nobles, and the army all   115

Will see your actions in another light.
Our noble lord grew fearful of this Turk,
And thus departed secretly from here.
Since Gazhdahám has warned us of Sohráb,
We must abandon all Irán at once.   120
When brave Rostám flees from the battlefield,
It's not for you and me to stay and fight.
I've heard much comment on Kavús's rage
At court, and of his hasty words and deeds,
But all there speak with wonder of Sohráb.   125
Don't turn your back upon our royal shah.
Your name has grown renowned throughout the world,
Don't bring it low by turning now to flight.
What's more, the enemy is at our gate.
Do not endanger more this crown and throne."   130
Gudárz thus spoke his reasons to Rostám,
Who heard them with astonishment and shame.
He said, "If fear afflicts my heart, then I've
No use for it. I'll tear it from my chest."

---

6. One of the names of God.

He turned aside from shame, took to the road,   135
And galloped swiftly back toward the shah.
And when he strode into the court, Kavús
Stood up and asked forgiveness of Rostám.
"I am by nature rash in speech and act,
And one must be as God created him.   140
This unexpected foe oppressed my heart
Till like the moon, it grew both pale and weak.
To find some remedy I sent for you.
When you were slow to come, I grew enraged.
But when you were distressed, Piltán, I felt   145

Remorse, and shame has filled my mouth with dust."
Rostám replied, "Oh, shah, the world is yours.
We are your subjects. Yours is sovereignty.
I've come to court to be at your command.
May the wisdom of your soul be never less."   150
Kavús replied, "Today let's choose instead
To celebrate. Tomorrow we'll make war."
A place was then prepared, fit for a shah;
The palace was adorned like verdant spring.
And there they drank their wine while pale-   155
Cheeked beauties waited on the shah, and to
The sound of silken strings and plaintive reeds,
The sweet-voiced minstrels filled the night with song.

The Iranians Make War

Next day at dawn he ordered Giv and Tus
To bind the war drums on the elephants.
He opened wide his treasury's doors, gave out
Supplies, and loaded up the baggage train.
A hundred thousand men, all bearing shields   5
And wearing mail, assembled for the march.
Then from the court, an army rode to war
Whose dust rose up and blotted out the sun.
When camped, it spread its tents and canopies
For miles, and carpeted the earth with hooves.   10
The hills were dark as ebony, the air
Like indigo. The river boiled with drumbeats,
And as the troops proceeded stage by stage,
The world turned dark and night obscured the day.
The flash of spears and lances through the dust   15
Were like bright flames seen through a deep blue haze.
There were so many flags and shining spears,
So many golden shields and gilded boots,
It seemed a cloud as dark as ebony
Had formed, and rained down drops of yellow pitch.   20
In all the world there was no day or night;
The heavens and the Pleiades both were gone.
Thus they proceeded to the fortress gates.
The army hid the earth and stones from view.

The shouts of lookouts on the fortress walls,   25
Informed Sohráb the army had arrived.
And when he heard the lookout's cry, Sohráb
Stood on its lofty walls to view his foe.
He showed Humán this vast and fearsome host,
The margins of whose camp could not be seen.   30
And when Humán looked down upon the foe,
His heart was filled with terror and he groaned.
But thus the brave Sohráb encouraged him,
"Relieve your heart of all these fearful thoughts.
In all this endless army you'll not see   35
One warrior, one wielder of the heavy mace,
Who dares approach me on the field of war,
Not even with the aid of sun and moon.
Arms there are in rich array, and many proud
And noble men, all quite unknown to me.   40
But now, thanks to the great Afrasiyáb,
I'll fill this plain with rivers of their blood."
Sohráb descended lightly from the wall,
His heart untroubled by the thought of war.
While on that side, before the fortress walls,   45
They pitched the royal tents upon the plain.
So many tents and men were gathered there,
No inch of plain or mountain could be seen.

Summary   Rostám approaches the Turkish camp at night to spy on it. By mischance, he slays the one retainer of Sohráb, Zhende Razm, who can identify him. Meanwhile, in the Turkish camp, Sohráb asks Hojir to identify the Iranian heroes, especially Rostám, who are camped before him. Hojir, fearing that Rostám is no match for Sohráb, misidentifies Rostám as an unknown Chinese prince. Sohráb is enraged by this deception, and slays Hojir.

The Challenge

* * *

Then [Sohráb] sought his tent.
There like the wind, he donned his coat of mail   5
And on his head he placed his Chinese casque.
His rage had made the blood boil in his veins.
He seized his lance, mounted his swift-paced steed,
Then roaring in his fury like a maddened
Elephant, he rushed onto the field.   10
There was no famous hero of Irán
Who even dared to look upon Sohráb—
That sturdy foot and thigh, that hand and rein,
Those mighty arms, that finely polished lance.
The stalwarts of Irán assembled there.   15
"This surely is the pahlaván Rostám,"
They said, "one almost fears to look on him.
Who here will dare to challenge him to fight?"
And then Sohráb the hero roared once more,
And poured his curses on Kavús the shah.   20

The noble youth, Sohráb, addressed him thus,
"What business do you have upon this field?
Why do you call yourself Kavús the shah?
When in a fight you've neither strength nor pluck.
I'll spit your body on this lance, 25
And set the stars to weeping with one blow.
The night they slew brave Zhende Razm, I swore
A solemn oath to seek revenge in war.
Here in Irán I'll spare no one who bears
A lance, and Shah Kavús I'll crucify. 30
Of all Irán's swift-handed pahlaváns,
Do you have one to face me here and fight?"
Sohráb spoke thus, his words boiled up with rage,
But from Irán none rose to answer him.
He roared aloud and set upon their camp; 35
A tethered horse he drove off with his lance,
Then bending low, he used its sharpened tip
To pluck some seventy pegs out of the earth.
At once the palace tent came crashing down,
And from all sides the buglers blew retreat. 40
The army of Irán fled from Sohráb
Like onagers who flee the lion's claws.
In his distress Kavús cried out,
"Choose one among the well-born notables
And send him to Rostám with news of this. 45
Tell him that fear has struck our heroes dumb.
I've not one horseman who's the equal of
This dreadful Turk, not one to challenge him."
    Tus rushed to tell Rostám the shah's command,
Reciting for him what Kavús had said. 50
Rostám replied, "The other shahs who've called
On me when they'd some pressing need, sometimes
Invited me to battle, sometimes to feast.
Kavús has shown me but the pain of war."
He ordered that they saddle Rakhsh and that 55
His horsemen now set frowns upon their brows.
Then from his tent Rostám looked out and saw
The noble Giv was galloping toward
The battlefield. He put his saddle on
The shining Rakhsh. Gorgín urged him to haste. 60
Rohám made tight the cinch while noble Tus
Was swiftly buckling on its coat of mail.
And each one urged the other to be quick.
Within his tent, Rostám could hear the fight.
"This is the work of Ahrimán,"[7] he thought, 65
"This turmoil's not the work of just one man."
He quickly seized his tiger-skin cuirass,
And tied the royal belt around his waist,
Then mounted Rakhsh and rode to war. The host
He left his brother, Zavaré, to guard. 70
They bore his banner at his side, and as
He rode along, rage mounted in his heart.

7. The god of darkness.

When he could see Sohráb, his neck and arms,
His chest as broad as that of warlike Sam,
He called to him, "Let's move a little way   75
Apart, and face each other on the field."
Sohráb just rubbed his hands together and
Moved off to wait before the battle lines.
He told Rostám, "I've shown my readiness
For war. It's you who now must choose to fight.   80
Don't look to any in Irán for help.
It is enough when you and I are here.
You don't belong upon the battlefield.
You can't withstand a single blow of mine.
Although you're tall in stature and you have   85
A mighty chest, your wings now droop with age."
Rostám looked on that noble mien, that fist
And neck, that massive leg, and said with warmth,
"Oh, savage youth. Your speech is full of heat.
Alas, the earth is dry and cold. In my   90
Long years I've looked on many battlefields,
And many foes I've stretched upon the ground.
Not few the demons I've slain with my two hands,
And nowhere have I ever known defeat.
Look on me now. When you have fought with me,   95
And lived, you need not fear the crocodile.
The mountains and the sea know what I've done
To all the bravest heroes of Turán.
The stars bear witness too. In manliness
And bravery the world is at my feet.   100
Sohráb replied, "I have a single question,
But you must answer it with truth. I think
That you must be Rostám, or that you are
The seed of Narimán. Is this not so?"
Rostám thus answered him, "I am not he,   105
Nor descended from great Sam or Narimán.
Rostám's a pahlaván, I'm less than he.
I have no throne, no palace, and no crown."
From hope Sohráb was cast into despair.
The day's bright face turned to the darkest night.   110

The First Battle

He rode onto the battlefield, armed with
His lance and wondering at his mother's words.
Upon the field of war they chose a narrow
Space to meet and fought with shortened lance.
When neither points nor bindings held,   5
They reined their horses in and turned aside,
And then with Indian swords renewed their fight,
Sparks pouring from their iron blades like rain.
With blows they shattered both their polished swords.
Such blows as these will fall on Judgment Day.   10
And then each hero seized his heavy mace.
The battle had now wearied both their arms.
Although their mounts were panting and both heroes

Were in pain, they bent them with their might.
The armor flew from their two steeds; the links   15
That held their coats of mail burst wide apart.
Both mounts stood still; nor could their masters move.
Not one could lift a hand or arm to fight.
Their bodies ran with sweat, dirt filled their mouths,
And heat and thirst had split their tongues. Once more   20
They faced each other on that plain—the son
Exhausted and the father weak with pain.
Oh, world! How strange your workings are! From you
Comes both what's broken and what's whole as well.
Of these two men, not one was stirred by love.   25
Wisdom was far off, the face of love not seen.
The fishes in the sea, the mustangs on
The plain, all beasts can recognize their young.
But man who's blinded by his wretched pride,
Alas, cannot distinguish son from foe.   30
    Rostám said to himself, "I've never seen
A warlike crocodile that fought like this.
My battle with the Div Sepíd[8] seems nothing now.
Today my heart despaired of my own strength.
While these two armies watched us here,   35
A youth who's seen but little of the world,
And who is neither noble nor well known,
Has made me weary of my destiny."
When both their steeds had rested and they had
Recovered from the pain and shame of war,   40
These mighty warriors, one ancient and
The other still a youth, both strung their bows.
But since each wore a breast plate and a tiger-
Skin cuirass, their arrows could not penetrate.
Although each now despaired before his foe,   45
They closed and seized each other round the waist.
Rostám, who in the heat of battle could wrench
Stones from the flinty earth with his bare hands,
Now grasped Sohráb around the waist,
And sought with all his strength to wrest him from   50
His horse's back. The youth budged not at all.
The hero's mighty grip left him unmoved.
These lion-slayers both grew weary then.
They paused to rest and ease their wounds awhile.
And then once more Sohráb drew out his mace,   55
And pressed his thighs into his horse's flanks.
He struck Rostám upon the shoulder once,
A fearful blow that made him wince with pain.
Sohráb just laughed at him, "Oh, pahlaván!
It seems you cannot bear a warrior's blow.   60
This steed of yours in battle is an ass.
Or is it that his master's hands grow weak?
Although you're tall as any cypress tree,
An ancient who would play the youth's a fool."

---

8. The White Demon of the kingdom of Mazandarán (see n. 8, p. 902).

But each was wearied by the other now.   65
The earth seemed strait to them, the end unsure.
They turned their steeds aside and left the field,
Abandoning their hearts and souls to grief.
Great Tahamtán attacked the Turkish host
Just like a leopard when he spies his prey.   70
And when that wolf appeared within their ranks,
The army of Turán all turned and fled.
Sohráb had turned his horse toward Irán,
And fell upon their camp in swift assault.
He launched himself into their very midst.   75
And slaughtered many heroes with his mace.
Rostám grew anxious when he learned of this.
He thought that he would surely harm Kavús—
This wondrous Turk who had so suddenly
Appeared with trunk and arms adorned for war.   80
He galloped swiftly to his army's camp,
So greatly was Rostám distressed.
Within the army's heart he saw Sohráb,
The earth beneath him ran with blood like wine.
His spear was drenched in gore, his breast and arms   85
As well. He seemed a hunter drunk with sport.
Rostám grew sick at heart as he looked on,
And lionlike he roared his rage.
"You cruel bloodthirsty Turk! Which of the men
Assembled here has challenged you to fight?   90
Why did you raise your hand in war to them?
Why slaughter them, a wolf among the flock?"
Sohráb replied, "The army of Turán
Was blameless in this fight as well. You first
Attacked, though none was keen to challenge you."   95
"The day's grown dark," Rostám replied, "but when
Once more the world-illuming sun's bright blade
Appears, there'll be a gibbet and a throne
Set side by side upon this plain of war.
The whole bright world now lies beneath the sword.   100
Although your blade's familiar with the smell
Of milk, may you live long and never die.
Let us return at dawn with our keen swords.
Go now; await the World Creator's wish."

The Interval

They left and then the sky turned black. The circling
Sphere looked down and wondered at Sohráb.
It seemed that he'd been formed for war and strife.
He rested not a moment from attack.
The steed he rode was made of steel, his soul   5
A wonder, and his body hardened brass.
Sohráb came to his camp in dark of night,
His body scoured with wounds. He asked Humán,
"Today the rising sun filled all the world

With weapons and the sounds of war. Tell me,   10
What damage did he wreak upon our host,
That horseman with a hero's neck and lion's charge?"
Humán replied, "The shah's command to me
Was that the army should not stir from here.
We were quite unprepared. We had not looked   15
To fight at all today. When suddenly
A fierce and warlike man approached our camp,
And turned to face this broad-ranged company,
It seemed he'd just returned from drinking or
From battling singlehanded with some foe."   20
Sohráb replied, "And yet he did not slay
A single man from all this numerous host,
While I slew many heroes from Irán,
And made that campground muddy with their blood.
But now it's time to spread the board and feast.   25
Come, let's ease our hearts with ruby wine."
      While on the other side, Rostám reviewed
His troops and spoke a while with Giv. "How did
The battle-tried Sohráb fare here today?
Did he attack the camp? How did he fight?"   30
Heroic Giv thus answered Tahamtán,
"I've never seen a hero quite like him.
He galloped to the army's very heart.
And there within that host made straight for Tus,
For he was armed and mounted, lance in hand.   35
And while Gorgín dismounted, he sat firm.
He came and when he saw him with his lance,
He galloped toward him like a raging lion.
He bent his heavy mace upon his chest.
Its force unloosed his helmet from his head.   40
Tus saw that he must fail, and turned and fled.
Then many other warriors challenged him,
But none among those heroes had his strength.
Only Piltán's the equal of this youth.
And yet we still held fast our ancient rule,   45
And stood the army in a single rank.
No horseman went to fight with him alone.
While he paraded on the field of war."
Rostám was grieved at this report. He turned
His face toward the camp of Shah Kavús.   50
      When Kay Kavús saw him approach his tent,
He sat the pahlaván close by his throne.
Rostám described Sohráb to him, and spoke
At length of his great stature and his strength.
"None in this world has ever seen a child   55
Half grown who is so brave, so lionlike.
His head brushes against the stars above,
The earth below bends at his body's weight.
His arms and thighs are like a camel's limbs,
And yet to me they seemed more massive still.   60
We fought at length with heavy mace and sword,
With bow and arrow, and with lasso too.

No feint or weapon did we leave untried.
And finally I said, 'Before this time
I've lifted many heroes from their seats,'   65
And seized him round the waist and grasped his belt.
I thought to pluck him from his horse's back
And hurl him like the others to the ground.
The hurricane that shakes a granite peak
Would not disturb that worthy in his seat.   70
Tomorrow when he rides into the field,
My only hope's to fight him hand to hand.
And though I'll strive, I don't know who will win.
Nor do I know what choice Yazdán will make.
Strength, victory, and fame all come from Him   75
Who has created both the sun and moon."
Kavús replied, "Then may the Pure Lord split
In two the hearts of all who wish you ill!
Tonight before the Maker of the World
I'll press my brow and cheeks against the earth.   80
For strength and greatness come from Him alone.
By His command the moon sends down its light.
Once more may He renew your hopes, and raise
Your name aloft in triumph to the sun."
Rostám then said, "By the glory of the shah,   85
May the hopes of those who wish him well be heard."
    Then Tahamtán returned to camp, his soul
Distressed, his mind prepared for war.
His brother, Zavaré approached him with
An anxious heart. "How did you fare today?"   90
Rostám first called for food, and ate his fill,
Then purged his heart of all his grief and fear.
He spoke to Zavaré, advising him,
"Be vigilant of heart, do nothing rash.
Tomorrow, just at dawn, when I must meet   95
That warlike Turk in battle once again,
You bring the army and my standard to
The field, my throne and golden boots as well.
Be standing at the door of my pavilion
When the shining sun begins to rise.   100
If in this fight I gain the victory,
I will not linger on the battlefield.
But should the matter turn out otherwise,
Don't weep for me, and do not seek revenge.
Neither enter the field to fight alone,   105
Nor yet prepare yourself for general war.
Return together to Zabolestán,
Once you are there, seek out my father, Zal.
Then you must try to ease my mother's heart.
This fate, alas, Yazdán decreed for me.   110
Tell her she should not mourn for me too long,
For she will do herself no good by that.
No one has lived for all eternity.
I've no complaint against the circling sphere.
In battle have I strangled many demons,   115

And lions, crocodiles, and leopards too.
I've leveled forts and towers to the ground,
And there's no man who's ever vanquished me.
The man who mounts a horse and gallops off
To fight, is he not knocking on death's door?   120
And if you live a thousand years, or more,
At last, the end of all will be the same.
When she's content, then tell Dastán, 'Don't turn
Your back upon the monarch of the world.
Should he make war, do not be slack in your   125
Support, obey his word in everything.
We all are mortal, young and old alike.
There's none who lives for all eternity.' "
For half that night their words were of Sohráb.
The other half they spent in restful sleep.   130
    And on that side Sohráb with all his friends
Had passed the night with wine and minstrelsy.
Thus to Humán he said, "This lion who
Engages me so fiercely on the field,
Is not one whit less tall than I, and when   135
Engaged in single combat has no fear.
His shoulders, chest, and neck are so like mine,
It seems more craftsman marked them with a rule.
I see in him the signs my mother told
Me of, what's more, my heart is drawn to him.   140
I think that he must be Rostám, for in
This world few pahlaváns can equal him.
I must not in confusion rush to meet
My father here in combat face to face."
Humán replied, "I've met Rostám in war,   145
And seen him battle many times. I've heard
How that brave hero used his heavy mace
When he was fighting in Mazandarán.
This horse of his is very like Rostám's,
But he has not the hoof or rump of Rakhsh."   150

The Second Day

The shining sun spread wide its radiance,
The raven tucked its head beneath its wings,
Tahamtán put on his tiger-skin cuirass,
And sat astride his huge, fierce elephant.
To his seat he bound his rope in sixty coils,   5
And in his hand he grasped an Indian sword.
He galloped to the field, the place where they
Would fight, and there put on his iron helm.
All bitterness is born of precedence,
Alas when it is yoked to greedy pride!   10
    Sohráb stood up and armed himself. His head
Was filled with war, his heart with revelry.
Shouting his cry he rode into the field,
Within his hand, he held his bullhide mace.

He greeted him, a smile upon his lips,   15
As though they'd spent the night in company.
"How did you sleep? How do you feel today?
And how have you prepared yourself to fight?
Let's put aside this mace and sword of war.
Cast strife and wrong down to the ground.   20
Let us dismount and sit together now,
And smooth our brows with wine. And let us make
A pact before the World Preserving Lord,
That we'll repent of all our warlike plans.
Until another comes who's keen to fight,   25
Make peace with me and let us celebrate.
My heart is ever moved by love for you,
And wets my face with tears of modesty.
I'm sure you're from a noble line, come then,
Recite for me the line of your descent.   30
Aren't you the son of brave Dastán, the son
Of Sam? Aren't you the pahlaván Rostám?"
Rostám replied, "Oh, shrewd ambitious youth,
Before this hour we never spoke like this.
Last night our words were of the coming fray.   35
Your tricks won't work with me; don't try again.
Though you are but a youth, I am no child,
And I'm prepared to fight you hand to hand.
So let's begin our strife. Its end will be
As the Keeper of the World commands it should.   40
I've traveled long through hills and valleys too.
And I'm no man for guile, deceits, and lies."
Sohráb replied, "Such words do not befit
A warrior who's so advanced in years.
I wished that you might die upon your bed,   45
And that your soul would leave in its own time;
That those you leave behind could keep your bones,
Immure your flesh, but let your spirit fly.[9]
But if your life is in my grasp, then as
Yazdán commands, let us lock hands and fight."   50
    They both dismounted from their battle steeds.
In casque and tunic they approached with care,
And to a stone they tied their steeds of war.
They then advanced, their hearts as cold as earth.
Each seized the other and they grappled till   55
Their bodies ran with sweat and blood. Sohráb
Was like a maddened elephant; he struck
Rostám a blow that felled him to the earth.
Then like a lion in the hunt whose claws
Have thrown a mighty stallion to the ground,   60
Sohráb sat firmly on the chest of huge
Rostám, fist, face, and mouth all smeared with dirt,
And from his belt he drew his polished blade.
As he bent down to sever head from trunk,

---

9. A reference to the Zoroastrian practice of leaving the dead exposed in walled enclosures until their skeletons have been picked clean by vultures. The bones are then collected and placed in an ossuary. In this way neither earth, air, fire, nor water is defiled by the dead.

Rostám looked up and said, "Oh, lion-slaying   65
Chief, and master of the sword and mace and rope!
The custom of our nation is not thus.
Our faith commands us to another way.
Whoever in a wrestling match first throws
His noble adversary to the ground,   70
And pins him to the earth, may not cut off
His head, not even if he seeks revenge.
But if he fells him twice, he's earned that right,
And all will call him Lion if he does."
By that deceit he shrewdly sought to free   75
Himself from this fierce dragon's mortal grip.
     The brave youth bowed his head and yielded
To the old man's words, and said no more,
But loosed his grip and rushed off to the plain,
A lion who has seen a deer race by.   80
He hunted eagerly and gave no thought
To him with whom he'd fought so recently.
When it grew late, Humán came swiftly to
The field and asked him how the battle'd gone.
Sohráb then told Humán all that had passed,   85
And what Rostám had said to him. The brave
Humán just heaved a sigh and said, "Dear youth,
I see that you've grown weary of your life.
I fear for this stout neck and arms and chest,
This hero's waist and royal legs and feet.   90
You caught a tiger firm within your trap,
Then spoiled your work by letting him escape.
You'll see what consequence this foolish act
Of yours will have when next you meet to fight."
He spoke, despairing of his life. He turned   95
His steed aside, still wondering at his deed.
     Sohráb returned toward his army's camp,
Perplexed at heart and angry with himself.
A shah once wisely spoke a proverb on
This point, "Despise no foe, however mean."   100
Rostám, when he'd escaped from his foe's hand,
Sprang up just like a blade of steel, and rushed
Off to a flowing stream that was nearby,
For he was like a man who'd been reborn.
He drank his fill, and when he'd washed his face   105
And limbs, he bowed before his Lord in prayer.
He asked for strength and victory; he did
Not know what sun and moon might hold in store,
Or if the heavens as they wheeled above
Would wish to snatch the crown from off his head.   110
     Then pale of face and with an anxious heart,
He left the stream to meet his foe once more.
While like a maddened elephant, Sohráb
With bow and lasso galloped on the plain.
He wheeled and shouted as he chased his prey;   115
His yellow steed leaped high and tore the earth.
Rostám could not but stand in awe of him;

He sought to take his measure for the fight.
And when the lion-slayer saw him there,
The arrogance of youth boiled up in him.   120
"Hail him who fled the lion's claws,
And kept himself apart from his fierce blows."

The Death of Sohráb

Again they firmly hitched their steeds, as ill-
Intentioned fate revolved above their heads.
Once more they grappled hand to hand. Each seized
The other's belt and sought to throw him down.
Whenever evil fortune shows its wrath,   5
It makes a block of granite soft as wax.
Sohráb had mighty arms, and yet it seemed
The skies above had bound them fast. He paused
In fear; Rostám stretched out his hands and seized
That warlike leopard by his chest and arms.   10
He bent that strong and youthful back, and with
A lion's speed, he threw him to the ground.
Sohráb had not the strength; his time had come.
Rostám knew well he'd not stay down for long.
He swiftly drew a dagger from his belt   15
And tore the breast of that stout-hearted youth.
He writhed upon the ground; groaned once aloud,
Then thought no more of good and ill. He told
Rostám, "This was the fate allotted me.
The heavens gave my key into your hand.   20
It's not your fault. It was this hunchback fate,
Who raised me up then quickly cast me down.
While boys my age still spent their time in games,
My neck and shoulders stretched up to the clouds.
My mother told me who my father was.   25
My love for him has ended in my death.
Whenever you should thirst for someone's blood,
And stain your silver dagger with his gore,
Then Fate may thirst for yours as well, and make
Each hair upon your trunk a sharpened blade.   30
Now should you, fishlike, plunge into the sea,
Or cloak yourself in darkness like the night,
Or like a star take refuge in the sky,
And sever from the earth your shining light,
Still when he learns that earth's my pillow now,   35
My father will avenge my death on you.
A hero from among this noble band
Will take this seal and show it to Rostám.
'Sohráb's been slain, and humbled to the earth,'
He'll say, 'This happened while he searched for you.'"   40
    When he heard this, Rostám was near to faint.
The world around grew dark before his eyes.
And when Rostám regained his wits once more,

He asked Sohráb with sighs of grief and pain,
"What sign have you from him—Rostám? Oh, may   45
His name be lost to proud and noble men!"
"If you're Rostám," he said, "you slew me while
Some evil humor had confused your mind.
I tried in every way to draw you forth,
But not an atom of your love was stirred.   50
When first they beat the war drums at my door,
My mother came to me with bloody cheeks.[1]
Her soul was racked by grief to see me go.
She bound a seal upon my arm, and said,
'This is your father's gift, preserve it well.   55
A day will come when it will be of use.'
Alas, its day has come when mine has passed.
The son's abased before his father's eyes.
My mother with great wisdom thought to send
With me a worthy pahlaván as guide.   60
The noble warrior's name was Zhende Razm,
A man both wise in action and in speech.
He was to point my father out to me,
And ask for him among all groups of men.
But Zhende Razm, that worthy man, was slain.   65
And at his death my star declined as well.
Now loose the binding of my coat of mail,
And look upon my naked, shining flesh."
When he unloosed his armor's ties and saw
That seal, he tore his clothes and wept.   70
"Oh, brave and noble youth, and praised among
All men, whom I have slain with my own hand!"
He wept a bloody stream and tore his hair;
His brow was dark with dust, tears filled his eyes.
Sohráb then said, "But this is even worse.   75
You must not fill your eyes with tears. For now
It does no good to slay yourself with grief.
What's happened here is what was meant to be."
     When the radiant sun had left the sky,
And Tahamtán had not returned to camp,   80
Some twenty cavaliers rode off to see
How matters stood upon the field of war.
They saw two horses standing on the plain,
Both caked with dirt. Rostám was somewhere else.
Because they did not see his massive form   85
Upon the battlefield and mounted on
His steed, the heroes thought that he'd been slain.
The nobles all grew fearful and perplexed.
They sent a message swiftly to the shah,
"The throne of majesty has lost Rostám."   90
From end to end the army cried aloud,
And suddenly confusion filled the air.
Kavús commanded that the horns and drums
Be sounded, and his marshal, Tus, approached.

---

1. In Persian poetry intense grief is indicated by bloody tears.

Then Kavús spoke, "Be quick, and send a scout   95
From here to view the battlefield
And see how matters stand with bold Sohráb.
Must we lament the passing of Irán?
If by his hand the brave Rostám's been slain,
Who from Irán will dare approach this foe?   100
We now must strike a wide and general blow;
We dare not tarry long upon this field."
    And while a tumult rose within their camp,
Sohráb was speaking thus with Tahamtán,
"The situation of the Turks has changed   105
In every way, now that my days are done.
Be kind to them, and do not let the shah
Pursue this war or urge his army on.
It was for me the Turkish troops rose up,
And mounted this campaign against Irán.   110
I it was who promised victory, and I
Who strove in every way to give them hope.
They should not suffer now as they retreat.
Be generous with them, and let them go."
    Rostám then mounted Rakhsh, as swift as dust.   115
His eyes bled tears, his lips were chilled with sighs.
He wept as he approached the army's camp,
His heart was filled with pain at what he'd done.
When they first spied his face, the army of Irán
Fell prostrate to the earth in gratitude,   120
And loudly praised the Maker of the World,
That he'd returned alive and well from war.
But when they saw him thus, his chest and clothes
All torn, his body heavy and his face
Begrimed by dust, they asked him all at once,   125
"What does this mean? Why are you sad at heart?"
He told them of his strange and baffling deed,
Of how he'd slain the one he held most dear.
They all began to weep and mourn with him,
And filled the earth and sky with loud lament.   130
At last he told the nobles gathered there,
"It seems my heart is gone, my body too.
Do not pursue this battle with the Turks.
The evil I have done is quite enough."
And when he left that place, the pahlaván   135
Returned with weary heart to where he lay.
The noble lords accompanied their chief,
Men like Gudárz and Tus and Gostahám.
The army all together loosed their tongues,
And gave advice and counsel to Rostám,   140
"Yazdán alone can remedy this wound;
He yet may ease this burden's weight for you."
He grasped a dagger in his hand, and made
To cut his worthless head from his own trunk.
The nobles hung upon his arm and hand, and tears   145
Of blood poured from the lashes of their eyes.
Gudárz said to Rostám, "What gain is there

If by your death you set the world in flames?[2]
Were you to give yourself a hundred wounds,
How would that ease the pain of brave Sohráb?   150
If some time yet remains for him on earth,
He'll live, and you'll remain with him, at peace.
But if this youth is destined to depart,
Look on the world, who's there that does not die?
The head that wears a helmet and the head   155
That wears a crown, to death we all are prey."

[Sohráb dies]

Rostám Mourns Sohráb

Rostám commanded that a servant bring
A robe and spread it by the river's bank.
He gently laid Sohráb upon the robe,
Then mounted Rakhsh and rode toward the shah.
But as he rode, his face toward the court,   5
They overtook him swiftly with the news,
"Sohráb has passed from this wide world; he'll need
A coffin from you now, and not a crown.
'Father!' he cried, then sighed an icy wind,
Then wept aloud and closed his eyes at last."   10
    Rostám dismounted from his steed at once.
Dark dust replaced the helmet on his head.
He wept and cried aloud, "Oh, noble youth,
And proud, courageous seed of pahlaváns!
The sun and moon won't see your like again,   15
No more will shield or mail, nor throne or crown.
Who else has been afflicted as I've been?
That I should slay a youth in my old age
Who is the grandson of world-conquering Sam,
Whose mother's seed's from famous men as well.   20
It would be right to sever these two hands.
No seat be mine henceforth save darkest earth.
What father's ever done a deed like this?
I now deserve abuse and icy scorn.
Who else in all this world has slain his son,   25
His wise, courageous, youthful son?
How Zal the golden will rebuke me now,
He and the virtuous Rudabé as well.
What can I offer them as my excuse?
What plea of mine will satisfy their hearts?   30
What will the heroes and the warriors say
When word of this is carried to their ears?
And when his mother learns, what shall I say?
How can I send a messenger to her?
What can I say? Why did I slay him when   35
He'd done no crime? Why blacken all his days?

2. That is, warfare and chaos would result from Rostám's death, because there would be no one to
defend the shah.

How will her sire, that worthy pahlaván,
Report this to his pure and youthful child?
He'll call this seed of Sam a godless wretch,
And heap his curses on my ancient head.   40
Alas, who could have known this precious child
Would quickly grow to cypress height, or that
He'd raise this host and think of arms and war,
Or that he'd turn my shining day to night."
Rostám commanded that the body of   45
His son be covered with a royal robe.
He'd longed to sit upon the throne and rule;
His portion was a coffin's narrow walls.
The coffin of Sohráb was carried from
The field. Rostám returned to his own tent.   50
They set aflame Sohráb's pavilion while
His army cast dark dust upon their heads.
They threw his tents of many colored silk,
His precious throne and leopard saddle cloth
Into the flames, and tumult filled the air.   55
He cried aloud, "Oh, youthful conqueror!
Alas, that stature and that noble face!
Alas, that wisdom and that manliness!
Alas, what sorrow and heart-rending loss—
No mother near, heart pierced by father's blade!"   60
His eyes wept bloody tears, he tore the earth,
And rent the kingly garments on his back.
Then all the pahlaváns and Shah Kavús
Sat with him in the dust beside the road.
They spoke to him with counsel and advice—   65
In grief Rostám was like one driven mad—
"This is the way of fortune's wheel. It holds
A lasso in this hand, a crown in that.
As one sits happily upon his throne,
A loop of rope will snatch him from his place.   70
Why is it we should hold the world so dear?
We and our fellows must depart this road.
The longer we have thought about our wealth,
The sooner we must face that earthy door.
If heaven's wheel knows anything of this,   75
Or if its mind is empty of our fate,
The turning of the wheel it cannot know,
Nor can it understand the reason why.
One must lament that he should leave this world,
Yet what this means at last, I do not know."   80

Summary   Kay Kavús, at Rostám's request, lets Sohráb's troops return home in peace. Rostám takes his son's body to Zabolestán for burial.

Thus spoke Bahrám the wise and eloquent,
"Don't bind yourself too closely to the dead,
For you yourself will not remain here long.
Prepare yourself to leave, and don't be slow.

One day your sire gave you a turn at life.   55
The turn is now your son's, that's only right.
That's how it is, the secret why's unknown.
The door is locked; nor will the key be found.
You won't discover it, why even try?
And if you should, you'll spend your life in vain."   60
  It is a tale that's filled with tears and grief.
The tender heart will rage against Rostám.

THE THOUSAND AND ONE NIGHTS
fourteenth century

The Thousand and One Nights is rich in paradoxes. An anonymous work, it is
nevertheless more widely known in the Arab world than any other work of Arabic
literature. It is almost as well known in Europe, and so far is the only work of
Arabic letters to become a permanent part of European and, indeed, of world
literature. Despite this great popularity, and despite its shaping influence on modern literature, traditional Arabic literary scholars have never recognized it as a
work of serious literature, and it is still occasionally banned as immoral by Arab
governments—most recently by Egypt in 1989.

The history of *The Thousand and One Nights* is vague, and its shape as hard to
pin down as a cloud's. The starting point of the work in Arabic was probably a
collection of tales in Middle Persian called the "thousand stories" that had been
translated or adapted from Sanskrit in the time of the Sassanids (226–652), the last
pre-Islamic Iranian dynasty. During the ninth and tenth centuries a great deal of
Persian literature, both popular and courtly, was translated into Arabic, particularly
at the caliphal court in Baghdad. The tales that became the core of the *Nights*
were probably among them. The Perso-Indian origins of the prologue and other
tales are suggested by the Persian personal names—Shahrayar, Shahzaman, Shahrazad—and place names—Indo-China, Samarkand—of the prologue. Stories set
in the Baghdad of the late eighth century—those that mention the caliph Haroun
al-Rashid and his vizier Ja'far the Barmakid, for instance—indicate that the original translator, or later copyists, felt free to add local tales to the originals. From
Baghdad, manuscripts of this original translation circulated widely to other parts
of the Islamic world, especially Syria and Egypt. The tales were also transmitted
orally and adapted and translated into other languages of the region. Indeed, the
initial translation into Arabic may have been an oral one—the work of a Persian
storyteller who came to the great metropolis of Baghdad and adapted his wares to
the language of his audience. What we know for certain is that written and oral
transmissions of the tales have intermingled down to the present day. Oral versions
were written down and written tales were memorized and added to oral repertories.

We can discern two quite distinct branches in the written transmission of the
Nights. The earliest manuscript, which dates from thirteenth-century Syria,
belongs to the more conservative branch. Later manuscripts derived from it adhere
closely to it in substance, form, and style. Others, known collectively as the Egyptian branch, depart widely from it, deleting some of the original stories and adding
others from Indian, Persian, Turkish, and Egyptian sources. The story of Sindbad
is one of the earliest such additions, and that of Aladdin and the magic lamp one
of the latest. At times it seems that the copyists were determined to expand the
number of tales to fit the fanciful "one thousand and one" of the title. The first
European translator of the *Nights*, the French scholar and traveler Jean Antoine

Galland (1646–1715) followed the example of the copyists in the Egyptian branch, translating whatever stories he could find. The great success of his work encouraged other European translators, notably Sir Richard Burton (1821–1890), to do likewise. Some of the tales that Galland and Burton translated from oral sources were retranslated from French or English back into Arabic for new Arabic printings of the *Nights*, and the original character of the *Nights* was distorted almost beyond recognition. The first scholarly edition of *The Thousand and One Nights*, the first, that is, to be based on the thirteenth-century Syrian manuscript, was completed only in 1984, and the selection printed here was translated from it.

From the very beginning classical Arabic literature was unable to find a place for the *Nights*. It was a work neither of history nor of useful knowledge and moral instruction. It was not composed in an elegant, poetic style but in ordinary prose that was very close to common speech. It was filled with magical and fantastic stories that were clearly untrue. While such extravagant and improbable fabrications might be tolerated in poetry, they were unacceptable in a work of prose, since prose was expected to be more serious and substantial than poetry. The qualities that exclude the *Nights* from the canon of classical Arabic are, of course, the very ones that ensure its wide popular acceptance. It is a brilliantly entertaining work, and its stories vary from lighthearted and frivolous to touchingly romantic or terrifying and painful. The themes set forth in the prologue—lust, madness, violence, justice, retribution, and heroism—are weighty ones, and they are grounded in the stuff of everyday life. But they are told with great artistry and made magical by luxurious settings, fantastic adventures, magical turns of fortune, and the timely intervention of demons and sorcerers.

In the selections printed here, Shahrayar is a monarch driven mad by the infidelity of his wife. To ensure that another such humiliation will not occur, he has decided to marry a new young woman each night and murder her the next morning—before she has a chance to betray him. Three years pass in this way and Shahrayar has drastically depleted the number of marriageable young women in the kingdom. His chief vizier has been unable to think of a way to dissuade his monarch from this mad, self-destructive policy, but the vizier's elder daughter, Shahrazad, a young woman of exceptional learning and courage, has a plan. She will voluntarily marry Shahrayar and then use her skill as a storyteller to manipulate him into deferring her death endlessly. Her father tries, unsuccessfully, to dissuade her by telling her tales that are both irrelevant and unpersuasive, but she launches her scheme with the help of her sister, Dinarzad. Each night Shahrazad tells Shahrayar stories to while away the long hours, stopping each sunrise just before some crisis and counting on Shahrayar's eagerness to hear the end of the story to dissuade him from having her executed. In this way, she is able to hold his murderous impulses in check until he at last pardons her and and abandons his policy.

To Western readers, the *Nights* most resembles such other famous collections of tales as Chaucer's *Canterbury Tales*, Boccaccio's *Decameron*, and Marguerite de Navarre's *Heptameron*. Like these, its tales are set within the frame of another, larger tale. The prologue of the *Nights* does not surround or frame the tales it includes, however. There are examples of such framed collections within the *Nights*, starting with the first set that Shahrazad recites, but the *Prologue* is a frame tale with a difference. It has a single narrator, not many; and as a consequence there is none of the interplay between narrators, or between narrators and the tales they tell, that marks these other collections. That is, while there are many narrators, and tales within tales, all the stories are ultimately recounted by Shahrazad. Moreover, her motive throughout is the single and compelling one of preventing the destruction of herself and the other young women of her community. The formulaic exchange between Shahrazad, Shahrayar, and Dinarzad that is repeated

each dawn and evening reminds us that Shahrazad is not telling tales simply to while away the time.

The image of Shahrazad deftly employing her skills as a narrator to buy her life a day at a time has captured the fancy of all who have read the *Nights*, but there may be more to her tales than an endlessly deferred conclusion. That is, her tales can also be read as a means of healing the wound inflicted on him by his wife's infidelity, and of teaching him that not all women wish him ill. That she may have cure in mind as much as delay is suggested by the neat fit between the first set of tales she tells and her own plight. In the first story, for example, a demon sets a precedent for allowing Shahrazad to purchase her life with her tales by allowing three old men to pay the merchant's blood price with theirs. This story also suggests that the demon is too harsh in threatening to kill the merchant for a crime that is at worst accidental. How much more innocent of any wrongdoing are the young women of Shahrayar's realm? In each of the tales a benign but powerful woman undoes the harm caused by an ill-intentioned one. The wicked characters are punished according to their crimes, and never by death. All this suggests that Shahrazad is not simply distracting Shahrayar with her tales, she is educating him or, better, attempting to cure him of his madness. Her choice of a cure may suggest that these tales were shaped by female narrators as well as male or at least by narrators who had an understanding and appreciation of women. A more characteristically male solution to the problem that Shahrayar poses might have been to depose or destroy him.

For those who wish to do more reading in the *Nights*, Husain Haddawy, *The Arabian Nights* (1990), is a complete translation of the text of Muhsin Mahdi's critical edition of the Syrian manuscript. The translations by Edward William Lane, *The Thousand and One Nights* (1838), and Richard Burton, *The Book of a Thousand Nights and a Night* (1885), are based on later, heterogeneous manuscripts. Burton's is the better known but Lane's is closer to the original (though it bowdlerizes the erotic scenes). N. J. Dawood, *Tales from the Thousand and One Nights* (1973), is more readable than either Lane and Burton and includes famous stories like Sindbad and Aladdin that are not in the Mahdi edition. Mia Gerhardt, *The Art of Storytelling: A Literary Study of the Thousand and One Nights* (1963), is virtually the only interpretive study of the whole of *The Thousand and One Nights* in English. It contains an excellent discussion of European interest in the work but is less satisfactory for individual stories. Ferial Jabouri Ghazoul, *The Arabian Nights: A Structural Analysis* (1980), focuses on several stories and groups of stories, among them the *Prologue*. She also argues the central importance of the feminine in the *Nights*. Tzvetan Todorov, "Narrative—Men" in *The Poetics of Prose* (1977), has a provocative discussion of the masculine role in the tales. Bruno Bettelheim, *The Uses of Enchantment: The Meaning and Importance of Fairy Tales* (1976), includes a brief discussion of Shahrazad in his study of the therapeutic role of fairy tales.

PRONOUNCING GLOSSARY

The following list uses common English syllables and stress accents to provide rough equivalents of selected words whose pronunciation may be unfamiliar to the general reader.

Dinarzad: *dee-nar-zahd'*

Haroun al-Rashid: *ha-roon' ar–ra-sheed'*

Ja'far the Barmakid: *juh-far' the bar'-muh-kid*

Sa'd al-Din Mas'ud: *sad' ad–deen mass-ood'*

Shahrazad: *shah-ruh-zahd'*

Shahrayar: *shah-ruh-yahr'*

Shahzaman: *shah-zuh-mahn'*

From The Thousand and One Nights[1]

Prologue

[The Story of King Shahrayar and Shahrazad, His Vizier's Daughter][2]

It is related—but God knows and sees best what lies hidden in the old accounts of bygone peoples and times—that long ago, during the time of the Sasanid dynasty,[3] in the peninsulas of India and Indochina, there lived two kings who were brothers. The older brother was named Shahrayar, the younger Shahzaman. The older, Shahrayar, was a towering knight and a daring champion, invincible, energetic, and implacable. His power reached the remotest corners of the land and its people, so that the country was loyal to him, and his subjects obeyed him. Shahrayar himself lived and ruled in India and Indochina, while to his brother he gave the land of Samarkand[4] to rule as king.

Ten years went by, when one day Shahrayar felt a longing for his brother the king, summoned his vizier (who had two daughters, one called Shahrazad, the other Dinarzad) and bade him go to his brother. Having made preparations, the vizier journeyed day and night until he reached Samarkand. When Shahzaman heard of the vizier's arrival, he went out with his retainers to meet him. He dismounted, embraced him, and asked him for news from his older brother, Shahrayar. The vizier replied that he was well, and that he had sent him to request his brother to visit him. Shahzaman complied with his brother's request and proceeded to make preparations for the journey. In the meantime, he had the vizier camp on the outskirts of the city, and took care of his needs. He sent him what he required of food and fodder, slaughtered many sheep in his honor, and provided him with money and supplies, as well as many horses and camels.

For ten full days he prepared himself for the journey; then he appointed a chamberlain in his place, and left the city to spend the night in his tent, near the vizier. At midnight he returned to his palace in the city, to bid his wife good-bye. But when he entered the palace, he found his wife lying in the arms of one of the kitchen boys. When he saw them, the world turned dark before his eyes and, shaking his head, he said to himself, "I am still here, and this is what she has done when I was barely outside the city. How will it be and what will happen behind my back when I go to visit my brother in India? No. Women are not to be trusted." He got exceedingly angry, adding, "By God, I am king and sovereign in Samarkand, yet my wife has betrayed me and has inflicted this on me." As his anger boiled, he drew his sword and struck both his wife and the cook. Then he dragged them by the heels and threw them from the top of the palace to the trench below. He then left the city and going to the vizier

---

1. All selections translated by Husain Haddawy except for *The Third Old Man's Tale*, translated by Jerome W. Clinton.   2. One who bears burdens (literal trans.); the highest state official or administrator under a caliph or shah.   3. The last pre-Islamic dynasty (ruled 226–652).   4. A city and province in central Asia, now in Uzbekistan.

ordered that they depart that very hour. The drum was struck, and they set out on their journey, while Shahzaman's heart was on fire because of what his wife had done to him and how she had betrayed him with some cook, some kitchen boy. They journeyed hurriedly, day and night, through deserts and wilds, until they reached the land of King Shahrayar, who had gone out to receive them.

When Shahrayar met them, he embraced his brother, showed him favors, and treated him generously. He offered him quarters in a palace adjoining his own, for King Shahrayar had built two beautiful towering palaces in his garden, one for the guests, the other for the women and members of his household. He gave the guest house to his brother, Shahzaman, after the attendants had gone to scrub it, dry it, furnish it, and open its windows, which overlooked the garden. Thereafter, Shahzaman would spend the whole day at his brother's, return at night to sleep at the palace, then go back to his brother the next morning. But whenever he found himself alone and thought of his ordeal with his wife, he would sigh deeply, then stifle his grief, and say, "Alas, that this great misfortune should have happened to one in my position!" Then he would fret with anxiety, his spirit would sag, and he would say, "None has seen what I have seen." In his depression, he ate less and less, grew pale, and his health deteriorated. He neglected everything, wasted away, and looked ill.

When King Shahrayar looked at his brother and saw how day after day he lost weight and grew thin, pale, ashen, and sickly, he thought that this was because of his expatriation and homesickness for his country and his family, and he said to himself, "My brother is not happy here. I should prepare a goodly gift for him and send him home." For a month he gathered gifts for his brother; then he invited him to see him and said, "Brother, I would like you to know that I intend to go hunting and pursue the roaming deer, for ten days. Then I shall return to prepare you for your journey home. Would you like to go hunting with me?" Shahzaman replied, "Brother, I feel distracted and depressed. Leave me here and go with God's blessing and help." When Shahrayar heard his brother, he thought that his dejection was because of his homesickness for his country. Not wishing to coerce him, he left him behind, and set out with his retainers and men. When they entered the wilderness, he deployed his men in a circle to begin trapping and hunting.

After his brother's departure, Shahzaman stayed in the palace and, from the window overlooking the garden, watched the birds and trees as he thought of his wife and what she had done to him, and sighed in sorrow. While he agonized over his misfortune, gazing at the heavens and turning a distracted eye on the garden, the private gate of his brother's palace opened, and there emerged, strutting like a dark-eyed deer, the lady, his brother's wife, with twenty slave-girls, ten white and ten black. While Shahzaman looked at them, without being seen, they continued to walk until they stopped below his window, without looking in his direction, thinking that he had gone to the hunt with his brother. Then they sat down, took off their clothes, and suddenly there were ten slave-girls and ten black slaves dressed in the same clothes as the girls. Then the ten black slaves mounted the ten girls, while the lady called, "Mas'ud, Mas'ud!" and

a black slave jumped from the tree to the ground, rushed to her, and, raising her legs, went between her thighs and made love to her. Mas'ud topped the lady, while the ten slaves topped the ten girls, and they carried on till noon. When they were done with their business, they got up and washed themselves. Then the ten slaves put on the same clothes again, mingled with the girls, and once more there appeared to be twenty slave-girls. Mas'ud himself jumped over the garden wall and disappeared, while the slave-girls and the lady sauntered to the private gate, went in and, locking the gate behind them, went their way.

All of this happened under King Shahzaman's eyes. When he saw this spectacle of the wife and the women of his brother the great king—how ten slaves put on women's clothes and slept with his brother's paramours and concubines and what Mas'ud did with his brother's wife, in his very palace—and pondered over this calamity and great misfortune, his care and sorrow left him and he said to himself, "This is our common lot. Even though my brother is king and master of the whole world, he cannot protect what is his, his wife and his concubines, and suffers misfortune in his very home. What happened to me is little by comparison. I used to think that I was the only one who has suffered, but from what I have seen, everyone suffers. By God, my misfortune is lighter than that of my brother." He kept marveling and blaming life, whose trials none can escape, and he began to find consolation in his own affliction and forget his grief. When supper came, he ate and drank with relish and zest and, feeling better, kept eating and drinking, enjoying himself and feeling happy. He thought to himself, "I am no longer alone in my misery; I am well."

For ten days, he continued to enjoy his food and drink, and when his brother, King Shahrayar, came back from the hunt, he met him happily, treated him attentively, and greeted him cheerfully. His brother, King Shahrayar, who had missed him, said, "By God, brother, I missed you on this trip and wished you were with me." Shahzaman thanked him and sat down to carouse with him, and when night fell, and food was brought before them, the two ate and drank, and again Shahzaman ate and drank with zest. As time went by, he continued to eat and drink with appetite, and became lighthearted and carefree. His face regained color and became ruddy, and his body gained weight, as his blood circulated and he regained his energy; he was himself again, or even better. King Shahrayar noticed his brother's condition, how he used to be and how he had improved, but kept it to himself until he took him aside one day and said, "My brother Shahzaman, I would like you to do something for me, to satisfy a wish, to answer a question truthfully." Shahzaman asked, "What is it, brother?" He replied, "When you first came to stay with me, I noticed that you kept losing weight, day after day, until your looks changed, your health deteriorated, and your energy sagged. As you continued like this, I thought that what ailed you was your homesickness for your family and your country, but even though I kept noticing that you were wasting away and looking ill, I refrained from questioning you and hid my feelings from you. Then I went hunting, and when I came back, I found that you had recovered and had regained your health. Now I want you to tell me every-

thing and to explain the cause of your deterioration and the cause of your subsequent recovery, without hiding anything from me." When Shahzaman heard what King Shahrayar said, he bowed his head, then said, "As for the cause of my recovery, that I cannot tell you, and I wish that you would excuse me from telling you." The king was greatly astonished at his brother's reply and, burning with curiosity, said, "You must tell me. For now, at least, explain the first cause."

Then Shahzaman related to his brother what happened to him with his own wife, on the night of his departure, from beginning to end, and concluded, "Thus all the while I was with you, great King, whenever I thought of the event and the misfortune that had befallen me, I felt troubled, careworn, and unhappy, and my health deteriorated. This then is the cause." Then he grew silent. When King Shahrayar heard his brother's explanation, he shook his head, greatly amazed at the deceit of women, and prayed to God to protect him from their wickedness, saying, "Brother, you were fortunate in killing your wife and her lover, who gave you good reason to feel troubled, careworn, and ill. In my opinion, what happened to you has never happened to anyone else. By God, had I been in your place, I would have killed at least a hundred or even a thousand women. I would have been furious; I would have gone mad. Now praise be to God who has delivered you from sorrow and distress. But tell me what has caused you to forget your sorrow and regain your health?" Shahzaman replied, "King, I wish that for God's sake you would excuse me from telling you." Shahrayar said, "You must." Shahzaman replied, "I fear that you will feel even more troubled and careworn than I." Shahrayar asked, "How could that be, brother? I insist on hearing your explanation."

Shahzaman then told him about what he had seen from the palace window and the calamity in his very home—how ten slaves, dressed like women, were sleeping with his women and concubines, day and night. He told him everything from beginning to end (but there is no point in repeating that). Then he concluded, "When I saw your own misfortune, I felt better—and said to myself, 'My brother is king of the world, yet such a misfortune has happened to him, and in his very home.' As a result I forgot my care and sorrow, relaxed, and began to eat and drink. This is the cause of my cheer and good spirits."

When King Shahrayar heard what his brother said and found out what had happened to him, he was furious and his blood boiled. He said, "Brother, I can't believe what you say unless I see it with my own eyes." When Shahzaman saw that his brother was in a rage, he said to him, "If you do not believe me, unless you see your misfortune with your own eyes, announce that you plan to go hunting. Then you and I shall set out with your troops, and when we get outside the city, we shall leave our tents and camp with the men behind, enter the city secretly, and go together to your palace. Then the next morning you can see with your own eyes."

King Shahrayar realized that his brother had a good plan and ordered his army to prepare for the trip. He spent the night with his brother, and when God's morning broke, the two rode out of the city with their army, preceded by the camp attendants, who had gone to drive the poles and pitch the tents where the king and his army were to camp. At nightfall

King Shahrayar summoned his chief chamberlain and bade him take his place. He entrusted him with the army and ordered that for three days no one was to enter the city. Then he and his brother disguised themselves and entered the city in the dark. They went directly to the palace where Shahzaman resided and slept there till the morning. When they awoke, they sat at the palace window, watching the garden and chatting, until the light broke, the day dawned, and the sun rose. As they watched, the private gate opened, and there emerged as usual the wife of King Shahrayar, walking among twenty slave-girls. They made their way under the trees until they stood below the palace window where the two kings sat. Then they took off their women's clothes, and suddenly there were ten slaves, who mounted the ten girls and made love to them. As for the lady, she called, "Mas'ud, Mas'ud," and a black slave jumped from the tree to the ground, came to her, and said, "What do you want, you slut? Here is Sa'ad al-Din Mas'ud." She laughed and fell on her back, while the slave mounted her and like the others did his business with her. Then the black slaves got up, washed themselves, and, putting on the same clothes, mingled with the girls. Then they walked away, entered the palace, and locked the gate behind them. As for Mas'ud, he jumped over the fence to the road and went on his way.

When King Shahrayar saw the spectacle of his wife and the slave-girls, he went out of his mind, and when he and his brother came down from upstairs, he said, "No one is safe in this world. Such doings are going on in my kingdom, and in my very palace. Perish the world and perish life! This is a great calamity, indeed." Then he turned to his brother and asked, "Would you like to follow me in what I shall do?" Shahzaman answered, "Yes. I will." Shahrayar said, "Let us leave our royal state and roam the world for the love of the Supreme Lord. If we should find one whose misfortune is greater than ours, we shall return. Otherwise, we shall continue to journey through the land, without need for the trappings of royalty." Shahzaman replied, "This is an excellent idea. I shall follow you."

Then they left by the private gate, took a side road, and departed, journeying till nightfall. They slept over their sorrows, and in the morning resumed their day journey until they came to a meadow by the seashore. While they sat in the meadow amid the thick plants and trees, discussing their misfortunes and the recent events, they suddenly heard a shout and a great cry coming from the middle of the sea. They trembled with fear, thinking that the sky had fallen on the earth. Then the sea parted, and there emerged a black pillar that, as it swayed forward, got taller and taller, until it touched the clouds. Shahrayar and Shahzaman were petrified; then they ran in terror and, climbing a very tall tree, sat hiding in its foliage. When they looked again, they saw that the black pillar was cleaving the sea, wading in the water toward the green meadow, until it touched the shore. When they looked again, they saw that it was a black demon, carrying on his head a large glass chest with four steel locks. He came out, walked into the meadow, and where should he stop but under the very tree where the two kings were hiding. The demon sat down and placed the glass chest on the ground. He took out four keys and, opening the locks of the chest, pulled out a full-grown woman. She had a beautiful

figure, and a face like the full moon, and a lovely smile. He took her out, laid her under the tree, and looked at her, saying, "Mistress of all noble women, you whom I carried away on your wedding night, I would like to sleep a little." Then he placed his head on the young woman's lap, stretched his legs to the sea, sank into sleep, and began to snore.

Meanwhile, the woman looked up at the tree and, turning her head by chance, saw King Shahrayar and King Shahzaman. She lifted the demon's head from her lap and placed it on the ground. Then she came and stood under the tree and motioned to them with her hand, as if to say, "Come down slowly to me." When they realized that she had seen them, they were frightened, and they begged her and implored her, in the name of the Creator of the heavens, to excuse them from climbing down. She replied, "You must come down to me." They motioned to her, saying, "This sleeping demon is the enemy of mankind. For God's sake, leave us alone." She replied, "You must come down, and if you don't, I shall wake the demon and have him kill you." She kept gesturing and pressing, until they climbed down very slowly and stood before her. Then she lay on her back, raised her legs, and said, "Make love to me and satisfy my need, or else I shall wake the demon, and he will kill you." They replied, "For God's sake, mistress, don't do this to us, for at this moment we feel nothing but dismay and fear of this demon. Please, excuse us." She replied, "You must," and insisted, swearing, "By God who created the heavens, if you don't do it, I shall wake my husband the demon and ask him to kill you and throw you into the sea." As she persisted, they could no longer resist and they made love to her, first the older brother, then the younger. When they were done and withdrew from her, she said to them, "Give me your rings," and, pulling out from the folds of her dress a small purse, opened it, and shook out ninety-eight rings of different fashions and colors. Then she asked them, "Do you know what these rings are?" They answered, "No." She said, "All the owners of these rings slept with me, for whenever one of them made love to me, I took a ring from him. Since you two have slept with me, give me your rings, so that I may add them to the rest, and make a full hundred. A hundred men have known me under the very horns of this filthy, monstrous cuckold, who has imprisoned me in this chest, locked it with four locks, and kept me in the middle of this raging, roaring sea. He has guarded me and tried to keep me pure and chaste, not realizing that nothing can prevent or alter what is predestined and that when a woman desires something, no one can stop her." When Shahrayar and Shahzaman heard what the young woman said, they were greatly amazed, danced with joy, and said, "O God, O God! There is no power and no strength, save in God the Almighty, the Magnificent. Great is women's cunning." Then each of them took off his ring and handed it to her. She took them and put them with the rest in the purse. Then sitting again by the demon, she lifted his head, placed it back on her lap, and motioned to them, "Go on your way, or else I shall wake him."

They turned their backs and took to the road. Then Shahrayar turned to his brother and said, "My brother Shahzaman, look at this sorry plight. By God, it is worse than ours. This is no less than a demon who has carried a young woman away on her wedding night, imprisoned her in a glass

chest, locked her up with four locks, and kept her in the middle of the sea, thinking that he could guard her from what God had foreordained, and you saw how she has managed to sleep with ninety-eight men, and added the two of us to make a hundred. Brother, let us go back to our kingdoms and our cities, never to marry a woman again. As for myself, I shall show you what I will do."

Then the two brothers headed home and journeyed till nightfall. On the morning of the third day, they reached their camp and men, entered their tent, and sat on their thrones. The chamberlains, deputies, princes, and viziers came to attend King Shahrayar, while he gave orders and bestowed robes of honor, as well as other gifts. Then at his command everyone returned to the city, and he went to his own palace and ordered his chief vizier, the father of the two girls Shahrazad and Dinarzad, who will be mentioned below, and said to him, "Take that wife of mine and put her to death." Then Shahrayar went to her himself, bound her, and handed her over to the vizier, who took her out and put her to death. Then King Shahrayar grabbed his sword, brandished it, and, entering the palace chambers, killed every one of his slave-girls and replaced them with others. He then swore to marry for one night only and kill the woman the next morning, in order to save himself from the wickedness and cunning of women, saying, "There is not a single chaste woman anywhere on the entire face of the earth." Shortly thereafter he provided his brother Shahzaman with supplies for his journey and sent him back to his own country with gifts, rarities, and money. The brother bade him good-bye and set out for home.

Shahrayar sat on his throne and ordered his vizier, the father of the two girls, to find him a wife from among the princes' daughters. The vizier found him one, and he slept with her and was done with her, and the next morning he ordered the vizier to put her to death. That very night he took one of his army officers' daughters, slept with her, and the next morning ordered the vizier to put her to death. The vizier, who could not disobey him, put her to death. The third night he took one of the merchants' daughters, slept with her till the morning, then ordered his vizier to put her to death, and the vizier did so. It became King Shahrayar's custom to take every night the daughter of a merchant or a commoner, spend the night with her, then have her put to death the next morning. He continued to do this until all the girls perished, their mothers mourned, and there arose a clamor among the fathers and mothers, who called the plague upon his head, complained to the Creator of the heavens, and called for help on Him who hears and answers prayers.

Now, as mentioned earlier, the vizier, who put the girls to death, had an older daughter called Shahrazad and a younger one called Dinarzad. The older daughter, Shahrazad, had read the books of literature, philosophy, and medicine. She knew poetry by heart, had studied historical reports, and was acquainted with the sayings of men and the maxims of sages and kings. She was intelligent, knowledgeable, wise, and refined. She had read and learned. One day she said to her father, "Father, I will tell you what is in my mind." He asked, "What is it?" She answered, "I would like you to marry me to King Shahrayar, so that I may either suc-

ceed in saving the people or perish and die like the rest." When the vizier heard what his daughter Shahrazad said, he got angry and said to her, "Foolish one, don't you know that King Shahrayar has sworn to spend but one night with a girl and have her put to death the next morning? If I give you to him, he will sleep with you for one night and will ask me to put you to death the next morning, and I shall have to do it, since I cannot disobey him." She said, "Father, you must give me to him, even if he kills me." He asked, "What has possessed you that you wish to imperil yourself?" She replied, "Father, you must give me to him. This is absolute and final." Her father the vizier became furious and said to her, "Daughter, 'He who misbehaves, ends up in trouble,' and 'He who considers not the end, the world is not his friend.' As the popular saying goes, 'I would be sitting pretty, but for my curiosity.' I am afraid that what happened to the donkey and the ox with the merchant will happen to you." She asked, "Father, what happened to the donkey, the ox, and the merchant?" He said:

[The Tale of the Ox and the Donkey]

There was a prosperous and wealthy merchant who lived in the country-side and labored on a farm. He owned many camels and herds of cattle and employed many men, and he had a wife and many grown-up as well as little children. This merchant was taught the language of the beasts, on condition that if he revealed his secret to anyone, he would die; therefore, even though he knew the language of every kind of animal, he did not let anyone know, for fear of death. One day, as he sat, with his wife beside him and his children playing before him, he glanced at an ox and a don-key he kept at the farmhouse, tied to adjacent troughs, and heard the ox say to the donkey, "Watchful one, I hope that you are enjoying the comfort and the service you are getting. Your ground is swept and watered, and they serve you, feed you sifted barley, and offer you clear, cool water to drink. I, on the contrary, am taken out to plow in the middle of the night. They clamp on my neck something they call yoke and plow, push me all day under the whip to plow the field, and drive me beyond my endurance until my sides are lacerated, and my neck is flayed. They work me from nighttime to nighttime, take me back in the dark, offer me beans soiled with mud and hay mixed with chaff, and let me spend the night lying in urine and dung. Meanwhile you rest on well-swept, watered, and smoothed ground, with a clean trough full of hay. You stand in comfort, save for the rare occasion when our master the merchant rides you to do a brief errand and returns. You are comfortable, while I am weary; you sleep, while I keep awake."

When the ox finished, the donkey turned to him and said, "Greenhorn, they were right in calling you ox, for you ox harbor no deceit, malice, or meanness. Being sincere, you exert and exhaust yourself to comfort others. Have you not heard the saying 'Out of bad luck, they hastened on the road'? You go into the field from early morning to endure your torture at the plow to the point of exhaustion. When the plowman takes you back and ties you to the trough, you go on butting and beating with your horns,

kicking with your hoofs, and bellowing for the beans, until they toss them to you; then you begin to eat. Next time, when they bring them to you, don't eat or even touch them, but smell them, then draw back and lie down on the hay and straw. If you do this, life will be better and kinder to you, and you will find relief."

As the ox listened, he was sure that the donkey had given him good advice. He thanked him, commended him to God, and invoked His blessing on him, and said, "May you stay safe from harm, watchful one." All of this conversation took place, daughter, while the merchant listened and understood. On the following day, the plowman came to the merchant's house and, taking the ox, placed the yoke upon his neck and worked him at the plow, but the ox lagged behind. The plowman hit him, but following the donkey's advice, the ox, dissembling, fell on his belly, and the plowman hit him again. Thus the ox kept getting up and falling until nightfall, when the plowman took him home and tied him to the trough. But this time the ox did not bellow or kick the ground with his hoofs. Instead, he withdrew, away from the trough. Astonished, the plowman brought him his beans and fodder, but the ox only smelled the fodder and pulled back and lay down at a distance with the hay and straw, complaining till the morning. When the plowman arrived, he found the trough as he had left it, full of beans and fodder, and saw the ox lying on his back, hardly breathing, his belly puffed, and his legs raised in the air. The plowman felt sorry for him and said to himself, "By God, he did seem weak and unable to work." Then he went to the merchant and said, "Master, last night, the ox refused to eat or touch his fodder."

The merchant, who knew what was going on, said to the plowman, "Go to the wily donkey, put him to the plow, and work him hard until he finishes the ox's task." The plowman left, took the donkey, and placed the yoke upon his neck. Then he took him out to the field and drove him with blows until he finished the ox's work, all the while driving him with blows and beating him until his sides were lacerated and his neck was flayed. At nightfall he took him home, barely able to drag his legs under his tired body and his drooping ears. Meanwhile the ox spent his day resting. He ate all his food, drank his water, and lay quietly, chewing his cud in comfort. All day long he kept praising the donkey's advice and invoking God's blessing on him. When the donkey came back at night, the ox stood up to greet him saying, "Good evening, watchful one! You have done me a favor beyond description, for I have been sitting in comfort. God bless you for my sake." Seething with anger, the donkey did not reply, but said to himself, "All this happened to me because of my miscalculation. 'I would be sitting pretty, but for my curiosity.' If I don't find a way to return this ox to his former situation, I will perish." Then he went to his trough and lay down, while the ox continued to chew his cud and invoke God's blessing on him.

"You, my daughter, will likewise perish because of your miscalculation. Desist, sit quietly, and don't expose yourself to peril. I advise you out of compassion for you." She replied, "Father, I must go to the king, and you must give me to him." He said, "Don't do it." She insisted, "I must." He

replied, "If you don't desist, I will do to you what the merchant did to his wife." She asked, "Father, what did the merchant do to his wife?" He said:

[The Tale of the Merchant and His Wife]

After what had happened to the donkey and the ox, the merchant and his wife went out in the moonlight to the stable, and he heard the donkey ask the ox in his own language, "Listen, ox, what are you going to do tomorrow morning, and what will you do when the plowman brings you your fodder?" The ox replied, "What shall I do but follow your advice and stick to it? If he brings me my fodder, I will pretend to be ill, lie down, and puff my belly." The donkey shook his head, and said, "Don't do it. Do you know what I heard our master the merchant say to the plowman?" The ox asked, "What?" The donkey replied, "He said that if the ox failed to get up and eat his fodder, he would call the butcher to slaughter him and skin him and would distribute the meat for alms and use the skin for a mat. I am afraid for you, but good advice is a matter of faith; therefore, if he brings you your fodder, eat it and look alert lest they cut your throat and skin you." The ox farted and bellowed.

The merchant got up and laughed loudly at the conversation between the donkey and the ox, and his wife asked him, "What are you laughing at? Are you making fun of me?" He said, "No." She said, "Tell me what made you laugh." He replied, "I cannot tell you. I am afraid to disclose the secret conversation of the animals." She asked, "And what prevents you from telling me?" He answered, "The fear of death." His wife said, "By God, you are lying. This is nothing but an excuse. I swear by God, the Lord of heaven, that if you don't tell me and explain the cause of your laughter, I will leave you. You must tell me." Then she went back to the house crying, and she continued to cry till the morning. The merchant said, "Damn it! Tell me why you are crying. Ask for God's forgiveness, and stop questioning and leave me in peace." She said, "I insist and will not desist." Amazed at her, he replied, "You insist! If I tell you what the donkey said to the ox, which made me laugh, I shall die." She said, "Yes, I insist, even if you have to die." He replied, "Then call your family," and she called their two daughters, her parents and relatives, and some neighbors. The merchant told them that he was about to die, and everyone, young and old, his children, the farmhands, and the servants began to cry until the house became a place of mourning. Then he summoned legal witnesses, wrote a will, leaving his wife and children their due portions, freed his slave-girls, and bid his family good-bye, while everybody, even the witnesses, wept. Then the wife's parents approached her and said, "Desist, for if your husband had not known for certain that he would die if he revealed his secret, he wouldn't have gone through all this." She replied, "I will not change my mind," and everybody cried and prepared to mourn his death.

Well, my daughter Shahrazad, it happened that the farmer kept fifty hens and a rooster at home, and while he felt sad to depart this world and leave his children and relatives behind, pondering and about to reveal and utter his secret, he overheard a dog of his say something in dog language

to the rooster, who, beating and clapping his wings, had jumped on a hen and, finishing with her, jumped down and jumped on another. The merchant heard and understood what the dog said in his own language to the rooster, "Shameless, no-good rooster. Aren't you ashamed to do such a thing on a day like this?" The rooster asked, "What is special about this day?" The dog replied, "Don't you know that our master and friend is in mourning today? His wife is demanding that he disclose his secret, and when he discloses it, he will surely die. He is in this predicament, about to interpret to her the language of the animals, and all of us are mourning for him, while you clap your wings and get off one hen and jump on another. Aren't you ashamed?" The merchant heard the rooster reply, "You fool, you lunatic! Our master and friend claims to be wise, but he is foolish, for he has only one wife, yet he does not know how to manage her." The dog asked, "What should he do with her?"

The rooster replied, "He should take an oak branch, push her into a room, lock the door, and fall on her with the stick, beating her mercilessly until he breaks her arms and legs and she cries out, 'I no longer want you to tell me or explain anything.' He should go on beating her until he cures her for life, and she will never oppose him in anything. If he does this, he will live, and live in peace, and there will be no more grief, but he does not know how to manage." Well, my daughter Shahrazad, when the merchant heard the conversation between the dog and the rooster, he jumped up and, taking an oak branch, pushed his wife into a room, got in with her, and locked the door. Then he began to beat her mercilessly on her chest and shoulders and kept beating her until she cried for mercy, screaming, "No, no, I don't want to know anything. Leave me alone, leave me alone. I don't want to know anything," until he got tired of hitting her and opened the door. The wife emerged penitent, the husband learned good management, and everybody was happy, and the mourning turned into a celebration.

"If you don't relent, I shall do to you what the merchant did to his wife." She said, "Such tales don't deter me from my request. If you wish, I can tell you many such tales. In the end, if you don't take me to King Shahrayar, I shall go to him by myself behind your back and tell him that you have refused to give me to one like him and that you have begrudged your master one like me." The vizier asked, "Must you really do this?" She replied, "Yes, I must."

Tired and exhausted, the vizier went to King Shahrayar and, kissing the ground before him, told him about his daughter, adding that he would give her to him that very night. The king was astonished and said to him, "Vizier, how is it that you have found it possible to give me your daughter, knowing that I will, by God, the Creator of heaven, ask you to put her to death the next morning and that if you refuse, I will have you put to death too?" He replied, "My King and Lord, I have told her everything and explained all this to her, but she refuses and insists on being with you tonight." The king was delighted and said, "Go to her, prepare her, and bring her to me early in the evening."

The vizier went down, repeated the king's message to his daughter, and

said, "May God not deprive me of you." She was very happy and, after preparing herself and packing what she needed, went to her younger sister, Dinarzad, and said, "Sister, listen well to what I am telling you. When I go to the king, I will send for you, and when you come and see that the king has finished with me, say, 'Sister, if you are not sleepy, tell us a story.' Then I will begin to tell a story, and it will cause the king to stop his practice, save myself, and deliver the people." Dinarzad replied, "Very well."

At nightfall the vizier took Shahrazad and went with her to the great King Shahrayar. But when Shahrayar took her to bed and began to fondle her, she wept, and when he asked her, "Why are you crying?" she replied, "I have a sister, and I wish to bid her good-bye before daybreak." Then the king sent for the sister, who came and went to sleep under the bed. When the night wore on, she woke up and waited until the king had satisfied himself with her sister Shahrazad and they were by now all fully awake. Then Dinarzad cleared her throat and said, "Sister, if you are not sleepy, tell us one of your lovely little tales to while away the night, before I bid you good-bye at daybreak, for I don't know what will happen to you tomorrow." Shahrazad turned to King Shahrayar and said, "May I have your permission to tell a story?" He replied, "Yes," and Shahrazad was very happy and said, "Listen":

[The Story of the Merchant and the Demon]

THE FIRST NIGHT

It is said, O wise and happy King, that once there was a prosperous merchant who had abundant wealth and investments and commitments in every country. He had many women and children and kept many servants and slaves. One day, having resolved to visit another country, he took provisions, filling his saddlebag with loaves of bread and with dates, mounted his horse, and set out on his journey. For many days and nights, he journeyed under God's care until he reached his destination. When he finished his business, he turned back to his home and family. He journeyed for three days, and on the fourth day, chancing to come to an orchard, went in to avoid the heat and shade himself from the sun of the open country. He came to a spring under a walnut tree and, tying his horse, sat by the spring, pulled out from the saddlebag some loaves of bread and a handful of dates, and began to eat, throwing the date pits right and left until he had had enough. Then he got up, performed his ablutions, and performed his prayers.

But hardly had he finished when he saw an old demon, with sword in hand, standing with his feet on the ground and his head in the clouds. The demon approached until he stood before him and screamed, saying, "Get up, so that I may kill you with this sword, just as you have killed my son." When the merchant saw and heard the demon, he was terrified and awestricken. He asked, "Master, for what crime do you wish to kill me?" The demon replied, "I wish to kill you because you have killed my son." The merchant asked, "Who has killed your son?" The demon replied, "You have killed my son." The merchant said, "By God, I did not kill your

son. When and how could that have been?" The demon said, "Didn't you
sit down, take out some dates from your saddlebag, and eat, throwing the
pits right and left?" The merchant replied, "Yes, I did." The demon said,
"You killed my son, for as you were throwing the stones right and left, my
son happened to be walking by and was struck and killed by one of them,
and I must now kill you." The merchant said, "O my lord, please don't
kill me." The demon replied, "I must kill you as you killed him—blood
for blood." The merchant said, "To God we belong and to God we turn.
There is no power or strength, save in God the Almighty, the Magnificent.
If I killed him, I did it by mistake. Please forgive me." The demon replied,
"By God, I must kill you, as you killed my son." Then he seized him, and
throwing him to the ground, raised the sword to strike him. The merchant
began to weep and mourn his family and his wife and children. Again,
the demon raised his sword to strike, while the merchant cried until he
was drenched with tears, saying, "There is no power or strength, save in
God the Almighty, the Magnificent." Then he began to recite the following verses:

> Life has two days: one peace, one wariness,
> And has two sides: worry and happiness.
> Ask him who taunts us with adversity,
> "Does fate, save those worthy of note, oppress?
> Don't you see that the blowing, raging storms   5
> Only the tallest of the trees beset,
> And of earth's many green and barren lots,
> Only the ones with fruits with stones are hit,
> And of the countless stars in heaven's vault
> None is eclipsed except the moon and sun?   10
> You thought well of the days, when they were good,
> Oblivious to the ills destined for one.
> You were deluded by the peaceful nights,
> Yet in the peace of night does sorrow stun."

When the merchant finished and stopped weeping, the demon said, "By
God, I must kill you, as you killed my son, even if you weep blood." The
merchant asked, "Must you?" The demon replied, "I must," and raised his
sword to strike.

*But morning overtook Shahrazad, and she lapsed into silence, leaving
King Shahrayar burning with curiosity to hear the rest of the story. Then
Dinarzad said to her sister Shahrazad, "What a strange and lovely story!"
Shahrazad replied, "What is this compared with what I shall tell you tomorrow night if the king spares me and lets me live? It will be even better and
more entertaining." The king thought to himself, "I will spare her until I
hear the rest of the story; then I will have her put to death the next day."
When morning broke, the day dawned, and the sun rose; the king left to
attend to the affairs of the kingdom, and the vizier, Shahrazad's father, was
amazed and delighted. King Shahrayar governed all day and returned home
at night to his quarters and got into bed with Shahrazad. Then Dinarzad
said to her sister Shahrazad, "Please, sister, if you are not sleepy, tell us one
of your lovely little tales to while away the night." The king added, "Let it*

*be the conclusion of the story of the demon and the merchant, for I would
like to hear it." Shahrazad replied, "With the greatest pleasure, dear, happy
King":*

THE SECOND NIGHT

It is related, O wise and happy King, that when the demon raised his
sword, the merchant asked the demon again, "Must you kill me?" and the
demon replied, "Yes." Then the merchant said, "Please give me time to
say good-bye to my family and my wife and children, divide my property
among them, and appoint guardians. Then I shall come back, so that you
may kill me." The demon replied, "I am afraid that if I release you and
grant you time, you will go and do what you wish, but will not come
back." The merchant said, "I swear to keep my pledge to come back, as
the God of Heaven and earth is my witness." The demon asked, "How
much time do you need?" The merchant replied, "One year, so that I may
see enough of my children, bit my wife good-bye, discharge my obligations
to people, and come back on New Year's Day." The demon asked, "Do
you swear to God that if I let you go, you will come back on New Year's
Day?" The merchant replied, "Yes, I swear to God."

After the merchant swore, the demon released him, and he mounted
his horse sadly and went on his way. He journeyed until he reached his
home and came to his wife and children. When he saw them, he wept
bitterly, and when his family saw his sorrow and grief, they began to
reproach him for his behavior, and his wife said, "Husband, what is the
matter with you? Why do you mourn, when we are happy, celebrating
your return?" He replied, "Why not mourn when I have only one year to
live?" Then he told her of his encounter with the demon and informed
her that he had sworn to return on New Year's Day, so that the demon
might kill him.

When they heard what he said, everyone began to cry. His wife struck
her face in lamentation and cut her hair, his daughters wailed, and his
little children cried. It was a day of mourning, as all the children gathered
around their father to weep and exchange good-byes. The next day he
wrote his will, dividing his property, discharged his obligations to people,
left bequests and gifts, distributed alms, and engaged reciters to read portions of the Quran in his house. Then he summoned legal witnesses and
in their presence freed his slaves and slave-girls, divided among his elder
children their shares of the property, appointed guardians for his little
ones, and gave his wife her share, according to her marriage contract. He
spent the rest of the time with his family, and when the year came to an
end, save for the time needed for the journey, he performed his ablutions,
performed his prayers, and, carrying his burial shroud, began to bid his
family good-bye. His sons hung around his neck, his daughters wept, and
his wife wailed. Their mourning scared him, and he began to weep, as he
embraced and kissed his children good-bye. He said to them, "Children,
this is God's will and decree, for man was created to die." Then he turned
away and, mounting his horse, journeyed day and night until he reached
the orchard on New Year's Day.

He sat at the place where he had eaten the dates, waiting for the demon, with a heavy heart and tearful eyes. As he waited, an old man, leading a deer on a leash, approached and greeted him, and he returned the greeting. The old man inquired, "Friend, why do you sit here in this place of demons and devils? For in this haunted orchard none come to good." The merchant replied by telling him what had happened to him and the demon, from beginning to end. The old man was amazed at the merchant's fidelity and said, "Yours is a magnificent pledge," adding, "By God, I shall not leave until I see what will happen to you with the demon." Then he sat down beside him and chatted with him. As they talked . . .

But morning overtook Shahrazad, and she lapsed into silence. As the day dawned, and it was light, her sister Dinarzad said, "What a strange and wonderful story!" Shahrazad replied, "Tomorrow night I shall tell something even stranger and more wonderful than this."

THE THIRD NIGHT

When it was night and Shahrazad was in bed with the king, Dinarzad said to her sister Shahrazad, "Please, if you are not sleepy, tell us one of your lovely little tales to while away the night." The king added, "Let it be the conclusion of the merchant's story." Shahrazad replied, "As you wish":

I heard, O happy King, that as the merchant and the man with the deer sat talking, another old man approached, with two black hounds, and when he reached them, he greeted them, and they returned his greeting. Then he asked them about themselves, and the man with the deer told him the story of the merchant and the demon, how the merchant had sworn to return on New Year's Day, and how the demon was waiting to kill him. He added that when he himself heard the story, he swore never to leave until he saw what would happen between the merchant and the demon. When the man with the two dogs heard the story, he was amazed, and he too swore never to leave them until he saw what would happen between them. Then he questioned the merchant, and the merchant repeated to him what had happened to him with the demon.

While they were engaged in conversation, a third old man approached and greeted them, and they returned his greeting. He asked, "Why do I see the two of you sitting here, with this merchant between you, looking abject, sad, and dejected?" They told him the merchant's story and explained that they were sitting and waiting to see what would happen to him with the demon. When he heard the story, he sat down with them, saying, "By God, I too like you will not leave, until I see what happens to this man with the demon." As they sat, conversing with one another, they suddenly saw the dust rising from the open country, and when it cleared, they saw the demon approaching, with a drawn steel sword in his hand. He stood before them without greeting them, yanked the merchant with his left hand, and, holding him fast before him, said, "Get ready to die." The merchant and the three old men began to weep and wail.

But dawn broke and morning overtook Shahrazad, and she lapsed into silence. Then Dinarzad said, "Sister, what a lovely story!" Shahrazad

replied, "What is this compared with what I shall tell you tomorrow night?
It will be even better; it will be more wonderful, delightful, entertaining, and
delectable if the king spares me and lets me live." The king was all curiosity
to hear the rest of the story and said to himself, "By God, I will not have her
put to death until I hear the rest of the story and find out what happened
to the merchant with the demon. Then I will have her put to death the next
morning, as I did with the others." Then he went out to attend to the affairs
of his kingdom, and when he saw Shahrazad's father, he treated him kindly
and showed him favors, and the vizier was amazed. When night came, the
king went home, and when he was in bed with Shahrazad, Dinarzad said,
"Sister, if you are not sleepy, tell us one of your lovely little tales to while
away the night." Shahrazad replied, "With the greatest pleasure":

THE FOURTH NIGHT

It is related, O happy King, that the first old man with the deer
approached the demon and, kissing his hands and feet, said, "Fiend and
King of the demon kings, if I tell you what happened to me and that deer,
and you find it strange and amazing, indeed stranger and more amazing
than what happened to you and the merchant, will you grant me a third
of your claim on him for his crime and guilt?" The demon replied, "I
will." The old man said:

[The First Old Man's Tale]

Demon, this deer is my cousin, my flesh and blood. I married her when
I was very young, and she a girl of twelve, who reached womanhood only
afterward. For thirty years we lived together, but I was not blessed with
children, for she bore neither boy nor girl. Yet I continued to be kind to
her, to care for her, and to treat her generously. Then I took a mistress,
and she bore me a son, who grew up to look like a slice of the moon.[5]
Meanwhile, my wife grew jealous of my mistress and my son. One day,
when he was ten, I had to go on a journey. I entrusted my wife, this one
here, with my mistress and son, bade her take good care of them, and was
gone for a whole year. In my absence my wife, this cousin of mine, learned
soothsaying and magic and cast a spell on my son and turned him into a
young bull. Then she summoned my shepherd, gave my son to him, and
said, "Tend this bull with the rest of the cattle." The shepherd took him
and tended him for a while. Then she cast a spell on the mother, turning
her into a cow, and gave her also to the shepherd.

When I came back, after all this was done, and inquired about my
mistress and my son, she answered, "Your mistress died, and your son ran
away two months ago, and I have had no news from him ever since."
When I heard her, I grieved for my mistress, and with an anguished heart
I mourned for my son for nearly a year. When the Great Feast of the
Immolation[6] drew near, I summoned the shepherd and ordered him to
bring me a fat cow for the sacrifice. The cow he brought me was in reality

5. The moon is a symbol of beauty for men and women.   6. Celebrates the pilgrimage of Mecca; it
lasts four days, during which sheep and cattle are sacrificed to God.

my enchanted mistress. When I bound her and pressed against her to cut her throat, she wept and cried, as if saying, "My son, my son," and her tears coursed down her cheeks. Astonished and seized with pity, I turned away and asked the shepherd to bring me a different cow. But my wife shouted, "Go on. Butcher her, for he has none better or fatter. Let us enjoy her meat at feast time." I approached the cow to cut her throat, and again she cried, as if saying, "My son, my son." Then I turned away from her and said to the shepherd, "Butcher her for me." The shepherd butchered her, and when he skinned her, he found neither meat nor fat but only skin and bone. I regretted having her butchered and said to the shepherd, "Take her all for yourself, or give her as alms to whomever you wish, and find me a fat young bull from among the flock." The shepherd took her away and disappeared, and I never knew what he did with her.

Then he brought me my son, my heartblood, in the guise of a fat young bull. Then my son saw me, he shook his head loose from the rope, ran toward me, and, throwing himself at my feet, kept rubbing his head against me. I was astonished and touched with sympathy, pity, and mercy, for the blood hearkened to the blood and the divine bond, and my heart throbbed within me when I saw the tears coursing over the cheeks of my son the young bull, as he dug the earth with his hoofs. I turned away and said to the shepherd, "Let him go with the rest of the flock, and be kind to him, for I have decided to spare him. Bring me another one instead of him." My wife, this very deer, shouted, "You shall sacrifice none but this bull." I got angry and replied, "I listened to you and butchered the cow uselessly. I will not listen to you and kill this bull, for I have decided to spare him." But she pressed me, saying, "You must butcher this bull," and I bound him and took the knife . . .

But dawn broke, and morning overtook Shahrazad, and she lapsed into silence, leaving the king all curiosity for the rest of the story. Then her sister Dinarzad said, "What an entertaining story!" Shahrazad replied, "Tomorrow night I shall tell you something even stranger, more wonderful, and more entertaining if the king spares me and lets me live."

THE FIFTH NIGHT

The following night, Dinarzad said to her sister Shahrazad, "Please, sister, if you are not sleepy, tell us one of your little tales." Shahrazad replied, "With the greatest pleasure":

I heard, dear King, that the old man with the deer said to the demon and to his companions:

I took the knife and as I turned to slaughter my son, he wept, bellowed, rolled at my feet, and motioned toward me with his tongue. I suspected something, began to waver with trepidation and pity, and finally released him, saying to my wife, "I have decided to spare him, and I commit him to your care." Then I tried to appease and please my wife, this very deer, by slaughtering another bull, promising her to slaughter this one next season. We slept that night, and when God's dawn broke, the shepherd came to me without letting my wife know, and said, "Give me credit for bringing

you good news." I replied, "Tell me, and the credit is yours." He said, "Master, I have a daughter who is fond of soothsaying and magic and who is adept at the art of oaths and spells. Yesterday I took home with me the bull you had spared, to let him graze with the cattle, and when my daughter saw him, she laughed and cried at the same time. When I asked her why she laughed and cried, she answered that she laughed because the bull was in reality the son of our master the cattle owner, put under a spell by his step-mother, and that she cried because his father had slaughtered the son's mother. I could hardly wait till daybreak to bring you the good news about your son."

Demon, when I heard that, I uttered a cry and fainted, and when I came to myself, I accompanied the shepherd to his home, went to my son, and threw myself at him, kissing him and crying. He turned his head toward me, his tears coursing over his cheeks, and dangled his tongue, as if to say, "Look at my plight." Then I turned to the shepherd's daughter and asked, "Can you release him from the spell? If you do, I will give you all my cattle and all my possessions." She smiled and replied, "Master, I have no desire for your wealth, cattle, or possessions. I will deliver him, but on two conditions: first, that you let me marry him; second, that you let me cast a spell on her who had cast a spell on him, in order to control her and guard against her evil power." I replied, "Do whatever you wish and more. My possessions are for you and my son. As for my wife, who has done this to my son and made me slaughter his mother, her life is forfeit to you." She said, "No, but I will let her taste what she has inflicted on others." Then the shepherd's daughter filled a bowl of water, uttered an incantation and an oath, and said to my son, "Bull, if you have been created in this image by the All-Conquering, Almighty Lord, stay as you are, but if you have been treacherously put under a spell, change back to your human form, by the will of God, Creator of the wide world." Then she sprinkled him with the water, and he shook himself and changed from a bull back to his human form.

As I rushed to him, I fainted, and when I came to myself, he told me what my wife, this very deer, had done to him and to his mother. I said to him, "Son, God has sent us someone who will pay her back for what you and your mother and I have suffered at her hands." Then, O demon, I gave my son in marriage to the shepherd's daughter, who turned my wife into this very deer, saying to me, "To me this is a pretty form, for she will be with us day and night, and it is better to turn her into a pretty deer than to suffer her sinister looks." Thus she stayed with us, while the days and nights followed one another, and the months and years went by. Then one day the shepherd's daughter died, and my son went to the country of this very man with whom you have had your encounter. Some time later I took my wife, this very deer, with me, set out to find out what had happened to my son, and chanced to stop here. This is my story, my strange and amazing story.

The demon assented, saying, "I grant you one-third of this man's life."

Then, O King Shahrayar, the second old man with the two black dogs approached the demon and said, "I too shall tell you what happened to

me and to these two dogs, and if I tell it to you and you find it stranger
and more amazing than this man's story will you grant me one-third of
this man's life?" The demon replied, "I will." Then the old man began to
tell his story, saying . . .

*But dawn broke, and morning overtook Shahrazad, and she lapsed into
silence. Then Dinarzad said, "This is an amazing story," and Shahrazad
replied, "What is this compared with what I shall tell you tomorrow night if
the king spares me and lets me live!" The king said to himself, "By God, I
will not have her put to death until I find out what happened to the man
with the two black dogs. Then I will have her put to death, God the
Almighty willing."*

THE SIXTH NIGHT

*When the following night arrived and Shahrazad was in bed with King
Shahrayar, her sister Dinarzad said, "Sister, if you are not sleepy, tell us a
little tale. Finish the one you started." Shahrazad replied, "With the greatest
pleasure":*

I heard, O happy King, that the second old man with the two dogs said:

[*The Second Old Man's Tale*]

Demon, as for my story, these are the details. These two dogs are my
brothers. When our father died, he left behind three sons, and left us three
thousand dinars,[7] with which each of us opened a shop and became a
shopkeeper. Soon my older brother, one of these very dogs, went and sold
the contents of his shop for a thousand dinars, bought trading goods, and,
having prepared himself for his trading trip, left us. A full year went by,
when one day, as I sat in my shop, a beggar stopped by to beg. When I
refused him, he tearfully asked, "Don't you recognize me?" and when I
looked at him closely, I recognized my brother. I embraced him and took
him into the shop, and when I asked him about his plight, he replied,
"The money is gone, and the situation is bad." Then I took him to the
public bath, clothed him in one of my robes, and took him home with
me. Then I examined my books and checked my balance, and found out
that I had made a thousand dinars and that my net worth was two thousand
dinars. I divided the amount between my brother and myself, and said to
him, "Think as if you have never been away." He gladly took the money
and opened another shop.

Soon afterward my second brother, this other dog, went and sold his
merchandise and collected his money, intending to go on a trading trip.
We tried to dissuade him, but he did not listen. Instead, he bought merchandise and trading goods, joined a group of travelers, and was gone for
a full year. Then he came back, just like his older brother. I said to him,
"Brother, didn't I advise you not to go?" He replied tearfully, "Brother, it
was foreordained. Now I am poor and penniless, without even a shirt on
my back." Demon, I took him to the public bath, clothed him in one of

---

7. Gold coins; the basic Muslim money units [Translator's note].

my new robes, and took him back to the shop. After we had something to eat, I said to him, "Brother, I shall do my business accounts, calculate my net worth for the year, and after subtracting the capital, whatever the profit happens to be, I shall divide it equally between you and myself. When I examined my books and subtracted the capital, I found out that my profit was two thousand dinars, and I thanked God and felt very happy. Then I divided the money, giving him a thousand dinars and keeping a thousand for myself. With that money he opened another shop, and the three of us stayed together for a while. Then my two brothers asked me to go on a trading journey with them, but I refused, saying, "What did you gain from your ventures that I can gain?"

They dropped the matter, and for six years we worked in our stores, buying and selling. Yet every year they asked me to go on a trading journey with them, but I refused, until I finally gave in. I said, "Brothers, I am ready to go with you. How much money do you have?" I found out that they had eaten and drunk and squandered everything they had, but I said nothing to them and did not reproach them. Then I took inventory, gathered all I had together, and sold everything. I was pleased to discover that the sale netted six thousand dinars. Then I divided the money into two parts, and said to my brothers, "The sum of three thousand dinars is for you and myself to use on our trading journey. The other three thousand I shall bury in the ground, in case what happened to you happens to me, so that when we return, we will find three thousand dinars to reopen our shops." They replied, "This is an excellent idea." Then, demon, I divided my money and buried three thousand dinars. Of the remaining three I gave each of my brothers a thousand and kept a thousand for myself. After I closed my shop, we bought merchandise and trading goods, rented a large seafaring boat, and after loading it with our goods and provisions, sailed day and night, for a month.

But morning overtook Shahrazad, and she lapsed into silence. Then her sister Dinarzad said, "Sister, what a lovely story!" Shahrazad replied, "Tomorrow night I shall tell you something even lovelier, stranger, and more wonderful if I live, the Almighty God willing."

THE SEVENTH NIGHT

The following night Dinarzad said to her sister Shahrazad, "For God's sake, sister, if you are not sleepy, tell us a little tale." The king added, "Let it be the completion of the story of the merchant and the demon." Shahrazad replied, "With the greatest pleasure":

I heard, O happy King, that the second old man said to the demon:

For a month my brothers, these very dogs, and I sailed the salty sea, until we came to a port city. We entered the city and sold our goods, earning ten dinars for every dinar. Then we bought other goods, and when we got to the seashore to embark, I met a girl who was dressed in tatters. She kissed my hands and said, "O my lord, be charitable and do me a favor, and I believe that I shall be able to reward you for it." I replied, "I

am willing to do you a favor regardless of any reward." She said, "O my lord, marry me, clothe me, and take me home with you on this boat, as your wife, for I wish to give myself to you. I, in turn, will reward you for your kindness and charity, the Almighty God willing. Don't be misled by my poverty and present condition." When I heard her words, I felt pity for her, and guided by what God the Most High had intended for me, I consented. I clothed her with an expensive dress and married her. Then I took her to the boat, spread the bed for her, and consummated our marriage. We sailed many days and nights, and I, feeling love for her, stayed with her day and night, neglecting my brothers. In the meantime they, these very dogs, grew jealous of me, envied me for my increasing merchandise and wealth, and coveted all our possessions. At last they decided to betray me and, tempted by the Devil, plotted to kill me. One night they waited until I was asleep beside my wife; then they carried the two of us and threw us into the sea.

When we awoke, my wife turned into a she-demon and carried me out of the sea to an island. When it was morning, she said, "Husband, I have rewarded you by saving you from drowning, for I am one of the demons who believe in God.[8] When I saw you by the seashore, I felt love for you and came to you in the guise in which you saw me, and when I expressed my love for you, you accepted me. Now I must kill your brothers." When I heard what she said, I was amazed and I thanked her and said, "As for destroying my brothers, this I do not wish, for I will not behave like them." Then I related to her what had happened to me and them, from beginning to end. When she heard my story, she got very angry at them, and said, "I shall fly to them now, drown their boat, and let them all perish." I entreated her, saying, "For God's sake, don't. The proverb advises 'Be kind to those who hurt you.' No matter what, they are my brothers after all." In this manner, I entreated her and pacified her. Afterward, she took me and flew away with me until she brought me home and put me down on the roof of my house. I climbed down, threw the doors open, and dug up the money I had buried. Then I went out and, greeting the people in the market, reopened my shop. When I came home in the evening, I found these two dogs tied up, and when they saw me, they came to me, wept, and rubbed themselves against me. I started, when I suddenly heard my wife say, "O my lord, these are your brothers." I asked, "Who has done this to them?" She replied, "I sent to my sister and asked her to do it. They will stay in this condition for ten years, after which they may be delivered." Then she told me where to find her and departed. The ten years have passed, and I was with my brothers on my way to her to have the spell lifted, when I met this man, together with this old man with the deer. When I asked him about himself, he told me about his encounter with you, and I resolved not to leave until I found out what would happen between you and him. This is my story. Isn't it amazing?

The demon replied, "By God, it is strange and amazing. I grant you one-third of my claim on him for his crime."

8. According to the Koran, God created both humans and demons (jinns), some of whom accepted Islam.

Then the third old man said, "Demon, don't disappoint me. If I told you a story that is stranger and more amazing than the first two would you grant me one-third of your claim on him for his crime?" The demon replied, "I will." Then the old man said, "Demon, listen":

But morning overtook Shahrazad, and she lapsed into silence. Then her sister said, "What an amazing story!" Shahrazad replied, "The rest is even more amazing." The king said to himself, "I will not have her put to death until I hear what happened to the old man and the demon; then I will have her put to death, as is my custom with the others."

THE EIGHTH NIGHT

The following night Dinarzad said to her sister Shahrazad, "For God's sake, sister, if you are not sleepy, tell us one of your lovely little tales to while away the night." Shahrazad replied, "With the greatest pleasure":

[The Third Old Man's Tale]⁹

The demon said, "This is a wonderful story, and I grant you a third of my claim on the merchant's life."

The third sheikh approached and said to the demon, "I will tell you a story more wonderful than these two if you will grant me a third of your claim on his life, O demon!"

To which the demon agreed.

So the sheikh began:

O sultan and chief of the demons, this mule was my wife. I had gone off on a journey and was absent from her for a whole year. At last I came to the end of my journey and returned home late one night. When I entered the house I saw a black slave lying in bed with her. They were chatting and dallying and laughing and kissing and quarreling together. When she saw me my wife leaped out of bed, ran to the water jug, recited a spell over it, then splashed me with some of the water and said, "Leave this form for the form of a dog."

Immediately I became a dog and she chased me out of the house. I ran out of the gate and didn't stop running until I reached a butcher's shop. I entered it and fell to eating the bones lying about. When the owner of the shop saw me, he grabbed me and carried me into his house. When his daughter saw me, she hid her face and said, "Why are you bringing this strange man in with you?"

"What man?" her father asked.

"This dog is a man whose wife has put a spell on him," she said, "but I can set him free again." She took a jug of water, recited a spell over it, then splashed a little water from it on me, and said, "Leave this shape for your original one."

And I became myself again. I kissed her hand and said, "I want to cast a spell on my wife as she did on me. Please give me a little of that water."

---

9. Because the earliest manuscript does not include a story for the third sheikh, later narrators supplied one. This brief anecdote comes from a manuscript found in the library of the Royal Academy in Madrid.

"Gladly," she said, "if you find her asleep, sprinkle a few drops on her and she will become whatever you wish."

Well, I did find her asleep, and I sprinkled some water on her and said, "Leave this shape for the shape of a she mule." She at once became the very mule you see here, oh sultan and chief of the demons."

The demon then turned to him and asked, "Is this really true?"

"Yes," he answered, nodding his head vigorously, "it's all true."

When the sheikh had finished his story, the demon shook with laughter and granted him a third of his claim on the merchant's blood.

Then the demon released the merchant and departed. The merchant turned to the three old men and thanked them, and they congratulated him on his deliverance and bade him good-bye. Then they separated, and each of them went on his way. The merchant himself went back home to his family, his wife, and his children, and he lived with them until the day he died. But this story is not as strange or as amazing as the story of the fisherman.

Dinarzad asked, "Please, sister, what is the story of the fisherman?" Shahrazad said: . . .

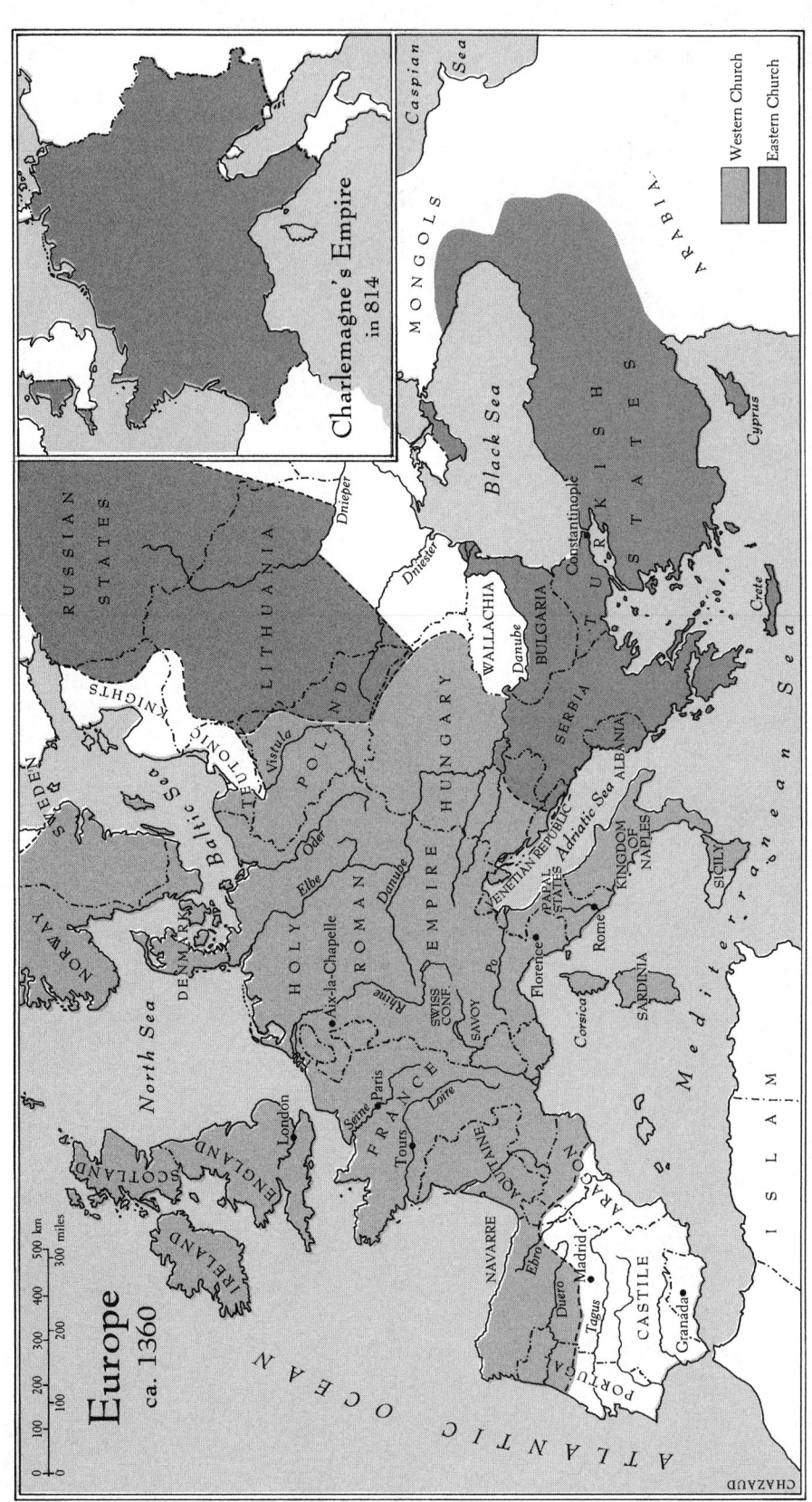

Europe
ca. 1360

300 miles

500 km

ATLANTIC OCEAN

IRELAND

SCOTLAND

ENGLAND

London

North Sea

NORWAY

SWEDEN

DENMARK

Baltic Sea

TEUTONIC KNIGHTS

RUSSIAN STATES

LITHUANIA

Dnieper

Dniester

POLAND

Vistula

Oder

Elbe

HOLY

ROMAN

EMPIRE

Aix-la-Chapelle

Rhine

HUNGARY

Danube

WALLACHIA

BULGARIA

Danube

Black Sea

Constantinople

T U R K I S H

S T A T E S

MONGOLS

Caspian Sea

ARABIA

SERBIA

ALBANIA

VENETIAN REPUBLIC

Adriatic Sea

PAPAL STATES

Florence

Po

SWISS CONF.

SAVOY

FRANCE

Seine

Paris

Loire

Tours

AQUITAINE

NAVARRE

ARAGON

Ebro

CASTILE

Duero

Madrid

Tagus

Granada

PORTUGAL

ISLAM

Mediterranean Sea

SARDINIA

Corsica

KINGDOM OF NAPLES

Rome

SICILY

Crete

Cyprus

Charlemagne's Empire
in 814

Western Church

Eastern Church

CHAZAUD

tors, and countless others skilled in the graphic and plastic arts; the biblical stories and scenes had the same meaning in every country. The stories of Charlemagne, Roland, Arthur, Aeneas, Troy, and Thebes were European literary property. They were handled and rehandled, copied, translated, adapted, expanded, condensed, and in general appropriated by innumerable authors, writing in various languages, with no thought of property rights or misgivings about plagiarism. There were no copyright regulations and no author's royalties to motivate insistence on individuality of authorship; there was comparatively little concern about the identity of the artist. Many medieval poems and tales are anonymous, including some of the greatest.

The submergence of the artist in the work is accounted for in part, at least, by the medieval system of human values. The dominant hierarchy of values—we have seen that it did not dominate universally, especially in the literature of northern Europe—was based on the Christian view of humanity. Men and women, in this conception, are creatures of God, toward whom they are inevitably oriented but from whom they are separated by the world in which they must live their earthly, mortal lives. Civilization under Christian direction may be regarded as ideally designed—even if not actually so functioning—to assist all people on their way to union with God. This is the criterion according to which the institutions of society and the patterns of its culture should ultimately be evaluated. Hence derive the scale, the order, the hierarchical categories of medieval life and thought. Because the spiritual side of humanity transcends the material, the saint becomes the ideal. The saint is one whose life is most fully subdued, assimilated, and ordered to the spiritual. On earth he or she may be a hermit, like Cuthbert; an abbess, like Hilda; a reformer of monasteries, like Bernard; a philosopher and a theologian, like Aquinas; a mystic, like Catharine of Siena; a king, like Louis IX of France; or a humble citizen in private life. As a whole, medieval literature is a study in human life judged according to this scale of values. The scale is represented clearly in Dante's *Divine Comedy*. Secular-value patterns may be assimilated to it, as in *The Song of Roland*, or it may be taken for granted without much emphasis, as in the works of Chaucer. For the modern reader it supplies a focus for the adequate reading and understanding of most of the literature of the Middle Ages.

FURTHER READING

Robert S. Hoyt, *Europe in the Middle Ages* (1957), is a general historical survey. For a view of medieval thought and culture as a whole, the standard older work is H. O. Taylor, *The Mediaeval Mind* (1925). E. K. Rand, *Founders of the Middle Ages* (1928), vividly portrays central figures from Ambrose and Jerome to Augustine. R. L. Fox, *Pagans and Christians* (1987), traces in full and lively detail the struggle between the religious orientations of the contending parties. C. S. Lewis, *The Discarded Image* (1964), offers an illuminating survey of the basic assumptions and outlook of medieval people. C. W. Previté-Orton, *Shorter Cambridge Medieval History* (1952), is an authoritative account of the period as a whole. Norman Daniel, *The Arabs and Medieval Europe* (1975), is a good introduction to Muslim influences on European thought and culture.

THE FORMATION OF A WESTERN LITERATURE

TEXTS	CONTEXTS
	732 Arab conquest of Europe blocked at Battle of Tours
8th century *Beowulf* • *The Wanderer* • *The Story of Deirdre*	**8th century** Chinese invention of gunpowder
	1009 Arab conquest of Jerusalem
	1066 Norman conquest of Britain
	1099 Knights of the First Crusade retake Jerusalem
12th century Marie de France, *Eliduc* • *The Song of Roland*	**12th century** Guido d'Arezzo invents first musical clef signs to denote pitch
	1187 Arabs recover Jerusalem
	1187–1192 Third Crusade fails to recapture the city, as do six later Crusades through the 13th century
	13th century Chinese invent movable type • Mongols under Jenghiz Khan establish vast empire embracing all of China and much of present-day Iran, Russia, and Turkey
	1215 King John of England forced by his barons to sign Magna Carta
1300s *Sir Gawain and the Green Knight* **1301–1321** Dante, *The Divine Comedy* **1353** Boccaccio, *The Decameron* finished **1390–1400** Chaucer, *Canterbury Tales* **1400s?** *Aucassin and Nicolette*	**14th century** Gunpowder introduced into Europe • Age of the great cathedrals • Duccio, Cimabue, and Giotto initiate a Golden Age of Italian painting • The Black Death (transmitted by fleas from infected rats) sweeps Europe and parts of Asia, killing more than half the population
	1453 Muslim Turks take Constantinople; flight of many scholars and manuscripts to the west

TEXTS	CONTEXTS
	1454 First dated European document from movable type is a papal indulgence printed in Mainz
1485? *Everyman*	**1455** Gutenberg prints the Bible, the first printed book

THE SONG OF ROLAND
twelfth century

With some literal inaccuracy, but with substantial truth, it has been said that French literature begins with *The Song of Roland*. Certainly it is the first great narrative poem in that language. Of unknown authorship and date, it was apparently composed in the decade or decades after 1100. Imbued with the spirit of the First Crusade, it seems to reproduce some details of the campaigns and expeditions to capture and hold the Holy Land for Christendom. The story it tells was developed from a historical incident in the career of Charlemagne (Charles the Great). As Charlemagne was returning from a successful war in northern Spain, the Gascons attacked his baggage train and rear guard in the mountain passes of the Pyrenees. The rear guard perished, including Roland, the prefect of the Breton March. These events occurred in 778. The poet of the twelfth century has transformed them—somewhat as Geoffrey of Monmouth, Chrétien de Troyes, and Malory transformed incidents involving the (probably also historical) Arthur, his exploits, and the deeds of his warriors. The Charles of the *Roland*, a magnificent figure, is white haired and venerable and not without a touch of the miraculous; though still valiant in fight, he is reputed among the enemy to be two hundred years old, or more. He is served especially by a choice band of leaders, the twelve peers, of whom the chief is Roland, his nephew—a relationship that in Heroic narrative intensifies either loyalty or disloyalty. The enemy, too, has been changed. Not a few border Gascons or Basques, but enormous Saracen armies fight against Roland and the emperor. Thus we have a holy war; all the motives of a Crusade are invoked in this struggle of Christians against Muslims. Keeping the emperor as the central *background* figure, the poet has concentrated his efforts on Roland as the hero, the central *foreground* character. Close beside him stand Oliver, the wise and faithful friend, and Ganelon, whose hatred of Roland leads him to treason against Charles.

The world of the poem is an idealization of feudal society in the early twelfth century. This society was headed by proud barons—a hereditary nobility—whose independent spirit found liberal scope in valiant action, fierce devotion, and bitter personal antagonism. A man was esteemed for his prowess in battle, for his loyalty to his king or other feudal chief, and for his wisdom, as the portrait of Oliver reminds us. The action of the poem is infused with a warm glow of patriotic feeling—not the flag-waving variety but a cherishing love of the homeland, "sweet France." It might be called regional rather than political patriotism, for in a feudal regime a man's binding obligations are to his lord rather than to the country as a whole. Yet the larger issue enters, in a special way: in the second half of the poem, Ganelon is finally condemned and punished because in compassing the destruction of Roland he has injured the king and the French nation; the poet denies Ganelon's claim that these are separable things.

The present volume includes only part of the first half of the poem, but this portion has a satisfactory completeness. We see the anger of Ganelon at Roland, out of which grows his treachery and the attack of the Saracens; the valor of Roland, and the rest, in battle; and their heroic death. The second half of the poem relates the vengeance taken by Charles against the Saracens—in two separate battles—and the trial and execution of Ganelon. Although *The Song of Roland* was the work, and probably the *written* work, of a well-educated man, during the period immediately following its composition, it was sung or chanted. It is divided into strophes averaging fourteen lines, each of ten (or eleven) syllables.

It is easy to see why modern French readers and critics assign the *Roland* a high place in their national literature. Inherent in its structure and texture are the qualities especially esteemed in the French literary tradition—clarity of focus, lucidity in exposition and narration, definite design, and mastery of technical detail. In the poem as a whole—even in the abridgment printed here—scale and proportion are evident. The succession of quarrels, treachery, and battles is only the raw material out of which the poet has built a highly wrought work of art. The emphasis on action—on what Roland, Ganelon, and Oliver do and say—has been recognized since Aristotle as the right method for a poet. But mere action is the formula of the adventure story. The great-literature standard requires that the action have significance—which the author of the *Roland* has provided in rich and ordered variety. The acts of the hero, of his friend, and of his foe are presented as part of the total character of each; they grow out of the whole man, including his temperament and personality. But they are also presented against an ethical and social background. Every act, every decision, bears a relation to the feudal code of conduct, of right and wrong, and hence is an indication of human good or evil. Courage rather than cowardice, loyalty rather than treachery, judgment rather than folly—a belief in these criteria is implicit or explicit in the presentation of each action. And they apply to the outermost frame within which the poet has placed the specific events of the narrative—the contest between Christianity and paganism. For to the author and his audience the Christian cause is just, the Saracen, unjust. Roland, fighting for the crusading emperor, is *right*; Ganelon, aiding the heathen enemy against his brother-in-arms, is doubly *wrong*.

The man who brings about the death of Roland and twenty thousand Franks is no mean and petty villain. The husband of the emperor's sister and the stepfather of Roland, he holds a very high place in Charles's council. Nor does he lack the ability or the personality to sustain this position. He has no hesitation in speaking against Roland in the first discussion of the Saracen proposals; his nomination as envoy to King Marsile is readily accepted by Charles, and his success in his treachery is a brilliant feat. To accomplish it he must first provoke the now peacefully inclined Marsile to wrath and then turn this anger against Roland. To this end he takes a calculated risk for the sake of a calculated—but far from guaranteed—result. Insulting Marsile deliberately, in the name of the emperor, he makes himself the first target of the Saracen king's fury and certainly endangers his own life. Luckily for him, the king's hand is stayed, and the Saracen nobles applaud Ganelon's magnificent courage. The rest is comparatively easy—though everything now depends on Ganelon's success in getting Roland placed in command of the rear guard. That he succeeds is the more credible because it was Roland who previously nominated Ganelon for the embassy: Roland and Charles may be expected to act, as in fact they do, on the principle that turn about is fair play.

To the twelfth-century poet and his audience of proud knights the question of motive in Ganelon's hatred of Roland doubtless presented little difficulty. Indeed, if Ganelon had not resorted to treason, a tenable defense of his attitude could be established. For it may well be that he is honestly opposed to the policy of relentless war against the Saracens. His speech at the first council, urging acceptance of Marsile's proposals, wins the support of the wise counselor Naimes and carries the day. An advocate of peace would obviously regard the uncompromising spokesman of the war party—Roland—as his opponent. Later, talking with the Saracen envoy Blancandrin, Ganelon plausibly represents Roland as the chief obstacle to pacific relations between the two peoples. To be sure, Ganelon is now plotting against Roland, but that should not blind us to the possibility that he honestly differs with Roland about this question of the emperor's foreign policy. When we have said this and when we have recognized the faults in Roland's personality that might

normally vex another powerful, but less powerful, courtier, we have said all that can be said in defense of Ganelon. His acts put him quite beyond the possibility of moral justification. But justifying him is one thing; understanding him is quite another, and this the author has enabled us to do.

In Roland the poet has created one of the great heroes of European literature. Like Achilles, Aeneas, and Hamlet, he is the embodiment of a definite ideal of humanity. The ideal that Roland incarnates is that of feudal chivalry. Roland exhibits in superlative degree the traits and attitudes that feudal society and institutions sought to produce in a whole class. He is a supremely valiant fighter, a completely faithful vassal, and a warmly affectionate friend, and because his creator lived in the early twelfth century, his fervent Christianity bears the Crusader's stamp. His words to his friend Oliver before the battle epitomize his vocation as he sees it:

> A man must bear some hardships for his lord,
> stand everything, the great heat, the great cold,
> lose the hide and hair on him for his good lord.
> Now let each man make sure to strike hard here:
> let them not sing a bad song about us!
> Pagans are wrong and Christians are right!
> They'll make no bad example of me this day!

This is the code of a man of action, of one to whom action appears as duty. Neither here nor elsewhere in the poem is Roland touched by any sense of the "doubtful doom of human kind" that haunts Aeneas. Nor is he ever plagued by Hamlet's doubts. In assurance and self-reliance he is much closer to Achilles, except that Achilles fought essentially for himself—certainly not for Agamemnon! In Roland the man is wholly assimilated to the vassal. The ceiling above him is lower, the pattern he follows is more limited, than those of Achilles, Aeneas, and Hamlet; yet within his pattern Roland achieves perfection, as they do in theirs.

Roland's feats in battle require no analysis; they are bright and glorious; they outshine the great deeds of his noble comrades. This superiority is no more than the poet has led us to expect. It is the hero's weakness—weakness counterpoised to his greatness—that gives the poem depth and produces the tension that commands our interest. Roland's defect has been called the excess of his special virtue—confidence, courage, bravery; if assurance outstrips prudence, then bravery becomes recklessness, which can bring disaster on the hero and those for whom he is responsible. The author carefully shows us that Roland has no habit or instinct of caution to match his marvelous courage. Charles notes the vindictive manner in which Ganelon proposes Roland for the rear guard, and though at a loss to divine its meaning, is moved to assign half his entire army to Roland. But Roland either has not noticed the gleam of triumph in Ganelon's eye or, if he has, loftily disregards it and firmly refuses to take more than twenty thousand men, a relatively small force.

So far Roland has done nothing definitely wrong, though he has revealed a certain lack of perception and of intuitive prudence. But he does do wrong when, surprised by an army of a hundred thousand Saracens, he refuses to blow the horn that would summon Charles to the rescue. The error is emphasized by the repetition in Oliver's effort to persuade him, and the relationship between Roland's refusal and his rashness of character is made apparent both through his answers and through the contrast with Oliver. Roland fears that asking for help would make him look foolish among the Franks—instead, he will slay the foe himself; he will not leave his kin at home open to reproach because of him; if, as Oliver

says, the rear guard is hopelessly outnumbered, then death is better than disgrace. Actually, Roland is confident of victory despite the odds. His judgment is not equal to his daring. As the poet summarizes, "Roland is fierce and Oliver wise."

The result is catastrophe. But it is catastrophe redeemed by glorious heroism, as well as self-sacrificing penitence. When, despite tremendous exploits of the Franks, especially by Roland, all but a handful of the rear guard have been slain, Roland wishes to sound the horn to let the emperor know what has happened. But now Oliver dissents on the ground of honor: Roland had refused to summon Charles to a rescue, and it would be shameful to summon him only to witness a disaster. The repetitions in this scene balance those of the earlier one. Though the question is decided by Archbishop Turpin, the argument has embittered Oliver against Roland. Hence it is that when, blinded by his own blood, Oliver later strikes Roland, his comrade has to ask whether the blow was intentional. Roland's humility here is a part of his penitence, a penitence never put into words but sublimely revealed in deeds. Exhausted by battle as he is, his superhuman and repeated blasts on the horn burst his temples. The angels and archangels who receive his soul in Paradise are functional symbols of his final triumph in defeat. The poet does not remit the penalty of Roland's error, which is paid by his death. But his victory combines an epic with a tragic conclusion; atonement and redemption, not merely death, is the end, as it is in another profoundly Christian poem of action, Milton's *Samson Agonistes*.

The best summary in English of information about the origin and nature of the poem is contained in the introduction to the edition by T. A. Jenkins, *La Chanson de Roland* (1924). For discussion against the background of the *chanson de geste* in general, see Urban Tigner Holmes, *A History of Old French Literature* (1938). P. le Gentil, *The "Chanson de Roland"* (1969), provides technical information in the first half and a more general commentary in the second. J. J. Duggan, *The Song of Roland* (1979), makes the strongest case for it as the work of an oral poet. Frederick Goldin, *The Song of Roland* (1978), contains a valuable introduction. Another excellent book for the general reader is Eugene Vance, *Reading the Song of Roland* (1970). The most comprehensive and detailed recent scholarly work is Gerald S. Brault, *The Song of Roland: An Analytical Edition* (1978), 2 vols. Also to be consulted is R. F. Cook, *The Sense of the Song of Roland* (1987).

PRONOUNCING GLOSSARY

The following list uses common English syllables to provide rough equivalents of selected words whose pronunciation may be unfamiliar to the general reader.

Aquitaine: *ah-kee-ten*	Haltille: *ahl-tee-yuh*
Blancandrin: *blanh-cahn-drinh*	Marsilion: *mahr-see-lyonh'*
Durendal: *dur-ahn-dahl*	Munjoie: *munh-zhwah*
Gerer: *zhehr-air'*	Ogier: *oh-zhyay*
Gerin: *zhehr-anh'*	Roland: *roh-lanh*
Halteclere: *ahl-te-clehr'*	Veillantif: *ve-yanh-teef*

From The Song of Roland[1]

1

Charles the King, our Emperor, the Great,
has been in Spain for seven full years,
has conquered the high land down to the sea.
There is no castle that stands against him now,
no wall, no citadel left to break down—   5
except Saragossa, high on a mountain.[2]
King Marsilion holds it, who does not love God,
who serves Mahumet and prays to Apollin.[3]
He cannot save himself: his ruin will find him there. AOI.[4]

2

King Marsilion was in Saragossa.   10
He has gone forth into a grove, beneath its shade,
and he lies down on a block of blue marble,
twenty thousand men, and more, all around him.
He calls aloud to his dukes and his counts:
"Listen, my lords, to the troubles we have.   15
The Emperor Charles of the sweet land of France
has come into this country to destroy us.
I have no army able to give him battle,
I do not have the force to break his force.
Now act like my wise men: give me counsel,   20
save me, save me from death, save me from shame!"
No pagan there has one word to say to him
except Blancandrin, of the castle of Valfunde.

3

One of the wisest pagans was Blancandrin,
brave and loyal, a great mounted warrior,   25
a useful man, the man to aid his lord;
said to the King: "Do not give way to panic.
Do this: send Charles, that wild, terrible man,
tokens of loyal service and great friendship:
you will give him bears and lions and dogs,   30
seven hundred camels, a thousand molted hawks,
four hundred mules weighed down with gold and silver,
and fifty carts, to cart it all away:
he'll have good wages for his men who fight for pay.
Say he's made war long enough in this land: 35
let him go home, to France, to Aix, at last—
come Michaelmas[5] you will follow him there,
say you will take their faith, become a Christian,

---

1. Translated by Frederick Goldin. Many of Goldin's notes have been adapted for use here.   2. Saragossa, in northeastern Spain, is not actually on a mountaintop. The poet's geography is not always accurate.   3. The Greek god Apollo; but the poet is mistaken, for these people worship only one god, Allah. *Mahumet:* Muhammed, founder of the Islamic religion.   4. These three mysterious letters appear at certain moments throughout the text, 180 times in all. No one has ever adequately explained them, though every reader feels their effect.   5. The feast of St. Michael, September 29. Aix: Aix-la-Chapelle, or Aachen, was the capital of Charlemagne's empire.

and be his man with honor, with all you have.
If he wants hostages, why, you'll send them,   40
ten, or twenty, to give him security.
Let us send him the sons our wives have borne.
I'll send my son with all the others named to die.
It is better that they should lose their heads[6]
than that we, Lord, should lose our dignity   45
and our honors—and be turned into beggars!" AOI.

4

Said Blancandrin: "By this right hand of mine
and by this beard that flutters on my chest,
you will soon see the French army disband,
the Franks will go to their own land, to France.   50
When each of them is in his dearest home,
King Charles will be in Aix, in his chapel.
At Michaelmas he will hold a great feast—
that day will come, and then our time runs out,
he'll hear no news, he'll get no word from us.   55
This King is wild, the heart in him is cruel:
he'll take the heads of the hostages we gave.
It is better, Lord, that they lose their heads
than that we lose our bright, our beautiful Spain—
and nothing more for us but misery and pain!"   60
The pagans say: "It may be as he says."

6

Marsilion brought his council to an end,
said to his men: "Lords, you will go on now,
and remember: olive branches in your hands;   80
and in my name tell Charlemagne the King
for his god's sake to have pity on me—
he will not see a month from this day pass
before I come with a thousand faithful;
say I will take that Christian religion   85
and be his man in love and loyalty.
If he wants hostages, why, he'll have them."
Said Blancandrin: "Now you will get good terms." AOI.

7

King Marsilion had ten white mules led out,
sent to him once by the King of Suatilie,[7]   90
with golden bits and saddles wrought with silver.
The men are mounted, the men who brought the message,
and in their hands they carry olive branches.
They came to Charles, who has France in his keeping.
He cannot prevent it: they will fool him. AOI.   95

6. The speaker expects that the hostages will be killed by the French when the deception becomes
clear. Sometime before, hostages sent by the French had been similarly slain (see lines 207–9).   7. A
subordinate king, owing allegiance to Marsilion.

8

The Emperor is secure and jubilant:
he has taken Cordres, broken the walls,
knocked down the towers with his catapults.
And what tremendous spoils his knights have won—
gold and silver, precious arms, equipment.   100
In the city not one pagan remained
who is not killed or turned into a Christian.
The Emperor is in an ample grove,
Roland and Oliver are with him there,
Samson the Duke and Ansëis the fierce,   105
Geoffrey d'Anjou, the King's own standard-bearer;
and Gerin and Gerer, these two together always,
and the others, the simple knights, in force:
fifteen thousand from the sweet land of France.
The warriors sit on bright brocaded silk;   110
they are playing at tables to pass the time,
the old and the wisest men sitting at chess,
the young light-footed men fencing with swords.
Beneath a pine, beside a wild sweet-briar,
there was a throne, every inch of pure gold.   115
There sits the King, who rules over sweet France.
His beard is white, his hair flowering white.
That lordly body! the proud fierce look of him!—
If someone should come here asking for him,
      there'd be no need to point out the King of France.
The messengers dismounted, and on their feet   120
they greeted him in all love and good faith.

9

Blancandrin spoke, he was the first to speak,
said to the King: "Greetings, and God save you,
that glorious God whom we all must adore.
Here is the word of the great king Marsilion: 125
he has looked into this law of salvation,
wants to give you a great part of his wealth,
bears and lions and hunting dogs on chains,
seven hundred camels, a thousand molted hawks,
four hundred mules packed tight with gold and silver,   130
and fifty carts, to cart it all away;
and there will be so many fine gold bezants,[8]
you'll have good wages for the men in your pay.
You have stayed long—long enough!—in this land,
it is time to go home, to France, to Aix.   135
My master swears he will follow you there."
The Emperor holds out his hands toward God,
bows down his head, begins to meditate. AOI.

8. Gold coins; the name is derived from Byzantium.

10

The Emperor held his head bowed down;
never was he too hasty with his words: 140
his custom is to speak in his good time.
When his head rises, how fierce the look of him;
he said to them: "You have spoken quite well.
King Marsilion is my great enemy.
Now all these words that you have spoken here— 145
how far can I trust them? How can I be sure?"
The Saracen: "He wants to give you hostages.
How many will you want? ten? fifteen? twenty?
I'll put my son with the others named to die.[9]
You will get some, I think, still better born. 150
When you are at home in your high royal palace,
at the great feast of Saint Michael-in-Peril,[1]
the lord who nurtures me will follow you,
and in those baths[2]—the baths God made for you—
my lord will come and want to be made Christian." 155
King Charles replies: "He may yet save his soul." AOI.

11

Late in the day it was fair, the sun was bright.
Charles has them put the ten mules into stables.
The King commands a tent pitched in the broad grove,
and there he has the ten messengers lodged; 160
twelve serving men took splendid care of them.
There they remained that night till the bright day.
The Emperor rose early in the morning,
the King of France, and heard the mass and matins.
And then the King went forth beneath a pine, 165
calls for his barons to complete his council:
he will proceed only with the men of France. AOI.

13

"Barons, my lords," said Charles the Emperor, 180
"King Marsilion has sent me messengers,
wants to give me a great mass of his wealth,
bears and lions and hunting dogs on chains,
seven hundred camels, a thousand molting hawks,
four hundred mules packed with gold of Araby, 185
and with all that, more than fifty great carts;
but also asks that I go back to France:
he'll follow me to Aix, my residence,
and take our faith, the one redeeming faith,
become a Christian, hold his march[3] lands from me. 190
But what lies in his heart? I do not know."
And the French say: "We must be on our guard!" AOI.

9. That is, if the promise is broken. *Saracen:* the usual term for the enemy.   1. The epithet "in peril of the sea" was applied to the famous sanctuary Mont-St.-Michel off the Normandy coast because it could be reached on foot only at low tide, and pilgrims were endangered by the incoming tide. Eventually, the phrase was applied to the saint himself.   2. Famous healing springs at Aix-la-Chapelle.
3. A frontier province or territory.

14

The Emperor has told them what was proposed.
Roland the Count will never assent to that,
gets to his feet, comes forth to speak against it;   195
says to the King: "Trust Marsilion—and suffer!
We came to Spain seven long years ago,
I won Noples for you, I won Commibles,
I took Valterne and all the land of Pine,
and Balaguer and Tudela and Seville.   200
And then this king, Marsilion, played the traitor:
he sent you men, fifteen of his pagans—
and sure enough, each held an olive branch;
and they recited just these same words to you.
You took counsel with all your men of France;   205
they counseled you to a bit of madness:
you sent two Counts across to the Pagans,
one was Basan, the other was Basile.
On the hills below Haltille, he took their heads.
They were your men. Fight the war you came to fight!   210
Lead the army you summoned on to Saragossa!
Lay siege to it all the rest of your life!
Avenge the men that this criminal murdered!" AOI.

15

The Emperor held his head bowed down with this,
and stroked his beard, and smoothed his mustache down,   215
and speaks no word, good or bad, to his nephew.
The French keep still, all except Ganelon:
he gets to his feet and, come before King Charles,
how fierce he is as he begins his speech;
said to the King: "Believe a fool—me or   220
another—and suffer! Protect your interest!
When Marsilion the King sends you his word
that he will join his hands[4] and be your man,
and hold all Spain as a gift from your hands
and then receive the faith that we uphold—   225
whoever urges that we refuse this peace,
that man does not care, Lord, what death we die.
That wild man's counsel must not win the day here—
let us leave fools, let us hold with wise men!" AOI.

16

And after that there came Naimon the Duke—   230
no greater vassal in that court than Naimon—
said to the King: "You've heard it clearly now,
Count Ganelon has given you your answer:
let it be heeded, there is wisdom in it.
King Marsilion is beaten in this war,   235
you have taken every one of his castles,
broken his walls with your catapults,

---

4. Part of the gesture of homage; the lord enclosed the joined hands of his vassal with his own.

burnt his cities and defeated his men.
Now when he sends to ask you to have mercy,
it would be a sin to do still more to him.   240
Since he'll give you hostages as guarantee,
this great war must not go on, it is not right."
And the French say: "The Duke has spoken well." AOI.

20

"My noble knights," said the Emperor Charles,
"choose me one man: a baron from my march,[5]   275
to bring my message to King Marsilion."
And Roland said: "Ganelon, my stepfather."
The French respond: "Why, that's the very man!
pass this man by and you won't send a wiser."
And hearing this Count Ganelon began to choke,   280
pulls from his neck the great furs of marten
and stands there now, in his silken tunic,
eyes full of lights, the look on him of fury,
he has the body, the great chest of a lord;
stood there so fair, all his peers gazed on him;   285
said to Roland: "Madman, what makes you rave?
Every man knows I am your stepfather,
yet you named me to go to Marsilion.
Now if God grants that I come back from there,
you will have trouble: I'll start a feud with you,   290
it will go on till the end of your life."
Roland replies: "What wild words—all that blustering!
Every man knows that threats don't worry me.
But we need a wise man to bring the message:
if the King wills, I'll gladly go in your place."   295

21

Ganelon answers: "You will not go for me. AOI.
You're not my man, and I am not your lord.
Charles commands me to perform this service:
I'll go to Marsilion in Saragossa.
And I tell you, I'll play a few wild tricks   300
before I cool the anger in me now."

*   *   *

25

The Emperor offers him his right glove.
But Ganelon would have liked not to be there.
When he had to take it, it fell to the ground.
"God!" say the French, "What's that going to mean?
What disaster will this message bring us!"   335
Said Ganelon: "Lords, you'll be hearing news."

---

5. Charlemagne wants them to choose a baron from an outlying region and not one of the Twelve
Peers, the circle of his dearest men.

26

Said Ganelon: "Lord, give me leave to go,
since go I must, there's no reason to linger."
And the King said: "In Jesus' name and mine,"
absolved him and blessed him with his right hand.   340
Then he gave him the letter and the staff.

27

Count Ganelon goes away to his camp.
He chooses, with great care, his battle-gear,
picks the most precious arms that he can find.
The spurs he fastened on were golden spurs;   345
he girds his sword, Murgleis, upon his side;
he has mounted Tachebrun, his battle horse,
his uncle, Guinemer, held the stirrup.
And there you would have seen brave men in tears,
his men, who say: "Baron, what bad luck for you!   350
All your long years in the court of the King,
always proclaimed a great and noble vassal!
Whoever it was doomed you to go down there—
Charlemagne himself will not protect that man.
Roland the Count should not have thought of this—   355
and you the living issue of a mighty line!"
And then they say: "Lord, take us there with you!"
Ganelon answers: "May the Lord God forbid!
It is better that I alone should die
        than so many good men and noble knights.
You will be going back, Lords, to sweet France: 360
go to my wife and greet her in my name,
and Pinabel, my dear friend and peer,
and Baldewin, my son, whom you all know:
give him your aid, and hold him as your lord."
And he starts down the road; he is on his way. AOI.   365

28

Ganelon rides to a tall olive tree,
there he has joined the pagan messengers.
And here is Blancandrin, who slows down for him:
and what great art they speak to one another.
Said Blancandrin: "An amazing man, Charles!   370
conquered Apulia, conquered all of Calabria,
crossed the salt sea on his way into England,
won its tribute,[6] got Peter's pence[7] for Rome:
what does he want from us here in our march?"
Ganelon answers: "That is the heart in him.   375
There'll never be a man the like of him." AOI.

---

6. Although begun perhaps as early as the 8th century, the tribute was not the result of any effort of
Charlemagne, who did not in fact visit England.   7. A tribute of one penny per house "for the use of
Saint Peter," that is, for the Pope in Rome.

29

Said Blancandrin: "The Franks are a great people.
Now what great harm all those dukes and counts do
to their own lord when they give him such counsel:
they torment him, they'll destroy him, and others."   380
Ganelon answers: "Well, now, I know no such man
except Roland, who'll suffer for it yet.
One day the Emperor was sitting in the shade:
his nephew came, still wearing his hauberk,
he had gone plundering near Carcassonne;   385
and in his hand he held a bright red apple:
'Dear Lord, here, take,' said Roland to his uncle;
'I offer you the crowns of all earth's kings.'
Yes, Lord, that pride of his will destroy him,
for every day he goes riding at death.   390
And *should* someone kill him, we would have peace." AOI.

30

Said Blancandrin: "A wild man, this Roland!
wants to make every nation beg for his mercy
and claims a right to every land on earth!
But what men support him, if that is his aim?"   395
Ganelon answers: "Why, Lord, the men of France.
They love him so, they will never fail him.
He gives them gifts, masses of gold and silver,
mules, battle horses, brocaded silks, supplies.
And it is all as the Emperor desires: 400
he'll win the lands from here to the Orient." AOI.

31

Ganelon and Blancandrin rode on until
each pledged his faith to the other and swore
they'd find a way to have Count Roland killed.

* * *

32

Blancandrin came before Marsilion,
his hand around the fist of Ganelon,   415
said to the King: "May Mahumet save you,
and Apollin, whose sacred laws we keep!
We delivered your message to Charlemagne:
when we finished, he raised up both his hands
and praised his god. He made no other answer.   420
Here he sends you one of his noble barons,
a man of France, and very powerful.
You'll learn from him whether or not you'll have peace."
"Let him speak, we shall hear him," Marsilion answers. AOI.

33

But Ganelon had it all well thought out.   425
With what great art he commences his speech,
a man who knows his way about these things;
said to the King: "May the Lord God save you,
that glorious God, whom we must all adore.
Here is the word of Charlemagne the King: 430
you are to take the holy Christian faith;
he will give you one half of Spain in fief.
If you refuse, if you reject this peace,
you will be taken by force, put into chains,
and then led forth to the King's seat at Aix;   435
you will be tried; you will be put to death:
you will die there, in shame, vilely, degraded."
King Marsilion, hearing this, was much shaken.
In his hand was a spear, with golden feathers.
He would have struck, had they not held him back. AOI.   440

36

Now Ganelon drew closer to the King
and said to him: "You are wrong to get angry,
for Charles, who rules all France, sends you this word: 470
you are to take the Christian people's faith;
he will give you one half of Spain in fief,
the other half goes to his nephew: Roland—
quite a partner you will be getting there!
If you refuse, if you reject this peace,   475
he will come and lay siege to Saragossa;
you will be taken by force, put into chains,
and brought straight on to Aix, the capital.
No saddle horse, no war horse for you then,
no he-mule, no she-mule for you to ride: 480
you will be thrown on some miserable dray;
you will be tried, and you will lose your head.
Our Emperor sends you this letter."
He put the letter in the pagan's right fist.

39

Said Marsilion: "My dear Lord Ganelon,
that was foolish, what I just did to you,
I showed my anger, even tried to strike you.
Here's a pledge of good faith, these sable furs,   515
the gold alone worth over five hundred pounds:
I'll make it all up before tomorrow night."
Ganelon answers: "I will not refuse it.
May it please God to reward you for it." AOI.

42

Said the pagan: "Truly, how I must marvel   550
at Charlemagne, who is so gray and white—

over two hundred years, from what I hear;
gone through so many lands a conqueror,
and borne so many blows from strong sharp spears,
killed and conquered so many mighty kings: 555
when will he lose the heart for making war?"
"Never," said Ganelon, "while one man lives: Roland!
no man like him from here to the Orient!
There's his companion, Oliver, a brave man.
And the Twelve Peers, whom Charles holds very dear,   560
form the vanguard, with twenty thousand Franks.
Charles is secure, he fears no man alive." AOI.

43

"Dear Lord Ganelon," said Marsilion the King,
"I have my army, you won't find one more handsome:
I can muster four hundred thousand knights!   565
With this host, now, can I fight Charles and the French?"
Ganelon answers: "No, no, don't try that now,
you'd take a loss: thousands of your pagans!
Forget such foolishness, listen to wisdom:
send the Emperor so many gifts   570
there'll be no Frenchman there who does not marvel.
For twenty hostages—those you'll be sending—
he will go home: home again to sweet France!
And he will leave his rear-guard behind him.
There will be Roland, I do believe, his nephew,   575
and Oliver, brave man, born to the court.
These Counts are dead, if anyone trusts me.
Then Charles will see that great pride of his go down,
he'll have no heart to make war on you again." AOI.

44

"Dear Lord Ganelon," said Marsilion the King,   580
"What must I do to kill Roland the Count?"
Ganelon answers: "Now I can tell you that.
The King will be at Cize,[8] in the great passes,
he will have placed his rear-guard at his back:
there'll be his nephew, Count Roland, that great man,   585
and Oliver, in whom he puts such faith,
and twenty thousand Franks in their company.
Now send one hundred thousand of your pagans
against the French—let them give the first battle.
The French army will be hit hard and shaken.   590
I must tell you: your men will be martyred.
Give them a second battle, then, like the first.
One will get him, Roland will not escape.
Then you'll have done a deed, a noble deed,
and no more war for the rest of your life!" AOI.   595

---

8. The pass through the Pyrenees.

45

"If someone can bring about the death of Roland,
then Charles would lose the right arm of his body,
that marvelous army would disappear—
never again could Charles gather such forces.
Then peace at last for the Land of Fathers!"[9] 600
When Marsilion heard that, he kissed his neck.
Then he begins to open up his treasures. AOI.

47

There stood a throne made all of ivory.
Marsilion commands them bring forth a book: 610
it was the law of Mahum and Tervagant.[1]
This is the vow sworn by the Saracen of Spain:
if he shall find Roland in the rear-guard,
he shall fight him, all his men shall fight him,
and once he finds Roland, Roland will die. 615
Says Ganelon: "May it be as you will." AOI.

52

Marsilion took Ganelon by the shoulder
and said to him: "You're a brave man, a wise man.
Now by that faith you think will save your soul,
take care you do not turn your heart from us. 650
I will give you a great mass of my wealth,
ten mules weighed down with fine Arabian gold;
and come each year, I'll do the same again.
Now you take these, the keys to this vast city:
present King Charles with all of its great treasure; 655
then get me Roland picked for the rear-guard.
Let me find him in some defile or pass,
I will fight him, a battle to the death."
Ganelon answers: "It's high time that I go."
Now he is mounted, and he is on his way. AOI. 660

54

The Emperor rose early in the morning,
the King of France, and has heard mass and matins. 670
On the green grass he stood before his tent.
Roland was there, and Oliver, brave man,
Naimon the Duke, and many other knights.
Ganelon came, the traitor, the foresworn.
With what great cunning he commences his speech; 675
said to the King: "May the Lord God save you!
Here I bring you the keys to Saragossa.
And I bring you great treasure from that city,
and twenty hostages, have them well guarded.

---

9. *Tere Major*, in the original; it can mean either "the great land" or "the land of fathers, ancestors." It always refers to France.   1. A fictitious deity whom the poet mistakenly says the Saracens worshiped.

And good King Marsilion sends you this word: 680
Do not blame him concerning the Algalife:
I saw it all myself, with my own eyes:
      four hundred thousand men, and all in arms,
their hauberks on, some with their helms laced on,
swords on their belts, the hilts enameled gold,
who went with him to the edge of the sea.   685
They are in flight: it is the Christian faith—
they do not want it, they will not keep its law.
They had not sailed four full leagues out to sea
when a high wind, a tempest swept them up.
They were all drowned; you will never see them;   690
if he were still alive, I'd have brought him.
As for the pagan King, Lord, believe this:
before you see one month from this day pass,
he'll follow you to the Kingdom of France
and take the faith—he will take your faith, Lord,   695
and join his hands and become your vassal.
He will hold Spain as a fief from your hand."
Then the King said: "May God be thanked for this.
You have done well, you will be well rewarded."
Throughout the host they sound a thousand trumpets.   700
The French break camp, strap their gear on their pack-horses.
They take the road to the sweet land of France. AOI.

55

King Charlemagne laid waste the land of Spain,
stormed its castles, ravaged its citadels.
The King declares his war is at an end.   705
The Emperor rides toward the land of sweet France.
Roland the Count affixed the gonfanon,[8]
raised it toward heaven on the height of a hill;
the men of France make camp across that country.
Pagans are riding up through these great valleys,   710
their hauberks on, their tunics of double mail,
their helms laced on, their swords fixed on their belts,
shields on their necks, lances trimmed with their banners.
In a forest high in the hills they gathered:
four hundred thousand men waiting for dawn.   715
God, the pity of it! the French do not know! AOI.

58

The day goes by, and the bright dawn arises.
Throughout that host. . . .[3]
The Emperor rides forth with such fierce pride.
"Barons, my lords," said the Emperor Charles,   740
"look at those passes, at those narrow defiles—
pick me a man to command the rear-guard."
Ganelon answers: "Roland, here, my stepson.
You have no baron as great and brave as Roland."

---

2. Pennant.   3. Rest of line unintelligible in the manuscript.

When he hears that, the King stares at him in fury;   745
and said to him: "You are the living devil,
a mad dog—the murderous rage in you!
And who will precede me, in the vanguard?"
Ganelon answers, "Why, Ogier of Denmark,
you have no baron who could lead it so well."   750

59

Roland the Count, when he heard himself named,
knew what to say, and spoke as a knight must speak:
"Lord Stepfather, I have to cherish you!
You have had the rear-guard assigned to me.
Charles will not lose, this great King who rules France,   755
I swear it now, one palfrey, one war horse—
    while I'm alive and know what's happening—
one he-mule, one she-mule that he might ride,
Charles will not lose one sumpter, not one pack horse
that has not first been bought and paid for with swords."
Ganelon answers: "You speak the truth, I know." AOI.   760

61

"Just Emperor," said Roland, that great man,
"give me the bow that you hold in your hand.
And no man here, I think, will say in reproach
I let it drop, as Ganelon let the staff drop[4]
from his right hand, when he should have taken it."   770
The Emperor bowed down his head with this,
he pulled his beard, he twisted his mustache,
cannot hold back, tears fill his eyes, he weeps.

62

And after that there came Naimon the Duke,
no greater vassal in the court than Naimon,   775
said to the King: "You've heard it clearly now:
it is Count Roland. How furious he is.
He is the one to whom the rear-guard falls,
no baron here can ever change that now.
Give him the bow that you have stretched and bent,   780
and then find him good men to stand with him."
The King gives him the bow; Roland has it now.

63

The Emperor calls forth Roland the Count:
"My lord, my dear nephew, of course you know
I will give you half my men, they are yours.   785
Let them serve you, it is your salvation."
"None of that!" said the Count. "May God strike me
if I discredit the history of my line.

---

4. In this *laisse* a reviser tried to make the text more consistent by adding the reference to the staff.

I'll keep twenty thousand Franks—they are good men.
Go your way through the passes, you will be safe.   790
You must not fear any man while I live."

68

King Charles the Great cannot keep from weeping.
A hundred thousand Franks feel pity for him;
and for Roland, an amazing fear.
Ganelon the criminal has betrayed him;
got gifts for it from the pagan king,   845
gold and silver, cloths of silk, gold brocade,
mules and horses and camels and lions.
Marsilion sends for the barons of Spain,
counts and viscounts and dukes and almaçurs,
and the emirs,[5] and the sons of great lords: 850
four hundred thousand assembled in three days.
In Saragossa he has them beat the drums,
they raise Mahumet upon the highest tower:
no pagan now who does not worship him
and adore him. Then they ride, racing each other,   855
search through the land, the valleys, the mountains;
and then they saw the banners of the French.
The rear-guard of the Twelve Companions
will not fail now, they'll give the pagans battle.

80

Oliver climbs to the top of a hill,
looks to his right, across a grassy vale,
sees the pagan army on its way there;
and called down to Roland, his companion: 1020
"That way, toward Spain: the uproar I see coming!
All their hauberks, all blazing, helmets like flames!
It will be a bitter thing for our French.
Ganelon knew, that criminal, that traitor,
when he marked us out before the Emperor."   1025
"Be still, Oliver," Roland the Count replies.
"He is my stepfather—my stepfather.
    I won't have you speak one word against him."

82

Said Oliver: "I saw the Saracens,
no man on earth ever saw more of them—   1040
one hundred thousand, with their shields, up in front,
helmets laced on, hauberks blazing on them,
the shafts straight up, the iron heads like flames—
you'll get a battle, nothing like it before.
My lords, my French, may God give you the strength.   1045
Hold your ground now! Let them not defeat us!"
And the French say: "God hate the man who runs!
We may die here, but no man will fail you." AOI.

5. All lords of high rank.

83

Said Oliver: "The pagan force is great;
from what I see, our French here are too few.
Roland, my companion, sound your horn then,   1050
Charles will hear it, the army will come back."
Roland replies: "I'd be a fool to do it.
I would lose my good name all through sweet France.
I will strike now, I'll strike with Durendal,   1055
the blade will be bloody to the gold from striking!
These pagan traitors came to these passes doomed!
I promise you, they are marked men, they'll die." AOI.

86

Said Oliver: "I see no blame in it—
I watched the Saracens coming from Spain,
the valleys and mountains covered with them,
every hillside and every plain all covered,   1085
hosts and hosts everywhere of those strange men—
and here we have a little company."
Roland replies: "That whets my appetite.
May it not please God and his angels and saints
to let France lose its glory because of me—   1090
let me not end in shame, let me die first.
The Emperor loves us when we fight well."

87

Roland is good, and Oliver is wise,
both these vassals men of amazing courage:
once they are armed and mounted on their horses,   1095
they will not run, though they die for it, from battle.
Good men, these Counts, and their words full of spirit.
Traitor pagans are riding up in fury.
Said Oliver: "Roland, look—the first ones,
on top of us—and Charles is far away.   1100
You did not think it right to sound your olifant:
if the King were here, we'd come out without losses.
Now look up there, toward the passes of Aspre—
you can see the rear-guard: it will suffer.
No man in that detail will be in another."   1105
Roland replies: "Don't speak such foolishness—
shame on the heart gone coward in the chest.
We'll hold our ground, we'll stand firm—we're the ones!
We'll fight with spears, we'll fight them hand to hand!" AOI.

88

When Roland sees that there will be a battle,   1110
it makes him fiercer than a lion or leopard;
shouts to the French, calls out to Oliver:
"Lord, companion: friend, do not say such things.
The Emperor, who left us these good French,
had set apart these twenty thousand men: 1115

he knew there was no coward in their ranks.
A man must meet great troubles for his lord,
stand up to the great heat and the great cold,
give up some flesh and blood—it is his duty.
Strike with the lance, I'll strike with Durendal—   1120
it was the King who gave me this good sword!
If I die here, the man who gets it can say:
it was a noble's, a vassal's, a good man's sword."

89

And now there comes the Archbishop Turpin.
He spurs his horse, goes up into a mountain,   1125
summons the French; and he preached them a sermon:
"Barons, my lords, Charles left us in this place.
We know our duty: to die like good men for our King.
Fight to defend the holy Christian faith.
Now you will have a battle, you know it now,   1130
you see the Saracens with your own eyes.
Confess your sins, pray to the Lord for mercy.
I will absolve you all, to save your souls.
If you die here, you will stand up holy martyrs,
you will have seats in highest Paradise."   1135
The French dismount, cast themselves on the ground;
the Archbishop blesses them in God's name.
He commands them to do one penance: strike.

90

The French arise, stand on their feet again;
they are absolved, released from all their sins: 1140
the Archbishop has blessed them in God's name.
Now they are mounted on their swift battle horses,
bearing their arms like faithful warriors;
and every man stands ready for the battle.
Roland the Count calls out to Oliver: 1145
"Lord, Companion, you knew it, you were right,
Ganelon watched for his chance to betray us,
got gold for it, got goods for it, and money.
The Emperor will have to avenge us now.
King Marsilion made a bargain for our lives,   1150
but still must pay, and that must be with swords." AOI.

92

Said Oliver: "I will waste no more words.   1170
You did not think it right to sound your olifant,
there'll be no Charles coming to your aid now.
He knows nothing, brave man, he's done no wrong;
those men down there—they have no blame in this.
Well, then, ride now, and ride with all your might!   1175
Lords, you brave men, stand your ground, hold the field!
Make up your minds, I beg you in God's name,

to strike some blows, take them and give them back!
Here we must not forget Charlemagne's war cry."
And with that word the men of France cried out.   1180
A man who heard that shout: Munjoie! Munjoie![6]
would always remember what manhood is.
Then they ride, God! Look at their pride and spirit!
and they spur hard, to ride with all their speed,
come on to strike—what else would these men do?   1185
The Saracens kept coming, never fearing them.
Franks and pagans, here they are, at each other.

93

Marsilion's nephew is named Aëlroth.
He rides in front, at the head of the army,
comes on shouting insults against our French: 1190
"French criminals, today you fight our men.
One man should have saved you: he betrayed you.
A fool, your King, to leave you in these passes.
This is the day sweet France will lose its name,
and Charlemagne the right arm of his body."   1195
When he hears that—God!—Roland is outraged!
He spurs his horse, gives Veillantif its head.
The Count comes on to strike with all his might,
smashes his shield, breaks his hauberk apart,
and drives: rips through his chest, shatters the bones,   1200
knocks the whole backbone out of his back,
casts out the soul of Aëlroth with his lance;
which he thrusts deep, makes the whole body shake,
throws him down dead, lance straight out,[7] from his horse;
he has broken his neck; broken it in two.   1205
There is something, he says, he must tell him:
"Clown! Nobody! Now you know Charles is no fool,
he never was the man to love treason.
It took his valor to leave us in these passes!
France will not lose its name, sweet France! today.   1210
Brave men of France, strike hard! The first blow is ours!
We're in the right, and these swine in the wrong!" AOI.

94

A duke is there whose name is Falsaron,
he was the brother of King Marsilion,
held the wild land of Dathan and Abiram;[8]   1215
under heaven, no criminal more vile;
a tremendous forehead between his eyes—
a good half-foot long, if you had measured it.
His pain is bitter to see his nephew dead;

---

6. According to Littré, a mountjoy (or montjoie) was a mound or cairn of stones set up to mark the site of a victory. The old French war cry "Montjoie St.-Denis!" (or, briefly, "Montjoie!") derived from the cairn set up at St.-Denis on the site of the saint's martyrdom (his spiritual victory). Others derive the word from the Hill of Rama, called "Mons Gaudii," from which pilgrims obtained their first view of Jerusalem.   7. The lance is held, not thrown, and used to knock the enemy from his horse. To throw one's weapons is savage and ignoble. See *laisses* 154 and 160 and the outlandish names of the things the pagans throw at Roland, Gautier, and Turpin.   8. See Numbers 16:1–35.

rides out alone, baits the foe with his body,   1220
and riding shouts the war cry of the pagans,
full of hate and insults against the French:
"This is the day sweet France will lose its honor!"
Oliver hears, and it fills him with fury,
digs with his golden spurs into his horse,   1225
comes on to strike the blow a baron strikes,
smashes his shield, breaks his hauberk apart,
thrusts into him the long streamers of his gonfalon,
knocks him down, dead, lance straight out, from the saddle;
looks to the ground and sees the swine stretched out,   1230
and spoke these words—proud words, terrible words:
"You nobody, what are your threats to me!
Men of France, strike! Strike and we will beat them!"
Munjoie! he shouts—the war cry of King Charles. AOI.

104

The battle is fearful and wonderful   1320
and everywhere. Roland never spares himself,
strikes with his lance as long as the wood lasts:
the fifteenth blow he struck, it broke, was lost.
Then he draws Durendal, his good sword, bare,
and spurs his horse, comes on to strike Chernuble,   1325
smashes his helmet, carbuncles shed their light,
cuts through the coif, through the hair on his head,
cut through his eyes, through his face, through that look,
the bright, shining hauberk with its fine rings,
down through the trunk to the fork of his legs,   1330
through the saddle, adorned with beaten gold,
into the horse; and the sword came to rest:
cut through the spine, never felt for the joint;
knocks him down, dead, on the rich grass of the meadow;
then said to him: "You were doomed when you started,   1335
Clown! Nobody! Let Mahum help you now.
No pagan swine will win this field today."

105

Roland the Count comes riding through the field,
holds Durendal, that sword! it carves its way!
and brings terrible slaughter down on the pagans.   1340
To have seen him cast one man dead on another,
the bright red blood pouring out on the ground,
his hauberk, his two arms, running with blood,
his good horse—neck and shoulders running with blood!
And Oliver does not linger, he strikes!   1345
and the Twelve Peers, no man could reproach them;
and the brave French, they fight with lance and sword.
The pagans die, some simply faint away!
Said the Archbishop: "Bless our band of brave men!"
Munjoie! he shouts—the war cry of King Charles. AOI.   1350

106

Oliver rides into that battle-storm,
his lance is broken, he holds only the stump;
comes on to strike a pagan, Malsarun;
and he smashes his shield, all flowers and gold,
sends his two eyes flying out of his head,   1355
and his brains come pouring down to his feet;
casts him down, dead, with seven hundred others.
Now he has killed Turgis and Esturguz,
and the shaft bursts, shivers down to his fists.
Count Roland said: "Companion, what are you doing?   1360
Why bother with a stick in such a battle?
Iron and steel will do much better work!
Where is your sword, your Halteclere—that name!
Where is that crystal hilt, that golden guard?"
"Haven't had any time to draw it out,   1365
been so busy fighting," said Oliver. AOI.

107

Lord Oliver has drawn out his good sword—
that sword his companion had longed to see—
and showed him how a good man uses it:
strikes a pagan, Justin of Val Ferrée,   1370
and comes down through his head, cuts through the center,
through his body, his hauberk sewn with brass,
the good saddle beset with gems in gold,
into the horse, the backbone cut in two;
knocks him down, dead, before him on the meadow.   1375
Count Roland said: "Now I know it's you, Brother.
The Emperor loves us for blows like that."
Munjoie! that cry! goes up on every side. AOI.

109

In the meantime, the fighting grew bitter.
Franks and pagans, the fearful blows they strike—
those who attack, those who defend themselves;
so many lances broken, running with blood,
the gonfanons in shreds, the ensigns torn,   1400
so many good French fallen, their young lives lost:
they will not see their mothers or wives again,
or the men of France who wait for them at the passes. AOI.
Charlemagne waits and weeps and wails for them.
What does that matter? They'll get no help from him.   1405
Ganelon served him ill that day he sold,
in Saragossa, the barons of his house.
He lost his life and limbs for what he did:
was doomed to hang in the great trial at Aix,
and thirty of his kin were doomed with him,   1410
who never expected to die that death. AOI.

110

The battle is fearful and full of grief.
Oliver and Roland strike like good men,
the Archbishop, more than a thousand blows,
and the Twelve Peers do not hang back, they strike!   1415
the French fight side by side, all as one man.
The pagans die by hundreds, by thousands:
whoever does not flee finds no refuge from death,
like it or not, there he ends all his days.
And there the men of France lose their greatest arms;   1420
they will not see their fathers, their kin again,
or Charlemagne, who looks for them in the passes.
Tremendous torment now comes forth in France,
a mighty whirlwind, tempests of wind and thunder,
rains and hailstones, great and immeasurable,   1425
bolts of lightning hurtling and hurtling down:
it is, in truth, a trembling of the earth.
From Saint Michael-in-Peril to the Saints,
from Besançon to the port of Wissant,
there is no house whose veil of walls does not crumble.   1430
A great darkness at noon falls on the land,
there is no light but when the heavens crack.
No man sees this who is not terrified,
and many say: "The Last Day! Judgment Day!
The end! The end of the world is upon us!"   1435
They do not know, they do not speak the truth:
it is the worldwide grief for the death of Roland.

111

The French have fought with all their hearts and strength,
pagans are dead by the thousands, in droves:
of one hundred thousand, not two are saved.   1440
Said the Archbishop: "Our men! What valiant fighters!
No king under heaven could have better.
It is written in the Gesta Francorum:[9]
our Emperor's vassals were all good men."
They walk over the field to seek their dead,   1445
they weep, tears fill their eyes, in grief and pity
for their kindred, with love, with all their hearts.
Marsilion the King, with all his men
     in that great host, rises up before them. AOI.

112

King Marsilion comes along a valley
with all his men, the great host he assembled: 1450
twenty divisions, formed and numbered by the King,
helmets ablaze with gems beset in gold,
and those bright shields, those hauberks sewn with brass.
Seven thousand clarions sound the pursuit,
and the great noise resounds across that country.   1455

9. "The Deeds of the French" (Latin), title of an account of these events which has not survived.

Said Roland then: "Oliver, Companion, Brother,
that traitor Ganelon has sworn our deaths:
it is treason, it cannot stay hidden,
the Emperor will take his terrible revenge.
We have this battle now, it will be bitter,   1460
no man has ever seen the like of it.
I will fight here with Durendal, this sword,
and you, my companion, with Halteclere —
we've fought with them before, in many lands!
how many battles have we won with these two!   1465
Let no one sing a bad song of our swords." AOI.

125

Marsilion sees his people's martyrdom.
He commands them: sound his horns and trumpets;
and he rides now with the great host he has gathered.   1630
At their head rides the Saracen Abisme:
no worse criminal rides in that company,
stained with the marks of his crimes and great treasons,
lacking the faith in God, Saint Mary's son.
And he is black, as black as melted pitch,   1635
a man who loves murder and treason more
than all the gold of rich Galicia,
no living man ever saw him play or laugh;
a great fighter, a wild man, mad with pride,
and therefore dear to that criminal king;   1640
holds high his dragon,[1] where all his people gather.
The Archbishop will never love that man,
no sooner saw than wanted to strike him;
considered quietly, said to himself:
"That Saracen — a heretic, I'll wager.   1645
Now let me die if I do not kill him —
I never loved cowards or cowards' ways." AOI.

126

Turpin the Archbishop begins the battle.
He rides the horse that he took from Grossaille,
who was a king this priest once killed in Denmark.   1650
Now this war horse is quick and spirited,
his hooves high-arched, the quick legs long and flat,
short in the thigh, wide in the rump, long in the flanks,
and the backbone so high, a battle horse!
and that white tail, the yellow mane on him,   1655
the little ears on him, the tawny head!
No beast on earth could ever run with him.
The Archbishop — that valiant man! — spurs hard,
he will attack Abisme, he will not falter,
strikes on his shield, a miraculous blow: 1660
a shield of stones, of amethysts, topazes,
esterminals,[2] carbuncles all on fire —

---

1. Banner.   2. Precious ornaments.

a gift from a devil, in Val Metas,
sent on to him by the Amiral Galafre.
There Turpin strikes, he does not treat it gently—   1665
after that blow, I'd not give one cent for it;
cut through his body, from one side to the other,
and casts him down dead in a barren place.
And the French say: "A fighter, that Archbishop!
Look at him there, saving souls with that crozier!"   1670

127

Roland the Count calls out to Oliver:
"Lord, Companion, now you have to agree
the Archbishop is a good man on horse,
there's none better on earth or under heaven,
he knows his way with a lance and a spear."   1675
The Count replies: "Right! Let us help him then."
And with these words the Franks began anew,
the blows strike hard, and the fighting is bitter;
there is a painful loss of Christian men.
To have seen them, Roland and Oliver,   1680
these fighting men, striking down with their swords,
the Archbishop with them, striking with his lance!
One can recount the number these three killed:
it is written—in charters, in documents;
the Geste tells it: it was more than four thousand.   1685
Through four assaults all went well with our men;
then comes the fifth, and that one crushes them.
They are all killed, all these warriors of France,
all but sixty, whom the Lord God has spared:
they will die too, but first sell themselves dear. AOI.   1690

128

Count Roland sees the great loss of his men,
calls on his companion, on Oliver:
"Lord, Companion, in God's name, what would you do?
All these good men you see stretched on the ground.
We can mourn for sweet France, fair land of France!   1695
a desert now, stripped of such great vassals.
Oh King, and friend, if only you were here!
Oliver, Brother, how shall we manage it?
What shall we do to get word to the King?"
Said Oliver: "I don't see any way.   1700
I would rather die now than hear us shamed." AOI.

129

And Roland said: "I'll sound the olifant,
Charles will hear it, drawing through the passes,
I promise you, the Franks will return at once."
Said Oliver: "That would be a great disgrace,   1705
a dishonor and reproach to all your kin,
the shame of it would last them all their lives.

When I urged it, you would not hear of it;
you will not do it now with my consent.
It is not acting bravely to sound it now—
look at your arms, they are covered with blood."   1710
The Count replies: "I've fought here like a lord."[3] AOI.

130

And Roland says: "We are in a rough battle.
I'll sound the olifant, Charles will hear it."
Said Oliver: "No good vassal would do it.   1715
When I urged it, friend, you did not think it right.
If Charles were here, we'd come out with no losses.
Those men down there—no blame can fall on them."
Oliver said: "Now by this beard of mine,
If I can see my noble sister, Aude,   1720
once more, you will never lie in her arms!"[4] AOI.

131

And Roland said: "Why are you angry at me?"
Oliver answers: "Companion, it is your doing.
I will tell you what makes a vassal good:
    it is judgment, it is never madness;
restraint is worth more than the raw nerve of a fool.   1725
Frenchmen are dead because of your wildness.
And what service will Charles ever have from us?
If you had trusted me, my lord would be here,
we would have fought this battle through to the end,
Marsilion would be dead, or our prisoner.   1730
Roland, your prowess—had we never seen it!
    And now, dear friend, we've seen the last of it.
No more aid from us now for Charlemagne,
a man without equal till Judgment Day,
you will die here, and your death will shame France.
We kept faith, you and I, we were companions;
    and everything we were will end today.   1735
We part before evening, and it will be hard." AOI.

132

Turpin the Archbishop hears their bitter words,
digs hard into his horse with golden spurs
and rides to them; begins to set them right:
"You, Lord Roland, and you, Lord Oliver,   1740
I beg you in God's name do not quarrel.
To sound the horn could not help us now, true,
but still it is far better that you do it:
let the King come, he can avenge us then—
these men of Spain must not go home exulting!   1745

---

3. Some have found lines 1710–12 difficult. Oliver means, "We have fought this far—look at the enemy's blood on your arms: It is too late, it would be a disgrace to summon help when there is no longer any chance of being saved." But Roland thinks that that is the one time when it is not a disgrace.
4. Aude had been betrothed to Roland.

Our French will come, they'll get down on their feet,
and find us here—we'll be dead, cut to pieces.
They will lift us into coffins on the backs of mules,
and weep for us, in rage and pain and grief,
and bury us in the courts of churches;   1750
and we will not be eaten by wolves or pigs or dogs."
Roland replies, "Lord, you have spoken well." AOI.

134

And now the mighty effort of Roland the Count:
he sounds his olifant; his pain is great,
and from his mouth the bright blood comes leaping out,
and the temple bursts in his forehead.
That horn, in Roland's hands, has a mighty voice: 1765
King Charles hears it drawing through the passes.
Naimon heard it, the Franks listen to it.
And the King said: "I hear Count Roland's horn;
he'd never sound it unless he had a battle."
Says Ganelon: "Now no more talk of battles!   1770
You are old now, your hair is white as snow,
the things you say make you sound like a child.
You know Roland and that wild pride of his—
what a wonder God has suffered it so long!
Remember? he took Noples without your command: 1775
the Saracens rode out, to break the siege;
they fought with him, the great vassal Roland.
Afterwards he used the streams to wash the blood
from the meadows: so that nothing would show.
He blasts his horn all day to catch a rabbit,   1780
he's strutting now before his peers and bragging—
who under heaven would dare meet him on the field?
So now: ride on! Why do you keep on stopping?
The Land of Fathers lies far ahead of us." AOI.

135

The blood leaping from Count Roland's mouth,   1785
the temple broken with effort in his forehead,
he sounds his horn in great travail and pain.
King Charles heard it, and his French listen hard.
And the King said: "That horn has a long breath!"
Naimon answers: "It is a baron's breath.   1790
There is a battle there, I know there is.
He betrayed him! and now asks you to fail him!
Put on your armor! Lord, shout your battle cry,
and save the noble barons of your house!
You hear Roland's call. He is in trouble."   1795

136

The Emperor commanded the horns to sound,
the French dismount, and they put on their armor:
their hauberks, their helmets, their gold-dressed swords,

their handsome shields; and take up their great lances,
the gonfalons of white and red and blue.   1800
The barons of that host mount their war horses
and spur them hard the whole length of the pass;
and every man of them says to the other:
"If only we find Roland before he's killed,
we'll stand with him, and then we'll do some fighting!"   1805
What does it matter what they say? They are too late.

137

It is the end of day, and full of light,
arms and armor are ablaze in the sun,
and fire flashes from hauberks and helmets,
and from those shields, painted fair with flowers,   1810
and from those lances, those gold-dressed gonfanons.
The Emperor rides on in rage and sorrow,
the men of France indignant and full of grief.
There is no man of them who does not weep,
they are in fear for the life of Roland.   1815
The King commands: seize Ganelon the Count!
and gave him over to the cooks of his house;
summons the master cook, their chief, Besgun:
"Guard him for me like the traitor he is:
he has betrayed the barons of my house."   1820
Besgun takes him, sets his kitchen comrades,
a hundred men, the best, the worst, on him;
and they tear out his beard and his mustache,
each one strikes him four good blows with his fist;
and they lay into him with cudgels and sticks,   1825
put an iron collar around his neck
and chain him up, as they would chain a bear;
dumped him, in dishonor, on a packhorse,
and guard him well till they give him back to Charles.

139

King Charles the Great rides on, a man in wrath,
his great white beard spread out upon his hauberk.[5]
All the barons of France ride spurring hard,
there is no man who does not wail, furious   1845
not to be with Roland, the captain count,
who stands and fights the Saracens of Spain,
so set upon, I cannot think his soul abides.
God! those sixty men who stand with him, what men!
No king, no captain ever stood with better. AOI.   1850

140

Roland looks up on the mountains and slopes,
sees the French dead, so many good men fallen,
and weeps for them, as a great warrior weeps:
"Barons, my lords, may God give you his grace,

---

5. A gesture of defiance toward the enemy.

may he grant Paradise to all your souls,   1855
make them lie down among the holy flowers.
I never saw better vassals than you.
All the years you've served me, and all the times,
the mighty lands you conquered for Charles our King!
The Emperor raised you for this terrible hour!   1860
Land of France, how sweet you are, native land,
laid waste this day, ravaged, made a desert.
Barons of France, I see you die for me,
and I, your lord—I cannot protect you.
May *God* come to your aid, that God who never failed.   1865
Oliver, brother, now I will not fail *you*.
I will die here—of grief, if no man kills me.
Lord, Companion, let us return and fight."

142

When a man knows there'll be no prisoners,
what will that man not do to defend himself!
And so the Franks fight with the fury of lions.
Now Marsilion, the image of a baron,
mounted on that war horse he calls Gaignun,   1890
digs in his spurs, comes on to strike Bevon,
who was the lord of Beaune and of Dijon;
smashes his shield, rips apart his hauberk,
knocks him down, dead, no need to wound him more.
And then he killed Yvorie and Yvon,   1895
and more: he killed Gerard of Rousillon.
Roland the Count is not far away now,
said to the pagan: "The Lord God's curse on you!
You kill my companions, how you wrong me!
You'll feel the pain of it before we part,   1900
you will learn my sword's name by heart today";
comes on to strike—the image of a baron.
He has cut off Marsilion's right fist;
now takes the head of Jurfaleu the blond—
the head of Jurfaleu! Marsilion's son.   1905
The pagans cry: "Help, Mahumet! Help us!
Vengeance, our gods, on Charles! the man who set
these criminals on us in our own land,
they will not quit the field, they'll stand and die!"
And one said to the other: "Let *us* run then."   1910
And with that word, some hundred thousand flee.
Now try to call them back: they won't return. AOI.

143

What does it matter? If Marsilion has fled,
his uncle has remained: the Algalife,[6]
who holds Carthage, Alfrere, and Garmalie,   1915
and Ethiopia: a land accursed;
holds its immense black race under his power,

---

6. The Caliph, Marsilion's uncle, whom Ganelon lied about to Charlemagne (see lines 680–91).

the huge noses, the enormous ears on them;
and they number more than fifty thousand.
These are the men who come riding in fury,   1920
and now they shout that pagan battle cry.
And Roland said: "Here comes our martyrdom;
I see it now: we have not long to live.
But let the world call any man a traitor
        who does not make them pay before he dies!
My lords, attack! Use those bright shining swords!   1925
Fight a good fight for your deaths and your lives,
let no shame touch sweet France because of us!
When Charles my lord comes to this battlefield
and sees how well we punished these Saracens,
finds fifteen of their dead for one of ours,   1930
I'll tell you what he will do: he will bless us." AOI.

145

The Saracens, when they saw these few French,   1940
looked at each other, took courage, and presumed,
telling themselves: "The Emperor is wrong!"
The Algalife rides a great sorrel horse,
digs into it with his spurs of fine gold,
strikes Oliver, from behind, in the back,   1945
shattered the white hauberk upon his flesh,
drove his spear through the middle of his chest;
and speaks to him: "Now you feel you've been struck!
Your great Charles doomed you when he left you in this pass.
That man wronged us, he must not boast of it.   1950
I've avenged all our dead in you alone!"

146

Oliver feels: he has been struck to death;
grips Halteclere, that steel blade shining, strikes
on the gold-dressed pointed helm of the Algalife,
sends jewels and flowers crackling down to the earth,   1955
into the head, into the little teeth;
draws up his flashing sword, casts him down, dead,
and then he says: "Pagan, a curse on you!
If only I could say Charles has lost nothing—
but no woman, no lady you ever knew   1960
will hear you boast, in the land you came from,
that you could take one thing worth a cent from me,
or do me harm, or do any man harm";
then cries out to Roland to come to his aid. AOI.

147

Oliver feels he is wounded to death,   1965
will never have his fill of vengeance, strikes,
as a baron strikes, where they are thickest,
cuts through their lances, cuts through those buckled shields,
through feet, through fists, through saddles, and through flanks.

Had you seen him, cutting the pagans limb   1970
from limb, casting one corpse down on another,
you would remember a brave man keeping faith.
Never would he forget Charles' battle-cry,
Munjoie! he shouts, that mighty voice ringing;
calls to Roland, to his friend and his peer: 1975
"Lord, Companion, come stand beside me now.
We must part from each other in pain today." AOI.

148

Roland looks hard into Oliver's face,
it is ashen, all its color is gone,
the bright red blood streams down upon his body,   1980
Oliver's blood spattering on the earth.
"God!" said the Count, "I don't know what to do,
Lord, Companion, your fight is finished now.
There'll never be a man the like of you.
Sweet land of France, today you will be stripped   1985
of good vassals, laid low, a fallen land!
The Emperor will suffer the great loss";
faints with that word, mounted upon his horse. AOI.

149

Here is Roland, lords, fainted on his horse,
and Oliver the Count, wounded to death:
he has lost so much blood, his eyes are darkened—   1990
he cannot see, near or far, well enough
to recognize a friend or enemy:
struck when he came upon his companion,
strikes on his helm, adorned with gems in gold,
cuts down straight through, from the point to the nasal,[7]   1995
but never harmed him, he never touched his head.
Under this blow, Count Roland looked at him;
and gently, softly now, he asks of him:
"Lord, Companion, do you mean to do this?   2000
It is Roland, who always loved you greatly.
You never declared that we were enemies."
Said Oliver: "Now I hear it is you—
I don't see you, may the Lord God see you.
Was it you that I struck? Forgive me then."   2005
Roland replies: "I am not harmed, not harmed,
I forgive you, Friend, here and before God."
And with that word, each bowed to the other.
And this is the love, lords, in which they parted.

151

Roland the Count, when he sees his friend dead,
lying stretched out, his face against the earth,   2025
softly, gently, begins to speak the regret:[8]

7. The nosepiece protruding down from the cone-shaped helmet.   8. What follows is a formal and customary lament for the dead.

"Lord, Companion, you were brave and died for it.
We have stood side by side through days and years,
you never caused me harm, I never wronged you;
when you are dead, to be alive pains me."   2030
And with that word the lord of marches faints
upon his horse, which he calls Veillantif.
He is held firm by his spurs of fine gold,
whichever way he leans, he cannot fall.

152

Before Roland could recover his senses   2035
and come out of his faint, and be aware,
a great disaster had come forth before him:
the French are dead, he has lost every man
except the Archbishop, and Gautier de l'Hum,
who has come back, down from that high mountain: 2040
he has fought well, he fought those men of Spain.
His men are dead, the pagans finished them;
flees now down to these valleys, he has no choice,
and calls on Count Roland to come to his aid:
"My noble Count, my brave lord, where are you?   2045
I never feared whenever you were there.
It is Walter: I conquered Maëlgut,
my uncle is Droün, old and gray: your Walter
and always dear to you for the way I fought;
and I have fought this time: my lance is shattered,   2050
my good shield pierced, my hauberk's meshes broken;
and I am wounded, a lance struck through my body.
I will die soon, but I sold myself dear."
And with that word, Count Roland has heard him,
he spurs his horse, rides spurring to his man. AOI.   2055

153

Roland in pain, maddened with grief and rage:
rushes where they are thickest and strikes again,
strikes twenty men of Spain, strikes twenty dead,
and Walter six, and the Archbishop five.
The pagans say: "Look at those criminals!   2060
Now take care, Lords, they don't get out alive,
only a traitor will not attack them now!
Only a coward will let them save their skins!"
And then they raise their hue and cry once more,
rush in on them, once more, from every side. AOI.   2065

154

Count Roland was always a noble warrior,
Gautier de l'Hum is a fine mounted man,
the Archbishop, a good man tried and proved:
not one of them will ever leave the others;
strike, where they are thickest, at the pagans.   2070
A thousand Saracens get down on foot,

and forty thousand more are on their mounts:
and I tell you, not one will dare come close,
they throw, and from afar, lances and spears,
wigars and darts, mizraks, javelins, pikes.   2075
With the first blows they killed Gautier de l'Hum
and struck Turpin of Reims, pierced through his shield,
broke the helmet on him, wounded his head;
ripped his hauberk, shattered its rings of mail,
and pierced him with four spears in his body,   2080
the war horse killed under him; and now there comes
great pain and rage when the Archbishop falls. AOI.

155

Turpin of Reims, when he feels he is unhorsed,
struck to the earth with four spears in his body,
quickly, brave man, leaps to his feet again;   2085
his eyes find Roland now, he runs to him
and says one word: "See! I'm not finished yet!
What good vassal ever gives up alive!";
and draws Almace, his sword, that shining steel!
and strikes, where they are thickest, a thousand blows, and more.   2090
Later, Charles said: Turpin had spared no one;
he found four hundred men prostrate around him,
some of them wounded, some pierced from front to back,
some with their heads hacked off. So says the Geste,
and so says one who was there, on that field,   2095
the baron Saint Gilles,[9] for whom God performs miracles,
who made the charter setting forth these great things
      in the Church of Laon. Now any man
who does not know this much understands nothing.

156

Roland the Count fights well and with great skill,
but he is hot, his body soaked with sweat;   2100
has a great wound in his head, and much pain,
his temple broken because he blew the horn.
But he must know whether King Charles will come;
draws out the olifant, sounds it, so feebly.
The Emperor drew to a halt, listened.   2105
"Seigneurs," he said, "it goes badly for us—
My nephew Roland falls from our ranks today.
I hear it in the horn's voice: he hasn't long.
Let every man who wants to be with Roland
ride fast! Sound trumpets! Every trumpet in this host!"   2110
Sixty thousand, on these words, sound, so high
the mountains sound, and the valleys resound.
The pagans hear: it is no joke to them;
cry to each other: "We're getting Charles on us!"

9. St. Gilles of Provence. These lines explain how the story of Rencesvals could be told after all who
had fought there died.

157

The pagans say: "The Emperor is coming, AOI.   2115
listen to their trumpets—it is the French!
If Charles comes back, it's all over for us,
if Roland lives, this war begins again
and we have lost our land, we have lost Spain."
Some four hundred, helmets laced on, assemble,   2120
some of the best, as they think, on that field.
They storm Roland, in one fierce, bitter attack.
And now Count Roland has some work on his hands. AOI.

158

Roland the Count, when he sees them coming,
how strong and fierce and alert he becomes!   2125
He will not yield to them, not while he lives.
He rides the horse they call Veillantif, spurs,
digs into it with his spurs of fine gold,
and rushes at them all where they are thickest,
the Archbishop—that Turpin!—at his side.   2130
Said one man to the other: "Go at it, friend.
The horns we heard were the horns of the French,
King Charles is coming back with all his strength."[1]

159

Roland the Count never loved a coward,
a blusterer, an evil-natured man,   2135
a man on horse who was not a good vassal.
And now he called to Archbishop Turpin:
"You are on foot, Lord, and here I am mounted,
and so, here I take my stand: for love of you.
We'll take whatever comes, the good and bad,   2140
together, Lord: no one can make me leave you.
They will learn our swords' names today in battle,
the name of Almace, the name of Durendal!"
Said the Archbishop: "Let us strike or be shamed!
Charles is returning, and he brings our revenge."   2145

160

Say the pagans: "We were all born unlucky!
The evil day that dawned for us today!
We have lost our lords and peers, and now comes Charles—
that Charlemagne!—with his great host. Those trumpets!
that shrill sound on us—the trumpets of the French!   2150
And the loud roar of that Munjoie! This Roland
is a wild man, he is too great a fighter—
What man of flesh and blood can ever hope
to bring him down? Let us cast at him, and leave him there."
And so they did: arrows, wigars, darts,   2155
lances and spears, javelots dressed with feathers;

1. The lines could be spoken either by Roland and the archbishop or by the pagans.

struck Roland's shield, pierced it, broke it to pieces,
ripped his hauberk, shattered its rings of mail,
but never touched his body, never his flesh.
They wounded Veillantif in thirty places,   2160
struck him dead, from afar, under the Count.
The pagans flee, they leave the field to him.
Roland the Count stood alone, on his feet. AOI.

161

The pagans flee, in bitterness and rage,
strain every nerve running headlong toward Spain,   2165
and Count Roland has no way to chase them,
he has lost Veillantif, his battle horse;
he has no choice, left alone there on foot.
He went to the aid of Archbishop Turpin,
unlaced the gold-dressed helmet, raised it from his head, 2170
lifted away his bright, light coat of mail,
cut his under tunic into some lengths,
stilled his great wounds with thrusting on the strips;
then held him in his arms, against his chest,
and laid him down, gently, on the green grass;   2175
and softly now Roland entreated him:
"My noble lord, I beg you, give me leave:
our companions, whom we have loved so dearly,
are all dead now, we must not abandon them.
I want to look for them, know them once more,   2180
and set them in ranks, side by side, before you."
Said the Archbishop: "Go then, go and come back.
The field is ours, thanks be to God, yours and mine."

162

So Roland leaves him, walks the field all alone,
seeks in the valleys, and seeks in the mountains.   2185
He found Gerin, and Gerer his companion,
and then he found Berenger and Otun,
Anseïs and Sansun, and on that field
he found Gerard the old of Roussillon;
and carried them, brave man, all, one by one,   2190
came back to the Archbishop with these French dead,
and set them down in ranks before his knees.
The Archbishop cannot keep from weeping,
raises his hand and makes his benediction;
and said: "Lords, Lords, it was your terrible hour.   2195
May the Glorious God set all your souls
among the holy flowers of Paradise!
Here is my own death, Lords, pressing on me,
I shall not see our mighty Emperor."

163

And Roland leaves, seeks in the field again;   2200
he has found Oliver, his companion,

held him tight in his arms against his chest;
came back to the Archbishop, laid Oliver
down on a shield among the other dead.
The Archbishop absolved him, signed him with the Cross.   2205
And pity now and rage and grief increase;
and Roland says: "Oliver, dear companion,
you were the son of the great duke Renier,
who held the march of the vale of Runers.
Lord, for shattering lances, for breaking shields,   2210
for making men great with presumption weak with fright,
for giving life and counsel to good men,
for striking fear in that unbelieving race,
no warrior on earth surpasses you."

164

Roland the Count, when he sees his peers dead,   2215
and Oliver, whom he had good cause to love,
felt such grief and pity, he begins to weep;
and his face lost its color with what he felt:
a pain so great he cannot keep on standing,
he has no choice, falls fainting to the ground.   2220
Said the Archbishop: "Baron, what grief for you."

165

The Archbishop, when he saw Roland faint,
felt such pain then as he had never felt;
stretched out his hand and grasped the olifant.
At Rencesvals there is a running stream: 2225
he will go there and fetch some water for Roland;
and turns that way, with small steps, staggering;
he is too weak, he cannot go ahead,
he has no strength: all the blood he has lost.
In less time than a man takes to cross a little field   2230
that great heart fails, he falls forward, falls down;
and Turpin's death comes crushing down on him.

166

Roland the Count recovers from his faint,
gets to his feet, but stands with pain and grief;
looks down the valley, looks up the mountain, sees: 2235
on the green grass, beyond his companions,
that great and noble man down on the ground,
the Archbishop, whom God sent in His name;
who confesses his sins, lifts up his eyes,
holds up his hands joined together to heaven,   2240
and prays to God: grant him that Paradise.
Turpin is dead, King Charles' good warrior.
In great battles, in beautiful sermons
he was ever a champion against the pagans.
Now God grant Turpin's soul His holy blessing. AOI.   2245

167

Roland the Count sees the Archbishop down,
sees the bowels fallen out of his body,
and the brain boiling down from his forehead.
Turpin has crossed his hands upon his chest
beneath the collarbone, those fine white hands. 2250
Roland speaks the lament, after the custom
followed in his land: aloud, with all his heart:
"My noble lord, you great and well-born warrior,
I commend you today to the God of Glory,
whom none will ever serve with a sweeter will. 2255
Since the Apostles no prophet the like of you[2]
arose to keep the faith and draw men to it.
May your soul know no suffering or want,
and behold the gate open to Paradise."

168

Now Roland feels that death is very near. 2260
His brain comes spilling out through his two ears;
prays to God for his peers: let them be called;
and for himself, to the angel Gabriel;
took the olifant: there must be no reproach!
took Durendal his sword in his other hand, 2265
and farther than a crossbow's farthest shot
he walks toward Spain, into a fallow land,
and climbs a hill: there beneath two fine trees
stand four great blocks of stone, all are of marble;
and he fell back, to earth, on the green grass, 2270
has fainted there, for death is very near.

169

High are the hills, and high, high are the trees;
there stand four blocks of stone, gleaming of marble.
Count Roland falls fainting on the green grass,
and is watched, all this time, by a Saracen: 2275
who has feigned death and lies now with the others,
has smeared blood on his face and on his body;
and quickly now gets to his feet and runs—
a handsome man, strong, brave, and so crazed with pride
that he does something mad and dies for it: 2280
laid hands on Roland, and on the arms of Roland,
and cried: "Conquered! Charles's nephew conquered!
I'll carry this sword home to Arabia!"
As he draws it, the Count begins to come round.

170

Now Roland feels: *someone taking his sword!* 2285
opened his eyes, and had one word for him:

---

2. Compare Deuteronomy 34:10, on the death of Moses: "And there arose not a prophet since in Israel like unto Moses, whom the Lord knew face to face."

"I don't know you, you aren't one of ours";
grasps that olifant that he will never lose,
strikes on the helm beset with gems in gold,
shatters the steel, and the head, and the bones,   2290
sent his two eyes flying out of his head,
dumped him over stretched out at his feet dead;
and said: "You nobody! how could you dare
lay hands on me—rightly or wrongly: how?
Who'll hear of this and not call you a fool?   2295
Ah! the bell-mouth of the olifant is smashed,
the crystal and the gold fallen away."

171

Now Roland the Count feels: his sight is gone;
gets on his feet, draws on his final strength,
the color on his face lost now for good.   2300
Before him stands a rock; and on that dark rock
in rage and bitterness he strikes ten blows:
the steel blade grates, it will not break, it stands unmarked.
"Ah!" said the Count, "Blessed Mary, your help!
Ah Durendal, good sword, your unlucky day,   2305
for I am lost and cannot keep you in my care.
The battles I have won, fighting with you,
the mighty lands that holding you I conquered,
that Charles rules now, our King, whose beard is white!
Now you fall to another: it must not be
    a man who'd run before another man!   2310
For a long while a good vassal held you:
there'll never be the like in France's holy land."

172

Roland strikes down on that rock of Cerritania:
the steel blade grates, will not break, stands unmarked.
Now when he sees he can never break that sword,   2315
Roland speaks the lament, in his own presence:
"Ah Durendal, how beautiful and bright!
so full of light, all on fire in the sun!
King Charles was in the vales of Moriane
when God sent his angel and commanded him,   2320
from heaven, to give you to a captain count.
That great and noble King girded it on me.
And with this sword I won Anjou and Brittany,
I won Poitou, I won Le Maine for Charles,
and Normandy, that land where men are free,   2325
I won Provence and Aquitaine with this,
and Lombardy, and every field of Romagna,
I won Bavaria, and all of Flanders,
all of Poland, and Bulgaria, for Charles,
Constantinople, which pledged him loyalty,   2330
and Saxony, where he does as he wills;
and with this sword I won Scotland and Ireland,
and England, his chamber, his own domain—

the lands, the nations I conquered with this sword,
for Charles, who rules them now, whose beard is white!   2335
Now, for this sword, I am pained with grief and rage:
Let it not fall to pagans! Let me die first!
Our Father God, save France from that dishonor."

173

Roland the Count strikes down on a dark rock,
and the rock breaks, breaks more than I can tell,   2340
and the blade grates, but Durendal will not break,
the sword leaped up, rebounded toward the sky.
The Count, when he sees that sword will not be broken,
softly, in his own presence, speaks the lament:
"Ah Durendal, beautiful, and most sacred,   2345
the holy relics in this golden pommel!
Saint Peter's tooth and blood of Saint Basile,
a lock of hair of my lord Saint Denis,
and a fragment of blessed Mary's robe:
your power must not fall to the pagans,   2350
you must be served by Christian warriors.
May no coward ever come to hold you!
It was with you I conquered those great lands
that Charles has in his keeping, whose beard is white,
the Emperor's lands, that make him rich and strong."   2355

174

Now Roland feels: death coming over him,
death descending from his temples to his heart.
He came running underneath a pine tree
and there stretched out, face down, on the green grass,
lays beneath him his sword and the olifant.   2360
He turned his head toward the Saracen hosts,
and this is why: with all his heart he wants
King Charles the Great and all his men to say,
he died, that noble Count, a conqueror;
makes confession, beats his breast often, so feebly,   2365
offers his glove, for all his sins, to God. AOI.

175

Now Roland feels that his time has run out;
he lies on a steep hill, his face toward Spain;
and with one of his hands he beat his breast:
"Almighty God, *mea culpa* in thy sight,[3]   2370
forgive my sins, both the great and the small,
sins I committed from the hour I was born
until this day, in which I lie struck down."
And then he held his right glove out to God.
Angels descend from heaven and stand by him. AOI.   2375

---

3. See Psalm 51:4: "Against thee, thee only, have I sinned, and done this evil in thy sight."

176

Count Roland lay stretched out beneath a pine;
he turned his face toward the land of Spain,
began to remember many things now:
how many lands, brave man, he had conquered;
and he remembered: sweet France, the men of his line,   2380
remembered Charles, his lord, who fostered him:
cannot keep, remembering, from weeping, sighing;
but would not be unmindful of himself:
he confesses his sins, prays God for mercy:
"Loyal Father, you who never failed us,   2385
who resurrected Saint Lazarus from the dead,
and saved your servant Daniel from the lions:[4]
now save the soul of me from every peril
for the sins I committed while I still lived."
Then he held out his right glove to his Lord: 2390
Saint Gabriel took the glove from his hand.
He held his head bowed down upon his arm,
he is gone, his two hands joined, to his end.
Then God sent him his angel Cherubin[5]
and Saint Michael, angel of the sea's Peril;   2395
and with these two there came Saint Gabriel:
they bear Count Roland's soul to Paradise.

*   *   *

4. See Daniel 6:12–23. For the raising of Lazarus, see John 11:1–44.   5. The poet seems to have regarded this as the name of a single angel.

MARIE DE FRANCE
twelfth century

The first woman known to write poetry in French was Marie de France, who lived in the last third of the twelfth century. As often with medieval authors, the name does not identify her with any specific historical figure, but it indicates that she was a French native. Her works show that she was associated in some way with the court of King Henry II of England, husband of the famous Queen Eleanor of Aquitaine. Marie was probably familiar with English as well as Latin and French. A versatile writer, she produced works in three varieties of literature: fables, visions of purgatory, and *lais*. She may or may not have been the first author of Breton *lais* and thus have given a designation to the genre. These were comparatively short narratives based in varying degrees on a story or song circulated by traveling entertainers (*jongleurs*) from the northwestern province of France known as Brittany. They were presumably in Breton, originally the Celtic language of Brittany, but none have come down to us. For French and English poets, a Breton *lai* was a narrative of moderate length recounting an event remarkable in some way, often associated with the magical or miraculous; most often, the "adventure" involves what we should call romantic love. Thus *Eliduc*, the longest of Marie's dozen *lais*, has been called a story of a man with two wives. In that respect it recalls the better-known story of Tristan and the two Isoldes. As Marie rightly says, her

tale centers on the two women; it's a pity that her change of the title to *Guildelüec and Guilliadun* has not prevailed in literary history.

Marie's handling of the plot precludes any dismissal of Eliduc as a mere villain, an exploiter of women. The reader's sympathy is engaged by his loyalty to the lord in his home country (where he suffers baseless slander) whom Eliduc returns to help in a time of need—and also by his faithful service to the lord of the country to which he goes. He is an honorable knight, exceptionally able and dependable. There is nothing said to his discredit about his relationship to Guildelüec, his wife in his home country, before he goes into exile. And there is no doubt about the reality or strength of his love for Guilliadun in the new country. This is made quite clear in the narrtive—by his clandestine return to take her with him to his homeland and by his inconsolable grief when he believes her dead—to say nothing of their later long and happy life together. On the other hand, it is a selfish affection, and it leads to dishonesty in his treatment of both the princess and her father. He does not tell her that he already has a wife in his home country, and in taking her away secretly he betrays the trust that her father has clearly placed in him. We are told that these considerations disturb Eliduc—but they do not deter him. The penalty is not long delayed: the storm at sea, the harsh revelation of Eliduc's marital state by the sailor on the ship, and Guilliadun's apparent death from shock.

In Guilliadun, the author presents a young, inexperienced, and rather naive woman—but one determined to have what she wants. From the beginning she is obsessed by her love of Eliduc. It is she who makes all the advances, she who begs, "Take me with you," at the decisive moment. (This may serve to mitigate our judgment of Eliduc's conduct, though it does not, in the end, justify it.) Guilliadun seems undisturbed by her violation of the trust of an apparently affectionate father; he might or might not have forbidden the alliance, but she gives him no chance to say. As we have seen, retribution strikes the lovers together, but its impact is more drastic for Guilliadun than for Eliduc. She suffers two shocks at once: the news that Eliduc already has a wife and the sailor's proposal to throw her overboard as a means of calming the storm. (In the stress of the moment she cannot know whether this is a real danger or not.) The combined effect of the two is overwhelming; no wonder that it seems fatal—and a miracle is necessary to restore her to life.

In Eliduc and Guilliadun the author examines the moral or ethical defects of an exclusive, self-regarding love; in Guildelüec she presents a contrast to that kind of love—a paragon of "good" love. Guildelüec's affection for Eliduc is genuine and strong. She grieves at his going into exile; her life in his absence is flawless, but she is distressed when his coldness on his first return might suggest otherwise and offers to answer any possible accusations. Later, on his second return, she seeks to understand his grief and sorrow to relieve them if she can. This love is never in conflict with other claims on her loyalty; it never leads her into unjust treatment of other people. That is, she has it under control, as the others do not have theirs. When, through her own assiduity, she comes to understand the relationship that has developed between Eliduc and Guilliadun, she does all she can to promote their happiness. With the help of the weasel's miraculous flower she restores Guilliadun from apparent death to life, reassures her of Eliduc's devotion, organizes a search for him, and finally reunites the pair. Then, so that they can be married and live in accord with the laws of God and man, she voluntarily renounces her status as Eliduc's wife and becomes a nun. Thus she does not allow "sexual" love to undermine or preclude the love that is traditionally known as *charity*—that is, devotion to the welfare of others. It might also be said that here the two are combined: she loves Eliduc enough to renounce him.

Robert Hanning and Joan Ferrante, *The Lais of Marie de France* (1982), contains translations of all twelve *lais*, with a lengthy introduction and an excellent bibliography. A convenient edition of the twelfth-century French text is Jeanne Lods, *Les Lais de Marie de France* (1959), in the series *Les Classiques Français du moyen âge*.

PRONOUNCING GLOSSARY

The following list uses common English syllables to provide rough equivalents of selected words whose pronunciation may be unfamiliar to the general reader.

Eliduc: *ay-lee-duk*　　　　　　　Guilliandun: *ghee-yuh-doon*

Guildelüec: *gheel-duh-lu-ek*　　　lais: *lai*

Eliduc[1]

I am going to give you the full story of a very old Celtic tale, at least as I've been able to understand the truth of it.

In Brittany there was once a knight called Eliduc. He was a model of his type, one of the bravest men in the country, and he had a wife of excellent and influential family, as finely bred as she was faithful to him. They lived happily for several years, since it was a marriage of truth and love. But then a war broke out and he went away to join the fighting. There he fell in love with a girl, a ravishingly pretty princess called Guilliadun. The Celtic name of the wife who stayed at home was Guildelüec, and so the story is called *Guildelüec and Guilliadun* after their names. Its original title was *Eliduc*, but it was changed because it's really about the two women. Now I'll tell you exactly how it all happened.

Eliduc's overlord was the king of Brittany, who was very fond of the knight and looked after his interests. Eliduc served him faithfully—whenever the king had to go abroad, Eliduc was left in charge of his territories, and kept them safe by his military skills. He got many favors in return. He was allowed to hunt in the royal forests. No gamekeeper, even the most resolute, dared stand in his way or complain about him. But other people's envy of his good luck did its usual work. He was slandered and traduced, and brought into bad relations with the king. Finally he was dismissed from the court without any reason. Left in the dark, Eliduc repeatedly asked to be allowed to defend himself before the king—the slanders were lies, he had served the king well, and happily so. But no answer came from the court. Convinced he would never get a hearing, Eliduc decided to go into exile. So he went home and called together all his friends. He told them how things lay with the king, of the anger toward him. Eliduc had done the best he could and there was no justice in the royal resentment. When the plowman gets the rough edge of his master's tongue, the peasants have a proverb: *Never trust a great man's love.* If someone in

---

1. Translated by John Fowles. The ellipses do not indicate omissions from this text.

Eliduc's position is sensible, he puts more trust in the love of his neighbors. So now he says[2] he's sick of Brittany, he'll cross the sea to England and amuse himself there for a while. He'll leave his wife at home; have his servants take care of her, along with his friends.

Once it was made, he kept to this decision. He fitted himself—and the ten horsemen he took with him—out handsomely for the journey. His friends were very sad to see him go, and as for his wife . . . she accompanied him for the first part of the journey, in tears that she was losing him. But he swore solemnly that he would stay true to her. Then he says goodbye and rides straight on to the sea. There he takes ship, crosses successfully and arrives at the port of Totnes.[3]

There were several kings in that part of England, and they were at war. Toward Exeter in this country there lived a very powerful old man. He had no male heir, simply an unmarried daughter. This explained the present war: because he had refused her hand to an equal from another dynasty, the other king was putting all his land to the sack. He had trapped the old king in one of his fortified cities.[4] No one there had the courage to go out and join combat, general or single, with the invader. Eliduc heard about all this and decided that since there was war he would stay in those parts instead of going on. He wanted to help the besieged king, who was getting into worse and worse trouble and faced with ruin and disaster. He would hire himself out as a mercenary.[5]

He sent messengers to the king, explaining in a letter that he had left his own country and had come to help him; but he was at the king's disposal and if he didn't want Eliduc's services, then Eliduc asked only for safe-conduct through his lands, so that he could go and offer his fighting abilities somewhere else. When the king saw the messengers, he was delighted and welcomed them warmly. He summoned the castle commander and ordered that an escort be provided immediately for Eliduc and that he should be brought to him. Then the king had lodgings arranged. All that was necessary for a month's stay was also provided.

The escort were armed and horsed and sent to fetch Eliduc. He was received with great honor, having made the journey without trouble. His lodging was with a rich townsman, a decent and well-mannered man who gave up his tapestry-hung best room to the knight. Eliduc had a good meal prepared and invited to it all the other anxious[6] knights who were quartered in the city. He forbade his own men, even the most grabbing, to accept any gift or wages for the first forty days.

On his third day at Exeter the cry ran through the city that the enemy had arrived and were all over the surrounding countryside—and already preparing an attack on the city gates. Eliduc heard the uproar from the panicking townspeople and immediately donned armor. His companions

2. The shifts to the narrative present (like those into dialogue) are all in the original [Translator's note].
3. On the southern coast of England.   4. The text says "in a castle," but it seems clear that Exeter, then a walled city, is meant. Marie would have known of its importance in West Saxon times and of William the Conqueror's siege of 1068 [Translator's note].   5. . . . *en soudees remaneir.* The knight *soudoyer* has to be understood (at least in romance) in a far more honorable—and honor driven—sense than in the contemporary or even the Renaissance use of "mercenary." Perhaps the Japanese samurai is the best equivalent [Translator's note]. Similarly, the Knight of Chaucer's *Canterbury Tales* was an honorable mercenary (see *General Prologue* lines 46–65).   6. Because of their precarious or uncertain status.

did the same. There were fourteen other knights capable of fighting in the town, the rest being wounded, or captured. Seeing Eliduc mount his horse, they go to their lodgings and put on their own armor as well. They won't wait to be called, they'll go out of the gates with him.

"We'll ride with you, sir," they now say. "And whatever you do, we'll do the same."

Eliduc answers. "My thanks. Is there anyone here who knows an ambush place? A defile? Somewhere where we might catch them hopping? If we wait here, we'll get a good fight. But we have no advantage. Has anyone a better plan?"

"There's a narrow cart road, sir. Beside that wood by the flax field over there. When they've got enough loot, they'll return by it. They ride back carelessly from such work, as a rule. Like that they're asking for a quick death."

It could be over in a flash; and much damage done.

"My friends," said Eliduc, "one thing for certain. Nothing venture, even when things look hopeless, then nothing gain—either in war or reputation. You're all the king's men, you owe him complete loyalty. So follow me, wherever I go, and do as I do. I promise you there won't be setbacks if I can help it. We may not get any loot. But we'll never be forgotten if we beat the enemy today."

His confidence spread to the other knights and they led him to the wood. There they hid by the road and waited for the enemy to return from their raid. Eliduc had planned everything, showed them how they should charge at the gallop and what to cry. When the enemy reached the narrow place, Eliduc shouted the battle challenge, then cried to his friends to fight well. They struck hard, and gave no quarter. Taken by surprise, the enemy were soon broken and put to flight. The engagement was brief. They captured the officer in command and many other knights, whom they entrust to their squires. Eliduc's side had had twenty-five men, and they took thirty of the enemy. They also took a great deal of armor, and a quantity of other valuable things. Now they return triumphantly to the city, full of this splendid victory. The king was there on a tower, desperately anxious for his men. He complained bitterly, having convinced himself that Eliduc was a traitor and had lost him all his knights.

They come in a crowd, some laden, others bound—many more on the return than at the going out, which was why the king was misled and stayed in doubt and suspense. He orders the city gates closed and the people up on the walls, bows and other weapons at the ready. But they have no need of them. Eliduc's party had sent a squire galloping on ahead to explain what had happened. The man told the king about the Breton mercenary, how he had driven the enemy away, how well he had conducted himself. There was never a better handler of arms on horseback. He had personally captured the enemy commander and taken twenty-nine prisoners, besides wounding and killing many others.

When the king hears the good news, he's beside himself with joy. He came down from the tower and went to meet Eliduc; then thanked him for all he had done and gave him all the prisoners for ransoming. Eliduc shared out the armor among the other knights, keeping no more for his

own men than three horses that had been allocated to them. He distributed everything else, even his own rightful part as well, among the prisoners and the other people.

After this exploit the king made Eliduc his favorite. He retained him
and his companions for a whole year and Eliduc gave his oath of faithful
service. He then became the protector of the king's lands.

The king's young daughter heard all about Eliduc and his splendid
actions—how good-looking he was, such a proud knight, how civilized
and openhanded. She sent one of her personal pages to request, to *beg*
Eliduc to come and amuse her. They must talk, get to know each other,
and she would be very hurt if he didn't come. Eliduc replies: of course
he'll come, he looks forward very much to meeting her. He got on his
horse; and taking a servant with him, he goes to chat with the girl. When
he's at the door of her room, he sends the page ahead. He doesn't barge
in, but waits a little, till the page comes back. Then with gentle expression,
sincere face and perfect good manners he addressed the young lady formally and thanked her for having invited him to visit her. Guilliadun was
very pretty, and she took him by the hand and led him to a couch, where
they sat and talked of this and that. She kept stealing looks at him . . . his
face, his body, his every expression . . . and said to herself how attractive
he was, how close to her ideal man. Love fires his arrow, she falls headlong
in love. She goes pale, she sighs, but she can't declare herself, in case he
despises her for it.

Eliduc stayed a long time, but in the end took his leave and went away.
Guilliadun was very unwilling to let him go, but there it was. He returned
to his lodgings, unsmiling and very thoughtful. The girl alarmed him,
since she was the king's daughter and he the king's servant. She had
seemed so shy, yet subtly accused him of something. He feels badly done
by[7]—to have been so long in the country, yet not to have seen her once
till now. Yet when he said that to himself, he felt ashamed. He remembered his wife, and how he had promised to behave as a husband should.

Now she had met him, the girl wanted to make Eliduc her lover. She
had never liked a man more—if only she can, if only he'll agree. All night
she was awake thinking of him, and had neither rest nor sleep. The next
morning she got up at dawn and went to a window and called down to
her page. Then she revealed everything to him.

"Dear God," she says, "I'm in such a state, I've fallen into such a trap. I
love the new mercenary. Eliduc. Who's fought so brilliantly. I haven't
slept a wink all night, my eyes just wouldn't shut. If he's really in love with
me, if he'll only show he's serious, I'll do anything he likes. And there's so
much to hope for—he could be king here one day. I'm mad about him.
He's so intelligent, so easy-mannered. If he doesn't love me, I'll die of
despair."

When he'd heard all she had to say, the young page gave her good
advice: no need to give up hope so soon.

"My lady, if you're in love with him, then let him know it. Send him a
belt or a ribbon—or a ring. To see if it pleases him. If he's happy to accept

---

7. The Old French is less specific: it is too bad it turned out they had not met.

the gift, looks glad to have heard from you, then you're in. He loves you. And show me an emperor who wouldn't dance for joy if he knew you fancied him."

The girl mulled over this advice.

"But how shall I know just by a gift whether he really wants me? You don't realize. A gentleman has to accept, whether he likes the sender or not. One has to take such things with good grace. I should loathe it if he made fun of me. But perhaps you could learn something from his expression. So get ready. Quickly. And go."

"I am ready."

"Take him this gold ring. And here, give him my belt. And be very warm when you greet him for me."

The page turned away, leaving her in such a state that she very nearly calls him back. Nevertheless she lets him go—and then begins to rave to herself.

"Oh God, I've fallen in love with a foreigner! I don't even know if he's of good family. Whether he won't suddenly disappear. I shall be left in despair. I'm insane to have made it all so obvious. I'd never even spoken with him before yesterday, and now I'm throwing myself at him. I think he'll just despise me. No he won't, if he's nice he'll like me for it. It's all in the lap of the gods now. If he doesn't care for me at all, I shall feel such a fool. I'll never be happy again, as long as I live."

Meanwhile, as she agonized on like that, the page rode fast on his way. He found Eliduc and gave him in private the kind of greetings the girl had asked. Then he handed him the little ring and the belt. The knight had thanked him, then put the ring on his finger and fastened the belt[8] around his waist. But he said nothing else to the page, asked him nothing—except that he offered him his own ring and belt in return. But the page didn't accept them and went away back to his young mistress. He found her in her room; then passed on Eliduc's return of greetings and thanks.

"For pity's sake, don't hide the truth. Does he really love me?"

"I think so. He wouldn't deceive you. In my opinion he's playing polite and being shrewd—he knows how to hide his feelings. I said hallo to him for you and gave him the presents. He put the belt on himself, and was rather careful to get it right. Then the ring on his finger. I didn't say anything else to him. Or he to me."

"But did he realize what it meant? Because if he didn't, I'm lost!"

"I honestly don't know. But if you must have my solemn opinion, then, well, since he didn't turn up his nose at what you sent, he doesn't exactly . . . hate you?"

"Stop teasing me, you cheeky boy! I'm perfectly well aware he doesn't hate me. How could I ever hurt him? Except by loving him so much. But if he does, he deserves to die. Until I've spoken with him myself, I won't have anything to do with him. Either through you or anyone else. I'll show him myself how wanting him tears me apart. But if only I knew how long he was staying here!"

8. The fashionable belt of the Middle Ages had links, with a hook at one end. It was fastened with a free end left hanging at the side.

"Lady, the king has him under contract for a year. That ought to be time enough to show him how you feel?"

When she heard Eliduc wasn't going away, Guilliadun was in ecstasy: how wonderful that he must stay! What she didn't know was the torment Eliduc had been in from the moment he set eyes on her. Fear had dealt him a cruel hand—that promise to his wife when he left home, that he'd never look at another woman. Now his heart was in a vise. He wanted to stay faithful. But nothing could hide the fact that he had hopelessly fallen for Guilliadun and her prettiness. To see her again and talk with her, kiss her and hold her in his arms . . . yet he could never show her this longing, which would disgrace him—on the one hand for breaking his promise to his wife, on the other because of his relationship with the king. He was torn in two; then mounted his horse, and wavered no more. He calls his friends to him, then goes to the castle to speak to the king. If it can be managed, he will see the girl—and that is why he hurries so.

The king has just risen from table and gone to his daughter's rooms, and now he's begun to play chess with a knight from overseas. On the other side of the chessboard, his daughter had to show the moves. Eliduc came forward. The king greeted him kindly and made Eliduc sit beside him. He spoke to his daughter.

"My dear, you must get to know this gentleman. And pay him every honor. There's no finer knight in the country."

The girl was delighted to hear this command from her father. She stands up, invites Eliduc to sit with her well away from the others. Both are struck dumb with love. She dared not explain herself to him, and he was afraid to speak as well . . . except to thank her for the presents she had sent him: he had never liked a present so much. She tells him she is pleased that he is pleased. Then suddenly why she sent him the ring, and her belt as well—that her body was his, she couldn't resist, she loved him to madness, she gave herself to his every wish. If she couldn't have him, he knew, he must know it was true, no other man would ever have her.

Now it was Eliduc's turn.

"Princess, I'm so happy that you love me. All joy. That you should like me so much—how could I feel otherwise? I shan't ever forget it. You know I'm promised to your father for a year, under oath that I shan't leave till the war's ended. Then I shall go home. Provided you'll let me. I don't want to stay here."

"Eliduc, I'm so grateful for your frankness. You're so honest, you know such a lot. Long before you go you'll have decided what to do with me. I love you, I trust you more than anything else in the world."

They knew now that they were sure of each other; and on that occasion no more was said.

Eliduc goes back to his lodgings, enchanted at how well things have turned out. He can talk as often as he likes with Guilliadun, they're wildly in love.

He now occupied himself so well with the war that he captured the enemy king, and liberated the old king's country. His military reputation grew, as did that of his ingenuity and public generosity. On this side of his life everything went very well.

But during this same time the king of Brittany had sent three messengers over the sea to find Eliduc. Things at home were in a very bad way, and getting worse. All his strong points were under siege, his lands being put to the sword. With increasing bitterness, the king regretted having driven Eliduc away. His judgment had been distorted by the malicious advice he had listened to. Already he had thrown the treacherous clique who had blackened Eliduc and intrigued against him into permanent exile. Now, in his hour of great need, he commanded, he summoned, he begged Eliduc—in the name of the trust that had existed between them ever since the knight first paid homage to him—to come and save the situation. He was in the direst straits.

Eliduc read this news. It distressed him deeply. He thought of Guilliadun. He loved her now to the anguished depths of his being, and she felt the same for him. But there had been no madness between them—nothing improper, theirs was no casual affair. Caressing and talking, giving each other lovely presents—the passionate feeling between them hadn't gone beyond that. She kept it so on purpose, because of what she hoped. She thought he'd be entirely hers, and hers alone, if she played her cards right.

She did not know there was a wife.

"Alas," thinks Eliduc to himself, "I've gone astray. I've stayed too long here. It was cursed, the day I first set eyes on this country. I've fallen head over heels in love. And she with me. If I have to say farewell to her now, one of us will die. Perhaps both. And yet I must go, the king of Brittany's letter commands it, and there's my promise to him. To say nothing of the one I swore my wife. I must pull myself together. I can't stay any longer, I have no alternative. If I were to marry Guilliadun, the Church would never stand for it. In all ways it's a mess. And oh God, to think of never seeing her again! I must be open with her, whatever the cost. I'll do whatever she wants, whichever way she sees it. Her father has got a decent peace, no one wants war with him anymore. I'll plead the king of Brittany's need and ask for permission to leave before the day's out. It was what was agreed—I'd go to him as soon as we had peace here. I'll see Guilliadun and explain the whole business. Then she can tell me what she wants, and I'll do my best to make it come true."

Without further delay, Eliduc went to the king to seek leave. He explained the situation in Brittany and showed him the letter the king there had sent him—the cry for help. The old king reads the command and realizes he will lose Eliduc. He is very upset and worried. He offered him a share of his possessions, a third of his heritage, his treasury—if he'll only stay, he'll do so much for him that Eliduc will be eternally grateful.

But Eliduc stayed firm.

"At this juncture, since my king's in danger and he's taken such trouble to find me, I must go to his assistance. Nothing would make me stop here. But if you ever need my services again, I'll willingly return—and bring plenty of other knights with me."

At that the king thanked him and gave him leave to go without further argument. He puts all his household possessions at Eliduc's disposal—

gold and silver, hounds and horses and beautiful silk. Eliduc took no more
than he needed. Then he politely told the king that he would like very
much to speak with his daughter, if it were allowed.

"Consent is a pleasure," said the king.

Eliduc sends a young lady ahead to open the door of Guilliadun's room.
Then he goes in to speak with her. When she saw him, she cried out his
name and passionately clung to him. Then they discussed his problem,
and he explained briefly the necessity for his journey. But when he had
made it all clear, and yet pointedly still not asked for her permission to
leave, for his freedom, she nearly fainted with the shock. Her face went
white. When Eliduc sees the agony she is in, he begins to go mad. He
keeps kissing her mouth and begins to cry in sympathy. At last he takes
her in his arms and holds her until she recovers.

"You sweetest thing, oh God, listen—you're life and death to me, you're
my whole existence. That's why I've come. So that we can talk about it,
and trust each other. I must go home. I've got your father's permission.
But I'll do whatever you want. Whatever may happen to me."

"Then take me with you, if you don't want to stay! If you don't, I'll kill
myself. Nothing good or happy will ever happen to me again."

Gently Eliduc tells her how much he loves her; how beautiful she is.
"But I've solemnly sworn to obey your father. If I take you away with me
I'll be breaking my oath to him before its term is over. I swear, I promise
you with all my heart that if you'll let me leave you now for a while, but
name a day on which I must come back, then nothing on earth will stop
me doing so—as long as I'm alive and in good health. My life's entirely in
your hands."

She loved him so much. So she gave him a final date, a day by which
he must return and take her away. They parted in tears and misery,
exchanging their gold rings and tenderly kissing each other.

Eliduc rode to the sea. The wind was good and the crossing quick.
When he gets home, the king of Brittany is overjoyed, and so are Eliduc's
relations and friends and everyone else—and especially his wife, who
remained as attractive and worthy of him as ever. But all the time Eliduc
stayed turned in on himself, because of the shock of his love affair in
England. Nothing he saw gave him any pleasure, he wouldn't smile—
he'll never be happy till he sees Guilliadun again. His wife was very
depressed by his secretive behavior, since she had no idea what caused it.
She felt sorry for herself; kept asking if he hadn't heard from someone
that she'd misbehaved while he was abroad. She'll willingly defend herself
before the world, whenever he wants.

"My lady, no one's accused you of anything bad. But I've solemnly
sworn to the king in the country where I've been that I shall return to him.
He has great need of me. I told him I'd be on my way within a week, as
soon as the king of Brittany had peace. I've got a huge task ahead of me
before I can return. I can't take pleasure in anything at all until I've got
back there. I *will* not break promises."

And that was all he told his wife. He went to join the king of Brittany
and helped him greatly. The king adopted his strategy and saved his kingdom. But when the date approached that Guilliadun had named, Eliduc

intervened to make peace. He agreed to all the terms the enemy wanted,[9] then he got ready to travel and picked his companions—two nephews he was fond of and one of his pages, a boy who had known what was going on and had carried messages between Eliduc and Guilliadun. Besides them, only his squires; he didn't want anyone else. He made these companions swear to keep the secret.

He waits no longer, puts to sea and soon arrives in Totnes. At last he was back where he was so longed for. Eliduc was very cunning. He found an inn well away from the harbor, since he was very anxious not to be seen . . . traced and recognized. He got his page ready and sent him to Guilliadun to tell her he had returned and kept strictly to his promise. By night, when darkness had fallen, she must slip out of the city; the page would escort her and Eliduc come to meet her. The boy changed into a disguise and went all the way on foot straight to Exeter. He cleverly found a way to get into her private apartments; then greeted the princess and told her her lover had come back. He found her sad and hopeless, but when she hears the news she breaks down and begins to cry, then kisses and kisses the page. He told her she must leave with him that evening; and they spent the whole day planning their escape in every detail.

When night had come, they stole cautiously out of the city alone together. They were terrified someone might see them. She wore a silk dress delicately embroidered in gold and a short cloak.

About a bowshot from the city gate there was a copse enclosed in a fine garden. Eliduc, who had come to fetch her, waited under the hedge. The page led her to the place. Eliduc sprang down from his horse and kissed her: such joy to meet again. He helped her onto a horse, then mounted his own and took her bridle. They rode quickly away, back to the port of Totnes, and boarded the ship at once: no other passengers but Eliduc's men and his beloved Guilliadun. They had favorable winds and settled weather, but when they came near the coast of Brittany they ran into a storm. A contrary wind drove them out away from the harbor. Then the mast split and broke, and they lost all the sails. They prayed in despair— to God, to St. Nicholas and St. Clement—to Our Lady, that she might invoke Christ's protection for them, save them from drowning and bring them to land. Backward and forward they were driven along the coast, the storm raging around them. One of the sailors began to shout.

"What are we doing? My lord, it's the girl you've brought aboard who's going to drown us all. We'll never reach land. You have a proper wife at home. But now you want another woman. It's against God and the law. Against all decency and religion. So let's throw her in the sea, and save our skins."

Eliduc hears what the man cries, and nearly goes berserk.

"You son of a whore, you fiend, you rat—shut your mouth! If she goes into the sea, I'll make you pay for it!"

He held Guilliadun in his arms, gave her what comfort he could. She was seasick, and riven by what she'd just heard: that her lover had a wife at home. She fainted and fell to the deck, deathly pale; and stayed like

---

9. The Old French says that he reconciled the enemy (to the king).

that, without breath or sign of consciousness. Eliduc knew she was only there because of him, and sincerely thought she was dead. He was in agony. He stood up and rushed at the sailor and struck him down with an oar. The man collapsed to the deck and Eliduc kicked the body over the side, where the waves took it away. As soon as he had done that, he went to the helm. There he steered and held the ship so well that they came to the harbor and land. When they were safely in, he cast anchor and had the gangway let down. Still Guilliadun lay unconscious, her only appearance that of death. Eliduc wept without stop—if he had had his way, he would have been dead with her. He asked his companions their advice, where he could carry her. He refused to leave her side until she was buried with every honor and full ritual, and laid to rest in holy ground. She was a king's daughter, it was her due. But his men were at a loss and could suggest nothing. Eliduc began to think for himself. His own house was not far from the sea, not a day's ride away. There was a forest around it, some thirty miles across. A saintly hermit had lived there for forty years and had a chapel. Eliduc had often spoken with him.

I'll take her there, Eliduc said to himself, I'll bury her in his chapel. Then bestow land and found an abbey or a monastery. Nuns or canons, who can pray for her every day, may God have mercy on her soul.

He had horses brought and ordered everyone to mount, then made them promise they would never betray him. He carried Guilliadun's body in front of him, on his own horse. They took the most direct road and soon entered the forest. At last they came to the chapel, and called and knocked. But no voice answered and the door stayed closed. Eliduc made one of his men climb in and open it. They found a fresh tomb: the pure and saintly hermit had died that previous week. They stood there sad and dismayed. The men wanted to prepare the grave in which Eliduc must leave Guilliadun forever, but he made them withdraw outside the chapel.

"This isn't right. I need advice first from the experts on how I can glorify this place with an abbey or a convent. For now we'll lay Guilliadun before the altar and leave her in God's care."

He had bedding brought and they quickly made a resting place for the girl; then laid her there, and left her for dead. But when Eliduc came to leave the chapel, he thought he would die of pain. He kissed her eyes, her face.

"Darling heart, may it please God I'll never bear arms again or live in the outer world. I damn the day you ever saw me. Dear gentle thing, why did you come with me? Not even a queen could have loved me more trustingly. More deeply. My heart breaks for you. On the day I bury you, I'll enter a monastery. Then come here every day and weep all my desolation out on your tomb."

Abruptly then he turned from the girl's body and closed the chapel door.

He had sent a messenger on ahead to tell his wife he was coming, but tired and worn. Full of happiness at the news, she dressed to meet him; and welcomed him back affectionately. But she had little joy of it. Eliduc gave her not a single smile or a kind word. No one dared to ask why. He stayed like that for a couple of days—each early morning, having heard

mass, he took the road to the forest and the chapel where Guilliadun lay
. . . still unconscious, without breathing, no sign of life. Yet something
greatly puzzled him: she had hardly lost color, her skin stayed pink and
white, only very faintly pale. In profound despair, Eliduc wept and prayed
for her soul. Then having done that, he returned home.

The following day, when he came out of the church after mass, there
was a spy—a young servant his wife had promised horses and arms to if he
could follow at a distance and see which way his master went. The lad did
as she ordered. He rides into the forest after Eliduc without being seen.
He watched well, saw how Eliduc went into the chapel, and heard the
state he was in. As soon as Eliduc came out, the servant went home and
told his mistress everything—all the sounds of anguish her husband had
made inside the chapel. From being resentful, she now felt touched.

"We'll go there as soon as possible and search the place. Your master
must be off soon to court, to confer with the king. The hermit died some
time ago. I know Eliduc was very fond of him, but that wouldn't make
him behave like this. Not show such grief."

Thus for the time being she left the mystery.

That very same afternoon Eliduc set off to speak with the king of Brittany. His wife took the servant with her and he led her to the hermitage
chapel. As soon as she went in she saw the bed and the girl lying on it, as
fresh as a first rose. She pulled back the covering and revealed the slender
body, the slim arms, the white hands with their long and delicately
smooth-skinned fingers. She knew the truth at once—why Eliduc had his
tragic face. She called the servant forward and showed him the miraculous
corpse.

"Do you see this girl? She's as lovely as a jewel. She's my husband's
mistress. That's why he's so miserable. Somehow it doesn't shock me. So
pretty . . . to have died so young. I feel only pity for her. And I still love
him. It's a tragedy for us all."

She began to cry, in sympathy for Guilliadun. But as she sat by the
deathbed with tears in her eyes a weasel darts out from beneath the altar.
The servant struck at it with a stick to stop it running over the corpse. He
killed it, then threw the small body into the middle of the chancel floor.
It had not been there long when its mate appeared and saw where it lay.
The living animal ran around the dead one's head and touched it several
times with a foot. But when this failed, it seemed distressed. Suddenly it
ran out of the chapel into the forest grass. There it picked a deep red
flower with its teeth, then carried it quickly back and placed it in the
mouth of the weasel the servant had killed. Instantly the animal came
back to life. The wife had watched all this, and now she cried out to the
servant.

"Catch it! Throw, boy! Don't let it escape!"

He hurled his stick and hit the weasel. The blossom fell from between
its teeth. Eliduc's wife went and picked it up, then returned and placed the
exquisite red flower in Guilliadun's mouth. For a second or two nothing
happened, but then the girl stirred, sighed, and opened her eyes.[1]

---

1. Abundant parallels from folklore represent an animal as having the gift of immortality—or being able
to restore life after apparent death.

"Good lord," she murmured, "how long I've slept!"

When the wife heard her speak, she thanked heaven. Then she asked Guilliadun who she was.

"My lady, I'm British born, the daughter of a king there. I fell hopelessly in love with a knight, a brave mercenary called Eliduc. He eloped with me. But he was wicked, he deceived me. He had a wife all the time. He never told me, never gave me the least hint. When I heard the truth, I fainted with the agony of it. Now he's brutally left me helpless here in a foreign country. He tricked me, I don't know what will become of me. Women are mad to trust in men."

"My dear," said the lady, "he's been quite inconsolable. I can assure you of that. He thinks you're dead, he's been mad with grief. He's come here to look at you every day. But obviously you've always been unconscious. I'm his real wife, and I'm deeply sorry for him. He was so unhappy . . . I wanted to find out where he was disappearing to, so I had him followed, and that's how I found you. And now I'm glad you're alive after all. I'm going to take you away with me. And give you back to him. I'll tell the world he's not to blame for anything. Then I shall take the veil."

She spoke so comfortingly that Guilliadun went home with her. The wife made the servant get ready and sent him after Eliduc. He rode hard and soon came up with him. The lad greeted Eliduc respectfully, then tells him the whole story. Eliduc leaps on a horse, without waiting for his friends. That same night he was home, and found Guilliadun restored to life. He gently thanks his wife, he's in his seventh heaven, he's never known such happiness. He can't stop kissing Guilliadun; and she keeps kissing him shyly back. They can't hide their joy at being reunited. When Eliduc's wife saw how things stood, she told her husband her plans. She asked his formal permission for a separation, she wished to become a nun and serve God. He must give her some of his land and she would found an abbey on it. And then he must marry the girl he loved so much, since it was neither decent nor proper, besides being against the law, to live with two wives. Eliduc did not try to argue with her; he'll do exactly as she wants and give her the land.

In the same woodlands near the castle that held the hermitage chapel he had a church built, and all the other offices of a nunnery. Then he settled a great deal of property and other possessions on it. When everything was ready, his wife took the veil, along with thirty other nuns. Thus she established her order and her new way of life.

Eliduc married Guilliadun. The wedding was celebrated with great pomp and circumstance, and for a long time they lived happily together in a perfect harmony of love. They gave a great deal away and performed many good deeds, so much so that in the end they also turned religious. After great deliberation and forethought, Eliduc had a church built on the other side of his castle and endowed it with all his money and the greater part of his estate. He appointed servants and other religious people to look after the order and its buildings. When all was ready, he delays no more: he surrenders himself with his servants to omnipotent God. And Guilliadun, whom he loved so much, he sent to join his first wife. Guildelüec received her as if she were her own sister and did her great honor, teaching

her how to serve God and live the religious life of the order. They prayed for the salvation of Eliduc's soul, and in his turn he prayed for both of them. He found out by messengers how they were, how they comforted each other. All three tried in their own ways to love God with true faith; and in the end, by the mercy of God in whom all truth reposes, each died a peaceful death.

The noble Celts composed this story long ago to enshrine the strange adventure of these three. May it never be forgotten!

DANTE ALIGHIERI
1265–1321

The greatest poem of the Middle Ages, called by its author a comedy and designated in later centuries *The Divine Comedy (La divina commedia)*, was written in the early fourteenth century. The poet, Dante Alighieri, was born in late May 1265, in Florence, Italy. In 1291 he married Gemma Donati, by whom he had two sons and one or two daughters. In 1295 he was a member of the "people's council" of Florence and in 1300 served for two months, the usual term, as one of the six priors, or magistrates, of Florence. In 1302 the Blacks, opponents of the Whites (a political group with which Dante was affiliated), seized power in Florence, and he, with other White leaders, was exiled. Dante had gone to Rome on a mission to Pope Boniface in 1301, and as the decree of banishment was soon coupled with a condemnation to execution by fire (on false charges of corruption in office), he never returned to his native city. The last twenty years of his life were spent in exile in various parts of Italy and possibly elsewhere. He died at Ravenna in September 1321.

The New Life (Vita nuova) was probably written about 1292. It consists of sonnets and odes with a prose account and running commentary by the poet; the poems were mostly inspired by Beatrice Portinari (1266–1290), Dante's first love, who appears in the *Commedia* as a heavenly guide whose name signifies blessedness or salvation. *The Banquet* (of uncertain date and unfinished) is a work of encyclopedic scope in the form of a prose commentary on a series of the poet's odes (*canzoni*). *On the Vernacular Language*, in Latin prose (of uncertain date and unfinished), is an essay on language and poetry, especially on the dialects of Italy and Provence; it is of great linguistic and literary interest. *On Single Government* (of uncertain date), in Latin prose, presents a closely reasoned defense of world government, together with an attempt to demonstrate the independent status of the Holy Roman Empire and the papacy.

The Divine Comedy (begun ca. 1301) was apparently finished shortly before Dante's death in 1321. The poem is in many ways both the supreme and the centrally representative expression of the medieval mind in European imaginative literature. But to appreciate the poem adequately in this light the reader must know it in its entirety, since it is an organic whole designed with the utmost symmetry. The selection printed here includes the entire *Inferno*. It will be best to look rapidly at the general plan and then concentrate on the part included here.

The three great divisions of the poem—Hell (*Inferno*), Purgatory (*Purgatorio*), and Paradise (*Paradiso*)—are of identical length; each of the last two has thirty-three cantos, and the first, the *Inferno*, has thirty-four; but the opening canto is a

prologue to the entire poem. The total, one hundred, is the square of ten, regarded in the thought of the time as a perfect number. The three divisions correspond in number to the Trinity. Nine, the square of three, figures centrally in the interior structure of each of the three divisions. In Hell, the lost souls are arranged in three main groups and occupy nine circles. Most of the circles are themselves subdivided. Hell itself is a funnel-shaped opening in the earth extending from the surface to the center. Dante's journey thus takes him steadily downward through the nine concentric circles. The progression is from the least to the greatest types of evil; all the souls are irrevocably condemned, but all are not intrinsically equal in the degree or nature of their sin. Thus, as we follow Dante in his descent, we find first an ante-Hell, the abode of those who refused to choose between right and wrong; then the boundary river, Acheron; then a circle for virtuous pagans who did not know Christ; and then a series of circles occupied by those guilty of sins of self-indulgence, or Incontinence, of all kinds. These include the illicit lovers, the gluttons, the hoarders and spendthrifts, and those of violent or sullen disposition. Comparable classes and subclasses are found within the other two main groups of sinners, those guilty respectively of Violence and of Fraud, the latter including treachery and treason. At the bottom is the fallen Angel, Satan, or Lucifer.

Purgatory is situated on a lofty mountain rising on an island in the sea. It is divided into the ante-Purgatory, which is the lower half of the mountain; Purgatory proper, just above; and the Earthly Paradise, or Garden of Eden, at the summit. Purgatory proper is arranged in a series of seven ledges encircling the mountain, each devoted to the purification of souls from particular kinds of sinful disposition—Pride, Envy, Anger, Sloth, Avarice, Gluttony, and Illicit Love. These seven divisions, plus the ante-Purgatory and the Earthly Paradise, make a total of nine.

The *Paradise* takes us, in ascending order, through the circles of the seven planets of medieval astronomy, the moon, Mercury, Venus, the sun, Mars, Jupiter, and Saturn; then through the circles of the fixed stars and the *primum mobile*, or outermost circle, which moves the others; and finally to the Empyrean, or Heaven itself, the abode of God, the angels, and the redeemed souls. Again we have nine circles, besides the Empyrean, inclusion of which would give a total of ten. Such is the vast design and scope of *The Divine Comedy* as a whole.

INFERNO

The poem itself begins with action, not outline; explanations appear in suitable places; they are part of the traveler's experience. We shall do well to follow the hint. The incidents recounted in Canto I of the *Inferno* are concrete and definite; their literal meaning is perfectly plain. As critics have often said, Dante is a highly visual poet; he gives us clear pictures or images. Beginning with a man lost in a wood, hindered by three beasts from escape by his own effort, the canto might well be the start of a tale of unusual but quite earthly adventures. But when the stranger Dante meets identifies himself as the shade of the poet Virgil and offers to conduct him through realms that, though not named, can only be Hell and Purgatory, we realize that there is a meaning beyond the one that appears on the surface. We recognize that the wood, the mountain, the sun, and the three beasts, though casually introduced, are not casual features of the scene. They represent something other than themselves; they are symbols. In the light of the entire poem, it is usually possible to determine, at least in a general sense, what they signify, and in this volume the headnotes and footnotes identify them. Occasionally, however, there is doubt. What do the three beasts stand for? A lack of certainty is not a serious disadvantage to readers; they should regard it as a challenge to reach a decision for themselves. Indeed, if they go on to read the entire poem, they may

arrive at an identification that seems sounder and more consistent with the work as a whole than those proposed here. Meanwhile, there is no ambiguity about the animals themselves; they are the satisfying and specific images of poetry.

The simple style of this first canto may surprise readers who have been told that *The Divine Comedy* is one of the five or six great poems of European literature, especially if they assume that it will sound like an epic. For Dante begins with neither the splendor of Homer nor the stateliness of Virgil nor the grandeur of Milton. Indeed, except for the use of verse, Canto I seems more like a narrative by Daniel Defoe or Jonathan Swift, particularly at the outset. It is quiet, factual, economical; it convinces us by its air of serious simplicity. Dante called the poem a comedy, in accordance with the use of the term in his day, not only because it began in misery and ended in happiness but also because in that literary form a sustained loftiness of style was not requisite. In other words, he is free to use the whole range of style, from the humblest, including the colloquial and the humorous, to the highest. There is, indeed, a great variety of tone in the poem. Yet readers will doubtless eventually agree that Dante strikes the right note *for him* at the beginning. Variation will result chiefly from change in intensity, achieved by differing degrees of concentration and repetition—rather than from a shift to the "grand style." This unpretentious manner is, we see, most suitable to a prolonged work of serious fiction in which the author is the central character. For *The Divine Comedy* is not primarily a Cook's tour of the world of the dead; it is an account of the effect of such a journey on the man who takes it—Dante. It is a record of his moral and spiritual experience of illumination, regeneration, and beatitude. We are interested partly because of the unique and individual character of the traveler—Dante as the man he was, the man revealed in the poem—and partly because the experience of the author is imaginatively available and meaningful to all of us.

In Canto IV we come to the first of the nine concentric circles of Hell. Here are the noble heroes, wise philosophers, and inspired poets of the ancient—and medieval—pagan world. They are excluded from Heaven because they knew nothing of Christ and His religion. This fate may seem harsh to us, but the orthodox view recognized only one gate to Heaven. These spirits suffer no punishment, Virgil (who is one of them) tells Dante, only "without hope, we live on in desire." Here Dante's fervent pity and sympathy at once nourish and mirror the reader's; but there is no rebellion against God's decree. Further explanation, and thereby justification, in Dante's view, will come as the poem progresses toward its goal.

With Canto V we reach the second circle, the first of those containing souls guilty of active sin unrepented at the time of death. Here, therefore, is found the contemptuous and monstrous judge Minos, another figure taken from classical myth and freely adapted to Dante's purposes. The souls assigned to the second circle are those guilty of unlawful love. The poet's method here, as throughout the journey, is first to point out a number of prominent figures who would be familiar to his fourteenth-century readers, and then to concentrate attention on a very few, one or two in each circle, telling more about them and eliciting their stories. In general, Dante lets the place and condition in which the sinners are found serve as a minimum essential of information. For the penalties in the various circles are of many different kinds. Their fundamental characteristic is appropriateness to the particular sin; this is one of the principal differences between the punishments in Dante's Hell and the miscellaneous and arbitrary horrors of many accounts of the place. In Dante the penalties symbolize the sin. Thus the illicit lovers of the second circle are continually blown about by storm winds, for their sin consisted in the surrender of reason to lawless passions.

Here we find Paolo and Francesca, the best-known figures of the entire *Divine Comedy*. Like all the human beings presented in the poem, they actually existed.

They lived in Italy about the time of Dante's childhood and early youth, and were slain by Francesca's husband, a brother of Paolo. Dante's method, it is hence clear, is not to build up an allegorical cast of personified abstractions. Instead of, say, Passion and Rebellion, he portrays Paolo and Francesca. They represent, or symbolize, sinful love by example. They show how an intrinsically noble emotion, love, if contrary to God's law, can bring two essentially fine persons to damnation and spiritual ruin. The tenderness and the sympathy with which the story is told are famous. But its pathos, and Dante's personal response of overwhelming pity, should not blind us to the *justice* of the penalty. The poet who describes himself as fainting at the end of Francesca's recital is the same man who consigned her to Hell. His purpose is partly to portray the attractiveness of sin, an especially congenial theme when *this* is the sin involved—both for Dante and for most readers. But although Dante allows the lovers the bitter sweetness of inseparability in Hell, the modern "romantic" idea that union anywhere is sufficient happiness for lovers does not even occur to him. Paolo and Francesca indeed have their love; but they have lost God and thus corrupted their personalities—their inmost selves—from order into anarchy; they can hardly be considered happy. In a sense, they have what they wanted; they continue in the lawless condition that they chose on earth. But that condition, seen from the point of view of eternity, is not bliss.

In Canto X we are among the heretics in their flaming tomb in the sixth circle. Situated within the walled city of Dis—the capital, as it were, of Hell—this circle is a kind of border between the upper Hell (devoted to punishments for Incontinence) and the lower (concerned with Violence and Fraud). Here Dante portrays the proud aristocrat Farinata and his associate, the elder Cavalcante, father of Dante's closest friend. Their crime is heresy, a flagrant aspect of intellectual pride. But there is a nobility in Farinata's pride; Dante, like the reader, admires the splendid self-sufficiency of a man who, in this situation, can seem "to hold all Hell in disrespect." And the essence of the aristocratic nature is distilled in his address to Dante as "the great soul stared almost contemptuously, / before he asked: 'Of what line do you come?' " and in his abrupt resumption of the conversation interrupted by Cavalcante. Alongside the haughtiness of Farinata, Dante sets the pathetic—and mistaken—grief of Cavalcante for his son; each portrait gains in effect by the extreme contrast.

Canto XIII shows us one group of those guilty of Violence; for the suicides have been violent against themselves. Here they are turned into monstrous trees, their misery finding expression when a bough is torn or plucked. In the eyes of the Church, suicide was murder, in no way diminished by the fact that the slayer and the victim were the same. By representing in Pier delle Vigne a man who had every human motive to end his life, Dante achieves the deepest pathos and evokes our shuddering pity. As Francesca displays in her dramatic monologue the charm and the potential weakness of her character, as Farinata's manner of speech reveals his nature, so Pier delle Vigne by his exact and legal-sounding language lets us see the careful, methodical counselor whose sense of logic and sense of justice were so outraged that he saw no point in enduring life any longer. His judgment is still unimpaired; he does not reproach his king, only the jealous courtiers who misled him. The Wood of the Suicides is one of the greatest—among many admirable—examples of landscape in Hell assimilated to theme and situation.

Canto XV describes the meeting of Dante and his venerable teacher and adviser, the scholar Brunetto Latini. We are in another ring of the seventh circle, among more of those who have sinned through Violence. The impact of this scene results from the contrast between the dignity of the man and the indignity of his condition in hell, and by the tact with which both he and Dante ignore it for the moment. Brunetto, with the others guilty of homosexual "vice," must move continually along a sandy desert under a rain of fire. Dante accords him the utmost

respect and expresses his gratitude in the warmest terms; and something like their earthly relationship of teacher and pupil is reenacted, for Brunetto is keenly interested in Dante's prospects in life. In the final image of Brunetto running, not like the loser, but like the winner of a race, Dante extracts dignity and victory out of indignity itself.

The presence of such people as these will remind the reader that Hell is not reserved exclusively for arrant scoundrels. They are there, of course; but so are many charming, and some noble and great, men and women. These are in Hell because they preferred something else—no matter what—to God; at the moment of death they were therefore in rebellion against Him. God and Heaven would not be congenial to them, *as they are and as He is*; and there is no acceptable repentance after death. Hence they go on unchanged—only now experiencing the harsher aspects of the sin in which they chose to live.

In Canto XVII the travelers are carried on the back of the flying monster Geryon down the deep descent from the seventh to the eighth circle. With the face of a just man and the body of a serpent, Geryon symbolizes Fraud. He is one of the most exciting figures in Hell. In an age before Ferris wheels and airplanes, he gives our poets a ride that anticipates some of the terrifying thrill that a young child may feel in an airplane journey. The eighth circle is subdivided into ten chasms or trenches (Malebolge), each with its own kind of sinners: seducers and panderers, flatterers, simoniacs (buyers and sellers of appointments in the Church), sorcerers, grafters, hypocrites, thieves, evil counselors, troublemakers, forgers, and impostors.

Most readers will agree that the punishments fit the crimes of the eighth circle. It is a long catalog of iniquity; much, but not all, is sordid. Dante has avoided monotony not only by the vividness and intensity of the separate scenes but also by their ingenious variety and by the frequent changes of pace in the narrative. The satirical situation and fierce denunciation of the simoniacs is followed by the quiet horror of the sorcerers with twisted necks. The hilarious episode of the grafters precedes the encounter with the solemn, slow-walking hypocrites; and these are succeeded by the macabre serpent-transformations of the thieves. Nevertheless, our slow descent in Hell gradually produces a sense of oppressiveness. This is appropriate and deliberate; it is a part of Dante's total design. But he recognizes the need of momentary relief, a breath of fresh air, a reminder of the world above. These he provides, for example, in the long simile describing the shipyard in Venice (the opening of Canto XXI) or the picture of the peasant and his two sallies outside on a winter morning (the opening of Canto XXIV).

The episode of the grafters (Cantos XXI and XXII) probably has biographical relevance for Dante. During his absence from Florence on business of state, the opposing political party seized power and sentenced Dante to death if he should return to Florence. The quite unfounded charge against him was misappropriation of public funds. In these cantos Dante cuts a ludicrous figure: fearful, cowering, in constant danger from the demons. He escapes their clutches, first by a distraction and then by belated vigilance. The whole sequence affords an oblique and amusing view of an actual episode. It is worth noting also that here, and here only, in the poem, we find ourselves in the kind of Hell known in popular lore and anecdote, with winged devils playing rough jokes on their human prey. Scenes, style, and language alike here show one extreme of the range of the poem—the "low" comic. Dante very unobtrusively indicates his awareness of this by the contrasting allusions found in Canto XX.113 and Canto XXI.2.

Cantos XXVI and XXVII take us among the wicked counselors, who occupy the eighth chasm, or subdivision, of the eighth circle. Appearing at a distance like fireflies in a summer valley, these souls are wrapped in individual, or occasionally

twin, flames. Fire is a fit punishment for those who used the flame of intellect to accomplish evil. When the two poets approach more closely, Virgil identifies one flame as that of Ulysses (Odysseus) and Diomede, who burn together. Among the deceptions devised by Ulysses was the wooden horse, which made possible the capture of Troy. It will strike the reader as strange that a man should suffer for his powers as a military tactician. But the Greeks were enemies of the Trojans, whom the Romans and later most of the nations of western Europe regarded as their ancestors. Ulysses was on the wrong side and was responsible for his deeds, but Dante mingles with his condemnation an admiration of the man's mental powers. Ulysses remains aloof; he does not converse with Dante, like most of the souls we have met. Instead, as Dorothy Sayers puts it in the notes to her translation of the poem, Virgil conjures the flame into monologue. Thus we are told how Ulysses determined not to return home after the Trojan War but to explore the western ocean instead. In this narrative, apparently invented by Dante, Ulysses becomes the type of the adventuring and searching spirit of man; the voyage is an act of the mind and soul as well as the body. When he has sailed within sight of a mountainous island, his ship is wrecked by a storm and he perishes. Since, as other parts of the poem indicate, this is the island of Purgatory, the episode clearly has symbolic significance. On this island is the Earthly Paradise, or Garden of Eden, lost to us by the sin of Adam. People, unassisted by divine grace—pagans, represented by Ulysses—cannot regain it by their own intelligence, although the effort toward that end is noble in itself.

The other evil counselor, Guido da Montefeltro, speaks fluently in Canto XXVII; he shows a quite earthly eagerness for news, crafty, garrulous old intriguer that he is. It is a neat irony that, in spite of Guido's deserved reputation for cleverness, Dante shows him twice deceived: first on earth, as he himself relates, and now in Hell—he does not want his story known and is convinced that Dante will never return to earth to tell it. He sketches in detail, with recollective acidity, the steps by which the pope led him, an aging and reformed man, to return for a moment to his old ways. He even includes the contest of St. Francis and the Devil for his soul at his death, along with the Devil's bitter witticism: you didn't think I was a logician, perhaps!

In Cantos XXXII and XXXIII the poet reaches the ninth and last circle, where the traitors are immersed in ice that symbolizes their unfeeling hearts. At the end of one canto we are shown the horror of Ugolino gnawing the skull of his enemy Ruggieri, both partly fastened in the ice. Dante does not concentrate on the acts that have put either man in Hell. Instead he lets Ugolino tell us, in the next canto, why his hatred of Ruggieri is so implacable. The fearful pathos, the power, and at the same time the restraint and compression of this narrative make it one of the finest episodes in the poem.

The last canto, Canto XXXIV, shows us the enormous shape of the fallen Angel, Satan, fixed at the bottom of Hell, where the motion of his wings freezes the ice in which we have found the traitors immersed. In one of his three mouths he holds Judas Iscariot, who betrayed Christ; in the other two are Brutus and Cassius, who plotted the assassination of Julius Caesar. Dante did not regard them, as we generally do today, as perhaps misguided patriots; to him they were the destroyers of a providentially ordained ruler. Readers who remember John Milton's *Paradise Lost* may be surprised at the absence of any interior presentation of Satan. One critic regrets that his suffering is not shown as different from that of the other inhabitants of Hell. But the fact is that his suffering is not presented at all; he is not a person, to Dante, but an object, a part of the machinery and geography of Hell. For *The Divine Comedy* is occupied exclusively with human sin, human redemption, and human beatitude.

DANTE IN ITALIAN

The translator of the selections printed here is the American poet John Ciardi. As with some other poems in this volume, the reader may find it interesting to have a brief look at the original text, so here are the opening lines of the *Inferno* in the Italian.

> Nel mezzo del cammin di nostra vita
> mi retrovai per una selva oscura
> ché la diritta via era smarrita.
>
> Ah, quanto a dir qual era è cosa dura
> esta selva selvaggia e aspra e forte   5
> che nel pensier rinova la paura!
>
> Tant'è amara che poco è più morte;
> ma per trattar del ben ch'io vi trovai,
> dirò dell'altre cose ch'i' v'ho scorte.
>
> Io non so ben ridir com'io v'entrai,   10
> tant'era pieno di sonno a quel punto
> che la verace via abbandonai.

The individual lines are metrically similar to most lines in Chaucer and Shakespeare; they regularly have five metrical feet, each consisting of an unstressed syllable followed by a stressed one, or vice versa, with the possibility of an additional unstressed syllable or two somewhere within the line. But the most notable metrical feature of the *Divine Comedy* is the pattern of rhymes, or the *terza rima*. Thus the lines form groups of three: *vita* in the first line rhymes with the last two syllables of *smarrita* in the third line, while *oscura* in the second line rhymes with *dura* in line four and *paura* in line six of the next group. The groups are independent units interlocked by the sequence of rhymes. This overall structure reminds the reader of the Christian Trinity: God the Father, Son, and Holy Spirit; it is one expression of the poet's religious devotion. In his translation Ciardi maintains the separation into groups of three lines: *astray* in the first line rhymes with *I say* in the third. But he does not keep the interlocking rhyme scheme: *myself* in line two of the first group does not rhyme with *drear* and *fear* in the second group. The sound structure of the Italian language makes Dante's rhyme patterns easier than this arrangement would be in an English poem. Attempts to reproduce it entirely have not been very successful in English.

For biographical information, the general reader will find Michele Barbi, *Life of Dante* (1954), readable and convenient. Also helpful for background is Dorothy Sayers, *Introductory Papers on Dante* (1954), as well as her *Further Papers on Dante* (1957). T. G. Bergin, *Dante's Divine Comedy* (1971), is a valuable overall account. The series of *Dante Studies* (1956) by Charles S. Singleton is intensive and demanding. Important studies of particular topics are Erich Auerbach, *Dante, Poet of the Secular World* (1961) and John Freccero, ed., *Dante: A Collection of Critical Essays* (1965). Freccero is also the author of *Dante, The Poetics of Conversion* (1986). The most helpful introduction for the newcomer to the *Inferno* is Wallace Fowlie, *A Reading of Dante's Inferno* (1981).

A broader context of study and interpretation is attempted in K. Vossler, *Medieval Culture: An Introduction to Dante and his Times* (1929), and E. R. Curtius, *European Literature and the Latin Middle Ages* (1953). A still broader context can be found in George Santayana, "Dante," in *Three Philosophical Poets* (1910), and T. S. Eliot, "Dante," in *Selected Essays* (1932).

PRONOUNCING GLOSSARY

The following list uses common English syllables and stress accents to provide rough equivalents of selected words whose pronunciation may be unfamiliar to the general reader.

Alessio: *ah-les'-syoh*

Arezzo: *ah-rets'-soh*

Argenti: *ar-jen'-tee*

Bacchiglione: *bahk-kee-yoh'-nay*

Beatrice: *bay-ah-tree'-chay*

Borsiere: *bor-syeh'-ray*

Brescia: *bre'-shah*

Casalodi: *cah-zah-loh'-dee*

Cecina: *chay-chee'-nah*

Chiarentana: *kyahr-en-tah'-nah*

Ciacco: *chahk'-koh*

Jacopo: *yah'-coh-poh*

luce: *loo'-chay*

Puccio: *poo'-chyoh*

Pugliese: *poo-lyay'-zay*

Rusticucci: *roo-stee-koo'-chee*

Schicchi: *skee'-kee*

Sciancato: *shahn-kah'-toh*

Tegghiaio: *teg-gyai'-oh*

Verruchio: *vehr-roo'-chyoh*

Zanche: *tsahn'-kay*

From The Divine Comedy[1]

Inferno

CANTO I

The Dark Wood of Error

Midway in his allotted threescore years and ten, Dante comes to himself with a start and realizes that he has strayed from the True Way into the Dark Wood of Error (Worldliness). As soon as he has realized his loss, Dante lifts his eyes and sees the first light of the sunrise (the Sun is the Symbol of Divine Illumination) lighting the shoulders of a little hill (The Mount of Joy). It is the Easter Season, the time of resurrection, and the sun is in its equinoctial rebirth. This juxtaposition of joyous symbols fills Dante with hope and he sets out at once to climb directly up the Mount of Joy, but almost immediately his way is blocked by the Three Beasts of Worldliness: The Leopard of Malice and Fraud, The Lion of Violence and Ambition, and The She-Wolf of Incontinence. These beasts, and especially the She-Wolf, drive him back despairing into the darkness of error. But just as all seems lost, a figure appears to him. It is the shade of Virgil, Dante's symbol of Human Reason.

Virgil explains that he has been sent to lead Dante from error. There can, however, be no direct ascent past the beasts: the man who would escape them must go a longer and harder way. First he must descend through Hell (The Recognition of Sin), then he must ascend through Purgatory (The Renunciation of Sin), and only then may he reach the pinnacle of joy and come to the Light of God. Virgil offers to guide Dante, but only as far as Human Reason can go. Another guide (Beatrice, symbol

---

1. Translated, with notes and commentary, by John Ciardi.

of Divine Love) must take over for the final ascent, for Human Reason is self-limited. Dante submits himself joyously to Virgil's guidance and they move off.

The Slope of Hell

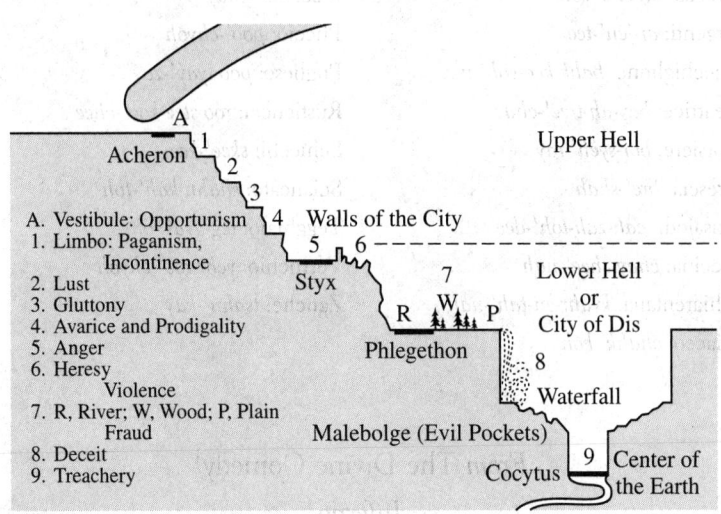

A. Vestibule: Opportunism
1. Limbo: Paganism, Incontinence
2. Lust
3. Gluttony
4. Avarice and Prodigality
5. Anger
6. Heresy
   Violence
7. R, River; W, Wood; P, Plain
   Fraud
8. Deceit
9. Treachery

Upper Hell
Walls of the City
Lower Hell
or
City of Dis
Phlegethon
Waterfall
Malebolge (Evil Pockets)
Cocytus
Center of the Earth

Hell is entirely below the surface of the earth; Dante moves steadily downward until he reaches earth's center at the bottom of hell. There is a corresponding gradation or hierarchy of evil—from bad to worse to worst.

Midway in our life's journey,[2] I went astray
　from the straight road and woke to find myself
　alone in a dark wood. How shall I say
what wood that was! I never saw so drear,
　so rank, so arduous a wilderness!
　Its very memory gives a shape to fear.　　　　　　　　　　5
Death could scarce be more bitter than that place!
　But since it came to good, I will recount
　all that I found revealed there by God's grace.
How I came to it I cannot rightly say,　　　　　　　　　　10
　so drugged and loose with sleep had I become
　when I first wandered there from the True Way.
But at the far end of that valley of evil
　whose maze had sapped my very heart with fear,
　I found myself before a little hill　　　　　　　　　　　15
and lifted up my eyes. Its shoulders glowed
　already with the sweet rays of that planet[3]
　whose virtue leads men straight on every road,
and the shining strengthened me against the fright
　whose agony had wracked the lake of my heart　　　　　20
　through all the terrors of that piteous night.
Just as a swimmer, who with his last breath

---

2. The biblical life span is three-score years and ten (seventy years). The action opens in Dante's thirty-fifth year, i.e., 1300 A.D.　　3. The sun. Ptolemaic astronomers considered it a planet. It is also symbolic of God as He who lights the way.

flounders ashore from perilous seas, might turn
to memorize the wide water of his death—
so did I turn, my soul still fugitive   25
from death's surviving image, to stare down
that pass that none had ever left alive.
And there I lay to rest from my heart's race
till calm and breath returned to me. Then rose
and pushed up that dead slope at such a pace   30
each footfall rose above the last.[4] And lo!
almost at the beginning of the rise
I faced a spotted Leopard, all tremor and flow
and gaudy pelt. And it would not pass, but stood
so blocking my every turn that time and again   35
I was on the verge of turning back to the wood.
This fell at the first widening of the dawn
as the sun was climbing Aries with those stars
that rode with him to light the new creation.[5]
Thus the holy hour and the sweet season   40
of commemoration did much to arm my fear
of that bright murderous beast with their good omen.
Yet not so much but what I shook with dread
at sight of a great Lion that broke upon me
raging with hunger, its enormous head   45
held high as if to strike a mortal terror
into the very air. And down his track,
a She-Wolf drove upon me, a starved horror
ravening and wasted beyond all belief.[6]
She seemed a rack for avarice, gaunt and craving.   50
Oh many the souls she has brought to endless grief!
She brought such heaviness upon my spirit
at sight of her savagery and desperation,
I died from every hope of that high summit.
And like a miser—eager in acquisition   55
but desperate in self-reproach when Fortune's wheel
turns to the hour of his loss—all tears and attrition
I wavered back; and still the beast pursued,
forcing herself against me bit by bit
till I slid back into the sunless wood.   60
And as I fell to my soul's ruin, a presence
gathered before me on the discolored air,
the figure of one who seemed hoarse from long silence.
At sight of him in that friendless waste I cried:

4. The literal rendering would be: "So that the fixed foot was ever the lower." "Fixed" has often been translated "right" and an ingenious reasoning can support that reading, but a simpler explanation offers itself and seems more competent: Dante is saying that he climbed with such zeal and haste that every footfall carried him above the last despite the steepness of the climb. At a slow pace, on the other hand, the rear foot might be brought up only as far as the forward foot.   5. The medieval tradition had it that the sun was in Aries at the time of the Creation. The significance of the astronomical and religious conjunction is an important part of Dante's intended allegory. It is just before dawn of Good Friday 1300 A.D. when he awakens in the Dark Wood. Thus his new life begins under Aries, the sign of creation, at dawn (rebirth) and in the Easter season (resurrection). Moreover the moon is full and the sun is in the equinox, conditions that did not fall together on any Friday of 1300. Dante is obviously constructing poetically the perfect Easter as a symbol of his new awakening.   6. These three beasts undoubtedly are taken from Jeremiah v, 6. Many additional and incidental interpretations have been advanced for them, but the central interpretation must remain as noted. They foreshadow the three divisions of Hell (incontinence, violence, and fraud) which Virgil explains at length in Canto XI, 16–111.

"Have pity on me, whatever thing you are,   65
    whether shade or living man." And it replied:
"Not man, though man I once was, and my blood
    was Lombard, both my parents Mantuan.
    I was born, though late, *sub Julio*,[7] and bred
in Rome under Augustus in the noon   70
    of the false and lying gods. I was a poet
    and sang of old Anchises' noble son[8]
who came to Rome after the burning of Troy.
    But you—why do *you* return to these distresses
    instead of climbing that shining Mount of Joy   75
which is the seat and first cause of man's bliss?"
    "And are you then that Virgil and that fountain
    of purest speech?" My voice grew tremulous:
"Glory and light of poets! now may that zeal
    and love's apprenticeship that I poured out   80
    on your heroic verses serve me well!
For you are my true master and first author,
    the sole maker from whom I drew the breath
    of that sweet style whose measures have brought me honor.
See there, immortal sage, the beast I flee.   85
    For my soul's salvation, I beg you, guard me from her,
    for she has struck a mortal tremor through me."
And he replied, seeing my soul in tears:
    "He must go by another way who would escape
    this wilderness, for that mad beast that fleers   90
before you there, suffers no man to pass.
    She tracks down all, kills all, and knows no glut,
    but, feeding, she grows hungrier than she was.
She mates with any beast, and will mate with more
    before the Greyhound[9] comes to hunt her down.   95
    He will not feed on lands nor loot, but honor
and love and wisdom will make straight his way.
    He will rise between Feltro and Feltro, and in him
    shall be the resurrection and new day
of that sad Italy for which Nisus died,   100
    and Turnus, and Euryalus, and the maid Camilla.[1]
    He shall hunt her through every nation of sick pride
till she is driven back forever to Hell
    whence Envy first released her on the world.
    Therefore, for your own good, I think it well   105
you follow me and I will be your guide
    and lead you forth through an eternal place.
    There you shall see the ancient spirits tried
in endless pain, and hear their lamentation
    as each bemoans the second death[2] of souls.   110
    Next you shall see upon a burning mountain

---

7. In the reign of Julius Caesar.   8. Aeneas.   9. Almost certainly refers to Can Grande della Scala
(1290–1329), great Italian leader born in Verona, which lies between the towns of Feltre and Montefeltro.   1. All were killed in the war between the Trojans and the Latians when, according to legend,
Aeneas led the survivors of Troy into Italy. Nisus and Euryalus (*Aeneid* IX) were Trojan comrades-in-
arms who died together. Camilla (*Aeneid* XI) was the daughter of the Latian king and one of the warrior
women. She was killed in a horse charge against the Trojans after displaying great gallantry. Turnus
(*Aeneid* XII) was killed by Aeneas in a duel.   2. Damnation. "This is the second death, even the lake
of fire" (Revelation xx, 14).

souls in fire and yet content in fire,
    knowing that whensoever it may be
    they yet will mount into the blessed choir.
To which, if it is still your wish to climb,   115
    a worthier spirit shall be sent to guide you.
    With her shall I leave you, for the King of Time,
who reigns on high, forbids me to come there
    since, living, I rebelled against his law.[3]
    He rules the waters and the land and air   120
and there holds court, his city and his throne.
    Oh blessed are they he chooses!" And I to him:
    "Poet, by that God to you unknown,
lead me this way. Beyond this present ill
    and worse to dread, lead me to Peter's gate[4]   125
    and be my guide through the sad halls of Hell."
And he then: "Follow." And he moved ahead
in silence, and I followed where he led.

CANTO II

The Descent

It is evening of the first day (Friday). Dante is following Virgil and finds himself tired and despairing. How can he be worthy of such a vision as Virgil has described? He hesitates and seems about to abandon his first purpose.

To comfort him Virgil explains how Beatrice descended to him in Limbo and told him of her concern for Dante. It is she, the symbol of Divine Love, who sends Virgil to lead Dante from error. She has come into Hell itself on this errand, for Dante cannot come to Divine Love unaided; Reason must lead him. Moreover Beatrice has been sent with the prayers of the Virgin Mary (Compassion), and of Saint Lucia (Divine Light). Rachel (The Contemplative Life) also figures in the heavenly scene which Virgil recounts.

Virgil explains all this and reproaches Dante: how can he hesitate longer when such heavenly powers are concerned for him, and Virgil himself has promised to lead him safely?

Dante understands at once that such forces cannot fail him, and his spirits rise in joyous anticipation.

The light was departing. The brown air drew down
    all the earth's creatures, calling them to rest
    from their day-roving, as I, one man alone,
prepared myself to face the double war
    of the journey and the pity, which memory   5
    shall here set down, nor hesitate, nor err.

---

3. Salvation is only through Christ in Dante's theology. Virgil lived and died before the establishment of Christ's teachings in Rome, and cannot therefore enter Heaven.   **4.** The gate of Purgatory. (*Purgatorio* IX, 76 ff.) The gate is guarded by an angel with a gleaming sword. The angel is Peter's vicar (Peter, the first Pope, symbolized all Popes; i.e., Christ's vicar on earth) and is entrusted with the two great keys. Some commentators argue that this is the gate of Paradise, but Dante mentions no gate beyond this one in his ascent to Heaven. It should be remembered, too, that those who pass the gate of Purgatory have effectively entered Heaven.

O Muses! O High Genius! Be my aid!
  O Memory, recorder of the vision,
  here shall your true nobility be displayed!
Thus I began: "Poet, you who must guide me,   10
  before you trust me to that arduous passage,
  look to me and look through me—can I be worthy?
You sang how the father of Sylvius,[5] while still
  in corruptible flesh won to that other world,
  crossing with mortal sense the immortal sill.   15
But if the Adversary of all Evil
  weighing his consequence and who and what
  should issue from him, treated him so well—
that cannot seem unfitting to thinking men,
  since he was chosen father of Mother Rome   20
  and of her Empire by God's will and token.
Both, to speak strictly, were founded and foreknown
  as the established Seat of Holiness
  for the successors of Great Peter's throne.
In that quest, which your verses celebrate,   25
  he learned those mysteries from which arose
  his victory and Rome's apostolate.
There later came the chosen vessel, Paul,
  bearing the confirmation of that Faith
  which is the one true door to life eternal.   30
But I—how should I dare? By whose permission?
  I am not Aeneas. I am not Paul.
  Who could believe me worthy of the vision?
How, then, may I presume to this high quest
  and not fear my own brashness? You are wise   35
  and will grasp what my poor words can but suggest."
As one who unwills what he wills, will stay
  strong purposes with feeble second thoughts
  until he spells all his first zeal away—
so I hung back and balked on that dim coast   40
  till thinking had worn out my enterprise,
  so stout at starting and so early lost.
"I understand from your words and the look in your eyes,"
  that shadow of magnificence answered me,
  "your soul is sunken in that cowardice   45
that bears down many men, turning their course
  and resolution by imagined perils,
  as his own shadow turns the frightened horse.
To free you of this dread I will tell you all

5. Aeneas. Lines 13–30 are a fair example of the way in which Dante absorbed pagan themes into his
Catholicism. According to Virgil, Aeneas is the son of mortal Anchises and of Venus. Venus, in her
son's interest, secures a prophecy and a promise from Jove to the effect that Aeneas is to found a royal
line that shall rule the world. After the burning of Troy, Aeneas is directed by various signs to sail for
the Latian lands (Italy) where his destiny awaits him. After many misadventures, he is compelled (like
Dante) to descend to the underworld of the dead. There he finds his father's shade, and there he is
shown the shades of the great kings that are to stem from him. (*Aeneid* VI, 921 ff.) Among them are
Romulus, Julius Caesar, and Augustus Caesar. The full glory of the Roman Empire is also foreshadowed
to him.
    Dante, however, continues the Virgilian theme and includes in the predestination not only the
Roman Empire but the Holy Roman Empire and its Church. Thus what Virgil presented as an arrangement of Jove, a concession to the son of Venus, becomes part of the divine scheme of the Catholic
God, and Aeneas is cast as a direct forerunner of Peter and Paul.

in this infected light." At which the Sage:
"All this shall be made known to you when we stand
  on the joyless beach of Acheron." And I
  cast down my eyes, sensing a reprimand   75
in what he said, and so walked at his side
  in silence and ashamed until we came
  through the dead cavern to that sunless tide.
There, steering toward us in an ancient ferry
  came an old man⁵ with a white bush of hair,   80
  bellowing: "Woe to you depraved souls! Bury
here and forever all hope of Paradise:
  I come to lead you to the other shore,
  into eternal dark, into fire and ice.
And you who are living yet, I say begone   85
  from these who are dead." But when he saw me stand
  against his violence he began again:
"By other windings and by other steerage
  shall you cross to that other shore. Not here! Not here!
  A lighter craft than mine must give you passage."⁶   90
And my Guide to him: "Charon, bite back your spleen:
  this has been willed where what is willed must be,
  and is not yours to ask what it may mean."
The steersman of that marsh of ruined souls,
  who wore a wheel of flame around each eye,   95
  stifled the rage that shook his woolly jowls.
But those unmanned and naked spirits there
  turned pale with fear and their teeth began to chatter
  at sound of his crude bellow. In despair
they blasphemed God,⁷ their parents, their time on earth,   100
  the race of Adam, and the day and the hour
  and the place and the seed and the womb that gave them birth.
But all together they drew to that grim shore
  where all must come who lose the fear of God.
  Weeping and cursing they come for evermore,   105
and demon Charon with eyes like burning coals
  herds them in, and with a whistling oar
  flails on the stragglers to his wake of souls.
As leaves in autumn loosen and stream down
  until the branch stands bare above its tatters   110
  spread on the rustling ground, so one by one
the evil seed of Adam in its Fall
  cast themselves, at his signal, from the shore
  and streamed away like birds who hear their call.
So they are gone over that shadowy water,   115
  and always before they reach the other shore
  a new noise stirs on this, and new throngs gather.
"My son," the courteous Master said to me,
  "all who die in the shadow of God's wrath
  converge to this from every clime and country.   120

---

5. Charon. He is the ferryman of dead souls across the Acheron in all classical mythology.   6. Charon recognizes Dante not only as a living man but as a soul in grace, and knows, therefore, that the Infernal Ferry was not intended for him. He is probably referring to the fact that souls destined for Purgatory and Heaven assemble not at his ferry point, but on the banks of the Tiber, from which they are transported by an angel.   7. The souls of the damned are not permitted to repent, for repentance is a divine grace.

And all pass over eagerly, for here
   Divine Justice transforms and spurs them so
   their dread turns wish: they yearn for what they fear.[8]
No soul in Grace comes ever to this crossing;
   therefore if Charon rages at your presence   125
   you will understand the reason for his cursing."
When he had spoken, all the twilight country
   shook so violently, the terror of it
   bathes me with sweat even in memory:
the tear-soaked ground gave out a sigh of wind   130
   that spewed itself in flame on a red sky,
   and all my shuttered senses left me. Blind,
like one whom sleep comes over in a swoon,
I stumbled into darkness and went down.[9]

CANTO IV

Circle One: Limbo   The Virtuous Pagans

   Dante wakes to find himself across Acheron. The Poets are now on the brink of Hell itself, which Dante conceives as a great funnel-shaped cave lying below the northern hemisphere with its bottom point at the earth's center. Around this great circular depression runs a series of ledges, each of which Dante calls a *Circle*. Each circle is assigned to the punishment of one category of sin.

   As soon as Dante's strength returns, the Poets begin to cross the First Circle. Here they find the Virtuous Pagans. They were born without the light of Christ's revelation, and, therefore, they cannot come into the light of God, but they are not tormented. Their only pain is that they have no hope.

   Ahead of them Dante sights a great dome of light, and a voice trumpets through the darkness welcoming Virgil back, for this is his eternal place in Hell. Immediately the great Poets of all time appear—Homer, Horace, Ovid, and Lucan. They greet Virgil, and they make Dante a sixth in their company.

   With them Dante enters the Citadel of Human Reason and sees before his eyes the Master Souls of Pagan Antiquity gathered on a green, and illuminated by the radiance of Human Reason. This is the highest state man can achieve without God, and the glory of it dazzles Dante, but he knows also that it is nothing compared to the glory of God.

A monstrous clap of thunder broke apart
   the swoon that stuffed my head; like one awakened
   by violent hands, I leaped up with a start.
And having risen; rested and renewed,

---

8. Hell (allegorically Sin) is what the souls of the damned really wish for. Hell is their actual and deliberate choice, for divine grace is denied to none who wish for it in their hearts. The damned must, in fact, deliberately harden their hearts to God in order to become damned. Christ's grace is sufficient to save all who wish for it.   9. This device (repeated at the end of Canto V) serves a double purpose. The first is technical: Dante uses it to cover a transition. We are never told how he crossed Acheron, for that would involve certain narrative matters he can better deal with when he crosses Styx in Canto VII. The second is to provide a point of departure for a theme that is carried through the entire descent: the theme of Dante's emotional reaction to Hell. These two swoons early in the descent show him most susceptible to the grief about him. As he descends, pity leaves him, and he even goes so far as to add to the torments of one sinner. The allegory is clear: we must harden ourselves against every sympathy for sin.

I studied out the landmarks of the gloom   5
  to find my bearings there as best I could.
And I found I stood on the very brink of the valley
  called the Dolorous Abyss, the desolate chasm
  where rolls the thunder of Hell's eternal cry,
so depthless-deep and nebulous and dim   10
  that stare as I might into its frightful pit
  it gave me back no feature and no bottom.
Death-pale,[1] the Poet spoke: "Now let us go
  into the blind world waiting here below us.
  I will lead the way and you shall follow."   15
And I, sick with alarm at his new pallor,
  cried out, "How can I go this way when you
  who are my strength in doubt turn pale with terror?"
And he: "The pain of these below us here,
  drains the color from my face for pity,   20
  and leaves this pallor you mistake for fear.
Now let us go, for a long road awaits us."
  So he entered and so he led me in
  to the first circle and ledge of the abyss.
No tortured wailing rose to greet us here   25
  but sounds of sighing rose from every side,
  sending a tremor through the timeless air,
a grief breathed out of untormented sadness,
  the passive state of those who dwelled apart,
  men, women, children—a dim and endless congress.   30
And the Master said to me: "You do not question
  what souls these are that suffer here before you?
  I wish you to know before you travel on
that these were sinless. And still their merits fail,
  for they lacked Baptism's grace, which is the door   35
  of the true faith you were born to. Their birth fell
before the age of the Christian mysteries,
  and so they did not worship God's Trinity
  in fullest duty. I am one of these.
For such defects are we lost, though spared the fire   40
  and suffering Hell in one affliction only:
  that without hope we live on in desire."
I thought how many worthy souls there were
  suspended in that Limbo, and a weight
  closed on my heart for what the noblest suffer.   45
"Instruct me, Master and most noble Sir,"
  I prayed him then, "better to understand
  the perfect creed that conquers every error:
has any, by his own or another's merit,
  gone ever from this place to blessedness?"   50
  He sensed my inner question and answered it:
"I was still new to this estate of tears
  when a Mighty One[2] descended here among us,

1. Virgil is most likely affected here by the return to his own place in Hell. "The pain of these below,"
then (line 19), would be the pain of his own group in Limbo (the Virtuous Pagans) rather than the
total of Hell's suffering.   2. Christ. His name is never directly uttered in Hell. *Descended here:* the
legend of the Harrowing of Hell is Apocryphal. It is based on I Peter iii, 19: "He went and preached
unto the spirits in prison." The legend is that Christ in the glory of His resurrection descended into
Limbo and took with Him to Heaven the first human souls to be saved. The event would, accordingly,
have occurred in 33 or 34 A.D.. Virgil died in 19 B.C.

crowned with the sign of His victorious years.
He took from us the shade of our first parent,[3]   55
    of Abel, his pure son, of ancient Noah,
    of Moses, the bringer of law, the obedient.
Father Abraham, David the King,
    Israel[4] with his father and his children,
    Rachel,[5] the holy vessel of His blessing,   60
and many more He chose for elevation
    among the elect. And before these, you must know,
    no human soul had ever won salvation."
We had not paused as he spoke, but held our road
    and passed meanwhile beyond a press of souls   65
    crowded about like trees in a thick wood.
And we had not traveled far from where I woke
    when I made out a radiance before us
    that struck away a hemisphere of dark.
We were still some distance back in the long night,   70
    yet near enough that I half-saw, half-sensed,
    what quality of souls lived in that light.
"O ornament of wisdom and of art,
    what souls are these whose merit lights their way
    even in Hell. What joy sets them apart?"   75
And he to me: "The signature of honor
    they left on earth is recognized in Heaven
    and wins them ease in Hell out of God's favor."
And as he spoke a voice rang on the air:
    "Honor the Prince of Poets; the soul and glory   80
    that went from us returns. He is here! He is here!"
The cry ceased and the echo passed from hearing;
    I saw four mighty presences come toward us
    with neither joy nor sorrow in their bearing.
"Note well," my Master said as they came on,   85
    "that soul that leads the rest with sword in hand
    as if he were their captain and champion.
It is Homer, singing master of the earth.
    Next after him is Horace, the satirist,
    Ovid is third, and Lucan is the fourth.   90
Since all of these have part in the high name
    the voice proclaimed, calling me Prince of Poets,
    the honor that they do me honors them."
So I saw gathered at the edge of light
    the masters of that highest school whose song   95
    outsoars all others like an eagle's flight.
And after they had talked together a while,
    they turned and welcomed me most graciously,
    at which I saw my approving Master smile.
And they honored me far beyond courtesy,   100
    for they included me in their own number,
    making me sixth in that high company.
So we moved toward the light, and as we passed
    we spoke of things as well omitted here

3. Adam.   4. Another name for Jacob; his father was Isaac.   5. Wife of Jacob.

as it was sweet to touch on there. At last   105
we reached the base of a great Citadel
   circled by seven towering battlements
   and by a sweet brook flowing round them all.[6]
This we passed over as if it were firm ground.[7]
   Through seven gates I entered with those sages   110
   and came to a green meadow blooming round.
There with a solemn and majestic poise
   stood many people gathered in the light,
   speaking infrequently and with muted voice.
Past that enameled green we six withdrew   115
   into a luminous and open height
   from which each soul among them stood in view.
And there directly before me on the green
   the master souls of time were shown to me.
   I glory in the glory I have seen![8]   120
Electra stood in a great company
   among whom I saw Hector and Aeneas
   and Caesar in armor with his falcon's eye.
I saw Camilla, and the Queen Amazon
   across the field. I saw the Latian King   125
   seated there with his daughter by his throne.
And the good Brutus who overthrew the Tarquin:
   Lucrezia, Julia, Marcia, and Cornelia;
   and, by himself apart, the Saladin.
And raising my eyes a little I saw on high   130
   Aristotle, the master of those who know,
   ringed by the great souls of philosophy.

6. The most likely allegory is that the Citadel represents philosophy (that is, human reason without the light of God) surrounded by seven walls which represent the seven liberal arts, or the seven sciences, or the seven virtues. Note that Human Reason makes a light of its own, but that it is a light in darkness and forever separated from the glory of God's light. The *sweet brook flowing round them all* has been interpreted in many ways. Clearly fundamental, however, is the fact that it divides those in the Citadel (those who wish to know) from those in the outer darkness.   7. Since Dante still has his body, and since all others in Hell are incorporeal shades, there is a recurring narrative problem in the *Inferno* (and through the rest of the *Commedia*): how does flesh act in contact with spirit? In the *Purgatorio* Dante attempts to embrace the spirit of Casella and his arms pass through him as if he were empty air. In the Third Circle, below (Canto VI, 34–36), Dante steps on some of the spirits lying in the slush and his foot passes right through them. (The original lines offer several possible readings of which I have preferred this one.) And at other times Virgil, also a spirit, picks Dante up and carries him bodily.
It is clear, too, that Dante means the spirits of Hell to be weightless. When Virgil steps into Phlegyas's bark (Canto VIII) it does not settle into the water, but it does when Dante's living body steps aboard. There is no narrative reason why Dante should not sink into the waters of this stream and Dante follows no fixed rule in dealing with such phenomena, often suiting the physical action to the allegorical need. Here, the moat probably symbolizes some requirement (The Will to Know) which he and the other poets meet without difficulty.   8. The inhabitants of the Citadel fall into three main groups: 1. *The heroes and heroines:* All of these it must be noted were associated with the Trojans and their Roman descendants. ... The Electra Dante mentions here is not the sister of Orestes (see Euripides' *Electra*) but the daughter of Atlas and the mother of Dardanus, the founder of Troy. 2. *The philosophers:* Most of this group is made up of philosophers whose teachings were, at least in part, acceptable to church scholarship. Democritus, however, "who ascribed the world to chance," would clearly be an exception. The group is best interpreted, therefore, as representing the highest achievements of Human Reason unaided by Divine Love. *Plato and Aristotle:* Through a considerable part of the Middle Ages Plato was held to be the fountainhead of all scholarship, but in Dante's time practically all learning was based on Aristotelian theory as interpreted through the many commentaries. *Linus:* the Italian is "Lino" and for it some commentators read "Livio" (Livy). 3. *The naturalists:* They are less well known today. In Dante's time their place in scholarship more or less corresponded to the role of the theoretician and historian of science in our universities. *Avicenna* (his major work was in the eleventh century) and *Averrhoës* (twelfth century) were Arabian philosophers and physicians especially famous in Dante's time for their commentaries on Aristotle. *Great Commentary:* has the force of a title, i.e., The Great Commentary as distinguished from many lesser commentaries. *The Saladin:* This is the famous Saladin who was defeated by Richard the Lion-Heart, and whose great qualities as a ruler became a legend in medieval Europe.

All wait upon him for their honor and his.
 I saw Socrates and Plato at his side
 before all others there. Democritus   135
who ascribes the world to chance, Diogenes,
 and with him there Thales, Anaxagoras,
 Zeno, Heraclitus, Empedocles.
And I saw the wise collector and analyst—
 Dioscorides I mean. I saw Orpheus there,   140
 Tully, Linus, Seneca the moralist,
Euclid the geometer, and Ptolemy,
 Hippocrates, Galen, Avicenna,
 and Averrhoës of the Great Commentary.
I cannot count so much nobility;   145
 my longer theme pursues me so that often
 the word falls short of the reality.
The company of six is reduced by four.
 My Master leads me by another road
 out of that serenity to the roar   150
and trembling air of Hell. I pass from light
into the kingdom of eternal night.

CANTO V

Circle Two The Carnal

 The Poets leave Limbo and enter the Second Circle. Here begin the
torments of Hell proper, and here, blocking the way, sits Minos, the dread
and semi-bestial judge of the damned who assigns to each soul its eternal
torment. He orders the Poets back; but Virgil silences him as he earlier
silenced Charon, and the Poets move on.
 They find themselves on a dark ledge swept by a great whirlwind, which
spins within it the souls of the Carnal, those who betrayed reason to their
appetites. Their sin was to abandon themselves to the tempest of their
passions: so they are swept forever in the tempest of Hell, forever denied
the light of reason and of God. Virgil identifies many among them. Semiramis is there, and Dido, Cleopatra, Helen, Achilles, Paris, and Tristan.
Dante sees Paolo and Francesca swept together, and in the name of love
he calls to them to tell their sad story. They pause from their eternal flight
to come to him, and Francesca tells their history while Paolo weeps at her
side. Dante is so stricken by compassion at their tragic tale that he swoons
once again.

So we went down to the second ledge alone;
 a smaller circle[9] of so much greater pain
 the voice of the damned rose in a bestial moan.
There Minos[1] sits, grinning, grotesque, and hale.

---

9. The pit of Hell tapers like a funnel. The circles of ledges accordingly grow smaller as they descend.
1. The son of Europa and of Zeus, who descended to her in the form of a bull. Minos became a
mythological king of Crete, so famous for his wisdom and justice that after death his soul was made
judge of the dead. Virgil presents him fulfilling the same office at Aeneas' descent to the underworld.
Dante, however, transforms him into an irate and hideous monster with a tail. The transformation may
have been suggested by the form Zeus assumed for the rape of Europa—the monster is certainly bullish
enough here—but the obvious purpose of the brutalization is to present a figure symbolic of the guilty
conscience of the wretches who come before it to make their confessions.

He examines each lost soul as it arrives   5
and delivers his verdict with his coiling tail.
That is to say, when the ill-fated soul
    appears before him it confesses all,
    and that grim sorter of the dark and foul
decides which place in Hell shall be its end,   10
    then wraps his twitching tail about himself
    one coil for each degree it must descend.
The soul descends and others take its place:
    each crowds in its turn to judgment, each confesses,
    each hears its doom and falls away through space.   15
"O you who come into this camp of woe,"
    cried Minos when he saw me turn away
    without awaiting his judgment, "watch where you go
once you have entered here, and to whom you turn!
    Do not be misled by that wide and easy passage!"   20
And my Guide to him: "That is not your concern;
it is his fate to enter every door.
    This has been willed where what is willed must be,
    and is not yours to question. Say no more."
Now the choir of anguish, like a wound,   25
    strikes through the tortured air. Now I have come
    to Hell's full lamentation, sound beyond sound.
I came to a place stripped bare of every light
    and roaring on the naked dark like seas
    wracked by a war of winds. Their hellish flight   30
of storm and counterstorm through time foregone,
    sweeps the souls of the damned before its charge.
    Whirling and battering it drives them on,
and when they pass the ruined gap of Hell[2]
    through which we had come, their shrieks begin anew.   35
    There they blaspheme the power of God eternal.
And this, I learned, was the never ending flight
    of those who sinned in the flesh, the carnal and lusty
    who betrayed reason to their appetite.
As the wings of wintering starlings bear them on   40
    in their great wheeling flights, just so the blast
    wherries these evil souls through time foregone.
Here, there, up, down, they whirl and, whirling, strain
    with never a hope of hope to comfort them,
    not of release, but even of less pain.   45
As cranes go over sounding their harsh cry,
    leaving the long streak of their flight in air,
    so come these spirits, wailing as they fly.
And watching their shadows lashed by wind, I cried:
    "Master, what souls are these the very air   50
    lashes with its black whips from side to side?"
"The first of these whose history you would know,"
    he answered me, "was Empress of many tongues.[3]
    Mad sensuality corrupted her so

2. See note to Canto IV, 53. At the time of the Harrowing of Hell a great earthquake shook the
underworld shattering rocks and cliffs. Ruins resulting from the same shock are noted in Canto XII, 34,
and Canto XXI, 112 ff. At the beginning of Canto XXIV, the Poets leave the *bolgia* of the Hypocrites
by climbing the ruined slabs of a bridge that was shattered by this earthquake. 3. Semiramis, a
legendary queen of Assyria who assumed full power at the death of her husband, Ninus.

that to hide the guilt of her debauchery   55
   she licensed all depravity alike,
   and lust and law were one in her decree.
She is Semiramis of whom the tale is told
   how she married Ninus and succeeded him
   to the throne of that wide land the Sultans hold.   60
The other is Dido;[4] faithless to the ashes
   of Sichaeus, she killed herself for love.
The next whom the eternal tempest lashes
is sense-drugged Cleopatra. See Helen[5] there,
   from whom such ill arose. And great Achilles,[6]   65
   who fought at last with love in the house of prayer.
And Paris. And Tristan." As they whirled above
   he pointed out more than a thousand shades
   of those torn from the mortal life by love.
I stood there while my Teacher one by one   70
   named the great knights and ladies of dim time;
   and I was swept by pity and confusion.
At last I spoke: "Poet, I should be glad
   to speak a word with those two swept together
   so lightly on the wind and still so sad."[7]   75
And he to me: "Watch them. When next they pass,
   call to them in the name of love that drives
   and damns them here. In that name they will pause."
Thus, as soon as the wind in its wild course
   brought them around, I called: "O wearied souls!   80
   if none forbid it, pause and speak to us."
As mating doves that love calls to their nest
   glide through the air with motionless raised wings,
   borne by the sweet desire that fills each breast—
Just so those spirits turned on the torn sky   85
   from the band where Dido whirls across the air;
   such was the power of pity in my cry.
"O living creature, gracious, kind, and good,
   going this pilgrimage through the sick night,
   visiting us who stained the earth with blood,   90
were the King of Time our friend, we would pray His peace
   on you who have pitied us. As long as the wind
   will let us pause, ask of us what you please.
The town where I was born lies by the shore

---

4. Queen and founder of Carthage. She had vowed to remain faithful to her husband, Sichaeus, but she fell in love with Aeneas. When Aeneas abandoned her she stabbed herself on a funeral pyre she had had prepared. According to Dante's own system of punishments, she should be in the Seventh Circle (Canto XIII) with the suicides. The only clue Dante gives to the tempering of her punishment is his statement that "she killed herself for love." Dante always seems readiest to forgive in that name. 5. She was held responsible for the Trojan War; the wife of King Meneleus of Sparta, she ran away with the visiting Prince Paris from Troy.   6. He is placed among this company because of his passion for Polyxena, the daughter of Priam. For love of her, he agreed to desert the Greeks and to join the Trojans, but when he went to the temple for the wedding (according to the legend Dante has followed) he was killed by Paris.   7. Paolo and Francesca. In 1275 Giovanni Malatesta of Rimini, called Giovanni the Lame, a somewhat deformed but brave and powerful warrior, made a political marriage with Francesca, daughter of Guido da Polenta of Ravenna. Francesca came to Rimini and there an amour grew between her and Giovanni's younger brother Paolo. Despite the fact that Paolo had married in 1269 and had become the father of two daughters by 1275, his affair with Francesca continued for many years. It was sometime between 1283 and 1286 that Giovanni surprised them in Francesca's bedroom and killed both of them.
   Around these facts the legend has grown that Paolo was sent by Giovanni as his proxy to the marriage, that Francesca thought he was her real bridegroom and accordingly gave him her heart irrevocably at first sight. The legend obviously increases the pathos, but nothing in Dante gives it support.

where the Po descends into its ocean rest   95
  with its attendant streams in one long murmur.
Love, which in gentlest hearts will soonest bloom
  seized my lover with passion for that sweet body
  from which I was torn unshriven to my doom.
Love, which permits no loved one not to love,   100
  took me so strongly with delight in him
  that we are one in Hell, as we were above.[8]
Love led us to one death. In the depths of Hell
  Caïna waits for him[9] who took our lives."
  This was the piteous tale they stopped to tell.   105
And when I had heard those world-offended lovers
  I bowed my head. At last the Poet spoke:
  "What painful thoughts are these your lowered brow covers?"
When at length I answered, I began: "Alas!
  What sweetest thoughts, what green and young desire   110
  led these two lovers to this sorry pass."
Then turning to those spirits once again,
  I said: "Francesca, what you suffer here
  melts me to tears of pity and of pain.
But tell me: in the time of your sweet sighs   115
  by what appearances found love the way
  to lure you to his perilous paradise?"
And she: "The double grief of a lost bliss
  is to recall its happy hour in pain.
  Your Guide and Teacher knows the truth of this.   120
But if there is indeed a soul in Hell
  to ask of the beginning of our love
  out of his pity, I will weep and tell:
On a day for dalliance we read the rhyme
  of Lancelot,[1] how love had mastered him.   125
  We were alone with innocence and dim time.[2]
Pause after pause that high old story drew
  our eyes together while we blushed and paled;
  but it was one soft passage overthrew
our caution and our hearts. For when we read   130
  how her fond smile was kissed by such a lover,
  he who is one with me alive and dead
breathed on my lips the tremor of his kiss.
  That book, and he who wrote it, was a pander.[3]
  That day we read no further." As she said this,   135
the other spirit, who stood by her, wept

8. At many points of the *Inferno* Dante makes clear the principle that the souls of the damned are locked so blindly into their own guilt that none can feel sympathy for another, or find any pleasure in the presence of another. The temptation of many readers is to interpret this line romantically: *i.e.*, that the love of Paolo and Francesca survives Hell itself. The more Dantean interpretation, however, is that they add to one another's anguish (a) as mutual reminders of their sin, and (b) as insubstantial shades of the bodies for which they once felt such great passion.   9. Giovanni Malatesta was still alive at the writing. His fate is already decided, however, and upon his death, his soul will fall to Caïna, the first ring of the last circle (Canto XXXII), where lie those who performed acts of treachery against their kin. 1. The story of Lancelot and Guinevere (of Arthurian legend) exists in many forms. The details Dante makes use of are from an Old French version.   2. The original simply reads "We were alone, suspecting nothing." "Dim time" is rhyme-forced, but not wholly outside the legitimate implications of the original, I hope. The old courtly romance may well be thought of as happening in the dim ancient days. The apology, of course, comes after the fact: one does the possible then argues for justification, and there probably is none.   3. "Galeotto," the Italian word for "pander," is also the Italian rendering of the name of Gallehault, who, in the French Romance Dante refers to here, urged Lancelot and Guinevere on to love.

so piteously, I felt my senses reel
   and faint away with anguish. I was swept
by such a swoon as death is, and I fell,
as a corpse might fall, to the dead floor of Hell.   140

CANTO VI

Circle Three   The Gluttons

Dante recovers from his swoon and finds himself in the Third Circle.
A great storm of putrefaction falls incessantly, a mixture of stinking snow
and freezing rain, which forms into a vile slush underfoot. Everything
about this Circle suggests a gigantic garbage dump. The souls of the
damned lie in the icy paste, swollen and obscene, and Cerberus, the ravenous three-headed dog of Hell, stands guard over them, ripping and tearing them with his claws and teeth.

These are the Gluttons. In life they made no higher use of the gifts of
God than to wallow in food and drink, producers of nothing but garbage
and offal. Here they lie through all eternity, themselves like garbage, half-
buried in fetid slush, while Cerberus slavers over them as they in life
slavered over their food.

As the Poets pass, one of the speakers sits up and addresses Dante. He
is Ciacco, The Hog, a citizen of Dante's own Florence. He recognizes
Dante and asks eagerly for news of what is happening there. With the
foreknowledge of the damned, Ciacco then utters the first of the political
prophecies that are to become a recurring theme of the *Inferno*. The poets
then move on toward the next Circle, at the edge of which they encounter
the monster Plutus.

My senses had reeled from me out of pity
   for the sorrow of those kinsmen and lost lovers.
   Now they return, and waking gradually,
I see new torments and new souls in pain
   about me everywhere. Wherever I turn   5
   away from grief I turn to grief again.
I am in the Third Circle of the torments.
   Here to all time with neither pause nor change
   the frozen rain of Hell descends in torrents.
Huge hailstones, dirty water, and black snow   10
   pour from the dismal air to putrefy
   the putrid slush that waits for them below.
Here monstrous Cerberus,[4] the ravening beast,
   howls through his triple throats like a mad dog
   over the spirits sunk in that foul paste.   15
His eyes are red, his beard is greased with phlegm,
   his belly is swollen, and his hands are claws
   to rip the wretches and flay and mangle them.
And they, too, howl like dogs in the freezing storm,

---

4. In classical mythology Cerberus appears as a three-headed dog. His master was Pluto, king of the
Underworld. Cerberus was placed at the Gate of the Underworld to allow all to enter, but none to
escape. His three heads and his ravenous disposition make him an apt symbol of gluttony. *Like a mad
dog:* Dante seems clearly to have visualized him as a half-human monster. The beard (line 16) suggests
that at least one of his three heads is human, and many illuminated manuscripts so represent him.

turning and turning from it as if they thought   20
   one naked side could keep the other warm.
When Cerberus discovered us in that swill
   his dragon-jaws yawned wide, his lips drew back
   in a grin of fangs. No limb of him was still.
My Guide bent down and seized in either fist   25
   a clod of the stinking dirt that festered there
   and flung them down the gullet of the beast.
As a hungry cur will set the echoes raving
   and then fall still when he is thrown a bone,
   all of his clamor being in his craving,   30
so the three ugly heads of Cerberus,
   whose yowling at those wretches deafened them,
   choked on their putrid sops and stopped their fuss.
We made our way across the sodden mess
   of souls the rain beat down, and when our steps   35
   fell on a body, they sank through emptiness.
All those illusions of being seemed to lie
   drowned in the slush; until one wraith among them
   sat up abruptly and called as I passed by:
"O you who are led this journey through the shade   40
   of Hell's abyss, do you recall this face?
   You had been made before I was unmade."[5]
And I: "Perhaps the pain you suffer here
   distorts your image from my recollection.
   I do not know you as you now appear."   45
And he to me: "Your own city, so rife
   with hatred that the bitter cup flows over
   was mine too in that other, clearer life.
Your citizens nicknamed me Ciacco, The Hog:
   gluttony was my offense, and for it   50
   I lie here rotting like a swollen log.
Nor am I lost in this alone; all these
   you see about you in this painful death
   have wallowed in the same indecencies."
I answered him: "Ciacco, your agony   55
   weighs on my heart and calls my soul to tears;
   But tell me, if you can, what is to be
for the citizens of that divided state,
   and whether there are honest men among them,
   and for what reasons we are torn by hate."   60
And he then: "After many words given and taken
   it shall come to blood; White shall rise over Black
   and rout the dark lord's force, battered and shaken.
Then it shall come to pass within three suns
   that the fallen shall arise, and by the power   65
   of one now gripped by many hesitations
Black shall ride on White for many years,
   loading it down with burdens and oppressions
   and humbling of proud names and helpless tears.
Two are honest, but none will heed them. There,   70

---

5. That is, "you were born before I died." The further implication is that they must have seen one another in Florence, a city one can still walk across in twenty minutes, and around in a very few hours. Dante certainly would have known everyone in Florence.

pride, avarice, and envy are the tongues
men know and heed, a Babel of despair."[6]
Here he broke off his mournful prophecy.
　And I to him: "Still let me urge you on
　to speak a little further and instruct me: 75
Farinata and Tegghiaio, men of good blood,
　Jacopo Rusticucci, Arrigo, Mosca,[7]
　and the others who set their hearts on doing good—
where are they now whose high deeds might be-gem
　the crown of kings? I long to know their fate.   80
　Does Heaven soothe or Hell envenom them?"
And he: "They lie below in a blacker lair.
　A heavier guilt draws them to greater pain.
　If you descend so far you may see them there.
But when you move again among the living,   85
　oh speak my name to the memory of men![8]
　Having answered all, I say no more." And giving
his head a shake, he looked up at my face
　cross-eyed, then bowed his head and fell away
　among the other blind souls of that place.   90
And my Guide to me: "He will not wake again
　until the angel trumpet sounds the day
　on which the host shall come to judge all men.
Then shall each soul before the seat of Mercy
　return to its sad grave and flesh and form   95
　to hear the edict of Eternity."
So we picked our slow way among the shades
　and the filthy rain, speaking of life to come.
　"Master," I said, "when the great clarion fades
into the voice of thundering Omniscience,   100
　what of these agonies? Will they be the same,
　or more, or less, after the final sentence?"
And he to me: "Look to your science[9] again
　where it is written: the more a thing is perfect
　the more it feels of pleasure and of pain.   105
As for these souls, though they can never soar
　to true perfection, still in the new time
　they will be nearer it than they were before."

6. This is the first of the political prophecies that are to become a recurring theme of the *Inferno*. (It is the second if we include the political symbolism of the Greyhound in Canto I.) Dante is, of course, writing after these events have all taken place. At Easter time of 1300, however, the events were in the future. The Whites and the Blacks of Ciacco's prophecy should not be confused with the Guelphs and the Ghibellines. The internal strife between the Guelphs and the Ghibellines ended with the total defeat of the Ghibellines. By the end of the 13th century that strife had passed. But very shortly a new feud began in Florence between White Guelphs and Black Guelphs. A rather gruesome murder perpetrated by Focaccio de' Cancellieri became the cause of new strife between two branches of the Cancellieri family. On May 1 of 1300 the White Guelphs (Dante's party) drove the Black Guelphs from Florence in bloody fighting. Two years later, however ("within three suns"), the Blacks, aided by Dante's detested Boniface VIII, returned and expelled most of the prominent Whites, among them Dante; for he had been a member of the Priorate (City Council) that issued a decree banishing the leaders of both sides. This was the beginning of Dante's long exile from Florence.   7. Farinata will appear in Canto X among the Heretics: Tegghiaio and Jacopo Rusticucci, in Canto XVI with the homosexuals, Mosca in Canto XXVIII with the sowers of discord. Arrigo does not appear again and he has not been positively identified. Dante probably refers here to Arrigo (or Oderigo) dei Fifanti, one of those who took part in the murder of Buondelmonte (Canto XXVIII, line 107, note).   8. Excepting those shades in the lowest depths of Hell whose sins are so shameful that they wish only to be forgotten, all of the damned are eager to be remembered on earth. The concept of the family name and of its survival in the memories of men were matters of first importance among Italians of Dante's time, and expressions of essentially the same attitude are common in Italy today.   9. "Science" to the learnèd of Dante's time meant specifically "the writings of Aristotle and the commentaries upon them.

And so we walked the rim of the great ledge
   speaking of pain and joy, and of much more   110
   that I will not repeat, and reached the edge
where the descent begins. There, suddenly,
   we came on Plutus, the great enemy.

CANTO VII

Circle Four   The Hoarders and the Wasters
Circle Five   The Wrathful and the Sullen

Plutus menaces the Poets, but once more Virgil shows himself more
powerful than the rages of Hell's monsters. The Poets enter the Fourth
Circle and find what seems to be a war in progress.

The sinners are divided into two raging mobs, each soul among them
straining madly at a great boulder-like weight. The two mobs meet, clashing their weights against one another, after which they separate, pushing
the great weights apart, and begin over again.

One mob is made up of the Hoarders, the other of the Wasters. In life,
they lacked all moderation in regulating their expenses; they destroyed the
light of God within themselves by thinking of nothing but money. Thus
in death, their souls are encumbered by dead weights (mundanity) and
one excess serves to punish the other. Their souls, moreover, have become
so dimmed and awry in their fruitless rages that there is no hope of recognizing any among them.

The Poets pass on while Virgil explains the function of Dame Fortune
in the Divine Scheme. As he finishes (it is past midnight now of Good
Friday) they reach the inner edge of the ledge and come to a Black Spring
which bubbles murkily over the rocks to form the Marsh of Styx, which is
the Fifth Circle, the last station of the Upper Hell.

Across the marsh they see countless souls attacking one another in the
foul slime. These are the Wrathful and the symbolism of their punishment
is obvious. Virgil also points out to Dante certain bubbles rising from the
slime and informs him that below that mud lie entombed the souls of the
Sullen. In life they refused to welcome the sweet light of the Sun (Divine
Illumination) and in death they are buried forever below the stinking
waters of the Styx, gargling the words of an endless chant in a grotesque
parody of singing a hymn.

"Papa Satán, Papa Satán, aleppy,"[1]
   Plutus[2] clucked and stuttered in his rage;
   and my all-knowing Guide, to comfort me:

1. Virgil, the all-knowing, may understand these words, but no one familiar with merely human languages has deciphered them. In Canto XXXI the monster Nimrod utters a similar meaningless jargon,
and Virgil there cites it as evidence of the dimness of his mind. Gibberish is certainly a characteristic
appropriate to monsters, and since Dante takes pains to make the reference to Satan apparent in the
gibberish, it is obviously infernal and debased, and that is almost certainly all he intended. The word
"papa" as used here probably means "Pope" rather than "father." "Il papa santo" is the Pope. "Papa
Satán" would be his opposite number. In the original the last word is "aleppe." On the assumption that
jargon translates jargon I have twisted it a bit to rhyme with "me."   2. In Greek mythology, Plutus
was the God of Wealth. Many commentators suggest that Dante confused him with Pluto, the son of
Saturn and God of the Underworld. But in that case, Plutus would be identical with Lucifer himself
and would require a central place in Hell, whereas the classical function of Plutus as God of Material
Wealth makes him the ideal overseer of the miserly and the prodigal.

"Do not be startled, for no power of his,
    however he may lord it over the damned,   5
    may hinder your descent through this abyss."
And turning to that carnival of bloat
    cried: "Peace, you wolf of Hell. Choke back your bile
    and let its venom blister your own throat.
Our passage through this pit is willed on high   10
    by that same Throne that loosed the angel wrath
    of Michael on ambition and mutiny."
As puffed out sails fall when the mast gives way
    and flutter to a self-convulsing heap—
    so collapsed Plutus into that dead clay.   15
Thus we descended the dark scarp of Hell
    to which all the evil of the Universe
    comes home at last, into the Fourth Great Circle
and ledge of the abyss. O Holy Justice,
    who could relate the agonies I saw!   20
    What guilt is man that he can come to this?
Just as the surge Charybdis[3] hurls to sea
    crashes and breaks upon its countersurge,
    so these shades dance and crash eternally.
Here, too, I saw a nation of lost souls,   25
    far more than were above: they strained their chests
    against enormous weights, and with mad howls
rolled them at one another. Then in haste
    they rolled them back, one party shouting out:
    "Why do you hoard?" and the other: "Why do you waste?"   30
So back around that ring they puff and blow,
    each faction to its course, until they reach
    opposite sides, and screaming as they go
the madmen turn and start their weights again
    to crash against the maniacs. And I,   35
    watching, felt my heart contract with pain.
"Master," I said, "what people can these be?
    And all those tonsured ones there on our left—
    is it possible they *all* were of the clergy?"
And he: "In the first life beneath the sun   40
    they were so skewed and squinteyed in their minds
    their misering or extravagance mocked all reason.
The voice of each clamors its own excess
    when lust meets lust at the two points of the circle
    where opposite guilts meet in their wretchedness.   45
These tonsured wraiths of greed were priests indeed,
    and popes and cardinals, for it is in these
    the weed of avarice sows its rankest seed."
And I to him: "Master, among this crew
    surely I should be able to make out   50
    the fallen image of some soul I knew."
And he to me: "This is a lost ambition.
    In their sordid lives they labored to be blind,
    and now their souls have dimmed past recognition.
All their eternity is to butt and bray: 55
    one crew will stand tight-fisted, the other stripped

---

3. A famous whirlpool in the Straits of Sicily.

of its very hair at the bar of Judgment Day.
Hoarding and squandering wasted all their light
   and brought them screaming to this brawl of wraiths.
   You need no words of mine to grasp their plight.   60
Now may you see the fleeting vanity
   of the goods of Fortune for which men tear down
   all that they are, to build a mockery.
Not all the gold that is or ever was
   under the sky could buy for one of these   65
   exhausted souls the fraction of a pause."
"Master," I said, "tell me—now that you touch
   on this Dame Fortune[4]—what *is* she, that she holds
   the good things of the world within her clutch?"
And he to me: "O credulous mankind,   70
   is there one error that has wooed and lost you?
   Now listen, and strike error from your mind:
That king whose perfect wisdom transcends all,
   made the heavens and posted angels on them
   to guide the eternal light that it might fall   75
from every sphere to every sphere the same.
   He made earth's splendors by a like decree
   and posted as their minister this high Dame,
the Lady of Permutations. All earth's gear
   she changes from nation to nation, from house to house,   80
   in changeless change through every turning year.
No mortal power may stay her spinning wheel.
   The nations rise and fall by her decree.
   None may foresee where she will set her heel:[5]
she passes, and things pass. Man's mortal reason   85
   cannot encompass her. She rules her sphere
   as the other gods[6] rule theirs. Season by season
her changes change her changes endlessly,
   and those whose turn has come press on her so,
   she must be swift by hard necessity.   90
And this is she so railed at and reviled
   that even her debtors in the joys of time
   blaspheme her name. Their oaths are bitter and wild,
but she in her beatitude does not hear.
   Among the Primal Beings of God's joy   95
   she breathes her blessedness and wheels her sphere.
But the stars that marked our starting fall away.[7]
   We must go deeper into greater pain,
   for it is not permitted that we stay."
And crossing over to the chasm's edge   100
   we came to a spring[8] that boiled and overflowed
   through a great crevice worn into the ledge.
By that foul water, black from its very source,

---

4. A central figure in medieval mythology. She is almost invariably represented as a female figure holding an ever-revolving wheel symbolic of Chance. Dante incorporates her into his scheme of the Universe, ranking her among the angels, and giving her a special office in the service of the Catholic God.   5. A literal translation of the original would be "She is hidden like a snake in the grass." To avoid the comic overtone of that figure in English, I have substituted another figure which I believe expresses Dante's intent without destroying his tone.   6. Dante can only mean here "the other angels and ministers of God."   7. It is now past midnight of Good Friday.   8. All the waters of Hell derive from one source (see Canto XIV, lines 12 following). This black spring must therefore be the waters of Acheron boiling out of some subterranean passage.

we found a nightmare path among the rocks
and followed the dark stream along its course.   105
Beyond its rocky race and wild descent
   the river floods and forms a marsh called Styx,[9]
   a dreary swampland, vaporous and malignant.
And I, intent on all our passage touched,
   made out a swarm of spirits in that bog   110
   savage with anger, naked, slime-besmutched.
They thumped at one another in that slime
   with hands and feet, and they butted, and they bit
   as if each would tear the other limb from limb.
And my kind Sage: "My son, behold the souls   115
   of those who lived in wrath. And do you see
   the broken surfaces of those water-holes
on every hand, boiling as if in pain?
   There are souls beneath that water. Fixed in slime
   they speak their piece, end it, and start again: 120
'Sullen were we in the air made sweet by the Sun;
   in the glory of his shining our hearts poured
   a bitter smoke. Sullen were we begun;
sullen we lie forever in this ditch.'
   This litany they gargle in their throats   125
   as if they sang, but lacked the words and pitch."
Then circling on along that filthy wallow,
   we picked our way between the bank and fen,
   keeping our eyes on those foul souls that swallow
the slime of Hell. And so at last we came   130
to foot of a Great Tower that has no name.[1]

CANTO VIII

Circle Five: Styx   The Wrathful, Phlegyas
Circle Six: Dis   The Fallen Angels

The Poets stand at the edge of the swamp, and a mysterious signal flames from the great tower. It is answered from the darkness of the other side, and almost immediately the Poets see Phlegyas, the Boatman of Styx, racing toward them across the water, fast as a flying arrow. He comes avidly, thinking to find new souls for torment, and he howls with rage when he discovers the Poets. Once again, however, Virgil conquers wrath with a word and Phlegyas reluctantly gives them passage.

As they are crossing, a muddy soul rises before them. It is Filippo Argenti, one of the Wrathful. Dante recognizes him despite the filth with which he is covered, and he berates him soundly, even wishing to see him tormented further. Virgil approves Dante's disdain and, as if in answer to Dante's wrath, Argenti is suddenly set upon by all the other sinners present, who fall upon him and rip him to pieces.

9. The river Styx figures variously in classic mythology, but usually (and in later myths always) as a river of the Underworld. Dante, to heighten his symbolism, makes it a filthy marsh. This marsh marks the first great division of Hell. Between Acheron and Styx are punished the sins of Incontinence (the Sins of the She-Wolf). This is the Upper Hell. Beyond Styx rise the flaming walls of the infernal city of Dis, within which are punished Violence and Fraud (the Sins of the Lion, and the Sins of the Leopard). 1. No special significance need be attributed to the Tower. It serves as a signaling point for calling the ferryman from Dis.

The boat meanwhile has sped on, and before Argenti's screams have
died away, Dante sees the flaming red towers of Dis, the Capital of Hell.
The great walls of the iron city block the way to the Lower Hell. Properly
speaking, all the rest of Hell lies within the city walls, which separate the
Upper and the Lower Hell.

Phlegyas deposits them at a great Iron Gate which they find to be
guarded by the Rebellious Angels. These creatures of Ultimate Evil, rebels
against God Himself, refuse to let the Poets pass. Even Virgil is powerless
against them, for Human Reason by itself cannot cope with the essence of
Evil. Only Divine Aid can bring hope. Virgil accordingly sends up a prayer
for assistance and waits anxiously for a Heavenly Messenger to appear.

Returning to my theme,[2] I say we came
   to the foot of a Great Tower; but long before
   we reached it through the marsh, two horns of flame
flared from the summit, one from either side,
   and then, far off, so far we scarce could see it   5
   across the mist, another flame replied.
I turned to that sea of all intelligence
   saying: "What is this signal and counter-signal?
   Who is it speaks with fire across this distance?"
And he then: "Look across the filthy slew: 10
   you may already see the one they summon,
   if the swamp vapors do not hide him from you."
No twanging bowspring ever shot an arrow
   that bored the air it rode dead to the mark
   more swiftly than the flying skiff whose prow   15
shot toward us over the polluted channel
   with a single steersman at the helm who called:
   "So, do I have you at last, you whelp of Hell?"
"Phlegyas, Phlegyas,"[3] said my Lord and Guide,
   "this time you waste your breath: you have us only   20
   for the time it takes to cross to the other side."
Phlegyas, the madman, blew his rage among
   those muddy marshes like a cheat deceived,
   or like a fool at some imagined wrong.
My Guide, whom all the fiend's noise could not nettle,   25
   boarded the skiff, motioning me to follow:
   and not till I stepped aboard did it seem to settle[4]
into the water. At once we left the shore,
   that ancient hull riding more heavily
   than it had ridden in all of time before   30
And as we ran on that dead swamp, the slime
   rose before me, and from it a voice cried:

2. There is evidence that Dante stopped writing for a longer or shorter period between the seventh and
eighth Cantos. None of the evidence is conclusive but it is quite clear that the plan of the *Inferno*
changes from here on. Up to this point the Circles have been described in one canto apiece. If this was
Dante's original plan, Hell would have been concluded in five more cantos, since there are only Nine
Circles in all. But in the later journey the Eighth Circle alone occupies thirteen Cantos. Dante's phrase
may be simply transitional, but it certainly marks a change in the plan of the poem.   3. Mythological
King of Boeotia. He was the son of Ares (Mars) by a human mother. Angry at Apollo, who had seduced
his daughter (Aesculapius was born of this union), he set fire to Apollo's temple at Delphi. For this
offense, the God killed him and threw his soul into Hades under sentence of eternal torment. Dante's
choice of a ferryman is especially apt. Phlegyas is the link between the Wrathful (to whom his paternity
relates him) and the Rebellious Angels who menaced God (as he menaced Apollo).   4. Because of
his living weight.

"Who are you that come here before your time?"
And I replied: "If I come, I do not remain.
  But you, who are *you*, so fallen and so foul?"   35
And he: "I am one who weeps." And I then:
"May you weep and wail to all eternity,
  for I know you, hell-dog, filthy as you are."[5]
Then he stretched both hands to the boat, but warily
the Master shoved him back, crying, "Down! Down!   40
  with the other dogs!" Then he embraced me saying:
"Indignant spirit, I kiss you as you frown.
Blessed be she who bore you.[6] In world and time
  this one was haughtier yet. Not one unbending
  graces his memory. Here is his shadow in slime.   45
How many living now, chancellors of wrath,
  shall come to lie here in this pigmire,
  leaving a curse to be their aftermath!"
And I: "Master, it would suit my whim
  to see the wretch scrubbed down into the swill   50
  before we leave this stinking sink and him."
And he to me: "Before the other side
  shows through the mist, you shall have all you ask.
  This is a wish that should be gratified."
And shortly after, I saw the loathsome spirit   55
  so mangled by a swarm of muddy wraiths
  that to this day I praise and thank God for it.
"After Filippo Argenti!" all cried together.
  The maddog Florentine wheeled at their cry
  and bit himself for rage. I saw them gather.   60
And there we left him. And I say no more.
  But such a wailing beat upon my ears,
  I strained my eyes ahead to the far shore.
"My son," the Master said, "the City called Dis[7]
  lies just ahead, the heavy citizens,   65
  the swarming crowds of Hell's metropolis."
And I then: "Master, I already see
  the glow of its red mosques,[8] as if they came
  hot from the forge to smolder in this valley."
And my all-knowing Guide: "They are eternal   70
  flues to eternal fire that rages in them
  and makes them glow across this lower Hell."
And as he spoke we entered the vast moat

---

5. Filippo Argenti was one of the Adimari family, who were bitter political enemies of Dante. Dante's savagery toward him was probably intended in part as an insult to the family. He pays them off again in the *Paradiso* when he has Cacciaguida call them "The insolent gang that makes itself a dragon to chase those who run away, but is sweet as a lamb to any who show their teeth—or their purse."   6. These were Luke's words to Christ. To have Virgil apply them to Dante after such violence seems shocking, even though the expression is reasonably common in Italian. But Dante does not use such devices lightly. The *Commedia*, it must be remembered, is a vision of the progress of man's soul toward perfection. In being contemptuous of Wrath, Dante is purging it from his soul. He is thereby growing nearer to perfection, and Virgil, who has said nothing in the past when Dante showed pity for other sinners (though Virgil will later take him to task for daring to pity those whom God has shut off from pity), welcomes this sign of relentless rejection. Only by a ruthless enmity toward evil may the soul be purified.
7. Pluto, King of the Underworld of ancient mythology, was sometimes called Dis. This, then, is his city, the metropolis of Satan.   8. To a European of Dante's time a mosque would seem the perversion of a church, the impious counterpart of the House of God, just as Satan is God's impious counterpart.

of the sepulchre. Its wall seemed made of iron
and towered above us in our little boat.   75
We circled through what seemed an endless distance
     before the boatman ran his prow ashore
     crying: "Out! Out! Get out! This is the entrance."
Above the gates more than a thousand shades
     of spirits purged from Heaven[9] for its glory   80
     cried angrily: "Who is it that invades
Death's Kingdom in his life?" My Lord and Guide
     advanced a step before me with a sign
     that he wished to speak to some of them aside.
They quieted somewhat, and one called, "Come,   85
     but come alone. And tell that other one,
     who thought to walk so blithely through death's kingdom,
he may go back along the same fool's way
     he came by. Let him try his living luck.
     You who are dead can come only to stay."   90
Reader, judge for yourself, how each black word
     fell on my ears to sink into my heart:
     I lost hope of returning to the world.
"O my beloved Master, my Guide in peril,
     who time and time again[1] have seen me safely   95
     along this way, and turned the power of evil,
stand by me now," I cried, "in my heart's fright.
     And if the dead forbid our journey to them,
     let us go back together toward the light."
My Guide then, in the greatness of his spirit: 100
     "Take heart. Nothing can take our passage from us
     when such a power has given warrant for it.
Wait here and feed your soul while I am gone
     on comfort and good hope; I will not leave you
     to wander in this underworld alone."   105
So the sweet Guide and Father leaves[2] me here,
     and I stay on in doubt with yes and no
     dividing all my heart to hope and fear.
I could not hear my Lord's words, but the pack
     that gathered round him suddenly broke away   110
     howling and jostling and went pouring back,
slamming the towering gate hard in his face.
     That great Soul stood alone outside the wall.
     Then he came back; his pain showed in his pace.
His eyes were fixed upon the ground, his brow   115
     had sagged from its assurance. He sighed aloud:
     "Who has forbidden me the halls of sorrow?"
And to me he said: "You need not be cast down
     by my vexation, for whatever plot
     these fiends may lay against us, we will go on.   120
This insolence of theirs is nothing new:

---

9. The Rebellious Angels. We have already seen, on the other side of Acheron, the angels who sinned
by refusing to take sides.   1. A literal translation of the original would read "more than seven times."
"Seven" is used here as an indeterminate number indicating simply "quite a number of times." Italian
makes rather free use of such numbers.   2. Dante shifts tenses more freely than English readers are
accustomed to.

they showed it once at a less secret gate[3]
  that still stands open for all that they could do—
the same gate where you read the dead inscription;
  and through it at this moment a Great One[4] comes.   125
  Already he has passed it and moves down
ledge by dark ledge. He is one who needs no guide,
and at his touch all gates must spring aside."

CANTO IX

Circle Six   The Heretics

At the Gate of Dis the Poets wait in dread. Virgil tries to hide his anxiety
from Dante, but both realize that without Divine Aid they will surely be
lost. To add to their terrors Three Infernal Furies, symbols of Eternal
Remorse, appear on a near-by tower, from which they threaten the Poets
and call for Medusa to come and change them to stone. Virgil at once
commands Dante to turn and shut his eyes. To make doubly sure, Virgil
himself places his hands over Dante's eyes, for there is an Evil upon which
man must not look if he is to be saved.

But at the moment of greatest anxiety a storm shakes the dirty air of
Hell and the sinners in the marsh begin to scatter like frightened Frogs.
The Heavenly Messenger is approaching. He appears walking majestically
through Hell, looking neither to right nor to left. With a touch he throws
open the Gate of Dis while his words scatter the Rebellious Angels. Then
he returns as he came.

The Poets now enter the gate unopposed and find themselves in the
Sixth Circle. Here they find a countryside like a vast cemetery. Tombs of
every size stretch out before them, each with its lid lying beside it, and
each wrapped in flames. Cries of anguish sound endlessly from the
entombed dead.

This is the torment of the Heretics of every cult. By Heretic, Dante
means specifically those who did violence to God by denying immortality.
Since they taught that the soul dies with the body, so their punishment is
an eternal grave in the fiery morgue of God's wrath.

My face had paled to a mask of cowardice
  when I saw my Guide turn back. The sight of it
  the sooner brought the color back to his.
He stood apart like one who strains to hear
  what he cannot see, for the eye could not reach far   5
  across the vapors of that midnight air.
"Yet surely we were meant to pass these tombs,"
  he said aloud. "If not . . . so much was promised . . .
  Oh how time hangs and drags till our aid comes!"
I saw too well how the words with which he ended   10

---

3. The Gate of Hell. According to an early medieval tradition, these demons gathered at the outer gate
to oppose the descent of Christ into Limbo at the time of the Harrowing of Hell, but Christ broke the
door open and it has remained so ever since. The service of the Mass for Holy Saturday still sings *Hodie
portas mortis et seras pariter Salvator noster disrupit.* (On this day our Saviour broke open the door of
the dead and its lock as well.)   4. A Messenger of Heaven. He is described in the next Canto.

covered his start, and even perhaps I drew
a worse conclusion from that than he intended.
"Tell me, Master, does anyone ever come
    from the first ledge,[5] whose only punishment
    is hope cut off, into this dreary bottom?"   15
I put this question to him, still in fear
    of what his broken speech might mean; and he:
    "Rarely do any of us enter here.
Once before, it is true, I crossed through Hell
    conjured by cruel Erichtho[6] who recalled   20
    the spirits to their bodies. Her dark spell
forced me, newly stripped of my mortal part,
    to enter through this gate and summon out
    a spirit from Judaïca.[7] Take heart,
That is the last depth and the darkest lair   25
    and the farthest from Heaven which encircles all,
    and at that time I came back even from there.
The marsh from which the stinking gasses bubble
    lies all about this capital of sorrow
    whose gates we may not pass now without trouble."   30
All this and more he expounded; but the rest
    was lost on me, for suddenly my attention
    was drawn to the turret with the fiery crest
where all at once three hellish and inhuman
    Furies[8] sprang to view, bloodstained and wild.   35
    Their limbs and gestures hinted they were women.
Belts of greenest hydras wound and wound
    about their waists, and snakes and horned serpents
    grew from their heads like matted hair and bound
their horrid brows. My Master, who well knew   40
    the handmaids of the Queen of Woe,[9] cried: "Look:
    the terrible Erinyes of Hecate's crew.
That is Megaera to the left of the tower.
    Alecto is the one who raves on the right.
    Tisiphone stands between." And he said no more.   45
With their palms they beat their brows, with their nails they clawed
    their bleeding breasts. And such mad wails broke from them
    that I drew close to the Poet, overawed.
And all together screamed, looking down at me:
    "Call Medusa that we may change him to stone!   50
    Too lightly we let Theseus go free."[1]
"Turn your back and keep your eyes shut tight;
    for should the Gorgon come and you look at her,

---

5. Limbo.   6. A sorceress drawn from Lucan (*Pharsalia* VI, 508ff.).   7. Judaïca (or Judecca) is the final pit of Hell. Erichtho called up the spirit in order to foretell the outcome of the campaign between Pompey and Caesar. There is no trace of the legend in which Virgil is chosen for the descent; Virgil, in fact, was still alive at the time of the battle of Pharsalia.   8. Or Erinyes. In classical mythology they were especially malignant spirits who pursued and tormented those who had violated fundamental taboos (desecration of temples, murder of kin, etc.). They are apt symbols of the guilty conscience of the damned.   9. Proserpine (or Hecate) was the wife of Pluto, and therefore Queen of the Underworld. 1. Theseus and Pirithous tried to kidnap Hecate. Pirithous was killed in the attempt and Theseus was punished by being chained to a great rock. He was later set free by Hercules, who descended to his rescue in defiance of all the powers of Hell. The meaning of the Furies' cry is that Dante must be made an example of. Had they punished Theseus properly, men would have acquired more respect for their powers and would not still be attempting to invade the Underworld. *The Gorgon:* She turned to stone whoever looked at her.

never again would you return to the light."
This was my Guide's command. And he turned me about   55
   himself, and would not trust my hands alone,
   but, with his placed on mine, held my eyes shut.
Men of sound intellect and probity,
   weigh with good understanding what lies hidden
   behind the veil of my strange allegory![2]   60
Suddenly there broke on the dirty swell
   of the dark marsh a squall of terrible sound
   that sent a tremor through both shores of Hell;
a sound as if two continents of air,
   one frigid and one scorching, clashed head on   65
   in a war of winds that stripped the forests bare,
ripped off whole boughs and blew them helter skelter
   along the range of dust it raised before it
   making the beasts and shepherds run for shelter.
The Master freed my eyes. "Now turn," he said,   70
   "and fix your nerve of vision on the foam
   there where the smoke is thickest and most acrid."
As frogs before the snake that hunts them down
   churn up their pond in flight, until the last
   squats on the bottom as if turned to stone—   75
so I saw more than a thousand ruined souls
   scatter away from one who crossed dry-shod
   the Stygian marsh into Hell's burning bowels.
With his left hand he fanned away the dreary
   vapors of that sink as he approached;   80
   and only of that annoyance did he seem weary.
Clearly he was a Messenger from God's Throne,
   and I turned to my Guide; but he made me a sign
   that I should keep my silence and bow down.
Ah, what scorn breathed from that Angel-presence!   85
   He reached the gate of Dis and with a wand
   he waved it open, for there was no resistance.
"Outcasts of Heaven, you twice-loathsome crew,"
   he cried upon that terrible sill of Hell,
   "how does this insolence still live in you?   90
Why do you set yourselves against that Throne
   whose Will none can deny, and which, times past,
   has added to your pain for each rebellion?
Why do you butt against Fate's ordinance?
   Your Cerberus, if you recall, still wears   95
   his throat and chin peeled for such arrogance."[3]
Then he turned back through the same filthy tide
   by which he had come. He did not speak to us,
   but went his way like one preoccupied
by other presences than those before him.   100
   And we moved toward the city, fearing nothing
   after his holy words. Straight through the dim

2. Most commentators take this to mean the allegory of the Three Furies, but the lines apply as aptly to the allegory that follows. Dante probably meant both. Almost certainly, too, "my strange allegory" refers to the whole *Commedia*.   3. When Cerberus opposed the fated entrance of Hercules into Hell, Hercules threw a chain about his neck and dragged him to the upperworld. Cerberus's throat, according to Dante, is still peeled raw from it.

and open gate we entered unopposed.
    And I, eager to learn what new estate
    of Hell those burning fortress walls enclosed,   105
began to look about the very moment
    we were inside, and I saw on every hand
    a countryside of sorrow and new torment.
As at Arles where the Rhone sinks into stagnant marshes,
    as at Pola[4] by the Quarnaro Gulf, whose waters   110
    close Italy and wash her farthest reaches,
the uneven tombs cover the even plain—
    such fields I saw here, spread in all directions,
    except that here the tombs were chests of pain:
for, in a ring around each tomb, great fires   115
    raised every wall to a red heat. No smith
    works hotter iron in his forge. The biers
stood with their lids upraised, and from their pits
    an anguished moaning rose on the dead air
    from the desolation of tormented spirits.   120
And I: "Master, what shades are these who lie
    buried in these chests and fill the air
    with such a painful and unending cry?"
"These are the arch-heretics of all cults,
    with all their followers," he replied. "Far more   125
    than you would think lie stuffed into these vaults.
Like lies with like in every heresy,
    and the monuments are fired, some more, some less;
    to each depravity its own degree."
He turned then, and I followed through that night   130
between the wall and the torments, bearing right.[5]

CANTO X

Circle Six   The Heretics

As the Poets pass on, one of the damned hears Dante speaking, recognizes him as a Tuscan, and calls to him from one of the fiery tombs. A moment later he appears. He is Farinata degli Uberti, a great war-chief of the Tuscan Ghibellines. The majesty and power of his bearing seem to diminish Hell itself. He asks Dante's lineage and recognizes him as an enemy. They begin to talk politics, but are interrupted by another shade, who rises from the same tomb.

This one is Cavalcante dei Cavalcanti, father of Guido Cavalcanti, a contemporary poet. If it is genius that leads Dante on his great journey, the shade asks, why is Guido not with him? Can Dante presume to a greater genius than Guido's? Dante replies that he comes this way only with the aid of powers Guido has not sought. His reply is a classic example

---

4. *Arles . . . Pola:* Situated as indicated on the Rhone and the Quarnaro Gulf respectively, these cities were the sites of great cemeteries dating back to the time of Rome. The Quarnaro Gulf is the body of water on which Fiume is situated.   5. Through all of Hell the Poets bear left in their descent with only two exceptions, the first in their approach to the Heretics, the second in their approach to Geryon, the monster of fraud (see XVII, 29n). Note that both these exceptions occur at a major division of the *Inferno.* There is no satisfactory explanation of Dante's allegorical intent in making these exceptions.

of many-leveled symbolism as well as an overt criticism of a rival poet. The senior Cavalcanti mistakenly infers from Dante's reply that Guido is dead, and swoons back into the flames.

Farinata, who has not deigned to notice his fellow-sinner, continues from the exact point at which he had been interrupted. It is as if he refuses to recognize the flames in which he is shrouded. He proceeds to prophesy Dante's banishment from Florence, he defends his part in Florentine politics, and then, in answer to Dante's question, he explains how it is that the damned can foresee the future but have no knowledge of the present. He then names others who share his tomb, and Dante takes his leave with considerable respect for his great enemy, pausing only long enough to leave word for Cavalcanti that Guido is still alive.

We go by a secret path along the rim
   of the dark city, between the wall and the torments.
   My Master leads me and I follow him.
"Supreme Virtue, who through this impious land
   wheel me at will down these dark gyres," I said,   5
   "speak to me, for I wish to understand.
Tell me, Master, is it permitted to see
   the souls within these tombs? The lids are raised,
   and no one stands on guard." And he to me:
"All shall be sealed forever on the day   10
   these souls return here from Jehosaphat[6]
   with the bodies they have given once to clay.
In this dark corner of the morgue of wrath
   lie Epicurus[7] and his followers,
   who make the soul share in the body's death.   15
And here you shall be granted presently
   not only your spoken wish, but that other as well,[8]
   which you had thought perhaps to hide from me."
And I: "Except to speak my thoughts in few
   and modest words, as I learned from your example,   20
   dear Guide, I do not hide my heart from you."
"O Tuscan, who go living through this place
   speaking so decorously,[9] may it please you pause
   a moment on your way, for by the grace
of that high speech in which I hear your birth,   25
   I know you for a son of that noble city
   which perhaps I vexed too much in my time on earth."
These words broke without warning from inside
   one of the burning arks. Caught by surprise,

6. A valley outside Jerusalem. The popular belief that it would serve as the scene of the Last Judgment was based on Joel iii, 2, 12.   7. The Greek philosopher. The central aim of his philosophy was to achieve happiness, which he defined as the absence of pain. For Dante this doctrine meant the denial of the Eternal life, since the whole aim of the Epicurean was temporal happiness.   8. "All knowing" Virgil is frequently presented as being able to read Dante's mind. The "other wish" is almost certainly Dante's desire to speak to someone from Florence with whom he could discuss politics. Many prominent Florentines were Epicureans.   9. Florence lies in the province of Tuscany. Italian, to an extent unknown in America, is a language of dialects, all of them readily identifiable even when they are not well understood by the hearer. Dante's native Tuscan has become the main source of modern official Italian. Two very common sayings still current in Italy are: "*Lingua toscana, lingua di Dio*" (the Tuscan tongue is the language of God) and—to express the perfection of Italian speech—"*Lingua toscana in bocca romana* (the Tuscan tongue in a Roman mouth).

I turned in fear and drew close to my Guide.   30
And he: "Turn around. What are you doing? Look there:
  it is Farinata[1] rising from the flames.
  From the waist up his shade will be made clear."
My eyes were fixed on him already. Erect,
  he rose above the flame, great chest, great brow;   35
  he seemed to hold all Hell in disrespect.
My Guide's prompt hands urged me among the dim
  and smoking sepulchres to that great figure,
  and he said to me: "Mind how you speak to him."
And when I stood alone at the foot of the tomb,   40
  the great soul stared almost contemptuously,
  before he asked: "Of what line do you come?"
Because I wished to obey, I did not hide
  anything from him: whereupon, as he listened,
  he raised his brows a little, then replied: 45
"Bitter enemies were they to me,
  to my fathers, and to my party, so that twice
  I sent them scattering from high Italy."
"If they were scattered, still from every part
  they formed again and returned both times," I answered,   50
  "but yours have not yet wholly learned that art."
At this another shade[2] rose gradually,
  visible to the chin. It had raised itself,
  I think, upon its knees, and it looked around me
as if it expected to find through that black air   55
  that blew about me, another traveler.
  And weeping when it found no other there,
turned back. "And if," it cried, "you travel through
  this dungeon of the blind by power of genius,
  where is my son? why is he not with you?"   60
And I to him: "Not by myself[3] am I borne
  this terrible way. I am led by him who waits there,
  and whom perhaps your Guido held in scorn."
For by his words and the manner of his torment
  I knew his name already, and could, therefore,   65
  answer both what he asked and what he meant.
Instantly he rose to his full height:
  "He *held*? What is it you say? Is he dead, then?
  Do his eyes no longer fill with that sweet light?"
And when he saw that I delayed a bit   70
  in answering his question, he fell backwards

---

1. Farinata degli Uberti was head of the ancient noble house of the Uberti. He became leader of the
Ghibellines of Florence in 1239, and played a large part in expelling the Guelphs in 1248. The Guelphs
returned in 1251, but Farinata remained. His arrogant desire to rule singlehanded led to difficulties,
however, and he was expelled in 1258. With the aid of the Manfredi of Siena, he gathered a large force
and defeated the Guelphs at Montaperti on the River Arbia in 1260. Re-entering Florence in triumph,
he again expelled the Guelphs, but at the Diet of Empoli, held by the victors after the battle of Montaperti, he alone rose in open counsel to resist the general sentiment that Florence should be razed. He
died in Florence in 1264. In 1266 the Guelphs once more returned and crushed forever the power of
the Uberti, destroying their palaces and issuing special decrees against persons of the Uberti line. In
1283 a decree of heresy was published against Farinata.   2. Cavalcante dei Cavalcanti was a famous
Epicurean ("like lies with like"). He was the father of Guido Cavalcanti, a poet and friend of Dante.
Guido was also Farinata's son-in-law.   3. Cavalcanti assumes that the resources of human genius are
all that are necessary for such a journey. (It is an assumption that well fits his character as an Epicurean.)
Dante replies as a man of religion that other aid is necessary.

into the flame, and rose no more from it.
But that majestic spirit at whose call
    I had first paused there, did not change expression,
    nor so much as turn his face to watch him fall.   75
"And if," going on from his last words, he said,
    "men of my line have yet to learn that art,
    that burns me deeper than this flaming bed.
But the face of her who reigns in Hell[4] shall not
    be fifty times rekindled in its course   80
    before you learn what griefs attend that art.
And as you hope to find the world again,
    tell me: why is that populace[5] so savage
    in the edicts they pronounce against my strain?"
And I to him: "The havoc and the carnage   85
    that dyed the Arbia red at Montaperti
    have caused these angry cries in our assemblage."
He sighed and shook his head. "I was not alone
    in that affair," he said, "nor certainly
    would I have joined the rest without good reason.   90
But I *was* alone at that time when every other
    consented to the death of Florence; I
    alone with open face defended her."
"Ah, so may your soul sometime have rest,"
    I begged him, "solve the riddle that pursues me   95
    through this dark place and leaves my mind perplexed:
you seem to see in advance all time's intent,
    if I have heard and understood correctly;
    but you seem to lack all knowledge of the present."
"We see asquint, like those whose twisted sight   100
    can make out only the far-off," he said,
    "for the King of All still grants us that much light.
When things draw near, or happen, we perceive
    nothing of them. Except what others bring us
    we have no news of those who are alive.   105
So may you understand that all we know
    will be dead forever from that day and hour
    when the Portal of the Future is swung to."
Then, as if stricken by regret, I said:
    "Now, therefore, will you tell that fallen one   110
    who asked about his son, that he is not dead,
and that, if I did not reply more quickly,
    it was because my mind was occupied
    with this confusion you have solved for me."
And now my Guide was calling me. In haste,   115
    therefore, I begged that mighty shade to name
    the others who lay with him in that chest.
And he: "More than a thousand cram this tomb.
    The second Frederick[6] is here, and the Cardinal

---

4. Hecate or Proserpine. She is also the moon goddess. The sense of this prophecy, therefore, is that Dante will be exiled within fifty full moons. Dante was banished from Florence in 1302, well within the fifty months of the prophecy.   5. The Florentines.   6. The Emperor Frederick II. In Canto XIII Dante has Pier delle Vigne speak of him as one worthy of honor, but he was commonly reputed to be an Epicurean.

of the Ubaldini.[7] Of the rest let us be dumb."   120
And he disappeared without more said, and I
   turned back and made my way to the ancient Poet,
   pondering the words of the dark prophecy.
He moved along, and then, when we had started,
   he turned and said to me, "What troubles you?   125
   Why do you look so vacant and downhearted?"
And I told him. And he replied: "Well may you bear
   those words in mind." Then, pausing, raised a finger:
   "Now pay attention to what I tell you here:
when finally you stand before the ray   130
   of that Sweet Lady[8] whose bright eye sees all,
   from her you will learn the turnings of your way."
So saying, he bore left, turning his back
   on the flaming walls, and we passed deeper yet
   into the city of pain, along a track   135
that plunged down like a scar into a sink
which sickened us already with its stink.

CANTO XI

Circle Six   The Heretics

   The Poets reach the inner edge of the Sixth Circle and find a great
jumble of rocks that had once been a cliff, but which has fallen into rubble
as the result of the great earthquake that shook Hell when Christ died.
Below them lies the Seventh Circle, and so fetid is the air that arises from
it that the Poets cower for shelter behind a great tomb until their breaths
can grow accustomed to the stench.

   Dante finds an inscription on the lid of the tomb labeling it as the place
in Hell of Pope Anastasius.

   Virgil takes advantage of the delay to outline in detail The Division of
the Lower Hell, a theological discourse based on *The Ethics* and *The Physics* of Aristotle with subsequent medieval interpretations. Virgil explains
also why it is that the Incontinent are not punished within the walls of
Dis, and rather ingeniously sets forth the reasons why Usury is an act of
violence against Art, which is the child of Nature and hence the Grandchild of God. (By "Art," Dante means the arts and crafts by which man
draws from nature, i.e., Industry.)

   As he concludes he rises and urges Dante on. By means known only to
Virgil, he is aware of the motion of the stars and from them he sees that it
is about two hours before Sunrise of Holy Saturday.

We came to the edge of an enormous sink
   rimmed by a circle of great broken boulders.[9]

---

7. In the original Dante refers to him simply as "il Cardinale." Ottaviano degli Ubaldini (born *circa*
1209, died 1273) became a Cardinal in 1245, but his energies seem to have been directed exclusively
to money and political intrigue. When he was refused an important loan by the Ghibellines, he is
reported by many historians as having remarked: "I may say that if I have a soul, I have lost it in the
cause of the Ghibellines, and no one of them will help me now." The words "If I have a soul" would
be enough to make him guilty in Dante's eyes of the charge of heresy.   8. Beatrice.   9. These
boulders were broken from the earthquake that shook Hell at the death of Christ.

Here we found ghastlier gangs. And here the stink
thrown up by the abyss so overpowered us
   that we drew back, cowering behind the wall   5
   of one of the great tombs; and standing thus,
I saw an inscription in the stone, and read:
   "I guard Anastasius, once Pope,
   he whom Photinus[1] led from the straight road."
"Before we travel on to that blind pit   10
   we must delay until our sense grows used
   to its foul breath, and then we will not mind it,"
my Master said. And I then: "Let us find
   some compensation for the time of waiting."
And he: "You shall see I have just that in mind.   15
My son," he began, "there are below this wall
   three smaller circles,[2] each in its degree
   like those you are about to leave, and all
are crammed with God's accurst. Accordingly,
   that you may understand their sins at sight,   20
   I will explain how each is prisoned, and why.
Malice is the sin most hated by God.
   And the aim of malice is to injure others
   whether by fraud or violence. But since fraud
is the vice of which man alone is capable,   25
   God loathes it most. Therefore, the fraudulent
   are placed below, and their torment is more painful.
The first below are the violent. But as violence
   sins in three persons, so is that circle formed
   of three descending rounds of crueler torments.   30
Against God, self, and neighbor is violence shown.
   Against their persons and their goods, I say,
   as you shall hear set forth with open reason.
Murder and mayhem are the violation
   of the person of one's neighbor: and of his goods;   35
   harassment, plunder, arson, and extortion.
Therefore, homicides, and those who strike
   in malice—destroyers and plunderers—all lie
   in that first round, and like suffers with like.
A man may lay violent hands upon his own   40
   person and substance; so in that second round
   eternally in vain repentance moan
the suicides and all who gamble away
   and waste the good and substance of their lives
   and weep in that sweet time when they should be gay.   45
Violence may be offered the deity
   in the heart that blasphemes and refuses Him
   and scorns the gifts of Nature, her beauty and bounty.

1. Anastasius II was Pope from 496 to 498. This was the time of schism between the Eastern (Greek) and Western (Roman) churches. Photinus, deacon of Thessalonica, was of the Greek church and held to the Acacian heresy, which denied the divine paternity of Christ. Dante follows the report that Anastasius gave communion to Photinus, thereby countenancing his heresy. Dante's sources, however, had probably confused Anastasius II, the Pope, with Anastasius I, who was Emperor from 491 to 518. It was the Emperor Anastasius who was persuaded by Photinus to accept the Acacian heresy.   2. The Poets are now at the cliff that bounds the Sixth Circle. Below them lie Circles Seven, Eight, and Nine. They are smaller in circumference, being closer to the center, but they are all intricately subdivided, and will be treated at much greater length than were the Circles of Upper Hell.

Therefore, the smallest round brands with its mark
  both Sodom and Cahors,[3] and all who rail   50
    at God and His commands in their hearts' dark.
Fraud, which is a canker to every conscience,
  may be practiced by a man on those who trust him,
    and on those who have reposed no confidence.
The latter mode seems only to deny   55
  the bond of love which all men have from Nature;
    therefore within the second circle lie
simoniacs, sycophants, and hypocrites,
  falsifiers, thieves, and sorcerers,
    grafters, pimps, and all such filthy cheats.   60
The former mode of fraud not only denies
  the bond of Nature, but the special trust
    added by bonds of friendship or blood-ties.
Hence, at the center point of all creation,[4]
  in the smallest circle, on which Dis is founded,   65
    the traitors lie in endless expiation."
"Master," I said, "the clarity of your mind
  impresses all you touch; I see quite clearly
    the orders of this dark pit of the blind.
But tell me: those who lie in the swamp's bowels,   70
  those the wind blows about, those the rain beats,
    and those who meet and clash with such mad howls[5]—
why are *they* not punished in the rust-red city[6]
  if God's wrath be upon them? and if it is not,
    why must they grieve through all eternity?"   75
And he: "Why does your understanding stray
  so far from its own habit? or can it be
    your thoughts are turned along some other way?
Have you forgotten that your *Ethics*[7] states
  the three main dispositions of the soul   80
    that lead to those offenses Heaven hates—
incontinence, malice, and bestiality?
  and how incontinence offends God least
    and earns least blame from Justice and Charity?
Now if you weigh this doctrine and recall   85
  exactly who they are whose punishment
    lies in that upper Hell outside the wall,
you will understand at once why they are confined
  apart from these fierce wraiths, and why less anger
    beats down on them from the Eternal Mind."   90
"O sun which clears all mists from troubled sight,
  such joy attends your rising that I feel
    as grateful to the dark as to the light.
Go back a little further," I said, "to where
  you spoke of usury as an offense   95
    against God's goodness. How is that made clear?"

3. Both these cities are used as symbols for the sins that are said to have flourished within them. Sodom (Genesis xix) is, of course, identified with unnatural sex practices. Cahors, a city in southern France, was notorious in the Middle Ages for its usurers.   4. In the Ptolemaic system the earth was the center of the Universe. In Dante's geography, the bottom of Hell is the center of the earth.   5. These are, of course, the sinners of the Upper Hell.   6. Dis. All of Lower Hell is within the city walls.   7. *The Ethics* of Aristotle.

"Philosophy makes plain by many reasons,"
   he answered me, "to those who heed her teachings,
   how all of Nature,—her laws, her fruits, her seasons,—
springs from the Ultimate Intellect and Its art: 100
   and if you read your *Physics*[8] with due care,
   you will note, not many pages from the start,
that Art strives after her by imitation,
   as the disciple imitates the master;
   Art, as it were, is the Grandchild of Creation.   105
By this, recalling the Old Testament
   near the beginning of Genesis, you will see
   that in the will of Providence, man was meant
to labor and to prosper. But usurers,
   by seeking their increase in other ways,   110
   scorn Nature in herself and her followers.
But come, for it is my wish now to go on:
   the wheel turns and the Wain lies over Caurus,[9]
   the Fish are quivering low on the horizon,
and there beyond us runs the road we go   115
down the dark scarp into the depths below."

CANTO XII

Circle Seven: Round One   The Violent Against Neighbors

   The Poets begin the descent of the fallen rock wall, having first to evade the Minotaur, who menaces them. Virgil tricks him and the Poets hurry by.

   Below them they see the River of Blood, which marks the First Round of the Seventh Circle as detailed in the previous Canto. Here are punished the Violent Against Their Neighbors, great war-makers, cruel tyrants, highwaymen—all who shed the blood of their fellowmen. As they wallowed in blood during their lives, so they are immersed in the boiling blood forever, each according to the degree of his guilt, while fierce Centaurs patrol the banks, ready to shoot with their arrows any sinner who raises himself out of the boiling blood beyond the limits permitted him. Alexander the Great is here, up to his lashes in the blood, and with him Attila, The Scourge of God. They are immersed in the deepest part of the river, which grows shallower as it circles to the other side of the ledge, then deepens again.

   The Poets are challenged by the Centaurs, but Virgil wins a safe conduct from Chiron, their chief, who assigns Nessus to guide them and to bear them across the shallows of the boiling blood. Nessus carries them across at the point where it is only ankle deep and immediately leaves them and returns to his patrol.

---

8. *The Physics* of Aristotle.   9. The Wain is the constellation of the Great Bear. Caurus was the northwest wind in classical mythology. Hence the constellation of the Great Bear now lies in the northwest. The Fish is the constellation and zodiacal sign of Pisces. It is just appearing over the horizon. The next sign of the zodiac is Aries. We know from Canto I that the sun is in Aries, and since the twelve signs of the zodiac each cover two hours of the day, it must now be about two hours before dawn. It is, therefore, approximately 4:00 A.M. *of Holy Saturday.* The stars are not visible in Hell, but throughout the *Inferno* Virgil reads them by some special power which Dante does not explain.

The scene that opened from the edge of the pit
 was mountainous, and such a desolation
 that every eye would shun the sight of it:
a ruin like the Slides of Mark[1] near Trent
 on the bank of the Adige, the result of an earthquake   5
 or of some massive fault in the escarpment—
for, from the point on the peak where the mountain split
 to the plain below, the rock is so badly shattered
 a man at the top might make a rough stair of it.[2]
Such was the passage down the steep, and there   10
 at the very top, at the edge of the broken cleft,
 lay spread the Infamy of Crete,[3] the heir
of bestiality and the lecherous queen
 who hid in a wooden cow. And when he saw us,
 he gnawed his own flesh in a fit of spleen.   15
And my Master mocked: "How you do pump your breath!
 Do you think, perhaps, it is the Duke of Athens,
 who in the world above served up your death?
Off with you, monster; this one does not come
 instructed by your sister, but of himself   20
 to observe your punishment in the lost kingdom."
As a bull that breaks its chains just when the knife
 has struck its death-blow, cannot stand nor run
 but leaps from side to side with its last life—
so danced the Minotaur, and my shrewd Guide   25
 cried out: "Run now! While he is blind with rage!
 Into the pass, quick, and get over the side!"
So we went down across the shale and slate
 of that ruined rock, which often slid and shifted
 under me at the touch of living weight.   30
I moved on, deep in thought; and my Guide to me:
 "You are wondering perhaps about this ruin
 which is guarded by the beast upon whose fury
I played just now. I should tell you that when last
 I came this dark way to the depths of Hell,   35
 this rock had not yet felt the ruinous blast.[4]
But certainly, if I am not mistaken,
 it was just before the coming of Him who took
 the souls from Limbo, that all Hell was shaken
so that I thought the universe felt love   40

---

1. *Li Slavoni di Marco* are about two miles from Rovereto (between Verona and Trent) on the left bank of the River Adige. 2. I am defeated in all attempts to convey Dante's emphasis in any sort of a verse line. The sense of the original: "It might provide some sort of a way down for one who started at the top, but (by implication) would not be climbable from below." 3. This is the infamous Minotaur of classical mythology. His mother was Pasiphaë, wife of Minos, the King of Crete. She conceived an unnatural passion for a bull, and in order to mate with it, she crept into a wooden cow. From this union the Minotaur was born, half-man, half-beast. King Minos kept him in an ingenious labyrinth from which he could not escape. When Androgeos, the son of King Minos, was killed by the Athenians, Minos exacted an annual tribute of seven maidens and seven youths. These were annually turned into the labyrinth and there were devoured by the Minotaur. The monster was finally killed by Theseus, duke of Athens. He was aided by Ariadne, daughter of Minos (and half-sister of the monster). She gave Theseus a ball of cord to unwind as he entered the labyrinth and a sword with which to kill the Minotaur. 4. According to Matthew xxvii, 51, an earthquake shook the earth at the moment of Christ's death. These stones, Dante lets us know, were broken off in that earthquake. We shall find other effects of the same shock in the Eighth Circle. It is worth noting also that both the Upper (See Canto V, 34) and the Lower Hell begin with evidences of this ruin. For details of Virgil's first descent see notes to Canto IX.

and all its elements moved toward harmony,
   whereby the world of matter, as some believe,
has often plunged to chaos.[5] It was then,
   that here and elsewhere in the pits of Hell,
   the ancient rock was stricken and broke open.   45
But turn your eyes to the valley; there we shall find
   the river of boiling blood[6] in which are steeped
   all who struck down their fellow men." Oh blind!
Oh ignorant, self-seeking cupidity
   which spurs us so in the short mortal life   50
   and steeps us so through all eternity!
I saw an arching fosse that was the bed
   of a winding river circling through the plain
   exactly as my Guide and Lord had said.
A file of Centaurs[7] galloped in the space   55
   between the bank and the cliff, well armed with arrows,
   riding as once on earth they rode to the chase.
And seeing us descend, that straggling band
   halted, and three of them moved out toward us,
   their long bows and their shafts already in hand.   60
And one of them cried out while still below:
   "To what pain are you sent down that dark coast?
   Answer from where you stand, or I draw the bow!"
"Chiron[8] is standing there hard by your side;
   our answer will be to him. This wrath of yours   65
   was always your own worst fate," my Guide replied.
And to me he said: "That is Nessus, who died in the wood
   for insulting Dejanira.[9] At his death
   he plotted his revenge in his own blood.
The one in the middle staring at his chest   70
   is the mighty Chiron, he who nursed Achilles:
   the other is Pholus,[1] fiercer than all the rest.
They run by that stream in thousands, snapping their bows
   at any wraith who dares to raise himself
   out of the blood more than his guilt allows."   75
We drew near those swift beasts. In a thoughtful pause
   Chiron drew an arrow, and with its notch
   he pushed his great beard back along his jaws.
And when he had thus uncovered the huge pouches

---

5. The Greek philosopher, Empedocles, taught that the universe existed by the counter-balance (discord or mutual repulsion) of its elements. Should the elemental matter feel harmony (love or mutual attraction) all would fly together into chaos.   6. This is Phlegethon, the river that circles through the First Round of the Seventh Circle, then sluices through the wood of the suicides (the Second Round) and the burning sands (Third Round) to spew over the Great Cliff into the Eighth Circle, and so, eventually, to the bottom of Hell (Cocytus).   7. Creatures of classical mythology, half-horse, half-men. They were skilled and savage hunters, creatures of passion and violence. Like the Minotaur, they are symbols of the bestial-human, and as such, they are fittingly chosen as the tormentors of these sinners. 8. The son of Saturn and of the nymph Philira. He was the wisest and most just of the Centaurs and reputedly was the teacher of Achilles and of other Greek heroes to whom he imparted great skill in bearing arms, medicine, astronomy, music, and augury. Dante places him far down in Hell with the others of his kind, but though he draws Chiron's coarseness, he also grants him a kind of majestic understanding.   9. Nessus carried travelers across the River Evenus for hire. He was hired to ferry Dejanira, the wife of Hercules, and tried to abduct her, but Hercules killed him with a poisoned arrow. While Nessus was dying, he whispered to Dejanira that a shirt stained with his poisoned blood would act as a love charm should Hercules' affections stray. When Hercules fell in love with Iole, Dejanira sent him a shirt stained with the Centaur's blood. The shirt poisoned Hercules and he died in agony. 1. A number of classical poets mention Pholus, but very little else is known of him.

of his lips, he said to his fellows: "Have you noticed   80
how the one who walks behind moves what he touches?"
That is not how the dead go." My good Guide,
   already standing by the monstrous breast
   in which the two mixed natures joined, replied:
"It is true he lives; in his necessity   85
   I alone must lead him through this valley.
   Fate brings him here, not curiosity.
From singing Alleluia the sublime
   spirit[2] who sends me came. He is no bandit.
   Nor am I one who ever stooped to crime.   90
But in the name of the Power by which I go
   this sunken way across the floor of Hell,
   assign us one of your troop whom we may follow,
that he may guide us to the ford, and there
   carry across on his back the one I lead,   95
   for he is not a spirit to move through air."
Chiron turned his head on his right breast[3]
   and said to Nessus: "Go with them, and guide them,
   and turn back any others that would contest
their passage." So we moved beside our guide   100
   along the bank of the scalding purple river
   in which the shrieking wraiths were boiled and dyed.
Some stood up to their lashes in that torrent,
   and as we passed them the huge Centaur said:
   "These were the kings of bloodshed and despoilment.   105
Here they pay for their ferocity.
   Here is Alexander.[4] And Dionysius,
   who brought long years of grief to Sicily.
That brow you see with the hair as black as night
   is Azzolino;[5] and that beside him, the blonde,   110
   is Opizzo da Esti,[6] who had his mortal light
blown out by his own stepson." I turned then
   to speak to the Poet but he raised a hand:
   "Let him be the teacher now, and I will listen."
Further on, the Centaur stopped beside   115
   a group of spirits steeped as far as the throat
   in the race of boiling blood, and there our guide
pointed out a sinner who stood alone:
   "That one before God's altar pierced a heart
   still honored on the Thames."[7] And he passed on.   120
We came in sight of some who were allowed
   to raise the head and all the chest from the river,

2. Beatrice.   3. The right is the side of virtue and honor. In Chiron it probably signifies his human side as opposed to his bestial side.   4. Alexander the Great. *Dionysius:* Dionysius I (died 367 B.C.) and his son, Dionysius II (died 343), were tyrants of Sicily. Both were infamous as prototypes of the bloodthirsty and exorbitant ruler. Dante may intend either or both.   5. Ezzelino da Romano, Count of Onora (1194–1259). The cruelest of the Ghibelline tyrants. In 1236 Frederick II appointed Ezzelino his vicar in Padua. Ezzelino became especially infamous for his bloody treatment of the Paduans, whom he slaughtered in great numbers.   6. Marquis of Ferrara (1264–1293). The account of his life is confused. One must accept Dante's facts as given.   7. The sinner indicated is Guy de Montfort. His father, Simon de Montfort, was a leader of the barons who rebelled against Henry III and was killed at the battle of Evesham (1265) by Prince Edward (later Edward I). In 1271, Guy (then Vicar General of Tuscany) avenged his father's death by murdering Henry's nephew (who was also named Henry). The crime was openly committed in a church at Viterbo. The murdered Henry's heart was sealed in a casket and sent to London, where it was accorded various honors.

and I recognized many there. Thus, as we followed
along the stream of blood, its level fell
   until it cooked no more than the feet of the damned.   125
   And here we crossed the ford to deeper Hell.
"Just as you see the boiling stream grow shallow
   along this side," the Centaur said to us
   when we stood on the other bank, "I would have you know
that on the other, the bottom sinks anew   130
   more and more, until it comes again
   full circle to the place where the tyrants stew.
It is there that Holy Justice spends its wrath
   on Sextus[8] and Pyrrhus through eternity,
   and on Attila,[9] who was a scourge on earth: 135
and everlastingly milks out the tears
   of Rinier da Corento and Rinier Pazzo,[1]
   those two assassins who for many years
stalked the highways, bloody and abhorred."
And with that he started back across the ford.   140

CANTO XIII

Circle Seven: Round Two   The Violent Against Themselves

Nessus carries the Poets across the river of boiling blood and leaves
them in the Second Round of the Seventh Circle, The Wood of the Suicides. Here are punished those who destroyed their own lives and those
who destroyed their substance.

The souls of the Suicides are encased in thorny trees whose leaves are
eaten by the odious Harpies, the overseers of these damned. When the
Harpies feed upon them, damaging their leaves and limbs, the wound
bleeds. Only as long as the blood flows are the souls of the trees able to
speak. Thus, they who destroyed their own bodies are denied a human
form; and just as the supreme expression of their lives was self-destruction,
so they are permitted to speak only through that which tears and destroys
them. Only through their own blood do they find voice. And to add one
more dimension to the symbolism, it is the Harpies—defilers of all they
touch—who give them their eternally recurring wounds.

The Poets pause before one tree and speak with the soul of Pier delle
Vigne. In the same wood they see Jacomo da Sant' Andrea, and Lano da
Siena, two famous Squanderers and Destroyers of Goods pursued by a
pack of savage hounds. The hounds overtake Sant' Andrea, tear him to
pieces and go off carrying his limbs in their teeth, a self-evident symbolic
retribution for the violence with which these sinners destroyed their substance in the world. After this scene of horror, Dante speaks to an
Unknown Florentine Suicide whose soul is inside the bush which was
torn by the hound pack when it leaped upon Sant' Andrea.

---

8. Probably the younger son of Pompey the Great. His piracy is mentioned in Lucan (*Pharsalia* VI,
420–422). *Pyrrhus:* Pyrrhus, the son of Achilles, was especially bloodthirsty at the sack of Troy. Pyrrhus,
King of Epirus (319–372 B.C.), waged relentless and bloody war against the Greeks and Romans. Either
may be intended.   9. King of the Huns from 433 to 453. He was called the Scourge of God.
1. Both were especially bloodthirsty robber-barons of the thirteenth century.

Nessus had not yet reached the other shore
   when we moved on into a pathless wood
   that twisted upward from Hell's broken floor.
Its foliage was not verdant, but nearly black.
   The unhealthy branches, gnarled and warped and tangled,   5
   bore poison thorns instead of fruit. The track
of those wild beasts that shun the open spaces
   men till between Cecina and Corneto
   runs through no rougher nor more tangled places.[2]
Here nest the odious Harpies[3] of whom my Master   10
   wrote how they drove Aeneas and his companions
   from the Strophades with prophecies of disaster.
Their wings are wide, their feet clawed, their huge bellies
   covered with feathers, their necks and faces human.
   They croak eternally in the unnatural trees.   15
"Before going on, I would have you understand,"
   my Guide began, "we are in the second round
   and shall be till we reach the burning sand.[4]
Therefore look carefully and you will see
   things in this wood, which, if I told them to you   20
   would shake the confidence you have placed in me."
I heard cries of lamentation rise and spill
   on every hand, but saw no souls in pain
   in all that waste; and, puzzled, I stood still.
I think perhaps he thought that I was thinking[5]   25
   those cries rose from among the twisted roots
   through which the spirits of the damned were slinking
to hide from us. Therefore my Master said:
   "If you break off a twig, what you will learn
   will drive what you are thinking from your head."   30
Puzzled, I raised my hand a bit and slowly
   broke off a branchlet from an enormous thorn:
   and the great trunk of it cried: "Why do you break me?"
And after blood had darkened all the bowl
   of the wound, it cried again: "Why do you tear me?   35
   Is there no pity left in any soul?
Men we were, and now we are changed to sticks;
   well might your hand have been more merciful
   were we no more than souls of lice and ticks."
As a green branch with one end all aflame   40
   will hiss and sputter sap out of the other
   as the air escapes—so from that trunk there came
words and blood together, gout by gout.

2. The reference here is to the Maremma district of Tuscany which lies between the mountains and the sea. The river Cecina is the northern boundary of this district; Corneto is on the river Marta, which forms the southern boundary. It is a wild district of marsh and forest.   3. These hideous birds with the faces of malign women were often associated with the Erinyes (Furies). Their original function in mythology was to snatch away the souls of men at the command of the Gods. Later, they were portrayed as defilers of food, and, by extension, of everything they touched. The islands of the Strophades were their legendary abode. Aeneas and his men landed there and fought with the Harpies, who drove them back and pronounced a prophecy of unbearable famine upon them.   4. The Third Round of this Circle.   5. The original is "Cred' io ch'ei credette ch'io credesse." This sort of word play was considered quite elegant by medieval rhetoricians and by the ornate Sicilian School of Poetry. Dante's style is based on a rejection of all such devices in favor of a sparse and direct diction. The best explanation of this unusual instance seems to be that Dante is anticipating his talk with Pier delle Vigne, a rhetorician who, as we shall see, delights in this sort of locution.

Startled, I dropped the branch that I was holding
and stood transfixed by fear, half turned about   45
to my Master, who replied: "O wounded soul,
    could he have believed before what he has seen
    in my verses only,[6] you would yet be whole,
for his hand would never have been raised against you.
    But knowing this truth could never be believed   50
    till it was seen, I urged him on to do
what grieves me now; and I beg to know your name,
    that to make you some amends in the sweet world
    when he returns, he may refresh your fame."
And the trunk: "So sweet those words to me that I   55
    cannot be still, and may it not annoy you
    if I seem somewhat lengthy in reply.
I am he who held both keys to Frederick's heart,[7]
    locking, unlocking with so deft a touch
    that scarce another soul had any part   60
in his most secret thoughts. Through every strife
    I was so faithful to my glorious office
    that for it I gave up both sleep and life.
That harlot, Envy, who on Caesar's[8] face
    keeps fixed forever her adulterous stare,   65
    the common plague and vice of court and palace,
inflamed all minds against me. These inflamed
    so inflamed him that all my happy honors
    were changed to mourning. Then, unjustly blamed,
my soul, in scorn, and thinking to be free   70
    of scorn in death, made me at last, though just,
    unjust to myself. By the new roots[9] of this tree
I swear to you that never in word or spirit
    did I break faith to my lord and emperor
    who was so worthy of honor in his merit.   75
If either of you return to the world, speak for me,
    to vindicate in the memory of men
    one who lies prostrate from the blows of Envy."
The Poet stood. Then turned. "Since he is silent,"
    he said to me, "do not you waste this hour,   80
    if you wish to ask about his life or torment."
And I replied: "Question him for my part,
    on whatever you think I would do well to hear;
    I could not, such compassion chokes my heart."

---

6. The *Aeneid*, Book III, describes a similar bleeding plant. There, Aeneas pulls at a myrtle growing on a Thracian hillside. It bleeds where he breaks it and a voice cries out of the ground. It is the voice of Polydorus, son of Priam and friend of Aeneas. He had been treacherously murdered by the Thracian king.   7. Pier delle Vigne, 1190–1249. A famous and once-powerful minister of Emperor Frederick II. He enjoyed Frederick's whole confidence until 1247 when he was accused of treachery and was imprisoned and blinded. He committed suicide to escape further torture. (For Frederick see Canto X.) Pier delle Vigne was famous for his eloquence and for his mastery of the ornate Provençal-inspired Sicilian School of Italian Poetry, and Dante styles his speech accordingly. . . . It is worth noting, however, that the style changes abruptly in the middle of line 72. There, his courtly preamble finished, delle Vigne speaks from the heart, simply and passionately. *Who held both keys:* The phrasing unmistakably suggests the Papal keys; delle Vigne may be suggesting that he was to Frederick as the Pope is to God.   8. Frederick II was of course Caesar of the Roman Empire, but in this generalized context "Caesar" seems to be used as a generic term for any great ruler, *i.e.*, "The harlot, Envy, never turns her attention from those in power."   9. Pier delle Vigne had only been in Hell fifty-one years, a short enough time on the scale of eternity.

The Poet began again: "That this man may   85
    with all his heart do for you what your words
    entreat him to, imprisoned spirit, I pray,
tell us how the soul is bound and bent
    into these knots, and whether any ever
    frees itself from such imprisonment."   90
At that the trunk blew powerfully, and then
    the wind became a voice that spoke these words:
    "Briefly is the answer given: when
out of the flesh from which it tore itself,
    the violent spirit comes to punishment,   95
    Minos assigns it to the seventh shelf.
It falls into the wood, and landing there,
    wherever fortune flings it,[1] it strikes root,
    and there it sprouts, lusty as any tare,
shoots up a sapling, and becomes a tree.   100
    The Harpies, feeding on its leaves then, give it
    pain and pain's outlet simultaneously.[2]
Like the rest, we shall go for our husks on Judgment Day,
    but not that we may wear them, for it is not just
    that a man be given what he throws away.   105
Here shall we drag them and in this mournful glade
    our bodies will dangle to the end of time,
    each on the thorns of its tormented shade."
We waited by the trunk, but it said no more;
    and waiting, we were startled by a noise   110
    that grew through all the wood. Just such a roar
and trembling as one feels when the boar and chase
    approach his stand, the beasts and branches crashing
    and clashing in the heat of the fierce race.
And there on the left, running so violently   115
    they broke off every twig in the dark wood,
    two torn and naked wraiths went plunging by me.
The leader cried, "Come now, O Death! Come now!"
    And the other, seeing that he was outrun,
    cried out: "Your legs were not so ready, Lano,[3]   120
in the jousts at the Toppo." And suddenly in his rush,
    perhaps because his breath was failing him,
    he hid himself inside a thorny bush
and cowered among its leaves. Then at his back,
    the wood leaped with black bitches, swift as greyhounds   125
    escaping from their leash, and all the pack
sprang on him; with their fangs they opened him
    and tore him savagely, and then withdrew,
    carrying his body with them, limb by limb.
Then, taking me by the hand across the wood,   130
    my Master led me toward the bush. Lamenting,
    all its fractures blew out words and blood:

1. Just as the soul of the suicide refused to accept divine regulation of its mortal life span, so eternal justice takes no special heed of where the soul falls.   2. Suicide also gives pain and its outlet simultaneously.   3. Lano da Siena, a famous squanderer. He died at the ford of the river Toppo near Arezzo in 1287 in a battle against the Aretines. Boccaccio writes that he deliberately courted death having squandered all his great wealth and being unwilling to live on in poverty. Thus his companion's jeer probably means: "You were not so ready to run then, Lano: why are you running now?"

"O Jacomo da Sant' Andrea!"[4] it said,
    "what have you gained in making me your screen?
    What part had I in the foul life you led?"   135
And when my Master had drawn up to it
    he said: "Who were you, who through all your wounds
    blow out your blood with your lament, sad spirit?"
And he to us: "You who have come to see
    how the outrageous mangling of these hounds   140
    has torn my boughs and stripped my leaves from me,
O heap them round my ruin! I was born
    in the city that tore down Mars and raised the Baptist.[5]
    On that account the God of War has sworn
her sorrow shall not end. And were it not   145
    that something of his image still survives
    on the bridge across the Arno, some have thought
those citizens who of their love and pain
    afterwards rebuilt it from the ashes
    left by Attila,[6] would have worked in vain.   150
I am one who has no tale to tell:
I made myself a gibbet of my own lintel."

CANTO XIV

Circle Seven: Round Three   The Violent Against God, Nature, and Art

Dante, in pity, restores the torn leaves to the soul of his countryman
and the Poets move on to the next round, a great Plain of Burning Sand
upon which there descends an eternal slow Rain of Fire. Here, scorched
by fire from above and below, are three classes of sinners suffering differing degrees of exposure to the fire. The Blasphemers (The Violent
against God) are stretched supine upon the sand, the Sodomites (The
Violent against Nature) run in endless circles, and the Usurers (The Violent against Art, which is the Grandchild of God) huddle on the sands.

The Poets find Capaneus stretched out on the sands, the chief sinner
of that place. He is still blaspheming God. They continue along the edge
of the Wood of the Suicides and come to a blood-red rill which flows
boiling from the Wood and crosses the burning plain. Virgil explains the
miraculous power of its waters and discourses on the Old Man of Crete
and the origin of all the rivers of Hell.

The symbolism of the burning plain is obviously centered in sterility
(the desert image) and wrath (the fire image). Blasphemy, sodomy, and
usury are all unnatural and sterile actions: thus the unbearing desert is the

4. A Paduan with an infamous lust for laying waste his own goods and those of his neighbors. Arson
was his favorite prank. On one occasion, to celebrate the arrival of certain noble guests, he set fire to all
the workers' huts and outbuildings of his estate. He was murdered in 1239, probably by assassins hired
by Ezzolino (for whom see Canto XII).   5. Florence. Mars was the first patron of the city and when
the Florentines were converted to Christianity they pulled down his equestrian statue and built a church
on the site of his temple. The statue of Mars was placed on a tower beside the Arno. When Totila (see
note to line 150) destroyed Florence, the tower fell into the Arno and the statue with it. Legend has it
that Florence could never have been rebuilt had not the mutilated statue been rescued. It was placed
on the Ponte Vecchio but was carried away in the flood of 1333.   6. Dante confuses Attila with
Totila, King of the Ostrogoths (died 552). He destroyed Florence in 542. Attila (died 453), King of the
Huns, destroyed many cities of northern Italy, but not Florence.

eternity of these sinners; and thus the rain, which in nature should be
fertile and cool, descends as fire. Capaneus, moreover, is subjected not
only to the wrath of nature (the sands below) and the wrath of God (the
fire from above), but is tortured most by his own inner violence, which is
the root of blasphemy.

Love of that land that was our common source
   moved me to tears; I gathered up the leaves
   and gave them back. He was already hoarse.
We came to the edge of the forest where one goes
   from the second round to the third, and there we saw   5
   what fearful arts the hand of Justice knows.
To make these new things wholly clear, I say
   we came to a plain whose soil repels all roots.
   The wood of misery rings it the same way
the wood itself is ringed by the red fosse.   10
   We paused at its edge: the ground was burning sand,
   just such a waste as Cato marched across.[7]
O endless wrath of God: how utterly
   thou shouldst become a terror to all men
   who read the frightful truths revealed to me!   15
Enormous herds of naked souls I saw,
   lamenting till their eyes were burned of tears;
   they seemed condemned by an unequal law,
for some were stretched supine upon the ground,
   some squatted with their arms about themselves,   20
   and others without pause roamed round and round.
Most numerous were those that roamed the plain.
   Far fewer were the souls stretched on the sand,
   but moved to louder cries by greater pain.
And over all that sand on which they lay   25
   or crouched or roamed, great flakes of flame fell slowly
   as snow falls in the Alps on a windless day.
Like those Alexander met in the hot regions
   of India, flames raining from the sky
   to fall still unextinguished on his legions: 30
whereat he formed his ranks, and at their head
   set the example, trampling the hot ground
   for fear the tongues of fire might join and spread[8] —
just so in Hell descended the long rain
   upon the damned, kindling the sand like tinder   35
   under a flint and steel, doubling the pain.
In a never-ending fit upon those sands,
   the arms of the damned twitched all about their bodies,
   now here, now there, brushing away the brands.
"Poet," I said, "master of every dread   40
   we have encountered, other than those fiends
   who sallied from the last gate of the dead —
who is that wraith who lies along the rim

---

7. In 47 B.C., Cato of Utica led an army across the Libyan desert. Lucan described the march in
Pharsalia IX, 587 ff.   8. This incident of Alexander the Great's campaign in India is described in *De
Meteoris* of Albertus Magnus and was taken by him with considerable alteration from a letter reputedly
sent to Aristotle by Alexander.

and sets his face against the fire in scorn,
  so that the rain seems not to mellow him?"   45
And he himself,[9] hearing what I had said
  to my Guide and Lord concerning him, replied:
  "What I was living, the same am I now, dead.
Though Jupiter wear out his sooty smith
  from whom on my last day he snatched in anger   50
  the jagged thunderbolt he pierced me with;
though he wear out the others one by one
  who labor at the forge at Mongibello[1]
  crying again 'Help! Help! Help me, good Vulcan!'
as he did at Phlegra[2] and hurl down endlessly   55
  with all the power of Heaven in his arm,
  small satisfaction would he win from me."
At this my Guide spoke with such vehemence
  as I had not heard from him in all of Hell:
  "O Capaneus, by your insolence   60
you are made to suffer as much fire inside
  as falls upon you. Only your own rage
  could be fit torment for your sullen pride."
Then he turned to me more gently. "That," he said,
  "was one of the Seven who laid siege to Thebes.   65
  Living, he scorned God, and among the dead
he scorns Him yet. He thinks he may detest
  God's power too easily, but as I told him,
  his slobber is a fit badge for his breast.
Now follow me; and mind for your own good   70
  you do not step upon the burning sand,
  but keep well back along the edge of the wood."
We walked in silence then till we reached a rill
  that gushes from the wood;[3] it ran so red
  the memory sends a shudder through me still.   75
As from the Bulicame[4] springs the stream
  the sinful women keep to their own use;
  so down the sand the rill flowed out in steam.
The bed and both its banks were petrified,
  as were its margins; thus I knew at once   80
  our passage through the sand lay by its side.
"Among all other wonders I have shown you
  since we came through the gate denied to none,
  nothing your eyes have seen is equal to
the marvel of the rill by which we stand,   85
  for it stifles all the flames above its course

---

9. Capaneus, one of the seven captains who warred on Thebes. As he scaled the walls of Thebes,
Capaneus defied Jove to protect them. Jove replied with a thunderbolt that killed the blasphemer with
his blasphemy still on his lips. (Statius, *Thebiad* x, 845 ff.) **1.** Mt. Etna. Vulcan was believed to have
his smithy inside the volcano. **2.** At the battle of Phlegra in Thessaly the Titans tried to storm Olympus. Jove drove them back with the help of the thunderbolts Vulcan forged for him. **3.** The rill, still
blood-red and still boiling, is the overflow of Phlegethon which descends across the Wood of the Suicides and the Burning Plain to plunge over the Great Cliff into the Eighth Circle. It is clearly a water
of marvels, for it not only petrifies the sands over which it flows, but its clouds of steam quench all the
flames above its course. **4.** A hot sulphur spring near Viterbo. The choice is strikingly apt, for the
waters of the Bulicame not only boil and steam but have a distinctly reddish tint as a consequence of
their mineral content. A part of the Bulicame flows out through what was once a quarter reserved to
prostitutes; and they were given special rights to the water, since they were not permitted to use the
public baths.

as it flows out across the burning sand."
So spoke my Guide across the flickering light,
    and I begged him to bestow on me the food
    for which he had given me the appetite.   90
"In the middle of the sea, and gone to waste,
    there lies a country known as Crete," he said,
    "under whose king the ancient world was chaste.
Once Rhea[5] chose it as the secret crypt
    and cradle of her son; and better to hide him,   95
    her Corybantes raised a din when he wept.
An ancient giant[6] stands in the mountain's core.
    He keeps his shoulder turned toward Damietta,
    and looks toward Rome as if it were his mirror.
His head is made of gold; of silverwork   100
    his breast and both his arms, of polished brass
    the rest of his great torso to the fork.
He is of chosen iron from there down,
    except that his right foot is terra cotta;
    it is this foot he rests more weight upon.   105
Every part except the gold is split
    by a great fissure from which endless tears
    drip down and hollow out the mountain's pit.
Their course sinks to this pit from stone to stone,
    becoming Acheron, Phlegethon, and Styx.   110
    Then by this narrow sluice they hurtle down
to the end of all descent, and disappear
    into Cocytus.[7] You shall see what sink that is
    with your own eyes. I pass it in silence here."
And I to him: "But if these waters flow   115
    from the world above, why is this rill met only
    along this shelf?" And he to me: "You know
the place is round, and though you have come deep
    into the valley through the many circles,
    always bearing left along the steep,   120
you have not traveled any circle through
    its total round; hence when new things appear
    from time to time, that hardly should surprise you."

5. Wife of Saturn (Cronos) and mother of Jove (Zeus). It had been prophesied to Saturn that one of his own children would dethrone him. To nullify the prophecy Saturn devoured each of his children at birth. On the birth of Jove, Rhea duped Saturn by letting him bolt down a stone wrapped in baby clothes. After this tribute to her husband's appetite she hid the infant on Mount Ida in Crete. There she posted her Corybantes (or Bacchantes) as guards and instructed them to set up a great din whenever the baby cried. Thus Saturn would not hear him. The Corybantic dances of the ancient Greeks were based on the frenzied shouting and clashing of swords on shields with which the Corybantes protected the infant Jove.   **6.** This is the Old Man of Crete. The original of this figure occurs in Daniel ii, 32–34, where it is told by Daniel as Nebuchadnezzar's dream. Dante follows the details of the original closely but adds a few of his own and a totally different interpretation. In Dante each metal represents one of the ages of humanity, each deteriorating from the Golden Age of Innocence. The left foot, terminating the Age of Iron, is the Holy Roman Empire. The right foot, of terra cotta, is the Roman Catholic Church, a more fragile base than the left, but the one upon which the greater weight descends. The tears of the woes of humanity are a Dantean detail: they flow down the great fissure that defaces all but the Golden Age. Thus, starting in man's decline, they flow through humanity's decline, into the hollow of the mountain and become the waters of all Hell. Dante's other major addition is the site and position of the figure: equidistant from the three continents, the Old Man stands at a sort of center of Time, his back turned to Damietta in Egypt (here symbolizing the East, the past, the birth of religion) and fixes his gaze upon Rome (the West, the future, the Catholic Church). It is certainly the most elaborately worked single symbol in the *Inferno*.   **7.** The frozen lake that lies at the bottom of Hell. (See Cantos XXXII–XXXIII.)

And I: "Where shall we find Phlegethon's course?
   And Lethe's? One you omit, and of the other   125
   you only say the tear-flood is its source."
"In all you ask of me you please me truly,"
   he answered, "but the red and boiling water
   should answer the first question you put to me,
and you shall stand by Lethe, but far hence: 130
   there, where the spirits go to wash themselves
   when their guilt has been removed by penitence."
And then he said: "Now it is time to quit
   this edge of shade: follow close after me
   along the rill, and do not stray from it;   135
for the unburning margins form a lane,
and by them we may cross the burning plain."

CANTO XV

Circle Seven: Round Three   The Violent Against Nature

Protected by the marvelous powers of the boiling rill, the Poets walk
along its banks across the burning plain. The Wood of the Suicides is
behind them; the Great Cliff at whose foot lies the Eighth Circle is before
them.

They pass one of the roving bands of Sodomites. One of the sinners
stops Dante, and with great difficulty the Poet recognizes him under his
baked features as Ser Brunetto Latino. This is a reunion with a dearly
loved man and writer, one who had considerably influenced Dante's own
development, and Dante addresses him with great and sorrowful affection,
paying him the highest tribute offered to any sinner in the *Inferno*. Brunetto prophesies Dante's sufferings at the hands of the Florentines, gives
an account of the souls that move with him through the fire, and finally,
under Divine Compulsion, races off across the plain.

We go by one of the stone margins now
   and the steam of the rivulet makes a shade above it,
   guarding the stream and banks from the flaming snow.
As the Flemings in the lowland between Bruges
   and Wissant, under constant threat of the sea,   5
   erect their great dikes to hold back the deluge;[8]
as the Paduans along the shores of the Brent
   build levees to protect their towns and castles
   lest Chiarentana drown in the spring torrent—
to the same plan, though not so wide nor high,[9]   10
   did the engineer, whoever he may have been,
   design the margin we were crossing by.
Already we were so far from the wood
   that even had I turned to look at it,

---

8. Dante compares the banks of the rill of Phlegethon to the dikes built by the Flemings to hold back
the sea, and to those built by the Paduans to hold back the spring floods of the river Brent. Chiarentana
(Latin: Clarentana) was a Duchy of the Middle Ages. Its territory included the headwaters of the Brent
(Brenta).   9. Their width is never precisely specified, but we shall see when Dante walks along speaking to Ser Brunetto (line 40) that their height is about that of a man.

I could not have made it out from where I stood,   15
when a company of shades came into sight
  walking beside the bank. They stared at us
  as men at evening by the new moon's light
stare at one another when they pass by
  on a dark road, pointing their eyebrows toward us   20
  as an old tailor squints at his needle's eye.
Stared at so closely by that ghostly crew,
  I was recognized by one who seized the hem
  of my skirt and said: "Wonder of wonders! You?"
And I, when he stretched out his arm to me,   25
  searched his baked features closely, till at last
  I traced his image from my memory
in spite of the burnt crust, and bending near
  to put my face closer to his, at last
  I answered: "Ser Brunetto,[1] are *you* here?"   30
"O my son! may it not displease you," he cried,
  "if Brunetto Latino leave his company
  and turn and walk a little by your side."
And I to him: "With all my soul I ask it.
  Or let us sit together, if it please him   35
  who is my Guide and leads me through this pit."
"My son!" he said, "whoever of this train
  pauses a moment, must lie a hundred years
  forbidden to brush off the burning rain.
Therefore, go on; I will walk at your hem,[2]   40
  and then rejoin my company, which goes
  mourning eternal loss in eternal flame."
I did not dare descend to his own level
  but kept my head inclined, as one who walks
  in reverence meditating good and evil.   45
"What brings you here before your own last day?
  What fortune or what destiny?" he began.
  "And who is he that leads you this dark way?"
"Up there in the happy life I went astray
  in a valley," I replied, "before I had reached   50
  the fullness of my years. Only yesterday
at dawn I turned from it. This spirit showed
  himself to me as I was turning back,
  and guides me home again along this road."
And he: "Follow your star, for if in all   55
  of the sweet life I saw one truth shine clearly,
  you cannot miss your glorious arrival.
And had I lived to do what I meant to do,
  I would have cheered and seconded your work,

---

1. A prominent Florentine Guelph (1212?–1294) who held, among many other posts, that of notary, whence the title *Ser* (sometimes *Sere*). He was not Dante's schoolmaster as many have supposed—he was much too busy and important a man for that. Dante's use of the word "master" is to indicate spiritual indebtedness to Brunetto and his works. It is worth noting that Dante addresses him in Italian as "voi" instead of using the less respectful "tu" form. Farinata is the only other sinner so addressed in the *Inferno*. Brunetto's two principal books, both of which Dante admired, were the prose *Livre dou Tresor (The Book of the Treasure)* and the poetic *Tesoretta (The Little Treasure).* Dante learned a number of his devices from the allegorical journey which forms the *Tesoretto.*   2. Dante is standing on the dike at approximately the level of Brunetto's head and he cannot descend because of the rain of fire and the burning sands.

observing Heaven so well disposed toward you.   60
But that ungrateful and malignant stock
   that came down from Fiesole of old
   and still smacks of the mountain and the rock,
for your good works will be your enemy.[3]
   And there is cause: the sweet fig is not meant   65
   to bear its fruit beside the bitter sorb-tree.[4]
Even the old adage calls them blind,[5]
   an envious, proud, and avaricious people:
   see that you root their customs from your mind.
It is written in your stars, and will come to pass,   70
   that your honours shall make both sides hunger for you:[6]
   but the goat shall never reach to crop that grass.
Let the beasts of Fiesole[7] devour their get
   like sows, but never let them touch the plant,
   if among their rankness any springs up yet,   75
in which is born again the holy seed
   of the Romans who remained among their rabble
   when Florence made a new nest for their greed."
"Ah, had I all my wish," I answered then,
   "you would not yet be banished from the world   80
   in which you were a radiance among men,
for that sweet image, gentle and paternal,
   you were to me in the world when hour by hour
   you taught me how man makes himself eternal,
lives in my mind, and now strikes to my heart;   85
   and while I live, the gratitude I owe it
   will speak to men out of my life and art.
What you have told me of my course, I write
   by another text I save to show a Lady[8]
   who will judge these matters, if I reach her height.   90
This much I would have you know: so long, I say,
   as nothing in my conscience troubles me
   I am prepared for Fortune, come what may.
Twice already in the eternal shade
   I have heard this prophecy;[9] but let Fortune turn   95
   her wheel as she please, and the countryman his spade."
My guiding spirit paused at my last word
   and, turning right about, stood eye to eye
   to say to me: "Well heeded is well heard."
But I did not reply to him, going on   100

3. The ancient Etruscan city of Fiesole was situated on a hill about three miles north of the present site of Florence. According to legend, Fiesole had taken the side of Catiline in his war with Julius Caesar. Caesar destroyed the town and set up a new city called Florence on the Arno, peopling it with Romans and Fiesolans. The Romans were the aristocracy of the new city, but the Fiesolans were a majority. Dante ascribes the endless bloody conflicts of Florence largely to the internal strife between these two strains. His scorn of the Fiesolans is obvious in this passage. Dante proudly proclaimed his descent from the Roman strain.   4. A species of tart apple.   5. The source of this proverbial expression, "Blind as a Florentine," can no longer be traced with any assurance, though many incidents from Florentine history suggest possible sources.   6. Brunetto can scarcely mean that both sides will hunger to welcome the support of a man of Dante's distinction. Rather, that both sides will hunger to destroy him. (See also lines 94–95. Dante obviously accepts this as another dark prophecy.)   7. The Fiesolans themselves.   8. Beatrice.   9. The prophecies of Ciacco (Canto VI) and of Farinata (Canto X) are the other two places at which Dante's exile and suffering are foretold. Dante replies that come what may he will remain true to his purpose through all affliction; and Virgil turns to look proudly at his pupil, uttering a proverb: "*Bene ascolta chi la nota,*" i.e., "Well heeded is well heard."

with Ser Brunetto to ask him who was with him
in the hot sands, the best-born and best known.
And he to me: "Of some who share this walk
    it is good to know; of the rest let us say nothing,
    for the time would be too short for so much talk.   105
In brief, we all were clerks and men of worth,
    great men of letters, scholars of renown;
    all by the one same crime defiled on earth.
Priscian[1] moves there along the wearisome
    sad way, and Francesco d'Accorso,[2] and also there,   110
    if you had any longing for such scum,
you might have seen that one the Servant of Servants[3]
    sent from the Arno to the Bacchiglione
    where he left his unnatural organ[4] wrapped in cerements.
I would say more, but there across the sand   115
    a new smoke rises and new people come,
    and I must run to be with my own band.
Remember my *Treasure*, in which I still live on:
    I ask no more." He turned then, and he seemed,
    across that plain, like one of those who run   120
for the green cloth at Verona;[5] and of those,
more like the one who wins, than those who lose.

CANTO XVI

Circle Seven: Round Three   The Violent Against Nature and Art

The Poets arrive within hearing of the waterfall that plunges over the
Great Cliff into the Eighth Circle. The sound is still a distant throbbing
when three wraiths, recognizing Dante's Florentine dress, detach themselves from their band and come running toward him. They are Jacopo
Rusticucci, Guido Guerra, and Tegghiaio Aldobrandi, all of them Florentines whose policies and personalities Dante admired. Rusticucci and Tegghiaio have already been mentioned in a highly complimentary way in
Dante's talk with Ciacco (Canto VI).

The sinners ask for news of Florence, and Dante replies with a passionate lament for her present degradation. The three wraiths return to their
band and the Poets continue to the top of the falls. Here, at Virgil's command, Dante removes a Cord from about his waist and Virgil drops it over
the edge of the abyss. As if in answer to a signal, a great distorted shape
comes swimming up through the dirty air of the pit.

1. Latin grammarian and poet of the first half of the sixth century.   2. A Florentine scholar. He
served as a professor at Bologna and, from 1273 to 1280, at Oxford. He died in Bologna in 1294.
3. Dante's old enemy, Boniface VIII [died 1303]. *Servus servorum* is technically a correct papal title,
but there is certainly a touch of irony in Dante's application of it in this context. In 1295 Boniface
transferred Bishop Andrea de'Mozzi from the Bishopric of Florence (on the Arno) to that of Vicenza
(on the Bacchiglione). The transference was reputedly brought about at the request of the Bishop's
brother, Tommaso de' Mozzi of Florence, who wished to remove from his sight the spectacle of his
brother's stupidity and unnatural vices.   4. The original, *mal protesi nervi*, contains an untranslatable
word-play. *Nervi* may be taken as "the male organ" and *protesi* for "erected"; thus the organ aroused to
passion for unnatural purposes (*mal*). Or *nervi* may be taken as "nerves" and *mal protesi* for "dissolute."
Taken in context, the first rendering strikes me as more Dantean.   5. On the first Sunday of Lent all
the young men of Verona ran a race for the prize of green cloth. The last runner in was given a live
rooster and was required to carry it through the town.

We could already hear the rumbling drive
   of the waterfall in its plunge to the next circle,
   a murmur like the throbbing of a hive,
when three shades turned together on the plain,
   breaking toward us from a company   5
   that went its way to torture in that rain.
They cried with one voice as they ran toward me:
   "Wait, oh wait, for by your dress you seem
   a voyager from our own tainted country."
Ah! what wounds I saw, some new, some old,   10
   branded upon their bodies! Even now
   the pain of it in memory turns me cold.
My Teacher heard their cries, and turning-to,
   stood face to face. "Do as they ask," he said,
   "for these are souls to whom respect is due;   15
and were it not for the darting flames that hem
   our narrow passage in, I should have said
   it were more fitting you ran after them."
We paused, and they began their ancient wail
   over again, and when they stood below us   20
   they formed themselves into a moving wheel.
As naked and anointed champions do
   in feeling out their grasp and their advantage
   before they close in for the thrust or blow—
so circling, each one stared up at my height,   25
   and as their feet moved left around the circle,
   their necks kept turning backward to the right.
"If the misery of this place, and our unkempt
   and scorched appearance," one of them began,
   "bring us and what we pray into contempt,   30
still may our earthly fame move you to tell
   who and what you are, who so securely
   set your live feet to the dead dusts of Hell.
This peeled and naked soul who runs before me
   around this wheel, was higher than you think   35
   there in the world, in honor and degree.
Guido Guerra[6] was the name he bore,
   the good Gualdrada's[7] grandson. In his life
   he won great fame in counsel and in war.
The other who behind me treads this sand   40
   was Tegghiaio Aldobrandi,[8] whose good counsels

---

6. (around 1220–1272). A valiant leader of the Guelphs (hence his name which signifies Guido of War) despite his Ghibelline origin as one of the counts of Guidi. It is a curious fact, considering the prominence of Guido, that Dante is the only writer to label him a sodomite.   7. The legend of "the good Gualdrada," Guido Guerra's grandmother, is a typical example of the medieval talent for embroidery. She was the daughter of Bellincione Berti de' Ravignana. The legend is that Emperor Otto IV saw her in church and, attracted by her beauty, asked who she was. Bellincione replied that she was the daughter of one whose soul would be made glad to have the Emperor salute her with a kiss. The young-lady-of-all-virtues, hearing her father's words, declared that no man might kiss her unless he were her husband. Otto was so impressed by the modesty and propriety of this remark that he married her to one of his noblemen and settled a large estate upon the couple. It was from this marriage that the counts Guidi de Modigliano (among them Guido Guerra) were said to descend. Unfortunately for the legend, Otto's first visit to Italy was in 1209, and surviving records show that Count Guido had already had two children by his wife Gualdrada as early as 1202.   8. Date of birth unknown. He died shortly before 1266. A valiant knight of the family degli Adimari of the Guelph nobles. With Guido Guerra he advised the Florentines not to move against the Sienese at the disastrous battle of Montaperti (See Farinata,

the world would have done well to understand.
And I who share their torment, in my life
   was Jacopo Rusticucci;[9] above all
   I owe my sorrows to a savage wife."   45
I would have thrown myself to the plain below
   had I been sheltered from the falling fire;
   and I think my Teacher would have let me go.
But seeing I should be burned and cooked, my fear
   overcame the first impulse of my heart   50
   to leap down and embrace them then and there.
"Not contempt," I said, "but the compassion
   that seizes on my soul and memory
   at the thought of you tormented in this fashion—
it was grief that choked my speech when through the scorching 55
   air of this pit my Lord announced to me
   that such men as you are might be approaching.
I am of your own land, and I have always
   heard with affection and rehearsed with honor
   your name and the good deeds of your happier days.   60
Led by my Guide and his truth, I leave the gall
   and go for the sweet apples of delight.
   But first I must descend to the center of all."
"So may your soul and body long continue
   together on the way you go," he answered,   65
   "and the honor of your days shine after you—
tell me if courtesy and valor raise
   their banners in our city as of old,
   or has the glory faded from its days?
For Borsiere,[1] who is newly come among us   70
   and yonder goes with our companions in pain,
   taunts us with such reports, and his words have stung us."
"O Florence! your sudden wealth and your upstart
   rabble, dissolute and overweening,
   already set you weeping in your heart!"   75
I cried with face upraised, and on the sand
   those three sad spirits looked at one another
   like men who hear the truth and understand.
"If this be your manner of speaking, and if you can
   satisfy others with such ease and grace,"   80
   they said as one, "we hail a happy man.
Therefore, if you win through this gloomy pass
   and climb again to see the heaven of stars;
   when it rejoices you to say 'I was',
speak of us to the living." They parted then,   85
   breaking their turning wheel, and as they vanished
   over the plain, their legs seemed wings. "Amen"

Canto X), knowing that the Sienese had been heavily reinforced by mercenaries. It is probably these good counsels that "the world would have done well to understand." This is another case in which Dante is the only writer to bring the charge of sodomy.   9. Dates of birth and death unknown, but mention of him exists in Florentine records of 1235, 1236, 1254, and 1266. A rich and respected Florentine knight. Dante's account of his sin and of its cause is the only record and it remains unsupported: no details of his life are known.   1. "Borsiere" in Italian means "pursemaker," and the legend has grown without verification or likelihood that this was his origin. He was a courtier, a peacemaker, and an arranger of marriages. Boccaccio speaks of him in highly honorable terms in the Eighth Tale of the First Day of the *Decameron*.

could not have been pronounced between their start
   and their disappearance over the rim of sand.
   And then it pleased my Master to depart.   90
A little way beyond we felt the quiver
   and roar of the cascade, so close that speech
   would have been drowned in thunder. As that river[2] —
the first one on the left of the Apennines
   to have a path of its own from Monte Veso   95
   to the Adriatic Sea — which, as it twines
is called the Acquacheta from its source
   until it nears Forli, and then is known
   as the Montone in its further course —
resounds from the mountain in a single leap   100
   there above San Benedetto dell'Alpe
   where a thousand falls might fit into the steep;
so down from a sheer bank, in one enormous
   plunge, the tainted water roared so loud
   a little longer there would have deafened us.   105
I had a cord bound round me like a belt[3]
   which I had once thought I might put to use
   to snare the leopard with the gaudy pelt.
When at my Guide's command I had unbound
   its loops from about my habit, I gathered it   110
   and held it out to him all coiled and wound.
He bent far back to his right, and throwing it
   out from the edge, sent it in a long arc
   into the bottomless darkness of the pit.
"Now surely some unusual event,"   115
   I said to myself, "must follow this new signal
   upon which my good Guide is so intent."
Ah, how cautiously a man should breathe
   near those who see not only what we do,
   but have the sense which reads the mind beneath!   120
He said to me: "You will soon see arise
   what I await, and what you wonder at;
   soon you will see the thing before your eyes."
To the truth which will seem falsehood every man
   who would not be called a liar while speaking fact   125
   should learn to seal his lips as best he can.
But here I cannot be still: Reader, I swear
   by the lines of my Comedy — so may it live —
   that I saw swimming up through that foul air
a shape to astonish the most doughty soul,   130

---

2. The water course described by Dante and made up of the Acquacheta and the Montone flows directly into the sea without draining into the Po. The placement of it as "first on the left of the Apennines" has been shown by Casella to result from the peculiar orientation of the maps of Dante's time. The "river" has its source and course along a line running almost exactly northwest from Florence. San Benedetto dell' Alpe is a small monastery situated on that line about twenty-five miles from Florence. 3. As might be expected, many ingenious explanations have been advanced to account for the sudden appearance of this cord. It is frequently claimed, but without proof, that Dante had been a minor friar of the Franciscans but had left without taking vows. The explanation continues that he had clung to the habit of wearing the white cord of the Franciscans, which he now produces with the information that he had once intended to use it to snare the Leopard. One invention is probably as good as another. What seems obvious is that the narrative required some sort of device for signaling the monster, and that to meet his narrative need, Dante suddenly invented the business of the cord.

a shape like one returning through the sea
　from working loose an anchor run afoul
of something on the bottom—so it rose,
its arms spread upward and its feet drawn close.

CANTO XVII

Circle Seven: Round Three   The Violent Against Art. Geryon

The monstrous shape lands on the brink and Virgil salutes it ironically.
It is Geryon, the Monster of Fraud. Virgil announces that they must fly
down from the cliff on the back of this monster. While Virgil negotiates
for their passage, Dante is sent to examine the Usurers (The Violent
against Art).

These sinners sit in a crouch along the edge of the burning plain that
approaches the cliff. Each of them has a leather purse around his neck,
and each purse is blazoned with a coat of arms. Their eyes, gushing with
tears, are forever fixed on these purses. Dante recognizes none of these
sinners, but their coats of arms are unmistakably those of well-known Florentine families.

Having understood who they are and the reason for their present condition, Dante cuts short his excursion and returns to find Virgil mounted on
the back of Geryon. Dante joins his Master and they fly down from the
great cliff.

Their flight carries them from the Hell of the Violent and the Bestial
(The Sins of the Lion) into the Hell of the Fraudulent and Malicious
(The Sins of the Leopard).

"Now see the sharp-tailed beast that mounts the brink.
　He passes mountains, breaks through walls and weapons.
　Behold the beast that makes the whole world stink."[4]
These were the words my Master spoke to me;
　then signaled the weird beast to come to ground   5
　close to the sheer end of our rocky levee.
The filthy prototype of Fraud drew near
　and settled his head and breast upon the edge
　of the dark cliff, but let his tail hang clear.
His face was innocent of every guile,   10
　benign and just in feature and expression;
　and under it his body was half reptile.
His two great paws were hairy to the armpits;
　all his back and breast and both his flanks
　were figured with bright knots and subtle circlets: 15

4. [Geryon], a mythical king of Spain represented as a giant with three heads and three bodies. He was
killed by Hercules, who coveted the king's cattle. A later tradition represents him as killing and robbing
strangers whom he lured into his realm. It is probably on this account that Dante chose him as the
prototype of fraud, though in a radically altered bodily form. Some of the details of Dante's Geryon may
be drawn from Revelation ix, 9–20, but most of them are almost certainly his own invention: a monster
with the general shape of a dragon but with the tail of a scorpion, hairy arms, a gaudily-marked reptilian
body, and the face of a just and honest man.

never was such a tapestry of bloom
   woven on earth by Tartar or by Turk,[5]
   nor by Arachne[6] at her flowering loom.
As a ferry sometimes lies along the strand,
   part beached and part afloat; and as the beaver,[7]   20
   up yonder in the guzzling Germans' land,
squats halfway up the bank when a fight is on—
   just so lay that most ravenous of beasts
   on the rim which bounds the burning sand with stone.
His tail twitched in the void beyond that lip,   25
   thrashing, and twisting up the envenomed fork
   which, like a scorpion's stinger, armed the tip.
My Guide said: "It is time now we drew near
   that monster." And descending on the right[8]
   we moved ten paces outward to be clear   30
of sand and flames. And when we were beside him,
   I saw upon the sand a bit beyond us
   some people crouching close beside the brim.[9]
The Master paused. "That you may take with you
   the full experience of this round," he said,   35
   "go now and see the last state of that crew.
But let your talk be brief, and I will stay
   and reason with this beast till you return,
   that his strong back may serve us on our way."
So further yet along the outer edge   40
   of the seventh circle I moved on alone.
   And came to the sad people of the ledge.
Their eyes burst with their grief; their smoking hands
   jerked about their bodies, warding off
   now the flames and now the burning sands.   45
Dogs in summer bit by fleas and gadflies,
   jerking their snouts about, twitching their paws
   now here, now there, behave no otherwise.
I examined several faces there among
   that sooty throng, and I saw none I knew;   50
   but I observed that from each neck there hung
an enormous purse, each marked with its own beast
   and its own colors like a coat of arms.
   On these their streaming eyes appeared to feast.
Looking about, I saw one purse display   55
   azure on or, a kind of lion;[1] another,

---

5. These were the most skilled weavers of Dante's time.   6. She was so famous as a spinner and weaver that she challenged Minerva to a weaving contest. There are various accounts of what happened in the contest, but all of them end with the goddess so moved to anger that she changed Arachne into a spider.   7. Dante's description of the beaver is probably drawn from some old bestiary or natural history. It may be based on the medieval belief that the beaver fished by crouching on the bank, scooping the fish out with its tail. *The guzzling Germans:* The heavy drinking of the Germans was proverbial in the Middle Ages and far back into antiquity.   8. The Poets had crossed on the right bank of the rill. In the course of Geryon's flight they will be carried to the other side of the falls, thus continuing their course to the left. It should be noted that inside the walls of Dis, approaching the second great division of Hell (as here the third) they also moved to the right. No satisfactory reason can be given for these exceptions.   9. The Usurers. Virgil explains in Canto XI why they sin against Art, which is the Grandchild of God. They are the third and final category of the Violent against God and His works.   1. The arms of the Gianfigliazzi of Florence were a lion azure on a field of gold. The sinner bearing this purse must be Catello di Rosso Gianfigliazzi, who set up as a usurer in France and was made a knight on his return to Florence.

on a blood red field, a goose whiter than whey.[2]
And one that bore a huge and swollen sow
    azure on field argent[3] said to me:
    "What are you doing in this pit of sorrow?   60
Leave us alone! And since you have not yet died,
    I'll have you know my neighbor Vitaliano[4]
    has a place reserved for him here at my side.
A Paduan among Florentines, I sit here
    while hour by hour they nearly deafen me   65
    shouting: 'Send us the sovereign cavalier
with the purse of the three goats!' "[5] He half arose,
    twisted his mouth, and darted out his tongue
    for all the world like an ox licking its nose.
And I, afraid that any longer stay   70
    would anger him who had warned me to be brief,
    left those exhausted souls without delay.
Returned, I found my Guide already mounted
    upon the rump of that monstrosity.
    He said to me: "Now must you be undaunted: 75
this beast must be our stairway to the pit:
    mount it in front, and I will ride between
    you and the tail, lest you be poisoned by it."
Like one so close to the quartanary chill[6]
    that his nails are already pale and his flesh trembles   80
    at the very sight of shade or a cool rill—
so did I tremble at each frightful word.
    But his scolding filled me with that shame that makes
    the servant brave in the presence of his lord.
I mounted the great shoulders of that freak   85
    and tried to say "Now help me to hold on!"
    But my voice clicked in my throat and I could not speak.
But no sooner had I settled where he placed me
    than he, my stay, my comfort, and my courage
    in other perils, gathered and embraced me.   90
Then he called out: "Now, Geryon, we are ready:
    bear well in mind that his is living weight
    and make your circles wide and your flight steady."
As a small ship slides from a beaching or its pier,
    backward, backward—so that monster slipped   95
    back from the rim. And when he had drawn clear
he swung about, and stretching out his tail
    he worked it like an eel, and with his paws
    he gathered in the air, while I turned pale.
I think there was no greater fear the day   100

2. A white goose on a red field was the arms of the noble Ghibelline family of the Ubriachi, or Ebriachi, of Florence. The wearer is probably Ciappo Ubriachi, a notorious usurer.   3. These are the arms of the Scrovegni of Padua. The bearer is probably Reginaldo Scrovegni.   4. Vitaliano di Iacopo Vitaliani, another Paduan.   5. Giovanni di Buiamonte was esteemed in Florence as "the sovereign cavalier" and was chosen for many high offices. He was a usurer and a gambler who lost great sums at play. Dante's intent is clearly to bewail the decay of standards which permits Florence to honor so highly a man for whom Hell is waiting so dismally. Buiamonte was of the Becchi family whose arms were three black goats on a gold field. "Becchi" in Italian is the plural form of the word for "goat." 6. Quartan fever is an ague that runs a four-day cycle with symptoms roughly like those of malaria. At the approach of the chill, Dante intends his figure to say, any thought of coolness strikes terror into the shivering victim.

Phaeton[7] let loose the reins and burned the sky
  along the great scar of the Milky Way,
nor when Icarus, too close to the sun's track
  felt the wax melt, unfeathering his loins,
  and heard his father cry "Turn back! Turn back!"[8]—   105
than I felt when I found myself in air,
  afloat in space with nothing visible
  but the enormous beast that bore me there.
Slowly, slowly, he swims on through space,
  wheels and descends, but I can sense it only   110
  by the way the wind blows upward past my face.
Already on the right I heard the swell
  and thunder of the whirlpool. Looking down
  I leaned my head out and stared into Hell.
I trembled again at the prospect of dismounting   115
  and cowered in on myself, for I saw fires
  on every hand, and I heard a long lamenting.
And then I saw—till then I had but felt it—
  the course of our down-spiral to the horrors
  that rose to us from all sides of the pit.   120
As a flight-worn falcon sinks down wearily
  though neither bird nor lure has signalled it,[9]
  the falconer crying out: "What! spent already!"—
then turns and in a hundred spinning gyres
  sulks from her master's call, sullen and proud—   125
  so to that bottom lit by endless fires
the monster Geryon circled and fell,
  setting us down at the foot of the precipice
  of ragged rock on the eighth shelf of Hell.
And once freed of our weight, he shot from there   130
into the dark like an arrow into air.

CANTO XVIII

Circle Eight (Malebolge)   *The Fraudulent and Malicious*
Bolgia One   *The Panderers and Seducers*
Bolgia Two   *The Flatterers*

    Dismounted from Geryon, the Poets find themselves in the Eighth Circle, called Malebolge (The Evil Ditches). This is the upper half of the Hell of the Fraudulent and Malicious. Malebolge is a great circle of stone that slopes like an amphitheater. The slopes are divided into ten concentric ditches; and within these ditches, each with his own kind, are punished those guilty of Simple Fraud.

---

7. Son of Apollo who drove the chariot of the sun. Phaeton begged his father for a chance to drive the chariot himself but he lost control of the horses and Zeus killed him with a thunderbolt for fear the whole earth would catch fire. The scar left in the sky by the runaway horses is marked by the Milky Way.   8. Daedalus, the father of Icarus, made wings for himself and his son and they flew into the sky, but Icarus, ignoring his father's commands, flew too close to the sun. The heat melted the wax with which the wings were fastened and Icarus fell into the Aegean and was drowned.   9. Falcons, when sent aloft, were trained to circle until sighting a bird, or until signaled back by the lure (a stuffed bird). Flight-weary, Dante's metaphoric falcon sinks bit by bit, rebelling against his training and sulking away from his master in wide slow circles.

A series of stone dikes runs like spokes from the edge of the great cliff face to the center of the place, and these serve as bridges.

The Poets bear left toward the first ditch, and Dante observes below him and to his right the sinners of the first bolgia, the Panderers and Seducers. These make two files, one along either bank of the ditch, and are driven at an endless fast walk by horned demons who hurry them along with great lashes. In life these sinners goaded others on to serve their own foul purposes; so in Hell are they driven in their turn. The horned demons who drive them symbolize the sinners' own vicious natures, embodiments of their own guilty consciences. Dante may or may not have intended the horns of the demons to symbolize cuckoldry and adultery.

The Poets see Venedico Caccianemico and Jason in the first pit, and pass on to the second, where they find the souls of the Flatterers sunk in excrement, the true equivalent of their false flatteries on earth. They observe Alessio Interminelli and Thaïs, and pass on.

There is in Hell a vast and sloping ground
   called Malebolge,[1] a lost place of stone
   as black as the great cliff that seals it round.
Precisely in the center of that space
   there yawns a well extremely wide and deep.[2]   5
   I shall discuss it in its proper place.
The border that remains between the well-pit
   and the great cliff forms an enormous circle,
   and ten descending troughs are cut in it,
offering a general prospect like the ground   10
   that lies around one of those ancient castles
   whose walls are girded many times around
by concentric moats. And just as, from the portal,
   the castle's bridges run from moat to moat
   to the last bank; so from the great rock wall   15
across the embankments and the ditches, high
   and narrow cliffs run to the central well,
   which cuts and gathers them like radii.
Here, shaken from the back of Geryon,
   we found ourselves. My Guide kept to the left   20
   and I walked after him. So we moved on.
Below, on my right, and filling the first ditch
   along both banks, new souls in pain appeared,
   new torments, and new devils black as pitch.
All of these sinners were naked; on our side   25
   of the middle they walked toward us; on the other,
   in our direction, but with swifter stride.
Just so the Romans, because of the great throng
   in the year of the Jubilee, divide the bridge[3]

1. *Bolgia* in Italian equals "ditch" or "pouch." That combination of meanings is not possible in a single English word, but it is well to bear in mind that Dante intended both meanings: not only a ditch of evil, but a pouch full of it, a filthy treasure of ill-gotten souls.   2. This is the final pit of Hell, and in it are punished the Treacherous (those Guilty of Compound Fraud). Cantos XXIX–XXXIV will deal with this part of Hell.   3. Boniface VIII had proclaimed 1300 a Jubilee Year, and consequently throngs of pilgrims had come to Rome. Since the date of the vision is also 1300, the Roman throngs are moving back and forth across the Tiber via Ponte Castello Sant' Angelo at the very time Dante is watching the sinners in Hell.

in order that the crowds may pass along,   30
so that all face the Castle as they go
   on one side toward St. Peter's, while on the other,
   all move along facing toward Mount Giordano.
And everywhere along that hideous track
   I saw horned demons with enormous lashes   35
   move through those souls, scourging them on the back.
Ah, how the stragglers of that long rout stirred
   their legs quick-march at the first crack of the lash!
   Certainly no one waited a second, or third!
As we went on, one face in that procession   40
   caught my eye and I said: "That sinner there:
   It is certainly not the first time I've seen that one."
I stopped, therefore, to study him, and my Guide
   out of his kindness waited, and even allowed me
   to walk back a few steps at the sinner's side.   45
And that flayed spirit, seeing me turn around,
   thought to hide his face, but I called to him:
   "You there, that walk along with your eyes on the ground—
if those are not false features, then I know you
   as Venedico Caccianemico of Bologna:[4]   50
   what brings you here among this pretty crew?"
And he replied: "I speak unwillingly,
   but something in your living voice, in which
   I hear the world again, stirs and compels me.
It was I who brought the fair Ghisola 'round   55
   to serve the will and lust of the Marquis,
   however sordid that old tale may sound.
There are many more from Bologna who weep away
   eternity in this ditch; we fill it so
   there are not as many tongues that are taught to say   60
'sipa'[5] in all the land that lies between
   the Reno and the Saveno, as you must know
   from the many tales of our avarice and spleen."
And as he spoke, one of those lashes fell
   across his back, and a demon cried, "Move on,   65
   you pimp, there are no women here to sell."
Turning away then, I rejoined my Guide.
   We came in a few steps to a raised ridge
   that made a passage to the other side.
This we climbed easily, and turning right   70
   along the jagged crest, we left behind
   the eternal circling of those souls in flight.
And when we reached the part at which the stone
   was tunneled for the passage of the scourged,
   my Guide said, "Stop a minute and look down   75
on these other misbegotten wraiths of sin.
   You have not seen their faces, for they moved
   in the same direction we were headed in."

---

4. To win the favor of the Marquis Obbizo da Este of Ferrara, Caccianemico acted as the procurer of
his own sister Ghisola, called "la bella" or "Ghisolabella."   5. Bolognese dialect for *si*, i.e., "yes."
Bologna lies between the Savena and the Reno. This is a master taunt at Bologna as a city of panderers
and seducers, for it clearly means that the Bolognese then living on earth were fewer in number than
the Bolognese dead who had been assigned to this *bolgia*.

So from that bridge we looked down on the throng
    that hurried toward us on the other side.   80
    Here, too, the whiplash hurried them along.
And the good Master, studying that train,
    said: "Look there, at that great soul that approaches
    and seems to shed no tears for all his pain—
what kingliness moves with him even in Hell!   85
    It is Jason,[6] who by courage and good advice
    made off with the Colchian Ram. Later it fell
that he passed Lemnos, where the women of wrath,
    enraged by Venus' curse that drove their lovers
    out of their arms, put all their males to death.   90
There with his honeyed tongue and his dishonest
    lover's wiles, he gulled Hypsipyle,
    who, in the slaughter, had gulled all the rest.
And there he left her, pregnant and forsaken.
    Such guilt condemns him to such punishment;   95
    and also for Medea is vengeance taken.
All seducers march here to the whip.
    And let us say no more about this valley
    and those it closes in its stony grip."
We had already come to where the walk   100
    crosses the second bank, from which it lifts
    another arch, spanning from rock to rock.
Here we heard people whine in the next chasm,
    and knock and thump themselves with open palms,
    and blubber through their snouts as if in a spasm.   105
Steaming from that pit, a vapour rose
    over the banks, crusting them with a slime
    that sickened my eyes and hammered at my nose.
That chasm sinks so deep we could not sight
    its bottom anywhere until we climbed   110
    along the rock arch to its greatest height.
Once there, I peered down; and I saw long lines
    of people in a river of excrement
    that seemed the overflow of the world's latrines.
I saw among the felons of that pit   115
    one wraith who might or might not have been tonsured—
    one could not tell, he was so smeared with shit.
He bellowed: "You there, why do you stare at me
    more than at all the others in this stew?"
    And I to him: "Because if memory   120
serves me, I knew you when your hair was dry.
    You are Alessio Interminelli da Lucca.[7]
    That's why I pick you from this filthy fry."

---

6. Leader of the Argonauts. He carried off the Colchian Ram (i.e., The Golden Fleece). "The good advice" that helped him win the fleece was given by Medea, daughter of the King of Colchis, whom Jason took with him and later abandoned for Creusa ("Also for Medea is vengeance taken.") In the course of his very Grecian life, Jason had previously seduced Hypsipyle and deserted her to continue his voyage after the fleece. She was one of the women of Lemnos whom Aphrodite, because they no longer worshiped her, cursed with a foul smell which made them unbearable to their husbands and lovers. The women took their epic revenge by banding together to kill all their males, but Hypsipyle managed to save her father, King Thoas, by pretending to the women that she had already killed him.
7. One of the noble family of the Interminelli or Interminei, a prominent White family of Lucca. About all that is known of Alessio is the fact that he was still alive in 1295.

And he then, beating himself on his clown's head:
  "Down to this have the flatteries I sold   125
  the living sunk me here among the dead."
And my Guide prompted then: "Lean forward a bit
  and look beyond him, there—do you see that one
  scratching herself with dungy nails, the strumpet
who fidgets to her feet, then to a crouch?   130
  It is the whore Thaïs[8] who told her lover
  when he sent to ask her, 'Do you thank me much?'
'Much? Nay, past all believing!' And with this

CANTO XIX

Circle Eight: Bolgia Three   The Simoniacs

Dante comes upon the Simoniacs (sellers of ecclesiastic favors and offices) and his heart overflows with the wrath he feels against those who corrupt the things of God. This bolgia is lined with round tube-like holes and the sinners are placed in them upside down with the soles of their feet ablaze. The heat of the blaze is proportioned to their guilt.

The holes in which these sinners are placed are debased equivalents of the baptismal fonts common in the cities of Northern Italy and the sinners' confinement in them is temporary: as new sinners arrive, the souls drop through the bottom of their holes and disappear eternally into the crevices of the rock.

As always, the punishment is a symbolic retribution. Just as the Simoniacs made a mock of holy office, so are they turned upside down in a mockery of the baptismal font. Just as they made a mockery of the holy water of baptism, so is their hellish baptism by fire, after which they are wholly immersed in the crevices below. The oily fire that licks at their soles may also suggest a travesty on the oil used in Extreme Unction (last rites for the dying).

Virgil carries Dante down an almost sheer ledge and lets him speak to one who is the chief sinner of that place, Pope Nicholas III. Dante delivers himself of another stirring denunciation of those who have corrupted church office, and Virgil carries him back up the steep ledge toward the Fourth Bolgia.

O Simon Magus![9] O you wretched crew
  who follow him, pandering for silver and gold
  the things of God which should be wedded to
love and righteousness! O thieves for hire,
  now must the trump of judgment sound your doom   5
  here in the third fosse of the rim of fire!

---

8. The flattery uttered by Thaïs is put into her mouth by Terence in his *Eunuchus* (Act III, 1:1–2). Thaïs' lover had sent her a slave, and later sent a servant to ask if she thanked him much. *Magnas vero agere gratias Thais mihi?* The servant reported her as answering *Ingentes!* Cicero later commented on the passage as an example of immoderate flattery, and Dante's conception of Thaïs probably springs from this source. (*De Amicitia*, 26.)   9. Simon the Samarian magician (see Acts viii, 9–24) from whom the word "Simony" derives. Upon his conversion to Christianity he offered to buy the power to administer the Holy Ghost and was severely rebuked by Peter.

We had already made our way across
   to the next grave, and to that part of the bridge[1]
   which hangs above the mid-point of the fosse.
O Sovereign Wisdom, how Thine art doth shine   10
   in Heaven, on Earth, and in the Evil World![2]
   How justly doth Thy power judge and assign!
I saw along the walls and on the ground
   long rows of holes cut in the livid stone;
   all were cut to a size, and all were round.   15
They seemed to be exactly the same size
   as those in the font of my beautiful San Giovanni,
   built to protect the priests who come to baptize;[3]
(one of which, not so long since, I broke open
   to rescue a boy who was wedged and drowning in it.   20
   Be this enough to undeceive all men.)[4]
From every mouth a sinner's legs stuck out
   as far as the calf. The soles were all ablaze
   and the joints of the legs quivered and writhed about.
Withes and tethers would have snapped in their throes.   25
   As oiled things blaze upon the surface only,
   so did they burn from the heels to the points of their toes.
"Master," I said, "who is that one in the fire
   who writhes and quivers more than all the others?[5]
   From him the ruddy flames seem to leap higher."   30
And he to me: "If you wish me to carry you down
   along that lower bank, you may learn from him
   who he is, and the evil he has done."
And I: "What you will, I will. You are my lord
   and know I depart in nothing from your wish;   35
   and you know my mind beyond my spoken word."
We moved to the fourth ridge, and turning left
   my Guide descended by a jagged path
   into the strait and perforated cleft.
Thus the good Master bore me down the dim   40
   and rocky slope, and did not put me down
   till we reached the one whose legs did penance for him.
"Whoever you are, sad spirit," I began,
   "who lie here with your head below your heels
   and planted like a stake—speak if you can."   45
I stood like a friar who gives the sacrament
   to a hired assassin, who, fixed in the hole,
   recalls him, and delays his death a moment.[6]

---

1. The center point . . . obviously the best observation point. *The next grave*: the next *bolgia*.   2. Hell.
3. It was the custom in Dante's time to baptize only on Holy Saturday and on Pentecost. These occasions were naturally thronged, therefore, and to protect the priests a special font was built in the Baptistry of San Giovanni with marble stands for the priests, who were thus protected from both the crowds and the water in which they immersed those to be baptized. The Baptistry is still standing, but the font is no longer in it. A similar font still exists, however, in the Baptistry at Pisa.   4. In these lines Dante is replying to a charge of sacrilege that had been rumored against him. One day a boy playing in the baptismal font became jammed in the marble tube and could not be extricated. To save the boy from drowning, Dante took it upon himself to smash the tube.   5. The fire is proportioned to the guilt of the sinner. These are obviously the feet of the chief sinner of this *bolgia*. In a moment we shall discover that he is Pope Nicholas III.   6. Persons convicted of murdering for hire were sometimes executed by being buried alive upside down. If the friar were called back at the last moment, he should have to bend over the hole in which the man is fixed upside down awaiting the first shovelful of earth.

"Are you there already, Boniface?[7] Are you there
   already?" he cried. "By several years the writ   50
   has lied. And all that gold, and all that care—
are you already sated with the treasure
   for which you dared to turn on the Sweet Lady
   and trick and pluck and bleed her at your pleasure?"
I stood like one caught in some raillery,   55
   not understanding what is said to him,
   lost for an answer to such mockery.
Then Virgil said. "Say to him: 'I am not he,
   I am not who you think.' " And I replied
   as my good Master had instructed me.   60
The sinner's feet jerked madly; then again
   his voice rose, this time choked with sighs and tears,
   and said at last: "What do you want of me then?
If to know who I am drives you so fearfully
   that you descend the bank to ask it, know   65
   that the Great Mantle[8] was once hung upon me.
And in truth I was a son of the She-Bear,[9]
   so sly and eager to push my whelps ahead,
   that I pursed wealth above, and myself here.[1]
Beneath my head are dragged all who have gone   70
   before me in buying and selling holy office;
   there they cower in fissures of the stone.
I too shall be plunged down when that great cheat
   for whom I took you comes here in his turn.
   Longer already have I baked my feet   75
and been planted upside-down, than he shall be
   before the west sends down a lawless Shepherd[2]
   of uglier deeds to cover him and me.
He will be a new Jason of the Maccabees;
   and just as that king bent to his high priests' will,   80
   so shall the French king do as this one please."
Maybe—I cannot say—I grew too brash
   at this point, for when he had finished speaking
   I said: "Indeed! Now tell me how much cash
our Lord required of Peter in guarantee   85
   before he put the keys into his keeping?
   Surely he asked nothing but 'Follow me!'
Nor did Peter, nor the others, ask silver or gold
   of Matthew when they chose him for the place

7. The speaker is Pope Nicholas III, Giovanni Gaetano degli Orsini, Pope from 1277 to 1280. His
presence here is self-explanatory. He is awaiting the arrival of his successor, Boniface VIII, who will take
his place in the stone tube and who will in turn be replaced by Clement V, a Pope even more corrupt
than Boniface. With the foresight of the damned he had read the date of Boniface's death (1303) in the
Book of Fate. Mistaking Dante for Boniface, he thinks his foresight has erred by three years, since it is
now 1300.   8. Of the Papacy.   9. Nicholas' family name, degli Orsini, means in Italian "of the bear
cubs."   1. A play on the second meaning of *bolgia* (i.e., "purse"). "Just as I put wealth in my purse
when alive, so am I put in this foul purse now that I am dead."   2. Clement V, Pope from 1305 to
1314. He came from Gascony (the West) and was involved in many intrigues with the King of France.
It was Clement V who moved the Papal See to Avignon where it remained until 1377. He is compared
to Jason (see Maccabees iv, 7ff.) who bought an appointment as High Priest of the Jews from King
Antiochus and thereupon introduced pagan and venal practices into the office in much the same way
as Clement used his influence with Philip of France to secure and corrupt his high office. Clement
will succeed Boniface in Hell because Boniface's successor, Benedictus XI (1303–1304), was a good
and holy man.

the despicable and damned apostle sold.[3]   90
Therefore stay as you are; this hole well fits you—
    and keep a good guard on the ill-won wealth
    that once made you so bold toward Charles of Anjou.[4]
And were it not that I am still constrained
    by the reverence I owe to the Great Keys[5]   95
    you held in life, I should not have refrained
from using other words and sharper still;
    for this avarice of yours grieves all the world,
    tramples the virtuous, and exalts the evil.
Of such as you was the Evangelist's[6] vision   100
    when he saw She who Sits upon the Waters
    locked with the Kings of earth in fornication.
She was born with seven heads and ten enormous
    and shining horns strengthened and made her glad
    as long as love and virtue pleased her spouse.   105
Gold and silver are the gods you adore!
    In what are you different from the idolater,
    save that he worships one, and you a score?
Ah Constantine, what evil marked the hour—
    not of your conversion, but of the fee   110
    the first rich Father[7] took from you in dower!"
And as I sang him this tune, he began to twitch
    and kick both feet out wildly, as if in rage
    or gnawed by conscience—little matter which.
And I think, indeed, it pleased my Guide: his look   115
    was all approval as he stood beside me
    intent upon each word of truth I spoke.
He approached, and with both arms he lifted me,
    and when he had gathered me against his breast,
    remounted the rocky path out of the valley,   120
nor did he tire of holding me clasped to him,
    until we reached the topmost point of the arch
    which crosses from the fourth to the fifth rim
of the pits of woe. Arrived upon the bridge,
    he tenderly set down the heavy burden   125
    he had been pleased to carry up that ledge
which would have been hard climbing for a goat.
Here I looked down on still another moat.

3. Upon the expulsion of Judas from the band of Apostles, Matthias was chosen in his place.   4. The seventh son of Louis VIII of France. Charles became King of Naples and of Sicily largely through the good offices of Pope Urban IV and later of Clement IV. Nicholas III withdrew the high favor his predecessors had shown Charles, but the exact nature and extent of his opposition are open to dispute. Dante probably believed, as did many of his contemporaries, that Nicholas instigated the massacre called the Sicilian Vespers, in which the Sicilians overthrew the rule of Charles and held a general slaughter of the French who had been their masters. The Sicilian Vespers, however, was a popular and spontaneous uprising, and it did not occur until Nicholas had been dead for two years.   5. Of the Papacy.   6. St. John the Evangelist. His vision of Her who sits upon the waters is set forth in Revelation xvii. The Evangelist intended it as a vision of Pagan Rome, but Dante interprets it as a vision of the Roman Church in its simoniacal corruption. The seven heads are the seven sacraments; the ten horns, the ten commandments.   7. Silvester (Pope from 314 to 355). Before him the Popes possessed nothing, but when Constantine was converted and Catholicism became the official religion of the Empire, the church began to acquire wealth. Dante and the scholars of his time believed, according to a document called "The Donation of Constantine," that the Emperor had moved his Empire to the East in order to leave sovereignty of the West to the Church. The document was not shown to be a forgery until the fifteenth century.

CANTO XX

Circle Eight: Bolgia Four   The Fortune Tellers and Diviners

Dante stands in the middle of the bridge over the Fourth Bolgia and
looks down at the souls of the Fortune Tellers and Diviners. Here are the
souls of all those who attempted by forbidden arts to look into the future.
Among these damned are: Amphiareus, Tiresias, Aruns, Manto, Eurypylus, Michael Scott, Guido Bonatti, and Asdente.

Characteristically, the sin of these wretches is reversed upon them: their
punishment is to have their heads turned backwards on their bodies and
to be compelled to walk backwards through all eternity, their eyes blinded
with tears. Thus, those who sought to penetrate the future cannot even see
in front of themselves; they attempted to move themselves forward in time,
so must they go backwards through all eternity; and as the arts of sorcery
are a distortion of God's law, so are their bodies distorted in Hell.

No more need be said of them: Dante names them, and passes on to
fill the Canto with a lengthy account of the founding of Virgil's native city
of Mantua.

Now must I sing new griefs, and my verses strain
    to form the matter of the Twentieth Canto
    of Canticle One,[8] the Canticle of Pain.
My vantage point[9] permitted a clear view
    of the depths of the pit below: a desolation   5
    bathed with the tears of its tormented crew,
who moved about the circle of the pit
    at about the pace of a litany procession.[1]
    Silent and weeping, they wound round and round it.
And when I looked down from their faces,[2] I saw   10
    that each of them was hideously distorted
    between the top of the chest and the lines of the jaw;
for the face was reversed on the neck, and they came on
    backwards, staring backwards at their loins,[3]
    for to look before them was forbidden. Someone,   15
sometime, in the grip of a palsy may have been
    distorted so, but never to my knowledge;
    nor do I believe the like was ever seen.
Reader, so may God grant you to understand
    my poem and profit from it, ask yourself   20
    how I could check my tears, when near at hand
I saw the image of our humanity
    distorted so that the tears that burst from their eyes
    ran down the cleft of their buttocks. Certainly
I wept. I leaned against the jagged face   25

8. The *Inferno*. The other Canticles are, of course, the *Purgatorio* and the *Paradiso*.   9. Virgil, it will
be recalled, had set Dante down on the bridge across the Fourth Bolgia.   1. The litanies are chanted
not only in church (before the mass), but sometimes in procession, the priest chanting the prayers and
the marchers the response. As one might gather from the context, the processions move very slowly.
2. A typically Dantean conception. Dante often writes as if the eye pin-pointed on one feature of a
figure seen at a distance. The pin-point must then be deliberately shifted before the next feature can be
observed. As far as I know, this stylistic device is peculiar to Dante.   3. General usage seems to have
lost sight of the fact that the first meaning of "loin" is "that part of a human being or quadruped on
either side of the spinal column between the hipbone and the false ribs." (Webster.)

of a rock and wept so that my Guide said: "Still?
    Still like the other fools? There is no place
for pity here. Who is more arrogant
    within his soul, who is more impious
    than one who dares to sorrow at God's judgment?   30
Lift up your eyes, lift up your eyes and see
    him the earth swallowed before all the Thebans,
    at which they cried out: 'Whither do you flee,
Amphiareus?[4] Why do you leave the field?'
    And he fell headlong through the gaping earth   35
    to the feet of Minos, where all sin must yield.
Observe how he has made a breast of his back.
    In life he wished to see too far before him,
    and now he must crab backwards round this track.
And see Tiresias,[5] who by his arts   40
    succeeded in changing himself from man to woman,
    transforming all his limbs and all his parts;
later he had to strike the two twined serpents
    once again with his conjurer's wand before
    he could resume his manly lineaments.   45
And there is Aruns,[6] his back to that one's belly,
    the same who in the mountains of the Luni
    tilled by the people of Carrara's valley,
made a white marble cave his den, and there
    with unobstructed view observed the sea   50
    and the turning constellations year by year.
And she whose unbound hair flows back to hide
    her breasts—which you cannot see—and who also wears
    all of her hairy parts on that other side,
was Manto, who searched countries far and near,   55
    then settled where I was born.[7] In that connection
    there is a story I would have you hear.
Tiresias was her sire. After his death,
    Thebes, the city of Bacchus, became enslaved,
    and for many years she roamed about the earth.   60
High in sweet Italy, under the Alps that shut
    the Tyrolean gate of Germany, there lies
    a lake known as Benacus[8] roundabout.
Through endless falls, more than a thousand and one,
    Mount Appennine from Garda to Val Cammonica   65
    is freshened by the waters that flow down
into that lake. At its center is a place

---

4. Another of the seven Captains who fought against Thebes (v. Capaneus, Canto XIV). Statius (*Thebaid* VII, 690 ff. and VIII, 8 ff.) tells how he foresaw his own death in this war, and attempted to run away from it, but was swallowed in his flight by an earthquake. I have Romanized his name from "Amphiaraus."   5. A Theban diviner and magician. Ovid (*Metamorphoses* III) tells how he came on two twined serpents, struck them apart with his stick, and was thereupon transformed into a woman. Seven years later he came on two serpents similarly entwined, struck them apart, and was changed back.
6. An Etruscan soothsayer (see Lucan, *Pharsalia*, I, 580 ff.). He foretold the war between Pompey and Julius Caesar, and also that it would end with Caesar's victory and Pompey's death. *Luni*: Also *Luna*. An ancient Etruscan city. *Carrara's valley*: The Carrarese valley is famous for its white (Carrara) marble.
7. Dante's version of the founding of Mantua is based on a reference in the *Aeneid* X, 198–200.
8. The ancient name for the famous Lago di Garda, which lies a short distance north of Mantua. The other places named in this passage lie around Lago di Garda. On an island in the lake the three dioceses mentioned in line 68 conjoined. All three bishops, therefore, had jurisdiction on the island.

where the Bishops of Brescia, Trentine, and Verona
   might all give benediction with equal grace.
Peschiera, the beautiful fortress, strong in war   70
   against the Brescians and the Bergamese,
   sits at the lowest point along that shore.
There, the waters Benacus cannot hold
   within its bosom, spill and form a river
   that winds away through pastures green and gold.   75
But once the water gathers its full flow,
   it is called Mincius rather than Benacus
   from there to Governo, where it joins the Po.
Still near its source, it strikes a plain, and there
   it slows and spreads, forming an ancient marsh   80
   which in the summer heats pollutes the air.
The terrible virgin, passing there by chance,
   saw dry land at the center of the mire,
   untilled, devoid of all inhabitants.
There, shunning all communion with mankind,   85
   she settled with the ministers of her arts,
   and there she lived, and there she left behind
her vacant corpse. Later the scattered men
   who lived nearby assembled on that spot
   since it was well defended by the fen.   90
Over those whited bones they raised the city,
   and for her who had chosen the place before all others
   they named it—with no further augury—
Mantua. Far more people lived there once—
   before sheer madness prompted Casalodi   95
   to let Pinamonte play him for a dunce.[9]
Therefore, I charge you, should you ever hear
   other accounts of this, to let no falsehood
   confuse the truth which I have just made clear."
And I to him: "Master, within my soul   100
   your word is certainty, and any other
   would seem like the dead lumps of burned out coal.
But tell me of those people moving down
   to join the rest. Are any worth my noting?
   For my mind keeps coming back to that alone."   105
And he: "That one whose beard spreads like a fleece
   over his swarthy shoulders, was an augur
   in the days when so few males remained in Greece
that even the cradles were all but empty of sons.
   He chose the time for cutting the cable at Aulis,   110
   and Calchas joined him in those divinations.
He is Eurypylus.[1] I sing him somewhere

9. Albert, Count of Casalodi and Lord of Mantua, let himself be persuaded by Pinamonte de Buonac-
corsi to banish the nobles from Mantua as a source of danger to his rule. Once the nobles had departed,
Pinamonte headed a rebellion against the weakened lord and took over the city himself.   **1.** According
to Greek custom an augur was summoned before each voyage to choose the exact propitious moment
for departure (cutting the cables). Dante has Virgil imply that Eurypylus and Calchas were selected to
choose the moment for Agamemnon's departure from Aulis to Troy. Actually, according to the *Aeneid*,
Eurypylus was not at Aulis. The *Aeneid* (II, 110 ff.) tells how Eurypylus and Calchas were both consulted
in choosing the moment for the departure from Troy. Dante seems to have confused the two incidents.
Even the cradles were all but empty of sons: At the time of the Trojan Wars, Greece was said to be so
empty of males that scarcely any were to be found even in the cradles.

in my High Tragedy; you will know the place
who know the whole of it. The other there,
the one beside him with the skinny shanks   115
     was Michael Scott,[2] who mastered every trick
     of magic fraud, a prince of mountebanks.
See Guido Bonatti[3] there; and see Asdente,
     who now would be wishing he had stuck to his last,
     but repents too late, though he repents aplenty.   120
And see on every hand the wretched hags
     who left their spinning and sewing for soothsaying
     and casting of spells with herbs, and dolls, and rags.
But come: Cain with his bush of thorns[4] appears
     already on the wave below Seville,   125
     above the boundary of the hemispheres;
and the moon was full already yesternight.
     as you must well remember from the wood,
     for it certainly did not harm you when its light
shone down upon your way before the dawn."   130
And as he spoke to me, we traveled on.

CANTO XXI

Circle Eight: Bolgia Five   The Grafters

The Poets move on, talking as they go, and arrive at the Fifth Bolgia.
Here the Grafters are sunk in boiling pitch and guarded by Demons, who
tear them to pieces with claws and grappling hooks if they catch them
above the surface of the pitch.

The sticky pitch is symbolic of the sticky fingers of the Grafters. It serves
also to hide them from sight, as their sinful dealings on earth were hidden
from men's eyes. The demons, too, suggest symbolic possibilities, for they
are armed with grappling hooks and are forever ready to rend and tear all
they can get their hands on.

The Poets watch a demon arrive with a grafting Senator of Lucca and
fling him into the pitch where the demons set upon him.

To protect Dante from their wrath, Virgil hides him behind some jagged rocks and goes ahead alone to negotiate with the demons. They set
upon him like a pack of mastiffs, but Virgil secures a safe-conduct from
their leader, Malacoda. Thereupon Virgil calls Dante from hiding, and
they are about to set off when they discover that the Bridge Across the
Sixth Bolgia lies shattered. Malacoda tells them there is another further
on and sends a squad of demons to escort them. Their adventures with
the demons continue through the next Canto.

These two Cantos may conveniently be remembered as the Gargoyle

---

2. An Irish scholar of the first half of the thirteenth century. His studies were largely in the occult. Sir
Walter Scott refers to him in *The Lay of the Last Minstrel.*   3. A thirteenth-century astrologer of Forli.
He was court astrologer to Guido da Montefeltro (see Canto XXVII) advising him in his wars. *Asdente:*
A shoemaker of Parma who turned diviner and won wide fame for his forecastings in the last half of the
thirteenth century.   4. The Moon. Cain with a bush of thorns was the medieval equivalent of our
Man in the Moon. Dante seems to mean by "Seville" the whole area of Spain and the Straits of
Gibraltar (Pillars of Hercules), which were believed to be the western limit of the world. The moon is
setting (*i.e.*, it appears on the western waves) on the morning of Holy Saturday, 1300.

Cantos. If the total Commedia is built like a cathedral (as so many critics have suggested), it is here certainly that Dante attaches his grotesqueries. At no other point in the Commedia does Dante give such free rein to his coarsest style.

Thus talking of things which my Comedy does not care
    to sing, we passed from one arch to the next
    until we stood upon its summit. There
we checked our steps to study the next fosse
    and the next vain lamentations of Malebolge;   5
    awesomely dark and desolate it was.
As in the Venetian arsenal,[5] the winter through
    there boils the sticky pitch to caulk the seams
    of the sea-battered bottoms when no crew
can put to sea—instead of which, one starts   10
    to build its ship anew, one plugs the planks
    which have been sprung in many foreign parts;
some hammer at a mast, some at a rib;
    some make new oars, some braid and coil new lines;
    one patches up the mainsail, one the jib—   15
so, but by Art Divine and not by fire,
    a viscid pitch boiled in the fosse below
    and coated all the bank with gluey mire.
I saw the pitch; but I saw nothing in it
    except the enormous bubbles of its boiling,   20
    which swelled and sank, like breathing, through all the pit.
And as I stood and stared into that sink,
    my Master cried, "Take care!" and drew me back
    from my exposed position on the brink.
I turned like one who cannot wait to see   25
    the thing he dreads, and who, in sudden fright,
    runs while he looks, his curiosity
competing with his terror—and at my back
    I saw a figure that came running toward us
    across the ridge, a Demon huge and black.   30
Ah what a face he had, all hate and wildness!
    Galloping so, with his great wings outspread
    he seemed the embodiment of all bitterness.
Across each high-hunched shoulder he had thrown
    one haunch of a sinner, whom he held in place   35
    with a great talon round each ankle bone.
"Blacktalons[6] of our bridge," he began to roar,
    "I bring you one of Santa Zita's[7] Elders!
    Scrub him down while I go back for more:
I planted a harvest of them in that city: 40
    everyone there is a grafter except Bonturo.[8]

5. The arsenal was not only an arms manufactory but a great center of shipbuilding and repairing.
6. The original is Malebranche, i.e., "Evil Claws."   7. The patron saint of the city of Lucca. "One of Santa Zita's Elders" would therefore equal "One of Lucca's Senators" (i.e., Aldermen). Commentators have searched the records of Luccan Aldermen who died on Holy Saturday of 1300, and one Martino Bottaio has been suggested as the newcomer, but there is no evidence that Dante had a specific man in mind. More probably he meant simply to underscore the fact that Lucca was a city of grafters, just as Bologna was represented as a city of panderers and seducers.   8. Bonturo Dati, a politician of Lucca. The phrase is ironic: Bonturo was the most avid grafter of them all.

There 'Yes' is 'No' and 'No' is 'Yes' for a fee."
Down the sinner plunged, and at once the Demon
    spun from the cliff; no mastiff ever sprang
    more eager from the leash to chase a felon.   45
Down plunged the sinner and sank to reappear
    with his backside arched and his face and both his feet
    glued to the pitch, almost as if in prayer.
But the Demons under the bridge, who guard that place
    and the sinners who are thrown to them, bawled out: 50
    "You're out of bounds here for the Sacred Face:[9]
this is no dip in the Serchio: take your look
    and then get down in the pitch. And stay below
    unless you want a taste of a grappling hook."
Then they raked him with more than a hundred hooks   55
    bellowing: "Here you dance below the covers.
    Graft all you can there: no one checks your books."
They dipped him down into that pitch exactly
    as a chef makes scullery boys dip meat in a boiler,
    holding it with their hooks from floating free.   60
And the Master said: "You had best not be seen[1]
    by these Fiends till I am ready. Crouch down here.
    One of these rocks will serve you as a screen.
And whatever violence you see done to me,
    you have no cause to fear. I know these matters: 65
    I have been through this once and come back safely."
With that, he walked on past the end of the bridge;
    and it wanted all his courage to look calm
    from the moment he arrived on the sixth ridge.
With that same storm and fury that arouses   70
    all the house when the hounds leap at a tramp
    who suddenly falls to pleading where he pauses—
so rushed those Fiends from below, and all the pack
    pointed their gleaming pitchforks at my Guide.
But he stood fast and cried to them: "Stand back!   75
Before those hooks and grapples make too free,
    send up one of your crew to hear me out,
    then ask yourselves if you still care to rip me."
All cried as one: "Let Malacoda[2] go."
    So the pack stood and one of them came forward,   80
    saying: "What good does he think this will do?"
"Do you think, Malacoda," my good Master said,
    "you would see me here, having arrived this far
    already, safe from you and every dread,
without Divine Will and propitious Fate?   85
    Let me pass on, for it is willed in Heaven
    that I must show another this dread state."

9. *Il volto santo* was an ancient wooden image of Christ venerated by the Luccanese. These ironies and
the grotesqueness of the Elder's appearance mark the beginning of the gargoyle dance that swells and
rolls through this Canto and the next. *Serchio*: A river near Lucca.   1. It is only in the passage through
this Bolgia, out of the total journey, that Dante presents himself as being in physical danger. Since his
dismissal from office and his exile from Florence (on pain of death if he return) was based on a false
charge of grafting, the reference is pointedly autobiographical.   2. The name equals "Bad Tail," or
"Evil Tail." He is the captain of these grim and semi-military police. I have not translated his name as
I have those of the other fiends, since I cannot see that it offers any real difficulty to an English
reader.

The Demon stood there on the flinty brim,
    so taken aback he let his pitchfork drop;
    then said to the others: "Take care not to harm him!"   90
"O you crouched like a cat," my Guide called to me,
    "among the jagged rock piles of the bridge,
    come down to me, for now you may come safely."
Hearing him, I hurried down the ledge;
    and the Demons all pressed forward when I appeared,   95
    so that I feared they might not keep their pledge.
So once I saw the Pisan infantry
    march out under truce from the fortress at Caprona,
    staring in fright at the ranks of the enemy.[3]
I pressed the whole of my body against my Guide,   100
    and not for an instant did I take my eyes
    from those black fiends who scowled on every side.
They swung their forks saying to one another:
    "Shall I give him a touch in the rump?" and answering:
    "Sure; give him a taste to pay him for his bother."   105
But the Demon who was talking to my Guide
    turned round and cried to him: "At ease there, Snatcher!"
    And then to us: "There's no road on this side:
the arch lies all in pieces in the pit.
    If you *must* go on, follow along this ridge;   110
    there's another cliff to cross by just beyond it.[4]
In just five hours it will be, since the bridge fell,
    a thousand two hundred sixty-six years and a day;[5]
    that was the time the big quake shook all Hell.
I'll send a squad of my boys along that way   115
    to see if anyone's airing himself below:
    you can go with them: there will be no foul play.
Front and center here, Grizzly and Hellken,"
    he began to order them. "You too, Deaddog.
    Curlybeard, take charge of a squad of ten.   120
Take Grafter and Dragontooth along with you.
    Pigtusk, Catclaw, Cramper, and Crazyred.
    Keep a sharp lookout on the boiling glue
as you move along, and see that these gentlemen
    are not molested until they reach the crag   125
    where they can find a way across the den."
"In the name of heaven, Master," I cried, "what sort
    of guides are these? Let us go on alone
    if you know the way. Who can trust such an escort!

---

3. A Tuscan army attacked the fortress of Caprona near Pisa in 1289 and after fierce fighting the Pisan defenders were promised a safe-conduct if they would surrender. Dante was probably serving with the Tuscans (the opening lines of the next Canto certainly suggest that he had seen military service). In some accounts it is reported that the Tuscans massacred the Pisans despite their promised safe-conduct—an ominous analogy if true. In any case the emerging Pisans would be sufficiently familiar with the treacheries of Italian politics to feel profoundly uneasy at being surrounded by their enemies under such conditions.   4. Malacoda is lying, as the Poets will discover: all the bridges across the Sixth Bolgia have fallen as a result of the earthquake that shook Hell at the death of Christ.   5. Christ died on Good Friday of the year 34, and it is now Holy Saturday of the year 1300, five hours before the hour of his death. Many commentators (and Dante himself in the *Convivio*) place the hour of Christ's death at exactly noon. Accordingly, it would now be 7:00 A.M. of Holy Saturday—exactly eight minutes since the Poets left the bridge over the Fourth Bolgia (at moonset). In the gospels of Matthew, Mark, and Luke, however, the hour of Christ's death is precisely stated as 3:00 P.M. Dante would certainly be familiar with the Synoptic Gospels, and on that authority it would now be 10:00 A.M.

If you are as wary as you used to be   130
   you surely see them grind their teeth at us,
   and knot their beetle brows so threateningly."
And he: "I do not like this fear in you.
   Let them gnash and knot as they please; they menace only
   the sticky wretches simmering in that stew."   135
They turned along the left bank in a line;
   but not before they formed a single rank
   had stuck their pointed tongues out as a sign
to their Captain that they wished permission to pass,
and he had made a trumpet of his ass.   140

CANTO XXII

Circle Eight: Bolgia Five   The Grafters

The poets set off with their escorts of demons. Dante sees the Grafters lying in the pitch like frogs in water with only their muzzles out. They disappear as soon as they sight the demons and only a ripple on the surface betrays their presence.

One of the Grafters, an Unidentified Navarrese, ducks too late and is seized by the demons who are about to claw him, but Curlybeard holds them back while Virgil questions him. The wretch speaks of his fellow sinners, Friar Gomita and Michel Zanche, while the uncontrollable demons rake him from time to time with their hooks.

The Navarrese offers to lure some of his fellow sufferers into the hands of the demons, and when his plan is accepted he plunges into the pitch and escapes. Hellken and Grizzly fly after him, but too late. They start a brawl in mid-air and fall into the pitch themselves. Curlybeard immediately organizes a rescue party and the Poets, fearing the bad temper of the frustrated demons, take advantage of the confusion to slip away.

I have seen horsemen breaking camp. I have seen
   the beginning of the assault, the march and muster,
   and at times the retreat and riot. I have been
where chargers trampled your land, O Aretines![6]
   I have seen columns of foragers, shocks of tourney,   5
   and running of tilts.[7] I have seen the endless lines
march to bells,[8] drums, trumpets, from far and near.
   I have seen them march on signals from a castle.[9]
   I have seen them march with native and foreign gear.
But never yet have I seen horse or foot,   10
   nor ship in range of land nor sight of star,
   take its direction from so low a toot.

---

6. The people of Arezzo. In 1289 the Guelphs of Florence and Lucca defeated the Ghibellines of Arrezo at Campaldino. Dante was present with the Guelphs, though probably as an observer and not as a warrior.   7. A tourney was contested by groups of knights in a field; a tilt by individuals who tried to unhorse one another across a barrier.   8. The army of each town was equipped with a chariot on which bells were mounted. Signals could be given by the bells and special decorations made the chariot stand out in battle. It served therefore as a rallying point.   9. When troops were in sight of their castle their movements could be directed from the towers—by banners in daytime and by fires at night, much as some naval signals are still given today.

We went with the ten Fiends—ah, savage crew!—
   but "In church with saints; with stewpots in the tavern,"
   as the old proverb wisely bids us do.   15
All my attention was fixed upon the pitch:
   to observe the people who were boiling in it,
   and the customs and the punishments of that ditch.
As dolphins surface and begin to flip
   their arched backs from the sea, warning the sailors   20
   to fall-to and begin to secure ship[1]—
So now and then, some soul, to ease his pain.
   showed us a glimpse of his back above the pitch
   and quick as lightning disappeared again.
And as, at the edge of a ditch, frogs squat about   25
   hiding their feet and bodies in the water,
   leaving only their muzzles sticking out—
so stood the sinners in that dismal ditch;
   but as Curlybeard approached, only a ripple
   showed where they had ducked back into the pitch.   30
I saw—the dread of it haunts me to this day—
   one linger a bit too long, as it sometimes happens
   one frog remains when another spurts away;
and Catclaw, who was nearest, ran a hook
   through the sinner's pitchy hair and hauled him in.   35
   He looked like an otter dripping from the brook.
I knew the names of all the Fiends by then;
   I had made a note of them at the first muster,
   and, marching, had listened and checked them over again.
"Hey, Crazyred," the crew of Demons cried   40
   all together, "give him a taste of your claws.
   Dig him open a little. Off with his hide."
And I then: "Master, can you find out, please,
   the name and history of that luckless one
   who has fallen into the hands of his enemies?"   45
My Guide approached that wraith from the hot tar
   and asked him whence he came. The wretch replied:
   "I was born and raised in the Kingdom of Navarre.
My mother placed me in service to a knight;
   for she had borne me to a squanderer   50
   who killed himself when he ran through his birthright.
Then I became a domestic in the service
   of good King Thibault.[2] There I began to graft,
   and I account for it in this hot crevice."
And Pigtusk, who at the ends of his lower lip   55
   shot forth two teeth more terrible than a boar's,
   made the wretch feel how one of them could rip.
The mouse had come among bad cats, but here
   Curlybeard locked arms around him crying:
   "While I've got hold of him the rest stand clear!"   60
And turning his face to my Guide: "If you want to ask him
   anything else," he added, "ask away

---

1. It was a common belief that when dolphins began to leap around a ship they were warning the sailors of an approaching storm.   2. Thibault II was King of Navarre, a realm that lay in what is now northern Spain.

before the others tear him limb from limb."
And my Guide to the sinner; "I should like to know
  if among the other souls beneath the pitch   65
  are any Italians'?"[3] And the wretch: "Just now
I left a shade who came from parts near by.
  Would I were still in the pitch with him, for then
  these hooks would not be giving me cause to cry."
And suddenly Grafter bellowed in great heat: 70
  "We've stood enough!" And he hooked the sinner's arm
  and, raking it, ripped off a chunk of meat.
Then Dragontooth wanted to play, too, reaching down
  for a catch at the sinner's legs; but Curlybeard
  wheeled round and round with a terrifying frown,   75
and when the Fiends had somewhat given ground
  and calmed a little, my Guide, without delay,
  asked the wretch, who was staring at his wound:
"Who was the sinner from whom you say you made
  your evil-starred departure to come ashore   80
  among these Fiends?" And the wretch: "It was the shade
of Friar Gomita of Gallura,[4] the crooked stem
  of every Fraud: when his master's enemies
  were in his hands, he won high praise from them.
He took their money without case or docket,   85
  and let them go. He was in all his dealings
  no petty bursar, but a kingly pocket.
With him, his endless crony in the fosse,
  is Don Michel Zanche of Logodoro;[5]
  they babble about Sardinia without pause.   90
But look! See that fiend grinning at your side!
  There is much more that I should like to tell you,
  but oh, I think he means to grate my hide!"
But their grim sergeant wheeled, sensing foul play,
  and turning on Cramper, who seemed set to strike,   95
  ordered: "Clear off, you buzzard. Clear off, I say!"
"If either of you would like to see and hear
  Tuscans or Lombards," the pale sinner said,
  "I can lure them out of hiding if you'll stand clear
and let me sit here at the edge of the ditch,   100
  and get all these Blacktalons out of sight;
  for while they're here, no one will leave the pitch.
In exchange for myself, I can fish you up as pretty
  a mess of souls as you like. I have only to whistle
  the way we do when one of us gets free."   105
Deaddog raised his snout as he listened to him;
  then, shaking his head, said, "Listen to the grafter

---

3. Dante uses the term *Latino*—strictly speaking, a person from the area of ancient Latium, now (roughly) Lazio, the province in which Rome is located. It was against the Latians that Aeneas fought on coming to Italy. More generally, Dante uses the term for any southern Italian. Here, however, the usage seems precise, since the sinner refers to "points near by" and means Sardinia. Rome is the point in Italy closest to Sardinia.   4. In 1300 Sardinia was a Pisan possession, and was divided into four districts, of which Gallura was the northeast. Friar Gomita administered Gallura for his own considerable profit. He was hanged by the Pisan governor when he was found guilty of taking bribes to let prisoners escape.   5. He was made Vicar of Logodoro when the King of Sardinia went off to war. The King was captured and did not return. Michel maneuvered a divorce for the Queen and married her himself. About 1290 he was murdered by his son-in-law, Branca d'Oria (see Canto XXXIII).

spinning his tricks so he can jump from the brim!"
And the sticky wretch, who was all treachery:
   "Oh I am more than tricky when there's a chance   110
   to see my friends in greater misery."
Hellken, against the will of all the crew,
   could hold no longer. "If you jump," he said
   to the scheming wretch, "I won't come after you
at a gallop, but like a hawk after a mouse.   115
   We'll clear the edge and hide behind the bank:
   let's see if you're trickster enough for all of us."
Reader, here is new game! The Fiends withdrew
   from the bank's edge, and Deaddog, who at first
   was most against it, led the savage crew.   120
The Navarrese chose his moment carefully:
   and planting both his feet against the ground,
   he leaped, and in an instant he was free.
The Fiends were stung with shame, and of the lot
   Hellken most, who had been the cause of it.   125
   He leaped out madly bellowing: "You're caught!"
but little good it did him; terror pressed
   harder than wings; the sinner dove from sight
   and the Fiend in full flight had to raise his breast.
A duck, when the falcon dives, will disappear   130
   exactly so, all in a flash, while he
   returns defeated and weary up the air.
Grizzly, in a rage at the sinner's flight,
   flew after Hellken, hoping the wraith would escape,
   so he might find an excuse to start a fight.   135
And as soon as the grafter sank below the pitch,
   Grizzly turned his talons against Hellken,
   locked with him claw to claw above the ditch.
But Hellken was sparrowhawk enough for two
   and clawed him well; and ripping one another,   140
   they plunged together into the hot stew.
The heat broke up the brawl immediately,
   but their wings were smeared with pitch and they could not rise.
   Curlybeard, upset as his company,
commanded four to fly to the other coast   145
   at once with all their grapples. At top speed
   the Fiends divided, each one to his post.
Some on the near edge, some along the far,
   they stretched their hooks out to the clotted pair
   who were already cooked deep through the scar   150
of their first burn. And turning to one side
we slipped off, leaving them thus occupied.

CANTO XXIII

Circle Eight: Bolgia Six   The Hypocrites

  The Poets are pursued by the Fiends and escape them by sliding down
the sloping bank of the next pit. They are now in the Sixth Bolgia. Here
the Hypocrites, weighted down by great leaden robes, walk eternally round

and round a narrow track. The robes are brilliantly gilded on the outside
and are shaped like a monk's habit, for the hypocrite's outward appearance
shines brightly and passes for holiness, but under that show lies the terrible
weight of his deceit which the soul must bear through all eternity.

The Poets talk to Two Jovial Friars and come upon Caiaphas, the chief
sinner of that place. Caiaphas was the High Priest of the Jews who counseled the Pharisees to crucify Jesus in the name of public expedience. He
is punished by being himself crucified to the floor of Hell by three great
stakes, and in such a position that every passing sinner must walk upon
him. Thus he must suffer upon his own body the weight of all the world's
hypocrisy, as Christ suffered upon his body the pain of all the world's sins.

The Jovial Friars tell Virgil how he may climb from the pit, and Virgil
discovers that Malacoda lied to him about the bridges over the Sixth
Bolgia.

Silent, apart, and unattended we went
   as Minor Friars go when they walk abroad,
   one following the other. The incident
recalled the fable of the Mouse and the Frog
   that Aesop tells.[6] For compared attentively   5
   point by point, "pig" is no closer to "hog"
than the one case to the other. And as one thought
   springs from another, so the comparison
   gave birth to a new concern, at which I caught
my breath in fear. This thought ran through my mind: 10
   "These Fiends, through us, have been made ridiculous,
   and have suffered insult and injury of a kind
to make them smart. Unless we take good care—
   now rage is added to their natural spleen—
   they will hunt us down as greyhounds hunt the hare."   15
Already I felt my scalp grow tight with fear.
   I was staring back in terror as I said:
   "Master, unless we find concealment here
and soon, I dread the rage of the Fiends: already
   they are yelping on our trail: I imagine them   20
   so vividly I can hear them now." And he:
"Were I a pane of leaded glass,[7] I could not
   summon your outward look more instantly
   into myself, than I do your inner thought.
Your fears were mixed already with my own   25
   with the same suggestion and the same dark look;
   so that of both I form one resolution:
the right bank may be sloping: in that case
   we may find some way down to the next pit

6. The fable was not by Aesop, but was attributed to him in Dante's time: A mouse comes to a body of
water and wonders how to cross. A frog, thinking to drown the mouse, offers to ferry him, but the mouse
is afraid he will fall off. The frog thereupon suggests that the mouse tie himself to one of the frog's feet.
In this way they start across, but in the middle the frog dives from under the mouse, who struggles
desperately to stay afloat while the frog tries to pull him under. A hawk sees the mouse struggling and
swoops down and seizes him; but since the frog is tied to the mouse, it too is carried away, and so both
of them are devoured. The mouse would be the Navarrese Grafter. The frog would be the two fiends,
Grizzly and Hellken. By seeking to harm the Navarrese they came to grief themselves.   7. A mirror.
Mirrors were backed with lead in Dante's time.

and so escape from the imagined chase."   30
He had not finished answering me thus
    when, not far off, their giant wings outspread,
    I saw the Fiends come charging after us.
Seizing me instantly in his arms, my Guide—
    like a mother wakened by a midnight noise   35
    to find a wall of flame at her bedside
(who takes her child and runs, and more concerned
    for him than for herself, does not pause even
    to throw a wrap about her) raised me, turned,
and down the rugged bank from the high summit   40
    flung himself down supine onto the slope
    which walls the upper side of the next pit.
Water that turns the great wheel of a land-mill
    never ran faster through the end of a sluice
    at the point nearest the paddles[8]—as down that hill   45
my Guide and Master bore me on his breast,
    as if I were not a companion, but a son.
    And the soles of his feet had hardly come to rest
on the bed of the depth below, when on the height
    we had just left, the Fiends beat their great wings.   50
    But now they gave my Guide no cause for fright;
for the Providence that gave them the fifth pit
    to govern as the ministers of Its will,
    takes from their souls the power of leaving it.
About us now in the depth of the pit we found   55
    a painted people, weary and defeated.
    Slowly, in pain, they paced it round and round.
All wore great cloaks cut to as ample a size
    as those worn by the Benedictines of Cluny.[9]
    The enormous hoods were drawn over their eyes.   60
The outside is all dazzle, golden and fair;
    the inside, lead, so heavy that Frederick's capes,[1]
    compared to these, would seem as light as air.
O weary mantle for eternity!
    We turned to the left again along their course,   65
    listening to their moans of misery,
but they moved so slowly down that barren strip,
    tired by their burden, that our company
    was changed at every movement of the hip.
And walking thus, I said: "As we go on,   70
    may it please you to look about among these people
    for any whose name or history may be known."
And one who understood Tuscan cried to us there
    as we hurried past: "I pray you check your speed.
    you who run so fast through the sick air: 75
it may be I am one who will fit your case."

---

8. The sharp drop of the sluice makes the water run faster at the point at which it hits the wheel. *Land-mill:* As distinguished from the floating mills common in Dante's time and up to the advent of the steam engine. These were built on rafts that were anchored in the swift-flowing rivers of Northern Italy. 9. The habit of these monks was especially ample and elegant. St. Bernard once wrote ironically to a nephew who had entered this monastery: "If length of sleeves and amplitude of hood made for holiness, what could hold me back from following [your lead]."   1. Frederick II executed persons found guilty of treason by fastening them into a sort of leaden shell. The doomed man was then placed in a cauldron over a fire and the lead was melted around him.

And at his words my Master turned and said:
"Wait now, then go with him at his own pace."
I waited there, and saw along that track
   two souls who seemed in haste to be with me;   80
   but the narrow way and their burden held them back.
When they had reached me down that narrow way
   they stared at me in silence and amazement,
   then turned to one another. I heard one say:
"This one seems, by the motion of his throat,   85
   to be alive; and if they are dead, how is it
   they are allowed to shed the leaden coat?"
And then to me: "O Tuscan, come so far
   to the college of the sorry hypocrites,
   do not disdain to tell us who you are."   90
And I: "I was born and raised a Florentine
   on the green and lovely banks of Arno's waters,
   I go with the body that was always mine.
But who are *you*, who sighing as you go
   distill in floods of tears that drown your cheeks?   95
   What punishment is this that glitters so?"
"These burnished robes are of thick lead," said one,
   "and are hung on us like counterweights, so heavy
   that we, their weary fulcrums, creak and groan.
Jovial Friars[2] and Bolognese were we.   100
   We were chosen jointly by your Florentines
   to keep the peace,[3] an office usually
held by a single man; near the Gardingo[4]
   one still may see the sort of peace we kept.
   I was called Catalano, he, Loderingo."   105
I began: "O Friars, your evil . . ." —and then I saw
   a figure crucified upon the ground[5]
   by three great stakes, and I fell still in awe.
When he saw me there, he began to puff great sighs
   into his beard, convulsing all his body;   110
   and Friar Catalano, following my eyes,
said to me: "That one nailed across the road
   counselled the Pharisees that it was fitting
   one man be tortured for the public good.
Naked he lies fixed there, as you see,   115
   in the path of all who pass; there he must feel
   the weight of all through all eternity.

2. A nickname given to the military monks of the order of the Glorious Virgin Mary founded at Bologna in 1261. Their original aim was to serve as peacemakers, enforcers of order, and protectors of the weak, but their observance of their rules became so scandalously lax, and their management of worldly affairs so self-seeking, that the order was disbanded by Papal decree.   3. Catalano dei Malavolti (ca. 1210–1285), a Guelph, and Loderingo degli Andolo (ca. 1210–1293), a Ghibelline, were both Bolognese and, as brothers of the Jovial Friars, both had served as *podestà* (the chief officer charged with keeping the peace) of many cities for varying terms. In 1266 they were jointly appointed to the office of *podestà* of Florence on the theory that a bipartisan administration by men of God would bring peace to the city. Their tenure of office was marked by great violence, however; and they were forced to leave in a matter of months. Modern scholarship has established the fact that they served as instruments of Clement IV's policy in Florence, working at his orders to overthrow the Ghibellines under the guise of an impartial administration.   4. The site of the palace of the Ghibelline family degli Uberti. In the riots resulting from the maladministration of the two Jovial Friars, the Ghibellines were forced out of the city and the Uberti palace was razed.   5. Caiaphas. His words were: "It is expedient that one man shall die for the people and that the whole nation perish not." (John xi, 50).

His father-in-law[6] and the others of the Council
   which was a seed of wrath to all the Jews,
   are similarly staked for the same evil."   120
Then I saw Virgil marvel[7] for a while
   over that soul so ignominiously
   stretched on the cross in Hell's eternal exile.
Then, turning, he asked the Friar: "If your law permit,
   can you tell us if somewhere along the right   125
   there is some gap in the stone wall of the pit
through which we two may climb to the next brink
   without the need of summoning the Black Angels
   and forcing them to raise us from this sink?"
He: "Nearer than you hope, there is a bridge   130
   that runs from the great circle of the scarp
   and crosses every ditch from ridge to ridge,
except that in this it is broken; but with care
   you can mount the ruins which lie along the slope
   and make a heap on the bottom." My Guide stood there   135
motionless for a while with a dark look.
   At last he said: "He[8] lied about this business
   who spears the sinners yonder with his hook."
And the Friar: "Once at Bologna I heard the wise
   discussing the Devil's sins; among them I heard   140
   that he is a liar and the father of lies."
When the sinner had finished speaking, I saw the face
   of my sweet Master darken a bit with anger:
   he set off at a great stride from that place,
and I turned from that weighted hypocrite   145
to follow in the prints of his dear feet.

CANTO XXIV

Circle Eight: Bolgia Seven   The Thieves

   The Poets climb the right bank laboriously, cross the bridge of the Seventh Bolgia and descend the far bank to observe the Thieves. They find the pit full of monstrous reptiles who curl themselves about the sinners like living coils of rope, binding each sinner's hands behind his back, and knotting themselves through the loins. Other reptiles dart about the place, and the Poets see one of them fly through the air and pierce the jugular vein of one sinner who immediately bursts into flames until only ashes remain. From the ashes the sinner reforms painfully.

   These are Dante's first observations of the Thieves and will be carried further in the next Canto, but the first allegorical retribution is immediately apparent. Thievery is reptilian in its secrecy; therefore it is punished by reptiles. The hands of the thieves are the agents of their crimes; therefore they are bound forever. And as the thief destroys his fellow men by making their substance disappear, so is he painfully destroyed and made to disappear, not once but over and over again.

---

6. Annas, father-in-law of Caiaphas, was the first before whom Jesus was led upon his arrest. (John xviii, 13). He had Jesus bound and delivered to Caiaphas.   7. Caiaphas had not been there on Virgil's first descent into Hell.   8. Malacoda.

The sinner who has risen from his own ashes reluctantly identifies himself as Vanni Fucci. He tells his story, and to revenge himself for having been forced to reveal his identity he utters a dark prophecy against Dante.

In the turning season of the youthful year,
    when the sun is warming his rays beneath Aquarius[9]
    and the days and nights already begin to near
their perfect balance; the hoar-frost copies then
    the image of his white sister on the ground,   5
    but the first sun wipes away the work of his pen.[1]
The peasants who lack fodder then arise
    and look about and see the fields all white,
    and hear their lambs bleat; then they smite their thighs,[2]
go back into the house, walk here and there,   10
    pacing, fretting, wondering what to do,
    then come out doors again, and there, despair
falls from them when they see how the earth's face
    has changed in so little time, and they take their staffs
    and drive their lambs to feed—so in that place   15
when I saw my Guide and Master's eyebrows lower,
    my spirits fell and I was sorely vexed;
    and as quickly came the plaster to the sore:
for when he had reached the ruined bridge, he stood
    and turned on me that sweet and open look   20
    with which he had greeted me in the dark wood.
When he had paused and studied carefully
    the heap of stones, he seemed to reach some plan,
    for he turned and opened his arms and lifted me.
Like one who works and calculates ahead,   25
    and is always ready for what happens next—
    so, raising me above that dismal bed
to the top of one great slab of the fallen slate,
    he chose another saying: "Climb here, but first
    test it to see if it will hold your weight."   30
It was no climb for a lead-hung hypocrite:
    for scarcely we—he light and I assisted—
    could crawl handhold by handhold from the pit;
and were it not that the bank along this side
    was lower than the one down which we had slid,   35
    I at least—I will not speak for my Guide—
would have turned back. But as all of the vast rim
    of Malebolge leans toward the lowest well,
    so each succeeding valley and each brim
is lower than the last. We climbed the face   40
    and arrived by great exertion to the point
    where the last rock had fallen from its place.
My lungs were pumping as if they could not stop;
    I thought I could not go on, and I sat exhausted

---

9. The zodiacal sign for the period from January 21 to February 21. The sun is moving north then to approach the vernal equinox (March 21), at which point the days and the nights are equal. The Italian spring comes early, and the first warm days would normally occur under Aquarius. 1. The hoar-frost looks like snow but melts away as soon as the sun strikes it. 2. A common Italian gesture of vexation, about equivalent to smiting the forehead with the palm of the hand.

the instant I had clambered to the top.   45
"Up on your feet! This is no time to tire!"
    my Master cried. "The man who lies asleep
    will never waken fame, and his desire
and all his life drift past him like a dream,
    and the traces of his memory fade from time   50
    like smoke in air, or ripples on a stream.
Now, therefore, rise. Control your breath, and call
    upon the strength of soul that wins all battles
    unless it sink in the gross body's fall.
There is a longer ladder yet to climb: 55
    this much is not enough. If you understand me,
    show that you mean to profit from your time."
I rose and made my breath appear more steady
    than it really was, and I replied: "Lead on
    as it pleases you to go: I am strong and ready."   60
We picked our way up the cliff, a painful climb,[3]
    for it was narrower, steeper, and more jagged
    than any we had crossed up to that time.
I moved along, talking to hide my faintness,
    when a voice that seemed unable to form words   65
    rose from the depths of the next chasm's darkness.
I do not know what it said, though by then the Sage
    had led me to the top of the next arch;
    but the speaker seemed in a tremendous rage.
I was bending over the brim, but living eyes   70
    could not plumb to the bottom of that dark;
    therefore I said, "Master, let me advise
that we cross over and climb down the wall:
    for just as I hear the voice without understanding,
    so I look down and make out nothing at all."   75
"I make no other answer than the act,
    the Master said: "the only fit reply
    to a fit request is silence and the fact."
So we moved down the bridge to the stone pier
    that shores the end of the arch on the eighth bank,   80
    and there I saw the chasm's depths made clear;
and there great coils of serpents met my sight,
    so hideous a mass that even now
    the memory makes my blood run cold with fright.
Let Libya[4] boast no longer, for though its sands   85
    breed chelidrids, jaculi, and phareans,
    cenchriads, and two-headed amphisbands,
it never bred such a variety
    of vipers, no, not with all Ethiopia
    and all the lands that lie by the Red Sea.   90
Amid that swarm, naked and without hope,

3. The "top" Dante mentions in line 45 must obviously have been the top of the fallen stone that was
once the bridge. There remains the difficult climb up the remainder of the cliff.   4. *Libya . . . Ethiopia . . . lands that lie by the Red Sea:* The desert areas of the Mediterranean shores. Lucan's *Pharsalia*
describes the assortment of monsters listed here by Dante. I have rendered their names from Latin to
English jabberwocky to avoid problems of pronunciation. In Lucan *chelydri* make their trails smoke and
burn, they are amphibious; *jaculi* fly through the air like darts piercing what they hit; *pharese* plow the
ground with their tails; *cenchri* waver from side to side when they move; and *amphisboenae* have a head
at each end.

people ran terrified, not even dreaming
   of a hole to hide in, or of heliotrope.[5]
Their hands were bound behind by coils of serpents
   which thrust their heads and tails between the loins   95
   and bunched in front, a mass of knotted torments.
One of the damned came racing round a boulder,
   and as he passed us, a great snake shot up
   and bit him where the neck joins with the shoulder.
No mortal pen—however fast it flash   100
   over the page—could write down o or i
   as quickly as he flamed and fell in ash;
and when he was dissolved into a heap
   upon the ground, the dust rose of itself
   and immediately resumed its former shape.   105
Precisely so, philosophers declare,
   the Phoenix dies and then is born again
   when it approaches its five hundredth year.[6]
It lives on tears of balsam and of incense;
   in all its life it eats no herb or grain,   110
   and nard and precious myrrh sweeten its cerements.
And as a person fallen in a fit,
   possessed by a Demon or some other seizure
   that fetters him without his knowing it,
struggles up to his feet and blinks his eyes   115
   (still stupefied by the great agony
   he has just passed), and, looking round him, sighs—
such was the sinner when at last he rose.
   O Power of God! How dreadful is Thy will
   which in its vengeance rains such fearful blows.   120
Then my Guide asked him who he was. And he
   answered reluctantly: "Not long ago
   I rained into this gullet from Tuscany.
I am Vanni Fucci,[7] the beast. A mule among men,
   I chose the bestial life above the human.   125
   Savage Pistoia was my fitting den."
And I to my Guide: "Detain him a bit longer
   and ask what crime it was that sent him here;
   I knew him as a man of blood and anger."[8]
The sinner, hearing me, seemed discomforted,   130
   but he turned and fixed his eyes upon my face
   with a look of dismal shame; at length he said:
"That you have found me out among the strife
   and misery of this place, grieves my heart more
   than did the day that cut me from my life.   135
But I am forced to answer truthfully:

5. Not the flower, but the bloodstone, a spotted chalcedony. It was believed to make the wearer invisible.   6. The fabulous Phoenix of Arabia was the only one of its kind in the world. Every five hundred years it built a nest of spices and incense which took fire from the heat of the sun and the beating of the Phoenix's wings. The Phoenix was thereupon cremated and was then reborn from its ashes. 7. The bastard son of Fuccio de Lazzeri, a nobleman (Black) of Pistoia. In 1293 with two accomplices he stole the treasure of San Jacopo in the Duomo of San Zeno. Others were accused, and one man spent a year in jail on this charge before the guilty persons were discovered. Vanni Fucci had escaped from Pistoia by then, but his accomplices were convicted.   8. Dante (the traveler within the narrative rather than Dante the author) claims that he did not know Fucci was a thief, but only that he was a man of blood and violence. He should therefore be punished in the Seventh Circle.

I am put down so low because it was I
  who stole the treasure from the Sacristy,
for which others once were blamed. But that you may
  find less to gloat about if you escape here,   140
  prick up your ears and listen to what I say:
First Pistoia is emptied of the Black,
  then Florence changes her party and her laws.
  From Valdimagra the God of War brings back
a fiery vapor wrapped in turbid air: 145
  then in a storm of battle at Piceno
  the vapor breaks apart the mist, and there
every White shall feel his wounds anew.
And I have told you this that it may grieve you."[9]

CANTO XXV

Circle Eight: Bolgia Seven   The Thieves

Vanni's rage mounts to the point where he hurls an ultimate obscenity
at God, and the serpents immediately swarm over him, driving him off in
great pain. The Centaur, Cacus, his back covered with serpents and a fire-
eating dragon, also gives chase to punish the wretch.

  Dante then meets Five Noble Thieves of Florence and sees the further
retribution visited upon the sinners. Some of the thieves appear first in
human form, others as reptiles. All but one of them suffer a painful transformation before Dante's eyes. Agnello appears in human form and is
merged with Cianfa, who appears as a six-legged lizard. Buoso appears as
a man and changes form with Francesco, who first appears as a tiny reptile.
Only Puccio Sciancato remains unchanged, though we are made to
understand that his turn will come.

  For endless and painful transformation is the final state of the thieves.
In life they took the substance of others, transforming it into their own. So
in Hell their very bodies are constantly being taken from them, and they
are left to steal back a human form from some other sinner. Thus they
waver constantly between man and reptile, and no sinner knows what to
call his own.

When he had finished, the thief—to his disgrace—
  raised his hands with both fists making figs,[1]
  and cried: "Here, God! I throw them in your face!"
Thereat the snakes became my friends, for one
  coiled itself about the wretch's neck   5
  as if it were saying: "You shall not go on!"
and another tied his arms behind him again,

9. In May of 1301 the Whites of Florence joined with the Whites of Pistoia to expel the Pistoian Blacks
and destroy their houses. The ejected Blacks fled to Florence and joined forces with the Florentine
Blacks. On November 1st of the same year, Charles of Valois took Florence and helped the Blacks drive
out the Whites. Piceno was the scene of a battle in which the Blacks of Florence and Lucca combined
in 1302 to capture Serravalle, a White strong point near Pistoia.   1. An obscene gesture made by
closing the hand into a fist with the thumb protruding between the first and second fingers. The fig is
an ancient symbol for the vulva, and the protruding thumb is an obvious phallic symbol. The gesture is
still current in Italy and has lost none of its obscene significance since Dante's time.

knotting its head and tail between his loins
so tight he could not move a finger in pain.
Pistoia! Pistoia! why have you not decreed   10
to turn yourself to ashes and end your days,
rather than spread the evil of your seed!
In all of Hell's corrupt and sunken halls
I found no shade so arrogant toward God,
not even him who fell from the Theban walls!   15
Without another word, he fled; and there
I saw a furious Centaur race up, roaring:
"Where is the insolent blasphemer? Where?"
I do not think as many serpents swarm
in all the Maremma as he bore on his back   20
from the haunch to the first sign of our human form.
Upon his shoulders, just behind his head
a snorting dragon whose hot breath set fire
to all it touched, lay with its wings outspread.
My Guide said: "That is Cacus.[2] Time and again   25
in the shadow of Mount Aventine he made
a lake of blood upon the Roman plain.
He does not go with his kin by the blood-red fosse
because of the cunning fraud with which he stole
the cattle of Hercules. And thus it was   30
his thieving stopped, for Hercules found his den
and gave him perhaps a hundred blows with his club,
and of them he did not feel the first ten."
Meanwhile, the Centaur passed along his way,
and three wraiths came. Neither my Guide nor I   35
knew they were there until we heard them say:
"You there—who are you?" There our talk fell still
and we turned to stare at them. I did not know them,
but by chance it happened, as it often will,
one named another. "Where is Cianfa?" he cried;   40
"Why has he fallen back?" I placed a finger
across my lips as a signal to my Guide.
Reader, should you doubt what next I tell,
it will be no wonder, for though I saw it happen,
I can scarce believe it possible, even in Hell.   45
For suddenly, as I watched, I saw a lizard
come darting forward on six great taloned feet
and fasten itself to a sinner from crotch to gizzard.
Its middle feet sank in the sweat and grime
of the wretch's paunch, its forefeet clamped his arms,   50
its teeth bit through both cheeks. At the same time
its hind feet fastened on the sinner's thighs:
its tail thrust through his legs and closed its coil
over his loins. I saw it with my own eyes!
No ivy ever grew about a tree   55

---

2. The son of Vulcan. He lived in a cave at the foot of Mount Aventine, from which he raided the
herds of the cattle of Hercules, which pastured on the Roman plain. Hercules clubbed him to death for
his thievery, beating him in rage long after he was dead. Cacus is condemned to the lower pit for his
greater crime, instead of guarding Phlegethon with his brother centaurs. Virgil, however, did not
describe him as a centaur (V. *Aeneid* VIII, 193–267). Dante's interpretation of him is probably based on
the fact that Virgil referred to him as "half-human."

as tightly as that monster wove itself
   limb by limb about the sinner's body;
they fused like hot wax, and their colors ran
   together until neither wretch nor monster
   appeared what he had been when he began: 60
just so, before the running edge of the heat
   on a burning page, a brown discoloration
   changes to black as the white dies from the sheet.
The other two cried out as they looked on:
   "Alas! Alas! Agnello, how you change!   65
   Already you are neither two nor one!"
The two heads had already blurred and blended;
   now two new semblances appeared and faded,
   one face where neither face began nor ended.
From the four upper limbs of man and beast   70
   two arms were made, then members never seen
   grew from the thighs and legs, belly and breast.
Their former likenesses mottled and sank
   to something that was both of them and neither;
   and so transformed, it slowly left our bank.   75
As lizards at high noon of a hot day
   dart out from hedge to hedge, from shade to shade,
   and flash like lightning when they cross the way,
so toward the bowels of the other two,
   shot a small monster; livid, furious,   80
   and black as a pepper corn. Its lunge bit through
that part[3] of one of them from which man receives
   his earliest nourishment; then it fell back
   and lay sprawled out in front of the two thieves.
Its victim stared at it but did not speak: 85
   indeed, he stood there like a post, and yawned
   as if lack of sleep, or a fever, had left him weak.
The reptile stared at him, he at the reptile;
   from the wound of one and from the other's mouth
   two smokes poured out and mingled, dark and vile.   90
Now let Lucan be still with his history
   of poor Sabellus and Nassidius,[4]
   and wait to hear what next appeared to me.
Of Cadmus and Arethusa be Ovid silent.
   I have no need to envy him those verses   95
   where he makes one a fountain, and one a serpent:
for he never transformed two beings face to face
   in such a way that both their natures yielded
   their elements each to each, as in this case.
Responding sympathetically to each other,   100
   the reptile cleft his tail into a fork,
   and the wounded sinner drew his feet together.
The sinner's legs and thighs began to join:
   they grew together so, that soon no trace

---

3. The navel.   4. In *Pharsalia* (IX, 761 ff.) Lucan relates how Sabellus and Nassidius, two soldiers of the army Cato led across the Libyan desert, were bitten by monsters. Sabellus melted into a puddle and Nassidius swelled until he popped his coat of mail. In his *Metamorphoses*, Ovid wrote how Cadmus was changed into a serpent (IV, 562–603) and how Arethusa was changed into a fountain (V, 572–661).

of juncture could be seen from toe to loin.   105
Point by point the reptile's cloven tail
  grew to the form of what the sinner lost;
  one skin began to soften, one to scale.
The armpits swallowed the arms, and the short shank
  of the reptile's forefeet simultaneously   110
  lengthened by as much as the man's arms shrank.
Its hind feet twisted round themselves and grew
  the member man conceals; meanwhile the wretch
  from his one member generated two.
The smoke swelled up about them all the while: 115
  it tanned one skin and bleached the other; it stripped
  the hair from the man and grew it on the reptile.
While one fell to his belly, the other rose
  without once shifting the locked evil eyes
  below which they changed snouts as they changed pose.   120
The face of the standing one drew up and in
  toward the temples, and from the excess matter
  that gathered there, ears grew from the smooth skin;
while of the matter left below the eyes
  the excess became a nose, at the same time   125
  forming the lips to an appropriate size.
Here the face of the prostrate felon slips,
  sharpens into a snout, and withdraws its ears
  as a snail pulls in its horns. Between its lips
the tongue, once formed for speech, thrusts out a fork;   130
  the forked tongue of the other heals and draws
  into his mouth. The smoke has done its work.
The soul that had become a beast went flitting
  and hissing over the stones, and after it
  the other walked along talking and spitting.   135
Then turning his new shoulders, said to the one
  that still remained: "It is Buoso's turn to go
  crawling along this road as I have done."
Thus did the ballast of the seventh hold
  shift and reshift; and may the strangeness of it   140
  excuse my pen if the tale is strangely told.
And though all this confused me, they did not flee
  so cunningly but what I was aware
  that it was Puccio Sciancato alone of the three
that first appeared, who kept his old form still.   145
The other was he for whom you weep, Gaville.[5]

CANTO XXVI

Circle Eight: Bolgia Eight   The Evil Counselors

Dante turns from the Thieves toward the Evil Counselors of the next
Bolgia, and between the two he addresses a passionate lament to Florence

---

5. Francesco dei Cavalcanti. He was killed by the people of Gaville (a village in the Valley of the
Arno). His kin rallied immediately to avenge his death, and many of the townspeople of Gaville were
killed in the resulting feud.

prophesying the griefs that will befall her from these two sins. At the purported time of the Vision, it will be recalled, Dante was a Chief Magistrate of Florence and was forced into exile by men he had reason to consider both thieves and evil counselors. He seems prompted, in fact, to say much more on this score, but he restrains himself when he comes in sight of the sinners of the next Bolgia, for they are a moral symbolism, all men of gift who abused their genius, perverting it to wiles and stratagems. Seeing them in Hell he knows his must be another road: his way shall not be by deception.

So the Poets move on and Dante observes the Eighth Bolgia in detail. Here the Evil Counselors move about endlessly, hidden from view inside great flames. Their sin was to abuse the gifts of the Almighty, to steal his virtues for low purposes. And as they stole from God in their lives and worked by hidden ways, so are they stolen from sight and hidden in the great flames which are their own guilty consciences. And as, in most instances at least, they sinned by glibness of tongue, so are the flames made into a fiery travesty of tongues.

Among the others, the Poets see a great doubleheaded flame, and discover that Ulysses and Diomede are punished together within it. Virgil addresses the flame, and through its wavering tongue Ulysses narrates an unforgettable tale of his last voyage and death.

Joy to you, Florence, that your banners swell,
    beating their proud wings over land and sea,
    and that your name expands through all of Hell!
Among the thieves I found five who had been
    your citizens, to my shame; nor yet shall you   5
    mount to great honor peopling such a den!
But if the truth is dreamed of toward the morning,[6]
    you soon shall feel what Prato[7] and the others
    wish for you. And were that day of mourning
already come it would not be too soon.   10
    So may it come, since it must! for it will weigh
    more heavily on me as I pass my noon.
We left that place. My Guide climbed stone by stone
    the natural stair by which we had descended
    and drew me after him. So we passed on,   15
and going our lonely way through that dead land
    among the crags and crevices of the cliff,
    the foot could make no way without the hand.
I mourned among those rocks, and I mourn again
    when memory returns to what I saw: 20
    and more than usually I curb the strain
of my genius, lest it stray from Virtue's course;

6. A semi-proverbial expression. It was a common belief that those dreams that occur just before waking foretell the future. "Morning" here would equal both "the rude awakening" and the potential "dawn of a new day."   7. Not the neighboring town (which was on good terms with Florence) but Cardinal Niccolò da Prato, papal legate from Benedict XI to Florence. In 1304 he tried to reconcile the warring factions, but found that neither side would accept mediation. Since none would be blessed, he cursed all impartially and laid the city under an interdict (i.e., forbade the offering of the sacraments). Shortly after this rejection by the Church, a bridge collapsed in Florence, and later a great fire broke out. Both disasters cost many lives, and both were promptly attributed to the Papal curse.

so if some star, or a better thing, grant me merit,
may I not find the gift cause for remorse.
As many fireflies as the peasant sees   25
  when he rests on a hill and looks into the valley
  (where he tills or gathers grapes or prunes his trees)
in that sweet season when the face of him
  who lights the world rides north, and at the hour
  when the fly yields to the gnat and the air grows dim—   30
such myriads of flames I saw shine through
  the gloom of the eighth abyss when I arrived
  at the rim from which its bed comes into view.
As he the bears avenged[8] so fearfully
  beheld Elijah's chariot depart—   35
  the horses rise toward heaven—but could not see
more than the flame, a cloudlet in the sky,
  once it had risen—so within the fosse
  only those flames, forever passing by
were visible, ahead, to right, to left;   40
  for though each steals a sinner's soul from view
  not one among them leaves a trace of the theft.
I stood on the bridge, and leaned out from the edge;
  so far, that but for a jut of rock I held to
  I should have been sent hurtling from the ledge   45
without being pushed. And seeing me so intent,
  my Guide said: "There are souls within those flames;
  each sinner swathes himself in his own torment."
"Master," I said, "your words make me more sure,
  but I had seen already that it was so   50
  and meant to ask what spirit must endure
the pains of that great flame which splits away
  in two great horns, as if it rose from the pyre
  where Eteocles and Polynices lay?"[9]
He answered me: "Forever round this path   55
  Ulysses and Diomede[1] move in such dress,
  united in pain as once they were in wrath;
there they lament the ambush of the Horse
  which was the door through which the noble seed
  of the Romans issued from its holy source;   60
there they mourn that for Achilles slain

---

8. Elisha saw Elijah transported to Heaven in a fiery chariot. Later he was mocked by some children, who called out tauntingly that he should "Go up" as Elijah had. Elisha cursed the children in the name of the Lord, and bears came suddenly upon the children and devoured them. (2 Kings ii, 11–24.)
9. Eteocles and Polynices, sons of Oedipus, succeeded jointly to the throne of Thebes, and came to an agreement whereby each one would rule separately for a year at a time. Eteocles ruled the first year and when he refused to surrender the throne at the appointed time, Polynices led the Seven against Thebes in a bloody war. In single combat the two brothers killed one another. Statius (*Thebaid* XII, 429 ff.) wrote that their mutual hatred was so great that when they were placed on the same funeral pyre the very flame of their burning drew apart in two great raging horns.   1. They suffer here for their joint guilt in counseling and carrying out many stratagems which Dante considered evil, though a narrator who was less passionately a partisan of the Trojans might have thought their actions justifiable methods of warfare. . . .
      Their first sin was the stratagem of the Wooden Horse, as a result of which Troy fell and Aeneas went forth to found the Roman line. The second evil occurred at Scyros. There Ulysses discovered Achilles in female disguise, hidden by his mother, Thetis, so that he would not be taken off to the war. Deidamia was in love with Achilles and had borne him a son. When Ulysses persuaded her lover to sail for Troy, she died of grief. The third count is Ulysses' theft of the sacred statue of Pallas from the Palladium. Upon the statue, it was believed, depended the fate of Troy. Its theft, therefore, would result in Troy's downfall.

sweet Deidamia weeps even in death;
  there they recall the Palladium in their pain."
"Master," I cried, "I pray you and repray
  till my prayer becomes a thousand—if these souls   65
  can still speak from the fire, oh let me stay
until the flame draws near! Do not deny me:
  You see how fervently I long for it!"
  And he to me: "Since what you ask is worthy,
it shall be. But be still and let me speak;   70
  for I know your mind already, and they perhaps
  might scorn your manner of speaking, since they were Greek."
And when the flame had come where time and place
  seemed fitting to my Guide, I heard him say
  these words to it: "O you two souls who pace   75
together in one flame!—if my days above
  won favor in your eyes, if I have earned
  however much or little of your love
in writing my High Verses, do not pass by,
  but let one of you[2] be pleased to tell where he,   80
  having disappeared from the known world, went to die."
As if it fought the wind, the greater prong
  of the ancient flame began to quiver and hum;
  then moving its tip as if it were the tongue
that spoke, gave out a voice above the roar.   85
  "When I left Circe,"[3] it said, "who more than a year
  detained me near Gaëta long before
Aeneas came and gave the place that name,
  not fondness for my son, nor reverence
  for my aged father, nor Penelope's[4] claim   90
to the joys of love, could drive out of my mind
  the lust to experience the far-flung world
  and the failings and felicities of mankind.
I put out on the high and open sea
  with a single ship and only those few souls   95
  who stayed true when the rest deserted me.
As far as Morocco and as far as Spain
  I saw both shores;[5] and I saw Sardinia
  and the other islands of the open main.
I and my men were stiff and slow with age   100
  when we sailed at last into the narrow pass[6]
  where, warning all men back from further voyage,
Hercules' Pillars rose upon our sight.
  Already I had left Ceuta on the left;
  Seville[7] now sank behind me on the right.   105
'Shipmates,' I said, 'who through a hundred thousand
  perils have reached the West, do not deny

2. Ulysses. He is the figure in the larger horn of the flame (which symbolizes that his guilt, as leader, is greater than that of Diomede). His memorable account of his last voyage and death is purely Dante's invention.   3. She changed Ulysses' men to swine and kept him a prisoner, though with rather exceptional accommodations. *Gaëta*: Southeastern Italian coastal town. According to Virgil (*Aeneid* VII, 1 ff.) it was earlier named Caieta by Aeneas in honor of his aged nurse.   4. Ulysses' wife.   5. Of the Mediterranean.   6. The Straits of Gilbraltar, formerly called the Pillars of Hercules. They were presumed to be the Western limit beyond which no man could navigate.   7. In Dante's time this was the name given to the general region of Spain. Having passed through the Straits, the men are now in the Atlantic. *Ceuta*: In Africa, opposite Gibraltar.

to the brief remaining watch our senses stand
experience of the world beyond the sun.
  Greeks! You were not born to live like brutes,   110
  but to press on toward manhood and recognition!
With this brief exhortation I made my crew
  so eager for the voyage I could hardly
  have held them back from it when I was through;
and turning our stern toward morning, our bow toward night,   115
  we bore southwest out of the world of man;
  we made wings of our oars for our fool's flight.
That night we raised the other pole ahead
  with all its stars, and ours had so declined
  it did not rise out of its ocean bed.[8]   120
Five times since we had dipped our bending oars
  beyond the world, the light beneath the moon
  had waxed and waned, when dead upon our course
we sighted, dark in space, a peak so tall
  I doubted any man had seen the like.[9]   125
  Our cheers were hardly sounded, when a squall
broke hard upon our bow from the new land:
  three times it sucked the ship and the sea about
  as it pleased Another to order and command.
At the fourth, the poop rose and the bow went down   130
till the sea closed over us and the light was gone."

CANTO XXVII

Circle Eight: Bolgia Eight   The Evil Counselors

The double flame departs at a word from Virgil and behind it appears
another which contains the soul of Count Guido da Montefeltro, a Lord
of Romagna. He had overheard Virgil speaking Italian, and the entire
flame in which his soul is wrapped quivers with his eagerness to hear
recent news of his wartorn country. (As Farinata has already explained,
the spirits of the damned have prophetic powers, but lose all track of events
as they approach.)

Dante replies with a stately and tragic summary of how things stand in
the cities of Romagna. When he has finished, he asks Guido for his story,
and Guido recounts his life, and how Boniface VIII persuaded him to sin.

When it had finished speaking, the great flame
  stood tall and shook no more. Now, as it left us
  with the sweet Poet's license, another[1] came
along that track and our attention turned
  to the new flame: a strange and muffled roar   5
  rose from the single tip to which it burned.

---

8. They drove south across the equator, observed the southern stars, and found that the North Star had
sunk below the horizon.   9. Purgatory. They sight it after five months of passage. According to Dante's
geography, the Northern hemisphere is land and the Southern is all water except for the Mountain of
Purgatory which rises above the surface at a point directly opposite Jerusalem.   1. Guido da Montefeltro (1223–1298). As head of the Ghibellines of Romagna, he was reputed the wisest and cunningest
man in Italy.

As the Sicilian bull[2]—that brazen spit
  which bellowed first (and properly enough)
  with the lament of him whose file had tuned it—
was made to bellow by its victim's cries   10
  in such a way, that though it was of brass,
  it seemed itself to howl and agonize:
so lacking any way through or around
  the fire that sealed them in, the mournful words
  were changed into its language. When they found   15
their way up the tip, imparting to it
  the same vibration given them in their passage
  over the tongue of the concealed sad spirit,
we heard it say: "O you at whom I aim
  my voice, and who were speaking Lombard, saying: 20
  'Go now, I ask no more,'[3] just as I came—
though I may come a bit late to my turn,
  may it not annoy you to pause and speak a while:
  you see it does not annoy me—and I burn.
If you have fallen only recently   25
  to this blind world from that sweet Italy
  where I acquired my guilt, I pray you, tell me:
is there peace or war in Romagna? for on earth
  I too was of those hills between Urbino
  and the fold from which the Tiber springs to birth."[4]   30
I was still staring at it from the dim
  edge of the pit when my Guide nudged me, saying:
  "This one is Italian; *you* speak to him."
My answer was framed already; without pause
  I spoke these words to it: "O hidden soul,   35
  your sad Romagna is not and never was
without war in her tyrants' raging blood;
  but none flared openly when I left just now.
  Ravenna's fortunes stand as they have stood
these many years: Polenta's eagles brood   40
  over her walls, and their pinions cover Cervia.[5]
  The city that so valiantly withstood
the French, and raised a mountain of their dead,
  feels the Green Claws again.[6] Still in Verrucchio
  the Aged Mastiff and his Pup, who shed   45
Montagna's blood, raven in their old ranges.[7]
  The cities of Lamone and Santerno

2. In the sixth century B.C. Perillus of Athens constructed for Phalaris, Tyrant of Sicily, a metal bull to be used as an instrument of torture. When victims were placed inside it and roasted to death, their screams passed through certain tuned pipes and emerged as a burlesque bellowing of the bull. Phalaris accepted delivery and showed his gratitude by appointing the inventor the bull's first victim. Later Phalaris was overthrown, and he, too, took his turn inside the bull.   3. These are the words with which Virgil dismisses Ulysses and Diomede, his "license."   4. Romagna is the district that runs south from the Po along the east side of the Apennines. Urbino is due east of Florence and roughly south of Rimini. Between Urbino and Florence rise the Coronaro Mountains which contain the headwaters of the Tiber.   5. In 1300 Ravenna was ruled by Guido Vecchio da Polenta, father of Francesca da Rimini. His arms bore an eagle and his domain included the small city of Cervia about twelve miles south of Ravenna.   6. The city is Forlì. In 1282 Guido da Montefeltro defended Forlì from the French, but in 1300 it was under the despotic rule of Sinibaldo degli Ordelaffi, whose arms were a green lion.   7. Verrucchio was the castle of Malatesta and his son Malatestino, Lords of Rimini, whom Dante calls dogs for their cruelty. Montagna de' Parcitati, the leader of Rimini's Ghibellines, was captured by Malatesta in 1295 and murdered in captivity by Malatestino.

are led by the white den's Lion, he who changes
his politics with the compass.[8] And as the city
    the Savio washes[9] lies between plain and mountain,   50
    so it lives between freedom and tyranny.
Now, I beg you, let us know your name;
    do not be harder than one has been to you;
    so, too, you will preserve your earthly fame."
And when the flame had roared a while beneath   55
    the ledge on which we stood, it swayed its tip
    to and fro, and then gave forth this breath:
"If I believed that my reply were made
    to one who could ever climb to the world again,
    this flame would shake no more. But since no shade   60
ever returned—if what I am told is true—
    from this blind world into the living light,
    without fear of dishonor I answer you.
I was a man of arms: then took the rope
    of the Franciscans, hoping to make amends: 65
    and surely I should have won to all my hope
but for the Great Priest[1]—may he rot in Hell!—
    who brought me back to all my earlier sins;
    and how and why it happened I wish to tell
in my own words: while I was still encased   70
    in the pulp and bone my mother bore, my deeds
    were not of the lion but of the fox: I raced
through tangled ways; all wiles were mine from birth,
    and I won to such advantage with my arts
    that rumor of me reached the ends of the earth.   75
But when I saw before me all the signs
    of the time of life that cautions every man
    to lower his sail and gather in his lines,
that which had pleased me once, troubled my spirit,
    and penitent and confessed, I became a monk.   80
    Alas! What joy I might have had of it!
It was then the Prince of the New Pharisees[2] drew
    his sword and marched upon the Lateran—
    and not against the Saracen or the Jew,
for every man that stood against his hand   85
    was a Christian soul: not one had warred on Acre,
    nor been a trader in the Sultan's land.[3]
It was he abused his sacred vows and mine:
    his Office and the Cord I wore, which once
    made those it girded leaner. As Constantine   90

---

8. Maginardo de' Pagani (died 1302) ruled Faenza, on the River Lamone, and Imola, close by the
River Santerno. His arms were a blue lion on a white field (hence "the Lion from the white den"). He
supported the Ghibellines in the north, but the Guelphs in the south (Florence), changing his politics
according to the direction in which he was facing.   9. Cesena. It ruled itself for a number of years,
but was taken over by Malatestino in 1314. It lies between Forlì and Rimini.   1. Boniface VIII, so
called as Pope.   2. Also Boniface. *Marched upon the Lateran*: Boniface had had a long-standing feud
with the Colonna family. In 1297 the Colonna walled themselves in a castle twenty-five miles east of
Rome at Penestrino (now called Palestrina) in the Lateran. On Guido's advice the Pope offered a fair-
sounding amnesty which he had no intention of observing. When the Colonna accepted the terms and
left the castle, the Pope destroyed it, leaving the Colonna without a refuge.   3. It was the Saracens
who opposed the crusaders at Acre, the Jews who traded in the Sultan's land.

sent for Silvestro to cure his leprosy,[4]
    seeking him out among Soracte's cells;
    so this one from his great throne sent for me
to cure the fever of pride that burned his blood.
    He demanded my advice, and I kept silent   95
    for his words seemed drunken to me. So it stood
until he said: 'Your soul need fear no wound;
    I absolve your guilt beforehand; and now teach me
    how to smash Penestrino to the ground.
The Gates of Heaven, as you know, are mine   100
    to open and shut, for I hold the two Great Keys
    so easily let go by Celestine.'[5]
His weighty arguments led me to fear
    silence was worse than sin. Therefore, I said:
    'Holy Father, since you clean me here   105
of the guilt into which I fall, let it be done:
    long promise and short observance[6] is the road
    that leads to the sure triumph of your throne.'
Later, when I was dead, St. Francis came
    to claim my soul,[7] but one of the Black Angels   110
    said: 'Leave him. Do not wrong me. This one's name
went into my book the moment he resolved
    to give false counsel. Since then he has been mine,
    for who does not repent cannot be absolved;
nor can we admit the possibility   115
    of repenting a thing at the same time it is willed,
    for the two acts are contradictory.'
Miserable me! with what contrition
    I shuddered when he lifted me, saying: 'Perhaps
    you hadn't heard that I was a logician.'   120
He carried me to Minos: eight times round
    his scabby back the monster coiled his tail,
    then biting it in rage he pawed the ground
and cried: 'This one is for the thievish fire!'
    And, as you see, I am lost accordingly,   125
    grieving in heart as I go in this attire."
His story told, the flame began to toss
    and writhe its horn. And so it left, and we
    crossed over to the arch of the next fosse
where from the iron treasury of the Lord   130
the fee of wrath is paid the Sowers of Discord.[8]

---

4. In the persecutions of the Christians by the Emperor Constantine, Pope Sylvester I took refuge in the caves of Mount Soracte near Rome. (It is now called Santo Oreste.) Later, according to legend, Constantine was stricken by leprosy and sent for Sylvester, who cured him and converted him to Christianity, in return for which the Emperor was believed to have made the famous "Donation of Constantine." (See Canto XIX.)   5. Celestine V under the persuasion of Boniface abdicated the Papacy. (See Canto III notes.)   6. This is the advice upon which Boniface acted in trapping the Colonna with his hypocritical amnesty.   7. To gather in the soul of one of his monks. *Black Angel:* A devil. 8. I have taken liberties with these lines in the hope of achieving a reasonably tonic final couplet. The literal reading is: "In which the fee is paid to those who, sowing discord, acquire weight (of guilt and pain)."

CANTO XXVIII

Circle Eight: Bolgia Nine   The Sowers of Discord

The Poets come to the edge of the Ninth Bolgia and look down at a parade of hideously mutilated souls. These are the Sowers of Discord, and just as their sin was to rend asunder what God had meant to be united, so are they hacked and torn through all eternity by a great demon with a bloody sword. After each mutilation the souls are compelled to drag their broken bodies around the pit and to return to the demon, for in the course of the circuit their wounds knit in time to be inflicted anew. Thus is the law of retribution observed, each sinner suffering according to his degree.

Among them Dante distinguishes three classes with varying degrees of guilt within each class. First come the Sowers of Religious Discord. Mahomet is chief among them, and appears first, cleft from crotch to chin, with his internal organs dangling between his legs. His son-in-law, Ali, drags on ahead of him, cleft from topknot to chin. These reciprocal wounds symbolize Dante's judgment that, between them, these two sum up the total schism between Christianity and Mohammedanism. The revolting details of Mahomet's condition clearly imply Dante's opinon of that doctrine. Mahomet issues an ironic warning to another schismatic, Fra Dolcino.

Next come the Sowers of Political Discord, among them Pier da Medicina, the Tribune Curio, and Mosca dei Lamberti, each mutilated according to the nature of his sin.

Last of all is Bertrand de Born, Sower of Discord Between Kinsmen. He separated father from son, and for that offense carries his head separated from his body, holding it with one hand by the hair, and swinging it as if it were a lantern to light his dark and endless way. The image of Bertrand raising his head at arm's length in order that it might speak more clearly to the Poets on the ridge is one of the most memorable in the *Inferno*. For some reason that cannot be ascertained, Dante makes these sinners quite eager to be remembered in the world, despite the fact that many who lie above them in Hell were unwilling to be recognized.

Who could describe, even in words set free
   of metric and rhyme and a thousand times retold,
   the blood and wounds that now were shown to me!
At grief so deep the tongue must wag in vain;
   the language of our sense and memory   5
   lacks the vocabulary of such pain.
If one could gather all those who have stood
   through all of time on Puglia's[9] fateful soil
   and wept for the red running of their blood
in the war of the Trojans;[1] and in that long war   10
   which left so vast a spoil of golden rings,

9. I have used the modern name but some of the events Dante narrates took place in the ancient province of Apulia. The southeastern area of Italy is the scene of all the fighting Dante mentions in the following passage. It is certainly a bloody total of slaughter that Dante calls upon to illustrate his scene.
1. The Romans (descended from the Trojans) fought the native Samnites in a long series of raids and skirmishes from 343–290 B.C.

as we find written in Livy, who does not err;[2]
along with those whose bodies felt the wet
    and gaping wounds of Robert Guiscard's lances;[3]
    with all the rest whose bones are gathered yet   15
at Ceperano where every last Pugliese
    turned traitor;[4] and with those from Tagliacozzo
    where Alardo won without weapons[5] — if all these
were gathered, and one showed his limbs run through,
    another his lopped off, that could not equal   20
    the mutilations of the ninth pit's crew.
A wine tun when a stave or cant-bar starts
    does not split open as wide as one I saw
    split from his chin to the mouth with which man farts.
Between his legs all of his red guts hung   25
    with the heart, the lungs, the liver, the gall bladder,
    and the shriveled sac that passes shit to the bung.
I stood and stared at him from the stone shelf;
    he noticed me and opening his own breast
    with both hands cried: "See how I rip myself!   30
See how Mahomet's mangled and split open!
    Ahead of me walks Ali[6] in his tears,
    his head cleft from the top-knot to the chin.
And all the other souls that bleed and mourn
    along this ditch were sowers of scandal and schism: 35
    as they tore others apart, so are they torn.
Behind us, warden of our mangled horde,
    the devil who butchers us and sends us marching
    waits to renew our wounds with his long sword
when we have made the circuit of the pit;   40
    for by the time we stand again before him
    all the wounds he gave us last have knit.
But who are you that gawk down from that sill —
    probably to put off your own descent
    to the pit you are sentenced to for your own evil?"   45
"Death has not come for him, guilt does not drive
    his soul to torment," my sweet Guide replied.
    "That he may experience all while yet alive
I, who am dead, must lead him through the drear
    and darkened halls of Hell, from round to round: 50
    and this is true as my own standing here."
More than a hundred wraiths who were marching under
    the sill on which we stood, paused at his words

---

2. The Punic Wars (264–146 B.C.). Livy writes that in the battle of Cannae (216 B.C.) so many Romans fell that Hannibal gathered three bushels of gold rings from the fingers of the dead and produced them before the Senate at Carthage.   3. Dante places Guiscard (1015–1085) in the *Paradiso* among the Warriors of God. He fought the Greeks and Saracens in their attempted invasion of Italy.   4. In 1266 the Pugliese under Manfred, King of Sicily, were charged with holding the pass at Ceperano against Charles of Anjou. The Pugliese, probably under Papal pressure, allowed the French free passage, and Charles went on to defeat Manfred at Benevento. Manfred himself was killed in that battle.   5. At Tagliacozzo (1268) in a continuation of the same strife, Charles of Anjou used a stratagem suggested to him by Alard de Valéry and defeated Conradin, nephew of Manfred. "Won without weapons" is certainly an overstatement: what Alardo suggested was a simple but effective concealment of reserve troops. When Conradin seemed to have carried the day and was driving his foes before him, the reserve troops broke on his flank and rear, and defeated Conradin's out-positioned forces.   6. Ali succeeded Mahomet to the Caliphate, but not until three of the disciples had preceded him. Mahomet died in 632, and Ali did not assume the Caliphate until 656.

and stared at me, forgetting pain in wonder.
"And if you do indeed return to see   55
    the sun again, and soon, tell Fra Dolcino[7]
    unless he longs to come and march with me
he would do well to check his groceries
    before the winter drives him from the hills
    and gives the victory to the Novarese."   60
Mahomet, one foot raised, had paused to say
    these words to me. When he had finished speaking
    he stretched it out and down, and moved away.
Another—he had his throat slit, and his nose
    slashed off as far as the eyebrows, and a wound   65
    where one of his ears had been—standing with those
who stared at me in wonder from the pit,
    opened the grinning wound of his red gullet
    as if it were a mouth, and said through it:
"O soul unforfeited to misery   70
    and whom—unless I take you for another—
    I have seen above in our sweet Italy;
if ever again you see the gentle plain
    that slopes down from Vercelli to Marcabò,[8]
    remember Pier da Medicina in pain,   75
and announce this warning to the noblest two
    of Fano, Messers Guido and Angiolello:
    that unless our foresight sees what is not true
they shall be thrown from their ships into the sea
    and drown in the raging tides near La Cattolica   80
    to satisfy a tyrant's treachery.[9]
Neptune never saw so gross a crime
    in all the seas from Cyprus to Majorca,
    not even in pirate raids, nor the Argive time.[1]
The one-eyed traitor,[2] lord of the demesne   85
    whose hill and streams one who walks here beside me
    will wish eternally he had never seen,
will call them to a parley, but behind
    sweet invitations he will work it so
    they need not pray against Focara's wind."   90
And I to him: "If you would have me bear
    your name to time, show me the one who found
    the sight of that land so harsh, and let me hear
his story and his name." He touched the cheek
    of one nearby, forcing the jaws apart,   95
    and said: "This is the one; he cannot speak.

7. In 1300 Fra Dolcino took over the reformist order called the Apostolic Brothers, who preached, among other things, the community of property and of women. Clement V declared them heretical and ordered a crusade against them. The brotherhood retired with its women to an impregnable position in the hills between Novara and Vercelli, but their supplies gave out in the course of a year-long siege, and they were finally starved out in March of 1307. Dolcino and Margaret of Trent, his "Sister in Christ," were burned at the stake at Vercelli the following June.   8. Vercelli is the most western town in Lombardy. Marcabò stands near the mouth of the Po.   9. Malatestino da Rimini (see preceding Canto), in a move to annex the city of Fano, invited Guido del Cassero and Angioletto da Carignano, leading citizens of Fano, to a conference at La Cattolica, a point on the Adriatic midway between Fano and Rimini. At Malatestino's orders the two were thrown overboard off Focara, a headland swept by such dangerous currents that approaching sailors used to offer prayers for a safe crossing.   1. The Greeks were raiders and pirates. Cyprus . . . Majorca: these islands are at opposite ends of the Mediterranean.   2. Malatestino.

This outcast settled Caesar's doubts that day
  beside the Rubicon by telling him:
    'A man prepared is a man hurt by delay.' "
Ah, how wretched Curio[3] seemed to me   100
  with a bloody stump in his throat in place of the tongue
  which once had dared to speak so recklessly!
And one among them with both arms hacked through
  cried out, raising his stumps on the foul air
  while the blood bedaubed his face: "Remember, too, 105
Mosca dei Lamberti,[4] alas, who said
  'A thing done has an end!' and with those words
  planted the fields of war with Tuscan dead."
"And brought about the death of all your clan!"
  I said, and he, stung by new pain on pain,   110
  ran off; and in his grief he seemed a madman.
I stayed to watch those broken instruments,
  and I saw a thing so strange I should not dare
  to mention it without more evidence
but that my own clear conscience strengthens me, 115
  that good companion that upholds a man
  within the armor of his purity.
I saw it there; I seem to see it still—
  a body without a head, that moved along
  like all the others in that spew and spill.   120
It held the severed head by its own hair,
  swinging it like a lantern in its hand;
  and the head looked at us and wept in its despair.
It made itself a lamp of its own head,
  and they were two in one and one in two;   125
  how this can be, He knows who so commanded.
And when it stood directly under us
  it raised the head at arm's length toward our bridge
  the better to be heard, and swaying thus
it cried: "O living soul in this abyss,   130
  see what a sentence has been passed upon me,
  and search all Hell for one to equal this!
When you return to the world, remember me:
  I am Bertrand de Born,[5] and it was I
  who set the young king on to mutiny,   135
son against father, father against son
  as Achitophel[6] set Absalom and David;
  and since I parted those who should be one
in duty and in love, I bear my brain

3. This is the Roman Tribune Curio, who was banished from Rome by Pompey and joined Caesar's forces, advising him to cross the Rubicon, which was then the boundary between Gaul and the Roman Republic. The crossing constituted invasion, and thus began the Roman Civil War. The Rubicon flows near Rimini.   **4.** Dante had asked Ciacco (Canto VI) for news of Mosca as a man of good works. Now he finds him, his merit canceled by his greater sin. Buondelmonte dei Buondelmonti had insulted the honor of the Amidei by breaking off his engagement to a daughter of that line in favor of a girl of the Donati. When the Amidei met to discuss what should be done, Mosca spoke for the death of Buondelmonte. The Amidei acted upon his advice and from that murder sprang the bloody feud between the Guelphs and Ghibellines of Florence.   **5.** Bertrand de Born (1140–1215), a great knight and master of the troubadours of Provence. He is said to have instigated a quarrel between Henry II of England and his son Prince Henry, called "The Young King" because he was crowned within his father's lifetime.   **6.** One of David's counselors, who deserted him to assist the rebellious Absalom. (II Samuel, xv–xvii.)

divided from its source within this trunk;   140
and walk here where my evil turns to pain,
an eye for an eye to all eternity:
thus is the law of Hell observed in me."

CANTO XXIX

Circle Eight: Bolgia Ten   The Falsifiers (Class I, Alchemists)

Dante lingers on the edge of the Ninth Bolgia expecting to see one of
his kinsmen, Geri del Bello, among the Sowers of Discord. Virgil, however, hurries him on, since time is short, and as they cross the bridge over
the Tenth Bolgia, Virgil explains that he had a glimpse of Geri among the
crowd near the bridge and that he had been making threatening gestures
at Dante.

The Poets now look into the last Bolgia of the Eighth Circle and see
The Falsifiers. They are punished by afflictions of every sense: by darkness,
stench, thirst, filth, loathsome diseases, and a shrieking din. Some of them,
moreover, run ravening through the pit, tearing others to pieces. Just as in
life they corrupted society by their falsifications, so in death these sinners
are subjected to a sum of corruptions. In one sense they figure forth what
society would be if all falsifiers succeeded—a place where the senses are
an affliction (since falsification deceives the senses) rather than a guide,
where even the body has no honesty, and where some lie prostrate while
others run ravening to prey upon them.

Not all of these details are made clear until the next Canto, for Dante
distinguishes four classes of Falsifiers, and in the present Canto we meet
only the first class, The Alchemists, the Falsifiers of Things. Of this class
are Griffolino D'Arezzo and Capocchio, with both of whom Dante speaks.

The sight of that parade of broken dead
   had left my eyes so sotted with their tears
   I longed to stay and weep, but Virgil said:
"What are you waiting for? Why do you stare
   as if you could not tear your eyes away   5
   from the mutilated shadows passing there?
You did not act so in the other pits.
   Consider—if you mean perhaps to count them—
   this valley and its train of dismal spirits.
winds twenty-two miles round.[7] The moon already   10
   is under our feet;[8] the time we have is short,
   and there is much that you have yet to see."
"Had you known what I was seeking," I replied,
   "you might perhaps have given me permission
   to stay on longer." (As I spoke, my Guide   15
had started off already, and I in turn
   had moved along behind him; thus, I answered
   as we moved along the cliff.) "Within that cavern

---

7. Another instance of "poetic" rather than "literal" detail. Dante's measurements cannot be made to
fit together on any scale map.   8. If the moon, nearly at full, is under their feet, the sun must be
overhead. It is therefore approximately noon of Holy Saturday.

upon whose brim I stood so long to stare,
   I think a spirit of my own blood mourns   20
   the guilt that sinners find so costly there."
And the Master then: "Hereafter let your mind
   turn its attention to more worthy matters
   and leave him to his fate among the blind;
for by the bridge and among that shapeless crew   25
   I saw him point to you with threatening gestures,
   and I heard him called Geri del Bello.[9] You
were occupied at the time with that headless one
   who in his life was master of Altaforte,[1]
   and did not look that way; so he moved on."   30
"O my sweet Guide," I answered, "his death came
   by violence and is not yet avenged
   by those who share his blood, and, thus, his shame.
For this he surely hates his kin, and, therefore,
   as I suppose, he would not speak to me;   35
   and in that he makes me pity him the more."
We spoke of this until we reached the edge
   from which, had there been light, we could have seen
   the floor of the next pit. Out from that ledge
Malebolge's final cloister lay outspread,   40
   and all of its lay brethren might have been
   in sight but for the murk; and from those dead
such shrieks and strangled agonies shrilled through me
   like shafts, but barbed with pity, that my hands
   flew to my ears. If all the misery   45
that crams the hospitals of pestilence
   in Maremma, Valdichiano, and Sardinia[2]
   in the summer months when death sits like a presence
on the marsh air, were dumped into one trench —
   that might suggest their pain. And through the screams,   50
   putrid flesh spread up its sickening stench.
Still bearing left we passed from the long sill
   to the last bridge of Malebolge. There
   the reeking bottom was more visible.
There, High Justice, sacred ministress   55
   of the First Father, reigns eternally
   over the falsifiers in their distress.
I doubt it could have been such pain to bear
   the sight of the Aeginian people dying[3]
   that time when such malignance rode the air   60
that every beast down to the smallest worm
   shriveled and died (it was after that great plague
   that the Ancient People, as the poets affirm,
were reborn from the ants) — as it was to see

9. A cousin of Dante's father. He became embroiled in a quarrel with the Sacchetti of Florence and was murdered. At the time of the writing he had not been avenged by his kinsmen in accord with the clan code of a life for a life.   1. Bertrand de Born was Lord of Hautefort.   2. Malarial plague areas. Valdichiano and Maremma were swamp areas of eastern and western Tuscany.   3. Juno, incensed that the nymph Aegina let Jove possess her, set a plague upon the island that bore her name. Every animal and every human died until only Aeacus, the son born to Aegina of Jove, was left. He prayed to his father for aid and Jove repopulated the island by transforming the ants at his son's feet into men. The Aeginians have since been called Myrmidons, from the Greek word for ant (Ovid, *Metamorphoses* VII, 523–660).

the spirits lying heaped on one another   65
in the dank bottom of that fetid valley.
One lay gasping on another's shoulder,
one on another's belly; and some were crawling
on hands and knees among the broken boulders.
Silent, slow step by step, we moved ahead   70
looking at and listening to those souls
too weak to raise themselves from their stone bed.
I saw two there like pans that are put
one against the other to hold their warmth.
They were covered with great scabs from head to foot.   75
No stable boy in a hurry to go home,[4]
or for whom his master waits impatiently,
ever scrubbed harder with his currycomb
than those two spirits of the stinking ditch
scrubbed at themselves with their own bloody claws   80
to ease the furious burning of the itch.
And as they scrubbed and clawed themselves, their nails
drew down the scabs the way a knife scrapes bream
or some other fish with even larger scales.
"O you," my Guide called out to one, "you there   85
who rip your scabby mail as if your fingers
were claws and pincers; tell us if this lair
counts any Italians among those who lurk
in its dark depths; so may your busy nails
eternally suffice you for your work."   90
"We both are Italian whose unending loss
you see before you," he replied in tears.
"But who are you who come to question us?"
"I am a shade," my Guide and Master said,
"who leads this living man from pit to pit   95
to show him Hell as I have been commanded."
The sinners broke apart as he replied
and turned convulsively to look at me,
as others did who overheard my Guide.
My Master, then, ever concerned for me,   100
turned and said: "Ask them whatever you wish."
And I said to those two wraiths of misery:
"So may the memory of your names and actions
not die forever from the minds of men
in that first world, but live for many suns,   105
tell me who you are and of what city;
do not be shamed by your nauseous punishment
into concealing your identity."
"I was a man of Arezzo,"[5] one replied,
"and Albert of Siena had me burned;   110
but I am not here for the deed for which I died.

---

4. The literal text would be confusing here. I have translated one possible interpretation of it as offered
by Giuseppe Vandelli. The original line is "ne da colui che mal volentier vegghia" ("nor by one who
unwillingly stays awake," or less literally, but with better force: "nor by one who fights off sleep").
5. Griffolino D'Arezzo, an alchemist who extracted large sums of money from Alberto da Siena on the
promise of teaching him to fly like Daedalus. When the Sienese oaf finally discovered he had been
tricked, he had his "father," the Bishop of Siena, burn Griffolino as a sorcerer. Griffolino, however, is
not punished for sorcery, but for falsification of silver and gold through alchemy.

It is true that jokingly I said to him once:
   'I know how to raise myself and fly through air';
   and he—with all the eagerness of a dunce—
wanted to learn. Because I could not make   115
   a Daedalus of him—for no other reason—
   he had his father burn me at the stake.
But Minos, the infallible, had me hurled
   here to the final bolgia of the ten
   for the alchemy I practiced in the world."   120
And I to the Poet: "Was there ever a race
   more vain than the Sienese? Even the French,
   compared to them, seem full of modest grace."
And the other leper answered mockingly:
   "Excepting Stricca, who by careful planning   125
   managed to live and spend so moderately;
and Niccolò, who in his time above
   was first of all the shoots in that rank garden
   to discover the costly uses of the clove;
and excepting the brilliant company of talents   130
   in which Caccia squandered his vineyards and his woods,
   and Abbagliato displayed his intelligence.[6]
But if you wish to know who joins your cry
   against the Sienese, study my face
   with care and let it make its own reply.   135
So you will see I am the suffering shadow
   of Capocchio,[7] who, by practicing alchemy,
   falsified the metals, and you must know,
unless my mortal recollection strays
how good an ape I was of Nature's ways."   140

CANTO XXX

*Circle Eight: Bolgia Ten   The Falsifiers (The Remaining Three Classes:
Evil Impersonators, Counterfeiters, False Witnesses)*

    Just as Capocchio finishes speaking, two ravenous spirits come racing
through the pit; and one of them, sinking his tusks into Capocchio's neck,
drags him away like prey. Capocchio's companion, Griffolino, identifies
the two as Gianni Schicchi and Myrrha, who run ravening through the
pit through all eternity, snatching at other souls and rending them. These
are the Evil Impersonators, Falsifiers of Persons. In life they seized upon
the appearance of others, and in death they must run with never a pause,
seizing upon the infernal apparition of these souls, while they in turn are
preyed upon by their own furies.

    Next the Poets encounter Master Adam, a sinner of the third class, a
Falsifier of Money, i.e., a Counterfeiter. Like the alchemists, he is punished by a loathsome disease and he cannot move from where he lies, but

---

6. *Stricca . . . Niccolò . . . Caccia . . . Abbagliato:* All of these Sienese noblemen were members of the
Spendthrift Brigade and wasted their substance in competitions of riotous living. Lano (Canto XIII) was
also of this company. Niccolò dei Salimbeni discovered some recipe (details unknown) prepared with
fabulously expensive spices.   7. Reputedly a Florentine friend of Dante's student days. For practicing
alchemy he was burned at the stake at Siena in 1293.

his disease is compounded by other afflictions, including an eternity of unbearable thirst. Master Adam identifies two spirits lying beside him as Potiphar's Wife and Sinon the Greek, sinners of the fourth class, The False Witnesses, i.e., Falsifiers of Words.

Sinon, angered by Master Adam's identification of him, strikes him across the belly with the one arm he is able to move. Master Adam replies in kind, and Dante, fascinated by their continuing exchange of abuse, stands staring at them until Virgil turns on him in great anger, for "The wish to hear such baseness is degrading." Dante burns with shame, and Virgil immediately forgives him because of his great and genuine repentance.

At the time when Juno took her furious
   revenge for Semele, striking in rage
   again and again at the Theban royal house,[8]
King Athamas, by her contrivance, grew
   so mad, that seeing his wife out for an airing   5
   with his two sons, he cried to his retinue:
"Out with the nets there! Nets across the pass!
   for I will take this lioness and her cubs!"
   And spread his talons, mad and merciless,
and seizing his son Learchus, whirled him round   10
   and brained him on a rock; at which the mother
   leaped into the sea with her other son and drowned.
And when the Wheel of Fortune spun about
   to humble the all-daring Trojan's pride
   so that both king and kingdom were wiped out;   15
Hecuba[9]—mourning, wretched, and a slave—
   having seen Polyxena sacrificed,
   and Polydorus dead without a grave;
lost and alone, beside an alien sea,
   began to bark and growl like a dog   20
   in the mad seizure of her misery.
But never in Thebes nor Troy were Furies seen
   to strike at man or beast in such mad rage
   as two I saw, pale, naked, and unclean,
who suddenly came running toward us then,   25
   snapping their teeth as they ran, like hungry swine
   let out to feed after a night in the pen.
One of them sank his tusks so savagely
   into Capocchio's neck, that when he dragged him,
   the ditch's rocky bottom tore his belly.   30
And the Aretine,[1] left trembling by me, said:

8. As in the case of the Aeginians, Jove begot a son (Bacchus) upon a mortal (Semele, daughter of King Cadmus of Thebes); and Juno, who obviously could not cope with her husband's excursions directly, turned her fury upon the mortals in a number of godlike ways, among them inducing the madness of King Athamas (Semele's brother-in-law) which Ovid recounts in *Metamorphoses* IV. 512ff.   9. Wife of King Priam. When Troy fell she was taken to Greece as a slave. En route she was forced to witness the sacrifice of her daughter and to look upon her son lying murdered and unburied. She went mad in her affliction and fell to howling like a dog. Ovid (*Metamorphoses* XIII, 568 ff.) describes her anguish but does not say she was changed into a dog.   1. Capocchio's companion, Griffolino.

"That incubus, in life, was Gianni Schicchi;[2]
  here he runs rabid, mangling the other dead."
"So!" I answered, "and so may the other one
  not sink its teeth in you, be pleased to tell us   35
  what shade it is before it races on."
And he: "That ancient shade in time above
  was Myrrha,[3] vicious daughter of Cinyras
  who loved her father with more than rightful love.
She falsified another's form and came   40
  disguised to sin with him just as that other
  who runs with her, in order that he might claim
the fabulous lead-mare, lay under disguise
  on Buoso Donati's death bed and dictated
  a spurious testament to the notaries."   45
And when the rabid pair had passed from sight,
  I turned to observe the other misbegotten
  spirits that lay about to left and right.
And there I saw another husk of sin,
  who, had his legs been trimmed away at the groin,   50
  would have looked for all the world like a mandolin.
The dropsy's heavy humors, which so bunch
  and spread the limbs, had disproportioned him
  till his face seemed much too small for his swollen paunch.
He strained his lips apart and thrust them forward   55
  the way a sick man, feverish with thirst,
  curls one lip toward the chin and the other upward.
"O you exempt from every punishment
  of this grim world (I know not why)," he cried,
  "look well upon the misery and debasement   60
of him who was Master Adam.[4] In my first
  life's time, I had enough to please me: here,
  I lack a drop of water for my thirst.
The rivulets that run from the green flanks
  of Casentino[5] to the Arno's flood,   65
  spreading their cool sweet moisture through their banks,
run constantly before me, and their plash
  and ripple in imagination dries me
  more than the disease that eats my flesh.
Inflexible Justice that has forked and spread   70
  my soul like hay, to search it the more closely,
  finds in the country where my guilt was bred
this increase of my grief; for there I learned,
  there in Romena, to stamp the Baptist's image[6]
  on alloyed gold—till I was bound and burned.   75

2. Of the Cavalcanti of Florence. When Buoso di Donati (see Canto XXV) died, his son, Simone,
persuaded Schicchi to impersonate the dead man and to dictate a will in Simone's favor. Buoso was
removed from the death bed, Schicchi took his place in disguise, and the will was dictated to a notary
as if Buoso were still alive. Schicchi took advantage of the occasion to make several bequests to himself,
including one of a famous and highly prized mare.   3. Moved by an incestuous passion for her father,
the King of Cyprus, she disguised herself and slipped into his bed. After he had mated with her, the
king discovered who she was and threatened to kill her but she ran away and was changed into a myrtle
[tree]. Adonis was born from her trunk. (Ovid, *Metamorphoses* X, 298 ff.)   4. Of Brescia. Under the
orders of the Counts Guidi of Romena, he counterfeited Florentine florins of twenty-one rather than
twenty-four carat gold, and on such a scale that a currency crisis arose in Northern Italy. He was burned
at the stake by the Florentines in 1281.   5. A mountainous district in which the Arno rises.   6. John
the Baptist's. As patron of Florence, his image was stamped on the florins.

But could I see the soul of Guido here,
  or of Alessandro, or of their filthy brother,[7]
  I would not trade that sight for all the clear
cool flow of Branda's fountain.[8] One of the three—
  if those wild wraiths who run here are not lying—   80
  is here already.[9] But small good it does me
when my legs are useless! Were I light enough
  to move as much as an inch in a hundred years,
  long before this I would have started off
to cull him from the freaks that fill this fosse,   85
  although it winds on for eleven miles
  and is no less than half a mile across.
Because of them I lie here in this pig-pen;
  it was they persuaded me to stamp the florins
  with three carats of alloy." And I then: 90
"Who are those wretched two sprawled alongside
  your right-hand borders, and who seem to smoke
  as a washed hand smokes in winter?" He replied:
"They were here when I first rained into this gully,
  and have not changed position since, nor may they,   95
  as I believe, to all eternity.
One is the liar who charged young Joseph wrongly:[1]
  the other, Sinon,[2] the false Greek from Troy.
  A burning fever makes them reek so strongly."
And one of the false pair, perhaps offended   100
  by the manner of Master Adam's presentation,
  punched him in the rigid and distended
belly—it thundered like a drum—and he
  retorted with an arm blow to the face
  that seemed delivered no whit less politely,   105
saying to him: "Although I cannot stir
  my swollen legs, I still have a free arm
  to use at times when nothing else will answer."
And the other wretch said: "It was not so free
  on your last walk to the stake, free as it was   110
  when you were coining." And he of the dropsy:
"That's true enough, but there was less truth in you
  when they questioned you at Troy." And Sinon then:
  "For every word I uttered that was not true
you uttered enough false coins to fill a bushel: 115
  I am put down here for a single crime,
  but you for more than any Fiend in Hell."[3]
"Think of the Horse," replied the swollen shade,
  "and may it torture you, perjurer, to recall
  that all the world knows the foul part you played."   120
"And to you the torture of the thirst that fries
  and cracks your tongue," said the Greek, "and of the water
  that swells your gut like a hedge before your eyes."
And the coiner: "So is your own mouth clogged

7. The Counts Guidi.   8. A spring near Romena. The famous fountain of Branda is in Siena, but Adam is speaking of his home country and must mean the spring.   9. Guido died before 1300. 1. Potiphar's wife bore false witness against Joseph (Genesis xxxix, 6–23).   2. The Greek who glibly talked the Trojans into taking the Horse inside the city walls. (Aeneid II, 57–194.)   3. Dante must reckon each false florin as a separate sin.

with the filth that stuffs and sickens it as always;   125
  if I am parched while my paunch is waterlogged,
you have the fever and your cankered brain;
  and were you asked to lap Narcissus' mirror[4]
  you would not wait to be invited again."
I was still standing, fixed upon those two   130
  when the Master said to me: "Now keep on looking
  a little longer and I quarrel with you."
When I heard my Master raise his voice to me,
  I wheeled about with such a start of shame
  that I grow pale yet at the memory.   135
As one trapped in a nightmare that has caught
  his sleeping mind, wishes within the dream
  that it were all a dream, as if it were not—
such I became: my voice could not win through
  my shame to ask his pardon; while my shame   140
  already won more pardon than I knew.
"Less shame," my Guide said, ever just and kind,
  "would wash away a greater fault than yours.
Therefore, put back all sorrow from your mind;
and never forget that I am always by you   145
  should it occur again, as we walk on,
  that we find ourselves where others of this crew
fall to such petty wrangling and upbraiding.
The wish to hear such baseness is degrading."

CANTO XXXI

The Central Pit of Malebolge   The Giants

Dante's spirits rise again as the Poets approach the Central Pit, a great
well, at the bottom of which lies Cocytus, the Ninth and final circle of
Hell. Through the darkness Dante sees what appears to be a city of great
towers, but as he draws near he discovers that the great shapes he has seen
are the Giants and Titans who stand perpetual guard inside the well-pit
with the upper halves of their bodies rising above the rim.

Among the Giants, Virgil identifies Nimrod, builder of the Tower of
Babel; Ephialtes and Briareus, who warred against the Gods; and Tityos
and Typhon, who insulted Jupiter. Also here, but for no specific offense,
is Antaeus, and his presence makes it clear that the Giants are placed here
less for their particular sins than for their general natures.

These are the sons of earth, embodiments of elemental forces unbal-
anced by love, desire without restraint and without acknowledgment of
moral and theological law. They are symbols of the earth-trace that every
devout man must clear from his soul, the unchecked passions of the beast.
Raised from the earth, they make the very gods tremble. Now they are
returned to the darkness of their origins, guardians of earth's last depth.

---

4. A pool of water. Ovid (*Metamorphoses* III, 407–510) tells how the young Narcissus fell in love with
his own reflection in a pool. He remained bent over the reflection till he wasted away and was changed
into a flower.

At Virgil's persuasion, Antaeus takes the Poets in his huge palm and
lowers them gently to the final floor of Hell.

One and the same tongue had first wounded me
    so that the blood came rushing to my cheeks,
    and then supplied the soothing remedy.
Just so, as I have heard, the magic steel
    of the lance that was Achilles' and his father's   5
    could wound at a touch, and, at another, heal.[5]
We turned our backs on the valley and climbed from it
    to the top of the stony bank that walls it round,
    crossing in silence to the central pit.
Here it was less than night and less than day;   10
    my eyes could make out little through the gloom,
    but I heard the shrill note of a trumpet bray
louder than any thunder. As if by force,
    it drew my eyes; I stared into the gloom
    along the path of the sound back to its source.   15
After the bloody rout when Charlemagne
    had lost the band of Holy Knights, Roland[6]
    blew no more terribly for all his pain.
And as I stared through that obscurity,
    I saw what seemed a cluster of great towers,   20
    whereat I cried: "Master, what is this city?"
And he: "You are still too far back in the dark
    to make out clearly what you think you see;
    it is natural that you should miss the mark:
you will see clearly when you reach that place   25
    how much your eyes mislead you at a distance;
    I urge you, therefore, to increase your pace."
Then taking my hand in his, my Master said:
    "The better to prepare you for strange truth,
    let me explain those shapes you see ahead: 30
they are not towers but giants. They stand in the well
    from the navel down; and stationed round its bank
    they mount guard on the final pit of Hell."
Just as a man in a fog that starts to clear
    begins little by little to piece together   35
    the shapes the vapor crowded from the air—
so, when those shapes grew clearer as I drew
    across the darkness to the central brink,
    error fled from me; and my terror grew.
For just as at Montereggione[7] the great towers   40

---

5. Peleus, father of Achilles, left this magic lance to his son. (Ovid, *Metamorphoses* XIII. 171ff.) Sonnet-
eers of Dante's time made frequent metaphoric use of this lance: just as the lance could wound and
then heal, so could the lady's look destroy with love and her kiss make whole.   6. Nephew of Charlemagne, hero of *The Song of Roland* (above, p. 956). He protected the rear of Charlemagne's column
on the return march through the Pyrenees from a war against the Saracens. When he was attacked he
was too proud to blow his horn as a signal for help, but as he was dying he blew so prodigious a blast
that it was heard by Charlemagne eight miles away. *Band of Holy Knights:* The original is *"la santa
gesta,"* which may be interpreted as "the holy undertaking." *"Gesta,"* however, can also mean "a sworn
band or fellowship of men at arms" (such as the Knights of the Round Table), and since it was his
Knights, rather than his undertaking, that Charlemagne lost, the second rendering seems more apt in
context.   7. A castle in Val d'Elsa near Siena built in 1213. Its walls had a circumference of more
than half a kilometer and were crowned by fourteen great towers, most of which are now destroyed.

crown the encircling wall; so the grim giants
  whom Jove still threatens when the thunder roars
raised from the rim of stone about that well
  the upper halves of their bodies, which loomed up
  like turrets through the murky air of Hell.   45
I had drawn close enough to one already
  to make out the great arms along his sides,
  the face, the shoulders, the breast, and most of the belly.
Nature, when she destroyed the last exemplars
  on which she formed those beasts, surely did well   50
  to take such executioners from Mars.
And if she has not repented the creation
  of whales and elephants, the thinking man
  will see in that her justice and discretion:
for where the instrument of intelligence   55
  is added to brute power and evil will,
  mankind is powerless in its own defense.
His face, it seemed to me, was quite as high
  and wide as the bronze pine cone in St. Peter's[8]
  with the rest of him proportioned accordingly: 60
so that the bank, which made an apron for him
  from the waist down, still left so much exposed
  that three Frieslanders[9] standing on the rim,
one on another, could not have reached his hair;
  for to that point at which men's capes are buckled,   65
  thirty good hand-spans[1] of brute bulk rose clear.
"Rafel mahee amek zabi almit,"[2]
  began a bellowed chant from the brute mouth
  for which no sweeter psalmody was fit.
And my Guide in his direction: "Babbling fool,   70
  stick to your horn and vent yourself with it
  when rage or passion stir your stupid soul.
Feel there around your neck, you muddle-head,
  and find the cord; and there's the horn itself,
  there on your overgrown chest." To me he said: 75
"His very babbling testifies the wrong
  he did on earth: he is Nimrod,[3] through whose evil
  mankind no longer speaks a common tongue.
Waste no words on him: it would be foolish.
  To him all speech is meaningless; as his own,   80
  which no one understands, is simply gibberish."
We moved on, bearing left along the pit,
  and a crossbow-shot away we found the next one,
  an even huger and more savage spirit.
What master could have bound so gross a beast   85
  I cannot say, but he had his right arm pinned
  behind his back, and the left across his breast

---

8. Originally a part of a fountain. In Dante's time it stood in front of the Basilica of St. Peter. It is now inside the Vatican. It stands about thirteen feet high (Scartazzini-Vandelli give the height as four meters) but shows signs of mutilation that indicate it was once higher.   9. The men of Friesland were reputed to be the tallest in Europe.   1. Dante uses the word "palma," which in Italian signifies the spread of the open hand.   2. This line, as Virgil explains below, is Nimrod's gibberish.   3. The first king of Babylon, supposed to have built the Tower of Babel, for which he is punished, in part, by the confusion of his own tongue and understanding. Nothing in the biblical reference portrays him as one of the earth-giants.

by an enormous chain that wound about him
　　from the neck down, completing five great turns
　　before it spiraled down below the rim.　　　　　　　　90
"This piece of arrogance," said my Guide to me,
　　"dared try his strength against the power of Jove;
　　for which he is rewarded as you see.
He is Ephialtes,[4] who made the great endeavour
　　with the other giants who alarmed the Gods;　　　　95
　　the arms he raised then, now are bound forever."
"Were it possible, I should like to take with me,"
　　I said to him, "the memory of seeing
　　the immeasurable Briareus."[5] And he:
"Nearer to hand, you may observe Antaeus[6]　　　　　100
　　who is able to speak to us, and is not bound.
　　It is he will set us down in Cocytus,[7]
the bottom of all guilt. The other hulk
　　stands far beyond our road. He too, is bound
　　and looks like this one, but with a fiercer sulk."　　105
No earthquake in the fury of its shock
　　ever seized a tower more violently,
　　than Ephialtes, hearing, began to rock.
Then I dreaded death as never before;
　　and I think I could have died for very fear　　　　110
　　had I not seen what manacles he wore.
We left the monster, and not far from him
　　we reached Antaeus, who to his shoulders alone
　　soared up a good five ells above the rim.
"O soul who once in Zama's fateful vale —　　　　　115
　　where Scipio became the heir of glory
　　when Hannibal and all his troops turned tail —
took more than a thousand lions for your prey;
　　and in whose memory many still believe
　　the sons of earth would yet have won the day　　　120
had you joined with them against High Olympus —
　　do not disdain to do us a small service,
　　but set us down where the cold grips Cocytus.
Would you have us go to Tityos or Typhon?[8] —
　　this man can give you what is longed for here:　　125
　　therefore do not refuse him, but bend down.
For he can still make new your memory:
　　he lives, and awaits long life, unless Grace call him
　　before his time to his felicity."
Thus my Master to that Tower of Pride;　　　　　　130

4. Son of Neptune (the sea) and Iphimedia. With his brother, Otus, he warred against the Gods striving
to pile Mt. Ossa on Mt. Olympus, and Mt. Pelion on Mt. Ossa. Apollo restored good order by killing
the two brothers.　　5. Another of the giants who rose against the Olympian Gods. Virgil speaks of him
as having a hundred arms and fifty heads (*Aeneid* X), but Dante has need only of his size, and of his
sin, which he seems to view as a kind of revolt of the angels, just as the action of Ephialtes and Otus
may be read as a pagan distortion of the Tower of Babel legend. He was the son of Uranus and Tellus.
6. The son of Neptune and Tellus (the earth). In battle, his strength grew every time he touched the
earth, his mother. He was accordingly invincible until Hercules killed him by lifting him over his head
and strangling him in midair. Lucan (*Pharsalia* IV, 595–660) describes Antaeus's great lion-hunting feat
in the valley of Zama where, in a later era, Scipio defeated Hannibal. Antaeus did not join in the
rebellion against the Gods and therefore he is not chained.　　7. The final pit of Hell.　　8. Also sons
of Tellus. They offended Jupiter, who had them hurled into the crater of Etna, below which the Lake
Tartarus was supposed to lie.

and the giant without delay reached out the hands
  which Hercules had felt, and raised my Guide.
Virgil, when he felt himself so grasped,
  called to me: "Come, and I will hold you safe."
  And he took me in his arms and held me clasped.   135
The way the Carisenda[9] seems to one
  who looks up from the leaning side when clouds
  are going over it from that direction,
making the whole tower seem to topple—so
  Antaeus seemed to me in the fraught moment   140
  when I stood clinging, watching from below
as he bent down; while I with heart and soul
  wished we had gone some other way, but gently
  he set us down inside the final hole
whose ice holds Judas and Lucifer in its grip.   145
Then straightened like a mast above a ship.

CANTO XXXII

Circle Nine: Cocytus   Compound Fraud
Round One: Caïna   The Treacherous to Kin
Round Two: Antenora   The Treacherous to Country

At the bottom of the well Dante finds himself on a huge frozen lake.
This is Cocytus, the Ninth Circle, the fourth and last great water of Hell,
and here, fixed in the ice, each according to his guilt, are punished sinners
guilty of Treachery Against Those to Whom They Were Bound by Special
Ties. The ice is divided into four concentric rings marked only by the
different positions of the damned within the ice.

This is Dante's symbolic equivalent of the final guilt. The treacheries
of these souls were denials of love (which is God) and of all human
warmth. Only the remorseless dead center of the ice will serve to express
their natures. As they denied God's love, so are they furthest removed from
the light and warmth of His Sun. As they denied all human ties, so are
they bound only by the unyielding ice.

The first round is Caïna, named for Cain. Here lie those who were
treacherous against blood ties. They have their necks and heads out of the
ice and are permitted to bow their heads—a double boon since it allows
them some protection from the freezing gale and, further, allows their
tears to fall without freezing their eyes shut. Here Dante sees Alessandro
and Napoleone degli Alberti, and he speaks to Camicion, who identifies
other sinners of this round.

The second round is Antenora, named for Antenor, the Trojan who was
believed to have betrayed his city to the Greeks. Here lie those guilty of
Treachery to Country. They, too, have their heads above the ice, but they
cannot bend their necks, which are gripped by the ice. Here Dante accidentally kicks the head of Bocca Degli Abbati and then proceeds to treat
him with a savagery he had shown to no other soul in Hell. Bocca names
some of his fellow traitors, and the Poets pass on to discover two heads

---

9. A leaning tower of Bologna.

frozen together in one hole. One of them is gnawing the nape of the
other's neck.

If I had rhymes as harsh and horrible
   as the hard fact of that final dismal hole
   which bears the weight of all the steeps of Hell,
I might more fully press the sap and substance
   from my conception; but since I must do   5
   without them, I begin with some reluctance.
For it is no easy undertaking, I say,
   to describe the bottom of the Universe;
   nor is it for tongues that only babble child's play.
But may those Ladies of the Heavenly Spring[1]   10
   who helped Amphion wall Thebes, assist my verse,
   that the word may be the mirror of the thing.
O most miscreant rabble, you who keep
   the stations of that place whose name is pain,
   better had you been born as goats or sheep!   15
We stood now in the dark pit of the well,
   far down the slope below the Giant's feet,
   and while I still stared up at the great wall,
I heard a voice cry: "Watch which way you turn:
   take care you do not trample on the heads   20
   of the forworn and miserable brethren."
Whereat I turned and saw beneath my feet
   and stretching out ahead, a lake so frozen
   it seemed to be made of glass. So thick a sheet
never yet hid the Danube's winter course,   25
   nor, far away beneath the frigid sky,
   locked the Don up in its frozen source:
for were Tanbernick and the enormous peak
   of Pietrapana[2] to crash down on it,
   not even the edges would so much as creak.   30
The way frogs sit to croak, their muzzles leaning
   out of the water, at the time and season
   when the peasant woman dreams of her day's gleaning[3] —
Just so the livid dead are sealed in place
   up to the part at which they blushed for shame,   35
   and they beat their teeth like storks. Each holds his face
bowed toward the ice, each of them testifies
   to the cold with his chattering mouth, to his heart's grief
   with tears that flood forever from his eyes.
When I had stared about me, I looked down   40
   and at my feet I saw two clamped together
   so tightly that the hair of their heads had grown
together. "Who are you," I said, "who lie
   so tightly breast to breast?" They strained their necks,
   and when they had raised their heads as if to reply,   45
the tears their eyes had managed to contain

---

1. The Muses. They so inspired Amphion's hand upon the lyre that the music charmed blocks of stone
out of Mount Cithaeron, and the blocks formed themselves into the walls of Thebes.   2. There is no
agreement on the location of the mountain Dante called Tanbernick. Pietrapana, today known as *la
Pania*, is in Tuscany.   3. The summer.

   up to that time gushed out, and the cold froze them
    between the lids, sealing them shut again
tighter than any clamp grips wood to wood,
    and mad with pain, they fell to butting heads   50
    like billy-goats in a sudden savage mood.
And a wraith who lay to one side and below,
    and who had lost both ears to frostbite, said,
    his head still bowed: "Why do you watch us so?
If you wish to know who they are[4] who share one doom,   55
    they owned the Bisenzio's valley with their father,
    whose name was Albert. They spring from one womb,
and you may search through all Caïna's crew
    without discovering in all this waste
    a squab more fit for the aspic than these two;   60
not him whose breast and shadow a single blow
    of the great lance of King Arthur pierced with light;[5]
    nor yet Focaccia[6] nor this one fastened so
into the ice that his head is all I see,
    and whom, if you are Tuscan, you know well—   65
    his name on the earth was Sassol Mascheroni.[7]
And I—to tell you all and so be through—
    was Camicion de' Pazzi.[8] I wait for Carlin
    beside whose guilt my sins will shine like virtue."
And leaving him,[9] I saw a thousand faces   70
    discolored so by cold, I shudder yet
    and always will when I think of those frozen places.
As we approached the center of all weight,
    where I went shivering in eternal shade,
    whether it was my will, or chance, or fate,   75
I cannot say, but as I trailed my Guide
    among those heads, my foot struck violently
    against the face of one.[1] Weeping, it cried:
"Why do you kick me? If you were not sent
    to wreak a further vengeance for Montaperti,   80
    why do you add this to my other torment?"
"Master," I said, "grant me a moment's pause
    to rid myself of a doubt concerning this one;
    then you may hurry me at your own pace."
The Master stopped at once, and through the volley   85
    of foul abuse the wretch poured out, I said:
    "Who are you who curse others so?" And he:

4. Alessandro and Napoleone, Counts of Mangona. Among other holdings, they inherited a castle in the Val di Bisenzio. They seemed to have been at odds on all things and finally killed one another in a squabble over their inheritance and their politics (Alessandro was a Guelph and Napoleone a Ghibelline).   5. Mordred, King Arthur's traitorous nephew. He tried to kill Arthur, but the king struck him a single blow of his lance, and when it was withdrawn, a shaft of light passed through the gaping wound and split the shadow of the falling traitor.   6. Of the Cancellieri of Pistoia. He murdered his cousin (among others) and may have been the principal cause of a great feud that divided the Cancellieri, and split the Guelphs into the White and Black parties.   7. Of the Toschi of Florence. He was appointed guardian of one of his nephews and murdered him to get the inheritance for himself.   8. Alberto Camicion de' Pazzi of Valdarno. He murdered a kinsman. Carlin: Carlino de' Pazzi, relative of Alberto. He was charged with defending for the Whites the castle of Piantravigne in Valdarno but surrendered it for a bribe. He belongs therefore in the next lower circle, Antenora, as a traitor to his country, and when he arrives there his greater sin will make Alberto seem almost virtuous by comparison.   9. These words mark the departure from Caïna to Antenora.   1. Bocca degli Abbati, a traitorous Florentine. At the battle of Montaperti (cf. Farinata, Canto X) he hacked off the hand of the Florentine standard bearer. The cavalry, lacking a standard around which it could rally, was soon routed.

"And who are *you* who go through the dead larder
  of Antenora kicking the cheeks of others
  so hard, that were you alive, you could not kick harder?"   90
"I *am* alive," I said, "and if you seek fame,
  it may be precious to you above all else
  that my notes on this descent include your name."
"Exactly the opposite is my wish and hope,"
  he answered. "Let me be; for it's little you know   95
  of how to flatter on this icy slope."
I grabbed the hair of his dog's-ruff and I said:
  "Either you tell me truly who you are,
  or you won't have a hair left on your head."
And he: "Not though you snatch me bald. I swear   100
  I will not tell my name nor show my face.
  Not though you rip until my brain lies bare."
I had a good grip on his hair; already
  I had yanked out more than one fistful of it,
  while the wretch yelped, but kept his face turned from me;   105
when another said: "Bocca, what is it ails you?
  What the Hell's wrong?[2] Isn't it bad enough
  to hear you bang your jaws? Must you bark too?"
"Now filthy traitor, say no more!" I cried,
  "for to your shame, be sure I shall bear back   110
  a true report of you." The wretch replied:
"Say anything you please but go away.
  And if you *do* get back, don't overlook
  that pretty one who had so much to say
just now. Here he laments the Frenchman's price.   115
  'I saw Buoso da Duera,'[3] you can report,
  'where the bad salad is kept crisp on ice.'
And if you're asked who else was wintering here,
  Beccheria,[4] whose throat was slit by Florence,
  is there beside you. Gianni de' Soldanier[5]   120
is further down, I think, with Ganelon,[6]
  and Tebaldello,[7] who opened the gates of Faenza
  and let Bologna steal in with the dawn."
Leaving him then, I saw two souls together
  in a single hole, and so pinched in by the ice   125
  that one head made a helmet for the other.
As a famished man chews crusts—so the one sinner
  sank his teeth into the other's nape

2. In the circumstances, a monstrous pun. The original is *"qual diavolo ti tocca?"* (what devil touches, or molests, you?), a standard colloquialism for "what's the matter with you?" A similar pun occurs in line 117: "kept crisp (cool) on ice." Colloquially *"stare fresco"* (to be or to remain cool) equals "to be left out in the cold," i.e., to be out of luck.   3. Of Cremona. In 1265 Charles of Anjou marched against Manfred and Naples (see Canto XIX), and Buoso da Duera was sent out in charge of a Ghibelline army to oppose the passage of one of Charles's armies, but accepted a bribe and let the French pass unopposed. The event took place near Parma.   4. Tesauro dei Beccheria of Pavia, Abbot of Vallombrosa and Papal Legate (of Alexander IV) in Tuscany. The Florentine Guelphs cut off his head in 1258 for plotting with the expelled Ghibellines.   5. A Florentine Ghibelline of ancient and noble family. In 1265, however, during the riots that occurred under the Two Jovial Friars, he deserted his party and became a leader of the commoners (Guelphs). In placing him in Antenora, Dante makes no distinction between turning on one's country and turning on one's political party, not at least if the end is simply for power.   6. It was Ganelon who betrayed Roland to the Saracens. (See Canto XXXI.) 7. Tebaldello de' Zambrasi of Faenza. At dawn on November 13, 1280, he opened the city gates and delivered Faenza to the Bolognese Guelphs in order to revenge himself on the Ghibelline family of the Lambertazzi, who, in 1274, had fled from Bologna to take refuge in Faenza.

at the base of the skull, gnawing his loathsome dinner.
Tydeus in his final raging hour   130
    gnawed Menalippus' head[8] with no more fury
    than this one gnawed at skull and dripping gore.
"You there," I said, "who show so odiously
    your hatred for that other, tell me why
    on this condition: that if in what you tell me   135
you seem to have a reasonable complaint
    against him you devour with such foul relish,
    I, knowing who you are, and his soul's taint,
may speak your cause to living memory,
God willing the power of speech be left to me."   140

CANTO XXXIII

Circle Nine: Cocytus Compound Fraud
Round Two: Antenora The Treacherous to Country
Round Three: Ptolomea The Treacherous to Guests and Hosts

In reply to Dante's exhortation, the sinner who is gnawing his companion's head looks up, wipes his bloody mouth on his victim's hair, and tells
his harrowing story. He is Count Ugolino and the wretch he gnaws is
Archbishop Ruggieri. Both are in Antenora for treason. In life they had
once plotted together. Then Ruggieri betrayed his fellow-plotter and
caused his death, by starvation, along with his four "sons." In the most
pathetic and dramatic passage of the *Inferno*, Ugolino details how their
prison was sealed and how his "sons" dropped dead before him one by
one, weeping for food. His terrible tale serves only to renew his grief and
hatred, and he has hardly finished it before he begins to gnaw Ruggieri
again with renewed fury. In the immutable Law of Hell, the killer-by-
starvation becomes the food of his victim.

The Poets leave Ugolino and enter Ptolomea, so named for the Ptolo-
maeus of Maccabees, who murdered his father-in-law at a banquet. Here
are punished those who were Treacherous Against the Ties of Hospitality.
They lie with only half their faces above the ice and their tears freeze in
their eye sockets, sealing them with little crystal visors. Thus even the
comfort of tears is denied them. Here Dante finds Friar Alberigo and
Branca D'Oria, and discovers the terrible power of Ptolomea: so great is
its sin that the souls of the guilty fall to its torments even before they die,
leaving their bodies still on earth, inhabited by Demons.

The sinner raised his mouth from his grim repast
    and wiped it on the hair of the bloody head
    whose nape he had all but eaten away. At last
he began to speak: "You ask me to renew
    a grief so desperate that the very thought   5
    of speaking of it tears my heart in two.

---

8. Statius recounts in the *Thebaid* that Tydeus killed Menalippus in battle but fell himself mortally
wounded. As he lay dying he had Menalippus's head brought to him and fell to gnawing it in his dying
rage.

But if my words may be a seed that bears
   the fruit of infamy for him I gnaw,
   I shall weep, but tell my story through my tears.
Who you may be, and by what powers you reach   10
   into this underworld, I cannot guess,
   but you seem to me a Florentine by your speech.
I was Count Ugolino,[9] I must explain;
   this reverend grace is the Archbishop Ruggieri:
   now I will tell you why I gnaw his brain.   15
That I, who trusted him, had to undergo
   imprisonment and death through his treachery,
   you will know already.[1] What you cannot know—
that is, the lingering inhumanity
   of the death I suffered—you shall hear in full: 20
   then judge for yourself if he has injured me.
A narrow window in that coop[2] of stone
   now called the Tower of Hunger for my sake
   (within which others yet must pace alone)
had shown me several waning moons already[3]   25
   between its bars, when I slept the evil sleep
   in which the veil of the future parted for me.
This beast[4] appeared as master of a hunt
   chasing the wolf and his whelps across the mountain
   that hides Lucca from Pisa.[5] Out in front   30
of the starved and shrewd and avid pack he had placed
   Gualandi and Sismondi and Lanfranchi[6]
   to point his prey. The father and sons had raced
a brief course only when they failed of breath
   and seemed to weaken; then I thought I saw   35
   their flanks ripped open by the hounds' fierce teeth.
Before the dawn, the dream still in my head,
   I woke and heard my sons,[7] who were there with me,
   cry from their troubled sleep, asking for bread.
You are cruelty itself if you can keep   40
   your tears back at the thought of what foreboding
   stirred in my heart; and if you do not weep,
at what are you used to weeping?—The hour when food
   used to be brought, drew near. They were now awake,
   and each was anxious from his dream's dark mood.   45
And from the base of that horrible tower I heard
   the sound of hammers nailing up the gates:

9. Count of Donoratico and a member of the Guelph family della Gherardesca. He and his nephew, Nino de' Visconti, led the two Guelph factions of Pisa. In 1288 Ugolino intrigued with Archbishop Ruggieri degli Ubaldini, leader of the Ghibellines, to get rid of Visconti and to take over the command of all the Pisan Guelphs. The plan worked, but in the consequent weakening of the Guelphs, Ruggieri saw his chance and betrayed Ugolino, throwing him into prison with his sons and his grandsons. In the following year the prison was sealed up and they were left to starve to death.   1. News of Ugolino's imprisonment and death would certainly have reached Florence. *What you cannot know:* No living man could know what happened after Ugolino and his sons were sealed in the prison and abandoned.   2. Dante uses the word *muda*, in Italian signifying a stone tower in which falcons were kept in the dark to moult. From the time of Ugolino's death it became known as The Tower of Hunger.   3. Ugolino was jailed late in 1288. He was sealed in to starve early in 1289.   4. Ruggieri.   5. These two cities would be in view of one another were it not for Monte San Giuliano.   6. Three Pisan nobles, Ghibellines and friends of the Archbishop.   7. Actually two of the boys were grandsons and all were considerably older than one would gather from Dante's account. Anselm, the younger grandson, was fifteen. The others were really young men and were certainly old enough for guilt despite Dante's charge in line 90.

I stared at my sons' faces without a word.
'I did not weep: I had turned stone inside.
  They wept. 'What ails you, Father, you look so strange,'   50
  my little Anselm, youngest of them, cried.
But I did not speak a word nor shed a tear:
  not all that day nor all that endless night,
  until I saw another sun appear.
When a tiny ray leaked into that dark prison   55
  and I saw staring back from their four faces
  the terror and the wasting of my own,
I bit my hands in helpless grief. And they,
  thinking I chewed myself for hunger, rose
  suddenly together. I heard them say: 60
'Father, it would give us much less pain
  if you ate us: it was you who put upon us
  this sorry flesh; now strip it off again.'
I calmed myself to spare them. Ah! hard earth,
  why did you not yawn open? All that day   65
  and the next we sat in silence. On the fourth,
Gaddo, the eldest, fell before me and cried,
  stretched at my feet upon that prison floor:
  'Father, why don't you help me?' There he died.
And just as you see me, I saw them fall   70
  one by one on the fifth day and the sixth.
  Then, already blind, I began to crawl
from body to body shaking them frantically.
  Two days I called their names, and they were dead.
  Then fasting overcame my grief and me."[8]   75
His eyes narrowed to slits when he was done,
  and he seized the skull again between his teeth
  grinding it as a mastiff grinds a bone.
Ah, Pisa! foulest blemish on the land
  where "si" sounds sweet and clear,[9] since those nearby you   80
  are slow to blast the ground on which you stand,
may Caprara and Gorgona[1] drift from place
  and dam the flooding Arno at its mouth
  until it drowns the last of your foul race!
For if to Ugolino falls the censure   85
  for having betrayed your castles,[2] you for your part
  should not have put his sons to such a torture:
you modern Thebes![3] those tender lives you spilt—
  Brigata, Uguccione, and the others
  I mentioned earlier—were too young for guilt!   90

8. I.e., he died. Some interpret the line to mean that Ugolino's hunger drove him to cannibalism. Ugolino's present occupation in Hell would certainly support that interpretation but the fact is that cannibalism is the one major sin Dante does not assign a place to in Hell. So monstrous would it have seemed to him that he must certainly have established a special punishment for it. Certainly he could hardly have relegated it to an ambiguity. Moreover, it would be a sin of bestiality rather than of fraud, and as such it would be punished in the Seventh Circle.   9. Italy.   1. These two islands near the mouth of the Arno were Pisan possessions in 1300.   2. In 1284, Ugolino gave up certain castles to Lucca and Florence. He was at war with Genoa at the time and it is quite likely that he ceded the castles to buy the neutrality of these two cities, for they were technically allied with Genoa. Dante, however, must certainly consider the action as treasonable, for otherwise Ugolino would be in Caïna for his treachery to Visconti.   3. Thebes, as a number of the foregoing notes will already have made clear, was the site of some of the most hideous crimes of antiquity.

We passed on further,[4] where the frozen mine
  entombs another crew in greater pain;
  these wraiths are not bent over, but lie supine.
Their very weeping closes up their eyes;
  and the grief that finds no outlet for its tears   95
  turns inward to increase their agonies:
for the first tears that they shed knot instantly
  in their eye-sockets, and as they freeze they form
  a crystal visor above the cavity.
And despite the fact that standing in that place   100
  I had become as numb as any callus,
  and all sensation had faded from my face,
somehow I felt a wind begin to blow,
  whereat I said: "Master, what stirs this wind?
  Is not all heat extinguished here below?"[5]   105
And the Master said to me: "Soon you will be
  where your own eyes will see the source and cause
  and give you their own answer to the mystery."
And one of those locked in that icy mall
  cried out to us as we passed: "O souls so cruel   110
  that you are sent to the last post of all,
relieve me for a little from the pain
  of this hard veil; let my heart weep a while
  before the weeping freeze my eyes again."
And I to him: "If you would have my service,   115
  tell me your name; then if I do not help you
  may I descend to the last rim of the ice."[6]
"I am Friar Alberigo,"[7] he answered therefore,
  "the same who called for the fruits from the bad garden.
  Here I am given dates for figs full store."   120
"What! Are you dead already?" I said to him.
  And he then: "How my body stands in the world
  I do not know. So privileged is this rim
of Ptolomea, that often souls fall to it
  before dark Atropos[8] has cut their thread.   125
  And that you may more willingly free my spirit
of this glaze of frozen tears that shrouds my face,
  I will tell you this: when a soul betrays as I did,
  it falls from flesh, and a demon takes its place,
ruling the body till its time is spent.   130
  The ruined soul rains down into this cistern.
  So, I believe, there is still evident
in the world above, all that is fair and mortal
  of this black shade who winters here behind me.
  If you have only recently crossed the portal   135

---

4. Marks the passage into Ptolomea.   5. Dante believed (rather accurately, by chance) that all winds resulted from "exhalations of heat." Cocytus, however, is conceived as wholly devoid of heat, a metaphysical absolute zero. The source of the wind, as we discover in the next Canto, is Satan himself. 6. Dante is not taking any chances; he has to go on to the last rim in any case. The sinner, however, believes him to be another damned soul and would interpret the oath quite otherwise than as Dante meant it.   7. Of the Manfredi of Faenza. He was another Jovial Friar. In 1284 his brother Manfred struck him in the course of an argument. Alberigo pretended to let it pass, but in 1285 he invited Manfred and his son to a banquet and had them murdered. The signal to the assassins was the words: "Bring in the fruit." "Friar Alberigo's bad fruit" became a proverbial saying.   8. The Fate who cuts the thread of life.

from that sweet world, you surely must have known
 his body: Branca D'Oria[9] is its name,
 and many years have passed since he rained down."
"I think you are trying to take me in," I said,
 "Ser Branca D'Oria is a living man;   140
 he eats, he drinks, he fills his clothes and his bed."
"Michel Zanche had not yet reached the ditch
 of the Black Talons," the frozen wraith replied,
 "there where the sinners thicken in hot pitch,
when this one left his body to a devil,   145
 as did his nephew and second in treachery,
 and plumbed like lead through space to this dead level.
But now reach out your hand, and let me cry."
 And I did not keep the promise I had made,
 for to be rude to him was courtesy.   150
Ah, men of Genoa! souls of little worth,
 corrupted from all custom of righteousness,
 why have you not been driven from the earth?
For there beside the blackest soul of all
 Romagna's evil plain, lies one of yours   155
 bathing his filthy soul in the eternal
glacier of Cocytus for his foul crime,
 while he seems yet alive in world and time!

CANTO XXXIV

Ninth Circle: Cocytus Compound Fraud
Round Four: Judecca The Treacherous to Their Masters
The Center: Satan

"On march the banners of the King," Virgil begins as the Poets face the last depth. He is quoting a medieval hymn, and to it he adds the distortion and perversion of all that lies about him. "On march the banners of the King—of Hell." And there before them, in an infernal parody of Godhead, they see Satan in the distance, his great wings beating like a windmill. It is their beating that is the source of the icy wind of Cocytus, the exhalation of all evil.

All about him in the ice are strewn the sinners of the last round, Judecca, named for Judas Iscariot. These are the Treacherous to Their Masters. They lie completely sealed in the ice, twisted and distorted into every conceivable posture. It is impossible to speak to them, and the Poets move on to observe Satan.

He is fixed into the ice at the center to which flow all the rivers of guilt; and as he beats his great wings as if to escape, their icy wind only freezes him more surely into the polluted ice. In a grotesque parody of the Trinity, he has three faces, each a different color, and in each mouth he clamps a sinner whom he rips eternally with his teeth. Judas Iscariot is in the central mouth: Brutus and Cassius in the mouths on either side.

Having seen all, the Poets now climb through the center, grappling

---

9. A Genoese Ghibelline. His sin is identical in kind to that of Friar Alberigo. In 1275 he invited his father-in-law, Michel Zanche (see Canto XXII), to a banquet and had him and his companions cut to pieces. He was assisted in the butchery by his nephew.

hand over hand down the hairy flank of Satan himself—a last supremely
symbolic action—and at last, when they have passed the center of all gravity, they emerge from Hell. A long climb from the earth's center to the
Mount of Purgatory awaits them, and they push on without rest, ascending
along the sides of the river Lethe, till they emerge once more to see the
stars of Heaven, just before dawn on Easter Sunday.

"On march the banners of the King of Hell,"[1]
    my Master said. "Toward us. Look straight ahead:
    can you make him out at the core of the frozen shell?"
Like a whirling windmill seen afar at twilight,
    or when a mist has risen from the ground—   5
    just such an engine rose upon my sight
stirring up such a wild and bitter wind
    I cowered for shelter at my Master's back,
    there being no other windbreak I could find.
I stood now where the souls of the last class   10
    (with fear my verses tell it) were covered wholly;
    they shone below the ice like straws in glass.
Some lie stretched out; others are fixed in place
    upright, some on their heads, some on their soles;
    another, like a bow, bends foot to face.   15
When we had gone so far across the ice
    that it pleased my Guide to show me the foul creature[2]
    which once had worn the grace of Paradise,
he made me stop, and, stepping aside, he said:
    "Now see the face of Dis! This is the place   20
    where you must arm your soul against all dread."
Do not ask, Reader, how my blood ran cold
    and my voice choked up with fear. I cannot write it:
    this is a terror that cannot be told.
I did not die, and yet I lost life's breath: 25
    imagine for yourself what I became,
    deprived at once of both my life and death.
The Emperor of the Universe of Pain
    jutted his upper chest above the ice;
    and I am closer in size to the great mountain   30
the Titans make around the central pit,
    than they to his arms. Now, starting from this part,
    imagine the whole that corresponds to it!
If he was once as beautiful as now
    he is hideous, and still turned on his Maker,   35
    well may he be the source of every woe!
With what a sense of awe I saw his head
    towering above me! for it had three faces:
    one was in front, and it was fiery red;
the other two, as weirdly wonderful,   40
    merged with it from the middle of each shoulder
    to the point where all converged at the top of the skull;

1. The hymn (Vexilla regis prodeunt) was written in the sixth century by Venantius Fortunatus, Bishop
of Poitiers. The original celebrates the Holy Cross, and is part of the service for Good Friday to be sung
at the moment of uncovering the Cross.   2. Satan.

the right was something between white and bile;
   the left was about the color that one finds
   on those who live along the banks of the Nile.   45
Under each head two wings rose terribly,
   their span proportioned to so gross a bird:
   I never saw such sails upon the sea.
They were not feathers—their texture and their form
   were like a bat's wings—and he beat them so   50
   that three winds blew from him in one great storm:
it is these winds that freeze all Cocytus.
   He wept from his six eyes, and down three chins
   the tears ran mixed with bloody froth and pus.[3]
In every mouth he worked a broken sinner   55
   between his rake-like teeth. Thus he kept three
   in eternal pain at his eternal dinner.
For the one in front the biting seemed to play
   no part at all compared to the ripping: at times
   the whole skin of his back was flayed away.   60
"That soul that suffers most," explained my Guide,
   "is Judas Iscariot, he who kicks his legs
   on the fiery chin and has his head inside.
Of the other two, who have their heads thrust forward,
   the one who dangles down from the black face   65
   is Brutus: note how he writhes without a word.
And there, with the huge and sinewy arms,[4] is the soul
   of Cassius.—But the night is coming on[5]
   and we must go, for we have seen the whole."
Then, as he bade, I clasped his neck, and he,   70
   watching for a moment when the wings
   were opened wide, reached over dexterously
and seized the shaggy coat of the king demon;
   then grappling matted hair and frozen crusts
   from one tuft to another, clambered down.   75
When we had reached the joint where the great thigh
   merges into the swelling of the haunch,
   my Guide and Master, straining terribly,
turned his head to where his feet had been
   and began to grip the hair as if he were climbing;   80
   so that I thought we moved toward Hell again.
"Hold fast!" my Guide said, and his breath came shrill[6]
   with labor and exhaustion. "There is no way
   but by such stairs to rise above such evil."
At last he climbed out through an opening   85
   in the central rock, and he seated me on the rim;
   then joined me with a nimble backward spring.
I looked up, thinking to see Lucifer
   as I had left him, and I saw instead
   his legs projecting high into the air.   90

---

3. The gore of the sinners he chews, which is mixed with his slaver.   **4.** The Cassius who betrayed Caesar was more generally described in terms of Shakespeare's "lean and hungry look." Another Cassius is described by Cicero (*Catiline* III) as huge and sinewy. Dante probably confused the two.   **5.** It is now Saturday evening.   **6.** Cf. Canto XXIII, 85, where the fact that Dante breathes indicates to the Hypocrites that he is alive. Virgil's breathing is certainly a contradiction.

Now let all those whose dull minds are still vexed
  by failure to understand what point it was
  I had passed through, judge if I was perplexed.
"Get up. Up on your feet," my Master said.
  "The sun already mounts to middle tierce,[7]   95
  and a long road and hard climbing lie ahead."
It was no hall of state we had found there,
  but a natural animal pit hollowed from rock
  with a broken floor and a close and sunless air.
"Before I tear myself from the Abyss,"   100
  I said when I had risen, "O my Master,
  explain to me my error in all this:
where is the ice? and Lucifer—how has he
  been turned from top to bottom: and how can the sun
  have gone from night to day so suddenly?"   105
And he to me: "You imagine you are still
  on the other side of the center where I grasped
  the shaggy flank of the Great Worm of Evil
which bores through the world—you *were* while I climbed down,
  but when I turned myself about, you passed   110
  the point to which all gravities are drawn.
You are under the other hemisphere where you stand;
  the sky above us is the half opposed
  to that which canopies the great dry land.
Under the mid-point of that other sky   115
  the Man who was born sinless and who lived
  beyond all blemish, came to suffer and die.
You have your feet upon a little sphere
  which forms the other face of the Judecca.
  There it is evening when it is morning here.   120
And this gross Fiend and Image of all Evil
  who made a stairway for us with his hide
  is pinched and prisoned in the ice-pack still.
On this side he plunged down from heaven's height,
  and the land that spread here once hid in the sea   125
  and fled North to our hemisphere for fright;
and it may be that moved by that same fear,
  the one peak[8] that still rises on this side
  fled upward leaving this great cavern here.
Down there, beginning at the further bound   130
  of Beelzebub's dim tomb, there is a space
  not known by sight, but only by the sound
of a little stream[9] descending through the hollow
  it has eroded from the massive stone
  in its endlessly entwining lazy flow.   135
My Guide and I crossed over and began
  to mount that little known and lightless road
  to ascend into the shining world again.

7. In the canonical day tierce is the period from about six to nine A.M. Middle tierce, therefore, is seven-thirty. In going through the center point, they have gone from night to day. They have moved ahead twelve hours.   8. The Mount of Purgatory.   9. Lethe. In classical mythology, the river of forgetfulness, from which souls drank before being born. In Dante's symbolism it flows down from Purgatory, where it has washed away the memory of sin from the souls who are undergoing purification. That memory it delivers to Hell, which draws all sin to itself.

He first, I second, without thought of rest
    we climbed the dark until we reached the point   140
    where a round opening brought in sight the blest
and beauteous shining of the Heavenly cars.
And we walked out once more beneath the Stars.[1]

1. Dante ends each of the three divisions of the *Commedia* with this word. Every conclusion of the upward soul is toward the stars, God's shining symbols of hope and virtue. It is just before dawn of Easter Sunday that the Poets emerge.

GIOVANNI BOCCACCIO

1313–1375

The tales of Giovanni Boccaccio's *Decameron* (completed about 1353) constitute the greatest achievement of prose fiction in a vernacular language of southern Europe during the medieval period. In his hundred stories the Italian author presents a great variety of people and situations, aptly and often acutely characterized, and abundant dialogue of great liveliness and realism.

Born in 1313 in Paris, Boccaccio was the son of a Florentine businessman and a Frenchwoman. He was apparently taken to Italy in infancy, and in 1328 was sent to Naples to learn commerce in the office of his father's partner; but after six years, bored with business, he turned to the study of canon law. In 1336 Boccaccio saw Maria d'Aquino in a church at Naples; she is represented as Fiammetta in several of his works, including the *Decameron*. A romantic affair ended in Maria's desertion of her lover and finally in her death in the plague of 1348. In 1341 Boccaccio returned to Florence. After 1351 he was greatly influenced by Petrarch, and turned in his writing from Italian poetry and prose fiction to Latin works of a scholarly nature. He sheltered Leon Pilatus, inducing him to make the first translation of Homer from Greek. Unlike Petrarch, Boccaccio was devoted to the study of Dante, of whom he wrote a biography; in 1373 he was appointed to a Dante chair or lectureship in Florence.

Like Chaucer, who wrote his *Canterbury Tales* several decades later, Boccaccio provides a dramatic framework for his narrations. But his storytellers are not miscellaneous pilgrims traveling to a famous shrine; they are seven young ladies and three young gentlemen who have withdrawn from Florence to the countryside, to escape the Black Death, or plague, of 1348.* They engage in gay banter and good-natured raillery, but as they are all refined and cultivated young people with no occupational bias or ingrained prejudices, their relationships are polite rather than boisterous and lack the force and depth and vitality of those portrayed in *The Canterbury Tales*. They agree on a plan of storytelling—and adhere to it (with slight changes). Here there is no drunken miller, such as interrupts Chaucer's pilgrims, to upset the seemly orderliness acceptable to gentlefolk, for there are no other folk present. Each member of the company is to tell a tale each day; on some days a general topic is assigned, on others each narrator follows his or her own taste and judgment.

The story about Brother Alberto and his impersonation of the angel Gabriel, a bawdy tale of amorous intrigue and deception, exemplifies what most modern

---

* The exact nature of the Black Plague is not known, but an epidemic swept over western Europe about this time. Perhaps a fourth of the population died from it. Other epidemics are known from other centuries as well, notably the 17th century. In its deadly effect it might be compared with the epidemic of influenza in Europe, America, and elsewhere in 1918–19.

readers regard as typical of the *Decameron*. Like Chaucer's *Miller's Tale*, it presents a (moderately) clever person successfully deceiving a very foolish one, but eventually punished for his trickery. In the present story, the man is the trickster and the woman is the foolish dupe, but these roles are often reversed in other stories of the *Decameron*; indeed, Boccaccio digresses during the introduction to the fourth day to assert his devotion to women—the Muses, after all, were women—and, indeed, the women storytellers outnumber the men. He nonetheless knew that some women are foolish, just as he knew, though he was a devout Christian, that some priests and friars fall short of their vocation. Like other authors of his time, he saw nothing wrong in acknowledging these facts and turning them to artistic use.

If reduced to the bare essentials of its plot, this tale could be told far more briefly, as a mere anecdote, a joke. Indeed, it may well have been in circulation as an anecdote both before and after Boccaccio. But he gives it literary value by the way he handles it. He makes the reader see the successive scenes in vivid detail, he creates memorable and amusing characters, and he relates the incidents of the narrative closely to the personalities of those characters. Lisetta is not only credulous but also inordinately vain—her credulity derives from her vanity—and it is because of these qualities that she can be taken in by Brother Alberto's preposterous account of the angel's interest in her. The reader also notices the tacit perception of Lisetta's woman friend, who at once sees through the friar's scheme but, instead of disabusing her foolish friend, leads her on and then gleefully reveals the whole story to the outside world. And Alberto, though clever, is not as cautious as he should be. Otherwise, once warned, he would not have exposed himself to discovery and disgrace.

The story of Federigo and his falcon is told on a day devoted to accounts of love that turns out happily after difficulties on the way. It presents the courtly love relationship—or one of the possible relationships—in a remarkable combination of realism and nobility. Federigo's conduct perfectly fulfills the code; he devotes himself completely to Monna Giovanna, and his failure to receive anything in return in no way disturbs the pattern of that devotion. He never repines or complains; his lady's married or widowed condition is all one to him; and, having spent his fortune in the futile effort to attract her, he lives with resignation on his tiny estate. But Federigo is genuinely high-minded and noble; he has absorbed the ideals and not merely the etiquette of courtly love. His declaration, when Giovanna comes to call, that he has gained and not lost by his service to her, might be politeness learned out of a book—a romance, for example. But his sacrifice of the falcon to provide her with a good meal is a splendid and magnificent folly that could come only from an almost unbelievably generous heart. His grief at the outcome is probably sharper than Giovanna's, despite the painful disappointment that it produces for her.

Giovanna's dignity and charm and sensitivity are as clear to us as they evidently are to Federigo. Unwilling, whether as wife or widow, to have a romance with Federigo, she does not encourage him. Yet she knows that he loves her and that he has squandered his wealth on her account. We see her distress at having to ask him for anything, let alone the falcon, his most cherished possession. But when love for her young son, mortally ill, forces her to it, she acts with grace and decorum. And with something more; for she has discerned the nobleness of temper in Federigo through his consistently courteous behavior. It is that to which she appeals, not to any obligation of a courtly lover to please his lady. Later, when her brothers convince her that she should remarry, she also shows both generosity and independence of character. She gives Federigo his reward by marrying him—and seeing that his new fortune is not wasted! The happy ending is agreeable; but the notable achievement of the story is the brief but complete and poignant depiction

of the dilemmas faced by the two against a background of preliminary characterization which gives their decision full significance.

Two good biographies are T. C. Chubb, *The Life of Giovanni Boccaccio* (1930),
and Edward Hutton, *Giovanni Boccaccio* (1910). Interesting and sensitive criticism
is to be found in Charles G. Osgood, *Boccaccio on Poetry* (1930). John Addington
Symonds, *Giovanni Boccaccio* (1968), has been reissued. A. D. Scaglione, *Nature
and Love in the Middle Ages* (1963), is a useful discussion of the *Decameron* as is
G. Mazzotta, *The World at Play in Boccaccio's Decameron* (1986). Twenty-one of
the tales from the *Decameron* can be found in Mark Musa and Peter E. Bondanella, *Giovanni Boccaccio: The Decameron, A New Translation* (1977).

PRONOUNCING GLOSSARY

The following list uses common English syllables and stress accents to provide rough equivalents of selected words whose pronunciation may be unfamiliar to the general reader.

Alberighi: *al-behr-ee'-gee*   Filomena: *fee-loh-may'-nah*

Boccaccio: *boh-cah'-chyoh*   Filostrato: *fee-loh-strah'-toh*

Dioneo: *dee-oh-nay'-oh*   Neifile: *nay-ee-fee'-le*

Fiammetta: *fyahm-met'-tah*   Pampinea: *pahm-pee-nay'-ah*

The Decameron[1]

THE FIRST DAY

Thirteen hundred and forty-eight years had already passed after the fruitful
Incarnation of the Son of God when into the distinguished city of Florence, more noble than any other Italian city, there came the deadly pestilence. It started in the East, either because of the influence of heavenly
bodies or because of God's just wrath as a punishment to mortals for our
wicked deeds, and it killed an infinite number of people. Without pause
it spread from one place and it stretched its miserable length over the
West. And against this pestilence no human wisdom or foresight was of
any avail; quantities of filth were removed from the city by officials
charged with this task; the entry of any sick person into the city was prohibited; and many directives were issued concerning the maintenance of
good health. Nor were the humble supplications, rendered not once but
many times to God by pious people, through public processions or by
other means, efficacious; for almost at the beginning of springtime of the
year in question the plague began to show its sorrowful effects in an
extraordinary manner. It did not act as it had done in the East, where
bleeding from the nose was a manifest sign of inevitable death, but it
began in both men and women with certain swellings either in the groin
or under the armpits, some of which grew to the size of a normal apple
and others to the size of an egg (more or less), and the people called them
buboes. And from the two parts of the body already mentioned, within a
brief space of time, the said deadly buboes began to spread indiscrimi-

1. Translated by Mark Musa and Peter E. Bondanella.

nately over every part of the body; and after this, the symptoms of the illness changed to black or livid spots appearing on the arms and thighs, and on every part of the body, some large ones and sometimes many little ones scattered all around. And just as the buboes were originally, and still are, a very certain indication of impending death, in like manner these spots came to mean the same thing for whoever had them. Neither a doctor's advice nor the strength of medicine could do anything to cure this illness; on the contrary, either the nature of the illness was such that it afforded no cure, or else the doctors were so ignorant that they did not recognize its cause and, as a result, could not prescribe the proper remedy (in fact, the number of doctors, other than the well-trained, was increased by a large number of men and women who had never had any medical training); at any rate, few of the sick were ever cured, and almost all died after the third day of the appearance of the previously described symptoms (some sooner, others later), and most of them died without fever or any other side effects.

This pestilence was so powerful that it was communicated to the healthy by contact with the sick, the way a fire close to dry or oily things will set them aflame. And the evil of the plague went even further: not only did talking to or being around the sick bring infection and a common death, but also touching the clothes of the sick or anything touched or used by them seemed to communicate this very disease to the person involved. What I am about to say is incredible to hear, and if I and others had not witnessed it with our own eyes, I should not dare believe it (let alone write about it), no matter how trustworthy a person I might have heard it from. Let me say, then, that the power of the plague described here was of such virulence in spreading from one person to another that not only did it pass from one man to the next, but, what's more, it was often transmitted from the garments of a sick or dead man to animals that not only became contaminated by the disease, but also died within a brief period of time. My own eyes, as I said earlier, witnessed such a thing one day: when the rags of a poor man who died of this disease were thrown into the public street, two pigs came upon them, as they are wont to do, and first with their snouts and then with their teeth they took the rags and shook them around; and within a short time, after a number of convulsions, both pigs fell dead upon the ill-fated rags, as if they had been poisoned. From these and many similar or worse occurrences there came about such fear and such fantastic notions among those who remained alive that almost all of them took a very cruel attitude in the matter; that is, they completely avoided the sick and their possessions; and in so doing, each one believed that he was protecting his good health.

There were some people who thought that living moderately and avoiding all superfluity might help a great deal in resisting this disease, and so, they gathered in small groups and lived entirely apart from everyone else. They shut themselves up in those houses where there were no sick people and where one could live well by eating the most delicate of foods and drinking the finest of wines (doing so always in moderation), allowing no one to speak about or listen to anything said about the sick and the dead outside; these people lived, spending their time with music

and other pleasures that they could arrange. Others thought the opposite: they believed that drinking too much, enjoying life, going about singing and celebrating, satisfying in every way the appetites as best one could, laughing, and making light of everything that happened was the best medicine for such a disease; so they practiced to the fullest what they believed by going from one tavern to another all day and night, drinking to excess; and often they would make merry in private homes, doing everything that pleased or amused them the most. This they were able to do easily, for everyone felt he was doomed to die and, as a result, abandoned his property, so that most of the houses had become common property, and any stranger who came upon them used them as if he were their rightful owner. In addition to this bestial behavior, they always managed to avoid the sick as best they could. And in this great affliction and misery of our city the revered authority of the laws, both divine and human, had fallen and almost completely disappeared, for, like other men, the ministers and executors of the laws were either dead or sick or so short of help that it was impossible for them to fulfill their duties; as a result, everybody was free to do as he pleased.

Many others adopted a middle course between the two attitudes just described: neither did they restrict their food or drink so much as the first group nor did they fall into such dissoluteness and drunkenness as the second; rather, they satisfied their appetites to a moderate degree. They did not shut themselves up, but went around carrying in their hands flowers, or sweet-smelling herbs, or various kinds of spices; and often they would put these things to their noses, believing that such smells were a wonderful means of purifying the brain, for all the air seemed infected with the stench of dead bodies, sickness, and medicines.

Others were of a crueler opinion (though it was, perhaps, a safer one): they maintained that there was no better medicine against the plague than to flee from it; and convinced of this reasoning, not caring about anything but themselves, men and women in great numbers abandoned their city, their houses, their farms, their relatives, and their possessions and sought other places, and they went at least as far away as the Florentine countryside—as if the wrath of God could not pursue them with this pestilence wherever they went but would only strike those it found within the walls of the city! Or perhaps they thought that Florence's last hour had come and that no one in the city would remain alive.

And not all those who adopted these diverse opinions died, nor did they all escape with their lives; on the contrary, many of those who thought this way were falling sick everywhere, and since they had given, when they were healthy, the bad example of avoiding the sick, they, in turn, were abandoned and left to languish away without care. The fact was that one citizen avoided another, that almost no one cared for his neighbor, and that relatives rarely or hardly ever visited each other—they stayed far apart. This disaster had struck such fear into the hearts of men and women that brother abandoned brother, uncle abandoned nephew, sister left brother, and very often wife abandoned husband, and—even worse, almost unbelievable—fathers and mothers neglected to tend and care for their children, as if they were not their own.

Thus, for the countless multitude of men and women who fell sick, there remained no support except the charity of their friends (and these were few) or the avarice of servants, who worked for inflated salaries and indecent periods of time and who, in spite of this, were few and far between; and those few were men or women of little wit (most of them not trained for such service) who did little else but hand different things to the sick when requested to do so or watch over them while they died, and in this service, they very often lost their own lives and their profits. And since the sick were abandoned by their neighbors, their parents, and their friends and there was a scarcity of servants, a practice that was almost unheard of before spread through the city: when a woman fell sick, no matter how attractive or beautiful or noble she might be, she did not mind having a manservant (whoever he might be, no matter how young or old he was), and she had no shame whatsoever in revealing any part of her body to him—the way she would have done to a woman—when the necessity of her sickness required her to do so. This practice was, perhaps, in the days that followed the pestilence, the cause of looser morals in the women who survived the plague. And so, many people died who, by chance, might have survived if they had been attended to. Between the lack of competent attendants, which the sick were unable to obtain, and the violence of the pestilence, there were so many, many people who died in the city both day and night that it was incredible just to hear this described, not to mention seeing it! Therefore, out of sheer necessity, there arose among those who remained alive customs which were contrary to the established practices of the time.

It was the custom, as it is again today, for the women, relatives, and neighbors to gather together in the house of a dead person and there to mourn with the women who had been dearest to him; on the other hand, in front of the deceased's home, his male relatives would gather together with his male neighbors and other citizens, and the clergy also came (many of them, or sometimes just a few) depending upon the social class of the dead man. Then, upon the shoulders of his equals, he was carried to the church chosen by him before death with the funeral pomp of candles and chants. With the fury of the pestilence increasing, this custom, for the most part, died out and other practices took its place. And so, not only did people die without having a number of women around them, but there were many who passed away without even having a single witness present, and very few were granted the piteous laments and bitter tears of their relatives; on the contrary, most relatives were somewhere else, laughing, joking, and amusing themselves; even the women learned this practice too well, having put aside, for the most part, their womanly compassion for their own safety. Very few were the dead whose bodies were accompanied to the church by more than ten or twelve of their neighbors, and these dead bodies were not even carried on the shoulders of honored and reputable citizens but rather by gravediggers from the lower classes that were called *becchini*. Working for pay, they would pick up the bier and hurry it off, not to the church the dead man had chosen before his death but, in most cases, to the church closest by, accompanied by four or six churchmen with just a few candles, and often none at all.

With the help of these *becchini*, the churchmen would place the body as fast as they could in whatever unoccupied grave they could find, without going to the trouble of saying long or solemn burial services.

The plight of the lower class and, perhaps, a large part of the middle class, was even more pathetic: most of them stayed in their homes or neighborhoods either because of their poverty or their hopes for remaining safe, and every day they fell sick by the thousands; and not having servants or attendants of any kind, they almost always died. Many ended their lives in the public streets, during the day or at night, while many others who died in their homes were discovered dead by their neighbors only by the smell of their decomposing bodies. The city was full of corpses. The dead were usually given the same treatment by their neighbors, who were moved more by the fear that the decomposing corpses would contaminate them than by any charity they might have felt towards the deceased: either by themselves or with the assistance of porters (when they were available), they would drag the corpse out of the home and place it in front of the doorstep where, usually in the morning, quantities of dead bodies could be seen by any passerby; then, they were laid out on biers, or for lack of biers, on a plank. Nor did a bier carry only one corpse; sometimes it was used for two or three at a time. More than once, a single bier would serve for a wife and husband, two or three brothers, a father or son, or other relatives, all at the same time. And countless times it happened that two priests, each with a cross, would be on their way to bury someone, when porters carrying three or four biers would just follow along behind them; and where these priests thought they had just one dead man to bury, they had, in fact, six or eight and sometimes more. Moreover, the dead were honored with no tears or candles or funeral mourners but worse: things had reached such a point that the people who died were cared for as we care for goats today. Thus, it became quite obvious that what the wise had not been able to endure with patience through the few calamities of every-day life now became a matter of indifference to even the most simple-minded people as a result of this colossal misfortune.

So many corpses would arrive in front of a church every day and at every hour that the amount of holy ground for burials was certainly insuf-ficient for the ancient custom of giving each body its individual place; when all the graves were full, huge trenches were dug in all of the ceme-teries of the churches and into them the new arrivals were dumped by the hundreds; and they were packed in there with dirt, one on top of another, like a ship's cargo, until the trench was filled.

But instead of going over every detail of the past miseries which befell our city, let me say that the same unfriendly weather there did not, because of this, spare the surrounding countryside any evil; there, not to speak of the towns which, on a smaller scale, were like the city, in the scattered villages and in the fields the poor, miserable peasants and their families, without any medical assistance or aid of servants, died on the roads and in their fields and in their homes, as many by day as by night, and they died not like men but more like wild animals. Because of this they, like the city dwellers, became careless in their ways and did not look after their possessions or their businesses; furthermore, when they saw that

death was upon them, completely neglecting the future fruits of their past labors, their livestock, their property, they did their best to consume what they already had at hand. So, it came about that oxen, donkeys, sheep, pigs, chickens and even dogs, man's most faithful companion, were driven from their homes into the fields, where the wheat was left not only unharvested but also unreaped, and they were allowed to roam where they wished; and many of these animals, almost as if they were rational beings, returned at night to their homes without any guidance from a shepherd, satiated after a good day's meal.

Leaving the countryside and returning to the city, what more can one say, except that so great was the cruelty of Heaven, and, perhaps, also that of man, that from March to July of the same year, between the fury of the pestiferous sickness and the fact that many of the sick were badly treated or abandoned in need because of the fear that the healthy had, more than one hundred thousand human beings are believed to have lost their lives for certain inside the walls of the city of Florence whereas, before the deadly plague, one would not have estimated that there were actually that many people dwelling in that city.

Oh, how many great palaces, beautiful homes, and noble dwellings, once filled with families, gentlemen, and ladies, were now emptied, down to the last servant! How many notable families, vast domains, and famous fortunes remained without legitimate heir! How many valiant men, beautiful women, and charming young men, who might have been pronounced very healthy by Galen, Hippocrates, and Aesculapius[2] (not to mention lesser physicians), dined in the morning with their relatives, companions, and friends and then in the evening took supper with their ancestors in the other world!

Reflecting upon so many miseries makes me very sad; therefore, since I wish to pass over as many as I can, let me say that as our city was in this condition, almost emptied of inhabitants, it happened (as I heard it later from a person worthy of trust) that one Tuesday morning in the venerable church of Santa Maria Novella there was hardly any congregation there to hear the holy services except for seven young women, all dressed in garments of mourning as the times demanded, each of whom was a friend, neighbor, or relative of the other, and none of whom had passed her twenty-eighth year, nor was any of them younger than eighteen; all were educated and of noble birth and beautiful to look at, well-mannered and gracefully modest. I would tell you their real names, if I did not have a good reason for not doing so, which is this: I do not wish any of them to be embarrassed in the future because of the things that they said to each other and what they listened to—all of which I shall later recount. Today the laws regarding pleasure are again strict, more so than at that time (for the reasons mentioned above when they were very lax), not only for women of their age but even for those who were older; nor would I wish to give an opportunity to the envious, who are always ready to attack every

---

2. Roman god of medicine and healing, often identified with Asclepius, Apollo's son, who was the Greek god of medicine. Galen (A.D. 130?–201?), a Greek anatomist and physician. Hippocrates (460?–377? B.C.), a Greek physician to whom the Hippocratic oath, administered to new physicians, is attributed.

praiseworthy life, to diminish in any way with their indecent talk the dignity of these worthy ladies. But, so that you may understand clearly what each of them had to say, I intend to call them by names which are either completely or in part appropriate to their personalities. We shall call the first and the oldest Pampinea and the second Fiammetta, the third Filomena, and the fourth Emilia, and we shall name the fifth Lauretta and the sixth Neifile, and the last, not without reason, we shall call Elissa.[3] Not by prior agreement, but purely by chance, they gathered together in one part of the church and were seated almost in a circle, saying their rosaries; after many sighs, they began to discuss among themselves various matters concerning the nature of the times, and after a while, as the others fell silent, Pampinea began to speak in this manner:

"My dear ladies, you have often heard, as I have, how a proper use of one's reason does harm to no one. It is only natural for everyone born on this earth to aid, preserve, and defend his own life to the best of his ability; this is a right so taken for granted that it has, at times, permitted men to kill each other without blame in order to defend their own lives. And if the laws dealing with the welfare of every human being permit such a thing, how much more lawful, and with no harm to anyone, is it for us, or anyone else, to take all possible precautions to preserve our own lives! When I consider what we have been doing this morning and in the past days and what we have spoken about, I understand, and you must understand too, that each one of us is afraid for her life; nor does this surprise me in the least—rather I am greatly amazed that since each of us has the natural feelings of a woman, we do not find some remedy for ourselves to cure what each one of us dreads. We live in the city, in my opinion, for no other reason than to bear witness to the number of dead bodies that are carried to burial, or to listen whether the friars (whose number has been reduced to almost nothing) chant their offices at the prescribed hours, or to demonstrate to anyone who comes here the quality and the quantity of our miseries by our garments of mourning. And if we leave the church, either we see dead or sick bodies being carried all about, or we see those who were once condemned to exile for their crimes by the authority of the public laws making sport of these laws, running about wildly through the city, because they know that the executors of these laws are either dead or dying; or we see the scum of our city, avid for our blood, who call themselves *becchini* and who ride about on horseback torturing us by deriding everything, making our losses more bitter with their disgusting songs. Nor do we hear anything but 'So-and-so is dead,' and 'So-and-so is dying'; and if there were anyone left to mourn, we should hear nothing but piteous laments everywhere. I do not know if what happens to me also happens to you in your homes, but when I go home I find no one there except my maid, and I become so afraid that my hair stands on end, and wherever I go or sit in my house, I seem to see the shadows of those who have passed away, not with the faces that I remember, but with horrible expressions that terrify me. For these reasons, I am uncomfortable

---

3. Perhaps the reason is that, like her namesake, the Carthaginian queen, who is better known as Dido, Boccaccio's Elissa is dominated by a violent passion.

here, outside, and in my home, and the more so since it appears that no one like ourselves, who is well off and who has some other place to go, has remained here except us. And if there are any who remain, according to what I hear and see, they do whatever their hearts desire, making no distinction between what is proper and what is not, whether they are alone or with others, by day or by night; and not only laymen but also those who are cloistered in convents have broken their vows of obedience and have given themselves over to carnal pleasures, for they have made themselves believe that these things are permissible for them and are improper for others, and thinking that they will escape with their lives in this fashion, they have become wanton and dissolute.

"If this is the case, and plainly it is, what are we doing here? What are we waiting for? What are we dreaming about? Why are we slower to protect our health than all the rest of the citizens? Do we hold ourselves less dear than all the others? Or do we believe that our own lives are tied by stronger chains to our bodies than those of others and, therefore, that we need not worry about anything which might have the power to harm them? We are mistaken and deceived, and we are mad if we believe it. We shall have clear proof of this if we just call to mind how many young men and ladies have been struck down by this cruel pestilence. I do not know if you agree with me, but I think that, in order not to fall prey, out of laziness or presumption, to what we might well avoid, it might be a good idea for all of us to leave this city, just as many others before us have done and are still doing. Let us avoid like death itself the ugly examples of others, and go to live in a more dignified fashion in our country houses (of which we all have several) and there let us take what enjoyment, what happiness, and what pleasure we can, without going beyond the rules of reason in any way. There we can hear the birds sing, and we can see the hills and the pastures turning green, the wheat fields moving like the sea, and a thousand kinds of trees; and we shall be able to see the heavens more clearly which, though they still may be cruel, nonetheless will not deny to us their eternal beauties, which are much more pleasing to look at than the empty walls of our city. Besides all this, there in the country the air is much fresher, and the necessities for living in such times as these are plentiful there, and there are just fewer troubles in general; though the peasants are dying there even as the townspeople here, the displeasure is the less in that there are fewer houses and inhabitants than in the city. Here on the other hand, if I judge correctly, we would not be abandoning anyone; on the contrary, we can honestly say it is we ourselves that have been abandoned, for our loved ones are either dead or have fled and have left us alone in such affliction as though we did not belong to them. No reproach, therefore, can come to us if we follow this course of action, whereas sorrow, worry, and perhaps even death can come if we do not follow this course. So, whenever you like, I think it would be well to take our servants, have all our necessary things sent after us, and go from one place one day to another the next, enjoying what happiness and merriment these times permit; let us live in this manner (unless we are overtaken first by death) until we see what ending Heaven has reserved for these horrible times. And remember that it is no more forbidden for us

to go away virtuously than it is for most other women to remain here dishonorably."

When they had listened to what Pampinea had said, the other women not only praised her advice but were so anxious to follow it that they had already begun discussing among themselves the details, as if they were going to leave that very instant. But Filomena, who was most discerning, said:

"Ladies, regardless of how convincing Pampinea's arguments are, that is no reason to rush into things, as you seem to wish to do. Remember that we are all women, and any young girl can tell you that women do not know how to reason in a group when they are without the guidance of some man who knows how to control them. We are changeable, quarrelsome, suspicious, timid, and fearful, because of which I suspect that this company will soon break up without honor to any of us if we do not take a guide other than ourselves. We would do well to resolve this matter before we depart."

Then Elissa said:

"Men are truly the leaders of women, and without their guidance, our actions rarely end successfully. But how are we to find any men? We all know that the majority of our relatives are dead and those who remain alive are scattered here and there in various groups, not knowing where we are (they, too, are fleeing precisely what we seek to avoid), and since taking up with strangers would be unbecoming to us, we must, if we wish to leave for the sake of our health, find a means of arranging it so that while going for our own pleasure and repose, no trouble or scandal follow us."

While the ladies were discussing this, three young men came into the church, none of whom was less than twenty-five years of age. Neither the perversity of the times nor the loss of friends or parents, nor fear for their own lives had been able to cool, much less extinguish, the love those lovers bore in their hearts. One of them was called Panfilo, another Filostrato, and the last Dioneo, each one very charming and well-bred; and in those turbulent times they sought their greatest consolation in the sight of the ladies they loved, all three of whom happened to be among the seven ladies previously mentioned, while the others were close relatives of one or the other of the three men. No sooner had they sighted the ladies than they were seen by them, whereupon Pampinea smiled and said:

"See how Fortune favors our plans and has provided us with these discreet and virtuous young men, who would gladly be our guides and servants if we do not hesitate to accept them for such service."

Then Neifile's face blushed out of embarrassment, for she was one of those who was loved by one of the young men, and she said:

"Pampinea, for the love of God, be careful what you say! I realize very well that nothing but good can be said of any of them, and I believe that they are capable of doing much more than that task and, likewise, that their good and worthy company would be fitting not only for us but for ladies much more beautiful and attractive than we are, but it is quite obvious that some of them are in love with some of us who are here pres-

ent, and I fear that if we take them with us, slander and disapproval will follow, through no fault of ours or of theirs."

Then Filomena said:

"That does not matter at all; as long as I live with dignity and have no remorse of conscience about anything, let anyone who wishes say what he likes to the contrary: God and Truth will take up arms in my defense. Now, if they were just prepared to come with us, as Pampinea says, we could truly say that Fortune was favorable to our departure."

When the others heard her speak in such a manner, the argument was ended, and they all agreed that the young men should be called over, told about their intentions, and asked if they would be so kind as to accompany the ladies on such a journey. Without further discussion, then, Pampinea, who was related to one of the men, rose to her feet and made her way to where they stood gazing at the ladies, and she greeted them with a cheerful expression, outlined their plan to them, and begged them, in everyone's name, to keep them company in the spirit of pure and brotherly affection.

At first the young men thought they were being mocked, but when they saw that the lady was speaking seriously, they gladly consented; and in order to start without delay and put the plan into action, before leaving the church they agreed upon what preparations must be made for their departure. And when everything had been arranged and word had been sent on to the place they intended to go, the following morning (that is, Wednesday) at the break of dawn the ladies with some of their servants and the three young men with three of their servants left the city and set out on their way; they had traveled no further than two short miles when they arrived at the first stop they had agreed upon.

The place was somewhere on a little mountain, at some distance away from our roads, full of various shrubs and plants with rich, green foliage — most pleasant to look at; at the top there was a country mansion with a beautiful large inner courtyard with open collonades, halls, and bedrooms, all of them beautiful in themselves and decorated with cheerful and interesting paintings; it was surrounded by meadows and marvelous gardens, with wells of fresh water and cellars full of the most precious wines, the likes of which were more suitable for expert drinkers than for sober and dignified ladies. And the group discovered, to their delight, that the entire palace had been cleaned and the beds made in the bedchambers, and that fresh flowers and rushes had been strewn everywhere. Soon after they arrived and were resting, Dioneo, who was more attractive and wittier than either of the other young men, said:

"Ladies, more than our preparations, it was your intelligence that guided us here. I do not know what you intend to do with your thoughts, but I left mine inside the city walls when I passed through them in your company a little while ago; and so, you must either make up your minds to enjoy yourselves and laugh and sing with me (as much, let me say, as your dignity permits), or you must give me leave to return to my worries and to remain in our troubled city."

To this Pampinea, who had driven away her sad thoughts in the same way, replied happily:

"Dioneo, you speak very well: let us live happily, for after all it was unhappiness that made us flee the city. But when things are not organized they cannot long endure, and since I began the discussions which brought this fine company together, and since I desire the continuation of our happiness, I think it is necessary that we choose a leader from among us, whom we shall honor and obey as our superior and whose every thought shall be to keep us living happily. And in order that each one of us may feel the weight of this responsibility together with the pleasure of its authority, so that no one of us who has not experienced it can envy the others, let me say that both the weight and the honor should be granted to each one of us in turn for a day; the first will be chosen by election; the others that follow will be whomever he or she that will have the rule for that day chooses as the hour of vespers[4] approaches; this ruler, as long as his reign endures, will organize and arrange the place and the manner in which we will spend our time."

These words greatly pleased everyone, and they unanimously elected Pampinea queen for the first day; Filomena quickly ran to a laurel bush, whose leaves she had always heard were worthy of praise and bestowed great honor upon those crowned with them; she plucked several branches from it and wove them into a handsome garland of honor. And when it would be placed upon the head of any one of them, it was to be to all in the group a clear symbol of royal rule and authority over the rest of them for as long as their company stayed together.

After she had been chosen queen, Pampinea ordered everyone to refrain from talking; then, she sent for the four servants of the ladies and for those of the three young men, and as they stood before her in silence, she said:

"Since I must set the first example for you all in order that it may be bettered and thus allow our company to live in order and in pleasure, and without any shame, and so that it may last as long as we wish, I first appoint Parmeno, Dioneo's servant, as my steward, and I commit to his care and management all our household and everything which pertains to the services of the dining hall. I wish Sirisco, the servant of Panfilo, to act as our buyer and treasurer and follow the orders of Parmeno. Tindaro, who is in the service of Filostrato, shall wait on Filostrato and Dioneo and Panfilo in their bedchambers when the other two are occupied with their other duties and cannot do so. Misia, my servant, and Licisca, Filomena's, will be occupied in the kitchen and will prepare those dishes which are ordered by Parmeno. Chimera, Lauretta's servant, and Stratilia, Fiammetta's servant, will take care of the bedchambers of the ladies and the cleaning of those places we use. And in general, we desire and command each of you, if you value our favor and good graces, to be sure—no matter where you go or come from, no matter what you hear or see—to bring us back nothing but pleasant news."

And when these orders, praised by all present, were delivered, Pampinea rose happily to her feet and said:

"Here there are gardens and meadows and many other pleasant places,

---

4. Late afternoon; the sixth of the seven times of day set aside for prayer by canon law.

which all of us can wander about in and enjoy as we like; but at the hour of tierce[5] let everyone be here so that we can eat in the cool of the morning."

After the merry group had been given the new queen's permission, the young men, together with the beautiful ladies, set off slowly through a garden, discussing pleasant matters, making themselves beautiful garlands of various leaves and singing love songs. After the time granted them by the queen had elapsed, they returned home and found Parmeno busy carrying out the duties of his task; for as they entered a hall on the ground floor, they saw the tables set with the whitest of linens and with glasses that shone like silver and everything decorated with broom blossoms; then, they washed their hands and, at the queen's command, they all sat down in the places assigned them by Parmeno. The delicately cooked foods were brought in and very fine wines were served; the three servants in silence served the tables. Everyone was delighted to see everything so beautiful and well arranged, and they ate merrily and with pleasant conversation. Since all the ladies and young men knew how to dance (and some of them even knew how to play and sing very well), when the tables had been cleared, the queen ordered that instruments be brought, and on her command, Dioneo took a lute and Fiammetta a viola, and they began softly playing a dance tune. After the queen had sent the servants off to eat, she began to dance together with the other ladies and two of the young men; and when that was over, they all began to sing carefree and gay songs. In this manner they continued until the queen felt that it was time to retire; therefore, at the queen's request, the three young men went off to their chambers (which were separate from those of the ladies), where they found their beds prepared and the rooms as full of flowers as the halls; the ladies, too, discovered their chambers decorated in like fashion. Then they all undressed and fell asleep.

Not long after the hour of nones, the queen arose and had the other ladies and young men awakened, stating that too much sleep in the daytime was harmful;[6] then they went out onto a lawn of thick, green grass, where no ray of the sun could penetrate; and there, with a gentle breeze caressing them, they all sat in a circle upon the green grass, as was the wish of their queen. Then she spoke to them in this manner:

"As you see, the sun is high, the heat is great, and nothing can be heard except the cicadas in the olive groves; therefore, to wander about at this hour would be, indeed, foolish. Here it is cool and fresh and, as you see, there are games and chessboards with which all of you can amuse yourselves to your liking. But if you take my advice in this matter, I suggest we spend this hot part of the day not in playing games (a pastime which of necessity disturbs the player who loses without providing much pleasure either for his opponents or for those who watch) but rather in telling stories, for this way one person, by telling a story, can provide amusement for the entire company. In the time it takes for the sun to set and the heat to become less oppressive, you will each have told a little story, and then we

---

5. The third canonical hour, nine A.M. 6. They had been taking a siesta. *Nones:* the fifth canonical hour, three P.M.

can go wherever we like to amuse ourselves; so, if what I say pleases you (and in this I am willing to follow your pleasure), then, let us do it; if not, then let everyone do as he pleases until the hour of vespers."

The entire group of men and women liked the idea of telling stories.

"Then," said the queen, "if this is your wish, for this first day I order each of you to tell a story about any subject he likes."

And turning to Panfilo, who sat on her right, she ordered him in a gracious manner to begin with one of his tales; whereupon, hearing her command, Panfilo, while everyone listened, began at once as follows:

*   *   *

THE SECOND TALE OF THE FOURTH DAY[7]

Gracious ladies, there was once in Imola a man of wicked and corrupt ways named Berto della Massa, whose evil deeds were so well known by the people of Imola that nobody there would believe him when he told the truth, not to mention when he lied. Realizing that his tricks would no longer work there, in desperation he moved to Venice, that receptacle of all forms of wickedness, thinking that he would adopt a different style of trickery there from what he had used anywhere else before. And almost as if his conscience were struck with remorse for his evil deeds committed in the past, he gave every sign of a man who had become truly humble and most religious; in fact, he went and turned himself into a minor friar, taking the name of Brother Alberto da Imola; and in this disguise he pretended to lead an ascetic life, praising repentance and abstinence, and never eating meat nor drinking wine unless they were of a quality good enough for him.

Never before had such a thief, pimp, forger, and murderer become so great a preacher without having abandoned these vices, even while he may have been practicing them in secret. And besides this, after he became a priest, whenever he celebrated the mass at the altar, in view of all the congregation, he would weep when it came to the Passion of Our Savior, for he was a man to whom tears cost very little when they were called for. And in short, between his sermons and his tears, he managed to beguile the Venetians to such an extent that he was almost always made the trustee and guardian of every will that was made, the keeper of many people's money, and confessor and advisor to the majority of men and women; and acting in this way, he changed from a wolf into a shepherd, and his reputation for sanctity in those parts was far greater than St. Francis's was in Assisi.

Now it happened that there was a foolish and silly young woman named Madonna Lisetta da Ca' Quirino (the wife of a great merchant who had gone with his galleys to Flanders) who, along with other ladies, went to be confessed by this holy friar. She was kneeling at his feet and, being a Venetian (and, as such, a gossip like all of them), she was asked by Brother Alberto halfway through her confession if she had a lover. To this question she crossly replied:

---

7. Told by Pampinea. On the fourth day, in Filostrato's reign, the friends were to tell love stories with unhappy endings.

"What, my dear brother, don't you have eyes in your head? Do my charms appear to you to be like all those of other women? I could have even more lovers than I want, but my beauty is not to be enjoyed by just anyone. How many ladies do you know who possess such charms as mine, charms which would make me beautiful even in paradise?"

And then she kept on saying so many things about her beauty that it became boring to listen to her. Brother Alberto realized immediately that she was a simpleton, and since he thought she was just the right terrain for plowing, he fell passionately in love with her right then and there; but putting aside his flatteries for a more appropriate time, and reassuming his saintly manner, he began to reproach her and to tell her that her attitude was vainglorious and other such things; and so the lady told him that he was a beast and that he did not know one beauty from another; and because he did not want to upset her too much, Brother Alberto, after having confessed her, let her go off with the other women.

After a few days, he went with a trusted companion to Madonna Liset-ta's home and taking her into a room where they could be seen by no one, he threw himself on his knees before her and said:

"My lady, I beg you in God's name to forgive me for speaking to you as I did last Sunday about your beauty, for I was so soundly punished the following night that I have not been able to get up until today."

"And who punished you in this way?" asked Lady Halfwit.

"I shall tell you," replied Brother Alberto. "As I was praying that night in my cell, as I always do, I suddenly saw a glowing light, and before I was able to turn around to see what it was, I saw a very beautiful young man with a large stick in his hand who took me by the collar, dragged me to my feet, and gave me so many blows that he broke practically everything in my body. I asked him why he had done this and he replied:

'Because yesterday you presumed to reproach the celestial beauty of Madonna Lisetta whom I love more than anything else except God.'

"And then I asked: 'Who are you?'

"He replied that he was the angel Gabriel.

" 'Oh My Lord,' I said, 'I beg you to forgive me.'

" 'I shall forgive you on one condition,' he said, 'that you go to her as soon as you are able and beg her forgiveness; and if she does not pardon you, I shall return here and beat you so soundly that you will be sorry for the rest of your life.' "

Lady Lighthead, who was as smart as salt is sweet, enjoyed hearing all these words and believed them all, and after a moment she said:

"I told you, Brother Alberto, that my charms were heavenly; but, God help me, I feel sorry for you, and from now on, in order to spare you more harm, I forgive you on condition that you tell me what the angel said next."

Brother Alberto said: "My lady, since you have forgiven me, I shall gladly tell you, but I remind you of one thing: you must not tell what I tell you to anyone in the world, otherwise you will spoil everything, you who are the most fortunate woman in the world today. The angel Gabriel told me that I was to tell you that you are so pleasing to him that often he would have come to pass the night with you if he had not thought it might

frighten you. Now he sends me here with a message that he would like to come to you one night and spend some time with you; but since he is an angel and you would not be able to touch him in the form of an angel, he says that for your pleasure he would like to come as a human being, and he asks when you would have him come and in whose shape should he come, and he will come; therefore you, more than any other woman alive, should consider yourself blessed."

Lady Silly then said that it pleased her very much that the angel Gabriel was in love with her, for she loved him as well and never failed to light a cheap candle in his honor whenever she found a painting of him in church; and whenever he wished to come to her, he would be very welcome, and he would find her all alone in her room, and he could come on the condition that he would not leave her for the Virgin Mary, whom, it was said, he loved very much, and it was obviously true, because everywhere she saw him, he was always on his knees before her;[8] and besides this, she said that he could appear in whatever shape or form he wished — she would not be afraid.

"My Lady," Brother Alberto then said, "you speak wisely, and I shall arrange everything with him as you have said. And you could do me a great favor which will cost you nothing; and the favor is this: that you allow him to come to you in my body. Let me tell you how you would be doing me a favor: he will take my soul from my body and place it in paradise, and he will enter my body, and as long as he is with you my soul will be in paradise."

Then Lady Dimwit replied: "That pleases me; I wish you to have this consolation for the beating he gave you on my account."

Brother Alberto then said: "Now arrange for him to find the door of your house open tonight so that he can come inside; since he will be arriving in the form of a man, he cannot enter unless he uses the door."

The lady replied that it would be done. Brother Alberto departed, and she was so delighted by the whole affair that, jumping for joy, she could hardly keep her skirts over her ass, and it seemed like a thousand years to her waiting for the angel Gabriel to come. Brother Alberto, who was thinking more about getting in the saddle than of being an angel that evening, began to fortify himself with sweetmeats and other delicacies so that he would not be easily thrown from his horse; and then he got permission to stay out that night and, as soon as it was dark, he went with a trusted companion to the house of a lady friend of his, which on other occasions he had used as his point of departure whenever he went to ride the mares; and from there, when the time seemed ripe to him, he went in disguise to the lady's house, and went inside; and, having changed himself into an angel with the different odds and ends he brought with him, he climbed the stairs, and entered the lady's bedroom.

When she saw this white object approaching, she threw herself on her knees in front of him, and the angel blessed her and raised her to her feet, and made a sign for her to get into bed; and she, most anxious to obey, did

8. Gabriel told the Virgin Mary that she was to bear the Son of God, and so the two are invariably shown together in paintings of the Annunciation, which Lisetta would often have seen in church.

so immediately, and the angel lay down alongside his devout worshipper. Brother Alberto was a handsome young man with a robust, well-built body; Lady Lisetta was all fresh and soft, and she discovered that his ride was altogether different from that of her husband. He flew many times that night without his wings, which caused the lady to cry aloud with delight and, in addition, he told her many things about the glory of heaven. Then as day broke, having made another appointment to meet her, he gathered his equipment and returned to his companion, who had struck up a friendly relationship with the good woman of the house so that she would not be afraid of sleeping alone.

When the lady had finished breakfast, she went with one of her attendants to Brother Alberto's and told him the story of the angel Gabriel and of what she had heard from him about the glory of the eternal life and of how he looked, adding all sorts of incredible tales to her story. To this Brother Alberto said:

"My lady, I do not know how you were with him; I only know that last night, when he came to me and I delivered your message to him, in an instant he transported my soul to a place where there were more flowers and roses than I have ever seen before, and he left my soul in this most delightful spot until this morning at the hour of early prayer. What happened to my body I know not."

"But did I not tell you?" replied the lady. "Your body passed the entire night in my arms with the angel Gabriel inside it; and if you do not believe me, look under your left nipple, where I gave the angel such a passionate kiss that he will carry its mark for some days!"

Then Brother Alberto said: "Today I shall perform an act that I have not done for some time—I shall undress myself to see if what you say is true."

And after much more chatter, the lady returned home; and Brother Alberto, without the slightest problem, often went to visit her, disguised as an angel. One day, however, Madonna Lisetta was discussing the nature of beauty with one of her neighbors, and she, showing off and being the silly goose she was, said: "You would not talk about any other women if you knew who it is that loves my beauty."

Her neighbor, anxious to hear more about this and knowing very well the kind of woman Lisetta was, replied: "Madame, you may be right; but as I do not know to whom you are referring, I cannot change my opinion so easily."

"Neighbor," replied Madonna Lisetta, who was easily excited, "he does not want it to be known, but my lover is the angel Gabriel, and he loves me more than himself, and he tells me that this is because I am the most beautiful woman that there is in the world or even in the Maremma."[9]

Her neighbor had the urge to break into laughter right then, but she held herself back in order to make her friend continue talking, and she said: "God's faith, Madame, if the angel Gabriel is your lover and he tells you this, it must really be so; but I did not realize that angels did such things."

9. A small, marshy region of Tuscany.

"Neighbor," replied the lady, "that is where you are wrong; by God's wounds, he does it better than my husband, and he tells me that they do it up there as well; but since he thinks I am more beautiful than anyone in heaven, he fell in love with me and comes to be with me very often. Now do you see?"

When the neighbor had left Madonna Lisetta, it seemed to her as if a thousand years had passed before she was able to repeat what she had learned; and at a large gathering of women, she told them the whole story. These women told it to their husbands and to other women, who passed it on to others, and thus in less than two days it was the talk of all Venice. But among those whom this story reached were also the woman's in-laws, and they decided, without telling her a word, to find this angel and to see if he knew how to fly; and they kept watch for him for several nights. It just happened that some hint of this got back to Brother Alberto, so he went there one night to reprove the lady, and no sooner was he undressed than her in-laws, who had seen him arrive, were at the door of the bedroom ready to open it. When Brother Alberto heard this and realized what was going on, he jumped up, and seeing no other means of escape, he flung open a window which looked out on the Grand Canal and threw himself into the water.

The water was deep there, but he knew how to swim well, and so he did not hurt himself; after he swam to the other side of the canal, he immediately entered a home that was opened to him and begged the good man inside, for the love of God, to save his life, as he made up a story to explain why he was there at that hour and in the nude. The good man, moved to pity, gave him his own bed, since he had some affairs of his own to attend to, and he told him to remain there until he returned; and having locked him in, he went about his business.

When the lady's in-laws opened the door to her bedroom and entered, they found that the angel Gabriel had flown away, leaving his wings behind him; they abused the lady no end and finally, leaving her alone, all distressed, they returned to their home with the angel's equipment. In the meanwhile, at daybreak, while the good man was on the Rialto, he heard talk about how the angel Gabriel had gone to bed that night with Madonna Lisetta and had been discovered there by her in-laws, and how he had thrown himself into the canal out of fear, and how no one knew what had happened to him; immediately he realized that the man in his house was the man in question. Returning home and identifying him, after much discussion, he came to an agreement with the friar: he would not give him over to the in-laws if he would pay him fifty ducats; and this was done.

When Brother Alberto wished to leave the place, the good man told him:

"There is only one way out, if you agree to it. Today we are celebrating a festival in which men are led around dressed as bears, others dressed as wild men, and others in one costume or another, and a hunt is put on in St. Mark's Square, and with that the festival is ended; then everyone goes away, with whomever he led there, to wherever they please; and if you wish, so that no one will discover you, I am willing to lead you to wherever

you like; otherwise, I don't see any way for you to escape from here without being recognized; and the in-laws of the lady, knowing that you have hidden yourself somewhere around here, have posted guards everywhere to trap you."

Though it seemed rough to Brother Alberto to have to go in such a disguise, his fear of the lady's relatives induced him to agree, and he told the man where he would like to go and that in whatever way he might choose to lead him there, he would be happy. The man smeared him completely with honey, covered him up with feathers, put a chain around his neck and a mask on his head; in one of his hands he put a large club and in the other two great dogs which he had brought from the butcher; at the same time he sent someone to the Rialto to announce that whoever wished to see the angel Gabriel should go to St. Mark's Square. And this is what they call good old Venetian honesty!

And when this was done, he took the friar outside and had him take the lead, holding him by a chain from behind; and many bystanders kept asking: "Who is it? What is it?" Thus he led him up to the piazza where, between those who had followed him and those who had heard the announcement and had come from the Rialto, a huge crowd gathered. When he arrived there, he tied his wild man up to a column in a conspicuous and elevated spot, pretending to wait for the hunt; meanwhile, the flies and horseflies were giving Brother Alberto a great deal of trouble, for he was covered with honey. But when the good man saw that the piazza was full, pretending to unchain his wild man, he tore the mask from his face and announced:

"Ladies and gentlemen, since the pig has not come to the hunt, and since there is no hunt, I would not want you to have come in vain; therefore I should like you to see the angel Gabriel, who descends from heaven to earth to console the Venetian women by night."

When his mask was removed, Brother Alberto was instantly recognized by everybody, and everyone cried out against him and shouted the most insulting words that were ever directed at a scoundrel; besides this, one by one they all started throwing garbage in his face, keeping him occupied this way for a long time until, by chance, the news reached his brother friars; six of them came, and throwing a cloak over him, they unchained him, and in the midst of a great commotion, they led him back to their monastery, where he was locked up, and after a miserable life he is believed to have died there.

Thus a man who was thought to be good and who acted evilly, not recognized for what he really was, dared to turn himself into the angel Gabriel, and instead was converted into a wild man, and, finally, was cursed at as he deserved and made to lament in vain for the sins he had committed. May it please God that the same thing happen to all others like him!

*   *   *

THE NINTH TALE OF THE FIFTH DAY[1]

There was once in Florence a young man named Federigo, the son of Messer Filippo Alberighi, renowned above all other men in Tuscany for his prowess in arms and for his courtliness. As often happens to most gentlemen, he fell in love with a lady named Monna Giovanna, in her day considered to be one of the most beautiful and one of the most charming women that ever there was in Florence; and in order to win her love, he participated in jousts and tournaments, organized and gave feasts, and spent his money without restraint; but she, no less virtuous than beautiful, cared little for these things done on her behalf, nor did she care for him who did them. Now, as Federigo was spending far beyond his means and was taking nothing in, as easily happens he lost his wealth and became poor, with nothing but his little farm to his name (from whose revenues he lived very meagerly) and one falcon which was among the best in the world.

More in love than ever, but knowing that he would never be able to live the way he wished to in the city, he went to live at Campi, where his farm was. There he passed his time hawking whenever he could, asked nothing of anyone, and endured his poverty patiently. Now, during the time that Federigo was reduced to dire need, it happened that the husband of Monna Giovanna fell ill, and realizing death was near, he made his last will: he was very rich, and he made his son, who was growing up, his heir, and, since he had loved Monna Giovanna very much, he made her his heir should his son die without a legitimate heir; and then he died.

Monna Giovanna was now a widow, and as is the custom among our women, she went to the country with her son to spend a year on one of her possessions very close by to Federigo's farm, and it happened that this young boy became friends with Federigo and began to enjoy birds and hunting dogs; and after he had seen Federigo's falcon fly many times, it pleased him so much that he very much wished it were his own, but he did not dare to ask for it, for he could see how dear it was to Federigo. And during this time, it happened that the young boy took ill, and his mother was much grieved, for he was her only child and she loved him enormously; she would spend the entire day by his side, never ceasing to comfort him, and often asking him if there was anything he desired, begging him to tell her what it might be, for if it were possible to obtain it, she would certainly do everything possible to get it. After the young boy had heard her make this offer many times, he said:

"Mother, if you can arrange for me to have Federigo's falcon, I think I would be well very soon."

When the lady heard this, she was taken aback for a moment, and she began to think what she should do. She knew that Federigo had loved her for a long while, in spite of the fact that he never received a single glance from her, and so, she said to herself:

"How can I send or go and ask for this falcon of his which is, as I have heard tell, the best that ever flew, and besides this, his only means of

---

1. Told by Dioneo. On the fifth day, in Fiammetta's reign, the friends were to tell love stories that end happily after a period of misfortune.

support? And how can I be so insensitive as to wish to take away from this
gentleman the only pleasure which is left to him?"

And involved in these thoughts, knowing that she was certain to have
the bird if she asked for it, but not knowing what to say to her son, she
stood there without answering him. Finally the love she bore her son persuaded her that she should make him happy, and no matter what the
consequences might be, she would not send for the bird, but rather go
herself for it and bring it back to him; so she answered her son:

"My son, take comfort and think only of getting well, for I promise you
that the first thing I shall do tomorrow morning is to go for it and bring it
back to you."

The child was so happy that he showed some improvement that very
day. The following morning, the lady, accompanied by another woman,
as if going for a stroll, went to Federigo's modest house and asked for him.
Since it was not the season for it, Federigo had not been hawking for some
days and was in his orchard, attending to certain tasks; when he heard that
Monna Giovanna was asking for him at the door, he was very surprised
and happy to run there; as she saw him coming, she greeted him with
feminine charm, and once Federigo had welcomed her courteously, she
said:

"Greetings, Federigo!" Then she continued: "I have come to compensate you for the harm you have suffered on my account by loving me
more than you needed to; and the compensation is this: I, along with this
companion of mine, intend to dine with you—a simple meal—this very
day."

To this Federigo humbly replied: "Madonna, I never remember having
suffered any harm because of you; on the contrary: so much good have I
received from you that if ever I have been worth anything, it has been
because of your merit and the love I bore for you; and your generous visit
is certainly so dear to me that I would spend all over again that which I
spent in the past; but you have come to a poor host."

And having said this, he received her into his home humbly, and from
there he led her into his garden, and since he had no one there to keep
her company, he said:

"My lady, since there is no one else, this good woman here, the wife of
this workman, will keep you company while I go to set the table."

Though he was very poor, Federigo, until now, had never before realized to what extent he had wasted his wealth; but this morning, the fact
that he found nothing with which he could honor the lady for the love of
whom he had once entertained countless men in the past gave him cause
to reflect: in great anguish, he cursed himself and his fortune and, like a
man beside himself, he started running here and there, but could find
neither money nor a pawnable object. The hour was late and his desire to
honor the gracious lady was great, but not wishing to turn for help to
others (not even to his own workman), he set his eyes upon his good
falcon, perched in a small room; and since he had nowhere else to turn,
he took the bird, and finding it plump, he decided that it would be a
worthy food for such a lady. So, without further thought, he wrung its
neck and quickly gave it to his servant girl to pluck, prepare, and place on

a spit to be roasted with care; and when he had set the table with the whitest of tablecloths (a few of which he still had left), he returned, with a cheerful face, to the lady in his garden, saying that the meal he was able to prepare for her was ready.

The lady and her companion rose, went to the table together with Federigo, who waited upon them with the greatest devotion, and they ate the good falcon without knowing what it was they were eating. And having left the table and spent some time in pleasant conversation, the lady thought it time now to say what she had come to say, and so she spoke these kind words to Federigo:

"Federigo, if you recall your past life and my virtue, which you perhaps mistook for harshness and cruelty, I do not doubt at all that you will be amazed by my presumption when you hear what my main reason for coming here is; but if you had children, through whom you might have experienced the power of parental love, it seems certain to me that you would, at least in part, forgive me. But, just as you have no child, I do have one, and I cannot escape the common laws of other mothers; the force of such laws compels me to follow them, against my own will and against good manners and duty, and to ask of you a gift which I know is most precious to you; and it is naturally so, since your extreme condition has left you no other delight, no other pleasure, no other consolation; and this gift is your falcon, which my son is so taken by that if I do not bring it to him, I fear his sickness will grow so much worse that I may lose him. And therefore I beg you, not because of the love that you bear for me, which does not oblige you in the least, but because of your own nobility, which you have shown to be greater than that of all others in practicing courtliness, that you be pleased to give it to me, so that I may say that I have saved the life of my son by means of this gift, and because of it I have placed him in your debt forever."

When he heard what the lady requested and knew that he could not oblige her since he had given her the falcon to eat, Federigo began to weep in her presence, for he could not utter a word in reply. The lady, at first, thought his tears were caused more by the sorrow of having to part with the good falcon than by anything else, and she was on the verge of telling him she no longer wished it, but she held back and waited for Federigo's reply after he stopped weeping. And he said:

"My lady, ever since it pleased God for me to place my love in you, I have felt that Fortune has been hostile to me in many things, and I have complained of her, but all this is nothing compared to what she has just done to me, and I must never be at peace with her again, thinking about how you have come here to my poor home where, while it was rich, you never deigned to come, and you requested a small gift, and Fortune worked to make it impossible for me to give it to you; and why this is so I shall tell you briefly. When I heard that you, out of your kindness, wished to dine with me, I considered it fitting and right, taking into account your excellence and your worthiness, that I should honor you, according to my possibilities, with a more precious food than that which I usually serve to other people; therefore, remembering the falcon that you requested and its value, I judged it a food worthy of you, and this very day you had it

roasted and served to you as best I could; but seeing now that you desired it in another way, my sorrow in not being able to serve you is so great that I shall never be able to console myself again."

And after he had said this, he laid the feathers, the feet, and the beak of the bird before her as proof. When the lady heard and saw this, she first reproached him for having killed such a falcon to serve as a meal to a woman; but then to herself she commended the greatness of his spirit, which no poverty was able or would be able to diminish; then, having lost all hope of getting the falcon and, perhaps because of this, of improving the health of her son as well, she thanked Federigo both for the honor paid to her and for his good will, and she left in grief, and returned to her son. To his mother's extreme sorrow, either because of his disappointment that he could not have the falcon, or because his illness must have necessarily led to it, the boy passed from this life only a few days later.

After the period of her mourning and bitterness had passed, the lady was repeatedly urged by her brothers to remarry, since she was very rich and was still young; and although she did not wish to do so, they became so insistent that she remembered the merits of Federigo and his last act of generosity—that is, to have killed such a falcon to do her honor—and she said to her brothers:

"I would prefer to remain a widow, if that would please you; but if you wish me to take a husband, you may rest assured that I shall take no man but Federigo degli Alberighi."

In answer to this, making fun of her, her brothers replied:

"You foolish woman, what are you saying? How can you want him; he hasn't a penny to his name?"

To this she replied: "My brothers, I am well aware of what you say, but I would rather have a man who needs money than money that needs a man."

Her brothers, seeing that she was determined and knowing Federigo to be of noble birth, no matter how poor he was, accepted her wishes and gave her in marriage to him with all her riches; when he found himself the husband of such a great lady, whom he had loved so much and who was so wealthy besides, he managed his financial affairs with more prudence than in the past and lived with her happily the rest of his days.

*   *   *

GEOFFREY CHAUCER
1340?–1400

Although the French produced the richest and most influential body of vernacular literature in the Middle Ages, the greatest writers of the period were an Italian, Dante, and an Englishman, Geoffrey Chaucer. The Florentine poet and the Londoner both wrote their most important works in the fourteenth century, the former in its early decades, the latter in its latest. In origin and background, both represent

the point of view of the upper middle class or the lesser gentry, groups that were not sharply separated in the urban life of Italy and of London in the later medieval centuries. Both were active in public affairs; both on occasion were envoys of their respective governments. Dante was once responsible for widening a street in Florence, and Chaucer for a time held a post comparable to that of an undersecretary of the interior in the cabinet of the United States. If Dante had sharper political convictions and a greater theoretical interest in the philosophy of government, Chaucer held a wider variety of offices—and held them longer.

Chaucer was born in 1340 or a few years later, the son of a London wine merchant. In 1357 he apparently became a page in the household of the countess of Ulster, wife of Lionel, a son of King Edward III. In 1359, in military service with the English in France, he was captured by the French and ransomed with royal funds. Between 1368 and 1378 Chaucer made several journeys to France and Italy as the king's envoy or courier. In 1374 he received a pension from John of Gaunt, a son of Edward III, and became comptroller of customs in the port of London; about 1385 he moved to Kent, where he was elected knight of the shire in 1386, and sat in Parliament for one term. In 1389 he became clerk of the King's Works (under Richard II), in 1391 deputy forester of the royal forest of North Petherton in Somerset, and in 1399 pensioner of King Henry IV.

Chaucer's early works include *The Romance of the Rose*, a translation (probably never finished) of the *Roman de la Rose*; the *Book of the Duchess*; the *House of Fame*; and the *Parliament of Fowls*—all in English verse. He also translated *A Treatise on the Astrolabe* and Boethius' *Consolation of Philosophy* into English prose. His major works are *Troilus and Criseyde*, completed about 1385, and *The Canterbury Tales*, composed largely in the 1390s but with some use of earlier material.

Both Dante and Chaucer probably lived out their lives as laymen; their view of the world is free from the bias of a clerical vocation. Yet both were orthodox in religion and theology. Dante was severe with heretics and schismatics, and Chaucer was neither a Wycliffite nor a sympathizer with the Peasants' Revolt. With the partial exception of Dante's insistence on the equal status of the Holy Roman Empire and the papacy, alike providentially sponsored, it may be said that both poets found themselves in harmony with the traditional institutions and patterns of medieval civilization. Both were keenly aware of injustices resulting from abuses of the system; each exposed scoundrels and frauds with enthusiasm—Dante with bitterness, Chaucer with amusement. But their denunciation of wicked rulers and their satire directed against the worldliness of bishops and abbots and the corruptness of friars and pardoners do not show either writer to be a rebel against the established institutions of Church or State. The background against which abuses are portrayed is always, implicitly or explicitly, the ideal pattern for the king or priest or monk—not some utopian or revolutionary social order that would dispense with or radically alter the patterns themselves.

On the ultimate issues of human life, as in these questions of the structure of civilization, the two greatest literary geniuses of the Middle Ages were in agreement with each other and with their contemporaries. For each, God was the center of the universe, as humanity and our earth were the center of the cosmic order. Our life's goal was union with God; if we attained it—after this short earthly life—we would spend eternity in Heaven; if we missed it, then Hell awaited us. For our direction and guidance toward the good in this life and the next, there were the divinely ordained religion and its Church, and the divinely approved hierarchy of society on earth. As men of independent intelligence, of education— and of essentially middle-class origin—both Dante and Chaucer insisted that true nobility depends on intrinsic character, not the accident of birth. But the modern conceptions of political, social, and economic equality as well as complete reli-

gious freedom, would have appeared to them as anarchy. They had fundamental faith in the quite different patterns of institutional hierarchy and authority.

If Dante chose the life after death as the theme of the greatest medieval poem, Chaucer chose a religious pilgrimage as the framework of the richest portrayal of medieval men and women in the earthly scene. Chaucer's pilgrims are very much alive; they are on their way to thank St. Thomas of Canterbury for his help in keeping them that way! Yet the twenty-nine travelers, including those described in the course of the pilgrimage, are not incomparable in number or vividness to the characters presented with similar fullness in *The Divine Comedy*. Both poets— when they wish—make the individual stand out clearly and distinctly; both— when they choose—present fully the background, the milieu, the occupational or moral setting from which the individual emerges and in terms of which he or she is to be estimated. Both poets sketch the portraits with extraordinary insight, discrimination, and perception of the subtle mixture of good and bad in humanity. It would be interesting to attempt the assignment of Chaucer's pilgrims to their proper places in *The Divine Comedy*—assuming that each of them dies in the condition described in the *General Prologue*.

With the Knight, the Parson, his brother the Plowman, the Clerk of Oxford, and the Nun's Priest (who is characterized in the course of the journey) we should have no trouble. Though thoroughly human, flesh-and-blood people, these are all wholly excellent and admirable men. Moral and ethical nobility is a part of their personal and vocational perfection. They embody—not merely personify as abstractions—the ideal characteristics of men in their several stations in life; they are models as well as individuals. But these individuals are living men on earth. We recognize in the portrait of the Clerk, for instance, an ingredient of tacit humor hardly duplicated in Dante's presentation of the blessed. The Clerk's unique traits of temperament and taste—the concise habit of speech, the aloofness, the ardent book collecting—might be a little irrelevant in Heaven, while eminently suited to his portrait in this world.

The scoundrels, likewise, would be easy to deal with. The Friar, the Pardoner, the Summoner—and perhaps also the Shipman, the Reeve, the Manciple, and the Miller—would easily find their respective niches in the circles of Hell—most of them in the ten subdivisions of the eighth circle, in which those guilty of various kinds of fraud are punished. Dante might have made each of them tell his story in much the same terms as Chaucer used. He would have done it with as much gusto; indeed, his work includes parallels to most of them. But denunciation and contempt would have replaced Chaucer's detached delight in the cleverness and success of their rascality. Again, the vantage point dictates an appropriate difference of treatment; time and our earth are a different background from eternity and Hell. Both Dante's and Chaucer's portraits achieve symmetry. But Dante's are more decisive, more limited, more exclusively concentrated on ethical definition; Chaucer's have room for more mundane, personal, and morally neutral detail.

We should have great difficulty in classifying some of the other pilgrims. The exquisite Prioress is doubtless destined for Heaven. But should we expect to find her, fairly soon, among the blessed in one of the three lowest spheres—the moon, Mercury, or Venus? Is she, like Piccarda, a soul whose unquestionably genuine devotion is linked with an intrinsically limited spiritual capacity—limited in a way suggested by her unmonastic fondness for pet dogs, nice clothes, and fashionable manners? Or is her sensibility an outward sign of great spiritual endowment, so that, after some time on the terraces of Purgatory, she will be found among the higher spheres of the celestial hierarchy? Dante had to decide such questions concerning his characters, and his portraits naturally show how they fit the classifications. Chaucer did not have to decide; his pilgrims still belong to the earth, and some of their portraits are executed without conclusive moral definition. The

worldly, hunting Monk—will he take his place among the avaricious or the hypo-crites in Hell? Or will he purge his worldliness, like Pope Adrian, on the fifth ledge of the mountain?

In general, Chaucer shows a large "middle" group of people, confirmed perhaps in neither wickedness nor holiness but absorbed in the things of this world. Such an absorption exposes the professed cleric, secular or monastic, to ironical satire; for the religious vocation involves renunciation of the world. This is why many of the pilgrims connected with the Church are obvious targets. But laymen also run the risk of ridicule if their absorption in worldly matters leads to excessive egotism or affectation or limitation of perspective. Thus the Sergeant of the Law, whose days are, in fact, full, *seems* even busier than he is; the Merchant apparently talks entirely about profits; and the Physician's financial astuteness is not unmixed with complacency. The Franklin's pride in his hospitality and fine table is a more attractive form of egotism—although one might hesitate to become his cook! Traits such as these, casually mentioned in the Prologue, would be valuable hints as to where on the terraces of Purgatory the several pilgrims might be expected to spend some time. Meanwhile, it is just such qualities, the weaknesses, foibles, excesses, and limitations, that endow them with distinctness and poignancy in this world—in short, with individuality and personality.

It is often said that the characters in the Prologue are delineated in terms of the superlative—each of the pilgrims is the best, or worst, representative of his particu-lar kind. To some degree this is true. Yet it is also true that Chaucer finds far less to say about some than about others. He is, in fact, interested in them in different ways. Thus the Knight is described at length; occupationally, ethically, and other-wise he emerges as an individual member of a class. His son, the young Squire, is presented primarily as a fine but standard specimen of his type, the fashionable young warrior and politely cultivated "lover." And in their servant, the Yeoman, we see a yet smaller segment of the whole character: he is simply an expert woods-man. Other pilgrims, like the five Guildsmen, receive only a collective portrait; they all share in the pride of their crafts and their organized "fraternity," in the garb of which they are handsomely turned out. A few of the company are not described at all in the Prologue.

Evidently Chaucer has allowed himself a margin of freedom in his account of this imaginary company as they present themselves to the imaginary observer and fellow traveler, the poet. With the future possibilities of the pilgrimage in mind, he readily leaves a few members of the group undeveloped; one of these, the Nun's Priest, does emerge in full characterization as the tales proceed. But in the Pro-logue itself Chaucer gives us the fullest, the most varied, and the liveliest, pan-orama of men and women in medieval literature. The portraits are usually fairly complete and satisfying in themselves, though, as we have noted, some are minia-tures and some large canvases, some are full face, some profile, and a few quarter face. Yet the portraits are not merely lively in themselves; they are dynamic; they prepare us for the highly dramatic relationships that develop among the pilgrims in the course of the journey.

THE MILLER'S TALE

At the end of the *General Prologue* we are told that the Knight will tell the first tale. This narrative, not included here, is a fine example of medieval metrical romance—with important variations from the standard types. As we learn from the Words between the Host and the Miller, the latter, now drunk, refuses to follow the decorous order preferred by the Host; he insists on matching the Knight right now with his tale. When he goes on to say that it will be a story of an old carpenter, his wife, and her student lover, we anticipate, rightly, that it will be the opposite of the Knight's courtly romance. Like the medieval reader, we expect a tale of

amorous intrigue and trickery involving people of considerably less than noble rank, in short, a fabliau. But the carpenter's wife, Alison, has not only a husband, John, and a lover, Nicholas; there is also a would-be lover, the parish clerk, Absalom. There is thus a double-triangle plot, with Alison at the apex of both triangles; and the denouement comes when one triangle crashes down on the other.

This addition to the traditional fabliau plot is one part of Chaucer's vast enrichment of what must have been a fairly stereotyped narrative. In mediocre tales of this sort, the plot is almost everything; they are comic anecdotes. But Chaucer has lavished as much effort on characterization and depiction of scenes as one expects in the best serious literature. We get to know the clever, opportunistic, cynical Nicholas very well indeed. His rival, Absalom, is a complete contrast. He is theatrical, sentimental, and silly; his "love" songs are an amusing parody of the poetic pleas of chivalric suitors. (Nicholas is much too practical and hardheaded to go in for amorous complaints; he keeps his eye on the main chance—and he is right; he knows how to get what he wants, as Absalom does not.)

The vivid, detailed description of Alison, rich in comparisons and fresh images, would remind the medieval reader of traditional portraits of ladies in romances— by difference rather than similarity. Instead of the standard noble lady, looking out placidly from a castle window, we have Alison, painted in a series of modest similes: "a coin," "a swallow," a "mouth . . . as sweet as honey-ale," "skittish as an untrained colt." The personality of John, the carpenter, is similarly altered. Here the prototype was an old husband married to a young wife; he was jealous and suspicious. Chaucer's John is a great deal more than this. He is genuinely devoted to his wife—he dotes on her; he is fond of Nicholas, his student lodger, though he also believes in the commonsense advantages of the ordinary man (himself) over the scholar; and he is attractively gullible—he embraces the plan for dealing with the flood with great gusto.

The denouement of *The Miller's Tale* does not satisfy the requirements of poetic justice; it does not reward the good and punish the wicked, at least not consistently. Instead, it penalizes stupidity and vindicates cleverness. Moreover, characterization and plot reinforce each other: the various individuals do the kinds of things that we are willing to believe these kinds of people would do. And there is room for variation within the basic pattern: The ingenuity of Nicholas is duly rewarded, but when overconfidence leads him to overreach himself a bit (both metaphorically and literally), he suffers in the end. Alison's cleverness is not flawed by such excess—and she escapes.

THE PARDONER'S TALE

The Pardoner is one of the liveliest rascals on the Canterbury pilgrimage. His crookedness is so complete that it may be difficult for us to realize just what a pardoner was properly or ideally like in the fourteenth century. For one thing, a legitimate pardoner did not go about "pardoning" people for their sins. Many such men were not—and were not expected to be—priests, in the proper sense of the term, at all. Many doubtless were in what is called minor orders, extending up to subdeacon. Such men were not qualified or authorized to hear confession or grant absolution. The legitimate activity of a pardoner consisted in making available to devout persons a certificate of ecclesiastical "indulgence." The charge made for this constituted a gift or offering to God and the Church. The purchase was therefore considered a worthy act in the sight of God that might benefit the soul of the purchaser (as well as relatives or friends if they were doing penance in Purgatory, but *not* if they had been sent to Hell).

No doubt there were many perfectly honest and worthy pardoners in medieval Europe. But the opportunities for personal profit are evident, and there must have been some who exploited these opportunities unscrupulously. Besides distributing

indulgences of doubtful validity, Chaucer's Pardoner preaches in country churches, intimidating the congregation so that they will not fail to put money in the collection plate, and he makes a good profit out of fake relics. Far from being ashamed of these vices, he is proud of his skill in dishonesty. He tells us all about it in the prologue to his tale.

The Pardoner's Tale itself is a sample of his preaching. The text of the sermon is his favorite: Covetousness is the root of evil. It is ironical, of course, that such a man should preach so regularly and strenuously against his own greatest sin. His sermon, as Chaucer presents it, is really a very old and simple story about three men who went in search of Death and found him unexpectedly. The Pardoner dramatizes the narrative with great energy and imagination. In addition, he embroiders it with brief anecdotes which are really digressions. Before he has really entered into the story, moreover, he takes time out for a ringing denunciation of gluttony (including drunkenness), gambling, and swearing—complete with examples of each.

CHAUCER IN MIDDLE ENGLISH

Chaucer is presented here in a Modern English version by Theodore Morrison, which is remarkably clear, accurate, and easy to read. But, to get some idea of Chaucer's original language, we may profitably compare the first eighteen lines of the *General Prologue* in the two forms. It will be possible to point out only a few of the changes that have occurred in pronunciation, in grammatical forms, and sometimes in the use and meaning of words.

> Whan that Aprille with his shoures sote
> The droghte of Marche hath perced to the rote,
> And bathed every veyne in swich licour,
> Of which vertu engendred is the flour;
> When Zephirus eek with his swete breeth   5
> Inspired hath in every holt and heeth
> The tendre croppes, and the yonge sonne
> Hath in the Ram his halfe cours y-ronne,
> And smale fowles maken melodye,
> That slepen al the night with open yë,   10
> So priketh hem nature in hir corages:
> Than longen folk to goon on pilgrimages
> And palmers for to seken straunge strandes
> To ferne halwes, couthe in sondry landes;
> And specially, from every shires ende   15
> Of Engeland, to Caunterbury they wende,
> The holy blisful martir for to seke,
> That hem hath holpen, whan that they were seke.

In Middle English of the late fourteenth century, the letters representing the stressed vowels were pronounced about as they are in Spanish or Italian in our time. Thus the A of *Aprille* sounded like *a* in our *father;* the first *e* in *swete* (line 5) was like the *a* in modern English *late;* and the second *i* in *Inspired* (line 6) was like *i* in our *machine.* In verbs, the third person singular ended in *-th*, not *-s*, as in *hath* (line 2); and the plural ending, either *-en* or *-e*, formed a separate syllable, as in *maken* (line 9), *slepen* (line 10), and *wende* (line 16). Among the pronouns and pronominal adjectives, Chaucer's language did not have our *its, their,* or *them.* Instead, the corresponding forms were, respectively, *his* (line 1), *hir(e)* (line 11), and *hem* (line 18). Changes in the meaning or use of words may compel a substitution. Thus Chaucer's *couthe* (line 14) has become obsolete and hence is translated

as *renowned* instead; so also *corages* (line 11) becomes *hearts*, and *ferne halwes* (line 14) becomes *foreign shrines*.

It will be noted that both the original and the translation have lines regularly rhyming in couplets. Sometimes the translator has been able to keep the same rhyming words (with some difference of pronunciation) as in lines 7 and 8 and lines 13 and 14. In other places he has found it necessary to substitute a new rhyming pair of his own, as in lines 1 and 2 and lines 17 and 18—although in the first instance the translator keeps one of the original rhyming words but not the other.

The standard edition of Chaucer's works is Larry D. Benson, ed., *The Riverside Chaucer*, (1987). This book provides a fully annotated text in the original Middle English, with a glossary, ample introductions, and other apparatus. Among the large number of good books about Chaucer, here are a few that may be especially helpful to our readers. For an overall view, G. L. Kittredge, *Chaucer and his Poetry* (1915), is still important. The artistic development of the poet is traced in Derek S. Brewer, *Chaucer* (1953). A survey of critical problems is presented in Derek A. Pearsall, *The Canterbury Tales* (1985). A variety of topics and points of view will be found in Edward Wagenknecht, ed., *Chaucer: Modern Essays in Criticism* (1959), and for a lively discussion of Chaucer's comic techniques, see L. Kendrick, *Chaucerian Play: Comedy and Control in the Canterbury Tales* (1988).

PRONOUNCING GLOSSARY

The following list uses common English syllables and stress accents to provide rough equivalents of selected words whose pronunciation may be unfamiliar to the general reader.

Berwick: *behr'-ik*   Southwark: *suth'-ark*

The Canterbury Tales[1]

General Prologue

As soon as April pierces to the root
The drought of March, and bathes each bud and shoot
Through every vein of sap with gentle showers
From whose engendering liquor spring the flowers;
When zephyrs[2] have breathed softly all about   5
Inspiring every wood and field to sprout,
And in the zodiac the youthful sun
His journey halfway through the Ram[3] has run;
When little birds are busy with their song
Who sleep with open eyes the whole night long   10
Life stirs their hearts and tingles in them so,
Then off as pilgrims people long to go,
And palmers[4] to set out for distant strands
And foreign shrines renowned in many lands.
And specially in England people ride   15
To Canterbury from every countryside

---

1. Translated and edited by Theodore Morrison.   2. The west wind.   3. A sign of the zodiac (Aries); the sun is in the Ram from March 12 to April 11.   4. Pilgrims, who, originally, brought back palm leaves from the Holy Land.

To visit there the blessed martyred saint[5]
Who gave them strength when they were sick and faint.
   In Southwark at the Tabard[6] one spring day
It happened, as I stopped there on my way,   20
Myself a pilgrim with a heart devout
Ready for Canterbury to set out,
At night came all of twenty-nine assorted
Travelers, and to that same inn resorted,
Who by a turn of fortune chanced to fall   25
In fellowship together, and they were all
Pilgrims who had it in their minds to ride
Toward Canterbury. The stable doors were wide,
The rooms were large, and we enjoyed the best,
And shortly, when the sun had gone to rest,   30
I had so talked with each that presently
I was a member of their company
And promised to rise early the next day
To start, as I shall show, upon our way.
   But none the less, while I have time and space,   35
Before this tale has gone a further pace,
I should in reason tell you the condition
Of each of them, his rank and his position,
And also what array they all were in;
And so then, with a knight I will begin.   40
   A Knight was with us, and an excellent man,
Who from the earliest moment he began
To follow his career loved chivalry,
Truth, openhandedness, and courtesy.
He was a stout man in the king's campaigns   45
And in that cause had gripped his horse's reins
In Christian lands and pagan through the earth,
None farther, and always honored for his worth.
He was on hand at Alexandria's[7] fall.
He had often sat in precedence to all   50
The nations at the banquet board in Prussia.
He had fought in Lithuania and in Russia,
No Christian knight more often; he had been
In Moorish Africa at Benmarin,
At the siege of Algeciras in Granada,   55
And sailed in many a glorious armada
In the Mediterranean, and fought as well
At Ayas and Attalia when they fell
In Armenia and on Asia Minor's coast.
Of fifteen deadly battles he could boast,   60
And in Algeria, at Tremessen,
Fought for the faith and killed three separate men

---

5. St. Thomas à Becket, slain in Canterbury cathedral in 1170.   6. An inn at Southwark, across the
river Thames from London.   7. In Egypt, captured in 1365 by King Peter of Cyprus.

In single combat. He had done good work
Joining against another pagan Turk
With the king of Palathia. And he was wise,   65
Despite his prowess, honored in men's eyes,
Meek as a girl and gentle in his ways.
He had never spoken ignobly all his days
To any man by even a rude inflection.
He was a knight in all things to perfection.   70
He rode a good horse, but his gear was plain,
For he had lately served on a campaign.
His tunic was still spattered by the rust
Left by his coat of mail, for he had just
Returned and set out on his pilgrimage.   75
    His son was with him, a young Squire, in age
Some twenty years as near as I could guess.
His hair curled as if taken from a press.
He was a lover and would become a knight.
In stature he was of a moderate height   80
But powerful and wonderfully quick.
He had been in Flanders, riding in the thick
Of forays in Artois and Picardy,
And bore up well for one so young as he,
Still hoping by his exploits in such places   85
To stand the better in his lady's graces.
He wore embroidered flowers, red and white,
And blazed like a spring meadow to the sight.
He sang or played his flute the livelong day.
He was as lusty as the month of May.   90
His coat was short, its sleeves were long and wide.
He sat his horse well, and knew how to ride,
And how to make a song and use his lance,
And he could write and draw well, too, and dance.
So hot his love that when the moon rose pale   95
He got no more sleep than a nightingale.
He was modest, and helped whomever he was able,
And carved as his father's squire at the table.
    But one more servant had the Knight beside,
Choosing thus simply for the time to ride: 100
A Yeoman, in a coat and hood of green.
His peacock-feathered arrows, bright and keen,
He carried under his belt in tidy fashion.
For well-kept gear he had a yeoman's passion,
No draggled feather might his arrows show,   105
And in his hand he held a mighty bow.
He kept his hair close-cropped, his face was brown.
He knew the lore of woodcraft up and down.
His arm was guarded from the bowstring's whip
By a bracer, gaily trimmed. He had at hip   110
A sword and buckler, and at his other side

A dagger whose fine mounting was his pride,
Sharp-pointed as a spear. His horn he bore
In a sling of green, and on his chest he wore
A silver image of St. Christopher,   115
His patron, since he was a forester.
    There was also a Nun, a Prioress,
Whose smile was gentle and full of guilelessness.
"By St. Loy!"[8] was the worst oath she would say.
She sang mass well, in a becoming way,   120
Intoning through her nose the words divine,
And she was known as Madame Eglantine.
She spoke good French, as taught at Stratford-Bow[9]
For the Parisian French she did not know.
She was schooled to eat so primly and so well   125
That from her lips no morsel ever fell.
She wet her fingers lightly in the dish
Of sauce, for courtesy was her first wish.
With every bite she did her skillful best
To see that no drop fell upon her breast.   130
She always wiped her upper lip so clean
That in her cup was never to be seen
A hint of grease when she had drunk her share.
She reached out for her meat with comely air.
She was a great delight, and always tried   135
To imitate court ways, and had her pride,
Both amiable and gracious in her dealings.
As for her charity and tender feelings,
She melted at whatever was piteous.
She would weep if she but came upon a mouse   140
Caught in a trap, if it were dead or bleeding.
Some little dogs that she took pleasure feeding
On roasted meat or milk or good wheat bread
She had, but how she wept to find one dead
Or yelping from a blow that made it smart,   145
And all was sympathy and loving heart.
Neat was her wimple in its every plait,
Her nose well formed, her eyes as gray as slate.
Her mouth was very small and soft and red.
She had so wide a brow I think her head   150
Was nearly a span broad, for certainly
She was not undergrown, as all could see.
She wore her cloak with dignity and charm,
And had her rosary about her arm,
The small beads coral and the larger green,   155
And from them hung a brooch of golden sheen,
On it a large A and a crown above;

---

8. Perhaps St. Eligius, apparently a popular saint at this time.   9. In Middlesex, near London, where
there was a nunnery.

Beneath, "All things are subject unto love."
   A Priest accompanied her toward Canterbury,
And an attendant Nun, her secretary.   160
   There was a Monk, and nowhere was his peer,
A hunter, and a roving overseer.
He was a manly man, and fully able
To be an abbot. He kept a hunting stable,
And when he rode the neighborhood could hear   165
His bridle jingling in the wind as clear
And loud as if it were a chapel bell.
Wherever he was master of a cell
The principles of good St. Benedict,[1]
For being a little old and somewhat strict,   170
Were honored in the breach, as past their prime.
He lived by the fashion of a newer time.
He would have swapped that text for a plucked hen
Which says that hunters are not holy men,
Or a monk outside his discipline and rule   175
Is too much like a fish outside his pool;
That is to say, a monk outside his cloister.
But such a text he deemed not worth an oyster.
I told him his opinion made me glad.
Why should he study always and go mad,   180
Mewed in his cell with only a book for neighbor?
Or why, as Augustine commanded, labor
And sweat his hands? How shall the world be served?
To Augustine be all such toil reserved!
And so he hunted, as was only right.   185
He had greyhounds as swift as birds in flight.
His taste was all for tracking down the hare,
And what his sport might cost he did not care.
His sleeves I noticed, where they met his hand,
Trimmed with gray fur, the finest in the land.   190
His hood was fastened with a curious pin
Made of wrought gold and clasped beneath his chin,
A love knot at the tip. His head might pass,
Bald as it was, for a lump of shining glass,
And his face was glistening as if anointed.   195
Fat as a lord he was, and well appointed.
His eyes were large, and rolled inside his head
As if they gleamed from a furnace of hot lead.
His boots were supple, his horse superbly kept.
He was a prelate to dream of while you slept.   200
He was not pale nor peaked like a ghost.
He relished a plump swan as his favorite roast.
He rode a palfrey brown as a ripe berry.
   A Friar was with us, a gay dog and a merry,

1. Monastic rules, authored by St. Maurus and St. Benedict in the 6th century.

Who begged his district with a jolly air.   205
No friar in all four orders could compare
With him for gallantry; his tongue was wooing.
Many a girl was married by his doing,
And at his own cost it was often done.
He was a pillar, and a noble one,   210
To his whole order. In his neighborhood
Rich franklins[2] knew him well, who served good food,
And worthy women welcomed him to town;
For the license that his order handed down,
He said himself, conferred on him possession   215
Of more than a curate's power of confession.
Sweetly the list of frailties he heard,
Assigning penance with a pleasant word.
He was an easy man for absolution
Where he looked forward to a contribution,   220
For if to a poor order a man has given
It signifies that he has been well shriven,
And if a sinner let his purse be dented
The Friar would stake his oath he had repented.
For many men become so hard of heart   225
They cannot weep, though conscience makes them smart.
Instead of tears and prayers, then, let the sinner
Supply the poor friars with the price of dinner.
For pretty women he had more than shrift.
His cape was stuffed with many a little gift,   230
As knives and pins and suchlike. He could sing
A merry note, and pluck a tender string,
And had no rival at all in balladry.
His neck was whiter than a fleur-de-lis,[3]
And yet he could have knocked a strong man down.   235
He knew the taverns well in every town.
The barmaids and innkeepers pleased his mind
Better than beggars and lepers and their kind.
In his position it was unbecoming
Among the wretched lepers to go slumming.   240
It mocks all decency, it sews no stitch
To deal with such riffraff, but with the rich,
With sellers of victuals, that's another thing.
Wherever he saw some hope of profiting,
None so polite, so humble. He was good,   245
The champion beggar of his brotherhood.
Should a woman have no shoes against the snow,
So pleasant was his *"In principio"*[4]
He would have her widow's mite before he went.
He took in far more than he paid in rent   250

2. Landowners or country squires, not belonging to the nobility.   3. Lily.   4. In the beginning
(Latin); the opening phrase of a famous passage in the New Testament (John 1:1–16), which the friar
recites in Latin as a devotional exercise to awe the ignorant and extract their alms.

For his right of begging within certain bounds.
None of his brethren trespassed on his grounds!
He loved as freely as a half-grown whelp.
On arbitration-days[5] he gave great help,
For his cloak was never shiny nor threadbare   255
Like a poor cloistered scholar's. He had an air
As if he were a doctor or a pope.
It took stout wool to make his semicope[6]
That plumped out like a bell for portliness.
He lisped a little in his rakishness   260
To make his English sweeter on his tongue,
And twanging his harp to end some song he'd sung
His eyes would twinkle in his head as bright
As the stars twinkle on a frosty night.
Hubert this gallant Friar was by name.   265
　　Among the rest a Merchant also came.
He wore a forked beard and a beaver hat
From Flanders. High up in the saddle he sat,
In figured cloth, his boots clasped handsomely,
Delivering his opinions pompously,   270
Always on how his gains might be increased.
At all costs he desired the sea policed[7]
From Middleburg in Holland to Orwell.[8]
He knew the exchange rates, and the time to sell
French currency, and there was never yet   275
A man who could have told he was in debt
So grave he seemed and hid so well his feelings
With all his shrewd engagements and close dealings.
You'd find no better man at any turn;
But what his name was I could never learn.   280
　　There was an Oxford Student too, it chanced,
Already in his logic well advanced.
He rode a mount as skinny as a rake,
And he was hardly fat. For learning's sake
He let himself look hollow and sober enough.   285
He wore an outer coat of threadbare stuff,
For he had no benefice for his enjoyment
And was too unworldly for some lay employment.
He much preferred to have beside his bed
His twenty volumes bound in black or red   290
All packed with Aristotle from end to middle
Than a sumptuous wardrobe or a merry fiddle.
For though he knew what learning had to offer
There was little coin to jingle in his coffer.
Whatever he got by touching up a friend   295
On books and learning he would promptly spend

---

5. Days appointed for the adjustment of disputes.　6. A short cape.　7. For protection from piracy.
8. An English port near Harwich.

And busily pray for the soul of anybody
Who furnished him the wherewithal for study.
His scholarship was what he truly heeded.
He never spoke a word more than was needed,   300
And that was said with dignity and force,
And quick and brief. He was of grave discourse
Giving new weight to virtue by his speech,
And gladly would he learn and gladly teach.

   There was a Lawyer, cunning and discreet,   305
Who had often been to St. Paul's porch[9] to meet
His clients. He was a Sergeant of the Law,
A man deserving to be held in awe,
Or so he seemed, his manner was so wise.
He had often served as Justice of Assize   310
By the king's appointment, with a broad commission,
For his knowledge and his eminent position.
He had many a handsome gift by way of fee.
There was no buyer of land as shrewd as he.
All ownership to him became fee simple.[1]   315
His titles were never faulty by a pimple.
None was so busy as he with case and cause,
And yet he seemed much busier than he was.
In all cases and decisions he was schooled
That were of record since King William[2] ruled.   320
No one could pick a loophole or a flaw
In any lease or contract he might draw.
Each statute on the books he knew by rote.
He traveled in a plain, silk-belted coat.

   A Franklin traveled in his company.   325
Whiter could never daisy petal[3] be
Than was his beard. His ruddy face gave sign
He liked his morning sop of toast in wine.
He lived in comfort, as he would assure us,
For he was a true son of Epicurus[4]   330
Who held the opinion that the only measure
Of perfect happiness was simply pleasure.
Such hospitality did he provide,
He was St. Julian[5] to his countryside.
His bread and ale were always up to scratch.   335
He had a cellar none on earth could match.
There was no lack of pasties in his house,
Both fish and flesh, and that so plenteous
That where he lived it snowed of meat and drink.
With every dish of which a man can think,   340

---

9. A meeting place for lawyers and their clients in the porch of St. Paul's Cathedral, London.
1. Owned outright without legal impediments.   2. The Conqueror (reigned 1066–1087).   3. The
English daisy, a small white flower; not the same as the American.   4. Greek philosopher whose
teaching (presented here in a somewhat debased form) is believed to make pleasure the goal of life.
5. Patron saint of hospitality.

After the various seasons of the year,
He changed his diet for his better cheer.
He had coops of partridges as fat as cream,
He had a fishpond stocked with pike and bream.
Woe to his cook for an unready pot   345
Or a sauce that wasn't seasoned and spiced hot!
A table in his hall stood on display
Prepared and covered through the livelong day.
He presided at court sessions for his bounty
And sat in Parliament often for his county.   350
A well-wrought dagger and a purse of silk
Hung at his belt, as white as morning milk.
He had been a sheriff and county auditor.
On earth was no such rich proprietor!
    There were five Guildsmen, in the livery   355
Of one august and great fraternity,
A Weaver, a Dyer, and a Carpenter,
A Tapestry-maker and a Haberdasher.
Their gear was furbished new and clean as glass.
The mountings of their knives were not of brass   360
But silver. Their pouches were well made and neat,
And each of them, it seemed, deserved a seat
On the platform at the Guildhall, for each one
Was likely timber to make an alderman.
They had goods enough, and money to be spent,   365
Also their wives would willingly consent
And would have been at fault if they had not.
For to be "Madamed" is a pleasant lot,
And to march in first at feasts for being well married,
And royally to have their mantles carried.   370
    For the pilgrimage these Guildsmen brought their own
Cook to boil their chicken and marrow bone
With seasoning powder and capers and sharp spice.
In judging London ale his taste was nice.
He well knew how to roast and broil and fry,   375
To mix a stew, and bake a good meat pie,
Or capon creamed with almond, rice, and egg.
Pity he had an ulcer on his leg!
    A Skipper was with us, his home far in the west.
He came from the port of Dartmouth, as I guessed.   380
He sat his carthorse pretty much at sea
In a coarse smock that joggled on his knee.
From his neck a dagger on a string hung down
Under his arm. His face was burnished brown
By the summer sun. He was a true good fellow.   385
Many a time he had tapped a wine cask mellow
Sailing from Bordeaux while the owner slept.
Too nice a point of honor he never kept.
In a sea fight, if he got the upper hand,

Drowned prisoners floated home to every land.   390
But in navigation, whether reckoning tides,
Currents, or what might threaten him besides,
Harborage, pilotage, or the moon's demeanor,
None was his like from Hull to Cartagena.[6]
He knew each harbor and the anchorage there   395
From Gotland to the Cape of Finisterre[7]
And every creek in Brittany and Spain,
And he had called his ship the *Madeleine*.
    With us came also an astute Physician.
There was none like him for a disquisition   400
On the art of medicine or surgery,
For he was grounded in astrology.
He kept his patient long in observation,
Choosing the proper hour for application
Of charms and images by intuition   405
Of magic, and the planets' best position.
For he was one who understood the laws
That rule the humors, and could tell the cause
That brought on every human malady,
Whether of hot or cold, or moist or dry.   410
He was a perfect medico, for sure.
The cause once known, he would prescribe the cure
For he had his druggists ready at a motion
To provide the sick man with some pill or potion—
A game of mutual aid, with each one winning.   415
Their partnership was hardly just beginning!
He was well versed in his authorities,
Old Aesculapius, Dioscorides,
Rufus, and old Hippocrates, and Galen,
Haly, and Rhazes, and Serapion,   420
Averroës, Bernard, Johannes Damascenus,
Avicenna, Gilbert, Gaddesden, Constantinus.[8]
He urged a moderate fare on principle,
But rich in nourishment, digestible;
Of nothing in excess would he admit.   425
He gave but little heed to Holy Writ.
His clothes were lined with taffeta; their hue
Was all of blood red and of Persian blue,
Yet he was far from careless of expense.
He saved his fees from times of pestilence,   430
For gold is a cordial, as physicians hold,
And so he had a special love for gold.
    A worthy woman there was from near the city
Of Bath,[9] but somewhat deaf, and more's the pity.
For weaving she possessed so great a bent   435

---

6. A Spanish port. *Hull:* an English port.   7. On the Spanish coast. *Gotland:* a Swedish island.
8. Eminent medical authorities from ancient Greece, ancient and medieval Arabic civilization, and
England in the 13th and 14th centuries.   9. A town in southwest England.

She outdid the people of Ypres and of Ghent.[1]
No other woman dreamed of such a thing
As to precede her at the offering,
Or if any did, she fell in such a wrath
She dried up all the charity in Bath.   440
She wore fine kerchiefs of old-fashioned air,
And on a Sunday morning, I could swear,
She had ten pounds of linen on her head.
Her stockings were of finest scarlet-red,
Laced tightly, and her shoes were soft and new.   445
Bold was her face, and fair, and red in hue.
She had been an excellent woman all her life
Five men in turn had taken her to wife,
Omitting other youthful company—
But let that pass for now! Over the sea   450
She had traveled freely; many a distant stream
She crossed, and visited Jerusalem
Three times. She had been at Rome and at Boulogne,
At the shrine of Compostella, and at Cologne.[2]
She had wandered by the way through many a scene.   455
Her teeth were set with little gaps between.[3]
Easily on her ambling horse she sat.
She was well wimpled, and she wore a hat
As wide in circuit as a shield or targe.[4]
A skirt swathed up her hips, and they were large.   460
Upon her feet she wore sharp-roweled spurs.
She was a good fellow; a ready tongue was hers.
All remedies of love she knew by name,[5]
For she had all the tricks of that old game.
        There was a good man of the priests' vocation,   465
A poor town Parson of true consecration,
But he was rich in holy thought and work.
Learned he was, in the truest sense a clerk
Who meant Christ's gospel faithfully to preach
And truly his parishioners to teach.   470
He was a kind man, full of industry,
Many times tested by adversity
And always patient. If tithes[6] were in arrears,
He was loth to threaten any man with fears
Of excommunication; past a doubt   475
He would rather spread his offering about
To his poor flock, or spend his property.
To him a little meant sufficiency.
Wide was his parish, with houses far asunder,
But he would not be kept by rain or thunder,   480

1. Towns in Flanders famous for their cloth.   2. Sites of shrines much visited by pilgrims.   3. I.e.,
gap-toothed; in a woman considered a sign of sexual prowess.   4. A small shield.   5. Chaucer has
Ovid's *Love Cures* (*Remedia Amoris*) in mind.   6. Payments due to the priest, usually a tenth of
annual income.

If any had suffered a sickness or a blow,
From visiting the farthest, high or low
Plodding his way on foot, his staff in hand.
He was a model his flock could understand,
For first he did and afterward he taught.   485
That precept from the Gospel he had caught,
And he added as a metaphor thereto,
"If the gold rusts, what will the iron do?"
For if a priest is foul, in whom we trust,
No wonder a layman shows a little rust.   490
A priest should take to heart the shameful scene
Of shepherds filthy while the sheep are clean.
By his own purity a priest should give
The example to his sheep, how they should live.
He did not rent his benefice for hire,[7]   495
Leaving his flock to flounder in the mire,
And run to London, happiest of goals,
To sing paid masses in St. Paul's for souls,
Or as chaplain from some rich guild take his keep,
But dwelt at home and guarded well his sheep   500
So that no wolf should make his flock miscarry.
He was a shepherd, and not a mercenary.
And though himself a man of strict vocation
He was not harsh to weak souls in temptation,
Not overbearing nor haughty in his speech,   505
But wise and kind in all he tried to teach.
By good example and just words to turn
Sinners to heaven was his whole concern.
But should a man in truth prove obstinate,
Whoever he was, of rich or mean estate,   510
The Parson would give him a snub to meet the case.
I doubt there was a priest in any place
His better. He did not stand on dignity
Nor affect in conscience too much nicety,
But Christ's and his disciples' words he sought   515
To teach, and first he followed what he taught.
    There was a Plowman with him on the road,
His brother, who had forked up many a load
Of good manure. A hearty worker he,
Living in peace and perfect charity.   520
Whether his fortune made him smart or smile,
He loved God with his whole heart all the while
And his neighbor as himself. He would undertake,
For every luckless poor man, for the sake
Of Christ to thresh and ditch and dig by the hour   525
And with no wage, if it was in his power.
His tithes on goods and earnings he paid fair.

---

7. Rent out his appointment to a substitute.

He wore a coarse, rough coat and rode a mare.
    There also were a Manciple, a Miller,
A Reeve, a Summoner, and a Pardoner,[8]
And I—this makes our company complete.   530
    As tough a yokel as you care to meet
The Miller was. His big-beefed arms and thighs
Took many a ram put up as wrestling prize.
He was a thick, squat-shouldered lump of sins.   535
No door but he could heave it off its pins
Or break it running at it with his head.
His beard was broader than a shovel, and red
As a fat sow or fox. A wart stood clear
Atop his nose, and red as a pig's ear   540
A tuft of bristles on it. Black and wide
His nostrils were. He carried at his side
A sword and buckler. His mouth would open out
Like a great furnace, and he would sing and shout
His ballads and jokes of harlotries and crimes.   545
He could steal corn and charge for it three times,
And yet was honest enough, as millers come,
For a miller, as they say, has a golden thumb.
In white coat and blue hood this lusty clown,
Blowing his bagpipes, brought us out of town.   550
    The Manciple was of a lawyers' college,
And other buyers might have used his knowledge
How to be shrewd provisioners, for whether
He bought on cash or credit, altogether
He managed that the end should be the same: 555
He came out more than even with the game.
Now isn't it an instance of God's grace
How a man of little knowledge can keep pace
In wit with a whole school of learned men?
He had masters to the number of three times ten   560
Who knew each twist of equity and tort;
A dozen in that very Inn of Court
Were worthy to be steward of the estate
To any of England's lords, however great,
And keep him to his income well confined   565
And free from debt, unless he lost his mind,
Or let him scrimp, if he were mean in bounty;
They could have given help to a whole county
In any sort of case that might befall;
And yet this Manciple could cheat them all!   570
    The Reeve was a slender, fiery-tempered man.
He shaved as closely as a razor can.
His hair was cropped about his ears, and shorn

---

8. Dispenser of papal pardons. *Manciple:* an officer in charge of supplies. *Reeve:* farm overseer. *Summoner:* he summoned people to appear before the church court (presided over by the archdeacon) and in general acted as a kind of deputy sheriff of the court.

Above his forehead as a priest's is worn.
His legs were very long and very lean. 575
No calf on his lank spindles could be seen.
But he knew how to keep a barn or bin,
He could play the game with auditors and win.
He knew well how to judge by drought and rain
The harvest of his seed and of his grain. 580
His master's cattle, swine, and poultry flock,
Horses and sheep and dairy, all his stock,
Were altogether in this Reeve's control.
And by agreement, he had given the sole
Accounting since his lord reached twenty years. 585
No man could ever catch him in arrears.
There wasn't a bailiff, shepherd, or farmer working
But the Reeve knew all his tricks of cheating and shirking.
He would not let him draw an easy breath.
They feared him as they feared the very death. 590
He lived in a good house on an open space,
Well shaded by green trees, a pleasant place.
He was shrewder in acquisition than his lord.
With private riches he was amply stored.
He had learned a good trade young by work and will. 595
He was a carpenter of first-rate skill.
On a fine mount, a stallion, dappled gray.
Whose name was Scot, he rode along the way.
He wore a long blue coat hitched up and tied
As if it were a friar's, and at his side 600
A sword with rusty blade was hanging down.
He came from Norfolk, from nearby the town
That men call Bawdswell. As we rode the while,
The Reeve kept always hindmost in our file.
　　A Summoner in our company had his place. 605
Red as the fiery cherubim[9] his face.
He was pocked and pimpled, and his eyes were narrow.
He was lecherous and hot as a cock sparrow.
His brows were scabby and black, and thin his beard.
His was a face that little children feared. 610
Brimstone or litharge bought in any quarter,
Quicksilver, ceruse, borax, oil of tartar,
No salve nor ointment that will cleanse or bite
Could cure him of his blotches, livid white,
Or the nobs and nubbins sitting on his cheeks. 615
He loved his garlic, his onions, and his leeks.
He loved to drink the strong wine down blood-red.
Then would he bellow as if he had lost his head.
And when he had drunk enough to parch his drouth,
Nothing but Latin issued from his mouth. 620

---

9. An order of angels; represented with red faces in medieval art.

He had smattered up a few terms, two or three,
That he had gathered out of some decree —
No wonder; he heard law Latin all the day,
And everyone knows a parrot or a jay
Can cry out "Wat" or "Poll" as well as the pope;   625
But give him a strange term, he began to grope.
His little store of learning was paid out,
So *"Questio quod juris"*[1] he would shout.
He was a goodhearted bastard and a kind one.
If there were better, it was hard to find one.   630
He would let a good fellow, for a quart of wine,
The whole year round enjoy his concubine
Scot-free from summons, hearing, fine, or bail,
And on the sly he too could flush a quail.
If he liked a scoundrel, no matter for church law.   635
He would teach him that he need not stand in awe
If the archdeacon threatened with his curse —
That is, unless his soul was in his purse,
For in his purse he would be punished well.
"The purse," he said, "is the archdeacon's hell."   640
Of course I know he lied in what he said.
There is nothing a guilty man should so much dread
As the curse that damns his soul, when, without fail,
The church can save him, or send him off to jail.[2]
He had the young men and girls in his control   645
Throughout the diocese; he knew the soul
Of youth, and heard their every last design.
A garland big enough to be the sign
Above an alehouse balanced on his head,
And he made a shield of a great round loaf of bread.   650
    There was a Pardoner of Rouncivalle[3]
With him, of the blessed Mary's hospital,
But now come straight from Rome (or so said he).
Loudly he sang, "Come hither, love, to me,"
While the Summoner's counterbass trolled out profound —   655
No trumpet blew with half so vast a sound.
This Pardoner had hair as yellow as wax,
But it hung as smoothly as a hank of flax.
His locks trailed down in bunches from his head,
And he let the ends about his shoulders spread,   660
But in thin clusters, lying one by one.
Of hood, for rakishness, he would have none,
For in his wallet he kept it safely stowed.
He traveled, as he thought, in the latest mode,

---

1. The question is, what (part) of the law [applies] (Latin).   2. Lines 643–44 attempt to render the sense and tone of a passage in which Chaucer says literally that a guilty man should be in dread "because a curse will slay just as absolution saves, and he should also beware of a Significavit." This word, according to Robinson, was the first word of a writ remanding an excommunicated person to prison [Translator's note].   3. A religious house near Charing Cross, now part of London.

Disheveled. Save for his cap, his head was bare,   665
And in his eyes he glittered like a hare.
A Veronica[4] was stitched upon his cap
His wallet lay before him in his lap
Brimful of pardons from the very seat
In Rome. He had a voice like a goat's bleat.   670
He was beardless and would never have a beard.
His cheek was always smooth as if just sheared.
I think he was a gelding or a mare;
But in this trade, from Berwick down to Ware,
No pardoner could beat him in the race,   675
For in his wallet he had a pillow case
Which he represented as Our Lady's veil;
He said he had a piece of the very sail
St. Peter, when he fished in Galilee
Before Christ caught him, used upon the sea.   680
He had a latten[5] cross embossed with stones
And in a glass he carried some pig's bones,
And with these holy relics, when he found
Some village parson grubbing his poor ground,
He would get more money in a single day   685
Than in two months would come the parson's way.
Thus with his flattery and his trumped-up stock
He made dupes of the parson and his flock.
But though his conscience was a little plastic
He was in church a noble ecclesiastic.   690
Well could he read the Scripture or saint's story,
But best of all he sang the offertory,
For he understood that when this song was sung,
Then he must preach, and sharpen up his tongue
To rake in cash, as well he knew the art,   695
And so he sang out gaily, with full heart.
Now I have set down briefly, as it was,
Our rank, our dress, our number, and the cause
That many our sundry fellowship begin
In Southwark, at this hospitable inn   700
Known as the Tabard, nor far from the Bell.
But what we did that night I ought to tell,
And after that our journey, stage by stage,
And the whole story of our pilgrimage.
But first, in justice, do not look askance   705
I plead, nor lay it to my ignorance
If in this matter I should use plain speech
And tell you just the words and style of each,
Reporting all their language faithfully.
For it must be known to you as well as me   710

4. A reproduction of the handkerchief bearing the miraculous impression of Christ's face, said to have
been impressed on the handkerchief that St. Veronica gave Him to wipe His face with on the way to
His Crucifixion.   5. An alloy of copper and zinc made to resemble brass.

That whoever tells a story after a man
Must follow him as closely as he can.
If he takes the tale in charge, he must be true
To every word, unless he would find new
Or else invent a thing or falsify.   715
Better some breadth of language than a lie!
He may not spare the truth to save his brother.
He might as well use one word as another.
In Holy Writ Christ spoke in a broad sense
And surely his word is without offense.   720
Plato, if his pages you can read,
Says let the word be cousin to the deed.
So I petition your indulgence for it
If I have cut the cloth just as men wore it,
Here in this tale, and shown its very weave.   725
My wits are none too sharp, you must believe.
    Our Host gave each of us a cheerful greeting
And promptly of our supper had us eating.
The victuals that he served us were his best.
The wine was potent, and we drank with zest.   730
Our Host cut such a figure, all in all,
He might have been a marshal in a hall.
He was a big man, and his eyes bulged wide.
No sturdier citizen lived in all Cheapside,[6]
Lacking no trace of manhood, bold in speech,   735
Prudent, and well versed in what life can teach,
And with all this he was a jovial man.
And so when supper ended he began
To jolly us, when all our debts were clear.
"Welcome," he said. "I have not seen this year   740
So merry a company in this tavern as now,
And I would give you pleasure if I knew how.
And just this very minute a plan has crossed
My mind that might amuse you at no cost.
    "You go to Canterbury—may the Lord   745
Speed you, and may the martyred saint reward
Your journey! And to while the time away
You mean to talk and pass the time of day,
For you would be as cheerful all alone
As riding on your journey dumb as stone.   750
Therefore, if you'll abide by what I say,
Tomorrow, when you ride off on your way,
Now, by my father's soul, and he is dead,
If you don't enjoy yourselves, cut off my head!
Hold up your hands, if you accept my speech."   755
    Our counsel did not take us long to reach.
We bade him give his orders at his will.

6. A London street.

"Well, sirs," he said, "then do not take it ill,
But hear me in good part, and for your sport.
Each one of you, to make our journey short,   760
Shall tell two stories, as we ride, I mean,
Toward Canterbury; and coming home again
Shall tell two other tales he may have heard
Of happenings that some time have occurred.
And the one of you whose stories please us most,   765
Here in this tavern, sitting by this post
Shall sup at our expense while we make merry
When we come riding home from Canterbury.
And to cheer you still the more, I too will ride
With you at my own cost, and be your guide.   770
And if anyone my judgment shall gainsay
He must pay for all we spend along the way.
If you agree, no need to stand and reason.
Tell me, and I'll be stirring in good season."
     This thing was granted, and we swore our pledge   775
To take his judgment on our pilgrimage,
His verdict on our tales, and his advice.
He was to plan a supper at a price
Agreed upon; and so we all assented
To his command, and we were well contented.   780
The wine was fetched; we drank, and went to rest.
     Next morning, when the dawn was in the east,
Up spring our Host, who acted as our cock,
And gathered us together in a flock,
And off we rode, till presently our pace   785
Had brought us to St. Thomas' watering place.
And there our Host began to check his horse.
"Good sirs," he said, "you know your promise, of course.
Shall I remind you what it was about?
If evensong and matins don't fall out,   790
We'll soon find who shall tell us the first tale.
But as I hope to drink my wine and ale,
Whoever won't accept what I decide
Pays everything we spend along the ride.
Draw lots, before we're farther from the Inn.   795
Whoever draws the shortest shall begin.
Sir Knight," said he, "my master, choose your straw.
Come here, my lady Prioress, and draw,
And you, Sir Scholar, don't look thoughtful, man!
Pitch in now, everyone!" So all began   800
To draw the lots, and as the luck would fall
The draw went to the Knight, which pleased us all.
And when this excellent man saw how it stood,
Ready to keep his promise, he said, "Good!
Since it appears that I must start the game,   805
Why then, the draw is welcome, in God's name.

Now let's ride on, and listen, what I say."
And with that word we rode forth on our way,
And he, with his courteous manner and good cheer,
Began to tell his tale, as you shall hear.   810

The Miller's Prologue and Tale

THE PROLOGUE

When the Knight had finished,[7] no one, young or old,
In the whole company, but said he had told
A noble story, one that ought to be
Preserved and kept alive in memory,
Especially the gentlefolk, each one.   5
Our good Host laughed, and swore, "The game's begun,
The ball is rolling! This is going well.
Let's see who has another tale to tell.
Come, match the Knight's tale if you can, Sir Monk!"
    The Miller, who by this time was so drunk   10
He looked quite bloodless, and who hardly sat
His horse, he was never one to doff his hat
Or stand on courtesy for any man.
Like Pilate in the Church plays[8] he began
To bellow. "Arms and blood and bones," he swore,   15
"I know a yarn that will even up the score,
A noble one, I'll pay off the Knight's tale!"
    Our Host could see that he was drunk on ale.
"Robin," he said, "hold on a minute, brother.
Some better man shall come first with another.   20
Let's do this right. You tell yours by and by."
    "God's soul," the Miller told him, "that won't I!
Either I'll speak, or go on my own way."
    "The devil with you! Say what you have to say,"
Answered our Host. "You are a fool. Your head   25
Is overpowered."
                    "Now," the Miller said,
"Everyone listen! But first I will propound
That I am drunk, I know it by my sound.
If I can't get my words out, put the blame
On Southwark ale, I ask you, in God's name!   30
For I'll tell a golden legend and a life
Both of a carpenter and of his wife,
How a student put horns on the fellow's head."
    "Shut up and stop your racket," the Reeve said.
"Forget your ignorant drunken bawdiness.   35
It is a sin and a great foolishness

---

7. *The Knight's Tale* is the first told, immediately following the *General Prologue*.   8. Miracle plays
represented Pilate as a braggart and loudmouth. His lines were marked by frequent alliteration.

To injure any man by defamation
And to give women such a reputation.
Tell us of other things; you'll find no lack."

    Promptly this drunken Miller answered back: 40
"Oswald, my brother, true as babes are suckled,
The man who has no wife, he is no cuckold.
I don't say for this reason that you are.
There are plenty of faithful wives, both near and far,
Always a thousand good for every bad,   45
And you know this yourself, unless you're mad.
I see you are angry with my tale, but why?
You have a wife; no less, by God, do I.
But I wouldn't, for the oxen in my plow,
Shoulder more than I need by thinking how   50
I may myself, for aught I know, be one.
I'll certainly believe that I am none.
A husband mustn't be curious, for his life,
About God's secrets or about his wife.
If she gives him plenty and he's in the clover,   55
No need to worry about what's left over."

    The Miller, to make the best of it I can,
Refused to hold his tongue for any man,
But told his tale like any low-born clown.
I am sorry that I have to set it down,   60
And all you people, for God's love, I pray,
Whose taste is higher, do not think I say
A word with evil purpose; I must rehearse
Their stories one and all, both better and worse,
Or play false with my matter, that is clear.   65
Whoever, therefore, may not wish to hear,
Turn over the page and choose another tale;
For small and great, he'll find enough, no fail,
Of things from history, touching courtliness,
And virtue too, and also holiness.   70
If you choose wrong, don't lay it on my head.
You know the Miller couldn't be called well bred.
So with the Reeve, and many more as well,
And both of them had bawdy tales to tell.
Reflect a little, and don't hold me to blame.   75
There's no sense making earnest out of game.

THE TALE

There used to be a rich old oaf who made
His home at Oxford, a carpenter by trade,
And took in boarders. With him used to dwell
A student who had done his studies well,
But he was poor; for all that he had learned,   5
It was toward astrology his fancy turned.

He knew a number of figures and constructions
By which he could supply men with deductions
If they should ask him at a given hour
Whether to look for sunshine or for shower,   10
Or want to know whatever might befall,
Events of all sorts, I can't count them all.
    He was known as handy Nicholas,[9] this student.
Well versed in love, he knew how to be prudent,
Going about unnoticed, sly, and sure.   15
In looks no girl was ever more demure.
Lodged at this carpenter's, he lived alone;
He had a room there that he made his own,
Festooned with herbs, and he was sweet himself
As licorice or ginger. On a shelf   20
Above his bed's head, neatly stowed apart,
He kept the trappings that went with his art,
His astrolabe, his books—among the rest,
Thick ones and thin ones, lay his *Almagest*[1] —
And the counters for his abacus as well.   25
Over his cupboard a red curtain fell
And up above a pretty zither lay
On which at night so sweetly would he play
That with the music the whole room would ring.
"Angelus to the Virgin" he would sing   30
And then the song that's known as "The King's Note."
Blessings were called down on his merry throat!
So this sweet scholar passed his time, his end
Being to eat and live upon his friend.
    This carpenter had newly wed a wife   35
And loved her better than he loved his life.
He was jealous, for she was eighteen in age;
He tried to keep her close as in a cage,
For she was wild and young, and old was he
And guessed that he might smack of cuckoldry.   40
His ignorant wits had never chanced to strike
On Cato's[2] word, that man should wed his like;
Men ought to wed where their conditions point,
For youth and age are often out of joint.
But now, since he had fallen in the snare,   45
He must, like other men, endure his care.
    Fair this young woman was, her body trim
As any mink, so graceful and so slim.
She wore a striped belt that was all of silk;
A piece-work apron, white as morning milk,   50
About her loins and down her lap she wore.

---

9. Chaucer's word is hendë, implying, I take it, both *ready to hand* and *ingratiating*. Nicholas was a Johnny-on-the-spot and also had a way with him [Translator's note].   1. A 2nd-century treatise by Ptolemy, an astronomy textbook.   2. Dionysius Cato, the supposed author of a book of maxims employed in elementary education.

White was her smock, her collar both before
And on the back embroidered all about
In coal-black silk, inside as well as out.
And like her collar, her white-laundered bonnet   55
Had ribbons of the same embroidery on it.
Wide was her silken fillet, worn up high,
And for a fact she had a willing eye.
She plucked each brow into a little bow,
And each one was as black as any sloe.   60
She was a prettier sight to see by far
Than the blossoms of the early pear tree are,
And softer than the wool of an old wether.
Down from her belt there hung a purse of leather
With silken tassels and with studs of brass.   65
No man so wise, wherever people pass,
Who could imagine in this world at all
A wench like her, the pretty little doll!
Far brighter was the dazzle of her hue
Than a coin struck in the Tower,[3] fresh and new.   70
As for her song, it twittered from her head
Sharp as a swallow perching on a shed.
And she could skip and sport as a young ram
Or calf will gambol, following his dam.
Her mouth was sweet as honey-ale or mead   75
Or apples in the hay, stored up for need.
She was as skittish as an untrained colt,
Slim as a mast and straighter than a bolt.
On her simple collar she wore a big brooch-pin
Wide as a shield's boss underneath her chin.   80
High up along her legs she laced her shoes.
She was a pigsney, she was a primrose
For any lord to tumble in his bed
Or a good yeoman honestly to wed.
     Now sir, and again sir, this is how it was: 85
A day came round when handy Nicholas,
While her husband was at Oseney,[4] well away,
Began to fool with this young wife, and play.
These students always have a wily head.
He caught her in between the legs, and said,   90
"Sweetheart, unless I have my will with you
I'll die for stifled love, by all that's true,"
And held her by the haunches, hard. "I vow
I'll die unless you love me here and now,
Sure as my soul," he said, "is God's to save."   95
     She shied just as a colt does in the trave,[5]
And turned her head hard from him, this young wife,

---

3. Minted in the Tower of London.   4. A town near Oxford.   5. A wooden frame confining a horse
being shod.

And said, "I will not kiss you, on my life.
Why, stop it now," she said, "stop, Nicholas,
Or I will cry out 'Help, help,' and 'Alas!'   100
Be good enough to take your hands away."
   "Mercy," this Nicholas began to pray,
And spoke so well and poured it on so fast
She promised she would be his love at last,
And swore by Thomas à Becket, saint of Kent,   105
That she would serve him when she could invent
Or spy out some good opportunity.
"My husband is so full of jealousy
You must be watchful and take care," she said,
"Or well I know I'll be as good as dead.   110
You must go secretly about this business."
   "Don't give a thought to that," said Nicholas.
"A student has been wasting time at school
If he can't make a carpenter a fool."
And so they were agreed, these two, and swore   115
To watch their chance, as I have said before.
When Nicholas had spanked her haunches neatly
And done all I have spoken of, he sweetly
Gave her a kiss, and then he took his zither
And loudly played, and sang his music with her.   120
   Now in her Christian duty, one saint's day,
To the parish church this good wife made her way,
And as she went her forehead cast a glow
As bright as noon, for she had washed it so
It glistened when she finished with her work.   125
   Serving this church there was a parish clerk
Whose name was Absolom, a ruddy man
With goose-gray eyes and curls like a great fan
That shone like gold on his neatly parted head.
His tunic was light blue and his nose red,   130
And he had patterns that had been cut through
Like the windows of St. Paul's in either shoe.
He wore above his tunic, fresh and gay,
A surplice white as a blossom on a spray.
A merry devil, as true as God can save,   135
He knew how to let blood, trim hair, and shave,
Or write a deed of land in proper phrase,
And he could dance in twenty different ways
In the Oxford fashion, and sometimes he would sing
A loud falsetto to his fiddle string   140
Or his guitar. No tavern anywhere
But he had furnished entertainment there.
Yet his speech was delicate, and for his part
He was a little squeamish toward a fart.
   This Absolom, so jolly and so gay,   145
With a censer went about on the saint's day

Censing the parish women one and all.
Many the doting look that he let fall,
And specially on this carpenter's young wife.
To look at her, he thought, was a good life,   150
She was so trim, so sweetly lecherous.
I dare say that if she had been a mouse
And he a cat, he would have made short work
Of catching her. This jolly parish clerk
Had such a heartful of love-hankerings   155
He would not take the women's offerings;
No, no, he said, it would not be polite.
      The moon, when darkness fell, shone full and bright
And Absolom was ready for love's sake
With his guitar to be up and awake,   160
And toward the carpenter's, brisk and amorous,
He made his way until he reached the house
A little after the cocks began to crow.
Under a casement he sang sweet and low,
"Dear lady, by your will, be kind to me,"   165
And strummed on his guitar in harmony.
This lovelorn singing woke the carpenter
Who said to his wife, "What, Alison, don't you hear
Absolom singing under our bedroom wall?"
      "Yes, God knows, John," she answered, "I hear it all."   170
      What would you like? In this way things went on
Till jolly Absolom was woebegone
For wooing her, awake all night and day.
He combed his curls and made himself look gay.
He swore to be her slave and used all means   175
To court her with his gifts and go-betweens.
He sang and quavered like a nightingale.
He sent her sweet spiced wine and seasoned ale,
Cakes that were piping hot, mead sweet with honey,
And since she was town-bred, he proffered money.   180
For some are won by wealth, and some no less
By blows, and others yet by gentleness.
      Sometimes, to keep his talents in her gaze,
He acted Herod[6] in the mystery plays
High on the stage. But what can help his case?   185
For she so loves this handy Nicholas
That Absolom is living in a bubble.
He has nothing but a laugh for all his trouble.
She leaves his earnestness for scorn to cool
And makes this Absolom her proper fool.   190
For this is a true proverb, and no lie;
"It always happens that the nigh and sly
Will let the absent suffer." So 'tis said,

---

6. A role traditionally played as a bully in the Miracle plays.

And Absolom may rage or lose his head
But just because he was farther from her sight   195
This nearby Nicholas got in his light.
    Now hold your chin up, handy Nicholas,
For Absolom may wail and sing "Alas!"
One Saturday when the carpenter had gone
To Oseney, Nicholas and Alison   200
Agreed that he should use his wit and guile
This simple jealous husband to beguile.
And if it happened that the game went right
She would sleep in his arms the livelong night,
For this was his desire and hers as well.   205
At once, with no more words, this Nicholas fell
To working out his plan. He would not tarry,
But quietly to his room began to carry
Both food and drink to last him out a day,
Or more than one, and told her what to say   210
If her husband asked her about Nicholas.
She must say she had no notion where he was;
She hadn't laid eyes on him all day long;
He must be sick, or something must be wrong;
No matter how her maid had called and cried   215
He wouldn't answer, whatever might betide.
    This was the plan, and Nicholas kept away,
Shut in his room, for that whole Saturday.
He ate and slept or did as he thought best
Till Sunday, when the sun was going to rest,   220
This carpenter began to wonder greatly
Where Nicholas was and what might ail him lately,
"Now, by St. Thomas, I begin to dread
All isn't right with Nicholas," he said.
"He hasn't, God forbid, died suddenly!   225
The world is ticklish these days, certainly.
Today I saw a corpse to church go past,
A man that I saw working Monday last!
Go up," he told his chore-boy, "call and shout,
Knock with a stone, find what it's all about   230
And let me know."
                        The boy went up and pounded
And yelled as if his wits had been confounded.
"What, how, what's doing, Master Nicholas?
How can you sleep all day?" But all his fuss
Was wasted, for he could not hear a word.   235
He noticed at the bottom of a board
A hole the cat used when she wished to creep
Into the room, and through it looked in deep
And finally of Nicholas caught sight.
This Nicholas sat gaping there upright   240
As though his wits were addled by the moon

When it was new. The boy went down, and soon
Had told his master how he had seen the man.
   The carpenter, when he heard this news, began
To cross himself. "Help us, St. Frideswide!   245
Little can we foresee what may betide!
The man's astronomy has turned his wit,
Or else he's in some agonizing fit.
I always knew that it would turn out so.
What God has hidden is not for men to know.   250
Aye, blessed is the ignorant man indeed,
Blessed is he that only knows his creed!
So fared another scholar of the sky,
For walking in the meadows once to spy
Upon the stars and what they might foretell,   255
Down in a clay-pit suddenly he fell!
He overlooked that! By St. Thomas, though,
I'm sorry for handy Nicholas. I'll go
And scold him roundly for his studying
If so I may, by Jesus, heaven's king!   260
Give me a staff, I'll pry up from the floor
While you, Robin, are heaving at the door.
He'll quit his books, I think."
                     He took his stand
Outside the room. The boy had a strong hand
And by the hasp he heaved it off at once.   265
The door fell flat. With gaping countenance
This Nicholas sat studying the air
As still as stone. He was in black despair,
The carpenter believed, and hard about
The shoulders caught and shook him, and cried out   270
Rudely, "What, how! What is it? Look down at us!
Wake up, think of Christ's passion, Nicholas!
I'll sign you with the cross to keep away
These elves and things!" And he began to say,
Facing the quarters of the house, each side,   275
And on the threshold of the door outside,
The night-spell: "Jesu and St. Benedict
From every wicked thing this house protect . . ."
   Choosing his time, this handy Nicholas
Produced a dreadful sigh, and said, "Alas,   280
This world, must it be all destroyed straightway?"
   "What," asked the carpenter, "what's that you say?
Do as we do, we working men; and think
Of God."
        Nicholas answered, "Get me a drink,
And afterwards I'll tell you privately   285
Of something that concerns us, you and me.
I'll tell you only, you among all men."
   This carpenter went down and came again

With a draught of mighty ale, a generous quart.
As soon as each of them had drunk his part   290
Nicholas shut the door and made it fast
And sat down by the carpenter at last
And spoke to him. "My host," he said, "John dear,
You must swear by all that you hold sacred here
That not to any man will you betray   295
My confidence. What I'm about to say
Is Christ's own secret. If you tell a soul
You are undone, and this will be the toll:
If you betray me, you shall go stark mad."
    "Now Christ forbid it, by His holy blood,"   300
Answered this simple man. "I don't go blabbing.
If I say it myself, I have no taste for gabbing.
Speak up just as you like, I'll never tell,
Not wife nor child, by Him that harrowed hell."[7]
    "Now, John," said Nicholas, "this is no lie.   305
I have discovered through astrology,
And studying the moon that shines so bright
That Monday next, a quarter through the night,
A rain will fall, and such a mad, wild spate
That Noah's flood was never half so great.   310
This world," he said, "in less time than an hour
Shall drown entirely in that hideous shower.
Yes, every man shall drown and lose his life."
    "Alas," the carpenter answered, "for my wife!
Alas, my Alison! And shall she drown?"   315
For grief at this he nearly tumbled down,
And said, "But is there nothing to be done?"
    "Why, happily there is, for anyone
Who will take advice," this handy Nicholas said.
"You mustn't expect to follow your own head.   320
For what said Solomon, whose words were true?
'Proceed by counsel, and you'll never rue.'
If you will act on good advice, no fail,
I'll promise, and without a mast or sail,
To see that she's preserved, and you and I.   325
Haven't you heard how Noah was kept dry
When, warned by Christ beforehand, he discovered
That the whole earth with water should be covered?"
    "Yes," said the carpenter, "long, long ago."
    "And then again," said Nicholas, "don't you know   330
The grief they all had trying to embark
Till Noah could get his wife into the Ark?[8]
That was a time when Noah, I dare say,

---

7. I.e., Christ, who descended into Hell and led away Adam, Eve, the Patriarchs, John the Baptist, and others, redeeming and releasing them. It was the subject of a number of Miracle plays. The original story comes from the Apocryphal New Testament. 8. A stock comedy scene in the mystery plays, of which the carpenter would have been an avid spectator [Translator's note].

Would gladly have given his best black wethers away
If she could have had a ship herself alone.   335
And therefore do you know what must be done?
This demands haste, and with a hasty thing
People can't stop for talk and tarrying.
    "Start out and get into the house right off
For each of us a tub or kneading-trough,   340
Above all making sure that they are large,
In which we'll float away as in a barge.
And put in food enough to last a day.
Beyond won't matter; the flood will fall away
Early next morning. Take care not to spill   345
A word to your boy Robin, nor to Jill
Your maid. I cannot save her, don't ask why.
I will not tell God's secrets, no, not I.
Let it be enough, unless your wits are mad,
To have as good a grace as Noah had.   350
I'll save your wife for certain, never doubt it.
Now go along, and make good time about it.
    "But when you have, for her and you and me,
Brought to the house these kneading-tubs, all three,
Then you must hang them under the roof, up high,   355
To keep our plans from any watchful eye.
When you have done exactly as I've said,
And put in snug our victuals and our bread,
Also an ax to cut the ropes apart
So when the rain comes we can make our start,   360
And when you've broken a hole high in the gable
Facing the garden plot, above the stable,
To give us a free passage out, each one,
Then, soon as the great fall of rain is done,
You'll swim as merrily, I undertake,   365
As the white duck paddles along behind her drake.
Then I shall call, 'How, Alison! How, John!
Be cheerful, for the flood will soon be gone.'
And 'Master Nicholas, what ho!' you'll say.
'Good morning, I see you clearly, for it's day.'   370
Then we shall lord it for the rest of life
Over the world, like Noah and his wife.
    "But one thing I must warn you of downright.
Use every care that on that selfsame night
When we have taken ship and climbed aboard,   375
No one of us must speak a single word,
Nor call, nor cry, but pray with all his heart.
It is God's will. You must hang far apart,
You and your wife, for there must be no sin
Between you, no more in a look than in   380
The very deed. Go now, the plans are drawn.
Go, set to work, and may God spur you on!

Tomorrow night when all men are asleep
Into our kneading-troughs we three shall creep
And sit there waiting, and abide God's grace.   385
Go along now, this isn't the time or place
For me to talk at length or sermonize.
The proverb says, 'Don't waste words on the wise.'
You are so wise there is no need to teach you.
Go, save our lives—that's all that I beseech you!"   390
   This simple carpenter went on his way.
Many a time he said, "Alack the day,"
And to his wife he laid the secret bare.
She knew it better than he; she was aware
What this quaint bargain was designed to buy.   395
She carried on as if about to die,
And said, "Alas, go get this business done.
Help us escape, or we are dead, each one.
I am your true, your faithful wedded wife.
Go, my dear husband, save us, limb and life!"   400
   Great things, in all truth, can the emotions be!
A man can perish through credulity
So deep the print imagination makes.
This simple carpenter, he quails and quakes.
He really sees, according to his notion,   405
Noah's flood come wallowing like an ocean
To drown his Alison, his pet, his dear.
He weeps and wails, and gone is his good cheer,
And wretchedly he sighs. But he goes off
And gets himself a tub, a kneading-trough,   410
Another tub, and has them on the sly
Sent home, and there in secret hangs them high
Beneath the roof. He made three ladders, these
With his own hands, and stowed in bread and cheese
And a jug of good ale, plenty for a day.   415
Before all this was done, he sent away
His chore-boy Robin and his wench likewise
To London on some trumped-up enterprise,
And so on Monday, when it drew toward night,
He shut the door without a candlelight   420
And saw that all was just as it should be,
And shortly they went clambering up, all three.
They sat there still, and let a moment pass.
   "Now then, 'Our Father,' mum!" said Nicholas,
And "Mum!" said John, and "Mum!" said Alison,   425
And piously this carpenter went on
Saying his prayers. He sat there still and straining,
Trying to make out whether he heard it raining.
   The dead of sleep, for very weariness,
Fell on this carpenter, as I should guess,   430
At about curfew time, or little more.

His head was twisted, and that made him snore.
His spirit groaned in its uneasiness.
Down from his ladder slipped this Nicholas,
And Alison too, downward she softly sped   435
And without further word they went to bed
Where the carpenter himself slept other nights.
There were the revels, there were the delights!
And so this Alison and Nicholas lay
Busy about their solace and their play   440
Until the bell for lauds began to ring
And in the chancel friars began to sing.
   Now on this Monday, woebegone and glum
For love, this parish clerk, this Absolom
Was with some friends at Oseney, and while there   445
Inquired after John the carpenter.
A member of the cloister drew him away
Out of the church, and told him, "I can't say.
I haven't seen him working hereabout
Since Saturday. The abbot sent him out   450
For timber, I suppose. He'll often go
And stay at the granary a day or so.
Or else he's at his own house, possibly.
I can't for certain say where he may be."
   Absolom at once felt jolly and light,   455
And thought, "Time now to be awake all night,
For certainly I haven't seen him making
A stir about his door since day was breaking.
Don't call me a man if when I hear the cock
Begin to crow I don't slip up and knock   460
On the low window by his bedroom wall.
To Alison at last I'll pour out all
My love-pangs, for at this point I can't miss,
Whatever happens, at the least a kiss.
Some comfort, by my word, will come my way.   465
I've felt my mouth itch the whole livelong day,
And that's a sign of kissing at the least.
I dreamed all night that I was at a feast.
So now I'll go and sleep an hour or two,
And then I'll wake and play the whole night through."   470
   When the first cockcrow through the dark had come
Up rose this jolly lover Absolom
And dressed up smartly. He was not remiss
About the least point. He chewed licorice
And cardamom to smell sweet, even before   475
He combed his hair. Beneath his tongue he bore
A sprig of Paris[9] like a truelove knot.
He strolled off to the carpenter's house, and got

9. A cloverlike plant.

Beneath the window. It came so near the ground
It reached his chest. Softly, with half a sound,   480
He coughed, "My honeycomb, sweet Alison,
What are you doing, my sweet cinnamon?
Awake, my sweetheart and my pretty bird,
Awake, and give me from your lips a word!
Little enough you care for all my woe,   485
How for your love I sweat wherever I go!
No wonder I sweat and faint and cannot eat
More than a girl; as a lamb does for the teat
I pine. Yes, truly, I so long for love
I mourn as if I were a turtledove."   490
     Said she, "You jack-fool, get away from here!
So help me God, I won't sing 'Kiss me, dear!'
I love another more than you. Get on,
For Christ's sake, Absolom, or I'll throw a stone.
The devil with you! Go and let me sleep."   495
     "Ah, that true love should ever have to reap
So evil a fortune," Absolom said. "A kiss,
At least, if it can be no more than this,
Give me, for love of Jesus and of me."
     "And will you go away for that?" said she.   500
     "Yes, truly, sweetheart," answered Absolom.
     "Get ready then," she said, "for here I come,"
And softly said to Nicholas, "Keep still,
And in a minute you can laugh your fill."
This Absolom got down upon his knee   505
And said, "I am a lord of pure degree,
For after this, I hope, comes more to savor.
Sweetheart, your grace, and pretty bird, your favor!"
     She undid the window quickly. "That will do,"
She said. "Be quick about it, and get through,   510
For fear the neighbors will look out and spy."
     Absolom wiped his mouth to make it dry.
The night was pitch dark, coal-black all about.
Her rear end through the window she thrust out.
He got no better or worse, did Absolom,   515
Than to kiss her with his mouth on the bare bum
Before he had caught on, a smacking kiss.
     He jumped back, thinking something was amiss.
A woman had no beard, he was well aware,
But what he felt was rough and had long hair.   520
     "Alas," he cried, "what have you made me do?"
     "Te-hee!" she said, and banged the window to.
     Absolom backed away a sorry pace.
     "You've bearded him!" said handy Nicholas.
"God's body, this is going fair and fit!"   525
     This luckless Absolom heard every bit,
And gnawed his mouth, so angry he became.

He said to himself, "I'll square you, all the same."
    But who now scrubs and rubs, who chafes his lips
With dust, with sand, with straw, with cloth and chips   530
If not this Absolom? "The devil," says he,
"Welcome my soul if I wouldn't rather be
Revenged than have the whole town in a sack!
Alas," he cries, "if only I'd held back!"
His hot love had become all cold and ashen.   535
He didn't have a curse to spare for passion
From the moment when he kissed her on the ass.
That was the cure to make his sickness pass!
He cried as a child does after being whipped;
He railed at love. Then quietly he slipped   540
Across the street to a smith who was forging out
Parts that the farmers needed round about.
He was busy sharpening colter[1] and plowshare
When Absolom knocked as though without a care.
    "Undo the door, Jervice, and let me come."   545
    "What? Who are you?"
                        "It is I, Absolom."
    "Absolom, is it! By Christ's precious tree,
Why are you up so early? Lord bless me,
What's ailing you? Some gay girl has the power
To bring you out, God knows, at such an hour!   550
Yes, by St. Neot, you know well what I mean!"
    Absolom thought his jokes not worth a bean.
Without a word he let them all go by.
He had another kind of fish to fry
Than Jervice guessed. "Lend me this colter here   555
That's hot in the chimney, friend," he said. "Don't fear,
I'll bring it back right off when I am through.
I need it for a job I have to do."
    "Of course," said Jervice. "Why, if it were gold
Or coins in a sack, uncounted and untold,   560
As I'm a rightful smith, I wouldn't refuse it.
But, Christ's foot! how on earth do you mean to use it?"
    "Let that," said Absolom, "be as it may.
I'll let you know tomorrow or next day,"
And took the colter where the steel was cold   565
And slipped out with it safely in his hold
And softly over to the carpenter's wall.
He coughed and then he rapped the window, all
As he had done before.
                  "Who's knocking there?"
Said Alison. "It is a thief, I swear."   570
    "No, no," said he. "God knows, my sugarplum,
My bird, my darling, it's your Absolom.

---

1. A turf cutter on a plow.

I've brought a golden ring my mother gave me,
Fine and well cut, as I hope that God will save me.
It's yours, if you will let me have a kiss."   575
   Nicholas had got up to take a piss
And thought he would improve the whole affair.
This clerk, before he got away from there,
Should give *his* ass a smack; and hastily
He opened the window, and thrust out quietly,   580
Buttocks and haunches, all the way, his bum.
Up spoke this clerk, this jolly Absolom:
"Speak, for I don't know where you are, sweetheart."
   Nicholas promptly let fly with a fart
As loud as if a clap of thunder broke,   585
So great he was nearly blinded by the stroke,
And ready with his hot iron to make a pass,
Absolom caught him fairly on the ass.
   Off flew the skin, a good handbreadth of fat
Lay bare, the iron so scorched him where he sat.   590
As for the pain, he thought that he would die,
And like a madman he began to cry.
"Help! Water! Water! Help, for God's own heart!"
   At this the carpenter came to with a start.
He heard a man cry "Water!" as if mad.   595
"It's coming now," was the first thought he had.
"It's Noah's flood, alas, God be our hope!"
He sat up with his ax and chopped the rope
And down at once the whole contraption fell.
He didn't take time out to buy or sell   600
Till he hit the floor and lay there in a swoon.
   Then up jumped Nicholas and Alison
And in the street began to cry, "Help, ho!"
The neighbors all came running, high and low,
And poured into the house to see the sight.   605
The man still lay there, passed out cold and white,
For in his tumble he had broken an arm.
But he himself brought on his greatest harm,
For when he spoke he was at once outdone
By handy Nicholas and Alison   610
Who told them one and all that he was mad.
So great a fear of Noah's flood he had,
By some delusion, that in his vanity
He had bought himself these kneading-troughs, all three.
And hung them from the roof there, up above,   615
And he had pleaded with them, for God's love,
To sit there in the loft for company.
   The neighbors laughed at such a fantasy,
And round the loft began to pry and poke
And turned his whole disaster to a joke.   620
He found it was no use to say a word.

Whatever reason he offered, no one heard.
With oaths and curses people swore him down
Until he passed for mad in the whole town.
Wit, clerk, and student all stood by each other.   625
They said, "It's clear the man is crazy, brother."
Everyone had his laugh about this feud.
So Alison, the carpenter's wife, got screwed
For all the jealous watching he could try,
And Absolom, he kissed her nether eye,   630
And Nicholas got his bottom roasted well.
God save this troop! That's all I have to tell.

The Pardoner's Prologue and Tale

THE PROLOGUE

"In churches," said the Pardoner, "when I preach,
I use, milords, a lofty style of speech
And ring it out as roundly as a bell,
Knowing by rote all that I have to tell.
My text is ever the same, and ever was: 5
Radix malorum est cupiditas.[2]
    "First I inform them whence I come; that done,
I then display my papal bulls, each one.
I show my license first, my body's warrant,
Sealed by the bishop, for it would be abhorrent   10
If any man made bold, though priest or clerk,
To interrupt me in Christ's holy work.
And after that I give myself full scope.
Bulls in the name of cardinal and pope,
Of bishops and of patriarchs I show.   15
I say in Latin some few words or so
To spice my sermon; it flavors my appeal
And stirs my listeners to greater zeal.
Then I display my cases made of glass
Crammed to the top with rags and bones. They pass   20
For relics with all the people in the place.
I have a shoulder bone in a metal case,
Part of a sheep owned by a holy Jew.
'Good men,' I say, 'heed what I'm telling you:
Just let this bone be dipped in any well   25
And if cow, calf, or sheep, or ox should swell
From eating a worm, or by a worm be stung,
Take water from this well and wash its tongue
And it is healed at once. And furthermore
Of scab and ulcers and of every sore   30
Shall every sheep be cured, and that straightway,
That drinks from the same well. Heed what I say:

---

2. The root of evil is greed (Latin).

If the good man who owns the beasts will go,
Fasting, each week, and drink before cockcrow
Out of this well, his cattle shall be brought   35
To multiply—that holy Jew so taught
Our elders—and his property increase.
    " 'Moreover, sirs, this bone cures jealousies.
Though into a jealous madness a man fell,
Let him cook his soup in water from this well,   40
He'll never, though for truth he knew her sin,
Suspect his wife again, though she took in
A priest, or even two of them or three.
    " 'Now here's a mitten that you all can see.
Whoever puts his hand in it shall gain,   45
When he sows his land, increasing crops of grain,
Be it wheat or oats, provided that he bring
His penny or so to make his offering.
    " 'There is one word of warning I must say,
Good men and women. If any here today   50
Has done a sin so horrible to name
He daren't be shriven of it for the shame,
Or if any woman, young or old, is here
Who has cuckolded her husband, be it clear
They may not make an offering in that case   55
To these my relics; they have no power nor grace.
But any who is free of such dire blame,
Let him come up and offer in God's name
And I'll absolve him through the authority
That by the pope's bull has been granted me.'   60
    "By such hornswoggling I've won, year by year,
A hundred marks[3] since being a pardoner.
I stand in my pulpit like a true divine,
And when the people sit I preach my line
To ignorant souls, as you have heard before,   65
And tell skullduggeries by the hundred more.
Then I take care to stretch my neck well out
And over the people I nod and peer about
Just like a pigeon perching on a shed.
My hands fly and my tongue wags in my head   70
So busily that to watch me is a joy.
Avarice is the theme that I employ
In all my sermons, to make the people free
In giving pennies—especially to me.
My mind is fixed on what I stand to win   75
And not at all upon correcting sin.
I do not care, when they are in the grave,
If souls go berry-picking that I could save.
Truth is that evil purposes determine,

---

3. Probably the equivalent of several thousand dollars.

And many a time, the origin of a sermon: 80
Some to please people and by flattery
To gain advancement through hypocrisy,
Some for vainglory, some again for hate.
For when I daren't fight otherwise, I wait
And give him a tongue-lashing when I preach.   85
No man escapes or gets beyond the reach
Of my defaming tongue, supposing he
Has done a wrong to my brethren or to me.
For though I do not tell his proper name,
People will recognize him all the same.   90
By sign and circumstance I let them learn.
Thus I serve those who have done us an ill turn.
Thus I spit out my venom under hue
Of sanctity, and seem devout and true!
   "But to put my purpose briefly, I confess   95
I preach for nothing but for covetousness.
That's why my text is still and ever was
Radix malorum est cupiditas.
For by this text I can denounce, indeed,
The very vice I practice, which is greed.   100
But though that sin is lodged in my own heart,
I am able to make other people part
From avarice, and sorely to repent,
Though that is not my principal intent.
   "Then I bring in examples, many a one,   105
And tell them many a tale of days long done.
Plain folk love tales that come down from of old.
Such things their minds can well report and hold.
Do you think that while I have the power to preach
And take in silver and gold for what I teach   110
I shall ever live in willful poverty?
No, no, that never was my thought, certainly.
I mean to preach and beg in sundry lands.
I won't do any labor with my hands,
Nor live by making baskets. I don't intend   115
To beg for nothing; that is not my end.
I won't ape the apostles; I must eat,
I must have money, wool, and cheese, and wheat,
Though I took it from the meanest wretch's tillage
Or from the poorest widow in a village,   120
Yes, though her children starved for want. In fine,
I mean to drink the liquor of the vine
And have a jolly wench in every town.
But, in conclusion, lords, I will get down
To business: you would have me tell a tale.   125
Now that I've had a drink of corny ale,
By God, I hope the thing I'm going to tell
Is one that you'll have reason to like well.

For though myself a very sinful man,
I can tell a moral tale, indeed I can,   130
One that I use to bring the profits in
While preaching. Now be still, and I'll begin."

THE TALE

There was a company of young folk living
One time in Flanders, who were bent on giving
Their lives to follies and extravagances,
Brothels and taverns, where they held their dances
With lutes, harps, and guitars, diced at all hours,   5
And also ate and drank beyond their powers,
Through which they paid the devil sacrifice
In the devil's temple with their drink and dice,
Their abominable excess and dissipation.
They swore oaths that were worthy of damnation;   10
It was grisly to be listening when they swore.
The blessed body of our Lord they tore—
The Jews, it seemed to them, had failed to rend
His body enough—and each laughed at his friend
And fellow in sin. To encourage their pursuits   15
Came comely dancing girls, peddlers of fruits,
Singers with harps, bawds and confectioners
Who are the very devil's officers
To kindle and blow the fire of lechery
That is the follower of gluttony.   20
    Witness the Bible, if licentiousness
Does not reside in wine and drunkenness!
Recall how drunken Lot, unnaturally,
With his two daughters lay unwittingly,
So drunk he had no notion what he did.[4]   25
    Herod, the stories tell us, God forbid,
When full of liquor at his banquet board
Right at his very table gave the word
To kill the Baptist, John, though guiltless he.[5]
    Seneca says a good word, certainly.   30
He says there is no difference he can find
Between a man who has gone out of his mind
And one who carries drinking to excess,
Only that madness outlasts drunkenness.[6]
O gluttony, first cause of mankind's fall,[7]   35
Of our damnation the cursed original
Until Christ bought us with his blood again!
How dearly paid for by the race of men
Was this detestable iniquity!
This whole world was destroyed through gluttony.   40

---

4. Genesis 19:33–35.   5. Matthew 14:1–11; Mark 6:14–28.   6. Seneca's *Epistles* 83.   7. Since
the Fall was caused by eating the forbidden fruit.

Adam our father and his wife also
From paradise to labor and to woe
Were driven for that selfsame vice, indeed.
As long as Adam fasted—so I read—
He was in heaven; but as soon as he   45
Devoured the fruit of that forbidden tree
Then he was driven out in sorrow and pain.
Of gluttony well ought we to complain!
Could a man know how many maladies
Follow indulgences and gluttonies   50
He would keep his diet under stricter measure
And sit at table with more temperate pleasure.
The throat is short and tender is the mouth,
And hence men toil east, west, and north, and south,
In earth, and air, and water—alas to think—   55
Fetching a glutton dainty meat and drink.
    This is a theme, O Paul, that you well treat:
"Meat unto belly, and belly unto meat,
God shall destroy them both," as Paul has said.[8]
When a man drinks the white wine and the red—   60
This is a foul word, by my soul, to say,
And fouler is the deed in every way—
He makes his throat his privy through excess.
    The Apostle says, weeping for piteousness,
"There are many of whom I told you—at a loss   65
I say it, weeping—enemies of Christ's cross,
Whose belly is their god; their end is death."[9]
O cursed belly! Sack of stinking breath
In which corruption lodges, dung abounds!
At either end of you come forth foul sounds.   70
Great cost it is to fill you, and great pain!
These cooks, how they must grind and pound and strain
And transform substance into accident[1]
To please your cravings, though exorbitant!
From the hard bones they knock the marrow out.   75
They'll find a use for everything, past doubt,
That down the gullet sweet and soft will glide.
The spiceries of leaf and root provide
Sauces that are concocted for delight,
To give a man a second appetite.   80
But truly, he whom gluttonies entice
Is dead, while he continues in that vice.
    O drunken man, disfigured is your face,
Sour is your breath, foul are you to embrace!
You seem to mutter through your drunken nose   85
The sound of "Samson, Samson," yet God knows

8. I Corinthians 6:13.   9. Philippians 3:18–19.   1. A distinction was made in philosophy between "substance," the real nature of a thing, and "accident," its merely sensory qualities, such as flavor (see also Dante's *Paradiso* xxxiii.88 ff.).

That Samson never indulged himself in wine.[2]
Your tongue is lost, you fall like a stuck swine,
And all the self-respect that you possess
Is gone, for of man's judgment, drunkenness   90
Is the very sepulcher and annihilation.
A man whom drink has under domination
Can never keep a secret in his head.
Now steer away from both the white and red,
And most of all from that white wine keep wide   95
That comes from Lepe.[3] They sell it in Cheapside
And Fish Street. It's a Spanish wine, and sly
To creep in other wines that grow nearby,
And such a vapor it has that with three drinks
It takes a man to Spain; although he thinks   100
He is home in Cheapside, he is far away
At Lepe. Then "Samson, Samson" will he say!
 By God himself, who is omnipotent,
All the great exploits in the Old Testament
Were done in abstinence, I say, and prayer.   105
Look in the Bible, you may learn it there.
 Attila,[4] conqueror of many a place,
Died in his sleep in shame and in disgrace
Bleeding out of his nose in drunkenness.
A captain ought to live in temperateness!   110
And more than this, I say, remember well
The injunction that was laid on Lemuel[5] —
Not Samuel, but Lemuel, I say!
Read in the Bible; in the plainest way
Wine is forbidden to judges and to kings.   115
This will suffice; no more upon these things.
 Now that I've shown what gluttony will do,
Now I will warn you against gambling, too;
Gambling, the very mother of low scheming,
Of lying and forswearing and blaspheming   120
Against Christ's name, of murder and waste as well
Alike of goods and time; and, truth to tell,
With honor and renown it cannot suit
To be held a common gambler by repute.
The higher a gambler stands in power and place,   125
The more his name is lowered in disgrace.
If a prince gambles, whatever his kingdom be,
In his whole government and policy
He is, in all the general estimation,
Considered so much less in reputation.   130
 Stilbon, who was a wise ambassador,
From Lacedaemon once to Corinth bore

---

2. Judges 13:4.   3. A town in Spain noted for strong wines.   4. Leader of the Hun invasion of
Europe, 5th century.   5. Proverbs 31:4–7.

A mission of alliance. When he came
It happened that he found there at a game
Of hazard all the great ones of the land,   135
And so, as quickly as it could be planned,
He stole back, saying, "I will not lose my name
Nor have my reputation put to shame
Allying you with gamblers. You may send
Other wise emissaries to gain your end,   140
For by my honor, rather than ally
My countrymen to gamblers, I will die.
For you that are so gloriously renowned
Shall never with this gambling race be bound
By will of mine or treaty I prepare."   145
Thus did this wise philosopher declare.
     Remember also how the Parthians' lord
Sent King Demetrius, as the books record,
A pair of golden dice, by this proclaiming
His scorn, because that king was known for gaming,   150
And the king of Parthia therefore held his crown
Devoid of glory, value, or renown.
Lords can discover other means of play
More suitable to while the time away.
     Now about oaths I'll say a word or two,   155
Great oaths and false oaths, as the old books do.
Great swearing is a thing abominable,
And false oaths yet more reprehensible.
Almighty God forbade swearing at all,
Matthew be witness;[6] but specially I call   160
The holy Jeremiah on this head.
"Swear thine oaths truly, do not lie," he said.
"Swear under judgment, and in righteousness."[7]
But idle swearing is a great wickedness.
Consult and see, and he that understands   165
In the first table of the Lord's commands
Will find the second of his commandments this:
"Take not the Lord's name idly or amiss."
If a man's oaths and curses are extreme,
Vengeance shall find his house, both roof and beam.   170
"By the precious heart of God," and "By his nails"—
"My chance is seven,[8] by Christ's blood at Hailes,[9]
Yours five and three." "Cheat me, and if you do,
By God's arms, with this knife I'll run you through!"—
Such fruit comes from the bones,[1] that pair of bitches: 175
Oaths broken, treachery, murder. For the riches
Of Christ's love, give up curses, without fail,
Both great and small!—Now, sirs, I'll tell my tale.
     These three young roisterers of whom I tell

---

6. Matthew 5:34.   7. Jeremiah 4:2.   8. That is, "My lucky number is seven."   9. An abbey in
Gloucestershire, where some of Christ's blood was believed to be preserved.   1. Dice.

Long before prime had rung from any bell 180
Were seated in a tavern at their drinking,
And as they sat, they heard a bell go clinking
Before a corpse being carried to his grave.
One of these roisterers, when he heard it, gave
An order to his boy: "Go out and try 185
To learn whose corpse is being carried by.
Get me his name, and get it right. Take heed."
   "Sir," said the boy, "there isn't any need.
I learned before you came here, by two hours.
He was, it happens, an old friend of yours, 190
And all at once, there on his bench upright
As he was sitting drunk, he was killed last night.
A sly thief, Death men call him, who deprives
All the people in this country of their lives,
Came with his spear and smiting his heart in two 195
Went on his business with no more ado.
A thousand have been slaughtered by his hand
During this plague. And, sir, before you stand
Within his presence, it should be necessary,
It seems to me, to know your adversary. 200
Be evermore prepared to meet this foe.
My mother taught me thus; that's all I know."
   "Now by St. Mary," said the innkeeper,
"This child speaks truth. Man, woman, laborer,
Servant, and child the thief has slain this year 205
In a big village a mile or more from here.
I think it is his place of habitation.
It would be wise to make some preparation
Before he brought a man into disgrace."
   "God's arms!" this roisterer said. "So that's the case! 210
Is it so dangerous with this thief to meet?
I'll look for him by every path and street,
I vow it, by God's holy bones! Hear me,
Fellows of mine, we are all one, we three.
Let each of us hold up his hand to the other 215
And each of us become his fellow's brother.
We'll slay this Death, who slaughters and betrays.
He shall be slain whose hand so many slays,
By the dignity of God, before tonight!"
   The three together set about to plight 220
Their oaths to live and die each for the other
Just as though each had been to each born brother,
And in their drunken frenzy up they get
And toward the village off at once they set
Which the innkeeper had spoken of before, 225
And many were the grisly oaths they swore.
They rent Christ's precious body limb from limb—
Death shall be dead, if they lay hands on him!

When they had hardly gone the first half mile,
Just as they were about to cross a stile, 230
An old man, poor and humble, met them there.
The old man greeted them with a meek air
And said, "God bless you, lords, and be your guide."
　"What's this?" the proudest of the three replied.
"Old beggar, I hope you meet with evil grace! 235
Why are you all wrapped up except your face?
What are you doing alive so many a year?"
　The old man at these words began to peer
Into this gambler's face. "Because I can,
Though I should walk to India, find no man," 240
He said, "in any village or any town,
Who for my age is willing to lay down
His youth. So I must keep my old age still
For as long a time as it may be God's will.
Nor will Death take my life from me, alas! 245
Thus like a restless prisoner I pass
And on the ground, which is my mother's gate,
I walk and with my staff both early and late
I knock and say, 'Dear mother, let me in!
See how I vanish, flesh, and blood, and skin! 250
Alas, when shall my bones be laid to rest?
I would exchange with you my clothing chest,
Mother, that in my chamber long has been
For an old haircloth rag to wrap me in.'
And yet she still refuses me that grace. 255
All white, therefore, and withered is my face.
　"But, sirs, you do yourselves no courtesy
To speak to an old man so churlishly
Unless he had wronged you either in word or deed.
As you yourselves in Holy Writ may read, 260
'Before an aged man whose head is hoar
Men ought to rise.'[2] I counsel you, therefore,
No harm nor wrong here to an old man do,
No more than you would have men do to you
In your old age, if you so long abide. 265
And God be with you, whether you walk or ride!
I must go yonder where I have to go."
　"No, you old beggar, by St. John, not so,"
Said another of these gamblers. "As for me,
By God, you won't get off so easily! 270
You spoke just now of that false traitor, Death,
Who in this land robs all our friends of breath.
Tell where he is, since you must be his spy,
Or you will suffer for it, so say I
By God and by the holy sacrament. 275

---

2. Leviticus 19:32.

You are in league with him, false thief, and bent
On killing us young folk, that's clear to my mind."
  "If you are so impatient, sirs, to find
Death," he replied, "turn up this crooked way,
For in that grove I left him, truth to say,   280
Beneath a tree, and there he will abide.
No boast of yours will make him run and hide.
Do you see that oak tree? Just there you will find
This Death, and God, who bought again mankind,
Save and amend you!" So said this old man;   285
And promptly each of these three gamblers ran
Until he reached the tree, and there they found
Florins of fine gold, minted bright and round,
Nearly eight bushels of them, as they thought.
And after Death no longer then they sought.   290
Each of them was so ravished at the sight,
So fair the florins glittered and so bright,
That down they sat beside the precious hoard.
The worst of them, he uttered the first word.
  "Brothers," he told them, "listen to what I say.   295
My head is sharp, for all I joke and play.
Fortune has given us this pile of treasure
To set us up in lives of ease and pleasure.
Lightly it comes, lightly we'll make it go.
God's precious dignity! Who was to know   300
We'd ever tumble on such luck today?
If we could only carry this gold away,
Home to my house, or either one of yours—
For well you know that all this gold is ours—
We'd touch the summit of felicity.   305
But still, by daylight that can hardly be.
People would call us thieves, too bold for stealth,
And they would have us hanged for our own wealth.
It must be done by night, that's our best plan,
As prudently and slyly as we can.   310
Hence my proposal is that we should all
Draw lots, and let's see where the lot will fall,
And the one of us who draws the shortest stick
Shall run back to the town, and make it quick,
And bring us bread and wine here on the sly,   315
And two of us will keep a watchful eye
Over this gold; and if he doesn't stay
Too long in town, we'll carry this gold away
By night, wherever we all agree it's best."
  One of them held the cut out in his fist   320
And had them draw to see where it would fall,
And the cut fell on the youngest of them all.
At once he set off on his way to town,
And the very moment after he was gone

The one who urged this plan said to the other: 325
"You know that by sworn oath you are my brother.
I'll tell you something you can profit by.
Our friend has gone, that's clear to any eye,
And here is gold, abundant as can be,
That we propose to share alike, we three.   330
But if I worked it out, as I could do,
So that it could be shared between us two,
Wouldn't that be a favor, a friendly one?"
     The other answered, "How that can be done,
I don't quite see. He knows we have the gold.   335
What shall we do, or what shall he be told?"
     "Will you keep the secret tucked inside your head?
And in a few words," the first scoundrel said,
"I'll tell you how to bring this end about."
     "Granted," the other told him. "Never doubt,   340
I won't betray you, that you can believe."
     "Now," said the first, "we are two, as you perceive,
And two of us must have more strength than one.
When he sits down, get up as if in fun
And wrestle with him. While you play this game   345
I'll run him through the ribs. You do the same
With your dagger there, and then this gold shall be
Divided, dear friend, between you and me.
Then all that we desire we can fulfill,
And both of us can roll the dice at will."   350
Thus in agreement these two scoundrels fell
To slay the third, as you have heard me tell.
     The youngest, who had started off to town,
Within his heart kept rolling up and down
The beauty of those florins, new and bright.   355
"O Lord," he thought, "were there some way I might
Have all this treasure to myself alone,
There isn't a man who dwells beneath God's throne
Could live a life as merry as mine should be!"
And so at last the fiend, our enemy,   360
Put in his head that he could gain his ends
If he bought poison to kill off his friends.
Finding his life in such a sinful state,
The devil was allowed to seal his fate.
For it was altogether his intent   365
To kill his friends, and never to repent.
So off he set, no longer would he tarry,
Into the town, to an apothecary,
And begged for poison; he wanted it because
He meant to kill his rats; besides, there was   370
A polecat living in his hedge, he said,
Who killed his capons; and when he went to bed
He wanted to take vengeance, if he might,

On vermin that devoured him by night.

The apothecary answered, "You shall have   375
A drug that as I hope the Lord will save
My soul, no living thing in all creation,
Eating or drinking of this preparation
A dose no bigger than a grain of wheat,
But promptly with his death-stroke he shall meet.   380
Die, that he will, and in a briefer while
Than you can walk the distance of a mile,
This poison is so strong and virulent."

Taking the poison, off the scoundrel went,
Holding it in a box, and next he ran   385
To the neighboring street, and borrowed from a man
Three generous flagons. He emptied out his drug
In two of them, and kept the other jug
For his own drink; he let no poison lurk
In that! And so all night he meant to work   390
Carrying off the gold. Such was his plan,
And when he had filled them, this accursed man
Retraced his path, still following his design,
Back to his friends with his three jugs of wine.

But why dilate upon it any more?   395
For just as they had planned his death before,
Just so they killed him, and with no delay.
When it was finished, one spoke up to say:
"Now let's sit down and drink, and we can bury
His body later on. First we'll be merry,"   400
And as he said the words, he took the jug
That, as it happened, held the poisonous drug,
And drank, and gave his friend a drink as well,
And promptly they both died. But truth to tell,
In all that Avicenna[3] ever wrote   405
He never described in chapter, rule, or note
More marvelous signs of poisoning, I suppose,
Than appeared in these two wretches at the close.
Thus they both perished for their homicide,
And thus the traitorous poisoner also died.   410

O sin accursed above all cursedness,
O treacherous murder, O foul wickedness,
O gambling, lustfulness, and gluttony,
Traducer of Christ's name by blasphemy
And monstrous oaths, through habit and through pride!   415
Alas, mankind! Ah, how may it betide
That you to your Creator, he that wrought you
And even with his precious heart's blood bought you,
So falsely and ungratefully can live?
And now, good men, your sins may God forgive   420

---

3. An Arab physician.

And keep you specially from avarice!
My holy pardon will avail in this,
For it can heal each one of you that brings
His pennies, silver brooches, spoons, or rings.
Come, bow your head under this holy bull!   425
You wives, come offer up your cloth or wool!
I write your names here in my roll, just so.
Into the bliss of heaven you shall go!
I will absolve you here by my high power,
You that will offer, as clean as in the hour   430
When you were born.—Sirs, thus I preach. And now
Christ Jesus, our souls' healer, show you how
Within his pardon evermore to rest,
For that, I will not lie to you, is best.

    But in my tale, sirs, I forgot one thing.   435
The relics and the pardons that I bring
Here in my pouch, no man in the whole land
Has finer, given me by the pope's own hand.
If any of you devoutly wants to offer
And have my absolution, come and proffer   440
Whatever you have to give. Kneel down right here,
Humbly, and take my pardon, full and clear,
Or have a new, fresh pardon if you like
At the end of every mile of road we strike,
As long as you keep offering ever newly   445
Good coins, not counterfeit, but minted truly.
Indeed it is an honor I confer
On each of you, an authentic pardoner
Going along to absolve you as you ride.
For in the country mishaps may betide—   450
One or another of you in due course
May break his neck by falling from his horse.
Think what security it gives you all
That in this company I chanced to fall
Who can absolve you each, both low and high,   455
When the soul, alas, shall from the body fly!
By my advice, our Host here shall begin,
For he's the man enveloped most by sin.
Come, offer first, Sir Host, and once that's done,
Then you shall kiss the relics, every one,   460
Yes, for a penny! Come, undo your purse!

    "No, no," said he. "Then I should have Christ's curse!
I'll do nothing of the sort, for love or riches!
You'd make me kiss a piece of your old britches
And for a saintly relic make it pass   465
Although it had the tincture of your ass.
By the cross St. Helen[4] found in the Holy Land,

---

4. Mother of Constantine the Great; believed to have found the True Cross.

I wish I had your balls here in my hand
For relics! Cut 'em off, and I'll be bound
If I don't help you carry them around. 470
I'll have the things enshrined in a hog's turd!"
    The Pardoner did not answer; not a word,
He was so angry, could he find to say.
    "Now," said our Host, "I will not try to play
With you, nor any other angry man." 475
    Immediately the worthy Knight began,
When he saw that all the people laughed, "No more,
This has gone far enough. Now as before,
Sir Pardoner, be gay, look cheerfully,
And you, Sir Host, who are so dear to me, 480
Come, kiss the Pardoner, I beg of you,
And Pardoner, draw near, and let us do
As we've been doing, let us laugh and play."
And so they kissed, and rode along their way.

SIR GAWAIN AND THE GREEN KNIGHT
fourteenth century

Sir Gawain and the Green Knight is the best English example of the medieval romance, a narrative poem presenting, usually, knightly adventures and "courtly" love. The adventures typically involve the hero in fighting or jousting with other knights and often also in encounters with giants or monsters. No medieval reader or listener would be surprised by the frequent occurrence of magical or supernatural elements. *Courtly love* is the modern term for the relationship between men and women usually depicted in medieval romances. Here the woman—or, rather, the lady—is sovereign; the man (the knight—but never her husband) is the humble suppliant or petitioner for her favors. (In this situation, with the woman on a pedestal but effectively immobilized, and the man looking up to her but with both feet firmly on the ground, may be found an early version of a classic sexual stereotype; it is probably more noticeable in this summary than in the poem itself.) The relationship, though usually adulterous, is carried on with careful regard for the conventions and manners of aristocratic (courtly) society.

The poem's first audience, men and women of the late fourteenth century, might well have recognized both of the main plots of the story, the "Beheading Game" and the "Temptation," which also appear in earlier romances. This would more have pleased than troubled them, as originality per se was not so important then as now—indeed, the anonymous poet himself claims only to be repeating the story "As I heard it in hall." But many members of that first audience, as they listened or read, would also have noticed some of the original features of the poem that intrigue us as well.

To begin with, the hero, Gawain, must prove his courage not by fighting or jousting in the usual way but by accepting an exchange of blows that seems almost certain to kill him. Then, at Bertilak's castle, by another inversion, it is the lady who takes the initiative and woos; and the knight, because of his unusual situation, must resist. Thus Gawain, traditionally the model of the knightly warrior and courtly lover, cannot show his prowess in the traditional way. Indeed, he is tested

in the most extreme way, for his fears and desires must be dealt with not in action but by strength of spirit alone. He is prevented, moreover, by the overall design of the double plot from knowing what is really going on until the very end of the story.

The structure of the *Gawain* narrative is also far tighter and more symmetrical than that of most romances. The story begins at King Arthur's court during a Christmas holiday and ends, almost exactly a year later, in the same place. At Bertilak's castle, the three days of hunting are matched by the three visits of the lady to Gawain's bedroom; each day follows the same pattern, beginning with the start of a hunt, continuing with a wooing scene, returning to the hunt, and concluding with evening festivities. The hunting and wooing are also bound together by the agreement between Bertilak and Gawain to exchange winnings at the end of each day.

Mood and atmosphere depend in large part on the premise that it is all a Christmas *game* (a word that recurs often in the poem). The Green Knight declares that he comes in peace, that he asks not for battle but for sport. But, as all realize, it is a grim and dangerous sport, for the Green Knight is clearly a magical being, and behind his apparently absurd challenge lie two threats: death to anyone who accepts it, disgrace to anyone who does not. Gawain's devotion to King Arthur and to the honor of the court compel him to offer himself for the deadly game, and later his high sense of personal obligation leads him to journey through many perils to find the Green Knight and receive the return stroke of the ax. His faithfulness to his word, his honor, are also at stake in the exchange of gifts at Bertilak's castle. A story that began as a Christmas entertainment has become a series of tests of knightly and Christian virtues.

Keeping to the spirit of the game, we might better appreciate the skill of the author if we try to answer some questions about the poem. What is the significance of the many parallels in it? For example, is there any broad similarity between Bertilak's third hunt—of the fox—and the lady's third visit to Gawain? Turning to the conclusion of the poem, what *is* Gawain's fault? Of what does he accuse himself in the final talk with Bertilak? Why are his chagrin and self-disgust so intense? What is Bertilak's view of the matter? Does the poet agree with Gawain or with Bertilak, or can their attitudes be reconciled?

A word about the language of the poem and our modern English version of it: it was originally written by a contemporary of Chaucer but in a very different dialect than his, that of the English Midlands near the site of modern Birmingham. Furthermore, except at the end of each stanza, the form depends not on rhyme but on the older device of alliteration: two or more words of every line begin with the same sound. The translation reproduces this pattern with great skill and fidelity. One result of this is the occasional use of unusual words or of ordinary words in slightly unaccustomed senses; some of these have been glossed, while the meanings of others may be surmised from the context or, if necessary, found in a dictionary.

The standard edition of the original poem (in Middle English) is by J. R. R. Tolkien and E. V. Gordon (1967). Some interpretations are M. Boroff, *Sir Gawain and the Green Knight, A Stylistic and Metrical Study* (1962); Larry D. Benson, *Art and Tradition in Sir Gawain and the Green Knight* (1965); and J. A Burrow, *A Reading of Sir Gawain and the Green Knight* (1965). Donald R. Howard and Christian K. Zacher, eds., *Critical Studies of Sir Gawain and the Green Knight* (1968), is an excellent collection. Other studies include L. S. Johnson, *The Voice of the Gawain Poet* (1984), and W. Clein, *Concepts of Chivalry in Sir Gawain and the Green Knight* (1987).

PRONOUNCING GLOSSARY

The following list uses common English syllables and stress accents to provide rough equivalents of selected words whose pronunciation may be unfamiliar to the general reader.

Bertilak: *behr-tee-lak'*   Sauvage: *soh-vazh'*

Sir Gawain and the Green Knight[1]

PART I

Since the siege and the assault was ceased at Troy,
The walls breached and burnt down to brands and ashes,
The knight that had knotted the nets of deceit
Was impeached for his perfidy,[2] proven most true,
It was high-born Aeneas and his haughty race   5
That since prevailed over provinces, and proudly reigned
Over well-nigh all the wealth of the West Isles.[3]
Great Romulus[4] to Rome repairs in haste;
With boast and with bravery builds he that city
And names it with his own name, that it now bears.   10
Ticius to Tuscany,[5] and towers raises,
Langobard[6] in Lombardy lays out homes,
And far over the French Sea,[7] Felix Brutus
On many broad hills and high Britain he sets,[8]
                    most fair.   15
          Where war and wrack and wonder
          By shifts have sojourned there,
          And bliss by turns with blunder
          In that land's lot had share.

And since this Britain was built by this baron great,   20
Bold boys bred there, in broils delighting,
That did in their day many a deed most dire.
More marvels have happened in this merry land
Than in any other I know, since that olden time,
But of those that here built, of British kings,   25
King Arthur was counted most courteous of all,
Wherefore an adventure I aim to unfold,
That a marvel of might some men think it,
And one unmatched among Arthur's wonders.

---

1. Translated by Marie Borroff. Many of the notes are by E. Talbot Donaldson.   2. The treacherous knight is either Aeneas himself or Antenor, both of whom were, according to medieval tradition, traitors to their city Troy; but Aeneas was actually tried ("impeached") by the Greeks for his refusal to hand over to them his sister Polyxena.   3. Perhaps western Europe.   4. The legendary founder of Rome is here given Trojan ancestry, like Aeneas.   5. A region north of Rome; modern Florence is located in it. *Ticius:* not otherwise known.   6. The reputed founder of Lombardy, a region in the north centered on modern Milan.   7. The North Sea, including the English Channel. *Felix Brutus:* great-grandson of Aeneas and legendary founder of Britain; not elsewhere given the name Felix (Latin "happy").   8. Establishes.

If you will listen to my lay but a little while,   30
As I heard it in hall, I shall hasten to tell
                    anew,
                    As it was fashioned featly
                    In tale of derring-do,
                    And linked in measures meetly[9]   35
                    By letters tried and true.

This king lay at Camelot[1] at Christmastide;
Many good knights and gay his guests were there,
Arrayed of the Round Table rightful brothers,[2]
With feasting and fellowship and carefree mirth.   40
There true men contended in tournaments many,
Joined there in jousting these gentle knights,
Then came to the court for carol-dancing,
For the feast was in force full fifteen days,
With all the meat and the mirth that men could devise,   45
Such gaiety and glee, glorious to hear,
Brave din by day, dancing by night.
High were their hearts in halls and chambers,
These lords and these ladies, for life was sweet.
In peerless pleasures passed they their days,   50
The most noble knights known under Christ,
And the loveliest ladies that lived on earth ever,
And he the comeliest king, that that court holds,
For all this fair folk in their first age
                    were still.   55
                    Happiest of mortal kind,
                    King noblest famed of will;
                    You would now go far to find
                    So hardy a host on hill.

While the New Year was new, but yesternight come,   60
This fair folk at feast two-fold was served,
When the king and his company were come in together,
The chanting in chapel achieved and ended.
Clerics and all the court acclaimed the glad season,
Cried Noel anew, good news to men;   65
Then gallants gather gaily, hand-gifts to make,
Called them out clearly, claimed them by hand,
Bickered long and busily about those gifts.
Ladies laughed aloud, though losers they were,
And he that won was not angered, as well you will know.[3]   70
All this mirth they made until meat was served;
When they had washed them worthily, they went to their seats,

---

9. Suitably.   1. Capital of Arthur's kingdom, presumably located in southwest England or southern
Wales.   2. According to legend, the Round Table was made by Merlin, the wise magician who had
helped Arthur become King after a dispute broke out among Arthur's knights about precedence: it
seated 100 knights. The table described in the poem is not round.   3. The dispensing of New Year's
gifts seems to have involved kissing.

The best seated above, as best it beseemed,
Guenevere the goodly queen gay in the midst
On a dais well-decked and duly arrayed   75
With costly silk curtains, a canopy over,
Of Toulouse and Turkestan tapestries rich,
All broidered and bordered with the best gems
Ever brought into Britain, with bright pennies
      to pay.   80
   Fair queen, without a flaw,
   She glanced with eyes of grey.
   A seemlier[4] that once he saw,
   In truth, no man could say.

But Arthur would not eat till all were served;   85
So light was his lordly heart, and a little boyish;
His life he liked lively—the less he cared
To be lying for long, or long to sit,
So busy his young blood, his brain so wild.
And also a point of pride pricked him in heart,   90
For he nobly had willed, he would never eat
On so high a holiday, till he had heard first
Of some fair feat or fray, some far-borne tale,
Of some marvel of might, that he might trust,
By champions of chivalry achieved in arms,   95
Or some suppliant came seeking some single knight
To join with him in jousting, in jeopardy each
To lay life for life, and leave it to fortune
To afford him on field fair hap[5] or other.
Such is the king's custom, when his court he holds   100
At each far-famed feast amid his fair host
      so dear.
   The stout king stands in state
   Till a wonder shall appear;
   He leads, with heart elate,   105
   High mirth in the New Year.

So he stands there in state, the stout young king,
Talking before the high table[6] of trifles fair.
There Gawain the good knight by Guenevere sits,
With Agravain à la dure main[7] on his other side,   110
Both knights of renown, and nephews of the king.
Bishop Baldwin above begins the table,
And Yvain, son of Urien, ate with him there.
These few with the fair queen were fittingly served;
At the side-tables sat many stalwart knights.   115
Then the first course comes, with clamor of trumpets
That were bravely bedecked with bannerets bright,

---

4. More suitable and pleasing (queen).   5. Good luck.   6. The high table is on a dais; the side
tables (line 115) are on the main floor and run along the walls at a right angle to the high table.
7. Of the hard hand.

With noise of new drums and the noble pipes.
Wild were the warbles that wakened that day
In strains that stirred many strong men's hearts.   120
There dainties were dealt out, dishes rare,
Choice fare to choose, on chargers so many
That scarce was there space to set before the people
The service of silver, with sundry meats,
　　　　　　　　　　on cloth.   125
　　　　　　Each fair guest freely there
　　　　　　Partakes, and nothing loth;[8]
　　　　　　Twelve dishes before each pair;
　　　　　　Good beer and bright wine both.

Of the service itself I need say no more,   130
For well you will know no tittle was wanting.
Another noise and a new was well-nigh at hand,
That the lord might have leave his life to nourish;
For scarce were the sweet strains still in the hall,
And the first course come to that company fair,   135
There hurtles in at the hall-door an unknown rider,
One the greatest on ground in growth of his frame:
From broad neck to buttocks so bulky and thick,
And his loins and his legs so long and so great,
Half a giant on earth I hold him to be,   140
But believe him no less than the largest of men,
And that the seemliest in his stature to see, as he rides,
For in back and in breast though his body was grim,
His waist in its width was worthily small,
And formed with every feature in fair accord   145
　　　　　　　　　　was he.
　　　　　　Great wonder grew in hall
　　　　　　At his hue most strange to see,
　　　　　　For man and gear and all
　　　　　　Were green as green could be.   150

And in guise all of green, the gear and the man:
A coat cut close, that clung to his sides,
And a mantle to match, made with a lining
Of furs cut and fitted—the fabric was noble,
Embellished all with ermine, and his hood beside,   155
That was loosed from his locks, and laid on his shoulders.
With trim hose and tight, the same tint of green,
His great calves were girt, and gold spurs under
He bore on silk bands that embellished his heels,
And footgear well-fashioned, for riding most fit.   160
And all his vesture verily was verdant green;
Both the bosses[9] on his belt and other bright gems
That were richly ranged on his raiment noble

8. Not unwillingly.　　9. Ornamental knobs.

About himself and his saddle, set upon silk,
That to tell half the trifles would tax my wits,   165
The butterflies and birds embroidered thereon
In green of the gayest, with many a gold thread.
The pendants of the breast-band, the princely crupper,[1]
And the bars of the bit were brightly enameled;
The stout stirrups were green, that steadied his feet,   170
And the bows of the saddle and the side-panels both,
That gleamed all and glinted with green gems about.
The steed he bestrides of that same green
                              so bright.
              A green horse great and thick;   175
              A headstrong steed of might;
              In broidered bridle quick,
              Mount matched man aright.

Gay was this goodly man in guise all of green,
And the hair of his head to his horse suited;   180
Fair flowing tresses enfold his shoulders;
A beard big as a bush on his breast hangs,
That with his heavy hair, that from his head falls,
Was evened all about above both his elbows,
That half his arms thereunder were hid in the fashion   185
Of a king's cap-à-dos,[2] that covers his throat.
The mane of that mighty horse much to it like,
Well curled and becombed, and cunningly knotted
With filaments of fine gold amid the fair green,
Here a strand of the hair, here one of gold;   190
His tail and his foretop twin in their hue,
And bound both with a band of a bright green
That was decked adown the dock[3] with dazzling stones
And tied tight at the top with a triple knot
Where many bells well burnished rang bright and clear.   195
Such a mount in his might, nor man on him riding,
None had seen, I dare swear, with sight in that hall
                              so grand.
              As lightning quick and light
              He looked to all at hand;   200
              It seemed that no man might
              His deadly dints withstand.

Yet had he no helm, nor hauberk[4] neither,
Nor plate, nor appurtenance appending to arms,
Nor shaft pointed sharp, nor shield for defense,   205
But in his one hand he had a holly bob
That is goodliest in green when groves are bare,
And an ax in his other, a huge and immense,

---

1. *Breast-band . . . crupper:* parts of the horse's harness.   2. Or *capados,* interpreted by the translator as a garment covering its wearer "from head to back."   3. The solid part of the tail.   4. Tunic of chain mail.

A wicked piece of work in words to expound:
The head on its haft was an ell[5] long; 210
The spike of green steel, resplendent with gold;
The blade burnished bright, with a broad edge,
As well shaped to shear as a sharp razor;
Stout was the stave in the strong man's gripe,
That was wound all with iron to the weapon's end, 215
With engravings in green of goodliest work.
A lace lightly about, that led to a knot,
Was looped in by lengths along the fair haft,
And tassels thereto attached in a row,
With buttons of bright green, brave to behold. 220
This horseman hurtles in, and the hall enters;
Riding to the high dais, recked he no danger;
Not a greeting he gave as the guests he o'erlooked,
Nor wasted his words, but "Where is," he said,
"The captain of this crowd? Keenly I wish 225
To see that sire with sight, and to himself say
              my say."
              He swaggered all about
              To scan the host so gay;
              He halted, as if in doubt 230
              Who in that hall held sway.

There were stares on all sides as the stranger spoke,
For much did they marvel what it might mean
That a horseman and a horse should have such a hue,
Grow green as the grass, and greener, it seemed, 235
Than green fused on gold more glorious by far.
All the onlookers eyed him, and edged nearer,
And awaited in wonder what he would do,
For many sights had they seen, but such a one never,
So that phantom and faerie the folk there deemed it, 240
Therefore chary of answer was many a champion bold,
And stunned at his strong words stone-still they sat
In a swooning silence in the stately hall.
As all were slipped into sleep, so slackened their speech
              apace 245
              Not all, I think, for dread,
              But some of courteous grace
              Let him who was their head
              Be spokesman in that place.

Then Arthur before the high dais that entrance beholds, 250
And hailed him, as behooved, for he had no fear,
And said "Fellow, in faith you have found fair welcome;
The head of this hostelry Arthur am I;
Leap lightly down, and linger, I pray,

5. Three or four feet long.

And the tale of your intent you shall tell us after." 255
"Nay, so help me," said the other, "He that on high sits,
To tarry here any time, 'twas not mine errand;
But as the praise of you, prince, is puffed up so high,
And your court and your company are counted the best,
Stoutest under steel-gear on steeds to ride, 260
Worthiest of their works the wide world over,
And peerless to prove in passages of arms,
And courtesy here is carried to its height,
And so at this season I have sought you out.
You may be certain by the branch that I bear in hand 265
That I pass here in peace, and would part friends,
For had I come to this court on combat bent,
I have a hauberk at home, and a helm beside,
A shield and a sharp spear, shining bright,
And other weapons to wield, I ween[6] well, to boot, 270
But as I willed no war, I wore no metal.
But if you be so bold as all men believe,
You will graciously grant the game that I ask
          by right."
        Arthur answer gave 275
        And said, "Sir courteous knight,
        If contest here you crave,
        You shall not fail to fight."

"Nay, to fight, in good faith, is far from my thought;
There are about on these benches but beardless children, 280
Were I here in full arms on a haughty steed,
For measured against mine, their might is puny.
And so I call in this court for a Christmas game,
For 'tis Yule and New Year, and many young bloods about;
If any in this house such hardihood claims, 285
Be so bold in his blood, his brain so wild,
As stoutly to strike one stroke for another,
I shall give him as my gift this gisarme[7] noble,
This ax, that is heavy enough, to handle as he likes,
And I shall bide[8] the first blow, as bare as I sit. 290
If there be one so wilful my words to assay,
Let him leap hither lightly, lay hold of this weapon;
I quitclaim it forever, keep it[9] as his own,
And I shall stand him a stroke, steady on this floor,
So you grant me the guerdon[1] to give him another, 295
          sans[2] blame.
        In a twelvemonth and a day
        He shall have of me the same;
        Now be it seen straightway
        Who dares take up the game." 300

6. Believe.   7. Weapon.   8. Endure.   9. I.e., let him keep it.   1. Reward.   2. Without.

If he astonished them at first, stiller were then
All that household in hall, the high and the low;
The stranger on his green steed stirred in the saddle,
And roisterously his red eyes he rolled all about,
Bent his bristling brows, that were bright green, 305
Wagged his beard as he watched who would arise.
When the court kept its counsel he coughed aloud,
And cleared his throat coolly, the clearer to speak:
"What, is this Arthur's house," said that horseman then,
"Whose fame is so fair in far realms and wide? 310
Where is now your arrogance and your awesome deeds,
Your valor and your victories and your vaunting words?
Now are the revel and renown of the Round Table
Overwhelmed with a word of one man's speech,
For all cower and quake, and no cut felt!" 315
With this he laughs so loud that the lord grieved;
The blood for sheer shame shot to his face,

and pride.
With rage his face flushed red,
And so did all beside. 320
Then the king as bold man bred
Toward the stranger took a stride.

And said "Sir, now we see you will say but folly,
Which whoso has sought, it suits that he find.
No guest here is aghast of your great words. 325
Give to me your gisarme, in God's own name,
And the boon you have begged shall straight be granted."
He leaps to him lightly, lays hold of his weapon;
The green fellow on foot fiercely alights.
Now has Arthur his ax, and the haft grips, 330
And sternly stirs it about, on striking bent.
The stranger before him stood there erect,
Higher than any in the house by a head and more;
With stern look as he stood, he stroked his beard,
And with undaunted countenance drew down his coat, 335
No more moved nor dismayed for his mighty dints
Than any bold man on bench had brought him a drink

of wine.
Gawain by Guenevere
Toward the king doth now incline: 340
"I beseech, before all here,
That this melee may be mine."

"Would you grant me the grace," said Gawain to the king,
"To be gone from this bench and stand by you there,
If I without discourtesy might quit this board, 345
And if my liege lady[3] misliked it not,

---

3. Lady entitled to the knight's feudal service.

I would come to your counsel before your court noble.
For I find it not fit, as in faith it is known,
When such a boon is begged before all these knights,
Though you be tempted thereto, to take it on yourself   350
While so bold men about upon benches sit,
That no host under heaven is hardier of will,
Nor better brothers-in-arms where battle is joined;
I am the weakest, well I know, and of wit feeblest;
And the loss of my life would be least of any;   355
That I have you for uncle is my only praise;
My body, but for your blood, is barren of worth;
And for that this folly befits not a king,
And 'tis I that have asked it, it ought to be mine,
And if my claim be not comely let all this court judge,   360
                              in sight."
                    The court assays the claim,
                    And in counsel all unite
                    To give Gawain the game
                    And release the king outright.   365

Then the king called the knight to come to his side,
And he rose up readily, and reached him with speed,
Bows low to his lord, lays hold of the weapon,
And he releases it lightly, and lifts up his hand,
And gives him God's blessing, and graciously prays   370
That his heart and his hand may be hardy both.
"Keep, cousin," said the king, "what you cut with this day,
And if you rule it aright, then readily, I know,
You shall stand the stroke it will strike after."
Gawain goes to the guest with gisarme in hand,   375
And boldly he bides there, abashed not a whit.
Then hails he Sir Gawain, the horseman in green:
"Recount we our contract, ere you come further.
First I ask and adjure you, how you are called
That you tell me true, so that trust it I may."   380
"In good faith," said the good knight, "Gawain am I
Whose buffet befalls you, whate'er betide after,
And at this time twelvemonth take from you another
With what weapon you will, and with no man else
                              alive."   385
                    The other nods assent:
                    "Sir Gawain, as I may thrive,
                    I am wondrous well content
                    That you this dint shall drive."

"Sir Gawain," said the Green Knight, "By God, I rejoice   390
That your fist shall fetch this favor I seek,
And you have readily rehearsed, and in right terms,
Each clause of my covenant with the king your lord,
Save that you shall assure me, sir, upon oath,

That you shall seek me yourself, wheresoever you deem   395
My lodgings may lie, and look for such wages
As you have offered me here before all this host."
"What is the way there?" said Gawain, "Where do you dwell?
I heard never of your house, by Him that made me,
Nor I know you not, knight, your name nor your court.   400
But tell me truly thereof, and teach me your name,
And I shall fare forth to find you, so far as I may,
And this I say in good certain, and swear upon oath."
"That is enough in New Year, you need say no more,"
Said the knight in the green to Gawain the noble,   405
"If I tell you true, when I have taken your knock,
And if you handily have hit, you shall hear straightway
Of my house and my home and my own name;
Then follow in my footsteps by faithful accord.
And if I spend no speech, you shall speed the better: 410
You can feast with your friends, nor further trace
                         my tracks.
               Now hold your grim tool steady
               And show us how it hacks."
               "Gladly, sir; all ready,"   415
               Says Gawain; he strokes the ax.

The Green Knight upon ground girds him with care:
Bows a bit with his head, and bares his flesh:
His long lovely locks he laid over his crown,
Let the naked nape for the need be shown.   420
Gawain grips to his ax and gathers it aloft—
The left foot on the floor before him he set—
Brought it down deftly upon the bare neck,
That the shock of the sharp blow shivered the bones
And cut the flesh cleanly and clove it in twain,   425
That the blade of bright steel bit into the ground.
The head was hewn off and fell to the floor;
Many found it at their feet, as forth it rolled;
The blood gushed from the body, bright on the green,
Yet fell not the fellow, nor faltered a whit,   430
But stoutly he starts forth upon stiff shanks,
And as all stood staring he stretched forth his hand,
Laid hold of his head and heaved it aloft,
Then goes to the green steed, grasps the bridle,
Steps into the stirrup, bestrides his mount,   435
And his head by the hair in his hand holds,
And as steady he sits in the stately saddle
As he had met with no mishap, nor missing were
                         his head.
               His bulk about he haled,[4]   440
               That fearsome body that bled;

4. Hauled.

> There were many in the court that quailed
> Before all his say was said.

For the head in his hand he holds right up;
Toward the first on the dais directs he the face,   445
And it lifted up its lids, and looked with wide eyes,
And said as much with its mouth as now you may hear:
"Sir Gawain, forget not to go as agreed,
And cease not to seek till me, sir, you find,
As you promised in the presence of these proud knights.   450
To the Green Chapel come, I charge you, to take
Such a dint as you have dealt—you have well deserved
That your neck should have a knock on New Year's morn.
The Knight of the Green Chapel I am well-known to many,
Wherefore you cannot fail to find me at last;   455
Therefore come, or be counted a recreant[5] knight."
With a roisterous rush he flings round the reins,
Hurtles out at the hall-door, his head in his hand,
That the flint-fire flew from the flashing hooves.
Which way he went, not one of them knew   460
Nor whence he was come in the wide world
> so fair.
>> The king and Gawain gay
>> Make game of the Green Knight there,
>> Yet all who saw it say   465
>> 'Twas a wonder past compare.

Though high-born Arthur at heart had wonder,
He let no sign be seen, but said aloud
To the comely queen, with courteous speech,
"Dear dame, on this day dismay you no whit;   470
Such crafts are becoming at Christmastide,
Laughing at interludes, light songs and mirth,
Amid dancing of damsels with doughty knights.
Nevertheless of my meat now let me partake,
For I have met with a marvel, I may not deny."   475
He glanced at Sir Gawain, and gaily he said,
"Now, sir, hang up your ax, that has hewn enough,"
And over the high dais it was hung on the wall
That men in amazement might on it look,
And tell in true terms the tale of the wonder.   480
Then they turned toward the table, these two together,
The good king and Gawain, and made great feast,
With all dainties double, dishes rare,
With all manner of meat and minstrelsy both,
Such happiness wholly had they that day   485
> in hold.
>> Now take care, Sir Gawain,

5. Cowardly.

> That your courage wax not cold
> When you must turn again
> To your enterprise foretold.   490

PART II

This adventure had Arthur of handsels[6] first
When young was the year, for he yearned to hear tales;
Though they wanted for words when they went to sup,
Now are fierce deeds to follow, their fists stuffed full.
Gawain was glad to begin those games in hall,   495
But if the end be harsher, hold it no wonder,
For though men are merry in mind after much drink,
A year passes apace, and proves ever new:
First things and final conform but seldom.
And so this Yule to the young year yielded place,   500
And each season ensued at its set time;
After Christmas there came the cold cheer of Lent,
When with fish and plainer fare our flesh we reprove;
But then the world's weather with winter contends:
The keen cold lessens, the low clouds lift;   505
Fresh falls the rain in fostering showers
On the face of the fields; flowers appear.
The ground and the groves wear gowns of green;
Birds build their nests, and blithely sing
That solace of all sorrow with summer comes   510
>   ere long.
>> And blossoms day by day
>> Bloom rich and rife in throng;
>> Then every grove so gay
>> Of the greenwood rings with song.   515

And then the season of summer with the soft winds,
When Zephyr sighs low over seeds and shoots;
Glad is the green plant growing abroad,
When the dew at dawn drops from the leaves,
To get a gracious glance from the golden sun.   520
But harvest with harsher winds follows hard after,
Warns him to ripen well ere winter comes;
Drives forth the dust in the droughty season,
From the face of the fields to fly high in air.
Wroth winds in the welkin[7] wrestle with the sun,   525
The leaves launch from the linden and light on the ground,
And the grass turns to gray, that once grew green.
Then all ripens and rots that rose up at first,
And so the year moves on in yesterdays many,
And winter once more, by the world's law,   530
>   draws nigh.

---

6. Gifts to mark the New Year.   7. The heavens.

At Michaelmas[8] the moon
Hangs wintry pale in sky;
Sir Gawain girds him soon
For travails yet to try.   535

Till All-Hallows' Day[9] with Arthur he dwells,
And he held a high feast to honor that knight
With great revels and rich, of the Round Table.
Then ladies lovely and lords debonair
With sorrow for Sir Gawain were sore at heart;   540
Yet they covered their care with countenance glad:
Many a mournful man made mirth for his sake.
So after supper soberly he speaks to his uncle
Of the hard hour at hand, and openly says,
"Now, liege lord of my life, my leave I take;   545
The terms of this task too well you know—
To count the cost over concerns me nothing.
But I am bound forth betimes[1] to bear a stroke
From the grim man in green, as God may direct."
Then the first and foremost came forth in throng: 550
Yvain and Eric and others of note,
Sir Dodinal le Sauvage, the Duke of Clarence,
Lionel and Lancelot and Lucan the good,
Sir Bors and Sir Bedivere, big men both,
And many manly knights more, with Mador de la Porte.   555
All this courtly company comes to the king
To counsel their comrade, with care in their hearts;
There was much secret sorrow suffered that day
That one so good as Gawain must go in such wise
To bear a bitter blow, and his bright sword   560
          lay by.
          He said, "Why should I tarry?"
          And smiled with tranquil eye;
          "In destinies sad or merry,
          True men can but try."   565

He dwelt there all that day, and dressed in the morning;
Asked early for his arms, and all were brought.
First a carpet of rare cost was cast on the floor
Where much goodly gear gleamed golden bright;
He takes his place promptly and picks up the steel,   570
Attired in a tight coat of Turkestan silk
And a kingly cap-à-dos, closed at the throat,
That was lavishly lined with a lustrous fur.
Then they set the steel shoes on his sturdy feet
And clad his calves about with comely greaves,   575
And plate well-polished protected his knees,
Affixed with fastenings of the finest gold.

8. September 29.   9. November 1.   1. Soon.

Fair cuisses enclosed, that were cunningly wrought,
His thick-thewed thighs, with thongs bound fast,
And massy chain-mail of many a steel ring   580
He bore on his body, above the best cloth,
With brace burnished bright upon both his arms,
Good couters[2] and gay, and gloves of plate,
And all the goodly gear to grace him well
                      that tide.   585
          His surcoat[3] blazoned bold;
          Sharp spurs to prick with pride;
          And a brave silk band to hold
          The broadsword at his side.

When he had on his arms, his harness was rich,   590
The least latchet or loop laden with gold;
So armored as he was, he heard a mass,
Honored God humbly at the high altar.
Then he comes to the king and his comrades-in-arms,
Takes his leave at last of lords and ladies,   595
And they clasped and kissed him, commending him to Christ.
By then Gringolet[4] was girt with a great saddle
That was gaily agleam with fine gilt fringe,
New-furbished for the need with nail-heads bright;
The bridle and the bars bedecked all with gold;   600
The breast-plate, the saddlebow, the side-panels both,
The caparison and the crupper accorded in hue,
And all ranged on the red the resplendent studs
That glittered and glowed like the glorious sun.
His helm now he holds up and hastily kisses,   605
Well-closed with iron clinches, and cushioned within;
It was high on his head, with a hasp behind,
And a covering of cloth to encase the visor,
All bound and embroidered with the best gems
On broad bands of silk, and bordered with birds,   610
Parrots and popinjays preening their wings,
Lovebirds and love-knots as lavishly wrought
As many women had worked seven winters thereon,
                    entire.
          The diadem costlier yet   615
          That crowned that comely sire,
          With diamonds richly set,
          That flashed as if on fire.

Then they showed forth the shield, that shone all red,
With the pentangle[5] portrayed in purest gold.   620
About his broad neck by the baldric[6] he casts it,

---

2. Armor for the elbows.   3. Cloth tunic worn over the armor.   4. Gawain's horse.   5. A five-
pointed star, formed by five lines which are drawn without lifting the pen, supposed to have mystical
significance; as Solomon's sign (line 625), it was enclosed in a circle.   6. Belt worn diagonally across
the chest.

That was meet for the man, and matched him well.
And why the pentangle is proper to that peerless prince
I intend now to tell, though detain me it must.
It is a sign by Solomon sagely devised   625
To be a token of truth, by its title of old,
For it is a figure formed of five points,
And each line is linked and locked with the next
For ever and ever, and hence it is called
In all England, as I hear, the endless knot.   630
And well may he wear it on his worthy arms,
For ever faithful five-fold in five-fold fashion
Was Gawain in good works, as gold unalloyed,
Devoid of all villainy, with virtues adorned
                     in sight.   635
        On shield and coat in view
        He bore that emblem bright,
        As to his word most true
        And in speech most courteous knight.

And first, he was faultless in his five senses,   640
Nor found ever to fail in his five fingers,
And all his fealty was fixed upon the five wounds
That Christ got on the cross, as the creed tells;
And wherever this man in melee took part,
His one thought was of this, past all things else,   645
That all his force was founded on the five joys[7]
That the high Queen of heaven had in her child.
And therefore, as I find, he fittingly had
On the inner part of his shield her image portrayed,
That when his look on it lighted, he never lost heart.   650
The fifth of the five fives followed by this knight
Were beneficence boundless and brotherly love
And pure mind and manners, that none might impeach,
And compassion most precious—these peerless five
Were forged and made fast in him, foremost of men.   655
Now all these five fives were confirmed in this knight,
And each linked in other, that end there was none,
And fixed to five points, whose force never failed,
Nor assembled all on a side, nor asunder either,
Nor anywhere at an end, but whole and entire   660
However the pattern proceeded or played out its course.
And so on his shining shield shaped was the knot
Royally in red gold against red gules,[8]
That is the peerless pentangle, prized of old
                    in lore.   665

---

7. These were the annunciation to Mary that she was to bear the Son of God, Christ's Nativity, Resurrection, and Ascension into Heaven, and the "Assumption" or bodily taking up of Mary into Heaven to join Him.   8. Background (*gules* is the heraldic name for red).

Now armed is Gawain gay,
And bears his lance before,
And soberly said good day,
He thought forevermore.

He struck his steed with the spurs and sped on his way   670
So fast that the flint-fire flashed from the stones.
When they saw him set forth they were sore aggrieved,
And all sighed softly, and said to each other,
Fearing for their fellow, "Ill fortune it is
That you, man, must be marred, that most are worthy!   675
His equal on this earth can hardly be found;
To have dealt more discreetly had done less harm,
And have dubbed him a duke, with all due honor.
A great leader of lords he was like to become,
And better so to have been than battered to bits,   680
Beheaded by an elf-man,[9] for empty pride!
Who would credit that a king could be counseled so,
And caught in a cavil in a Christmas game?"
Many were the warm tears they wept from their eyes
When goodly Sir Gawain was gone from the court   685
that day.
No longer he abode,
But speedily went his way
Over many a wandering road,
As I heard my author say.   690

Now he rides in his array through the realm of Logres,[1]
Sir Gawain, God knows, though it gave him small joy!
All alone must he lodge through many a long night
Where the food that he fancied was far from his plate;
He had no mate but his mount, over mountain and plain,   695
Nor man to say his mind to but almighty God,
Till he had wandered well-nigh into North Wales.
All the islands of Anglesey he holds on his left,
And follows, as he fares, the fords by the coast,
Comes over at Holy Head, and enters next   700
The Wilderness of Wirral[2]—few were within
That had great good will toward God or man.
And earnestly he asked of each mortal he met
If he had ever heard aught of a knight all green,
Or of a Green Chapel, on ground thereabouts,   705
And all said the same, and solemnly swore
They saw no such knight all solely green
in hue.

9. Supernatural being, in this case obviously not small.   1. Another name for Arthur's kingdom.
2. *North Wales . . . Wirral:* Gawain went from Camelot north to the northern coast of Wales, opposite
the islands of Anglesey; there he turned east across the river Dee to the forest of Wirral, near what is
now Liverpool.

Over country wild and strange
The knight sets off anew;   710
Often his course must change
Ere the Chapel comes in view.

Many a cliff must he climb in country wild;
Far off from all his friends, forlorn must he ride;
At each strand or stream where the stalwart passed   715
'Twere a marvel if he met not some monstrous foe,
And that so fierce and forbidding that fight he must.
So many were the wonders he wandered among
That to tell but the tenth part would tax my wits.
Now with serpents he wars, now with savage wolves,   720
Now with wild men of the woods, that watched from the rocks,
Both with bulls and with bears, and with boars besides,
And giants that came gibbering from the jagged steeps.
Had he not borne himself bravely, and been on God's side,
He had met with many mishaps and mortal harms.   725
And if the wars were unwelcome, the winter was worse,
When the cold clear rains rushed from the clouds
And froze before they could fall to the frosty earth.
Near slain by the sleet he sleeps in his irons
More nights than enough, among naked rocks,   730
Where clattering from the crest the cold stream ran
And hung in hard icicles high overhead.
Thus in peril and pain and predicaments dire
He rides across country till Christmas Eve,
                           our knight.   735
And at that holy tide
He prays with all his might
That Mary may be his guide
Till a dwelling comes in sight.

By a mountain next morning he makes his way   740
Into a forest fastness, fearsome and wild;
High hills on either hand, with hoar woods below,
Oaks old and huge by the hundred together.
The hazel and the hawthorn were all intertwined
With rough raveled moss, that raggedly hung,   745
With many birds unblithe upon bare twigs
That peeped most piteously for pain of the cold.
The good knight on Gringolet glides thereunder
Through many a marsh and mire, a man all alone;
He feared for his default, should he fail to see   750
The service of that Sire that on that same night
Was born of a bright maid, to bring us His peace.
And therefore sighing he said, "I beseech of Thee, Lord,
And Mary, thou mildest mother so dear,
Some harborage where haply I might hear mass   755
And Thy matins tomorrow—meekly I ask it,

And thereto proffer and pray my pater and ave[3]
                and creed."
      He said his prayer with sighs,
      Lamenting his misdeed;   760
      He crosses himself, and cries
      On Christ in his great need.

No sooner had Sir Gawain signed himself[4] thrice
Than he was ware, in the wood, of a wondrous dwelling,
Within a moat, on a mound, bright amid boughs   765
Of many a tree great of girth that grew by the water—
A castle as comely as a knight could own,
On grounds fair and green, in a goodly park
With a palisade of palings planted about
For two miles and more, round many a fair tree.   770
The stout knight stared at that stronghold great
As it shimmered and shone amid shining leaves,
Then with helmet in hand he offers his thanks
To Jesus and Saint Julian,[5] that are gentle both,
That in courteous accord had inclined to his prayer;   775
"Now fair harbor," said he, "I humbly beseech!"
Then he pricks his proud steed with the plated spurs,
And by chance he has chosen the chief path
That brought the bold knight to the bridge's end
                in haste.   780
      The bridge hung high in air;
      The gates were bolted fast;
      The walls well-framed to bear
      The fury of the blast.

The man on his mount remained on the bank   785
Of the deep double moat that defended the place.
The wall went in the water wondrous deep,
And a long way aloft it loomed overhead.
It was built of stone blocks to the battlements' height,
With corbels under cornices[6] in comeliest style;   790
Watch-towers trusty protected the gate,
With many a lean loophole, to look from within:
A better-made barbican the knight beheld never.
And behind it there hoved[7] a great hall and fair:
Turrets rising in tiers, with tines at their tops,   795
Spires set beside them, splendidly long,
With finials well-fashioned, as filigree fine.
Chalk-white chimneys over chambers high
Gleamed in gay array upon gables and roofs;
The pinnacles in panoply, pointing in air,   800
So vied there for his view that verily it seemed

---

3. Two prayers, the Pater Noster ("Our Father," the Lord's Prayer) and Ave Maria ("Hail, Mary").
4. Made the Sign of the Cross over his own chest.   5. Patron saint of hospitality.   6. Ornamental projections supporting the top courses of stone.   7. Arose. *Tines*: sharp points.

A castle cut of paper for a king's feast.
The good knight on Gringolet thought it great luck
If he could but contrive to come there within
To keep the Christmas feast in that castle fair   805
           and bright.
           There answered to his call
           A porter most polite;
           From his station on the wall
           He greets the errant knight.   810

"Good sir," said Gawain, "Wouldst go to inquire
If your lord would allow me to lodge here a space?"
"Peter!"[8] said the porter, "For my part, I think
So noble a knight will not want for a welcome!"
Then he bustles off briskly, and comes back straight,   815
And many servants beside, to receive him the better.
They let down the drawbridge and duly went forth
And kneeled down on their knees on the naked earth
To welcome this warrior as best they were able.
They proffered him passage — the portals stood wide —   820
And he beckoned them to rise, and rode over the bridge.
Men steadied his saddle as he stepped to the ground,
And there stabled his steed many stalwart folk.
Now come the knights and the noble squires
To bring him with bliss into the bright hall.   825
When his high helm was off, there hied forth a throng
Of attendants to take it, and see to its care;
They bore away his brand[9] and his blazoned shield;
Then graciously he greeted those gallants each one,
And many a noble drew near, to do the knight honor.   830
All in his armor into hall he was led,
Where fire on a fair hearth fiercely blazed.
And soon the lord himself descends from his chamber
To meet with good manners the man on his floor.
He said, "To this house you are heartily welcome: 835
What is here is wholly yours, to have in your power
           and sway."
           "Many thanks," said Sir Gawain;
           "May Christ your pains repay!"
           The two embrace amain   840
           As men well met that day.

Gawain gazed on the host that greeted him there,
And a lusty fellow he looked, the lord of that place:
A man of massive mold, and of middle age;
Broad, bright was his beard, of a beaver's hue,   845
Strong, steady his stance, upon stalwart shanks,

---

8. I.e., "By Saint Peter!"   9. Sword.

His face fierce as fire, fair-spoken withal,
And well-suited he seemed in Sir Gawain's sight
To be a master of men in a mighty keep.
They pass into a parlor, where promptly the host   850
Has a servant assigned him to see to his needs,
And there came upon his call many courteous folk
That brought him to a bower where bedding was noble,
With heavy silk hangings hemmed all in gold,
Coverlets and counterpanes curiously wrought,   855
A canopy over the couch, clad all with fur,
Curtains running on cords, caught to gold rings,
Woven rugs on the walls of eastern work,
And the floor, under foot, well-furnished with the same.
With light talk and laughter they loosed from him then   860
His war-dress of weight and his worthy clothes.
Robes richly wrought they brought him right soon,
To change there in chamber and choose what he would.
When he had found one he fancied, and flung it about,
Well-fashioned for his frame, with flowing skirts,   865
His face fair and fresh as the flowers of spring,
All the good folk agreed, that gazed on him then,
His limbs arrayed royally in radiant hues,
That so comely a mortal never Christ made
                    as he.   870
           Whatever his place of birth,
           It seemed he well might be
           Without a peer on earth
           In martial rivalry.

A couch before the fire, where fresh coals burned,   875
They spread for Sir Gawain splendidly now
With quilts quaintly stitched, and cushions beside,
And then a costly cloak they cast on his shoulders
Of bright silk, embroidered on borders and hems,
With furs of the finest well-furnished within,   880
And bound about with ermine, both mantle and hood;
And he sat at that fireside in sumptuous estate
And warmed himself well, and soon he waxed merry.
Then attendants set a table upon trestles broad,
And lustrous white linen they laid thereupon,   885
A saltcellar of silver, spoons of the same.
He washed himself well and went to his place,
Men set his fare before him in fashion most fit.
There were soups of all sorts, seasoned with skill,
Double-sized servings, and sundry fish,   890
Some baked, some breaded, some broiled on the coals,
Some simmered, some in stews, steaming with spice,
And with sauces to sup that suited his taste.
He confesses it a feast with free words and fair;

They requite him as kindly with courteous jests,   895
     well-sped.
   "Tonight you fast and pray;
   Tomorrow we'll see you fed."
   The knight grows wondrous gay
   As the wine goes to his head.   900

Then at times and by turns, as at table he sat,
They questioned him quietly, with queries discreet,
And he courteously confessed that he comes from the court,
And owns him of the brotherhood of high-famed Arthur,
The right royal ruler of the Round Table,   905
And the guest by their fireside is Gawain himself,
Who has happened on their house at that holy feast.
When the name of the knight was made known to the lord,
Then loudly he laughed, so elated he was,
And the men in that household made haste with joy   910
To appear in his presence promptly that day,
That of courage ever-constant, and customs pure,
Is pattern and paragon, and praised without end:
Of all knights on earth most honored is he.
Each said solemnly aside to his brother,   915
"Now displays of deportment shall dazzle our eyes
And the polished pearls of impeccable speech;
The high art of eloquence is ours to pursue
Since the father of fine manners is found in our midst.
Great is God's grace, and goodly indeed,   920
That a guest such as Gawain he guides to us here
When men sit and sing of their Savior's birth
     in view.
   With command of manners pure
   He shall each heart imbue;   925
   Who shares his converse, sure,
   Shall learn love's language true."

When the knight had done dining and duly arose,
The dark was drawing on; the day nigh ended.
Chaplains in chapels and churches about   930
Rang the bells aright, reminding all men
Of the holy evensong of the high feast.
The lord attends alone; his fair lady sits
In a comely closet, secluded from sight.
Gawain in gay attire goes thither soon;   935
The lord catches his coat, and calls him by name,
And has him sit beside him, and says in good faith
No guest on God's earth would he gladlier greet.
For that Gawain thanked him; the two then embraced
And sat together soberly the service through.   940
Then the lady, that longed to look on the knight,
Came forth from her closet with her comely maids.

The fair hues of her flesh, her face and her hair
And her body and her bearing were beyond praise,
And excelled the queen herself, as Sir Gawain thought.   945
He goes forth to greet her with gracious intent;
Another lady led her by the left hand
That was older than she—an ancient, it seemed,
And held in high honor by all men about.
But unlike to look upon, those ladies were,   950
For if the one was fresh, the other was faded:
Bedecked in bright red was the body of one;
Flesh hung in folds on the face of the other;
On one a high headdress, hung all with pearls;
Her bright throat and bosom fair to behold,   955
Fresh as the first snow fallen upon hills;
A wimple[1] the other one wore round her throat;
Her swart chin well swaddled, swathed all in white;
Her forehead enfolded in flounces of silk
That framed a fair fillet,[2] of fashion ornate,   960
And nothing bare beneath save the black brows,
The two eyes and the nose, the naked lips,
And they unsightly to see, and sorrily bleared.
A beldame, by God, she may well be deemed,
                of pride!   965
        She was short and thick of waist,
        Her buttocks round and wide;
        More toothsome, to his taste,
        Was the beauty by her side.

When Gawain had gazed on that gay lady,   970
With leave of her lord, he politely approached;
To the elder in homage he humbly bows;
The lovelier he salutes with a light embrace.
He claims a comely kiss, and courteously he speaks;
They welcome him warmly, and straightway he asks   975
To be received as their servant, if they so desire.
They take him between them; with talking they bring him
Beside a bright fire; bade then that spices
Be freely fetched forth, to refresh them the better,
And the good wine therewith, to warm their hearts.   980
The lord leaps about in light-hearted mood;
Contrives entertainments and timely sports;
Takes his hood from his head and hangs it on a spear,
And offers him openly the honor thereof
Who should promote the most mirth at that Christmas feast;   985
"And I shall try for it, trust me—contend with the best,
Ere I go without my headgear by grace of my friends!"
Thus with light talk and laughter the lord makes merry

1. A garment covering the neck and sides of the head.   2. Ornamental ribbon or headband.

To gladden the guest he had greeted in hall
                              that day.   990
                    At the last he called for light
                    The company to convey;
                    Gawain says goodnight
                    And retires to bed straightway.

On the morn when each man is mindful in heart   995
That God's son was sent down to suffer our death,
No household but is blithe for His blessed sake;
So was it there on that day, with many delights.
Both at larger meals and less they were lavishly served
By doughty lads on dais, with delicate fare;   1000
The old ancient lady, highest she sits;
The lord at her left hand leaned, as I hear;
Sir Gawain in the center, beside the gay lady,
Where the food was brought first to that festive board,
And thence throughout the hall, as they held most fit,   1005
To each man was offered in order of rank.
There was meat, there was mirth, there was much joy,
That to tell all the tale would tax my wits,
Though I pained me, perchance, to paint it with care;
But yet I know that our knight and the noble lady   1010
Were accorded so closely in company there,
With the seemly solace of their secret words,
With speeches well-sped, spotless and pure,
That each prince's pastime their pleasures far
                              outshone.   1015
                    Sweet pipes beguile their cares,
                    And the trumpet of martial tone;
                    Each tends his affairs
                    And those two tend their own.

That day and all the next, their disport was noble,   1020
And the third day, I think, pleased them no less;
The joys of St. John's Day³ were justly praised,
And were the last of their like for those lords and ladies;
Then guests were to go in the gray morning,
Wherefore they whiled the night away with wine and with mirth,   1025
Moved to the measures of many a blithe carol;
At last, when it was late, took leave of each other,
Each one of those worthies, to wend his way.
Gawain bids goodbye to his goodly host
Who brings him to his chamber, the chimney beside,   1030
And detains him in talk, and tenders his thanks
And holds it an honor to him and his people
That he has harbored in his house at that holy time
And embellished his abode with his inborn grace.

3. December 27.

"As long as I may live, my luck is the better   1035
That Gawain was my guest at God's own feast!"
"Noble sir," said the knight, "I cannot but think
All the honor is your own—may heaven requite it!
And your man to command I account myself here
As I am bound and beholden, and shall be, come   1040
                    what may."
                The lord with all his might
                Entreats his guest to stay;
                Brief answer makes the knight:
                Next morning he must away.   1045

Then the lord of that land politely inquired
What dire affair had forced him, at that festive time,
So far from the king's court to fare forth alone
Ere the holidays wholly had ended in hall.
"In good faith," said Gawain, "you have guessed the truth: 1050
On a high errand and urgent I hastened away,
For I am summoned by myself to seek for a place—
I would I knew whither, or where it might be!
Far rather would I find it before the New Year
Than own the land of Logres, so help me our Lord!   1055
Wherefore, sir, in friendship this favor I ask,
That you say in sober earnest, if something you know
Of the Green Chapel, on ground far or near,
Or the lone knight that lives there, of like hue of green.
A certain day was set by assent of us both   1060
To meet at that landmark, if I might last,
And from now to the New Year is nothing too long,
And I would greet the Green Knight there, would God but allow,
More gladly, by God's Son, than gain the world's wealth!
And I must set forth to search, as soon as I may;   1065
To be about the business I have but three days
And would as soon sink down dead as desist from my errand."
Then smiling said the lord, "Your search, sir, is done,
For we shall see you to that site by the set time.
Let Gawain grieve no more over the Green Chapel;   1070
You shall be in your own bed, in blissful ease,
All the forenoon, and fare forth the first of the year,
And make the goal by midmorn, to mind your affairs,
                    no fear!
                Tarry till the fourth day   1075
                And ride on the first of the year.
                We shall set you on your way;
                It is not two miles from here."

Then Gawain was glad, and gleefully he laughed:
"Now I thank you for this, past all things else!   1080
Now my goal is here at hand! With a glad heart I shall
Both tarry, and undertake any task you devise."

Then the host seized his arm and seated him there;
Let the ladies be brought, to delight them the better,
And in fellowship fair by the fireside they sit;   1085
So gay waxed the good host, so giddy his words,
All waited in wonder what next he would say.
Then he stares on the stout knight, and sternly he speaks:
"You have bound yourself boldly my bidding to do—
Will you stand by that boast, and obey me this once?"   1090
"I shall do so indeed," said the doughty knight;
"While I lie in your lodging, your laws will I follow."
"As you have had," said the host, "many hardships abroad
And little sleep of late, you are lacking, I judge,
Both in nourishment needful and nightly rest;   1095
You shall lie abed late in your lofty chamber
Tomorrow until mass, and meet then to dine
When you will, with my wife, who will sit by your side
And talk with you at table, the better to cheer
      our guest.   1100
    A-hunting I will go
    While you lie late and rest."
    The knight, inclining low,
    Assents to each behest.

"And Gawain," said the good host, "agree now to this: 1105
Whatever I win in the woods I will give you at eve,
And all you have earned you must offer to me;
Swear now, sweet friend, to swap as I say,
Whether hands, in the end, be empty or better."
"By God," said Sir Gawain, "I grant it forthwith!   1110
If you find the game good, I shall gladly take part."
"Let the bright wine be brought, and our bargain is done,"
Said the lord of that land—the two laughed together.
Then they drank and they dallied and doffed all constraint,
These lords and these ladies, as late as they chose,   1115
And then with gaiety and gallantries and graceful adieux
They talked in low tones, and tarried at parting.
With compliments comely they kiss at the last;
There were brisk lads about with blazing torches
To see them safe to bed, for soft repose   1120
      long due.
    Their covenants, yet awhile,
    They repeat, and pledge anew;
    That lord could well beguile
    Men's hearts, with mirth in view.   1125

PART III

Long before daylight they left their beds;
Guests that wished to go gave word to their grooms,

And they set about briskly to bind on saddles,
Tend to their tackle, tie up trunks.
The proud lords appear, appareled to ride,   1130
Leap lightly astride, lay hold of their bridles,
Each one on his way to his worthy house.
The liege lord of the land was not the last
Arrayed there to ride, with retainers many;
He had a bite to eat when he had heard mass;   1135
With horn to the hills he hastens amain.
By the dawn of that day over the dim earth,
Master and men were mounted and ready.
Then they harnessed in couples the keen-scented hounds,
Cast wide the kennel-door and called them forth,   1140
Blew upon their bugles bold blasts three;
The dogs began to bay with a deafening din,
And they quieted them quickly and called them to heel,
A hundred brave huntsmen, as I have heard tell,
                              together.   1145
          Men at stations meet;
          From the hounds they slip the tether;
          The echoing horns repeat,
          Clear in the merry weather.

At the clamor of the quest, the quarry trembled;   1150
Deer dashed through the dale, dazed with dread;
Hastened to the high ground, only to be
Turned back by the beaters, who boldly shouted.
They harmed not the harts, with their high heads,
Let the bucks go by, with their broad antlers,   1155
For it was counted a crime, in the close[4] season,
If a man of that demesne should molest the male deer.
The hinds were headed up, with "Hey!" and "Ware!"
The does with great din were driven to the valleys.
Then you were ware, as they went, of the whistling of arrows; 1160
At each bend under boughs the bright shafts flew
That tore the tawny hide with their tapered heads.
Ah! They bray and they bleed, on banks they die,
And ever the pack pell-mell comes panting behind;
Hunters with shrill horns hot on their heels—   1165
Like the cracking of cliffs their cries resounded.
What game got away from the gallant archers
Was promptly picked off at the posts below
When they were harried on the heights and herded to the streams:
The watchers were so wary at the waiting-stations,   1170
And the greyhounds so huge, that eagerly snatched,
And finished them off as fast as folk could see
                         with sight.

---

4. Or closed.

> The lord, now here, now there,
> Spurs forth in sheer delight.   1175
> And drives, with pleasures rare,
> The day to the dark night.

So the lord in the linden-wood leads the hunt
And Gawain the good knight in gay bed lies,
Lingered late alone, till daylight gleamed,   1180
Under coverlet costly, curtained about.
And as he slips into slumber, slyly there comes
A little din at his door, and the latch lifted,
And he holds up his heavy head out of the clothes;
A corner of the curtain he caught back a little   1185
And waited there warily, to see what befell.
Lo! it was the lady, loveliest to behold,
That drew the door behind her deftly and still
And was bound for his bed—abashed was the knight,
And laid his head low again in likeness of sleep;   1190
And she stepped stealthily, and stole to his bed,
Cast aside the curtain and came within,
And set herself softly on the bedside there,
And lingered at her leisure, to look on his waking.
The fair knight lay feigning for a long while,   1195
Conning in his conscience what his case might
Mean or amount to—a marvel he thought it.
But yet he said within himself, "More seemly it were
To try her intent by talking a little."
So he started and stretched, as startled from sleep,   1200
Lifts wide his lids in likeness of wonder,
And signs himself swiftly, as safer to be,
>   with art.
> Sweetly does she speak
> And kindling glances dart,   1205
> Blent white and red on cheek
> And laughing lips apart.

"Good morning, Sir Gawain," said that gay lady,
"A slack sleeper you are, to let one slip in!
Now you are taken in a trice—a truce we must make,   1210
Or I shall bind you in your bed, of that be assured."
Thus laughing lightly that lady jested.
"Good morning, good lady," said Gawain the blithe,
"Be it with me as you will; I am well content!
For I surrender myself, and sue for your grace,   1215
And that is best, I believe, and behooves me now."
Thus jested in answer that gentle knight.
"But if, lovely lady, you misliked it not,
And were pleased to permit your prisoner to rise,
I should quit this couch and accoutre me better,   1220
And be clad in more comfort for converse here."

"Nay, not so, sweet sir," said the smiling lady;
"You shall not rise from your bed; I direct you better:
I shall hem and hold you on either hand,
And keep company awhile with my captive knight.   1225
For as certain as I sit here, Sir Gawain you are,
Whom all the world worships, whereso you ride;
Your honor, your courtesy are highest acclaimed
By lords and by ladies, by all living men;
And lo! we are alone here, and left to ourselves: 1230
My lord and his liegemen are long departed,
The household asleep, my handmaids too,
The door drawn, and held by a well-driven bolt,
And since I have in this house him whom all love,
I shall while the time away with mirthful speech   1235
                at will.
             My body is here at hand,
             Your each wish to fulfill;
             Your servant to command
             I am, and shall be still."   1240

"In good faith," said Gawain, "my gain is the greater,
Though I am not he of whom you have heard;
To arrive at such reverence as you recount here
I am one all unworthy, and well do I know it.
By heaven, I would hold me the happiest of men   1245
If by word or by work I once might aspire
To the prize of your praise—'twere a pure joy!"
"In good faith, Sir Gawain," said that gay lady,
"The well-proven prowess that pleases all others,
Did I scant or scout⁵ it, 'twere scarce becoming.   1250
But there are ladies, believe me, that had liefer far⁶
Have thee here in their hold, as I have today,
To pass an hour in pastime with pleasant words,
Assuage all their sorrows and solace their hearts,
Than much of the goodly gems and gold they possess.   1255
But laud be to the Lord of the lofty skies,
For here in my hands all hearts' desire
                doth lie."
             Great welcome got he there
             From the lady who sat him by;   1260
             With fitting speech and fair
             The good knight makes reply.

"Madame," said the merry man, "Mary reward you!
For in good faith, I find your beneficence noble.
And the fame of fair deeds runs far and wide,   1265
But the praise you report pertains not to me,
But comes of your courtesy and kindness of heart."

5. Mock.   6. Would much rather.

"By the high Queen of heaven" (said she) "I count it not so,
For were I worth all the women in this world alive,
And all wealth and all worship were in my hands,   1270
And I should hunt high and low, a husband to take,
For the nurture I have noted in thee, knight, here,
The comeliness and courtesies and courtly mirth—
And so I had ever heard, and now hold it true—
No other on this earth should have me for wife."   1275
"You are bound to a better man," the bold knight said,
"Yet I prize the praise you have proffered me here,
And soberly your servant, my sovereign I hold you,
And acknowledge me your knight, in the name of Christ."
So they talked of this and that until 'twas nigh noon,   1280
And ever the lady languishing in likeness of love.
With feat[7] words and fair he framed his defence,
For were she never so winsome, the warrior had
The less will to woo, for the wound that his bane
                         must be.   1285
         He must bear the blinding blow,
         For such is fate's decree;
         The lady asks leave to go;
         He grants it full and free.

Then she gaily said goodbye, and glanced at him, laughing,   1290
And as she stood, she astonished him with a stern speech:
"Now may the Giver of all good words these glad hours repay!
But our guest is not Gawain—forgot is that thought."
"How so?" said the other, and asks in some haste,
For he feared he had been at fault in the forms of his speech.   1295
But she held up her hand, and made answer thus:
"So good a knight as Gawain is given out to be,
And the model of fair demeanor and manners pure,
Had he lain so long at a lady's side,
Would have claimed a kiss, by his courtesy,   1300
Through some touch or trick of phrase at some tale's end."
Said Gawain, "Good lady, I grant it at once!
I shall kiss at your command, as becomes a knight,
And more, lest you mislike, so let be, I pray."
With that she turns toward him, takes him in her arms,   1305
Leans down her lovely head, and lo! he is kissed.
They commend each other to Christ with comely words,
He sees her forth safely, in silence they part,
And then he lies no later in his lofty bed,
But calls to his chamberlain, chooses his clothes,   1310
Goes in those garments gladly to mass,
Then takes his way to table, where attendants wait,
And made merry all day, till the moon rose
                in view

7. Fitting.

Was never knight beset   1315
'Twixt worthier ladies two:
The crone and the coquette;
Fair pastimes they pursue.

And the lord of the land rides late and long,
Hunting the barren hind[8] over the broad heath.   1320
He had slain such a sum, when the sun sank low,
Of does and other deer, as would dizzy one's wits.
Then they trooped in together in triumph at last,
And the count of the quarry quickly they take.
The lords lent a hand with their liegemen many,   1325
Picked out the plumpest and put them together
And duly dressed the deer, as the deed requires.
Some were assigned the assay of the fat:
Two fingers'-width fully they found on the leanest.
Then they slit the slot[9] open and searched out the paunch,   1330
Trimmed it with trencher-knives and tied it up tight.
They flayed the fair hide from the legs and trunk,
Then broke open the belly and laid bare the bowels,
Deftly detaching and drawing them forth.
And next at the neck they neatly parted   1335
The weasand[1] from the windpipe, and cast away the guts.
At the shoulders with sharp blades they showed their skill,
Boning them from beneath, lest the sides be marred;
They breached the broad breast and broke it in twain,
And again at the gullet they begin with their knives,   1340
Cleave down the carcass clear to the breach;
Two tender morsels they take from the throat,
Then round the inner ribs they rid off a layer
And carve out the kidney-fat, close to the spine,
Hewing down to the haunch, that all hung together,   1345
And held it up whole, and hacked it free,
And this they named the numbles,[2] that knew such terms
                    of art.
        They divide the crotch in two,
        And straightway then they start   1350
        To cut the backbone through
        And cleave the trunk apart.

With hard strokes they hewed off the head and the neck,
Then swiftly from the sides they severed the chine,
And the corbie's bone[3] they cast on a branch.   1355
Then they pierced the plump sides, impaled either one
With the hock of the hind foot, and hung it aloft,
To each person his portion most proper and fit.
On a hide of a hind the hounds they fed

---

8. Female deer that are not pregnant.   9. The hollow above the breastbone.   1. Esophagus.
2. Other internal organs.   3. A bit of gristle for the ravens ("corbies").

With the liver and the lights,[4] the leathery paunches,   1360
And bread soaked in blood well blended therewith.
High horns and shrill set hounds a-baying,
Then merrily with their meat they make their way home,
Blowing on their bugles many a brave blast.
Ere dark had descended, that doughty band   1365
Was come within the walls where Gawain waits
                              at leisure.
          Bliss and hearth-fire bright
          Await the master's pleasure;
          When the two men met that night,   1370
          Joy surpassed all measure.

Then the host in the hall his household assembles,
With the dames of high degree and their damsels fair.
In the presence of the people, a party he sends
To convey him his venison in view of the knight.   1375
And in high good-humor he hails him then,
Counts over the kill, the cuts on the tallies,[5]
Holds high the hewn ribs, heavy with fat.
"What·think you, sir, of this? Have I thriven well?
Have I won with my woodcraft a worthy prize?"   1380
"In good earnest," said Gawain, "this game is the finest
I have seen in seven years in the season of winter."
"And I give it to you, Gawain," said the goodly host,
"For according to our covenant, you claim it as your own."
"That is so," said Sir Gawain, "the same say I: 1385
What I worthily have won within these fair walls,
Herewith I as willingly award it to you."
He embraces his broad neck with both his arms,
And confers on him a kiss in the comeliest style.
"Have here my profit, it proved no better;   1390
Ungrudging do I grant it, were it greater far."
"Such a gift," said the good host, "I gladly accept—
Yet it might be all the better, would you but say
Where you won this same award, by your wits alone."
"That was no part of the pact; press me no further,   1395
For you have had what behooves; all other claims
                              forbear."
          With jest and compliment
          They conversed, and cast off care;
          To the table soon they went;   1400
          Fresh dainties wait them there.

And then by the chimney-side they chat at their ease;
The best wine was brought them, and bounteously served;
And after in their jesting they jointly accord
To do on the second day the deeds of the first: 1405

---

4. Lungs.   5. Notched sticks were used to count the animals taken in the hunt.

That the two men should trade, betide as it may,
What each had taken in, at eve when they met.
They seal the pact solemnly in sight of the court;
Their cups were filled afresh to confirm the jest;
Then at last they took their leave, for late was the hour,   1410
Each to his own bed hastening away.
Before the barnyard cock had crowed but thrice
The lord had leapt from his rest, his liegemen as well.
Both of mass and their meal they made short work:
By the dim light of dawn they were deep in the woods   1415
             away.
          With huntsmen and with horns
          Over plains they pass that day;
          They release, amid the thorns,
          Swift hounds that run and bay.   1420

Soon some were on a scent by the side of a marsh;
When the hounds opened cry, the head of the hunt
Rallied them with rough words, raised a great noise.
The hounds that had heard it came hurrying straight
And followed along with their fellows, forty together.   1425
Then such a clamor and cry of coursing hounds
Arose, that the rocks resounded again.
Hunters exhorted them with horn and with voice;
Then all in a body bore off together
Between a mere[6] in the marsh and a menacing crag,   1430
To a rise where the rock stood rugged and steep,
And boulders lay about, that blocked their approach.
Then the company in consort closed on their prey:
They surrounded the rise and the rocks both,
For well they were aware that it waited within,   1435
The beast that the bloodhounds boldly proclaimed.
Then they beat on the bushes and bade him appear,
And he made a murderous rush in the midst of them all;
The best of all boars broke from his cover,
That had ranged long unrivaled, a renegade old,   1440
For of tough-brawned boars he was biggest far,
Most grim when he grunted—then grieved were many,
For three at the first thrust he threw to the earth,
And dashed away at once without more damage.
With "Hi!" "Hi!" and "Hey!" "Hey!" the others followed,   1445
Had horns at their lips, blew high and clear.
Merry was the music of men and of hounds
That were bound after this boar, his bloodthirsty heart
            to quell.
          Often he stands at bay,   1450
          Then scatters the pack pell-mell;

6. Pool.

>He hurts the hounds, and they
>Most dolefully yowl and yell.

Men then with mighty bows moved in to shoot,
Aimed at him with their arrows and often hit,   1455
But the points had no power to pierce through his hide,
And the barbs were brushed aside by his bristly brow;
Though the shank of the shaft shivered in pieces,
The head hopped away, wheresoever it struck.
But when their stubborn strokes had stung him at last,   1460
Then, foaming in his frenzy, fiercely he charges,
Hies at them headlong that hindered his flight,
And many feared for their lives, and fell back a little.
But the lord on a lively horse leads the chase;
As a high-mettled huntsman his horn he blows;   1465
He sounds the assembly and sweeps through the brush,
Pursuing this wild swine till the sunlight slanted.
All day with this deed they drive forth the time
While our lone knight so lovesome lies in his bed,
Sir Gawain safe at home, in silken bower   1470
>so gay.
>The lady, with guile in heart,
>Came early where he lay;
>She was at him with all her art
>To turn his mind her way.   1475

She comes to the curtain and coyly peeps in;
Gawain thought it good to greet her at once,
And she richly repays him with her ready words,
Settles softly at his side, and suddenly she laughs,
And with a gracious glance, she begins on him thus: 1480
"Sir, if you be Gawain, it seems a great wonder—
A man so well-meaning, and mannerly disposed,
And cannot act in company as courtesy bids,
And if one takes the trouble to teach him, 'tis all in vain.
That lesson learned lately is lightly forgot,   1485
Though I painted it as plain as my poor wit allowed."
"What lesson, dear lady?" he asked all alarmed;
"I have been much to blame, if your story be true."
"Yet my counsel was of kissing," came her answer then,
"Where favor has been found, freely to claim   1490
As accords with the conduct of courteous knights."
"My dear," said the doughty man," dismiss that thought;
Such freedom, I fear, might offend you much;
It were rude to request if the right were denied."
"But none can deny you," said the noble dame,   1495
"You are stout enough to constrain with strength, if you choose,
Were any so ungracious as to grudge you aught."
"By heaven," said he, "you have answered well,
But threats never throve among those of my land,

Nor any gift not freely given, good though it be.   1500
I am yours to command, to kiss when you please;
You may lay on as you like, and leave off at will."

With this,
The lady lightly bends
And graciously gives him a kiss;   1505
The two converse as friends
Of true love's trials and bliss.

"I should like, by your leave," said the lovely lady,
"If it did not annoy you, to know for what cause
So brisk and so bold a young blood as you,   1510
And acclaimed for all courtesies becoming a knight—
And name what knight you will, they are noblest esteemed
For loyal faith in love, in life as in story;
For to tell the tribulations of these true hearts,
Why, 'tis the very title and text of their deeds,   1515
How bold knights for beauty have braved many a foe,
Suffered heavy sorrows out of secret love,
And then valorously avenged them on villainous churls
And made happy ever after the hearts of their ladies.
And you are the noblest knight known in your time;   1520
No household under heaven but has heard of your fame,
And here by your side I have sat for two days
Yet never has a fair phrase fallen from your lips
.Of the language of love, not one little word!
And you, that with sweet vows sway women's hearts,   1525
Should show your winsome ways, and woo a young thing,
And teach by some tokens the craft of true love.
How! are you artless, whom all men praise?
Or do you deem me so dull, or deaf to such words?

Fie! Fie!   1530
In hope of pastimes new
I have come where none can spy;
Instruct me a little, do,
While my husband is not nearby."

"God love you, gracious lady!" said Gawain then;   1535
"It is a pleasure surpassing, and a peerless joy,
That one so worthy as you would willingly come
And take the time and trouble to talk with your knight
And content you with his company—it comforts my heart.
But to take to myself the task of telling of love,   1540
And touch upon its texts, and treat of its themes
To one that, I know well, wields more power
In that art, by a half, than a hundred such
As I am where I live, or am like to become,
It were folly, fair dame, in the first degree!   1545
In all that I am able, my aim is to please,
As in honor behooves me, and am evermore

Your servant heart and soul, so save me our Lord!"
Thus she tested his temper and tried many a time,
Whatever her true intent, to entice him to sin,   1550
But so fair was his defense that no fault appeared,
Nor evil on either hand, but only bliss
                they knew.
          They linger and laugh awhile;
          She kisses the knight so true,   1555
          Takes leave in comeliest style
          And departs without more ado.

Then he rose from his rest and made ready for mass,
And then a meal was set and served, in sumptuous style;
He dallied at home all day with the dear ladies,   1560
But the lord lingered late at his lusty sport;
Pursued his sorry swine, that swerved as he fled,
And bit asunder the backs of the best of his hounds
When they brought him to bay, till the bowmen appeared
And soon forced him forth, though he fought for dear life,   1565
So sharp were the shafts they shot at him there.
But yet the boldest drew back from his battering head,
Till at last he was so tired he could travel no more,
But in as much haste as he might, he makes his retreat
To a rise on rocky ground, by a rushing stream.   1570
With the bank at his back he scrapes the bare earth,
The froth foams at his jaws, frightful to see.
He whets his white tusks—then weary were all
Those hunters so hardy that hoved[7] round about
Of aiming from afar, but ever they mistrust   1575
               his mood.
          He had hurt so many by then
          That none had hardihood
          To be torn by his tusks again,
          That was brainsick, and out for blood.   1580

Till the lord came at last on his lofty steed,
Beheld him there at bay before all his folk;
Lightly he leaps down, leaves his courser,
Bares his bright sword, and boldly advances;
Straight into the stream he strides towards his foe.   1585
The wild thing was wary of weapon and man;
His hackles rose high; so hotly he snorts
That many watched with alarm, lest the worst befall.
The boar makes for the man with a mighty bound
So that he and his hunter came headlong together   1590
Where the water ran wildest—the worse for the beast,
For the man, when they first met, marked him with care,
Sights well the slot, slips in the blade,

---

7. Hovered.

Shoves it home to the hilt, and the heart shattered,
And he falls in his fury and floats down the water,   1595
         ill-sped.
           Hounds hasten by the score
           To maul him, hide and head;
           Men drag him in to shore
           And dogs pronounce him dead.   1600

With many a brave blast they boast of their prize,
All hallooed in high glee, that had their wind;
The hounds bayed their best, as the bold men bade
That were charged with chief rank in that chase of renown.
Then one wise in woodcraft, and worthily skilled,   1605
Began to dress the boar in becoming style:
He severs the savage head and sets it aloft,
Then rends the body roughly right down the spine;
Takes the bowels from the belly, broils them on coals,
Blends them well with bread to bestow on the hounds.   1610
Then he breaks out the brawn in fair broad flitches,
And the innards to be eaten in order he takes.
The two sides, attached to each other all whole,
He suspended from a spar that was springy and tough;
And so with this swine they set out for home;   1615
The boar's head was borne before the same man
That had stabbed him in the stream with his strong arm,
           right through.
           He thought it long indeed
           Till he had the knight in view;   1620
           At his call, he comes with speed
           To claim his payment due.

The lord laughed aloud, with many a light word,
When he greeted Sir Gawain—with good cheer he speaks.
They fetch the fair dames and the folk of the house;   1625
He brings forth the brawn, and begins the tale
Of the great length and girth, the grim rage as well,
Of the battle of the boar they beset in the wood.
The other men meetly commended his deeds
And praised well the prize of his princely sport,   1630
For the brawn of that boar, the bold knight said,
And the sides of that swine surpassed all others.
Then they handled the huge head; he owns it a wonder,
And eyes it with abhorrence, to heighten his praise.
"Now, Gawain," said the good man, "this game becomes yours   1635
By those fair terms we fixed, as you know full well."
"That is true," returned the knight, "and trust me, fair friend,
All my gains, as agreed, I shall give you forthwith."
He clasps him and kisses him in courteous style,
Then serves him with the same fare a second time.   1640
"Now we are even," said he, "at this evening feast,

And clear is every claim incurred here to date,
                              and debt."
                    "By Saint Giles!" the host replies,
                    "You're the best I ever met!   1645
                    If your profits are all this size,
                    We'll see you wealthy yet!"

Then attendants set tables on trestles about,
And laid them with linen; light shone forth,
Wakened along the walls in waxen torches.   1650
The service was set and the supper brought;
Royal were the revels that rose then in hall
At that feast by the fire, with many fair sports:
Amid the meal and after, melody sweet,
Carol-dances comely and Christmas songs,   1655
With all the mannerly mirth my tongue may describe.
And ever our gallant knight beside the gay lady;
So uncommonly kind and complaisant was she,
With sweet stolen glances, that stirred his stout heart,
That he was at his wits' end, and wondrous vexed;   1660
But he could not in conscience her courtship repay,
Yet took pains to please her, though the plan might
                              go wrong.
                    When they to heart's delight
                    Had reveled there in throng,   1665
                    To his chamber he calls the knight,
                    And thither they go along.

And there they dallied and drank, and deemed it good sport
To enact their play anew on New Year's Eve,
But Gawain asked again to go on the morrow,   1670
For the time until his tryst was not two days.
The host hindered that, and urged him to stay,
And said, "On my honor, my oath here I take
That you shall get to the Green Chapel to begin your chores
By dawn on New Year's Day, if you so desire.   1675
Wherefore lie at your leisure in your lofty bed,
And I shall hunt hereabouts, and hold to our terms,
And we shall trade winnings when once more we meet,
For I have tested you twice, and true have I found you;
Now think this tomorrow: the third pays for all;   1680
Be we merry while we may, and mindful of joy,
For heaviness of heart can be had for the asking."
This is gravely agreed on and Gawain will stay.
They drink a last draught and with torches depart
                              to rest.   1685
                    To bed Sir Gawain went;
                    His sleep was of the best;
                    The lord, on his craft intent,
                    Was early up and dressed.

After mass, with his men, a morsel he takes;   1690
Clear and crisp the morning; he calls for his mount;
The folk that were to follow him afield that day
Were high astride their horses before the hall gates.
Wondrous fair were the fields, for the frost was light;
The sun rises red amid radiant clouds,   1695
Sails into the sky, and sends forth his beams.
They let loose the hounds by a leafy wood;
The rocks all around re-echo to their horns;
Soon some have set off in pursuit of the fox,
Cast about with craft for a clearer scent;   1700
A young dog yaps, and is yelled at in turn;
His fellows fall to sniffing, and follow his lead,
Running in a rabble on the right track,
And he scampers all before; they discover him soon,
And when they see him with sight they pursue him the faster,   1705
Railing at him rudely with a wrathful din.
Often he reverses over rough terrain,
Or loops back to listen in the lee of a hedge;
At last, by a little ditch, he leaps over the brush,
Comes into a clearing at a cautious pace,   1710
Then he thought through his wiles to have thrown off the hounds
Till he was ware, as he went, of a waiting-station
Where three athwart his path threatened him at once,
          all gray.
          Quick as a flash he wheels   1715
          And darts off in dismay;
          With hard luck at his heels
          He is off to the wood away.

Then it was heaven on earth to hark to the hounds
When they had come on their quarry, coursing together!   1720
Such harsh cries and howls they hurled at his head
As all the cliffs with a crash had come down at once.
Here he was hailed, when huntsmen met him;
Yonder they yelled at him, yapping and snarling;
There they cried "Thief!" and threatened his life,   1725
And ever the harriers at his heels, that he had no rest.
Often he was menaced when he made for the open,
And often rushed in again, for Reynard was wily;
And so he leads them a merry chase, the lord and his men,
In this manner on the mountains, till midday or near,   1730
While our hero lies at home in wholesome sleep
Within the comely curtains on the cold morning.
But the lady, as love would allow her no rest,
And pursuing ever the purpose that pricked her heart,
Was awake with the dawn, and went to his chamber   1735
In a fair flowing mantle that fell to the earth,
All edged and embellished with ermines fine;

No hood on her head, but heavy with gems
Were her fillet and the fret[8] that confined her tresses;
Her face and her fair throat freely displayed;   1740
Her bosom all but bare, and her back as well.
She comes in at the chamber-door, and closes it with care,
Throws wide a window—then waits no longer,
But hails him thus airily with her artful words,
                    with cheer: 1745
          "Ah, man, how can you sleep?
          The morning is so clear!"
          Though dreams have drowned him deep,
          He cannot choose but hear.

Deep in his dreams he darkly mutters   1750
As a man may that mourns, with many grim thoughts
Of that day when destiny shall deal him his doom
When he greets his grim host at the Green Chapel
And must bow to his buffet, bating all strife.
But when he sees her at his side he summons his wits,   1755
Breaks from the black dreams, and blithely answers.
That lovely lady comes laughing sweet,
Sinks down at his side, and salutes him with a kiss.
He accords her fair welcome in courtliest style;
He sees her so glorious, so gaily attired,   1760
So faultless her features, so fair and so bright,
His heart swelled swiftly with surging joys.
They melt into mirth with many a fond smile,
And there was bliss beyond telling between those two,
                    at height.   1765
          Good were their words of greeting;
          Each joyed in other's sight;
          Great peril attends that meeting
          Should Mary forget her knight.

For that high-born beauty so hemmed him about,   1770
Made so plain her meaning, the man must needs
Either take her tendered love or distastefully refuse.
His courtesy concerned him, lest crass he appear,
But more his soul's mischief, should he commit sin
And belie his loyal oath to the lord of that house.   1775
"God forbid!" said the bold knight, "That shall not befall!"
With a little fond laughter he lightly let pass
All the words of special weight that were sped his way;
"I find you much at fault," the fair one said,
"Who can be cold toward a creature so close by your side,   1780
Of all women in this world most wounded in heart,
Unless you have a sweetheart, one you hold dearer,
And allegiance to that lady so loyally knit

8. Ornamental net.

That you will never love another, as now I believe.
And, sir, if it be so, then say it, I beg you;   1785
By all your heart holds dear, hide it no longer
               with guile."
        "Lady, by Saint John,"
        He answers with a smile,
        "Lover have I none,   1790
        Nor will have, yet awhile."

"Those words," said the woman, "are the worst of all,
But I have had my answer, and hard do I find it!
Kiss me now kindly; I can but go hence
To lament my life long like a maid lovelorn."   1795
She inclines her head quickly and kisses the knight,
Then straightens with a sigh, and says as she stands,
"Now, dear, ere I depart, do me this pleasure:
Give me some little gift, your glove or the like,
That I may think on you, man, and mourn the less."   1800
"Now by heaven," said he, "I wish I had here
My most precious possession, to put it in your hands,
For your deeds, beyond doubt, have often deserved
A repayment far passing my power to bestow.
But a love-token, lady, were of little avail;   1805
It is not to your honor to have at this time
A glove as a guerdon from Gawain's hand,
And I am here on an errand in unknown realms
And have no bearers with baggage with becoming gifts,
Which distresses me, madame, for your dear sake.   1810
A man must keep within his compass: account it neither grief
               nor slight."
        "Nay, noblest knight alive,"
        Said that beauty of body white,
        "Though you be loath to give,   1815
        Yet you shall take, by right."

She reached out a rich ring, wrought all of gold,
With a splendid stone displayed on the band
That flashed before his eyes like a fiery sun;
It was worth a king's wealth, you may well believe.   1820
But he waved it away with these ready words:
"Before God, good lady, I forego all gifts;
None have I to offer, nor any will I take."
And she urged it on him eagerly, and ever he refused,
And vowed in very earnest, prevail she would not.   1825
And she sad to find it so, and said to him then,
"If my ring is refused for its rich cost—
You would not be my debtor for so dear a thing—
I shall give you my girdle;[9] you gain less thereby."

9. Belt.

She released a knot lightly, and loosened a belt   1830
That was caught about her kirtle, the bright cloak beneath,
Of a gay green silk, with gold overwrought,
And the borders all bound with embroidery fine,
And this she presses upon him, and pleads with a smile,
Unworthy though it were, that it would not be scorned.   1835
But the man still maintains that he means to accept
Neither gold nor any gift, till by God's grace
The fate that lay before him was fully achieved.
"And be not offended, fair lady, I beg,
And give over your offer, for ever I must   1840
     decline.
    I am grateful for favor shown
    Past all deserts of mine,
    And ever shall be your own
    True servant, rain or shine."   1845

 "Now does my present displease you," she promptly inquired,
"Because it seems in your sight so simple a thing?
And belike, as it is little, it is less to praise,
But if the virtue that invests it were verily known,
It would be held, I hope, in higher esteem.   1850
For the man that possesses this piece of silk,
If he bore it on his body, belted about,
There is no hand under heaven that could hew him down,
For he could not be killed by any craft on earth."
Then the man began to muse, and mainly he thought   1855
It was a pearl for his plight, the peril to come
When he gains the Green Chapel to get his reward:
Could he escape unscathed, the scheme were noble!
Then he bore with her words and withstood them no more,
And she repeated her petition and pleaded anew,   1860
And he granted it, and gladly she gave him the belt,
And besought him for her sake to conceal it well,
Lest the noble lord should know—and the knight agrees
That not a soul save themselves shall see it thenceforth
     with sight.   1865
    He thanked her with fervent heart,
    As often as ever he might;
    Three times, before they part,
    She has kissed the stalwart knight.

Then the lady took her leave, and left him there,   1870
For more mirth with that man she might not have.
When she was gone, Sir Gawain got from his bed,
Arose and arrayed him in his rich attire;
Tucked away the token the temptress had left,
Laid it reliably where he looked for it after.   1875
And then with good cheer to the chapel he goes,
Approached a priest in private, and prayed to be taught

To lead a better life and lift up his mind,
Lest he be among the lost when he must leave this world.
And shamefaced at shrift[1] he showed his misdeeds   1880
From the largest to the least, and asked the Lord's mercy,
And called on his confessor to cleanse his soul,
And he absolved him of his sins as safe and as clean
As if the dread Day of Judgment should dawn on the morrow.
And then he made merry amid the fine ladies   1885
With deft-footed dances and dalliance light,
As never until now, while the afternoon wore
               away.
        He delighted all around him,
        And all agreed, that day,   1890
        They never before had found him
        So gracious and so gay.

   Now peaceful be his pasture, and love play him fair!
The host is on horseback, hunting afield;
He has finished off this fox that he followed so long: 1895
As he leapt a low hedge to look for the villain
Where he heard all the hounds in hot pursuit,
Reynard comes racing out of a rough thicket,
And all the rabble in a rush, right at his heels.
The man beholds the beast, and bides his time,   1900
And bares his bright sword, and brings it down hard,
And he blenches from the blade, and backward he starts;
A hound hurries up and hinders that move,
And before the horse's feet they fell on him at once
And ripped the rascal's throat with a wrathful din.   1905
The lord soon alighted and lifted him free,
Swiftly snatched him up from the snapping jaws,
Holds him over his head, halloos with a will,
And the dogs bayed the dirge, that had done him to death.
Hunters hastened thither with horns at their lips,   1910
Sounding the assembly till they saw him at last.
When that comely company was come in together,
All that bore bugles blew them at once,
And the others all hallooed, that had no horns.
It was the merriest medley that ever a man heard,   1915
The racket that they raised for Sir Reynard's soul
               that died.
        Their hounds they praised and fed,
        Fondling their heads with pride,
        And they took Reynard the Red   1920
        And stripped away his hide.

And then they headed homeward, for evening had come,
Blowing many a blast on their bugles bright.

_____

1. Confession.

The lord at long last alights at his house,
Finds fire on the hearth where the fair knight waits,   1925
Sir Gawain the good, that was glad in heart.
With the ladies, that loved him, he lingered at ease;
He wore a rich robe of blue, that reached to the earth
And a surcoat lined softly with sumptuous furs;
A hood of the same hue hung on his shoulders;   1930
With bands of bright ermine embellished were both.
He comes to meet the man amid all the folk,
And greets him good-humoredly, and gaily he says,
"I shall follow forthwith the form of our pledge
That we framed to good effect amid fresh-filled cups."   1935
He clasps him accordingly and kisses him thrice,
As amiably and as earnestly as ever he could.
"By heaven," said the host, "you have had some luck
Since you took up this trade, if the terms were good."
"Never trouble about the terms," he returned at once,   1940
"Since all that I owe here is openly paid."
"Marry!" said the other man, "mine is much less,
For I have hunted all day, and nought have I got
But this foul fox pelt, the fiend take the goods!
Which but poorly repays those precious things   1945
That you have cordially conferred, those kisses three
        so good."
        "Enough!" said Sir Gawain;
        "I thank you, by the rood!"[2]
        And how the fox was slain   1950
        He told him, as they stood.

With minstrelsy and mirth, with all manner of meats,
They made as much merriment as any men might
(Amid laughing of ladies and light-hearted girls,
So gay grew Sir Gawain and the goodly host)   1955
Unless they had been besotted, or brainless fools.
The knight joined in jesting with that joyous folk,
Until at last it was late; ere long they must part,
And be off to their beds, as behooved them each one.
Then politely his leave of the lord of the house   1960
Our noble knight takes, and renews his thanks:
"The courtesies countless accorded me here,
Your kindness at this Christmas, may heaven's King repay!
Henceforth, if you will have me, I hold you my liege,
And so, as I have said, I must set forth tomorrow,   1965
If I may take some trusty man to teach, as you promised,
The way to the Green Chapel, that as God allows
I shall see my fate fulfilled on the first of the year."
"In good faith," said the good man, "with a good will

2. Cross.

Every promise on my part shall be fully performed."   1970
He assigns him a servant to set him on the path,
To see him safe and sound over the snowy hills,
To follow the fastest way through forest green
                              and grove.
                    Gawain thanks him again,   1975
                    So kind his favors prove,
                    And of the ladies then
                    He takes his leave, with love.

Courteously he kissed them, with care in his heart,
And often wished them well, with warmest thanks,   1980
Which they for their part were prompt to repay.
They commend him to Christ with disconsolate sighs;
And then in that hall with the household he parts—
Each man that he met, he remembered to thank
or his deeds of devotion and diligent pains,   1985
And the trouble he had taken to tend to his needs;
And each one as woeful, that watched him depart,
As he had lived with him loyally all his life long.
By lads bearing lights he was led to his chamber
And blithely brought to his bed, to be at his rest.   1990
How soundly he slept, I presume not to say,
For there were matters of moment his thoughts might well
                              pursue.
                    Let him lie and wait;
                    He has little more to do,   1995
                    Then listen, while I relate
                    How they kept their rendezvous.

                              PART IV

Now the New Year draws near, and the night passes,
The day dispels the dark, by the Lord's decree;
But wild weather awoke in the world without: 2000
The clouds in the cold sky cast down their snow
With great gusts from the north, grievous to bear.
Sleet showered aslant upon shivering beasts;
The wind warbled wild as it whipped from aloft,
And drove the drifts deep in the dales below.   2005
Long and well he listens, that lies in his bed;
Though he lifts not his eyelids, little he sleeps;
Each crow of the cock he counts without fail.
Readily from his rest he rose before dawn,
For a lamp had been left him, that lighted his chamber.   2010
He called to his chamberlain, who quickly appeared,
And bade him get him his gear, and gird his good steed,
And he sets about briskly to bring in his arms,
And makes ready his master in manner most fit.

First he clad him in his clothes, to keep out the cold,   2015
And then his other harness, made handsome anew,
His plate-armor of proof, polished with pains,
The rings of his rich mail rid of their rust,
And all was fresh as at first, and for this he gave thanks
                indeed.   2020
        With pride he wears each piece,
        New-furbished for his need:
        No gayer from here to Greece;
        He bids them bring his steed.

In his richest raiment he robed himself then: 2025
His crested coat-armor, close-stitched with craft,
With stones of strange virtue on silk velvet set;
All bound with embroidery on borders and seams
And lined warmly and well with furs of the best.
Yet he left not his love-gift, the lady's girdle;   2030
Gawain, for his own good, forgot not that:
When the bright sword was belted and bound on his haunches,
Then twice with that token he twined him about.
Sweetly did he swathe him in that swatch of silk,
That girdle of green so goodly to see,   2035
That against the gay red showed gorgeous bright.
Yet he wore not for its wealth that wondrous girdle,
Nor pride in its pendants, though polished they were,
Though glittering gold gleamed at the ends,
But to keep himself safe when consent he must   2040
To endure a deadly dint, and all defense
                denied.
        And now the bold knight came
        Into the courtyard wide;
        That folk of worthy fame   2045
        He thanks on every side.

Then was Gringolet girt, that was great and huge,
And had sojourned safe and sound, and savored his fare;
He pawed the earth in his pride, that princely steed.
The good knight draws near him and notes well his look,   2050
And says sagely to himself, and soberly swears,
"Here is a household in hall that upholds the right!
The man that maintains it, may happiness be his!
Likewise the dear lady, may love betide her!
If thus they in charity cherish a guest   2055
That are honored here on earth, may they have His reward
That reigns high in heaven—and also you all;
And were I to live in this land but a little while,
I should willingly reward you, and well, if I might."
Then he steps into the stirrup and bestrides his mount;   2060
His shield is shown forth; on his shoulder he casts it;

Strikes the side of his steed with his steel spurs,
And he starts across the stones, nor stands any longer
     to prance.
    On horseback was the swain   2065
    That bore his spear and lance;
    "May Christ this house maintain
    And guard it from mischance!"

The bridge was brought down, and the broad gates
Unbarred and carried back upon both sides;   2070
He commended him[3] to Christ, and crossed over the planks;
Praised the noble porter, who prayed on his knees
That God save Sir Gawain, and bade him good day,
And went on his way alone with the man
That was to lead him ere long to that luckless place   2075
Where the dolorous dint must be dealt him at last.
Under bare boughs they ride, where steep banks rise,
Over high cliffs they climb, where cold snow clings;
The heavens held aloof, but heavy thereunder
Mist mantled the moors, moved on the slopes.   2080
Each hill had a hat, a huge cape of cloud;
Brooks bubbled and broke over broken rocks,
Flashing in freshets that waterfalls fed.
Roundabout was the road that ran through the wood
Till the sun at that season was soon to rise,   2085
     that day.
    They were on a hilltop high;
    The white snow round them lay;
    The man that rode nearby
    Now bade his master stay.   2090

"For I have seen you here safe at the set time,
And now you are not far from that notable place
That you have sought for so long with such special pains.
But this I say for certain, since I know you, sir knight,
And have your good at heart, and hold you dear—   2095
Would you heed well my words, it were worth your while—
You are rushing into risks that you reck not of:
There is a villain in yon valley, the veriest on earth,
For he is rugged and rude, and ready with fists,
And most immense in his mold of mortals alive,   2100
And his body bigger than the best four
That are in Arthur's house, Hector[4] or any.
He gets his grim way at the Green Chapel;
None passes by that place so proud in his arms
That he does not dash him down with his deadly blows,   2105
For he is heartless wholly, and heedless of right,
For be it chaplain or churl that by the Chapel rides,

---

3. I.e., himself. 4. Either the Trojan hero or one of Arthur's knights.

Monk or mass-priest or any man else,
He would as soon strike him dead as stand on two feet.
Wherefore I say, just as certain as you sit there astride,   2110
You cannot but be killed, if his counsel holds,
For he would trounce you in a trice, had you twenty lives
                              for sale.
                    He has lived long in this land
                    And dealt out deadly bale;   2115
                    Against his heavy hand
                    Your power cannot prevail.

"And so, good Sir Gawain, let the grim man be;
Go off by some other road, in God's own name!
Leave by some other land, for the love of Christ,   2120
And I shall get me home again, and give you my word
That I shall swear by God's self and the saints above,
By heaven and by my halidom⁵ and other oaths more,
To conceal this day's deed, nor say to a soul
That ever you fled for fear from any that I knew."   2125
"Many thanks!" said the other man—and demurring he speaks—
"Fair fortune befall you for your friendly words!
And conceal this day's deed I doubt not you would,
But though you never told the tale, if I turned back now,
Forsook this place for fear, and fled, as you say,   2130
I were a caitiff⁶ coward; I could not be excused.
But I must to the Chapel to chance my luck
And say to that same man such words as I please,
Befall what may befall through Fortune's will
                              or whim.   2135
                    Though he be a quarrelsome knave
                    With a cudgel great and grim,
                    The Lord is strong to save:
                    His servants trust in Him."

"Marry," said the man, "since you tell me so much,   2140
And I see you are set to seek your own harm,
If you crave a quick death, let me keep you no longer!
Put your helm on your head, your hand on your lance,
And ride the narrow road down yon rocky slope
Till it brings you to the bottom of the broad valley.   2145
Then look a little ahead, on your left hand,
And you will soon see before you that self-same Chapel,
And the man of great might that is master there.
Now goodbye in God's name, Gawain the noble!
For all the world's wealth I would not stay here,   2150
Or go with you in this wood one footstep further!"
He tarried no more to talk, but turned his bridle,
Hit his horse with his heels as hard as he might,

---

5. Holiness or, more likely, patron saints.   6. Despicable.

Leaves the knight alone, and off like the wind
goes leaping. 2155
"By God," said Gawain then,
"I shall not give way to weeping;
God's will be done, amen!
I commend me to His keeping."

He puts his heels to his horse, and picks up the path; 2160
Goes in beside a grove where the ground is steep,
Rides down the rough slope right to the valley;
And then he looked a little about him—the landscape was wild,
And not a soul to be seen, nor sign of a dwelling,
But high banks on either hand hemmed it about, 2165
With many a ragged rock and rough-hewn crag;
The skies seemed scored by the scowling peaks.
Then he halted his horse, and hoved there a space,
And sought on every side for a sight of the Chapel,
But no such place appeared, which puzzled him sore, 2170
Yet he saw some way off what seemed like a mound,
A hillock high and broad, hard by the water,
Where the stream fell in foam down the face of the steep
And bubbled as if it boiled on its bed below.
The knight urges his horse, and heads for the knoll; 2175
Leaps lightly to earth; loops well the rein
Of his steed to a stout branch, and stations him there.
He strides straight to the mound, and strolls all about,
Much wondering what it was, but no whit the wiser;
It had a hole at one end, and on either side, 2180
And was covered with coarse grass in clumps all without,
And hollow all within, like some old cave,
Or a crevice of an old crag—he could not discern
aright.
"Can this be the Chapel Green? 2185
Alack!" said the man, "Here might
The devil himself be seen
Saying matins[7] at black midnight!"

"Now by heaven," said he, "it is bleak hereabouts;
This prayer-house is hideous, half-covered with grass! 2190
Well may the grim man mantled in green
Hold here his orisons, in hell's own style!
Now I feel it is the Fiend, in my five wits,
That has tempted me to this tryst, to take my life;
This is a Chapel of mischance, may the mischief take it! 2195
As accursed a country church as I came upon ever!"
With his helm on his head, his lance in his hand,
He stalks toward the steep wall of that strange house.
Then he heard, on the hill, behind a hard rock,

---

7. Morning prayers.

Beyond the brook, from the bank, a most barbarous din: 2200
Lord! it clattered in the cliff fit to cleave it in two,
As one upon a grindstone ground a great scythe!
Lord! it whirred like a mill-wheel whirling about!
Lord! it echoed loud and long, lamentable to hear!
Then "By heaven," said the bold knight, "That business up there   2205
Is arranged for my arrival, or else I am much
                  misled.
        Let God work! Ah me!
        All hope of help has fled!
        Forfeit my life may be   2210
        But noise I do not dread."

Then he listened no longer, but loudly he called,
"Who has power in this place, high parley to hold?
For none greets Sir Gawain, or gives him good day;
If any would a word with him, let him walk forth   2215
And speak now or never, to speed his affairs."
"Abide," said one on the bank above over his head,
"And what I promised you once shall straightway be given."
Yet he stayed not his grindstone, nor stinted its noise,
But worked awhile at his whetting before he would rest,   2220
And then he comes around a crag, from a cave in the rocks,
Hurtling out of hiding with a hateful weapon,
A Danish ax devised for that day's deed,
With a broad blade and bright, bent in a curve,
Filed to a fine edge—four feet it measured   2225
By the length of the lace that was looped round the haft.
And in form as at first, the fellow all green,
His lordly face and his legs, his locks and his beard,
Save that firm upon two feet forward he strides,
Sets a hand on the ax-head, the haft to the earth;   2230
When he came to the cold stream, and cared not to wade,
He vaults over on his ax, and advances amain
On a broad bank of snow, overbearing and brisk
                  of mood.
        Little did the knight incline   2235
        When face to face they stood;
        Said the other man, "Friend mine,
        It seems your word holds good!"

"God love you, Sir Gawain!" said the Green Knight then,
"And well met this morning, man, at my place!   2240
And you have followed me faithfully and found me betimes,[8]
And on the business between us we both are agreed:
Twelve months ago today you took what was yours,
And you at this New Year must yield me the same.
And we have met in these mountains, remote from all eyes: 2245

8. In good time.

There is none here to halt us or hinder our sport;
Unhasp your high helm, and have here your wages;
Make no more demur than I did myself
When you hacked off my head with one hard blow."
"No, by God," said Sir Gawain, "that granted me life,   2250
I shall grudge not the guerdon, grim though it prove;
Bestow but one stroke, and I shall stand still,
And you may lay on as you like till the last of my part
                    be paid."
                He proffered, with good grace,   2255
                His bare neck to the blade,
                And feigned a cheerful face:
                He scorned to seem afraid.

Then the grim man in green gathers his strength,
Heaves high the heavy ax to hit him the blow.   2260
With all the force in his frame he fetches it aloft,
With a grimace as grim as he would grind him to bits;
Had the blow he bestowed been as big as he threatened,
A good knight and gallant had gone to his grave.
But Gawain at the great ax glanced up aside   2265
As down it descended with death-dealing force,
And his shoulders shrank a little from the sharp iron.
Abruptly the brawny man breaks off the stroke,
And then reproved with proud words that prince among knights.
"You are not Gawain the glorious," the green man said,   2270
"That never fell back on field in the face of the foe,
And now you flee for fear, and have felt no harm:
Such news of that knight I never heard yet!
I moved not a muscle when you made to strike,
Nor caviled at the cut in King Arthur's house;   2275
My head fell to my feet, yet steadfast I stood,
And you, all unharmed, are wholly dismayed—
Wherefore the better man I, by all odds,
                    must be."
                Said Gawain, "Strike once more;   2280
                I shall neither flinch nor flee;
                But if my head falls to the floor
                There is no mending me!"

"But go on, man, in God's name, and get to the point!
Deliver me my destiny, and do it out of hand,   2285
For I shall stand to the stroke and stir not an inch
Till your ax has hit home—on my honor I swear it!"
"Have at thee then!" said the other, and heaves it aloft,
And glares down as grimly as he had gone mad.
He made a mighty feint, but marred not his hide;   2290
Withdrew the ax adroitly before it did damage.
Gawain gave no ground, nor glanced up aside,
But stood still as a stone, or else a stout stump

That is held in hard earth by a hundred roots.
Then merrily does he mock him, the man all in green: 2295
"So now you have your nerve again, I needs must strike;
Uphold the high knighthood that Arthur bestowed,
And keep your neck-bone clear, if this cut allows!"
Then was Gawain gripped with rage, and grimly he said,
"Why, thrash away, tyrant, I tire of your threats;   2300
You make such a scene, you must frighten yourself."
Said the green fellow, "In faith, so fiercely you speak
That I shall finish this affair, nor further grace
                          allow."
            He stands prepared to strike   2305
            And scowls with both lip and brow;
            No marvel if the man mislike
            Who can hope no rescue now.

He gathered up the grim ax and guided it well:
Let the barb at the blade's end brush the bare throat;   2310
He hammered down hard, yet harmed him no whit
Save a scratch on one side, that severed the skin;
The end of the hooked edge entered the flesh,
And a little blood lightly leapt to the earth.
And when the man beheld his own blood bright on the snow,   2315
He sprang a spear's length with feet spread wide,
Seized his high helm, and set it on his head,
Shoved before his shoulders the shield at his back,
Bares his trusty blade, and boldly he speaks—
Not since he was a babe born of his mother   2320
Was he once in this world one-half so blithe—
"Have done with your hacking—harry me no more!
I have borne, as behooved, one blow in this place;
If you make another move I shall meet it midway
And promptly, I promise you, pay back each blow   2325
                          with brand.
            One stroke acquits me here;
            So did our covenant stand
            In Arthur's court last year—
            Wherefore, sir, hold your hand!"   2330

He lowers the long ax and leans on it there,
Sets his arms on the head, the haft on the earth,
And beholds the bold knight that bides there afoot,
How he faces him fearless, fierce in full arms,
And plies him with proud words—it pleases him well.   2335
Then once again gaily to Gawain he calls,
And in a loud voice and lusty, delivers these words:
"Bold fellow, on this field your anger forbear!
No man has made demands here in manner uncouth,
Nor done, save as duly determined at court.   2340

I owed you a hit and you have it; be happy therewith!
The rest of my rights here I freely resign.
Had I been a bit busier, a buffet, perhaps,
I could have dealt more directly, and done you some harm.
First I flourished with a feint, in frolicsome mood,   2345
And left your hide unhurt—and here I did well
By the fair terms we fixed on the first night;
And fully and faithfully you followed accord:
Gave over all your gains as a good man should.
A second feint, sir, I assigned for the morning   2350
You kissed my comely wife—each kiss you restored.
For both of these there behooved but two feigned blows
                  by right.
           True men pay what they owe;
           No danger then in sight.   2355
           You failed at the third throw,
           So take my tap, sir knight.

"For that is my belt about you, that same braided girdle,
My wife it was that wore it; I know well the tale,
And the count of your kisses and your conduct too,   2360
And the wooing of my wife—it was all my scheme!
She made trial of a man most faultless by far
Of all that ever walked over the wide earth;
As pearls to white peas, more precious and prized,
So is Gawain, in good faith, to other gay knights.   2365
Yet you lacked, sir, a little in loyalty there,
But the cause was not cunning, nor courtship either,
But that you loved your own life; the less, then, to blame."
The other stout knight in a study stood a long while,
So gripped with grim rage that his great heart shook.   2370
All the blood of his body burned in his face
As he shrank back in shame from the man's sharp speech.
The first words that fell from the fair knight's lips:
"Accursed be a cowardly and covetous heart!
In you is villainy and vice, and virtue laid low!"   2375
Then he grasps the green girdle and lets go the knot,
Hands it over in haste, and hotly he says:
"Behold there my falsehood, ill hap betide it!
Your cut taught me cowardice, care for my life,
And coveting came after, contrary both   2380
To largesse and loyalty belonging to knights.
Now am I faulty and false, that fearful was ever
Of disloyalty and lies, bad luck to them both!
                 and greed.
           I confess, knight, in this place,   2385
           Most dire is my misdeed;
           Let me gain back your good grace,
           And thereafter I shall take heed."

Then the other laughed aloud, and lightly he said,
"Such harm as I have had, I hold it quite healed.   2390
You are so fully confessed, your failings made known,
And bear the plain penance of the point of my blade,
I hold you polished as a pearl, as pure and as bright
As you had lived free of fault since first you were born.
And I give you, sir, this girdle that is gold-hemmed   2395
And green as my garments, that, Gawain, you may
Be mindful of this meeting when you mingle in throng
With nobles of renown—and known by this token
How it chanced at the Green Chapel, to chivalrous knights.
And you shall in this New Year come yet again   2400
And we shall finish out our feast in my fair hall,
                              with cheer."
                    He urged the knight to stay,
                    And said, "With my wife so dear
                    We shall see you friends this day,   2405
                    Whose enmity touched you near."

"Indeed," said the doughty knight, and doffed his high helm,
And held it in his hands as he offered his thanks,
"I have lingered long enough—may good luck be yours,
And He reward you well that all worship bestows!   2410
And commend me to that comely one, your courteous wife,
Both herself and that other, my honoured ladies,
That have trapped their true knight in their trammels so quaint.
But if a dullard should dote, deem it no wonder,
And through the wiles of a woman be wooed into sorrow,   2415
For so was Adam by one, when the world began,
And Solomon by many more, and Samson the mighty—
Delilah was his doom, and David thereafter
Was beguiled by Bathsheba, and bore much distress;
Now these were vexed by their devices—'twere a very joy   2420
Could one but learn to love, and believe them not.
For these were proud princes, most prosperous of old,
Past all lovers lucky, that languished under heaven,
                              bemused.
                    And one and all fell prey   2425
                    To women that they had used;
                    If I be led astray,
                    Methinks I may be excused.

"But your girdle, God love you! I gladly shall take
And be pleased to possess, not for the pure gold,   2430
Nor the bright belt itself, nor the beauteous pendants,
Nor for wealth, nor worldly state, nor workmanship fine,
But a sign of excess it shall seem oftentimes
When I ride in renown, and remember with shame
The faults and the frailty of the flesh perverse,   2435
How its tenderness entices the foul taint of sin;

And so when praise and high prowess have pleased my heart,
A look at this love-lace will lower my pride.
But one thing would I learn, if you were not loath,
Since you are lord of yonder land where I have long sojourned   2440
With honor in your house—may you have His reward
That upholds all the heavens, highest on throne!
How runs your right name?—and let the rest go."
"That shall I give you gladly," said the Green Knight then;
"Bertilak de Hautdesert, this barony I hold.   2445
Through the might of Morgan le Fay,[9] that lodges at my house,
By subtleties of science and sorcerers' arts,
The mistress of Merlin, she has caught many a man,
For sweet love in secret she shared sometime
With that wizard, that knows well each one of your knights   2450
              and you.
              Morgan the Goddess, she,
              So styled by title true;
              None holds so high degree
              That her arts cannot subdue.   2455

"She guided me in this guise to your glorious hall,
To assay, if such it were, the surfeit of pride
That is rumored of the retinue of the Round Table.
She put this shape upon me to puzzle your wits,
To afflict the fair queen, and frighten her to death   2460
With awe of that elvish man that eerily spoke
With his head in his hand before the high table.
She was with my wife at home, that old withered lady,
Your own aunt is she,[1] Arthur's half-sister,
The Duchess' daughter of Tintagel, that dear King Uther   2465
Got Arthur on after, that honored is now.
And therefore, good friend, come feast with your aunt;
Make merry in my house; my men hold you dear,
And I wish you as well, sir, with all my heart,
As any mortal man, for your matchless faith."   2470
But the knight said him nay, that he might by no means.
They clasped then and kissed, and commended each other
To the Prince of Paradise, and parted with one
              assent.
              Gawain sets out anew;   2475
              Toward the court his course is bent;
              And the knight all green in hue,
              Wheresoever he wished, he went.

Wild ways in the world our worthy knight rides
On Gringolet, that by grace had been granted his life.   2480
He harbored often in houses, and often abroad,
And with many valiant adventures verily he met

9. Arthur's half-sister, an enchantress ("Faye," fairy) who sometimes abetted him, sometimes made trouble for him.   1. Morgan was the daughter of Igraine, Duchess of Tintagel, and her husband, the Duke. Igraine conceived Arthur when his father, Uther, lay with her through one of Merlin's trickeries.

That I shall not take time to tell in this story.
The hurt was whole that he had had in his neck,
And the bright green belt on his body he bore,   2485
Oblique, like a baldric, bound at his side,
Below his left shoulder, laced in a knot,
In betokening of the blame he had borne for his fault;
And so to court in due course he comes safe and sound.
Bliss abounded in hall when the high-born heard   2490
That good Gawain was come; glad tidings they thought it.
The king kisses the knight, and the queen as well,
And many a comrade came to clasp him in arms,
And eagerly they asked, and awesomely he told,
Confessed all his cares and discomfitures many,   2495
How it chanced at the Chapel, what cheer made the knight,
The love of the lady, the green lace at last.
The nick on his neck he naked displayed
That he got in his disgrace at the Green Knight's hands,
                alone.   2500
        With rage in heart he speaks,
        And grieves with many a groan;
        The blood burns in his cheeks
        For shame at what must be shown.

"Behold, sir," said he, and handles the belt,   2505
"This is the blazon of the blemish that I bear on my neck;
This is the sign of sore loss that I have suffered there
For the cowardice and coveting that I came to there;
This is the badge of false faith that I was found in there,
And I must bear it on my body till I breathe my last.   2510
For one may keep a deed dark, but undo it no whit,
For where a fault is made fast, it is fixed evermore."
The king comforts the knight, and the court all together
Agree with gay laughter and gracious intent
That the lords and the ladies belonging to the Table,   2515
Each brother of that band, a baldric should have,
A belt borne oblique, of a bright green,
To be worn with one accord for that worthy's sake.
So that was taken as a token by the Table Round,
And he honored that had it, evermore after,   2520
As the best book of knighthood bids it be known.
In the old days of Arthur this happening befell;
The books of Brutus' deeds bear witness thereto
Since Brutus, the bold knight, embarked for this land
After the siege ceased at Troy and the city fared   2525
                amiss.
        Many such, ere we were born,
        Have befallen here, ere this.
        May He that was crowned with thorn
        Bring all men to His bliss! Amen.   2530

HONY SOYT QUI MAL PENCE

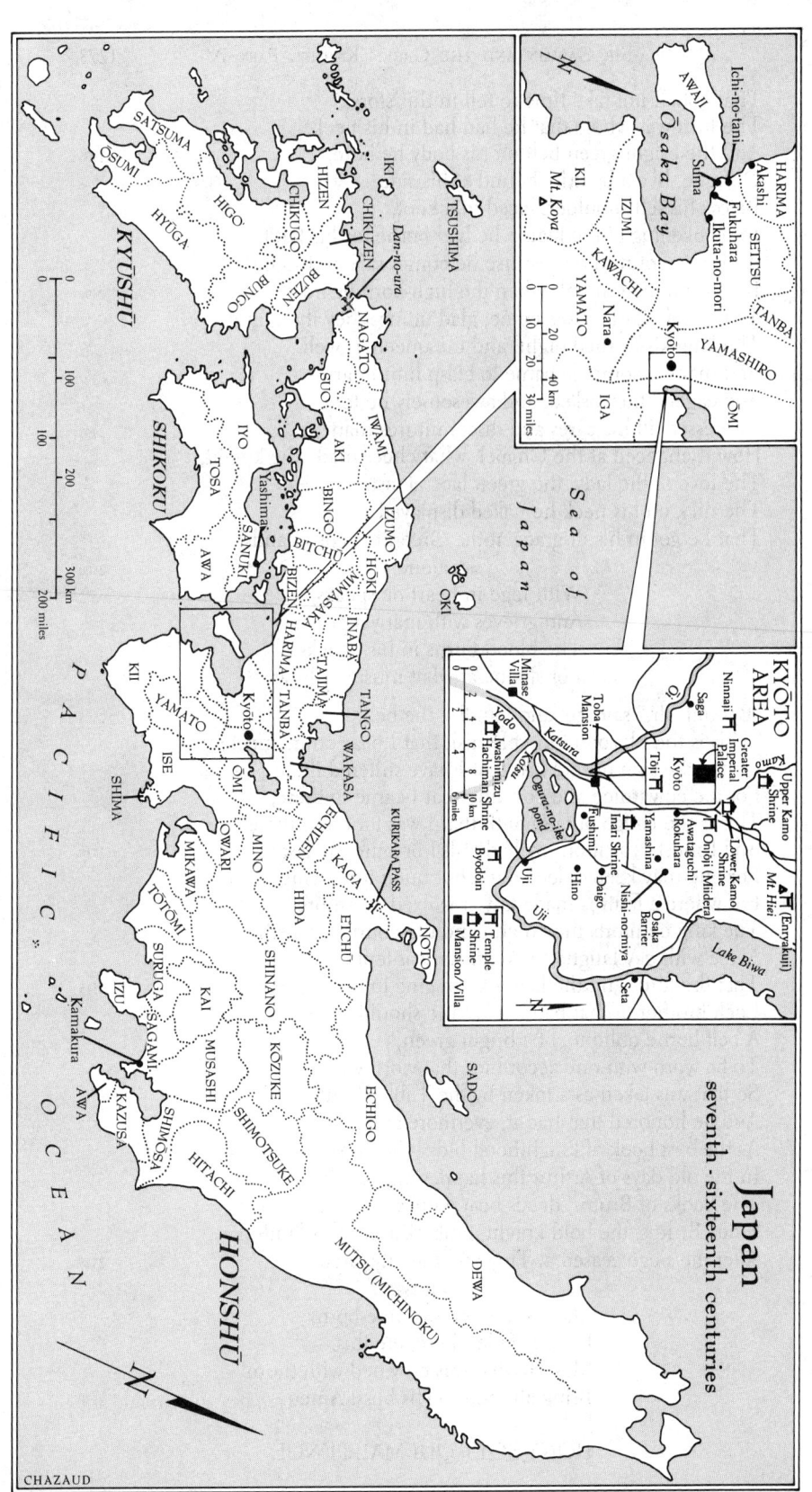

Japan
seventh · sixteenth centuries

CHAZAUD

The Golden Age of Japanese Culture

Japan today looms large in the Western consciousness. Its economy is one of the miracles of modern times. This single fact impinges so forcefully on our material lives, however, that it tends to crowd out all other considerations of Japan. Due in part to the barrier of language and, for much of history, a degree of geographical isolation, it is less well known that Japan has also produced one of the world's richest cultures. The first novel was written in Japan almost a thousand years ago. *The Tale of Genji* is a work that can still stand beside the finest accomplishments in fiction. One of poetry's most evocative and influential forms, *haiku*—a flash of insight expressed in a sliver of verse—is also a Japanese creation. Japanese wood-block prints had a profound influence on the French Impressionists, and the design of the traditional Japanese house, when discovered by Le Corbusier, Frank Lloyd Wright, and others in this century, helped determine the course of modern architecture.

Yet despite Japan's cultural achievements and their worldwide impact, two clichés still govern our thinking about Japan. The first is that Japan is a small country with a homogeneous population. Japan is small only in one sense. The total land mass of the Japanese archipelago, which consists of four principal islands plus some thousand smaller ones, altogether would not fill the state of California. The gross national product, on the other hand, is the second largest in the world, and Japan's population, 125 million, is half as big as that of the United States. A common myth about these 125 million people (and a myth to which the Japanese themselves subscribe) is that they constitute a singularly homogeneous group, one "tribe" moving in lockstep. Although Japan may lack the racial and ethnic diversity of a country like the United States, by no means are its citizens all cast from the same mold. As the selections printed here will demonstrate, the Japanese speak with many voices, and the weight of their cultural output down through the centuries makes their voices anything but small.

The second stereotype is that Japan is a nation of imitators. This commonplace derives from the fact that it has been Japan's peculiar destiny to have lived at the edge of two great and contrasting traditions—Chinese civilization from the sixth century until the mid-nineteenth and Western modernity thereafter—always managing to accommodate influence while retaining the stamp of its own identity. Far from being a cultural parasite, Japan has demonstrated a certain genius for knowing when and what to learn from others. Furthermore, the Japanese have always been too vigorous a people to sit back and let someone else invent their culture for them. The same streak of perfectionism that has made Japanese quality control the envy of every American manufacturer seems to have compelled Japan to improve perpetually on the original, whether it be Confucian theories of government or Henry Ford's assembly line. Nor should we let this agility as a cultural transformer obscure Japan's own creativity. The tea ceremony, the multicolor woodblock print, *kabuki*, *haiku*, and *sumo* all spring from native soil.

Yet in the sweep of history this is a newcomer, and twice in its existence Japan has found itself having to catch up. While the empires of Mesopotamia and ancient Egypt rose and fell and the civilizations of Greece, India, and China came to flower, the inhabitants of the Japanese islands remained hunters and gatherers. Their ancestors probably migrated to Japan in several waves, some from the Asian continent and others from the islands to the south. In the third century B.C. a new influx brought rice cultivation, and the Japanese exchanged a nomadic way of life for an agricultural one; they settled villages in the miniature plains nestled between the mountains and the sea. But the wanderers' past left its mark on Japanese civilization: an ingrained sense of the impermanence of things; an acute awareness of the changes brought by the seasons; a taste for the spare, the unrefined, the natural—even when prodigious artifice would sometimes be required to produce something "natural."

The new techniques of cultivating wet rice, one of the world's most labor-intensive crops, taught the Japanese people economy in the use of space and the advantages of cooperation. The latter, in turn, gave rise to the long-standing ideal in Japan that it is best to submit individual will to the greater needs of the group—the origin, perhaps, of the notion that the Japanese form a homogeneous and harmonious whole. This was no more true in 300 B.C. than it is today, for along with agriculture came bronze and iron; along with metallurgy came weapons; and with weapons, war. In other words, very early on another trait of Japanese culture surfaced: rule by warrior elites, precursors of the *samurai*. A class of martial aristocrats competed for power over the thickly settled countryside of the southern and central islands, until one clan succeeded in asserting its predominance, thereby establishing the imperial line.

The new governors quickly imported the superior fruits of Chinese civilization, which, by the seventh and eighth centuries, represented the most powerful, most advanced, and best administered country in the world. Having consolidated their hold over rival clans, the fledgling rulers claimed authority by absorbing Chinese theories of sovereignty and a centralized state, along with the economic and political apparatus—land surveys, districting, taxation, law codes, and bureaucratic management—to make their bold ambition work.

In many ways, the Japanese succeeded, though the political history of premodern Japan is ultimately the story of how the Chinese model proved a poor fit. It was a system that has been described by historians as a form of agricultural communism, with land divided equally among the population (and taxed uniformly) to ensure maximum returns. China's theory of government was profoundly egalitarian. The emperor reigned as an absolute sovereign, but his administrators were chosen on the basis of ability through an examination system that not only emphasized learning but fostered a true meritocracy. The emperor's bureaucrats thus provided the talent and diversity to help him rule impartially.

But the temperament and earliest traditions of the Japanese inclined them in a very different direction. Kinship ties from tribal times persisted in the emphasis of family and lineage, so that when Japan decided to adapt the Chinese model of bureaucracy, administrative positions went as a matter of course to those of good pedigree. There was no examination or open competition, because government was the right of the aristocracy. A system based on family connections rather than ability may strike us as unfair; it is also inherently unstable. Family fortunes wax and wane, and therein lies not only the formula for the political, economic, and military vicissitudes of premodern Japanese history but also the subject for much of Japan's best literature. Heroes are launched on fictional adventures when clan rivalries cost them imperial favor. The most popular tale of the classical era recounts the rise and fall of an overweening family. A kind of Japanese *Gone with*

the Wind (but better as literature), *The Tale of the Heike* follows a powerful house of warrior-aristocrats through the glory days of bending even the emperor to their whims until the family's star inevitably falls, civil war comes, and a world of pride and elegant pursuits vanishes.

Life in premodern Japan, indeed the earthly realm, was seen as impermanent, transitory, almost a dream. This was a central teaching of Buddhism, which Japan committed to memory during its Chinese tutelage. Buddhism had an exorbitant impact on Japanese civilization, and is the best example of how much more enduring were some of the intellectual, artistic, and material influences that crossed the China Sea along with statecraft. The new religion was obviously congenial to the Japanese mind. While it is true that the native faith, Shinto, was little more than an amorphous and naive belief in the protective or baneful effect of supernatural powers—local divinities and the mythical creators of Japan—completely lacking in creed, scripture, or a developed metaphysic, these deficiencies alone do not account for the success of Buddhism among the Japanese. In a country where earthquakes and typhoons are common occurrences and where people lived close to nature in all its changing aspects, the doctrine of universal impermanence spoke to Japanese experience. More important, Buddhism brought meaning to that discordant experience. Precisely because human existence is fleeting and illusory, life is but dissatisfaction. So long as one clings to the things of this world, one is bound to suffer. Buddhism offered hope of escape, however, because it taught that we all hold the possibility of Buddhahood within us. To realize this Buddha nature and end the painful cycle of rebirth into worlds of continued suffering, we have only to stop our grasping.

Here is the kernel of a great literature. It would sprout in Japan as luxuriantly as anywhere Buddhism ever touched: a literature that takes as its main ambition to plumb the depths of longing. If the Japanese have not been the world's metaphysicians and have proved inhospitable to the schematizing that in China elevated a taste for the symmetric almost to a national tic, they have been thinkers of another kind. Like the ancient Romans, the Japanese have always been a profoundly practical people. While they may never have distinguished themselves in abstract speculation, through art and literature rather than philosophy they have addressed, albeit more obliquely, the large questions of life: the nature of emotional attachment, the human need for affection, the clash between passion and reason, the curse of worldly ambition, the demon of the self, what courage means, what beauty is, where wisdom lies, the weight of the past, the true meaning of time.

In an astonishing series of masterpieces the Japanese developed one of their great gifts—for the play of words. That the medium employed was a foreign vessel, the Chinese writing system assimilated along with Buddhism, remains insignificant. The presence of a mentor should never obscure the accomplishments of the student.

PRONOUNCING GLOSSARY

The following list uses common English syllables to provide rough equivalents of selected words whose pronunciation may be unfamiliar to the general reader.

Genji: *gen-jee* kabuki: *kah-boo-kee*

haiku: *hai-koo* samurai: *sah-moo-rai*

Heike: *hay-kay* sumo: *soo-moh*

THE MAN'YŌSHŪ
eighth century

The first monument of Japanese literature, and some would say its greatest, is a large collection of poetry whose range, complexity, and force still speak to us, more than one thousand years later, of the exuberance of a people experiencing literacy and cultural animation for the first time. Known as *The Man'yōshū* (The collection of ten thousand leaves), this earliest extant collection of Japanese poetry appears to have been intended as an anthology of anthologies. The compilers repeatedly refer to older anthologies, no longer existing, from which they have culled their selections. Furthermore, the "leaves" of the title refer not only to the poems but to future generations of readers, because, by tradition, the character for *leaf* also meant "age," or "generation." The anthologizers were proclaiming, then, that this "collection of ten thousand poems" (4,516 to be precise) was to serve as a "collection for ten thousand ages."

Such a claim might seem the height of audacity, given the circumstances. At the time that the last specifically dated poem in the collection was completed in 759, Japan had only recently emerged from a primitive preliterate past. A loose confederation of competing clans, who drew their wealth from the cultivation of rice and whose principal cultural accomplishment was the erection of enormous burial mounds equipped with clay statuary, had remade itself into a society with a national identity, a ruling imperial family, an elaborate government administration, a complex system of religious beliefs, a command of letters, and the other accouterments of civilization.

All this had been realized within the span of a mere century or two, as Japan worked frenetically to catch up with the world's exemplar of cultural sophistication: China. Once the Japanese comprehended the chasm separating them from this much older civilization, which by every standard—economic, political, and philosophical—threw their unseasoned situation into bold relief, national ambition and competitive pride propelled a stunning process of assimiliation. Where before there had been paddy fields and simple thatched-roof shrines intended to placate spirits residing in the rivers and mountains of the vicinity, now there were vast road networks, irrigation works, ports, and courier service and, in the capital, a hierarchy of court ranks, fine silks and brocades, and lacquered pagodas whose rooftops soared like the wings of a great bird gliding in mid-flight. These were all visible signs of the material progress Japan had accomplished as the diligent student of China.

But perhaps the most fateful decision that the Japanese made in their importation of Chinese culture was the bending of the Chinese writing system to the needs of their own very different language. The Chinese script, known as characters, had originated as a system of pictograms, evolving over time to incorporate pictographic, ideographic, and phonetic elements. Because it was designed solely to record the Chinese language and lacked the pliancy of a phonetic writing system—an alphabet or syllabary—the Chinese script required cumbersome manipulation before it could serve to record another language.

That the Japanese chose to borrow rather than invent a writing system makes them no different from most other peoples. The Greek alphabet, for example, is but a mutation of the Phoenician script, and the Roman alphabet merely the Greek slightly modified. What may set the Japanese apart, however (and would later become a cliché), is the ingenuity of their adaptation. The poems of *The Man'yōshū* were recorded using Chinese characters in three different ways: for

meaning, for sound when read in Chinese, and for sound when read in Japanese. The character denoting "person," for instance, could naturally be used for its semantic value when the poet wanted to write the word *person*. But it could also be used to approximate the sound of its original Chinese pronunciation, *jen*, which Japanese phonology rendered *jin*, or *nin*. Or it could be used in an altogether different way. Because the Japanese word for "person" is *hito*, the character could represent that native sound in another word. For example, Hitomaro, the name of the first of the poets in the selections printed here, came to be written with the "person" character signifying the "Hito" element. The sheer perversity of this system (for there were thousands of Chinese characters to be mastered and the number had then to be multiplied by three) is a testament to the overwhelming desire of the Japanese people of the seventh and eighth centuries to express their new experiences through the written word.

Indeed the range of experience the early poets chronicled is one of the qualities that later generations of Japanese would prize in *The Man'yōshū*. Other qualities are its passion and sincerity, together with an innocence, vigor, and seeming artlessness that stand in marked contrast to the controlled, more self-conscious polish that would define Japanese poetry throughout the subsequent classical era. In the age of *The Man'yōshū*, the aristocratic customs of the court had yet to solidify into the weight of convention. And the cultural situation in Japan was still fluid enough that the aristocracy did not yet dominate.

In fact, one finds a surprising number of poems in *The Man'yōshū* by people completely outside court circles, whose literacy itself is surprising. The anonymous poems in the collection, nearly two thousand, far outnumber those by any of the known poets. There are rustic poems that tell of life in the wilderness of the eastern frontier, poems purportedly by fishers, poems recording local dialects, farewell poems by military conscripts, and even poems by travelers to Korea. Of course, one must allow for the possibility that aristocrats chose to romanticize rustic life, and no doubt some of the poems in a common voice are a reworking of folk elements. Nonetheless, in many cases sufficient internal evidence remains to convince scholars that a substantial number of the anonymous poems are the product of the ordinary citizen.

Authorship, however, is only one indication of the breadth of *The Man'yōshū*. Those poets who came from the privileged class and whose names we do know also ranged widely in their chosen topics. Kakinomoto Hitomaro* (flourished ca. 680–700), the undisputed master of the collection, captures the profound sadness of parting, the warrior's bravery, the shock of sudden death, the pageantry of the imperial institution, the burdens of travel, and the mysteries of the human fate. The three sets of poems included here by Hitomaro are representative of his genius. In the first he broods on the passing of time and the evanescence of worldly glory as he views the ruins of the ancient capital. In the second he laments the loneliness of parting from his wife. He depicts their union through the sensual imagery of stems of "sleek seaweed" that once "swayed toward" each other and intertwined but after too few nights have been sundered; the seaweed now grows alone "on the desolate shore."

Like so many of his best poems, it is a highly visual presentation. When the poet describes looking back through the falling leaves for a final glimpse of his wife, not only do we clearly see the sad autumn scene but we can picture the poet's wife disappearing before his (and our) eyes:

> And so I look back,
> still thinking of her . . .

---

* Names are given in the Japanese order, with surname first.

> but in the storm
> of fallen scarlet leaves
> on Mount Watari,
> crossed as on
>   a great ship,
> I cannot make out the sleeves
> she waves in farewell.
> For she, alas,
> is slowly hidden
> like the moon
>   in its crossing
>   between the clouds.

The same visual force is apparent in the third set of poems by Hitomaro, perhaps his most famous, inspired by the sight of a dead man lying amid the rocks on the forsaken shore of a distant island. Having traveled there through a storm that nearly cost him his own life, Hitomaro understandably identifies with the fate of the dead man. Through his rich use of imagistic language deployed in the lyric equivalent of narration, he makes us identify as well. In poems like these, Hitomaro perfected the techniques of the earliest Japanese poetry, still marked by the formulaic style of an oral tradition, and raised them to a poetry of high artistry.

What constituted that artistry is deceptively simple. Because the sound system of Japanese employs no stress accent, each syllable is pronounced with virtually equal emphasis, and the forms of meter based on stress that we associate with English poetry do not occur. Nor does rhyme figure in Japanese prosody. Most syllables consist of a single vowel or a consonant (or consonant cluster) followed by a vowel. With only five vowel sounds, given Japanese word structure, a poetry based on rhyme would be akin, as Robert Frost once said of free verse, to playing tennis without a net. Instead, Japanese poetry depended from its inception on the rhythm created by alternating phrases of long and short syllable counts. Japan's most archaic songs employ this pattern of alternation, which originally varied from combinations of phrases with four syllables paired with those of six to alternations of phrases of five syllables with those of three. Eventually, by the mid-seventh century the accepted pattern became an alternation of five and seven syllables, establishing a rhythm that would reign until the modern day.

The poets of *The Man'yōshū* compose in two principal forms. The *chōka*, or long poem, consists of an indeterminate number of lines of alternating five- and seven-syllable phrases, culminating in a couplet of two seven-syllable phrases. The *tanka*, or short poem, is identical in form to the last five lines of a *chōka*, that is, it is a thirty-one-syllable poem arranged in lines whose syllable counts are 5, 7, 5, 7, 7.

The long poems in *The Man'yōshū* are by far the rarest, and in fact the *chōka* disappears as a viable poetic form after *The Man'yōshū*. Approximately 4,200 of the 4,516 poems in the collection are *tanka*. Even most of the *chōka* have satellite *tanka* known as "envoys" that serve as a summing up or expand an imagistic or emotive theme from the original *chōka* to a fuller, still more lyrical realization.

Despite their numerical inferiority within the *The Man'yōshū* the longer poems by Hitomaro and others are what many readers remember best. No doubt their very scarcity makes them stand out against the subsequent history of a more confined form of poetry. At the same time, this mingling of *chōka* and *tanka* is yet another indication of the anthology's unusual range.

Among the finest *tanka* in the collection are the ironic poems in praise of wine by Ōtomo Tabito (665–731). Unlike Hitomaro, of whose extraliterary life we unfortunately know nothing, Tabito is a political figure with a well-documented

government career. His affection for Chinese literature also sets him apart from Hitomaro, and his bibulous poems printed here are an excellent example of his expert handling of Chinese themes. Like his friend Tabito, Yamanoue Okura (660–ca. 733), author of the last two sets of poems included here, was a devotee of Chinese culture. But the stances the two poets assume are completely different. If Tabito speaks as the Taoist epicure detached from the stress of life, Okura is the old Confucian gentleman, moralistic, with a strong sense of outrage at the ills of society. His poems on the impermanence of life treat a theme that had already become familiar in Japanese literature, but his poems on poverty depart radically from the norm. They become somewhat less radical, it is true, when we compare them with Chinese treatments of social injustice. Still, Okura's humble, earthy style, the vigor of his language, his genuine compassion, and the humorous, loving voice that breaks through his austere pose are all distinctive.

Owing to its amazing variety, The Man'yōshū has been all things to all readers. To some, it is proof that the earliest Japanese literature is derivative. For others, it is the repository of the essential Japanese identity: wholehearted, sincere, robust, and unaffected. It is important, however, to keep perspective. Susceptibility to influence does not preclude creative invention, and the Chinese example can best be viewed as a fertilizing one. Furthermore, a careful reading of The Man'yōshū reveals a work of considerable complexity, in which confidence in the artistic effect that language creates has overshadowed preliterate belief in the sheer incantatory power of words. Finally, it is one of the ironies of literary history that in the later generations invoked in the very title of the collection—for whom the poetic art was intended to endure—poetry was appropriated as the exclusive property of one group, the aristocracy. Compared with the later poetry of Japan's classical age, The Man'yōshū, in its diverse forms and multiplicity of voices, can rightly be viewed as the mirror of an entire nation.

Two good partial translations of The Man'yōshū exist in English: Nippon Gakujutsu Shinkōkai, The Manyōshū (1965), and Ian Hideo Levy, The Ten Thousand Leaves (1981). Both have informative introductions. Levy has also produced a detailed study of one poet, Hitomaro and the Birth of Japanese Lyricism (1984). The best overall study of The Man'yōshū is contained in Robert H. Brower and Earl Miner, Japanese Court Poetry (1961). For a concise history of Japan see John Whitney Hall, Japan: From Prehistory to Modern Times (1991), and for a short, general introduction to Japanese literature see Donald Keene, The Pleasures of Japanese Literature (1988).

PRONOUNCING GLOSSARY

The following list uses common English syllables to provide rough equivalents of selected words whose pronunciation may be unfamiliar to the general reader.

chōka: *choh-kah*

Dazaifu: *dah-zai-foo*

Iwami: *ee-wah-mee*

Izanagi: *ee-zah-nah-gee*

Izanami: *ee-zah-nah-mee*

Jinmu: *jeen-moo*

Kakinomoto Hitomaro: *kah-kee-noh-moh-toh hee-toh-mah-roh*

Kashiwara: *kah-shee-wah-rah*

Kyūshū: *kyoo-shoo*

Man'yōshū: *mahn-yoh-shoo*

Ōmi: *oh-mee*

Ōtomo Tabito: *oh-toh-moh tah-bee-toh*

Ōtsu: *oh-tsoo*

Samine: *sah-mee-ne*

Sanuki: *sah-noo-kee*

Sasanami: *sah-sah-nah-mee*   Watari: *wah-tah-ree*

Shikoko: *shee-koh-ku*   Yamanoue Okura: *yah-mah-noh-oo-e*

tanka: *tahn-kah*   *oh-koo-rah*

Unebi: *oo-ne-bee*   Yamato: *yah-mah-toh*

FROM THE MAN'YŌSHŪ[1]

29–31

Poem written by Kakinomoto Hitomaro when he passed the ruined capital at Ōmi[2]

Since the reign of the Master of the Sun[3]
at Kashiwara by Unebi Mountain,
   where the maidens
     wear strands of jewels,
all gods who have been born   5
have ruled the realm under heaven,
each following each
like generations of the spruce,
     in Yamato[4]
that spreads to the sky.   10

What was in his mind
that he would leave it
and cross beyond the hills of Nara,
   beautiful in blue earth?
Though a barbarous place   15
at the far reach of the heavens,
here in the land of Ōmi
where the waters race on stone,
at the Ōtsu Palace
in Sasanami   20
   by the rippling waves,
the Emperor, divine Prince,
ruled the realm under heaven.

Though I hear
this was the great palace,   25
though they tell me
here were the mighty halls,
now it is rank with spring grasses.
Mist rises, and the spring sun is dimmed.

---

1. All selections translated by and with notes adapted from Ian Hideo Levy.   2. Because of the
ancient Japanese belief that death polluted a dwelling, when the sovereign died it was customary for his
successor to take up residence in a new palace. The capital shifted from place to place among the
central provinces, until an edict in 646 called for the establishment of a permanent center of government.   3. Emperor Jinmu, in legend the founding sovereign of Japan, credited with subduing rival
chieftains to create the first Japanese state.   4. An archaic name for Japan, which originally referred
to the area around present-day Nara.

Gazing on the ruins of the great palace, 30
its walls once thick with wood and stone,
I am filled with sorrow.

ENVOYS

Cape Kara in Shiga
at Sasanami
 by the rippling waves, 35
you are as before, but I
wait for courtiers' boats in vain.

Waters, you are quiet
in deep bends of Shiga's lake
at Sasanami 40
 by the rippling waves,
but never again may I
meet the men of ancient times.

135–137

*Poem written by Kakinomoto Hitomaro when he parted from his wife in
the land of Iwami and came up to the capital*

At Cape Kara
on the Sea of Iwami,
where the vines
 crawl on the rocks,
rockweed of the deep 5
grows on the reefs
and sleek seaweed
grows on the desolate shore.
As deeply do I
think of my wife 10
who swayed toward me in sleep
 like the lithe seaweed.
Yet few were the nights
we had slept together
before we were parted 15
like crawling vines uncurled.
And so I look back,
still thinking of her
with painful heart,
this clench of inner flesh, 20
but in the storm
of fallen scarlet leaves
on Mount Watari,[1]
crossed as on
 a great ship, 25
I cannot make out the sleeves
she waves in farewell.

---

1. Watari means "crossing"; thus the leaves fall at the very spot where the poet might have caught one
last glimpse of his wife.

For she, alas,
is slowly hidden
like the moon   30
    in its crossing
        between the clouds
over Yagami Mountain
just as the evening sun
coursing through the heavens   35
has begun to glow,
            and even I
who thought I was a brave man
find the sleeves
of my well-woven robe   40
drenched with tears.

ENVOYS

The quick gallop
of my dapple-blue steed
races me to the clouds,
passing far away   45
from where my wife dwells.

O scarlet leaves
falling on the autumn mountainside:
stop, for a while, the storm
your strewing makes, that I might glimpse   50
the place where my wife dwells.

220–222

*Poem written by Kakinomoto Hitomaro upon seeing a dead man lying
among the rocks on the island of Samine in Sanuki*

The land of Sanuki,[1]
    fine in sleek seaweed:
is it for the beauty of the land
that we do not tire
        to gaze upon it?   5
Is it for its divinity
that we deem it most noble?
Eternally flourishing,
    with the heavens
        and the earth,   10
    with the sun
        and the moon,
the very face of a god —
so it has come down
        through the ages.   15

1. In Japan's creation myth Sanuki (part of the island now called Shikoku) was one of the first places
to be formed by the union of the gods Izanagi and Izanami.

Casting off
from Naka harbor,
we came rowing.
Then tide winds
blew through the clouds;   20
on the offing
we saw the rustled waves,
on the strand
we saw the roaring crests.
Fearing the whale-hunted seas,   25
our ship plunged through —
we bent those oars!
Many were the islands
near and far,
but we beached on Samine —   30
        beautiful its name —
and built a shelter
            on the rugged shore.

Looking around,
            we saw you   35
lying there
on a jagged bed of stones,
the beach
        for your finely woven pillow,
by the breakers' roar.   40
        If I knew your home,
I would go and tell them.
If your wife knew,
she would come and seek you out.
But she does not even know the road,   45
    straight as a jade spear.
Does she not wait for you,
    worrying and longing,
your beloved wife?

                    ENVOYS

If your wife were here,   50
she would gather and feed you
the starwort that grows
on the Sami hillsides,
but is its season not past?

Making a finely woven pillow   55
of the rocky shore
        where waves from the offing
                draw near,
you, who sleep there!

338–350

Thirteen poems in praise of wine by Lord Ōtomo Tabito, the Commander of the Dazaifu[1]

Rather than engaging
in useless worries,
it's better to down a cup
of raw wine.

Great sages of the past
gave the name of "sage"[2] to wine.
How well they spoke!

What the Seven Wise Men[3]
    of ancient times
wanted, it seems,
    was wine.

Rather than making pronouncements
    with an air of wisdom,
it's better to down the wine
and sob drunken tears.

What is most noble,
    beyond all words
    and beyond all deeds,
is wine.

Rather than be half-heartedly human,
I wish I could be a jug of wine
and be soaked in it!

How ugly!
    those men who,
        with airs of wisdom,
            refuse to drink wine.
Take a good look,
and they resemble apes.

How could even
a priceless treasure
be better than a cup
    of raw wine?

How could even a gem
that glitters in the night

---

1. Government headquarters in Kyūshū, southernmost of the four main islands of Japan, an important outpost for regulating contacts with China and Korea. In Tabito's time the flourishing city was nick-named "the distant capital."   2. So-called by those who drank it secretly during the brief time in ancient China when wine was prohibited by the emperor.   3. The Seven Sages of the Bamboo Grove of 3rd-century China, a Taoist coterie of wealthy dissidents who expressed their social and political disaffection by withdrawing into a kind of intellectual hedonism, given over to tippling, poetastering, and philosophical debate. One of the sages set the style for the group by employing an attendant who carried a wine jug in one hand to quench his master's thirst and a spade in the other to bury him if he fell dead.

be as good as drinking wine
and cleansing the heart?

Here in this life,
on these roads of pleasure,
it is fun to sob drunken tears.

As long as I have fun
    in this life,
let me be an insect or a bird
    in the next.[4]

Since all who live
must finally die,
let's have fun
while we're still alive.

Smug and silent airs of wisdom
are still not as good
as downing a cup of wine
and sobbing drunken tears.

804–805[1]

Poem sorrowing on the impermanence of life in this world

PREFACE

Easy to gather and difficult to dispel are the eight great hardships.[2] Difficult to fully enjoy and easy to expend are the pleasures of life's century span. So the ancients lamented, and so today our grief finds the same cause. Therefore I have composed a poem, and with it hope to dispel the sorrow of my black hair marked with white. My poem:

Our helplessness in this life
is like the streaming away
of the months and years.
Again and again
misfortune tracks us down   5
and assaults us with a hundred ills.
We cannot hold time
    in its blossoming:
            when young girls,
to be maidenly,   10
wrapped Chinese jewels
around their wrists
and, hand in hand
with companions of their age,
must once have played.   15

4. The poet adheres to the Buddhist belief in reincarnation, in which present deeds determine one's future life. 1. By Yamanoue Okura. 2. In Buddhism, birth, old age, sickness, death, separation, anger, coveting, and the so-called pain of five passions—the suffering derived from one's attachment to the five elemental aggregates of which the body, mind, and environment are formed (perception, conception, volition, consciousness, and form).

When has frost fallen
on hair as black
as the guts of river snails?
From where do wrinkles come
to crease those crimson faces?   20
We have let time go.
        Once strong young men,
to be manly,
girt their waists
with great swords   25
and, tossing saddles
with cloth embroidered
        in Yamato patterns
on their red-maned steeds,
mounted and rode for sport—   30
how could it last forever?
Few were the nights
I pushed apart the wooden doors
that young girls creak open and shut
and, groping to their side,   35
slept arm in jewelled arm,
arm in truly jewelled arm!
But now I walk
with a cane gripped in my hand
and propped against my waist.   40
Going this way,
        I am despised.
Going that way,
        I am hated.
Such, it seems,   45
is the fate of old men.
Though I regret the passing
of my life,
        that swelled with spirit,
there is nothing I can do.   50

ENVOY

Like the unchanging cliffs,
I would remain just as I am.
But I am living in this world
and cannot hold time back.

892–893[1]

Dialog of the Destitute

"On nights when rain falls,
        mixed with wind,
on nights when snow falls,
        mixed with rain,

1. By Yamanoue Okura.

I am cold   5
And the cold.
      leaves me helpless:
I lick black lumps of salt
and suck up melted dregs of *sake*.[2]
Coughing and sniffling,   10
I smooth my uncertain wisps
           of beard.
I am proud—
      I know no man
         is better than me.   15
But I am cold.
I pull up my hempen nightclothes
and throw on every scrap
of cloth shirt that I own.
But the night is cold.   20
And I wonder how a man like you,
        even poorer than myself,
with his father and mother
starving and freezing,
with his wife and children   25
begging and begging
        through their tears,
can get through the world alive
        at times like this."

"Wide, they say,   30
        are heaven and earth—
but have they shrunk for me?
Bright, they say,
        are the sun and moon—
but do they refuse to shine for me?   35
Is it thus for all men,
        or for me alone?
Above all, I was born human,[3]
I too toil for my keep—
as much as the next man—   40
yet on my shoulders hangs
a cloth shirt
not even lined with cotton,
these tattered rags
thin as strips of seaweed.   45
In my groveling hut,
   my tilting hut,
sleeping on straw
cut and spread right on the ground,
with my father and mother   50
      huddled at my pillow
and my wife and children
      huddled at my feet,
I grieve and lament.

2. A brewed alcoholic beverage made from fermented rice.   3. In the Buddhist doctrine of reincarnation one could not achieve enlightenment, thereby escaping the cyclical chain of rebirth, without first attaining the human level. In this, at least, he is fortunate.

Not a spark rises in the stove,   55
and in the pot
a spider has drawn its web.
I have forgotten
what it is to cook rice!
As I lie here,   60
a thin cry tearing from my throat—
          a   tiger   thrush's
moan—
then, as they say,
to slice the ends
of a thing already too short,   65
to our rough bed
comes the scream of the villadman
                    with   his   tax   collecting
whip.
Is it so helpless and desperate,
the way of life in this world?"   70

ENVOY

I find this world
a hard and shameful place.
But I cannot fly away—
I am not a bird.

MURASAKI SHIKIBU

ca. 973–1016

The Tale of Genji is the undisputed masterpiece of Japanese prose and the first great novel in the history of world literature. It was written in the early eleventh century by Murasaki Shikibu, a woman of the lower reaches of the aristocracy. Murasaki was the daughter of a provincial governor, but her service as lady-in-waiting to the empress allowed her the most intimate glimpse of the social and political doings of the imperial court. Unlike the fanciful romances that preceded it, *The Tale of Genji* (ca. 1001–13) is revered for its psychological insight, capturing a world that, however remote it might eventually become in time, has always retained the sharp authenticity of real life.

Vast in scale and peopled by hundreds of characters, this thousand-page novel has a plot of supreme simplicity. It depicts the lives and loves of a former prince and, following his death, the lives and loves of his descendants. But in a novel in which everything is finely calibrated, things are seldom really simple. To begin with, why is the hero a *former* prince? Though he is cherished by his father, the emperor, political exigencies force his removal from the imperial line. The family name *Genji* is bestowed on him, along with the sobriquet "the shining one" and generous emoluments. Nonetheless, before the first chapter is even over, the young hero has already lost the most important attribute of a man of his rank: the chance to rule someday as emperor.

Because political concerns were of little interest to the author except implicitly,

she is not about to dissect the career of a favorite son as he rises through the ranks of the government. She is interested instead in how one compensates, substitutes, and replaces and in larger issues than worldly success: fate, retribution, sexual attraction, and the emotional depth of human experience.

What begins as the story of a glittering existence darkens with time. The sensitive aristocrat discovers more of life, including failure. Yet this is no ordinary story of age bringing wisdom or of the past repeating itself. As Murasaki augments her tale (which seems to have grown more by accretion than by blueprint), she questions, attenuates, and sometimes undermines the fundamental presumptions of its earlier portions.

By the time Genji dies two-thirds of the way through the book, a deep pessimism has taken over. We have entered a world diminished, not only because Genji is gone but because his survivors are somehow smaller people, flawed fragments of their forebears. Murasaki now follows the hapless lives of Genji's two descendants, but here again things are not as simple as they appear. One of the two possesses the ultimate flaw of inauthenticity. He is only passing as Genji's son, being in fact, the issue of an illicit union between Genji's wife and the son of Genji's best friend. In their different ways, the two scions represent a sad falling off. The real grandson is frivolous and inconsequential, and the putative son is so wracked by neurotic indecision that he has been dubbed world literature's first antihero.

Though the armature supporting this long story lies in the lives of three men, it is fundamentally a work of women's literature. To a degree that would have been the envy of European women writers as recently as Virginia Woolf, Murasaki thrived in a culture where women had the leisure, financial security, and intellectual freedom to become writers of significance. "A woman must have money and a room of her own if she wants to write fiction," Virginia Woolf said in 1929. She was lamenting the fact that until the late eighteenth century such favorable conditions were usually wanting and Western literature was the poorer for its slender pantheon of women writers.

The situation in Murasaki's day, courtly Japan of nearly a thousand years earlier, could not have been more different. True, women led a circumscribed existence. The role of a lady was to marry and bear children, and if she came of a suitably good family, she was apt to find herself a pawn in the marriage politics of the imperial court. The most influential family of the time, the Fujiwara, had attained its influence by marrying daughters to emperors, who produced new emperors who could be dominated by their maternal grandfathers. (Murasaki was herself a member of a subsidiary branch of the Fujiwara family.) A noblewoman's days were spent behind curtains and screens, hidden from the world (or from the male world). The verb *to see* constituted an act of possession and was synonymous with having sexual relations. Proper ladies were not seen casually. Nor did they enjoy the same mobility as men or have careers, except as ladies-in-waiting.

They did, however, have the requisite leisure that Virginia Woolf specified. And they had the income. Although at this time Japan was a polygamous society, women of the aristocracy retained a degree of independence, thanks to a system of matrilineal inheritance, so that a well-born woman was not solely dependent on her husband for financial support.

Most important of all, the women of Murasaki's circle had the intellectual attainments to produce literature. Theirs was an education by default, but it was an education all the same. As is so often the case in early Japanese literature, the issue of language becomes crucial. Despite the development of a new native writing system by the mid-ninth century and the birth of an indigenous Japanese literature, both Chinese script and the Chinese language retained tremendous authority in eleventh-century Japan. Chinese, not Japanese, was the official language of the government, whose organization and institutions were themselves

based on the model of China. The bureaucracy, the legal codes, political theory, even the calendar were of Chinese origin. To prepare for a career in the administration of the government—the only career for a male aristocrat—required a thorough education in the Chinese classics (for example, the *Book of Songs*, p. 534), which made Chinese both the language of the practical, workaday world of men and the medium of intellection, like Latin in medieval Europe.

A command of Chinese was considered irrelevant to a woman's life, and if she happened to pick it up, this "mannish" attainment was best concealed. In her diary, Murasaki tells us this:

> When my brother, Secretary at the Ministry of Ceremonial, was a young boy learning the Chinese classics, I was in the habit of listening to him and I became unusually proficient at understanding those passages which he found too difficult to grasp. Father, a most learned man, was always regretting the fact: "Just my luck!" he would say. "What a pity she was not born a man!"[*]

After that, Murasaki feigned ignorance and turned her attention to the native language.

Left to their own devices and with plenty of time on their hands, Murasaki and her female contemporaries explored the potential of their own language and discovered it to be a supple instrument for a literature of introspection. One of the remarkable aspects of *The Tale of Genji* and other great works by women writers of Murasaki's time is that they appeared so early in the development of the native literature. Or put another way, it is astonishing that the prestige of the Chinese classics, which permeated every official element of Japanese life, should have proved a less formidable obstacle than the Greek and Latin precedent did in Europe to the rise of a vernacular literature. All evidence suggests that this was mainly thanks to women like Murasaki, whose talent and passion for expression were indomitable.

And what was it Murasaki wanted to express in writing *The Tale of Genji?* This is a question the Japanese have spent nearly a millennium answering, not because the novel is opaque but because it is so various. Perhaps the most obvious reading of the tale is to see it as a sexual poetics, a study of the distinctive features of love— its language, forms, and conventions. This is not to suggest that *Genji* is in any way an erotic novel. In the customs of the time, men took principal wives and secondary wives, akin to concubines, as well as the occasional lover. Men moved about with a great degree of sexual freedom. Women did not; they waited. It was not only attention and affection they sat waiting for behind their screens but a definition of themselves, which depended entirely on male recognition.

The whole process was fraught with uncertainty. If a man came, would he come again? A woman's position depended more on the frequency of the man's visits than on any formal arrangements. And even marriage, that is to say as the principal wife, was no guarantee of domestic security. A man's first wife usually remained with her parents, and he visited. Secondary wives also tended to live separately from their husbands. The man, then, was often elsewhere, and the tension that this produced on the woman's part in the form of longing, loneliness, insecurity, jealousy, resentment, and other vulnerabilities was balanced on the man's part by the unhappy fate of being forever on the outside looking in (or trying to), the endless traveler, the incessant aggressor. Both sides were condemned to a world of physical separation, with all its attendant agonies. And this is what Murasaki is really interested in: the dynamics of love at the emotional and psychological level, not the physical. Courtship and seduction might seem to form the central

---

[*] Richard Bowring, *Murasaki Shikibu: Her Diary and Poetic Memoirs* (1982) 139.

theme of the novel, but the real theme is the longing to connect with another person.

That is why Genji's life and the lives of his successors are presented as a search for the ideal woman. Like a symphony unfolding with its themes and variations, the novel announces early on its main motif. In the second chapter, *The Broom Tree* (the first of the selections printed here), the seventeen-year-old Genji and his friends while away a rainy night in his quarters at the palace debating what makes the perfect woman. In the process, the young men trade stories of their experiences with women, which, to their credit, involve fewer conquests than failures. But they remain undeterred to a man, and the rest of the long novel continues the quest for fulfilment in love.

Thus, in the manner of music, this early chapter anticipates episodes to follow, which in turn generate other episodes and further repercussions. The characters are unaware of it, but when Genji's best friend, Tō no Chūjō, mentions his most memorable affair, he describes the very woman with whom Genji will soon fall in love and whose death will be caused by the jealousy it inspires in a rival. These events appear in Chapter 4, *Evening Faces*. And they too have repercussions later in the novel (see *Fireflies*), when Genji, now thirty-six, pursues the daughter of this same woman. In a twist of fate emblematic of the novel's pattern, the young lady, Tamakazura, is the child of Tō no Chūjō, and the product of the affair he recounted some twenty years before when the young courtiers spent their rainy night trying to define perfect love.

Gradually, through age and experience, the once-charmed Genji begins to comprehend that there is no such thing. The tale of his life may be read as a progress from youthful idealism (involving its share of insensitivity) to disillusion and then on to the edges of insight. It may further be read, in the lives of Genji's incomplete descendants, as an ironic comment on the novel's own earlier ideals—a parable about the process of maturing and the realization that all human bonds are by nature defective.

If the lives of the heroes represent a fruitless quest for the perfect woman, Murasaki's chronicle seems also a quest, ultimately abandoned, for the perfect man. One can easily imagine Murasaki in the tedium of slow-moving days at court, or perhaps on her own long rainy night, amusing herself and her empress by conjuring up a man who would not disappoint them. In the early pages of the novel, Genji possesses every manly virtue. "He had grown into a lad of such beauty," we are told, "that he hardly seemed meant for this world—and indeed one almost feared that he might only briefly be a part of it." He is witty, artistic, amusing, sophisticated, influential, generous, and more than any of his peers, understanding of women—in short, irresistible. Even his learning takes the breath away: "When he was seven he went through the ceremonial reading of the Chinese classics, and never before had there been so fine a performance. Again a tremor of apprehension passed over the emperor—might it be that such a prodigy was not to be long for this world?"

In fact, Genji endures into his early fifties (a ripe enough age for the era), and there is ample time to see him fall short of perfection. Very quickly Murasaki forsook romance, the tale's antecedent, in favor of realism. At the start, it is a cheerful sort of realism, but it darkens as the novel progresses, and we can detect this already in *Suma* and *Akashi*. The twin chapters are numbers twelve and thirteen of the novel, relatively early in a work of fifty-four chapters. Even so, the idealization of Genji that we saw in *The Broom Tree* has been muted by now. Genji has transgressed, and he is exiled. His expansive appetite for life has finally got him into real trouble.

The proximate cause of exile is an unwise affair with the daughter of a rival family, which Genji's enemies use as a pretext to remove him from the capital.

But the actual, or moral, cause is a serious misstep. Genji has also had an affair with his father's consort, Fujitsubo, and the secret liaison has produced a child. While, strictly speaking, he has not violated the taboo on sexual relations between close family members, since Fujitsubo is his stepmother, Genji has come perilously close, and he has disturbed the imperial succession. His transgression is rooted in a central theme of the novel: repetition and substitution. Things that happen once have an uncanny tendency to recur under a slightly different guise. In Buddhist belief life is a wheel; as it spins we confront situations that echo our past, or the fates of those before us. But this sense of repetition is also partly an illusion. Nothing is exactly the same, much as we sometimes want it to be. And this is Genji's problem. His desire for a mother he lost when still a child has led him to seek substitutions. His father's consort is the closest substitute of all, since the grief-stricken emperor had originally selected the woman precisely because of her resemblance to Genji's mother.

Murasaki understands not only the sheer recklessness of her protagonist but also Genji's complex psychological makeup. When Genji trifles with the incest taboo, it is not only lust that drives him. It is the lure of the forbidden, intertwined with the persistent need for a symbolic repossession of his mother and perhaps even an unconscious will to disrupt the political order. It could well be that Genji's "theft" of the emperor's wife is the subliminal revenge of a fallen prince who lost paradise too young to recall it with equanimity. In any case, Murasaki fully appreciates how seductive prohibition can be. And she continually observes in her novel the multifarious ways that obsession demands to be reincarnated.

In exile, Genji has time to ruminate on his failings, but also to seek new substitutes for the women he has left behind in the capital. The wheel of life keeps turning. Genji pursues women to replace other women. In time, he himself sees the pattern. Eventually, his own wife is unfaithful. He cannot help remembering his father and wondering if, though the emperor remained silent, he knew. Genji's youthful misdeeds have come back to haunt him. By the end of his life he comprehends what unhappiness he has caused others.

Charming and handsome, gifted and ardent, rakish but faithful in his own way (unlike other men, he never abandons any woman he has loved), Genji is a charismatic figure. Yet he is also one of the most problematic of literary characters. All the world loves a lover perhaps, but even when he brings pain and suffering to so many of his loves? Genji may intend only the best for these women—he is inherently kind and noble—but his generous intentions are clouded by an impetuous, self-centered streak that lingers long after youth might have excused it. A man of taste he may be, gregarious and totally alive; Genji is also a past master of lechery, hypocrisy, and self-deceit. His sexual connoisseurship can seem positively arrogant, though not so different from the reported behavior of some of our own heroes in the twentieth century, from rock stars to politicians. Readers may hate Genji or adore him or fall somewhere in between, but we can hardly deny that his creator has fashioned a character both larger than life and believably human.

In a certain way, one ends up feeling sorry for Genji. The eleventh-century Japanese version of machismo was as emotionally confining for a man of his delicate sentiment as court conventions were physically restricting for women. Both sexes paid the price of membership in a beautiful, exclusive little world. If the Buddhist wheel is turning, it is on a very short axis. Even the aristocrat's privileged myopia cannot obscure, finally, the ways actions have consequences—which are, if anything, magnified by the tight compass of their closed circle. Murasaki understands, as her characters do not, that narrow horizons bring their own penalties.

Loss, substitution, repetition. Transgression and retribution. In a work as oceanic as the Bible, here too the sins of the father are visited on the children. If Genji is flawed, his descendants are imperfection intensified. Time is succession,

and life itself substitution. Just as youth will not return, neither will youthful assumptions. The full measure of the story's profundity is not merely its extraordinary insights into human nature, but its subversion of its own earlier suppositions. For many people *The Tale of Genji* has been a discovery. The novel's continually expanding reflection and self-scrutiny have shown them a way to look at themselves. For such readers, *Genji* is more than a book, it is an experience of life.

Nonetheless, a full appreciation of this work will elude us if we fail to comprehend some of the fundamental practical aspects and assumptions underpinning eleventh-century Japanese society. In many ways, the world of the imperial court might seem by our standards a misogynistic one. It was probably no more so, however, than European society in the Middle Ages or the Renaissance, or even the Victorian era. Its patriarchal hierarchies that denied women a formal education or a public role (except for the empress) and relegated them to a life of seclusion find their disconcerting echo in traditional Western attitudes. It is worth remembering that American women did not win the right to vote until 1919. If Buddhist doctrine held that women were inferior creatures who must first be reborn as men before attaining enlightenment or salvation, the Bible also made clear where women have customarily fit in the pecking order. Genesis asserts that the female body was created from the male and 1 Corinthians 11.3 that "the head of every man is Christ, and the head of the woman is the man."

Life for European women in the eleventh century may have been every bit as confining as it was for their Japanese sisters. Western women of the Middle Ages were also expected to live behind walls, either at home or in a convent. Even to stand by an open window was to venture too close to the outside world—the world of men—and thus risk corruption. When religious faith or family obligations made an excursion necessary, a woman was to be escorted by a servant or family member and told to keep her eyes "so low that nothing but where you put your feet matters to you."* She was instructed not to laugh, and if she must smile not to show her teeth. If she was discouraged by this world of repression, the appropriate response was not to sob or wring her hands but to suffer, predictably, in silence.

In eleventh-century Japan, however, neither laughter nor tears nor sexuality were denied women. On the contrary, the Japanese view of sex was relatively liberated. Stemming perhaps from the ancient Chinese belief that sexual intercourse was physically beneficial, the Japanese of the time attached no sense of sin to carnal relations or undue value to virginity. A woman of the upper classes was expected to be sexually alive, but this does not mean that she was licentious. In a society as stratified as the imperial court, relations between the sexes were highly regulated. Yet the underlying economic and political imperatives of a clan-based aristocracy sanctioned polygamous intermarriage, and a certain amount of premarital experimentation was deemed necessary to ensure sexual compatibility and thus progeniture. As in most polygamous societies, however, the actual number of wives kept by a Japanese aristocrat was small, usually no more than two or three—hardly harems—for the saying went that to keep many wives was to suffer many troubles.

A man's first marriage normally took place when he was, in today's view, still a boy of twelve or thirteen; women were a year or two younger. Because of the ages of the spouses and the fact that the first marriage in particular tended to be a political and economic arrangement, both husband and wife were eventually apt to seek love elsewhere. Until modern times the Japanese have not expected marriage, romance, and erotic love to weave a seamless whole. The purpose of marriage was procreation, continuation of the family line, and the striking of advantageous alliances with other families. Love had other purposes, and sexual gratification, far from being "the abomination of the flesh" that medieval Chris-

---

* Christiane Klapisch-Zuber, ed., *A History of Women*, Vol. 2 (1992) 95.

tianity condemned, was but another natural need. So long as its fulfillment did not compete with a man's responsibilities to his family, society tolerated his amours. Sometimes he found them in his other marriages. Sometimes these too were political arrangements, and the romantic type would have to seek his bliss in a discreet affair.

The possibility of forming such a liaison had much to do with the living arrangements of the time. Ordinarily a man's several wives lived in different establishments. His first wife would typically remain in her parent's house. Initially, the young husband might take up residence there or merely visit. Sometimes her parents would furnish the newlyweds with a house of their own, though this was less common when the couple married at a young age, since the maternal grandparents would then assume many of the child-rearing duties. If in time a man took a second or third wife he would usually live with his first (and main) wife and commute among the separate residences. His periodic absence obviously created a certain leeway. Thus a woman in eleventh-century Japan had greater liberty than her counterpart in medieval Europe, but it was definitely the man who moved about, while the woman stayed rooted to her spot.

Among the practical ramifications of this multiple marriage system was the custom for the children of the first, or principal, wife to receive favored support from their father, although he remained a distant figure in their upbringing. Because the primary responsibility for child-rearing lay with the mother and her family and because a daughter usually inherited her parents' house (in addition sometimes to other property, including, perhaps, rights to income from provincial estates), a typical household in aristocratic Japanese society had a strong matriarchal component, despite its patriarchal clan affiliation. From the European perspective, Japanese noblewomen were surprisingly independent—economically and, to a certain extent, sexually. Yet the porous nature of marriage, which could be dissolved by the simple cessation of relations, left women emotionally vulnerable, as *The Tale of Genji* repeatedly demonstrates.

The tale also demonstrates a seemingly casual attitude toward what current Western convention would regard as incest, particularly Genji's affair with his stepmother, Fujitsubo, and his marriage to Murasaki*, whom he first treats as an adopted daughter. The young Murasaki is distressed and bewildered when Genji forces himself on her, but it is significant that none of her attendants are especially surprised, and there are those who assume that the two are already married. In the eleventh-century Japanese practice of endogamy, in this case intermarriage within one's own aristocratic clique, the only unions apparently considered incestuous were those between biological parents and children or between brothers and sisters. If the young Murasaki finds Genji's sudden advances "gross and unscrupulous," it is not because his actions amount to incest but because she is experiencing, unprepared, the disconcerting awakening of sexuality in a manner that shows Genji at his most selfish. The world of Genji will continue to startle, if not shock, us unless we remember that prohibitions governing one culture will not necessarily govern another. Just as we may be astonished by what did or did not constitute incest in Murasaki's society, Murasaki might well have been amazed to be told, for example, that in ancient Egypt and Persia marriage between the closest blood relatives was required by law.

The assumptions of societies, then, are not universal. A good example of this is the Japanese conception of time. Since 1873 Japan has followed the Gregorian calendar of the West, but the official calendar employed in Japan in the eleventh

---

*The origin of the nickname court circles eventually gave Murasaki Shikibu (no doubt because the character is Genji's favorite). The second element of her name, Shikibu, refers to her father's official title.

century derived from China and was divided into twelve lunations (months) of twenty-nine or thirty days. The resulting lunar year was approximately eleven days shorter than a solar year, which required the insertion of a thirteenth intercalary month every third year or thereabout to align the calendrical year with the solar. In addition, by custom the Japanese year began slightly later than the Western, so that New Year's Day fell anywhere from January 15 to February 15. The beginning of the new year also marked an increase in one's age, in contrast to the Western practice of reckoning age by birthdays. A child born in the twelfth month, for instance, would turn two with the new year.

Years were numbered serially from the year when a reigning emperor ascended the throne. In the modern period (beginning in 1868) the reign of an emperor has one name for its duration. For example, the reign of Emperor Hirohito is called the Shōwa ("enlightened peace") era, which lasted from his ascension in 1926 until his death in 1989. In addition to following the Western practice of numbering years by the Gregorian calendar, the year 1930, say, is reckoned as Shōwa 5. In the premodern period, rather than having one name throughout, an emperor's reign was usually divided into various eras, each with its own name.

In the eleventh century, both the months and the hours of the day were designated by the signs of the Chinese zodiac. The day was divided into twelve units, each equivalent to 120 minutes:

Hour	Modern Equivalent
1 Rat	11 P.M.–1 A.M.
2 Ox	1 A.M.–3 A.M.
3 Tiger	3 A.M.–5 A.M.
4 Rabbit	5 A.M.–7 A.M.
5 Dragon	7 A.M.–9 A.M.
6 Snake	9 A.M.–11 A.M.
7 Horse	11 A.M.–1 P.M.
8 Ram	1 P.M.–3 P.M.
9 Monkey	3 P.M.–5 P.M.
10 Rooster	5 P.M.–7 P.M.
11 Dog	7 P.M.–9 P.M.
12 Boar	9 P.M.–11 P.M.

These hours were carefully measured at court with the use of a water clock to ensure that official rites, changes of the palace guard, and so forth could be observed accurately. Beyond the court, time keeping was less precise. In *The Tale of Genji*, when characters are at court, Murasaki cites the exact time, say the hour of the horse, but when they are away from court she gives only an approximation, like "the sun was high."

As you read *The Tale of Genji* you will quickly notice that poetry figures extensively in the lives of Genji and his fellow courtiers. Occasionally, they quote an existing poem. Knowledge of the canon was a necessary accomplishment for any self-respecting aristocrat. Most of the time, however, members of the nobility composed their own, original poems, peppered with traditional allusions. The thirty-one-syllable *tanka* was the verbal repository of court etiquette and cultural values. It was also the principal means of communication—the equivalent of a letter of condolence, a holiday greeting, a farewell note, a postcard, a eulogy, an invitation, a toast, a love letter. With this in mind, it is not surprising that poetry occurs so frequently in the text, although you may be surprised to see it rendered by the translator in couplets rather than in the conventional five lines of the poems in *The Kokinshū*.

There are two English translations of *The Tale of Genji*, and both have their partisans. The older translation, first published in installments between 1925 and 1933, is by Arthur Waley, *The Tale of Genji* (1960). A recent translation in a more contemporary idiom is by Edward G. Seidensticker, *The Tale of Genji* (1976). The Seidensticker translation, chosen here, is generally acknowledged to be the more faithful. Of the secondary works, the best brief introduction is Richard Bowring, *The Tale of Genji* (1988). Two excellent longer studies are Norma Field, *The Splendor of Longing in the "Tale of Genji"* (1987), and Haruo Shirane, *The Bridge of Dreams: A Poetics of "The Tale of Genji"* (1987). A collection of essays on the last part of the novel representative of recent American scholarship is Andrew Pekarik, ed., *Ukifune: Love in "The Tale of Genji"* (1982). For a glimpse into the life of the author see Richard Bowring, *Murasaki Shikibu: Her Diary and Poetic Memoirs* (1982).

PRONOUNCING GLOSSARY

The following list uses common English syllables to provide rough equivalents of selected words whose pronunciation may be unfamiliar to the general reader.

Akashi: *ah-kah-shee*

Akikonomu: *ah-kee-koh-noh-moo*

Aoi: *ah-oy*

Asagao: *ah-sah-gah-oh*

Atemiya: *ah-te-mee-yah*

aware: *ah-wah-re*

Chūjō: *choo-joh*

Chūnagon: *choo-nah-gohn*

Fujitsubo: *foo-jee-tsoo-boh*

Fujiwara: *foo-jee-wah-rah*

Genji: *gen-jee*

Gojō: *goh-joh*

Gosechi: *goh-se-chee*

Hiei: *hee-ay*

Higekuro: *hee-ge-koo-roh*

Hirohito: *hee-roh-hee-toh*

Hitachi: *hee-tah-chee*

Hotaru: *hoh-tah-roo*

hototogisu: *hoh-toh-toh-gee-soo*

Kamo: *kah-moh*

Kaoru: *kah-oh-roo*

Kashiwagi: *kah-shee-wah-gee*

Kasugano: *kah-soo-gah-noh*

Katano: *kah-tah-noh*

Kii: *kee-ee*

Kokiden: *koh-kee-den*

Koremitsu: *koh-ray-mee-tsoo*

Kumano: *koo-mah-noh*

Kumoinokari: *koo-moy-noh-kah-ree*

Matsushima: *mah-tsoo-shee-mah*

Matsuyama: *mah-tsoo-yah-mah*

Mitake: *mee-tah-ke*

Murasaki Shikibu: *moo-rah-sah-kee shee-kee-boo*

Nakatsukasa: *nah-kah-tsoo-kah-sah*

Nijō: *nee-joh*

Niou: *nee-oh*

Oborozukiyo: *oh-boh-roh-zoo-kee-yoh*

Oe: *oh-ay*

Omyōbu: *oh-myoh-boo*

Reikeiden: *ray-kay-den*

Reizei: *ray-zay*

Rokujō: *roh-koo-joh*

Saishō: *sai-shoh*

Sanjō: *sahn-joh*

Shōnagon: *shoh-nah-gohn*

Shōwa: *shoh-wah*

Sumiyoshi: *soo-mee-yoh-shee*

Tamakazura: *tah-mah-kah-zoo-rah*

Tanabata: *tanh-ah-bah-tah*

Tatsuta: *tah-tsoo-tah*

Tō no Chūjō: *toh no choo-joh*

Uji: *oo-jee*	wasuregusa: *wah-soo-re-goo-sah*
Ukifune: *oo-kee-foo-ne*	Yoshikiyo: *yoh-shee-kee-yoh*
Ukon: *oo-kohn*	Yūgiri: *yoo-gee-ree*
warekara: *wah-re-kah-rah*	Yukihira: *yoo-kee-hee-rah*

From The Tale of Genji[1]

Summary   *The Tale of Genji* opens with the flavor of an old romance, in which the adventure is set in the distant past and the idealized characters dwell in an almost enchanted setting:

> In a certain reign there was a lady not of the first rank whom the emperor loved more than any of the others. The grand ladies with high ambitions thought her a presumptuous upstart, and lesser ladies were still more resentful. Everything she did offended someone. Probably aware of what was happening, she fell seriously ill and came to spend more time at home than at court. The emperor's pity and affection quite passed bounds. No longer caring what his ladies and courtiers might say, he behaved as if intent upon stirring gossip.

In time, a child is born to the woman, which makes the emperor even more devoted, but which also stirs the wrath of her rival, Kokiden, a powerful senior wife. The poor woman is persecuted, and, weakened from the strain, she dies. The emperor is devastated by her death. As solace, he takes some delight in his beautiful and brilliant son. As further solace, he installs in the palace a woman who he has heard bears a striking resemblance to his beloved. This proves true, and the new lady, Fujitsubo, wins the emperor's affections.

Meanwhile, his young son continues to dazzle almost everyone. The emperor would like to designate the boy crown prince, but he lacks political support. Furthermore, a Korean soothsayer warns that disaster will befall the country if the boy becomes emperor. Reluctantly, the emperor decides to reduce his son to the status of a mere subject, albeit a nobleman, ensuring that at least the boy will have an official career. He confers the name *Genji* on his son.

At the age of twelve, Genji undergoes the initiation into manhood. On the night of the initiation ceremonies Genji is married to Aoi, the daughter of a powerful minister of state. She is four years older than Genji, however, and they do not take a fancy to each other. Instead Genji finds himself drawn to Fujitsubo, his father's consort. "He could not remember his own mother," the narrator tells us, "and it moved him deeply to learn, from the lady who had first told the emperor of Fujitsubo, that the resemblance was striking. He wanted to be near her always."

With Genji's marriage off to a rocky start, he occupies the palace apartments that had belonged to his mother. As the handsome young man moves through the court, he becomes known as "the shining Genji."

CHAPTER 2

The Broom Tree

"The shining Genji": it was almost too grand a name. Yet he did not escape criticism for numerous little adventures. It seemed indeed that his

---

1. Translated by and with notes adapted from Edward G. Seidensticker.

indiscretions might give him a name for frivolity, and he did what he could to hide them. But his most secret affairs (such is the malicious work of the gossips) became common talk. If, on the other hand, he were to go through life concerned only for his name and avoid all these interesting and amusing little affairs, then he would be laughed to shame by the likes of the lieutenant of Katano.[2]

Still a guards captain, Genji spent most of his time at the palace, going infrequently to the Sanjō mansion of his father-in-law. The people there feared that he might have been stained by the lavender of Kasugano.[3] Though in fact he had an instinctive dislike for the promiscuity he saw all around him, he had a way of sometimes turning against his own better inclinations and causing unhappiness.

The summer rains came, the court was in retreat, and an even longer interval than usual had passed since his last visit to Sanjō. Though the minister and his family were much put out, they spared no effort to make him feel welcome. The minister's sons were more attentive than to the emperor himself. Genji was on particularly good terms with Tō no Chūjō.[4] They enjoyed music together and more frivolous diversions as well. Tō no Chūjō was of an amorous nature and not at all comfortable in the apartments which his father-in-law, the Minister of the Right,[5] had at great expense provided for him. At Sanjō with his own family, on the other hand, he took very good care of his rooms, and when Genji came and went the two of them were always together. They were a good match for each other in study and at play. Reserve quite disappeared between them.

It had been raining all day. There were fewer courtiers than usual in the royal presence. Back in his own palace quarters, also unusually quiet, Genji pulled a lamp near and sought to while away the time with his books. He had Tō no Chūjō with him. Numerous pieces of colored paper, obviously letters, lay on a shelf. Tō no Chūjō made no attempt to hide his curiosity.

"Well," said Genji, "there are some I might let you see. But there are some I think it better not to."

"You miss the point. The ones I want to see are precisely the ones you want to hide. The ordinary ones—I'm not much of a hand at the game, you know, but even I am up to the ordinary give and take. But the ones from ladies who think you are not doing right by them, who sit alone through an evening and wait for you to come—those are the ones I want to see."

It was not likely that really delicate letters would be left scattered on a

<hr>

2. Evidently the hero of a romance now lost.   3. Alludes to a poem from another tale: "Kasugano lavender stains my robe, / In deep disorder, like my secret loves." (Lavender suggests a romantic affinity.) Note that throughout this translation of *The Tale of Genji* Seidensticker renders the *tanka*, or classical Japanese poem, as an unrhymed couplet. However, these thirty-one-syllable compositions in metric patterns of 5, 7, 5, 7, 7 are conventionally viewed as comprising five lines and are usually so translated. 4. Brother of Genji's wife Aoi; he becomes Genji's closest friend.   5. One of the highest officials in the government. In rank, only the emperor, regent, chancellor, and minister of the left stood above him. The minister of the left was the legal head of government, responsible for the operation of the emperor's cabinet, known as the council of state. When he was absent, the minister of the right assumed his duties. Genji's father-in-law is, therefore, a powerful figure.

shelf, and it may be assumed that the papers treated so carelessly were the less important ones.

"You do have a variety of them," said Tō no Chūjō, reading the correspondence through piece by piece. This will be from her, and this will be from *her*, he would say. Sometimes he guessed correctly and sometimes he was far afield, to Genji's great amusement. Genji was brief with his replies and let out no secrets.

"It is I who should be asking to see *your* collection. No doubt it is huge. When I have seen it I shall be happy to throw my files open to you."

"I fear there is nothing that would interest you." Tō no Chūjō was in a contemplative mood. "It is with women as it is with everything else: the flawless ones are very few indeed. This is a sad fact which I have learned over the years. All manner of women seem presentable enough at first. Little notes, replies to this and that, they all suggest sensibility and cultivation. But when you begin sorting out the really superior ones you find that there are not many who have to be on your list. Each has her little tricks and she makes the most of them, getting in her slights at rivals, so broad sometimes that you almost have to blush. Hidden away by loving parents who build brilliant futures for them, they let word get out of this little talent and that little accomplishment and you are all in a stir. They are young and pretty and amiable and carefree, and in their boredom they begin to pick up a little from their elders, and in the natural course of things they begin to concentrate on one particular hobby and make something of it. A woman tells you all about it and hides the weak points and brings out the strong ones as if they were everything, and you can't very well call her a liar. So you begin keeping company, and it is always the same. The fact is not up to the advance notices."

Tō no Chūjō sighed, a sigh clearly based on experience. Some of what he had said, though not all, accorded with Genji's own experience. "And have you come upon any," said Genji, smiling, "who would seem to have nothing at all to recommend them?"

"Who would be fool enough to notice such a woman? And in any case, I should imagine that women with no merits are as rare as women with no faults. If a woman is of good family and well taken care of, then the things she is less than proud of are hidden and she gets by well enough. When you come to the middle ranks, each woman has her own little inclinations and there are thousands of ways to separate one from another. And when you come to the lowest—well, who really pays much attention?"

He appeared to know everything. Genji was by now deeply interested.

"You speak of three ranks," he said, "but is it so easy to make the division? There are well-born ladies who fall in the world and there are people of no background who rise to the higher ranks and build themselves fine houses as if intended for them all along. How would you fit such people into your system?"

At this point two young courtiers, a guards officer and a functionary in the ministry of rites, appeared on the scene, to attend the emperor in his retreat. Both were devotees of the way of love and both were good talkers. Tō no Chūjō, as if he had been waiting for them, invited their views on

the question that had just been asked. The discussion progressed, and included a number of rather unconvincing points.

"Those who have just arrived at high position," said one of the newcomers, "do not attract the same sort of notice as those who were born to it. And those who were born to the highest rank but somehow do not have the right backing—in spirit they may be as proud and noble as ever, but they cannot hide their deficiencies. And so I think that they should both be put in your middle rank.

"There are those whose families are not quite of the highest rank but who go off and work hard in the provinces. They have their place in the world, though there are all sorts of little differences among them. Some of them would belong on anyone's list. So it is these days. Myself, I would take a woman from a middling family over one who has rank and nothing else. Let us say someone whose father is almost but not quite a councillor. Someone who has a decent enough reputation and comes from a decent enough family and can live in some luxury. Such people can be very pleasant. There is nothing wrong with the household arrangements, and indeed a daughter can sometimes be set out in a way that dazzles you. I can think of several such women it would be hard to find fault with. When they go into court service, they are the ones the unexpected favors have a way of falling on. I have seen cases enough of it, I can tell you."

Genji smiled. "And so a person should limit himself to girls with money?"

"That does not sound like you," said Tō no Chūjō.

"When a woman has the highest rank and a spotless reputation," continued the other, "but something has gone wrong with her upbringing, something is wrong in the way she puts herself forward, you wonder how it can possibly have been allowed to happen. But when all the conditions are right and the girl herself is pretty enough, she is taken for granted. There is no cause for the least surprise. Such ladies are beyond the likes of me, and so I leave them where they are, the highest of the high. There are surprisingly pretty ladies wasting away behind tangles of weeds, and hardly anyone even knows of their existence. The first surprise is hard to forget. There she is, a girl with a fat, sloppy old father and boorish brothers and a house that seems common at best. Off in the women's rooms is a proud lady who has acquired bits and snatches of this and that. You get wind of them, however small the accomplishments may be, and they take hold of your imagination. She is not the equal of the one who has everything, of course, but she has her charm. She is not easy to pass by."

He looked at his companion, the young man from the ministry of rites. The latter was silent, wondering if the reference might be to his sisters, just then coming into their own as subjects for conversation. Genji, it would seem, was thinking that on the highest levels there were sadly few ladies to bestow much thought upon. He was wearing several soft white singlets with an informal court robe thrown loosely over them. As he sat in the lamplight leaning against an armrest, his companions almost wished that he were a woman. Even the "highest of the high" might seem an inadequate match for him.

They talked on, of the varieties of women.

"A man sees women, all manner of them, who seem beyond reproach," said the guards officer, "but when it comes to picking the wife who must be everything, matters are not simple. The emperor has trouble, after all, finding the minister who has all the qualifications. A man may be very wise, but no man can govern by himself. Superior is helped by subordinate, subordinate defers to superior, and so affairs proceed by agreement and concession. But when it comes to choosing the woman who is to be in charge of your house, the qualifications are altogether too many. A merit is balanced by a defect, there is this good point and that bad point, and even women who though not perfect can be made to do are not easy to find. I would not like to have you think me a profligate who has to try them all. But it is a question of the woman who must be everything, and it seems best, other things being equal, to find someone who does not require shaping and training, someone who has most of the qualifications from the start. The man who begins his search with all this in mind must be reconciled to searching for a very long time.

"He comes upon a woman not completely and in every way to his liking but he makes certain promises and finds her hard to give up. The world praises him for his honest heart and begins to note good points in the woman too; and why not? But I have seen them all, and I doubt that there are any genuinely superior specimens among them. What about you gentlemen so far above us? How is it with you when you set out to choose your ladies?

"There are those who are young enough and pretty enough and who take care of themselves as if no particle of dust were allowed to fall upon them. When they write letters they choose the most inoffensive words, and the ink is so faint a man can scarcely read them. He goes to visit, hoping for a real answer. She keeps him waiting and finally lets him have a word or two in an almost inaudible whisper. They are clever, I can tell you, at hiding their defects.

"The soft, feminine ones are likely to assume a great deal. The man seeks to please, and the result is that the woman is presently looking elsewhere. That is the first difficulty in a woman.

"In the most important matter, the matter of running his household, a man can find that his wife has too much sensibility, an elegant word and device for every occasion. But what of the too domestic sort, the wife who bustles around the house the whole day long, her hair tucked up behind her ears, no attention to her appearance, making sure that everything is in order? There are things on his mind, things he has seen and heard in his comings and goings, the private and public demeanor of his colleagues, happy things and sad things. Is he to talk of them to an outsider? Of course not. He would much prefer someone near at hand, someone who will immediately understand. A smile passes over his face, tears well up. Or some event at court has angered him, things are too much for him. What good is it to talk to such a woman? He turns his back on her, and smiles, and sighs, and murmurs something to himself. 'I beg your pardon?' she says, finally noticing. Her blank expression is hardly what he is looking for.

"When a man picks a gentle, childlike wife, he of course must see to

training her and making up for her inadequacies. Even if at times she seems a bit unsteady, he may feel that his efforts have not been wasted. When she is there beside him her gentle charm makes him forget her defects. But when he is away and sends asking her to perform various services, it becomes clear, however small the service, that she has no thoughts of her own in the matter. Her uselessness can be trying.

"I wonder if a woman who is a bit chilly and unfeeling cannot at times seem preferable."

His manner said that he had known them all; and he sighed at his inability to hand down a firm decision.

"No, let us not worry too much about rank and beauty. Let us be satisfied if a woman is not too demanding and eccentric. It is best to settle on a quiet, steady girl. If she proves to have unusual talent and discrimination—well, count them an unexpected premium. Do not, on the other hand, worry too much about remedying her defects. If she seems steady and not given to tantrums, then the charms will emerge of their own accord.

"There are those who display a womanly reticence to the world, as if they had never heard of complaining. They seem utterly calm. And then when their thoughts are too much for them they leave behind the most horrendous notes, the most flamboyant poems, the sort of keepsakes certain to call up dreadful memories, and off they go into the mountains or to some remote seashore. When I was a child I would hear the women reading romantic stories, and I would join them in their sniffling and think it all very sad, all very profound and moving. Now I am afraid that it suggests certain pretenses.

"It is very stupid really, to run off and leave a perfectly kind and sympathetic man. He may have been guilty of some minor dereliction, but to run off with no understanding at all of his true feelings, with no purpose other than to attract attention and hope to upset him—it is an unpleasant sort of memory to have to live with. She gets drunk with admiration for herself and there she is, a nun. When she enters her convent she is sure that she has found enlightenment and has no regrets for the vulgar world.

"Her women come to see her. 'How very touching,' they say. 'How brave of you.'

"But she no longer feels quite as pleased with herself. The man, who has not lost his affection for her, hears of what has happened and weeps, and certain of her old attendants pass this intelligence on to her. 'He is a man of great feeling, you see. What a pity that it should have come to this.' The woman can only brush aside her newly cropped hair to reveal a face on the edge of tears. She tries to hold them back and cannot, such are her regrets for the life she has left behind; and the Buddha is not likely to think her one who has cleansed her heart of passion. Probably she is in more danger of brimstone now in this fragile vocation than if she had stayed with us in our sullied world.

"The bond between husband and wife is a strong one. Suppose the man had hunted her out and brought her back. The memory of her acts would still be there, and inevitably, sooner or later, it would be cause for rancor. When there are crises, incidents, a woman should try to overlook them,

for better or for worse, and make the bond into something durable. The wounds will remain, with the woman and with the man, when there are crises such as I have described. It is very foolish for a woman to let a little dalliance upset her so much that she shows her resentment openly. He has his adventures—but if he has fond memories of their early days together, his and hers, she may be sure that she matters. A commotion means the end of everything. She should be quiet and generous, and when something comes up that quite properly arouses her resentment she should make it known by delicate hints. The man will feel guilty and with tactful guidance he will mend his ways. Too much lenience can make a woman seem charmingly docile and trusting, but it can also make her seem somewhat wanting in substance. We have had instances enough of boats abandoned to the winds and waves. Do you not agree?"

Tō no Chūjō nodded. "It may be difficult when someone you are especially fond of, someone beautiful and charming, has been guilty of an indiscretion, but magnanimity produces wonders. They may not always work, but generosity and reasonableness and patience do on the whole seem best."

His own sister was a case in point, he was thinking, and he was somewhat annoyed to note that Genji was silent because he had fallen asleep. Meanwhile the young guards officer talked on, a dedicated student of his subject. Tō no Chūjō was determined to hear him out.

"Let us make some comparisons," said the guardsman. "Let us think of the cabinetmaker. He shapes pieces as he feels like shaping them. They may be only playthings, with no real plan or pattern. They may all the same have a certain style for what they are—they may take on a certain novelty as times change and be very interesting. But when it comes to the genuine object, something of such undeniable value that a man wants to have it always with him—the perfection of the form announces that it is from the hand of a master.

"Or let us look at painting. There are any number of masters in the academy. It is not easy to separate the good from the bad among those who work on the basic sketches. But let color be added. The painter of things no one ever sees, of paradises, of fish in angry seas, raging beasts in foreign lands, devils and demons—the painter abandons himself to his fancies and paints to terrify and astonish. What does it matter if the results seem somewhat remote from real life? It is not so with the things we know, mountains, streams, houses near and like our own. The soft, unspoiled, wooded hills must be painted layer on layer, the details added gently, quietly, to give a sense of affectionate familiarity. And the foreground too, the garden inside the walls, the arrangement of the stones and grasses and waters. It is here that the master has his own power. There are details a lesser painter cannot imitate.

"Or let us look at calligraphy. A man without any great skill can stretch out this line and that in the cursive style and give an appearance of boldness and distinction. The man who has mastered the principles and writes with concentration may, on the other hand, have none of the eyecatching tricks; but when you take the trouble to compare the two the real thing is the real thing.

"So it is with trivialities like painting and calligraphy. How much more so with matters of the heart! I put no trust in the showy sort of affection that is quick to come forth when a suitable occasion presents itself. Let me tell you of something that happened to me a long time ago. You may find the story a touch wanton, but hear me through all the same."

He drew close to Genji, who awoke from his slumber. Tō no Chūjō, chin in hand, sat opposite, listening with the greatest admiration and attention. There was in the young man's manner something slightly comical, as if he were a sage expostulating upon the deepest truths of the universe, but at such times a young man is not inclined to conceal his most intimate secrets.

"It happened when I was very young, hardly more than a page. I was attracted to a woman. She was of a sort I have mentioned before, not the most beautiful in the world. In my youthful frivolity, I did not at first think of making her my wife. She was someone to visit, not someone who deserved my full attention. Other places interested me more. She was violently jealous. If only she could be a little more understanding, I thought, wanting to be away from the interminable quarreling. And on the other hand it sometimes struck me as a little sad that she should be so worried about a man of so little account as myself. In the course of time I began to mend my ways.

"For my sake, she would try to do things for which her talent and nature did not suit her, and she was determined not to seem inferior even in matters for which she had no great aptitude. She served me diligently in everything. She did not want to be guilty of the smallest thing that might go against my wishes. I had at first thought her rather strong-willed, but she proved to be docile and pliant. She thought constantly about hiding her less favorable qualities, afraid that they might put me off, and she did what she could to avoid displaying herself and causing me embarrassment. She was a model of devotion. In a word, there was nothing wrong with her—save the one thing I found so trying.

"I told myself that she was devoted to the point of fear, and that if I led her to think I might be giving her up she might be a little less suspicious and given to nagging. I had had almost all I could stand. If she really wanted to be with me and I suggested that a break was near, then she might reform. I behaved with studied coldness, and when, as always, her resentment exploded, I said to her: 'Not even the strongest bond between husband and wife can stand an unlimited amount of this sort of thing. It will eventually break, and he will not see her again. If you want to bring matters to such a pass, then go on doubting me as you have. If you would like to be with me for the years that lie ahead of us, then bear the trials as they come, difficult though they may be, and think them the way of the world. If you manage to overcome your jealousy, my affection is certain to grow. It seems likely that I will move ahead into an office of some distinction, and you will go with me and have no one you need think of as a rival.' I was very pleased with myself. I had performed brilliantly as a preceptor.

"But she only smiled. 'Oh, it won't be all that much trouble to put up with your want of consequence and wait till you are important. It will be

much harder to pass the months and the years in the barely discernible hope that you will settle down and mend your fickle ways. Maybe you are right. Maybe this is the time to part.'

"I was furious, and I said so, and she answered in kind. Then, suddenly, she took my hand and bit my finger.

"I reproved her somewhat extravagantly. 'You insult me, and now you have wounded me. Do you think I can go to court like this? I am, as you say, a person of no consequence, and now, mutilated as I am, what is to help me get ahead in the world? There is nothing left for me but to become a monk.' That meeting must be our last, I said, and departed, flexing my wounded finger.

> " 'I count them over, the many things between us.
> One finger does not, alas, count the sum of your failures.'

"I left the verse behind, adding that now she had nothing to complain about.

"She had a verse of her own. There were tears in her eyes.

> " 'I have counted them up myself, be assured, my failures.
> For one bitten finger must all be bitten away?'

"I did not really mean to leave her, but my days were occupied in wanderings here and there, and I sent her no message. Then, late one evening toward the end of the year — it was an evening of rehearsals for the Kamo festival — a sleet was falling as we all started for home. Home. It came to me that I really had nowhere to go but her house. It would be no pleasure to sleep alone at the palace, and if I visited a woman of sensibility I would be kept freezing while she admired the snow. I would go look in upon *her*, and see what sort of mood she might be in. And so, brushing away the sleet, I made my way to her house. I felt just a little shy, but told myself that the sleet melting from my coat should melt her resentment. There was a dim light turned toward the wall, and a comfortable old robe of thick silk lay spread out to warm. The curtains were raised, everything suggested that she was waiting for me. I felt that I had done rather well.

"But she was nowhere in sight. She had gone that evening to stay with her parents, said the women who had been left behind. I had been feeling somewhat unhappy that she had maintained such a chilly silence, sending no amorous poems or queries. I wondered, though not very seriously, whether her shrillness and her jealousy might not have been intended for the precise purpose of disposing of me; but now I found clothes laid out with more attention to color and pattern than usual, exactly as she knew I liked them. She was seeing to my needs even now that I had apparently discarded her.

"And so, despite this strange state of affairs, I was convinced that she did not mean to do without me. I continued to send messages, and she neither protested nor gave an impression of wanting to annoy me by staying out of sight, and in her answers she was always careful not to anger or hurt me. Yet she went on saying that she could not forgive the behavior I had been guilty of in the past. If I would settle down she would be very happy to keep company with me. Sure that we would not part, I thought I would

give her another lesson or two. I told her I had no intention of reforming, and made a great show of independence. She was sad, I gathered, and then without warning she died. And the game I had been playing came to seem rather inappropriate.

"She was a woman of such accomplishments that I could leave everything to her. I continue to regret what I had done. I could discuss trivial things with her and important things. For her skills in dyeing she might have been compared to Princess Tatsuta and the comparison would not have seemed ridiculous, and in sewing she could have held her own with Princess Tanabata."[6]

The young man sighed and sighed again.

Tō no Chūjō nodded. "Leaving her accomplishments as a seamstress aside, I should imagine you were looking for someone as faithful as Princess Tanabata.[7] And if she could embroider like Princess Tatsuta, well, it does not seem likely that you will come on her equal again. When the colors of a robe do not match the seasons, the flowers of spring and the autumn tints, when they are somehow vague and muddy, then the whole effort is as futile as the dew. So it is with women. It is not easy in this world to find a perfect wife. We are all pursuing the ideal and failing to find it."

The guards officer talked on. "There was another one. I was seeing her at about the same time. She was more amiable than the one I have just described to you. Everything about her told of refinement. Her poems, her handwriting when she dashed off a letter, the koto[8] she plucked a note on—everything seemed right. She was clever with her hands and clever with words. And her looks were adequate. The jealous woman's house had come to seem the place I could really call mine, and I went in secret to the other woman from time to time and became very fond of her. The jealous one died, I wondered what to do next. I was sad, of course, but a man cannot go on being sad forever. I visited the other more often. But there was something a little too aggressive, a little too sensuous about her. As I came to know her well and to think her a not very dependable sort, I called less often. And I learned that I was not her only secret visitor.

"One bright moonlit autumn night I chanced to leave court with a friend. He got in with me as I started for my father's. He was much concerned, he said, about a house where he was sure someone would be waiting. It happened to be on my way.

"Through gaps in a neglected wall I could see the moon shining on a pond. It seemed a pity not to linger a moment at a spot where the moon seemed so much at home, and so I climbed out after my friend. It would appear that this was not his first visit. He proceeded briskly to the veranda and took a seat near the gate and looked up at the moon for a time. The chrysanthemums were at their best, very slightly touched by the frost, and the red leaves were beautiful in the autumn wind. He took out a flute and played a tune on it, and sang 'The Well of Asuka'[9] and several other songs. Blending nicely with the flute came the mellow tones of a Japanese koto. It had been tuned in advance, apparently, and was waiting. The *ritsu*

6. The goddess Tanabata was the patron of sewing and weaving. Tatsuta was the patron of autumn and, therefore, of dyeing.   7. Tanabata and her lover the Herdsman (the stars Altair and Vega) met annually on the seventh night of the Seventh Month.   8. A thirteen-stringed zither.   9. A folk song.

scale[1] had a pleasant modern sound to it, right for a soft, womanly touch from behind blinds, and right for the clear moonlight too. I can assure you that the effect was not at all unpleasant.

"Delighted, my friend went up to the blinds.

" 'I see that no one has yet broken a path through your fallen leaves,' he said, somewhat sarcastically. He broke off a chrysanthemum and pushed it under the blinds.

> " 'Uncommonly fine this house, for moon, for koto.
> Does it bring to itself indifferent callers as well?

> " 'Excuse me for asking. You must not be parsimonious with your music. You have a by no means indifferent listener.'

"He was very playful indeed. The woman's voice, when she offered a verse of her own, was suggestive and equally playful.

> " 'No match the leaves for the angry winter winds.
> Am I to detain the flute that joins those winds?'

"Naturally unaware of resentment so near at hand, she changed to a Chinese koto in an elegant *banjiki*.[2] Though I had to admit that she had talent, I was very annoyed. It is amusing enough, if you let things go no further, to exchange jokes from time to time with fickle and frivolous ladies; but as a place to take seriously, even for an occasional visit, matters here seemed to have gone too far. I made the events of that evening my excuse for leaving her.

"I see, as I look back on the two affairs, that young though I was the second of the two women did not seem the kind to put my trust in. I have no doubt that the wariness will grow as the years go by. The dear, uncertain ones—the dew that will fall when the *hagi*[3] branch is bent, the speck of frost that will melt when it is lifted from the bamboo leaf—no doubt they can be interesting for a time. You have seven years to go before you are my age," he said to Genji. "Just wait and you will understand. Perhaps you can take the advice of a person of no importance, and avoid the uncertain ones. They stumble sooner or later, and do a man's name no good when they do."

Tō no Chūjō nodded, as always. Genji, though he only smiled, seemed to agree.

"Neither of the tales you have given us has been a very happy one," he said.

"Let me tell you a story about a foolish woman I once knew," said Tō no Chūjō. "I was seeing her in secret, and I did not think that the affair was likely to last very long. But she was very beautiful, and as time passed I came to think that I must go on seeing her, if only infrequently. I sensed that she had come to depend on me. I expected signs of jealousy. There were none. She did not seem to feel the resentment a man expects from a woman he visits so seldom. She waited quietly, morning and night. My affection grew, and I let it be known that she did indeed have a man she

---

1. A pentatonic scale (that is, having five tones to an octave), resembling the Western minor without its half-steps.   2. The note B in ancient Japanese music.   3. Japanese bush clover.

could depend on. There was something very appealing about her (she was an orphan), letting me know that I was all she had.

"She seemed content. Untroubled, I stayed away for rather a long time. Then—I heard of it only later—my wife found a roundabout way to be objectionable. I did not know that I had become a cause of pain. I had not forgotten, but I let a long time pass without writing. The woman was desperately lonely and worried for the child she had borne. One day she sent me a letter attached to a wild carnation." His voice trembled.

"And what did it say?" Genji urged him on.

"Nothing very remarkable. I do remember her poem, though:

> " 'The fence of the mountain rustic may fall to the ground.
> Rest gently, O dew, upon the wild carnation.'

"I went to see her again. The talk was open and easy, as always, but she seemed pensive as she looked out at the dewy garden from the neglected house. She seemed to be weeping, joining her laments to the songs of the autumn insects. It could have been a scene from an old romance. I whispered a verse:

> " 'No bloom in this wild array would I wish to slight.
> But dearest of all to me is the wild carnation.'

"Her carnation had been the child. I made it clear that my own was the lady herself, the wild carnation no dust falls upon.[4]

"She answered:

> " 'Dew wets the sleeve that brushes the wild carnation.
> The tempest rages. Now comes autumn too.'

"She spoke quietly all the same, and she did not seem really angry. She did shed a tear from time to time, but she seemed ashamed of herself, and anxious to avoid difficult moments. I went away feeling much relieved. It was clear that she did not want to show any sign of anger at my neglect. And so once more I stayed away for rather a long time.

"And when I looked in on her again she had disappeared.

"If she is still living, it must be in very unhappy circumstances. She need not have suffered so if she had asserted herself a little more in the days when we were together. She need not have put up with my absences, and I would have seen to her needs over the years. The child was a very pretty little girl. I was fond of her, and I have not been able to find any trace of her.

"She must be listed among your reticent ones, I suppose? She let me have no hint of jealousy. Unaware of what was going on, I had no intention of giving her up. But the result was hopeless yearning, quite as if I had given her up. I am beginning to forget; and how is it with her? She must remember me sometimes, I should think, with regret, because she must remember too that it was not I who abandoned her. She was, I fear, not the sort of woman one finds it possible to keep for very long.

---

4. Alludes to a poem in *The Kokinshū:* "Let no dust fall upon the wild carnation, / Upon the couch where lie my love and I." For the pink, or wild, carnation, she has used a word that can also mean "child." He has shifted to a synonym, the first two syllables of which mean "bed."

"Your jealous woman must be interesting enough to remember, but she must have been a bit wearying. And the other one, all her skill on the koto cannot have been much compensation for the undependability. And the one I have described to you—her very lack of jealousy might have brought a suspicion that there was another man in her life. Well, such is the way with the world—you cannot give your unqualified approval to any of them. Where are you to go for the woman who has no defects and who combines the virtues of all three? You might choose Our Lady of Felicity[5]—and find yourself married to unspeakable holiness."

The others laughed.

Tō no Chūjō turned to the young man from the ministry of rites. "You must have interesting stories too."

"Oh, please. How could the lowest of the low hope to hold your attention?"

"You must not keep us waiting."

"Let me think a minute." He seemed to be sorting out memories. "When I was still a student I knew a remarkably wise woman. She was the sort worth consulting about public affairs, and she had a good mind too for the little tangles that come into your private life. Her erudition would have put any ordinary sage to shame. In a word, I was awed into silence.

"I was studying under a learned scholar. I had heard that he had many daughters, and on some occasion or other I had made the acquaintance of this one. The father learned of the affair. Taking out wedding cups, he made reference, among other things, to a Chinese poem about the merits of an impoverished wife.[6] Although not exactly enamored of the woman, I had developed a certain fondness for her, and felt somewhat deferential toward the father. She was most attentive to my needs. I learned many estimable things from her, to add to my store of erudition and help me with my work. Her letters were lucidity itself, in the purest Chinese. None of this Japanese nonsense for her. I found it hard to think of giving her up, and under her tutelage I managed to turn out a few things in passable Chinese myself. And yet—though I would not wish to seem wanting in gratitude, it is undeniable that a man of no learning is somewhat daunted at the thought of being forever his wife's inferior. So it is in any case with an ignorant one like me; and what possible use could you gentlemen have for so formidable a wife? A stupid, senseless affair, a man tells himself, and yet he is dragged on against his will, as if there might have been a bond in some other life."

"She seems a most unusual woman." Genji and Tō no Chūjō were eager to hear more.

Quite aware that the great gentlemen were amusing themselves at his expense, he smiled somewhat impishly. "One day when I had not seen her for rather a long time I had some reason or other for calling. She was not in the room where we had been in the habit of meeting. She insisted on talking to me through a very obtrusive screen. I thought she might be sulking, and it all seemed very silly. And then again—if she was going to be so petty, I might have my excuse for leaving her. But no. She was not

---

5. A Buddhist deity who confers happiness and virtue.   6. *On Marriage*, a poem by Po Chü-i (772–846), the first of *Ten Poems Composed at Ch'ang-an.*

a person to let her jealousy show. She knew too much of the world. Her explanation of what was happening poured forth at great length, all of it very well reasoned.

" 'I have been indisposed with a malady known as coryza.[7] Discommoded to an uncommon degree, I have been imbibing of a steeped potion made from bulbaceous herbs. Because of the noisome odor, I will not find it possible to admit of greater propinquity. If you have certain random matters for my attention, perhaps you can deposit the relevant materials where you are.'

" 'Is that so?' I said. I could think of nothing else to say.

"I started to leave. Perhaps feeling a little lonely, she called after me, somewhat shrilly. "When I have disencumbered myself of this aroma, we can meet once more.'

"It seemed cruel to rush off, but the time was not right for a quiet visit. And it was as she said: her odor was rather high. Again I started out, pausing long enough to compose a verse:

" 'The spider[8] must have told you I would come.
      Then why am I asked to keep company with garlic?'

"I did not take time to accuse her of deliberately putting me off.

"She was quicker than I. She chased after me with an answer.

" 'Were we two who kept company every night,
      What would be wrong with garlic in the daytime?'[9]

"You must admit she was quick with her answers." He had quietly finished his story.

The two gentlemen, Genji and his friend, would have none of it. "A complete fabrication, from start to finish. Where could you find such a woman? Better to have a quiet evening with a witch." They thought it an outrageous story, and asked if he could come up with nothing more acceptable.

"Surely you would not wish for a more unusual sort of story?"

The guards officer took up again. "In women as in men, there is no one worse than the one who tries to display her scanty knowledge in full. It is among the least endearing of accomplishments for a woman to have delved into the Three Histories and the Five Classics;[1] and who, on the other hand, can go through life without absorbing something of public affairs and private? A reasonably alert woman does not need to be a scholar to see and hear a great many things. The very worst are the ones who scribble off Chinese characters at such a rate that they fill a good half of letters where they are most out of place, letters to other women. 'What a bore,' you say. 'If only she had mastered a few of the feminine things.' She cannot of course intend it to be so, but the words read aloud seem muscular and unyielding, and in the end hopelessly mannered. I fear that even our highest of the high are too often guilty of the fault.

7. That is, the common cold, which she would have said if she were not flaunting her superior knowledge.   8. It was believed that a busy spider foretold a visit from one's lover.   9. The word for "daytime" is homophonous with a word for numbers of strongly scented roots.   1. Ancient Chinese histories and the canonical works of early Chinese thought: *The Book of Poetry, The Book of History, The Book of Divination (I Ching), Spring and Autumn Annals,* and *The Book of Rites.*

"Then there is the one who fancies herself a poetess. She immerses herself in the anthologies, and brings antique references into her very first line, interesting enough in themselves but inappropriate. A man has had enough with that first line, but he is called heartless if he does not answer, and cannot claim the honors if he does not answer in a similar vein. On the Day of the Iris he is frantic to get off to court and has no eye for irises, and there she is with subtle references to iris roots. On the Day of the Chrysanthemum,[2] his mind has no room for anything but the Chinese poem he must come up with in the course of the day, and there she is with something about the dew upon the chrysanthemum. A poem that might have been amusing and even moving on a less frantic day has been badly timed and must therefore be rejected. A woman who dashes off a poem at an unpoetic moment cannot be called a woman of taste.

"For someone who is not alive to the particular quality of each moment and each occasion, it is safer not to make a great show of taste and elegance; and from someone who is alive to it all, a man wants restraint. She should feign a certain ignorance, she should keep back a little of what she is prepared to say."

Through all the talk Genji's thoughts were on a single lady. His heart was filled with her. She answered every requirement, he thought. She had none of the defects, was guilty of none of the excesses, that had emerged from the discussion.

The talk went on and came to no conclusion, and as the rainy night gave way to dawn the stories became more and more improbable.

It appeared that the weather would be fine. Fearing that his father-in-law might resent his secluding himself in the palace, Genji set off for Sanjō. The mansion itself, his wife—every detail was admirable and in the best of taste. Nowhere did he find a trace of disorder. Here was a lady whom his friends must count among the truly dependable ones, the indispensable ones. And yet—she was too finished in her perfection, she was so cool and self-possessed that she made him uncomfortable. He turned to playful conversation with Chūnagon and Nakatsukasa and other pretty young women among her attendants. Because it was very warm, he loosened his dress, and they thought him even handsomer.

The minister came to pay his respects. Seeing Genji thus in dishabille, he made his greetings from behind a conveniently placed curtain. Though somewhat annoyed at having to receive such a distinguished visitor on such a warm day, Genji made it clear to the women that they were not to smile at his discomfort. He was a very calm, self-possessed young gentleman.

As evening approached, the women reminded him that his route from the palace had transgressed upon the domain of the Lord of the Center.[3] He must not spend the night here.

"To be sure. But my own house lies in the same direction. And I am

2. The Day of the Chrysanthemum fell on the ninth of the Ninth Month. The Day of the Iris fell on the fifth of the Fifth Month.   3. A god who changed his abode periodically and did not permit trespassers. Superstition influenced many aspects of Japanese life in the 11th century, with directional taboos among the most important. There were three main types of directional taboo. The northeast was regarded as a perpetually unlucky direction. Other directions were unfavorable during certain periods of one's life, so that at sixteen, for example, one might have to avoid the northwest. Still other directions

very tired." He lay down as if he meant in spite of everything to stay the night.

"It simply will not do, my lord."

"The governor of Kii here," said one of Genji's men, pointing to another. "He has dammed the Inner River[4] and brought it into his garden, and the waters are very cool, very pleasant."

"An excellent idea. I really am very tired, and perhaps we can send ahead to see whether we might drive into the garden."

There were no doubt all sorts of secret places to which he could have gone to avoid the taboo. He had come to Sanjō, and after a considerable absence. The minister might suspect that he had purposely chosen a night on which he must leave early.

The governor of Kii was cordial enough with his invitation, but when he withdrew he mentioned certain misgivings to Genji's men. Ritual purification,[5] he said, had required all the women to be away from his father's house, and unfortunately they were all crowded into his own, a cramped enough place at best. He feared that Genji would be inconvenienced.

"Nothing of the sort," said Genji, who had overheard. "It is good to have people around. There is nothing worse than a night away from home with no ladies about. Just let me have a little corner behind their curtains."

"If that is what you want," said his men, "then the governor's place should be perfect."

And so they sent runners ahead. Genji set off immediately, though in secret, thinking that no great ceremony was called for. He did not tell the minister where he was going, and took only his nearest retainers. The governor grumbled that they were in rather too much of a hurry. No one listened.

The east rooms of the main hall had been cleaned and made presentable. The waters were as they had been described, a most pleasing arrangement. A fence of wattles, of a deliberately rustic appearance, enclosed the garden, and much care had gone into the plantings. The wind was cool. Insects were humming, one scarcely knew where, fireflies drew innumerable lines of light, and all in all the time and the place could not have been more to his liking. His men were already tippling, out where they could admire a brook flowing under a gallery. The governor seemed to have "hurried off for viands."[6] Gazing calmly about him, Genji concluded that the house would be of the young guardsman's favored in-between category. Having heard that his host's stepmother, who would be in residence, was a high-spirited lady, he listened for signs of her presence. There were signs of someone's presence immediately to the west. He heard a swishing of silk and young voices that were not at all displeasing. Young ladies seemed to be giggling self-consciously and trying to contain themselves. The shutters were raised, it seemed, but upon a word from the governor they were lowered. There was a faint light over the sliding doors. Genji

---

were universally but temporarily inauspicious, caused by the transit of deities, whose descent from the heavens could close a sector to human traffic. A taboo of the third category is what affects Genji on this evening.   4. Marks the eastern limits of the capital.   5. Various purification rituals were conducted to ward off bad luck and to remove the polluting effects of sickness or a death in the family.   6. Reference to a folk song: "The jeweled flask is here. / But where is our host, what of our host? / He has hurried off for viands, / Off to the beach for viands, / To Koyurugi for seaweed."

went for a look, but could find no opening large enough to see through. Listening for a time, he concluded that the women had gathered in the main room, next to his.

The whispered discussion seemed to be about Genji himself.

"He is dreadfully serious, they say, and has made a fine match for himself. And still so young. Don't you imagine he might be a little lonely? But they say he finds time for a quiet little adventure now and then."

Genji was startled. There was but one lady on his mind, day after day. So this was what the gossips were saying; and what if, in it all, there was evidence that rumors of his real love had spread abroad? But the talk seemed harmless enough, and after a time he wearied of it. Someone misquoted a poem he had sent to his cousin Asagao,[7] attached to a morning glory. Their standards seemed not of the most rigorous. A misquoted poem for every occasion. He feared he might be disappointed when he saw the woman.

The governor had more lights set out at the eaves, and turned up those in the room. He had refreshments brought.

"And are the curtains all hung?"[8] asked Genji. "You hardly qualify as a host if they are not."

"And what will you feast upon?" rejoined the governor, somewhat stiffly. "Nothing so very elaborate, I fear."

Genji found a cool place out near the veranda and lay down. His men were quiet. Several young boys were present, all very sprucely dressed, sons of the host and of his father, the governor of Iyo.[9] There was one particularly attractive lad of perhaps twelve or thirteen. Asking who were the sons of whom, Genji learned that the boy was the younger brother of the host's stepmother, son of a guards officer no longer living. His father had had great hopes for the boy and had died while he was still very young. He had come to this house upon his sister's marriage to the governor of Iyo. He seemed to have some aptitude for the classics, said the host, and was of a quiet, pleasant disposition; but he was young and without backing, and his prospects at court were not good.

"A pity. The sister, then, is your stepmother?"

"Yes."

"A very young stepmother. My father had thought of inviting her to court. He was asking just the other day what might have happened to her. Life," he added with a solemnity rather beyond his years, "is uncertain."

"It happened almost by accident. Yes, you are right: it is a very uncertain world, and it always has been, particularly for women. They are like bits of driftwood."

"Your father is no doubt very alert to her needs. Perhaps, indeed, one has trouble knowing who is the master?"

"He quite worships her. The rest of us are not entirely happy with the arrangements he has made."

"But you cannot expect him to let you young gallants have everything.

---

7. The word for various morning flowers, including the morning glory.   8. Reference to a folk song: "The curtains all are hung. / Come and be my bridegroom. / And what will you feast upon? / Abalone, turbo, / And sea urchins too."   9. He is sometimes called the governor and sometimes the vice governor.

He has a name in that regard himself, you know. And where might the lady be?"

"They have all been told to spend the night in the porter's lodge, but they don't seem in a hurry to go."

The wine was having its effect, and his men were falling asleep on the veranda.

Genji lay wide awake, not pleased at the prospect of sleeping alone. He sensed that there was someone in the room to the north. It would be the lady of whom they had spoken. Holding his breath, he went to the door and listened.

"Where are you?" The pleasantly husky voice was that of the boy who had caught his eye.

"Over here." It would be the sister. The two voices, very sleepy, resembled each other. "And where is our guest? I had thought he might be somewhere near, but he seems to have gone away."

"He's in the east room." The boy's voice was low. "I saw him. He is every bit as handsome as everyone says."

"If it were daylight I might have a look at him myself." The sister yawned, and seemed to draw the bedclothes over her face.

Genji was a little annoyed. She might have questioned her brother more energetically.

"I'll sleep out toward the veranda. But we should have more light." The boy turned up the lamp. The lady apparently lay at a diagonal remove from Genji. "And where is Chūjō? I don't like being left alone."

"She went to have a bath. She said she'd be right back." He spoke from out near the veranda.

All was quiet again. Genji slipped the latch open and tried the doors. They had not been bolted. A curtain had been set up just inside, and in the dim light he could make out Chinese chests and other furniture scattered in some disorder. He made his way through to her side. She lay by herself, a slight little figure. Though vaguely annoyed at being disturbed, she evidently took him for the woman Chūjō until he pulled back the covers.

"I heard you summoning a captain," he said, "and I thought my prayers over the months had been answered."[1]

She gave a little gasp. It was muffled by the bedclothes and no one else heard.

"You are perfectly correct if you think me unable to control myself. But I wish you to know that I have been thinking of you for a very long time. And the fact that I have finally found my opportunity and am taking advantage of it should show that my feelings are by no means shallow."

His manner was so gently persuasive that devils and demons could not have gainsaid him. The lady would have liked to announce to the world that a strange man had invaded her boudoir.

"I think you have mistaken me for someone else," she said, outraged, though the remark was under her breath.

---

1. *Chūjō* means "captain," the rank Genji holds. Women's names were often derived from the titles of their fathers; hence the lady's companion is called Chūjō.

The little figure, pathetically fragile and as if on the point of expiring from the shock, seemed to him very beautiful.

"I am driven by thoughts so powerful that a mistake is completely out of the question. It is cruel of you to pretend otherwise. I promise you that I will do nothing unseemly. I must ask you to listen to a little of what is on my mind."

She was so small that he lifted her easily. As he passed through the doors to his own room, he came upon the Chūjō who had been summoned earlier. He called out in surprise. Surprised in turn, Chūjō peered into the darkness. The perfume that came from his robes like a cloud of smoke told her who he was. She stood in confusion, unable to speak. Had he been a more ordinary intruder she might have ripped her mistress away by main force. But she would not have wished to raise an alarm all through the house.

She followed after, but Genji was quite unmoved by her pleas.

"Come for her in the morning," he said, sliding the doors closed.

The lady was bathed in perspiration and quite beside herself at the thought of what Chūjō, and the others too, would be thinking. Genji had to feel sorry for her. Yet the sweet words poured forth, the whole gamut of pretty devices for making a woman surrender.

She was not to be placated. "Can it be true? Can I be asked to believe that you are not making fun of me? Women of low estate should have husbands of low estate."

He was sorry for her and somewhat ashamed of himself, but his answer was careful and sober. "You take me for one of the young profligates you see around? I must protest. I am very young and know nothing of the estates which concern you so. You have heard of me, surely, and you must know that I do not go in for adventures. I must ask what unhappy entanglement imposes this upon me. You are making a fool of me, and nothing should surprise me, not even the tumultuous emotions that do in fact surprise me."

But now his very splendor made her resist. He might think her obstinate and insensitive, but her unfriendliness must make him dismiss her from further consideration. Naturally soft and pliant, she was suddenly firm. It was as with the young bamboo: she bent but was not to be broken. She was weeping. He had his hands full but would not for the world have missed the experience.

"Why must you so dislike me?" he asked with a sigh, unable to stop the weeping. "Don't you know that the unexpected encounters are the ones we were fated for? Really, my dear, you do seem to know altogether too little of the world."

"If I had met you before I came to this," she replied, and he had to admit the truth of it, "then I might have consoled myself with the thought—it might have been no more than self-deception, of course— that you would someday come to think fondly of me. But this is hopeless, worse than I can tell you. Well, it has happened. Say no to those who ask if you have seen me."[2]

2. An allusion to a poem in *The Kokinshū*: "As one small mark of your love, if such there be, / Say no to those who ask if you have seen me."

One may imagine that he found many kind promises with which to comfort her.

The first cock was crowing and Genji's men were awake.

"Did you sleep well? I certainly did."

"Let's get the carriage ready."

Some of the women were heard asking whether people who were avoiding taboos were expected to leave again in the middle of the night.

Genji was very unhappy. He feared he could not find an excuse for another meeting. He did not see how he could visit her, and he did not see how they could write. Chūjō came out, also very unhappy. He let the lady go and then took her back again.

"How shall I write to you? Your feelings and my own—they are not shallow, and we may expect deep memories. Has anything ever been so strange?" He was in tears, which made him yet handsomer. The cocks were now crowing insistently. He was feeling somewhat harried as he composed his farewell verse:

"Why must they startle with their dawn alarums
When hours are yet required to thaw the ice?"

The lady was ashamed of herself that she had caught the eye of a man so far above her. His kind words had little effect. She was thinking of her husband, whom for the most part she considered a clown and a dolt. She trembled to think that a dream might have told him of the night's happenings.

This was the verse with which she replied:

"Day has broken without an end to my tears.
To my cries of sorrow are added the calls of the cocks."

It was lighter by the moment. He saw her to her door, for the house was coming to life. A barrier had fallen between them. In casual court dress, he leaned for a time against the south railing and looked out at the garden. Shutters were being raised along the west side of the house. Women seemed to be looking out at him, beyond a low screen at the veranda. He no doubt brought shivers of delight. The moon still bright in the dawn sky added to the beauty of the morning. The sky, without heart itself, can at these times be friendly or sad, as the beholder sees it. Genji was in anguish. He knew that there would be no way even to exchange notes. He cast many a glance backward as he left.

At Sanjō once more, he was unable to sleep. If the thought that they would not meet again so pained him, what must it do to the lady? She was no beauty, but she had seemed pretty and cultivated. Of the middling rank, he said to himself. The guards officer who had seen them all knew what he was talking about.

Spending most of his time now at Sanjō, he thought sadly of the unapproachable lady. At last he summoned her stepson, the governor of Kii.

"The boy I saw the other night, your foster uncle. He seemed a promising lad. I think I might have a place for him. I might even introduce him to my father."

"Your gracious words quite overpower me. Perhaps I should take the matter up with his sister."

Genji's heart leaped at the mention of the lady. "Does she have children?"

"No. She and my father have been married for two years now, but I gather that she is not happy. Her father meant to send her to court."

"How sad for her. Rumor has it that she is a beauty. Might rumor be correct?"

"Mistaken, I fear. But of course stepsons do not see a great deal of stepmothers."

Several days later he brought the boy to Genji. Examined in detail the boy was not perfect, but he had considerable charm and grace. Genji addressed him in a most friendly manner, which both confused and pleased him. Questioning him about his sister, Genji did not learn a great deal. The answers were ready enough while they were on safe ground, but the boy's self-possession was a little disconcerting. Genji hinted rather broadly at what had taken place. The boy was startled. He guessed the truth but was not old enough to pursue the matter.

Genji gave him a letter for his sister. Tears came to her eyes. How much had her brother been told? she wondered, spreading the letter to hide her flushed cheeks.

It was very long, and concluded with a poem:

"I yearn to dream again the dream of that night.
The nights go by in lonely wakefulness.

"There are no nights of sleep."[3]

The hand was splendid, but she could only weep at the yet stranger turn her life had taken.

The next day Genji sent for the boy.

Where was her answer? the boy asked his sister.

"Tell him you found no one to give his letter to."

"Oh, please." The boy smiled knowingly. "How can I tell him that? I have learned enough to be sure there is no mistake."

She was horrified. It was clear that Genji had told everything.

"I don't know why you must always be so clever. Perhaps it would be better if you didn't go at all."

"But he sent for me." And the boy departed.

The governor of Kii was beginning to take an interest in his pretty young stepmother, and paying insistent court. His attention turned to the brother, who became his frequent companion.

"I waited for you all day yesterday," said Genji. "Clearly I am not as much on your mind as you are on mine."

The boy flushed.

"Where is her answer?" And when the boy told him: "A fine messenger. I had hoped for something better."

---

3. Alludes to a classical poem, "Where shall I find comfort in my longing? / There are no dreams, for there are no nights of sleep."

There were other letters.

"But didn't you know?" he said to the boy. "I knew her before that old man she married. She thought me feeble and useless, it seems, and looked for a stouter support. Well, she may spurn me, but you needn't. You will be my son. The gentleman you are looking to for help won't be with us long."

The boy seemed to be thinking what a nuisance his sister's husband was. Genji was amused.

He treated the boy like a son, making him a constant companion, giving him clothes from his own wardrobe, taking him to court. He continued to write to the lady. She feared that with so inexperienced a messenger the secret might leak out and add suspicions of promiscuity to her other worries. These were very grand messages, but something more in keeping with her station seemed called for. Her answers were stiff and formal when she answered at all. She could not forget his extraordinary good looks and elegance, so dimly seen that night. But she belonged to another, and nothing was to be gained by trying to interest him. His longing was undiminished. He could not forget how touchingly fragile and confused she had With so many people around, another invasion of her boudoir was not likely to go unnoticed, and the results would be sad.

One evening after he had been at court for some days he found an excuse: his mansion again lay in a forbidden direction. Pretending to set off for Sanjō, he went instead to the house of the governor of Kii. The governor was delighted, thinking that those well-designed brooks and lakes had made an impression. Genji had consulted with the boy, always in earnest attendance. The lady had been informed of the visit. She must admit that they seemed powerful, the urges that forced him to such machinations. But if she were to receive him and display herself openly, what could she expect save the anguish of the other night, a repetition of that nightmare? No, the shame would be too much.

The brother having gone off upon a summons from Genji, she called several of her women. "I think it might be in bad taste to stay too near. I am not feeling at all well, and perhaps a massage might help, somewhere far enough away that we won't disturb him."

The woman Chūjō had rooms on a secluded gallery. They would be her refuge.

It was as she had feared. Genji sent his men to bed early and dispatched his messenger. The boy could not find her. He looked everywhere and finally, at the end of his wits, came upon her in the gallery.

He was almost in tears. "But he will think me completely useless."

"And what do you propose to be doing? You are a child, and it is quite improper for you to be carrying such messages. Tell him I have not been feeling well and have kept some of my women to massage me. You should not be here. They will think it very odd."

She spoke with great firmness, but her thoughts were far from firm. How happy she might have been if she had not made this unfortunate marriage, and were still in the house filled with memories of her dead parents. Then she could have awaited his visits, however infrequent. And the coldness she must force herself to display—he must think her

quite unaware of her place in the world. She had done what she thought best, and she was in anguish. Well, it all was hard fact, about which she had no choice. She must continue to play the cold and insensitive woman.

Genji lay wondering what blandishments the boy might be using. He was not sanguine, for the boy was very young. Presently he came back to report his mission a failure. What an uncommonly strong woman! Genji feared he must seem a bit feckless beside her. He heaved a deep sigh. This evidence of despondency had the boy on the point of tears.

Genji sent the lady a poem:

> "I wander lost in the Sonohara moorlands,
>   For I did not know the deceiving ways of the broom tree.[4]

"How am I to describe my sorrow?"
She too lay sleepless. This was her answer:

> "Here and not here, I lie in my shabby hut.
>   Would that I might like the broom tree vanish away."

The boy traveled back and forth with messages, a wish to be helpful driving sleep from his thoughts. His sister beseeched him to consider what the others might think.

Genji's men were snoring away. He lay alone with his discontent. This unique stubbornness was no broom tree. It refused to vanish away. The stubbornness was what interested him. But he had had enough. Let her do as she wished. And yet—not even this simple decision was easy.

"At least take me to her."

"She is shut up in a very dirty room and there are all sorts of women with her. I do not think it would be wise." The boy would have liked to be more helpful.

"Well, you at least must not abandon me." Genji pulled the boy down beside him.

The boy was delighted, such were Genji's youthful charms. Genji, for his part, or so one is informed, found the boy more attractive than his chilly sister.

Summary Genji continues to yearn for the woman he met in the last chapter, the wife of the governor of Iyo. He pays another visit to the house where she is staying and steals into the lady's quarters. She eludes him by slipping out of the room, and unaware of this, Genji makes love to her stepdaughter, whom she has left behind. The governor's wife will reappear in future episodes, where she is called the lady of the locust shell, a reference to the light summer singlet she discards, like a locust shedding its shell, when she avoids Genji in this chapter.

---

4. Alludes to a poem: "O broom tree of Fuseya in Sonohara, / You seem to be there, and yet I cannot find you." The broom tree of Sonohara was said to disappear or change shape when one approached. *Fuseya* means "hut," which the lady employs in her response to Genji.

CHAPTER 4

Evening Faces

On his way from court to pay one of his calls at Rokujō,[5] Genji stopped to inquire after his old nurse, Koremitsu's[6] mother, at her house in Gojō. Gravely ill, she had become a nun. The carriage entrance was closed. He sent for Koremitsu and while he was waiting looked up and down the dirty, cluttered street. Beside the nurse's house was a new fence of plaited cypress. The four or five narrow shutters above had been raised, and new blinds, white and clean, hung in the apertures. He caught outlines of pretty foreheads beyond. He would have judged, as they moved about, that they belonged to rather tall women. What sort of women might they be? His carriage was simple and unadorned and he had no outrunners. Quite certain that he would not be recognized, he leaned out for a closer look. The hanging gate, of something like trelliswork, was propped on a pole, and he could see that the house was tiny and flimsy. He felt a little sorry for the occupants of such a place—and then asked himself who in this world had more than a temporary shelter.[7] A hut, a jeweled pavilion, they were the same. A pleasantly green vine was climbing a board wall. The white flowers, he thought, had a rather self-satisfied look about them.

" 'I needs must ask the lady far off yonder,' "[8] he said, as if to himself.

An attendant came up, bowing deeply. "The white flowers far off yonder are known as 'evening faces.' " he said. "A very human sort of name—and what a shabby place they have picked to bloom in."

It was as the man said. The neighborhood was a poor one, chiefly of small houses. Some were leaning precariously, and there were "evening faces" at the sagging eaves.

"A hapless sort of flower. Pick one off for me, would you?"

The man went inside the raised gate and broke off a flower. A pretty little girl in long, unlined yellow trousers of raw silk came out through a sliding door that seemed too good for the surroundings. Beckoning to the man, she handed him a heavily scented white fan.

"Put it on this. It isn't much of a fan, but then it isn't much of a flower either."

Koremitsu, coming out of the gate, passed it on to Genji.

"They lost the key, and I have had to keep you waiting. You aren't likely to be recognized in such a neighborhood, but it's not a very nice neighborhood to keep you waiting in."

Genji's carriage was pulled in and he dismounted. Besides Koremitsu, a son and a daughter, the former an eminent cleric, and the daughter's husband, the governor of Mikawa, were in attendance upon the old woman. They thanked him profusely for his visit.

The old woman got up to receive him. "I did not at all mind leaving the world, except for the thought that I would no longer be able to see

---

5. The sixth ward; one of Genji's loves lives there and thus her name, the Rokujō lady. Daughter of an influential minister and widow of a crown prince, she is one of Genji's most demanding women. Although the reader does not learn much about her until chap. 9, she begins to make her presence felt here.   6. Genji's servant and confidant.   7. Alludes to a poem in *The Kokinshū*: "Where in all this world shall I call home? / A temporary shelter is my home."   8. Another allusion to *The Kokinshū*: "I needs must ask the lady far off yonder / What flower is off there that blooms so white."

you as I am seeing you now. My vows seem to have given me a new lease on life, and this visit makes me certain that I shall receive the radiance of Lord Amitābha[9] with a serene and tranquil heart." And she collapsed in tears.

Genji was near tears himself. "It has worried me enormously that you should be taking so long to recover, and I was very sad to learn that you have withdrawn from the world. You must live a long life and see the career I make for myself. I am sure that if you do you will be reborn upon the highest summits of the Pure Land. I am told that it is important to rid oneself of the smallest regret for this world."

Fond of the child she has reared, a nurse tends to look upon him as a paragon even if he is a half-wit. How much prouder was the old woman, who somehow gained stature, who thought of herself as eminent in her own right for having been permitted to serve him. The tears flowed on.

Her children were ashamed for her. They exchanged glances. It would not do to have these contortions taken as signs of a lingering affection for the world.

Genji was deeply touched. "The people who were fond of me left me when I was very young. Others have come along, it is true, to take care of me, but you are the only one I am really attached to. In recent years there have been restrictions upon my movements, and I have not been able to look in upon you morning and evening as I would have wished, or indeed to have a good visit with you. Yet I become very depressed when the days go by and I do not see you. 'Would that there were on this earth no final partings.' "[1] He spoke with great solemnity, and the scent of his sleeve, as he brushed away a tear, quite flooded the room.

Yes, thought the children, who had been silently reproaching their mother for her want of control, the fates had been kind to her. They too were now in tears.

Genji left orders that prayers and services be resumed. As he went out he asked for a torch, and in its light examined the fan on which the "evening face" had rested. It was permeated with a lady's perfume, elegant and alluring. On it was a poem in a disguised cursive hand that suggested breeding and taste. He was interested.

> "I think I need not ask whose face it is,
>   So bright, this evening face, in the shining dew."

"Who is living in the house to the west?" he asked Koremitsu. "Have you perhaps had occasion to inquire?"

At it again, thought Koremitsu. He spoke somewhat tartly. "I must confess that these last few days I have been too busy with my mother to think about her neighbors."

"You are annoyed with me. But this fan has the appearance of something it might be interesting to look into. Make inquiries, if you will, please, of someone who knows the neighborhood."

Koremitsu went in to ask his mother's steward, and emerged with the

---

9. The Buddha of Infinite Light, into whose paradise, the Pure Land, the faithful are reborn.
1. Alludes to a poem by Ariwara Narihira in *The Kokinshū:* "Would that my mother might live a thousand years. / Would there were on this earth no final partings."

information that the house belonged to a certain honorary vice-governor. "The husband is away in the country, and the wife seems to be a young woman of taste. Her sisters are out in service here and there. They often come visiting. I suspect the fellow is too poorly placed to know the details."

His poetess would be one of the sisters, thought Genji. A rather practiced and forward young person, and, were he to meet her, perhaps vulgar as well—but the easy familiarity of the poem had not been at all unpleasant, not something to be pushed away in disdain. His amative propensities, it will be seen, were having their way once more.

Carefully disguising his hand, he jotted down a reply on a piece of notepaper and sent it in by the attendant who had earlier been of service.

> "Come a bit nearer, please. Then might you know
> Whose was the evening face so dim in the twilight."

Thinking it a familiar profile, the lady had not lost the opportunity to surprise him with a letter, and when time passed and there was no answer she was left feeling somewhat embarrassed and disconsolate. Now came a poem by special messenger. Her women became quite giddy as they turned their minds to the problem of replying. Rather bored with it all, the messenger returned empty-handed. Genji made a quiet departure, lighted by very few torches. The shutters next door had been lowered. There was something sad about the light, dimmer than fireflies, that came through the cracks.

At the Rokujō house, the trees and the plantings had a quiet dignity. The lady herself was strangely cold and withdrawn. Thoughts of the "evening faces" quite left him. He overslept, and the sun was rising when he took his leave. He presented such a fine figure in the morning light that the women of the place understood well enough why he should be so universally admired. On his way he again passed those shutters, as he had no doubt done many times before. Because of that small incident he now looked at the house carefully, wondering who might be within.

"My mother is not doing at all well, and I have been with her," said Koremitsu some days later. And, coming nearer: "Because you seemed so interested, I called someone who knows about the house next door and had him questioned. His story was not completely clear. He said that in the Fifth Month or so someone came very quietly to live in the house, but that not even the domestics had been told who she might be. I have looked through the fence from time to time myself and had glimpses through blinds of several young women. Something about their dress suggests that they are in the service of someone of higher rank. Yesterday, when the evening light was coming directly through, I saw the lady herself writing a letter. She is very beautiful. She seemed lost in thought, and the women around her were weeping."

Genji had suspected something of the sort. He must find out more.

Koremitsu's view was that while Genji was undeniably someone the whole world took seriously, his youth and the fact that women found him attractive meant that to refrain from these little affairs would be less than

human. It was not realistic to hold that certain people were beyond temptation.

"Looking for a chance to do a bit of exploring, I found a small pretext for writing to her. She answered immediately, in a good, practiced hand. Some of her women do not seem at all beneath contempt."

"Explore very thoroughly, if you will. I will not be satisfied until you do."

The house was what the guardsman would have described as the lowest of the low, but Genji was interested. What hidden charms might he not come upon!

He had thought the coldness of the governor's wife, the lady of "the locust shell," quite unique. Yet if she had proved amenable to his persuasions the affair would no doubt have been dropped as a sad mistake after that one encounter. As matters were, the resentment and the distinct possibility of final defeat never left his mind. The discussion that rainy night would seem to have made him curious about the several ranks. There had been a time when such a lady would not have been worth his notice. Yes, it had been broadening, that discussion! He had not found the willing and available one, the governor of Iyo's daughter, entirely uninteresting, but the thought that the stepmother must have been listening coolly to the interview was excruciating. He must await some sign of her real intentions.

The governor of Iyo returned to the city. He came immediately to Genji's mansion. Somewhat sunburned, his travel robes rumpled from the sea voyage, he was a rather heavy and displeasing sort of person. He was of good lineage, however, and, though aging, he still had good manners. As they spoke of his province, Genji wanted to ask the full count of those hot springs,[2] but he was somewhat confused to find memories chasing one another through his head. How foolish that he should be so uncomfortable before the honest old man! He remembered the guardsman's warning that such affairs are unwise, and he felt sorry for the governor. Though he resented the wife's coldness, he could see that from the husband's point of view it was admirable. He was upset to learn that the governor meant to find a suitable husband for his daughter and take his wife to the provinces. He consulted the lady's young brother upon the possibility of another meeting. It would have been difficult even with the lady's cooperation, however, and she was of the view that to receive a gentleman so far above her would be extremely unwise.

Yet she did not want him to forget her entirely. Her answers to his notes on this and that occasion were pleasant enough, and contained casual little touches that made him pause in admiration. He resented her chilliness, but she interested him. As for the stepdaughter, he was certain that she would receive him hospitably enough however formidable a husband she might acquire. Reports upon her arrangements disturbed him not at all.

Autumn came. He was kept busy and unhappy by affairs of his own making, and he visited Sanjō infrequently. There was resentment.

As for the affair at Rokujō, he had overcome the lady's resistance and

---

2. The province was noted for its hot springs.

had his way, and, alas, he had cooled toward her. People thought it worthy of comment that his passions should seem so much more governable than before he had made her his. She was subject to fits of despondency, more intense on sleepless nights when she awaited him in vain. She feared that if rumors were to spread the gossips would make much of the difference in their ages.

On a morning of heavy mists, insistently roused by the lady, who was determined that he be on his way, Genji emerged yawning and sighing and looking very sleepy. Chūjō, one of her women, raised a shutter and pulled a curtain aside as if urging her lady to come forward and see him off. The lady lifted her head from her pillow. He was an incomparably handsome figure as he paused to admire the profusion of flowers below the veranda. Chūjō followed him down a gallery. In an aster robe that matched the season pleasantly and a gossamer train worn with clean elegance, she was a pretty, graceful woman. Glancing back, he asked her to sit with him for a time at the corner railing. The ceremonious precision of the seated figure and the hair flowing over her robes were very fine.

He took her hand.

"Though loath to be taxed with seeking fresher blooms,
I feel impelled to pluck this morning glory.

"Why should it be?"

She answered with practiced alacrity, making it seem that she was speaking not for herself but for her lady:

"In haste to plunge into the morning mists,
You seem to have no heart for the blossoms here."

A pretty little page boy, especially decked out for the occasion, it would seem, walked out among the flowers. His trousers wet with dew, he broke off a morning glory for Genji. He made a picture that called out to be painted.

Even persons to whom Genji was nothing were drawn to him. No doubt even rough mountain men wanted to pause for a time in the shade of the flowering tree, and those who had basked even briefly in his radiance had thought, each in accordance with his rank, of a daughter who might be taken into his service, a not ill-formed sister who might perform some humble service for him. One need not be surprised, then, that people with a measure of sensibility among those who had on some occasion received a little poem from him or been treated to some little kindness found him much on their minds. No doubt it distressed them not to be always with him.

I had forgotten: Koremitsu gave a good account of the fence peeping to which he had been assigned. "I am unable to identify her. She seems determined to hide herself from the world. In their boredom her women and girls go out to the long gallery at the street, the one with the shutters, and watch for carriages. Sometimes the lady who seems to be their mistress comes quietly out to join them. I've not had a good look at her, but she seems very pretty indeed. One day a carriage with outrunners went by. The little girls shouted to a person named Ukon that she must come in a

hurry. The captain[3] was going by, they said. An older woman came out
and motioned to them to be quiet. How did they know? she asked, coming
out toward the gallery. The passage from the main house is by a sort of
makeshift bridge. She was hurrying and her skirt caught on something,
and she stumbled and almost fell off. 'The sort of thing the god of Katsuragi[4] might do,' she said, and seems to have lost interest in sightseeing.
They told her that the man in the carriage was wearing casual court dress
and that he had a retinue. They mentioned several names, and all of them
were undeniably Lord Tō no Chūjō's guards and pages."

"I wish you had made positive identification." Might she be the lady of
whom Tō no Chūjō had spoken so regretfully that rainy night?

Koremitsu went on, smiling at this open curiosity. "I have as a matter
of fact made the proper overtures and learned all about the place. I come
and go as if I did not know that they are not all equals. They think they
are hiding the truth and try to insist that there is no one there but themselves when one of the little girls makes a slip."

"Let me have a peep for myself when I call on your mother."

Even if she was only in temporary lodgings, the woman would seem to
be of the lower class for which his friend had indicated such contempt
that rainy evening. Yet something might come of it all. Determined not
to go against his master's wishes in the smallest detail and himself driven
by very considerable excitement, Koremitsu searched diligently for a
chance to let Genji into the house. But the details are tiresome, and I
shall not go into them.

Genji did not know who the lady was and he did not want her to know
who he was. In very shabby disguise, he set out to visit her on foot. He
must be taking her very seriously, thought Koremitsu, who offered his
horse and himself went on foot.

"Though I do not think that our gentleman will look very good with
tramps for servants."

To make quite certain that the expedition remained secret, Genji took
with him only the man who had been his intermediary in the matter of
the "evening faces" and a page whom no one was likely to recognize. Lest
he be found out even so, he did not stop to see his nurse.

The lady had his messengers followed to see how he made his way
home and tried by every means to learn where he lived; but her efforts
came to nothing. For all his secretiveness, Genji had grown fond of her
and felt that he must go on seeing her. They were of such different ranks,
he tried to tell himself, and it was altogether too frivolous. Yet his visits
were frequent. In affairs of this sort, which can muddle the senses of the
most serious and honest of men, he had always kept himself under tight
control and avoided any occasion for censure. Now, to a most astonishing
degree, he would be asking himself as he returned in the morning from a
visit how he could wait through the day for the next. And then he would
rebuke himself. It was madness, it was not an affair he should let disturb
him. She was of an extraordinarily gentle and quiet nature. Though there

3. Tō no Chūjō.   4. Tradition held that he was very ugly and built a bridge that he used only at
night. Katsuragi is south of Nara.

was a certain vagueness about her, and indeed an almost childlike quality, it was clear that she knew something about men. She did not appear to be of very good family. What was there about her, he asked himself over and over again, that so drew him to her?

He took great pains to hide his rank and always wore travel dress, and he did not allow her to see his face. He came late at night when everyone was asleep. She was frightened, as if he were an apparition from an old story. She did not need to see his face to know that he was a fine gentleman. But who might he be? Her suspicions turned to Koremitsu. It was that young gallant, surely, who had brought the strange visitor. But Koremitsu pursued his own little affairs unremittingly, careful to feign indifference to and ignorance of this other affair. What could it all mean? The lady was lost in unfamiliar speculations.

Genji had his own worries. If, having lowered his guard with an appearance of complete unreserve, she were to slip away and hide, where would he seek her? This seemed to be but a temporary residence, and he could not be sure when she would choose to change it, and for what other. He hoped that he might reconcile himself to what must be and forget the affair as just another dalliance; but he was not confident.

On days when, to avoid attracting notice, he refrained from visiting her, his fretfulness came near anguish. Suppose he were to move her in secret to Nijō. If troublesome rumors were to arise, well, he could say that they had been fated from the start. He wondered what bond in a former life might have produced an infatuation such as he had not known before.

"Let's have a good talk," he said to her, "where we can be quite at our ease."

"It's all so strange. What you say is reasonable enough, but what you do is so strange. And rather frightening."

Yes, she might well be frightened. Something childlike in her fright brought a smile to his lips. "Which of us is the mischievous fox spirit?[5] I wonder. Just be quiet and give yourself up to its persuasions."

Won over by his gentle warmth, she was indeed inclined to let him have his way. She seemed such a pliant little creature, likely to submit absolutely to the most outrageous demands. He thought again of Tō no Chūjō's "wild carnation," of the equable nature his friend had described that rainy night. Fearing that it would be useless, he did not try very hard to question her. She did not seem likely to indulge in dramatics and suddenly run off and hide herself, and so the fault must have been Tō no Chūjō's. Genji himself would not be guilty of such negligence—though it did occur to him that a bit of infidelity might make her more interesting.

The bright full moon of the Eighth Month came flooding in through chinks in the roof. It was not the sort of dwelling he was used to, and he was fascinated. Toward dawn he was awakened by plebeian voices in the shabby houses down the street.

"Freezing, that's what it is, freezing. There's not much business this

---

5. According to popular superstition, foxes played havoc with people by taking human form and deceiving them.

year, and when you can't get out into the country you feel like giving up.
Do you hear me, neighbor?"

He could make out every word. It embarrassed the woman that, so near
at hand, there should be this clamor of preparation as people set forth on
their sad little enterprises. Had she been one of the stylish ladies of the
world, she would have wanted to shrivel up and disappear. She was a
placid sort, however, and she seemed to take nothing, painful or embarrassing or unpleasant, too seriously. Her manner elegant and yet girlish,
she did not seem to know what the rather awful clamor up and down the
street might mean. He much preferred this easygoing bewilderment to a
show of consternation, a face scarlet with embarrassment. As if at his very
pillow, there came the booming of a foot pestle, more fearsome than the
stamping of the thunder god, genuinely earsplitting. He did not know
what device the sound came from, but he did know that it was enough to
awaken the dead. From this direction and that there came the faint thump
of fulling hammers against coarse cloth; and mingled with it—these were
sounds to call forth the deepest emotions—were the calls of geese flying
overhead. He slid a door open and they looked out. They had been lying
near the veranda. There were tasteful clumps of black bamboo just outside
and the dew shone as in more familiar places. Autumn insects sang busily,
as if only inches from an ear used to wall crickets at considerable distances.
It was all very clamorous, and also rather wonderful. Countless details
could be overlooked in the singleness of his affection for the girl. She was
pretty and fragile in a soft, modest cloak of lavender and a lined white
robe. She had no single feature that struck him as especially beautiful,
and yet, slender and fragile, she seemed so delicately beautiful that he was
almost afraid to hear her voice. He might have wished her to be a little
more assertive, but he wanted only to be near her, and yet nearer.

"Let's go off somewhere and enjoy the rest of the night. This is too
much."

"But how is that possible?" She spoke very quietly. "You keep taking me
by surprise."

There was a newly confiding response to his offer of his services as
guardian in this world and the next. She was a strange little thing. He
found it hard to believe that she had had much experience of men. He no
longer cared what people might think. He asked Ukon to summon his
man, who got the carriage ready. The women of the house, though
uneasy, sensed the depth of his feelings and were inclined to put their
trust in him.

Dawn approached. No cocks were crowing. There was only the voice
of an old man making deep obeisance to a Buddha, in preparation, it
would seem, for a pilgrimage to Mitake. He seemed to be prostrating himself repeatedly and with much difficulty. All very sad. In a life itself like
the morning dew, what could he desire so earnestly?

"Praise to the Messiah to come," intoned the voice.

"Listen," said Genji. "He is thinking of another world.

"This pious one shall lead us on our way
     As we plight our troth for all the lives to come."

The vow exchanged by the Chinese emperor and Yang Kuei-fei[6] seemed to bode ill, and so he preferred to invoke Lord Maitreya, the Buddha of the Future; but such promises are rash.

> "So heavy the burden I bring with me from the past,
> I doubt that I should make these vows for the future."

It was a reply that suggested doubts about his "lives to come."

The moon was low over the western hills. She was reluctant to go with him. As he sought to persuade her, the moon suddenly disappeared behind clouds in a lovely dawn sky. Always in a hurry to be off before daylight exposed him, he lifted her easily into his carriage and took her to a nearby villa. Ukon was with them. Waiting for the caretaker to be summoned, Genji looked up at the rotting gate and the ferns that trailed thickly down over it. The groves beyond were still dark, and the mist and the dews were heavy. Genji's sleeve was soaking, for he had raised the blinds of the carriage.

"This is a novel adventure, and I must say that it seems like a lot of trouble.

> "And did it confuse them too, the men of old,
> This road through the dawn, for me so new and strange?

"How does it seem to you?"

She turned shyly away.

> "And is the moon, unsure of the hills it approaches,
> Foredoomed to lose its way in the empty skies?

"I am afraid."

She did seem frightened, and bewildered. She was so used to all those swarms of people, he thought with a smile.

The carriage was brought in and its traces propped against the veranda while a room was made ready in the west wing. Much excited, Ukon was thinking about earlier adventures. The furious energy with which the caretaker saw to preparations made her suspect who Genji was. It was almost daylight when they alighted from the carriage. The room was clean and pleasant, for all the haste with which it had been readied.

"There are unfortunately no women here to wait upon His Lordship." The man, who addressed him through Ukon, was a lesser steward who had served in the Sanjō mansion of Genji's father-in-law. "Shall I send for someone?"

"The last thing I want. I came here because I wanted to be in complete solitude, away from all possible visitors. You are not to tell a soul."

The man put together a hurried breakfast, but he was, as he had said, without serving women to help him.

Genji told the girl that he meant to show her a love as dependable as "the patient river of the loons."[7] He could do little else in these strange lodgings.

---

6. The emperor's concubine, whose execution during a rebellion in 756 drove the heartbroken emperor to abdicate.   7. An allusion to a poem in *The Man'yōshū:* "The patient river of the patient loons / Will not run dry. My love will still outlast it."

The sun was high when he arose. He opened the shutters. All through the badly neglected grounds not a person was to be seen. The groves were rank and overgrown. The flowers and grasses in the foreground were a drab monotone, an autumn moor. The pond was choked with weeds, and all in all it was a forbidding place. An outbuilding seemed to be fitted with rooms for the caretaker, but it was some distance away.

"It is a forbidding place," said Genji. "But I am sure that whatever devils emerge will pass me by."

He was still in disguise. She thought it unkind of him to be so secretive, and he had to agree that their relationship had gone beyond such furtiveness.

> "Because of one chance meeting by the wayside
> The flower now opens in the evening dew.

"And how does it look to you?"

> "The face seemed quite to shine in the evening dew,
> But I was dazzled by the evening light."

Her eyes turned away. She spoke in a whisper.

To him it may have seemed an interesting poem.

As a matter of fact, she found him handsomer than her poem suggested, indeed frighteningly handsome, given the setting.

"I hid my name from you because I thought it altogether too unkind of you to be keeping your name from me. Do please tell me now. This silence makes me feel that something awful might be coming."

"Call me the fisherman's daughter."[8] Still hiding her name, she was like a little child.

"I see. I brought it all on myself? A case of *warekara?*"[9]

And so, sometimes affectionately, sometimes reproachfully, they talked the hours away.

Koremitsu had found them out and brought provisions. Feeling a little guilty about the way he had treated Ukon, he did not come near. He thought it amusing that Genji should thus be wandering the streets, and concluded that the girl must provide sufficient cause. And he could have had her himself, had he not been so generous.

Genji and the girl looked out at an evening sky of the utmost calm. Because she found the darkness in the recesses of the house frightening, he raised the blinds at the veranda and they lay side by side. As they gazed at each other in the gathering dusk, it all seemed very strange to her, unbelievably strange. Memories of past wrongs quite left her. She was more at ease with him now, and he thought her charming. Beside him all through the day, starting up in fright at each little noise, she seemed delightfully childlike. He lowered the shutters early and had lights brought.

"You seem comfortable enough with me, and yet you raise difficulties."

8. Alludes to a poem: "A fisherman's daughter, I spend my life by the waves, / The waves that tell us nothing. I have no home."   9. Alludes to a poem in *The Kokinshū:* "The grass the fishermen take, the *warekara:* / 'I did it myself.' I shall weep but I shall not hate you." *Warekara* is both the fishermen's catch (skeleton shrimp) and a homonym meaning "I did it myself."

At court everyone would be frantic. Where would the search be directed? He thought what a strange love it was, and he thought of the turmoil the Rokujō lady was certain to be in. She had every right to be resentful, and yet her jealous ways were not pleasant. It was that sad lady to whom his thoughts first turned. Here was the girl beside him, so simple and undemanding; and the other was so impossibly forceful in her demands. How he wished he might in some measure have his freedom.

It was past midnight. He had been asleep for a time when an exceedingly beautiful woman appeared by his pillow.

"You do not even think of visiting me, when you are so much on my mind. Instead you go running off with someone who has nothing to recommend her, and raise a great stir over her. It is cruel, intolerable." She seemed about to shake the girl from her sleep. He awoke, feeling as if he were in the power of some malign being. The light had gone out. In great alarm, he pulled his sword to his pillow and awakened Ukon. She too seemed frightened.

"Go out to the gallery and wake the guard. Have him bring a light."

"It's much too dark."

He forced a smile. "You're behaving like a child."

He clapped his hands and a hollow echo answered. No one seemed to hear. The girl was trembling violently. She was bathed in sweat and as if in a trance, quite bereft of her senses.

"She is such a timid little thing," said Ukon, "frightened when there is nothing at all to be frightened of. This must be dreadful for her."

Yes, poor thing, thought Genji. She did seem so fragile, and she had spent the whole day gazing up at the sky.

"I'll go get someone. What a frightful echo. You stay here with her." He pulled Ukon to the girl's side.

The lights in the west gallery had gone out. There was a gentle wind. He had few people with him, and they were asleep. They were three in number: a young man who was one of his intimates and who was the son of the steward here, a court page, and the man who had been his intermediary in the matter of the "evening faces." He called out. Someone answered and came up to him.

"Bring a light. Wake the other, and shout and twang your bowstrings. What do you mean, going to sleep in a deserted house? I believe Lord Koremitsu was here."

"He was. But he said he had no orders and would come again at dawn."

An elite guardsman, the man was very adept at bow twanging. He went off with a shouting as of a fire watch. At court, thought Genji, the courtiers on night duty would have announced themselves, and the guard would be changing. It was not so very late.

He felt his way back inside. The girl was as before, and Ukon lay face down at her side.

"What is this? You're a fool to let yourself be so frightened. Are you worried about the fox spirits that come out and play tricks in deserted houses? But you needn't worry. They won't come near me." He pulled her to her knees.

"I'm not feeling at all well. That's why I was lying down. My poor lady must be terrified."

"She is indeed. And I can't think why."

He reached for the girl. She was not breathing. He lifted her and she was limp in his arms. There was no sign of life. She had seemed as defenseless as a child, and no doubt some evil power had taken possession of her. He could think of nothing to do. A man came with a torch. Ukon was not prepared to move, and Genji himself pulled up curtain frames to hide the girl.

"Bring the light closer."

It was a most unusual order. Not ordinarily permitted at Genji's side, the man hesitated to cross the threshold.

"Come, come, bring it here! There is a time and place for ceremony."

In the torchlight he had a fleeting glimpse of a figure by the girl's pillow. It was the woman in his dream. It faded away like an apparition in an old romance. In all the fright and horror, his confused thoughts centered upon the girl. There was no room for thoughts of himself.

He knelt over her and called out to her, but she was cold and had stopped breathing. It was too horrible. He had no confidant to whom he could turn for advice. It was the clergy one thought of first on such occasions. He had been so brave and confident, but he was young, and this was too much for him. He clung to the lifeless body.

"Come back, my dear, my dear. Don't do this awful thing to me." But she was cold and no longer seemed human.

The first paralyzing terror had left Ukon. Now she was writhing and wailing. Genji remembered a devil a certain minister had encountered in the Grand Hall.

"She can't possibly be dead." He found the strength to speak sharply. "All this noise in the middle of the night—you must try to be a little quieter." But it had been too sudden.

He turned again to the torchbearer. "There is someone here who seems to have had a very strange seizure. Tell your friend to find out where Lord Koremitsu is spending the night and have him come immediately. If the holy man is still at his mother's house, give him word, very quietly, that he is to come too. His mother and the people with her are not to hear. She does not approve of this sort of adventure."

He spoke calmly enough, but his mind was in a turmoil. Added to grief at the loss of the girl was horror, quite beyond describing, at this desolate place. It would be past midnight. The wind was higher and whistled more dolefully in the pines. There came a strange, hollow call of a bird. Might it be an owl? All was silence, terrifying solitude. He should not have chosen such a place—but it was too late now. Trembling violently, Ukon clung to him. He held her in his arms, wondering if she might be about to follow her lady. He was the only rational one present, and he could think of nothing to do. The flickering light wandered here and there. The upper parts of the screens behind them were in darkness, the lower parts fitfully in the light. There was a persistent creaking, as of someone coming up behind them. If only Koremitsu would come. But Koremitsu was a nocturnal wanderer without a fixed abode, and the man had to search for

him in numerous places. The wait for dawn was like the passage of a thousand nights. Finally he heard a distant crowing. What legacy from a former life could have brought him to this mortal peril? He was being punished for a guilty love, his fault and no one else's, and his story would be remembered in infamy through all the ages to come. There were no secrets, strive though one might to have them. Soon everyone would know, from his royal father down, and the lowest court pages would be talking; and he would gain immortality as the model of the complete fool.

Finally Lord Koremitsu came. He was the perfect servant who did not go against his master's wishes in anything at any time; and Genji was angry that on this night of all nights he should have been away, and slow in answering the summons. Calling him inside even so, he could not immediately find the strength to say what must be said. Ukon burst into tears, the full horror of it all coming back to her at the sight of Koremitsu. Genji too lost control of himself. The only sane and rational one present, he had held Ukon in his arms, but now he gave himself up to his grief.

"Something very strange has happened," he said after a time. "Strange—'unbelievable' would not be too strong a word. I wanted a priest—one does when these things happen—and asked your reverend brother to come."

"He went back up the mountain yesterday. Yes, it is very strange indeed. Had there been anything wrong with her?"

"Nothing."

He was so handsome in his grief that Koremitsu wanted to weep. An older man who has had everything happen to him and knows what to expect can be depended upon in a crisis; but they were both young, and neither had anything to suggest.

Koremitsu finally spoke. "We must not let the caretaker know. He may be dependable enough himself, but he is sure to have relatives who will talk. We must get away from this place."

"You aren't suggesting that we could find a place where we would be less likely to be seen?"

"No, I suppose not. And the women at her house will scream and wail when they hear about it, and they live in a crowded neighborhood, and all the mob around will hear, and that will be that. But mountain temples are used to this sort of thing.[1] There would not be much danger of attracting attention." He reflected on the problem for a time. "There is a woman I used to know. She has gone into a nunnery up in the eastern hills. She is very old, my father's nurse, as a matter of fact. The district seems to be rather heavily populated, but the nunnery is off by itself."

It was not yet full daylight. Koremitsu had the carriage brought up. Since Genji seemed incapable of the task, he wrapped the body in a covering and lifted it into the carriage. It was very tiny and very pretty, and not at all repellent. The wrapping was loose and the hair streamed forth, as if to darken the world before Genji's eyes.

He wanted to see the last rites through to the end, but Koremitsu would

---

1. Corpses were brought to temples for burial.

not hear of it. "Take my horse and go back to Nijō, now while the streets are still quiet."

He helped Ukon into the carriage and himself proceeded on foot, the skirts of his robe hitched up. It was a strange, bedraggled sort of funeral procession, he thought, but in the face of such anguish he was prepared to risk his life. Barely conscious, Genji made his way back to Nijō.

"Where have you been?" asked the women. "You are not looking at all well."

He did not answer. Alone in his room, he pressed a hand to his heart. Why had he not gone with the others? What would she think if she were to come back to life? She would think that he had abandoned her. Self-reproach filled his heart to breaking. He had a headache and feared he had a fever. Might he too be dying? The sun was high and still he did not emerge. Thinking it all very strange, the women pressed breakfast upon him. He could not eat. A messenger reported that the emperor had been troubled by his failure to appear the day before.

His brothers-in-law came calling.

"Come in, please, just for a moment." He received only Tō no Chūjō and kept a blind between them. "My old nurse fell seriously ill and took her vows in the Fifth Month or so. Perhaps because of them, she seemed to recover. But recently she had a relapse. Someone came to ask if I would not call on her at least once more. I thought I really must go and see an old and dear servant who was on her deathbed, and so I went. One of her servants was ailing, and quite suddenly, before he had time to leave, he died. Out of deference to me they waited until night to take the body away. All this I learned later. It would be very improper of me to go to court with all these festivities coming up,[2] I thought, and so I stayed away. I have had a headache since early this morning—perhaps I have caught cold. I must apologize."

"I see. I shall so inform your father. He sent out a search party during the concert last night, and really seemed very upset." Tō no Chūjō turned to go, and abruptly turned back. "Come now. What sort of brush did you really have? I don't believe a word of it."

Genji was startled, but managed a show of nonchalance. "You needn't go into the details. Just say that I suffered an unexpected defilement. Very unexpected, really."

Despite his cool manner, he was not up to facing people. He asked a younger brother-in-law to explain in detail his reasons for not going to court. He got off a note to Sanjō with a similar explanation.

Koremitsu came in the evening. Having announced that he had suffered a defilement, Genji had callers remain outside, and there were few people in the house. He received Koremitsu immediately.

"Are you sure she is dead?" He pressed a sleeve to his eyes.

Koremitsu too was in tears. "Yes, I fear she is most certainly dead. I could not stay shut up in a temple indefinitely, and so I have made arrangements with a venerable priest whom I happen to know rather well. Tomorrow is a good day for funerals."

---

2. There were many Shinto rites during the Ninth Month.

"And the other woman?"

"She has seemed on the point of death herself. She does not want to be left behind by her lady. I was afraid this morning that she might throw herself over a cliff. She wanted to tell the people at Gojō, but I persuaded her to let us have a little more time."

"I am feeling rather awful myself and almost fear the worst."

"Come, now. There is nothing to be done and no point in torturing yourself. You must tell yourself that what must be must be. I shall let absolutely no one know, and I am personally taking care of everything."

"Yes, to be sure. Everything is fated. So I tell myself. But it is terrible to think that I have sent a lady to her death. You are not to tell your sister, and you must be very sure that your mother does not hear. I would not survive the scolding I would get from her."

"And the priests too: I have told them a plausible story." Koremitsu exuded confidence.

The women had caught a hint of what was going on and were more puzzled than ever. He had said that he had suffered a defilement, and he was staying away from court; but why these muffled lamentations?

Genji gave instructions for the funeral. "You must make sure that nothing goes wrong."

"Of course. No great ceremony seems called for."

Koremitsu turned to leave.

"I know you won't approve," said Genji, a fresh wave of grief sweeping over him, "but I will regret it forever if I don't see her again. I'll go on horseback."

"Very well, if you must." In fact Koremitsu thought the proposal very ill advised. "Go immediately and be back while it is still early."

Genji set out in the travel robes he had kept ready for his recent amorous excursions. He was in the bleakest despair. He was on a strange mission and the terrors of the night before made him consider turning back. Grief urged him on. If he did not see her once more, when, in another world, might he hope to see her as she had been? He had with him only Koremitsu and the attendant of that first encounter. The road seemed a long one.

The moon came out, two nights past full. They reached the river. In the dim torchlight, the darkness off towards Mount Toribe was ominous and forbidding; but Genji was too dazed with grief to be frightened. And so they reached the temple.

It was a harsh, unfriendly region at best. The board hut and chapel where the nun pursued her austerities were lonely beyond description. The light at the altar came dimly through cracks. Inside the hut a woman was weeping. In the outer chamber two or three priests were conversing and invoking the holy name in low voices. Vespers seemed to have ended in several temples nearby. Everything was quiet. There were lights and there seemed to be clusters of people in the direction of Kiyomizu. The grand tones in which the worthy monk, the son of the nun, was reading a sutra brought on what Genji thought must be the full flood tide of his tears.

He went inside. The light was turned away from the corpse. Ukon lay

behind a screen. It must be very terrible for her, thought Genji. The girl's face was unchanged and very pretty.

"Won't you let me hear your voice again?" He took her hand. "What was it that made me give you all my love, for so short a time, and then made you leave me to this misery?" He was weeping uncontrollably.

The priests did not know who he was. They sensed something remarkable, however, and felt their eyes mist over.

"Come with me to Nijō," he said to Ukon.

"We have been together since I was very young. I never left her side, not for a single moment. Where am I to go now? I will have to tell the others what has happened. As if this weren't enough, I will have to put up with their accusations." She was sobbing. "I want to go with her."

"That is only natural. But it is the way of the world. Parting is always sad. Our lives must end, early or late. Try to put your trust in me." He comforted her with the usual homilies, but presently his real feelings came out. "Put your trust in me—when I fear I have not long to live myself." He did not after all seem likely to be much help.

"It will soon be light," said Koremitsu. "We must be on our way."

Looking back and looking back again, his heart near breaking, Genji went out. The way was heavy with dew and the morning mists were thick. He scarcely knew where he was. The girl was exactly as she had been that night. They had exchanged robes and she had on a red singlet of his. What might it have been in other lives that had brought them together? He managed only with great difficulty to stay in his saddle. Koremitsu was at the reins. As they came to the river Genji fell from his horse and was unable to remount.

"So I am to die by the wayside? I doubt that I can go on."

Koremitsu was in a panic. He should not have permitted this expedition, however strong Genji's wishes. Dipping his hands in the river, he turned and made supplication to Kiyomizu. Genji somehow pulled himself together. Silently invoking the holy name, he was seen back to Nijō.

The women were much upset by these untimely wanderings. "Very bad, very bad. He has been so restless lately. And why should he have gone out again when he was not feeling well?"

Now genuinely ill, he took to his bed. Two or three days passed and he was visibly thinner. The emperor heard of the illness and was much alarmed. Continuous prayers were ordered in this shrine and that temple. The varied rites, Shinto and Confucian and Buddhist, were beyond counting. Genji's good looks had been such as to arouse forebodings. All through the court it was feared that he would not live much longer. Despite his illness, he summoned Ukon to Nijō and assigned her rooms near his own. Koremitsu composed himself sufficiently to be of service to her, for he could see that she had no one else to turn to. Choosing times when he was feeling better, Genji would summon her for a talk, and she soon was accustomed to life at Nijō. Dressed in deep mourning, she was a somewhat stern and forbidding young woman, but not without her good points.

"It lasted such a very little while. I fear that I will be taken too. It must be dreadful for you, losing your only support. I had thought that as long

as I lived I would see to all your needs, and it seems sad and ironical that I should be on the point of following her." He spoke softly and there were tears in his eyes. For Ukon the old grief had been hard enough to bear, and now she feared that a new grief might be added to it.

All through the Nijō mansion there was a sense of helplessness. Emissaries from court were thicker than raindrops. Not wanting to worry his father, Genji fought to control himself. His father-in-law was extremely solicitous and came to Nijō every day. Perhaps because of all the prayers and rites the crisis passed—it had lasted some twenty days—and left no ill effects. Genji's full recovery coincided with the final cleansing of the defilement. With the unhappiness he had caused his father much on his mind, he set off for his apartments at court. For a time he felt out of things, as if he had come back to a strange new world.

By the end of the Ninth Month he was his old self once more. He had lost weight, but emaciation only made him handsomer. He spent a great deal of time gazing into space, and sometimes he would weep aloud. He must be in the clutches of some malign spirit, thought the women. It was all most peculiar.

He would summon Ukon on quiet evenings. "I don't understand it at all. Why did she so insist on keeping her name from me? Even if she *was* a fisherman's daughter it was cruel of her to be so uncommunicative. It was as if she did not know how much I loved her."

"There was no reason for keeping it secret. But why should she tell you about her insignificant self? Your attitude seemed so strange from the beginning. She used to say that she hardly knew whether she was waking or dreaming. Your refusal to identify yourself, you know, helped her guess who you were. It hurt her that you should belittle her by keeping your name from her."

"An unfortunate contest of wills. I did not want anything to stand between us; but I must always be worrying about what people will say. I must refrain from things my father and all the rest of them might take me to task for. I am not permitted the smallest indiscretion. Everything is exaggerated so. The little incident of the 'evening faces' affected me strangely and I went to very great trouble to see her. There must have been a bond between us. A love doomed from the start to be fleeting— why should it have taken such complete possession of me and made me find her so precious? You must tell me everything. What point is there in keeping secrets now? I mean to make offerings every week, and I want to know in whose name I am making them."

"Yes, of course—why have secrets now? It is only that I do not want to slight what she made so much of. Her parents are dead. Her father was a guards captain. She was his special pet, but his career did not go well and his life came to an early and disappointing end. She somehow got to know Lord Tō no Chūjō—it was when he was still a lieutenant. He was very attentive for three years or so, and then about last autumn there was a rather awful threat from his father-in-law's house. She was ridiculously timid and it frightened her beyond all reason. She ran off and hid herself at her nurse's in the western part of the city. It was a wretched little hovel of a place. She wanted to go off into the hills, but the direction she had

in mind has been taboo since New Year's. So she moved to the odd place where she was so upset to have you find her. She was more reserved and withdrawn than most people, and I fear that her unwillingness to show her emotions may have seemed cold."

So it was true. Affection and pity welled up yet more strongly.

"He once told me of a lost child. Was there such a one?"

"Yes, a very pretty little girl, born two years ago last spring."

"Where is she? Bring her to me without letting anyone know. It would be such a comfort. I should tell my friend Tō no Chūjō, I suppose, but why invite criticism? I doubt that anyone could reprove me for taking in the child. You must think up a way to get around the nurse."

"It would make me very happy if you were to take the child. I would hate to have her left where she is. She is there because we had no competent nurses in the house where you found us."

The evening sky was serenely beautiful. The flowers below the veranda were withered, the songs of the insects were dying too, and autumn tints were coming over the maples. Looking out upon the scene, which might have been a painting, Ukon thought what a lovely asylum she had found herself. She wanted to avert her eyes at the thought of the house of the "evening faces." A pigeon called, somewhat discordantly, from a bamboo thicket. Remembering how the same call had frightened the girl in that deserted villa, Genji could see the little figure as if an apparition were there before him.

"How old was she? She seemed so delicate, because she was not long for this world, I suppose?"

"Nineteen, perhaps? My mother, who was her nurse, died and left me behind. Her father took a fancy to me, and so we grew up together, and I never once left her side. I wonder how I can go on without her. I am almost sorry that we were so close. She seemed so weak, but I can see now that she was a source of strength."

"The weak ones do have a power over us. The clear, forceful ones I can do without. I am weak and indecisive by nature myself, and a woman who is quiet and withdrawn and follows the wishes of a man even to the point of letting herself be used has much the greater appeal. A man can shape and mold her as he wishes, and becomes fonder of her all the while."

"She was exactly what you would have wished, sir." Ukon was in tears. "That thought makes the loss seem greater."

The sky had clouded over and a chilly wind had come up. Gazing off into the distance, Genji said softly:

"One sees the clouds as smoke that rose from the pyre,
And suddenly the evening sky seems nearer."

Ukon was unable to answer. If only her lady were here! For Genji even the memory of those fulling blocks was sweet.

"In the Eighth Month, the Ninth Month, the nights are long,"[3] he whispered, and lay down.

The young page, brother of the lady of the locust shell, came to Nijō

---

3. Alludes to the Chinese poem *The Fulling Blocks at Night*, by Po Chü-i.

from time to time, but Genji no longer sent messages for his sister. She was sorry that he seemed angry with her and sorry to hear of his illness. The prospect of accompanying her husband to his distant province was a dreary one. She sent off a note to see whether Genji had forgotten her.

"They tell me you have not been well.

> "Time goes by, you ask not why I ask not.
> Think if you will how lonely a life is mine.

"I might make reference to Masuda Pond."[4]

This was a surprise; and indeed he had not forgotten her. The uncertain hand in which he set down his reply had its own beauty.

"Who, I wonder, lives the more aimless life.

> "Hollow though it was, the shell of the locust
> Gave me strength to face a gloomy world.

"But only precariously."

So he still remembered "the shell of the locust." She was sad and at the same time amused. It was good that they could correspond without rancor. She wished no further intimacy, and she did not want him to despise her.

As for the other, her stepdaughter, Genji heard that she had married a guards lieutenant. He thought it a strange marriage and he felt a certain pity for the lieutenant. Curious to know something of her feelings, he sent a note by his young messenger.

"Did you know that thoughts of you had brought me to the point of expiring?

> "I bound them loosely, the reeds beneath the eaves,[5]
> And reprove them now for having come undone."

He attached it to a long reed.

The boy was to deliver it in secret, he said. But he thought that the lieutenant would be forgiving if he were to see it, for he would guess who the sender was. One may detect here a note of self-satisfaction.

Her husband was away. She was confused, but delighted that he should have remembered her. She sent off in reply a poem the only excuse for which was the alacrity with which it was composed:

> "The wind brings words, all softly, to the reed,
> And the under leaves are nipped again by the frost."

It might have been cleverer and in better taste not to have disguised the clumsy handwriting. He thought of the face he had seen by lamplight. He could forget neither of them, the governor's wife, seated so primly before him, or the younger woman, chattering on so contentedly, without the smallest suggestion of reserve. The stirrings of a susceptible heart suggested that he still had important lessons to learn.

Quietly, forty-ninth-day services[6] were held for the dead lady in the Lotus Hall on Mount Hiei. There was careful attention to all the details,

---

4. Alludes to a poem: "Long the roots of the Masuda waters shield, / Longer still the aimless, sleepless nights."   5. The girl is traditionally called Nokiba-no-ogi, The Reeds Beneath the Eaves.   6. Held to pray for the woman's successful rebirth. Buddhist doctrine maintains that the spirit of the dead leads an indeterminate existence for forty-nine days, after which it begins a new incarnation.

the priestly robes and the scrolls and the altar decorations. Koremitsu's older brother was a priest of considerable renown, and his conduct of the services was beyond reproach. Genji summoned a doctor of letters with whom he was friendly and who was his tutor in Chinese poetry and asked him to prepare a final version of the memorial petition. Genji had prepared a draft. In moving language he committed the one he had loved and lost, though he did not mention her name, to the mercy of Amitābha.

"It is perfect, just as it is. Not a word needs to be changed." Noting the tears that refused to be held back, the doctor wondered who might be the subject of these prayers. That Genji should not reveal the name, and that he should be in such open grief—someone, no doubt, who had brought a very large bounty of grace from earlier lives.

Genji attached a poem to a pair of lady's trousers which were among his secret offerings:

"I weep and weep as today I tie this cord.
It will be untied in an unknown world to come."

He invoked the holy name with great feeling. Her spirit had wandered uncertainly these last weeks. Today it would set off down one of the ways of the future.

His heart raced each time he saw Tō no Chūjō. He longed to tell his friend that "the wild carnation" was alive and well; but there was no point in calling forth reproaches.

In the house of the "evening faces," the women were at a loss to know what had happened to their lady. They had no way of inquiring. And Ukon too had disappeared. They whispered among themselves that they had been right about that gentleman, and they hinted at their suspicions to Koremitsu. He feigned complete ignorance, however, and continued to pursue his little affairs. For the poor women it was all like a nightmare. Perhaps the wanton son of some governor, fearing Tō no Chūjō, had spirited her off to the country? The owner of the house was her nurse's daughter. She was one of three children and related to Ukon. She could only long for her lady and lament that Ukon had not chosen to enlighten them. Ukon for her part was loath to raise a stir, and Genji did not want gossip at this late date. Ukon could not even inquire after the child. And so the days went by bringing no light on the terrible mystery.

Genji longed for a glimpse of the dead girl, if only in a dream. On the day after the services he did have a fleeting dream of the woman who had appeared that fatal night. He concluded, and the thought filled him with horror, that he had attracted the attention of an evil spirit haunting the neglected villa.

Early in the Tenth Month the governor of Iyo left for his post, taking the lady of the locust shell with him. Genji chose his farewell presents with great care. For the lady there were numerous fans, and combs of beautiful workmanship, and pieces of cloth (she could see that he had had them dyed specially) for the wayside gods. He also returned her robe, "the shell of the locust."

"A keepsake till we meet again, I had hoped,
And see, my tears have rotted the sleeves away."

There were other things too, but it would be tedious to describe them. His messenger returned empty-handed. It was through her brother that she answered his poem.

"Autumn comes, the wings of the locust are shed.
A summer robe returns, and I weep aloud."

She had remarkable singleness of purpose, whatever else she might have. It was the first day of winter. There were chilly showers, as if to mark the occasion, and the skies were dark. He spent the day lost in thought.

"The one has gone, to the other I saw farewell.
They go their unknown ways. The end of autumn."

He knew how painful a secret love can be.

I had hoped, out of deference to him, to conceal these difficult matters; but I have been accused of romancing, of pretending that because he was the son of an emperor he had no faults. Now, perhaps, I shall be accused of having revealed too much.

Summary Nine years elapse in the chapters between *Evening Faces* and *Suma*, and many things happen. Genji meets Murasaki, a ten-year-old child, whom he grooms as his future wife, and in due course they marry. Of all the women he will know, throughout his life Genji remains supremely devoted to this one.

Although relations have been chilly with his first wife, Aoi, she bears him a son, Yūgiri, only to die soon after. It is following the period of mourning for Aoi that Genji consummates his union with Murasaki.

Despite his new love, Genji's eye continues to wander. Unwisely, he allows his obsession with Fujitsubo to run away with him. She becomes pregnant as a result, and although the emperor is delighted with the thought of an heir, Genji and Fujitsubo are greatly troubled. A son is born, a future emperor, and Fujitsubo is elevated to the rank of empress.

In the meantime, Genji has also become enamored of Oborozukiyo, the sister of his greatest enemy, his mother's old rival, Kokiden. When Kokiden discovers her sister's affair, in her fury she vows to drive Genji from the court. The death of his father abruptly alters the climate for Genji. Kokiden, with her son on the throne, is now in control. And Fujitsubo, remorseful over her actions, which have violated both her husband's trust and the sanctity of the imperial institution, renounces the world and becomes a nun. Everything has changed. It would seem that for Genji the palmy days are over.

CHAPTER 12

Suma[7]

For Genji life had become an unbroken succession of reverses and afflictions. He must consider what to do next. If he went on pretending that nothing was amiss, then even worse things might lie ahead. He thought of the Suma coast. People of worth had once lived there, he was told, but now it was deserted save for the huts of fishermen, and even they

---

7. The village on the Inland Sea, southwest of the capital, where Genji goes into exile.

were few. The alternative was worse, to go on living this public life, so to speak, with people streaming in and out of his house. Yet he would hate to leave, and affairs at court would continue to be much on his mind if he did leave. This irresolution was making life difficult for his people.

Unsettling thoughts of the past and the future chased one another through his mind. The thought of leaving the city aroused a train of regrets, led by the image of a grieving Murasaki. It was very well to tell himself that somehow, someday, by some route they would come together again. Even when they were separated for a day or two Genji was beside himself with worry and Murasaki's gloom was beyond describing. It was not as if they would be parting for a fixed span of years; and if they had only the possibility of a reunion on some unnamed day with which to comfort themselves, well, life is uncertain, and they might be parting forever. He thought of consulting no one and taking her with him, but the inappropriateness of subjecting such a fragile lady to the rigors of life on that harsh coast, where the only callers would be the wind and the waves, was too obvious. Having her with him would only add to his worries. She guessed his thoughts and was unhappy. She let it be known that she did not want to be left behind, however forbidding the journey and life at the end of it.

Then there was the lady of the orange blossoms.[8] He did not visit her often, it is true, but he was her only support and comfort, and she would have every right to feel lonely and insecure. And there were women who, after the most fleeting affairs with him, went on nursing their various secret sorrows.

Fujitsubo, though always worried about rumors, wrote frequently. It struck him as bitterly ironical that she had not returned his affection earlier, but he told himself that a fate which they had shared from other lives must require that they know the full range of sorrows.

He left the city late in the Third Month. He made no announcement of his departure, which was very inconspicuous, and had only seven or eight trusted retainers with him. He did write to certain people who should know of the event. I have no doubt that there were many fine passages in the letters with which he saddened the lives of his many ladies, but, grief-stricken myself, I did not listen as carefully as I might have.

Two or three days before his departure he visited his father-in-law. It was sad, indeed rather eerie, to see the care he took not to attract notice. His carriage, a humble one covered with cypress basketwork, might have been mistaken for a woman's. The apartments of his late wife wore a lonely, neglected aspect. At the arrival of this wondrous and unexpected guest, the little boy's nurse and all the other women who had not taken positions elsewhere gathered for a last look. Even the shallowest of the younger women were moved to tears at the awareness he brought of transience and mutability. Yūgiri, the little boy, was very pretty indeed, and indefatigably noisy.

"It has been so long. I am touched that he has not forgotten me." He took the boy on his knee and seemed about to weep.

8. One of Genji's lesser loves.

The minister, his father-in-law, came in. "I know that you are shut up at home with little to occupy you, and I had been thinking I would like to call on you and have a good talk. I talk on and on when once I let myself get started. But I have told them I am ill and have been staying away from court, and I have even resigned my offices; and I know what they would say if I were to stretch my twisted old legs for my own pleasure. I hardly need to worry about such things any more, of course, but I am still capable of being upset by false accusations. When I see how things are with you, I know all too painfully what a sad day I have come on at the end of too long a life. I would have expected the world to end before this was allowed to happen, and I see not a ray of light in it all."

"Dear sir, we must accept the disabilities we bring from other lives. Everything that has happened to me is a result of my own inadequacy. I have heard that in other lands as well as our own an offense which does not, like mine, call for dismissal from office is thought to become far graver if the culprit goes on happily living his old life. And when exile is considered, as I believe it is in my case, the offense must have been thought more serious. Though I know I am innocent, I know too what insults I may look forward to if I stay, and so I think that I will forestall them by leaving."

Brushing away tears, the minister talked of old times, of Genji's father, and all he had said and thought. Genji too was weeping. The little boy scrambled and rolled about the room, now pouncing upon his father and now making demands upon his grandfather.

"I have gone on grieving for my daughter. And then I think what agony all this would have been to her, and am grateful that she lived such a short life and was spared the nightmare. So I try to tell myself, in any event. My chief sorrows and worries are for our little man here. He must grow up among us dotards, and the days and months will go by without the advantage of your company. It used to be that even people who were guilty of serious crimes escaped this sort of punishment; and I suppose we must call it fate, in our land and other lands too, that punishment should come all the same. But one does want to know what the charges are. In your case they quite defy the imagination."

Tō no Chūjō came in. They drank until very late, and Genji was induced to stay the night. He summoned Aoi's various women. Chūnagon was the one whom he had most admired, albeit in secret. He went on talking to her after everything was quiet, and it would seem to have been because of her that he was prevailed upon to spend the night. Dawn was at hand when he got up to leave. The moon in the first suggestions of daylight was very beautiful. The cherry blossoms were past their prime, and the light through the few that remained flooded the garden silver. Everything faded together into a gentle mist, sadder and more moving than on a night in autumn. He sat for a time leaning against the railing at a corner of the veranda. Chūnagon was waiting at the door as if to see him off.

"I wonder when we will be permitted to meet again." He paused, choking with tears. "Never did I dream that this would happen, and I neglected you in the days when it would have been so easy to see you."

Saishō, Yūgiri's nurse, came with a message from Princess Omiya.[9] "I would have liked to say goodbye in person, but I have waited in hope that the turmoil of my thoughts might quiet a little. And now I hear that you are leaving, and it is still so early. Everything seems changed, completely wrong. It is a pity that you cannot at least wait until our little sleepyhead is up and about."

Weeping softly, Genji whispered to himself, not precisely by way of reply:

"There on the shore, the salt burners' fires await me.
Will their smoke be as the smoke over Toribe Moor?

Is this the parting at dawn we are always hearing of? No doubt there are those who know.

"I have always hated the word 'farewell,'" said Saishō, whose grief seemed quite unfeigned. "And our farewells today are unlike any others."

"Over and over again," he sent back to Princess Omiya, "I have thought of all the things I would have liked to say to you; and I hope you will understand and forgive my muteness. As for our little sleepyhead, I fear that if I were to see him I would wish to stay on even in this hostile city, and so I shall collect myself and be on my way."

All the women were there to see him go. He looked more elegant and handsome than ever in the light of the setting moon, and his dejection would have reduced tigers and wolves to tears. These were women who had served him since he was very young. It was a sad day for them.

There was a poem from Princess Omiya:

"Farther retreats the day when we bade her goodbye,
For now you depart the skies that received the smoke."[1]

Sorrow was added to sorrow, and the tears almost seemed to invite further misfortunes.

He returned to Nijō. The women, awake the whole night through, it seemed, were gathered in sad clusters. There was no one in the guardroom. The men closest to him, reconciled to going with him, were making their own personal farewells. As for other court functionaries, there had been ominous hints of sanctions were they to come calling, and so the grounds, once crowded with horses and carriages, were empty and silent. He knew again what a hostile world it had become. There was dust on the tables, cushions had been put away. And what would be the extremes of waste and the neglect when he was gone?

He went to Murasaki's wing of the house. She had been up all night, not even lowering the shutters. Out near the verandas little girls[2] were noisily bestirring themselves. They were so pretty in their night dress—and presently, no doubt, they would find the loneliness too much, and go their various ways. Such thoughts had not before been a part of his life.

He told Murasaki what had kept him at Sanjō. "And I suppose you are filled with the usual odd suspicions. I have wanted to be with you every moment I am still in the city, but there are things that force me to go out.

---

9. Mother of Aoi and Tō no Chūjō.   1. Refers to Aoi's cremation.   2. Murasaki's companions in Genji's absence.

Life is uncertain enough at best, and I would not want to seem cold and unfeeling."

"And what should be 'odd' now except that you are going away?"

That she should feel these sad events more cruelly than any of the others was not surprising. From her childhood she had been closer to Genji than to her own father, who now bowed to public opinion and had not offered a word of sympathy. His coldness had caused talk among her women. She was beginning to wish that they had kept him in ignorance of her whereabouts.

Someone reported what her stepmother was saying: "She had a sudden stroke of good luck, and now just as suddenly everything goes wrong. It makes a person shiver. One after another, each in his own way, they all run out on her."

This was too much. There was nothing more she wished to say to them. Henceforth she would have only Genji.

"If the years go by and I am still an outcast," he continued, "I will come for you and bring you to my 'cave among the rocks.'[3] But we must not be hasty. A man who is out of favor at court is not permitted the light of the sun and the moon, and it is thought a great crime, I am told, for him to go on being happy. The cause of it all is a great mystery to me, but I must accept it as fate. There seems to be no precedent for sharing exile with a lady, and I am sure that to suggest it would be to invite worse insanity from an insane world."

He slept until almost noon.

Tō no Chūjō and Genji's brother, Prince Hotaru, came calling. Since he was now without rank and office, he changed to informal dress of unfigured silk, more elegant, and even somehow grand, for its simplicity. As he combed his hair he could not help noticing that loss of weight had made him even handsomer.

"I am skin and bones," he said to Murasaki, who sat gazing at him, tears in her eyes. "Can I really be as emaciated as this mirror makes me? I am a little sorry for myself.

"I now must go into exile. In this mirror
An image of me will yet remain beside you."

Huddling against a pillar to hide her tears, she replied as if to herself:

"If when we part an image yet remains,
Then will I find some comfort in my sorrow."

Yes, she was unique—a new awareness of that fact stabbed at his heart.

Prince Hotaru kept him affectionate company through the day and left in the evening.

It was not hard to imagine the loneliness that brought frequent notes from the house of the falling orange blossoms. Fearing that he would seem unkind if he did not visit the ladies again, he resigned himself to spending yet another night away from home. It was very late before he gathered himself for the effort.

---

3. Alludes to a poem in *The Kokinshū*: "Where shall I go, to what cave among the rocks, / To be free of tidings of this gloomy world?"

"We are honored that you should consider us worth a visit," said Lady Reikeiden—and it would be difficult to record the rest of the interview.

They lived precarious lives, completely dependent on Genji. So lonely indeed was their mansion that he could imagine the desolation awaiting it once he himself was gone; and the heavily wooded hill rising dimly beyond the wide pond in misty moonlight made him wonder whether the "cave among the rocks" at Suma would be such a place.

He went to the younger sister's room, at the west side of the house. She had been in deep despondency, almost certain that he would not find time for a visit. Then, in the soft, sad lights of the moon, his robes giving off an indescribable fragrance, he made his way in. She came to the veranda and looked up at the moon. They talked until dawn.

"What a short night it has been. I think how difficult it will be for us to meet again, and I am filled with regrets for the days I wasted. I fear I worried too much about the precedents I might be setting."

A cock was crowing busily as he talked on about the past. He made a hasty departure, fearful of attracting notice. The setting moon is always sad, and he was prompted to think its situation rather like his own. Catching the deep purple of the lady's robe, the moon itself seemed to be weeping.[4]

"Narrow these sleeves, now lodging for the moonlight.
Would they might keep a light which I do not tire of."

Sad himself, Genji sought to comfort her.

"The moon will shine upon this house once more.
Do not look at the clouds which now conceal it.

"I wish I were really sure it is so, and find the unknown future clouding my heart."

He left as dawn was coming over the sky.

His affairs were in order. He assigned all the greater and lesser affairs of the Nijō mansion to trusted retainers who had not been swept up in the currents of the times, and he selected others to go with him to Suma. He would take only the simplest essentials for a rustic life, among them a book chest, selected writings of Po Chü-i and other poets, and a seven-stringed Chinese koto. He carefully refrained from anything which in its ostentation might not become a nameless rustic.

Assigning all the women to Murasaki's west wing, he left behind deeds to pastures and manors and the like and made provision for all his various warehouses and storerooms. Confident of Shōnagon's perspicacity he gave her careful instructions and put stewards at her disposal. He had been somewhat brisk and businesslike toward his own serving women, but they had had security—and now what was to become of them?

"I shall be back, I know, if I live long enough. Do what you can in the west wing, please, those of you who are prepared to wait."

And so they all began a new life.

---

4. Alludes to a poem by Lady Ise in *The Kokinshū*: "Catching the drops on my sleeves as I lay in thought, / The moonlight seemed to be shedding tears of its own."

To Yūgiri's nurse and maids and to the lady of the orange blossoms he sent elegant parting gifts and plain, useful everyday provisions as well.

He even wrote to Oborozukiyo. "I know that I have no right to expect a letter from you; but I am not up to describing the gloom and the bitterness of leaving this life behind.

> "Snagged upon the shoals of this river of tears,
> I cannot see you. Deeper waters await me.

"Remembering is the crime to which I cannot plead innocent."

He wrote nothing more, for there was a danger that his letter would be intercepted.

Though she fought to maintain her composure, there was nothing she could do about the tears that wet her sleeves.

> "The foam on the river of tears will disappear
> Short of the shoals of meeting that wait downstream."

There was something very fine about the hand disordered by grief.

He longed to see her again, but she had too many relatives who wished him ill. Discretion forbade further correspondence.

On the night before his departure he visited his father's grave in the northern hills. Since the moon would be coming up shortly before dawn, he went first to take leave of Fujitsubo. Receiving him in person, she spoke of her worries for the crown prince. It cannot have been, so complicated were matters between them, a less than deeply felt interview. Her dignity and beauty were as always. He would have liked to hint at old resentments; but why, at this late date, invite further unpleasantness, and risk adding to his own agitation?

He only said, and it was reasonable enough: "I can think of a single offense for which I must undergo this strange, sad punishment, and because of it I tremble before the heavens. Though I would not care in the least if my own unworthy self were to vanish away, I only hope that the crown prince's reign is without unhappy event."

She knew too well what he meant, and was unable to reply. He was almost too handsome as at last he succumbed to tears.

"I am going to pay my respects at His Majesty's grave. Do you have a message?"

She was silent for a time, seeking to control herself.

> "The one whom I served is gone, the other must go.
> Farewell to the world was no farewell to its sorrows."

But for both of them the sorrow was beyond words.

He replied:

> "The worst of grief for him should long have passed.
> And now I must leave the world where dwells the child."

The moon had risen and he set out. He was on horseback and had only five or six attendants, all of them trusted friends. I need scarcely say that it was a far different procession from those of old. Among his men was that guards officer who had been his special attendant at the Kamo lustration

services.[5] The promotion he might have expected had long since passed him by, and now his right of access to the royal presence and his offices had been taken away. Remembering that day as they came in sight of the Lower Kamo Shrine, he dismounted and took Genji's bridle.

"There was heartvine[6] in our caps. I led your horse.
And now at this jeweled fence I berate the gods."

Yes, the memory must be painful, for the young man had been the most resplendent in Genji's retinue. Dismounting, Genji bowed toward the shrine and said as if by way of farewell:

"I leave this world of gloom. I leave my name
To the offices of the god who rectifies."[7]

The guards officer, an impressionable young man, gazed at him in wonder and admiration.

Coming to the grave, Genji almost thought he could see his father before him. Power and position were nothing once a man was gone. He wept and silently told his story, but there came no answer, no judgment upon it. And all those careful instructions and admonitions had served no purpose at all?

Grasses overgrew the path to the grave, the dew seemed to gather weight as he made his way through. The moon had gone behind a cloud and the groves were dark and somehow terrible. It was as if he might lose his way upon turning back. As he bowed in farewell, a chill came over him, for he seemed to see his father as he once had been.

"And how does he look upon me? I raise my eyes,
And the moon now vanishes behind the clouds."

Back at Nijō at daybreak, he sent a last message to the crown prince. Tying it to a cherry branch from which the blossoms had fallen, he addressed it to Omyōbu, whom Fujitsubo had put in charge of her son's affairs. "Today I must leave. I regret more than anything that I cannot see you again. Imagine my feelings, if you will, and pass them on to the prince.

"When shall I, a ragged, rustic outcast,
See again the blossoms of the city?"

She explained everything to the crown prince. He gazed at her solemnly.

"How shall I answer?" Omyōbu asked.

"I am sad when he is away for a little, and he is going so far, and how—tell him that, please."

A sad little answer, thought Omyōbu.[8]

All the details of that unhappy love came back to her. The two of them

---

5. Held to inaugurate the shrines' new high priestess. The Kamo shrines were two of the most important Shinto shrines. In the novel, the entire imperial court turns out to observe the ceremonial procession. During the procession the retainers of Genji's wife Aoi tangle with those of the Rokujō lady, who is humiliated.   6. A pun that suggests Genji's wife Aoi, whose name can be translated as "heartvine," or "hollyhock."   7. Tadasu no Kami, who has his abode in the Lower Kamo Shrine.   8. The crown prince's answer breaks into seven-syllable lines, as if he were trying to compose a poem.

should have led placid, tranquil lives, and she felt as if she and she alone had been the cause of all the troubles.

"I can think of nothing to say." It was clear to him that her answer had indeed been composed with great difficulty. "I passed your message on to the prince, and was sadder than ever to see how sad it made him.

"Quickly the blossoms fall. Though spring departs,
You will come again, I know, to a city of flowers."

There was sad talk all through the crown prince's apartments in the wake of the letter, and there were sounds of weeping. Even people who scarcely knew him were caught up in the sorrow. As for people in his regular service, even scullery maids of whose existence he can hardly have been aware were sad at the thought that they must for a time do without his presence.

So it was all through the court. Deep sorrow prevailed. He had been with his father day and night from his seventh year, and, since nothing he had said to his father had failed to have an effect, almost everyone was in his debt. A cheerful sense of gratitude should have been common in the upper ranks of the court and the ministries, and omnipresent in the lower ranks. It was there, no doubt; but the world had become a place of quick punishments. A pity, people said, silently reproving the great ones whose power was now absolute; but what was to be accomplished by playing the martyr? Not that everyone was satisfied with passive acceptance. If he had not known before, Genji knew now that the human race is not perfect.

He spent a quiet day with Murasaki and late in the night set out in rough travel dress.

"The moon is coming up. Do please come out and see me off. I know that later I will think of any number of things I wanted to say to you. My gloom strikes me as ridiculous when I am away from you for even a day or two."

He raised the blinds and urged her to come forward. Trying not to weep, she at length obeyed. She was very beautiful in the moonlight. What sort of home would this unkind, inconstant city be for her now? But she was sad enough already, and these thoughts were best kept to himself.

He said with forced lightness:

"At least for this life we might make our vows, we thought.
And so we vowed that nothing would ever part us.

How silly we were!"

This was her answer:

"I would give a life for which I have no regrets
If it might postpone for a little the time of parting."

They were not empty words, he knew; but he must be off, for he did not want the city to see him in broad daylight.

Her face was with him the whole of the journey. In great sorrow he boarded the boat that would take him to Suma. It was a long spring day and there was a tail wind, and by late afternoon he had reached the strand where he was to live. He had never before been on such a journey, how-

ever short. All the sad, exotic things along the way were new to him. The Oe station[9] was in ruins, with only a grove of pines to show where it had stood.

> "More remote, I fear, my place of exile
> Than storied ones in lands beyond the seas."

The surf came in and went out again. "I envy the waves," he whispered to himself.[1] It was a familiar poem, but it seemed new to those who heard him, and sad as never before. Looking back toward the city, he saw that the mountains were enshrouded in mist. It was as though he had indeed come "three thousand leagues."[2] The spray from the oars brought thoughts scarcely to be borne.

> "Mountain mists cut off that ancient village.
> Is the sky I see the sky that shelters it?"

Not far away Yukihira had lived in exile, "dripping brine from the sea grass."[3] Genji's new house was some distance from the coast, in mountains utterly lonely and desolate. The fences and everything within were new and strange. The grass-roofed cottages, the reed-roofed galleries—or so they seemed—were interesting enough in their way. It was a dwelling proper to a remote littoral, and different from any he had known. Having once had a taste for out-of-the-way places, he might have enjoyed this Suma had the occasion been different.

Yoshikiyo had appointed himself a sort of confidential steward. He summoned the overseers of Genji's several manors in the region and assigned them to necessary tasks. Genji watched admiringly. In very quick order he had a rather charming new house. A deep brook flowed through the garden with a pleasing murmur, new plantings were set out; and when finally he was beginning to feel a little at home he could scarcely believe that it all was real. The governor of the province, an old retainer, discreetly performed numerous services. All in all it was a brighter and livelier place than he had a right to expect, although the fact that there was no one whom he could really talk to kept him from forgetting that it was a house of exile, strange and alien. How was he to get through the months and years ahead?

The rainy season came. His thoughts traveled back to the distant city. There were people whom he longed to see, chief among them the lady at Nijō, whose forlorn figure was still before him. He thought too of the crown prince, and of little Yūgiri, running so happily, that last day, from father to grandfather and back again. He sent off letters to the city. Some of them, especially those to Murasaki and to Fujitsubo, took a great deal of time, for his eyes clouded over repeatedly.

This is what he wrote to Fujitsubo:

9. In the heart of present-day Osaka; it was used by high priestesses on their way to and from the Ise Shrine.   1. Alludes to a poem by Ariwara Narihira: "Strong my yearning for what I have left behind. / I envy the waves that go back whence they came."   2. Alludes to Po Chü-i's poem *Lines Written on the Winter Solstice, in the Arbutus Hall.*   3. From a poem by Ariwara Yukihira in *The Kokinshū:* "If someone should inquire for me, reply: / 'He idles at Suma, dripping brine from the sea grass.' " Yukihira was himself exiled at Suma.

"Briny our sleeves on the Suma strand; and yours
In the fisher cots of thatch at Matsushima?"[4]

"My eyes are dark as I think of what is gone and what is to come, and
'the waters rise.' "[5]

His letter to Oborozukiyo he sent as always to Chūnagon, as if it were a
private matter between the two of them. "With nothing else to occupy me,
I find memories of the past coming back.

"At Suma, unchastened, one longs for the deep-lying sea pine.
And she, the fisher lady burning salt?"

I shall leave the others, among them letters to his father-in-law and
Yūgiri's nurse, to the reader's imagination. They reached their several des-
tinations and gave rise to many sad and troubled thoughts.

Murasaki had taken to her bed. Her women, doing everything they
could think of to comfort her, feared that in her grief and longing she
might fall into a fatal decline. Brooding over the familiar things he had
left behind, the koto, the perfumed robes, she almost seemed on the point
of departing the world. Her women were beside themselves. Shōnagon
sent asking that the bishop, her uncle, pray for her. He did so, and to
double purpose, that she be relieved of her present sorrows and that she
one day be permitted a tranquil life with Genji.

She sent bedding and other supplies to Suma. The robes and trousers
of stiff, unfigured white silk brought new pangs of sorrow, for they were
unlike anything he had worn before. She kept always with her the mirror
to which he had addressed his farewell poem, though it was not acquitting
itself of the duty he had assigned to it. The door through which he had
come and gone, the cypress pillar at his favorite seat—everything brought
sad memories. So it is even for people hardened and seasoned by trials,
and how much more for her, to whom he had been father and mother!
"Grasses of forgetfulness"[6] might have sprung up had he quite vanished
from the earth; but he was at Suma, not so very far away, she had heard.
She could not know when he would return.

For Fujitsubo, sorrow was added to uncertainty about her son. And how,
at the thought of the fate that had joined them, could her feelings for
Genji be of a bland and ordinary kind? Fearful of gossips, she had coldly
turned away each small show of affection, she had become more and more
cautious and secretive, and she had given him little sign that she sensed
the depth of his affection. He had been uncommonly careful himself.
Gossips are cruelly attentive people (it was a fact she knew too well), but
they seemed to have caught no suspicion of the affair. He had kept himself
under tight control and preserved the most careful appearances. How then
could she not, in this extremity, have fond thoughts for him?

Her reply was more affectionate than usual.

"The nun of Matsushima burns the brine
And fuels the fires with the logs of her lamenting,

now more than ever."

---

4. A very common pun makes *Matsushima* "The isle of one who waits." 5. Another poetic allusion:
"The sorrow of parting brings such flood of tears / That the waters of this river must surely rise."
6. The literal translation of *wasuregusa*, "day lilies."

Enclosed with Chūnagon's letter was a brief reply from Oborozukiyo:

> "The fisherwife burns salt and hides her fires
> And strangles, for the smoke has no escape.

"I shall not write of things which at this late date need no saying."
Chūnagon wrote in detail of her lady's sorrows. There were tears in his
eyes as he read her letter.

And Murasaki's reply was of course deeply moving. There was this
poem:

> "Taking brine on that strand, let him compare
> His dripping sleeves with these night sleeves of mine."

The robes that came with it were beautifully dyed and tailored. She did
everything so well. At Suma there were no silly and frivolous distractions,
and it seemed a pity that they could not enjoy the quiet life together.
Thoughts of her, day and night, became next to unbearable. Should he
send for her in secret? But no: his task in this gloomy situation must be to
make amends for past misdoings. He began a fast and spent his days in
prayer and meditation.

There were also messages about his little boy, Yūgiri. They of course
filled him with longing; but he would see the boy again one day, and in
the meantime he was in good hands. Yet a father must, however he tries,
"wander lost in thoughts upon his child."[7]

In the confusion I had forgotten: he had sent off a message to the
Rokujō lady, and she on her own initiative had sent a messenger to seek
out his place of exile. Her letter was replete with statements of the deepest
affection. The style and the calligraphy, superior to those of anyone else
he knew, showed unique breeding and cultivation.

"Having been told of the unthinkable place in which you find yourself,
I feel as if I were wandering in an endless nightmare. I should imagine
that you will be returning to the city before long, but it will be a very long
time before I, so lost in sin, will be permitted to see you.

> "Imagine, at Suma of the dripping brine,
> The woman of Ise,[8] gathering briny sea grass.

"And what is to become of one, in a world where everything conspires
to bring new sorrow?" It was a long letter.

> "The tide recedes along the coast of Ise.
> No hope, no promise in the empty shells."

Laying down her brush as emotion overcame her and then beginning
again, she finally sent off some four or five sheets of white Chinese paper.
The gradations of ink were marvelous. He had been fond of her, and it
had been wrong to make so much of that one incident.[9] She had turned
against him and presently left him. It all seemed such a waste. The letter
itself and the occasion for it so moved him that he even felt a certain

---

7. Alludes to a poem: "The heart of a parent is not darkness, and yet / He wanders lost in thoughts
upon his child."   8. She has gone to Ise, where her daughter serves as high priestess.   9. It was the
Rokujō lady's jealousy, in the form of a vengeful spirit, that killed the lady in chap. 4.

affection for the messenger, an intelligent young man in her daughter's service. Detaining him for several days, he heard about life at Ise. The house being rather small, the messenger was able to observe Genji at close range. He was moved to tears of admiration by what he saw.

The reader may be left to imagine Genji's reply. He said among other things: "Had I known I was destined to leave the city, it would have been better, I tell myself in the tedium and loneliness here, to go off with you to Ise.

> "With the lady of Ise I might have ridden small boats
> That row the waves, and avoided dark sea tangles.[1]

> "How long, dripping brine on driftwood logs,
> On logs of lament, must I gaze at this Suma coast?

"I cannot know when I will see you again."

But at least his letters brought the comfort of knowing that he was well.

There came letters, sad and yet comforting, from the lady of the orange blossoms and her sister.

> "Ferns of remembrance weigh our eaves ever more,
> And heavily falls the dew upon our sleeves."

There was no one, he feared, whom they might now ask to clear away the rank growth. Hearing that the long rains had damaged their garden walls, he sent off orders to the city that people from nearby manors see to repairs.

Oborozukiyo had delighted the scandalmongers, and she was now in very deep gloom. Her father, the minister, for she was his favorite daughter, sought to intercede on her behalf with the emperor and Kokiden. The emperor was moved to forgive her. She had been severely punished, it was true, for her grave offense, but not as severely as if she had been one of the companions of the royal bedchamber. In the Seventh Month she was permitted to return to court. She continued to long for Genji. Much of the emperor's old love remained, and he chose to ignore criticism and keep her near him, now berating her and now making impassioned vows. He was a handsome man and he groomed himself well, and it was something of an affront that old memories should be so much with her.

"Things do not seem right now that he is gone," he said one evening when they were at music together. "I am sure that there are many who feel the loss even more strongly than I do. I cannot put away the fear that I have gone against Father's last wishes and that it is a dereliction for which I must one day suffer." There were tears in his eyes and she too was weeping. "I have awakened to the stupidity of the world and I do not feel that I wish to remain in it much longer. And how would you feel if I were to die? I hate to think that you would grieve less for me gone forever than for him gone so briefly such a short distance away. The poet[2] who said that we love while we live did not know a great deal about love." Tears were streaming from Oborozukiyo's eyes. "And whom might you be weep-

---

1. From the folk song "Men of Ise": "Oh, the men of Ise are strange ones. / How so? How are they strange? / They ride small boats that row the waves, / That row the waves, they do." 2. Unidentified.

ing for? It is sad that we have no children. I would like to follow Father's instructions and adopt the crown prince, but people will raise innumerable objections. It all seems very sad."

There were some whose ideas of government did not accord with his own, but he was too young to impose his will. He passed his days in helpless anger and sorrow.

At Suma, melancholy autumn winds were blowing. Genji's house was some distance from the sea, but at night the wind that blew over the barriers, now as in Yukihira's day, seemed to bring the surf to his bedside. Autumn was hushed and lonely at a place of exile. He had few companions. One night when they were all asleep he raised his head from his pillow and listened to the roar of the wind and of the waves, as if at his ears. Though he was unaware that he wept, his tears were enough to set his pillow afloat. He plucked a few notes on his koto, but the sound only made him sadder.

"The waves on the strand, like moans of helpless longing.
The winds—like messengers from those who grieve?"

He had awakened the others. They sat up, and one by one they were in tears.

This would not do. Because of him they had been swept into exile, leaving families from whom they had never before been parted. It must be very difficult for them, and his own gloom could scarcely be making things easier. So he set about cheering them. During the day he would invent games and make jokes, and set down this and that poem on multicolored patchwork, and paint pictures on fine specimens of figured Chinese silk. Some of his larger paintings were masterpieces. He had long ago been told of this Suma coast and these hills and had formed a picture of them in his mind, and he found now that his imagination had fallen short of the actuality. What a pity, said his men, that they could not summon Tsunenori and Chieda and other famous painters of the day to add colors to Genji's monochromes. This resolute cheerfulness had the proper effect. His men, four or five of whom were always with him, would not have dreamed of leaving him.

There was a profusion of flowers in the garden. Genji came out, when the evening colors were at their best, to a gallery from which he had a good view of the coast. His men felt chills of apprehension as they watched him, for the loneliness of the setting made him seem like a visitor from another world. In a dark robe tied loosely over singlets of figured white and aster-colored trousers, he announced himself as "a disciple of the Buddha" and slowly intoned a sutra, and his men thought that they had never heard a finer voice. From offshore came the voices of fishermen raised in song. The barely visible boats were like little seafowl on an utterly lonely sea, and as he brushed away a tear induced by the splashing of oars and the calls of wild geese overhead, the white of his hand against the jet black of his rosary was enough to bring comfort to men who had left their families behind.

"Might they be companions of those I long for?
Their cries ring sadly through the sky of their journey."

This was Yoshikiyo's reply:

> "I know not why they bring these thoughts of old,
> These wandering geese. They were not then my comrades."

And Koremitsu's:

> "No colleagues of mine, these geese beyond the clouds.
> They chose to leave their homes, and I did not."

And that of the guards officer who had cut such a proud figure on the day of the Kamo lustration:

> "Sad are their cries as they wing their way from home.
> They still find solace, for they still have comrades.

It is cruel to lose one's comrades."

His father had been posted to Hitachi, but he himself had come with Genji. He contrived, for all that must have been on his mind, to seem cheerful.

A radiant moon had come out. They were reminded that it was the harvest full moon. Genji could not take his eyes from it. On other such nights there had been concerts at court, and perhaps they of whom he was thinking would be gazing at this same moon and thinking of him. "My thoughts are of you, old friend," he sang, "two thousand leagues away."[3] His men were in tears.

His longing was intense at the memory of Fujitsubo's farewell poem, and as other memories came back, one after another, he had to turn away to hide his tears. It was very late, said his men, but still he did not come inside.

> "So long as I look upon it I find comfort,
> The moon which comes again to the distant city."

He thought of the emperor and how much he had resembled their father, that last night when they had talked so fondly of old times. "I still have with me the robe which my lord gave me,"[4] he whispered, going inside. He did in fact have a robe that was a gift from the emperor, and he kept it always beside him.

> "Not bitter thoughts alone does this singlet bring.
> Its sleeves are damp with tears of affection too."

The assistant viceroy of Kyushu was returning to the capital. He had a large family and was especially well provided with daughters, and since progress by land would have been difficult he had sent his wife and the daughters by boat. They proceeded by easy stages, putting in here and there along the coast. The scenery at Suma was especially pleasing, and the news that Genji was in residence produced blushes and sighs far out at sea. The Gosechi dancer[5] would have liked to cut the tow rope and

---

3. From Po Chü-i's poem *On the Evening of the Full Moon of the Eighth Month.*   4. From a poem by Sugawara Michizane (9th century), scholar, poet, and bureaucrat; he was in exile.   5. Gosechi dances were part of a festival held in the Eleventh Month, usually performed by the young daughters of noble families. The appearance of the Gosechi dancer here is abrupt and puzzling. See n. 2, p. 1382.

drift ashore. The sound of a koto came faint from the distance, the sadness of it joined to a sad setting and sad memories. The more sensitive members of the party were in tears.

The assistant viceroy sent a message. "I had hoped to call on you immediately upon returning to the city from my distant post, and when, to my surprise, I found myself passing your house, I was filled with the most intense feelings of sorrow and regret. Various acquaintances who might have been expected to come from the city have done so, and our party has become so numerous that it would be out of the question to call on you. I shall hope to do so soon."

His son, the governor of Chikuzen, brought the message. Genji had taken notice of the youth and obtained an appointment for him in the imperial secretariat. He was sad to see his patron in such straits, but people were watching and had a way of talking, and he stayed only briefly.

"It was kind of you to come," said Genji. "I do not often see old friends these days."

His reply to the assistant viceroy was in a similar vein. Everyone in the Kyushu party and in the party newly arrived from the city as well was deeply moved by the governor's description of what he had seen. The tears of sympathy almost seemed to invite worse misfortunes.

The Gosechi dancer contrived to send him a note.

> "Now taut, now slack, like my unruly heart,
>   The tow rope is suddenly still at the sound of a koto.

"Scolding will not improve me."[6]

He smiled, so handsome a smile that his men felt rather inadequate.

> "Why, if indeed your heart is like the two rope,
>   Unheeding must you pass this strand of Suma?

"I had not expected to leave you for these wilds."[7]

There once was a man who, passing Akashi on his way into exile,[8] brought pleasure into an innkeeper's life with an impromptu Chinese poem. For the Gosechi dancer the pleasure was such that she would have liked to make Suma her home.

As time passed, the people back in the city, and even the emperor himself, found that Genji was more and more in their thoughts. The crown prince was the saddest of all. His nurse and Omyōbu would find him weeping in a corner and search helplessly for ways to comfort him. Once so fearful of rumors and their possible effect on this child of hers and Genji's, Fujitsubo now grieved that Genji must be away.

In the early days of his exile he corresponded with his brothers and with important friends at court. Some of his Chinese poems were widely praised.

Kokiden flew into a rage. "A man out of favor with His Majesty is expected to have trouble feeding himself. And here he is living in a fine

---

6. Alludes to a poem in *The Kokinshū:* "My heart is like a ship upon the seas. / I am easily moved. Scolding will not improve me."   7. An allusion to *The Kokinshū:* "I had not expected to leave you for these wilds. / A fisherman's net is mine, an angler's line."   8. Sugawara Michizane.

stylish house and saying awful things about all of us. No doubt the grovelers around him are assuring him that a deer is a horse.[9]

And so writing to Genji came to be rather too much to ask of people, and letters stopped coming.

The months went by, and Murasaki was never really happy. All the women from the other wings of the house were now in her service. They had been of the view that she was beneath their notice, but as they came to observe her gentleness, her magnanimity in household matters, her thoughtfulness, they changed their minds, and not one of them departed her service. Among them were women of good family. A glimpse of her was enough to make them admit that she deserved Genji's altogether remarkable affection.

And as time went by at Suma, Genji began to feel that he could bear to be away from her no longer. But he dismissed the thought of sending for her: this cruel punishment was for himself alone. He was seeing a little of plebeian life, and he thought it very odd and, he must say, rather dirty. The smoke near at hand would, he supposed, be the smoke of the salt burners' fires. In fact, someone was trying to light wet kindling just behind the house.

> "Over and over the rural ones light fires.
> Not so unflagging the urban ones with their visits."

It was winter, and the snowy skies were wild. He beguiled the tedium with music, playing the koto himself and setting Koremitsu to the flute, with Yoshikiyo to sing for them. When he lost himself in a particularly moving strain the others would fall silent, tears in their eyes.

He thought of the lady the Chinese emperor sent off to the Huns.[1] How must the emperor have felt, how would Genji himself feel, in so disposing of a beautiful lady? He shuddered, as if some such task might be approaching, "at the end of a frosty night's dream."[2]

A bright moon flooded in, lighting the shallow-eaved cottage to the farthest corners. He was able to imitate the poet's feat of looking up at the night sky without going to the veranda.[3] There was a weird sadness in the setting moon. "The moon goes always to the west,"[4] he whispered.

> "All aimless is my journey through the clouds.
> It shames me that the unswerving moon should see me."

He recited it silently to himself. Sleepless as always, he heard the sad calls of the plovers in the dawn and (the others were not yet awake) repeated several times to himself:

> "Cries of plovers in the dawn bring comfort
> To one who awakens in a lonely bed."

---

9. It is recorded in the *Shih chi* (historical records) of ancient China that a eunuch planning a rebellion showed the high courtiers a deer and required them to call it a horse, ensuring that they feared him. 1. Wang Chao-chün was dispatched to the Huns from the harem of the Han emperor Yüan-ti because she had failed to bribe the artists who did portraits of court ladies, and the emperor therefore thought her ill-favored. 2. From a poem about the unlucky Wang Chao-chün. 3. Alludes to a poem written in Chinese, in which the poet describes a view of the night sky from within a ruined palace. 4. From *To the Moon*, a poem by Sugawara Michizane.

His practice of going through his prayers and ablutions in the deep of night seemed strange and wonderful to his men. Far from being tempted to leave him, they did not return even for brief visits to their families.

The Akashi coast was a very short distance away. Yoshikiyo remembered the daughter of the former governor, now a monk, and wrote to her. She did not answer.

"I would like to see you for a few moments sometime at your convenience," came a note from her father. "There is something I want to ask you."

Yoshikiyo was not encouraged. He would look very silly if he went to Akashi only to be turned away. He did not go.

The former governor was an extremely proud and intractable man. The incumbent governor was all-powerful in the province, but the eccentric old man had no wish to marry his daughter to such an upstart. He learned of Genji's presence at Suma.

"I hear that the shining Genji is out of favor," he said to his wife, "and that he has come to Suma. What a rare stroke of luck—the chance we have been waiting for. We must offer our girl."

"Completely out of the question. People from the city tell me that he has any number of fine ladies of his own and that he has reached out for one of the emperor's. That is why the scandal. What interest can he possibly take in a country lump like her?"

"You don't understand the first thing about it. My own views couldn't be more different. We must make our plans. We must watch for a chance to bring him here." His mind was quite made up, and he had the look of someone whose plans were not easily changed. The finery which he had lavished upon house and daughter quite dazzled the eye.

"He may be ever so grand a grand gentleman," persisted the mother, "but it hardly seems the right and sensible thing to choose of all people a man who has been sent into exile for a serious crime. It might just possibly be different if he were likely to look at her—but no. You must be joking."

"A serious crime! Why in China too exactly this sort of thing happens to every single person who has remarkable talents and stands out from the crowd. And who do you think he is? His late mother was the daughter of my uncle, the Lord Inspector. She had talent and made a name for herself, and when there wasn't enough of the royal love to go around, the others were jealous, and finally they killed her. But she left behind a son who was a royal joy and comfort. Ladies should have pride and high ambitions. I may be a bumpkin myself, but I doubt that he will think her entirely beneath contempt."

Though the girl was no great beauty, she was intelligent and sensitive and had a gentle grace of which someone of far higher rank would have been proud. She was reconciled to her sad lot. No one among the great persons of the land was likely to think her worth a glance. The prospect of marrying someone nearer her station in life revolted her. If she was left behind by those on whom she depended, she would become a nun, or perhaps throw herself into the sea.

Her father had done everything for her. He sent her twice a year to the Sumiyoshi Shrine, hoping that the god might be persuaded to notice her.

The New Year came to Suma, the days were longer, and time went by slowly. The sapling cherry Genji had planted the year before sent out a scattering of blossoms, the air was soft and warm, and memories flooded back, bringing him often to tears. He thought longingly of the ladies for whom he had wept when, toward the end of the Second Month the year before, he had prepared to depart the city. The cherries would now be in bloom before the Grand Hall. He thought of that memorable cherry-blossom festival, and his father, and the extraordinarily handsome figure his brother, now the emperor, had presented, and he remembered how his brother had favored him by reciting his Chinese poem.

A Japanese poem[5] formed in his mind:

> "Fond thoughts I have of the noble ones on high,
> And the day of the flowered caps has come again."

Tō no Chūjō was now a councillor. He was a man of such fine character that everyone wished him well, but he was not happy. Everything made him think of Genji. Finally he decided that he did not care what rumors might arise and what misdeeds he might be accused of and hurried off to Suma. The sight of Genji brought tears of joy and sadness. Genji's house seemed very strange and exotic. The surroundings were such that he would have liked to paint them. The fence was of plaited bamboo and the pillars were of pine and the stairs of stone.[6] It was a rustic, provincial sort of dwelling, and very interesting.

Genji's dress too was somewhat rustic. Over a singlet dyed lightly in a yellowish color denoting no rank or office he wore a hunting robe and trousers of greenish gray. It was plain garb and intentionally countrified, but it so became the wearer as to bring an immediate smile of pleasure to his friend's lips. Genji's personal utensils and accessories were of a makeshift nature, and his room was open to anyone who wished to look in. The gaming boards and stones were also of rustic make. The religious objects that lay about told of earnest devotion. The food was very palatable and very much in the local taste. For his friend's amusement, Genji had fishermen bring fish and shells. Tō no Chūjō had them questioned about their maritime life, and learned of perils and tribulations. Their speech was as incomprehensible as the chirping of birds, but no doubt their feelings were like his own. He brightened their lives with clothes and other gifts. The stables being nearby, fodder was brought from a granary or something of the sort beyond, and the feeding process was as novel and interesting as everything else. Tō no Chūjō hummed the passage from "The Well of Asuka"[7] about the well-fed horses.

Weeping and laughing, they talked of all that had happened over the months.

"Yūgiri quite rips the house to pieces, and Father worries and worries about him."

Genji was of course sorry to hear it; but since I am not capable of recording the whole of the long conversation, I should perhaps refrain from recording any part of it. They composed Chinese poetry all through

5. The poem he remembers was written in Chinese. The poem he composes is in Japanese.   6. Giving the house a Chinese aspect.   7. A folk song popular with the nobility.

the night. Tō no Chūjō had come in defiance of the gossips and slanderers, but they intimidated him all the same. His stay was a brief one.

Wine was brought in, and their toast was from Po Chü-i:

> "Sad topers we. Our springtime cups flow with tears."

The tears were general, for it had been too brief a meeting.

A line of geese flew over in the dawn sky.

> "In what spring tide will I see again my old village?
> I envy the geese, returning whence they came."

Sorrier than ever that he must go, Tō no Chūjō replied:

> "Sad are the geese to leave their winter's lodging.
> Dark my way of return to the flowery city."

He had brought gifts from the city, both elegant and practical. Genji gave him in return a black pony, a proper gift for a traveler.

"Considering its origins, you may fear that it will bring bad luck; but you will find that it neighs into the northern winds."[8]

It was a fine beast.

"To remember me by," said Tō no Chūjō, giving in return what was recognized to be a very fine flute. The situation demanded a certain reticence in the giving of gifts.

The sun was high, and Tō no Chūjō's men were becoming restive. He looked back and looked back, and Genji almost felt that no visit at all would have been better than such a brief one.

"And when will we meet again? It is impossible to believe that you will be here forever."

> "Look down upon me, cranes who skim the clouds,
> And see me unsullied as this cloudless day.

"Yes, I do hope to go back, someday. But when I think how difficult it has been for even the most remarkable men to pick up their old lives, I am no longer sure that I want to see the city again."

> "Lonely the voice of the crane among the clouds.
> Gone the comrade that once flew at its side.

"I have been closer to you than ever I have deserved. My regrets for what has happened are bitter."

They scarcely felt that they had had time to renew their friendship. For Genji the loneliness was unrelieved after his friend's departure.

It was the day of the serpent, the first such day in the Third Month.

"The day when a man who has worries goes down and washes them away," said one of his men, admirably informed, it would seem, in all the annual observances.

Wishing to have a look at the seashore, Genji set forth. Plain, rough curtains were strung up among the trees, and a soothsayer who was doing the circuit of the province was summoned to perform the lustration.

---

8. Alludes to a Chinese poem: "The Tartar pony faces towards the north. / The Annamese bird nests on the southern branch."

Genji thought he could see something of himself in the rather large doll being cast off to sea, bearing away sins and tribulations.

"Cast away to drift on an alien vastness,
I grieve for more than a doll cast out to sea."

The bright, open seashore showed him to wonderful advantage. The sea stretched placid into measureless distances. He thought of all that had happened to him, and all that was still to come.

"You eight hundred myriad gods must surely help me,
For well you know that blameless I stand before you."

Suddenly a wind came up and even before the services were finished the sky was black. Genji's men rushed about in confusion. Rain came pouring down, completely without warning. Though the obvious course would have been to return straightway to the house, there had been no time to send for umbrellas. The wind was now a howling tempest, everything that had not been tied down was scuttling off across the beach. The surf was biting at their feet. The sea was white, as if spread over with white linen. Fearful every moment of being struck down, they finally made their way back to the house.

"I've never seen anything like it," said one of the men. "Winds do come up from time to time, but not without warning. It is all very strange and very terrible."

The lightning and thunder seemed to announce the end of the world, and the rain to beat its way into the ground; and Genji sat calmly reading a sutra. The thunder subsided in the evening, but the wind went on through the night.

"Our prayers seem to have been answered. A little more and we would have been carried off. I've heard that tidal waves do carry people off before they know what is happening to them, but I've not seen anything like this."

Towards dawn sleep was at length possible. A man whom he did not recognize came to Genji in a dream.

"The court summons you." He seemed to be reaching for Genji. "Why do you not go?"

It would be the king of the sea, who was known to have a partiality for handsome men. Genji decided that he could stay no longer at Suma.

CHAPTER 13

Akashi[9]

The days went by and the thunder and rain continued. What was Genji to do? People would laugh if, in this extremity, out of favor at court, he were to return to the city. Should he then seek a mountain retreat? But if it were to be noised about that a storm had driven him away, then he would cut a ridiculous figure in history.

---

9. A coastal village on the Inland Sea, approximately six miles west of Suma.

His dreams were haunted by that same apparition. Messages from the city almost entirely ceased coming as the days went by without a break in the storms. Might he end his days at Suma? No one was likely to come calling in these tempests.

A messenger did come from Murasaki, a sad, sodden creature. Had they passed in the street, Genji would scarcely have known whether he was man or beast, and of course would not have thought of inviting him to come near. Now the man brought a surge of pleasure and affection—though Genji could not help asking himself whether the storm had weakened his moorings.

Murasaki's letter, long and melancholy, said in part: "The terrifying deluge goes on without a break, day after day. Even the skies are closed off, and I am denied the comfort of gazing in your direction.

"What do they work, the sea winds down at Suma?
At home, my sleeves are assaulted by wave after wave."

Tears so darkened his eyes that it was as if they were inviting the waters to rise higher.

The man said that the storms had been fierce in the city too, and that a special reading of the Prajñāpāramitā Sutra[1] had been ordered. "The streets are all closed and the great gentlemen can't get to court, and everything has closed down."

The man spoke clumsily and haltingly, but he did bring news. Genji summoned him near and had him questioned.

"It's not the way it usually is. You don't usually have rain going on for days without a break and the wind howling on and on. Everyone is terrified. But it's worse here. They haven't had this hail beating right through the ground and thunder going on and on and not letting a body think." The terror written so plainly on his face did nothing to improve the spirits of the people at Suma.

Might it be the end of the world? From dawn the next day the wind was so fierce and the tide so high and the surf so loud that it was as if the crags and the mountains must fall. The horror of the thunder and lightning was beyond description. Panic spread at each new flash. For what sins, Genji's men asked, were they being punished? Were they to perish without another glimpse of their mothers and fathers, their dear wives and children?

Genji tried to tell himself that he had been guilty of no misdeed for which he must perish here on the seashore. Such were the panic and confusion around him, however, that he bolstered his confidence with special offerings to the god of Sumiyoshi.[2]

"O you of Sumiyoshi who protect the lands about: if indeed you are an avatar of the Blessed One, then you must save us."

His men were of course fearful for their lives; but the thought that so fine a gentleman (and in these deplorable circumstances) might be swept

---

1. "The Wisdom Sutra," which sets forth the Buddhist doctrine of Śūnyatā ("void" or "nothingness" or "relativity"): there is no such thing as static existence, since life is flux, causal factors change by the moment and all phenomena are relative and interdependent.   2. Deity venerated at a Shinto shrine in the Sumiyoshi ward of Osaka, a kind of patron saint of mariners and fishermen.

beneath the waters seemed altogether too tragic. The less distraught among them prayed in loud voices to this and that favored deity, Buddhist and Shinto, that their own lives be taken if it meant that his might be spared.

They faced Sumiyoshi and prayed and made vows: "Our lord was reared deep in the fastnesses of the palace, and all blessings were his. You who, in the abundance of your mercy, have brought strength through these lands to all who have sunk beneath the weight of their troubles: in punishment for what crimes do you call forth these howling waves? Judge his case if you will, you gods of heaven and earth. Guiltless, he is accused of a crime, stripped of his offices, driven from his house and city, left as you see him with no relief from the torture and the lamentation. And now these horrors, and even his life seems threatened. Why? we must ask. Because of sins in some other life, because of crimes in this one? If your vision is clear, O you gods, then take all this away."

Genji offered prayers to the king of the sea and countless other gods as well. The thunder was increasingly more terrible, and finally the gallery adjoining his rooms was struck by lightning. Flames sprang up and the gallery was destroyed. The confusion was immense; the whole world seemed to have gone mad. Genji was moved to a building out in back, a kitchen or something of the sort it seemed to be. It was crowded with people of every station and rank. The clamor was almost enough to drown out the lightning and thunder. Night descended over a sky already as black as ink.

Presently the wind and rain subsided and stars began to come out. The kitchen being altogether too mean a place, a move back to the main hall was suggested. The charred remains of the gallery were an ugly sight, however, and the hall had been badly muddied and all the blinds and curtains blown away. Perhaps, Genji's men suggested somewhat tentatively, it might be better to wait until dawn. Genji sought to concentrate upon the holy name, but his agitation continued to be very great.

He opened a wattled door and looked out. The moon had come up. The line left by the waves was white and dangerously near, and the surf was still high. There was no one here whom he could turn to, no student of the deeper truths who could discourse upon past and present and perhaps explain these wild events. All the fisherfolk had gathered at what they had heard was the house of a great gentleman from the city. They were as noisy and impossible to communicate with as a flock of birds, but no one thought of telling them to leave.

"If the wind had kept up just a little longer," someone said, "absolutely everything would have been swept under. The gods did well by us."

There are no words—"lonely" and "forlorn" seem much too weak—to describe his feelings.

"Without the staying hand of the king of the sea
The roar of the eight hundred waves would have taken us under."

Genji was as exhausted as if all the buffets and fires of the tempest had been aimed at him personally. He dozed off, his head against some nondescript piece of furniture.

The old emperor came to him, quite as when he had lived. "And why are you in this wretched place?" He took Genji's hand and pulled him to his feet. "You must do as the god of Sumiyoshi tells you. You must put out to sea immediately. You must leave this shore behind."

"Since I last saw you, sir," said Genji, overjoyed, "I have suffered an unbroken series of misfortunes. I had thought of throwing myself into the sea."

"That you must not do. You are undergoing brief punishment for certain sins. I myself did not commit any conscious crimes while I reigned, but a person is guilty of transgressions and oversights without his being aware of them. I am doing penance and have no time to look back towards this world. But an echo of your troubles came to me and I could not stand idle. I fought my way through the sea and up to this shore and I am very tired; but now that I am here I must see to a matter in the city." And he disappeared.

Genji called after him, begging to be taken along. He looked around him. There was only the bright face of the moon. His father's presence had been too real for a dream, so real that he must still be here. Clouds traced sad lines across the sky. It had been clear and palpable, the figure he had so longed to see even in a dream, so clear that he could almost catch an afterimage. His father had come through the skies to help him in what had seemed the last extremity of his sufferings. He was deeply grateful, even to the tempests; and in the aftermath of the dream he was happy.

Quite different emotions now ruffled his serenity. He forgot his immediate troubles and only regretted that his father had not stayed longer. Perhaps he would come again. Genji would have liked to go back to sleep, but he lay wakeful until daylight.

A little boat had pulled in at the shore and two or three men came up.

"The revered monk who was once governor of Harima has come from Akashi. If the former Minamoto councillor, Lord Yoshikiyo, is here, we wonder if we might trouble him to come down and hear the details of our mission."

Yoshikiyo pretended to be surprised and puzzled. "He was once among my closer acquaintances here in Harima, but we had a falling out and it has been some time since we last exchanged letters. What can have brought him through such seas in that little boat?"

Genji's dream had given intimations. He sent Yoshikiyo down to the boat immediately. Yoshikiyo marveled that it could even have been launched upon such a sea.

These were the details of the mission, from the mouth of the old governor: "Early this month a strange figure came to me in a dream. I listened, though somewhat incredulously, and was told that on the thirteenth there would be a clear and present sign. I was to ready a boat and make for this shore when the waves subsided. I did ready a boat, and then came this savage wind and lightning. I thought of numerous foreign sovereigns who have received instructions in dreams on how to save their lands, and I concluded that even at the risk of incurring his ridicule I must on the day appointed inform your lord of the import of the dream. And so I did

indeed put out to sea. A strange jet blew all the way and brought us to this shore. I cannot think of it except as divine intervention. And might I ask whether there have been corresponding manifestations here? I do hate to trouble you, but might I ask you to communicate all of this to your lord?"

Yoshikiyo quietly relayed the message, which brought new considerations. There had been these various unsettling signs conveyed to Genji dreaming and waking. The possibility of being laughed at for having departed these shores under threat now seemed the lesser risk. To turn his back on what might be a real offer of help from the gods would be to ask for still worse misfortunes. It was not easy to reject ordinary advice, and personal reservations counted for little when the advice came from great eminences. "Defer to them; they will cause you no reproaches," a wise man of old once said. He could scarcely face worse misfortunes by deferring than by not deferring, and he did not seem likely to gain great merit and profit by hesitating out of concern for his brave name. Had not his own father come to him? What room was there for doubts?

He sent back his answer: "I have been through a great deal in this strange place, and I hear nothing at all from the city. I but gaze upon a sun and moon going I know not where as comrades from my old home; and now comes this angler's boat, happy tidings on an angry wind.[3] Might there be a place along your Akashi coast where I can hide myself?"

The old man was delighted. Genji's men pressed him to set out even before sunrise. Taking along only four or five of his closest attendants, he boarded the boat. That strange wind came up again and they were at Akashi as if they had flown. It was very near, within crawling distance, so to speak; but still the workings of the wind were strange and marvelous.

The Akashi coast was every bit as beautiful as he had been told it was. He would have preferred fewer people, but on the whole he was pleased. Along the coast and in the hills the old monk had put up numerous buildings with which to take advantage of the four seasons: a reed-roofed beach cottage with fine seasonal vistas; beside a mountain stream a chapel of some grandeur and dignity, suitable for rites and meditation and invocation of the holy name; and rows of storehouses where the harvest was put away and a bountiful life assured for the years that remained. Fearful of the high tides, the old monk had sent his daughter and her women off to the hills. The house on the beach was at Genji's disposal.

The sun was rising as Genji left the boat and got into a carriage. This first look by daylight at his new guest brought a happy smile to the old man's lips. He felt as if the accumulated years were falling away and as if new years had been granted him. He gave silent thanks to the god of Sumiyoshi. He might have seemed ridiculous as he bustled around seeing to Genji's needs, as if the radiance of the sun and the moon had become his private property; but no one laughed at him.

I need not describe the beauty of the Akashi coast. The careful attention that had gone into the house and the rocks and plantings of the garden, the graceful line of the coast—it was infinitely pleasanter than Suma, and

---

3. Alludes to a poem by Ki no Tsurayuki: "An angler's boat upon the waves that pound us, / Happy tidings on an angry wind."

one would not have wished to ask a less than profoundly sensitive painter to paint it. The house was in quiet good taste. The old man's way of life was as Genji had heard it described, hardly more rustic than that of the grandees at court. In sheer luxury, indeed, he rather outdid them.

When Genji had rested for a time he got off messages to the city. He summoned Murasaki's messenger, who was still at Suma recovering from the horrors of his journey. Loaded with rewards for his services, he now set out again for the city. It would seem that Genji sent off a description of his perils to priests and others of whose services he regularly made use, but he told only Fujitsubo how narrow his escape had in fact been. He repeatedly laid down his brush as he sought to answer that very affectionate letter from Murasaki.

"I feel that I have run the whole gamut of horrors and then run it again, and more than ever I would like to renounce the world; but though everything else has fled away, the image which you entrusted to the mirror has not for an instant left me. I think that I might not see you again.

"Yet farther away, upon the beach at Akashi,
    My thoughts of a distant city, and of you.

"I am still half dazed, which fact will I fear be too apparent in the confusion and disorder of this letter."

Though it was true that his letter was somewhat disordered, his men thought it splendid. How very fond he must be of their lady! It would seem that they sent off descriptions of their own perils.

The apparently interminable rains had at last stopped and the sky was bright far into the distance. The fishermen radiated good spirits. Suma had been a lonely place with only a few huts scattered among the rocks. It was true that the crowds here at Akashi were not entirely to Genji's liking, but it was a pleasant spot with much to interest him and take his mind from his troubles.

The old man's devotion to the religious life was rather wonderful. Only one matter interfered with it: worry about his daughter. He told Genji a little of his concern for the girl. Genji was sympathetic. He had heard that she was very handsome and wondered if there might not be some bond between them,[4] that he should have come upon her in this strange place. But no; here he was in the remote provinces, and he must think of nothing but his own prayers. He would be unable to face Murasaki if he were to depart from the promises he had made her. Yet he continued to be interested in the girl. Everything suggested that her nature and appearance were very far from ordinary.

Reluctant to intrude himself, the old man had moved to an outbuilding. He was restless and unhappy when away from Genji, however, and he prayed more fervently than ever to the gods and Buddhas that his unlikely hope might be realized. Though in his sixties he had taken good care of himself and was young for his age. The religious life and the fact that he was of proud lineage may have had something to do with the matter. He was stubborn and intractable, as old people often are, but he was well

---

4. Essentially a Buddhist conception, that their fates might be linked from former lives.

versed in antiquities and not without a certain subtlety. His stories of old times did a great deal to dispel Genji's boredom. Genji had been too busy himself for the sort of erudition, the lore about customs and precedents, which he now had in bits and installments, and he told himself that it would have been a great loss if he had not known Akashi and its venerable master.

In a sense they were friends, but Genji rather overawed the old man. Though he had seemed so confident when he told his wife of his hopes, he hesitated, unable to broach the matter, now that the time for action had come, and seemed capable only of bemoaning his weakness and inadequacy. As for the daughter, she rarely saw a passable man here in the country among people of her own rank; and now she had had a glimpse of a man the like of whom she had not suspected to exist. She was a shy, modest girl, and she thought him quite beyond her reach. She had had hints of her father's ambitions and thought them wildly inappropriate, and her discomfort was greater for having Genji near.

It was the Fourth Month. The old man had all the curtains and fixtures of Genji's rooms changed for fresh summery ones. Genji was touched and a little embarrassed, feeling that the old man's attentions were perhaps a bit overdone; but he would not have wished for the world to offend so proud a nature.

A great many messages now came from the city inquiring after his safety. On a quiet moonlit night when the sea stretched off into the distance under a cloudless sky, he almost felt that he was looking at the familiar waters of his own garden. Overcome with longing, he was like a solitary, nameless wanderer. "Awaji, distant foam,"[5] he whispered to himself.

> "Awaji: in your name is all my sadness,
> And clear you stand in the light of the moon tonight."

He took out the seven-stringed koto, long neglected, which he had brought from the city and spread a train of sad thoughts through the house as he plucked out a few tentative notes. He exhausted all his skills on "The Wide Barrow,"[6] and the sound reached the house in the hills on a sighing of wind and waves. Sensitive young ladies heard it and were moved. Lowly rustics, though they could not have identified the music, were lured out into the sea winds, there to catch cold.

The old man could not sit still. Casting aside his beads, he came running over to the main house.

"I feel as if a world I had thrown away were coming back," he said, breathless and tearful. "It is a night such as to make one feel that the blessed world for which one longs must be even so."

Genji played on in a reverie, a flood of memories of concerts over the years, of this gentleman and that lady on flute and koto, of voices raised in song, of times when he and they had been the center of attention,

---

5. Alludes to a poem: "Awaji in the moonlight, like distant foam: / From these cloudy sovereign heights it seems so near." The place name *Awaji* contains the word *awa*, "foam," and also suggests the Japanese word *aware*, an exclamation of vague and undefined sadness.   6. A Chinese composition, apparently, which does not survive.

recipients of praise and favors from the emperor himself. Sending to the house on the hill for a lute and a thirteen-stringed koto, the old man now seemed to change roles and become one of these priestly mendicants who make their living by the lute. He played a most interesting and affecting strain. Genji played a few notes on the thirteen-stringed koto which the old man pressed on him and was thought an uncommonly impressive performer on both sorts of koto. Even the most ordinary music can seem remarkable if the time and place are right; and here on the wide seacoast, open far into the distance, the groves seemed to come alive in colors richer than the bloom of spring or the change of autumn, and the calls of the water rails were as if they were pounding on the door and demanding to be admitted.

The old man had a delicate style to which the instruments were beautifully suited and which delighted Genji. "One likes to see a gentle lady quite at her ease with a koto," said Genji, as if with nothing specific in mind.

The old man smiled. "And where, sir, is one likely to find a gentler, more refined musician than yourself? On the koto I am in the third generation from the emperor Daigo. I have left the great world for the rustic surroundings in which you have found me, and sometimes when I have been more gloomy than usual I have taken out a koto and picked away at it; and, curiously, there has been someone who has imitated me. Her playing has come quite naturally to resemble my master's. Or perhaps it has only seemed so to the degenerate ear of the mountain monk who has only the pine winds for company. I wonder if it might be possible to let you hear a strain, in the greatest secrecy of course." He brushed away a tear.

"I have been rash and impertinent. My playing must have sounded like no playing at all." Genji turned away from the koto. "I do not know why, but it has always been the case that ladies have taken especially well to the koto. One hears that with her father to teach her the fifth daughter of the emperor Saga was a great master of the instrument, but it would seem that she had no successors. The people who set themselves up as masters these days are quite ordinary performers with no real grounding at all. How fascinating that someone who still holds to the grand style should be hidden away on this coast. Do let me hear her."

"No difficulty at all, if that is what you wish. If you really wish it, I can summon her. There was once a poet,[7] you will remember, who was much pleased at the lute of a tradesman's wife. While we are on the subject of lutes, there were not many even in the old days who could bring out the best in the instrument. Yet it would seem that the person of whom I speak plays with a certain sureness and manages to affect a rather pleasing delicacy. I have no idea where she might have acquired these skills. It seems wrong that she should be asked to compete with the wild waves, but sometimes in my gloom I do have her strike up a tune."

He spoke with such spirit that Genji, much interested, pushed the lute toward him.

7. Po Chü-i's *The Lutist.*

He did indeed play beautifully, adding decorations that have gone out of fashion. There was a Chinese elegance in his touch, and he was able to induce a particularly solemn tremolo from the instrument. Though it might have been argued that the setting was wrong, an adept among his retainers was persuaded to sing for them about the clean shore of Ise.[8] Tapping out the rhythm, Genji would join in from time to time, and the old man would pause to offer a word of praise. Refreshments were brought in, very prettily arranged. The old man was most assiduous in seeing that the cups were kept full, and it became the sort of evening when troubles are forgotten.

Late in the night the sea breezes were cool and the moon seemed brighter and clearer as it sank towards the west. All was quiet. In pieces and fragments the old man told about himself, from his feelings upon taking up residence on this Akashi coast to his hopes for the future life and the prospects which his devotions seemed to be opening. He added, unsolicited, an account of his daughter. Genji listened with interest and sympathy.

"It is not easy for me to say it, sir, but the fact that you are here even briefly in what must be for you strange and quite unexpected surroundings, and the fact that you are being asked to undergo trials new to your experience—I wonder if it might not be that the powers to whom an aged monk has so fervently prayed for so many years have taken pity on him. It is now eighteen years since I first prayed and made vows to the god of Sumiyoshi. I have had certain hopes for my daughter since she was very young, and every spring and autumn I have taken her to Sumiyoshi. At each of my six daily services, three of them in the daytime and three at night, I have put aside my own wishes for salvation and ventured a suggestion that my hopes for the girl be noticed. I have sunk to this provincial obscurity because I brought an unhappy destiny with me into this life. My father was a minister, and you see what I have become. If my family is to follow the same road in the future, I ask myself, then where will it end? But I have had high hopes for her since she was born. I have been determined that she go to some noble gentleman in the city. I have been accused of arrogance and unworthy ambitions and subjected to some rather unpleasant treatment. I have not let it worry me. I have said to her that while I live I will do what I can for her, limited though my resources may be; and that if I die before my hopes are realized she is to throw herself into the sea." He was weeping. It had taken great resolve for him to speak so openly.

Genji wept easily these days. "I had been feeling put upon, bundled off to this strange place because of crimes I was not aware of having committed. Your story makes me feel that there is a bond between us. Why did you not tell me earlier? Nothing has seemed quite real since I came here, and I have given myself up to prayers to the exclusion of everything else, and so I fear that I will have struck you as spiritless. Though reports had reached me of the lady of whom you have spoken, I had feared that she

---

8. Refers to the folk song "The Sea of Ise": "On the clean shore of Ise, / Let us gather shells in the tide. / Let us gather shells and jewels."

would want to have nothing to do with an outcast like myself. You will be my guide and intermediary? May I look forward to company these lonely evenings?"

The old man was thoroughly delighted.

"Do you too know the sadness of the nights
On the shore of Akashi with only thoughts for companions?"

"Imagine, if you will, how it has been for us through the long months and years." He faltered, though with no loss of dignity, and his voice was trembling.

"But you, sir, are used to this seacoast.

"The traveler passes fretful nights at Akashi.
The grass which he reaps for his pillow reaps no dreams."

His openness delighted the old man, who talked on and on—and became rather tiresome, I fear. In my impatience I may have allowed inaccuracies to creep in, and exaggerated his eccentricities.

In any event, he felt a clean happiness sweep over him. A beginning had been made.

At about noon the next day Genji got off a note to the house on the hill. A real treasure might lie buried in this unlikely spot. He took a great deal of trouble with his note, which was on a fine saffron-colored Korean paper.

"Do I catch, as I gaze into unresponsive skies,
A glimpse of a grove of which I have had certain tidings?

"My resolve has been quite dissipated."[9]

And was that all? one wonders.

The old man had been waiting. Genji's messenger came staggering back down the hill, for he had been hospitably received.

But the girl was taking time with her reply. The old man rushed to her rooms and urged haste, but to no avail. She thought her hand quite unequal to the task, and awareness of the difference in their stations dismayed her. She was not feeling well, she said, and lay down.

Though he would certainly have wished it otherwise, the old man finally answered in her place. "Her rustic sleeves are too narrow to encompass such awesome tidings, it would seem, and indeed she seems to have found herself incapable of even reading your letter.

"She gazes into the skies into which you gaze.
May they bring your thoughts and hers into some accord.

"But I fear that I will seem impertinent and forward."

It was in a most uncompromisingly old-fashioned hand, on sturdy Michinoku paper; but there was something spruce and dashing about it too. Yes, "forward" was the proper word. Indeed, Genji was rather startled. He gave the messenger a "bejeweled apron," an appropriate gift, he thought, from a beach cottage.[1]

9. Alludes to a poem in *The Kokinshū:* "Resolve that I would keep them to myself, / These thoughts of you, has been quite dissipated."   1. There is a pun on *tamamo,* "jeweled apron" (an elegant word for "apron") and a kind of seaweed.

He got off another message the next day, beautifully written on soft, delicate paper. "I am not accustomed to receiving letters from ladies' secretaries.

> "Unwillingly reticent about my sorrows
> I still must be—for no one makes inquiry.

"Though it is difficult to say just what I mean."

There would have been something unnatural about a girl who refused to be interested in such a letter. She thought it splendid, but she also thought it impossibly out of her reach. Notice from such supreme heights had the perverse effect of reducing her to tears and inaction.

She was finally badgered into setting something down. She chose delicately perfumed lavender paper and took great care with the gradations of her ink.

> "Unwillingly reticent—how can it be so?
> How can you sorrow for someone you have not met?"

The diction and the handwriting would have done credit to any of the fine ladies at court. He fell into a deep reverie, for he was reminded of days back in the city. But he did not want to attract attention, and presently shook it off.

Every other day or so, choosing times when he was not likely to be noticed, and when he imagined that her thoughts might be similar to his—a quiet, uneventful evening, a lonely dawn—he would get off a note to her. There was a proud reserve in her answers which made him want more than ever to meet her. But there was Yoshikiyo to think of. He had spoken of the lady as if he thought her his property, and Genji did not wish to contravene these long-standing claims. If her parents persisted in offering her to him, he would make that fact his excuse, and seek to pursue the affair as quietly as possible. Not that she was making things easy for him. She seemed prouder and more aloof than the proudest lady at court; and so the days went by in a contest of wills.

The city was more than ever on his mind now that he had moved beyond the Suma barrier. He feared that not even in jest[2] could he do without Murasaki. Again he was asking himself if he might not bring her quietly to Akashi, and he was on the point of doing just that. But he did not expect to be here very much longer, and nothing was to be gained by inviting criticism at this late date.

In the city it had been a year of omens and disturbances. On the thirteenth day of the Third Month, as the thunder and winds mounted to new fury, the emperor had a dream. His father stood glowering at the stairs to the royal bedchamber and had a great deal to say, all of it, apparently, about Genji. Deeply troubled, the emperor described the dream to his mother.

"On stormy nights a person has a way of dreaming about the things that are on his mind," she said. "If I were you I would not give it a second thought."

---

2. Alludes to a poem in *The Kokinshū:* "I wondered if even in jest I could do without you. / I gave it a try, to which I proved unequal."

Perhaps because his eyes had met the angry eyes of his father, he came down with a very painful eye ailment. Retreat and fasting were ordered for the whole court, even Kokiden's household. Then the minister, her father, died. He was of such years that his death need have surprised no one, but Kokiden too was unwell, and worse as the days went by; and the emperor had a great deal to worry about. So long as an innocent Genji was off in the wilderness, he feared, he must suffer. He ventured from time to time a suggestion that Genji be restored to his old rank and offices.

His mother sternly advised against it. "People will tax you with shallowness and indecision. Can you really think of having a man go into exile and then bringing him back before the minimum three years have gone by?"

And so he hesitated, and he and his mother were in increasingly poor health.

At Akashi it was the season when cold winds blow from the sea to make a lonely bed even lonelier.

Genji sometimes spoke to the old man. "If you were perhaps to bring her here when no one is looking?"

He thought that he could hardly be expected to visit her. She had her own ideas. She knew that rustic maidens should come running at a word from a city gentleman who happened to be briefly in the vicinity. No, she did not belong to his world, and she would only be inviting grief if she pretended that she did. Her parents had impossible hopes, it seemed, and were asking the unthinkable and building a future on nothing. What they were really doing was inviting endless trouble. It was good fortune enough to exchange notes with him for so long as he stayed on this shore. Her own prayers had been modest: that she be permitted a glimpse of the gentleman of whom she had heard so much. She had had her glimpse, from a distance, to be sure, and, brought in on the wind, she had also caught hints of his unmatched skill (of this too she had heard) on the koto. She had learned rather a great deal about him these past days, and she was satisfied. Indeed a nameless woman lost among the fishermen's huts had no right to expect even this. She was acutely embarrassed at any suggestion that he be invited nearer.

Her father too was uneasy. Now that his prayers were being answered he began to have thoughts of failure. It would be very sad for the girl, offered heedlessly to Genji, to learn that he did not want her. Rejection was painful at the hands of the finest gentleman. His unquestioning faith in all the invisible gods had perhaps led him to overlook human inclinations and probabilities.

"How pleasant," Genji kept saying, "if I could hear that koto to the singing of the waves. It is the season for such things. We should not let it pass."

Dismissing his wife's reservations and saying nothing to his disciples, the old man selected an auspicious day. He bustled around making preparations, the results of which were dazzling. The moon was near full. He sent off a note which said only: "This night that should not be wasted."[3]

3. Alludes to a poem: "If only I could show them to someone who knows, / This moon, these flowers, this night that should not be wasted."

It seemed a bit arch, but Genji changed to informal court dress and set forth late in the night. He had a carriage decked out most resplendently, and then, deciding that it might seem ostentatious, went on horseback instead. The lady's house was some distance back in the hills. The coast lay in full view below, the bay silver in the moonlight. He would have liked to show it to Murasaki. The temptation was strong to turn his horse's head and gallop on to the city.

> "Race on through the moonlit sky, O roan-colored horse,
> And let me be briefly with her for whom I long."[4]

The house was a fine one, set in a grove of trees. Careful attention had gone into all the details. In contrast to the solid dignity of the house on the beach, this house in the hills had a certain fragility about it, and he could imagine the melancholy thoughts that must come to one who lived here. There was sadness in the sound of the temple bells borne in on pine breezes from a hall of meditation nearby. Even the pines seemed to be asking for something as they sent their roots out over the crags. All manner of autumn insects were singing in the garden. He looked about him and saw a pavilion finer than the others. The cypress door upon which the moonlight seemed to focus was slightly open.

He hesitated and then spoke. There was no answer. She had resolved to admit him no nearer. All very aristocratic, thought Genji. Even ladies so wellborn that they were sheltered from sudden visitors usually tried to make conversation when the visitor was Genji. Perhaps she was letting him know that he was under a cloud. He was annoyed and thought of leaving. It would run against the mood of things to force himself upon her, and on the other hand he would look rather silly if it were to seem that she had bested him at this contest of wills. One would indeed have wished to show him, the picture of dejection, "to someone who knows."[5]

A curtain string brushed against a koto, to tell him that she had been passing a quiet evening at her music.

"And will you not play for me on the koto of which I have heard so much?

> "Would there were someone with whom I might share my thoughts
> And so dispel some part of these sad dreams."

> "You speak to one for whom the night has no end.
> How can she tell the dreaming from the waking?"

The almost inaudible whisper reminded him strongly of the Rokujō lady.

This lady had not been prepared for an incursion and could not cope with it. She fled to an inner room. How she could have contrived to bar it he could not tell, but it was very firmly barred indeed. Though he did not exactly force his way through, it is not to be imagined that he left matters as they were. Delicate, slender—she was almost too beautiful. Pleasure was mingled with pity at the thought that he was imposing himself upon

---

4. A play on words gives a roan horse a special affinity with moonlight.   5. See n. 3, p. 1375.

her. She was even more pleasing than reports from afar had had her. The autumn night, usually so long, was over in a trice. Not wishing to be seen, he hurried out, leaving affectionate assurances behind.

He got off an unobtrusive note later in the morning. Perhaps he was feeling twinges of conscience. The old monk was equally intent upon secrecy, and sorry that he was impelled to treat the messenger rather coolly.

Genji called in secret from time to time. The two houses being some distance apart, he feared being seen by fishermen, who were known to relish a good rumor, and sometimes several days would elapse between his visits. Exactly as she had expected, thought the girl. Her father, forgetting that enlightenment was his goal, quite gave his prayers over to silent queries as to when Genji might be expected to come again; and so (and it seems a pity) a tranquillity very laboriously attained was disturbed at a very late date.

Genji dreaded having Murasaki learn of the affair. He still loved her more than anyone, and he did not want her to make even joking reference to it. She was a quiet, docile lady, but she had more than once been unhappy with him. Why, for the sake of brief pleasure, had he caused her pain? He wished it were all his to do over again. The sight of the Akashi lady only brought new longing for the other lady.

He got off a more earnest and affectionate letter than usual, at the end of which he said: "I am in anguish at the thought that, because of foolish occurrences for which I have been responsible but have had little heart, might appear in a guise distasteful to you. There has been a strange, fleeting encounter. That I should volunteer this story will make you see, I hope, how little I wish to have secrets from you. Let the gods be my judges.

"It was but the fisherman's brush with the salty sea pine
Followed by a tide of tears of longing."

Her reply was gentle and unreproachful, and at the end of it she said: "That you should have deigned to tell me a dreamlike story which you could not keep to yourself calls to mind numbers of earlier instances.

"Naïve of me, perhaps; yet we did make our vows.
And now see the waves that wash the Mountain of Waiting!"[6]

It was the one note of reproach in a quiet, undemanding letter. He found it hard to put down, and for some nights he stayed away from the house in the hills.

The Akashi lady was convinced once more that her fears had become actuality. Now seemed the time to throw herself into the sea. She had only her parents to turn to and they were very old. She had had no ambitions for herself, no thought of making a respectable marriage. Yet the years had gone by happily enough, without storms or tears. Now she saw that the world can be very cruel. She managed to conceal her worries, however,

6. Alludes to a poem in *The Kokinshū*: "On the day that I am unfaithful to my vows, / May the waves break over the Mountain of Waiting of Sué." A very common pun makes *Matsuyama*, "Mount of Pines," also "Mountain of Waiting."

and to do nothing that might annoy Genji. He was more and more pleased with her as time went by.

But there was the other, the lady in the city, waiting and waiting for his return. He did not want to do anything that would make her unhappy, and he spent his nights alone. He sent sketchbooks off to her, adding poems calculated to provoke replies. No doubt her women were delighted with them; and when the sorrow was too much for her (and as if by thought transference) she too would make sketches and set down notes which came to resemble a journal.

And what did the future have in store for the two of them?

The New Year came, the emperor was ill, and a pall settled over court life. There was a son, by Lady Shōkyōden, daughter of the Minister of the Right, but the child was only two, far too young for the throne. The obvious course was to abdicate in favor of the crown prince. As the emperor turned over in his mind the problem of advice and counsel for his successor, he thought it more than ever a pity that Genji should be off in the provinces. Finally he went against Kokiden's injunctions and issued an amnesty. Kokiden had been ill from the previous year, the victim of a malign spirit, it seemed, and numerous other dire omens had disturbed the court. Though the emperor's eye ailment had for a time improved, perhaps because of strict fasting, it was worse again. Late in the Seventh Month, in deep despondency, he issued a second order, summoning Genji back to the city.

Genji had been sure that a pardon would presently come, but he also knew that life is uncertain. That it should come so soon was of course pleasing. At the same time the thought of leaving this Akashi coast filled him with regret. The old monk, though granting that it was most proper and just, was upset at the news. He managed all the same to tell himself that Genji's prosperity was in his own best interest. Genji visited the lady every night and sought to console her. From about the Sixth Month she had shown symptoms such as to make their relations more complex. A sad, ironical affair seemed at the same time to come to a climax and to disintegrate. He wondered at the perverseness of fates that seemed always to be bringing new surprises. The lady, and one could scarcely have blamed her, was sunk in the deepest gloom. Genji had set forth on a strange, dark journey with a comforting certainty that he would one day return to the city; and he now lamented that he would not see this Akashi again.

His men, in their several ways, were delighted. An escort came from the city, there was a joyous stir of preparation, and the master of the house was lost in tears. So the month came to an end. It was a season for sadness in any case, and sad thoughts accosted Genji. Why, now and long ago, had he abandoned himself, heedlessly but of his own accord, to random, profitless affairs of the heart?

"What a great deal of trouble he does cause," said those who knew the secret. "The same thing all over again. For almost a year he didn't tell anyone and he didn't seem to care the first thing about her. And now just when he ought to be letting well enough alone he makes things worse."

Yoshikiyo was the uncomfortable one. He knew what his fellows were saying: that he had talked too much and started it all.

Two days before his departure Genji visited his lady, setting out earlier than usual. This first really careful look at her revealed an astonishingly proud beauty. He comforted her with promises that he would choose an opportune time to bring her to the city. I shall not comment again upon his own good looks. He was thinner from fasting, and emaciation seemed to add the final touches to the picture. He made tearful vows. The lady replied in her heart that this small measure of affection was all she wanted and deserved, and that his radiance only emphasized her own dullness. The waves moaned in the autumn winds, and smoke from the salt burners' fires drew faint lines across the sky, and all the symbols of loneliness seemed to gather together.

"Even though we now must part for a time,
The smoke from these briny fires will follow me."

"Smoldering thoughts like the sea grass burned on these shores.
And what good now to ask for anything more?"

She fell silent, weeping softly, and a rather conventional poem seemed to say a great deal.

She had not, through it all, played for him on the koto of which he had heard so much.

"Do let me hear it. Let it be a memento."

Sending for the seven-stringed koto he had brought from the city, he played an unusual strain, quiet but wonderfully clear on the midnight air. Unable to restrain himself, the old man pushed a thirteen-stringed koto toward his daughter. She was apparently in a mood for music. Softly she tuned the instrument, and her touch suggested very great polish and elegance. He had thought Fujitsubo's playing quite incomparable. It was in the modern style, and enough to bring cries of wonder from anyone who knew a little about music. For him it was like Fujitsubo herself, the essence of all her delicate awareness. The koto of the lady before him was quiet and calm, and so rich in overtones as almost to arouse envy. She left off playing just as the connoisseur who was her listener had passed the first stages of surprise and become eager attention. Disappointment and regret succeeded pleasure. He had been here for nearly a year. Why had he not insisted that she play for him, time after time? All he could do now was repeat the old vows.

"Take this koto," he said, "to remember me by. Someday we will play together."

Her reply was soft and almost casual:

"One heedless word, one koto, to set me at rest.
In the sound of it the sound of my weeping, forever."

He could not let it pass.

"Do not change the middle string[7] of this koto.
Unchanging I shall be till we meet again.

---

7. There are various theories about what this expression means. The most plausible is that the middle string remains unaltered during tuning, although the translator does not follow this interpretation.

"And we will meet again before it has slipped out of tune."

Yet it was not unnatural that the parting should seem more real than the reunion.

On the last morning Genji was up and ready before daybreak. Though he had little time to himself in all the stir, he contrived to write to her:

> "Sad the retreating waves at leaving this shore.
> Sad I am for you, remaining after."

> "You leave, my reed-roofed hut will fall to ruin.
> Would that I might go out with these waves."

It was an honest poem, and in spite of himself he was weeping. One could, after all, become fond of a hostile place, said those who did not know the secret. Those who did, Yoshikiyo and others, were a little jealous, concluding that it must have been a rather successful affair.

There were tears, for all the joy; but I shall not dwell upon them.

The old man had arranged the grandest of farewell ceremonies. He had splendid travel robes for everyone, even the lowliest footmen. One marveled that he had found time to collect them all. The gifts for Genji himself were of course the finest, chests and chests of them, borne by a retinue which he attached to Genji's. Some of them would make very suitable gifts in the city. He had overlooked nothing.

The lady had pinned a poem to a travel robe:

> "I made it for you, but the surging brine has wet it.
> And might you find it unpleasant and cast it off?"

Despite the confusion, he sent one of his own robes in return, and with it a note:

"It was very thoughtful of you.

> "Take it, this middle robe, let it be the symbol
> Of days uncounted but few between now and then."

Something else, no doubt, to put in her chest of memories. It was a fine robe and it bore a most remarkable fragrance. How could it fail to move her?

The old monk, his face like one of the twisted shells on the beach, was meanwhile making some of the younger people smile. "I have quite renounced the world," he said, "but the thought that I may not see you back to the city—

> "Though weary of life, seasoned by salty winds,
> I am not able to leave this shore behind,

and I wander lost in thoughts upon my child.[8] Do let me see you at least as far as the border. It may seem forward of me, but if something should from time to time call up thoughts of her, do please let her hear from you."

"It is an impossibility, sir, for very particular reasons, that I can ever forget her. You will very quickly be made to see my real intentions. If I seem dispirited, it is only because I am sad to leave all this behind.

8. See n. 7, p. 1355.

"I wept upon leaving the city in the spring.
I weep in the autumn on leaving this home by the sea.

"What else can I do?" And he brushed away a tear.

The old man seemed on the point of expiring.

The lady did not want anyone to guess the intensity of her grief, but it was there, and with it sorrow at the lowly rank (she knew that she could not complain) that had made this parting inevitable. His image remained before her, and she seemed capable only of weeping.

Her mother tried everything to console her. "What could we have been thinking of? You have such odd ideas," she said to her husband, "and I should have been more careful."

"Enough, enough. There are reasons why he cannot abandon her. I have no doubt that he has already made his plans. Stop worrying, mix yourself a dose of something or other. This wailing will do no good." But he was sitting disconsolate in a corner.

The women of the house, the mother and the nurse and the rest, went on charging him with unreasonable methods. "We had hoped and prayed over the years that she might have the sort of life any girl wants, and things finally seemed to be going well—and now see what has happened."

It was true. Old age suddenly advanced and subdued him, and he spent his days in bed. But when night came he was up and alert.

"What can have happened to my beads?"

Unable to find them, he brought empty hands together in supplication. His disciples giggled. They giggled again when he set forth on a moonlight peregrination and managed to fall into the brook and bruise his hip on one of the garden stones he had chosen so carefully. For a time pain drove away, or at least obscured, his worries.

Genji went through lustration ceremonies at Naniwa and sent a messenger to Sumiyoshi with thanks that he had come thus far and a promise to visit at a later date in fulfillment of his vows. His retinue had grown to an army and did not permit side excursions. He made his way directly back to the city. At Nijō the reunion was like a dream. Tears of joy flowed so freely as almost to seem inauspicious. Murasaki, for whom life had come to seem of as little value as her farewell poem had suggested it to be, shared in the joy. She had matured and was more beautiful than ever. Her hair had been almost too rich and thick. Worry and sorrow had thinned it somewhat and thereby improved it. And now, thought Genji, a deep peace coming over him, they would be together. And in that instant there came to him the image of the one whom he had not been ready to leave. It seemed that his life must go on being complicated.

He told Murasaki about the other lady. A pensive, dreamy look passed over his face, and she whispered, as if to dismiss the matter: "For myself I do not worry."[9]

He smiled. It was a charmingly gentle reproof. Unable to take his eyes from her now that he had her before him, he could not think how he had survived so many months and years without her. All the old bitterness

9. Alludes to a poem, "For myself, who am forgotten, I do not worry, / But for him who vowed fidelity while he lived."

came back. He was restored to his former rank and made a supernumerary councillor. All his followers were similarly rehabilitated. It was as if spring had come to a withered tree.

The emperor summoned him and as they made their formal greetings thought how exile had improved him. Courtiers looked on with curiosity, wondering what the years in the provinces would have done to him. For the elderly women who had been in service since the reign of his late father, regret gave way to noisy rejoicing. The emperor had felt rather shy at the prospect of receiving Genji and had taken great pains with his dress. He seemed pale and sickly, though he had felt somewhat better these last few days. They talked fondly of this and that, and presently it was night. A full moon flooded the tranquil scene. There were tears in the emperor's eyes.

"We have not had music here of late," he said, "and it has been a very long time since I last heard any of the old songs."

Genji replied:

"Cast out upon the sea, I passed the years
As useless as the leech child of the gods."[1]

The emperor was touched and embarrassed.

"The leech child's parents met beyond the pillar.
We meet again to forget the spring of parting."

He was a man of delicate grace and charm.

Genji's first task was to commission a grand reading of the Lotus Sutra in his father's memory. He called on the crown prince, who had grown in his absence, and was touched that the boy should be so pleased to see him. He had done so well with his studies that there need be no misgivings about his competence to rule. It would seem that Genji also called on Fujitsubo, and managed to control himself sufficiently for a quiet and affectionate conversation.

I had forgotten: he sent a note with the retinue which, like a returning wave, returned to Akashi. Very tender, it had been composed when no one was watching.

"And how is it with you these nights when the waves roll in?

"I wonder, do the morning mists yet rise,
There at Akashi of the lonely nights?"

The Kyushu Gosechi dancer[2] had had fond thoughts of the exiled Genji, and she was vaguely disappointed to learn that he was back in the city and once more in the emperor's good graces. She sent a note, with instructions that the messenger was to say nothing of its origin:

"There once came tidings from a boat at Suma,
From one who now might show you sodden sleeves."

1. Refers to the native creation myth, in which the leech child, among the Sun Goddess's siblings, lives approximately the period of Genji's exile before being cast out to sea. It is at a pillar (see the emperor's answering poem) that both the leech and the Sun Goddess are conceived.   2. See n. 5, p. 1358. The translator asserts that this is not the dancer mentioned in chap. 12, but the "charming girl, the daughter of the assistant viceroy of Kyushu" (mentioned in an earlier chapter), with whom Genji had a dalliance.

Her hand had improved, though not enough to keep him from guessing whose it was.

"It is I, not you, from whom the complaints should come.
My sleeves have refused to dry since last you wrote."

He had not seen enough of her, and her letter brought fond memories. But he was not going to embark upon new adventures.

To the lady of the orange blossoms he sent only a note, cause more for disappointment than for pleasure.

Summary   Eight years pass in the novel before we come to Chapter 25, *Fireflies*. When Genji returns to the capital, he is quickly restored to his former glory. And when his son by Fujitsubo assumes the throne as Emperor Reizei (although neither the emperor himself nor the world at large knows his true parentage), Genji's position could hardly be more secure. Genji is promoted to minister, his father-in-law is made prime minister, and his supporters reign supreme.

In his personal life, things are as eventful as ever. The Akashi lady gives birth to a baby girl. Though jealous at first, Murasaki is persuaded by Genji to adopt the child, an act to which the Akashi lady accedes in the interests of her daughter's future. Now in his early thirties, however, Genji loses a woman of whom he had always been fixated and with whom he shares a terrible secret. After a grave illness, Fujitsubo succumbs, and Genji is plunged into mourning.

Even worse, once the funeral observances end, a meddling priest informs the emperor who his real father is. Shocked and feeling somehow guilty himself, Emperor Reizei considers abdicating, though Genji argues against it.

In the meantime, Genji's other son, by Aoi, is rising nicely in the world. Yūgiri completes his education and is named chamberlain, a prestigious post, if not in the very upper reaches of administration.

In his mid-thirties, Genji turns his attention to constructing a proper mansion for his various ladies—a kind of surrogate palace for the man who will never be emperor and the women who will never be his imperial consorts. It is a splendid building, particularly the gardens, which are organized in seasonal progression. Pride of place, the spring compound, naturally goes to Murasaki.

But in the summer wing Genji establishes a newcomer, Tamakazura, the twenty-year-old daughter of the woman he once loved briefly (told in Chapter 4). Genji has just discovered her, and with parental interest that quickly raises the suspicions of both Tamakazura and Murasaki, he installs her in his new palace. She is so much like her mother that Genji cannot bear it. When he confesses his feelings, however, Tamakazura rebuffs him, and for once, Genji appears abashed. "He knew that this impetuous behavior did not become his age and eminence. Collecting himself, he withdrew before the lateness of the hour brought her women to mistaken conclusions." Many a courtier would like to woo the lovely Tamakazura, but Genji, who still nurses his own unrequited affection, will allow only three contenders: Kashiwagi, the son of his old friend Tō no Chūjō; a nobleman named Higekuro; and his own brother, Prince Hotaru, whose name—literally Fireflies—makes up the title of the next chapter.

CHAPTER 25

Fireflies

Genji was famous and life was secure and peaceful. His ladies had in their several ways made their own lives and were happy. There was an

exception, Tamakazura, who faced a new crisis and was wondering what to do next. She was not as genuinely frightened of him, of course, as she had been of the Higo man;[3] but since few people could possibly know what had happened, she must keep her disquiet to herself, and her growing sense of isolation. Old enough to know a little of the world, she saw more than ever what a handicap it was not to have a mother.

Genji had made his confession. The result was that his longing increased. Fearful of being overheard, however, he found the subject a difficult one to approach, even gingerly. His visits were very frequent. Choosing times when she was likely to have few people with her, he would hint at his feelings, and she would be in an agony of embarrassment. Since she was not in a position to turn him away, she could only pretend that she did not know what was happening.

She was of a cheerful, affectionate disposition. Though she was also of a cautious and conservative nature, the chief impression she gave was of a delicate, winsome girlishness.

Prince Hotaru continued to pay energetic court. His labors had not yet gone on for very long when he had the early-summer rains to be resentful of.

"Admit me a little nearer, please," he wrote. "I will feel better if I can unburden myself of even part of what is in my heart."

Genji saw the letter. "Princes," he said, "should be listened to. Aloofness is not permitted. You must let him have an occasional answer." He even told her what to say.

But he only made things worse. She said that she was not feeling well and did not answer.

There were few really highborn women in her household. She did have a cousin called Saishō, daughter of a maternal uncle who had held a seat on the council. Genji had heard that she had been having a difficult time since her father's death, and had put her in Tamakazura's service. She wrote a passable hand and seemed generally capable and well informed. He assigned her the task of composing replies to gentlemen who deserved them. It was she whom he summoned today. One may imagine that he was curious to see all of his brother's letters. Tamakazura herself had been reading them with more interest since that shocking evening. It must not be thought that she had fallen in love with Hotaru, but he did seem to offer a way of evading Genji. She was learning rapidly.

Unaware that Genji himself was eagerly awaiting him, Hotaru was delighted at what seemed a positive invitation and quietly came calling. A seat was put out for him near the corner doors, where she received him with only a curtain between them. Genji had given close attention to the incense, which was mysterious and seductive—rather more attention, indeed, than a guardian might have felt that his duty demanded. One had to admire the results, whatever the motive. Saishō was at a loss to reply to

---

3. An uncouth suitor of the past. After her mother's death (in chap. 4) Tamakazura is taken by her nurse to the distant southern province of Higo, where the nurse's husband has been appointed an official. She grows up there, and in due course a rustic official *(the Higo man)* pursues her. He is powerful and persistent, but a little crude. Finally, under cover of darkness, Tamakazura and her nurse flee, setting sail for the capital.

Hotaru's overtures. Genji pinched her gently to remind her that her mistress must not behave like an unfeeling lump, and only added to her discomfiture. The dark nights of the new moon were over and there was a bland quarter-moon in the cloudy sky. Calm and dignified, the prince was very handsome indeed. Genji's own very special perfume mixed with the incense that drifted through the room as people moved about. More interesting than he would have expected, thought the prince. In calm control of himself all the while (and in pleasant contrast to certain other people), he made his avowals.

Tamakazura withdrew to the east penthouse and lay down. Genji followed Saishō as she brought a new message from the prince.

"You are not being kind," he said to Tamakazura. "A person should behave as the occasion demands. You are unnecessarily coy. You should not be sending a messenger back and forth over such distances. If you do not wish him to hear your voice, very well, but at least you should move a little nearer."

She was in despair. She suspected that his real motive was to impose himself upon her, and each course open to her seemed worse than all the others. She slipped away and lay down at a curtain between the penthouse and the main hall.

She was sunk in thought, unable to answer the prince's outpourings. Genji came up beside her and lifted the curtain back over its frame. There was a flash of light. She looked up startled. Had someone lighted a torch? No—Genji had earlier in the evening put a large number of fireflies in a cloth bag. Now, letting no one guess what he was about, he released them. Tamakazura brought a fan to her face. Her profile was very beautiful.

Genji had worked everything out very carefully. Prince Hotaru[4] was certain to look in her direction. He was making a show of passion, Genji suspected, because he thought her Genji's daughter, and not because he had guessed what a beauty she was. Now he would see, and be genuinely excited. Genji would not have gone to such trouble if she had in fact been his daughter. It all seems rather perverse of him.

He slipped out through another door and returned to his part of the house.

The prince had guessed where the lady would be. Now he sensed that she was perhaps a little nearer. His heart racing, he looked through an opening in the rich gossamer curtains. Suddenly, some six or seven feet away, there was a flash of light—and such beauty as was revealed in it! Darkness was quickly restored, but for the brief glimpse he had had was the sort of thing that makes for romance. The figure at the curtains may have been indistinct but it most certainly was slim and tall and graceful. Genji would not have been disappointed at the interest it had inspired.

> "You put out this silent fire to no avail.
> Can you extinguish the fire in the human heart?

"I hope I make myself understood."

Speed was the important thing in answering such a poem.

---

4. It is from this episode that the prince obtains his name, Hotaru (Firefly).

"The firefly but burns and makes no comment.
Silence sometimes tells of deeper thoughts."

It was a brisk sort of reply, and having made it, she was gone. His lament about this chilly treatment was rather wordy, but he would not have wished to overdo it by staying the night. It was late when he braved the dripping eaves (and tears as well) and went out. I have no doubt that a cuckoo sent him on his way,[5] but did not trouble myself to learn all the details.

So handsome, so poised, said the women—so very much like Genji. Not knowing their lady's secret, they were filled with gratitude for Genji's attentions. Why, not even her mother could have done more for her.

Unwelcome attentions, the lady was thinking. If she had been recognized by her father and her situation were nearer the ordinary, then they need not be entirely unwelcome. She had had wretched luck, and she lived in dread of rumors.

Genji too was determined to avoid rumors. Yet he continued to have his ways. Can one really be sure, for instance, that he no longer had designs upon Akikonomu?[6] There was something different about his manner when he was with her, something especially charming and seductive. But she was beyond the reach of direct overtures. Tamakazura was a modern sort of girl, and approachable. Sometimes dangerously near losing control of himself, he would do things which, had they been noticed, might have aroused suspicions. It was a difficult and complicated relationship indeed, and he must be given credit for the fact that he held back from the final line.

On the fifth day of the Fifth Month, the Day of the Iris, he stopped by her apartments on his way to the equestrian grounds.

"What happened? Did he stay late? You must be careful with him. He is not to be trusted—not that there are very many men these days a girl really can trust."

He praised his brother and blamed him. He seemed very young and was very handsome as he offered this word of caution. As for his clothes, the singlets and the robe thrown casually over them glowed in such rich and pleasing colors that they seemed to brim over and seek more space. One wondered whether a supernatural hand might not have had some part in the dyeing. The colors themselves were familiar enough, but the woven patterns were as if everything had pointed to this day of flowers.[7] The lady was sure she would have been quite intoxicated with the perfumes burned into them had she not had these worries.

A letter came from Prince Hotaru, on white tissue paper in a fine, aristocratic hand. At first sight the contents seemed very interesting, but somehow they became ordinary upon repeating.

5. The narrator slips into the mode of pathetic fallacy, attributing feelings of sympathy for Genji to the cuckoo (hototogisu), a bird whose poetic overtones are lost in translation; nightingale would be closer to the mood.   6. Like Tamakazura, the daughter of a former love (the Rokujō lady). Genji has also posed as her father and been erotically attracted. She is now married to the current emperor, Genji's illegitimate son with Fujitsubo, and is thus empress.   7. Ayame means both "iris" and "patterns." The pun is repeated several times in the following passage, as for instance in Hotaru's poem, in which ayame suggests something like "discernment."

"Even today the iris is neglected.
Its roots, my cries, are lost among the waters."[8]

It was attached to an iris root certain to be much talked of.

"You must get off an answer," said Genji, preparing to leave.

Her women argued that she had no choice.

Whatever she may have meant to suggest by it, this was her answer, a simple one set down in a faint, delicate hand:

"It might have flourished better in concealment,
The iris root washed purposelessly away.

"Exposure seems rather unwise."

A connoisseur, the prince thought that the hand could just possibly be improved.

Gifts of medicinal herbs[9] in decorative packets came from this and that well-wisher. The festive brightness did much to make her forget earlier unhappiness and hope that she might come uninjured through this new trial.

Genji also called on the lady of the orange blossoms, in the east wing of the same northeast quarter.

"Yūgiri is to bring some friends around after the archery meet. I should imagine it will still be daylight. I have never understood why our efforts to avoid attention always end in failure. The princes and the rest of them hear that something is up and come around to see, and so we have a much noisier party than we had planned on. We must in any event be ready."

The equestrian stands were very near the galleries of the northeast quarter.

"Come, girls," he said. "Open all the doors and enjoy yourselves. Have a look at all the handsome officers. The ones in the Left Guards are especially handsome, several cuts above the common run at court."

They had a delightful time. Tamakazura joined them. There were fresh green blinds all along the galleries, and new curtains too, the rich colors at the hems fading, as is the fashion these days, to white above. Women and little girls clustered at all the doors. The girls in green robes and trains of purple gossamer seemed to be from Tamakazura's wing. There were four of them, all very pretty and well behaved. Her women too were in festive dress, trains blending from lavender at the waist down to deeper purple and formal jackets the color of carnation shoots.

The lady of the orange blossoms had her little girls in very dignified dress, singlets of deep pink and trains of red lined with green. It was very amusing to see all the women striking new poses as they draped their finery about them. The young courtiers noticed and seemed to be striking poses of their own.

Genji went out to the stands toward midafternoon. All the princes were there, as he had predicted. The equestrian archery was freer and more varied than at the palace. The officers of the guard joined in, and everyone sat entranced through the afternoon. The women may not have under-

8. There is a pun on *ne*, which means both "root" and "cry" or "sob."   9. Conventional on the Day of the Iris.

stood all the finer points, but the uniforms of even the common guardsmen were magnificent and the horsemanship was complicated and exciting. The grounds were very wide, fronting also on Murasaki's southeast quarter, where young women were watching. There was music and dancing, Chinese polo music and the Korean dragon dance. As night came on, the triumphal music rang out high and wild. The guardsmen were richly rewarded according to their several ranks. It was very late when the assembly dispersed.

Genji spent the night with the lady of the orange blossoms.

"Prince Hotaru is a man of parts," he said. "He may not be the handsomest man in the world, but everything about him tells of breeding and cultivation, and he is excellent company. Did you chance to catch a glimpse of him? He has many good points, as I have said, but it may be that in the final analysis there is something just a bit lacking in him."

"He is younger than you but I thought he looked older. I have heard that he never misses a chance to come calling. I saw him once long ago at court and had not really seen him again until today. He has improved. Prince Sochi[1] is a very fine gentleman too, but somehow he does not quite look like royalty."

Genji smiled. Her judgment was quick and sure. But he kept his own counsel. This sort of open appraisal of people still living was not to his taste. He could not understand why the world had such a high opinion of Higekuro and would not have been pleased to receive him into the family, but these views too he kept to himself.

They were good friends, he and she, and no more, and they went to separate beds. Genji wondered when they had begun to drift apart. She never let fall the tiniest hint of jealousy. It had been the usual thing over the years for reports of such festivities to come to her through others. The events of the day seemed to bring new recognition to her and her household.

She said softly:

> "You honor the iris on the bank to which
> No pony comes to taste of withered grasses?"[2]

One could scarcely have called it a masterpiece, but he was touched:

> "This pony, like the love grebe, wants a comrade.
> Shall it forget the iris on the bank?"

Nor was his a very exciting poem.

"I do not see as much of you as I would wish, but I do enjoy you." There was a certain irony in the words, from his bed to hers, but also affection. She was a dear, gentle lady. She had let him have her bed and spread quilts for herself outside the curtains. She had in the course of time come to accept such arrangements as proper, and he did not suggest changing them.

The rains of early summer continued without a break, even gloomier than in most years. The ladies at Rokujō amused themselves with illus-

---

1. One of Genji's brothers.   2. Alludes to a poem in *The Kokinshū:* "Withered is the grass of Oaraki, / No pony comes for it, no harvester."

trated romances. The Akashi lady, a talented painter, sent pictures to her daughter.

Tamakazura was the most avid reader of all. She quite lost herself in pictures and stories and would spend whole days with them. Several of her young women were well informed in literary matters. She came upon all sorts of interesting and shocking incidents (she could not be sure whether they were true or not), but she found little that resembled her own unfortunate career. There was *The Tale of Sumiyoshi*,[3] popular in its day, of course, and still well thought of. She compared the plight of the heroine, within a hairbreadth of being taken by the chief accountant, with her own escape from the Higo person.

Genji could not help noticing the clutter of pictures and manuscripts. "What a nuisance this all is," he said one day. "Women seem to have been born to be cheerfully deceived. They know perfectly well that in all these old stories there is scarcely a shred of truth, and yet they are captured and made sport of by the whole range of trivialities and go on scribbling them down, quite unaware that in these warm rains their hair is all dank and knotted."

He smiled. "What would we do if there were not these old romances to relieve our boredom? But amid all the fabrication I must admit that I do find real emotions and plausible chains of events. We can be quite aware of the frivolity and the idleness and still be moved. We have to feel a little sorry for a charming princess in the depths of gloom. Sometimes a series of absurd and grotesque incidents which we know to be quite improbable holds our interest, and afterwards we must blush that it was so. Yet even then we can see what it was that held us. Sometimes I stand and listen to the stories they read to my daughter, and I think to myself that there certainly are good talkers in the world. I think that these yarns must come from people much practiced in lying. But perhaps that is not the whole of the story?"

She pushed away her inkstone. "I can see that that would be the view of someone much given to lying himself. For my part, I am convinced of their truthfulness."

He laughed. "I have been rude and unfair to your romances, haven't I. They have set down and preserved happenings from the age of the gods to our own. *The Chronicles of Japan*[4] and the rest are a mere fragment of the whole truth. It is your romances that fill in the details.

"We are not told of things that happened to specific people exactly as they happened; but the beginning is when there are good things and bad things, things that happen in this life which one never tires of seeing and hearing about, things which one cannot bear not to tell of and must pass on for all generations. If the storyteller wishes to speak well, then he chooses the good things; and if he wishes to hold the reader's attention he chooses bad things, extraordinarily bad things. Good things and bad things alike, they are things of this world and no other.

---

3. Does not survive except in a 13th-century revision, which is a Japanese equivalent of the Cinderella story. If the revision is faithful to the original tale, Tamakazura might well have identified with the heroine, whose stepmother plots to have her kidnapped by a man not at all to her liking, and so she runs away with her nurse (as Tamakazura fled Higo) to hide in Sumiyoshi, now part of Osaka.   4. One of the early histories.

"Writers in other countries approach the matter differently. Old stories in our own are different from new. There are differences in the degree of seriousness. But to dismiss them as lies is itself to depart from the truth. Even in the writ which the Buddha drew from his noble heart are parables, devices for pointing obliquely at the truth. To the ignorant they may seem to operate at cross purposes. The Greater Vehicle[5] is full of them, but the general burden is always the same. The difference between enlightenment and confusion is of about the same order as the difference between the good and the bad in a romance. If one takes the generous view, then nothing is empty and useless."

He now seemed bent on establishing the uses of fiction.

"But tell me: is there in any of your old stories a proper, upright fool like myself?" He came closer. "I doubt that even among the most unworldly of your heroines there is one who manages to be as distant and unnoticing as you are. Suppose the two of us set down our story and give the world a really interesting one."

"I think it very likely that the world will take notice of our curious story even if we do not go to the trouble." She hid her face in her sleeves.

"Our curious story? Yes, incomparably curious, I should think." Smiling and playful, he pressed nearer.

"Beside myself, I search through all the books,
And come upon no daughter so unfilial.

"You are breaking one of the commandments."

He stroked her hair as he spoke, but she refused to look up. Presently, however, she managed a reply:

"So too it is with me. I too have searched,
And found no cases quite so unparental."

Somewhat chastened, he pursued the matter no further. Yet one worried. What was to become of her?

Murasaki too had become addicted to romances. Her excuse was that Genji's little daughter[6] insisted on being read to.

"Just see what a fine one this is," she said, showing Genji an illustration for *The Tale of Kumano*.[7] The young girl in tranquil and confident slumber made her think of her own younger self. "How precocious even very little children seem to have been. I suppose I might have set myself up as a specimen of the slow, plodding variety. I would have won that competition easily."

Genji might have been the hero of some rather more eccentric stories.

"You must not read love stories to her. I doubt that clandestine affairs would arouse her unduly, but we would not want her to think them commonplace."

What would Tamakazura have made of the difference between his remarks to her and these remarks to Murasaki?

5. Mahayana Buddhism, the later form of the religion that prevailed in Tibet, China, and Japan.
6. Genji's daughter by the Akashi lady, whom Murasaki has been raising.   7. Or *The Tale of Komano*. It does not survive.

"I would not of course offer the wanton ones as a model," replied Murasaki, "but I would have doubts too about the other sort. Lady Atemiya in *The Tale of the Hollow Tree*,[8] for instance. She is always very brisk and efficient and in control of things, and she never makes mistakes; but there is something unwomanly about her cool manner and clipped speech."

"I should imagine that it is in real life as in fiction. We are all human and we all have our ways. It is not easy to be unerringly right. Proper, well-educated parents go to great trouble over a daughter's education and tell themselves that they have done well if something quiet and demure emerges. It seems a pity when defects come to light one after another and people start asking what her good parents can possibly have been up to. Yet the rewards are very great when a girl's manner and behavior seem just right for her station. Even then empty praise is not satisfying. One knows that the girl is not perfect and looks at her more critically than before. I would not wish my own daughter to be praised by people who have no standards."

He was genuinely concerned that she acquit herself well in the tests that lay before her.

Wicked stepmothers are of course standard fare for the romancers, and he did not want them poisoning relations between Murasaki and the child. He spent a great deal of time selecting romances he thought suitable, and ordered them copied and illustrated.

He kept Yūgiri from Murasaki but encouraged him to be friends with the girl. While he himself was alive it might not matter a great deal one way or the other, but if they were good friends now their affection was likely to deepen after he was dead. He permitted Yūgiri inside the front room, though the inner rooms were forbidden. Having so few children, he had ample time for Yūgiri, who was a sober lad and seemed completely dependable. The girl was still devoted to her dolls. They made Yūgiri think of his own childhood games with Kumoinokari.[9] Sometimes as he waited in earnest attendance upon a doll princess, tears would come to his eyes. He sometimes joked with ladies of a certain standing, but he was careful not to lead them too far. Even those who might have expected more had to make do with a joke. The thing that really concerned him and never left his mind was getting back at the nurse who had sneered at his blue sleeves. He was fairly sure that he could better Tō no Chūjō at a contest of wills, but sometimes the old anger and chagrin came back and he wanted more.[1] He wanted to make Tō no Chūjō genuinely regretful for what he had done. He revealed these feelings only to Kumoinokari. Before everyone else he was a model of cool composure.

Her brothers sometimes thought him rather conceited. Kashiwagi, the oldest, was greatly interested these days in Tamakazura. Lacking a better intermediary, he came sighing to Yūgiri. The friendship of the first generation was being repeated in the second.

---

8. A late 10th-century work of fiction. The tale describes, among other things, the efforts of several suitors to win the hand of the beautiful Atemiya, their disappointment when she marries the crown prince, and the ensuing power struggle over imperial succession.   9. Tō no Chūjō's daughter; she is Yūgiri's childhood playmate and eventually his wife.   1. Tō no Chūjō has so far thwarted Yūgiri's desire to wed Kumoinokari.

"One does not undertake to plead another's case," replied Yūgiri quietly.

Tō no Chūjō was a very important man, and his many sons were embarked upon promising careers, as became their several pedigrees and inclinations. He had only two daughters. The one who had gone to court had been a disappointment. The prospect of having the other do poorly did not of course please him. He had not forgotten the lady of the evening faces. He often spoke of her, and he went on wondering what had happened to the child. The lady had put him off guard with her gentleness and appearance of helplessness, and so he had lost a daughter. A man must not under any circumstances let a woman out of his sight. Suppose the girl were to turn up now in some outlandish guise and stridently announce herself as his daughter—well, he would take her in.

"Do not dismiss anyone who says she is my daughter," he told his sons. "In my younger days I did many things I ought not to have done. There was a lady of not entirely contemptible birth who lost patience with me over some triviality or other, and so I lost a daughter, and I have so few."

There had been a time when he had almost forgotten the lady. Then he began to see what great things his friends were doing for their daughters, and to feel resentful that he had been granted so few.

One night he had a dream. He called in a famous seer and asked for an interpretation.

"Might it be that you will hear of a long-lost child who has been taken in by someone else?"

This was very puzzling. He could think of no daughters whom he had put out for adoption. He began to wonder about Tamakazura.

Summary   Twenty-nine chapters follow Chapter 25. Eventually Tamakazura marries Higekuro, and Genji, for political reasons, agrees to marry the favorite daughter of a retired emperor. Murasaki worries that Genji's new wife will supplant her in Genji's affections, but what happens is something else altogether. The new wife is unfaithful. After a liaison with Tō no Chūjō's son, she gives birth to the boy Kaoru. Genji learns the truth and remains indifferent to mother and child. The incident reminds Genji of his own transgression. He has no choice but to suffer in silence, mindful of the wrong he did his father.

In the meantime, Murasaki becomes ill. Before long she dies, and Genji is inconsolable. His grief is made worse when he realizes how his recent marriage had distressed Murasaki. Late in life, once again Genji confronts the unhappiness he has caused others. Sensing that his own end is near, the fifty-two-year-old Genji begins to put his affairs in order. And then, suddenly, we are told that he is dead:

> The shining Genji was dead, and there was no one quite like him. . . . Niou [his grandson], the third son of the present emperor, and Kaoru, the young son of Genji's [wife, the] Third Princess, had grown up in the same house and were both thought by the world to be uncommonly handsome, but somehow they did not shine with the same radiance. They were but sensitive, cultivated young men, and the fact that they were rather more loudly acclaimed than Genji had been at their age was very probably because they had been so close to him.

They will never equal him, however, and the rest of the novel, the account of their rivalry for the affections of three sisters, is the story of their failure to do so.

Niou is a brash, carefree sort, inclined to take his pleasure where he finds it. One cannot avoid the conclusion that he is a coarser version of his grandfather. Kaoru, while not in fact descended from Genji, seems to represent the extreme form of one of Genji's most admirable traits: sensitivity gone pathological. Both men are exaggerations of qualities that in Genji were "shining," like two halves—Kaoru's deference and Niou's impetuousness—that, if fused, might approximate the whole of Genji.

Instead we have their misadventures, which take place for the most part in a world removed from the capital, a forsaken spot called Uji. The very name means gloom or melancholy, and this is the tone for the balance of the tale. In search of love off the beaten path, the two men pursue an ideal first articulated at the beginning of the novel (Chapter 2): the affair of the heart unsullied by court intrigue. Unfortunately, intrigue and discontent are what Niou and Kaoru bring to the three women in the hinterlands. One dies of anxiousness, the second languishes in an unhappy marriage to Niou, and the third tries to kill herself; when she fails, she vows to have nothing more to do with men.

Not knowing whether she is dead or alive, Kaoru keeps searching for the third sister. The novel ends enigmatically, when he thinks he may have located her. His messenger is rebuffed, however, and the last, inconclusive lines of *The Tale of Genji* leave our antihero wondering, his life more unresolved than ever:

> It would seem that, as he examined the several possibilities, a suspicion crossed his mind: the memory of how he himself had behaved in earlier days made him ask whether someone might be hiding her from the world.

Nō Drama

Nō, the classical theater of Japan, is the world's oldest extant professional theater. It is also among the world's gravest and most stylized. Performed on an austere, undecorated stage of polished cypress, with no scenery and virtually no props, the ritual-like poetic dance-dramas of the *nō* have been described as a theater free of the artifice of stagecraft. But it would be more accurate to characterize the *nō* as a theater elevating stagecraft to the *n*th power. The absence of illusory scrims, revolving sets, or cyclorama floodlights is only the absence of the most obvious artifice. The word *nō* may be translated as "talent," "skill," or "accomplishment." And the ways that "accomplishment" has been cultivated by *nō* actors (all *nō* performers are male) demonstrate how fundamental, in fact, artifice, or stratagem, has always been to the tradition of the *nō*.

In Japan's medieval period, when *nō* coalesced from disparate origins—mystery plays, rice-planting rituals, classical poetry, carnival tricks, myth, and Buddhist liturgy—Zeami Motokiyo, master actor, playwright, and critic of the *nō*, analyzed the actor's art in a series of treatises as rigorous and self-conscious as the pronouncements of Stanislavsky, progenitor of the twentieth-century school of "method acting." Zeami's dissection of acting technique reveals both a practical and philosophical command of his craft. It also demonstrates the indissoluble link between *nō* and Zen Buddhism.

Let's begin first with the practical. Because *nō* shunned the trappings of representational theater, the actor's own talent or accomplishment (that is, his *nō*) became paramount. While over time the practice developed of incorporating a chorus and musical instruments to assist the actor, he had nonetheless little but

his own artistry to convey the reality of his performance. The stately pace of *nō* drama and its highly conventionalized formal and thematic patterns may distance some audiences today, but the *nō* actor's subtle if stylized stage business can express an astonishing artistry. This artistry rejects theatricality. It also avoids both improvisation and the actor's deployment of personal experience to flesh out or give psychological depth to his characterization. (In fact, as we will see, the Western concept of "characterization" has little utility in the realm of *nō*.)

Instead, in Zeami's conception, the ideal *nō* actor combines a commonsense approach to performing ("If an actor thinks he has attained a higher level of skill than he has reached . . . he will lose even the level he has achieved") with a less-is-more view of art that today sounds curiously modern. "The expression 'when you feel ten in your heart, express seven in your movements,' " he tells us, refers to the necessity of underplaying. "When a beginner . . . learns to gesture . . . he will use all his energies to perform. . . . Later he will learn to move less. . . . No matter how slight a bodily action, if the motion is more restrained than the emotion behind it, the emotion will become the Substance and the movement of the body its Function, thus moving his audience."*

To these technical concerns of the impresario Zeami weds some of the more abstruse values of medieval Japanese aesthetics. *Yūgen* is the key criterion, a complex term with a web of meanings: mystery, depth, darkness, but also beauty and elegance, all tinged with the sadness of the ephemeral. The word *yūgen* originated in China (*yu hsüan*), where it described an object concealed from view, something that lay hidden too deep to be either seen or comprehended. *Yūgen* developed in Japan as a poetic principle denoting the profound. Poetry capturing the spirit of *yūgen* expressed emotions so delicate or subtle that they could only be implied. This taste for implication embodied in *yūgen* influenced all the major arts of medieval Japan, not only poetry and drama but also painting, calligraphy, ceramics, and even architecture. In the visual arts, the *yūgen* aesthetic preferred monochrome to color, and the evocative ink landscapes of the fourteenth century—in which a still mountain ridge appears and disappears within the mist, creating from the illusion of vast space a sense of infinity—testify to the fact that a monochromatic work can suggest more than the richest palette. In defining too well, color proves oddly restrictive. But with monochrome, there are no limits to what can be evoked through suggestion.

A famous anecdote about the sixteenth-century warlord Hideyoshi will demonstrate how central the suggestive component of *yūgen* has been to Japanese cultural identity. Hideyoshi was a brute foot soldier who, having risen to unify Japan through prowess and cunning, sought culture under the tutelage of a man of superior taste, Rikyū the tea master. The two men met often to perform the tea ceremony. One afternoon Hideyoshi asked Rikyū to show him his garden, which was famous for its morning glories. Rikyū demurred, but when Hideyoshi persisted Rikyū invited him to return the following morning. Hideyoshi arrived at the appointed hour, only to find that all the morning glories had been removed from the garden. A man with a hot temper who was accustomed to having his way, Hideyoshi stormed over to the tea hut, where he knew Rikyū would be waiting. He slid back the little door to the hut and entered. Before he could demand an explanation, however, he saw that the tea master had placed a single morning glory in the alcove. The one blossom was the essence of all morning glories. To Hideyoshi it was a revelation.

In the same manner, *yūgen*'s powers of suggestion were for Zeami the apex of the theatrical art of *nō*, what he calls "the art of the flower of mystery." This can

---

*Zeami Motokiyo, *On the Art of Nō Drama*, trans. J. Thomas Rimer and Yamazaki Masakazu (1984) 7, 75.

by symbolized, he says, by the paradoxical phrase "In Silla* at midnight the sun is bright." Zeami elaborates:

> It is impossible to express in words or even to grasp in the mind the mystery of this art. When one speaks of the sun rising at midnight, the words themselves do not explain anything; thus too, in the art of nō, the yūgen of a supreme actor defies our attempts to praise it. We are so deeply impressed that we do not know what to single out as being of special excellence, and, if we attempt to assign it a rank, we discover that it is peerless artistry which transcends any degrees. This kind of artistic expression, which is invisible to ordinary eyes, may be what is termed the Art of the Flower of Mystery."†

The profundity of nō, according to Zeami, is ineffable. Nō must pierce the brittle surface of everyday reality and reach for the truth that lies hidden underneath. Distilled to its essence, yūgen is truth, and nō's quest for the truth marks this theater as the literary progeny of Zen. Both see outward reality as illusory and ultimate reality as beyond words, beyond the senses. Both adhere to the doctrine of karma and the transmigration of souls. All human beings are born into an endless cycle of reincarnation. In this life we sow the seeds for the next. But flawed by our appetite for worldly things, each successive existence is steeped in delusion, suffering, and discontent. There is only one escape: satori, or enlightenment, the realization that material phenomena are fancies, not facts. This discovery frees us to let go of illusory attachments, whether love, passion, hatred, ambition, or greed. It is a discovery to be made in our own backyard, as it were. In Zen, enlightenment has nothing to do with cerebration, and everything to do with uncovering the meaning hidden in the particulars of daily experience. Illumination is apt to be sudden, mystical, even accidental.

At the same time, paradoxically, great discipline is demanded of the Zen aspirant, and considerable effort goes into achieving effortlessness. The initiate must submit to the grueling practice of zazen, or "meditation sitting," assuming a tortuous yogic position and contemplating an intractable riddle assigned by the Zen master. These riddles vary from seemingly unanswerable questions (What is the sound of one hand clapping?) to gnomic conundrums (A flag waved in the air. Two monks disputed whether the flag was moving or the wind was moving. A third monk retorted, "It is not the wind that is moving; it is not the flag that is moving; it is your mind that is moving!"). Whether such mental exercises strike one as intriguing or exasperating, the persistent meditation of Zen puzzles, when it succeeds, is thought to enable the aspirant to break free of the constraints of logic, to cast off the conceptualization we learn to superimpose on the flow of life's encounters, and thus to experience intuitive insight: enlightenment.

A further refinement of Zen, with important implications for the nō theater, was the belief that enlightenment did not occur in a vacuum, that the profane world at all times intrudes on Zen. The secular arts—archery, nō, calligraphy, swordsmanship, and the tea ceremony—were seen as a means of spiritual training. This endeared Zen to the ruling samurai class, who were the patrons of the nō. Because there was no distinction, or antagonism, between enlightenment and empirical existence and because the anti-intellectual strain in Zen held that an aspirant does not so much ignore the everyday, or the material, as work through it, it was possible for a samurai to live the illuminated life within his secular station. Discipline and dedication were required, to be sure, but in the discourse of the times these were already the defining attributes of the samurai.

The warrior schooled in the austerities of military training and Zen meditation

---

* A kingdom in ancient Korea, founded in 57 B.C.   † Donald Keene, Nō: The Classical Theatre of Japan (1973) 23.

found the severe aspects of *nō* to his liking. The bare stage, the ritualistic disregard for verisimilitude, the harsh musical accompaniment—hardly melodic and more like a dolorous Gregorian chant, in which the shrill flute and irregular drumbeats seem to puncture the performance more than they accompany it—all were the perfect correlates to the theatrical paring away that is *nō*.

Considering the many dramatic elements that *nō* does not possess, at least from a Eurocentric perspective, one might be forgiven the punning thought that perhaps this is the reason it is called *nō* theater. Where, one might ask, is the conflict that drives a Western play, the touchstone of dramaturgy since Aeschylus? *Nō* plays seldom offer a confrontation between dramatic equals. Instead one figure, the *shite* (literally, the "doer"), dominates the stage. If this is the protagonist, the *shite* lacks any foil with enough dramatic heft to weight in as a viable antagonist. The other actors, the *waki* ("sideman") and the *tsure* ("companion"), are mere observers. And what they observe can hardly be called the action. That took place a long time ago—in what Hollywood would call the "backstory." To continue in the current idiom, one might characterize present time on stage as the depiction of an obsession precisely about "the action" of the past. The play portrays an emotion, and the *shite* is nothing other than the embodiment of that emotion. Just as the tea master needed only one morning glory to convey the essence of all morning glories, the *nō* play needs only the present moment—stripped of the impedimenta of theatrical realism—to capture the essence of an emotion. At first glance *nō* may appear an abbreviation, but in fact it is a concentration.

The typical play opens with the entrance of the *waki*, often in the role of a priest. He proceeds down the bridge, or runway, at the audience's left, which connects the stage to the greenroom, and announces the circumstances of the play: the season, the place, and the central theme (see illustration). The statement of the theme is repeated in a poem or chant by the chorus of six or eight men, who, together with the "orchestra" of flute player and one or two drummers, have preceded the *waki* on stage. (The musicians sit along the back of the stage under the lone pine tree painted on the wall, the single and unvarying decoration for all *nō* plays. The chorus sits on a veranda at the side of the stage, to the audience's right.) The *waki* moves onto the stage proper and states his name and his intentions. "I am Kumagai no Naozane," declaims the *waki* in *Atsumori*, a *nō* play, "a man of the country of Musashi. I have left my home and call myself the priest

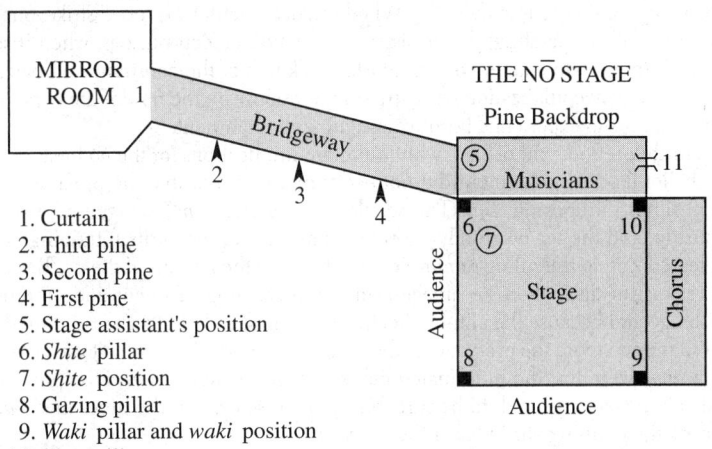

MIRROR ROOM 1   THE NŌ STAGE

Bridgeway   Pine Backdrop

⑤ Musicians   11

2   3   4

1. Curtain
2. Third pine
3. Second pine
4. First pine
5. Stage assistant's position
6. *Shite* pillar
7. *Shite* position
8. Gazing pillar
9. *Waki* pillar and *waki* position
10. Flute pillar
11. Slit door

Audience   ⑥ ⑦   10   Stage   Chorus   8   9

Audience

Rensei; this I have done because of my grief at the death of Atsumori, who fell in battle by my hand. Hence it comes that I am dressed in priestly guise. And now I am going to Ichi-no-Tani to pray for the salvation of Atsumori's soul." As he trails across the stage, intoning a travel song, his slow progress represents his journey. When he reaches the opposite side of the stage, he announces his arrival at his destination, "I have come so fast that here I am already at Ichi-no-Tani, in the country of Tsu." With this, the first, or introductory, movement of the play concludes.

The second, expository, movement opens with the appearance of the *shite*, the principal actor, who is usually followed by his companion, the *tsure*. Advancing down the bridge in slow-motion and making his way onto the stage, the *shite* sings an entrance song that describes his current situation without revealing who he really is. The *shite* in *Atsumori* first appears as a young reaper. He and his companion enter chanting,

> To the music of the reaper's flute
> No song is sung
> But the sighing of wind in the fields.

And the *shite* adds,

> They that were reaping,
> Reaping on that hill,
> Walk now through the fields
> Homeward, for it is dusk.

Soon the *shite* encounters the *waki*, who, being a stranger to the region, asks various questions, first about the locality and then about the identity of the *shite*. The chorus elaborates this dialogue in a song of poetic allusion. By now the *waki* begins to realize that there is something odd about the *shite*, and the *shite* tries to evade him. Agitated, the *shite* begins to dance, which in the *nō* is always a sign of emotional excitement. The *shite* implores the priest to pray for him. As the chorus reiterates his plea for help, the *shite* moves onto the bridge and departs, concluding the second movement.

An interlude precedes the third and final movement of the play. An actor identified as a "man of the place" appears to recount the "backstory," which, in this play, would make up the events of Atsumori's death on the battlefield. Note, however, that the translator does not include the entr'acte, since, as he explains, "These interludes are subject to variation and are not considered part of the literary text." Audiences today regard this portion of the play as an intermission, during which they are free to whisper, or rustle through their programs, or slip out for a cup of tea.

After the interlude comes the climax, or *kyū*, a "rushing to the end," which begins with the *waki*'s "waiting song," an admission of willingness to pray for the deliverance of the *shite*. Soon the *shite* reappears, but in a different guise. He has changed his costume and mask to reveal his true self. "Would you like to know who I am?" asks the *shite*. "Listen, Rensei, I am Atsumori," he says—the very Atsumori whom Rensei, or Kumagai, had slain in the wars between the Heike and the Genji, the ghost of a restless spirit unable to free itself from an obsession with past defeat, bound to this world through fixation on the last moments of final battle, incapable of letting go, and so perpetually deprived of enlightenment.

Atsumori now rehearses the elements of his obsession. He recounts the disasters that befell his clan, the Taira, or Heike, whereupon the chorus assists him, as though it were an extension of Atsumori's anxious mind:

> Yet their prosperity lasted but for a day;
> It was like the flower of the convolvulus.
> There was none to tell them
> That glory flashes like sparks from flint-stone,
> And after,—darkness.

But perhaps Atsumori is on the verge of a breakthrough, for he begins to comprehend the darker side of the Taira clan. He admits,

> When they were on high they afflicted the humble;
> When they were rich they were reckless in pride.

Pride led inevitably to war, and war to the trauma that haunts him. As Atsumori revisits the ordeals of war, he works himself into a frenzy, until frenzy bursts into dance. In this final dance, he relives his mortal struggle with Kumagai, narrated by the chorus:

> He looks behind him and sees
> That Kumagai pursues him;
> He cannot escape.
> Then Atsumori turns his horse
> Knee-deep in the lashing waves,
> And draws his sword.
> Twice, three times he strikes; then, still saddled,
> In close fight they twine; roll headlong together
> Among the surf of the shore.
> So Atsumori fell.

But fate seems to have given Atsumori a second chance. He comes out of his dance as from a seizure. The enemy stands before him; revenge is his. Atsumori lifts his sword. Suddenly, however, something strange happens. What he sees is neither a foe nor a warrior, but a priest intoning the name of Buddha. "No," Atsumori understands, "Rensei is not my enemy." The play ends as he asks the priest to pray for him. The audience sits riveted. Slowly, Atsumori makes his final exit. The *shite* glides along the bridge like an apparition fading from sight or a soul on the way to salvation.

Given the subject of *nō*, it should not come as a surprise that many of the plays are peopled by ghosts, for, in the world of *nō*, ghosts represent emotion unreconciled, the mind caught in the spiral of material illusion. Technically, there are five categories of *nō* plays in a repertoire of some 240 dramas: celebratory "god plays," in which the *shite* appears first in human form and later as the deity it really is, performed at New Year's and on other felicitous occasions; plays like *Atsumori*, about the ghosts of warriors doomed to eternal battle, unless a priest will pray to release them from their suffering; "wig plays," in which the *shite* portrays the spirit of an angry woman, often obsessed with unhappy love; "mundane plays" (assuming ghosts are mundane), which make up almost half the repertoire and tend to focus on derangement, a woman driven mad by the loss of a lover or child, or a husband distraught over the death of his wife (the play printed here belongs to this group); and "demon plays," depicting supernatural creatures, devils in particular, who threaten to overwhelm the forces of good.

Clearly, in the majority of plays, the *shite* embodies the human mind, and this psychological dimension is one of the things that has given *nō* a new lease on life in the present century. While the protagonist of a *nō* play is never a fully wrought character, endowed with a complex temperament or granted realistic substance

through individualistic detail, the dramatization of an obsession takes on fresh, contemporary relevance in the wake of Freud and Jung. The psychology of *nō*, combined with its Zen astringency, sloughing off both the decorative and the mimetic, appealed to W. B. Yeats, Ezra Pound, and other writers of an experimental bent, for whom realism was an outdated bourgeois convention. The very things *nō* lacked were seen by the modernists as its strong suit. Its bold simplicity was a near relation to the new calligraphic line in abstract painting. Its nuanced precision was preferable to traditional Western theater, in which, in the opinion of Pound, "subtlety must give way; where every fineness of word or of word-cadence is sacrificed to the 'broad effect'; where the paint must be put on with a broom." Pound, more than any other, idealized the *nō*, but under his tutorship *nō*'s rich fusion of poetry and prose, creating a compact collage of fragmentary images and complex allusions, helped revivify twentieth-century British and American poetry. We see this particularly in the poetry of Yeats, who drew inspiration from *nō*'s reliance on a single symbol (in *Atsumori*, for example, the flute) to strive for a similar metaphoric unity. Yeats's encounter with the *nō* even led him to write his own brand of *nō* plays, in which he attempted to mine the legends and layered literary traditions of Western culture as Zeami had done with those of Japan.

The play offered here is attributed to Zeami's grandnephew, Kanze Kojirō Nobumitsu. *Dōjōji* is one of the most dramatic *nō* plays. It is based on a legend included in a collection of Buddhist miracle stories compiled around 1040. In the original tale, a handsome young priest has the misfortune of attracting the attentions of a very lustful widow. He eludes her by departing on a pilgrimage, though not before placating her with the promise to spend the night on his return. When she realizes that he has no intention of keeping his promise, the wrath of the spurned woman is so intense that it transforms her into a serpent. The snake sets off in pursuit of the priest, and the results are not happy.

The *nō* version of this story elicits greater sympathy, and at the same time heightens the drama, by recasting the oversexed woman as a young girl. Now it is her innocence rather than her appetite, combined with her father's careless sense of humor, that precipitates disaster. *Dōjōji* is an unusual *nō* play in several respects. It is one of the few to rely on an elaborate prop: the huge bell that becomes a powerful part of the climax. And *Dōjōji* creates something closer to what we would call a dramatic situation; with more animation on stage than in most plays, the poetry of the text must compete with the spectacle.

Where are we, then, when we are left only with the text and none of the spectacle? Something is definitely lost. *Nō* may be spare, but it is highly visual: the rich brocade costumes; the shrinelike atmosphere of the stage; the mad, climactic dances of ghostly characters; the evocative masks worn by the *shite*. And no flute will sound, unless you use your imagination, though, of course, imagination has always been an important part of *nō*. Perhaps this is the key to appreciating *nō* as literature. Imagine yourself as a Zen master. The actors are gone. The chorus is gone. The musicians are gone. The stage is gone. The audience is gone. The words remain—diminishment or essence?

The most accessible introduction to the *nō* is by Donald Keene, *Nō: The Classical Theatre of Japan* (1973), which is also valuable for its photographs. Zeami's theories of drama are available in English in J. Thomas Rimer and Yamazaki Masakazu, *On the Art of Nō Drama: The Major Treatises of Zeami* (1894). Two excellent technical works are P. G. O'Neill, *Early Nō Drama* (1974), and Thomas Blenman Hare, *Zeami's Style: The Noh Plays of Zeami Motokiyo* (1986). Appraisals of the *nō* by Pound and Yeats will be found in a collection of translated plays: Ezra Pound and Ernest Fenollosa, *The Classic Noh Theatre of Japan* (1959). Other collections of translations include Arthur Waley, *The Nō Plays of Japan* (1921);

Donald Keene, ed., *Twenty Plays of the Nō Theatre* (1970); Nippon Gakujutsu Shinkōkai, *The Noh Drama* (1973); Kenneth Yasuda, *Masterworks of the Nō Theatre* (1989); and Royall Tyler, *Japanese Nō Dramas* (1992).

PRONOUNCING GLOSSARY

The following list uses common English syllables to provide rough equivalents of selected words whose pronunciation may be unfamiliar to the general reader.

Atsumori: *ah-tsoo-moh-ree*

Dōjōji: *doh-joh-jee*

ei tō: *ay-toh*

ei ya: *ay-yah*

Hideyoshi: *hee-de-yoh-shee*

Ichi-no-Tani: *ee-chee–noh–tah-nee*

Kanze Kojirō Nobumitsu: *kahn-ze koh-*
    jee-roh noh-boo-mee-tsoo

kotsuzumi: *koh-tsoo-zoo-mee*

Kumagai no Naozane: *koo-mah-gai noh*
    nah-oh-zah-ne

Michinari: *mee-chee-nah-ree*

Musashi: *moo-sah-shee*

nō: *noh*

rambyōshi: *rahm-byoh-shee*

Rensei: *ren-say*

Rikyū: *ree-kyoo*

shite: *shee-te*

Tsu: *tsoo*

tsure: *tsoo-re*

yamabushi: *yah-mah-boo-shee*

yūgen: *yoo-gen*

zazen: *zah-zen*

Zeami Motokiyo: *ze-ah-mee moh-toh-*
    kee-yoh

KANZE KOJIRŌ NOBUMITSU

1435–1516

Dōjōji[1]

PERSONS

The ABBOT of Dōjōji
Two PRIESTS of the Temple
Two Temple SERVANTS
A DANCER
The Serpent DEMON
CHORUS

As the opening flute is played the ABBOT, *the two* PRIESTS, *and the* FIRST SERVANT *enter. The* PRIESTS *and the* SERVANT *kneel on the bridgeway, but the* ABBOT *continues on to the stage.*

ABBOT: I am the abbot of Dōjōji, a temple in the Province of Kii. For many years no bell has hung in the belfry tower of the temple, and for a good reason. I have decided lately to restore the ancient cus-

---

1. Translated by and with notes adapted from Donald Keene.

tom and at my order a new bell has been cast. In the calendar today
is a day of good omen. I have ordered that the bell be raised into 5
the tower and that there be a service of dedication.

[*He calls towards the bridgeway.*]

Servant!

FIRST SERVANT: Here I am, sir.

ABBOT: Today is marked in the calendar as a lucky day, and I want you to
hoist the bell into the belfry. 10

FIRST SERVANT: Yes, certainly, sir.

[*As the* SERVANT *stands the two* PRIESTS *enter the stage from the
bridgeway and sit at the waki-position[2] behind the waki. The* SERVANT
leaves the bridgeway but returns shortly with another SERVANT. *They
carry between them on bamboo poles the prop, a huge bell. Two
stage assistants help them.*]

FIRST SERVANT: *Ei tō, ei tō.*[3]

SECOND SERVANT: *Ei ya, ei ya.*

FIRST SERVANT: *Ei tō, ei tō.*

SECOND SERVANT: *Ei ya, ei ya.* 15

[*Groaning under the strain, they lower the bell halfway down the
bridgeway.*]

FIRST SERVANT: Let's rest a while.

SECOND SERVANT: A good idea.

FIRST SERVANT: It's certainly a heavy bell.

SECOND SERVANT: Amazingly heavy.

FIRST SERVANT: Well, shall we lift it again? 20

SECOND SERVANT: All right.

[*They lift the bell again.*]

FIRST SERVANT: *Ei tō, ei tō.*

SECOND SERVANT: *Ei ya, ei ya.*

FIRST SERVANT: *Ei tō, ei tō.*

SECOND SERVANT: *Ei ya, ei ya.* 25

[*They reach the middle of the stage.*]

FIRST SERVANT: Let's put it down right here.

SECOND SERVANT: Right you are.

FIRST SERVANT: Everything under control?

SECOND SERVANT: Everything's going fine.

[*With appropriate cries they set the bell down.*]

FIRST SERVANT: Now for hoisting it into the belfry. 30

SECOND SERVANT: Right you are.

[*The two* SERVANTS, *helped by the stage assistants, use poles to thread
the rope of the prop through the ring set in the ceiling. Then, with
rhythmic shouts they hoist the prop to the appropriate height.*]

FIRST SERVANT: It looks more impressive than ever, now that we've
hoisted it up there.

SECOND SERVANT: That's right. It's certainly an impressive sight.

FIRST SERVANT: Let's waste no time in telling the Abbot about this. 35

---

2. Front, stage left, near the chorus. 3. The servants shout rhythmic but meaningless sounds to
encourage each other as they carry the big bell.

[*The* FIRST SERVANT *goes before the gazing-pillar*[4] *and addresses the* ABBOT.]

FIRST SERVANT: Excuse me, sir. We've raised the bell into the belfry.

ABBOT: You've raised it, you say?

FIRST SERVANT: Yes, that's just what I said, sir.

ABBOT: Then we will hold the dedication service today. For certain reasons best known to me, women are not to be admitted to the   45 courtyard where the ceremonies are held. Make sure that everyone understands this.

FIRST SERVANT: Your orders shall be obeyed.

[*He goes to the naming-place*[5] *where he addresses people offstage.*]
Listen, you people! The new bell of the Dōjōji is to be dedicated today. All who wish to attend the ceremony are welcome. However,   50 for reasons known only to himself, the Abbot has ordered that women are not to be allowed inside the courtyard where the service will take place. Take care you all obey his orders!

[*He goes to kneel before the flute player. The* DANCER *enters. She wears the fukai mask,*[6] *a long wig, a brocade outer robe, an inner kimono with a fish-scale pattern, and a crested garment tied around her waist. She stands at the shite-position*[7] *and faces the area before the musicians.*]

DANCER:

> My sin, my guilt, will melt away,
> My sin, my guilt, will melt away,   55
> I will go to the service for the bell.

[*She faces forward.*]
I am a dancer who lives in a remote village of this Province of Kii. I have heard that a bell is to be dedicated at the Dōjōji, and so I am hurrying there now, in the hopes of improving my chances of salvation.   60

> The moon will soon be sinking;
> As I pass the groves of little pines
> The rising tide weaves veils of mist around them.
> But look—can it be my heart's impatience?—

[*She takes a few steps to the right, then returns to her original position. This indicates she has reached the temple.*]

> Dusk has not yet fallen, the sun's still high,   65
> But I have already arrived:
> I am here at the Temple of Dōjōji.

[*She faces forward.*]
My journey has been swift, and now I have reached the temple. I shall go at once to watch the ceremony.

[*She moves towards the center of the stage. The* FIRST SERVANT *rises.*]

FIRST SERVANT: Stop! You can't go into the courtyard. Women aren't   70 allowed.

---

4. Front, stage right.   5. Rear, stage right, near the bridge, or runway.   6. Worn to portray a woman who has begun to age.   7. Same as the naming-place.

DANCER: But I'm not like other women. I'm only a dancer. I live nearby and I am to perform a dance at the dedication of the bell. Please let me see the ceremony.

FIRST SERVANT: [*To himself.*] A dancer? That's right, I suppose she   75
doesn't count as an ordinary woman. [*To the* DANCER.] Very well, I'll let you into the courtyard on my own, but in return you must dance for me. [*He goes before flute player, picks up a tall court cap lying on the stage, and brings it to the* DANCER.] Here, take this hat.[8] It just happened to be around. Put it on and let's see you   80
dance.

DANCER: With pleasure. I'll dance for you as best I can.

[*She retires to stage assistant's position*[9] *to alter her costume. The* SERVANT *returns to his original place and sits. The* DANCER *puts on the hat and goes to the first pine on the bridgeway. She looks beyond the pillar at the bell, then glides onto the stage to the suddenly stepped-up tempo of large drum. She stops just past the shite-pillar.*[1]]

DANCER: How happy you have made me! I will dance for you. [*She describes her actions.*] Borrowing for a moment a courtier's hat, she puts it on her head.   85

> Her feet already stamp the rhythm.
> Apart from cherry blossoms,
> There are only the pines,
> Apart from cherry blossoms,
> There are only the pines.   90
> When the darkness starts to fall
> The temple bell will resound.

[*She lifts the hem of her robe a little with her left hand, and dances the following passage as if she were climbing step by step up to the bell. This is the famous rambyōshi dance, accompanied by the weird cries and pounding of the kotsuzumi drum.*[2]]

> Prince Michinari, at the imperial command,
> First raised these sacred walls.
> And because the temple was his work,   95
> Tachibana no Michinari,
> They called it Dōjōji.[3]

[*The rhythm of the dance grows more rapid and intense.*]

CHORUS: [*For the* DANCER.]

> To a temple in the mountains
> Now, on this evening in spring,
> I have come, I have seen   100
> The blossoms scattered with the evening bell,
> The blossoms scatter, the blossoms fall.

---

8. It was customary for professional women dancers to wear a tall ceremonial court cap when they performed.   9. Extreme rear corner, stage right.   1. At the corner where the bridge joins the rear stage. In front of the bridge are three potted young pine trees spaced at intervals along a pebble moat. The first pine, where she stands, is toward the end of the bridge nearest the stage.   2. A small hand drum. *Rambyōshi dance:* characterized by slight movements of the feet made in time to single drumbeats at long intervals.   3. The temple of Michinari; the name *Michinari* is pronounced in Sino-Japanese as Dōjō.

DANCER:

> And all the while,
> And all the while,
> At temples everywhere across the land   105
> The sinking moon strikes the bell.
> The birds sing, and frost and snow fill the sky;
> Soon the swelling tide will recede.
> The peaceful fishers will show their lights
> In villages along the river banks—   110
> And if the watchers sleep when danger threatens
> I'll not let my chances pass me by!

[*The* SERVANTS *have become hypnotized by the rhythm of the dance.
The* DANCER *looks at the* ABBOT *and the* PRIESTS. *The* CHORUS
describes her actions.]

CHORUS:

> Up to the bell she stealthily creeps
> Pretending to go on with her dance.

[*She holds her fan and looks at the bell.*]

> She starts to strike it!   115

[*She swings the fan back and forth like a bell-hammer.*]

> This loathsome bell, now I remember it!

[*She unfastens the cords of her hat, then strikes the hat from her
hand with a blow of her fan. She stands under the bell.*]

> Placing her hand on the dragon-head boss,[4]
> She seems to fly upward into the bell.
> She wraps the bell around her,
> She has disappeared.   120

[*At the words, "Placing her hand," the* DANCER *rests her hand on the
edge of the bell, then leaps up into it. At the same moment the stage
assistant loosens the rope and drops the bell over her. The* SERVANTS,
*who have been drowsing, hypnotized by the dance, wake up, startled
by the noise of the bell falling. The* FIRST SERVANT *tumbles in confusion on the stage; the* SECOND SERVANT *falls on the bridgeway.*]

BOTH SERVANTS: [*Variously.*] Ho! Hi! What was that frightful noise?
That awful crashing racket? I'm so frightened I don't know what
I'm doing!

FIRST SERVANT: That certainly was a terrible crash. I wonder where
the other fellow went. [*He sees the* SECOND SERVANT.] Hey there,   125
are you all right?

SECOND SERVANT: How about you?

FIRST SERVANT: I still don't know yet.

SECOND SERVANT: No wonder. We got so carried away by her dance
we dozed off. Then came that awful bang. What do you think that   130
was?

---

4. A metal ornament on the bell, in the shape of a dragon's head.

FIRST SERVANT: Do you suppose it was thunder? If it was thunder, there should have been some sort of warning—a little clap or two before the big one. Strange, very strange.

SECOND SERVANT: Yes, you're right. Whatever it was, the earth shook something terrible. 135

FIRST SERVANT: I don't think it was an earthquake. Look—come over here. [*He discovers the bell and claps his hands in recognition.*] Here's what made the noise.

SECOND SERVANT: You're right! 140

FIRST SERVANT: I hung it up very carefully, but the loop must've snapped. How else could it fall?

SECOND SERVANT: No. Look. The loop's all right. Nothing's broken. It's certainly a mystery. [*He touches the bell.*] Oww! This bell is scorching hot! 145

FIRST SERVANT: Why should falling make it hot? [*He too touches the bell.*] Oww! Boiling hot!

SECOND SERVANT: It's a problem, all right. What do you suppose it can mean? It's beyond me. Well, we'd better report what's happened. We can't leave things this way. 150

FIRST SERVANT: That's a good idea. Too bad if the Abbot heard about it from anyone but us! We've got to do something. But I don't think I should be the one to tell. You tell him.

SECOND SERVANT: Telling him is no problem, but it would look peculiar if I went. You tell him—you were left in charge. 155

FIRST SERVANT: That's what makes it so hard! You tell him, please.
    [*He pushes the SECOND SERVANT forward.*]

SECOND SERVANT: No, it's not my business to tell him. *You* tell him. Hurry!
    [*He pushes the FIRST SERVANT.*]

FIRST SERVANT: Please, I beg of you, as a favor. You tell him.

SECOND SERVANT: Why should I? You tell him. I don't know anything about it. 160
    [*The SECOND SERVANT leaves. The FIRST SERVANT watches him go.*]

FIRST SERVANT: He's gone! Now I have no choice. I'll have to tell the Abbot, and it's going to get me into trouble. Well, I'll get it over with. [*He goes up to the ABBOT.*] It fell down.

ABBOT: What fell down? 165

FIRST SERVANT: The bell. It fell from the belfry.

ABBOT: What? Our bell? From the belfry?

FIRST SERVANT: Yes, Master.

ABBOT: What caused it?

FIRST SERVANT: I fastened it very carefully, but all the same it fell 170 down. Ah! That reminds me. There was a dancer here a little while ago. She said she lives nearby, and asked me to let her into the courtyard to see the dedication of the bell. Of course I told her that it wasn't allowed, but she said she wasn't an ordinary woman, and that she was going to offer a dance. So I let her in. I wonder if she 175 had something to do with this?

ABBOT: You idiot! What a stupid thing to do! I knew this would hap-

pen. That's why I forbade you strictly to allow any women in here! You blundering fool!

FIRST SERVANT: Ahhhh. [*He bows to the ground.*]   180

ABBOT: I suppose I must go now and take a look.

FIRST SERVANT: Yes, Master. Please hurry. Help! Help!

[*He exits, still crying for help.*]

ABBOT [*To the* PRIESTS.] Priests, come with me. [*They stand and go to the bell.*] Do you know why I gave the order that no woman was to be permitted to enter the temple during the dedication of the   185
bell?

PRIESTS: No, Master. We have no idea.

ABBOT: Then I will tell you.

PRIESTS: Yes, please tell us the whole story.

ABBOT: Many years ago there lived in this region a man who was the   190
steward of the manor of Manago,[5] and he had an only daughter. In those days too there was a certain *yamabushi*[6] priest who came here every year from the northern provinces on his way to worship at the shrine of Kumano,[7] and he would always stay with this same steward. The priest never forgot to bring charming little presents for the   195
steward's daughter, and the steward, who doted on the girl, as a joke once told her, "Some day that priest will be your husband, and you will be his wife!" In her childish innocence the girl thought he was speaking the truth, and for months and years she waited.

Time passed and once again the priest came to the landlord's   200
house. Late one night, after everyone else was asleep, the girl went to his bedroom and chided him: "Do you intend to leave me here forever? Claim me soon as your wife."

Amazed to hear these words, the priest turned the girl away with a joking answer. That night he crept out into the darkness and   205
came to this temple, imploring us to hide him. But having nowhere else we could hide him, we lowered the bell and hid him inside. Soon the girl followed, swearing she would never let him go. At that time the River Hitaka was swollen to a furious flood and the girl could not cross over. She ran up and down the bank, wild with   210
rage, until at last her jealous fury turned her into a venomous snake, and she easily swam across the river.

The serpent glided here, to the Temple of Dōjōji, and searched here and there until her suspicions were aroused by the lowered bell. Taking the metal loop between her teeth, she coiled herself   215
around the bell in seven coils. Then, breathing smoke and flames, she lashed the bell with her tail. At once the bronze grew hot, boiling hot, and the monk, hidden inside, was roasted alive. [*To the* PRIESTS.] Isn't that a horrible story?

---

5. Name of the owner of the manor.   6. Mountain ascetic who practiced austerities to attain holy or magical powers.   7. A complex of three Shinto shrines whose local divinities were identified as manifestations of Buddhist deities; they were venerated for prolonging life and assisting rebirth in paradise. The Kumano district, in Kii Province (now Wakayama Prefecture) south of both Kyoto and Nara, is a mountainous area overlooking the sea, long believed the dwelling place of native gods. Kumano was thus a popular site of pilgrimage and the center of the mountain asceticism practiced by the *yamabushi*.

PRIEST: Unspeakable! The worst I have ever heard!   220

ABBOT: I have felt her jealous ghost about here, and I feared she might bring some harm to our new bell. All of our austerities and penances have been for strength in this moment. Pray with all your hearts. Let us try to raise the bell again.

PRIEST: We will, Master.   225

[*The* ABBOT *and the* PRIESTS *stand on either side of the bell, facing it.*]

ABBOT:

> Though the waters of Hitaka River seethe and dry up,
> Though the sands of its shores run out,
> Can the sacred strength of our holy order fail?

[*They pray, their rosaries clasped in their hands.*]

PRIESTS: [*Describing their actions.*] All raise their voices together.

ABBOT: To the East, the Guardian King, Conqueror of the Three   230
Realms;

PRIESTS: To the South, the Guardian King, Conqueror of the Demons;

ABBOT: To the West, the Guardian King, Conqueror of Evil Serpents and Dragons;   235

PRIESTS: To the North, the Guardian King, Conqueror of Frightful Monsters;

ABBOT: And you in the Center, Messenger of the Sun, All Holy Immovable One,[8]

TOGETHER:

> Will you make the bell move?   240
> Show us the power of your avenging noose!
> *Namaku Samanda Basarada*
> *Senda Makaroshana Sowataya*
> *Un Tarata Kamman*
> "I dedicate myself to the universal diamond,   245
> May this raging fury be destroyed!"[9]
> "He who hearkens to My Law shall gain enlightenment,
> He who knows My Heart will be a Buddha in this flesh."[1]
> Now that we have prayed
> For the serpent's salvation,   250
> What rancor could it bear us?
> As the moon at daybreak

ABBOT: Strikes the hanging bell—

CHORUS:

> Look! Look! It moves!
> Pray with all your hearts!   255
> Pray to raise the bell!

[*They rub their rosaries frantically. The stage assistant lifts the bell a little and the* DEMON *shakes it from within.*]

---

8. These lines are a prayer favored by *yamabushi* priests for invoking the five fierce deities who serve as the guardian kings, messengers of the Buddha's wrath against evil spirits.   9. This mantra is dedicated to Fudō, one of the five guardian kings.   1. Part of the vow of Fudō.

Here the Priests, joining hands,
Invoke the sacred spell of the Thousand-Handed-One,
The Song of Salvation of the Guardian King,
The Immovable One, the Flaming One.[2]   260
Black smoke rises from their frantic prayers.
And as they pray,
And as they pray,
Though no one strikes the bell, it sounds!
[The DEMON *inside the bell strikes cymbals.*]

Though no one tugs the rope, the bell begins to dance!   265
[*The stage assistant pulls the bell up farther, and the* DEMON *shakes it.*]

Soon it rises to the belfry tower,
Look! A serpent form emerges!
[*The stage assistant lifts the bell completely. The* DANCER, *now transformed into a* DEMON, *wears the hannya mask.[3] She has removed her outer brocade robe. When she is clear of the bell she takes up her mallet, then picks up her outer robe in both hands and wraps it around her waist. She stands and tries to drive the* ABBOT *away. The* ABBOT *and* PRIESTS *pray, trying to subdue her. The* DEMON *is driven onto the bridgeway where she drops her outer robe. Then she is forced back as far as the curtain,[4] only to turn on the* ABBOT *again, this time compelling him to withdraw. She stands with her back to the shite-pillar,[5] throws one arm around it, pauses, and then invades the stage again. She tries to pull the bell down, but the* ABBOT *forces her to the ground with the power of his rosary. The* DEMON *rises again, and during the following passage sung by the* CHORUS, *she and the* ABBOT *struggle.*]

CHORUS:

Humbly we ask the help of the Green-bodied,
The Green Dragon of the East;
Humbly we ask the help of the White-bodied,   270
The White Dragon of the West;
Humbly we ask the help of the Yellow-bodied,
The Yellow Dragon of the Center,
All ye countless Dragon Kings of the three thousand worlds:
Have mercy, hear our prayers![6]   275
If now you show your mercy, your benevolence,
What refuge can the serpent find?
And as we pray,
Defeated by our prayers,
Behold the serpent fall!   280
[*She staggers back under the pressure of the* ABBOT'S *prayers and drops to the ground.*]

2. All are Buddhist deities.   3. A female demon mask, which is horned and contorted to suggest a
jealous rage.   4. Leading from the bridge into the dressing room, known as the mirror room.
5. The demon has made its way back down the bridge and onto the stage.   6. This is an invocation
of the five dragon kings, who in folk belief were each a different color and held sway over a different
direction — north, south, east, west, and center. Here, north and south have been omitted.

Again she springs to her feet,
The breath she vomits at the bell
Has turned to raging flames.
[*She rises and rushes to the bridgeway.*]

Her body burns in her own fire.
She leaps into the river pool,   285
[*She rushes through the curtain.*]

Into the waves of the River Hitaka,
And there she vanishes.
The Priests, their prayers granted,
Return to the temple,
Return to the temple.   290

[*The* ABBOT *gives a final stamp of the foot near the shite-pillar.*]

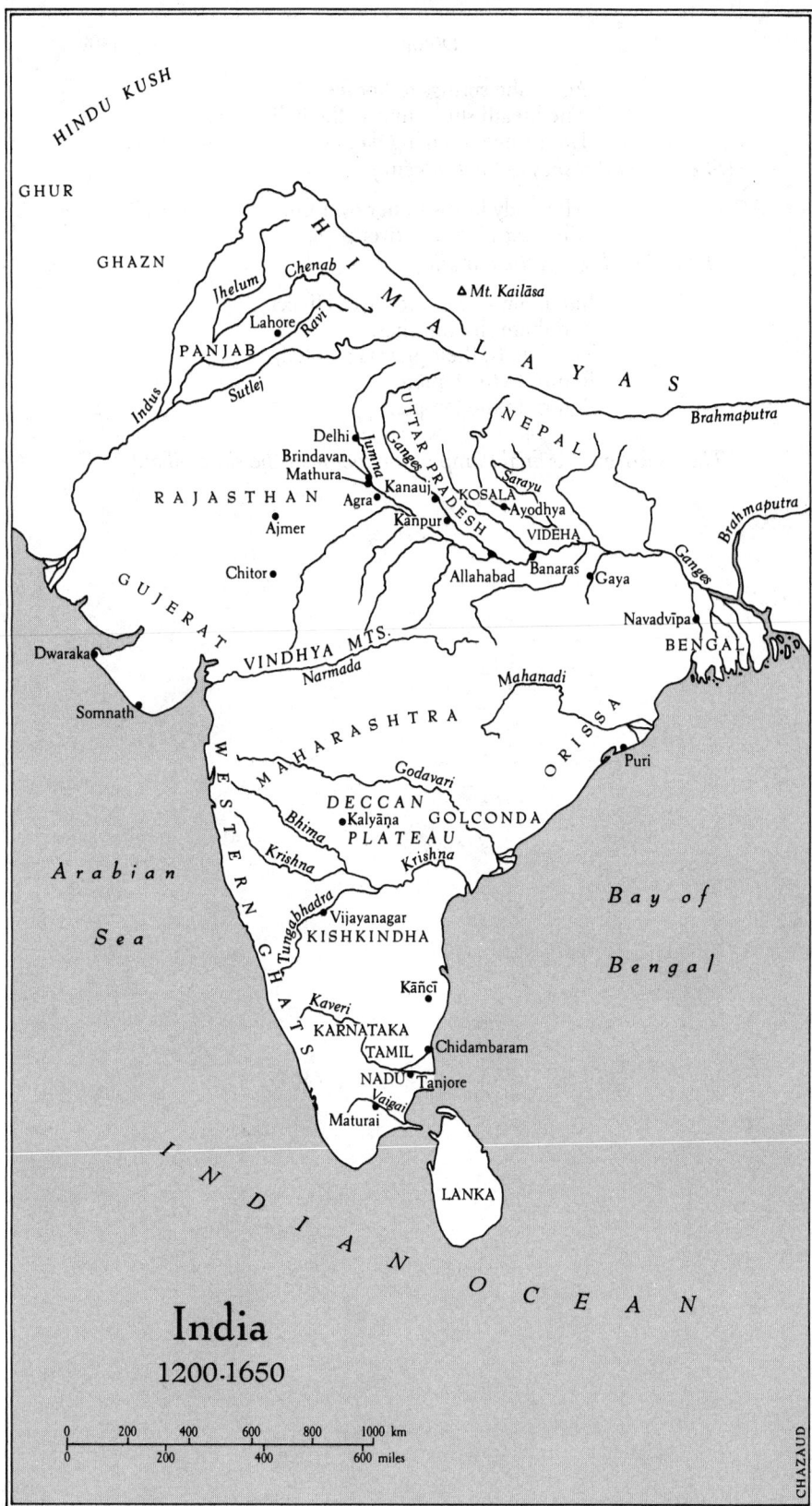

HINDU KUSH

GHUR

GHAZN

HIMALAYAS

△ Mt. Kailāsa

Jhelum *Chenab*

Lahore

PANJAB *Ravi*

Indus *Sutlej*

NEPAL *Brahmaputra*

UTTAR PRADESH

Delhi

Brindavan *Jumna* *Ganges*

Mathura Kanauj *Brahmaputra*

RAJASTHAN Agra *Sarayu* *Ganges*

KOSALA

Ajmer Kānpur Ayodhya

VIDEHA

Chitor Allahabad Banaras Gaya

Navadvīpa

GUJERAT BENGAL

Dwaraka VINDHYA MTS.

Narmada *Mahanadi*

Somnath

MAHARASHTRA

Godavari ORISSA

DECCAN Puri

Bhima Kalyāṇa GOLCONDA

PLATEAU

Krishna *Krishna*

Arabian *Tungabhadra* Vijayanagar

Sea KISHKINDHA

Kaveri Kāñcī

KARNATAKA

TAMIL Chidambaram

NADU Tanjore

Vaigai

Maturai

LANKA

INDIAN

OCEAN

India

1200-1650

0   200   400   600   800   1000 km

0   200   400   600 miles

CHAZAUD

Arabian Sea

Bay of Bengal

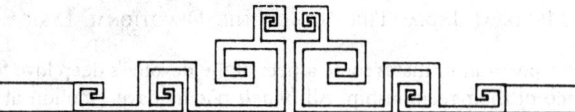

Medieval India: The Age of the Devotional Lyric

The period between the eleventh and eighteenth centuries in India saw the rise of regional kingdoms with distinct identities based on growing differences in language and culture. While the reign of the Tamil kings continued in the south, a succession of Hindu and Muslim dynasties, the latter mostly of Turkish and Afghan origin, ruled over parts of north India. Sizable Hindu and Muslim kingdoms flourished in central India as well. It was during this period that rapidly evolving regional languages—including both the Sanskrit-related tongues and the Dravidian languages related to Tamil in the south—developed literary traditions of their own. While these literatures are as diverse as the languages and subcultures they represent, the quintessential genre of the medieval era is the Hindu lyric poetry devoted to *bhakti*, the religion of personal devotion to God.

The earliest *bhakti* poems are the Tamil hymns of the Vaiṣṇava and Śaiva poets (sixth to ninth centuries) who led devotional movements in the Tamil region, focusing on Śiva and Viṣṇu, the chief Hindu gods. In the nine hundred years that followed, each of the more than sixteen other major languages of India acquired a substantial body of *bhakti* poems, devotional songs associated with regional cults of the preeminent Hindu deities, especially Śiva, Viṣṇu (in his incarnations as Krishna and Rāma), and the great goddess. The authors of the *bhakti* lyrics are celebrated as saints—exemplary religious figures—and their poems, preserved as sacred literature in oral as well as written traditions, were and are familiar to people from all walks of life.

Though many factors contributed to the rise of devotionalism as a religious ideology in Hinduism, *bhakti* religion and literature are essentially populist in character. Already in the first century, in an attempt to meet the challenge of the more egalitarian Buddhism and Jainism, the author of the *Bhagavad-Gītā*, a key text of Hinduism, had validated the dignity of all the castes and classes in Hindu society and the personal worship of God regardless of social status. Nevertheless, the *Gītā* is a philosophical text, one written by and for the elite classes in Sanskrit, the classical language. Medieval *bhakti* poems, by contrast, are lyrics in the spoken mother tongue, authored by poet-saints who came from high as well as low castes and classes, including women and "untouchables" (persons born into castes considered ritually impure). The *Gītā*'s author extols *bhakti* as an attitude of devotion, but the medieval poems are actual expressions of devotion by a diverse group of people who practiced this form of religion in a popular context.

Unlike classical Sanskrit and Tamil poems, which strive for an impersonal tone, *bhakti* poems are intensely personal and emotional. In some the poet directly addresses God; in others he or she describes to an implied audience his or her feelings toward God and the world. Often, these poems of the medieval saints are read as spiritual autobiography. True to the spirit of the concept of *bhakti*, which connotes an intimate, loving relationship between God and devotee (*bhaj*, the root from which the Sanskrit word *bhakti* is derived, literally means "to participate, to

share"), every poem illuminates some aspect of the devotee's deep love for God or some nuance of their relationship. All *bhakti* poems have emotion at the core; most are intense, passionate, expressing a range of emotions from joy and peace to pain and despair. Most *bhakti* poems end with a line or verse in which the poet either names himself or herself or employs an expression or epithet that becomes a "signature." In each poem, too, the public mythology and iconography of the deity are shaped by the poet's personal vision, language, and imagery.

Despite devotional religion's emphasis on the mystical, interior aspects of religious experience, public and social dimensions are integral to *bhakti* poetry. *Bhakti* poets view themselves as members of a community of devotees, often addressing their songs to their own. *Bhakti* poetry also celebrates public, exuberantly expressive modes of devotion, including dance and song. At another level, the public aspect of *bhakti* poems derives from the role of the saint as the exemplary devotee. In these poems the metaphors for the saints' relationship with God are drawn from the entire range of intimate human relationships, with the devotee and God playing the roles of son and father or mother, parent and child, servant and master, friends, lovers, spouses. Hindu communities respond deeply to these relational metaphors for the love of God, seeing in each poet-saint's life and lyrics a paradigm for one of the ways in which devotion may be experienced and expressed.

Although the *Bhagavad-Gītā* celebrates *bhakti* as a relationship of love between an adoring devotee and a gracious God, the text's social message is essentially conservative. *Bhakti* poems, by contrast, are always on the brink of social revolution. Not all *bhakti* poets advocate real social change, but many speak of having defied societal norms to practice their religion, while others use metaphors of social transgression to describe the nature of their relationship with God, and all hold out visions of an ideal community of devotees who are entirely equal in the eyes of God. Out of these statements of defiance and transgression, the popular audience of *bhakti* poems has constructed heroic biographies for the poet-saints, who have thus become models and symbols of social liberation as well as of spiritual perfection. Regardless of the intention of the poets themselves, *bhakti* poems have traditionally served the Hindu masses as instruments with which to question and challenge not only the canonical and elite biases of Hindu religious practice but the very premises of the religion's social hierarchy.

It is in *bhakti* poetry that the voices of suppressed, marginalized, and excluded groups in Indian society are first heard. Not only do poets and saints of lowly origins—cobblers, potters, and outcastes—rank high in the long list of *bhakti* saints, but also the oppressed and the lowly become the models for the highest kind of devotion. Women and people of low caste are the most heroic of devotees, because they risk the most in claiming, through devotional practice, freedom, equality, and a voice in society. By the same logic, the upper-class man becomes a true devotee by imitating women and men of low status. The ideal *bhakti* saint is thus one who rejects his or her traditional role in society, defying the norms of behavior dictated by *dharma*, the Hindu code of social and moral order.

The rejection of *dharma* and conventional markers of identity takes many forms in the *bhakti* poets represented here. Himself a brahman (a member of the highest caste) and a king's minister, Basavaṇṇa, a poet of the south Indian Vīraśaiva (literally, "militant devotees of Śiva") sect, lashes out against caste distinctions, ritualism, and the convention of gender itself: "Look here, dear fellow: / I wear these men's clothes / only for you." "O lord of the meeting rivers / I'll make wars for you / but I'll be your devotees' bride." Declaring that she has taken her beloved God Śiva for her husband, the Vīraśaiva saint Mahādēviyakka cries, "Take these husbands who die, / decay, and feed them / to your kitchen fires!"—an unthinkable statement for a woman in Hindu society, where marriage and unquestioning

allegiance to the husband are the norms. The poems and traditional narratives of the life of Mīrābāī, a renowned north Indian woman poet, exhibit striking commonalities with those of Mahādēviyakka. Each is portrayed as rejecting a real-life marriage to pursue a passionate love relationship with God (depicted as her lover or husband), each declares her freedom not only from marriage but from all familial and domestic responsibilities, and each is shown triumphing over men who harrass her and ultimately achieving mystical union with the beloved God.

The feminization of the subject in *bhakti* lyrics is motivated, however, by more than a desire to question societal norms. Of the various models for the love between God and devotee, none has so captivated practitioners of *bhakti* religion as that of the erotic love between a man and woman. In the discourse of *bhakti*, the devotee is most often a woman who longs for her male lover. In some *bhakti* traditions, the highest love is adulterous, with the devotee portrayed as a woman trapped in a loveless marriage, but striving to unite with God, her true love. Seen as the social group that has been most denied personal freedom, women were also thought to have the ability to love more deeply and more unselfishly than men and to risk all for love in a manner that no man can.

It is easy to understand the tremendous appeal that *bhakti* poetry, a poetry that exalts women and celebrates the oppressed, holds for the Hindu masses. But it appears that the elites have also found it attractive, especially because the most radical elements of the social philosophy of *bhakti* religion are couched in terms of fantasy and metaphor and contained in the sphere of personal religion. This explains why such strikingly different poetic sensibilities and social visions as those of Kabīr and Tulsīdās, two of north India's most famous *bhakti* saints, both writing in Hindi in the late medieval period, could be encompassed by the rubric of *bhakti*. It is uncertain whether Kabīr, born into the low caste of weavers, was a Muslim or a Hindu. Nevertheless, he excoriates with equal vehemence ritualism, hypocrisy, and social injustice in both Hinduism and Islam, opting for a mystical relationship with a God whose personality is not apprehensible in sectarian terms. In contrast, Tulsīdās, who flourished about a century after Kabīr, wrote a version of the *Rāmāyaṇa* epic, a text whose hero is the exemplar of the man who lives by the Hindu code of *dharma*. Even while bypassing the issues of social hierarchy and inequality, Tulsīdās in his own way subverts the classical view of *dharma*. He portrays the divine incarnation Rāma as God in a humane and accessible form and depicts the relationships between Rāma and other characters in the epic, especially those low in the social hierarchy, such as the monkey servant, Hanumān, as relationships of boundless love.

Although manuscript editions of *bhakti* poems have been carefully preserved, it is as popular songs that they have gained widespread currency. All over India *bhakti* songs are sung by communities of devotees (*bhakta*) in congregational sessions called *bhajan* or *kīrtan*. All *bhakti* poets use colloquial language and imagery, folk song meters, refrains, and other elements of oral composition in their poems. Some, like Kabīr the weaver, came from genuinely humble backgrounds. Others were learned men and women who adopted the idiom of simplicity. Indeed, the portrayal of the love of God on the model of erotic love in *bhakti* poetry is based on the conventions and metaphors of classical Indian love poetry. In their depiction of the love affair between the god Krishna and his herdswoman-lover Rādhā the Bengali Vaiṣṇava (literally, "devotee of Viṣṇu") poets transpose in minute detail the conventions and imagery of secular erotic poems in the tradition of Sanskrit court poetry. The female voice of *bhakti* lyrics evolved from the woman's voice in classical Tamil love poems. *Bhakti* poems skillfully synthesize and transform the means and content of classical as well as genuinely "folk" poetic forms.

The poetry of some of the best-known *bhakti* poets is partly based on sectarian

teachings that are transmitted by spiritual teachers *(gurus)* to their initiated disciples. A prime example of a *bhakti* poet whose work is pervaded with esoteric ideas is Kabīr; his lyrics, not included here, nevertheless deserve mention. Something of the enigmatic attraction of Kabīr's poems may be discerned in the following sample (translated by Linda Hess and Shukdev Singh):

> If seed is form is god,
> then, pandit,
> what can you ask?
> Where is the intellect? ego? heart?
> the three qualities?
> Nectar and poison bloom,
> fruits ripen,
> the Vedas show many ways
> to cross the sea.
> Kabir says, what do I know
> of you or me,
> of who gets caught
> and who goes free?

The visionary, riddlelike quality of this poem is characteristic of Kabīr's style. Here the poet challenges the brahman scholar-priest's *(paṇḍit)* doctrine of liberation from *karma* rebirth, the standard problem of all Indian philosophies. But a full appreciation of the poem would require knowledge of the occult lore of the Nāth school of *yogīs* (adepts in the philosophy of *yoga*) and a sense for Kabīr's personal use of *ulaṭbhāṣā* ("inverted or upside-down language"), the Nāth philosophers' esoteric manipulation of the symbolic vocabularies of mainstream philosophies.

Direct, brief, and passionate, even *bhakti* lyrics with an arcane content are accessible to the devotees. *Bhakti* poems speak to the heart. It is the deep emotion animating lyrics as varied as Kabīr's poems of social critique and Mīrābāī's love songs to Krishna that constitutes their powerful appeal to their audience. *Bhakti* poems ushered into Indian literature a whole new poetic, one that celebrates personal emotion and an equally personal response, in stark opposition to the classical Sanskrit and Tamil poetics of depersonalized mood and universalized emotion. These poems are powerful because they portray an all-consuming love that crosses the boundaries of the secular and the sacred.

FURTHER READING

Excellent introductions to *bhakti* religion as well as translations of a range of *bhakti* poems in their north and south Indian variants are available in A. K. Ramanujan, *Speaking of Śiva* (1973) and *Hymns for the Drowning* (1981), and John Stratton Hawley and Mark Juergensmeyer, *Songs of the Saints of India* (1988). For a study and translation of Kabīr, see Linda Hess and Shukdev Singh, *The Bījak of Kabir* (1986). On women poets in *bhakti* literature, see Susie Tharu and K. Lalitha, eds., *Women Writing in India*, Vol. 1 (1991), and Margaret Macnicol, *Poems by Indian Women* (1923).

PRONOUNCING GLOSSARY

The following list uses common English syllables and stress accents to provide rough equivalents of selected words whose pronunciation may be unfamiliar to the general reader.

Basavaṇṇa: *buh'-suh-vuhn-nuh*   bhaj: *buhj*

Bhagavad-Gītā: *buh'-guh-vuhd–gee'-*   bhajan: *buh'-juhn*
    tah   bhakta: *buhk'-tuh*

bhakti: *buhk'-tee*

dharma: *duhr'-muh*

Hanumān: *huh'-noo-mahn*

Kabīr: *kuh-beer'*

kīrtan: *keer'-tuhn*

Krishna: *kreesh'-nuh*

Mahādēviyakka: *muh-hah-day'-vee-yuhk'-kuh*

Mīrābāī: *mee'-rah-bah'-yee*

Nāth: *nahth*

paṇḍit: *puhn'-deet*

Rādhā: *rahd'-hah*

Rāma: *rah'-muh*

Rāmāyaṇa: *rah-mah'-yuh-nuh*

Śaiva: *shai'-vuh*

Śiva: *shee'-vuh*

Tulsīdās: *tool'-see-dahs*

ulaṭbhāṣā: *oo-luht'-bah'-shah*

Vaiṣṇava: *vaish'-nuh-vuh*

Vīraśaiva: *veeh'-ruh-shai'-vuh*

Viṣṇu: *veesh'-noo*

MEDIEVAL INDIA: THE AGE OF THE DEVOTIONAL LYRIC

TEXTS	CONTEXTS
1100–1200 Basavaṇṇa and Mahādēvi-yakka, leaders of the Vīraśaiva Hindu religious movement, write poems *(vacana)* of social criticism and devotion to God in Kannada, a major spoken language of South India	
ca. 1275 Amir Khusrau, a Muslim Sufi (mystic) poet from Deccan in central India, writes poetry in Urdu	
	1288 Venetian traveler Marco Polo visits India
14th–16th centuries Vidyāpati and other poets of the Vaiṣṇava religious sect of Bengal write *bhakti* (devotional) lyric poems in Bengali on the love of the god Krishna and the herdswoman Rādhā	**ca. 1336** Vijayanagara, last major Hindu kingdom in India, is founded in central India
	1350 Thai kingdom of Ayuthia, named after Ayodhya, the capital of the Hindu epic hero Rāma, is established
	1398 Central Asian conqueror Timur (Tamerlane) sacks Delhi
1399 Krittivāsa's version of the ancient Hindu epic *The Rāmāyana* in the Bengali language	
ca. 1400–1448 Mystic poet Kabīr writes poems of social criticism and spiritual quest in Hindi, the major spoken language of north India	1400 Paper is introduced from Persia
	1498 Portuguese explorer Vasco da Gama arrives in India, signaling the beginning of the European commercial and colonial presence there
16th century One of India's most popular poets, Rajput woman saint-mystic Mīrabāi, writes lyric songs of love for the Hindu god Krishna	**ca. 1500** Guru Nanak founds Sikhism, a monotheistic religion synthesizing elements of Hinduism and Islam, in north India
	ca. 1500–1533 Mystical teacher Chaitanya of Bengal spreads the cult of devotion to the Hindu God Krishna in north India

TEXTS	CONTEXTS
	1510 The Portuguese establish a colony at Goa in western India
	ca. 1526 Central Asian Muslim invader Babar seizes power in Delhi and establishes the Mogul empire in north India
	1542 Jesuit Francis Xavier reaches India
	1556–1605 Jalaluddin Akbar, preeminent Mogul emperor, patronizes miniature painting and translations of texts from Indian languages to Persian, and proclaims Din-e-Ilahi a new universal religion
late 16th century The scriptures of the Sikh religion are compiled in the *Adi Granth*	1565 The fall of the Hindu kingdom of Vijayanagar
1574 Tulsīdās begins *Rāmcaritmānas* (Sacred lake of the deeds of Ram), India's most popular version of *The Rāmāyaṇa*, in a dialect of Hindi	
1580–1588 The Mogul emperor Akbar commissions illustrated Persian translations of the Sanskrit epics *The Rāmāyaṇa* and *The Mahābhārata* and the Sanskrit animal fable collection *Pañcatantra* • Akbar's court poet Abu'l Fazl writes the Persian *Akbar-Nāmā* (The chronicle of Akbar)	
	1600 Queen Elizabeth grants the British East India Company a charter for trade in India

POEMS OF THE VĪRAŚAIVA SAINTS

Mahādēviyakka is among the preeminent poet-saints of the Vīraśaiva (literally, "militant devotees of Śiva") *bhakti* sect that arose in the Karnataka region in southern India in the eleventh and twelfth centuries. Her poems, known as *vacanas* ("utterances"), are among the earliest literary works in Kannada, the language of Karnataka. While the colloquial language and the simple rhythms of these brief, epigrammatical poems link them to everyday speech, the bold, often shocking ideas expressed in them, combined with their vivid imagery, place them among the most thought-provoking poems in Indian literature.

The *akka* in Mahādēviyakka's name makes her "elder sister" to all her fellow devotees. Initiated by a Śaiva ("Śiva worshiping") *guru* at the age of ten, Mahādēvī (or Mahādēviyakka) proceeded to put the principles of her personal religion to practice. This included leaving a royal husband (after he tried to force himself on her); wandering naked in the countryside, pausing only to keep company with the Lord's men and women; and of course, voicing her passionate thoughts on God, love, and the world in beautiful *vacanas*.

In her 350 poems Mahādēvī expresses her conviction that it is only by going against societal norms that she can achieve spiritual fulfillment as a true devotee of Śiva. Total devotion to God means giving up the conventional coverings that society requires for the female body: "When all the world is the eye of the lord, / onlooking everywhere, what can you / cover and conceal?" For her, a woman born into a society in which marriage and chastity are the definitive frames for women's lives, a total relationship with God means rejecting men and declaring: "I'm the woman of love / for my lord, white as jasmine." Mahādēvī's metaphor for the ultimate act of defiance of social taboos is a sexual one: she is determined to "go cuckold my husband with Hara [Śiva] my Lord." In the context of *bhakti* religion, Mahādēvī becomes a "saint" by doing and fearlessly speaking of precisely those things that are forbidden to ordinary women.

A. K. Ramanujan, *Speaking of Śiva* (1973), contains fine poetic translations of the poems of Mahādēvī and other Vīraśaiva poets, along with an introduction to *bhakti* religion and appendices on Vīraśaivism.

PRONOUNCING GLOSSARY

The following list uses common English syllables and stress accents to provide rough equivalents of selected words whose pronunciation may be unfamiliar to the general reader.

bhakti: *buhk'-tee*

Kalyāṇa: *kuhl-yah'-nuh*

Karnataka: *kuhr-nah'-tuh-kuh*

Mahādēviyakka: *muh-hah-day'-vee-yuhk-kuh*

Śaiva: *shai'-vuh*

Vīraśaiva: *veeh-ruh-shai'-vuh*

MAHĀDĒVIYAKKA

twelfth century

17[1]

Like a silkworm weaving
her house with love
from her marrow,[2]
    and dying
in her body's threads   5
winding tight, round
and round,
    I burn
desiring what the heart desires.

Cut through, O lord,   10
my heart's greed,
and show me
your way out,

O lord white as jasmine.[3]

114

Husband inside,
lover outside.
I can't manage them both.

This world
and that other,   5
cannot manage them both.

O lord white as jasmine

I cannot hold in one hand
both the round nut
and the long bow.[4]   10

119

What's to come tomorrow
let it come today.
What's to come today
let it come right now.

Lord white as jasmine,   5
don't give us your *nows* and *thens!*

1. All selections translated by A. K. Ramanujan.   2. A variation of the classical Indian image of the spider and her web, representing the soul's self-deception by means of illusory notions.   3. This signature phrase is an epithet of Śiva in the temple at Mahadēvī's birthplace.   4. The reference here is obscure.

124

You can confiscate
money in hand;
can you confiscate
the body's glory?

Or peel away every strip   5
you wear,
but can you peel
the Nothing, the Nakedness
that covers and veils?

To the shameless girl   10
wearing the White Jasmine Lord's
light of morning,
you fool,
where's the need for cover and jewel?

283

I love the Handsome One:
he has no death
decay nor form
no place or side
no end nor birthmarks.   5
I love him O mother. Listen.

I love the Beautiful One
with no bond nor fear
no clan no land
no landmarks   10
for his beauty.

So my lord, white as jasmine, is my husband.

Take these husbands who die,
decay, and feed them
to your kitchen fires!   15

294

O brothers,[5] why do you talk
to this woman,
hair loose,
face withered,
body shrunk?   5

O fathers, why do you bother
with this woman?
She has no strength of limb,
has lost the world,

---

5. The men who tried to molest her.

lost power of will,   10
turned devotee,

she has lain down
with the Lord, white as jasmine,
and has lost caste.

336

Look at
love's marvellous
ways:

if you shoot an arrow
plant it   5
till no feather shows;

if you hug
a body, bones
must crunch and crumble;

weld,   10
the welding must vanish.

Love is then
our lord's love.

THE BENGALI VAIṢṆAVA SAINTS' SONGS OF DEVOTION TO KRISHNA

The poems of the Bengali Vaiṣṇava saints, written in medieval dialects of Bengali, an important language of eastern India, are among the most beautiful *bhakti* songs devoted to Viṣṇu in his popular incarnation as Krishna. Vidyāpati and Chaṇḍidāsa, the major poets of this group, were brahman court poets who lived in the Bengal area in the fourteenth and fifteenth centuries, respectively. Govindadāsa lived in the sixteenth century and belonged to what had by then developed, under the leadership of the charismatic saint Śrī Krishna Chaitanya (1486–1533), into a flourishing devotional sect celebrating Krishna.

No other Hindu god has captured the popular imagination as has Krishna, and the aspect of Krishna mythology most emphasized in *bhakti* literature is the god's love idyll with married herdswomen (*gopīs*), especially with a *gopī* named Rādhā, in the cowherd village of Brindāvan in Braj. Current in the Tamil area as early as the sixth century, by the twelfth century the Rādhā-Krishna myth had spread to Bengal and Orissa in eastern India. There it became the central theme of Jayadeva's *Gītagovinda* (Krishna in song), an extended lyric-dramatic court poem in Sanskrit, and later, of the short lyric poems of the Bengali Vaiṣṇava saints composed Bengali folk song meters. These songs are still sung in communal sessions called *kīrtan* ("singing of God"). Indeed, according to a popular saying in Bengal, "Without Krishna there is no song."

In the *Gītagovinda* Jayadeva delineates the love affair of Rādhā and Krishna in

terms of the conventions of classical Sanskrit love poetry. After a brief period of happiness, the lovers become estranged because of Krishna's dalliance with other women, but they are eventually reunited with the help of Rādhā's female companion, the sakhī. Admired for its exquisite depiction of romantic love and its vivid descriptions of the lovemaking of Rādhā and Krishna, Jayadeva's poem is understood as an allegory of the devotee's separation and union with his or her beloved God.

Influenced as they are by the Sanskrit poet's masterful treatment of the Rādhā and Krishna theme, Govindadāsa and the other Vaiṣṇava poets approach it quite differently. Like Jayadeva, they portray Rādhā and Krishna as courtly lovers, equals engaged in a relationship; not only does Rādhā adore Krishna but he reciprocates her adoration, and both lovers suffer the pain of separation and rejection and are overwhelmed by the bliss of union. However, the Vaiṣṇava poets focus on the adulterous nature of the love affair, a feature implicit in the myth but ignored by Jayadeva. In poem after poem Rādhā speaks of the passion that drives her to leave her husband and family and flee to her cowherd lover Krishna in his forest retreat. She is drawn by his love and enchanted by his beauty and the call of his bamboo flute, and she is ready to face slander and punishment for breaking the rules by which an Indian woman is expected to live.

Why did the allegory of an adulterous liaison between an incarnate god and a herdswoman become the paradigm for the experience of bhakti in Bengali Vaiṣṇavism? For one thing, this myth of forbidden love provided the Vaiṣṇava saints with the model for the situation of the human soul in relation to God. At one level, Rādhā is the ideal devotee because her love is spontaneous and sincere and its purity gives her the courage to defy society. Seen from a slightly different perspective, God and the human soul desire each other like Rādhā and Krishna; like the lovers, too, they suffer greatly from inevitable separation, which heightens their passion for each other, deepening at the same time the joy of their moments of union. Finally, far from hindering spirituality, Rādhā and Krishna's sensuous apprehension of each other, as a manifestation of divine love on the physical plane, becomes the devotee's vehicle to a true understanding of God's nature and the fullest experience of a relationship of mutual love with him.

This idea—of the sensuous relationship as a way to God—forms the basis of the poetics of the Bengali bhakti poems. While the Sanskrit courtly love poems lead the reader to an experience of the erotic mood (rasa), a universalized flavor of sexual passion and the emotional states connected with passion, the Bengali Krishna poems plunge the reader/listener into emotion (bhāva) itself, with the qualification that "the emotion of sweet delight" that results from savoring the delineation of the love of Rādhā and Krishna is not mundane and the experience of it is the devotee's ultimate goal.

Autobiography is not as important an element in the understanding of the Bengali saints' songs as it is in the Vīraśaiva poems. In the Bengali Krishna poems the quasi-historical identity of the poet is deliberately replaced by a fluid persona that partakes of the emotions of the characters in the drama of Rādhā and Krishna's love. In these poems the bhakti framework in which male poets articulate their love of God by identifying themselves with a female self is further complicated by the allegorical structure of the Rādhā and Krishna myth. In some poems the poet speaks in Rādhā's voice, in others in Krishna's, and in yet others as a commentator on the lovers and their love. The songs are addressed variously to Krishna, to the poet's own self, to Rādhā's girlfriend, and to a nameless audience. The greatest complexity is reached in the concluding lines of each poem, which constitute the bhaṇita, or "poet's signature." In a song in which Rādhā and Krishna's relationship is described by a series of analogies and that ends with a question voiced by Rādhā—"Mādhava, beloved, / who are you? / Who are you really?"—the

bhaṇita takes the form of a single line in which the poet's voice "answers" Rādhā's question: *"Vidyāpati says, they are one another."* Some *bhaṇitas* raise questions or overturn propositions established in the preceding lines; others simply comment on the emotional landscape of the song; but all separate the poet's voice from those that have figured in the dramatic situation in the poem and offer a new perspective on it. This plurality of vision is perhaps the Bengali Vaiṣṇava poets' distinctive contribution to *bhakti* literature.

Edward C. Dimock's collaboration with the poet Denise Levertov has resulted in a slim volume containing the best translations of Bengali Vaiṣṇava poetry to date: Dimock and Levertov, *In Praise of Krishna* (1967). Translations of the poems of Vidyāpati and Chaṇḍidāsa, along with seventeenth- and eighteenth-century miniature paintings on the Rādhā and Krishna theme, may be found in Deben Bhattacharya's *Love Songs of Vidyapati* (1963) and *Love-songs of Chandidas* (1967). For a fine translation and study of Jayadeva's *Gītagovinda*, see Barbara Miller, *Love Song of the Dark Lord* (1977). W. G. Archer, *The Loves of Krishna in Indian Painting and Poetry* (1957), discusses the Rādhā and Krishna myth.

PRONOUNCING GLOSSARY

The following list uses common English syllables and stress accents to provide rough equivalents of selected words whose pronunciation may be unfamiliar to the general reader.

anchal: *ahn'-chuhl*

bhakti: *buhk'-tee*

bhaṇita: *bhuh'-nee-tuh*

Brindāvan: *breen-dah'-vuhn*

Chaṇḍidāsa: *chuhn'-dee-dah'-suh*

Gītagovinda: *gee'-tuh-goh-veen'-duh*

Govindadāsa: *goh-veen'-duh-dah'-suh*

Jayadeva: *juh-yuh-day'-vuh*

Krishna: *krish'-nuh*

kunja: *koon'-juh*

Mādhava: *mahd'-huh-vuh*

Rādhā: *rahd'-hah*

sakhī: *suhk'-heeh*

Shyāma: *shyah'-muh*

Śrī Krishna Chaitanya: *shree kreesh'- nuh chai-tuhn'-yuh*

Vaiṣṇava: *vaish'-nuh-vuh*

Vidyāpati: *veed-yah'-puh-tee*

Viṣṇu: *vish'-noo*

GOVINDADĀSA

fifteenth century

[O Mādhava, how shall I tell you of my terror?][1]

O Mādhava,[2] how shall I tell you of my terror?
I could not describe my coming here
if I had a million tongues.
When I left my room and saw the darkness

---

1. All selections translated by Edward C. Dimock and Denise Levertov.   2. Krishna, suggesting his mighty persona as a slayer of demons.

I trembled: 5
I could not see the path,
there were snakes that writhed round my ankles!

I was alone, a woman; the night was so dark,
the forest so dense and gloomy,
and I had so far to go.   10
The rain was pouring down—
which path should I take?³
My feet were muddy
and burning where thorns had scratched them.
But I had the hope of seeing you, none of it mattered,   15
and now my terror seems far away . . .
When the sound of your flute reaches my ears
it compels me to leave my home, my friends,
it draws me into the dark toward you.

I no longer count the pain of coming here,   20
says Govindadāsa.

[When they had made love]

When they had made love
she lay in his arms in the *kunja* grove.⁴
Suddenly she called his name
and wept—as if she burned in the fire of
separation.⁵   5
        The gold was in her *anchal*⁶
        but she looked afar for it!
—Where has he gone? Where has my love gone?
O why has he left me alone?
And she writhed on the ground in despair,   10
only her pain kept her from fainting.
Krishna was astonished
and could not speak.

*Taking her beloved friend by the hand,*⁷
Govindadāsa led her softly away.   15

[Let the earth of my body be mixed with the earth]

SHE SPEAKS:

Let the earth of my body be mixed with the earth
my beloved walks on.

3. This poem builds on a convention of classical Sanskrit love poetry, in which a woman—usually a married woman—braves strange roads and the danger of discovery to meet her lover on a rainy night at a prearranged spot. The rainy season is the time of lovers' union.   4. A bower of flowering plants and creepers in the woods, the arena of Rādhā and Krishna's lovemaking.   5. It is the premise of Vaiṣṇava theology as well as of classical Sanskrit love poetry that separation is latent in lovers' union and that brief moments of bliss merely intensify the pain of separation.   6. The free-hanging end of the sari (a garment worn by Bengali and Indian women) in which coins and valuables are carried.   7. Here Govindadāsa takes the part of a *gopī*, one of the herdswomen with whom Krishna dallies as a young man. *Gopīs* are often depicted as witnesses to Rādhā and Krishna's love play. The *beloved friend* is the conventional character of the *sakhī*, the heroine's female friend who acts as a go-between, both in the classical court poetry and in Rādhā-Krishna love poems.

Let the fire of my body be the brightness
in the mirror that reflects his face.   5
Let the water of my body join the waters
of the lotus pool he bathes in.
Let the breath of my body be air
lapping his tired limbs.
Let me be sky, and moving through me   10
that cloud-dark Shyāma,[8] my beloved.

Govindadāsa says, O golden one,
Could he of the emerald body[9] let you go?

8. Krishna; he has a dark complexion—thus here he is called "the dark one." 9. Krishna; another reference to his complexion.

MĪRĀBĀĪ
sixteenth century

Mīrābāī (or Mīrā), a devotee of Krishna who flourished in the sixteenth century,
is one of the most popular of the north Indian *bhakti* poets writing in Hindi, and
the only woman among them. Born in Rajasthan in western India, Mīrā is said to
have achieved fame as a saint during her own lifetime and to have spent the end of
her life in the north Indian village Brindavan (the locale of the myths of Krishna's
lovemaking with herdswomen), which had become the principal center of Krishna
worship under the leadership of the Bengali saint Chaitanya (p. 1421). The majority of the fourteen hundred *bhakti* songs attributed to Mīrā are in Brajbhāṣā, a
dialect of Hindi, the major language of north India; the rest of the poems are in a
form of Gujerati, a western Indian language. Mīrā's songs are sung all over India,
including the south, where the dominant languages are not related to Hindi.

Mīrā's poetry and the reception of her songs and life have been profoundly
colored by her identity as a woman. According to the traditional biographies, born
a princess of one Rajput clan and married into another, Mīrā abandoned her royal
husband and family to sing songs about her love for Krishna. For her audience the
voice of Krishna's female lover in Mīrā's poetry is no mere persona or metaphor,
but Mīrā's own voice. Her songs bring the poignancy and authenticity of a woman's real-life experience to the archetypal *bhakti* myth of the lovelorn woman pining for a beloved God.

The central theme of Mīrā's poetry is that of breaking away from husband and
family to engage in an erotic, romantic relationship with Krishna. In many poems
Mīrā speaks of her mother-in-law and sisters-in-law tormenting her and of being
imprisoned by the king, who may have been her father-in-law or her husband.
When the king sends her a cup of poison, she drinks it without being harmed.
Mīrā's poems repeatedly evoke trangressions of the rules of modesty, chastity, and
seclusion prescribed for married women, especially among the Rajput noble families, whose men considered any infringement of these rules an insult to family
honor. The defiant Mīrā speaks of tearing off the veil *(pardā)*, which is supposed
to help guard her modesty, and of wandering in the streets, singing, in defiance of
the custom of female seclusion. In a society in which only courtesans—women
who are sexually free—may practice the art of dance, Mīrā dances in public with
bells on her ankles, celebrating her love for Krishna. She is "mad" with desire for

her God, and she is "colored with the color" of the Lord. In an image that repeatedly appears in her poems, she lies "on the couch of love" with her beloved Krishna as his bride or lover. The distinctly personal sensibility informing the sensuous, subversive language and imagery of Mīrā's poems is quite different from that of the male authors of Krishnaite devotional literature, who evoke the myths of Krishna's love affair with the herdswoman Rādhā or his riotous love play with the herdswomen on the banks of the river Jumna.

An important feature of Mīrā's songs is their closeness to women's songs and folk traditions. Women in north India sing songs to each other at women's festivals and rites throughout the year, especially to mark the cycle of the seasons. In the folk tradition the monsoon season, a time of continuous rainfall, is a time for songs expressing the pain of separation from one's lover, while the songs of Holi, a rite of spring, celebrate the joy of lovers' union. Mīrā's monsoon songs about Krishna share much with women's songs of the rainy season, and her image of being "dyed in Krishna's color" (Krishna has a dark complexion) is taken from the festival of Holi, in which men and women spray each other with colored water or throw colored powder on each other in a carnivalesque frenzy. Many of Mīrā's poems are addressed to a girlfriend or to an implied audience of women, suggesting kinship with the women's song traditions, in which, even when an absent lover is addressed, the songs are usually sung to an audience of women. Paradoxically, however, in the context of devotion to Krishna, the feminine sensibility and the language of desire and defiance of social norms that permeate Mīrā's songs are the very qualities that make them speak to men and women alike.

John Stratton Hawley and Mark Juergensmeyer, *Songs of the Saints of India* (1988), offers an insightful discussion of Mīrā's life and excellent translations of her poems. For a larger selection of poems, see A. J. Alston, *The Devotional Poems of Mīrābāī* (1980).

PRONOUNCING GLOSSARY

The following list uses common English syllables and stress accents to provide rough equivalents of selected words whose pronunciation may be unfamiliar to the general reader.

bhakti: *buhk'-tee*

Brajbhāṣā: *bruhj-b-hah'-shah*

Brindavan: *breend-dah'-vuhn*

Chaitanya: *chai-tuhn'-yuh*

Gujerati: *goo-juh-rah'-teeh*

Mīrābāī: *meeh'-rah-bah'-yee*

Murali: *moo'-ruh-lee*

Rādhā: *rahd'-hah*

Rajasthan: *rah'-juhs-than*

Rajput: *rahj'-pooht*

37[1]

I'm colored with the color of dusk, oh *rana*,[2]
    colored with the color of my Lord.
Drumming out the rhythm on the drums, I danced,
    dancing in the presence of the saints,[3]
        colored with the color of my Lord.   5
They thought me mad for the Maddening One,[4]

---

1. All selections translated by John Stratton Hawley and Mark Juergensmeyer. 2. King. *Color of dusk:* Krishna has a blue-black complexion. 3. Devotees of Krishna. 4. Here, Krishna; "the one who maddens" is more often the love god Kāma.

raw for my dear dark love,
   colored with the color of my Lord.
The *rana* sent me a poison cup:
   I didn't look, I drank it up,   10
   colored with the color of my Lord.
The clever Mountain Lifter is the lord of Mira.[5]
   Life after life he's true—
   colored with the color of my Lord.

42

Life without Hari[6] is no life, friend,
And though my mother-in-law fights,
   my sister-in-law teases,
   the *rana*[7] is angered,
A guard is stationed on a stool outside,   5
   and a lock is mounted on the door,
How can I abandon the love I have loved
   in life after life?
Mira's Lord is the clever Mountain Lifter:
   Why would I want anyone else?   10

82

I saw the dark clouds burst,
       dark Lord,[8]
Saw the clouds and tumbling down
In black and yellow streams
       they thicken,   5
Rain and rain two hours long.
See—
   my eyes see only rain and water,
   watering the thirsty earth green.
Me—   10
   my love's in a distant land
   and wet, I stubbornly stand at the door,[9]
For Hari is indelibly green,[1]
       Mira's Lord,
And he has invited a standing,   15
       stubborn love.

84

Hey love bird, crying cuckoo,
   don't make your crying coos,

5. Mīrā's signature phrase. *Clever:* civilized, gallant. *Mountain Lifter:* a reference to a feat of Krishna's youth, in which he lifted a mountain to shelter the entire cowherd village from torrential rain. 6. Krishna.   7. King.   8. Krishna.   9. Evokes the feelings of a woman waiting for her lover to come to her, the theme of poems about the monsoon season in women's folk songs.   1. One of the meanings of the word *Hari* (a name for Krishna).

for I who am crying, cut off from my love,
   will cut off your crying beak
   and twist off your flying wings   5
   and pour black salt in the wounds.

Hey, I am my love's and my love is mine.
   How do you dare cry love?
   But if my love were restored today
   your love call would be a joy.   10
   I would gild your crying beak with gold
   and you would be my crown.

Hey, I'll write my love a note,
   crying crow, now take it away[2]
   and tell him that his separated love   15
   can't eat a single grain.
   His servant Mira's mind's in a mess.
   She wastes her time crying coos.

Come quick, my Lord,
   the one who sees inside;   20
   without you nothing remains.

153

Go to where my loved one lives,
   go where he lives and tell him
     if he says so, I'll color my sari red;
     if he says so, I'll wear the godly yellow garb;[3]
     if he says so, I'll drape the part in my hair with pearls;   5
     if he says so, I'll let my hair grow wild.[4]
Mira's Lord is the clever Mountain Lifter:
   listen to the praises of that king.

166

Murali[5] sounds on the banks of the Jumna,
Murali snatches away my mind;
My senses cut loose from their moorings—
Dark waters, dark garments, dark Lord.[6]
I listen close to the sounds of Murali   5
And my body withers away—
Lost thoughts, lost even the power to think.
   Mira's Lord, clever Mountain Lifter,
   Come quick, and snatch away my pain.

---

2. Modeled on folk songs in which a lovelorn woman speaks to birds and asks them to take a message to her lover.   3. The yellow robes worn by monks and nuns in contrast to the red saris worn by Hindu brides.   4. The ascetic's matted hair in contrast to the bride's hairstyle adorned with pearls.   5. Krishna's enchanting bamboo flute.   6. Krishna, who has a dark complexion. *Dark waters*: Jumna River. *Dark garments*: Krishna's cloak.

193

Let us go to a realm beyond going,
Where death is afraid to go,
Where the high-flying birds alight and play,
Afloat in the full lake[7] of love.
There they gather—the good, the true—   5
To strengthen an inner regimen,
To focus on the dark form of the Lord
And refine their minds like fire.
Garbed in goodness—their ankle bells—
They dance the dance of contentment   10
And deck themselves with the sixteen signs
Of beauty,[8] and a golden crown—
There where the love of the Dark One[9] comes first
And everything else is last.

---

7. A traditional mystical image of pure souls as swans or wild geese and spiritual perfection as a sacred lake.
8. Conventional adornments for a woman.   9. Krishna.

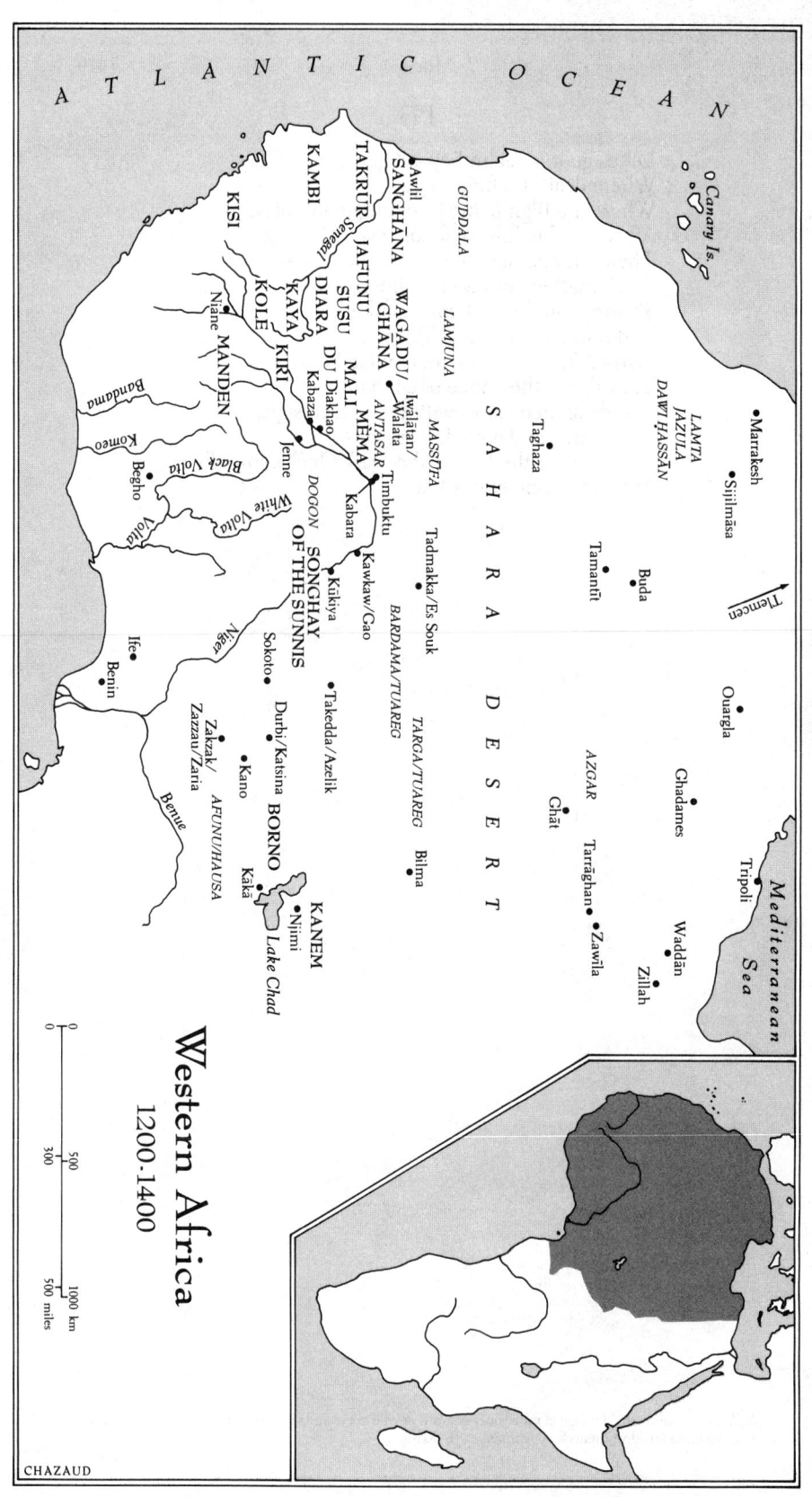

Western Africa
1200·1400

Africa: The Mali Epic of
Son-Jara

late thirteenth–early fourteenth century

The epic of *Son-Jara* is the national epic of the Manding people, who inhabit what may be called the heartland of West Africa. The greater part of this area is in the savanna belt, in present-day Mali, but it also embraces, to the west and southwest, considerable parts of the coastal region bordering the Atlantic, in the modern states of Senegal, the Gambia, and Guinea. The people of this extensive area, which cuts across the boundaries established since the late nineteenth century by French and British colonial administrations, share a common history and culture deriving from a continuing sense of affiliation to the ancient, precolonial empire of Mali.

The founding of the Mali empire in the mid-thirteenth century is attributed to Son-Jara Keita, whose life and exploits are celebrated in the epic and whose hold on the feelings and imagination of the Manding people it has helped in no small measure to sustain to this day. In its oral form (as it is still performed all over the Manding area) the epic is considered to be not only the record of great events that led to the formation of the empire in the distant past—a factual recollection of its auspicious beginnings—but also a repository of the values of the society itself, even in its present circumstance. The epic thus functions for the Manding as a significant cultural reference, similar in this respect to the *Iliad* in ancient Greece and the *Rāmāyaṇa* in India.

The personality of Son-Jara (also known as Sundiata) is shrouded in mystery. All we know about him has had to be reconstructed from the oral tradition of the Manding—the epic itself forming the principal element of this tradition—and various Arab historical records concerning ancient Mali, which refer to its founder as "Mari Jata." Some of these records date from the very beginnings of the empire, but the most important historical account is the work of Ibn Khaldoun, whose fifteenth-century descriptions of the imperial court and the political and social life of the empire include a dynastic list of the rulers, traced back in every case to Son-Jara. Thus, although he has been transformed in the oral tradition into a figure of myth and legend, like the warriors of the Greek expedition to Troy, there seems no doubt about his historical existence. Nor is there doubt about his determining role in the establishment of Mali, initially as a centralized monarchical state and subsequently as a powerful empire that welded the various ethnic groups in the West African savanna into a distinctive national community.

The rise of ancient Mali in the thirteenth century represents an important stage in the process of state formation in West Africa, a process closely associated with the spread of Islam into the region, which began as early as the seventh century. The literacy Islam introduced enabled the formation (during the period that corresponds to the European Middle Ages) of an elite educated in Arabic, whose services to the early rulers made possible the establishment of their rule over ever-widening territories and fostered the emergence of the three best-known West African medieval empires: Songhai, Ghana, and Mali.

To understand the association of these early West African states with Islam, it is important to observe that in the oral tradition Son-Jara Keita is held to be the descendant of Bilal, a companion of Muhammad and a religious leader. Bilal's family is said to have migrated from the Near East and settled in the region, founding a religious community in the Manden, which proved to be the nucleus of ancient Mali. The version of the Son-Jara epic printed here begins with an invocation in which the hero is assimilated to Adam, the first man in both the Bible and the Koran, and thus underlines their common status as founding figures. Moreover, despite the fact that the epic's outlook on the world is essentially pagan, the invocation, which incorporates an allusion to Bilal as a close associate of Muhammad, and the many other references to Islam throughout the epic lend the sanction of an established world religion to the commemoration of the hero. The invocation thus intimates and prefigures the subsequent interaction between the practices and tenets of Islam and local Manding beliefs and customs. This cultural fusion within the poem mirrors the way in which a literate culture bound to Islam and the Arabic language was appropriated and integrated into the forms of an indigenous African orality.

Although the epic of *Son-Jara* has been recorded and transcribed by literary scholars in recent times, and thus carried one more stage into the realm of writing, it remains an integral part of the oral tradition in Africa. This tradition comprises various expressive forms—folk tales, legends, myths, and poetry—through which the imaginative impulse of preliterate societies takes shape. A conscious elaboration of language in these forms, managed through imagery and structural devices, distinguishes them from ordinary speech and gives them an aesthetic function above and beyond any referential content. Moreover, it is often the case that over the years oral cultures evolve a consecrated body of texts, a term that in oral literature applies to any extensive expression of experience in a *settled* art form. The generation, performance, and oral transmission of such texts endow them with a life of their own, so that they come to represent the literary monuments of the culture. In this respect, they function for oral societies in the same way that written literature does for literate societies.

The principal custodians of the oral tradition among the Manding are professional bards, known variously as *dyeli, belein-tigui,* or more commonly by the French term *griot.* They are specially trained oral performers who in former times were attached to the imperial court (and to its local replications across the Mali empire) as well as to members of the aristocracy. Their role was to recite from memory, on great occasions of state, the oral chronicles and family history of their patrons. In this capacity, they were expected not merely to recall the bare historical narrative as handed down by tradition but also, as poets and wordsmiths, to endow their recitations with all the power of language they could command, thus creating an ever-developing imaginative expression of the community's historical consciousness. It is to these "masters of the word" that we owe the persistence of the oral tradition and especially, among the Manding, the continued existence of the epic of *Son-Jara.*

The epic probably originated in a series of praise poems addressed to Son-Jara during his reign; their allusions to his virtues and exploits were developed later into an extended narrative of his life and heroic achievement. This development by accretion, together with the oral transmission of the resulting narrative, may explain why the epic exists not as a fixed text but rather as a fusion of three distinct generic layers.

Most important is the narrative framework. This is the overarching "master text" in which the movement of the epic is broadly formulated. This framework is composed of structural episodes, and it is the narrator's immediate task to recall these in appropriate sequence. He is, however, at liberty to expand on them in whatever

way best suits the context of performance and the character of the audience, employing in the process a number of formulaic devices not only as props to memory but as building blocks in his recreation of the epic story. The interplay between core elements of the text, which are relatively fixed (for example, genealogies of families and clans), and the performer's free improvisations (often involving digressions and general reflections as well as anachronistic references and topical allusions), generates a profound sense that the story, though established by tradition, is at the same time constantly renewed in performance. Thus if orality implies limitations, it also implies creative possibilities, apparent in the many differing versions of the epic recorded by individual *griots*.

The other two generic layers derive from the conditions of oral performance outlined above. The many passages of praise poetry with which the epic is interspersed stand in a close formal relationship to the formulaic plan of the narrative. Their shape attests to their independent existence before they were integrated into the epic we have today, and they are still on occasion recited outside its narrative framework. As generally with praise poems in oral literature, they are composed of strings of epithets, often hyperbolic, emphasizing the uncommon attributes—the heroic essence as it were—of their subject. Finally, in the third layer are the songs. These function as interludes within the epic narrative but, like the praise poems, are often performed as autonomous pieces to the accompaniment of the *kora*, an elaborate stringed instrument with tonal qualities comparable to those of the harp.

Performance of the epic is highly rhythmic, with breath stops, often accentuated by tonal patterns, rather than meter or rhyme, determining the verse lines. This basic register frequently intensifies into a chanting mode, notably for the praise poems. The song mode, in which musical instruments intervene, is another resource available to performers of the epic. To these effects must be added movement and gesture, with which the narrator dramatizes action or provides a visual delineation of character. Such extraliterary aspects of epic performance represent crucial factors and subtly evoke that direct relationship of the *griot* to his audience without which it would have been difficult, if not impossible, to sustain the cultural vitality of the epic. In short, the *griot's* task consists far less in reproducing an exact text of the epic from one performance to the other—a text with which the audience is usually familiar—than in bringing to life the master text: the epic narrative prescribed by tradition, as actualized, through his living agency, in a dramatic reenactment.

The epic of *Son-Jara* is primarily a political poem, centered on the rivalry of two brothers for succession to their father's throne, a theme exemplified by the conflict between Cain and Abel and Jacob and Esau in the Bible and that between Polynices and Eteocles in Sophocles' *Antigone*. This rivalry develops later into a wider contest between two rival chieftains for territorial control. Its ideological function as a myth to legitimize the ruling dynasty of ancient Mali is apparent not only from the heroic glorification of its historical founder but also from the motifs that structure the epic narrative. As in many early epics, psychological interest is limited and the hero's character is simply sketched; it is, however, endowed with symbolic significance. The story is essentially a relation of Son-Jara's trials, which he overcomes through his personal qualities—his piety, his filial devotion to his mother, his courage and tenacity. His final victory is also presented in moral terms as a triumph of good over evil. Fa-Koli's disaffection from the Susu Sumamuru (his uncle and Son-Jara's rival), which leads to his defection to Son-Jara—an act that proves decisive for the outcome of the struggle between Sumamuru and Son-Jara—is prompted by his sense of wrong. The moral implication of this episode, identifying Son-Jara's cause with that of universal justice, confirms the political and ideological thrust of the epic on a note that is distinctly personal and human.

The ideological function of the epic needs, however, to be placed in a broader

perspective, that of the construction of a Manding collective identity around the figure of their founding hero. In its relation to the process of state formation in the West African savanna region, the epic of *Son-Jara* serves as the essential medium of the collective memory of the Manding people, keeping alive not only a sense of their historical continuities but also of the integrity of their communal values. The epic is thus the repository not merely of the achievements of an outstanding individual but of the growth of a national consciousness.

Although a singular work in many respects, the epic of *Son-Jara* is representative of the heritage of oral poetry in Africa. Scholarly research has made it increasingly evident that this heritage is more diversified than was thought; that it goes beyond folktales; and especially, that it includes extended forms, of which the epic genre — exemplified by the Son-Jara epic and other African narratives such as *Kabili, Da Monzon of Segou*, the *Mwindo* epic, and the *Ozidi* saga — forms an integral part. Beyond their intrinsic interest as outstanding forms of imaginative expression, these products of the African oral tradition point to a universal heritage — that literature seems almost everywhere (with few exceptions, notably China and Japan) to have had its beginnings in heroic song.

The epic of *Son-Jara* represents a communal resource, whose various versions are associated with individual *griots*. The earliest published version is the prose adaptation brought out in French in 1968 by the Malian historian, Djibril Tamsir Niane, *Sundiata, an Epic of Old Mali* (1989). This adaptation, undertaken as part of the nationalist reclamation of the African past, brought the work into the limelight and has remained its best-known version. While it presents a faithful rendering of the action, it fails to capture the epic's heroic movement and the atmosphere of performance essential to its character. Three further versions have been collected by Gordon Innes, *Sunjata: Three Madinka Versions* (1974), a work of interest mainly for comparative purposes. More recent is a prose adaptation by the Guinean novelist Camara Laye, *The Guardian of the Word* (1980), a controversial version in its highly personal reinterpretation as well as, in the view of many scholars, its distortion of the material. The version printed here was transcribed from a recital performed by the *griot* Fa-Digi Sisoko and translated by John William Johnson. More than any published version, this version conveys a sense of the epic's tone and movement as well as of the dynamics of its performance.

For a comprehensive discussion, from a cross-cultural perspective, of the epic genre in Africa, see Isidore Okpewho, *The Epic in Africa* (1979). The translation printed here is John William Johnson, *The Epic of Son-Jara: A West African Tradition* (1992), which contains a valuable introduction. Adu Boahen, *Topics in West African History* (1990), provides in a succinct and readable form the general historical background. On the specific role of Islam as a historical and cultural factor in West Africa, see J. Spencer Trimingham, *A History of Islam in West Africa* (1970).

PRONOUNCING GLOSSARY

The following list uses common English syllables to provide rough equivalents of selected words whose pronunciation may be unfamiliar to the general reader.

belein-tigui: *bay-len–tee-ghee*

Bintanyan Kamalan: *been-tah-yarn kah-mah-lan*

Bugu Turu: *boo-goo too-roo*

Dankaran Tuman: *dahn-kah-ran too-man*

Dan Mansa Wulandin: *dahn man-sah woo-lahn-deen*

Dan Mansa Wulanba: *dahn man-sah woo-lahn-bah*

Dòka: *doh-kah*

Du Kamisa: *do kah-mee-sah*

Dun Fayiri: *doon fah-yee-ree*

dyeli: *jay-lee*

Fa-Digi Sisoko: *fah–dee-gee see-soh-koh*

Fata Magan: *fah-tah mah-gahn*

Genu: *gay-noo*

griot: *gree-oh*

Kamasiga: *kah-mah-see-gah*

Kanu Simbon: *kah-noo seem-bon*

Kukuba: *koo-koo-bah*

Kulu-Kòrò: *koo-loo–koh-roh*

Kuyatè: *koo-yah-tay*

Magan Jata Kòndè: *mah-gahn jah-ta kon-day*

Mane: *ma-nay*

Nakana Tiliba: *nah-kah-nah tee-lee-bah*

Nare Magan Kònatè: *nah-ray mah-gan koh-nah-tay*

Nyani (Niane): *neer-nee*

Saman Berete: *sah-mahn bay-ray-tay*

Sane: *sah-nay*

Sasagalò: *sah-sag-gah-loh*

Son-Jara Keita: *sawn–jah-rah kay-ee-tah*

Sugulun Kòndè: *soo-goo-loon kon-day*

Sundiata: *soon-jah-tah*

Tanimunari: *tah-nee-moo-nah-ree*

Tarawere: *tah-rah-way-ray*

Tura Magan: *too-rah mah-gahn*

TEXTS	CONTEXTS
ca. A.D. 300 Development of the Geez Script	
	A.D. 200–350 Introduction and spread of Christianity in North Africa
397 Augustine begins *Confessions*	
	500–1495 Rise of the West African Savanna Empires: Ghana in the northwest (ca. 500), Kanem around Lake Chad (ca. 900), Mali (ca. 1200), and Songhay in the Middle Niger (ca. 1495)
	600–1000 Introduction and spread of Islam in East and West Africa
13th–14th centuries *The Epic of Son-Jara*	
	1300–1500 Rise of the Kongo kingdom on the lower Zaire (Congo) River, including present-day Angola, in Central Africa; rise of Benin in West African forest belt, in the hinterland of the Niger Delta (ca. 1400); and rise of Monomotapa ("Great Zimbabwe") in Southern Africa, north of the Limpopo River (ca. 1500)
1352 *Arab Chronicles*: Ibn Battuta on ancient Mali	
	1450–1600 Portuguese explorers on the West and Central African coasts
ca. 1513 Leo Africanus, *History and Description of Africa*	
	late 16th–mid 19th century The Atlantic slave trade

From The Epic of Son-Jara[1]

FROM EPISODE 1

Prologue in Paradise

Nare Magan Kònatè![2]
Sorcerer-Seizing-Sorcerer![3]
A man of power is hard to find.
And four mastersingers.   (Indeed)
5   O Kala Jula Sangoyi[4]
Sorcerer-Seizing-Sorcerer!   (Mmm)

It is of Adam that I sing.
Of Adam,
Ben Adam.[5]   ('Tis true)
10 As you succeeded some,
So shall you have successors![6]
It is of Adam that I sing, of Adam.   (Indeed)

I sing of Biribiriba![7]   (Indeed)
Of Nare Magan Kònatè!
15 Sorcerer-Seizing Sorcerer!   (True)
From Fatiyataligara
All the way to Sokoto,[8]   (Indeed)
Belonged to Magan Son-Jara.   (Indeed)
Africans call that, my father,[9]
20 The Republic of Mali,[1]   (Indeed)
The Maninka[2] realm: (Mmm, 'tis true)
That's the meaning of Mali.
Magan Son-Jara,
He slayed Bambara-of-the-Border;[3]
25 Settling on the border[4] does not suit the weak. (Indeed)
And slayed Bambara-the-Lizard;[5]

1. Text by Fa-Digi Sisoko; translated by John William Johnson. The words in parentheses at the right
are interjections made by members of the audience, principally by Bèmba.   2. Son-Jara. This praise
name combines a reference to his place of origin *(Nare)* with his royal title *(Magan,* "king" or "lord";
the title of the emperor of ancient Ghana was *Kaya Magan). Kònatè* is Son-Jara's clan.   3. This praise
name refers to Son-Jara's superior magical powers.   4. A bard reputed to be the originator of the epic;
he can thus be considered the equivalent of Homer with respect to the *Iliad.* He is invoked here in
homage to the artistic ancestor of Fa-Digi Sisoko, the bard who is re-creating the epic on this occasion.
The exact reference of l. 4 is obscure, but its allusion to the bard's professional status is clearly related
to the invocation of Kala Jula Sangoyi.   5. The Adam of Genesis.   6. A formulaic device employed
by the bard at various points in the epic; here it stresses the unbroken continuity of Son-Jara's dynastic
line.   7. This praise name for Son-Jara conveys his immense physical prowess.   8. An ancient city
in northern Nigeria, several hundred miles east of the Manding area. The city was the capital of the
Fulani empire, which by the early 19th century had embraced most of the area in the Niger-Benue
basin and was conquered by the British in the early years of this century. Fayitaligara can no longer be
identified. The bard means the extent of the old Mali empire from west to east.   9. A term of reverence; here an aside addressed to the older members of the audience.   1. That is, present-day Mali;
the name of the ancient empire was revived in 1960, when the modern republic achieved independence
from France.   2. Manding or Mandenka; the term covers many more ethnic groups than are found
in the present Republic of Mali.   3. That is, Sumamuru, Son-Jara's principal antagonist, who was a
Susu, an ethnic group related to the Bambara of present-day Mali.   4. All areas beyond the safe limits
of human settlement. The implication is that it requires an intrepid character, such as that associated
with the professional hunter, to venture beyond these limits and confront the dangers of the wilderness.
5. A derogatory term, which alludes to the fact that young boys start to practice hunting with lizards;
hence the reptile is associated with the weak and uninitiated.

No weak one should call himself lizard.   (Indeed)
And slayed Bambara-of-the-Backwoods;
Settling the backwoods does not suit the weak.   (Indeed)
30   All this by the hand of Nare Magan Kònatè.
Sorcerer-Seizing-Sorcerer!
Simbon, Lion-Born-of-the-Cat.[6]   ('Tis true)

Summary   Fa-Digi Sisoko follows this opening invocation with a lengthy
account of the Genesis story, in a version that incorporates a cosmological myth
and the origin of the races of the world. This provides a background to the epic
recall, in the next section, of the original migration of Bilal from the Middle East
with his band of followers, and their settlement among and interaction with the
indigenous peoples in the West African savannah. This reconstruction of the early
history of the region is directly linked to Son-Jara's genealogy, traced from Bilal
right down to Son-Jara's father, Fata Magan the Handsome, who settles in a place
called Kamalen, destined to be the center of the Manding kingdom. The bard
recounts Fata Magan's marriage to Saman Berete, who will later bear him a son,
in the confused circumstances that will pit this son against Son-Jara, his half
brother, in a struggle for succession to the thone.
    Having thus established Son-Jara's paternal line of descent, the bard next traces
the origins of his maternal clan, the Kòndès. He recounts the quarrel between the
leader of the clan and his aunt, Du Kamisa, over her exclusion from a family
ritual. Du Kamisa is enraged and transforms herself into a wild buffalo who ravages
the countryside and kills many of the hunters sent after her. At this point, two
brothers, Dan Mansa Wulandin and Dan Mansa Wulanba, hunters from another
clan, the Taraweres, enter the story. As much by sheer skill and courage as by
supernatural help, the younger brother Dan Wulandin succeeds in killing the
buffalo, and is rewarded for this exploit with the gift of a maiden of the clan,
Sugulun Kòndè. The Tarawere brothers continue on their journey, seeking further
adventures, and finally arrive at the town founded by Fata Magan the Handsome.
Dan Mansa Wulanba attempts to consumate his marriage with Sugulun Kòndè
who repulses him, saying, "My husband is in the Manden." Thus, her virginity is
preserved for her future husband, Fata Magan the Handsome, for whom she will
bear her first child, Son-Jara. The episode that follows recounts the circumstances
in which Sugulun Kòndè enters Fata Magan's household, and the events that
ensue.

FROM EPISODE 4

The Manden

Now, Fata Magan, the Handsome was about to leave that
        town.
He was leaving to trade in a far market.   (Mmm)
1000   But a jinn came and laid a hand on him:[7]   (Mmm)
"Stay right here!   (Indeed)
"Two youths have come amongst us,   (Mmm)
"Two youths with an ugly young maid.   (Mmm)
"Should you come by that ugly maid,   (Mmm)

---

6. Compare with "Lion Heart," which became attached to the name of the medieval king of England,
Richard. *Simbon:* hunter; the ideal of manhood in traditional African societies.   7. Implying that the
jinn is an agent of providence.

1005	"She will bear you a son.	(Indeed)
	"The Manden will belong to him."	(Indeed)

O! Bèmba!   (Indeed)
I sing of the Sorcerer's future;   (Mmm, that's true)
Of the life ahead of Son-Jara!
1010   There were two ways to greet in the Manden
of Old   (Mmm)
Brave young men said, "Ilu tuntun!"   (That's true)
To which the reply, "Tuntun bèrè!"
The women said, "Ilu kònkòn!"
To which the reply, "Kònkòn lògòsò!"   (Indeed)
1015   The Taraweres came forward: (True)
"I tuntun!"
He answered them, "Tuntun bèrè!   (Mmm)
"Where do you come from?
"Where are you going?"
1020   "We have come from the land of Du.
"We go to Bintanya Kamalen."
"Whose people are you?"   (Mmm)
"We are Taraweres."
"O Taraweres,
1025   "Were this young prince to find the right wife,   (Mmm)
"She would be the reward of a Tarawere struggle.   (True)

"My flesh-and-blood sister is here,   (Indeed)
"Nakana Tiliba.   (Indeed)
"I will give her to you.
1030   "You must give me your ugly maid.   (Mmm)
"My forefather Bilal,   (Indeed)
"When he departed from the Messenger of God,   (True)
"He designed a certain token,   (Mmm)
"Saying that his ninth descendant,   (Indeed)
1035   "Having taken his first wife,   (True)
"When he takes his second wife,   (Indeed)
"Must add that token to that marriage.   (Mmm)
"I am adding that token
"Together with Nakana Tiliba,   (Mmm)
1040   "And giving them to you,[8]
"You must give me your ugly little maid."
That token was added to Nakana Tiliba,
Exchanging her for Sugulun Kòndè.   (Indeed)
It is said that Fata Magan, the Handsome
1045   Took the Kòndè maiden to bed.   (Mmm)
His Berete wife became pregnant.   (Indeed)
His Kòndè wife became pregnant.   (Indeed)

One day as dawn was breaking,   (Indeed)
The Berete woman give birth to a son.   (Indeed)
She cried out, "Ha! Old Women!   (Indeed)
1050   "That which causes co-wife conflict
"Is nothing but the co-wife's child.[9]   (True)

---

8. Fata Magan's readiness to part with the token inherited from his ancestor Bilal emphasizes the importance to him of securing Sugulun Kòndè for a wife.   9. Rivalry between co-wives and their offspring in polygamous households is a common theme in African folktales.

"Go forth and tell my husband   (Indeed)
"His first wife has borne him a son."   (Indeed)

1055   The old women came up running.   (Indeed)
"Alu kònkòn!"   (Mmm)
They replied to them, "Kònkòn dògòsò!
"Come let us eat."   (Mmm)
They fixed their eyes on one another:
1060   "Ah! Man must swallow his saliva!"[1]   (True)
They sat down around the food.   (Indeed)
The Kòndè woman then bore a son.   (Indeed)
They sent the Kuyatè matriarch, Tumu Maniya: (Indeed)
"Tumu Maniya, go tell it,   (True)
1065   "Tell Fata Magan, the Handsome,
"Say, 'the Tarawere trip to Du was good.'   (True)
"Say, 'the ugly maid they brought with them,'
"Say, 'that woman has just borne a son.' "   (True)

The Kuyatè matriarch came forward: (True)
1070   "Alu kònkòn!"   (Mmm)
They replied to her, "Kònkòn dògòsò!   (Indeed)
"Come and let us eat."

[The female bard Tumu Maniya goes to find the king and, like the old women
who preceded her, is also invited to eat, but she rejects the food until her message
is delivered. The announcing of the birth of Son-Jara first, though he was actually
born second, causes the father to designate him as first-born. The old women then
burst out their message of the Berete woman's child, but alas, they are too late.
The reversal of announcements is viewed as theft of birthright, and the Berete
woman is understandably furious at the old women, who flop their hands about
nervously.][2]

Some just flopped their hands about:
"I will not hear of this from anyone!
1075   "I spent a sleepless night.
"The lids of my eyes are dried out,
    bèrè-bèrè-bèrè.[3]   (That's true)
"But I will not hear of this from anyone!"
Some just clasped their hands together.
What travail it had become!
1080   Ha! The old woman had forgotten her message
And abandoned it for a meal.
Those-Caught-by-their-Craws![4]
That was the first day of battle in the Manden.
Pandemonium broke loose! bòkòlen![5]

1. To placate their hunger. The food the women are offered is presumably too tempting to be ignored,
hence their delay in announcing the birth of the Berete woman's child; this leads to the confusion
about the order of precedence between him and Son-Jara and to dissension in the family.   2. Johnson's summary. He noted that Fa-Digi Sisoko broke off his performance at this point to answer the call
of nature and that he resumed the narration at a point further along in the story.   3. Ideophone for
the distraught state of the women.   4. Derogatory term for the women.   5. Ideophone summing up
the pandemonium.

* * *

Both women were confined in one hut.
Pandemonium broke loose! bòkòlen!   (Indeed)
Saman Berete,
1100   The daughter of Tall Magan Berete-of-the Ruins,
Saman Berete,   (Indeed)
Still bloodstained, she came out.   (Indeed)
"What happened then!
"O Messengers, what happened?   (Indeed)
1105   "O Messengers, what became of the message?"   (Indeed)

The Kuyatè matriarch spoke out:
"Nothing happened at all.   (Indeed)
"I was the first to pronounce myself.   (Indeed)
"Your husband said the first name heard,
1110   "Said, he would be the elder,   (Indeed)
"And thus yours became the younger."   (Indeed)
She[6] cried out, "Old women,   (Indeed)
"Now you have really reached the limit!   (True)
"I was the first to marry my husband,
1115   "And the first to bear him a son.   (Indeed)
"Now you have made him the younger.   (Indeed)
"You have really reached your limit!"
She spoke then to her younger co-wife,   (Indeed)
"Oh Lucky Karunga,[7]   (Indeed)
1120   "For you marriage has turned sweet.   (Indeed)
"A first son birth is the work of old,
"And yours has become the elder."[8]   (That's the truth)

The infants were bathed.   (Indeed)
Both were laid beneath a cloth.   (Indeed)
1125   The grandmother[9] had gone to fetch firewood.   (Indeed)
The old mother had gone to fe . . . , to
fetch firewood.   (Indeed)
She then quit the firewood-fetching place,
And came and left her load of wood.   (Indeed)
She came into the hut.   (Indeed)
1130   She cast her eye on the Berete woman,   (Indeed)
And cast her eye on the Kòndè woman,   (Indeed)
And looked the Berete woman over,
And looked the Kòndè woman over.   (Indeed)

She lifted the edge of the cloth.
1135   And examined the child of the Berete woman,
And lifted again the edge of the cloth,
And examined the child of the Kòndè woman.   (Indeed)
From the very top of Son-Jara's head,   (Indeed)
To the very tip of his toes, all hair![1]   (Indeed)

1140   The old mother went outside.   (Indeed)
She laughed out: "Ha! Birth-givers! Hurrah!

6. Saman Berete.   7. Sugulun Kòndè.   8. A bitter comment on what Saman Berete perceives as
an ironic reversal of situations.   9. Son-Jara's paternal grandmother.   1. An extraordinary circumstance that earns him his praise name of Lion-Born-of-the-Cat.

"The little mother has borne a lion thief."   (That's true)
Thus gave the old mother Son-Jara his name.   (Indeed)
"Givers of birth, Hurrah!
1145   "The little mother has borne a lion thief.   (That's true)
"Hurrah! The mother has given birth to a lion thief."
        Biribiriba!   (Indeed)
        And thus they say of him,
        Son-Jara. Nare Magan Kònatè.   (Indeed)
1150   Simbon. Lion-Born-of-the-Cat.   (Indeed)
The Berete woman,
She summoned to her a holy-man,
Charging him to pray to God,   (Indeed)
So Son-Jara would not walk.   (Indeed)
1155   And summoned to her an Omen Master,   (Indeed)
For him to read the signs in sand,   (Indeed)
So Son-Jara would not walk.   (Indeed)

For nine years, Son-Jara crawled upon the ground. (Indeed)
Magan Kònatè could not rise.   (Indeed)
1160   The benefactor of the Kòndè woman's child,
It was a jinn Magan Son-Jara had.   (Indeed)
His name was Tanimunari.
Tanimunari,   (Indeed)
He took the lame Son-Jara   (Indeed)
1165   And made the hājj[2]   (Indeed)
To the gates of the Kaabah.[3]   (Indeed)
Have you never heard this warrant of his hājj?   (Indeed)
        "Ah! God!   (Indeed)
        "I am the man for the morrow.   (Indeed)
1170   "I am the man for the day to follow.   (Indeed)
        "I will rule over the bards,   (Indeed)
        "And the three and thirty warrior clans.
        "I will rule over all these people.   (Indeed)
        "The Manden shall be mine!"[4]   (Indeed)
1175   That is how he made the hājj.
He[5] took him up still lame,
And brought him back to Bintanya Kamalen.   (Indeed)
In the month before Dònba,   (Indeed)
On the twenty-fifth day,
1180   The Berete woman's Omen Master emerged from
        retreat:[6]   (Indeed)
        "Damn! My fingers are worn out!   (Indeed)
        "My buttocks are worn out!   (Indeed)
        "A tragic thing will come to pass in the Manden. (Indeed)
        "There is no remedy to stop it.
1185   "There is no sacrifice to halt it.
        "Its cause cannot be ascertained,   (Indeed)
        "Until two rams be sacrificed.   (Indeed)

---

2. The pilgrimage to Mecca that Muslims are obliged by the tenets of their religion to undertake at least once in their lifetime.   3. The mosque in Mecca that contains the sacred stone, draped in black, around which a special ceremony takes place during the month of the pilgrimage.   4. An ambition attributed by the bard to Son-Jara even in his youth.   5. Tanimunari.   6. His place of seclusion, where he has been preparing magical charms for Saman Berete.

"The one for Son-Jara, a black-headed ram.   (True)
"Dankaran Tuma, an all white ram.[7]   (Indeed)
1190 "Have them do battle this very day."   (Indeed)
By the time of the midday meal,
Son-Jara's ram had won.   (Indeed)
They slaughtered both the rams.   (Indeed)
And cast them down a well,
1195 So the deed would not be known.   (Indeed)
But known it did become.   (Indeed)
    Knowing never fails its time,
    Except its day not come.   (That's true, eh,
                                                Fa-Digi, that's true)

In the month before Dònba   (That's true)
1200 On the twenty-seventh day,   (Indeed)
The holy-man emerged from his retreat!   (Indeed)
"Hey! A tragic thing will come to pass in the
      Manden.   (Indeed)
"There is no remedy to stop it.
"There is no sacrifice to halt it.   (Indeed)
1205 "Its cause cannot be ascertained,
"Until a toothless dog be sacrificed."[8]
Now whoever saw a toothless dog in the Manden?   (Indeed)
They went forth to Kong,[9]   (Indeed)
And bought a snub-nosed dog,   (Indeed)
1210 A little spotted dog,
And pulled its teeth with pliers,
And mixed a potion for its mouth,   (Indeed)
And brought it back to the Manden,
Saying, with this toothless dog,   (Indeed)
1215 Saying, Magan Kònatè should not walk.   (Indeed)
Son-Jara should not rise!

                        *   *   *

Ah! Bèmba!   (Indeed)
They made a sacrifice of the spotted dog   (Indeed)
So that the Wizard would not walk.   (Indeed)
1255 In the month of Dòmba,   (Indeed)
The very, very, very first day,   (Indeed)
Son-Jara's Muslim jinn came forward: (Indeed)
"That which God has said to me,   (Indeed)
"To me Tanimunari,   (Indeed)
1260 "That which God has said to me,   (Indeed)
"So it will be done.   (Indeed)
"When the month of Dòmba is ten days old,   (Indeed)
"Son-Jara will rise and walk."   (Indeed)
In the month of Dòmba,   (Indeed)
1265 On its twelfth day,   (Indeed)
The Messenger of God was born.   (Indeed)

7. The contrasting colors of the two animals represent the sharp opposition between the brothers. Dankaran Tuma is Saman Berete's son.   8. The bizarre and desperate nature of this stipulation is brought out in the lines that follow.   9. A town in present-day Ivory Coast.

On the thirteenth day,   (Indeed)
Jòn Bilal was born.   (Indeed)
On its tenth day,   (Indeed)
1270 Was the day for Son-Jara to walk.[1]

        O Nare Magan Kònatè!   (That's true)
        . . .
        Master and Warrior Master!
        O Nare Magan Kònatè!
1275   O Sorcerer-Seizing-Sorcerer!
        A man of power is hard to find.   (Mmm)
        All people with their empty words,
        They all seek to be men of power.   (That's true)
        Ministers, deputies and presidents,   (Indeed)
1280   All of them seek after power,
        But there is no easy way to power.   (That's true)

        Here in our Mali,
        We have found our freedom.   (Indeed)
        Though a person find no gold,
1285   Though he find no silver,   (Indeed)
        Should he find his freedom,
        Then noble will he be.   (That's the truth)
        A man of power is hard to find.   (Mmm)
        Ah! Bèmba!

1290 On the tenth day of Dòmba,   (Indeed)
      The Wizard's mother cooked some couscous,[2]   (Indeed)
      Sacrificial couscous for Son-Jara.
      Whatever woman's door she went to,   (Indeed)
      The Wizard's mother would cry: (Indeed)
1295 "Give me some sauce of baobab leaf."[3]   (Indeed)
      The woman would retort,
      "I have some sauce of baobab leaf,
      "But it is not to give to you.
      "Go tell that cripple child of yours
1300 "That he should harvest some for you.   (Mmm)
      " 'Twas my son harvested these for me."   (True)

      And bitterly did she weep: bilika bilika.[4]
      She went to another woman's door;   (Mmm)
      That one too did say: (Mmm)
1305 "I have some sauce of baobab leaf,
      "But it is not to give to you.
      "Go tell that cripple child of yours
      "That he should harvest some for you.
      " 'Twas my son harvested these for me."   (True)

1310 With bitter tears, the Kòndè woman
            came back, bilika bilika.
            "King of Nyani, King of Nyani,[5]

---

1. The bard makes an explicit connection between the hero's rising to his feet and the sense of origins that underlies the epic.   2. Here a meal, similar in texture to the North African couscous, made from millet grain; it is brownish red in color.   3. A huge tree that grows in the semidesert conditions of the West African savanna; its leaves are eaten as a vegetable. The tree is associated with nobility. 4. Ideophone for the weeping.   5. Her ambition for her son.

     "Will you never rise?   (Mmm)
     "King of Nyani, King of Nyani,
     "Will you never rise?   (Mmm)
1315   "King of Nyani with helm of mail,
     "He says he fears no man.
     "Will you never rise?
     "Rise up, O King of Nyani!   (That's true)

     "King of Nyani, King of Nyani,
1320   "Will you never rise?
     "King of Nyani with shirt of mail,
     "He says he fears no man,
     "Will you never rise?
     "Rise up, O King of Nyani!   (True)

1325   "O Wizard,I have failed!"   (True)
     "Ah, my mother,
     "There is a thickener, I hear, called black *lele*.[6]   (True)
     "Why not put some in my sauce?
     " 'Tis the thickener grown in gravel."

1330   She put black *lele* in the couscous.
     The Wizard ate of it.
     Ma'an[7] Kònatè ate his fill: (True)
     "My mother,   (Indeed)
     "Go to the home of the blacksmith patriarchs,   (Indeed)
1335   "To Dun Fayiri and Nun Fayiri.   (Indeed)
     "Have them shape a staff, seven-fold forged,
     "So that Magan Kònatè may rise up."   (Indeed)
     The blacksmith patriarchs shaped a staff, seven-fold
        forged.   (Indeed)
     The Wizard came forward.   (Indeed)
1340   He put his right hand o'er his left,
     And upwards drew himself,   (Indeed)
     And upwards drew himself.
     He had but reached the halfway point.   (Indeed)
     "Take this staff away from me!"
1345   Magan Kònatè did not rise.   (True)

     In misery his mother wept: bilika bilika: (Indeed)
     "Giving birth has made me suffer!"   (Mmm)
     "Ah, my mother,   (Mmm)
     "Return to the blacksmith patriarchs.   (Indeed)
1350   "Ask that they forge that staff anew,   (Indeed)
     "And shape it twice again in size.   (Mmm)
     "Today I arise, my holy-man said."   (Mmm)

     The patriarchs of the smiths forged the staff,
     Shaping it twice again in size.   (True)
1355   They forged that staff,
     And gave it to Ma'an Kònatè.   (Indeed)
     He put his right hand o'er his left,   (Indeed)
     And upwards Son-Jara drew himself.   (Indeed)
     Upwards Nare Magan Kònatè drew himself.   (Indeed)

6. A seasoning.   7. Short for Magan (Son-Jara's name).

1360 Again he reached the halfway point: (Mmm)
      "Take this staff away from me!"
      Ma'an Kònatè did not rise.
      He sat back down again.   (Indeed)
      His mother wrung her hands atop her head,
1365 And wailed: "dèndèlen!
      "Giving birth has made me suffer!"   (True)
      "Ah, my mother,   (Mmm)
      "Whate'er has come twixt you and God,   (Indeed)
      "Go and speak to God about it now!"[8]   (Indeed)

1370 On that, his mother left,
      And went to the east of Bintanya,   (Indeed)
      To seek a custard apple tree.   (Indeed)

      Ah! Bèmba!   (Indeed)
      And found some custard apple trees,[9]   (Indeed)
1375 And cut one down,   (Indeed)
      And trimmed it level to her breast,   (Indeed)
      And stood as if in prayer: (Indeed)
          "O God!
          "For Son-Jara I have made this staff.   (Indeed)
1380   "If he be the man for the morrow,   (Indeed)
          "If he be the man for the day to follow,   (Indeed)
          "If he is to rule the bards,   (Indeed)
          "If he is to rule the smiths,   (Indeed)
          "The three and thirty warrior clans,   (Indeed)
1385   "If he is to rule all those,   (Indeed)
          "When this staff I give to Nare Magan Kònatè,   (Indeed)
          "Let Magan Kònatè arise.   (True)
          "If he be not the man for the morrow,   (Indeed)
          "If he be not the man for the day to follow,   (Indeed)
1390   "If he is not to rule the bards,   (Indeed)
          "If he is not to rule the smiths,   (Indeed)
          "When this staff I give to the King of Nyani,
          "Let Son-Jara not arise.
          "O God, from the day of my creation,   (Indeed)
1395   "If I have known another man,
          "Save Fata Magan, the Handsome alone,
          "When this staff I give to the King of Nyani,
          "Let Son-Jara arise.   (Indeed)
          "From the day of my creation,   (True)
1400   "If I have known a second man,
          "And not just Fata Magan, the Handsome,   (Indeed)
          "Let Ma'an Kònatè not arise!"   (True)

      She cut down that staff,
      Going to give it to Nare Magan Kònatè,
1405 To the Kòndè woman's child, the Answerer-of
          Needs!   (True)
      The Wizard took the staff,   (Mmm)
      And put his right hand o'er his left,   (Indeed)

8. Son-Jara insinuates that his inability to walk may be God's punishment for some act of infidelity on
his mother's part. This is made clear in Sugulun Kòndè's prayer a few lines below.   9. Trees that bear
a fruit with fleshy white pulp that is believed to have magical potency.

And upwards drew himself,   (Indeed)
And upwards drew himself.
1410   Magan Kònatè rose up!   (Mmm)
Running, his mother came forward,
And clasped his legs
And squeezed them,   (Indeed)
And squeezed them: (True)
1415   "This home of ours,
           "The home of happiness.   (Indeed)
           "Happiness did not pass us by.
           "Magan Kònatè has risen!"   (Indeed)
           "Oh! Today!   (Indeed)
1420   "Today is sweet!   (Indeed)
           "God the King ne'er made today's equal!   (Indeed)
           "Ma'an Kònatè has risen!"   (Indeed)
           "There is no way of standing without worth.
           "Behold his way of standing: danka!¹
1425   "O Kapok Tree and Flame Tree!"²   (Fa-Digi, that's true)
       "My mother,   (Mmm)
       "That baobab there in Manden country,
       "That baobab from which the best sauce comes,   (Indeed)
       "Where is that baobab, my mother?"   (Indeed)
1430   "Ah, my lame one,   (Indeed)
       "You have yet to walk."   (Indeed)

The Wizard took his right foot,
And put it before his left.   (Indeed)
His mother followed behind him,
1435   And sang these songs for him: (Indeed)
           "Tunyu Tanya!³   (Indeed)
           "Brave men fit well among warriors!   (Indeed)
           "Tunyu tanya!   (Indeed)
           "Brave men fit well among warriors!   (Indeed)
1440   "Ma'an Kònatè, you have risen!"   (Indeed)

           "Muddy water,   (Indeed)
           "Do not compare yourself to water among the stones. (Indeed)
           "That among the stones is pure, wasili!⁴   (Indeed)
           " . . .   (Indeed)
1445   " . . .   (Indeed)
           "And a good reputation.   (Indeed)
           "Khalif Magan Kònatè has risen.   (True)

           "Great snake, O great snake,   (Indeed)
           "I will tolerate you.   (Indeed)
1450   "Should you confront me, toleration.   (Indeed)
           "O great snake upon the path,   (Indeed)
           "Whatever confronts me, I will tolerate."⁵ (Indeed)

1. Ideophone to emphasize the words said.   2. Both trees rise tall and straight and hence provide an
image of the hero.   3. Ideophones, depicting the unsteady movement of the child learning to walk.
4. A somewhat onomatopoeic ideophone for movement of water; the three lines of this part of Sugulun
Kòndè's song convey the idea that her son is superior to other children.   5. She will brave any danger
for her son's sake.

	"Arrow-shaft of happiness.	(Indeed)
	"It is in one hundred.	(Indeed)
1455	"The one hundred dead,	
	"All but Son-Jara.	(True)
	"The higher stones get crushed![6]	(Indeed)
	"Who can mistake the Destroyer-of-Origins!	
	"And this by the hand of Nare Magan Kònatè!"	

	Hey! Biribiriba came forward.	(Indeed)
1460	He shook the baobab tree.	(Indeed)
	A young boy fell out.	
	His leg was broken.	
	The bards thus sing, "Leg-Crushing-Ruler!	
1465	"Magan Kònatè has risen!"	(Indeed)
	He shook the baobab again.	(Indeed)
	Another young boy fell out.	
	His arm was broken.	(Indeed)
	The bards thus sing, "Arm-Breaking-Ruler!	
1470	"Magan Kònatè has risen!"	(Indeed)
	He shook the baobab again.	(Indeed)
	Another young boy fell out.	(Indeed)
	His neck was broken.	(Indeed)
	And thus the bards sing, "Neck-Breaking-Ruler!	
1475	"Magan Kònatè has risen!"	(Indeed)
	The Wizard uprooted the baobab tree,	
	And laid it across his shoulder.	(Mmm)
	Nare Magan Kònatè rose up.[7]	(Indeed)

*   *   *

	Biribiriba came forward.	(Mmm)
	He planted the baobab behind his mother's house:	
	"In and about the Manden,	(Mmm)
1520	"From my mother they must seek these leaves!"	(Mmm)
	To which his mother said, "I do not think I	
	heard."	(Mmm)
	"Ah, my mother,	(Indeed)
	"Now all the Manden baobabs are yours."	
	"I do not think I heard."	
1525	"Ah, my mother,	(Indeed)
	"All those women who refused you leaves,	
	"They all must seek those leaves from you."	(Indeed)
	His mother fell upon her knees, gejebu![8]	
	On both her knees,	
1530	And laid her head aside the baobab.	(Indeed)
	"For years and years,	
	"My ear was deaf.	(Indeed)
	"Only this year	
	"Has my ear heard news.	
1535	"Khalif Magan Kònatè has risen!"	(That's true)
	Biribiriba!	(Indeed)

---

6. An image of Son-Jara storming the heights of power and overcoming them.   7. The series of mishaps caused by the hero in these lines prefigures his later prowess in war and explains the praise names he thus earns.   8. An exclamation.

Since he began to walk,   (Indeed)
Whenever he went into the bush,   (Mmm)
Were he to kill some game,   (Indeed)
1540 He would give his elder the tail.[9]
And think no more of it.
...   (Indeed)

Took up the bow!
Simbon, Master-of-the-Bush!
1545 *Took up the bow!*
Took up the bow!   (Indeed)
Ruler of bards and smiths
Took up the bow!
Took up the bow!
1550 *The Kòndè woman's child,*
Answerer-of-Needs,
He took up the bow.
Sugulun's Ma'an took up the bow!

The Wizard has risen!
1555 *King of Nyani, Nare Magan Kònatè!*
The Wizard has risen!   (Indeed)
Ah! Bèmba!   (Indeed)
Whenever he went to the bush,   (Indeed)
Were he to kill some game,   (Indeed)
1560 He would give to his elder the tail,
And think no more of it.
...   (Indeed)
As Biribiriba walked forth one day,   (That's true)
A jinn came upon him,
1565 And laid his hand on Son-Jara's shoulder:
"O Son-Jara!   (Mmm)
"In the Manden, there's a plot against you.   (Mmm)
"That spotted dog you see before you,[1]   (Indeed)
"Is an offering made against you,   (Indeed)
1570 "So that you not rule the bards,   (Indeed)
"So that you not rule the smiths,
"So, the three and thirty warrior clans,
"That you rule over none of them.   (Mmm)
"When you go forth today,   (Mmm)
1575 "Make an offering of a safo-dog,[2]   (Indeed)
"Should God will it,
"The Manden will be yours!"   (Indeed)

Ah! Bèmba!
On that, Biribiriba went forth, my father,
1580 And made an offering of a safo-dog,
And hung a weight around its neck,[3]
And fastened an iron chain about it.   (Indeed)
Even tomorrow morning,
The Europeans will imitate him.

---

9. Considered a delicacy. This detail emphasizes Son-Jara's generous disposition toward his brother, despite the conflict between them.   1. The toothless dog (line 1206).   2. A dog consecrated for ritual sacrifice.   3. To restrain the dog's ferocity.

1585   Whenever the Europeans leave a dog,   (Mmm)
        Its neck weight,
        They fasten that dog with an iron chain, Manden!   (Indeed)

        O! Bèmba!
        He hung a weight around the dog's neck,
1590   And fastened it with a chain.   (Mmm)
        That done, whatever home he passed before,   (Indeed)
        The people stood gaping at him:
        "Causer-of-Loss![4]   (Indeed)
        "A cow with its neckweight,
1595   "But a dog with a neckweight?"   (Indeed)
        To which the Wizard did retort:
        "Leave me be!   (True)
        "Cast your eyes on the dog of the prince.[5]
        "There's not a tooth in that dog's mouth!
1600   "But there are teeth in my dog's mouth,
        "My commoner's[6] dog. Leave me be!   (Indeed)
        "My dog's name is Tomorrow's Affair."

        Son-Jara's sacrificial dog,
        That dog was called Tomorrow's Affair.[7]

1605   From his neckwright he broke loose,
        And also from his chain,   (Indeed)
        And charged the dog of Dankaran Tuman,   (Indeed)
        And ripped him into shreads, fèsè fèsè fèsè![8]   (Indeed)
        And stacked one piece atop the other.   (Indeed)
1610   The mother of Dankaran Tuman, she wrung her hands
                atop her head,
        And gave a piercing cry: "dèndèlen!   (Indeed)
        "That a dog would bite a dog,   (Indeed)
        "A natural thing in the Manden.   (Indeed)
        "That a dog would kill a dog.
1615   "The natural thing in the Manden.
        "That a dog shred another like an old cloth,
        "My mother, there must be something with his master!"[9]
        Dankaran Tuman replied, "Ah! my mother,   (Mmm)
        "I called my dog Younger-Leave-Me-Be.   (Mmm)
1620   "Ah! My mother, do not sever the bonds of family.[1] (True)
        "My mother!   (Indeed)
        "That is the dog that stalked the bush
        "To go and kill some game,
        "Bringing it back to me, my mother.   (True)
1625   "Do not sever the bonds of family, my mother!"   (True)

---

4. That is, to his enemies; the praise name anticipates Son-Jara's later deeds.   5. That is, Dankaran Tuman, considered the heir apparent.   6. By referring to himself as a commoner, Son-Jara seems here to concede his half-brother's birthright.   7. Compare Du Kamisa's *A thing for tomorrow* (line 343). The implication is that he counts on the future to bring a change to his fortunes.   8. Ideophone evocative of the action described.   9. That is, Son-Jara must have superior magical power. The words carry a note of deep apprehension.   1. It is apparent from these words and from Son-Jara's attitude toward his half-brother (see n. 9, p. 1449) that the primary source of the conflict between the princes is the rivalry between their mothers.

The mother of Dankaran Tuman had no answer:[2]   (Indeed)
"One afternoon, the time will come for Son-Jara
    to depart.   (Mmm)
"Indeed what the wise men have said,   (Mmm)
"His time is for the morrow.[3]   (Mmm)
1630   "The one that I have borne,   (Mmm)
"He is being left behind without explanation.   (Mmm)
"Son-Jara,   (Mmm)
"The Kòndè woman's offspring,   (Mmm)
"He will take the Manden tribute,   (Mmm)
1635   "And he will rule the bards,   (Mmm)
"And he will rule the smiths,   (Indeed)
"And rule the funès[4] and the cordwainers.   (Indeed)
"The Manden will be his.
"That time will yet arrive,   (Indeed)
1640   "And that by the hand of Nare Magan Kònatè.
"Nothing leaves its time behind."
    O Biribiriba!
    Kirikisa, Spear-of-Access, Spear-of-Service!
    People of Kaya, Son-Jara entered Kaya.
1645   All this by the hand of Nare Magan Kònatè.
    Gaining power is not easy!   (Indeed)
Ah! Bèmba!   (Indeed)
The mother of King Dankaran Tuman,   (Indeed)
When the Wizard had left the bush,   (Indeed)
1650   And offered his flesh-and-blood-brother the tail,   (Indeed)
And when he said, "Here take the tail,"[5]
She retorted: "Your mother, Sugulun Kòndè, will take
    the tail!   (Indeed)
"And your younger sister, Sugulun Kulukan,   (Indeed)
"And your younger brother, Manden Bukari.   (Indeed)
1655   "Go and seek a place to die,   (Indeed)
"If not, I will chop through your necks,
"Cutting a handspan down into the ground.
"Be it so; you'll never return to the Manden again."   (Indeed)
Son-Jara bitterly wept, bilika bilika!   (Indeed)
1660   And went to tell his mother.   (Indeed)
His mother said,   (Indeed)
"Ah! My child,   (Indeed)
"Be calm. Salute your brother.   (Indeed)
"Had he banished you as a cripple,
1665   "Where would you have gone?
"Let us at least agree on that.
"Let us depart.
"What sitting will not solve,
"Travel will resolve."   (That's true)

---

2. She remains insensitive to her son's entreaty.   3. Saman Berete woman is credited with a foresight
that contradicts her deepest sentiment. This is, however, only a narrative effect, the result of the bard's
identification with Son-Jara and his anticipation of events.   4. A subclass of *griots* who only recite and
do not play musical instruments.   5. There is a play on words in the original text, so that the phrase
is interpreted by Saman Berete as an injunction to leave.

FROM EPISODE 5

MÈMA

1670	They rose up	(Mmm)
	The Kuyatè matriarch took up the iron rasp.[6]	(Mmm)
	She sang a hunter's song for Nare Magan Kònatè:	
	"Took up the bow!	(Indeed)
	"Simbon, Master-of-the-Bush!	
1675	"Took up the bow!	
	"Took up the bow!	(Indeed)
	"Simbon, Master-of-Wild-Beasts!	
	"Took up the bow!	(Indeed)
	"Took up the bow!	(Indeed)
1680	"Warrior and Master-of-Slaves!	
	"Took up the bow!	(Indeed)
	"The Kòndè woman's child,	
	"Answerer-of-Needs,	(Indeed)
	"Took up the bow.	(Indeed)
1685	"Sugulan's Ma'an took up the bow.	(Indeed)
	You seized him, O Lion!	(Indeed)
	"And the Wizard killed him!	
	"O Simbon, that, the sound of your chords."	(True)
	He fled from suffering	(Mmm)
1690	To seek refuge with the blacksmith patriarch,[7]	(Indeed)
	Because of the hardships of rivalry.	(Mmm)
	But they counted out one measure of gold,[8]	(Mmm)
	And gave it to the blacksmith patriarch,	(Indeed)
	Saying, were he not to cast the Wizard out,	(Indeed)
1695	Saying, he would jeopardize the land,	(Indeed)
	Saying, the Manden would be the Wizard's,	(Indeed)
	Because of the hardships of rivalry.	(Indeed)
	The Wizard fled anew from suffering.	(Mmm)
	He went to seek refute with the Karanga patriarch.	(Indeed)
1700	Do you not know that person's name?	(Mmm)
	Jobi, the Seer.	(Indeed)
	The Karanga patriarch was Jobi, the Seer.	(I did not know that until you told me)

Because of the hardships of rivalry,
He cast the Wizard out.

[Son-Jara and his mother wander from town to town seeking refuge and are cast out in the same manner everywhere. In desperation, they turn for help to a company of women who represent the forces of evil. Meanwhile, Son-Jara's half-brother succeeds to the throne, but the Manden is now threatened by a powerful neighbor, the Susu king Sumamuru.]

Biribiriba went on to seek refuge
With the nine Queens-of-Darkness.[9]

6. A musical instrument. *Kuyatè matriarch:* Tumu Maniya, the female bard who announced Son-Jara's birth to his father.   7. His profession indicates that he is of lowly station. By seeking refuge with him, Son-Jara thus accepts a humiliated condition.   8. To reward the blacksmith for casting out Son-Jara and his mother. The reward is paid by Dankaran Tuman's people *(they).*   9. Probably a cult of women devoted to the practice of magic.

1770   "What brought you here?" they asked of him.   (Mmm)
        "Have you not heard that none come here?   (Indeed)
        "What brought you here?"   (Indeed)
        The Sorcerer spoke out.
        "Ah! Those who are feared by all,
1775   "If you join them, you are spared.
        "It is that which made me come here."
        He sat down.   (Indeed)
        His flesh-and-blood elder, King Dankaran Tuman,   (Indeed)
        He took his first-born daughter,   (Indeed)
1780   Caress-of-Hot-Fire,[1]   (Indeed)
        And gave her to the Kuyatè patriarch, Dòka the Cat,[2]   (Indeed)
        Saying, "Give her to Susu Mountain Sumamuru,"[3]   (Indeed)
        Saying, "Should he not slay the King of Nyani,"
        Saying, "He's gone to seek refuge with the nine
            Queens-of-Darkness,"
1785   Saying, "The folk have lost their faith in him."   (True)

        At that time, the bards did not have balaphones,[4]   (True)
        Nor had the smiths a balaphone,
        Nor had the funès a balaphone,
        Nor did the cordwainers have one,   (Indeed)
1790   None but Susu Mountain Sumamuru.   (Indeed)
            Sori Kantè the Tall,   (Indeed)
            Who begat Bala Kantè of Susu,   (Indeed)
            And who begat Kabani Kantè,   (True)
            And who begat Kankuba Kantè,
1795   And who begat Susu Mountain Sumamuru Kantè.[5]
        The village where Sumamuru was,
        That village was called Dark Forest.[6]   (True)

        It was there he came forth, my father,   (Indeed)
        Ah! Bèmba!   (Indeed)
1800   He came in Sumamuru's absence,   (Indeed)
        Dòka the Cat,   (Indeed)
        He asked for Sumamuru.[7]   (Indeed)
        They said, "If you seek Sumamuru,
        "Ask of the hawk!"   (Mmm)
1805   The balaphone of seven keys,   (Mmm)
        After Sumamuru had played that balaphone,   (Indeed)
        The mallets of the balaphone he would take,
        And give them to the hawk.   (Indeed)
        It would fly up high in a Flame Tree,
1810   And there in the depths of Susu Forest sit.   (Indeed)
        Dòka the Cat called to the hawk.   (Indeed)
        The balaphone mallets it delivered to him.   (Indeed)

---

1. So-named because of her sexual prowess. By giving his daughter to Sumamuru in marriage, Dankaran Tuman hopes to placate the Susu king and to enlist his aid in eliminating Son-Jara, who remains a threat even in exile.   2. Son-Jara's personal bard, whom he had to leave behind in the Manden, has been appropriated by Dankaran Tuman.   3. Son-Jara's principal antagonist is introduced here for the first time. His massive physical aspect is denoted in the sobriquet *Mountain* that has become attached to his name.   4. Musical instruments, akin to the xylophone, with boards of varying length laid out for the different notes.   5. These lines are a rapid summary of Sumamuru's genealogy.   6. The name of the village identifies Sumamuru with paganism, as opposed to the Muslim affiliations of Son-Jara.   7. Dòka the Cat's motive in seeking out Sumamuru, who is ravaging the Manden, is not made clear, for it soon becomes apparent he has no intention of entering his service.

"Dun Fayiri, Nun Fayiri!   (Indeed)
"Manda Kantè and Sama Kantè!   (Indeed)
1815   *"Sori Kantè, the Tall!*[8]   (Mmm)
"Susu Mountain Sumamuru Kantè!   (Indeed)
"Salute Sumamuru!   (Indeed)
"Sumamuru came amongst us,
"His pants of human skin.[9]   (Indeed)
1820   *"Sumamuru came amongst us,*
"His coat of human skin.   (Indeed)
"Sumamuru came amongst us,
"His helm of human skin.   (Indeed)
"The first and ancient king,
1825   *"The King of yesteryear.*[1]   (Indeed)
"So, respite does not end resolve.
"Sumamuru, I found you gone.
"Oh! Glorious Janjon!"[2]

Sumamuru was off doing battle,
1830   With pants of human skin,
And coat of human skin.
Whenever he would mount a hill,
Down another he would go.
Up one and down another.
1835   Was it God or man?[3]
He approached the Kuyatè patriarch, Dòka the
        Cat: (Mmm)
"God or man?"   (Indeed)
"I am a man," the reply.
"Where do you hail from?"   (Mmm)
1840   "I come," he said, "from the Manden.   (Indeed)
"I am from Nyani."   (Indeed)

"Play something for me to hear," he said.   (Indeed)
He took up the balaphone: (Indeed)
"Kukuba and Bantanba!
1845   *"Nyani-nyani and Kamasiga!"*[4]
"Brave child of the warrior!
"And Deliverer-of-the-Benign.
"Sumamuru came amongst us
"With pants of human skin.
1850   *"Sumamuru came amongst us,*
"With coat of human skin.
"Sumamuru came amongst us
"With helm of human skin.
"The first and ancient king,
1855   *"The king of yesteryear.*
"So, respite does not end resolve!

8. These are the names of Sumamuru's ancestors, invoked in his praise song.   9. Symbolic of his savage ferocity.   1. As addressed by Dòka the Cat to Sumamuru, this praise epithet is shot through with ambivalence. It may refer to the sanction bestowed by the years on Sumamuru's ancestry and reign, but it also suggests that the addressee belongs to a past age that is to be superseded by a new one, that of Son-Jara.   2. War song, a genre of oral poetry in the Manding.   3. As the notes of his balaphone reach his ears, Sumamuru wonders who is playing the instrument.   4. These are place names in the Manden.

"Sumamuru, I found you gone.
"Oh! Glorious Janjon!"

	He[5] said, "Ah! What is your name?"	
1860	"My name is Dòka, the Cat."	(Mmm)
	"Will you not remain with me?"	
	"Not I! Two kings I cannot praise.	
	"I am Son-Jara's bard.	
	"From the Manden I have come,	
1865	"And to the Manden I must return."	(True)

	He laid hold of the Kuyatè patriarch,	
	And severed both Achilles tendons,[6]	
	And by the Susu balaphone set him.	(Indeed)
	"Now what is your name?"	(Indeed)
1870	"Dòka, the Cat is still my name."	(Indeed)
	"Dòka, the Cat will no longer do."	(Indeed)
	He drew water and poured it over his head,	(Indeed)
	And shaved it clean,[7]	(Indeed)
	And gave him the name Bala Faseke Kuyatè.	
1875	That Bala Faseke Kuyatè,	(Indeed)
	He fathered three children,	(Indeed)
	Musa and Mansa Magan,	(Indeed)
	Making Baturu, the Holy his last-born son in the	
	Manden.	(Indeed)
	Those were the Kuyatès.	

	And this by the hand of Sumamuru.	
1880	He sent forth a messenger,	
	Saying, "Go tell King Dankaran Tuman,"	(Indeed)
	Saying, "If you kill your own vicious dog,"	
	Saying, "Another man's will surely bite you."[8]	(Indeed, that's
		the truth)

	With this he declared war, my father,	
1885	And went forth from Susu.	
	Going to fall on King Dankaran Tuman,	(Indeed)
	Breaking the Manden like an old pot,	(Indeed)
	Breaking the Manden like an old gourd,	(Indeed)
1890	Slaying the nine and ninety Masters-of-Shadow,[9]	
	Slaying the nine and ninety royal princes,	
	And ousting King Dankaran Tuman.	
	He fled to Nsèrè-kòrò,[1]	
	Saying, "I was spared.	(Indeed)
1895	"From your torment, I was spared.	(True)
	From death, I have been spared."	(Indeed)
	And thus he settled there.	
	The sons he there begat, my father,	(Indeed)
	They became the Kisi[2] people.	
1900	They are all in Masanta.[3]	

5. Sumamuru.   6. In other versions of the epic, this violation of his bard is presented as Son-Jara's principal grievance against Sumamuru.   7. As with a newborn child at its naming ceremony. The shaving of the bard's hair and his new name signify his rededication to a new service.   8. The meaning is that Dankaran Tuman can expect to suffer the same fate he inflicted on Son-Jara.   9. Diviners in the royal household.   1. In present-day Guinea.   2. An ethnic group spread along the coast from Guinea to Senegal.   3. An area farther inland, to the north.

They had come from the Manden.	
Their family name, it is Gindo.	(Indeed)

Ah! Bèmba!	(Indeed)
O Biribiriba!	

1905   He put gourds in the mouths[4]
      of the poor and the powerful.
This by the hand of Susu Mountain Sumamuru,   (Indeed)
Saying each must speak into his gourd,
Saying there is no pleasure in weakness,[5]
Saying the Manden was now his.

1910   He summoned Kankira-of-Silver   (Indeed)
And Kankira-of-Gold,[6]   (Indeed)
The latter, the Saginugu patriarch,   (Indeed)
And one red[7] bull did give to them,   (Indeed)
Saying they should offer it
1915   To the nine Queens-of-Darkness,   (Indeed)
Asking them to slay Son-Jara,   (Mmm)
That he not enter the Manden again,
To say that the Manden be his,
Saying they have slain the
      nine and ninety Masters-of-Shadow,
1920   Saying they have slain the nine and
      ninety royal princes,
And put gourds o'er the mouths
      of the poor and the powerful,   (Indeed)
Saying that they should slay him,   (Indeed)
So he not enter the Manden again   (Mmm)
To say that the Manden be his.   (Indeed)

1925   Those messengers arrived.   (Indeed)
They came upon the witches there: (Indeed)
"Ilu tuntun!"   (Indeed)
The witches did not speak.   (Mmm)
"Peace be unto you."   (Mmm)
1930   The witches did not speak.
"Alu tuntun!"
The witches did not speak.
"Peace be with you!"
The witches did not speak.   (That's true)

1935   "The slaughtered bull,   (Indeed)
"Lay it out in nine piles."   (Indeed)
Nakana Tiliba[8] then said to the witches,
"Each must either take her own,   (Indeed)
"Questions without end looking for trouble,[9]   (That's true)
1940   "Then take the meat and be off,   (Indeed)
"Or," Nakana Tiliba continued,   (Indeed)
"You must not take the meat.

---

4. Metaphor to denote Sumamuru's repressive rule.   5. Expressive of the arrogance of power.
6. Silversmith and Goldsmith; they belong to a special caste of craftsmen.   7. In many African societies, the red symbolizes the supernatural world.   8. Son-Jara's paternal aunt, previously given by Fata
Magan the Handsome to the Tarawere brothers in exchange for Sugulun Kòndè (see line 1028). She is
now the principal queen of darkness.   9. That is, each must take her part without argument.

"O Son-Jara,   (Indeed)
"A message has come from the Manden,   (Indeed)
1945   "From Susu Mountain Sumamuru,   (Indeed)
"Saying to come and tell us,   (Indeed)
"Saying we should slay you,   (Indeed)
"So that you not enter the Manden again,
"Saying, the folk have lost their faith in you.   (Indeed)
1950   "Saying, he has slain the nine and ninety
       Masters-of-the-Shadow,   (Indeed)
"Saying, he has slain the nine and ninety royal
       princes.   (Indeed)
"Nine were the times he razed the Manden,
"And nine were the times he rebuilt it,   (Indeed)
Saying, he put gourds on the mouths of the poor and the
       powerful,   (Indeed)
1955   "Saying, all must speak into their gourds,
"Saying, there is no pleasure in weakness,
Saying, he has ousted King Dankaran Tuman,
Saying, who has fled to Nsèrè-kòrò,
"Saying, we should slay you,
1960   "So that you not enter the Manden again,
"And that is the reason for this meat."
"Then kill me," his reply.
"A person flees to be spared,
"But should one not be spared, then kill me!"[1]   (True)
1965   Biribiriba!   (Mmm)
He went to the back of the house.
Into a lion he transformed himself,   (Mmm)
A lion seizing no one,[2]
Before he had sounded a roar.   (Mmm)
1970   He went and seized a buffalo,
And came back and laid it down,
And went and seized another,
And came and laid it down,
And went and seized another,
1975   And came and laid it down.
"Nine water buffalos, nine witches!   (Mmm)
"Each take your own!"   (True)
The witches then replied to him,
"Let us hold a council.
1980   "The town where people hold no council,
"There will living not be good."
They went to hold their council,
"From the Manden and its neighbors,   (Indeed)
"All of it together, and only one red bull!   (Indeed)
1985   "Son-Jara, you alone, nine buffalos!
"It is to him the Manden must belong!
"Let us then release him!"   (True)
They trimmed a branch of the custard apple tree: (Indeed)
"When you leave the land of the nine
       Queens-of-Darkness,   (Indeed)

1. Note the equanimity with which Son-Jara receives Nakana Tiliba's words.   2. That is, one that does not bother any human being, because he is only after game.

1990   "You will see no village,   (Mmm)
        "Until you see Jula Fundu,   (Mmm)
        "The original town of the Mossi³ patriarch,   (Indeed)
        "Jula Fundu and Wagadugu,   (Indeed)
        "In Mèma Farin Tunkara's land of Mèma."
1995   They stacked the bull meat in one pile,   (Mmm)
        And upon it laid its skin,
        And upon this placed its head.   (Mmm)
        "All of you witches, say your verses!   (Indeed)

        "All of you witches, read your signs!"   (Indeed)
2000   Nakana Tiliba,
        From her head she took her scarf,
        And tied three knots⁴ into it,
        And laid it o'er the meat,
        Saying, "Rise up!
2005   "Kitibili Kintin!⁵   (Indeed)
        " 'Twas a man that puts us in conflict.
        "A matter of truth is not to be feared."⁶
        The bull rose up and stretched.   (Mmm)
        It bellowed to Muhammad.⁷   (Mmm)
2010   The Messenger of God was thus evoked.   (That's true)

        That bull rose up and stretched.   (Indeed)
        Ah! Bèmba!   (Indeed)
        Son-Jara came forth: (Indeed)
        "O Kankira-of-Silver and Kankira-of-Gold,   (Indeed)
2015   "A messenger is not to be whipped.   (Indeed)
        "A messenger is not to be defiled.⁸   (Indeed)
        "When you go forth from here,
        "You should go tell Susu Mountain Sumamuru,   (Indeed)
        "When you go forth from here,   (Indeed)
2020   "You should go tell Susu Mountain Sumamuru: (Indeed)
        " 'The cowherd offers naught of the cow,'
        " 'But the milk of Friday past.'
        " 'No matter how loving the wet nurse,'
        " 'The child will never be hers.'
2025   "Say, 'A child may be first-born, but that does not always
            make him the elder.'
        "Say, 'Today may belong to some,'
        " 'Tomorrow will belong to another.'
        "Say, 'As you succeeded some,'
        " 'So shall you have successors.'
2030   "Say, 'I am off to seek refuge with Mèma's Prince Tunkara,'
        " 'In the land of Mèma.' "⁹

        He took the shape of a hawk.
        You took it, Nare Magan Kònatè.

3. An ethnic group in Burkina Faso. Nothing more is known about Jula Fundu (founder of the Mossi).
4. To give it magical potency.   5. An incantation.   6. Or telling the truth is a moral obligation,
even if it means offending the powerful.   7. An example of the mix of religions that occasionally
surfaces in the epic. It is obvious, however, that invocation of Muhammad is out of keeping with the
atmosphere of the scene described here.   8. By tradition, a messenger enjoys absolute immunity, even
if sent by an enemy.   9. Thus Son-Jara and his mother chose to seek refuge in Mèma.

Biribiriba and Bow-of-the-Bush . . . ,
2035   . . . fled because of suffering.
Gaining power is not easy.

Ah! Bèmba!
Son-Jara went to seek refuge in Mèma,
In a town of the Tunkaras, my father, in Mèma.   (Indeed)

[There follows a long account of a ritual ordeal Son-Jara must undergo before he is allowed by Prince Burama, the ruler of Mèma, to settle in the town. Mèma Sira, Prince Burama's eldest daughter, who has fallen in love with Son-Jara, reveals the secret of the ordeal to him so that he passes it without difficulty. With his mother, brother, and sister, Son-Jara settles in Mèma, practicing his profession as a hunter, while waiting for a chance to return to the Manden, which is meanwhile being devastated by Sumamuru.]

2410   Son-Jara had a certain fetish   (Indeed)
Accepting no sacrifice save shea butter.   (Indeed)
There were no shea trees there in Mèma.   (Indeed)
O Mansa Magan!   (Indeed)
Wherever you sacrifice to the shea tree,   (Indeed)
2415   That town must be in Mandenland.   (Indeed)

All of them are in the Manden.   (Indeed)
No shea trees were there in Mèma.   (Indeed)
Save one old dry Shea tree in Mèma.   (Indeed)
Son-Jara's mother came forward:[1]   (Indeed)
2420   "Ah! God!   (Indeed)
"Let Son-Jara go to the Manden.   (Indeed)
"He is the man for the morrow.   (Indeed)
"He is the man for the day to follow.   (Indeed)
"He is to rule o'er the bards,   (Indeed)
2425   "He is to rule o'er the smiths,   (Indeed)
"And the three and thirty warrior clans.   (Indeed)
"He will rule o'er all those people.   (Indeed)
"Ah, God!   (Indeed)
"Before the break of day,   (Indeed)
2430   "That dried up shea tree here,   (Indeed)
"Let it bear leaf and fruit.   (Indeed)
"Let the fruit fall down to earth,   (Indeed)
"So that Son-Jara may gather the fruit,
"From it to make shea butter,   (Indeed)
2435   "To offer his fetish.   (Indeed, yes, Fa-Digi)

"Ah, God!   (Indeed)
"Let Son-Jara go to the Manden.   (Indeed)
"He is the man for the morrow.
"He is the man for the day to follow.   (Indeed)
2440   "He will rule the bards and smiths.   (Indeed)
"The Manden belongs to the Wizard.   (Indeed)
"Before the break of day,   (Indeed)
"Let me change my dwelling,[2]   (Indeed)

1. Because they were running out of the oil they had brought with them from the Manden, Sugulun Kòndè prays for the rejuvenation of this lone shea tree.   2. That is, depart this world for the next.

      "Old am I and cannot travel.   (Indeed)
2445   "Let Nare Magan Kònatè go home."   (Indeed)
     When the day was dawning,   (Indeed)
     The dried up shea tree did bear leaf.   (Indeed)
     Its fruit did fall to earth.   (Indeed)
     Son-Jara looked in on the Kòndè woman, (Indeed)
2450   But the Kòndè woman had abandoned the world. (Indeed)
     He washed his mother's body,   (Indeed)
     And then he dug her grave,   (Indeed)
     And wrapped her in a shroud,   (Indeed)
     And laid his mother in the earth,   (Indeed)
2455   And then chopped down a kapok tree,   (Indeed)
     And wrapped it in a shroud,   (Indeed)
     And laid it in the house,   (Indeed)
     And laid a blanket over it.   (Indeed)
     And sent a messenger to Prince Birama,
2460   Asking of him a grant of land,   (Indeed)
     In order to bury his mother in Mèma,
     So that he could return to the Manden. (Indeed)
     This answer they did give to him
     That no land could he have,
2465   Unless he were to pay its price.   (Indeed)

     Prince Birama decreed,   (Indeed)
     Saying he could have no land,   (Indeed)
     Unless he were to pay its price.   (Indeed)
     He[3] took feathers of Guinea fowl and partridge, (Indeed)
2470   And took some leaves of arrow-shaft plant, (Indeed)
     And took some leaves of wild grass reed, (Indeed)
     And took some red fanda-vines,   (Indeed)
     And took one measure of shot,   (Indeed)
     And took a haftless knife,   (Indeed)
2475   And added a cornerstone fetish[4] to that, (Indeed)
     And put it all in a leather pouch,   (Indeed)
     Saying go give it to Prince Birama,   (Indeed)
     Saying it was the price of his land.   (Indeed, ha, Fa-Digi)

     That person gave it to Prince Birama.   (Indeed)
2480   Prince Birama summoned his three sages,[5] (Indeed)
     All-Knowing Sage,   (Indeed)
     All-Seeing-Sage,   (Indeed)
     All-Saying-Sage.   (Indeed)
     The three sages counseled Prince Birama. (Indeed)
2485   He said, "O Sages!   (Indeed)
     "The forest by the river is never empty.[6] (Indeed)
     "You also should take this.[7]   (Indeed)
     "That which came first,   (Indeed)
     "I will not take it.   (Indeed)
2490   "Tis yours."[8]   (Indeed)
     O Garan!   (Indeed)

---

3. Son-Jara.   4. The allusion is obscure, but this is probably a fetish object.   5. To explain the meaning of Son-Jara's gesture.   6. There is more to this than meets the eye.   7. Look into this for me.   8. Within your domain as seers.

	All-Seeing-Sage,	
	All-Saying-Sage,	
	All-Knowing-Sage,	(Indeed)
2495	They untied the mouth of the pouch,	
	And shook its contents out.	(Indeed)
	The All-Seeing Sage exclaimed,	(Indeed)
	"Anyone can see that!	(Indeed)
	"I am going home!"[9]	(Indeed)
2500	The All-Knowing-Sage exclaimed,	(Indeed)
	"Everybody knows that!	(Indeed)
	"I am going home."	(Indeed)
	All-Saying-Sage exclaimed,	(Indeed)
	"Everyone knows that?	(Indeed)
2505	"That is a lie!	(Indeed)
	"Everyone sees that?	(Indeed)
	"That is a lie!	(Indeed)
	"There may be something one may see,	
	"Be it ne'er explained to him,	
2510	"He will never know it.	(Indeed)

	"Prince Birama,	(Indeed)
	"Did you not see feathers of Guinea fowl and partridge?	
	"They are the things of ruins.[1]	(Indeed)
	"Did you not see the leaf of arrow-shaft plant?	
2515	"That is a thing of ruins.	(Indeed)
	"Was not your eye on the wild grass reed?	(Indeed)
	"That is a thing of ruins.	(Indeed)
	"Did you not see those broken shards?	(Indeed)
	"They are the things of ruins.	(Indeed)
2520	"Did you not see that measure of shot?[2]	(Indeed)
	"The annihilator of Mèma![3]	(Indeed)
	"Did you not see that haftless knife?	(Indeed)
	"The warrior-head-severing blade!	(Indeed)
	"Was not your eye on the red fanda-vine?[4]	(Indeed)
2525	"The warrior-head-severing blood!	(Indeed)
	"If you do not give the land to him,	(Indeed)
	"That cornerstone fetish your eye beheld,	
	"It is the warrior's thunder shot!	(Indeed)
	"If you do not give the land to him,	
2530	"To Nare Magan Kònatè,	
	"The Wizard will reduce the town to ruin.	(Indeed)
	"Son-Jara is to return to the Manden!"	(That's the truth)

	They gave the land to the Sorcerer,	(Indeed)
	He buried his mother in Mèma's earth.	
2535	He rose up.	
	That which sitting will not solve,	
	Travel will resolve.	(Indeed)

9. The matter is too trivial to detain him. It is an ironic comment on the self-importance of seers.
1. In other words, a threat of destruction.   2. An anachronism.   3. Son-Jara, if his request is not
granted.   4. An unidentified creeping plant.

FROM EPISODE 6

Kulu-Kòrò

*   *   *

2575	O Biribiriba!	(Indeed)
	When he and his mother were going to Mèma,	(Indeed)
	She took her silver bracelet off,	
	And gave it to the Boatman patriarch,	
	To Sasagalò, the Tall.	(Indeed)
2580	The ancestor of the boatman was Sasagalò, the Tall.	
	She took her silver bracelet off:	(Indeed)
	"When one digs a distant-day well,	
	"Should a distant-day thirst descend, then drink!"[5]	(Indeed)
	A partridge was sent to deliver the message[6]	(Indeed)
2585	To Susu Mountain Sumamuru:	(Indeed)
	"Manda and Sama Kantè!	(Indeed)
	"Susu Bala Kantè!	
	"Kukuba and Bantanba!	
	"Nyani-nyani and Kamasiga!	(Indeed)
2590	*"Brave child of the warrior!*	
	"And Deliverer-of-the-Benign!	
	"Sumamuru came among us	
	"With pants of human skin!	(Indeed)
	"Sumamuru came among us	
2595	*"With coat of human skin.*	(Indeed)
	"Applaud him!	(Indeed)
	"Susu Mountain Sumamuru!	
	"The Sorcerer with his army has left Mèma.	(Indeed)
	"He has entered the Manden!"[7]	(Indeed)
2600	Susu Mountain Sumamuru,	(Indeed)
	He took four measures of gold,	(Indeed)
	To the Boatman patriarch,	
	Sasagalò, the Tall, did give them,	(Indeed)
	Saying, "That army coming from Mèma,	(Indeed)
2605	"That army must not cross!"	(Indeed)
	For one entire month,	(Indeed)
	Son-Jara and his army by the riverbank sat.	(Indeed)
	He wandered up and down.	(Indeed)
	One day Son-Jara rose up	
2610	And followed up the river:	(Indeed)
	"Being good, a bane.	(Indeed)
	"Not being good, a bane.	(Indeed)
	"When my mother and I were going to Mèma,	(Indeed)
	"She took her silver bracelet off,	(Indeed)
2615	"And gave it to a person here,	(Indeed)
	Saying when you dig a distant-day well,	

5. A proverb counseling foresight.   6. It is not clear whether Son-Jara sends this message to challenge Sumumaru or whether it is a general report by the latter's retainers and spies. *Partridge:* birds were often used to carry messages over long distances in earlier societies and in Europe even as late as the 19th century. The partridge, however, was never used for this purpose; thus it is not clear whether the reference here is intended as a realistic detail or is merely symbolic.   7. This announcement marks the point at which Son-Jara's campaign for recovery of his kingdom begins.

"When a distant-day thirst descends, then drink.   (Indeed)
"Thus have I come with my army,   (Indeed)
"And we have not yet made a crossing."[8]   (Indeed)
2620   The Boatman patriarch responded: (Indeed)
"Ah! Is it you who are Son-Jara?"   (Indeed)
The reply, "It is I who am Son-Jara."   (Indeed)
"You are Son-Jara?"   (Indeed)
"Indeed I am Son-Jara!"   (Indeed)
2625   "It is you who are Nare Magan Kònatè?   (Indeed)
"If God wills,
"With the break of day,
"Tomorrow will the army cross."   (Indeed)

At the break of day,   (Indeed)
2630   The Boatman patriarch, Sasagalò the Tall,   (Indeed)
He brought Son-Jara across.   (Indeed)
The Wizard advanced with his army.   (Indeed)
They fell upon Sumamuru at Dark Forest.   (Indeed)
But he drove them off.   (Indeed)
2635   Susu Mountain Sumamuru drove Son-Jara off.   (Indeed)
He went and founded a town called Anguish.[9]   (Indeed)
Of which the bards did sing:
     "We will not move to Anguish.   (Indeed)
     "Should one go to Anguish.
2640   "Should not anguish he endure.   (Indeed)
     "Then nothing would he reap.   (Indeed)
     "We will not move to Anguish."   (Indeed)

That Anguish,   (Indeed)
The Maninka sing this of it, my father:
2645   "There is no joy in you."   (Indeed)
Our name for that town is Anguish (Nyani).   (Indeed)

The Wizard advanced with his army.   (Indeed)
They went to fall on Susu Mountain Sumamuru.   (Indeed)
He drove Son-Jara off again.   (Indeed)
2650   He went to found the town called Resolve.   (Indeed)
The bards thus sing of it:
     "We will not move to Resolve.
     "Should one move to Resolve,
     "Should not resolve he entertain,
2655   "Then nothing would he reap.   (Indeed)
     "We will not move to Resolve."   (Indeed)
The Wizard advanced again.   (Indeed)
He with his bards advanced.   (Indeed)
They went to fall on Susu Mountain Sumamuru.   (Indeed)
2660   Sumamuru drove him off with his bards.   (Indeed)
They went to found the town called Sharing.[1]   (Indeed)
And they sang:
     Let us move to the Wizard's town, my father.
     "To Sharing,   (Indeed)

8. Son-Jara reproaches Sasagalò the Tall for not keeping his part of the bargain with his mother.
9. A metaphor for Son-Jara's mental condition as a result of his setback. The names of the other locations he founds have a more general moral significance.   1. That is, partial success.

2665   "The town where sharing is not done,
          "Founding that town is not easy."   (Indeed)
          They went to found the town called Sharing.   (Indeed)

          Son-Jara's flesh-and-blood-sister, Sugulun
              Kulunkan,   (Indeed)
          She said, "O Magan Son-Jara,   (Indeed)
2670   "One person cannot fight this war.[2]   (Indeed)
          "Let me go seek Sumamuru.   (Indeed)
          "Were I then to reach him,
          "To you I will deliver him,   (Indeed)
          "So that the folk of the Manden be yours,   (Indeed)
2675   "And all the Mandenland you shield."   (Indeed)
          Sugulun Kulunkan arose,   (Indeed)
          And went up to the gates of Sumamuru's fortress: (Indeed)
              "Manda and Sama Kantè!   (Indeed)
              "Kukuba and Bantamba
2680   *"Nyani-nyani and Kamasiga!*   (Indeed)
              "Brave child of the Warrior,
              "And Deliverer-of-the Benign.   (Indeed)
              "Sumamuru came amongst us
              "With pants of human skin.   (Indeed)
2685   *"Sumamuru came amongst us*
              "With shirt of human skin.   (Indeed)
              "Sumamuru came amongst us
              "With helm of human skin.   (Indeed)
          "Come open the gates, Susu Mountain
              Sumamuru!   (Indeed)

2690   "Come make me your bed companion!"   (Indeed)
          Sumamuru came to the gates: (Indeed)
          "What manner of person are you?"   (Indeed)
          "It is I Sugulun Kulunkan!"   (Indeed)
          "Well, now, Sugulun Kulunkan,   (Indeed)
2695   "If you have come to trap me,   (Indeed)
          "To turn me over to some person,   (Indeed)
          "Know that none can ever vanquish me.   (Indeed)
          "I have found the Manden secret,   (Indeed)
          "And made the Manden sacrifice,   (Indeed)
2700   "And in five score millet stalks placed it,   (Indeed)
          "And buried them here in the earth.   (Indeed)
          " 'Tis I who found the Manden secret,   (Indeed)
          "And made the Manden sacrifice,   (Indeed)
          "And in a red piebald bull did place it,   (Indeed)
2705   "And buried it here in the earth.   (Indeed)
          "Know that none can vanquish me.   (Indeed)
          " 'Tis I who found the Manden secret   (Indeed)
          "And made a sacrifice to it.   (Indeed)
          "And in a pure white cock did place it.   (Indeed)
2710   "Were you to kill it,   (Indeed)
          "And uproot some barren groundnut plants,   (Indeed)
          "And strip them of their leaves,

2. It cannot be won by arms alone. Like Judith and Dalila in the Bible, Son-Jara's sister intends to
employ her feminine charms in the struggle against her brother's enemy.

"And spread them round the fortress,   (Indeed)
"And uproot more barren peanut plants,   (Indeed)
2715 "And fling them into the fortress,   (Indeed)
"Only then can I be vanquished,"[3]   (Indeed)
His mother sprang forward at that: (Indeed)
"Heh! Susu Mountain Sumamuru!   (Indeed)
"Never tell all to a woman,
2720 "To a one-night woman!   (Indeed)
"The woman is not safe, Sumamuru."   (Indeed)
Sumamuru sprang towards his mother,   (Indeed)
And came and seized his mother,   (Indeed)
And slashed off her breast with a knife, magasi![4]   (Indeed)
2725 She went and got the old menstrual cloth.   (Indeed)
"Ah! Sumamuru!" she swore.   (Indeed)
"If your birth was ever a fact,
"I have cut your old menstrual cloth!"[5]

O Kalajula Sangoyi Mamunaka!   (Indeed)
2730 He lay Sugulun Kulunkan down on the bed.   (Indeed)
After one week had gone by,
Sugulun Kulunkan spoke up: (Indeed)
"Ah, my husband,   (Indeed)
"Will you not let me go to the Manden,   (Indeed)
2735 "That I may get my bowls and spoons,[6]
"For me to build my household here?   (Indeed)
From that day to this,
Should you marry a woman in Mandenland,   (Indeed)
When the first week has passed,
2740 She will take a backward glance,   (Indeed)
And this is what that custom means.   (Yes, Fa-Digi, that's
                    the truth)

Sugulun returned to reveal those secrets
To her flesh-and-blood-brother, Son-Jara.   (Indeed)
The sacrifices did Son-Jara thus discover.   (Indeed)
2745 The sacrifices did he thus discover.[7]   (Indeed)
Now five score wives had Susu Mountain Sumamuru,   (Indeed)
One hundred wives had he.   (Indeed)
His nephew, Fa-Koli, had but one,[8]   (Indeed)
. . .   (Mmm)
2750 And Sumamuru, five score!   (Indeed)
When a hundred bowls they would cook
To make the warriors' meal,   (Indeed)
Fa-Koli's wife alone would one hundred cook
To make the warriors' meal,   (That's the truth, eh,
                    Fa-Digi, indeed, indeed)
2755 "Let the fonio[9] increase!   (Indeed)
"Let the rice increase!   (Indeed)

---

3. Sumamuru's bravado here is in keeping with his vaingloriousness as it comes through in the narrative.   4. The same words used for Jata Magan Kòndè's treatment of his sister, Du Kamisa.   5. The cloth in which he was wrapped at his birth, stained with the blood of parturition. By tearing it up, she disowns her son.   6. It is customary among the Manding for a new bride to return to her home a last time to collect her belongings before settling into her new life. The passage traces the custom to the incident recounted here.   7. To be acted on later.   8. In contrast to Sumamuru's *five score*, which emphasizes his sexual desire.   9. A cereal.

"Let the groundnuts increase!   (Indeed)
"Let the groundpeas increase!   (Indeed)
"Let the beans increase!"[1]   (Indeed)
2760   She took them all one by one,   (Indeed)
       And put them all in one pot,   (Indeed)
       And in that pot they all were cooked,   (Indeed)
       And served it all in her calabash,   (Indeed)
       And all of this for Fa-Koli.   (Indeed)

[Sumamuru takes Fa-Koli's wife, causing a rift between him and his nephew, who defects to Son-Jara.]

2770   Hero-of-the-Original-Clans and Magan
          Sukudana![2]   (Indeed)
       Son-Jara called out,   (Indeed)
       "Who in the Manden will make this sacrifice?"[3]   (Indeed)
       "I shall!" Fa-Koli's reply.   (Indeed)
       "The thing that drove me away,   (Indeed)
2775   "And took my only wife from me,
       "So that not even a weak wife have I now,   (Indeed)
       "I shall make the whole sacrifice!"   (Indeed)
       Fa-Koli thus made the whole sacrifice.   (Indeed)
       He came and reported to the Wizard.
2780   Son-Jara then called out: (Indeed)
       "Who will bring us face to face,
       "That we may join in battle?"   (Indeed)
       "I shall," Fa-Koli's reply.   (Indeed)
       On that Fa-Koli rose up.   (Indeed)
2785   He arrived in Dark Forest.   (Indeed)
       As he espied the rooftops of Sumamuru's city, Dark
          Forest,   (Indeed)
       With every single step he took,   (Indeed)
       He thrust a dart[4] into the earth,   (Indeed)
       And in a tree fork laid another.   (Indeed, yes, Fa-Digi)
2790   With every single step he took,   (Indeed)
       He thrust a dart into the earth,   (Indeed)
       And in a tree fork laid another,[5]   (That's the truth)
       Until he entered the very gates,
       Until he entered the city.   (Indeed)
2795   O, Garan!   (Indeed)
       The daughter given by King Dankaran Tuman,[6]   (Indeed)
       Given to Susu Mountain Sumamuru,   (Indeed)
       That he should go and kill Son-Jara,   (Indeed)
       Fa-Koli went and seized that maiden,   (Indeed)
2800   "Come! Your uncle has left Mèma!   (Indeed)
       "Your uncle has summoned you.   (Indeed)
       "Your uncle has now come. He has left Mèma!" (Indeed)
       The people of Susu pursued them: biri biri biri. (Indeed)
       They came attacking after them: yrrrrrr!   (Indeed)
2805   With every single step he took,   (Indeed)

1. Fa-Koli's wife's incantations over the food she has prepared.   2. Praise name of Fa-Koli.
3. Revealed by Son-Jara's sister (see line 2742).   4. It will soon be clear that this is a magic dart.
5. The motif here is a heroicized variant of the Hansel and Gretel story.   6. Caress-of-Hot-Fire.

He drew a war dart from the earth,
And hurled it at the Susu,   (Indeed)
And from a tree fork grabbed another,   (Indeed)
And hurled it at the Susu,   (Indeed)
2810   "Heh! Come to my aid!   (Indeed)
"Heaven and Earth, come aid me!
"Susu Mountain Sumamuru is after
        me!"   (Indeed, yes, father)
He retreated on and on.[7]
He drew a war dart from the earth,
2815   And hurled it at the Susu,   (Indeed)
And from a tree fork grabbed another,   (Indeed)
And fired it at the Susu.   (Indeed)
"Heh! Come to my aid!   (Indeed)
"Heaven and Earth, come to my aid!
2820   "Susu Mountain Sumamuru is after me!"   (That's the truth)

At that, the Susu said, my father,   (Indeed)
"If we do not fall back from Fa-Koli,   (Indeed)
"Fa-Koli will bring all our folk to an end![8]   (Indeed)
"Let us fall back from Fa-Koli!   (Indeed)
2825   Hero-of-the-Original-Clans and Magan Sukudana.
        . . .   (That's the truth)
And thus they fell back from Fa-Koli.   (Indeed)
They readied themselves for battle.   (Indeed)
Susu Mountain Sumamuru came forward.   (Indeed)
2830   And taking his favorite wife,
On the saddle's cantle sat her,   (Indeed)
With golden ladle and silver ladle.   (Indeed)
Son-Jara attacked and encircled the walls.   (Indeed)
He had split the enemy army,[9]   (Indeed)
2835   And taken the fortress gates.   (Indeed)
Susu Mountain Sumamuru charged out at a gallop.[1] (Indeed)
Fa-Koli,   (Indeed)
With Tura-Magan-and-Kanke-jan,   (Indeed)
And Bee-King-of-the-Wilderness,   (Indeed)
2840   And Fa-Kanda Tunandi,   (Indeed)
And Sura, the Jawara patriarch,   (Indeed)
And Son-Jara,   (Indeed)
They all chased after Sumamuru.   (True)
They arrived at Kukuba.   (Indeed)
2845   He told them, "I am not ready!"   (Indeed)
They let him go:[2]   (Indeed)
"Prepare yourself!"   (Indeed)
They arrived at Kamasiga,[3]   (Indeed)
"I am not ready."   (Indeed)
2850   They let him go: (Indeed)
"Prepare yourself!"   (Indeed)
They arrived at Nyani-Nyani.   (Indeed)
Said, "I am not ready."   (Indeed)

---

7. Clearly as a diversionary tactic to draw out the enemy lines.   8. He is single-handedly destroying the enemy ranks with his magic dart.   9. Thanks to Fa-Koli.   1. Forcefully breaking out of the siege laid to his fortress.   2. This can only mean that Sumamuru escaped their clutches.   3. The places named are the scenes of the successive engagements between the two armies.

	They let him go again:	
2855	"Prepare yourself!"	(Indeed)
	They arrived at Bantanba,	(Indeed)
	"I am not ready."	(Indeed)
	And again they let him go:	
	"Prepare yourself!"	(Indeed)
2860	And still they attacked him from behind,	
	Behind Susu Mountain Sumamuru.	(That's the truth, yes, Fa-Digi)

Sumamuru crossed the river at Kulu-Kòrò,[4]   (Indeed)
And had his favored wife dismount,   (Indeed)
And gave her the ladle of gold,
2865   Saying that he would drink,   (Indeed)
Saying else the thirst would kill him.   (That's the truth)
The favored wife took the ladle of gold,   (Indeed)
And filled it up with water,   (Indeed)
And to Sumamuru stretched her hand,
2870   And passed the water to him.   (Indeed)
Fa-Koli with his darts charged up:
"O Colossus,   (Indeed)
"We have taken you!   (That's the truth)
"We have taken you, Colossus!
2875   "We have taken you, Colossus!
"We have taken you!"   (Indeed)
Tura Magan held him at bladepoint.   (Indeed)
Sura, the Jawara patriarch held him at bladepoint.   (Indeed)
Fa-Koli came up and held him at bladepoint.
2880   Son-Jara held him at bladepoint:[5]   (Indeed)
"We have taken you, Colossus!   (That's the truth)
"We have taken you!"   (Indeed)
Sumamuru dried up on the spot: nyònyòwu![6]   (Indeed)
He has become the sacred fetish of Kulu-Kòrò.   (Indeed)
2885   The Bambara worship that now,[7] my father.
Susu Mountain Sumamuru,
He became that sacred fetish.   (That's the truth, indeed, father, yes, yes, yes, yes)

FROM EPISODE 7

Kanbi

Biribiriba turned back, Son-Jara!   (Indeed)
Stranger-in-the-Morning, Chief-in-the
         Afternoon![8]   (Indeed)
2890   Great-Host-Slaying-Stranger!
Stump-in-the-Dark-of-Night!   (Indeed)
Should you bump against it,
It will bump against you!   (That's the truth)

---

4. A village near Bamako, on the river Niger. In some versions of the epic, Sumamuru disappears into the hillside on a site near this village.   5. We must imagine the warriors crowding in on Sumamuru from various directions. Note too that they are all given credit for his final defeat.   6. Ideophone for the drying up.   7. Sumamuru is still revered among his people, who have kept his memory alive in a counterepic devoted to him as well as in various forms of ritual.   8. With his victory, Son-Jara is suddenly transformed from a homeless vagrant into a powerful ruler.

The Granary Guard Dog.   (Indeed)
2895   The thing discerning not the stranger,
           Nor the familiar.
           Should it come upon any person,
           He will be bitten.   (That's the truth)
           Kirikara Watita!   (Indeed)
2900   Adversity's true place!
           Man's reason and woman's are not the same.
           Pretty words and truth are not the
                same.   (That's the truth)
           No matter how long the road,
           It always comes out at someone's home.[9]   (Indeed)
2905   The Nyani king with his army came forward, (Indeed)
           Saying the Manden belonged to him,   (That's the truth)
           Saying no more was he rival to any,   (That's the truth)
           Saying the Manden belonged to him.   (That's the truth)

           He found the Kuyatè patriarch[1] with tendons cut, (Indeed)
2910   And beckoned him to rise, "Let us go!   (Indeed)
           "Bala Faseke Kuyatè, arise. Let us go!" (Indeed)
           He lurched forward.   (Indeed)
           Saying he would rise.
           He fell back to the ground again,   (Indeed)
2915   His two Achilles tendons cut: (Indeed)
           "O Nare Magan Kònatè!"   (Indeed)
           "Arise and let us go!   (Indeed)
           I have no rival in Mandenland now!   (That's the truth)
           "The Manden is mine alone."   (Indeed)
2920   He lurched forward,   (Indeed)
           Saying that he would rise.   (Indeed)
           He fell back to the ground again.   (Indeed)
           "Had Sumamuru no child?" they queried.   (Indeed)
           "Here is his first born son," the reply. (Indeed)
2925   "What is his name?"   (Indeed)
           "His name is Mansa Saman."   (Indeed)
           They summoned Mansa Saman   (Indeed)
           And brought forth Dòka the Cat,
           And placed him on Mansa Saman's shoulders,[2] (Indeed)
2930   Laying the balaphone on his head, serew! (Indeed)
           He followed after the Wizard: (Indeed)
                "Biribiriba!   (Indeed)
                "O Nare Magan Kònatè!   (Indeed)
                "Entered Kaya,
2935   "Son-Jara entered Kaya.   (That's the truth)
                "Entered Kaya,
                "Sugulun's Ma'an entered Kaya.[3]   (Yes, Fa-Digi)
                "If they took no gold,   (Indeed)
                "If they took no measure of gold for the
                     Wizard,   (Indeed)
2940   "The reason for Son-Jara's coming to the Manden,
                "To stabilize the Manden,

9. A proverb: everything has a beginning and an end.   1. Bala Faseke.   2. As a sign of his humiliation.   3. The refrain of a song celebrating Son-Jara's triumphal return to the Manden.

"To improve the people's lot:[4] jon jon!   (That's the truth)
"O Sorcerer, you have come for the Manden
    people!   (Indeed)
"O Nare Magan Kònatè,   (Indeed)
2945   "O Khalif Magan Kònatè!"   (That's the truth)
They arrived back in the Manden.   (Indeed)
The Sorcerer ruled over everyone.   (Indeed)
He continued on at that.[5]   (Indeed)

[Although he has regained his homeland, Son-Jara still must establish his authority
over the neighboring territories. A quarrel with the Jolof king provides him with a
pretext for a new campaign for the expansion of his domain. The Jolof king has
seized a large herd of horses Son-Jara has sent his retainers to collect within Jolof
territory and sends him instead a pack of dogs, with the message that he knows
Son-Jara not as king but only as a mere hunter ("a runner of dogs"). This challenge
angers Son-Jara, who summons his generals to a council of war.]

In turn, the warriors swore their fealty:[6]   (Indeed)
"Let me the battle-master be!"   (Indeed)
Fa-Koli and Tura Magan swore their fealty.   (Indeed)
"Let me lead the army!" Fa-Koli
    adjured.   (That's the truth)

3000   "Let me lead the army!" Tura Magan adjured. (Indeed)
Son-Jara finally spoke,   (Indeed)
" 'Tis I who will lead the army,   (Indeed)
"And go to Dark Jòlòf land."   (Indeed)
O Nare Magan Kònatè!   (Indeed)
3005   Tura Magan plunged into grief,   (Indeed)
And went to the graveyard to dig his grave,   (Indeed)
And laid himself down in his grave.[7]   (Indeed)
The bards came forth: "O Nare Magan Kònatè,   (Indeed)
"If you don't go see Tura Magan,   (Indeed)
3010   "Your army will not succeed!"   (Indeed)
He sent the bards forth
That they should summon Tura Magan.
And so the bards went forth.   (Indeed)
But Tura Magan they could not find.   (That's the truth)
3015   Son-Jara came and stood in the graveyard: (Indeed)
    "*Bugu Turu and Bugu Bò!*   (Indeed)
    "*Muke Musa and Muke Dantuman!*   (Indeed)
    "*Juru Kèta and Juru Moriba!*   (Indeed)
    "*Tunbila the Manden Slave!*   (Indeed)
3020   "*Kalabila, the Manden Slave!*   (Indeed)
    "*Sana Fa-Buren, Danka Fa-Buren!*   (Indeed)
    "*Dark-Pilgrim and Light-Pilgrim!*[8]   (Indeed)
"Ah! Bards,   (Indeed)
"Let us give the army to Tura Magan,   (Indeed)

4. The ideological function of the epic becomes fully evident here.   5. That is, until the end of his
reign.   6. Made necessary by the defiance of the Jolof king.   7. A sign of his disappointment.
8. This passage is a reference to the pilgrimage he is reputed to have made to Mecca, from which he
is also said to have brought magical powers. The names are of Tura Magan's ancestors, invoked by Son-
Jara in appealing to him.

3025   "To the Slave-of-the-Tomb,[9] Tura Magan,   (Indeed)
       "O Tura Magan-and-Kanke-jan!"   (That's the truth)

       Tura Magan spoke out,   (Indeed)
       "That is the best of all things to my ear!"   (Indeed)
       To Tura Magan they gave quiver and bow.   (Indeed)
3030   Tura Magan advanced to cross the river here, (Indeed)
       At the Passage-of-Tura-Magan.[1]   (Indeed)
       A member of the troop cried out,   (Indeed)
       "Hey! The war to which we go,   (Indeed)
       "That war will not be easy!   (Indeed)
3035   "Ninety iron drums has the Dark Jòlòf King.   (Indeed)
       "No drum like this has the Manden.   (Indeed)
       "Nor balaphone has the Manden.   (Indeed)
       "There is no such thing in the Manden,   (Indeed)
       "Save the Jawara patriarch, Sita Fata,   (Indeed)
3040   "Save when he puffs out his cheeks,   (Indeed)
       "Making with them like drum and balaphone,[2]
       "To go awaken the Nyani King.   (Indeed)
       "This battle will not be easy!"   (Indeed)
       But they drove this agitator off.   (Indeed)
3045   Saying better in the bush a frightened brave
       Than a loudmouthed agitator.   (That's the truth)
       He went back across the river,   (Indeed)
       At the place they call Salakan,[3]   (Indeed)
       And Ford-of-the-Frightened.   (Indeed)
3050   The Ford-of-the-Frightened-Braves.   (Indeed)
       Tura Magan with battle met.   (Indeed)
       He slayed that dog-giving king,[4]   (Indeed)
       Saying he was but running the dogs.[5]   (That's the truth)
       Tura Magan with army marched on,   (Indeed)
3055   He went to slay Nyani Mansa,
       Saying he was but running the dogs.   (That's the truth)
       Tura Magan with the army marched on, (Indeed)
       He slayed the Sanumu King,
       Saying that he was but running the dogs, (Indeed)
3060   He slayed Ba-dugu King   (Indeed)
       Saying he was but running the dogs,   (Indeed)
       And marched on thus through Jòlòf land.[6] (Indeed)
       Their name for stone is Jòlòf.   (Indeed)
       Once there was this king . . . ,   (Indeed)
3065   The stone there that is red,   (Indeed)
       The Wòlòf call it Jòlòf.   (Indeed)
       There once was a king in that country, my father,
       Called King of Dark Jòlòfland.   (Indeed)
       And that is the meaning of this.   (That's the truth)
3070   He slayed that Dark Jòlòf King,   (Indeed)
       Severing his great head at his shoulders, (Indeed)

---

9. This is the *Manden Slave* mentioned in line 3020.   1. A ford across the Senegal River.   2. The inspirational role of bards is once again affirmed.   3. A ford whose name and significance are explained in lines 3049–50.   4. A reference to the Jolof king's insult.   5. That is, out hunting with his dogs. A pun on the previous line, expressing Tura Magan's pleasure in waging war.   6. In present-day Senegal, to the west of the original Manden homeland. Note the way the repetitions give a terse economy to the narration.

From whence comes the Wòlòf name, Njòp![7]   (Indeed)
They are Taraweres.   (Indeed)
Sane and Mane,[8]   (Indeed)
3075 They are Taraweres.   (Indeed)
Mayga, they are Taraweres.   (Indeed)
Magaraga, they are Taraweres.   (Indeed)
Tura Magan-and-Kanke-jan,   (Indeed)
He with the army marched on,
3080 To destroy the golden sword and the tall
        throne.[9]   (That's the truth)
This by the hand of Tura Magan-and-Kanke-jan.
    Kirikisa, Spear-of-Access, Spear-of Service!   (Indeed)
Ah! Garan!   (Indeed)
Let us leave the words[1] right here.   (That's the truth,
                                           indeed, it's over now!)

---

7. A common Wòlòf surname. This is an example of folk etymology. *Njòp* can also be spelled "Diop" and "Dyob," and in Gambia, "Job."   8. Two important clans in Senegal and in Gambia; the names often serve as surnames.   9. Emblems of the Jolof king.   1. In many African languages the word *word* refers not only to ordinary speech but also to reflective thought in general, especially as conveyed in a proverb or a story.

Part III

1500 TO 1650

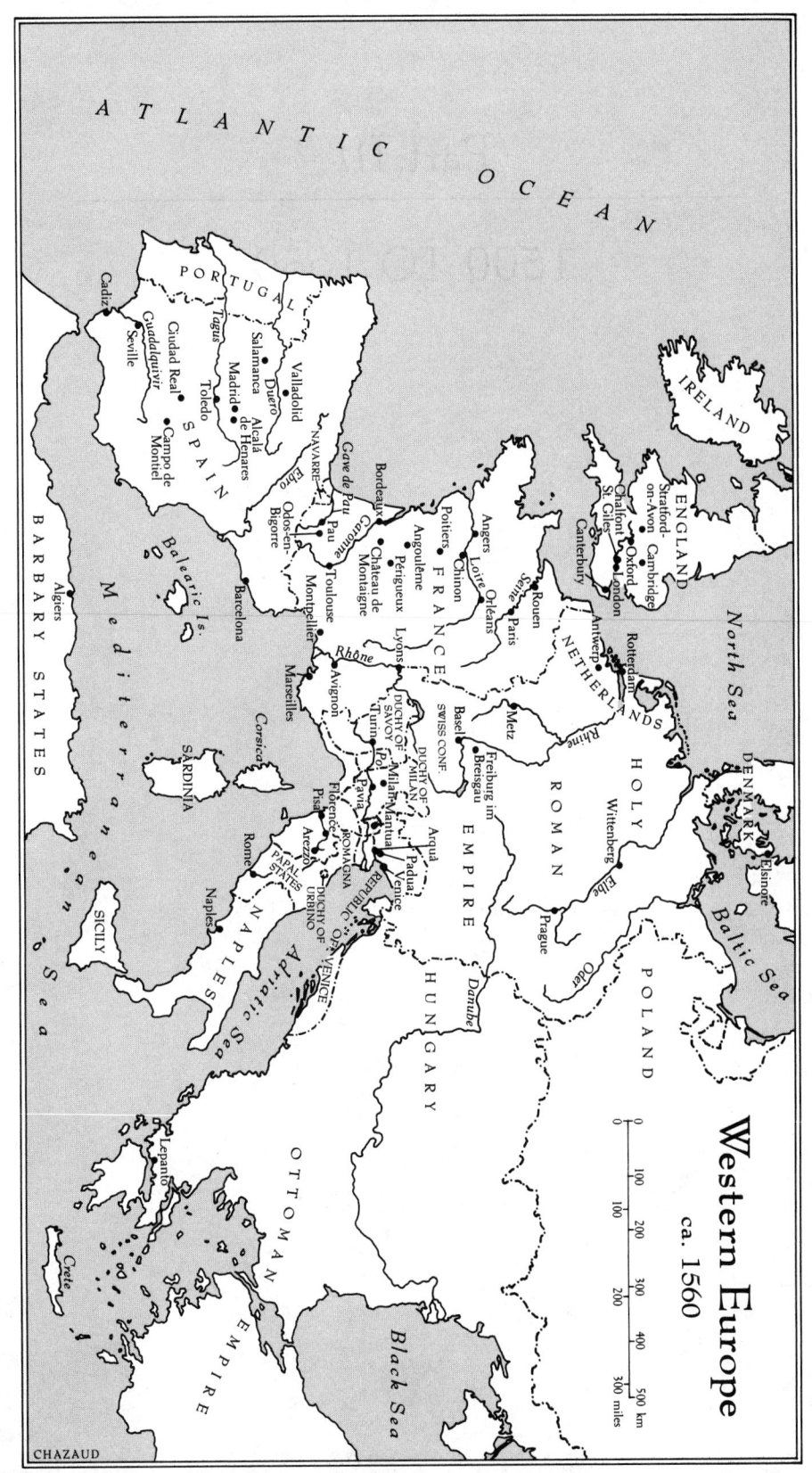

Western Europe ca. 1560

The Renaissance in Europe

We meet in Renaissance literature some of the most resonant, thought-provoking characters that literary genius has ever produced: Marlowe's Dr. Faustus, Shakespeare's Hamlet, Rabelais's Gargantua, Cervantes's Quixote, Milton's Adam and Eve. These characters no longer move, as most of Chaucer's do, through a life conceived as pilgrimage within a world of ideas and feelings for the most part firmly structured by religious, feudal, and chivalric values. Renaissance characters tend to be more like us: baffled as to exactly what *is* the structure that contains them (if any), seeking sometimes to feel it out (like Hamlet), sometimes—if they think they already know—rebelling against it (like Faustus or Adam and Eve), and sometimes (like Gargantua) happy to replace it with a giantized image of fleshly freedoms, or (like Quixote) with an idiosyncratic view of things uncontestably their own. Chaucer's populous and well-worn route between the Tabard Inn and Canterbury Cathedral gives way to a crisscross of dimly sensed paths.

As with other terms that have currency in cultural history (for instance, *Romanticism*), the usefulness of the term *Renaissance* depends on its keeping a certain degree of elasticity. The literal meaning of the word—"rebirth"—suggests that one impulse toward the great intellectual and artistic achievements of the period came from the example of ancient culture or, even better, from a certain vision that the artists and intellectuals of the Renaissance possessed of the world of antiquity, which was "reborn" through their work. Especially in the more mature phase of the Renaissance, these individuals were aware of having brought about a vigorous renewal, which they openly associated with the cult of antiquity. The restoration of ancient canons was regarded as a glorious achievement to be set beside the thrilling discoveries of their own age. "For now," Rabelais writes through his Gargantua,

> all courses of study have been restored, and the acquisition of languages has become supremely honorable: Greek, without which it is shameful for any man to be called a scholar; Hebrew; Chaldean; Latin. And in my time we have learned how to produce wonderfully elegant and accurate printed books, just as, on the other hand, we have also learned (by diabolic suggestion) how to make cannon and other such fearful weapons.

Machiavelli, whose infatuation with antiquity is as typical a trait as his better-advertised political realism, suggests in the opening of his *Discourses on the First Ten Books of Livy* (1513–1521) that rulers should be as keen on the imitation of ancient "virtues" as are artists, lawyers, and the scientists: "The civil laws are nothing but decisions given by the ancient jurisconsults. . . . And what is the science of medicine, but the experience of ancient physicians, which their successors have taken for their guide?"

Elasticity should likewise be maintained in regard to the chronological span of the Renaissance as a "movement" extending through varying periods of years, and as including phases and traits of the epoch that is otherwise known as the Middle Ages (and vice versa). The peak of the Renaissance can be shown to have occurred

at different times in different countries, the "movement" having had its inception
in Italy, where its impact was at first most remarkable in the visual arts, while in
England, for instance, it developed later, and its main achievements were in literature, particularly drama. The meaning of the term also has, in the course of time,
widened considerably. Nowadays it conveys, to say the least, a general notion of
artistic creativity, of extraordinary zest for life and knowledge, of sensory delight
in opulence and magnificence, of spectacular individual achievement, thus
extending far beyond the literal meaning of rebirth and the strict idea of a revival
and imitation of antiquity.

Even in its stricter sense, however, the term continues to have its function. The
degree to which European intellectuals of the period possessed and were possessed
by the writings of the ancient world is difficult for the average modern reader to
realize. For these writers references to classical mythology, philosophy, and literature are not ornaments or affectations. Along with references to the Scriptures they
are part, and a major part, of their mental equipment and way of thinking. When
Erasmus through his *Praise of Folly* speaks in a cluster of classical allusions, or
when Machiavelli writes to a friend: "I get up before daylight, prepare my birdlime, and go out with a bundle of cages on my back, so that I look like Geta when
he came back from the harbor with the books of Amphitryo," the words have by
no means the sound of erudite self-gratification that they might have nowadays.
They are wholly natural, familiar, unassuming.

When we are overcome by sudden emotion, our first exclamations are likely to
be in the language most familiar to us—our dialect, if we happen to have one.
Montaigne relates of himself that when once his father unexpectedly fell back in
his arms in a swoon, the first words he uttered under the emotion of that experience were in Latin. Similarly Benvenuto Cellini, the Italian sculptor, goldsmith,
and autobiographer, talking to his patron and expressing admiration of a Greek
statue, establishes with the ancient artist an immediate contact, a proud familiarity:

> I cried to the Duke: "My lord, this is a statue in Greek marble, and it is a
> miracle of beauty. . . . If your Excellency permits, I should like to restore it—
> head and arms and feet. . . . It is certainly not my business to patch up statues,
> that being the trade of botchers, who do it in all conscience villainously ill;
> yet the art displayed by this great master of antiquity cries out to me to help
> him."

Those who, starting at about the middle of the fourteenth century, gave new
impulse to this emulation of the classics are often referred to as humanists. The
word in that sense is related to what we call the humanities, and the humanities
at that time were Latin and Greek. Every cultivated person wrote and spoke Latin,
with the result that a Western community of intellectuals could exist, a spiritual
"republic of letters" above individual nations. There was also a considerable
amount of individual contact among humanists. In glancing at the biographies of
the authors included in this section, the extensiveness of their travels may strike us
as a remarkable or even surprising fact, considering the hardships and slowness of
traveling during those centuries.

The archetype of literature as a vocation is often said to be Petrarch—the first
author in this sweep—who anticipated certain ideals of the high Renaissance: a
lofty conception of the literary art, a taste for the good life, a basic pacifism, and a
strong sense of the memories and glories of antiquity. In this last respect, what
should be emphasized is the imaginative quality, the visionary impulse with which
the writers of the period looked at those memories—the same vision and imagination with which they regarded such contemporary heroes as the great navigators
and astronomers. The Renaissance view of the cultural monuments of antiquity
was far from being that of the philologist and the antiquarian; indeed, familiarity

was facilitated by the very lack of a scientific sense of history. We find the visionary and imaginative element not only in the creations of poets and dramatists (Shakespeare's Romans, to give an obvious example) but also in the works of political writers; as when Machiavelli describes himself entering, through his reading, the

> ancient courts of ancient men, where, being lovingly received, I feed on that food which alone is mine, and which I was born for; I am not ashamed to speak with them and to ask the reasons for their actions, and they courteously answer me. For . . . hours I feel no boredom and forget every worry; I do not fear poverty, and death does not terrify me. I give myself completely over to the ancients.

Imitation of antiquity acquires, in Machiavelli and many others, a special quality; between mere "academic" imitation and the Renaissance approach there is as much difference as between the impulse to learn and the impulse to *be*.

The vision of an ancient age of glorious intellectual achievement that is "now" brought to life again, implies of course, however roughly, the idea of an intervening "middle" time, by comparison ignorant and dark. The hackneyed notion that the "light" of the Renaissance broke through a long "night" of the Middle Ages may be vastly inaccurate. Yet it is inevitable to remember that this view was not devised by subsequent "enlightened" centuries; it was held by the people of the Renaissance themselves. In his genealogy of giants from Grangousier to Gargantua to Pantagruel, Rabelais conveniently represents the generations of modern learning with their varying degrees of enlightenment. Thus Gargantua writes to his son:

> Though my late father of worthy memory, Grandgousier, devoted all his energy to those things of which I might take the fullest advantage, and from which I might acquire the most sensible knowledge, and though my own effort matched his—or even surpassed it—still, as you know very well, it was neither so fit nor so right a time for learning as exists today, nor was there an abundance of such teachers as you have had. It was still a murky, dark time, oppressed by the misery, unhappiness, and disasters of the Goths, who destroyed all worthwhile literature of every sort. But divine goodness has let me live to see light and dignity returned to humanistic studies, and to see such an improvement, indeed, that it would be hard for me to qualify for the very first class of little schoolboys—I who, in my prime, had the reputation (and not in error) of the most learned man of my day.

Definitions of the Renaissance must also take account of the period's preoccupation with this life rather than with the life beyond. The contrast of an ideal Medieval man or woman, whose mode of action is basically oriented toward the thought of the afterlife—and who therefore conceives of life on earth as transient and preparatory—with an ideal Renaissance man or woman, possessing and cherishing earthly interests so concrete and self-sufficient that the very realization of the ephemeral quality of life is to him or her nothing but an added spur to its immediate enjoyment—this is a useful contrast, even though it represents an enormous oversimplification of the facts.

The same emphasis on the immediate and tangible is reflected in the earthly, amoral, and aesthetic character of what we may call the Renaissance code of behavior. According to this code, human action is judged not in terms of right and wrong, of good and evil (as it is judged when life is viewed as a moral test, with reward or punishment in the afterlife), but in terms of its present concrete validity and effectiveness, of the delight it affords, of its memorability, and of its beauty. In that sense a good deal that is typical of the Renaissance, from architecture to poetry, from sculpture to rhetoric, may be related to a taste for the harmonious and the memorable, for the spectacular effect, for the successful striking of a pose.

Individual human action, seeking as it were in itself its own reward, finds justification in its formal appropriateness; in its being a well-rounded achievement, perfect of its kind; in the zest and gusto with which it is, here and now, performed; and finally, in its proving worthy of remaining as a testimony to the performer's power on earth.

A convenient way to illustrate this emphasis is to consider certain words especially expressive of the interests of the period — *virtue, fame, glory. Virtue,* particularly in its Italian form, *virtù,* is to be understood in a wide sense. As we may see even now in some relics of its older meanings, the word (from the Latin *vir,* "man") connotes active power — the intrinsic force and ability of a person or thing (the "virtue" of a law or of a medicine) — and hence, also, technical skill (the capacity of the "virtuoso"). The Machiavellian prince's "virtues," therefore, are not necessarily goodness, temperance, clemency, and the like; they are whatever forces and skills may help him in the efficient management and preservation of his princely powers. The idealistic, intangible part of the prince's success is consigned to such concepts as *fame* and *glory,* but even in this case the dimension within which human action is considered is still an earthly one. These concepts connote the hero's success and reputation with his contemporaries or look forward to splendid recognition from posterity, on earth.

In this sense (though completely pure examples of such an attitude are rare) the purpose of life is the unrestrained and self-sufficient practice of one's "virtue," the competent and delighted exercise of one's skill. At the same time there is no reason to forget that such virtues and skills are God's gift. The worldview of even some of the most clearly earthbound Renaissance writers was hardly godless; Machiavelli, Rabelais, and Cellini take for granted the presence of God in their own and in their heroes' lives:

> We have before our eyes extraordinary and unexampled means prepared by God. The sea has been divided. A cloud has guided you on your way. The rock has given forth water. Manna has fallen. Everything has united to make you great. The rest is for you to do. God does not intend to do everything, lest he deprive us of our free will and the share of glory that belongs to us. (Machiavelli)

> And then Gargantua and Powerbrain would briefly recapitulate, according to the Pythagorean fashion, everything Gargantua had read and seen and understood, everything he had done and heard, all day long.
> They would both pray to God their Creator, worshiping, reaffirming their faith, glorifying Him for His immense goodness and thanking Him for all they had been given, and forever placing themselves in His hands.
> And then they would go to sleep. (Rabelais)

> I found that all the bronze my furnace contained had been exhausted in the head of this figure [of the statue of Perseus]. It was a miracle to observe that not one fragment remained in the orifice of the channel, and that nothing was wanting to the statue. In my great astonishment I seemed to see in this the hand of God arranging and controlling all. (Cellini)

Yet if we compare the attitudes of these authors with the view of the world and of the value of human action that emerges from the major literary work of the Middle Ages, the *Divine Comedy,* and with the manner in which human action is there seen within a grand extratemporal design, the presence of God in the Renaissance writers cited above appears marginal and perfunctory.

In any attempt to discuss the religious temper of the Renaissance, we should not lose sight of certain basic historical facts: the papacy was not only a spiritual power but a political and military one as well; furthermore, the European Renais-

sance was a period of violent religious strife. The consequences of the Protestant Reformation (Lutheranism, Zwinglianism, Calvinism) were not only theological and ideological debates but also armed conflict and bloodshed, as is apparent from the biographies of several of the writers presented here (Erasmus, Rabelais, and Montaigne). It is also apparent that the position of the intellectual generally was not one of militant partisanship or, conversely, of retreat to an "ivory tower" but was characterized by wisdom and attempts at conciliation.

Much about the religious temper of the age is expressed in its art, particularly in Italian painting, where Renaissance Madonnas often make it difficult, as the saying goes, to recite a properly devout Hail Mary—serving as celebrations of earthly beauty rather than exhortations to contrite thoughts and mystical hopes of salvation. Castiglione in the first pages of the *Courtier* pays homage to the memory of the late lord of Montefeltro, in whose palace at Urbino the book's personages hold their lofty debate on the idea of a perfect gentleman (an earlier Montefeltro appears in Dante's Hell, another in Dante's Purgatory), but Castiglione praises him only for his achievements as a man of arms and a promoter of the arts. There is no thought of either the salvation or the damnation of his soul (though the general tone of the work would seem to imply his salvation); he is exalted instead for military victories and even more warmly for having built a splendid palace— the tangible symbol of his earthly glory, for it is both the mark of political and social power and a work of art.

Thus the popular view that associates the idea of the Renaissance especially with the flourishing of the arts is correct. The leaders of the period saw in a work of art the clearest instance of beautiful, harmonious, and self-justified performance. To create such a work became the valuable occupation par excellence, the most satisfactory display of *virtù*. The Renaissance view of antiquity exemplifies this attitude. The artists and intellectuals of the period not only drew on antiquity for certain practices and forms but also found there a recognition of the place of the arts among outstanding modes of human action. In this way, the concepts of fame and glory became particularly associated with the art of poetry, because the Renaissance drew from antiquity the idea of the poet as celebrator of high deeds, the "dispenser of glory."*

There is, then, an important part of the Renaissance mind that sees terrestrial life as positive fulfillment. This is especially clear when there is a close association between the practical and the intellectual, as in the exercise of political power, the act of scientific discovery, and the creation of works of art. The Renaissance assumption is that there are things highly worth doing, within a strictly temporal pattern. By doing them, humanity proves its privileged position in creation and, therefore, incidentally follows God's intent. The often cited phrase "the dignity of man" describes this positive, strongly affirmed awareness of the intellectual and physical "virtues" of the human being, and of the individual's place in creation.

It is important, however, to see this fact about the Renaissance in the light of another phenomenon. Where there is a singularly high capacity for feeling the delight of earthly achievement, there is a possibility that its ultimate worth will also be questioned profoundly. What (the Renaissance mind usually seems to ask at some point) is the purpose of all this activity? What meaningful relation does it bear to any all-inclusive, cosmic pattern? The Renaissance coincided with, and perhaps to some extent occasioned, a loss of firm belief in the final unity and the final intelligibility of the universe, such belief as underlies, for example, the *Divine Comedy*, enabling Dante to say in Paradise:

---

* And, of course, a typical guarantee of memorability was having oneself portrayed—perhaps at various stages in life—by some of the magnificent and highly honored painters of the period.

> I saw within Its depth how It conceives
> all things in a single volume bound by Love,
> of which the universe is the scattered leaves;
> substance, accident, and their relation
> so fused that all I say could do no more
> than yield a glimpse of that bright revelation.

Once the notion of this grand unity of design has lost its authority, certainty about the final value of human actions is no longer to be found. For some minds, indeed, the sense of void becomes so strong as to paralyze all aspiration to power or thirst for knowledge or delight in beauty; the resulting attitude we may call Renaissance melancholy, whether it is openly shown (as by some characters in Elizabethan drama) or provides an undercurrent of sadness or means some sort of wise adjustment (as in Erasmus or Montaigne). The legend of Faust—"Dr." Faustus—a great amasser of knowledge doomed to frustration by his perception of the vanity of science, for which he finds at one point desperate substitutes in pseudoscience and the devil's arts, is one illustration of this sense of vanity. Shakespeare's *Hamlet* is another, a play in which the very word *thought* seems to acquire a troubled connotation: "the pale cast of thought," "thought and affliction, passion, hell itself." In these instances, the intellectual excitement of understanding, the zest and pride of achievement through intellect, seem not so much lost as inverted.

Thus while on one, and perhaps the better-known, side of the picture human intellect in Renaissance literature enthusiastically expatiates over the realms of knowledge and unveils the mysteries of the universe, on the other it is beset by puzzling doubts and a profound mistrust of its own powers. Our moral nature is seen as only a little lower than the angels' but also scarcely above the beasts'. Earthly power—a favorite theme because Renaissance literature was so largely produced in the courts or with a vivid sense of courtly ideas—is the crown of human aspirations ("How sweet a thing it is to wear a crown, / Within whose circuit is Elysium"), but it is also the death's head ("Imperious Caesar, dead and turn'd to clay, / Might stop a hole to keep the wind away").

Much of Renaissance literature takes its character and strength from the tensions generated by this simultaneous exaltation and pessimism about the human condition.

FURTHER READING

Richard L. DeMolen, ed., *The Meaning of Renaissance and Reformation* (1974), is a collection of essays by experts on the Renaissance and Reformation, with maps and illustrations. A. J. Krailsheimer, *The Continental Renaissance, 1500–1600* (1978), is one of the reliable Pelican Guides to European literature. Paul Oskar Kristeller's lecture series on the Renaissance is printed in *Renaissance Thought: The Classic, Scholastic, and Humanist Strains* (1961). A solid, well-written, general historical and cultural presentation is Eugene F. Rice Jr., *The Foundations of Early Modern Europe, 1460–1559* (1970), with illustrations, facsimiles, maps, and bibliographic references. Lewis W. Spitz gives a reliable historical presentation of the period, taking into account literary and artistic trends in *The Renaissance and Reformation Movements* (1971). Jean R. Brink and William F. Gentrup, eds., *Renaissance Culture in Context: Theory and Practice* (1993), is a recent collection of essays.

On English literature of the Renaissance, see C. S. Lewis, *English Literature in the Sixteenth Century Excluding Drama* (1954) and D. Bush, *English Literature in the Earlier Seventeenth Century 1600–1660* (1962). On Italian literature of the Renaissance, see the appropriate chapters in Eugenio Donadoni, *A History of Italian Literature* (1969), a standard, reliable work widely used as a textbook in Italian

schools, and Ernest Hatch Wilkins, *History of Italian Literature* (rev. ed., 1974), one of the best of the few histories of Italian literature written in English. Américo Castro, *An Idea of History: Selected Essays of Américo Castro* (1977), includes the chapter "The Problem of the Renaissance in Spain." On French literature of the Renaissance, see John Cruickshank, ed., *French Literature and Its Background* (1968), particularly vol. 1, *The Sixteenth Century*.

PRONOUNCING GLOSSARY

The following list uses common English syllables and stress accents to provide rough equivalents of selected words whose pronunciation may be unfamiliar to the general reader.

Canzoniere: *cant-son-ye'-ray*

Castiglione: *cas-teel-yoh'-nay*

Grandgousier: *gran-goo-zyeh'*

Montaigne: *mon-ten'*

Rabelais: *ra-blay'*

virtù: *veer-too'*

THE RENAISSANCE IN EUROPE

TEXTS	CONTEXTS
1335 Petrarch's poems to Laura, including *Sonnets,* underway (published 1360)	
	1338–1453 Hundred Years' War
	1348–1350 The Black Death: Petrarch's Laura dies in the plague
1349–1353 Boccaccio's *Decameron* in progress	
1387–1399 Chaucer's *The Canterbury Tales* in progress; he dies in 1400	
	1428 Joan of Arc liberates Orléans from the British; she is burned at the stake for heresy in 1431
	1453 Constantinople falls to the Turks, increasing dissemination of Greek culture in Western Europe
	1492 Columbus, in the service of Spain, lands in the Bahamas • Moorish kingdom of Granada falls to the Spanish • Jews expelled from Spain
	1495 da Vinci, *The Last Supper*
	1502 Michelangelo, *David*
1508–1516 Castiglione's *Book of the Courtier* in progress; published 1528	
1509 Erasmus's *The Praise of Folly*	
1513 Machiavelli's *The Prince* in progress; published 1532	
	1517 Martin Luther's Ninety-five Theses denouncing abuses of the Roman church
1532–1534 Rabelais's *Gargantua and Pantagruel* (parts 1 and 2) published • Martin Luther's translation of the Bible into German published	

TEXTS	CONTEXTS
1551 First English translation of More's *Utopia*; More had been executed for high treason by Henry VIII in 1535	
1558 Marguerite de Navarre's *Heptameron* published	**1558–1603** Reign of Elizabeth I of England
1571? Montaigne's *Essays* in progress; books I and II published 1580; complete publication 1588	**1571** Battle of Lepanto; European powers defeat Muslims
ca. 1586 Thomas Kyd's *Spanish Tragedy*, which published; first performance of *Hamlet* (published 1603)	
1597–1604 Cervantes's *Don Quixote* in progress; part 1 published in 1605, part 2 in 1615	
1601 Marlowe's *Dr. Faustus*	
1611 King James version of the Bible published	
	1620 Colony founded by Pilgrims at Plymouth (Massachusetts)
	1633 Galileo forced by the Inquisition to repudiate Copernican theory that Earth rotates around the sun
1633 Donne's *Songs and Sonnets* published	
1636 Calderón's *Life Is a Dream* published	
	1643–1715 Reign of Louis XIV of France, "the Sun King"
	1645–1649 England's Charles I surrenders to antimonarchical forces of Oliver Cromwell, is executed, and monarchy is abolished
1655(?) Milton's *Paradise Lost* in progress; published 1667	
	1660 Charles II restores the English monarchy

FRANCIS PETRARCH

1304–1374

Francesco Petrarca, forty years younger than Dante, was born in Arezzo on July 13, 1304. His father, like Dante, was exiled from Florence for political reasons and in 1312 moved with his family to Avignon with hopes of employment at the papal court, which had been transferred there in 1309 by a pope of French nationality—Clement V (Bertrand de Got). Following his father's wish, Petrarch studied law at Montpellier and Bologna for a brief period. A highly cultivated man of the world, he was well received, on his return to Avignon, by the brilliant and refined society that moved around the papal court. It was in Avignon, in the church of St. Clare, on April 6, 1327, that he saw for the first time Laura, who would become the object and image of his love poetry. Soon after this momentous event, he began to travel widely (in France, Flanders, and Germany), not only as a diplomat but also, and perhaps more relevantly, as a man of letters and humanist in search of manuscripts from classical antiquity.

In 1338 he made his first trip to Rome, a twofold spiritual capital for him as a classical scholar and as a Christian. Later that same year, at his home in Vaucluse near Avignon, Petrarch attempted to revive the ancient ideal of spiritually active relaxation, or *otium*. He was so imbued with the idea of a renovation of classical antiquity that he expected his major glory as a poet from the work he began at this time—*Africa*, an epic poem in Latin hexameters that has for its central figure Scipio Africanus, conceived by the poet as the model of the valiant and pious Roman hero. No less characteristic of his devotion to classical ideals is the fact that when in 1340 he received invitations from both Paris and Rome to be crowned poet laureate, he chose Rome, and received the crown in the capitol.

There was in his life, as in Dante's, a pattern of moral dissipation followed by spiritual conflict and repentance. This conflict, which is reflected in Petrarch's autobiographical treatise in Latin, *Secretum*, may have been enhanced by his brother Gherardo's decision to enter a monastery and by the news of Laura's death by plague, which he received in 1348 while traveling in Italy. She died on April 6, the very day of the month on which he had first seen her, and the day of Christ's passion as well. Thus Laura remained an image of exclusively spiritual love, in contrast to Petrarch's more earthly attachments, evidenced by the birth of two illegitimate children, Giovanni, in 1337, and Francesca, in 1343.

As a pilgrim on his way to Rome for the Papal Jubilee of 1350, Petrarch stopped at Florence as a guest of Boccaccio, the great Florentine storyteller and fellow humanist. Most of the years between 1353 and 1361 Petrarch spent in Milan, where he was entrusted by the ruling Visconti family with various diplomatic missions (to Venice, to Prague, to the king of France). He alternated such duties with intense literary work, including a complete edition of his lyric poetry in Italian, letters and treatises in Latin, and progress on his great unfinished *terza rima* allegory, *The Triumphs*. To avoid the plague, in 1361 he moved to Padua, spending much of his time in a nearby country house in the Euganean hills at Arquà, now called Arquà Petrarca. He died there in 1374, on the eve of his seventieth birthday, working until the very end on the refinement and ordering of his work and on the careful creation of what we would call today his "public image," polishing for posterity with exquisite care his poems and letters (the letter was then an established literary form). Even accidental events in his life seem to have been inspired by his taste for the harmonious and well-rounded gesture. He came within a few

hours of reaching the "perfect" life span, three score and ten, and frequently used April 6, as in sonnet 3, to symbolize his own drama of passion.

If we compare Petrarch with the standard image of the Medieval character, what first strikes us as new is the self-centered quality of his work. A comparison between him and Dante points to this quality, and the contrast is made sharper by certain analogies in their situations. Both illustrate the same basic motif, the quest for salvation. But while Dante as hero of the quest focused dramatically on himself only on a few enormously effective and severe occasions (his exchange with Brunetto in *Inferno* XV, for example), Petrarch was continuously at work on his personal drama, its lights and shades, its subtle modulations of feeling.

A different way of getting at the distinction between Renaissance and Medieval characters may be found in Petrarch's conception of the literary profession and the status of the poet. His attitude toward classical antiquity makes him "the first writer of the Renaissance," rather than a writer of the Middle Ages. As a self-aware man of letters he modeled his work on classical examples—the texts that, as a humanistic scholar, he had sometimes helped rediscover and bring back to life. In 1333 at Liège, for example, he found a manuscript of Cicero's oration *Pro Archia*, a Roman "defense of poetry," celebrating the role of artist and thinker as creators of value, legislators of virtuous behavior, and dispensers of fame: the program to which Petrarch was to devote his life. It would be difficult to overestimate his importance for European culture in establishing the model of the poet, scholar, and member of the "republic of letters" that remains today an ideal of Western civilization.

But however important this aspect of his work may have been, the prevailing Petrarchan image in literary history is the drama of his love for Laura, both in life and in death. Of course there would be no drama in that love without an element of the tragic—his sense of its sinfulness and vanity. Thus he sounds a "medieval" note, but in a new context: that of the ever-changing, ambiguous attractions of mortal beauty and earthly values. One even surmises that these values might have been less attractive to him had they not kept the taint of vanity, for without it they would have afforded a less rich and complex life. Thus he sings in sonnet 61 of his first encounter with Laura, the source of his torment. Even though calling him a Romantic may stretch the meaning of the term to the point of uselessness, we can say that his definition of love as sorrow has had a yet wider influence than those striking verbal inventions that inspired European poetry for a century and more before degenerating into "Petrarchism," the arsenal of conceits, witticisms, and hyperboles on which much popular twentieth-century songwriting still draws.

Another essential part of Petrarch's drama is the death of his lady and her role as mediator between the penitent poet and divine grace. Here again, the inevitable comparison with Dante makes the differences between the two poets stand clear. The shift in tone between Petrarch's poems for Laura "in life" and the ones for her "in death" is less relevant than the similarity of the two sections of the *Canzoniere* (Songbook). A sensuous quality pervades both groups of poems, suggesting an earthly relationship even when the beloved woman is dead. Thus, in sonnet 292, written after Laura's death, the larger part of the octave is devoted to the living woman's physical appearance. In other sonnets Laura herself, in heaven, refers to her mortal body as her "beautiful veil." In sonnet 333 the poet implores her to come to him at the moment of his death and guide him to "the blessèd place." His poetry has made the world know and love her, and the implication is that he has thus become worthy of her succor. Hence Petrarch is not only a repentant sinner but also a literary master turning autobiography and confession into art. However strong his sense of the vanity and fallaciousness of human attachments, he seems to have no doubt about the validity of one particular manifestation of *virtù*: the sensuous, expert handling of words, the poetic art itself.

A thorough account of Petrarch's life with many quotations from his writing may be found in Morris Bishop's *Petrarch and His World* (1963). Peter Hainsworth's *Petrarch the Poet: An Introduction to the Rerum Vulgarium Fragmenta* (1988) provides "critical and historical interpretation" of Petrarch's major work in Italian. Marjorie O'Rourke's *Petrarch's Genius: Pentimento and Prophecy* (1991) is an innovative study. Nicholas Mann's *Petrarch* (1984) is a clear, cogent analysis of Petrarch's life and works. Two other worthwhile biographical studies are J. H. Whitfield's *Petrarch and the Renaissance* (1966) and Ernest Hatch Wilkins's *Life of Petrarch* (1961).

Sonnets

3[1]

It was the morning of that blessèd day[2]
Whereon the Sun in pity veiled his glare
For the Lord's agony, that, unaware,
I fell a captive, Lady, to the sway

Of your swift eyes: that seemed no time to stay　　　　5
The strokes of Love: I stepped into the snare
Secure, with no suspicion: then, and there
I found my cue in man's most tragic play.

Love caught me naked to his shaft, his sheaf,
The entrance for his ambush and surprise　　　　10
Against the heart wide open through the eyes,[3]

The constant gate and fountain of my grief:
How craven so to strike me stricken so,[4]
Yet from you fully armed conceal his bow!

61[5]

Blest be the day, and blest the month and year,
Season and hour[6] and very moment blest,
The lovely land and place[7] where first possessed
By two pure eyes I found me prisoner;

And blest the first sweet pain, the first most dear,　　　　5
Which burnt my heart when Love came in as guest;
And blest the bow, the shafts which shook my breast,
And even the wounds which Love delivered there.

Blest be the words and voices which filled grove
And glen with echoes of my lady's name;　　　　10
The sighs, the tears, the fierce despair of love;

1. Translated by Joseph Auslander.　2. In sonnet 211 Petrarch gives the date as April 6, 1327, a Monday. Here too the day is apparently intended to be the day of Christ's death (April 6) rather than Good Friday, 1327.　3. The image of the eyes as the gateway to the heart had been a poetic commonplace since pre-Dante days.　4. With grief on commemorating the Passion of Christ.　5. Translated by Joseph Auslander.　6. "Upon the first hour" (sonnet 211), sunrise. *Season:* spring.　7. The church of Saint Clare at Avignon.

And blest the sonnet-sources of my fame;
And blest that thought of thoughts which is her own,
Of her, her only, of herself alone!

90[8]

She used to let her golden hair fly free
For the wind to toy and tangle and molest;
Her eyes were brighter than the radiant west.
(Seldom they shine so now.) I used to see

Pity look out of those deep eyes on me.   5
("It was false pity," you would now protest.)
I had love's tinder heaped within my breast;
What wonder that the flame burned furiously?

She did not walk in any mortal way,
But with angelic progress; when she spoke,   10
Unearthly voices sang in unison.

She seemed divine among the dreary folk
Of earth. You say she is not so today?
Well, though the bow's unbent, the wound bleeds on.

292[9]

The eyes that drew from me such fervent praise,
The arms and hands and feet and countenance
Which made me a stranger in my own romance
And set me apart from the well-trodden ways;

The gleaming golden curly hair, the rays   5
Flashing from a smiling angel's glance
Which moved the world in paradisal dance,
Are grains of dust, insensibilities.

And I live on, but in grief and self-contempt,
Left here without the light I loved so much,   10
In a great tempest and with shrouds unkempt.

No more love songs, then, I have done with such;
My old skill now runs thin at each attempt,
And tears are heard within the harp I touch.[1]

333[2]

Go, grieving rimes of mine, to that hard stone
Whereunder lies my darling, lies my dear,
And cry to her to speak from heaven's sphere.
Her mortal part with grass is overgrown.

---

8. Translated by Morris Bishop.   **9.** Translated by Edwin Morgan. All the poems in the canon from number 267 on were written to commemorate Laura. She died in Avignon on April 6, 1348.   **1.** Compare Job 30:31: "My harp also is turned to mourning, and my organ into the voice of them that weep."
2. Translated by Morris Bishop.

Tell her, I'm sick of living; that I'm blown   5
By winds of grief from the course I ought to steer,
That praise of her is all my purpose here
And all my business; that of her alone

Do I go telling, that how she lived and died
And lives again in immortality,   10
All men may know, and love my Laura's grace.

Oh, may she deign to stand at my bedside
When I come to die; and may she call to me
And draw me to her in the blessèd place!

NICCOLÒ MACHIAVELLI
1469–1527

The most famous and controversial political writer and theorist of his time—indeed, possibly of all time—Niccolò Machiavelli was born in Florence on May 3, 1469. Little is known of his schooling, but it is obvious from his works that he knew the Latin and Italian writers well. He entered public life in 1494 as a clerk and from 1498 to 1512 was secretary to the second chancery of the commune of Florence, whose magistrates were in charge of internal and war affairs. During the conflict between Florence and Pisa, he dealt with military problems firsthand. Thus he had a direct experience of war as well as of diplomacy; he was entrusted with many missions—among others, to King Louis XII of France in 1500 and in 1502 to Cesare Borgia, duke of Valentinois or "il duca Valentino," the favorite son of Pope Alexander VI. Machiavelli described the duke's ruthless methods in crushing a conspiracy during his conquest of the Romagna region in a terse booklet *Of the Method Followed by Duke Valentino in Killing Vitellozzo Vitelli*, which already shows direct insight into the type of the amoral and technically efficient "prince." In 1506 Machiavelli went on a mission to Pope Julius II, whose expedition into Romagna (an old name for north-central Italy) he followed closely. From this and other missions—to Emperor Maximilian (1508) and again to the king of France (1509)—Machiavelli drew his two books of observations or *Portraits* of the affairs of those territories, written in 1508 and 1510.

Preeminently a student of politics and an acute observer of historical events, Machiavelli endeavored to apply his experience of other states to the strengthening of his own, the Florentine republic, and busied himself in 1507 with the establishment of a Florentine militia, encountering great difficulties. When the republican regime came to an end, he lost his post and was exiled from the city proper, though forbidden to leave Florentine territory. The new regime of the Medici accused him unjustly of conspiracy, and he was released only after a period of imprisonment and torture. To the period of his exile (spent near San Casciano, a few miles from Florence, where he retired with his wife, Marietta Corsini, and his five children), we owe his major works: the *Discourses on the First Ten Books of Livy* (1513–21) and *The Prince*, written in 1513 with the hope of obtaining public office from the Medici. In 1520 Machiavelli was commissioned to write a history of Florence, which he presented in 1525 to Pope Clement VII (Giulio de' Medici). The following year, conscious of imminent dangers, he took part in the work to improve the military fortifications of Florence. The fate of the city at this point depended on the outcome of the larger struggle between Francis I of France and

the Holy Roman emperor, Charles V. Pope Clement's siding with the king of France led to the disastrous "Sack of Rome" by Charles V in 1527, and the result for Florence was the collapse of Medici domination. Machiavelli's hopes, briefly raised by the reestablishment of the republic, came to naught, because he was now regarded as a Medici sympathizer. This last disappointment may have accelerated his end. He died on June 22, 1527, and was buried in the church of Santa Croce.

Though Machiavelli has a place in literary history for a short novel and two plays, one of which, *La mandragola* (The mandrake), first performed in the early 1520s, belongs in the upper rank of Italian comedies of intrigue, his world reputation is based on *The Prince*. This "handbook" on how to obtain and keep political power consists of twenty-six chapters. The first eleven deal with different types of dominions and the ways in which they are acquired and preserved — the early title of the whole book, in Latin, was *De principatibus* (Of Princedoms) — and the twelfth to fourteenth chapters focus particularly on problems of military power. The book's astounding fame, however, is based on the final part (from chapter fifteen to the end), which deals primarily with the attributes and "virtues" of the prince himself. In other words, despite its reputation for cool, precise realism, the work presents a hypothetical type, the idealized portrait of a certain kind of person.

Manuals of this sort may be classified, in one sense, as pedagogical literature. Because of their merits of form and of vivid, if stylized, characterization they can be considered works of art, but their overt purpose is to codify a certain set of manners and rules of conduct; the authors, therefore, present themselves as especially wise, experts in the field, "minds" offering advice to the executive "arm." Machiavelli is a clear example of this approach. His fervor, the dramatic, oratorical way he confronts his reader, the wealth and pertinence of his illustrations are all essential qualities of his pedagogical *persona*: "Either you are already a prince, or you are on the way to become one. In the first case liberality is dangerous; in the second it is very necessary to be thought liberal. Caesar was one of those. . . . Somebody may answer . . . I answer." Relying on his direct knowledge of politics, he uses examples he can personally vouch for:

> Men are so simple and so subject to present needs that he who deceives in this way will always find those who will let themselves be deceived.
> I do not wish to keep still about one of the recent instances. Alexander VI did nothing else than deceive men, and had no other intention.

The implied tone of *I know, I have seen such things myself* adds a special immediacy to Machiavelli's prose. His view of the practical world may have been an especially startling one, but the sensation caused by his work would have been far less without the rhetorical power, the drama of argumentation, that makes *The Prince* a unique example of "the art of persuasion."

The view of humanity in Machiavelli is not at all cheerful. Indeed, the pessimistic notion that humanity is evil is not so much Machiavelli's conclusion about human nature as his premise; it is the point of departure of all subsequent reasoning on the course for a ruler to follow. The very fact of its being given as a premise, however, tends to qualify it; it is not a firm philosophical judgment, but a stratagem, dictated by the facts as they are seen by a lucid observer of the here and now. The author is committed to his view of the human being not as a philosopher or as a religious man but as a practical politician. He indicates the rules of the game as his experience shows it must, under the circumstances, be played.

> A prudent ruler . . . cannot and should not observe faith when such observance is to his disadvantage and the causes that made him give his promise

have vanished. If men were all good, this advice would not be good, but since men are wicked and do not keep their promises to you, you likewise do not have to keep yours to them.

A basic question in the study of Machiavelli, therefore, is "How much of a realist is he?" His picture of the perfectly efficient ruler has something of the quality of an abstraction; it shows, though much less clearly than Castiglione's portrayal of the courtier, the well-known Renaissance tendency toward "perfected" form. Machiavelli's abandonment of complex actualities in favor of an ideal vision is shown most clearly at the conclusion of the book, particularly in the last chapter. This is where he offers what amounts to the greatest of his illustrations as the prince's preceptor and counselor: the ideal ruler, now technically equipped by his pedagogue, is to undertake a mission—the liberation of Machiavelli's Italy. If we regard the last chapter of *The Prince* as a culmination of Machiavelli's discussion rather than as a dissonant addition to it, we are likely to feel at that point not only that Machiavelli's realistic method is ultimately directed toward an ideal task but also that his conception of that task, far from being based on immediate realities, is founded on cultural and poetic myths. Machiavelli's method here becomes imaginative rather than scientific. His exhortation to liberate Italy, and his final prophecy, belong to the tradition of poetic visions in which a present state of decay is lamented, and a hope of future redemption is expressed (as in Dante's *Purgatory*, Canto VI). And a very significant part of this hope is presented not in terms of technical political considerations (choice of the opportune moment, evaluation of military power) but in terms of a poetic justice for which precedents are sought in religious and ancient history and in mythology:

> . . . if it was necessary to make clear the ability of Moses that the people of Israel should be enslaved in Egypt, and to reveal Cyrus's greatness of mind that the Persians should be oppressed by the Medes, and to demonstrate the excellence of Theseus that the Athenians should be scattered, so at the present time. . . . Everything is now fully disposed for the work . . . if only your House adopts the methods of those I have set forth as examples. Moreover, we have before our eyes extraordinary and unexampled means prepared by God. The sea has been divided. . . . Manna has fallen.

Machiavelli's Italy, as he observed in chapter 25, is now a country "without dykes and without any wall of defence." It has suffered from "deluges," and its present rule, a "barbarian" one, "stinks in every nostril." Something is rotten in it, in short, as in Hamlet's Denmark. And we become more and more detached even from the particular example, Italy, as we recognize in the situation a pattern frequently exemplified in tragedy: the desire for communal regeneration, for the cleansing of the city-state, the *polis*. Of this cleansing, Italy on the one side and the imaginary prince on the other may be taken as symbols. The envisaged redemption is identified with antiquity and Roman virtue, while the realism of the political observer is here drowned out by the cry of the humanist dreaming of ancient glories.

Peter E. Bondanella focuses on the literary aspects of Machiavelli's works in *Machiavelli and the Art of Renaissance History* (1973). Sebastian De Grazia, *Machiavelli in Hell* (1989), on politics in *The Prince*, contains indexes and a bibliography. J. R. Hale's biography, *Machiavelli and Renaissance Italy* (1972), places Machiavelli in a historical perspective. A political analysis is provided by Anthony Parel in *The Political Calculus. Essays on Machiavelli's Political Philosophy* (1972). Roberto Ridolfi, *The Life of Niccolò Machiavelli* (1963), is still considered the best and most accurate biography. Silvia Ruffo-Fiore, *Niccolò Machiavelli* (1982), is a useful comprehensive guide for the beginning student.

PRONOUNCING GLOSSARY

The following list uses common English syllables and stress accents to provide rough equivalents of selected words whose pronunciation may be unfamiliar to the general reader.

Borgia: *bor'-juh*   Pistoia: *pees-toh'-yah*

Chiron: *kai'-ron*   San Casciano: *san ka-shah'-noh*

de' Medici: *day may'-dee-chee*   Santa Croce: *san'-tuh croh'-chay*

Machiavelli: *ma-kee-ah-vel'-lee*

From The Prince[1]

[*Princely Virtues*]

FROM CHAPTER 15

On the Things for Which Men, and Especially Princes, Are Praised or Censured

* * * Because I know that many have written on this topic, I fear that when I too write I shall be thought presumptuous, because, in discussing it, I break away completely from the principles laid down by my predecessors. But since it is my purpose to write something useful to an attentive reader, I think it more effective to go back to the practical truth of the subject than to depend on my fancies about it. And many have imagined republics and principalities that never have been seen or known to exist in reality. For there is such a difference between the way men live and the way they ought to live, that anybody who abandons what is for what ought to be will learn something that will ruin rather than preserve him, because anyone who determines to act in all circumstances the part of a good man must come to ruin among so many who are not good. Hence, if a prince wishes to maintain himself, he must learn how to be not good, and to use that ability or not as is required.

Leaving out of account, then, things about an imaginary prince, and considering things that are true, I say that all men, when they are spoken of, and especially princes, because they are set higher, are marked with some of the qualities that bring them either blame or praise. To wit, one man is thought liberal, another stingy (using a Tuscan word, because *avaricious* in our language is still applied to one who desires to get things through violence, but *stingy* we apply to him who refrains too much from using his own property); one is thought open-handed, another grasping; one cruel, the other compassionate; one is a breaker of faith, the other reliable; one is effeminate and cowardly, the other vigorous and spirited; one is philanthropic, the other egotistic; one is lascivious, the other chaste; one is straight-forward, the other crafty; one hard, the other easy to deal with; one is firm, the other unsettled; one is religious, the other unbelieving; and so on.

And I know that everybody will admit that it would be very praiseworthy for a prince to possess all of the above-mentioned qualities that are consid-

1. Translated by Allan H. Gilbert.

ered good. But since he is not able to have them or to observe them completely, because human conditions do not allow him to, it is necessary that he be prudent enough to understand how to avoid getting a bad name because he is given to those vices that will deprive him of his position. He should also, if he can, guard himself from those vices that will not take his place away from him, but if he cannot do it, he can with less anxiety let them go. Moreover, he should not be troubled if he gets a bad name because of vices without which it will be difficult for him to preserve his position. I say this because, if everything is considered, it will be seen that some things seem to be virtuous, but if they are put into practice will be ruinous to him; other things seem to be vices, yet if put into practice will bring the prince security and well-being.

FROM CHAPTER 16

On Liberality and Parsimony

Beginning, then, with the first of the above-mentioned qualities, I assert that it is good to be thought liberal.[2] Yet liberality, practiced in such a way that you get a reputation for it, is damaging to you, for the following reasons: If you use it wisely and as it ought to be used, it will not become known, and you will not escape being censured for the opposite vice. Hence, if you wish to have men call you liberal, it is necessary not to omit any sort of lavishness. A prince who does this will always be obliged to use up all his property in lavish actions; he will then, if he wishes to keep the name of liberal, be forced to lay heavy taxes on his people and exact money from them, and do everything he can to raise money. This will begin to make his subjects hate him, and as he grows poor he will be little esteemed by anybody. So it comes about that because of this liberality of his, with which he has damaged a large number and been of advantage to but a few, he is affected by every petty annoyance and is in peril from every slight danger. If he recognizes this and wishes to draw back, he quickly gets a bad name for stinginess.

Since, then, a prince cannot without harming himself practice this virtue of liberality to such an extent that it will be recognized, he will, if he is prudent, not care about being called stingy. As time goes on he will be thought more and more liberal, for the people will see that because of his economy his income is enough for him, that he can defend himself from those who make war against him, and that he can enter upon undertakings without burdening his people. Such a prince is in the end liberal to all those from whom he takes nothing, and they are numerous; he is stingy to those to whom he does not give, and they are few. In our times we have seen big things done only by those who have been looked on as stingy; the others have utterly failed. Pope Julius II,[3] though he made use of a reputation for liberality to attain the papacy, did not then try to maintain it, because he wished to be able to make war. The present King of France[4] has carried on great wars without laying unusually heavy taxes on his peo-

2. Generous, openhanded.   3. Giuliano della Róvere (1443–1513), elected to the papacy in 1503 at the death of Pius III, who had been successor to Alexander VI (Rodrigo Borgia). Alexander VI is discussed in chap. 18. Julius II's character is discussed in chap. 25.   4. Louis XII (1462–1515).

ple, merely because his long economy has made provision for heavy expenditures. The present King of Spain,[5] if he had continued liberal, would not have carried on or completed so many undertakings.

Therefore a prince ought to care little about getting called stingy, if as a result he does not have to rob his subjects, is able to defend himself, does not become poor and contemptible, and is not obliged to become grasping. For this vice of stinginess is one of those that enables him to rule. Somebody may say: Caesar, by means of his liberality became emperor, and many others have come to high positions because they have been liberal and have been thought so. I answer: Either you are already prince, or you are on the way to become one. In the first case liberality is dangerous; in the second it is very necessary to be thought liberal. Caesar was one of those who wished to attain dominion over Rome. But if, when he had attained it, he had lived for a long time and had not moderated his expenses, he would have destroyed his authority. Somebody may answer: Many who have been thought very liberal have been princes and done great things with their armies. I answer: The prince spends either his own property and that of his subjects or that of others. In the first case he ought to be frugal; in the second he ought to abstain from no sort of liberality. When he marches with his army and lives on plunder, loot, and ransom, a prince controls the property of others. To him liberality is essential, for without it his soldiers would not follow him. You can be a free giver of what does not belong to you or your subjects, as were Cyrus, Caesar, and Alexander, because to spend the money of others does not decrease your reputation but adds to it. It is only the spending of your own money that hurts you.

There is nothing that eats itself up as fast as does liberality, for when you practice it you lose the power to practice it, and become poor and contemptible, or else to escape poverty you become rapacious and therefore are hated. And of all the things against which a prince must guard himself, the first is being an object of contempt and hatred. Liberality leads you to both of these. Hence there is more wisdom in keeping a name for stinginess, which produces a bad reputation without hatred, than in striving for the name of liberal, only to be forced to get the name of rapacious, which brings forth both bad reputation and hatred.

FROM CHAPTER 17

On Cruelty and Pity, and Whether It Is Better to Be Loved or to Be Feared, and Vice Versa

Coming then to the other qualities already mentioned, I say that every prince should wish to be thought compassionate and not cruel; still, he should be careful not to make a bad use of the pity he feels. Cesare Borgia[6] was considered cruel, yet this cruelty of his pacified the Romagna, united it, and changed its condition to that of peace and loyalty. If the matter is well considered, it will be seen that Cesare was much more compassionate

---

5. Ferdinand II, "the Catholic" (1452–1516).   6. Son of Pope Alexander VI and duke of Valentinois and Romagna. His skillful and merciless subjugation of the local lords of Romagna occurred between 1499 and 1502.

than the people of Florence, for in order to escape the name of cruel they allowed Pistoia to be destroyed.[7] Hence a prince ought not to be troubled by the stigma of cruelty, acquired in keeping his subjects united and faithful. By giving a very few examples of cruelty he can be more truly compassionate than those who through too much compassion allow disturbances to continue, from which arise murders or acts of plunder. Lawless acts are injurious to a large group, but the executions ordered by the prince injure a single person. The new prince, above all other princes, cannot possibly avoid the name of cruel, because new states are full of perils. Dido in Vergil puts it thus: "Hard circumstances and the newness of my realm force me to do such things, and to keep watch and ward over all my lands."[8]

All the same, he should be slow in believing and acting, and should make no one afraid of him; his procedure should be so tempered with prudence and humanity that too much confidence does not make him incautious, and too much suspicion does not make him unbearable.

All this gives rise to a question for debate: Is it better to be loved than to be feared, or the reverse? I answer that a prince should wish for both. But because it is difficult to reconcile them, I hold that it is much more secure to be feared than to be loved, if one of them must be given up. The reason for my answer is that one must say of men generally that they are ungrateful, mutable, pretenders and dissemblers, prone to avoid danger, thirsty for gain. So long as you benefit them they are all yours; as I said above, they offer you their blood, their property, their lives, their children, when the need for such things is remote. But when need comes upon you, they turn around. So if a prince has relied wholly on their words, and is lacking in other preparations, he falls. For friendships that are gained with money, and not with greatness and nobility of spirit, are deserved but not possessed, and in the nick of time one cannot avail himself of them. Men hesitate less to injure a man who makes himself loved than to injure one who makes himself feared, for their love is held by a chain of obligation, which, because of men's wickedness, is broken on every occasion for the sake of selfish profit; but their fear is secured by a dread of punishment which never fails you.

Nevertheless the prince should make himself feared in such a way that, if he does not win love, he escapes hatred. This is possible, for to be feared and not to be hated can easily coexist. In fact it is always possible, if the ruler abstains from the property of his citizens and subjects, and from their women. And if, as sometimes happens, he finds that he must inflict the penalty of death, he should do it when he has proper justification and evident reason. But above all he must refrain from taking property, for men forget the death of a father more quickly than the loss of their patrimony. Further, causes for taking property are never lacking, and he who begins to live on plunder is always finding cause to seize what belongs to others. But on the contrary, reasons for taking life are rare and fail sooner.

But when a prince is with his army and has a great number of soldiers

7. By internal dissensions, because the Florentines, Machiavelli contends, failed to treat the leaders of the dissenting parties with an iron hand.   8. *Aeneid* I.563–64.

under his command, then above all he must pay no heed to being called cruel, because if he does not have that name he cannot keep his army united or ready for duty. It should be numbered among the wonderful feats of Hannibal that he led to war in foreign lands a large army, made up of countless types of men, yet never suffered from dissension, either among the soldiers or against the general, in either bad or good fortune. His success resulted from nothing else than his inhuman cruelty, which, when added to his numerous other strong qualities, made him respected and terrible in the sight of his soldiers. Yet without his cruelty his other qualities would not have been adequate. So it seems that those writers have not thought very deeply who on one side admire his accomplishment and on the other condemn the chief cause for it.

The truth that his other qualities alone would not have been adequate may be learned from Scipio,[9] a man of the most unusual powers not only in his own times but in all ages we know of. When he was in Spain his armies mutinied. This resulted from nothing other than his compassion, which had allowed his soldiers more license than befits military discipline. This fault was censured before the Senate by Fabius Maximus, and Scipio was called by him the corrupter of the Roman soldiery. The Locrians[1] were destroyed by a lieutenant of Scipio's, yet he did not avenge them or punish the disobedience of that lieutenant. This all came from his easy nature, which was so well understood that one who wished to excuse him in the Senate said there were many men who knew better how not to err than how to punish errors. This easy nature would in time have overthrown the fame and glory of Scipio if, in spite of this weakness, he had kept on in independent command. But since he was under the orders of the Senate, this bad quality was not merely concealed but was a glory to him.

Returning, then, to the debate on being loved and feared, I conclude that since men love as they please and fear as the prince pleases, a wise prince will evidently rely on what is in his own power and not on what is in the power of another. As I have said, he need only take pains to avoid hatred.

FROM CHAPTER 18

In What Way Faith Should Be Kept by Princes

Everybody knows how laudable it is in a prince to keep his faith and to be an honest man and not a trickster. Nevertheless, the experience of our times shows that the princes who have done great things are the ones who have taken little account of their promises and who have known how to addle the brains of men with craft. In the end they have conquered those who have put their reliance on good faith.

You must realize, then, that there are two ways to fight. In one kind the laws are used, in the other, force. The first is suitable to man, the second to animals. But because the first often falls short, one has to turn to the

9. Publius Cornelius Scipio Africanus the Elder (235–183 B.C.). The episode of the mutiny occurred in 206 B.C.   1. Citizens of Locri, in Sicily.

second. Hence a prince must know perfectly how to act like a beast and like a man. This truth was covertly taught to princes by ancient authors, who write that Achilles and many other ancient princes[2] were turned over for their up-bringing to Chiron the centaur, that he might keep them under his tuition. To have as teacher one who is half beast and half man means nothing else than that a prince needs to know how to use the qualities of both creatures. The one without the other will not last long.

Since, then, it is necessary for a prince to understand how to make good use of the conduct of the animals, he should select among them the fox and the lion, because the lion cannot protect himself from traps, and the fox cannot protect himself from the wolves. So the prince needs to be a fox that he may know how to deal with traps, and a lion that he may frighten the wolves. Those who act like the lion alone do not understand their business. A prudent ruler, therefore, cannot and should not observe faith when such observance is to his disadvantage and the causes that made him give his promise have vanished. If men were all good, this advice would not be good, but since men are wicked and do not keep their promises to you, you likewise do not have to keep yours to them. Lawful reasons to excuse his failure to keep them will never be lacking to a prince. It would be possible to give innumerable modern examples of this and to show many treaties and promises that have been made null and void by the faithlessness of princes. And the prince who has best known how to act as a fox has come out best. But one who has this capacity must understand how to keep it covered, and be a skilful pretender and dissembler. Men are so simple and so subject to present needs that he who deceives in this way will always find those who will let themselves be deceived.

I do not wish to keep still about one of the recent instances. Alexander VI[3] did nothing else than deceive men, and had no other intention; yet he always found a subject to work on. There never was a man more effective in swearing that things were true, and the greater the oaths with which he made a promise, the less he observed it. Nonetheless his deceptions always succeeded to his wish, because he thoroughly understood this aspect of the world.

It is not necessary, then, for a prince really to have all the virtues mentioned above, but it is very necessary to seem to have them. I will even venture to say that they damage a prince who possesses them and always observes them, but if he seems to have them they are useful. I mean that he should seem compassionate, trustworthy, humane, honest, and religious, and actually be so; but yet he should have his mind so trained that, when it is necessary not to practice these virtues, he can change to the opposite, and do it skilfully. It is to be understood that a prince, especially a new prince, cannot observe all the things because of which men are considered good, because he is often obliged, if he wishes to maintain his government, to act contrary to faith, contrary to charity, contrary to humanity, contrary to religion. It is therefore necessary that he have a

2. For example, Theseus, Jason, and Hercules.   3. Pope from 1492 to 1503; father of Cesare Borgia.

mind capable of turning in whatever direction the winds of Fortune and the variations of affairs require, and, as I said above, that he should not depart from what is morally right, if he can observe it, but should know how to adopt what is bad, when he is obliged to.

A prince, then, should be very careful that there does not issue from his mouth anything that is not full of the above-mentioned five qualities. To those who see and hear him he should seem all compassion, all faith, all honesty, all humanity, all religion. There is nothing more necessary to make a show of possessing than this last quality. For men in general judge more by their eyes than by their hands; everybody is fitted to see, few to understand. Everybody sees what you appear to be; few make out what you really are. And these few do not dare to oppose the opinion of the many, who have the majesty of the state to confirm their view. In the actions of all men, and especially those of princes, where there is no court to which to appeal, people think of the outcome. A prince needs only to conquer and to maintain his position. The means he has used will always be judged honorable and will be praised by everybody, because the crowd is always caught by appearance and by the outcome of events, and the crowd is all there is in the world; there is no place for the few when the many have room enough. A certain prince[4] of the present day, whom it is not good to name, preaches nothing else than peace and faith, and is wholly opposed to both of them, and both of them, if he had observed them, would many times have taken from him either his reputation or his throne.

["*Fortune Is a Woman*"]

FROM CHAPTER 25

The Power of Fortune in Human Affairs, and to What Extent She Should Be Relied On

It is not unknown to me that many have been and still are of the opinion that the affairs of this world are so under the direction of Fortune and of God that man's prudence cannot control them; in fact, that man has no resource against them. For this reason many think there is no use in sweating much over such matters, but that one might as well let Chance take control. This opinion has been the more accepted in our times, because of the great changes in the state of the world that have been and now are seen every day, beyond all human surmise. And I myself, when thinking on these things, have now and then in some measure inclined to their view. Nevertheless, because the freedom of the will should not be wholly annulled, I think it may be true that Fortune is arbiter of half of our actions, but that she still leaves the control of the other half, or about that, to us.

I liken her to one of those raging streams that, when they go mad, flood the plains, ruin the trees and the buildings, and take away the fields from

---

4. Ferdinand II. In refraining from mentioning him, Machiavelli apparently had in mind the good relations existing between Spain and the house of Medici.

one bank and put them down on the other. Everybody flees before them; everybody yields to their onrush without being able to resist anywhere. And though this is their nature, it does not cease to be true that, in calm weather, men can make some provisions against them with walls and dykes, so that, when the streams swell, their waters will go off through a canal, or their currents will not be so wild and do so much damage. The same is true of Fortune. She shows her power where there is no wise preparation for resisting her, and turns her fury where she knows that no walls and dykes have been made to hold her in. And if you consider Italy— the place where these variations occur and the cause that has set them in motion—you will see that she is a country without dykes and without any wall of defence. If, like Germany, Spain, and France, she had had a sufficient bulwark of military vigor, this flood would not have made the great changes it has, or would not have come at all.

And this, I think, is all I need to say on opposing oneself to Fortune, in general. But limiting myself more to particulars, I say that a prince may be seen prospering today and falling in ruin tomorrow, though it does not appear that he has changed in his nature or any of his qualities. I believe this comes, in the first place, from the causes that have been discussed at length in preceding chapters. That is, if a prince bases himself entirely on Fortune, he will fall when she varies. I also believe that a ruler will be successful who adapts his mode of procedure to the quality of the times, and likewise that he will be unsuccessful if the times are out of accord with his procedure. Because it may be seen that in things leading to the end each has before him, namely glory and riches, men proceed differently. One acts with caution, another rashly; one with violence, another with skill; one with patience, another with its opposite; yet with these different methods each one attains his end. Still further, two cautious men will be seen, of whom one comes to his goal, the other does not. Likewise you will see two who succeed with two different methods, one of them being cautious and the other rash. These results are caused by nothing else than the nature of the times, which is or is not in harmony with the procedure of men. It also accounts for what I have mentioned, namely, that two persons, working differently, chance to arrive at the same result; and that of two who work in the same way, one attains his end, but the other does not.

On the nature of the times also depends the variability of the best method. If a man conducts himself with caution and patience, times and affairs may come around in such a way that his procedure is good, and he goes on successfully. But if times and circumstances change, he is ruined, because he does not change his method of action. There is no man so prudent as to understand how to fit himself to this condition, either because he is unable to deviate from the course to which nature inclines him, or because, having always prospered by walking in one path, he cannot persuade himself to leave it. So the cautious man, when the time comes to go at a reckless pace, does not know how to do it. Hence he comes to ruin. Yet if he could change his nature with the times and with circumstances, his fortune would not be altered.

Pope Julius II proceeded rashly in all his actions, and found the times

and circumstances so harmonious with his mode of procedure that he was always so lucky as to succeed. Consider the first enterprise he engaged in, that of Bologna, while messer Giovanni Bentivogli[5] was still alive. The Venetians were not pleased with it; the King of Spain felt the same way; the Pope was debating such an enterprise with the King of France. Nevertheless, in his courage and rashness Julius personally undertook that expedition. This movement made the King of Spain and the Venetians stand irresolute and motionless, the latter for fear, and the King because of his wish to recover the entire kingdom of Naples. On the other side, the King of France was dragged behind Julius, because the King, seeing that the Pope had moved and wishing to make him a friend in order to put down the Venetians, judged he could not refuse him soldiers without doing him open injury. Julius, then, with his rash movement, attained what no other pontiff, with the utmost human prudence, would have attained. If he had waited to leave Rome until the agreements were fixed and everything arranged, as any other pontiff would have done, he would never have succeeded, for the King of France would have had a thousand excuses, and the others would have raised a thousand fears. I wish to omit his other acts, which are all of the same sort, and all succeeded perfectly. The brevity of his life did not allow him to know anything different. Yet if times had come in which it was necessary to act with caution, they would have ruined him, for he would never have deviated from the methods to which nature inclined him.

I conclude, then, that since Fortune is variable and men are set in their ways, they are successful when they are in harmony with Fortune and unsuccessful when they disagree with her. Yet I am of the opinion that it is better to be rash than over-cautious, because Fortune is a woman and, if you wish to keep her down, you must beat her and pound her. It is evident that she allows herself to be overcome by men who treat her in that way rather than by those who proceed coldly. For that reason, like a woman, she is always the friend of young men, because they are less cautious, and more courageous, and command her with more boldness.

[The Roman Dream]

FROM CHAPTER 26

An Exhortation to Take Hold of Italy and Restore Her to Liberty from the Barbarians

Having considered all the things discussed above, I have been turning over in my own mind whether at present in Italy the time is ripe for a new prince to win prestige, and whether conditions there give a wise and vigorous ruler occasion to introduce methods that will do him honor, and bring good to the mass of the people of the land. It appears to me that so many things unite for the advantage of a new prince, that I do not know of any time that has ever been more suited for this. And, as I said, if it was neces-

---

5. Of the ruling family Bentivogli. The pope undertook to dislodge him from Bologna in 1506. *Messer:* My lord.

sary to make clear the ability of Moses that the people of Israel should be enslaved in Egypt, and to reveal Cyrus's greatness of mind that the Persians should be oppressed by the Medes, and to demonstrate the excellence of Theseus that the Athenians should be scattered, so at the present time, in order to make known the greatness of an Italian soul, Italy had to be brought down to her present position, to be more a slave than the Hebrews, more a servant than the Persians, more scattered than the Athenians; without head, without government; defeated, plundered, torn asunder, overrun; subject to every sort of disaster.

And though before this, certain persons[6] have showed signs from which it could be inferred that they were chosen by God for the redemption of Italy, nevertheless it has afterwards been seen that in the full current of action they have been cast off by Fortune. So Italy remains without life and awaits the man, whoever he may be, who is to heal her wounds, put an end to the plundering of Lombardy and the tribute laid on Tuscany and the kingdom of Naples, and cure her of those sores that have long been suppurating. She may be seen praying God to send some one to redeem her from these cruel and barbarous insults. She is evidently ready and willing to follow a banner, if only some one will raise it. Nor is there at present anyone to be seen in whom she can put more hope than in your illustrious House, because its fortune and vigor, and the favor of God and of the Church, which it now governs,[7] enable it to be the leader in such a redemption. This will not be very difficult, as you will see if you will bring to mind the actions and lives of those I have named above. And though these men were striking exceptions, yet they were men, and each of them had less opportunity than the present gives; their enterprises were not more just than this, nor easier, nor was God their friend more than he is yours. Here justice is complete. "A way is just to those to whom it is necessary, and arms are holy to him who has no hope save in arms."[8] Everything is now fully disposed for the work, and when that is true an undertaking cannot be difficult, if only your House adopts the methods of those I have set forth as examples. Moreover, we have before our eyes extraordinary and unexampled means prepared by God. The sea has been divided. A cloud has guided you on your way. The rock has given forth water. Manna has fallen.[9] Everything has united to make you great. The rest is for you to do. God does not intend to do everything, lest he deprive us of our free will and the share of glory that belongs to us.

It is no wonder if no one of the above-named Italians[1] has been able to do what we hope your illustrious House can. Nor is it strange if in the many revolutions and military enterprises of Italy, the martial vigor of the land always appears to be exhausted. This is because the old military customs were not good, and there has been nobody able to find new ones. Yet nothing brings so much honor to a man who rises to new power, as the new laws and new methods he discovers. These things, when they are

6. Possibly Cesare Borgia and Francesco Sforza, who were discussed earlier in the book.   7. Pope Leo X (1475–1521) was a Medici (Giovanni de' Medici). *House:* of Medici. *The Prince* was first meant for Giuliano de' Medici. After Giuliano's death it was dedicated to his nephew Lorenzo, later duke of Urbino.   8. Livy's *History* IX.1, para. 10.   9. Another allusion to Moses.   1. Perhaps another reference to Borgia and Sforza.

well founded and have greatness in them, make him revered and worthy of admiration. And in Italy matter is not lacking on which to impress forms of every sort. There is great vigor in the limbs if only it is not lacking in the heads. You may see that in duels and combats between small numbers, the Italians have been much superior in force, skill, and intelligence. But when it is a matter of armies, Italians cannot be compared with foreigners. All this comes from the weakness of the heads, because those who know are not obeyed, and each man thinks he knows. Nor up to this time has there been a man able to raise himself so high, through both ability and fortune, that the others would yield to him. The result is that for the past twenty years, in all the wars that have been fought when there has been an army entirely Italian, it has always made a bad showing. Proof of this was given first at the Taro, and then at Alessandria, Capua, Genoa, Vailà, Bologna, and Mestri.[2]

If your illustrious House, then, wishes to imitate those excellent men who redeemed their countries, it is necessary, before everything else, to furnish yourself with your own army, as the true foundation of every enterprise. You cannot have more faithful, nor truer, nor better soldiers. And though every individual of these may be good, they become better as a body when they see that they are commanded by their prince, and honored and trusted by him. It is necessary, therefore, that your House should be prepared with such forces, in order that it may be able to defend itself against the foreigners with Italian courage.

And though the Swiss and the Spanish infantry are properly estimated as terribly effective, yet both have defects. Hence a third type would be able not merely to oppose them but to feel sure of overcoming them. The fact is that the Spaniards are not able to resist cavalry, and the Swiss have reason to fear infantry, when they meet any as determined in battle as themselves. For this reason it has been seen and will be seen in experience that the Spaniards are unable to resist the French cavalry, and the Swiss are overthrown by Spanish infantry. And though of this last a clear instance has not been observed, yet an approach to it appeared in the battle of Ravenna,[3] when the Spanish infantry met the German battalions, who use the same methods as the Swiss. There the Spanish, through their ability and the assistance given by their shields, got within the points of the spears from below, and slew their enemies in security, while the Germans could find no means of resistance. If the cavalry had not charged the Spanish, they would have annihilated the Germans. It is possible, then, for one who realizes the defects of these two types, to equip infantry in a new manner, so that it can resist cavalry and not be afraid of foot-soldiers; but to gain this end they must have weapons of the right sorts, and adopt varied methods of combat. These are some of the things which, when they are put into service as novelties, give reputation and greatness to a new ruler.[4]

This opportunity, then, should not be allowed to pass, in order that after so long a time Italy may see her redeemer. I am unable to express with what love he would be received in all the provinces that have suffered

2. Sites of battles occurring between the end of the 15th century and 1513. 3. Between Spain and France in April 1512. 4. Machiavelli was subsequently the author of the treatise *Art of War* (1521).

from these foreign deluges; with what thirst for vengeance, what firm faith, what piety, what tears! What gates would be shut against him? what peoples would deny him obedience? what envy would oppose itself to him? what Italian would refuse to follow him? This barbarian rule stinks in every nostril. May your illustrious House, then, undertake this charge with the spirit and the hope with which all just enterprises are taken up, in order that, beneath its ensign, our native land may be ennobled, and, under its auspices, that saying of Petrarch may come true: "Manhood[5] will take arms against fury, and the combat will be short, because in Italian hearts the ancient valor is not yet dead."

5. An etymological translation of the original *virtù* (from the Latin *vir*, "man"). The quotation is from the *canzone* "My Italy."

MICHEL DE MONTAIGNE

1533–1592

Michel Eyquem de Montaigne was representative of his age and unique at the same time. Though involved in the political and religious conflicts of the day, he yet maintained an unmistakable sense of individuality and a considerable degree of detachment. These same qualities characterize his writing.

Montaigne was born on February 28, 1533, in the castle of Montaigne (in the wine-rich Bordeaux region), from which his family of traders derived their surname. His father, Pierre Eyquem, was for two terms mayor of Bordeaux and had fought in Italy under Francis I. Montaigne's inclination to tolerance and naturalness may have had its origin in his background and early training; his mother, of Spanish-Jewish descent, was a Protestant, as were his brother Beauregard and his sister Jeanne. The third of nine children, Michel himself, like his other brothers and sisters, was raised a Catholic. His father, though no man of learning, had unconventional ideas of upbringing; Michel, who had a peasant nurse and peasant godparents, was awakened in the morning by the sound of music and had Latin taught him as his mother tongue by a German tutor. At six he went to the famous Collège de Guienne at Bordeaux; later he studied law, probably at Toulouse. In his youth he already had firsthand experience of court life. (At the court celebrations at Rouen for the coming of age of Charles IX in 1560, he saw cannibals, brought from Brazil, who became the subject of the famous essay printed here.) In 1557 he was a member of the Bordeaux parliament. In 1565 he married Françoise de la Chassaigne, daughter of a colleague in the Bordeaux parliament, and the object of his temperate love. It is possible that disappointed political ambitions contributed to Montaigne's decision to "retire" at the age of thirty-eight to his castle of Montaigne and devote himself to meditation and writing. His stay there, however, had various interruptions. France was split between the Protestants, led by Henry of Navarre, and two Catholic factions, those faithful to the reigning kings of the house of Valois (first Charles IX and then Henry III) and the "leaguers," i.e., the followers of the house of Guise. Though his sympathies went to the unfanatical Navarre, the future founder of the Bourbon dynasty as Henry IV, Montaigne's attitude was balanced and conservative (both Henry III of Valois and Henry of Navarre bestowed honors on him), and in 1574 Montaigne attempted to mediate an agreement between Henry and the duke of Guise.

In 1580 he undertook a journey through Switzerland, Germany, and Italy (partly to cure his gallstones); while in Italy he received news that he had been appointed mayor of Bordeaux, an office he held competently for two terms (1581–1585). Toward the end of his life he began an important friendship with the intelligent and ardently devoted Marie de Gournay, who became a kind of adopted daughter and was his literary executrix. When Henry of Navarre, who had visited him twice in his castle, became King Henry IV, Montaigne expressed his joy, though he refused Henry's offers of money; he did not live to witness in Paris, as he probably would have, the entry of the king turned Catholic ("Paris," Henry said, "is well worth a Mass"), for he died on September 13, 1592, and was buried in a church in Bordeaux.

Montaigne's major claim to fame, the *Essays*, were started as a collection of interesting quotations, observations, recordings of remarkable events, and the like and slowly developed to their large form and bulk. Of the three books, I and II were first published in 1580; III (together with I and II revised and amplified) appeared in 1588. A posthumous edition prepared by de Gournay, and containing some further additions, appeared in 1595. A noteworthy early English translation by John Florio was published in 1603.

Although the quality of Montaigne's *Essays* can be fully appreciated only by a direct experience of them, let us attempt to describe this unique genre and place it within the context of its time. If one accepts the common view that in the Renaissance the individual human being was exalted, and therefore, a special emphasis was placed on the study of our "virtues" and singularities, it might be appropriate to think of Montaigne as a typical product of that new emphasis. Indeed, of the writers presented in this anthology, Montaigne is the one who most openly speaks in his own right, clearly and unabashedly as himself. Montaigne's characteristic and somewhat rambling prose is in the simplest and most quintessential first person. Perhaps at no other time in literature—certainly not in the nineteenth-century age of Romanticism, where in spite of widespread notions about the "free" expression of individual feelings writers so often wrapped themselves in an alter ego or a heroic mask—has a writer so thoroughly attempted to present himself or herself without in the least assuming a pose, of falling into a type.

> Authors communicate themselves to the world by some special and extrinsic mark; I am the first to do so by my general being, as Michel de Montaigne, not as a grammarian or a poet or a lawyer. If the world finds fault with me for speaking too much of myself, I find fault with the world for not even thinking of itself.

Yet nothing would be more erroneous than to suppose that Montaigne's focusing on his individual self implies a sense of the extraordinary importance of humanity, of our central place in the world, or of the special power of our understanding. The contrary is true. In the first place, in temperament Montaigne is singularly opposed to assuming an attitude of importance; one of the keynotes of his writing, and one of his premises in undertaking it, is that the subject is average, "mediocre." He declares that he has "but a private and family end in view," and in that sense, in fact, the way he introduces himself to the reader shows a nobly elegant and perhaps vaguely ironic humbleness—not to mention a considerable degree of the artfulness he disclaims! "So, Reader, I am myself the subject of my book; it is not reasonable to expect you to waste your leisure on a matter so frivolous and empty."

But, more important, in deciding to probe, to "essay," his own nature, his serious implication is that this is the only subject on which one can speak with any degree of certainty. So this writer whose work is the most acute exposure of an individual personality in the literature of the Renaissance is at the same time one of the highest illustrations of the ironic awareness of our intellectual limits.

With all this, Montaigne's work remains an outstanding assertion of an individuality, even though it is an assertion of doubt, contradiction, and change. As always the quality and novelty of the work should be experienced in the actual text, in terms of "style." Montaigne's style conjoins a solid classical manner, reflected in certain elements of the syntactical structure and in the continuous support of classical quotations, with the variety, the apparent disconnectedness, and the dramatic assertiveness of someone who is continuously analyzing a constantly changing subject, and—his modesty notwithstanding—a singularly attractive one.

> Others form man; I describe him, and portray a particular, very ill-made one, who, if I had to fashion him anew, should indeed be very different from what he is. But now it is done. . . . The world is but a perennial see-saw. All things in it are incessantly on the swing, the earth, the rocks of the Caucasus, the Egyptian pyramids. . . . Even fixedness is nothing but a more sluggish motion. I cannot fix my object; it is befogged, and reels with a natural intoxication. . . . I do not portray the thing in itself. I portray the passage.

In spite of what may often seem a leisurely gait, Montaigne is permanently on the alert, listening to the promptings of his thought, his sensibility, his imagination—and recording them.

Montaigne writes about one individual, and with a fairly obvious abhorrence of any sort of classification or description of human types in the manner of conventional moralists. Yet a powerfully keen observation of humanity in general emerges from his writings—an observation of our nature, intellectual power, and capacity for coherent action; of our place on earth among other beings; and of our place in creation.

If we keep in mind the broad range of European Renaissance literature, poised between positive and negative, enthusiasm and melancholy, we shall probably find that the general temper of Montaigne's assertions of doubt, and his consciousness of vanity, by no means imply an attitude of despair and gloom. His attitude is positive and negative in the same breath; it is a rich and fruitful sense of the relativity of everything. Thus if he examines and essays the human capacity to act purposefully and coherently (see *Of the Inconsistency of Our Actions*, included here), his implicit verdict is not that our action is absolutely futile. Rather, he refuses to attribute to the human personality a coherence it does not possess and that, we may be tempted to surmise, would rather impoverish it. "Our actions are nothing but a patchwork. . . . There is as much difference between us and ourselves as between us and others." And he sustains his arguments, as usual, with a wealth of examples and anecdotes. Emperor Augustus, to mention one, pleases him because his character has "slipped through the fingers of even the most daring critics."

A sense of relativity and a balanced outlook are apparent also from Montaigne's observation of the individual in relation to his or her fellow human beings. In the famous essay *Of Cannibals*, in which a comparison is made between the behavioral codes of primitive tribes and those of "ourselves," the basic idea is not a disparagement of our civilization but a relativistic warning, for "each man calls barbarism whatever is not in his own practice." The enlightening sense of relativity—rather than a more extreme and totally paradoxical view of the "nobility" of savages—permits Montaigne to see and admire what he detects as superior elements in the customs of the cannibals—for instance, their conception of valor for valor's sake. "The honor of valor consists in combating, not in beating," Montaigne writes. Acceptance of this notion of pure *virtù*, practiced for no material purposes, may well be, for writers like Montaigne, the way to preserve their admiration for the warrior's code of courage and valor in spite of the basically pacifist tendencies of their temperaments and their revulsion from the spectacles of conflict and bloodshed witnessed in their own time.

Naturally, an even larger sense of relativity emerges from Montaigne's writing when he examines our place in a more universal framework, as he does, in an outstanding instance, in *Apology for Raymond Sebond*. The notion of our privileged position in creation is eloquently questioned: Who has persuaded him that that admirable motion of the celestial vault, the eternal light of those torches rolling so proudly above his head, the fearful movements of that infinite sea, were established and have lasted so many centuries for his convenience and his service? In many other writers a similar anxiety about our smallness and ignorance casts a light of tragic vanity on the human condition. If Montaigne asks questions that involve, to say the very least, the whole Renaissance conception of human "dignity," our impression is never really one of negation and gloom. While our advantages over other beings are quietly evaluated and discredited ("this licence of thought . . . is an advantage sold to him very dearly. . . . For from it springs the principal source of . . . sin, sickness, irresolution, affliction, despair"), Montaigne maintains a balanced and often humorous tone in which even the frivolous aside of the personal essayist is not dissonant, but characteristic: "When I play with my cat, who knows if I am not a pastime to her more than she is to me?" So while his view of the "mediocrity" of the human race among other beings debunks any form of intellectual conceit, on the other hand an all-encompassing sense of natural fellowship presides over his view of our place in creation as well as over his conception of the moral individual in relation to others. See the end of *Of Repentance*, where the practice of goodness—as, in other instances, that of valor—is seen as a beautiful and self-rewarding act of "virtue":

> There is . . . no good deed that does not rejoice a wellborn nature. . . . It is no slight pleasure to feel oneself preserved from the contagion of so depraved an age, and to say to oneself: "If anyone should see right into my soul, still he would not find me guilty either of anyone's affliction or ruin. . . ." These testimonies of conscience give us pleasure; and this natural rejoicing is a great boon to us, and the only payment that never fails us.

In conclusion—and difficult as it is to reduce Montaigne's views to short and abstract statements—we are left with the impression that here Montaigne's vision of humanity, and of the possibility of a good life, is nearer to hopefulness than to despair. It is based on a balance between the "natural" and the intellectual, between instinct and reason. He belittles, at times even scornfully, the power of the human intellect, and he points to instinctive simplicity of mind as being more conducive to happiness and even to true knowledge; but on the other hand the whole tone of his work, its intellectual sophistication, its very bulk, and the loving manner with which he attended to it show that his own thought was not something that "sicklied o'er" his life, but something that gave it sustenance and delight. Thus we see in him some of the basic contrasts of the Renaissance mind—the acceptance and the rejection of our intellectual dignity—leading not to disruption but to temperately positive results. In passages like the one cited above, some kind of pattern of the truly virtuous individual seems to emerge unobtrusively. And though it is not imposed on the audience, any reader is free to think that conforming to this pattern would result in better spiritual balance in the individual and a more harmonious and sensible fellowship in society. Montaigne does not preach ("Others form man; I describe him"), because his code of conduct is one that cannot be taught but only experienced. He limits himself to exemplifying it in his own wise and unheroic self.

Donald M. Frame, *Montaigne: A Biography* (1965), is a modern work by one of the leading modern scholars of French literature. Frame is also author of *Mon-*

taigne's Essais: A Study (1969), a brief, clear, cogent account. A classic study is André Gide, *Montaigne: An Essay in Two Parts* (1929). Philip Paul Hallie's *Montaigne and Philosophy as Self-Portraiture* (1966) and Frederick Rider, *The Dialectic of Selfhood in Montaigne* (1973), assess Montaigne's creation of his self-image in the *Essays*. Marcel Tetel, *Montaigne* (1990), part of the Twayne's World Authors series, is a comprehensive view of Montaigne by a leading scholar of French literature.

PRONOUNCING GLOSSARY

The following list uses common English syllables and stress accents to provide rough equivalents of selected words whose pronunciation may be unfamiliar to the general reader.

de la Chassaigne: *duh lah shah-sen'*   Sebond: *se-bon'*

Dordogne: *dor-don'*   Suidas: *swee'-dahs*

Guise: *geez*   Valois: *val-wah'*

Montaigne: *mon-ten'*   Villegaignon: *veel-gahn-yonh'*

From Essays[1]

TO THE READER

This book was written in good faith, reader. It warns you from the outset that in it I have set myself no goal but a domestic and private one. I have had no thought of serving either you or my own glory. My powers are inadequate for such a purpose. I have dedicated it to the private convenience of my relatives and friends, so that when they have lost me (as soon they must), they may recover here some features of my habits and temperament, and by this means keep the knowledge they have had of me more complete and alive.

If I had written to seek the world's favor, I should have bedecked myself better, and should present myself in a studied posture. I want to be seen here in my simple, natural, ordinary fashion, without straining or artifice; for it is myself that I portray. My defects will here be read to the life, and also my natural form, as far as respect for the public has allowed. Had I been placed among those nations which are said to live still in the sweet freedom of nature's first laws, I assure you I should very gladly have portrayed myself here entire and wholly naked.

Thus, reader, I am myself the matter of my book; you would be unreasonable to spend your leisure on so frivolous and vain a subject.

So farewell. Montaigne, this first day of March, fifteen hundred and eighty.

OF CANNIBALS

When King Pyrrhus[2] passed over into Italy, after he had reconnoitered the formation of the army that the Romans were sending to meet him, he

---

1. Translated by Donald Frame.   2. King of Epirus (in Greece) who fought the Romans in Italy in 280 B.C.

said: "I do not know what barbarians these are" (for so the Greeks called all foreign nations), "but the formation of this army that I see is not at all barbarous." The Greeks said as much of the army that Flamininus brought into their country, and so did Philip, seeing from a knoll the order and distribution of the Roman camp, in his kingdom, under Publius Sulpicius Galba.[3] Thus we should beware of clinging to vulgar opinions, and judge things by reason's way, not by popular say.

I had with me for a long time a man who had lived for ten or twelve years in that other world which has been discovered in our century, in the place where Villegaignon landed, and which he called Antarctic France.[4] This discovery of a boundless country seems worthy of consideration. I don't know if I can guarantee that some other such discovery will not be made in the future, so many personages greater than ourselves having been mistaken about this one. I am afraid we have eyes bigger than our stomachs, and more curiosity than capacity. We embrace everything, but we clasp only wind.

Plato brings in Solon,[5] telling how he had learned from the priests of the city of Saïs in Egypt that in days of old, before the Flood, there was a great island named Atlantis, right at the mouth of the Strait of Gibraltar, which contained more land than Africa and Asia put together, and that the kings of that country, who not only possessed that island but had stretched out so far on the mainland that they held the breadth of Africa as far as Egypt, and the length of Europe as far as Tuscany, undertook to step over into Asia and subjugate all the nations that border on the Mediterranean, as far as the Black Sea; and for this purpose crossed the Spains, Gaul, Italy, as far as Greece, where the Athenians checked them; but that some time after, both the Athenians and themselves and their island were swallowed up by the Flood.

It is quite likely that that extreme devastation of waters made amazing changes in the habitations of the earth, as people maintain that the sea cut off Sicily from Italy—

> 'Tis said an earthquake once asunder tore
> These lands with dreadful havoc, which before
> Formed but one land, one coast
> > VIRGIL[6]

—Cyprus from Syria, the island of Euboea from the mainland of Boeotia; and elsewhere joined lands that were divided, filling the channels between them with sand and mud:

> A sterile marsh, long fit for rowing, now
> Feeds neighbor towns, and feels the heavy plow.
> > HORACE[7]

But there is no great likelihood that that island was the new world which we have just discovered; for it almost touched Spain, and it would be an incredible result of a flood to have forced it away as far as it is, more than

---

3. Both Titus Quinctius Flaminius and Publius Sulpicius Galba were Roman statesmen and generals who fought Philip V of Macedon in the early years of the 2nd century B.C.   4. In Brazil. Villegaignon landed there in 1557.   5. In his *Timaeus*.   6. *Aeneid* III.414–15.   7. *Art of Poetry*, lines 65–66.

twelve hundred leagues; besides, the travels of the moderns have already almost revealed that it is not an island, but a mainland connected with the East Indies on one side, and elsewhere with the lands under the two poles; or, if it is separated from them, it is by so narrow a strait and interval that it does not deserve to be called an island on that account.

It seems that there are movements, some natural, others feverish, in these great bodies, just as in our own. When I consider the inroads that my river, the Dordogne, is making in my lifetime into the right bank in its descent, and that in twenty years it has gained so much ground and stolen away the foundations of several buildings, I clearly see that this is an extraordinary disturbance; for if it had always gone at this rate, or was to do so in the future, the face of the world would be turned topsy-turvy. But rivers are subject to changes: now they overflow in one direction, now in another, now they keep to their course. I am not speaking of the sudden inundations whose causes are manifest. In Médoc, along the seashore, my brother, the sieur d'Arsac, can see an estate of his buried under the sands that the sea spews forth; the tops of some buildings are still visible; his farms and domains have changed into very thin pasturage. The inhabitants say that for some time the sea has been pushing toward them so hard that they have lost four leagues of land. These sands are its harbingers; and we see great dunes of moving sand that march half a league ahead of it and keep conquering land.

The other testimony of antiquity with which some would connect this discovery is in Aristotle, at least if that little book *Of Unheard-of Wonders* is by him. He there relates that certain Carthaginians, after setting out upon the Atlantic Ocean from the Strait of Gibraltar and sailing a long time, at last discovered a great fertile island, all clothed in woods and watered by great deep rivers, far remote from any mainland; and that they, and others since, attracted by the goodness and fertility of the soil, went there with their wives and children, and began to settle there. The lords of Carthage, seeing that their country was gradually becoming depopulated, expressly forbade anyone to go there any more, on pain of death, and drove out these new inhabitants, fearing, it is said, that in course of time they might come to multiply so greatly as to supplant their former masters and ruin their state. This story of Aristotle does not fit our new lands any better than the other.

This man I had was a simple, crude fellow—a character fit to bear true witness; for clever people observe more things and more curiously, but they interpret them; and to lend weight and conviction to their interpretation, they cannot help altering history a little. They never show you things as they are, but bend and disguise them according to the way they have seen them; and to give credence to their judgment and attract you to it, they are prone to add something to their matter, to stretch it out and amplify it. We need a man either very honest, or so simple that he has not the stuff to build up false inventions and give them plausibility; and wedded to no theory. Such was my man; and besides this, he at various times brought sailors and merchants, whom he had known on that trip, to see me. So I content myself with his information, without inquiring what the cosmographers say about it.

We ought to have topographers who would give us an exact account of the places where they have been. But because they have over us the advantage of having seen Palestine, they want to enjoy the privilege of telling us news about all the rest of the world. I would like everyone to write what he knows, and as much as he knows, not only in this, but in all other subjects; for a man may have some special knowledge and experience of the nature of a river or a fountain, who in other matters knows only what everybody knows. However, to circulate this little scrap of knowledge, he will undertake to write the whole of physics. From this vice spring many great abuses.

Now, to return to my subject, I think there is nothing barbarous and savage in that nation, from what I have been told, except that each man calls barbarism whatever is not his own practice; for indeed it seems we have no other test of truth and reason than the example and pattern of the opinions and customs of the country we live in. *There* is always the perfect religion, the perfect government, the perfect and accomplished manners in all things. Those people are wild, just as we call wild the fruits that Nature has produced by herself and in her normal course; whereas really it is those that we have changed artificially and led astray from the common order, that we should rather call wild. The former retain alive and vigorous their genuine, their most useful and natural, virtues and properties, which we have debased in the latter in adapting them to gratify our corrupted taste. And yet for all that, the savor and delicacy of some uncultivated fruits of those countries is quite as excellent, even to our taste, as that of our own. It is not reasonable that art should win the place of honor over our great and powerful mother Nature. We have so overloaded the beauty and richness of her works by our inventions that we have quite smothered her. Yet wherever her purity shines forth, she wonderfully puts to shame our vain and frivolous attempts:

> Ivy comes readier without our care;
> In lonely caves the arbutus grows more fair;
> No art with artless bird song can compare.
>   PROPERTIUS[8]

All our efforts cannot even succeed in reproducing the nest of the tiniest little bird, its contexture, its beauty and convenience; or even the web of the puny spider. All things, says Plato,[9] are produced by nature, by fortune, or by art; the greatest and most beautiful by one or the other of the first two, the least and most imperfect by the last.

These nations, then, seem to me barbarous in this sense, that they have been fashioned very little by the human mind, and are still very close to their original naturalness. The laws of nature still rule them, very little corrupted by ours; and they are in such a state of purity that I am sometimes vexed that they were unknown earlier, in the days when there were men able to judge them better than we. I am sorry that Lycurgus[1] and Plato did not know of them; for it seems to me that what we actually see in these nations surpasses not only all the pictures in which poets have

---

8. *Elegies* I.2.10–12.   9. See his *Laws*.   1. The half-legendary Spartan lawgiver (9th century B.C.).

idealized the golden age and all their inventions in imagining a happy state of man, but also the conceptions and the very desire of philosophy. They could not imagine a naturalness so pure and simple as we see by experience; nor could they believe that our society could be maintained with so little artifice and human solder. This is a nation, I should say to Plato, in which there is no sort of traffic, no knowledge of letters, no science of numbers, no name for a magistrate or for political superiority, no custom of servitude, no riches or poverty, no contracts, no successions, no partitions, no occupations but leisure ones, no care for any but common kinship, no clothes, no agriculture, no metal, no use of wine or wheat.[2] The very words that signify lying, treachery, dissimulation, avarice, envy, belittling, pardon—unheard of. How far from this perfection would he find the republic that he imagined: *Men fresh sprung from the gods* [Seneca].[3]

These manners nature first ordained.
                                        VIRGIL[4]

For the rest, they live in a country with a very pleasant and temperate climate, so that according to my witnesses it is rare to see a sick man there; and they have assured me that they never saw one palsied, bleary-eyed, toothless, or bent with age. They are settled along the sea and shut in on the land side by great high mountains, with a stretch about a hundred leagues wide in between. They have a great abundance of fish and flesh which bear no resemblance to ours, and they eat them with no other artifice than cooking. The first man who rode a horse there, though he had had dealings with them on several other trips, so horrified them in this posture that they shot him dead with arrows before they could recognize him.

Their buildings are very long, with a capacity of two or three hundred souls; they are covered with the bark of great trees, the strips reaching to the ground at one end and supporting and leaning on one another at the top, in the manner of some of our barns, whose covering hangs down to the ground and acts as a side. They have wood so hard that they cut with it and make of it their swords and grills to cook their food. Their beds are of a cotton weave, hung from the roof like those in our ships, each man having his own; for the wives sleep apart from their husbands.

They get up with the sun, and eat immediately upon rising, to last them through the day; for they take no other meal than that one. Like some other Eastern peoples, of whom Suidas[5] tells us, who drank apart from meals, they do not drink then; but they drink several times a day, and to capacity. Their drink is made of some root, and is of the color of our claret wines. They drink it only lukewarm. This beverage keeps only two or three days; it has a slightly sharp taste, is not at all heady, is good for the stomach, and has a laxative effect upon those who are not used to it; it is a very pleasant drink for anyone who is accustomed to it. In place of bread they use a certain white substance like preserved coriander. I have tried it; it tastes sweet and a little flat.

---

2. This passage is always compared with Shakespeare's *The Tempest* 2.1.154ff.   3. *Epistles* 90.
4. *Georgics* II.20.   5. A Byzantine lexicographer.

The whole day is spent in dancing. The younger men go to hunt animals with bows. Some of the women busy themselves meanwhile with warming their drink, which is their chief duty. Some one of the old men, in the morning before they begin to eat, preaches to the whole barnful in common, walking from one end to the other, and repeating one single sentence several times until he has completed the circuit (for the buildings are fully a hundred paces long). He recommends to them only two things: valor against the enemy and love for their wives. And they never fail to point out this obligation, as their refrain, that it is their wives who keep their drink warm and seasoned.

There may be seen in several places, including my own house, specimens of their beds, of their ropes, of their wooden swords and the bracelets with which they cover their wrists in combats, and of the big canes, open at one end, by whose sound they keep time in their dances. They are close shaven all over, and shave themselves much more cleanly than we, with nothing but a wooden or stone razor. They believe that souls are immortal, and that those who have deserved well of the gods are lodged in that part of heaven where the sun rises, and the damned in the west.

They have some sort of priests and prophets, but they rarely appear before the people, having their home in the mountains. On their arrival there is a great feast and solemn assembly of several villages—each barn, as I have described it, makes up a village, and they are about one French league[6] from each other. The prophet speaks to them in public, exhorting them to virtue and their duty; but their whole ethical science contains only these two articles: resoluteness in war and affection for their wives. He prophesies to them things to come and the results they are to expect from their undertakings, and urges them to war or holds them back from it; but this is on the condition that when he fails to prophesy correctly, and if things turn out otherwise than he has predicted, he is cut into a thousand pieces if they catch him, and condemned as a false prophet. For this reason, the prophet who has once been mistaken is never seen again.

Divination is a gift of God; that is why its abuse should be punished as imposture. Among the Scythians, when the soothsayers failed to hit the mark, they were laid, chained hand and foot, on carts full of heather and drawn by oxen, on which they were burned. Those who handle matters subject to the control of human capacity are excusable if they do the best they can. But these others who come and trick us with assurances of an extraordinary faculty that is beyond our ken, should they not be punished for not making good their promise, and for the temerity of their imposture?

They have their wars with the nations beyond the mountains, further inland, to which they go quite naked, with no other arms than bows or wooden swords ending in a sharp point, in the manner of the tongues of our boar spears. It is astonishing what firmness they show in their combats, which never end but in slaughter and bloodshed; for as to routs and terror, they know nothing of either.

Each man brings back his trophy the head of the enemy he has killed, and sets it up at the entrance to his dwelling. After they have treated their

6. About 2.49 miles.

prisoners well for a long time with all the hospitality they can think of, each man who has a prisoner calls a great assembly of his acquaintances. He ties a rope to one of the prisoner's arms, by the end of which he holds him, a few steps away, for fear of being hurt, and gives his dearest friend the other arm to hold in the same way; and these two, in the presence of the whole assembly, kill him with their swords. This done, they roast him and eat him in common and send some pieces to their absent friends. This is not, as people think, for nourishment, as of old the Scythians used to do; it is to betoken an extreme revenge. And the proof of this came when they saw the Portuguese, who had joined forces with their adversaries, inflict a different kind of death on them when they took them prisoner, which was to bury them up to the waist, shoot the rest of their body full of arrows, and afterward hang them. They thought that these people from the other world, being men who had sown the knowledge of many vices among their neighbors and were much greater masters than themselves in every sort of wickedness, did not adopt this sort of vengeance without some reason, and that it must be more painful than their own; so they began to give up their old method and to follow this one.

I am not sorry that we notice the barbarous horror of such acts, but I am heartily sorry that, judging their faults rightly, we should be so blind to our own. I think there is more barbarity in eating a man alive than in eating him dead; and in tearing by tortures and the rack a body still full of feeling, in roasting a man bit by bit, in having him bitten and mangled by dogs and swine (as we have not only read but seen within fresh memory, not among ancient enemies, but among neighbors and fellow citizens, and what is worse, on the pretext of piety and religion),[7] than in roasting and eating him after he is dead.

Indeed, Chrysippus and Zeno, heads of the Stoic sect, thought there was nothing wrong in using our carcasses for any purpose in case of need, and getting nourishment from them; just as our ancestors,[8] when besieged by Caesar in the city of Alésia, resolved to relieve their famine by eating old men, women, and other people useless for fighting.

> The Gascons once, 'tis said, their life renewed
> By eating of such food.
>
> JUVENAL[9]

And physicians do not fear to use human flesh in all sorts of ways for our health, applying it either inwardly or outwardly. But there never was any opinion so disordered as to excuse treachery, disloyalty, tyranny, and cruelty, which are our ordinary vices.

So we may well call these people barbarians, in respect to the rules of reason, but not in respect to ourselves, who surpass them in every kind of barbarity.

Their warfare is wholly noble and generous, and as excusable and beautiful as this human disease can be; its only basis among them is their rivalry in valor. They are not fighting for the conquest of new lands, for they still enjoy that natural abundance that provides them without toil and

---

7. The allusion is to the spectacles of religious warfare that Montaigne himself had witnessed in his time and country.   8. The Gauls.   9. *Satires* 15.93–94.

trouble with all necessary things in such profusion that they have no wish to enlarge their boundaries. They are still in that happy state of desiring only as much as their natural needs demand; anything beyond that is superfluous to them.

They generally call those of the same age, brothers; those who are younger, children; and the old men are fathers to all the others. These leave to their heirs in common the full possession of their property, without division or any other title at all than just the one that Nature gives to her creatures in bringing them into the world.

If their neighbors cross the mountains to attack them and win a victory, the gain of the victor is glory, and the advantage of having proved the master in valor and virtue; for apart from this they have no use for the goods of the vanquished, and they return to their own country, where they lack neither anything necessary nor that great thing, the knowledge of how to enjoy their condition happily and be content with it. These men of ours do the same in their turn. They demand of their prisoners no other ransom than that they confess and acknowledge their defeat. But there is not one in a whole century who does not choose to die rather than to relax a single bit, by word or look, from the grandeur of an invincible courage; not one who would not rather be killed and eaten than so much as ask not to be. They treat them very freely, so that life may be all the dearer to them, and usually entertain them with threats of their coming death, of the torments they will have to suffer, the preparations that are being made for the purpose, the cutting up of their limbs, and the feast that will be made at their expense. All this is done for the sole purpose of extorting from their lips some weak or base word, or making them want to flee, so as to gain the advantage of having terrified them and broken down their firmness. For indeed, if you take it the right way, it is in this point alone that true victory lies:

> It is no victory
> Unless the vanquished foe admits your mastery.
> CLAUDIAN[1]

The Hungarians, very bellicose fighters, did not in olden times pursue their advantage beyond putting the enemy at their mercy. For having wrung a confession from him to this effect, they let him go unharmed and unransomed, except, at most, for exacting his promise never again to take up arms against them.

We win enough advantages over our enemies that are borrowed advantages, not really our own. It is the quality of a porter, not of valor, to have sturdier arms and legs; agility is a dead and corporeal quality; it is a stroke of luck to make our enemy stumble, or dazzle his eyes by the sunlight; it is a trick of art and technique, which may be found in a worthless coward, to be an able fencer. The worth and value of a man is in his heart and his will; there lies his real honor. Valor is the strength, not of legs and arms, but of heart and soul; it consists not in the worth of our horse or our

---

1. *Of the Sixth Consulate of Honorius*, lines 248–49.

weapons, but in our own. He who falls obstinate in his courage, *if he has fallen, he fights on his knees* [Seneca].[2] He who relaxes none of his assurance, no matter how great the danger of imminent death; who, giving up his soul, still looks firmly and scornfully at his enemy—he is beaten not by us, but by fortune; he is killed, not conquered.

The most valiant are sometimes the most unfortunate. Thus there are triumphant defeats that rival victories. Nor did those four sister victories, the fairest that the sun ever set eyes on—Salamis, Plataea, Mycale, and Sicily[3]—ever dare match all their combined glory against the glory of the annihilation of King Leonidas and his men at the pass of Thermopylae.[4]

Who ever hastened with more glorious and ambitious desire to win a battle than Captain Ischolas to lose one? Who ever secured his safety more ingeniously and painstakingly than he did his destruction? He was charged to defend a certain pass in the Peloponnesus against the Arcadians. Finding himself wholly incapable of doing this, in view of the nature of the place and the inequality of the forces, he made up his mind that all who confronted the enemy would necessarily have to remain on the field. On the other hand, deeming it unworthy both of his own virtue and magnanimity and of the Lacedaemonian name to fail in his charge, he took a middle course between these two extremes, in this way. The youngest and fittest of his band he preserved for the defense and service of their country, and sent them home; and with those whose loss was less important, he determined to hold this pass, and by their death to make the enemy buy their entry as dearly as he could. And so it turned out. For he was presently surrounded on all sides by the Arcadians, and after slaughtering a large number of them, he and his men were all put to the sword. Is there a trophy dedicated to victors that would not be more due to these vanquished? The role of true victory is in fighting, not in coming off safely; and the honor of valor consists in combating, not in beating.

To return to our story. These prisoners are so far from giving in, in spite of all that is done to them, that on the contrary, during the two or three months that they are kept, they wear a gay expression; they urge their captors to hurry and put them to the test; they defy them, insult them, reproach them with their cowardice and the number of battles they have lost to the prisoners' own people.

I have a song composed by a prisoner which contains this challenge, that they should all come boldly and gather to dine off him, for they will be eating at the same time their own fathers and grandfathers, who have served to feed and nourish his body. "These muscles," he says, "this flesh and these veins are your own, poor fools that you are. You do not recognize that the substance of your ancestors' limbs is still contained in them. Savor them well; you will find in them the taste of your own flesh." An idea that certainly does not smack of barbarity. Those that paint these people dying, and who show the execution, portray the prisoner spitting in the face of his slayers and scowling at them. Indeed, to the last gasp they never stop braving and defying their enemies by word and look. Truly here are real

2. *Of Providence* II.   3. References to the famous Greek victories against the Persians and (at Himera, Sicily) against the Carthaginians in or about 480 B.C.   4. The Spartan king Leonidas's defense here also took place in 480 B.C., during the war against the Persians.

savages by our standards; for either they must be thoroughly so, or we must be; there is an amazing distance between their character and ours.

The men there have several wives, and the higher their reputation for valor the more wives they have. It is a remarkably beautiful thing about their marriages that the same jealousy our wives have to keep us from the affection and kindness of other women, theirs have to win this for them. Being more concerned for their husbands' honor than for anything else, they strive and scheme to have as many companions as they can, since that is a sign of their husbands' valor.

Our wives will cry "Miracle!" but it is no miracle. It is a properly matrimonial virtue, but one of the highest order. In the Bible, Leah, Rachel, Sarah, and Jacob's wives gave their beautiful handmaids to their husbands; and Livia seconded the appetites of Augustus to her own disadvantage; and Stratonice, the wife of King Deiotarus,[5] not only lent her husband for his use a very beautiful young chambermaid in her service, but carefully brought up her children, and backed them up to succeed to their father's estates.

And lest it be thought that all this is done through a simple and servile bondage to usage and through the pressure of the authority of their ancient customs, without reasoning or judgment, and because their minds are so stupid that they cannot take any other course, I must cite some examples of their capacity. Besides the warlike song I have just quoted, I have another, a love song, which begins in this vein: "Adder, stay; stay, adder, that from the pattern of your coloring my sister may draw the fashion and the workmanship of a rich girdle that I may give to my love; so may your beauty and your pattern be forever preferred to all other serpents." This first couplet is the refrain of the song. Now I am familiar enough with poetry to be a judge of this: not only is there nothing barbarous in this fancy, but it is altogether Anacreontic.[6] Their language, moreover, is a soft language, with an agreeable sound, somewhat like Greek in its endings.

Three of these men, ignorant of the price they will pay some day, in loss of repose and happiness, for gaining knowledge of the corruptions of this side of the ocean; ignorant also of the fact that of this intercourse will come their ruin (which I suppose is already well advanced: poor wretches, to let themselves be tricked by the desire for new things, and to have left the serenity of their own sky to come and see ours!)—three of these men were at Rouen, at the time the late King Charles IX was there. The king talked to them for a long time; they were shown our ways, our splendor, the aspect of a fine city. After that, someone asked their opinion, and wanted to know what they had found most amazing. They mentioned three things, of which I have forgotten the third, and I am very sorry for it; but I still remember two of them. They said that in the first place they thought it very strange that so many grown men, bearded, strong, and armed, who were around the king (it is likely that they were talking about the Swiss of his guard) should submit to obey a child, and that one of them was not chosen to command instead. Second (they have a way in

---

5. Tetrarch of Galatia, in Asia Minor.   6. Worthy of Anacreon (572?–488? B.C.), major Greek writer of amatory lyrics.

their language of speaking of men as halves of one another), they had noticed that there were among us men full and gorged with all sorts of good things, and that their other halves were beggars at their doors, emaciated with hunger and poverty; and they thought it strange that these needy halves could endure such an injustice, and did not take the others by the throat, or set fire to their houses.

I had a very long talk with one of them; but I had an interpreter who followed my meaning so badly, and who was so hindered by his stupidity in taking in my ideas, that I could get hardly any satisfaction from the man. When I asked him what profit he gained from his superior position among his people (for he was a captain, and our sailors called him king), he told me that it was to march foremost in war. How many men followed him? He pointed to a piece of ground, to signify as many as such a space could hold; it might have been four or five thousand men. Did all this authority expire with the war? He said that this much remained, that when he visited the villages dependent on him, they made paths for him through the underbrush by which he might pass quite comfortably.

All this is not too bad—but what's the use? They don't wear breeches.

OF THE INCONSISTENCY OF OUR ACTIONS

Those who make a practice of comparing human actions are never so perplexed as when they try to see them as a whole and in the same light; for they commonly contradict each other so strangely that it seems impossible that they have come from the same shop. One moment young Marius is a son of Mars, another moment a son of Venus.[7] Pope Boniface VIII, they say, entered office like a fox, behaved in it like a lion, and died like a dog. And who would believe that it was Nero, that living image of cruelty, who said, when they brought him in customary fashion the sentence of a condemned criminal to sign: "Would to God I had never learned to write!" So much his heart was wrung at condemning a man to death!

Everything is so full of such examples—each man, in fact, can supply himself with so many—that I find it strange to see intelligent men sometimes going to great pains to match these pieces; seeing that irresolution seems to me the most common and apparent defect of our nature, as witness that famous line of Publilius, the farce writer:

> Bad is the plan that never can be changed.
>   PUBLILIUS SYRUS[8]

There is some justification for basing a judgment of a man on the most ordinary acts of his life; but in view of the natural instability of our conduct and opinions, it has often seemed to me that even good authors are wrong to insist on fashioning a consistent and solid fabric out of us. They choose one general characteristic, and go and arrange and interpret all a man's actions to fit their picture; and if they cannot twist them enough, they go and set them down to dissimulation. Augustus has escaped them; for there is in this man throughout the course of his life such an obvious, abrupt,

---

7. Goddess of love. Marius was the nephew of the older and better-known Marius. Montaigne's source is Plutarch's *Life of Marius*. Mars was the god of war.   8. *Apothegms (Sententiae)*, line 362.

and continual variety of actions that even the boldest judges have had to let him go, intact and unsolved. Nothing is harder for me than to believe in men's consistency, nothing easier than to believe in their inconsistency. He who would judge them in detail and distinctly, bit by bit, would more often hit upon the truth.

In all antiquity it is hard to pick out a dozen men who set their lives to a certain and constant course, which is the principal goal of wisdom. For, to comprise all wisdom in a word, says an ancient [Seneca], and to embrace all the rules of our life in one, it is "always to will the same things, and always to oppose the same things."[9] I would not deign, he says, to add "provided the will is just"; for if it is not just, it cannot always be whole.

In truth, I once learned that vice is only unruliness and lack of moderation, and that consequently consistency cannot be attributed to it. It is a maxim of Demosthenes, they say, that the beginning of all virtue is consultation and deliberation; and the end and perfection, consistency. If it were by reasoning that we settled on a particular course of action, we would choose the fairest course—but no one has thought of that:

> He spurns the thing he sought, and seeks anew
> What he just spurned; he seethes, his life's askew.
> HORACE[1]

Our ordinary practice is to follow the inclinations of our appetite, to the left, to the right, uphill and down, as the wind of circumstance carries us. We think of what we want only at the moment we want it, and we change like that animal which takes the color of the place you set it on. What we have just now planned, we presently change, and presently again we retrace our steps: nothing but oscillation and inconsistency:

> Like puppets we are moved by outside strings.
> HORACE[2]

We do not go; we are carried away, like floating objects, now gently, now violently, according as the water is angry or calm:

> Do we not see all humans unaware
> Of what they want, and always searching everywhere,
> And changing place, as if to drop the load they bear?
> LUCRETIUS[3]

Every day a new fancy, and our humors shift with the shifts in the weather:

> Such are the minds of men, as is the fertile light
> That Father Jove himself sends down to make earth bright.
> HOMER[4]

We float between different states of mind; we wish nothing freely, nothing absolutely, nothing constantly. If any man could prescribe and establish definite laws and a definite organization in his head, we should see shining throughout his life an evenness of habits, an order, and an infallible relation between his principles and his practice.

9. *Epistles* 20.   1. *Epistles* I.1.98–99.   2. *Satires* II.7.82.   3. *On the Nature of Things* III.1057–59.   4. *Odyssey* XVIII.135–36, 152–53 in the Fitzgerald translation.

Empedocles noticed this inconsistency in the Agrigentines, that they abandoned themselves to pleasures as if they were to die on the morrow, and built as if they were never to die.[5]

This man would be easy to understand, as is shown by the example of the younger Cato:[6] he who has touched one chord of him has touched all; he is a harmony of perfectly concordant sounds, which cannot conflict. With us, it is the opposite: for so many actions, we need so many individual judgments. The surest thing, in my opinion, would be to trace our actions to the neighboring circumstances, without getting into any further research and without drawing from them any other conclusions.

During the disorders of our poor country,[7] I was told that a girl, living near where I then was, had thrown herself out of a high window to avoid the violence of a knavish soldier quartered in her house. Not killed by the fall, she reasserted her purpose by trying to cut her throat with a knife. From this she was prevented, but only after wounding herself gravely. She herself confessed that the soldier had as yet pressed her only with requests, solicitations, and gifts; but she had been afraid, she said, that he would finally resort to force. And all this with such words, such expressions, not to mention the blood that testified to her virtue, as would have become another Lucrece.[8] Now, I learned that as a matter of fact, both before and since, she was a wench not so hard to come to terms with. As the story[9] says: Handsome and gentlemanly as you may be, when you have had no luck, do not promptly conclude that your mistress is inviolably chaste; for all you know, the mule driver may get his will with her.

Antigonus,[1] having taken a liking to one of his soldiers for his virtue and valor, ordered his physicians to treat the man for a persistent internal malady that had long tormented him. After his cure, his master noticed that he was going about his business much less warmly, and asked him what had changed him so and made him such a coward. "You yourself, Sire," he answered, "by delivering me from the ills that made my life indifferent to me." A soldier of Lucullus[2] who had been robbed of everything by the enemy made a bold attack on them to get revenge. When he had retrieved his loss, Lucullus, having formed a good opinion of him, urged him to some dangerous exploit with all the fine expostulations he could think of,

> With words that might have stirred a coward's heart.
> HORACE[3]

"Urge some poor soldier who has been robbed to do it," he replied;

> Though but a rustic lout,
> "That man will go who's lost his money," he called out;
> HORACE[4]

and resolutely refused to go.

We read that Sultan Mohammed outrageously berated Hassan, leader

---

5. From Diogenes Laertius's life of the Greek philosopher Empedocles (5th century).   6. Cato "Uticensis (1st century B.C.), a philosopher. He is traditionally considered the epitome of moral and intellectual integrity.   7. See n. 7, p. 1512.   8. The legendary, virtuous Roman who stabbed herself after being raped by King Tarquinius Superbus's son.   9. A common folk tale.   1. Macedonian king (382–301 B.C.).   2. Roman general (1st century B.C.).   3. *Epistles* II.2.36.   4. *Epistles* II.2.39–40.

of his Janissaries, because he saw his troops giving way to the Hungarians and Hassan himself behaving like a coward in the fight, Hassan's only reply was to go and hurl himself furiously—alone, just as he was, arms in hand—into the first body of enemies that he met, by whom he was promptly swallowed up; this was perhaps not so much self-justification as a change of mood, nor so much his natural valor as fresh spite.

That man whom you saw so adventurous yesterday, do not think it strange to find him just as cowardly today: either anger, or necessity, or company, or wine, or the sound of a trumpet, had put his heart in his belly. His was a courage formed not by reason, but by one of these circumstances; it is no wonder if he has now been made different by other, contrary circumstances.

These supple variations and contradictions that are seen in us have made some imagine that we have two souls, and others that two powers accompany us and drive us, each in its own way, one toward good, the other toward evil; for such sudden diversity cannot well be reconciled with a simple subject.

Not only does the wind of accident move me at will, but, besides, I am moved and disturbed as a result merely of my own unstable posture; and anyone who observes carefully can hardly find himself twice in the same state. I give my soul now one face, now another, according to which direction I turn it. If I speak of myself in different ways, that is because I look at myself in different ways. All contradictions may be found in me by some twist and in some fashion. Bashful, insolent; chaste, lascivious; talkative, taciturn; tough, delicate; clever, stupid; surly, affable; lying, truthful; learned, ignorant; liberal, miserly, and prodigal: all this I see in myself to some extent according to how I turn; and whoever studies himself really attentively finds in himself, yes, even in his judgment, this gyration and discord. I have nothing to say about myself absolutely, simply, and solidly, without confusion and without mixture, or in one word. *Distinguo*[5] is the most universal member of my logic.

Although I am always minded to say good of what is good, and inclined to interpret favorably anything that can be so interpreted, still it is true that the strangeness of our condition makes it happen that we are often driven to do good by vice itself—were it not that doing good is judged by intention alone.

Therefore one courageous deed must not be taken to prove a man valiant; a man who was really valiant would be so always and on all occasions. If valor were a habit of virtue, and not a sally, it would make a man equally resolute in any contingency, the same alone as in company, the same in single combat as in battle; for, whatever they say, there is not one valor for the pavement and another for the camp. As bravely would he bear an illness in his bed as a wound in camp, and he would fear death no more in his home than in an assault. We would not see the same man charging into the breach with brave assurance, and later tormenting himself, like a woman, over the loss of a lawsuit or a son. When, though a coward against infamy, he is firm against poverty; when, though weak against the sur-

---

5. I distinguish (Latin)—that is, I separate into its components.

geons' knives, he is steadfast against the enemy's swords, the action is praiseworthy, not the man.

Many Greeks, says Cicero, cannot look at the enemy, and are brave in sickness; the Cimbrians and Celtiberians, just the opposite; *for nothing can be uniform that does not spring from a firm principle* [Cicero].[6]

There is no more extreme valor of its kind than Alexander's; but it is only of one kind, and not complete and universal enough. Incomparable though it is, it still has its blemishes; which is why we see him worry so frantically when he conceives the slightest suspicion that his men are plotting against his life, and why he behaves in such matters with such violent and indiscriminate injustice and with a fear that subverts his natural reason. Also superstition, with which he was so strongly tainted, bears some stamp of pusillanimity. And the excessiveness of the penance he did for the murder of Clytus[7] is also evidence of the unevenness of his temper.

Our actions are nothing but a patchwork—*they despise pleasure, but are too cowardly in pain; they are indifferent to glory, but infamy breaks their spirit* [Cicero][8]—and we want to gain honor under false colors. Virtue will not be followed except for her own sake; and if we sometimes borrow her mask for some other purpose, she promptly snatches it from our face. It is a strong and vivid dye, once the soul is steeped in it, and will not go without taking the fabric with it. That is why, to judge a man, we must follow his traces long and carefully. If he does not maintain consistency for its own sake, *with a way of life that has been well considered and preconcerted* [Cicero];[9] if changing circumstances makes him change his pace (I mean his path, for his pace may be hastened or slowed), let him go: that man goes before the wind, as the motto of our Talbot[1] says.

It is no wonder, says an ancient [Seneca], that chance has so much power over us, since we live by chance.[2] A man who has not directed his life as a whole toward a definite goal cannot possibly set his particular actions in order. A man who does not have a picture of the whole in his head cannot possibly arrange the pieces. What good does it do a man to lay in a supply of paints if he does not know what he is to paint? No one makes a definite plan of his life; we think about it only piecemeal. The archer must first know what he is aiming at, and then set his hand, his bow, his string, his arrow, and his movements for that goal. Our plans go astray because they have no direction and no aim. No wind works for the man who has no port of destination.

I do not agree with the judgment given in favor of Sophocles, on the strength of seeing one of his tragedies, that it proved him competent to manage his domestic affairs, against the accusation of his son. Nor do I think that the conjecture of the Parians sent to reform the Milesians was sufficient ground for the conclusion they drew. Visiting the island, they noticed the best-cultivated lands and the best-run country houses, and noted down the names of their owners. Then they assembled the citizens in the town and appointed these owners the new governors and magis-

6. *Tusculan Disputations* II, chap. 27.   7. A commander in Alexander's army who was killed by him during an argument, an act Alexander immediately and bitterly regretted, as related by Plutarch in his *Life of Alexander*, chaps. 50–52.   8. *Of Duties (De officiis)* I, chap. 21.   9. *Paradoxes* 5.   1. An English captain who fought in France and died there in 1453.   2. *Epistles* 71.

trates, judging that they, who were careful of their private affairs, would be careful of those of the public.

We are all patchwork, and so shapeless and diverse in composition that each bit, each moment, plays its own game. And there is as much difference between us and ourselves as between us and others. *Consider it a great thing to play the part of one single man* [Seneca].[3] Ambition can teach men valor, and temperance, and liberality, and even justice. Greed can implant in the heart of a shop apprentice, brought up in obscurity and idleness, the confidence to cast himself far from hearth and home, in a frail boat at the mercy of the waves and angry Neptune; it also teaches discretion and wisdom. Venus herself supplies resolution and boldness to boys still subject to discipline and the rod, and arms the tender hearts of virgins who are still in their mothers' laps:

> Furtively passing sleeping guards, with Love as guide,
> Alone by night the girl comes to the young man's side.
> TIBULLUS[4]

In view of this, a sound intellect will refuse to judge men simply by their outward actions; we must probe the inside and discover what springs set men in motion. But since this is an arduous and hazardous undertaking, I wish fewer people would meddle with it.

OF REPENTANCE

["These Testimonies of a Good Conscience"]

Others form man; I tell of him, and portray a particular one, very ill-formed, whom I should really make very different from what he is if I had to fashion him over again. But now it is done.

Now the lines of my painting do not go astray, though they change and vary. The world is but a perennial movement. All things in it are in constant motion—the earth, the rocks of the Caucasus, the pyramids of Egypt—both with the common motion and with their own. Stability itself is nothing but a more languid motion.

I cannot keep my subject still. It goes along befuddled and staggering, with a natural drunkenness. I take it in this condition, just as it is at the moment I give my attention to it. I do not portray being: I portray passing. Not the passing from one age to another, or, as the people say, from seven years to seven years,[5] but from day to day, from minute to minute. My history needs to be adapted to the moment. I may presently change, not only by chance, but also by intention. This is a record of various and changeable occurrences, and of irresolute and, when it so befalls, contradictory ideas: whether I am different myself, or whether I take hold of my subjects in different circumstances and aspects. So, all in all, I may indeed contradict myself now and then; but truth, as Demades[6] said, I do not contradict. If my mind could gain a firm footing, I would not make essays, I would make decisions; but it is always in apprenticeship and on trial.

I set forth a humble and inglorious life; that does not matter. You can

---

3. *Epistles* 120.   4. *Elegies* II.1.75–76.   5. An allusion to the popular notion that the human body is completely renewed every seven years.   6. Greek orator and politician (4th century B.C.).

tie up all moral philosophy with a common and private life just as well as with a life of richer stuff. Each man bears the entire form of man's estate.

Authors communicate with the people by some special extrinsic mark; I am the first to do so by my entire being, as Michel de Montaigne, not as a grammarian or a poet or a jurist. If the world complains that I speak too much of myself, I complain that it does not even think of itself.

But is it reasonable that I, so fond of privacy in actual life, should aspire to publicity in the knowledge of me? Is it reasonable too that I should set forth to the world, where fashioning and art have so much credit and authority, some crude and simple products of nature, and of a very feeble nature at that? Is it not making a wall without stone, or something like that, to construct books without knowledge and without art? Musical fancies are guided by art, mine by chance.

At least I have one thing according to the rules: that no man ever treated a subject he knew and understood better than I do the subject I have undertaken; and that in this I am the most learned man alive. Secondly, that no man ever penetrated more deeply into his material, or plucked its limbs and consequences cleaner, or reached more accurately and fully the goal he had set for his work. To accomplish it, I need only bring it to fidelity; and that is in it, as sincere and pure as can be found. I speak the truth, not my fill of it, but as much as I dare speak; and I dare to do so a little more as I grow old, for it seems that custom allows old age more freedom to prate and more indiscretion in talking about oneself. It cannot happen here as I see it happening often, that the craftsman and his work contradict each other: "Has a man whose conversation is so good written such a stupid book?" or "Have such learned writings come from a man whose conversation is so feeble?"

If a man is commonplace in conversation and rare in writing, that means that his capacity is in the place from which he borrows it, and not in himself. A learned man is not learned in all matters; but the capable man is capable in all matters, even in ignorance.

In this case we go hand in hand and at the same pace, my book and I. In other cases one may commend or blame the work apart from the workman; not so here; he who touches the one, touches the other. He who judges it without knowing it will injure himself more than me; he who has known it will completely satisfy me. Happy beyond my deserts if I have just this share of public approval, that I make men of understanding feel that I was capable of profiting by knowledge, if I had had any, and that I deserved better assistance from my memory.

Let me here excuse what I often say, that I rarely repent and that my conscience is content with itself—not as the conscience of an angel or a horse, but as the conscience of a man; always adding this refrain, not perfunctorily but in sincere and complete submission: that I speak as an ignorant inquirer, referring the decision purely and simply to the common and authorized beliefs. I do not teach, I tell.

There is no vice truly a vice which is not offensive, and which a sound judgement does not condemn; for its ugliness and painfulness is so apparent that perhaps the people are right who say it is chiefly produced by stupidity and ignorance. So hard it is to imagine anyone knowing it without hating it.

Malice sucks up the greater part of its own venom, and poisons itself with it. Vice leaves repentance in the soul, like an ulcer in the flesh, which is always scratching itself and drawing blood. For reason effaces other griefs and sorrows; but it engenders that of repentance, which is all the more grievous because it springs from within, as the cold and heat of fevers is sharper than that which comes from outside. I consider as vices (but each one according to its measure) not only those that reason and nature condemn, but also those that man's opinion has created, even false and erroneous opinion, if it is authorized by laws and customs.

There is likewise no good deed that does not rejoice a wellborn nature. Indeed there is a sort of gratification in doing good which makes us rejoice in ourselves, and a generous pride that accompanies a good conscience. A boldly vicious soul may perhaps arm itself with security, but with this complacency and satisfaction it cannot provide itself. It is no slight pleasure to feel oneself preserved from the contagion of so depraved an age, and to say to oneself: "If anyone should see right into my soul, still he would not find me guilty either of anyone's affliction or ruin, or of vengeance or envy, or of public offense against the laws, or of innovation and disturbance, or of failing in my word; and in spite of what the license of the times allows and teaches each man, still I have not put my hand either upon the property or into the purse of any Frenchman, and have lived only on my own, both in war and in peace; nor have I used any man's work without paying his wages." These testimonies of conscience give us pleasure; and this natural rejoicing is a great boon to us, and the only payment that never fails us.

MIGUEL DE CERVANTES
1547–1616

The author of Don Quixote's extravagant adventures himself had a most unusual and adventurous life. The son of an apothecary, Miguel de Cervantes Saavedra was born in Alcalá de Henares, a university town near Madrid. Almost nothing is known of his childhood and early education. Only in 1569 is he mentioned as a favorite pupil by a Madrid humanist, Juan López. Records indicate that by the end of that year he had left Spain and was living in Rome, for a time in the service of Giulio Acquaviva, who later became a cardinal. We know that he enlisted in the Spanish fleet under the command of Don John of Austria and that he took part in the struggle of the allied forces of Christendom against the Turks. He was at the crucial Battle of Lepanto (1571), where in spite of fever he fought valiantly and received three gunshot wounds, one of which permanently impaired the use of his left hand, "for the greater glory of the right." After further military action and garrison duty at Palermo and Naples, he and his brother Rodrigo, bearing testimonials from Don John and from the viceroy of Sicily, began the journey back to Spain, where Miguel hoped to obtain a captaincy. In September 1575 their ship was captured near the Marseille coast by Barbary pirates, and the two brothers were taken as prisoners to Algiers. Cervantes's captors, considering him a person of some consequence, held him as a slave for a high ransom. He repeatedly attempted to escape, and his daring and fortitude excited the admiration of Hassan Pasha, the viceroy of Algiers, who bought him for five hundred crowns after five years of captivity.

Cervantes was freed on September 15, 1580, and reached Madrid in December of that year. There his literary career began rather inauspiciously; he wrote twenty or thirty plays, with little success, and in 1585 published a pastoral romance, *Galatea*. At about this time he had a daughter with Ana Franca de Rojas, and during the same period married Catalina de Salazar, who was eighteen years his junior. Seeking nonliterary employment, he obtained a position in the navy, requisitioning and collecting supplies for the "Invincible Armada." Irregularities in his administration, for which he was held responsible if not directly guilty, caused him to spend more time in prison. In 1590 he tried unsuccessfully to obtain colonial employment in the New World. Later he served as tax collector in the province of Granada but was dismissed from government service in 1597.

The following years of Cervantes's life are the most obscure; there is a legend that *Don Quixote* was first conceived and planned while its author was in prison in Seville. In 1604 he was in Valladolid, then the temporary capital of Spain, living in sordid surroundings with the numerous women of his family (his wife, daughter, niece, and two sisters). It was in Valladolid, in late 1604, that he obtained the official license for the publication of *Don Quixote* (Part I). The book appeared in 1605 and was a popular success. Cervantes followed the Spanish court when it returned to Madrid, where he continued to live poorly in spite of a popularity with readers that quickly made proverbial figures of his heroes. A false sequel to his book appeared, prompting him to write his own continuation, *Don Quixote*, Part II, published in 1615. His *Exemplary Tales* had appeared in 1613. He died on April 23, 1616, and was buried in the convent of the Barefooted Trinitarian nuns. *Persiles and Sigismunda*, his last novel, was published posthumously in 1617.

Although, as we have indicated, *The Ingenious Gentleman Don Quixote de la Mancha* was a popular success from the time Part I was published in 1605, it was only later recognized as an important work of literature. This delay was due partly to the fact that in a period of established and well-defined literary genres such as the epic, the tragedy, and the pastoral romance (Cervantes himself had tried his hand at some of these forms), the unconventional combination of elements in *Don Quixote* resulted in a work of considerable novelty, with the serious aspects hidden under a mocking surface.

The initial and overt purpose of the book was to satirize the romances of chivalry. In those long yarns—which had to do with the Carolingian and Arthurian legends and which were full of supernatural deeds of valor, implausible and complicated adventures, duels, and enchantments—the literature that had expressed the medieval spirit of chivalry and romance had degenerated to the same extent to which, in our day, certain conventions of romantic literature have degenerated in "pulp" fiction and film melodrama. Up to a point, then, what Cervantes set out to do was to produce a parody, a caricature of a literary type. But neither the nature of his genius nor the particular method he chose allowed him to limit himself to such a relatively simple and direct undertaking. The actual method he followed to expose the silliness of the romances of chivalry was to show to what extraordinary consequences they would lead a man insanely infatuated with them, once this man set out to live "now" according to their patterns of action and belief.

So what we have is not mere parody or caricature; for there is a great deal of difference between presenting a remote and more or less imaginary world and presenting an individual deciding to live by the standards of that world in a modern and realistic context. The first consequence is a mingling of genres. On the one hand much of the book has the color and intonation of the world of medieval chivalry as its poets had portrayed it. The fact that that vision and that tone depend for their existence in the book on the self-deception of the hero makes them no less operative artistically and adds, in fact, an important element of idealization. On the other hand the chivalric world is continuously jostled by elements of contemporary life evoked by the narrator—the realities of landscape and speech, peasants and nobles, inns and highways. So the author can draw on two sources, roughly the realistic and the romantic, truth and vision, practical facts and lofty values. In this respect—having found a way to bring together concrete actuality and highly ideal values—Cervantes can be said to have created the modern novel.

The consequences of Cervantes's invention are more apparent when we begin to analyze a little more closely the nature of these worlds, romantic and realistic, and the kind of impact the first exerts on the second. The hero embodying the world of the romances is not, as we know, a cavalier; he is an impoverished country gentleman who embraces that code in the "modern" world. Chivalry is not directly satirized; it is simply placed in a context different from its native one. The result of that new association is a new whole, a new unity. The "code" is renovated; it is put into a different perspective, given another chance.

We should remember at this point that in the process of deterioration that the romances of chivalry had undergone, certain basically attractive ideals had become empty conventions—for instance, the ideal of love as devoted "service." In this connection, it may be especially interesting to observe that the treatment of love, and Don Quixote's conception of it, are not limited to his well-known admiration for his purely fantastic lady Dulcinea but are also dealt with from a feminine point of view. Don Quixote warmly admires Marcela's elaborate, logical, and poetic speech in which the noble shepherdess defends herself against the accusation of being "a wild beast and a basilisk" for having caused Grisóstomo's death and proclaims her right to choose her particular kind of freedom in nature, where "these mountain trees are my company, the clear running waters in these brooks are my mirror" (Part I, chapter 14).

No less relevant are Quixote's ideals of adventurousness, of loyalty to high concepts of valor and generosity. In the new context those values are reexamined. Cervantes may well have gained a practical sense of them in his own life while still a youth, for instance at the Battle of Lepanto (the great victory of the European coalition against the "infidels") and as a pirate's captive. Because he began writing Don Quixote in his late fifties, a vantage point from which the adventures of his youth must have appeared impossibly remote, a factor of nostalgia—which could hardly have been present in a pure satire—may well have entered into his work. Furthermore, had he undertaken a direct caricature of the romance genre, the serious and noble values of chivalry could not have been made apparent except negatively, whereas in the context devised by him in Don Quixote they find a way to assert themselves positively as well.

The book in its development is, to a considerable extent, the story of that assertion—of the impact that Don Quixote's revitalization of the chivalric code has on a contemporary world. We must remember, of course, that there is ambiguity in the way the assertion is made; it works slowly on the reader, as his or her own discovery rather than as the narrator's overt suggestion. Actually, whatever attraction the chivalric world of his hero's vision may have had for Cervantes, he does not openly support Don Quixote at all. He even seems at times to go further in repudiating him than he needs to, for the hero is officially insane, and the narrator never tires of reminding us of this. One critic has described the attitude Cervantes affects toward his creature as "animosity." Nevertheless, by the very magniloquence and, often, the extraordinary coherence and beauty that the narrator allows his hero to display in his speeches in defense of his vision and his code, we are gradually led to discover for ourselves the serious and important elements these contain. For instance, Don Quixote's speech evoking the lost Golden Age and justifying the institution of knight-errantry (in Part I, Chapter 11) is described by the narrator—after Don Quixote has delivered it—as a "futile harangue" that "might very well have been dispensed with"; but there it is, in all of its fervor and effectiveness. Thus the narrator's so-called animosity ultimately does nothing but intensify our interest in Don Quixote and our sympathy for him. And in that process we are, as audience, simply repeating the experience many characters have on the "stage" of the book, in their relationships with him.

Generally speaking, the encounters between the ordinary world and Don Quixote are encounters between the world of reality and that of illusion, between reason and imagination, and ultimately between the world in which action is prompted by material considerations and interests and a world in which action is prompted by ideal motives. The selections printed here illustrate these aspects of the experience. Among the first adventures are some that have most contributed to the popularity of the Don Quixote legend: he sees windmills and decides they are giants, and country inns become castles. Though the conclusions of such episodes often have the ludicrousness of slapstick comedy, there is a powerfully imposing quality about Don Quixote's insanity; his madness always has method, a commanding persistence and coherence. And there is perhaps an inevitable sense of moral grandeur in the spectacle of anyone remaining so unflinchingly faithful to his or her own vision. The world of "reason" may win in point of fact, but we come to wonder whether from a moral point of view Quixote is not the victor.

Furthermore, we increasingly realize that Quixote's own manner of action has greatness in itself, and not only the greatness of persistence: his purpose is to redress wrongs, to come to the aid of the afflicted, to offer generous help, to challenge danger, and to practice valor. And we finally feel the impact of the arguments that sustain his action—for example, in the episode of the lions in which he expounds "the meaning of valor." The ridiculousness of the situation is counterbalanced by the basic seriousness of Quixote's motives; his notion of courage for its own sake appears, and is recognized, as singularly noble, a sort of generous display of integrity in a world usually ruled by lower standards. Thus the distinction between reason and madness, truth and illusion, becomes, to say the least, ambiguous. The hero's delusions are indeed exposed when they come up against hard facts, but the authority of such facts is seen to be morally questionable.

The effectiveness of Don Quixote's conduct and vision is seen most clearly in his relationship with his "squire" Sancho Panza. It would be a crude oversimplification to say that Don Quixote and Sancho represent illusion and reality, the insane code of knight-errantry versus down-to-earth practicalities. Actually Sancho—though his nature is strongly defined by such elements as his common sense, his earthy speech, his simple phrases studded with proverbs set against the hero's magniloquence—is mainly characterized in his development by the degree to which he believes in his master. He is caught in the snare of Don Quixote's vision; the seeds of the imaginative life are successfully implanted in him.

The impact of Quixote's view of life on Sancho serves, therefore, to illustrate one of the important qualities of the protagonist and, we may finally say, one of the important aspects of Renaissance literature: the attempt, ultimately frustrated but extremely attractive as long as it lasts, of the individual mind to produce a vision and a system of its own in a world that often seems to have lost a universal frame of reference and a fully satisfactory sense of the value and meaning of action. What Don Quixote presents is a vision of a world that, for all its aberrant qualities, appears generally to be more colorful and more thrilling and also, incidentally, to be inspired by more honorable rules of conduct than the world of ordinary people, "realism," current affairs, private interests, easy jibes, and petty pranks. It is a world in which actions are performed out of a sense of their beauty and excitement, not for the sake of their usefulness. It is, again, the world as stage, animated by "folly"; in this case the lights go out at the end, an end that is "reasonable" and, therefore, gloomy. Sancho provides the main example of one who is exposed to that vision and absorbs that light while it lasts. How successfully he has done so is seen during Don Quixote's death scene, in which Sancho begs his master not to die but to continue the play, as has been suggested, in a new costume—that of shepherds in an Arcadian setting. But at that final point the hero is "cured" and killed, and Sancho is restored to the petty interests of the world as he can see it by his own lights, after the cord connecting him to his imaginative master is cut by the latter's "repentance" and death.

William Byron, *Cervantes: A Biography* (1978), is very thorough. The more advanced student of *Don Quixote* will find useful Stephen Gilman's *The Novel According to Cervantes* (1989) and Howard Mancing's detailed study, *The Chivalric World of Don Quijote: Style, Structure, and Narrative Technique* (1982). Lowry Nelson, ed., *Cervantes: A Collection of Critical Essays* (1969), offers the views of eminent scholars and authors.

PRONOUNCING GLOSSARY

The following list uses common English syllables and stress accents to provide rough equivalents of selected words whose pronunciation may be unfamiliar to the general reader.

Acquaviva: *ahk-wah-vee'-vah*

Benengeli: *ben-en-hel'-ee*

Boiardo: *boy-ar'-doh*

Eugenio: *yoo-hen'-yoh*

Orbaneja: *or-bah-nay'hah*

Periquillo: *pehr-i-kee'-yoh*

Quejana: *kay-hah'-nah*

Quesada: *kay-sah'-dah*

Quijada: *kee-hah'-dah*

Quintanar: *kin-ta-nar'*

real: *ray-al'*

Roque: *ro'kay*

From Don Quixote[1]

From *Part I*

[*"I Know Who I Am, and Who I May Be, If I Choose"*]

CHAPTER 1

Which treats of the station in life and the pursuits of the famous gentleman, Don Quixote de la Mancha.

In a village of La Mancha[2] the name of which I have no desire to recall, there lived not so long ago one of those gentlemen who always have a lance in the rack, an ancient buckler, a skinny nag, and a greyhound for the chase. A stew with more beef than mutton in it, chopped meat for his evening meal, scraps for a Saturday, lentils on Friday, and a young pigeon as a special delicacy for Sunday, went to account for three-quarters of his

---

1. Translated by Samuel Putnam.   2. Efforts at identifying the village have proved inconclusive. La Mancha is a section of Spain south of Madrid.

income. The rest of it he laid out on a broadcloth greatcoat and velvet stockings for feast days, with slippers to match, while the other days of the week he cut a figure in a suit of the finest homespun. Living with him were a housekeeper in her forties, a niece who was not yet twenty, and a lad of the field and market place who saddled his horse for him and wielded the pruning knife.

This gentleman of ours was close on to fifty, of a robust constitution but with little flesh on his bones and a face that was lean and gaunt. He was noted for his early rising, being very fond of the hunt. They will try to tell you that his surname was Quijada or Quesada—there is some difference of opinion among those who have written on the subject—but according to the most likely conjectures we are to understand that it was really Quejana. But all this means very little so far as our story is concerned, providing that in the telling of it we do not depart one iota from the truth.

You may know, then, that the aforesaid gentleman, on those occasions when he was at leisure, which was most of the year around, was in the habit of reading books of chivalry with such pleasure and devotion as to lead him almost wholly to forget the life of a hunter and even the administration of his estate. So great was his curiosity and infatuation in this regard that he even sold many acres of tillable land in order to be able to buy and read the books that he loved, and he would carry home with him as many of them as he could obtain.

Of all those that he thus devoured none pleased him so well as the ones that had been composed by the famous Feliciano de Silva,[3] whose lucid prose style and involved conceits were as precious to him as pearls; especially when he came to read those tales of love and amorous challenges that are to be met with in many places, such a passage as the following, for example: "The reason of the unreason that afflicts my reason, in such a manner weakens my reason that I with reason lament me of your comeliness." And he was similarly affected when his eyes fell upon such lines as these: ". . . the high Heaven of your divinity divinely fortifies you with the stars and renders you deserving of that desert your greatness doth deserve."

The poor fellow used to lie awake nights in an effort to disentangle the meaning and make sense out of passages such as these, although Aristotle himself would not have been able to understand them, even if he had been resurrected for that sole purpose. He was not at ease in his mind over those wounds that Don Belianís[4] gave and received; for no matter how great the surgeons who treated him, the poor fellow must have been left with his face and his entire body covered with marks and scars. Nevertheless, he was grateful to the author for closing the book with the promise of an interminable adventure to come; many a time he was tempted to take up his pen and literally finish the tale as had been promised, and he undoubtedly would have done so, and would have succeeded at it very well, if his thoughts had not been constantly occupied with other things of greater moment.

3. Author of romances (16th century); the lines that follow are from his *Don Florisel de Niguea*.
4. The allusion is to a romance by Jeronimo Fernández.

He often talked it over with the village curate, who was a learned man, a graduate of Sigüenza,[5] and they would hold long discussions as to who had been the better knight, Palmerin of England or Amadis of Gaul; but Master Nicholas, the barber of the same village, was in the habit of saying that no one could come up to the Knight of Phoebus,[6] and that if anyone *could* compare with him it was Don Galaor, brother of Amadis of Gaul, for Galaor was ready for anything—he was none of your finical knights, who went around whimpering as his brother did, and in point of valor he did not lag behind him.

In short, our gentleman became so immersed in his reading that he spent whole nights from sundown to sunup and his days from dawn to dusk in poring over his books, until, finally, from so little sleeping and so much reading, his brain dried up and he went completely out of his mind. He had filled his imagination with everything that he had read, with enchantments, knightly encounters, battles, challenges, wounds, with tales of love and its torments, and all sorts of impossible things, and as a result had come to believe that all these fictitious happenings were true; they were more real to him than anything else in the world. He would remark that the Cid Ruy Díaz had been a very good knight, but there was no comparison between him and the Knight of the Flaming Sword, who with a single backward stroke had cut in half two fierce and monstrous giants. He preferred Bernardo del Carpio, who at Roncesvalles had slain Roland despite the charm the latter bore, availing himself of the stratagem which Hercules employed when he strangled Antaeus,[7] the son of Earth, in his arms.

He had much good to say for Morgante[8] who, though he belonged to the haughty, overbearing race of giants, was of an affable disposition and well brought up. But, above all, he cherished an admiration for Rinaldo of Montalbán,[9] especially as he beheld him sallying forth from his castle to rob all those that crossed his path, or when he thought of him overseas stealing the image of Mohammed which, so the story has it, was all of gold. And he would have liked very well to have had his fill of kicking that traitor Galalón,[1] a privilege for which he would have given his housekeeper with his niece thrown into the bargain.

At last, when his wits were gone beyond repair, he came to conceive the strangest idea that ever occurred to any madman in this world. It now appeared to him fitting and necessary, in order to win a greater amount of honor for himself and serve his country at the same time, to become a knight-errant and roam the world on horseback, in a suit of armor; he would go in quest of adventures, by way of putting into practice all that he had read in his books; he would right every manner of wrong, placing himself in situations of the greatest peril such as would redound to the

5. Ironical, for Sigüenza was the seat of a minor and discredited university.   6. Or Knight of the Sun. Heroes of romances customarily adopted emblematic names and also changed them according to circumstances. *Palmerin . . . Amadis:* each a hero of a very famous romance of chivalry.   7. The mythological Antaeus was invulnerable as long as he maintained contact with his mother, Earth. Hercules killed him while holding him raised in his arms. *Charm:* the magic gift of invulnerability.   8. In Pulci's *Morgante maggiore,* a comic-epic poem of the Italian Renaissance.   9. Roland's cousin. In Boiardo's *Roland in Love* (*Orlando innamorato*) and Ariosto's *Roland Mad* (*Orlando furioso*), romantic and comic-epic poems of the Italian Renaissance.   1. Ganelón, the villain in the Charlemagne legend who betrayed the French at Roncesvalles.

eternal glory of his name. As a reward for his valor and the might of his arm, the poor fellow could already see himself crowned Emperor of Trebizond at the very least; and so, carried away by the strange pleasure that he found in such thoughts as these, he at once set about putting his plan into effect.

The first thing he did was to burnish up some old pieces of armor, left him by his great-grandfather, which for ages had lain in a corner, moldering and forgotten. He polished and adjusted them as best he could, and then he noticed that one very important thing was lacking: there was no closed helmet, but only a morion, or visorless headpiece, with turned up brim of the kind foot soldiers wore. His ingenuity, however, enabled him to remedy this, and he proceeded to fashion out of cardboard a kind of half-helmet, which, when attached to the morion, gave the appearance of a whole one. True, when he went to see if it was strong enough to withstand a good slashing blow, he was somewhat disappointed; for when he drew his sword and gave it a couple of thrusts, he succeeded only in undoing a whole week's labor. The ease with which he had hewed it to bits disturbed him no little, and he decided to make it over. This time he placed a few strips of iron on the inside, and then, convinced that it was strong enough, refrained from putting it to any further test; instead, he adopted it then and there as the finest helmet ever made.

After this, he went out to have a look at his nag; and although the animal had more *cuartos*, or cracks, in its hoof than there are quarters in a real,[2] and more blemishes than Gonela's steed which *tantum pellis et ossa fuit*,[3] it nonetheless looked to its master like a far better horse than Alexander's Bucephalus or the Babieca of the Cid.[4] He spent all of four days in trying to think up a name for his mount; for—so he told himself—seeing that it belonged to so famous and worthy a knight, there was no reason why it should not have a name of equal renown. The kind of name he wanted was one that would at once indicate what the nag had been before it came to belong to a knight-errant and what its present status was; for it stood to reason that, when the master's worldly condition changed, his horse also ought to have a famous, high-sounding appellation, one suited to the new order of things and the new profession that it was to follow.

After he in his memory and imagination had made up, struck out, and discarded many names, now adding to and now subtracting from the list, he finally hit upon "Rocinante," a name that impressed him as being sonorous and at the same time indicative of what the steed had been when it was but a hack, whereas now it was nothing other than the first and foremost of all the hacks[5] in the world.

Having found a name for his horse that pleased his fancy, he then desired to do as much for himself, and this required another week, and by the end of that period he had made up his mind that he was henceforth to be known as Don Quixote, which, as has been stated, has led the authors of this veracious history to assume that his real name must

---

2. A coin (about five cents). *Cuarto:* one-eighth of a *real.*   3. Was so much skin and bones (Latin).
4. The chief (Spanish)—that is, Ruy Diaz, celebrated hero of *Poema del Cid* (12th century).   5. In Spanish, *rocin.*

undoubtedly have been Quijada, and not Quesada as others would have it. But remembering that the valiant Amadis was not content to call himself that and nothing more, but added the name of his kingdom and fatherland that he might make it famous also, and thus came to take the name Amadis of Gaul, so our good knight chose to add his place of origin and become "Don Quixote de la Mancha"; for by this means, as he saw it, he was making very plain his lineage and was conferring honor upon his country by taking its name as his own.

And so, having polished up his armor and made the morion over into a closed helmet, and having given himself and his horse a name, he naturally found but one thing lacking still: he must seek out a lady of whom he could become enamored; for a knight-errant without a lady-love was like a tree without leaves or fruit, a body without a soul.

"If," he said to himself, "as a punishment for my sins or by a stroke of fortune I should come upon some giant hereabouts, a thing that very commonly happens to knights-errant, and if I should slay him in a hand-to-hand encounter or perhaps cut him in two, or, finally, if I should vanquish and subdue him, would it not be well to have someone to whom I may send him as a present, in order that he, if he is living, may come in, fall upon his knees in front of my sweet lady, and say in a humble and submissive tone of voice, 'I, lady, am the giant Caraculiambro, lord of the island Malindrania, who has been overcome in single combat by that knight who never can be praised enough, Don Quixote de la Mancha, the same who sent me to present myself before your Grace that your Highness may dispose of me as you see fit'?"

Oh, how our good knight reveled in this speech, and more than ever when he came to think of the name that he should give his lady! As the story goes, there was a very good-looking farm girl who lived near by, with whom he had once been smitten, although it is generally believed that she never knew or suspected it. Her name was Aldonza Lorenzo, and it seemed to him that she was the one upon whom he should bestow the title of mistress of his thoughts. For her he wished a name that should not be incongruous with his own and that would convey the suggestion of a princess or a great lady; and, accordingly, he resolved to call her "Dulcinea del Toboso," she being a native of that place. A musical name to his ears, out of the ordinary and significant, like the others he had chosen for himself and his appurtenances.

CHAPTER 2

Which treats of the first sally that the ingenious Don Quixote made from his native heath.

Having, then, made all these preparations, he did not wish to lose any time in putting his plan into effect, for he could not but blame himself for what the world was losing by his delay, so many were the wrongs that were to be righted, the grievances to be redressed, the abuses to be done away with, and the duties to be performed. Accordingly, without informing anyone of his intention and without letting anyone see him, he set out one morning before daybreak on one of those very hot days in July. Donning all his armor, mounting Rocinante, adjusting his ill-contrived helmet, bracing his shield on his arm, and taking up his lance, he sallied forth by the back gate of his stable yard into the open countryside. It was with great contentment and joy that he saw how easily he had made a beginning toward the fulfillment of his desire.

No sooner was he out on the plain, however, than a terrible thought assailed him, one that all but caused him to abandon the enterprise he had undertaken. This occurred when he suddenly remembered that he had never formally been dubbed a knight, and so, in accordance with the law of knighthood, was not permitted to bear arms against one who had a right to that title. And even if he had been, as a novice knight he would have had to wear white armor, without any device on his shield, until he should have earned one by his exploits. These thoughts led him to waver in his purpose, but, madness prevailing over reason, he resolved to have himself knighted by the first person he met, as many others had done if what he had read in those books that he had at home was true. And so far as white armor was concerned, he would scour his own the first chance that offered until it shone whiter than any ermine. With this he became more tranquil and continued on his way, letting his horse take whatever path it chose, for he believed that therein lay the very essence of adventures.

And so we find our newly fledged adventurer jogging along and talking to himself. "Undoubtedly," he is saying, "in the days to come, when the true history of my famous deeds is published, the learned chronicler who records them, when he comes to describe my first sally so early in the morning, will put down something like this: 'No sooner had the rubicund Apollo spread over the face of the broad and spacious earth the gilded filaments of his beauteous locks, and no sooner had the little singing birds of painted plumage greeted with their sweet and mellifluous harmony the coming of the Dawn, who, leaving the soft couch of her jealous spouse, now showed herself to mortals at all the doors and balconies of the horizon that bounds La Mancha—no sooner had this happened than the famous knight, Don Quixote de la Mancha, forsaking his own downy bed and mounting his famous steed, Rocinante, fared forth and began riding over the ancient and famous Campo de Montiel.'"[6]

And this was the truth, for he was indeed riding over that stretch of plain.

"O happy age and happy century," he went on, "in which my famous exploits shall be published, exploits worthy of being engraved in bronze, sculptured in marble, and depicted in paintings for the benefit of posterity. O wise magician, whoever you be, to whom shall fall the task of chronicling this extraordinary history of mine! I beg of you not to forget my good Rocinante, eternal companion of my wayfarings and my wanderings."

Then, as though he really had been in love: "O Princess Dulcinea, lady of this captive heart! Much wrong have you done me in thus sending me forth with your reproaches and sternly commanding me not to appear in

6. The scene of a battle in 1369.

your beauteous presence. O lady, deign to be mindful of this your subject who endures so many woes for the love of you."

And so he went on, stringing together absurdities, all of a kind that his books had taught him, imitating insofar as he was able the language of their authors. He rode slowly, and the sun came up so swiftly and with so much heat that it would have been sufficient to melt his brains if he had had any. He had been on the road almost the entire day without anything happening that is worthy of being set down here; and he was on the verge of despair, for he wished to meet someone at once with whom he might try the valor of his good right arm. Certain authors say that his first adventure was that of Puerto Lápice, while others state that it was that of the windmills; but in this particular instance I am in a position to affirm what I have read in the annals of La Mancha; and that is to the effect that he went all that day until nightfall, when he and his hack found themselves tired to death and famished. Gazing all around him to see if he could discover some castle or shepherd's hut where he might take shelter and attend to his pressing needs, he caught sight of an inn not far off the road along which they were traveling, and this to him was like a star guiding him not merely to the gates, but rather, let us say, to the palace of redemption. Quickening his pace, he came up to it just as night was falling.

By chance there stood in the doorway two lasses of the sort known as "of the district"; they were on their way to Seville in the company of some mule drivers who were spending the night in the inn. Now, everything that this adventurer of ours thought, saw, or imagined seemed to him to be directly out of one of the storybooks he had read, and so, when he caught sight of the inn, it at once became a castle with its four turrets and its pinnacles of gleaming silver, not to speak of the drawbridge and moat and all the other things that are commonly supposed to go with a castle. As he rode up to it, he accordingly reined in Rocinante and sat there waiting for a dwarf to appear upon the battlements and blow his trumpet by way of announcing the arrival of a knight. The dwarf, however, was slow in coming, and as Rocinante was anxious to reach the stable, Don Quixote drew up to the door of the hostelry and surveyed the two merry maidens, who to him were a pair of beauteous damsels or gracious ladies taking their ease at the castle gate.

And then a swineherd came along, engaged in rounding up his drove of hogs—for, without any apology, that is what they were. He gave a blast on his horn to bring them together, and this at once became for Don Quixote just what he wished it to be: some dwarf who was heralding his coming; and so it was with a vast deal of satisfaction that he presented himself before the ladies in question, who, upon beholding a man in full armor like this, with lance and buckler, were filled with fright and made as if to flee indoors. Realizing that they were afraid, Don Quixote raised his pasteboard visor and revealed his withered, dust-covered face.

"Do not flee, your Ladyships," he said to them in a courteous manner and gentle voice. "You need not fear that any wrong will be done you, for it is not in accordance with the order of knighthood which I profess to wrong anyone, much less such highborn damsels as your appearance shows you to be."

The girls looked at him, endeavoring to scan his face, which was half hidden by his ill-made visor. Never having heard women of their profession called damsels before, they were unable to restrain their laughter, at which Don Quixote took offense.

"Modesty," he observed, "well becomes those with the dower of beauty, and, moreover, laughter that has not good cause is a very foolish thing. But I do not say this to be discourteous or to hurt your feelings; my only desire is to serve you."

The ladies did not understand what he was talking about, but felt more than ever like laughing at our knight's unprepossessing figure. This increased his annoyance, and there is no telling what would have happened if at that moment the innkeeper had not come out. He was very fat and very peaceably inclined; but upon sighting this grotesque personage clad in bits of armor that were quite as oddly matched as were his bridle, lance, buckler, and corselet, mine host was not at all indisposed to join the lasses in their merriment. He was suspicious, however, of all this paraphernalia and decided that it would be better to keep a civil tongue in his head.

"If, Sir Knight," he said, "your Grace desires a lodging, aside from a bed—for there is none to be had in this inn—you will find all else that you may want in great abundance."

When Don Quixote saw how humble the governor of the castle was— for he took the innkeeper and his inn to be no less than that—he replied, "For me, Sir Castellan,[7] anything will do, since

> Arms are my only ornament,
> My only rest the fight, etc."

The landlord thought that the knight had called him a castellan because he took him for one of those worthies of Castile, whereas the truth was, he was an Andalusian from the beach of Sanlúcar, no less a thief than Cacus[8] himself, and as full of tricks as a student or a page boy.

"In that case," he said,

> "Your bed will be the solid rock,
> Your sleep: to watch all night.

This being so, you may be assured of finding beneath this roof enough to keep you awake for a whole year, to say nothing of a single night."

With this, he went up to hold the stirrup for Don Quixote, who encountered much difficulty in dismounting, not having broken his fast all day long. The knight then directed his host to take good care of his steed, as it was the best piece of horseflesh in all the world. The innkeeper looked it over, and it did not impress him as being half as good as Don Quixote had said it was. Having stabled the animal, he came back to see what his guest would have and found the latter being relieved of his armor by the damsels, who by now had made their peace with the new arrival. They had already removed his breastplate and backpiece but had no idea how they

---

7. The Spanish, *castellano*, means both "castellan" and "Castilian."   8. In Roman mythology he stole some of the cattle of Hercules, concealing the theft by having them walk backward into his cave; he was finally discovered and slain.

were going to open his gorget or get his improvised helmet off. That piece of armor had been tied on with green ribbons which it would be necessary to cut, since the knots could not be undone, but he would not hear of this, and so spent all the rest of that night with his headpiece in place, which gave him the weirdest, most laughable appearance that could be imagined.

Don Quixote fancied that these wenches who were assisting him must surely be the chatelaine and other ladies of the castle, and so proceeded to address them very gracefully and with much wit:

> Never was knight so served
> By any noble dame
> As was Don Quixote
> When from his village he came,
> With damsels to wait on his every need
> While princesses cared for his hack . . .

"By hack," he explained, "is meant my steed Rocinante, for that is his name, and mine is Don Quixote de la Mancha. I had no intention of revealing my identity until my exploits done in your service should have made me known to you; but the necessity of adapting to present circumstances that old ballad of Lancelot has led to your becoming acquainted with it prematurely. However, the time will come when your Ladyships shall command and I will obey and with the valor of my good right arm show you how eager I am to serve you."

The young women were not used to listening to speeches like this and had not a word to say, but merely asked him if he desired to eat anything.

"I could eat a bite of something, yes," replied Don Quixote. "Indeed, I feel that a little food would go very nicely just now."

He thereupon learned that, since it was Friday, there was nothing to be had in all the inn except a few portions of codfish, which in Castile is called *abadejo*, in Andalusia *bacalao*, in some places *curadillo*, and elsewhere *truchuella* or small trout. Would his Grace, then, have some small trout, seeing that was all there was that they could offer him?

"If there are enough of them," said Don Quixote, "they will take the place of a trout, for it is all one to me whether I am given in change eight reales or one piece of eight. What is more, those small trout may be like veal, which is better than beef, or like kid, which is better than goat. But however that may be, bring them on at once, for the weight and burden of arms is not to be borne without inner sustenance."

Placing the table at the door of the hostelry, in the open air, they brought the guest a portion of badly soaked and worse cooked codfish and a piece of bread as black and moldy as the suit of armor that he wore. It was a mirth-provoking sight to see him eat, for he still had his helmet on with his visor fastened, which made it impossible for him to put anything into his mouth with his hands, and so it was necessary for one of the girls to feed him. As for giving him anything to drink, that would have been out of the question if the innkeeper had not hollowed out a reed, placing one end in Don Quixote's mouth while through the other end he poured the wine. All this the knight bore very patiently rather than have them cut the ribbons of his helmet.

At this point a gelder of pigs approached the inn, announcing his arrival with four or five blasts on his horn, all of which confirmed Don Quixote in the belief that this was indeed a famous castle, for what was this if not music that they were playing for him? The fish was trout, the bread was the finest, the wenches were ladies, and the innkeeper was the castellan. He was convinced that he had been right in his resolve to sally forth and roam the world at large, but there was one thing that still distressed him greatly, and that was the fact that he had not as yet been dubbed a knight; as he saw it, he could not legitimately engage in any adventure until he had received the order of knighthood.

CHAPTER 3

Of the amusing manner in which Don Quixote had himself dubbed a knight.

Wearied of his thoughts, Don Quixote lost no time over the scanty repast which the inn afforded him. When he had finished, he summoned the landlord and, taking him out to the stable, closed the doors and fell on his knees in front of him.

"Never, valiant knight," he said, "shall I arise from here until you have courteously granted me the boon I seek, one which will redound to your praise and to the good of the human race."

Seeing his guest at his feet and hearing him utter such words as these, the innkeeper could only stare at him in bewilderment, not knowing what to say or do. It was in vain that he entreated him to rise, for Don Quixote refused to do so until his request had been granted.

"I expected nothing less of your great magnificence, my lord," the latter then continued, "and so I may tell you that the boon I asked and which you have so generously conceded me is that tomorrow morning you dub me a knight. Until that time, in the chapel of this your castle, I will watch over my armor, and when morning comes, as I have said, that which I so desire shall then be done, in order that I may lawfully go to the four corners of the earth in quest of adventures and to succor the needy, which is the chivalrous duty of all knights-errant such as I who long to engage in deeds of high emprise."

The innkeeper, as we have said, was a sharp fellow. He already had a suspicion that his guest was not quite right in the head, and he was now convinced of it as he listened to such remarks as these. However, just for the sport of it, he determined to humor him; and so he went on to assure Don Quixote that he was fully justified in his request and that such a desire and purpose was only natural on the part of so distinguished a knight as his gallant bearing plainly showed him to be.

He himself, the landlord added, when he was a young man, had followed the same honorable calling. He had gone through various parts of the world seeking adventures, among the places he had visited being the Percheles of Málaga, the Isles of Riarán, the District of Seville, the Little

Market Place of Segovia, the Olivera of Valencia, the Rondilla of Granada, the beach of Sanlúcar, the Horse Fountain of Cordova, the Small Taverns of Toledo,[9] and numerous other localities where his nimble feet and light fingers had found much exercise. He had done many wrongs, cheated many widows, ruined many maidens, and swindled not a few minors until he had finally come to be known in almost all the courts and tribunals that are to be found in the whole of Spain.

At last he had retired to his castle here, where he lived upon his own income and the property of others; and here it was that he received all knights-errant of whatever quality and condition, simply out of the great affection that he bore them and that they might share with him their possessions in payment of his good will. Unfortunately, in this castle there was no chapel where Don Quixote might keep watch over his arms, for the old chapel had been torn down to make way for a new one; but in case of necessity, he felt quite sure that such a vigil could be maintained anywhere, and for the present occasion the courtyard of the castle would do; and then in the morning, please God, the requisite ceremony could be performed and his guest be duly dubbed a knight, as much a knight as anyone ever was.

He then inquired if Don Quixote had any money on his person, and the latter replied that he had not a cent, for in all the storybooks he had never read of knights-errant carrying any. But the innkeeper told him he was mistaken on this point: supposing the authors of those stories had not set down the fact in black and white, that was because they did not deem it necessary to speak of things as indispensable as money and a clean shirt, and one was not to assume for that reason that those knights-errant of whom the books were so full did not have any. He looked upon it as an absolute certainty that they all had well-stuffed purses, that they might be prepared for any emergency; and they also carried shirts and a little box of ointment for healing the wounds that they received.

For when they had been wounded in combat on the plains and in desert places, there was not always someone at hand to treat them, unless they had some skilled enchanter for a friend who then would succor them, bringing to them through the air, upon a cloud, some damsel or dwarf bearing a vial of water of such virtue that one had but to taste a drop of it and at once his wounds were healed and he was as sound as if he had never received any.

But even if this was not the case, knights in times past saw to it that their squires were well provided with money and other necessities, such as lint and ointment for healing purposes; and if they had no squires — which happened very rarely — they themselves carried these objects in a pair of saddlebags very cleverly attached to their horses' croups in such a manner as to be scarcely noticeable, as if they held something of greater importance than that, for among the knights-errant saddlebags as a rule were not favored. Accordingly, he would advise the novice before him, and inasmuch as the latter was soon to be his godson, he might even command him, that henceforth he should not go without money and a

---

9. All reputed to be haunts of robbers and rogues.

supply of those things that have been mentioned, as he would find that they came in useful at a time when he least expected it.

Don Quixote promised to follow his host's advice punctiliously; and so it was arranged that he should watch his armor in a large barnyard at one side of the inn. He gathered up all the pieces, placed them in a horse trough that stood near the well, and, bracing his shield on his arm, took up his lance and with stately demeanor began pacing up and down in front of the trough even as night was closing in.

The innkeeper informed his other guests of what was going on, of Don Quixote's vigil and his expectation of being dubbed a knight; and, marveling greatly at so extraordinary a variety of madness, they all went out to see for themselves and stood there watching from a distance. For a while the knight-to-be, with tranquil mien, would merely walk up and down; then, leaning on his lance, he would pause to survey his armor, gazing fixedly at it for a considerable length of time. As has been said, it was night now, but the brightness of the moon, which well might rival that of Him who lent it, was such that everything the novice knight did was plainly visible to all.

At this point one of the mule drivers who were stopping at the inn came out to water his drove, and in order to do this it was necessary to remove the armor from the trough.

As he saw the man approaching, Don Quixote cried out to him, "O bold knight, whoever you may be, who thus would dare to lay hands upon the accouterments of the most valiant man of arms that ever girded on a sword, look well what you do and desist if you do not wish to pay with your life for your insolence!"

The muleteer gave no heed to these words—it would have been better for his own sake had he done so—but, taking it up by the straps, tossed the armor some distance from him. When he beheld this, Don Quixote rolled his eyes heavenward and with his thoughts apparently upon his Dulcinea exclaimed, "Succor, O lady mine, this vassal heart in this my first encounter; let not your favor and protection fail me in the peril in which for the first time I now find myself."

With these and other similar words, he loosed his buckler, grasped his lance in both his hands, and let the mule driver have such a blow on the head that the man fell to the ground stunned; and had it been followed by another one, he would have had no need of a surgeon to treat him. Having done this, Don Quixote gathered up his armor and resumed his pacing up and down with the same calm manner as before. Not long afterward, without knowing what had happened—for the first muleteer was still lying there unconscious—another came out with the same intention of watering his mules, and he too was about to remove the armor from the trough when the knight, without saying a word or asking favor of anyone, once more adjusted his buckler and raised his lance, and if he did not break the second mule driver's head to bits, he made more than three pieces of it by dividing it into quarters. At the sound of the fracas everybody in the inn came running out, among them the innkeeper; whereupon Don Quixote again lifted his buckler and laid his hand on his sword.

"O lady of beauty," he said, "strength and vigor of this fainting heart of mine! Now is the time to turn the eyes of your greatness upon this captive knight of yours who must face so formidable an adventure."

By this time he had worked himself up to such a pitch of anger that if all the mule drivers in the world had attacked him he would not have taken one step backward. The comrades of the wounded men, seeing the plight those two were in, now began showering stones on Don Quixote, who shielded himself as best he could with his buckler, although he did not dare stir from the trough for fear of leaving his armor unprotected. The landlord, meanwhile, kept calling for them to stop, for he had told them that this was a madman who would be sure to go free even though he killed them all. The knight was shouting louder than ever, calling them knaves and traitors. As for the lord of the castle, who allowed knights-errant to be treated in this fashion, he was a lowborn villain, and if he, Don Quixote, had but received the order of knighthood, he would make him pay for his treachery.

"As for you others, vile and filthy rabble, I take no account of you; you may stone me or come forward and attack me all you like; you shall see what the reward of your folly and insolence will be."

He spoke so vigorously and was so undaunted in bearing as to strike terror in those who would assail him; and for this reason, and owing also to the persuasions of the innkeeper, they ceased stoning him. He then permitted them to carry away the wounded, and went back to watching his armor with the same tranquil, unconcerned air that he had previously displayed.

The landlord was none too well pleased with these mad pranks on the part of his guest and determined to confer upon him that accursed order of knighthood before something else happened. Going up to him, he begged Don Quixote's pardon for the insolence which, without his knowledge, had been shown the knight by those of low degree. They, however, had been well punished for their impudence. As he had said, there was no chapel in this castle, but for that which remained to be done there was no need of any. According to what he had read of the ceremonial of the order, there was nothing to this business of being dubbed a knight except a slap on the neck and one across the shoulder, and that could be performed in the middle of a field as well as anywhere else. All that was required was for the knight-to-be to keep watch over his armor for a couple of hours, and Don Quixote had been at it more than four. The latter believed all this and announced that he was ready to obey and get the matter over with as speedily as possible. Once dubbed a knight, if he were attacked one more time, he did not think that he would leave a single person in the castle alive, save such as he might command be spared, at the bidding of his host and out of respect to him.

Thus warned, and fearful that it might occur, the castellan brought out the book in which he had jotted down the hay and barley for which the mule drivers owed him, and, accompanied by a lad bearing the butt of a candle and the two aforesaid damsels, he came up to where Don Quixote stood and commanded him to kneel. Reading from the account book—as if he had been saying a prayer—he raised his hand and, with the knight's own sword, gave him a good thwack upon the neck and another lusty one upon the shoulder, muttering all the while between his teeth. He then directed one of the ladies to gird on Don Quixote's sword, which she did with much gravity and composure; for it was all they could do to keep from laughing at every point of the ceremony, but the thought of the knight's prowess which they had already witnessed was sufficient to restrain their mirth.

"May God give your Grace much good fortune," said the worthy lady as she attached the blade, "and prosper you in battle."

Don Quixote thereupon inquired her name, for he desired to know to whom it was he was indebted for the favor he had just received, that he might share with her some of the honor which his strong right arm was sure to bring him. She replied very humbly that her name was Tolosa and that she was the daughter of a shoemaker, a native of Toledo who lived in the stalls of Sancho Bicnaya.[1] To this the knight replied that she would do him a very great favor if from then on she would call herself Doña Tolosa, and she promised to do so. The other girl then helped him on with his spurs, and practically the same conversation was repeated. When asked her name, she stated that it was La Molinera and added that she was the daughter of a respectable miller of Antequera. Don Quixote likewise requested her to assume the "don" and become Doña Molinera and offered to render her further services and favors.

These unheard-of ceremonies having been dispatched in great haste, Don Quixote could scarcely wait to be astride his horse and sally forth on his quest for adventures. Saddling and mounting Rocinante, he embraced his host, thanking him for the favor of having dubbed him a knight and saying such strange things that it would be quite impossible to record them here. The innkeeper, who was only too glad to be rid of him, answered with a speech that was no less flowery, though somewhat shorter, and he did not so much as ask him for the price of a lodging, so glad was he to see him go.

CHAPTER 4

Of what happened to our knight when he sallied forth from the inn.

Day was dawning when Don Quixote left the inn, so well satisfied with himself, so gay, so exhilarated, that the very girths of his steed all but burst with joy. But remembering the advice which his host had given him concerning the stock of necessary provisions that he should carry with him, especially money and shirts, he decided to turn back home and supply himself with whatever he needed, and with a squire as well; he had in mind a farmer who was a neighbor of his, a poor man and the father of a family but very well suited to fulfill the duties of squire to a man of arms. With this thought in mind he guided Rocinante toward the village once more, and that animal, realizing that he was homeward bound, began stepping out at so lively a gait that it seemed as if his feet barely touched the ground.

1. An old square in Toledo.

The knight had not gone far when from a hedge on his right hand he heard the sound of faint moans as of someone in distress.

"Thanks be to Heaven," he at once exclaimed, "for the favor it has shown me by providing me so soon with an opportunity to fulfill the obligations that I owe to my profession, a chance to pluck the fruit of my worthy desires. Those, undoubtedly, are the cries of someone in distress, who stands in need of my favor and assistance."

Turning Rocinante's head, he rode back to the place from which the cries appeared to be coming. Entering the wood, he had gone but a few paces when he saw a mare attached to an oak, while bound to another tree was a lad of fifteen or thereabouts, naked from the waist up. It was he who was uttering the cries, and not without reason, for there in front of him was a lusty farmer with a girdle who was giving him many lashes, each one accompanied by a reproof and a command, "Hold your tongue and keep your eyes open"; and the lad was saying, "I won't do it again, sir; by God's Passion, I won't do it again. I promise you that after this I'll take better care of the flock."

When he saw what was going on, Don Quixote was very angry. "Discourteous knight," he said, "it ill becomes you to strike one who is powerless to defend himself. Mount your steed and take your lance in hand" — for there was a lance leaning against the oak to which the mare was tied — "and I will show you what a coward you are."

The farmer, seeing before him this figure all clad in armor and brandishing a lance, decided that he was as good as done for. "Sir Knight," he said, speaking very mildly, "this lad that I am punishing here is my servant; he tends a flock of sheep which I have in these parts and he is so careless that every day one of them shows up missing. And when I punish him for his carelessness or his roguery, he says it is just because I am a miser and do not want to pay him the wages that I owe him, but I swear to God and upon my soul that he lies."

"It is you who lie, base lout," said Don Quixote, "and in my presence; and by the sun that gives us light, I am minded to run you through with this lance. Pay him and say no more about it, or else, by the God who rules us, I will make an end of you and annihilate you here and now. Release him at once."

The farmer hung his head and without a word untied his servant. Don Quixote then asked the boy how much has master owed him. For nine months' work, the lad told him, at seven reales the month. The knight did a little reckoning and found that this came to sixty-three reales; whereupon he ordered the farmer to pay over the money immediately, as he valued his life. The cowardly bumpkin replied that, facing death as he was and by the oath that he had sworn — he had not sworn any oath as yet — it did not amount to as much as that; for there were three pairs of shoes which he had given the lad that were to be deducted and taken into account, and a real for two blood-lettings when his servant was ill.

"That," said Don Quixote, "is all very well; but let the shoes and the blood-lettings go for the undeserved lashings which you have given him; if he has worn out the leather of the shoes that you paid for, you have taken the hide off his body, and if the barber let a little blood for him when he was sick,[2] you have done the same when he was well; and so far as that goes, he owes you nothing."

"But the trouble is, Sir Knight, that I have no money with me. Come along home with me, Andrés, and I will pay you real for real."

"I go home with him!" cried the lad. "Never in the world! No, sir, I would not even think of it; for once he has me alone he'll flay me like a St. Bartholomew."

"He will do nothing of the sort," said Don Quixote. "It is sufficient for me to command, and he out of respect will obey. Since he has sworn to me by the order of knighthood which he has received, I shall let him go free and I will guarantee that you will be paid."

"But look, your Grace," the lad remonstrated, "my master is no knight; he has never received any order of knighthood whatsoever. He is Juan Haldudo, a rich man and a resident of Quintanar."

"That makes little difference," declared Don Quixote, "for there may well be knights among the Haldudos, all the more so in view of the fact that every man is the son of his works."

"That is true enough," said Andrés, "but this master of mine—of what works is he the son, seeing that he refuses me the pay for my sweat and labor?"

"I do not refuse you, brother Andrés," said the farmer. "Do me the favor of coming with me, and I swear to you by all the orders of knighthood that there are in this world to pay you, as I have said, real for real, and perfumed at that."

"You can dispense with the perfume," said Don Quixote; "just give him the reales and I shall be satisfied. And see to it that you keep your oath, or by the one that I myself have sworn I shall return to seek you out and chastise you, and I shall find you though you be as well hidden as a lizard. In case you would like to know who it is that is giving you this command in order that you may feel the more obliged to comply with it, I may tell you that I am the valorous Don Quixote de la Mancha, righter of wrongs and injustices; and so, God be with you, and do not fail to do as you have promised, under that penalty that I have pronounced."

As he said this, he put spurs to Rocinante and was off. The farmer watched him go, and when he saw that Don Quixote was out of the wood and out of sight, he turned to his servant, Andrés.

"Come here, my son," he said. "I want to pay you what I owe you as that righter of wrongs has commanded me."

"Take my word for it," replied Andrés, "your Grace would do well to observe the command of that good knight—may he live a thousand years; for as he is valorous and a righteous judge, if you don't pay me then, by Rocque,[3] he will come back and do just what he said!"

"And I will give you my word as well," said the farmer; "but seeing that I am so fond of you, I wish to increase the debt, that I may owe you all the more." And with this he seized the lad's arm and bound him to the tree again and flogged him within an inch of his life. "There, Master Andrés, you may call on that righter of wrongs if you like and you will see

---

2. Barbers were also surgeons.   3. The origin of this oath is unknown.

whether or not he rights this one. I do not think I have quite finished with you yet, for I have a good mind to flay you alive as you feared."

Finally, however, he unbound him and told him he might go look for that judge of his to carry out the sentence that had been pronounced. Andrés left, rather down in the mouth, swearing that he would indeed go look for the brave Don Quixote de la Mancha; he would relate to him everything that had happened, point by point, and the farmer would have to pay for it seven times over. But for all that, he went away weeping, and his master stood laughing at him.

Such was the manner in which the valorous knight righted this particular wrong. Don Quixote was quite content with the way everything had turned out; it seemed to him that he had made a very fortunate and noble beginning with his deeds of chivalry, and he was very well satisfied with himself as he jogged along in the direction of his native village, talking to himself in a low voice all the while.

"Well may'st thou call thyself fortunate today, above all other women on earth, O fairest of the fair, Dulcinea del Toboso! Seeing that it has fallen to thy lot to hold subject and submissive to thine every wish and pleasure so valiant and renowned a knight as Don Quixote de la Mancha is and shall be, who, as everyone knows, yesterday received the order of knighthood and this day has righted the greatest wrong and grievance that injustice ever conceived or cruelty ever perpetrated, by snatching the lash from the hand of the merciless foeman who was so unreasonably flogging that tender child."

At this point he came to a road that forked off in four directions, and at once he thought of those crossroads where knights-errant would pause to consider which path they should take. By way of imitating them, he halted there for a while; and when he had given the subject much thought, he slackened Rocinante's rein and let the hack follow its inclination. The animal's first impulse was to make straight for its own stable. After they had gone a couple of miles or so Don Quixote caught sight of what appeared to be a great throng of people, who, as was afterward learned, were certain merchants of Toledo on their way to purchase silk at Murcia. There were six of them altogether with their sunshades, accompanied by four attendants on horseback and three mule drivers on foot.

No sooner had he sighted them than Don Quixote imagined that he was on the brink of some fresh adventure. He was eager to imitate those passages at arms of which he had read in his books, and here, so it seemed to him, was one made to order. And so, with bold and knightly bearing, he settled himself firmly in the stirrups, couched his lance, covered himself with his shield, and took up a position in the middle of the road, where he paused to wait for those other knights-errant (for such he took them to be) to come up to him. When they were near enough to see and hear plainly, Don Quixote raised his voice and made a haughty gesture.

"Let everyone," he cried, "stand where he is, unless everyone will confess that there is not in all the world a more beauteous damsel than the Empress of La Mancha, the peerless Dulcinea del Toboso."

Upon hearing these words and beholding the weird figure who uttered them, the merchants stopped short. From the knight's appearance and his speech they knew at once that they had to deal with a madman; but they were curious to know what was meant by that confession that was demanded of them, and one of their number who was somewhat of a jester and a very clever fellow raised his voice.

"Sir Knight," he said, "we do not know who this beauteous lady is of whom you speak. Show her to us, and if she is as beautiful as you say, then we will right willingly and without any compulsion confess the truth as you have asked of us."

"If I were to show her to you," replied Don Quixote, "what merit would there be in your confessing a truth so self-evident? The important thing is for you, without seeing her, to believe, confess, affirm, swear, and defend that truth. Otherwise, monstrous and arrogant creatures that you are, you shall do battle with me. Come on, then, one by one, as the order of knighthood prescribes; or all of you together, if you will have it so, as is the sorry custom of those of your breed. Come on, and I will await you here, for I am confident that my cause is just."

"Sir Knight," responded the merchant, "I beg your Grace, in the name of all the princes here present, in order that we may not have upon our consciences the burden of confessing a thing which we have never seen nor heard, and one, moreover, so prejudicial to the empresses and queens of Alcarria and Estremadura,[4] that your Grace will show us some portrait of this lady, even though it be no larger than a grain of wheat, for by the thread one comes to the ball of yarn; and with this we shall remain satisfied and assured, and your Grace will likewise be content and satisfied. The truth is, I believe that we are already so much of your way of thinking that though it should show her to be blind of one eye and distilling vermilion and brimstone from the other, nevertheless, to please your Grace, we would say in her behalf all that you desire."

"She distills nothing of the sort, infamous rabble!" shouted Don Quixote, for his wrath was kindling now. "I tell you, she does not distill what you say at all, but amber and civet[5] wrapped in cotton; and she is neither one-eyed nor hunchbacked but straighter than a spindle that comes from Guadarrama. You shall pay for the great blasphemy which you have uttered against such a beauty as is my lady!"

Saying this, he came on with lowered lance against the one who had spoken, charging with such wrath and fury that if fortune had not caused Rocinante to stumble and fall in mid-career, things would have gone badly with the merchant and he would have paid for his insolent gibe. As it was, Don Quixote went rolling over the plain for some little distance, and when he tried to get to his feet, found that he was unable to do so, being too encumbered with his lance, shield, spurs, helmet, and the weight of that ancient suit of armor.

"Do not flee, cowardly ones," he cried even as he struggled to rise. "Stay, cravens, for it is not my fault but that of my steed that I am stretched out here."

One of the muleteers, who must have been an ill-natured lad, upon

---

4. Ironical, because both were known as particularly backward regions.   5. A musky substance used in perfume, imported from Africa in cotton packings.

hearing the poor fallen knight speak so arrogantly, could not refrain from giving him an answer in the ribs. Going up to him, he took the knight's lance and broke it into bits, and then with a companion proceeded to belabor him so mercilessly that in spite of his armor they milled him like a hopper of wheat. The merchants called to them not to lay on so hard, saying that was enough and they should desist, but the mule driver by this time had warmed up to the sport and would not stop until he had vented his wrath, and, snatching up the broken pieces of the lance, he began hurling them at the wretched victim as he lay there on the ground. And through all this tempest of sticks that rained upon him Don Quixote never once closed his mouth nor ceased threatening Heaven and earth and these ruffians, for such he took them to be, who were thus mishandling him.

Finally the lad grew tired, and the merchants went their way with a good story to tell about the poor fellow who had had such a cudgeling. Finding himself alone, the knight endeavored to see if he could rise; but if this was a feat that he could not accomplish when he was sound and whole, how was he to achieve it when he had been thrashed and pounded to a pulp? Yet nonetheless he considered himself fortunate; for as he saw it, misfortunes such as this were common to knights-errant, and he put all the blame upon his horse; and if he was unable to rise, that was because his body was so bruised and battered all over.

CHAPTER 5

In which is continued the narrative of the misfortune that befell our knight.

Seeing, then, that he was indeed unable to stir, he decided to fall back upon a favorite remedy of his, which was to think of some passage or other in his books; and as it happened, the one that he in his madness now recalled was the story of Baldwin and the Marquis of Mantua, when Carloto left the former wounded upon the mountainside,[6] a tale that is known to children, not unknown to young men, celebrated and believed in by the old, and, for all of that, not any truer than the miracles of Mohammed. Moreover, it impressed him as being especially suited to the straits in which he found himself; and, accordingly, with a great show of feeling, he began rolling and tossing on the ground as he feebly gasped out the lines which the wounded knight of the wood is supposed to have uttered:

> "Where art thou, lady mine,
> That thou dost not grieve for my woe?
> Either thou art disloyal,
> Or my grief thou dost not know."

He went on reciting the old ballad until he came to the following verses:

> "O noble Marquis of Mantua,
> My uncle and liege lord true!"

6. The allusion is to an old ballad about Charlemagne's son Charlot (Carloto) wounding Baldwin, nephew of the Marquis of Mantua.

He had reached this point when down the road came a farmer of the same village, a neighbor of his, who had been to the mill with a load of wheat. Seeing a man lying there stretched out like that, he went up to him and inquired who he was and what was the trouble that caused him to utter such mournful complaints. Thinking that this must undoubtedly be his uncle, the Marquis of Mantua, Don Quixote did not answer but went on with his recitation of the ballad, giving an account of the Marquis' misfortunes and the amours of his wife and the emperor's son, exactly as the ballad has it.

The farmer was astounded at hearing all these absurdities, and after removing the knight's visor which had been battered to pieces by the blows it had received, the good man bathed the victim's face, only to discover, once the dust was off, that he knew him very well.

"Señor Quejana," he said (for such must have been Don Quixote's real name when he was in his right senses and before he had given up the life of a quiet country gentleman to become a knight-errant), "who is responsible for your Grace's being in such a plight as this?"

But the knight merely went on with his ballad in response to all the questions asked of him. Perceiving that it was impossible to obtain any information from him, the farmer as best he could relieved him of his breastplate and backpiece to see if he had any wounds, but there was no blood and no mark of any sort. He then tried to lift him from the ground, and with a great deal of effort finally managed to get him astride the ass, which appeared to be the easier mount for him. Gathering up the armor, including even the splinters from the lance, he made a bundle and tied it on Rocinante's back, and, taking the horse by the reins and the ass by the halter, he started out for the village. He was worried in his mind at hearing all the foolish things that Don Quixote said, and that individual himself was far from being at ease. Unable by reason of his bruises and his soreness to sit upright on the donkey, our knight-errant kept sighing to Heaven, which led the farmer to ask him once more what it was that ailed him.

It must have been the devil himself who caused him to remember those tales that seemed to fit his own case; for at this point he forgot all about Baldwin and recalled Abindarráez, and how the governor of Antequera, Rodrigo de Narváez, had taken him prisoner and carried him off captive to his castle. Accordingly, when the countryman turned to inquire how he was and what was troubling him, Don Quixote replied with the very same words and phrases that the captive Abindarráez used in answering Rodrigo, just as he had read in the story Diana of Jorge de Montemayor,[7] where it is all written down, applying them very aptly to the present circumstances as the farmer went along cursing his luck for having to listen to such a lot of nonsense. Realizing that his neighbor was quite mad, he made haste to reach the village that he might not have to be annoyed any longer by Don Quixote's tiresome harangue.

"Señor Don Rodrigo de Narváez," the knight was saying, "I may inform your Grace that this beautiful Jarifa of whom I speak is not the lovely

---

7. The reference is to the tale of the love of Abindarráez, a captive Moor, for the beautiful Jarifa, included in the 2nd edition of Jorge de Montemayor's Diana, a pastoral romance.

Dulcinea del Toboso, in whose behalf I have done, am doing, and shall do the most famous deeds of chivalry that ever have been or will be seen in all the world."

"But, sir," replied the farmer, "sinner that I am, cannot your Grace see that I am not Don Rodrigo de Narváez nor the Marquis of Mantua, but Pedro Alonso, your neighbor? And your Grace is neither Baldwin nor Abindarráez but a respectable gentleman by the name of Señor Quijana."

"I know who I am," said Don Quixote, "and who I may be, if I choose: not only those I have mentioned but all the Twelve Peers of France and the Nine Worthies[8] as well; for the exploits of all of them together, or separately, cannot compare with mine."

With such talk as this they reached their destination just as night was falling; but the farmer decided to wait until it was a little darker in order that the badly battered gentleman might not be seen arriving in such a condition and mounted on an ass. When he thought the proper time had come, they entered the village and proceeded to Don Quixote's house, where they found everything in confusion. The curate and the barber were there, for they were great friends of the knight, and the housekeeper was speaking to them.

"Señor Licentiate Pero Pérez," she was saying, for that was the manner in which she addressed the curate, "what does your Grace think could have happened to my master? Three days now, and not a word of him, nor the hack, nor the buckler, nor the lance, nor the suit of armor. Ah, poor me! I am as certain as I am that I was born to die that it is those cursed books of chivalry he is always reading that have turned his head; for now that I recall, I have often heard him muttering to himself that he must become a knight-errant and go through the world in search of adventures. May such books as those be consigned to Satan and Barabbas,[9] for they have sent to perdition the finest mind in all La Mancha."

The niece was of the same opinion. "I may tell you, Señor Master Nicholas," she said, for that was the barber's name, "that many times my uncle would sit reading those impious tales of misadventure for two whole days and nights at a stretch; and when he was through, he would toss the book aside, lay his hand on his sword, and begin slashing at the walls. When he was completely exhausted, he would tell us that he had just killed four giants as big as castle towers, while the sweat that poured off him was blood from the wounds that he had received in battle. He would then drink a big jug of cold water, after which he would be very calm and peaceful, saying that the water was the most precious liquid which the wise Esquife, a great magician and his friend, had brought to him. But I blame myself for everything. I should have advised your Worships of my uncle's nonsensical actions so that you could have done something about it by burning those damnable books of his before things came to such a pass; for he has many that ought to be burned as if they were heretics."

8. In French medieval epics, the Twelve Peers (Roland, Olivier, and so on) were warriors all equal in rank, forming a kind of guard of honor around Charlemagne. In a tradition originating in France, the Nine Worthies consisted of three biblical, three classical, and three Christian figures (David, Hector, Alexander, Charlemagne, and so on).   9. The thief whose release, rather than that of Jesus, the crowd requested when Pilate, conforming to Passover custom, was ready to have one prisoner set free.

"I agree with you," said the curate, "and before tomorrow's sun has set there shall be a public *auto da fé*, and those works shall be condemned to the flames that they may not lead some other who reads them to follow the example of my good friend."

Don Quixote and the farmer overheard all this, and it was then that the latter came to understand the nature of his neighbor's affliction.

"Open the door, your Worships," the good man cried. "Open for Sir Baldwin and the Marquis of Mantua, who comes badly wounded, and for Señor Abindarráez the Moor whom the valiant Rodrigo de Narváez, governor of Antequera, brings captive."

At the sound of his voice they all ran out, recognizing at once friend, master, and uncle, who as yet was unable to get down off the donkey's back. They all ran up to embrace him.

"Wait, all of you," said Don Quixote, "for I am sorely wounded through fault of my steed. Bear me to my couch and summon, if it be possible, the wise Urganda to treat and care for my wounds."

"There!" exclaimed the housekeeper. "Plague take it! Did not my heart tell me right as to which foot my master limped on? To bed with your Grace at once, and we will take care of you without sending for that Urganda of yours. A curse, I say, and a hundred other curses, on those books of chivalry that have brought your Grace to this."

And so they carried him off to bed, but when they went to look for his wounds, they found none at all. He told them it was all the result of a great fall he had taken with Rocinante, his horse, while engaged in combating ten giants, the hugest and most insolent that were ever heard of in all the world.

"Tut, tut," said the curate. "So there are giants in the dance now, are there? Then, by the sign of the cross, I'll have them burned before nightfall tomorrow."

They had a thousand questions to put to Don Quixote, but his only answer was that they should give him something to eat and let him sleep, for that was the most important thing of all; so they humored him in this. The curate then interrogated the farmer at great length concerning the conversation he had had with his neighbor. The peasant told him everything, all the absurd things their friend had said when he found him lying there and afterward on the way home, all of which made the licentiate more anxious than ever to do what he did the following day,[1] when he summoned Master Nicholas and went with him to Don Quixote's house.

[*Fighting the Windmills and a Choleric Biscayan*]

CHAPTER 7

Of the second sally of our good knight, Don Quixote de la Mancha.

* * * After that he remained at home very tranquilly for a couple of weeks, without giving sign of any desire to repeat his former madness. During that time he had the most pleasant conversations with his two old

---

1. He and the barber burned most of Don Quixote's library.

friends, the curate and the barber, on the point he had raised to the effect that what the world needed most was knights-errant and a revival of chivalry. The curate would occasionally contradict him and again would give in, for it was only by means of this artifice that he could carry on a conversation with him at all.

In the meanwhile Don Quixote was bringing his powers of persuasion to bear upon a farmer who lived near by, a good man—if this title may be applied to one who is poor—but with very few wits in his head. The short of it is, by pleas and promises, he got the hapless rustic to agree to ride forth with him and serve him as his squire. Among other things, Don Quixote told him that he ought to be more than willing to go, because no telling what adventure might occur which would win them an island, and then he (the farmer) would be left to be the governor of it. As a result of these and other similar assurances, Sancho Panza forsook his wife and children and consented to take upon himself the duties of squire to his neighbor.

Next, Don Quixote set out to raise some money, and by selling this thing and pawning that and getting the worst of the bargain always, he finally scraped together a reasonable amount. He also asked a friend of his for the loan of a buckler and patched up his broken helmet as well as he could. He advised his squire, Sancho, of the day and hour when they were to take to the road and told him to see to laying in a supply of those things that were most necessary, and, above all, not to forget the saddlebags. Sancho replied that he would see to all this and added that he was also thinking of taking along with him a very good ass that he had, as he was not much used to going on foot.

With regard to the ass, Don Quixote had to do a little thinking, trying to recall if any knight-errant had ever had a squire thus asininely mounted. He could not think of any, but nevertheless he decided to take Sancho with the intention of providing him with a nobler steed as soon as occasion offered; he had but to appropriate the horse of the first discourteous knight he met. Having furnished himself with shirts and all the other things that the innkeeper had recommended, he and Panza rode forth one night unseen by anyone and without taking leave of wife and children, housekeeper or niece. They went so far that by the time morning came they were safe from discovery had a hunt been started for them.

Mounted on his ass, Sancho Panza rode along like a patriarch, with saddlebags and flask, his mind set upon becoming governor of that island that his master had promised him. Don Quixote determined to take the same route and road over the Campo de Montiel that he had followed on his first journey; but he was not so uncomfortable this time, for it was early morning and the sun's rays fell upon them slantingly and accordingly did not tire them too much.

"Look, Sir Knight-errant," said Sancho, "your Grace should not forget that island you promised me; for no matter how big it is, I'll be able to govern it right enough."

"I would have you know, friend Sancho Panza," replied Don Quixote, "that among the knights-errant of old it was a very common custom to make their squires governors of the islands or the kingdoms that they won, and I am resolved that in my case so pleasing a usage shall not fall into desuetude. I even mean to go them one better; for they very often, perhaps most of the time, waited until their squires were old men who had had their fill of serving their masters during bad days and worse nights, whereupon they would give them the title of count, or marquis at most, of some valley or province more or less. But if you live and I live, it well may be that within a week I shall win some kingdom with others dependent upon it, and it will be the easiest thing in the world to crown you king of one of them. You need not marvel at this, for all sorts of unforeseen things happen to knights like me, and I may readily be able to give you even more than I have promised."

"In that case," said Sancho Panza, "if by one of those miracles of which your Grace was speaking I should become king, I would certainly send for Juana Gutiérrez, my old lady, to come and be my queen, and the young ones could be infantes."

"There is no doubt about it," Don Quixote assured him.

"Well, I doubt it," said Sancho, "for I think that even if God were to rain kingdoms upon the earth, no crown would sit well on the head of Mari Gutiérrez,[2] for I am telling you, sir, as a queen she is not worth two maravedis.[3] She would do better as a countess, God help her."

"Leave everything to God, Sancho," said Don Quixote, "and he will give you whatever is most fitting; but I trust you will not be so pusillanimous as to be content with anything less than the title of viceroy."

"That I will not," said Sancho Panza, "especially seeing that I have in your Grace so illustrious a master who can give me all that is suitable to me and all that I can manage."

CHAPTER 8

Of the good fortune which the valorous Don Quixote had in the terrifying and never-before-imagined adventure of the windmills, along with other events that deserve to be suitably recorded.

At this point they caught sight of thirty or forty windmills which were standing on the plain there, and no sooner had Don Quixote laid eyes upon them than he turned to his squire and said, "Fortune is guiding our affairs better than we could have wished; for you see there before you, friend Sancho Panza, some thirty or more lawless giants with whom I mean to do battle. I shall deprive them of their lives, and with the spoils from this encounter we shall begin to enrich ourselves; for this is righteous warfare, and it is a great service to God to remove so accursed a breed from the face of the earth."

"What giants?" said Sancho Panza.

"Those that you see there," replied his master, "those with the long arms some of which are as much as two leagues in length."

"But look, your Grace, those are not giants but windmills, and what appear to be arms are their wings which, when whirled in the breeze, cause the millstone to go."

---

2. Sancho's wife, Juana Gutiérrez.   3. Coin worth one–thirty-fourth of a *real*.

"It is plain to be seen," said Don Quixote, "that you have had little experience in this matter of adventures. If you are afraid, go off to one side and say your prayers while I am engaging them in fierce, unequal combat."

Saying this, he gave spurs to his steed Rocinante, without paying any heed to Sancho's warning that these were truly windmills and not giants that he was riding forth to attack. Nor even when he was close upon them did he perceive what they really were, but shouted at the top of his lungs, "Do not seek to flee, cowards and vile creatures that you are, for it is but a single knight with whom you have to deal!"

At that moment a little wind came up and the big wings began turning. "Though you flourish as many arms as did the giant Briareus,"[4] said Don Quixote when he perceived this, "you still shall have to answer to me."

He thereupon commended himself with all his heart to his lady Dulcinea, beseeching her to succor him in this peril; and, being well covered with his shield and with his lance at rest, he bore down upon them at a full gallop and fell upon the first mill that stood in his way, giving a thrust at the wing, which was whirling at such a speed that his lance was broken into bits and both horse and horseman went rolling over the plain, very much battered indeed. Sancho upon his donkey came hurrying to his master's assistance as fast as he could, but when he reached the spot, the knight was unable to move, so great was the shock with which he and Rocinante had hit the ground.

"God help us!" exclaimed Sancho, "did I not tell your Grace to look well, that those were nothing but windmills, a fact which no one could fail to see unless he had other mills of the same sort in his head?"

"Be quiet, friend Sancho," said Don Quixote. "Such are the fortunes of war, which more than any other are subject to constant change. What is more, when I come to think of it, I am sure that this must be the work of that magician Frestón, the one who robbed me of my study and my books,[5] and who has thus changed the giants into windmills in order to deprive me of the glory of overcoming them, so great is the enmity that he bears me; but in the end his evil arts shall not prevail against this trusty sword of mine."

"May God's will be done," was Sancho Panza's response. And with the aid of his squire the knight was once more mounted on Rocinante, who stood there with one shoulder half out of joint. And so, speaking of the adventure that had just befallen them, they continued along the Puerto Lápice highway; for there, Don Quixote said, they could not fail to find many and varied adventures, this being a much traveled thoroughfare. The only thing was, the knight was exceedingly downcast over the loss of his lance.

"I remember," he said to his squire, "having read of a Spanish knight by the name of Diego Pérez de Vargas, who, having broken his sword in battle, tore from an oak a heavy bough or branch and with it did such feats

4. Mythological giant with a hundred arms.   5. Don Quixote had promptly attributed the ruin of his library to magical intervention (see n. 1, p. 1548).

of valor that day, and pounded so many Moors, that he came to be known as Machuca,[6] and he and his descendants from that day forth have been called Vargas y Machuca. I tell you this because I too intend to provide myself with just such a bough as the one he wielded, and with it I propose to do such exploits that you shall deem yourself fortunate to have been found worthy to come with me and behold and witness things that are almost beyond belief."

"God's will be done," said Sancho. "I believe everything that your Grace says; but straighten yourself up in the saddle a little, for you seem to be slipping down on one side, owing, no doubt, to the shaking-up that you received in your fall."

"Ah, that is the truth," replied Don Quixote, "and if I do not speak of my sufferings, it is for the reason that it is not permitted knights-errant to complain of any wound whatsoever, even though their bowels may be dropping out."

"If that is the way it is," said Sancho, "I have nothing more to say; but, God knows, it would suit me better if your Grace did complain when something hurts him. I can assure you that I mean to do so, over the least little thing that ails me—that is, unless the same rule applies to squires as well."

Don Quixote laughed long and heartily over Sancho's simplicity, telling him that he might complain as much as he liked and where and when he liked, whether he had good cause or not; for he had read nothing to the contrary in the ordinances of chivalry. Sancho then called his master's attention to the fact that it was time to eat. The knight replied that he himself had no need of food at the moment, but his squire might eat whenever he chose. Having been granted this permission, Sancho seated himself as best he could upon his beast, and, taking out from his saddle-bags the provisions that he had stored there, he rode along leisurely behind his master, munching his victuals and taking a good, hearty swig now and then at the leather flask in a manner that might well have caused the biggest-bellied tavernkeeper of Málaga to envy him. Between draughts he gave not so much as a thought to any promise that his master might have made him, nor did he look upon it as any hardship, but rather as good sport, to go in quest of adventures however hazardous they might be.

The short of the matter is, they spent the night under some trees, from one of which Don Quixote tore off a withered bough to serve him as a lance, placing it in the lance head from which he had removed the broken one. He did not sleep all night long for thinking of his lady Dulcinea; for this was in accordance with what he had read in his books, of men of arms in the forest or desert places who kept a wakeful vigil, sustained by the memory of their ladies fair. Not so with Sancho, whose stomach was full, and not with chicory water. He fell into a dreamless slumber, and had not his master called him, he would not have been awakened either by the rays of the sun in his face or by the many birds who greeted the coming of the new day with their merry song. Upon arising, he had another go at the flask, finding it somewhat more

6. "The Crusher," the hero of a folk ballad.

flaccid then it had been the night before, a circumstance which grieved his heart, for he could not see that they were on the way to remedying the deficiency within any very short space of time. Don Quixote did not wish any breakfast; for, as has been said, he was in the habit of nourishing himself on savorous memories. They then set out once more along the road to Puerto Lápice, and around three in the afternoon they came in sight of the pass that bears that name.

"There," said Don Quixote as his eyes fell upon it, "we may plunge our arms up to the elbow in what are known as adventures. But I must warn you that even though you see me in the greatest peril in the world, you are not to lay hand upon your sword to defend me, unless it be that those who attack me are rabble and men of low degree, in which case you may very well come to my aid; but if they be gentlemen, it is in no wise permitted by the laws of chivalry that you should assist me until you yourself shall have been dubbed a knight."

"Most certainly, sir," replied Sancho, "your Grace shall be very well obeyed in this; all the more so for the reason that I myself am of a peaceful disposition and not fond of meddling in the quarrels and feuds of others. However, when it comes to protecting my own person, I shall not take account of those laws of which you speak, seeing that all laws, human and divine, permit each one to defend himself whenever he is attacked."

"I am willing to grant you that," assented Don Quixote, "but in this matter of defending me against gentlemen you must restrain your natural impulses."

"I promise you I shall do so," said Sancho. "I will observe this precept as I would the Sabbath day."

As they were conversing in this manner, there appeared in the road in front of them two friars of the Order of St. Benedict, mounted upon dromedaries—for the she-mules they rode were certainly no smaller than that. The friars wore travelers' spectacles and carried sunshades, and behind them came a coach accompanied by four or five men on horseback and a couple of muleteers on foot. In the coach, as was afterwards learned, was a lady of Biscay, on her way to Seville to bid farewell to her husband, who had been appointed to some high post in the Indies. The religious were not of her company although they were going by the same road.

The instant Don Quixote laid eyes upon them he turned to his squire. "Either I am mistaken or this is going to be the most famous adventure that ever was seen; for those black-clad figures that you behold must be, and without any doubt are, certain enchanters who are bearing with them a captive princess in that coach, and I must do all I can to right this wrong."

"It will be worse than the windmills," declared Sancho. "Look you, sir, those are Benedictine friars and the coach must be that of some travelers. Mark well what I say and what I do, lest the devil lead you astray."

"I have already told you, Sancho," replied Don Quixote, "that you know little where the subject of adventures is concerned. What I am saying to you is the truth, as you shall now see."

With this, he rode forward and took up a position in the middle of the road along which the friars were coming, and as soon as they appeared to be within earshot he cried out to them in a loud voice, "O devilish and monstrous beings, set free at once the highborn princesses whom you bear captive in that coach, or else prepare at once to meet your death as the just punishment of your evil deeds."

The friars drew rein and sat there in astonishment, marveling as much at Don Quixote's appearance as at the words he spoke. "Sir Knight," they answered him, "we are neither devilish nor monstrous but religious of the Order of St. Benedict who are merely going our way. We know nothing of those who are in that coach, nor of any captive princesses either."

"Soft words," said Don Quixote, "have no effect on me. I know you for what you are, lying rabble!" And without waiting for any further parley he gave spur to Rocinante and, with lowered lance, bore down upon the first friar with such fury and intrepidity that, had not the fellow tumbled from his mule of his own accord, he would have been hurled to the ground and either killed or badly wounded. The second religious, seeing how his companion had been treated, dug his legs into his she-mule's flanks and scurried away over the countryside faster than the wind.

Seeing the friar upon the ground, Sancho Panza slipped lightly from his mount and, falling upon him, began stripping him of his habit. The two mule drivers accompanying the religious thereupon came running up and asked Sancho why he was doing this. The latter replied that the friar's garments belonged to him as legitimate spoils of the battle that his master Don Quixote had just won. The muleteers, however, were lads with no sense of humor, nor did they know what all this talk of spoils and battles was about; but, perceiving that Don Quixote had ridden off to one side to converse with those inside the coach, they pounced upon Sancho, threw him to the ground, and proceeded to pull out the hair of his beard and kick him to a pulp, after which they went off and left him stretched out there, bereft at once of breath and sense.

Without losing any time, they then assisted the friar to remount. The good brother was trembling all over from fright, and there was not a speck of color in his face, but when he found himself in the saddle once more, he quickly spurred his beast to where his companion, at some little distance, sat watching and waiting to see what the result of the encounter would be. Having no curiosity as to the final outcome of the fray, the two of them now resumed their journey, making more signs of the cross than the devil would be able to carry upon his back.

Meanwhile Don Quixote, as we have said, was speaking to the lady in the coach.

"Your beauty, my lady, may now dispose of your person as best may please you, for the arrogance of your abductors lies upon the ground, overthrown by this good arm of mine; and in order that you may not pine to know the name of your liberator, I may inform you that I am Don Quixote de la Mancha, knight-errant and adventurer and captive of the peerless and beauteous Doña Dulcinea del Toboso. In payment of the favor which you have received from me, I ask nothing other than that you return to El Toboso and on my behalf pay your respects to this lady, telling her that it was I who set you free."

One of the squires accompanying those in the coach, a Biscayan,[7] was listening to Don Quixote's words, and when he saw that the knight did not propose to let the coach proceed upon its way but was bent upon having it turn back to El Toboso, he promptly went up to him, seized his lance, and said to him in bad Castilian and worse Biscayan, "Go, *caballero*, and bad luck go with you; for by the God that created me, if you do not let this coach pass, me kill you or me no Biscayan."

Don Quixote heard him attentively enough and answered him very mildly, "If you were a *caballero*,[8] which you are not, I should already have chastised you, wretched creature, for your foolhardiness and your impudence."

"Me no *caballero*." cried the Biscayan "Me swear to God, you lie like a Christian. If you will but lay aside your lance and unsheath your sword, you will soon see that you are carrying water to the cat![9] Biscayan on land, gentleman at sea, but a gentleman in spite of the devil, and you lie if you say otherwise."

" 'You shall see as to that presently,' said Agrajes,"[1] Don Quixote quoted. He cast his lance to the earth, drew his sword, and, taking his buckler on his arm, attacked the Biscayan with intent to slay him. The latter, when he saw his adversary approaching, would have liked to dismount from his mule, for she was one of the worthless sort that are let for hire and he had no confidence in her; but there was no time for this, and so he had no choice but to draw his own sword in turn and make the best of it. However, he was near enough to the coach to be able to snatch a cushion from it to serve him as a shield; and then they fell upon each other as though they were mortal enemies. The rest of those present sought to make peace between them but did not succeed, for the Biscayan with his disjointed phrases kept muttering that if they did not let him finish the battle then he himself would have to kill his mistress and anyone else who tried to stop him.

The lady inside the carriage, amazed by it all and trembling at what she saw, directed her coachman to drive on a little way; and there from a distance she watched the deadly combat, in the course of which the Biscayan came down with a great blow on Don Quixote's shoulder, over the top of the latter's shield, and had not the knight been clad in armor, it would have split him to the waist.

Feeling the weight of this blow, Don Quixote cried out, "O lady of my soul, Dulcinea, flower of beauty, succor this your champion who out of gratitude for your many favors finds himself in so perilous a plight!" To utter these words, lay hold of his sword, cover himself with his buckler, and attack the Biscayan was but the work of a moment; for he was now resolved to risk everything upon a single stroke.

As he saw Don Quixote approaching with so dauntless a bearing, the Biscayan was well aware of his adversary's courage and forthwith determined to imitate the example thus set him. He kept himself protected with his cushion, but he was unable to get his she-mule to budge to one

7. From the Basque region.   8. Knight, gentleman (Spanish).   9. An inversion of a proverbial phrase: "carrying the cat to the water."   1. A violent character in the romance *Amadis de Gaul.* His challenging phrase is the conventional opener of a fight.

side or the other, for the beast, out of sheer exhaustion and being, more-over, unused to such childish play, was incapable of taking a single step. And so, then, as has been stated, Don Quixote was approaching the wary Biscayan, his sword raised on high and with the firm resolve of cleaving his enemy in two; and the Biscayan was awaiting the knight in the same posture, cushion in front of him and with uplifted sword. All the bystand-ers were trembling with suspense at what would happen as a result of the terrible blows that were threatened, and the lady in the coach and her maids were making a thousand vows and offerings to all the images and shrines in Spain, praying that God would save them all and the lady's squire from this great peril that confronted them.

But the unfortunate part of the matter is that at this very point the author of the history breaks off and leaves the battle pending, excusing himself upon the ground that he has been unable to find anything else in writing concerning the exploits of Don Quixote beyond those already set forth. It is true, on the other hand, that the second author[2] of this work could not bring himself to believe that so unusual a chronicle would have been consigned to oblivion, nor that the learned ones of La Mancha were pos-sessed of so little curiosity as not to be able to discover in their archives or registry offices certain papers that have to do with this famous knight. Being convinced of this, he did not despair of coming upon the end of this pleasing story. * * *

CHAPTER 9

In which is concluded and brought to an end the stupendous battle between the gallant Biscayan and the valiant Knight of La Mancha.

* * * We left the valorous Biscayan and the famous Don Quixote with swords unsheathed and raised aloft, about to let fall furious slashing blows which, had they been delivered fairly and squarely, would at the very least have split them in two and laid them wide open from top to bottom like a pomegranate; and it was at this doubtful point that the pleasing chronicle came to a halt and broke off, without the author's informing us as to where the rest of it might be found.

I was deeply grieved by such a circumstance, and the pleasure I had had in reading so slight a portion was turned into annoyance as I thought of how difficult it would be to come upon the greater part which it seemed to me must still be missing. It appeared impossible and contrary to all good precedent that so worthy a knight should not have had some scribe to take upon himself the task of writing an account of these unheard-of exploits; for that was something that had happened to none of the knights-errant who, as the saying has it, had gone forth in quest of adventures, seeing that each of them had one or two chroniclers, as if ready at hand, who not only had set down their deeds, but had depicted their most trivial thoughts and amiable weaknesses, however well concealed they might be. The good knight of La Mancha surely could not have been so unfortunate

---

2. Cervantes himself, adopting here—with tongue in cheek—a device used in the romances of chivalry to create suspense.

as to have lacked what Platir and others like him had in abundance. And so I could not bring myself to believe that this gallant history could have remained thus lopped off and mutilated, and I could not but lay the blame upon the malignity of time, that devourer and consumer of all things, which must either have consumed it or kept it hidden.

On the other hand, I reflected that inasmuch as among the knight's books had been found such modern works as *The Disenchantments of Jealousy* and *The Nymphs and Shepherds of Henares*, his story likewise must be modern, and that even though it might not have been written down, it must remain in the memory of the good folk of his village and the surrounding ones. This thought left me somewhat confused and more than ever desirous of knowing the real and true story, the whole story, of the life and wondrous deeds of our famous Spaniard, Don Quixote, light and mirror of the chivalry of La Mancha, the first in our age and in these calamitous times to devote himself to the hardships and exercises of knight-errantry and to go about righting wrongs, succoring widows, and protecting damsels—damsels such as those who, mounted upon their palfreys and with riding-whip in hand, in full possession of their virginity, were in the habit of going from mountain to mountain and from valley to valley; for unless there were some villain, some rustic with an ax and hood, or some monstrous giant to force them, there were in times past maiden ladies who at the end of eighty years, during all which time they had not slept for a single day beneath a roof, would go to their graves as virginal as when their mothers had borne them.

If I speak of these things, it is for the reason that in this and in all other respects our gallant Quixote is deserving of constant memory and praise, and even I am not to be denied my share of it for my diligence and the labor to which I put myself in searching out the conclusion of this agreeable narrative; although if heaven, luck, and circumstance had not aided me, the world would have had to do without the pleasure and the pastime which anyone may enjoy who will read this work attentively for an hour or two. The manner in which it came about was as follows:

I was standing one day in the Alcaná, or market place, of Toledo when a lad came up to sell some old notebooks and other papers to a silk weaver who was there. As I am extremely fond of reading anything, even though it be but the scraps of paper in the streets, I followed my natural inclination and took one of the books, whereupon I at once perceived that it was written in characters which I recognized as Arabic. I recognized them, but reading them was another thing; and so I began looking around to see if there was any Spanish-speaking Moor near by who would be able to read them for me. It was not very hard to find such an interpreter, nor would it have been even if the tongue in question had been an older and a better one.[3] To make a long story short, chance brought a fellow my way; and when I told him what it was I wished and placed the book in his hands, he opened it in the middle and began reading and at once fell to laughing. When I asked him what the cause of his laughter was, he replied that it was a note which had been written in the margin.

---

3. That is, Hebrew.

I besought him to tell me the content of the note, and he, laughing still, went on, "As I told you, it is something in the margin here: 'This Dulcinea del Toboso, so often referred to, is said to have been the best hand at salting pigs of any woman in all La Mancha.'"

No sooner had I heard the name Dulcinea del Toboso than I was astonished and held in suspense, for at once the thought occurred to me that those notebooks must contain the history of Don Quixote. With this in mind I urged him to read me the title, and he proceeded to do so, turning the Arabic into Castilian upon the spot: *History of Don Quixote de la Mancha, Written by Cid Hamete Benengeli[4] Arabic Historian*. It was all I could do to conceal my satisfaction and, snatching them from the silk weaver, I bought from the lad all the papers and notebooks that he had for half a real; but if he had known or suspected how very much I wanted them, he might well have had more than six reales for them.

The Moor and I then betook ourselves to the cathedral cloister, where I requested him to translate for me into the Castilian tongue all the books that had to do with Don Quixote, adding nothing and subtracting nothing; and I offered him whatever payment he desired. He was content with two arrobas of raisins and two fanegas[5] of wheat and promised to translate them well and faithfully and with all dispatch. However, in order to facilitate matters, and also because I did not wish to let such a find as this out of my hands, I took the fellow home with me, where in a little more than a month and a half he translated the whole of the work just as you will find it set down here.

In the first of the books there was a very lifelike picture of the battle between Don Quixote and the Biscayan, the two being in precisely the same posture as described in the history, their swords upraised, the one covered by his buckler, the other with his cushion. As for the Biscayan's mule, you could see at the distance of a crossbow shot that it was one for hire. Beneath the Biscayan there was a rubric which read: "Don Sancho de Azpeitia," which must undoubtedly have been his name; while beneath the feet of Rocinante was another inscription: "Don Quixote." Rocinante was marvelously portrayed: so long and lank, so lean and flabby, so extremely consumptivelooking that one could well understand the justness and propriety with which the name of "hack" had been bestowed upon him.

Alongside Rocinante stood Sancho Panza, holding the halter of his ass, and below was the legend: "Sancho Zancas." The picture showed him with a big belly, a short body and long shanks, and that must have been where he got the names of Panza y Zancas[6] by which he is a number of times called in the course of the history. There are other small details that might be mentioned, but they are of little importance and have nothing to do with the truth of the story—and no story is bad so long as it is true.

If there is any objection to be raised against the veracity of the present one, it can be only that the author was an Arab, and that nation is known for its lying propensities; but even though they be our enemies, it may

---

4. Citing some ancient chronicle as the author's source and authority is very much in the tradition of the romances. *Benengeli*: eggplant (Arabic).   5. About fifty pounds. *Two arrobas*: three bushels.   6. Paunch and Shanks (Spanish).

readily be understood that they would more likely have detracted from, rather than added to, the chronicle. So it seems to me, at any rate; for whenever he might and should deploy the resources of his pen in praise of so worthy a knight, the author appears to take pains to pass over the matter in silence; all of which in my opinion is ill done and ill conceived, for it should be the duty of historians to be exact, truthful, and dispassionate, and neither interest nor fear nor rancor nor affection should swerve them from the path of truth, whose mother is history, rival of time, depository of deeds, witness of the past, exemplar and adviser to the present, and the future's counselor. In this work, I am sure, will be found all that could be desired in the way of pleasant reading; and if it is lacking in any way, I maintain that this is the fault of that hound of an author rather than of the subject.

But to come to the point, the second part, according to the translation, began as follows:

As the two valorous and enraged combatants stood there, swords upraised and poised on high, it seemed from their bold mien as if they must surely be threatening heaven, earth, and hell itself. The first to let fall a blow was the choleric Biscayan, and he came down with such force and fury that, had not his sword been deflected in mid-air, that single stroke would have sufficed to put an end to this fearful combat and to all our knight's adventures at the same time; but fortune, which was reserving him for greater things, turned aside his adversary's blade in such a manner that, even though it fell upon his left shoulder, it did him no other damage than to strip him completely of his armor on that side, carrying with it a good part of his helmet along with half an ear, the headpiece clattering to the ground with a dreadful din, leaving its wearer in a sorry state.

Heaven help me! Who could properly describe the rage that now entered the heart of our hero of La Mancha as he saw himself treated in this fashion? It may merely be said that he once more reared himself in the stirrups, laid hold of his sword with both hands, and dealt the Biscayan such a blow, over the cushion and upon the head, that, even so good a defense proving useless, it was as if a mountain had fallen upon his enemy. The latter now began bleeding through the mouth, nose, and ears; he seemed about to fall from his mule, and would have fallen, no doubt, if he had not grasped the beast about the neck, but at that moment his feet slipped from the stirrups and his arms let go, and the mule, frightened by the terrible blow, began running across the plain, hurling its rider to the earth with a few quick plunges.

Don Quixote stood watching all this very calmly. When he saw his enemy fall, he leaped from his horse, ran over very nimbly, and thrust the point of his sword into the Biscayan's eyes, calling upon him at the same time to surrender or otherwise he would cut off his head. The Biscayan was so bewildered that he was unable to utter a single word in reply, and things would have gone badly with him, so blind was Don Quixote in his rage, if the ladies of the coach, who up to then had watched the struggle in dismay, had not come up to him at this point and begged him with many blandishments to do them the very great favor of sparing their squire's life.

To which Don Quixote replied with much haughtiness and dignity, "Most certainly, lovely ladies, I shall be very happy to do that which you ask of me, but upon one conditon and understanding, and that is that this knight promise me that he will go to El Toboso and present himself in my behalf before Doña Dulcinea, in order that she may do with him as she may see fit."

Trembling and disconsolate, the ladies did not pause to discuss Don Quixote's request, but without so much as inquiring who Dulcinea might be they promised him that the squire would fulfill that which was commanded of him.

"Very well, then, trusting in your word, I will do him no further harm, even though he has well deserved it."

CHAPTER 10

Of the pleasing conversation that took place between Don Quixote and Sancho Panza, his squire.

By this time Sancho Panza had got to his feet, somewhat the worse for wear as the result of the treatment he had received from the friars' lads. He had been watching the battle attentively and praying God in his heart to give the victory to his master, Don Quixote, in order that he, Sancho, might gain some island where he could go to be governor as had been promised him. Seeing now that the combat was over and the knight was returning to mount Rocinante once more, he went up to hold the stirrup for him; but first he fell on his knees in front of him and, taking his hand, kissed it and said, "May your Grace be pleased, Señor Don Quixote, to grant me the governorship of that island which you have won in this deadly affray; for however large it may be, I feel that I am indeed capable of governing it as well as any man in this world has ever done."

To which Don Quixote replied, "Be advised, brother Sancho, that this adventure and other similar ones have nothing to do with islands; they are affairs of the crossroads in which one gains nothing more than a broken head or an ear the less. Be patient, for there will be others which will not only make you a governor, but more than that."

Sancho thanked him very much and, kissing his hand again and the skirt of his cuirass, he assisted him up on Rocinante's back, after which the squire bestraddled his own mount and started jogging along behind his master, who was now going at a good clip. Without pausing for any further converse with those in the coach, the knight made for a near-by wood, with Sancho following as fast as his beast could trot; but Rocinante was making such speed that the ass and its rider were left behind, and it was necessary to call out to Don Quixote to pull up and wait for them. He did so, reining in Rocinante until the weary Sancho had drawn abreast of him.

"It strikes me, sir," said the squire as he reached his master's side, "that it would be better for us to take refuge in some church; for in view of the way you have treated that one with whom you were fighting, it would be small wonder if they did not lay the matter before the Holy Brotherhood[7] and have us arrested; and faith, if they do that, we shall have to sweat a-plenty before we come out of jail."

"Be quiet," said Don Quixote. "And where have you ever seen, or read of, a knight being brought to justice no matter how many homicides he might have committed?"

"I know nothing about omecils,"[8] replied Sancho, "nor ever in my life did I bear one to anybody; all I know is that the Holy Brotherhood has something to say about those who go around fighting on the highway, and I want nothing of it."

"Do not let it worry you," said Don Quixote, "for I will rescue you from the hands of the Chaldeans, not to speak of the Brotherhood. But answer me upon your life: have you ever seen a more valorous knight than I on all the known face of the earth? Have you ever read in the histories of any other who had more mettle in the attack, more perseverance in sustaining it, more dexterity in wounding his enemy, or more skill in overthrowing him?"

"The truth is," said Sancho, "I have never read any history whatsoever, for I do not know how to read or write; but what I would wager is that in all the days of my life I have never served a more courageous master than your Grace; I only hope your courage is not paid for in the place that I have mentioned. What I would suggest is that your Grace allow me to do something for that ear, for there is much blood coming from it, and I have here in my saddlebags some lint and a little white ointment."

"We could well dispense with all that," said Don Quixote, "if only I had remembered to bring along a vial of Fierabrás's[9] balm, a single drop of which saves time and medicines."

"What vial and what balm is that?" inquired Sancho Panza.

"It is a balm the receipt[1] for which I know by heart; with it one need have no fear of death nor think of dying from any wound. I shall make some of it and give it to you; and thereafter, whenever in any battle you see my body cut in two—as very often happens—all that is necessary is for you to take the part that lies on the ground, before the blood has congealed, and fit it very neatly and with great nicety upon the other part that remains in the saddle, taking care to adjust it evenly and exactly. Then you will give me but a couple of swallows of the balm of which I have told you, and you will see me sounder than an apple in no time at all."

"If that is so," said Panza, "I herewith renounce the governorship of the island you promised me and ask nothing other in payment of my many and faithful services than that your Grace give me the receipt for this wonderful potion, for I am sure that it would be worth more than two reales the ounce anywhere, and that is all I need for a life of ease and honor. But may I be so bold as to ask how much it costs to make it?"

"For less than three reales you can make something like six quarts," Don Quixote told him.

---

7. A tribunal instituted by Ferdinand and Isabella at the end of the 15th century to punish highway robbers.   8. In Spanish a word play on *homecidio-omecillo*. Not to bear an *omecillo* to anybody means not to bear a grudge, and good-natured Sancho does not.   9. A giant Saracen healer in the medieval epics of the Twelve Peers (see n. 8, p. 1547).   1. Recipe.

"Sinner that I am!" exclaimed Sancho. "Then why does your Grace not make some at once and teach me also?"

"Hush, my friend," said the knight, "I mean to teach you greater secrets than that and do you greater favors; but, for the present, let us look after this ear of mine, for it is hurting me more than I like."

Sancho thereupon took the lint and the ointment from his saddlebags; but when Don Quixote caught a glimpse of his helmet, he almost went out of his mind and, laying his hand upon his sword and lifting his eyes heavenward, he cried, "I make a vow to the Creator of all things and to the four holy Gospels in all their fullness of meaning that I will lead from now on the life that the great Marquis of Mantua did after he had sworn to avenge the death of his nephew Baldwin: not to eat bread of a table-cloth, not to embrace his wife, and other things which, although I am unable to recall them, we will look upon as understood—all this until I shall have wreaked an utter vengeance upon the one who has perpetrated such an outrage upon me."

"But let me remind your Grace," said Sancho when he heard these words, "that if the knight fulfills that which was commanded of him, by going to present himself before my lady Dulcinea del Toboso, then he will have paid his debt to you and merits no further punishment at your hands, unless it be for some fresh offense."

"You have spoken very well and to the point," said Don Quixote, "and so I annul the vow I have just made insofar as it has to do with any further vengeance, but I make it and confirm it anew so far as leading the life of which I have spoken is concerned, until such time as I shall have obtained by force of arms from some other knight another headpiece as good as this. And do not think, Sancho, that I am making smoke out of straw; there is one whom I well may imitate in this matter, for the same thing happened in all literalness in the case of Mambrino's helmet[2] which cost Sacripante so dear."

"I wish," said Sancho, "that your Grace would send all such oaths to the devil, for they are very bad for the health and harmful for the conscience as well. Tell me, please; supposing that for many days to come we meet no man wearing a helmet, then what are we to do? Must you still keep your vow in spite of all the inconveniences and discomforts, such as sleeping with your clothes on, not sleeping in any town, and a thousand other penances contained in the oath of that old madman of a Marquis of Mantua, an oath which you would now revive? Mark you, sir, along all these roads you meet no men of arms but only muleteers and carters, who not only do not wear helmets but quite likely have never heard tell of them in all their livelong days."

"In that you are wrong," said Don Quixote, "for we shall not be at these crossroads for the space of two hours before we shall see more men of arms than came to Albraca to win the fair Angélica."[3] "Very well, then," said Sancho, "so be it, and pray God that all turns out for the best so that

---

2. The enchanted helmet of Mambrino, a Moorish king, is stolen by Rinaldo in Bioardo's *Roland in Love*.   3. Another allusion to *Roland in Love*.

I may at last win that island that is costing me so dearly, and then let me die."

"I have already told you, Sancho, that you are to give no thought to that; should the island fail, there is the kingdom of Denmark or that of Sobradisa, which would fit you like a ring on your finger, and you ought, moreover, to be happy to be on *terra firma*.[4] But let us leave all this for some other time, while you look and see if you have something in those saddlebags for us to eat, after which we will go in search of some castle where we may lodge for the night and prepare that balm of which I was telling you, for I swear to God that my ear is paining me greatly."

"I have here an onion, a little cheese, and a few crusts of bread," said Sancho, "but they are not victuals fit for a valiant knight like your grace."

"How little you know about it!" replied Don Quixote. "I would inform you, Sancho, that it is a point of honor with knights-errant to go for a month at a time without eating, and when they do eat, it is whatever may be at hand. You would certainly know that if you had read the histories as I have. There are many of them, and in none have I found any mention of knights eating unless it was by chance or at some sumptuous banquet that was tendered them; on other days they fasted. And even though it is well understood that, being men like us, they could not go without food entirely, any more than they could fail to satisfy the other necessities of nature, nevertheless, since they spent the greater part of their lives in forest and desert places without any cook to prepare their meals, their diet ordinarily consisted of rustic viands such as those that you now offer me. And so, Sancho my friend, do not be grieved at that which pleases me, nor seek to make the world over, nor to unhinge the institution of knight-errantry."

"Pardon me, your Grace," said Sancho, "but seeing that, as I have told you I do not know how to read or write, I am consequently not familiar with the rules of the knightly calling. Hereafter, I will stuff my saddlebags with all manner of dried fruit for your Grace, but inasmuch as I am not a knight, I shall lay in for myself a stock of fowls and other more substantial fare."

"I am not saying, Sancho, that it is incumbent upon knights-errant to eat only those fruits of which you speak; what I am saying is that their ordinary sustenance should consist of fruit and a few herbs such as are to be found in the fields and with which they are well acquainted, as am I myself."

"It is a good thing," said Sancho, "to know those herbs, for, so far as I can see, we are going to have need of that knowledge one of these days."

With this, he brought out the articles he had mentioned, and the two of them ate in peace, and most companionably. Being desirous, however, of seeking a lodging for the night, they did not tarry long over their humble and unsavory repast. They then mounted and made what haste they could that they might arrive at a shelter before nightfall but the sun failed them,

---

4. Solid earth (Latin, literal trans.), here Firm Island, an imaginary final destination for the squires of knights-errant. Sobradisa is an imaginary realm.

and with it went the hope of attaining their wish. As the day ended they found themselves beside some goatherds' huts, and they accordingly decided to spend the night there. Sancho was as much disappointed at their not having reached a town as his master was content with sleeping under the open sky; for it seemed to Don Quixote that every time this happened it merely provided him with yet another opportunity to establish his claim to the title of knight-errant.

["*To Right Wrongs and Come to the Aid of the Wretched*"]

CHAPTER 22

Of how Don Quixote freed many unfortunate ones who, much against their will, were being taken where they did not wish to go.

Cid Hamete Benengeli, the Arabic and Manchegan[5] author, in the course of this most grave, high-sounding, minute, delightful, and imaginative history, informs us that, following the remarks that were exchanged between Don Quixote de la Mancha and Sancho Panza, his squire, . . . the knight looked up and saw coming toward them down the road which they were following a dozen or so men on foot, strung together by their necks like beads on an iron chain and all of them wearing handcuffs. They were accompanied by two men on horseback and two on foot, the former carrying wheel-lock muskets while the other two were armed with swords and javelins.

"That," said Sancho as soon as he saw them, "is a chain of galley slaves, people on their way to the galleys where by order of the king they are forced to labor."

"What do you mean by 'forced'?" asked Don Quixote. "Is it possible that the king uses force on anyone?"

"I did not say that," replied Sancho. "What I did say was that these are folks who have been condemned for their crimes to forced labor in the galleys for his Majesty the King."

"The short of it is," said the knight, "whichever way you put it, these people are being taken there by force and not of their own free will."

"That is the way it is," said Sancho.

"Well, in that case," said his master, "now is the time for me to fulfill the duties of my calling, which is to right wrongs and come to the aid of the wretched."

"But take note, your Grace," said Sancho, "that justice, that is to say, the king himself, is not using any force upon, or doing any wrong to, people like these, but is merely punishing them for the crimes they have committed."

The chain of galley slaves had come up to them by this time, whereupon Don Quixote very courteously requested the guards to inform him of the reason or reasons why they were conducting these people in such a manner as this. One of the men on horseback then replied that the men

---

5. Of La Mancha.

were prisoners who had been condemned by his Majesty to serve in the galleys, whither they were bound, and that was all there was to be said about it and all that he, Don Quixote, need know.

"Nevertheless," said the latter, "I should like to inquire of each one of them, individually, the cause of his misfortune." And he went on speaking so very politely in an effort to persuade them to tell him what he wanted to know that the other mounted guard finally said, "Although we have here the record and certificate of sentence of each one of these wretches, we have not the time to get them out and read them to you; and so your Grace may come over and ask the prisoners themselves, and they will tell you if they choose, and you may be sure that they will, for these fellows take a delight in their knavish exploits and in boasting of them afterward."

With this permission, even though he would have done so if it had not been granted him, Don Quixote went up to the chain of prisoners and asked the first whom he encountered what sins had brought him to so sorry a plight. The man replied that it was for being a lover that he found himself in that line.

"For that and nothing more?" said Don Quixote. "And do they, then, send lovers to the galleys? If so, I should have been rowing there long ago."

"But it was not the kind of love that your Grace has in mind," the prisoner went on. "I loved a wash basket full of white linen so well and hugged it so tightly that, if they had not taken it away from me by force, I would never of my own choice have let go of it to this very minute. I was caught in the act, there was no need to torture me, the case was soon disposed of, and they supplied me with a hundred lashes across the shoulders and, in addition, a three-year stretch in the *gurapas*, and that's all there is to tell."

"What are *gurapas*?" asked Don Quixote.

"*Gurapas* are the galleys," replied the prisoner. He was a lad of around twenty-four and stated that he was a native of Piedrahita.

The knight then put the same question to a second man, who appeared to be very downcast and melancholy and did not have a word to say. The first man answered for him.

"This one, sir," he said, "is going as a canary—I mean, as a musician and singer."

"How is that?" Don Quixote wanted to know. "Do musicians and singers go to the galleys too?"

"Yes, sir; and there is nothing worse than singing when you're in trouble."

"On the contrary," said Don Quixote, "I have heard it said that he who sings frightens away his sorrows."

"It is just the opposite," said the prisoner; "for he who sings once weeps all his life long."

"I do not understand," said the knight.

One of the guards then explained. "Sir Knight, with this *non sancta*[6] tribe, to sing when you're in trouble means to confess under torture. This

6. Unholy (Latin).

singer was put to the torture and confessed his crime, which was that of being a *cuatrero*, or cattle thief, and as a result of his confession he was condemned to six years in the galleys in addition to two hundred lashes which he took on his shoulders; and so it is he is always downcast and moody, for the other thieves, those back where he came from and the ones here, mistreat, snub, ridicule, and despise him for having confessed and for not having had the courage to deny his guilt. They are in the habit of saying that the word no has the same number of letters as the word *sí*, and that a culprit is in luck when his life or death depends on his own tongue and not that of witnesses or upon evidence; and, in my opinion, they are not very far wrong."

"And I," said Don Quixote, "feel the same way about it." He then went on to a third prisoner and repeated his question.

The fellow answered at once, quite unconcernedly. "I'm going to my ladies, the *gurapas*, for five years, for the lack of five ducats."

"I would gladly give twenty," said Don Quixote, "to get you out of this."

"That," said the prisoner, "reminds me of the man in the middle of the ocean who has money and is dying of hunger because there is no place to buy what he needs. I say this for the reason that if I had had, at the right time, those twenty ducats your Grace is now offering me, I'd have greased the notary's quill and freshened up the attorney's wit with them, and I'd now be living in the middle of Zocodover Square in Toledo instead of being here on this highway coupled like a greyhound. But God is great; patience, and that's enough of it."

Don Quixote went on to a fourth prisoner, a venerable-looking old fellow with a white beard that fell over his bosom. When asked how he came to be there, this one began weeping and made no reply, but a fifth comrade spoke up in his behalf.

"This worthy man," he said, "is on his way to the galleys after having made the usual rounds clad in a robe of state and on horseback."[7]

"That means, I take it," said Sancho, "that he has been put to shame in public."

"That is it," said the prisoner, "and the offense for which he is being punished is that of having been an ear broker, or, better, a body broker. By that I mean to say, in short, that the gentleman is a pimp, and besides, he has his points as a sorcerer."

"If that point had not been thrown in," said Don Quixote, "he would not deserve, for merely being a pimp, to have to row in the galleys, but rather should be the general and give orders there. For the office of pimp is not an indifferent one; it is a function to be performed by persons of discretion and is most necessary in a well-ordered state; it is a profession that should be followed only by the wellborn, and there should, moreover, be a supervisor or examiner as in the case of other offices, and the number of practitioners should be fixed by law as is done with brokers on the exchange. In that way many evils would be averted that arise when this office is filled and this calling practiced by stupid folk and those with little sense, such as silly women and pages or mountebanks with few years and

---

7. After having been flogged in public, with all the ceremony that accompanied that punishment.

less experience to their credit, who, on the most pressing occasions, when it is necessary to use one's wits, let the crumbs freeze between their hand and their mouth and do not know which is their right hand and which is the left.

"I would go on and give reasons why it is fitting to choose carefully those who are to fulfill so necessary a state function, but this is not the place for it. One of these days I will speak of the matter to someone who is able to do something about it. I will say here only that the pain I felt at seeing those white hairs and this venerable countenance in such a plight, and all for his having been a pimp, has been offset for me by the additional information you have given me, to the effect that he is a sorcerer as well; for I am convinced that there are no sorcerers in the world who can move and compel the will, as some simple-minded persons think, but that our will is free and no herb or charm can force it.[8] All that certain foolish women and cunning tricksters do is to compound a few mixtures and poisons with which they deprive men of their senses while pretending that they have the power to make them loved, although, as I have just said, one cannot affect another's will in that manner."

"That is so," said the worthy old man; "but the truth is, sir, I am not guilty on the sorcery charge. As for being a pimp, that is something I cannot deny. I never thought there was any harm in it, however, my only desire being that everyone should enjoy himself and live in peace and quiet, without any quarrels or troubles. But these good intentions on my part cannot prevent me from going where I do not want to go, to a place from which I do not expect to return; for my years are heavy upon me and an affection of the urine that I have will not give me a moment's rest."

With this, he began weeping once more, and Sancho was so touched by it that he took a four-real piece from his bosom and gave it to him as an act of charity.

Don Quixote then went on and asked another what his offense was. The fellow answered him, not with less, but with much more, briskness than the preceding one had shown.

"I am here," he said, "for the reason that I carried a joke too far with a couple of cousins-german of mine and a couple of others who were not mine, and I ended by jesting with all of them to such an extent that the devil himself would never be able to straighten out the relationship. They proved everything on me, there was no one to show me favor, I had no money, I came near swinging for it, they sentenced me to the galleys for six years, and I accepted the sentence as the punishment that was due me. I am young yet, and if I live long enough, everything will come out all right. If, Sir Knight, your Grace has anything with which to aid these poor creatures that you see before you, God will reward you in Heaven, and we here on earth will make it a point to ask God in our prayers to grant you long life and good health, as long and as good as your amiable presence deserves."

---

8. Here Don Quixote despises charms and love potions, although often elsewhere, in his own vision of himself as a knight-errant, he accepts enchantments and spells as part of his world of fantasy.

This man was dressed as a student, and one of the guards told Don Quixote that he was a great talker and a very fine Latinist.

Back of these came a man around thirty years of age and of very good appearance, except that when he looked at you his eyes were seen to be a little crossed. He was shackled in a different manner from the others, for he dragged behind a chain so huge that it was wrapped all around his body, with two rings at the throat, one of which was attached to the chain while the other was fastened to what is known as a keep-friend or friend's foot, from which two irons hung down to his waist, ending in handcuffs secured by a heavy padlock in such a manner that he could neither raise his hands to his mouth nor lower his head to reach his hands.

When Don Quixote asked why this man was so much more heavily chained than the others, the guard replied that it was because he had more crimes against him than all the others put together, and he was so bold and cunning that, even though they had him chained like this, they were by no means sure of him but feared that he might escape from them.

"What crimes could he have committed," asked the knight, "if he has merited a punishment no greater than that of being sent to the galleys?"

"He is being sent there for ten years," replied the guard, "and that is equivalent to civil death. I need tell you no more than that this good man is the famous Ginés de Pasamonte, otherwise known as Ginesillo de Parapilla."

"Señor Commissary," spoke up the prisoner at this point, "go easy there and let us not be so free with names and surnames. My just name is Ginés and not Ginesillo; and Pasamonte, not Parapilla as you make it out to be, is my family name. Let each one mind his own affairs and he will have his hands full."

"Speak a little more respectfully, you big thief, you," said the commissary, "unless you want me to make you be quiet in a way you won't like."

"Man goes as God pleases, that is plain to be seen," replied the galley slave, "but someday someone will know whether my name is Ginesillo de Parapilla or not."

"But, you liar, isn't that what they call you?"

"Yes," said Ginés, "they do call me that; but I'll put a stop to it, or else I'll skin their you-know-what. And you, sir, if you have anything to give us, give it and may God go with you, for I am tired of all this prying into other people's lives. If you want to know anything about my life, know that I am Ginés de Pasamonte whose life story has been written down by these fingers that you see here."

"He speaks the truth," said the commissary, "for he has himself written his story, as big as you please, and has left the book in the prison, having pawned it for two hundred reales."

"And I mean to redeem it," said Ginés, "even if it costs me two hundred ducats."

"Is it as good as that?" inquired Don Quixote.

"It is so good," replied Ginés, "that it will cast into the shade *Lazarillo de Tormes*[9] and all others of that sort that have been or will be written.

---

9. A picaresque or rogue novel, published anonymously about the middle of the 15th century.

What I would tell you is that it deals with facts, and facts so interesting and amusing that no lies could equal them."

"And what is the title of the book?" asked Don Quixote.

"The Life of Ginés de Pasamonte."

"Is it finished?"

"How could it be finished," said Ginés, "when my life is not finished as yet? What I have written thus far is an account of what happened to me from the time I was born up to the last time that they sent me to the galleys."

"Then you have been there before?"

"In the service of God and the king I was there four years, and I know what the biscuit and the cowhide are like. I don't mind going very much, for there I will have a chance to finish my book. I still have many things to say, and in the Spanish galleys I shall have all the leisure that I need, though I don't need much, since I know by heart what it is I want to write."

"You seem to be a clever fellow," said Don Quixote.

"And an unfortunate one," said Ginés; "for misfortunes always pursue men of genius."

"They pursue rogues," said the commissary.

"I have told you to go easy, Señor Commissary," said Pasamonte, "for their Lordships did not give you that staff in order that you might mistreat us poor devils with it, but they intended that you should guide and conduct us in accordance with his Majesty's command. Otherwise, by the life of— But enough. It may be that someday the stains made in the inn will come out in the wash. Meanwhile, let everyone hold his tongue, behave well, and speak better, and let us be on our way. We've had enough of this foolishness."

At this point the commissary raised his staff as if to let Pasamonte have it in answer to his threats, but Don Quixote placed himself between them and begged the officer not to abuse the man; for it was not to be wondered at if one who had his hands so bound should be a trifle free with his tongue. With this, he turned and addressed them all.

"From all that you have told me, my dearest brothers," he said, "one thing stands out clearly for me, and that is the fact that, even though it is a punishment for offenses which you have committed, the penalty you are about to pay is not greatly to your liking and you are going to the galleys very much against your own will and desire. It may be that the lack of spirit which one of you displayed under torture, the lack of money on the part of another, the lack of influential friends, or, finally, warped judgment on the part of the magistrate, was the thing that led to your downfall; and, as a result, justice was not done you. All of which presents itself to my mind in such a fashion that I am at this moment engaged in trying to persuade and even force myself to show you what the purpose was for which Heaven sent me into this world, why it was it led me to adopt the calling of knighthood which I profess and take the knightly vow to favor the needy and aid those who are oppressed by the powerful.

"However, knowing as I do that it is not the part of prudence to do by foul means what can be accomplished by fair ones, I propose to ask these

gentlemen, your guards, and the commissary to be so good as to unshackle
you and permit you to go in peace. There will be no dearth of others to
serve his Majesty under more propitious circumstances; and it does not
appear to me to be just to make slaves of those whom God created as
free men. What is more, gentlemen of the guard, these poor fellows have
committed no offense against you. Up there, each of us will have to answer
for his own sins; for God in Heaven will not fail to punish the evil and
reward the good; and it is not good for self-respecting men to be executioners of their fellow-men in something that does not concern them. And so,
I ask this of you, gently and quietly, in order that, if you comply with my
request, I shall have reason to thank you; and if you do not do so of your
own accord, then this lance and this sword and the valor of my arm shall
compel you to do it by force."

"A fine lot of foolishness!" exclaimed the commissary. "So he comes
out at last with this nonsense! He would have us let the prisoners of the
king go free, as if we had any authority to do so or he any right to command it! Be on your way, sir, at once; straighten that basin that you have
on your head, and do not go looking for three feet on a cat."[1]

"You," replied Don Quixote, "are the cat and the rat and the rascal!"
And, saying this, he charged the commissary so quickly that the latter had
no chance to defend himself but fell to the ground badly wounded by the
lance blow. The other guards were astounded by this unexpected occurrence; but, recovering their self-possession, those on horseback drew their
swords, those on foot leveled their javelins, and all bore down on Don
Quixote, who stood waiting for them very calmly. Things undoubtedly
would have gone badly for him if the galley slaves, seeing an opportunity
to gain their freedom, had not succeeded in breaking the chain that linked
them together. Such was the confusion that the guards, now running to
fall upon the prisoners and now attacking Don Quixote, who in turn was
attacking them, accomplished nothing that was of any use.

Sancho for his part aided Ginés de Pasamonte to free himself, and that
individual was the first to drop his chains and leap out onto the field,
where, attacking the fallen commissary, he took away that officer's sword
and musket; and as he stood there, aiming first at one and then at another,
though without firing, the plain was soon cleared of guards, for they had
taken to their heels, fleeing at once Pasamonte's weapon and the stones
which the galley slaves, freed now, were hurling at them. Sancho, meanwhile, was very much disturbed over this unfortunate event, as he felt sure
that the fugitives would report the matter to the Holy Brotherhood, which,
to the ringing of the alarm bell, would come out to search for the guilty
parties. He said as much to his master, telling him that they should leave
at once and go into hiding in the near-by mountains.

"That is all very well," said Don Quixote, "but I know what had best be
done now." He then summoned all the prisoners, who, running riot, had
by this time despoiled the commissary of everything that he had, down to
his skin, and as they gathered around to hear what he had to say, he
addressed them as follows:

---

1. Looking for the impossible ("five feet" is the more usual form of the proverb).

"It is fitting that those who are wellborn should give thanks for the benefits they have received, and one of the sins with which God is most offended is that of ingratitude. I say this, gentlemen, for the reason that you have seen and had manifest proof of what you owe to me; and now that you are free of the yoke which I have removed from about your necks, it is my will and desire that you should set out and proceed to the city of El Toboso and there present yourselves before the lady Dulcinea del Toboso and say to her that her champion, the Knight of the Mournful Countenance, has sent you; and then you will relate to her, point by point, the whole of this famous adventure which has won you your longed-for freedom. Having done that, you may go where you like, and may good luck go with you."

To this Ginés de Pasamonte replied in behalf of all of them, "It is absolutely impossible, your Grace, our liberator, for us to do what you have commanded. We cannot go down the highway all together but must separate and go singly, each in his own direction, endeavoring to hide ourselves in the bowels of the earth in order not to be found by the Holy Brotherhood, which undoubtedly will come out to search for us. What your Grace can do, and it is right that you should do so, is to change this service and toll that you require of us in connection with the lady Dulcinea del Toboso into a certain number of Credos and Hail Marys which we will say for your Grace's intention, as this is something that can be accomplished by day or night, fleeing or resting, in peace or in war. To imagine, on the other hand, that we are going to return to the fleshpots of Egypt, by which I mean, take up our chains again by setting out along the highway for El Toboso, is to believe that it is night now instead of ten o'clock in the morning and is to ask of us something that is the same as asking pears of the elm tree."

"Then by all that's holy!" exclaimed Don Quixote, whose wrath was now aroused, "you, Don Son of a Whore, Don Ginesillo de Parapilla, or whatever your name is, you shall go alone, your tail between your legs and the whole chain on your back."

Pasamonte, who was by no means a long-suffering individual, was by this time convinced that Don Quixote was not quite right in the head, seeing that he had been guilty of such a folly as that of desiring to free them; and so, when he heard himself insulted in this manner, he merely gave the wink to his companions and, going off to one side, began raining so many stones upon the knight that the latter was wholly unable to protect himself with his buckler, while poor Rocinante paid no more attention to the spur than if he had been made of brass. As for Sancho, he took refuge behind his donkey as a protection against the cloud and shower of rocks that was falling on both of them, but Don Quixote was not able to shield himself so well, and there is no telling how many struck his body, with such force as to unhorse and bring him to the ground.

No sooner had he fallen than the student was upon him. Seizing the basin from the knight's head, he struck him three or four blows with it across the shoulders and banged it against the ground an equal number of times until it was fairly shattered to bits. They then stripped Don Quixote of the doublet which he wore over his armor, and would have taken his hose as well, if his greaves had not prevented them from doing so, and made off with Sancho's greatcoat, leaving him naked; after which, dividing the rest of the battle spoils amongst themselves, each of them went his own way, being a good deal more concerned with eluding the dreaded Holy Brotherhood than they were with burdening themselves with a chain or going to present themselves before the lady Dulcinea del Toboso.

They were left alone now—the ass and Rocinante, Sancho and Don Quixote: the ass, crestfallen and pensive, wagging its ears now and then, being under the impression that the hurricane of stones that had raged about them was not yet over; Rocinante, stretched alongside his master, for the hack also had been felled by a stone; Sancho, naked and fearful of the Holy Brotherhood; and Don Quixote, making wry faces at seeing himself so mishandled by those to whom he had done so much good.

[*"Set Free at Once That Lovely Lady"*]

CHAPTER 52

Of the quarrel that Don Quixote had with the goatherd, together with the rare adventure of the penitents, which the knight by the sweat of his brow brought to a happy conclusion.[2]

All those who had listened to it were greatly pleased with the goatherd's story, especially the canon,[3] who was more than usually interested in noting the manner in which it had been told. Far from being a mere rustic herdsman, the narrator seemed rather a cultured city dweller; and the canon accordingly remarked that the curate had been quite right in saying that the mountain groves bred men of learning. They all now offered their services to Eugenio, and Don Quixote was the most generous of any in this regard.

"Most assuredly, brother goatherd," he said, "if it were possible for me to undertake any adventure just now, I would set out at once to aid you and would take Leandra out of that convent, where she is undoubtedly being held against her will, in spite of the abbess and all the others who might try to prevent me, after which I would place her in your hands to do with as you liked, with due respect, however, for the laws of chivalry, which command that no violence be offered to any damsel. But I trust in God, Our Lord, that the power of one malicious enchanter is not so great that another magician may not prove still more powerful, and then I promise you my favor and my aid, as my calling obliges me to do, since it is none other than that of succoring the weak and those who are in distress."

The goatherd stared at him, observing in some astonishment the knight's unprepossessing appearance.

2. Last chapter of Part I. Through various devices, including the use of Don Quixote's own belief in enchantments and spells, the curate and the barber have persuaded the knight to let himself be taken home in an ox cart.   3. A canon from Toledo who has joined Don Quixote and his guardians on the way; conversing about chivalry with the knight, he has had cause to be "astonished at Don Quixote's well-reasoned nonsense." Eugenio, a very literate goatherd met on the way, has just told them the story of his unhappy love for Leandra. The girl, instead of choosing one of her local suitors, had eloped with a flashy and crooked soldier; robbed and abandoned by him, she had been put by her father in a convent.

"Sir," he said, turning to the barber who sat beside him, "who is this man who looks so strange and talks in this way?"

"Who should it be," the barber replied, "if not the famous Don Quixote de la Mancha, righter of wrongs, avenger of injustices, protector of damsels, terror of giants, and champion of battles?"

"That," said the goatherd, "sounds to me like the sort of thing you read of in books of chivalry, where they do all those things that your Grace has mentioned in connection with this man. But if you ask me, either your Grace is joking or this worthy gentleman must have a number of rooms to let inside his head."

"You are the greatest villain that ever was!" cried Don Quixote when he heard this. "It is you who are the empty one; I am fuller than the bitch that bore you ever was." Saying this, he snatched up a loaf of bread that was lying beside him and hurled it straight in the goatherd's face with such force as to flatten the man's nose. Upon finding himself thus mistreated in earnest, Eugenio, who did not understand this kind of joke, forgot all about the carpet, the tablecloth, and the other diners and leaped upon Don Quixote. Seizing him by the throat with both hands, he would no doubt have strangled him if Sancho Panza, who now came running up, had not grasped him by the shoulders and flung him backward over the table, smashing plates and cups and spilling and scattering all the food and drink that was there. Thus freed of his assailant, Don Quixote then threw himself upon the shepherd, who, with bleeding face and very much battered by Sancho's feet, was creeping about on his hands and knees in search of a table knife with which to exact a sanguinary vengeance, a purpose which the canon and the curate prevented him from carrying out. The barber, however, so contrived it that the goatherd came down on top of his opponent, upon whom he now showered so many blows that the poor knight's countenance was soon as bloody as his own.

As all this went on, the canon and the curate were laughing fit to burst, the troopers[4] were dancing with glee, and they all hissed on the pair as men do at a dog fight. Sancho Panza alone was in despair, being unable to free himself of one of the canon's servants who held him back from going to his master's aid. And then, just as they were all enjoying themselves hugely, with the exception of the two who were mauling each other, the note of a trumpet fell upon their ears, a sound so mournful that it caused them all to turn their heads in the direction from which it came. The one who was most excited by it was Don Quixote; who, very much against his will and more than a little bruised, was lying pinned beneath the goatherd.

"Brother Demon," he now said to the shepherd, "for you could not possibly be anything but a demon, seeing that you have shown a strength and valor greater than mine, I request you to call a truce for no more than an hour; for the doleful sound of that trumpet that we hear seems to me to be some new adventure that is calling me."

Tired of mauling and being mauled, the goatherd let him up at once.

---

4. Law officers from the Holy Brotherhood. They had wanted to arrest Don Quixote on account of his having attempted the liberation of the galley slaves but had been persuaded not to do so, considering the knight's state of insanity.

As he rose to his feet and turned his head in the direction of the sound,
Don Quixote then saw, coming down the slope of a hill, a large number
of persons clad in white after the fashion of penitents; for, as it happened,
the clouds that year had denied their moisture to the earth, and in all
the villages of that district processions for prayer and penance were being
organized with the purpose of beseeching God to have mercy and send
rain. With this object in view, the good folk from a near-by town were
making a pilgrimage to a devout hermit who dwelt on these slopes. Upon
beholding the strange costumes that the penitents wore, without pausing
to think how many times he had seen them before, Don Quixote imagined
that this must be some adventure or other, and that it was for him alone
as a knight-errant to undertake it. He was strengthened in this belief by
the sight of a covered image that they bore, as it seemed to him this must
be some highborn lady whom these scoundrelly and discourteous brigands
were forcibly carrying off; and no sooner did this idea occur to him than
he made for Rocinante, who was grazing not far away.

Taking the bridle and his buckler from off the saddletree, he had the
bridle adjusted in no time, and then, asking Sancho for his sword, he
climbed into the saddle, braced his shield upon his arm, and cried out to
those present, "And now, valorous company, you shall see how important
it is to have in the world those who follow the profession of knight-errantry.
You have but to watch how I shall set at liberty that worthy lady who there
goes captive, and then you may tell me whether or not such knights are to
be esteemed."

As he said this, he dug his legs into Rocinante's flanks, since he had no
spurs, and at a fast trot (for nowhere in this veracious history are we ever
told that the hack ran full speed) he bore down on the penitents in spite
of all that the canon, the curate, and the barber could do to restrain him —
their efforts were as vain as were the pleadings of his squire.

"Where are you bound for, Señor Don Quixote?" Sancho called after
him. "What evil spirits in your bosom spur you on to go against our Catholic faith? Plague take me, can't you see that's a procession of penitents and
that lady they're carrying on the litter is the most blessed image of the
Immaculate Virgin? Look well what you're doing, my master, for this time
it may be said that you really do not know."

His exertions were in vain, however, for his master was so bent upon
having it out with the sheeted figures and freeing the lady clad in mourning that he did not hear a word, nor would he have turned back if he had,
though the king himself might have commanded it. Having reached the
procession, he reined in Rocinante, who by this time was wanting a little
rest, and in a hoarse, excited voice he shouted, "You who go there with
your faces covered, out of shame, it may be, listen well to what I have to
say to you."

The first to come to a halt were those who carried the image; and then
one of the four clerics who were intoning the litanies, upon beholding
Don Quixote's weird figure, his bony nag, and other amusing appurtenances, spoke up in reply.

"Brother, if you have something to say to us, say it quickly, for these
brethren are engaged in macerating their flesh, and we cannot stop to hear

anything, nor is it fitting that we should, unless it is capable of being said in a couple of words."

"I will say it to you in one word," Don Quixote answered, "and that word is the following: 'Set free at once that lovely lady whose tears and mournful countenance show plainly that you are carrying her away against her will and that you have done her some shameful wrong. I will not consent to your going one step farther until you shall have given her the freedom that should be hers.'"

Hearing these words, they all thought that Don Quixote must be some madman or other and began laughing heartily; but their laughter proved to be gunpowder to his wrath, and without saying another word he drew his sword and fell upon the litter. One of those who bore the image, leaving his share of the burden to his companions, then sallied forth to meet the knight, flourishing a forked stick that he used to support the Virgin while he was resting; and upon this stick he now received a mighty slash that Don Quixote dealt him, one that shattered it in two, but with the piece about a third long that remained in his hand he came down on the shoulder of his opponent's sword arm, left unprotected by the buckler, with so much force that the poor fellow sank to the ground sorely battered and bruised.

Sancho Panza, who was puffing along close behind his master, upon seeing him fall cried out to the attacker not to deal another blow, as this was an unfortunate knight who was under a magic spell but who had never in all the days of his life done any harm to anyone. But the thing that stopped the rustic was not Sancho's words; it was, rather, the sight of Don Quixote lying there without moving hand or foot. And so, thinking that he had killed him, he hastily girded up his tunic and took to his heels across the countryside like a deer.

By this time all of Don Quixote's companions had come running up to where he lay; and the penitents, when they observed this, and especially when they caught sight of the officers of the Brotherhood with their crossbows, at once rallied around the image, where they raised their hoods and grasped their whips as the priests raised their tapers aloft in expectations of an assault; for they were resolved to defend themselves and even, if possible, to take the offensive against their assailants, but, as luck would have it, things turned out better than they had hoped. Sancho, meanwhile, believing Don Quixote to be dead, had flung himself across his master's body and was weeping and wailing in the most lugubrious and, at the same time, the most laughable fashion that could be imagined; and the curate had discovered among those who marched in the procession another curate whom he knew, their recognition of each other serving to allay the fears of all parties concerned. The first curate then gave the second a very brief account of who Don Quixote was, whereupon all the penitents came up to see if the poor knight was dead. And as they did so, they heard Sancho Panza speaking with tears in his eyes.

"O flower of chivalry,"[5] he was saying, "the course of whose well-spent years has been brought to an end by a single blow of a club! O honor of

---

5. Note how Sancho has absorbed some of his master's speech mannerisms.

your line, honor and glory of all La Mancha and of all the world, which, with you absent from it, will be full of evil-doers who will not fear being punished for their deeds! O master more generous than all the Alexanders, who after only eight months of service presented me with the best island that the sea washes and surrounds! Humble with the proud, haughty with the humble, brave in facing dangers, long-suffering under outrages, in love without reason, imitator of the good, scourge of the wicked, enemy of the mean—in a word, a knight-errant, which is all there is to say."

At the sound of Sancho's cries and moans, Don Quixote revived, and the first thing he said was, "He who lives apart from thee, O fairest Dulcinea, is subject to greater woes than those I now endure. Friend Sancho, help me onto that enchanted cart, as I am in no condition to sit in Rocinante's saddle with this shoulder of mine knocked to pieces the way it is."

"That I will gladly do, my master," replied Sancho, "and we will go back to my village in the company of these gentlemen who are concerned for your welfare, and there we will arrange for another sally and one, let us hope, that will bring us more profit and fame than this one has."

"Well spoken, Sancho," said Don Quixote, "for it will be an act of great prudence to wait until the present evil influence of the stars has passed."

The canon, the curate, and the barber all assured him that he would be wise in doing this; and so, much amused by Sancho Panza's simplicity, they placed Don Quixote upon the cart as before, while the procession of penitents re-formed and continued on its way. The goatherd took leave of all of them, and the curate paid the troopers what was coming to them, since they did not wish to go any farther. The canon requested the priest to inform him of the outcome of Don Quixote's madness, as to whether it yielded to treatment or not; and with this he begged permission to resume his journey. In short, the party broke up and separated, leaving only the curate and the barber, Don Quixote and Panza, and the good Rocinante, who looked upon everything that he had seen with the same resignation as his master. Yoking his oxen, the carter made the knight comfortable upon a bale of hay, and then at his customary slow pace proceeded to follow the road that the curate directed him to take. At the end of the six days they reached Don Quixote's village, making their entrance at noon of a Sunday, when the square was filled with a crowd of people through which the cart had to pass.

They all came running to see who it was, and when they recognized their townsman, they were vastly astonished. One lad sped to bring the news to the knight's housekeeper and his niece, telling them that their master had returned lean and jaundiced and lying stretched out upon a bale of hay on an ox-cart. It was pitiful to hear the good ladies' screams, to behold the way in which they beat their breasts, and to listen to the curses which they once more heaped upon those damnable books of chivalry, and this demonstration increased as they saw Don Quixote coming through the doorway.

At news of the knight's return, Sancho Panza's wife had hurried to the scene, for she had some while since learned that her husband had accompanied him as his squire; and now, as soon as she laid eyes upon her man, the first question she asked was if all was well with the ass, to which Sancho replied that the beast was better off than his master.

"Thank God," she exclaimed, "for all his blessings! But tell me now, my dear, what have you brought me from all your squirings? A new cloak to wear? Or shoes for the young ones?"

"I've brought you nothing of the sort, good wife," said Sancho, "but other things of greater value and importance."

"I'm glad to hear that," she replied. "Show me those things of greater value and importance, my dear. I'd like a sight of them just to cheer this heart of mine which has been so sad and unhappy all the centuries that you've been gone."

"I will show them to you at home, wife," said Sancho. "For the present be satisfied that if, God willing, we set out on another journey in search of adventures, you will see me in no time a count or the governor of an island, and not one of those around here, but the best that is to be had."

"I hope to Heaven it's true, my husband, for we certainly need it. But tell me, what is all this about islands? I don't understand."

"Honey," replied Sancho, "is not for the mouth of an ass. You will find out in good time, woman; and you're going to be surprised to hear yourself called 'my Ladyship' by all your vassals."

"What's this you are saying, Sancho, about ladyships, islands, and vassals?" Juana Panza insisted on knowing—for such was the name of Sancho's wife, although they were not blood relatives, it being the custom in La Mancha for wives to take their husbands' surnames.

"Do not be in such a hurry to know all this, Juana," he said. "It is enough that I am telling you the truth. Sew up your mouth, then; for all I will say, in passing, is that there is nothing in the world that is more pleasant than being a respected man, squire to a knight-errant who goes in search of adventures. It is true that most of the adventures you meet with do not come out the way you'd like them to, for ninety-nine out of a hundred will prove to be all twisted and crosswise. I know that from experience, for I've come out of some of them blanketed and out of others beaten to a pulp. But, all the same, it's a fine thing to go along waiting for what will happen next, crossing mountains, making your way through woods, climbing over cliffs, visiting castles, and putting up at inns free of charge, and the devil take the maravedi that is to pay."

Such was the conversation that took place between Sancho Panza and Juana Panza, his wife, as Don Quixote's housekeeper and niece were taking him in, stripping him, and stretching him out on his old-time bed. He gazed at them blankly, being unable to make out where he was. The curate charged the niece to take great care to see that her uncle was comfortable and to keep close watch over him so that he would not slip away from them another time. He then told them of what it had been necessary to do in order to get him home, at which they once more screamed to Heaven and began cursing the books of chivalry all over again, praying God to plunge the authors of such lying nonsense into the center of the bottomless pit. In short, they scarcely knew what to do, for they were very much afraid that their master and uncle would give them the slip once more, the moment he was a little better, and it turned out just the way they feared it might.

From *Part II*

["Put into a Book"]

CHAPTER 3

*Of the laughable conversation that took place between Don Quixote,
Sancho Panza, and the bachelor Sansón Carrasco.*

Don Quixote remained in a thoughtful mood as he waited for the bachelor Carrasco,[6] from whom he hoped to hear the news as to how he had
been put into a book, as Sancho had said. He could not bring himself to
believe that any such history existed, since the blood of the enemies he
had slain was not yet dry on the blade of his sword; and here they were
trying to tell him that his high deeds of chivalry were already circulating
in printed form. But, for that matter, he imagined that some sage, either
friend or enemy, must have seen to the printing of them through the art
of magic. If the chronicler was a friend, he must have undertaken the task
in order to magnify and exalt Don Quixote's exploits above the most notable ones achieved by knights-errant of old. If an enemy, his purpose would
have been to make them out as nothing at all, by debasing them below
the meanest acts ever recorded of any mean squire. The only thing was,
the knight reflected, the exploits of squires never were set down in writing.
If it was true that such a history existed, being about a knight-errant, then
it must be eloquent and lofty in tone, a splendid and distinguished piece
of work and veracious in its details.

This consoled him somewhat, although he was a bit put out at the
thought that the author was a Moor, if the appellation "Cid" was to be
taken as an indication,[7] and from the Moors you could never hope for any
word of truth, seeing that they are all of them cheats, forgers, and schem-
ers. He feared lest his love should not have been treated with becoming
modesty but rather in a way that would reflect upon the virtue of his lady
Dulcinea del Toboso. He hoped that his fidelity had been made clear,
and the respect he had always shown her, and that something had been
said as to how he had spurned queens, empresses, and damsels of every
rank while keeping a rein upon those impulses that are natural to a man.
He was still wrapped up in these and many other similar thoughts when
Sancho returned with Carrasco.

Don Quixote received the bachelor very amiably. The latter, although
his name was Sansón, or Samson, was not very big so far as bodily size
went, but he was a great joker, with a sallow complexion and a ready wit.
He was going on twenty-four and had a round face, a snub nose, and a
large mouth, all of which showed him to be of a mischievous disposition
and fond of jests and witticisms. This became apparent when, as soon as
he saw Don Quixote, he fell upon his knees and addressed the knight as
follows:

6. The bachelor of arts Sansón Carrasco, an important new character who appears at the beginning of
Part II and will play a considerable role in the story with his attempts at "curing" Don Quixote. Just
now he has been telling Sancho about a book relating the adventures of Don Quixote and his squire,
by which the two have been made famous; the book is, of course, *Don Quixote,* Part I.   7. The
allusion is to Cid Hamete Benengeli (see n. 4, p. 1558). The word *cid* is of Arabic derivation.

"O mighty Don Quixote de la Mancha, give me your hands; for by the habit of St. Peter that I wear[8]—though I have received but the first four orders—your Grace is one of the most famous knights-errant that ever have been or ever will be anywhere on this earth. Blessings upon Cid Hamete Benengeli who wrote down the history of your great achievements, and upon that curious-minded one who was at pains to have it translated from the Arabic into our Castilian vulgate for the universal entertainment of the people."

Don Quixote bade him rise. "Is it true, then," he asked, "that there is a book about me and that it was some Moorish sage who composed it?"

"By way of showing you how true it is," replied Sansón, "I may tell you that it is my belief that there are in existence today more than twelve thousand copies of that history. If you do not believe me, you have but to make inquiries in Portugal, Barcelona, and Valencia, where editions have been brought out, and there is even a report to the effect that one edition was printed at Antwerp. In short, I feel certain that there will soon not be a nation that does not know it or a language into which it has not been translated."

"One of the things," remarked Don Quixote, "that should give most satisfaction to a virtuous and eminent man is to see his good name spread abroad during his own lifetime, by means of the printing press, through translations into the languages of the various peoples. I have said 'good name,' for if he has any other kind, his fate is worse than death."

"If it is a matter of good name and good reputation," said the bachelor, "your Grace bears off the palm from all the knights-errant in the world; for the Moor in his tongue and the Christian in his have most vividly depicted your Grace's gallantry, your courage in facing dangers, your patience in adversity and suffering, whether the suffering be due to wounds or to misfortunes of another sort, and your virtue and continence in love, in connection with that platonic relationship that exists between your Grace and my lady Doña Dulcinea del Toboso."

At this point Sancho spoke up. "Never in my life," he said, "have I heard my lady Dulcinea called 'Doña,' but only 'la Señora Dulcinea del Toboso'; so on that point, already, the history is wrong."

"That is not important," said Carrasco.

"No, certainly not," Don Quixote agreed. "But tell me, Señor Bachelor, what adventures of mine as set down in this book have made the deepest impression?"

"As to that," the bachelor answered, "opinions differ, for it is a matter of individual taste. There are some who are very fond of the adventure of the windmills—those windmills which to your Grace appeared to be so many Briareuses and giants. Others like the episode at the fulling mill. One relishes the story of the two armies which took on the appearance of droves of sheep, while another fancies the tale of the dead man whom they were taking to Segovia for burial. One will assert that the freeing of the galley slaves is the best of all, and yet another will maintain that noth-

---

8. The dress of one of the minor clerical orders.

ing can come up to the Benedictine giants and the encounter with the valiant Biscayan."

Again Sancho interrupted him. "Tell me, Señor Bachelor," he said, "does the book say anything about the adventure with the Yanguesans, that time our good Rocinante took it into his head to go looking for tidbits in the sea?"

"The sage," replied Sansón, "has left nothing in the inkwell. He has told everything and to the point, even to the capers which the worthy Sancho cut as they tossed him in the blanket."

"I cut no capers in the blanket," objected Sancho, "but I did in the air, and more than I liked."

"I imagine," said Don Quixote, "that there is no history in the world, dealing with humankind, that does not have its ups and downs, and this is particularly true of those that have to do with deeds of chivalry, for they can never be filled with happy incidents alone."

"Nevertheless," the bachelor went on, "there are some who have read the book who say that they would have been glad if the authors had forgotten a few of the innumerable cudgelings which Señor Don Quixote received in the course of his various encounters."

"But that is where the truth of the story comes in," Sancho protested.

"For all of that," observed Don Quixote, "they might well have said nothing about them; for there is no need of recording those events that do not alter the veracity of the chronicle, when they tend only to lessen the reader's respect for the hero. You may be sure that Aeneas was not as pious as Vergil would have us believe, nor was Ulysses as wise as Homer depicts him."

"That is true enough," replied Sansón, "but it is one thing to write as a poet and another as a historian. The former may narrate or sing of things not as they were but as they should have been; the latter must describe them not as they should have been but as they were, without adding to or detracting from the truth in any degree whatsoever."

"Well," said Sancho, "if this Moorish gentleman is bent upon telling the truth, I have no doubt that among my master's thrashings my own will be found; for they never took the measure of his Grace's shoulders without measuring my whole body. But I don't wonder at that; for as my master himself says, when there's an ache in the head the members have to share it."

"You are a sly fox, Sancho," said Don Quixote. "My word, but you can remember things well enough when you choose to do so!"

"Even if I wanted to forget the whacks they gave me," Sancho answered him, "the welts on my ribs wouldn't let me, for they are still fresh."

"Be quiet, Sancho," his master admonished him, "and do not interrupt the bachelor. I beg him to go on and tell me what is said of me in this book."

"And what it says about me, too," put in Sancho, "for I have heard that I am one of the main presonages in it—"

"*Personages*, not *presonages*, Sancho my friend," said Sansón.

"So we have another one who catches you up on everything you say," was Sancho's retort. "If we go on at this rate, we'll never be through in a lifetime."

"May God put a curse on *my* life," the bachelor told him, "if you are not the second most important person in the story; and there are some who would rather listen to you talk than to anyone else in the book. It is true, there are those who say that you are too gullible in believing it to be the truth that you could become the governor of that island that was offered you by Señor Don Quixote, here present."

"There is still sun on the top of the wall," said Don Quixote, "and when Sancho is a little older, with the experience that the years bring, he will be wiser and better fitted to be a governor than he is at the present time."

"By God, master," said Sancho, "the island that I couldn't govern right now I'd never be able to govern if I lived to be as old as Methuselah. The trouble is, I don't know where that island we are talking about is located; it is not due to any lack of noddle on my part."

"Leave it to God, Sancho," was Don Quixote's advice, "and everything will come out all right, perhaps even better than you think; for not a leaf on the tree stirs except by His will."

"Yes," said Sansón, "if it be God's will, Sancho will not lack a thousand islands to govern, not to speak of one island alone."

"I have seen governors around here," said Sancho, "that are not to be compared to the sole of my shoe, and yet they call them 'your Lordship' and serve them on silver plate."

"Those are not the same kind of governors," Sansón informed him. "Their task is a good deal easier. The ones that govern islands must at least know grammar."

"I could make out well enough with the *gram*," replied Sancho, "but with the *mar* I want nothing to do, for I don't understand it at all. But leaving this business of the governorship in God's hands—for He will send me wherever I can best serve Him—I will tell you, Señor Bachelor Sansón Carrasco, that I am very much pleased that the author of the history should have spoken of me in such a way as does not offend me; for, upon the word of a faithful squire, if he had said anything about me that was not becoming to an old Christian, the deaf would have heard of it."

"That would be to work miracles," said Sansón.

"Miracles or no miracles," was the answer, "let everyone take care as to what he says or writes about people and not be setting down the first thing that pops into his head."

"One of the faults that is found with the book," continued the bachelor, "is that the author has inserted in it a story entitled *The One Who Was Too Curious for His Own Good*. It is not that the story in itself is a bad one or badly written; it is simply that it is out of place there, having nothing to do with the story of his Grace, Señor Don Quixote."[9]

"I will bet you," said Sancho, "that the son of a dog has mixed the cabbages with the baskets."[1]

9. The story, a tragic tale about a jealousy-ridden husband, occupies several chapters of Part I. Here, as elsewhere in this chapter, Cervantes echoes criticism currently aimed at his book.   1. Has jumbled together things of different kinds.

"And I will say right now," declared Don Quixote, "that the author of this book was not a sage but some ignorant prattler who at haphazard and without any method set about the writing of it, being content to let things turn out as they might. In the same manner, Orbaneja,[2] the painter of Ubeda, when asked what he was painting would reply, 'Whatever it turns out to be.' Sometimes it would be a cock, in which case he would have to write alongside it, in Gothic letters, 'This is a cock.' And so it must be with my story, which will need a commentary to make it understandable."

"No," replied Sansón, "that it will not; for it is so clearly written that none can fail to understand it. Little children leaf through it, young people read it, adults appreciate it, and the aged sing its praises. In short, it is so thumbed and read and so well known to persons of every walk in life that no sooner do folks see some skinny nag than they at once cry, 'There goes Rocinante!' Those that like it best of all are the pages; for there is no lord's antechamber where a *Don Quixote* is not to be found. If one lays it down, another will pick it up; one will pounce upon it, and another will beg for it. It affords the pleasantest and least harmful reading of any book that has been published up to now. In the whole of it there is not to be found an indecent word or a thought that is other than Catholic."

"To write in any other manner," observed Don Quixote, "would be to write lies and not the truth. Those historians who make use of falsehoods ought to be burned like the makers of counterfeit money. I do not know what could have led the author to introduce stories and episodes that are foreign to the subject matter when he had so much to write about in describing my adventures. He must, undoubtedly, have been inspired by the old saying, 'With straw or with hay[3] . . .' For, in truth, all he had to do was to record my thoughts, my sighs, my tears, my lofty purposes, and my undertakings, and he would have had a volume bigger or at least as big as that which the works of El Tostado[4] would make. To sum the matter up, Señor Bachelor, it is my opinion that, in composing histories or books of any sort, a great deal of judgment and ripe understanding is called for. To say and write witty and amusing things is the mark of great genius. The cleverest character in a comedy is the clown, since he who would make himself out to be a simpleton cannot be one. History is a near-sacred thing, for it must be true, and where the truth is, there is God. And yet there are those who compose books and toss them out into the world as if they were no more than fritters."

"There is no book so bad," opined the bachelor, "that there is not some good in it."

"Doubtless that is so," replied Don Quixote, "but it very often happens that those who have won in advance a great and well-deserved reputation for their writings, lose it in whole or in part when they give their works to the printer."

"The reason for it," said Sansón, "is that, printed works being read at leisure, their faults are the more readily apparent, and the greater the reputation of the author the more closely are they scrutinized. Men famous for their genius, great poets, illustrious historians, are almost always envied by

---

2. Unidentified.   3. The proverb concludes either "the mattress is filled" or "I fill my belly."
4. Alonso de Madrigal, bishop of Avila, a prolific author of devotional works.

those who take a special delight in criticizing the writings of others without having produced anything of their own."

"That is not to be wondered at," said Don Quixote, "for there are many theologians who are not good enough for the pulpit but who are very good indeed when it comes to detecting the faults or excesses of those who preach."

"All of this is very true, Señor Don Quixote," replied Carrasco, "but, all the same, I could wish that these self-appointed censors were a bit more forbearing and less hypercritical; I wish they would pay a little less attention to the spots on the bright sun of the work that occasions their fault-finding. For if *aliquando bonus dormitat Homerus*,[5] let them consider how much of his time he spent awake, shedding the light of his genius with a minimum of shade. It well may be that what to them seems a flaw is but one of those moles which sometimes add to the beauty of a face. In any event, I insist that he who has a book printed runs a very great risk, inasmuch as it is an utter impossibility to write it in such a manner that it will please all who read it."

"This book about me must have pleased very few," remarked Don Quixote.

"Quite the contrary," said Sansón, "for just as *stultorum infinitus est numerus*,[6] so the number of those who have enjoyed this history is likewise infinite. Some, to be sure, have complained of the author's forgetfulness, seeing that he neglected to make it plain who the thief was who stole Sancho's gray;[7] for it is not stated there, but merely implied, that the ass was stolen; and, a little further on, we find the knight mounted on the same beast, although it has not made its reappearance in the story. They also say that the author forgot to tell us what Sancho did with those hundred crowns that he found in the valise on the Sierra Morena, as nothing more is said of them and there are many who would like to know how he disposed of the money or how he spent it. This is one of the serious omissions to be found in the work."

To this Sancho replied, "I, Señor Sansón, do not feel like giving any account or accounting just now; for I feel a little weak in my stomach, and if I don't do something about it by taking a few swigs of the old stuff, I'll be sitting on St. Lucy's thorn.[8] I have some of it at home, and my old woman is waiting for me. After I've had my dinner, I'll come back and answer any questions your Grace or anybody else wants to ask me, whether it's about the loss of the ass or the spending of the hundred crowns."

And without waiting for a reply or saying another word, he went on home. Don Quixote urged the bachelor to stay and take potluck with him, and Sansón accepted the invitation and remained. In addition to the knight's ordinary fare, they had a couple of pigeons, and at table their talk was of chivalry and feats of arms.

---

5. Good Homer sometimes nods too (Latin), Horace, *Art of Poetry*, line 359.   6. Infinite is the number of fools (Latin).   7. In Part I, chap. 23.   8. I shall be weak and exhausted.

[*A Victorious Duel*]

CHAPTER 12

*Of the strange adventure that befell the valiant Don Quixote with the
fearless Knight of the Mirrors.*[9]

The night following the encounter with Death was spent by Don Quixote and his squire beneath some tall and shady trees,[1] the knight having been persuaded to eat a little from the stock of provisions carried by the gray.

"Sir," said Sancho, in the course of their repast, "how foolish I'd have been if I had chosen the spoils from your Grace's first adventure rather than the foals from the three mares.[2] Truly, truly, a sparrow in the hand is worth more than a vulture on the wing."[3]

"And yet, Sancho," replied Don Quixote, "if you had but let me attack them as I wished to do, you would at least have had as spoils the Empress's gold crown and Cupid's painted wings;[4] for I should have taken them whether or no and placed them in your hands."

"The crowns and scepters of stage emperors," remarked Sancho, "were never known to be of pure gold; they are always of tinsel or tinplate."

"That is the truth," said Don Quixote, "for it is only right that the accessories of a drama should be fictitious and not real, like the play itself. Speaking of that, Sancho, I would have you look kindly upon the art of the theater and, as a consequence, upon those who write the pieces and perform in them, for they all render a service of great value to the State by holding up a mirror for us at each step that we take, wherein we may observe, vividly depicted, all the varied aspects of human life; and I may add that there is nothing that shows us more clearly, by similitude, what we are and what we ought to be than do plays and players.

"Tell me, have you not seen some comedy in which kings, emperors, pontiffs, knights, ladies, and numerous other characters are introduced? One plays the ruffian, another the cheat, this one a merchant and that one a soldier, while yet another is the fool who is not so foolish as he appears, and still another the one of whom love has made a fool. Yet when the play is over and they have taken off their players' garments, all the actors are once more equal."

"Yes," replied Sancho, "I have seen all that."

"Well," continued Don Quixote, "the same thing happens in the comedy that we call life, where some play the part of emperors, others that of pontiffs—in short, all the characters that a drama may have—but when it

---

9. Until he earns this title (in chap. 15), he will be referred to as the Knight of the Wood.   1. Don Quixote and his squire are now in the woody region around El Toboso, Dulcinea's town. Sancho has been sent to look for his knight's lady and has saved the day by pretending to see the beautiful damsel in a "village wench, and not a pretty one at that, for she was round-faced and snub-nosed." But by his imaginative lie he has succeeded, as he had planned, in setting in motion Don Quixote's belief in spells and enchantments: enemy magicians, envious of him, have hidden his lady's splendor only from his sight. While the knight was still under the shock of this experience, farther along their way he and his squire have met a group of itinerant players dressed in their proper costumes for a religious play, *The Parliament of Death*.   2. Don Quixote has promised them to Sancho as a reward for bringing news of Dulcinea.   3. That is, a bird in the hand is worth two in the bush.   4. The Empress and Cupid were characters in *The Parliament of Death*.

is all over, that is to say, when life is done, death takes from each the garb that differentiates him, and all at last are equal in the grave."

"It is a fine comparison," Sancho admitted, "though not so new but that I have heard it many times before. It reminds me of that other one, about the game of chess. So long as the game lasts, each piece has its special qualities, but when it is over they are all mixed and jumbled together and put into a bag, which is to the chess pieces what the grave is to life."

"Every day, Sancho," said Don Quixote, "you are becoming less stupid and more sensible."

"It must be that some of your Grace's good sense is sticking to me," was Sancho's answer. "I am like a piece of land that of itself is dry and barren, but if you scatter manure over it and cultivate it, it will bear good fruit. By this I mean to say that your Grace's conversation is the manure that has been cast upon the barren land of my dry wit; the time that I spend in your service, associating with you, does the cultivating; and as a result of it all, I hope to bring forth blessed fruits by not departing, slipping, or sliding, from those paths of good breeding which your Grace has marked out for me in my parched understanding."

Don Quixote had to laugh at this affected speech of Sancho's, but he could not help perceiving that what the squire had said about his improvement was true enough; for every now and then the servant would speak in a manner that astonished his master. It must be admitted, however, that most of the time when he tried to use fine language, he would tumble from the mountain of his simple-mindedness into the abyss of his ignorance. It was when he was quoting old saws and sayings, whether or not they had anything to do with the subject under discussion, that he was at his best, displaying upon such occasions a prodigious memory, as will already have been seen and noted in the course of this history.

With such talk as this they spent a good part of the night. Then Sancho felt a desire to draw down the curtains of his eyes, as he was in the habit of saying when he wished to sleep, and, unsaddling his mount, he turned him loose to graze at will on the abundant grass. If he did not remove Rocinante's saddle, this was due to his master's express command; for when they had taken the field and were not sleeping under a roof, the hack was under no circumstances to be stripped. This was in accordance with an old and established custom which knights-errant faithfully observed: the bridle and saddlebow might be removed, but beware of touching the saddle itself! Guided by this precept, Sancho now gave Rocinante the same freedom that the ass enjoyed.

The close friendship that existed between the two animals was a most unusual one, so remarkable indeed that it has become a tradition handed down from father to son, and the author of this veracious chronicle even wrote a number of special chapters on the subject, although, in order to preserve the decency and decorum that are fitting in so heroic an account, he chose to omit them in the final version. But he forgets himself once in a while and goes on to tell us how the two beasts when they were together would hasten to scratch each other, and how, when they were tired and their bellies were full, Rocinante would lay his long neck over that of the ass—it extended more than a half a yard on the other side—and the pair would then stand there gazing pensively at the ground for as much as three whole days at a time, or at least until someone came for them or hunger compelled them to seek nourishment.

I may tell you that I have heard it said that the author of this history, in one of his writings, has compared the friendship of Rocinante and the gray to that of Nisus and Euryalus and that of Pylades and Orestes;[5] and if this be true, it shows for the edification of all what great friends these two peace-loving animals were, and should be enough to make men ashamed, who are so inept at preserving friendship with one another. For this reason it has been said:

> There is no friend for friend,
> Reeds to lances turn[6] . . .

And there was the other poet who sang:

> Between friend and friend the bug[7] . . .

Let no one think that the author has gone out of his way in comparing the friendship of animals with that of men; for human beings have received valuable lessons from the beasts and have learned many important things from them. From the stork they have learned the use of clysters; the dog has taught them the salutary effects of vomiting as well as a lesson in gratitude; the cranes have taught them vigilance, the ants foresight, the elephants modesty, and the horse loyalty.[8]

Sancho had at last fallen asleep at the foot of a cork tree, while Don Quixote was slumbering beneath a sturdy oak. Very little time had passed when the knight was awakened by a noise behind him, and, starting up, he began looking about him and listening to see if he could make out where it came from. Then he caught sight of two men on horseback, one of whom, slipping down from the saddle, said to the other, "Dismount, my friend, and unbridle the horses; for there seems to be plenty of grass around here for them and sufficient silence and solitude for my amorous thoughts."

Saying this, he stretched himself out on the ground, and as he flung himself down the armor that he wore made such a noise that Don Quixote knew at once, for a certainty, that he must be a knight-errant. Going over to Sancho, who was still sleeping, he shook him by the arm and with no little effort managed to get him awake.

"Brother Sancho," he said to him in a low voice, "we have an adventure on our hands."

"God give us a good one," said Sancho. "And where, my master, may her Ladyship, Mistress Adventure, be?"

"Where, Sancho?" replied Don Quixote. "Turn your eyes and look, and you will see stretched out over there a knight-errant who, so far as I can make out, is not any too happy; for I saw him fling himself from his horse to the ground with a certain show of despondency, and as he fell his armor rattled."

---

5. Famous examples of friendship in Virgil's *Aeneid* and in Greek tradition and drama.   6. From a popular ballad.   7. The Spanish "a bug in the eye" implies keeping a watchful eye on somebody.
8. All folkloristic beliefs about the virtues of animals.

"Well," said Sancho, "and how does your Grace make this out to be an adventure?"

"I would not say," the knight answered him, "that this is an adventure in itself, but rather the beginning of one, for that is the way they start. But listen; he seems to be tuning a lute or guitar, and from the way he is spitting and clearing his throat he must be getting ready to sing something."

"Faith, so he is," said Sancho. "He must be some lovesick knight."

"There are no knights-errant that are not lovesick," Don Quixote informed him. "Let us listen to him, and the thread of his song will lead us to the yarn-ball of his thoughts; for out of the abundance of the heart the mouth speaketh."

Sancho would have liked to reply to his master, but the voice of the Knight of the Wood, which was neither very good nor very bad, kept him from it; and as the two of them listened attentively, they heard the following:

Sonnet

Show me, O lady, the pattern of thy will,
That mine may take that very form and shape;
For my will in thine own I fain would drape,
Each slightest wish of thine I would fulfill.
If thou wouldst have me silence this dead ill   5
Of which I'm dying now, prepare the crape!
Or if I must another manner ape,
Then let Love's self display his rhyming skill.
Of opposites I am made, that's manifest:
In part soft wax, in part hard-diamond fire;   10
Yet to Love's laws my heart I do adjust,
And, hard or soft, I offer thee this breast:
Print or engrave there what thou may'st desire,
And I'll preserve it in eternal trust.[9]

With an *Ay!* that appeared to be wrung from the very depths of his heart, the Knight of the Wood brought his song to a close, and then after a brief pause began speaking in a grief-stricken voice that was piteous to hear.

"O most beautiful and most ungrateful woman in all the world!" he cried, "how is it possible, O most serene Casildea de Vandalia,[1] for you to permit this captive knight of yours to waste away and perish in constant wanderings, amid rude toils and bitter hardships? Is it not enough that I have compelled all the knights of Navarre, all those of León, all the Tartessians and Castilians, and, finally, all those of La Mancha, to confess that there is no beauty anywhere that can rival yours?"

"That is not so!" cried Don Quixote at this point. "I am of La Mancha, and I have never confessed, I never could nor would confess a thing so prejudicial to the beauty of my lady. The knight whom you see there, Sancho, is raving; but let us listen and perhaps he will tell us more."

---

9. The poem intentionally follows affected conventions of the time.   1. The Knight of the Wood's counterpart to Don Quixote's Dulcinea del Toboso.

"That he will," replied Sancho, "for at the rate he is carrying on, he is good for a month at a stretch."

This did not prove to be the case, however; for when the Knight of the Wood heard voices near him, he cut short his lamentations and rose to his feet.

"Who goes there?" he called in a loud but courteous tone. "What kind of people are you? Are you, perchance, numbered among the happy or among the afflicted?"

"Among the afflicted," was Don Quixote's response.

"Then come to me," said the one of the Wood, "and, in doing so, know that you come to sorrow's self and the very essence of affliction."

Upon receiving so gentle and courteous an answer, Don Quixote and Sancho as well went over to him, whereupon the sorrowing one took the Manchegan's arm.

"Sit down here, Sir Knight," he continued, "for in order to know that you are one of those who follow the profession of knight-errantry, it is enough for me to have found you in this place where solitude and serenity keep you company, such a spot being the natural bed and proper dwelling of wandering men of arms."

"A knight I am," replied Don Quixote, "and of the profession that you mention; and though sorrows, troubles, and misfortunes have made my heart their abode, this does not mean that compassion for the woes of others has been banished from it. From your song a while ago I gather that your misfortunes are due to love—the love you bear that ungrateful fair one whom you named in your lamentations."

As they conversed in this manner, they sat together upon the hard earth, very peaceably and companionably, as if at daybreak they were not going to break each other's heads.

"Sir Knight," inquired the one of the Wood, "are you by any chance in love?"

"By mischance I am," said Don Quixote, "although the ills that come from well-placed affection should be looked upon as favors rather than as misfortunes."

"That is the truth," the Knight of the Wood agreed, "if it were not that the loved one's scorn disturbs our reason and understanding; for when it is excessive scorn appears as vengeance."

"I was never scorned by my lady," said Don Quixote.

"No, certainly not," said Sancho, who was standing near by, "for my lady is gentle as a ewe lamb and soft as butter."

"Is he your squire?" asked the one of the Wood.

"He is," replied Don Quixote.

"I never saw a squire," said the one of the Wood, "who dared to speak while his master was talking. At least, there is mine over there; he is as big as your father, and it cannot be proved that he has ever opened his lips while I was conversing."

"Well, upon my word," said Sancho, "I have spoken, and I will speak in front of any other as good—but never mind; it only makes it worse to stir it."

The Knight of the Wood's squire now seized Sancho's arm. "Come along," he said, "let the two of us go where we can talk all we like, squire fashion, and leave these gentlemen our masters to come to lance blows as they tell each other the story of their loves; for you may rest assured, daybreak will find them still at it."

"Let us, by all means," said Sancho, "and I will tell your Grace who I am, so that you may be able to see for yourself whether or not I am to be numbered among the dozen most talkative squires."

With this, the pair went off to one side, and there then took place between them a conversation that was as droll as the one between their masters was solemn.

CHAPTER 13

In which is continued the adventure of the Knight of the Wood, together with the shrewd, highly original, and amicable conversation that took place between the two squires.

The knights and the squires had now separated, the latter to tell their life stories, the former to talk of their loves; but the history first relates the conversation of the servants and then goes on to report that of the masters. We are told that, after they had gone some little distance from where the others were, the one who served the Knight of the Wood began speaking to Sancho as follows:

"It is a hard life that we lead and live, *Señor mio*, those of us who are squires to knights-errant. It is certainly true that we eat our bread in the sweat of our faces, which is one of the curses that God put upon our first parents."[2]

"It might also be said," added Sancho, "that we eat it in the chill of our bodies, for who endures more heat and cold than we wretched ones who wait upon these wandering men of arms? It would not be so bad if we did eat once in a while, for troubles are less where there is bread; but as it is, we sometimes go for a day or two without breaking our fast, unless we feed on the wind that blows."

"But all this," said the other, "may very well be put up with, by reason of the hope we have of being rewarded; for if a knight is not too unlucky, his squire after a little while will find himself the governor of some fine island or prosperous earldom."

"I," replied Sancho, "have told my master that I would be satisfied with the governorship of an island, and he is so noble and so generous that he has promised it to me on many different occasions."

"In return for my services," said the Squire of the Wood, "I'd be content with a canonry. My master has already appointed me to one—and what a canonry!"

"Then he must be a churchly knight," said Sancho, "and in a position to grant favors of that sort to his faithful squire; but mine is a layman, pure and simple, although, as I recall, certain shrewd and, as I see it, scheming persons did advise him to try to become an archbishop. However, he did

---

2. Compare Genesis 3:19: "In the sweat of thy face shalt thou eat bread, till thou return unto the ground."

not want to be anything but an emperor. And there I was, all the time trembling for fear he would take it into his head to enter the Church, since I was not educated enough to hold any benefices. For I may as well tell your Grace that, though I look like a man, I am no more than a beast where holy orders are concerned."

"That is where you are making a mistake," the Squire of the Wood assured him. "Not all island governments are desirable. Some of them are misshapen bits of land, some are poor, others are gloomy, and, in short, the best of them lays a heavy burden of care and trouble upon the shoulders of the unfortunate one to whose lot it falls. It would be far better if we who follow this cursed trade were to go back to our homes and there engage in pleasanter occupations, such as hunting or fishing, for example; for where is there in this world a squire so poor that he does not have a hack, a couple of greyhounds, and a fishing rod to provide him with sport in his own village?"

"I don't lack any of those," replied Sancho. "It is true, I have no hack, but I do have an ass that is worth twice as much as my master's horse. God send me a bad Easter, and let it be the next one that comes, if I would make a trade, even though he gave me four fanegas³ of barley to boot. Your Grace will laugh at the price I put on my gray—for that is the color of the beast. As to greyhounds, I shan't want for them, as there are plenty and to spare in my village. And, anyway, there is more pleasure in hunting when someone else pays for it."

"Really and truly, Sir Squire," said the one of the Wood, "I have made up my mind and resolved to have no more to do with the mad whims of these knights; I intend to retire to my village and bring up my little ones— I have three of them, and they are like oriental pearls."

"I have two of them," said Sancho, "that might be presented to the Pope in person, especially one of my girls that I am bringing up to be a countess, God willing, in spite of what her mother says."

"And how old is this young lady that is destined to be a countess?"

"Fifteen," replied Sancho, "or a couple of years more or less. But she is tall as a lance, fresh as an April morning, and strong as a porter."

"Those," remarked the one of the Wood, "are qualifications that fit her to be not merely a countess but a nymph of the verdant wildwood. O whore's daughter of a whore! What strength the she-rogue must have!"

Sancho was a bit put out by this. "She is not a whore," he said, "nor was her mother before her, nor will either of them ever be, please God, so long as I live. And you might speak more courteously. For one who has been brought up among knights-errant, who are the soul of courtesy, those words are not very becoming."

"Oh, how little your Grace knows about compliments, Sir Squire!" the one of the Wood exclaimed. "Are you not aware that when some knight gives a good lance thrust to the bull in the plaza, or when a person does anything remarkably well, it is the custom for the crowd to cry out, 'Well done, whoreson rascal!' and that what appears to be vituperation in such a case is in reality high praise? Sir, I would bid you disown those sons or

---

3. About 1.6 bushels.

daughters who do nothing to cause such praise to be bestowed upon their parents."

"I would indeed disown them if they didn't," replied Sancho, "and so your Grace may go ahead and call me, my children, and my wife all the whores in the world if you like, for everything that they say and do deserves the very highest praise. And in order that I may see them all again, I pray God to deliver me from mortal sin, or, what amounts to the same thing, from this dangerous calling of squire, seeing that I have fallen into it a second time, decoyed and deceived by a purse of a hundred ducats that I found one day in the heart of the Sierra Morena.[4] The devil is always holding up a bag full of doubloons in front of my eyes, here, there—no, not here, but there—everywhere, until it seems to me at every step I take that I am touching it with my hand, hugging it, carrying it off home with me, investing it, drawing an income from it, and living on it like a prince. And while I am thinking such thoughts, all the hardships I have to put up with serving this crackbrained master of mine, who is more of a madman than a knight, seem to me light and easy to bear."

"That," observed the Squire of the Wood, "is why it is they say that avarice bursts the bag. But, speaking of madmen, there is no greater one in all this world than my master; for he is one of those of whom it is said, 'The cares of others kill the ass.' Because another knight has lost his senses, he has to play mad too[5] and go hunting for that which, when he finds it, may fly up in his snout."

"Is he in love, maybe?"

"Yes, with a certain Casildea de Vandalia, the rawest[6] and best-roasted lady to be found anywhere on earth; but her rawness is not the foot he limps on, for he has other and greater schemes rumbling in his bowels, as you will hear tell before many hours have gone by."

"There is no road so smooth," said Sancho, "that it does not have some hole or rut to make you stumble. In other houses they cook horse beans, in mine they boil them by the kettleful.[7] Madness has more companions and attendants than good sense does. But if it is true what they say, that company in trouble brings relief, I may take comfort from your Grace, since you serve a master as foolish as my own."

"Foolish but brave," the one of the Wood corrected him, "and more of a rogue than anything else."

"That is not true of my master," replied Sancho. "I can assure you there is nothing of the rogue about him; he is as open and aboveboard as a wine pitcher and would not harm anyone but does good to all. There is no malice in his make-up, and a child could make him believe it was night at midday. For that very reason I love him with all my heart and cannot bring myself to leave him, no matter how many foolish things he does."

"But, nevertheless, good sir and brother," said the Squire of the Wood, "with the blind leading the blind, both are in danger of falling into the pit. It would be better for us to get out of all this as quickly as we can and

---

4. When Don Quixote retired there in Part I, chap. 23.   5. In the Sierra Morena, Don Quixote had decided to imitate Amadis de Gaul and Ariosto's Roland "by playing the part of a desperate and raving madman" as a consequence of love.   6. The Spanish has a pun on *crudo*, meaning both "raw" and "cruel."   7. Meaning that his misfortunes always come in large quantities.

return to our old haunts; for those that go seeking adventures do not always find good ones."

Sancho kept clearing his throat from time to time, and his saliva seemed rather viscous and dry; seeing which, the woodland squire said to him, "It looks to me as if we have been talking so much that our tongues are cleaving to our palates, but I have a loosener over there, hanging from the bow of my saddle, and a pretty good one it is." With this, he got up and went over to his horse and came back a moment later with a big flask of wine and a meat pie half a yard in diameter. This is no exaggeration, for the pasty in question was made of a hutch-rabbit of such a size that Sancho took it to be a goat, or at the very least a kid.

"And are you in the habit of carrying this with you, Señor?" he asked.

"What do you think?" replied the other. "Am I by any chance one of your wood-and-water[8] squires? I carry better rations on the flanks of my horse than a general does when he takes the field."

Sancho ate without any urging, gulping down mouthfuls that were like the knots on a tether, as they sat there in the dark.

"You are a squire of the right sort," he said, "loyal and true, and you live in grand style as shown by this feast, which I would almost say was produced by magic. You are not like me, poor wretch, who have in my saddlebags only a morsel of cheese so hard you could crack a giant's skull with it, three or four dozen carob beans, and a few nuts. For this I have my master to thank, who believes in observing the rule that knights-errant should nourish and sustain themselves on nothing but dried fruits and the herbs of the field."

"Upon my word, brother," said the other squire, "my stomach was not made for thistles, wild pears, and woodland herbs. Let our masters observe those knightly laws and traditions and eat what their rules prescribe; I carry a hamper of food and a flask on my saddlebow, whether they like it or not. And speaking of that flask, how I love it! There is scarcely a minute in the day that I'm not hugging and kissing it, over and over again."

As he said this, he placed the wine bag in Sancho's hands, who put it to his mouth, threw his head back, and sat there gazing up at the stars for a quarter of an hour. Then, when he had finished drinking, he let his head loll on one side and heaved a deep sigh.

"The whoreson rascal!" he exclaimed, "that's a fine vintage for you!"

"There!" cried the Squire of the Wood, as he heard the epithet Sancho had used, "do you see how you have praised this wine by calling it 'whoreson'?"

"I grant you," replied Sancho, "that it is no insult to call anyone a son of a whore so long as you really do mean to praise him. But tell me, sir, in the name of what you love most, is this the wine of Ciudad Real?"[9]

"What a winetaster you are! It comes from nowhere else, and it's a few years old, at that."

"Leave it to me," said Sancho, "and never fear, I'll show you how much I know about it. Would you believe me, Sir Squire, I have such a great natural instinct in this matter of wines that I have but to smell a vintage

---

8. Of low quality.   9. The main town in La Mancha and the center of a wine region.

and I will tell you the country where it was grown, from what kind of grapes, what it tastes like, and how good it is, and everything that has to do with it. There is nothing so unusual about this, however, seeing that on my father's side were two of the best winetasters La Mancha has known in many a year, in proof of which, listen to the story of what happened to them.

"The two were given a sample of wine from a certain vat and asked to state its condition and quality and determine whether it was good or bad. One of them tasted it with the tip of his tongue while the other merely brought it up to his nose. The first man said that it tasted of iron, the second that it smelled of Cordovan leather. The owner insisted that the vat was clean and that there could be nothing in the wine to give it a flavor of leather or of iron, but, nevertheless, the two famous winetasters stood their ground. Time went by, and when they came to clean out the vat they found in it a small key attached to a leather strap. And so your Grace may see for yourself whether or not one who comes of that kind of stock has a right to give his opinion in such cases."

"And for that very reason," said the Squire of the Wood, "I maintain that we ought to stop going about in search of adventures. Seeing that we have loaves, let us not go looking for cakes, but return to our cottages, for God will find us there if He so wills."

"I mean to stay with my master," Sancho replied, "until he reaches Saragossa, but after that we will come to an understanding."

The short of the matter is, the two worthy squires talked so much and drank so much that sleep had to tie their tongues and moderate their thirst, since to quench the latter was impossible. Clinging to the wine flask, which was almost empty by now, and with half-chewed morsels of food in their mouths, they both slept peacefully; and we shall leave them there as we go on to relate what took place between the Knight of the Wood and the Knight of the Mournful Countenance.

CHAPTER 14

Wherein is continued the adventure of the Knight of the Wood.

In the course of the long conversation that took place between Don Quixote and the Knight of the Wood, the history informs us that the latter addressed the following remarks to the Manchegan:

"In short, Sir Knight, I would have you know that my destiny, or, more properly speaking, my own free choice, has led me to fall in love with the peerless Casildea de Vandalia. I call her peerless for the reason that she has no equal as regards either her bodily proportions or her very great beauty. This Casildea, then, of whom I am telling you, repaid my worthy affections and honorable intentions by forcing me, as Hercules[1] was forced by his stepmother, to incur many and diverse perils; and each time as I overcame one of them she would promise me that with the next one I should have that which I desired; but instead my labors have continued,

---

1. Son of Zeus and Alcmena; he was persecuted by Zeus's wife, Hera.

forming a chain whose links I am no longer able to count, nor can I say which will be the last one, that shall mark the beginning of the realization of my hopes.

"One time she sent me forth to challenge that famous giantess of Seville, known as La Giralda,[2] who is as strong and brave as if made of brass, and who without moving from the spot where she stands is the most changeable and fickle woman in the world. I came, I saw, I conquered her, I made her stand still and point in one direction only, and for more than a week nothing but north winds blew. Then, there was that other time when Casildea sent me to lift those ancient stones, the mighty Bulls of Guisando,[3] an enterprise that had better have been entrusted to porters than to knights. On another occasion she commanded me to hurl myself down into the Cabra chasm[4]—an unheard-of and terribly dangerous undertaking—and bring her back a detailed account of what lay concealed in that deep and gloomy pit. I rendered La Giralda motionless, I lifted the Bulls of Guisando, and I threw myself into the abyss and brought to light what was hidden in its depths; yet my hopes are dead—how dead!—while her commands and her scorn are as lively as can be.

"Finally, she commanded me to ride through all the provinces of Spain and compel all the knights-errant whom I met with to confess that she is the most beautiful woman now living and that I am the most enamored man of arms that is to be found anywhere in the world. In fulfillment of this behest I have already traveled over the greater part of these realms and have vanquished many knights who have dared to contradict me. But the one whom I am proudest to have overcome in single combat is that famous gentleman, Don Quixote de la Mancha; for I made him confess that my Casildea is more beautiful than his Dulcinea, and by achieving such a conquest I reckon that I have conquered all the others on the face of the earth, seeing that this same Don Quixote had himself routed them. Accordingly, when I vanquished him, his fame, glory, and honor passed over and were transferred to my person.

> The brighter is the conquered one's lost crown,
> The greater is the conqueror's renown.[5]

Thus, the innumerable exploits of the said Don Quixote are now set down to my account and are indeed my own."

Don Quixote was astounded as he listened to the Knight of the Wood, and was about to tell him any number of times that he lied; the words were on the tip of his tongue, but he held them back as best he could, thinking that he would bring the other to confess with his own lips that what he had said was a lie. And so it was quite calmly that he now replied to him.

"Sir Knight," he began, "as to the assertion that your Grace has conquered most of the knights-errant in Spain and even in all the world, I have nothing to say, but that you have vanquished Don Quixote de la

---

2. Actually a statue on the Moorish belfry of the cathedral at Seville.   3. Statues representing animals and supposedly marking a place where Caesar defeated Pompey.   4. Possibly an ancient mine in the Sierra de Cabra near Cordova.   5. From Alonso de Ercilla y Zúñiga's *Araucana*, a poem about the Spanish struggle against the Araucanian Indians of Chile.

Mancha, I am inclined to doubt. It may be that it was someone else who resembled him, although there are very few that do."

"What do you mean?" replied the one of the Wood. "I swear by the heavens above that I did fight with Don Quixote and that I overcame him and forced him to yield. He is a tall man, with a dried-up face, long, lean legs, graying hair, an eagle-like nose somewhat hooked, and a big, black, drooping mustache. He takes the field under the name of the Knight of the Mournful Countenance, he has for squire a peasant named Sancho Panza, and he rides a famous steed called Rocinante. Lastly, the lady of his heart is a certain Dulcinea del Toboso, once upon a time known as Aldonza Lorenzo, just as my own lady, whose name is Casildea and who is an Andalusian by birth, is called by me Casildea de Vandalia. If all this is not sufficient to show that I speak the truth, here is my sword which shall make incredulity itself believe."

"Calm yourself, Sir Knight," replied Don Quixote, "and listen to what I have to say to you. You must know that this Don Quixote of whom you speak is the best friend that I have in the world, so great a friend that I may say that I feel toward him as I do toward my own self; and from all that you have told me, the very definite and accurate details that you have given me, I cannot doubt that he is the one whom you have conquered. On the other hand, the sight of my eyes and the touch of my hands assure me that he could not possibly be the one, unless some enchanter who is his enemy—for he has many, and one in particular who delights in persecuting him—may have assumed the knight's form and then permitted himself to be routed, by way of defrauding Don Quixote of the fame which his high deeds of chivalry have earned for him throughout the known world. To show you how true this may be, I will inform you that not more than a couple of days ago those same enemy magicians transformed the figure and person of the beauteous Dulcinea del Toboso into a low and mean village lass, and it is possible that they have done something of the same sort to the knight who is her lover. And if all this does not suffice to convince you of the truth of what I say, here is Don Quixote himself who will maintain it by force of arms, on foot or on horseback, or in any way you like."

Saying this, he rose and laid hold of his sword, and waited to see what the Knight of the Wood's decision would be. That worthy now replied in a voice as calm as the one Don Quixote had used.

"Pledges," he said, "do not distress one who is sure of his ability to pay. He who was able to overcome you when you were transformed, Señor Don Quixote, may hope to bring you to your knees when you are your own proper self. But inasmuch as it is not fitting that knights should perform their feats of arms in the darkness, like ruffians and highwaymen, let us wait until it is day in order that the sun may behold what we do. And the condition governing our encounter shall be that the one who is vanquished must submit to the will of his conqueror and perform all those things that are commanded of him, provided they are such as are in keeping with the state of knighthood."

"With that condition and understanding," said Don Quixote, "I shall be satisfied."

With this, they went off to where their squires were, only to find them snoring away as hard as when sleep had first overtaken them. Awakening the pair, they ordered them to look to the horses; for as soon as the sun was up the two knights meant to stage an arduous and bloody single-handed combat. At this news Sancho was astonished and terrified, since, as a result of what the other squire had told him of the Knight of the Wood's prowess, he was led to fear for his master's safety. Nevertheless, he and his friend now went to seek the mounts without saying a word, and they found the animals all together, for by this time the two horses and the ass had smelled one another out. On the way the Squire of the Wood turned to Sancho and addressed him as follows:

"I must inform you, brother, that it is the custom of the fighters of Andalusia, when they are godfathers in any combat, not to remain idly by, with folded hands, while their godsons fight it out. I tell you this by way of warning you that while our masters are settling matters, we, too, shall have to come to blows and hack each other to bits."

"The custom, Sir Squire," replied Sancho, "may be all very well among the fighters and ruffians that you mention, but with the squires of knights-errant it is not to be thought of. At least, I have never heard my master speak of any such custom, and he knows all the laws of chivalry by heart. But granting that it is true and that there is a law which states in so many words that squires must fight while their masters do, I have no intention of obeying it but rather will pay whatever penalty is laid on peaceable-minded ones like myself, for I am sure it cannot be more than a couple of pounds of wax,[6] and that would be less expensive than the lint which it would take to heal my head—I can already see it split in two. What's more, it's out of the question for me to fight since I have no sword nor did I ever in my life carry one."

"That," said the one of the Wood, "is something that is easily remedied. I have here two linen bags of the same size. You take one and I'll take the other and we will fight that way, on equal terms."

"So be it, by all means," said Sancho, "for that will simply knock the dust out of us without wounding us."

"But that's not the way it's to be," said the other squire. "Inside the bags, to keep the wind from blowing them away, we will put a half-dozen nice smooth pebbles of the same weight, and so we'll be able to give each other a good pounding without doing ourselves any real harm or damage."

"Body of my father!" cried Sancho, "just look, will you, at the marten and sable and wads of carded cotton that he's stuffing into those bags so that we won't get our heads cracked or our bones crushed to a pulp. But I am telling you, Señor mio, that even though you fill them with silken pellets, I don't mean to fight. Let our masters fight and make the best of it, but as for us, let us drink and live; for time will see to ending our lives without any help on our part by way of bringing them to a close before they have reached their proper season and fall from ripeness."

"Nevertheless," replied the Squire of the Wood, "fight we must, if only for half an hour."

---

6. In some confraternities, penalties were paid in wax, presumably to make church candles.

"No," Sancho insisted, "that I will not do. I will not be so impolite or so ungrateful as to pick any quarrel however slight with one whose food and drink I've shared. And, moreover, who in the devil could bring himself to fight in cold blood, when he's not angry or vexed in any way?"

"I can take care of that, right enough," said the one of the Wood. "Before we begin, I will come up to your Grace as nicely as you please and give you three or four punches that will stretch you out at my feet; and that will surely be enough to awaken your anger, even though it's sleeping sounder than a dormouse."

"And I," said Sancho, "have another idea that's every bit as good as yours. I will take a big club, and before your Grace has had a chance to awaken my anger I will put yours to sleep with such mighty whacks that if it wakes at all it will be in the other world; for it is known there that I am not the man to let my face be mussed by anyone, and let each look out for the arrow.[7] But the best thing to do would be to leave one's anger to its slumbers, for no one knows the heart of any other, he who comes for wool may go back shorn, and God bless peace and curse all strife. If a hunted cat when surrounded and cornered turns into a lion, God knows what I who am a man might not become. And so from this time forth I am warning you, Sir Squire, that all the harm and damage that may result from our quarrel will be upon your head."

"Very well," the one of the Wood replied, "God will send the dawn and we shall make out somehow."

At that moment gay-colored birds of all sorts began warbling in the trees and with their merry and varied songs appeared to be greeting and welcoming the fresh-dawning day, which already at the gates and on the balconies of the east was revealing its beautiful face as it shook out from its hair an infinite number of liquid pearls. Bathed in this gentle moisture, the grass seemed to shed a pearly spray, the willows distilled a savory manna, the fountains laughed, the brooks murmured, the woods were glad, and the meadows put on their finest raiment. The first thing that Sancho Panza beheld, as soon as it was light enough to tell one object from another, was the Squire of the Wood's nose, which was so big as to cast into the shade all the rest of his body. In addition to being of enormous size, it is said to have been hooked in the middle and all covered with warts of a mulberry hue, like eggplant; it hung down for a couple of inches below his mouth, and the size, color, warts, and shape of this organ gave his face so ugly an appearance that Sancho began trembling hand and foot like a child with convulsions and made up his mind then and there that he would take a couple of hundred punches before he would let his anger be awakened to a point where he would fight with this monster.

Don Quixote in the meanwhile was surveying his opponent, who had already adjusted and closed his helmet so that it was impossible to make out what he looked like. It was apparent, however, that he was not very tall and was stockily built. Over his armor he wore a coat of some kind or

---

7. A proverbial expression from archery: let each one take care of his or her own arrow. Other obviously proverbial expressions follow, as is typical of Sancho's speech.

other made of what appeared to be the finest cloth of gold, all bespangled with glittering mirrors that resembled little moons and that gave him a most gallant and festive air, while above his helmet were a large number of waving plumes, green, white, and yellow in color. His lance, which was leaning against a tree, was very long and stout and had a steel point of more than a palm in length. Don Quixote took all this in, and from what he observed concluded that his opponent must be of tremendous strength, but he was not for this reason filled with fear as Sancho Panza was. Rather, he proceeded to address the Knight of the Mirrors, quite boldly and in a highbred manner.

"Sir Knight," he said, "if in your eagerness to fight you have not lost your courtesy, I would beg you to be so good as to raise your visor a little in order that I may see if your face is as handsome as your trappings."

"Whether you come out of this emprise the victor or the vanquished, Sir Knight," he of the Mirrors replied, "there will be ample time and opportunity for you to have a sight of me. If I do not now gratify your desire, it is because it seems to me that I should be doing a very great wrong to the beauteous Casildea de Vandalia by wasting the time it would take me to raise my visor before having forced you to confess that I am right in my contention, with which you are well acquainted."

"Well, then," said Don Quixote, "while we are mounting our steeds you might at least inform me if I am that knight of La Mancha whom you say you conquered."

"To that our[8] answer," said he of the Mirrors, "is that you are as like the knight I overcame as one egg is like another; but since you assert that you are persecuted by enchanters, I should not venture to state positively that you are the one in question."

"All of which," said Don Quixote, "is sufficient to convince me that you are laboring under a misapprehension; but in order to relieve you of it once and for all, let them bring our steeds, and in less time than you would spend in lifting your visor, if God, my lady, and my arm give me strength, I will see your face and you shall see that I am not the vanquished knight you take me to be."

With this, they cut short their conversation and mounted, and, turning Rocinante around, Don Quixote began measuring off the proper length of field for a run against his opponent as he of the Mirrors did the same. But the Knight of La Mancha had not gone twenty paces when he heard his adversary calling to him, whereupon each of them turned halfway and he of the Mirrors spoke.

"I must remind you, Sir Knight," he said, "of the condition under which we fight, which is that the vanquished, as I have said before, shall place himself wholly at the disposition of the victor."

"I am aware of that," replied Don Quixote, "not forgetting the provision that the behest laid upon the vanquished shall not exceed the bounds of chivalry."

"Agreed," said the Knight of the Mirrors.

At that moment Don Quixote caught sight of the other squire's weird

---

8. Note the dignified, "majestic" plural form.

nose and was as greatly astonished by it as Sancho had been. Indeed, he took the fellow for some monster, or some new kind of human being wholly unlike those that people this world. As he saw his master riding away down the field preparatory to the tilt, Sancho was alarmed; for he did not like to be left alone with the big-nosed individual, fearing that one powerful swipe of that protuberance against his own nose would end the battle so far as he was concerned and he would be lying stretched out on the ground, from fear if not from the force of the blow.

He accordingly ran after the knight, clinging to one of Rocinante's stirrup straps, and when he thought it was time for Don Quixote to whirl about and bear down upon his opponent, he called to him and said, "Señor mio, I beg your Grace, before you turn for the charge, to help me up into that cork tree yonder where I can watch the encounter which your Grace is going to have with this knight better than I can from the ground and in a way that is much more to my liking."

"I rather think, Sancho," said Don Quixote, "that what you wish to do is to mount a platform where you can see the bulls without any danger to yourself."

"The truth of the matter is," Sancho admitted, "the monstrous nose on that squire has given me such a fright that I don't dare stay near him."

"It is indeed of such a sort," his master assured him, "that if I were not the person I am, I myself should be frightened. And so, come, I will help you up."

While Don Quixote tarried to see Sancho ensconced in the cork tree, the Knight of the Mirrors measured as much ground as seemed to him necessary and then, assuming that his adversary had done the same, without waiting for sound of trumpet or any other signal, he wheeled his horse, which was no swifter nor any more impressive-looking than Rocinante, and bore down upon his enemy at a mild trot; but when he saw that the Manchegan was busy helping his squire, he reined in his mount and came to a stop midway in his course, for which his horse was extremely grateful, being no longer able to stir a single step. To Don Quixote, on the other hand, it seemed as if his enemy was flying, and digging his spurs with all his might into Rocinante's lean flanks he caused that animal to run a bit for the first and only time, according to the history, for on all other occasions a simple trot had represented his utmost speed. And so it was that, with an unheard-of-fury, the Knight of the Mournful Countenance came down upon the Knight of the Mirrors as the latter sat there sinking his spurs all the way up to the buttons without being able to persuade his horse to budge a single inch from the spot where he had come to a sudden standstill.

It was at this fortunate moment, while his adversary was in such a predicament, that Don Quixote fell upon him, quite unmindful of the fact that the other knight was having trouble with his mount and either was unable or did not have time to put his lance at rest. The upshot of it was, he encountered him with such force that, much against his will, the Knight of the Mirrors went rolling over his horse's flanks and tumbled to the ground, where as a result of his terrific fall he lay as if dead, without moving hand or foot.

No sooner did Sancho perceive what had happened than he slipped down from the cork tree and ran up as fast as he could to where his master was. Dismounting from Rocinante, Don Quixote now stood over the Knight of the Mirrors, and undoing the helmet straps to see if the man was dead, or to give him air in case he was alive, he beheld—who can say what he beheld without creating astonishment, wonder, and amazement in those who hear the tale? The history tells us that it was the very countenance, form, aspect, physiognomy, effigy, and image of the bachelor Sansón Carrasco!

"Come, Sancho," he cried in a loud voice, "and see what is to be seen but is not to be believed. Hasten, my son, and learn what magic can do and how great is the power of wizards and enchanters."

Sancho came, and the moment his eyes fell on the bachelor Carrasco's face he began crossing and blessing himself a countless number of times. Meanwhile, the overthrown knight gave no signs of life.

"If you ask me, master," said Sancho, "I would say that the best thing for your Grace to do is to run his sword down the mouth of this one who appears to be the bachelor Carrasco; maybe by so doing you would be killing one of your enemies, the enchanters."

"That is not a bad idea," replied Don Quixote, "for the fewer enemies the better." And, drawing his sword, he was about to act upon Sancho's advice and counsel when the Knight of the Mirrors' squire came up to them, now minus the nose which had made him so ugly.

"Look well what you are doing, Don Quixote!" he cried. "The one who lies there at your feet is your Grace's friend, the bachelor Sansón Carrasco, and I am his squire."

"And where is your nose?" inquired Sancho, who was surprised to see him without that deformity.

"Here in my pocket," was the reply. And, thrusting his hand into his coat, he drew out a nose of varnished pasteboard of the make that has been described. Studying him more and more closely, Sancho finally exclaimed, in a voice that was filled with amazement, "Holy Mary preserve me! And is this not my neighbor and crony, Tomé Cecial?"

"That is who I am!" replied the de-nosed squire, "your good friend Tomé Cecial, Sancho Panza. I will tell you presently of the means and snares and falsehoods that brought me here. But, for the present, I beg and entreat your master not to lay hands on, mistreat, wound, or slay the Knight of the Mirrors whom he now has at his feet; for without any doubt it is the rash and ill-advised bachelor Sansón Carrasco, our fellow villager."

The Knight of the Mirrors now recovered consciousness, and, seeing this, Don Quixote at once placed the naked point of his sword above the face of the vanquished one.

"Dead you are, knight," he said, "unless you confess that the peerless Dulcinea del Toboso is more beautiful than your Casildea de Vandalia. And what is more, you will have to promise that, should you survive this encounter and the fall you have had, you will go to the city of El Toboso and present yourself to her in my behalf, that she may do with you as she may see fit. And in case she leaves you free to follow your own will, you are to return to seek me out—the trail of my exploits will serve as a guide to bring you wherever I may be—and tell me all that has taken place between you and her. These conditions are in conformity with those that we arranged before our combat and they do not go beyond the bounds of knight-errantry."

"I confess," said the fallen knight, "that the tattered and filthy shoe of the lady Dulcinea del Toboso is of greater worth than the badly combed if clean beard of Casildea, and I promise to go to her presence and return to yours and to give you a complete and detailed account concerning anything you may wish to know."

"Another thing," added Don Quixote, "that you will have to confess and believe is that the knight you conquered was not and could not have been Don Quixote de la Mancha, but was some other that resembled him, just as I am convinced that you, though you appear to be the bachelor Sansón Carrasco, are another person in his form and likeness who has been put here by my enemies to induce me to restrain and moderate the impetuosity of my wrath and make a gentle use of my glorious victory."

"I confess, think, and feel as you feel, think, and believe," replied the lamed knight. "Permit me to rise, I beg of you, if the jolt I received in my fall will let me do so, for I am in very bad shape."

Don Quixote and Tomé Cecial the squire now helped him to his feet. As for Sancho, he could not take his eyes off Tomé but kept asking him one question after another, and although the answers he received afforded clear enough proof that the man was really his fellow townsman, the fear that had been aroused in him by his master's words—about the enchanters' having transformed the Knight of the Mirrors into the bachelor Sansón Carrasco—prevented him from believing the truth that was apparent to his eyes. The short of it is, both master and servant were left with this delusion as the other ill-errant knight and his squire, in no pleasant state of mind, took their departure with the object of looking for some village where they might be able to apply poultices and splints to the bachelor's battered ribs.

Don Quixote and Sancho then resumed their journey along the road to Saragossa, and here for the time being the history leaves them in order to give an account of who the Knight of the Mirrors and his long-nosed squire really were.

CHAPTER 15

Wherein is told and revealed who the Knight of the Mirrors and his squire were.

Don Quixote went off very happy, self-satisfied, and vainglorious at having achieved a victory over so valiant a knight as he imagined the one of the Mirrors to be, from whose knightly word he hoped to learn whether or not the spell which had been put upon his lady was still in effect; for, unless he chose to forfeit his honor, the vanquished contender must of necessity return and give an account of what had happened in the course of his interview with her. But Don Quixote was of one mind, the Knight of the Mirrors of another, for, as has been stated, the latter's only thought at the moment was to find some village where plasters were available.

The history goes on to state that when the bachelor Sansón Carrasco advised Don Quixote to resume his feats of chivalry, after having desisted from them for a while, this action was taken as the result of a conference which he had held with the curate and the barber as to the means to be adopted in persuading the knight to remain quietly at home and cease agitating himself over his unfortunate adventures. It had been Carrasco's suggestion, to which they had unanimously agreed, that they let Don Quixote sally forth, since it appeared to be impossible to prevent his doing so, and that Sansón should then take to the road as a knight-errant and pick a quarrel and do battle with him. There would be no difficulty about finding a pretext, and then the bachelor knight would overcome him (which was looked upon as easy of accomplishment), having first entered into a pact to the effect that the vanquished should remain at the mercy and bidding of his conqueror. The behest in this case was to be that the fallen one should return to his village and home and not leave it for the space of two years or until further orders were given him, it being a certainty that, once having been overcome, Don Quixote would fulfill the agreement, in order not to contravene or fail to obey the laws of chivalry. And it was possible that in the course of his seclusion he would forget his fancies, or they would at least have an opportunity to seek some suitable cure for his madness.

Sansón agreed to undertake this, and Tomé Cecial, Sancho's friend and neighbor, a merry but featherbrained chap, offered to go along as squire. Sansón then proceeded to arm himself in the manner that has been described, while Tomé disguised his nose with the aforementioned mask so that his crony would not recognize him when they met. Thus equipped, they followed the same route as Don Quixote and had almost caught up with him by the time he had the adventure with the Cart of Death. They finally overtook him in the wood, where those events occurred with which the attentive reader is already familiar; and if it had not been for the knight's extraordinary fancies, which led him to believe that the bachelor was not the bachelor, the said bachelor might have been prevented from ever attaining his degree of licentiate, as a result of having found no nests where he thought to find birds.

Seeing how ill they had succeeded in their undertaking and what an end they had reached, Tomé Cecial now addressed his master.

"Surely, Señor Sansón Carrasco," he said, "we have had our deserts. It is easy enough to plan and embark upon an enterprise, but most of the time it's hard to get out of it. Don Quixote is a madman and we are sane, yet he goes away sound and laughing while your Grace is left here, battered and sorrowful. I wish you would tell me now who is the crazier: the one who is so because he cannot help it, or he who turns crazy of his own free will?"

"The difference between the two," replied Sansón, "lies in this: that the one who cannot help being crazy will be so always, whereas the one who is a madman by choice can leave off being one whenever he so desires."

"Well," said Tomé Cecial, "since that is the way it is, and since I chose to be crazy when I became your Grace's squire, by the same reasoning I now choose to stop being insane and to return to my home."

"That is your affair," said Sansón, "but to imagine that I am going back before I have given Don Quixote a good thrashing is senseless; and what will urge me on now is not any desire to see him recover his wits, but rather a thirst for vengeance; for with the terrible pain that I have in my ribs, you can't expect me to feel very charitable."

Conversing in this manner they kept on until they reached a village where it was their luck to find a bonesetter to take care of poor Sansón. Tomé Cecial then left him and returned home, while the bachelor meditated plans for revenge. The history has more to say of him in due time, but for the present it goes on to make merry with Don Quixote.

CHAPTER 16

Of what happened to Don Quixote upon his meeting with a prudent gentleman of La Mancha.

With that feeling of happiness and vainglorious self-satisfaction that has been mentioned, Don Quixote continued on his way, imagining himself to be, as a result of the victory he had just achieved, the most valiant knight-errant of the age. Whatever adventures might befall him from then on he regarded as already accomplished and brought to a fortunate conclusion. He thought little now of enchanters and enchantments and was unmindful of the innumerable beatings he had received in the course of his knightly wanderings, of the volley of pebbles that had knocked out half his teeth, of the ungratefulness of the galley slaves and the audacity of the Yanguesans whose poles had fallen upon his body like rain. In short, he told himself, if he could but find the means, manner, or way of freeing his lady Dulcinea of the spell that had been put upon her, he would not envy the greatest good fortune that the most fortunate of knights-errant in ages past had ever by any possibility attained.

He was still wholly wrapped up in these thoughts when Sancho spoke to him.

"Isn't it strange, sir, that I can still see in front of my eyes the huge and monstrous nose of my old crony, Tomé Cecial?"

"And do you by any chance believe, Sancho, that the Knight of the Mirrors was the bachelor Sansón Carrasco and that his squire was your friend Tomé?"

"I don't know what to say to that," replied Sancho. "All I know is that the things he told me about my home, my wife and young ones, could not have come from anybody else; and the face, too, once you took the nose away, was the same as Tomé Cecial's, which I have seen many times in our village, right next door to my own house, and the tone of voice was the same also."

"Let us reason the matter out, Sancho," said Don Quixote. "Look at it this way: how can it be thought that the bachelor Sansón Carrasco would come as a knight-errant, equipped with offensive and defensive armor, to contend with me? Am I, perchance, his enemy? Have I given him any occasion to cherish a grudge against me? Am I a rival of his? Or can it be jealousy of the fame I have acquired that has led him to take up the profession of arms?"

"Well, then, sir," Sancho answered him, "how are we to explain the fact that the knight was so like the bachelor and his squire like my friend? And if this was a magic spell, as your Grace has said, was there no other pair in the world whose likeness they might have taken?"

"It is all a scheme and a plot," replied Don Quixote, "on the part of those wicked magicians who are persecuting me and who, foreseeing that I would be the victor in the combat, saw to it that the conquered knight should display the face of my friend the bachelor, so that the affection which I bear him would come between my fallen enemy and the edge of my sword and might of my arm, to temper the righteous indignation of my heart. In that way, he who had sought by falsehood and deceits to take my life, would be left to go on living. As proof of all this, Sancho, experience, which neither lies nor deceives, has already taught you how easy it is for enchanters to change one countenance into another, making the beautiful ugly and the ugly beautiful. It was not two days ago that you beheld the peerless Dulcinea's beauty and elegance in its entirety and natural form, while I saw only the repulsive features of a low and ignorant peasant girl with cataracts over her eyes and a foul smell in her mouth. And if the perverse enchanter was bold enough to effect so vile a transformation as this, there is certainly no cause for wonderment at what he has done in the case of Sansón Carrasco and your friend, all by way of snatching my glorious victory out of my hands. But in spite of it all, I find consolation in the fact that, whatever the shape he may have chosen to assume, I have laid my enemy low."

"God knows what the truth of it all may be," was Sancho's comment. Knowing as he did that Dulcinea's transformation had been due to his own scheming and plotting, he was not taken in by his master's delusions. He was at a loss for a reply, however, lest he say something that would reveal his own trickery.

As they were carrying on this conversation, they were overtaken by a man who, following the same road, was coming along behind them. He was mounted on a handsome flea-bitten mare and wore a hooded great-coat of fine green cloth trimmed in tawny velvet and a cap of the same material, while the trappings of his steed, which was accoutered for the field, were green and mulberry in hue, his saddle being of the *jineta*[9] mode. From his broad green and gold shoulder strap there dangled a Moorish cutlass, and his half-boots were of the same make as the baldric. His spurs were not gilded but were covered with highly polished green lacquer, so that harmonizing as they did with the rest of his apparel, they seemed more appropriate than if they had been of purest gold. As he came up, he greeted the pair courteously and, spurring his mare, was about to ride on past when Don Quixote called to him.

"Gallant sir," he said, "If your Grace is going our way and is not in a hurry, it would be a favor to us if we might travel together."

"The truth is," replied the stranger, "I should not have ridden past you if I had not been afraid that the company of my mare would excite your horse."

9. It has a high pommel and short stirrups.

"In that case, sir," Sancho spoke up, "you may as well rein in, for this horse of ours is the most virtuous and well mannered of any that there is. Never on such an occasion has he done anything that was not right—the only time he did misbehave, my master and I suffered for it aplenty. And so, I say again, your Grace may slow up if you like; for even if you offered him your mare on a couple of platters, he'd never try to mount her."

With this, the other traveler drew rein, being greatly astonished at Don Quixote's face and figure. For the knight was now riding along without his helmet, which was carried by Sancho like a piece of luggage on the back of his gray, in front of the packsaddle. If the green-clad gentleman stared hard at his new-found companion, the latter returned his gaze with an even greater intensity. He impressed Don Quixote as being a man of good judgment, around fifty years of age, with hair that was slightly graying and an aquiline nose, while the expression of his countenance was half humorous, half serious. In short, both his person and his accouterments indicated that he was an individual of some worth.

As for the man in green's impression of Don Quixote de la Mancha, he was thinking that he had never before seen any human being that resembled this one. He could not but marvel at the knight's long neck, his tall frame, and the leanness and the sallowness of his face, as well as his armor and his grave bearing, the whole constituting a sight such as had not been seen for many a day in those parts. Don Quixote in turn was quite conscious of the attentiveness with which the traveler was studying him and could tell from the man's astonished look how curious he was; and so, being very courteous and fond of pleasing everyone, he proceeded to anticipate any questions that might be asked him.

"I am aware," he said, "that my appearance must strike your Grace as being very strange and out of the ordinary, and for that reason I am not surprised at your wonderment. But your Grace will cease to wonder when I tell you, as I am telling you now, that I am a knight, one of those

> Of whom it is folks say,
> They to adventures go.

I have left my native heath, mortgaged my estate, given up my comfortable life, and cast myself into fortune's arms for her to do with me what she will. It has been my desire to revive a knight-errantry that is now dead, and for some time past, stumbling here and falling there, now throwing myself down headlong and then rising up once more, I have been able in good part to carry out my design by succoring widows, protecting damsels, and aiding the fallen, the orphans, and the young, all of which is the proper and natural duty of knights-errant. As a result, owing to my many valiant and Christian exploits, I have been deemed worthy of visiting in printed form nearly all the nations of the world. Thirty thousand copies of my history have been published, and, unless Heaven forbid, they will print thirty million of them.

"In short, to put it all into a few words, or even one, I will tell you that I am Don Quixote de la Mancha, otherwise known as the Knight of the Mournful Countenance. Granted that self-praise is degrading, there still are times when I must praise myself, that is to say, when there is no one else present to speak in my behalf. And so, good sir, neither this steed nor this lance nor this buckler nor this squire of mine, nor all the armor that I wear and arms I carry, nor the sallowness of my complexion, nor my leanness and gauntness, should any longer astonish you, now that you know who I am and what the profession is that I follow."

Having thus spoken, Don Quixote fell silent, and the man in green was so slow in replying that it seemed as if he was at a loss for words. Finally, however, after a considerable while, he brought himself to the point of speaking.

"You were correct, Sir Knight," he said, "about my astonishment and my curiosity, but you have not succeeded in removing the wonderment that the sight of you has aroused in me. You say that, knowing who you are, I should not wonder any more, but such is not the case, for I am now more amazed than ever. How can it be that there are knights-errant in the world today and that histories of them are actually printed? I find it hard to convince myself that at the present time there is anyone on earth who goes about aiding widows, protecting damsels, defending the honor of wives, and succoring orphans, and I should never have believed it had I not beheld your Grace with my own eyes. Thank Heaven for that book that your Grace tells me has been published concerning your true and exalted deeds of chivalry, as it should cast into oblivion all the innumerable stories of fictitious knights-errant with which the world is filled, greatly to the detriment of good morals and the prejudice and discredit of legitimate histories."

"As to whether the stories of knights-errant are fictitious or not," observed Don Quixote, "there is much that remains to be said."

"Why," replied the gentleman in green, "is there anyone who can doubt that such tales are false?"

"I doubt it," was the knight's answer, "but let the matter rest there. If our journey lasts long enough, I trust with God's help to be able to show your Grace that you are wrong in going along with those who hold it to be a certainty that they are not true."

From this last remark the traveler was led to suspect that Don Quixote must be some kind of crackbrain, and he was waiting for him to confirm the impression by further observations of the same sort; but before they could get off on another subject, the knight, seeing that he had given an account of his own station in life, turned to the stranger and politely inquired who his companion might be.

"I, Sir Knight of the Mournful Countenance," replied the one in the green-colored greatcoat, "am a gentleman, and a native of the village where, please God, we are going to dine today. I am more than moderately rich, and my name is Don Diego de Miranda. I spend my life with my wife and children and with my friends. My occupations are hunting and fishing, though I keep neither falcon nor hounds but only a tame partridge[1] and a bold ferret or two. I am the owner of about six dozen books, some of them in Spanish, others in Latin, including both histories and devotional works. As for books of chivalry, they have not as yet crossed the

---

1. Used as a decoy.

threshold of my door. My own preference is for profane rather than devotional writings, such as afford an innocent amusement, charming us by their style and arousing and holding our interest by their inventiveness, although I must say there are very few of that sort to be found in Spain.

"Sometimes," the man in green continued, "I dine with my friends and neighbors, and I often invite them to my house. My meals are wholesome and well prepared and there is always plenty to eat. I do not care for gossip, nor will I permit it in my presence. I am not lynx-eyed and do not pry into the lives and doings of others. I hear mass every day and share my substance with the poor, but make no parade of my good works lest hypocrisy and vainglory, those enemies that so imperceptibly take possession of the most modest heart, should find their way into mine. I try to make peace between those who are at strife. I am the devoted servant of Our Lady, and my trust is in the infinite mercy of God Our Savior."

Sancho had listened most attentively to the gentleman's account of his mode of life, and inasmuch as it seemed to him that this was a good and holy way to live and that the one who followed such a pattern ought to be able to work miracles, he now jumped down from his gray's back and, running over to seize the stranger's right stirrup, began kissing the feet of the man in green with a show of devotion that bordered on tears.

"Why are you doing that, brother?" the gentleman asked him. "What is the meaning of these kisses?"

"Let me kiss your feet," Sancho insisted, "for if I am not mistaken, your Grace is the first saint riding *jineta* fashion that I have seen in all the days of my life."

"I am not a saint," the gentleman assured him, "but a great sinner. It is you, brother, who are the saint; for you must be a good man, judging by the simplicity of heart that you show."

Sancho then went back to his packsaddle, having evoked a laugh from the depths of his master's melancholy and given Don Diego fresh cause for astonishment.

Don Quixote thereupon inquired of the newcomer how many children he had, remarking as he did so that the ancient philosophers, who were without a true knowledge of God, believed that mankind's greatest good lay in the gifts of nature, in those of fortune, and in having many friends and many and worthy sons.

"I, Señor Don Quixote," replied the gentleman, "have a son without whom I should, perhaps, be happier than I am. It is not that he is bad, but rather that he is not as good as I should like him to be. He is eighteen years old, and for six of those years he has been at Salamanca studying the Greek and Latin languages. When I desired him to pass on to other branches of learning, I found him so immersed in the science of Poetry (if it can be called such) that it was not possible to interest him in the Law, which I wanted him to study, nor in Theology, the queen of them all. My wish was that he might be an honor to his family; for in this age in which we are living our monarchs are in the habit of highly rewarding those forms of learning that are good and virtuous, since learning without virtue is like pearls on a dunghill. But he spends the whole day trying to decide whether such and such a verse of Homer's *Iliad* is well conceived or not, whether or not Martial is immodest in a certain epigram, whether certain lines of Vergil are to be understood in this way or in that. In short, he spends all of his time with the books written by those poets whom I have mentioned and with those of Horace, Persius, Juvenal, and Tibullus. As for our own moderns, he sets little store by them, and yet, for all his disdain of Spanish poetry, he is at this moment racking his brains in an effort to compose a gloss on a quatrain that was sent him from Salamanca and which, I fancy, is for some literary tournament."

To all this Don Quixote made the following answer:

"Children, sir, are out of their parents' bowels and so are to be loved whether they be good or bad, just as we love those that gave us life. It is for parents to bring up their offspring, from the time they are infants, in the paths of virtue, good breeding, proper conduct, and Christian morality, in order that, when they are grown, they may be a staff to the old age of the ones that bore them and an honor to their own posterity. As to compelling them to study a particular branch of learning, I am not so sure as to that, though there may be no harm in trying to persuade them to do so. But where there is no need to study *pane lucrando*[2]—where Heaven has provided them with parents that can supply their daily bread—I should be in favor of permitting them to follow that course to which they are most inclined; and although poetry may be more pleasurable than useful, it is not one of those pursuits that bring dishonor upon those who engage in them.

"Poetry in my opinion, my dear sir," he went on, "is a young and tender maid of surpassing beauty, who has many other damsels (that is to say, the other disciplines) whose duty it is to bedeck, embellish, and adorn her. She may call upon all of them for service, and all of them in turn depend upon her nod. She is not one to be rudely handled, nor dragged through the streets, nor exposed at street corners, in the market place, or in the private nooks of palaces. She is fashioned through an alchemy of such power that he who knows how to make use of it will be able to convert her into the purest gold of inestimable price. Possessing her, he must keep her within bounds and not permit her to run wild in bawdy satires or soulless sonnets. She is not to be put up for sale in any manner, unless it be in the form of heroic poems, pity-inspiring tragedies, or pleasing and ingenious comedies. Let mountebanks keep hands off her, and the ignorant mob as well, which is incapable of recognizing or appreciating the treasures that are locked within her. And do not think, sir, that I apply that term 'mob' solely to plebeians and those of low estate; for anyone who is ignorant, whether he be lord or prince, may, and should, be included in the vulgar herd.

"But," Don Quixote continued, "he who possesses the gift of poetry and who makes the use of it that I have indicated, shall become famous and his name shall be honored among all the civilized nations of the world. You have stated, sir, that your son does not greatly care for poetry written in our Spanish tongue, and in that I am inclined to think he is somewhat

2. Earning one's bread (Latin).

mistaken. My reason for saying so is this: the great Homer did not write in Latin, for the reason that he was a Greek, and Vergil did not write in Greek since he was a Latin. In a word, all the poets of antiquity wrote in the language which they had imbibed with their mother's milk and did not go searching after foreign ones to express their loftiest conceptions. This being so, it would be well if the same custom were to be adopted by all nations, the German poet being no longer looked down upon because he writes in German, nor the Castilian or the Basque for employing his native speech.

"As for your son, I fancy, sir, that his quarrel is not so much with Spanish poetry as with those poets who have no other tongue or discipline at their command such as would help to awaken their natural gift; and yet, here, too, he may be wrong. There is an opinion, and a true one, to the effect that 'the poet is born,' that is to say, it is as a poet that he comes forth from his mother's womb, and with the propensity that has been bestowed upon him by Heaven, without study or artifice, he produces those compositions that attest the truth of the line: 'Est deus in nobis,'[3] etc. I further maintain that the born poet who is aided by art will have a great advantage over the one who by art alone would become a poet, the reason being that art does not go beyond, but merely perfects, nature; and so it is that, by combining nature with art and art with nature, the finished poet is produced.

"In conclusion, then, my dear sir, my advice to you would be to let your son go where his star beckons him; for being a good student as he must be, and having already successfully mounted the first step on the stairway of learning, which is that of languages, he will be able to continue of his own accord to the very peak of humane letters, an accomplishment that is altogether becoming in a gentleman, one that adorns, honors, and distinguishes him as much as the miter does the bishop or his flowing robe the learned jurisconsult. Your Grace well may reprove your son, should he compose satires that reflect upon the honor of other persons; in that case, punish him and tear them up. But should he compose discourses in the manner of Horace, in which he reprehends vice in general as that poet so elegantly does, then praise him by all means; for it is permitted the poet to write verses in which he inveighs against envy and the other vices as well, and to lash out at the vicious without, however, designating any particular individual. On the other hand, there are poets who for the sake of uttering something malicious would run the risk of being banished to the shores of Pontus.[4]

"If the poet be chaste where his own manners are concerned, he would likewise be modest in his verses, for the pen is the tongue of the mind, and whatever thoughts are engendered there are bound to appear in his writings. When kings and princes behold the marvelous art of poetry as practiced by prudent, virtuous, and serious-minded subjects of their realm, they honor, esteem, and reward those persons and crown them with the leaves of the tree that is never struck by lightning[5] — as if to show that those

---

3. There is a god in us (Latin), Ovid's *Fasti* VI.5.   4. As Ovid was by Augustus in A.D. 8.   5. The laurel.

who are crowned and adorned with such wreaths are not to be assailed by anyone."

The gentleman in the green-colored greatcoat was vastly astonished by this speech of Don Quixote's and was rapidly altering the opinion he had previously held, to the effect that his companion was but a crackbrain. In the middle of the long discourse, which was not greatly to his liking, Sancho had left the highway to go seek a little milk from some shepherds who were draining the udders of their ewes near by. Extremely well pleased with the knight's sound sense and excellent reasoning, the gentleman was about to resume the conversation when, raising his head, Don Quixote caught sight of a cart flying royal flags that was coming toward them down the road and, thinking it must be a fresh adventure, began calling to Sancho in a loud voice to bring him his helmet. Whereupon Sancho hastily left the shepherds and spurred his gray until he was once more alongside his master, who was now about to encounter a dreadful and bewildering ordeal.

["For I Well Know the Meaning of Valor"]
CHAPTER 17

Wherein Don Quixote's unimaginable courage reaches its highest point, together with the adventure of the lions and its happy ending.

The history relates that, when Don Quixote called to Sancho to bring him his helmet, the squire was busy buying some curds from the shepherds and, flustered by his master's great haste, did not know what to do with them or how to carry them. Having already paid for the curds, he did not care to lose them, and so he decided to put them into the headpiece, and, acting upon this happy inspiration, he returned to see what was wanted of him.

"Give me that helmet," said the knight; "for either I know little about adventures or here is one where I am going to need my armor."

Upon hearing this, the gentleman in the green-colored greatcoat looked around in all directions but could see nothing except the cart that was approaching them, decked out with two or three flags which indicated that the vehicle in question must be conveying his Majesty's property. He remarked as much to Don Quixote, but the latter paid no attention, for he was always convinced that whatever happened to him meant adventures and more adventures.

"Forewarned is forearmed," he said. "I lose nothing by being prepared, knowing as I do that I have enemies both visible and invisible and cannot tell when or where or in what form they will attack me."

Turning to Sancho, he asked for his helmet again, and as there was no time to shake out the curds, the squire had to hand it to him as it was. Don Quixote took it and, without noticing what was in it, hastily clapped it on his head; and forthwith, as a result of the pressure on the curds, the whey began running down all over his face and beard, at which he was very much startled.

"What is this, Sancho?" he cried. "I think my head must be softening or my brains melting, or else I am sweating from head to foot. If sweat it be, I assure you it is not from fear, though I can well believe that the adventure which now awaits me is a terrible one indeed. Give me something with which to wipe my face, if you have anything, for this perspiration is so abundant that it blinds me."

Sancho said nothing but gave him a cloth and at the same time gave thanks to God that his master had not discovered what the trouble was. Don Quixote wiped his face and then took off his helmet to see what it was that made his head feel so cool. Catching sight of that watery white mass, he lifted it to his nose and smelled it.

"By the life of my lady Dulcinea del Toboso!" he exclaimed. "Those are curds that you have put there, you treacherous, brazen, ill-mannered squire!"

To this Sancho replied, very calmly and with a straight face, "If they are curds, give them to me, your Grace, so that I can eat them. But no, let the devil eat them, for he must be the one who did it. Do you think I would be so bold as to soil your Grace's helmet? Upon my word, master, by the understanding that God has given me, I, too, must have enchanters who are persecuting me as your Grace's creature and one of his members, and they are the ones who put that filthy mess there to make you lose your patience and your temper and cause you to whack my ribs as you are in the habit of doing. Well, this time, I must say, they have missed the mark; for I trust my master's good sense to tell him that I have neither curds nor milk nor anything of the kind, and if I did have, I'd put it in my stomach and not in that helmet."

"That may very well be," said Don Quixote.

Don Diego was observing all this and was more astonished than ever, especially when, after he had wiped his head, face, beard, and helmet, Don Quixote once more donned the piece of armor and, settling himself in the stirrups, proceeded to adjust his sword and fix his lance.

"Come what may, here I stand, ready to take on Satan himself in person!" shouted the knight.

The cart with the flags had come up to them by this time, accompanied only by a driver riding one of the mules and a man seated up in front.

"Where are you going, brothers?" Don Quixote called out as he placed himself in the path of the cart. "What conveyance is this, what do you carry in it, and what is the meaning of those flags?"

"The cart is mine," replied the driver, "and in it are two fierce lions in cages which the governor of Oran is sending to court as a present for his Majesty. The flags are those of our lord the King, as a sign that his property goes here."

"And are the lions large?" inquired Don Quixote.

It was the man sitting at the door of the cage who answered him. "The largest," he said, "that ever were sent from Africa to Spain. I am the lion-keeper and I have brought back others, but never any like these. They are male and female. The male is in this first cage, the female in the one behind. They are hungry right now, for they have had nothing to eat today; and so we'd be obliged if your Grace would get out of the way, for we must hasten on to the place where we are to feed them."

"Lion whelps against me?" said Don Quixote with a slight smile. "Lion whelps against me? And at such an hour? Then, by God, those gentlemen who sent them shall see whether I am the man to be frightened by lions. Get down, my good fellow, and since you are the lionkeeper, open the cages and turn those beasts out for me; and in the middle of this plain I will teach them who Don Quixote de la Mancha is, notwithstanding and in spite of the enchanters who are responsible for their being here."

"So," said the gentleman to himself as he heard this, "our worthy knight has revealed himself. It must indeed be true that the curds have softened his skull and mellowed his brains."

At this point Sancho approached him. "For God's sake, sir," he said, "do something to keep my master from fighting those lions. For if he does, they're going to tear us all to bits."

"Is your master, then, so insane," the gentleman asked, "that you fear and believe he means to tackle those fierce animals?"

"It is not that he is insane," replied Sancho, "but, rather, foolhardy."

"Very well," said the gentleman, "I will put a stop to it." And going up to Don Quixote, who was still urging the lionkeeper to open the cages, he said, "Sir Knight, knights-errant should undertake only those adventures that afford some hope of a successful outcome, not those that are utterly hopeless to begin with; for valor when it turns to temerity has in it more of madness than of bravery. Moreover, these lions have no thought of attacking your Grace but are a present to his Majesty, and it would not be well to detain them or interfere with their journey."

"My dear sir," answered Don Quixote, "you had best go mind your tame partridge and that bold ferret of yours and let each one attend to his own business. This is my affair, and I know whether these gentlemen, the lions, have come to attack me or not." He then turned to the lionkeeper. "I swear, Sir Rascal, if you do not open those cages at once, I'll pin you to the cart with this lance!"

Perceiving how determined the armed phantom was, the driver now spoke up. "Good sir," he said, "will your Grace please be so kind as to let me unhitch the mules and take them to a safe place before you turn those lions loose? For if they kill them for me, I am ruined for life, since the mules and cart are all the property I own."

"O man of little faith!" said Don Quixote. "Get down and unhitch your mules if you like, but you will soon see that it was quite unnecessary and that you might have spared yourself the trouble."

The driver did so, in great haste, as the lionkeeper began shouting, "I want you all to witness that I am being compelled against my will to open the cages and turn the lions out, and I further warn this gentleman that he will be responsible for all the harm and damage the beasts may do, plus my wages and my fees. You other gentlemen take cover before I open the doors; I am sure they will not do any harm to me."

Once more Don Diego sought to persuade his companion not to commit such an act of madness, as it was tempting God to undertake anything so foolish as that; but Don Quixote's only answer was that he knew what he was doing. And when the gentleman in green insisted that he was sure the knight was laboring under a delusion and ought to consider the matter well, the latter cut him short.

"Well, then, sir," he said, "if your Grace does not care to be a spectator at what you believe is going to turn out to be a tragedy, all you have to do is to spur your flea-bitten mare and seek safety."

Hearing this, Sancho with tears in his eyes again begged him to give up the undertaking, in comparison with which the adventure of the windmills and the dreadful one at the fulling mills—indeed, all the exploits his master had ever in the course of his life undertaken—were but bread and cakes.

"Look, sir," Sancho went on, "there is no enchantment here nor anything of the sort. Through the bars and chinks of that cage I have seen a real lion's claw, and judging by the size of it, the lion that it belongs to is bigger than a mountain."

"Fear, at any rate," said Don Quixote, "will make him look bigger to you than half the world. Retire, Sancho, and leave me, and if I die here, you know our ancient pact: you are to repair to Dulcinea—I say no more."

To this he added other remarks that took away any hope they had that he might not go through with his insane plan. The gentleman in the green-colored greatcoat was of a mind to resist him but saw that he was no match for the knight in the matter of arms. Then, too, it did not seem to him the part of wisdom to fight it out with a madman; for Don Quixote now impressed him as being quite mad in every way. Accordingly, while the knight was repeating his threats to the lionkeeper, Don Diego spurred his mare, Sancho his gray, and the driver his mules, all of them seeking to put as great a distance as possible between themselves and the cart before the lions broke loose.

Sancho already was bewailing his master's death, which he was convinced was bound to come from the lions' claws, and at the same time he cursed his fate and called it an unlucky hour in which he had taken it into his head to serve such a one. But despite his tears and lamentations, he did not leave off thrashing his gray in an effort to leave the cart behind them. When the lionkeeper saw that those who had fled were a good distance away, he once more entreated and warned Don Quixote as he had warned and entreated him before, but the answer he received was that he might save his breath as it would do him no good and he had best hurry and obey. In the space of time that it took the keeper to open the first cage, Don Quixote considered the question as to whether it would be well to give battle on foot or on horseback. He finally decided that he would do better on foot, as he feared that Rocinante would become frightened at sight of the lions; and so, leaping down from his horse, he fixed his lance, braced his buckler, and drew his sword, and then advanced with marvelous daring and great resoluteness until he stood directly in front of the cart, meanwhile commending himself to God with all his heart and then to his lady Dulcinea.

Upon reaching this point, the reader should know, the author of our veracious history indulges in the following exclamatory passage:

"O great-souled Don Quixote de la Mancha, thou whose courage is beyond all praise, mirror wherein all the valiant of the world may behold themselves, a new and second Don Manuel de León,[6] once the glory and the honor of Spanish knighthood! With what words shall I relate thy terrifying exploit, how render it credible to the ages that are to come? What eulogies do not belong to thee of right, even though they consist of hyperbole piled upon hyperbole? On foot and singlehanded, intrepid and with greathearted valor, armed but with a sword, and not one of the keenedged Little Dog[7] make, and with a shield that was not of gleaming and polished steel, thou didst stand and wait for the two fiercest lions that ever the African forests bred! Thy deeds shall be thy praise, O valorous Manchegan; I leave them to speak for thee, since words fail me with which to extol them."

Here the author leaves off his exclamations and resumes the thread of the story.

Seeing Don Quixote posed there before him and perceiving that, unless he wished to incur the bold knight's indignation there was nothing for him to do but release the male lion, the keeper now opened the first cage, and it could be seen at once how extraordinarily big and horribly ugly the beast was. The first thing the recumbent animal did was to turn round, put out a claw, and stretch himself all over. Then he opened his mouth and yawned very slowly, after which he put out a tongue that was nearly two palms in length and with it licked the dust out of his eyes and washed his face. Having done this, he stuck his head outside the cage and gazed about him in all directions. His eyes were now like live coals and his appearance and demeanor were such as to strike terror in temerity itself. But Don Quixote merely stared at him attentively, waiting for him to descend from the cart so that they could come to grips, for the knight was determined to hack the brute to pieces, such was the extent of his unheard-of madness.

The lion, however, proved to be courteous rather than arrogant and was in no mood for childish bravado. After having gazed first in one direction and then in another, as has been said, he turned his back and presented his hind parts to Don Quixote and then very calmly and peaceably lay down and stretched himself out once more in his cage. At this, Don Quixote ordered the keeper to stir him up with a stick in order to irritate him and drive him out.

"That I will not do," the keeper replied, "for if I stir him, I will be the first one he will tear to bits. Be satisfied with what you have already accomplished, Sir Knight, which leaves nothing more to be said on the score of valor, and do not go tempting your fortune a second time. The door was open and the lion could have gone out if he had chosen; since he has not done so up to now, that means he will stay where he is all day long. Your Grace's stoutheartedness has been well established; for no brave fighter, as I see it, is obliged to do more than challenge his enemy and wait for him in the field; his adversary, if he does not come, is the one who is disgraced and the one who awaits him gains the crown of victory."

"That is the truth," said Don Quixote. "Shut the door, my friend, and

---

6. Don Manuel Ponce de León, a paragon of gallantry and courtesy, from the time of Ferdinand and Isabella.   7. The trademark of a famous armorer of Toledo and Saragossa.

bear me witness as best you can with regard to what you have seen me do here. I would have you certify: that you opened the door for the lion, that I waited for him and he did not come out, that I continued to wait and still he stayed there, and finally went back and lay down. I am under no further obligation. Away with enchantments, and God uphold the right, the truth, and true chivalry! So close the door, as I have told you, while I signal to the fugitives in order that they who were not present may hear of this exploit from your lips."

The keeper did as he was commanded, and Don Quixote, taking the cloth with which he had dried his face after the rain of curds, fastened it to the point of his lance and began summoning the runaways, who, all in a body with the gentleman in green bringing up the rear, were still fleeing and turning around to look back at every step. Sancho was the first to see the white cloth.

"May they slay me," he said, "if my master hasn't conquered those fierce beasts, for he's calling to us."

They all stopped and made sure that the one who was doing the signaling was indeed Don Quixote, and then, losing some of their fear, they little by little made their way back to a point where they could distinctly hear what the knight was saying. At last they returned to the cart, and as they drew near Don Quixote spoke to the driver.

"You may come back, brother, hitch your mules, and continue your journey. And you, Sancho, may give each of them two gold crowns to recompense them for the delay they have suffered on my account."

"That I will, right enough," said Sancho. "But what has become of the lions? Are they dead or alive?"

The keeper thereupon, in leisurely fashion and in full detail, proceeded to tell them how the encounter had ended, taking pains to stress to the best of his ability the valor displayed by Don Quixote, at sight of whom the lion had been so cowed that he was unwilling to leave his cage, though the door had been left open quite a while. The fellow went on to state that the knight had wanted him to stir the lion up and force him out, but had finally been convinced that this would be tempting God and so, much to his displeasure and against his will, had permitted the door to be closed.

"What do you think of that, Sancho?" asked Don Quixote. "Are there any spells that can withstand true gallantry? The enchanters may take my luck away, but to deprive me of my strength and courage is an impossibility."

Sancho then bestowed the crowns, the driver hitched his mules, and the lionkeeper kissed Don Quixote's hands for the favor received, promising that, when he reached the court, he would relate this brave exploit to the king himself.

"In that case," replied Don Quixote, "if his Majesty by any chance should inquire who it was that performed it, you are to say that it was the Knight of the Lions; for that is the name by which I wish to be known from now on, thus changing, exchanging, altering, and converting the one I have previously borne, that of Knight of the Mournful Countenance; in which respect I am but following the old custom of knights-errant, who changed their names whenever they liked or found it convenient to do so."

With this, the cart continued on its way, and Don Quixote, Sancho, and the gentleman in the green-colored greatcoat likewise resumed their journey. During all this time Don Diego de Miranda had not uttered a word but was wholly taken up with observing what Don Quixote did and listening to what he had to say. The knight impressed him as being a crazy sane man and an insane one on the verge of sanity. The gentleman did not happen to be familiar with the first part of our history, but if he had read it he would have ceased to wonder at such talk and conduct, for he would then have known what kind of madness this was. Remaining as he did in ignorance of his companion's malady, he took him now for a sensible individual and now for a madman, since what Don Quixote said was coherent, elegantly phrased, and to the point, whereas his actions were nonsensical, foolhardy, and downright silly. What greater madness could there be, Don Diego asked himself, than to don a helmet filled with curds and then persuade oneself that enchanters were softening one's cranium? What could be more rashly absurd than to wish to fight lions by sheer strength alone? He was roused from these thoughts, this inward soliloquy, by the sound of Don Quixote's voice.

"Undoubtedly, Señor Don Diego de Miranda, your Grace must take me for a fool and a madman, am I not right? And it would be small wonder if such were the case, seeing that my deeds give evidence of nothing else. But, nevertheless, I would advise your Grace that I am neither so mad nor so lacking in wit as I must appear to you to be. A gaily caparisoned knight giving a fortunate lance thrust to a fierce bull in the middle of a great square makes a pleasing appearance in the eyes of his king. The same is true of a knight clad in shining armor as he paces the lists in front of the ladies in some joyous tournament. It is true of all those knights who, by means of military exercises or what appear to be such, divert and entertain and, if one may say so, honor the courts of princes. But the best showing of all is made by a knight-errant who, traversing deserts and solitudes, crossroads, forests, and mountains, goes seeking dangerous adventures with the intention of bringing them to a happy and successful conclusion, and solely for the purpose of winning a glorious and enduring renown.

"More impressive, I repeat, is the knight-errant succoring a widow in some unpopulated place than a courtly man of arms making love to a damsel in the city. All knights have their special callings: let the courtier wait upon the ladies and lend luster by his liveries to his sovereign's palace; let him nourish impoverished gentlemen with the splendid fare of his table; let him give tourneys and show himself truly great, generous, and magnificent and a good Christian above all, thus fulfilling his particular obligations. But the knight-errant's case is different.

"Let the latter seek out the nooks and corners of the world; let him enter into the most intricate of labyrinths; let him attempt the impossible at every step; let him endure on desolate highlands the burning rays of the midsummer sun and in winter the harsh inclemencies of wind and frost; let no lions inspire him with fear, no monsters frighten him, no dragons terrify him, for to seek them out, attack them, and conquer them all is his chief and legitimate occupation. Accordingly, I whose lot it is to be numbered among the knights-errant cannot fail to attempt anything that appears to me to fall within the scope of my duties, just as I attacked those lions a while ago even though I knew it to be an exceedingly rash thing to do, for that was a matter that directly concerned me.

"For I well know the meaning of valor: namely, a virtue that lies between the two extremes of cowardice on the one hand and temerity on the other. It is, nonetheless, better for the brave man to carry his bravery to the point of rashness than for him to sink into cowardice. Even as it is easier for the prodigal to become a generous man than it is for the miser, so is it easier for the foolhardy to become truly brave than it is for the coward to attain valor. And in this matter of adventures, you may believe me, Señor Don Diego, it is better to lose by a card too many than a card too few, and 'Such and such a knight is temerarious and overbold' sounds better to the ear than 'That knight is timid and a coward.' "

"I must assure you, Señor Don Quixote," replied Don Diego, "that everything your Grace has said and done will stand the test of reason; and it is my opinion that if the laws and ordinances of knight-errantry were to be lost, they would be found again in your Grace's bosom, which is their depository and storehouse. But it is growing late; let us hasten to my village and my home, where your Grace shall rest from your recent exertions; for if the body is not tired the spirit may be, and that sometimes results in bodily fatigue."

"I accept your offer as a great favor and an honor, Señor Don Diego," was the knight's reply. And, by spurring their mounts more than they had up to then, they arrived at the village around two in the afternoon and came to the house that was occupied by Don Diego, whom Don Quixote had dubbed the Knight of the Green-colored Greatcoat.

[Last Duel]

CHAPTER 64

Which treats of the adventure that caused Don Quixote the most sorrow of all those that have thus far befallen him.

* * * One morning, as Don Quixote went for a ride along the beach,[8] clad in full armor—for, as he was fond of saying, that was his only ornament, his only rest the fight, and, accordingly, he was never without it for a moment—he saw approaching him a horseman similarly arrayed from head to foot and with a brightly shining moon blazoned upon his shield.

As soon as he had come within earshot the stranger cried out to Don Quixote in a loud voice. "O illustrious knight, the never to be sufficiently praised Don Quixote de la Mancha, I am the Knight of the White Moon whose incomparable exploits you will perhaps recall. I come to contend

8. Don Quixote and Sancho, after numberless encounters and experiences (of which the most prominent have been Don Quixote's descent into the cave of Montesinos and their residence at the castle of the playful ducal couple who give Sancho the "governorship of an island" for ten days), are now in Barcelona. Famous as they are, they meet the viceroy and the nobles; their host is Don Antonio Moreno, "a gentleman of wealth and discernment who was fond of amusing himself in an innocent and kindly way."

with you and try the might of my arm, with the purpose of having you acknowledge and confess that my lady, whoever she may be, is beyond comparison more beautiful than your own Dulcinea del Toboso. If you will admit the truth of this fully and freely, you will escape death and I shall be spared the trouble of inflicting it upon you. On the other hand, if you choose to fight and I should overcome you, I ask no other satisfaction than that, laying down your arms and seeking no further adventures, you retire to your own village for the space of a year, during which time you are not to lay hand to sword but are to dwell peacefully and tranquilly, enjoying a beneficial rest that shall redound to the betterment of your worldly fortunes and the salvation of your soul. But if you are the victor, then my head shall be at your disposal, my arms and steed shall be the spoils, and the fame of my exploits shall go to increase your own renown. Consider well which is the better course and let me have your answer at once, for today is all the time I have for the dispatching of this business."

Don Quixote was amazed at the knight's arrogance as well as at the nature of the challenge, but it was with a calm and stern demeanor that he replied to him.

"Knight of the White Moon," he said, "of whose exploits up to now I have never heard, I will venture to take an oath that you have not once laid eyes upon the illustrious Dulcinea; for I am quite certain that if you had beheld her you would not be staking your all upon such an issue, since the sight of her would have convinced you that there never has been, and never can be, any beauty to compare with hers. I do not say that you lie, I simply say that you are mistaken; and so I accept your challenge with the conditions you have laid down, and at once, before this day you have fixed upon shall have ended. The only exception I make is with regard to the fame of your deeds being added to my renown, since I do not know what the character of your exploits has been and am quite content with my own, such as they are. Take, then, whichever side of the field you like, and I will take up my position, and may St. Peter bless what God may give."

Now, as it happened, the Knight of the White Moon was seen by some of the townspeople, who informed the viceroy that he was there, talking to Don Quixote de la Mancha. Believing this to be a new adventure arranged by Don Antonio Moreno or some other gentleman of the place, the viceroy at once hastened down to the beach, accompanied by a large retinue, including Don Antonio, and they arrived just as Don Quixote was wheeling Rocinante to measure off the necessary stretch of field. When the viceroy perceived that they were about to engage in combat, he at once interposed and inquired of them what it was that impelled them thus to do battle all of a sudden.

The Knight of the White Moon replied that it was a matter of beauty and precedence and briefly repeated what he had said to Don Quixote, explaining the terms to which both parties had agreed. The viceroy then went up to Don Antonio and asked him if he knew any such knight as this or if it was some joke that they were playing, but the answer that he received left him more puzzled than ever; for Don Antonio did not know who the knight was, nor could he say as to whether this was a real encounter or not. The viceroy, accordingly, was doubtful about letting them proceed, but inasmuch as he could not bring himself to believe that it was anything more than a jest, he withdrew to one side, saying, "Sir Knights, if there is nothing for it but to confess or die, and if Señor Don Quixote's mind is made up and your Grace, the Knight of the White Moon, is even more firmly resolved, then fall to it in the name of God and may He bestow the victory."

The Knight of the White Moon thanked the viceroy most courteously and in well-chosen words for the permission which had been granted them, and Don Quixote did the same, whereupon the latter, commending himself with all his heart to Heaven and to his lady Dulcinea, as was his custom at the beginning of a fray, fell back a little farther down the field as he saw his adversary doing the same. And then, without blare of trumpet or other warlike instrument to give them the signal for the attack, both at the same instant wheeled their steeds about and returned for the charge. Being mounted upon the swifter horse, the Knight of the White Moon met Don Quixote two-thirds of the way and with such tremendous force that, without touching his opponent with his lance (which, it seemed, he deliberately held aloft) he brought both Rocinante and his rider to the ground in an exceedingly perilous fall. At once the victor leaped down and placed his lance at Don Quixote's visor.

"You are vanquished, O knight! Nay, more, you are dead unless you make confession in accordance with the conditions governing our encounter."

Stunned and battered, Don Quixote did not so much as raise his visor but in a faint, wan voice, as if speaking from the grave, he said, "Dulcinea del Toboso is the most beautiful woman in the world and I the most unhappy knight upon the face of this earth. It is not right that my weakness should serve to defraud the truth. Drive home your lance, O knight, and take my life since you already have deprived me of my honor."

"That I most certainly shall not do," said the one of the White Moon. "Let the fame of my lady Dulcinea del Toboso's beauty live on undiminished. As for me, I shall be content if the great Don Quixote will retire to his village for a year or until such a time as I may specify, as was agreed upon between us before joining battle."

The viceroy, Don Antonio, and all the many others who were present heard this, and they also heard Don Quixote's response, which was to the effect that, seeing nothing was asked of him that was prejudicial to Dulcinea, he would fulfill all the other conditions like a true and punctilious knight. The one of the White Moon thereupon turned and with a bow to the viceroy rode back to the city at a mild canter. The viceroy promptly dispatched Don Antonio to follow him and make every effort to find out who he was; and, in the meanwhile, they lifted Don Quixote up and uncovered his face, which held no sign of color and was bathed in perspiration. Rocinante, however, was in so sorry a state that he was unable to stir for the present.

Brokenhearted over the turn that events had taken, Sancho did not know what to say or do. It seemed to him that all this was something that was happening in a dream and that everything was the result of magic. He saw his master surrender, heard him consent not to take up arms again for a year to come as the light of his glorious exploits faded into darkness. At the same time his own hopes, based upon the fresh promises that had been made him, were whirled away like smoke before the wind. He feared that Rocinante was maimed for life, his master's bones permanently dislocated—it would have been a bit of luck if his madness also had been jolted out of him.[9]

Finally, in a hand litter which the viceroy had them bring, they bore the knight back to town. The viceroy himself then returned, for he was very anxious to ascertain who the Knight of the White Moon was who had left Don Quixote in so lamentable a condition.

CHAPTER 65

Wherein is revealed who the Knight of the White Moon was.

The Knight of the White Moon was followed not only by Don Antonio Moreno, but by a throng of small boys as well, who kept after him until the doors of one of the city's hostelries had closed behind him. A squire came out to meet him and remove his armor, for which purpose the victor proceeded to shut himself up in a lower room, in the company of Don Antonio, who had also entered the inn and whose bread would not bake until he had learned the knight's identity. Perceiving that the gentleman had no intention of leaving him, he of the White Moon then spoke.

"Sir," he said, "I am well aware that you have come to find out who I am; and, seeing that there is no denying you the information that you seek, while my servant here is removing my armor I will tell you the exact truth of the matter. I would have you know, sir, that I am the bachelor Sansón Carrasco from the same village as Don Quixote de la Mancha, whose madness and absurdities inspire pity in all of us who know him and in none more than me. And so, being convinced that his salvation lay in his returning home for a period of rest in his own house, I formed a plan for bringing him back.

"It was three months ago that I took to the road as a knight-errant, calling myself the Knight of the Mirrors, with the object of fighting and overcoming him without doing him any harm, intending first to lay down the condition that the vanquished was to yield to the victor's will. What I meant to ask of him—for I looked upon him as conquered from the start— was that he should return to his village and not leave it for a whole year, in the course of which time he might be cured. Fate, however, ordained things otherwise; for he was the one who conquered me and overthrew me from my horse, and thus my plan came to naught. He continued on his wanderings, and I went home, defeated, humiliated, and bruised from my fall, which was quite a dangerous one. But I did not for this reason give up the idea of hunting him up once more and vanquishing him as you have seen me do today.

"Since he is the soul of honor when it comes to observing the ordi-

9. The Spanish has an untranslatable pun on *deslocado*, which means "out of joint" ("dislocated") and also "cured of madness" (from *loco*, "mad").

nances of knight-errantry, there is not the slightest doubt that he will keep the promise he has given me and fulfill his obligations. And that, sir, is all that I need to tell you concerning what has happened. I beg you not to disclose my secret or reveal my identity to Don Quixote, in order that my well-intentioned scheme may be carried out and a man of excellent judgment be brought back to his senses—for a sensible man he would be, once rid of the follies of chivalry."

"My dear sir," exclaimed Don Antonio, "may God forgive you for the wrong you have done the world by seeking to deprive it of its most charming madman! Do you not see that the benefit accomplished by restoring Don Quixote to his senses can never equal the pleasure which others derive from his vagaries? But it is my opinion that all the trouble to which the Señor Bachelor has put himself will not suffice to cure a man who is so hopelessly insane; and if it were not uncharitable, I would say let Don Quixote never be cured, since with his return to health we lose not only his own drolleries but also those of his squire, Sancho Panza, for either of the two is capable of turning melancholy itself into joy and merriment. Nevertheless, I will keep silent and tell him nothing, that I may see whether or not I am right in my suspicion that Señor Carrasco's efforts will prove to have been of no avail."

The bachelor replied that, all in all, things looked very favorable and he hoped for a fortunate outcome. With this, he took his leave of Don Antonio, after offering to render him any service that he could; and, having had his armor tied up and placed upon a mule's back, he rode out of the city that same day on the same horse on which he had gone into battle, returning to his native province without anything happening to him that is worthy of being set down in this veracious chronicle.

[Homecoming and Death]

CHAPTER 73

*Of the omens that Don Quixote encountered upon entering his village,
with other incidents that embellish and lend credence to this great
history.*

As they entered the village, Cid Hamete informs us, Don Quixote caught sight of two lads on the communal threshing floor who were engaged in a dispute.

"Don't let it worry you, Periquillo," one of them was saying to the other; "you'll never lay eyes on it again as long as you live."

Hearing this, Don Quixote turned to Sancho. "Did you mark what that boy said, my friend?" he asked. " 'You'll never lay eyes on it[1] again . . .' "

"Well," replied Sancho, "what difference does it make what he said?"

"What difference?" said Don Quixote. "Don't you see that, applied to the one I love, it means I shall never again see Dulcinea."

Sancho was about to answer him when his attention was distracted by a hare that came flying across the fields pursued by a large number of hunt-

---

1. The same as *her* in the Spanish, because the reference is to a cricket cage, which is a feminine noun. Hence Don Quixote's inference concerning Dulcinea.

ers with their greyhounds. The frightened animal took refuge by huddling down beneath the donkey, whereupon Sancho reached out his hand and caught it and presented it to his master.

"*Malum signum, malum signum,*"[2] the knight was muttering to himself. "A hare flees, the hounds pursue it, Dulcinea appears not."

"It is very strange to hear your Grace talk like that," said Sancho. "Let us suppose that this hare *is* Dulcinea del Toboso and the hounds pursuing it are those wicked enchanters that transformed her into a peasant lass; she flees, I catch her and turn her over to your Grace, you hold her in your arms and caress her. Is that a bad sign? What ill omen can you find in it?"

The two lads who had been quarreling now came up to have a look at the hare, and Sancho asked them what their dispute was about. To this the one who had uttered the words "You'll never lay eyes on it again as long as you live," replied that he had taken a cricket cage from the other boy and had no intention of returning it ever. Sancho then brought out from his pocket four cuartos and gave them to the lad in exchange for the cage, which he placed in Don Quixote's hands.

"There, master," he said, "these omens are broken and destroyed, and to my way of thinking, even though I may be a dunce, they have no more to do with what is going to happen to us than the clouds of yesteryear. If I am not mistaken, I have heard our curate say that sensible persons of the Christian faith should pay no heed to such foolish things, and you yourself in the past have given me to understand that all those Christians who are guided by omens are fools. But there is no need to waste a lot of words on the subject; come, let us go on and enter our village."

The hunters at this point came up and asked for the hare, and Don Quixote gave it to them. Continuing on their way, the returning pair encountered the curate and the bachelor Carrrasco, who were strolling in a small meadow on the outskirts of the town as they read their breviaries. And here it should be mentioned that Sancho Panza, by way of sumpter cloth, had thrown over his gray and the bundle of armor it bore the flame-covered buckram robe in which they had dressed the squire at the duke's castle, on the night that witnessed Altisidora's[3] resurrection; and he had also fitted the miter over the donkey's head, the result being the weirdest transformation and the most bizarrely appareled ass that ever were seen in this world. The curate and the bachelor recognized the pair at once and came forward to receive them with open arms. Don Quixote dismounted and gave them both a warm embrace; meanwhile, the small boys (boys are like lynxes in that nothing escapes them), having spied the ass's miter, ran up for a closer view.

"Come, lads," they cried, "and see Sancho Panza's ass trigged out finer than Mingo,[4] and Don Quixote's beast is skinnier than ever!"

Finally, surrounded by the urchins and accompanied by the curate and the bachelor, they entered the village and made their way to Don Quixote's house, where they found the housekeeper and the niece standing in

2. Meeting a hare is considered an ill omen (Latin)—that is, a bad sign.   3. A girl in the duke's castle where Don Quixote and Sancho were guests for a time. She dramatically pretended to be in love with Don Quixote.   4. The allusion is to the opening lines of *Mingo Revulgo* (15th century), a satire.

the doorway, for the news of their return had preceded them. Teresa Panza, Sancho's wife, had also heard of it, and, half naked and disheveled, dragging her daughter Sanchica by the hand, she hastened to greet her husband and was disappointed when she saw him, for he did not look to her as well fitted out as a governor ought to be.

"How does it come, my husband," she said, "that you return like this, tramping and footsore? You look more like a vagabond than you do like a governor."

"Be quiet, Teresa," Sancho admonished her, "for very often there are stakes where there is no bacon. Come on home with me and you will hear marvels. I am bringing money with me, which is the thing that matters, money earned by my own efforts and without harm to anyone."

"You just bring along the money, my good husband," said Teresa, "and whether you got it here or there, or by whatever means, you will not be introducing any new custom into the world."

Sanchica then embraced her father and asked him if he had brought her anything, for she had been looking forward to his coming as to the showers in May. And so, with his wife holding him by the hand while his daughter kept one arm about his waist and at the same time led the gray, Sancho went home, leaving Don Quixote under his own roof in the company of niece and housekeeper, the curate and the barber.

Without regard to time or season, the knight at once drew his guests to one side and in a few words informed them of how he had been overcome in battle and had given his promise not to leave his village for a year, a promise that he meant to observe most scrupulously, without violating it in the slightest degree, as every knight-errant was obliged to do by the laws of chivalry. He accordingly meant to spend that year as a shepherd,[5] he said, amid the solitude of the fields, where he might give free rein to his amorous fancies as he practiced the virtues of the pastoral life; and he further begged them, if they were not too greatly occupied and more urgent matters did not prevent their doing so, to consent to be his companions. He would purchase a flock sufficiently large to justify their calling themselves shepherds; and, moreover, he would have them know, the most important thing of all had been taken care of, for he had hit upon names that would suit them marvelously well. When the curate asked him what these names were, Don Quixote replied that he himself would be known as "the shepherd Quixotiz," the bachelor as "the shepherd Carrascón," the curate as "the shepherd Curiambro," and Sancho Panza as "the shepherd Pancino."

Both his listeners were dismayed at the new form which his madness had assumed. However, in order that he might not go faring forth from the village on another of his expeditions (for they hoped that in the course of the year he would be cured), they decided to fall in with his new plan and approve it as being a wise one, and they even agreed to be his companions in the calling he proposed to adopt.

---

5. Because the knight-errant's life has been forbidden him by his defeat, Don Quixote for a time plans to live according to another and no less "literary" code, that of the pastoral. The following paragraphs, especially through the bachelor Carrasco, refer humorously to some of the conventions of pastoral literature.

"What's more," remarked Sansón Carrasco, "I am a very famous poet, as everyone knows, and at every turn I will be composing pastoral or courtly verses or whatever may come to mind, by way of a diversion for us as we wander in those lonely places; but what is most necessary of all, my dear sirs, is that each one of us should choose the name of the shepherd lass to whom he means to dedicate his songs, so that we may not leave a tree, however hard its bark may be, where their names are not inscribed and engraved as is the custom with lovelorn shepherds."

"That is exactly what we should do," replied Don Quixote, "although, for my part, I am relieved of the necessity of looking for an imaginary shepherdess, seeing that I have the peerless Dulcinea del Toboso, glory of these brookside regions, adornment of these meadows, beauty's mainstay, cream of the Graces—in short, one to whom all praise is well becoming however hyperbolical it may be."

"That is right," said the curate, "but we will seek out some shepherd maids that are easily handled, who if they do not square with us will fit in the corners."

"And," added Sansón Carrasco, "if we run out of names we will give them those that we find printed in books the world over: such as Fílida, Amarilis, Diana, Flérida, Galatea, and Belisarda; for since these are for sale in the market place, we can buy them and make them our own. If my lady, or, rather, my shepherdess, should be chance be called Ana, I will celebrate her charms under the name of Anarda; if she is Francisca, she will become Francenia; if Lucía, Luscinda; for it all amounts to the same thing. And Sancho Panza, if he enters this confraternity, may compose verses to his wife, Teresa Panza, under the name of Teresaina."

Don Quixote had to laugh at this, and the curate then went on to heap extravagant praise upon him for his noble resolution which did him so much credit, and once again he offered to keep the knight company whenever he could spare the time from the duties of his office. With this, they took their leave of him, advising and beseeching him to take care of his health and to eat plentifully of the proper food.

As fate would have it, the niece and the housekeeper had overheard the conversation of the three men, and as soon as the visitors had left they both descended upon Don Quixote.

"What is the meaning of this, my uncle? Here we were thinking your Grace had come home to lead a quiet and respectable life, and do you mean to tell us you are going to get yourself involved in fresh complications—

Young shepherd, thou who comest here,
Young shepherd, thou who goest there . . .[6]

For, to tell the truth, the barley is too hard now to make shepherds' pipes of it."[7]

"And how," said the housekeeper, "is your Grace going to stand the midday heat in summer, the winter cold, the howling of the wolves out there in the fields? You certainly cannot endure it. That is an occupation

6. From a ballad.   7. A proverb.

for robust men, cut out and bred for such a calling almost from their swaddling clothes. Setting one evil over against another, it is better to be a knight-errant than a shepherd. Look, sir, take my advice, for I am not stuffed with bread and wine when I give it to you but am fasting and am going on fifty years of age: stay at home, attend to your affairs, go often to confession, be charitable to the poor, and let it be upon my soul if any harm comes to you as a result of it."

"Be quiet, daughters," said Don Quixote. "I know very well what I must do. Take me up to bed, for I do not feel very well; and you may be sure of one thing: whether I am a knight-errant now or a shepherd to be, I never will fail to look after your needs as you will see when the time comes."

And good daughters that they unquestionably were, the housekeeper and the niece helped him up to bed, where they gave him something to eat and made him as comfortable as they could.

CHAPTER 74

Of how Don Quixote fell sick, of the will that he made, and of the manner of his death.

Inasmuch as nothing that is human is eternal but is ever declining from its beginning to its close, this being especially true of the lives of men, and since Don Quixote was not endowed by Heaven with the privilege of staying the downward course of things, his own end came when he was least expecting it. Whether it was owing to melancholy occasioned by the defeat he had suffered, or was, simply, the will of Heaven which had so ordained it, he was taken with a fever that kept him in bed for a week, during which time his friends, the curate, the bachelor, and the barber, visited him frequently, while Sancho Panza, his faithful squire, never left his bedside.

Believing that the knight's condition was due to sorrow over his downfall and disappointment at not having been able to accomplish the disenchantment and liberation of Dulcinea, Sancho and the others endeavored to cheer him up in every possible way. The bachelor urged him to take heart and get up from bed that he might begin his pastoral life, adding that he himself had already composed an eclogue that would cast in the shade all that Sannazaro[8] had ever written, and had purchased with his own money from a herdsman of Quintanar two fine dogs to guard the flock, one of them named Barcino and the other Butrón. All this, however, did not serve to relieve Don Quixote's sadness; whereupon his friends called in the doctor, who took his pulse and was not very well satisfied with it. In any case, the physician told them, they should attend to the health of his soul as that of his body was in grave danger.

Don Quixote received this news calmly enough, but not so his housekeeper, niece, and squire, who began weeping bitterly, as if he were already lying dead in front of them. It was the doctor's opinion that melancholy and depression were putting an end to his patient's life. The knight

---

8. Jacopo Sannazaro (1456?–1530), Italian poet whose *Arcadia* is one of the milestones in the pastoral tradition.

then requested them to leave him alone as he wished to sleep a little, and they complied. He slept for more than six hours at a stretch, as the saying is, and so soundly that the housekeeper and niece thought he would never wake.

At last he did, however, and at once cried out in a loud voice, "Blessed be Almighty God who has given me so many blessings! Truly His mercy is boundless and is not limited or restrained by the sins of men."

The niece listened carefully to what her uncle said, and it seemed to her that he was speaking more rationally than was his wont, at least during his illness.

"Sir," she said to him, "what does your Grace mean? Has something occurred that we know nothing about? What is this talk of mercy and sins?"

"The mercy that I speak of," replied Don Quixote, "is that which God is showing me at this moment—in spite of my sins, as I have said. My mind now is clear, unencumbered by those misty shadows of ignorance that were cast over it by my bitter and continual reading of those hateful books of chivalry. I see through all the nonsense and fraud contained in them, and my only regret is that my disillusionment has come so late, leaving me no time to make any sort of amends by reading those that are the light of the soul. I find myself, niece, at the point of death, and I would die in such a way as not to leave the impression of a life so bad that I shall be remembered as a madman; for even though I have been one, I do not wish to confirm it on my deathbed. And so, my dear, call in my good friends: the curate, the bachelor Sansón Carrasco, and Master Nicholas the barber; for I want to confess my sins and make my last will and testament."

The niece, however, was relieved of this errand, for the three of them came in just then.

"I have good news for you, kind sirs," said Don Quixote the moment he saw them. "I am no longer Don Quixote de la Mancha but Alonso Quijano, whose mode of life won for him the name of 'Good.' I am the enemy of Amadis of Gaul and all his innumerable progeny; for those profane stories dealing with knight-errantry are odious to me, and I realize how foolish I was and the danger I courted in reading them; but I am in my right senses now and I abominate them."

Hearing this, they all three were convinced that some new kind of madness must have laid hold of him.

"Why, Señor Don Quixote!" exclaimed Sansón. "What makes you talk like that, just when we have received news that my lady Dulcinea is disenchanted? And just when we are on the verge of becoming shepherds so that we may spend the rest of our lives in singing like a lot of princes, why does your Grace choose to turn hermit? Say no more, in Heaven's name, but be sensible and forget these idle tales."

"Tales of that kind," said Don Quixote, "have been the truth for me in the past, and to my detriment, but with Heaven's aid I trust to turn them to my profit now that I am dying. For I feel, gentlemen, that death is very near; so, leave all jesting aside and bring me a confessor for my sins and a notary to draw up my will. In such straits as these a man cannot trifle with his soul. Accordingly, while the Señor Curate is hearing my confession, let the notary be summoned."

Amazed at his words, they gazed at one another in some perplexity, yet they could not but believe him. One of the signs that led them to think he was dying was this quick return from madness to sanity and all the additional things he had to say, so well reasoned and well put and so becoming in a Christian that none of them could any longer doubt that he was in full possession of his faculties. Sending the others out of the room, the curate stayed behind to confess him, and before long the bachelor returned with the notary and Sancho Panza, who had been informed of his master's condition, and who, finding the housekeeper and the niece in tears, began weeping with them. When the confession was over, the curate came out.

"It is true enough," he said, "that Alonso Quijano the Good is dying, and it is also true that he is a sane man. It would be well for us to go in now while he makes his will."

At this news the housekeeper, niece, and the good squire Sancho Panza were so overcome with emotion that the tears burst forth from their eyes and their bosoms heaved with sobs; for, as has been stated more than once, whether Don Quixote was plain Alonso Quijano the Good or Don Quixote de la Mancha, he was always of a kindly and pleasant disposition and for this reason was beloved not only by the members of his household but by all who knew him.

The notary had entered along with the others, and as soon as the preamble had been attended to and the dying man had commended his soul to his Maker with all those Christian formalities that are called for in such a case, they came to the matter of bequests, with Don Quixote dictating as follows:

"ITEM. With regard to Sancho Panza, whom, in my madness, I appointed to be my squire, and who has in his possession a certain sum of money belonging to me: inasmuch as there has been a standing account between us, of debits and credits, it is my will that he shall not be asked to give any accounting whatsoever of this sum, but if any be left over after he has had payment for what I owe him, the balance, which will amount to very little, shall be his, and much good may it do him. If when I was mad I was responsible for his being given the governorship of an island, now that I am of sound mind I would present him with a kingdom if it were in my power, for his simplicity of mind and loyal conduct merit no less."

At this point he turned to Sancho. "Forgive me, my friend," he said, "for having caused you to appear as mad as I by leading you to fall into the same error, that of believing that there are still knights-errant in the world."

"Ah, master," cried Sancho through his tears, "don't die, your Grace, but take my advice and go on living for many years to come; for the greatest madness that a man can be guilty of in this life is to die without good reason, without anyone's killing him, slain only by the hands of melancholy. Look you, don't be lazy but get up from this bed and let us go out into the fields clad as shepherds as we agreed to do. Who knows but behind some bush we may come upon the lady Dulcinea, as disenchanted as you could wish. If it is because of worry over your defeat that you are dying, put the blame on me by saying that the reason for your being overthrown was that I had not properly fastened Rocinante's girth. For the matter of that, your Grace knows from reading your books of chivalry that it is a common thing for certain knights to overthrow others, and he who is vanquished today will be the victor tomorrow."

"That is right," said Sansón, "the worthy Sancho speaks the truth."

"Not so fast, gentlemen," said Don Quixote. "In last year's nests there are no birds this year. I was mad and now I am sane; I was Don Quixote de la Mancha, and now I am, as I have said, Alonso Quijano the Good. May my repentance and the truth I now speak restore to me the place I once held in your esteem. And now, let the notary proceed:

"ITEM. I bequeath my entire estate, without reservation, to my niece Antonia Quijana, here present, after the necessary deductions shall have been made from the most available portion of it to satisfy the bequests that I have stipulated. The first payment shall be to my housekeeper for the wages due her, with twenty ducats over to buy her a dress. And I hereby appoint the Señor Curate and the Señor Bachelor Sansón Carrasco to be my executors.

"ITEM. It is my will that if my niece Antonia Quijana should see fit to marry, it shall be to a man who does not know what books of chivalry are; and if it shall be established that he is acquainted with such books and my niece still insists on marrying him, then she shall lose all that I have bequeathed her and my executors shall apply her portion to works of charity as they may see fit.

"ITEM. I entreat the aforementioned gentlemen, my executors, if by good fortune they should come to know the author who is said to have composed a history now going the rounds under the title of *Second Part of the Exploits of Don Quixote de la Mancha*, to beg his forgiveness in my behalf, as earnestly as they can, since it was I who unthinkingly led him to set down so many and such great absurdities as are to be found in it; for I leave this life with a feeling of remorse at having provided him with the occasion for putting them into writing."

The will ended here, and Don Quixote, stretching himself at length in the bed, fainted away. They all were alarmed at this and hastened to aid him. The same thing happened very frequently in the course of the three days of life that remained to him after he had made his will. The household was in a state of excitement, but with it all the niece continued to eat her meals, the housekeeper had her drink, and Sancho Panza was in good spirits; for this business of inheriting property effaces or mitigates the sorrow which the heir ought to feel and causes him to forget.

Death came at last for Don Quixote, after he had received all the sacraments and once more, with many forceful arguments, had expressed his abomination of books of chivalry. The notary who was present remarked that in none of those books had he read of any knight-errant dying in his own bed so peacefully and in so Christian a manner. And thus, amid the tears and lamentations of those present, he gave up the ghost; that is to say, he died. Perceiving that their friend was no more, the curate asked the notary to be a witness to the fact that Alonso Quijano the Good, commonly known as Don Quixote, was truly dead, this being necessary in order that some author other than Cid Hamete Benengeli might not have the opportunity of falsely resurrecting him and writing endless histories of his exploits.

Such was the end of the Ingenious Gentleman of La Mancha, whose birthplace Cid Hamete was unwilling to designate exactly in order that all the towns and villages of La Mancha might contend among themselves for the right to adopt him and claim him as their own, just as the seven cities of Greece did in the case of Homer. The lamentations of Sancho and those of Don Quixote's niece and his housekeeper, as well as the original epitaphs that were composed for his tomb, will not be recorded here, but mention may be made of the verses by Sansón Carrasco:

> Here lies a gentleman bold
> Who was so very brave
> He went to lengths untold,
> And on the brink of the grave
> Death had on him no hold.
> By the world he set small store —
> He frightened it to the core —
> Yet somehow, by Fate's plan,
> Though he'd lived a crazy man,
> When he died he was sane once more.

WILLIAM SHAKESPEARE
1564–1616

When William Shakespeare was born in April 1564 at Stratford-on-Avon in Warwickshire, Stratford was a rural community with a population of less than two thousand—of which his father, John Shakespeare, was a prominent and prosperous member. Little is known of Shakespeare's early life beyond conjecture or legend; he probably received the education offered by the good local grammar school, with emphasis on Latin; at eighteen he married a farmer's daughter, Anne Hathaway, seven or eight years his senior; there are baptismal records of their children, Susanna (1583) and the twins Hamnet and Judith (1585). After a gap of seven years, records show Shakespeare in 1592 already a successful and many-talented playwright in London; in 1594 he was a shareholder in a prominent players' company of which the Lord Chamberlain was patron and the famous actors Burbage and Kempe were members, while literary distinction of a type that was then more highly respected came from successful poems (*Venus and Adonis*, 1593; *The Rape of Lucrece*, 1594). By 1596, of his now best-known plays he had written *The Taming of the Shrew, Richard III, Romeo and Juliet*, and *The Merchant of Venice*; in 1597–1598, with the two parts of *Henry IV* he added Falstaff to his growing list of famous characters.

The Chamberlain's Company had been playing at the Theatre, north of the city of London, and later at the Curtain; in 1598 the Theatre was demolished, and the Globe, a large playhouse south of the Thames, was built; Shakespeare shared in the expenses. Increased prosperity had brought social advancement: in 1596 the College of Heralds had sanctioned Shakespeare's claim to a gentleman's station by recognizing the family's coat of arms; in the same period he had bought New Place, a large house in his hometown. In 1599, *Henry V*, the last of the plays centering on the Lancastrian kings, was followed by the first of the great Roman tragedies, *Julius Caesar*. The Globe period saw most of Shakespeare's mature work; this is a usual dating of the most famous plays: *Hamlet*, 1601; *Othello*, 1603–1604; *King Lear*, 1605; *Macbeth*, 1606; *Antony and Cleopatra*, 1607; and *The Tempest*, 1611. Queen Elizabeth had favored the players, and her successor, James I, directly patronized them; the Lord Chamberlain's company thus became the King's Men. In 1608, besides the Globe, they acquired an enclosed playhouse in Blackfriars, in the city of London, for winter entertainment. At about that time Shakespeare seems to have retired from the stage, and certainly from then on he wrote fewer plays. He lived most of the time at Stratford until his death there on April 23, 1616.

Shakespeare's plays constitute the most important body of dramatic work in the history of literature, and no character in literature is more familiar to world audiences than Hamlet. He belongs to the world also in the sense that some of the influential interpretations of his character have been developed outside the country and language of his origin, the most famous being the one offered by Goethe in *Wilhelm Meister*. The unparalleled reputation of the work may also have certain nonliterary causes. For instance, it is a play whose central role is singularly cherished by actors in all languages as the test of their skill, and conversely, audiences sometimes content themselves with a rather vague notion of the work as a whole and concentrate on the attractively problematical and eloquent hero and on the actor impersonating him, waiting for his famous soliloquies as a certain type of operagoer waits for the next aria of a favorite singer. But along with the impact of the protagonist, there are other and deeper reasons why the world should naturally have given *Hamlet* its leading place in our literary heritage. Though it is a drama that concerns personages of superior station and the conflicts and problems associated with men and women of high degree, it reveals these problems in terms of a particular family, presenting an individual and domestic dimension along with a public one—the pattern of family conflict within the larger pattern of the *polis*—like the plays of antiquity that deal with the Theban myth, such as *Oedipus* and *Antigone*.

This public dimension of *Hamlet* helps us see it, for our present purposes, in relation to the literature of the Renaissance—for the framework within which the characters are presented and come into conflict is a court. In spite of the Danish locale and the relatively remote period of the action, it is plainly a Renaissance court exhibiting the structure of interests to which Machiavelli's *Prince* has potently drawn our attention. There is a ruler holding power, and much of the action is related to questions concerning the nature of that power—the way in which he had acquired it and the ways in which it can be preserved. Moreover, there is a courtly structure: the king has several courtiers around him, among whom Hamlet, the heir apparent, is only the most prominent.

We have seen some of the forms of the Renaissance court pattern earlier in Machiavelli. The court, the ruling nucleus of the community, was also an arena for conflicts of interest and of wit, a setting for the cultivation and codification of aristocratic virtues (valor, physical and intellectual brilliance, "courtesy"). The positive view of human achievement on earth, so prominent in the Renaissance, was given in courtly life its characteristic setting and testing ground. And as we have observed, the negative view (melancholy, sense of void and purposelessness) also emerged there.

Examining *Hamlet*, we soon realize that its temper belongs more to the negative than to the positive Renaissance outlook. Certain outstanding forms of human endeavor (the establishment of earthly power, the display of gallantry, the confident attempt of the mind to acquire knowledge and to inspire purposeful action), which elsewhere are presented as highly worthwhile, or are at least soberly discussed in terms of their value and limits, seem to be caught here in a condition of disorder and imbued with a sense of vanity and emptiness.

The way in which the state and the court of Denmark are presented in *Hamlet* is significant: they are shown in images of disease and rottenness. And here again, excessive stress on the protagonist himself must be avoided. His position as denouncer of the prevailing decadence, and the major basis for his denunciation—the murder of his father, which leads to his desire to obtain revenge and purify the court by destroying the present king—are central elements in the play, but they are not the *whole* play. The public situation is indicated, and Marcellus has pronounced his famous "Something is rotten" before Hamlet has talked to the Ghost and learned the Ghost's version of events. Moreover, the sense of outside dangers and internal disruption everywhere transcends the personal story of Hamlet, of his revenge, of Claudius's crime; these are rather the signs of the breakdown, portents of a general situation. In this sense, we may tentatively say that the general theme of the play has to do with a kingdom, a society, a *polis*, going to pieces—or even more, with its realization that it has already gone to pieces. Concomitant with this is a sense of the vanity of those forms of human endeavor and power of which the kingdom and the court are symbols.

The tone Shakespeare wants to establish is evident from the opening scenes: the night air is full of dread premonitions; sentinels turn their eyes toward the threatening outside world; meanwhile, the Ghost has already made his appearance, a sinister omen. The kingdom, as we proceed, is presented in terms that are an almost point by point reversal of the ideal. Claudius, the *pater patriae* and *pater familias*, whether we believe the Ghost's indictment or not (Hamlet does not necessarily, and some of his famous indecision has been attributed to his seeking evidence of the Ghost's truthfulness before acting), has by marrying the queen committed an act that by Elizabethan standards is incestuous. There is an overwhelming sense of disintegration in the body of the state, evident in the first court assembly and in all subsequent ones. In their various ways the two courtiers, Hamlet and Laertes, are strangers, contemplating departure; they offer, around their king, a picture quite unlike that of the conventional paladins, supports of the throne, in a well-manned and well-mannered court.

On the other hand, as in all late and decadent phases of a social or artistic structure (the court in a sense is both), we have semblance instead of substance, ornate and empty facades, of which the more enlightened members of the group are mockingly aware. Thus Polonius, who after Hamlet is the major figure in the king's retinue, is presented satirically in his empty formalities of speech and conventional patterns of behavior. And there are numerous instances (e.g., Osric) of manners being replaced by mannerisms. Hence the way courtly life is depicted in the play suggests always the hollow, the fractured, and the crooked. The traditional forms and institutions of gentle living and all the pomp and solemnity are marred by corruption and distortion. Courtship and love are reduced to Hamlet's mockery of a "civil conversation" in the play scene, his phrases presenting not the Platonic loftiness and the repartee of "gentilesse" of Baldesar Castiglione, but punning undercurrents of bawdiness. The theater, a traditional institution of court life, is "politically" used by the hero as a device to expose the king's crime. There are elements of macabre caricature in Shakespeare's treatment of the solemn theme of death (see, for instance, the manner of Polonius's death, which is a sort of sarcastic version of a cloak-and-dagger scene, or the effect of the clownish gravediggers' talk). Finally, the arms tournament, the typical occasion for the display of courtiers' gallantry in front of their king, is here turned by the scheming of the king himself into the play's conclusive scene of carnage. And the person who, on the king's behalf, invites Hamlet to that feast is Osric, the "waterfly," the caricature of the hollow courtier.

This sense of corruption and decadence dominates the temper of the play and obviously qualifies the character of Hamlet, his indecision, and his sense of vanity and disenchantment with the world in which he lives. In Hamlet the relation between thought and deed, intent and realization, is confused in the same way the norms and institutions that would regulate the life of a well-ordered court have been deprived of their original purpose and beauty. He and the king are "mighty opposites," and it can be argued that against Hamlet's indecision and negativism the king presents a more positive scheme of action, at least in the purely Machiavellian sense, at the level of practical power politics. But even this conclusion will prove only partly true. There are indeed moments in which all that the king seems to wish for himself is to forget the past and rule honorably. He advises Hamlet not to mourn his father excessively, for melancholy is not in accord with "nature." On various occasions the king shows a high and competent conception of his office: a culminating instance is the courageous and cunning way in which he confronts and handles Laertes's wrath. The point can be made that since his life is obviously threatened by Hamlet (who was seeking to kill him when by mistake he killed Polonius instead), the king acts within a legitimate pattern of politics in wanting to have Hamlet liquidated. But this argument cannot be carried so far as to demonstrate that he represents a fully positive attitude toward life and the world, even in the strictly amoral terms of political technique. For in fact his action is corroded by an element alien to that technique—the vexations of his own conscience. In spite of his energy and his extrovert qualities he too becomes part of the negative picture of disruption and lacks concentration of purpose. The images of decay and putrescence that characterize his court extend to his own speech: his "offense," in his own words, "smells to heaven."

To conclude, *Hamlet* as a Renaissance tragedy presents a world particularly "out of joint," a world that, having long ago lost the sense of a grand extratemporal design that was so important in medieval times (to Hamlet the thought of the afterlife is even more puzzling and dark than that of this life), looks with an even greater sense of disenchantment at the circle of temporal action symbolized by the kingdom and the court. These structures could have offered certain codes of conduct and objects of allegiance that would have given individual action a purposeful meaning. But now their order has been destroyed. Ideals that once had power and freshness have lost their vigor under the impact of satiety, doubt, and melancholy.

Because communal values are so degraded, it is natural to ask in the end whether some alternative attempt at a settlement could be imagined, with Hamlet—like other Renaissance heroes—adopting an individual code of conduct, however extravagant. On the whole, Hamlet seems too steeped in his own hopelessness and in the courtly mechanism to which he inevitably belongs to be able to find personal intellectual and moral compromise or his own version of total escape or total dream; for his "antic disposition" is a strategy, his "folly" is politically motivated. Still, the tone of his brooding and often moralizing speech, his melancholy and dissatisfaction, his very desire for revenge do seem to imply an aspiration toward some form of moral beauty, a nostalgia for a world—as his father's must have been—of clean allegiances and respected codes of honor. One thing worth examining in this connection is Hamlet's attitude toward Fortinbras. Fortinbras is a marginal character, but our attention is emphatically drawn to him both at the very opening and at the very close of the play. There is no doubt that while in the play certain positive virtues—such as friendship, loyalty, and truthfulness—are represented by the very prominent Horatio, who will live on to give a true report of Hamlet, in Fortinbras the ideals of gallant knighthood, which in the present court have been so corrupted and lost, seem to be presented at their purest. And he has, of course, Hamlet's "dying voice." In act 4, scene 4, Hamlet saw Fortinbras move with his army toward an enterprise characterized by the flimsiness of its material rewards. In a world where all matter seems corrupt, Hamlet's qualified sympathy for that gratuitous display of honor for honor's sake, of valor "even for an eggshell," of death braved "for a fantasy," calls to mind some of the serious aspects of the Quixotic code.

William Shakespeare's "Hamlet" (1986), edited by Harold Bloom, contains some unconventional critical approaches. A biography placing Shakespeare in his social context is M. C. Bradbrook, *Shakespeare the Poet in His World* (1978), while E. K. Chambers, *William Shakespeare, A Study of Facts and Problems*, 2 vols. (1930), is considered the most fully documented biography. Paul Arthur Cantor, *Shakespeare, "Hamlet"* (1989), is an in-depth study of the tragedy. The student will find several views in *Shakespeare: Modern Essays in Criticism* (1957), edited by Leonard F. Dean. More advanced interpretations and critical methods are presented in Paul Gottschalk, *The Meanings of "Hamlet." Modes of Literary Interpretation Since Bradley* (1972). Another valuable work is Harry Levin, *The Question of "Hamlet"* (1959). Cedric Watts, *Hamlet* (1988), besides critical interpretation, offers stage history, critical history, and a selected bibliography. Bert O. States, *"Hamlet" and the Concept of Character* (1992), focuses on characters and characteristics in the play.

Hamlet, Prince of Denmark

CHARACTERS

CLAUDIUS, *king of Denmark*
HAMLET, *son to the late, and*
   nephew to the present king
POLONIUS, *lord chamberlain*
HORATIO, *friend to Hamlet*
LAERTES, *son of Polonius*
PRIEST
MARCELLUS,⎫ *officers*
BERNARDO, ⎭
FRANCISCO, *a soldier*
REYNALDO, *servant to Polonius*
PLAYERS
TWO CLOWNS, *grave-diggers*
FORTINBRAS, *prince of Norway*
CAPTAIN

VOLTIMAND,
CORNELIUS,
ROSENCRANTZ,
GUILDENSTERN, ⎱ *courtiers*
OSRIC,
GENTLEMAN,
ENGLISH AMBASSADORS
GERTRUDE, *queen of Denmark,*
   and mother to Hamlet
OPHELIA, *daughter of Polonius*
LORDS, LADIES, OFFICERS, SOL-
   DIERS, SAILORS, MESSENGERS,
   and OTHER ATTENDANTS
GHOST OF HAMLET'S FATHER

SCENE—*Denmark.*

Act I

SCENE 1

Elsinore. A platform before the castle.

[FRANCISCO *at his post. Enter to him* BERNARDO.]
BERNARDO: Who's there?
FRANCISCO: Nay, answer me: stand, and unfold yourself.
BERNARDO: Long live the king!
FRANCISCO: Bernardo?
BERNARDO: He.   5
FRANCISCO: You come most carefully upon your hour.
BERNARDO: 'Tis now struck twelve; get thee to bed, Francisco.
FRANCISCO: For this relief much thanks: 'tis bitter cold,
   And I am sick at heart.
BERNARDO: Have you had quiet guard?
FRANCISCO: Not a mouse stirring.   10
BERNARDO: Well, good night.
   If you do meet Horatio and Marcellus,
   The rivals[1] of my watch, bid them make haste.
FRANCISCO: I think I hear them. Stand, ho! Who is there?
   [*Enter* HORATIO *and* MARCELLUS.]
HORATIO: Friends to this ground.
MARCELLUS: And liegemen to the Dane.[2]   15
FRANCISCO: Give you good night.
MARCELLUS: O, farewell, honest soldier:
   Who hath relieved you?
FRANCISCO: Bernardo hath my place.
   Give you good night.
   [*Exit.*]
MARCELLUS: Holla! Bernardo!
BERNARDO: Say,
   What, is Horatio there?
HORATIO: A piece of him.
BERNARDO: Welcome, Horatio; welcome, good Marcellus.   20
MARCELLUS: What, has this thing appeared again to-night?
BERNARDO: I have seen nothing.
MARCELLUS: Horatio says 'tis but our fantasy,
   And will not let belief take hold of him
   Touching this dreaded sight, twice seen of us: 25
   Therefore I have entreated him along
   With us to watch the minutes of this night,
   That if again this apparition come,
   He may approve our eyes[3] and speak to it.
HORATIO: Tush, tush, 'twill not appear.
BERNARDO: Sit down a while;   30
   And let us once again assail your ears,

1. Partners.   2. The king of Denmark.   3. Confirm what we saw.

That are so fortified against our story,
What we have two nights seen.
HORATIO: Well, sit we down,
    And let us hear Bernardo speak of this.
BERNARDO: Last night of all,   35
    When yond same star that's westward from the pole
    Had made his course to illume that part of heaven
    Where now it burns, Marcellus and myself,
    The bell then beating one,—
        [*Enter* GHOST.]
MARCELLUS: Peace, break thee off; look, where it comes again!   40
BERNARDO: In the same figure, like the king that's dead.
MARCELLUS: Thou art a scholar; speak to it, Horatio.
BERNARDO: Looks it not like the king? mark it, Horatio.
HORATIO: Most like it: it harrows me with fear and wonder.
BERNARDO: It would be spoke to.
MARCELLUS: Question it, Horatio.   45
HORATIO: What art thou, that usurp'st this time of night,
    Together with that fair and warlike form
    In which the majesty of buried Denmark
    Did sometimes[4] march? by heaven I charge thee, speak!
MARCELLUS: It is offended.
BERNARDO: See, it stalks away!   50
HORATIO: Stay! speak, speak! I charge thee, speak!
        [*Exit* GHOST.]
MARCELLUS: 'Tis gone, and will not answer.
BERNARDO: How now, Horatio! you tremble and look pale:
    Is not this something more than fantasy?
    What think you on't?   55
HORATIO: Before my God, I might not this believe
    Without the sensible and true avouch
    Of mine own eyes.
MARCELLUS: Is it not like the king?
HORATIO: As thou art to thyself:
    Such was the very armor he had on   60
    When he the ambitious Norway[5] combated;
    So frown'd he once, when, in an angry parle,
    He smote the sledded[6] Polacks on the ice.
    'Tis strange.
MARCELLUS: Thus twice before, and jump[7] at this dead hour,   65
    With martial stalk hath he gone by our watch.
HORATIO: In what particular thought to work I know not;
    But, in the gross and scope of my opinion,[8]
    This bodes some strange eruption to our state.
MARCELLUS: Good now, sit down, and tell me, he that knows,   70
    Why this same strict and most observant watch

---

4. Formerly. *Denmark:* the king of Denmark.   5. The king of Norway (the elder Fortinbras).
6. They travel in sledges. *Parle:* parley.   7. Just.   8. Taking a general view.

So nightly toils the subject[9] of the land,
And why such daily cast of brazen cannon,
And foreign mart for implements of war;
Why such impress of shipwrights,[1] whose sore task   75
Does not divide the Sunday from the week;
What might be toward,[2] that this sweaty haste
Doth make the night joint-laborer with the day:
Who is't that can inform me?
HORATIO: That can I;
     At least the whisper goes so. Our last king,   80
     Whose image even but now appear'd to us,
     Was, as you know, by Fortinbras of Norway,
     Thereto pricked on by a most emulate pride,
     Dared to the combat; in which our valiant Hamlet—
     For so this side of our known world esteem'd him—   85
     Did slay this Fortinbras; who by a seal'd compact
     Well ratified by law and heraldry,[3]
     Did forfeit, with his life, all those his lands
     Which he stood seized of, to the conqueror:
     Against the which, a moiety competent   90
     Was gagèd[4] by our king; which had returned
     To the inheritance of Fortinbras,
     Had he been vanquisher; as, by the same covenant
     And carriage[5] of the article design'd,
     His fell to Hamlet. Now, sir, young Fortinbras,   95
     Of unimprovèd metal hot and full,
     Hath in the skirts[6] of Norway here and there
     Shark'd up a list of lawless resolutes,
     For food and diet, to some enterprise
     That hath a stomach in't:[7] which is no other—   100
     As it doth well appear unto our state—
     But to recover of us, by strong hand
     And terms compulsatory, those foresaid lands
     So by his father lost: and this, I take it,
     Is the main motive of our preparations,   105
     The source of this our watch and the chief head
     Of this post-haste and romage[8] in the land.
BERNARDO: I think it be no other but e'en so:
     Well may it sort,[9] that this portentous figure
     Comes armèd through our watch, so like the king   110
     That was and is the question of these wars.
HORATIO: A mote it is to trouble the mind's eye.
     In the most high and palmy state of Rome,
     A little ere the mightiest Julius fell,
     The graves stood tenantless, and the sheeted dead   115

9. The people.   1. Ship carpenters. *Mart:* trading. *Impress:* pressing into service.   2. Impending.
3. Duly ratified and proclaimed through heralds.   4. Pledged. *Seized:* possessed. *Moiety competent:*
equal share.   5. Purport.   6. Outskirts, border regions. *Unimprovèd:* untested.   7. Calls for courage.   8. Bustle. *Head:* origin, cause.   9. Fit with the other signs of war.

Did squeak and gibber in the Roman streets:
As stars with trains of fire and dews of blood,
Disasters in the sun; and the moist star,
Upon whose influence Neptune's empire stands,[1]
Was sick almost to doomsday with eclipse: 120
And even the like precurse[2] of fierce events,
As harbingers preceding still the fates
And prologue to the omen coming on,
Have heaven and earth together demonstrated
Unto our climatures[3] and countrymen.   125
    [*Re-enter* GHOST.]
But soft, behold! lo, where it comes again!
I'll cross it, though it blast me. Stay, illusion!
If thou hast any sound, or use of voice,
Speak to me:
If there be any good thing to be done,   130
That may to thee do ease and grace to me,
Speak to me:
If thou art privy to thy country's fate,
Which, happily, foreknowing may avoid,
O, speak!   135
Or if thou hast uphoarded in thy life
Extorted treasure in the womb of earth,
For which, they say, you spirits oft walk in death,
Speak of it: stay, and speak! [*The cock crows.*] Stop it, Marcellus.
MARCELLUS: Shall I strike at it with my partisan?   140
HORATIO: Do, if it will not stand.
BERNARDO: 'Tis here!
HORATIO: 'Tis here!
    [*Exit* GHOST.]
MARCELLUS: 'Tis gone!
We do it wrong, being so majestical,
To offer it the show of violence;
For it is, as the air, invulnerable,   145
And our vain blows malicious mockery.
BERNARDO: It was about to speak, when the cock crew.
HORATIO: And then it started like a guilty thing
Upon a fearful summons. I have heard
The cock, that is the trumpet to the morn,   150
Doth with his lofty and shrill-sounding throat
Awake the god of day, and at his warning,
Whether in sea or fire, in earth or air,
The extravagant[4] and erring spirit hies
To his confine: and of the truth herein   155
This present object made probation.[5]
MARCELLUS: It faded on the crowing of the cock.

---

1. The moon (*moist star*) regulates the sea's tides. *Disasters:* Ill omens.   **2.** Foreboding.
3. Regions.   **4.** Wandering out of its confines.   **5.** Gave proof.

Some say that ever 'gainst[6] that season comes
Wherein our Saviour's birth is celebrated,
The bird of dawning singeth all night long: 160
And then, they say, no spirit dare stir abroad,
The nights are wholesome, then no planets strike,
No fairy takes nor witch hath power to charm,
So hallowed and so gracious[7] is the time.
HORATIO: So have I heard and do in part believe it.   165
But look, the morn, in russet mantle clad,
Walks o'er the dew of yon high eastward hill:
Break we our watch up; and by my advice,
Let us impart what we have seen to-night
Unto young Hamlet; for, upon my life,   170
This spirit, dumb to us, will speak to him:
Do you consent we shall acquaint him with it,
As needful in our loves, fitting our duty?
MARCELLUS: Let's do't, I pray; and I this morning know
Where we shall find him most conveniently.   175
   [Exeunt.]

SCENE 2

A room of state in the castle.

[*Flourish. Enter the* KING, QUEEN, HAMLET, POLONIUS, LAERTES, VOL-
TIMAND, CORNELIUS, LORDS, *and* ATTENDANTS.]
KING: Though yet of Hamlet our dear brother's death
The memory be green, and that it us befitted
To bear our hearts in grief and our whole kingdom
To be contracted in one brow of woe,
Yet so far hath discretion[8] fought with nature   5
That we with wisest sorrow think on him,
Together with remembrance of ourselves.
Therefore our sometime sister, now our queen,
The imperial jointress to this warlike state,
Have we, as 'twere with a defeated joy, —   10
With an auspicious and a dropping eye,
With mirth in funeral and with dirge in marriage,
In equal scale weighing delight and dole, —
Taken to wife: nor have we herein barr'd[9]
Your better wisdoms, which have freely gone   15
With this affair along. For all, our thanks.
Now follows, that[1] you know, young Fortinbras,
Holding a weak supposal of our worth,
Or thinking by our late dear brother's death
Our state to be disjoint and out of frame,   20
Colleaguèd with this dream[2] of his advantage,

6. Just before.   7. Full of blessing. *Strike:* exercise evil influence (compare "moonstruck"). *Fairy
takes:* bewitches.   8. Restraint (on grief).   9. Ignored. *Dole:* grief.   1. What.   2. Combined
with this fantastic notion.

He hath not failed to pester us with message,
Importing the surrender of those lands
Lost by his father, with all bonds of law,
To our most valiant brother. So much for him. 25
Now for ourself, and for this time of meeting:
Thus much the business is: we have here writ
To Norway, uncle of young Fortinbras,—
Who, impotent and bed-rid, scarcely hears
Of this his nephew's purpose,—to suppress 30
His further gait herein; in that the levies,
The lists and full proportions,³ are all made
Out of his subject: and we here dispatch
You, good Cornelius, and you, Voltimand,
For bearers of this greeting to old Norway, 35
Giving to you no further personal power
To business with the king more than the scope
Of these delated⁴ articles allow.
Farewell, and let your haste commend your duty.

CORNELIUS: ⎫ In that and all things will we show our duty. 40
VOLTIMAND: ⎭

KING: We doubt it nothing: heartily farewell.

    [*Exeunt* VOLTIMAND *and* CORNELIUS.]

And now, Laertes, what's the news with you?
You told us of some suit; what is't, Laertes?
You cannot speak of reason to the Dane,
And lose your voice: what wouldst thou beg, Laertes, 45
That shall not be my offer, not thy asking?
The head is not more native to⁵ the heart,
The hand more instrumental to the mouth,
Than is the throne of Denmark to thy father.
What wouldst thou have, Laertes?

LAERTES: My dread lord, 50
Your leave and favor to return to France,
From whence though willingly I came to Denmark,
To show my duty in your coronation,
Yet now, I must confess, that duty done,
My thoughts and wishes bend again toward France 55
And bow them to your gracious leave and pardon.

KING: Have you your father's leave? What says Polonius?

POLONIUS: He hath, my lord, wrung from me my slow leave
By laborsome petition, and at last
Upon his will I sealed my hard consent: 60
I do beseech you, give him leave to go.

KING: Take thy fair hour, Laertes; time be thine,
And thy best graces spend it at thy will!
But now, my cousin Hamlet, and my son,—

HAMLET: [*Aside.*] A little more than kin, and less than kind. 65

---

3. Amounts of forces and supplies. *Gait:* proceeding.   4. Detailed.   5. Naturally bound to.

KING: How is it that the clouds still hang on you?
HAMLET: Not so, my lord; I am too much i' the sun.[6]
QUEEN: Good Hamlet, cast thy nighted color off,
    And let thine eye look like a friend on Denmark.
    Do not for ever with thy vailèd[7] lids   70
    Seek for thy noble father in the dust:
    Thou know'st 'tis common; all that lives must die,
    Passing through nature to eternity.
HAMLET: Aye, madam, it is common.
QUEEN: If it be,
    Why seems it so particular with thee?   75
HAMLET: Seems, madam! nay, it is; I know not 'seems.'
    'Tis not alone my inky cloak, good mother,
    Nor customary suits of solemn black,
    Nor windy suspiration of forced breath,
    No, nor the fruitful river in the eye,   80
    Nor the dejected havior of the visage,
    Together with all forms, moods, shapes of grief,
    That can denote me truly: these indeed seem,
    For they are actions that a man might play:
    But I have that within which passeth show;   85
    These but the trappings and the suits of woe.
KING: 'Tis sweet and cómmendàble in your nature, Hamlet,
    To give these mourning duties to your father:
    But, you must know, your father lost a father,
    That father lost, lost his, and the survivor bound   90
    In filial obligation for some term
    To do obsequious[8] sorrow: but to persevere
    In obstinate condolement is a course
    Of impious stubborness; 'tis unmanly grief:
    It shows a will most incorrect[9] to heaven,   95
    A heart unfortified, a mind impatient,
    An understanding simple and unschool'd:
    For what we know must be and is as common
    As any the most vulgar thing to sense,
    Why should we in our peevish opposition   100
    Take it to heart? Fie! 'tis a fault to heaven,
    A fault against the dead, a fault to nature,
    To reason most absurd, whose common theme
    Is death of fathers, and who still hath cried,
    From the first corse till he that died to-day,   105
    'This must be so.' We pray you, throw to earth
    This unprevailing[1] woe, and think of us
    As of a father: for let the world take note,
    You are the most immediate to our throne,
    And with no less nobility of love   110

6. The cue to Hamlet's irony is given by the King's "my cousin . . . my son" (line 64). Hamlet is punning on *son*.   7. Downcast.   8. Dutiful, especially concerning funeral rites (obsequies).
9. Not subdued.   1. Useless.

Than that which dearest father bears his son
Do I impart toward you. For your intent
In going back to school in Wittenberg,
It is most retrograde[2] to our desire:
And we beseech you, bend you to remain   115
Here in the cheer and comfort of our eye,
Our chiefest courtier, cousin and our son.
QUEEN: Let not thy mother lose her prayers, Hamlet:
I pray thee, stay with us; go not to Wittenberg.
HAMLET: I shall in all my best obey you, madam.   120
KING: Why, 'tis a loving and a fair reply:
Be as ourself in Denmark. Madam, come;
This gentle and unforced accord of Hamlet
Sits smiling to my heart: in grace whereof,
No jocund health that Denmark drinks to-day,   125
But the great cannon to the clouds shall tell,
And the king's rouse the heaven shall bruit[3] again,
Re-speaking earthly thunder. Come away.
    [*Flourish. Exeunt all but* HAMLET.]
HAMLET: O, that this too too sullied flesh would melt,
Thaw and resolve itself into a dew!   130
Or that the Everlasting had not fixed
His canon[4] 'gainst self-slaughter! O God! God!
How weary, stale, flat and unprofitable
Seem to me all the uses of this world!
Fie on't! ah fie! 'tis an unweeded garden,   135
That grows to seed; things rank and gross in nature
Possess it merely. That it should come to this!
But two months dead! nay, not so much, not two:
So excellent a king; that was, to this,
Hyperion to a satyr: so loving to my mother,   140
That he might not beteem[5] the winds of heaven
Visit her face too roughly. Heaven and earth!
Must I remember? why, she would hang on him,
As if increase of appetite had grown
By what it fed on: and yet, within a month—   145
Let me not think on't—Frailty, thy name is woman!—
A little month, or ere those shoes were old
With which she followed my poor father's body,
Like Niobe,[6] all tears:—why she, even she,—
O God! a beast that wants discourse[7] of reason   150
Would have mourned longer,—married with my uncle,
My father's brother, but no more like my father
Than I to Hercules: within a month;

---

2. Opposed. *Wittenberg:* the seat of a university; at the peak of fame in Shakespeare's time because of its connection with Martin Luther.   3. Proclaim, echo. *Rouse:* carousal, revel.   4. Law.   5. Allow. Hyperion is the sun god.   6. A proud mother who boasted of having more children than Leto; her seven sons and seven daughters were slain by Apollo and Artemis, children of Leto. The grieving Niobe was changed by Zeus into a continually weeping stone.   7. Lacks the faculty.

Ere yet the salt of most unrighteous tears
Had left the flushing in her gallèd[8] eyes,   155
She married. O, most wicked speed, to post
With such dexterity to incestuous sheets![9]
It is not, nor it cannot come to good:
But break, my heart, for I must hold my tongue!

[*Enter* HORATIO, MARCELLUS, *and* BERNARDO.]

HORATIO: Hail to your lordship!
HAMLET: I am glad to see you well: 160
  Horatio,— or I do forget myself.
HORATIO: The same, my lord, and your poor servant ever.
HAMLET: Sir, my good friend; I'll change[1] that name with you:
  And what make you from Wittenberg, Horatio?
  Marcellus?   165
MARCELLUS: My good lord?
HAMLET: I am very glad to see you. [*To* BERNARDO.] Good even, sir.
  But what, in faith, make you from Wittenberg?
HORATIO: A truant disposition, good my lord.
HAMLET: I would not hear your enemy say so,   170
  Nor shall you do my ear that violence,
  To make it truster of your own report
  Against yourself: I know you are no truant.
  But what is your affair in Elsinore?
  We'll teach you to drink deep ere you depart.   175
HORATIO: My lord, I came to see your father's funeral.
HAMLET: I pray thee, do not mock me, fellow-student;
  I think it was to see my mother's wedding.
HORATIO: Indeed, my lord, it followed hard upon.
HAMLET: Thrift, thrift, Horatio! the funeral baked-meats   180
  Did coldly furnish forth the marriage tables.
  Would I had met my dearest[2] foe in heaven
  Or ever I had seen that day, Horatio!
  My father!—methinks I see my father.
HORATIO: O where, my lord?
HAMLET: In my mind's eye, Horatio.   185
HORATIO: I saw him once; he was a goodly king.
HAMLET: He was a man, take him for all in all,
  I shall not look upon his like again.
HORATIO: My lord, I think I saw him yesternight.
HAMLET: Saw? who?
HORATIO: My lord, the king your father.   190
HAMLET: The king my father!
HORATIO: Season your admiration[3] for a while
  With an attent ear, till I may deliver,
  Upon the witness of these gentlemen,
  This marvel to you.

8. Inflamed.   9. According to principles that Hamlet accepts, marrying one's brother's widow is
incest.   1. Exchange.   2. Bitterest.   3. Restrain your astonishment.

HAMLET: For God's love, let me hear.   195
HORATIO: Two nights together had these gentlemen,
    Marcellus and Bernardo, on their watch,
    In the dead vast and middle of the night,
    Been thus encountered. A figure like your father,
    Armed at point exactly, cap-a-pe,[4]   200
    Appears before them, and with solemn march
    Goes slow and stately by them: thrice he walked
    By their oppressed and fear-surprisèd eyes,
    Within his truncheon's length; whilst they, distilled
    Almost to jelly with the act of fear,   205
    Stand dumb, and speak not to him. This to me
    In dreadful secrecy impart they did;
    And I with them the third night kept the watch:
    Where, as they had delivered, both in time,
    Form of the thing, each word made true and good,   210
    The apparition comes: I knew your father;
    These hands were not more like.
HAMLET: But where was this?
MARCELLUS: My lord, upon the platform where we watched.
HAMLET: Did you not speak to it?
HORATIO: My lord, I did.
    But answer made it none: yet once methought   215
    It lifted up its head and did address
    Itself to motion, like as it would speak:
    But even then the morning cock crew loud,
    And at the sound it shrunk in haste away
    And vanished from our sight.
HAMLET: 'Tis very strange.   220
HORATIO: As I do live, my honored lord, 'tis true,
    And we did think it writ down in our duty
    To let you know of it.
HAMLET: Indeed, indeed, sirs, but this troubles me.
    Hold you the watch to-night?
MARCELLUS: ⎫
BERNARDO: ⎭   We do, my lord.   225
HAMLET: Armed, say you?
MARCELLUS: ⎫
BERNARDO: ⎭   Armed, my lord.
HAMLET: From top to toe?
MARCELLUS: ⎫
BERNARDO: ⎭   My lord, from head to foot.
HAMLET: Then saw you not his face?
HORATIO: O, yes, my lord; he wore his beaver[5] up.
HAMLET: What, looked he frowningly?   230
HORATIO: A countenance more in sorrow than in anger.
HAMLET: Pale, or red?

---

4. From head to foot. At *point*: completely.   5. Visor.

HORATIO: Nay, very pale.
HAMLET: And fixed his eyes upon you?
HORATIO: Most constantly.
HAMLET: I would I had been there.
HORATIO: It would have much amazed you.   235
HAMLET: Very like, very like. Stayed it long?
HORATIO: While one with moderate haste might tell[6] a hundred.
MARCELLUS: ⎫
BERNARDO: ⎭ Longer, longer.
HORATIO: Not when I saw't.
HAMLET: His beard was grizzled?[7] no?
HORATIO: It was, as I have seen it in his life,   240
    A sable silvered.[8]
HAMLET: I will watch to-night;
    Perchance 'twill walk again.
HORATIO: I warrant it will.
HAMLET: If it assume my noble father's person,
    I'll speak to it, though hell itself should gape
    And bid me hold my peace. I pray you all,   245
    If you have hitherto concealed this sight,
    Let it be tenable in your silence still,[9]
    And whatsoever else shall hap to-night,
    Give it an understanding, but no tongue:
    I will requite your loves. So fare you well: 250
    Upon the platform, 'twixt eleven and twelve,
    I'll visit you.
ALL: Our duty to your honor.
HAMLET: Your loves, as mine to you: farewell.
    [Exeunt all but HAMLET.]
    My father's spirit in arms! all is not well;
    I doubt[1] some foul play: would the night were come!   255
    Till then sit still, my soul: foul deeds will rise,
    Though all the earth o'erwhelm them, to men's eyes.
    [Exit.]

SCENE 3

A room in Polonius's house.

[Enter LAERTES and OPHELIA.]
LAERTES: My necessaries are embarked: farewell:
    And, sister, as the winds give benefit
    And convoy[2] is assistant, do not sleep,
    But let me hear from you.
OPHELIA: Do you doubt that?
LAERTES: For Hamlet, and the trifling of his favor,   5
    Hold it a fashion, and a toy in blood,

---

6. Count.   7. Gray.   8. Black and white.   9. Consider it still a secret.   1. Suspect.   2. Conveyance, means of transport.

A violet in the youth of primy nature,
Forward,[3] not permanent, sweet, not lasting,
The perfume and suppliance of a minute;
No more.   10
OPHELIA: No more but so?
LAERTES: Think it no more:
  For nature crescent does not grow alone
  In thews and bulk; but, as this temple[4] waxes,
  The inward service of the mind and soul   15
  Grows wide withal. Perhaps he loves you now;
  And now no soil nor cautel[5] doth besmirch
  The virtue of his will: but you must fear,
  His greatness weighed,[6] his will is not his own;
  For he himself is subject to his birth: 20
  He may not, as unvalued persons do,
  Carve for himself, for on his choice depends
  The safety and health of this whole state,
  And therefore must his choice be circumscribed
  Unto the voice and yielding[7] of that body   25
  Whereof he is the head. Then if he says he loves you,
  It fits your wisdom so far to believe it
  As he in his particular act and place
  May give his saying deed; which is no further
  Than the main voice of Denmark goes withal.[8]   30
  Then weigh what loss your honor may sustain,
  If with too credent ear you list his songs,
  Or lose your heart, or your chaste treasure open
  To his unmastered importunity.
  Fear it, Ophelia, fear it, my dear sister,   35
  And keep you in the rear of your affection,
  Out of the shot and danger of desire.
  The chariest maid is prodigal enough
  If she unmask her beauty to the moon:
  Virtue itself 'scapes not calumnious strokes: 40
  The canker galls the infants of the spring
  Too oft before their buttons be disclosed,
  And in the morn and liquid dew of youth
  Contagious blastments[9] are most imminent.
  Be wary then; best safety lies in fear: 45
  Youth to itself[1] rebels, though none else near.
OPHELIA: I shall the effect of this good lesson keep,
  As watchman to my heart. But, good my brother,
  Do not, as some ungracious pastors do,
  Show me the steep and thorny way to heaven,   50
  Whilst, like a puffed and reckless libertine,

---

3. Early. *Fashion:* passing mood. *Primy:* early, young.   4. The body. *Crescent:* growing.   5. No foul
or deceitful thoughts.   6. When you consider his rank. *Will:* desire.   7. Assent.   8. Goes along
with, agrees. *Main:* powerful.   9. Blights.   1. Against its better self.

Himself the primrose path of dalliance treads
And recks not his own rede.[2]

LAERTES: O, fear me not.
I stay too long; but here my father comes.

[Enter POLONIUS.]

A double blessing is a double grace;   55
Occasion smiles upon a second leave.

POLONIUS: Yet here, Laertes! Aboard, aboard, for shame!
The wind sits in the shoulder of your sail,
And you are stayed for. There; my blessing with thee!
And these few precepts in thy memory   60
See thou charácter.[3] Give thy thoughts no tongue,
Nor any unproportioned[4] thought his act.
Be thou familiar, but by no means vulgar.
Those friends thou hast, and their adoption tried,
Grapple them to thy soul with hoops of steel,   65
But do not dull thy palm[5] with entertainment
Of each new-hatched unfledged comrade. Beware
Of entrance to a quarrel; but being in,
Bear't, that the opposèd may beware of thee.
Give every man thy ear, but few thy voice: 70
Take each man's censure,[6] but reserve thy judgment.
Costly thy habit as thy purse can buy,
But not expressed in fancy; rich, not gaudy:
For the apparel oft proclaims the man;
And they in France of the best rank and station   75
Are of a most select and generous chief[7] in that.
Neither a borrower nor a lender be:
For loan oft loses both itself and friend,
And borrowing dulls the edge of husbandry.[8]
This above all: to thine own self be true,   80
And it must follow, as the night the day,
Thou canst not then be false to any man.
Farewell: my blessing season[9] this in thee!

LAERTES: Most humbly do I take my leave, my lord.
POLONIUS: The time invites you; go, your servants tend.[1]   85
LAERTES: Farewell, Ophelia, and remember well
What I have said to you.

OPHELIA: 'Tis in my memory locked,
And you yourself shall keep the key of it.

LAERTES: Farewell.

     [Exit.]

POLONIUS: What is't, Ophelia, he hath said to you?
OPHELIA: So please you, something touching the Lord Hamlet.   90
POLONIUS: Marry, well bethought:
'Tis told me, he hath very oft of late

---

2. Does not follow his own advice.   3. Engrave in your memory.   4. Unsuitable.   5. Make the
palm of your hand callous (by indiscriminate handshaking).   6. Opinion.   7. Preeminence.
8. Thriftiness.   9. Ripen.   1. Wait.

Given private time to you, and you yourself
Have of your audience been most free and bounteous:
If it be so—as so 'tis put on me,   95
And that in way of caution—I must tell you,
You do not understand yourself so clearly
As it behoves my daughter and your honor.
What is between you? give me up the truth.

OPHELIA: He hath, my lord, of late made many tenders   100
Of his affection to me.

POLONIUS: Affection! pooh! you speak like a green girl,
Unsifted[2] in such perilous circumstance.
Do you believe his tenders, as you call them?

OPHELIA: I do not know, my lord, what I should think.   105

POLONIUS: Marry, I'll teach you: think yourself a baby,
That you have ta'en these tenders for true pay,
Which are not sterling. Tender[3] yourself more dearly;
Or—not to crack the wind of the poor phrase,
Running it thus—you'll tender me a fool.[4]   110

OPHELIA: My lord, he hath importuned me with love
In honorable fashion.

POLONIUS: Aye, fashion you may call it; go to, go to.

OPHELIA: And hath given countenance[5] to his speech, my lord,
With almost all the holy vows of heaven.   115

POLONIUS: Aye, springes to catch woodcocks. I do know,
When the blood burns, how prodigal the soul
Lends the tongue vows: these blazes, daughter,
Giving more light than heat, extinct in both,
Even in their promise, as it is a-making,   120
You must not take for fire. From this time
Be something scanter of your maiden presence;
Set your entreatments[6] at a higher rate
Than a command to parley. For Lord Hamlet,
Believe so much in him, that he is young,   125
And with a larger tether may he walk
Than may be given you: in few, Ophelia,
Do not believe his vows; for they are brokers,
Not of that dye which their investments[7] show,
But mere implorators of unholy suits,   130
Breathing like sanctified and pious bawds,
The better to beguile. This is for all:
I would not, in plain terms, from this time forth,
Have you so slander any moment[8] leisure,
As to give words or talk with the Lord Hamlet.   135
Look to't, I charge you: come your ways.

OPHELIA: I shall obey, my lord.
    [Exeunt.]

---

2. Untested.   3. Regard.   4. You'll furnish me with a fool (a foolish daughter).   5. Authority.
6. Conversation, company.   7. Clothes. *Brokers*: procurers, panders.   8. Use badly any momentary.

SCENE 4

The platform.

[*Enter* HAMLET, HORATIO, *and* MARCELLUS.]
HAMLET: The air bites shrewdly; it is very cold.
HORATIO: It is a nipping and an eager[9] air.
HAMLET: What hour now?
HORATIO: I think it lacks of twelve.
MARCELLUS: No, it is struck.
HORATIO: Indeed? I heard it not: it then draws near the season   5
    Wherein the spirit held his wont to walk.
    [*A flourish of trumpets, and ordnance shot off within.*]
    What doth this mean, my lord?
HAMLET: The king doth wake to-night, and takes his rouse,
    Keeps wassail, and the swaggering up-spring reels;
    And as he drains his draughts of Rhenish[1] down,   10
    The kettle-drum and trumpet thus bray out
    The triumph of his pledge.[2]
HORATIO: Is it a custom?
HAMLET: Aye, marry, is't:
    But to my mind, though I am native here
    And to the manner born, it is a custom   15
    More honored[3] in the breach than the observance.
    This heavy-headed revel east and west
    Makes us traduced and taxed of other nations:
    They clepe us drunkards, and with swinish phrase
    Soil our addition;[4] and indeed it takes   20
    From our achievements, though performed at height,[5]
    The pith and marrow of our attribute.[6]
    So, oft it chances in particular men,
    That for some vicious mole of nature in them,
    As, in their birth,—wherein they are not guilty,   25
    Since nature cannot choose his origin,—
    By the o'ergrowth of some complexion,[7]
    Oft breaking down the pales and forts of reason,
    Or by some habit that too much o'er-leavens[8]
    The form of plausive[9] manners, that these men,—   30
    Carrying, I say, the stamp of one defect,
    Being nature's livery, or fortune's star,—
    Their virtues else[1]—be they as pure as grace,
    As infinite as man may undergo—
    Shall in the general censure take corruption   35
    From that particular fault: the dram of evil
    Doth all the noble substance often dout
    To his own scandal.[2]

9. Sharp.   1. Rhine wine. *Up-spring reels:* wild dances.   2. In downing the cup in one draught.
3. Honorable.   4. Reputation. *Taxed:* blamed. *Clepe:* call.   5. Done in the best possible manner.
6. Reputation.   7. Excess in one side of their temperament.   8. Modifies, as yeast changes dough.
9. Agreeable.   1. The rest of their qualities.   2. To its own harm. *Dout:* extinguish, nullify.

[*Enter* GHOST.]
HORATIO: Look, my lord it comes!
HAMLET: Angels and ministers of grace defend us!
  Be thou a spirit of health or goblin damned,   40
  Bring with thee airs from heaven or blasts from hell,
  Be thy intents wicked or charitable,
  Thou comest in such a questionable shape
  That I will speak to thee: I'll call thee Hamlet,
  King, father, royal Dane: O, answer me!   45
  Let me not burst in ignorance; but tell
  Why thy canónized bones, hearsèd in death,
  Have burst their cerements; why the sepulchre,
  Wherein we saw thee quietly inurned,
  Hath oped his ponderous and marble jaws,   50
  To cast thee up again. What may this mean,
  That thou, dead corse, again, in complete steel,
  Revisit'st thus the glimpses of the moon,
  Making night hideous; and we fools of nature
  So horridly to shake our disposition   55
  With thoughts beyond the reaches of our souls?
  Say, why is this? Wherefore? what should we do?
    [GHOST *beckons* HAMLET.]
HORATIO: It beckons you to go away with it,
  As if it some impartment did desire
  To you alone.   60
MARCELLUS: Look, with what courteous action
  It waves you to a more removèd ground:
  But do not go with it.
HORATIO: No, by no means.
HAMLET: It will not speak; then I will follow it.
HORATIO: Do not, my lord.
HAMLET: Why, what should be the fear?   65
  I do not set my life at a pin's fee;
  And for my soul, what can it do to that,
  Being a thing immortal as itself?
  It waves me forth again: I'll follow it.
HORATIO: What if it tempt you toward the flood, my lord,   70
  Or to the dreadful summit of the cliff
  That beetles o'er[3] his base into the sea,
  And there assume some other horrible form,
  Which might deprive your sovereignty of reason
  And draw you into madness? think of it: 75
  The very place puts toys[4] of desperation,
  Without more motive, into every brain
  That looks so many fathoms to the sea
  And hears it roar beneath.
HAMLET: It waves me still.

3. Juts over.   4. Fancies.

Go on; I'll follow thee.   80
MARCELLUS: You shall not go, my lord.
HAMLET: Hold off your hands.
HORATIO: Be ruled; you shall not go.
HAMLET: My fate cries out,
And makes each petty artery in this body
As hardy as the Nemean lion's nerve.[5]
Still am I called, unhand me, gentlemen;   85
By heaven, I'll make a ghost of him that lets[6] me:
I say, away! Go on; I'll follow thee.
    [*Exeunt* GHOST *and* HAMLET.]
HORATIO: He waxes desperate with imagination.
MARCELLUS: Let's follow; 'tis not fit thus to obey him.
HORATIO: Have after. To what issue will this come?   90
MARCELLUS: Something is rotten in the state of Denmark.
HORATIO: Heaven will direct it.
MARCELLUS: Nay, let's follow him.
    [*Exeunt.*]

SCENE 5

Another part of the platform.

[*Enter* GHOST *and* HAMLET.]
HAMLET: Whither wilt thou lead me? speak; I'll go no further.
GHOST: Mark me.
HAMLET: I will.
GHOST: My hour is almost come,
When I to sulphurous and tormenting flames[7]
Must render up myself.
HAMLET: Alas, poor ghost!
GHOST: Pity me not, but lend thy serious hearing   5
    To what I shall unfold.
HAMLET: Speak; I am bound to hear.
GHOST: So art thou to revenge, when thou shalt hear.
HAMLET: What?
GHOST: I am thy father's spirit;
    Doomed for a certain term to walk the night,   10
    And for the day confined to fast in fires,
    Till the foul crimes done in my days of nature
    Are burnt and purged away. But that I am forbid
    To tell the secrets of my prison-house,
    I could a tale unfold whose lightest word   15
    Would harrow up thy soul, freeze thy young blood,
    Make thy two eyes, like stars, start from their spheres,[8]
    Thy knotted and combinèd locks to part
    And each particular hair to stand on end,

---

5. Sinew, muscle. The Nemean lion was slain by Hercules as one of his twelve labors.   6. Hinders.
7. Of purgatory.   8. Transparent revolving shells in each of which, according to Ptolemaic astronomy,
a planet or other heavenly body was placed.

Like quills upon the fretful porpentine: 20
But this eternal blazon[9] must not be
To ears of flesh and blood. List, list, O, list!
If thou didst ever thy dear father love —
HAMLET: O God!
GHOST: Revenge his foul and most unnatural murder.   25
HAMLET: Murder!
GHOST: Murder most foul, as in the best it is,
But this most foul, strange, and unnatural.
HAMLET: Haste me to know't, that I, with wings as swift
As meditation or the thoughts of love,   30
May sweep to my revenge.
GHOST: I find thee apt;
And duller shouldst thou be than the fat weed
That roots itself in ease on Lethe[1] wharf,
Wouldst thou not stir in this. Now, Hamlet, hear:
'Tis given out that, sleeping in my orchard,   35
A serpent stung me; so the whole ear of Denmark
Is by a forgèd process of my death
Rankly abused: but know, thou noble youth,
The serpent that did sting thy father's life
Now wears his crown.
HAMLET: O my prophetic soul!   40
My uncle!
GHOST: Aye, that incestuous, that adulterate beast,
With witchcraft of his wit, with traitorous gifts, —
O wicked wit and gifts, that have the power
So to seduce! — won to his shameful lust   45
The will of my most seeming-virtuous queen:
O Hamlet, what a falling-off was there!
From me, whose love was of that dignity
That it went hand in hand even with the vow
I made to her in marriage; and to decline   50
Upon a wretch, whose natural gifts were poor
To those of mine!
But virtue, as it never will be moved,
Though lewdness court it in a shape of heaven,[2]
So lust, though to a radiant angel linked,   55
Will sate itself in a celestial bed
And prey on garbage.
But, soft! methinks I scent the morning air;
Brief let me be. Sleeping within my orchard,
My custom always of the afternoon,   60
Upon my secure hour thy uncle stole,
With juice of cursed hebenon[3] in a vial,
And in the porches of my ears did pour

9. Publication of the secrets of the other world (of eternity). *Porpentine:* porcupine.   1. The river of forgetfulness in Hades.   2. A heavenly, angelic form.   3. Henbane, a very poisonous herb.

The leperous distilment; whose effect
Holds such an enmity with blood of man   65
That swift as quicksilver it courses through
The natural gates and alleys of the body;
And with a sudden vigor it doth posset
And curd, like eager⁴ droppings into milk,
The thin and wholesome blood: so did it mine;   70
And a most instant tetter barked about,⁵
Most lazar-like,⁶ with vile and loathsome crust,
All my smooth body.
Thus was I, sleeping, by a brother's hand
Of life, of crown, of queen, at once dispatched: 75
Cut off even in the blossoms of my sin,
Unhouseled, disappointed, unaneled;⁷
No reckoning made, but sent to my account
With all my imperfections on my head:
O, horrible! O, horrible! most horrible!   80
If thou hast nature in thee, bear it not;
Let not the royal bed of Denmark be
A couch for luxury and damned incest.
But, howsoever thou pursuest this act,
Taint not thy mind, nor let thy soul contrive   85
Against thy mother aught: leave her to heaven,
And to those thorns that in her bosom lodge,
To prick and sting her. Fare thee well at once!
The glow-worm shows the matin to be near,
And 'gins to pale his uneffectual fire: 90
Adieu, adieu, adieu! remember me.
    [*Exit.*]
HAMLET: O all you host of heaven! O earth! what else?
And shall I couple hell? O, fie! Hold, hold, my heart;
And you, my sinews, grow not instant old,
But bear me stiffly up. Remember thee!   95
Aye, thou poor ghost, while memory holds a seat
In this distracted globe. Remember thee!
Yea, from the table⁸ of my memory
I'll wipe away all trivial fond records,
All saws of books, all forms, all pressures past,   100
That youth and observation copied there:
And thy commandment all alone shall live
Within the book and volume of my brain,
Unmixed with baser matter: yes, by heaven!
O most pernicious woman!   105
O villain, villain, smiling, damnèd villain!
My tables,—meet it is I set it down,
That one may smile, and smile, and be a villain;

---

4. *Posset*: coagulate. Sour.   5. The skin immediately became thick like the bark of a tree.
6. Leper-like (from the beggar Lazarus, "full of sores," in Luke 16:20).   7. Without sacrament, unprepared, without extreme unction.   8. Writing tablet; used in the same sense in line 107. *Globe*: head.

At least I'm sure it may be so in Denmark.
  [*Writing.*]
So, uncle, there you are. Now to my word;   110
It is 'Adieu, adieu! remember me.'
I have sworn't.

HORATIO: } [*Within.*] My lord, my lord!
MARCELLUS:
  [*Enter* HORATIO *and* MARCELLUS.]

MARCELLUS: Lord Hamlet!
HORATIO: Heaven secure him!
HAMLET: So be it!
MARCELLUS: Illo,[9] ho, ho, my lord!   115
HAMLET: Hillo, ho, ho, boy! come, bird, come.
MARCELLUS: How is't, my noble lord?
HORATIO: What news, my lord?
HAMLET: O, wonderful!
HORATIO: Good my lord, tell it.
HAMLET: No; you will reveal it.
HORATIO: Not I, my lord, by heaven.
MARCELLUS: Nor I, my lord.   120
HAMLET: How say you, then; would heart of man once think it?
  But you'll be secret?
HORATIO: }
              }   Aye, by heaven, my lord.
MARCELLUS: }
HAMLET: There's ne'er a villain dwelling in all Denmark
  But he's an arrant knave.
HORATIO: There needs no ghost, my lord, come from the grave   125
  To tell us this.
HAMLET: Why, right; you are i' the right;
  And so, without more circumstance[1] at all,
  I hold it fit that we shake hands and part:
  You, as your business and desire shall point you;
  For every man hath business and desire,   130
  Such as it is; and for my own poor part,
  Look you, I'll go pray.
HORATIO: These are but wild and whirling words, my lord.
HAMLET: I'm sorry they offend you, heartily;
  Yes, faith, heartily.
HORATIO: There's no offense, my lord.   135
HAMLET: Yes, by Saint Patrick, but there is, Horatio,
  And much offense too. Touching this vision here,
  It is an honest[2] ghost, that let me tell you:
  For your desire to know what is between us,
  O'ermaster't as you may. And now, good friends,   140
  As you are friends, scholars and soldiers,
  Give me one poor request.
HORATIO: What is't, my lord? we will.

9. A falconer's call.   1. Ceremony.   2. Genuine.

HAMLET: Never make known what you have seen tonight.

MARCELLUS:
HORATIO: } My lord, we will not.

HAMLET: Nay, but swear't.

HORATIO: In faith,
My lord, not I.

MARCELLUS: Nor I, my lord, in faith. 145

HAMLET: Upon my sword.

MARCELLUS: We have sworn, my lord, already.

HAMLET: Indeed, upon my sword, indeed.

GHOST: [*Beneath.*] Swear.

HAMLET: Ah, ha, boy! say'st thou so? art thou there, true-penny?[3]
Come on: you hear this fellow in the cellarage:
Consent to swear.

HORATIO: Propose the oath, my lord. 150

HAMLET: Never to speak of this that you have seen,
Swear by my sword.

GHOST: [*Beneath.*] Swear.

HAMLET: Hic et ubique?[4] then we'll shift our ground.
Come hither, gentlemen, 155
And lay your hands again upon my sword:
Never to speak of this that you have heard,
Swear by my sword.

GHOST: [*Beneath.*] Swear.

HAMLET: Well said, old mole! canst work i' the earth so fast? 160
A worthy pioner![5] Once more remove, good friends.

HORATIO: O day and night, but this is wondrous strange!

HAMLET: And therefore as a stranger give it welcome.
There are more things in heaven and earth, Horatio,
Than are dreamt of in your philosophy. 165
But come;
Here, as before, never, so help you mercy,
How strange or odd soe'er I bear myself,
As I perchance hereafter shall think meet
To put an antic[6] disposition on, 170
That you, at such times seeing me, never shall,
With arms encumbered[7] thus, or this head-shake,
Or by pronouncing of some doubtful phrase,
As 'Well, well, we know,' or 'We could, an if we would,'
Or 'If we list to speak,' or 'There be, an if they might,' 175
Or such ambiguous giving out, to note
That you know aught of me: this not to do,
So grace and mercy at your most need help you,
Swear.

GHOST: [*Beneath.*] Swear. 180

HAMLET: Rest, rest, perturbèd spirit!
[*They swear.*]

3. Honest fellow. 4. Here and everywhere (Latin). 5. Miner. 6. Odd, fantastic. 7. Folded.

So, gentlemen,
With all my love I do commend[8] me to you:
And what so poor a man as Hamlet is
May do, to express his love and friending to you,   185
God willing, shall not lack. Let us go in together;
And still your fingers on your lips, I pray.
The time is out of joint: O cursèd spite,
That ever I was born to set it right!
Nay, come, let's go together.   190
    [*Exeunt.*]

Act II

SCENE 1

A room in Polonius's house.

[*Enter* POLONIUS *and* REYNALDO.]
POLONIUS: Give him this money and these notes, Reynaldo.
REYNALDO: I will, my lord.
POLONIUS: You shall do marvelous wisely, good Reynaldo,
  Before you visit him, to make inquire
  Of his behavior.
REYNALDO: My lord, I did intend it.   5
POLONIUS: Marry, well said, very well said. Look you, sir,
  Inquire me first what Danskers are in Paris,
  And how, and who, what means, and where they keep,[9]
  What company, at what expense, and finding
  By this encompassment[1] and drift of question   10
  That they do know my son, come you more nearer
  Than your particular demands will touch it:
  Take you, as 'twere, some distant knowledge of him,
  As thus, 'I know his father and his friends,
  And in part him': do you mark this, Reynaldo?   15
REYNALDO: Aye, very well, my lord.
POLONIUS: 'And in part him; but,' you may say, 'not well:
  But if 't be he I mean, he's very wild,
  Addicted so and so'; and there put on him
  What forgeries you please; marry, none so rank   20
  As may dishonor him; take heed of that;
  But, sir, such wanton, wild and usual slips
  As are companions noted and most known
  To youth and liberty.
REYNALDO: As gaming, my lord.
POLONIUS: Aye, or drinking, fencing, swearing, quarreling,   25
  Drabbing:[2] you may go so far.
REYNALDO: My lord, that would dishonor him.

---

8. Entrust.   9. Dwell. *Danskers:* Danes.   1. Roundabout way.   2. Whoring.

POLONIUS: Faith, no; as you may season it in the charge.[3]
 You must not put another scandal on him,
 That he is open to incontinency;   30
 That's not my meaning: but breathe his faults so quaintly[4]
 That they may seem the taints of liberty,
 The flash and outbreak of a fiery mind,
 A savageness in unreclaimèd blood,
 Of general assault.[5]
REYNALDO: But, my good lord,—   35
POLONIUS: Wherefore should you do this?
REYNALDO: Aye, my lord,
 I would know that.
POLONIUS: Marry, sir, here's my drift,
 And I believe it is a fetch of warrant:[6]
 You laying these slight sullies on my son,
 As 'twere a thing a little soiled i' the working,   40
 Mark you,
 Your party in converse, him you would sound,
 Having ever seen in the prenominate[7] crimes
 The youth you breathe of guilty, be assured
 He closes with you in this consequence;[8]   45
 'Good sir,' or so, or 'friend,' or 'gentleman,'
 According to the phrase or the addition[9]
 Of man and country.
REYNALDO: Very good, my lord.
POLONIUS: And then, sir, does he this—he does—what was I about to
 say? By the mass, I was about to say something: where did I leave?   50
REYNALDO: At 'closes in the consequence,' at 'friend or so,' and 'gen-
 tleman.'
POLONIUS: At 'closes in the consequence,' aye, marry;
 He closes with you thus: 'I know the gentleman;
 I saw him yesterday, or t' other day,   55
 Or then, or then, with such, or such, and, as you say,
 There was a' gaming, there o'ertook in 's rouse,[1]
 There falling out at tennis': or perchance,
 'I saw him enter such a house of sale,'
 Videlicet,[2] a brothel, or so forth.   60
 See you now;
 Your bait of falsehood takes this carp of truth:
 And thus do we of wisdom and of reach,[3]
 With windlasses and with assays of bias,[4]
 By indirections find directions out: 65
 So, by my former lecture and advice,
 Shall you my son. You have me, have you not?

---

3. Qualify it in making the accusation. 4. Delicately, skillfully. *Incontinency:* extreme sensuality.
5. Assailing all. *Unreclaimèd:* untamed. 6. Allowable stratagem. 7. Aforementioned. *Having ever:*
if he has ever. 8. You may be sure he will agree in this conclusion. 9. Title. 1. Intoxicated in
his reveling. 2. Namely. 3. Wise and farsighted. 4. Sending the ball indirectly (in bowling),
devious attacks. *Windlasses:* winding ways, roundabout courses.

REYNALDO: My lord, I have.

POLONIUS: God be wi' ye; fare ye well.

REYNALDO: Good my lord!

POLONIUS: Observe his inclination in yourself.[5]   70

REYNALDO: I shall, my lord.

POLONIUS: And let him ply his music.

REYNALDO: Well, my lord.

POLONIUS: Farewell!

    [*Exit* REYNALDO. — *Enter* OPHELIA.]

    How now, Ophelia! what's the matter?

OPHELIA: O, my lord, I have been so affrighted!   75

POLONIUS: With what, i' the name of God?

OPHELIA: My lord, as I was sewing in my closet,
    Lord Hamlet, with his doublet[6] all unbraced,
    No hat upon his head, his stockings fouled,
    Ungartered and down-gyvèd[7] to his ankle;   80
    Pale as his shirt, his knees knocking each other,
    And with a look so piteous in purport
    As if he had been loosèd out of hell
    To speak of horrors, he comes before me.

POLONIUS: Mad for thy love?

OPHELIA: My lord, I do not know,   85
    But truly I do fear it.

POLONIUS: What said he?

OPHELIA: He took me by the wrist and held me hard;
    Then goes he to the length of all his arm,
    And with his other hand thus o'er his brow,
    He falls to such perusal of my face   90
    As he would draw it. Long stayed he so;
    At last, a little shaking of mine arm,
    And thrice his head thus waving up and down,
    He raised a sigh so piteous and profound
    As it did seem to shatter all his bulk   95
    And end his being: that done, he lets me go:
    And with his head over his shoulder turned,
    He seemed to find his way without his eyes;
    For out o' doors he went without their help,
    And to the last bended their light on me.   100

POLONIUS: Come, go with me: I will go seek the king.
    This is the very ecstasy of love;
    Whose violent property fordoes itself[8]
    And leads the will to desperate undertakings
    As oft as any passion under heaven   105
    That does afflict our natures. I am sorry.
    What, have you given him any hard words of late?

OPHELIA: No, my good lord, but, as you did command,

---

5. Ways of procedure by yourself.   6. Jacket. *Closet:* private room.   7. Pulled down like fetters on
a prisoner's leg.   8. Which, when violent, destroys itself. *Ecstasy:* madness.

I did repel his letters and denied
His access to me.

POLONIUS: That hath made him mad.   110
   I am sorry that with better heed and judgment
   I had not quoted him: I fear'd he did but trifle
   And meant to wreck thee; but beshrew my jealousy![9]
   By heaven, it is as proper to our age
   To cast beyond ourselves[1] in our opinions   115
   As it is common for the younger sort
   To lack discretion. Come, go we to the king:
   This must be known; which, being kept close, might move
   More grief to hide than hate to utter love.[2]
   Come.   120
      [*Exeunt.*]

SCENE 2

A room in the castle.

[*Flourish. Enter* KING, QUEEN, ROSENCRANTZ, GUILDENSTERN, *and*
ATTENDANTS.]

KING: Welcome, dear Rosencrantz and Guildenstern!
   Moreover that we much did long to see you,
   The need we have to use you did provoke
   Our hasty sending. Something have you heard
   Of Hamlet's transformation; so call it,   5
   Sith[3] nor the exterior nor the inward man
   Resembles that it was. What it should be,
   More than his father's death, that thus hath put him
   So much from the understanding of himself,
   I cannot dream of: I entreat you both,   10
   That, being of so young days brought up with him
   And sith so neighbored to his youth and behavior,
   That you vouchsafe your rest[4] here in our court
   Some little time: so by your companies
   To draw him on to pleasures, and to gather   15
   So much as from occasion you may glean,
   Whether aught to us unknown afflicts him thus,
   That opened[5] lies within our remedy.

QUEEN: Good gentlemen, he hath much talked of you,
   And sure I am two men there are not living   20
   To whom he more adheres.[6] If it will please you
   To show us so much gentry[7] and good will
   As to expend your time with us awhile
   For the supply and profit of our hope,
   Your visitation shall receive such thanks   25
   As fits a king's remembrance.

---

9. Curse my suspicion. *Quoted:* noted.   1. Overshoot, go too far.   2. If Hamlet's love is revealed.
To hide: if kept hidden.   3. Since.   4. Consent to stay.   5. Once revealed.   6. Is more
attached.   7. Courtesy.

ROSENCRANTZ: Both your majesties
  Might, by the sovereign power you have of us,
  Put your dread pleasures more into[8] command
  Than to entreaty.
GUILDENSTERN: But we both obey,
  And here give up ourselves, in the full bent[9]   30
  To lay our service freely at your feet,
  To be commanded.
KING: Thanks, Rosencrantz and gentle Guildenstern.
QUEEN: Thanks, Guildenstern and gentle Rosencrantz:
  And I beseech you instantly to visit   35
  My too much changéd son. Go, some of you,
  And bring these gentlemen where Hamlet is.
GUILDENSTERN: Heavens make our presence and our practices
  Pleasant and helpful to him!
QUEEN: Aye, amen!
  [*Exeunt* ROSENCRANTZ, GUILDENSTERN, *and some* ATTENDANTS.—
  Enter POLONIUS.]
POLONIUS: The ambassadors from Norway, my good lord,   40
  Are joyfully returned.
KING: Thou still[1] hast been the father of good news.
POLONIUS: Have I, my lord? I assure my good liege,
  I hold my duty as I hold my soul,
  Both to my God and to my gracious king: 45
  And I do think, or else this brain of mine
  Hunts not the trail of policy so sure
  As it hath used to do, that I have found
  The very cause of Hamlet's lunacy.
KING: O, speak of that; that do I long to hear.   50
POLONIUS: Give first admittance to the ambassadors;
  My news shall be the fruit to that great feast.
KING: Thyself do grace[2] to them, and bring them in.
  [*Exit* POLONIUS.]
  He tells me, my dear Gertrude, he hath found
  The head and source of all your son's distemper.   55
QUEEN: I doubt it is no other but the main;
  His father's death and our o'erhasty marriage.
KING: Well, we shall sift him.
  [*Re-enter* POLONIUS, *with* VOLTIMAND *and* CORNELIUS.]
                          Welcome, my good friends!
  Say, Voltimand, what from our brother Norway?
VOLTIMAND: Most fair return of greetings and desires.   60
  Upon our first,[3] he sent out to suppress
  His nephew's levies, which to him appeared
  To be a preparation 'gainst the Polack,
  But better looked into, he truly found

8. Give your sovereign wishes the form of.   9. Bent (as a bow) to the limit.   1. Always.
2. Honor. *Fruit*: dessert.   3. As soon as we made the request.

It was against your highness: whereat grieved,   65
That so his sickness, age and impotence
Was falsely borne in hand,[4] sends out arrests
On Fortinbras; which he, in brief, obeys,
Receives rebuke from Norway, and in fine[5]
Makes vow before his uncle never more   70
To give the assay[6] of arms against your majesty.
Whereon old Norway, overcome with joy,
Gives him three thousand crowns in annual fee
And his commission to employ those soldiers,
So levied as before, against the Polack: 75
With an entreaty, herein further shown,
　　　[Giving a paper.]
That it might please you to give quiet pass
Through your dominions for this enterprise,
On such regards of safety and allowance
As therein are set down.
KING:　　　　　　　　　　It likes us well,   80
And at our more considered time we'll read,
Answer, and think upon this business.
Meantime we thank you for your well-took labor:
Go to your rest; at night we'll feast together:
Most welcome home!
　　　[Exeunt VOLTIMAND and CORNELIUS.]
POLONIUS:　　　　　　　This business is well ended.   85
My liege, and madam, to expostulate
What majesty should be, what duty is,
Why day is day, night night, and time is time,
Were nothing but to waste night, day and time.
Therefore, since brevity is the soul of wit   90
And tediousness the limbs and outward flourishes,
I will be brief. Your noble son is mad:
Mad call I it; for, to define true madness,
What is 't but to be nothing else but mad?
But let that go.
QUEEN:　　　　　More matter, with less art.   95
POLONIUS: Madam, I swear I use no art at all.
That he is mad, 'tis true: 'tis true 'tis pity,
And pity 'tis 'tis true: a foolish figure;[7]
But farewell it, for I will use no art.
Mad let us grant him then: and now remains   100
That we find out the cause of this effect,
Or rather say, the cause of this defect,
For this effect defective comes by cause:
Thus it remains and the remainder thus.
Perpend.[8]   105
I have a daughter,—have while she is mine,—

4. Deceived, deluded.　5. Finally.　6. Test.　7. Of speech.　8. Consider.

Who in her duty and obedience, mark,
Hath given me this: now gather and surmise.
[*Reads.*] 'To the celestial, and my soul's idol, the most beautified
Ophelia,'—That's an ill phrase, a vile phrase; 'beautified' is a vile   110
phrase; but you shall hear. Thus:
    [*Reads.*] 'In her excellent white bosom, these,' &c.
QUEEN: Came this from Hamlet to her?
POLONIUS: Good madam, stay awhile; I will be faithful.
    [*Reads.*]   'Doubt thou the stars are fire;   115
              Doubt that the sun doth move;
              Doubt truth to be a liar;
              But never doubt I love.
'O dear Ophelia, I am ill at these numbers;[9] I have not art to reckon
my groans: but that I love thee best, O most best, believe it. Adieu.   120
            'Thine evermore, most dear lady, whilst this
                machine is to him,[1] HAMLET.'
This in obedience hath my daughter shown me;
And more above,[2] hath his solicitings,
As they fell out by time, by means and place,   125
All given to mine ear.
KING: But how hath she
Received his love?
POLONIUS: What do you think of me?
KING: As of a man faithful and honorable.
POLONIUS: I would fain prove so. But what might you think,
When I had seen this hot love on the wing,—   130
As I perceived it, I must tell you that,
Before my daughter told me,—what might you,
Or my dear majesty your queen here, think,
If I had played the desk or table-book,[3]
Or given my heart a winking,[4] mute and dumb,   135
Or looked upon this love with idle sight;
What might you think? No, I went round[5] to work,
And my young mistress thus I did bespeak:
'Lord Hamlet is a prince, out of thy star;[6]
This must not be:' and then I prescripts gave her,   140
That she should lock herself from his resort,
Admit no messengers, receive no tokens.
Which done, she took the fruits of my advice;
And he repulsed, a short tale to make,
Fell into a sadness, then into a fast,   145
Thence to a watch, thence into a weakness,
Thence to a lightness,[7] and by this declension
Into the madness wherein now he raves
And all we mourn for.
KING: Do you think this?

---

9. Verses.   1. Body is attached.   2. Moreover.   3. If I had acted as a desk or notebook (in keeping the matter secret).   4. Shut my heart's eye.   5. Straight.   6. Sphere.   7. Light-headedness.
Watch: insomnia.

QUEEN: It may be, very like.   150
POLONIUS: Hath there been such a time, I'ld fain know that,
    That I have positively said ' 'tis so,'
    When it proved otherwise?
KING: Not that I know.
POLONIUS: [*Pointing to his head and shoulder.*] Take this, from this,
    if this be otherwise: 155
    If circumstances lead me, I will find
    Where truth is hid, though it were hid indeed
    Within the center.[8]
                           How may we try it further?
KING: POLONIUS: You know, sometimes he walks for hours together
    Here in the lobby.
QUEEN: So he does, indeed.   160
POLONIUS: At such a time I'll loose my daughter to him:
    Be you and I behind an arras then;
    Mark the encounter: if he love her not,
    And be not from his reason fall'n thereon,[9]
    Let me be no assistant for a state,   165
    But keep a farm and carters.
KING: We will try it.
QUEEN: But look where sadly the poor wretch comes reading.
POLONIUS: Away, I do beseech you, both away:
    I'll board him presently.[1]
        [*Exeunt* KING, QUEEN, *and* ATTENDANTS. —*Enter* HAMLET, *reading.*]
    O, give me leave: how does my good Lord Hamlet?   170
HAMLET: Well, God-a-mercy.
POLONIUS: Do you know me, my lord?
HAMLET: Excellent well; you are a fishmonger.[2]
POLONIUS: Not I, my lord.
HAMLET: Then I would you were so honest a man.   175
POLONIUS: Honest, my lord!
HAMLET: Aye, sir; to be honest, as this world goes, is to be one man
    picked out of ten thousand.
POLONIUS: That's very true, my lord.
HAMLET: For if the sun breed maggots in a dead dog, being a good   180
    kissing carrion[3] — Have you a daughter?
POLONIUS: I have, my lord.
HAMLET: Let her not walk i' the sun: conception is a blessing; but as
    your daughter may conceive, —friend, look to 't.
POLONIUS: [*Aside.*] How say you by that? Still harping on my daughter: 185
    yet he knew me not at first; he said I was a fishmonger: he is far
    gone: and truly in my youth I suffered much extremity for love;
    very near this. I'll speak to him again. —What do you read, my lord?
HAMLET: Words, words, words.

---

8. Of the earth.   9. For that reason.   1. Approach him at once.   2. Fish seller but also slang for
procurer.   3. Good bit of flesh for kissing.

POLONIUS: What is the matter,[4] my lord?   190

HAMLET: Between who?

POLONIUS: I mean, the matter that you read, my lord.

HAMLET: Slanders, sir: for the satirical rogue says here that old men
have gray beards, that their faces are wrinkled, their eyes purging
thick amber and plum-tree gum, and that they have a plentiful lack   195
of wit, together with most weak hams: all which, sir, though I most
powerfully and potently believe, yet I hold it not honesty to have it
thus set down; for yourself, sir, shall grow old as I am, if like a crab
you could go backward.

POLONIUS: [Aside.] Though this be madness, yet there is method in   200
't. — Will you walk out of the air, my lord?

HAMLET: Into my grave.

POLONIUS: Indeed, that's out of the air.
    [Aside.]
How pregnant sometimes his replies are! a happiness[5] that often
madness hits on, which reason and sanity could not so prosperously   205
be delivered of. I will leave him, and suddenly contrive the means
of meeting between him and my daughter. — My honorable lord, I
will most humbly take my leave of you.

HAMLET: You cannot, sir, take from me any thing that I will more
willingly part withal: except my life, except my life, except my life.   210

POLONIUS: Fare you well, my lord.

HAMLET: These tedious old fools.
    [Re-enter ROSENCRANTZ and GUILDENSTERN.]

POLONIUS: You go to seek the Lord Hamlet; there he is.

ROSENCRANTZ: [To POLONIUS.] God save you, sir!
    [Exit POLONIUS.]

GUILDENSTERN: My honored lord!   215

ROSENCRANTZ: My most dear lord!

HAMLET: My excellent good friends! How dost thou, Guildenstern?
Ah, Rosencrantz! Good lads, how do you both?

ROSENCRANTZ: As the indifferent[6] children of the earth.

GUILDENSTERN: Happy, in that we are not over-happy;   220
On Fortune's cap we are not the very button.[7]

HAMLET: Nor the soles of her shoe?

ROSENCRANTZ: Neither, my lord.

HAMLET: Then you live about her waist, or in the middle of her favors?

GUILDENSTERN: Faith, her privates[8] we.   225

HAMLET: In the secret parts of Fortune? O, most true; she is a strumpet. What's the news?

ROSENCRANTZ: None, my lord, but that the world's grown honest.

HAMLET: Then is doomsday near: but your news is not true. Let me
question more in particular: what have you, my good friends, de-   230
served at the hands of Fortune, that she sends you to prison hither?

GUILDENSTERN: Prison, my lord!

---

4. The subject matter of the book. Hamlet responds as if he referred to the subject of a quarrel.   5. Apt-
ness of expression.   6. Average.   7. Top.   8. Ordinary men (with obvious play on the sexual term
private parts).

HAMLET: Denmark's a prison.

ROSENCRANTZ: Then is the world one.

HAMLET: A goodly one; in which there are many confines, wards[9] and   235
dungeons, Denmark being one o' the worst.

ROSENCRANTZ: We think not so, my lord.

HAMLET: Why, then, 'tis none to you; for there is nothing either good
or bad, but thinking makes it so: to me it is a prison.

ROSENCRANTZ: Why, then your ambition makes it one; 'tis too narrow   240
for your mind.

HAMLET: O God, I could be bounded in a nut-shell and count myself
a king of infinite space, were it not that I have bad dreams.

GUILDENSTERN: Which dreams indeed are ambition; for the very substance of the ambitious is merely the shadow of a dream.   245

HAMLET: A dream itself is but a shadow.

ROSENCRANTZ: Truly, and I hold ambition of so airy and light a quality
that it is but a shadow's shadow.

HAMLET: Then are our beggars bodies, and our monarchs and outstretched heroes the beggars' shadows. Shall we to the court? for,   250
by my fay, I cannot reason.

ROSENCRANTZ: ⎫
GUILDENSTERN: ⎬ We'll wait upon you.

HAMLET: No such matter: I will not sort you[1] with the rest of my
servants; for, to speak to you like an honest man, I am most dreadfully attended. But, in the beaten way of friendship, what make you   255
at Elsinore?

ROSENCRANTZ: To visit you, my lord; no other occasion.

HAMLET: Beggar that I am, I am even poor in thanks; but I thank you:
and sure, dear friends, my thanks are too dear a halfpenny.[2] Were
you not sent for? Is it your own inclining? Is it a free visitation?   260
Come, deal justly[3] with me: come, come; nay, speak.

GUILDENSTERN: What should we say, my lord?

HAMLET: Why, any thing, but to the purpose. You were sent for; and
there is a kind of confession in your looks, which your modesties
have not craft enough to color: I know the good king and queen   265
have sent for you.

ROSENCRANTZ: To what end, my lord?

HAMLET: That you must teach me. But let me conjure you, by the
rights of our fellowship, by the consonancy of our youth, by the
obligation of our ever-preserved love, and by what more dear a bet-   270
ter proposer[4] could charge you withal, be even and direct with me,
whether you were sent for, or no.

ROSENCRANTZ: [Aside to GUILDENSTERN.] What say you?

HAMLET: [Aside.] Nay then, I have an eye of[5] you.—If you love me,
hold not off.   275

GUILDENSTERN: My lord, we were sent for.

HAMLET: I will tell you why; so shall my anticipation prevent your

9. Cells. Confines: places of confinement.   1. Put you together.   2. If priced at a halfpenny.
3. Honestly.   4. Speaker.   5. On.

discovery,[6] and your secrecy to the king and queen moult no
feather. I have of late—but wherefore I know not—lost all my
mirth, forgone all custom of exercises; and indeed it goes so heav-   280
ily with my disposition that this goodly frame, the earth, seems to
me a sterile promontory; this most excellent canopy, the air, look
you, this brave o'erhanging firmament, this majestical roof fretted[7]
with golden fire, why, it appears no other thing to me than a foul
and pestilent congregation of vapors. What a piece of work is a   285
man! how noble in reason! how infinite in faculty! in form and
moving how express[8] and admirable! in action how like an angel!
in apprehension how like a god! the beauty of the world! the paragon of animals! And yet, to me, what is this quintessence of dust?
man delights not me; no, nor woman neither, though by your smil-   290
ing you seem to say so.

ROSENCRANTZ: My lord, there was no such stuff in my thoughts.

HAMLET: Why did you laugh then, when I said 'man delights not me'?

ROSENCRANTZ: To think, my lord, if you delight not in man, what
lenten entertainment the players shall receive from you: we coted[9]   295
them on the way; and hither are they coming, to offer you service.

HAMLET: He that plays the king shall be welcome; his majesty shall
have tribute of me; the adventurous knight shall use his foil and
target; the lover shall not sigh gratis; the humorous[1] man shall end
his part in peace; the clown shall make those laugh whose lungs   300
are tickle o' the sere,[2] and the lady shall say her mind freely, or the
blank verse shall halt for 't. What players are they?

ROSENCRANTZ: Even those you were wont to take such delight in, the
tragedians of the city.

HAMLET: How chances it they travel? their residence, both in reputa-   305
tion and profit, was better both ways.

ROSENCRANTZ: I think their inhibition comes by means of the late
innovation.[3]

HAMLET: Do they hold the same estimation they did when I was in
the city? are they so followed?   310

ROSENCRANTZ: No, indeed, are they not.

HAMLET: How comes it? do they grow rusty?

ROSENCRANTZ: Nay, their endeavor keeps in the wonted pace: but
there is, sir, an eyrie of children, little eyases,[4] that cry out on the
top of question[5] and are most tyrannically clapped for 't: these are   315
now the fashion, and so berattle[6] the common stages—so they call
them—that many wearing rapiers are afraid of goose-quills,[7] and
dare scarce come thither.

HAMLET: What, are they children? who maintains 'em? how are they
escoted? Will they pursue the quality[8] no longer than they can   320
sing? will they not say afterwards, if they should grow themselves to

---

6. Precede your disclosure.   7. Adorned.   8. Precise.   9. Overtook.   1. Eccentric, whimsical.
2. Ready to shoot off at a touch.   3. The introduction of the children (line 314), as Rosencrantz
explains in his subsequent replies to Hamlet. *Inhibition:* prohibition.   4. Nestling hawks. *Eyrie:* nest.
5. Above others on matter of dispute.   6. Berate.   7. Gentlemen are afraid of pens (that is, of poets
satirizing the "common stages").   8. Profession of acting. *Escoted:* financially supported.

common players—as it is most like, if their means are no better,— their writers do them wrong, to make them exclaim against their own succession?[9]

ROSENCRANTZ: Faith, there has been much to-do on both sides, and 325 the nation holds it no sin to tarre[1] them to controversy: there was for a while no money bid for argument unless the poet and the player went to cuffs in the question.[2]

HAMLET: Is 't possible?

GUILDENSTERN: O, there has been much throwing about of brains. 330

HAMLET: Do the boys carry it away?[3]

ROSENCRANTZ: Aye, that they do, my lord; Hercules and his load too.[4]

HAMLET: It is not very strange; for my uncle is king of Denmark, and those that would make mows[5] at him while my father lived, give twenty, forty, fifty, a hundred ducats a-piece, for his picture in lit- 335 tle. 'Sblood, there is something in this more than natural, if philoso- phy could find it out.

[Flourish of trumpets within.]

GUILDENSTERN: There are the players.

HAMLET: Gentlemen, you are welcome to Elsinore. Your hands, come then: the appurtenance of welcome is fashion and ceremony: let 340 me comply with you in this garb, lest my extent[6] to the players, which, I tell you, must show fairly outwards, should more appear like entertainment[7] than yours. You are welcome: but my uncle- father and aunt-mother are deceived.

GUILDENSTERN: In what, my dear lord? 345

HAMLET: I am but mad north-north-west: when the wind is southerly I know a hawk from a handsaw.[8]

[Re-enter POLONIUS.]

POLONIUS: Well be with you, gentlemen!

HAMLET: Hark you, Guildenstern; and you too: at each ear a hearer: that great baby you see there is not yet out of his swaddling clouts.[9] 350

ROSENCRANTZ: Happily he's the second time come to them; for they say an old man is twice a child.

HAMLET: I will prophesy he comes to tell me of the players; mark it. You say right, sir: o' Monday morning; 'twas so, indeed.[1]

POLONIUS: My lord, I have news to tell you. 355

HAMLET: My lord, I have news to tell you. When Roscius[2] was an actor in Rome,—

POLONIUS: The actors are come hither, my lord.

HAMLET: Buz, buz![3]

POLONIUS: Upon my honor,— 360

HAMLET: Then came each actor on his ass,—

POLONIUS: The best actors in the world, either for tragedy, comedy,

---

9. Recite satiric pieces against what they are themselves likely to become, common players. 1. Incite. 2. No offer to buy a plot for a play if it did not contain a quarrel between poet and player on that subject. 3. Win out. 4. The sign in front of the Globe theater showed Hercules bearing the world on his shoulders. 5. Faces, grimaces. 6. Welcoming behavior. *Garb*: style. 7. Welcome. 8. A hawk from a heron as well as a kind of ax from a handsaw. 9. Clothes. 1. Hamlet, for Polonius's sake, pretends he is deep in talk with Rosencrantz. 2. A famous Roman comic actor (126?–62? B.C.). 3. An expression used to stop the teller of a stale story.

history, pastoral, pastoral-comical, historical-pastoral, tragical-his-
torical, tragical-comical-historical-pastoral, scene individable, or
poem unlimited:[4] Seneca cannot be too heavy, nor Plautus too light.   365
For the law of writ and the liberty,[5] these are the only men.

HAMLET: O Jephthah,[6] judge of Israel, what a treasure hadst thou!

POLONIUS: What a treasure had he, my lord?

HAMLET: Why,
        'One fair daughter, and no more,   370
         The which he lovèd passing well.'[7]

POLONIUS: [Aside.] Still on my daughter.

HAMLET: Am I not i' the right, old Jephthah?

POLONIUS: If you call me Jephthah, my lord, I have a daughter that I
love passing well.   375

HAMLET: Nay, that follows not.

POLONIUS: What follows, then, my lord?

HAMLET: Why,
        'As by lot, God wot.'
and then you know,
        'It came to pass, as most like it was,' —   380
the first row of the pious chanson will show you more; for look,
where my abridgment[8] comes.

    [Enter four or five PLAYERS.]

You are welcome, masters; welcome, all. I am glad to see thee well.
Welcome, good friends. O, my old friend! Why thy face is valanced[9]
since I saw thee last; comest thou to beard me in Denmark? What,   385
my young lady and mistress! By'r lady, your ladyship is nearer to
heaven than when I saw you last, by the altitude of a chopine. Pray
God, your voice, like a piece of uncurrent gold, be not cracked
within the ring.[1] Masters, you are all welcome. We'll e'en to 't like
French falconers, fly at any thing we see: we'll have a speech straight: 390
come, give us a taste of your quality; come, a passionate speech.

FIRST PLAYER: What speech, my good lord?

HAMLET: I heard thee speak me a speech once, but it was never acted;
or, if it was, not above once; for the play, I remember, pleased not
the million; 'twas caviare to the general:[2] but it was — as I received   395
it, and others, whose judgments in such matters cried in the top of
mine[3] — an excellent play, well digested in the scenes, set down
with as much modesty as cunning. I remember, one said there were
no sallets in the lines to make the matter savory, nor no matter in
the phrase that might indict the author of affection;[4] but called it   400
an honest method, as wholesome as sweet, and by very much more
handsome than fine.[5] One speech in it I chiefly loved: 'twas Æneas'

---

4. For plays governed and those not governed by classical rules.   5. Possibly, for both written and
extemporized plays. Seneca (ca. 4 B.C.–A.D. 65) was a Roman who wrote tragedies. Plautus (ca. 254–184
B.C.) was a Roman who wrote comedies.   6. Who was compelled to sacrifice a dearly beloved daughter (Judges 11).   7. From an old ballad about Jephthah.   8. That is, the players interrupting him.
Row: stanza. Chanson: song.   9. Draped (with a beard).   1. A pun on the ring of the voice and the
ring around the king's head on a coin. Chopine: a thick-soled shoe. Uncurrent: unfit for currency.
2. A delicacy wasted on the general public.   3. Were louder (more authoritative than) mine.   4. Affectation. Sallets: salads (that is, relish, spicy passages).   5. More elegant than showy.

tale to Dido; and thereabout of it especially, where he speaks of
Priam's slaughter:[6] it live in your memory, begin at this line; let me
see, let me see;   405
'The rugged Pyrrhus, like th' Hyrcanian beast,'[7] —
It is not so: it begins with 'Pyrrhus.'
'The rugged Pyrrhus, he whose sable arms,
Black as his purpose, did the night resemble
When he lay couchèd in the ominous horse,[8]   410
Hath now this dread and black complexion smeared
With heraldry more dismal: head to foot
Now is he total gules; horridly tricked[9]
With the blood of fathers, mothers, daughters, sons,
Baked and impasted with the parching streets,   415
That lend a tyrannous[1] and a damnèd light
To their lord's murder: roasted in wrath and fire,
And thus o'er-sizèd[2] with coagulate gore,
With eyes like carbuncles, the hellish Pyrrhus
Old grandsire Priam seeks.'   420
So, proceed you.

POLONIUS: 'Fore God, my lord, well spoken, with good accent and
good discretion.

FIRST PLAYER: 'Anon he finds him
Striking too short at Greeks; his antique sword,   425
Rebellious to his arm, lies where it falls,
Repugnant to command: unequal matched,
Pyrrhus at Priam drives; in rage strikes wide;
But with the whiff and wind of his fell sword
The unnervèd father falls. Then senseless Ilium,[3]   430
Seeming to feel this blow, with flaming top
Stoops to his base, and with a hideous crash
Takes prisoner Pyrrhus' ear: for, lo! his sword,
Which was declining on the milky[4] head
Of reverend Priam seemed i' the air to stick: 435
So, as a painted tyrant, Pyrrhus stood,
And like a neutral to his will and matter,
Did nothing.
But as we often see, against some storm,
A silence in the heavens, the rack[5] stand still,   440
The bold winds speechless and the orb below
As hush as death, anon the dreadful thunder
Doth rend the region, so after Pyrrhus' pause
Aroused vengeance sets him new a-work;
And never did the Cyclops'[6] hammers fall   445
On Mars's armor, forged for proof[7] eterne,
With less remorse than Pyrrhus' bleeding sword

---

6. The story of the fall of Troy, told by Aeneas to Queen Dido. Priam was the king of Troy.   7. Tiger.
Pyrrhus was Achilles' son (also called Neoptolemus).   8. The wooden horse in which Greek warriors
were smuggled into Troy.   9. Adorned. *Gules:* heraldic term for red.   1. Savage.   2. Glued over.
3. Troy's citadel.   4. White-haired.   5. Clouds. *Against:* just before.   6. The gigantic workmen
of Hephaestus (Vulcan), god of blacksmiths and fire.   7. Protection.

Now falls on Priam.
Out, thou strumpet, Fortune! All you gods,
In general synod take away her power,   450
Break all the spokes and fellies from her wheel,
And bowl the round nave[8] down the hill of heaven
As low as to the fiends!

POLONIUS: This is too long.

HAMLET: It shall to the barber's, with your beard. Prithee, say on: he's   455
for a jig[9] or a tale of bawdry, or he sleeps: say on: come to Hecuba.

FIRST PLAYER: 'But who, O, who had seen the mobled[1] queen—'

HAMLET: 'The mobled queen'?

POLONIUS: That's good; 'mobled queen' is good.

FIRST PLAYER: 'Run barefoot up and down, threatening the flames   460
With bisson rheum; a clout[2] upon that head
Where late the diadem stood; and for a robe,
About her lank and all o'er-teemèd loins,[3]
A blanket, in the alarm of fear caught up:
Who this had seen, with tongue in venom steeped   465
'Gainst Fortune's state[4] would treason have pronounced:
But if the gods themselves did see her then,
When she saw Pyrrhus make malicious sport
In mincing with his sword her husband's limbs,
The instant burst of clamor that she made,   470
Unless things mortal move them[5] not at all,
Would have made milch the burning eyes of heaven[6]
And passion in the gods.'

POLONIUS: Look, whether he has not turned his color and has tears in
's eyes. Prithee, no more.   475

HAMLET: 'Tis well; I'll have thee speak out the rest of this soon. Good
my lord, will you see the players well bestowed?[7] Do you hear, let
them be well used, for they are the abstracts and brief chronicles of
the time: after your death you were better have a bad epitaph than
their ill report while you live.   480

POLONIUS: My lord, I will use them according to their desert.

HAMLET: God's bodykins,[8] man, much better: use every man after his
desert, and who shall 'scape whipping? Use them after your own
honor and dignity: the less they deserve, the more merit is in your
bounty. Take them in.   485

POLONIUS: Come, sirs.

HAMLET: Follow him, friends: we'll hear a play to-morrow. [Exit
POLONIUS with all the PLAYERS but the first.] Dost thou hear me,
old friend; can you play the Murder of Gonzago?

FIRST PLAYER: Aye, my lord.   490

HAMLET: We'll ha 't to-morrow night. You could, for a need, study a
speech of some dozen or sixteen lines, which I would set down and
insert in 't, could you not?

---

8. Hub. *Fellies:* rims.   9. Ludicrous sung dialogue, short farce.   1. Muffled.   2. Cloth. *Bisson
rheum:* blinding moisture, tears.   3. Worn out by childbearing.   4. Government.   5. The gods.
6. The stars. *Milch:* moist (milk-giving).   7. Taken care of, lodged.   8. By God's little body.

FIRST PLAYER: Aye, my lord.

HAMLET: Very well. Follow that lord; and look you mock him not. 495
[*Exit* FIRST PLAYER.] My good friends, I'll leave you till night: you
are welcome to Elsinore.

ROSENCRANTZ: Good my lord!

HAMLET: Aye, so, God be wi' ye! [*Exeunt* ROSENCRANTZ *and* GUILDEN-
STERN.] Now I am alone. 500
O, what a rogue and peasant slave am I!
Is it not monstrous that this player here,
But in a fiction, in a dream of passion,
Could force his soul so to his own conceit
That from her[9] working all his visage wanned; 505
Tears in his eyes, distraction in 's aspect,
A broken voice, and his whole function[1] suiting
With forms to his conceit? and all for nothing!
For Hecuba![2]
What's Hecuba to him, or he to Hecuba, 510
That he should weep for her? What would he do,
Had he the motive and the cue for passion
That I have? He would drown the stage with tears
And cleave the general air with horrid speech,
Make mad the guilty and appal the free, 515
Confound the ignorant, and amaze indeed
The very faculties of eyes and ears.
Yet I,
A dull and muddy-mettled rascal, peak,[3]
Like John-a-dreams, unpregnant of my cause,[4] 520
And can say nothing; no, not for a king,
Upon whose property and most dear life
A damn'd defeat was made. Am I a coward?
Who calls me villain? breaks my pate across?
Plucks off my beard, and blows it in my face? 525
Tweaks me by the nose? gives me the lie i' the throat,
As deep as to the lungs? who does me this?
Ha!
'Swounds, I should take it: for it cannot be
But I am pigeon-livered and lack gall 530
To make oppression bitter, or ere this
I should have fatted all the region kites[5]
With this slave's offal: bloody, bawdy villain!
Remorseless, treacherous, lecherous, kindless[6] villain!
O, vengeance! 535
Why, what an ass am I! This is most brave,
That I, the son of a dear father murdered,

9. His soul's.   1. Bodily action.   2. Queen of Troy, Priam's wife. *Conceit:* imagination, conception
of the role played.   3. Mope. *Muddy-mettled:* of poor metal (spirit, temper), dull-spirited.   4. Not
really conscious of my cause, unquickened by it. *John-a-dreams:* a dreamy, absentminded character.
5. Kites (hawks) of the air.   6. Unnatural.

Prompted to my revenge by heaven and hell,
Must, like a whore, unpack my heart with words,
And fall a-cursing, like a very drab,   540
A scullion!
Fie upon 't! About,[7] my brain! Hum, I have heard
That guilty creatures, sitting at a play,
Have by the very cunning of the scene
Been struck so to the soul that presently   545
They have proclaimed their malefactions;
For murder, though it have no tongue, will speak
With most miraculous organ. I'll have these players
Play something like the murder of my father
Before mine uncle: I'll observe his looks;   550
I'll tent him to the quick: if he but blench,[8]
I know my course. The spirit that I have seen
May be the devil; and the devil hath power
To assume a pleasing shape; yea, and perhaps
Out of my weakness and my melancholy,   555
As he is very potent with such spirits,
Abuses me to damn me. I'll have grounds
More relative[9] than this. The play's the thing
Wherein I'll catch the conscience of the king.
     [*Exit.*]

Act III

SCENE 1

A room in the castle.

[*Enter* KING, QUEEN, POLONIUS, OPHELIA, ROSENCRANTZ, *and* GUILDE-
NSTERN.]

KING: And can you, by no drift of circumstance,[1]
     Get from him why he puts on this confusion,
     Grating so harshly all his days of quiet
     With turbulent and dangerous lunacy?
ROSENCRANTZ: He does confess he feels himself distracted,   5
     But from what cause he will by no means speak.
GUILDENSTERN: Nor do we find him forward to be sounded;
     But, with a crafty madness, keeps aloof,
     When we would bring him on to some confession
     Of his true state.
QUEEN: Did he receive you well?   10
ROSENCRANTZ: Most like a gentleman.
GUILDENSTERN: But with much forcing of his disposition.
ROSENCRANTZ: Niggard of question, but of our demands
     Most free in his reply.

---

7. To work!   8. Flinch. *Tent:* probe.   9. Relevant.   1. Turn of talk, or roundabout way.

QUEEN: Did you assay[2] him
  To any pastime?   15
ROSENCRANTZ: Madam, it so fell out that certain players
  We o'er-raught[3] on the way: of these we told him,
  And there did seem in him a kind of joy
  To hear of it: they are about the court,
  And, as I think, they have already order   20
  This night to play before him.
POLONIUS: 'Tis most true:
  And he beseeched me to entreat your majesties
  To hear and see the matter.
KING: With all my heart; and it doth much content me
  To hear him so inclined.   25
  Good gentlemen, give him a further edge,[4]
  And drive his purpose on to these delights.
ROSENCRANTZ: We shall, my lord.
    [*Exeunt* ROSENCRANTZ *and* GUILDENSTERN.]
KING: Sweet Gertrude, leave us too;
  For we have closely[5] sent for Hamlet hither,
  That he, as 'twere by accident, may here   30
  Affront Ophelia:
  Her father and myself, lawful espials,
  Will so bestow[6] ourselves that, seeing unseen,
  We may of their encounter frankly judge,
  And gather by him, as he is behaved,   35
  If 't be the affliction of his love or no
  That thus he suffers for.
QUEEN: I shall obey you:
  And for your part, Ophelia, I do wish
  That your good beauties be the happy cause
  Of Hamlet's wildness: so shall I hope your virtues   40
  Will bring him to his wonted way again,
  To both your honors.
OPHELIA: Madam, I wish it may.
    [*Exit* QUEEN.]
POLONIUS: Ophelia, walk you here. Gracious, so please you,
  We will bestow ourselves. [*To* OPHELIA.] Read on this book;
  That show of such an exercise may color[7]   45
  Your loneliness. We are oft to blame in this,—
  'Tis too much proved—that with devotion's visage
  And pious action we do sugar o'er
  The devil himself.
KING: [*Aside.*]   O, 'tis too true!
  How smart a lash that speech doth give my conscience!   50
  The harlot's cheek, beautied with plastering art,
  Is not more ugly to the thing that helps it

---

2. Try to attract him.   3. Overtook.   4. Incitement.   5. Privately.   6. Place. *Affront*: confront.
Espials: spies.   7. Excuse.

Than is my deed to my most painted word:
O heavy burthen!

POLONIUS: I hear him coming: let's withdraw, my lord.   55
   [*Exeunt* KING *and* POLONIUS. — *Enter* HAMLET.]

HAMLET: To be, or not to be: that is the question:
Whether 'tis nobler in the mind to suffer
The slings and arrows of outrageous fortune,
Or to take arms against a sea of troubles,
And by opposing end them. To die: to sleep;   60
No more; and by a sleep to say we end
The heart-ache, and the thousand natural shocks
That flesh is heir to, 'tis a consummation[8]
Devoutly to be wished. To die, to sleep;
To sleep: perchance to dream: aye, there's the rub;[9]   65
For in that sleep of death what dreams may come,
When we have shuffled off this mortal coil,[1]
Must give us pause: there's the respect
That makes calamity of so long life;[2]
For who would bear the whips and scorns of time,   70
The oppressor's wrong, the proud man's contumely,
The pangs of despisèd love, the law's delay,
The insolence of office, and the spurns
That patient merit of the unworthy takes,
When he himself might his quietus make   75
With a bare bodkin? who would fardels[3] bear,
To grunt and sweat under a weary life,
But that the dread of something after death,
The undiscovered country from whose bourn[4]
No traveler returns, puzzles the will,   80
And makes us rather bear those ills we have
Than fly to others that we know not of?
Thus conscience does make cowards of us all,
And thus the native hue of resolution
Is sicklied o'er with the pale cast of thought,   85
And enterprises of great pitch[5] and moment
With this regard their currents turn awry
And lose the name of action. Soft you now!
The fair Ophelia! Nymph, in thy orisons[6]
Be all my sins remembered.

OPHELIA: Good my lord,   90
How does your honor for this many a day?

HAMLET: I humbly thank you: well, well, well.

OPHELIA: My lord, I have remembrances of yours,
That I have longed to re-deliver;
I pray you, now receive them.

---

8. Final settlement.   9. The impediment (a bowling term).   1. Have rid ourselves of the turmoil
of mortal life.   2. So long-lived. *Respect*: consideration.   3. Burdens. *Bodkin*: poniard, dagger.
4. Boundary.   5. Height.   6. Prayers.

HAMLET: No, not I;   95
I never gave you aught.

OPHELIA: My honored lord, you know right well you did;
And with them words of so sweet breath composed
As made the things more rich: their perfume lost,
Take these again; for to the noble mind   100
Rich gifts wax poor when givers prove unkind.
There, my lord.

HAMLET: Ha, ha! are you honest?

OPHELIA: My lord?

HAMLET: Are you fair?   105

OPHELIA: What means your lordship?

HAMLET: That if you be honest and fair, your honesty should admit
no discourse to your beauty.

OPHELIA: Could beauty, my lord, have better commerce⁷ than with
honesty?   110

HAMLET: Aye, truly; for the power of beauty will sooner transform honesty from what it is to a bawd than the force of honesty can translate
beauty into his⁸ likeness: this was sometime a paradox, but now the
time gives it proof.⁹ I did love you once.

OPHELIA: Indeed, my lord, you made me believe so.   115

HAMLET: You should not have believed me; for virtue cannot so inoculate our old stock, but we shall relish¹ of it: I loved you not.

OPHELIA: I was the more deceived.

HAMLET: Get thee to a nunnery: why wouldst thou be a breeder of
sinners? I am myself indifferent honest; but yet I could accuse me   120
of such things that it were better my mother had not borne me: I
am very proud, revengeful, ambitious; with more offenses at my
beck than I have thoughts to put them in, imagination to give them
shape, or time to act them in. What should such fellows as I do
crawling between heaven and earth! We are arrant knaves all; believe   125
none of us. Go thy ways to a nunnery. Where's your father?

OPHELIA: At home, my lord.

HAMLET: Let the doors be shut upon him, that he may play the fool
no where but in 's own house. Farewell.

OPHELIA: O, help him, you sweet heavens!   130

HAMLET: If thou dost marry, I'll give thee this plague for thy dowry: be
thou as chaste as ice, as pure as snow, thou shalt not escape calumny. Get thee to a nunnery, go: farewell. Or, if thou wilt needs
marry, marry a fool; for wise men know well enough what monsters²
you make of them. To a nunnery, go; and quickly too. Farewell.   135

OPHELIA: O heavenly powers, restore him!

HAMLET: I have heard of your paintings too, well enough; God hath
given you one face, and you make yourselves another: you jig, you
amble, and you lisp, and nick-name God's creatures, and make

---

7. Intercourse.   8. Its.   9. In his mother's adultery.   1. Retain the flavor of. *Inoculate*: graft itself
onto.   2. Cuckolds bear imaginary horns and "a horned man's a monster" (*Othello* IV.1).

your wantonness your ignorance.[3] Go to, I'll no more on 't; it hath   140
made me mad. I say, we will have no more marriages: those that
are married already, all but one, shall live; the rest shall keep as
they are. To a nunnery, go.
     [*Exit.*]

OPHELIA: O, what a noble mind is here o'erthrown!
     The courtier's, soldier's, scholar's, eye, tongue, sword: 145
     The expectancy and rose of the fair state,
     The glass of fashion and the mould of form.[4]
     The observed of all observers, quite, quite down!
     And I, of ladies most deject and wretched,
     That sucked the honey of his music vows,   150
     Now see that noble and most sovereign reason,
     Like sweet bells jangled, out of tune and harsh;
     That unmatched form and feature of blown[5] youth
     Blasted with ecstasy: O, woe is me,
     To have seen what I have seen, see what I see!   155
     [*Re-enter* KING *and* POLONIUS.]

KING: Love! his affections do not that way tend;
     Nor what he spake, though it lacked form a little,
     Was not like madness. There's something in his soul
     O'er which his melancholy sits on brood,
     And I do doubt[6] the hatch and the disclose   160
     Will be some danger: which for to prevent,
     I have in quick determination
     Thus set it down: — he shall with speed to England,
     For the demand of our neglected tribute:
     Haply the seas and countries different   165
     With variable objects shall expel
     This something-settled matter in his heart,
     Whereon his brains still beating puts him thus
     From fashion of himself.[7] What think you on 't?

POLONIUS: It shall do well: but yet do I believe   170
     The origin and commencement of his grief
     Sprung from neglected love. How now, Ophelia!
     You need not tell us what Lord Hamlet said;
     We heard it all. My lord, do as you please;
     But, if you hold it fit, after the play,   175
     Let his queen mother all alone entreat him
     To show his grief: let her be round[8] with him;
     And I'll be placed, so please you, in the ear
     Of all their conference. If she find him not,
     To England send him, or confine him where   180
     Your wisdom best shall think.

KING: It shall be so:

---

3. Misname (out of affection) the most natural things, and pretend that this is due to ignorance
instead of affection.   4. The mirror of fashion and the model of behavior.   5. In full bloom.
6. Fear.   7. Makes him behave unusually.   8. Direct.

Madness in great ones must not unwatched go.
[*Exeunt.*]

SCENE 2

A hall in the castle.

[*Enter* HAMLET *and* PLAYERS.]

HAMLET: Speak the speech, I pray you, as I pronounced it to you,
trippingly on the tongue: but if you mouth it, as many of your players do, I had as lief the town-crier spoke my lines. Nor do not saw
the air too much with your hand, thus; but use all gently: for in the
very torrent, tempest, and, as I may say, whirlwind of your   5
passion, you must acquire and beget a temperance that may give it
smoothness. O, it offends me to the soul to hear a robustious peri-
wig-pated fellow tear a passion to tatters, to very rags, to split the
ears of the groundlings,[9] who, for the most part, are capable of
nothing but inexplicable dumb-shows and noise: I would have such   10
a fellow whipped for o'er doing Termagant;[1] it out-herods Herod:
pray you, avoid it.

FIRST PLAYER: I warrant your honor.

HAMLET: Be not too tame neither, but let your own discretion be your
tutor: suit the action to the word, the word to the action; with this   15
special observance, that you o'erstep not the modesty[2] of nature: for
anything so overdone is from the purpose of playing, whose end,
both at the first and now, was and is, to hold, as 'twere, the mirror
up to nature; to show virtue her own feature, scorn her own image,
and the very age and body of the time his form and pressure.[3] Now   20
this overdone or come tardy off, though it make the unskillful
laugh, cannot but make the judicious grieve; the censure of the
which one must in your allowance o'erweigh a whole theater of
others. O, there be players that I have seen play, and heard others
praise, and that highly, not to speak it profanely,[4] that neither hav-   25
ing the accent of Christians nor the gait of Christian, pagan, nor
man, have so strutted and bellowed, that I have thought some of
nature's journeymen had made men, and not made them well, they
imitated humanity so abominably.

FIRST PLAYER: I hope we have reformed that indifferently[5] with us, sir.   30

HAMLET: O, reform it altogether. And let those that play your clowns
speak no more than is set down for them: for there be of them that
will themselves laugh, to set on some quantity of barren[6] spectators
to laugh too, though in the mean time some necessary question of
the play be then to be considered: that's villainous, and shows a   35
most pitiful ambition in the fool that uses it. Go, make you ready.

[*Exeunt* PLAYERS. —*Enter* POLONIUS, ROSENCRANTZ, *and* GUILDEN-
STERN.]

---

9. Spectators in the pit, where admission was cheapest.   1. God of the Mohammedans in old
romances and morality plays; he was portrayed as being noisy and excitable.   2. Moderation.
3. Impress, shape. *Feature:* form. *His:* its.   4. Hamlet apologizes for the profane implication that there
could be men not of God's making.   5. Pretty well.   6. Silly.

How now, my lord! will the king hear this piece of work?
POLONIUS: And the queen too, and that presently.
HAMLET: Bid the players make haste.

  [*Exit* POLONIUS.]

Will you two help to hasten them?   40

ROSENCRANTZ: ⎫
GUILDENSTERN: ⎬ We will, my lord.

  [*Exeunt* ROSENCRANTZ *and* GUILDENSTERN.]

HAMLET: What ho! Horatio!

  [*Enter* HORATIO.]

HORATIO: Here, sweet lord, at your service.
HAMLET: Horatio, thou art e'en as just a man
  As e'er my conversation coped withal.[7]   45
HORATIO: O, my dear lord,—
HAMLET: Nay, do not think I flatter;
  For what advancement may I hope from thee,
  That no revenue hast but thy good spirits,
  To feed and clothe thee? Why should the poor be flattered?
  No, let the candied tongue lick absurd pomp,   50
  And crook the pregnant hinges of the knee
  Where thrift may follow fawning.[8] Dost thou hear?
  Since my dear soul was mistress of her choice,
  And could of men distinguish, her election
  Hath sealed thee for herself: for thou hast been   55
  As one, in suffering all, that suffers nothing;
  A man that fortune's buffets and rewards
  Hast ta'en with equal thanks: and blest are those
  Whose blood and judgment[9] are so well commingled
  That they are not a pipe for fortune's finger   60
  To sound what stop she please.[1] Give me that man
  That is not passion's slave, and I will wear him
  In my heart's core, ay, in my heart of heart,
  As I do thee. Something too much of this.
  There is a play to-night before the king;   65
  One scene of it comes near the circumstance
  Which I have told thee of my father's death:
  I prithee, when thou sees that act a-foot,
  Even with the very comment of thy soul[2]
  Observe my uncle: if his occulted guilt   70
  Do not itself unkennel in one speech
  It is a damned ghost that we have seen,
  And my imaginations are as foul
  As Vulcan's stithy.[3] Give him heedful note;
  For I mine eyes will rivet to his face,   75
  And after we will both our judgments join
  In censure of his seeming.[4]

---

7. As I ever associated with.   8. Material profit may be derived from cringing. *Pregnant hinges:* supple joints.   9. Passion and reason.   1. For Fortune to put her finger on any windhole of the pipe she wants.   2. With all your powers of observation.   3. Smithy.   4. To judge his behavior.

HORATIO: Well, my lord:
If he steal aught the whilst this play is playing,
And 'scape detecting. I will pay the theft.
HAMLET: They are coming to the play: I must be idle:[5]   80
Get you a place.
   [*Danish march. A flourish. Enter* KING, QUEEN, POLONIUS, OPHELIA,
   ROSENCRANTZ, GUILDENSTERN, *and other* LORDS *attendant, with the*
   GUARD *carrying torches.*]
KING: How fares our cousin Hamlet?
HAMLET: Excellent, i' faith; of the chameleon's dish: I eat the air,[6]
promise-crammed: you cannot feed capons so.
KING: I have nothing with this answer, Hamlet; these words are not   85
mine.[7]
HAMLET: No, nor mine now. [*To* POLONIUS.] My lord, you played
once i' the university, you say?
POLONIUS: That did I, my lord, and was accounted a good actor.
HAMLET: What did you enact?   90
POLONIUS: I did enact Julius Cæsar: I was killed i' the Capitol; Brutus
killed me.
HAMLET: It was a brute part of him to kill so capital a calf there. Be
the players ready?
ROSENCRANTZ: Aye, my lord; they stay upon your patience.   95
QUEEN: Come hither, my dear Hamlet, sit by me.
HAMLET: No, good mother, here's metal more attractive.
POLONIUS: [*To the* KING.] O, ho! do you mark that?
HAMLET: Lady, shall I lie in your lap? [*Lying down at* OPHELIA's *feet.*]
OPHELIA: No, my lord.   100
HAMLET: I mean, my head upon your lap?
OPHELIA: Aye, my lord.
HAMLET: Do you think I meant country matters?
OPHELIA: I think nothing, my lord.
HAMLET: That's a fair thought to lie between maids' legs.   105
OPHELIA: What is, my lord?
HAMLET: Nothing.[8]
OPHELIA: You are merry, my lord.
HAMLET: Who, I?
OPHELIA: Aye, my lord.   110
HAMLET: O God, your only jig-maker.[9] What should a man do but be
merry? for, look you, how cheerfully my mother looks, and my
father died within 's two hours.
OPHELIA: Nay, 'tis twice two months, my lord.
HAMLET: So long? Nay then, let the devil wear black, for I'll have a   115
suit of sables.[1] O heavens! die two months ago, and not forgotten
yet? Then there's hope a great man's memory may outlive his life
half a year: but, by 'r lady, he must build churches then; or else

---

5. Crazy.   6. The chameleon was supposed to feed on air.   7. Have nothing to do with my question.   8. A sexual pun: no thing.   9. Maker of comic songs.   1. Hamlet notes sarcastically the
lack of mourning for his father in the fancy dress of court and king.

shall he suffer not thinking on, with the hobby-horse,[2] whose epitaph is, 'For, O, for, O, the hobby-horse is forgot.'   120
[*Hautboys play. The dumb-show enters. —Enter a King and a Queen
very lovingly; the Queen embracing him and he her. She kneels, and
makes show of protestation unto him. He takes her up, and declines
his head upon her neck; lays him down upon a bank of flowers: she,
seeing him asleep, leaves him. Anon comes in a fellow, takes off his
crown, kisses it, and pours poison in the King's ears, and exits. The
Queen returns; finds the King dead, and makes passionate action.
The Poisoner, with some two or three Mutes comes in again, seeming
to lament with her. The dead body is carried away. The Poisoner
woos the Queen with gifts: she seems loath and unwilling awhile, but
in the end accepts his love. —Exeunt.*]
OPHELIA: What means this, my lord?
HAMLET: Marry, this is miching mallecho;[3] it means mischief.
OPHELIA: Belike this show imports the argument of the play.
     [*Enter* PROLOGUE.]
HAMLET: We shall know by this fellow: the players cannot keep coun-
sel;[4] they'll tell all.   125
OPHELIA: Will he tell us what this show meant?
HAMLET: Aye, or any show that you'll show him: be not you ashamed
to show, he'll not shame to tell you what it means.
OPHELIA: You are naught,[5] you are naught: I'll mark the play.
PROLOGUE: For us, and for our tragedy,   130
          Here stooping to your clemency,
          We beg your hearing patiently.
HAMLET: Is this a prologue, or the posy[6] of a ring?
OPHELIA: 'Tis brief, my lord.
HAMLET: As woman's love.   135
     [*Enter two* PLAYERS, KING *and* QUEEN.]
PLAYER KING: Full thirty times hath Phœbus' cart[7] gone round
     Neptune's salt wash and Tellus' orbed ground,
     And thirty dozen moons with borrowed sheen
     About the world have times twelve thirties been,
     Since love our hearts and Hymen did our hands   140
     Unite commutual in most sacred bands.
PLAYER QUEEN: So many journeys may the sun and moon
     Make us again count o'er ere love be done!
     But, woe is me, you are so sick of late,
     So far from cheer and from your former state,   145
     That I distrust you.[8] Yet, though I distrust,
     Discomfort you, my lord, it nothing must:
     For women's fear and love holds quantity,[9]
     In neither aught, or in extremity.
     Now, what my love is, proof hath made you know,   150
     And as my love is sized, my fear is so:

2. A figure in the old May Day games and Morris dances.   3. Sneaking misdeed.   4. A secret.
5. Naughty, improper.   6. Motto, inscription.   7. The chariot of the sun.   8. I am worried about
you.   9. Maintain mutual balance.

Where love is great, the littlest doubts are fear,
Where little fears grow great, great love grows there.

PLAYER KING: Faith, I must leave thee, love, and shortly too;
My operant powers their functions leave[1] to do: 155
And thou shalt live in this fair world behind,
Honored, beloved; and haply one as kind
For husband shalt thou—

PLAYER QUEEN: O, confound the rest!
Such love must needs be treason in my breast:
In second husband let me be accurst!   160
None wed the second but who killed the first.

HAMLET: [Aside.] Wormwood, wormwood.

PLAYER QUEEN: The instances that second marriage move
Are base respects of thrift,[2] but none of love:
A second time I kill my husband dead,   165
When second husband kisses me in bed.

PLAYER KING: I do believe you think what now you speak,
But what we do determine oft we break.
Purpose is but the slave to memory,
Of violent birth but poor validity: 170
Which now, like fruit unripe, sticks on the tree,
But fall unshaken when they mellow be.
Most necessary 'tis that we forget
To pay ourselves what to ourselves is debt:
What to ourselves in passion we propose,   175
The passion ending, both the purpose lose.
The violence of either grief or joy
Their own enactures[3] with themselves destroy:
Where joy most revels, grief doth most lament;
Grief joys, joy grieves, on slender accident.   180
This world is not for aye, nor 'tis not strange
That even our loves should with our fortunes change,
For 'tis a question left us yet to prove,
Whether love lead fortune or else fortune love.
The great man down, you mark his favorite flies;   185
The poor advanced makes friends of enemies:
And hitherto doth love on fortune tend;
For who not needs shall never lack a friend,
And who in want a hollow friend doth try
Directly seasons[4] him his enemy.   190
But, orderly to end where I begun,
Our wills and fates do so contrary run,
That our devices still are overthrown,
Our thoughts are ours, their ends none of our own:
So think thou wilt no second husband wed,   195
But die thy thoughts when thy first lord is dead.

PLAYER QUEEN: Nor earth to me give food nor heaven light!

1. Cease.   2. Considerations of material profit. *Instances:* motives.   3. Their own fulfillment in action.   4. Matures.

Sport and repose lock from me day and night!
To desperation turn my trust and hope!
An anchor's cheer in prison be my scope!   200
Each opposite, that blanks[5] the face of joy,
Meet what I would have well and it destroy!
Both here and hence pursue me lasting strife,
If, once a widow, ever I be wife!

HAMLET: If she should break it now!   205

PLAYER KING: 'Tis deeply sworn. Sweet, leave me here a while;
My spirits grow dull, and fain I would beguile
The tedious day with sleep.
    [Sleeps.]

PLAYER QUEEN: Sleep rock thy brain;
And never come mischance between us twain!
    [Exit.]

HAMLET: Madam, how like you this play?   210

QUEEN: The lady doth protest[6] too much, methinks.

HAMLET: O, but she'll keep her word.

KING: Have you heard the argument?[7] Is there no offense in 't?

HAMLET: No, no, they do but jest, poison in jest; no offense i' the
world.   215

KING: What do you call the play?

HAMLET: The Mouse-Trap. Marry, how? Tropically.[8] This play is the
image of a murder done in Vienna: Gonzago is the duke's name;
his wife, Baptista: you shall see anon; 'tis a knavish piece of work;
but what o' that? your majesty, and we that have free souls, it   220
touches us not: let the galled jade wince, our withers are unwrung.[9]
    [Enter LUCIANUS.]
This is one Lucianus, nephew to the king.

OPHELIA: You are as good as a chorus, my lord.

HAMLET: I could interpret[1] between you and your love, if I could see
the puppets dallying.   225

OPHELIA: You are keen,[2] my lord, you are keen.

HAMLET: It would cost you a groaning to take off my edge.

OPHELIA: Still better and worse.

HAMLET: So you must take[3] your husbands. Begin, murderer; pox,
leave thy damnable faces, and begin. Come: the croaking raven   230
doth bellow for revenge.

LUCIANUS: Thoughts black, hands apt, drugs fit, and time agreeing;
Confederate season, else no creature seeing;
Thou mixture rank, of midnight weeds collected,
With Hecate's ban[4] thrice blasted, thrice infected,   235
Thy natural magic and dire property,
On wholesome life usurp immediately.

---

5. Makes pale. Anchor's cheer: hermit's, or anchorite's, fare.   6. Promise.   7. Plot of the play in
outline.   8. By a trope, figuratively.   9. Not wrenched. Galled jade: injured horse. Withers: the area
between a horse's shoulders.   1. Act as interpreter (regular feature in puppet shows).   2. Bitter, but
Hamlet chooses to take the word sexually.   3. That is, for better or for worse, as in the marriage
service—but in fact you "mis-take," deceive them.   4. Goddess of witchcraft's curse. Confederate:
favorable.

[*Pours the poison into the sleeper's ear.*]

HAMLET: He poisons him i' the garden for his estate. His name's Gonzago: the story is extant, and written in very choice Italian: you shall
see anon how the murderer gets the love of Gonzago's wife.   240

OPHELIA: The king rises.

HAMLET: What, frighted with false fire![5]

QUEEN: How fares my lord?

POLONIUS: Give o'er the play.

KING: Give me some light. Away!   245

POLONIUS: Lights, lights, lights!

[*Exeunt all but* HAMLET *and* HORATIO.]

HAMLET: Why, let the stricken deer go weep,
      The hart ungallèd play;
    For some must watch, while some must sleep:
      Thus runs the world away.   250
  Would not this, sir, and a forest of feathers—if the rest of my fortunes turn Turk with me—with two Provincial roses on my razed
shoes, get me a fellowship in a cry[6] of players, sir?

HORATIO: Half a share.

HAMLET: A whole one, I.   255
    For thou dost know, O Damon dear,
        This realm dismantled was
      Of Jove himself; and now reigns here
        A very, very—pajock.

HORATIO: You might have rhymed.[7]   260

HAMLET: O good Horatio, I'll take the ghost's word for a thousand
pound. Didst perceive?

HORATIO: Very well, my lord.

HAMLET: Upon the talk of the poisoning?

HORATIO: I did very well note him.   265

HAMLET: Ah, ha! Come, some music! come, the recorders!
    For if the king like not the comedy,
      Why then, belike, he likes it not, perdy.[8]
  Come, some music!

[*Re-enter* ROSENCRANTZ *and* GUILDENSTERN.]

GUILDENSTERN: Good my lord, vouchsafe me a word with you.   270

HAMLET: Sir, a whole history.

GUILDENSTERN: The king, sir—

HAMLET: Aye, sir, what of him?

GUILDENSTERN: Is in his retirement marvelous distempered.

HAMLET: With drink, sir?   275

GUILDENSTERN: No, my lord, rather with choler.[9]

HAMLET: Your wisdom should show itself more richer to signify this
to the doctor; for, for me to put him to his purgation would perhaps
plunge him into far more choler.

GUILDENSTERN: Good my lord, put your discourse into some frame,   280

---

5. Blank shot.   6. Company; a term generally used with hounds. *Turk with:* betray. *Razed shoes:*
sometimes worn by actors.   7. *Ass* would have rhymed. *Pajock:* peacock.   8. By God (*per Dieu*).
9. Bile, anger.

and start not so wildly from my affair.

HAMLET: I am tame, sir: pronounce.

GUILDENSTERN: The queen, your mother, in most great affliction of spirit, hath sent me to you.

HAMLET: You are welcome.   285

GUILDENSTERN: Nay, good my lord, this courtesy is not of the right breed. If it shall please you to make me a wholesome[1] answer, I will do your mother's commandment: if not, your pardon and my return shall be the end of my business.

HAMLET: Sir, I cannot.   290

GUILDENSTERN: What, my lord?

HAMLET: Make you a wholesome answer; my wit's diseased: but, sir, such answer as I can make, you shall command; or rather, as you say, my mother: therefore no more, but to the matter: my mother, you say,—   295

ROSENCRANTZ: Then thus she says; your behavior hath struck her into amazement and admiration.[2]

HAMLET: O wonderful son, that can so astonish a mother! But is there no sequel at the heels of this mother's admiration? Impart.

ROSENCRANTZ: She desires to speak with you in her closet, ere you go   300
to bed.

HAMLET: We shall obey, were she ten times our mother. Have you any further trade with us?

ROSENCRANTZ: My lord, you once did love me.

HAMLET: So I do still, by these pickers and stealers.[3]   305

ROSENCRANTZ: Good my lord, what is your cause of distemper? you do surely bar the door upon your own liberty, if you deny your griefs to your friend.

HAMLET: Sir, I lack advancement.[4]

ROSENCRANTZ: How can that be, when you have the voice of the king   310
himself for your succession in Denmark?

HAMLET: Aye, sir, but 'while the grass grows,'[5]—the proverb is something musty.

[Re-enter PLAYERS with recorders.]
O, the recorders! let me see one. To withdraw with you:—why do
you go about to recover the wind of me, as if you would drive me   315
into a toil?[6]

GUILDENSTERN: O, my lord, if my duty be too bold, my love is too unmannerly.

HAMLET: I do not well understand that. Will you play upon this pipe?

GUILDENSTERN: My lord, I cannot.   320

HAMLET: I pray you.

GUILDENSTERN: Believe me, I cannot.

HAMLET: I do beseech you.

GUILDENSTERN: I know no touch of it, my lord.

HAMLET: It is as easy as lying: govern these ventages[7] with your fingers   325

---

1. Sensible.   2. Confusion and surprise.   3. The hands.   4. Hamlet pretends that the cause of his "distemper" is frustrated ambition.   5. The proverb ends: "oft starves the silly steed."   6. Snare. Withdraw: retire, talk in private. Recover the wind of: get to the windward.   7. Windholes.

and thumb, give it breath with your mouth, and it will discourse
most eloquent music. Look you, these are the stops.

GUILDENSTERN: But these cannot I command to any utterance of harmony; I have not the skill.

HAMLET: Why, look you now, how unworthy a thing you make of me!   330
You would play upon me; you would seem to know my stops; you
would pluck out the heart of my mystery; you would sound me
from my lowest note to the top of my compass: and there is much
music, excellent voice, in this little organ; yet cannot you make it
speak. 'Sblood, do you think I am easier to be played on than a   335
pipe? Call me what instrument you will, though you can fret[8] me,
yet you cannot play upon me.

    [*Re-enter* POLONIUS.]

    God bless you, sir!

POLONIUS: My lord, the queen would speak with you, and presently.

HAMLET: Do you see yonder cloud that's almost in shape of a camel?   340

POLONIUS: By the mass, and 'tis like a camel, indeed.

HAMLET: Methinks it is like a weasel.

POLONIUS: It is backed like a weasel.

HAMLET: Or like a whale?

POLONIUS: Very like a whale.   345

HAMLET: Then I will come to my mother by and by. They fool me to
the top of my bent. I will come by and by.

POLONIUS: I will say so.

    [*Exit* POLONIUS.]

HAMLET: 'By and by' is easily said. Leave me, friends.

    [*Exeunt all but* HAMLET.]

    'tis now the very witching time of night,   350
When churchyards yawn, and hell itself breathes out
Contagion to this world: now could I drink hot blood,
And do such bitter business as the day
Would quake to look on. Soft! now to my mother.
O heart, lose not thy nature; let not ever   355
The soul of Nero[9] enter this firm bosom:
Let me be cruel, not unnatural:
I will speak daggers to her, but use none;
My tongue and soul in this be hypocrites;
How in my words soever she be shent,   360
To give them seals[1] never, my soul, consent!

    [*Exit.*]

SCENE 3

A room in the castle.

[*Enter* KING, ROSENCRANTZ, *and* GUILDENSTERN.]

KING: I like him not, nor stands it safe with us

---

8. Vex, with a pun on *frets*, meaning the ridges placed across the finger board of a guitar to regulate
the fingering.   9. A Roman emperor (A.D. 37–68) who murdered his mother.   1. Ratify them by
action. *Shent:* reproached.

To let his madness range. Therefore prepare you;
I your commission will forthwith dispatch,
And he to England shall along with you:
The terms of our estate[2] may not endure   5
Hazard so near us as doth hourly grow
Out of his lunacies.
GUILDENSTERN: We will ourselves provide:
  Most holy and religious fear it is
  To keep those many many bodies safe
  That live and feed upon your majesty.   10
ROSENCRANTZ: The single and peculiar[3] life is bound
  With all the strength and armor of the mind
  To keep itself from noyance; but much more
  That spirit upon whose weal depends and rests
  The lives of many. The cease[4] of majesty   15
  Dies not alone, but like a gulf doth draw
  What 's near it with it; it is a massy wheel,
  Fixed on the summit of the highest mount,
  To whose huge spokes ten thousand lesser things
  Are mortised[5] and adjoined; which, when it falls,   20
  Each small annexment, petty consequence,
  Attends the boisterous ruin. Never alone
  Did the king sigh, but with a general groan.
KING: Arm you, I pray you, to this speedy voyage,
  For we will fetters put about this fear,   25
  Which now goes too free-footed.
ROSENCRANTZ: ⎱
GUILDENSTERN: ⎰ We will haste us.
        [*Exeunt* ROSENCRANTZ *and* GUILDENSTERN. — *Enter* POLONIUS.]
POLONIUS: My lord, he's going to his mother's closet:
  Behind the arras I'll convey myself,
  To hear the process: I'll warrant she'll tax him home:[6]   30
  And, as you said, and wisely was it said
  'Tis meet that some more audience than a mother,
  Since nature makes them partial, should o'erhear
  The speech, of vantage.[7] Fare you well, my liege:
  I'll call upon you ere you go to bed,   35
  And tell you what I know.
KING: Thanks, dear my lord.
        [*Exit* POLONIUS.]
  O, my offense is rank, it smells to heaven;
  It hath the primal eldest curse[8] upon 't,
  A brother's murder. Pray can I not,
  Though inclination be as sharp as will: 40
  My stronger guilt defeats my strong intent,
  And like a man to double business bound,
  I stand in pause where I shall first begin,

2. My position as king.   3. Individual.   4. Decease, extinction.   5. Fastened.   6. Take him to
task thoroughly.   7. From a vantage point.   8. The curse of Cain.

And both neglect. What if this cursed hand
Were thicker than itself with brother's blood,   45
Is there not rain enough in the sweet heavens
To wash it white as snow? Whereto serves mercy
But to confront the visage of offense?[9]
And what's in prayer but this twofold force,
To be forestalled ere we come to fall,   50
Or pardoned being down? Then I'll look up;
My fault is past. But O, what form of prayer
Can serve my turn? 'Forgive me my foul murder?'
That cannot be, since I am still possessed
Of those effects for which I did the murder,   55
My crown, mine own ambition and my queen.
May one be pardoned and retain the offense?[1]
In the corrupted currents of this world
Offense's gilded hand may shove by justice,
And oft 'tis seen the wicked prize itself   60
Buys out the law:[2] but 'tis not so above;
There is no shuffling, there the action lies
In his[3] true nature, and we ourselves compelled
Even to the teeth and forehead of our faults
To give in evidence. What then? what rests?[4]   65
Try what repentance can: what can it not?
Yet what can it when one can not repent?
O wretched state! O bosom black as death!
O limèd soul, that struggling to be free
Art more engaged! Help, angels! make assay![5]   70
Bow, stubborn knees, and, heart with strings of steel,
Be soft as sinews of the new-born babe!
All may be well.
       [*Retires and kneels.* —*Enter* HAMLET.]
HAMLET: Now might I do it pat,[6] now he is praying
And now I'll do 't: and so he goes to heaven: 75
And so am I revenged. That would be scanned;[7]
A villain kills my father; and for that,
I, his sole son, do this same villain send
To heaven.
O, this is hire and salary, not revenge.   80
He took my father grossly, full of bread,
With all his crimes broad blown, as flush as May;
And how his audit[8] stands who knows save heaven?
But in our circumstance and course of thought,
'Tis heavy with him: and am I then revenged,   85
To take him in the purging of his soul,
When he is fit and seasoned[9] for his passage?

---

9. Guilt.   1. The things obtained through the offense.   2. The wealth unduly acquired is used for bribery.   3. Its.   4. What remains?   5. Make the attempt! *Limèd:* caught as with birdlime. 6. Conveniently.   7. Would have to be considered carefully.   8. Account. *Broad blown:* in full bloom.   9. Ripe, ready.

No.
Up, sword, and know thou a more horrid hent:[1]
When he is drunk asleep, or in his rage,   90
Or, in the incestuous pleasure of his bed;
At game, a-swearing, or about some act
That has no relish of salvation in 't;
Then trip him, that his heels may kick at heaven
And that his soul may be as damned and black   95
As hell, whereto it goes. My mother stays:
This physic but prolongs thy sickly days.
     [*Exit.*]
KING: [*Rising.*] My words fly up, my thoughts remain below:
     Words without thoughts never to heaven go.
     [*Exit.*]

SCENE 4

The Queen's closet.

[*Enter* QUEEN *and* POLONIUS.]
POLONIUS: He will come straight. Look you lay home to him:
     Tell him his pranks have been too broad[2] to bear with,
     And that your grace hath screen'd and stood between
     Much heat and him. I'll sconce me even here.
     Pray you, be round[3] with him.
HAMLET: [*Within.*]   Mother, mother, mother!   5
QUEEN: I'll warrant you; fear me not. Withdraw,
     I hear him coming.
     [POLONIUS *hides behind the arras.* —*Enter* HAMLET.]
HAMLET: Now, mother, what's the matter?
QUEEN: Hamlet, thou hast thy father much offended.
HAMLET: Mother, you have my father much offended.   10
QUEEN: Come, come, you answer with an idle tongue.
HAMLET: Go, go, you question with a wicked tongue.
QUEEN: Why, how now, Hamlet!
HAMLET: What's the matter now?
QUEEN: Have you forgot me?
HAMLET: No, by the rood,[4] not so:
     You are the queen, your husband's brother's wife;   15
     And—would it were not so!—you are my mother.
QUEEN: Nay, then, I'll set those to you that can speak.
HAMLET: Come, come, and sit you down; you shall not budge:
     You go not till I set you up a glass[5]
     Where you may see the inmost part of you.   20
QUEEN: What wilt thou do? thou wilt not murder me?
     Help, help, ho!
POLONIUS: [*Behind.*] What, ho! help, help, help!

---

1. Grip.   2. Unrestrained. *Lay home:* give him a stern lesson.   3. Straightforward.   4. Cross.
5. Mirror.

HAMLET: [*Drawing.*] How now! a rat? Dead, for a ducat, dead!
   [*Makes a pass through the arras.*]
POLONIUS: [*Behind.*] O, I am slain!
   [*Falls and dies.*]
QUEEN: O me, what hast thou done?   25
HAMLET: Nay, I know not: is it the king?
QUEEN: O, what a rash and bloody deed is this!
HAMLET: A bloody deed! almost as bad, good mother,
   As kill a king, and marry with his brother.
QUEEN: As kill a king!
HAMLET: Aye, lady, 'twas my word.   30
   [*Lifts up the arras and discovers* POLONIUS.]
   Thou wretched, rash, intruding fool, farewell!
   I took thee for thy better: take thy fortune;
   Thou find'st to be too busy[6] is some danger.
   Leave wringing of your hands: peace! sit you down,
   And let me wring your heart: for so I shall,   35
   If it be made of penetrable stuff;
   If damned custom have not brassed it so,
   That it be proof and bulwark against sense.[7]
QUEEN: What have I done, that thou darest wag thy tongue
   In noise so rude against me?
HAMLET: Such an act   40
   That blurs the grace and blush of modesty,
   Calls virtue hypocrite, takes off the rose
   From the fair forehead of an innocent love,
   And sets a blister there; makes marriage vows
   As false as dicers' oaths: O, such a deed   45
   As from the body of contraction[8] plucks
   The very soul, and sweet religion makes
   A rhapsody of words: heaven's face doth glow;[9]
   Yea, this solidity and compound mass,
   With tristful visage, as against the doom,[1]   50
   Is thought-sick at the act.
QUEEN: Aye me, what act,
   That roars so loud and thunders in the index?[2]
HAMLET: Look here, upon this picture, and on this,
   The counterfeit presentment[3] of two brothers.   55
   See what a grace was seated on this brow;
   Hyperion's curls, the front of Jove himself,
   An eye like Mars, to threaten and command;
   A station[4] like the herald Mercury
   New-lighted on a heaven-kissing hill;   60
   A combination and a form indeed,
   Where every god did seem to set his seal
   To give the world assurance of a man:

---

6. Too much of a busybody.   7. Feeling.   8. Duty to the marriage contract.   9. Blush with
shame.   1. Doomsday. *Tristful*: sad.   2. Prologue, table of contents.   3. Portrait.   4. Posture.

This was your husband. Look you now, what follows:
Here is your husband; like a mildewed ear,[5]   65
Blasting his wholesome brother. Have you eyes?
Could you on this fair mountain leave to feed,
And batten[6] on this moor? Ha! have you eyes?
You cannot call it love, for at your age
The hey-day in the blood is tame, it's humble,   70
And waits upon[7] the judgment: and what judgment
Would step from this to this? Sense sure you have,
Else could you not have motion: but sure that sense
Is apoplexed: for madness would not err,
Nor sense to ecstasy was ne'er so thralled   75
But it reserved some quantity of choice,
To serve in such a difference. What devil was 't
That thus hath cozened you at hoodman-blind?[8]
Eyes without feeling, feeling without sight,
Ears without hands or eyes, smelling sans[9] all,   80
Or but a sickly part of one true sense
Could not so mope.[1]
O shame! where is thy blush? Rebellious hell,
If thou canst mutine in a matron's bones,
To flaming youth let virtue be as wax   85
And melt in her own fire: proclaim no shame
When the compulsive ardor gives the charge,[2]
Since frost itself as actively doth burn,
And reason panders[3] will.
QUEEN: O Hamlet, speak no more:
Thou turn'st mine eyes into my very soul,   90
And there I see such black and grained spots
As will not leave their tinct.[4]
HAMLET: Nay, but to live
In the rank sweat of an enseamèd[5] bed,
Stew'd in corruption, honeying and making love
Over the nasty sty,—
QUEEN: O, speak to me no more;   95
These words like daggers enter in my ears;
No more, sweet Hamlet!
HAMLET: A murderer and a villain;
A slave that is not twentieth part the tithe[6]
Of your precédent lord; a vice of kings;
A cutpurse[7] of the empire and the rule,   100
That from a shelf the precious diadem stole
And put it in his pocket!
QUEEN: No more!
HAMLET: A king of shreds and patches—

---

5. Of corn.   6. Gorge, fatten. *Leave*: cease.   7. Is subordinated to.   8. Blindman's buff. *Cozened*:
tricked.   9. Without.   1. Be stupid.   2. Attack.   3. Becomes subservient to.   4. Lose their
color. *Grained*: dyed in.   5. Greasy.   6. Tenth.   7. Pickpocket. *Vice*: clown, from the custom in
the old morality plays of having a buffoon take the part of Vice or of a particular vice.

[*Enter* GHOST.]
Save me, and hover o'er me with your wings,
You heavenly guards! What would your gracious figure?   105
QUEEN: Alas, he's mad!
HAMLET: Do you not come your tardy son to chide,
   That, lapsed in time and passion, lets go by
   The important acting of your dread command?
   O, say!
GHOST: Do not forget: this visitation   110
   Is but to whet thy almost blunted purpose.
   But look, amazement on thy mother sits:
   O, step between her and her fighting soul:
   Conceit[8] in weakest bodies strongest works:
   Speak to her, Hamlet.
HAMLET: How is it with you, lady?   115
QUEEN: Alas, how is 't with you,
   That you do bend your eye on vacancy
   And with the incorporal air do hold discourse?
   Forth at your eyes your spirits wildly peep;
   And, as the sleeping soldiers in the alarm,   120
   Your bedded hairs, like life in excrements,[9]
   Start up and stand on end. O gentle son,
   Upon the heat and flame of thy distemper
   Sprinkle cool patience. Whereon do you look?
HAMLET: On him, on him! Look you how pale he glares!   125
   His form and cause conjoined, preaching to stones,
   Would make them capable.[1] Do not look upon me,
   Lest with this piteous action you convert
   My stern effects:[2] then what I have to do
   Will want true color; tears perchance for[3] blood.   130
QUEEN: To whom do you speak this?
HAMLET: Do you see nothing there?
QUEEN: Nothing at all; yet all that is I see.
HAMLET: Nor did you nothing hear?
QUEEN: No, nothing but ourselves.
HAMLET: Why, look you there! look, how it steals away!
   My father, in his habit as he lived!   135
   Look, where he goes, even now, out at the portal!
      [*Exit* GHOST.]
QUEEN: This is the very coinage of your brain:
   This bodiless creation ecstasy
   Is very cunning in.
HAMLET: Ecstasy!
   My pulse, as yours, doth temperately keep time,   140
   And makes as healthful music: it is not madness
   That I have uttered: bring me to the test,
   And I the matter will re-word, which madness

---

8. Imagination.   9. Outgrowths. *Alarm:* call to arms.   1. Of feeling.   2. You make me change
my purpose.   3. Instead of.

Would gambol from. Mother, for love of grace,
Lay not that flattering unction to your soul,   145
That not your trespass but my madness speaks:
It will but skin and film the ulcerous place,
Whiles rank corruption, mining all within,
Infects unseen. Confess yourself to heaven;
Repent what's past, avoid what is to come,   150
And do not spread the compost on the weeds,
To make them ranker. Forgive me this my virtue,
For in the fatness of these pursy[4] times
Virtue itself of vice must pardon beg.
Yea, curb[5] and woo for leave to do him good.   155
QUEEN: O Hamlet, thou hast cleft my heart in twain.
HAMLET: O, throw away the worser part of it,
   And live the purer with the other half.
   Good night: but go not to my uncle's bed;
   Assume a virtue, if you have it not.   160
   That monster, custom, who all sense doth eat,
   Of habits devil, is angel yet in this,
   That to the use of actions fair and good
   He likewise gives a frock or livery,
   That aptly is put on.[6] Refrain to-night,   165
   And that shall lend a kind of easiness
   To the next abstinence; the next more easy;
   For use almost can change the stamp[7] of nature,
   And either curb the devil, or throw him out
   With wondrous potency. Once more, good night: 170
   And when you are desirous to be blest,
   I'll blessing beg of you. For this same lord,
     [*Pointing to* POLONIUS.]
   I do repent: but heaven hath pleased it so,
   To punish me with this, and this with me,
   That I must be their scourge and minister.   175
   I will bestow[8] him, and will answer well
   The death I gave him. So, again, good night.
   I must be cruel, only to be kind:
   Thus bad begins, and worse remains behind.
   One word more, good lady.
QUEEN: What shall I do?   180
HAMLET: Not this, by no means, that I bid you do:
   Let the bloat[9] king tempt you again to bed;
   Pinch wanton on your cheek, call you his mouse;
   And let him, for a pair of reechy[1] kisses,
   Or paddling in your neck with his damned fingers,   185
   Make you to ravel all this matter out,
   That I essentially am not in madness,

---

4. Swollen from pampering.   5. Bow.   6. That is, habit, although like a devil in establishing evil ways in us, is like an angel in doing the same for virtues. *Aptly:* easily.   7. Cast, form. *Use:* habit. 8. Stow away. *Minister:* agent of punishment.   9. Bloated with drink.   1. Fetid.

But mad in craft.[2] 'Twere good you let him know;
For who, that's but a queen, fair, sober, wise,
Would from a paddock, from a bat, a gib,   190
Such dear concernings[3] hide? who would do so?
No, in despite of sense and secrecy,
Unpeg the basket on the house's top,
Let the birds fly, and like the famous ape,[4]
To try conclusions, in the basket creep   195
And break your own neck down.
QUEEN: Be thou assured, if words be made of breath
  And breath of life, I have no life to breathe
  What thou hast said to me.
HAMLET: I must to England; you know that?
QUEEN: Alack,   200
  I had forgot: 'tis so concluded on.
HAMLET: There's letters sealed: and my two schoolfellows,
  Whom I will trust as I will adders fanged,
  They bear the mandate; they must sweep my way,
  And marshal me to knavery. Let it work;   205
  For 'tis the sport to have the enginer
  Hoist with his own petar:[5] and 't shall go hard
  But I will delve one yard below their mines,
  And blow them at the moon: I, 'tis most sweet
  When in one line two crafts directly meet.   210
  This man shall set me packing:
  I'll lug the guts into the neighbor room.
  Mother, good night. Indeed this counselor
  Is now most still, most secret and most grave,[6]
  Who was in life a foolish prating knave.   215
  Come, sir, to draw toward an end with you.
  Good night, mother.
    [*Exeunt severally;* HAMLET *dragging in* POLONIUS.]

Act IV

SCENE 1

A room in the castle.

[*Enter* KING, QUEEN, ROSENCRANTZ, *and* GUILDENSTERN]
KING: There's matter in these sighs, these profound heaves:
  You must translate: 'tis fit we understand them.
  Where is your son?
QUEEN: Bestow this place on us[7] a little while.

---

2. Simulation.   3. Matters with which one is closely concerned. *Paddock:* toad. *Gib:* tomcat.
4. The ape in the unidentified animal fable to which Hamlet alludes; apparently the animal saw birds fly out of a basket and drew the conclusion that by placing himself in a basket he could fly too.
5. Petard, a variety of bomb. *Marshal:* lead. *Enginer:* military engineer. *Hoist:* blow up.   6. Hamlet is punning on the word.   7. Leave us alone.

[*Exeunt* ROSENCRANTZ *and* GUILDENSTERN.]
Ah, mine own lord, what have I seen to-night!   5
KING: What, Gertrude? How does Hamlet?
QUEEN: Mad as the sea and wind, when both contend
   Which is the mightier: in his lawless fit,
   Behind the arras hearing something stir,
   Whips out his rapier, cries 'A rat, a rat!'   10
   And in this brainish apprehension[8] kills
   The unseen good old man.
KING: O heavy deed!
   It had been so with us, had we been there:
   His liberty is full of threats to all,
   To you yourself, to us, to every one.   15
   Alas, how shall this bloody deed be answered?
   It will be laid to us, whose providence
   Should have kept short,[9] restrained and out of haunt,
   This mad young man: but so much was our love,
   We would not understand what was most fit,   20
   But, like the owner of a foul disease,
   To keep it from divulging, let it feed
   Even on the pith of life. Where is he gone?
QUEEN: To draw apart the body he hath killed:
   O'er whom his very madness, like some ore   25
   Among a mineral[1] of metals base,
   Shows itself pure; he weeps for what is done.
KING: O Gertrude, come away!
   The sun no sooner shall the mountains touch,
   But we will ship him hence: and this vile deed   30
   We must, with all our majesty and skill,
   Both countenance[2] and excuse. Ho, Guildenstern!
      [*Re-enter* ROSENCRANTZ *and* GUILDENSTERN.]
   Friends both, go join you with some further aid:
   Hamlet in madness hath Polonius slain,
   And from his mother's closet hath he dragged him: 35
   Go seek him out; speak fair, and bring the body
   Into the chapel. I pray you, haste in this.
      [*Exeunt* ROSENCRANTZ *and* GUILDENSTERN.]
   Come, Gertrude, we'll call up our wisest friends;
   And let them know, both what we mean to do,
   And what's untimely done. . . .[3]   40
   Whose whisper o'er the world's diameter
   As level as the cannon to his blank[4]
   Transports his poisoned shot, may miss our name
   And hit the woundless air. O, come away!
   My soul is full of discord and dismay.   45
      [*Exeunt.*]

---

8. Imaginary notion.   9. Under close watch.   1. Mine. *Ore*: gold.   2. Recognize.   3. This gap
in the text has been guessingly filled in with "So envious slander."   4. His target.

SCENE 2

Another room in the castle.

[*Enter* HAMLET.]

HAMLET: Safely stowed.

ROSENCRANTZ: ⎱ [*Within.*] Hamlet! Lord Hamlet!
GUILDENSTERN: ⎰

HAMLET: But soft, what noise? who calls on Hamlet?
   O, here they come.

[*Enter* ROSENCRANTZ *and* GUILDENSTERN.]

ROSENCRANTZ: What have you done, my lord, with the dead body?   5
HAMLET: Compounded[5] it with dust, whereto 'tis kin.
ROSENCRANTZ: Tell us where 'tis, that we may take it thence
   And bear it to the chapel.
HAMLET: Do not believe it.
ROSENCRANTZ: Believe what?   10
HAMLET: That I can keep your counsel and not mine own. Besides, to
   be demanded of a sponge! what replication[6] should be made by the
   son of a king?
ROSENCRANTZ: Take you me for a sponge, my lord?
HAMLET: Aye, sir; that soaks up the king's countenance,[7] his rewards,   15
   his authorities. But such officers do the king best service in the end:
   he keeps them, like an ape, in the corner of his jaw; first mouthed,
   to be last swallowed: when he needs what you have gleaned, it is
   but squeezing you, and sponge, you shall be dry again.
ROSENCRANTZ: I understand you not, my lord.   20
HAMLET: I am glad of it: a knavish speech sleeps in a foolish ear.
ROSENCRANTZ: My lord, you must tell us where the body is, and go
   with us to the king.
HAMLET: The body is with the king, but the king is not with the body.
   The king is a thing—   25
GUILDENSTERN: A thing, my lord?
HAMLET: Of nothing: bring me to him. Hide fox, and all after.[8]
   [*Exeunt.*]

SCENE 3

Another room in the castle.

[*Enter* KING, *attended.*]

KING: I have sent to seek him, and to find the body.
   How dangerous is it that this man goes loose!
   Yet must not we put the strong law on him:
   He's loved of the distracted multitude,
   Who like not in their judgment, but their eyes;   5
   And where 'tis so, the offender's scourge is weighed,
   But never the offense. To bear[9] all smooth and even,

---

5. Mixed.   6. Formal reply. *Demanded:* questioned by.   7. Favor.   8. A children's game.
9. Conduct. *Scourge:* punishment.

This sudden sending away must seem
Deliberate pause: diseases desperate grown
By desperate appliance[1] are relieved,   10
Or not at all.
    [*Enter* ROSENCRANTZ.]
             How now! what hath befall'n?
ROSENCRANTZ: Where the dead body is bestowed, my lord,
  We cannot get from him.
KING: But where is he?
ROSENCRANTZ: Without, my lord; guarded, to know your pleasure.
KING: Bring him before us.   15
ROSENCRANTZ: Ho, Guildenstern! bring in my lord.
    [*Enter* HAMLET *and* GUILDENSTERN.]
KING: Now, Hamlet, where's Polonius?
HAMLET: At supper.
KING: At supper! where?
HAMLET: Not where he eats, but where he is eaten: a certain convo-   20
  cation of public worms are e'en at him. Your worm is your only
  emperor for diet:[2] we fat all creatures else to fat us, and we fat
  ourselves for maggots: your fat king and your lean beggar is but
  variable service,[3] two dishes, but to one table: that's the end.
KING: Alas, alas!   25
HAMLET: A man may fish with the worm that hath eat of a king, and
  eat of the fish that hath fed of that worm.
KING: What dost thou mean by this?
HAMLET: Nothing but to show you how a king may go a progress[4]
  through the guts of a beggar.   30
KING: Where is Polonius?
HAMLET: In heaven; send thither to see: if your messenger find him
  not there, seek him i' the other place yourself. But indeed, if you
  find him not within this month, you shall nose[5] him as you go up
  the stairs into the lobby.   35
KING: [*To some* ATTENDANTS.] Go seek him there.
HAMLET: He will stay till you come.
    [*Exeunt* ATTENDANTS.]
KING: Hamlet, this deed, for thine especial safety,
  Which we do tender,[6] as we dearly grieve
  For that which thou hast done, must send thee hence   40
  With fiery quickness: therefore prepare thyself;
  The bark is ready and the wind at help,
  The associates tend, and every thing is bent
  For England.
HAMLET: For England?
KING: Aye, Hamlet.
HAMLET: Good.

---

1. Treatment. *Deliberate pause:* the result of careful argument.   2. Possibly a punning reference to
the Diet (assembly) of the Holy Roman Empire at Worms.   3. That is, the service varies, not the
food.   4. Royal state journey.   5. Smell.   6. Care for.

KING: So is it, if thou knew'st our purposes.   45
HAMLET: I see a cherub that sees them. But, come; for England!
   Farewell, dear mother.
KING: Thy loving father, Hamlet.
HAMLET: My mother: father and mother is man and wife; man and
   wife is one flesh, and so, my mother. Come, for England!   50
   [*Exit.*]
KING: Follow him at foot;[7] tempt him with speed aboard;
   Delay it not; I'll have him hence to-night:
   Away! for every thing is sealed and done
   That else leans on[8] the affair: pray you, make haste.
   [*Exeunt* ROSENCRANTZ *and* GUILDENSTERN.]
   And, England,[9] if my love thou hold'st at aught—   55
   As my great power thereof may give thee sense,
   Since yet thy cicatrice looks raw and red
   After the Danish sword, and thy free awe
   Pays homage to us—thou mayst not coldly set[1]
   Our sovereign process; which imports at full,   60
   By letters conjuring[2] to that effect,
   The present death of Hamlet. Do it, England;
   For like the hectic[3] in my blood he rages,
   And thou must cure me; till I know 'tis done,
   Howe'er my haps, my joys were ne'er begun.   65
   [*Exit.*]

SCENE 4

A plain in Denmark.

[*Enter* FORTINBRAS, *a* CAPTAIN *and* SOLDIERS, *marching.*]
FORTINBRAS: Go, captain, from me greet the Danish king;
   Tell him that by his license Fortinbras
   Craves the conveyance[4] of a promised march
   Over his kingdom. You know the rendezvous.
   If that his majesty would aught with us,   5
   We shall express our duty in his eye;[5]
   And let him know so.
CAPTAIN: I will do 't, my lord.
FORTINBRAS: Go softly on.
   [*Exeunt* FORTINBRAS *and* SOLDIERS. — *Enter* HAMLET, ROSENCRANTZ,
   GUILDENSTERN, *and others.*]
HAMLET: Good sir, whose powers[6] are these?
CAPTAIN: They are of Norway, sir.   10
HAMLET: How purposed, sir, I pray you?
CAPTAIN: Against some part of Poland.
HAMLET: Who commands them, sir?

---

7. At his heels.   8. Pertains to.   9. The king of England.   1. Regard with indifference.
2. Enjoining.   3. Fever.   4. Convoy.   5. Presence.   6. Armed forces.

CAPTAIN: The nephew to Old Norway, Fortinbras.

HAMLET: Goes it against the main[7] of Poland, sir,   15
    Or for some frontier?

CAPTAIN: Truly to speak, and with no addition,
    We go to gain a little patch of ground
    That hath in it no profit but the name.
    To pay five ducats, five, I would not farm it;   20
    Nor will it yield to Norway or the Pole
    A ranker rate, should it be sold in fee.[8]

HAMLET: Why, then the Polack never will defend it.

CAPTAIN: Yes, it is already garrisoned.

HAMLET: Two thousand souls and twenty thousand ducats   25
    Will not debate the question of this straw!
    This is the imposthume[9] of much wealth and peace,
    That inward breaks, and shows no cause without
    Why the man dies. I humbly thank you, sir.

CAPTAIN: God be wi' you, sir.
    [Exit.]

ROSENCRANTZ: Will 't please you go, my lord?   30

HAMLET: I'll be with you straight. Go a little before.
    [Exeunt all but HAMLET.]
    How all occasions do inform against[1] me,
    And spur my dull revenge! What is a man,
    If his chief good and market[2] of his time
    Be but to sleep and feed? a beast, no more.   35
    Sure, he that made us with such large discourse,[3]
    Looking before and after, gave us not
    That capability and god-like reason
    To fust[4] in us unused. Now, whether it be
    Bestial oblivion, or some craven scruple   40
    Of thinking too precisely on the event,[5]—
    A thought which, quartered, hath but one part wisdom
    And ever three parts coward,—I do not know
    Why yet I live to say 'this thing's to do,'
    Sith I have cause, and will, and strength, and means,   45
    To do 't. Examples gross as earth exhort me:
    Witness this army, of such mass and charge,[6]
    Led by a delicate and tender prince,
    Whose spirit with divine ambition puffed
    Makes mouths[7] at the invisible event,   50
    Exposing what is mortal and unsure
    To all that fortune, death, and danger dare,
    Even for an egg-shell. Rightly to be great
    Is not to stir without great argument,
    But greatly to find quarrel in a straw   55
    When honor's at the stake. How stand I then,

7. The whole of.   8. For absolute possession. *Ranker:* higher.   9. Ulcer.   1. Denounce.
2. Payment for, reward.   3. Reasoning power.   4. Become moldy, taste of the cask.   5. Outcome.   6. Cost.   7. Laughs at.

That have a father killed, a mother stained,
Excitements of my reason and my blood,
And let all sleep, while to my shame I see
The imminent death of twenty thousand men,   60
That for a fantasy and trick[8] of fame
Go to their graves like beds, fight for a plot
Whereon the numbers cannot try the cause,[9]
Which is not tomb enough and continent[1]
To hide the slain? O, from this time forth,   65
My thoughts be bloody, or be nothing worth!
    [*Exit.*]

SCENE 5

Elsinore. A room in the castle.

[*Enter* QUEEN, HORATIO, *and a* GENTLEMAN.]
QUEEN: I will not speak with her.
GENTLEMAN: She is importunate, indeed distract:
    Her mood will needs be pitied.
QUEEN: What would she have?
GENTLEMAN: She speaks much of her father, says she hears
    There's tricks i' the world, and hems and beats her heart,   5
    Spurns enviously at straws;[2] speaks things in doubt,
    That carry but half sense: her speech is nothing,
    Yet the unshapèd use of it doth move
    The hearers to collection; they aim[3] at it,
    And botch[4] the words up fit to their own thoughts;   10
    Which, as her winks and nods and gestures yield them,
    Indeed would make one think there might be thought,
    Though nothing sure, yet much unhappily.
HORATIO: 'Twere good she were spoken with, for she may strew
    Dangerous conjectures in ill-breeding minds.[5]   15
QUEEN: Let her come in.
    [*Exit* GENTLEMAN.]
    [*Aside.*] To my sick soul, as sin's true nature is,
Each toy seems prologue to some great amiss:
So full of artless jealousy[6] is guilt,
It spills itself in fearing to be spilt.   20
    [*Re-enter* GENTLEMAN, *with* OPHELIA.]
OPHELIA: Where is the beauteous majesty of Denmark?
QUEEN: How now, Ophelia!
OPHELIA: [*Sings.*] How should I your true love know
          From another one?
          By his cockle hat and staff   25
          And his sandal shoon.[7]

---

8. Trifle of.   9. So small that it cannot hold the men who fight for it.   1. Container.   2. Gets angry at trifles.   3. Guess. *Collection:* gathering up her words and trying to make sense of them. 4. Patch.   5. Minds breeding evil thoughts.   6. Uncontrolled suspicion. *Toy:* trifle. *Amiss:* misfortune.   7. Shoes. These are all typical signs of pilgrims traveling to places of devotion.

QUEEN: Alas, sweet lady, what imports this song?
OPHELIA: Say you? nay, pray you, mark.
  [*Sings.*] He is dead and gone, lady,
          He is dead and gone;   30
        At his head a grass-green turf,
          At his heels a stone.
    Oh, oh!
QUEEN: Nay, but Ophelia,—
OPHELIA: Pray you, mark.
  [*Sings.*] White his shroud as the mountain snow,—
    [*Enter* KING.]
QUEEN: Alas, look here, my lord.   35
OPHELIA: [*Sings.*]   Larded[8] with sweet flowers;
          Which bewept to the grave did—not—go
            With true-love showers.
KING: How do you, pretty lady?
OPHELIA: Well, God 'ild[9] you! They say the owl was a baker's daugh-   40
  ter. Lord, we know what we are, but know not what we may be.[1]
  God be at your table!
KING: Conceit upon her father.
OPHELIA: Pray you, let's have no words of this; but when they ask you
  what it means, say you this: 45
  [*Sings.*] To-morrow is Saint Valentine's day
          All in the morning betime,
        And I a maid at your window,
          To be your Valentine.
        Then up he rose, and donned his clothes,   50
          And dupped[2] the chamber-door;
        Let in the maid, that out a maid
          Never departed more.
KING: Pretty Ophelia!
OPHELIA: Indeed, la, without an oath, I'll make an end on 't: 55
  [*Sings.*] By Gis[3] and by Saint Charity,
          Alack, and fie for shame!
        Young men will do 't, if they come to 't;
          By Cock,[4] they are to blame.
        Quoth she, before you tumbled me,   60
          You promised me to wed.
    He answers:
        So would I ha' done, by yonder sun,
          An thou hadst not come to my bed.
KING: How long hath she been thus?   65
OPHELIA: I hope all will be well. We must be patient: but I cannot
  choose but weep, to think they should lay him i' the cold ground.
  My brother shall know of it: and so I thank you for your good coun-

---

8. Garnished.   9. Yield—that is, repay.   1. An allusion to a folk tale about a baker's daughter
changed into an owl for having shown no charity to those in need.   2. Opened.   3. By Jesus.
4. Corruption of *God*, but with a sexual undermeaning.

sel. Come, my coach! Good night, ladies; good night, sweet ladies; good night, good night.   70
    [*Exit.*]
KING: Follow her close; give her good watch, I pray you.
    [*Exit* HORATIO.]
O, this is the poison of deep grief; it springs
All from her father's death. O Gertrude, Gertrude,
When sorrows come, they come not single spies,
But in battalions! First, her father slain: 75
Next, your son gone; and he most violent author
Of his own just remove: the people muddied,⁵
Thick and unwholesome in their thoughts and whispers,
For good Polonius' death; and we have done but greenly
In hugger-mugger⁶ to inter him: poor Ophelia   80
Divided from herself and her fair judgment,
Without the which we are pictures, or mere beasts:
Last, and as much containing as all these,
Her brother is in secret come from France,
Feeds on his wonder,⁷ keeps himself in clouds,   85
And wants not buzzers⁸ to infect his ear
With pestilent speeches of his father's death;
Wherein necessity, of matter beggared,⁹
Will nothing stick our person to arraign¹
In ear and ear. O my dear Gertrude, this,   90
Like to a murdering-piece,² in many places
Gives me superfluous death.
    [*A noise within.*]
QUEEN: Alack, what noise is this?
KING: Where are my Switzers?³ Let them guard the door.
    [*Enter another* GENTLEMAN.]
What is the matter?
GENTLEMAN: Save yourself, my lord:
The ocean, overpeering of his list,⁴   95
Eats not the flats with more impetuous haste
Than young Laertes, in a riotous head,⁵
O'erbears your officers. The rabble call him lord;
And, as the world were now but to begin,
Antiquity forgot, custom not known,   100
The ratifiers and props of every word,
They cry 'Choose we; Laertes shall be king!'
Caps, hands and tongues applaud it to the clouds,
'Laertes shall be king, Laertes king!'
QUEEN: How cheerfully on the false trail they cry!   105

---

5. Confused, their thoughts made turbid (as water by mud).   6. Hasty secrecy. *Greenly:* foolishly.
7. Broods, keeps wondering.   8. Lacks not tale-bearers.   9. The necessity to build up a story without the materials for doing so.   1. Will not hesitate to accuse me.   2. A variety of cannon that scattered its shot in many directions.   3. Swiss guards.   4. Overflowing above the high-water mark.
5. Group of rebels.

O, this is counter,[6] you false Danish dogs!
  [*Noise within.*]
KING: The doors are broke.
  [*Enter* LAERTES, *armed;* DANES *following.*]
LAERTES: Where is this king? Sirs, stand you all without.
DANES: No, let's come in.
LAERTES: I pray you, give me leave.
DANES: We will, we will.   110
  [*They retire without the door.*]
LAERTES: I thank you: keep the door. O thou vile king,
  Give me my father!
QUEEN: Calmly, good Laertes.
LAERTES: That drop of blood that's calm proclaims me bastard;
  Cries cuckold to my father; brands the harlot
  Even here, between the chaste unsmirchèd brows   115
  Of my true mother.
KING: What is the cause, Laertes,
  That thy rebellion looks so giant-like?
  Let him go, Gertrude; do not fear[7] our person:
  There's such divinity doth hedge a king,
  That treason can but peep to what it would,[8]   120
  Acts little of his[9] will. Tell me, Laertes,
  Why thou art thus incensed: let him go, Gertrude:
  Speak, man.
LAERTES: Where is my father?
KING: Dead.
QUEEN: But not by him.
KING: Let him demand his fill.   125
LAERTES: How came he dead? I'll not be juggled with:
  To hell, allegiance! vows, to the blackest devil!
  Conscience and grace, to the profoundest pit
  I dare damnation: to this point I stand,
  That both the worlds I give to negligence,[1]   130
  Let come what comes; only I'll be revenged
  Most thoroughly for my father.
KING: Who shall stay you?
LAERTES: My will, not all the world:
  And for my means, I'll husband them so well,
  They shall go far with little.
KING: Good Laertes,   135
  If you desire to know the certainty
  Of your dear father's death, is 't writ in your revenge
  That, swoopstake,[2] you will draw both friend and foe,
  Winner and loser?
LAERTES: None but his enemies.
KING: Will you know them then?   140

6. Following the scent in the wrong direction.   7. Fear for.   8. Look from a distance at what it desires.   9. Its.   1. I don't care what may happen to me in either this world or the next.   2. Without making any distinction, as the winner takes the whole stake in a card game.

LAERTES: To his good friends thus wide I'll ope my arms;
And, like the kind life-rendering pelican,[3]
Repast them with my blood.

KING: Why, now you speak
Like a good child and a true gentleman.
That I am guiltless of your father's death,   145
And am most sensibly in grief for it,
It shall as level to your judgment pierce
As day does to your eye.

DANES: [*Within.*]   Let her come in.

LAERTES: How now! what noise is that?

    [*Re-enter* OPHELIA.]

O heat, dry up my brains! tears seven times salt,   150
Burn out the sense and virtue[4] of mine eye!
By heaven, thy madness shall be paid with weight,
Till our scale turn the beam. O rose of May!
Dear maid, kind sister, sweet Ophelia!
O heavens! is 't possible a young maid's wits   155
Should be as mortal as an old man's life?
Nature is fine in love, and where 'tis fine
It sends some precious instance[5] of itself
After the thing it loves.

OPHELIA: [*Sings.*] They bore him barefaced on the bier: 160
              Hey non nonny, nonny, hey nonny:
                   And in his grave rained many a tear,—
Fare you well, my dove!

LAERTES: Hadst thou thy wits, and didst persuade revenge,
It could not move thus.   165

OPHELIA: [*Sings.*] You must sing down a-down,
              An you call him a-down-a.
O, how the wheel becomes it! It is the false steward,[6] that stole his
master's daughter.

LAERTES: This nothing's more than matter.[7]   170

OPHELIA: There's rosemary, that's for remembrance: pray you, love,
remember: and there is pansies, that's for thoughts.

LAERTES: A document[8] in madness; thoughts and remembrance fitted.

OPHELIA: There's fennel for you, and columbines: there's rue for you:
and here's some for me: we may call it herbs of grace o' Sundays: 175
O, you must wear your rue with a difference. There's a daisy: I
would give you some violets,[9] but they withered all when my father
died: they say he made a good end,—
[*Sings.*] For bonnie sweet Robin is all my joy.

LAERTES: Thought and affliction, passion, hell itself,   180

---

3. In myth, the pelican is supposed to feed its young with its own blood.   4. Power, faculty.
5. Sample, token. *Fine*: refined.   6. An allusion (probably to a lost ballad) further expressing Ophelia's preoccupation with betrayal, lost love, and death. *How the wheel becomes it*: that is, how well the refrain fits.   7. This nonsense is more indicative than sane speech.   8. Lesson. Traditionally, flowers and herbs have symbolic meanings. Here rosemary is the symbol for remembrance and pansies symbolize thoughts.   9. Violets symbolize faithfulness. Fennel stands for flattery, columbines for cuckoldom, and rue for sorrow and repentance (compare the verb *rue*).

She turns to favor[1] and to prettiness.
OPHELIA: [*Sings.*] And will he not come again?
         And will he not come again?
           No, no, he is dead,
             Go to thy death-bed,   185
          He never will come again.
          His beard was as white as snow,
          All flaxen was his poll:
           He is gone, he is gone,
            And we cast away moan: 190
            God ha' mercy on his soul!
And of all Christian souls, I pray God. God be wi' you.
    [*Exit.*]
LAERTES: Do you see this, O God?
KING: Laertes, I must commune with your grief,
Or you deny me right. Go but apart,   195
Make choice of whom your wisest friends you will.
And they shall hear and judge 'twixt you and me:
If by direct or by collateral hand
They find us touched,[2] we will our kingdom give,
Our crown, our life, and all that we call ours,   200
To you in satisfaction; but if not,
Be you content to lend your patience to us,
And we shall jointly labor with your soul
To give it due content.
LAERTES: Let this be so;
His means of death, his obscure funeral,   205
No trophy, sword, nor hatchment[3] o'er his bones,
No noble rite nor formal ostentation,
Cry to be heard, as 'twere from heaven to earth,
That I must call 't in question.
KING: So you shall;
And where the offense is let the great axe fall.   210
I pray you, go with me.
    [*Exeunt.*]

SCENE 6

Another room in the castle.

[*Enter* HORATIO *and a* SERVANT.]
HORATIO: What are they that would speak with me?
SERVANT: Sea-faring men, sir: they say they have letters for you.
HORATIO: Let them come in.
    [*Exit* SERVANT.]
I do not know from what part of the world
I should be greeted, if not from Lord Hamlet.   5
    [*Enter* SAILORS.]

---

1. Charm.   2. Involved (in the murder). *Collateral:* indirect.   3. Coat of arms.

FIRST SAILOR: God bless you, sir.

HORATIO: Let him bless thee too.

FIRST SAILOR: He shall, sir, an 't please him.
There's a letter for you, sir; it comes from the ambassador that was
bound for England; if your name be Horatio, as I am let to know it   10
is.

HORATIO: [*Reads.*] 'Horatio, when thou shalt have overlooked[4] this,
give these fellows some means to the king: they have letters for him.
Ere we were two days old at sea, a pirate of very warlike appointment gave us chase. Finding ourselves too slow of sail, we put on a   15
compelled valor, and in the grapple I boarded them: on the instant
they got clear of our ship; so I alone became their prisoner. They
have dealt with me like thieves of mercy:[5] but they knew what they
did; I am to do a good turn for them. Let the king have the letters I
have sent; and repair thou to me with as much speed as thou wouldst   20
fly death. I have words to speak in thine ear will make thee dumb;
yet are they much too light for the bore[6] of the matter. These good
fellows will bring thee where I am. Rosencrantz and Guildenstern
hold their course for England: of them I have much to tell thee.
Farewell.   25
        'He that thou knowest thine, HAMLET.'
Come, I will make you way for these your letters;
And do 't the speedier, that you may direct me
To him from whom you brought them.
        [*Exeunt.*]

SCENE 7

Another room in the castle.

[*Enter* KING *and* LAERTES.]

KING: Now must your conscience my acquittance seal,
And you must put me in your heart for friend,
Sith you have heard, and with a knowing ear,
That he which hath your noble father slain
Pursued my life.

LAERTES: It well appears: but tell me   5
Why you proceeded not against these feats,
So crimeful and so capital in nature,
As by your safety, wisdom, all things else,
You mainly[7] were stirred up.

KING: O, for two special reasons,
Which may to you perhaps seem much unsinewed,[8]   10
But yet to me they're strong. The queen his mother
Lives almost by his looks; and for myself—
My virtue or my plague, be it either which—
She's so conjunctive[9] to my life and soul,

---

4. Read over.   5. Merciful.   6. Caliber, that is, importance.   7. Powerfully.   8. Weak.
9. Closely joined.

That, as the star moves not but in his sphere,   15
I could not but by her. The other motive,
Why to a public count I might not go,
Is the great love the general gender¹ bear him;
Who, dipping all his faults in their affection,
Would, like the spring that turneth wood to stone,   20
Convert his gyves² to graces; so that my arrows,
Too slightly timber'd for so loud a wind,
Would have reverted to my bow again
And not where I had aim'd them.

LAERTES: And so have I a noble father lost;   25
A sister driven into desperate terms,
Whose worth, if praises may go back again,
Stood challenger on mount of³ all the age
For her perfections: but my revenge will come.

KING: Break not your sleeps for that: you must not think   30
That we are made of stuff so flat and dull
That we can let our beard be shook with danger
And think it pastime. You shortly shall hear more:
I loved your father, and we love ourself;
And that, I hope, will teach you to imagine—   35
    [Enter a MESSENGER, with letters.]
How now! what news?

MESSENGER: Letters, my lord, from Hamlet:
This to your majesty; this to the queen.

KING: From Hamlet! who brought them?

MESSENGER: Sailors, my lord, they say; I saw them not:
They were given me by Claudio; he received them   40
Of him that brought them.

KING: Laertes, you shall hear them.
Leave us.
    [Exit MESSENGER.]
    [Reads.] 'High and mighty, you shall know I am set naked on your
kingdom. To-morrow shall I beg leave to see your kingly eyes: when
I shall, first asking your pardon thereunto, recount the occasion of   45
my sudden and more strange return.   HAMLET.'
What should this mean? Are all the rest come back?
Or is it some abuse, and no such thing?⁴

LAERTES: Know you the hand?

KING: 'Tis Hamlet's character.⁵ 'Naked'!   50
And in a postscript here, he says 'alone.'
Can you advise me?

LAERTES: I'm lost in it, my lord. But let him come;
It warms the very sickness in my heart,
That I shall live and tell him to his teeth,   55
'Thus diddest thou.'

---

1. Common people. *Count:* accounting, trial.   2. Leg irons (shames).   3. Above. *Go back:* to what
she was before her madness.   4. A delusion, not a reality.   5. Handwriting.

KING: If it be so, Laertes,—
    As how should it be so? how otherwise?—
    Will you be ruled by me?

LAERTES: Aye, my lord;
    So you will not o'errule me to a peace.

KING: To thine own peace. If he be now returned,   60
    As checking[6] at his voyage, and that he means
    No more to undertake it, I will work him
    To an exploit now ripe in my device,
    Under the which he shall not choose but fall:
    And for his death no wind of blame shall breathe;   65
    But even his mother shall uncharge the practice,[7]
    call it accident.

LAERTES: My lord, I will be ruled;
    The rather, if you could devise it so
    That I might be the organ.[8]

KING: It falls right.
    You have been talked of since your travel much,   70
    And that in Hamlet's hearing, for a quality
    Wherein, they say, you shine; your sum of parts[9]
    Did not together pluck such envy from him,
    As did that one, and that in my regard
    Of the unworthiest siege.[1]

LAERTES: What part is that, my lord?   75

KING: A very riband in the cap of youth,
    Yet needful too; for youth no less becomes[2]
    The light and careless livery that it wears
    Than settled age his sables and his weeds,[3]
    Importing health and graveness. Two months since   80
    Here was a gentleman of Normandy:—
    I've seen myself, and served against, the French,
    And they can well on horseback: but this gallant
    Had witchcraft in 't; he grew unto his seat,
    And to such wondrous doing brought his horse   85
    As had he been incorpsed and demi-natured[4]
    With the brave beast: so far he topped my thought
    That I, in forgery of shapes and tricks,[5]
    Come short of what he did.

LAERTES: A Norman was 't?

KING: A Norman.   90

LAERTES: Upon my life, Lamord.

KING: The very same.

LAERTES: I know him well: he is the brooch[6] indeed
    And gem of all the nation.

KING: He made confession of you,

---

6. Changing the course of, refusing to continue.   7. Not recognize it as a plot.   8. Instrument.
9. The sum of your gifts.   1. Seat, that is, rank.   2. Is the appropriate age for. *Riband:* ribbon,
ornament.   3. Furs (also meaning "blacks," dark colors) and robes.   4. Incorporated and split his
nature in two.   5. In imagining methods and skills of horsemanship.   6. Ornament.

And gave you such a masterly report, 95
For art and exercise in your defense,[7]
And for your rapier most especial,
That he cried out, 'twould be a sight indeed
If one could match you: the scrimers[8] of their nation,
He swore, had neither motion, guard, nor eye, 100
If you opposed them. Sir, this report of his
Did Hamlet so envenom with his envy
That he could nothing do but wish and beg
Your sudden coming o'er, to play with him.
Now, out of this—

LAERTES: What out of this, my lord? 105

KING: Laertes, was your father dear to you?
Or are you like the painting of a sorrow,
A face without a heart?

LAERTES: Why ask you this?

KING: Not that I think you did not love your father,
But that I know love is begun by time, 110
And that I see, in passages of proof,[9]
Time qualifies[1] the spark and fire of it.
There lives within the very flame of love
A kind of wick or snuff[2] that will abate it;
And nothing is at a like goodness still, 115
For goodness, growing to a plurisy,[3]
Dies in his own too much: that we would do
We should do when we would; for this 'would' changes
And hath abatements and delays as many
As there are tongues, are hands, are accidents, 120
And then this 'should' is like a spendthrift sigh,
That hurts by easing.[4] But, to the quick o' the ulcer:
Hamlet comes back: what would you undertake,
To show yourself your father's son in deed
More than in words?

LAERTES: To cut his throat i' the church. 125

KING: No place indeed should murder sanctuarize;
Revenge should have no bounds. But, good Laertes,
Will you do this, keep close within your chamber.
Hamlet returned shall know you are come home:
We'll put on[5] those shall praise your excellence 130
And set a double varnish on the fame
The Frenchman gave you; bring you in fine together
And wager on your heads: he, being remiss,[6]
Most generous and free from all contriving,
Will not peruse[7] the foils, so that with ease, 135

---

7. Report of your mastery in the theory and practice of fencing.   8. Fencers.   9. Instances that prove it.   1. Weakens.   2. Charred part of the wick.   3. Excess. *Still:* constantly.   4. A sigh that gives relief but is harmful (according to an old notion that it draws blood from the heart).   5. Instigate.   6. Careless. *In fine:* finally.   7. Examine closely.

Or with a little shuffling, you may choose
A sword unbated, and in a pass of practice[8]
Requite him for your father.

LAERTES: I will do 't;
    And for that purpose I'll anoint my sword.
    I bought an unction of a mountebank,[9]   140
    So mortal that but dip a knife in it,
    Where it draws blood no cataplasm so rare,
    Collected from all simples[1] that have virtue
    Under the moon, can save the thing from death
    That is but scratched withal: I'll touch my point   145
    With this contagion, that, if I gall[2] him slightly,
    It may be death.

KING: Let's further think of this;
    Weigh what convenience both of time and means
    May fit us to our shape: if this should fail,
    And that our drift look through[3] our bad performance,   150
    'Twere better not assayed: therefore this project
    Should have a back or second, that might hold
    If this did blast in proof.[4] Soft! let me see:
    We'll make a solemn wager on your cunnings:
    I ha 't: 155
    When in your motion you are hot and dry—
    As make your bouts more violent to that end—
    And that he calls for drink, I'll have prepared him
    A chalice for the nonce;[5] whereon but sipping,
    If he by chance escape your venomed stuck,[6]   160
    Our purpose may hold there. But stay, what noise?
        [Enter QUEEN.]
    How now, sweet queen!

QUEEN: One woe doth tread upon another's heel,
    So fast they follow: your sister's drowned, Laertes.

LAERTES: Drowned! O, where?   165

QUEEN: There is a willow grows aslant[7] a brook,
    That shows his hoar leaves in the glassy stream;
    There with fantastic garlands did she come
    Of crow-flowers, nettles, daisies, and long purples,
    That liberal shepherds give a grosser name,   170
    But our cold maids do dead men's fingers call them:
    There, on the pendent boughs her coronet weeds
    Clambering to hang, an envious sliver[8] broke;
    When down her weedy trophies and herself
    Fell in the weeping brook. Her clothes spread wide,   175
    And mermaid-like a while they bore her up:

8. Treacherous thrust. *Unbated:* not blunted (as a rapier for exercise ordinarily would be).   9. Ointment of a peddler of quack medicines.   1. Healing herbs. *Cataplasm:* plaster.   2. Scratch.
3. Our design should show through. *Shape:* plan.   4. Burst (like a new firearm) once it is put to the
test.   5. For that particular occasion.   6. Thrust.   7. Across.   8. Malicious bough.

Which time she chanted snatches of old tunes,
As one incapable of[9] her own distress,
Or like a creature native and indued[1]
Unto that element: but long it could not be   180
Till that her garments, heavy with their drink,
Pulled the poor wretch from her melodious lay
To muddy death.

LAERTES: Alas, then she is drowned!

QUEEN: Drowned, drowned.

LAERTES: Too much of water hast thou, poor Ophelia,   185
And therefore I forbid my tears: but yet
It is our trick;[2] nature her custom holds,
Let shame say what it will: when these are gone,
The woman[3] will be out. Adieu, my lord:
I have a speech of fire that fain would blaze,   190
But that this folly douts[4] it.
[Exit.]

KING: Let's follow, Gertrude:
How much I had to do to calm his rage!
Now fear I this will give it start again;
Therefore let's follow.
[Exeunt.]

Act V

SCENE 1

A churchyard.

[Enter two CLOWNS, with spades, etc.]

FIRST CLOWN: Is she to be buried in Christian burial that willfully
seeks her own salvation?

SECOND CLOWN: I tell thee she is; and therefore make her grave
straight: the crowner[5] hath sat on her, and finds it Christian burial.

FIRST CLOWN: How can that be, unless she drowned herself in her   5
own defense?

SECOND CLOWN: Why, 'tis found so.

FIRST CLOWN: It must be 'se offendendo;'[6] it cannot be else. For here
lies the point: if I drown myself wittingly, it argues an act: and an
act hath three branches; it is, to act, to do, to perform: argal,[7] she   10
drowned herself wittingly.

SECOND CLOWN: Nay, but hear you, goodman delver.

FIRST CLOWN: Give me leave. Here lies the water; good: here stands
the man; good: if the man go to this water and drown himself, it is,
will he, nill he,[8] he goes; mark you that; but if the water come to   15

9. Insensitive to.   1. Adapted, in harmony with.   2. Peculiar trait.   3. The softer qualities, the
woman in me.   4. Extinguishes.   5. Coroner. *Straight:* right away.   6. The Clown's blunder for
se defendendo: "in self-defense" (Latin).   7. Blunder for *ergo:* "therefore" (Latin).   8. Willy-nilly.

him and drown him, he drowns not himself: argal, he that is not
guilty of his own death shortens not his own life.

SECOND CLOWN: But is this law?

FIRST CLOWN: Aye, marry, is 't; crowner's quest[9] law.

SECOND CLOWN: Will you ha' the truth on 't? If this had not been a   20
gentlewoman, she should have been buried out o' Christian burial.

FIRST CLOWN: Why, there thou say'st: and the more pity that great folk
should have countenance[1] in this world to drown or hang themselves, more than their even[2] Christian. Come, my spade. There is
no ancient gentlemen but gardeners, ditchers and gravemakers: 25
they hold up Adam's profession.

SECOND CLOWN: Was he a gentleman?

FIRST CLOWN: A' was the first that ever bore arms.

SECOND CLOWN: Why, he had none.

FIRST CLOWN: What, art a heathen? How dost thou understand the   30
Scripture? The Scripture says Adam digged: could he dig without
arms? I'll put another question to thee: if thou answerest me not to
the purpose, confess thyself—

SECOND CLOWN: Go to.

FIRST CLOWN: What is he that builds stronger than either the mason,   35
the shipwright, or the carpenter?

SECOND CLOWN: The gallows-maker; for that frame outlives a thousand tenants.

FIRST CLOWN: I like thy wit well, in good faith: the gallows does well;
but how does it well? it does well to those that do ill: now, thou dost   40
ill to say the gallows is built stronger than the church: argal, the gallows may do well to thee. To 't again, come.

SECOND CLOWN: 'Who builds stronger than a mason, a shipwright, or
a carpenter?'

FIRST CLOWN: Aye, tell me that, and unyoke.[3]   45

SECOND CLOWN: Marry, now I can tell.

FIRST CLOWN: To 't.

SECOND CLOWN: Mass, I cannot tell.

> [*Enter* HAMLET *and* HORATIO, *afar off.*]

FIRST CLOWN: Cudgel thy brains no more about it, for your dull ass
will not mend his pace with beating, and when you are asked this   50
question next, say 'a grave-maker:' the houses that he makes last till
doomsday. Go, get thee to Yaughan; fetch me a stoup[4] of liquor.

> [*Exit* SECOND CLOWN.—FIRST CLOWN *digs and sings.*]

In youth, when I did love, did love,
    Methought it was very sweet,
To contract, O, the time, for-a my behove,   55
    O, methought, there-a was nothing-a meet.[5]

HAMLET: Has this fellow no feeling of his business that he sings at
grave-making?

---

9. Inquest.   1. Sanction.   2. Fellow.   3. Call it a day.   4. Mug. *Yaughan:* apparently a tavern
keeper's name.   5. Fitting. *Contract:* shorten. *Behove:* profit.

HORATIO: Custom hath made it in him a property of easiness.[6]

HAMLET: 'Tis e'en so: the hand of little employment hath the daintier[7]   60
sense.

FIRST CLOWN: [*Sings.*] But age, with his stealing steps,
                              Hath clowed me in his clutch,
                              And hath shipped me intil[8] the land,
                              As if I had never been such.   65
      [*Throws up a skull.*]

HAMLET: That skull had a tongue in it, and could sing once: how the
knave jowls it to the ground, as if it were Cain's jaw-bone, that did
the first murder! It might be the pate of a politician,[9] which this ass
now o'er-reaches;[1] one that would circumvent God, might it not?

HORATIO: It might, my lord.   70

HAMLET: Or of a courtier, which could say, 'Good morrow, sweet lord!
How dost thou, sweet lord?' This might be my lord such-a-one, that
praised my lord such-a-one's horse, when he meant to beg it; might
it not?

HORATIO: Aye, my lord.   75

HAMLET: Why, e'en so: and now my Lady Worm's; chapless, and
knocked about the mazzard[2] with a sexton's spade: here's fine revolution, an we had the trick to see 't. Did these bones cost no more
the breeding, but to play at loggats[3] with 'em? mine ache to think
on 't.   80

FIRST CLOWN: [*Sings.*] A pick-axe, and a spade, a spade,
                              For a shrouding sheet:
                              O, a pit of clay for to be made
                              For such a guest is meet.
      [*Throws up another skull.*]

HAMLET: There's another: why may not that be the skull of a lawyer?   85
Where be his quiddities now, his quillets, his cases, his tenures,[4]
and his tricks? why does he suffer this rude knave now to knock
him about the sconce with a dirty shovel, and will not tell him of
his action of battery?[5] Hum! This fellow might be in 's time a great
buyer of land, with his statutes, his recognizances,[6] his fines, his   90
double vouchers, his recoveries: is this the fine[7] of his fines and the
recovery of his recoveries, to have his fine pate full of fine dirt? will
his vouchers vouch him no more of his purchases, and double ones
too, than the length and breadth of a pair of indentures? The very
conveyances[8] of his lands will hardly lie in this box; and must the   95
inheritor himself have no more, ha?

HORATIO: Not a jot more, my lord.

HAMLET: Is not parchment made of sheep-skins?

---

6. Has made it a matter of indifference to him.   7. Finer sensitivity. *Of little employment:* that does
little labor.   8. Into.   9. In a pejorative sense. *Jowls:* knocks. *First murder:* possibly an allusion to
the legend that Cain slew Abel with an ass's jawbone.   1. Outwits.   2. Pate. *Chapless:* the lower
jawbone missing.   3. A game resembling bowls. *Trick:* faculty.   4. Real estate holdings. *Quiddities:*
subtle definitions. *Quillets:* quibbles.   5. Assault. *Sconce:* head.   6. Varieties of bonds. This passage
contains legal terms relating to the transfer of estates.   7. End. Hamlet is punning on the legal and
nonlegal meanings of the word.   8. Deeds. *Indentures:* contracts drawn in duplicate on the same
piece of parchment; the two copies were separated by an indented line.

HORATIO: Aye, my lord, and of calf-skins too.

HAMLET: They are sheep and calves which seek out assurance[9] in that.   100
I will speak to this fellow. Whose grave's this, sirrah?

FIRST CLOWN: Mine, sir.

[*Sings.*] O, a pit of clay for to be made
      For such a guest is meet.

HAMLET: I think it be thine indeed, for thou liest in 't.   105

FIRST CLOWN: You lie out on 't, sir, and therefore 'tis not yours: for my
part, I do not lie in 't, and yet it is mine.

HAMLET: Thou dost lie in 't, to be in 't and say it is thine: 'tis for the
dead, not for the quick;[1] therefore thou liest.

FIRST CLOWN: 'Tis a quick lie, sir; 'twill away again, from me to you.   110

HAMLET: What man dost thou dig it for?

FIRST CLOWN: For no man, sir.

HAMLET: What woman then?

FIRST CLOWN: For none neither.

HAMLET: Who is to be buried in 't?   115

FIRST CLOWN: One that was a woman, sir; but, rest her soul, she's
dead.

HAMLET: How absolute the knave is! we must speak by the card,[2] or
equivocation will undo us. By the Lord, Horatio, these three years
I have taken note of it; the age is grown so picked[3] that the toe of   120
the peasant comes so near the heel of the courtier, he galls his
kibe.[4] How long hast thou been a grave-maker?

FIRST CLOWN: Of all the days i' the year, I came to 't that day that our
last King Hamlet o'ercame Fortinbras.

HAMLET: How long is that since?   125

FIRST CLOWN: Cannot you tell that? every fool can tell that: it was that
very day that young Hamlet was born: he that is mad, and sent into
England.

HAMLET: Aye, marry, why was he sent into England?

FIRST CLOWN: Why, because a' was mad; a' shall recover his wits there: 130
or, if a' do not, 'tis no great matter there.

HAMLET: Why?

FIRST CLOWN: 'Twill not be seen in him there; there the men are as
mad as he.

HAMLET: How came he mad?   135

FIRST CLOWN: Very strangely, they say.

HAMLET: How 'strangely'?

FIRST CLOWN: Faith, e'en with losing his wits.

HAMLET: Upon what ground?

FIRST CLOWN: Why, here in Denmark: I have been sexton here, man   140
and boy, thirty years.

HAMLET: How long will a man lie i' the earth ere he rot?

FIRST CLOWN: I' faith, if a' be not rotten before a' die—as we have
many pocky corses now-a-days, that will scarce hold the laying

---

9. Security; another pun, because the word is also a legal term.   1. Living.   2. By the chart, that
is, exactness. *Absolute*: positive.   3. Choice, fastidious.   4. Hurts the chilblain on the courtier's
heel.

in[5]—a' will last you some eight year or nine year: a tanner will last   145
    you nine year.
HAMLET: Why he more than another?
FIRST CLOWN: Why, sir, his hide is so tanned with his trade that a' will
    keep out water a great while; and your water is a sore decayer of
    your whoreson dead body. Here's a skull now: this skull has lain in   150
    the earth three and twenty years.
HAMLET: Whose was it?
FIRST CLOWN: A whoreson mad fellow's it was: whose do you think it
    was?
HAMLET: Nay, I know not.   155
FIRST CLOWN: A pestilence on him for a mad rogue! a' poured a flagon
    of Rhenish on my head once. This same skull, sir, was Yorick's
    skull, the king's jester.
HAMLET: This?
FIRST CLOWN: E'en that.   160
HAMLET: Let me see. [*Takes the skull.*] Alas, poor Yorick! I knew him,
    Horatio: a fellow of infinite jest, of most excellent fancy: he hath
    borne me on his back a thousand times; and now how abhorred in
    my imagination it is! my gorge rises at it. Here hung those lips that
    I have kissed I know not how oft. Where be your gibes now? your   165
    gambols? your songs? your flashes of merriment, that were wont to
    set the table on a roar? Not one now, to mock your own grinning?
    quite chop-fallen?[6] Now get you to my lady's chamber, and tell her,
    let her paint an inch thick, to this favor[7] she must come; make her
    laugh at that. Prithee, Horatio, tell me one thing.   170
HORATIO: What's that, my lord?
HAMLET: Dost thou think Alexander looked o' this fashion i' the earth?
HORATIO: E'en so.
HAMLET: And smelt so? pah!
    [*Puts down the skull.*]
HORATIO: E'en so, my lord.   175
HAMLET: To what base uses we may return, Horatio! Why may not
    imagination trace the noble dust of Alexander, till he find it stop-
    ping a bung-hole?
HORATIO: 'Twere to consider too curiously, to consider so.
HAMLET: No, faith, not a jot; but to follow him thither with modesty   180
    enough[8] and likelihood to lead it: as thus: Alexander died, Alexan-
    der was buried, Alexander returneth into dust; the dust is earth; of
    earth we make loam; and why of that loam, whereto he was con-
    verted, might they not stop a beer-barrel?
        Imperious Caesar, dead and turned to clay,   185
        Might stop a hole to keep the wind away:
        O, that that earth, which kept the world in awe,
        Should patch a wall to expel the winter's flaw!

---

5. Hold together till they are buried. *Pocky:* with marks of disease (from "pox").   6. The lower jaw
fallen down, hence dejected.   7. Appearance.   8. Without exaggeration.

But soft! but soft! aside: here comes the king.
  [*Enter* PRIESTS *etc., in procession; the Corpse of Ophelia,* LAERTES
  and MOURNERS *following;* KING, QUEEN, *their trains, etc.*]
The queen, the courtiers: who is this they follow? 190
And with such maimèd rites?[9] This doth betoken
The corse they follow did with desperate hand
Fordo its own life: 'twas of some estate.[1]
Couch we awhile, and mark.
  [*Retiring with* HORATIO.]
LAERTES: What ceremony else? 195
HAMLET: That is Laertes, a very noble youth: mark.
LAERTES: What ceremony else?
FIRST PRIEST: Her obsequies have been as far enlarged
  As we have warranty: her death was doubtful;
  And, but that great command o'ersways the order[2] 200
  She should in ground unsanctified have lodged
  Till the last trumpet; for[3] charitable prayers,
  Shards, flints and pebbles should be thrown on her:
  Yet here she is allowed her virgin crants,
  Her maiden strewments and the bringing home[4] 205
  Of bell and burial.
LAERTES: Must there no more be done?
FIRST PRIEST: No more be done:
  We should profane the service of the dead
  To sing a requiem and such rest to her
  As to peace-parted souls.
LAERTES: Lay her i' the earth: 210
  And from her fair and unpolluted flesh
  May violets spring! I tell thee, churlish priest,
  A ministering angel shall my sister be,
  When thou liest howling.
HAMLET: What, the fair Ophelia!
QUEEN: [*Scattering flowers.*] Sweets to the sweet: farewell! 215
  I hoped thou shouldst have been my Hamlet's wife;
  I thought thy bride-bed to have decked, sweet maid,
  And not have strewed thy grave.
LAERTES: O, treble woe
  Fall ten times treble on that cursed head
  Whose wicked deed thy most ingenious sense 220
  Deprived thee of! Hold off the earth a while,
  Till I have caught her once more in mine arms.
  [*Leaps into the grave.*]
  Now pile your dust upon the quick and dead,
  Till of this flat a mountain you have made

9. Incomplete, mutilated ritual. 1. Rank. *Fordo:* destroy. 2. The king's command prevails against ordinary rules. *Doubtful:* of uncertain cause (that is, accident or suicide). 3. Instead of. 4. Laying to rest. *Crants:* garlands. *Strewments:* strews the grave with flowers.

To o'ertop old Pelion[5] or the skyish head   225
Of blue Olympus.
HAMLET: [*Advancing.*] What is he whose grief
  Bears such an emphasis? whose phrase of sorrow
  Conjures the wandering stars and makes them stand
  Like wonder-wounded hearers? This is I,   230
  Hamlet the Dane.
    [*Leaps into the grave.*]
LAERTES: The devil take thy soul!
    [*Grappling with him.*]
HAMLET: Thou pray'st not well.
  I prithee, take thy fingers from my throat;
  For, though I am not splenitive[6] and rash,
  Yet have I in me something dangerous,   235
  Which let thy wisdom fear. Hold off thy hand.
KING: Pluck them asunder.
QUEEN: Hamlet, Hamlet!
ALL: Gentlemen,—
HORATIO: Good my lord, be quiet.
    [*The* ATTENDANTS *part them, and they come out of the grave.*]
HAMLET: Why, I will fight with him upon this theme
  Until my eyelids will no longer wag.   240
QUEEN: O my son, what theme?
HAMLET: I loved Ophelia: forty thousand brothers
  Could not, with all their quantity of love,
  Make up my sum. What wilt thou do for her?
KING: O, he is mad, Laertes.   245
QUEEN: For love of God, forbear him.
HAMLET: 'Swounds, show me what thou 'lt do:
  Woo't weep? woo't fight? woo't fast? woo't tear thyself?
  Woo't drink up eisel?[7] eat a crocodile?
  I'll do't. Dost thou come here to whine?   250
  To outface me with leaping in her grave?
  Be buried quick with her, and so will I:
  And, if thou prate of mountains, let them throw
  Millions of acres on us, till our ground,
  Singeing his pate against the burning zone,   255
  Make Ossa like a wart! Nay, an thou 'lt mouth,
  I'll rant as well as thou.
QUEEN: This is mere madness:
  And thus a while the fit will work on him;
  Anon, as patient as the female dove
  When that her golden couplets are disclosed,[8]   260
  His silence will sit drooping.
HAMLET: Hear you, sir;

---

5. The mountain on which the Aloadae, two rebellious giants in Greek mythology, piled up Mount Ossa in their attempt to reach Olympus.   6. Easily moved to anger.   7. Vinegar (the bitter drink given to Christ). *Woo't*: wilt thou.   8. Twins are hatched.

What is the reason that you use me thus?
I loved you ever: but it is no matter;
Let Hercules himself do what he may,
The cat will mew, and dog will have his day.   265
    [*Exit.*]
KING: I pray thee, good Horatio, wait upon him.
    [*Exit* HORATIO.]
[*To* LAERTES.] Strengthen your patience in our last night's speech;
We'll put the matter to the present push.[9]
Good Gertrude, set some watch over your son.
This grave shall have a living monument: 270
An hour of quiet shortly shall we see;
Till then, in patience our proceeding be.
    [*Exeunt.*]

SCENE 2

A hall in the castle.

[*Enter* HAMLET *and* HORATIO.]
HAMLET: So much for this, sir: now shall you see the other;
    You do remember all the circumstance?
HORATIO: Remember it, my lord?
HAMLET: Sir, in my heart there was a kind of fighting,
    That would not let me sleep: methought I lay   5
    Worse than the mutines in the bilboes.[1] Rashly,
    And praised be rashness for it, let us know,
    Our indiscretion sometime serves us well
    When our deep plots do pall;[2] and that should learn us
    There's a divinity that shapes our ends,   10
    Rough-hew them how we will.
HORATIO: That is most certain.
HAMLET: Up from my cabin,
    My sea-gown scarfed about me, in the dark
    Groped I to find out them; had my desire,
    Fingered their packet, and in fine withdrew   15
    To mine own room again; making so bold,
    My fears forgetting manners, to unseal
    Their grand commission; where I found, Horatio,—
    O royal knavery!—an exact command,
    Larded with many several sorts of reasons,   20
    Importing[3] Denmark's health and England's too,
    With, ho! such bugs and goblins in my life,
    That, on the supervise, no leisure bated,[4]
    No, not to stay the grinding of the axe,
    My head should be struck off.

---

9. We'll push the matter on immediately.   1. Mutineers in iron fetters.   2. Become useless.
3. Concerning.   4. As soon as the message was read, with no time subtracted for leisure. *Bugs:* imaginary horrors to be expected if I lived.

HORATIO: Is't possible?   25
HAMLET: Here's the commission: read it at more leisure.
  But wilt thou hear now how I did proceed?
HORATIO: I beseech you.
HAMLET: Being thus be-netted round with villainies, —
  Ere I could make a prologue to my brains,   30
  They had begun the play, — I sat me down;
  Devised a new commission; wrote it fair:
  I once did hold it, as our statists[5] do,
  A baseness to write fair, and labored much
  How to forget that learning; but, sir, now   35
  It did me yeoman's service:[6] wilt thou know
  The effect of what I wrote?
HORATIO: Aye, good my lord.
HAMLET: An earnest conjuration from the king,
  As England was his faithful tributary,
  As love between them like the palm might flourish,   40
  As peace should still her wheaten garland wear
  And stand a comma[7] 'tween their amities,
  And many such-like 'As'es of great charge,[8]
  That, on the view and knowing of these contents,
  Without debatement further, more or less,   45
  He should the bearers put to sudden death,
  Not shriving-time[9] allowed.
HORATIO: How was this sealed?
HAMLET: Why, even in that was heaven ordinant.[1]
  I had my father's signet in my purse,
  Which was the model of that Danish seal: 50
  Folded the writ up in the form of the other;
  Subscribed it; gave 't the impression;[2] placed it safely,
  The changeling never known. Now, the next day
  Was our sea-fight; and what to this was sequent
  Thou know'st already.   55
HORATIO: So Guildenstern and Rosencrantz go to 't.
HAMLET: Why, man, they did make love to this employment;
  They are not near my conscience; their defeat
  Does by their own insinuation[3] grow:
  'Tis dangerous when the baser nature comes   60
  Between the pass and fell[4]-incensèd points
  Of mighty opposites.
HORATIO: Why, what a king is this!
HAMLET: Does it not, think'st thee, stand me now upon[5] —
  He that hath killed my king, and whored my mother;
  Popped in between the election and my hopes;   65

---

5. Statesmen.   6. Excellent service.   7. Connecting element.   8. As'es: a pun on *as* and *ass,*
which extends to *of great charge,* signifying both "moral weight" and "ass's burden."   9. Time for
confession and absolution.   1. Ordaining.   2. Of the seal.   3. Meddling. *Defeat:* destruction.
4. Fiercely. *Baser:* lower in rank than the king and Prince Hamlet. *Pass:* thrust.   5. Is it not my duty
now?

Thrown out his angle for my proper life,[6]
And with such cozenage—is't not perfect conscience,
To quit[7] him with this arm? and is't not to be damned,
To let this canker of our nature come
In further evil?   70
HORATIO: It must be shortly known to him from England
What is the issue of the business there.
HAMLET: It will be short: the interim is mine;
And a man's life's no more than to say 'One.'
But I am very sorry, good Horatio,   75
That to Laertes I forgot myself;
For, by the image of my cause, I see
The portraiture of his: I'll court his favors:
But, sure, the bravery[8] of his grief did put me
Into a towering passion.
HORATIO: Peace! who comes here?   80
       [Enter OSRIC.]
OSRIC: Your lordship is right welcome back to Denmark.
HAMLET: I humbly thank you, sir. Dost know this waterfly?
HORATIO: No, my good lord.
HAMLET: Thy state is the more gracious, for 'tis a vice to know him.
He hath much land, and fertile: let a beast be lord of beasts, and   85
his crib shall stand at the king's mess: 'tis a chough,[9] but, as I say,
spacious in the possession of dirt.
OSRIC: Sweet lord, if your lordship were at leisure, I should impart a
thing to you from his majesty.
HAMLET: I will receive it, sir, with all diligence of spirit. Put your   90
bonnet to his right use; 'tis for the head.
OSRIC: I thank your lordship, it is very hot.
HAMLET: No, believe me, 'tis very cold; the wind is northerly.
OSRIC: It is indifferent[1] cold, my lord, indeed.
HAMLET: But yet methinks it is very sultry and hot, or my complex-   95
ion—
OSRIC: Exceedingly, my lord; it is very sultry, as 'twere,—I cannot tell
how. But, my lord, his majesty bade me signify to you that he has
laid a great wager on your head: sir, this is the matter—
HAMLET: I beseech you, remember—   100
       [HAMLET moves him to put on his hat.]
OSRIC: Nay, good my lord; for mine ease, in good faith. Sir, here is
newly come to court Laertes; believe me, an absolute gentleman,
full of most excellent differences, of very soft society and great
showing:[2] indeed, to speak feelingly of him, he is the card or calendar of gentry,[3] for you shall find in him the continent of what part[4]   105
a gentleman would see.
HAMLET: Sir, his definement suffers no perdition in you; though, I

6. An angling line for my own life.   7. Pay back.   8. Ostentation, bravado.   9. Jackdaw. Mess:
table.   1. Fairly.   2. Agreeable company, handsome in appearance. Differences: distinctions.
3. Chart and model of gentlemanly manners.   4. Whatever quality. Continent: container.

know, to divide him inventorially would dizzy the arithmetic[5] of
memory, and yet but yaw neither, in respect of his quick sail.[6] But
in the verity of extolment, I take him to be a soul of great article,   110
and his infusion[7] of such dearth and rareness, as, to make true diction of him, his semblable is his mirror, and who else would trace
him, his umbrage,[8] nothing more.

OSRIC: Your lordship speaks most infallibly of him.

HAMLET: The concernancy, sir? why do we wrap the gentleman[9] in   115
our more rawer breath?

OSRIC: Sir?

HORATIO: Is 't not possible to understand in another tongue?[1] You will
do 't, sir, really.

HAMLET: What imports the nomination of this gentleman?   120

OSRIC: Of Laertes?

HORATIO: His purse is empty already; all 's golden words are spent.

HAMLET: Of him, sir.

OSRIC: I know you are not ignorant—

HAMLET: I would you did, sir; yet, in faith, if you did, it would not   125
much approve me.[2] Well, sir?

OSRIC: You are not ignorant of what excellence Laertes is—

HAMLET: I dare not confess that, lest I should compare with him in
excellence; but, to know a man well, were to know himself.[3]

OSRIC: I mean, sir, for his weapon; but in the imputation laid on him   130
by them, in his meed he 's unfellowed.[4]

HAMLET: What 's his weapon?

OSRIC: Rapier and dagger.

HAMLET: That 's two of his weapons: but, well.

OSRIC: The king, sir, hath wagered with him six Barbary horses: against 135
the which he has imponed, as I take it, six French rapiers and pon-
iards, with their assigns,[5] as girdle, hanger, and so: three of the
carriages, in faith, are very dear to fancy, very responsive[6] to the
hilts, most delicate carriages, and of very liberal conceit.[7]

HAMLET: What call you the carriages?   140

HORATIO: I knew you must be edified by the margent[8] ere you had
done.

OSRIC: The carriages, sir, are the hangers.

HAMLET: The phrase would be more germane to the matter if we could
carry a cannon by our sides:[9] I would it might be hangers till then.   145
But, on: six Barbary horses against six French swords, their assigns,
and three liberal-conceited carriages; that 's the French bet against
the Danish. Why is this 'imponed,' as you call it?

5. Arithmetical power. *Definement:* definition. *Perdition:* loss. *Inventorially:* make an inventory of his
virtues.   6. And yet would only be able to steer unsteadily (unable to catch up with the *sail* of Laertes's
virtues).   7. The virtues infused into him. *Verify of extolment:* to prize Laertes truthfully. *Article:*
importance.   8. Keep pace with him, his shadow.   9. Laertes. *Concernancy:* meaning.   1. In a
less affected jargon or in the same jargon when spoken by another (that is, Hamlet's) tongue.   2. Be
to my credit.   3. To know others one has to know oneself.   4. In the reputation given him by
his weapons, his merit is unparalleled.   5. Appendages. *Imponed:* wagered.   6. Closely matched.
Carriages: ornamented straps by which the rapiers hung from the belt. *Very dear to fancy:* agreeable to
the taste.   7. Elegant design.   8. Instructed by the marginal note.   9. Hamlet is playfully criticizing Osric's affected application of the term *carriage*, more properly used to mean "gun carriage."

OSRIC: The king, sir, hath laid, sir, that in a dozen passes between
yourself and him, he shall not exceed you three hits: he hath laid   150
on twelve for nine; and it would come to immediate trial, if your
lordship would vouchsafe the answer.[1]

HAMLET: How if I answer 'no'?

OSRIC: I mean, my lord, the opposition of your person in trial.

HAMLET: Sir, I will walk here in the hall: if it please his majesty, it is   155
the breathing time[2] of day with me; let the foils be brought, the
gentleman willing, and the king hold his purpose, I will win for
him an I can; if not, I will gain nothing but my shame and the
odd hits.

OSRIC: Shall I redeliver you e'en so?[3]   160

HAMLET: To this effect, sir, after what flourish your nature will.

OSRIC: I commend my duty to your lordship.

HAMLET: Yours, yours. [*Exit* OSRIC.] He does well to commend it
himself; there are no tongues else for's turn.

HORATIO: This lapwing[4] runs away with the shell on his head.   165

HAMLET: He did comply with his dug before he sucked it. Thus has
he—and many more of the same breed that I know the drossy[5]
age dotes on—only got the tune of the time and outward habit of
encounter; a kind of yesty[6] collection, which carries them through
and through the most fond and winnowed opinions;[7] and do but   170
blow them to their trial, the bubbles are out.

   [*Enter a* LORD.]

LORD: My lord, his majesty commended him[8] to you by young Osric,
who brings back to him, that you attend him in the hall: he sends
to know if your pleasure hold to play with Laertes, or that you will
take longer time.   175

HAMLET: I am constant to my purposes; they follow the king's pleasure: if his fitness speaks, mine is ready; now or whensoever, provided I be so able as now.

LORD: The king and queen and all are coming down.

HAMLET: In happy time.   180

LORD: The queen desires you to use some gentle entertainment[9] to
Laertes before you fall to play.

HAMLET: She well instructs me.

   [*Exit* LORD.]

HORATIO: You will lose this wager, my lord.

HAMLET: I do not think so; since he went into France, I have been in   185
continual practice; I shall win at the odds. But thou wouldst not
think how ill all's here about my heart: but it is no matter.

HORATIO: Nay, good my lord,—

HAMLET: It is but foolery; but it is such a kind of gaingiving[1] as would
perhaps trouble a woman.   190

---

1. The terms of this wager have never been satisfactorily clarified.   2. Time for exercise.   3. Is that
the reply you want me to carry back?   4. A bird supposedly able to run as soon as it is out of its shell.
5. Degenerate. *Comply:* use ceremony.   6. Frothy.   7. Makes them pass the test of the most refined
judgment.   8. Sent his regards.   9. Kind word of greeting.   1. Misgiving.

HORATIO: If your mind dislike anything, obey it. I will forestall their
repair[2] hither, and say you are not fit.

HAMLET: Not a whit; we defy augury: there is special providence in the
fall of a sparrow. If it be now, 'tis not to come; if it be not to come,
it will be now; if it be not now, yet it will come: the readiness is   195
all; since no man has aught of what he leaves, what is't to leave
betimes?[3] Let be.

[*Enter* KING, QUEEN, LAERTES, *and* LORDS, OSRIC *and other* ATTEN-
DANTS *with foils and gauntlets; a table and flagons of wine on it.*]

KING: Come, Hamlet, come, and take this hand from me.

[*The* KING *puts* LAERTES' *hand into* HAMLET'*s.*]

HAMLET: Give me your pardon, sir: I've done you wrong;
But pardon't, as you are a gentleman.   200
This presence[4] knows,
And you must needs have heard, how I am punished
With sore distraction. What I have done,
That might your nature, honor and exception[5]
Roughly awake, I here proclaim was madness.   205
Was't Hamlet wronged Laertes? Never Hamlet:
If Hamlet from himself be ta'en away,
And when he's not himself does wrong Laertes,
Then Hamlet does it not, Hamlet denies it.
Who does it then? His madness: if't be so,   210
Hamlet is of the faction that is wronged;
His madness is poor Hamlet's enemy.
Sir, in this audience,
Let my disclaiming from a purposed evil
Free me so far in your most generous thoughts,   215
That I have shot mine arrow o'er the house,
And hurt my brother.

LAERTES: I am satisfied in nature,
Whose motive, in this case, should stir me most
To my revenge: but in my terms of honor[6]
I stand aloof, and will no reconcilement,   220
Till by some elder masters of known honor
I have a voice and precedent of peace,
To keep my name ungored.[7] But till that time
I do receive your offered love like love
And will not wrong it.

HAMLET: I embrace it freely,   225
And will this brother's wager frankly play.
Give us the foils. Come on.

LAERTES: Come, one for me.

HAMLET: I'll be your foil,[8] Laertes: in mine ignorance

2. Coming.   3. What is wrong with dying early (leaving *betimes*), because man knows nothing of life
(*what he leaves*)?   4. Audience.   5. Objection.   6. Laertes answers separately each of the two
points brought up by Hamlet in line 86. *Nature* is Laertes's natural feeling toward his father. *Honor* is
the code of honor with its conventional rules.   7. Unwounded. A *voice and:* an opinion based on.
8. A pun, because *foil* means both "rapier" and "a thing that sets off another to advantage" (as gold leaf
under a jewel).

Your skill shall, like a star i' the darkest night,
Stick fiery off[9] indeed.
LAERTES: You mock me, sir.   230
HAMLET: No, by this hand.
KING: Give them the foils, young Osric. Cousin Hamlet,
You know the wager?
HAMLET: Very well, my lord;
Your grace has laid the odds o' the weaker side.
KING: I do not fear it; I have seen you both: 235
But since he is bettered, we have therefore odds.
LAERTES: This is too heavy; let me see another.
HAMLET: This likes me well. These foils have all a length?
    [*They prepare to play.*]
OSRIC: Aye, my good lord.
KING: Set me the stoups[1] of wine upon that table.   240
If Hamlet give the first or second hit,
Or quit in answer of the third exchange,[2]
Let all the battlements their ordnance fire;
The king shall drink to Hamlet's better breath;
And in the cup an union[3] shall he throw,   245
Richer than that which four successive kings
In Denmark's crown have worn. Give me the cups;
And let the kettle[4] to the trumpet speak,
The trumpet to the cannoneer without,
The cannons to the heavens, the heaven to earth,   250
'Now the king drinks to Hamlet.' Come, begin;
And you, the judges, bear a wary eye.
HAMLET: Come on, sir.
LAERTES: Come, my lord.
    [*They play.*]
HAMLET: One.
LAERTES: No.
HAMLET: Judgment.
OSRIC: A hit, a very palpable hit.
LAERTES: Well; again.
KING: Stay; give me drink. Hamlet, this pearl is thine;   255
Here's to thy health.
    [*Trumpets sound, and cannon shot off within.*]
                        Give him the cup.
HAMLET: I'll play this bout first; set it by awhile.
Come. [*They play.*] Another hit; what say you?
LAERTES: A touch, a touch, I do confess.
KING: Our son shall win.
QUEEN: He's fat and scant of breath.   260
Here, Hamlet, take my napkin,[5] rub thy brows:
The queen carouses to thy fortune, Hamlet.

9. Stand out brilliantly.   1. Cups.   2. Requite, or repay (by scoring a hit) on the third bout.   3. A
large pearl.   4. Kettledrum.   5. Handkerchief. *Fat*: sweaty, or soft, because out of training.

HAMLET: Good madam!
KING: Gertrude, do not drink.
QUEEN: I will, my lord; I pray you, pardon me.
KING: [*Aside.*] It is the poisoned cup; it is too late.   265
QUEEN: Come, let me wipe thy face.
LAERTES: My lord, I'll hit him now.
KING: I do not think't.
LAERTES: [*Aside.*] And yet it is almost against my conscience.
HAMLET: Come, for the third, Laertes: you but dally;
    I pray you, pass with your best violence;   270
    I am afeard you make a wanton[6] of me.
LAERTES: Say you so? come on.
    [*They play.*]
OSRIC: Nothing, neither way.
LAERTES: Have at you now!
    [LAERTES *wounds* HAMLET; *then, in scuffling, they change rapiers,*
    and HAMLET *wounds* LAERTES.]
KING: Part them; they are incensed.
HAMLET: Nay, come, again.
    [*The* QUEEN *falls.*]
OSRIC: Look to the queen there, ho!   275
HORATIO: They bleed on both sides. How is it, my lord?
OSRIC: How is't, Laertes?
LAERTES: Why, as a woodcock to mine own springe,[7] Osric;
    I am justly killed with mine own treachery.
HAMLET: How does the queen?   280
KING: She swounds to see them bleed.
QUEEN: No, no, the drink, the drink,—O my dear Hamlet,—
    The drink, the drink! I am poisoned.
    [*Dies.*]
HAMLET: O villainy! Ho! let the door be locked:
    Treachery! seek it out.   285
    [LAERTES *falls.*]
LAERTES: It is here, Hamlet: Hamlet, thou art slain;
    No medicine in the world can do thee good,
    In thee there is not half an hour of life;
    The treacherous instrument is in thy hand,
    Unbated and envenomed: the foul practice[8]   290
    Hath turned itself on me; lo, here I lie,
    Never to rise again: thy mother's poisoned:
    I can no more: the king, the king's to blame.
HAMLET: The point envenomed too!
    Then, venom, to thy work.   295
    [*Stabs the* KING.]
ALL: Treason! treason!
KING: O, yet defend me, friends; I am but hurt.
HAMLET: Here, thou incestuous, murderous, damnèd Dane,

6. Weakling, spoiled child.   7. Snare.   8. Plot.

Drink off this potion: is thy union here?
Follow my mother.
   [KING *dies*.]

LAERTES: He is justly served;   300
It is a poison tempered[9] by himself.
Exchange forgiveness with me, noble Hamlet:
Mine and my father's death come not upon thee,
Nor thine on me!
   [*Dies*.]

HAMLET: Heaven make thee free of it! I follow thee.   305
I am dead, Horatio. Wretched queen, adieu!
You that look pale and tremble at this chance,
That are but mutes or audience to this act,
Had I but time—as this fell sergeant, death,
Is strict in his arrest—O, I could tell you—   310
But let it be. Horatio, I am dead;
Thou livest; report me and my cause aright
To the unsatisfied.

HORATIO: Never believe it:
I am more an antique Roman than a Dane:
Here's yet some liquor left.

HAMLET: As thou'rt a man,   315
Give me the cup: let go; by heaven, I'll have 't.
O good Horatio, what a wounded name,
Things standing thus unknown, shall live behind me!
If thou didst ever hold me in thy heart,
Absent thee from felicity a while,   320
And in this harsh world draw thy breath in pain,
To tell my story.
   [*March afar off, and shot within*.]
                What warlike noise is this?

OSRIC: Young Fortinbras, with conquest come from Poland,
To the ambassadors of England gives
This warlike volley.

HAMLET: O, I die, Horatio;   325
The potent poison quite o'er-crows[1] my spirit:
I cannot live to hear the news from England;
But I do prophesy the election lights
On Fortinbras: he has my dying voice;
So tell him, with the occurrents, more and less,   330
Which have solicited.[2] The rest is silence.
   [*Dies*.]

HORATIO: Now cracks a noble heart. Good night sweet prince,
And flights of angels sing thee to thy rest;
   [*March within*.]
Why does the drum come hither?

---

9. Compounded. 1. Overcomes. 2. Which have brought all this about. *Occurrents*: occurrences.

[*Enter* FORTINBRAS, *and the* ENGLISH AMBASSADORS, *with drum, colors, and* ATTENDANTS.]

FORTINBRAS: Where is this sight?

HORATIO: What is it you would see?   335
If aught of woe or wonder, cease your search.

FORTINBRAS: This quarry cries on havoc.[3] O proud death,
What feast is toward[4] in thine eternal cell,
That thou so many princes at a shot
So bloodily hast struck?

FIRST AMBASSADOR: The sight is dismal;   340
And our affairs from England come too late:
The ears are senseless that should give us hearing,
To tell him his commandment is fulfilled,
That Rosencrantz and Guildenstern are dead:
Where should we have our thanks?

HORATIO: Not from his mouth   345
Had it the ability of life to thank you:
He never gave commandment for their death.
But since, so jump upon[5] this bloody question,
You from the Polack wars, and you from England
Are here arrived, give order that these bodies   350
High on a stage be placèd to the view;
And let me speak to the yet unknowing world
How these things came about; so shall you hear
Of carnal, bloody and unnatural acts,
Of accidental judgments, casual slaughters,   355
Of deaths put on[6] by cunning and forced cause,
And, in this upshot, purposes mistook
Fall'n on the inventors' heads: all this can I
Truly deliver.

FORTINBRAS: Let us haste to hear it,
And call the noblest to the audience.   360
For me, with sorrow I embrace my fortune:
I have some rights of memory in this kingdom,
Which now to claim my vantage[7] doth invite me.

HORATIO: Of that I shall have also cause to speak,
And from his mouth whose voice will draw on more:[8]   365
But let this same be presently performed,
Even while men's minds are wild; lest more mischance
On[9] plots and errors happen.

FORTINBRAS: Let four captains
Bear Hamlet, like a soldier, to the stage;   370
For he was likely, had he been put on,[1]
To have proved most royal: and, for his passage,[2]
The soldiers' music and the rites of war

3. This heap of corpses proclaims a carnage.   4. Imminent.   5. So immediately on.
6. Prompted. *Casual:* chance.   7. Advantageous position, opportunity. *Have some rights of memory:* am still remembered.   8. More voices.   9. Following on.   1. Tried (as a king).   2. Death.

Speak loudly for him.
Take up the bodies: such a sight as this   375
Becomes the field, but here shows much amiss.
Go, bid the soldiers shoot.
   [*A dead march. Exeunt, bearing off the bodies: after which a peal of ordnance is shot off.*]

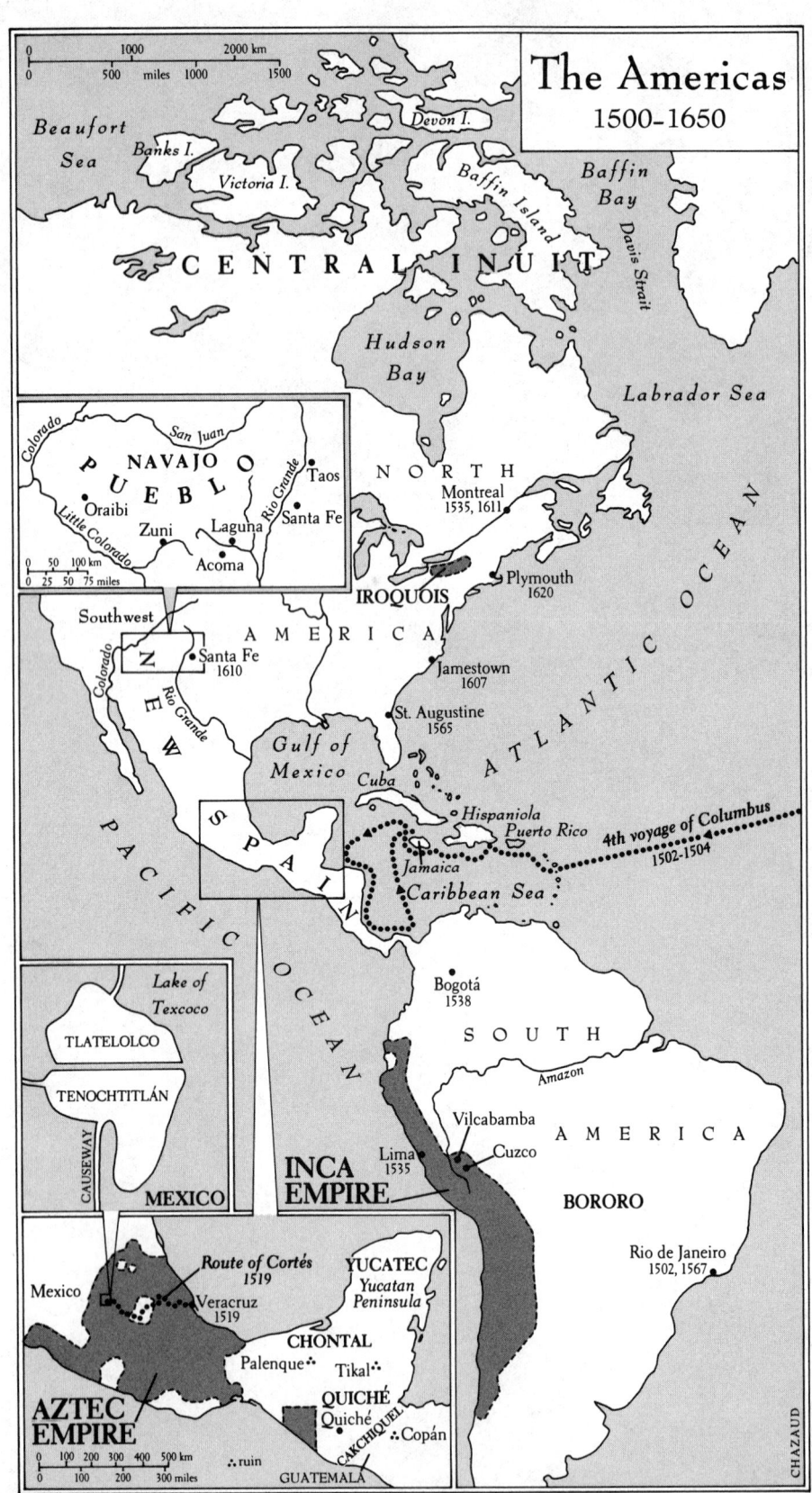

The Americas
1500–1650

Beaufort Sea

Banks I.

Victoria I.

Devon I.

Baffin Island

Baffin Bay

Davis Strait

CENTRAL INUIT

Hudson Bay

Labrador Sea

1000 2000 km
500 1000 1500
miles

Colorado
San Juan
NAVAJO
P U E B L O
Little Colorado
Oraibi
Zuni
Laguna
Acoma
Rio Grande
Taos
Santa Fe

0 50 100 km
0 25 50 75 miles

Southwest

N O R T H

Montreal
1535, 1611

Plymouth
1620

IROQUOIS

ATLANTIC OCEAN

A M E R I C A

N
E
W

Colorado

Rio Grande

Santa Fe
1610

Jamestown
1607

St. Augustine
1565

Gulf of Mexico

Cuba

Hispaniola

Puerto Rico

4th voyage of Columbus
1502-1504

S
P
A
I
N

Jamaica

Caribbean Sea

P A C I F I C   O C E A N

Bogotá
1538

S O U T H

Amazon

A M E R I C A

Lake of Texcoco

TLATELOLCO

TENOCHTITLÁN

CAUSEWAY

MEXICO

Vilcabamba

Lima
1535

Cuzco

INCA EMPIRE

BORORO

Rio de Janeiro
1502, 1567

Mexico

Route of Cortés
1519

Veracruz
1519

YUCATEC
Yucatan Peninsula

CHONTAL

Palenque

Tikal

AZTEC EMPIRE

QUICHÉ
Quiché
CAKCHIQUEL
Copán

0 100 200 300 400 500 km
0 100 200 300 miles

ruin

GUATEMALA

CHAZAUD

Native America
and Europe
in the New World

The definitive meeting between alien cultures, an event unmatched in world history, took place the morning of November 8, 1519, as the conquistador Hernán Cortés with his band of four hundred soldiers entered the Aztec capital of Tenochtitlán. To be sure, there had been earlier expeditions, Columbus's among them, that had brought Europeans into contact with native Americans—but none that could produce the far-reaching shock of Cortés's introduction to the Aztec emperor Moteuczoma (better known in the English-speaking world as Montezuma).

The encounter provided one of the rare moments in history when life seems to imitate art. Surrounded by the dazzling architecture of a city larger than Rome, the newly arrived Spaniards compared the scene before them to the fantasies of which they had read in *Amadis of Gaul* (one of the chivalric romances to be satirized a century later in Cervantes's *Don Quixote*). In the words of the soldier-chronicler Bernal Díaz del Castillo: "We said it seemed like the things of enchantment told in the book of Amadis" and wondered aloud "if this were a dream."

As for the reluctant hosts, forewarned by couriers from the Gulf Coast, a decision had already been made that the newcomers were spirits stepped out of the pages of the Quetzalcoatl (Plumed Serpent) cycle, a body of narrative chronicling the deeds of a hero god who had fled eastward in deep disgrace but had promised to return. The interview itself was conducted in Nahuatl, the language of the Aztecs, with Cortés assisted by a pair of interpreters to get him from Spanish to Chontal (a Gulf Coast language) and from Chontal to Nahuatl. According to native records, the proceeding began with these phrases:

> CORTÉS: *Cuix ahmo teh? Cuix ahmo yeh teh? Yeh teh in tiMoteuczomah?* (Is it not you? Are you not he? Are you Montezuma?)
> MONTEZUMA: *Ca quemahca, ca nehhuatl. Toteucyoe!* (Yes, it is I. O Our Lord [i.e., Quetzalcoatl]!)

The sequence of events that preceded and followed this meeting, leading to the conquest of 1521, would be painstakingly re-created in Spanish chronicles, in the celebrated letters of Cortés, in the native-language Florentine Codex, and, for readers of English, in William H. Prescott's *History of the Conquest of Mexico* (1843), a constellation of works that would come to be esteemed for their literary as well as their historical value.

The immediate consequence of the fall of Tenochtitlán was the dismantling of an empire that had stretched from the Gulf Coast to the Pacific and from what is now the state of San Luis Potosí in central Mexico eastward to just within the present boundary of Guatemala. In due course, Tenochtitlán, or Tenochtitlán

Mexico (now Mexico City), became the base from which further conquests were launched, reaching to the upper Rio Grande Valley and deep into Central America. Cortés's example inspired a generation of opportunistic intruders, notably Francisco Pizarro, whose conquest of the Inca empire of Peru was completed in 1533. Exploration by other European nations, including Britain and Portugal, had begun even before Cortés, and within a hundred years European outposts would be implanted all along the eastern rim of the Americas.

Devastating to native people and permanently disruptive to long-established cultures, the conquests nevertheless prepared the way for exchange. Wheat, livestock, horses, and firearms entered the so-called New World. From the Americas came tomatoes, chocolate, chilies, avocados (the names are all from the Nahuatl: *tomatl, xocolatl, chilli, ahuacatl*), not to mention tobacco, corn, potatoes, and the near-legendary gold and silver that heated the economy of Europe through the sixteenth century.

There were intellectual exchanges as well. In Aztec territory Spaniards, especially members of the clergy, learned Nahuatl, while native people became proficient in Spanish. Founded in 1536, the Royal College of Santa Cruz in the borough of Tlatelolco (part of Mexico City) taught young Aztec men to read and write Spanish and Nahuatl and even Latin. This Franciscan-run academy proved to be the principal training ground for what in retrospect would be recognized as the great era of Nahuatl letters, extending to about 1650. During this period Aesop's Fables, the Life of St. Francis, portions of the Bible, and writings by St. Augustine, Calderón de la Barca, Lope de Vega, and other authors were translated into Nahuatl.

At the same time works of Aztec verbal art were recorded for posterity in the alphabetic script of western Europe and, in some cases at least, translated into Spanish. Among the most noteworthy of these are the creation epic known as Legend of the Suns, the massive Florentine Codex (including traditional narratives, oratory, and the history of the Spanish Conquest), and the song compilation called Cantares Mexicanos. Owing to censorship and the fear of encouraging native religion, however, none of these works, whether in the native language or in translation, could be published in its own time.

The native literary materials were prepared in manuscript and stored in libraries on both sides of the Atlantic. In some cases missionary-scholars served as the recorders, writing from the dictation of a knowledgeable elder. In other cases native scribes took the lead, either writing from live recitals or transcribing, so to speak, from the old pictorial books. These often magnificent volumes were bark-paper screen-folds that opened to form a lengthy streamer, crowded with illustrations typically read from right to left. Although the pictures contained a few phonetic features, they were essentially mnemonic, intended to call forth a text that had been learned orally.

On a somewhat smaller scale, literary activity of the same sort was initiated in Maya territory in the mid-1500s. There was no academy of Maya-Spanish-Latin learning on the level of the College of Santa Cruz. But in local monasteries and in church schools gifted Maya quickly learned the new script and began preparing native-language documents for their own use. Transcriptions in the full sense of the word might have been possible using the old bark-paper books, because Maya writing—in many communities at least—had been fully phonetic.

Though the Mayan languages are entirely different from Nahuatl and comprise a linguistic family in themselves (including Chontal, spoken in the Mexican state of Tabasco; Quiché, one of many Mayan languages of the Guatemalan highlands; and the widespread Yucatec Maya of the Yucatán peninsula), both cultures developed in the Mexican-Central American region known to modern anthropologists as Mesoamerica. Both show such distinguishing traits as stepped pyramids, floating gardens, specialized markets, an eighteen-month calendar, and screen-fold books. And in their verbal arts both have themes and genres in common, in particular a sacred book, or world history, in which the creation of the earth and the deeds of gods and kings are narrated in chronological sequence. The Popol Vuh of the Quiché Maya is the best-known work of this type.

The pattern of literary preservation set by the Aztec example and matched in sixteenth- and seventeenth-century Maya communities was to be repeated over the centuries and throughout the hemisphere. Again and again, after contact with Europeans, one or a few exceptional individuals would cooperate with outsiders to make a permanent record of historical narratives, prayers, song texts, or other matter. In many cases native intellectuals took a leading role or even worked on their own, independent of a missionary's or an anthropologist's agenda. The result of this activity is a vast and still growing native literature, preserved in the Western European, or Latin, script and generally available to the world through translations into European languages, especially English and Spanish but also German, French, Portuguese, and Italian. (It is fascinating to contemplate what might have been the outcome had the Americas joined the Old World through contact with Asia or Africa instead of Europe.)

In view of the written record, one may speak of native American *literature* in the strict sense of the term. The works have become texts. Still it should be kept in mind that the language arts of the Maya, Zuni, Navajo, and other American cultures have continued to live in oral tradition, and even those works that have been written down and published must be regarded as mere variants, possibly to be contradicted, perhaps improved, by later recordings. Therefore, the term *oral literature*, suggesting change and spontaneous creation, is often used by students of native American speech arts, even if particular renderings may be singled out as masterworks.

The texts themselves are intimately linked to the languages from which they spring, and it is essential to recognize the uniqueness of each linguistic tradition. Estimates have placed the number of American languages spoken at the beginning of the sixteenth century at approximately two thousand, of which several hundred are still in use. Moreover, these languages have served a variety of cultures, ranging from small nomadic bands and village communities to complex, stratified societies like the Aztec, Maya, and Inca, which formerly gave rise to city-states and empires.

But in spite of differing cultures, native peoples have not lived in isolation. They have been accomplished linguists and traders and have borrowed freely across cultural boundaries, disseminating literary themes and genres and even figures of speech. As a starting point toward grasping the unity of native literature, the anthropologist Donald Bahr has proposed three basic genres: song, narrative, and oratory.

Song tends to be the most perfectly memorized of the genres, with texts sometimes varying not at all from one performer to the next. Divorced from music, as is seldom or never the case in native performance, the texts by themselves do not exhibit meter or rhyme. But the interjection of vocables, or song syllables, create patterns, and stanzas are often paired.

Narrative, by contrast, is improvised by the performer, who, while following a prescribed plot line, adds details at will. The English terms *myth* and *folktale* reflect a division recognized in many native cultures, where a more serious, more sacred, or more "ancient" kind of story is contrasted with less serious narratives felt to be "new" or "false" (that is, fictional).

Oratory, a genre more significant in native American (and African) than in European lore, encompasses prayer, educational monologues, ceremonial colloquy, and the magical prose poems, or formulas, calculated to bring about a desired result by coercion. Composed of set phrases, whose sequence may be varied considerably, oratory falls between the strictness of song and the freedom of narrative.

Obviously the most expansive of the genres is narrative, the principle vehicle for relating the deeds of deities and heroes (more rarely heroines). In many cases the hero is a trickster or has tricksterlike attributes, which means that he is gullible, clownish, ribald, conniving, or a combination of all four. Often the tale tells of twin heroes, who either aid or antagonize one another. Human in their foibles (like the Greek Olympians), these figures may also be the divine creators of the universe and of social institutions.

Mixed genres are not uncommon. Often a narrative will be punctuated by short songs. The Aztec story of Quetzalcoatl, noted earlier, tells how the ill-fated king and all his pages were tricked by sorcerers, who not only caused the priestly ruler to become drunk but steered him toward an incestuous embrace with his sister, necessitating his flight from the brilliant palace appointed with red shell and decorated with the plumage of such brilliant birds as the quetzal and the troupial:

> When the sorcerers had gotten them completely drunk, they said to Quetzalcoatl, "My child, may it please you to sing, and here's a song for you to recite." Then Ihuimecatl [one of the sorcerers] recited it for him.

> I must leave my
> house of quetzal, of quetzal,
> my house of troupial,
> my house of redshell.

> When he had gotten into a happy mood, he said, "Go get my sister Quetzalpetlatl. Let the two of us be drunk together."

Narratives interlaced with song are especially typical of Mexico and the North American Southwest. In a variation of the mixed-genre style, narratives may be punctuated by oratory. In many if not most native traditions, the stories are joined in lengthy sequences to form what may be called epics. Finally, the epic as a whole may be condensed into song or oratory for ritualized performance at winter solstice gatherings, at funerals, or on other ceremonial occasions.

In approaching this literature, the question of cultural barriers comes to the fore. Is it possible for outsiders to make meaningful contact with traditions so far removed from their own? Without doubt, the challenge is there, but so is the opportunity. The planet holds no other land mass that could have given rise to cultures (and literatures) both so varied and so completely isolated from the sphere of Europe, Africa, and Asia that has come to dominate world thinking. For the student of literature, native America reintroduces—in ways that are distinctly fresh—the role of supernatural power, the problem of humanity versus nature, and the great themes centering on social obligation and the development of the individual.

Despite its reliance on symbolism and imagery, native American literature may be regarded as essentially technological, or functional, rather than aesthetic. For the individual its function is medicinal—to facilitate safe progress toward old age and to weaken destructive powers, especially those of disease and death. For society it functions to reinforce mores drawn from the timeless realm of deities; it also reorders the natural world so as to assign the human community its proper place, at the same time preserving a link to untamed nature as the source of livelihood and power. Such considerations may be suspended as native audiences submit to the charms of music or enjoy the antics of the trickster or the deeds of the monster slayer. Close juxtaposition of the divine and the irreverent, the awe-inspiring and the comic, is one of the hallmarks of native traditions. The important point is that this literature in its own setting is not an afterthought or an amenity; it is a necessary component of individual and social well-being.

FURTHER READING

Fernando Horcasitas, *The Aztecs Then and Now* (1979), offers a concise summary of Aztec history and culture from pre-Aztec times to the mid-twentieth century. The Maya are surveyed in Michael D. Coe, *The Maya* (1993). Harold E. Driver's comprehensive *Indians of North America* (1969) remains a standard work in its field. Diego Durán, *The Aztecs* (1964), is a readable, richly detailed sixteenth-century source on the history of Tenochtitlán. John Bierhorst's three-volume series—*The Mythology of North America* (1985), *The Mythology of South America* (1988), and *The Mythology of Mexico and Central America* (1990)—presents an overview of native American narrative traditions. Munro S. Edmonson, ed., *Literatures* (*Supplement to the Handbook of Middle American Indians*, edited by Victoria Reifler Bricker, vol. 3, 1985), consists of survey articles on Nahuatl and four Maya literatures.

PRONOUNCING GLOSSARY

The following list uses common English syllables and stress accents to provide rough equivalents of selected words whose pronunciation may be unfamiliar to the general reader.

Cantares Mexicanos: *kahn-tah'-rays may-hee-kah'-nohs*

Cortés: *kohr-tays'*

Ihuimecatl: *ee-wee-may'-kahtl*

matasanos: *mah-tah-sáh-nohs*

Mexico: *may-shee'-koh* (in English: *meks'-ee-koh*)

Moteuczoma: *moh-tayk-soo'-mah*

Nahuatl: *nah'-wahtl*

Popol vuh: *poh-pohl' woo* (in English: *poh'-puhl voo*)

Quetzalcoatl: *kay-tzahl-koh'-ahtl*

Quetzalpetlatl: *kay-tzahl-pay'-tlahtl*

Quiché: *kee-chay'*

Tenochtitlán: *tay-nohch-tee-tlahn'*

Tlatelolco: *tlah-tel-ohl'-koh*

NATIVE AMERICA AND EUROPE IN THE NEW WORLD

TEXTS	CONTEXTS
	1500 Pedro Alvares Cabral sights the coast of Brazil and claims it for Portugal
	1502 Montezuma II ascends the throne of Tenochtitlán • Maya trading canoe contacted in Bay of Honduras during fourth voyage of Columbus
1508 Rodríguez de Montalvo, *Amadis of Gaul,* a chivalric romance that inspired the future conquistadors of Mexico	
1519–1526 Hernán Cortés, six letters to Charles I of Spain on the conquest of Mexico, with descriptions of Aztec warfare, statecraft, and daily life	**1519–1522** Voyage of Ferdinand Magellan around the world
	1521 Fall of Tenochtitlán, conquered for Spain by Hernán Cortés
	1524 Fall of Quiché, conquered for Spain by Pedro de Alvarado
	1525 Execution of Cuauhtemoc, last Aztec emperor, hanged by order of Cortés
1528 Annals of Tlatelolco, earliest Latin-script chronicle in the Aztec language	**1528** Beginning of civil war between Huascar and Atahualpa, rivals for the Inca throne
	1533 Fall of the Inca empire, conquered for Spain by Francisco Pizarro
1547–1579 Florentine Codex, the encyclopedic compilation of Aztec lore and literature	
1550–1581 Cantares Mexicanos, principal source of Aztec poetry	
1554–1558 Popol Vuh, sacred book of the Quiché Maya of Guatemala	
1556– Books of Chilam Balam, native compilations of Maya lore, including histories, prayers, and prophecies, still in use in the Yucatán	
1558 *Legend of the Suns,* history of the world according to the Aztecs, written in the Aztec language by an anonymous scribe	

TEXTS	CONTEXTS
	1572 Fall of Vilcabamba, last outpost of the Inca empire
	1588 England defeats the Spanish Armada
1590s? Aesop's *Fables* translated into Aztec	**1598** Beginning of Spanish settlement in New Mexico
	1607 Founding of Jamestown, first permanent English settlement in North America
1609–1617 Garcilaso de la Vega, El Inca, *Royal Commentaries of the Incas*, history of pre-Conquest Peru by an author who was himself a son of the Incas	
1611 Shakespeare, *The Tempest*, inspired in part by Silvester Jourdain's *A Discovery of the Bermudas* and thus the first major European work of imaginative literature to touch on a New World theme	
	1619 Beginning of African slavery in North America
	1620 Arrival of the *Mayflower* at Plymouth (Massachusetts), bringing English Puritans
1632 Bernal Díaz del Castillo, *True History of the Conquest of New Spain*	**1630s** League of the Iroquois, in existence since the 1400s, enters recorded history
1640 Plays by Calderón de la Barca and Lope de Vega translated into Aztec	
1649 Luis Lasso de la Vega, *Huei Tlamahuiçoltica* . . . (By means of a great miracle . . .), legend of the Virgin of Guadalupe, a cornerstone of Mexican nationalism, published in the Aztec language, Mexico City	

FLORENTINE CODEX

1547–1579

Compiled over three decades, the encyclopedic Florentine Codex represents the joint effort of the Franciscan missionary-ethnographer Bernardino de Sahagún and the knowledgeable Aztec elders and scribes who labored with him to produce a permanent record of Aztec culture. There had never been a document quite like this, and there have been few since. In view of its linguistic precision, its scope, and its objectivity, it emerges as the first work of modern anthropology.

The name Florentine Codex, it should be pointed out, is merely a latter-day scholar's designation for the most finished version of a corpus properly known as *General History of the Things of New Spain*. Several versions of the *History* have survived. But the manuscript now at the Laurentian Library in Florence, although it lacks some texts preserved in the so-called Madrid codices, is the copy that best deserves to be called complete.

Written in paired columns, with Aztec (that is, Nahuatl) on the left and a Spanish paraphrase on the right, the Codex's twelve books begin with descriptions of the preconquest gods and ceremonies, followed by detailed expositions of native astronomy, botany, zoology, commerce, industry, medicine, time counting, prophecy, and other topics. The final book is devoted to a native history of the Spanish Conquest.

Of particular interest for the study of literature is Book 6, containing what Sahagún called "rhetoric." Voluminous and varied, it is the single richest body of native American oratory ever assembled. Here, in native text, are the speeches used by kings on state occasions, the great prayer to the rain god Tlaloc, the admonitions addressed by fathers to their sons and by mothers to their daughters, the marriage counsels, the prayers for schoolchildren—and the remarkable sequence of midwifery orations, from which selections have been printed here.

According to the texts on midwifery, which include not only the orations but the associated customs, the midwife is chosen by the married couple's parents during the woman's seventh or eighth month of pregnancy. Shortly thereafter a party of kinswomen visit the candidate, flattering her with set speeches, calling her "artisan" and "expert," begging her to accept the contract. In response she protests, she is unworthy, others are more skilled. After seeming to disqualify herself, she abruptly relents, announcing, "Let the water be boiled."

From that moment on the expectant woman is in the care of the midwife, who now represents Night Midwife, the tutelary spirit of her profession. Similarly, the patient becomes identified with the deity Cihuacoatl Quilaztli, progenitor of the human race. Such titles are frequently invoked in the orations used as the midwife assumes her duties and prepares the "flower house," or birthing room. When the time arrives she exhorts the expectant woman, urging her to emulate Cihuacoatl Quilaztli.

If the fetus should die in the womb, the midwife removes it surgically, using an extreme form of curettage. Should the woman herself die in labor, the midwife addresses her in one of the most eloquent of the orations, initiating her into the company of the celestial soldiers and thereby conferring the highest honor of which Aztec society can conceive. The woman in labor is imagined as a warrior, seeking to bring a live captive into the world—just as the male warrior in battle seeks not to kill but to bring home a prisoner (who will be ceremonially sacrificed to the gods). Should the male lose his life in battle he joins the company of slain warriors in the eastern sky who greet the sun each morning and conduct it to the zenith; at the zenith it is handed over to the women who have died in childbirth, and it is they who lead the sun downward to the western horizon. Thus the male and female roles are mirror images of one another.

Should the woman deliver successfully, the midwife addresses her as one would greet a victorious warrior. But again, as elsewhere in the orations (and in Aztec deportment generally), humility is the watchword. The new mother must not be "boastful" of the child, respecting the will of the Creator, the supreme spirit, who both gives and takes away.

Sahagún's *History* has been published in a thirteen-part English-Nahuatl edition, *Florentine Codex* (1950–1582), edited by Arthur J. O. Anderson and Charles E. Dibble; the introductory volume (Part 1) includes background data and a subject guide; Part 7 (Book 6) has the complete oratory. Articles on various aspects of Sahagún's *History*, including the oratory, are included in Munro S. Edmonson, ed., *Sixteenth-Century Mexico: The Work of Sahagún* (1974). More of the midwifery orations are in Thelma Sullivan's *A Scattering of Jades: Stories, Poems, and Prayers of the Aztecs* (1994), edited by T. J. Knab.

PRONOUNCING GLOSSARY

The following list uses common English syllables and stress accents to provide rough equivalents of selected words whose pronunciation may be unfamiliar to the general reader.

Cihuacoatl Quilaztli: *see-wah-koh'-aht kee-lahs'-tlee*

Nahuatl: *nah'-waht*

Sahagún: *sah-ah-goon'*

Tlaloc: *tlahl'-ohk*

Tloque Nahuaque: *tloh'-kay nah-wah' kay*

FLORENTINE CODEX

[The Midwife Addresses the Woman Who Has Died in Childbirth][1]

The woman who dies in childbirth, of whom it is said she stands up as a woman, when she dies they say she becomes a god. Then the midwife calls to her, greets her, prays to her, while she is still lying there, while she is still stretched out, saying:

Precious feather, child,
Eagle woman, dear one,
Dove, darling daughter,[2]
You have labored, you have toiled,
Your task is finished.   5
You came to the aid of your Mother, the noble lady, Cihuacoatl
    Quilaztli.[3]
You received, raised up, and held the shield, the little buckler that she
    laid in your hands: she your Mother, the noble lady, Cihuacoatl
    Quilaztli.

1. Translated by John Bierhorst.   2. Terms of endearment. *Eagle woman:* implies valor.   3. Cihuacoatl (Woman Serpent) and Quilaztli (untranslatable) are names for the principle female deity.

Now wake! Rise! Stand up!
Comes the daylight, the daybreak:
Dawn's house has risen crimson, it comes up standing.   10
The crimson swifts, the crimson swallows, sing,
And all the crimson swans[4] are calling.
Get up, stand up! Dress yourself!
Go! Go seek the good place, the perfect place, the home of your Mother,
    your Father, the Sun,[5]
The place of happiness, joy,   15
Delight, rejoicing.
Go! Go follow your Mother, your Father, the Sun.
May his elder sisters bring you to him: they the exalted, the celestial
    women,[6] who always and forever know happiness, joy, delight, and
    rejoicing, in the company and in the presence of our Mother, our
    Father, the Sun; who make him happy with their shouting.
My child, darling daughter, lady,
You spent yourself, you labored manfully: 20
You made yourself a victor, a warrior for Our Lord, though not without
    consuming all your strength; you sacrificed yourself.
Yet you earned a compensation, a reward: a good, perfect, precious death.
By no means did you die in vain.
And are you truly dead? You have made a sacrifice. Yet how else could
    you have become worthy of what you now deserve?
You will live forever, you will be happy, you will rejoice in the company
    and in the presence of our holy ones, the exalted women. Farewell,
    my daughter, my child. Go be with them, join them. Let them hold
    you and take you in.   25
May you join them as they cheer him and shout to him: our Mother, our
    Father, the Sun;
And may you be with them always, wherever they go in their rejoicing.

But my little child, my daughter, my lady,
You went away and left us, you deserted us, and we are but old men and
    old women.
You have cast aside your mother and your father.   30
Was this your wish? No, you were summoned, you were called.
Yet without you, how can we survive?
How painful will it be, this hard old age?
Down what alleys or in what doorways will we perish?
Dear lady, do not forget us! Remember the hardships that we see, that we
    suffer, here on earth: 35
The heat of the sun presses against us; also the wind, icy and cold:
This flesh, this clay of ours, is starved and trembling. And we, poor
    prisoners of our stomachs! There is nothing we can do.
Remember us, my precious daughter, O eagle woman, O lady!
You lie beyond in happiness. In the good place, the perfect place,
You live.   40
In the company and in the presence of our lord,
You live.
You as living flesh can see him, you as living flesh can call to him.
Pray to him for us!

---

4. Male warriors slain in battle, now in the eastern sky with the sun.   5. The sun is both mother and
father.   6. Women who have died in childbirth, now in the western sky.

Call to him for us! 45
This is the end,
We leave the rest to you.

[The Midwife Addresses the Newly Delivered Woman][1]

O my daughter, O valiant woman, you worked, you toiled.
You soared like an eagle, you sprang like a jaguar,
you put all your strength behind the shield, behind the buckler;
you endured.
You went forth into battle, you emulated Our Mother,
    Cihuacoatl Quilaztli, 5
and now our lord has seated you on the Eagle Mat, the Jaguar
    Mat.[2]
You have spent yourself, O my daughter, now be tranquil.
What does our lord Tloque Nahuaque[3] will?
Shall he bestow his favors upon each of you separately, in separate
    places? 10
Perhaps you shall go off and leave behind the child that has arrived.
Perhaps, small as he is the Creator will summon him, will call out
    to him,
or perhaps he shall come to take you.
Do not be boastful of [the child].
Do not consider yourself worthy of it. 15
Call out humbly to our lord, Tloque Nahuaque.

1. Translated by Thelma Sullivan.   2. Warriors' seat of honor.   3. Ever Present, Ever Near, the supreme spirit.

CANTARES MEXICANOS
1550–1581

Taken from the lips of singers by native scribes during the second half of the sixteenth century, the Cantares Mexicanos ("songs of the Aztecs") is the principal surviving source of Aztec poetry and one of the monuments of native American literature. Voluminous and fascinating, if difficult to decipher, it has attracted a modern following of scholars and poets determined to distill its essence and make fresh versions for new audiences. It is one of those bodies of work that for itself alone prompts the dedicated to study a difficult language.

The songs are composed in grammatical Nahuatl, or Aztec. But they are not immediately accessible, even to fluent speakers. Replete with tropes and word distortions, the Cantares diction, though some of its imagery is shared by oratory, belongs to a special genre called *netotiliztli* (freely, "dance associated with worldly entertainment"). Interspersed song syllables, coupled metaphors, and kennings comparable to those in Norse and Old English verse abound. And yet, even if textually obscure, the *netotiliztli* as performed in sixteenth-century Mexico were well calculated to chill the blood of European eavesdroppers. As correctly noted by the Spanish academician Francisco Cervantes de Salazar, drawing on observations made in the 1550s and 1560s, "In these songs they speak of conspiracy against ourselves."

A native document, prepared without missionary interference, the Cantares, nevertheless, is more than native. A better term is *nativistic*, implying work that aggressively reasserts — and to an extent reformulates — the values of a people under stress. In fact some of the songs defiantly rehearse the Spanish Conquest of 1521 in ways that hint at native retribution; others introduce Christian themes overlaid by Aztec interpretations that were deeply disturbing to missionaries. No doubt a number of the pieces in the repertory had been used before the Conquest, possibly to intimidate enemy ambassadors or to inspire martial ardor or, in the case of the many satirical pieces, simply to entertain. Thus the genre has deep roots, even if reshaped by mid-sixteenth-century concerns.

War, the taking of captives, the immortalizing of slain warriors by means of song, the nature of song itself, the valor of dead kings, and the taunting of enemies and laggard soldiers are the pervasive themes. For all its hyperaesthetic imagery devoted to birds and flowers, this is an intensely masculine, militarist poetry, from which women, either as composers or performers, were apparently excluded. (It may come as no surprise to the psychoanalytically minded that the corpus includes a homosexual song and several pieces in which the male monologuist assumes female, even lesbian, roles.)

The two selections printed here are among the least taxing interpretively yet provide a full-blown taste of the sensuous imagery for which the genre is renowned. In the first, a singer reveals his version of the Aztec theory—also expounded in surviving narratives—by which music is a sky world phenomenon reproduced on earth. The related theme of musical intoxication, much treated in the Cantares, is also introduced. In the second selection, a singer exhorts the faint-hearted, inspiring them to emulate slain comrades now enjoying immortality in the sky. In both pieces the supreme spirit is identified as Tloque Nahuaque (Ever Present, Ever Near), a name often associated with the great god Tezcatlipoca in unacculturated lore. In the Cantares, however, the "ever present" is identified with *Dios* (God), permitting one to say, albeit with understatement, that the two songs express a modified Christianity.

In performance such texts were accompanied by the *huehuetl*, or upright skin drum (played with bare hands), and the horizontal two-toned *teponaztli*, or slit drum (played with mallets). Gongs, flutes, whistles, and other instruments might also be present, as the singer intones his phrases, punctuated by the cries of dancers in military attire. Although the program for any particular song text cannot be reconstructed, contemporary descriptions allow one to imagine a lively scene, staged as an outdoor theatrical complete with its ominous drumming and the sight of glistening unsheathed weapons.

The only complete edition of the Cantares Mexicanos is John Bierhorst, *Cantares Mexicanos: Songs of the Aztecs* (1985), which includes extensive commentary. Robert Stevenson, *Music in Aztec and Inca Territory* (1968), gives useful background on instrumentation and performance. Modern poetry inspired by the Cantares can be found in William Carlos Williams, *Pictures from Brueghel and Other Poems* (1949); Stephen Berg, *Nothing in the Word* (1972); and Ernesto Cardenal, *Los Ovnis de Oro/Golden UFOs* (1992).

PRONOUNCING GLOSSARY

The following list uses common English syllables and stress accents to provide rough equivalents of selected words whose pronunciation may be unfamiliar to the general reader.

Cantares Mexicanos: *kahn-tah'-rays*
   may-hee-kah'-nohs
Ce Olintzin: *say oh-leen'-tzeen*
huehuetl: *way'-wayt*
Nahuatl: *nah'-waht*
netotiliztli: *nay-toh-tee-lees'-tlee*

Otomi: *oh-doh-mee'*
teponaztli: *tay-poh-nahs'-tlee*
Tezcatlipoca: *tays-kahtl-ee-poh'-kah*
Tloque Nahuaque: *tloh'-kay nah-wah'-kay*

CANTARES MEXICANOS[1]

Song IV

Mexican Otomi[2] Song

Burnishing them as sunshot jades, mounting them as trogon feathers, I recall the root songs, I, the singer, composing good songs as troupials:[3] I've scattered them as precious jades, producing a flower brilliance to entertain the Ever Present, the Ever Near.[4]

As precious troupial feathers, as trogons, as roseate swans, I design my songs. Gold jingles are my songs. I, a parrot corn-tassel bird,[5] I sing, and they resound. In this place of scattering flowers I lift them up before the Ever Present, the Ever Near.

Delicious are the root songs, as I, the parrot corn-tassel bird, lift them through a conch of gold, the sky songs passing through my lips: like sunshot jades I make the good songs glow, lifting fumes of flower fire, a singer making fragrance before the Ever Present, the Ever Near.

The spirit swans[6] are echoing me as I sing, shrilling like bells from the Place of Good Song. As jewel mats, shot with jade and emerald sunray, the Green Place[7] flower songs are radiating green. A flower incense, flaming all around, spreads sky aroma, filled with sunshot mist, *as I, the singer, in this gentle rain of flowers sing before the Ever Present, the Ever Near.*[8]

As colors I devise them. I strew them as flowers in the Place of Good Song. *As jewel mats, shot with jade and emerald sunray, the Green Place flower songs are radiating green. A flower incense, flaming all around, spreads sky aroma, filled with sunshot mist, as I, the singer, in this gentle rain of flowers sing before the Ever Present, the Ever Near.*

I exalt him, rejoice him with heart-pleasing flowers in this place of song. With narcotic fumes my heart is pleasured. I soften my heart, inhaling them. My soul grows dizzy with the fragrance, inhaling good flowers in this place of enjoyment. My soul is drunk with flowers.

---

1. Translated by John Bierhorst.   2. Here an Aztec warrior class distinguished by superior achievement; usually the name of a non-Aztec ethnic group.   3. Tropical orioles. *Trogon:* a brilliant tropical bird.   4. Tezcatlipoca, the all-powerful Aztec deity.   5. A tiny yellow songbird not otherwise identified; here joined with the parrot, implying that the singer resembles either or both. *Roseate swans:* roseate spoonbills or their feathers.   6. Gorgeous birds of the sky world, formerly warriors on earth.   7. Evidently the sky world, but terms such as *Good Song* and *Green Place* may also designate the singer's earthly locale, beautified by music, war deeds, or both.   8. Passages in italics indicate the translator is filling out an "et cetera" in the text.

Song XII

Song for Admonishing Those Who Seek No Honor in War

Clever with a song, I beat my drum to wake our friends, rousing them to
arrow deeds, whose never dawning hearts know nothing, whose
hearts lie dead asleep in war, who praise themselves in shadows, in
darkness. Not in vain do I say, "They are poor." Let them come and
hear the flower dawn songs drizzling down incessantly beside the
drum.

Sacred flowers of the dawn are blooming in the rainy place of flowers that
belongs to him the Ever Present, the Ever Near. The heart pleasers
are laden with sunstruck dew. Come and see them: they blossom
uselessly for those who are disdainful. Doesn't anybody crave them?
O friends, not useless flowers are the life-colored honey flowers.

They that intoxicate one's soul with life lie only there, they blossom only
there, within the city of the eagles, inside the circle, in the middle of
the field, where flood and blaze are spreading, where the spirit eagle
shines, the jaguar growls, and all the precious bracelet stones[1] are
scattered, all the precious noble lords dismembered, where the
princes lie broken, lie shattered.

These princes are the ones who greatly crave the dawn flowers. So that all
will enter in, he causes them to be desirous, he who lies within the
sky, he, Ce Olintzin,[2] ah the noble one, who makes them drizzle
down, giving a gift of flower brilliance to the eagle-jaguar princes,
making them drunk with the flower dew of life.

If, my friend, you think the flowers are useless that you crave here on
earth, how will you acquire them, how will you create them, you that
are poor, you that gaze on the princes at their flowers, at their songs?
Come look: do they rouse themselves to arrow deeds for nothing?
There beyond, the princes, all of them, are troupials, spirit swans,
trogons, roseate swans: they live in beauty, they that know the middle
of the field.

With shield flowers, with eagle-trophy flowers, the princes are rejoicing in
their bravery, adorned with necklaces of pine flowers. Songs of
beauty, flowers of beauty, glorify their blood-and-shoulder toil. They
who have accepted flood and blaze become our Black Mountain
friends, with whom we rise warlike on the great road.[3] Offer your
shield, stand up, you eagle jaguar!

---

1. *Eagle, jaguar,* and *bracelet stones* denote the noble warrior. *City of the eagles* and *the circle* signify
the battlefield.   2. One Movement, a calendrical sign, or the tutelary spirit of that sign, that is, Tezcatlipoca.   3. Here the sun's road to the sky. Black Mountain represents, perhaps, paradise. The ordinary
meaning is: Our comrades with whom we march down the causeway (*great road*) that leads from the
Mexican capital (which was surrounded by water) to Black Mountain (a town traditionally at war with
Mexico).

POPOL VUH

1554–1558

A compendium of stories cherished by the ancient, the colonial, and even the
modern Maya, the Popol Vuh of the sixteenth-century Quiché people of Guatemala has been compared with the *Odyssey* of the Greeks and the *Mahābhārata* of

India. Such omnibus compositions, repeatedly mined by the artist and the moralist, serve as cultural touchstones; they dramatize the life of a nation and help bind it together. In the case of the Popol Vuh, as with similar works, the stories have been woven together to form an epic, with threads of continuity that may be called novelistic. On account of this seemingly modern feature, rare in New World literatures, the Quiché book strikes nonnative observers as the single most significant work of native American verbal art. Viewed from yet another perspective, focusing on its lofty account of world creation and tribal origins, it has been called America's Bible.

But if the Popol Vuh is comparable, it is also different. By Western standards it might be judged too formal—and at the same time too earthy. Derived from a fascination with numbers, its formalism is expressed stylistically in the pairing, tripling, and quadrupling of phrases. Major characters, likewise, are paired, acting almost as duplicates of one another; deities also are paired, occasionally tripled, with a strong suggestion that they are the same. The structure of the work itself is reiterative, fitted to a traditional pattern of four successive worlds, or creations: the first three are said to have ended in failure, our own is the fourth. Yet against this stately patterning, the hero-gods appear as light-hearted boys, even as tricksters. Their adventures—from which ribaldry is not excluded—have a playful, anecdotal quality. For the uninitiated reader willing to accept this juxtaposition of the sacred and the profane, the high and the low, an experience both rewarding and unusual lies in wait.

Despite the best efforts of scholarship, the author of the Popol Vuh remains anonymous. It has been generally assumed that he is a man—since known scribes of the period are male—and, with less agreement, that he is a lone composer who uses the authorial we (some have conjectured a team of authors). Evidently, he is a native of the town variously called Utatlán, Rotten Cane, or Quiché, political center of the pre-Columbian confederacy that controlled most of the Guatemalan highlands.

Inevitably, following the conquest of Mexico in 1521, Spanish imperialism cast its eye toward Guatemala, and in 1524, after a brief struggle, Quiché fell to Spanish and Mexican troops under the command of the red-haired conquistador Pedro de Alvarado (called "the sun" by native people). By the 1530s, Quiché scribes, presumably including the Popol Vuh author, were being trained to use alphabetic writing. From internal evidence in the manuscript, coordinated with other records, the date of the Popol Vuh has been tentatively fixed at 1554–1558.

In the text itself the author hints at the existence of a certain "council book" (popol vuh), presumably a pre-Columbian screen-fold that served him as a source. The sixteenth-century Quiché were well acquainted with books of this sort, some dating from the classic period of Maya culture (A.D. 100–900), which saw the rise of such imposing centers as Tikal, Copán, and Palenque. By the time of European contact those important sites, abandoned in the mysterious collapse of Maya civilization ca. A.D. 900, lay in ruins. But Maya learning survived along the rim of the now-depopulated central area, notably in southern Guatemala among the Quiché and their neighbors, also in the northern part of the Yucatán peninsula. As Mayanists have recently demonstrated, the old books do contain phonetic writing. But judging from the few examples that have been preserved, it is likely that even during the classic period extended narratives were transmitted orally, with the picture-filled books acting only as prompts. The conclusion usually drawn is that the Popol Vuh is by no means a transcription of ancient screen-folds; yet it no doubt borrows from them.

Though not so indicated in the manuscript, the Popol Vuh falls naturally into four parts, as most translators have recognized. The first three attempts at creation—that is, the creation of humans—are compressed into Part 1, saving the climactic dawning of the sun, preceded by the fourth, successful creation of humans, for the opening passages of Part 4.

The first sunrise, typically, is the defining event in Mesoamerican chronology. Prior to it, the world is in darkness or is lit by mere substitute suns. The earth's surface, moreover, is said to be soft and moist; it does not harden until the sun finally comes up. During the dark, or soft, time all things are possible. Thus Parts 1, 2, and 3 of the Popol Vuh relate the events of a formative age. History, it may be said, begins with Part 4. In the version printed here the translator has chosen to set off the concluding passages of Part 4, labeling the most recent phase of history "Part 5." Selections have been made so as to represent each of these five parts.

As the author plainly states in the preamble that begins Part 1, "We shall write about this now amid the preaching of God, in Christendom now." Admittedly, then, the Popol Vuh is a latter-day work. But the question of missionary influence is not easy to settle. Most critics have assumed that the account of the earth's creation that immediately follows the preamble owes something to the Book of Genesis. If so, the material has been thoroughly assimilated to the Maya pantheon and to the native American concept of primordial water. Comparisons with Aztec accounts, in which a company of gods (including the deity Plumed Serpent, named also in the Quiché text) deliberates, then places the earth on the surface of a preexisting sea, are just as applicable as comparisons with Genesis.

Part 1 continues with a description of the first three efforts at creating humans, in line with a widespread pattern shared by Aztec and other Mesoamerican traditions. As Part 1 ends, the narrative changes gears, moving directly into the exploits of the divine heroes Hunahpu and Xbalanque. The work of these two heroes may be said to prepare the world for society and for the well-being of individuals within society. Thus Part 2 deals with the problem of human arrogance; Part 3 confronts the scourge of death.

The cycle of trickster tales that makes up Part 2 appears to be purely Central American, not shared by Aztec lore. Here the twin heroes bring low the overproud Seven Macaw and, in further adventures not included here, defeat his two "self-magnifying" sons, Zipacna and Earthquake.

In the cycle of tales that comprises Part 3, the most celebrated portion of the Popol Vuh, Hunahpu and Xbalanque vanquish the lords of the Maya underworld, called Xibalba (a term of obscure etymology, provisionally translated "place of fright"). This material, likewise, is Central American—and quintessentially Mayan. Scenes from the story are preserved on painted vases of the classic period, recovered by archaeologists from Maya burial chambers. Evidently, the sequence of events, in which the heroes' twin fathers, One Hunahpu and Seven Hunahpu, are undone by Xibalba and are ultimately avenged by their two sons, served as a paradigm for the dying and the dead, promising them victory over the powers of the afterworld. From the archaeological evidence, the story told in Part 3 of the Popol Vuh must have aided the Maya in their journey through the realms of death somewhat as the *Book of the Dead* comforted the ancient Egyptians. Indeed, the vase paintings as a whole, with their depictions of underworld lords and the trials of the twin heroes, have lately been called the "Maya Book of the Dead."

Parts 4 and 5 complete the vast epic, relating the connected stories of the origin of humans, the discovery of corn, the birth of the sun, and the history of the Quiché tribes and their royal lineages down to the time of the Spanish Conquest and, subsequently, to the 1550s.

Old as the stories are, they are also new. Narratives of the origin and destruction of early humans can still be heard in traditional Maya storytelling sessions. The traditional account of the discovery of corn continues to be widely told; and tales of the trickster Zipacna and of exploits identical to those of the hero twins also persist, even if much abbreviated and without the grand continuity of the Popol Vuh.

Beyond the native community, knowledge of the Popol Vuh among Central Americans is not only widespread but taken for granted. When the Nicaraguan poet Pablo Antonio Cuadra writes (in *The Calabash Tree*, 1978), "A hero struggled against the lords of the House of Bats, / against the lords of the House of Darkness," his readers understand that although he refers to a contemporary revolutionary figure he is also alluding to the ordeal of Hunahpu and Xbalanque. For the Salvadoran novelist Manlio Argueta (*Cuzcatlán*, 1986) the story of the origin of humans from corn as told in the Popol Vuh is a reminder, in Argueta's words, that "the species will not perish"—a theme equally detectable (and inspired by the same source) in the title of the 1949 novel *Men of Maize* by the Guatemalan Nobel laureate Miguel Angel Asturias.

In the translation printed here, wherever the text solidifies into a string of three or more couplets the passage is set apart as though it were a poem. This is a device of the translator. It is not meant to imply that the lines were chanted but rather to show off the more pronounced moments of formalism in a prose that borders on oratory.

Dennis Tedlock's translation, satisfyingly annotated, is published as *Popol Vuh: The Mayan Book of the Dawn of Life* (1985). Older translations with useful introductions are Adrián Recinos, Delia Goetz, and Sylvanus Morley, *Popol Vuh: The Sacred Book of the Ancient Quiché Maya* (1950); and Munro S. Edmonson, *The Book of Counsel: The Popol Vuh of the Quiche Maya of Guatemala* (1971). Edmonson's is the only Quiché-English edition. Essays on the Popol Vuh and related topics are in Tedlock's *The Spoken Word and the Work of Interpretation* (1983). Maya vase paintings related to Part 3 of the Popol Vuh are illustrated and discussed in Michael D. Coe, *Lords of the Underworld: Masterpieces of Classic Maya Ceramics* (1978).

PRONOUNCING GLOSSARY

The following list uses common English syllables and stress accents to provide rough equivalents of selected words whose pronunciation may be unfamiliar to the general reader.

anonas: *ah-noh'-nahs*

Auilix: *ah-wee-leesh'*

Cauiztan Copal: *kah-weez-tahn' koh-pahl'*

Chimalmat: *chee-mahl-maht'*

Hacauitz: *hah-kah-weets'*

Hunahpu: *hoo-nah-poo'*

jocotes: *hoh-koh'-tays*

Mahucutah: *mah-hoo-koo-tah'*

matasanos: *mah-tah-sah'-nohs*

Mixtam Copal: *meesh-tahm' koh-pahl'*

nance: *nahn'-say*

naual: *nah'-wahl*

Palenque: *puh-leng'-kay*

pataxte: *pah-tahsh'-tay*

Popol Vuh: *poh-pohl' woo* (in English: *poh'-puhl voo*)

Quiché: *kee-chay'*

Quitze: *kee-tsay'*

Tikal: *tee-kahl'*

Tohil: *toh-heel'*

Xbalanque: *shbah-lahn-kay'*

Xibalba: *shee-bahl-bah'*

Xmucane: *shmoo-kah-nay'*

Xpiyacoc: *shpee-yah-kok'*

zapotes: *sah-poh'-tays*

Zipacna: *see-pahk-nah'*

Popol Vuh[1]

FROM PART 1

[Prologue, Creation]

This is the beginning of the Ancient Word, here in this place called Quiché. Here we shall inscribe, we shall implant the Ancient Word, the potential and source for everything done in the citadel of Quiché, in the nation of Quiché people.

And here we shall take up the demonstration, revelation, and account of how things were put in shadow and brought to light

> by the Maker, Modeler, named Bearer, Begetter,
> Hunahpu Possum, Hunahpu Coyote,
> Great White Peccary, Tapir,
> Sovereign Plumed Serpent,
> Heart of the Lake, Heart of the Sea,
> Maker of the Blue-Green Plate,
> Maker of the Blue-Green Bowl,[2]

as they are called, also named, also described as

> the midwife, matchmaker
> named Xpiyacoc, Xmucane,
> defender, protector,[3]
> twice a midwife, twice a matchmaker,

as is said in the words of Quiché. They accounted for everything—and did it, too—as enlightened beings, in enlightened words. We shall write about this now amid the preaching of God, in Christendom now. We shall bring it out because there is no longer a place to see it, a Council Book,

> a place to see "The Light That Came from
>   Across the Sea,"
> the account of "Our Place in the Shadows,"
> a place to see "The Dawn of Life,"

as it is called. There is the original book and ancient writing, but he who reads and ponders it hides his face.[4] It takes a long performance and account to complete the emergence of all the sky-earth:

> the fourfold siding, fourfold cornering,
> measuring, fourfold staking,

---

1. Translated by Dennis Tedlock. 2. All thirteen names refer to the Creator or to a company of creators, a designation applicable clearly to the first four names and *Sovereign Plumed Serpent. Heart of the Lake* and *Heart of the Sea* also apply, since the creators will later be described as "in the water," and somewhat obscurely, so does the last pair of names (*Plate* and *Bowl* may be read as "earth" and "sky," respectively). *Hunahpu Possum, Hunahpu Coyote, Great White Peccary,* and *Tapir* refer specifically to the grandparents of the gods, usually called Xpiyacoc and Xmucane. 3. Four names for Xpiyacoc and Xmucane. 4. The hieroglyphic source (*Council Book*) was suppressed by missionaries; it was said to have been brought to Quiché in ancient times from the far side of a lagoon (*Sea*). The reader *hides his face* to avoid the missionaries.

> halving the cord, stretching the cord
> in the sky, on the earth,
> the four sides, the four corners,[5]

as it is said,

> by the Maker, Modeler,
> mother-father of life, of humankind,
> giver of breath, giver of heart,
> bearer, upbringer in the light that lasts
> of those born in the light, begotten in the light;
> worrier, knower of everything, whatever there is:
> sky-earth, lake-sea.

This is the account, here it is:

Now it still ripples, now it still murmurs, ripples, it still sighs, still hums, and it is empty under the sky.

Here follow the first words, the first eloquence:

There is not yet one person, one animal, bird, fish, crab, tree, rock, hollow, canyon, meadow, forest. Only the sky alone is there; the face of the earth is not clear. Only the sea alone is pooled under all the sky; there is nothing whatever gathered together. It is at rest; not a single thing stirs. It is held back, kept at rest under the sky.

Whatever there is that might be is simply not there: only the pooled water, only the calm sea, only it alone is pooled.

Whatever might be is simply not there: only murmurs, ripples, in the dark, in the night. Only the Maker, Modeler alone, Sovereign Plumed Serpent, the Bearers, Begetters are in the water, a glittering light. They are there, they are enclosed in quetzal feathers, in blue-green.

Thus the name, "Plumed Serpent." They are great knowers, great thinkers in their very being.

And of course there is the sky, and there is also the Heart of Sky. This is the name of the god, as it is spoken.

And then came his word, he came here to the Sovereign Plumed Serpent, here in the blackness, in the early dawn. He spoke with the Sovereign Plumed Serpent, and they talked, then they thought, then they worried. They agreed with each other, they joined their words, their thoughts. Then it was clear, then they reached accord in the light, and then humanity was clear, when they conceived the growth, the generation of trees, of bushes, and the growth of life, of humankind, in the blackness, in the early dawn, all because of the Heart of Sky, named Hurricane. Thunderbolt Hurricane comes first, the second is Newborn Thunderbolt, and the third is Raw Thunderbolt.[6]

So there were three of them, as Heart of Sky, who came to the Sovereign Plumed Serpent, when the dawn of life was conceived:

"How should it be sown, how should it dawn? Who is to be the provider, nurturer?"[7]

---

5. As though a farmer were measuring and staking a cornfield.   6. Alternate names for Heart of Sky, the deity who cooperates with Sovereign Plumed Serpent. The triple naming adapts the Christian trinity to native theology, perhaps more in the spirit of defiant preemption than of conciliation.   7. That is, humanity, which alone is capable of *nurturing* the gods with sacrifices.

"Let it be this way, think about it: this water should be removed, emptied out for the formation of the earth's own plate and platform, then comes the sowing, the dawning of the sky-earth. But there will be no high days and no bright praise for our work, our design, until the rise of the human work, the human design," they said.

And then the earth arose because of them, it was simply their word that brought it forth. For the forming of the earth they said "Earth." It arose suddenly, just like a cloud, like a mist, now forming, unfolding. Then the mountains were separated from the water, all at once the great mountains came forth. By their genius alone, by their cutting edge[8] alone they carried out the conception of the mountain-plain, whose face grew instant groves of cypress and pine.

And the Plumed Serpent was pleased with this:

"It was good that you came, Heart of Sky, Hurricane, and Newborn Thunderbolt, Raw Thunderbolt. Our work, our design will turn out well," they said.

And the earth was formed first, the mountain-plain. The channels of water were separated; their branches wound their ways among the mountains. The waters were divided when the great mountains appeared.

Such was the formation of the earth when it was brought forth by the Heart of Sky, Heart of Earth, as they are called, since they were the first to think of it. The sky was set apart, and the earth was set apart in the midst of the waters.

Such was their plan when they thought, when they worried about the completion of their work.[9]

FROM PART 2

[The Twins Defeat Seven Macaw]

Here is the beginning of the defeat and destruction of The day of Seven Macaw by the two boys, the first named Hunahpu and the second named Xbalanque.[1] Being gods, the two of them saw evil in his attempt at self-magnification before the Heart of Sky.

*   *   *

This is the great tree of Seven Macaw, a nance,[2] and this is the food of Seven Macaw. In order to eat the fruit of the nance he goes up the tree every day. Since Hunahpu and Xbalanque have seen where he feeds, they are now hiding beneath the tree of Seven Macaw, they are keeping quiet here, the two boys are in the leaves of the tree.

And when Seven Macaw arrived, perching over his meal, the nance, it was then that he was shot by Hunahpu. The blowgun shot went right to

---

8. When used together, *puz* ("cutting edge" or "sacrifice") and *naual* ("genius") are metonyms for shamanic power, referring to the ability to make genius or spiritual essence visible or audible by means of ritual [Translator's note].   9. That is, the creation of humans; an account of the first three, unsuccessful, attempts at creating humans occupies the remainder of Part 1.   1. First mention of the twin hero gods (their origin is recounted in Part 3). Here they confront the false god Seven Macaw, who has arisen during the time of primordial darkness, boasting, "My eyes are of metal; my teeth just glitter with jewels, and turquoise as well. . . . I am like the sun and the moon." Note that all the characters in Parts 1, 2, and 3 are supernatural; humans are not created until Part 4.   2. A pickle tree (*Byrsonima crassifolia*).

his jaw, breaking his mouth. Then he went up over the tree and fell flat on the ground. Suddenly Hunahpu appeared, running. He set out to grab him, but actually it was the arm of Hunahpu that was seized by Seven Macaw. He yanked it straight back, he bent it back at the shoulder. Then Seven Macaw tore it right out of Hunahpu. Even so, the boys did well: the first round was not their defeat by Seven Macaw.

And when Seven Macaw had taken the arm of Hunahpu, he went home. Holding his jaw very carefully, he arrived:

"What have you got there?" said Chimalmat, the wife of Seven Macaw.

"What is it but those two tricksters! They've shot me, they've dislocated my jaw.[3] All my teeth are just loose, now they ache. But once what I've got is over the fire—hanging there, dangling over the fire—then they can just come and get it. They're real tricksters!" said Seven Macaw, then he hung up the arm of Hunahpu.

Meanwhile Hunahpu and Xbalanque were thinking. And then they invoked a grandfather, a truly white-haired grandfather, and a grandmother, a truly humble grandmother—just bent-over, elderly people. Great White Peccary is the name of the grandfather, and Great White Tapir is the name of the grandmother.[4] The boys said to the grandmother and grandfather:

"Please travel with us when we go to get our arm from Seven Macaw; we'll just follow right behind you. You'll tell him:

'Do forgive us our grandchildren, who travel with us. Their mother and father are dead, and so they follow along there, behind us. Perhaps we should give them away, since all we do is pull worms out of teeth.' So we'll seem like children to Seven Macaw, even though we're giving you the instructions," the two boys told them.

"Very well," they replied.

After that they approached the place where Seven Macaw was in front of his home. When the grandmother and grandfather passed by, the two boys were romping along behind them. When they passed below the lord's house, Seven Macaw was yelling his mouth off because of his teeth. And when Seven Macaw saw the grandfather and grandmother traveling with them:

"Where are you headed, our grandfather?" said the lord.

"We're just making our living, your lordship," they replied.

"Why are you working for a living? Aren't those your children traveling with you?"

"No, they're not, your lordship. They're our grandchildren, our descendants, but it is nevertheless we who take pity on them. The bit of food they get is the portion we give them, your lordship," replied the grandmother and grandfather. Since the lord is getting done in by the pain in his teeth, it is only with great effort that he speaks again:

"I implore you, please take pity on me! What sweets can you make, what poisons[5] can you cure? said the lord.

---

3. This is obviously the origin of the way a macaw's beak looks, with a huge upper mandible and a much smaller and retreating lower one [Translator's note].   4. Animal names of the divine grandparents, Xpiyacoc and Xmucane, who are also the twins' genealogical grandparents.   5. Play on words as *qui* is translated as both "sweet" and "poison."

"We just pull the worms out of teeth, and we just cure eyes. We just set bones, your lordship," they replied.

"Very well, please cure my teeth. They really ache, every day. It's insufferable! I get no sleep because of them—and my eyes. They just shot me, those two tricksters! Ever since it started I haven't eaten because of it. Therefore take pity on me! Perhaps it's because my teeth are loose now."

"Very well, your lordship. It's a worm, gnawing at the bone.[6] It's merely a matter of putting in a replacement and taking the teeth out, sir."

"But perhaps it's not good for my teeth to come out—since I am, after all, a lord. My finery is in my teeth—and my eyes."

"But then we'll put in a replacement. Ground bone will be put back in." And this is the "ground bone": it's only white corn.

"Very well. Yank them out! Give me some help here!" he replied.

And when the teeth of Seven Macaw came out, it was only white corn that went in as a replacement for his teeth—just a coating shining white, that corn in his mouth. His face fell at once, he no longer looked like a lord. The last of his teeth came out, the jewels that had stood out blue from his mouth.

And then the eyes of Seven Macaw were cured. When his eyes were trimmed back the last of his metal came out.[7] Still he felt no pain; he just looked on while the last of his greatness left him. It was just as Hunahpu and Xbalanque had intended.

And when Seven Macaw died, Hunahpu got back his arm. And Chimalmat, the wife of Seven Macaw, also died.

Such was the loss of the riches of Seven Macaw: only the doctors got the jewels and gems that had made him arrogant, here on the face of the earth. The genius of the grandmother, the genius of the grandfather did its work when they took back their arm: it was implanted and the break got well again. Just as they had wished the death of Seven Macaw, so they brought it about. They had seen evil in his self-magnification.

After this the two boys went on again. What they did was simply the word of the Heart of Sky.

FROM PART 3

[Victory over the Underworld]

And now we shall name the name of the father of Hunahpu and Xbalanque. Let's drink to him, and let's just drink to the telling and accounting of the begetting of Hunahpu and Xbalanque. We shall tell just half of it, just a part of the account of their father. Here follows the account.

These are the names: One Hunahpu and Seven Hunahpu,[8] as they are called.

* * *

6. The present-day Quiché retain the notion that a toothache is caused by a worm gnawing at the bone [Translator's note].   7. This is clearly meant to be the origin of the large white eye patch and very small eyes of the scarlet macaw [Translator's note].   8. Twin sons of Xpiyacoc and Xmucane; the elder of these twins, One Hunahpu, will become the father of Hunahpu and Xbalanque. "As for Seven Hunahpu," according to the text, "he has no wife. He's just a partner and just secondary; he just remains a boy."

And One and Seven Hunahpu went inside Dark House.[9] And then their torch was brought, only one torch, already lit, sent by One and Seven Death, along with a cigar for each of them, also already lit, sent by the lords. When these were brought to One and Seven Hunahpu they were cowering, here in the dark. When the bearer of their torch and cigars arrived, the torch was bright as it entered; their torch and both of their cigars were burning. The bearer spoke:

" 'They must be sure to return them in the morning—not finished, but just as they look now. They must return them intact,' the lords say to you," they were told, and they were defeated. They finished the torch and they finished the cigars that had been brought to them.

And Xibalba is packed with tests, heaps and piles of tests.

This is the first one: the Dark House, with darkness alone inside.

And the second is named Rattling House, heavy with cold inside, whistling with drafts, clattering with hail. A deep chill comes inside here.

And the third is named Jaguar House, with jaguars alone inside, jostling one another, crowding together, with gnashing teeth. They're scratching around; these jaguars are shut inside the house.

Bat House is the name of the fourth test, with bats alone inside the house, squeaking, shrieking, darting through the house. The bats are shut inside; they can't get out.

And the fifth is named Razor House, with blades alone inside. The blades are moving back and forth, ripping, slashing through the house.

These are the first tests of Xibalba, but One and Seven Hunahpu never entered into them, except for the one named earlier, the specified test house.

And when One and Seven Hunahpu went back before One and Seven Death, they were asked:

"Where are my cigars? What of my torch? They were brought to you last night!"

"We finished them, your lordship."

"Very well. This very day, your day is finished, you will die, you will disappear, and we shall break you off. Here you will hide your faces: you are to be sacrificed!" said One and Seven Death.

And then they were sacrificed and buried. They were buried at the Place of Ball Game Sacrifice,[1] as it is called. The head of One Hunahpu was cut off; only his body was buried with his younger brother.

"Put his head in the fork of the tree that stands by the road," said One and Seven Death.

And when his head was put in the fork of the tree, the tree bore fruit. It would not have had any fruit, had not the head of One Hunahpu been put in the fork of the tree.

This is the calabash tree, as we call it today, or "the head of One Hunahpu," as it is said.

9. The first of the "test" houses in Xibalba (the underworld) to which One and Seven Hunahpu, avid ballplayers, have been lured by the underworld lords, One and Seven Death; the lords have promised them a challenging ball game. The Mesoamerican ball game, remotely comparable to both basketball and soccer, was played on a rectangular court, using a ball of native rubber.   1. Probably not a place name, but rather a name for the altar where losing ball players were sacrificed [Translator's note].

And then One and Seven Death were amazed at the fruit of the tree. The fruit grows out everywhere, and it isn't clear where the head of One Hunahpu is; now it looks just the way the calabashes look. All the Xibalbans see this, when they come to look.

The state of the tree loomed large in their thoughts, because it came about at the same time the head of One Hunahpu was put in the fork. The Xibalbans said among themselves:

"No one is to pick the fruit, nor is anyone to go beneath the tree," they said. They restricted themselves; all of Xibalba held back.

It isn't clear which is the head of One Hunahpu; now it's exactly the same as the fruit of the tree. Calabash tree came to be its name, and much was said about it. A maiden heard about it, and here we shall tell of her arrival.

And here is the account of a maiden, the daughter of a lord named Blood Gatherer.[2]

And this is when a maiden heard of it, the daughter of a lord. Blood Gatherer is the name of her father, and Blood Woman is the name of the maiden.

And when he heard the account of the fruit of the tree, her father retold it. And she was amazed at the account:

"I'm not acquainted with that tree they talk about. ' "Its fruit is truly sweet!" they say,' I hear," she said.

Next, she went all alone and arrived where the tree stood. It stood at the Place of Ball Game Sacrifice:

"What? Well! What's the fruit of this tree? Shouldn't this tree bear something sweet? They shouldn't die, they shouldn't be wasted. Should I pick one?" said the maiden.

And then the bone spoke; it was here in the fork of the tree:

"Why do you want a mere bone, a round thing in the branches of a tree?" said the head of One Hunahpu when it spoke to the maiden. "You don't want it," she was told.

"I do want it," said the maiden.

"Very well. Stretch out your right hand here, so I can see it," said the bone.

"Yes," said the maiden. She stretched out her right hand, up there in front of the bone.

And then the bone spit out its saliva, which landed squarely in the hand of the maiden.

And then she looked in her hand, she inspected it right away, but the bone's saliva wasn't in her hand.

"It is just a sign I have given you, my saliva, my spittle. This, my head, has nothing on it—just bone, nothing of meat. It's just the same with the head of a great lord: it's just the flesh that makes his face look good. And when he dies, people get frightened by his bones. After that, his son is like his saliva, his spittle, in his being, whether it be the son of a lord or the son of a craftsman, an orator. The father does not disappear, but goes on being fulfilled. Neither dimmed nor destroyed is the face of a lord, a war-

---

2. Fourth-ranking lord of Xibalba, whose commission is to draw blood from people.

rior, craftsman, orator. Rather, he will leave his daughters and sons. So it is that I have done likewise through you. Now go up there on the face of the earth; you will not die. Keep the word. So be it," said the head of One and Seven Hunahpu—they were of one mind when they did it.

This was the word Hurricane, Newborn Thunderbolt, Raw Thunderbolt had given them. In the same way, by the time the maiden returned to her home, she had been given many instructions. Right away something was generated in her belly, from the saliva alone, and this was the generation of Hunahpu and Xbalanque.

And when the maiden got home and six months had passed, she was found out by her father. Blood Gatherer is the name of her father.

*   *   *

And they came to the lords.[3] Feigning great humility, they bowed their heads all the way to the ground when they arrived. They brought themselves low, doubled over, flattened out, down to the rags, to the tatters. They really looked like vagabonds when they arrived.

So then they were asked what their mountain[4] and tribe were, and they were also asked about their mother and father:

"Where do you come from?" they were asked.

"We've never known, lord. We don't know the identity of our mother and father. We must've been small when they died," was all they said. They didn't give any names.

"Very well. Please entertain us, then. What do you want us to give you in payment?" they were asked.

"Well, we don't want anything. To tell the truth, we're afraid," they told the lord.

"Don't be afraid. Don't be ashamed. Just dance this way: first you'll dance to sacrifice yourselves, you'll set fire to my house after that, you'll act out all the things you know. We want to be entertained. This is our heart's desire, the reason you had to be sent for, dear vagabonds. We'll give you payment," they were told.

So then they began their songs and dances, and then all the Xibalbans arrived, the spectators crowded the floor, and they danced everything: they danced the Weasel, they danced the Poorwill,[5] they danced the Armadillo. Then the lord said to them:

"Sacrifice my dog, then bring him back to life again," they were told.

"Yes," they said.

> When they sacrificed the dog
> he then came back to life.
> And that dog was really happy
> when he came back to life.

---

3. Forced to flee the underworld the maiden (Blood Woman) finds refuge on earth with Xmucane. There she gives birth to the twins, who, like their father and uncle, become ballplayers and are enticed to the underworld. Surviving the Dark House and other tests, they disguise themselves as vagabonds and earn a reputation as clever entertainers among the denizens of Xibalba; as such they are summoned to entertain the high lords.   4. A metonym for almost any settlement, but especially a fortified town or citadel, located on a defensible elevation [Translator's note].   5. The goatsucker. The dances apparently were imitations of these animals and birds.

Back and forth he wagged his tail
when he came back to life.

And the lord said to them:

"Well, you have yet to set my home on fire," they were told next, so then they set fire to the home of the lord. The house was packed with all the lords, but they were not burned. They quickly fixed it back again, lest the house of One Death be consumed all at once, and all the lords were amazed, and they went on dancing this way. They were overjoyed.

And then they were asked by the lord:

"You have yet to kill a person! Make a sacrifice without death!" they were told.

"Very well," they said.

And then they took hold of a human sacrifice.

And they held up a human heart on high.

And they showed its roundness to the lords.

And now One and Seven Death admired it, and now that person was brought right back to life. His heart was overjoyed when he came back to life, and the lords were amazed:

"Sacrifice yet again, even do it to yourselves! Let's see it! At heart, that's the dance we really want from you," the lords said now.

"Very well, lord," they replied, and then they sacrificed themselves.

And this is the sacrifice of Hunahpu by Xbalanque. One by one his legs, his arms were spread wide. His head came off, rolled far away outside. His heart, dug out, was smothered in a leaf,[6] and all the Xibalbans went crazy at the sight.

So now, only one of them was dancing there: Xbalanque.

"Get up!" he said, and Hunahpu came back to life. The two of them were overjoyed at this—and likewise the lords rejoiced, as if they were doing it themselves. One and Seven Death were as glad at heart as if they themselves were actually doing the dance.

And then the hearts of the lords were filled with longing, with yearning for the dance of Hunahpu and Xbalanque, so then came these words from One and Seven Death:

"Do it to us! Sacrifice us!" they said. "Sacrifice both of us!" said One and Seven Death to Hunahpu and Xbalanque.

"Very well. You ought to come back to life. After all, aren't you Death?[7] And aren't we making you happy, along with the vassals of your domain?" they told the lords.

And this one was the first to be sacrificed: the lord at the very top, the one whose name is One Death, the ruler of Xibalba.

And with One Death dead, the next to be taken was Seven Death. They did not come back to life.

And then the Xibalbans were getting up to leave, those who had seen the lords die. They underwent heart sacrifice there, and the heart sacrifice was performed on the two lords only for the purpose of destroying them.

---

6. As a tamale is wrapped. In the typical Mesoamerican heart sacrifice, the victim's arms and legs were stretched wide and the heart was excised and offered to a deity.   7. Evident sarcasm.

once. Perfectly they saw, perfectly they knew everything under the sky, whenever they looked. The moment they turned around and looked around in the sky, on the earth, everything was seen without any obstruction. They didn't have to walk around before they could see what was under the sky; they just stayed where they were.

As they looked, their knowledge became intense. Their sight passed through trees, through rocks, through lakes, through seas, through mountains, through plains. Jaguar Quitze, Jaguar Night, Mahucutah, and True Jaguar were truly gifted people.

And then they were asked by the builder and mason:

"What do you know about your being? Don't you look, don't you listen? Isn't your speech good, and your walk? So you must look, to see out under the sky. Don't you see the mountain-plain clearly? So try it," they were told.

And then they saw everything under the sky perfectly. After that, they thanked the Maker, Modeler:

> "Truly now,
> double thanks, triple thanks
> that we've been formed, we've been given
> our mouths, our faces,
> we speak, we listen,
> we wonder, we move,
> our knowledge is good, we've understood
> what is far and near,
> and we've seen what is great and small
> under the sky, on the earth.
> Thanks to you we've been formed,
> we've come to be made and modeled,
> our grandmother, our grandfather,"

they said when they gave thanks for having been made and modeled. They understood everything perfectly, they sighted the four sides, the four corners in the sky, on the earth, and this didn't sound good to the builder and sculptor:

"What our works and designs have said is no good:

'We have understood everything, great and small,' they say." And so the Bearer, Begetter took back their knowledge:

"What should we do with them now? Their vision should at least reach nearby, they should see at least a small part of the face of the earth, but what they're saying isn't good. Aren't they merely 'works' and 'designs' in their very names? Yet they'll become as great as gods, unless they procreate, proliferate at the sowing, the dawning, unless they increase."

"Let it be this way: now we'll take them apart just a little, that's what we need. What we've found out isn't good. Their deeds would become equal to ours, just because their knowledge reaches so far. They see everything," so said

> the Heart of Sky, Hurricane,
> Newborn Thunderbolt, Raw Thunderbolt,
> Sovereign Plumed Serpent,

Part IV

1650 TO 1800

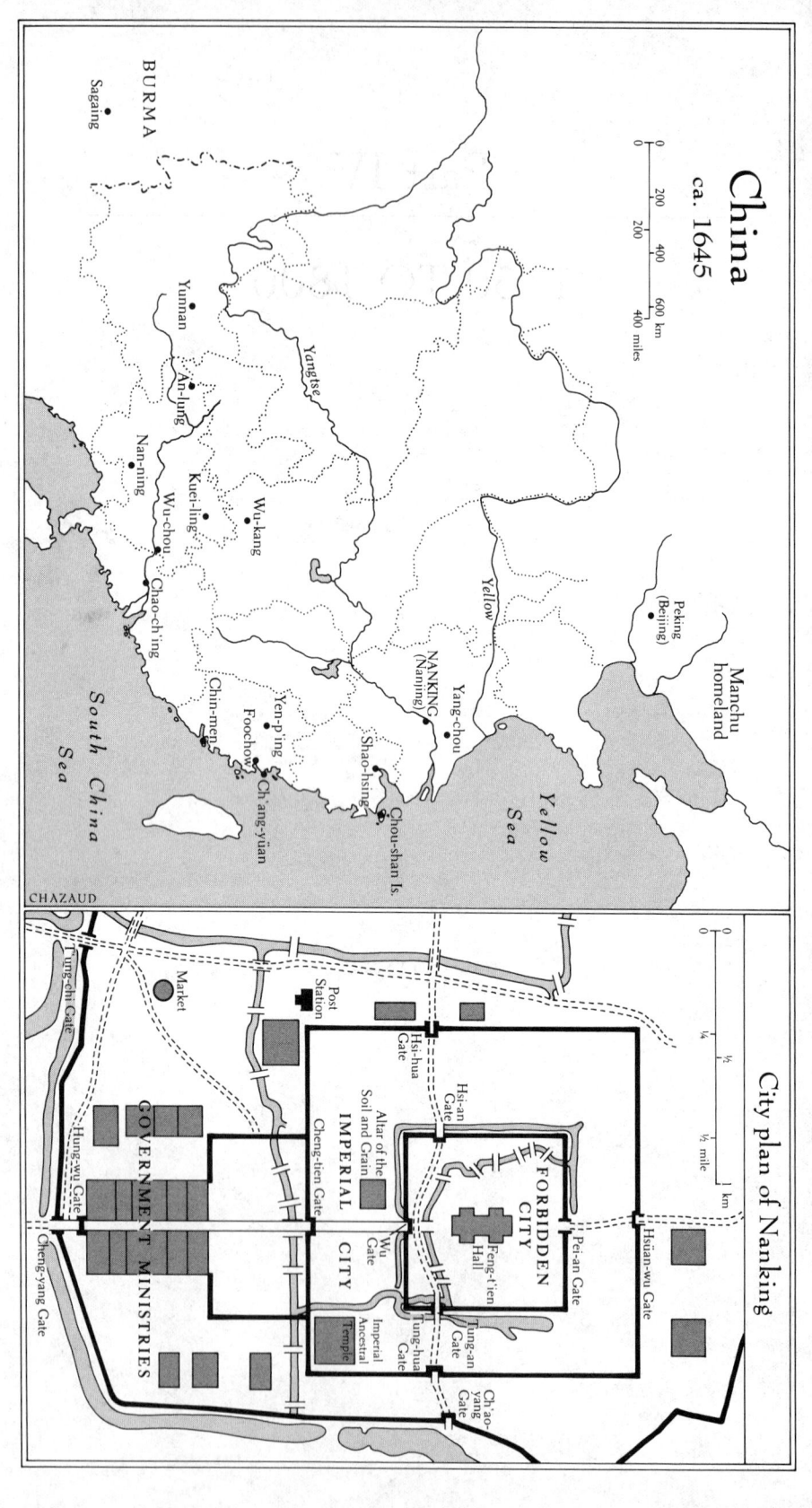

China
ca. 1645

BURMA

Sagaing

Yunnan

An-lung

Nan-ning

Kuei-ling

Wu-chou

Chao-ch'ing

Wu-kang

Chin-men

Yen-p'ing

Foochow

Ch'ang-yüan

Shao-hsing

Chou-shan Is.

NANKING
(Nanjing)

Yang-chou

Peking
(Beijing)

Manchu
homeland

Yangtse

Yellow

Yellow
Sea

South
China
Sea

CHAZAUD

0   200   400   600 km
0   200   400 miles

City plan of Nanking

Tung-chi Gate

Market

Post
Station

Hsi-hua
Gate

Hsi-an
Gate

Altar of the
Soil and Grain

Cheng-tien Gate

GOVERNMENT MINISTRIES

Hung-wu Gate

Cheng-yang Gate

IMPERIAL

CITY

Wu
Gate

FORBIDDEN
CITY

Feng-t'ien
Hall

Pei-an Gate

Tung-an
Gate

Tung-hua
Gate

Hüan-wu Gate

Ch'ao-
yang
Gate

Imperial
Ancestral
Temple

0   ¼   ½   ¾   1 km
0   ¼   ½   mile

Vernacular Literature in China

Several decades after completing the conquest of north China, Mongol armies crossed the Yangtse River and conquered the Southern Sung Dynasty in 1279. At the time their empire stretched across all of Asia, but as a Chinese dynasty the Mongols were known as the Yüan. Although they assumed a Chinese dynastic title and some of the trappings of Chinese imperial government, the Mongols did not base their state on Confucian principles, for which they had the greatest contempt. To the everlasting shock of Chinese intellectuals, the Mongols suspended the examination system, by which members of the educated elite were recruited for government service. The long-established link between classical literature (poetry and nonfiction prose), an education in the Confucian classics, and service in the government was temporarily broken. Even after the civil service examinations were reestablished later in the dynasty, classical literature never regained its place as the core around which public, social, and private life was organized. Through the rest of the imperial period, classical literature remained an important part of the life of intellectuals, but its general role had been diminished to something like that of literature in Western civilization, an important adjunct of social life but not at its core.

As classical literature lost its importance, literature in vernacular Chinese (plays, verse romances, and prose fiction) began to be published. The steady rise of the bourgeoisie in the great cities and the spread of literacy in urban areas created a market for written versions of literary forms that already flourished in performance. In Europe and Great Britain the authority of classical drama could be used to defend the validity of Renaissance drama in the vernacular tongues. Greek and Latin prose romance, though with lesser prestige than drama, likewise informed the development of vernacular narrative prose. In China, by contrast, there was no ancient drama, and classical prose fiction was generally considered pure entertainment.

In the cities of China, however, rich traditions of theater, oral verse romance, and storytelling flourished. The thirteenth and fourteenth centuries produced the first published versions of these forms, with each written form carefully preserving the ambience of performance. Some intellectuals were fascinated by this urban popular literature, and what survives of it is the result of their efforts. Such literature grew steadily in volume and importance through the Ming Dynasty (1368–1644).

Although Yüan and Ming vernacular literature lacked the subtlety of classical literature, much that had been repressed in classical literature burst forth in the vernacular: sex, violence, satire, and humor. Plays, verse romances, and prose stories were often elaborations of some source in the classical language, spinning out a few pages into thirty or a thousand. This was a literature whose strength lay not in inventing plots but in filling in details and saying what had been omitted. In that strength, it became something different in kind from classical literature, with new virtues and new failings.

Chinese popular literature is largely a vast tissue of interrelated stories. The illiterate and semiliterate population had learned history from storytellers, who took a time period and elaborated it in the spoken tongue, including poems and songs. A dramatist might take one incident from a story cycle and develop it into a play. A fiction writer might cover an entire story cycle in a novel. A number of these historical romances survive, the most famous being *The Romance of the Three Kingdoms* (*San-kuo chih yen-yi*)—attributed to Lo Kuan-chung (earliest printed version 1522)—an elaboration of the official history of the period in which the Han Dynasty disintegrated, around the turn of the third century A.D. In *The Romance of the Three Kingdoms*, the somewhat dry historical account was transformed into a dazzling saga of battles and clever stratagems.

Popular literature worked with other materials as well. Murder mysteries, often based on recent cases, circulated, in which the wise magistrate, "Judge Pao," played a role equivalent to that of the modern detective. Stories of a famous group of twelfth-century bandits, like Robin Hood representing justice against corrupt authority, developed into the novel *Water Margin* (*Shui-hu chuan*) (early 1500s). One small incident in *Water Margin* was elaborated into the saga of a corrupt sensualist whose greed and sexual escapades give a vivid if skewed portrait of urban life in Ming China; this is *Golden Lotus* (*Chin P'ing Mei*) (1617). And the story of the Buddhist monk Hsuan Tsang who went west to India to get scriptures, guarded by a band of fantastic creatures headed by a wily monkey possessed of supernatural powers, became the novel *Monkey* (*Hsi-yu chi*) (1592).

As literature lost its role in public life, the vital link between literature and Confucian intellectual culture also gave way. High culture favored neo-Confucianism, at best prim and at worst dogmatic. Neo-Confucianism was an attempt to discover the philosophical grounds of the Confucian classics, and it developed into a system of private and social ethics that was to guide all aspects of life. Its rigid strictures on self-cultivation and ethical behavior failed in basic ways to address the complexities of human nature and the pressures of living in an increasingly complex world. Except among a very few committed thinkers, it was a philosophical position that invited gross hypocrisy. Vernacular literature, on the other hand, celebrated liberty, violent energy, and passion. Though such works often contained elements of neo-Confucian ethics and were later given pious neo-Confucian interpretations, by and large they either voiced qualities that neo-Confucianism sought to repress or savagely attacked society as a world of false appearances and secret evils.

In 1644 Manchu armies from the northeast descended into China and established a new dynasty, the Ch'ing, which would rule China until the revolution in 1911. Once again under non-Chinese rule and forced to wear the Manchu queue, a long ponytail, as a mark of submission, many Chinese harbored strong anti-Manchu sentiments. The Manchus, for their part, became very sensitive to native opposition. Censors set to survey current writings for hostility to the regime continually discovered slights, both real and imagined, against the dynasty. The late seventeenth and eighteenth centuries, known as the "literary inquisition," had a chilling effect on writing, especially in classical Chinese.

Such political realities may strongly affect, but do not entirely determine the intellectual and literary climate of an era. Ch'ing intellectual culture was a strong reaction against the radical individualism of the last part of the Ming, when personal freedom was celebrated at the expense of social responsibility. Early Ch'ing intellectuals held this late Ming ethos responsible for the decline of the Ming Dynasty. In the latter part of the seventeenth century and into the eighteenth century intellectuals turned away from Ming "subjectivism," the belief that each individual contained within himself or herself the grounds to make moral decisions and to interpret the authoritative texts of the tradition. The reaction saw not only a conservative public morality but also a new historical and philological rigor in the interpretation of early texts. This was closely analogous to the contemporary

Western conflict in biblical studies between subjectivist "liberty of interpretation" and the development of historical philology—that is, the understanding of early texts by close study of how words were used at the time when the text was written. The new emphasis on historical scholarship had profound consequences for both China and the West, each of which had depended to some degree on the authority of received texts. This historical and philological approach to early texts was a form of empiricism, basing judgments on evidence and proof rather than tradition or private inclination. In China, as in the West at the same time, such empiricism in scholarship became linked to other forms of empiricism, such as interest in the natural sciences.

Ming subjectivist thought had found its strongest literary manifestation in a fascination with dreams, a world of illusion that was both a prominent theme in and a metaphor for the theater. And like Shakespeare, Chinese dramatists also observed that "all the world's a stage" and thus also a dream, as did the Spanish dramatist Calderon in his play *Life Is a Dream*. Drama, far more than prose fiction, dominated the literary world, both in the theater and in published texts. Social rituals and ceremonies had been one of the pillars of Confucian society, and these came increasingly to be represented in terms of theatrical performance. What had been norms of behavior became "roles," strongly suggesting awareness of their unreality and the presence of an individual who was only "playing" a role.

The eighteenth century was the last period of glory and self-confidence for traditional Chinese civilization. Although China had been in continuous contact with Europe since the sixteenth century, in the early nineteenth century European colonial powers began to make major inroads on Chinese autonomy. The opium trade, dominated by British merchants, drained away silver while producing a major social problem. In their campaign to stop the drug trade, the Chinese fired on a ship flying the British flag. From this followed the Opium War (1840–42), in which Great Britain inflicted a series of humiliating defeats on Chinese forces. In the treaty that followed, Hong Kong was ceded to Great Britain and five so-called treaty ports were established, subject to British law and control. Other European powers rushed to carve out their own enclaves. Christian missionaries, protected by treaty, spread throughout the country. One consequence was the T'ai-p'ing T'ien-kuo, the "Heavenly Kingdom of Great Peace," a political movement and religious sect that mingled Christianity and native Chinese beliefs. The T'ai-p'ing T'ien-kuo rose in rebellion against the Ch'ing government, and between 1850 and 1864 carried out a war that left central China in desolation.

Humiliated and exhausted, the Ch'ing government found itself unable to adapt, either culturally or technologically, to the world that had been thrust on it. Through the latter half of the nineteenth century and first decade of the twentieth, the Ch'ing Dynasty slowly disintegrated, until it was overthrown with remarkable ease in 1911, when the Republic of China was established.

FURTHER READING

A basic survey of the history of Chinese drama can be found in William Dolby, *A History of Chinese Drama* (1976). C. T. Hsia, *The Classic Chinese Novel: A Critical Introduction* (1968), remains one of the most readable introductions to the major novels. Patrick Hanan, *The Chinese Vernacular Story* (1981), provides an insightful study of the cultural background of vernacular fiction.

VERNACULAR LITERATURE IN CHINA

TEXTS	CONTEXTS
1300–1350 Earliest printed versions of vernacular drama ca. 1350 Earliest publication of vernacular short stories	
	1368 Ming Dynasty is established with the capital at Nanking
	1405–1421 Ming admiral Cheng Ho explores southeast Asia, Sri Lanka, and the coast of Africa
	1421 The capital is moved to Peking
early 16th century Earliest edition of *Water Margin*, an episodic novel about a band of outlaws	
1522 Earliest edition of *Romance of the Three Kingdoms*, a long historical novel about the fall of the Han dynasty	
1550–1617 T'ang Hsien-tsu, a major dramatist who developed the long *ch'uan-ch'i* play into a literary form	
1574–1646 Feng Meng-lung, collector and author of vernacular stories and popular songs, important in raising the status of vernacular literature	1580–1644 Late Ming, a period of radical subjectivism and questioning of authority of tradition
	1583–1610 Matteo Ricci, Jesuit missionary, serves in China
1592 Earliest extant edition of *Monkey* (*Journey to the West*)	
1611–1680 Li Yü, comic dramatist, story writer, and champion of vernacular literature	
1617 Earliest edition of *Chin P'ing Mei* (Golden lotus), a satirical novel of manners about a corrupt sensualist	
	1644–1645 Manchus conquer China • Ch'ing Dynasty is established • All Chinese males are forced to cut their hair and wear the queue

TEXTS	CONTEXTS
1648–1718 K'ung Shang-jen, author of *The Peach Blossom Fan* (1699)	
1715–1763 Cao Xueqin, author of *The Story of the Stone* (1740–50)	
	1736–1794 "Literary inquisition": earlier works are censored and many writers imprisoned for suspected critical references to the Ch'ing Dynasty
ca. 1750 *Ju-lin wai-shih* (The scholars), a satirical novel; first extant edition 1803	
1788 The completion of the *Ssu-k'u ch'üan-shu*, a massive collection of all important earlier literature	

CAO XUEQIN (TS'AO HSÜEH-CH'IN)

1715–1763

Of all the world's novels perhaps only *Don Quixote* rivals *The Story of the Stone* as the embodiment of a nation's cultural identity in recent times, much as the epic once embodied cultural identity in the ancient world. For Chinese readers of the past two centuries *The Story of the Stone* (also known as the *Dream of the Red Chamber*) has come to represent the best and worst of traditional China in its final phase. It is the story of an extended family, centered around its women, and of the relationships within the family. Even after nearly a century of war, revolution, and social experiment, a century that has seen the dissolution of the traditional extended family, *The Story of the Stone* has retained its hold on the Chinese imagination.

As the title tells us, the novel is also, on a basic level, the story of a magical and conscious stone, the one block left over when the goddess Nü-wa repaired the damaged vault of the sky in the mythic past. Transported into the mortal world by a pair of priests, one Buddhist and one Taoist, Stone is destined to find enlightenment by suffering the pains of love, loss, and disillusion as a human being. In his incarnation, Stone is born as the sole legitimate male heir of a wealthy and powerful household, the Jias, which is about to pass from the height of prosperity into decline. Miraculously, the baby is born with an inscribed piece of jade in his mouth, from which he is given his name Bao-yu (Precious Jade) and which he wears always.

The novel itself has a peculiar genesis. The first eighty chapters are the work of Cao Xueqin, himself the scion of a once-wealthy family fallen on hard times. It is believed that he wrote the novel, in at least five drafts, between 1740 and 1750. There is another figure in the process of the novel's composition, someone who used the pseudonym "Red Inkstone" (or more properly "He of Red Inkstone Studio") and who added commentary and made corrections to the manuscript versions. He was obviously a close friend or relative of Cao Xueqin and acted the role of virtual collaborator. His comments suggest that the characters in the main portion of the novel are based on real people.

The novel was left unfinished and probably was never intended for publication, but it did circulate widely in Peking in manuscript copies, whose many variations show a complex process of revision. One version of the manuscript came into the hands of the writer Gao E (ca. 1740–ca. 1815), who completed the story by adding another 40 chapters, publishing the full 120-chapter version in 1791, about a half century after Cao Xueqin began to write. The transformations of the novel in its manuscript versions, the role of the mysterious Red Inkstone (and of another early commentator who calls himself "Odd Tablet"), and the relation of the characters to Cao's life are questions that continue to engage professional and amateur scholars.

Chinese novels are, as a rule, very long, and *The Story of the Stone* is longer than most, taking up five substantial volumes in its complete English translation. The narrative is impossible to summarize and difficult to excerpt. It has a huge cast of characters, both major and minor, who appear and disappear in intricately interwoven incidents. But, in part because of its very magnitude, the novel gradually draws its readers into the details of everyday life and the complexities of human relationships, occasionally punctuated by reminders that the intense emotions and the values given to things are all illusory. That sense of illusion is underscored by the family name Jia, a real Chinese surname that happens to be homophonous with another character meaning "false" or "feigned."

In addition to Bao-yu, the human metamorphosis of Stone, one other central character originates in the supernatural frame story and its fanciful landscape. This is Crimson Pearl Flower, a semidivine plant that grew near the Rock of Rebirth. In the opening chapter, while Stone is serving at the court of the goddess Disenchantment, he takes a fancy to this flower and waters it with sweet dew. This eventually brings the flower to life in the form of a fairy girl, who is obsessed with repaying the kindness of Stone, and for his gift of sweet dew she owes him the "debt of tears." This character is born as Bao-yu's cousin, the delicate and high-strung Lin Dai-yu (*Dai-yu* means "Black Jade").

The early chapters are devoted to the supernatural frame story and to bringing the characters together. In chapters seventeen and eighteen, Bao-yu's elder sister, an imperial concubine, has been permitted to pay a visit to her home. The women of the emperor's harem were usually confined to the palace; in permitting her to return, the emperor is displaying his favor to her and to her family. In her honor a huge garden (Prospect Garden) is constructed on the grounds of the family compound. After the imperial concubine's departure, the adolescent girls of the extended family are allowed to take up residence in the various buildings in the garden, and by special permission Bao-yu is also permitted to live there with his maids. The world of the garden is one of adolescent love in full flower, though we never forget the violent and ugly world outside, a world that often creeps into the garden world.

The adolescent love between Bao-yu and Dai-yu forms the core of the novel. Each is intensely sensitive to the other, and neither can express what he or she feels. Communication between them often depends on subtle gestures with implicit meanings, meanings that are inevitably misunderstood. Both, and particularly Dai-yu, believe in a perfect understanding of hearts, but even in the charmed world of the garden, closeness eludes them. The novel often juxtaposes brutish characters (usually male) with those possessed of a finer sensibility; but in the case of Dai-yu, sensibility is carried to the extreme. Dai-yu's relation to Bao-yu is balanced by that of another distant relation, Xue Bao-chai, whose plump good looks and gentle common sense are the very opposite of Dai-yu's frailty and histrionic morbidity. Bao-chai ("Precious Hairpin") has a golden locket with an inscription that matches Bao-yu's jade, and the marriage of "jade and gold" is a possibility seriously considered by older members of the family. Eventually, in Gao E's ending for the novel, as Dai-yu is dying of consumption, Bao-yu will be tricked into marrying Bao-chai. Bao-yu will finally carry out his obligation to continue the family line and at last renounce the world to become a Buddhist monk.

Although the triangle of Bao-yu, Dai-yu, and Bao-chai stands at the center of the novel, scores of subplots involve characters of all types. *The Story of the Stone* is, as noted, a novel about family, its internal relationships and its place in the larger social world. The reader easily becomes absorbed in the intensity of the family's internal relationships, always to be reminded how those relationships touch and are touched by the world outside. Because this family has social power, the actions taken by family members to serve its interests and loyalties can also be seen as corruption. In some cases the corruption is obvious, but in a far subtler way the reader comes to identify with the family and takes many acts of power and privilege for granted. At the same time, the outside world has the capacity to impinge on the protected space of the family, and the reader sees these forces from the point of view of the insider, as intrusions. It is a world of concentric circles of proximity, both of kinship and affinity. Petty details and private loves and hates grow larger and larger as they approach the center. And above this is the Buddhist and Taoist lesson about the illusion of care, of a world driven by blind but powerful emotions that at last cause only suffering, both to self and others.

The reader will find much unfamiliar about the Jia household, a vast establishment of close and distant family members, personal maids, and servants, each with his or her own level of status. Although the personal maids had some responsibilities, it will be obvious that the number of maids attached to each family member was primarily a mark of status. For a girl from a poor family, the position of personal maid was very desirable, providing room, board, and income to send to her own family. Bao-yu often flirts with his maids, but he has sexual relations only with his chief maid, Aroma.

The selection printed here includes part of the opening frame story and a series of chapters on Bao-yu and his female relations in Prospect Garden, with the blossoming of the love between him and Dai-yu.

There is a complete translation of *The Story of the Stone* in five volumes (1973–82), the first three volumes by David Hawkes and the last two by John Minford. Andrew Plaks, *Archetype and Allegory in the Dream of the Red Chamber* (1976), is a useful study.

PRONOUNCING GLOSSARY

The following list uses common English syllables to provide rough equivalents of selected words whose pronunciation may be unfamiliar to the general reader.

Cao Xueqin: *tsao shueh-chin*

Feng-shi: *fuhng–shir*

Feng Zi-ying: *fuhng dzuh–ying*

Gao E: *gau uh*

Jia Yu-cun: *jyah yow–tswuhn*

Jia Zheng: *jyah juhng*

Kong Mei-xi: *koong may–shee*

　　qiang: *chyahng*

Shi Xiang-yun: *shir shyahng–yoon*

Wang Ji-ren: *wahng jee–ruhn*

Wu Yu-feng: *woo yow–fuhng*

Xi-feng: *shee–fuhng*

Xue Bao-chai: *shooeh bau–chai*

Ying-lian: *ying–lyen*

Zhao: *jau*

Zhen Shi-yin: *juhn shir–yin*

Zhi-xiao: *juhr–shyau*

From The Story of the Stone[1]
From *Volume 1*

CHAPTER 1

Zhen Shi-yin makes the Stone's acquaintance in a dream
And Jia Yu-cun finds that poverty is not incompatible with romantic
feelings

Gentle Reader,

What, you may ask, was the origin of this book?

Though the answer to this question may at first seem to border on the absurd, reflection will show that there is a good deal more in it than meets the eye.

---

1. Translated by David Hawkes. Note that Hawkes used the pinyin system of spelling (whereas this volume usually uses the Wade-Giles system).

Long ago, when the goddess Nü-wa was repairing the sky, she melted down a great quantity of rock and, on the Incredible Crags of the Great Fable Mountains, moulded the amalgam into thirty-six thousand, five hundred and one large building blocks, each measuring seventy-two feet by a hundred and forty-four feet square. She used thirty-six thousand five hundred of these blocks in the course of her building operations, leaving a single odd block unused, which lay, all on its own, at the foot of Greensickness Peak in the aforementioned mountains.

Now this block of stone, having undergone the melting and moulding of a goddess, possessed magic powers. It could move about at will and could grow or shrink to any size it wanted. Observing that all the other blocks had been used for celestial repairs and that it was the only one to have been rejected as unworthy, it became filled with shame and resentment and passed its days in sorrow and lamentation.

One day, in the midst of its lamentings, it saw a monk and a Taoist approaching from a great distance, each of them remarkable for certain eccentricities of manner and appearance. When they arrived at the foot of Greensickness Peak, they sat down on the ground and began to talk. The monk, catching sight of a lustrous, translucent stone—it was in fact the rejected building block which had now shrunk itself to the size of a fan-pendant[2] and looked very attractive in its new shape—took it up on the palm of his hand and addressed it with a smile:

"Ha, I see you have magical properties! But nothing to recommend you. I shall have to cut a few words on you so that anyone seeing you will know at once that you are something special. After that I shall take you to a certain

>brilliant
>successful
>poetical
>cultivated
>aristocratic
>elegant
>delectable
>luxurious
>opulent
>locality on a little trip."

The stone was delighted.

"What words will you cut? Where is this place you will take me to? I beg to be enlightened."

"Do not ask," replied the monk with a laugh. "You will know soon enough when the time comes."

And with that he slipped the stone into his sleeve and set off at a great pace with the Taoist. But where they both went to I have no idea.

Countless aeons went by and a certain Taoist called Vanitas in quest of the secret of immortality chanced to be passing below that same Greensickness Peak in the Incredible Crags of the Great Fable Mountains when

---

2. Jade decoration strung from the bottom of a fan.

he caught sight of a large stone standing there, on which the characters of a long inscription were clearly discernible.

Vanitas read the inscription through from beginning to end and learned that this was a once lifeless stone block which had been found unworthy to repair the sky, but which had magically transformed its shape and been taken down by the Buddhist mahāsattva[3] Impervioso and the Taoist illuminate Mysterioso into the world of mortals, where it had lived out the life of a man before finally attaining nirvana and returning to the other shore.[4] The inscription named the country where it had been born, and went into considerable detail about its domestic life, youthful amours, and even the verses, mottoes and riddles it had written. All it lacked was the authentication of a dynasty and date. On the back of the stone was inscribed the following quatrain:

> Found unfit to repair the azure sky
> Long years a foolish mortal man was I.
> My life in both worlds on this stone is writ:
> Pray who will copy out and publish it?

From his reading of the inscription Vanitas realized that this was a stone of some consequence. Accordingly he addressed himself to it in the following manner:

"Brother Stone, according to what you yourself seem to imply in these verses, this story of yours contains matter of sufficient interest to merit publication and has been carved here with that end in view. But as far as I can see (a) it has no discoverable dynastic period, and (b) it contains no examples of moral grandeur among its characters—no statesmanship, no social message of any kind. All I can find in it, in fact, are a number of females, conspicuous, if at all, only for their passion or folly or for some trifling talent or insignificant virtue. Even if I were to copy all this out, I cannot see that it would make a very remarkable book."

"Come, your reverence," said the stone (for Vanitas had been correct in assuming that it could speak) "must you be so obtuse? All the romances ever written have an artificial period setting—Han or Tang for the most part. In refusing to make use of that stale old convention and telling my *Story of the Stone* exactly as it occurred, it seems to me that, far from *depriving* it of anything, I have given it a freshness these other books do not have.

"Your so-called 'historical romances,' consisting, as they do, of scandalous anecdotes about statesmen and emperors of bygone days and scabrous attacks on the reputations of long-dead gentlewomen, contain more wickedness and immorality than I care to mention. Still worse is the 'erotic novel,' by whose filthy obscenities our young folk are all too easily corrupted. And the 'boudoir romances,' those dreary stereotypes with their volume after volume all pitched on the same note and their different characters undistinguishable except by name (all those ideally beautiful young ladies and ideally eligible young bachelors)—even they seem unable to avoid descending sooner or later into indecency.

---

3. Wise man.   4. That is, achieving enlightenment and passing beyond the cycles of rebirth.

"The trouble with this last kind of romance is that it only gets written in the first place because the author requires a framework in which to show off his love-poems. He goes about constructing this framework quite mechanically, beginning with the names of his pair of young lovers and invariably adding a third character, a servant or the like, to make mischief between them, like the *chou*[5] in a comedy.

"What makes these romances even more detestable is the stilted, bombastic language — inanities dressed in pompous rhetoric, remote alike from nature and common sense and teeming with the grossest absurdities.

"Surely my 'number of females,' whom I spent half a lifetime studying with my own eyes and ears, are preferable to this kind of stuff? I do not claim that they are better people than the ones who appear in books written before my time; I am only saying that the contemplation of their actions and motives may prove a more effective antidote to boredom and melancholy. And even the inelegant verses with which my story is interlarded could serve to entertain and amuse on those convivial occasions when rhymes and riddles are in demand.

"All that my story narrates, the meetings and partings, the joys and sorrows, the ups and downs of fortune, are recorded exactly as they happened. I have not dared to add the tiniest bit of touching-up, for fear of losing the true picture.

"My only wish is that men in the world below may sometimes pick up this tale when they are recovering from sleep or drunkenness, or when they wish to escape from business worries or a fit of the dumps, and in doing so find not only mental refreshment but even perhaps, if they will heed its lesson and abandon their vain and frivolous pursuits, some small arrest in the deterioration of their vital forces. What does your reverence say to that?"

For a long time Vanitas stood lost in thought, pondering this speech. He then subjected *The Story of the Stone* to a careful second reading. He could see that its main theme was love; that it consisted quite simply of a true record of real events; and that it was entirely free from any tendency to deprave and corrupt. He therefore copied it all out from beginning to end and took it back with him to look for a publisher.

As a consequence of all this, Vanitas, starting off in the Void (which is Truth) came to the contemplation of Form (which is Illusion); and from Form engendered Passion; and by communicating Passion, entered again into Form; and from Form awoke to the Void (which is Truth). He therefore changed his name from Vanitas to Brother Amor, or the Passionate Monk, (because he had approached Truth by way of Passion), and changed the title of the book from *The Story of the Stone* to *The Tale of Brother Amor*.

Old Kong Mei-xi from the homeland of Confucius called the book *A Mirror for the Romantic*. Wu Yu-feng called it *A Dream of Golden Days*. Cao Xueqin in his Nostalgia Studio worked on it for ten years, in the course of which he rewrote it no less than five times, dividing it into chapters, composing chapter headings, renaming it *The Twelve Beauties of Jin-*

---

5. The stock role of the clown in a play.

ling, and adding an introductory quatrain. Red Inkstone restored the original title when he recopied the book and added his second set of annotations to it.

This, then, is a true account of how *The Story of the Stone* came to be written.

> Pages full of idle words
> Penned with hot and bitter tears:
> All men call the author fool;
> None his secret message hears.

The origin of *The Story of the Stone* has now been made clear. The same cannot, however, be said of the characters and events which it recorded. Gentle reader, have patience! This is how the inscription began:

Long, long ago the world was tilted downwards towards the south-east; and in that lower-lying south-easterly part of the earth there is a city called Soochow; and in Soochow the district around the Chang-men Gate is reckoned one of the two or three wealthiest and most fashionable quarters in the world of men. Outside the Chang-men Gate is a wide thoroughfare called Worldly Way; and somewhere off Worldly Way is an area called Carnal Lane. There is an old temple in the Carnal Lane area which, because of the way it is bottled up inside a narrow *cul-de-sac*, is referred to locally as Bottle-gourd Temple. Next door to Bottle-gourd Temple lived a gentleman of private means called Zhen Shi-yin and his wife Feng-shi, a kind, good woman with a profound sense of decency and decorum. The household was not a particularly wealthy one, but they were nevertheless looked up to by all and sundry as the leading family in the neighbourhood.

Zhen Shi-yin himself was by nature a quiet and totally unambitious person. He devoted his time to his garden and to the pleasures of wine and poetry. Except for a single flaw, his existence could, indeed, have been described as an idyllic one. The flaw was that, although already past fifty, he had no son, only a little girl, just two years old, whose name was Ying-lian.

Once, during the tedium of a burning summer's day, Shi-yin was sitting idly in his study. The book had slipped from his nerveless grasp and his head had nodded down onto the desk in a doze. While in this drowsy state he seemed to drift off to some place he could not identify, where he became aware of a monk and a Taoist walking along and talking as they went.

"Where do you intend to take that thing you are carrying?" the Taoist was asking.

"Don't you worry about him!" replied the monk with a laugh. "There is a batch of lovesick souls awaiting incarnation in the world below whose fate is due to be decided this very day. I intend to take advantage of this opportunity to slip our little friend in amongst them and let him have a taste of human life along with the rest."

"Well, well, so another lot of these amorous wretches is about to enter the vale of tears," said the Taoist. "How did all this begin? And where are the souls to be reborn?"

"You will laugh when I tell you," said the monk. "When this stone was left unused by the goddess, he found himself at a loose end and took to wandering about all over the place for want of better to do, until one day his wanderings took him to the place where the fairy Disenchantment lives.

"Now Disenchantment could tell that there was something unusual about this stone, so she kept him there in her Sunset Glow Palace and gave him the honorary title of Divine Luminescent Stone-in-Waiting in the Court of Sunset Glow.

"But most of his time he spent west of Sunset Glow exploring the banks of the Magic River. There, by the Rock of Rebirth, he found the beautiful Crimson Pearl Flower, for which he conceived such a fancy that he took to watering her every day with sweet dew, thereby conferring on her the gift of life.

"Crimson Pearl's substance was composed of the purest cosmic essences, so she was already half-divine; and now, thanks to the vitalizing effect of the sweet dew, she was able to shed her vegetable shape and assume the form of a girl.

"This fairy girl wandered about outside the Realm of Separation, eating the Secret Passion Fruit when she was hungry and drinking from the Pool of Sadness when she was thirsty. The consciousness that she owed the stone something for his kindness in watering her began to prey on her mind and ended by becoming an obsession.

" 'I have no sweet dew here that I can repay him with,' she would say to herself. 'The only way in which I could perhaps repay him would be with the tears shed during the whole of a mortal lifetime if he and I were ever to be reborn as humans in the world below.'

"Because of this strange affair, Disenchantment has got together a group of amorous young souls, of which Crimson Pearl is one, and intends to send them down into the world to take part in the great illusion of human life. And as today happens to be the day on which this stone is fated to go into the world too, I am taking him with me to Disenchantment's tribunal for the purpose of getting him registered and sent down to earth with the rest of these romantic creatures."

"How very amusing!" said the Taoist. "I have certainly never heard of a debt of tears before. Why shouldn't the two of us take advantage of this opportunity to go down into the world ourselves and save a few souls? It would be a work of merit."

"That is exactly what I was thinking," said the monk. "Come with me to Disenchantment's palace to get this absurd creature cleared. Then, when this last batch of romantic idiots goes down, you and I can go down with them. At present about half have already been born. They await this last batch to make up the number."

"Very good, I will go with you then," said the Taoist. Shi-yin heard all this conversation quite clearly, and curiosity impelled him to go forward and greet the two reverend gentlemen. They returned his greeting and asked him what he wanted.

"It is not often that one has the opportunity of listening to a discussion of the operations of *karma*[6] such as the one I have just been privileged to overhear," said Shi-yin. "Unfortunately I am a man of very limited understanding and have not been able to derive the full benefit from your conversation. If you would have the very great kindness to enlighten my benighted understanding with a somewhat fuller account of what you were discussing, I can promise you the most devout attention. I feel sure that your teaching would have a salutary effect on me and—who knows—might save me from the pains of hell."

The reverend gentlemen laughed. "These are heavenly mysteries and may not be divulged. But if you wish to escape from the fiery pit, you have only to remember us when the time comes, and all will be well."

Shi-yin saw that it would be useless to press them. "Heavenly mysteries must not, of course, be revealed. But might one perhaps inquire what the 'absurd creature' is that you were talking about? Is it possible that I might be allowed to see it?"

"Oh, as for that," said the monk: "I think it is on the cards for you to have a look at *him*," and he took the object from his sleeve and handed it to Shi-yin.

Shi-yin took the object from him and saw that it was a clear, beautiful jade on one side of which were carved the words "Magic Jade." There were several columns of smaller characters on the back, which Shi-yin was just going to examine more closely when the monk, with a cry of "Here we are, at the frontier of Illusion," snatched the stone from him and disappeared, with the Taoist, through a big stone archway above which

THE LAND OF ILLUSION

was written in large characters. A couplet in smaller characters was inscribed vertically on either side of the arch:

> Truth becomes fiction when the fiction's true;
> Real becomes not-real where the unreal's real.

Shi-yin was on the point of following them through the archway when suddenly a great clap of thunder seemed to shake the earth to its very foundations, making him cry out in alarm.

And there he was sitting in his study, the contents of his dream already half forgotten, with the sun still blazing on the ever-rustling plantains outside, and the wet-nurse at the door with his little daughter Ying-lian in her arms. Her delicate little pink-and-white face seemed dearer to him than ever at that moment, and he stretched out his arms to take her and hugged her to him.

*　　*　　*

Chapters 1 to 25 Summary   After waking from his dream in the middle of the first chapter, Zhen Shi-yin meets the monk and the Taoist in the flesh, and they seek to take his daughter Ying-lian from him, informing him that otherwise

6. The accumulation of good and bad deeds that determines a soul's future lives.

share. What makes me so angry is that people like Skybright and Mackerel should count as top grade when everyone knows they're only put there to curry favour with Bao-yu. Doesn't it make you angry?"

"I don't see much point in getting angry," said Crimson. "You know what they said about the mile-wide marquee: 'Even the longest party must have an end'? Well, none of us is here for ever, you know. Another four or five years from now when we've each gone our different ways it won't *matter* any longer what all the rest of us are doing."

Little Melilot found this talk of parting and impermanence vaguely affecting and a slight moisture was to be observed about her eyes. She thought shame to cry without good cause, however, and masked her emotion with a smile:

"That's perfectly true. Only yesterday Bao-yu was going on about all the things he's going to do to his rooms and the clothes he's going to have made and everything, just as if he had a hundred or two years ahead of him with nothing to do but kill time in."

Crimson laughed scornfully, though whether at Melilot's simplicity or at Bao-yu's improvidence is unclear, since just as she was about to comment, a little maid came running in, so young that her hair was still done up in two little girl's horns. She was carrying some patterns and sheets of paper.

"You're to copy out these two patterns."

She threw them in Crimson's direction and straightway darted out again. Crimson shouted after her:

"Who are they for, then? You might at least finish your message before rushing off. What are you in such a tearing hurry about? Is someone steaming wheatcakes for you and you're afraid they'll get cold?"

"They're for Mackerel." The little maid paused long enough to bawl an answer through the window, then picking up her heels, went pounding off, *plim-plam, plim-plam, plim-plam,* as fast as she had come.

Crimson threw the patterns crossly to one side and went to hunt in her drawer for a brush to trace them with. After rummaging for several minutes she had only succeeded in finding a few worn-out ones, too moulted for use.

"Funny!" she said. "I could have sworn I put a new one in there the other day . . ."

She thought a bit, then laughed at herself as she remembered:

"Of course. Oriole[4] took it, the evening before last." She turned to Melilot. "Would you go and get it for me, then?"

"I'm afraid I can't," said Melilot. "Miss Aroma's waiting for me to fetch some boxes for her. You'll have to get it yourself."

"If Aroma's waiting for you, why have you been sitting here gossiping all this time?" said Crimson. "If I hadn't asked you to go and get it, she wouldn't have been waiting, would she? Lazy little beast!"

She left the room and walked out of the gate of Green Delights and in the direction of Bao-chai's courtyard. She was just passing by Drenched Blossoms Pavilion when she caught sight of Bao-yu's old wet-nurse, Nan-

---

4. One of Bao-chai's maids.

nie Li, coming from the opposite direction and stood respectfully aside to
wait for her.

"Where have you been, Mrs. Li?" she asked her. "I didn't expect to see
you here."

Nannie Li made a flapping gesture with her hand:

"What do you think, my dear: His Nibs has taken a fancy to the young
fellow who does the tree-planting—'Yin' or 'Yun' or whatever his name
is—so Nannie has to go and ask him in. Let's hope Their Ladyships don't
find out about it. There'll be trouble if they do."

"Are you really going to ask him in?"

"Yes. Why?"

Crimson laughed:

"If your Mr. Yun knows what's good for him, he won't agree to come."

"He's no fool," said Nannie Li. "Why shouldn't he?"

"Any way, if he *does* come in," said Crimson, ignoring her question,
"you can't just bring him in and then leave him, Mrs. Li. You'll have to
take him back again yourself afterwards. You don't want him wandering
off on his own. There's no knowing *who* he might bump into."

(Crimson herself, was the secret hope.)

"Gracious me! I haven't got *that* much spare time," said Nannie Li.
"All I've done is just to tell him that he's got to come. I'll send someone
else to fetch him in when I get back presently—one of the girls, or one of
the older women, maybe."

She hobbled off on her stick, leaving Crimson standing there in a muse,
her mission to fetch the tracing-brush momentarily forgotten. She was still
standing there a minute or two later when a little maid came along, who,
seeing that it was Crimson, asked her what she was doing there. Crimson
looked up. It was Trinket, another of the maids from Green Delights.

"Where are you going?" Crimson asked her.

"I've been sent to fetch Mr. Yun," said Trinket. "I have to bring him
inside to meet Master Bao."

She ran off on her way.

At the gate to Wasp Waist Bridge Crimson ran into Trinket again, this
time with Jia Yun in tow. His eyes sought Crimson's; and hers, as she
made pretence of conversing with Trinket, sought his. Their two pairs of
eyes met and briefly skirmished; then Crimson felt herself blushing, and
turning away abruptly, she made off for Allspice Court.

Our narrative now follows Jia Yun and Trinket along the winding pathway
to the House of Green Delights. Soon they were at the courtyard gate and
Jia Yun waited outside while she went in to announce his arrival. She
returned presently to lead him inside.

There were a few scattered rocks in the courtyard and some clumps of
jade-green plantain. Two storks stood in the shadow of a pine-tree, preening themselves with their long bills. The gallery surrounding the courtyard
was hung with cages of unusual design in which perched or fluttered a
wide variety of birds, some of them gay-plumaged exotic ones. Above the
steps was a little five-frame[5] penthouse building with a glimpse of deli-

5. A unit for measuring space in a building; a *five-frame* building is relatively small.

cately-carved partitions visible through the open doorway, above which a horizontal board hung, inscribed with the words

CRIMSON JOYS AND GREEN DELIGHTS

"So that's why it's called 'The House of Green Delights,' " Jia Yun told himself. "The name is taken from the inscription."

A laughing voice addressed him from behind one of the silk gauze casements:

"Come on in! It must be two or three months since I first forgot our appointment!"

Jia Yun recognized the voice as Bao-yu's and hurried up the steps inside. He looked about him, dazzled by the brilliance of gold and semi-precious inlay-work and the richness of the ornaments and furnishings, but unable to see Bao-yu in the midst of it all. To the left of him was a full-length mirror from behind which two girls now emerged, both about fifteen or sixteen years old and of much the same build and height. They addressed him by name and asked him to come inside. Slightly overawed, he muttered something in reply and hurried after them, not daring to take more than a furtive glance at them from the corner of his eye. They ushered him into a tent-like summer "cabinet" of green net, whose principal furniture was a tiny lacquered bed with crimson hangings heavily patterned in gold. On this Bao-yu, wearing everyday clothes and a pair of bedroom slippers, was reclining, book in hand. He threw the book down as Jia Yun entered and rose to his feet with a welcoming smile. Jia Yun swiftly dropped knee and hand to floor in greeting. Bidden to sit, he modestly placed himself on a bedside chair.

"After I invited you round to my study that day," said Bao-yu, "a whole lot of things seemed to happen one after the other, and I'm afraid I quite forgot about your visit."[6]

Jia Yun returned his smile:

"Let's just say that it wasn't my luck to see you then. But you have been ill since then, Uncle Bao. Are you quite better now?"

"Quite better, thank you. I hear you've been very busy these last few days."

"That's as it should be,' said Jia Yun. "But I'm glad you are better, Uncle. That's a piece of good fortune for *all* of us."

As they chatted, a maid came in with some tea. Jia Yun was talking to Bao-yu as she approached, but his eyes were on her. She was tall and rather thin with a long oval face, and she was wearing a rose-pink dress over a closely pleated white satin skirt and a black satin sleeveless jacket over the dress.

In the course of his brief sojourn among them in the early days of Bao-yu's illness, Jia Yun had got by heart the names of most of the principal females of Bao-yu's establishment. He knew at a glance that the maid now serving him tea was Aroma. He was also aware that she was in some way more important than the other maids and that to be waited on by her in

---

6. Earlier, Jia Yun had been invited to pay a visit on Bao-yu.

the seated presence of her master was an honour. Jumping hastily to his feet he addressed her with a modest smile:

"You shouldn't pour tea for *me*, Miss! I'm not like a visitor here. You should let me pour for myself!"

"Oh *do* sit down!" said Bao-yu. "You don't have to be like that in front of the *maids*!"

"I know," said Jia Yun. "But a body-servant![7] I don't like to presume."

He sat down, nevertheless, and sipped his tea while Bao-yu made conversation on a number of unimportant topics. He told him which household kept the best troupe of players, which had the finest gardens, whose maids were the prettiest, who gave the best parties, and who had the best collection of curiosities or the strangest pets. Jia Yun did his best to keep up with him. After a while Bao-yu showed signs of flagging, and when Jia Yun, observing what appeared to be fatigue, rose to take his leave, he did not very strongly press him to stay.

"You must come again when you can spare the time," said Bao-yu, and ordered Trinket to see him out of the Garden.

Once outside the gateway of Green Delights, Jia Yun looked around him on all sides, and having ascertained that there was no one else about, slowed down to a more dawdling pace so that he could ask Trinket a few questions. Indeed, the little maid was subjected to quite a catechism: How old was she? What was her name? What did her father and mother do? How many years had she been working for his Uncle Bao? How much pay did she get a month? How many girls were there working for him altogether? Trinket seemed to have no objection, however, and answered each question as it came.

"That girl you were talking to on the way in," he said, "isn't her name 'Crimson'?"

Trinket laughed:

"Yes. Why do you ask?"

"I heard her asking you about a handkerchief. Only it just so happens that I picked one up."

Trinket showed interest.

"She's asked me about that handkerchief of hers a number of times. I told her, I've got better things to do with my time than go looking for people's handkerchiefs. But when she asked me about it again today, she said that if I could find it for her, she'd give me a reward. Come to think of it, you were there when she said that, weren't you? It was when we were outside the gate of Allspice Court. So you can bear me out. Oh Mr. Jia, please let me have it if you've picked it up and I'll be able to see what she will give me for it!"

Jia Yun had picked up a silk handkerchief a month previously at the time when his tree-planting activities had just started. He knew that it must have been dropped by one or another of the female inmates of the Garden, but not knowing which, had not so far ventured to do anything about his discovery. When earlier on he had heard Crimson question Trinket about her loss, he had realized, with a thrill of pleasure, that the

---

7. A personal servant of higher status than maids.

handkerchief he had picked up must have been hers. Trinket's request now gave him just the opening he required. He drew a handkerchief of his own from inside his sleeve and held it up in front of her with a smile:

"I'll give it to you on one condition. If she lets you have this reward you were speaking of, you've *got* to let me know. No cheating, mind!"

Trinket received the handkerchief with eager assurances that he would be informed of the outcome, and having seen him out of the Garden, went back again to look for Crimson.

Our narrative returns now to Bao-yu.

After disposing of Jia Yun, Bao-yu continued to feel extremely lethargic and lay back on the bed with every appearance of being about to doze off to sleep. Aroma hurried over to him and, sitting on the edge of the bed, roused him with a shake:

"Come on! Surely you are not going to sleep *again?* You need some fresh air. Why don't you go outside and walk around for a bit?"

Bao-yu took her by the hand and smiled at her.

"I'd like to go," he said, "but I don't want to leave you."

"Silly!" said Aroma with a laugh. "Don't say what you don't mean!"

She hoicked[8] him to his feet.

"Well, where am I going to go then?" said Bao-yu. "I just feel so *bored*."

"Never mind where, just go out!" said Aroma. "If you stay moping indoors like this, you'll get even more bored."

Bao-yu followed her advice, albeit half-heartedly, and went out into the courtyard. After visiting the cages in the gallery and playing for a bit with the birds, he ambled out of the courtyard into the Garden and along the bank of Drenched Blossoms Stream, pausing for a while to look at the goldfish in the water. As he did so, a pair of fawns came running like the wind from the hillside opposite. Bao-yu was puzzled. There seemed to be no reason for their mysterious terror. But just then little Jia Lan came running down the same slope after them, a tiny bow clutched in his hand. Seeing his uncle ahead of him, he stood politely to attention and greeted him cheerfully:

"Hello, Uncle. I didn't know you were at home. I thought you'd gone out."

"Mischievous little blighter, aren't you?" said Bao-yu. "What do you want to go shooting them for, poor little things?"

"I've got no reading to do today," said Jia Lan, "and I don't like to hang about doing nothing, so I thought I'd practise my archery and equitation."[9]

"Goodness! You'd better not waste time jawing, then," said Bao-yu, and left the young toxophilite[1] to his pursuits.

Moving on, without much thinking where he was going, he came presently to the gate of a courtyard.

> Denser than feathers on the phoenix' tail
> The stirred leaves murmured with a pent dragon's moan.

The multitudinous bamboos and the board above the gate confirmed that his feet had, without conscious direction, carried him to the Naiad's

8. Yanked.   9. Horseback riding.   1. Archer.

House. Of their own accord they now carried him through the gateway and into the courtyard.

The House seemed silent and deserted, its bamboo door-blind hanging unrolled to the ground; but as he approached the window, he detected a faint sweetness in the air, traceable to a thin curl of incense smoke which drifted out through the green gauze of the casement. He pressed his face to the gauze; but before his eyes could distinguish anything, his ear became aware of a long, languorous sigh and the sound of a voice speaking:

> "Each day in a drowsy waking dream of love."

Bao-yu felt a sudden yearning for the speaker. He could see her now. It was Dai-yu, of course, lying on her bed, stretching herself and yawning luxuriously.

He laughed:

"Why 'each day in a drowsy waking dream of love'?" he asked through the window (the words were from his beloved *Western Chamber*[2]); then going to the doorway he lifted up the door-blind and walked into the room.

Dai-yu realized that she had been caught off her guard. She covered her burning face with her sleeve, and turning over towards the wall, pretended to be asleep. Bao-yu went over intending to turn her back again, but just at that moment Dai-yu's old wet-nurse came hurrying in with two other old women at her heels:

"Miss Lin's asleep, sir. Would you mind coming back again after she's woken up?"

Dai-yu at once turned over and sat up with a laugh:

"Who's asleep?"

The three old women laughed apologetically.

"Sorry, miss. We thought you were asleep. Nightingale! Come inside now! Your mistress is awake."

Having shouted for Nightingale, the three guardians of morality retired.

"What do you mean by coming into people's rooms when they're asleep?" said Dai-yu, smiling up at Bao-yu as she sat on the bed's edge patting her hair into shape.

At the sight of those soft cheeks so adorably flushed and the starry eyes a little misted with sleep a wave of emotion passed over him. He sank into a chair and smiled back at her:

"What was that you were saying just now before I came in?"

"I didn't say anything," said Dai-yu.

Bao-yu laughed and snapped his fingers at her:

"Put that on your tongue, girl! I heard you say it."

While they were talking to one another, Nightingale came in.

"Nightingale," said Bao-yu, "what about a cup of that excellent tea of yours?"

"Excellent tea?" said Nightingale. "There's nothing very special about

2. A 13th-century romantic play.

the tea we drink here. If nothing but the best will do, you'd better wait for Aroma to come."

"Never mind about *him!*" said Dai-yu. "First go and get me some water!"

"He *is* our guest," said Nightingale. "I can't fetch you any water until I've given him his tea." And she went to pour him a cup.

"Good girl!" said Bao-yu.

"If with your amorous mistress I should wed,
'Tis you, sweet maid, must make our bridal bed."

The words, like Dai-yu's languorous line, were from *Western Chamber*, but in somewhat dubious taste. Dai-yu was dreadfully offended by them. In an instant the smile had vanished from her face.

"*What* was that you said?"

He laughed:

"I didn't say anything."

Dai-yu began to cry.

"This is your latest amusement, I suppose. Every time you hear some coarse expression outside or read some crude, disgusting book, you have to come back here and give me the benefit of it. I am to become a source of entertainment for the *menfolk* now, it seems."

She rose, weeping, from the bed and went outside. Bao-yu followed her in alarm.

"Dearest coz, it was very wrong of me to say that, but it just slipped out without thinking. Please don't go and tell! I promise never to say anything like that again. May my mouth rot and my tongue decay if I do!"

Just at that moment Aroma came hurrying up:

"Quick!" she said. "You must come back and change. The Master[3] wants to see you."

The descent of this thunderbolt drove all else from his mind and he rushed off in a panic. As soon as he had changed, he hurried out of the Garden. Tealeaf[4] was waiting for him outside the inner gate.

"I suppose you don't know what he wants to see me about?" Bao-yu asked him.

"I should hurry up, if I were you," said Tealeaf. "All I know is that he wants to see you. You'll find out why soon enough when you get there."

He hustled him along as he spoke.

They had passed round the main hall, Bao-yu still in a state of fluttering apprehensiveness, when there was a loud guffaw from a corner of the wall. It was Xue Pan,[5] clapping his hands and stamping his feet in mirth.

"Ho! Ho! Ho! You'd never have come this quickly if you hadn't been told that Uncle wanted you!"

Tealeaf, also laughing, fell on his knees. Bao-yu stood there looking puzzled. It was some moments before it dawned on him that he had been hoaxed. Xue Pan was by this time being apologetic—bowing repeatedly and pumping his hands to show how sorry he was:

3. Jia Sheng, Bao-yu's father.   4. One of Bao-yu's male pages.   5. A troublemaker, Xue Bao-chai's brother.

"Don't blame the lad!" he said. "It wasn't his fault. I talked him into it."

Bao-yu saw that he could do nothing, and might as well accept with a good grace.

"I don't mind being made a fool of," he said, "but I think it was going a bit far to bring my father into it. I think perhaps I'd better tell Aunt Xue and see what *she* thinks about it all."

"Now look here, old chap," said Xue Pan, getting agitated, "it was only because I wanted to fetch you out a bit quicker. I admit it was very wrong of me to make free with your Parent, but after all, you've only got to mention *my* father next time you want to fool *me* and we'll be quits!"

"Aiyo!" said Bao-yu. "Worse and worse!" He turned to Tealeaf: "Treacherous little beast! What are you still kneeling for?"

Tealeaf kotowed and rose to his feet.

"Look," said Xue Pan. "I wouldn't have troubled you otherwise, only it's my birthday on the third of next month and old Hu and old Cheng and a couple of the others, I don't know where they got them from but they've given me:

> a piece of fresh lotus root, ever so crisp and crunchy, as thick as that, look, and as long as that;
> a huge great melon, look, as big as that;
> a freshly-caught sturgeon as big as that;
> and a cypress-smoked Siamese sucking-pig as big as that that came in the tribute from Siam.

Don't you think it was clever of them to get me those things? Maybe not so much the sturgeon and the sucking-pig. They're just expensive. But where would you go to get a piece of lotus root or a melon like that? However did they get them to *grow* so big? I've given some of the stuff to Mother, and while I was about it I sent some round to your grandmother and Auntie Wang, but I've still got a lot left over. I can't eat it all myself: it would be unlucky. But apart from me, the only person I can think of who is *worthy* to eat a present like this is you. That's why I came over specially to invite you. And we're lucky, because we've got a little chap who sings coming round as well. So you and I will be able to sit down and make a day of it, eh? Really enjoy ourselves."

Xue Pan, still talking, conducted Bao-yu to his "study," where Zhan Guang, Cheng Ri-xing, Hu Si-lai and Dan Ping-ren (the four donors of the feast) and the young singer he had mentioned were already waiting. They rose to welcome Bao-yu as he entered. When the bowings and courtesies were over and tea had been taken, Xue Pan called for his servants to lay.[6] A tremendous bustle ensued, which seemed to go on for quite a long time before everything was finally ready and the diners were able to take their places at the table.

Bao-yu noticed sliced melon and lotus root among the dishes, both of unusual quality and size.

"It seems wrong to be sharing your presents with you before I have given you anything myself," he said jokingly.

---

6. That is, to set the table.

"Yes," said Xue Pan. "What are you planning to give me for my birthday next month? Something new and out of the ordinary, I hope."

"I haven't really *got* anything much to give you," said Bao-yu. "Things like money and food and clothing I don't want for, but they're not really mine to give. The only way I could give you something that would *really* be mine would be by doing some calligraphy or painting a picture for you."

"Talking of pictures," said Xue Pan genially, "that's reminded me. I saw a set of dirty pictures in someone's house the other day. They were real beauties. There was a lot of writing on top that I didn't pay much attention to, but I did notice the signature. I think it was 'Geng Huang,' the man who painted them. They were really good!"

Bao-yu was puzzled. His knowledge of the masters of painting and calligraphy both past and present was not inconsiderable, but he had never in all his experience come across a "Geng Huang." After racking his brains for some moments he suddenly began to chuckle and called for a writing-brush. A writing-brush having been produced by one of the servants, he wrote two characters with it in the palm of his hand.

"Are you quite *sure* the signature you saw was 'Geng Huang'?" he asked Xue Pan.

"What do you mean?" said Xue Pan. "Of course I'm sure."

Bao-yu opened his hand and held it up for Xue Pan to see:

"You sure it wasn't these two characters? They *are* quite similar."

The others crowded round to look. They all laughed when they saw what he had written:

"Yes, it must have been 'Tang Yin.'[7] Mr. Xue couldn't have been seeing straight that day. Ha! Ha! Ha!"

Xue Pan realized that he had made a fool of himself, but passed it off with an embarrassed laugh:

"Oh, Tankin' or wankin'," he said, "what difference does it make, anyway?"

Just then "Mr. Feng" was announced by one of the servants, which Bao-yu knew could only mean General Feng Tang's son, Feng Zi-ying. Xue Pan and the rest told the boy to bring him in immediately, but Feng Zi-ying was already striding in, talking and laughing as he went. The others hurriedly rose and invited him to take a seat.

"Ha!" said Feng Zi-ying. "No need to go out then. Enjoyin' yourselves at home, eh? Very nice too!"

"It's a long time since we've seen you around," said Bao-yu. "How's the General?"

"Fahver's in good health, thank you very much," said Feng Zi-ying, "but Muvver hasn't been too well lately. Caught a chill or somethin'."

Observing with glee that Feng Zi-ying was sporting a black eye, Xue Pan asked him how he had come by it:

"Been having a dust-up, then? Who was it this time? Looks as if he left his signature!"

Feng Zi-ying laughed:

---

7. This joke shows Xue Pan's ignorance: he has misread the Chinese characters for one of the most famous of all Ming painters.

"Don't use the mitts any more nowadays—not since that time I laid into Colonel Chou's son and did him an injury. That was a lesson to me. I've learned to keep my temper since then. No, this happened the other day durin' a huntin' expedition in the Iron Net Mountains. I got flicked by a goshawk's wing."

"When was this?" Bao-yu asked him.

"We left on the twenty-eighth of last month," said Feng Zi-ying. "Didn't get back till a few days ago."

"Ah, that explains why I didn't see you at Shen's party earlier this month," said Bao-yu. "I meant at the time to ask why you weren't there, but I forgot. Did you go alone on this expedition or was the General there with you?"

"Fahver most certainly *was* there," said Feng Zi-ying. "I was practically dragged along in tow. Do you think I'm mad enough to go rushin' off in pursuit of hideous hardships when I could be sittin' comfortably at home eatin' good food and drinkin' good wine and listenin' to the odd song or two? Still, some good came of it. It was a lucky accident."

As he had now finished his tea, Xue Pan urged him to join them at table and tell them his story at leisure, but Feng Zi-ying rose to his feet again and declined.

"I ought by rights to stay and drink a few cups with you," he said, "but there's somethin' very important I've got to see Fahver about now, so I'm afraid I really must refuse."

But Xue Pan, Bao-yu and the rest were by no means content to let him get away with this excuse and propelled him insistently towards the table.

"Now look here, this is too bad!" Feng Zi-ying good-humouredly protested. "All the years we've been knockin' around togevver we've never before insisted that a fellow should have to stay if he don't want to. The fact is, I really *can't.* Oh well, if I *must* have a drink, fetch some decent-sized cups and I'll just put down a couple of quick ones!"

This was clearly the most he would concede and the others perforce acquiesced. Two sconce-cups were brought and ceremoniously filled, Bao-yu holding the cups and Xue Pan pouring from the wine-kettle.[8] Feng Zi-ying drank them standing, one after the other, each in a single breath.

"Now come on," said Bao-yu, "let's hear about this 'lucky accident' before you go!"

Feng Zi-ying laughed:

"Couldn't tell it properly just now," he said. "It's somethin' that needs a special party all to itself. I'll invite you all round to my place another day and you shall have the details then. There's a favour I want to ask too, by the bye, so we'll be able to talk about that then as well."

He made a determined movement towards the door.

"Now you've got us all peeing ourselves with curiosity!" said Xue Pan. "You might at least tell us when this party is going to be, to put us out of our suspense."

"Not more than ten days' time and not less than eight," said Feng Zi-

---

8. Chinese wine was heated before it was drunk. *Sconce-cups:* large wine cups.

ying; and going out into the courtyard, he jumped on his horse and clattered away.

Having seen him off, the others went in again, reseated themselves at table, and resumed their potations. When the party finally broke up, Bao-yu returned to the Garden in a state of cheerful inebriation. Aroma, who had had no idea what the summons from Jia Zheng might portend and was still wondering anxiously what had become of him, at once demanded to know the cause of his condition. He gave her a full account of what had happened.

"Well really!" said Aroma. "Here were we practically beside ourselves with anxiety, and all the time you were there enjoying yourself! You might at least have sent word to let us know you were all right."

"I was going to send word," said Bao-yu. "Of course I was. But then old Feng arrived and it put it out of my mind."

At that moment Bao-chai walked in, all smiles.

"I hear you've made a start on the famous present," she said.

"But surely you and your family must have had some already?" said Bao-yu.

Bao-chai shook her head:

"Pan was very pressing that I should have some, but I refused. I told him to save it for other people. I know I'm not really the right sort of person for such superior delicacies. If I were to eat any, I should be afraid of some frightful nemesis overtaking me."

A maid poured tea for her as she spoke, and conversation of a desultory kind proceeded between sips.

Our narrative returns now to Dai-yu.

Having been present when Bao-yu received his summons, Dai-yu, too, was greatly worried about him—the more so as the day advanced and he had still not returned. Then in the evening, some time after dinner, she heard that he had just got back and resolved to go over and ask him exactly what had happened. She was sauntering along on the way there when she caught sight of Bao-chai some distance ahead of her, just entering Bao-yu's courtyard. Continuing to amble on, she came presently to Drenched Blossoms Bridge, from which a large number of different kinds of fish were to be seen swimming about in the water below. Dai-yu did not know what kinds of fish they were, but they were so beautiful that she had to stop and admire them, and by the time she reached the House of Green Delights, the courtyard gate had been shut for the night and she was obliged to knock for admittance.

Now it so happened that Skybright had just been having a quarrel with Emerald, and being thoroughly out of temper, was venting some of her ill-humour on the lately arrived Bao-chai, complaining *sotto voce* behind her back about "people who were always inventing excuses to come dropping in and who kept other people staying up half the night when they would like to be in bed." A knock at the gate coming in the midst of these resentful mutterings was enough to make her really angry.

"They've all gone to bed," she shouted, not even bothering to inquire who the caller was. "Come again tomorrow!"

Dai-yu was aware that Bao-yu's maids often played tricks on one another, and it occurred to her that the girl in the courtyard, not recognizing her voice, might have mistaken her for another maid and be keeping her locked out for a joke. She therefore called out again, this time somewhat louder than before:

"Come on! Open up, please! It's me."

Unfortunately Skybright had still not recognized the voice.

"I don't care who you are," she replied bad-temperedly. "Master Bao's orders are that I'm not to let *anyone* in."

Dumbfounded by her insolence, Dai-yu stood outside the gate in silence. She could not, however much she felt like it, give vent to her anger in noisy expostulation. "Although they are always telling me to treat my Uncle's house as my own," she reflected, "I am still really an outsider. And now that Mother and Father are both dead and I am on my own, to make a fuss about a thing like this when I am living in someone else's house could only lead to further unpleasantness."

A big tear coursed, unregarded, down her cheek.

She was still standing there irresolute, unable to decide whether to go or stay, when a sudden volley of talk and laughter reached her from inside. It resolved itself, as she listened attentively, into the voices of Bao-yu and Bao-chai. An even bitterer sense of chagrin took possession of her. Suddenly, as she hunted in her mind for some possible reason for her exclusion, she remembered the events of the morning and concluded that Bao-yu must think she had told on him to his parents and was punishing her for her betrayal.

"But I would never betray you!" she expostulated with him in her mind. "Why couldn't you have asked first, before letting your resentment carry you to such lengths? If you won't see me today, does that mean that from now on we are going to stop seeing each other altogether?"

The more she thought about it the more distressed she became.

> Chill was the green moss pearled with dew
> And chill was the wind in the avenue;

but Dai-yu, all unmindful of the unwholesome damp, had withdrawn into the shadow of a flowering fruit-tree by the corner of the wall, and grieving now in real earnest, began to cry as though her heart would break. And as if Nature herself were affected by the grief of so beautiful a creature, the crows who had been roosting in the trees round about flew up with a great commotion and removed themselves to another part of the Garden, unable to endure the sorrow of her weeping.

> Tears filled each flower and grief their hearts perturbed,
> And silly birds were from their nests disturbed.

The author of the preceding couplet has given us a quatrain in much the same vein:

> Few in this world fair Frowner's looks surpassed,
> None matched her store of sweetness unexpressed.
> The first sob scarcely from her lips had passed
> When blossoms fell and birds flew off distressed.

As Dai-yu continued weeping there alone, the courtyard door suddenly opened with a loud creak and someone came out.

But in order to find out who it was, you will have to wait for the next chapter.

From *Volume 2*

CHAPTER 27

*Beauty Perspiring sports with butterflies
by the Raindrop Pavilion
And Beauty Suspiring weeps for fallen blossoms
by the Flowers' Grave*

As Dai-yu stood there weeping, there was a sudden creak of the courtyard gate and Bao-chai walked out, accompanied by Bao-yu with Aroma and a bevy of other maids who had come out to see her off. Dai-yu was on the point of stepping forward to question Bao-yu, but shrank from embarrassing him in front of so many people. Instead she slipped back into the shadows to let Bao-chai pass, emerging only when Bao-yu and the rest were back inside and the gate was once more barred. She stood for a while facing it, and shed a few silent tears; then, realizing that it was pointless to remain standing there, she turned and went back to her room and began, in a listless, mechanical manner, to take off her ornaments and prepare herself for the night.

Nightingale and Snowgoose had long since become habituated to Dai-yu's moody temperament; they were used to her unaccountable fits of depression, when she would sit, the picture of misery, in gloomy silence broken only by an occasional gusty sigh, and to her mysterious, perpetual weeping, that was occasioned by no observable cause. At first they had tried to reason with her, or, imagining that she must be grieving for her parents or that she was feeling homesick or had been upset by some unkindness, they would do their best to comfort her. But as the months lengthened into years and she still continued exactly the same as before, they gradually became accustomed and no longer sought reasons for her behaviour. That was why they ignored her on this occasion and left her alone to her misery, remaining where they were in the outer room and continuing to occupy themselves with their own affairs.

She sat, motionless as a statue, leaning against the back of the bed, her hands clasped about her knees, her eyes full of tears. It had already been dark for some hours when she finally lay down to sleep.

Our story passes over the rest of that night in silence.

Next day was the twenty-sixth of the fourth month, the day on which, this year, the festival of Grain in Ear was due to fall. To be precise, the festival's official commencement was on the twenty-sixth day of the fourth month at two o'clock in the afternoon. It has been the custom from time immemorial to make offerings to the flower fairies on this day. For Grain in Ear marks the beginning of summer; it is about this time that the blossom begins to fall; and tradition has it that the flowerspirits, their work now completed, go away on this day and do not return until the following year. The offerings are therefore thought of as a sort of farewell party for the flowers.

This charming custom of "speeding the fairies" is a special favourite with the fair sex, and in Prospect Garden all the girls were up betimes on this day making little coaches and palanquins[9] out of willow-twigs and flowers and little banners and pennants from scraps of brocade and any other pretty material they could find, which they fastened with threads of coloured silk to the tops of flowering trees and shrubs. Soon every plant and tree was decorated and the whole garden had become a shimmering sea of nodding blossoms and fluttering coloured streamers. Moving about in the midst of it all, the girls in their brilliant summer dresses, beside which the most vivid hues of plant and plumage became faint with envy, added the final touch of brightness to a scene of indescribable gaiety and colour.

All the young people—Bao-chai, Ying-chun, Tan-chun, Xi-chun, Li Wan, Xi-feng[1] and her little girl and Caltrop, and all the maids from all the different apartments—were outside in the Garden enjoying themselves—all, that is, except Dai-yu, whose absence, beginning to be noticed, was first commented on by Ying-chun:

"What's happened to Cousin Lin? Lazy girl! Surely she can't *still* be in bed at this hour?"

Bao-chai volunteered to go and fetch her:

"'The rest of you wait here; I'll go and rout her out for you," she said; and breaking away from the others, she made off in the direction of the Naiad's House.

While she was on her way, she caught sight of Élégante and the eleven other little actresses, evidently on their way to join in the fun. They came up and greeted her, and for a while she stood and chatted with them. As she was leaving them, she turned back and pointed in the direction from which she had just come:

"You'll find the others somewhere over there," she said. "I'm on my way to get Miss Lin. I'll join the rest of you presently."

She continued, by the circuitous route that the garden's contours obliged her to take, on her way to the Naiad's House. Raising her eyes as she approached it, she suddenly became aware that the figure ahead of her just disappearing inside it was Bao-yu. She stopped and lowered her eyes pensively again to the ground.

"Bao-yu and Dai-yu have known each other since they were little," she reflected. "They are used to behaving uninhibitedly when they are alone together. They don't seem to care what they say to one another; and one is never quite sure what sort of mood one is going to find them in. And Dai-yu, at the best of times, is always so touchy and suspicious. If I go in now after him, *he* is sure to feel embarrassed and *she* is sure to start imagining things. It would be better to go back without seeing her."

Her mind made up, she turned round and began to retrace her steps,

---

9. Sedan chairs, carried on poles by bearers.   1. The wife of Bao-yu's uncle; she manages the household.

intending to go back to the other girls; but just at that moment she noticed two enormous turquoise-coloured butterflies a little way ahead of her, each as large as a child's fan, fluttering and dancing on the breeze. She watched them fascinated and thought she would like to play a game with them. Taking a fan from inside her sleeve and holding it outspread in front of her, she followed them off the path and into the grass.

To and fro fluttered the pair of butterflies, sometimes alighting for a moment, but always flying off again before she could reach them. Once they seemed on the point of flying across the little river that flowed through the midst of the garden and Bao-chai had to stalk them with bated breath for fear of startling them out on to the water. By the time she had reached the Raindrop Pavilion she was perspiring freely and her interest in the butterflies was beginning to evaporate. She was about to turn back when she became aware of a low murmur of voices coming from inside the pavilion.

Raindrop Pavilion was built in such a way that it projected into the middle of the pool into which the little watercourse widened out at this point, so that on three of its sides it looked out on to the water. It was surrounded by a verandah, whose railing followed the many angles formed by the bays and projections of the base. In each of its wooden walls there was a large paper-covered casement of elegantly patterned lattice-work.

Hearing voices inside the pavilion, Bao-chai halted and inclined her ear to listen.

"Are you *sure* this is your handkerchief?" one of the voices was saying. "If it is, take it; but if it isn't, I must return it to Mr. Yun."

"Of course it's mine," said the second voice. "Come on, let me have it!"

"Are you going to give me a reward? I hope I haven't taken all this trouble for nothing."

"I promised you I would give you a reward, and so I shall. Surely you don't think I was deceiving you?"

"All right, I get a reward for bringing it to you. But what about the person who picked it up? Doesn't *he* get anything?"

"Don't talk nonsense," said the second voice. "He's one of the masters. A master picking up something belonging to one of us should give it back as a matter of course. How can there be any question of *rewarding* him?"

"If you don't intend to reward him, what am I supposed to tell him when I see him? He was most insistent that I wasn't to give you the hand-kerchief unless you gave him a reward."

There was a long pause, after which the second voice replied:

"Oh, all right. Let him have this other handkerchief of mine then. That will have to do as his reward—But you must swear a solemn oath not to tell anyone else about this."

"May my mouth rot and may I die a horrible death if I ever tell anyone else about this, amen!" said the first voice.

"Goodness!" said the second voice again. "Here we are talking away, and all the time someone could be creeping up outside and listening to every word we say. We had better open these casements;[2] then even if anyone outside sees us, they'll think we are having an ordinary conversation; and *we* shall be able to see *them* and know in time when to stop."

Bao-chai, listening outside, gave a start.

"No wonder they say 'venery and thievery sharpen the wits,' " she thought. "If they open those windows and see me here, they are going to feel terribly embarrassed. And one of those voices sounds like that proud, peculiar girl Crimson who works in Bao-yu's room. If a girl like that knows that I have overheard her doing something she shouldn't be doing, it will be a case of 'the desperate dog will jump a wall, the desperate man will hazard all': there'll be a great deal of trouble and *I* shall be involved in it. There isn't time to hide. I shall have to do as the cicada does when he jumps out of his skin: give them something to put them off the scent—"

There was a loud creak as the casement yielded. Bao-chai advanced with deliberately noisy tread.

"Frowner!" she called out gaily. "*I* know where you're hiding."

Inside the pavilion Crimson and Trinket, who heard her say this and saw her advancing towards them just as they were opening the casement, were speechless with amazement; but Bao-chai ignored their confusion and addressed them genially:

"Have you two got Miss Lin hidden away in there?"

"I haven't *seen* Miss Lin," said Trinket.

"I saw her just now from the river-bank," said Bao-chai. "She was squatting down over here playing with something in the water. I was going to creep up and surprise her, but she spotted me before I could get up to her and disappeared round this corner. Are you *sure* she's not hiding in there?"

She made a point of going inside the pavilion and searching; then, coming out again, she said in a voice loud enough for them to hear:

"If she's not in the pavilion, she must have crept into that grotto. Oh well, if she's not afraid of being bitten by a snake—!"

As she walked away she laughed inwardly at the ease with which she had extricated herself from a difficult situation.

"I think I'm fairly safely out of *that* one," she thought. "I wonder what those two will make of it."

What indeed! Crimson believed every word that Bao-chai had said, and as soon as the latter was at a distance, she seized hold of Trinket in alarm:

"Oh, how terrible! If Miss Lin was squatting there, she must have heard what we said before she went away."

Her companion was silent.

"Oh dear! What do you think she'll *do?*" said Crimson.

"Well, suppose she *did* hear," said Trinket, "it's not *her* backache. If we mind our business and she minds hers, there's no reason why anything should come of it."

"If it were Miss Bao that had heard us, I don't suppose anything *would,*" said Crimson; "but Miss Lin is so critical and so intolerant. If *she* heard it and it gets about—oh dear!"

2. That is, casement windows.

But just at that moment Caltrop, Advent, Chess and Scribe were seen approaching the pavilion, and Crimson and Trinket had to drop the subject in a hurry and join in a general conversation. Crimson noticed Xi-feng standing half-way up the rockery above the little grotto, beckoning. Breaking away from the others, she bounded up to her with a smiling face:

"What can I do for you, madam?"

Xi-feng ran an appraising eye over her. A neat, pretty, pleasantly-spoken girl, she decided, and smiled at her graciously:

"I have come here without my maids and need someone to take a message back to my apartment. I wonder if you are clever enough to get it right."

"Tell me the message, madam. If I don't get it right and make a mess of it, it will be up to you to punish me."

"Which of the young ladies do you work for?" said Xi-feng. "I'd better know, so that I can explain to her if she asks for you while you are doing my errand."

"I work for Master Bao," said Crimson.

Xi-feng laughed.

"Ah ha! You work for Master Bao. No wonder. Very well, then, if he asks for you while you are away, I shall explain. I want you to go to my apartment and tell Patience that there is a roll of money under the stand of the Ru-ware dish on the table in the outside room. There are a hundred and twenty taels[3] of silver in it to pay the embroiderers with. Tell her that when Zhang Cai's wife comes for it, she is to weigh it out in front of her before handing it over. And there's one other thing. There's a little purse at the head of the bed in my inside room. I want you to bring it to me."

"Yes madam," said Crimson, and hurried off.

Returning shortly afterwards, she found that Xi-feng was no longer on the rockery; but Chess had just emerged from the little grotto beneath it and was standing there doing up her sash. Crimson ran down to speak to her:

"Excuse me, did you see where Mrs. Lian went to?"

" 'Fraid I didn't notice," said Chess.

Crimson looked around her. Bao-chai and Tan-chun were standing at the edge of the pool looking at the fish. She went up to them:

"Excuse me, does either of you young ladies happen to know where Mrs. Lian went to just now, please?"

"Try Mrs. Zhu's place," said Tan-chun.

Crimson hurried off in the direction of Sweet-rice Village. On her way she ran head-on into a party of maids consisting of Skybright, Mackerel, Emerald, Ripple, Musk, Scribe, Picture and Oriole.

"Here, what are you gadding about like this for?" said Skybright as soon as she saw who it was. "The flowers want watering; the birds need feeding; the stove for the tea-water needs seeing to. You've no business to go wandering around outside!"

"Master Bao gave orders yesterday that the flowers were only to be

---

3. A unit of currency. Ru-ware: fine porcelain.

watered every other day," said Crimson. "I fed the birds when you were still fast asleep in bed."

"What about the stove?" said Emerald.

"It isn't my day for the stove," said Crimson. "The tea-water today has nothing to do with me."

"Listen to Miss Pert!" said Mackerel. "I wouldn't bother about her, if I were you—just leave her to wander about as she pleases."

"I'm *not* 'wandering about,' if you really want to know," said Crimson. "If you really want to know, Mrs. Lian sent me outside to take a message and to fetch something for her."

She held up the purse for them to see; at which they were silent. But when they had passed each other, Skybright laughed sneeringly:

"You can see why she's so uppity. She's on the climb again. Look at her—all cock-a-hoop because someone's given her a little message to carry! And she probably doesn't even know who it's about. Well, one little message isn't going to get her very far. It's what happens in the long run that counts. Now if she were clever enough to climb her way right out of this Garden and stay there, that would be really something!"

These words were spoken for Crimson to hear, but in such a way that she was unable to answer them. She had to swallow her anger and hurry on to look for Xi-feng.

Xi-feng was in Li Wan's room, as Tan-chun had predicted, and Crimson found the two of them in conversation. She went up to Xi-feng and delivered her message:

"Patience says that she found the silver just after you had gone and took care of it; and she says that when Zhang Cai's wife came for it she did weigh it out in front of her before giving it to her to take away."

Crimson now produced the purse and handed it to Xi-feng.

Then she added:

"Patience told me to tell you that Brightie has just been in to inquire what your instructions were for his visit, and she said that she gave him a message to take based on the things she thought you would want him to say."

"Oh?" said Xi-feng, amused. "And what *was* this message 'based on the things she thought I would want him to say'?"

"She said he was to tell them: 'Our lady hopes your lady is well and she says that the Master is away at present and may not be back for another day or two, but your lady is not to worry; and when the lady from West Lane is better, our lady will come with their lady to see your lady. And our lady says that the lady from West Lane sent someone the other day with a message from the *elder* Lady Wang[4] saying that she hopes our lady is well and will she please see if *our* Lady Wang can let her have a few of her Golden Myriad Macrobiotic Pills; and if she can, will our lady please send someone with them to *her*, because someone will be going from there to the *elder* Lady Wang's in a few days' time and they will be able to take them for her—'"

---

4. Lady Wang's mother and Bao-yu's grandmother.

Crimson was still in full spate when Li Wan interrupted her with a laugh:

"What an extraordinary number of 'ladies'! I hope you can understand what it's all about, Feng. I'm sure *I* can't!"

"I'm not surprised," said Xi-feng. "There are four or five different households involved in that message." She smiled graciously at Crimson. "You're a clever girl, my dear, to have got it all right—not like the simpering little ninnies I usually have to put up with. You have no idea, cousin," she said, turning to Li Wan again. "Apart from the one or two girls and one or two older women that I always keep about me, I just dread talking to servants nowadays. They take such an *interminable* time to tell you anything—so long-winded! And the airs and graces they give themselves! and the simpering! and the um-ing and ah-ing! If they only knew how it makes me *fume!* Our Patience used to be like that when she first came to me. I used to say to her, 'Do you think it makes you seem glamorous, all that affected humming?—like a little gnat!' I had to talk to her several times about it before she would mend her ways."

Li Wan laughed.

"I suppose if they were all peppercorns like you, it would be all right."

"This girl's all right," said Xi-feng. "Those two messages she gave me just now may not have been very long ones, but you could see how clear-cut her delivery of them was."

She smiled at Crimson again.

"How would you like to come and work for me and be my god-daughter? With a little grooming from me you could go far."

Crimson suppressed a giggle.

"Why do you laugh?" said Xi-feng. "I suppose you think I'm too young to be your god-mother. You're very silly if you think that. You just ask around a bit: there are plenty much older than you who'd give their ears to be my god-daughter. What I'm offering you is a very special favour."

Crimson smiled.

"I wasn't laughing because of that, madam. I was laughing because you had got the generation wrong. My mother is your god-daughter already. If you made me your god-daughter too, I should be my own mother's sister!"

"Who *is* your mother?" said Xi-feng.

"Do you mean to say that you don't know who this girl is that you've been talking to all this time?" said Li Wan. "This is Lin Zhi-xiao's daughter."

Xi-feng registered surprise:

"You mean to tell me that this is the *Lins'* daughter?" She laughed. "*That* couple of old sticks? I can never get a peep out of either of them. I've always maintained that Lin Zhi-xiao and his wife were the perfect match: one *hears* nothing and the other *says* nothing. Well! To think they should have produced a bright little thing like this between them!—How old are you?" she asked Crimson.

"Sixteen."

"And what's your name?"

" 'Crimson,' madam. I used to be called 'Jade,' but they made me change it on account of Master Bao."

Xi-feng looked away with a frown of displeasure.

"I should think so too," she muttered. "Odious people! One can hear them saying it: 'We've got a "Jade" in our family the same as you,' or some such impertinence."

She turned to Li Wan again:

"I don't think you know, Wan, but I told this girl's mother that as Lai Da's wife is so busy nowadays that she doesn't even know who half the girls in the household *are* any longer, I wanted *her* to pick out a couple of likely-looking girls to work under me. Now she promised that she would do this; but you see, not only has she not done so, but she's actually gone and sent her own daughter to work for someone else. Do you suppose she *really* thinks her girl would have had such a terrible time with me?"

"Don't be so touchy," said Li Wan. "Her mother is not to blame. The girl had already started service in the Garden before you ever spoke to her about it."

"Oh well, in that case," said Xi-feng, recovering her good humour, "I'll have a word with Bao-yu about it tomorrow. I'll tell him to find someone else and let me have this girl to work under *me*. Still—" she turned to Crimson, "perhaps we ought to ask the party most concerned if she is willing."

Crimson smiled.

"As to being willing or not, madam, I don't think it's my place to say. But I do know this: that if I was to work for you, I should get to know what's what and all the inside and outside of household management. I'm sure it would be wonderful experience."

Just then a maid arrived from Lady Wang's asking for Xi-feng, who promptly excused herself to Li Wan and left. Crimson returned to Green Delights—where our story now leaves her.

We now return to Dai-yu, who, having slept so little the night before, was very late getting up on the morning of the festival. Hearing that the other girls were all out in the garden "speeding the fairies" and fearing to be teased by them for her lazy habits, she hurried over her toilet and went out as soon as it was completed. A smiling Bao-yu appeared in the gateway as she was stepping down into the courtyard.

"Well, coz," he said, "I hope you *didn't* tell on me yesterday. You had me worrying about it all last night."

Dai-yu turned back, ignoring him, to address Nightingale inside:

"When you do the room, leave one of the casements open so that the parent swallows can get in. And put the lion doorstop on the bottom of the blind to stop it flapping. And don't forget to put the cover back on the burner after you've lighted the incense."

She made her way across the courtyard, still ignoring him.

Bao-yu, who knew nothing of the little drama that had taken place outside his gate the night before, assumed that she was still angry about his unfortunate lapse earlier on that same day, when he had offended her susceptibilities with a somewhat risqué quotation from *The Western Chamber*. He offered her now, with energetic bowing and hand-pumping, the apologies that the previous day's emergency had caused him to neglect. But Dai-yu walked straight past him and out of the gate, not deigning so much as a glance in his direction, and stalked off in search of the others.

Bao-yu was nonplussed. He began to suspect that something more than he had first imagined must be wrong.

"Surely it can't only be because of yesterday lunchtime that she's carrying on in this fashion? There must be something else. On the other hand, I didn't get back until late and I didn't see her again last night, so how *could* I have offended her?"

Preoccupied with these reflections, he followed her at some distance behind.

Not far ahead Bao-chai and Tan-chun were watching the ungainly courtship dance of some storks. When they saw Dai-yu coming, they invited her to join them, and the three girls stood together and chatted. Then Bao-yu arrived. Tan-chun greeted him with sisterly concern:

"How have you been keeping, Bao? It's three whole days since I saw you last."

Bao-yu smiled back at her.

"How have *you* been keeping, sis? I was asking Cousin Wan about you the day before yesterday."

"Come over here a minute," said Tan-chun. "I want to talk to you."

He followed her into the shade of a pomegranate tree a little way apart from the other two.

"Has Father asked to see you at all during this last day or two?" Tan-chun began.

"No."

"I thought I heard someone say yesterday that he had been asking for you."

"No," said Bao-yu, smiling at her concern. "Whoever it was was mistaken. He certainly hasn't asked for *me*."

Tan-chun smiled and changed the subject.

"During the past few months," she said, "I've managed to save up another ten strings or so of cash.[5] I'd like you to take it again like you did last time, and next time you go out, if you see a nice painting or calligraphic scroll or some amusing little thing that would do for my room, I'd like you to buy it for me."

"Well, I don't know," said Bao-yu. "In the trips I make to bazaars and temple fairs, whether it's inside the city or round about, I can't say that I ever see anything *really* nice or out of the ordinary. It's all bronzes and jades and porcelain and that sort of stuff. Apart from that it's mostly dressmaking materials and clothes and things to eat."

"Now what would I want things like that for?" said Tan-chun. "No, I mean something like that little wickerwork basket you bought me last time, or the little box carved out of bamboo root, or the little clay burner. I thought they were sweet. Unfortunately the others took such a fancy to them that they carried them off as loot and wouldn't give them back to me again."

---

5. Chinese copper coins had holes in the center and thus could be strung together.

"Oh, if *those* are the sort of things you want," said Bao-yu laughing, "it's very simple. Just give a few strings of cash to one of the boys and he'll bring you back a whole cartload of them."

"What do the boys know about it?" said Tan-chun. "I need someone who can pick out the interesting things and the ones that are in good taste. You get me lots of nice little things, and I'll embroider a pair of slippers for you like the ones I made for you last time—only this time I'll do them more carefully."

"Talking of those slippers reminds me," said Bao-yu. "I happened to run into Father once when I was wearing them. He was Most Displeased. When he asked me who made them, I naturally didn't dare to tell him that *you* had, so I said that Aunt Wang had given them to me as a birthday present a few days before. There wasn't much he could do about it when he heard that they came from Aunt Wang; so after a very long pause he just said, 'What a pointless waste of human effort and valuable material, to produce things like that!' I told this to Aroma when I got back, and she said, 'Oh, that's nothing! You should have heard your Aunt Zhao complaining about those slippers. She was *furious* when she heard about them: "Her own natural brother so down at heel he scarcely dares show his face to people, and she spends her time making things like that!" ' "

Tan-chun's smile had vanished:

"How *can* she talk such nonsense? Why should *I* be the one to make shoes for him? Huan[6] gets a clothing allowance, doesn't he? He gets his clothing and footwear provided for the same as all the rest of us. And fancy saying a thing like that in front of a roomful of servants! For whose benefit was this remark made, I wonder? I make an occasional pair of slippers just for something to do in my spare time; and if I give a pair to someone I particularly like, that's my own affair. Surely no one else has any business to start telling me who I should give them to? Oh, she's so *petty!*"

Bao-yu shook his head:

"Perhaps you're being a bit hard on her. She's probably got her reasons."

This made Tan-chun really angry. Her chin went up defiantly:

"Now you're being as stupid as her. Of *course* she's got her reasons; but they are ignorant, stupid reasons. But she can think what she likes: as far as *I* am concerned, Sir Jia is my father and Lady Wang is my mother, and who was born in whose room doesn't interest me—the way I choose my friends inside the family has nothing to do with that. Oh, I know I shouldn't talk about her like this; but she is *so* idiotic about these things. As a matter of fact I can give you an even better example than your story of the slippers. That last time I gave you my savings to get something for me, she saw me a few days afterwards and started telling me how short of money she was and how difficult things were for her. I took no notice, of course. But later, when the maids were out of the room, she began attacking me for giving the money I'd saved to other people instead of giving it to Huan. Really! I didn't know whether to laugh or get angry with her. In the end I just walked out of the room and went round to see Mother."

---

6. Jia Huan, Bao-yu's half-brother, born to his father and the concubine Aunt Zhao.

There was an amused interruption at this point from Bao-chai, who was still standing where they had left her a few minutes before:

"Do finish your talking and come back soon! It's easy to see that you two are brother and sister. As soon as you see each other, you get into a huddle and start talking about family secrets. Would it *really* be such a disaster if anything you are saying were to be overheard?"

Tan-chun and Bao-yu rejoined her, laughing.

Not seeing Dai-yu, Bao-yu realized that she must have slipped off elsewhere while he was talking.

"Better leave it a day or two," he told himself on reflection. "Wait until her anger has calmed down a bit."

While he was looking downwards and meditating, he noticed that the ground where they were standing was carpeted with a bright profusion of wind-blown flowers — pomegranate and balsam for the most part.

"You can see she's upset," he thought ruefully. "She's neglecting her flowers. I'll bury this lot for her and remind her about it next time I see her."

He became aware that Bao-chai was arranging for him and Tan-chun to go with her outside.

"I'll join you two presently," he said, and waited until they were a little way off before stooping down to gather the fallen blossoms into the skirt of his gown. It was quite a way from where he was to the place where Dai-yu had buried the peach-blossom on that previous occasion,[7] but he made his way towards it, over rocks and bridges and through plantations of trees and flowers. When he had almost reached his destination and there was only the spur of a miniature "mountain" between him and the burial-place of the flowers, he heard the sound of a voice, coming from the other side of the rock, whose continuous, gentle chiding was occasionally broken by the most pitiable and heart-rending sobs.

"It must be a maid from one of the apartments," thought Bao-yu. "Someone has been ill-treating her, and she has run here to cry on her own."

He stood still and endeavoured to catch what the weeping girl was saying. She appeared to be reciting something:

> The blossoms fade and falling fill the air,
> Of fragrance and bright hues bereft and bare.
> Floss drifts and flutters round the Maiden's bower,
> Or softly strikes against her curtained door.
>
> The Maid, grieved by these signs of spring's decease,
> Seeking some means her sorrow to express,
> Has rake in hand into the garden gone,
> Before the fallen flowers are trampled on.
>
> Elm-pods and willow-floss are fragrant too;
> Why care, Maid, where the fallen flowers blew?
> Next year, when peach and plum-tree bloom again,
> Which of your sweet companions will remain?

---

7. A reference to an incident in Chap. 23. Dai-yu explains that she is burying the blossoms to return them to the earth, rather than letting them be simply swept away. Because beautiful women were commonly compared to flowers, this foreshadows her own death.

This spring the heartless swallow built his nest
Beneath the eaves of mud with flowers compressed.
Next year the flowers will blossom as before,
But swallow, nest, and Maid will be no more.

Three hundred and three-score the year's full tale:
From swords of frost and from the slaughtering gale
How can the lovely flowers long stay intact,
Or, once loosed, from their drifting fate draw back?

Blooming so steadfast, fallen so hard to find!
Beside the flowers' grave, with sorrowing mind,
The solitary Maid sheds many a tear,
Which on the boughs as bloody drops appear.

At twilight, when the cuckoo sings no more,
The Maiden with her rake goes in at door
And lays her down between the lamplit walls,
While a chill rain against the window falls.

I know not why my heart's so strangely sad,
Half grieving for the spring and yet half glad:
Glad that it came, grieved it so soon was spent.
So soft it came, so silently it went!

Last night, outside, a mournful sound was heard:
The spirits of the flowers and of the bird.
But neither bird nor flowers would long delay,
Bird lacking speech, and flowers too shy to stay.

And then I wished that I had wings to fly
After the drifting flowers across the sky:
Across the sky to the world's farthest end,
The flowers' last fragrant resting-place to find.

But better their remains in silk to lay
And bury underneath the wholesome clay,
Pure substances the pure earth to enrich,
Than leave to soak and stink in some foul ditch.

Can I, that these flowers' obsequies attend,
Divine how soon or late *my* life will end?
Let others laugh flower-burial to see:
Another year who will be burying me?

As petals drop and spring begins to fail,
The bloom of youth, too, sickens and turns pale.
One day, when spring has gone and youth has fled.
The Maiden and the flowers will both be dead.

All this was uttered in a voice half-choked with sobs; for the words recited seemed only to inflame the grief of the reciter—indeed, Bao-yu, listening on the other side of the rock, was so overcome by them that he had already flung himself weeping upon the ground.

But the sequel to this painful scene will be told in the following chapter.

CHAPTER 28

A crimson cummerbund becomes a pledge of friendship
And a chaplet of medicine-beads becomes a source of
embarrassment

On the night before the festival, it may be remembered, Lin Dai-yu had mistakenly supposed Bao-yu responsible for Skybright's refusal to open the gate for her. The ceremonial farewell to the flowers of the following morning had transformed her pent-up and still smouldering resentment into a more generalized and seasonable sorrow. This had finally found its expression in a violent outburst of grief as she was burying the latest collection of fallen blossoms in her flower-grave. Meditation on the fate of flowers had led her to a contemplation of her own sad and orphaned lot; she had burst into tears, and soon after had begun a recitation of the poem whose words we recorded in the preceding chapter.

Unknown to her, Bao-yu was listening to this recitation from the slope of the near-by rockery. At first he merely nodded and sighed sympathetically; but when he heard the words

> "Can I, that these flowers' obsequies attend,
> Divine how soon or late *my* life will end?"

and, a little later,

> "One day when spring has gone and youth has fled,
> The Maiden and the flowers will both be dead."

he flung himself on the ground in a fit of weeping, scattering the earth all about him with the flowers he had been carrying in the skirt of his gown.

Lin Dai-yu dead! A world from which that delicate, flower-like countenance had irrevocably departed! It was unutterable anguish to think of it. Yet his sensitized imagination *did* now consider it—went on, indeed, to consider a world from which the others, too—Bao-chai, Caltrop, Aroma and the rest—had also irrevocably departed. Where would *he* be then? What would have become of him? And what of the Garden, the rocks, the flowers, the trees? To whom would they belong when he and the girls were no longer there to enjoy them? Passing from loss to loss in his imagination, he plunged deeper and deeper into a grief that seemed inconsolable. As the poet says:

> Flowers in my eyes and bird-song in my ears
> Augment my loss and mock my bitter tears.

Dai-yu, then, as she stood plunged in her own private sorrowing, suddenly heard the sound of another person crying bitterly on the rocks above her.

"The others are always telling me I'm a 'case,' " she thought. "Surely there can't be another 'case' up there?"

But on looking up she saw that it was Bao-yu.

"Pshaw!" she said crossly to herself. "I thought it was another girl, but all the time it was that cruel, hate—"

"Hateful" she had been going to say, but clapped her mouth shut before uttering it. She sighed instead and began to walk away.

By the time Bao-yu's weeping was over, Dai-yu was no longer there. He realized that she must have seen him and have gone away in order to avoid him. Feeling suddenly rather foolish, he rose to his feet and brushed the earth from his clothes. Then he descended from the rockery and began to retrace his steps in the direction of Green Delights. Quite by coincidence Dai-yu was walking along the same path a little way ahead.

"Stop a minute!" he cried, hurrying forward to catch up with her. "I know you are not taking any notice of me, but I only want to ask you one simple question, and then you need never have anything more to do with me."

Dai-yu had turned back to see who it was. When she saw that it was Bao-yu still, she was going to ignore him again; but hearing him say that he only wanted to ask her one question, she told him that he might do so.

Bao-yu could not resist teasing her a little.

"How about *two* questions? Would you wait for two?"

Dai-yu set her face forwards and began walking on again.

Bao-yu sighed.

"If it has to be like this now," he said, as if to himself, "it's a pity it was ever like it was in the beginning."

Dai-yu's curiosity got the better of her. She stopped walking and turned once more towards him.

"Like *what* in the beginning?" she asked. "And like what now?"

"Oh, the *beginning!*" said Bao-yu. "In the *beginning,* when you first came here, I was your faithful companion in all your games. Anything I had, even the thing most dear to me, was yours for the asking. If there was something to eat that I specially liked, I had only to hear that you were fond of it too and I would religiously hoard it away to share with you when you got back, not daring even to touch it until you came. We ate at the same table. We slept in the same bed. I used to think that because we were so close then, there would be something special about our relationship when we grew up—that even if we weren't particularly affectionate, we should at least have more understanding and forbearance for each other than the rest. But how wrong I was! Now that you *have* grown up, you seem only to have grown more touchy. You don't seem to care about *me* any more at all. You spend all your time brooding about outsiders like Feng and Chai. I haven't got any *real* brothers and sisters left here now. There are Huan and Tan, of course; but as you know, they're only my half-brother and half-sister: they aren't my mother's children. I'm on my own, like you. I should have thought we had so much in common—But what's the use? I try and try, but it gets me nowhere; and nobody knows or cares."

At this point—in spite of himself—he burst into tears.

The palpable evidence of her own eyes and ears had by now wrought a considerable softening on Dai-yu's heart. A sympathetic tear stole down her own cheek, and she hung her head and said nothing. Bao-yu could see that he had moved her.

"I know I'm not much use nowadays," he continued, "but however bad you may think me, I would never wittingly do anything in your presence to offend you. If I *do* ever slip up in some way, you ought to tell me off

about it and warn me not to do it again, or shout at me—hit me, even, if
you feel like it; I shouldn't mind. But you don't do that. You just ignore
me. You leave me utterly at a loss to know what I'm supposed to have
done wrong, so that I'm driven half frantic wondering what I ought to do
to make up for it. If I were to die now, I should die with a grievance, and
all the masses and exorcisms in the world wouldn't lay my ghost. Only
when you explained what your reason was for ignoring me should I cease
from haunting you and be reborn into another life."

Dai-yu's resentment for the gate incident had by now completely evapo-
rated. She merely said:

"Oh well, in that case why did you tell your maids not to let me in
when I came to call on you?"

"I honestly don't know what you are referring to," said Bao-yu in surprise. "Strike me dead if I ever did any such thing!"

"Hush!" said Dai-yu. "Talking about death at this time of the morning!
You should be more careful what you say. If you did, you did. If you didn't,
you didn't. There's no need for these horrible oaths."

"I really and truly didn't know you had called," said Bao-yu. "Cousin
Bao came and sat with me a few minutes last night and then went away
again. That's the only call I know about."

Dai-yu reflected for a moment or two, then smiled.

"Yes, it must have been the maids being lazy. Certainly they can be
very disagreeable at such times."

"Yes, I'm sure that's what it was," said Bao-yu. "When I get back, I'll
find out who it was and give her a good talking-to."

"I think some of your young ladies could *do* with a good talking-to,"
said Dai-yu, "—though it's not really for me to say so. It's a good job it was
only me they were rude to. If Miss Bao or Miss Cow were to call and they
behaved like that to *her*, that would be really serious."

She giggled mischievously. Bao-yu didn't know whether to laugh with
her or grind his teeth. But just at that moment a maid came up to ask
them both to lunch and the two of them went together out of the Garden
and through into the front part of the mansion, calling in at Lady Wang's[8]
on the way.

"How did you get on with that medicine of Dr. Bao's," Lady Wang
asked Dai-yu as soon as she saw her, "—the Court Physician? Do you
think you are any better for it?"

"It didn't seem to make very much difference," said Dai-yu. "Grandmother has put me back on Dr. Wang's prescription."

"Cousin Lin has got a naturally weak constitution, Mother," said Bao-
yu. "She takes cold very easily. These strong decoctions are all very well
provided she only takes one or two to dispel the cold. For regular treatment it's probably best if she sticks to pills."

"The doctor was telling me about some pills for her the other day," said
Lady Wang, "but I just can't remember the name."

"I know the names of most of those pills," said Bao-yu. "I expect he
wanted her to take Ginseng Tonic Pills."[9]

---

8. Bao-yu's mother.   9. This passage plays on the fantastic names of Chinese medicines.

"No, that wasn't it," said Lady Wang.

"Eight Gem Motherwort Pills?" said Bao-yu. "Zhang's Dextrals? Zhang's Sinistrals? If it wasn't any of them, it was probably Dr. Cui's Adenophora Kidney Pills."

"No," said Lady Wang, "it was none of those. All I can remember is that there was a 'Vajra'[1] in it."

Bao-yu gave a hoot and clapped his hands:

"I've never heard of 'Vajra Pills.' If there are 'Vajra Pills,' I suppose there must be 'Buddha Boluses'!"[2]

The others all laughed. Bao-chai looked at him mockingly.

"I should think it was probably 'The Deva-king Cardiac Elixir Pills,'" she said.

"Yes, yes, that's it!" said Lady Wang."Of course! How stupid of me!"

"No, Mother, not stupid," said Bao-yu. "It's the strain. All those Vajra-kings and Bodhisattvas have been overworking you!"

"You're a naughty boy to make fun of your poor mother," said Lady Wang. "A good whipping from your Pa is what you need."

"Oh, Father doesn't whip me for that sort of thing nowadays," said Bao-yu.

"Now that we know the name of the pills, we must get them to buy some for your Cousin Lin," said Lady Wang.

"None of those things are any good," said Bao-yu. "You give me three hundred and sixty taels of silver and I'll make up some pills for Cousin Lin that I guarantee will have her completely cured before she has finished the first boxful."

"Stuff!" said Lady Wang. "Whoever heard of a medicine that cost so much?"

"No, honestly!" said Bao-yu. "This prescription is a very unusual one with very special ingredients. I can't remember all of them, but I know they include

the caul[3] of a first-born child;
a ginseng root shaped like a man, with the leaves still on it;
a turtle-sized polygonum[4] root;

and

lycoperdon from the stump of a thousand-year-old pine-tree.

—Actually, though, there's nothing so *very* special about those ingredients. They're all in the standard pharmacopoeia. For 'sovereign remedies' they use ingredients that would *really* make you jump. I once gave the prescription for one to Cousin Xue. He was more than a year begging me for it before I would give it to him, and it took him another two or three years and nearly a thousand taels of silver to get all the ingredients together. Ask Bao-chai if you don't believe me, Mother."

"I know nothing about it," said Bao-chai. "I've never heard it mentioned. It's no good telling Aunt to ask *me*."

1. The thunderbolt of the Indian god Indra, a conventional image for something hard and powerful.
2. A large pill given to a horse.　3. The membrane around the newborn.　4. The translator is using the Latin names of the plants used in the prescription.

"You see! Bao-chai is a *good* girl. *She* doesn't tell lies," said Lady Wang.

Bao-yu was standing in the middle of the floor below the kang. He clapped his hands at this and turned to the others appealingly.

"But it's the *truth* I'm telling you. This is no lie."

As he turned, he happened to catch sight of Dai-yu, who was sitting behind Bao-chai, smiling mockingly and stroking her cheek with her finger—which in sign-language means, "You are a great big liar and you ought to be ashamed of yourself."

But Xi-feng, who happened to be in the inner room supervising the laying of the table and had overheard the preceding remarks, now emerged into the outer room to corroborate:

"It's quite true, what Bao says. I don't think he *is* making it up," she said. "Not so long ago Cousin Xue came to me asking for some pearls, and when I asked him what he wanted them for, he said, 'To make medicine with.' Then he started grumbling about the trouble he was having in getting the right ingredients and how he had half a mind not to make this medicine up after all. I said, 'What medicine?' and he told me that it was a prescription that Cousin Bao had given him and reeled off a lot of ingredients—I can't remember them now. 'Of course,' he said, 'I could easily enough *buy* a few pearls; only these have to be ones that have been worn. That's why I'm asking *you* for them. If you haven't got any loose ones,' he said, 'a few pearls broken off a bit of jewellery would do. I'd get you something nice to replace it with.' He was so insistent that in the end I had to break up two of my ornaments for him. Then he wanted a yard of Imperial red gauze. That was to put over the mortar to pound the pearls through. He said they had to be ground until they were as fine as flour.'

"You see!" "You see!" Bao-yu kept interjecting throughout this recital.

"Incidentally, Mother," he said, when it was ended, "even *that* was only a substitute. According to the prescription, the pearls ought really to have come from an ancient grave. They should really have been pearls taken from jewellery on the corpse of a long-buried noblewoman. But as one can't very well go digging up graves and rifling tombs every time one wants to make this medicine, the prescription allows pearls worn by the living as a second-best."

"Blessed name of the Lord!" said Lady Wang. "What a *dreadful* idea! Even if you *did* get them from a grave, I can't believe that a medicine made from pearls that had been come by so wickedly—desecrating people's bones that had been lying peacefully in the ground all those hundreds of years—could possibly do you any good."

Bao-yu turned to Dai-yu.

"Did you hear what Feng said?" he asked her. "I hope you're not going to say that *she* was lying."

Although the remark was addressed to Dai-yu, he winked at Bao-chai as he made it.

Dai-yu clung to Lady Wang.

"Listen to him, Aunt!" she wailed. "Bao-chai won't be a party to his lies, but he still expects *me* to be."

"Bao-yu, you are very unkind to your cousin," said Lady Wang.

Bao-yu only laughed.

"You don't know the reason, Mother. Bao-chai didn't know a half of what Cousin Xue got up to, even when she was living with her mother outside; and now that she's moved into the Garden, she knows even less. When she said she didn't know, she *really* didn't know: she wasn't giving me the lie. What you don't realize is that Cousin Lin was all the time sitting behind her making signs to show that she didn't believe me."

Just then a maid came from Grandmother Jia's apartment to fetch Bao-yu and Dai-yu to lunch.

Without saying a word to Bao-yu, Dai-yu got up and, taking the maid's hand, began to go. But the maid was reluctant.

"Let's wait for Master Bao and we can go together."

"He's not eating lunch today," said Dai-yu. "Come on, let's go!"

"Whether he's eating lunch or not," said the maid, "he'd better come with us, so that he can explain to Her Old Ladyship about it when she asks."

"All right, you wait for him then," said Dai-yu. "I'm going on ahead." And off she went.

"I think I'd rather eat with *you* today, Mother," said Bao-yu.

"No, no, you can't," said Lady Wang. "Today is one of my fast-days:[5] I shall only be eating vegetables. You go and have a proper meal with your Grandma."

"I shall share your vegetables," said Bao-yu. "Go on, you can go," he said, dismissing the maid; and rushing up to the table, he sat himself down at it in readiness.

"You others had better get on with your own lunch," Lady Wang said to Bao-chai and the girls. "Let him do as he likes."

"You really ought to go," Bao-chai said to Bao-yu. "Whether you have lunch there or not, you ought to keep Cousin Lin company. She is very upset, you know. Why don't you?"

"Oh, leave her alone!" said Bao-yu. "She'll be all right presently."

Soon they had finished eating, and Bao-yu, afraid that Grandmother Jia might be worrying and at the same time anxious to rejoin Dai-yu, hurriedly demanded tea to rinse his mouth with. Tan-chun and Xi-chun were much amused.

"Why are you always in such a hurry, Bao?" they asked him. "Even your eating and drinking all seems to be done in a rush."

"You should let him finish quickly, so that he can get back to his Dai-yu," said Bao-chai blandly. "Don't make him waste time here with us."

Bao-yu left as soon as he had drunk his tea, and made straight for the west courtyard where his Grandmother Jia's apartment was. But as he was passing by the gateway of Xi-feng's courtyard, it happened that Xi-feng herself was standing in her doorway with one foot on the threshold, grooming her teeth with an ear-cleaner and keeping a watchful eye on nine or ten pages who were moving potted plants about under her direction.

"Ah, just the person I wanted to see!" she said, as soon as she caught

---

5. Days when no meat is eaten; a Buddhist practice.

sight of Bao-yu. "Come inside. I want you to write something down for me."

Bao-yu was obliged to follow her indoors. Xi-feng called for some paper, an inkstone and a brush, and at once began dictating:

"Crimson lining-damask forty lengths, dragonet figured satin forty lengths, miscellaneous Imperial gauze one hundred lengths, gold necklets four, — "

"Here, what *is* this?" said Bao-yu. "It isn't an invoice and it isn't a presentation list. How am I supposed to write it?"

"Never you mind about that," said Xi-feng. "As long as *I* know what it is, that's all that matters. Just put it down anyhow."

Bao-yu wrote down the four items. As soon as he had done so, Xi-feng took up the paper and folded it away.

"Now," she said, smiling pleasantly, "there's something I want to talk to you about. I don't know whether you'll agree to this or not, but there's a girl in your room called 'Crimson' whom I'd like to work for me. If I find you someone to replace her with, will you let me have her?"

"There are so many girls in my room," said Bao-yu. "Please take any you have a fancy to. You really don't need to ask me about it."

"In that case," said Xi-feng, "I'll send for her straight away."

"Please do," said Bao-yu, and started to go.

"Hey, come back!" said Xi-feng. "I haven't finished with you yet."

"I've got to see Grandma now," said Bao-yu. "If you've got anything else to say, you can tell me on my way back."

When he got to Grandmother Jia's apartment, they had all just finished lunch. Grandmother Jia asked him if he had had anything nice to eat with his mother.

"There wasn't anything nice," he said. "But I had an extra bowl of rice."

Then, after the briefest pause:

"Where's Cousin Lin?"

"In the inner room," said Grandmother Jia.

In the inner room a maid stood below the kang[6] blowing on a flat-iron. Up on the kang two maids were marking some material with a chalked string, while Dai-yu, her head bent low over her work, was engaged in cutting something from it with her shears.

"What are you making?" he asked her. "You'll give yourself a headache, stooping down like that immediately after your lunch."

Dai-yu took no notice and went on cutting.

"That corner looks a bit creased still," said one of the maids. "It will have to be ironed again."

"*Leave it alone!*" said Dai-yu, laying down her shears. "*It will be all right presently.*"

Bao-yu found her reply puzzling.

Bao-chai, Tan-chun and the rest had now arrived in the outer room and were talking to Grandmother Jia. Presently Bao-chai drifted inside and asked Dai-yu what she was doing; then, when she saw that she was cutting material, she exclaimed admiringly.

---

6. A brick platform, heated by a small fire underneath, that could be used for sitting on or as a bed.

drunk in no time without giving us any real enjoyment. I've got a good new drinking-game for you. Let me first drink the M.C.'s starting-cup,[9] and I'll tell you the rules. After that, anyone who doesn't toe the line will be made to drink ten sconce-cups straight off as a forfeit, give up his seat at the party, and spend the rest of the time pouring out drinks for the rest of us."

Feng Zi-ying and Jiang Yu-han agreed enthusiastically, and Bao-yu picked up one of the extra large cups that had now been provided and drained its contents at a single draught.

"Now," he said. "We're going to take four words—let's say 'upset,' 'glum,' 'blest' and 'content.' You have to begin by saying 'The girl is—,' and then you say one of the four words. That's your first line. The next line has to rhyme with the first line and it has to give the reason why the girl is whatever it says—'upset' or 'glum' or 'blest' or 'content.' When you've done all four, you're entitled to drink the wine in front of you. Only, before drinking it, you've first got to sing some new popular song; and *after* you've drunk it, you've got to choose some animal or vegetable object from the things in front of us and recite a line from a well-known poem, or an old couplet, or a quotation from the classics—"

Before he could finish, Xue Pan was on his feet, protesting vigorously:

"You can count *me* out of this. *I'm* taking no part in this. This is just to make a fool of me, isn't it?"

Nuageuse, too, stood up and attempted to push him back into his seat:

"What are you so afraid of, a practised drinker like you? You can't be any worse at this sort of thing than I am, and *I'm* going to have a go when *my* turn comes. If you do it all right, you've got nothing to worry about, and even if you can't, you'll only be made to drink a few cups of wine; whereas if you refuse to follow the rules at the very outset, you'll have to drink ten sconces straight off in a row and then be thrown out of the party and made to pour drinks for the rest of us."

"Bravo!" cried the others, clapping; and Xue Pan, seeing them united against him, subsided.

Bao-yu now began his own turn:

> "The girl's upset:
>   The years pass by, but no one's claimed her yet.
> The girl looks glum:
>   Her true-love's gone to follow ambition's drum.
> The girl feels blest:
>   The mirror shows her looks are at their best.
> The girl's content:
>   Long summer days in pleasant pastimes spent."

The others all applauded, except Xue Pan, who shook his head disapprovingly:

"No good, no good!" he said. "Pay the forfeit."

"Why, what's wrong with it?" they asked him.

"I couldn't understand a word of it."

Nuageuse gave him a pinch:

---

9. Bao-yu is going to set up the drinking games, so he drinks first.

"Keep quiet and try to think what *you*'re going to say," she advised him; "otherwise you'll have nothing ready when your own turn comes and you'll have to pay the forfeit yourself."

Thereupon she picked up her lute and accompanied Bao-yu as he sang the following song:

> "Still weeping tears of blood about our separation:
> Little red love-beans of my desolation.
> Still blooming flowers I see outside my window growing.
> Still awake in the dark I hear the wind a-blowing.
> Still oh still I can't forget those old hopes and fears.
> Still can't swallow food and drink, 'cos I'm choked with tears.
> Mirror, mirror on the wall, tell me it's not true:
> Do I look so thin and pale, do I look so blue?
> Mirror, mirror, this long night how shall I get through?
>   Oh—oh—oh!
> Blue as the mist upon the distant mountains,
> Blue as the water in the ever-flowing fountains."

General applause—except from Xue Pan, who objected that there was "no rhythm."

Bao-yu now drank his well-earned cup—the "pass cup" as they call it—and, picking up a slice of pear from the table, concluded his turn with the following quotation:

> "Rain whips the pear-tree, shut fast the door."

Now it was Feng Zi-ying's turn:

> "The girl's upset:
>   Her husband's ill and she's in debt.
> The girl looks glum:
>   The gale has turned her room into a slum.
> The girl feels blest:
>   She's got twin babies at the breast.
> The girl's content:
>   Waiting a certain pleasurable event."

Next, holding up his cupful of wine in readiness to drink, he sang this song:

> "You're so exciting,
>   And so inviting;
> You're my Mary Contrary;
>   You're a crazy, mad thing.
> You're my goddess, but oh! you're deaf to my praying:
> Why won't you listen to what I am saying?
> If you don't believe me, make a small investigation:
> You will soon find out the true depth of my admiration."

Then he drained his bumper and, picking up a piece of chicken from one of the dishes, ended the performance, prior to popping it into his mouth, with a line from Wen Ting-yun:[1]

---

1. Poet (9th century).

"From moonlit cot the cry of chanticleer."

Next it was the turn of Nuageuse:

"The girl's upset:"

she began,

"Not knowing how the future's to be met—"

Xue Pan laughed noisily.

"That's all right, my darling, don't you worry! Your Uncle Xue will take care of you."

"Shush!" said the others. "Don't confuse her."

She continued:

"The girl looks glum:
Nothing but blows and hard words from her Mum—"

"I saw that Mum of yours the other day," said Xue Pan, "and I particularly told her that she wasn't to beat you."

"Another word from you," said the others, "and you'll be made to drink ten cups as a punishment."

Xue Pan gave his own face a slap.

"Sorry! I forgot. Won't do it again."

"The girl feels blest:"

said Nuageuse,

"Her young man's rich and beautifully dressed.
The girl's content:
She's been performing in a big event."

Next Nuageuse sang her song:

"A flower began to open in the month of May.
Along came a honey-bee to sport and play.
He pushed and he squeezed to get inside,
But he couldn't get in however hard he tried.
So on the flower's lip he just hung around,
A-playing the see-saw up and down.
Oh my honey-sweet,
Oh my sweets of sin,
If I don't open up,
How will you get in?"

After drinking her "pass cup," she picked up a peach:

"So bonny blooms the peach-tree-o."[2]

It was now Xue Pan's turn.

"Ah yes, now, let's see! *I* have to say something now, don't I?"

"The girl's upset—"

But nothing followed.

---

2. From the *Book of Songs.*

"All right, what's she upset about then?" said Feng Zi-ying with a laugh. "Buck up!"

Xue Pan appeared to be engaged in a species of mental effort so frightful that his eyes seemed about to pop out of his head. After glaring fixedly for an unconscionable time, he said:

"The girl's upset—"

He coughed a couple of times. Then at last it came:

"The girl's upset:
She's married to a marmoset."

The others greeted this with a roar of laughter.

"What are you laughing at?" said Xue Pan. "That's perfectly reasonable, isn't it? If a girl was expecting a proper husband and he turned out to be one of *them*, she'd have cause to be upset, wouldn't she?"

His audience were by now doubled up.

"That's perfectly true," they conceded. "Very good. Now what about the next bit?"

Xue Pan glared a while very concentratedly, then:

"The girl looks glum—"

But after that was silence.

"Come on!" said the others. "Why was she glum?"

"His dad's a baboon with a big red bum."

"Ho! Ho! Ho! Pay the forfeit," they cried. "The first one was bad enough. We really can't let this one go."

The more officious of them even began filling the sconce-cups for him. But Bao-yu allowed the line.

"As long as it rhymes," he said, "we'll let it pass."

"There you are!" said Xue Pan. "The M.C. says it's all right. What are the rest of you making such a fuss about?"

At this the others desisted.

"The next two are even harder," said Nuageuse. "Shall I do them for you, dear?"

"Piss off!" said Xue Pan. "D'you think I haven't got any good lines of my own? Listen to this:

The girl feels blest:
In bridal bower she takes her rest."

The others stared at him in amazement:

"I say, old chap, that's a bit poetical for you, isn't it?"

Xue Pan continued unconcernedly:

"The girl's content:
She's got a big prick up her vent."

The others looked away with expressions of disgust.

"Oh dear, oh dear! Hurry up and get on with the song, then."

"One little gnat went hum hum hum,"

Xue Pan began tunelessly. The others looked at him open-mouthed:
"What sort of song is that?"

Xue Pan droned on, ignoring the question:

> "Two little flies went bum bum bum,
>   Three little—"

"Stop!" shouted the others.

"Sod you lot!" said Xue Pan. "This is the very latest new hit. It's called the Hum-bum Song. If you can't be bothered to listen to it, you'll have to let me off the other thing. I'll agree not to sing the rest of the song on that condition."

"Yes, yes, we'll let you off," they said. "Just don't interfere with the rest of us, that's all we ask."

This meant that it was now Jiang Yu-han's turn to perform. This is what he said:

> "The girl's upset:
>   Her man's away, she fears he will forget.
> The girl looks glum:
>   So short of cash she can't afford a crumb.
> The girl feels blest:
>   Her lampwick's got a lucky crest.
> The girl's content:
>   She's married to a perfect gent."

Then he sang this song:

> "A mischievous bundle of charm and love,
> Or an angel come down from the skies above?
>   Sweet sixteen
>   And so very green,
> Yet eager to see all there is to be seen.
>   Aie aie aie
>   The galaxy's high
>   In the roof of the sky,
> And the drum from the tower
>   Sounds the midnight hour.
> So trim the lamp, love, and come with me
> Inside the bed-curtains, and you shall see!"

He raised the pass cup to his lips, but before drinking it, smiled round at his auditors and made this little speech:

"I'm afraid my knowledge of poetry is strictly limited. However, I happened to see a couplet on someone's wall yesterday which has stuck in my mind; and as one line in it is about something I can see here, I shall use it to finish my turn with."

So saying, he drained the cup and then, picking up a spray of cassia, recited the following line:

> "The flowers' aroma breathes of hotter days."

The others all accepted this as a satisfactory conclusion of the performance. Not so Xue Pan, however, who leaped to his feet and began protesting noisily:

"Terrible! Pay the forfeit. Where's the little doll? I can't see any doll on the table."

"I didn't say anything about a doll," said Jiang Yu-han. "What are you talking about?"

"Come on, don't try to wriggle out of it!" said Xue Pan. "Say what you said just now again."

"The flowers' aroma breathes of hotter days."

"There you are!" said Xue Pan. " 'Aroma.' That's the name of a little doll.[3] Ask *him* if you don't believe me." — He pointed to Bao-yu.

Bao-yu looked embarrassed.

"Cousin Xue, this time I think you *do* have to pay the forfeit."

"All right, all right!" said Xue Pan. "I'll drink."

And he picked up the wine in front of him and drained it at a gulp.

Feng Zi-ying and Jiang Yu-han were still puzzled and asked him what this was all about. But it was Nuageuse who explained. Immediately Jiang Yu-han was on his feet apologizing. The others reassured him.

"It's not your fault. 'Ignorance excuses all,' " they said.

Shortly after this Bao-yu had to take temporary leave of the company to ease his bladder and Jiang Yu-han followed him outside. As the two of them stood side by side under the eaves, Jiang Yu-han once more offered Bao-yu his apologies. Much taken with the actor's winsome looks and gentleness of manner, Bao-yu impulsively took his hand and gave it a squeeze.

"Do come round to our place some time when you are free," he said. "There's something I want to ask you about. You have an actor in your company called 'Bijou' whom everyone is talking about lately. I should so much like to meet him, but so far I haven't had an opportunity."

"That's me!" said Jiang Yu-han. " 'Bijou' is my stage-name."

Bao-yu stamped with delight.

"But this is wonderful! I must say, you fully deserve your reputation. Oh dear! What am I going to do about a First Meeting present?"[4]

He thought for a bit, then took a fan from his sleeve and broke off its jade pendant.

"Here you are," he said, handing it to Bijou. "It's not much of a present, I'm afraid, but it will do to remind you of our meeting."

Bijou smiled and accepted it ceremoniously:

"I have done nothing to deserve this favour. It is too great an honour. Well, thank you. There's rather an unusual thing I'm wearing — I put it on today for the first time, so it's still fairly new: I wonder if you will allow me to give it to you as a token of my warm feelings towards you?"

He opened up his gown, undid the crimson cummerbund with which his trousers were fastened, and handed it to Bao-yu.

"It comes from the tribute sent by the Queen of the Madder Islands. It's for wearing in summer. It makes you smell nice and it doesn't show perspiration stains. I was given it yesterday by the Prince of Bei-jing, and today is the first time it's ever been worn. I wouldn't give a thing like this

---

3. Aroma is also the name of Bao-yu's chief maid.   4. Exchanged when people become friends.

to anyone else, but I'd like *you* to have it. Will you take your own sash off, please, so that I can put it on instead?"

Bao-yu received the crimson cummerbund with delight and quickly took off his own viridian-coloured sash to give to Bijou in exchange. They had just finished fastening the sashes on again when Xue Pan jumped out from behind and seized hold of them both.

"What are you two up to, leaving the party and sneaking off like this?" he said. "Come on, take 'em out again and let's have a look!"

It was useless for them to protest that the situation was not what he imagined. Xue Pan continued to force his unwelcome attentions upon them until Feng Zi-ying came out and rescued them. After that they returned to the party and continued drinking until the evening.

Back in his own apartment in the Garden, Bao-yu took off his outer clothes[5] and relaxed with a cup of tea. While he did so, Aroma noticed that the pendant of his fan was missing and asked him what had become of it. Bao-yu told her that it had come off while he was riding, and she gave the matter no more thought. But later, when he was going to bed, she saw the magnificent blood-red sash round his waist and began to put two and two together.

"Since you've got a better sash now," she said, "do you think I could have mine back, please?"

Bao-yu remembered, too late, that the viridian sash had been Aroma's and that he ought never to have given it away. He now very much regretted having done so, but instead of apologizing, attempted to pass it off with a laugh.

"I'll get you another," he told her lightly.

Aroma shook her head and sighed.

"I knew you still got up to these tricks,"[6] she said, "but at least you might refrain from giving *my* things to those disgusting creatures. I'm surprised you haven't got more sense."

She was going to say more, but checked herself for fear of provoking an explosion while he was in his cups.[7] And since there was nothing else she could do, she went to bed.

She awoke at first daylight next morning to find Bao-yu smiling down at her:

"We might have been burgled last night for all you'd have known about it—Look at your trousers!"

Looking down, Aroma saw the sash that Bao-yu had been wearing yesterday tied round her own waist, and knew that he must have exchanged it for hers during the night. She tore it off impatiently.

"*I* don't want the horrible thing. The sooner you take it away the better."

Bao-yu was anxious that she should keep it, and after a great deal of coaxing she consented, very reluctantly, to tie it on again. But she took it off once and for all as soon as he was out of the room and threw it into an empty chest, having first found another one of her own to put on in its place.

---

5. Clothes were worn in multiple layers.   6. This may suggest that Aroma suspects him of engaging in homosexual acts.   7. That is, he was drunk.

Bao-yu made no comment on the change when they were together again. He merely inquired whether anything had happened the day before, while he was out.

"Mrs. Lian sent someone round to fetch Crimson," said Aroma. "She wanted to wait for you; but it seemed to me that it wasn't all that important, so I took it on myself to send her off straight away."

"Quite right," said Bao-yu. "I already knew about it. There was no need to wait till I got back."

Aroma continued:

"Her Grace[8] sent that Mr. Xia of the Imperial Bedchamber yesterday with a hundred and twenty taels of silver to pay for a three-day *Pro Viventibus* by the Taoists of the Lunar Queen temple starting on the first of next month. There are to be plays performed as part of the Offering, and Mr. Zhen and all the other gentlemen are to go there to burn incense. Oh, and Her Grace's presents for the Double Fifth[9] have arrived."

She ordered a little maid to get out Bao-yu's share of the things sent. There were two Palace fans of exquisite workmanship, two strings of red musk-scented medicine-beads, two lengths of maidenhair chiffon and a grass-woven "lotus" mat to lie on in the hot weather.

"Did the others all get the same?" he asked.

"Her Old Ladyship's presents were the same as yours with the addition of a perfume-sceptre and an agate head-rest, and Sir Zheng's, Lady Wang's and Mrs. Xue's were the same as Her Old Ladyship's but without the head-rest; Miss Bao's were exactly the same as yours; Miss Lin, Miss Ying-chun, Miss Tan-chun and Miss Xi-chun got only the fans and the beads; and Mrs. Zhu and Mrs. Lian both got two lengths of gauze, two lengths of chiffon, two perfume sachets and two moulded medicine-cakes."

"Funny!" said Bao-yu. "I wonder why Miss Lin didn't get the same as me and why only Miss Bao's and mine were the same. There must have been some mistake, surely?"

"When they unpacked them yesterday, the separate lots were all labelled," said Aroma. "I don't see how there could have been any mistake. Your share was in Her Old Ladyship's room and I went round there to get it for you. Her Old Ladyship says she wants you to go to Court at four o'clock tomorrow morning to give thanks."

"Yes, of course," said Bao-yu inattentively, and gave Ripple instructions to take his presents round to Dai-yu:

"Tell Miss Lin that I got these things yesterday and that if there's anything there she fancies, I should like her to keep it."

Ripple went off with the presents. She was back in a very short time, however.

"Miss Lin says she got some yesterday too, and will you please keep these for yourself."

Bao-yu told her to put them away. As soon as he had washed, he left to pay his morning call on Grandmother Jia; but just as he was going out he saw Dai-yu coming towards him and hurried forward to meet her.

---

8. Bao-yu's elder sister, the imperial concubine.   9. A holiday that falls on the fifth day of the Fifth Month.

"Why didn't you choose anything from the things I sent you?"

Yesterday's resentments were now quite forgotten; today Dai-yu had fresh matter to occupy her mind.

"I'm not equal to the honour," she said. "You forget, I'm not in the gold and jade class like you and your Cousin Bao. I'm only a common little wall-flower!"

The reference to gold and jade immediately aroused Bao-yu's suspicions.

"I don't know what anyone else may have been saying on the subject," he said, "but if any such thought ever so much as crossed *my* mind, may Heaven strike me dead, and may I never be reborn as a human being!"

Seeing him genuinely bewildered, Dai-yu smiled in what was meant to be a reassuring manner.

"I wish you wouldn't make these horrible oaths. It's so disagreeable. Who *cares* about your silly old 'gold and jade,' anyway?"

"It's hard to make you *see* what is in my heart," said Bao-yu. "One day perhaps you will know. But I can tell you this. My heart has room for four people only. Grannie and my parents are three of them and Cousin Dai is the fourth. I swear to you there isn't a fifth."

"There's no need for you to swear," said Dai-yu. "I know very well that Cousin Dai has a place in your heart. The trouble is that as soon as Cousin Chai comes along, Cousin Dai gets forgotten."

"You imagine these things," said Bao-yu. "It really isn't as you say."

"Yesterday when Little Miss Bao wouldn't tell lies for you, why did you turn to *me* and expect *me* to? How would you like it if I did that sort of thing to you?"

Bao-chai happened to come along while they were still talking and the two of them moved aside to avoid her. Bao-chai saw this clearly, but pretended not to notice and hurried by with lowered eyes. She went and sat with Lady Wang for a while and from there went on to Grandmother Jia's. Bao-yu was already at his grandmother's when she got there.

Bao-chai had on more than one occasion heard her mother telling Lady Wang and other people that the golden locket she wore had been given her by a monk, who had insisted that when she grew up the person she married must be someone who had "a jade to match the gold." This was one of the reasons why she tended to keep aloof from Bao-yu. The slight embarrassment she always felt as a result of her mother's chatter had yesterday been greatly intensified when Yuan-chun singled her out as the only girl to receive the same selection of presents as Bao-yu. She was relieved to think that Bao-yu, so wrapped up in Dai-yu that his thoughts were only of her, was unaware of her embarrassment.

But now here was Bao-yu smiling at her with sudden interest.

"Cousin Bao, may I have a look at your medicine-beads?"

She happened to be wearing one of the little chaplets[1] on her left wrist and began to pull it off now in obedience to his request. But Bao-chai was inclined to plumpness and perspired easily, and for a moment or two it would not come off. While she was struggling with it, Bao-yu had ample

---

1. Strings of beads.

opportunity to observe her snow-white arm, and a feeling rather warmer than admiration was kindled inside him.

"If that arm were growing on Cousin Lin's body," he speculated, "I might hope one day to touch it. What a pity it's hers! Now I shall never have that good fortune."

Suddenly he thought of the curious coincidence of the gold and jade talismans and their matching inscriptions, which Dai-yu's remark had reminded him of. He looked again at Bao-chai —

> that face like the full moon's argent bowl;
> those eyes like sloes;
> those lips whose carmine hue no Art contrived;
> and brows by none but Nature's pencil lined.

This was beauty of quite a different order from Dai-yu's. Fascinated by it, he continued to stare at her with a somewhat dazed expression, so that when she handed him the chaplet, which she had now succeeded in getting off her wrist, he failed to take it from her.

Seeing that he had gone off into one of his trances, Bao-chai threw down the chaplet in embarrassment and turned to go. But Dai-yu was standing on the threshold, biting a corner of her handkerchief, convulsed with silent laughter.

"I thought you were so delicate," said Bao-chai. "What are you standing there in the draught for?"

"I've been in the room all the time," said Dai-yu. "I just this moment went to have a look outside because I heard the sound of something in the sky. It was a gawping goose."

"Where?" said Bao-chai. "Let *me* have a look."

"Oh," said Dai-yu, "as soon as I went outside he flew away with a *whir-r-r—*"

She flicked her long handkerchief as she said this in the direction of Bao-yu's face.

"Ow!" he exclaimed—She had flicked him in the eye.

The extent of the damage will be examined in the following chapter.

CHAPTER 29

In which the greatly blessed pray for yet greater blessings
And the highly strung rise to new heights of passion

We told in the last chapter how, as Bao-yu was standing lost in one of his trances, Dai-yu flicked her handkerchief at him and made him jump by inadvertently catching him in the eye with it.

"Who did that?" he asked.

Dai-yu laughingly shook her head.

"I'm sorry. I didn't mean to. Bao-chai wanted to look at a *gawping goose,* and I accidently flicked you while I was showing her how it went."

Bao-yu rubbed his eye. He appeared to be about to say something, but then thought better of it.

And so the matter passed.

Shortly after this incident Xi-feng arrived and began talking about the
arrangements that had been made for the purification ceremonies, due to
begin on the first of next month at the Taoist temple of the Lunar Goddess. She invited Bao-chai, Bao-yu and Dai-yu to go with her there to
watch the plays.

"Oh no!" said Bao-chai. "It's too *hot*. Even if they were to do something
we haven't seen before—which isn't likely—I think I should still not want
to go."

"But it's *cool* there," said Xi-feng. "There are upstairs galleries on all
three sides that you can watch from in the shade. And if we go, I shall
send someone a day or two in advance to turn the Taoists out of that part
of the temple and make it nice and clean for us and get them to put up
blinds.[2] And I'll ask them not to let any other visitors in on that day. I've
already told Lady Wang I'm going, so if you others won't come with me,
I shall go by myself. I'm so bored lately. And it's such a business when we
put on our own plays at home, that I can never enjoy them properly."

"All right then, *I'll* come," said Grandmother Jia, who had been listening.

"*You'll* come, Grannie? Well that's splendid, isn't it! That means it will
be just as bad for me as it would be if I were watching here at home."

"Now look here," said Grandmother Jia, "I shan't want you to stand and
wait on me. Let me take the gallery facing the stage and you can have one
of the side galleries all to yourself; then you can sit down and enjoy yourself in comfort."

Xi-feng was touched.

"*Do* come!" Grandmother Jia said to Bao-chai. "I'll see that your mother
comes too. The days are so long now, and there's nothing to do at home
except go to sleep."

Bao-chai had to promise that she would go.

Grandmother Jia now sent someone to invite Aunt Xue. The messenger
was to call in on the way at Lady Wang's and ask her if the girls might go
as well.

Lady Wang had already made it clear that she would not be going herself, partly because she was not feeling very well, and partly because she
wanted to be at home in case any further messages arrived from Yuan-
chun; but when she learned of Grandmother Jia's enthusiasm, she had
word carried into the Garden that not just the girls but anyone else who
wanted to might go along with Grandmother Jia's party on the first.

When this exciting news had been transmitted throughout the Garden,
the maids—some of whom hardly set foot outside their own courtyards
from one year's end to the next—were all dying to go, and those whose
mistresses showed a lethargic disinclination to accept employed a hundred
different wiles to make sure that they did so. The result was that in the
end *all* the Garden's inhabitants said that they would be going. Grandmother Jia was quite elated and at once issued orders for the cleaning and
preparation of the temple theatre.

---

2. Although Taoist religious observances were respected, Taoist priests themselves were rarely of high
status. When an important family like the Jias visited the temple, it had to be specially cleaned and a
large section was set off.

But these are details with which we need not concern ourselves.

On the morning of the first sedans,[3] carriages, horses and people filled all the roadway outside Rong-guo[4] House. The stewards in charge knew that the occasion of this outing was a *Pro Viventibus* ordered by Her Grace the Imperial Concubine and that Her Old Ladyship was going in person to burn incense—quite apart from the fact that this was the first day of the month and the first day of the Summer Festival; consequently the turnout was as splendid as they could make it and far exceeded anything that had been seen on previous occasions.

Presently Grandmother Jia appeared, seated, in solitary splendour, in a large palanquin carried by eight bearers. Li Wan, Xi-feng and Aunt Xue followed, each in a palanquin with four bearers. After them came Bao-chai and Dai-yu sharing a carriage with a splendid turquoise-coloured canopy trimmed with pearls. The carriage after them, in which Ying-chun, Tan-chun and Xi-chun sat, had vermilion-painted wheels and was shaded with a large embroidered umbrella. After them rode Grandmother Jia's maids, Faithful, Parrot, Amber and Pearl; after them Lin Dai-yu's maids, Nightingale, Snowgoose and Delicate; then Bao-chai's maids, Oriole and Apricot; then Ying-chun's maids, Chess and Tangerine; then Tan-chun's maids, Scribe and Ebony; then Xi-chun's maids, Picture and Landscape; then Aunt Xue's maids, Providence and Prosper, sharing a carriage with Caltrop and Caltrop's own maid, Advent; then Li Wan's maids, Candida and Casta; then Xi-feng's own maids, Patience, Felicity and Crimson, with two of Lady Wang's maids, Golden and Suncloud, whom Xi-feng had agreed to take with her, in the carriage behind. In the carriage after them sat another couple of maids and a nurse holding Xi-feng's little girl. Yet more carriages followed carrying the nannies and old women from the various apartments and the women whose duty it was to act as duennas when the ladies of the household went out of doors. The street was packed with carriages as far as the eye could see in either direction, and Grandmother Jia's palanquin was well on the way to the temple before the last passengers in the rear had finished taking their places. A confused hubbub of laughter and chatter rose from the line of carriages while they were doing so, punctuated by an occasional louder and more distinctly audible protest, such as:

"I'm not sitting next to *you!*"

or,

"You're squashing the Mistress's bundle!"

or,

"Look, you've trodden on my spray!"

or,

"You've ruined my fan, clumsy!"

Zhou Rui's wife walked up and down calling for some order:

"Girls! Girls! You're out in the street now, where people can see you. A little behaviour, *please!*"

She had to do this several times before the clamour subsided somewhat. The footmen and insignia-bearers at the front of the procession had

---

3. That is, sedan chairs.   4. The branch of the Jia clan to which Bao-yu belongs.

now reached the temple, and as the files of their column opened out to range themselves on either side of the gateway, the onlookers lining the sides of the street were able to see Bao-yu on a splendidly caparisoned white horse riding at the head of the procession immediately in front of his grandmother's great palanquin with its eight bearers. As Grandmother Jia and her party approached the temple, there was a crash of drums and cymbals from the roadside. It was the Taoists of the temple come out to welcome them, with old Abbot Zhang at their head, resplendent in cope and vestments and with a burning joss-stick[5] in his hand.

The palanquin passed through the gateway and into the first courtyard. From her seat inside it Grandmother Jia could see the terrifying painted images of the temple guardians, one on each side of the inner gate, flanked by that equally ferocious pair, Thousand League Eye with his blue face and Favourable Wind Ear with his green one, and farther on, the benigner forms of the City God and the little Local Gods. She ordered the bearers to halt, and Cousin Zhen[6] at the head of the younger male members of the clan came forward from the inner courtyard to meet her.

Xi-feng, whose palanquin was nearest to Grandmother Jia's, realized that Faithful and the other maids were too far back in the procession to be able to reach the old lady in time to help her out, and hurried forward to perform this service herself. Unfortunately a little eleven- or twelve-year-old acolyte, who had been going round with a pair of snuffers trimming the wicks of the numerous candles that were burning everywhere and whom the arrival of the procession had caught unawares, chose this very moment to attempt a getaway and ran head-on into her. Out flew Xi-feng's hand and dealt him a resounding smack on the face that sent him flying.

"Clumsy brat!" she shouted. "Look where you're going!"

The little acolyte picked himself up and, leaving his snuffers where they had fallen, darted off in the direction of the gate. But by now Bao-chai and the other young ladies were getting down from their carriages and a phalanx of women-servants clustered all round them, making egress impossible. Seeing a little Taoist running towards them, the women began to scream and shout:

"Catch him! Catch him! Hit him! Hit him!"

"What is it?" asked Grandmother Jia in alarm, hearing this hubbub behind her, and Cousin Zhen went forward to investigate.

"It's one of the young acolytes," said Xi-feng as she helped the old lady from her conveyance. "He was snuffing the candles and didn't get away in time and now he's rushing around trying to find a way out."

"Bring him to me, poor little thing!" said Grandmother Jia. "And don't frighten him. These children from poorer families have generally been rather spoiled. You can't expect them to stand up to great occasions like this. It would be a shame to frighten the poor little thing out of his wits. Think how upset his mother and father would be. Go on!" she said to Cousin Zhen. "Go and fetch him yourself."

Cousin Zhen was obliged to retrieve the little Taoist in person and led

5. A stick of incense.   6. Jia Zhen is the acting head of a branch of the Jia clan, one to which Bao-yu does not belong.

him by the hand to Grandmother Jia. The boy knelt down in front of her, the snuffers—now restored to him—clutched in one hand, trembling like a leaf. Grandmother Jia asked Cousin Zhen to raise him to his feet.

"Don't be afraid," she told the boy. "How old are you?"

But the little boy's mouth was hurting him too badly to speak.

"*Poor* little thing!" said Grandmother Jia. "You'd better take him away, Zhen. Give him some money to buy sweeties with and tell the others that they are not to grumble at him."

Cousin Zhen had to promise, and led the boy away, while the old lady led *her* party inside to begin a systematic tour of the shrines.

The pages in the outer courtyard, who had a moment before witnessed Grandmother Jia and her train trooping through the gateway that led into the inner courtyard, were surprised to see Cousin Zhen now emerging from it again with a little Taoist in tow. They heard him say that the boy was to be taken out and given a few hundred cash and that he was to be treated kindly. A few of them came forward and led the child away in obedience to his instructions.

Still standing at the top of the steps to the inner gate, Cousin Zhen inquired what had become of the stewards.

"Steward! Steward!" shouted the pages in unison, and almost immediately Lin Zhi-xiao came running out from heaven knows where, adjusting his hat with one hand as he ran.

"This is a big place," said Cousin Zhen when Lin Zhi-xiao was standing in front of him, "and we weren't expecting so many here today. I want you to take all the people you need and stay here in this courtyard with them. Those you don't need here can wait in the second courtyard. And pick some reliable boys to go on this gate and the two posterns to pass word through to those outside if those inside need anything. Do you understand? All the ladies are here today and I don't want any outsiders to get in. Is that understood?"

"Yessir!" said Lin Zhi-xiao. "Sir!"

"Well get on with it!" said Cousin Zhen. "Where's Rong got to?"

The words were scarcely out of his mouth when Jia Rong came bounding out of the bell-tower, buttoning his jacket as he ran.

"Look at him!" said Cousin Zhen irately. "Enjoying himself in the cool while I am roasting down here! Spit at him, someone."

Long familiarity with Cousin Zhen's temper had taught the boys that he would brook no opposition when roused. One of them obediently stepped forward and spat in Jia Rong's face; then, as Cousin Zhen continued to glare at him, he rebuked Jia Rong for presuming to be cool while his father was still sweating outside in the sun. Jia Rong was obliged to stand with his arms hanging submissively at his sides throughout this public humiliation, not daring to utter a word.

The other members of Jia Rong's generation who were present—Jia Yun, Jia Ping, Jia Qin and the rest—were greatly alarmed by this outburst; indeed, even the clansmen of Cousin Zhen's own generation—the Jia Bins and Jia Huangs and Jia Qiongs—were to be seen putting their hats on and slinking out, one by one, from the shadow of the walls.

"What are you standing here for?" said Cousin Zhen to Jia Rong. "Why don't you get on your horse and go back home and tell your mother and that new wife of yours that Her Old Ladyship is here with all the Rong-guo girls. Tell them they must come here at once to wait on her."

Jia Rong ran outside and began bawling impatiently for his horse. "What on earth can have got into him that he should suddenly have picked on me like that?" he muttered to himself resentfully; then, as his horse had still not arrived, he shouted angrily at the grooms:

"Come on, bring that horse, damn you! Are your hands tied or something?"

He would have liked to send a boy in his place, but was afraid that if he did, his father would find out when he went back later to report; and so, when the horse arrived, he mounted and rode off home.

Cousin Zhen was about to turn and go in again when he discovered old Abbot Zhang at his elbow, smiling somewhat unnaturally.

"Perhaps I don't come in quite the same category as the others," said the old Taoist. "Perhaps I should be allowed inside to wait on Her Old Ladyship. However. In this inclement heat, and with so many young ladies about, I shouldn't like to presume. I will do whatever you say. I *did* just wonder whether Her Old Ladyship might ask for me, or whether she might require a guide to take her round the shrines . . . However. Perhaps it would be best if I waited here."

Cousin Zhen was aware that, though Abbot Zhang had started life a poor boy and entered the Taoist church as "proxy novice" of Grandmother Jia's late husband, a former Emperor had with his own Imperial lips conferred on him the title "Doctor Mysticus," and he now held the seals of the Board of Commissioners of the Taoist Church, had been awarded the title "Doctor Serenissimus"[7] by the reigning sovereign, and was addressed as "Holiness" by princes, dukes and governors of provinces. He was therefore not a man to be trifled with. Moreover he was constantly in and out of the two mansions and on familiar terms with most of the Jia ladies. Cousin Zhen at once became affable.

"Oh, *you*'re one of the family, Papa Zhang, so let's have no more of that kind of talk, or I'll take you by that old beard of yours and give it a good pull. Come on, follow me!"

Abbot Zhang followed him inside, laughing delightedly.

Having found Grandmother Jia, Cousin Zhen ducked and smiled deferentially.

"Papa Zhang has come to pay his respects, Grannie."

"Help him, then!" said Grandmother Jia; and Cousin Zhen hurried back to where Abbot Zhang was waiting a few yards behind him and supported him by an elbow into her presence. The abbot prefaced his greeting with a good deal of jovial laughter.

"Blessed Buddha of Boundless Life! And how has Your Old Ladyship been all this while? In rude good health, I trust? And Their Ladyships, and all the younger ladies?—also flourishing? It's quite a while since I was at the mansion to call on Your Old Ladyship, but I declare you look more blooming than ever!"

---

7. The translator is imitating the pompous titles of the Taoist clergy.

"And how are *you*, old Holy One?" Grandmother Jia asked him with a pleased smile.

"Thank Your Old Ladyship for asking. I still keep pretty fit. But never mind about that. What *I* want to know is, how's our young hero been keeping, eh? We were celebrating the blessed Nativity of the Veiled King[8] here on the twenty-sixth. Very select little gathering. Tasteful offerings. I thought our young friend might have enjoyed it; but when I sent round to invite him, they told me he was out."

"He really *was* out," said Grandmother Jia, and turned aside to summon the "young hero"; but Bao-yu had gone to the lavatory. He came hurrying forward presently.

"Hallo, Papa Zhang! How are you?"

The old Taoist embraced him affectionately and returned his greeting.

"He's beginning to fill out," he said, addressing Grandmother Jia.

"He looks well enough on the outside," said Grandmother Jia, "but underneath he's delicate. And his Pa doesn't improve matters by forcing him to study all the time. I'm afraid he'll end up by *making* the child ill."

"Lately I've been seeing calligraphy and poems of his in all kinds of places," said Abbot Zhang, "—all quite remarkably good. I really can't understand why Sir Zheng is concerned that the boy doesn't study enough. If you ask me, I think he's all right as he is." He sighed. "Of course, you know who this young man reminds me of, don't you? Whether it's his looks or the way he talks or the way he moves, to me he's the spit and image of Old Sir Jia."

The old man's eyes grew moist, and Grandmother Jia herself showed a disposition to be tearful.

"It's quite true," she said. "None of our children or our children's children turned out like him, except my Bao. Only my little Jade Boy is like his grandfather."

"Of course, your generation wouldn't remember Old Sir Jia," Abbot Zhang said, turning to Cousin Zhen. "It's before your time. In fact, I don't suppose even Sir She and Sir Zheng can have a very clear recollection of what their father was like in his prime."

He brightened as another topic occurred to him and once more quaked with laughter.

"I saw a most attractive young lady when I was out visiting the other day. Fourteen this year. Seeing her put me in mind of our young friend here. It must be about time we started thinking about a match for him, surely? In looks, intelligence, breeding, background this girl was ideally suited. What does Your Old Ladyship feel? I didn't want to rush matters. I thought I'd better first wait and see what Your Old Ladyship thought before saying anything to the family."

"A monk who once told the boy's fortune said that he was not to marry young," said Grandmother Jia; "so I think we had better wait until he is a little older before we arrange anything definite. But do by all means go on inquiring for us. It doesn't matter whether the family is wealthy or not; as long as the girl *looks* all right, you can let me know. Even if it's a poor

---

8. The Taoist pantheon was filled with literally thousands of deities with such grandiloquent names.

"Very well, look after this stuff for me, then," said Bao-yu to the servant, "and this evening you will distribute a largesse."

This being now settled, Abbot Zhang withdrew, and Grandmother Jia and her party went up to the galleries. Grandmother Jia sat with Bao-yu and the girls in the gallery facing the stage and Xi-feng and Li Wan sat in the east gallery. The maids all sat in the west gallery and took it in turns to go off and wait on their mistresses.

Not long after they were all seated, Cousin Zhen came upstairs to say that the gods had now chosen which plays were to be performed—by which was meant, of course, that the names had been shaken from a pot in front of the altar, since this was the only way in which the will of the gods could be known. The first play selected was *The White Serpent*.

"What's the story?" said Grandmother Jia.

Cousin Zhen explained that it was about the emperor Gao-zu, founder of the Han dynasty, who began his rise to greatness by decapitating a monstrous white snake.

The second choice was *A Heap of Honours*, which shows the sixtieth birthday party of the great Tang general Guo Zi-yi, attended by his seven sons and eight sons-in-law, all of whom held high office, the "heap of honours" of the title being a reference to the table in his reception-hall piled high with their insignia.

"It seems a bit conceited to have this second one played," said Grandmother Jia. "Still, if that's what the gods chose, I suppose we'd better have it. What's the third one going to be?"

"*The South Branch*,"[1] said Cousin Zhen.

Grandmother Jia was silent. She knew that *The South Branch* likens the world to an ant-heap and tells a tale of power and glory which turns out in the end to have been a dream.

Hearing no reply, Cousin Zhen went off downstairs again to see about the Offertory Scroll, which had to be ceremonially burnt in front of the holy images along with paper money and paper ingots before the theatrical performance could begin.

Our record omits any description of that ceremony and moves back to Bao-yu, who was sitting in the central gallery beside his grandmother, and who now called for a maid to bring the tray up so that he could put on his Magic Jade again. When he had done so, he began to pick over the other trinkets with which the tray was covered and to hand them one by one to Grandmother Jia for her inspection. Her attention was taken by a little red-gold kylin[2] with kingfisher-feather inlay. She stretched out her hand to take it.

"Now where have I seen something like this before?" she said. "I feel certain I've seen some girl wearing an ornament like this."

"Cousin Shi's got one," said Bao-chai. "It's the same as this one only a little smaller."

"Funny!" said Bao-yu. "All the times she's been to our house, I don't remember ever having seen it."

---

1. A play by T'ang Hsien-tsu (1550–1617).   2. A unicorn, considered good luck.

"Cousin Bao is observant," said Tan-chun. "No matter what it is, she remembers everything."

"Well, perhaps not quite *everything*," said Dai-yu wryly. "But she's certainly very observant where things like *this* are concerned."

Bao-chai turned her head away and pretended not to have heard.

Now that he knew the kylin on the tray was like one that Shi Xiang-yun[3] wore, Bao-yu hurriedly picked it up and thrust it inside his jacket. But no sooner had he done so than it occurred to him that his action might be misconstrued; so instead of dropping it into his inside pocket, he continued to hold it there, at the same time glancing about him furtively to see if he had been observed. None of the others seemed to have noticed except Dai-yu, who was staring at him fixedly and nodding her head in mock approval.

Bao-yu felt suddenly embarrassed. Drawing his hand out again with the ornament still in it, he returned her look and laughed sheepishly:

"It's rather nice, isn't it? I thought I'd keep it for you," he said. "When we get home we can thread it on a ribbon and you'll be able to wear it."

Dai-yu tossed her head.

"I don't want it!"

"If *you* don't want it, I'll keep it for myself, then," said Bao-yu, and popped it once more inside his jacket.

He was about to add something, but just at that moment Cousin Zhen's wife, You-shi, and his new daughter-in-law, Hu-shi, arrived and came upstairs to pay their respects to Grandmother Jia.

"Now why have *you* come here? You really shouldn't have bothered," said Grandmother Jia. "We only came to amuse ourselves. It isn't a formal visit."

No sooner had she said this than it was announced that representatives from General Feng's household had arrived. It appeared that Feng Zi-ying's mother, hearing that the Jia ladies were having a *Pro Viventibus* performed at the Taoist temple, had immediately prepared an offering of pork, mutton, incense, tea and cakes and sent it post-haste to the temple with her compliments. Xi-feng, hearing the announcement, came hurrying round to the central gallery. She clapped her hands and laughed.

"Dear oh dear! This is something I hadn't bargained for. My idea was a quiet little outing for us girls; but here is everyone sending offerings and behaving as if we'd come here for a high mass or something. It's all your fault, Grannie! And we haven't even got any vails[4] ready to give to the bearers."

Even as she said this, two stewardesses from the Feng household were already mounting the stairs. And before *they* had gone, other messengers arrived with offerings from Vice-president Zhao's lady. From then on it was a steady stream: friends, kinsmen, family connections, business associates—all who had heard that the Jia ladies were holding a *Pro Viventibus* sent their representatives along with offerings and complimentary messages. Grandmother Jia began to regret that she had ever come.

"It isn't as if we'd come here for the ceremony," she grumbled. "We

3. An orphaned great-niece of Grandmother Jia.   4. Tips.

only wanted to enjoy ourselves. But all we seem to have done is to have stirred up a lot of fuss."

Consequently, although she stayed and watched the plays for that day, she returned home fairly early in the afternoon and next day professed herself too lacking in energy to go again. Xi-feng reacted differently. "In for a penny, in for a pound" was her motto. They had already had the fuss; and since the players were there anyway, they might as well go again today and enjoy themselves in peace.

For Bao-yu the whole of the previous day had been spoilt by Abbot Zhang's proposal to Grandmother Jia to arrange a match for him. He came home in a thoroughly bad temper and kept telling everyone that he would "never see Abbot Zhang again as long as he lived." Not associating his ill-humour with the abbot's proposal, the others were mystified.

Grandmother Jia's unwillingness was further reinforced by the fact that Dai-yu, since her return home yesterday, had been suffering from mild sunstroke. What with one thing and another, the old lady declined absolutely to go again, and Xi-feng had to make up her own party and go by herself.

But Xi-feng's play-going does not concern us.

Bao-yu, believing that Dai-yu's sunstroke was serious and that she might even be in danger of her life, was so worried that he could not eat, and rushed round in the middle of the lunch-hour to see how she was. He found her neither as ill as he had feared nor as responsive as he might have hoped.

"Why don't you go and watch your plays?" she asked him. "What are you mooning about at home for?"

Abbot Zhang's recent attempt at match-making had profoundly distressed Bao-yu and he was shocked by her seeming indifference.

"I can forgive the others for not understanding what has upset me," he thought; "but that *she* should want to trifle with me at a time like this . . . !"

The sense that she had failed him made the annoyance he now felt with her a hundred times greater than it had been on any previous occasion. Never could any other person have stirred him to such depths of atrabilious[5] rage. Coming from other lips, her words would scarcely have touched him. Coming from hers, they put him in a passion. His face darkened.

"It's all along been a mistake, then," he said. "You're not what I took you for."

Dai-yu gave an unnatural little laugh.

"Not what you took me for? That's hardly surprising, is it? I haven't got that *little something* which would have made me worthy of you."

Bao-yu came right up to her and held his face close to hers:

"You do realize, don't you, that you are deliberately willing my death?"

Dai-yu could not for the moment understand what he was talking about.

"I swore an oath to you yesterday," he went on. "I said that I hoped

---

5. Literally "black bile"; here, dark mood.

Heaven might strike me dead if this 'gold and jade' business meant anything to me. Since you have now brought it up again, it's clear to me that you *want* me to die. Though what you hope to gain by my death I find it hard to imagine."

Dai-yu now remembered what had passed between them on the previous day. She knew that she was wrong to have spoken as she did, and felt both ashamed and a little frightened. Her shoulders started shaking and she began to cry.

"May Heaven strike *me* dead if I ever willed your death!" she said. "But I don't see what you have to get so worked up about. It's only because of what Abbot Zhang said about arranging a match for you. You're afraid he might interfere with your precious 'gold and jade' plans; and because you're angry about that, you have to come along and take it out on me — That's all it is, isn't it?"

Bao-yu had from early childhood manifested a streak of morbid sensibility, which being brought up in close proximity with a nature so closely in harmony with his own had done little to improve. Now that he had reached an age when both his experience and the reading of forbidden books had taught him something about "worldly matters," he had begun to take a rather more grown-up interest in girls. But although there were plenty of young ladies of outstanding beauty and breeding among the Jia family's numerous acquaintance, none of them, in his view, could remotely compare with Dai-yu. For some time now his feeling for her had been a very special one; but precisely because of this same morbid sensibility, he had shrunk from telling her about it. Instead, whenever he was feeling particularly happy or particularly cross, he would invent all sorts of ways of probing her to find out if this feeling for her was reciprocated. It was unfortunate for him that Dai-yu herself possessed a similar streak of morbid sensibility and disguised her real feelings, as he did his, while attempting to discover what *he* felt about *her.*

Here was a situation, then, in which both parties concealed their real emotions and assumed counterfeit ones in an endeavour to find out what the real feelings of the other party were. And because

> When false meets false the truth will oft-times out,

there was the constant possibility that the innumerable little frustrations that were engendered by all this concealment would eventually erupt into a quarrel.

Take the present instance. What Bao-yu was actually thinking at this moment was something like this:

"In my eyes and in my thoughts there is no one else but you. I can forgive the others for not knowing this, but surely *you* ought to realize? If at a time like this you can't share my anxiety — if you can think of nothing better to do than provoke me with that sort of silly talk, it shows that the concern I feel for you every waking minute of the day is wasted: that you just don't care about me at all."

This was what he *thought*; but of course he didn't *say* it. On her side Dai-yu's thoughts were somewhat as follows:

"I know you must care for me a little bit, and I'm sure you don't take this ridiculous 'gold and jade' talk seriously. But if you cared *only* for me and had absolutely no inclination at all in another direction, then every time I mentioned 'gold and jade' you would behave quite naturally and let it pass almost as if you hadn't noticed. How is it, then, that when I do refer to it you get so excited? It shows that it must be on your mind. You *pretend* to be upset in order to allay my suspicions."

Meanwhile a quite different thought was running through Bao-yu's mind:

"I would do anything—absolutely *anything*," he was thinking, "if only you would be nice to me. If you would be nice to me, I would gladly die for you this moment. It doesn't really matter whether you know what I feel for you or not. Just be nice to me, then at least we shall be a little closer to each other, instead of so horribly far apart."

At the same time Dai-yu was thinking:

"Never mind me. Just be your own natural self. If *you* were all right, *I* should be all right too. All these manoeuvrings to try and anticipate my feelings don't bring us any closer together; they merely draw us farther apart."

The percipient reader will no doubt observe that these two young people were already of one mind, but that the complicated procedures by which they sought to draw together were in fact having precisely the opposite effect. Complacent reader! Permit us to remind you that your correct understanding of the situation is due solely to the fact that we have been revealing to you the secret, innermost thoughts of those two young persons, which neither of them had so far ever felt able to express.

Let us now return from the contemplation of inner thoughts to the recording of outward appearances.

When Dai-yu, far from saying something nice to him, once more made reference to the "gold and jade," Bao-yu became so choked with rage that for a moment he was quite literally bereft of speech. Frenziedly snatching the "Magic Jade" from his neck and holding it by the end of its silken cord he gritted his teeth and dashed it against the floor with all the strength in his body.

"*Beastly* thing!" he shouted. "I'll smash you to pieces and put an end to this once and for all."

But the jade, being exceptionally hard and resistant, was not the tiniest bit damaged. Seeing that he had not broken it, Bao-yu began to look around for something to smash it with. Dai-yu, still crying, saw what he was going to do.

"Why smash a dumb, lifeless object?" she said. "If you want to smash something, let it be me."

The sound of their quarrelling brought Nightingale and Snowgoose hurrying in to keep the peace. They found Bao-yu apparently bent on destroying his jade and tried to wrest it from him. Failing to do so, and sensing that the quarrel was of more than usual dimensions, they went off to fetch Aroma. Aroma came back with them as fast as she could run and eventually succeeded in prising the jade from his hand. He glared at her scornfully.

"It's my own thing I'm smashing," he said. "What business is it of yours to interfere?"

Aroma saw that his face was white with anger and his eyes wild and dangerous. Never had she seen him in so terrible a rage. She took him gently by the hand:

"You shouldn't smash the jade just because of a disagreement with your cousin," she said. "What do you think she would feel like and what sort of position would it put her in if you really *were* to break it?"

Dai-yu heard these words through her sobs. They struck a responsive chord in her breast, and she wept all the harder to think that even Aroma seemed to understand her better than Bao-yu did. So much emotion was too much for her weak stomach. Suddenly there was a horrible retching noise and up came the tisane of elsholtzia[6] leaves she had taken only a short while before. Nightingale quickly held out her handkerchief to receive it and, while Snowgoose rubbed and pounded her back, Dai-yu continued to retch up wave upon wave of watery vomit, until the whole handkerchief was soaked with it.

"However cross you may be, Miss, you ought to have more regard for your health," said Nightingale. "You'd only just taken that medicine and you were beginning to feel a little bit better for it, and now because of your argument with Master Bao you've gone and brought it all up again. Suppose you were to be *really* ill as a consequence. How do you think Master Bao would feel?"

When Bao-yu heard these words they struck a responsive chord in *his* breast, and he reflected bitterly that even Nightingale seemed to understand him better than Dai-yu. But then he looked again at Dai-yu, who was sobbing and panting by turns, and whose red and swollen face was wet with perspiration and tears, and seeing how pitiably frail and ill she looked, his heart misgave him.

"I shouldn't have taken her up on that 'gold and jade' business," he thought. "I've got her into this state and now there's no way in which I can relieve her by sharing what she suffers." As he thought this, he, too, began to cry.

Now that Bao-yu and Dai-yu were both crying, Aroma instinctively drew towards her master to comfort him. A pang of pity for him passed through her and she squeezed his hand sympathetically. It was as cold as ice. She would have liked to tell him not to cry but hesitated, partly from the consideration that he might be suffering from some deep-concealed hurt which crying would do something to relieve, and partly from the fear that to do so in Dai-yu's presence might seem presumptuous. Torn between a desire to speak and fear of the possible consequences of speaking, she did what girls of her type often do when faced with a difficult decision: she avoided the necessity of making one by bursting into tears.

As for Nightingale, who had disposed of the handkerchief of vomited tisane and was now gently fanning her mistress with her fan, seeing the other three all standing there as quiet as mice with the tears streaming

---

6. Unidentified. *Tisane:* a tea or infusion.

down their faces, she was so affected by the sight that she too started crying and was obliged to have recourse to a second handkerchief.

There the four of them stood, then, facing each other; all of them crying; none of them saying a word. It was Aroma who broke the silence with a strained and nervous laugh.

"You ought not to quarrel with Miss Lin," she said to Bao-yu, "if only for the sake of this pretty cord she made you."

At these words Dai-yu, ill as she was, darted forward, grabbed the jade from Aroma's hand, and snatching up a pair of scissors that were lying nearby, began feverishly cutting at its silken cord with them. Before Aroma and Nightingale could stop her, she had already cut it into several pieces.

"It was a waste of time making it," she sobbed. "He doesn't really care for it. And there's someone else who'll no doubt make him a better one!"

"What a shame!" said Aroma, retrieving the jade. "It's all my silly fault. I should have kept my mouth shut."

"Go on! Cut away!" said Bao-yu. "I shan't be wearing the wretched thing again anyway, so it doesn't matter."

Preoccupied with the quarrel, the four of them had failed to notice several old women, who had been drawn by the sound of it to investigate. Apprehensive, when they saw Dai-yu hysterically weeping and vomiting and Bao-yu trying to smash his jade, of the dire consequences to be expected from a scene of such desperate passion, they had hurried off in a body to the front of the mansion to report the matter to Grandmother Jia and Lady Wang, hoping in this way to establish in advance that whatever the consequences might be, *they* were not responsible for them. From their precipitate entry and the grave tone of their announcement Grandmother Jia and Lady Wang assumed that some major catastrophe had befallen and hurried with them into the Garden to find out what it was.

Their arrival filled Aroma with alarm. "What did Nightingale want to go troubling Their Ladyships for?" she thought crossly, supposing that the talebearer had been sent to them by Nightingale; while Nightingale for her part was angry with Aroma, thinking that the talebearer must have been one of Aroma's minions.

Grandmother Jia and Lady Wang entered the room to find a silent Bao-yu and a silent Dai-yu, neither of whom, when questioned, would admit that anything at all was the matter. They therefore visited their wrath on the heads of the two unfortunate maids, insisting that it was entirely owing to their negligence that matters had got so much out of hand. Unable to defend themselves, the girls were obliged to endure a long and abusive dressing-down, after which Grandmother Jia concluded the affair by carrying Bao-yu off to her own apartment.

Next day, the third of the fifth month, was Xue Pan's birthday and there was a family party with plays, to which the Jias were all invited. Bao-yu, who had still not seen Dai-yu since his outburst—which he now deeply regretted—was feeling far too dispirited to care about seeing plays, and declined to go on the ground that he was feeling unwell.

Dai-yu, though somewhat overcome on the day previous to this by the sultry weather, had by no means been seriously ill. Arguing that if *she* was not ill, it was impossible that *he* should be, she felt sure, when she heard of Bao-yu's excuse that it must be a false one.

"He usually enjoys drinking and watching plays," she thought. "If he's not going, it must be because he is still angry about yesterday; or if it isn't that, it must be because he's heard that I'm not going and doesn't want to go without me. Oh! I should *never* have cut that cord! Now he won't ever wear his jade again—unless I make him another cord to wear it on."

So she, too, regretted the quarrel.

Grandmother Jia knew that Bao-yu and Dai-yu were angry with each other, but she had been assuming that they would see each other at the Xues' party and make it up there. When neither of them turned up at it, she became seriously upset.

"I'm a miserable old sinner," she grumbled. "It must be my punishment for something I did wrong in a past life to have to live with a pair of such obstinate, addle-headed little geese! I'm sure there isn't a day goes by without their giving me some fresh cause for anxiety. It must be fate. That's what it says in the proverb, after all:

> 'Tis Fate brings foes and lo'es[7] tegither.

I'll be glad when I've drawn my last breath and closed my old eyes for the last time; then the two of them can snap and snarl at each other to their hearts' content, for *I* shan't be there to see it, and 'what the eye doesn't see, the heart doesn't grieve.' The Lord knows, it's not *my* wish to drag on this wearisome life any longer!"

Amidst these muttered grumblings the old lady began to cry.

In due course her words were transmitted to Bao-yu and Dai-yu. It happened that neither of them had ever heard the saying

> 'Tis Fate brings foes and lo'es tegither,

and its impact on them, hearing it for the first time, was like that of a Zen "perception": something to be meditated on with bowed head and savoured with a gush of tears. Though they had still not made it up since their quarrel, the difference between them had now vanished completely:

> In Naiad's House one to the wind made moan,
> In Green Delights one to the moon complained,

to parody the well-known lines. Or, in homelier verses:

> Though each was in a different place,
> Their hearts in friendship beat as one.

On the second day after their quarrel Aroma deemed that the time was now ripe for urging a settlement.

"Whatever the rights and wrongs of all this may be," she said to Bao-yu, "*you* are certainly the one who is *most* to blame. Whenever in the past you've heard about a quarrel between one of the pages and one of the girls, you've always said that the boy was a brute for not understanding the girl's feelings better—yet here you are behaving in exactly the same way yourself! Tomorrow will be the Double Fifth. Her Old Ladyship will be

7. Loves.

really angry if the two of you are still at daggers drawn on the day of the festival, and that will make life difficult for *all* of us. Why not put your pride in your pocket and go and say you are sorry, so that we can all get back to normal again?"

But as to whether or not Bao-yu followed her advice, or, if he did so, what the effect of following it was—those questions will be dealt with in the following chapter.

CHAPTER 30

Bao-chai speaks of a fan and castigates her deriders
Charmante scratches a "qiang" and mystifies a beholder

Dai-yu, as we have shown, regretted her quarrel with Bao-yu almost as soon as it was over; but since there were no conceivable grounds on which she could run after him and tell him so, she continued, both day and night, in a state of unrelieved depression that made her feel almost as if a part of her was lost. Nightingale had a shrewd idea how it was with her and resolved at last to tackle her:

"I think the day before yesterday you were too hasty, Miss. We ought to know what things Master Bao is touchy about, if no one else does. Look at all the quarrels we've had with him in the past on account of that jade!"

"Poh!" said Dai-yu scornfully. "You are trying to make out that it was my fault because you have taken his side against me. Of course I wasn't too hasty."

Nightingale gave her a quizzical smile.

"No? Then why did you cut that cord up? If three parts of the blame was Bao-yu's, I'm sure at least seven parts of it was yours. From what I've seen of it, he's all right with you when you allow him to be; it's because you're so prickly with him and always trying to put him in the wrong that he gets worked up."

Dai-yu was about to retort when they heard someone at the courtyard gate calling to be let in. Nightingale turned to listen:

"That's Bao-yu's voice," she said. "I expect he has come to apologize."

"I forbid you to let him in," said Dai-yu.

"There you go again!" said Nightingale. "You're going to keep him standing outside in the blazing sun on a day like this. Surely *that*'s wrong, if nothing else is?"

She was moving outside, even as she said this, regardless of her mistress's injunction. Sure enough, it *was* Bao-yu. She unfastened the gate and welcomed him in with a friendly smile.

"Master Bao! I was beginning to think you weren't coming to see us any more. I certainly didn't expect to see you here again so soon."

"Oh, you've been making a mountain out of a molehill," said Bao-yu, returning her smile. "Why ever shouldn't I come? Even if I died, my *ghost* would be round here a hundred times a day. How is my cousin? Quite better now?"

"Physically she's better," said Nightingale, "but she's still in very poor spirits."

"Ah yes—I know she's upset."

This exchange took place as they were crossing the forecourt. He now entered the room. Dai-yu was sitting on the bed crying. She had not been crying to start with, but the bittersweet pang she experienced when she heard his arrival had started the tears rolling. Bao-yu went up to the bed and smiled down at her.

"How are you, coz? Quite better now?"

As Dai-yu seemed to be too busy wiping her eyes to make a reply, he sat down close beside her on the edge of the bed:

"I know you're not *really* angry with me," he said. "It's just that if the others noticed I wasn't coming here, they would think we had been quarrelling; and if we waited for them to interfere, we should be allowing other people to come between us. It would be better to hit me and shout at me now and get it over with, if you still bear any hard feelings, than to go on ignoring me. Coz dear! Coz dear!—"

He must have repeated those same two words in the same tone of passionate entreaty upwards of twenty times. Dai-yu had been meaning to ignore him, but what he had just been saying about other people "coming between" them seemed to prove that he must in *some* way feel closer to her than the rest, and she was unable to maintain her silence.

"You don't have to treat me like a child," she blurted out tearfully. "From now on I shall make no further claims on you. You can behave exactly as if I had gone away."

"Gone away?" said Bao-yu laughingly. "Where would you go to?"

"Back home."

"I'd follow you."

"As if I were dead then."

"If you died," he said, "I should become a monk."

Dai-yu's face darkened immediately:

"What an utterly idiotic thing to say! Suppose your own sisters were to die? Just how many times can one person become a monk? I think I had better see what the others think about that remark."

Bao-yu had realized at once that she would be offended; but the words were already out of his mouth before he could stop them. He turned very red and hung his head in silence. It was a good thing that no one else was in the room at that moment to see him. Dai-yu glared at him for some seconds—evidently too enraged to speak, for she made a sound somewhere between a snort and a sigh, but said nothing—then, seeing him almost purple in the face with suppressed emotion, she clenched her teeth, pointed her finger at him, and, with an indignant "Hmn!", stabbed the air quite savagely a few inches away from his forehead:

"You—!"

But whatever it was she had been going to call him never got said. She merely gave a sigh and began wiping her eyes again with her handkerchief.

Bao-yu had been in a highly emotional state when he came to see Dai-yu and it had further upset him to have inadvertently offended her so soon after his arrival. This angry gesture and the unsuccessful struggle, ending in sighs and tears, to say what she wanted to say now affected him so deeply that he, too, began to weep. In need of a handkerchief but finding that he had come out without one, he wiped his eyes on his sleeve.

Although Dai-yu was crying, the spectacle of Bao-yu using the sleeve of his brand-new lilac-coloured summer gown as a handkerchief had not escaped her, and while continuing to wipe her own eyes with one hand, she leaned over and reached with the other for the square of silk that was draped over the head-rest at the end of the bed. She lifted it off and threw it at him—all without uttering a word—then, once more burying her face in her own handkerchief, resumed her weeping. Bao-yu picked up the handkerchief she had thrown him and hurriedly wiped his eyes with it. When he had dried them, he drew up close to her again and took one of her hands in his own, smiling at her gently.

"I don't know why you go on crying," he said. "I feel as if all my insides were shattered. Come! Let's go and see Grandmother together."

Dai-yu flung off his hand.

"Take your hands off me! We're not children any more. You really can't go on mauling me about like this all the time. Don't you understand *anything*—?"

"Bravo!"

The shouted interruption startled them both. They spun round to look just as Xi-feng, full of smiles, came bustling into the room.

"Grandmother has been grumbling away something *awful*," she said. "She insisted that I should come over and see if you were both all right. 'Oh,' I said, 'there's no need to go and look, Grannie; they'll have made it up by now without any interference from *us*.' So she told me I was lazy. Well, here I am—and of course it's *exactly* as I said it would be. *I* don't know. I don't understand you two. What is it you find to argue about? For every three days that you're friends you must spend at least two days quarrelling. You really are a couple of babies. And the older you get, the worse you get. Look at you *now*—holding hands crying! And a couple of days ago you were glaring at each other like fighting-cocks. Come on! Come with me to see Grandmother. Let's put the old lady's mind at rest."

As she said this, she seized Dai-yu's hand and began marching off with her. Dai-yu turned back and called for her maids, but there was no response.

"What do you want to call *them* for?" said Xi-feng. "You've got *me* to wait on you, haven't you?"

She continued to walk away, still holding Dai-yu by the hand. Bao-yu followed a little way behind. They went out of the Garden and through into Grandmother Jia's apartment.

"I *told* you they could be left to themselves to make it up and that there was no need for you to worry," said Xi-feng to Grandmother Jia when they were all in the old lady's presence; "but you wouldn't believe me, would you? You insisted on my going there to act the peacemaker. Well, I went there; and what did I find? I found the two of them together *apologizing* to each other. It was like the kite and the kestrel[8] holding hands: they were positively *locked in a clinch*! No need of a peacemaker that *I* could see."

---

8. Two types of hawks.

There was a burst of laughter from all present. Bao-chai was among these, but Dai-yu slipped past her without speaking and took a seat next to Grandmother Jia. Bao-yu, rather at a loss for something to say, turned to Bao-chai.

"I'm afraid I wasn't very well on your brother's birthday; so apart from not giving him a present, I couldn't even make him a kotow this year. I'm afraid he may not have realized I was ill and thought that I was merely making excuses. If you can spare a moment next time you see him, I do hope you will explain to him for me."

Bao-chai looked amused.

"That seems a trifle excessive. I am sure he would have felt uncomfortable about your kotowing[9] to him, even if you had been able to come; so I'm quite sure he wouldn't have wanted you to come when you weren't feeling well. It would be rather unfriendly, surely, if cousins who see each other all the time were to start worrying about trifles like *that?*"

Bao-yu smiled.

"Well, as long as *you* understand, that's all right—But why aren't you watching the players?"

"I can't stand the heat," said Bao-chai. "I did watch a couple of acts of something, but it was so hot that I couldn't stay any longer. Unfortunately none of the guests showed any sign of going, so I had to pretend I was ill in order to get away."

"*Touché!*" thought Bao-yu; but he hid his embarrassment in a stupid laugh.

"No wonder they compare you to Yang Gui-fei,[1] cousin. You are well-covered like her, and they always say that plump people fear the heat."

The colour flew into Bao-chai's face. An angry retort was on her lips, but she could hardly make it in front of company. Yet reflection only made her angrier. Eventually, after a scornful sniff or two, she said:

"I may be like Yang Gui-fei in some respects, but I don't think there is much danger of my cousin becoming a Prime Minister."[2]

It happened that just at that moment a very young maid called "Pretti-kins" jokingly accused Bao-chai of having hidden a fan she was looking for.

"I *know* Miss Bao's hidden it," she said. "Come on, Miss! *Please* let me have it."

"You be careful," said Bao-chai, pointing at the girl angrily and speaking with unwonted stridency. "When did you last see *me* playing games of this sort with anyone? If there are other young ladies who are in the habit of *romping about* with you, you had better ask *them.*"

Prettikins fled.

Bao-yu realized that he had once again given offence by speaking thoughtlessly; and as this time it was in front of a lot of people, his embarrassment was correspondingly greater. He turned aside in confusion and began talking nervously to someone else.

9. Bowing the head to the ground, here as congratulations.   1. The favorite consort of the Tang emperor Xuan-zong, known for her plump beauty.   2. Yang Gui-fei's cousin became a corrupt prime minister. The comparison is a pointed reference to Bao-yu's neglect of his studies.

Bao-yu's rudeness to Bao-chai had given Dai-yu secret satisfaction. When Prettikins came in looking for her fan, she had been on the point of adding some facetiousness of her own at Bao-chai's expense; but Bao-chai's brief explosion caused her to drop the prepared witticism and ask instead what play the two acts were from that Bao-chai said she had just been watching.

Bao-chai had observed the smirk on Dai-yu's face and knew very well that Bao-yu's rudeness must have pleased her. The smiling answer she gave to Dai-yu's question was therefore not without a touch of malice.

"The play I saw was *Li Kui Abuses Song Jiang and Afterwards Has to Say He Is Sorry.*"

Bao-yu laughed.

"What a mouthful! Surely, with all your learning, cousin, you must know the proper name of that play? It's called *The Abject Apology.*"

"*The Abject Apology?*" said Bao-chai. "Well, no doubt you clever people know all there is to know about abject apology. I'm afraid it's something I wouldn't know about."

Her words touched Bao-yu and Dai-yu on a sensitive spot, and by the time she had finished, they were both blushing hotly with embarrassment.

Xi-feng was insufficiently educated to have understood all these nuances, but by studying the speakers' expressions she had formed a pretty good idea of what they were talking about.

"Rather hot weather to be eating raw ginger, isn't it?" she asked.

No one present could understand what she meant.

"No one's been eating raw ginger," they said.

Xi-feng affected great surprise and rubbed her cheek meaningfully with her hand:

"If no one's been eating raw ginger, then why are they looking so hot and bothered?"

At this Bao-yu and Dai-yu felt even more uncomfortable. Bao-chai was about to add something, but seeing the abject look on Bao-yu's face, she laughed and held her tongue. None of the others present had understood what the four of them were talking about and treated these exchanges as a joke.

Shortly after this, when Bao-chai and Xi-feng had gone out of the room, Dai-yu said to Bao-yu.

"You see? There are people even more dangerous to trifle with than I. If I weren't such a tongue-tied, slow-witted creature, you wouldn't get away with it quite so often, my friend."

Bao-yu was still smarting from Bao-chai's testiness. To be set upon now by Dai-yu as well seemed positively the last straw. But though he wanted to reply, he knew how easily she would take offence and controlled himself with an effort. Feeling in very low spirits, he left the room himself now and went off on his own.

It was the hottest part of the day. Lunch had long been over, and in every apartment mistress and maids alike had succumbed to the lassitude of the hour. As he sauntered slowly by, hands clasped behind his back, everywhere he went was hushed in the breathless silence of noon. From the back of Grandmother Jia's quarters he passed eastwards through the gallery that ended near the wall of Xi-feng's courtyard. He went up to the gate, but it was closed, and remembering that it was her invariable custom when the weather was hot to take two whole hours off in the middle of the day for her siesta, he thought he had better not go in. He continued, instead, through the corner gate that led into his parents' courtyard.

On entering his mother's apartment, he found several maids dozing over their embroidery. Lady Wang herself was lying on a summer-bed[3] in the inner room, apparently fast asleep. Her maid Golden, who was sitting beside her gently pounding her legs, also seemed half asleep, for her head was nodding and her half-closed eyes were blinking drowsily. Bao-yu tip-toed up to her and tweaked an ear-ring. She opened her eyes wide and saw that it was Bao-yu.

He smiled at her and whispered.

"So sleepy?"

Golden pursed her lips up in a smile, motioned to him with her hand to go away, and then closed her eyes again. But Bao-yu lingered, fasci-nated. Silently craning forward to make sure that Lady Wang's eyes were closed, he took a Fragrant Snow "quencher"[4] from the embroidered pouch at his waist and popped it between Golden's lips. Golden nibbled it dreamily without opening her eyes.

"Shall I ask Her Ladyship to let me have you, so that we can be together?" he whispered jokingly.

Golden made no reply.

"When she wakes up, I'll talk to her about it," he said.

Golden opened her eyes wide and gave him a little push.

"What's the hurry?" she said playfully. " 'Yours is yours, wherever it be,' as they said to the lady when she dropped her gold comb in the well. Haven't you ever heard that saying? — I'll tell you something to do, if you want a bit of fun. Go into the little east courtyard and you'll be able to catch Sunset and Huan together."

"Who cares about *them?*" said Bao-yu. "Let's talk about *us.*"

At this point Lady Wang sat bolt upright and dealt Golden a slap in the face.

"Shameless little harlot!" she cried, pointing at her wrathfully. "It's you and your like who corrupt our innocent young boys."

Bao-yu had slipped silently away as soon as his mother sat up. Golden, one of whose cheeks was now burning a fiery red, was left without a word to say. The other maids, hearing that their mistress was awake, came hur-rying into the room.

"Silver!" said Lady Wang. "Go and fetch your mother. I want her to take your sister Golden away."

Golden threw herself, weeping, upon her knees:

"No, Your Ladyship, please! Beat me and revile me as much as you like, but please, for pity's sake, don't send me away. I've been with Your Ladyship nigh on ten years now. How can I ever hold up my head again if you dismiss me?"

Lady Wang was not naturally unkind. On the contrary, she was an

---

3. A couch set up to catch the breeze.   4. A type of candy.

exceptionally lenient mistress. This was, in fact, the first time in her life that she had ever struck a maid. But the kind of "shamelessness" of which—in her view—Golden had just been guilty was the one thing she had always most abhorred. It was the uncontrollable anger of the morally outraged that had caused her to strike Golden and call her names; and though Golden now begged and pleaded, she refused to retract her dismissal. When Golden's mother, old Mrs. Bai, had eventually been fetched, the wretched girl, utterly crushed by her shame and humiliation, was led away.

But of her no more.

Embarrassed by his mother's awakening, Bao-yu had slipped hurriedly into the Garden.

The burning sun was now in the height of heaven, the contracted shadows were concentrated darkly beneath the trees, and the stillness of noon, filled with the harsh trilling of cicadas, was broken by no human voice; but as he approached the bamboo trellises of the rose-garden, a sound like a suppressed sob seemed to come from inside the pergola. Uncertain what it was that he had heard, he stopped to listen. Undoubtedly there was someone there.

This was the fifth month of the year, when the rambler roses are in fullest bloom. Peeping through the fragrant panicles[5] with which the pergola was smothered, he saw a girl crouching down on the other side of the trellis, scratching at the ground with one of those long, blunt pins that girls use for fastening their back hair with.

"Can this be some silly maid come here to bury flowers like Frowner?"[6] he wondered.

He was reminded of Zhuang-zi's story of the beautiful Xi-shi's ugly neighbour, whose endeavours to imitate the little frown that made Xi-shi captivating produced an aspect so hideous that people ran from her in terror. The recollection of it made him smile.

"This is 'imitating the Frowner' with a vengeance," he thought, "—if that is really what she is doing. Not merely unoriginal, but downright disgusting!"

"Don't imitate Miss Lin," he was about to shout; but a glimpse of the girl's face revealed to him just in time that this was no maid, but one of the twelve little actresses from Peartree Court—though which of them, since he had seen them only in their make-up on the stage, he was unable to make out. He stuck out his tongue in a grimace and clapped a hand to his mouth.

"Good job I didn't speak too soon," he thought. "I've been in trouble twice already today for doing that, once with Frowner and once with Chai. It only needs me to go and upset these twelve actresses as well and I shall be well and truly in the cart!"[7]

His efforts to identify the girl made him study her more closely. It was curious that he should have thought her an imitator of Dai-yu, for she had

5. Bunches of flowers.　　6. That is, Dai-yu.　　7. That is, in big trouble.

much of Dai-yu's ethereal grace in her looks: the same delicate face and frail, slender body; the same

> . . . brows like hills in spring,
> And eyes like autumn's limpid pools;

—even the same little frown that had often made him compare Dai-yu with Xi-shi of the legend.

It was now quite impossible for him to tear himself away. He watched her fascinated. As he watched, he began to see that what she was doing with the pin was not scratching a hole to bury flowers in, but writing. He followed the movements of her hand, and each vertical and horizontal stroke, each dot and hook that she made he copied with a finger on the palm of his hand. Altogether there were eighteen strokes. He thought for a moment. The character he had just written in his hand was QIANG. The name of the roses which covered the pergola contained the same character: "Qiang-wei."

"The sight of the roses has inspired her to write a poem," he thought. "Probably she's just thought of a good couplet and wants to write it down before she forgets it; or perhaps she has already composed several lines and wants to work on them a bit. Let's see what she writes next."

The girl went on writing, and he followed the movements of her hand as before. It was another QIANG. Again she wrote, and again he followed, and again it was a QIANG. It was as though she were under some sort of spell. As soon as she had finished writing one QIANG she began writing another.

QIANG QIANG QIANG QIANG QIANG QIANG QIANG . . .

He must have watched her write several dozen QIANG's in succession. He seemed to be as much affected by the spell on his side of the pergola as the girl herself was on hers, for his eyeballs continued to follow her pin long after he had learned to anticipate its movements.

"This girl must have something on her mind that she cannot tell anyone about to make her behave in this way," he thought. "One can see from her outward behaviour how much she must be suffering inwardly. And she looks so frail. Too frail for suffering. I wish I could bear some of it for you, my dear!"

In the stifling dog-days of summer the transition from clear to overcast is often sudden, and a little cloudlet can sometimes be the harbinger of a heavy shower. As Bao-yu watched the girl, a sudden gust of cool wind blew by, followed, within moments, by the hissing downpour of rain. He could see the water running off her head in streams and soaking into her clothes.

"Oh, it's raining! With her delicate constitution she ought not to be outside in a downpour like this."

In his anxiety he cried out to her involuntarily:

"Don't write any more. Look! You're getting soaked."

The girl looked up, startled, when she heard the voice. She could see someone amidst the roses saying "Don't write"; but partly because of Bao-yu's almost girlishly beautiful features, and partly because she could in any case only see about half of his face, everything above and below being hidden by flowers and foliage, she took him for a maid; so instead of rushing from his presence as she would have done if she had known that it was Bao-yu, she smiled up at him gratefully:

"Thank you for reminding me. But what about you? You must be getting wet too, surely?"

"Aiyo!"—her words made him suddenly aware that the whole of his body was icy cold, and when he looked down, he saw that he was soaked. "Oh lord!"

He rushed off in the direction of Green Delights; but all the time he was worrying about the girl, who had nowhere where she could shelter from the rain.

As this was the day before the Double Fifth festival, Élégante and the other little actresses—including the one whom Bao-yu had just been watching—had already started their holiday and had gone into the Garden to amuse themselves. Two of them, Trésor—one of the two members of the company who played Principal Boy parts—and Topaze—one of the company's two soubrettes[8]—happened to be in the House of Green Delights playing with Aroma when the rain started and prevented their leaving. They and the maids amused themselves by blocking up the gutters and letting the water collect in the courtyard. When it was nicely flooded, they rounded up a number of mallards, sheldrakes, mandarin ducks and other waterfowl, tied their wings together, and having first closed the courtyard gate, set them down in the water to swim about. Aroma and the girls were all in the outside gallery enjoying this spectacle when Bao-yu arrived at the gate. Finding it shut, he knocked on it for someone to come and open up for him. But there was little chance of a knock being heard above the excited laughter of the maids. He had to shout for some minutes and pound the gate till it shook before anyone heard him inside.

Aroma was not expecting him back so soon.

"I wonder who it can be at this time," she said. "Won't someone go and answer it?"

"It's *me!*" shouted Bao-yu.

"That's Miss Bao's voice," said Musk.

"Nonsense!" said Skybright. "What would *she* be doing visiting us at this time of day?"

"Let me just take a peep through the crack," said Aroma. "If I think it's all right, I'll let them in. We don't want to turn anyone away in the pouring rain."

Keeping under cover of the gallery, she made her way round to the gate and peered through the chink between the double doors. The sight of Bao-yu standing there like a bedraggled hen with the water running off him in streamlets was both alarming and—she could not help but feel—very funny. She opened the gate as quickly as she could, then, when she saw him fully, clapped her hands and doubled up with laughter.

8. Young actresses, who are often cast as maids.

"Master Bao! I *never* thought it would be you. What did you want to come running back in the pouring rain for?"

Bao-yu was by now in a thoroughly evil temper and had fully resolved to give whoever opened the gate a few kicks. As soon as it was open, therefore, he lashed out with his foot, not bothering to see who it was—for he assumed that the person answering it would be one of the younger maids—and dealt Aroma a mighty kick in the ribs that caused her to cry out in pain.

"Worthless lot!" he shouted. "Because I always treat you decently, you think you can get away with *anything*. I'm just your laughing-stock."

It was not until he looked down and saw Aroma crying that he realized he had kicked the wrong person.

"Aiyo! It's you! Where did I kick you?"

Up to this moment Aroma had never had so much as a harsh word from Bao-yu, and the combination of shame, anger and pain she now felt on being kicked and shouted at by him in front of so many people was well-nigh insupportable. Nevertheless she forced herself to bear it, reflecting that to have made an outcry would be like admitting that it was *her* he had meant to kick, which she knew was almost certainly not the case.

"You didn't; you missed me," she said. "Come in and get changed."

When Bao-yu had gone indoors and was changing his clothes, he said to her jokingly:

"In all these years this is the first time I've ever struck anyone in anger. Too bad that *you* should have been the one to get in the way of the blow!"

In spite of the pain, which it cost her some effort to master, Aroma was helping him with his changing. She smiled when he said this.

"I'm the person you always begin things with," she said. "Whether it's big things or little things or pleasant ones or unpleasant ones, it's only natural that you should try them out first on me. Only in this instance I hope that now you've hit me you won't from now on go around hitting other people."

"I didn't mean to kick *you*, you know," said Bao-yu.

"Who said you did?" said Aroma. "It's the younger ones who normally see to the gate; and they've grown so insolent nowadays, it's enough to put *anyone* in a rage. If you'd given one of *them* a few kicks and put the fear of God into them, it would have been a very good thing. No, it was my own silly fault. I should have made *them* open the gate and not gone to open it myself."

While they were speaking, the rain had stopped and Trésor and Topaze had left. The pain in Aroma's side was such that it was giving her a feeling of nausea and she could eat no dinner. At bedtime, when she took off her clothes, she saw a great black bruise the size of a rice-bowl spreading over the side of her chest. The extent of it frightened her, but she forbore to cry out. Nevertheless even her dreams that night were full of pain and she several times uttered an "Aiyo" in the midst of her sleep.

Although it was understood that he had not kicked her deliberately, Bao-yu had felt a little uneasy when he saw how sluggish Aroma seemed in her movements; and when, during the night, he heard her groaning in her sleep, he knew that he must have kicked her really hard. Getting out

of bed, he picked up a lamp and tiptoed over to have a look. Just as he
reached the foot of her bed, he heard her cough a couple of times and
spit out a mouthful of something.

"Aiyo!"

She opened her eyes wide and saw Bao-yu. Startled, she asked him what
he was doing there.

"You've been groaning in your sleep," he said. "I must have hurt you
badly. Let me have a look."

"My head feels giddy," said Aroma, "and I've got a sweet, sickly taste in
my throat. Have a look on the floor."

Bao-yu shone his lamp on the floor. Beside the bed, where she had spat,
there was a mouthful of bright red blood. He was horrified.

"Oh, help!"

Aroma looked too, and felt the grip of fear on her heart.

The outcome will be told in the following chapter.

CHAPTER 31

A torn fan is the price of silver laughter
And a lost kylin is the clue to a happy marriage

A cold fear came over Aroma when she saw the fresh blood on the floor.
She had often heard people say that if you spat blood when you were
young, you would die early, or at the very least be an invalid all your life;
and remembering this now, she felt all her bright, ambitious hopes for the
future turn into dust and ashes. Tears of misery ran down her cheeks. The
sight of them made Bao-yu, too, distressed.

"What is it?" he asked her.

"It's nothing." She forced herself to smile. "I'm all right."

Bao-yu was all for calling one of the maids and getting her to heat some
rice wine, so that Aroma could be given hot wine and Hainan kid's[9]-blood
pills; but Aroma, smiling through her tears, caught at his hand to restrain
him.

"It's all right for *you* to make a fuss," she said; "but if you go involving
the others, they are sure to accuse me of putting on airs. And besides, it
will do neither of us any good to draw attention to ourselves—especially
when so far no one seems to have noticed anything. The sensible thing
would be for you to send one of the boys round tomorrow to Dr. Wang's
and get me some medicine to take. I shall probably be all right again after
a few doses, without a single soul knowing anything about it. Surely that's
best, isn't it?"

Bao-yu knew that she was right and abandoned his intention of rousing
the others. Instead he poured her a cup of tea from a pot on the table and
gave it to her to rinse her mouth with. Aroma was uneasy about being
waited on by her master; but fearing that if she refused his services he
would insist on disturbing everybody, she lay back and allowed him to fuss
over her.

9. A kid is a young goat.

As soon as it was daylight, Bao-yu threw on his clothes and, without even waiting to wash or comb, went out of the Garden to his study in the front part of the mansion, whither he summoned the doctor Wang Ji-ren for detailed questioning. When this worthy had elicited the information that the haemorrhage inquired about had been caused by a blow, he seemed less disposed to take a serious view of the case, merely naming some pills and giving perfunctory instructions for taking them internally and for applying them in solution as a poultice. Bao-yu made a note of these instructions and went back into the Garden to carry them out.

But that is no part of our story.

It was now the festival of the Double Fifth. Sprays of calamus and artemisia crowned the doorways and everyone wore tiger amulets fastened on their clothing at the back. At noon Lady Wang gave a little party at which Aunt Xue and Bao-chai were the guests.

Bao-yu, finding Bao-chai somewhat glacial in her manner and evidently unwilling to talk to him, knew that it must be because of his rudeness to her of the day before.

Lady Wang, observing Bao-yu's dejected appearance, attributed it to embarrassment about yesterday's episode with Golden and ignored him even more pointedly than Bao-chai.

Dai-yu, seeing how morose Bao-yu looked assumed that it was because Bao-chai was offended with him and, feeling resentful that he should care, at once became as morose as he was.

Xi-feng, having been told all about Bao-yu and Golden the night before by Lady Wang, could scarcely be her usual laughing and joking self when she knew of her aunt's displeasure and, taking her cue from the latter, was if anything even more glacial than the others.

And Ying-chun, Tan-chun and Xi-chun, seeing everyone else so uncomfortable, soon began to feel just as uncomfortable themselves.

The result was that after sitting for only a very short time, the party broke up.

Dai-yu had a natural aversion to gatherings, which she rationalized by saying that since the inevitable consequence of getting together was parting, and since parting made people feel lonely and feeling lonely made them unhappy, *ergo* it was better for them not to get together in the first place. In the same way she argued that since the flowers, which give us so much pleasure when they open, only cause us a lot of extra sadness when they die, it would be better if they didn't come out at all.

Bao-yu was just the opposite. He always wanted the party to go on for ever and flowers to be in perpetual bloom; and when at last the party did end and the flowers did wither—well, it was infinitely sad and distressing, but it couldn't be helped.

And so today, while everyone else left the party with feelings of gloom, Dai-yu alone was completely unaffected. Bao-yu, on the other hand, returned to his room in a mood of black despondency, sighing and muttering as he went.

Unfortunately it was the sharp-tongued Skybright who came forward to help him change his clothes. With provoking carelessness she dropped a fan while she was doing so and snapped the bone fan-sticks by accidentally treading on it.

"Clumsy!" said Bao-yu reproachfully. "You won't be so careless with things when you have a household of your own."

Skybright gave a sardonic sniff.

"You're getting quite a temper lately, Master Bao. Almost every time we move nowadays we get a nasty look from you. Yesterday even Aroma caught it. Today you're finding fault with me, so I suppose I can expect a few kicks too. Well, kick away. But I must say, I shouldn't have thought treading on a *fan* was such a very terrible thing to do. In the past any number of glass bowls and agate cups have got broken without your turning a hair. Why this fuss about a fan, then? If you're not satisfied with my service, you ought to dismiss me and get someone better. Easy come, easy go. No need for beating about the bush."

By the time she had finished, Bao-yu was so angry that he was shaking all over.

"You'll *go* soon enough, don't you worry!" he said.

Aroma had heard all this from the adjoining room and now came hurrying in.

"Now what's all this about?" she said, addressing herself to Bao-yu. "Didn't I tell you? As soon as I turn my back there's trouble."

"If you knew that already," said Skybright, "it's a pity you couldn't have come in a bit sooner and saved me from provoking him. Of course, we all know that you're the only one who knows how to serve him properly. None of the rest of us knows how it's done. I suppose it's because you serve him so well that he gave you a kick in the ribs yesterday. Heaven knows what he's got in store for *me* for having served him so badly!"

Angry, and at the same time ashamed, Aroma was about to retort; but the sight of Bao-yu's face, now white with anger, made her restrain herself.

"Be a good girl—just go away and play for a bit. It's *we* who are in the wrong."

Skybright naturally assumed that "we" meant Aroma and Bao-yu. Her jealousy was further inflamed.

"What do you mean, 'we'?" she said. "You two make me feel ashamed for you, you really do—because you needn't think you deceive *me*. *I* know what goes on between you when you think no one is looking. But when all's said and done, in actual fact, when you come down to it, you're not even a 'Miss' by *rights*. By *rights* you're no better than any of the rest of us. I don't know where you get this 'we' from."

Aroma blushed and blushed with shame, until her face had become a dusky red colour. Too late she realized her slip. By "we" she had meant no more than "you and I"; not "Bao-yu and I" as Skybright imagined. But the pronoun had invited misunderstanding.

It was Bao-yu who retorted, however.

"I'll make her a 'Miss' then; I'll make her my chamber-wife[1] tomorrow, if that's all that's worrying you. You can spare your jealousy on *that* account."

---

1. A concubine, which would raise her status.

Aroma seized his hand impulsively.

"Don't argue with her, she's only a silly girl. In any case, you've put up with much worse than this in the past; why be so touchy today?"

Skybright gave a harsh little laugh.

"Oh, yes. I'm too stupid to talk to. I'm only a slave."

"Are you arguing with me, Miss, or with Master Bao?" said Aroma. "If it's me you've got it in for, you'd better address your remarks to me elsewhere. There's no cause to go quarrelling with me in front of Master Bao. But if it's Master Bao you want to quarrel with, then at least you might do it a bit more quietly and not let everyone else know about it. When I came in just now, it was for everyone's sake, so that we could have a bit of peace and quiet. I don't know why you had to turn on *me* and start picking on *my* shortcomings. It seems as if you can't make up your mind whether you're angry with me or with Master Bao. Slipping in a dig here and a dig there. I don't know what you think you're up to. Anyway, I shan't say any more; I'll just leave you here to get on with it."

She walked out.

"There's no need for you to be so angry," Bao-yu said to Skybright. "I can guess what it is that's bothering you. I shall go and tell Her Ladyship that you're old enough to leave us now and ask her to send you away. That's what you really want, isn't it?"

"I don't want to go away. Why should I want to go away?" said Skybright with tears in her eyes—now more upset than ever. "You're inventing this as a means of getting rid of me, aren't you, because I'm in your way? But you won't get away with it."

"Look, I've never had to put up with scenes like *this* before," said Bao-yu. "What other reason *can* there be but that you want to leave? I really think I *had* better go and see Her Ladyship about this."

He got up and began to go; but Aroma came in again and barred his way.

"Where are you off to?" she asked him smilingly.

"To see Her Ladyship."

"Oh, that's silly," said Aroma. "I wonder you're not ashamed to. Even if Skybright really does want to leave, there will be plenty of time to tell Her Ladyship about it when everyone has cooled down a bit and you are feeling calm and collected. If you go rushing off in your present state, Her Ladyship will suspect something."

"Her Ladyship won't suspect anything," said Bao-yu. "I shall tell her quite openly that Skybright has been agitating to leave."

"When have I ever agitated to leave?" said Skybright, weeping now in earnest. "Even if you're angry with me, you ought not to twist things round in order to get the better of me. But you go and tell her! I don't care if I have to beat my own brains out, I'm not going out of that door."

"Now that's really strange," said Bao-yu. "You don't want to go, yet at the same time you won't keep quiet. It's no good; I really can't stand this quarrelling. I shall really *have* to see Her Ladyship about this and get it over with."

This time he seemed quite determined to go.

Seeing that she was unable to hold him back, Aroma went down on her knees. Emerald, Ripple, Musk and the other maids, aware that a quarrel of more than usual magnitude was going on inside, were waiting together outside in breathless silence. When word reached them that Aroma was now on her knees interceding for Skybright, they came silently trooping in to kneel down behind her. Bao-yu raised Aroma to her feet, sighed, sat down on the edge of the bed, and told the other maids to get up.

"What do you want me to do?" he asked Aroma. "My heart is destroyed inside me, but none of you knows or cares."

Tears started from his eyes and rolled down his cheeks unheeded. Seeing his tears, Aroma too began to cry. Skybright, who stood crying beside them, was about to say something; but just at that moment Dai-yu walked in and she slipped outside.

Dai-yu beamed at the weeping pair:

"Crying on a holiday? What's all this about? Have you been quarrelling over the rice-cakes?"

Bao-yu and Aroma both burst out laughing.

"Well, if Cousin Bao won't tell me," she went on, "I'm sure that *you* will. Come!" she said, slapping Aroma familiarly on the shoulder. "Tell sis all about it. It's obvious that the two of you have been having an argument. Tell me what it's all about and I'll make it up between you."

"Oh, Miss!" Aroma gave her a push. "Don't carry on so! I'm only a maid; you shouldn't say such things to me."

"Only a maid?" said Dai-yu. "I always think of you as my sister-in-law."

"Don't you see that you're simply *encouraging* people to be nasty to her?" Bao-yu protested. "Even as it is, people already gossip about her. How can she stand up to them if *you* come along and lend your weight to what they are saying?"

"You don't know what I feel, Miss," said Aroma. "If I only knew how to stop breathing, I'd gladly die."

Dai-yu smiled.

"If you were to die, I don't know about anyone else, but I know that *I* should die of grief."

"I should become a monk," said Bao-yu.

"Try to be a bit more serious," said Aroma. "You and Miss Lin are both laughing at me."

Dai-yu held up two fingers and looked at Bao-yu with a quizzical expression.

"That's twice you're going to become a monk. From now on I'm keeping the score."

Bao-yu recognized the allusion to what he had said to her the day before. Fortunately he was able to pass it off with a laugh. Shortly after that, Dai-yu left them.

No sooner had Dai-yu gone than someone arrived with an invitation from Xue Pan. Bao-yu thought that this time he had better go. It turned out to be only a drinking-party, but Xue Pan refused to release him and kept him there until it was over. He returned home in the evening more than a little drunk.

As he came lurching into his courtyard, he saw that someone in quest of coolness had taken a bed outside and was lying down on it asleep.

Assuming that it must be Aroma, he sat down on the edge of it and gave her a push.

"Is the pain any better?"

"Can't you leave me alone?" she said, rising up wrathfully.

He looked again and saw that it was not Aroma after all but Skybright. Taking her by the hand, he drew her down on the bed beside him.

"You're getting so self-willed," he said laughingly. "When you trod on that fan this morning, I only made a harmless little remark, but look how you flew up in the air about it! And then when Aroma, out of the kindness of her heart, tried to reason with you, look how you pitched into *her*! Seriously, now, don't you think it was all a bit uncalled-for?"

"I'm so *hot*," said Skybright. "Do you *have* to maul me about like this? Suppose someone were to see us? Anyway, it's not right for me to be sitting here."

"If you know it's not right to be sitting here," he said teasingly, "what were you doing lying down?"

"Che-e-e!" Unable at once to reply, she gave a little laugh. Then she said:

"When you are not here it doesn't matter. It's *your* being here that makes it wrong. Anyway, let me get up now, because I want to have a bath. Aroma and Musk have had theirs already. I'll send *them* out to you."

"I've just had rather a lot to drink and I could do with a bath myself," said Bao-yu. "As you haven't had yours yet, bring the water out here and we'll have a bath together."

Skybright laughed and declined with a vigorous gesture of her hand.

"*Oh* no! I daren't start you off on that caper. I still remember that time you got Emerald to help you bath. You must have been two or three hours in there, so that we began to get quite worried. We didn't like to go in while you were there, but when we did go in to have a look afterwards, we found water all over the floor, pools of water round the legs of the bed, and even the mat on the bed had water splashed all over it. Heaven only knows what you'd been up to. We laughed about it for days afterwards. I haven't got time to fetch *that* amount of water. And in any case, you don't want to go taking baths with *me*. As a matter of fact it's cooler now, so I don't think I shall have a bath after all. Why don't you let me fetch you a bowl of water so that you can have a nice wash and comb your hair? Faithful just sent a lot of fruit round and we've got it soaking in iced water in the big glass bowl. I'll tell them to bring some out to you, shall I?"

"All right," said Bao-yu. "If you're not having a bath yourself, I'll just wash my hands; and you can get me some of that fruit to eat."

Skybright smiled.

"You've already told me once today how clumsy I am. I can't even drop a fan without treading on it. So I'm much too clumsy to get your fruit for you. Suppose I were to break a plate. That would be terrible!"

"If you *want* to break it, by all means break it," said Bao-yu. "These things are there for our use. What we use them *for* is a matter of individual taste. For example, fans are made for fanning with; but if you prefer to tear them up because it gives you pleasure, there's no reason why you shouldn't. What you *mustn't* do is to use them as objects to vent your anger on. It's the same with plates and cups. Plates and cups are made to put food and drink in. But if you want to smash them on purpose because you like the noise, it's perfectly all right to do so. As long as you don't get into a passion and start taking it out on *things*—that is the golden rule."

"All right then," said Skybright with a mischievous smile. "Give me your fan to tear. I love the sound of a fan being torn."

Bao-yu held it out to her. She took it eagerly and—*chah!*—promptly tore it in half. And again—*chah! chah! chah!*—she tore it several more times. Bao-yu, an appreciative onlooker, laughed and encouraged her.

"Well torn! Well torn! Now again—a really loud one!"

Just then Musk appeared. She stared at them indignantly.

"Don't do that!" she said. "It's *wicked* to waste things like that."

But Bao-yu leaped up to her, snatched the fan from her hand, and passed it to Skybright, who at once tore it into several pieces. The two of them, Bao-yu and Skybright, then burst into uproarious laughter.

"What do you think you're doing?" said Musk. "That's *my fan* you've just ruined."

"What's an old fan?" said Bao-yu. "Open up the fan box and get yourself another."

"If that's your attitude," said Musk, "we might as well carry out the whole boxful and let her tear away to her heart's content."

"All right. Go and get it," said Bao-yu.

"And be born a beggar in my next life?" said Musk. "No thank you! She hasn't broken her arm. Let her go and get it herself."

Skybright stretched back on the bed, smiling complacently.

"I'm rather tired just now. I think I shall tear some more tomorrow."

Bao-yu laughed.

"The ancients used to say that for one smile of a beautiful woman a thousand taels are well spent. For a few old fans it's cheap at the price!"

He called to Aroma, who had just finished changing into clean clothes, to come outside and join them. Little Melilot came and cleared away the broken bits of fan, and everyone sat for a while and enjoyed the cool.

But our narrative supplies no further details of that evening.

About noon next day, while Lady Wang, Bao-chai, Dai-yu and the girls were sitting in Grandmother Jia's room, someone came in to announce that "Miss Shi" had arrived. Shortly afterwards Shi Xiang-yun appeared in the courtyard, attended by a bevy of matrons and maids. Bao-chai, Dai-yu and the rest hurried out to the foot of the steps to welcome her.

For young girls like the cousins a reunion after a mere month's separation is an occasion for touching demonstrations of affection. After these initial transports, when they were all indoors and the greetings, introductions and salutations had been completed, Grandmother Jia suggested that, as the weather was so hot, Xiang-yun should remove her outer garments. Xiang-yun rose to her feet with alacrity and divested herself of one or two layers. Lady Wang was amused.

"Gracious, child! What a lot you have on! I don't think I've ever seen anyone wearing so much."

"It's my Aunt Shi who makes me wear it all," said Xiang-yun. "You wouldn't catch me wearing this stuff if I didn't have to."

"You don't know our Xiang-yun, Aunt," Bao-chai interposed. "She's really happiest in boy's clothes. That time she was here in the third or fourth month last year, I remember one day she dressed up in one of Bao-yu's gowns and put a pair of his boots on and one of his belts round her waist. At first glance she looked exactly like Cousin Bao. It was only the ear-rings that gave her away. When she stood behind that chair over there, Grandmother was completely taken in. She said, 'Bao-yu, come over here! You'll get the dust from that hanging lamp in your eyes if you're not careful.' But Xiang-yun just smiled and didn't move. It was only when everyone couldn't hold it in any longer and started laughing that Grandmother realized who it was and joined in the laugh. She told her that she made a very good-looking boy."

"That's nothing," said Dai-yu. "What about that time last year when she came to stay for a couple of days with us in the first month and it snowed? Grandma and Auntie Wang had just got back from somewhere—I think it was from visiting the ancestors' portraits[2]—and she saw Grandma's new scarlet felt rain-cape lying there and put it on when no one was looking. Of course, it was much too big and much too long for her, so she hitched it up and tied it round her waist with a sash and went out like that into the back courtyard to help the maids build a snowman. And then she slipped over in it and got covered all over with mud—"

The others all laughed at the recollection.

Bao-chai asked Xiang-yun's nurse, Mrs. Zhou, whether Xiang-yun was still as tomboyish as ever. Nurse Zhou laughed but said nothing.

"I don't mind her being tomboyish," said Ying-chun, "but I do wish she wasn't such a chatterbox. You wouldn't believe it—even when she's in bed at night it still goes on. Jabber-jabber, jabber-jabber. Then she laughs. Then she talks a bit more. Then she laughs again. And you never heard such a lot of rubbish in your life. I don't know where she gets it all from."

"Well, perhaps she'll have got over that by now," said Lady Wang. "I hear that someone was round the other day to talk about a betrothal. Now that there's a future mother-in-law to think about, she can't be *quite* as tomboyish as she used to be."

"Are you staying this time, or do you have to go back tonight?" asked Grandmother Jia.

"Your Old Ladyship hasn't seen all the clothes she's brought," said Nurse Zhou. "She'll be staying two days here at the very least."

"Isn't Bao at home?" said Xiang-yun.

"Listen to her!" said Bao-chai. "Cousin Bao is the only one she thinks about. He and she get on well together because they are both fond of mischief. You can see she hasn't really changed."

"Perhaps now that you're getting older you had better stop using baby-names," said Grandmother Jia, reminded by the talk of betrothal that her babies were rapidly turning into grown-ups.

Just then Bao-yu came in.

2. Kept in shrines and honored as part of Chinese ancestor worship.

"Ah! Hallo, Yun! Why didn't you come when we sent for you the other day?"

"Grandmother has just this moment been saying that it is time you all stopped using baby-names," said Lady Wang. "I must say, this isn't a very good beginning."

"Our cousin has got something nice to give you," said Dai-yu to Xiang-yun.

"Oh? What is it?" said Xiang-yun.

"Don't believe her," said Bao-yu. "Goodness! It's no time since you were here last, but you seem to have grown taller already."

Xiang-yun laughed.

"How's Aroma?"

"She's fine. Thank you for asking."

"I've brought something for her," said Xiang-yun. She produced a knotted-up silk handkerchief.

"What treasure have you got wrapped up in there?" said Bao-yu. "The best present you could have brought Aroma would have been a couple of those cheap agate rings like the ones you sent us the other day."

"What are these, then?"

With a triumphant smile she opened her little bundle and revealed four rings, each inset with the veined red agate they had so much admired on a previous occasion.

"What a girl!" said Dai-yu. "These are exactly the same as the ones you sent us the other day by messenger. Why didn't you get him to bring these too and save yourself some trouble? I thought you must have got some wonderful rarity tied up in that handkerchief, seeing that you'd gone to all the trouble of bringing it here yourself—and all the time it was only a few more of *those!* You really are rather a silly."

"Thilly yourthelf!" said Xiang-yun. "The others can decide which of us is the silly one when I have explained my reason. If I send things for you and the girls, it's assumed that they are for you without the messenger even needing to say anything; but if I send things for any of the maids, I have to explain very carefully to the messenger which ones I mean. Now if the messenger is someone intelligent, that's all right; but if it's someone not so bright who has difficulty in remembering names, they'll probably make such a mess of it that they'll get not only the maids' presents mixed up, but yours as well. Then again, if the messenger is a woman, it's not so bad; but the other day it was one of the boys—and you know how hopeless *they* are over girls' names. So you see, I thought it would be simpler if I delivered the maids' ones myself. There!"—she laid the rings down one after another on the table—"One for Aroma; one for Faithful; one for Golden; and one for Patience. Can you imagine one of the boys getting those four names right?"

The others laughed.

"Clever! Clever!" they said.

"You're always so eloquent," said Bao-yu. "No one else gets a chance."

"If she weren't so eloquent, she wouldn't be worthy of the gold kylin," said Dai-yu huffily, rising from her seat and walking off as she spoke.

Fortunately no one heard her but Bao-chai, who made a laughing grimace, and Bao-yu, who immediately regretted having once more spoken out of turn, but who, suddenly catching sight of Bao-chai's expression, could not help laughing himself. Seeing him laugh, Bao-chai at once rose from her seat and hurried off to joke with Dai-yu.

"When you've finished your tea and rested a bit," said Grandmother Jia to Xiang-yun, "you can go and see your married cousins. After that, you can amuse yourself in the Garden with the girls. It's nice and cool there."

Xiang-yun thanked her grandmother. She wrapped up three of the rings again, and after sitting a little longer, went off, attended by her nannies and maids, to call on Wang Xi-feng. After chatting a while with her, she went into the Garden and called on Li Wan. Then, after sitting a short while with Li Wan, she went off in the direction of Green Delights in quest of Aroma. Before doing so, however, she turned to dismiss her escort.

"You needn't stay with me any longer," she said. "You can go off now and visit your relations. I'll just keep Fishy to wait on me."

The others thanked her and went off to look for various kith and kin, leaving Xiang-yun alone with Kingfisher.

"Why aren't these water-lilies out yet?" said Kingfisher.

"It isn't time for them yet," said Xiang-yun.

"Look, they're going to be 'double-decker' ones, like the ones in our lily-pond at home," said Kingfisher.

"Our ones are better," said Xiang-yun.

"They've got a pomegranate-tree here which has four or five lots of flowers growing one above the other on each branch," said Kingfisher. "That's a double-double-double-decker. I wonder what makes them grow like that."

"Plants are the same as people," said Xiang-yun. "The healthier their constitution is, the better they grow."

"I don't believe that," said Kingfisher with a toss of her head. "If that were so, why don't we see people walking around with one head growing on top of the other?"

Xiang-yun was unable to avoid laughing at the girl's simplicity.

"I've told you before, you talk too much," she said. "Let's see: how can one answer a question like that? Everything in the world is moulded by the forces of Yin and Yang. That means that, besides the normal, the abnormal, the peculiar, the freakish—in fact all the thousands and thousands of different variations we find in things—are caused by different combinations of Yin and Yang. Even if something appears that is so rare that no one has ever seen it before, the principle is still the same."

"So according to what you say," said Kingfisher, "all the things that have ever existed, from the time the world began right up to the present moment, have just been a lot of Yins and Yangs."

"No, stupid!" said Xiang-yun. "The more you say, the sillier you get. 'Just a lot of Yins and Yangs' indeed! In any case, strictly speaking Yin and Yang are not two things but one and the same thing. By the time the Yang has become exhausted, it is Yin; and by the time the Yin has become exhausted, it is Yang. It isn't a case of one of them coming to an end and then the other one growing out of nothing."

"That's too deep for me," said Kingfisher. "What sort of thing is a Yin-yang, I'd like to know? No one's ever seen one. You just answer that, Miss. What does a Yin-yang look like?"

"Yin-yang is a sort of *force*," said Xiang-yun. "It's the force in things that gives them their distinctive forms. For example, the sky is Yang and the earth is Yin; water is Yin and fire is Yang; the sun is Yang and the moon is Yin."

"Ah yes! *Now* I understand," said Kingfisher happily. "That's why astrologers call the sun the 'Yang star' and the moon the 'Yin star.' "

"Holy name!" said Xiang-yun. "She understands."

"That's not so difficult," said Kingfisher. "But what about things like mosquitoes and fleas and midges and plants and flowers and bricks and tiles? Surely you are not going to say that they are all Yin-yang too?"

"Certainly they are!" said Xiang-yun. "Take the leaf of a tree, for example. That's divided into Yin and Yang. The side facing upwards towards the sky is Yang; the underside, facing towards the ground, is Yin."

Kingfisher nodded.

"I see. Yes. I can understand that. But take these fans we are holding. Surely *they* don't have Yin and Yang?"

"Yes they do. The front of the fan is Yang; the back of the fan is Yin."

Kingfisher nodded, satisfied. She tried to think of some other object to ask about, but being for the moment unable to, she began looking around her for inspiration. As she did so, her eye chanced to light on the gold kylin fastened in the intricate loopings of her mistress's girdle.

"Well, Miss," she said, pointing triumphantly to the kylin, "you're not going to say that *that's* got Yin and Yang?"

"Certainly. In the case of birds and beasts and males are Yang and the females are Yin."

"Is this a daddy one or a mummy one?" said Kingfisher.

" 'A daddy one or a mummy one'! Silly girl!"

"All right, then," said Kingfisher. "But why is it that everything else has Yin and Yang but we haven't?"

"Get along with you, naughty girl! What subject will you get on to next?"

"Why? Why can't you tell me?" said Kingfisher. "Anyway, I know; so there's no need for you to be so nasty to me."

Xiang-yun suppressed a giggle.

"You're Yang and I'm Yin," said Kingfisher.

Xiang-yun held her handkerchief to her mouth and laughed.

"Well, that's right, isn't it?" said Kingfisher. "What are you laughing at?"

"Yes, yes," said Xiang-yun. "That's quite right."

"That's what they always say," said Kingfisher: "the master is Yang and the servant is Yin. Even I can understand that principle."

"I'm sure you can," said Xiang-yun. "Very good."

While they were talking, a glittering golden object at the foot of the rose pergola caught Xiang-yun's eye. She pointed it out to Kingfisher.

"Go and see what it is."

Kingfisher bounded over and picked it up.

"Ah ha!" she said, examining the object in her hand. "Now we shall be able to see whether it's Yin or Yang."

She took hold of the kylin fastened to Xiang-yun's girdle and held it up to look at it more closely. Xiang-yun wanted to see what it was that she held in her hand, but Kingfisher wouldn't let her.

"It's *my* treasure," she said with a laugh. "I won't let you see it, Miss. Funny, though. I wonder where it came from. I've never seen anyone here wearing it."

"Come on! Let me look," said Xiang-yun.

"There you are, Miss!" Kingfisher opened her hand.

Xiang-yun looked. It was a beautiful, shining gold kylin, both larger and more ornate than the one she was wearing. Reaching out and taking it from Kingfisher, she held it on the palm of her hand and contemplated it for some moments in silence.

Whatever reverie the contemplation inspired was broken by the sudden arrival of Bao-yu.

"What are you doing, standing out here in the blazing sun?" he asked her. "Why don't you go and see Aroma?"

"We were on our way," said Xiang-yun, hurriedly concealing the gold kylin.

The three of them entered the courtyard of Green Delights together.

Aroma had gone outside to take the air and was leaning on the verandah railings at the foot of the front door steps. As soon as she caught sight of Xiang-yun, she hurried down into the courtyard to welcome her, and taking her by the hand, led her into the house, animatedly exchanging news with her as they went.

"You should have come sooner," said Bao-yu when they were indoors and Aroma had made Xiang-yun take a seat. "I've got something nice for you here and I've been waiting for you to come so that I could give it to you."

He had been hunting through his pockets as he said this. Not finding what he was searching for, he exclaimed in surprise.

"Aiyo!" He turned to Aroma. "Have you put it away somewhere?"

"Put what away?"

"That little kylin I got the other day."

"You've been carrying it around with you everywhere," said Aroma. "Why ask *me* about it?"

Bao-yu clapped his hands together in vexation.

"Oh, I've lost it! Wherever am I going to look for it?"

He got up to begin searching.

Xiang-yun now realized that it must have been Bao-yu who dropped the kylin she had only a few minutes earlier discovered outside.

"Since when have *you* had a kylin?" she asked him.

"Oh, several days now," said Bao-yu. "What a shame! I'll never get another one like that. And the trouble is, I don't know when I can have lost it. Oh dear! How stupid of me!"

"It's only an ornament you're getting so upset about," said Xiang-yun. "What a good job it wasn't something more serious!"

She opened her hand:
"Look! Is that it?"
Bao-yu looked and saw, with extravagant delight, that it was.
The remainder of this episode will be told in the following chapter.

CHAPTER 32

Bao-yu demonstrates confusion of mind by making
his declaration to the wrong person
And Golden shows an unconquerable spirit by ending
her humiliation in death

Our last chapter told of Bao-yu's delight at seeing the gold kylin again.
He reached out eagerly and took it from Xiang-yun's hand.

"Fancy *your* finding it!" he said. "How did you come to pick it up?"

"It's a good job it was only this you lost," she said. "One of these days it
will be your seal of office—and then it won't be quite so funny."[3]

"Oh, losing one's seal of office is nothing," said Bao-yu. "Losing a thing
like this is much more serious."

Aroma meanwhile was pouring tea.

"I heard your good news the other day," she said, handing Xiang-yun a
cup. "Congratulations!"

Xiang-yun bent low over the cup to hide her blushes and made no reply.

"Why so bashful, Miss?" said Aroma. "Have you forgotten the things
you used to tell me at night all those years ago, when we used to sleep
together in the little closet-bed[4] at Her Old Ladyship's? You weren't very
bashful then. What makes you so bashful with me now, all of a sudden?"

Xiang-yun's face became even redder. She gave a forced little laugh.

"Who's talking? That was a time when you and I were very close to each
other. Then I had to go back home when my uncle's first wife died and
you were given Cousin Bao to look after, and I don't know why, but whenever I came back here after that, you seemed somehow changed towards
me."

It was now Aroma's turn to blush and protest.

"When you first came to live here it was 'Pearl dear this' and 'Pearl dear
that' all the time. You were always coaxing me to do things for you—do
your hair, wash your face, or I don't know what. But now that's all
changed. Now you're the young lady, aren't you? You can't act the young
lady with me and expect me to stay on the same familiar terms as before."

"Holy name!" said Xiang-yun, now genuinely indignant. "That's *tho*
unfair. I wish I may die if I ever 'acted the young lady' with you, as you
put it. I come here in this frightful heat, and the very first person I want
to see when I get here is you. Ask Fishy if you don't believe me. *She* can
tell you. At home I'm *always* going on about you."

Aroma and Bao-yu both laughed.

---

3. The assumption is that Bao-yu will some day become a government official. All officials had seals
with which to stamp documents, and such stamps had authorizing power, like a signature. Hence the
loss of a seal was a serious matter.   4. A small temporary bed, like a cot.

"Don't take it to heart so, it was only a joke. You shouldn't be so excitable."

"Don't, whatever you do, admit that what *you* said was wounding," said Xiang-yun. "Say I'm 'excitable' and put *me* in the wrong!"

While she said this, she was undoing the knotted silk handkerchief and extracting one of the three rings from it. She handed it to Aroma. Aroma was greatly touched.

"I've got one like this already," she said. "It was given to me when you sent those ones the other day to the young ladies. But fancy your bringing this one here specially! Now I *know* you haven't forgotten me. It's little things like this that show you what a person really is. The ring itself isn't worth much, I know. It's the thought behind it."

"Who gave you the one you've already got?" said Xiang-yun.

"Miss Bao," said Aroma.

"Ah," said Xiang-yun, "Miss Bao. And I was thinking it must have been Miss Lin. Often when I'm at home I think to myself that of all my cousins Bao-chai is the one I like best. It's a pity we couldn't have been born of the same mother. With her for an elder sister it wouldn't matter so much being an orphan."

Her eyelids reddened as she said this and she seemed to be on the verge of tears.

"Now, now, now!" said Bao-yu. "Don't say things like that."

"And why not?" said Xiang-yun. "Oh, I know your trouble. You're afraid that Cousin Lin might hear and get angry with me again for praising Cousin Bao. That's what's worrying you, isn't it?"

Aroma giggled.

"Oh Miss Yun! You're just as outspoken as you used to be."

"Well, I've said that you lot are difficult to talk to," said Bao-yu, "and I was certainly right!"

"Don't make me sick," said Xiang-yun. "You say what you like to us. It's with your Cousin Lin that you have to be so careful."

"Never mind about that," said Aroma. "Joking apart, now: I want to ask you a favour."

"What is it?" said Xiang-yun.

"I've got a pair of slipper-tops here that I've already cut the openwork pattern in, but as I haven't been very well this last day or two, I haven't been able to sew them on to the backing material. Do you think you'd have time to do them for me?"

"That's rather a strange request," said Xiang-yun. "Quite apart from all the clever maids this household employs you have your own full-time tailors and embroiderers. Why ask *me* to do your sewing? You could give it to anyone here you liked. They could hardly refuse you."

"You can't be serious," said Aroma. "None of the sewing in this room is allowed to go outside.[5] Surely you knew that?"

Xiang-yun inferred from this that the slippers in question were for Bao-yu.

"Oh well," she said, "in that case I suppose I'd better do them for you.

---

5. Bao-yu wants all his sewing done by only those who are close to him.

On one condition, though: I'll do them if they are for *you* to wear, but if they are for anyone else, I'm afraid I can't."

"Get along with you!" said Aroma. "Ask you to make slippers for *me*? I wouldn't have the nerve. No, I'll be honest with you, they're not for me. Never mind who they're for. Just tell yourself that I'm the one you'll be doing the favour."

"It isn't *that*," said Xiang-yun. "In the past I've done lots of things for you. Surely you must *know* what makes me unwilling now?"

"I'm sorry, I don't," said Aroma.

"What about the person who got in a temper the other day when that fan-case I made for you was compared with hers and cut it up with a pair of scissors? *I* heard all about that, so don't start protesting. If you expect me to do sewing for you after *that*, you're just treating me as your drudge."

"I didn't know at the time it was you who made it," Bao-yu put in hurriedly.

"He really didn't," said Aroma. "I pretended there was someone outside we'd just discovered who could do very fine and original needlework. I told him I'd got them to do that fan-case for him as a sample. He believed what I said and went around showing it to everyone. Unfortunately while he was doing this he upset you know who and she took a pair of scissors and cut it in pieces. Afterwards he was very anxious to have some more work done by the same person, so I had to tell him who it really was. He was very upset when he heard that it was you."

"I still think this is a very strange request," said Xiang-yun. "If Miss Lin can cut things up, she can sew them for him, too. Why not ask *her* to do them for you?"

"Oh, *she* wouldn't want to do them," said Aroma. "And even if she did, Her Old Ladyship wouldn't let her, for fear of her tiring herself. The doctors say she needs rest and quiet. I wouldn't want to trouble *her* with them. Last year she took practically the whole year embroidering one little purse, and this last six months I don't think she's picked up a needle."

Their conversation was interrupted by a servant with a message:

"Mr. Jia of Rich Street is here. The Master says will Master Bao receive him, please?"

Recognizing the "Mr. Jia" of the message as Jia Yu-cun, Bao-yu was more than a little vexed. While Aroma hurried off for his going-out clothes, he sat pulling his boots on and grumbling.

"He's got Father to talk to, surely that's enough for him? Why does he always have to see me?"

Xiang-yun laughed at his disgruntlement:

"I'm sure you're very good at entertaining people," she said. "That's why Sir Zheng asks you to see him."

"That message didn't come from Father," said Bao-yu. "He'll have made it up himself."

" 'When the host is refined, the callers are frequent,' " said Xiang-yun. "There must be something about you that has impressed him, otherwise he wouldn't want to see you."

"I make no claim to being refined, thanks all the same," said Bao-yu.

"I'm as common as dirt. And furthermore I have no wish to mix with people of his sort."

"You're incorrigible," said Xiang-yun. "Now that you're older, you ought to be mixing with these officials and administrators as much as you can. Even if you don't want to take the Civil Service examinations and become an administrator yourself, you can learn a lot from talking to these people about the way the Empire is governed and the people who govern it that will stand you in good stead later on, when you come to manage your own affairs and take your place in society. You might even pick up one or two decent, respectable friends that way. You'll certainly never get anywhere if you spend all your time with us girls."

Bao-yu found such talk highly displeasing.

"I think perhaps you'd better go and sit in someone else's room," he said. "I wouldn't want a *decent, respectable* young lady like you to get contaminated."

"Don't try reasoning with him, Miss," Aroma put in hurriedly. "Last time Miss Bao tried it, he was just as rude to her. No consideration for her feelings whatever. He just said 'Hai!', picked up his heels, and walked out of the room, leaving her still half-way through her sentence. Poor Miss Bao! She was so embarrassed she turned bright red. She didn't know *what* to say. A good job it was her, though, and not Miss Lin. If it had been Miss Lin, there'd have been weeping and carrying on and I don't know what. I really admire the way Miss Bao behaved on that occasion. She just stood there a while collecting herself and then walked quietly out of the room. Myself, I was quite upset, thinking she must be offended. But not a bit of it. Next time she came round, it was just as if nothing had happened. A real little lady, Miss Bao—and generous-hearted, too. And yet the funny thing is that his lordship seems to have fallen out with her, whereas Miss Lin, who is always getting on her high horse and ignoring him, has him running round and apologizing to her all the time."

"Have you ever heard Miss Lin talking that sort of stupid rubbish?" said Bao-yu. "I'd long since have fallen out with *her* if she did."

Aroma and Xiang-yun shook their heads pityingly.

"So that's 'stupid rubbish,' is it?" they said, laughing.

Dai-yu rightly surmised that now Xiang-yun had arrived, Bao-yu would lose no time in telling her about his newly-acquired kylin.

Now Dai-yu had observed that in the romances which Bao-yu smuggled in to her and of which she was nowadays an avid consumer, it was always some trinket or small object of clothing or jewellery—a pair of lovebirds, a male and female phoenix, a jade ring, a gold buckle, a silken handkerchief, an embroidered belt or what not—that brought the heroes and heroines together. And since the fate and future happiness of those fortunate beings seemed to depend wholly on the instrumentality of such trifling objects, it was natural for her to suppose that Bao-yu's acquisition of the gold kylin would become the occasion of a dramatic rupture with *her* and the beginning of an association with Xiang-yun in which he and Xiang-yun would do together all those delightful things that she had read about in the romances.

It was with such apprehensions that she made her way stealthily towards Green Delights, her intention being to observe how the two of them were behaving and shape her own actions accordingly. Imagine her surprise when, just as she was about to enter, she heard Xiang-yun lecturing Bao-yu on his social obligations and Bao-yu telling Xiang-yun that "Cousin Lin never talked that sort of rubbish" and that if she did he would have "fallen out with her long ago." Mingled emotions of happiness, alarm, sorrow and regret assailed her.

Happiness:

Because after all (she thought) I wasn't mistaken in my judgement of you. I always thought of you as a true friend, and I was right.

Alarm:

Because if you praise me so unreservedly in front of other people, your warmth and affection are sure, sooner or later, to excite suspicion and be misunderstood.

Regret:

Because if you are my true friend, then I am yours and the two of us are a perfect match. But in that case why did there have to be all this talk of "the gold and the jade"? Alternatively, if there had to be all this talk of gold and jade, why weren't we the two to have them? Why did there have to be a Bao-chai with her golden locket?

Sorrow:

Because though there are things of burning importance to be said, without a father or a mother I have no one to say them for me. And besides, I feel so muzzy lately and I know that my illness is gradually gaining a hold on me. (The doctors say that the weakness and anaemia I suffer from may be the beginnings of a consumption.) So even if I *am* your true-love, I fear I may not be able to wait for you. And even though you are mine, you can do nothing to alter my fate.

At that point in her reflections she began to weep; and feeling in no fit state to be seen, she turned away from the door and began to make her way back again.

Bao-yu had finished his hasty dressing and now came out of the house. He saw Dai-yu slowly walking on ahead of him and, judging by her appearance from behind, wiping her eyes. He hurried forward to catch up with her.

"Where are you off to, coz? Are you crying again? Who has upset you this time?"

Dai-yu turned and saw that it was Bao-yu.

"I'm perfectly all right," she said, forcing a smile. "What would I be crying for?"

"Look at you! The tears are still wet on your face. How can you tell such fibs?"

Impulsively he stretched out his hand to wipe them. Dai-yu recoiled several paces:

"You'll get your head chopped off!" she said. "You really *must* keep your hands to yourself."

"I'm sorry. My feelings got the better of me. I'm afraid I wasn't thinking about my head."

"No, I forgot," said Dai-yu. "Losing your head is nothing, is it? It's losing your kylin—the famous *gold* kylin—that is really serious!"

Her words immediately put Bao-yu in a passion. He came up to her and held his face close to hers.

"Do you say these things to put a curse on me? or is it merely to make me angry that you say them?"

Remembering their recent quarrel, Dai-yu regretted her careless reintroduction of its theme and hastened to make amends:

"Now don't get excited. I shouldn't have said that—oh come now, it really isn't *that* important! Look at you! The veins are standing out on your forehead and your face is all covered with sweat."

She moved forward and wiped the perspiration from his brow. For some moments he stood there motionless, staring at her. Then he said:

"*Don't worry!*"

Hearing this, Dai-yu herself was silent for some moments.

"Why *should* I worry?" she said eventually. "I don't understand you. Would you mind telling me what you are talking about?"

Bao-yu sighed.

"Do you really not understand? Can I really have been all this time mistaken in my feelings towards you? If you don't even know your *own* mind, it's small wonder that you're always getting angry on *my* account."

"I really don't understand what you mean about not worrying," said Dai-yu.

Bao-yu sighed again and shook his head.

"My dear coz, don't think you can fool me. If you don't understand what I've just said, then not only have *my* feelings towards *you* been all along mistaken, but all that *you* have ever felt for *me* has been wasted, too. It's because you worry so much that you've made yourself ill. If only you could take things a bit easier, your illness wouldn't go on getting more and more serious all the time."

Dai-yu was thunderstruck. He had read her mind—had seen inside her more clearly than if she had plucked out her entrails and held them out for his inspection. And now there were a thousand things that she wanted to tell him; yet though she was dying to speak, she was unable to utter a single syllable and stood there like a simpleton, gazing at him in silence.

Bao-yu, too, had a thousand things to say, but he, too, stood mutely gazing at her, not knowing where to begin.

After the two of them had stared at each other for some considerable time in silence, Dai-yu heaved a deep sigh. The tears gushed from her eyes and she turned and walked away. Bao-yu hurried after her and caught at her dress.

"Coz dear, stop a moment! Just let me say one word."

As she wiped her eyes with one hand, Dai-yu pushed him away from her with the other.

"There's nothing to say. I already know what you want to tell me."

She said this without turning back her head, and having said it, passed swiftly on her way. Bao-yu remained where he was standing, gazing after her in silent stupefaction.

Now Bao-yu had left the apartment in such haste that he had forgotten to take his fan with him. Fearing that he would be very hot without it, Aroma hurried outside to give it to him, but when she noticed him standing some way ahead of her talking to Dai-yu, she halted. After a little while she saw Dai-yu walk away and Bao-yu continue standing motionless where he was. She chose this moment to go up and speak to him.

"You've gone out without your fan," she said. "It's a good job I noticed. Here you are. I ran out to give it to you."

Bao-yu, still in a muse, saw Aroma there talking to him, yet without clearly perceiving who it was. With the same glazed look in his eyes, he began to speak.

"Dearest coz! I've never before dared to tell you what I felt for you. Now at last I'm going to pluck up courage and tell you, and after that I don't care what becomes of me. Because of you I, too, have made myself ill—only I haven't dared tell anyone about it and have had to bear it all in silence. And the day that your illness is cured, I do believe that mine, too, will get better. Night and day, coz, sleeping and dreaming, you are never out of my mind."

Aroma listened to this declaration aghast.

"Holy saints preserve us!" she exclaimed. "He'll be the death of me."

She gave him a shake.

"What are you talking about? Are you bewitched? You'd better hurry."

Bao-yu seemed suddenly to waken from his trance and recognized the person he had been speaking to as Aroma. His face turned a deep red with embarrassment and he snatched the fan from her and fled.

After he had gone, Aroma began thinking about the words he had just said and realized that they must have been intended for Dai-yu. She reflected with some alarm that if things between them were as his words seemed to indicate, there was every likelihood of an ugly scandal developing, and wondered how she could arrange matters to prevent it. Preoccupied with these reflections, she stood as motionless and unseeing as her master had done a few moments before. Bao-chai found her in this state on her way back from the house.

"What are you brooding on, out in the burning sun?" she asked her, laughing.

Aroma laughed back.

"There were two little sparrows here having a fight. They were so funny, I had to stand and watch them."

"Where was Cousin Bao rushing off to just now, all dressed up for going out?" said Bao-chai. "I was going to call out and ask him, but he is getting so crotchety lately that I thought I had better not."

"The Master sent for him," said Aroma.

"Oh dear!" said Bao-chai. "I wonder why he should send for him in heat like this? I hope he hasn't thought of something to be angry about and called him over to be punished."

"No, it isn't that," said Aroma. "I think it's to receive a visitor."

"It must be a very tiresome visitor," said Bao-chai, "to go around bothering people on a boiling day like this instead of staying at home and trying to keep cool."

"You can say that again!" said Aroma.

"What's young Xiang-yun been doing at your place?" said Bao-chai, changing the subject.

"We were having a chat," said Aroma, "and after that she had a look at some slipper-tops that I've got ready pasted and have asked her to sew for me."

"You're an intelligent young woman," said Bao-chai, having first looked to right and left of her to make sure that no one else was about, "I should have thought you'd have sense enough to leave her a few moments in peace. I've been watching our Yun lately, and from what I've observed of her and various stray remarks I've heard, I get the impression that back at home she can barely call her soul her own. I know for a fact that they are too mean to pay for professional seamstresses and that nearly all the sewing has to be done by the women of the household, and I'm pretty sure that's why, whenever she's found herself alone with me on these last few visits, she's told me how tired she gets at home. When I press her for details, her eyes fill with tears and she answers evasively, as though she'd like to tell me but daren't. It must be very hard for her, losing both her parents when she was so young. It quite wrings my heart to see her so exploited."

Aroma smote her hands together as understanding dawned.

"Yes, I *see*. I see now why she was so slow with those ten butterfly bows I asked her to sew for me last month. It was ages before she sent them, and even then there was a message to say that she'd only been able to do them roughly. She told me I'd better use them on something else. 'If you want nice, even ones,' she said, 'you'll have to wait until next time I come to stay with you.' Now I can see why. She didn't like to refuse when I asked her, but I suppose she had to sit up till midnight doing them, poor thing. Oh, how stupid of me! I'd never have asked her if I'd realized."

"Last time she was here, she told me that it's quite normal for her to sit up sewing until midnight," said Bao-chai; "and if her aunt or the other women catch her doing the slightest bit of work for anyone else, they are angry with her."

"It's all the fault of that pig-headed young master of mine," said Aroma. "He refuses to let any of his sewing be done by the seamstresses outside. Every bit of work, large or small, has to be done in his room—and I just can't manage it all on my own."

Bao-chai laughed.

"Why do you take any notice of him? Why not simply give it to the seamstresses without telling him?"

"He's not so easy to fool," said Aroma. "He can tell the difference. I'm afraid there's nothing for it. I shall just have to work through it all gradually on my own."

"Now just a minute!" said Bao-chai. "We'll think of a way round this. Suppose I were to do some of it for you?"

"Would you really?" said Aroma. "I'd be so grateful if you would. I'll come over with some this evening then."

She had barely finished saying this when an old woman came rushing up to them in a state of great agitation.

"Isn't it dreadful? Miss Golden has drowned herself in the well."

"Which Golden?" said Aroma, startled.

"Which Golden?" said the old woman. "There aren't two Goldens that I know of. Golden from Her Ladyship's room, of course, that was dismissed the day before yesterday. She'd been crying and carrying on at home ever since, but nobody paid much attention to her. Then suddenly, when they went to look for her, she wasn't there, and just now someone going to fetch water from the well by the south-east corner found a body in it and rushed inside for help, and when they fished it out, they found that it was Golden. They did all they could to revive her, but it was too late. She was dead."

"How strange!" said Bao-chai.

Aroma shook her head wonderingly and a tear or two stole down her cheek. She and Golden had been like sisters to each other.

Bao-chai hurried off to Lady Wang's to offer her sympathy. Aroma went back to Green Delights.

When Bao-chai arrived at Lady Wang's apartment she found the whole place hushed and still and Lady Wang sitting in the inner room on her own, crying. Deeming it an unsuitable moment to raise the subject of her visit, Bao-chai sat down beside her in silence.

"Where have you just come from?" Lady Wang asked her.

"The Garden."

"The Garden," Lady Wang echoed. "Did you by any chance see your cousin Bao-yu there?"

"I saw him going out just now wearing his outdoor clothes, but I don't know where he was going to."

Lady Wang nodded and gave a sigh.

"I don't know if you've heard. Something very strange has happened. Golden has drowned herself in a well."

"That *is* strange," said Bao-chai. "Why ever did she do that?"

"The day before yesterday she broke something of mine," said Lady Wang, "and in a moment of anger I struck her a couple of times and sent her back to her mother's. I had only been meaning to leave her there a day or two to punish her. After that I would have had her back again. I never dreamed that she would be so angry with me as to drown herself. Now that she has, I feel that it is all my fault."

"It's only natural that a kind person like you should see it in that way," said Bao-chai, "but in my opinion Golden would never have drowned herself in anger. It's much more likely that she was playing about beside the well and slipped in accidentally. While she was in service her movements were restricted and it would be natural for her to go running around everywhere during her first day or two outside. There's no earthly reason why she should have felt angry enough with you to drown herself. If she did, all I can say is that she was a stupid person and not worth feeling sorry for!"

Lady Wang sighed and shook her head doubtfully.

"Well, it may be as you say, but I still feel very uneasy in my mind."

"I'm sure you have no cause, Aunt," said Bao-chai, "but if you feel *very* much distressed, I suggest that you simply give her family a little extra for the funeral. In that way you will more than fulfil any moral obligation you may have towards her as a mistress."

"I have just given her mother fifty taels," said Lady Wang. "I wanted to give her two new outfits as well from one of the girls' wardrobes, but it just so happens that at the moment none of them apart from your Cousin Lin has got anything new that would do. Your Cousin Lin has got two sets that we had made for her next birthday, but she is such a sensitive child and has had so much sickness and misfortune in her life that I'm afraid she would almost certainly feel superstitious about the clothes made for her birthday being used for dressing a corpse with, so I've had to ask the tailors to make up a couple in a hurry. Of course, if it were any other maid, I should have given the mother a few taels and that would have been the end of the matter. But though Golden was only a servant, she had been with me so long that she had become almost like a daughter to me."

She began to cry again as she said this.

"There's no need to hurry the tailors about this," said Bao-chai. "I've got two new outfits that I recently finished making for myself. Why not let her mother have *them* and save them the trouble? Golden once or twice wore old dresses of mine in the past, so I know they will fit her."

"That's very kind of you, but aren't you superstitious?" said Lady Wang.

Bao-chai laughed.

"Don't worry about *that*, Aunt. That sort of thing has never bothered me."

At that she rose and went off to fetch them. Lady Wang hurriedly ordered two of the servants to go after her.

When Bao-chai returned with the clothes, she found Bao-yu sitting beside his mother in tears. Lady Wang was evidently in the midst of rebuking him about something, but as soon as she caught sight of Bao-chai, she closed her mouth and fell silent. From the scene before her eyes and the word or two she had overheard, Bao-chai was able to form a pretty good idea of what had been happening. She handed the clothes over to Lady Wang and Lady Wang summoned Golden's mother to come and fetch them.

What happened after that will be told in the following chapter.

CHAPTER 33

*An envious younger brother puts in a malicious word or two
And a scapegrace elder brother receives a terrible chastisement*

Our story last told how Golden's mother was summoned to take away the clothing that Bao-chai had brought for Golden's laying-out. When she arrived, Lady Wang called her inside, and after making her an additional present of some jewellery, advised her to procure the services of some Buddhist monks to recite a *sūtra*[6] for the salvation of the dead girl's soul. Golden's mother kotowed her thanks and departed with the clothes and jewellery.

---

6. A Buddhist scripture.

The news that Golden's disgrace had driven her to take her own life had reached Bao-yu as he was returning from his interview with Jia Yu-cun, and he was already in a state of shock when he went in to see his mother, only to be subjected by her to a string of accusations and reproaches, to which he was unable to reply. He availed himself of the opportunity presented by Bao-chai's arrival to slip quietly out again, and wandered along, scarcely knowing where he was going, still in a state of shock, hands clasped behind him, head down low, and sighing as he went.

Without realizing it he was drifting towards the main reception hall, and was in fact just emerging from behind the screen-wall that masked the gateway leading from the inner to the outer part of the mansion, when he walked head-on into someone coming from the opposite direction.

"Stand where you are!" said this person in a harsh voice.

Bao-yu looked up with a start and saw that it was his father. He gave an involuntary gasp of fear and, dropping his hands to his sides, hastily assumed a more deferential posture.

"Now," said Jia Zheng, "will you kindly explain the meaning of these sighs and of this moping, hang-dog appearance? You took your time coming when Yu-cun called for you just now, and I gather that when you did eventually vouchsafe your presence, he found you dull and listless and without a lively word to say for yourself. And look at you now—sullenness and secret depravity written all over your face! What are these sighings and groanings supposed to indicate? What have *you* got to be discontented or displeased about? Come, sir! What is the meaning of this?"

Bao-yu was normally ready enough with his tongue, but on this occasion grief for Golden so occupied his mind (at that moment he would very willingly have changed places with her) that though he heard the words addressed to him by his father, he failed to take in their meaning and merely stared back at him stupidly.

Seeing him too hypnotized by fear—or so it appeared—to answer with his usual promptness, Jia Zheng, who had not been angry to start with, was now well on the way to becoming so; but the irate comment he was about to make was checked when a servant from the outer gate announced that a representative of "His Highness the Prince of Zhong-shun" had arrived.

Jia Zheng was puzzled.

"The Prince of Zhong-shun?" he thought. "I have never had any dealings with the Prince of Zhong-shun. I wonder why *he* should suddenly send someone to see me . . . ?"

He told the man to invite the prince's messenger to sit in the hall, while he himself hurried inside and changed into court dress. On entering the hall to receive his visitor, he found that it was the Prince of Zhong-shun's chamberlain who had come to see him. After an exchange of bows and verbal salutations, the two men sat down and tea was served. The chamberlain cut short the customary civilities by coming straight to the point.

"It would have been temerity on my part to have intruded on the leisure of an illustrious scholar in the privacy of his home, but in fact it is not for the purpose of paying a social call that I am here, but on orders from His Highness. His Highness has a small request to make of you. If you will be so good as to oblige him, not only will His Highness be extremely grateful himself, but I and my colleagues will also be very much beholden to you."

Jia Zheng was totally at a loss to imagine what the purpose of the man's visit might be; nevertheless he rose to his feet out of respect for the prince and smiled politely.

"You have orders from His Highness for me? I shall be happy to perform them if you will have the goodness to instruct me."

"I don't think any *performing* will be necessary," said the chamberlain drily. "All we want from you is a few words. A young actor called Bijou — a female impersonator — has gone missing from the palace. He hasn't been back now for four or five days; and though we have looked everywhere we can think of, we can't make out where he can have got to. However, in the course of the very extensive inquiries we have made both inside and outside the city, eight out of ten of the people we have spoken to say that he has recently been very thick with the young gentleman who was born with the jade in his mouth. Well, obviously we couldn't come inside here and search as we would have done if this had been anyone else's house, so we had to go back and report the matter to His Highness; and His Highness says that though he could view the loss of a hundred ordinary actors with equanimity, this Bijou is so skilled in anticipating his wishes and so essential to his peace of mind that it would be utterly impossible for him to dispense with his services. I have therefore come here to request you to ask your son if he will be good enough to let Bijou come back again. By doing so he will not only earn the undying gratitude of the Prince, but will also save me and my colleagues a great deal of tiring and disagreeable searching."

The chamberlain concluded with a sweeping bow.

Surprised and angered by what he had heard, Jia Zheng immediately sent for Bao-yu, who presently came hurrying in, ignorant of what the reason for his summons might be.

"Miserable scum!" said Jia Zheng. "It is not enough, apparently, that you should neglect your studies when you are at home. It seems that you must needs go perpetrating enormities outside. This Bijou I have been hearing about is under the patronage of His Royal Highness the Prince of Zhong-shun. How could you have the unspeakable effrontery to commit an act of enticement on his person — involving *me*, incidentally, in the consequences of your wrong-doing?"

The question made Bao-yu start.

"I honestly know nothing about this," he said. "I don't even know who or what 'Bijou' is, let alone what you mean by 'enticement.'"

Jia Zheng was about to exclaim, but the chamberlain forestalled him.

"There is really no point in concealment, young gentleman," he said coldly. "Even if you are not hiding him here, we are sure that you know where he is. In either case you had much better say straight out and save us a lot of trouble. I'd be greatly obliged if you would."

"I really don't know," said Bao-yu. "You must have been misinformed."

The chamberlain gave a sardonic laugh.

"I have, of course, got evidence for what I am saying and I'm afraid you are doing yourself little good by forcing me to mention it in front of your father. You say you don't know who Bijou is. Very well. Then will you kindly explain how his red cummerbund came to find its way around your waist?"

Bao-yu stared at him open-mouthed, too stunned to reply.

"If he knows even a private thing like that," he thought, "there's little likelihood of my being able to hoodwink him about anything else. I'd better get rid of him as quickly as possible, before he can say any more."

"Since you have managed to find out so much about him," he said, finding his tongue at last, "I'm surprised that so important a thing as buying a house should have escaped you. From what I've heard, he recently acquired a little villa and an acre or so of land at Fort Redwood, seven miles east of the walls. I suppose he could be there."

The chamberlain smiled.

"If you say so, then no doubt that is where we shall find him. I shall go and look there immediately. If I do find him there, you will hear no more from me; if not, I shall be back again for further instructions."

So saying, he hurriedly took his leave.

Jia Zheng, his eyes glaring and his mouth contorted with rage, went after the chamberlain to see him out. He turned briefly towards Bao-yu as he was leaving the hall.

"You stay where you are. I shall deal with you when I get back."

As he was on his way in again after seeing the chamberlain off the premises, Jia Huan with two or three pages at his heels came stampeding across the courtyard.

"Hit that boy!" Jia Zheng shouted, outraged. But Jia Huan, reduced to a quivering jelly of fear by the sight of his father, had already jolted to a halt and was standing with bowed head in front of him.

"And what is the meaning of this?" said Jia Zheng. "What has become of the people who are supposed to look after you? Why do they allow you to gallop around in this extraordinary fashion?" His voice rose to a shout: "Where are the people responsible for taking this boy to school?"

Jia Huan saw in his father's anger an opportunity of exercising his malice.

"I didn't mean to run, Father, but just as I was going by the well back there I saw the body of a maid who had drowned herself—all swollen up with water, and her head all swollen. It was *horrible*. I just couldn't help myself."

Jia Zheng heard him with incredulous horror.

"*What* are you saying? *Who* has drowned herself? Such a thing has never before happened in our family. Our family has always been lenient and considerate in its treatment of inferiors. It is one of our traditions. I suppose it is because I have been too neglectful of household matters during these last few years. Those in charge have felt encouraged to abuse their authority, until finally an appalling thing like this can happen— an innocent young life cut off by violence. What a terrible disgrace to our ancestors if this should get about!" He turned and shouted a command.

"Fetch Jia Lian and Lai Da!"

"Sir!" chorused the pages, and were on the point of doing so when Jia

Huan impulsively stepped forward, threw himself on his knees and clung to his father's skirts.

"Don't be angry with me, Father, but apart from the servants in Lady Wang's room, no one else knows anything about this. I heard my mother say—"

He broke off and glanced around behind him. Jia Zheng understood and signalled with his eyes to the pages, who obediently withdrew some distance back to either side of the courtyard. Jia Huan continued in a voice lowered almost to a whisper.

"My mother told me that the day before yesterday, in Lady Wang's room, my brother Bao-yu tried to rape one of Her Ladyship's maids called Golden, and when she wouldn't let him, he gave her a beating; and Golden was so upset that she threw herself in the well and was drowned—"

Jia Zheng, whose face had now turned to a ghastly gold-leaf colour, interrupted him with a dreadful cry.

"Fetch Bao-yu!"

He began to stride towards his study, shouting to all and sundry as he went.

"If anyone tries to stop me *this* time, I shall make over my house and property and my post at the Ministry and everything else I have to him and Bao-yu. I absolutely refuse to be responsible for the boy any longer. I shall cut off my few remaining hairs (those that worry and wretchedness have left me) and look for some clean and decent spot to end my days in. Perhaps in that way I shall escape the charge of having disgraced my ancestors by rearing this unnatural monster as my son."

When they saw the state he was in, the literary gentlemen and senior menservants who were waiting for him in the study, guessed that Bao-yu must be the cause of it and, looking at each other with various grimaces, biting their thumbs or sticking their tongues out, hastily retreated from the room. Jia Zheng entered it alone and sat down, stiffly upright, in a chair. He was breathing heavily and his face was bathed in tears. Presently, when he had regained his breath, he barked out a rapid series of commands:

"Bring Bao-yu here. Get a heavy bamboo. Get some rope to tie him with. Close the courtyard gates. If anyone tries to take word through inside, kill him!"

"Sir!—Sir!—Sir!" the terrified pages chorused in unison at each of his commands, and some of them went off to look for Bao-yu.

Jia Zheng's ominous "Stay where you are" as he went out with the chamberlain had warned Bao-yu that something dire was imminent— though just how much more dire as a result of Jia Huan's malicious intervention he could not have foreseen and as he stood where his father had left him, he twisted and turned himself about, anxiously looking for some passer-by who could take a message through to the womenfolk inside. But no one came. Even the omnipresent Tealeaf was on this occasion nowhere to be seen. Then suddenly, in answer to his prayers, an old woman appeared—a darling, precious treasure of an old woman (or so she seemed at that moment)—and he dashed forward and clung to her beseechingly.

"Quickly!" he said. "Go and tell them that Sir Zheng is going to beat me. Quickly! Quickly! Go and tell. GO AND TELL."

Partly because agitation had made him incoherent and partly because, as ill luck would have it, the old woman was deaf, almost everything he said had escaped her—except for the "Go and tell," which she misheard as "in the well." She smiled at him reassuringly.

"Let her jump in the well then, young master. Don't you worry your pretty head about it!"

Realizing that he had deafness, too, to contend with, he now became quite frantic.

"GO AND TELL MY PAGES."

"Her wages?" the old woman asked in some surprise. "Bless you, of course they paid her wages! Her Ladyship gave a whole lot of money towards the funeral as well. And clothes. Paid her wages, indeed!"

Bao-yu stamped his feet in a frenzy of impatience. He was still wondering despairingly how to make her understand when Jia Zheng's pages arrived and forced him to go with them to the study.

Jia Zheng turned a pair of wild and bloodshot eyes on him as he entered. Forgetting the "riotous and dissipated conduct abroad leading to the unseemly bestowal of impudicities on a theatrical performer" and the "neglect of proper pursuits and studies at home culminating in the attempted violation of a parent's maidservant" and all the other high-sounding charges he had been preparing to hurl against him, he shouted two brief orders to the pages.

"Gag his mouth. Beat him to death."

The pages were too frightened not to comply. Two held Bao-yu face downwards on a bench while a third lifted up the flattened bamboo sweep and began to strike him with it across the hams. After about a dozen blows Jia Zheng, not satisfied that his executioner was hitting hard enough, kicked him impatiently aside, wrested the bamboo from his grasp, and, gritting his teeth, brought it down with the utmost savagery on the places that had already been beaten.

At this point the literary gentlemen, sensing that Bao-yu was in serious danger of life and limb, came in again to remonstrate; but Jia Zheng refused to hear them.

"Ask him what he has done and then tell me if you think I should spare him," he said. "It is the encouragement of people like you that has corrupted him; and now, when things have come to this pass, you intercede for him. I suppose you would like me to wait until he commits parricide, or worse. Would you still intercede for him then?"

They could see from this reply that he was beside himself. Wasting no further time on words, they quickly withdrew and looked for someone to take a message through inside.

Lady Wang did not stop to tell Grandmother Jia when she received it. She snatched up an outer garment, pulled it about her, and, supported by a single maid, rushed off, not caring what menfolk might see her, to the outer study, bursting into it with such suddenness that the literary gentlemen and other males present were unable to avoid her.

Her entry provoked Jia Zheng to fresh transports of fury. Faster and harder fell the bamboo on the prostrate form of Bao-yu, which by now appeared to be unconscious, for when the boys holding it down relaxed their hold and fled from their Mistress's presence, it had long since ceased even to twitch. Even so Jia Zheng would have continued beating it had not Lady Wang clasped the bamboo to her bosom and prevented him.

"Enough!" said Jia Zheng. "Today you are determined, all of you, to drive me insane."

"No doubt Bao-yu deserved to be beaten," said Lady Wang tearfully, "but it is bad for you to get over-excited. Besides, you ought to have some consideration for Lady Jia. She is not at all well in this frightful heat. It may not seem to you of much consequence to kill Bao-yu, but think what the effect would be on *her*."

"Don't try that sort of talk with me!" said Jia Zheng bitterly. "Merely by fathering a monster like this I have proved myself an unfilial son; yet whenever in the past I have tried to discipline him, the rest of you have all conspired against me to protect him. Now that I have the opportunity at last, I may as well finish off what I have begun and put him down, like the vermin he is, before he can do any more damage."

So saying, he took up a rope and would have put his threat into execution, had not Lady Wang held her arms around him to prevent it.

"Of course you should discipline your son," she said, weeping, "but you have a wife too, Sir Zheng, don't forget. I am nearly fifty now and this wretched boy is the only son I have. If you insist on making an example of him, I dare not do much to dissuade you. But to kill him outright— that is deliberately to make me childless. Better strangle me first, if you are going to strangle him. Let the two of us die together. At least I shall have some support then in the world to come, if all support in this world is to be denied me!"

With these words she threw herself upon Bao-yu's body and, lifting up her voice, began weeping with noisy abandon. Jia Zheng, who had heard her with a sigh, sank into a chair and himself broke down in a fit of weeping.

Presently Lady Wang began to examine the body she was clasping. Bao-yu's face was ashen, his breathing was scarcely perceptible, and the trousers of thin green silk which clothed the lower part of his body were so soaked with blood that their colour was no longer recognizable. Feverishly she unfastened his waistband and drew them back. Everywhere, from the upper part of his buttocks down to his calves, was either raw and bloody or purplish black with bruises. Not an inch of sound flesh was to be seen. The sight made her cry out involuntarily.

"Oh my son! My unfortunate son!"

Once more she broke down into uncontrollable weeping.

Her own words reminded her of the son she had already lost, and now, with added bitterness, she began to call out his name.

"Oh, Zhu! Zhu! If only you had lived, I shouldn't have minded losing a *hundred* other sons!"

By this time news of Lady Wang's *démarche*[7] had circulated to the other

---

7. A strategically chosen course of action.

members of the inner mansion and Li Wan, Xi-feng, Ying-chun, Tan-chun and Xi-chun had come to join her. The invocation of her dead husband's name, painful to all of them, was altogether too much for Li Wan, who broke into loud sobs on hearing it. Jia Zheng himself was deeply affected, and tears as round as pumpkins rolled down both his cheeks. It was beginning to look as if they might all go on weeping there indefinitely, since no one would make a move; but just then there was a cry of "Her Old Ladyship—!" from one of the maids, interrupted by a quavering voice outside the window.

"Kill me first! You may as well kill both of us while you are about it!"

As much distressed by his mother's words as he was alarmed by her arrival, Jia Zheng hurried out to meet her. She was leaning on the shoulder of a little maid, her old head swaying from side to side with the effort of running, and panting as she ran.

Jia Zheng bowed down before her and his face assumed the semblance of a smile.

"Surely, Mother, in such hot weather as this there is no need for you to come here? If you have any instructions, you should call for me and let *me* come to *you*."

Grandmother Jia had stopped when she heard this voice and now stood panting for some moments while she regained her breath. When she spoke, her voice had an unnatural shrillness in it.

"Oh! Are you speaking to *me?*"—Yes, as a matter of fact I *have* got 'instructions,' as you put it; but as unfortunately I've never had a good son who cares for me, there's no one I can give them to."

Wounded in his most sensitive spot, Jia Zheng fell on his knees before her. The voice in which he replied to her was broken with tears.

"How can I bear it, Mother, if you speak to me like that? What I did to the boy I did for the honour of the family."

Grandmother Jia spat contemptuously.

"A single harsh word from me and you start whining that you can't bear it. How do you think Bao-yu could bear your cruel rod? And you say you've been punishing him for the honour of the family, but you just tell me this: did your own father ever punish *you* in such a way?—I think not."

She was weeping now herself.

"Don't upset yourself, Mother," said Jia Zheng, with the same forced smile. "I acted too hastily. From now on I'll never beat him again, if that's what you wish."

"Hoity-toity, keep your temper!" said Grandmother Jia. "He's your son. If you want to beat him, that's up to you. If we women are in your way, we'll leave you alone to get on with it." She turned to her attendants. "Call my carriage. Your Mistress and I and Bao-yu are going back to Nanking. We shall be leaving immediately."

The servants made a show of compliance.

"No need for you to cry," she said, turning to Lady Wang. "You love Bao-yu now that he's young, but when he's grown up and become an important official, he'll like enough forget that you're his mother. Much better force yourself not to love him now and save yourself some anguish later on."

you'd listened to me a bit in the past, it would never have come to *this*. Why, you might have been crippled for life. It doesn't bear thinking of."

Just then Bao-chai's arrival was announced by one of the maids. Since putting his trousers on again was out of the question, Aroma snatched up a lightweight coverlet and hurriedly threw it over him. Bao-chai came in carrying a large tablet of some sort of solid medicine which she instructed Aroma to pound up in wine and apply to Bao-yu's injuries in the evening.

"This is a decongestant," she said, handing it to her. "It will take away the inflammation by dispersing the bad blood in his bruises. After that, he should heal quite quickly."

She turned to Bao-yu.

"Are you feeling any better now?"

Bao-yu thanked her. "Yes," he said, he was feeling a little better, and invited her to sit down beside him. Bao-chai was relieved to see him with his eyes open and talking again. She shook her head sadly.

"If you had listened to what one said, this would never have happened. Everyone is so upset now. It isn't only Grandmother and Lady Wang, you know. Even—"

She checked herself abruptly, regretting that she had allowed her feelings to run away with her, and lowered her head, blushing. Bao-yu had sensed hidden depths of feeling in the passionate earnestness of her tone, and when she suddenly faltered and turned red, there was something so touching about the pretty air of confusion with which she dropped her head and played with the ends of her girdle, that his spirits soared and his pain was momentarily forgotten.

"What have I undergone but a few whacks of the bamboo?" he thought, "—yet already they are so sad and concerned about me! What dear, adorable, sweet, noble girls they are! Heaven knows how they would grieve for me if I were actually to die! It would be almost worth dying, just to find out. The loss of a life's ambitions would be a small price to pay, and I should be a peevish, ungrateful ghost if I did not feel proud and happy when such darling creatures were grieving for me."

He was roused from this reverie by the sound of Bao-chai's voice asking Aroma what it was that had moved his father to such violent anger against him. Aroma's low reply, in which she merely repeated what Tealeaf had told her, was his first inkling of the part that Jia Huan had played in his misfortune. Her mention of Xue Pan's involvement, however, made him apprehensive that Bao-chai might feel embarrassed, and he hastily interrupted Aroma to prevent her from saying more.

"Old Xue would never do a thing like that," he said. "It's silly to make these wild assertions."

Bao-chai knew that it was out of respect for her feelings that he was silencing Aroma, and she wondered at his considerateness.

"What delicacy of feeling!" she thought, "—after so terrible a beating and in spite of all the pain, to be still able to worry about the possibility of someone else's being offended! If only you could apply some of that thoughtfulness to the more important things of life, my friend, you would make my Uncle so happy; and then perhaps these awful things would never happen. And when all's said and done, this sensibility on my behalf is rather wasted. Do you *really* think I know my own brother so little that I am unaware of his unruly nature? Nothing has ever been allowed to stand in the way of Pan's desires. Look at the terrible trouble he made for you that time over Qin Zhong. That was a long time ago, and I am sure he has got much worse since then."

Those were her thoughts, but what she said was:

"There's really no need to look around for someone to blame. If you ask me, the mere fact that Cousin Bao has been willing to keep such company was in itself quite enough to make Uncle angry. And though my brother can be very tactless and may well have let something out about Cousin Bao in the course of conversation, I'm sure it wouldn't have been deliberate trouble-making on his part. In the first place, it is, after all, true, what he is supposed to have said: Cousin Bao *has* been going around with that actor. And in the second place, my brother simply hasn't got it in him to be discreet. You have lived all your life with sensitive, considerate people like Cousin Bao, my dear Aroma. You have never had to deal with a crude, forthright person like my brother—someone who says whatever comes into his head with complete disregard for the consequences."

When Bao-yu cut short her remarks about Xue Pan, Aroma had realized at once that she was being tactless and inwardly prayed that Bao-chai had not taken exception to them. To her, therefore, these words of Bao-chai's were a source of tongue-tied embarrassment. Bao-yu, on the other hand, could see in them only the refusal of a frank and generous nature to admit deviousness in others and a sensibility capable of matching and responding to his own. As a consequence his spirits soared yet higher. He was about to say something, but Bao-chai rose to her feet and anticipated him.

"I'll come and see you again tomorrow. You must rest now and give yourself a chance to get well. I've given Aroma something to make a lotion with. Get her to put it on for you in the evening. I can guarantee that it will hasten your recovery."

She was moving towards the door as she said this. When she was outside, Aroma hurried after her to see her off and to thank her for her trouble.

"As soon as he's better," she said, "Master Bao will come over and thank you himself, Miss."

"It's nothing at all," said Bao-chai, turning back to her with a smile. "Do tell him to rest properly, though, and not to brood. And if there's anything at all he wants, just quietly come round to my place for it. Don't go bothering Lady Jia or Lady Wang or any of the others, in case my uncle gets to hear of it. It probably wouldn't matter at the time, but it might do later on, next time there is any trouble."

With that she left, and Aroma turned back into the courtyard, her heart full of gratitude for Bao-chai's kindness. Re-entering Bao-yu's room, she found him lying back quietly, plunged in thought. From the look of it, he was already half asleep. Tiptoeing out again, she went off to wash her hair.

But it was difficult for Bao-yu to lie quietly for very long. The pain in his buttocks was like the stabbing and pricking of knives and needles and there was a burning sensation in them as if he were being grilled over a fire, so that the slightest movement made him cry out. Already it was growing late. Aroma appeared to have gone away, but two or three maids were still in attendance. As there was nothing that they could do for him, he told them that they might go off and prepare themselves for the night, provided that they remained within call. The maids accordingly withdrew, leaving him on his own.

He had dozed off. The shadowy form of Jiang Yu-han had come in to tell him of his capture by the Prince of Zhong-shun's men, followed, shortly after, by Golden, who gave him a tearful account of how she had drowned herself. In his half-dreaming, half-awake state he was having the greatest difficulty in attending to what they were saying, when suddenly he felt someone pushing him and became dimly aware of a sound of weeping in his ear. He gave a start. Fully awake now, he opened his eyes. It was Lin Dai-yu. Suspecting this, too, to be a dream, he raised his head to look. A pair of eyes swollen like peaches met his own, and a face that was glistening with tears. It was Dai-yu all right, no doubt about that. He would have looked longer, but the strain of raising himself was causing such excruciating pain in his nether parts, that he fell back again with a groan. The groan was followed by a sigh.

"Now what have *you* come for?" he said. "The sun's not long set and the ground must still be very hot underfoot. You could still get a heatstroke at this time of day, and that would be a fine how-do-you-do. Actually, in spite of the beating, I don't feel very much pain. This fuss I make is put on to fool the others. I'm hoping they'll spread the word around outside how badly I've been hurt, so that Father gets to hear of it. It's all shamming, really. You mustn't be taken in by it."

Dai-yu's sobbing had by this time ceased to be audible; but somehow her strangled, silent weeping was infinitely more pathetic than the most clamorous grief. At that moment volumes would have been inadequate to contain the things she wanted to say to him; yet all she could get out, after struggling for some time with her choking sobs, was:

"I suppose you'll change now."

Bao-yu gave a long sigh.

"Don't worry, I shan't change. People like that are worth dying for. I wouldn't change if he killed me."

The words were scarcely out of his mouth when they heard someone outside in the courtyard saying:

"Mrs. Lian has come."

Dai-yu had no wish to see Xi-feng, and rose to her feet hurriedly.

Bao-yu seized hold of her hand.

"Now that's funny. Why should you start being afraid of *her* all of a sudden?"

She stamped with impatience.

"Look at the state my eyes are in!" she said. "I don't want them all making fun of me again."

At that Bao-yu released her hand and she bounded round to the back of the bed, slipping into the rear courtyard just as Xi-feng was entering the room from the front.

"A bit better now?" said Xi-feng. "Is there anything you feel like eating yet? If there is, tell them to come round to my place and get it."

As soon as Xi-feng had gone, Bao-yu was visited by Aunt Xue, and shortly after that by someone whom his grandmother had sent to see how he was getting on. At lighting-up time, after taking a few mouthfuls of soup, he settled down into a fitful sleep.

Just then a new group of visitors arrived, consisting of Zhou Rui's wife, Wu Xin-deng's wife, Zheng Hao-shi's wife, and those other members of the mansion's female staff who had had most to do with Bao-yu in the past and who, having heard of his beating, were anxious to see how he was. Aroma came out smiling on to the verandah to welcome them.

"You're just too late to see him, ladies," she told them in a low voice. "He's just this minute dropped off."

She ushered them into the outer room, invited them to be seated, and served them with tea. After sitting there very quietly for several minutes, they got up to take their leave, requesting Aroma as they did so that she would inform Bao-yu when he waked that they had been round to ask about him. Aroma promised to do so and showed them out. Just as she was about to go in again, an old woman arrived from Lady Wang's to say that "Her Ladyship would like to see one of Master Bao's people." After reflecting for a moment, Aroma turned to the house and called softly to Skybright, Musk and Ripple inside.

"Her Ladyship wants to see someone, so I'm going over. Stay indoors and keep an eye on things while I'm away. I shan't be long."

Then she followed the old woman out of the Garden and round to Lady Wang's apartment in the central courtyard. She found Lady Wang sitting on a cane summer-bed and fanning herself with a palm-leaf fan. She appeared not entirely pleased when she saw that it was Aroma.

"You could have sent one of the others," she said. "There was no need for *you* to come and leave him unattended."

Aroma smiled reassuringly.

"Master Bao has just settled down for the night, Madam. If he *should* want anything, the others are nowadays quite capable of looking after him on their own. Your Ladyship has no need to worry. I thought I had better come myself and not send one of the others, in case Your Ladyship had something important to tell us. I was afraid that if I sent one of the others, they might not understand what you wanted."

"I have nothing in particular to tell you," said Lady Wang. "I merely wanted to ask about my son. How is the pain now?"

"Much better since I put on some of the lotion that Miss Bao brought for him," said Aroma. "It was so bad before that he couldn't lie still, but now he's sleeping quite soundly, so you can tell it must be better than it was."

"Has he had anything to eat yet?" said Lady Wang.

"He had a few sips of some soup Her Old Ladyship sent," said Aroma, "but that's all he would take. He kept complaining that he felt dry. He wanted me to give him plum bitters to drink, but of course that's an astringent, and I thought to myself that as he'd just had a beating and not been allowed to cry out during it, a lot of hot blood and hot poison must have been driven inwards and still be collected round his heart, and if he were to drink some of that stuff, it might stir them up and bring on a serious illness, so I talked him out of it. After a lot of persuading, I got him to take some rose syrup instead, that I mixed up in water for him; but after only half a cup of it he said it tasted sickly and he couldn't get it down."

"Oh dear, I wish you'd told me sooner," said Lady Wang. "We were sent some bottles of flavouring the other day that I could have let you have. As a matter of fact I *was* going to send him some of them, but then I thought that if I did they would probably only get wasted, so I didn't. If he can't manage the rose syrup, I can easily give you a few of them to take back with you. You need only mix a teaspoonful of essence in a cupful of water. The flavours are quite delicious." She called Suncloud to her. "Fetch me a few of those bottles of flavouring essence that were sent us the other day."

"Two will be enough," said Aroma, "otherwise it will only get wasted. If we run out, I can always come back for more later."

Suncloud was gone for a considerable time. Eventually she returned with two little glass bottles, each about three inches high, which she handed to Aroma. They had screw-on silver tops and yellow labels. One of them was labelled "Essence of Cassia Flower" and the other one "Essence of Roses."

"What tiny little bottles!" said Aroma. "They can't hold very much. I suppose the stuff inside them must be very precious."

"It was made specially for the Emperor," said Lady Wang. "That's what the yellow labels mean. Haven't you seen labels like that before? Mind you look after them and don't let the stuff in them get wasted."

Aroma promised to be careful and began to go.

"Just a minute!" said Lady Wang. "I've thought of something else that I wanted to ask you."

Aroma returned. Lady Wang first glanced about her to make sure that no one else was in the room, then she said:

"I think I heard someone say that Bao-yu's beating today was because of something that Huan had said to Sir Zheng. I suppose *you* don't happen to have heard anything about that?"

"No. I haven't heard anything about *that*," said Aroma. "What *I* heard was that it was because Master Bao had been going around with one of Prince Somebody-or-other's players and the Master was told about it by someone who called."

Lady Wang nodded her head mysteriously.

"Yes, that was one of the reasons. But there was another reason as well."

"I really know nothing about any other reason, Your Ladyship," said Aroma. She dropped her head and hesitated a moment before going on. "I wonder if I might be rather bold and say something very outspoken to Your Ladyship? Really and truly—" She faltered.

"Please go on."

"I will if Your Ladyship will promise not to be angry with me."

"That's all right," said Lady Wang. "Just tell me what you have to say."

"Well, really and truly," said Aroma, "Master Bao *needed* punishing. If the Master didn't keep an eye on him, there's no knowing *what* he mightn't get up to."

"My child," said Lady Wang with a warmth rarely seen in her, "those are exactly my own sentiments. How clever of you to have understood! Of course, I know perfectly well that Bao-yu is in need of discipline; and anyone who saw how strict I used to be with Mr. Zhu would realize that I am capable of exercising it. But I have my reasons. A woman of fifty cannot expect to bear any more children and Bao-yu is now the only son I have. He is not a very strong boy; and his Grannie dotes on him. I daren't *risk* being strict. I daren't risk losing another son. I daren't risk angering Her Old Ladyship and upsetting the whole household. I do once in a while have it out with him: but though I have argued and pleaded and wept, it doesn't do any good. He *seems* all right at the time, but he'll be just the same again a short while afterwards and I always know that I have failed to reach him. I am afraid he *has* to suffer before he can learn—but suppose it's too much for him?—suppose he doesn't get over *this* beating? What will become of *me?*"

She began to cry.

Seeing her mistress so distressed, Aroma herself was affected and began to cry too.

"I can understand Your Ladyship being so upset," she said, "when he's your own son. Even we servants that have been with him for a few years get worried about him. The most that *we* can ever hope for is to do our duty and get by without too much trouble—but even *that* won't be possible if he goes on the way he has been doing. I'm always telling him to change his ways. Every day—every hour—I tell him. But it's no use; he won't listen. Of course, if these people *will* make so much fuss of him, you can hardly blame him for going round with them—though it does make our job more difficult. But now that Your Ladyship has spoken like this, it puts me in mind of something that's been worrying me which I should like to have asked Your Ladyship's advice about, only I was afraid you might take it amiss, and then not only should I have spoken to no purpose, but I should leave myself without even a grave to lie in . . ."

It was evident to Lady Wang that what she was struggling to get out was a matter of some consequence.

"What is it you want to tell me, my child?" she said kindly. "I've heard a lot of people praising you recently, and I confess that I assumed it must be because you took special pains in serving Bao-yu or in making yourself agreeable to other people—little things of that sort. But I see that I was wrong. These are not at all little things that you have been talking about. What you have said so far makes very good sense and entirely accords with my own opinion of the matter. So if you have anything to tell me, I should like to hear it. But I must ask you not to discuss it with anyone else."

"All I really wanted to ask," said Aroma, "was if Your Ladyship could advise me how later on we can somehow or other contrive to get Master Bao moved back outside the Garden."

Lady Wang looked startled and clutched Aroma's hand in some alarm.

"I hope Bao-yu hasn't been doing something dreadful with one of the girls?"

"Oh no, Your Ladyship, please don't suspect that!" said Aroma hurriedly. "That wasn't my meaning at all. It's just that—if you'll allow me to say so—Master Bao and the young ladies are beginning to grow up now, and though they are all cousins, there is the difference of sex between them, which makes it very awkward sometimes when they are all living together, especially in the case of Miss Lin and Miss Bao, who aren't even of the same clan. One can't help feeling uneasy. Even to outsiders it looks like a very strange sort of family. They say 'where nothing happens, imagination is busiest,' and I'm sure lots of unaccountable misfortunes begin when some innocent little thing we did unthinkingly gets misconstrued in someone else's imagination and reported as something terrible. We just have to be on our guard against that sort of thing happening—especially when Master Bao has such a peculiar character, as Your Ladyship knows, and spends all his time with girls. He only has to make the tiniest slip in an unguarded moment, and whether he really did anything or not, with so many people about—and some of them no better than they should be—there is sure to be scandal. For you know what some of these people are like, Your Ladyship. If they feel well-disposed towards you, they'll make you out to be a saint; but if they're not, then Heaven help you! If Master Bao lives to be spoken well of, we can count ourselves lucky; but the way things are, it only needs someone to breathe a word of scandal and—I say nothing of what will happen to us servants—it's of no consequence if *we*'re all chopped up for mincemeat—but what's more important, Master Bao's reputation will be destroyed for life and all the care and worry Your Ladyship and Sir Zheng have had on his account will have been wasted. I know Your Ladyship is very busy and can't be expected to think of everything, and I probably shouldn't have thought of this myself, but once I *had* thought of it, it seemed to me that it would be wrong of me not to tell Your Ladyship, and it's been preying on my mind ever since. The only reason I haven't mentioned it before is because I was afraid Your Ladyship might be angry with me."

What Aroma had just been saying about misconstructions and scandals so exactly fitted what had in fact happened in the case of Golden that for a moment Lady Wang was quite taken aback. But on reflection she felt nothing but love and gratitude for this humble servant-girl who had shown so much solicitude on her behalf.

"It is very perceptive of you, my dear, to have thought it all out so carefully," she said. "I have, of course, thought about this matter myself, but other things have put it from my mind, and what you have just said has reminded me. It is most thoughtful of you. You are a very, very good girl—Well, you may go now. I think I now know what to do. There is just one thing before you go, though. Now that you have spoken to me like this, I am going to place Bao-yu entirely in your hands. Be very careful with him, won't you? Remember that anything you do for him you will be doing also for me. You will find that I am not ungrateful."

Aroma stood for a moment with bowed head, weighing the import of these words. Then she said:

"I will do what Your Ladyship has asked me to the utmost of my ability."

She left the apartment slowly and made her way back to Green Delights, pondering as she went. When she arrived, Bao-yu had just woken up, so she told him about the flavourings. He was pleased and made her mix some for him straight away. It was quite delicious. He kept thinking about Dai-yu and wanted to send someone over to see her, but he was afraid that Aroma would disapprove, so, as a means of getting her out of the way, he sent her over to Bao-chai's place to borrow a book. As soon as she had gone, he summoned Skybright.

"I want you to go to Miss Lin's for me," he said. "Just see what she's doing, and if she asks about me, tell her I'm all right."

"I can't go rushing in there bald-headed without a reason," said Skybright. "You'd better give me *some* kind of a message, just to give me an excuse for going there."

"I have none to give," said Bao-yu.

"Well, give me something to take, then," said Skybright, "or think of something I can ask her for. Otherwise it will look so silly."

Bao-yu thought for a bit and then, reaching out and picking up two of his old handkerchiefs, he tossed them towards her with a smile.

"All right. Tell her I said you were to give her these."

"That's an odd sort of present!" said Skybright. "What's she going to do with a pair of your old handkerchiefs? Most likely she'll think you're making fun of her and get upset again."

"No she won't," said Bao-yu. "She'll understand."

Skybright deemed it pointless to argue, so she picked up the handkerchiefs and went off to the Naiad's House. Little Delicate, who was hanging some towels out to dry on the verandah railings, saw her enter the courtyard and attempted to wave her away.

"She's gone to bed."

Skybright ignored her and went on inside. The lamps had not been lit and the room was in almost total darkness. The voice of Dai-yu, lying awake in bed, spoke to her out of the shadows.

"Who is it?"

"Skybright."

"What do you want?"

"Master Bao has sent me with some handkerchiefs, Miss."

Dai-yu seemed to hesitate. She found the gift puzzling and was wondering what it could mean.

"I suppose they must be very good ones," she said. "Probably someone gave them to him. Tell him to keep them and give them to somebody else. I have no use for them just now myself."

Skybright laughed.

"They're not new ones, Miss. They're two of his old, everyday ones."

This was even more puzzling. Dai-yu thought very hard for some moments. Then suddenly, in a flash, she understood.

"Put them down. You may go now."

Skybright did as she was bid and withdrew. All the way back to Green Delights she tried to make sense of what had happened, but it continued to mystify her.

Meanwhile the message that eluded Skybright had thrown Dai-yu into a turmoil of conflicting emotions.

"I feel so happy," she thought, "that in the midst of his own affliction he has been able to grasp the cause of all *my* trouble.

"And yet at the same time I am sad," she thought; "because how do I know that my trouble will end in the way I want it to?

"Actually, I feel rather amused," she thought. "Fancy his sending a pair of old handkerchiefs like that! Suppose I hadn't understood what he was getting at?

"But I feel alarmed that he should be sending presents to me in secret.

"Oh, and I feel so ashamed when I think how I am forever crying and quarrelling," she thought, "and all the time he has understood! . . ."

And her thoughts carried her this way and that, until the ferment of excitement within her cried out to be expressed. Careless of what the maids might think, she called for a lamp, sat herself down at her desk, ground some ink, softened her brush, and proceeded to compose the following quatrains, using the handkerchiefs themselves to write on:

1

Seeing my idle tears, you ask me why
These foolish drops fall from my teeming eye:
Then know, your gift, being by the merfolk[8] made,
In merman's currency must be repaid.

2

Jewelled drops by day in secret sorrow shed
Or, in the night-time, in my wakeful bed,
Lest sleeve or pillow they should spot or stain,
Shall on these gifts shower down their salty rain.

3

Yet silk preserves but ill the Naiad's tears:
Each salty trace of them fast disappears.
Only the speckled bamboo[9] stems that grow
Outside the window still her tear-marks show.

She had only half-filled the second handkerchief and was preparing to write another quatrain, when she became aware that her whole body was burning hot all over and her cheeks were afire. Going over to the dressing-table, she removed the brocade cover from the mirror and peered into it.

"Hmn! 'Brighter than the peach-flower's hue,' " she murmured complacently to the flushed face that stared out at her from the glass, and, little imagining that what she had been witnessing was the first symptom of a serious illness, went back to bed, her mind full of handkerchiefs.

* * *

---

8. Mythical beings who live in the sea. They were famous for the fine fabric they wove, and when they wept, their tears formed pearls.   9. This bamboo was supposed to have gotten its spots by the tears once shed on it by the two goddesses of the Hsiang River, who were lamenting the death of their husband, the sage-king Shun.

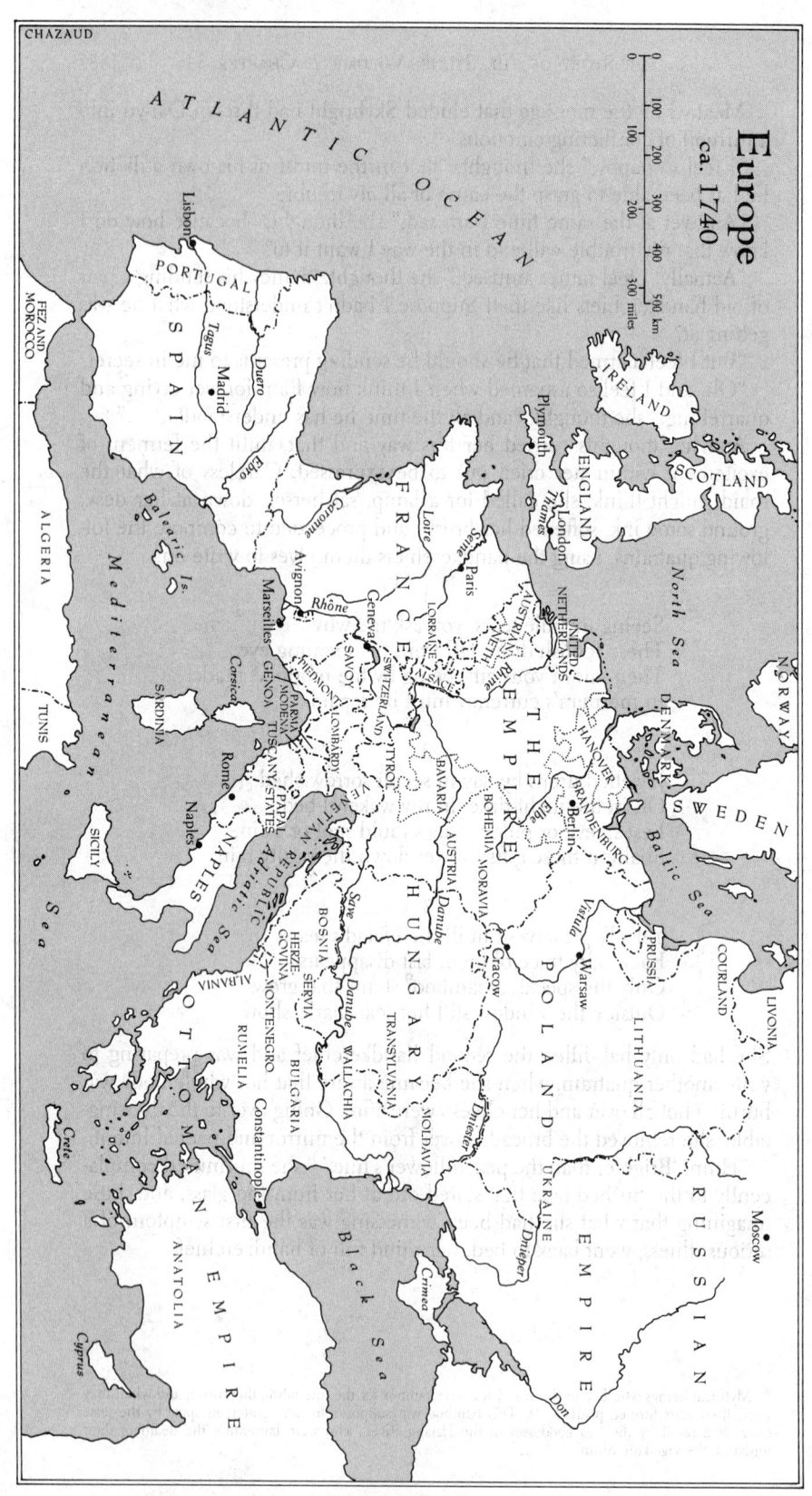

CHAZAUD

Europe
ca. 1740

The Enlightenment in Europe

"I wonder if it is not better to try to correct and moderate men's passions than to try to suppress them altogether." The sentence, from Jean-Baptiste Molière's 1669 preface to his biting comedy about religious hypocrisy, *Tartuffe*, captures something of the anxiety and the optimism of a period for which subsequent generations have found no adequate single designation. "The Neo-Classic Period," "The Age of Reason," "The Enlightenment": such labels suggest, accurately enough, that thinkers between (roughly) 1660 and 1770 emphasized the powers of the mind and turned to the Roman past for models. But these terms do not convey the awareness of limitation expressed in Molière's sentence, an awareness as typical of the historical period to which the sentence belongs as is the expressed aspiration toward correctness and moderation. The effort to correct and moderate the passions might prove less foolhardy than the effort to suppress them, but both endeavors would involve human nature's struggle with itself, a struggle necessarily perpetual. "On life's vast ocean diversely we sail, / Reason the card, but Passion is the gale," Alexander Pope's *Essay on Man* (1733) pointed out. One could hope to steer with reason as guide only by remembering the omnipresence of passion as impetus. Eighteenth-century thinkers analyzed and eighteenth-century imaginative writers dramatized intricate interchanges and conflicts between these aspects of our selves.

The drama of reason and passion played itself out in society, the system of association human beings had devised partly to control passion and institutionalize reason. Structured on the basis of a rigid class system, the traditional social order began to face incipient challenges in the eighteenth century as new commerce generated new wealth, whose possessors felt entitled to claim their own share of social power. The threat to established hierarchies extended even to kings. Thomas Hobbes, in *Leviathan* (1651), had argued for the secular origins of the social contract. Kings arise, he said, not by divine ordinance but out of human need; they exist to prevent what would otherwise be a war of all on all. Monarchs still presided over European nations in the eighteenth century, but with less security than before. The English had executed their ruler in 1649; the French would perform another royal decapitation before the end of the eighteenth century. The mortality of kings had become a political fact, a fact implying the conceivable instability of the social order over which kings presided.

A sense of the contingencies of the human condition impinged on many minds in a world where men and women no longer automatically assumed God's benign supervision of human affairs or the primacy of their own Christian obligations. The fierce strife between Protestants and Catholics lapsed into relative quiescence by the end of the seventeenth century, but the Protestant English deposed their king in 1688 because of his marriage to a Catholic princess and their fear of a Catholic dynasty; and in France Louis XIV in 1685 revoked the Edict of Nantes, which had granted religious toleration to Protestants. The overt English struggle of Cavaliers and Puritans ended with the restoration of Charles II to the throne in 1660. Religious differences now became translated into divisions of social class and of political conviction—divisions no less powerful for lacking the claim of supernatural authority. To England, the eighteenth century brought two unsuccessful but bitterly divisive rebellions on behalf of the deposed Stuart succession as well as the cataclysmic American Revolution. In France, the century ended in revolution. Throughout the eighteenth century, wars erupted over succession to European thrones and over nationalistic claims, although no fighting took place on such a scale as that of the devastating Thirty Years' War (1618–48). On the whole, divisions *within* nations (in France and England) assumed greater importance than those between nations.

Philosophers now turned their attention to defining the possibilities and limitations of the human position in the material universe. "I think, therefore I am," René Descartes pronounced, declaring the mind the source of individual being. But this idea proved less reassuring than it initially seemed. Subsequent philosophers, exploring the concept's implications, realized the possibility of the mind's isolation in its own constructions. Perhaps, Wilhelm Leibnitz suggested, no real communication can take place between one consciousness and another. Possibly, according to David Hume, the idea of individual identity itself derives from the mind's efforts to manufacture continuity out of discontinuous memories. Philosophers pointed out the impossibility of knowing for sure even the reality of the external world: the only certainty is that we think it exists. If contemplating the nature of human reason thus led philosophic skeptics to restrict severely the area of what we can know with certainty, other contemplations induced other thinkers to insist on the existence, beyond ourselves, of an entirely rational physical and moral universe. Isaac Newton's demonstrations of the order of natural law greatly encouraged this line of thought. The fullness and complexity of the perceived physical world testified, as many wrote, to the sublime rationality of a divine plan. The Planner, however, did not necessarily supervise the day-to-day operations of His arrangements; He might rather, as a popular analogy had it, resemble the watchmaker who winds the watch and leaves it running.

Deism, evoking a depersonalized deity, insisted on the logicality of the universe and encouraged the separation of ethics from religion. Ethics, too, could be understood as a matter of reason. "He that thinks reasonably must think morally," Samuel Johnson observed, echoing the noble horses Jonathan Swift had imagined in the fourth book of *Gulliver's Travels*. But such statements expressed wish more than perception. Awareness of the passions continued to haunt thinkers yearning for rationality. Swift's Houyhnhnms, creatures of his imagination, might achieve flawless rationality—with accompanying wisdom and benevolence—but actual human beings could only dream of such an ideal, while experiencing—as men and women have always experienced—the confusion of conflicting impulses often at war with the dictates of reason.

Although the social, economic, and political organizations in which the thinkers of this period participated hardly resemble our own, the questions they raised about the human condition have plagued the Western mind ever since. Though we no longer locate the solution to all problems in an unattainable ideal of "reason," we too struggle to find the limits of certainty, have problems of identity and isolation, and recognize the impossibility of altogether controlling internal forces now identified as "the unconscious" rather than "the passions." But we confront such issues largely from the position of isolated individuals. In the late seventeenth and early eighteenth centuries, in England and on the Continent, the sense of obligation to society had far more power than it possesses today. Society provided the standards and the instruments of control that might help to counter the tumult of individual impulse.

SOCIETY

Society, in this period, designates both a powerful idea and an omnipresent fact of experience. Prerevolutionary French society, like English society in the same period, depended on clear hierarchical structures. The literature of both countries issued from a small cultural elite, writing for others of their kind and assuming the rightness of their own knowledge of how people should feel and behave.

For the English and French upper classes, as for the ancient Romans they admired, public life mattered more than private. At one level, the *public* designated the realms of government and diplomacy: occupations allowing and encouraging oratory, frequent travel, negotiation, the exercise of political and economic power. In this sense, the public world belonged entirely to men, who determined the course of government, defined the limits of the important, enforced their sense of the fitness of things. By another definition, *public* might refer to the life of formal social intercourse. In France, such social life took place often in "salons," gatherings to engage in intellectual as well as frivolous conversation. Women typically presided over these salons, thus declaring both their intellectual authority and their capacity to combine high thought with high style. Until rather late in the eighteenth century, on the other hand, England allowed women no such commanding position; there, men controlled intellectual as well as political discourse. The male voice, accordingly, dominated English literature until the development of the novel provided new opportunities for women writers and for the articulation of domestic values.

Both the larger and the more limited "public" spheres depended on well-defined codes of behavior. The discrepancy between the forms of self-presentation dictated by these codes and the operations such forms might disguise—a specific form of the reason-passion conflict—provides one of the insistent themes of French and English literature in the century beginning around 1660. Molière, examining religious sham; Swift, lashing the English for institutionalized hypocrisy; Voltaire, sending a naive fictional protagonist to encounter the world's inconsistencies of profession and practice—such writers call attention to the deceptiveness and the possible misuses of social norms as well as to their necessity. None suggests that the codes themselves are at fault. If people lived up to what they profess, the world would be a better place; ideally, they would modify not their standards of behavior but their tendency to hide behind them.

We in the twentieth century have become accustomed to the notion of the sacredness of the individual, encouraged to believe in the high value of expressiveness, originality, specialness. Eighteenth-century writers, on the other hand, assumed the superior importance of the social group and of shared opinion. "Expressiveness," in their view, should provide an instrument for articulating the will of the community, not the eccentric desires of individuals. The mad astronomer in Johnson's *Rasselas*, who as a result of isolation develops an exaggerated sense of his own power, epitomizes the danger of allowing oneself to believe too readily in the self's specialness. Society implies subordination: not only class hierarchy but individual submission to the good of the group.

French writers of imaginative literature often used domestic situations as ways to examine larger problems. Marriage, an institution at once social and personal, provides a useful image for human relationship as social and emotional fact. The developing eighteenth-century novel, in England and France alike, would assume marriage as the normal goal for men and women; Molière and Racine, writing before the turn of the century, examine economic, psychological, moral, and social implications of specific imagined marriages. The sexual alliances of rulers, Racine's subject in *Phaedra*, have literal consequences far beyond the individuals involved. Molière evokes a private family to suggest how professed sentiment can obscure the operations of ambition. Both understand marriage as social micro-cosm, a society in miniature, not merely as a structure for fulfillment of personal desire.

In England, writers in genres other than the novel typically focus their attention on a broader panorama. Pope and Swift, like Voltaire satirists of the human scene, consider varied operations of social law and pressure. In *The Rape of the Lock*, Pope uses a card party to epitomize social structures. Swift fantasizes the horrifying consequences of venture capitalism in the processing of infants for food. Voltaire's world tourists witness and participate in a vast range of sobering experience. In general, women fill subordinate roles in the harsh social environments evoked by these satiric works. Johnson praised Shakespeare because he did not make love the only spring of action; other passions, Johnson suggested, more powerfully motivate human activity. As the evoked social scene widens, erotic love plays a less important part and the position of women becomes increasingly insignificant: women's sphere is the home, and home life matters less than does public life. It is perhaps not irrelevant to note that no work in this section (with the horrifying exception of *A Modest Proposal*) describes or evokes children. Only in adulthood do people assume social responsibility; only then do they provide interesting sub-stance for social commentary.

NATURE

Society establishes one locus of reality for eighteenth-century thinkers, although they understand it as a human construct. Nature comprises another assumed mea-sure of the real. The meanings of the word *nature* vary greatly in eighteenth-century usage, but two large senses are most relevant to the works here included: nature as the inherent order of things, including the physical universe, hence evidence of the deity's plan, and nature meaning specifically *human* nature.

Despite their pervasive awareness of natural contingency (vividly dramatized by Voltaire among others, in his account of the disastrous Lisbon earthquake), writers of this period locate their sense of permanence particularly in the idea of nature. The notion of a permanent, divinely ordained natural order offers a good deal of comfort to those aware of flaws in actual social arrangements. It embodies an ideal of harmony, of order in variety, which, although it cannot be fully grasped by human intelligence, can yet provide a model for social complexities. It posits a *system*, a structure of relationships that at some theoretical level necessarily makes sense; thus it provides an assumed substructure of rationality for all experience of irrationality. It supplies a means of valuing all appearances of the natural world: every flower, every minnow, has meaning beyond itself, as part of the great pattern. The ardency with which the period's thinkers cling to belief in such a pattern suggests once more a pervasive anxiety about what human reason could not do. Human beings create a vision of something at once sublimely reasonable and beyond reason's grasp to reassure themselves that the limits of the rational need not coincide with the limits of the human.

The permanence of the conceptual natural order corresponds to that of human nature, as conceived in the eighteenth century. Human nature, it was generally believed, remains in all times and places the same. Thus Racine could re-present a fable from Greek tragedy, using classical setting and characters, with complete assurance that his imagining of Phaedra's conflict and suffering would speak to his contemporaries without falsifying the classical original. Despite social divergen-cies, fundamental aspects of personality do in fact remain constant: all people hope and fear, feel envy and lust, possess the capacity to reason. All suffer loss, all face death. Thinkers of the Enlightenment emphasized these common aspects of humanity far more than they considered cultural divergencies. Readers and writers alike could draw on this conviction about universality. It provided a test of excellence: if an author's imagining of character failed to conform to what eighteenth-century readers understood as human nature, a work might be securely judged inadequate. Conversely, the idea of a constant human nature held out the hope of longevity for writers who successfully evoked it. Moral philosophers could define human obligation and possibility in the conviction that they too wrote for all time; ethical standards would never change. Like the vision of order in the physical universe, the notion of constancy in human nature provided bedrock for an increasingly secularized society.

CONVENTION AND AUTHORITY

Eighteenth-century society, like all societies, operated, and its literary figures wrote, on the basis of established conventions. Manners are social conventions: agreed-on systems of behavior declared appropriate for specific situations. Guides to manners proliferated in the eighteenth century, expressing a widespread sense that commitment to decorum helped to preserve society's important standards. Literary conventions—agreed-on systems of verbal behavior—served comparable purposes in another sphere. Like established codes of manners, such conventions declare continuity between present and past.

The literary conventions of the past, like outmoded manners or styles of dress, may strike the twentieth-century reader as antiquated and artificial. A woman who curtsied in a modern living room, a man who appeared in a wig, would seem to us ridiculous, even insane; but of course a young woman in jeans would affect our predecessors as equally perverse. The plaintive lyrics of current country music, say, are governed by highly restrictive conventions that affect their hearers as "natural" only because they are so familiar. Eighteenth-century writers had at their disposal an established set of conventions for every traditional literary genre. As the repetitive rhythms of the country ballad tell listeners what to expect, these literary conventions provided readers with clues about the kind of experience they could anticipate in a given poem or play.

Underlying all specific conventions was the classical assumption that literature existed to delight and to instruct its readers. The various genres represented in this period embody such belief in literature's dual function. Stage comedy and tragedy, the early novel, satire in prose and verse, didactic poetry, the philosophic tale: each form developed its own set of devices for involving audiences and readers in situations requiring moral choice as well as for creating pleasure. The insistence in drama on unity of time and place (stage action occupying no more time than its representation, with no change of scene) exemplifies one such set, intended to facilitate in audiences the kind of belief encouraging maximum emotional and moral effect. The elevated diction of the Pope's *Essay on Man* ("Mark how it mounts, to Man's imperial race, / From the green myriads in the peopled grass") and the two-dimensional characters of Voltaire's tales, although unfamiliar to us, provide signals about authorial intention and about anticipated reader response.

One dominant convention of twentieth-century poetry and prose is something we call "realism." In fiction, verse, and drama, writers often attempt to convey the literal feel of experience, the shape in which events actually occur in the world, the way people really talk. Racine, Pope, and Voltaire pursued no such goal. Despite their concern with permanent patterns of thought and feeling, they employed deliberate and obvious forms of artifice as modes of emphasis and of indirection. The sonorous verse in which Racine's characters reflect on their passions, for example ("I hate my life, abominate my lust; / Longing by death to rescue my good name / And hide my black love from the light of day"), embodies a form of stylization. Artistic transformation of life, the period's writers believed, involves the imposition of formal order on the endless flux of event and feeling. The formalities of this literature constitute part of its meaning: its statement that what experience shows as unstable, art makes stable.

Reliance on convention as a mode of control expressed an aspect of the period's constant effort toward elusive stability. The classical past, for many, provided an emblem of that stability, a standard of permanence. But some felt a problem inherent in the high valuing of the past, a problem dramatized by the so-called quarrel of Ancients and Moderns in England and in France. At stake in this controversy was the value of permanence as against the value of change. Proponents of the Ancients believed that the giants of Greece and Rome had not only established standards applicable to all subsequent accomplishment but provided models of achievement never to be excelled. Homer wrote the first great epics; subsequent endeavors in the same genre could only imitate him. Innovation came when it came by making the old new, as Pope makes a woman's dressing for conquest new by comparing it to the arming of Achilles. Moderns who valued originality for its own sake, who multiplied worthless publications, who claimed significance for what time had not tested thereby testified to their own inadequacies and their foolish pride.

Those proud to be Moderns, on the other hand, held that men (possibly even women) standing on the shoulders of the Ancients could see farther than their predecessors. The new conceivably exceeded in value the old; one might discover flaws even in revered figures of the classic past. Not everything had yet been accomplished; fresh possibilities remained always possible. This view, of course, corresponds to one widely current since the eighteenth century, but it did not triumph easily: many powerful thinkers of the late seventeenth and early eighteenth century adhered to the more conservative position.

Also at issue in this debate was the question of authority. What position should one assume who hoped to write and be read? Did authority reside only in tradition? If so, one must write in classical forms, rely on classical allusions. Until late in the eighteenth century, virtually all important writers attempted to ally themselves with the authority of tradition, declaring themselves part of a community extending through time as well as space. The problems of authority became particularly important in connection with satire, a popular Enlightenment form. Satire involves criticism of vice and folly; Molière, Swift, and Voltaire at least on occasion wrote in the satiric mode. To establish the right to criticize fellow men and women, the satirist must establish a rhetorical ascendancy such as the pulpit gives the priest—an ascendancy most readily obtained by at least implicit alliance with literary and moral tradition. The satirist, like the moral philosopher, cannot afford to seem idiosyncratic when prescribing and condemning the behavior of others. The fact that satire flourished so richly in this period suggests another version of the central conflict between reason and passion, the forces of stability and of instability. In its heightened description of the world (people eating babies, young women initiating epic battles over the loss of a lock of hair), satire calls attention to the powerful presence of the irrational, opposing to that presence the clarity of the satirist's own claim to reason and tradition. As it chastises human beings for their eruptions of passion, urging resistance and control, satire reminds its readers of the universality of the irrational as well as of opposition to it. The effort "to correct and moderate men's [and women's] passions," that great theme of the Enlightenment, can equally generate hope or despair: opposed moods richly expressed throughout this period.

FURTHER READING

Useful books on the Enlightenment include, for English background, H. Nicolson, *The Age of Reason: The Eighteenth Century* (1960); and for an opposed view,

D. Greene, *The Age of Exuberance: Backgrounds to Eighteenth-Century English Literature* (1970). For the intellectual and social situation in France, see L. Crocker, *An Age of Crisis: Man and World in Eighteenth-Century French Thought* (1959); L. Gossman, *French Society and Culture: Background for Eighteenth-Century Literature* (1972); and A. Adam, *Grandeur and Illusion: French Literature and Society, 1600–1715* (1972). An excellent treatment of the period's literature in England is M. Price, *To the Palace of Wisdom: Studies in Order and Energy from Dryden to Blake* (1964). M. Williamson, *Raising Their Voices, 1650–1750* (1990), discusses women's contributions to the English Enlightenment. A good introduction to the intellectual situation of eighteenth-century England is J. Sambrook, *The Eighteenth Century: The Intellectual and Cultural Context of English Literature, 1700–1789* (1986).

TEXTS	CONTEXTS
	1660 Civil War in England ends with Charles II's ascension to the throne (the "Restoration")
1664 Jean-Baptiste Poquelin Molière, *Tartuffe*	
1665 François de La Rochefoucauld, *Reflections*	
	1666 Isaac Newton uncovers laws of gravitation • London, already stricken by plague, is destroyed in the Great Fire and subsequently rebuilt in more orderly fashion
1667 Publication of John Milton's *Paradise Lost*	
1677 Jean Racine, *Phaedra*	
1678 Marie de la Vergne de La Fayette, *The Princess of Clèves*	
1690 John Locke, *Essay Concerning Human Understanding*, establishes psychological and philosophic principles of British philosophical empiricism	
1691 Sor Juana Inés de la Cruz, *Reply to Sor Filotea de la Cruz*	
	1694 Bank of England is chartered, forerunner of modern national banks and treasury systems; London stock exchange follows in 1698
	1697 Russian czar Peter the Great visits Western Europe and England, resolves to Westernize Russia
	1707 United Kingdom of Great Britain formed by union of England and Scotland
	1709 Up to 100,000 slaves a year cross the Atlantic, 20,000 to Britain's Caribbean colonies alone
1710 First British copyright law, transferring rights of property in a published work from publisher to author	
1717 Alexander Pope, *The Rape of the Lock*	
1719 Daniel Defoe publishes *Robinson Crusoe*, often called the first true novel in English	
	1721 J. S. Bach, *The Brandenburg Concertos*

TEXTS	CONTEXTS
1726 Jonathan Swift, *Gulliver's Travels*	
1729 Swift, *A Modest Proposal*	
1733–1734 Alexander Pope, *An Essay on Man*	
1740 Samuel Richardson, *Pamela*, arguably the first fully developed English novel	
1751 First edition of French *Encyclopédie*, edited by Denis Diderot	
1755 Samuel Johnson publishes the *Dictionary of the English Language*, the first comprehensive English dictionary on historical principles	1753 British Museum founded
1759 François-Marie Arouet de Voltaire, *Candide*	1756–1763 Seven Years' War, involving nine European powers; Britain acquires Canada and Florida, Spain gets Cuba and the Philippines, France wins colonies in India and Africa as well as Guadeloupe and Martinique
	1764 New British tax laws create American unrest • W. A. Mozart, eight years old, writes his first symphony
1771 First publication of *Encyclopedia Britannica* and complete French *Encyclopédie* testify to characteristic "Enlightenment" impulse to organize knowledge	1765 James Watt, a Scott, invents the steam engine, first in a series of mechanical innovations ushering in the Industrial Revolution
	1775–1783 American War of Independence; Declaration of Independence, 1776 • Constitution of the United States, 1787, the year of Mozart's opera *Don Giovanni*
1792 Mary Wollstonecraft, *Vindication of the Rights of Woman*, makes feminist case for female equality.	1789 French Revolution begins; French National Assembly adopts the Declaration of the Rights of Man
	1793 Captured by revolutionaries, Louis XVI and his queen, Marie Antoinette, are guillotined in Paris
	1799 After successful conquests throughout Europe, Napoleon Bonaparte becomes first consul—in effect, dictator—of France • Ludwig van Beethoven writes first symphony (1799–1800)

JEAN-BAPTISTE POQUELIN MOLIÈRE
1622–1673

Son of a prosperous Paris merchant, Jean-Baptiste Molière (originally named Poquelin) devoted his entire adult life to the creation of stage illusion, as playwright and as actor. At about the age of twenty-five, he joined a company of traveling players established by the Béjart family; with them he toured the provinces for about twelve years. In 1658 the company was ordered to perform for Louis XIV in Paris; a year later, Molière's first great success, *The High-Brow Ladies (Les Précieuses ridicules),* was produced. The theatrical company to which he belonged, patronized by the king, became increasingly successful, developing finally (1680) into the Comédie Française. In 1662, Molière married Armande Béjart. He died a few hours after performing in the lead role of his own play *The Imaginary Invalid.*

Molière wrote both broad farce and comedies of character, in which he caricatured some form of vice or folly by embodying it in a single figure. His targets included the miser, the aspiring but vulgar middle class, female would-be intellectuals, the hypochondriac, and in *Tartuffe,* the religious hypocrite.

In *Tartuffe* (1664), as in his other plays, Molière employs classic comic devices of plot and character—here, a foolish, stubborn father blocking the course of young love; an impudent servant commenting on her superiors' actions; a happy ending involving a marriage facilitated by implausible means. He often uses such devices, however, to comment on his own immediate social scene, imagining how universal patterns play themselves out in a specific historical context. *Tartuffe* had contemporary relevance so transparent that the Catholic Church forced the king to ban it, although Molière managed to have it published and produced once more by 1669.

The play's emotional energy derives not from the simple discrepancy of man and mask in Tartuffe ("Is not a face quite different from a mask?" inquires the normative character Cléante, who has no trouble making such distinctions) but from the struggle for erotic, psychic, and economic power in which people employ their masks. One can readily imagine modern equivalents for the stresses and strains within Orgon's family. Orgon, an aging man with grown children, seeks ways to preserve control. His mother, Madame Pernelle, encourages his efforts, thus fostering her illusion that *she* still runs things. Orgon identifies his own interests with those of the hypocritical Tartuffe, toward whom he plays a benevolent role. Because Tartuffe fulsomely hails him as benefactor, Orgon feels utterly powerful in relation to his fawning dependent. When he orders his passive daughter Mariane to marry Tartuffe, he reveals his vision of complete domestic autocracy. Tartuffe's lust, one of those passions forever eluding human mastery, disturbs Orgon's arrangements; in the end, the will of the offstage king orders everything, as though a benevolent god had intervened.

To make Tartuffe a specifically religious hypocrite is an act of inventive daring. Orgon, like his mother, conceals from himself his will to power by verbally subordinating himself to that divinity which Tartuffe too invokes. Although one may readily accept Molière's defense of his intentions (not to mock faith but to attack its misuse), it is not hard to see why the play might trouble religious authorities. Molière suggests how readily religious faith lends itself to misuse, how high-sounding pieties allow men and women to evade self-examination and immediate responsibilities. Tartuffe deceives others by his grandiosities of mortification ("Hang up my hair shirt") and charity; he encourages his victims in their own grandiosities. Orgon can indulge a fantasy of self-subordination (remarking of Tartuffe, "He guides our lives") at the same time that he furthers his more hidden desire for power. Religion offers ready justification for a course manifestly destructive as well as self-seeking.

Cléante, before he meets Tartuffe, claims (accurately) to understand him by his effects on others. Throughout the play, Cléante speaks in the voice of wisdom, counseling moderation, common sense, and self-control, calling attention to folly. More important, he emphasizes how the issues Molière examines in this comedy relate to dominant late seventeenth-century themes:

> Ah, Brother, man's a strangely fashioned creature
> Who seldom is content to follow Nature,
> But recklessly pursues his inclination
> Beyond the narrow bounds of moderation,
> And often, by transgressing Reason's laws,
> Perverts a lofty aim or noble cause.

To follow Nature means to act appropriately to the human situation in the created universe. Humankind occupies a middle position, between beasts and angels; such aspirations as Orgon's desire to control his daughter completely, or his apparent wish to submit himself absolutely to Tartuffe's claim of heavenly wisdom, imply a hope to surpass limitations inherent in the human condition. As Cléante's observations suggest, "to follow Nature," given the rationality of the universe, implies adherence to "Reason's laws." All transgression involves failure to submit to reason's dictates. Molière, with his stylized comic plot, makes that point as insistently as does Racine, who depicts grand passions and cataclysmic effects from them.

Although Cléante understands and can enunciate the principles of proper conduct, his wisdom has no direct effect on the play's action. In spite of the fact that the comedy suggests a social world in which women exist in utter subordination to fathers and husbands, in the plot, two women bring about the clarifications that unmask the villain. The virtuous wife Elmire, object of Tartuffe's lust, and the articulate servant girl Dorine confront the immediate situation with pragmatic inventiveness. Dorine goads others to response; Elmire encourages Tartuffe to play out his sexual fantasies before a hidden audience. Both women have a clear sense of right and wrong, although they express it in less resounding terms than does Cléante. Their concrete insistence on facing what is really going on, cutting through all obfuscation, rescues the men from entanglement in their own abstract formulations.

The women's clarifications, however, do not resolve the comedy's dilemmas. Suddenly the context shifts: economic terms replace erotic ones. It is as though Tartuffe were only playing in his attempt to seduce Elmire; now we get to what really matters: money. For all his claims of disinterestedness, Tartuffe has managed to get control of his dupe's property. Control of property, the action gradually reveals, amounts to power over life itself: prison threatens Orgon, and the prospect of expulsion from their home menaces him and his family alike. Only the convenient and ostentatious artifice of royal intervention rescues the victims and punishes their betrayer.

Comedies conventionally end in the restoration of order, declaring that good inevitably triumphs; rationality renews itself despite the temporary deviations of the foolish and the vicious. At the end of *Tartuffe*, Orgon and his mother have been chastened by revelation of their favorite's depravity; Mariane has been allowed to marry her lover; Tartuffe has been judged; the king's power and justice have reasserted themselves and been acknowledged. In the organization of family and nation (metaphorically a larger family), order reassumes dominion. Yet the arbitrary intervention of the king leaves a disturbing emotional residue. The play has demonstrated that Tartuffe's corrupt will to power (as opposed to Orgon's merely foolish will) can ruthlessly aggrandize itself. Money speaks, in Orgon's society as in ours; possession of wealth implies total control over others. Only a kind of miracle can save Orgon. The miracle occurs, given the benign world of comedy, but the play reminds its readers of the extreme precariousness with which reason finally triumphs, even given the presence of such reasonable people as Cléante and Elmire. Tartuffe's monstrous lust, for women, money, power, genuinely endangers the social structure. *Tartuffe* enforces recognition of the constant threats to rationality, of how much we have at stake in trying to use reason as principle of action.

K. Mantzius, *Molière* (1908), provides a good biographical introduction to Molière. Useful critical studies include J. D. Hubert, *Molière and the Comedy of Intellect* (1962); L. Gossman, *Men and Masks: A Study of Molière* (1963); Jacques Guicharnaud, ed., *Molière: A Collection of Critical Essays* (1964); and N. Gross, *From Gesture to Idea: Esthetics and Ethics in Molière's Comedy* (1982). An excellent treatment of Molière in his historical context is W. D. Howarth, *Molière: A Playwright and His Audience* (1984). Harold C. Knutson, *The Triumph of Wit* (1988), examines Molière in relation to Shakespeare and Ben Jonson.

PRONOUNCING GLOSSARY

The following list uses common English syllables and stress accents to provide rough equivalents of selected words whose pronunciation may be unfamiliar to the general reader.

Cléante: *clay-ahnt'*	Molière: *moh-lyar'*
Damis: *dah-mee'*	Orante: *oh-rahnt'*
Dorine: *do-reen'*	Orgon: *or-gohnh'*
Elmire: *el-meer'*	Pernelle: *payr-nel'*
Flipote: *flee'-pot*	Tartuffe: *tahr-toof'*
Laurent: *lor'-awn*	Valère: *vah-layr'*
Loyal: *lwah-yal'*	Vincennes: *vanh-s*

Tartuffe[1]

Preface

Here is a comedy that has excited a good deal of discussion and that has been under attack for a long time; and the persons who are mocked by it have made it plain that they are more powerful in France than all whom my plays have satirized up to this time. Noblemen, ladies of fashion, cuckolds, and doctors all kindly consented to their presentation, which they themselves seemed to enjoy along with everyone else; but hypocrites do not understand banter: they became angry at once, and found it strange that I was bold enough to represent their actions and to care to describe a profession shared by so many good men. This is a crime for which they cannot forgive me, and they have taken up arms against my comedy in a terrible rage. They were careful not to attack it at the point that had wounded them: they are too crafty for that and too clever to reveal their true character. In

---

1. Translated by Richard Wilbur. The first version of *Tartuffe* was performed in 1664 and the second in 1667. When a 2nd edition of the third version was printed in June 1669, Molière added his three petitions to Louis XIV; they follow the preface.

keeping with their lofty custom, they have used the cause of God to mask their private interests; and *Tartuffe*, they say, is a play that offends piety: it is filled with abominations from beginning to end, and nowhere is there a line that does not deserve to be burned. Every syllable is wicked, the very gestures are criminal, and the slightest glance, turn of the head, or step from right to left conceals mysteries that they are able to explain to my disadvantage. In vain did I submit the play to the criticism of my friends and the scrutiny of the public: all the corrections I could make, the judgment of the king and queen[2] who saw the play, the approval of great princes and ministers of state who honored it with their presence, the opinion of good men who found it worthwhile, all this did not help. They will not let go of their prey, and every day of the week they have pious zealots abusing me in public and damning me out of charity.

I would care very little about all they might say except that their devices make enemies of men whom I respect and gain the support of genuinely good men, whose faith they know and who, because of the warmth of their piety, readily accept the impressions that others present to them. And it is this which forces me to defend myself. Especially to the truly devout do I wish to vindicate my play, and I beg of them with all my heart not to condemn it before seeing it, to rid themselves of preconceptions, and not aid the cause of men dishonored by their actions.

If one takes the trouble to examine my comedy in good faith, he will surely see that my intentions are innocent throughout, and tend in no way to make fun of what men revere; that I have presented the subject with all the precautions that its delicacy imposes; and that I have used all the art and skill that I could to distinguish clearly the character of the hypocrite from that of the truly devout man. For that purpose I used two whole acts to prepare the appearance of my scoundrel. Never is there a moment's doubt about his character; he is known at once from the qualities I have given him; and from one end of the play to the other, he does not say a word, he does not perform an action which does not depict to the audience the character of a wicked man, and which does not bring out in sharp relief the character of the truly good man which I oppose to it.

I know full well that by way of reply, these gentlemen try to insinuate that it is not the role of the theater to speak of these matters; but with their permission, I ask them on what do they base this fine doctrine. It is a proposition they advance as no more than a supposition, for which they offer not a shred of proof; and surely it would not be difficult to show them that comedy, for the ancients, had its origin in religion and constituted a part of its ceremonies; that our neighbors, the Spaniards, have hardly a single holiday celebration in which a comedy is not a part; and that even here in France, it owes its birth to the efforts of a religious brotherhood who still own the Hôtel de Bourgogne, where the most important mystery plays of our faith were presented;[3] that you can still find comedies printed in gothic letters under the name of a learned doctor[4] of the Sorbonne; and without going so far, in our own day the religious dramas of Pierre Corneille[5] have been performed to the admiration of all France.

If the function of comedy is to correct men's vices, I do not see why any should be exempt. Such a condition in our society would be much more dangerous than the thing itself; and we have seen that the theater is admirably suited to provide correction. The most forceful lines of a serious moral statement are usually less powerful than those of satire; and nothing will reform most men better than the

---

2. Louis XIV was married to Marie Thérèse of Austria.   3. A reference to the *Confrérie de la Passion et Résurrection de Notre-Seigneur* (Fraternity of the passion and resurrection of our Savior), founded in 1402. The Hôtel de Bourgogne was a theater in rivalry with Molière's.   4. Probably Maître Jehán Michel, a medical doctor who wrote mystery plays.   5. Pierre Corneille (1606–1684) and Racine were France's two greatest writers of classic tragedy. The two dramas Molière doubtlessly had in mind were *Polyeucte* (1643) and *Théodore, vierge et martyre* (1645).

depiction of their faults. It is a vigorous blow to vices to expose them to public laughter. Criticism is taken lightly, but men will not tolerate satire. They are quite willing to be mean, but they never like to be ridiculed.

I have been attacked for having placed words of piety in the mouth of my impostor. Could I avoid doing so in order to represent properly the character of a hypocrite? It seemed to me sufficient to reveal the criminal motives which make him speak as he does, and I have eliminated all ceremonial phrases, which nonetheless he would not have been found using incorrectly. Yet some say that in the fourth act he sets forth a vicious morality; but is not this a morality which everyone has heard again and again? Does my comedy say anything new here? And is there any fear that ideas so thoroughly detested by everyone can make an impression on men's minds; that I make them dangerous by presenting them in the theater; that they acquire authority from the lips of a scoundrel? There is not the slightest suggestion of any of this; and one must either approve the comedy of *Tartuffe* or condemn all comedies in general.

This has indeed been done in a furious way for some time now, and never was the theater so much abused.[6] I cannot deny that there were Church Fathers who condemned comedy; but neither will it be denied me that there were some who looked on it somewhat more favorably. Thus authority, on which censure is supposed to depend, is destroyed by this disagreement; and the only conclusion that can be drawn from this difference of opinion among men enlightened by the same wisdom is that they viewed comedy in different ways, and that some considered it in its purity, while others regarded it in its corruption and confused it with all those wretched performances which have been rightly called performances of filth.

And in fact, since we should talk about things rather than words, and since most misunderstanding comes from including contrary notions in the same word, we need only to remove the veil of ambiguity and look at comedy in itself to see if it warrants condemnation. It will surely be recognized that as it is nothing more than a clever poem which corrects men's faults by means of agreeable lessons, it cannot be condemned without injustice. And if we listened to the voice of ancient times on this matter, it would tell us that its most famous philosophers have praised comedy—they who professed so austere a wisdom and who ceaselessly denounced the vices of their times. It would tell us that Aristotle spent his evenings at the theater[7] and took the trouble to reduce the art of making comedies to rules. It would tell us that some of its greatest and most honored men took pride in writing comedies themselves;[8] and that others did not disdain to recite them in public; that Greece expressed its admiration for this art by means of handsome prizes and magnificent theaters to honor it; and finally, that in Rome this same art also received extraordinary honors; I do not speak of Rome run riot under the license of the emperors, but of disciplined Rome, governed by the wisdom of the consuls, and in the age of the full vigor of Roman dignity.

I admit that there have been times when comedy became corrupt. And what do men not corrupt every day? There is nothing so innocent that men cannot turn it to crime; nothing so beneficial that its values cannot be reversed; nothing so good in itself that it cannot be put to bad uses. Medical knowledge benefits mankind and is revered as one of our most wonderful possessions; and yet there was a time when it fell into discredit, and was often used to poison men. Philosophy is a gift of Heaven; it has been given to us to bring us to the knowledge of a God by

---

6. Molière had in mind Nicole's two attacks on the theater: *Visionnaires* (1666) and *Traité de la Comédie* (1667) as well as the prince de Conti's *Traité de la Comédie* (1666).   7. A reference to Aristotle's *Poetics* (composed between 335 and 322 B.C., the year of his death).   8. Scipio Africanus Minor (ca. 185–129 B.C.), the Roman consul and general responsible for the final destruction of Carthage in 146 B.C., collaborated with Terence (Publius Terentius Afer, ca. 195 or 185–ca. 159 B.C.), a writer of comedies.

contemplating the wonders of nature; and yet we know that often it has been turned away from its function and has been used openly in support of impiety. Even the holiest of things are not immune from human corruption, and every day we see scoundrels who use and abuse piety, and wickedly make it serve the greatest of crimes. But this does not prevent one from making the necessary distinctions. We do not confuse in the same false inference the goodness of things that are corrupted with the wickedness of the corrupt. The function of an art is always distinguished from its misuse; and as medicine is not forbidden because it was banned in Rome,[9] nor philosophy because it was publicly condemned in Athens,[1] we should not suppress comedy simply because it has been condemned at certain times. This censure was justified then for reasons which no longer apply today; it was limited to what was then seen; and we should not seize on these limits, apply them more rigidly than is necessary, and include in our condemnation the innocent along with the guilty. The comedy that this censure attacked is in no way the comedy that we want to defend. We must be careful not to confuse the one with the other. There may be two persons whose morals may be completely different. They may have no resemblance to one another except in their names, and it would be a terrible injustice to want to condemn Olympia, who is a good woman, because there is also an Olympia who is lewd. Such procedures would make for great confusion everywhere. Everything under the sun would be condemned; now since this rigor is not applied to the countless instances of abuse we see every day, the same should hold for comedy, and those plays should be approved in which instruction and virtue reign supreme.

I know there are some so delicate that they cannot tolerate a comedy, who say that the most decent are the most dangerous, that the passions they present are all the more moving because they are virtuous, and that men's feelings are stirred by these presentations. I do not see what great crime it is to be affected by the sight of a generous passion; and this utter insensitivity to which they would lead us is indeed a high degree of virtue! I wonder if so great a perfection resides within the strength of human nature, and I wonder if it is not better to try to correct and moderate men's passions than to try to suppress them altogether. I grant that there are places better to visit than the theater; and if we want to condemn every single thing that does not bear directly on God and our salvation, it is right that comedy be included, and I should willingly grant that it be condemned along with everything else. But if we admit, as is in fact true, that the exercise of piety will permit interruptions, and that men need amusement, I maintain that there is none more innocent than comedy. I have dwelled too long on this matter. Let me finish with the words of a great prince on the comedy, *Tartuffe*.[2]

Eight days after it had been banned, a play called *Scaramouche the Hermit*[3] was performed before the court; and the king, on his way out, said to this great prince: "I should really like to know why the persons who make so much noise about Molière's comedy do not say a word about *Scaramouche*." To which the prince replied, "It is because the comedy of *Scaramouche* makes fun of Heaven and religion, which these gentlemen do not care about at all, but that of Molière makes fun of *them*, and that is what they cannot bear."

THE AUTHOR

---

9. Pliny the Elder says that the Romans expelled their doctors at the same time that the Greeks did theirs.   1. An allusion to Socrates' condemnation to death.   2. One of Molière's benefactors who liked the play was the prince de Condé; de Condé had *Tartuffe* read to him and also privately performed for him.   3. A troupe of Italian comedians had just performed the licentious farce, in which a hermit dressed as a monk makes love to a married woman, announcing that *questo e per mortificar la carne* ("this is to mortify the flesh").

FIRST PETITION[4]

(Presented to the King on the Comedy of Tartuffe)

Sire,

As the duty of comedy is to correct men by amusing them, I believed that in my occupation I could do nothing better than attack the vices of my age by making them ridiculous; and as hypocrisy is undoubtedly one of the most common, most improper, and most dangerous, I thought, Sire, that I would perform a service for all good men of your kingdom if I wrote a comedy which denounced hypocrites and placed in proper view all of the contrived poses of these incredibly virtuous men, all of the concealed villainies of these counterfeit believers who would trap others with a fraudulent piety and a pretended virtue.

I have written this comedy, Sire, with all the care and caution that the delicacy of the subject demands; and so as to maintain all the more properly the admiration and respect due to truly devout men, I have delineated my character as sharply as I could; I have left no room for doubt; I have removed all that might confuse good with evil, and have used for this painting only the specific colors and essential lines that make one instantly recognize a true and brazen hypocrite.

Nevertheless, all my precautions have been to no avail. Others have taken advantage of the delicacy of your feelings on religious matters, and they have been able to deceive you on the only side of your character which lies open to deception: your respect for holy things. By underhanded means, the Tartuffes have skillfully gained Your Majesty's favor, and the models have succeeded in eliminating the copy, no matter how innocent it may have been and no matter what resemblance was found between them.

Although the suppression of this work was a serious blow for me, my misfortune was nonetheless softened by the way in which Your Majesty explained his attitude on the matter; and I believed, Sire, that Your Majesty removed any cause I had for complaint, as you were kind enough to declare that you found nothing in this comedy that you would forbid me to present in public.

Yet, despite this glorious declaration of the greatest and most enlightened king in the world, despite the approval of the Papal Legate[5] and of most of our churchmen, all of whom, at private readings of my work, agreed with the views of Your Majesty, despite all this, a book has appeared by a certain priest[6] which boldly contradicts all of these noble judgments. Your Majesty expressed himself in vain, and the Papal Legate and churchmen gave their opinion to no avail: sight unseen, my comedy is diabolical, and so is my brain; I am a devil garbed in flesh and disguised

---

4. The first of the three *petitions* or *placets* to Louis XIV concerning the play. On May 12, 1664, *Tartuffe*—or at least the first three acts roughly as they now stand—was performed at Versailles. A cabal unfavorable to Molière, including the archbishop of Paris, Hardouin de Péréfixe, Queen Mother Anne of Austria, certain influential courtiers, and the Brotherhood or Company of the Holy Sacrament (formed in 1627 to enforce morality), arranged that the play be banned and Molière censured.   5. Cardinal Legate Chigi, nephew to Pope Alexander VII, heard a reading of *Tartuffe* at Fontainebleau on August 4, 1664.   6. Pierre Roullé, the curate of St. Barthélémy, who wrote a scathing attack on the play and sent his book to the king.

as a man,[7] a libertine, a disbeliever who deserves a punishment that will set an example. It is not enough that fire expiate my crime in public, for that would be letting me off too easily: the generous piety of this good man will not stop there; he will not allow me to find any mercy in the sight of God; he demands that I be damned, and that will settle the matter.

This book, Sire, was presented to Your Majesty; and I am sure that you see for yourself how unpleasant it is for me to be exposed daily to the insults of these gentlemen, what harm these abuses will do my reputation if they must be tolerated, and finally, how important it is for me to clear myself of these false charges and let the public know that my comedy is nothing more than what they want it to be. I will not ask, Sire, for what I need for the sake of my reputation and the innocence of my work: enlightened kings such as you do not need to be told what is wished of them; like God, they see what we need and know better than we what they should give us. It is enough for me to place my interests in Your Majesty's hands, and I respectfully await whatever you may care to command.

(August, 1664)

SECOND PETITION[8]

(Presented to the King in His Camp Before the City of Lille, in Flanders)

Sire,

It is bold indeed for me to ask a favor of a great monarch in the midst of his glorious victories; but in my present situation, Sire, where will I find protection anywhere but where I seek it, and to whom can I appeal against the authority of the power that crushes me,[9] if not to the source of power and authority, the just dispenser of absolute law, the sovereign judge and master of all?

My comedy, Sire, has not enjoyed the kindnesses of Your Majesty. All to no avail, I produced it under the title of *The Hypocrite* and disguised the principal character as a man of the world; in vain I gave him a little hat, long hair, a wide collar, a sword, and lace clothing,[1] softened the action and carefully eliminated all that I thought might provide even the shadow of grounds for discontent on the part of the famous models of the portrait I wished to present; nothing did any good. The conspiracy of opposition revived even at mere conjecture of what the play would be like. They found a way of persuading those who in all other matters plainly insist that they are not to be deceived. No sooner did my comedy appear than it was struck down by the very power which should impose respect; and all that I could do to save myself from the fury of this tempest was to

---

7. Molière took some of these phrases from Roullé.   8. On August 5, 1667, *Tartuffe* was performed at the Palais-Royal. The opposition—headed by the first president of parliament—brought in the police, and the play was stopped. Since Louis was campaigning in Flanders, friends of Molière brought the second *placet* to Lille. Louis had always been favorable toward the playwright; in August 1665 Molière's company, the *Troupe de Monsieur* (nominally sponsored by Louis's brother Philippe, duc d'Orléans), had become the *Troupe du Roi*.   9. President de Lanvignon, in charge of the Paris police. 1. There is evidence that in 1664 Tartuffe played his role dressed in a cassock, thus allying him more directly to the clergy.

say that Your Majesty had given me permission to present the play and I did not think it was necessary to ask this permission of others, since only Your Majesty could have refused it.

I have no doubt, Sire, that the men whom I depict in my comedy will employ every means possible to influence Your Majesty, and will use, as they have used already, those truly good men who are all the more easily deceived because they judge of others by themselves.[2] They know how to display all of their aims in the most favorable light; yet, no matter how pious they may seem, it is surely not the interests of God which stir them; they have proven this often enough in the comedies they have allowed to be performed hundreds of times without making the least objection. Those plays attacked only piety and religion, for which they care very little; but this play attacks and makes fun of them, and that is what they cannot bear. They will never forgive me for unmasking their hypocrisy in the eyes of everyone. And I am sure that they will not neglect to tell Your Majesty that people are shocked by my comedy. But the simple truth, Sire, is that all Paris is shocked only by its ban, that the most scrupulous persons have found its presentation worthwhile, and men are astounded that individuals of such known integrity should show so great a deference to people whom everyone should abominate and who are so clearly opposed to the true piety which they profess.

I respectfully await the judgment that Your Majesty will deign to pronounce: but it's certain, Sire, that I need not think of writing comedies if the Tartuffes are triumphant, if they thereby seize the right to persecute me more than ever, and find fault with even the most innocent lines that flow from my pen.

Let your goodness, Sire, give me protection against their envenomed rage, and allow me, at your return from so glorious a campaign, to relieve Your Majesty from the fatigue of his conquests, give him innocent pleasures after such noble accomplishments, and make the monarch laugh who makes all Europe tremble!

(*August, 1667*)

THIRD PETITION

(*Presented to the King*)

Sire,

A very honest doctor[3] whose patient I have the honor to be, promises and will legally contract to make me live another thirty years if I can obtain a favor for him from Your Majesty. I told him of his promise that I do not deserve so much, and that I should be glad to help him if he will merely agree not to kill me. This favor, Sire, is a post of canon at your royal chapel of Vincennes, made vacant by death.

May I dare to ask for this favor from Your Majesty on the very day of the glorious resurrection of *Tartuffe*, brought back to life by your goodness? By this first favor I have been reconciled with the devout, and the second will

---

2. Molière apparently did not know that de Lanvignon had been affiliated with the Company of the Holy Sacrament for the previous ten years.   3. A physician friend, M. de Mauvillain, who helped Molière with some of the medical details of *Le Malade imaginaire*.

reconcile me with the doctors.[4] Undoubtedly this would be too much grace for me at one time, but perhaps it would not be too much for Your Majesty, and I await your answer to my petition with respectful hope.

(*February*, 1669)

CHARACTERS[5]

MADAME PERNELLE, *Orgon's mother*
ORGON, *Elmire's husband*
ELMIRE, *Orgon's wife*
DAMIS, *Orgon's son, Elmire's stepson*
MARIANE, *Orgon's daughter, Elmire's stepdaughter, in love with Valère*

VALÈRE, *in love with Mariane*
CLÉANTE, *Orgon's brother-in-law*
TARTUFFE, *a hypocrite*
DORINE, *Mariane's lady's-maid*
M. LOYAL, *a bailiff*
A POLICE OFFICER
FLIPOTE, *Mme Pernelle's maid*

The SCENE *throughout: Orgon's house in Paris*

Act I

SCENE 1[6]

MADAME PERNELLE *and* FLIPOTE, *her maid*, ELMIRE,
MARIANE, DORINE, DAMIS, CLÉANTE

MADAME PERNELLE: Come, come, Flipote; it's time I left this place.
ELMIRE: I can't keep up, you walk at such a pace.
MADAME PERNELLE: Don't trouble, child; no need to show me out.
  It's not your manners I'm concerned about.
ELMIRE: We merely pay you the respect we owe.   5
  But, Mother, why this hurry? Must you go?
MADAME PERNELLE: I must. This house appals me. No one in it
  Will pay attention for a single minute.
  I offer good advice, but you won't hear it.
  Children, I take my leave much vexed in spirit.   10
  You all break in and chatter on and on.
  It's like a madhouse with the keeper gone.
DORINE: If . . .
MADAME PERNELLE:
      Girl, you talk too much, and I'm afraid
  You're far too saucy for a lady's-maid.
  You push in everywhere and have your say.   15
DAMIS: But . . .

---

4. Doctors are ridiculed to varying degrees in earlier plays of Molière: *Dom Juan, L'Amour médecin*, and *Le Médecin malgré lui*.   5. The name Tartuffe has been traced back to an older word associated with liar or charlatan: *truffer*, "to deceive" or "to cheat." Then there was also the Italian actor Tartufo, physically deformed and truffle shaped. Most of the other names are typical of this genre of court comedy and possess rather elegant connotations of pastoral and *bergerie*. Dorine would be a *demoiselle de compagne* and not a mere maid, that is, a female companion to Mariane of roughly the same social status. This in part accounts for the liberties she takes in conversation with Orgon, Madame Pernelle, and others. Her name is short for Théodorine.   6. In French drama, the scene changes every time a character enters or exits.

MADAME PERNELLE:
          You, boy, grow more foolish every day.
To think my grandson should be such a dunce!
I've said a hundred times, if I've said it once,
That if you keep the course on which you've started,
You'll leave your worthy father broken-hearted.   20
MARIANE: I think . . .
MADAME PERNELLE: And you, his sister, seem so pure,
So shy, so innocent, and so demure.
But you know what they say about still waters.
I pity parents with secretive daughters.
ELMIRE: Now, Mother . . .
MADAME PERNELLE: And as for you, child, let me add   25
That your behavior is extremely bad,
And a poor example for these children, too.
Their dear, dead mother did far better than you.
You're much too free with money, and I'm distressed
To see you so elaborately dressed.   30
When it's one's husband that one aims to please,
One has no need of costly fripperies.
CLÉANTE: Oh, Madam, really . . .
MADAME PERNELLE: You are her brother, Sir,
And I respect and love you; yet if I were
My son, this lady's good and pious spouse,   35
I wouldn't make you welcome in my house.
You're full of worldly counsels which, I fear,
Aren't suitable for decent folk to hear.
I've spoken bluntly, Sir; but it behooves us
Not to mince words when righteous fervor moves us.   40
DAMIS: Your man Tartuffe is full of holy speeches . . .
MADAME PERNELLE: And practises precisely what he preaches.
He's a fine man, and should be listened to.
I will not hear him mocked by fools like you.
DAMIS: Good God! Do you expect me to submit   45
To the tyranny of that carping hypocrite?
Must we forgo all joys and satisfactions
Because that bigot censures all our actions?
DORINE: To hear him talk—and he talks all the time—
There's nothing one can do that's not a crime.   50
He rails at everything, your dear Tartuffe.
MADAME PERNELLE: Whatever he reproves deserves reproof.
He's out to save your souls, and all of you
Must love him, as my son would have you do.
DAMIS: Ah no, Grandmother, I could never take   55
To such a rascal, even for my father's sake.
That's how I feel, and I shall not dissemble.
His every action makes me seethe and tremble
With helpless anger, and I have no doubt
That he and I will shortly have it out.   60

One never hears a word that's edifying:
Nothing but chaff and foolishness and lying,
As well as vicious gossip in which one's neighbor   155
Is cut to bits with épée, foil, and saber.
People of sense are driven half-insane
At such affairs, where noise and folly reign
And reputations perish thick and fast.
As a wise preacher said on Sunday last,   160
Parties are Towers of Babylon,[8] because
The guests all babble on with never a pause;
And then he told a story which, I think . . .
[*To* CLÉANTE.] I heard that laugh, Sir, and I saw that wink!
Go find your silly friends and laugh some more!   165
Enough; I'm going; don't show me to the door.
I leave this household much dismayed and vexed;
I cannot say when I shall see you next.
        [*Slapping* FLIPOTE.]
Wake up, don't stand there gaping into space!
I'll slap some sense into that stupid face.   170
Move, move, you slut.

SCENE 2

CLÉANTE, DORINE

CLÉANTE: I think I'll stay behind;
I want no further pieces of her mind.
How that old lady . . .
DORINE: Oh, what wouldn't she say
If she could hear you speak of her that way!
She'd thank you for the *lady,* but I'm sure   5
She'd find the *old* a little premature.
CLÉANTE: My, what a scene she made, and what a din!
And how this man Tartuffe has taken her in!
DORINE: Yes, but her son is even worse deceived;
His folly must be seen to be believed.   10
In the late troubles,[9] he played an able part
And served his king with wise and loyal heart,
But he's quite lost his senses since he fell
Beneath Tartuffe's infatuating spell.
He calls him brother, and loves him as his life,   15
Preferring him to mother, child, or wife.
In him and him alone will he confide;
He's made him his confessor and his guide;
He pets and pampers him with love more tender
Than any pretty maiden could engender,   20

---

8. Tower of Babel. Madame Pernelle's malapropism is the cause of Cléante's laughter.   9. A series
of political disturbances during the minority of Louis XIV. Specifically these consisted of the *Fronde*
("opposition") of the Parlement (1648–49) and the *Fronde* of the Princes (1650–53). Orgon is depicted
as supporting Louis XIV in these outbreaks and their resolution.

Gives him the place of honor when they dine,
Delights to see him gorging like a swine,
Stuffs him with dainties till his guts distend,
And when he belches, cries "God bless you, friend!"
In short, he's mad; he worships him; he dotes;   25
His deeds he marvels at, his words, he quotes,
Thinking each act a miracle, each word
Oracular as those that Moses heard.
Tartuffe, much pleased to find so easy a victim,
Has in a hundred ways beguiled and tricked him,   30
Milked him of money, and with his permission
Established here a sort of Inquisition.
Even Laurent, his lackey, dares to give
Us arrogant advice on how to live;
He sermonizes us in thundering tones   35
And confiscates our ribbons and colognes.
Last week he tore a kerchief into pieces
Because he found it pressed in a *Life of Jesus:*
He said it was a sin to juxtapose
Unholy vanities and holy prose.   40

SCENE 3

ELMIRE, MARIANE, DAMIS, CLÉANTE, DORINE

ELMIRE: [*To* CLÉANTE.] You did well not to follow; she stood in the door
And said *verbatim* all she'd said before.
I saw my husband coming. I think I'd best
Go upstairs now, and take a little rest.
CLÉANTE: I'll wait and greet him here; then I must go.   5
I've really only time to say hello.
DAMIS: Sound him about my sister's wedding, please.
I think Tartuffe's against it, and that he's
Been urging Father to withdraw his blessing.
As you well know, I'd find that most distressing.   10
Unless my sister and Valère can marry,
My hopes to wed *his* sister will miscarry.
And I'm determined . . .
DORINE: He's coming.

SCENE 4

ORGON, CLÉANTE, DORINE

ORGON: Ah, Brother, good-day.
CLÉANTE: Well, welcome back, I'm sorry I can't stay.
How was the country? Blooming, I trust, and green?
ORGON: Excuse me, Brother; just one moment.
[*To* DORINE.]   Dorine . . .
[*To* CLÉANTE.] To put my mind at rest, I always learn   5
The household news the moment I return.

[*To* DORINE.] Has all been well, these two days I've been gone?
   How are the family? What's been going on?
DORINE: Your wife, two days ago, had a bad fever,
   And a fierce headache which refused to leave her.   10
ORGON: Ah. And Tartuffe?
DORINE: Tartuffe? Why, he's round and red.
   Bursting with health, and excellently fed.
ORGON: Poor fellow!
DORINE: That night, the mistress was unable
   To take a single bite at the dinner-table.
   Her headache-pains, she said, were simply hellish.   15
ORGON: Ah. And Tartuffe?
DORINE: He ate his meal with relish,
   And zealously devoured in her presence
   A leg of mutton and a brace of pheasants.
ORGON: Poor fellow!
DORINE: Well, the pains continued strong,
   And so she tossed and tossed the whole night long,   20
   Now icy-cold, now burning like a flame.
   We sat beside her bed till morning came.
ORGON: Ah. And Tartuffe?
DORINE: Why, having eaten, he rose
   And sought his room, already in a doze,
   Got into his warm bed, and snored away   25
   In perfect peace until the break of day.
ORGON: Poor fellow!
DORINE: After much ado, we talked her
   Into dispatching someone for the doctor.
   He bled her, and the fever quickly fell.
ORGON: Ah. And Tartuffe?
DORINE: He bore it very well.   30
   To keep his cheerfulness at any cost,
   And make up for the blood Madame had lost,
   He drank, at lunch, four beakers full of port.
ORGON: Poor fellow.
DORINE: Both are doing well, in short.
   I'll go and tell Madame that you've expressed   35
   Keen sympathy and anxious interest.

SCENE 5

ORGON, CLÉANTE

CLÉANTE: That girl was laughing in your face, and though
   I've no wish to offend you, even so
   I'm bound to say that she had some excuse.
   How can you possibly be such a goose?
   Are you so dazed by this man's hocus-pocus   5
   That all the world, save him, is out of focus?
   You've given him clothing, shelter, food, and care;

Why must you also . . .

ORGON: Brother, stop right there.
 You do not know the man of whom you speak.

CLÉANTE: I grant you that. But my judgment's not so weak   10
 That I can't tell, by his effect on others . . .

ORGON: Ah, when you meet him, you two will be like brothers!
 There's been no loftier soul since time began.
 He is a man who . . . a man who . . . an excellent man.
 To keep his precepts is to be reborn,   15
 And view this dunghill of a world with scorn.
 Yes, thanks to him I'm a changed man indeed.
 Under his tutelage my soul's been freed
 From earthly loves, and every human tie:
 My mother, children, brother, and wife could die,   20
 And I'd not feel a single moment's pain.

CLÉANTE: That's a fine sentiment, Brother; most humane.

ORGON: Oh, had you seen Tartuffe as I first knew him,
 Your heart, like mine, would have surrendered to him.
 He used to come into our church each day   25
 And humbly kneel nearby, and start to pray.
 He'd draw the eyes of everybody there
 By the deep fervor of his heartfelt prayer;
 He'd sigh and weep, and sometimes with a sound
 Of rapture he would bend and kiss the ground;   30
 And when I rose to go, he'd run before
 To offer me holy-water at the door.
 His serving-man, no less devout than he,
 Informed me of his master's poverty;
 I gave him gifts, but in his humbleness   35
 He'd beg me every time to give him less.
 "Oh, that's too much," he'd cry, "too much by twice!
 I don't deserve it. The half, Sir, would suffice."
 And when I wouldn't take it back, he'd share
 Half of it with the poor, right then and there.   40
 At length, Heaven prompted me to take him in
 To dwell with us, and free our souls from sin.
 He guides our lives, and to protect my honor
 Stays by my wife, and keeps an eye upon her;
 He tells me whom she sees, and all she does,   45
 And seems more jealous than I ever was!
 And how austere he is! Why, he can detect
 A moral sin where you would least suspect;
 In smallest trifles, he's extremely strict.
 Last week, his conscience was severely pricked   50
 Because, while praying, he had caught a flea
 And killed it, so he felt, too wrathfully.[1]

---

1. In the *Golden Legend* (*Legenda sanctorum*), a popular collection of the lives of the saints written in the 13th century, it is said of St. Marcarius the Elder (died 390) that he dwelt naked in the desert for six months, a penance he felt appropriate for having killed a flea.

CLÉANTE: Good God, man! Have you lost your common sense —
Or is this all some joke at my expense?
How can you stand there and in all sobriety . . .   55
ORGON: Brother, your language savors of impiety.
Too much free-thinking's made your faith unsteady,
And as I've warned you many times already,
'Twill get you into trouble before you're through.
CLÉANTE: So I've been told before by dupes like you: 60
Being blind, you'd have all others blind as well;
The clear-eyed man you call an infidel,
And he who sees through humbug and pretense
Is charged, by you, with want of reverence.
Spare me your warnings, Brother; I have no fear   65
Of speaking out, for you and Heaven to hear,
Against affected zeal and pious knavery.
There's true and false in piety, as in bravery,
And just as those whose courage shines the most
In battle, are the least inclined to boast,   70
So those whose hearts are truly pure and lowly
Don't make a flashy show of being holy.
There's a vast difference, so it seems to me,
Between true piety and hypocrisy:
How do you fail to see it, may I ask?   75
Is not a face quite different from a mask?
Cannot sincerity and cunning art,
Reality and semblance, be told apart?
Are scarecrows just like men, and do you hold
That a false coin is just as good as gold?   80
Ah, Brother, man's a strangely fashioned creature
Who seldom is content to follow Nature,
But recklessly pursues his inclination
Beyond the narrow bounds of moderation,
And often, by transgressing Reason's laws,   85
Perverts a lofty aim or noble cause.
A passing observation, but it applies.
ORGON: I see, dear Brother, that you're profoundly wise;
You harbor all the insight of the age.
You are our one clear mind, our only sage,   90
The era's oracle, its Cato[2] too,
And all mankind are fools compared to you.
CLÉANTE: Brother, I don't pretend to be a sage,
Nor have I all the wisdom of the age.
There's just one insight I would dare to claim: 95
I know that true and false are not the same;
And just as there is nothing I more revere
Than a soul whose faith is steadfast and sincere,
Nothing that I more cherish and admire

---

2. Roman statesman (95–46 B.C.) with an enduring reputation for honesty and incorruptibility.

Than honest zeal and true religious fire,   100
So there is nothing that I find more base
Than specious piety's dishonest face —
Than these bold mountebanks, these histrios
Whose impious mummeries and hollow shows
Exploit our love of Heaven, and make a jest   105
Of all that men think holiest and best;
These calculating souls who offer prayers
Not to their Maker, but as public wares,
And seek to buy respect and reputation
With lifted eyes and sighs of exaltation;   110
These charlatans, I say, whose pilgrim souls
Proceed, by way of Heaven, toward earthly goals,
Who weep and pray and swindle and extort,
Who preach the monkish life, but haunt the court,
Who make their zeal the partner of their vice —   115
Such men are vengeful, sly, and cold as ice,
And when there is an enemy to defame
They cloak their spite in fair religion's name,
Their private spleen and malice being made
To seem a high and virtuous crusade,   120
Until, to mankind's reverent applause,
They crucify their foe in Heaven's cause.
Such knaves are all too common; yet, for the wise,
True piety isn't hard to recognize,
And, happily, these present times provide us   125
With bright examples to instruct and guide us.
Consider Ariston and Périandre;
Look at Oronte, Alcidamas, Clitandre;[3]
Their virtue is acknowledged; who could doubt it?
But you won't hear them beat the drum about it.   130
They're never ostentatious, never vain,
And their religion's moderate and humane;
It's not their way to criticize and chide:
They think censoriousness a mark of pride,
And therefore, letting others preach and rave,   135
They show, by deeds, how Christians should behave.
They think no evil of their fellow man,
But judge of him as kindly as they can.
They don't intrigue and wangle and conspire;
To lead a good life is their one desire;   140
The sinner wakes no rancorous hate in them;
It is the sin alone which they condemn;
Nor do they try to show a fiercer zeal
For Heaven's cause than Heaven itself could feel.
These men I honor, these men I advocate   145
As models for us all to emulate.

---

3. Vaguely Greek and Roman names derived from the elegant literature of the day.

Your man is not their sort at all, I fear:
And, while your praise of him is quite sincere,
I think that you've been dreadfully deluded.
ORGON: Now then, dear Brother, is your speech concluded?   150
CLÉANTE: Why, yes.
ORGON: Your servant, Sir.
     [*He turns to go.*]
CLÉANTE: No, Brother; wait.
There's one more matter. You agreed of late
That young Valère might have your daughter's hand.
ORGON: I did.
CLÉANTE: And set the date, I understand.
ORGON: Quite so.
CLÉANTE: You've now postponed it; is that true?   155
ORGON: No doubt.
CLÉANTE: The match no longer pleases you?
ORGON: Who knows?
CLÉANTE: D'you mean to go back on your word?
ORGON: I won't say that.
CLÉANTE: Has anything occurred
Which might entitle you to break your pledge?
ORGON: Perhaps.
CLÉANTE: Why must you hem, and haw, and hedge?   160
The boy asked me to sound you in this affair . . .
ORGON: It's been a pleasure.
CLÉANTE: But what shall I tell Valère?
ORGON. Whatever you like.
CLÉANTE: But what have you decided?
What are your plans?
ORGON: I plan, Sir, to be guided
By Heaven's will.
CLÉANTE: Come, Brother, don't talk rot.   165
You've given Valère your word; will you keep it, or not?
ORGON: Good day.
CLÉANTE: This looks like poor Valère's undoing;
I'll go and warn him that there's trouble brewing.

Act II

SCENE 1

ORGON, MARIANE

ORGON: Mariane.
MARIANE: Yes, Father?
ORGON: A word with you; come here.
MARIANE: What are you looking for?
ORGON: [*Peering into a small closet.*] Eavesdroppers, dear.
I'm making sure we shan't be overheard.

Someone in there could catch our every word.
Ah, good, we're safe. Now, Mariane, my child,   5
You're a sweet girl who's tractable and mild,
Whom I hold dear, and think most highly of.
MARIANE: I'm deeply grateful, Father, for your love.
ORGON: That's well said, Daughter; and you can repay me
If, in all things, you'll cheerfully obey me.   10
MARIANE: To please you, Sir, is what delights me best.
ORGON: Good, good. Now, what d'you think of Tartuffe, our guest?
MARIANE: I, Sir?
ORGON: Yes. Weigh your answer; think it through.
MARIANE: Oh, dear. I'll say whatever you wish me to.
ORGON: That's wisely said, my Daughter. Say of him, then,   15
That he's the very worthiest of men,
And that you're fond of him, and would rejoice
In being his wife, if that should be my choice.
Well?
MARIANE: What?
ORGON: What's that?
MARIANE: I . . .
ORGON: Well?
MARIANE: Forgive me, pray.
ORGON: Did you not hear me?
MARIANE: Of *whom*, Sir, must I say   20
That I am fond of him, and would rejoice
In being his wife, if that should be your choice?
ORGON: Why, of Tartuffe.
MARIANE: But, Father, that's false, you know.
Why would you have me say what isn't so?
ORGON: Because I am resolved it shall be true.   25
That it's my wish should be enough for you.
MARIANE: You can't mean, Father . . .
ORGON: Yes, Tartuffe shall be
Allied by marriage[4] to this family,
And he's to be your husband, is that clear?
It's a father's privilege   30

SCENE 2

DORINE, ORGON, MARIANE

ORGON: [*To* DORINE.]   What are you doing in here?
Is curiosity so fierce a passion
With you, that you must eavesdrop in this fashion?
DORINE: There's lately been a rumor going about—

---

4. This assertion is important and more than a mere device in the plot of the day. The second *placet* or petition insists that Tartuffe be costumed as a layman, and Orgon's plan for him to marry again asserts Tartuffe's position in the laity. In the 1664 version of the play Tartuffe had been dressed in a cassock suggestive of the priesthood, and Molière was now anxious to avoid any suggestion of this kind.

Based on some hunch or chance remark, no doubt—   5
That you mean Mariane to wed Tartuffe.
I've laughed it off, of course, as just a spoof.
ORGON: You find it so incredible?
DORINE: Yes, I do.
I won't accept that story, even from you.
ORGON: Well, you'll believe it when the thing is done.   10
DORINE: Yes, yes, of course. Go on and have your fun.
ORGON: I've never been more serious in my life.
DORINE: Ha!
ORGON: Daughter, I mean it; you're to be his wife.
DORINE: No, don't believe your father; it's all a hoax.
ORGON: See here, young woman . . .
DORINE: Come, Sir, no more jokes;   15
You can't fool us.
ORGON: How dare you talk that way?
DORINE: All right, then: we believe you, sad to say.
But how a man like you, who looks so wise
And wears a moustache of such splendid size,
Can be so foolish as to . . .
ORGON: Silence, please!   20
My girl, you take too many liberties.
I'm master here, as you must not forget.
DORINE: Do let's discuss this calmly; don't be upset.
You can't be serious, Sir, about this plan.
What should that bigot want with Mariane?   25
Praying and fasting ought to keep him busy.
And then, in terms of wealth and rank, what is he?
Why should a man of property like you
Pick out a beggar son-in-law?
ORGON: That will do.
Speak of his poverty with reverence.   30
His is a pure and saintly indigence
Which far transcends all worldly pride and pelf.
He lost his fortune, as he says himself,
Because he cared for Heaven alone, and so
Was careless of his interests here below.   35
I mean to get him out of his present straits
And help him to recover his estates—
Which, in his part of the world, have no small fame.
Poor though he is, he's a gentleman just the same.
DORINE: Yes, so he tells us; and, Sir, it seems to me   40
Such pride goes very ill with piety.
A man whose spirit spurns this dungy earth
Ought not to brag of lands and noble birth;
Such worldly arrogance will hardly square
With meek devotion and the life of prayer.   45
. . . But this approach, I see, has drawn a blank;
Let's speak, then, of his person, not his rank.

Doesn't it seem to you a trifle grim
To give a girl like her to a man like him?
When two are so ill-suited, can't you see   50
What the sad consequence is bound to be?
A young girl's virtue is imperilled, Sir,
When such a marriage is imposed on her;
For if one's bridegroom isn't to one's taste,
It's hardly an inducement to be chaste,   55
And many a man with horns upon his brow
Has made his wife the thing that she is now.
It's hard to be a faithful wife, in short,
To certain husbands of a certain sort,
And he who gives his daughter to a man she hates   60
Must answer for her sins at Heaven's gates.
Think, Sir, before you play so risky a role.
ORGON: This servant-girl presumes to save my soul!
DORINE: You would do well to ponder what I've said.
ORGON: Daughter, we'll disregard this dunderhead.   65
   Just trust your father's judgment. Oh, I'm aware
   That I once promised you to young Valère;
   But now I hear he gambles, which greatly shocks me;
   What's more, I've doubts about his orthodoxy.
   His visits to church, I note, are very few.   70
DORINE: Would you have him go at the same hours as you,
   And kneel nearby, to be sure of being seen?
ORGON: I can dispense with such remarks, Dorine.
   [*To* MARIANE.] Tartuffe, however, is sure of Heaven's blessing.
   And that's the only treasure worth possessing.   75
   This match will bring you joys beyond all measure;
   Your cup will overflow with every pleasure;
   You two will interchange your faithful loves
   Like two sweet cherubs, or two turtle-doves.
   No harsh word shall be heard, no frown be seen,   80
   And he shall make you happy as a queen.
DORINE: And she'll make him a cuckold, just wait and see.
ORGON: What language!
DORINE: Oh, he's a man of destiny;
   He's *made* for horns, and what the stars demand
   Your daughter's virtue surely can't withstand.   85
ORGON: Don't interrupt me further. Why can't you learn
   That certain things are none of your concern?
DORINE: It's for your own sake that I interfere.
   [*She repeatedly interrupts* ORGON *just as he is turning to speak to his
   daughter.*]
ORGON: Most kind of you. Now, hold your tongue, d'you hear?
DORINE: If I didn't love you . . .
ORGON: Spare me your affection.   90
DORINE: I'll love you, Sir, in spite of your objection.
ORGON: Blast!

DORINE: I can't bear, Sir, for your honor's sake,
To let you make this ludicrous mistake.
ORGON: You mean to go on talking?
DORINE: If I didn't protest
This sinful marriage, my conscience couldn't rest.   95
ORGON: If you don't hold your tongue, you little shrew . . .
DORINE: What, lost your temper? A pious man like you?
ORGON: Yes! Yes! You talk and talk. I'm maddened by it.
Once and for all, I tell you to be quiet.
DORINE: Well, I'll be quiet. But I'll be thinking hard.   100
ORGON: Think all you like, but you had better guard
That saucy tongue of yours, or I'll . . .
  [*Turning back to* MARIANE.]   Now, child,
I've weighed this matter fully.
DORINE: [*Aside.*]   It drives me wild
That I can't speak.
  [ORGON *turns his head, and she is silent.*]
ORGON: Tartuffe is no young dandy,
But, still, his person . . .
DORINE: [*Aside.*]   Is as sweet as candy.   105
ORGON: Is such that, even if you shouldn't care
For his other merits . . .
  [*He turns and stands facing* DORINE, *arms crossed.*]
DORINE: [*Aside.*]   They'll make a lovely pair.
If I were she, no man would marry me
Against my inclination, and go scot-free.
He'd learn, before the wedding-day was over,   110
How readily a wife can find a lover.
ORGON: [*To* DORINE.] It seems you treat my orders as a joke.
DORINE: Why, what's the matter? 'Twas not to you I spoke.
ORGON: What *were* you doing?
DORINE: Talking to myself, that's all.
ORGON: Ah! [*Aside.*] One more bit of impudence and gall,   115
And I shall give her a good slap in the face.
  [*He puts himself in position to slap her;* DORINE, *whenever he glances
  at her, stands immobile and silent.*]
Daughter, you shall accept, and with good grace,
The husband I've selected . . . Your wedding-day . . .
  [*To* DORINE.] Why don't you talk to yourself?
DORINE: I've nothing to say.
ORGON. Come, just one word.
DORINE: No thank you, Sir. I pass.   120
ORGON: Come, speak; I'm waiting.
DORINE: I'd not be such an ass.
ORGON. [*Turning to* MARIANE.]
In short, dear Daughter, I mean to be obeyed,
And you must bow to the sound choice I've made.
DORINE: [*Moving away.*] I'd not wed such a monster, even in jest.
  [ORGON *attempts to slap her, but misses.*]

ORGON: Daughter, that maid of yours is a thorough pest; 125
 She makes me sinfully annoyed and nettled.
 I can't speak further; my nerves are too unsettled.
 She's so upset me by her insolent talk,
 I'll calm myself by going for a walk.

SCENE 3

DORINE, MARIANE

DORINE: [*Returning.*] Well, have you lost your tongue, girl? Must I play
 Your part, and say the lines you ought to say?
 Faced with a fate so hideous and absurd,
 Can you not utter one dissenting word?
MARIANE: What good would it do? A father's power is great. 5
DORINE: Resist him now, or it will be too late.
MARIANE: But . . .
DORINE: Tell him one cannot love at a father's whim;
 That you shall marry for yourself, not him;
 That since it's you who are to be the bride,
 It's you, not he, who must be satisfied; 10
 And that if his Tartuffe is so sublime,
 He's free to marry him at any time.
MARIANE: I've bowed so long to Father's strict control,
 I couldn't oppose him now, to save my soul.
DORINE: Come, come, Mariane. Do listen to reason, won't you? 15
 Valère has asked your hand. Do you love him, or don't you?
MARIANE: Oh, how unjust of you! What can you mean
 By asking such a question, dear Dorine?
 You know the depth of my affection for him;
 I've told you a hundred times how I adore him. 20
DORINE: I don't believe in everything I hear;
 Who knows if your professions were sincere?
MARIANE: They were, Dorine, and you do me wrong to doubt it;
 Heaven knows that I've been all too frank about it.
DORINE: You love him, then?
MARIANE: Oh, more than I can express. 25
DORINE: And he, I take it, cares for you no less?
MARIANE: I think so.
DORINE: And you both, with equal fire,
 Burn to be married?
MARIANE: That is our one desire.
DORINE: What of Tartuffe, then? What of your father's plan?
MARIANE: I'll kill myself, if I'm forced to wed that man. 30
DORINE: I hadn't thought of that recourse. How splendid!
 Just die, and all your troubles will be ended!
 A fine solution. Oh, it maddens me
 To hear you talk in that self-pitying key.
MARIANE: Dorine, how harsh you are! It's most unfair. 35
 You have no sympathy for my despair.

DORINE: I've none at all for people who talk drivel
    And, faced with difficulties, whine and snivel.
MARIANE: No doubt I'm timid, but it would be wrong . . .
DORINE: True love requires a heart that's firm and strong.   40
MARIANE: I'm strong in my affection for Valère,
    But coping with my father is his affair.
DORINE: But if your father's brain has grown so cracked
    Over his dear Tartuffe that he can retract
    His blessing, though your wedding-day was named,   45
    It's surely not Valère who's to be blamed.
MARIANE: If I defied my father, as you suggest,
    Would it not seem unmaidenly, at best?
    Shall I defend my love at the expense
    Of brazenness and disobedience?   50
    Shall I parade my heart's desires, and flaunt . . .
DORINE: No, I ask nothing of you. Clearly you want
    To be Madame Tartuffe, and I feel bound
    Not to oppose a wish so very sound.
    What right have I to criticize the match?   55
    Indeed, my dear, the man's a brilliant catch.
    Monsieur Tartuffe! Now, there's a man of weight!
    Yes, yes, Monsieur Tartuffe, I'm bound to state,
    Is quite a person; that's not to be denied;
    'Twill be no little thing to be his bride.   60
    The world already rings with his renown;
    He's a great noble—in his native town;
    His ears are red, he has a pink complexion,
    And all in all, he'll suit you to perfection.
MARIANE: Dear God!
DORINE: Oh, how triumphant you will feel   65
    At having caught a husband so ideal!
MARIANE: Oh, do stop teasing, and use your cleverness
    To get me out of this appalling mess.
    Advise me, and I'll do whatever you say.
DORINE: Ah, no, a dutiful daughter must obey   70
    Her father, even if he weds her to an ape.
    You've a bright future; why struggle to escape?
    Tartuffe will take you back where his family lives,
    To a small town aswarm with relatives—
    Uncles and cousins whom you'll be charmed to meet.   75
    You'll be received at once by the elite,
    Calling upon the bailiff's[5] wife, no less—
    Even, perhaps, upon the mayoress,[6]
    Who'll sit you down in the *best* kitchen chair.[7]

---

5. A high-ranking official in the judiciary, not simply a sheriff's deputy as today.   6. The wife of a tax collector (*élue*), an important official controlling imports, elected by the Estates General.   7. In elegant society of Molière's day, there was a hierarchy of seats, and the use of each was determined by rank. The seats descended from *fauteuils* to *chaises, perroquets, tabourets,* and *pliants.* Thus Mariane would get the lowest seat in the room.

Then, once a year, you'll dance at the village fair   80
To the drone of bagpipes—two of them, in fact—
And see a puppet-show, or an animal act.[8]
Your husband . . .
MARIANE: Oh, you turn my blood to ice!
Stop torturing me, and give me your advice.
DORINE: [*Threatening to go.*]
Your servant, Madam.
MARIANE.   Dorine, I beg of you . . .   85
DORINE: No, you deserve it; this marriage must go through.
MARIANE: Dorine!
DORINE: No.
MARIANE: Not Tartuffe! You know I think him . . .
DORINE: Tartuffe's your cup of tea, and you shall drink him.
MARIANE: I've always told you everything, and relied . . .
DORINE: No. You deserve to be tartuffified.   90
MARIANE: Well, since you mock me and refuse to care,
I'll henceforth seek my solace in despair:
Despair shall be my counsellor and friend,
And help me bring my sorrows to an end. [*She starts to leave.*]
DORINE: There now, come back; my anger has subsided.   95
You do deserve some pity, I've decided.
MARIANE: Dorine, if Father makes me undergo
This dreadful martyrdom, I'll die, I know.
DORINE: Don't fret; it won't be difficult to discover
Some plan of action . . . But here's Valère, your lover.   100

SCENE 4

VALÈRE, MARIANE, DORINE

VALÈRE: Madam, I've just received some wondrous news
Regarding which I'd like to hear your views.
MARIANE: What news?
VALÈRE: You're marrying Tartuffe.
MARIANE: I find
That Father does have such a match in mind.
VALÈRE: Your father, Madam . . .
MARIANE: . . . has just this minute said   5
That it's Tartuffe he wishes me to wed.
VALÈRE: Can he be serious?
MARIANE: Oh, indeed he can;
He's clearly set his heart upon the plan.
VALÈRE: And what position do you propose to take,
Madam?
MARIANE: Why—I don't know.
VALÈRE: For heaven's sake—   10
You don't know?

8. In the original, *fagotin*, literally "a monkey dressed up in a man's clothing."

MARIANE: No.

VALÈRE: Well, well!

MARIANE: Advise me, do.

VALÈRE: Marry the man. That's my advice to you.

MARIANE: That's your advice?

VALÈRE: Yes.

MARIANE: Truly?

VALÈRE: Oh, absolutely.

You couldn't choose more wisely, more astutely.

MARIANE: Thanks for this counsel; I'll follow it, of course.   15

VALÈRE: Do, do; I'm sure 'twill cost you no remorse.

MARIANE: To give it didn't cause your heart to break.

VALÈRE: I gave it, Madam, only for your sake.

MARIANE: And it's for your sake that I take it, Sir.

DORINE: [*Withdrawing to the rear of the stage.*]

Let's see which fool will prove the stubborner.   20

VALÈRE: So! I am nothing to you, and it was flat

Deception when you . . .

MARIANE: Please, enough of that.

You've told me plainly that I should agree

To wed the man my father's chosen for me,

And since you've deigned to counsel me so wisely,   25

I promise, Sir, to do as you advise me.

VALÈRE: Ah, no, 'twas not by me that you were swayed.

No, your decision was already made;

Though now, to save appearances, you protest

That you're betraying me at my behest.   30

MARIANE: Just as you say.

VALÈRE: Quite so. And I now see

That you were never truly in love with me.

MARIANE: Alas, you're free to think so if you choose.

VALÈRE: I choose to think so, and here's a bit of news:

You've spurned my hand, but I know where to turn   35

For kinder treatment, as you shall quickly learn.

MARIANE: I'm sure you do. Your noble qualities

Inspire affection . . .

VALÈRE: Forget my qualities, please.

They don't inspire you overmuch, I find.

But there's another lady I have in mind   40

Whose sweet and generous nature will not scorn

To compensate me for the loss I've borne.

MARIANE: I'm no great loss, and I'm sure that you'll transfer

Your heart quite painlessly from me to her.

VALÈRE: I'll do my best to take it in my stride.   45

The pain I feel at being cast aside

Time and forgetfulness may put an end to.

Or if I can't forget, I shall pretend to.

No self-respecting person is expected

To go on loving once he's been rejected.   50

MARIANE: Now, that's a fine, high-minded sentiment.
VALÈRE: One to which any sane man would assent.
　　Would you prefer it if I pined away
　　In hopeless passion till my dying day?
　　Am I to yield you to a rival's arms   55
　　And not console myself with other charms?
MARIANE: Go then; console yourself; don't hesitate.
　　I wish you to; indeed, I cannot wait.
VALÈRE: You wish me to?
MARIANE:　　　　　　　　Yes.
VALÈRE:　　　　　　　　　　　That's the final straw.
　　Madam, farewell. Your wish shall be my law.   60
　　[He starts to leave, and then returns: this repeatedly.]
MARIANE: Splendid.
VALÈRE: [Coming back again.] This breach, remember, is of your making;
　　It's you who've driven me to the step I'm taking.
MARIANE: Of course.
VALÈRE: [Coming back again.] Remember, too, that I am merely
　　Following your example.
MARIANE:　　　　　　　　I see that clearly.
VALÈRE. Enough. I'll go and do your bidding, then.   65
MARIANE: Good.
VALÈRE: [Coming back again.] You shall never see my face again.
MARIANE: Excellent.
VALÈRE: [Walking to the door, then turning about.]
　　　　　　　　　　　Yes?
MARIANE:　　　　　　　What?
VALÈRE:　　　　　　　　　　　What's that? What did you say?
MARIANE: Nothing. You're dreaming.
VALÈRE:　　　　　　　　　　Ah. Well, I'm on my way.
　　Farewell, Madame.
　　[He moves slowly away.]
MARIANE:　　　　　　　Farewell.
DORINE: [To MARIANE.]　　　If you ask me,
　　Both of you are as mad as mad can be.   70
　　Do stop this nonsense, now. I've only let you
　　Squabble so long to see where it would get you.
　　Whoa there, Monsieur Valère!
　　[She goes and seizes VALÈRE by the arm; he makes a great show of
　　resistance.]
VALÈRE:　　　　　　　　　　What's this, Dorine?
DORINE: Come here.
VALÈRE:　　　　　　No, no, my heart's too full of spleen.
　　Don't hold me back; her wish must be obeyed.   75
DORINE: Stop!
VALÈRE:　　　It's too late now; my decision's made.
DORINE. Oh, pooh!
MARIANE: [Aside.] He hates the sight of me, that's plain.
　　I'll go, and so deliver him from pain.

DORINE: [*Leaving* VALÈRE, *running after* MARIANE.]
And now *you* run away! Come back.
MARIANE: No, no
Nothing you say will keep me here. Let go!   80
VALÈRE: [*Aside.*] She cannot bear my presence, I perceive.
To spare her further torment, I shall leave.
DORINE: [*Leaving* MARIANE, *running after* VALÈRE.]
Again! You'll not escape, Sir; don't you try it.
Come here, you two. Stop fussing and be quiet.
[*She takes* VALÈRE *by the hand, then* MARIANE, *and draws them together.*]
VALÈRE: [*To* DORINE.] What do you want of me?   85
MARIANE: [*To* DORINE.] What is the point of this?
DORINE. We're going to have a little armistice.
[*To* VALÈRE.] Now, weren't you silly to get so overheated?
VALÈRE: Didn't you see how badly I was treated?
DORINE: [*To* MARIANE.] Aren't you a simpleton, to have lost your head? 90
MARIANE: Didn't you hear the hateful things he said?
DORINE: [*To* VALÈRE.] You're both great fools. Her sole desire, Valère,
Is to be yours in marriage. To that I'll swear.
[*To* MARIANE.] He loves you only, and he wants no wife
But you, Mariane. On that I'll stake my life.   95
MARIANE. [*To* VALÈRE.] Then why you advised me so, I cannot see.
VALÈRE: [*To* MARIANE.] On such a question, why ask advice of *me*?
DORINE: Oh, you're impossible. Give me your hands, you two.
[*To* VALÈRE.] Yours first.
VALÈRE: [*Giving* DORINE *his hand.*] But why?
DORINE: [*To* MARIANE.]   And now a hand from you. 100
MARIANE: [*Also giving* DORINE *her hand.*]
What are you doing?
DORINE: There: a perfect fit.
You suit each other better than you'll admit.
[VALÈRE *and* MARIANE *hold hands for some time without looking at each other.*]
VALÈRE: [*Turning toward* MARIANE.]
Ah, come, don't be so haughty. Give a man
A look of kindness, won't you, Mariane?
[MARIANE *turns toward* VALÈRE *and smiles.*]
DORINE: I tell you, lovers are completely mad!   105
VALÈRE: [*To* MARIANE.] Now come, confess that you were very bad
To hurt my feelings as you did just now.
I have a just complaint, you must allow.
MARIANE: *You* must allow that you were most unpleasant . . .
DORINE: Let's table that discussion for the present;   110
Your father has a plan which must be stopped.
MARIANE: Advise us, then; what means must we adopt?
DORINE: We'll use all manner of means, and all at once.
[*To* MARIANE.] Your father's addled; he's acting like a dunce.
Therefore you'd better humor the old fossil.   115

Pretend to yield to him, be sweet and docile,
And then postpone, as often as necessary,
The day on which you have agreed to marry.
You'll thus gain time, and time will turn the trick.
Sometimes, for instance, you'll be taken sick,   120
And that will seem good reason for delay;
Or some bad omen will make you change the day—
You'll dream of muddy water, or you'll pass
A dead man's hearse, or break a looking-glass.
If all else fails, no man can marry you   125
Unless you take his ring and say "I do."
But now, let's separate. If they should find
Us talking here, our plot might be divined.
[*To* VALÈRE.] Go to your friends, and tell them what's occurred,
And have them urge her father to keep his word.   130
Meanwhile, we'll stir her brother into action,
And get Elmire,[9] as well, to join our faction.
Good-bye.
VALÈRE: [*To* MARIANE.] Though each of us will do his best,
It's your true heart on which my hopes shall rest.   135
MARIANE: [*To* VALÈRE.] Regardless of what Father may decide,
None but Valère shall claim me as his bride.
VALÈRE: Oh, how those words content me! Come what will . . .
DORINE: Oh, lovers, lovers! Their tongues are never still.
Be off, now.
VALÈRE: [*Turning to go, then turning back.*]
            One last word . . .
DORINE: No time to chat: 140
You leave by this door; and *you* leave by that.
[DORINE *pushes them, by the shoulders, toward opposing doors.*]

Act III

SCENE 1

DAMIS, DORINE

DAMIS: May lightning strike me even as I speak,
May all men call me cowardly and weak,
If any fear or scruple holds me back
From settling things, at once, with that great quack!
DORINE: Now, don't give way to violent emotion.   5
Your father's merely talked about this notion,
And words and deeds are far from being one.
Much that is talked about is never done.
DAMIS: No, I must stop that scoundrel's machinations;
I'll go and tell him off; I'm out of patience.   10

---

9. Orgon's second wife.

DORINE: Do calm down and be practical. I had rather
    My mistress dealt with him—and with your father.
    She has some influence with Tartuffe, I've noted.
    He hangs upon her words, seems most devoted,
    And may, indeed, be smitten by her charm.   15
    Pray Heaven it's true! 'Twould do our cause no harm.
    She sent for him, just now, to sound him out
    On this affair you're so incensed about;
    She'll find out where he stands, and tell him, too,
    What dreadful strife and trouble will ensue   20
    If he lends countenance to your father's plan.
    I couldn't get in to see him, but his man
    Says that he's almost finished with his prayers.
    Go, now. I'll catch him when he comes downstairs.
DAMIS: I want to hear this conference, and I will.   25
DORINE: No, they must be alone.
DAMIS: Oh, I'll keep still.
DORINE: Not you. I know your temper. You'd start a brawl,
    And shout and stamp your foot and spoil it all.
    Go on.
DAMIS: I won't; I have a perfect right . . .
DORINE: Lord, you're a nuisance! He's coming; get out of sight.   30
    [DAMIS *conceals himself in a closet at the rear of the stage.*]

SCENE 2

TARTUFFE, DORINE

TARTUFFE: [*Observing* DORINE, *and calling to his manservant off-stage.*]
    Hang up my hair-shirt, put my scourge in place,
    And pray, Laurent, for Heaven's perpetual grace.
    I'm going to the prison now, to share
    My last few coins with the poor wretches there.
DORINE: [*Aside.*] Dear God, what affectation! What a fake!   5
TARTUFFE: You wished to see me?
DORINE: Yes . . .
TARTUFFE. [*Taking a handkerchief from his pocket.*]
                          For mercy's sake,
    Please take this handkerchief, before you speak.
DORINE: What?
TARTUFFE: Cover that bosom,[1] girl. The flesh is weak.
    And unclean thoughts are difficult to control.
    Such sights as that can undermine the soul.   10
DORINE: Your soul, it seems, has very poor defenses,
    And flesh makes quite an impact on your senses.
    It's strange that you're so easily excited;
    My own desires are not so soon ignited,

1. The Brotherhood of the Holy Sacrament practiced alms giving to prisoners and kept a careful, censorious check on women's clothing if they deemed it lascivious. Thus Molière's audience would have identified Tartuffe as sympathetic—hypocritically—to the aims of the organization.

And if I saw you naked as a beast,   15
Not all your hide would tempt me in the least.
TARTUFFE: Girl, speak more modestly; unless you do,
I shall be forced to take my leave of you.
DORINE: Oh, no, it's I who must be on my way;
I've just one little message to convey.   20
Madame is coming down, and begs you, Sir,
To wait and have a word or two with her.
TARTUFFE: Gladly.
DORINE: [Aside.] That had a softening effect!
I think my guess about him was correct.
TARTUFFE: Will she be long?
DORINE: No: that's her step I hear.   25
Ah, here she is, and I shall disappear.

SCENE 3

ELMIRE, TARTUFFE

TARTUFFE: May Heaven, whose infinite goodness we adore,
Preserve your body and soul forevermore,
And bless your days, and answer thus the plea
Of one who is its humblest votary.
ELMIRE: I thank you for that pious wish. But please,   5
Do take a chair and let's be more at ease.
[They sit down.]
TARTUFFE: I trust that you are once more well and strong?
ELMIRE: Oh, yes: the fever didn't last for long.
TARTUFFE: My prayers are too unworthy, I am sure,
To have gained from Heaven this most gracious cure;   10
But lately, Madam, my every supplication
Has had for object your recuperation.
ELMIRE: You shouldn't have troubled so. I don't deserve it.
TARTUFFE: Your health is priceless, Madam, and to preserve it
I'd gladly give my own, in all sincerity.   15
ELMIRE: Sir, you outdo us all in Christian charity.
You've been most kind. I count myself your debtor.
TARTUFFE: 'Twas nothing, Madam. I long to serve you better.
ELMIRE: There's a private matter I'm anxious to discuss.
I'm glad there's no one here to hinder us.   20
TARTUFFE: I too am glad; it floods my heart with bliss
To find myself alone with you like this.
For just this chance I've prayed with all my power —
But prayed in vain, until this happy hour.
ELMIRE: This won't take long, Sir, and I hope you'll be   25
Entirely frank and unconstrained with me.
TARTUFFE: Indeed, there's nothing I had rather do
Than bare my inmost heart and soul to you.
First, let me say that what remarks I've made
About the constant visits you are paid   30

Were prompted not by any mean emotion,
But rather by a pure and deep devotion,
A fervent zeal . . .
ELMIRE: No need for explanation.
Your sole concern, I'm sure, was my salvation.
TARTUFFE: [*Taking* ELMIRE'S *hand and pressing her fingertips.*]
Quite so; and such great fervor do I feel . . .   35
ELMIRE: Ooh! Please! You're pinching!
TARTUFFE: 'Twas from excess of zeal.
I never meant to cause you pain, I swear.
I'd rather . . .
     [*He places his hand on* ELMIRE'S *knee.*]
ELMIRE: What can your hand be doing there?
TARTUFFE: Feeling your gown: what soft, fine-woven stuff!
ELMIRE: Please, I'm extremely ticklish. That's enough.   40
     [*She draws her chair away;* TARTUFFE *pulls his after her.*]
TARTUFFE: [*Fondling the lace collar of her gown.*]
My, my, what lovely lacework on your dress!
The workmanship's miraculous, no less.
I've not seen anything to equal it.
ELMIRE: Yes, quite. But let's talk business for a bit.
They say my husband means to break his word   45
And give his daughter to you, Sir. Had you heard?
TARTUFFE: He did once mention it. But I confess
I dream of quite a different happiness.
It's elsewhere, Madam, that my eyes discern
The promise of that bliss for which I yearn.   50
ELMIRE: I see: you care for nothing here below.
TARTUFFE: Ah, well—my heart's not made of stone, you know.
ELMIRE: All your desires mount heavenward, I'm sure,
In scorn of all that's earthly and impure.
TARTUFFE: A love of heavenly beauty does not preclude   55
A proper love for earthly pulchritude;
Our senses are quite rightly captivated
By perfect works our Maker has created.
Some glory clings to all that Heaven has made;
In you, all Heaven's marvels are displayed.   60
On that fair face, such beauties have been lavished,
The eyes are dazzled and the heart is ravished;
How could I look on you, O flawless creature,
And not adore the Author of all Nature,
Feeling a love both passionate and pure   65
For you, his triumph of self-portraiture?
At first, I trembled lest that love should be
A subtle snare that Hell had laid for me;
I vowed to flee the sight of you, eschewing
A rapture that might prove my soul's undoing;   70
But soon, fair being, I became aware
That my deep passion could be made to square

With rectitude, and with my bounden duty,
I thereupon surrendered to your beauty.
It is, I know, presumptuous on my part   75
To bring you this poor offering of my heart,
And it is not my merit, Heaven knows,
But your compassion on which my hopes repose.
You are my peace, my solace, my salvation;
On you depends my bliss—or desolation;   80
I bide your judgment and, as you think best,
I shall be either miserable or blest.

ELMIRE: Your declaration is most gallant, Sir,
But don't you think it's out of character?
You'd have done better to restrain your passion   85
And think before you spoke in such a fashion.
It ill becomes a pious man like you . . .

TARTUFFE: I may be pious, but I'm human too:
With your celestial charms before his eyes,
A man has not the power to be wise.   90
I know such words sound strangely, coming from me,
But I'm no angel, nor was meant to be,
And if you blame my passion, you must needs
Reproach as well the charms on which it feeds.
Your loveliness I had no sooner seen   95
Than you became my soul's unrivalled queen;
Before your seraph glance, divinely sweet,
My heart's defenses crumbled in defeat,
And nothing fasting, prayer, or tears might do
Could stay my spirit from adoring you.   100
My eyes, my sighs have told you in the past
What now my lips make bold to say at last,
And if, in your great goodness, you will deign
To look upon your slave, and ease his pain,—
If, in compassion for my soul's distress,   105
You'll stoop to comfort my unworthiness,
I'll raise to you, in thanks for that sweet manna,
An endless hymn, an infinite hosanna.
With me, of course, there need be no anxiety,
No fear of scandal or of notoriety.   110
These young court gallants, whom all the ladies fancy,
Are vain in speech, in action rash and chancy;
When they succeed in love, the world soon knows it;
No favor's granted them but they disclose it
And by the looseness of their tongues profane   115
The very altar where their hearts have lain.
Men of my sort, however, love discreetly,
And one may trust our reticence completely.
My keen concern for my good name insures
The absolute security of yours;   120
In short, I offer you, my dear Elmire,

Love without scandal, pleasure without fear.
ELMIRE: I've heard your well-turned speeches to the end,
    And what you urge I clearly apprehend.
    Aren't you afraid that I may take a notion   125
    To tell my husband of your warm devotion,
    And that, supposing he were duly told,
    His feelings toward you might grow rather cold?
TARTUFFE: I know, dear lady, that your exceeding charity
    Will lead your heart to pardon my temerity;   130
    That you'll excuse my violent affection
    As human weakness, human imperfection;
    And that—O fairest!— you will bear in mind
    That I'm but flesh and blood, and am not blind.
ELMIRE: Some women might do otherwise, perhaps,   135
    But I shall be discreet about your lapse;
    I'll tell my husband nothing of what's occurred
    If, in return, you'll give your solemn word
    To advocate as forcefully as you can
    The marriage of Valère and Mariane,   140
    Renouncing all desire to dispossess
    Another of his rightful happiness,
    And . . .

SCENE 4

DAMIS, ELMIRE, TARTUFFE

DAMIS: [*Emerging from the closet where he has been hiding.*]
       No! We'll not hush up this vile affair;
    I heard it all inside that closet there,
    Where Heaven, in order to confound the pride
    Of this great rascal, prompted me to hide.
    Ah, now I have my long-awaited chance   5
    To punish his deceit and arrogance,
    And give my father clear and shocking proof
    Of the black character of his dear Tartuffe.
ELMIRE: Ah no, Damis; I'll be content if he
    Will study to deserve my leniency.   10
    I've promised silence—don't make me break my word;
    To make a scandal would be too absurd.
    Good wives laugh off such trifles, and forget them;
    Why should they tell their husbands, and upset them?
DAMIS: You have your reasons for taking such a course,   15
    And I have reasons, too, of equal force.
    To spare him now would be insanely wrong.
    I've swallowed my just wrath for far too long
    And watched this insolent bigot bringing strife
    And bitterness into our family life.   20
    Too long he's meddled in my father's affairs,
    Thwarting my marriage-hopes, and poor Valère's.

It's high time that my father was undeceived,
And now I've proof that can't be disbelieved—
Proof that was furnished me by Heaven above.   25
It's too good not to take advantage of.
This is my chance, and I deserve to lose it
If, for one moment, I hesitate to use it.
ELMIRE: Damis . . .
DAMIS: No, I must do what I think right.
Madam, my heart is bursting with delight,   30
And, say whatever you will, I'll not consent
To lose the sweet revenge on which I'm bent.
I'll settle matters without more ado;
And here, most opportunely, is my cue.[2]

SCENE 5

ORGON, DAMIS, TARTUFFE, ELMIRE

DAMIS: Father, I'm glad you've joined us. Let us advise you
Of some fresh news which doubtless will surprise you.
You've just now been repaid with interest
For all your loving-kindness to our guest.
He's proved his warm and grateful feelings toward you;   5
It's with a pair of horns he would reward you.
Yes, I surprised him with your wife, and heard
His whole adulterous offer, every word.
She, with her all too gentle disposition,
Would not have told you of his proposition;   10
But I shall not make terms with brazen lechery,
And feel that not to tell you would be treachery.
ELMIRE: And I hold that one's husband's peace of mind
Should not be spoilt by tattle of this kind.
One's honor doesn't require it: to be proficient   15
In keeping men at bay is quite sufficient.
These are my sentiments, and I wish, Damis,
That you had heeded me and held your peace.

SCENE 6

ORGON, DAMIS, TARTUFFE

ORGON: Can it be true, this dreadful thing I hear?
TARTUFFE: Yes, Brother, I'm a wicked man, I fear:
A wretched sinner, all depraved and twisted,
The greatest villain that has ever existed.
My life's one heap of crimes, which grows each minute;   5
There's naught but foulness and corruption in it;
And I perceive that Heaven, outraged by me,

2. In the original stage directions, Tartuffe now reads silently from his breviary—in the Roman Catholic Church, the book containing the Divine Office for each day, which those in holy orders are required to recite.

Has chosen this occasion to mortify me.
Charge me with any deed you wish to name;
I'll not defend myself, but take the blame.   10
Believe what you are told, and drive Tartuffe
Like some base criminal from beneath your roof;
Yes, drive me hence, and with a parting curse:
I shan't protest, for I deserve far worse.
ORGON: [*To* DAMIS.] Ah, you deceitful boy, how dare you try   15
    To stain his purity with so foul a lie?
DAMIS: What! Are you taken in by such a fluff?
    Did you not hear . . .?
ORGON: Enough, you rogue, enough!
TARTUFFE: Ah, Brother, let him speak: you're being unjust.
    Believe his story; the boy deserves your trust.   20
    Why, after all, should you have faith in me?
    How can you know what I might do, or be?
    Is it on my good actions that you base
    Your favor? Do you trust my pious face?
    Ah, no, don't be deceived by hollow shows;   25
    I'm far, alas, from being what men suppose;
    Though the world takes me for a man of worth,
    I'm truly the most worthless man on earth.
    [*To* DAMIS.] Yes, my dear son, speak out now: call me the chief
    Of sinners, a wretch, a murderer, a thief;   30
    Load me with all the names men most abhor;
    I'll not complain; I've earned them all, and more;
    I'll kneel here while you pour them on my head
    As a just punishment for the life I've led.
ORGON: [*To* TARTUFFE.]
    This is too much, dear Brother.
    [*To* DAMIS.]   Have you no heart?   35
DAMIS: Are you so hoodwinked by this rascal's art . . .?
ORGON: Be still, you monster.
    [*To* TARTUFFE.]   Brother, I pray you, rise.
    [*To* DAMIS.] Villain!
DAMIS: But . . .
ORGON: Silence!
DAMIS: Can't you realize . . .?
ORGON: Just one word more, and I'll tear you limb from limb.
TARTUFFE: In God's name, Brother, don't be harsh with him.   40
    I'd rather far be tortured at the stake
    Than see him bear one scratch for my poor sake.
ORGON: [*To* DAMIS.] Ingrate!
TARTUFFE: If I must beg you, on bended knee,
    To pardon him . . .
ORGON: [*Falling to his knees, addressing* TARTUFFE.]
                    Such goodness cannot be!
    [*To* DAMIS.] Now, *there's* true charity!
DAMIS: What, you . . .?

ORGON: Villain, be still! 45
I know your motives; I know you wish him ill:
Yes, all of you—wife, children, servants, all—
Conspire against him and desire his fall,
Employing every shameful trick you can
To alienate me from this saintly man. 50
Ah, but the more you seek to drive him away,
The more I'll do to keep him. Without delay,
I'll spite this household and confound its pride
By giving him my daughter as his bride.

DAMIS: You're going to force her to accept his hand? 55

ORGON: Yes, and this very night, d'you understand?
I shall defy you all, and make it clear
That I'm the one who gives the orders here.
Come, wretch, kneel down and clasp his blessed feet,
And ask his pardon for your black deceit. 60

DAMIS: I ask that swindler's pardon? Why, I'd rather . . .

ORGON: So! You insult him, and defy your father!
A stick! A stick! [To TARTUFFE.] No, no—release me, do.
[To DAMIS.] Out of my house this minute! Be off with you,
And never dare set foot in it again. 65

DAMIS: Well, I shall go, but . . .

ORGON: Well, go quickly, then.
I disinherit you; an empty purse
Is all you'll get from me—except my curse!

SCENE 7

ORGON, TARTUFFE

ORGON: How he blasphemed your goodness! What a son!

TARTUFFE: Forgive him, Lord, as I've already done.
[To ORGON.] You can't know how it hurts when someone tries
To blacken me in my dear brother's eyes.

ORGON: Ahh!

TARTUFFE: The mere thought of such ingratitude 5
Plunges my soul into so dark a mood . . .
Such horror grips my heart . . . I gasp for breath,
And cannot speak, and feel myself near death.

ORGON: [He runs, in tears, to the door through which he has just driven
his son.]
You blackguard! Why did I spare you? Why did I not
Break you in little pieces on the spot? 10
Compose yourself, and don't be hurt, dear friend.

TARTUFFE: These scenes, these dreadful quarrels, have got to end.
I've much upset your household, and I perceive
That the best thing will be for me to leave.

ORGON: What are you saying!

TARTUFFE: They're all against me here; 15
They'd have you think me false and insincere.

ORGON: Ah, what of that? Have I ceased believing in you?
TARTUFFE: Their adverse talk will certainly continue,
　　And charges which you now repudiate
　　You may find credible at a later date.　　　　　　　20
ORGON: No, Brother, never.
TARTUFFE:　　　　　　　　　Brother, a wife can sway
　　Her husband's mind in many a subtle way.
ORGON: No, no.
TARTUFFE:　　　To leave at once is the solution;
　　Thus only can I end their persecution.
ORGON: No, no, I'll not allow it; you shall remain.　　25
TARTUFFE: Ah, well; 'twill mean much martyrdom and pain,
　　But if you wish it . . .
ORGON:　　　　　　　Ah!
TARTUFFE:　　　　　　Enough; so be it.
　　But one thing must be settled, as I see it.
　　For your dear honor, and for our friendship's sake,
　　There's one precaution I feel bound to take.　　　30
　　I shall avoid your wife, and keep away . . .
ORGON: No, you shall not, whatever they may say.
　　It pleases me to vex them, and for spite
　　I'd have them see you with her day and night.
　　What's more, I'm going to drive them to despair　　35
　　By making you my only son and heir;
　　This very day, I'll give to you alone
　　Clear deed and title to everything I own.
　　A dear, good friend and son-in-law-to-be
　　Is more than wife, or child, or kin to me.　　　　40
　　Will you accept my offer, dearest son?
TARTUFFE: In all things, let the will of Heaven be done.
ORGON: Poor fellow! Come, we'll go draw up the deed.
　　Then let them burst with disappointed greed!

Act IV

SCENE 1

CLÉANTE, TARTUFFE

CLÉANTE: Yes, all the town's discussing it, and truly,
　　Their comments do not flatter you unduly.
　　I'm glad we've met, Sir, and I'll give my view
　　Of this sad matter in a word or two.
　　As for who's guilty, that I shan't discuss;　　　　5
　　Let's say it was Damis who caused the fuss;
　　Assuming, then, that you have been ill-used
　　By young Damis, and groundlessly accused,
　　Ought not a Christian to forgive, and ought
　　He not to stifle every vengeful thought?　　　　10

Should you stand by and watch a father make
His only son an exile for your sake?
Again I tell you frankly, be advised:
The whole town, high and low, is scandalized;
This quarrel must be mended, and my advice is   15
Not to push matters to a further crisis.
No, sacrifice your wrath to God above,
And help Damis regain his father's love.
TARTUFFE: Alas, for my part I should take great joy
    In doing so. I've nothing against the boy.   20
    I pardon all, I harbor no resentment;
    To serve him would afford me much contentment.
    But Heaven's interest will not have it so:
    If he comes back, then I shall have to go.
    After his conduct—so extreme, so vicious—   25
    Our further intercourse would look suspicious.
    God knows what people would think! Why, they'd describe
    My goodness to him as a sort of bribe;
    They'd say that out of guilt I made pretense
    Of loving-kindness and benevolence—   30
    That, fearing my accuser's tongue, I strove
    To buy his silence with a show of love.
CLÉANTE: Your reasoning is badly warped and stretched,
    And these excuses, Sir, are most far-fetched.
    Why put yourself in charge of Heaven's cause?   35
    Does Heaven need our help to enforce its laws?
    Leave vengeance to the Lord, Sir; while we live,
    Our duty's not to punish, but forgive;
    And what the Lord commands, we should obey
    Without regard to what the world may say.   40
    What! Shall the fear of being misunderstood
    Prevent our doing what is right and good?
    No, no: let's simply do what Heaven ordains,
    And let no other thoughts perplex our brains.
TARTUFFE: Again, Sir, let me say that I've forgiven   45
    Damis, and thus obeyed the laws of Heaven;
    But I am not commanded by the Bible
    To live with one who smears my name with libel.
CLÉANTE: Were you commanded, Sir, to indulge the whim
    Of poor Orgon, and to encourage him   50
    In suddenly transferring to your name
    A large estate to which you have no claim?
TARTUFFE: 'Twould never occur to those who know me best
    To think I acted from self-interest.
    The treasures of this world I quite despise;   55
    Their specious glitter does not charm my eyes;
    And if I have resigned myself to taking
    The gift which my dear Brother insists on making,
    I do so only, as he well understands,

Lest so much wealth fall into wicked hands,   60
Lest those to whom it might descend in time
Turn it to purposes of sin and crime,
And not, as I shall do, make use of it
For Heaven's glory and mankind's benefit.
CLÉANTE: Forget these trumped-up fears. Your argument   65
Is one the rightful heir might well resent;
It *is* a moral burden to inherit
Such wealth, but give Damis a chance to bear it.
And would it not be worse to be accused
Of swindling, than to see that wealth misused?   70
I'm shocked that you allowed Orgon to broach
This matter, and that you feel no self-reproach;
Does true religion teach that lawful heirs
May freely be deprived of what is theirs?
And if the Lord has told you in your heart   75
That you and young Damis must dwell apart,
Would it not be the decent thing to beat
A generous and honorable retreat,
Rather than let the son of the house be sent,
For your convenience, into banishment?   80
Sir, if you wish to prove the honesty
Of your intentions . . . .
TARTUFFE: Sir, it is a half past three.
I've certain pious duties to attend to,
And hope my prompt departure won't offend you.
CLÉANTE: [*Alone.*] Damn.

SCENE 2

ELMIRE, MARIANE, CLÉANTE, DORINE

DORINE: Stay, Sir, and help Mariane, for Heaven's sake!
She's suffering so, I fear her heart will break.
Her father's plan to marry her off tonight
Has put the poor child in a desperate plight.
I hear him coming. Let's stand together, now,   5
And see if we can't change his mind, somehow,
About this match we all deplore and fear.

SCENE 3

ORGON, ELMIRE, MARIANE, CLÉANTE, DORINE

ORGON: Hah! Glad to find you all assembled here.
[*To* MARIANE.] This contract, child, contains your happiness,
And what it says I think your heart can guess.
MARIANE: [*Falling to her knees.*]
Sir, by that Heaven which sees me here distressed,
And by whatever else can move your breast,   5
Do not employ a father's power, I pray you,

To crush my heart and force it to obey you,
Nor by your harsh commands oppress me so
That I'll begrudge the duty which I owe—
And do not so embitter and enslave me   10
That I shall hate the very life you gave me.
If my sweet hopes must perish, if you refuse
To give me to the one I've dared to choose,
Spare me at least—I beg you, I implore—
The pain of wedding one whom I abhor;   15
And do not, by a heartless use of force,
Drive me to contemplate some desperate course.

ORGON: [*Feeling himself touched by her.*]
Be firm, my soul. No human weakness, now.

MARIANE: I don't resent your love for him. Allow
Your heart free rein, Sir; give him your property,   20
And if that's not enough, take mine from me;
He's welcome to my money; take it, do,
But don't, I pray, include my person too.
Spare me, I beg you; and let me end the tale
Of my sad days behind a convent veil.   25

ORGON: A convent! Hah! When crossed in their amours,
All lovesick girls have the same thought as yours.
Get up! The more you loathe the man, and dread him,
The more ennobling it will be to wed him.
Marry Tartuffe, and mortify your flesh!   30
Enough; don't start that whimpering afresh.

DORINE: But why . . . ?

ORGON: Be still, there. Speak when you're spoken to.
Not one more bit of impudence out of you.

CLÉANTE: If I may offer a word of counsel here . . .

ORGON: Brother, in counselling you have no peer;   35
All your advice is forceful, sound, and clever;
I don't propose to follow it, however.

ELMIRE: [*To* ORGON.] I am amazed, and don't know what to say;
Your blindness simply takes my breath away.
You are indeed bewitched, to take no warning   40
From our account of what occurred this morning.

ORGON: Madam, I know a few plain facts, and one
Is that you're partial to my rascal son;
Hence, when he sought to make Tartuffe the victim
Of a base lie, you dared not contradict him.   45
Ah, but you underplayed your part, my pet;
You should have looked more angry, more upset.

ELMIRE: When men make overtures, must we reply
With righteous anger and a battle-cry?
Must we turn back their amorous advances   50
With sharp reproaches and with fiery glances?
Myself, I find such offers merely amusing,
And make no scenes and fusses in refusing;

My taste is for good-natured rectitude,
And I dislike the savage sort of prude   55
Who guards her virtue with her teeth and claws,
And tears men's eyes out for the slightest cause:
The Lord preserve me from such honor as that,
Which bites and scratches like an alley-cat!
I've found that a polite and cool rebuff   60
Discourages a lover quite enough.
ORGON: I know the facts, and I shall not be shaken.
ELMIRE: I marvel at your power to be mistaken.
    Would it, I wonder, carry weight with you
    If I could *show* you that our tale was true?   65
ORGON: Show me?
ELMIRE: Yes.
ORGON: Rot.
ELMIRE: Come, what if I found a way
    To make you see the facts as plain as day?
ORGON: Nonsense.
ELMIRE: Do answer me; don't be absurd.
    I'm not now asking you to trust our word.
    Suppose that from some hiding-place in here   70
    You learned the whole sad truth by eye and ear—
    What would you say of your good friend, after that?
ORGON: Why, I'd say . . . nothing, by Jehoshaphat!
    It can't be true.
ELMIRE: You've been too long deceived,
    I'm quite tired of being disbelieved.   75
    Come now: let's put my statements to the test,
    And you shall see the truth made manifest.
ORGON: I'll take that challenge. Now do your uttermost.
    We'll see how you make good your empty boast.
ELMIRE: [*To* DORINE.] Send him to me.
DORINE: He's crafty; it may be hard   80
    To catch the cunning scoundrel off his guard.
ELMIRE: No, amorous men are gullible. Their conceit
    So blinds them that they're never hard to cheat.
    Have him come down.
    [*To* CLÉANTE *and* MARIANE.] Please leave us, for a bit.

SCENE 4

ELMIRE, ORGON

ELMIRE: Pull up this table, and get under it.
ORGON: What?
ELMIRE.   It's essential that you be well-hidden.
ORGON: Why there?
ELMIRE: Oh, Heavens! Just do as you are bidden.
    I have my plans; we'll soon see how they fare.
    Under the table, now; and once you're there,   5

Take care that you are neither seen nor heard.
ORGON: Well, I'll indulge you, since I gave my word
  To see you through this infantile charade.
ELMIRE: Once it is over, you'll be glad we played.
    [*To her husband, who is now under the table.*]
  I'm going to act quite strangely, now, and you   10
  Must not be shocked at anything I do.
  Whatever I may say, you must excuse
  As part of that deceit I'm forced to use.
  I shall employ sweet speeches in the task
  Of making that impostor drop his mask;   15
  I'll give encouragement to his bold desires,
  And furnish fuel to his amorous fires.
  Since it's for your sake, and for his destruction,
  That I shall seem to yield to his seduction,
  I'll gladly stop whenever you decide.   20
  That all your doubts are fully satisfied.
  I'll count on you, as soon as you have seen
  What sort of man he is, to intervene,
  And not expose me to his odious lust
  One moment longer than you feel you must.   25
  Remember: you're to save me from my plight
  Whenever . . . He's coming! Hush! Keep out of sight!

SCENE 5

TARTUFFE, ELMIRE, ORGON

TARTUFFE: You wish to have a word with me, I'm told.
ELMIRE: Yes, I've a little secret to unfold.
  Before I speak, however, it would be wise
  To close that door, and look about for spies.
    [TARTUFFE *goes to the door, closes it, and returns.*]
  The very last thing that must happen now   5
  Is a repetition of this morning's row.
  I've never been so badly caught off guard.
  Oh, how I feared for you! You saw how hard
  I tried to make that troublesome Damis
  Control his dreadful temper, and hold his peace.   10
  In my confusion, I didn't have the sense
  Simply to contradict his evidence;
  But as it happened, that was for the best,
  And all has worked out in our interest.
  This storm has only bettered your position;   15
  My husband doesn't have the least suspicion,
  And now, in mockery of those who do,
  He bids me be continually with you.
  And that is why, quite fearless of reproof,
  I now can be alone with my Tartuffe,   20

And why my heart—perhaps too quick to yield—
Feels free to let its passion be revealed.
TARTUFFE: Madam, your words confuse me. Not long ago,
    You spoke in quite a different style, you know.
ELMIRE: Ah, Sir, if that refusal made you smart,   25
    It's little that you know of woman's heart,
    Or what that heart is trying to convey
    When it resists in such a feeble way!
    Always, at first, our modesty prevents
    The frank avowal of tender sentiments: 30
    However high the passion which inflames us,
    Still, to confess its power somehow shames us.
    Thus we reluct, at first, yet in a tone
    Which tells you that our heart is overthrown,
    That what our lips deny, our pulse confesses,   35
    And that, in time, all noes will turn to yesses.
    I fear my words are all too frank and free,
    And a poor proof of woman's modesty;
    But since I'm started, tell me, if you will—
    Would I have tried to make Damis be still,   40
    Would I have listened, calm and unoffended,
    Until your lengthy offer of love was ended,
    And been so very mild in my reaction,
    Had your sweet words not given me satisfaction?
    And when I tried to force you to undo   45
    The marriage-plans my husband has in view,
    What did my urgent pleading signify
    If not that I admired you, and that I
    Deplored the thought that someone else might own
    Part of a heart I wished for mine alone?   50
TARTUFFE: Madam, no happiness is so complete
    As when, from lips we love, come words so sweet;
    Their nectar floods my every sense, and drains
    In honeyed rivulets through all my veins.
    To please you is my joy, my only goal;   55
    Your love is the restorer of my soul;
    And yet I must beg leave, now, to confess
    Some lingering doubts as to my happiness.
    Might this not be a trick? Might not the catch
    Be that you wish me to break off the match   60
    With Mariane, and so have feigned to love me?
    I shan't quite trust your fond opinion of me
    Until the feelings you've expressed so sweetly
    Are demonstrated somewhat more concretely,
    And you have shown, by certain kind concessions,   65
    That I may put my faith in your professions
ELMIRE: [*She coughs, to warn her husband.*]
    Why be in such a hurry? Must my heart
    Exhaust its bounty at the very start?

To make that sweet admission cost me dear,
But you'll not be content, it would appear,   70
Unless my store of favors is disbursed
To the last farthing, and at the very first.
TARTUFFE: The less we merit, the less we dare to hope,
And with our doubts, mere words can never cope.
We trust no promised bliss till we receive it;   75
Not till a joy is ours can we believe it.
I, who so little merit your esteem,
Can't credit this fulfillment of my dream,
And shan't believe it, Madam, until I savor
Some palpable assurance of your favor.   80
ELMIRE: My, how tyrannical your love can be,
And how it flusters and perplexes me!
How furiously you take one's heart in hand,
And make your every wish a fierce command!
Come, must you hound and harry me to death?   85
Will you not give me time to catch my breath?
Can it be right to press me with such force,
Give me no quarter, show me no remorse,
And take advantage, by your stern insistence,
Of the fond feelings which weaken my resistance?   90
TARTUFFE: Well, if you look with favor upon my love,
Why, then, begrudge me some clear proof thereof?
ELMIRE: But how can I consent without offense
To Heaven, toward which you feel such reverence?
TARTUFFE: If Heaven is all that holds you back, don't worry.   95
I can remove that hindrance in a hurry.
Nothing of that sort need obstruct our path.
ELMIRE: Must one not be afraid of Heaven's wrath?
TARTUFFE: Madam, forget such fears, and be my pupil,
And I shall teach you how to conquer scruple.   100
Some joys, it's true, are wrong in Heaven's eyes;
Yet Heaven is not averse to compromise;
There is a science, lately formulated,
Whereby one's conscience may be liberated,[3]
And any wrongful act you care to mention   105
May be redeemed by purity of intention.
I'll teach you, Madam, the secrets of that science;
Meanwhile, just place on me your full reliance.
Assuage my keen desires, and feel no dread:
The sin, if any, shall be on my head.   110
    [ELMIRE coughs, this time more loudly.]
You've a bad cough.
ELMIRE: Yes, yes, It's bad indeed.
TARTUFFE: [Producing a little paper bag.]
A bit of licorice may be what you need.

---

3. Molière created his own footnote to this line: "It is a scoundrel who speaks."

ELMIRE: No, I've a stubborn cold, it seems. I'm sure it
    Will take much more than licorice to cure it.
TARTUFFE: How aggravating.
ELMIRE: Oh, more than I can say.   115
TARTUFFE: If you're still troubled, think of things this way:
    No one shall know our joys, save us alone,
    And there's no evil till the act is known;
    It's scandal, Madam, which makes it an offense,
    And it's no sin to sin in confidence.   120
ELMIRE: [*Having coughed once more.*]
    Well, clearly I must do as you require,
    And yield to your importunate desire.
    It is apparent, now, that nothing less
    Will satisfy you, and so I acquiesce.
    To go so far is much against my will;   125
    I'm vexed that it should come to this; but still,
    Since you are so determined on it, since you
    Will not allow mere language to convince you,
    And since you ask for concrete evidence, I
    See nothing for it, now, but to comply.   130
    If this is sinful, if I'm wrong to do it,
    So much the worse for him who drove me to it.
    The fault can surely not be charged to me.
TARTUFFE: Madam, the fault is mine, if fault there be,
    And . . .
ELMIRE: Open the door a little, and peek out;   135
    I wouldn't want my husband poking about.
TARTUFFE: Why worry about the man? Each day he grows
    More gullible; one can lead him by the nose.
    To find us here would fill him with delight,
    And if he saw the worst, he'd doubt his sight.   140
ELMIRE: Nevertheless, do step out for a minute
    Into the hall, and see that no one's in it.

SCENE 6

ORGON, ELMIRE

ORGON: [*Coming out from under the table.*]
    That man's a perfect monster, I must admit!
    I'm simply stunned. I can't get over it.
ELMIRE: What, coming out so soon? How premature!
    Get back in hiding, and wait until you're sure.
    Stay till the end, and be convinced completely;   5
    We mustn't stop till things are proved concretely.
ORGON: Hell never harbored anything so vicious!
ELMIRE: Tut, don't be hasty. Try to be judicious.
    Wait, and be certain that there's no mistake.
    No jumping to conclusions, for Heaven's sake!   10
    [*She places* ORGON *behind her, as* TARTUFFE *re-enters.*]

SCENE 7

TARTUFFE, ELMIRE, ORGON

TARTUFFE: [*Not seeing* ORGON.]
 Madam, all things have worked out to perfection;
 I've given the neighboring rooms a full inspection;
 No one's about; and now I may at last . . .
ORGON: [*Intercepting him.*] Hold on, my passionate fellow, not so fast!
 I should advise a little more restraint.   5
 Well, so you thought you'd fool me, my dear saint!
 How soon you wearied of the saintly life—
 Wedding my daughter, and coveting my wife!
 I've long suspected you, and had a feeling
 That soon I'd catch you at your double-dealing.   10
 Just now, you've given me evidence galore;
 It's quite enough; I have no wish for more.
ELMIRE: [*To* TARTUFFE.] I'm sorry to have treated you so slyly,
 But circumstances forced me to be wily.
TARTUFFE: Brother, you can't think . . .
ORGON: No more talk from you;   15
 Just leave this household, without more ado.
TARTUFFE: What I intended . . .
ORGON: That seems fairly clear.
 Spare me your falsehoods and get out of here.
TARTUFFE: No, I'm the master, and you're the one to go!
 This house belongs to me, I'll have you know,   20
 And I shall show you that you can't hurt *me*
 By this contemptible conspiracy,
 That those who cross me know not what they do,
 And that I've means to expose and punish you,
 Avenge offended Heaven, and make you grieve   25
 That ever you dared order me to leave.

SCENE 8

ELMIRE, ORGON

ELMIRE: What was the point of all that angry chatter?
ORGON: Dear God, I'm worried. This is no laughing matter.
ELMIRE: How so?
ORGON: I fear I understood his drift.
 I'm much disturbed about that deed of gift.
ELMIRE: You gave him . . . ?
ORGON: Yes, it's all been drawn and signed. 5
 But one thing more is weighing on my mind.
ELMIRE: What's that?
ORGON: I'll tell you; but first let's see if there's
 A certain strong-box in his room upstairs.

Act V

SCENE 1

ORGON, CLÉANTE

CLÉANTE: Where are you going so fast?
ORGON: God knows!
CLÉANTE: Then wait;
  Let's have a conference, and deliberate
  On how this situation's to be met.
ORGON: That strong-box has me utterly upset;
  This is the worst of many, many shocks.   5
CLÉANTE: Is there some fearful mystery in that box?
ORGON: My poor friend Argas brought that box to me
  With his own hands, in utmost secrecy;
  'Twas on the very morning of his flight.
  It's full of papers which, if they came to light,   10
  Would ruin him—or such is my impression.
CLÉANTE: Then why did you let it out of your possession?
ORGON: Those papers vexed my conscience, and it seemed best
  To ask the counsel of my pious guest.
  The cunning scoundrel got me to agree   15
  To leave the strong-box in his custody,
  So that, in case of an investigation,
  I could employ a slight equivocation
  And swear I didn't have it, and thereby,
  At no expense to conscience, tell a lie.   20
CLÉANTE: It looks to me as if you're out on a limb.
  Trusting him with that box, and offering him
  That deed of gift, were actions of a kind
  Which scarcely indicate a prudent mind.
  With two such weapons, he has the upper hand,   25
  And since you're vulnerable, as matters stand,
  You erred once more in bringing him to bay.
  You should have acted in some subtler way.
ORGON: Just think of it: behind that fervent face,
  A heart so wicked, and a soul so base!   30
  I took him in, a hungry beggar, and then . . .
  Enough, by God! I'm through with pious men:
  Henceforth I'll hate the whole false brotherhood,
  And persecute them worse than Satan could.
CLÉANTE: Ah, there you go—extravagant as ever!   35
  Why can you not be rational? You never
  Manage to take the middle course, it seems,
  But jump, instead, between absurd extremes.
  You've recognized your recent grave mistake
  In falling victim to a pious fake;   40
  Now, to correct that error, must you embrace
  An even greater error in its place,

And judge our worthy neighbors as a whole
By what you've learned of one corrupted soul?
Come, just because one rascal made you swallow   45
A show of zeal which turned out to be hollow,
Shall you conclude that all men are deceivers,
And that, today, there are no true believers?
Let atheists make that foolish inference;
Learn to distinguish virtue from pretense,   50
Be cautious in bestowing admiration,
And cultivate a sober moderation.
Don't humor fraud, but also don't asperse
True piety; the latter fault is worse,
And it is best to err, if err one must,   55
As you have done, upon the side of trust.

SCENE 2

DAMIS, ORGON, CLÉANTE

DAMIS: Father, I hear that scoundrel's uttered threats
　　　Against you; that he pridefully forgets
　　　How, in his need, he was befriended by you,
　　　And means to use your gifts to crucify you.
ORGON: It's true, my boy. I'm too distressed for tears.   5
DAMIS: Leave it to me, Sir; let me trim his ears.
　　　Faced with such insolence, we must not waver.
　　　I shall rejoice in doing you the favor
　　　Of cutting short his life, and your distress.
CLÉANTE: What a display of young hotheadedness!   10
　　　Do learn to moderate your fits of rage.
　　　In this just kingdom, this enlightened age,
　　　One does not settle things by violence.

SCENE 3

MADAME PERNELLE, MARIANE, ELMIRE, DORINE, DAMIS,
ORGON, CLÉANTE

MADAME PERNELLE: I hear strange tales of very strange events.
ORGON: Yes, strange events which these two eyes beheld.
　　　The man's ingratitude is unparalleled.
　　　I save a wretched pauper from starvation,
　　　House him, and treat him like a blood relation,   5
　　　Shower him every day with my largesse,
　　　Give him my daughter, and all that I possess;
　　　And meanwhile the unconscionable knave
　　　Tries to induce my wife to misbehave;
　　　And not content with such extreme rascality,   10
　　　Now threatens me with my own liberality,
　　　And aims, by taking base advantage of
　　　The gifts I gave him out of Christian love,

To drive me from my house, a ruined man,
   And make me end a pauper, as he began.   15
DORINE: Poor fellow!
MADAME PERNELLE: No, my son, I'll never bring
   Myself to think him guilty of such a thing.
ORGON: How's that?
MADAME PERNELLE: The righteous always were maligned.
ORGON: Speak clearly, Mother. Say what's on your mind.
MADAME PERNELLE: I mean that I can smell a rat, my dear.   20
   You know how everybody hates him, here.
ORGON: That has no bearing on the case at all.
MADAME PERNELLE: I told you a hundred times, when you were small,
   That virtue in this world is hated ever;
   Malicious men may die, but malice never.   25
ORGON: No doubt that's true, but how does it apply?
MADAME PERNELLE: They've turned you against him by a clever lie.
ORGON: I've told you, I was there and saw it done.
MADAME PERNELLE: Ah, slanderers will stop at nothing, Son.
ORGON: Mother, I'll lose my temper . . . For the last time,   30
   I tell you I was witness to the crime.
MADAME PERNELLE: The tongues of spite are busy night and noon,
   And to their venom no man is immune.
ORGON: You're talking nonsense. Can't you realize
   I saw it; saw it; saw it with my eyes?   35
   Saw, do you understand me? Must I shout it
   Into your ears before you'll cease to doubt it?
MADAME PERNELLE: Appearances can deceive, my son. Dear me,
   We cannot always judge by what we see.
ORGON: Drat! Drat!
MADAME PERNELLE: One often interprets things awry;   40
   Good can seem evil to a suspicious eye.
ORGON: Was I to see his pawing at Elmire
   As an act of charity?
MADAME PERNELLE: Till his guilt is clear,
   A man deserves the benefit of the doubt.
   You should have waited, to see how things turned out.   45
ORGON: Great God in Heaven, what more proof did I need?
   Was I to sit there, watching, until he'd . . .
   You drive me to the brink of impropriety.
MADAME PERNELLE: No, no, a man of such surpassing piety
   Could not do such a thing. You cannot shake me.   50
   I don't believe it, and you shall not make me.
ORGON: You vex me so that, if you weren't my mother,
   I'd say to you . . . some dreadful thing or other.
DORINE: It's your turn now, Sir, not to be listened to;
   You'd not trust us, and now she won't trust you.   55
CLÉANTE: My friends, we're wasting time which should be spent
   In facing up to our predicament.
   I fear that scoundrel's threats weren't made in sport.

DAMIS: Do you think he'd have the nerve to go to court?

ELMIRE: I'm sure he won't: they'd find it all too crude　　　60
A case of swindling and ingratitude.

CLÉANTE: Don't be too sure. He won't be at a loss
To give his claims a high and righteous gloss;
And clever rogues with far less valid cause
Have trapped their victims in a web of laws.　　　65
I say again that to antagonize
A man so strongly armed was most unwise.

ORGON: I know it; but the man's appalling cheek
Outraged me so, I couldn't control my pique.

CLÉANTE: I wish to Heaven that we could devise　　　70
Some truce between you, or some compromise.

ELMIRE: If I had known what cards he held, I'd not
Have roused his anger by my little plot.

ORGON: [*To* DORINE, *as* M. LOYAL *enters.*]
What is that fellow looking for? Who is he?
Go talk to him—and tell him that I'm busy.　　　75

SCENE 4

MONSIEUR LOYAL, MADAME PERNELLE, ORGON, DAMIS, MARIANE, DORINE,
ELMIRE, CLÉANTE

MONSIEUR LOYAL: Good day, dear sister. Kindly let me see
Your master.

DORINE:　　　He's involved with company,
And cannot be disturbed just now, I fear.

MONSIEUR LOYAL: I hate to intrude; but what has brought me here
Will not disturb your master, in any event.　　　5
Indeed, my news will make him most content.

DORINE: Your name?

MONSIEUR LOYAL:　　　Just say that I bring greetings from
Monsieur Tartuffe, on whose behalf I've come.

DORINE: [*To* ORGON.] Sir, he's a very gracious man, and bears
A message from Tartuffe, which, he declares,　　　10
Will make you most content.

CLÉANTE:　　　　　　Upon my word,
I think this man had best be seen, and heard.

ORGON: Perhaps he has some settlement to suggest.
How shall I treat him? What manner would be best?

CLÉANTE: Control your anger, and if he should mention　　　15
Some fair adjustment, give him your full attention.

MONSIEUR LOYAL: Good health to you, good Sir. May Heaven confound
Your enemies, and may your joys abound.

ORGON: [*Aside, to* CLÉANTE.] A gentle salutation: it confirms
My guess that he is here to offer terms.　　　20

MONSIEUR LOYAL: I've always held your family most dear;
I served your father, Sir, for many a year.

ORGON: Sir, I must ask your pardon; to my shame,

I cannot now recall your face or name.

MONSIEUR LOYAL: Loyal's my name; I come from Normandy,   25
And I'm a bailiff, in all modesty.
For forty years, praise God, it's been my boast
To serve with honor in that vital post,
And I am here, Sir, if you will permit
The liberty, to serve you with this writ . . .   30

ORGON: To—*what?*

MONSIEUR LOYAL: Now, please, Sir, let us have no friction:
It's nothing but an order of eviction.
You are to move your goods and family out
And make way for new occupants, without
Deferment or delay, and give the keys . . .   35

ORGON: I? Leave this house?

MONSIEUR LOYAL: Why yes, Sir, if you please.
This house, Sir, from the cellar to the roof,
Belongs now to the good Monsieur Tartuffe,
And he is lord and master of your estate
By virtue of a deed of present date,   40
Drawn in due form, with clearest legal phrasing . . .

DAMIS: Your insolence is utterly amazing!

MONSIEUR LOYAL: Young man, my business here is not with you
But with your wise and temperate father, who,
Like every worthy citizen, stands in awe   45
Of justice, and would never obstruct the law.

ORGON: But . . .

MONSIEUR LOYAL: Not for a million, Sir, would you rebel
Against authority; I know that well.
You'll not make trouble, Sir, or interfere
With the execution of my duties here.   50

DAMIS: Someone may execute a smart tattoo
On that black jacket[4] of yours, before you're through.

MONSIEUR LOYAL: Sir, bid your son be silent. I'd much regret
Having to mention such a nasty threat
Of violence, in writing my report.   55

DORINE: [*Aside.*] This man Loyal's a most disloyal sort!

MONSIEUR LOYAL: I love all men of upright character,
And when I agreed to serve these papers, Sir,
It was your feelings that I had in mind.
I couldn't bear to see the case assigned   60
To someone else, who might esteem you less
And so subject you to unpleasantness.

ORGON: What's more unpleasant than telling a man to leave
His house and home?

MONSIEUR LOYAL: You'd like a short reprieve?
If you desire it, Sir, I shall not press you,   65
But wait until tomorrow to dispossess you.

---

4. In the original, *justaucorps à longues basques*, a close-fitting, long black coat with skirts, the customary dress of a bailiff.

Splendid. I'll come and spend the night here, then,
Most quietly, with half a score of men.
For form's sake, you might bring me, just before
You go to bed, the keys to the front door.   70
My men, I promise, will be on their best
Behavior, and will not disturb your rest.
But bright and early, Sir, you must be quick
And move out all your furniture, every stick:
The men I've chosen are both young and strong,   75
And with their help it shouldn't take you long.
In short, I'll make things pleasant and convenient,
And since I'm being so extremely lenient,
Please show me, Sir, a like consideration,
And give me your entire cooperation.   80
ORGON: [*Aside.*] I may be all but bankrupt, but I vow
I'd give a hundred louis, here and now,
Just for the pleasure of landing one good clout
Right on the end of that complacent snout.
CLÉANTE: Careful; don't make things worse.
DAMIS: My bootsole itches   85
To give that beggar a good kick in the breeches.
DORINE: Monsieur Loyal, I'd love to hear the whack
Of a stout stick across your fine broad back.
MONSIEUR LOYAL: Take care: a woman too may go to jail if
She uses threatening language to a bailiff.   90
CLÉANTE: Enough, enough, Sir. This must not go on.
Give me that paper, please, and then begone.
MONSIEUR LOYAL: Well, *au revoir*. God give you all good cheer!
ORGON: May God confound you, and him who sent you here!

SCENE 5

ORGON, CLÉANTE, MARIANE, ELMIRE, MADAME PERNELLE, DORINE, DAMIS

ORGON: Now, Mother, was I right or not? This writ
Should change your notion of Tartuffe a bit.
Do you perceive his villainy at last?
MADAME PERNELLE: I'm thunderstruck. I'm utterly aghast.
DORINE: Oh, come, be fair. You mustn't take offense   5
At this new proof of his benevolence.
He's acting out of selfless love, I know.
Material things enslave the soul, and so
He kindly has arranged your liberation
From all that might endanger your salvation.   10
ORGON: Will you not ever hold your tongue, you dunce?
CLÉANTE: Come, you must take some action, and at once.
ELMIRE: Go tell the world of the low trick he's tried.
The deed of gift is surely nullified
By such behavior, and public rage will not   15
Permit the wretch to carry out his plot.

SCENE 6

VALÈRE, ORGON, CLÉPANTE, ELMIRE, MARIANE, MADAME PERNELLE,
DAMIS, DORINE

VALÈRE: Sir, though I hate to bring you more bad news,
  Such is the danger that I cannot choose.
  A friend who is extremely close to me
  And knows my interest in your family
  Has, for my sake, presumed to violate   5
  The secrecy that's due to things of state,
  And sends me word that you are in a plight
  From which your one salvation lies in flight.
  That scoundrel who's imposed upon you so
  Denounced you to the King an hour ago   10
  And, as supporting evidence, displayed
  The strong-box of a certain renegade
  Whose secret papers, so he testified,
  You had disloyally agreed to hide.
  I don't know just what charges may be pressed, 15
  But there's a warrant out for your arrest;
  Tartuffe has been instructed, furthermore,
  To guide the arresting officer to your door.
CLÉANTE: He's clearly done this to facilitate
  His seizure of your house and your estate.   20
ORGON: That man, I must say, is a vicious beast!
VALÈRE: You can't afford to delay, Sir, in the least.
  My carriage is outside, to take you hence;
  This thousand louis should cover all expense.
  Let's lose no time, or you shall be undone;   25
  The sole defense, in this case, is to run.
  I shall go with you all the way, and place you
  In a safe refuge to which they'll never trace you.
ORGON: Alas, dear boy, I wish that I could show you
  My gratitude for everything I owe you.   30
  But now is not the time; I pray the Lord
  That I may live to give you your reward.
  Farewell, my dears; be careful . . .
CLÉANTE.   Brother, hurry.
  We shall take care of things; you needn't worry.

SCENE 7

The OFFICER, TARTUFFE, VALÈRE, ORGON, ELMIRE, MARIANE,
MADAME PERNELLE, DORINE, CLÉANTE, DAMIS

TARTUFFE: Gently, Sir, gently; stay right where you are.
  No need for haste; your lodging isn't far.
  You're off to prison, by order of the Prince.
ORGON: This is the crowning blow, you wretch; and since
  It means my total ruin and defeat,   5

Your villainy is now at last complete.

TARTUFFE: You needn't try to provoke me; it's no use.
  Those who serve Heaven must expect abuse.

CLÉANTE: You are indeed most patient, sweet, and blameless.

DORINE: How he exploits the name of Heaven! It's shameless.   10

TARTUFFE: Your taunts and mockeries are all for naught;
  To do my duty is my only thought.

MARIANE: Your love of duty is most meritorious,
  And what you've done is little short of glorious.

TARTUFFE: All deeds are glorious, Madam, which obey   15
  The sovereign prince who sent me here today.

ORGON: I rescued you when you were destitute;
  Have you forgotten that, you thankless brute?

TARTUFFE: No, no, I well remember everything;
  But my first duty is to serve my King.   20
  That obligation is so paramount
  That other claims, beside it, do not count;
  And for it I would sacrifice my wife,
  My family, my friend, or my own life.

ELMIRE: Hypocrite!

DORINE: All that we most revere, he uses   25
  To cloak his plots and camouflage his ruses.

CLÉANTE: If it is true that you are animated
  By pure and loyal zeal, as you have stated,
  Why was this zeal not roused until you'd sought
  To make Orgon a cuckold, and been caught?   30
  Why weren't you moved to give your evidence
  Until your outraged host had driven you hence?
  I shan't say that the gift of all his treasure
  Ought to have damped your zeal in any measure;
  But if he is a traitor, as you declare,   35
  How could you condescend to be his heir?

TARTUFFE: [To the OFFICER.]
  Sir, spare me all this clamor; it's growing shrill.
  Please carry out your orders, if you will.

OFFICER:[5] Yes, I've delayed too long, Sir. Thank you kindly.
  You're just the proper person to remind me.   40
  Come, you are off to join the other boarders
  In the King's prison, according to his orders.

TARTUFFE: Who? I, Sir?

OFFICER: Yes.

TARTUFFE: To prison? This can't be true!

OFFICER: I owe an explanation, but not to you.
  [To ORGON.] Sir, all is well; rest easy, and be grateful.   45
  We serve a Prince to whom all sham is hateful,
  A Prince who sees into our inmost hearts,

---

5. In the original, *un exempt.* He would actually have been a gentleman from the king's personal bodyguard with the rank of lieutenant colonel or "master of the camp."

And can't be fooled by any trickster's arts.
His royal soul, though generous and human,
Views all things with discernment and acumen;   50
His sovereign reason is not lightly swayed,
And all his judgments are discreetly weighed.
He honors righteous men of every kind,
And yet his zeal for virtue is not blind,
Nor does his love of piety numb his wits   55
And make him tolerant of hypocrites.
'Twas hardly likely that this man could cozen
A King who's foiled such liars by the dozen.
With one keen glance, the King perceived the whole
Perverseness and corruption of his soul,   60
And thus high Heaven's justice was displayed:
Betraying you, the rogue stood self-betrayed.
The King soon recognized Tartuffe as one
Notorious by another name, who'd done
So many vicious crimes that one could fill   65
Ten volumes with them, and be writing still.
But to be brief: our sovereign was appalled
By this man's treachery toward you, which he called
The last, worst villainy of a vile career,
And bade me follow the impostor here   70
To see how gross his impudence could be,
And force him to restore your property.
Your private papers, by the King's command,
I hereby seize and give into your hand.
The King, by royal order, invalidates   75
The deed which gave this rascal your estates,
And pardons, furthermore, your grave offense
In harboring an exile's documents.
By these decrees, our Prince rewards you for
Your loyal deeds in the late civil war,[6]   80
And shows how heartfelt is his satisfaction
In recompensing any worthy action,
How much he prizes merit, and how he makes
More of men's virtues than of their mistakes.
DORINE: Heaven be praised!
MADAME PERNELLE.   I breathe again, at last.   85
ELMIRE: We're safe.
MARIANE: I can't believe the danger's past.
ORGON: [*To* TARTUFFE.] Well, traitor, now you see . . .
CLÉANTE.   Ah, brother, please
Let's not descend to such indignities.
Leave the poor wretch to his unhappy fate,
And don't say anything to aggravate   90
His present woes; but rather hope that he

---

6. A reference to Orgon's role in supporting the king during the *Frondes.*

Will soon embrace an honest piety,
And mend his ways, and by a true repentance
Move our just King to moderate his sentence.
Meanwhile, go kneel before your sovereign's throne   95
And thank him for the mercies he has shown.
ORGON: Well said: let's go at once and, gladly kneeling,
Express the gratitude which all are feeling.
Then, when that first great duty has been done,
We'll turn with pleasure to a second one,   100
And give Valère, whose love has proven so true,
The wedded happiness which is his due.

JEAN RACINE
1639–1699

Jean Racine's capacity to communicate the full intensity of passion in tragedies marked by their formal decorum and their elevated tone gave him immediate and lasting fame among French dramatists. He brings to material adapted from classic texts an immediacy of psychological insight to which twentieth-century audiences readily respond.

Born into the family of a government official in the Valois district, eighty miles from Paris, Racine attended the College de Beauvais. Later (1655–59) he studied in the Jansenist center of Port-Royal. (Jansenism, a strict Catholic movement emphasizing moral self-examination and severely controlled conduct, exercised a profound influence on Racine.) In 1660, encouraged by the poet Jean de la Fontaine, Racine came to Paris, where his early plays failed, driving him to a period of seclusion in Provence. When he returned to Paris in 1663, however, the court and the nobility patronized him, and he rapidly developed a reputation as a major playwright. In 1677 he left Paris and returned to Port-Royal, an environment appropriate to his increasing interest in religious thought. He married Catherine de Romanet, with whom he had seven children, most of whom became nuns or priests. Remaining in the country, he wrote history, made short trips to Paris, and traveled as historiographer with Louis XIV's campaigns. Buried at Port-Royal, his body was exhumed in 1711 and reburied next to Pascal at the church of St. Étienne-du-Mont in Paris.

Only one of Racine's twelve plays, an early comedy, deviated from the tragic mode. His first tragedies imitated the work of his contemporary Pierre Corneille; later he chose biblical and classical models. *Phaedra* (1677) adapts, with new emphasis, the action of Euripides' *Hippolytus*, making the guilty woman rather than the relatively passive man the protagonist and using the highly charged sexual situation between the two to generate intense psychological drama. To twentieth-century readers, the play's most immediately obvious aspect may be its conventional formalities: long declamatory speeches, stylized exchanges in compressed half lines, the artificiality of conveying such complicated relationships and histories through the action of a single day. Such devices, however—which would have seemed as artificial to seventeenth-century audiences as they do to us, although more familiar—intensify the impact of the central characters' anguish and their desperate attempts to deal with it. If the play's surface is formal, its depths seethe with passion.

Passion, of course, is the subject of *Phaedra*. The conflict between reason and passion that preoccupied many thinkers in the late seventeenth and early eighteenth centuries—that conflict resolved on the side of reason at such great cost for the Princess of Clèves—here plays itself out with stark urgency. Passion triumphs, in *Phaedra*, over all principles of control, bringing death to the two central characters and misery to their survivors. As in Greek tragedy, although by rather different means, the reader feels not only the self-destructiveness of the human psyche but the pathos and the heroism of the doomed effort to transcend the limits of the given.

The play opens not with Phaedra herself but with Hippolytus, meditating about his heroic father, Theseus. Like Molière, Racine uses the family as microcosm of larger social orders, but the intense conflicts that throb beneath the surface in many real-life families here undergo no comic transformation. Hippolytus has his own problems, quite apart from Phaedra. Blessed and burdened with a larger-than-life father, he must choose whether to try to imitate that father or to seek other ways of being a man. "I sucked that pride which seems so strange to you / From an Amazonian mother," he tells his friend Theramenes, alluding to the "austere and proud / Persuasions" that have prevented him from feeling interest in any woman. But matters cannot remain so simple. Theseus has distinguished himself in two ways: by heroic womanizing (he leaves a trail of women behind him wherever he goes) and by heroic action, the conquering and destruction of monsters human and inhuman. As the play opens, Hippolytus acknowledges in himself the first incursions of love. No longer can his adolescent defense, his refusal of any resemblance to his father, serve him. When Theseus returns, Hippolytus will beg permission to seek his own heroism:

> Before you'd lived as long as I have done,
> More than one tyrant, monsters more than one
> Had felt your strength of arm, your sword's keen blade . . .
> Let me at long last show my courage.

He wants, he says, even by death to "prove to all the world I was your son." By the time he makes this plea, however, his innocent desire to prove his manhood, to declare his separateness from and worthiness of his father, has been overwhelmed by darker forces.

Phaedra's impulses are less innocent—less "natural," she suggests. In a poignant passage, she imagines Hippolytus and his youthful beloved, Aricia, expressing their love in a natural setting, themselves a part of the natural world. She understands her own sin as an internal revolution of feeling against control; she speaks of desperately seeking her "lost reason" in the entrails of sacrifices she makes to Venus, trying to avert her fate. Never does she excuse herself, never does she believe herself justified in loving the son of the man who kidnapped her into marriage. When Theseus is thought dead, Phaedra declares herself unworthy to rule a nation because she cannot rule herself. Yet such moral awareness fails to help her: knowing her sin, she continues to enact it, at least in feeling. The play evokes the full torment of such experience.

As for powerful Theseus, conqueror of women, defier of the supernatural, ally of Neptune—this kingly figure returns to find himself powerless at home. The son and wife who by social convention exist in utter subordination to him turn into enemies he has no capacity to master. First his wife's nurse tells him that his son has attempted to seduce Phaedra. The rivalry of sons and fathers lies deep: if sons fear they can never equal their fathers, fathers fear that the young necessarily overcome the old. Theseus believes the nurse's bare assertion, unsupported by substantial evidence. He banishes his son and invokes Neptune's power to destroy him. Then Aricia's hints lead him to suspect his wife, who confesses her own emotional sin while already on the verge of self-inflicted death. Theseus remains alone, bereft, his tyrannical impulse now devoid of domestic object. His own passions, too quickly fired—jealous possessiveness of his wife, jealous rivalry with his son—have deprived him of two beings he loved.

The play provides no villains. Phaedra, in some versions of the story a monster of lust, here becomes a woman struggling against her nature, as profoundly committed to standards of control as to the violent feelings that overthrow them. Hippolytus, in the process of self-discovery, at a delicate balance point between youth and maturity, cannot protect himself against the alternations of closely linked love and hate in a woman whose passions, and whose self-awareness, far exceed his. Theseus, in the ignorance of success, fails in comprehension, not understanding himself, his wife, or his son. All three exemplify the pathos and the dignity of the human struggle to be human.

Phaedra dies with the word *purity* on her lips, seeking self-purification in death, the only course now possible to her. Hippolytus dies in the beauty of his youth, deprived of age's suffering and fulfillment. Theseus lives to try once more to rule adequately, perhaps chastened by suffering into greater awareness. The names of the Greek gods survive in this drama: Aphrodite torments Phaedra, Neptune serves Theseus's impetuous will. But the gods now function as projections of human passion: Phaedra's sexual lust, Theseus's lust for power. Phaedra's torment suggests a Christian effort at purification, a Christian ideal of self-denial. The drama, in Racine's handling of the ancient story, projects on a giant screen conflicts all men and women undergo, the surge of feeling warring with the ideal of self-restraint. By concentrating the play of passions within a small family group and a confined space of time, while recalling connections between the characters' feelings and historical events that lie behind them; by giving Theseus and Phaedra heroic dignity and stature; by linking this family with the fate of nations, Racine forces his readers to feel the intensity and the large significance of feelings and happenings that might in other treatments seem merely sordid. He gives his characters timeless reality—speaking to his time, and to ours.

To translate Racine into English involves particularly difficult problems, since the French Alexandrine couplet, composed of twelve-syllable lines, does not adapt naturally to English verse. Richard Wilbur's version uses the common English pentameter, the ten-syllable line, to construct fluent, pointed, and dignified verse. His couplets by their formal elegance remind the reader steadily of the discipline that the play embodies and celebrates.

A useful biography of Racine is G. Brereton, *Jean Racine: A Critical Biography* (1951), which combines biography with literary criticism. Valuable critical insight is provided by O. de Mourgues, *Racine: Or, The Triumph of Relevance* (1967), and P. J. Yarrow, *Racine* (1978). A treatment of French tragic drama that includes extensive and valuable material on Racine is Albert Cook, *French Tragedy: The Power of Enactment* (1981). For an interpretation that includes stage history of Racine's plays, see D. Maskell, *Racine: A Theatrical Reading* (1991).

PRONOUNCING GLOSSARY

The following list uses common English syllables and stress accents to provide rough equivalents of selected words whose pronunciation may be unfamiliar to the general reader.

Acheron: *ah'-ker-awn*	Euripides: *yoo-rip'-uh-deez*
Ariadne: *ah-ree-ahd'-ne*	Hippolytus: *hip-pol'-i-tuhs*
Aricia: *ah-ree'-sha*	Ismene: *is-mee'-ne*
Cocytus: *cohs-i'-tuhs*	Medea: *me-dee'-a*

Mycenae: *mai-see'-nee*

Oenone: *ee-noh'-ne*

Panope: *pah'-no-pe*

Pasiphaë: *pa-si'-fa-ee*

Peirithous: *pay-rith'-oo-uhs*

Peloponnesus: *pel-luh-puh-nee'-suhs*

Phaedra: *fee'-drah*

Scythia: *sai'-thee-uh*

Taenarus: *ten'-a-ruhs*

Theramenes: *the-ram'-uh-neez*

Theseus: *thee'-see-uhs*

Troezen: *troh'-zen*

Phaedra[1]

CHARACTERS

THESEUS, *son of Aegeus, King of Athens*

PHAEDRA, *wife of Theseus, daughter of Minos and Pasiphaë*

HIPPOLYTUS, *son of Theseus and Antiope, Queen of the Amazons*

ARICIA, *princess of the blood royal of Athens*

THERAMENES, *Hippolytus' tutor*

OENONE, *Phaedra's nurse and confidante*

ISMENE, *Aricia's confidante*

PANOPE, *lady-in-waiting to Phaedra*

GUARDS

The action takes place within and without a palace at Troezen, a town in the Peloponnesus.

Act I

SCENE 1

HIPPOLYTUS, THERAMENES

HIPPOLYTUS: No, dear Theramenes, I've too long delayed
  In pleasant Troezen; my decision's made.
  I'm off; in my anxiety, I commence
  To tax myself with shameful indolence.
  My father has been gone six months and more,   5
  And yet I do not know what distant shore
  Now hides him, or what trials he now may bear.
THERAMENES: You'll go in search of him, my lord? But where?
  Already, to appease your fears, I've plied
  The seas which lie on Corinth's either side;   10
  I've asked for Theseus among tribes who dwell
  Where Acheron[2] goes plunging into Hell;
  Elis I've searched and, from Taenarus[3] bound,
  Reached even that sea where Icarus[4] was drowned.

---

1. Translated by Richard Wilbur.   2. A river that flows into Hades; across it Charon ferried the dead.
3. A point of land in southern Greece, near Sparta. Elis is a district of Greece on the west coast of the Peloponnesus.   4. Son of Daedalus. Escaping from Crete by means of wings made by his father, Icarus flew so high that the sun melted the wax holding his wings together, and he fell to his death.

In what fresh hope, in what unthought-of places,   15
Do you set out to find your father's traces?
Who knows, indeed, if he wants the truth about
His long, mysterious absence to come out,
And whether, while we tremble for him, he's
Not fondling some new conquest at his ease   20
And planning to deceive her like the rest? . . .

HIPPOLYTUS: Enough, Theramenes. In King Theseus' breast,
The foolish fires of youth have ceased to burn;
No tawdry dalliance hinders his return.
Phaedra need fear no rivals now; the King   25
Long since, for her sake, ceased philandering.
I go then, out of duty—and as a way
To flee a place in which I dare not stay.

THERAMENES: Since when, my lord, have you begun to fear
This peaceful place your childhood held so dear,   30
And which I've often known you to prefer
To Athens' court, with all its pomp and stir?
What danger or affliction drives you hence?

HIPPOLYTUS: Those happy times are gone. All's altered since
The Gods dispatched to us across the sea   35
The child of Minos and Pasiphaë.[5]

THERAMENES: Ah. Then it's Phaedra's presence in this place
That weighs on you. She'd hardly seen your face
When, as the King's new consort, she required
Your banishment, and got what she desired.   40
But now her hatred for you, once so great,
Has vanished, or has cooled, at any rate.
And why, my lord, should you feel threatened by
A dying woman who desires to die?
Sick unto death—with what, she will not say,   45
Weary of life and of the light of day,
Could Phaedra plot to do you any harm?

HIPPOLYTUS: Her vain hostility gives me no alarm.
It is, I own, another enemy.
The young Aricia, from whom I flee,   50
Last of a line which sought to overthrow
Our house.

THERAMENES: What! Will you also be her foe?
That gentle maiden, though of Pallas' line,
Had no part in her brothers' base design.[6]
If she is guiltless, why should you hate her, Sir?   55

HIPPOLYTUS: I would not flee her if I hated her.

THERAMENES: Dare I surmise, then, why you're leaving us?

---

5. Phaedra was the daughter of King Minos of Crete and of Pasiphaë, sister to Circe. Enamored of a white bull sent by Poseidon, Pasiphaë consequently gave birth to the Minotaur, the Cretan monster later killed by Theseus. Phaedra was thus half-sister to the Minotaur.   6. Theseus killed all fifty sons of Pallas because they threatened his kingdom of Athens. Aricia is Pallas's daughter.

Are you no longer that Hippolytus
Who spurned love's dictates and refused with scorn
The yoke which Theseus has so often borne?   60
Has Venus, long offended by your pride,
Contrived to see her Theseus justified
By making you confess her power divine
And bow, like other men, before her shrine?
Are you in love, Sir?

HIPPOLYTUS: What do you mean, dear man   65
You who have known me since my life began?
How can you wish that my austere and proud
Persuasions be so basely disvowed?
I sucked that pride which seems so strange to you
From an Amazonian mother,[7] and when I grew   70
To riper years, and knew myself, I thought
My given nature to be nobly wrought.
You then, devoted friend, instructed me
In all my father's brilliant history,
And you recall how glowingly I heard   75
His exploits, how I hung on every word
As you portrayed a sire whose deeds appease
Men's longing for another Hercules—
Those monsters slain, those brigands all undone,
Procrustes, Sciron, Sinis, Cercyon,—   80
The Epidaurian giant's scattered bones,
The Minotaur's foul blood on Cretan stones!
But when you told me of less glorious feats,
His far-flung chain of amorous deceits,
Helen of Sparta[8] kidnapped as a maid;   85
Sad Periboea[9] in Salamis betrayed;
Others, whose very names escape him now,
Too-trusting hearts, deceived by sigh and vow;
Wronged Ariadne,[1] telling the rocks her moan,
Phaedra abducted, though to grace a throne,—   90
You know how, loathing stories of that sort,
I begged you oftentimes to cut them short,
And wished posterity might never hear
The worser half of Theseus' great career.
Shall I, in my turn, be subjected so   95
To passion, by the Gods be brought so low—
The more disgraced because I cannot claim
Such honors as redeem King Theseus' name,
And have not, by the blood of monsters, won

---

7. Hippolytus's mother was Antiope, sister of Hippolyta, queen of the Amazons.   8. Daughter of Zeus
and Leda, later the wife of Menelaus of Sparta (and the cause of the Trojan War). In her girlhood she
was abducted by Theseus and Peirithoüs; her brothers rescued her and brought her back home.
9. The mother of Ajax, one of the women Theseus seduced and abandoned.   1. Phaedra's sister, who
was abandoned by Theseus on the island of Naxos after she rescued him from the Minotaur.

The right to trespass as my sire has done?   100
And even if my pride laid down its arms,
Could I surrender to Aricia's charms?
Would not my wayward passions heed the ban
Forbidding her to me, or any man?
The King's no friend to her, and has decreed   105
That she not keep alive her brothers' seed;
Fearing some new shoot from their guilty stem,
He wants her death to be the end of them;
For her, the nuptial torch shall never blaze;
He's doomed her to be single all her days.   110
Shall I take up her cause then, brave his rage,
Set a rebellious pattern for the age,
Commit my youth to love's delirium . . . ?
THERAMENES: Ah, Sir, if love's appointed hour has come,
It's vain to reason; Heaven will not hear.   115
What Theseus bans, he makes you hold more dear.
His hate for her but stirs your flames the more,
And lends new grace to her whom you adore.
Why fear, my lord, a love that's true and chaste?
Of what's so sweet, will you not dare to taste?   120
Shall timid scruples make your blood congeal?
What Hercules once felt, may you not feel?
What hearts has Venus' power failed to sway?
Where would you be, who strive with her today,
If fierce Antiope had not grown tame[2]   125
And loved king Theseus with a virtuous flame?
But come, my lord, why posture and debate?
Admit that you have changed, and that of late
You're seen less often, in your lonely pride,
Racing your chariot by the oceanside,   130
Or deftly using Neptune's[3] art to train
Some charger to obey the curb and rein.
The woods less often echo to our cries.
A secret fire burns in your heavy eyes.
No question of it: you're sick with love, you feel   135
A wasting passion which you would conceal.
Has fair Aricia wakened your desire?
HIPPOLYTUS: I'm off, Theramenes, to find my sire.
THERAMENES: Will you not see the Queen before you go,
My lord?
HIPPOLYTUS:
I mean to. You may tell her so.   140
Duty requires it of me. Ah, but here's
Her dear Oenone; what new grief prompts her tears?

---

2. As an Amazon, Hippolytus's mother, Antiope, was committed to chastity.   3. Or Poseidon, god of
the sea, who was also identified with Hippios, god of horses.

SCENE 2

HIPPOLYTUS, OENONE, THERAMENES

OENONE: Alas, my lord, what grief could equal mine?
The Queen has gone into a swift decline.
I nurse her, tend her day and night, but she
Is dying of some nameless malady.
Disorder rules within her heart and head.   5
A restless pain has dragged her from her bed;
She longs to see the light; but in her keen
Distress she is unwilling to be seen. . . .
She's coming.
HIPPOLYTUS: I understand, and I shall go.
My hated face would but increase her woe.   10

SCENE 3

PHAEDRA, OENONE

PHAEDRA: Let's go no farther; stay, Oenone dear.
I'm faint; my strength abandons me, I fear.
My eyes are blinded by the glare of day,
And now I feel my trembling knees give way.
Alas!
    [*She sits.*]
OENONE: O Gods, abate our misery!   5
PHAEDRA: These veils, these baubles, how they burden me!
What meddling hand has twined my hair, and made
Upon my brow so intricate a braid?
All things oppress me, vex me, do me ill.
OENONE: Her wishes war against each other still.   10
'Twas you who, full of self-reproach, just now
Insisted that our hands adorn your brow;
You who called back your strength so that you might
Come forth again and once more see the light.
Yet, seeing it, you all but turn and flee,   15
Hating the light which you came forth to see.
PHAEDRA: Founder of our sad race, bright god of fire,
You whom my mother dared to boast her sire,[4]
Who blush perhaps to see my wretched case,
For the last time, O Sun, I see your face.   20
OENONE: Can't you shake off that morbid wish? Must I
Forever hear you laying plans to die?
What is this pact with death which you have made?
PHAEDRA: Oh, to be sitting in the woods' deep shade!
When shall I witness, through a golden wrack   25
Of dust, a chariot flying down the track?
OENONE: What, Madam?

4. Helios, the sun god, was the father of Phaedra's mother, Pasiphaë.

PHAEDRA: Where am I? Madness! What did I say?
Where have I let my hankering senses stray?
The Gods have robbed me of my wits. A rush
Of shame, Oenone, causes me to blush.   30
I make my guilty torments all too plain.
My eyes, despite me, fill with tears of pain.

OENONE: If you must blush, then blush for your perverse
Silence, which only makes your sickness worse.
Spurning our care, and deaf to all we say—   35
Is it your cruel design to die this way?
What madness dooms your life in middle course?
What spell, what poison has dried up its source?
Three times the night has overrun the skies
Since sleep last visited your hollow eyes,   40
And thrice the day has made dim night retreat
Since you, though starving, have refused to eat.
What frightful evil does your heart intend?
What right have you to plot your own life's end?
You thereby wrong the Gods who authored you;   45
Betray the spouse to whom your faith is due;
Betray your children by the selfsame stroke,
And thrust their necks beneath a heavy yoke.
Yes, on the day their mother's life is done,
Proud hopes will stir in someone else's son—   50
Your foe, the foe of all your lineage, whom
An Amazon once carried in her womb:
Hippolytus . . .

PHAEDRA: Gods!

OENONE: My words strike home at last.

PHAEDRA: Oh, wretched woman, what was that name which passed
Your lips?

OENONE: Ah, now you're roused to anger. Good.   55
That name has made you shudder, as it should.
Live, then. Let love and duty fire your spirit.
Live, lest a Scythian's[5] son should disinherit
Your children, lest he crush the noblest fruit
Of Greece and of the Gods beneath his boot.   60
But lose no time; each moment now could cost
Your life; retrieve the strength that you have lost,
While still your feeble fires, which sink so low,
Smoulder and may be fanned into a glow.

PHAEDRA: Alas, my guilty flame has burnt too long.   65

OENONE: Come, what remorse can flay you so? What wrong
Can you have done to be so crushed with guilt?
There is no innocent blood your hands have spilt.

PHAEDRA: My hands, thank Heaven, are guiltless, as you say.
Gods! That my heart were innocent as they!   70

---

5. Scythia, home of the Amazons, was for the Greeks associated with barbarians.

OENONE: What fearful notion can your thoughts have bred
  So that your heart still shrinks from it in dread?
PHAEDRA: I've said enough, Oenone. Spare me the rest.
  I die, to keep that horror unconfessed.
OENONE: Then die, and keep your heartless silence, do;   75
  But someone else must close your eyes for you.
  Although your flickering life has all but fled,
  I shall go down before you to the dead.
  There are a thousand roads that travel there;
  I'll choose the shortest, in my just despair.   80
  O cruel mistress! When have I failed or grieved you?
  Remember: at your birth, these arms received you.
  For you I left my country, children, kin:
  Is this the prize my faithfulness should win?
PHAEDRA: What can you gain by this? Why rant and scold?   85
  You'd shake with terror if the truth were told.
OENONE: Great Gods! What words could match the terror I
  Must daily suffer as I watch you die?
PHAEDRA: When you have learnt my crime, my fate, my shame,
  I'll die no less, but with a guiltier name.   90
OENONE: My lady, by the tears which stain my face,
  And by your trembling knees which I embrace,
  Enlighten me; deliver me from doubt.
PHAEDRA: You've asked it. Rise.
OENONE: I'm listening. Come, speak out.
PHAEDRA: O Gods! What shall I say to her? Where shall I start?   95
OENONE: Speak, speak. Your hesitations wound my heart.
PHAEDRA: Alas, how Venus hates us! As Love's thrall,
  Into what vileness did my mother fall!
OENONE: Dear Queen, forget it; to the end of time
  Let silence shroud the memory of that crime.   100
PHAEDRA: O sister Ariadne! Through love, once more,
  You died abandoned on a barren shore![6]
OENONE: Madame, what's this? What anguish makes you trace
  So bitterly the tale of all your race?
PHAEDRA: And now, since Venus wills it, I must pine   105
  And die, the last of our accursèd line.
OENONE: You are in love?
PHAEDRA: I feel love's raging thirst.
OENONE: For whom?
PHAEDRA: Of all dire things, now hear the worst.
  I love . . . From that dread name I shrink, undone;
  I love . . .
OENONE: Whom?
PHAEDRA: Think of a Scythian woman's son,   110
  A prince I long ill-used and heaped with blame.
OENONE: Hippolytus? Gods!

---

6. Ariadne died on Naxos after Theseus's desertion of her.

PHAEDRA: 'Twas you who spoke his name.

OENONE: Just Heaven! All my blood begins to freeze.
   O crime, despair, most curst of families!
   Why did we voyage to this ill-starred land   115
   And set our feet upon its treacherous strand?

PHAEDRA: My ills began far earlier. Scarcely had I
   Pledged with Aegeus' son our marriage-tie,
   Secure in that sweet joy a bride should know,
   When I, in Athens, met my haughty foe.   120
   I stared, I blushed, I paled, beholding him;
   A sudden turmoil set my mind aswim;
   My eyes no longer saw, my lips were dumb;
   My body burned, and yet was cold and numb.
   I knew myself possessed by Venus, whose   125
   Fierce flames torment the quarry she pursues.
   I thought to appease her then by constant prayer,
   And built for her a temple, decked with care.
   I made continual sacrifice, and sought
   In entrails[7] for a spirit less distraught—   130
   But what could cure a lovesick soul like mine?
   In vain my hands burnt incense at her shrine:
   Though I invoked the Goddess' name, 'twas he
   I worshipped; I saw his image constantly,
   And even as I fed the altar's flame   135
   Made offering to a god I dared not name.
   I shunned him; but—O horror and disgrace!—
   My eyes beheld him in his father's face.
   At last I knew that I must act, must urge
   Myself, despite myself, to be his scourge.   140
   To rid me of the foe I loved, I feigned
   A harsh stepmother's malice, and obtained
   By ceaseless cries my wish that he be sent
   From home and father into banishment.
   I breathed once more, Oenone; once he was gone,   145
   My blameless days could flow more smoothly on.
   I hid my grief, was faithful to my spouse,
   And reared the offspring of our luckless vows.
   Ah, mocking Fate! What use was all my care?
   Brought by my spouse himself to Troezen, there   150
   I yet again beheld my exiled foe:
   My unhealed wound began once more to flow.
   Love hides no longer in these veins, at bay:
   Great Venus fastens on her helpless prey.
   I look with horror on my crime; I hate   155
   My life; my passion I abominate.
   I hoped by death to keep my honor bright,
   And hide so dark a flame from day's pure light;

---

7. Examining the entrails of an animal sacrifice was a means of prophecy.

Yet, yielding to your tearful argument,
I've told you all; of that I'll not repent   160
Provided you do not, as death draws near,
Pour more unjust reproaches in my ear,
Or seek once more in vain to fan a fire
Which flickers and is ready to expire.

SCENE 4

PHAEDRA, OENONE, PANOPE

PANOPE: Madam, there's grievous news which I'd withhold
  If I were able; but it must be told.
  Death's claimed your lord, who feared no other foe—
  Of which great loss you are the last to know.
OENONE: You tell us, Panope . . . ?
PANOPE: That the Queen in vain   5
  Prays for her Theseus to return again;
  That mariners have come to port, from whom
  Hippolytus has learned his father's doom.
PHAEDRA: Gods!
PANOPE: Who'll succeed him, Athens can't agree.
  The Prince your son commands much loyalty,   10
  My lady; yet, despite their country's laws,[8]
  Some make the alien woman's son their cause;
  Some plot, they say, to put in Theseus' place
  Aricia, the last of Pallas' race.
  Of both these threats I thought that you should know.   15
  Hippolytus has rigged his ship to go,
  And if, in Athens' ferment, he appeared,
  The fickle mob might back him, it is feared.
OENONE: Enough. The Queen has heard you. She'll give thought
  To these momentous tidings you have brought.   20

SCENE 5

PHAEDRA, OENONE

OENONE: Mistress, I'd ceased to urge you not to die;
  I thought to follow you to the grave, since my
  Dissuasions had no longer any force:
  But this dark news prescribes a change of course.
  Your destiny now wears a different face: 5
  The King is dead, and you must take his place.
  He leaves a son who needs your sheltering wing—
  A slave without you; if you live, a king.
  Who else will soothe his orphan sorrows, pray?
  If you are dead, who'll wipe his tears away?   10

---

8. Athenian law made the son of an Athenian and a non-Greek woman illegitimate. Hippolytus's
mother was Antiope the Amazon. It is not clear why Phaedra's children are not similarly classified.

His innocent cries, borne up to Heaven, will make
The Gods, his forebears, curse you for his sake.
Live, then: there's nothing now you're guilty of.
Your love's become like any other love.
With Theseus' death, those bonds exist no more   15
Which made your passion something to abhor.
Hippolytus need no longer cause you fear;
Seeing him now, your conscience can be clear.
Perhaps, convinced that you're his bitter foe,
He means to lead the rebels. Make him know   20
His error; win him over; stay his hand.
He's king, by right, of Troezen's pleasant land;
But as for bright Minerva's[9] citadel,
It is your son's by law, as he knows well.
You should, indeed, join forces, you and he: 25
Aricia is your common enemy.
PHAEDRA: So be it. By your advice I shall be led;
I'll live, if I can come back from the dead,
And if my mother-love still has the power
To rouse my weakened spirits in this hour.   30

Act II

SCENE 1

ARICIA, ISMENE

ARICIA: Hippolytus asks to see me? Can this be?
He seeks me out to take his leave of me?
There's no mistake, Ismene?
ISMENE: Indeed, there's not.
This shows how Theseus' death has changed your lot.
Expect now to receive from every side   5
The homage which, through him, you've been denied.
At last, Aricia rules her destiny;
Soon, at her feet, all Greece shall bend the knee.
ARICIA: This is no doubtful rumor, then? I've shed
The bonds of slavery? My oppressor's dead?   10
ISMENE: The Gods relent, my lady. It is so.
Theseus has joined your brothers' shades below.
ARICIA: And by what mishap did he come to grief?
ISMENE: The tales are many, and they strain belief.
Some say that he, abducting from her home   15
A new beloved, was swallowed by the foam.
It's even thought, as many tongues now tell,
That, faring with Pirithoüs down to Hell,[1]

---

9. The Greek goddess Athene, protector of Athens.   1. Theseus went to Hades with Pentithoüs, king of the Lapiths—with whom he had earlier abducted Helen—to help his friend steal Persephone. Hercules freed Theseus, whom the god Hades had imprisoned, but could not free Pentithoüs, who was later killed.

He walked alive amid the dusky ranks
Of souls, and saw Cocytus'[2] dismal banks,   20
But found himself a prisoner in that stern
Domain from which no mortal can return.
ARICIA: Shall I believe that, while he still draws breath,
    A man can penetrate the realms of death?
    What spell could lure him to that fearsome tract?   25
ISMENE: Theseus is dead. You, only, doubt the fact.
    All Athens grieves; the news was scarcely known
    When Troezen raised Hippolytus to its throne.
    Here in this palace, trembling for her son,
    Phaedra confers on what must now be done.   30
ARICIA: You think Hippolytus will be more kind
    Than Theseus was to me, that he'll unbind
    My chains, and show me pity?
ISMENE: Madam, I do.
ARICIA: Isn't the man's cold nature known to you?
    What makes you think that, scorning women, he   35
    Will yet show pity and respect to me?
    He long has shunned us, and as you well know
    Haunts just those places where we do not go.
ISMENE: He's called, I know, the most austere of men,
    But I have seen him in your presence, when,   40
    Intrigued by his repute, I thought to observe
    His celebrated pride and cold reserve.
    His manner contradicted all I'd heard:
    At your first glance, I saw him flushed and stirred.
    His eyes, already full of languor, tried   45
    To leave your face, but could not turn aside.
    He has, though love's a thing he may despise,
    If not a lover's tongue, a lover's eyes.
ARICIA: Ismene, how your words delight my ear!
    Even if baseless, they are sweet to hear.   50
    O you who know me, can you believe of me,
    Sad plaything of a ruthless destiny,
    Forever fed on tears and bitterness,
    That love could touch me, and its dear distress?
    Last offspring of that king whom Earth once bore,[3]   55
    I only have escaped the rage of war.
    I lost six brothers, young and fresh as May,
    In whom the hopes of our great lineage lay:
    The sharp sword reaped them all; Earth, soaked and red,
    Drank sadly what Erectheus' heirs had shed.   60
    You know that, since their death, a harsh decree
    Forbids all Greeks to pay their court to me,
    Lest, through my progeny, I should revive

2. River in Hades, tributary to Acheron.   3. Erectheus, their ancestor, son of Earth and reared by Athene.

My brothers' ashes, and keep their cause alive.
But you know too with what disdain I bore   65
The ban of our suspicious conqueror.
You know how I, a lifelong enemy
Of love, gave thanks for Theseus' tyranny,
Since he forbade what I was glad to shun.
But then . . . but then I had not seen his son.   70
Not that my eyes alone, charmed by his grace,
Have made me love him for his form or face,
Mere natural gifts for which he seems to care
But little, or of which he's unaware.
I find in him far nobler gifts than these —   75
His father's strengths, without his frailties.
I love, I own, a heart that's never bowed
Beneath Love's yoke, but stayed aloof and proud.
Small glory Phaedra gained from Theseus' sighs!
More proud than she, I spurn the easy prize   80
Of love-words said a thousand times before,
And of a heart that's like an open door.
Ah, but to move a heart that's firm as stone,
To teach it pangs which it has never known,
To bind my baffled captive in a chain   85
Against whose sweet constraint he strives in vain:
There's what excites me in Hippolytus; he's
A harder conquest than was Hercules,
Whose heart, so often vanquished and inflamed,
Less honored those by whom he had been tamed.   90
But, dear Ismene, how rashly I have talked!
My hopes may all too easily be balked,
And I may humbly grieve in future days
Because of that same pride which now I praise.
Of fortune can it be . . . ?

ISMENE: You'll shortly learn;   95
He's coming.

SCENE 2

HIPPOLYTUS, ARICIA, ISMENE

HIPPOLYTUS: Madam, I felt, ere leaving here,
That I should make your altered fortunes clear.
My sire is dead. My fears divined, alas,
By his long absence, what had come to pass.
Death only, ending all his feats and frays,   5
Could hide him from the world so many days.
The Gods have yielded to destroying Fate
Hercules' heir[4] and friend and battle-mate.

---

4. *Heir* in the sense of being, like Hercules, a destroyer of monsters.

Although you hated him, I trust that you
Do not begrudge such praise as was his due. 10
One thought, however, soothes my mortal grief:
I now may offer you a just relief,
Revoking the most cruel of decrees.
Your heart, your hand, bestow them as you please;
For here in Troezen, where I now shall reign, 15
Which was my grandsire Pittheus' domain,
And which with one voice gives its throne to me,
I make you free as I; indeed, more free.
ARICIA: Your goodness stuns me, Sir. By this excess
Of noble sympathy for my distress, 20
You leave me, more than you could dream, still yoked
By those strict laws which you have just revoked.
HIPPOLYTUS: Athens, unsure of who should rule, divides
'Twixt you and me, and the Queen's son besides.
ARICIA: They speak of *me?*
HIPPOLYTUS: Their laws, I'm well aware, 25
Would seem to void my claim as Theseus' heir,
Because an alien bore me. But if my one
Opponent were my brother, Phaedra's son,
I would, my lady, have the better cause,
And would contest those smug and foolish laws. 30
What checks me is a truer claim, your own;
I yield, or, rather, give you back, a throne
And scepter which your sires inherited
From that great mortal whom the Earth once bred.
Aegeus,[5] though adopted, took their crown. 35
Theseus, his son, enlarged the state, cast down
Her foes, and was the choice of everyone,
Leaving your brothers in oblivion.
Now Athens calls you back within her walls.
Too long she's grieved for these dynastic brawls; 40
Too long your kinsmen's blood has drenched her earth,
Rising in steam from fields which gave it birth.
Troezen is mine, then. The domain of Crete
Offers to Phaedra's son a rich retreat.
Athens is yours. I go now to combine 45
In your cause all your partisans and mine.
ARICIA: These words so daze me that I almost fear
Some dream, some fancy has deceived my ear.
Am I awake? This plan which you have wrought—
What god, what god inspired you with the thought? 50
How just that, everywhere, men praise your name!
And how the truth, my lord, exceeds your fame!

---

5. Pandion's son by adoption, and Theseus's father.

You'll press my claims, against your interest?
'Twas kind enough that you should not detest
My house and me, should not be governed by   55
Old hatreds. . . .
HIPPOLYTUS: Hate you, Princess? No, not I.
I'm counted rough and proud, but don't assume
That I'm the issue of some monster's womb.
What hate-filled heart, what brute however wild
Could look upon your face and not grow mild?   60
Could I withstand your sweet, beguiling spell?
ARICIA: What's this, my lord?
HIPPOLYTUS: I've said too much. Ah, well.
My reason can't rein in my heart, I see.
Since I have spoken thus impetuously,
I must go on, my lady, and make plain   65
A secret I no longer can contain.
You see before you a most sorry prince,
A signal case of blind conceit. I wince
To think how I, Love's enemy, long disdained
Its bonds, and all whom passion had enchained;   70
How, pitying poor storm-tossed fools, I swore
Ever to view such tempests from the shore;
And now, like common men, for all my pride,
Am lost to reason in a raging tide.
One moment saw my vain defenses fall: 75
My haughty spirit is at last in thrall.
For six months now, ashamed and in despair,
I've borne Love's piercing arrow everywhere;
I've striven with you, and with myself, and though
I shun you, you are everywhere I go;   80
In the deep woods, your image haunts my sight;
The light of day, the shadows of the night,
All things call up your charms before my eyes
And vie to make my rebel heart your prize.
What use to struggle? I am not as before: 85
I seek myself, and find myself no more.
My bow, my javelins and my chariot pall;
What Neptune taught me once, I can't recall;
My idle steeds forget the voice they've known,
And the woods echo to my plaints alone.   90
You blush, perhaps, for so uncouth a love
As you have caused, and which I tell you of.
What a rude offer of my heart I make!
How strange a captive does your beauty take!
Yet that should make my offering seem more rich.   95
Remember, it's an unknown tongue in which
I speak; don't scorn these words, so poorly turned,
Which, but for you, my lips had never learned.

SCENE 3

HIPPOLYTUS, ARICIA, THERAMENES, ISMENE

THERAMENES: My lord: the Queen, they tell me, comes this way.
  It's you she seeks.
HIPPOLYTUS: Me?
THERAMENES: Why, I cannot say.
  But Phaedra's sent ahead to let you know
  That she must speak with you before you go.
HIPPOLYTUS: I, talk with Phaedra? What should we talk about?   5
ARICIA: My lord, you can't refuse to hear her out.
  Malignant toward you as the Queen appears,
  You owe some pity to her widow's tears.
HIPPOLYTUS: But now you'll leave me! And I shall sail before
  I learn my fate from her whom I adore,   10
  And in whose hands I leave this heart of mine. . . .
ARICIA: Go, Prince; pursue your generous design.
  Make Athens subject to my royal sway.
  All of your gifts I gladly take this day.
  But that great empire, glorious though it be,   15
  Is not the offering most dear to me.

SCENE 4

HIPPOLYTUS, THERAMENES

HIPPOLYTUS: Are we ready, friend? But the Queen's coming: hark.
  Go, bid them trim our vessel; we soon embark.
  Quick, give the order and return, that you
  May free me from a vexing interview.

SCENE 5

PHAEDRA, HIPPOLYTUS, OENONE

PHAEDRA: [To OENONE, at stage rear.]
  He's here. Blood rushes to my heart: I'm weak,
  And can't recall the words I meant to speak.
OENONE: Think of your son, whose one hope rests with you.
PHAEDRA: My lord, they say you leave us. Before you do,
  I've come to join your sorrows and my tears,   5
  And tell you also of a mother's fears.
  My son now lacks a father; and he will learn
  Ere long that death has claimed me in my turn.
  A thousand foes already seek to end
  His hopes, which you, you only, can defend.   10
  Yet I've a guilty fear that I have made
  Your ears indifferent to his cries for aid.
  I tremble lest you visit on my son
  Your righteous wrath at what his mother's done.

HIPPOLYTUS: So base a thought I could not entertain. 15
PHAEDRA: Were you to hate me, I could not complain,
 My lord. You've seen me bent on hurting you,
 Though what was in my heart you never knew.
 I sought your enmity. I would not stand
 Your dwelling with me in the selfsame land. 20
 I vilified you, and did not feel free
 Till oceans separated you and me.
 I went so far, indeed, as to proclaim
 That none should, in my hearing, speak your name.
 Yet if the crime prescribes the culprit's fate, 25
 If I must hate you to have earned your hate,
 Never did woman more deserve, my lord,
 Your pity, or less deserve to be abhorred.
HIPPOLYTUS: It's common, Madam, that a mother spites
 The stepson who might claim her children's rights. 30
 I know that in a second marriage-bed
 Anxiety and mistrust are often bred.
 Another woman would have wished me ill
 As you have, and perhaps been harsher still.
PHAEDRA: Ah, Prince! The Gods, by whom I swear it, saw 35
 Fit to except me from that general law.
 By what a different care am I beset!
HIPPOLYTUS: My lady, don't give way to anguish yet.
 Your husband still may see the light of day;
 Heaven may hear us, and guide his sail this way. 40
 Neptune protects him, and that deity
 Will never fail to heed my father's plea.
PHAEDRA: No one goes twice among the dead; and since
 Theseus has seen those gloomy regions, Prince,
 No god will bring him back, hope though you may, 45
 Nor greedy Acheron yield up his prey.
 But no! He is not dead; he breathes in you.
 My husband still seems present to my view.
 I see him, speak with him . . . Ah, my lord, I feel
 Crazed with a passion which I can't conceal. 50
HIPPOLYTUS: In your strong love, what wondrous power lies!
 Theseus, though dead, appears before your eyes.
 For love of him your soul is still on fire.
PHAEDRA: Yes, Prince, I burn for him with starved desire,
 Though not as he was seen among the shades, 55
 The fickle worshiper of a thousand maids,
 Intent on cuckolding the King of Hell;
 But constant, proud, a little shy as well,
 Young, charming, irresistible, much as we
 Depict our Gods, or as you look to me. 60
 He had your eyes, your voice, your virile grace,
 It was your noble blush that tinged his face
 When, crossing on the waves, he came to Crete

And made the hearts of Minos' daughters[6] beat.
Where were you then? Why no Hippolytus   65
Among the flower of Greece he chose for us?
Why were you yet too young to join that band
Of heroes whom he brought to Minos' land?
You would have slain the Cretan monster then,
Despite the endless windings of his den.[7]   70
My sister would have armed you with a skein
Of thread, to lead you from that dark domain.
But no: I'd first have thought of that design,
Inspired by love; the plan would have been mine.
It's I who would have helped you solve the maze,   75
My Prince, and taught you all its twisting ways.
What I'd have done to save that charming head!
My love would not have trusted to a thread.
No, Phaedra would have wished to share with you
Your perils, would have wished to lead you through   80
The Labyrinth, and thence have side by side
Returned with you; or else, with you, have died.
HIPPOLYTUS: Gods! What are you saying, Madam? Is Theseus not
   Your husband, and my sire? Have you forgot?
PHAEDRA: You think that I forget those things? For shame,   85
   My lord. Have I no care for my good name?
HIPPOLYTUS: Forgive me, Madam. I blush to have misread
   The innocent intent of what you said.
   I'm too abashed to face you; I shall take
   My leave. . . .
PHAEDRA: Ah, cruel Prince, 'twas no mistake.   90
   You understood; my words were all too plain.
   Behold then Phaedra as she is, insane
   With love for you. Don't think that I'm content
   To be so, that I think it innocent,
   Or that by weak compliance I have fed   95
   The baneful love that clouds my heart and head.
   Poor victim that I am of Heaven's curse,[8]
   I loathe myself; you could not hate me worse.
   The Gods could tell how in this breast of mine
   They lit the flame that's tortured all my line,   100
   Those cruel Gods for whom it is but play
   To lead a feeble woman's heart astray.
   You too could bear me out; remember, do,
   How I not only shunned but banished you.
   I wanted to be odious in your sight;   105
   To balk my love, I sought to earn your spite.
   But what was gained by all of that distress?

6. Phaedra and Ariadne.   7. The Minotaur inhabited the heart of a maze. Ariadne provided Theseus with a ball of thread by which he left a trail behind him and could retrace his steps after killing the monster.   8. Phaedra feels herself a victim of Venus, the goddess of love; she loves Hippolytus against her will.

You hated me the more; I loved no less,
And what you suffered made you still more dear.
I pined, I withered, scorched by many a tear.   110
That what I say is true, your eyes could see
If for a moment they could look at me.
What have I said? Do you suppose I came
To tell, of my free will, this tale of shame?
No, anxious for a son I dared not fail,   115
I came to beg you not to hate him. Frail
Indeed the heart is that's consumed by love!
Alas, it's only you I've spoken of.
Avenge yourself, now; punish my foul desire.
Come, rid the world, like your heroic sire,   120
Of one more monster; do as he'd have done.
Shall Theseus' widow dare to love his son?
No, such a monster is too vile to spare.
Here is my heart. Your blade must pierce me there.
In haste to expiate its wicked lust,   125
My heart already leaps to meet your thrust.
Strike, then. Or if your hatred and disdain
Refuse me such a blow, so sweet a pain,
If you'll not stain your hand with my abhorred
And tainted blood, lend me at least your sword.   130
Give it to me!
OENONE: Just Gods! What's this, my Queen?
Someone is coming. You must not be seen.
Quick! Flee! You'll be disgraced if you delay.

SCENE 6

HIPPOLYTUS, THERAMENES

THERAMENES: Did I see Phaedra vanish, dragged away?
    Why do I find you pale and overcome?
    Where is your sword, Sir? Why are you stricken dumb?
HIPPOLYTUS: Theramenes, I'm staggered. Let's go in haste.
    I view myself with horror and distaste.   5
    Phaedra . . . but no, great Gods! This thing must not
    Be told, but ever buried and forgot.
THERAMENES: Sir, if you wish to sail, our ship's prepared.
    But Athens' choice already is declared.
    Her clans have all conferred; their leaders name   10
    Your brother; Phaedra has achieved her aim.
HIPPOLYTUS: Phaedra?
THERAMENES: A herald's come at their command
    To give the reins of state into her hand.
    Her son is king.
HIPPOLYTUS: Gods, what she is you know;
    Is it her virtue you've rewarded so?   15
THERAMENES: Meanwhile, it's rumored that the King's not dead,

That in Epirus he has shown his head.
But I, who searched that land, know well, my lord . . .
HIPPOLYTUS: No, let all clues be weighed, and none ignored.
We'll track this rumor down. Should it appear   20
Too insubstantial to detain us here,
We'll sail, and at whatever cost obtain
Great Athens' crown for one who's fit to reign.

Act III

SCENE 1

PHAEDRA, OENONE

PHAEDRA: Ah, let their honors deck some other brow.
Why urge me? How can I let them see me now?
D'you think to soothe my anguished heart with such
Vain solace? Hide me, rather. I've said too much.
My frenzied love's burst forth in act and word.   5
I've spoken what should never have been heard.
And how he heard me! How, with many a shift,
The brute pretended not to catch my drift!
How ardently he longed to turn and go!
And how his blushes caused my shame to grow!   10
Why did you come between my death and me?
Ah, when his sword-point neared my breast, did he
Turn pale with horror, and snatch back the blade?
No. I had touched it, and that touch had made
Him see it as a thing defiled and stained,   15
By which his pure hand must not be profaned.
OENONE: Dwelling like this on all you're grieved about,
You feed a flame which best were beaten out.
Would it not suit King Minos' child to find
In loftier concerns her peace of mind,   20
To flee an ingrate whom you love in vain,
Assume the conduct of the State, and reign?
PHAEDRA: I, reign? You'd trust the State to my control,
When reason rules no longer in my soul?
When passion's overthrown me? When, from the weight   25
Of shame I bear, I almost suffocate?
When I am dying?
OENONE: Flee him.
PHAEDRA: How could I? How?
OENONE: You once could banish him; can't you shun him now?
PHAEDRA: Too late. He knows what frenzy burns in me.
I've gone beyond the bounds of modesty.   30
My conqueror has heard my shame confessed,
And hope, despite me, has crept into my breast.
'Twas you who, when my life was near eclipse

And my last breath was fluttering on my lips,
Revived me with sweet lies that took me in.   35
You said that now my love was free of sin.
OENONE: Ah, whether or not your woes are on my head,
To save you, what would I not have done or said?
But if an insult ever roused your spleen,
How can you pardon his disdainful mien?   40
How stonily, and with what cold conceit
He saw you all but grovel at his feet!
Oh, but his arrogance was rude and raw!
Why did not Phaedra see the man I saw?
PHAEDRA: This arrogance which irks you may grow less.   45
Bred in the forests, he has their ruggedness,
And, trained in harsh pursuits since he was young,
Has never heard, till now, love's gentle tongue.
No doubt it was surprise which made him mute,
And we do wrong to take him for a brute.   50
OENONE: Remember that an Amazon gave him life.
PHAEDRA: True: yet she learned to love like any wife.
OENONE: He has a savage hate for womankind.
PHAEDRA: No fear of rivals, then, need plague my mind.
Enough. Your counsels now are out of season.   55
Oenone, serve my madness, not my reason.
His heart is armored against love; let's seek
Some point where his defenses may be weak.
Imperial rule was in his thoughts, I feel;
He wanted Athens; that he could not conceal;   60
His vessels' prows already pointed there,
With sails all set and flapping in the air.
Go in my name, then; find this ambitious boy;
Dangle the crown before him like a toy.
His be the sacred diadem; in its stead   65
I ask no honor but to crown his head,
And yield a power I cannot hold. He'll school
My son in princely arts, teach him to rule,
And play for him, perhaps, a father's role.
Both mother and son I yield to his control.   70
Sway him, Oenone, by every wile that's known:
Your words will please him better than my own.
Sigh, groan, harangue him; picture me as dying;
Make use of supplication and of crying;
I'll sanction all you say. Go. I shall find,   75
When you return, what fate I am assigned.

SCENE 2

PHAEDRA, *alone*

PHAEDRA: O you who see to what I have descended,
Implacable Venus, is your vengeance ended?

Your shafts have all struck home; your victory's
Complete; what need for further cruelties?
If you would prove your pitiless force anew,   5
Attack a foe who's more averse to you.
Hippolytus flouts you; braving your divine
Wrath, he has never knelt before your shrine.
His proud ears seem offended by your name.
Take vengeance, Goddess; our causes are the same.   10
Force him to love . . . Oenone! You've returned
So soon? He hates me, then; your words were spurned.

SCENE 3

PHAEDRA, OENONE

OENONE: Madam, your hopeless love must be suppressed.
  Call back the virtue which you once possessed.
  The King, whom all thought dead, will soon be here;
  Theseus has landed; Theseus is drawing near.
  His people rush to see him, rapturous.   5
  I'd just gone out to seek Hippolytus
  When a great cry went up on every hand. . . .
PHAEDRA: My husband lives, Oenone; I understand.
  I have confessed a love he will abhor.
  He lives, and I have wronged him. Say no more.   10
OENONE: What?
PHAEDRA: I foresaw this, but you changed my course.
  Your tears won out over my just remorse.
  I might have died this morning, mourned and chaste;
  I took your counsels, and I die disgraced.
OENONE: You die?
PHAEDRA: Just Heaven! Think what I have done!   15
  My husband's coming; with him will be his son.
  I'll see the witness of my vile desire
  Watch with what countenance I can greet his sire,
  My heart still heavy with rejected sighs,
  And tears which could not move him in my eyes.   20
  Mindful of Theseus' honor, will he conceal
  The scandal of my passion, do you feel,
  Deceiving both his sire and king? Will he
  Contain the horror that he feels for me?
  His silence would be vain. What ill I've done   25
  I know, Oenone, and I am not one
  Of those bold women who, at ease in crime,
  Are never seen to blush at any time.
  I know my mad deeds, I recall them all.
  I think that in this place each vault, each wall   30
  Can speak, and that, impatient to accuse,
  They wait to give my trusting spouse their news.
  I'll die, then; from these horrors I'll be free.

It is so sad a thing to cease to be?
Death is not fearful to a suffering mind.   35
My only fear's the name I leave behind.
For my poor children, what a dire bequest!
Each has the blood of Jove within his breast,
But whatsoever pride of blood they share,
A mother's crime's a heavy thing to bear.   40
I tremble lest—alas, too truly!—they
Be chided for their mother's guilt some day.
I tremble lest, befouled by such a stain,
Neither should dare to lift his head again.

OENONE: I pity both of them; you could not be   45
Be chided for their mother's guilt some day.
More justified in your anxiety.
But why expose them to such insult? Why
Witness against yourself? You've but to die,
And folk will say that Phaedra, having strayed
From virtue, flees the husband she betrayed.   50
Hippolytus will rejoice that, cutting short
Your days, you lend his charges your support.
How shall I answer your accuser? He
Will have no trouble in refuting me.
I'll watch him gloating hatefully, and hear   55
Him pour your shame in every listening ear.
Let Heaven's fire consume me ere I do!
But come, speak frankly; is he still dear to you?
How do you see this prince so full of pride?

PHAEDRA: I see a monster, of whom I'm terrified.   60

OENONE: Then why should he triumph, when all can be reversed?
You fear the man. Dare to accuse him first
Of that which he might charge you with today.
What could belie you? The facts all point his way:
The sword which by good chance he left behind,   65
Your past mistrust, your present anguished mind,
His sire long cautioned by your warning voice,
And he sent into exile by your choice.

PHAEDRA: I, charge an innocent man with doing ill?

OENONE: Trust to my zeal. You've only to be still.   70
Like you I tremble, and feel a sharp regret.
I'd sooner face a thousand deaths. And yet
Since, lacking this sad remedy, you'll perish;
Since, above all, it is your life I cherish,
I'll speak to Theseus. He will do no more   75
Than doom his son to exile, as before.
A sire, when he must punish, is still a sire;
A lenient sentence will appease his ire.
But even if guiltless blood must flow, the cost
Were less than if your honor should be lost.   80
That honor is too dear to risk; its cause
Is priceless, and its dictates are your laws.

You must give up, since honor is at stake,
Everything, even virtue, for its sake.
Ah! Here comes Theseus.

PHAEDRA: And Hippolytus, he   85
In whose cold eyes I read the end of me.
Do what you will; I yield myself to you.
In my confusion, I know not what to do.

SCENE 4

THESEUS, HIPPOLYTUS, PHAEDRA, OENONE, THERAMENES

THESEUS: Fortune has blessed me after long delay,
And in your arms, my lady . . .

PHAEDRA: Theseus, stay,
And don't profane the love those words express.
I am not worthy of your tenderness.
You have been wronged. Fortune or bitter fate   5
Did not, while you were absent, spare your mate.
Unfit to please you, or to be at your side,
Henceforth my only thought must be to hide.

SCENE 5

THESEUS, HIPPOLYTUS, THERAMENES

THESEUS: Why am I welcomed in this curious vein?
HIPPOLYTUS: That, Father, only Phaedra can explain.
But if my prayers can move you, grant me, Sir,
Never again to set my eyes on her.
Allow Hippolytus to say farewell   5
To any region where your wife may dwell.
THESEUS: Then you, my son, would leave me?
HIPPOLYTUS: I never sought her:
When to this land she came, 'twas you who brought her.
Yes, you, my lord, when last you left us, bore
Aricia and the Queen to Troezen's shore.   10
You bade me be their guardian then; but how
Should any duties here detain me now?
Too long my youthful skill's been thrown away
Amidst these woods, upon ignoble prey.
May I not flee my idle pastimes here   15
To stain with worthier blood my sword or spear?
Before you'd lived as long as I have done,
More than one tyrant, monsters more than one
Had felt your strength of arm, your sword's keen blade;
Already, scourging such as sack and raid,   20
You had made safe the coasts of either sea.
The traveler lost his fears of banditry,
And Hercules, to whom your fame was known,

Welcomed your toils, and rested from his own.
But I, the unknown son of such a sire, 25
Lack even the fame my mother's deeds inspire.[9]
Let me at long last show my courage, and,
If any monster has escaped your hand,
Bring back its pelt and lay it at your feet,
Or let me by a glorious death complete 30
A life that will defy oblivion
And prove to all the world I was your son.
THESEUS: What have I found? What horror fills this place,
And makes my family flee before my face?
If my unwished return makes all grow pale, 35
Why, Heaven, did you free me from my jail?
I'd one dear friend. He had a hankering
To steal the consort of Epirus'[1] king.
I joined his amorous plot, though somewhat loath;
But outraged Fate brought blindness on us both. 40
The tyrant caught me, unarmed and by surprise.
I saw Pirithoüs with my weeping eyes
Flung by the barbarous king to monsters then,
Fierce beasts who drink the blood of luckless men.
Me he confined where never light invades, 45
In caverns near the empire of the shades.
After six months, Heaven pitied my mischance.
Escaping from my guardians' vigilance,
I cleansed the world of one more fiend, and threw
To his own beasts the bloody corpse to chew. 50
But now when, joyful, I return to see
The dearest whom the Gods have left to me;
Now, when my spirits, glad once more and light,
Would feast again upon that cherished sight,
I'm met with shudders and with frightened faces; 55
All flee me, all deny me their embraces.
Touched by the very terror I beget,
I wish I were Epirus' prisoner yet.
Speak! Phaedra says that I've been wronged. By whom?
Why has the culprit not yet met his doom? 60
Has Greece, so often sheltered by my arm,
Chosen to shield this criminal from harm?
You're silent. Is my own son, if you please,
In some alliance with my enemies?
I shall go in, and end this maddening doubt. 65
Both crime and culprit must be rooted out,
And Phaedra tell why she is so distraught.

---

9. Hippolytus's mother, an Amazon, also performed brave deeds.   1. A district in western Greece, on the Ionian Sea.

SCENE 6

HIPPOLYTUS, THERAMENES

HIPPOLYTUS: How her words chilled me! What was in her thought?
   Will Phaedra, who is still her frenzy's prey,
   Accuse herself, and throw her life away?
   What will the King say? Gods! What love has done
   To poison all this house while he was gone!   5
   And I, who burn for one who bears his curse,
   Am altered in his sight, and for the worse!
   I've dark forebodings; something ill draws near.
   Yet surely innocence need never fear.
   Come, let's consider now how I may best   10
   Revive the kindness in my father's breast,
   And tell him of a love which he may take
   Amiss, but all his power cannot shake.

Act IV

SCENE 1

THESEUS, OENONE

THESEUS: What do I hear? How bold and treacherous
   To plot against his father's honor thus!
   How sternly you pursue me, Destiny!
   Where shall I turn? I know not. Where can I be?
   O love and kindness not repaid in kind!   5
   Outrageous scheme of a degenerate mind!
   To seek his lustful end he had recourse,
   Like any blackguard, to the use of force.
   I recognize the sword his passion drew—
   My gift, bestowed with nobler deeds in view.   10
   Why did our ties of blood prove no restraint?
   Why too did Phaedra make no prompt complaint?
   Was it to spare the culprit?
OENONE: It was rather
   That she, in pity, wished to spare his father.
   Ashamed because her beauty had begot   15
   So foul a passion, and so fierce a plot,
   By her own hand, my lord, she sought to die,
   And darken thus the pure light of her eye.
   I saw her raise her arm; to me you owe
   Her life, because I ran and stayed the blow.   20
   Now, pitying both her torment and your fears,
   I have, against my will, spelled out her tears.
THESEUS: The traitor! Ah, no wonder he turned pale.
   When first he sighted me, I saw him quail.
   'Twas strange to see no greeting in his face.   25

My heart was frozen by his cold embrace.
But did he, even in Athens, manifest
This guilty love by which he is possessed?
OENONE: The Queen, remember, could not tolerate him.
It was his infamous love which made her hate him. 30
THESEUS: That love, I take it, was rekindled here
In Troezen?
OENONE: I've told you all, my lord. I fear
I've left the Queen too long in mortal grief.
Let me now haste to bring her some relief.

SCENE 2

THESEUS, HIPPOLYTUS

THESEUS: Ah, here he comes. Gods! By that noble mien
What eye would not be duped, as mine has been!
Why must the brow of an adulterer
Be stamped with virtue's sacred character?
Should there not be clear signs by which one can 5
Divine the heart of a perfidious man?
HIPPOLYTUS: May I enquire what louring cloud obscures,
My lord, that royal countenance of yours?
Dare you entrust the secret to your son?
THESEUS: Dare you appear before me, treacherous one? 10
Monster, at whom Jove's thunder should be hurled!
Foul brigand, like those of whom I cleaned the world!
Now that your vile, unnatural love has led
You even to attempt your father's bed,
How dare you show your hated self to me 15
Here in the precincts of your infamy,
Rather than seek some unknown land where fame
Has never brought the tidings of my name?
Fly, wretch. Don't brave the hate which fills my soul,
Or tempt a wrath it pains me to control. 20
I've earned, forevermore, enough disgrace
By fathering one who'd do a deed so base,
Without your death upon my hands, to soil
A noble history of heroic toil.
Fly, and unless you wish to join the band 25
Of knaves who've met quick justice at my hand,
Take care lest by the sun's eye you be found
Setting an insolent foot upon this ground.
Now, never to return, be off; take flight;
Cleanse all my realms of your abhorrent sight. 30
And you, O Neptune, if by courage I
Once cleared your shores of murderers, hear my cry.
Recall that, as reward for that great task,
You swore to grant the first thing I should ask.
Pent in a cruel jail for endless hours, 35

I never called on your immortal powers.
I've hoarded up the aid you promised me
Till greater need should justify my plea.
I make it now. Avenge a father's wrong.
Seize on this traitor, and let your rage be strong.   40
Drown in his blood his brazen lust. I'll know
Your favor by the fury that you show.

HIPPOLYTUS: Phaedra accuses me of lust? I'm weak
With horror at the thought, and cannot speak;
By all these sudden blows I'm overcome;   45
They leave me stupefied, and stricken dumb.

THESEUS: Scoundrel, you thought that Phaedra'd be afraid
To tell of the depraved assault you made.
You should have wrested from her hands the hilt
Of the sharp sword that points now to your guilt;   50
Or, better, crowned your outrage of my wife
By robbing her at once of speech and life.

HIPPOLYTUS: In just resentment of so black a lie,
I might well let the truth be known, but I
Suppress what comes too near your heart. Approve,   55
My lord, a silence which bespeaks my love.
Restrain, as well, your mounting rage and woe:
Review my life; recall the son you know.
Great crimes grow out of small ones. If today
A man first oversteps the bounds, he may   60
Abuse in time all laws and sanctities;
For crime, like virtue, ripens by degrees;
But when has one seen innocence, in a trice,
So change as to embrace the ways of vice?
Not in a single day could time transmute   65
A virtuous man to an incestuous brute.
I had an Amazon mother, brave and chaste,
Whose noble blood my life has not debased.
And when I left her hands, 'twas Pitteus,[2] thought
Earth's wisest man, by whom my youth was taught.   70
I shall not vaunt such merits as I've got,
But if one virtue's fallen to my lot,
It is, my lord, a fierce antipathy
To just that vice imputed now to me.
It is for that Hippolytus is known   75
In Greece—for virtue cold and hard as stone.
By harsh austerity I am set apart.
The daylight is not purer than my heart.
Yet I, it's charged, consumed by lechery . . .

THESEUS: This very boast betrays your guilt. I see   80
What all your vaunted coldness signifies:

---

2. The most learned man of his age, Theseus's guardian. After marrying Phaedra, Theseus sent Hippolytus to Pitteus (or Pitheus), who had adopted him as heir to the throne of Troezen.

Phaedra alone could please your lustful eyes;
No other woman moved you, or could inspire
Your scornful heart with innocent desire.
HIPPOLYTUS: No Father: hear what it's time I told you of; 85
I have not scorned to feel a blameless love.
I here confess my only true misdeed:
I am in love, despite what you decreed.
Aricia has enslaved me; my heart is won,
And Pallas' daughter has subdued your son. 90
I worship her against your orders, Sir,
Nor could I burn or sigh except for her.
THESEUS: You love her? Gods! But no, I see your game.
You play the criminal to clear your name.
HIPPOLYTUS: Six months I've shunned her whom my heart adored. 95
I came in fear to tell you this, my lord.
Why must you be so stubbornly mistaken?
To win your trust, what great oath must be taken?
By Earth, and Heaven, and all the things that be . . .
THESEUS: A rascal never shrinks from perjury. 100
Cease now to weary me with sly discourse,
If your false virtue has but that resource.
HIPPOLYTUS: My virtue may seem false and sly to you,
But Phaedra has good cause to know it true.
THESEUS: Ah, how your impudence makes my temper boil! 105
HIPPOLYTUS: How long shall I be banished? On what soil?
THESEUS: Were you beyond Alcides' pillars,[3] I
Would think yet that a rogue was too nearby.
HIPPOLYTUS: Who will befriend me now—a man suspected
Of such a crime, by such a sire rejected? 110
THESEUS: Go look for friends who think adultery cause
For accolades, and incest for applause,
Yes, ingrates, traitors, to law and honor blind,
Fit to protect a blackguard of your kind.
HIPPOLYTUS: Incest! Adultery! Are these still your themes? 115
I'll say no more. Yet Phaedra's mother, it seems,
And, as you know, Sir, all of Phaedra's line
Knew more about such horrors than did mine.
THESEUS: So! You dare storm and rage before my face?
I tell you for the last time: leave this place. 120
Be off, before I'm roused to violence
And have you, in dishonor, driven hence.

SCENE 3

THESEUS, *alone*

THESEUS: Poor wretch, the path you take will end in blood.
What Neptune swore by Styx, that darkest flood

---

3. The Pillars of Hercules, the two points of land on either side of the Strait of Gibraltar, at the western end of the Mediterranean and thus representing one edge of the known world.

Which frights the Gods themselves, he'll surely do.
And none escapes when vengeful Gods' pursue.
I loved you; and in spite of what you've done,   5
I mourn your coming agonies, my son.
But you have all too well deserved my curse.
When was a father ever outraged worse?
Just Gods, who see this grief which drives me wild,
How could I father such a wicked child?   10

SCENE 4

PHAEDRA, THESEUS

PHAEDRA: My lord, I hasten to you, full of dread.
   I heard your threatening voice, and what it said.
   Pray Heaven no deed has followed on your threat.
   I beg you, if there is time to save him yet,
   To spare your son; spare me the dreadful sound   5
   Of blood, your own blood, crying from the ground.
   Do not impose on me the endless woe
   Of having caused your hand to make it flow.
THESEUS: No, Madam, my blood's not on my hands. But he,
   The thankless knave, has not escaped from me.   10
   A God's great hand will be his nemesis
   And your avenger. Neptune owes me this.
PHAEDRA: Neptune! And will your angry prayers be heard?
THESEUS: What! Are you fearful lest he keep his word?
   No, rather join me in my righteous pleas.   15
   Recount to me my son's black treacheries;
   Stir up my sluggish wrath, that's still too cold.
   He has done crimes of which you've not been told:
   Enraged at you, he slanders your good name:
   Your mouth is full of lies, he dares to claim;   20
   He states that heart and soul, his love is pledged
   To Aricia.
PHAEDRA: What, my lord!
THESEUS: So he alleged;
   But I saw through so obvious a trick.
   Let's hope that Neptune's justice will be quick.
   I go now to his altars, to implore   25
   A prompt fulfillment of the oath he swore.

SCENE 5

PHAEDRA, *alone*

PHAEDRA: He's gone. What news assails my ear? What ill-
   Extinguished fire flares in my bossom still?
   By what a thunderbolt I am undone!
   I'd flown here with one thought, to save his son.

Escaping from Oenone's arms by force,   5
I'd yielded to my torturing remorse.
How far I might have gone, I cannot guess.
Guilt might perhaps have driven me to confess.
Perhaps, had shock not caused my voice to fail,
I might have blurted out my hideous tale.   10
Hippolytus can feel, but not for me!
Aricia has his love, his loyalty!
Gods! When he steeled himself against my sighs
With that forbidding brow, those scornful eyes,
I thought his heart, which love-darts could not strike,   15
Was armed against all womankind alike.
And yet another's made his pride surrender;
Another's made his cruel eyes grow tender.
Perhaps his heart is easy to ensnare.
It's me, alone of women, he cannot bear!   20
Shall I defend a man by whom I'm spurned?

SCENE 6

PHAEDRA, OENONE

PHAEDRA: Oenone dear, do you know what I have learned?
OENONE: No, but in truth I'm quaking still with fear
    Of the wild urge that sent you rushing here:
    I feared some blunder fatally adverse.
PHAEDRA: I had a rival. Who would have thought it, Nurse?   5
OENONE: What?
PHAEDRA: Yes, Hippolytus is in love; it's true.
    That savage creature no one could subdue,
    Who scorned regard, who heard no lovers' pleas,
    That tiger whom I viewed with trembling knees,
    Is tame now, broken by a woman's art: 10
    Aricia's found the way into his heart.
OENONE: Aricia?
PHAEDRA: O pain I never felt before!
    What new, sharp torments have I kept in store!
    All that I've suffered—frenzies, fears, the dire
    Oppression of remorse, my heart on fire,   15
    The merciless rebuff he gave to me—
    All were but foretastes of this agony.
    They love each other! By what magic, then,
    Did they beguile me? Where did they meet, and when?
    You knew. Why did you keep me unaware,   20
    Deceived as to their furtive love-affair?
    Were they much seen together? Were they known
    To haunt the deep woods, so as to be alone?
    Alas, they'd perfect liberty to meet.

Heaven smiled on hearts so innocent and sweet; 25
Without remorse, they savored love's delight;
For them, each dawn arose serene and bright—
While I, creation's outcast, hid away
From the Sun's eye, and fled the light of day.
Death was the only God I dared implore. 30
I longed for him; I prayed to be no more.
Quenching my thirst with tears, and fed on gall,
Yet in my woe too closely watched by all,
I dared not weep and grieve in fullest measure;
I sipped in secret at that bitter pleasure; 35
And often, wearing a serene disguise,
I kept my pain from welling in my eyes.
OENONE: What will their love avail them? They will never
Meet again.
PHAEDRA: But they will love forever.
Even as I speak—ah, deadly thought!—they dare 40
To mock my crazed desire and my despair.
Despite this exile which will make them part,
They swear forever to be joined in heart.
No, no, their bliss I cannot tolerate,
Oenone. Take pity on my jealous hate. 45
Aricia must die. Her odious house
Must once more feel the anger of my spouse.
Nor can the penalty be light, for her
Misdeeds are darker than her brothers' were.
In my wild jealousy I will plead with him. 50
I'll what? Has my poor reason grown so dim?
I, jealous! And it's with Theseus I would plead!
My husband lives, and still my passions feed
On whom? Toward whom do all my wishes tend?
At every word, my hair stands up on end. 55
The measure of my crimes is now replete.
I foul the air with incest and deceit.
My murderous hands are itching to be stained
With innocent blood, that vengeance be obtained.
Wretch that I am, how can I live, how face 60
That sacred Sun, great elder of my race?
My grandsire was, of all the Gods, most high;
My forebears fill the world, and all the sky.
Where can I hide? For Hades' night I yearn.
No, there my father holds the dreadful urn 65
Entrusted to his hands by Fate, it's said:
There Minos judges all the ashen dead.
Ah, how his shade will tremble with surprise
To see his daughter brought before his eyes—
Forced to confess a throng of sins, to tell 70
Of crimes perhaps unheard of yet in Hell!

What will you say then, Father? As in a dream,
I see you drop the fearful urn;[4] you seem
To ponder some new torment fit for her,
Yourself become your own child's torturer.   75
Forgive me. A cruel God destroys your line;
Behold her hand in these mad deeds of mine.
My heart, alas! not once enjoyed the fruit
Of its dark, shameful crime. In fierce pursuit,
Misfortune dogs me till, with my last breath,   80
My sad life shall, in torments, yield to death.
OENONE: My lady, don't give in to needless terror.
Look freshly at your pardonable error.
You love. But who can conquer Destiny?
Lured by a fatal spell, you were not free.   85
Is that a marvel hitherto unknown?
Has Love entrapped no heart but yours alone?
Weakness is natural to us, is it not?
You are a mortal; accept your mortal lot.
To chafe against our frail estate is vain.   90
Even the Gods who on Olympus reign,
And with their thunders chasten men for crime,
Have felt illicit passions many a time.
PHAEDRA: Ah, what corrupting counsels do I hear?
Wretch! Will you pour such poison in my ear   95
Right to the end? Look how you've ruined me.
You dragged me back to all I sought to flee.
You blinded me to duty; called it no wrong
To see Hippolytus, whom I'd shunned so long.
Ah, meddling creature, why did your sinful tongue   100
Falsely accuse a soul so pure and young?
He'll die, it may be, if the Gods can bear
To grant his maddened father's impious prayer.
No, say no more. Go, monster whom I hate.
Go, let me face at last my own sad fate.   105
May Heaven reward you for your deeds! And may
Your punishment forever give dismay
To all who, like yourself, by servile arts
Nourish the weaknesses of princes' hearts,
Incline them to pursue the baser path,   110
And smooth for them the way to sin and wrath—
Accursèd flatterers, the worst of things
That Heaven's anger can bestow on kings!
OENONE: I've given my life to her. Ah, Gods! It hurts
To be thus thanked. Yet I have my just deserts.   115

---

4. After his death, Minos of Crete became, along with his brother Rhadamanthus, one of the judges of
souls in the underworld. The urn held the lots determining to what abode in the underworld the souls
of the dead were to be sent.

Act V

SCENE 1

HIPPOLYTUS, ARICIA

ARICIA: Come, in this mortal danger, will you not make
Your loving sire aware of his mistake?
If, scorning all my tears, you can consent
To parting and an endless banishment,
Go, leave Aricia in her life alone.   5
But first assure the safety of your own.
Defend your honor against a foul attack,
And force your sire to call his prayers back.
There yet is time. What moves you, if you please,
Not to contest Queen Phaedra's calumnies?   10
Tell Theseus the truth.
HIPPOLYTUS: What more should I
Have told him? How she smirched their marriage-tie?
How could I, by disclosing everything,
Humiliate my father and my king?
It's you alone I've told these horrors to.   15
I've bared my heart but to the Gods and you.
Judge of my love, which forced me to confide
What even from myself I wished to hide.
But, mind you, keep this secret ever sealed.
Forget, if possible, all that I've revealed,   20
And never let those pure lips part to bear
Witness, my lady, to this vile affair.
Let us rely upon the Gods' high laws:
Their honor binds them to defend my cause;
And Phaedra, sooner or later brought to book,   25
Will blush for crimes their justice cannot brook.
To that restraint I ask you to agree.
In all things else, just anger makes me free.
Come, break away from this, your slavish plight;
Dare follow me, dare join me in my flight;   30
Be quit of an accursèd country where
Virtue must breathe a foul and poisoned air.
Under the cover of this turbulence
Which my disfavor brings, slip quickly hence.
I can assure a safe escape for you.   35
Your only guards are of my retinue.
Strong states will champion us; upon our side
Is Sparta; Argos' arms are open wide:
Let's plead then to these friends our righteous case,
Lest Phaedra, profiting by our disgrace,   40
Deny our lineal claims to either throne,
And pledge her son my birthright and your own.
Come, let us seize the moment; we mustn't wait.

What holds you back? You seem to hesitate.
It's zeal for you that moves me to be bold.   45
When I am all on fire, what makes you cold?
Are you afraid to join a banished man?
ARICIA: Alas, my lord, how sweet to share that ban!
What deep delight, as partner of your lot,
To live with you, by all the world forgot!   50
But since no blessèd tie unites us two,
Can I, in honor, flee this land with you?
The sternest code, I know, would not deny
My right to break your father's bonds and fly;
I'd grieve no loving parents thus; I'm free,   55
As all are, to escape from tyranny.
But, Sir, you love me, and my fear of shame . . .
HIPPOLYTUS: Ah, never doubt my care for your good name.
It is a nobler plan that I propose:
Flee with your husband from our common foes.   60
Freed my mischance, since Heaven so commands,
We need no man's consent to join our hands.
Not every nuptial needs the torch's light.
At Troezen's gate, amidst that burial site
Where stand our princes' ancient sepulchers,   65
There is a temple feared by perjurers.
No man there dares to break his faith, on pain
Of instant doom, or swear an oath in vain;
There all deceivers, lest they surely die,
Bridle their tongues and are afraid to lie.   70
There, if you trust me, we will go, and of
Our own accord shall pledge eternal love;
The temple's God will witness to our oath;
We'll pray that he be father to us both.
I shall invoke all deities pure and just.   75
The chaste Diana, Juno[5] the august,
And all the Gods who know my faithfulness
Will guarantee the vows I shall profess.
ARICIA: The king is coming. Go, Prince, make no delay.
To cloak my own departure, I'll briefly stay.   80
Go, go; but leave with me some faithful guide
Who'll lead my timid footsteps to your side.

SCENE 2

THESEUS, ARICIA, ISMENE

THESEUS: O Gods, bring light into my troubled mind;
Show me the truth which I've come here to find.
ARICIA: Make ready for our flight, Ismene dear.

---

5. The wife of Jupiter and queen of the gods. Diana was goddess of the moon and of chastity.

SCENE 3

THESEUS, ARICIA

THESEUS: Your color changes, Madame, and you appear
   Confused. Why was Hippolytus here with you?
ARICIA: He came, my lord, to say a last adieu.
THESEUS: Ah, yes. You've tamed his heart, which none could capture.
   And taught his stubborn lips to sigh with rapture.   5
ARICIA: I shan't deny the truth, my lord. No, he
   Did not inherit your malignity,
   Nor treat me as a criminal, in your fashion.
THESEUS: I see. He's sworn, no doubt, eternal passion.
   Put no reliance on the vows of such   10
   A fickle lover. He's promised others as much.
ARICIA: He, Sir?
THESEUS: You should have taught him not to stray.
   How could you share his love in that base way?
ARICIA: How could you let a shameful lie besmear
   The stainless honor of his young career?   15
   Have you so little knowledge of his heart?
   Can't you tell sin and innocence apart?
   Must some black cloud bedim your eyes alone
   To the bright virtue for which your son is known?
   Shall slander ruin him? That were too much to bear.   20
   Turn back: repent now of your murderous prayer.
   Fear, my lord, fear lest the stern deities
   So hate you as to grant your wrathful pleas.
   Our sacrifices anger Heaven at times;
   Its gifts are often sent to scourge our crimes.   25
THESEUS: Your words can't cover up that sin of his:
   Love's blinded you to what the scoundrel is.
   But I've sure proofs on which I may rely:
   I have seen tears—yes, tears which could not lie.
ARICIA: Take care, my lord. You have, in many lands,   30
   Slain countless monsters with your conquering hands;
   But all are not destroyed; there still lives one
   Who . . . No, I am sworn to silence by your son.
   Knowing his wish to shield your honor, I'd
   Afflict him if I further testified.   35
   I'll imitate his reticence, and flee
   Your presence, lest the truth should burst from me.

SCENE 4

THESEUS, *alone*

THESEUS: What does she mean? These speeches which begin
   And then break off—what are they keeping in?
   Is this some sham those two have figured out?
   Have they conspired to torture me with doubt?

But I myself, despite my stern control—   5
What plaintive voice cries from my inmost soul?
I feel a secret pity, a surge of pain.
Oenone must be questioned once again.
I'll have more light on this. Not all is known.
Guards, go and bring Oenone here, alone.   10

SCENE 5

THESEUS, PANOPE

PANOPE: I don't know what the Queen may contemplate,
  My lord, but she is in a frightening state.
  Mortal despair is what her looks bespeak;
  Death's pallor is already on her cheek.
  Oenone, driven from her in disgrace,   5
  Has thrown herself into the sea's embrace.
  None knows what madness caused the thing she did;
  Beneath the waves she lies forever hid.
THESEUS: What do you tell me?
PANOPE: This death has left the Queen
  No calmer; her distraction grows more keen.   10
  At moments, to allay her dark unrest,
  She clasps her children, weeping, to her breast;
  Then, with a sudden horror, she will shove
  Them both away, and starve her mother-love.
  She wanders aimlessly about the floor;   15
  Her blank eye does not know us any more.
  Thrice she has written; and thrice, before she'd done,
  Torn up the letter which she had begun.
  We cannot help her. I beg you, Sire, to try.
THESEUS: Oenone's dead? And Phaedra wants to die?   20
  O bring me back my son, and let him clear
  His name! If he'll but speak, I now will hear.
  O Neptune, let your gifts not be conferred
  Too swiftly; let my prayers go unheard.
  Too much I've trusted what may not be true,   25
  Too quickly raised my cruel hands to you.
  How I'd despair if what I asked were done!

SCENE 6

THESEUS, THERAMENES

THESEUS: Is it you, Theramenes? Where have you left my son?
  You've been his mentor since his tenderest years.
  But why do I behold you drenched in tears?
  Where's my dear son?
THERAMENES: Too late, Sire, you restore
  Your love to him. Hippolytus is no more.   5
THESEUS: Gods!

THERAMENES: I have seen the best of mortals slain,
  My lord, and the least guilty, I maintain.
THESEUS: My son is dead? What! Just when I extend
  My arms to him, Heaven's haste has caused his end?
  What thunderbolt bereaved me? What was his fate?   10
THERAMENES: Scarcely had we emerged from Troezen's gate:
  He drove his chariot, and his soldiery
  Were ranged about him, mute and grave as he.
  Brooding, he headed toward Mycenae. Lax
  In his hands, the reins lay on his horses' backs.   15
  His haughty chargers, quick once to obey
  His voice, and give their noble spirits play,
  Now, with hung head and mournful eye, seemed part
  Of the sad thoughts that filled their master's heart.
  Out of the sea-deeps then a frightful cry   20
  Arose, to tear the quiet of the sky,
  And a dread voice from far beneath the ground
  Replies in groans to that appalling sound.
  Our hearts congeal; blood freezes in our veins.
  The horses, hearing, bristle up their manes.   25
  And now there rises from the sea's calm breast
  A liquid mountain with a seething crest.
  The wave approaches, breaks, and spews before
  Our eyes a raging monster on the shore.
  His huge brow's armed with horns; the spray unveils   30
  A body covered all with yellow scales;
  Half bull he is, half dragon; fiery, bold;
  His thrashing tail contorts in fold on fold.
  With echoing bellows now he shakes the strand.
  The sky, aghast, beholds him; he makes the land   35
  Shudder; his foul breath chokes the atmosphere;
  The wave which brought him in recoils in fear.
  All flee, and in a nearby temple save
  Their lives, since it is hopeless to be brave.
  Hippolytus alone dares make a stand.   40
  He checks his chargers, javelins in hand,
  Has at the monster and, with a sure-aimed throw,
  Pierces his flank: a great wound starts to flow.
  In rage and pain the beast makes one dread spring,
  Falls near the horses' feet, still bellowing,   45
  Rolls over toward them, with fiery throat takes aim
  And covers them with smoke and blood and flame.
  Sheer panic takes them; deaf now, they pay no heed
  To voice or curb, but bolt in full stampede;
  Their master strives to hold them back, in vain.   50
  A bloody slaver drips from bit and rein.
  It's said that, in that tumult, some caught sight
  Of a God who spurred those dusty flanks to flight.
  Fear drives them over rocks; the axletree

Screeches and breaks. The intrepid Prince must see   55
His chariot dashed to bits, for all his pains;
He falls at last, entangled in the reins.
Forgive my grief. That cruel sight will be
An everlasting source of tears for me.
I've seen, my lord, the heroic son you bred   60
Dragged by the horses which his hand had fed.
His shouts to them but make their fear more strong.
His body seems but one great wound, ere long.
The plain re-echoes to our cries of woe.
At last, their headlong fury starts to slow: 65
They stop, then, near that graveyard which contains,
In royal tombs, his forebears' cold remains.
I run to him in tears; his guards are led
By the bright trail of noble blood he shed;
The rocks are red with it; the briars bear   70
Their red and dripping trophies of his hair.
I reach him; speak his name; his hand seeks mine;
His eyelids lift a moment, then decline.
"Heaven takes," he says, "my innocent life away.
Protect my sad Aricia, I pray.   75
If ever, friend, my sire is disabused,
And mourns his son who falsely was accused,
Bid him appease my blood and plaintive shade
By dealing gently with that captive maid.
Let him restore . . ." His voice then died away,   80
And in my arms a mangled body lay
Which the God's wrath had claimed, a sorry prize
Which even his father would not recognize.
THESEUS: My son, dear hope whom folly made me kill!
O ruthless Gods, too well you did my will!   85
I'll henceforth be the brokenest of men.
THERAMENES: Upon this scene came shy Aricia then,
Fleeing your wrath, and ready to espouse
Your son before the Gods by holy vows.
She comes, and sees the red and steaming grass;   90
She sees—no sight for loving eyes, alas!—
Hippolytus sprawled there, lacking form or hue.
At first, she won't believe her loss is true.
Not recognizing her beloved, she
Both looks at him and asks where he may be.   95
At last she knows too well what's lying there;
She lifts to the Gods a sad, accusing stare;
Then, moaning, cold, and all but dead, the sweet
Maid drops unconscious at her lover's feet.
Ismene, weeping, kneels and seeks to bring   100
Her back to life—a life of suffering.
And I, my lord, have come, who now detest
This world, to bring a hero's last request,

And so perform the bitter embassy
Which, with his dying breath, he asked of me.   105
But look: his mortal enemy comes this way.

SCENE 7

THESEUS, PHAEDRA, THERAMENES, PANOPE, GUARDS

THESEUS: Well, Madam, my son's no more; you've won the day!
Ah, but what qualms I feel! What doubts torment
My heart, and plead that he was innocent!
But, madam, claim your victim. He is dead.
Enjoy his death, unjust or merited.   5
I'm willing to be evermore deceived.
You've called him guilty; let it be believed.
His death is grief enough for me to bear
Without my further probing this affair,
Which could not bring his dear life back again   10
And might perhaps but aggravate my pain.
No, far from you and Troezen, I shall flee
My dead son's torn and bloody memory.
It will pursue me ever, like a curse:
Would I were banished from the universe!   15
All seems to chide my wicked wrathfulness.
My very fame now adds to my distress.
How shall I hide, who have a name so great?
Even the Gods' high patronage I hate.
I go to mourn this murderous gift of theirs,   20
Nor trouble them again with useless prayers.
Do for me what they might, it could not pay
For what their deadly favor took away.
PHAEDRA: Theseus, my wrongful silence must be ended.
Your guiltless son must be at last defended.   25
He did no ill.
THESEUS: How curst a father am I!
I doomed him, trusting in your heartless lie!
Do you think to be excused for such a crime?
PHAEDRA: Hear me, my lord. I have but little time.
I was the lustful and incestuous one   30
Who dared desire your chaste and loyal son.
Heaven lit a fatal blaze within my breast.
Detestable Oenone did the rest.
She, fearing lest Hippolytus, who knew
Of my vile passion, might make it known to you,   35
Abused my weakness and, by a vicious ruse,
Made haste to be the first one to accuse.
For that she's paid; fleeing my wrath, she found
Too mild a death, and in the waves is drowned.
Much though I wished to die then by the sword,   40
Your son's pure name cried out to be restored.

That my remorse be told, I chose instead
A slower road that leads down to the dead.
I drank, to give my burning veins some peace,
A poison which Medea[6] brought to Greece.   45
Already, to my heart, the venom gives
An alien coldness, so that it scarcely lives;
Already, to my sight, all clouds and fades —
The sky, my spouse, the world my life degrades;
Death dims my eyes, which soiled what they could see,   50
Restoring to the light its purity.

PANOPE: She's dead, my lord!

THESEUS: Would that I could inter
The memory of her black misdeeds with her!
Let's go, since now my error's all too clear,
And mix my poor son's blood with many a tear,   55
Embrace his dear remains, and expiate
The fury of a prayer which now I hate.
To his great worth all honor shall be paid,
And, further to appease his angry shade,
Aricia, despite her brother's offense,   60
Shall be my daughter from this moment hence.

---

6. A sorceress who helped Jason get the Golden Fleece and later, deserted by him, killed her rival and her own children and burned her palace before fleeing to Athens. According to one legend, she tried to poison Theseus.

SOR JUANA INÉS DE LA CRUZ
1648–1695

One hardly expects to find a spirited defense of women's intellectual rights issuing from the pen of a seventeenth-century Mexican nun, but *Reply to Sor Filotea de la Cruz*, by Sister Juana Inés de la Cruz, is exactly that. In the guise of declaring her humility and her religious subordination, this nun manages to advance claims for her sex more far-reaching and profound than any previously offered.

Born into an upper-class family, Sister Juana in her teens served as lady-in-waiting at the Viceregal court. She soon took the veil, however; her *Reply* suggests a reason in her desire for a safe environment in which to pursue her intellectual interests. Religious vocation did not prevent her from writing in secular forms: lyric poetry and drama. Indeed, she achieved an important literary reputation, later coming to be known throughout the Spanish-speaking world as the "Tenth Muse." Since her religious superiors intermittently rebuked her for her worldly interests, however, she appears to have developed a powerful sense of guilt. It is said that the natural disasters — a solar eclipse, storms, and famine — plaguing Mexico City in the 1690s intensified her guilt; in 1694, she reaffirmed her faith, signing the statement in her own blood with the words, "I, Sister Juana Inés de la Cruz, the worst in the world." She died after nursing the sick in an epidemic.

The *Reply* stems directly from Sister Juana's venture into theological polemic. In 1690 she wrote a commentary on a sermon delivered forty years earlier by the Portuguese Jesuit Antonio de Vieyra, a sermon in which he disputed with St.

Augustine and St. Thomas about the nature of Christ's greatest expression of love at His life's end. Her commentary, in the form of a letter, was published, without her consent, by the bishop of Puebla. The bishop provided the title, *Athenagoric Letter*, or "letter worthy of the wisdom of Athena," but he also prefixed his own letter to Sister Juana, signed with the pseudonym "Filotea de la Cruz." Here he advised the nun to focus her attention and her talents more on religious matters. In her *Reply* (1691), she nominally accepted the bishop's rebuke; the smooth surface of her elegant prose, however, conceals both rage and determination to assert her right—and that of other women—to a fully realized life of the mind.

The artistry of this piece of self-defense demonstrates Sister Juana's powers and thus constitutes part of her justification. Systematically refusing to make any overt claims for herself, she declares her desire to do whatever her associates wish or demand of her. While asserting her own unimportance, she illustrates the range of her knowledge and of her rhetorical skill. The sheer abundance of her biblical allusions and of her quotations from theological texts, for instance, proves that she has mastered a large body of religious material and that she has not sacrificed religious to secular study. Her elaborate protestations of deference, her vocabulary of insignificance, her narrative of subservience: all show the verbal dexterity that enables her to achieve her own rhetorical ends even as she denies her commitment to purely personal goals.

If she acknowledges no self-seeking, she nevertheless declares and demonstrates her ungovernable passion for the life of the mind. She tells of how she joined the convent despite fears that the community "would intrude upon the peaceful silence of my books." "Certain learned persons," however, explained to her that her desire for solitary intellectual experience constituted "temptation." She therefore entered the religious life, believing, she says, "that I was fleeing from myself, but—wretch that I am!—I brought with me my worst enemy, my inclination, which I do not know whether to consider a gift or a punishment from Heaven; for once dimmed and encumbered by the many activities common to Religion, that inclination exploded in me like gunpowder." Although this sentence explicitly labels her intellectual inclinations her worst enemy and suggests that they might be considered divine punishment, the same sentence dramatizes the uncontrollable, explosive force of those inclinations and hints at the negative potential of religious experience, which dims and encumbers the mind. No matter how often Sister Juana admits that her longings amount to a form of "vice," she embodies in her prose the energy and the vividness they generate and makes her audience feel their positive weight.

The autobiographical aspects of Sister Juana's self-defense give it special immediacy for modern readers, who may recognize versions of their own dilemmas in her narrative of difficulties. Of course, girls no longer have to trick their way into learning or plead for permission to dress in boy's clothes to go to a university. But even twentieth-century young women have been known to experience the kind of hostility Sister Juana reports as the response to her remarkable achievement. Yet more recognizable as a frequent form of female anxiety is the nun's concern to proclaim her responsiveness to others, her "tender and affable nature," which causes the other nuns, she says, to hold her "in great affection." She insists that she fills all the responsibilities of a woman as well as displays the kinds of capacity more generally associated with men, and she performs her womanly and her religious duties *first*, reserving her scholarly pursuits for leisure hours.

But of course her larger argument depends on her utter denial that intelligence or a thirst for knowledge should be considered a sex-linked characteristic. She draws on history for evidence of female intellectual power; one may feel the irony of the fact that her list of female worthies requires so much annotation today. The names of these notable women have hardly become household words. Still, these names, these histories, do exist, providing powerful support for Sister Juana's position. Even more forceful is the testimony of her own experience: her account of how, deprived of books, she finds matter for intellectual inquiry everywhere—in the yolk of an egg, the spinning of a top, the reading of the Bible. This is, the reader comes to believe, a woman born to think. If she arouses uneasiness when she implicitly equates herself, as object of persecution, with Christ, she also makes one feel directly the horror of women's official exclusion, in the past, from intellectual pursuits.

Little has been written in English about Sister Juana. A volume in the Twayne series by Gerard Flynn, *Sor Juana Inés de la Cruz* (1971), provides a biographical, critical, and bibliographical introduction. She is also treated in histories of Latin American literature: for example, J. Franco, *An Introduction to Spanish-American Literature* (1969). This first English-language translation of the *Reply*, by Margaret Sayers Peden, was commissioned in 1981 by a small independent publisher in Salisbury, Connecticut (Lime Rock Press). An important critical work, belatedly translated into English, is Octavio Paz, *Sor Juana; Or, The Traps of Faith* (1988).

Reply to Sor Filotea de la Cruz[1]

My most illustrious *señora*, dear lady. It has not been my will, my poor health, or my justifiable apprehension that for so many days delayed my response. How could I write, considering that at my very first step my clumsy pen encountered two obstructions in its path? The first (and, for me, the most uncompromising) is to know how to reply to your most learned, most prudent, most holy, and most loving letter. For I recall that when Saint Thomas, the Angelic Doctor of Scholasticism, was asked about his silence regarding his teacher Albertus Magnus,[2] he replied that he had not spoken because he knew no words worthy of Albertus. With so much greater reason, must not I too be silent? Not, like the Saint, out of humility, but because in reality I know nothing I can say that is worthy of you. The second obstruction is to know how to express my appreciation for a favor as unexpected as extreme, for having my scribblings printed, a gift so immeasurable as to surpass my most ambitious aspiration, my most fervent desire, which even as an entity of reason never entered my thoughts. Yours was a kindness, finally, of such magnitude that words cannot express my gratitude, a kindness exceeding the bounds of appreciation, as great as it was unexpected—which is as Quintilian[3] said: *aspirations engender minor glory; benefices,[4] major.* To such a degree as to impose silence on the receiver.

When the blessedly sterile—that she might miraculously become fecund—Mother of John the Baptist saw in her house such an extraordinary visitor as the Mother of the Word, her reason became clouded and her speech deserted her; and thus, in the place of thanks, she burst out with doubts and questions: *And whence is to me [that the mother of my Lord should come to me?][5]* And whence cometh such a thing to me? And

---

1. Translated by Margaret Sayers Peden.   2. St. Albert the Great (1193?–1280), scholastic philosopher, called the Universal Doctor; he exercised great influence on his student Thomas Aquinas.   3. Marcus Fabius Quintilianus (ca. A.D. 35–100), born in Spain, became a famous Roman orator and wrote on rhetoric.   4. This word would be better understood as "good works."   5. Luke 1:43.

so also it fell to Saul when he found himself the chosen, the anointed, King of Israel: *Am I not a son of Jemini, of the least tribe of Israel, and my kindred the last among all the families of the tribe of Benjamin? Why then hast thou spoken this word to me?*[6] And thus say I, most honorable lady. Why do I receive such favor? By chance, am I other than an humble nun, the lowliest creature of the world, the most unworthy to occupy your attention? "Wherefore then speakest thou so to me?" "And whence is this to me?" Nor to the first obstruction do I have any response other than I am little worthy of your eyes; nor to the second, other than wonder, in the stead of thanks, saying that I am not capable of thanking you for the smallest part of that which I owe you. This is not pretended modesty, lady, but the simplest truth issuing from the depths of my heart, that when the letter which with propriety you called *Atenagórica*[7] reached my hands, in print, I burst into tears of confusion (withal, that tears do not come easily to me) because it seemed to me that your favor was but a remonstrance God made against the wrong I have committed, and that in the same way He corrects others with punishment He wishes to subject me with benefices, with this special favor for which I know myself to be myself to be His debtor, as for an infinitude of others from His boundless kindness. I looked upon this favor as a particular way to shame and confound me, it being the most exquisite means of castigation, that of causing me, by my own intellect, to be the judge who pronounces sentence and who denounces my ingratitude. And thus, when here in my solitude I think on these things, I am wont to say: Blessed art Thou, oh Lord, for Thou hast not chosen to place in the hands of others my judgment, nor yet in mine, but hast reserved that to Thy own, and freed me from myself, and from the necessity to sit in judgment on myself, which judgment, forced from my own intellect, could be no less than condemnation, but Thou hast reserved me to Thy mercy, because Thou lovest me more than I can love myself.

I beg you, lady, to forgive this digression to which I was drawn by the power of truth, and, if I am to confess all the truth, I shall confess that I cast about for some manner by which I might flee the difficulty of a reply, and was sorely tempted to take refuge in silence. But as silence is a negative thing, though it explains a great deal through the very stress of not explaining, we must assign some meaning to it that we may understand what the silence is intended to say, for if not, silence will say nothing, as that is its very office: *to say nothing*. The holy Chosen Vessel, Saint Paul, having been caught up into paradise, and having heard the arcane secrets of God, *heard secret words, which it is not granted to man to utter.*[8] He does not say what he heard; he says that he cannot say it. So that of things one cannot say, it is needful to say at least that they cannot be said, so that it may be understood that not speaking is not the same as having nothing to say, but rather being unable to express the many things there are to say. Saint John says that if all the marvels our Redeemer wrought "were written every one, the world itself, I think, would not be able to contain the books

---

6. 1 Samuel 9:21.   7. Sister Juana's letter criticizing Father Vieyra's sermon was retitled by the bishop *Carta Atenagórica* (Letter worthy of Athena). Athena was the Greek goddess of wisdom.   8. 2 Corinthians 12:4.

that should be written."[9] And Vieyra[1] says on this point that in this single phrase the Evangelist said more than in all else he wrote; and this same Lusitanian[2] Phoenix speaks well (but when does he not speak well, even when he does not speak well of others?) because in those words Saint John said everything left unsaid and expressed all that was left to be expressed. And thus I, lady, shall respond only that I do not know how to respond; I shall thank you in saying only that I am incapable of thanking you; and I shall say, through the indication of what I leave to silence, that it is only with the confidence of one who is favored and with the protection of one who is honorable that I presume to address your magnificence, and if this be folly, be forgiving of it, for folly may be good fortune, and in this manner I shall provide further occasion for your benignity and you will better shape my intellect.

Because he was halting of speech, Moses thought himself unworthy to speak with Pharaoh, but after he found himself highly favored of God, and thus inspired, he not only spoke with God Almighty but dared ask the impossible: *shew me thy face.*[3] In this same manner, lady, and in view of how you favor me, I no longer see as impossible the obstructions I posed in the beginning: for who was it who had my letter printed unbeknownst to me? Who entitled it, who bore the cost, who honored it, it being so unworthy in itself, and in its author? What will such a person not do, not pardon? What would he fail to do, or fail to pardon? And thus, based on the supposition that I speak under the safe-conduct of your favor, and with the assurance of your benignity, and with the knowledge that like a second Ahasuerus[4] you have offered to me to kiss the top of the golden scepter of your affection as a sign of conceding to me your benevolent license to speak and offer judgments in your exalted presence, I say to you that I have taken to heart your most holy admonition that I apply myself to the study of the Sacred Books, which, though it comes in the guise of counsel, will have for me the authority of a precept, but with the not insignificant consolation that even before your counsel I was disposed to obey your pastoral suggestion as your direction, which may be inferred from the premise and argument of my Letter. For I know well that your most sensible warning is not directed against it, but rather against those worldly matters of which I have written.[5] And thus I had hoped with the Letter to make amends for any lack of application you may (with great reason) have inferred from others of my writings; and, speaking more particularly, I confess to you with all the candor of which you are deserving, and with the truth and clarity which are the natural custom in me, that my not having written often of sacred matters was not caused by disaffection or by want of application, but by the abundant fear and reverence due those Sacred Letters, knowing myself incapable of their comprehension and unworthy of their employment. Always resounding in my ears, with no little horror, I hear God's threat and prohibition to sinners like myself.

9. John 21:25.   1. Antonio Vieira (1608–1697), author of the sermon that Sister Juana had earlier criticized, was a Portuguese ecclesiastic whose most important work was converting the Indians of Brazil. 2. Roman name for Portugal.   3. Exodus 33:13.   4. King of Persia, who stretched out his gold scepter to his queen, Esther, and said he would grant her whatever she wished (Esther 5:2–3).   5. Sister Juana had published secular poetry and drama.

Why dost thou declare my justices, and take my covenant in thy mouth?[6]
This question, as well as the knowledge that even learned men are forbidden to read the Canticle of Canticles[7] until they have passed thirty years of age, or even Genesis—the latter for its obscurity; the former in order that the sweetness of those epithalamia not serve as occasion for imprudent youth to transmute their meaning into carnal emotion, as borne out by my exalted Father Saint Jerome,[8] who ordered that these be the last verses to be studied, and for the same reason: *And finally, one may read without peril the Song of Songs, for if it is read one may suffer harm through not understanding those Epithalamia of the spiritual wedding which is expressed in carnal terms.* And Seneca[9] says: *In the early years the faith is dim.* For how then would I have dared take in my unworthy hands these verses, defying gender, age, and, above all, custom? And thus I confess that many times this fear has plucked my pen from my hand and has turned my thoughts back toward the very same reason from which they had wished to be born: which obstacle did not impinge upon profane matters, for a heresy against art is not punished by the Holy Office but by the judicious with derision, and by critics with censure, and censure, *just or unjust, is not to be feared,* as it does not forbid the taking of communion or hearing of mass, and offers me little or no cause for anxiety, because in the opinion of those who defame my art, I have neither the obligation to know nor the aptitude to triumph. If, then, I err, I suffer neither blame nor discredit: I suffer no blame, as I have no obligation; no discredit, as I have no possibility of triumphing—*and no one is obliged to do the impossible.* And, in truth, I have written nothing except when compelled and constrained, and then only to give pleasure to others; not alone without pleasure of my own, but with absolute repugnance, for I have never deemed myself one who has any worth in letters or the wit necessity demands of one who would write; and thus my customary response to those who press me, above all in sacred matters, is, what capacity of reason have I? what application? what resources? what rudimentary knowledge of such matters beyond that of the most superficial scholarly degrees? Leave these matters to those who understand them; I wish no quarrel with the Holy Office, for I am ignorant, and I tremble that I may express some proposition that will cause offense or twist the true meaning of some scripture. I do not study to write, even less to teach—which in one like myself were unseemly pride—but only to the end that if I study, I will be ignorant of less. This is my response, and these are my feelings.

have never written of my own choice, but at the urging of others, to whom with reason I might say, *You have compelled me.*[1] But one truth I shall not deny (first, because it is well-known to all, and second, because although it has not worked in my favor, God has granted me the mercy of loving truth above all else), which is that from the moment I was first illuminated by the light of reason, my inclination toward letters has been

---

6. Psalm 50:16.   7. Song of Songs (that is, Song of Solomon), which employs erotic imagery.
8. Eusebius Sophronius Hieronymus (ca. 342–420), ascetic and scholar, most learned of the Latin Church fathers, a prolific author of treaties and commentaries. Sister Juana belonged to a Jeronymite convent; Jerome had founded the order.   9. Lucius Annaeus Seneca (ca. 3 B.C.–A.D. 63), Roman philosopher and orator.   1. 2 Corinthians 12:11.

so vehement, so overpowering, that not even the admonitions of others—and I have suffered many—nor my own meditations—and they have not been few—have been sufficient to cause me to forswear this natural impulse that God placed in me: the Lord God knows why, and for what purpose. And He knows that I have prayed that He dim the light of my reason, leaving only that which is needed to keep His Law, for there are those who would say that all else is unwanted in a woman, and there are even those who would hold that such knowledge does injury. And my Holy Father knows too that as I have been unable to achieve this (my prayer has not been answered), I have sought to veil the light of my reason—along with my name—and to offer it up only to Him who bestowed it upon me, and He knows that none other was the cause of my entering into Religion, notwithstanding that the spiritual exercises and company of a community were repugnant to the freedom and quiet I desired for my studious endeavors. And later, in that community, the Lord God knows—and, in the world, only the one who must know[2]—how diligently I sought to obscure my name, and how this was not permitted, saying it was temptation: and so it would have been. If it were in my power, lady, to repay you in some part what I owe you, it might be done by telling you this thing which has never before passed my lips, except to be spoken to the one who should hear it. It is my hope that by having opened wide to you the doors of my heart, by having made patent to you its most deeply-hidden secrets, you will deem my confidence not unworthy of the debt I owe to your most august person and to your most uncommon favors.

Continuing the narrations of my inclinations, of which I wish to give you a thorough account, I will tell you that I was not yet three years old when my mother determined to send one of my elder sisters to learn to read at a school for girls we call the *Amigas*. Affection, and mischief, caused me to follow her, and when I observed how she was being taught her lessons I was so inflamed with the desire to know how to read, that deceiving—for so I knew it to be—the mistress, I told her that my mother had meant for me to have lessons too. She did not believe it, as it was little to be believed, but, to humour me, she acceded. I continued to go there, and she continued to teach me, but now, as experience had disabused her, with all seriousness; and I learned so quickly that before my mother knew of it I could already read, for my teacher had kept it from her in order to reveal the surprise and reap the reward at one and the same time. And I, you may be sure, kept the secret, fearing that I would be whipped for having acted without permission. The woman who taught me, may God bless and keep her, is still alive and can bear witness to all I say. I also remember that in those days, my tastes being those common to that age, I abstained from eating cheese because I had heard that it made one slow of wits, for in me the desire for learning was stronger than the desire for eating—as powerful as that is in children. When later, being six or seven, and having learned how to read and write, along with all the other skills of needlework and household arts that girls learn, it came to my attention that in Mexico City there were Schools, and a University, in which one

2. Presumably her confessor, Father Antonio Núñez.

studied the sciences. The moment I heard this, I began to plague my mother with insistent and importunate pleas: she should dress me in boy's clothing and send me to Mexico City to live with relatives, to study and be tutored at the University. She would not permit it, and she was wise, but I assuaged my disappointment by reading the many and varied books belonging to my grandfather, and there were not enough punishments, nor reprimands, to prevent me from reading: so that when I came to the city many marveled, not so much at my natural wit, as at my memory, and at the amount of learning I had mastered at an age when many have scarcely learned to speak well.

I began to study Latin grammar—in all, I believe, I had no more than twenty lessons—and so intense was my concern that though among women (especially a woman in the flower of her youth) the natural adornment of one's hair is held in such high esteem, I cut off mine to the breadth of some four to six fingers, measuring the place it had reached, and imposing upon myself the condition that if by the time it had again grown to that length I had not learned such and such a thing I had set for myself to learn while my hair was growing, I would again cut it off as punishment for being so slow-witted. And it did happen that my hair grew out and still I had not learned what I had set for myself—because my hair grew quickly and I learned slowly—and in fact I did cut it in punishment for such stupidity: for there seemed to me no cause for a head to be adorned with hair and naked of learning—which was the more desired embellishment. And so I entered the religious order, knowing that life there entailed certain conditions (I refer to superficial, and not fundamental, regards) most repugnant to my nature; but given the total antipathy I felt for marriage, I deemed convent life the least unsuitable and the most honorable I could elect if I were to insure my salvation. Working against that end, first (as, finally, the most important) was the matter of all the trivial aspects of my nature which nourished my pride, such as wishing to live alone, and wishing to have no obligatory occupation that would inhibit the freedom of my studies, nor the sounds of a community that would intrude upon the peaceful silence of my books. These desires caused me to falter some while in my decision, until certain learned persons enlightened me, explaining that they were temptation, and, with divine favor, I overcame them, and took upon myself the state which now so unworthily I hold. I believed that I was fleeing from myself, but— wretch that I am!—I brought with me my worst enemy, my inclination, which I do not know whether to consider a gift or a punishment from Heaven, for once dimmed and encumbered by the many activities common to Religion, that inclination exploded in me like gunpowder, proving how *privation is the source of appetite.*

I turned again (which is badly put, for I never ceased), I continued, then, in my studious endeavour (which for me was respite during those moments not occupied by my duties) of reading and more reading, of study and more study, with no teachers but my books. Thus I learned how difficult it is to study those soulless letters, lacking a human voice or the explication of a teacher. But I suffered this labor happily for my love of learning. Oh, had it only been for love of God, which were proper, how worthwhile it would have been! I strove mightily to elevate these studies, to dedicate them to His service, as the goal to which I aspired was to study Theology—it seeming to me debilitating for a Catholic not to know everything in this life of the Divine Mysteries that can be learned through natural means—and, being a nun and not a layperson, it was seemly that I profess my vows to learning through ecclesiastical channels; and especially, being a daughter of a Saint Jerome and a Saint Paula,[3] it was essential that such erudite parents not be shamed by a witless daughter. This is the argument I proposed to myself, and it seemed to me well-reasoned. It was, however (and this cannot be denied) merely glorification and approbation of my inclination, and enjoyment of it offered as justification. And so I continued, as I have said, directing the course of my studies toward the peak of Sacred Theology, it seeming necessary to me, in order to scale those heights, to climb the steps of the human sciences and arts; for how could one undertake the study of the Queen of Sciences if first one had not come to know her servants?

How, without Logic, could I be apprised of the general and specific way in which the Holy Scripture is written? How, without Rhetoric, could I understand its figures, its tropes, its locutions? How, without Physics,[4] so many innate questions concerning the nature of animals, their sacrifices, wherein exist so many symbols, many already declared, many still to be discovered? How should I know whether Saul's being refreshed by the sound of David's harp was due to the virtue and natural power of Music, or to a transcendent power God wished to place in David? How, without Arithmetic, could one understand the computations of the years, days, months, hours, those mysterious weeks communicated by Gabriel to Daniel,[5] and others for whose understanding one must know the nature, concordance, and properties of numbers? How, without Geometry, could one measure the Holy Arc of the Covenant and the Holy City of Jerusalem, whose mysterious measures are foursquare in their dimensions, as well as the miraculous proportions of all their parts? How, without Architecture, could one know the great Temple of Solomon, of which God Himself was the Author who conceived the disposition and the design, and the Wise King but the overseer who executed it, of which temple there was no foundation without mystery, no column without symbolism, no cornice without allusion, no architrave without significance; and similarly others of its parts, of which the least fillet was never intended solely for the service and complement of Art, but as symbol of greater things? How, without great knowledge of the laws and parts of which History is comprised, could one understand historical Books? Or those recapitulations in which many times what happened first is seen in the narrated account to have happened later? How, without great learning in Canon and Civil Law, could one understand Legal Books? How, without great erudition, could one apprehend the secular histories of which the Holy Scripture makes mention, such as the many customs of the Gentiles, their many rites, their

---

3. A Roman woman (died 404), converted to Christianity after her daughter's death, who founded a nunnery next to St. Jerome's monastery at Bethlehem and helped Jerome in his studies.   4. That is, physic, or medicine.   5. While Daniel was praying, Gabriel came to him to interpret, in great chronological detail, a vision Daniel had previously had (Daniel 9:21–27).

many ways of speaking? How without the abundant laws and lessons of the Holy Fathers could one understand the obscure lesson of the Prophets? And without being expert in Music, how could one understand the exquisite precision of the musical proportions that grace so many Scriptures, particularly those in which Abraham beseeches God in defense of the Cities,[6] asking whether He would spare the place were there but fifty just men therein; and then Abraham reduced that number to five less than fifty, forty-five, which is a ninth, and is as Mi to Re; then to forty, which is a tone, and is as Re to Mi; from forty to thirty, which is a diatessaron, the interval of the perfect fourth; from thirty to twenty, which is the perfect fifth; and from twenty to ten, which is the octave, the diapason; and as there are no further harmonic proportions, made no further reductions. How might one understand this without Music? And there in the Book of Job, God says to Job: *Shalt thou be able to join together the shining stars the Pleiades, or canst thou stop the turning about of Arcturus? Canst thou bring forth the day star in its time, and make the evening star to rise upon the children of the earth?*[7] Which message, without knowledge of Astrology, would be impossible to apprehend. And not only these noble sciences; there is no applied art that is not mentioned. And, finally, in consideration of the Book that comprises all books, and the Science in which all sciences are embraced, and for whose comprehension all sciences serve, and even after knowing them all (which we now see is not easy, nor even possible), there is one condition that takes precedence over all the rest, which is uninterrupted prayer and purity of life, that one may entreat of God that purgation of spirit and illumination of mind necessary for the understanding of such elevated matters: and if that be lacking, none of the aforesaid will have been of any purpose.

Of the Angelic Doctor Saint Thomas[8] the Church affirms: *When reading the most difficult passages of the Holy Scripture, he joined fast with prayer. And he was wont to say to his companion Brother Reginald that all he knew derived not so much from study or his own labor as from the grace of God.* How then should I—so lacking in virtue and so poorly read—find courage to write? But as I had acquired the rudiments of learning, I continued to study ceaselessly divers subjects, having for none any particular inclination, but for all in general; and having studied some more than others was not owing to preference, but to the chance that more books on certain subjects had fallen into my hands, causing the election of them through no discretion of my own. And as I was not directed by preference, nor, forced by the need to fulfill certain scholarly requirements, constrained by time in the pursuit of any subject, I found myself free to study numerous topics at the same time, or to leave some for others; although in this scheme some order was observed, for some I deigned[9] study and others diversion, and in the latter I found respite from the former. From which it follows that though I have studied many things I know nothing, as some have inhibited the learning of others. I speak specifically of the

---

6. Abraham beseeches God to save Sodom for the sake of its just inhabitants (Genesis 18:23–33).
7. Job 38:31–32.   8. Thomas Aquinas (ca. 1225–1274), Dominican theologian, author of *Summa Theologica* (ca. 1266), and for centuries the most important authority on Church doctrine.
9. Deemed, considered.

practical aspect of those arts that allow practice, because it is clear that when the pen moves the compass must lie idle, and while the harp is played the organ is stilled, *et sic de caeteris*.[1] And because much practice is required of one who would acquire facility, none who divides his interest among various exercises may reach perfection. Whereas in the formal and theoretical arts the contrary is true, and I would hope to persuade all with my experience, which is that one need not inhibit the other, but, in fact, each may illuminate and open the way to others, by nature of their variations and their hidden links, which were placed in this universal chain by the wisdom of their Author in such a way that they conform and are joined together with admirable unity and harmony. This is the very chain the ancients believed did issue from the mouth of Jupiter, from which were suspended all things linked one with another, as is demonstrated by the Reverend Father Athanasius Kircher[2] in his curious book, *De Magnate*. All things issue from God, Who is at once the center and the circumference from which and in which all lines begin and end.

I myself can affirm that what I have not understood in an author in one branch of knowledge I may understand in a second in a branch that seems remote from the first. And authors, in their elucidation, may suggest metaphorical examples in other arts: as when logicians say that to prove whether parts are equal, the means is to the extremes as a determined measure to two equidistant bodies; or in stating how the argument of the logician moves, in the manner of a straight line, along the shortest route, while that of the rhetorician moves as a curve, by the longest, but that both finally arrive at the same point. And similarly, as it is when they say that the Exegetes are like an open hand, and the Scholastics like a closed fist.[3] And thus it is no apology, nor do I offer it as such, to say that I have studied many subjects, seeing that each augments the other; but that I have not profited is the fault of my own ineptitude and the inadequacy of my intelligence, not the fault of the variety. But what may be offered as exoneration is that I undertook this great task without benefit of teacher, or fellow students with whom to confer and discuss, having for a master no other than a mute book, and for a colleague, an insentient inkwell; and in the stead of explication and exercise, many obstructions, not merely those of my religious obligations (for it is already known how useful and advantageous is the time employed in them), rather, all the attendant details of living in a community: how I might be reading, and those in the adjoining cell would wish to play their instruments, and sing; how I might be studying, and two servants who had quarreled would select me to judge their dispute; or how I might be writing, and a friend come to visit me, doing me no favor but with the best of will, at which time one must not only accept the inconvenience, but be grateful for the hurt. And such occurrences are the normal state of affairs, for as the times I set apart for study are those remaining after the ordinary duties of the community are fulfilled, they are the same moments available to my sisters, in which they may come to interrupt my labor; and only those who have experience of

1. And so for other things (Latin).   2. German Jesuit scientist (1601?–1680), author of *Magnes sive de arte magnetica* (The Magnet: or, of the magnetic science).   3. The Exegetes emphasized interpretation; the Scholastics, logic.

such a community will know how true this is, and how it is only the strength of my vocation that allows me happiness; that, and the great love existing between me and my beloved sisters, for as love is union, it knows no extremes of distance.

With this I confess how interminable has been my labor; and how I am unable to say what I have with envy heard others state—that they have not been plagued by the thirst for knowledge: blessed are they. For me, not the knowing (for still I do not know), merely the desiring to know, has been such torment that I can say, as has my Father Saint Jerome (although not with his accomplishment) . . . *my conscience is witness to what effort I have expended, what difficulties I have suffered, how many times I have despaired, how often I have ceased my labors and turned to them again, driven by the hunger for knowledge; my conscience is witness, and that of those who have lived beside me.* With the exception of the companions and witnesses (for I have been denied even this consolation), I can attest to the truth of these words. And to the fact that even so, my black inclination has been so great that it has conquered all else!

It has been my fortune that, among other benefices,[4] I owe to God a most tender and affable nature, and because of it my sisters (who being good women do not take note of my faults) hold me in great affection, and take pleasure in my company; and knowing this, and moved by the great love I hold for them—having greater reason than they—I enjoy even more *their* company. Thus I was wont in our rare idle moments to visit among them, offering them consolation and entertaining myself in their conversation. I could not help but note, however, that in these times I was neglecting my study, and I made a vow not to enter any cell unless obliged by obedience or charity; for without such a compelling constraint—the constraint of mere intention not being sufficient—my love would be more powerful than my will. I would (knowing well my frailty) make this vow for the period of a few weeks, or a month; and when that time had expired, I would allow myself a brief respite of a day or two before renewing it, using that time not so much for rest (for *not* studying has never been restful for me) as to assure that I not be deemed cold, remote, or ungrateful in the little-deserved affection of my dearest sisters.

In this practice one may recognize the strength of my inclination. I give thanks to God, Who willed that such an ungovernable force be turned toward letters and not to some other vice. From this it may also be inferred how obdurately against the current my poor studies have sailed (more accurately, have foundered). For still to be related is the most arduous of my difficulties—those mentioned until now, either compulsory or fortuitous, being merely tangential—and still unreported the more directly aimed slings and arrows that have acted to impede and prevent the exercise of my study. Who would have doubted, having witnessed such general approbation, that I sailed before the wind across calm seas, amid the laurels of widespread acclaim. But our Lord God knows that it has not been so; He knows how from amongst the blossoms of this very acclaim emerged such a number of aroused vipers, hissing their emulation and

4. Benefits or kindnesses.

their persecution, that one could not count them. But the most noxious, those who most deeply wounded me, have not been those who persecuted me with open loathing and malice, but rather those who in loving me and desiring my well-being (and who are deserving of God's blessing for their good intent) have mortified and tormented me more than those others with their abhorrence. "Such studies are not in conformity with sacred innocence; surely she will be lost; surely she will, by cause of her very perspicacity and acuity, grow heady at such exalted heights." How was I to endure? An uncommon sort of martyrdom in which I was both martyr and executioner. And for my (in me, twice hapless) facility in making verses, even though they be sacred verses, what sorrows have I not suffered? What sorrows not ceased to suffer? Be assured, lady, it is often that I have meditated on how one who distinguishes himself—or one on whom God chooses to confer distinction, for it is only He who may do so—is received as a common enemy, because it seems to some that he usurps the applause they deserve, or that he dams up the admiration to which they aspired, and so they persecute that person.

That politically barbaric law of Athens by which any person who excelled by cause of his natural gifts and virtues was exiled from his Republic in order that he not threaten the public freedom still endures, is still observed in our day, although not for the reasons held by the Athenians. Those reasons have been replaced by another, no less efficient though not as well founded, seeming, rather, a maxim more appropriate to that impious Machiavelli[5]—which is to abhor one who excels, because he deprives others of regard. And thus it happens, and thus it has always happened.

For if not, what was the cause of the rage and loathing the Pharisees[6] directed against Christ, there being so many reasons to love Him? If we behold His presence, what is more to be loved than that Divine beauty? What more powerful to stir one's heart? For if ordinary human beauty holds sway over strength of will, and is able to subdue it with tender and enticing vehemence, what power would Divine beauty exert, with all its prerogatives and sovereign endowments? What might move, what effect, what not move and not effect, such incomprehensible beauty, that beauteous face through which, as through a polished crystal, were diffused the rays of Divinity? What would not be moved by that semblance which beyond incomparable human perfections revealed Divine illuminations? If the visage of Moses, merely from conversation with God, caused men to fear to come near him,[7] how much finer must be the face of God-made-flesh? And among other virtues, what more to be loved than that celestial modesty? That sweetness and kindness disseminating mercy in every movement? That profound humility and gentleness? Those words of eternal life and eternal wisdom? How therefore is it possible that such beauty did not stir their souls, that they did not follow after Him, enamored and enlightened?

---

5. Niccolò Machiavelli (1469–1527), Italian statesman whose writings (notably *The Prince*) advocated political unscrupulousness.   6. The Pharisees, members of a strict Jewish sect that emphasized conformity to the law, were according to the New Testament of the Bible prominent in plotting the death of Jesus (Mark 3:6, John 11:47–57).   7. Exodus 34:30.

The Holy Mother, my Mother Teresa,[8] says that when she beheld the beauty of Christ never again was she inclined toward any human creature, for she saw nothing that was not ugliness compared to such beauty. How was it then that in men it engendered such contrary reactions? For although they were uncouth and vile and had no knowledge or appreciation of His perfections, not even as they might profit from them, how was it they were not moved by the many advantages of such benefices as He performed for them, healing the sick, resurrecting the dead, restoring those possessed of the devil? How was it they did not love Him? But God is witness that it was for these very acts they did not love Him, that they despised Him. As they themselves testified.

They gather together in their council and say: *What do we? for this man doth many miracles.*[9] Can this be cause? If they had said: here is an evil-doer, a transgressor of the law, a rabble-rouser who with deceit stirs up the populace, they would have lied—as they did indeed lie when they spoke these things. But there were more opposite reasons for effecting what they desired, which was to take His life; and to give as reason that he had performed wondrous deeds seems not befitting learned men, for such were the Pharisees. Thus it is that in the heat of passion learned men erupt with such irrelevancies; for we know it as truth that only for this reason was it determined that Christ should die. Oh, men, if men you may be called, being so like to brutes, what is the cause of so cruel a determination? Their only response is that "this man doth many miracles." May God forgive them. Then is performing signal deeds cause enough that one should die? This "he doth many miracles" evokes *the root of Jesse, who standeth for an ensign of the people,*[1] and that *and for a sign which shall be contradicted.*[2] He is a sign? Then He shall die. He excels? Then He shall suffer, for that is the reward for one who excels.

Often on the crest of temples are placed as adornment figures of the winds and of fame, and to defend them from the birds, they are covered with iron barbs; this appears to be in defense, but is in truth obligatory propriety: the figure thus elevated cannot survive without the very barbs that prick it; there on high is found the animosity of the air, on high the ferocity of the elements, on high is unleashed the anger of the thunderbolt, on high stands the target for slings and arrows. Oh unhappy eminence, exposed to such uncounted perils. Oh sign, become the target of envy and the butt of contradiction. Whatever eminence, whether that of dignity, nobility, riches, beauty, or science, must suffer this burden; but the eminence that undergoes the most severe attack is that of reason. First, because it is the most defenseless, for riches and power strike out against those who dare attack them; but not so reason, for while it is the greater it is more modest and long-suffering, and defends itself less. Second, as Gracian[3] stated so eruditely, *favors in man's reason are favors in his nature.*

For no other cause except that the angel is superior in reason is the angel above man; for no other cause does man stand above the beast but by his reason; and thus, as no one wishes to be lower than another, neither

8. St. Teresa de Ávila (1515–1582), a mystical writer, responsible for a great awakening of religious fervor.   9. John 11:47.   1. Isaiah 11:10.   2. Luke 2:34.   3. Baltasar Gracián (1601–1658), Spanish Jesuit philosopher.

does he confess that another is superior in reason, as reason is a consequence of being superior. One will abide, and will confess that another is nobler than he, that another is richer, more handsome, and even that he is more learned, but that another is richer in reason scarcely any will confess: *Rare is he who will concede genius.* That is why the assault against this virtue works to such profit.

When the soldiers mocked, made entertainment and diversion of our Lord Jesus Christ, they brought Him a worn purple garment and a hollow reed, and a crown of thorns to crown Him King of Fools.[4] But though the reed and the purple were an affront, they did not cause suffering. Why does only the crown give pain? Is it not enough that like the other emblems the crown was a symbol of ridicule and ignominy, as that was its intent? No. Because the sacred head of Christ and His divine intellect were the depository of wisdom, and the world is not satisfied for wisdom to be the object of mere ridicule, it must also be done injury and harm. A head that is a storehouse of wisdom can expect nothing but a crown of thorns. What garland may human wisdom expect when it is known what was bestowed on that divine wisdom? Roman pride crowned the many achievements of their Captains with many crowns: he who defended the city received the civic crown; he who fought his way into the hostile camp received the camp crown; he who scaled the wall, the mural;[5] he who liberated a beseiged city, or any army besieged either in the field or in the enemy camp, received the obsidional, the siege, crown; other feats were crowned with naval, ovation, or triumphal crowns, as described by Pliny and Aulus Gellius.[6] Observing so many and varied crowns, I debated as to which Christ's crown must have been, and determined that it was the siege crown, for (as well you know, lady) that was the most honored crown and was called obsidional after *obsidio,* which means siege; which crown was made not from gold, or silver, but from the leaves and grasses flourishing on the field where the feat was achieved. And as the heroic feat of Christ was to break the siege of the Prince of Darkness, who had laid siege to all the earth, as is told in the Book of Job, quoting Satan: *I have gone round about the earth, and walked through it,*[7] and as St. Peter says: *As a roaring lion, goeth about seeking whom he may devour.*[8] And our Master came and caused him to lift the siege: *Now shall the prince of this world be cast out.*[9] So the soldiers crowned Him not with gold or silver but with the natural fruit of the world, which was the field of battle—and which, after the curse *Thorns also and thistles shall it bring forth to thee,*[1] produced only thorns—and thus it was a most fitting crown for the courageous and wise Conqueror, with which His mother Synagogue crowned Him. And the daughters of Zion, weeping, came out to witness the sorrowful triumph,[2] as they had come rejoicing for the triumph of Solomon,[3] because the triumph of the wise is earned with sorrow and celebrated with weeping, which is the manner of the triumph of wisdom; and as Christ is

---

4. Matthew 27:28–31.   5. Pertaining to walls; the word *crown* is understood.   6. Latin writer (2nd century A.D.), author of *Noctes Atticae,* valuable for its quotations from lost works. Pliny the Younger (62?–ca. 113) was a Roman orator and statesman and author of well-known letters about Roman life. 7. Job 1:7.   8. 1 Peter 5:8.   9. John 12:31.   1. The curse on Adam and Eve after the Fall (Genesis 3:18).   2. Luke 23:27–28.   3. Song of Solomon 3:11.

the King of wisdom, He was the first to wear that crown; and as it was sanctified on His brow, it removed all fear and dread from those who are wise, for they know they need aspire to no other honor.

The Living Word, Life, wished to restore life to Lazarus, who was dead. His disciples did not know His purpose and they said to Him: *Rabbi, the Jews but now sought to stone thee; and goest thou thither again?* And the Redeemer calmed their fear: *Are there not twelve hours of the day?*[4] It seems they feared because there had been those who wished to stone Him when He rebuked them, calling them thieves and not shepherds of sheep.[5] And thus the disciples feared that if He returned to the same place—for even though rebukes be just, they are often badly received—He would be risking his life. But once having been disabused and having realized that He was setting forth to raise up Lazarus from the dead, what was it that caused Thomas, like Peter in the Garden, to say *Let us also go, that we may die with him?*[6] What say you, Sainted Apostle? The Lord does not go out to die; whence your misgiving? For Christ goes not to rebuke, but to work an act of mercy, and therefore they will do Him no harm. These same Jews could have assured you, for when He reproved those who wished to stone Him, *Many good works I have shewed you from my Father; for which of those works do you stone me?* they replied: *For a good work we stone thee not; but for blasphemy.*[7] And as they say they will not stone Him for doing good works, and now He goes to do a work so great as to raise up Lazarus from the dead, whence your misgiving? Why do you fear? Were it not better to say: let us go to gather the fruits of appreciation for the good work our Master is about to do; to see him lauded and applauded for His benefice; to see men marvel at His miracle. Why speak words seemingly so alien to the circumstance as *Let us also go?* Ah, woe, the Saint feared as a prudent man and spoke as an Apostle. Does Christ not go to work a miracle? Why, what *greater* peril? It is less to be suffered that pride endure rebukes than envy witness miracles. In all the above, most honored lady, I do not wish to say (nor is such folly to be found in me) that I have been persecuted for my wisdom, but merely for my love of wisdom and letters, having achieved neither one nor the other.

At one time even the Prince of the Apostles was very far from wisdom, as is emphasized in that *But Peter followed afar off.*[8] Very distant from the laurels of a learned man is one so little in his judgment that he was *Not knowing what he said.*[9] And being questioned on his mastery of wisdom, he himself was witness that he had not achieved the first measure: *But he denied him, saying: Woman, I know him not.*[1] And what becomes of him? We find that having this reputation of ignorance, he did not enjoy its good fortune, but, rather, the affliction of being taken for wise. And why? There was no other motive but: *This man also was with him*[2] He was fond of wisdom, it filled His heart, He followed after it, He prided himself as a pursuer and lover of wisdom; and although He followed from so *afar off* that He neither understood nor achieved it, His love for it was sufficient that He incur its torments. And there was present that soldier to cause

---

4. John 11:8–9.   5. John 10:1–31.   6. John 11:16.   7. John 10:32–33.   8. Luke 22:54.
9. Refers to Peter (Luke 9:33).   1. Luke 22:57.   2. A serving maid says this of Peter, who thereupon denies knowing Jesus (Luke 22:56).

Him distress, and a certain maid-servant to cause Him grief. I confess that I find myself very distant from the goals of wisdom, for all that I have desired to follow it, even from *afar off*. But in this I have been brought closer to the fire of persecution, to the crucible of torment, and to such lengths that they have asked that study be forbidden to me.

At one time this was achieved through the offices of a very saintly and ingenuous Abbess who believed that study was a thing of the Inquisition, who commanded me not to study. I obeyed her (the three some[3] months her power to command endured) in that I did not take up a book; but that I study not at all is not within my power to achieve, and this I could not obey, for though I did not study in books, I studied all the things that God had wrought, reading in them, as in writing and in books, all the workings of the universe. I looked on nothing without reflection; I heard nothing without meditation, even in the most minute and imperfect things; because as there is no creature, however lowly, in which one cannot recognize that *God made me*, there is none that does not astound reason, if properly meditated on. Thus, I reiterate, I saw and admired all things; so that even the very persons with whom I spoke, and the things they said, were cause for a thousand meditations. Whence the variety of genius and wit, being all of a single species? Which the temperaments and hidden qualities that occasioned such variety? If I saw a figure, I was forever combining the proportion of its lines and measuring it with my reason and reducing it to new proportions. Occasionally as I walked along the far wall of one of our dormitories (which is a most capacious room) I observed that though the lines of the two sides were parallel and the ceiling perfectly level, in my sight they were distorted, the lines seeming to incline toward one another, the ceiling seeming lower in the distance than in proximity: from which I inferred that *visual* lines run straight but not parallel, forming a pyramidal figure. I pondered whether this might not be the reason that caused the ancients to question whether the world were spherical. Because, although it so seems, this could be a deception of vision, suggesting concavities where possibly none existed.

This manner of reflection has always been my habit, and is quite beyond my will to control; on the contrary, I am wont to become vexed that my intellect makes me weary; and I believed that it was so with everyone, as well as making verses, until experience taught me otherwise; and it is so strong in me this nature, or custom, that I look at nothing without giving it further examination. Once in my presence two young girls were spinning a top and scarcely had I seen the motion and the figure described, when I began, out of this madness of mine, to meditate on the effortless *motus*[4] of the spherical form, and how the impulse persisted even when free and independent of its cause—for the top continued to dance even at some distance from the child's hand, which was the causal force. And not content with this, I had flour brought and sprinkled about, so that as the top danced one might learn whether these were perfect circles it described with its movement; and I found that they were not, but, rather, spiral lines that lost their circularity as the impetus declined. Other girls

3. That is, "the three or so."   4. Motion.

sat playing at spillikins[5] (surely the most frivolous game that children play); I walked closer to observe the figures they formed, and seeing that by chance three lay in a triangle, I set to joining one with another, recalling that this was said to be the form of the mysterious ring of Solomon,[6] in which he was able to see the distant splendor and images of the Holy Trinity, by virtue of which the ring worked such prodigies and marvels. And the same shape was said to form David's harp, and that is why Saul was refreshed at its sound; and harps today largely conserve that shape.

And what shall I tell you, lady, of the natural secrets I have discovered while cooking? I see that an egg holds together and fries in butter or in oil, but, on the contrary, in syrup shrivels into shreds; observe that to keep sugar in a liquid state one need only add a drop or two of water in which a quince or other bitter fruit has been soaked; observe that the yolk and the white of one egg are so dissimilar that each with sugar produces a result not obtainable with both together. I do not wish to weary you with such inconsequential matters, and make mention of them only to give you full notice of my nature, for I believe they will be occasion for laughter. But, lady, as women, what wisdom may be ours if not the philosophies of the kitchen? Lupercio Leonardo[7] spoke well when he said: how well one may philosophize when preparing dinner. And I often say, when observing these trivial details: had Aristotle prepared victuals, he would have written more. And pursuing the manner of my cogitations, I tell you that this process is so continuous in me that I have no need for books. And on one occasion, when because of a grave upset of the stomach the physicians forbade me to study, I passed thus some days, but then I proposed that it would be less harmful if they allowed me books, because so vigorous and vehement were my cogitations that my spirit was consumed more greatly in a quarter of an hour than in four days' studying books. And thus they were persuaded to allow me to read. And moreover, lady, not even have my dreams been excluded from this ceaseless agitation of my imagination; indeed, in dreams it is wont to work more freely and less encumbered, collating with greater clarity and calm the gleanings of the day, arguing and making verses, of which I could offer you an extended catalogue, as well as of some arguments and inventions that I have better achieved sleeping than awake. I relinquish this subject in order not to tire you, for the above is sufficient to allow your discretion and acuity to penetrate perfectly and perceive my nature, as well as the beginnings, the methods, and the present state of my studies.

Even, lady, were these merits (and I see them celebrated as such in men), they would not have been so in me, for I cannot but study. If they are faults, then, for the same reasons, I believe I have none. Nevertheless, I live always with so little confidence in myself that neither in my study, nor in any other thing, do I trust my judgment; and thus I remit the decision to your sovereign genius, submitting myself to whatever sentence you may bestow, without controversy, without reluctance, for I have wished

---

5. Jackstraws, or pick-up sticks.   6. It may, like Solomon's seal, have contained the image of the star of David, composed of triangles.   7. Lupercio Leonardo de Argensola (1559–1639), poet, playwright, and historian.

here only to present you with a simple narration of my inclination toward letters.

I confess, too, that though it is true, as I have stated, that I had no need of books, it is nonetheless also true that they have been no little inspiration, in divine as in human letters. Because I find a Debbora[8] administering the law, both military and political, and governing a people among whom there were many learned men. I find a most wise Queen of Saba,[9] so learned that she dares to challenge with hard questions the wisdom of the greatest of all wise men, without being reprimanded for doing so, but, rather, as a consequence, to judge unbelievers. I see many and illustrious women; some blessed with the gift of prophecy, like Abigail,[1] others of persuasion, like Esther;[2] others with pity, like Rehab;[3] others with perseverance, like Anna,[4] the mother of Samuel; and an infinite number of others, with divers gifts and virtues.

If I again turn to the Gentiles, the first I encounter are the Sibyls,[5] those women chosen by God to prophesy the principal mysteries of our Faith, and with learned and elegant verses that surpass admiration. I see adored as a goddess of the sciences a woman like Minerva,[6] the daughter of the first Jupiter and mistress over all the wisdom of Athens. I see a Polla Argentaria, who helped Lucan, her husband, write his epic *Pharsalia*.[7] I see the daughter of the divine Tiresias,[8] more learned than her father. I see a Zenobia, Queen of the Palmyrans,[9] as wise as she was valiant. An Arete, most learned daughter of Aristippus.[1] A Nicostrate,[2] framer of Latin verses and most erudite in Greek. An Aspasia Milesia, who taught philosophy and rhetoric, and who was a teacher of the philosopher Pericles. An Hypatia, who taught astrology, and studied many years in Alexandria. A Leontium, a Greek woman, who questioned the philosopher Theophrastus, and convinced him. A Julia, a Corinna, a Cornelia;[3] and, finally, a great throng of women deserving to be named, some as Greeks, some as muses, some as seers; for all were nothing more than learned women, held, and celebrated—and venerated as well—as such by antiquity. Without mentioning an infinity of other women whose names fill books. For example, I find the Egyptian Catherine,[4] studying and influencing the wisdom of all the wise men of Egypt. I see a Gertrudis[5] studying, writing, and teaching. And not to overlook examples close to home, I see my most

8. Or Deborah, a prophetess who judged the Israelites (Judges 4:4–14).   9. Or Sheba, who tested King Solomon with questions (1 Kings 10:1–3).   1. Wife of a surly husband, Nabal. After Nabal insulted King David, she went to the king with presents and prophesied his future triumphs, thus saving her husband's life (1 Samuel 25:2–35).   2. She persuaded her husband, King Ahasuerus, to protect the Jews (Esther 5–9).   3. Or Rahab, a harlot who protected two Israelites from the King of Jericho (Joshua 2:1–7).   4. Or Hannah, who after years of childlessness received the answer to her prayers in the birth of Samuel (1 Samuel 1:1–20).   5. Female prophets of the ancient world.   6. Or Athena, goddess of wisdom.   7. Epic poem on the civil war between Caesar and Pompey, properly called *Bellum Civile* (ca. A.D. 62–65).   8. Legendary blind Theban seer. His daughter was Manto, known for her skill in divination by fire.   9. Learned widow of Odenathus, she declared her independence from Rome and expanded the Middle-Eastern territory under her rule, naming herself Augusta, empress of Rome. She was finally defeated and captured in 272.   1. Greek philosopher (ca. 435–ca. 360 B.C.). 2. Or Carmentis, legendary daughter of Pallas, king of Arcadia, and (in legend) inventor of the Roman alphabet.   3. Noted for her devotion to her children's education after her husband's death (2nd century B.C.); she was the second daughter of Scipio Africanus and wife of Tiberius Sempronius Gracchus. Julia Domna (2nd century A.D.), wife of the Roman emperor Septimius Severus, known for her learning as Julia the Philosopher. Corinna (ca. 500? B.C.) was a lyric poet of Tanagra who wrote for a group of women.   4. St. Catherine (4th century?), allegedly so wise she could refute fifty philosophers at once. 5. St. Gertrude (died 1302), Benedictine nun and visionary, an important mystic.

holy mother Paula, learned in Hebrew, Greek, and Latin, and most able in interpreting the Scriptures. And what greater praise than, having as her chronicler a Jeronimus Maximus,[6] that Saint scarcely found himself competent for his task, and says, with that weighty deliberation and energetic precision with which he so well expressed himself: "If all the members of my body were tongues, they still would not be sufficient to proclaim the wisdom and virtue of Paula." Similarly praiseworthy was the widow Blesilla; also, the illustrious virgin Eustochium,[7] both daughters of this same saint; especially the second, who, for her knowledge, was called the Prodigy of the World. The Roman Fabiola[8] was most well-versed in the Holy Scripture. Proba Falconia, a Roman woman, wrote elegant centos,[9] containing verses from Virgil, about the mysteries of Our Holy Faith. It is well-known by all that Queen Isabel,[1] wife of the tenth Alfonso, wrote about astrology. Many others I do not list, out of the desire not merely to transcribe what others have said (a vice I have always abominated); and many are flourishing today, as witness Christina Alexandra,[2] Queen of Sweden, as learned as she is valiant and magnanimous, and the Most Honorable Ladies, the Duquesa of Abeyro and the Condesa of Villaumbrosa.

The venerable Doctor Arce[3] (by his virtue and learning a worthy teacher of the Scriptures) in his scholarly *Bibliorum* raises this question: *Is it permissible for women to dedicate themselves to the study of the Holy Scriptures, and to their interpretation?* and he offers as negative arguments the opinions of many saints, especially that of the Apostle: *Let women keep silence in the churches; for it is not permitted them to speak,* etc.[4] He later cites other opinions and, from the same Apostle, verses from his letter to Titus: *The aged women in like manner, in holy attire . . . teaching well,*[5] with interpretations by the Holy Fathers. Finally he resolves, with all prudence, that teaching publicly from a University chair, or preaching from the pulpit, is not permissible for women; but that to study, write, and teach privately not only is permissible, but most advantageous and useful. It is evident that this is not to be the case with all women, but with those to whom God may have granted special virtue and prudence, and who may be well advanced in learning, and having the essential talent and requisites for such a sacred calling. This view is indeed just, so much so that not only women, who are held to be so inept, but also men, who merely for being men believe they are wise, should be prohibited from interpreting the Sacred Word if they are not learned and virtuous and of gentle and well-inclined natures; that this is not so has been, I believe, at the root of so much sectarianism and so many heresies. For there are many who study but are ignorant, especially those who are in spirit arrogant, troubled, and proud, so eager for new interpretations of the Word (which itself rejects new interpretations) that merely for the sake of saying what no one else has said they speak a heresy, and even then are not content. Of these the Holy Spirit says: *For wisdom will not enter into a malicious soul.*[6] To such

---

6. St. Jerome.   7. Blesilla and Eustochium were daughters of St. Paula, and, like her, were taught by St. Jerome.   8. One of Jerome's disciples.   9. Compositions made up of verses from other authors. 1. Of Spain, wife of Alfonso X, Alfonso the Wise (1221–1284).   2. She attracted many scholars and artists to her court (1626–1689).   3. Juan Díaz de Arce (1594–1653), author of theological books. 4. 1 Corinthians 14:34.   5. Titus 2:3–5.   6. Book of Wisdom 1:4 (in the Apocrypha).

as these more harm results from knowing than from ignorance. A wise man has said: he who does not know Latin is not a complete fool; but he who knows it is well qualified to be.[7] And I would add that a fool may reach perfection (if ignorance may tolerate perfection) by having studied his tittle of philosophy and theology and by having some learning of tongues, by which he may be a fool in many sciences and languages: a great fool cannot be contained solely in his mother tongue.

For such as these, I reiterate, study is harmful, because it is as if to place a sword in the hands of a madman; which, though a most noble instrument for defense, is in his hands his own death and that of many others. So were the Divine Scriptures in the possession of the evil Pelagius[8] and the intractable Arius,[9] of the evil Luther,[1] and the other heresiarchs like our own Doctor (who was neither ours nor a doctor) Cazalla.[2] To these men, wisdom was harmful, although it is the greatest nourishment and the life of the soul; in the same way that in a stomach of sickly constitution and adulterated complexion, the finer the nourishment it receives, the more arid, fermented, and perverse are the humors it produces; thus these evil men: the more they study, the worse opinions they engender, their reason being obstructed with the very substance meant to nourish it, and they study much and digest little, exceeding the limits of the vessel of their reason. Of which the Apostle says: *For I say, by the grace that is given me, to all that are among you, not to be more wise than it behoveth to be wise, but to be wise unto sobriety, and according as God hath divided to every one the measure of faith.*[3] And in truth, the Apostle did not direct these words to women, but to men; and that *keep silence* is intended not only for women, but for *all* incompetents. If I desire to know as much, or more, than Aristotle or Saint Augustine, and if I have not the aptitude of Saint Augustine or Aristotle, though I study more than either, not only will I not achieve learning, but I will weaken and dull the workings of my feeble reason with the disproportionateness of the goal.

Oh, that each of us—I, being ignorant, the first—should take the measure of our talents before we study, or, more importantly, write, with the covetous ambition to equal and even surpass others, how little spirit we should have for it, and how many errors we should avoid, and how many tortured intellects of which we have experience, we should have had no experience! And I place my own ignorance in the forefront of all these, for if I knew all I should, I would not write. And I protest that I do so only to obey you; and with such apprehension that you owe me more that I have taken up my pen in fear than you would have owed had I presented you more perfect works. But it is well that they go to your correction. Cross them out, tear them up, reprove me, and I shall appreciate that more than all the vain applause others may offer. *That just men shall correct me in mercy, and shall reprove me; but let not the oil of the sinner fatten my head.*[4]

7. Alludes to the Spanish proverb "A fool, unless he knows Latin, is never a great fool."　8. Heretical monk (ca. 355–ca. 425) who taught that people do not need divine grace, since they have a natural tendency to seek the good.　9. Libyan theologian (ca. 256–336), founder of the Arian heresy that declared that Christ was neither eternal nor equal with God.　1. Martin Luther (1483–1546), German leader of the Protestant Reformation and, from Sister Juana's point of view, another heretic. 2. Augustino Cazallo (1510–1559), Spanish Protestant executed by the Inquisition for promulgating Lutheran doctrine.　3. Romans 12:3.　4. Psalm 141:5.

And returning again to our Arce, I say that in affirmation of his opinion he cites the words of my father, Saint Jerome: *To Leta, Upon the Education of Her Daughter.* Where he says: *Accustom her tongue, still young, to the sweetness of the Psalms. Even the names through which little by little she will become accustomed to form her phrases should not be chosen by chance, but selected and repeated with care; the prophets must be included, of course, and the apostles, as well, and all the Patriarchs beginning with Adam and down to Matthew and Luke, so that as she practices other things she will be readying her memory for the future. Let your daily task be taken from the flower of the Scriptures.* And if this Saint desired that a young girl scarcely beginning to talk be educated in this fashion, what would he desire for his nuns and his spiritual daughters? These beliefs are illustrated in the examples of the previously mentioned Eustochium and Fabiola, and Marcella, her sister, and Pacatula, and others whom the Saint honors in his epistles, exhorting them to this sacred exercise, as they are recognized in the epistle I cited, *Let your daily task . . .* , which is affirmation of and agreement with the *aged women . . . teaching well* of Saint Paul. My illustrious Father's *Let your daily task . . .* makes clear that the teacher of the child is to be Leta herself, the child's mother.

Oh, how much injury might have been avoided in our land if our aged women had been learned, as was Leta, and had they known how to instruct as directed by Saint Paul and by my Father, Saint Jerome. And failing this, and because of the considerable idleness to which our poor women have been relegated, if a father desires to provide his daughters with more than ordinary learning, he is forced by necessity, and by the absence of wise elder women, to bring men to teach the skills of reading, writing, counting, the playing of musical instruments, and other accomplishments, from which no little harm results, as is experienced every day in doleful examples of perilous association, because through the immediacy of contact and the intimacy born from the passage of time, what one may never have thought possible is easily accomplished. For which reason many prefer to leave their daughters unpolished and uncultured rather than to expose them to such notorious peril as that of familiarity with men, which quandary could be prevented if there were learned elder women, as Saint Paul wished to see, and if the teaching were handed down from one to another, as is the custom with domestic crafts and all other traditional skills.

For what objection can there be that an older woman, learned in letters and in sacred conversation and customs, have in her charge the education of young girls? This would prevent these girls being lost either for lack of instruction or for hesitating to offer instruction through such dangerous means as male teachers, for even when there is no greater risk of indecency than to seat beside a modest woman (who still may blush when her own father looks directly at her) a strange man who treats her as if he were a member of the household and with the authority of an intimate, the modesty demanded in interchange with men, and in conversation with them, is sufficient reason that such an arrangement not be permitted. For I do not find that the custom of men teaching women is without its peril, lest it be in the severe tribunal of the confessional, or from the remote decency of the pulpit, or in the distant learning of books—never in the personal contact of immediacy. And the world knows this is true; and, notwithstanding, it is permitted solely from the want of learned elder women. Then is it not detrimental, the lack of such women? This question should be addressed by those who, bound to that *Let women keep silence in the church*, say that it is blasphemy for women to learn and teach, as if it were not the Apostle himself who said: *The aged women . . . teaching well*. As well as the fact that this prohibition touches upon historical fact as reported by Eusebium:[5] which is that in the early Church, women were charged with teaching the doctrine to one another in the temples and the sound of this teaching caused confusion as the Apostles were preaching and this is the reason they were ordered to be silent; and even today, while the homilist is preaching, one does not pray aloud.

Who will argue that for the comprehension of many Scriptures one must be familiar with the history, customs, ceremonies, proverbs, and even the manners of speaking of those times in which they were written, if one is to apprehend the references and allusions of more than a few passages of the Holy Word. *And rend your heart and not your garments.*[6] Is this not a reference to the ceremony in which Hebrews rent their garments as a sign of grief, as did the evil pontiff when he said that Christ had blasphemed? In many scriptures the Apostle writes of succour for widows; did they not refer to the customs of those times? Does not the example of the valiant woman, *Her husband is honourable in the gates*,[7] allude to the fact that the tribunals of the judges were at the gates of the cities? That *Dare terram Deo*, give of your land to God, did that not mean to make some votive offering? And did they not call the public sinners *hiemantes*, those who endure the winter, because they made their penance in the open air instead of at a town gate as others did? And Christ's plaint to that Pharisee who had neither kissed him nor given him water for his feet,[8] was that not because it was the Jews' usual custom to offer these acts of hospitality? And we find an infinite number of additional instances not only in the Divine Letters, but human, as well, such as *adorate purpuram*, venerate the purple, which meant obey the King; *manumittere eum*, manumit them, alluding to the custom and ceremony of striking the slave with one's hand to signify his freedom. That *intonuit coelum*, heaven thundered, in Virgil, which alludes to the augury of thunder from the west, which was held to be good.[9] Martial's *tu nunquam leporem edisti*,[1] you never ate hare, has not only the wit of ambiguity in its *leporem*,[2] but, as well, the allusion to the reputed propensity of hares [to bless with beauty those who dine on them]. That proverb, *maleam legens, que sunt domi obliviscere*, to sail along the shore of Malia is to forget what one has at home, alludes to the great peril of the promontory of Laconia.[3] That chaste matron's response to the unwanted suit of her pretender: "the hinge-pins shall not be oiled for my sake, nor shall the torches blaze," meaning that she did not want

---

5. Probably Eusebius of Caesaria (ca. 263–339?), an early Church historian.   6. Joel 2:13.   7. Proverbs 31:23.   8. Luke 7:44–45.   9. Sister Juana possibly misremembers *Aeneid* 2.693: "thunder on the left."   1. Marcus Valerius Martialis (ca. 40–ca. 104), Roman epigrammatic poet; "Edisti numquam, Gellia, tu leporem" (*Epigrams* 5:29).   2. This word can also mean charm, grace, attractiveness.   3. The site of ancient Sparta, conquered by Macedonia in the 4th century B.C.

to marry, alluded to the ceremony of anointing the doorways with oils and lighting the nuptial torches in the wedding ceremony, as if now we would say, they shall not prepare the thirteen coins for my dowry, nor shall the priest invoke the blessing. And thus it is with many comments of Virgil and Homer and all the poets and orators. In addition, how many are the difficulties found even in the grammar of the Holy Scripture, such as writing a plural for a singular, or changing from the second to third persons, as in the Psalms, *Let him kiss me with the kiss of his mouth, for thy breasts are better than wine.*[4] Or placing adjectives in the genitive instead of the accusative, as in *Calicem salutaris accipiam,* I will take the chalice of salvation.[5] Or to replace the feminine with the masculine, and, in contrast, to call any sin adultery.

All this demands more investigation than some believe, who strictly as grammarians, or, at most, employing the four principles of applied logic, attempt to interpret the Scriptures while clinging to that *Let the women keep silence in the church,* not knowing how it is to be interpreted. As well as that other verse, *Let the women learn in silence.*[6] For this latter scripture works more to women's favor than their disfavor, as it commands them to learn; and it is only natural that they must maintain silence while they learn. And it is also written, *Hear, oh Israel, and be silent.*[7] Which addresses the entire congregation of men and women, commanding all to silence, because if one is to hear and learn, it is with good reason that he attend and be silent. And if it is not so, I would want these interpreters and expositors of Saint Paul to explain to me how they interpret that scripture, *Let the women keep silence in the church.* For either they must understand it to refer to the material church, that is the church of pulpits and cathedras,[8] or to the spiritual, the community of the faithful, which is the Church. If they understand it to be the former, which, in my opinion, is its true interpretation, then we see that if in fact it is not permitted of women to read publicly in church, nor preach, why do they censure those who study privately? And if they understand the latter, and wish that the prohibition of the Apostle be applied transcendentally—that not even in private are women to be permitted to write or study—how are we to view the fact that the Church permitted a Gertrudis, a Santa Teresa, a Saint Birgitta,[9] the Nun of Agreda,[1] and so many others, to write? And if they say to me that these women were saints, they speak the truth; but this poses no obstacle to my argument. First, because Saint Paul's proposition is absolute, and encompasses all women not excepting saints, as Martha and Mary,[2] Marcella,[3] Mary, mother of Jacob, and Salome,[4] all were in their time, and many other zealous women of the early church. But we see, too, that the Church allows women who are not saints to write, for the Nun of Agreda and Sor María de la Antigua[5] are not canonized, yet their writings are circulated. And when Santa Teresa and the others were

---

4. Song of Solomon 1:2.   5. Psalm 116:13.   6. 1 Timothy 2:11.   7. Not a biblical quotation. 8. The cathedra is the throne of the bishop in his church.   9. Or Bridget (1303–1373), of Sweden. 1. Maria de Agreda (1602–1635), Spanish Franciscan nun, author of *The Mystic City of God* (1670), a work allegedly divinely inspired.   2. Sisters. Mary anointed Jesus' feet (John 12:3). Martha was preoccupied with household tasks (Luke 10:40–42).   3. One of the women taught by Jerome.   4. In the King James Bible she is the mother of James and Salome, who came to the empty sepulcher to anoint Jesus' body (Mark 16:1).   5. Spanish nun (1544–1617).

writing, they were not as yet canonized. In which case, Saint Paul's prohibition was directed solely to the public office of the pulpit, for if the Apostle had forbidden women to write, the Church would not have allowed it. Now I do not make so bold as to teach—which in me would be excessively presumptuous—and as for writing, that requires a greater talent than mine, and serious reflection. As Saint Cyprian[6] says: *The things we write require most conscientious consideration.* I have desired to study that I might be ignorant of less; for (according to Saint Augustine[7]) some things are learned to be enacted and others only to be known: *We learn some things to know them, others, to do them.* Then, where is the offense to be found if even what is licit to women—which is to teach by writing—I do not perform, as I know that I am lacking in means, following the counsel of Quintilian: *Let each person learn not only from the precepts of others, but also let him reap counsel from his own nature.*

If the offense is to be found in the *Atenagórica* letter, was that letter anything other than the simple expression of my feeling, written with the implicit permission of our Holy Mother Church? For if the Church, in her most sacred authority, does not forbid it, why must others do so? That I proffered an opinion contrary to that of de Vieyra was audacious, but, as a Father, was it not audacious that he speak against the three Holy Fathers of the Church? My reason, such as it is, is it not as unfettered as his, as both issue from the same source? Is his opinion to be considered as a revelation, as a principle of the Holy Faith, that we must accept blindly? Furthermore, I maintained at all times the respect due such a virtuous man, a respect in which his defender was sadly wanting, ignoring the phrase of Titus Lucius:[8] *Respect is companion to the arts.* I did not touch a thread of the robes of the Society of Jesus; nor did I write for other than the consideration of the person who suggested that I write. And, according to Pliny, *how different the condition of one who writes from that of one who merely speaks.* Had I believed the letter was to be published I would not have been so inattentive. If, as the censor says, the letter is heretical, why does he not denounce it? And with that he would be avenged, and I content, for, which is only seemly, I esteem more highly my reputation as a Catholic and obedient daughter of the Holy Mother Church than all the approbation due a learned woman. If the letter is rash, and he does well to criticize it, then laugh, even if with the laugh of the rabbit, for I have not asked that he approve; as I was free to dissent from de Vieyra, so will anyone be free to oppose my opinion.

But how I have strayed, lady. None of this pertains here, nor is it intended for your ears, but as I was discussing my accusers I remembered the words of one that recently have appeared, and, though my intent was to speak in general, my pen, unbidden, slipped, and began to respond in particular. And so, returning to our Arce, he says that he knew in this city two nuns: one in the Convent of the Regina, who had so thoroughly committed the Breviary to memory that with the greatest promptitude and

6. Thascius Caecilius Cyprianus (ca. 200–258), one of the Church fathers, known for his efforts to enforce Church discipline.　7. Aurelius Augustinus (354–430), baptized by St. Ambrose in 387, author of *De Civitate Dei*, a vindication of the Church that long possessed great authority.　8. Better known as Saturantius Apuleius, greatly celebrated in his time (2d century A.D.) for eloquence.

propriety she applied in her conversation its verses, psalms, and maxims of saintly homilies. The other, in the Convent of the Conception, was so accustomed to reading the Epistles of my Father Saint Jerome, and the Locutions of this Saint, that Arce says, *It seemed I was listening to Saint Jerome himself, speaking in Spanish.* And of this latter woman he says that after her death he learned that she had translated these Epistles into the Spanish language. What pity that such talents could not have been employed in major studies with scientific principles. He does not give the name of either, although he offers these women as confirmation of his opinion, which is that not only is it licit, but most useful and essential for women to study the Holy Word, and even more essential for nuns; and that study is the very thing to which your wisdom exhorts me, and in which so many arguments concur.

Then if I turn my eyes to the oft-chastized faculty of making verses — which is in me so natural that I must discipline myself that even this letter not be written in that form — I might cite those lines, *All I wished to express took the form of verse.*[9] And seeing that so many condemn and criticize this ability, I have conscientiously sought to find what harm may be in it, and I have not found it, but, rather, I see verse acclaimed in the mouths of the Sibyls; sanctified in the pens of the Prophets, especially King David, of whom the exalted Expositor my beloved Father[1] says (explicating the measure of his meters): *in the manner of Horace and Pindar, now it hurries along in iambs, now it rings in alcaic, now swells in sapphic, then arrives in broken feet.* The greater part of the Holy Books are in meter, as is the Book of Moses; and those of Job (as Saint Isidore[2] states in his *Etymologiae*) are in heroic verse. Solomon wrote the Canticle of Canticles in verse; and Jeremias, his *Lamentations.* And so, says Cassiodorus:[3] *All poetic expression had as its source the Holy Scriptures.* For not only does our Catholic Church not disdain verse, it employs verse in its hymns, and recites the lines of Saint Ambrose,[4] Saint Thomas, Saint Isidore, and others. Saint Bonaventure[5] was so taken with verse that he writes scarcely a page where it does not appear. It is readily apparent that Saint Paul had studied verse, for he quotes and translates verses of Aratus: *For in him we live, and move, and are.*[6] And he quotes also that verse of Parmenides: *The Cretians are always liars, evil beasts, slothful bellies.*[7] Saint Gregory Nazianzen[8] argues in elegant verses the questions of matrimony and virginity. And, how should I tire? The Queen of Wisdom, Our Lady, with Her sacred lips, intoned the Canticle of the Magnificat;[9] and having brought forth this example, it would be offensive to add others that were profane, even those of the most serious and learned men, for this alone is more than sufficient confirmation; and even though Hebrew elegance could not be compressed into Latin measure, for which reason, although the sacred translator, more attentive to the importance of the meaning,

9. Ovid's *Tristia* 4.10.25ff.   1. Jerome.   2. Spanish archbishop (ca. 560–636), who helped organize the Church in Spain.   3. Flavius Magnus Aurelius Cassiodorus (ca. 485–ca.580), Roman monk and author of *Institutiones*, a course of studies for monks.   4. Bishop of Milan (339–397), who had an important share in the conversion of St. Augustine.   5. Franciscan bishop and cardinal (1221–1274), who preached the importance of study.   6. Acts 17:28.   7. Titus 1:12.   8. Gregorius Nazianzenus, bishop of Constantinople and associate of Jerome. The allusion is to the first of his forty moral poems, 732 lines eulogizing virginity.   9. Luke 1:46–55.

omitted the verse, the Psalms retain the number and divisions of verses, and what harm is to be found in them? For misuse is not the blame of art, but rather of the evil teacher who perverts the arts, making of them the snare of the devil; and this occurs in all the arts and sciences.

And if the evil is attributed to the fact that a woman employs them, we have seen how many have done so in praiseworthy fashion; what then is the evil in my being a woman? I confess openly my own baseness and meanness; but I judge that no couplet of mine has been deemed indecent. Furthermore, I have never written of my own will, but under the pleas and injunctions of others; to such a degree that the only piece I remember having written for my own pleasure was a little trifle they called *El sueño*.[1] That letter, lady, which you so greatly honored, I wrote more with repugnance than any other emotion; both by reason of the fact that it treated sacred matters, for which (as I have stated) I hold such reverent awe, and because it seems to wish to impugn, a practice for which I have natural aversion; and I believe that had I foreseen the blessed destiny to which it was fated—for like a second Moses I had set it adrift, naked, on the waters of the Nile of silence, where you, a princess, found and cherished it[2]—I believe, I reiterate, that had I known, the very hands of which it was born would have drowned it, out of the fear that these clumsy scribblings from my ignorance appear before the light of your great wisdom; by which one knows the munificence of your kindness, for your goodwill applauds precisely what your reason must wish to reject. For as fate cast it before your doors, so exposed, so orphaned, that it fell to you even to give it a name, I must lament that among other deformities it also bears the blemish of haste; both because of the unrelenting ill-health I suffer, and for the profusion of duties imposed on me by obedience, as well as the want of anyone to guide me in my writing and the need that it all come from my hand, and, finally, because the writing went against my nature and I wished only to keep my promise to one whom I could not disobey, I could not find the time to finish properly, and thus I failed to include whole treatises and many arguments that presented themselves to me, but which I omitted in order to put an end to the writing—many, that had I known the letter was to be printed, I would not have excluded, even if merely to satisfy some objections that have since arisen and which could have been refuted. But I shall not be so ill-mannered as to place such indecent objects before the purity of your eyes, for it is enough that my ignorance be an offense in your sight, without need of entrusting to it the effronteries of others. If they should wing your way (and they are of such little weight that this will happen), then you will command what I am to do; for, if it does not run contrary to your will, my defense shall be not to take up my pen, for I deem that one affront need not occasion another, if one recognizes the error in the very place it lies concealed. As my Father Saint Jerome says, *good discourse seeks not things*, and Saint Ambrose, *it is the nature of a guilty conscience to lie concealed*. Nor do I consider that I have been impugned, for one statute of the Law states: *An accusation will not endure*

---

1. *The Dream*, one of Sister Juana's best-known poems, which tells of the flight of her soul toward learning.   2. Because Pharaoh had ordered all male Hebrew infants killed, Moses' mother placed him in a basket by the Nile, where he was found and rescued by Pharaoh's daughter (Exodus 2:1–10).

unless nurtured by the person who brought it forth. What *is* a matter to be weighed is the effort spent in copying the accusation. A strange madness, to expend more effort in denying acclaim than in earning it! I, lady, have chosen not to respond (although others did so without my knowledge); it suffices that I have seen certain treatises, among them one so learned I send it to you so that reading it will compensate in part for the time you squandered on my writing. If, lady, you wish that I act contrary to what I have proposed here for your judgment and opinion, the merest indication of your desire will, as is seemly, countermand my inclination, which, as I have told you, is to be silent, for although Saint John Chrysostom[3] says, *those who slander must be refuted, and those who question, taught,* I know also that Saint Gregory[4] says, *It is no less a victory to tolerate enemies than to overcome them.* And that patience conquers by tolerating and triumphs by suffering. And if among the Roman Gentiles it was the custom when their captains were at the highest peak of glory—when returning triumphant from other nations, robed in purple and wreathed with laurel, crowned-but-conquered kings pulling their carriages in the stead of beasts, accompanied by the spoils of the riches of all the world, the conquering troops adorned with the insignia of their heroic feats, hearing the plaudits of the people who showered them with titles of honor and renown such as Fathers of the Nation, Columns of the Empire, Walls of Rome, Shelter of the Republic, and other glorious names—a soldier went before these captains in this moment of the supreme apogee of glory and human happiness crying out in a loud voice to the conqueror (by his consent and order of the Senate): Behold how you are mortal; behold how you have this or that defect, not excepting the most shameful, as happened in the triumph of Caesar, when the vilest soldiers clamored in his ear: *Beware, Romans, for we bring you the bald adulterer.* Which was done so that in the midst of such honor the conquerers not be swelled up with pride, and that the ballast of these insults act as counterweight to the bellying sails of such approbation, and that the ship of good judgment not founder amidst the winds of acclamation. If this, I say, was the practice among Gentiles, who knew only the light of Natural Law, how much might we Catholics, under the injunction to love our enemies, achieve by tolerating them? And in my own behalf I can attest that calumny has often mortified me, but never harmed me, being that I hold as a great fool one who having occasion to receive credit suffers the difficulty and loses the credit, as it is with those who do not resign themselves to death, but, in the end, die anyway, their resistance not having prevented death, but merely deprived them of the credit of resignation and caused them to die badly when they might have died well. And thus, lady, I believe these experiences do more good than harm, and I hold as greater the jeopardy of applause to human weakness, as we are wont to appropriate praise that is not our own, and must be ever watchful, and carry graven on our hearts those words of the Apostle: *Or what hast thou that thou hast not received? And if thou hast received, why doest thou glory as if thou hadst not received it?*[5] so that these words serve

---

3. Syrian prelate (ca. 347–407), known as the greatest orator of the Church, author of many homilies and treatises.   4. Gregory the Great (ca. 540–604), pope from 590, deeply concerned with the reformation of the Church.   5. 2 Corinthians 11:4.

as a shield to fend off the sharp barbs of commendations, which are as spears which when not attributed to God (whose they are), claim our lives and cause us to be thieves of God's honor and usurpers of the talents He bestowed on us and the gifts that He lent to us, for which we must give the most strict accounting. And thus, lady, I fear applause more than calumny, because the latter, with but the simple act of patience becomes gain, while the former requires many acts of reflection and humility and proper recognition so that it not become harm. And I know and recognize that it is by special favor of God that I know this, as it enables me in either instance to act in accord with the words of Saint Augustine: *One must believe neither the friend who praises nor the enemy who detracts.* Although most often I squander God's favor, or vitiate with such defects and imperfections that I spoil what, being His, was good. And thus in what little of mine that has been printed, neither the use of my name, nor even consent for the printing, was given by my own counsel, but by the license of another who lies outside my domain, as was also true with the printing of the *Atenagórica* letter, and only a few *Exercises of the Incarnation* and *Offerings of the Sorrow* were printed for public devotions with my pleasure, but without my name; of which I am sending some few copies that (if you so desire) you may distribute them among our sisters, the nuns of that holy community, as well as in that city. I send but one copy of the *Sorrows* because the others have been exhausted and I could find no other copy. I wrote them long ago, solely for the devotions of my sisters, and later they were spread abroad; and their contents are disproportionate as regards my unworthiness and my ignorance, and they profited that they touched on matters of our exalted Queen; for I cannot explain what it is that inflames the coldest heart when one refers to the Most Holy Mary. It is my only desire, esteemed lady, to remit to you works worthy of your virtue and wisdom; as the poet said: *Though strength may falter, good will must be praised. In this, I believe, the gods will be content.*

If ever I write again, my scribbling will always find its way to the haven of your holy feet and the certainty of your correction, for I have no other jewel with which to pay you, and, in the lament of Seneca, he who has once bestowed benefices has committed himself to continue; and so you must be repaid out of your own munificence, for only in this way shall I with dignity be freed from debt and avoid that the words of that same Seneca come to pass: *It is contemptible to be surpassed in benefices.*[6] For in his gallantry the generous creditor gives to the poor debtor the means to satisfy his debt. So God gave his gift to a world unable to repay Him: He gave his son that He be offered a recompense worthy of Him.

If, most venerable lady, the tone of this letter may not have seemed right and proper, I ask forgiveness for its homely familiarity, and the less than seemly respect in which by treating you as a nun, one of my sisters, I have lost sight of the remoteness of your most illustrious person; which, had I seen you without your veil, would never have occurred; but you in all your prudence and mercy will supplement or amend the language, and if you find unsuitable the *Vos* of the address I have employed, believing that for

6. *On Benefits* 5.2.1.

the reverence I owe you, Your Reverence seemed little reverent, modify it in whatever manner seems appropriate to your due, for I have not dared exceed the limits of your custom, nor transgress the boundary of your modesty.

And hold me in your grace, and entreat for me divine grace, of which the Lord God grant you large measure, and keep you, as I pray Him, and am needful. From this convent of our Father Saint Jerome in Mexico City, the first day of the month of March of sixteen hundred and ninety-one. Allow me to kiss your hand, your most favored

Juana Inés de la Cruz

JONATHAN SWIFT
1667–1745

In virtually all his writing, Jonathan Swift displays his gift for making other people uncomfortable. He makes us uneasy by making us aware of our own moral inadequacies, and by his wit, energy, and inventiveness, he actually compels us to enjoy the process of being brought to such awareness.

Born in Dublin to English parents, Swift was educated at Trinity College, Dublin. In 1689, the young man went to England, where he served as secretary to the statesman Sir William Temple. During his residence at Moor Park, Sir William's estate, Swift became friendly with Esther Johnson, daughter of the steward there; he remained on close terms with her for the rest of his life. (His playful, intimate letters to her—he used the name "Stella"—were published in a collection called *Journal to Stella*.) In 1692, Swift received an M.A. from Oxford University; three years later, he took orders, becoming a clergyman in the Anglican Church but continuing in Sir William's employ, although with intermittent stays in Ireland. Early in the eighteenth century, he began his career of political journalism; he also published brilliant satiric works, including *A Tale of a Tub* (1704), of which he is supposed to have said, late in his life, "What a genius I had when I composed that book!" Although he had hoped for church advancement in England, as a reward for his writings in the Tory cause, in 1713 he was instead named dean of St. Patrick's Cathedral, Dublin. He spent the rest of his life in Ireland (save for two brief visits to friends in England) writing passionately on behalf of the oppressed Irish people. In his final years, he was declared mentally incompetent, suffering, presumably, from senility. As he had prophesied in his verses *On the Death of Dr. Swift*, "He gave what little wealth he had / To build a house for fools and mad"; the mental hospital founded by his legacy still exists in Dublin.

Best known as the writer of *Gulliver's Travels* (1726), a book read both as children's fiction and as serious satire, Swift wrote effective satire in several genres (extended fiction, poetry, essay). Characteristically, he implicates the reader in often uncomfortable processes of judgment. *A Modest Proposal* (1729), his attack on the economic oppression of the Irish by the English, keeps the reader constantly off balance, trying to understand exactly who is being criticized and why. Swift is writing out of his firsthand awareness of the suffering caused by English policies in Ireland. Absentee landlords who never saw the actual situation of their tenants, British politicians who made policy at a distance, presumably did not know that Ireland had become a land of the starving. In Swift's view, however, the

Irish people collaborated by their apathy with the oppressors. In *A Modest Proposal*, he attacks English and Irish alike.

Even more emphatically than Gulliver, the nameless speaker in *A Modest Proposal* proves an undependable guide, tempting us to identify with his tone of rationality and compassion, only to reveal that his plausible economic orientation leads to advocacy of cannibalism. He offers a series of morally sound and economically feasible suggestions for solutions to Ireland's problems, but draws back immediately, declaring them impossible, since no one will put them in practice. The satire indicts the English for inhumanity, the Irish for passivity, and the economically oriented proposer of remedies for moral blindness. But it also reaches out to criticize the reader as representative of all who endure calmly the intolerable actuality in the world (but not, perhaps, where we have to see it ourselves) of our own inhumanity to our fellow human beings. Swift's self-chosen epitaph, on his tomb, may be translated, "Where fierce indignation no longer tears the heart." *A Modest Proposal* exemplifies the lacerating power of that indignation.

A good introduction to Swift's life and character is I. Ehrenpreis, *The Personality of Jonathan Swift* (1958). An interpretation of the writer in his intellectual context is K. Williams, *Jonathan Swift and the Age of Compromise* (1959). E. Zimmerman, *Swift's Narrative Satires: Author and Authority* (1983), provides acute interpretation of the prose satires. Useful and varied collections of essays about Swift include C. Probyn, ed., *Jonathan Swift: The Contemporary Background* (1978); C. Rawson, ed., *The Art of Swift's Satire: A Revised Focus* (1983); C. Rawson, ed., *Swift: A Collection of Critical Essays* (1994); and Harold Bloom, ed., *Jonathan Swift's Gulliver's Travels* (1986). R. A. Greenberg, ed., *Gulliver's Travels* (1970), is annotated and includes critical essays.

A Modest Proposal[1]

for Preventing the Children of poor People in Ireland, *from being a Burden to their Parents or Country; and for making them beneficial to the Publick.*

Written in the year 1729

It is a melancholy object to those who walk through this great town,[2] or travel in the country, when they see the streets, the roads, and cabin-doors crowded with beggars of the female sex, followed by three, four, or six children, all in rags, and importuning every passenger for an alms. These mothers, instead of being able to work for their honest livelihood, are forced to employ all their time in strolling to beg sustenance for their helpless infants: who, as they grow up, either turn thieves for want of work, or leave their dear native country to fight for the Pretender in Spain, or sell themselves to the Barbadoes.[3]

I think it is agreed by all parties, that this prodigious number of children in the arms, or on the backs, or at the heels of their mothers, and frequently of their fathers, is, in the present deplorable state of the kingdom, a very great additional grievance; and, therefore, whoever could find out a

---

1. The complete text edited by Herbert Davis.   2. Dublin.   3. At this time a British possession, with a prosperous sugar industry. Workers were needed in the sugar plantations. *The Pretender:* James Edward (1688–1766), son of the Catholic King James II of England, called the "Old Pretender" (in distinction to his son Charles, nine years old at the time of this work, called the "Young Pretender"). Many thought him a legitimate claimant to the throne.

fair, cheap, and easy method of making these children sound and useful members of the commonwealth, would deserve so well of the public, as to have his statue set up for a preserver of the nation.

But my intention is very far from being confined to provide only for the children of professed beggars; it is of a much greater extent, and shall take in the whole number of infants at a certain age, who are born of parents in effect as little able to support them as those who demand our charity in the streets.

As to my own part, having turned my thoughts for many years upon this important subject, and maturely weighed the several schemes of other projectors,[4] I have always found them grossly mistaken in their computation. It is true, a child, just dropped from its dam, may be supported by her milk for a solar year with little other nourishment; at most, not above the value of two shillings, which the mother may certainly get, or the value in scraps, by her lawful occupation of begging; and it is exactly at one year old that I propose to provide for them in such a manner, as, instead of being a charge upon their parents or the parish, or wanting food and raiment for the rest of their lives, they shall, on the contrary, contribute to the feeding, and partly to the clothing, of many thousands.

There is likewise another advantage in my scheme, that it will prevent those voluntary abortions, and that horrid practice of women murdering their bastard children, alas, too frequent among us, sacrificing the poor innocent babes, I doubt more to avoid the expense than the shame, which would move tears and pity in the most savage and inhuman breast.

The number of souls in this kingdom being usually reckoned one million and a half, of these I calculate there may be about two hundred thousand couple whose wives are breeders; from which number I subtract thirty thousand couple, who are able to maintain their own children (although I apprehend there cannot be so many, under the present distresses of the kingdom); but this being granted, there will remain an hundred and seventy thousand breeders. I again subtract fifty thousand for those women who miscarry, or whose children die by accident or disease within the year. There only remain a hundred and twenty thousand children of poor parents annually born. The question therefore is how this number shall be reared and provided for? which, as I have already said, under the present situation of affairs, is utterly impossible by all the methods hitherto proposed. For we can neither employ them in handicraft or agriculture; we neither build houses (I mean in the country) nor cultivate land: they can very seldom pick up a livelihood by stealing until they arrive at six years old, except where they are of towardly parts;[5] although I confess they learn the rudiments much earlier; during which time they can, however, be properly looked upon only as probationers; as I have been informed by a principal gentleman in the county of Cavan, who protested to me, that he never knew above one or two instances under the age of six, even in a part of the kingdom so renowned for the quickest proficiency in that art.

I am assured by our merchants that a boy or a girl before twelve years

4. Planners.   5. Particularly talented, unusually gifted.

old is no saleable commodity; and even when they come to this age they will not yield above three pounds or three pounds and half-a-crown at most, on the exchange; which cannot turn to account either to the parents or kingdom, the charge of nutriment and rags having been at least four times that value.

I shall now, therefore, humbly propose my own thoughts, which I hope will not be liable to the least objection.

I have been assured by a very knowing American of my acquaintance in London, that a young healthy child, well nursed, is, at a year old, a most delicious, nourishing, and wholesome food, whether stewed, roasted, baked, or boiled; and I make no doubt that it will equally serve in a fricassee or a ragout.

I do therefore humbly offer it to public consideration, that of the hundred and twenty thousand children already computed, twenty thousand may be reserved for breed, whereof only one-fourth part to be males; which is more than we allow to sheep, black cattle, or swine; and my reason is, that these children are seldom the fruits of marriage, a circumstance not much regarded by our savages, therefore one male will be sufficient to serve four females. That the remaining hundred thousand may, at a year old, be offered in sale to the persons of quality and fortune through the kingdom; always advising the mother to let them suck plentifully in the last month, so as to render them plump and fat for a good table. A child will make two dishes at an entertainment for friends; and when the family dines alone, the fore or hind quarter will make a reasonable dish, and, seasoned with a little pepper or salt, will be very good boiled on the fourth day, especially in winter.

I have reckoned, upon a medium,[6] that a child just born will weigh twelve pounds, and in a solar year, if tolerably nursed, increaseth to twenty-eight pounds.

I grant this food will be somewhat dear,[7] and therefore very proper for landlords, who, as they have already devoured most of the parents, seem to have the best title to the children.

Infants' flesh will be in season throughout the year, but more plentifully in March, and a little before and after: for we are told by a grave author, an eminent French physician,[8] that fish being a prolific diet, there are more children born in Roman Catholic countries about nine months after Lent than at any other season; therefore, reckoning a year after Lent, the markets will be more glutted than usual, because the number of popish infants is at least three to one in this kingdom; and therefore it will have one other collateral advantage, by lessening the number of papists among us.

I have already computed the charge of nursing a beggar's child (in which list I reckon all cottagers, labourers, and four-fifths of the farmers) to be about two shillings per annum,[9] rags included; and I believe no gentleman would repine to give ten shillings for the carcass of a good fat child, which, as I have said, will make four dishes of excellent nutritive

---

6. Average.   7. Expensive.   8. François Rabelais (1494?–1553), French satirist and author of *Gargantua and Pantagruel* (1532–52).   9. Per year.

meat, when he has only some particular friend, or his own family, to dine with him. Thus the squire will learn to be a good landlord, and grow popular among his tenants; the mother will have eight shillings net profit, and be fit for work till she produces another child.

Those who are more thrifty (as I must confess the times require) may flay the carcass; the skin of which, artificially dressed, will make admirable gloves for ladies, and summer-boots for fine gentlemen.

As to our city of Dublin, shambles[1] may be appointed for this purpose in the most convenient parts of it, and butchers we may be assured will not be wanting; although I rather recommend buying the children alive, and dressing them hot from the knife, as we do roasting pigs.

A very worthy person, a true lover of his country, and whose virtues I highly esteem, was lately pleased, in discoursing on this matter, to offer a refinement upon my scheme. He said, that many gentlemen of this kingdom, having of late destroyed their deer, he conceived that the want of venison might be well supplied by the bodies of young lads and maidens, not exceeding fourteen years of age, nor under twelve; so great a number of both sexes in every country being now ready to starve for want of work and service; and these to be disposed of by their parents, if alive, or otherwise by their nearest relations. But, with due deference to so excellent a friend, and so deserving a patriot, I cannot be altogether in his sentiments; for as to the males, my American acquaintance assured me from frequent experience, that their flesh was generally tough and lean, like that of our schoolboys, by continual exercise, and their taste disagreeable; and to fatten them would not answer the charge. Then as to the females, it would, I think, with humble submission, be a loss to the public, because they soon would become breeders themselves: and besides, it is not improbable that some scrupulous people might be apt to censure such a practice (although indeed very unjustly) as a little bordering upon cruelty; which, I confess hath always been with me the strongest objection against any project, how well soever intended.

But in order to justify my friend, he confessed that this expedient was put into his head by the famous Psalmanazar,[2] a native of the island Formosa, who came from thence to London above twenty years ago; and in conversation told my friend, that in his country, when any young person happened to be put to death, the executioner sold the carcass to persons of quality as a prime dainty; and that in his time the body of a plump girl of fifteen, who was crucified for an attempt to poison the emperor, was sold to his Imperial Majesty's prime minister of state, and other great mandarins of the court, in joints from the gibbet,[3] at four hundred crowns. Neither indeed can I deny, that if the same use were made of several plump young girls in this town, who, without one single groat to their fortunes, cannot stir abroad without a chair,[4] and appear at playhouse and

1. Slaughterhouses.   2. George Psalmanazar (1679?–1763), a literary impostor born in southern France who claimed to be a native of Formosa and a recent Christian convert. He published a catechism in an invented language that he called Formosan as well as a description of Formosa with an introductory autobiography.   3. The post from which the bodies of criminals were hung in chains after execution. *Joints*: portions of a carcass carved up by a butcher.   4. That is, a sedan chair, an enclosed seat carried on poles by men.

assemblies in foreign fineries which they never will pay for, the kingdom would not be the worse.

Some persons of a desponding spirit are in great concern about the vast number of poor people who are aged, diseased, or maimed; and I have been desired to employ my thoughts what course may be taken to ease the nation of so grievous an encumbrance. But I am not in the least pain upon that matter, because it is very well known, that they are every day dying, and rotting, by cold and famine, and filth and vermin, as fast as can be reasonably expected. And as to the younger labourers, they are now in almost as hopeful a condition: they cannot get work, and consequently pine away for want of nourishment, to a degree, that if at any time they are accidentally hired to common labour, they have not strength to perform it; and thus the country and themselves are happily delivered from the evils to come.

I have too long digressed, and therefore shall return to my subject. I think the advantages by the proposal which I have made are obvious and many, as well as of the highest importance.

For first, as I have already observed, it would greatly lessen the number of papists, with whom we are yearly overrun, being the principal breeders of the nation as well as our most dangerous enemies; and who stay at home on purpose with a design to deliver the kingdom to the Pretender, hoping to take their advantage by the absence of so many good Protestants, who have chosen rather to leave their country than stay at home and pay tithes against their conscience to an idolatrous Episcopal curate.

Secondly, the poorer tenants will have something valuable of their own, which by law may be made liable to distress,[5] and help to pay their landlord's rent; their corn and cattle being already seized, and money a thing unknown.

Thirdly, whereas the maintenance of an hundred thousand children, from two years old and upwards, cannot be computed at less than ten shillings a piece per annum, the nation's stock will be thereby increased fifty thousand pounds per annum; besides the profit of a new dish introduced to the tables of all gentlemen of fortune in the kingdom who have any refinement in taste. And the money will circulate among ourselves, the goods being entirely of our own growth and manufacture.

Fourthly, the constant breeders, besides the gain of eight shillings sterling per annum by the sale of their children, will be rid of the charge of maintaining them after the first year.

Fifthly, this food would likewise bring great custom to taverns; where the vinters will certainly be so prudent as to procure the best receipts[6] for dressing it to perfection, and, consequently, have their houses frequented by all the fine gentlemen, who justly value themselves upon their knowledge in good eating: and a skilful cook, who understands how to oblige his guests, will contrive to make it as expensive as they please.

Sixthly, this would be a great inducement to marriage, which all wise nations have either encouraged by rewards, or enforced by laws and penalties. It would increase the care and tenderness of mothers towards their

---

5. The legal seizing of goods to satisfy a debt, particularly for unpaid rent.   6. Recipes.

children, when they were sure of a settlement for life to the poor babes, provided in some sort by the public, to their annual profit instead of expense. We should soon see an honest emulation among the married women, which of them could bring the fattest child to the market. Men would become as fond of their wives during the time of their pregnancy, as they are now of their mares in foal, their cows in calf, or sows when they are ready to farrow; nor offer to beat or kick them (as is too frequent a practice) for fear of a miscarriage.

Many other advantages might be enumerated. For instance, the addition of some thousand carcasses in our exportation of barrelled beef; the propagation of swine's flesh, and improvement in the art of making good bacon, so much wanted among us by the great destruction of pigs, too frequent at our tables, which are no way comparable in taste or magnificence to a well-grown, fat yearling child, which, roasted whole, will make a considerable figure at a Lord Mayor's feast, or any other public entertainment. But this, and many others, I omit, being studious of brevity.

Supposing that one thousand families in this city would be constant customers for infants' flesh, besides others who might have it at merry meetings, particularly weddings and christenings. I compute that Dublin would take off annually about twenty thousand carcasses; and the rest of the kingdom (where probably they will be sold somewhat cheaper) the remaining eighty thousand.

I can think of no one objection that will possibly be raised against this proposal, unless it should be urged, that the number of people will be thereby much lessened in the kingdom. This I freely own, and it was indeed one principal design in offering it to the world. I desire the reader will observe that I calculate my remedy *for this one individual kingdom of Ireland, and for no other that ever was, is, or I think ever can be, upon earth.* Therefore let no man talk to me of other expedients: *of taxing our absentees at five shillings a pound: of using neither clothes nor household-furniture except what is of our own growth and manufacture: of utterly rejecting the materials and instruments that promote foreign luxury: of curing the expensiveness of pride, vanity, idleness, and gaming in our women; of introducing a vein of parsimony, prudence, and temperance: of learning to love our country, wherein we differ even from Laplanders, and the inhabitants of Topinamboo:*[7] *of quitting our animosities and factions, nor act any longer like the Jews,*[8] *who were murdering one another at the very moment their city was taken: of being a little cautious not to sell our country and consciences for nothing: of teaching landlords to have at least one degree of mercy towards their tenants: lastly, of putting a spirit of honesty, industry, and skill into our shopkeepers; who, if a resolution could now be taken to buy only our native goods, would immediately unite to cheat and exact upon us in the price, the measure, and the goodness, nor could ever yet be brought to make one fair proposal of just dealing, though often and earnestly invited to it.*[9]

Therefore I repeat, let no man talk to me of these and the like expedi-

---

7. In Brazil.   8. Referring to the factionalism under Herod Agrippa II at the time of the destruction of Jerusalem by the Roman emperor Titus.   9. The italicized proposals are Swift's serious suggestions for remedying the situation of Ireland.

ents, till he hath at least some glimpse of hope that there will ever be some hearty and sincere attempts to put them in practice.

But, as to myself, having been wearied out for many years with offering vain, idle, visionary thoughts, and at length utterly despairing of success, I fortunately fell upon this proposal; which, as it is wholly new, so it hath something solid and real, of no expense and little trouble, full in our own power, and whereby we can incur no danger in disobliging England. For this kind of commodity will not bear exportation, the flesh being of too tender a consistence to admit a long continuance in salt, although perhaps I could name a country[1] which would be glad to eat up our whole nation without it.

After all, I am not so violently bent upon my own opinion as to reject any offer proposed by wise men which shall be found equally innocent, cheap, easy, and effectual. But before something of that kind shall be advanced in contradiction to my scheme, and offering a better, I desire the author, or authors, will be pleased maturely to consider two points. First, as things now stand, how they will be able to find food and raiment for a hundred thousand useless mouths and backs? And, secondly, there being a round million of creatures in human figure throughout this kingdom, whose whole subsistence put into a common stock would leave them in debt two millions of pounds sterling, adding those who are beggars by profession, to the bulk of farmers, cottagers, and labourers, with the wives and children who are beggars in effect; I desire those politicians who dislike my overture, and may perhaps be so bold as to attempt an answer, that they will first ask the parents of these mortals, whether they would not at this day think it a great happiness to have been sold for food at a year old, in the manner I prescribe, and thereby have avoided such a perpetual scene of misfortunes as they have since gone through, by the oppression of landlords, the impossibility of paying rent without money or trade, the want of common sustenance, with neither house nor clothes to cover them from the inclemencies of weather, and the most inevitable prospect of entailing the like, or greater miseries, upon their breed for ever.

I profess, in the sincerity of my heart, that I have not the least personal interest in endeavouring to promote this necessary work, having no other motive than the public good of my country, by advancing our trade, providing for infants, relieving the poor, and giving some pleasure to the rich. I have no children by which I can propose to get a single penny; the youngest being nine years old, and my wife past child-bearing.

---

1. England.

FRANÇOIS-MARIE AROUET DE VOLTAIRE
1694–1778

Voltaire's *Candide* (1759) brings to near perfection the art of black comedy. It subjects its characters to an accumulation of horrors so bizarre that they provoke a

he insists that much of the order we claim to perceive itself comprises a comforting fiction, as he uses satire's fierce energies to challenge our complacencies, he reveals once more the underside of the Enlightenment ideal of reason. That we human beings have reason, Voltaire tells us, is no ground on which to flatter ourselves; rightly used, it exposes our insufficiencies.

Biographies and critical studies of Voltaire include R. Aldington, *Voltaire* (1934); G. Brandes, *The Life of Voltaire* (undated); I. O. Wade, *Voltaire and "Candide"* (1959); and T. Besterman, *Voltaire* (1969). A good general introduction is P. E. Richter and Ilona Ricardo, *Voltaire* (1980). A work placing Voltaire in a broad context is F. M. Keener, *The Chain of Becoming* (1983), on Voltaire and his English contemporaries. For a collection of essays by various writers, see M. Culler, ed., *Voltaire: The Enlightenment and the Comic Mode* (1990).

PRONOUNCING GLOSSARY

The following list uses common English syllables and stress accents to provide rough equivalents of selected words whose pronunciation may be unfamiliar to the general reader.

Abare: *a-bahr'*	Pangloss: *pan-gloos'*
Cacambo: *ka-kahm'-bo*	Paquette: *pah-ket'*
Candide: *kahn-deed'*	Pococurante: *poh-koh-ku-rahnt'*
Cunégonde: *koon-e-gond'*	Thunder-Ten-Tronckh: *tun-dayr'–ten–*
Giroflée: *jee-roh-flay'*	*trawnk*
Issachar: *ee-sah-shahr'*	

Candide, or Optimism[1]

translated from the German of Doctor Ralph with the additions which were found in the Doctor's pocket when he died at Minden in the Year of Our Lord 1759

CHAPTER 1

How Candide Was Brought up in a Fine Castle and How He Was Driven Therefrom

There lived in Westphalia,[2] in the castle of the Baron of Thunder-Ten-Tronckh, a young man on whom nature had bestowed the perfection of gentle manners. His features admirably expressed his soul; he combined an honest mind with great simplicity of heart; and I think it was for this reason that they called him Candide. The old servants of the house suspected that he was the son of the Baron's sister by a respectable, honest gentleman of the neighborhood, whom she had refused to marry because he could prove only seventy-one quarterings,[3] the rest of his family tree having been lost in the passage of time.

The Baron was one of the most mighty lords of Westphalia, for his castle

---

1. Translated and with notes by Robert M. Adams.   2. A province of western Germany, near Holland and the lower Rhineland. Flat, boggy, and drab, it is noted chiefly for its excellent ham. In a letter to his niece, written during his German expedition of 1750, Voltaire described the "vast, sad, sterile, detestable countryside of Westphalia."   3. Genealogical divisions of one's family-tree. Seventy-one of them is a grotesque number to have, representing something over 2,000 years of uninterrupted nobility.

had a door and windows. His great hall was even hung with a tapestry. The dogs of his courtyard made up a hunting pack on occasion, with the stableboys as huntsmen; the village priest was his grand almoner. They all called him "My Lord," and laughed at his stories.

The Baroness, who weighed in the neighborhood of three hundred and fifty pounds, was greatly respected for that reason, and did the honors of the house with a dignity which rendered her even more imposing. Her daughter Cunégonde,[4] aged seventeen, was a ruddy-cheeked girl, fresh, plump, and desirable. The Baron's son seemed in every way worthy of his father. The tutor Pangloss was the oracle of the household, and little Candide listened to his lectures with all the good faith of his age and character.

Pangloss gave instruction in metaphysico-theologico-cosmoloonig-ology.[5] He proved admirably that there cannot possibly be an effect without a cause and that in this best of all possible worlds the Baron's castle was the best of all castles and his wife the best of all possible Baronesses.

—It is clear, said he, that things cannot be otherwise than they are, for since everything is made to serve an end, everything necessarily serves the best end. Observe: noses were made to support spectacles, hence we have spectacles. Legs, as anyone can plainly see, were made to be breeched, and so we have breeches. Stones were made to be shaped and to build castles with; thus My Lord has a fine castle, for the greatest Baron in the province should have the finest house; and since pigs were made to be eaten, we eat pork all year round.[6] Consequently, those who say everything is well are uttering mere stupidities; they should say everything is for the best.

Candide listened attentively and believed implicitly; for he found Miss Cunégonde exceedingly pretty, though he never had the courage to tell her so. He decided that after the happiness of being born Baron of Thunder-Ten-Tronckh, the second order of happiness was to be Miss Cunégonde; the third was seeing her every day, and the fourth was listening to Master Pangloss, the greatest philosopher in the province and consequently in the entire world.

One day, while Cunégonde was walking near the castle in the little woods that they called a park, she saw Dr. Pangloss in the underbrush; he was giving a lesson in experimental physics to her mother's maid, a very attractive and obedient brunette. As Miss Cunégonde had a natural bent for the sciences, she watched breathlessly the repeated experiments which were going on; she saw clearly the doctor's sufficient reason, observed both cause and effect, and returned to the house in a distracted and pensive frame of mind, yearning for knowledge and dreaming that she might be the sufficient reason of young Candide—who might also be hers.

As she was returning to the castle, she met Candide, and blushed; Can-

---

4. Cunégonde gets her odd name from Kunigunda (wife to Emperor Henry II) who walked barefoot and blindfolded on red-hot irons to prove her chastity; Pangloss gets his name from Greek words meaning all-tongue. 5. The "looney" buried in this burlesque word corresponds to a buried *nigaud*— "booby" in the French. Christian Wolff, disciple of Leibniz, invented and popularized the word "cosmology." The catch phrases in the following sentence, echoed by popularizers of Leibniz, make reference to the determinism of his system, its linking of cause with effect, and its optimism. 6. The argument from design supposes that everything in this world exists for a specific reason; Voltaire objects not to the argument as a whole, but to the abuse of it.

dide blushed too. She greeted him in a faltering tone of voice; and Candide talked to her without knowing what he was saying. Next day, as everyone was rising from the dinner table, Cunégonde and Candide found themselves behind a screen; Cunégonde dropped her handkerchief, Candide picked it up; she held his hand quite innocently, he kissed her hand quite innocently with remarkable vivacity and emotion; their lips met, their eyes lit up, their knees trembled, their hands wandered. The Baron of Thunder-Ten-Tronckh passed by the screen and, taking note of this cause and this effect, drove Candide out of the castle by kicking him vigorously on the backside. Cunégonde fainted; as soon as she recovered, the Baroness slapped her face; and everything was confusion in the most beautiful and agreeable of all possible castles.

CHAPTER 2

What Happened to Candide Among the Bulgars[7]

Candide, ejected from the earthly paradise, wandered for a long time without knowing where he was going, weeping, raising his eyes to heaven, and gazing back frequently on the most beautiful of castles which contained the most beautiful of Baron's daughters. He slept without eating, in a furrow of a plowed field, while the snow drifted over him; next morning, numb with cold, he dragged himself into the neighboring village, which was called Waldberghoff-trarbk-dikdorff; he was penniless, famished, and exhausted. At the door of a tavern he paused forlornly. Two men dressed in blue[8] took note of him:

—Look, chum, said one of them, there's a likely young fellow of just about the right size.

They approached Candide and invited him very politely to dine with them.

—Gentlemen, Candide replied with charming modesty, I'm honored by your invitation, but I really don't have enough money to pay my share.

—My dear sir, said one of the blues, people of your appearance and your merit don't have to pay; aren't you five feet five inches tall?

—Yes, gentlemen, that is indeed my stature, said he, making a bow.

—Then, sir, you must be seated at once; not only will we pay your bill this time, we will never allow a man like you to be short of money; for men were made only to render one another mutual aid.

—You are quite right, said Candide; it is just as Dr. Pangloss always told me, and I see clearly that everything is for the best.

They beg him to accept a couple of crowns, he takes them, and offers an I.O.U.; they won't hear of it, and all sit down at table together.

—Don't you love dearly . . . ?

—I do indeed, says he, I dearly love Miss Cunégonde.

7. Voltaire chose this name to represent the Prussian troops of Frederick the Great because he wanted to make an insinuation of pederasty against both the soldiers and their master. Cf. French *bougre*, English "bugger."   8. The recruiting officers of Frederick the Great, much feared in eighteenth-century Europe, wore blue uniforms. Frederick had a passion for sorting out his soldiers by size; several of his regiments would accept only six-footers.

—No, no, says one of the gentlemen, we are asking if you don't love dearly the King of the Bulgars.

—Not in the least, says he, I never laid eyes on him.

—What's that you say? He's the most charming of kings, and we must drink his health.

—Oh, gladly, gentlemen; and he drinks.

—That will do, they tell him; you are now the bulwark, the support, the defender, the hero of the Bulgars; your fortune is made and your future assured.

Promptly they slip irons on his legs and lead him to the regiment. There they cause him to right face, left face, present arms, order arms, aim, fire, doubletime, and they give him thirty strokes of the rod. Next day he does the drill a little less awkwardly and gets only twenty strokes; the third day, they give him only ten, and he is regarded by his comrades as a prodigy.

Candide, quite thunderstruck, did not yet understand very clearly how he was a hero. One fine spring morning he took it into his head to go for a walk, stepping straight out as if it were a privilege of the human race, as of animals in general, to use his legs as he chose.[9] He had scarcely covered two leagues when four other heroes, each six feet tall, overtook him, bound him, and threw him into a dungeon. At the court-martial they asked which he preferred, to be flogged thirty-six times by the entire regiment or to receive summarily a dozen bullets in the brain. In vain did he argue that the human will is free and insist that he preferred neither alternative; he had to choose; by virtue of the divine gift called "liberty" he decided to run the gauntlet thirty-six times, and actually endured two floggings. The regiment was composed of two thousand men. That made four thousand strokes, which laid open every muscle and nerve from his nape to his butt. As they were preparing for the third beating, Candide, who could endure no more, begged as a special favor that they would have the goodness to smash his head. His plea was granted; they bandaged his eyes and made him kneel down. The King of the Bulgars, passing by at this moment, was told of the culprit's crime; and as this king had a rare genius, he understood, from everything they told him of Candide, that this was a young metaphysician, extremely ignorant of the ways of the world, so he granted his royal pardon, with a generosity which will be praised in every newspaper in every age. A worthy surgeon cured Candide in three weeks with the ointments described by Dioscorides.[1] He already had a bit of skin back and was able to walk when the King of the Bulgars went to war with the King of the Abares.[2]

9. This episode was suggested by the experience of a Frenchman named Courtilz, who had deserted from the Prussian army and been bastinadoed for it. Voltaire intervened with Frederick to gain his release. But it also reflects the story that Wolff, Leibniz's disciple, got into trouble with Frederick's father when someone reported that his doctrine denying free will had encouraged several soldiers to desert. "The argument of the grenadier," who was said to have pleaded preestablished harmony to justify his desertion, so infuriated the king that he had Wolff expelled from the country.   1. Dioscorides' treatise on *materia medica*, dating from the first century A.D., was not the most up to date.   2. A tribe of semicivilized Scythians, who might be supposed at war with the Bulgars; allegorically, the Abares are the French, who opposed the Prussians in the Seven Years' War (1756–63). According to the title page of 1761, "Doctor Ralph," the dummy author of *Candide*, himself perished at the battle of Minden (Westphalia) in 1759.

CHAPTER 3

How Candide Escaped from the Bulgars, and What Became of Him

Nothing could have been so fine, so brisk, so brilliant, so well-drilled as the two armies. The trumpets, the fifes, the oboes, the drums, and the cannon produced such a harmony as was never heard in hell. First the cannons battered down about six thousand men on each side; then volleys of musket fire removed from the best of worlds about nine or ten thousand rascals who were cluttering up its surface. The bayonet was a sufficient reason for the demise of several thousand others. Total casualties might well amount to thirty thousand men or so. Candide, who was trembling like a philosopher, hid himself as best he could while this heroic butchery was going on.

Finally, while the two kings in their respective camps celebrated the victory by having *Te Deums* sung, Candide undertook to do his reasoning of cause and effect somewhere else. Passing by mounds of the dead and dying, he came to a nearby village which had been burnt to the ground. It was an Abare village, which the Bulgars had burned, in strict accordance with the laws of war. Here old men, stunned from beatings, watched the last agonies of their butchered wives, who still clutched their infants to their bleeding breasts; there, disemboweled girls, who had first satisfied the natural needs of various heroes, breathed their last; others, half-scorched in the flames, begged for their death stroke. Scattered brains and severed limbs littered the ground.

Candide fled as fast as he could to another village; this one belonged to the Bulgars, and the heroes of the Abare cause had given it the same treatment. Climbing over ruins and stumbling over corpses, Candide finally made his way out of the war area, carrying a little food in his knapsack and never ceasing to dream of Miss Cunégonde. His supplies gave out when he reached Holland; but having heard that everyone in that country was rich and a Christian, he felt confident of being treated as well as he had been in the castle of the Baron before he was kicked out for the love of Miss Cunégonde.

He asked alms of several grave personages, who all told him that if he continued to beg, he would be shut up in a house of correction and set to hard labor.

Finally he approached a man who had just been talking to a large crowd for an hour on end; the topic was charity. Looking doubtfully at him, the orator demanded:

—What are you doing here? Are you here to serve the good cause?

—There is no effect without a cause, said Candide modestly; all events are linked by the chain of necessity and arranged for the best. I had to be driven away from Miss Cunégonde, I had to run the gauntlet, I have to beg my bread until I can earn it; none of this could have happened otherwise.

—Look here, friend, said the orator, do you think the Pope is Antichrist?[3]

---

3. Voltaire is satirizing extreme Protestant sects that have sometimes seemed to make hatred of Rome the sum and substance of their creed.

—I haven't considered the matter, said Candide; but whether he is or not, I'm in need of bread.

—You don't deserve any, said the other; away with you, you rascal, you rogue, never come near me as long as you live.

Meanwhile, the orator's wife had put her head out of the window, and, seeing a man who was not sure the Pope was Antichrist, emptied over his head a pot full of—— Scandalous! The excesses into which women are led by religious zeal!

A man who had never been baptized, a good Anabaptist[4] named Jacques, saw this cruel and heartless treatment being inflicted on one of his fellow creatures, a featherless biped possessing a soul;[5] he took Candide home with him, washed him off, gave him bread and beer, presented him with two florins, and even undertook to give him a job in his Persian-rug factory—for these items are widely manufactured in Holland. Candide, in an ecstasy of gratitude, cried out:

—Master Pangloss was right indeed when he told me everything is for the best in this world; for I am touched by your kindness far more than by the harshness of that black-coated gentleman and his wife.

Next day, while taking a stroll about town, he met a beggar who was covered with pustules, his eyes were sunken, the end of his nose rotted off, his mouth twisted, his teeth black, he had a croaking voice and a hacking cough, and spat a tooth every time he tried to speak.

CHAPTER 4

How Candide Met His Old Philosophy Tutor, Doctor Pangloss, and What Came of It

Candide, more touched by compassion even than by horror, gave this ghastly beggar the two florins that he himself had received from his honest Anabaptist friend Jacques. The phantom stared at him, burst into tears, and fell on his neck. Candide drew back in terror.

—Alas, said one wretch to the other, don't you recognize your dear Pangloss any more?

—What are you saying? You, my dear master! you, in this horrible condition? What misfortune has befallen you? Why are you no longer in the most beautiful of castles? What has happened to Miss Cunégonde, that pearl among young ladies, that masterpiece of Nature?

—I am perishing, said Pangloss.

Candide promptly led him into the Anabaptist's stable, where he gave him a crust of bread, and when he had recovered:—Well, said he, Cunégonde?

—Dead, said the other.

Candide fainted. His friend brought him around with a bit of sour vine-

---

4. Holland, as the home of religious liberty, had offered asylum to the Anabaptists, whose radical views on property and religious discipline had made them unpopular during the sixteenth century. Granted tolerance, they settled down into respectable burghers. Since this behavior confirmed some of Voltaire's major theses, he had a high opinion of contemporary Anabaptists.   5. Plato's famous minimal definition of man, which he corrected by the addition of a soul to distinguish man from a plucked chicken.

gar which happened to be in the stable. Candide opened his eyes.

—Cunégonde, dead! Ah, best of worlds, what's become of you now? But how did she die? It wasn't of grief at seeing me kicked out of her noble father's elegant castle?

—Not at all, said Pangloss; she was disemboweled by the Bulgar soldiers, after having been raped to the absolute limit of human endurance; they smashed the Baron's head when he tried to defend her, cut the Baroness to bits, and treated my poor pupil exactly like his sister. As for the castle, not one stone was left on another, not a shed, not a sheep, not a duck, not a tree; but we had the satisfaction of revenge, for the Abares did exactly the same thing to a nearby barony belonging to a Bulgar nobleman.

At this tale Candide fainted again; but having returned to his senses and said everything appropriate to the occasion, he asked about the cause and effect, the sufficient reason, which had reduced Pangloss to his present pitiful state.

—Alas, said he, it was love; love, the consolation of the human race, the preservative of the universe, the soul of all sensitive beings, love, gentle love.

—Unhappy man, said Candide, I too have had some experience of this love, the sovereign of hearts, the soul of our souls; and it never got me anything but a single kiss and twenty kicks in the rear. How could this lovely cause produce in you such a disgusting effect?

Pangloss replied as follows: —My dear Candide! you knew Paquette, that pretty maidservant to our august Baroness. In her arms I tasted the delights of paradise, which directly caused these torments of hell, from which I am now suffering. She was infected with the disease, and has perhaps died of it. Paquette received this present from an erudite Franciscan, who took the pains to trace it back to its source; for he had it from an elderly countess, who picked it up from a captain of cavalry, who acquired it from a marquise, who caught it from a page, who had received it from a Jesuit, who during his novitiate got it directly from one of the companions of Christopher Columbus. As for me, I shall not give it to anyone, for I am a dying man.

—Oh, Pangloss, cried Candide, that's a very strange genealogy. Isn't the devil at the root of the whole thing?

—Not at all, replied that great man; it's an indispensable part of the best of worlds, a necessary ingredient; if Columbus had not caught, on an American island, this sickness which attacks the source of generation and sometimes prevents generation entirely—which thus strikes at and defeats the greatest end of Nature herself—we should have neither chocolate nor cochineal. It must also be noted that until the present time this malady, like religious controversy, has been wholly confined to the continent of Europe. Turks, Indians, Persians, Chinese, Siamese, and Japanese know nothing of it as yet; but there is a sufficient reason for which they in turn will make its acquaintance in a couple of centuries. Meanwhile, it has made splendid progress among us, especially among those big armies of honest, well-trained mercenaries who decide the destinies of nations. You can be sure that when thirty thousand men fight a pitched battle against the same number of the enemy, there will be about twenty thousand with the pox on either side.

—Remarkable indeed, said Candide, but we must see about curing you.

—And how can I do that, said Pangloss, seeing I don't have a cent to my name? There's not a doctor in the whole world who will let your blood or give you an enema without demanding a fee. If you can't pay yourself, you must find someone to pay for you.

These last words decided Candide; he hastened to implore the help of his charitable Anabaptist, Jacques, and painted such a moving picture of his friend's wretched state that the good man did not hesitate to take in Pangloss and have him cured at his own expense. In the course of the cure, Pangloss lost only an eye and an ear. Since he wrote a fine hand and knew arithmetic, the Anabaptist made him his bookkeeper. At the end of two months, being obliged to go to Lisbon on business, he took his two philosophers on the boat with him. Pangloss still maintained that everything was for the best, but Jacques didn't agree with him.

—It must be, said he, that men have corrupted Nature, for they are not born wolves, yet that is what they become. God gave them neither twenty-four-pound cannon nor bayonets, yet they have manufactured both in order to destroy themselves. Bankruptcies have the same effect, and so does the justice which seizes the goods of bankrupts in order to prevent the creditors from getting them.[6]

—It was all indispensable, replied the one-eyed doctor, since private misfortunes make for public welfare, and therefore the more private misfortunes there are, the better everything is.

While he was reasoning, the air grew dark, the winds blew from all directions, and the vessel was attacked by a horrible tempest within sight of Lisbon harbor.

CHAPTER 5

Tempest, Shipwreck, Earthquake, and What Happened to Doctor Pangloss, Candide, and the Anabaptist, Jacques

Half of the passengers, weakened by the frightful anguish of seasickness and the distress of tossing about on stormy waters, were incapable of noticing their danger. The other half shrieked aloud and fell to their prayers, the sails were ripped to shreds, the masts snapped, the vessel opened at the seams. Everyone worked who could stir, nobody listened for orders or issued them. The Anabaptist was lending a hand in the after part of the ship when a frantic sailor struck him and knocked him to the deck; but just at that moment, the sailor lurched so violently that he fell head first over the side, where he hung, clutching a fragment of the broken mast. The good Jacques ran to his aid, and helped him to climb back on board, but in the process was himself thrown into the sea under the very eyes of the sailor, who allowed him to drown without even glancing at him. Candide rushed to the rail, and saw his benefactor rise for a moment to the surface, then sink forever. He wanted to dive to his rescue; but the philoso-

---

6. Voltaire had suffered losses from various bankruptcy proceedings.

pher Pangloss prevented him by proving that the bay of Lisbon had been formed expressly for this Anabaptist to drown in. While he was proving the point *a priori*, the vessel opened up and everyone perished except for Pangloss, Candide, and the brutal sailor who had caused the virtuous Anabaptist to drown; this rascal swam easily to shore, while Pangloss and Candide drifted there on a plank.

When they had recovered a bit of energy, they set out for Lisbon; they still had a little money with which they hoped to stave off hunger after escaping the storm.

Scarcely had they set foot in the town, still bewailing the loss of their benefactor, when they felt the earth quake underfoot; the sea was lashed to a froth, burst into the port, and smashed all the vessels lying at anchor there. Whirlwinds of fire and ash swirled through the streets and public squares; houses crumbled, roofs came crashing down on foundations, foundations split; thirty thousand inhabitants of every age and either sex were crushed in the ruins.[7] The sailor whistled through his teeth, and said with an oath: —There'll be something to pick up here.

—What can be the sufficient reason of this phenomenon? asked Pangloss.

—The Last Judgment is here, cried Candide.

But the sailor ran directly into the middle of the ruins, heedless of danger in his eagerness for gain; he found some money, laid violent hands on it, got drunk, and, having slept off his wine, bought the favors of the first streetwalker he could find amid the ruins of smashed houses, amid corpses and suffering victims on every hand. Pangloss however tugged at his sleeve.

—My friend, said he, this is not good form at all; your behavior falls short of that required by the universal reason; it's untimely, to say the least.

—Bloody hell, said the other, I'm a sailor, born in Batavia; I've been four times to Japan and stamped four times on the crucifix;[8] get out of here with your universal reason.

Some falling stonework had struck Candide; he lay prostrate in the street, covered with rubble, and calling to Pangloss: —For pity's sake bring me a little wine and oil; I'm dying.

—This earthquake is nothing novel, Pangloss replied; the city of Lima, in South America, underwent much the same sort of tremor, last year; same causes, same effects; there is surely a vein of sulphur under the earth's surface reaching from Lima to Lisbon.

—Nothing is more probable, said Candide; but, for God's sake, a little oil and wine.

—What do you mean, probable? replied the philosopher; I regard the case as proved.

Candide fainted and Pangloss brought him some water from a nearby fountain.

---

7. The great Lisbon earthquake and fire occurred on November 1, 1755; between thirty and forty thousand deaths resulted.   8. The Japanese, originally receptive to foreign visitors, grew fearful that priests and proselytizers were merely advance agents of empire and expelled both the Portuguese and Spanish early in the seventeenth century. Only the Dutch were allowed to retain a small foothold, under humiliating conditions, of which the notion of stamping on the crucifix is symbolic. It was never what Voltaire suggests here, an actual requirement for entering the country.

Next day, as they wandered amid the ruins, they found a little food which restored some of their strength. Then they fell to work like the others, bringing relief to those of the inhabitants who had escaped death. Some of the citizens whom they rescued gave them a dinner as good as was possible under the circumstances; it is true that the meal was a melancholy one, and the guests watered their bread with tears; but Pangloss consoled them by proving that things could not possibly be otherwise.

—For, said he, all this is for the best, since if there is a volcano at Lisbon, it cannot be somewhere else, since it is unthinkable that things should not be where they are, since everything is well.

A little man in black, an officer of the Inquisition,[9] who was sitting beside him, politely took up the question, and said: —It would seem that the gentleman does not believe in original sin, since if everything is for the best, man has not fallen and is not liable to eternal punishment.

—I most humbly beg pardon of your excellency, Pangloss answered, even more politely, but the fall of man and the curse of original sin entered necessarily into the best of all possible worlds.

—Then you do not believe in free will? said the officer.

—Your excellency must excuse me, said Pangloss; free will agrees very well with absolute necessity, for it was necessary that we should be free, since a will which is determined . . .

Pangloss was in the middle of his sentence, when the officer nodded significantly to the attendant who was pouring him a glass of port, or Oporto, wine.

CHAPTER 6

How They Made a Fine Auto-da-Fé to Prevent Earthquakes, and How Candide Was Whipped

After the earthquake had wiped out three quarters of Lisbon, the learned men of the land could find no more effective way of averting total destruction than to give the people a fine auto-da-fé;[1] the University of Coimbra had established that the spectacle of several persons being roasted over a slow fire with full ceremonial rites is an infallible specific against earthquakes.

In consequence, the authorities had rounded up a Biscayan convicted of marrying a woman who had stood godmother to his child, and two Portuguese who while eating a chicken had set aside a bit of bacon used for seasoning.[2] After dinner, men came with ropes to tie up Doctor Pangloss and his disciple Candide, one for talking and the other for listening with an air of approval; both were taken separately to a set of remarkably cool apartments, where the glare of the sun is never bothersome; eight days later they were both dressed in *san-benitos* and crowned with paper

9. Specifically, a *familier* or *poursuivant*, an undercover agent with powers of arrest.   1. Literally, "act of faith," a public ceremony of repentance and humiliation. Such an auto-da-fé was actually held in Lisbon, June 20, 1756.   2. The Biscayan's fault lay in marrying someone within the forbidden bounds of relationship, an act of spiritual incest. The men who declined pork or bacon were understood to be crypto-Jews.

mitres;[3] Candide's mitre and *san-benito* were decorated with inverted flames and with devils who had neither tails nor claws; but Pangloss's devils had both tails and claws, and his flames stood upright. Wearing these costumes, they marched in a procession, and listened to a very touching sermon, followed by a beautiful concert of plainsong. Candide was flogged in cadence to the music; the Biscayan and the two men who had avoided bacon were burned, and Pangloss was hanged, though hanging is not customary. On the same day there was another earthquake, causing frightful damage.[4]

Candide, stunned, stupefied, despairing, bleeding, trembling, said to himself: —If this is the best of all possible worlds, what are the others like? The flogging is not so bad, I was flogged by the Bulgars. But oh my dear Pangloss, greatest of philosophers, was it necessary for me to watch you being hanged, for no reason that I can see? Oh my dear Anabaptist, best of men, was it necessary that you should be drowned in the port? Oh Miss Cunégonde, pearl of young ladies, was it necessary that you should have your belly slit open?

He was being led away, barely able to stand, lectured, lashed, absolved, and blessed, when an old woman approached and said, —My son, be of good cheer and follow me.

CHAPTER 7

How an Old Woman Took Care of Candide, and How He Regained What He Loved

Candide was of very bad cheer, but he followed the old woman to a shanty; she gave him a jar of ointment to rub himself, left him food and drink; she showed him a tidy little bed; next to it was a suit of clothing.

—Eat, drink, sleep, she said; and may Our Lady of Atocha, Our Lord St. Anthony of Padua, and Our Lord St. James of Compostela watch over you. I will be back tomorrow.

Candide, still completely astonished by everything he had seen and suffered, and even more by the old woman's kindness, offered to kiss her hand.

—It's not *my* hand you should be kissing, said she. I'll be back tomorrow; rub yourself with the ointment, eat and sleep.

In spite of his many sufferings, Candide ate and slept. Next day the old woman returned bringing breakfast; she looked at his back and rubbed it herself with another ointment; she came back with lunch; and then she returned in the evening, bringing supper. Next day she repeated the same routine.

—Who are you? Candide asked continually. Who told you to be so kind to me? How can I ever repay you?

The good woman answered not a word; she returned in the evening, and without food.

—Come with me, says she, and don't speak a word.

3. The cone-shaped paper cap (intended to resemble a bishop's mitre) and flowing yellow cape were customary garb for those pleading before the Inquisition.   4. In fact, the second quake occurred December 21, 1755.

Taking him by the hand, she walks out into the countryside with him for about a quarter of a mile; they reach an isolated house, quite surrounded by gardens and ditches. The old woman knocks at a little gate, it opens. She takes Candide up a secret stairway to a gilded room furnished with a fine brocaded sofa; there she leaves him, closes the door, disappears. Candide stood as if entranced; his life, which had seemed like a nightmare so far, was now starting to look like a delightful dream.

Soon the old woman returned; on her feeble shoulder leaned a trembling woman, of a splendid figure, glittering in diamonds, and veiled.

—Remove the veil, said the old woman to Candide.

The young man stepped timidly forward, and lifted the veil. What an event! What a surprise! Could it be Miss Cunégonde? Yes, it really was! She herself! His knees give way, speech fails him, he falls at her feet, Cunégonde collapses on the sofa. The old woman plies them with brandy, they return to their senses, they exchange words. At first they could utter only broken phrases, questions and answers at cross purposes, sighs, tears, exclamations. The old woman warned them not to make too much noise, and left them alone.

—Then it's really you, said Candide, you're alive, I've found you again in Portugal. Then you never were raped? You never had your belly ripped open, as the philosopher Pangloss assured me?

—Oh yes, said the lovely Cunégonde, but one doesn't always die of these two accidents.

—But your father and mother were murdered then?

—All too true, said Cunégonde, in tears.

—And your brother?

—Killed too.

—And why are you in Portugal? and how did you know I was here? and by what device did you have me brought to this house?

—I shall tell you everything, the lady replied; but first you must tell me what has happened to you since that first innocent kiss we exchanged and the kicking you got because of it.

Candide obeyed her with profound respect; and though he was overcome, though his voice was weak and hesitant, though he still had twinges of pain from his beating, he described as simply as possible everything that had happened to him since the time of their separation. Cunégonde lifted her eyes to heaven; she wept at the death of the good Anabaptist and at that of Pangloss; after which she told the following story to Candide, who listened to every word while he gazed on her with hungry eyes.

CHAPTER 8

Cunégonde's Story

—I was in my bed and fast asleep when heaven chose to send the Bulgars into our castle of Thunder-Ten-Tronckh. They butchered my father and brother, and hacked my mother to bits. An enormous Bulgar, six feet tall, seeing that I had swooned from horror at the scene, set about raping me; at that I recovered my senses, I screamed and scratched, bit and fought, I tried to tear the eyes out of that big Bulgar—not realizing that everything which had happened in my father's castle was a mere matter of routine. The brute then stabbed me with a knife on my left thigh, where I still bear the scar.

—What a pity! I should very much like to see it, said the simple Candide.

—You shall, said Cunégonde; but shall I go on?

—Please do, said Candide.

So she took up the thread of her tale: —A Bulgar captain appeared, he saw me covered with blood and the soldier too intent to get up. Shocked by the monster's failure to come to attention, the captain killed him on my body. He then had my wound dressed, and took me off to his quarters, as a prisoner of war. I laundered his few shirts and did his cooking; he found me attractive, I confess it, and I won't deny that he was a handsome fellow, with a smooth, white skin; apart from that, however, little wit, little philosophical training; it was evident that he had not been brought up by Doctor Pangloss. After three months, he had lost all his money and grown sick of me; so he sold me to a Jew named Don Issachar, who traded in Holland and Portugal, and who was mad after women. This Jew developed a mighty passion for my person, but he got nowhere with it; I held him off better than I had done with the Bulgar soldier; for though a person of honor may be raped once, her virtue is only strengthened by the experience. In order to keep me hidden, the Jew brought me to his country house, which you see here. Till then I had thought there was nothing on earth so beautiful as the castle of Thunder-Ten-Tronckh; I was now undeceived.

—One day the Grand Inquisitor took notice of me at mass; he ogled me a good deal, and made known that he must talk to me on a matter of secret business. I was taken to his palace; I told him of my rank; he pointed out that it was beneath my dignity to belong to an Israelite. A suggestion was then conveyed to Don Issachar that he should turn me over to My Lord the Inquisitor. Don Issachar, who is court banker and a man of standing, refused out of hand. The inquisitor threatened him with an auto-da-fé. Finally my Jew, fearing for his life, struck a bargain by which the house and I would belong to both of them as joint tenants; the Jew would get Mondays, Wednesdays, and the Sabbath, the inquisitor would get the other days of the week. That has been the arrangement for six months now. There have been quarrels; sometimes it has not been clear whether the night from Saturday to Sunday belonged to the old or the new dispensation. For my part, I have so far been able to hold both of them off; and that, I think, is why they are both still in love with me.

—Finally, in order to avert further divine punishment by earthquake, and to terrify Don Issachar, My Lord the Inquisitor chose to celebrate an auto-da-fé. He did me the honor of inviting me to attend. I had an excellent seat; the ladies were served with refreshments between the mass and the execution. To tell you the truth, I was horrified to see them burn alive those two Jews and that decent Biscayan who had married his child's godmother; but what was my surprise, my terror, my grief, when I saw, huddled in a *san-benito* and wearing a mitre, someone who looked like Pangloss! I rubbed my eyes, I watched his every move, I saw him hanged;

and I fell back in a swoon. Scarcely had I come to my senses again, when I saw you stripped for the lash; that was the peak of my horror, consternation, grief, and despair. I may tell you, by the way, that your skin is even whiter and more delicate than that of my Bulgar captain. Seeing you, then, redoubled the torments which were already overwhelming me. I shrieked aloud, I wanted to call out, 'Let him go, you brutes!' but my voice died within me, and my cries would have been useless. When you had been thoroughly thrashed: 'How can it be,' I asked myself, 'that agreeable Candide and wise Pangloss have come to Lisbon, one to receive a hundred whiplashes, the other to be hanged by order of My Lord the Inquisitor, whose mistress I am? Pangloss must have deceived me cruelly when he told me that all is for the best in this world.'

—Frantic, exhausted, half out of my senses, and ready to die of weakness, I felt as if my mind were choked with the massacre of my father, my mother, my brother, with the arrogance of that ugly Bulgar soldier, with the knife slash he inflicted on me, my slavery, my cookery, my Bulgar captain, my nasty Don Issachar, my abominable inquisitor, with the hanging of Doctor Pangloss, with that great plainsong *miserere* which they sang while they flogged you—and above all, my mind was full of the kiss which I gave you behind the screen, on the day I saw you for the last time. I praised God, who had brought you back to me after so many trials. I asked my old woman to look out for you, and to bring you here as soon as she could. She did just as I asked; I have had the indescribable joy of seeing you again, hearing you and talking with you once more. But you must be frightfully hungry; I am, myself; let us begin with a dinner.

So then and there they sat down to table; and after dinner, they adjourned to that fine brocaded sofa, which has already been mentioned; and there they were when the eminent Don Issachar, one of the masters of the house, appeared. It was the day of the Sabbath; he was arriving to assert his rights and express his tender passion.

CHAPTER 9

What Happened to Cunégonde, Candide, the Grand Inquisitor, and a Jew

This Issachar was the most choleric Hebrew seen in Israel since the Babylonian captivity.

—What's this, says he, you bitch of a Christian, you're not satisfied with the Grand Inquisitor? Do I have to share you with this rascal, too?

So saying, he drew a long dagger, with which he always went armed, and, supposing his opponent defenceless, flung himself on Candide. But our good Westphalian had received from the old woman, along with his suit of clothes, a fine sword. Out it came, and though his manners were of the gentlest, in short order he laid the Israelite stiff and cold on the floor, at the feet of the lovely Cunégonde.

—Holy Virgin! she cried. What will become of me now? A man killed in my house! If the police find out, we're done for.

—If Pangloss had not been hanged, said Candide, he would give us good advice in this hour of need, for he was a great philosopher. Lacking him, let's ask the old woman.

She was a sensible body, and was just starting to give her opinion of the situation, when another little door opened. It was just one o'clock in the morning, Sunday morning. This day belonged to the inquisitor. In he came, and found the whipped Candide with a sword in his hand, a corpse at his feet, Cunégonde in terror, and an old woman giving them both good advice.

Here now is what passed through Candide's mind in this instant of time; this is how he reasoned: —If this holy man calls for help, he will certainly have me burned, and perhaps Cunégonde as well; he has already had me whipped without mercy; he is my rival; I have already killed once; why hesitate?

It was a quick, clear chain of reasoning; without giving the inquisitor time to recover from his surprise, he ran him through, and laid him beside the Jew.

—Here you've done it again, said Cunégonde; there's no hope for us now. We'll be excommunicated, our last hour has come. How is it that you, who were born so gentle, could kill in two minutes a Jew and a prelate?

—My dear girl, replied Candide, when a man is in love, jealous, and just whipped by the Inquisition, he is no longer himself.

The old woman now spoke up and said:—There are three Andalusian steeds in the stable, with their saddles and bridles; our brave Candide must get them ready: my lady has some gold coin and diamonds; let's take to horse at once, though I can only ride on one buttock; we will go to Cadiz. The weather is as fine as can be, and it is pleasant to travel in the cool of the evening.

Promptly, Candide saddled the three horses. Cunégonde, the old woman, and he covered thirty miles without a stop. While they were fleeing, the Holy Brotherhood[5] came to investigate the house; they buried the inquisitor in a fine church, and threw Issachar on the dunghill.

Candide, Cunégonde, and the old woman were already in the little town of Avacena, in the middle of the Sierra Morena; and there, as they sat in a country inn, they had this conversation.

CHAPTER 10

In Deep Distress, Candide, Cunégonde, and the Old Woman Reach Cadiz; They Put to Sea

—Who then could have robbed me of my gold and diamonds? said Cunégonde, in tears. How shall we live? what shall we do? where shall I find other inquisitors and Jews to give me some more?

—Ah, said the old woman, I strongly suspect that reverend Franciscan friar who shared the inn with us yesterday at Badajoz. God save me from judging him unfairly! But he came into our room twice, and he left long before us.

5. A semireligious order with police powers, very active in eighteenth-century Spain.

—Alas, said Candide, the good Pangloss often proved to me that the fruits of the earth are a common heritage of all, to which each man has equal right. On these principles, the Franciscan should at least have left us enough to finish our journey. You have nothing at all, my dear Cunégonde?

—Not a maravedi, said she.

—What to do? said Candide.

—We'll sell one of the horses, said the old woman; I'll ride on the croup behind my mistress, though only on one buttock, and so we will get to Cadiz.

There was in the same inn a Benedictine prior; he bought the horse cheap. Candide, Cunégonde, and the old woman passed through Lucena, Chillas, and Lebrixa, and finally reached Cadiz. There a fleet was being fitted out and an army assembled, to reason with the Jesuit fathers in Paraguay, who were accused of fomenting among their flock a revolt against the kings of Spain and Portugal near the town of St. Sacrement.[6] Candide, having served in the Bulgar army, performed the Bulgar manual of arms before the general of the little army with such grace, swiftness, dexterity, fire, and agility, that they gave him a company of infantry to command. So here he is, a captain; and off he sails with Miss Cunégonde, the old woman, two valets, and the two Andalusian steeds which had belonged to My Lord the Grand Inquisitor of Portugal.

Throughout the crossing, they spent a great deal of time reasoning about the philosophy of poor Pangloss.

—We are destined, in the end, for another universe, said Candide; no doubt that is the one where everything is well. For in this one, it must be admitted, there is some reason to grieve over our physical and moral state.

—I love you with all my heart, said Cunégonde; but my soul is still harrowed by thoughts of what I have seen and suffered.

—All will be well, replied Candide; the sea of this new world is already better than those of Europe, calmer and with steadier winds. Surely it is the New World which is the best of all possible worlds.

—God grant it, said Cunégonde; but I have been so horribly unhappy in the world so far, that my heart is almost dead to hope.

—You pity yourselves, the old woman told them; but you have had no such misfortunes as mine.

Cunégonde nearly broke out laughing; she found the old woman comic in pretending to be more unhappy than she.

—Ah, you poor old thing, said she, unless you've been raped by two Bulgars, been stabbed twice in the belly, seen two of your castles destroyed, witnessed the murder of two of your mothers and two of your fathers, and watched two of your lovers being whipped in an auto-da-fé, I do not see how you can have had it worse than me. Besides, I was born a baroness, with seventy-two quarterings, and I have worked in a scullery.

—My lady, replied the old woman, you do not know my birth and rank;

6. Actually, Colonia del Sacramento. Voltaire took great interest in the Jesuit role in Paraguay, which he has much oversimplified and largely misrepresented here in the interests of his satire. In 1750 they did, however, offer armed resistance to an agreement made between Spain and Portugal. They were subdued and expelled in 1769.

and if I showed you my rear end, you would not talk as you do, you might even speak with less assurance.

These words inspired great curiosity in Candide and Cunégonde, which the old woman satisfied with this story.

CHAPTER 11

The Old Woman's Story

—My eyes were not always bloodshot and red-rimmed, my nose did not always touch my chin, and I was not born a servant. I am in fact the daughter of Pope Urban the Tenth and the Princess of Palestrina.[7] Till the age of fourteen, I lived in a palace so splendid that all the castles of all your German barons would not have served it as a stable; a single one of my dresses was worth more than all the assembled magnificence of Westphalia. I grew in beauty, in charm, in talent, surrounded by pleasures, dignities, and glowing visions of the future. Already I was inspiring the young men to love; my breast was formed—and what a breast! white, firm, with the shape of the Venus de Medici; and what eyes! what lashes, what black brows! What fire flashed from my glances and outshone the glitter of the stars, as the local poets used to tell me! The women who helped me dress and undress fell into ecstasies, whether they looked at me from in front or behind; and all the men wanted to be in their place.

—I was engaged to the ruling prince of Massa-Carrara; and what a prince he was! as handsome as I, softness and charm compounded, brilliantly witty, and madly in love with me. I loved him in return as one loves for the first time, with a devotion approaching idolatry. The wedding preparations had been made, with a splendor and magnificence never heard of before; nothing but celebrations, masks, and comic operas, uninterruptedly; and all Italy composed in my honor sonnets of which not one was even passable. I had almost attained the very peak of bliss, when an old marquise who had been the mistress of my prince invited him to her house for a cup of chocolate. He died in less than two hours, amid horrifying convulsions. But that was only a trifle. My mother, in complete despair (though less afflicted than I), wished to escape for a while the oppressive atmosphere of grief. She owned a handsome property near Gaeta.[8] We embarked on a papal galley gilded like the altar of St. Peter's in Rome. Suddenly a pirate ship from Salé swept down and boarded us. Our soldiers defended themselves as papal troops usually do; falling on their knees and throwing down their arms, they begged of the corsair absolution *in articulo mortis.*[9]

—They were promptly stripped as naked as monkeys, and so was my mother, and so were our maids of honor, and so was I too. It's a very remarkable thing, the energy these gentlemen put into stripping people. But what surprised me even more was that they stuck their fingers in a

---

7. Voltaire left behind a comment on this passage, a note first published in 1829: "Note the extreme discretion of the author; hitherto there has never been a pope named Urban X; he avoided attributing a bastard to a known pope. What circumspection! what an exquisite conscience!"   8. About halfway between Rome and Naples.   9. Literally, when at the point of death. Absolution from a corsair in the act of murdering one is of very dubious validity.

place where we women usually admit only a syringe. This ceremony seemed a bit odd to me, as foreign usages always do when one hasn't traveled. They only wanted to see if we didn't have some diamonds hidden there; and I soon learned that it's a custom of long standing among the genteel folk who swarm the seas. I learned that my lords the very religious knights of Malta never overlook this ceremony when they capture Turks, whether male or female; it's one of those international laws which have never been questioned.

—I won't try to explain how painful it is for a young princess to be carried off into slavery in Morocco with her mother. You can imagine everything we had to suffer on the pirate ship. My mother was still very beautiful; our maids of honor, our mere chambermaids, were more charming than anything one could find in all Africa. As for myself, I was ravishing, I was loveliness and grace supreme, and I was a virgin. I did not remain so for long; the flower which had been kept for the handsome prince of Massa-Carrara was plucked by the corsair captain; he was an abominable negro, who thought he was doing me a great favor. My Lady the Princess of Palestrina and I must have been strong indeed to bear what we did during our journey to Morocco. But on with my story; these are such common matters that they are not worth describing.

—Morocco was knee deep in blood when we arrived. Of the fifty sons of the emperor Muley-Ismael,[1] each had his faction, which produced in effect fifty civil wars, of blacks against blacks, of blacks against browns, halfbreeds against halfbreeds; throughout the length and breadth of the empire, nothing but one continual carnage.

—Scarcely had we stepped ashore, when some negroes of a faction hostile to my captor arrived to take charge of his plunder. After the diamonds and gold, we women were the most prized possessions. I was now witness of a struggle such as you never see in the temperate climate of Europe. Northern people don't have hot blood; they don't feel the absolute fury for women which is common in Africa. Europeans seem to have milk in their veins; it is vitriol or liquid fire which pulses through these people around Mount Atlas. The fight for possession of us raged with the fury of the lions, tigers, and poisonous vipers of that land. A Moor snatched my mother by the right arm, the first mate held her by the left; a Moorish soldier grabbed one leg, one of our pirates the other. In a moment's time almost all our girls were being dragged four different ways. My captain held me behind him while with his scimitar he killed everyone who braved his fury. At last I saw all our Italian women, including my mother, torn to pieces, cut to bits, murdered by the monsters who were fighting over them. My captive companions, their captors, soldiers, sailors, blacks, browns, whites, mulattoes, and at last my captain, all were killed, and I remained half dead on a mountain of corpses. Similar scenes were occurring, as is well known, for more than three hundred leagues around, without anyone skimping on the five prayers a day decreed by Mohammed.

---

1. Having reigned for more than fifty years, a potent and ruthless sultan of Morocco, he died in 1727 and left his kingdom in much the condition described.

—With great pain, I untangled myself from this vast heap of bleeding bodies, and dragged myself under a great orange tree by a neighboring brook, where I collapsed, from terror, exhaustion, horror, despair, and hunger. Shortly, my weary mind surrendered to a sleep which was more of a swoon than a rest. I was in this state of weakness and languor, between life and death, when I felt myself touched by something which moved over my body. Opening my eyes, I saw a white man, rather attractive, who was groaning and saying under his breath: '*O che sciagura d'essere senza coglioni!*'[2]

CHAPTER 12

The Old Woman's Story Continued

—Amazed and delighted to hear my native tongue, and no less surprised by what this man was saying, I told him that there were worse evils than those he was complaining of. In a few words, I described to him the horrors I had undergone, and then fainted again. He carried me to a nearby house, put me to bed, gave me something to eat, served me, flattered me, comforted me, told me he had never seen anyone so lovely, and added that he had never before regretted so much the loss of what nobody could give him back.

'I was born at Naples, he told me, where they caponize two or three thousand children every year; some die of it, others acquire a voice more beautiful than any woman's, still others go on to become governors of kingdoms.[3] The operation was a great success with me, and I became court musician to the Princess of Palestrina . . .'

'Of my mother,' I exclaimed.

'Of your mother,' cried he, bursting into tears; 'then you must be the princess whom I raised till she was six, and who already gave promise of becoming as beautiful as you are now!'

'I am that very princess; my mother lies dead, not a hundred yards from here, buried under a pile of corpses.'

—I told him my adventures, he told me his: that he had been sent by a Christian power to the King of Morocco, to conclude a treaty granting him gunpowder, cannon, and ships with which to liquidate the traders of the other Christian powers.

'My mission is concluded,' said this honest eunuch; 'I shall take ship at Ceuta and bring you back to Italy. *Ma che sciagura d'essere senza coglioni!*'

—I thanked him with tears of gratitude, and instead of returning me to Italy, he took me to Algiers and sold me to the dey of that country. Hardly had the sale taken place, when that plague which has made the rounds of Africa, Asia, and Europe broke out in full fury at Algiers. You have seen earthquakes; but tell me, young lady, have you ever had the plague?

—Never, replied the baroness.

—If you had had it, said the old woman, you would agree that it is far worse than an earthquake. It is very frequent in Africa, and I had it. Imag-

---

2. "Oh what a misfortune to have no testicles!"   3. The castrato Farinelli (1705–1782), originally a singer, came to exercise considerable political influence on the kings of Spain, Philip V and Ferdinand VI.

ine, if you will, the situation of a pope's daughter, fifteen years old, who in three months' time had experienced poverty, slavery, had been raped almost every day, had seen her mother quartered, had suffered from famine and war, and who now was dying of pestilence in Algiers. As a matter of fact, I did not die; but the eunuch and the dey and nearly the entire seraglio of Algiers perished.

—When the first horrors of this ghastly plague had passed, the slaves of the dey were sold. A merchant bought me and took me to Tunis; there he sold me to another merchant, who resold me at Tripoli; from Tripoli I was sold to Alexandria, from Alexandria resold to Smyrna, from Smyrna to Constantinople. I ended by belonging to an aga of janizaries, who was shortly ordered to defend Azov against the besieging Russians.[4]

—The aga, who was a gallant soldier, took his whole seraglio with him, and established us in a little fort amid the Maeotian marshes,[5] guarded by two black eunuchs and twenty soldiers. Our side killed a prodigious number of Russians, but they paid us back nicely. Azov was put to fire and sword without respect for age or sex; only our little fort continued to resist, and the enemy determined to starve us out. The twenty janizaries had sworn never to surrender. Reduced to the last extremities of hunger, they were forced to eat our two eunuchs, lest they violate their oaths. After several more days, they decided to eat the women too.

—We had an imam,[6] very pious and sympathetic, who delivered an excellent sermon, persuading them not to kill us altogether.

'Just cut off a single rumpsteak from each of these ladies,' he said, 'and you'll have a fine meal. Then if you should need another, you can come back in a few days and have as much again; heaven will bless your charitable action, and you will be saved.'

—His eloquence was splendid, and he persuaded them. We underwent this horrible operation. The imam treated us all with the ointment that they use on newly circumcised children. We were at the point of death.

—Scarcely had the janizaries finished the meal for which we furnished the materials, when the Russians appeared in flat-bottomed boats; not a janizary escaped. The Russians paid no attention to the state we were in; but there are French physicians everywhere, and one of them, who knew his trade, took care of us. He cured us, and I shall remember all my life that when my wounds were healed, he made me a proposition. For the rest, he counselled us simply to have patience, assuring us that the same thing had happened in several other sieges, and that it was according to the laws of war.

—As soon as my companions could walk, we were herded off to Moscow. In the division of booty, I fell to a boyar who made me work in his garden, and gave me twenty whiplashes a day; but when he was broken on the wheel after about two years, with thirty other boyars, over some little court intrigue,[7] I seized the occasion; I ran away; I crossed all Russia;

---

4. Azov, near the mouth of the Don, was besieged by the Russians under Peter the Great in 1695–96. *Janizaries:* an elite corps of the Ottoman armies.   5. The Roman name of the so-called Sea of Azov, a shallow swampy lake near the town.   6. In effect, a chaplain.   7. Voltaire had in mind an ineffectual conspiracy against Peter the Great known as the "revolt of the streltsy" or musketeers, which took place in 1698. Though easily put down, it provoked from the emperor a massive and atrocious program of reprisals.

I was for a long time a chambermaid in Riga, then at Rostock, Vismara, Leipzig, Cassel, Utrecht, Leyden, The Hague, Rotterdam; I grew old in misery and shame, having only half a backside and remembering always that I was the daughter of a Pope; a hundred times I wanted to kill myself, but always I loved life more. This ridiculous weakness is perhaps one of our worst instincts; is anything more stupid than choosing to carry a burden that really one wants to cast on the ground? to hold existence in horror, and yet to cling to it? to fondle the serpent which devours us till it has eaten out our heart?

—In the countries through which I have been forced to wander, in the taverns where I have had to work, I have seen a vast number of people who hated their existence; but I never saw more than a dozen who deliberately put an end to their own misery: three negroes, four Englishmen, four Genevans, and a German professor named Robeck.[8] My last post was as servant to the Jew Don Issachar; he attached me to your service, my lovely one; and I attached myself to your destiny, till I have become more concerned with your fate than with my own. I would not even have mentioned my own misfortunes, if you had not irked me a bit, and if it weren't the custom, on shipboard, to pass the time with stories. In a word, my lady, I have had some experience of the world, I know it; why not try this diversion? Ask every passenger on this ship to tell you his story, and if you find a single one who has not often cursed the day of his birth, who has not often told himself that he is the most miserable of men, then you may throw me overboard head first.

CHAPTER 13

How Candide Was Forced to Leave the Lovely Cunégonde and the Old Woman

Having heard out the old woman's story, the lovely Cunégonde paid her the respects which were appropriate to a person of her rank and merit. She took up the wager as well, and got all the passengers, one after another, to tell her their adventures. She and Candide had to agree that the old woman had been right.

—It's certainly too bad, said Candide, that the wise Pangloss was hanged, contrary to the custom of autos-da-fé; he would have admirable things to say of the physical evil and moral evil which cover land and sea, and I might feel within me the impulse to dare to raise several polite objections.

As the passengers recited their stories, the boat made steady progress, and presently landed at Buenos Aires. Cunégonde, Captain Candide, and the old woman went to call on the governor, Don Fernando d'Ibaraa y Figueroa y Mascarenes y Lampourdos y Souza. This nobleman had the pride appropriate to a man with so many names. He addressed everyone with the most aristocratic disdain, pointing his nose so loftily, raising his voice so mercilessly, lording it so splendidly, and assuming so arrogant a pose, that everyone who met him wanted to kick him. He loved women

---

8. Johann Robeck (1672–1739) published a treatise advocating suicide and showed his conviction by drowning himself at the age of sixty-seven.

to the point of fury; and Cunégonde seemed to him the most beautiful creature he had ever seen. The first thing he did was to ask directly if she were the captain's wife. His manner of asking this question disturbed Candide; he did not dare say she was his wife, because in fact she was not; he did not dare say she was his sister, because she wasn't that either; and though this polite lie was once common enough among the ancients,[9] and sometimes serves moderns very well, he was too pure of heart to tell a lie.

—Miss Cunégonde, said he, is betrothed to me, and we humbly beg your excellency to perform the ceremony for us.

Don Fernando d'Ibaraa y Figueroa y Mascarenes y Lampourdos y Souza twirled his moustache, smiled sardonically, and ordered Captain Candide to go drill his company. Candide obeyed. Left alone with My Lady Cunégonde, the governor declared his passion, and protested that he would marry her tomorrow, in church or in any other manner, as it pleased her charming self. Cunégonde asked for a quarter-hour to collect herself, consult the old woman, and make up her mind.

The old woman said to Cunégonde: —My lady, you have seventy-two quarterings and not one penny; if you wish, you may be the wife of the greatest lord in South America, who has a really handsome moustache; are you going to insist on your absolute fidelity? You have already been raped by the Bulgars; a Jew and an inquisitor have enjoyed your favors; miseries entitle one to privileges. I assure you that in your position I would make no scruple of marrying My Lord the Governor, and making the fortune of Captain Candide.

While the old woman was talking with all the prudence of age and experience, there came into the harbor a small ship bearing an alcalde and some alguazils.[1] This is what had happened.

As the old woman had very shrewdly guessed, it was a long-sleeved Franciscan who stole Cunégonde's gold and jewels in the town of Badajoz, when she and Candide were in flight. The monk tried to sell some of the gems to a jeweler, who recognized them as belonging to the Grand Inquisitor. Before he was hanged, the Franciscan confessed that he had stolen them, indicating who his victims were and where they were going. The flight of Cunégonde and Candide was already known. They were traced to Cadiz, and a vessel was hastily dispatched in pursuit of them. This vessel was now in the port of Buenos Aires. The rumor spread that an alcalde was aboard, in pursuit of the murderers of My Lord the Grand Inquisitor. The shrewd old woman saw at once what was to be done.

—You cannot escape, she told Cunégonde, and you have nothing to fear. You are not the one who killed my lord, and, besides, the governor, who is in love with you, won't let you be mistreated. Sit tight.

And then she ran straight to Candide: —Get out of town, she said, or you'll be burned within the hour.

There was not a moment to lose; but how to leave Cunégonde, and where to go?

9. Voltaire has in mind Abraham's adventures with Sarah (Genesis 12) and Isaac's with Rebecca (Genesis 26).   1. Police officers.

CHAPTER 14

How Candide and Cacambo Were Received by the Jesuits of Paraguay

Candide had brought from Cadiz a valet of the type one often finds in the provinces of Spain and in the colonies. He was one quarter Spanish, son of a halfbreed in the Tucuman;[2] he had been choirboy, sacristan, sailor, monk, merchant, soldier, and lackey. His name was Cacambo, and he was very fond of his master because his master was a very good man. In hot haste he saddled the two Andalusian steeds.

—Hurry, master, do as the old woman says; let's get going and leave this town without a backward look.

Candide wept: —O my beloved Cunégonde! must I leave you now, just when the governor is about to marry us! Cunégonde, brought from so far, what will ever become of you?

—She'll become what she can, said Cacambo; women can always find something to do with themselves; God sees to it; let's get going.

—Where are you taking me? where are we going? what will we do without Cunégonde? said Candide.

—By Saint James of Compostela, said Cacambo, you were going to make war against the Jesuits, now we'll go make war for them. I know the roads pretty well, I'll bring you to their country, they will be delighted to have a captain who knows the Bulgar drill; you'll make a prodigious fortune. If you don't get your rights in one world, you will find them in another. And isn't it pleasant to see new things and do new things?

—Then you've already been in Paraguay? said Candide.

—Indeed I have, replied Cacambo; I was cook in the College of the Assumption, and I know the government of Los Padres[3] as I know the streets of Cadiz. It's an admirable thing, this government. The kingdom is more than three hundred leagues across; it is divided into thirty provinces. Los Padres own everything in it, and the people nothing; it's a masterpiece of reason and justice. I myself know nothing so wonderful as Los Padres, who in this hemisphere make war on the kings of Spain and Portugal, but in Europe hear their confessions; who kill Spaniards here, and in Madrid send them to heaven; that really tickles me; let's get moving, you're going to be the happiest of men. Won't Los Padres be delighted when they learn they have a captain who knows the Bulgar drill!

As soon as they reached the first barricade, Cacambo told the frontier guard that a captain wished to speak with My Lord the Commander. A Paraguayan officer ran to inform headquarters by laying the news at the feet of the commander. Candide and Cacambo were first disarmed and deprived of their Andalusian horses. They were then placed between two files of soldiers; the commander was at the end, his three-cornered hat on his head, his cassock drawn up, a sword at his side, and a pike in his hand. He nods, and twenty-four soldiers surround the newcomers. A sergeant then informs them that they must wait, that the commander cannot talk to them, since the reverend father provincial has forbidden all Spaniards

---

2. A province of Argentina, to the northwest of Buenos Aires.   3. The Jesuit fathers.

from speaking, except in his presence, and from remaining more than three hours in the country.

—And where is the reverend father provincial? says Cacambo.

—He is reviewing his troops after having said mass, the sergeant replies, and you'll only be able to kiss his spurs in three hours.

—But, says Cacambo, my master the captain, who, like me, is dying from hunger, is not Spanish at all, he is German; can't we have some breakfast while waiting for his reverence?

The sergeant promptly went off to report this speech to the commander.

—God be praised, said this worthy; since he is German, I can talk to him; bring him into my bower.

Candide was immediately led into a leafy nook surrounded by a handsome colonnade of green and gold marble and trellises amid which sported parrots, birds of paradise,[4] hummingbirds, guinea fowl, and all the rarest species of birds. An excellent breakfast was prepared in golden vessels; and while the Paraguayans ate corn out of wooden bowls in the open fields under the glare of the sun, the reverend father commander entered into his bower.

He was a very handsome young man, with an open face, rather blonde in coloring, with ruddy complexion, arched eyebrows, liquid eyes, pink ears, bright red lips, and an air of pride, but a pride somehow different from that of a Spaniard or a Jesuit. Their confiscated weapons were restored to Candide and Cacambo, as well as their Andalusian horses; Cacambo fed them oats alongside the bower, always keeping an eye on them for fear of an ambush.

First Candide kissed the hem of the commander's cassock, then they sat down at the table.

—So you are German? said the Jesuit, speaking in that language.

—Yes, your reverence, said Candide.

As they spoke these words, both men looked at one another with great surprise, and another emotion which they could not control.

—From what part of Germany do you come? said the Jesuit.

—From the nasty province of Westphalia, said Candide; I was born in the castle of Thunder-Ten-Tronckh.

—Merciful heavens! cries the commander. Is it possible?

—What a miracle! exclaims Candide.

—Can it be you? asks the commander.

—It's impossible, says Candide.

They both fall back in their chairs, they embrace, they shed streams of tears.

—What, can it be you, reverend father! you, the brother of the lovely Cunégonde! you, who were killed by the Bulgars! you, the son of My Lord the Baron! you, a Jesuit in Paraguay! It's a mad world, indeed it is. Oh, Pangloss! Pangloss! how happy you would be, if you hadn't been hanged.

---

4. In this passage and several later ones, Voltaire uses in conjunction two words, both of which mean hummingbird. The French system of classifying hummingbirds, based on the work of the celebrated Buffon, distinguishes *oiseaux-mouches* with straight bills from *colibris* with curved bills. This distinction is wholly fallacious. Hummingbirds have all manner of shaped bills, and the division of species must be made on other grounds entirely. At the expense of ornithological accuracy, I have therefore introduced birds of paradise to get the requisite sense of glitter and sheen.

The commander dismissed his negro slaves and the Paraguayans who served his drink in crystal goblets. He thanked God and Saint Ignatius a thousand times, he clasped Candide in his arms, their faces were bathed in tears.

—You would be even more astonished, even more delighted, even more beside yourself, said Candide, if I told you that My Lady Cunégonde, your sister, who you thought was disemboweled, is enjoying good health.

—Where?

—Not far from here, in the house of the governor of Buenos Aires; and to think that I came to make war on you!

Each word they spoke in this long conversation added another miracle. Their souls danced on their tongues, hung eagerly at their ears, glittered in their eyes. As they were Germans, they sat a long time at table, waiting for the reverend father provincial; and the commander spoke in these terms to his dear Candide.

CHAPTER 15

How Candide Killed the Brother of His Dear Cunégonde

—All my life long I shall remember the horrible day when I saw my father and mother murdered and my sister raped. When the Bulgars left, that adorable sister of mine was nowhere to be found; so they loaded a cart with my mother, my father, myself, two serving girls, and three little murdered boys, to carry us all off for burial in a Jesuit chapel some two leagues from our ancestral castle. A Jesuit sprinkled us with holy water; it was horribly salty, and a few drops got into my eyes; the father noticed that my lid made a little tremor; putting his hand on my heart, he felt it beat; I was rescued, and at the end of three weeks was as good as new. You know, my dear Candide, that I was a very pretty boy; I became even more so; the reverend father Croust,[5] superior of the abbey, conceived a most tender friendship for me; he accepted me as a novice, and shortly after, I was sent to Rome. The Father General had need of a resupply of young German Jesuits. The rulers of Paraguay accept as few Spanish Jesuits as they can; they prefer foreigners, whom they think they can control better. I was judged fit, by the Father General, to labor in this vineyard. So we set off, a Pole, a Tyrolean, and myself. Upon our arrival, I was honored with the posts of subdeacon and lieutenant; today I am a colonel and a priest. We are giving a vigorous reception to the King of Spain's men; I assure you they will be excommunicated as well as trounced on the battlefield. Providence has sent you to help us. But is it really true that my dear sister, Cunégonde, is in the neighborhood, with the governor of Buenos Aires?

Candide reassured him with a solemn oath that nothing could be more true. Their tears began to flow again.

The baron could not weary of embracing Candide; he called him his brother, his savior.

---

5. A Jesuit rector at Colmar with whom Voltaire had quarreled in 1754.

—Ah, my dear Candide, said he, maybe together we will be able to enter the town as conquerors, and be united with my sister Cunégonde.

—That is all I desire, said Candide; I was expecting to marry her, and I still hope to.

—You insolent dog, replied the baron, you would have the effrontery to marry my sister, who has seventy-two quarterings! It's a piece of presumption for you even to mention such a crazy project in my presence.

Candide, terrified by this speech, answered: —Most reverend father, all the quarterings in the world don't affect this case; I have rescued your sister out of the arms of a Jew and an inquisitor; she has many obligations to me, she wants to marry me. Master Pangloss always taught me that men are equal; and I shall certainly marry her.

—We'll see about that, you scoundrel, said the Jesuit baron of Thunder-Ten-Tronckh; and so saying, he gave him a blow across the face with the flat of his sword. Candide immediately drew his own sword and thrust it up to the hilt in the baron's belly; but as he drew it forth all dripping, he began to weep.

—Alas, dear God! said he, I have killed my old master, my friend, my brother-in-law; I am the best man in the world, and here are three men I've killed already, and two of the three were priests.

Cacambo, who was standing guard at the entry of the bower, came running.

—We can do nothing but sell our lives dearly, said his master; someone will certainly come; we must die fighting.

Cacambo, who had been in similar scrapes before, did not lose his head; he took the Jesuit's cassock, which the commander had been wearing, and put it on Candide; he stuck the dead man's square hat on Candide's head, and forced him onto horseback. Everything was done in the wink of an eye.

—Let's ride, master; everyone will take you for a Jesuit on his way to deliver orders; and we will have passed the frontier before anyone can come after us.

Even as he was pronouncing these words, he charged off, crying in Spanish: —Way, make way for the reverend father colonel!

CHAPTER 16

What Happened to the Two Travelers with Two Girls,
Two Monkeys, and the Savages Named Biglugs

Candide and his valet were over the frontier before anyone in the camp knew of the death of the German Jesuit. Foresighted Cacambo had taken care to fill his satchel with bread, chocolate, ham, fruit, and several bottles of wine. They pushed their Andalusian horses forward into unknown country, where there were no roads. Finally a broad prairie divided by several streams opened before them. Our two travelers turned their horses loose to graze; Cacambo suggested that they eat too, and promptly set the example. But Candide said: —How can you expect me to eat ham when I have killed the son of My Lord the Baron, and am now condemned never to see the lovely Cunégonde for the rest of my life? Why should I drag out my miserable days, since I must exist far from her in the depths of despair and remorse? And what will the *Journal de Trévoux*[6] say of all this?

Though he talked this way, he did not neglect the food. Night fell. The two wanderers heard a few weak cries which seemed to be voiced by women. They could not tell whether the cries expressed grief or joy; but they leaped at once to their feet, with that uneasy suspicion which one always feels in an unknown country. The outcry arose from two girls, completely naked, who were running swiftly along the edge of the meadow, pursued by two monkeys who snapped at their buttocks. Candide was moved to pity; he had learned marksmanship with the Bulgars, and could have knocked a nut off a bush without touching the leaves. He raised his Spanish rifle, fired twice, and killed the two monkeys.

—God be praised, my dear Cacambo! I've saved these two poor creatures from great danger. Though I committed a sin in killing an inquisitor and a Jesuit, I've redeemed myself by saving the lives of two girls. Perhaps they are two ladies of rank, and this good deed may gain us special advantages in the country.

He had more to say, but his mouth shut suddenly when he saw the girls embracing the monkeys tenderly, weeping over their bodies, and filling the air with lamentations.

—I wasn't looking for quite so much generosity of spirit, said he to Cacambo; the latter replied: —You've really fixed things this time, master; you've killed the two lovers of these young ladies.

—Their lovers! Impossible! You must be joking, Cacambo; how can I believe you?

—My dear master, Cacambo replied, you're always astonished by everything. Why do you think it so strange that in some countries monkeys succeed in obtaining the good graces of women? They are one quarter human, just as I am one quarter Spanish.

—Alas, Candide replied, I do remember now hearing Master Pangloss say that such things used to happen, and that from these mixtures there arose pans, fauns, and satyrs, and that these creatures had appeared to various grand figures of antiquity; but I took all that for fables.

—You should be convinced now, said Cacambo; it's true, and you see how people make mistakes who haven't received a measure of education. But what I fear is that these girls may get us into real trouble.

These sensible reflections led Candide to leave the field and to hide in a wood. There he dined with Cacambo; and there both of them, having duly cursed the inquisitor of Portugal, the governor of Buenos Aires, and the baron, went to sleep on a bed of moss. When they woke up, they found themselves unable to move; the reason was that during the night the Biglugs,[7] natives of the country, to whom the girls had complained of them, had tied them down with cords of bark. They were surrounded by

---

6. A newspaper published by the Jesuit order, founded in 1701 and consistently hostile to Voltaire.
7. Voltaire's name is "Oreillons" from Spanish "Orejones," a name mentioned in Garcilaso de Vega's *Historia General del Perú* (1609), on which Voltaire drew for many of the details in his picture of South America.

fifty naked Biglugs, armed with arrows, clubs, and stone axes. Some were boiling a caldron of water, others were preparing spits, and all cried out: — It's a Jesuit, a Jesuit! We'll be revenged and have a good meal; let's eat some Jesuit, eat some Jesuit!

—I told you, my dear master, said Cacambo sadly, I said those two girls would play us a dirty trick.

Candide, noting the caldron and spits, cried out: —We are surely going to be roasted or boiled. Ah, what would Master Pangloss say if he could see these men in a state of nature? All is for the best, I agree; but I must say it seems hard to have lost Miss Cunégonde and to be stuck on a spit by the Biglugs.

Cacambo did not lose his head.

—Don't give up hope, said he to the disconsolate Candide; I understand a little of the jargon these people speak, and I'm going to talk to them.

—Don't forget to remind them, said Candide, of the frightful inhumanity of eating their fellow men, and that Christian ethics forbid it.

—Gentlemen, said Cacambo, you have a mind to eat a Jesuit today? An excellent idea; nothing is more proper than to treat one's enemies so. Indeed, the law of nature teaches us to kill our neighbor, and that's how men behave the whole world over. Though we Europeans don't exercise our right to eat our neighbors, the reason is simply that we find it easy to get a good meal elsewhere; but you don't have our resources, and we certainly agree that it's better to eat your enemies than to let the crows and vultures have the fruit of your victory. But, gentlemen, you wouldn't want to eat your friends. You think you will be spitting a Jesuit, and it's your defender, the enemy of your enemies, whom you will be roasting. For my part, I was born in your country; the gentleman whom you see is my master, and far from being a Jesuit, he has just killed a Jesuit, the robe he is wearing was stripped from him; that's why you have taken a dislike to him. To prove that I am telling the truth, take his robe and bring it to the nearest frontier of the kingdom of Los Padres; find out for yourselves if my master didn't kill a Jesuit officer. It won't take long; if you find that I have lied, you can still eat us. But if I've told the truth, you know too well the principles of public justice, customs, and laws, not to spare our lives.

The Biglugs found this discourse perfectly reasonable; they appointed chiefs to go posthaste and find out the truth; the two messengers performed their task like men of sense, and quickly returned bringing good news. The Biglugs untied their two prisoners, treated them with great politeness, offered them girls, gave them refreshments, and led them back to the border of their state, crying joyously: —He isn't a Jesuit, he isn't a Jesuit!

Candide could not weary of exclaiming over his preservation.

—What a people! he said. What men! what customs! If I had not had the good luck to run a sword through the body of Miss Cunégonde's brother, I would have been eaten on the spot! But, after all, it seems that uncorrupted nature is good, since these folk, instead of eating me, showed me a thousand kindnesses as soon as they knew I was not a Jesuit.

CHAPTER 17

*Arrival of Candide and His Servant at the Country of Eldorado,
and What They Saw There*

When they were out of the land of the Biglugs, Cacambo said to Candide: —You see that this hemisphere is no better than the other; take my advice, and let's get back to Europe as soon as possible.

—How to get back, asked Candide, and where to go? If I go to my own land, the Bulgars and Abares are murdering everyone in sight; if I go to Portugal, they'll burn me alive; if we stay here, we risk being skewered any day. But how can I ever leave that part of the world where Miss Cunégonde lives?

—Let's go toward Cayenne, said Cacambo, we shall find some Frenchmen there, for they go all over the world; they can help us; perhaps God will take pity on us.

To get to Cayenne was not easy; they knew more or less which way to go, but mountains, rivers, cliffs, robbers, and savages obstructed the way everywhere. Their horses died of weariness; their food was eaten; they subsisted for one whole month on wild fruits, and at last they found themselves by a little river fringed with coconut trees, which gave them both life and hope.

Cacambo, who was as full of good advice as the old woman, said to Candide: —We can go no further, we've walked ourselves out; I see an abandoned canoe on the bank, let's fill it with coconuts, get into the boat, and float with the current; a river always leads to some inhabited spot or other. If we don't find anything pleasant, at least we may find something new.

—Let's go, said Candide, and let Providence be our guide.

They floated some leagues between banks sometimes flowery, sometimes sandy, now steep, now level. The river widened steadily; finally it disappeared into a chasm of frightful rocks that rose high into the heavens. The two travelers had the audacity to float with the current into this chasm. The river, narrowly confined, drove them onward with horrible speed and a fearful roar. After twenty-four hours, they saw daylight once more; but their canoe was smashed on the snags. They had to drag themselves from rock to rock for an entire league; at last they emerged to an immense horizon, ringed with remote mountains. The countryside was tended for pleasure as well as profit; everywhere the useful was joined to the agreeable. The roads were covered, or rather decorated, with elegantly shaped carriages made of a glittering material, carrying men and women of singular beauty, and drawn by great red sheep which were faster than the finest horses of Andalusia, Tetuan, and Mequinez.

—Here now, said Candide, is a country that's better than Westphalia.

Along with Cacambo, he climbed out of the river at the first village he could see. Some children of the town, dressed in rags of gold brocade, were playing quoits at the village gate; our two men from the other world paused to watch them; their quoits were rather large, yellow, red, and green, and they glittered with a singular luster. On a whim, the travelers picked up several; they were of gold, emeralds, and rubies, and the least of them would have been the greatest ornament of the Great Mogul's throne.

—Surely, said Cacambo, these quoit players are the children of the king of the country.

The village schoolmaster appeared at that moment, to call them back to school.

—And there, said Candide, is the tutor of the royal household.

The little rascals quickly gave up their game, leaving on the ground their quoits and playthings. Candide picked them up, ran to the school-master, and presented them to him humbly, giving him to understand by sign language that their royal highnesses had forgotten their gold and jewels. With a smile, the schoolmaster tossed them to the ground, glanced quickly but with great surprise at Candide's face, and went his way.

The travelers did not fail to pick up the gold, rubies, and emeralds.

—Where in the world are we? cried Candide. The children of this land must be well trained, since they are taught contempt for gold and jewels.

Cacambo was as much surprised as Candide. At last they came to the finest house of the village; it was built like a European palace. A crowd of people surrounded the door, and even more were in the entry; delightful music was heard, and a delicious aroma of cooking filled the air. Cacambo went up to the door, listened, and reported that they were talking Peruvian; that was his native language, for every reader must know that Cacambo was born in Tucuman, in a village where they talk that language exclusively.

—I'll act as interpreter, he told Candide; it's an hotel, let's go in.

Promptly two boys and two girls of the staff, dressed in cloth of gold, and wearing ribbons in their hair, invited them to sit at the host's table. The meal consisted of four soups, each one garnished with a brace of parakeets, a boiled condor which weighed two hundred pounds, two roast monkeys of an excellent flavor, three hundred birds of paradise in one dish and six hundred hummingbirds in another, exquisite stews, delicious pastries, the whole thing served up in plates of what looked like rock crystal. The boys and girls of the staff poured them various beverages made from sugar cane.

The diners were for the most part merchants and travelers, all extremely polite, who questioned Cacambo with the most discreet circumspection, and answered his questions very directly.

When the meal was over, Cacambo as well as Candide supposed he could settle his bill handsomely by tossing onto the table two of those big pieces of gold which they had picked up; but the host and hostess burst out laughing, and for a long time nearly split their sides. Finally they subsided.

—Gentlemen, said the host, we see clearly that you're foreigners; we don't meet many of you here. Please excuse our laughing when you offered us in payment a couple of pebbles from the roadside. No doubt you don't have any of our local currency, but you don't need it to eat here. All the hotels established for the promotion of commerce are maintained by the state. You have had meager entertainment here, for we are only a poor town; but everywhere else you will be given the sort of welcome you deserve.

Cacambo translated for Candide all the host's explanations, and Candide listened to them with the same admiration and astonishment that his friend Cacambo showed in reporting them.

—What is this country, then, said they to one another, unknown to the rest of the world, and where nature itself is so different from our own? This probably is the country where everything is for the best; for it's absolutely necessary that such a country should exist somewhere. And whatever Master Pangloss said of the matter, I have often had occasion to notice that things went badly in Westphalia.

CHAPTER 18

What They Saw in the Land of Eldorado

Cacambo revealed his curiosity to the host, and the host told him: —I am an ignorant man and content to remain so; but we have here an old man, retired from the court, who is the most knowing person in the kingdom, and the most talkative.

Thereupon he brought Cacambo to the old man's house. Candide now played second fiddle, and acted as servant to his own valet. They entered an austere little house, for the door was merely of silver and the paneling of the rooms was only gold, though so tastefully wrought that the finest paneling would not surpass it. If the truth must be told, the lobby was only decorated with rubies and emeralds; but the patterns in which they were arranged atoned for the extreme simplicity.

The old man received the two strangers on a sofa stuffed with bird-of-paradise feathers, and offered them several drinks in diamond carafes; then he satisfied their curiosity in these terms.

—I am a hundred and seventy-two years old, and I heard from my late father, who was liveryman to the king, about the astonishing revolutions in Peru which he had seen. Our land here was formerly part of the kingdom of the Incas, who rashly left it in order to conquer another part of the world, and who were ultimately destroyed by the Spaniards. The wisest princes of their house were those who had never left their native valley; they decreed, with the consent of the nation, that henceforth no inhabitant of our little kingdom should ever leave it; and this rule is what has preserved our innocence and our happiness. The Spaniards heard vague rumors about this land, they called it El Dorado;[8] and an English knight named Raleigh even came somewhere close to it about a hundred years ago; but as we are surrounded by unscalable mountains and precipices, we have managed so far to remain hidden from the rapacity of the European nations, who have an inconceivable rage for the pebbles and mud of our land, and who, in order to get some, would butcher us all to the last man.

8. The myth of this land of gold somewhere in Central or South America had been widespread since the sixteenth century. *The Discovery of Guiana*, published in 1595, described Sir Walter Ralegh's infatuation with the myth of Eldorado and served to spread the story still further.

The conversation was a long one; it turned on the form of the government, the national customs, on women, public shows, the arts. At last Candide, whose taste always ran to metaphysics, told Cacambo to ask if the country had any religion.

The old man grew a bit red.

—How's that? he said. Can you have any doubt of it? Do you suppose we are altogether thankless scoundrels?

Cacambo asked meekly what was the religion of Eldorado. The old man flushed again.

—Can there be two religions? he asked. I suppose our religion is the same as everyone's, we worship God from morning to evening.

—Then you worship a single deity? said Cacambo, who acted throughout as interpreter of the questions of Candide.

—It's obvious, said the old man, that there aren't two or three or four of them. I must say the people of your world ask very remarkable questions.

Candide could not weary of putting questions to this good old man; he wanted to know how the people of Eldorado prayed to God.

—We don't pray to him at all, said the good and respectable sage; we have nothing to ask him for, since everything we need has already been granted; we thank God continually.

Candide was interested in seeing the priests; he had Cacambo ask where they were. The old gentleman smiled.

—My friends, said he, we are all priests; the king and all the heads of household sing formal psalms of thanksgiving every morning, and five or six thousand voices accompany them.

—What! you have no monks to teach, argue, govern, intrigue, and burn at the stake everyone who disagrees with them?

—We should have to be mad, said the old man; here we are all of the same mind, and we don't understand what you're up to with your monks.

Candide was overjoyed at all these speeches, and said to himself: — This is very different from Westphalia and the castle of My Lord the Baron; if our friend Pangloss had seen Eldorado, he wouldn't have called the castle of Thunder-Ten-Tronckh the finest thing on earth; to know the world one must travel.

After this long conversation, the old gentleman ordered a carriage with six sheep made ready, and gave the two travelers twelve of his servants for their journey to the court.

—Excuse me, said he, if old age deprives me of the honor of accompanying you. The king will receive you after a style which will not altogether displease you, and you will doubtless make allowance for the customs of the country if there are any you do not like.

Candide and Cacambo climbed into the coach; the six sheep flew like the wind, and in less than four hours they reached the king's palace at the edge of the capital. The entryway was two hundred and twenty feet high and a hundred wide; it is impossible to describe all the materials of which it was made. But you can imagine how much finer it was than those pebbles and sand which we call gold and jewels.

Twenty beautiful girls of the guard detail welcomed Candide and Cacambo as they stepped from the carriage, took them to the baths, and dressed them in robes woven of hummingbird feathers; then the high officials of the crown, both male and female, led them to the royal chamber between two long lines, each of a thousand musicians, as is customary. As they approached the throne room, Cacambo asked an officer what was the proper method of greeting his majesty: if one fell to one's knees or on one's belly; if one put one's hands on one's head or on one's rear; if one licked up the dust of the earth—in a word, what was the proper form?[9]

—The ceremony, said the officer, is to embrace the king and kiss him on both cheeks.

Candide and Cacambo fell on the neck of his majesty, who received them with all the dignity imaginable, and asked them politely to dine.

In the interim, they were taken about to see the city, the public buildings rising to the clouds, the public markets and arcades, the fountains of pure water and of rose water, those of sugar cane liquors which flowed perpetually in the great plazas paved with a sort of stone which gave off odors of gillyflower and rose petals. Candide asked to see the supreme court and the hall of parliament; they told him there was no such thing, that lawsuits were unknown. He asked if there were prisons, and was told there were not. What surprised him more, and gave him most pleasure, was the palace of sciences, in which he saw a gallery two thousand paces long, entirely filled with mathematical and physical instruments.

Having passed the whole afternoon seeing only a thousandth part of the city, they returned to the king's palace. Candide sat down to dinner with his majesty, his own valet Cacambo, and several ladies. Never was better food served, and never did a host preside more jovially than his majesty. Cacambo explained the king's witty sayings to Candide, and even when translated they still seemed witty. Of all the things which astonished Candide, this was not, in his eyes, the least astonishing.

They passed a month in this refuge. Candide never tired of saying to Cacambo: —It's true, my friend, I'll say it again, the castle where I was born does not compare with the land where we now are; but Miss Cunégonde is not here, and you doubtless have a mistress somewhere in Europe. If we stay here, we shall be just like everybody else, whereas if we go back to our own world, taking with us just a dozen sheep loaded with Eldorado pebbles, we shall be richer than all the kings put together, we shall have no more inquisitors to fear, and we shall easily be able to retake Miss Cunégonde.

This harangue pleased Cacambo; wandering is such pleasure, it gives a man such prestige at home to be able to talk of what he has seen abroad, that the two happy men resolved to be so no longer, but to take their leave of his majesty.

—You are making a foolish mistake, the king told them; I know very well that my kingdom is nothing much; but when you are pretty comfortable somewhere, you had better stay there. Of course I have no right to keep strangers against their will, that sort of tyranny is not in keeping with

9. Candide's questions are probably derived from those of Gulliver on a similar occasion, in the third part of *Gulliver's Travels*.

our laws or our customs; all men are free; depart when you will, but the way out is very difficult. You cannot possibly go up the river by which you miraculously came; it runs too swiftly through its underground caves. The mountains which surround my land are ten thousand feet high, and steep as walls; each one is more than ten leagues across; the only way down is over precipices. But since you really must go, I shall order my engineers to make a machine which can carry you conveniently. When we take you over the mountains, nobody will be able to go with you, for my subjects have sworn never to leave their refuge, and they are too sensible to break their vows. Other than that, ask of me what you please.

—We only request of your majesty, Cacambo said, a few sheep loaded with provisions, some pebbles, and some of the mud of your country.

The king laughed.

—I simply can't understand, said he, the passion you Europeans have for our yellow mud; but take all you want, and much good may it do you.

He promptly gave orders to his technicians to make a machine for lifting these two extraordinary men out of his kingdom. Three thousand good physicists worked at the problem; the machine was ready in two weeks' time, and cost no more than twenty million pounds sterling, in the money of the country. Cacambo and Candide were placed in the machine; there were two great sheep, saddled and bridled to serve them as steeds when they had cleared the mountains, twenty pack sheep with provisions, thirty which carried presents consisting of the rarities of the country, and fifty loaded with gold, jewels, and diamonds. The king bade tender farewell to the two vagabonds.

It made a fine spectacle, their departure, and the ingenious way in which they were hoisted with their sheep up to the top of the mountains. The technicians bade them good-bye after bringing them to safety, and Candide had now no other desire and no other object than to go and present his sheep to Miss Cunégonde.

—We have, said he, enough to pay off the governor of Buenos Aires— if, indeed, a price can be placed on Miss Cunégonde. Let us go to Cayenne, take ship there, and then see what kingdom we can find to buy up.

CHAPTER 19

What Happened to Them at Surinam, and How Candide
Got to Know Martin

The first day was pleasant enough for our travelers. They were encouraged by the idea of possessing more treasures than Asia, Europe, and Africa could bring together. Candide, in transports, carved the name of Cunégonde on the trees. On the second day two of their sheep bogged down in a swamp and were lost with their loads; two other sheep died of fatigue a few days later; seven or eight others starved to death in a desert; still others fell, a little after, from precipices. Finally, after a hundred days' march, they had only two sheep left. Candide told Cacambo: —My friend, you see how the riches of this world are fleeting; the only solid things are virtue and the joy of seeing Miss Cunégonde again.

—I agree, said Cacambo, but we still have two sheep, laden with more treasure than the king of Spain will ever have; and I see in the distance a town which I suspect is Surinam; it belongs to the Dutch. We are at the end of our trials and on the threshold of our happiness.

As they drew near the town, they discovered a negro stretched on the ground with only half his clothes left, that is, a pair of blue drawers; the poor fellow was also missing his left leg and his right hand.

—Good Lord, said Candide in Dutch, what are you doing in that horrible condition, my friend?

—I am waiting for my master, Mr. Vanderdendur,[1] the famous merchant, answered the negro.

—Is Mr. Vanderdendur, Candide asked, the man who treated you this way?

—Yes, sir, said the negro, that's how things are around here. Twice a year we get a pair of linen drawers to wear. If we catch a finger in the sugar mill where we work, they cut off our hand; if we try to run away, they cut off our leg: I have undergone both these experiences. This is the price of the sugar you eat in Europe. And yet, when my mother sold me for ten Patagonian crowns on the coast of Guinea, she said to me: 'My dear child, bless our witch doctors, reverence them always, they will make your life happy; you have the honor of being a slave to our white masters, and in this way you are making the fortune of your father and mother.' Alas! I don't know if I made their fortunes, but they certainly did not make mine. The dogs, monkeys, and parrots are a thousand times less unhappy than we are. The Dutch witch doctors who converted me tell me every Sunday that we are all sons of Adam, black and white alike. I am no genealogist; but if these preachers are right, we must all be remote cousins; and you must admit no one could treat his own flesh and blood in a more horrible fashion.

—Oh Pangloss! cried Candide, you had no notion of these abominations! I'm through, I must give up your optimism after all.

—What's optimism? said Cacambo.

—Alas, said Candide, it is a mania for saying things are well when one is in hell.

And he shed bitter tears as he looked at this negro, and he was still weeping as he entered Surinam.

The first thing they asked was if there was not some vessel in port which could be sent to Buenos Aires. The man they asked was a Spanish merchant who undertook to make an honest bargain with them. They arranged to meet in a café; Candide and the faithful Cacambo, with their two sheep, went there to meet with him.

Candide, who always said exactly what was in his heart, told the Spaniard of his adventures, and confessed that he wanted to recapture Miss Cunégonde.

—I shall take good care *not* to send you to Buenos Aires, said the mer-

---

1. A name perhaps intended to suggest VanDuren, a Dutch bookseller with whom Voltaire had quarreled. In particular, the incident of gradually raising one's price recalls VanDuren, to whom Voltaire had successively offered 1,000, 1,500, 2,000, and 3,000 florins for the return of the manuscript of Frederick the Great's *Anti-Machiavel.*

chant; I should be hanged, and so would you. The lovely Cunégonde is his lordship's favorite mistress.

This was a thunderstroke for Candide; he wept for a long time; finally he drew Cacambo aside.

—Here, my friend, said he, is what you must do. Each one of us has in his pockets five or six millions' worth of diamonds; you are cleverer than I; go get Miss Cunégonde in Buenos Aires. If the governor makes a fuss, give him a million; if that doesn't convince him, give him two millions; you never killed an inquisitor, nobody will suspect you. I'll fit out another boat and go wait for you in Venice. That is a free country, where one need have no fear either of Bulgars or Abares or Jews or inquisitors.

Cacambo approved of this wise decision. He was in despair at leaving a good master who had become a bosom friend; but the pleasure of serving him overcame the grief of leaving him. They embraced, and shed a few tears; Candide urged him not to forget the good old woman. Cacambo departed that very same day; he was a very good fellow, that Cacambo.

Candide remained for some time in Surinam, waiting for another merchant to take him to Italy, along with the two sheep which were left him. He hired servants and bought everything necessary for the long voyage; finally Mr. Vanderdendur, master of a big ship, came calling.

—How much will you charge, Candide asked this man, to take me to Venice—myself, my servants, my luggage, and those two sheep over there?

The merchant set a price of ten thousand piastres; Candide did not blink an eye.

—Oh, ho, said the prudent Vanderdendur to himself, this stranger pays out ten thousand piastres at once, he must be pretty well fixed.

Then, returning a moment later, he made known that he could not set sail under twenty thousand.

—All right, you shall have them, said Candide.

—Whew, said the merchant softly to himself, this man gives twenty thousand piastres as easily as ten.

He came back again to say he could not go to Venice for less than thirty thousand piastres.

—All right, thirty then, said Candide.

—Ah ha, said the Dutch merchant, again speaking to himself; so thirty thousand piastres mean nothing to this man; no doubt the two sheep are loaded with immense treasures; let's say no more; we'll pick up the thirty thousand piastres first, and then we'll see.

Candide sold two little diamonds, the least of which was worth more than all the money demanded by the merchant. He paid him in advance. The two sheep were taken aboard. Candide followed in a little boat, to board the vessel at its anchorage. The merchant bides his time, sets sail, and makes his escape with a favoring wind. Candide, aghast and stupefied, soon loses him from view.

—Alas, he cries, now there is a trick worthy of the old world!

He returns to shore sunk in misery; for he had lost riches enough to make the fortunes of twenty monarchs.

Now he rushes to the house of the Dutch magistrate, and, being a bit disturbed, he knocks loudly at the door; goes in, tells the story of what happened, and shouts a bit louder than is customary. The judge begins by fining him ten thousand piastres for making such a racket; then he listens patiently to the story, promises to look into the matter as soon as the merchant comes back, and charges another ten thousand piastres as the costs of the hearing.

This legal proceeding completed the despair of Candide. In fact he had experienced miseries a thousand times more painful, but the coldness of the judge, and that of the merchant who had robbed him, roused his bile and plunged him into a black melancholy. The malice of men rose up before his spirit in all its ugliness, and his mind dwelt only on gloomy thoughts. Finally, when a French vessel was ready to leave for Bordeaux, since he had no more diamond-laden sheep to transport, he took a cabin at a fair price, and made it known in the town that he would pay passage and keep, plus two thousand piastres, to any honest man who wanted to make the journey with him, on condition that this man must be the most disgusted with his own condition and the most unhappy man in the province.

This drew such a crowd of applicants as a fleet could not have held. Candide wanted to choose among the leading candidates, so he picked out about twenty who seemed companionable enough, and of whom each pretended to be more miserable than all the others. He brought them together at his inn and gave them a dinner, on condition that each would swear to tell truthfully his entire history. He would select as his companion the most truly miserable and rightly discontented man, and among the others he would distribute various gifts.

The meeting lasted till four in the morning. Candide, as he listened to all the stories, remembered what the old woman had told him on the trip to Buenos Aires, and of the wager she had made, that there was nobody on the boat who had not undergone great misfortunes. At every story that was told him, he thought of Pangloss.

—That Pangloss, he said, would be hard put to prove his system. I wish he was here. Certainly if everything goes well, it is in Eldorado and not in the rest of the world.

At last he decided in favor of a poor scholar who had worked ten years for the booksellers of Amsterdam. He decided that there was no trade in the world with which one should be more disgusted.

This scholar, who was in fact a good man, had been robbed by his wife, beaten by his son, and deserted by his daughter, who had got herself abducted by a Portuguese. He had just been fired from the little job on which he existed; and the preachers of Surinam were persecuting him because they took him for a Socinian.[2] The others, it is true, were at least as unhappy as he, but Candide hoped the scholar would prove more amusing on the voyage. All his rivals declared that Candide was doing them a great injustice, but he pacified them with a hundred piastres apiece.

---

2. A follower of Faustus and Laelius Socinus, sixteenth-century Polish theologians, who proposed a form of "rational" Christianity which exalted the rational conscience and minimized such mysteries as the trinity. The Socinians, by a special irony, were vigorous optimists.

with fits and convulsions.[4] They say there are some very civilized people in that town; I'd like to think so.

—I myself have no desire to visit France, said Candide; you no doubt realize that when one has spent a month in Eldorado, there is nothing else on earth one wants to see, except Miss Cunégonde. I am going to wait for her at Venice; we will cross France simply to get to Italy; wouldn't you like to come with me?

—Gladly, said Martin; they say Venice is good only for the Venetian nobles, but that on the other hand they treat foreigners very well when they have plenty of money. I don't have any; you do, so I'll follow you anywhere.

—By the way, said Candide, do you believe the earth was originally all ocean, as they assure us in that big book belonging to the ship's captain?[5]

—I don't believe that stuff, said Martin, nor any of the dreams which people have been peddling for some time now.

—But why, then, was this world formed at all? asked Candide.

—To drive us mad, answered Martin.

—Aren't you astonished, Candide went on, at the love which those two girls showed for the monkeys in the land of the Biglugs that I told you about?

—Not at all, said Martin, I see nothing strange in these sentiments; I have seen so many extraordinary things that nothing seems extraordinary any more.

—Do you believe, asked Candide, that men have always massacred one another as they do today? That they have always been liars, traitors, ingrates, thieves, weaklings, sneaks, cowards, backbiters, gluttons, drunkards, misers, climbers, killers, calumniators, sensualists, fanatics, hypocrites, and fools?

—Do you believe, said Martin, that hawks have always eaten pigeons when they could get them?

—Of course, said Candide.

—Well, said Martin, if hawks have always had the same character, why do you suppose that men have changed?

—Oh, said Candide, there's a great deal of difference, because freedom of the will . . .

As they were disputing in this manner, they reached Bordeaux.

CHAPTER 22

What Happened in France to Candide and Martin

Candide paused in Bordeaux only long enough to sell a couple of Dorado pebbles and to fit himself out with a fine two-seater carriage, for he could no longer do without his philosopher Martin; only he was very unhappy to part with his sheep, which he left to the academy of science in Bordeaux. They proposed, as the theme of that year's prize contest, the

4. The Jansenists, a sect of strict Catholics, became notorious for spiritual ecstasies. Their public displays reached a height during the 1720s, and Voltaire described them in *Le Siècle de Louis XIV* (chap. 37), as well as in the article "Convulsions" in the *Philosophical Dictionary*.   5. The Bible: Genesis 1.

discovery of why the wool of the sheep was red; and the prize was awarded to a northern scholar[6] who demonstrated by A plus B minus C divided by Z that the sheep ought to be red and die of sheep rot.

But all the travelers with whom Candide talked in the roadside inns told him: —We are going to Paris.

This general consensus finally inspired in him too a desire to see the capital; it was not much out of his road to Venice.

He entered through the Faubourg Saint-Marceau,[7] and thought he was in the meanest village of Westphalia.

Scarcely was Candide in his hotel, when he came down with a mild illness caused by exhaustion. As he was wearing an enormous diamond ring, and people had noticed among his luggage a tremendously heavy safe, he soon found at his bedside two doctors whom he had not called, several intimate friends who never left him alone, and two pious ladies who helped to warm his broth. Martin said: —I remember that I too was ill on my first trip to Paris; I was very poor; and as I had neither friends, pious ladies, nor doctors, I got well.

However, as a result of medicines and bleedings, Candide's illness became serious. A resident of the neighborhood came to ask him politely to fill out a ticket, to be delivered to the porter of the other world.[8] Candide wanted nothing to do with it. The pious ladies assured him it was a new fashion; Candide replied that he wasn't a man of fashion. Martin wanted to throw the resident out the window. The cleric swore that without the ticket they wouldn't bury Candide. Martin swore that he would bury the cleric if he continued to be a nuisance. The quarrel grew heated; Martin took him by the shoulders and threw him bodily out the door; all of which caused a great scandal, from which developed a legal case.

Candide got better; and during his convalescence he had very good company in to dine. They played cards for money; and Candide was quite surprised that none of the aces were ever dealt to him, and Martin was not surprised at all.

Among those who did the honors of the town for Candide there was a little abbé from Perigord, one of those busy fellows, always bright, always useful, assured, obsequious, and obliging, who waylay passing strangers, tell them the scandal of the town, and offer them pleasures at any price they want to pay. This fellow first took Candide and Martin to the theatre. A new tragedy was being played. Candide found himself seated next to a group of wits. That did not keep him from shedding a few tears in the course of some perfectly played scenes. One of the commentators beside him remarked during the intermission: —You are quite mistaken to weep, this actress is very bad indeed; the actor who plays with her is even worse;

6. Maupertuis Le Lapon, philosopher and mathematician, whom Voltaire had accused of trying to adduce mathematical proofs of the existence of God.   7. A district on the left bank, notably grubby in the eighteenth century. "As I entered [Paris] through the Faubourg Saint-Marceau, I saw nothing but dirty stinking little streets, ugly black houses, a general air of squalor and poverty, beggars, carters, menders of clothes, sellers of herb-drinks and old hats." Jean-Jacques Rousseau, *Confessions*, Book IV. 8. In the middle of the eighteenth century, it became customary to require persons who were grievously ill to sign *billets de confession*, without which they could not be given absolution, admitted to the last sacraments, or buried in consecrated ground.

and the play is even worse than the actors in it. The author knows not a word of Arabic, though the action takes place in Arabia; and besides, he is a man who doesn't believe in innate ideas. Tomorrow I will show you twenty pamphlets written against him.

—Tell me, sir, said Candide to the abbé, how many plays are there for performance in France?

—Five or six thousand, replied the other.

—That's a lot, said Candide; how many of them are any good?

—Fifteen or sixteen, was the answer.

—That's a lot, said Martin.

Candide was very pleased with an actress who took the part of Queen Elizabeth in a rather dull tragedy[9] that still gets played from time to time.

—I like this actress very much, he said to Martin, she bears a slight resemblance to Miss Cunégonde; I should like to meet her.

The abbé from Perigord offered to introduce him. Candide, raised in Germany, asked what was the protocol, how one behaved in France with queens of England.

—You must distinguish, said the abbé; in the provinces, you take them to an inn; at Paris they are respected while still attractive, and thrown on the dunghill when they are dead.[1]

—Queens on the dunghill! said Candide.

—Yes indeed, said Martin, the abbé is right; I was in Paris when Miss Monime herself[2] passed, as they say, from this life to the other; she was refused what these folk call 'the honors of burial,' that is, the right to rot with all the beggars of the district in a dirty cemetery; she was buried all alone by her troupe at the corner of the Rue de Bourgogne; this must have been very disagreeable to her, for she had a noble character.

—That was extremely rude, said Candide.

—What do you expect? said Martin; that is how these folk are. Imagine all the contradictions, all the incompatibilities you can, and you will see them in the government, the courts, the churches, and the plays of this crazy nation.

—Is it true that they are always laughing in Paris? asked Candide.

—Yes, said the abbé, but with a kind of rage too; when people complain of things, they do so amid explosions of laughter; they even laugh as they perform the most detestable actions.

—Who was that fat swine, said Candide, who spoke so nastily about the play over which I was weeping, and the actors who gave me so much pleasure?

—He is a living illness, answered the abbé, who makes a business of slandering all the plays and books; he hates the successful ones, as eunuchs hate successful lovers; he's one of those literary snakes who live on filth and venom; he's a folliculator . . .

—What's this word *folliculator?* asked Candide.

---

9. *Le Comte d'Essex* by Thomas Corneille. 1. Voltaire engaged in a long and vigorous campaign against the rule that actors and actresses could not be buried in consecrated ground. The superstition probably arose from a feeling that by assuming false identities they drained their own souls. 2. Adrienne Lecouvreur (1690–1730), so called because she made her debut as Monime in Racine's *Mithridate.* Voltaire had assisted at her secret midnight funeral and wrote an indignant poem about it.

—It's a folio filler, said the abbé, a Fréron.[3]

It was after this fashion that Candide, Martin, and the abbé from Perigord chatted on the stairway as they watched the crowd leaving the theatre.

—Although I'm in a great hurry to see Miss Cunégonde again, said Candide, I would very much like to dine with Miss Clairon,[4] for she seemed to me admirable.

The abbé was not the man to approach Miss Clairon, who saw only good company.

—She has an engagement tonight, he said; but I shall have the honor of introducing you to a lady of quality, and there you will get to know Paris as if you had lived here for years.

Candide, who was curious by nature, allowed himself to be brought to the lady's house, in the depths of the Faubourg St.-Honoré; they were playing faro;[5] twelve melancholy punters held in their hands a little sheaf of cards, blank summaries of their bad luck. Silence reigned supreme, the punters were pallid, the banker uneasy; and the lady of the house, seated beside the pitiless banker, watched with the eyes of a lynx for the various illegal redoublings and bets at long odds which the players tried to signal by folding the corners of their cards; she had them unfolded with a determination which was severe but polite, and concealed her anger lest she lose her customers. The lady caused herself to be known as the Marquise of Parolignac.[6] Her daughter, fifteen years old, sat among the punters and tipped off her mother with a wink to the sharp practices of these unhappy players when they tried to recoup their losses. The abbé from Perigord, Candide, and Martin came in; nobody arose or greeted them or looked at them; all were lost in the study of their cards.

—My Lady the Baroness of Thunder-Ten-Tronckh was more civil, thought Candide.

However, the abbé whispered in the ear of the marquise, who, half rising, honored Candide with a gracious smile and Martin with a truly noble nod; she gave a seat and dealt a hand of cards to Candide, who lost fifty thousand francs in two turns; after which they had a very merry supper. Everyone was amazed that Candide was not upset over his losses; the lackeys, talking together in their usual lackey language, said: —He must be some English milord.

The supper was like most Parisian suppers: first silence, then an indistinguishable rush of words; then jokes, mostly insipid, false news, bad logic, a little politics, a great deal of malice. They even talked of new books.

—Have you seen the new novel by Dr. Gauchat, the theologian?[7] asked the abbé from Perigord.

—Oh yes, answered one of the guests; but I couldn't finish it. We have

3. A successful and popular journalist, who had attacked several of Voltaire's plays, including *Tancrède*.
4. Actually Claire Leris (1723–1803). She had played the lead role in *Tancrède* and was for many years a leading figure on the Paris stage.   5. A game of cards, about which it is necessary to know only that a number of punters play against a banker or dealer. The pack is dealt out two cards at a time, and each player may bet on any card as much as he pleases. The sharp practices of the punters consist essentially of tricks for increasing their winnings without corresponding risks.   6. A *paroli* is an illegal redoubling of one's bet; her name therefore implies a title grounded in cardsharping.   7. He had written against Voltaire, and Voltaire suspected him (wrongly) of having written the novel *L'Oracle des nouveaux philosophes*.

a horde of impudent scribblers nowadays, but all of them put together don't match the impudence of this Gauchat, this doctor of theology. I have been so struck by the enormous number of detestable books which are swamping us that I have taken up punting at faro.

—And the *Collected Essays* of Archdeacon T——[8] asked the abbé, what do you think of them?

—Ah, said Madame de Parolignac, what a frightful bore he is! He takes such pains to tell you what everyone knows; he discourses so learnedly on matters which aren't worth a casual remark! He plunders, and not even wittily, the wit of other people! He spoils what he plunders, he's disgusting! But he'll never disgust me again; a couple of pages of the archdeacon have been enough for me.

There was at table a man of learning and taste, who supported the marquise on this point. They talked next of tragedies; the lady asked why there were tragedies which played well enough but which were wholly unreadable. The man of taste explained very clearly how a play could have a certain interest and yet little merit otherwise; he showed succinctly that it was not enough to conduct a couple of intrigues, such as one can find in any novel, and which never fail to excite the spectator's interest; but that one must be new without being grotesque, frequently touch the sublime but never depart from the natural; that one must know the human heart and give it words; that one must be a great poet without allowing any character in the play to sound like a poet; and that one must know the language perfectly, speak it purely, and maintain a continual harmony without ever sacrificing sense to mere sound.

—Whoever, he added, does not observe all these rules may write one or two tragedies which succeed in the theatre, but he will never be ranked among the good writers; there are very few good tragedies; some are idylls in well-written, well-rhymed dialogue, others are political arguments which put the audience to sleep, or revolting pomposities; still others are the fantasies of enthusiasts, barbarous in style, incoherent in logic, full of long speeches to the gods because the author does not know how to address men, full of false maxims and emphatic commonplaces.

Candide listened attentively to this speech and conceived a high opinion of the speaker; and as the marquise had placed him by her side, he turned to ask her who was this man who spoke so well.

—He is a scholar, said the lady, who never plays cards and whom the abbé sometimes brings to my house for supper; he knows all about tragedies and books, and has himself written a tragedy that was hissed from the stage and a book, the only copy of which ever seen outside his publisher's office was dedicated to me.

—What a great man, said Candide, he's Pangloss all over.

Then, turning to him, he said: —Sir, you doubtless think everything is for the best in the physical as well as the moral universe, and that nothing could be otherwise than as it is?

—Not at all, sir, replied the scholar, I believe nothing of the sort. I find

---

8. His name was Trublet, and he had said, among other disagreeable things, that Voltaire's epic poem, the *Henriade*, made him yawn and that Voltaire's genius was "the perfection of mediocrity."

that everything goes wrong in our world; that nobody knows his place in society or his duty, what he's doing or what he ought to be doing, and that outside of mealtimes, which are cheerful and congenial enough, all the rest of the day is spent in useless quarrels, as of Jansenists against Molinists,[9] parliament-men against churchmen, literary men against literary men, courtiers against courtiers, financiers against the plebs, wives against husbands, relatives against relatives—it's one unending warfare.

Candide answered: —I have seen worse; but a wise man, who has since had the misfortune to be hanged, taught me that everything was marvelously well arranged. Troubles are just the shadows in a beautiful picture.

—Your hanged philosopher was joking, said Martin; the shadows are horrible ugly blots.

—It is human beings who make the blots, said Candide, and they can't do otherwise.

—Then it isn't their fault, said Martin.

Most of the faro players, who understood this sort of talk not at all, kept on drinking; Martin disputed with the scholar, and Candide told part of his story to the lady of the house.

After supper, the marquise brought Candide into her room and sat him down on a divan.

—Well, she said to him, are you still madly in love with Miss Cunégonde of Thunder-Ten-Tronckh?

—Yes, ma'am, replied Candide. The marquise turned upon him a tender smile.

—You answer like a young man of Westphalia, said she; a Frenchman would have told me: 'It is true that I have been in love with Miss Cunégonde; but since seeing you, madame, I fear that I love her no longer.'

—Alas, ma'am, said Candide, I will answer any way you want.

—Your passion for her, said the marquise, began when you picked up her handkerchief; I prefer that you should pick up my garter.

—Gladly, said Candide, and picked it up.

—But I also want you to put it back on, said the lady; and Candide put it on again.

—Look you now, said the lady, you are a foreigner; my Paris lovers I sometimes cause to languish for two weeks or so, but to you I surrender the very first night, because we must render the honors of the country to a young man from Westphalia.

The beauty, who had seen two enormous diamonds on the two hands of her young friend, praised them so sincerely that from the fingers of Candide they passed over to the fingers of the marquise.

As he returned home with his Perigord abbé, Candide felt some remorse at having been unfaithful to Miss Cunégonde; the abbé sympathized with his grief; he had only a small share in the fifty thousand francs which Candide lost at cards, and in the proceeds of the two diamonds which had been half-given, half-extorted. His scheme was to profit, as much as he could, from the advantage of knowing Candide. He spoke at

9. The Jansenists (from Corneille Jansen, 1585–1638) were a relatively strict party of religious reform; the Molinists (from Luis Molina) were the party of the Jesuits. Their central issue of controversy was the relative importance of divine grace and human will to the salvation of man.

length of Cunégonde, and Candide told him that he would beg forgiveness for his beloved for his infidelity when he met her at Venice.

The Perigordian overflowed with politeness and unction, taking a tender interest in everything Candide said, everything he did, and everything he wanted to do.

—Well, sir, said he, so you have an assignation at Venice?

—Yes indeed, sir, I do, said Candide; it is absolutely imperative that I go there to find Miss Cunégonde.

And then, carried away by the pleasure of talking about his love, he recounted, as he often did, a part of his adventures with that illustrious lady of Westphalia.

—I suppose, said the abbé, that Miss Cunégonde has a fine wit and writes charming letters.

—I never received a single letter from her, said Candide; for, as you can imagine, after being driven out of the castle for love of her, I couldn't write; shortly I learned that she was dead; then I rediscovered her; then I lost her again, and I have now sent, to a place more than twenty-five hundred leagues from here, a special agent whose return I am expecting.

The abbé listened carefully, and looked a bit dreamy. He soon took his leave of the two strangers, after embracing them tenderly. Next day Candide, when he woke up, received a letter, to the following effect:

—Dear sir, my very dear lover, I have been lying sick in this town for a week, I have just learned that you are here. I would fly to your arms if I could move. I heard that you had passed through Bordeaux; that was where I left the faithful Cacambo and the old woman, who are soon to follow me here. The governor of Buenos Aires took everything, but left me your heart. Come; your presence will either return me to life or cause me to die of joy.

This charming letter, coming so unexpectedly, filled Candide with inexpressible delight, while the illness of his dear Cunégonde covered him with grief. Torn between these two feelings, he took gold and diamonds, and had himself brought, with Martin, to the hotel where Miss Cunégonde was lodging. Trembling with emotion, he enters the room; his heart thumps, his voice breaks. He tries to open the curtains of the bed, he asks to have some lights.

—Absolutely forbidden, says the serving girl; light will be the death of her.

And abruptly she pulls shut the curtain.

—My dear Cunégonde, says Candide in tears, how are you feeling? If you can't see me, won't you at least speak to me?

—She can't talk, says the servant.

But then she draws forth from the bed a plump hand, over which Candide weeps a long time, and which he fills with diamonds, meanwhile leaving a bag of gold on the chair.

Amid his transports, there arrives a bailiff followed by the abbé from Perigord and a strong-arm squad.

—These here are the suspicious foreigners? says the officer; and he has them seized and orders his bullies to drag them off to jail.

—They don't treat visitors like this in Eldorado, says Candide.

—I am more a Manichee than ever, says Martin.

—But, please sir, where are you taking us? says Candide.

—To the lowest hole in the dungeons, says the bailiff.

Martin, having regained his self-possession, decided that the lady who pretended to be Cunégonde was a cheat, the abbé from Perigord was another cheat who had imposed on Candide's innocence, and the bailiff still another cheat, of whom it would be easy to get rid.

Rather than submit to the forms of justice, Candide, enlightened by Martin's advice and eager for his own part to see the real Cunégonde again, offered the bailiff three little diamonds worth about three thousand pistoles apiece.

—Ah, my dear sir! cried the man with the ivory staff, even if you have committed every crime imaginable, you are the most honest man in the world. Three diamonds! each one worth three thousand pistoles! My dear sir! I would gladly die for you, rather than take you to jail. All foreigners get arrested here; but let me manage it; I have a brother at Dieppe in Normandy; I'll take you to him; and if you have a bit of a diamond to give him, he'll take care of you, just like me.

—And why do they arrest all foreigners? asked Candide.

The abbé from Perigord spoke up and said: —It's because a beggar from Atrebatum[1] listened to some stupidities; that made him commit a parricide, not like the one of May, 1610, but like the one of December, 1594, much on the order of several other crimes committed in other years and other months by other beggars who had listened to stupidities.

The bailiff then explained what it was all about.[2]

—Foh! what beasts! cried Candide. What! monstrous behavior of this sort from a people who sing and dance? As soon as I can, let me get out of this country, where the monkeys provoke the tigers. In my own country I've lived with bears; only in Eldorado are there proper men. In the name of God, sir bailiff, get me to Venice where I can wait for Miss Cunégonde.

—I can only get you to Lower Normandy, said the guardsman.

He had the irons removed at once, said there had been a mistake, dismissed his gang, and took Candide and Martin to Dieppe, where he left them with his brother. There was a little Dutch ship at anchor. The Norman, changed by three more diamonds into the most helpful of men, put Candide and his people aboard the vessel, which was bound for Portsmouth in England. It wasn't on the way to Venice, but Candide felt like a man just let out of hell; and he hoped to get back on the road to Venice at the first possible occasion.

---

1. The Latin name for the district of Artois, from which came Robert-François Damiens, who tried to stab Louis XV in 1757. The assassination failed, like that of Châtel, who tried to kill Henri IV in 1594, but unlike that of Ravaillac, who succeeded in killing him in 1610.   2. The point, in fact, is not too clear since arresting foreigners is an indirect way at best to guard against homegrown fanatics, and the position of the abbé from Perigord in the whole transaction remains confused. Has he called in the officer just to get rid of Candide? If so, why is he sardonic about the very suspicions he is trying to foster? Candide's reaction is to the notion that Frenchmen should be capable of political assassination at all; it seems excessive.

CHAPTER 23

Candide and Martin Pass the Shores of England; What They See There

—Ah, Pangloss! Pangloss! Ah, Martin! Martin! Ah, my darling Cuné-gonde! What is this world of ours? sighed Candide on the Dutch vessel.

—Something crazy, something abominable, Martin replied.

—You have been in England; are people as crazy there as in France?

—It's a different sort of crazy, said Martin. You know that these two nations have been at war over a few acres of snow near Canada, and that they are spending on this fine struggle more than Canada itself is worth.[3] As for telling you if there are more people in one country or the other who need a strait jacket, that is a judgment too fine for my understanding; I know only that the people we are going to visit are eaten up with melancholy.

As they chatted thus, the vessel touched at Portsmouth. A multitude of people covered the shore, watching closely a rather bulky man who was kneeling, his eyes blindfolded, on the deck of a man-of-war. Four soldiers, stationed directly in front of this man, fired three bullets apiece into his brain, as peaceably as you would want; and the whole assemblage went home, in great satisfaction.[4]

—What's all this about? asked Candide. What devil is everywhere at work?

He asked who was that big man who had just been killed with so much ceremony.

—It was an admiral, they told him.

—And why kill this admiral?

—The reason, they told him, is that he didn't kill enough people; he gave battle to a French admiral, and it was found that he didn't get close enough to him.

—But, said Candide, the French admiral was just as far from the English admiral as the English admiral was from the French admiral.

—That's perfectly true, came the answer; but in this country it is useful from time to time to kill one admiral in order to encourage the others.

Candide was so stunned and shocked at what he saw and heard, that he would not even set foot ashore; he arranged with the Dutch merchant (without even caring if he was robbed, as at Surinam) to be taken forthwith to Venice.

The merchant was ready in two days; they coasted along France, they passed within sight of Lisbon, and Candide quivered. They entered the straits, crossed the Mediterranean, and finally landed at Venice.

—God be praised, said Candide, embracing Martin; here I shall recover the lovely Cunégonde. I trust Cacambo as I would myself. All is well, all goes well, all goes as well as possible.

---

3. The wars of the French and English over Canada dragged intermittently through the eighteenth century till the peace of Paris sealed England's conquest (1763). Voltaire thought the French should concentrate on developing Louisiana, where the Jesuit influence was less marked.   4. Candide has witnessed the execution of Admiral John Byng, defeated off Minorca by the French fleet under Galison-nière and executed by firing squad on March 14, 1757. Voltaire had intervened to avert the execution.

CHAPTER 24

About Paquette and Brother Giroflée

As soon as he was in Venice, he had a search made for Cacambo in all the inns, all the cafés, all the stews—and found no trace of him. Every day he sent to investigate the vessels and coastal traders; no news of Cacambo. —How's this? said he to Martin. I have had time to go from Surinam to Bordeaux, from Bordeaux to Paris, from Paris to Dieppe, from Dieppe to Portsmouth, to skirt Portugal and Spain, cross the Mediterranean, and spend several months at Venice—and the lovely Cunégonde has not come yet! In her place, I have met only that impersonator and that abbé from Perigord. Cunégonde is dead, without a doubt; and nothing remains for me too but death. Oh, it would have been better to stay in the earthly paradise of Eldorado than to return to this accursed Europe. How right you are, my dear Martin; all is but illusion and disaster.

He fell into a black melancholy, and refused to attend the fashionable operas or take part in the other diversions of the carnival season; not a single lady tempted him in the slightest. Martin told him: —You're a real simpleton if you think a half-breed valet with five or six millions in his pockets will go to the end of the world to get your mistress and bring her to Venice for you. If he finds her, he'll take her for himself; if he doesn't, he'll take another. I advise you to forget about your servant Cacambo and your mistress Cunégonde.

Martin was not very comforting. Candide's melancholy increased, and Martin never wearied of showing him that there is little virtue and little happiness on this earth, except perhaps in Eldorado, where nobody can go.

While they were discussing this important matter and still waiting for Cunégonde, Candide noticed in St. Mark's Square a young Theatine[5] monk who had given his arm to a girl. The Theatine seemed fresh, plump, and flourishing; his eyes were bright, his manner cocky, his glance brilliant, his step proud. The girl was very pretty, and singing aloud; she glanced lovingly at her Theatine, and from time to time pinched his plump cheeks.

—At least you must admit, said Candide to Martin, that these people are happy. Until now I have not found in the whole inhabited earth, except Eldorado, anything but miserable people. But this girl and this monk, I'd be willing to bet, are very happy creatures.

—I'll bet they aren't, said Martin.

—We have only to ask them to dinner, said Candide, and we'll find out if I'm wrong.

Promptly he approached them, made his compliments, and invited them to his inn for a meal of macaroni, Lombardy partridges, and caviar, washed down with wine from Montepulciano, Cyprus, and Samos, and some Lacrima Christi. The girl blushed but the Theatine accepted gladly, and the girl followed him, watching Candide with an expression of surprise and confusion, darkened by several tears. Scarcely had she entered

5. A Catholic order founded in 1524 by Cardinal Cajetan and G. P. Caraffa, later Pope Paul IV.

the room when she said to Candide: —What, can it be that Master Candide no longer knows Paquette?

At these words Candide, who had not yet looked carefully at her because he was preoccupied with Cunégonde, said to her: —Ah, my poor child! so you are the one who put Doctor Pangloss in the fine fix where I last saw him.

—Alas, sir, I was the one, said Paquette; I see you know all about it. I heard of the horrible misfortunes which befell the whole household of My Lady the Baroness and the lovely Cunégonde. I swear to you that my own fate has been just as unhappy. I was perfectly innocent when you knew me. A Franciscan, who was my confessor, easily seduced me. The consequences were frightful; shortly after My Lord the Baron had driven you out with great kicks on the backside, I too was forced to leave the castle. If a famous doctor had not taken pity on me, I would have died. Out of gratitude, I became for some time the mistress of this doctor. His wife, who was jealous to the point of frenzy, beat me mercilessly every day; she was a gorgon. The doctor was the ugliest of men, and I the most miserable creature on earth, being continually beaten for a man I did not love. You will understand, sir, how dangerous it is for a nagging woman to be married to a doctor. This man, enraged by his wife's ways, one day gave her as a cold cure a medicine so potent that in two hours' time she died amid horrible convulsions. Her relatives brought suit against the bereaved husband; he fled the country, and I was put in prison. My innocence would never have saved me if I had not been rather pretty. The judge set me free on condition that he should become the doctor's successor. I was shortly replaced in this post by another girl, dismissed without any payment, and obliged to continue this abominable trade which you men find so pleasant and which for us is nothing but a bottomless pit of misery. I went to ply the trade in Venice. Ah, my dear sir, if you could imagine what it is like to have to caress indiscriminately an old merchant, a lawyer, a monk, a gondolier, an abbé; to be subjected to every sort of insult and outrage; to be reduced, time and again, to borrowing a skirt in order to go have it lifted by some disgusting man; to be robbed by this fellow of what one has gained from that; to be shaken down by the police, and to have before one only the prospect of a hideous old age, a hospital, and a dunghill, you will conclude that I am one of the most miserable creatures in the world.

Thus Paquette poured forth her heart to the good Candide in a hotel room, while Martin sat listening nearby. At last he said to Candide: —You see, I've already won half my bet.

Brother Giroflée[6] had remained in the dining room, and was having a drink before dinner.

—But how's this? said Candide to Paquette. You looked so happy, so joyous, when I met you; you were singing, you caressed the Theatine with such a natural air of delight; you seemed to me just as happy as you now say you are miserable.

—Ah, sir, replied Paquette, that's another one of the miseries of this

6. His name means "carnation" and Paquette means "daisy."

business; yesterday I was robbed and beaten by an officer, and today I have to seem in good humor in order to please a monk.

Candide wanted no more; he conceded that Martin was right. They sat down to table with Paquette and the Theatine; the meal was amusing enough, and when it was over, the company spoke out among themselves with some frankness.

—Father, said Candide to the monk, you seem to me a man whom all the world might envy; the flower of health glows in your cheek, your features radiate pleasure; you have a pretty girl for your diversion, and you seem very happy with your life as a Theatine.

—Upon my word, sir, said Brother Giroflée, I wish that all the Theatines were at the bottom of the sea. A hundred times I have been tempted to set fire to my convent, and go turn Turk. My parents forced me, when I was fifteen years old, to put on this detestable robe, so they could leave more money to a cursed older brother of mine, may God confound him! Jealousy, faction, and fury spring up, by natural law, within the walls of convents. It is true, I have preached a few bad sermons which earned me a little money, half of which the prior stole from me; the remainder serves to keep me in girls. But when I have to go back to the monastery at night, I'm ready to smash my head against the walls of my cell; and all my fellow monks are in the same fix.

Martin turned to Candide and said with his customary coolness:

—Well, haven't I won the whole bet?

Candide gave two thousand piastres to Paquette and a thousand to Brother Giroflée.

—I assure you, said he, that with that they will be happy.

—I don't believe so, said Martin; your piastres may make them even more unhappy than they were before.

—That may be, said Candide; but one thing comforts me, I note that people often turn up whom one never expected to see again; it may well be that, having rediscovered my red sheep and Paquette, I will also rediscover Cunégonde.

—I hope, said Martin, that she will some day make you happy; but I very much doubt it.

—You're a hard man, said Candide.

—I've lived, said Martin.

—But look at these gondoliers, said Candide; aren't they always singing?

—You don't see them at home, said Martin, with their wives and squalling children. The doge has his troubles, the gondoliers theirs. It's true that on the whole one is better off as a gondolier than as a doge; but the difference is so slight, I don't suppose it's worth the trouble of discussing.

—There's a lot of talk here, said Candide, of this Senator Pococurante,[7] who has a fine palace on the Brenta and is hospitable to foreigners. They say he is a man who has never known a moment's grief.

—I'd like to see such a rare specimen, said Martin.

Candide promptly sent to Lord Pococurante, asking permission to call on him tomorrow.

---

7. His name means "small care."

CHAPTER 25

Visit to Lord Pococurante, Venetian Nobleman

Candide and Martin took a gondola on the Brenta, and soon reached the palace of the noble Pococurante. The gardens were large and filled with beautiful marble statues; the palace was handsomely designed. The master of the house, sixty years old and very rich, received his two inquisitive visitors perfectly politely, but with very little warmth; Candide was disconcerted and Martin not at all displeased.

First two pretty and neatly dressed girls served chocolate, which they whipped to a froth. Candide could not forbear praising their beauty, their grace, their skill.

—They are pretty good creatures, said Pococurante; I sometimes have them into my bed, for I'm tired of the ladies of the town, with their stupid tricks, quarrels, jealousies, fits of ill humor and petty pride, and all the sonnets one has to make or order for them; but, after all, these two girls are starting to bore me too.

After lunch, Candide strolled through a long gallery, and was amazed at the beauty of the pictures. He asked who was the painter of the two finest.

—They are by Raphael, said the senator; I bought them for a lot of money, out of vanity, some years ago; people say they're the finest in Italy, but they don't please me at all; the colors have all turned brown, the figures aren't well modeled and don't stand out enough, the draperies bear no resemblance to real cloth. In a word, whatever people may say, I don't find in them a real imitation of nature. I like a picture only when I can see in it a touch of nature itself, and there are none of this sort. I have many paintings, but I no longer look at them.

As they waited for dinner, Pococurante ordered a concerto performed. Candide found the music delightful.

—That noise? said Pococurante. It may amuse you for half an hour, but if it goes on any longer, it tires everybody though no one dares to admit it. Music today is only the art of performing difficult pieces, and what is merely difficult cannot please for long. Perhaps I should prefer the opera, if they had not found ways to make it revolting and monstrous. Anyone who likes bad tragedies set to music is welcome to them; in these performances the scenes serve only to introduce, inappropriately, two or three ridiculous songs designed to show off the actress's sound box. Anyone who wants to, or who can, is welcome to swoon with pleasure at the sight of a castrate wriggling through the role of Caesar or Cato, and strutting awkwardly about the stage. For my part, I have long since given up these paltry trifles which are called the glory of modern Italy, and for which monarchs pay such ruinous prices.

Candide argued a bit, but timidly; Martin was entirely of a mind with the senator.

They sat down to dinner, and after an excellent meal adjourned to the library. Candide, seeing a copy of Homer in a splendid binding, complimented the noble lord on his good taste.

—That is an author, said he, who was the special delight of great Pangloss, the best philosopher in all Germany.

—He's no special delight of mine, said Pococurante coldly. I was once made to believe that I took pleasure in reading him; but that constant recital of fights which are all alike, those gods who are always interfering but never decisively, that Helen who is the cause of the war and then scarcely takes any part in the story, that Troy which is always under siege and never taken—all that bores me to tears. I have sometimes asked scholars if reading it bored them as much as it bores me; everyone who answered frankly told me the book dropped from his hands like lead, but that they had to have it in their libraries as a monument of antiquity, like those old rusty coins which can't be used in real trade.

Your Excellence doesn't hold the same opinion of Virgil? said Candide.

—I concede, said Pococurante, that the second, fourth, and sixth books of his *Aeneid* are fine; but as for his pious Aeneas, and strong Cloanthes, and faithful Achates, and little Ascanius, and that imbecile King Latinus, and middle-class Amata, and insipid Lavinia, I don't suppose there was ever anything so cold and unpleasant. I prefer Tasso and those sleepwalkers' stories of Ariosto.

—Dare I ask, sir, said Candide, if you don't get great enjoyment from reading Horace?

—There are some maxims there, said Pococurante, from which a man of the world can profit, and which, because they are formed into vigorous couplets, are more easily remembered; but I care very little for his trip to Brindisi, his description of a bad dinner, or his account of a quibblers' squabble between some fellow Pupilus, whose words he says *were full of pus*, and another whose words *were full of vinegar*.[8] I feel nothing but extreme disgust at his verses against old women and witches; and I can't see what's so great in his telling his friend Maecenas that if he is raised by him to the ranks of lyric poets, he will strike the stars with his lofty forehead. Fools admire everything in a well-known author. I read only for my own pleasure; I like only what is in my style.

Candide, who had been trained never to judge for himself, was much astonished by what he heard; and Martin found Pococurante's way of thinking quite rational.

—Oh, here is a copy of Cicero, said Candide. Now this great man I suppose you're never tired of reading.

—I never read him at all, replied the Venetian. What do I care whether he pleaded for Rabirius or Cluentius? As a judge, I have my hands full of lawsuits. I might like his philosophical works better, but when I saw that he had doubts about everything, I concluded that I knew as much as he did, and that I needed no help to be ignorant.

—Ah, here are eighty volumes of collected papers from a scientific academy, cried Martin; maybe there is something good in them.

—There would be indeed, said Pococurante, if one of these silly authors

---

8. *Satires* I.vii; Pococurante, with gentlemanly negligence, has corrupted Rupilius to Pupilus. Horace's poems against witches are *Epodes* V, VIII, XII; the one about striking the stars with his lofty forehead is *Odes* I.i.

had merely discovered a new way of making pins; but in all those volumes there is nothing but empty systems, not a single useful discovery.

—What a lot of stage plays I see over there, said Candide, some in Italian, some in Spanish and French.

—Yes, said the senator, three thousand of them, and not three dozen good ones. As for those collections of sermons, which all together are not worth a page of Seneca, and all these heavy volumes of theology, you may be sure I never open them, nor does anybody else.

Martin noticed some shelves full of English books.

—I suppose, said he, that a republican must delight in most of these books written in the land of liberty.

—Yes, replied Pococurante, it's a fine thing to write as you think; it is mankind's privilege. In all our Italy, people write only what they do not think; men who inhabit the land of the Caesars and Antonines dare not have an idea without the permission of a Dominican. I would rejoice in the freedom that breathes through English genius, if partisan passions did not corrupt all that is good in that precious freedom.

Candide, noting a Milton, asked if he did not consider this author a great man.

—Who? said Pococurante. That barbarian who made a long commentary on the first chapter of Genesis in ten books of crabbed verse?[9] That clumsy imitator of the Greeks, who disfigures creation itself, and while Moses represents the eternal being as creating the world with a word, has the messiah take a big compass out of a heavenly cupboard in order to design his work? You expect me to admire the man who spoiled Tasso's hell and devil? who disguises Lucifer now as a toad, now as a pigmy? who makes him rehash the same arguments a hundred times over? who makes him argue theology? and who, taking seriously Ariosto's comic story of the invention of firearms, has the devils shooting off cannon in heaven? Neither I nor anyone else in Italy has been able to enjoy these gloomy extravagances. The marriage of Sin and Death, and the monster that Sin gives birth to, will nauseate any man whose taste is at all refined; and his long description of a hospital is good only for a gravedigger. This obscure, extravagant, and disgusting poem was despised at its birth; I treat it today as it was treated in its own country by its contemporaries. Anyhow, I say what I think, and care very little whether other people agree with me.

Candide was a little cast down by this speech; he respected Homer, and had a little affection for Milton.

—Alas, he said under his breath to Martin, I'm afraid this man will have a supreme contempt for our German poets.

—No harm in that, said Martin.

—Oh what a superior man, said Candide, still speaking softly, what a great genius this Pococurante must be! Nothing can please him.

Having thus looked over all the books, they went down into the garden. Candide praised its many beauties.

—I know nothing in such bad taste, said the master of the house; we

9. The first edition of *Paradise Lost* had ten books, which Milton later expanded to twelve.

have nothing but trifles here; tomorrow I am going to have one set out on a nobler design.

When the two visitors had taken leave of his excellency: —Well now, said Candide to Martin, you must agree that this was the happiest of all men, for he is superior to everything he possesses.

—Don't you see, said Martin, that he is disgusted with everything he possesses? Plato said, a long time ago, that the best stomachs are not those which refuse all food.

—But, said Candide, isn't there pleasure in criticizing everything, in seeing faults where other people think they see beauties?

—That is to say, Martin replied, that there's pleasure in having no pleasure?

—Oh well, said Candide, then I am the only happy man . . . or will be, when I see Miss Cunégonde again.

—It's always a good thing to have hope, said Martin.

But the days and the weeks slipped past; Cacambo did not come back, and Candide was so buried in his grief, that he did not even notice that Paquette and Brother Giroflée had neglected to come and thank him.

CHAPTER 26

About a Supper that Candide and Martin Had with Six Strangers, and Who They Were

One evening when Candide, accompanied by Martin, was about to sit down for dinner with the strangers staying in his hotel, a man with a soot-colored face came up behind him, took him by the arm, and said: —Be ready to leave with us, don't miss out.

He turned and saw Cacambo. Only the sight of Cunégonde could have astonished and pleased him more. He nearly went mad with joy. He embraced his dear friend.

—Cunégonde is here, no doubt? Where is she? Bring me to her, let me die of joy in her presence.

—Cunégonde is not here at all, said Cacambo, she is at Constantinople.

—Good Heavens, at Constantinople! but if she were in China, I must fly there, let's go.

—We will leave after supper, said Cacambo; I can tell you no more; I am a slave, my owner is looking for me, I must go wait on him at table; mum's the word; eat your supper and be prepared.

Candide, torn between joy and grief, delighted to have seen his faithful agent again, astonished to find him a slave, full of the idea of recovering his mistress, his heart in a turmoil, his mind in a whirl, sat down to eat with Martin, who was watching all these events coolly, and with six strangers who had come to pass the carnival season at Venice.

Cacambo, who was pouring wine for one of the strangers, leaned respectfully over his master at the end of the meal, and said to him: — Sire, Your Majesty may leave when he pleases, the vessel is ready.

Having said these words, he exited. The diners looked at one another in silent amazement, when another servant, approaching his master, said to him: —Sire, Your Majesty's litter is at Padua, and the bark awaits you.

The master nodded, and the servant vanished. All the diners looked at one another again, and the general amazement redoubled. A third servant, approaching a third stranger, said to him: —Sire, take my word for it, Your Majesty must stay here no longer; I shall get everything ready.

Then he too disappeared.

Candide and Martin had no doubt, now, that it was a carnival masquerade. A fourth servant spoke to a fourth master: —Your Majesty will leave when he pleases—and went out like the others. A fifth followed suit. But the sixth servant spoke differently to the sixth stranger, who sat next to Candide. He said: —My word, sire, they'll give no more credit to Your Majesty, nor to me either; we could very well spend the night in the lockup, you and I. I've got to look out for myself, so good-bye to you.

When all the servants had left, the six strangers, Candide, and Martin remained under a pall of silence. Finally Candide broke it.

—Gentlemen, said he, here's a funny kind of joke. Why are you all royalty? I assure you that Martin and I aren't.

Cacambo's master spoke up gravely then, and said in Italian: —This is no joke, my name is Achmet the Third.[1] I was grand sultan for several years; then, as I had dethroned my brother, my nephew dethroned me. My viziers had their throats cut; I was allowed to end my days in the old seraglio. My nephew, the Grand Sultan Mahmoud, sometimes lets me travel for my health; and I have come to spend the carnival season at Venice.

A young man who sat next to Achmet spoke after him, and said: —My name is Ivan; I was once emperor of all the Russias.[2] I was dethroned while still in my cradle; my father and mother were locked up, and I was raised in prison; I sometimes have permission to travel, though always under guard, and I have come to spend the carnival season at Venice.

The third said: —I am Charles Edward, king of England;[3] my father yielded me his rights to the kingdom, and I fought to uphold them; but they tore out the hearts of eight hundred of my partisans, and flung them in their faces. I have been in prison; now I am going to Rome, to visit the king, my father, dethroned like me and my grandfather; and I have come to pass the carnival season at Venice.

The fourth king then spoke up, and said: —I am a king of the Poles;[4] the luck of war has deprived me of my hereditary estates; my father suffered the same losses; I submit to Providence like Sultan Achmet, Emperor Ivan, and King Charles Edward, to whom I hope heaven grants long lives; and I have come to pass the carnival season at Venice.

The fifth said: —I too am a king of the Poles;[5] I lost my kingdom twice, but Providence gave me another state, in which I have been able to do

---

1. Ottoman ruler (1673–1736); he was deposed in 1730.   2. Ivan VI reigned from his birth in 1740 until 1756, then was confined in the Schlusselberg, and executed in 1764.   3. This is the Young Pretender (1720–1788), known to his supporters as Bonnie Prince Charlie. The defeat so theatrically described took place at Culloden, April 16, 1746.   4. Augustus III (1696–1763), Elector of Saxony and King of Poland, dethroned by Frederick the Great in 1756.   5. Stanislas Leczinski (1677–1766), father-in-law of Louis XV, who abdicated the throne of Poland in 1736, was made Duke of Lorraine and in that capacity befriended Voltaire.

more good than all the Sarmatian kings ever managed to do on the banks of the Vistula. I too have submitted to Providence, and I have come to pass the carnival season at Venice.

It remained for the sixth monarch to speak.

—Gentlemen, said he, I am no such great lord as you, but I have in fact been a king like any other. I am Theodore; I was elected king of Corsica.[6] People used to call me *Your Majesty*, and now they barely call me *Sir*; I used to coin currency, and now I don't have a cent; I used to have two secretaries of state, and now I scarcely have a valet; I have sat on a throne, and for a long time in London I was in jail, on the straw; and I may well be treated the same way here, though I have come, like your majesties, to pass the carnival season at Venice.

The five other kings listened to his story with noble compassion. Each one of them gave twenty sequins to King Theodore, so that he might buy a suit and some shirts; Candide gave him a diamond worth two thousand sequins.

—Who in the world, said the five kings, is this private citizen who is in a position to give a hundred times as much as any of us, and who actually gives it?[7]

Just as they were rising from dinner, there arrived at the same establishment four most serene highnesses, who had also lost their kingdoms through the luck of war, and who came to spend the rest of the carnival season at Venice. But Candide never bothered even to look at these newcomers because he was only concerned to go find his dear Cunégonde at Constantinople.

CHAPTER 27

Candide's Trip to Constantinople

Faithful Cacambo had already arranged with the Turkish captain who was returning Sultan Achmet to Constantinople to make room for Candide and Martin on board. Both men boarded ship after prostrating themselves before his miserable highness. On the way, Candide said to Martin: —Six dethroned kings that we had dinner with! and yet among those six there was one on whom I had to bestow charity! Perhaps there are other princes even more unfortunate. I myself have only lost a hundred sheep, and now I am flying to the arms of Cunégonde. My dear Martin, once again Pangloss is proved right, all is for the best.

—I hope so, said Martin.

6. Theodore von Neuhof (1690–1756), an authentic Westphalian, an adventurer and a soldier of fortune, who in 1736 was (for about eight months) the elected king of Corsica. He spent time in an Amsterdam as well as a London debtor's prison.   7. A late correction of Voltaire's makes this passage read:
—Who is this man who is in a position to give a hundred times as much as any of us, and who actually gives it? Are you a king too, sir?
—No, gentlemen, and I have no desire to be.
But this reading, though Voltaire's on good authority, produces a conflict with Candide's previous remark: —Why are you all royalty? I assure you that Martin and I aren't.
Thus, it has seemed better for literary reasons to follow an earlier reading. Voltaire was very conscious of his situation as a man richer than many princes; in 1758 he had money on loan to no fewer than three highnesses, Charles Eugene, Duke of Wurtemburg; Charles Theodore, Elector Palatine; and the Duke of Saxe-Gotha.

—But, said Candide, that was a most unlikely experience we had at Venice. Nobody ever saw, or heard tell of, six dethroned kings eating together at an inn.

—It is no more extraordinary, said Martin, than most of the things that have happened to us. Kings are frequently dethroned; and as for the honor we had from dining with them, that's a trifle which doesn't deserve our notice.[8]

Scarcely was Candide on board than he fell on the neck of his former servant, his friend Cacambo.

—Well! said he, what is Cunégonde doing? Is she still a marvel of beauty? Does she still love me? How is her health? No doubt you have bought her a palace at Constantinople.

—My dear master, answered Cacambo, Cunégonde is washing dishes on the shores of the Propontis, in the house of a prince who has very few dishes to wash; she is a slave in the house of a onetime king named Ragotski,[9] to whom the Great Turk allows three crowns a day in his exile; but, what is worse than all this, she has lost all her beauty and become horribly ugly.

—Ah, beautiful or ugly, said Candide, I am an honest man, and my duty is to love her forever. But how can she be reduced to this wretched state with the five or six millions that you had?

—All right, said Cacambo, didn't I have to give two millions to Señor don Fernando d'Ibaraa y Figueroa y Mascarenes y Lampourdos y Souza, governor of Buenos Aires, for his permission to carry off Miss Cunégonde? And didn't a pirate cleverly strip us of the rest? And didn't this pirate carry us off to Cape Matapan, to Melos, Nicaria, Samos, Petra, to the Dardanelles, Marmora, Scutari? Cunégonde and the old woman are working for the prince I told you about, and I am the slave of the dethroned sultan.

—What a lot of fearful calamities linked one to the other, said Candide. But after all, I still have a few diamonds, I shall easily deliver Cunégonde. What a pity that she's become so ugly!

Then, turning toward Martin, he asked: —Who in your opinion is more to be pitied, the Emperor Achmet, the Emperor Ivan, King Charles Edward, or myself?

—I have no idea, said Martin; I would have to enter your hearts in order to tell.

—Ah, said Candide, if Pangloss were here, he would know and he would tell us.

—I can't imagine, said Martin, what scales your Pangloss would use to weigh out the miseries of men and value their griefs. All I will venture is that the earth holds millions of men who deserve our pity a hundred times more than King Charles Edward, Emperor Ivan, or Sultan Achmet.

—You may well be right, said Candide.

In a few days they arrived at the Black Sea canal. Candide began by repurchasing Cacambo at an exorbitant price; then, without losing an

---

8. Another late change adds the following question: —*What does it matter whom you dine with as long as you fare well at table?* I have omitted it, again on literary grounds.   9. Francis Leopold Rakoczy (1676–1735), who was briefly king of Transylvania in the early eighteenth century. After 1720 he was interned in Turkey.

instant, he flung himself and his companions into a galley to go search out Cunégonde on the shores of Propontis, however ugly she might be.

There were in the chain gang two convicts who bent clumsily to the oar, and on whose bare shoulders the Levantine[1] captain delivered from time to time a few lashes with a bullwhip. Candide naturally noticed them more than the other galley slaves, and out of pity came closer to them. Certain features of their disfigured faces seemed to him to bear a slight resemblance to Pangloss and to that wretched Jesuit, that baron, that brother of Miss Cunégonde. The notion stirred and saddened him. He looked at them more closely.

—To tell you the truth, he said to Cacambo, if I hadn't seen Master Pangloss hanged, and if I hadn't been so miserable as to murder the baron, I should think they were rowing in this very galley.

At the names of 'baron' and 'Pangloss' the two convicts gave a great cry, sat still on their bench, and dropped their oars. The Levantine captain came running, and the bullwhip lashes redoubled.

—Stop, stop, captain, cried Candide. I'll give you as much money as you want.

—What, can it be Candide? cried one of the convicts.

—What, can it be Candide? cried the other.

—Is this a dream? said Candide. Am I awake or asleep? Am I in this galley? Is that My Lord the Baron, whom I killed? Is that Master Pangloss, whom I saw hanged?

—It is indeed, they replied.

—What, is that the great philosopher? said Martin.

—Now, sir, Mr. Levantine Captain, said Candide, how much money do you want for the ransom of My Lord Thunder-Ten-Tronckh, one of the first barons of the empire, and Master Pangloss, the deepest metaphysician in all Germany?

—Dog of a Christian, replied the Levantine captain, since these two dogs of Christian convicts are barons and metaphysicians, which is no doubt a great honor in their country, you will give me fifty thousand sequins for them.

—You shall have them, sir, take me back to Constantinople and you shall be paid on the spot. Or no, take me to Miss Cunégonde.

The Levantine captain, at Candide's first word, had turned his bow toward the town, and he had them rowed there as swiftly as a bird cleaves the air.

A hundred times Candide embraced the baron and Pangloss.

—And how does it happen I didn't kill you, my dear baron? and my dear Pangloss, how can you be alive after being hanged? and why are you both rowing in the galleys of Turkey?

—Is it really true that my dear sister is in this country? asked the baron.

—Yes, answered Cacambo.

—And do I really see again my dear Candide? cried Pangloss.

Candide introduced Martin and Cacambo. They all embraced; they all talked at once. The galley flew, already they were back in port. A Jew was

---

1. From the eastern Mediterranean.

called, and Candide sold him for fifty thousand sequins a diamond worth
a hundred thousand, while he protested by Abraham that he could not
possibly give more for it. Candide immediately ransomed the baron and
Pangloss. The latter threw himself at the feet of his liberator, and bathed
them with tears; the former thanked him with a nod, and promised to
repay this bit of money at the first opportunity.

—But is it really possible that my sister is in Turkey? said he.

—Nothing is more possible, replied Cacambo, since she is a dishwasher
in the house of a prince of Transylvania.

At once two more Jews were called; Candide sold some more diamonds;
and they all departed in another galley to the rescue of Cunégonde.

CHAPTER 28

What Happened to Candide, Cunégonde, Pangloss, Martin, &c.

—Let me beg your pardon once more, said Candide to the baron, pardon me, reverend father, for having run you through the body with my
sword.

—Don't mention it, replied the baron. I was a little too hasty myself,
I confess it; but since you want to know the misfortune which brought me
to the galleys, I'll tell you. After being cured of my wound by the brother
who was apothecary to the college, I was attacked and abducted by a Spanish raiding party; they jailed me in Buenos Aires at the time when my sister
had just left. I asked to be sent to Rome, to the father general. Instead,
I was named to serve as almoner in Constantinople, under the French
ambassador. I had not been a week on this job when I chanced one evening on a very handsome young ichoglan.[2] The evening was hot; the
young man wanted to take a swim; I seized the occasion, and went with
him. I did not know that it is a capital offense for a Christian to be found
naked with a young Moslem. A cadi sentenced me to receive a hundred
blows with a cane on the soles of my feet, and then to be sent to the galleys.
I don't suppose there was ever such a horrible miscarriage of justice. But
I would like to know why my sister is in the kitchen of a Transylvanian
king exiled among Turks.

—But how about you, my dear Pangloss, said Candide; how is it possible that we have met again?

—It is true, said Pangloss, that you saw me hanged; in the normal
course of things, I should have been burned, but you recall that a cloudburst occurred just as they were about to roast me. So much rain fell that
they despaired of lighting the fire; thus I was hanged, for lack of anything
better to do with me. A surgeon bought my body, carried me off to his
house, and dissected me. First he made a cross-shaped incision in me,
from the navel to the clavicle. No one could have been worse hanged
than I was. In fact, the executioner of the high ceremonials of the Holy
Inquisition, who was a subdeacon, burned people marvelously well, but
he was not in the way of hanging them. The rope was wet, and tightened

2. A page to the sultan.

badly; it caught on a knot; in short, I was still breathing. The cross-shaped incision made me scream so loudly that the surgeon fell over backwards; he thought he was dissecting the devil, fled in an agony of fear, and fell downstairs in his flight. His wife ran in, at the noise, from a nearby room; she found me stretched out on the table with my cross-shaped incision, was even more frightened than her husband, fled, and fell over him. When they had recovered a little, I heard her say to him: 'My dear, what were you thinking of, trying to dissect a heretic? Don't you know those people are always possessed of the devil? I'm going to get the priest and have him exorcised.' At these words, I shuddered, and collected my last remaining energies to cry: 'Have mercy on me!' At last the Portuguese barber³ took courage; he sewed me up again; his wife even nursed me; in two weeks I was up and about. The barber found me a job and made me lackey to a Knight of Malta who was going to Venice; and when this master could no longer pay me, I took service under a Venetian merchant, whom I followed to Constantinople.

—One day it occurred to me to enter a mosque; no one was there but an old imam and a very attractive young worshipper who was saying her prayers. Her bosom was completely bare; and between her two breasts she had a lovely bouquet of tulips, roses, anemones, buttercups, hyacinths, and primroses. She dropped her bouquet, I picked it up, and returned it to her with the most respectful attentions. I was so long getting it back in place that the imam grew angry, and, seeing that I was a Christian, he called the guard. They took me before the cadi, who sentenced me to receive a hundred blows with a cane on the soles of my feet, and then to be sent to the galleys. I was chained to the same galley and precisely the same bench as My Lord the Baron. There were in this galley four young fellows from Marseilles, five Neapolitan priests, and two Corfu monks, who assured us that these things happen every day. My Lord the Baron asserted that he had suffered a greater injustice than I; I, on the other hand, proposed that it was much more permissible to replace a bouquet in a bosom than to be found naked with an ichoglan. We were arguing the point continually, and getting twenty lashes a day with the bullwhip, when the chain of events within this universe brought you to our galley, and you ransomed us.

—Well, my dear Pangloss, Candide said to him, now that you have been hanged, dissected, beaten to a pulp, and sentenced to the galleys, do you still think everything is for the best in this world?

—I am still of my first opinion, replied Pangloss; for after all I am a philosopher, and it would not be right for me to recant since Leibniz could not possibly be wrong, and besides pre-established harmony is the finest notion in the world, like the plenum and subtle matter.⁴

---

3. The two callings of barber and surgeon, since they both involved sharp instruments, were inter-changeable in the early days of medicine.   4. Rigorous determinism requires that there be no empty spaces in the universe, so wherever it seems empty, one posits the existence of the "plenum." "Subtle matter" describes the soul, the mind, and all spiritual agencies—which can, therefore, be supposed subject to the influence and control of the great world machine, which is, of course, visibly material. Both are concepts needed to round out the system of optimistic determinism.

CHAPTER 29

How Candide Found Cunégonde and the Old Woman Again

While Candide, the baron, Pangloss, Martin, and Cacambo were tell-ing one another their stories, while they were disputing over the contin-gent or non-contingent events of this universe, while they were arguing over effects and causes, over moral evil and physical evil, over liberty and necessity, and over the consolations available to one in a Turkish galley, they arrived at the shores of Propontis and the house of the prince of Transylvania. The first sight to meet their eyes was Cunégonde and the old woman, who were hanging out towels on lines to dry.

The baron paled at what he saw. The tender lover Candide, seeing his lovely Cunégonde with her skin weathered, her eyes bloodshot, her breasts fallen, her cheeks seamed, her arms red and scaly, recoiled three steps in horror, and then advanced only out of politeness. She embraced Candide and her brother; everyone embraced the old woman; Candide ransomed them both.

There was a little farm in the neighborhood; the old woman suggested that Candide occupy it until some better fate should befall the group. Cunégonde did not know she was ugly, no one had told her; she reminded Candide of his promises in so firm a tone that the good Candide did not dare to refuse her. So he went to tell the baron that he was going to marry his sister.

—Never will I endure, said the baron, such baseness on her part, such insolence on yours; this shame at least I will not put up with; why, my sister's children would not be able to enter the Chapters in Germany.[5] No, my sister will never marry anyone but a baron of the empire.

Cunégonde threw herself at his feet, and bathed them with her tears; he was inflexible.

—You absolute idiot, Candide told him, I rescued you from the galleys, I paid your ransom, I paid your sister's; she was washing dishes, she is ugly, I am good enough to make her my wife, and you still presume to oppose it! If I followed my impulses, I would kill you all over again.

—You may kill me again, said the baron, but you will not marry my sister while I am alive.

CHAPTER 30

Conclusion

At heart, Candide had no real wish to marry Cunégonde; but the bar-on's extreme impertinence decided him in favor of the marriage, and Cunégonde was so eager for it that he could not back out. He consulted Pangloss, Martin, and the faithful Cacambo. Pangloss drew up a fine trea-tise, in which he proved that the baron had no right over his sister and that she could, according to all the laws of the empire, marry Candide morganatically.[6] Martin said they should throw the baron into the sea.

---

5. Knightly assemblies.   6. A morganatic marriage confers no rights on the partner of lower rank or on the offspring.

Cacambo thought they should send him back to the Levantine captain to finish his time in the galleys, and then send him to the father general in Rome by the first vessel. This seemed the best idea; the old woman approved, and nothing was said to his sister; the plan was executed, at modest expense, and they had the double pleasure of snaring a Jesuit and punishing the pride of a German baron.

It is quite natural to suppose that after so many misfortunes, Candide, married to his mistress, and living with the philosopher Pangloss, the philosopher Martin, the prudent Cacambo, and the old woman—having, besides, brought back so many diamonds from the land of the ancient Incas—must have led the most agreeable life in the world. But he was so cheated by the Jews[7] that nothing was left but his little farm; his wife, growing every day more ugly, became sour-tempered and insupportable; the old woman was ailing and even more ill-humored than Cunégonde. Cacambo, who worked in the garden and went into Constantinople to sell vegetables, was worn out with toil, and cursed his fate. Pangloss was in despair at being unable to shine in some German university. As for Martin, he was firmly persuaded that things are just as bad wherever you are; he endured in patience. Candide, Martin, and Pangloss sometimes argued over metaphysics and morals. Before the windows of the farmhouse they often watched the passage of boats bearing effendis, pashas, and cadis into exile on Lemnos, Mytilene, and Erzeroum; they saw other cadis, other pashas, other effendis coming, to take the place of the exiles and to be exiled in their turn. They saw various heads, neatly impaled, to be set up at the Sublime Porte.[8] These sights gave fresh impetus to their discussions; and when they were not arguing, the boredom was so fierce that one day the old woman ventured to say: —I should like to know which is worse, being raped a hundred times by negro pirates, having a buttock cut off, running the gauntlet in the Bulgar army, being flogged and hanged in an auto-da-fé, being dissected and rowing in the galleys—experiencing, in a word, all the miseries through which we have passed—or else just sitting here and doing nothing?

—It's a hard question, said Candide.

These words gave rise to new reflections, and Martin in particular concluded that man was bound to live either in convulsions of misery or in the lethargy of boredom. Candide did not agree, but expressed no positive opinion. Pangloss asserted that he had always suffered horribly; but having once declared that everything was marvelously well, he continued to repeat the opinion and didn't believe a word of it.

One thing served to confirm Martin in his detestable opinions, to make Candide hesitate more than ever, and to embarrass Pangloss. It was the arrival one day at their farm of Paquette and Brother Giroflée, who were in the last stages of misery. They had quickly run through their three thousand piastres, had split up, made up, quarreled, been jailed, escaped,

---

7. Voltaire's anti-Semitism, derived from various unhappy experiences with Jewish financiers, is not the most attractive aspect of his personality.   8. The gate of the sultan's palace is often used by extension to describe his government as a whole. But it was in fact a real gate where the heads of traitors and public enemies were gruesomely exposed.

and finally Brother Giroflée had turned Turk. Paquette continued to ply her trade everywhere, and no longer made any money at it.

—I told you, said Martin to Candide, that your gifts would soon be squandered and would only render them more unhappy. You have spent millions of piastres, you and Cacambo, and you are no more happy than Brother Giroflée and Paquette.

—Ah ha, said Pangloss to Paquette, so destiny has brought you back in our midst, my poor girl! Do you realize you cost me the end of my nose, one eye, and an ear? And look at you now! eh! what a world it is, after all!

This new adventure caused them to philosophize more than ever.

There was in the neighborhood a very famous dervish, who was said to be the best philosopher in Turkey; they went to ask his advice. Pangloss was spokesman, and he said: —Master, we have come to ask you to tell us why such a strange animal as man was created.

—What are you getting into? answered the dervish. Is it any of your business?

—But, reverend father, said Candide, there's a horrible lot of evil on the face of the earth.

—What does it matter, said the dervish, whether there's good or evil? When his highness sends a ship to Egypt, does he worry whether the mice on board are comfortable or not?

—What shall we do then? asked Pangloss.

—Hold your tongue, said the dervish.

—I had hoped, said Pangloss, to reason a while with you concerning effects and causes, the best of possible worlds, the origin of evil, the nature of the soul, and pre-established harmony.

At these words, the dervish slammed the door in their faces.

During this interview, word was spreading that at Constantinople they had just strangled two viziers of the divan,[9] as well as the mufti, and impaled several of their friends. This catastrophe made a great and general sensation for several hours. Pangloss, Candide, and Martin, as they returned to their little farm, passed a good old man who was enjoying the cool of the day at his doorstep under a grove of orange trees. Pangloss, who was as inquisitive as he was explanatory, asked the name of the mufti who had been strangled.

—I know nothing of it, said the good man, and I have never cared to know the name of a single mufti or vizier. I am completely ignorant of the episode you are discussing. I presume that in general those who meddle in public business sometimes perish miserably, and that they deserve their fate; but I never listen to the news from Constantinople; I am satisfied with sending the fruits of my garden to be sold there.

Having spoken these words, he asked the strangers into his house; his two daughters and two sons offered them various sherbets which they had made themselves, Turkish cream flavored with candied citron, orange, lemon, lime, pineapple, pistachio, and mocha coffee uncontaminated by the inferior coffee of Batavia and the East Indies. After which the two

---

9. Intimate advisers of the sultan.

daughters of this good Moslem perfumed the beards of Candide, Pangloss, and Martin.

—You must possess, Candide said to the Turk, an enormous and splendid property?

I have only twenty acres, replied the Turk; I cultivate them with my children, and the work keeps us from three great evils, boredom, vice, and poverty.

Candide, as he walked back to his farm, meditated deeply over the words of the Turk. He said to Pangloss and Martin: —This good old man seems to have found himself a fate preferable to that of the six kings with whom we had the honor of dining.

—Great place, said Pangloss, is very perilous in the judgment of all the philosophers; for, after all, Eglon, king of the Moabites, was murdered by Ehud; Absalom was hung up by the hair and pierced with three darts; King Nadab, son of Jeroboam, was killed by Baasha; King Elah by Zimri; Ahaziah by Jehu; Athaliah by Jehoiada; and Kings Jehoiakim, Jeconiah, and Zedekiah were enslaved. You know how death came to Croesus, Astyages, Darius, Dionysius of Syracuse, Pyrrhus, Perseus, Hannibal, Jugurtha, Ariovistus, Caesar, Pompey, Nero, Otho, Vitellius, Domitian, Richard II of England, Edward II, Henry VI, Richard III, Mary Stuart, Charles I, the three Henrys of France, and the Emperor Henry IV? You know . . .

—I know also, said Candide, that we must cultivate our garden.

—You are perfectly right, said Pangloss; for when man was put into the garden of Eden, he was put there *ut operaretur eum*, so that he should work it; this proves that man was not born to take his ease.

—Let's work without speculating, said Martin; it's the only way of rendering life bearable.

The whole little group entered into this laudable scheme; each one began to exercise his talents. The little plot yielded fine crops. Cunégonde was, to tell the truth, remarkably ugly; but she became an excellent pastry cook. Paquette took up embroidery; the old woman did the laundry. Everyone, down even to Brother Giroflée, did something useful; he became a very adequate carpenter, and even an honest man; and Pangloss sometimes used to say to Candide: —All events are linked together in the best of possible worlds; for, after all, if you had not been driven from a fine castle by being kicked in the backside for love of Miss Cunégonde, if you hadn't been sent before the Inquisition, if you hadn't traveled across America on foot, if you hadn't given a good sword thrust to the baron, if you hadn't lost all your sheep from the good land of Eldorado, you wouldn't be sitting here eating candied citron and pistachios.

—That is very well put, said Candide, but we must cultivate our garden.

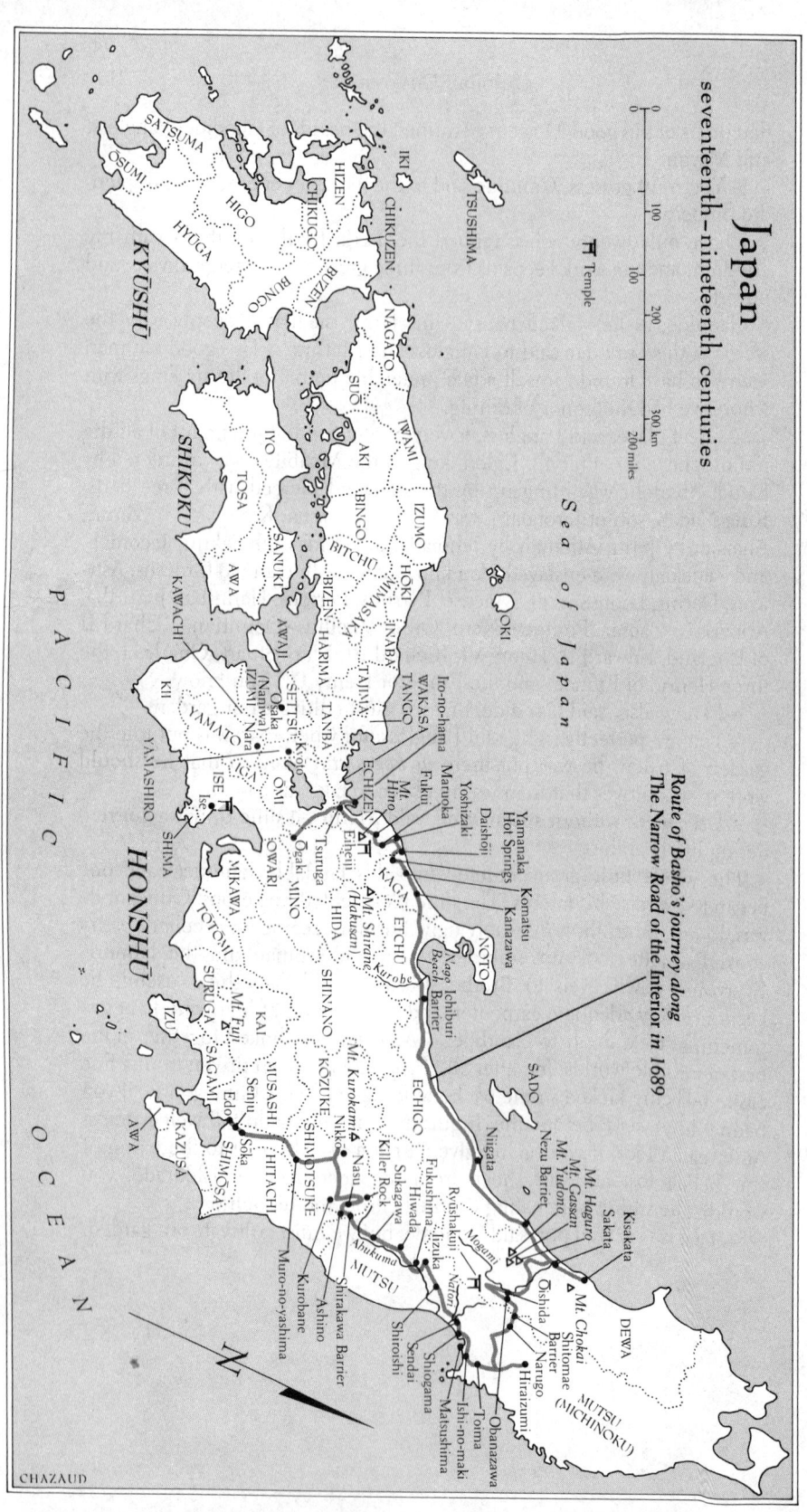

Japan

seventeenth–nineteenth centuries

⛩ Temple

0   100   200   300 km
0   100   200 miles

Route of Basho's journey along
The Narrow Road of the Interior in 1689

Sea of Japan

PACIFIC OCEAN

KYŪSHŪ

SATSUMA
OSUMI
HYŪGA
HIGO
CHIKUGO
BUNGO
CHIKUZEN
HIZEN
IKI
CHIKUZEN
TSUSHIMA
NAGATO
SUŌ

SHIKOKU
TOSA
IYO
SANUKI
AWA
KAWACHI
AWAJI

HONSHŪ

IWAMI
IZUMO
HŌKI
BINGO
MIMASAKA
BITCHŪ
BIZEN
INABA
TAJIMA
HARIMA
TANBA
TANGO
WAKASA
SETSU
Naniwa (Osaka)
Kyoto
IZUMI
YAMATO
Nara
IGA
ISE
Ise
SHIMA
OMI
OWARI
MINO
Tsuruga
ECHIZEN
Fukui
Maruoka
Mt. Hino
Yoshizaki
Daishoji
Komatsu
Kanazawa
KAGA
Mt. Shirane (Hakusan)
Eiheiji
Kurobe
ETCHŪ
NOTO
OKI
Natadera
Bach Barrier
Naga Ichiburi
SADO
Niigata
ECHIGO
Nezu Barrier
Mt. Haguro
Mt. Gassan
Mt. Yudono
Kisakata
Sakata
Mogami
Mt. Chokai
Shitomae Barrier
Narugo
Oishida
DEWA
Obanazawa
Ryushakuji
Yamanaka Hot Springs
MIKAWA
TOTOMI
SURUGA
Mt. Fuji
KAI
HIDA
SHINANO
Mt. Kurokami
Nikko
KŌZUKE
Killer Rock
Nasu
SHIMOTSUKE
Senju
Soka
Edo
MUSASHI
HITACHI
SHIMOSA
KAZUSA
AWA
SAGAMI
IZU
Kurobane
Ashino
Shirakawa Barrier
Muro-no-yashima
Abukuma
MUTSU (MICHINOKU)
Sukagawa
Hiwada
Fukushima
Iizuka
Kasashima
Shiroishi
Shiogama
Sendai
Shinobu
Matsushima
Ishi-no-maki
Toima
Hiraizumi

CHAZAUD

sive, iconoclastic, irrepressibly playful. Few here ever heard of the Enlightenment or the scientific revolution. The walled garden of Japan in the seventeenth and eighteenth centuries bloomed nicely without the irrigation of European currents.

A note on the Japanese calendar and time-keeping practices will be helpful in reading the following selection. Until 1873, when Japan adopted the Gregorian calendar of the West, the official calendar was derived from China and was divided into twelve lunations (months) of twenty-nine or thirty days. The resulting lunar year was approximately eleven days shorter than the solar year, which required the insertion of a thirteenth intercalary month every third year or thereabout to align the calendrical year with the solar. In addition, by custom the Japanese year began slightly later than the Western, so that New Year's Day fell anywhere from January 15 to February 15. The beginning of the new year also marked an increase in one's age, in contrast to the Western practice of reckoning age by birthdays. A child born in the twelfth month, for instance, would turn two with the new year.

Years were numbered serially from the year when a reigning emperor ascended the throne. In the modern period (beginning in 1868) the reign of an emperor has one name for its duration. For example, the reign of Emperor Hirohito is called the Shōwa ("enlightened peace") era, which lasted from his ascension in 1926 until his death in 1989. In addition to following the Western practice of numbering years by the Gregorian calendar, the year 1930, say, is reckoned as Shōwa 5. In the premodern period, rather than having one name throughout, an emperor's reign was usually divided into various eras, each with its own name.

Both the months and the hours of the day were designated by the signs of the Chinese zodiac. The day was divided into twelve units, each equivalent to 120 minutes:

Hour		Modern Equivalent
1	Rat	11 P.M.–1 A.M.
2	Ox	1 A.M.–3 A.M.
3	Tiger	3 A.M.–5 A.M.
4	Rabbit	5 A.M.–7 A.M.
5	Dragon	7 A.M.–9 A.M.
6	Snake	9 A.M.–11 A.M.
7	Horse	11 A.M.–1 P.M.
8	Ram	1 P.M.–3 P.M.
9	Monkey	3 P.M.–5 P.M.
10	Rooster	5 P.M.–7 P.M.
11	Dog	7 P.M.–9 P.M.
12	Boar	9 P.M.–11 P.M.

PRONOUNCING GLOSSARY

The following list uses common English syllables to provide rough equivalents of selected words whose pronunciation may be unfamiliar to the general reader.

haiku: *hai-koo*

Heike: *hay-kay*

kabuki: *kah-boo-kee*

nō: *noh*

Tokugawa: *toh-koo-gah-wah*

Zeami: *ze-ah-mee*

THE RISE OF POPULAR ARTS IN PREMODERN JAPAN

TEXTS	CONTEXTS
	1600–1868 Edo period: Tokugawa family establishes dynasty of shoguns who rule from Edo (present-day Tokyo)
1609 Commercial publishing begins in Japan	
	1616–1660 Imperial family commissions Katsura Detached Palace (icon of modernism for 20th-century architects)
	1620 The *Mayflower* carries Pilgrims to America
	ca. 1620–1716 Sōtatsu and Kōrin create masterpieces of Japanese screen painting
	1627 Korea becomes tributary state of China
1639 Aesop's *Fables* translated into Japanese	1639 Shogun proclaims policy of national isolation, expelling Portuguese and banning Christianity and foreign travel
1682 *The Life of a Sensuous Man* (Ihara Saikaku) launches comic realism and popular fiction	
1686 *The Barrelmaker Brimful of Love* published in Ihara Saikaku's collection *Five Women Who Loved Love*	
1690–1694 **The Narrow Road of the Interior** (Matsuo Bashō), verse inset in travel memoir by the foremost *haiku* poet	
1721 *The Love Suicides at Amijima* (Chikamatsu Monzaemon), masterpiece among tragedies of fatal love written for the puppet theater	
1745 *Haiku* poet Yosa Buson anticipates modern free verse with innovative poems in his *Elegy to Hokuju Rōsen*	

TEXTS	CONTEXTS
1748 *The Treasury of Loyal Retainers* (Takeda Izumo II), popular play immortalizing fealty of *samurai* who avenge their master's death	
1758–1801 Studies by Motoori Norinaga revive interest in **The Man'-yōshū** *(The Ten Thousand Leaves)*, **The Tale of Genji**, and other Japanese classics	
	1760s Harunobu inaugurates heyday of color woodblock print
	1769–1800 James Watt's refinements of the steam engine fuel Industrial Revolution
1770–1790 Center of literary activity shifts from Kyoto-Osaka area eastward to Edo (present-day Tokyo)	**1770–1790** Glory days of *kabuki* with actor Ichikawa Danjūrō V
ca. 1776 *Tales of Moonlight and Rain* (Ueda Akinari), a collection of supernatural stories, including *Bewitched*	**1776** American colonies adopt the Declaration of Independence
	1790 Utamaro's portraits of women add psychological depth to woodblock print tradition
	1810–1880 Landscapes by Hokusai and Hiroshige take art of woodblock print to its zenith

MATSUO BASHŌ
1644–1694

Until the seventeenth century, Japanese literature was privileged property. Court aristocrats and provincial warlords (and the occasional member of the Buddhist clergy) had exclusive access to "books": a narrow supply of manuscript copies. Even when the first printed books began to appear at the beginning of the seventeenth century, they were still luxury items. Connoisseurs underwrote lavishly illustrated printings of the Japanese classics available in limited editions, usually of no more than one hundred copies and intended not for sale but for presentation. Like the manuscripts they replaced, the first printed books were an indulgence. But when printing and publishing became commercial endeavors around the second decade of the new century, books changed from being rare works of art, whose mysteries were known only to the chosen few, into tools and pastimes for the multitude.

The diffusion of literacy, and thus education, was both a cause and an effect of the diffusion of the printed word. Print not only provided new channels of communication, a new medium for artists, and new commercial opportunities, it created for the first time in Japan the conditions necessary for that peculiarly modern phenomenon, celebrity.

The *haiku* poet Matsuo Bashō was an odd candidate for the new renown. Born in 1644 as the second son of a low-ranking provincial *samurai* who cobbled a living by teaching calligraphy, he had little in his background or early years that augured celebrity. Adult life commenced in the most ordinary way, when Bashō entered the service of a cadet branch of the local ruling military house. But he became close to his employer, the young heir, who was a devotee of linked verse, and Bashō too developed a taste for the popular poetry. Together they studied with Kitamura Kigin, one of the leading poets of the day, and they shared the excitement of seeing their compositions—two by Bashō and one by his patron—published in a poetry anthology in 1664. The easygoing days of poetastering and unchallenging service must have been very pleasant for Bashō and must have seemed the shape his days would take for the rest of his life.

But everything changed suddenly with the premature death in 1666 of his master. Bashō lost not only a friend and poetry companion but the protector who would have guaranteed him security and advancement in the ranks of the *samurai*. In 1672 Bashō left for Edo (now Tokyo), the expanding military capital of the shogun's new government, where he decided to make his career as a professional poet. To do so he had to build a following. With some thirty of his verses now in anthologies and his first book recently published, the twenty-eight-year-old Bashō must have conjectured that he had a better chance of establishing himself in a new city, where the competition for income as a teacher and corrector of poetry (an expert paid to correct other people's poetry) would be less intense than in the old capital of Kyoto or the seasoned commercial town of Osaka. This departure for the east was in its own quiet way daring. By leaving his home district and the employ of the local clan, he was forfeiting his status as a *samurai*, a member (however lowly) of the elite ruling class. In relocating to the boomtown of Edo, with a population already over six hundred thousand and growing, Bashō was in fact courting fame.

Not surprisingly, the first years in Edo were not easy. "Sometimes," he would later recall, "I grew weary of poetry and thought I would abandon it. Other times, I vowed to establish my name as the foremost poet. The two alternatives battled within, making me utterly restless." For a while, Bashō was forced to supplement his income with a post in the city's department of waterworks.

But ultimately he succeeded. Linked-verse anthologies sold well in the late seventeenth century, and Bashō's poems appeared in them with increasing frequency. Within eight years he had made a name for himself. He was asked to judge linked-verse competitions, and his published commentaries on these contests found a ready audience. Over time, he had gathered a stable of students large enough by 1680 for him to publish their best poems in an anthology. And Bashō's followers were so devoted that in the same year the more prosperous ones built a cottage for him in a quiet, still rural part of the city.

In front of this cottage, his students planted a banana tree. Its rare flowers were so small as to be unobtrusive, and the large, delicate leaves were easily torn when the wind blew in from the sea. The whole thing looked somehow lonesome. In a climate too cool for it to bear fruit, the tree was deprived of its purpose. Alone inside his hut, Bashō professed an affinity for his banana tree:

> Banana tree in autumn winds:
> a night passed hearing
> raindrops in a basin.

His persona was now complete: the lonely wayfarer who had traveled far from home, the man of simple tastes who had consecrated his life to poetry, the delicate sensibility as fragile as the leaves of a banana tree. It was only fitting that he took the word *banana*—Bashō—for his pen name.

One might well smile at Bashō's canniness. In the choice of his personal metaphor, he managed to join self-image and apparent, actual attributes with a public stance edited seamlessly into his literary product: like an actor so indistinguishable from his interchangeable roles that we think we know the "real" person. Bashō cast himself as a pilgrim, but the purpose of his frequent travels was a poetic devotion to nature—the beauty and truth it alone could reveal—not religious piety. Like a Zen monk, he shaved his head and donned the dark, drab garb of a cleric, setting off, as in *The Narrow Road of the Interior*, on paths by no means always certain, into wilderness not entirely safe. Whether home alone in his rustic cottage or enduring the ardors of the open road, Bashō sought an austere existence, as though he had taken a vow of poverty. *Economy* could have been his watchword.

In person and in art, he was the antithesis of Ihara Saikaku, a prosperous chronicler of rich, material life, and in fact Bashō appears to have disdained Saikaku's prolific literary output. To him, it was vulgar and excessive. (Not surprisingly, Bashō-the-perfectionist's entire oeuvre, about 1,000 *haiku*, is an afternoon's work for Saikaku, whose most frenzied single sitting of solo linked-verse composition yielded 23,500 poems in twenty-four hours!) Perhaps Saikaku in turn disdained Bashō's fastidiousness, endlessly revising a mere seventeen syllables. In the world of poetry, however, the tortoise won the race. Bashō's lapidary style perfected a kind of epigram that indeed seems to capture the universe in a grain of sand. His sympathy with nature, and particularly with its frailest elements, which speak of the transience and vulnerability of living things, was permanently accepted as the essence of Japanese poetic feeling.

The *haiku* was the perfect form for Bashō's art: a flash of lyric verse as fleeting as the momentary impression it encapsulates—a scene from nature or a natural object that evokes a truth larger than itself—expressed in cryptic, unrhymed lines of five, seven, and five syllables:

> Upon a bare branch
> a crow has descended—
> autumn in evening.

It is a form of poetry that looks effortless. Anyone can string together seventeen syllables and make them sound ponderous or picturesque, which is probably why *haiku* have become so popular (though syntactic differences between Japanese and English can sometimes defeat translation attempts that hold to the exact syllable count). Only a true poet can work within the slender margins of this constricted form and create something beyond aphorism. It was Bashō's gift to fuse the transitory and the eternal, both the moment observed and its greater significance. The crow landing on the branch of a withered tree is the "now" of the poem; time's passing and loneliness are the universals.

Actually, *haiku* began as part of linked verse, and in this respect too its apparent simplicity is deceptive. In the composition of linked poetry, resulting normally in sequences of thirty-six or one hundred verses (although they could stretch into one thousand verses or more), several poets worked in tandem. They took turns composing alternating links, or verses, in three lines with syllable counts of five, seven, and five (identical in form to *haiku*) and in two lines with syllable counts of seven each. Eventually, anthologies of linked poetry began to appear, excerpting the opening verses from various sequences. Thus these short poems in three lines of seventeen syllables, originally intended as the base to which subsequent lines of verse would be added, came to stand on their own. Poets began to write *haiku* as self-contained lyrics. But however independent they became, for a long time *haiku* retained a vestigial sense that they were somehow part of a larger matrix, or ought to be. This is one reason that poems in *The Narrow Road of the Interior* are embedded in a travel narrative, the prose equivalent of a linked sequence. By subtly following some of the structural principles of linked verse, Bashō's narrative achieves a kind of covert unity. And by including an occasional poem by his traveling companion, Sora, it retains something of the feel of linked verse. Once again poets were collaborating.

The Narrow Road of the Interior was written, or begun, in 1689, when Bashō embarked on his most ambitious journey. It would cover fifteen hundred miles of hinterland and take Bashō and Sora to the far corners of northern Japan. Although he is first thought of as a *haiku* poet, many of Bashō's best poems originally appeared in the five travel memoirs that he wrote in the final decade of his life. *The Narrow Road* is the last of these travel diaries, the longest, and the most esteemed. It also represents the climax of a venerable tradition in Japan, where the travel diary as poetic memoir enjoyed a distinguished eight-hundred-year history.

This fact too is an indication that Bashō's poetry involves more than meets the eye. The journey depicted in *The Narrow Road* is another pilgrimage through nature, but it is also a very conscious emulation of the conventions of the past. "Bewitched by the god of restlessness" Bashō describes himself as the trip gets under way. "Seduced by the call of history" would be just as accurate. Bashō, or his literary persona, sets off as the hero on a quest. His goal is to seek inspiration from remote places made famous by literature and history. Reputation, celebrity, tradition intertwine.

In 1943, some 250 years later, a second diary was published. This was Sora's account of their trip together, and it came like a thunderclap. The man who represented himself as a frail pilgrim at the mercy of nature and fate, and who was later deified by the Shinto religion, is described by Sora as a much more practical and wily figure, who altered the facts of his trip, abridged, and deleted to maintain the ascetic tone appropriate for a poetic saint, a man who saw himself as the successor to all poet-travelers of the past and was not about to reveal that among the motives for his trip were cultivating patrons and recruiting new students.

But *The Narrow Road of the Interior* is a literary creation. Its spare, supple prose anchors wise poetic insights. Its *haiku* transcend entertainment. The material has been shaped only by taking great pains, and that is the nature of artistry.

For another, more colloquial rendering of *The Narrow Road of the Interior*, translated by the poet Cid Corman in collaboration with Kamaike Susumu, see *Back Roads to Far Towns* (1986). All five of Bashō's travel journals are found in *The Narrow Road to the Deep North and Other Travel Sketches* (1966), translated by Nobuyuki Yuasa, whose re-creation of *haiku* as four-line poems seems less successful. For additional *haiku* by Bashō see Lucien Stryk, trans., *On Love and Barley* (1985). For examples of Bashō's linked poetry see Earl Miner and Hiroko Odagiri, trans., *The Monkey's Straw Raincoat* (1981). For more poems by Bashō and his followers see Steven D. Carter, *Traditional Japanese Poetry: An Anthology* (1991). Two excellent book-length introductions to Bashō, both by Makoto Ueda, are *Matsuo Bashō* (1982) and *Bashō and His Interpreters* (1991). Shorter introductions are found in two literary histories by Donald Keene: *World within Walls* (1976) and *Travelers of a Hundred Ages* (1989). For a general study of *haiku* see Kenneth Yasuda, *The Japanese Haiku* (1957), and for an anthology of *haiku* from Bashō to modern times see Harold G. Henderson, *An Introduction to Haiku* (1958).

PRONOUNCING GLOSSARY

The following list uses common English syllables to provide rough equivalents of selected words whose pronunciation may be unfamiliar to the general reader.

Atsumi: *ah-tsoo-mee*

Benkei: *ben-kay*

Butchō: *boot-choh*

Date: *dah-tay*

Echigo: *e-chee-goh*

Edo: *e-doh*

Fukuura: *foo-koo-oo-rah*

Genji: *gen-jee*

Genroku: *gen-roh-koo*

haikai: *hai-kai*

Heike: *hay-ke*

hototogisu: *hoh-toh-toh-gee-soo*

Ihara Saikaku: *ee-hah-rah sai-kah-koo*

Iizuka: *ee-ee-zoo-kah*

Ji: *jee*

Kanemori: *kah-ne-moh-ree*

Kawai: *kah-wai*

Kisakata: *kee-sah-kah-tah*

Kokinshū: *koh-keen-shoo*

konoshiro: *koh-noh-shee-roh*

koromogae: *koh-roh-moh-gah-e*

Kūkai: *koo-kai*

Kurokamiyama: *koo-roh-kah-mee-yah-mah*

Kyohaku: *kyoh-hah-koo*

Matsuo Bashō: *mah-tsoo-oh bah-shoh*

Minamidani: *mee-nah-mee-dah-nee*

Nikkō: *neek-koh*

Nōin: *noh-een*

Satō Shōji: *sah-toh shoh-jee*

Shinto: *sheen-toh*

Shiogoshi: *shee-oh-goh-shee*

Shirakawa: *shee-rah-kah-wah*

Sōgorō: *soh-goh-roh*

Tsuruga: *tsoo-roo-gah*

Yasuhira: *yah-soo-hee-rah*

Yoichi: *yoh-ee-chee*

Yudono: *yoo-doh-noh*

The Narrow Road of the Interior[1]

The sun and the moon are eternal voyagers; the years that come and go are travelers too. For those whose lives float away on boats, for those who greet old age with hands clasping the lead ropes of horses, travel is life, travel is home. And many are the men of old who have perished as they journeyed.

I myself fell prey to wanderlust some years ago, desiring nothing better than to be a vagrant cloud scudding before the wind. Only last autumn, after having drifted along the seashore for a time, had I swept away the old cobwebs from my dilapidated riverside hermitage. But the year ended before I knew it, and I found myself looking at hazy spring skies and thinking of crossing Shirakawa Barrier.[2] Bewitched by the god of restlessness, I lost my peace of mind; summoned by the spirits of the road, I felt unable to settle down to anything. By the time I had mended my torn trousers, put a new cord on my hat, and cauterized my legs with moxa,[3] I was thinking only of the moon at Matsushima. I turned over my dwelling to others, moved to a house belonging to Sanpū,[4] and affixed the initial page of a linked-verse sequence to one of the pillars at my cottage.

> Even my grass-thatched hut
> will have new occupants now:
> a display of dolls.[5]

It was the Twenty-seventh Day, almost the end of the Third Month. The wan morning moon retained little of its brilliance, but the silhouette of Mount Fuji was dimly visible in the first pale light of dawn. With a twinge of sadness, I wondered when I might see the flowering branches at Ueno and Yanaka again. My intimate friends, who had all assembled the night before, got on the boat to see me off.

We disembarked at Senju.[6] Transitory though I know this world to be, I shed tears when I came to the parting of the ways, overwhelmed by the prospect of the long journey ahead.

> Departing springtime:
> birds lament and fishes too
> have tears in their eyes.

With that as the initial entry in my journal, we started off, hard though it was to stride out in earnest. The others lined up part way along the road, apparently wanting to watch us out of sight.

That year was, I believe, the second of the Genroku[7] era [1689]. I had

---

1. Translated by Helen Craig McCullough and Steven D. Carter, with notes adapted from McCullough.   2. An old official checkpoint where travelers entered Mutsu Province.   3. A combustible substance used in traditional East Asian medicine. Moxa cones, made from pulverized plant leaves, were burned at specific therapeutic points on the skin, depending on the symptoms. The resulting heat was thought to adjust physical disorders by releasing energy obstructed at a crucial point and returning it to smooth circulation.   4. A disciple and patron.   5. It is the time of the Doll Festival, in the Third Month, when dolls representing the emperor, the empress, and their attendants are displayed in every household.   6. Near Edo (Tokyo). The path of Bashō's journey is traced on the map on p. 2102.   7. The era name. For information on the Japanese calendar, see the introduction "The Rise of Popular Arts in Premodern Japan" (p. 2105).

taken a sudden fancy to make the long pilgrimage on foot to Mutsu and Dewa[8]—to view places I had heard about but never seen, even at the cost of hardships severe enough to "whiten a man's hair under the skies of Wu."[9] The outlook was not reassuring, but I resolved to hope for the best and be content merely to return alive.

We barely managed to reach Sōka Post Station that night. My greatest trial was the pack I bore on my thin, bony shoulders. I had planned to set out with no baggage at all, but had ended by taking along a paper coat for cold nights, a cotton bath garment, rain gear, and ink and brushes, as well as certain farewell presents, impossible to discard, which simply had to be accepted as burdens on the way.

We went to pay our respects at Muro-no-yashima. Sora, my fellow pilgrim, said, "This shrine honors Ko-no-hana-sakuya-hime, the goddess worshipped at Mount Fuji. The name Muro-no-yashima is an allusion to the birth of Hohodemi-no-mikoto inside the sealed chamber the goddess entered and set ablaze in fulfillment of her vow. It is because of that same incident that poems about the shrine usually mention smoke. The passage in the shrine history telling of the prohibition against konoshiro fish[1] is also well known."

On the Thirtieth, we lodged at the foot of the Nikkō Mountains. "I am called Buddha Gozaemon," the master of the house informed us. "People have given me that title because I make it a point to be honest in all my dealings. You may rest here tonight with your minds at ease."

"What kind of Buddha is it who has manifested himself in this impure world to help humble travelers like us—mendicant monks, as it were, on a pious pilgrimage?" I wondered. By paying close attention to his behavior, I satisfied myself that he was indeed a man of stubborn integrity, devoid of shrewdness and calculation. He was one of those, "firm, resolute, simple, and modest, who are near virtue,"[2] and I found his honorable, unassuming nature wholly admirable.

On the First of the Fourth Month, we went to worship at the shrine. In antiquity, the name of that holy mountain was written Nikōsan [Two-Storm Mountain], but the Great Teacher Kūkai changed it to Nikkō [Sunlight] when he founded the temple. It is almost as though the Great Teacher had been able to see 1,000 years into the future, for today the shrine's radiance extends throughout the realm, its beneficence overflows in the eight directions, and the four classes[3] of people dwell in security and peace. This is an awesome subject of which I shall write no more.

Ah, awesome sight!
on summer leaves and spring leaves,
the radiance of the sun!

Kurokamiyama was veiled in haze, dotted with lingering patches of white snow. Sora composed this poem:

8. Two northern provinces.   9. An allusion to a Chinese poem written by someone seeing off a monk on his travels: "Your hat will be heavy with the snows of Wu; / Your boots will be fragrant with the fallen blossoms of Chu." Snow on a traveler's hat was associated with hardships and with whitening hair. 1. Gizzard shad. It was taboo to eat the fish because, when broiled, it gave off a smell like flesh burning. 2. From Confucius's Analects.   3. Samurai, farmer, artisan, and merchant. The shrine held the mausoleum of the founder of the Tokugawa shogunate.

> Black hair shaved off,
> at Kurokamiyama[4]
> I change to new robes.

Sora is of the Kawai family; he was formerly called Sōgorō. He lived in a house adjoining mine, almost under the leaves of the banana plant, and used to help me with the chores of hauling wood and drawing water. Delighted by the thought of seeing Matsushima and Kisakata with me on this trip, and eager also to spare me some of the hardships of the road, he shaved his head at dawn on the day of our departure, put on a monk's black robe, and changed his name to Sōgo. That is why he composed the Kurokamiyama poem. The word *koromogae* ["I change to new robes"][5] was most effective.

There is a waterfall half a league or so up the mountain. The stream leaps with tremendous force over outthrust rocks at the top and descends 100 feet into a dark green pool strewn with 1,000 rocks. Visitors squeeze into the space between the rocks and the cascade to view it from the rear, which is why it is called Urami-no-take [Rearview Falls].

> In brief seclusion
> at a waterfall—the start
> of a summer retreat.

I knew someone at Kurobane in Nasu, so we decided to head straight across the plain from there. It began to rain as we walked along, taking our bearings on a distant village, and the sun soon sank below the horizon. After borrowing accommodations for the night at a farmhouse, we started out across the plain again in the morning. A horse was grazing nearby. We appealed for help to a man who was cutting grass and found him by no means incapable of understanding other people's feelings, rustic though he was.

"What's the best thing to do, I wonder?" he said. "I can't leave my work. Still, inexperienced travelers are bound to get lost on this plain, what with all the trails branching off in every direction. Rather than see you go on alone, I'll let you take the horse. Send him back when he won't go any farther." With that, he lent us the animal.

Two small children came running behind the horse. One of them, a little girl, was called Kasane. Sora composed this poem:

> Kasane must be
> a name for a wild pink
> with double petals![6]

Before long, we arrived at a hamlet and turned the horse back with some money tied to the saddle.

We called on Jōbōji, the warden at Kurobane. Surprised and delighted to see us, he kept us in conversation day and night; and his younger brother, Tōsui, came morning and evening. We went with Tōsui to his

---

4. Or Mount Kurokami, homonymous with "black hair."   5. The first day of the Fourth Month was the date for changing from winter to summer clothing.   6. This poem uses wordplay. The name *Kasane* can mean "double." The word for "wild pink" (a flower) can also mean "beloved child."

own house and were also invited to the homes of various other relatives. So the time passed.

One day, we strolled into the outskirts of the town for a brief visit to the site of the old dog shoots, then pressed through the Nasu bamboo fields to Lady Tamamo's tumulus,[7] and went on to pay our respects at Hachiman Shrine. Someone told me that when Yoichi shot down the fan target, it was to this very shrine that he prayed, "and especially Shōhachiman, the tutelary deity of my province."[8] The thought of the divine response evoked deep emotion. We returned to Tōsui's house as darkness fell.

There was a mountain-cult temple, Kōmyōji, in the vicinity. We visited it by invitation and worshipped at the Ascetic's Hall.[9]

> Toward summer mountains
> we set off after prayers
> before the master's clogs.

The site of the Venerable Butchō's[1] hermitage was behind Unganji Temple in that province. Butchō once told me that he had used pine charcoal to inscribe a poem on a rock there:

> Ah, how I detest
> building any shelter at all,
> even a grass-thatched
> hovel less than five feet square!
> Were it not for the rainstorms . . .

Staff in hand, I prepared to set out for the temple to see what was left of the hermitage. A number of people encouraged one another to accompany me, and I acquired a group of young companions who kept up a lively chatter along the way. We reached the lower limits of the temple grounds in no time. The mountains created an impression of great depth. The valley road stretched far into the distance, pines and cryptomerias rose in dark masses, the moss dripped with moisture, and there was a bite to the air, even though it was the Fourth Month. We viewed all of the Ten Sights[2] and entered the main gate by way of a bridge.

Eager to locate the hermitage, I scrambled up the hill behind the temple to a tiny thatched structure on a rock, a lean-to built against a cave. It was like seeing the holy Yuanmiao's Death Gate or the monk Fayun's[3] rock chamber. I left an impromptu verse on a pillar:

> Even woodpeckers
> seem to spare the hermitage
> in the summer grove.

7. According to legend, Lady Tamamo was a fox-woman with whom an emperor fell in love. After having been unmasked by a diviner, she fled to Nasu, where local warriors shot her down. Her vindictive spirit survived as Killer Rock, a large boulder that releases poisonous fumes, which Bashō will soon visit on his journey. *Dog shoots:* for a brief time in the 13th century dog shooting had been a sport. 8. Refers to an episode in *The Tale of the Heike*. Yoichi is a minor *samurai* in the service of the Minamoto/Genji. An expert archer, he succeeds in shooting a fan suspended off the prow of an enemy ship, put there to taunt the Genji. Hachiman Shrine was dedicated to the god of war.   9. Dedicated to a miracle-working mountain ascetic of the 8th century, whose enshrined image is believed to have shown a holy man wearing high clogs (referred to in the following poem) and clothes made from leaves, holding a staff, and leaning against a rock.   1. A Zen master with whom Bashō had studied. 2. Various rocks, peaks, buildings, etc., within the temple precincts.   3. A Chinese priest; he lived in a hut perched atop a high rock. Yuanmiao was a Chinese priest who confined himself for fifteen years to a cave he called Death's Gate.

From Kurobane, I headed toward Killer Rock astride a horse lent us by the warden. When the groom asked if I would write a poem for him, I gave him this, surprised and impressed that he should exhibit such cultivated taste:

> A cuckoo[4] song:
> please make the horse angle off
> across the field.

Killer Rock stands in the shadow of a mountain near a hot spring. It still emits poisonous vapors: dead bees, butterflies, and other insects lie in heaps near it, hiding the color of the sand.

The willow "where fresh spring water flowed"[5] survives on a ridge between two ricefields in Ashino Village. The district officer there, a man called Kohō, had often expressed a desire to show me the tree, and I had wondered each time about its exact location—but on this day I rested in its shade.

> Ah, the willow tree:
> a whole rice paddy planted
> before I set out.

So the days of impatient travel had accumulated, until at last I had reached Shirakawa Barrier. It was there, for the first time, that I felt truly on the way. I could understand why Kanemori had been moved to say, "Would that there were a means somehow to send people word in the capital!"[6]

As one of the Three Barriers, Shirakawa has always attracted the notice of poets and other writers. An autumn wind seemed to sound in my ears, colored leaves seemed to appear before my eyes—but even the leafy summer branches were delightful in their own way. Wild roses bloomed alongside the whiteness of the deutzia, making us feel as though we were crossing snow. I believe one of Kiyosuke's writings preserves a story about a man of the past who straightened his hat and adjusted his dress there.[7] Sora composed this poem:

> With deutzia[8] flowers
> we adorn our hats—formal garb
> for the barrier.

We passed beyond the barrier and crossed the Abukuma River. To the left, the peak of Aizu soared; to the right, the districts of Iwaki, Sōma, and Mihara lay extended; to the rear, mountains formed boundaries with

---

4. In Japanese *hototogisu*; the name is an onomatopoeia derived from the bird's call: *ho-to-to*. Its song was deemed the quintessence of summer and is so beautiful that Bashō would like his horse to follow after it.   5. Refers to a verse by the famed poet-priest Saigyō (1118–1190): "On the wayside / where a clear spring flowed / in a willow's shade: / 'Just for a moment,' I thought, / but then I lingered there." Saigyō was an inveterate traveler and an important influence on Bashō.   6. Alludes to a poem by Kanemori (died 990): "Would there were means / to let them know, somehow, / the people of the capital: / 'Today I have crossed / Shirakawa Barrier.'"   7. Fujiwara Kiyosuke (1104–1177) was a court noble and a poet-scholar. The man's actions show respect to Nōin (998–1050?), a monk and early poet-traveler who established Shirakawa Barrier as a place with poetic associations. In earlier times, travelers approaching checkpoints between provinces adjusted their clothes before crossing the barrier.   8. A shrub of the saxifrage family, an ornamental bush with white or pink flowers. It blooms in the Fourth Month.

Hitachi and Shimotsuke provinces. We passed Kagenuma Pond, but the sky happened to be overcast that day, so there were no reflections.[9]

At the post town of Sukagawa, we visited a man called Tōkyū, who persuaded us to stay four or five days. His first act was to inquire, "How did you feel when you crossed Shirakawa Barrier?"

"What with the fatigue of the long, hard trip, the distractions of the scenery, and the stress of so many nostalgic associations, I couldn't manage to think of a decent poem," I said. "Still, it seemed a pity to cross with nothing to show for it . . .":

> A start for connoisseurs
> of poetry—rice-planting song
> of Michinoku.

We added a second verse and then a third, and continued until we had completed three sequences.

Under a great chestnut tree in the corner of the town, there lived a hermit monk. It seemed to me that his cottage, with its aura of lonely tranquility, must resemble that other place deep in the mountains where someone had gathered horse chestnuts.[1] I set down a few words:

To form the character "chestnut," we write "tree of the west."[2] I have heard, I believe, that the bodhisattva Gyōgi perceived an affinity between this tree and the Western Paradise,[3] and that he used its wood for staffs and pillars throughout his life:

> Chestnut at the eaves—
> here are blossoms unremarked
> by ordinary folk.

Asakayama is just beyond Hiwada Post Station, about five leagues from Tōkyū's house. It is close to the road, and there are numerous marshes in the vicinity. It was almost the season for reaping katsumi.[4] We kept asking, "Which plant is the flowering katsumi?" But nobody knew. We wandered about, scrutinizing marshes, questioning people, and seeking "katsumi, katsumi" until the sun sank to the rim of the hills.

We turned off to the right at Nihonmatsu, took a brief look at Kurozuka Cave,[5] and stopped for the night at Fukushima.

On the following day, we went to Shinobu in search of the Fern-print Rock,[6] which proved to be half buried under the soil of a remote hamlet in the shadow of a mountain. Some village urchins came up and told us, "In the old days, the rock used to be on top of that mountain, but the farmers got upset because the people who passed would destroy the young

---

9. The name of the pond is literally "Shadow Swamp"; with the sun obscured, it does not fulfill its reputation.　　1. Refers to Saigyō (see n. 5, p. 2116) and one of his poems: "In these remote hills, / I try to trap water / dripping onto the rocks; / I gather horse chestnuts / dropping to the ground."　　2. The character for "chestnut" consists of the character for "tree" surmounted by an element resembling the character for "west."　　3. One of the various "Buddha worlds" (Buddhist equivalents of Heaven); this one is located in the western sector of the universe and is presided over by Amida, the most popular Buddhist deity of the time. Bodhisattva: a person who attains enlightenment but compassionately refrains from entering paradise to save others, a future Buddha. Gyōgi (668–749) was a Buddhist monk known for his asceticism and charisma.　　4. Wild rice.　　5. Rich in folklore. A witch was said to be interred beneath Kurozuka, a hillock whose name means "black mound," and the nearby rocky cave was thought a goblins' lair.　　6. Said to have been used to imprint cloth with a moss-fern design, a specialty of the area.

grain so they could test it. They shoved it off into this valley; that's why it's lying upside down." A likely story, perhaps.

> Hands planting seedlings
> evoke Shinobu patterns
> of the distant past.

We crossed the river at Tsukinowa Ford and emerged at Senoue Post Station. Satō Shōji's[7] old home was about a league and a half away, near the mountains to the left. Told that we would find the site at Sabano in Iizuka Village, we went along, asking directions, until we came upon it at a place called Maruyama. That was where Shōji had had his house. I wept as someone explained that the front gate had been at the foot of the hill. Still standing at an old temple nearby were a number of stone monuments erected in memory of the family. It was especially moving to see the memorials to the two young wives.[8] "Women though they were, all the world knows of their bravery." The thought made me drench my sleeve. The Tablet of Tears[9] was not far to seek!

We entered the temple to ask for tea, and there we saw Yoshitsune's sword and Benkei's pannier,[1] preserved as treasures.

> Paper carp flying!
> Display pannier and sword, too,
> in the Fifth Month.

It was the First Day of the Fifth Month.

We lodged that night at Iizuka, taking advantage of the hot springs in the town to bathe before engaging a room. The hostelry turned out to be a wretched hovel, its straw mats spread over dirt floors. In the absence of a lamp, we prepared our beds and stretched out by the light from a fire-pit. Thunder rumbled during the night, and rain fell in torrents. What with the roof leaking right over my head and the fleas and mosquitoes biting, I got no sleep at all. To make matters worse, my old complaint[2] flared up, causing me such agony that I almost fainted.

At long last, the short night ended and we set out again. Still feeling the effects of the night, I rode a rented horse to Kōri Post Station. It was unsettling to fall prey to an infirmity while so great a distance remained ahead. But I told myself that I had deliberately planned this long pilgrimage to remote areas, a decision that meant renouncing worldly concerns and facing the fact of life's uncertainty. If I were to die on the road—very well, that would be Heaven's decree. Such reflections helped to restore my spirits a bit, and it was with a jaunty step that I passed through the Great Gate into the Date[3] domain.

We entered Kasajima District by way of Abumizuri and Shiraishi Castle. I asked someone about the Fujiwara Middle Captain Sanekata's[4] grave

7. A brave warrior and supporter of the Genji chieftain Yoshitsune (in *The Tale of the Heike*).   8. Of Satō Shōji's two sons, who died in battle. The young widows were said to have worn their husbands' suits of armor as a way of consoling their grieving mother-in-law, who still hoped to see her sons riding home victorious.   9. A memorial erected in China in honor of a virtuous official. All who saw it were said to weep.   1. A large basket. Yoshitsune is the great hero who leads his clan to victory in the war recounted in *The Tale of the Heike*. Benkei is his faithful lieutenant.   2. Bashō was troubled with stomachaches and hemorrhoids.   3. A clan that included some of the richest and most powerful provincial barons.   4. Fujiwara Sanekata (died 998) was a court poet whose quarrel with a clansman led to his exile in the northern provinces.

and was told, "Those two villages far off to the right at the edge of the hills are Minowa and Kasajima. The Road Goddess's shrine and the 'memento miscanthus' are still there."[5] The road was in a dreadful state from the recent early-summer rains, and I was exhausted, so we contented ourselves with looking in that direction as we trudged on. Because the names Minowa and Kasajima suggested the rainy season,[6] I composed this verse.

> Where is Rain Hat Isle?
> Somewhere down the muddy roads
> of the Fifth Month!

We lodged at Iwanuma. It was exciting to see the Takekuma Pine. The trunk forks a bit above the ground, and one knows instantly that this is just how the old tree must have looked. My first thought was of Nōin.[7] Did he compose the poem, "Not a trace this time of the pine" because a certain man, appointed long ago to serve as Governor of Mutsu, had felled the tree to get pilings for a bridge to span the Natori River? Someone told me that generations of people have been alternately cutting down the existing tree and planting a replacement. The present one is a magnificent specimen—quite capable, I should imagine, of living 1,000 years.

Kyohaku[8] had given me a poem as a farewell present:

> Late cherry blossoms:
> please show my friend the pine tree
> at Takekuma.

Thus:

> After three months:
> the twin-trunked pine awaited
> since the cherry trees bloomed.

We crossed the Natori River into Sendai on the day when people thatch their roofs with sweet-flag leaves.[9] We sought out a lodging and stayed four or five days.

I made the acquaintance of a local painter, Kaemon by name, who had been described to me as a man of cultivated taste. He told us he had devoted several years to locating famous old places that had become hard to identify, and took us to see some of them one day. The bush clover grew thick at Miyagino; I could imagine the sight in autumn. It was the season when the pieris[1] bloomed at Tamada, Yokono, and Tsutsuji-gaoka. We entered a pine grove where no sunlight penetrated—a place called Konoshita, according to Kaemon—and I thought it must have been the same kind of heavy moisture, dripping from those very trees long ago, that inspired the poem, "Suggest to your lord, attendants, that he wear his

---

5. Someone had planted a clump of miscanthus, a variety of ornamental grass, at Sanekata's grave in allusion to a memorial poem by Saigyō: "Only his name, / eternally unwithered, / has escaped decay: / we see, as a memento, / miscanthus on a dry plain." 6. *Mino* can mean "straw raincoat," and *kasa* can mean "rain hat." 7. See n. 7, p. 2116. 8. A disciple. 9. On Boys' Day, a holiday on the fifth day of the Fifth Month, it was the custom for families with sons to fly carp streamers, a symbol of vigor and success. On the day before, irises (*sweet-flag*), because they were thought to ward off evil, were hung from the eaves. The holiday was also known as the Iris Festival. 1. Japanese andromeda (*Pieris japonica*), a broad-leafed evergreen with drooping clusters of white flowers.

hat."[2] We paid our respects at the Yakushidō Hall and at Tenjin Shrine before the day ended.

Kaemon sent us off with a map on which he had drawn famous scenes of Shiogama and Matsushima. He also gave us two pairs of straw sandals, bound with dark blue cords, as a farewell present. The gifts showed him to be quite as cultivated as I had surmised.

> Let us bind sweet-flags
> to our feet, making of them
> cords for straw sandals.

Continuing on our way with the help of the map, we came to the *tofu* [ten-strand] sedge, growing at the base of the mountains where the "narrow road of the interior"[3] runs. I am told that the local people still make ten-strand mats every year for presentation to the provincial Governor.

We saw the Courtyard Monument Stone at Tagajō in Ichikawa Village. It was a little more than six feet tall and perhaps three feet wide. Some characters, faintly visible as depressions in the moss, listed distances to the provincial boundaries in the four directions. There was also an inscription: "This castle was erected in the first year of Jinki [724] by the Inspector-Garrison Commander Ōno no Ason Azumabito. It was rebuilt in the sixth year of Tenpyō Hōji [762] by the Consultant-Garrison Commander Emi no Ason Asakari. First Day, Twelfth Month." That was in the reign of Emperor Shōmu.

Although we hear about many places celebrated in verse since antiquity, most of them have vanished with the passing of time. Mountains have crumbled, rivers have entered unaccustomed channels, roads have followed new routes, stones have been buried and hidden underground, aged trees have given way to saplings. But this monument was a genuine souvenir from 1,000 years ago, and to see it before my eyes was to feel that I could understand the sentiments of the old poets. "This is a traveler's reward," I thought. "This is the joy of having survived into old age." Moved to tears, I forgot the hardships of the road.

From there, we went to see Noda-no-tamagawa and Oki-no-ishi. A temple, Masshōzan, had been built at Sue-no-matsuyama, and there were graves everywhere among the pine trees, saddening reminders that such must be the end of all vows to "interchange wings and link branches."[4] The evening bell was tolling as we entered Shiogama.

The perpetual overcast of the rainy season had lifted enough to reveal Magaki Island close at hand, faintly illuminated by the evening moon. A line of small fishing boats came rowing in. As I listened to the voices of the men dividing the catch, I felt that I understood the poet who sang, "There is deep pathos in a boat pulled by a rope," and my own emotion

---

2. A poem in the *Kokinshū* (Collection of ancient and modern times), the first of twenty-one imperially commissioned anthologies of classical Japanese poetry; it was completed around 905 and contains 1,111 poems. The poem referred to here is: "Suggest to your lord, / attendants, / that he wear his hat, / for beneath the trees of Miyagino / the dew comes down harder than the rain." 3. This road, the source of Bashō's title, extended from what is now northeastern Sendai to Tagajō City (see the map on p. 2102). 4. An allusion to the pledge exchanged by the Chinese emperor and his beloved in the *Song of Everlasting Sorrow* by Po Chü-i: "In heaven, may we be birds with shared wings; / On earth, may we be trees with linked branches." The places mentioned here are in the vicinity of Sendai.

deepened.[5] That night, a blind singer recited a Michinoku ballad[6] to the accompaniment of his lute. He performed not far from where I was trying to sleep, and I found his loud, countrified falsetto rather noisy—a chanting style quite different from either *Heike* recitation or the *kōwaka-mai*[7] ballad drama. But then I realized how admirable it was that the fine old customs were still preserved in that distant land.

Early the next day, we visited Shiogama Shrine, which had been restored by the provincial Governor. Its pillars stood firm and majestic, its painted rafters sparkled, its stone steps rose in flight after flight, and its sacred red fences gleamed in the morning sunlight. With profound reverence, I reflected that it is the way of our land for the miraculous powers of the gods to manifest themselves even in such remote, out-of-the-way places as this.

In front of the sanctuary, there was a splendid old lantern with an inscription on its iron door: "Presented as an offering by Izumi no Saburō in the third year of Bunji [1187]." It was rare, indeed, to see before one's eyes an object that had remained unchanged for 500 years. Izumi no Saburō was a brave, honorable, loyal, and filial warrior. His fame endures even today; there is no one who does not admire him. How true it is that men must strive to walk in the Way and uphold the right! "Fame will follow of itself."

Noon was already approaching when we engaged a boat for the crossing to Matsushima, a distance of a little more than two leagues. We landed at Ojima Beach.

Trite though it may seem to say so, Matsushima is the most beautiful spot in Japan, by no means inferior to Dongting Lake or West Lake.[8] The sea enters from the southeast into a bay extending for three leagues, its waters as ample as the flow of the Zhejiang Bore.[9] There are more islands than anyone could count. The tall ones rear up as though straining toward the sky; the flat ones crawl on their bellies over the waves. Some seem made of two layers, others of three folds. To the left, they appear separate; to the right, linked. Here and there, one carries another on its back or cradles it in its arms, as though caring for a beloved child or grandchild. The pines are deep green in color, and their branches, twisted by the salt gales, have assumed natural shapes so dramatic that they seem the work of human hands. The tranquil charm of the scene suggests a beautiful woman who has just completed her toilette. Truly, Matsushima might have been made by Ōyamazumi[1] in the ancient age of the mighty gods! What painter can reproduce, what author can describe the wonder of the creator's divine handiwork?

Ojima Island projects into the sea just offshore from the mainland. It is the site of the Venerable Ungo's[2] dwelling, and of the rock on which that holy man used to practice meditation. There also seemed to be a few

---

5. Reference to a poem in the *Kokinshū*: "However it may be elsewhere / in Michinoku, / there is deep pathos / in a boat pulled by a rope / along Shiogama shore." 6. A local ballad; Bashō is now in the province of Michinoku. 7. Dramatic ballad-dances recounting military episodes from *The Tale of the Heike* (originally performed as an oral narrative) and other warrior stories. *Kōwaka-mai* were one of the precursors of *nō* plays. 8. Chinese sites (which Bashō had never seen) famed for their beauty. 9. In China. 1. A mountain god who was son of the gods who created the Japanese islands. 2. A monk who rebuilt a temple at Matsushima. He was the teacher of Butchō, Bashō's Zen master.

recluses living among the pine trees. Upon seeing smoke rising from a fire of twigs and pine cones at one peaceful thatched hut, we could not help approaching the spot, even though we had no way of knowing what kind of man the occupant might be. Meanwhile, the moon began to shine on the water, transforming the scene from its daytime appearance.

We returned to the Matsushima shore to engage lodgings—a second-story room with a window on the sea. What marvelous exhilaration to spend the night so close to the winds and clouds! Sora recited this:

> Ah, Matsushima!
> Cuckoo, you ought to borrow
> the guise of the crane.[3]

I remained silent, trying without success to compose myself for sleep. At the time of my departure from the old hermitage, Sodō and Hara Anteki[4] had given me poems about Matsushima and Matsu-ga-urashima (the one in Chinese and the other in Japanese), and I got them out of my bag now to serve as companions for the evening. I also had some *hokku*, compositions by Sanpū and Jokushi.[5]

On the Eleventh, we visited Zuiganji.[6] Thirty-two generations ago, Makabe no Heishirō entered holy orders, went to China, and returned to found that temple. Later, through the virtuous influence of the Venerable Ungo, the seven old structures were transformed into a great religious center, a veritable earthly paradise, with dazzling golden walls and resplendent furnishings. I thought with respectful admiration of the holy Kenbutsu[7] and wondered where his place of worship might have been.

On the Twelfth, we left for Hiraizumi, choosing a little-frequented track used by hunters, grass-cutters, and woodchoppers, which was supposed to take us past the Aneha Pine and Odae Bridge. Blundering along, we lost our way and finally emerged at the port town of Ishino-maki. Kinkazan, the mountain of which the poet wrote, "Golden flowers have blossomed," was visible across the water.[8] Hundreds of coastal vessels rode together in the harbor, and smoke ascended everywhere from the cooking fires of houses jostling for space. Astonished to have stumbled on such a place, we looked for lodgings, but nobody seemed to have a room for rent, and we spent the night in a wretched shack.

The next morning, we set out again on an uncertain journey over strange roads, plodding along an interminable dike from which we could see Sode-no-watari, Obuchi-no-maki, and Mano-no-kayahara[9] in the distance. We walked beside a long, dismal marsh to a place called Toima,

---

3. The gist of the poem is: "Your song is appealing, cuckoo, but the stately white crane is the bird we expect to see at Matsushima [Pine Isles]." Pines and cranes were a conventional pair, both symbols of longevity. Sora's poem alludes to an old poem of uncertain provenance and unstable wording, one version of which reads in part: "[When snow falls] does the plover borrow / the crane's [white] plumage?" 4. Two friends of Bashō, both amateur poets. Hara was also a physician.   5. Bashō's disciples. *Hokku*: the first three lines of a linked-verse sequence, from which *haiku* evolved.   6. The temple restored by Ungo (see n. 2, p. 2121).   7. A monk who lived approximately six hundred years earlier and who confined himself to a small temple at Matsushima.   8. Refers to a poem in the *Man'yōshū* (The collection of ten thousand leaves), which was completed around 759 and is the earliest compilation of Japanese poetry, containing more than forty-five hundred poems. The poem referred to here was written when gold was discovered in the area: "For our sovereign's reign, / an auspicious augury: / among the mountains of Michinoku / in the east, / golden flowers have blossomed."   9. All are located between Ishi-no-maki and Toima and had associations with earlier poetry.

where we stopped overnight, and finally arrived in Hiraizumi. I think the distance was something over twenty leagues.

The glory of three generations[1] was but a dozing dream. Paddies and wild fields have claimed the land where Hidehira's mansion stood, a league beyond the site of the great gate, and only Mount Kinkeizan looks as it did in the past. My first act was to ascend to Takadachi. From there, I could see both the mighty Kitakami River, which flows down from Nanbu, and the Koromo River, which skirts Izumi Castle and empties into the larger stream below Takadachi. Yasuhira's[2] castle, on the near side of Koromo Barrier, seems to have guarded the Nanbu entrance against barbarian encroachments. There at Takadachi, Yoshitsune[3] shut himself up with a chosen band of loyal men—yet their heroic deeds lasted only a moment, and nothing remains but evanescent clumps of grass.

> The nation is destroyed; the mountains and rivers remain.
> Spring comes to the castle; the grasses are green.[4]

Sitting on my sedge hat with those lines running through my head, I wept for a long time.

> A dream of warriors,
> and after dreaming is done,
> the summer grasses.

> Ah, the white hair:
> vision of Kanefusa[5]
> in deutzia flowers.
> —Sora

The two halls of which we had heard so many impressive tales were open to visitors. The images of the three chieftains are preserved in the Sutra Hall, and in the Golden Hall there are the three coffins and the three sacred images.[6] In the past, the Golden Hall's seven precious substances were scattered and lost; gales ravaged the magnificent jewel-studded doors, and the golden pillars rotted in the frosts and snows. But just as it seemed that the whole building must collapse, leaving nothing but clumps of grass, new walls were put around it, and a roof was erected against the winds and rains. So it survives for a time, a memento of events that took place 1,000 years ago.

> Do the Fifth-Month rains
> stay away when they fall,
> sparing that Hall of Gold?

After journeying on with the Nanbu Road visible in the distance, we spent the night at Iwade-no-sato. From there, we passed Ogurazaki and Mizu-no-ojima and arrived at Shitomae Barrier by way of Narugo Hot

---

1. That is, of the powerful Fujiwara family—Kiyohira, Motohira, and Hidehira—who created the so-called golden age of the north in the 12th century.   2. Son of Fujiwara Hidehira, whose fight with his brother destroyed the clan's prosperity in the region. After killing his brother, Yasuhira was in turn killed by the Minamoto/Genji chieftain Yoritomo.   3. See n. 1, p. 2118.   4. A quote from the Chinese poet Tu Fu, lamenting the devastation caused by a rebellion in 755, from which the T'ang dynasty never fully recovered.   5. A loyal retainer of Yoshitsune.   6. Of Amida Buddha and his attendants Kannon and Seishi. The coffins contained the mummified remains of Hidehira, his father, and his grandfather.

Springs, intending to cross into Dewa Province. The road was so little frequented by travelers that we excited the guards' suspicions, and we barely managed to get through the checkpoint. The sun had already begun to set as we toiled upward through the mountains, so we asked for shelter when we saw a border guard's house. Then the wind howled and the rain poured for three days, trapping us in those miserable hills.

> The fleas and the lice—
> and next to my pillow,
> a pissing horse.

The master of the house told us that our route into Dewa was an ill-marked trail through high mountains; we would be wise to engage a guide to help us with the crossing. I took his advice and hired a fine, stalwart young fellow, who strode ahead with a short, curved sword tucked into his belt and an oak staff in his hand. As we followed him, I felt an uncomfortable presentiment that this would be the day on which we would come face to face with danger at last. Just as our host had said, the mountains were high and thickly wooded, their silence unbroken even by the chirp of a bird. It was like traveling at night to walk in the dim light under the dense canopy. Feeling as though dust must be blowing down from the edge of the clouds,[7] we pushed through bamboo, forded streams, and stumbled over rocks, all the time in a cold sweat, until we finally emerged at Mogami-no-shō. Our guide took his leave in high spirits, after having informed us that the path we had followed was one on which unpleasant things were always happening, and that it had been a great stroke of luck to bring us through safely. Even though the danger was past, his words made my heart pound.

At Obanazawa, we called on Seifū, a man whose tastes were not vulgar despite his wealth. As a frequent visitor to the capital, he understood what it meant to be a traveler, and he kept us for several days, trying in many kind ways to make us forget the hardships of the long journey.

> I sit at ease,
> taking this coolness
> as my lodging place.

> Come on, show yourself!
> Under the silkworm nursery
> the croak of a toad.

> In my mind's eye,
> a brush for someone's brows:
> the safflower blossom.

> The silkworm nurses—
> figures reminiscent
> of a distant past.[8]
>   —Sora

---

7. To emphasize the murkiness of the atmosphere, Bashō borrows from a poem in which Tu Fu compliments a princess by implying that she lives in the sky: "When I begin to ascend the breezy stone steps, / a dust storm blows down from the edge of the clouds."   8. The silkworm tenders (nurses) dress in an old style. Here, as Bashō does elsewhere, Sora expresses nostalgia for a way of life that had disappeared from the cities to the west.

In the Yamagata domain, there is a mountain temple called Ryū-sha-kuji, a serene, quiet seat of religion founded by the Great Teacher Jikaku.[9] Urged by others to see it, we retraced our steps some seven leagues from Obanazawa. We arrived before sundown, reserved accommodations in the pilgrims' hostel at the foot of the hill, and climbed to the halls above. The mountain consists of piles of massive rocks. Its pines and other evergreens bear the marks of many long years; its moss lies like velvet on the ancient rocks and soil. Not a sound emanated from the temple buildings at the summit, which all proved to be closed, but we skirted the cliffs and clambered over the rocks to view the halls. The quiet, lonely beauty of the environs purified the heart.

> Ah, tranquility!
> Penetrating the very rock,
> a cicada's voice.

At Ōishida, we awaited fair weather with a view to descending the Mogami River by boat. In that spot where the seeds of the old *haikai*[1] had fallen, some people still cherished the memory of the flowers. With hearts softened by poetry's civilizing touch, those onetime blowers of shrill reed flutes[2] had been groping for the correct way of practicing the art, so they told me, but had found it difficult to choose between the old styles and the new with no one to guide them. I felt myself under an obligation to leave them a sequence. Such was one result of this journey in pursuit of my art.

The Mogami River has its source deep in the northern mountains and its upper reaches in Yamagata. After presenting formidable hazards like Goten and Hayabusa,[3] it skirts Mount Itajiki on the north and finally empties into the sea at Sakata. Our boat descended amid luxuriant foliage, the mountains pressing overhead from the left and the right. It was probably similar craft, loaded with sheaves, that the old song meant when it spoke of rice boats.[4] Travelers can see the cascading waters of Shiraito Falls through gaps in the green leaves. The Sennindō Hall is there too, facing the bank.

The swollen waters made the journey hazardous:

> Bringing together
> the summer rains in swiftness:
> Mogami River!

On the Third of the Sixth Month, we climbed Mount Haguro. We called on Zushi Sakichi[5] and then were received by the Holy Teacher Egaku, the Abbot's deputy, who lodged us at the Minamidani Annex and treated us with great consideration.

---

9. Better known as Ennin (794–864), a famous priest who helped establish Buddhism in Japan. *Yama-gata domain:* from the early 17th century until 1868, Japan was divided into domains, or fiefdoms, held directly by the shogun and his family or by the feudal barons who, to one degree or another, supported him. Yamagata was in the province of Dewa.   1. Nonstandard, or eccentric, linked verse. Masters from two older *haikai* schools had spent time in the area.   2. That is, untutored country people.   3. Two treacherous spots in the river, one with rocks and the other with swift currents.   4. Refers to a folk song whose chief interest lies in its puns on the word *rice*.   5. A dyer by trade and an amateur poet.

On the Fourth, there was a *haikai* gathering at the Abbot's residence:

> Ah, what a delight!
> Cooled as by snow, the south wind
>   at Minamidani.

On the Fifth, we went to worship at Haguro Shrine. Nobody knows when the founder, the Great Teacher Nōjo, lived. The *Engi Canon*[6] mentions a shrine called "Satoyama in Dewa Province," which leads one to wonder if *sato* might be a copyist's error for *kuro*. Perhaps "Haguroyama" is a contraction of "Dewa no Kuroyama" [Kuroyama in Dewa Province]. I understand that the official gazetteer says Dewa acquired its name because the province used to present birds' feathers to the throne as tribute.[7]

Hagurosan, Gassan, and Yudono are known collectively as the Three Mountains. At Haguro, a subsidiary of Tōeizan Kan'eiji Temple in Edo, the moon of Tendai[8] enlightenment shines bright, and the lamp of the Law of perfect understanding and all-permeating vision burns high. The temple buildings stand roof to roof; the ascetics vie in the practice of rituals. We can but feel awe and trepidation before the miraculous powers of so holy a place, which may with justice be called a magnificent mountain, destined to flourish forever.

On the Eighth, we made the ascent of Gassan. Donning paper garlands, and with our heads wrapped in white turbans, we toiled upward for eight leagues, led by a porter guide through misty mountains with ice and snow underfoot. We could almost have believed ourselves to be entering the cloud barrier beyond which the sun and the moon traverse the heavens. The sun was setting and the moon had risen when we finally reached the summit, gasping for breath and numb with cold. We stretched out on beds of bamboo grass until dawn, and descended toward Yudono after the rising sun had dispersed the clouds.

Near a valley, we saw a swordsmith's cottage. The Dewa smiths, attracted by the miraculous waters, had purified themselves there before forging their famous blades, which they had identified by the carved signature, "Gassan."[9] I was reminded of the weapons tempered at Dragon Spring.[1] It also seemed to me that I could understand the dedication with which those men had striven to master their art, inspired by the ancient example of Gan Jiang and Moye.[2]

While seated on a rock for a brief rest, I noticed some half-opened buds on a cherry tree about three feet high. How admirable that those late blooms had remembered spring, despite the snowdrifts under which they had lain buried! They were like "plum blossoms in summer heat"[3] per-

---

6. An early collection of governmental regulations (compiled 905–927), designed to flesh out the broad administrative structure that was then being adapted from China.   7. The characters representing *sato* and *kuro* are similar in appearance, especially when written in cursive script. The *ha* of "Haguroyama" and the *wa* of "Dewa" can be written with the same phonetic symbol and were once the same sound. The connection between Dewa and birds' feathers is in the orthography: *wa* is written with the character for "feathers."   8. A Buddhist sect.   9. A famous swordsmith in the late 12th century.   1. A spring in China whose waters were used for tempering sword blades.   2. Gan Jiang was a Chinese swordsmith. He and his wife, Moye, forged two famous swords.   3. A Zen metaphor for the rare and unusual and, by extension, for passing beyond this world to enlightenment.

fuming the air. The memory of Archbishop Gyōson's touching poem[4] added to the little tree's charm.

It is a rule among ascetics not to give outsiders details about Mount Yudono, so I shall lay aside my brush and write no more.

When we returned to our lodgings, Egaku asked us to inscribe poem cards with verses suggested by our pilgrimage to the Three Mountains:

> Ah, what coolness!
> Under a crescent moon,
> Mount Haguro glimpsed.

> Mountain of the Moon:
> after how many cloud peaks
> had formed and crumbled?

> My sleeve was drenched
> at Yudono, the mountain
> of which none may speak.

> Yudonoyama:
> tears fall as I walk the path
> where feet tread on coins.[5]
> —Sora

After our departure from Haguro, we were invited to the warrior Naga-yama Shigeyuki's home, where we composed a sequence. (Sakichi accompanied us that far.) Then we boarded a river boat and traveled downstream to Sakata Harbor. We stayed with a physician, En'an Fugyoku.

> Evening cool!
> A view from Mount Atsumi
> to Fukuura.

> Mogami River—
> it has plunged the hot sun
> into the sea.

I had already enjoyed innumerable splendid views of rivers and mountains, ocean and land; now I set my heart on seeing Kisakata. It was a journey of ten leagues northeast from Sakata, across mountains and along sandy beaches. A wind from the sea stirred the white sand early in the afternoon, and Mount Chōkai disappeared behind misting rain. "Groping in the dark," we found "the view in the rain exceptional too."[6] The surroundings promised to be beautiful once the skies had cleared. We crawled into a fisherman's thatched shanty to await the end of the rain.

The next day was fine, and we launched forth onto the bay in a boat as

---

4. A reference to a poem that Gyōson (1055–1135), an ascetic, composed when he discovered cherries blooming out of season: "Let us sympathize / with one another, / cherry tree on the mountain: / were it not for your blossoms, / I would have no friend at all."   5. The coins have been strewn by pilgrims, but unlike the secular world, no one scrambles to pick them up. Sora sheds tears at this miraculous behavior, which he can only attribute to the power of the gods.   6. Bashō compares Kisakata to the famous West Lake in China, of which Su Tongbo (1037–1101) wrote: "The sparkling, brimming waters are beautiful in sunshine; / The view when a misty rain veils the mountains is exceptional too." "Groping in the dark": probably an allusion to a poem composed at the lake by a visiting Japanese monk, Sakugen (1501–1579): "The sun is setting beyond Yuhangmen; / All sights are indistinct, there is no view. / But I recall the poem, 'Exceptional in rain, beautiful in sunshine'; / Groping in the dark, I feel West Lake's charm."

the bright morning sun rose. First of all, we went to Nōinjima to visit the spot where Saigyō had lived in seclusion for three years. Then we disembarked on the opposite shore and saw a memento of the poet, the old cherry tree that had suggested the verse, "rowing over flowers."[7] Near the water's edge, we noticed a tomb that was said to be the grave of Empress Jingū,[8] together with a temple, Kanmanjuji. I had never heard that the Empress had gone to that place. I wonder how her grave happened to be there.

Seated in the temple's front apartment with the blinds raised, we commanded a panoramic view. To the south, Mount Chōkai propped up the sky, its image reflected in the bay; to the west, Muyamuya Barrier blocked the road; to the east, the Akita Road stretched far into the distance on an embankment; to the north, there loomed the majestic bulk of the sea, its waves entering the bay at a place called Shiogoshi.

The bay measures about a league in length and breadth. It resembles Matsushima in appearance but has a quality of its own: where Matsushima seems to smile, Kisakata droops in dejection. The lonely, melancholy scene suggests a troubled human spirit.

> Xi Shi's[9] drooping eyelids:
> mimosa in falling rain
> at Kisakata.

> At Shiogoshi
> crane legs drenched by high tide —
> and how cool the sea!

A festival:

> A shrine festival:
> what foods do worshippers eat
> at Kisakata?
> —Sora

> At fishers' houses,
> people lay down rain shutters,
> seeking evening cool.[1]
> —Teiji, a Mino merchant

Seeing an osprey nest on a rock:

> Might they have vowed,
> "Never shall waves cross here"[2] —
> those nesting ospreys?
> —Sora

7. From a poem attributed to Saigyō: "The cherry blossoms / at Kisakata / lie buried under waves: / seafolk in their fishing boat / go rowing over flowers."   8. Legendary empress said to have ruled in the second half of the 4th century.   9. A Chinese beauty of the 5th century B.C. Originally the consort of the king of Yue, she was later forced to wed her conqueror, the king of Wu.   1. That is, they remove the rain shutters from their houses and put them on the beach, where they sit, enjoying the evening cool.   2. This phrase constitutes a vow of eternal fidelity, derived from a poem in the *Kokinshū*: "Would I be the sort / to cast you aside / and turn to someone new? / Sooner would the waves traverse / Sue-no-matsu Mountain."

After several days of reluctant farewells to friends in Sakata, we set out under the clouds of the Northern Land Road, quailing before the prospect of the long journey ahead. It was reported to be 130 leagues to the castle town of the Kaga domain. Once past Nezu Barrier, we made our way on foot through Echigo Province to Ichiburi Barrier in Etchū Province, a tiring journey of nine miserably hot, rainy days. I felt too ill to write anything.

> In the Seventh Month,
> even the Sixth Day differs
> from ordinary nights.[3]

> Tumultuous seas:
> spanning the sky to Sado Isle,
> the Milky Way.

That night I drew up a pillow and lay down to sleep, exhausted after having traversed the most difficult stretches of road in all the north country—places with names like "Children Forget Parents," "Parents Forget Children," "Dogs Go Back," and "Horses Sent Back." The voices of young women drifted in from the adjoining room in front—two of them, it appeared, talking to an elderly man, whose voice was also audible. As I listened, I realized that they were prostitutes from Niigata in Echigo, bound on a pilgrimage to the Grand Shrines of Ise. The old man was to be sent home to Niigata in the morning, after having escorted them as far as this barrier, and they seemed to be writing letters and giving him inconsequential messages to take back. Adrift on "the shore where white breakers roll in," these "fishermen's daughters" had fallen low indeed, exchanging fleeting vows with every passerby.[4] How wretched the karma that had doomed them to such an existence! I fell asleep with their voices in my ears.

The next morning, the same two girls spoke to us as we were about to leave. "We're feeling terribly nervous and discouraged about going off on this hard trip over strange roads. Won't you let us join your party, even if we only stay close enough to catch a glimpse of you now and then? You wear the robes of mercy: please let us share the Buddha's compassion and form a bond with the Way," they said, weeping.

"I sympathize with you, but we'll be making frequent stops. Just follow others going to the same place; I'm sure the gods will see you there safely." We walked off without waiting for an answer, but it was some time before I could stop feeling sorry for them.

> Ladies of pleasure
> sleeping in the same hostel:
> bush clover and moon.[5]

---

3. Because people were preparing for the Tanabata Festival, which was held on the seventh day of the Seventh Month in honor of the stars Altair (the herd boy) and Vega (the weaver maiden). Legend held that the two lovers were separated by the Milky Way, except for this one night, when they would meet for their annual rendezvous. 4. Alludes to a classical poem: "I have no abode, / for I am but the daughter of a fisherman, / spending my life / on the shore / where white waves roll in." Prostitutes went out in small boats to greet in-coming vessels. 5. In this much-discussed poem Bashō is probably not making an invidious comparison between the prostitutes (showy, ephemeral flowers) and himself (the pure remote moon) but simply using aspects of the scene at the inn to comment in amusement on a

I recited those lines to Sora, who wrote them down.

After crossing the "forty-eight channels" of the Kurobe River and innumerable other streams, we reached the coast at Nago. Even though the season was not spring, it seemed a shame to miss the wisteria at Tako in early autumn. We asked someone how to get there, but the answer frightened us off. "Tako is five leagues along the beach from here, in the hollow of those mountains. The only houses are a few ramshackle thatched huts belonging to fishermen; you probably wouldn't find anyone to put you up for the night." Thus we went on into Kaga Province.

> Scent of ripening ears:[6]
> to the right as I push through,
> surf crashing onto rocks.

We arrived at Kanazawa on the Fifteenth of the Seventh Month, after crossing Unohana Mountain and Kurikara Valley. There we met the merchant Kasho,[7] who had come up from Ōsaka, and joined him in his lodgings. A certain Isshō had been living in Kanazawa—a man who had gradually come to be known as a serious student of poetry, and who had gained a reputation among the general public as well. I now learned that he had died last winter, still in the prime of life. At the Buddhist service arranged by his older brother:

> Stir, burial mound!
> The voice I raise in lament
> is the autumn wind.

On being invited to a thatched cottage:

> The cool of autumn:
> let's each of us peel his own
> melons and eggplant.

Composed on the way:

> Despite the red blaze
> of the pitiless sun—
> an autumn breeze.

At Komatsu [Young Pines]:

> An appealing name:
> The wind in Young Pines ruffles
> bush clover and miscanthus.

At Komatsu we visited Tada Shrine, which numbers among its treasures a helmet and a piece of brocade that once belonged to Sanemori.[8] We were told that the helmet was a gift from Lord Yoshitomo[9] in the old days when Sanemori served the Genji—and indeed it was no ordinary warrior's headgear. From visor to earflaps, it was decorated with a gold-filled chry-

---

chance encounter between two very different types of people. It has often been suggested that he may have recorded the meeting at the barrier—or possibly invented it—as a means of including a reference to love, a standard topic in linked verse.   6. That is, of the maturing rice crop.   7. Like others Bashō calls on during his journey, Kasho is an amateur poet.   8. Saitō Sanemori (1111–1183), a *samurai* in the service of the Minamoto/Genji who defects to the Taira/Heike.   9. See n. 1, p. 2118

santhemum arabesque in the Chinese style, and the front was surmounted by a dragon's head and a pair of horns. The shrine history tells in vivid language of how Kiso no Yoshinaka[1] presented a petition there after Sanemori's death in battle, and of how Higuchi no Jirō served as a messenger.

> A heartrending sound!
> Underneath the helmet,
> the cricket.

We could see Shirane's peaks behind us as we trudged toward Yamanaka Hot Springs. The Kannon Hall[2] stood at the base of the mountains to the left. Someone said the hall was founded by Retired Emperor Kazan, who enshrined an image of the bodhisattva there and named the spot Nata after completing a pious round of the Thirty-three Places. (The name Nata was explained to us as having been coined from Nachi and Tanigumi.[3]) It was a beautiful, impressive site, with many unusual rocks, rows of ancient pine trees, and a small thatched chapel, built on a rock against the cliff.

> Even whiter
> than the Ishiyama rocks—
> the wind of autumn.

We bathed in the hot springs, which were said to be second only to Ariake in efficacy.

> At Yamanaka,
> no need to pluck chrysanthemums:[4]
> the scent of the springs.

The master was a youth called Kumenosuke. His father, an amateur of *haikai*, had embarrassed Teishitsu[5] with his knowledge when the master visited Yamanaka from the capital as a young man. Teishitsu returned to the city, joined Teitoku's[6] school, and built up a reputation, but it is said that he never accepted money for reviewing the work of anyone from this village after he became famous. The story is an old one now.

Sora was suffering from a stomach complaint. Because he had relatives at Nagashima in Ise Province, he set off ahead of me. He wrote a poem as he was about to leave:

> Journeying onward:
> fall prostrate though I may—
> a bush-clover field!

The sorrow of the one who departed and the unhappiness of the one who remained resembled the feelings of a lapwing wandering lost in the clouds, separated from its friend.

1. Leader of the northern Genji forces in the war against the Heike.   2. In honor of Kannon, the bodhisattva of compassion and an attendant of the Buddha known as Amida.   3. Two towns in different provinces; they were the beginning and ending points on an eleven-province tour of thirty-three places sacred to Kannon.   4. These flowers were associated with longevity.   5. An adept of *haikai*.
6. Matsunaga Teitoku (1571–1653), one of the leading practitioners of linked verse.

From this day forward,
the legend will be erased:
dewdrops on the hat.[7]

Still in Kaga, I lodged at Zenshōji, a temple outside the castle town of Daishōji. Sora had stayed there the night before and left this poem:

All through the night,
listening to the autumn wind—
the mountain in back.

One night's separation is the same as 1,000 leagues. I too listened to the autumn wind as I lay in the guest dormitory. Toward dawn, I heard clear voices chanting a sutra, and then the sound of a gong beckoned me into the dining hall. I left the hall as quickly as possible, eager to reach Echizen Province that day, but a group of young monks pursued me to the foot of the stairs with paper and inkstone. Observing that some willow leaves had scattered in the courtyard, I stood there in my sandals and dashed off these lines:

To sweep your courtyard
of willow leaves, and then depart:
that would be my wish!

At the Echizen border, I crossed Lake Yoshizaki by boat for a visit to the Shiogoshi pines.

Inviting the gale
to carry the waves ashore
all through the night,
they drip moonlight from their boughs—
the pines of Shiogoshi!
—Saigyō

In that single verse, the poet captures the essence of the scene at Shiozaki. For anyone to say more would be like "sprouting a useless digit."
In Maruoka, I called on the Tenryūji Abbot, an old friend.
A certain Hokushi from Kanazawa had planned to see me off a short distance, but had finally come all the way to Maruoka, reluctant to say good-bye. Always intent on conveying the effect of beautiful scenery in verse, he had produced some excellent poems from time to time. Now that we were parting, I composed this:

Hard to say good-bye—
to tear apart the old fan
covered with scribbles.

I journeyed about a league and a half into the mountains to worship at Eiheiji, Dōgen's[8] temple. I believe I have heard that Dōgen had an admirable reason for avoiding the vicinity of the capital and founding his temple in those remote mountains.

---

7. A reference to a common practice when people traveled in pairs. They would write on their hats the phrase "Two persons following the same path."   8. Founder of one of the main sects of Zen Buddhism.

After the evening meal, I set out for Fukui, three leagues away. It was a tedious, uncertain journey in the twilight.

A man named Tōsai had been living in Fukui as a recluse for a long time. He had come to Edo and visited me once—I was not sure just when, but certainly more than ten years earlier. I thought he must be very old and feeble by now, or perhaps even dead, but someone assured me that he was very much alive. Following my informant's directions into a quiet corner of the town, I came upon a poor cottage, its walls covered with moonflower and snake-gourd vines, and its door hidden by cockscomb and goosefoot.[9] That would be it, I thought. A woman of humble appearance emerged when I rapped on the gate.

"Where are you from, Reverend Sir? The master has gone to see someone in the neighborhood. Please look for him there if you have business with him." She was apparently the housewife.

I hurried off to find Tōsai, feeling as though I had strayed into an old romance, and spent two nights at his house. Then I prepared to leave, hopeful of seeing the full moon at Tsuruga Harbor on the Fifteenth of the Eighth Month. Having volunteered to keep me company, Tōsai set out in high spirits as my guide, his skirts tucked jauntily into his sash.

The peaks of Shirane disappeared as Hina-ga-take came into view. We crossed Azamuzu Bridge, saw ears[1] on the reeds at Taema, journeyed beyond Uguisu Barrier and Yunoo Pass, heard the first wild geese of the season at Hiuchi Stronghold and Mount Kaeru, and took lodgings in Tsuruga at dusk on the Fourteenth. The sky was clear, the moon remarkably fine. When I asked if we might hope for the same weather on the following night, the landlord offered us wine, replying, "In the northern provinces, who knows whether the next night will be cloudy or fair?"

That night, I paid a visit to Kehi Shrine, the place where Emperor Chūai[2] is worshipped. An atmosphere of holiness pervaded the surroundings. Moonlight filtered in between the pine trees, and the white sand in front of the sanctuary glittered like frost. "Long ago, in pursuance of a great vow, the Second Pilgrim[3] himself cut grass and carried dirt and rock to fill a marsh that was a trial to worshippers going back and forth. The precedent is still observed; every new Pilgrim takes sand to the area in front of the shrine. The ceremony is called 'the Pilgrim's Carrying of the Sand,'" my landlord said.

> Shining on sand
> transported by pilgrims—
> pure light of the moon.

It rained on the Fifteenth, just as the landlord had warned it might.

> Night of the full moon:
> no predicting the weather
> in the northern lands.

9. A plant with small greenish blossoms. *Cockscomb:* a plant with fan-shaped clusters of red or yellow blossoms.   1. The spikes on a plant that contain the seeds.   2. According to tradition, the fourteenth emperor, married to Empress Jingū (see n. 8, p. 2128).   3. Taa Shōnin (1237–1319). *Pilgrim* was a title given to the patriarch of the Ji sect of Buddhism.

The weather was fine on the Sixteenth, so we went in a boat to Irono-hama Beach to gather red shells. It was seven leagues by sea. A man named Ten'ya provided us with all kinds of refreshments—compart-mented lunch boxes, wine flasks, and the like—and also ordered a number of servants to go along in the boat. A fair wind delivered us to our destina-tion in no time. The beach was deserted except for a few fishermen's shacks and a forlorn Nichiren[4] temple. As we drank tea and warmed wine at the temple, I struggled to control feelings evoked by the loneliness of the evening.

> Ah, what loneliness!
> More desolate than Suma,[5]
> this beach in autumn.

> Between wave and wave:
> mixed with small shells, the remains
> of bush-clover bloom.

I persuaded Tōsai to write a description of the day's outing to be left at the temple.

Rōtsu came to meet me at Tsuruga and accompanied me to Mino Prov-ince. Thus I arrived at Ōgaki, my journey eased by a horse. Sora came from Ise, Etsujin galloped in on horseback, and we all gathered at Jokō's house. Zensenji, Keikō, Keikō's sons, and other close friends called day and night, rejoicing and pampering me as though I had returned from the dead.

Despite my travel fatigue, I set out again by boat on the Sixth of the Ninth Month to witness the relocation of the Ise sanctuaries.[6]

> Off to Futami,
> loath to part as clam from shell
> in waning autumn.

---

4. Buddhist monk (1222–1282) and founder of a sect that bore his name.   5. A coastal town made famous as the hero's place of exile in *The Tale of Genji*.   6. The two sanctuaries at the Grand Shrines of Ise, dedicated to the ancestral gods of the imperial family, are rebuilt every twenty years as a kind of repurification.

Part V

1800 TO 1900

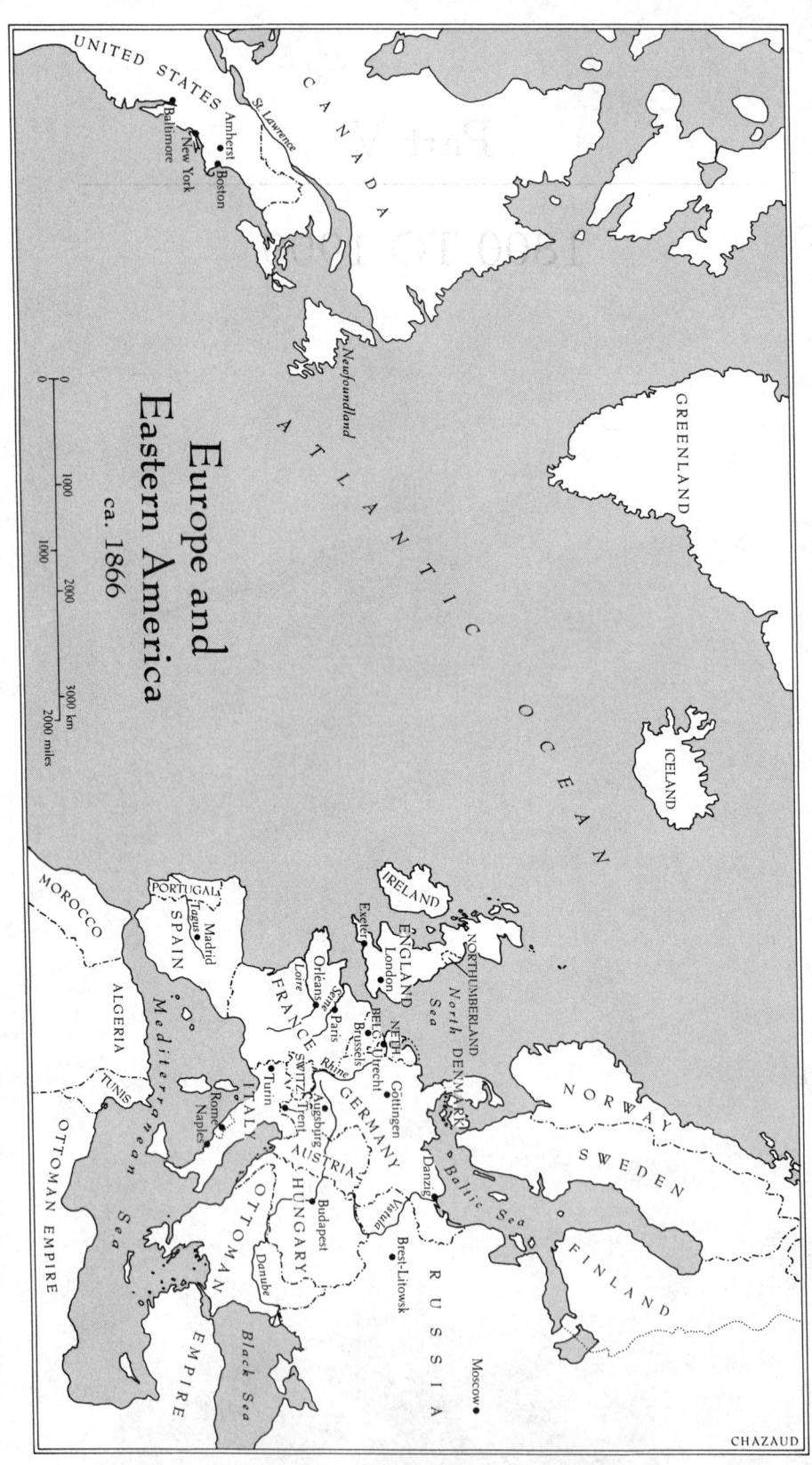

Europe and
Eastern America

ca. 1866

CHAZAUD

Revolution and Romanticism in Europe and America

"Bliss was it in that dawn to be alive, / But to be young was very heaven." William Wordsworth alludes here to his experience, at the age of seventeen, of the French Revolution. The possibility of referring to a national cataclysm in such terms suggests the remarkable shift in sensibility, in dominant assumptions, in intellectual preoccupations, that occurred late in the eighteenth century. We call the evidence of that shift "Romanticism"—a designation so grandly inclusive as to defy definition. If our terms for the late seventeenth and early eighteenth centuries ("Enlightenment," "Age of Reason") emphasize one aspect of the prevailing intellectual culture to the exclusion of others equally important, the label of "Romanticism" refers to so many cultural manifestations that one can hardly pin it down. In general, it implies new emphases on imagination, on feeling, on the value of the primitive and untrammeled, and particularly a narrowing of outlook from the universal to the particular, from humankind or "man" to nation or ethnic group and from the stability of community to the "fulfillment" of the individual. Such shifts have important political and philosophic as well as literary implications.

In the writings of individuals, one finds lines of continuity between the late and early parts of the eighteenth century; but when it comes to generalizations, all the important truths appear to have reversed themselves. In the middle of the century, reason was the guide to certainty; at the century's end, *feeling* tested authenticity. Earlier, tradition still anchored experience; now, the ideal of joyous liberation implied rejection of traditional authority. Wisdom had long associated itself with maturity, even with old age; by the 1790s, William Blake hinted at the child's superior insight, and Wordsworth openly claimed for the infant holy wisdom inevitably lost in the process of aging. Johnson had valued experience as a vital path to knowledge; at the beginning of the nineteenth century, innocence—in its nature evanescent—provided a more generally treasured resource.

Cause and effect, in such massive shifts of perspective, can never be ascertained. The French Revolution derived from new ideas about the sacredness of the individual; it also helped to generate such ideas. Without trying to distinguish causes from effects—indeed, with a strong suspicion that the period's striking phenomena constitute simultaneous causes and effects—one can specify a number of ways that the world appeared to change, as the eighteenth century approached the nineteenth, as well as ways that these changes both solidified themselves and evoked challenges later in the nineteenth century.

NEW AND OLD

The embattled farmers of Concord, Massachusetts, fired the shot heard round the world in 1775; fourteen years later, the Bastille fell. Both the American and the French revolutions developed out of strong convictions about the innate rights of individual human beings—in other words, Protestantism in political form. Those who developed revolutionary theory glimpsed new human possibility. The hope

2137

of salvation lay in the overturning of established institutions. Swift, in *Gulliver's Travels*, had made a clear distinction between institutions as ideal constructions of human reason and their corruption in practice. Lawyers might be a money-grubbing, hypocritical lot, but the idea of law, of a social structure designed to ensure the provision of justice, has its own inherent power. The theory of revolution implied radical assault on virtually all social institutions. Fundamental hierarchies of government, notions of sovereignty and of aristocracy, inherited systems of distinction—all fell. Old conventions, once emblems of social and of literary stability, now exemplified the dead hand of the past. Only a few years before, the old, the inherited, and the traditional embodied truth, its power attested by its survival. But the revolutionaries felt themselves to be originators; the newness of what they proposed gave it the almost religious authority suggested by Wordsworth's allusions to "bliss" and "Heaven."

The blessed state evoked by the new political thinkers embodied a sense of infinite possibility. Pope had written, in *An Essay on Man*, "The bliss of Man (could Pride that blessing find) / Is not to act or think beyond mankind." By the century's end, people were doing their best to "think beyond mankind"—or, at any rate, beyond what had been considered normal limitations. Evidence of this abounds, in revolutionary sermons preached from pulpits even in England, in writings by such flamboyant defenders of human rights as Thomas Paine, in the development, even, of a political theory about women's social position. Mary Wollstonecraft was not the first to note the oppression of women; a century before her, Mary Astell had suggested the need for broader female education, and outcries on the subject emerged sporadically even earlier in the seventeenth century. But Wollstonecraft's *Vindication of the Rights of Women* (1792) offered the first detailed argument that the ideal of fulfilled human possibility for men and for women demanded political acknowledgment of women's equality.

The very existence of such a work (which achieved a second edition in the year of its first publication) testifies to the atmosphere of political expectancy in which men and women could rethink "self-evident" principles. Replacing the ideal of hierarchy, for example, was the revolutionary notion of human brotherhood. Liberty, equality, and fraternity, the French proclaimed; the new American nation celebrated essentially the same ideals. In practice, though, "fraternity" turned out to involve the citizens specifically of France or of the new United States. The emphasis on individual uniqueness extended itself to national uniqueness. In America particularly, ideas of national character and of national destiny developed almost talismanic force. Although peace generally prevailed among nations in the early nineteenth century, the developing distinctions dividing one country imaginatively from another foretold future danger.

New ideas with massive practical consequences included more than the political. In 1776, Adam Smith published *The Wealth of Nations*, a theory of laissez-faire economics presaging the enormous importance of money in subsequent history. Matters of exchange and acquisition, Smith argued, could be left to regulate themselves—a doctrine behind which still lurked unobtrusively the confidence, expressed in market terms, that Pope had expressed in religious ones: "All Chance, Direction, which thou canst not see, / All Discord, Harmony, not understood." As manufacturing and trade developed increasing financial vitality, however, their importance as financial resources in fact heightened discord, through growing nationalism. Early in the century, at the end of *Windsor Forest* (1713), Pope had recognized in Britain's trade a form of power. A century later, the acceleration of this power would have astonished Pope. No longer did agriculture provide England's central economic resource. New forms of manufacture provided new substance for trade, generated new fortunes, produced a new social class—a "mid-

Browning, Emily Dickinson—all evoked intense passion in verse. In the Romantic novel, too, women excelled in the rendering of powerful feeling. The Brontë sisters, like George Eliot after them in England, like the equally passionate George Sand in France, wrote under male pseudonyms but established distinctively female visions of the struggle not only for love but also for freedom and power within a context of social restriction. Mary Shelley (daughter of Mary Wollstonecraft and married to the poet Shelley) in her eloquent fable of creativity, *Frankenstein* (1818), epitomizes the peculiar intensity of much women's writing in this period.

As the nineteenth century wore on, hope for a new terrestrial Eden faded. The efflorescence of commerce and the innovations of science turned out to have negative as well as positive consequences. As the novels of Charles Dickens and of William Thackeray insist, the new middle class frequently became the repository of moral mediocrity. The autocracy of money had effects more brutal than those of inherited privilege. Science, once the emblem of progress, began to generate theological confusion. Charles Darwin's *Origin of Species* (1859) stated clearly humanity's mean rather than transcendent origins: animal and plant species had evolved over the centuries, adapting themselves to their environment by the process of natural selection. Fossils found in rocks provided supporting evidence for this theory—an assertion troubling to many Christians because it contradicted the biblical account of Creation. Five years after Darwin's revolutionary work, Karl Marx published *Das Kapital*, with its dialectical theory of history and its vision of capitalism's eventual decay and of the working class inevitably triumphant. In the United States civil war raged from 1860 to 1865, its central issue the morality of slavery—that by-product of agricultural capitalism. Neither the making of money nor the effort to fathom natural law seemed merely reassuring.

In the face of history's threats—the menace of Marx's prophecy and of Darwin's biology, the chaos of civil war—to insist on the importance of private experience offered tentative security, a standing place, a temporary source of authority. The voices of blacks as well as, in increasing numbers, of women could now be heard: placing high value on the personal implied respecting all persons. The American Civil War made African-Americans for the first time truly visible to the society that both contained and denied them. Slave narratives—sometimes wholly or partly fictionized, sometimes entirely authentic renditions of often horrifying experience—provided useful propaganda for the abolitionist cause, the ideology opposed to the institution of slavery. They also opened a new emotional universe. In their typical emphasis, for instance, on the salvationary force of reading and writing (for most slaves officially forbidden knowledge), these narratives illuminated a new area of the taken-for-granted, thus extending the enterprise of Romantic poetry.

The capacity for revelatory illumination belonged, according to the dominant nineteenth-century view, to imagination, a mysterious and virtually sacred power of individual consciousness. When Samuel Johnson, in *Rasselas*, suggested that all predominance of imagination over reason constituted a degree of insanity, he intended, to put it crudely, an antithesis of true and false. Imagination, the faculty of generating images, had no necessary anchor in the communal, historical experience that tested truth. For Wordsworth and Coleridge and those who came after them, imagination was a visionary and unifying force (a new incarnation of the seventeenth century's inner light or candle of the Lord) through which the gifted person discovered and communicated new truth. As Coleridge wrote,

> from the soul itself must issue forth
> A light, a glory, a fair luminous cloud
> Enveloping the Earth—

Imagination derives from the soul, the aspect of human being that links the human with the eternal. Through it, men and women can transcend earthly limitations, can express high aspiration, can escape, and help one another escape, the dreariness of mortality without necessarily positing a life beyond the present one.

A corollary of the high value attached to creative imagination was a new concern with originality. The notion of "the genius," the man or woman so gifted as to operate by principles unknown to ordinary mortals, developed only in the late eighteenth century. Previously, a person *had* rather than *was* a genius: the term designated a particular tendency or gift (a genius for cooking, say) rather than a human being with vast creative power. Now the genius was revered for his or her extraordinary difference from others, idealized as a being set apart; and the literary or artistic products of genius, it could be assumed, would correspondingly differ from everything previously produced. Newness itself became as never before a measure of value. The language, the themes, the forms of the preceding century would no longer suffice. In the early eighteenth century, literary figures wishing to congratulate themselves and their contemporaries would compare their artistic situation to that of Rome under the benevolent patronage of Augustus Caesar. A hundred years later, the note of self-congratulation would express itself in the claim of an unprecedented situation, unprecedented kinds of accomplishment. John Keats, in a letter, characterized Wordsworth as representing "the egotistical sublime." Such sublimity—authority and grandeur emanating from a unique self still in touch with something beyond itself—was the nineteenth century's special achievement.

NATURE

Nature and nature's laws, the rationally ordered universe, provided the foundation for much early eighteenth-century thought. In the nineteenth century, nature's importance possibly increased—but *nature* now meant something new. *Wuthering Heights* (1847) creates a setting of windswept moors for its romantic lovers—both environment and metaphor of their love. Wordsworth could value a host of daffodils or fog-enveloped hills or an icy lake. The physical reality of the natural world, in its varied abundance, became a matter of absorbing interest for poets and novelists. Nature provided an alternative to the human, a possibility for imaginative as well as literal escape. Its imagery—flowers, clouds, ocean—became the common poetic stock. Workers still hastened from the country to the city, because the city housed possibilities of wealth; yet educated men and women increasingly declared their nostalgia for rural or sylvan landscapes embodying peace and beauty.

Nature, in the nineteenth-century mind, however, did not consist only in physical details. It also implied a totality, an enveloping whole greater than the sum of its parts, a vast unifying spirit. Wordsworth evokes

> a sense sublime
> Of something far more deeply interfused,
> Whose dwelling is the light of setting suns,
> And the round ocean and the living air,
> And the blue sky, and in the mind of man:
> A motion and a spirit, that impels
> All thinking things, all objects of all thought,
> And rolls through all things.

Coleridge and Shelley hint similar visions, vague yet comforting. The unifying whole, as Wordsworth's language suggests, depends less on rational system than on emotional association. Human beings link themselves with the infinite by what Wordsworth elsewhere terms "wise passiveness," the capacity to submit to feeling and be led by it to transcendence. Natural detail, too, acquires value by evoking and symbolizing emotion. Nature belongs to the realm of the nonrational, the superrational.

The idea of the natural can also imply the uncivilized, or precivilized. Philosophers have differed dramatically in their hypotheses about what humankind was like in its "natural" state. Thomas Hobbes, in the seventeenth century, argued that the natural human condition was one of conflict. Society developed to curb the violent impulses human beings would manifest without its restraint. The prevailing nineteenth-century view, on the other hand, made civilization the agent of corruption. Rousseau expounded the crippling effect of institutions. The child raised with the greatest possible freedom, he maintained, would develop in more admirable ways than one subjected to system. By the second half of the eighteenth century, a French novelist could contrast the decadent life of Europe unfavorably with existence on an unspoiled island (Bernardin de Saint-Pierre, *Paul and Virginia*, 1788); Thomas Chatterton, before committing suicide in 1770 at the age of eighteen, wrote poems rich in nostalgia for a more primitive stage of social development which he tried to pass off as medieval works; the forged Ossian poems (1760–63) of James Macpherson, purportedly ancient texts, attracted a large and enthusiastic audience. New interest manifested itself in ballads, poetic survivals of the primitive; Romantic poets imitated the form. The interest in a simpler past, a simpler life, continued throughout the nineteenth century: in Victorian England, Tennyson recast Arthurian legend in modern verse; the Pre-Raphaelites evoked the medieval in visual and verbal arts.

The revolutionary fervor of the late eighteenth century had generated a vision of infinite human possibility, political and personal. The escapist implications of the increasing emphasis on nature, the primitive, the uncomplicated past, suggest, however, a sense of alienation. Blake, Wordsworth, Shelley, all wrote poems of social protest. "Society" would not help the individual work out his or her salvation; on the contrary, it embodied forces opposed to individual development. Indeed, the word *society* had come to embody the impulses that desecrated nature and oppressed the poor in the interests of industry and "progress." Melancholy marked the Romantic hero (Lord Byron in his poetic self-manifestations; Heathcliff in fiction, for example) and tinged nineteenth-century poetry and fiction. The satiric spirit—that spirit of social reform—was in abeyance. Hope lay in the individual's separation from, not participation in, society. In the woods and mountains, one might feel free.

The Waste Land (1922), T. S. Eliot's twentieth-century epic, contains the line, "In the mountains, there you feel free," a line given complex ironic overtones by its context. Its occurrence, however, may remind us how powerfully ideas that came into currency in the late eighteenth and early nineteenth centuries survive into our own time. The world of the Romantic period specifically prefigures our own, despite all the differences dividing the two cultures. We have developed more fully important Romantic tendencies: stress on the sacredness of the individual, suspicion of social institutions, belief in expressed feeling as the sign of authenticity, nostalgia for simpler ways of being, faith in genius, valuing of originality and imagination, an ambivalent relation to science. Although Wordsworth and Dickinson and Melville employ vocabularies and use references partly strange to us, they speak directly to the preoccupations of our time. By attending closely to them, we may learn more about ourselves: not only in the common humanity that we share with all our predecessors but in our special historical situation as both direct heirs of nineteenth-century assumptions and rebels against them.

FURTHER READING

Useful introductions to the Romantic period include L. Furst, *Romanticism in Perspective: A Comparative Study of Aspects of the Romantic Movements in*

England, France, and Germany (1979); R. F. Gleckner and G. E. Enscoe, eds., *Romanticism: Points of View* (1962), a collection of essays by various contributors; R. W. Harris, *Romanticism and the Social Order, 1780–1830* (1969); and M. Butler, *Romantics, Rebels, and Reactionaries: English Literature and Its Background, 1760–1830* (1982). On French Romanticism, see P. T. Comeau, *Diehards and Innovators: The French Romantic Struggle, 1800–1830* (1988); on Germany, T. Ziolkowski, *German Romanticism and Its Institutions* (1990); on English and American developments, B. Taylor, R. Bain, and M. H. Abrams, *The Cast of Consciousness: Concepts of the Mind in British and American Romanticism* (1987); on the English and German situation, C. Jacobs, *Uncontainable Romanticism* (1989).

TEXTS	CONTEXTS
1781–1788 Jean-Jacques Rousseau, *Confessions*	
1794 William Blake, *Songs of Innocence and Experience*	
1798 William Wordsworth and Samuel Taylor Coleridge, *Lyrical Ballads*	
	1801 United Kingdom of Great Britain (England and Scotland) and Ireland established
1802 Coleridge, *Dejection: An Ode* • François René, Vicomte de Chateaubriand, *René*	
	1803 President Thomas Jefferson purchases French "Louisiana"
	1804 Napoleon crowned emperor of France
1808 Johann Wolfgang von Goethe, *Faust, Part I* (*Part II*, 1832)	
1812–1870 Charles Dickens, English novelist	
	1815 Battle of Waterloo, ending Napoleon's career
1816 Coleridge, *Kubla Khan* • John Keats, *On First Looking into Chapman's Homer*	
1818–1820 Lyrics by Percy Bysshe Shelley and John Keats	
1827 Heinrich Heine, *Book of Songs*	
1828 Victor Hugo, *Odes and Ballads*	
	1831 Invention of chloroform inaugurates a new medical era
1834 Alexander Sergeyevich Pushkin, *The Queen of Spades*	
1837 Giacomo Leopardi, *The Broom*	**1837** Victoria crowned queen of the United Kingdom

out awareness of the reality and integrity of others. Rousseau, in the *Confessions*, vividly expresses the narcissistic side of Romanticism.

Implicit in Rousseau's ways of understanding himself and his life are new moral assumptions as well. Honesty of a particular kind becomes the highest value; however disreputable his behavior, Rousseau can feel comfortable about it because he reports it accurately. What Johnson or Pope would see as self-indulgence, care exclusively for one's own pleasure, seems acceptable to Rousseau because of the minute, exacting attention devoted to it. The autobiographer examines each nuance of his own happiness, as if to know it fully constituted moral achievement. To take the self this seriously as subject—not in relation to a progress of education or of salvation, merely in its moment-to-moment being—implies belief in self-knowledge (knowledge of feeling, thought, action) as a high moral achievement. This is not the slowly achieved, arduous discipline recommended by Socrates but a somewhat more indulgent form of self-contemplation. To connect it, as Rousseau does, with morality conveys the view that self-absorption without self-judgment provides valuable and sufficient insight.

In his presentation of self, Rousseau contrasts vividly with his great predecessor, Montaigne. Rousseau insists on his uniqueness: "I am not made like any of those I have seen; I venture to believe that I am not made like any of those who are in existence." He presents himself for the reader's contemplation as a remarkable phenomenon. Montaigne, on the other hand, reminds us constantly of what author and reader (and humankind in general) have in common. "Not only does the wind of accidents stir me according to its blowing, but I am also stirred and troubled by the instability of my attitude; and he who examines himself closely will seldom find himself twice in the same state." The movement within the sentence from *I* to the universalizing *he* characterizes a more outward-looking mode.

It must be said, however, that the intensity of Rousseau's self-concentration makes his subject compelling for others as well. However distasteful one might find his obsessive focus, it is difficult to stop reading. The writer hints—makes us believe—that he will reveal all secrets about himself; and learning such secrets, despite Rousseau's insistence on his own uniqueness, tells us of human weakness, inconsistency, power, scope—tells us, therefore, something of ourselves.

F. C. Green, *Jean-Jacques Rousseau: A Critical Study of His Life and Writings* (1955), provides biography and criticism. I. Babbitt, *Rousseau and Romanticism* (1919), examines the relation of Rousseau's assumptions to those of the Romantic movement. A thorough modern evaluation of Rousseau's achievement is L. G. Crocker, *Jean-Jacques Rousseau: A New Interpretative Analysis of His Works* (1973). More directly focused on the *Confessions* is H. Williams, *Rousseau and Romantic Autobiography* (1983). Recent studies include T. M. Kavanagh, *Writing the Truth: Authority and Desire in the Works of Rousseau* (1987), and C. Kelly, *Rousseau's Exemplary Life: The Confessions as Political Philosophy* (1987). A collection of essays by various authors is H. Bloom, ed., *Jean-Jacques Rousseau* (1988).

PRONOUNCING GLOSSARY

The following list uses common English syllables and stress accents to provide rough equivalents of selected words whose pronunciation may be unfamiliar to the general reader.

de Vulson: *du vyu-saw'*
de Warens: *du vah-rahnh'*
Jean-Jacques Rousseau: *jahnh-jahk roo-soh'*

Lausanne: *loh-zahn'*
Montaigne: *mon-tenh'*
Nyon: *nee-yawnh'*
Saone: *sohn*

St. Marceau: *sanh mahr-soh'* Vaud: *voh*

Turin: *too-ranh'* Vévay: *vay-vay'*

From Confessions

Part I

BOOK I

[The Years 1712–1719]

I am commencing an undertaking, hitherto without precedent, and which will never find an imitator. I desire to set before my fellows the likeness of a man in all the truth of nature, and that man myself.

Myself alone! I know the feelings of my heart, and I know men. I am not made like any of those I have seen; I venture to believe that I am not made like any of those who are in existence. If I am not better, at least I am different. Whether Nature has acted rightly or wrongly in destroying the mould in which she cast me, can only be decided after I have been read.

Let the trumpet of the Day of Judgment sound when it will, I will present myself before the Sovereign Judge with this book in my hand. I will say boldly: "This is what I have done, what I have thought, what I was. I have told the good and the bad with equal frankness. I have neither omitted anything bad, nor interpolated anything good. If I have occasionally made use of some immaterial embellishments, this has only been in order to fill a gap caused by lack of memory. I may have assumed the truth of that which I knew might have been true, never of that which I knew to be false. I have shown myself as I was: mean and contemptible, good, high-minded and sublime, according as I was one or the other. I have unveiled my inmost self even as Thou hast seen it, O Eternal Being. Gather round me the countless host of my fellow-men; let them hear my confessions, lament for my unworthiness, and blush for my imperfections. Then let each of them in turn reveal, with the same frankness, the secrets of his heart at the foot of the Throne, and say, if he dare, *'I was better than that man!'* " * * *

I felt before I thought: this is the common lot of humanity. I experienced it more than others. I do not know what I did until I was five or six years old. I do not know how I learned to read; I only remember my earliest reading, and the effect it had upon me; from that time I date my uninterrupted self-consciousness. My mother had left some romances behind her, which my father and I began to read after supper. At first it was only a question of practising me in reading by the aid of amusing books; but soon the interest became so lively, that we used to read in turns without stopping, and spent whole nights in this occupation. We were unable to leave off until the volume was finished. Sometimes, my father, hearing the swallows begin to twitter in the early morning, would say, quite ashamed, "Let us go to bed; I am more of a child than yourself."

In a short time I acquired, by this dangerous method, not only extreme facility in reading and understanding what I read, but a knowledge of the passions that was unique in a child of my age. I had no idea of things in themselves, although all the feelings of actual life were already known to me. I had conceived nothing, but felt everything. These confused emotions which I felt one after the other, certainly did not warp the reasoning powers which I did not as yet possess; but they shaped them in me of a peculiar stamp, and gave me odd and romantic notions of human life, of which experience and reflection have never been able wholly to cure me. * * *

How could I become wicked, when I had nothing but examples of gentleness before my eyes, and none around me but the best people in the world? My father, my aunt, my nurse, my relations, our friends, our neighbours, all who surrounded me, did not, it is true, obey me, but they loved me; and I loved them in return. My wishes were so little excited and so little opposed, that it did not occur to me to have any. I can swear that, until I served under a master, I never knew what a fancy was. Except during the time I spent in reading or writing in my father's company, or when my nurse took me for a walk, I was always with my aunt, sitting or standing by her side, watching her at her embroidery or listening to her singing; and I was content. Her cheerfulness, her gentleness and her pleasant face have stamped so deep and lively an impression on my mind that I can still see her manner, look, and attitude; I remember her affectionate language: I could describe what clothes she wore and how her head was dressed, not forgetting the two little curls of black hair on her temples, which she wore in accordance with the fashion of the time.

I am convinced that it is to her I owe the taste, or rather passion, for music, which only became fully developed in me a long time afterwards. She knew a prodigious number of tunes and songs which she used to sing in a very thin, gentle voice. This excellent woman's cheerfulness of soul banished dreaminess and melancholy from herself and all around her. The attraction which her singing possessed for me was so great, that not only have several of her songs always remained in my memory, but even now, when I have lost her, and as I grow older, many of them, totally forgotten since the days of my childhood, return to my mind with inexpressible charm. Would anyone believe that I, an old dotard, eaten up by cares and troubles, sometimes find myself weeping like a child, when I mumble one of those little airs in a voice already broken and trembling?

* * * I have spent my life in idle longing, without saying a word, in the presence of those whom I loved most. Too bashful to declare my taste, I at least satisfied it in situations which had reference to it and kept up the idea of it. To lie at the feet of an imperious mistress, to obey her commands, to ask her forgiveness—this was for me a sweet enjoyment; and, the more my lively imagination heated my blood, the more I presented the appearance of a bashful lover. It may be easily imagined that this manner of making love does not lead to very speedy results, and is not very dangerous to the virtue of those who are its object. For this reason I have rarely possessed, but have none the less enjoyed myself in my own way— that is to say, in imagination. Thus it has happened that my senses, in

harmony with my timid disposition and my romantic spirit, have kept my sentiments pure and my morals blameless, owing to the very tastes which, combined with a little more impudence, might have plunged me into the most brutal sensuality. * * *

I am a man of very strong passions, and, while I am stirred by them, nothing can equal my impetuosity; I forget all discretion, all feelings of respect, fear and decency; I am cynical, impudent, violent and fearless; no feeling of shame keeps me back, no danger frightens me; with the exception of the single object which occupies my thoughts, the universe is nothing to me. But all this lasts only for a moment, and the following moment plunges me into complete annihilation. In my calmer moments I am indolence and timidity itself; everything frightens and discourages me; a fly, buzzing past, alarms me; a word which I have to say, a gesture which I have to make, terrifies my idleness; fear and shame overpower me to such an extent that I would gladly hide myself from the sight of my fellow-creatures. If I have to act, I do not know what to do; if I have to speak, I do not know what to say; if anyone looks at me, I am put out of countenance. When I am strongly moved I sometimes know how to find the right words, but in ordinary conversation I can find absolutely nothing, and my condition is unbearable for the simple reason that I am obliged to speak.

Add to this, that none of my prevailing tastes centre in things that can be bought. I want nothing but unadulterated pleasures, and money poisons all. For instance, I am fond of the pleasures of the table; but, as I cannot endure either the constraint of good society or the drunkenness of the tavern, I can only enjoy them with a friend; alone, I cannot do so, for my imagination then occupies itself with other things, and eating affords me no pleasure. If my heated blood longs for women, my excited heart longs still more for affection. Women who could be bought for money would lose for me all their charms; I even doubt whether it would be in me to make use of them. I find it the same with all pleasures within my reach; unless they cost me nothing, I find them insipid. I only love those enjoyments which belong to no one but the first man who knows how to enjoy them.

* * * I worship freedom; I abhor restraint, trouble, dependence. As long as the money in my purse lasts, it assures my independence; it relieves me of the trouble of finding expedients to replenish it, a necessity which always inspired me with dread; but the fear of seeing it exhausted makes me hoard it carefully. The money which a man possesses is the instrument of freedom; that which we eagerly pursue is the instrument of slavery. Therefore I hold fast to that which I have, and desire nothing.

My disinterestedness is, therefore, nothing but idleness; the pleasure of possession is not worth the trouble of acquisition. In like manner, my extravagance is nothing but idleness; when the opportunity of spending agreeably presents itself, it cannot be too profitably employed. Money tempts me less than things, because between money and the possession of the desired object there is always an intermediary, whereas between the thing itself and the enjoyment of it there is none. If I see the thing, it tempts me; if I only see the means of gaining possession of it, it does not. For this reason I have committed thefts, and even now I sometimes pilfer trifles which tempt me, and which I prefer to take rather than to ask for; but neither when a child nor a grown-up man do I ever remember to have robbed anyone of a farthing, except on one occasion, fifteen years ago, when I stole seven *livres* ten *sous*.

*   *   *

BOOK II

[The Years 1728–1731]

* * * I have drawn the great moral lesson, perhaps the only one of any practical value, to avoid those situations of life which bring our duties into conflict with our interests, and which show us our own advantage in the misfortunes of others; for it is certain that, in such situations, however sincere our love of virtue, we must, sooner or later, inevitably grow weak without perceiving it, and become unjust and wicked in act, without having ceased to be just and good in our hearts.

This principle, deeply imprinted on the bottom of my heart, which, although somewhat late, in practice guided my whole conduct, is one of those which have caused me to appear a very strange and foolish creature in the eyes of the world, and, above all, amongst my acquaintances. I have been reproached with wanting to pose as an original, and different from others. In reality, I have never troubled about acting like other people or differently from them. I sincerely desired to do what was right. I withdrew, as far as it lay in my power, from situations which opposed my interests to those of others, and might, consequently, inspire me with a secret, though involuntary, desire of injuring them.

* * * I loved too sincerely, too completely, I venture to say, to be able to be happy easily. Never have passions been at once more lively and purer than mine; never has love been tenderer, truer, more disinterested. I would have sacrificed my happiness a thousand times for that of the person whom I loved; her reputation was dearer to me than my life, and I would never have wished to endanger her repose for a single moment for all the pleasures of enjoyment. This feeling has made me employ such carefulness, such secrecy, and such precaution in my undertakings, that none of them have ever been successful. My want of success with women has always been caused by my excessive love for them.

*   *   *

BOOK III

[The Years 1731–1732]

* * * I only felt the full strength of my attachment when I no longer saw her.[1] When I saw her, I was only content; but, during her absence, my restlessness became painful. The need of living with her caused me outbreaks of tenderness which often ended in tears. I shall never forget how, on the day of a great festival, while she was at vespers, I went for a

---

1. Rousseau refers here to Françoise-Louise de Warens, whom he also calls "mamma."

walk outside the town, my heart full of her image and a burning desire to spend my life with her. I had sense enough to see that at present this was impossible, and that the happiness which I enjoyed so deeply could only be short. This gave to my reflections a tinge of melancholy, about which, however, there was nothing gloomy, and which was tempered by flattering hopes. The sound of the bells, which always singularly affects me, the song of the birds, the beauty of the daylight, the enchanting landscape, the scattered country dwellings in which my fancy placed our common home—all these produced upon me an impression so vivid, tender, melancholy and touching, that I saw myself transported, as it were, in ecstasy, into that happy time and place, wherein my heart, possessing all the happiness it could desire, tasted it with inexpressible rapture, without even a thought of sensual pleasure. I never remember to have plunged into the future with greater force and illusion than on that occasion; and what has struck me most in the recollection of this dream after it had been realised, is that I have found things again exactly as I had imagined them. If ever the dream of a man awake resembled a prophetic vision, it was assuredly that dream of mine. I was only deceived in the imaginary duration; for the days, the years, and our whole life were spent in serene and undisturbed tranquillity, whereas in reality it lasted only for a moment. Alas! my most lasting happiness belongs to a dream, the fulfilment of which was almost immediately followed by the awakening. * * *

Two things, almost incompatible, are united in me in a manner which I am unable to understand: a very ardent temperament, lively and tumultuous passions, and, at the same time, slowly developed and confused ideas, which never present themselves until it is too late. One might say that my heart and my mind do not belong to the same person. Feeling takes possession of my soul more rapidly than a flash of lightning; but, instead of illuminating, inflames and dazzles me. I feel everything and see nothing. I am carried away by my passions, but stupid; in order to think, I must be cool. The astonishing thing is that, notwithstanding, I exhibit tolerably sound judgment, penetration, even finesse, if I am not hurried; with sufficient leisure I can compose excellent impromptus; but I have never said or done anything worthy of notice on the spur of the moment. I could carry on a very clever conversation through the post, as the Spaniards are said to carry on a game of chess. When I read of that Duke of Savoy, who turned round on his journey, in order to cry, "At your throat, Parisian huckster," I said, "There you have myself!"

This sluggishness of thought, combined with such liveliness of feeling, not only enters into my conversation, but I feel it even when alone and at work. My ideas arrange themselves in my head with almost incredible difficulty; they circulate in it with uncertain sound, and ferment till they excite and heat me, and make my heart beat fast; and, in the midst of this excitement, I see nothing clearly and am unable to write a single word— I am obliged to wait. Imperceptibly this great agitation subsides, the confusion clears up, everything takes its proper place, but slowly, and only after a period of long and confused agitation.

* * *

BOOK IV

[The Years 1731–1732]

* * * I returned, not to Nyon, but to Lausanne. I wanted to sate myself with the sight of this beautiful lake, which is there seen in its greatest extent. Few of the secret motives which have determined me to act have been more rational. Things seen at a distance are rarely powerful enough to make me act. The uncertainty of the future has always made me look upon plans, which need considerable time to carry them out, as decoys for fools. I indulge in hopes like others, provided it costs me nothing to support them; but if they require continued attention, I have done with it. The least trifling pleasure which is within my reach tempts me more than the joys of Paradise. However, I make an exception of the pleasure which is followed by pain; this has no temptation for me, because I love only pure enjoyments, and these a man never has when he knows that he is preparing for himself repentance and regret. * * *

Why is it that, having found so many good people in my youth, I find so few in my later years? Is their race extinct? No; but the class in which I am obliged to look for them now, is no longer the same as that in which I found them. Among the people, where great passions only speak at intervals, the sentiments of nature make themselves more frequently heard; in the higher ranks they are absolutely stifled, and, under the mask of sentiment, it is only interest or vanity that speaks.

* * * Whenever I approach the Canton of Vaud, I am conscious of an impression in which the remembrance of Madame de Warens, who was born there, of my father who lived there, of Mademoiselle de Vulson who enjoyed the first fruits of my youthful love, of several pleasure trips which I made there when a child and, I believe, some other exciting cause, more mysterious and more powerful than all this, is combined. When the burning desire of this happy and peaceful life, which flees from me and for which I was born, inflames my imagination, it is always the Canton of Vaud, near the lake, in the midst of enchanting scenery, to which it draws me. I feel that I must have an orchard on the shore of this lake and no other, that I must have a loyal friend, a loving wife, a cow, and a little boat. I shall never enjoy perfect happiness on earth until I have all that. I laugh at the simplicity with which I have several times visited this country merely in search of this imaginary happiness. I was always surprised to find its inhabitants, especially the women, of quite a different character from that which I expected. How contradictory it appeared to me! The country and its inhabitants have never seemed to me made for each other.

During this journey to Vévay, walking along the beautiful shore, I abandoned myself to the sweetest melancholy. My heart eagerly flung itself into a thousand innocent raptures; I was filled with emotion, I sighed and wept like a child. How often have I stopped to weep to my heart's content, and, sitting on a large stone, amused myself with looking at my tears falling into the water! * * *

How greatly did the entrance into Paris belie the idea I had formed of it! The external decorations of Turin, the beauty of its streets, the symmetry and regularity of the houses, had made me look for something quite different in Paris. I had imagined to myself a city of most imposing aspect, as beautiful as it was large, where nothing was to be seen but splendid streets and palaces of gold and marble. Entering by the suburb of St. Marceau, I saw nothing but dirty and stinking little streets, ugly black houses, a general air of slovenliness and poverty, beggars, carters, menders of old clothes, criers of decoctions and old hats. All this, from the outset, struck me so forcibly, that all the real magnificence I have since seen in Paris has been unable to destroy this first impression, and I have always retained a secret dislike against residence in this capital. I may say that the whole time, during which I afterwards lived there, was employed solely in trying to find means to enable me to live away from it.

Such is the fruit of a too lively imagination, which exaggerates beyond human exaggeration, and is always ready to see more than it has been told to expect. I had heard Paris so much praised, that I had represented it to myself as the ancient Babylon, where, if I had ever visited it, I should, perhaps, have found as much to take off from the picture which I had drawn of it. The same thing happened to me at the Opera, whither I hastened to go the day after my arrival. The same thing happened to me later at Versailles; and again, when I saw the sea for the first time; and the same thing will always happen to me, when I see anything which has been too loudly announced; for it is impossible for men, and difficult for Nature herself, to surpass the exuberance of my imagination.

* * * The sight of the country, a succession of pleasant views, the open air, a good appetite, the sound health which walking gives me, the free life of the inns, the absence of all that makes me conscious of my dependent position, of all that reminds me of my condition—all this sets my soul free, gives me greater boldness of thought, throws me, so to speak, into the immensity of things, so that I can combine, select, and appropriate them at pleasure, without fear or restraint. I dispose of Nature in its entirety as its lord and master; my heart, roaming from object to object, mingles and identifies itself with those which soothe it, wraps itself up in charming fancies, and is intoxicated with delicious sensations. If, in order to render them permanent, I amuse myself by describing them by myself, what vigorous outlines, what fresh colouring, what power of expression I give them!

* * * At night I lay in the open air, and, stretched on the ground or on a bench, slept as calmly as upon a bed of roses. I remember, especially, that I spent a delightful night outside the city, on a road which ran by the side of the Rhône or Saône, I do not remember which. Raised gardens, with terraces, bordered the other side of the road. It had been very hot during the day; the evening was delightful; the dew moistened the parched grass; the night was calm, without a breath of wind; the air was fresh, without being cold; the sun, having gone down, had left in the sky red vapours, the reflection of which cast a rose-red tint upon the water; the trees on the terraces were full of nightingales answering one another. I walked on in a kind of ecstasy, abandoning my heart and senses to the enjoyment of all, only regretting, with a sigh, that I was obliged to enjoy it alone. Absorbed in my delightful reverie, I continued my walk late into the night, without noticing that I was tired. At last, I noticed it. I threw

myself with a feeling of delight upon the shelf of a sort of niche or false door let into a terrace wall; the canopy of my bed was formed by the tops of trees; a nightingale was perched just over my head, and lulled me to sleep with his song; my slumbers were sweet, my awaking was still sweeter. * * *

In relating my journeys, as in making them, I do not know how to stop. My heart beat with joy when I drew near to my dear mamma, but I walked no faster. I like to walk at my ease, and to stop when I like. A wandering life is what I want. To walk through a beautiful country in fine weather, without being obliged to hurry, and with a pleasant prospect at the end, is of all kinds of life the one most suited to my taste. My idea of a beautiful country is already known. No flat country, however beautiful, has ever seemed so to my eyes. I must have mountain torrents, rocks, firs, dark forests, mountains, steep roads to climb or descend, precipices at my side to frighten me.

*   *   *

BOOK V

[The Years 1732–1736]

* * * It is sometimes said that the sword wears out the scabbard. That is my history. My passions have made me live, and my passions have killed me. What passions? will be asked. Trifles, the most childish things in the world, which, however, excited me as much as if the possession of Helen or the throne of the universe had been at stake. In the first place—women. When I possessed one, my senses were calm; my heart, never. The needs of love devoured me in the midst of enjoyment; I had a tender mother, a dear friend; but I needed a mistress. I imagined one in her place; I represented her to myself in a thousand forms, in order to deceive myself. If I had thought that I held mamma in my arms when I embraced her, these embraces would have been no less lively, but all my desires would have been extinguished; I should have sobbed from affection, but I should never have felt any enjoyment. Enjoyment! Does this ever fall to the lot of man? If I had ever, a single time in my life, tasted all the delights of love in their fulness, I do not believe that my frail existence could have endured it; I should have died on the spot.

Thus I was burning with love, without an object; and it is this state, perhaps, that is most exhausting. I was restless, tormented by the hopeless condition of poor mamma's affairs, and her imprudent conduct, which were bound to ruin her completely at no distant date. My cruel imagination, which always anticipates misfortunes, exhibited this particular one to me continually, in all its extent and in all its results. I already saw myself compelled by want to separate from her to whom I had devoted my life, and without whom I could not enjoy it. Thus my soul was ever in a state of agitation; I was devoured alternately by desires and fears.

*   *   *

BOOK VI

[The Year 1736]

* * * At this period commences the brief happiness of my life; here approach the peaceful, but rapid moments which have given me the right to say, I have lived. Precious and regretted moments! Begin again for me your delightful course; and, if it be possible, pass more slowly in succession through my memory, than you did in your fugitive reality. What can I do, to prolong, as I should like, this touching and simple narrative, to repeat the same things over and over again, without wearying my readers by such repetition, any more than I was wearied of them myself, when I recommenced the life again and again? If all this consisted of facts, actions, and words, I could describe, and in a manner, give an idea of them; but how is it possible to describe what was neither said nor done, nor even thought, but enjoyed and felt, without being able to assign any other reason for my happiness than this simple feeling? I got up at sunrise, and was happy; I walked, and was happy; I saw mamma, and was happy; I left her, and was happy; I roamed the forests and hills, I wandered in the valleys, I read, I did nothing, I worked in the garden, I picked the fruit, I helped in the work of the house, and happiness followed me everywhere—happiness, which could not be referred to any definite object, but dwelt entirely within myself, and which never left me for a single instant. * * *

I should much like to know, whether the same childish ideas ever enter the hearts of other men as sometimes enter mine. In the midst of my studies, in the course of a life as blameless as a man could have led, the fear of hell still frequently troubled me. I asked myself: "In what state am I? If I were to die this moment, should I be damned?" According to my Jansenists,[2] there was no doubt about the matter; but, according to my conscience, I thought differently. Always fearful, and a prey to cruel uncertainty, I had recourse to the most laughable expedients to escape from it, for which I would unhesitatingly have anyone locked up as a madman if I saw him doing as I did. One day, while musing upon this melancholy subject, I mechanically amused myself by throwing stones against the trunks of trees with my usual good aim, that is to say, without hardly hitting one. While engaged in this useful exercise, it occurred to me to draw a prognostic from it to calm my anxiety. I said to myself: "I will throw this stone at the tree opposite; if I hit it, I am saved; if I miss it, I am damned." While speaking, I threw my stone with a trembling hand and a terrible palpitation of the heart, but with so successful an aim that it hit the tree right in the middle, which, to tell the truth, was no very difficult feat, for I had been careful to choose a tree with a thick trunk close at hand. From that time I have never had any doubt about my salvation! When I recall this characteristic incident, I do not know whether to laugh or cry at myself. You great men, who are most certainly laughing, may congratulate yourselves; but do not mock my wretchedness, for I swear to you that I feel it deeply. * * *

---

2. A sect of strict Catholics, named for Corneille Jansen (1585–1638). Voltaire mentions them in Candide, chaps. 21 and 22.

JOHANN WOLFGANG VON GOETHE

1749–1832

Recasting the ancient legend of Faust, Johann Wolfgang von Goethe created a powerful symbol of the Romantic imagination in all its aspiration and anxiety. Faust himself, central character of the epic drama, emerges as a Romantic hero, ever testing the limits of possibility. Yet to achieve his ends he must make a contract with the Devil: as if to say that giving full scope to imagination necessarily partakes of sin.

Goethe's *Faust* (Part I, 1808; Part II, 1832) constituted the crowning masterpiece of a life rich in achievement. Goethe exemplifies the nineteenth-century meaning of *genius*. Accomplished as poet, dramatist, novelist, and autobiographer, he also practiced law, served as a diplomat, and pursued scientific research. He had a happy childhood in Frankfurt, after which he studied law at Leipzig and then at Strasbourg, where in 1770–71 he met Gottfried Herder, leader of a new literary movement called the Sturm und Drang (Storm and Stress) movement. Participants in this movement emphasized the importance of revolt against established standards; they interested Goethe in such newly discovered forms as the folk song and in the literary vitality of Shakespeare, as opposed to more formally constricted writers.

During the brief period when he practiced law, after an unhappy love affair, Goethe wrote *The Sorrows of Young Werther* (1774), a novel of immense influence in establishing the image of the introspective, self-pitying, melancholy Romantic hero. In 1775 he accepted an invitation to the court of Charles Augustus, duke of Saxe-Weimar. He remained in Weimar for the rest of his life, for ten years serving the duke as chief minister. A trip to Italy from 1786 to 1788 aroused his interest in classic sources. He wrote dramas based on classic texts, most notably *Iphigenia* (1787); novels (for example, *Elective Affinities*, 1809) that pointed the way to the psychological novel; lyric poetry; and an important autobiography, *Poetry and Truth* (1811–33). He also did significant work in botany and physiology. Increasingly famous, he became in his own lifetime a legendary figure; all Europe flocked to Weimar to visit him.

The legend of Dr. Faustus (the real Johannes Faustus, a scholar, lived from 1480 to 1540), in most versions a seeker after forbidden knowledge, had attracted other writers before Goethe. The most important previous literary embodiment of the tale was Christopher Marlowe's *Doctor Faustus* (ca. 1588), a drama ending in its protagonist's damnation as a result of his search for illegitimate power through learning. Goethe's Faust meets no such fate. Pursuing not knowledge but experience, he embodies the ideal of limitless aspiration in all its glamour and danger. His contract with Mephistopheles provides that he will die at the moment he declares himself satisfied, content to rest in the present; he stakes his life and his salvation on his capacity ever to yearn for something beyond.

In Part I of Goethe's play, the protagonist's vision of the impossible locates itself specifically in the figure of Margaret (in German, *Margarete* or its diminutive, *Gretchen*), the simple, innocent girl whom he possesses physically but with whom he can never attain total union. In a speech epitomizing Romantic attitudes toward nature and toward emotion (especially the emotion of romantic love), Faust responds to his beloved's question, "Do you believe in God?"

> Does not the heaven vault above?
> Is the earth not firmly based down here?
> And do not, friendly,

Eternal stars arise?
Do we not look into each other's eyes,
And all in you is surging
To your head and heart,
And weaves in timeless mystery,
Unseeable, yet seen, around you?
Then let it fill your heart entirely,
And when your rapture in this feeling is complete,
Call it then as you will,
Call it bliss! heart! love! God!
I do not have a name
For this. Feeling is all.

The notion of *bliss*, for Pope associated with respect for limitation, for Wordsworth connected with revolutionary vision, here designates an unnameable feeling, derived from experience of nature and of romantic love, possibly identical with God, but valued partly for its very vagueness.

Modern readers may feel that Faust bullies Margaret, allowing her no reality except as instrument for his desires. In a poignant moment early in the play, interrupting Faust's rhapsody about her "meekness" and "humility," Margaret suggests, "If you should think of me one moment only . . ." Faust seems incapable of any such awareness, too busy inventing his loved one to see her as she is. He dramatically represents the "egotistical sublime," with a kind of imaginative grandeur inseparable from his utter absorption in the wonder of his own being, his own experience.

Yet the action of Part I turns on Faust's development of just that consciousness of another's reality which seemed impossible for him, and Margaret is the agent of his development. In the great final scene—Margaret in prison, intermittently mad, condemned to death for murdering her illegitimate child by Faust—the woman again appeals to the man to think about her, to *know* her: "Do you know, my love, *whom* you are setting free?" Her anguish, his responsibility for it, force themselves on Faust. He wishes he had never been born: his lust for experience has resulted in this terrible culpability, this agonizing loss. At the final moment of separation, with Margaret's spiritual redemption proclaimed from above, Faust implicitly acknowledges the full reality of the woman he has lost and thus, even though he departs with Mephistopheles, distinguishes himself from his Satanic mentor. Mephistopheles in his nature cannot grasp a reality utterly apart from his own; he can only recognize what belongs to him. Faust, at least fleetingly, realizes the otherness of the woman and the value of what he has lost.

Mephistopheles, at the outset witty and powerful in his own imagination, gradually reveals his limitations. In the *Prologue in Heaven*, the Devil seems energetic, perceptive, enterprising, fearless: as the Lord says, a "joker," apparently more playful than malign. His bargain with the Lord turns on his belief in the essentially "beastly" nature of humankind: like Gulliver's Houyhnhnm master, he emphasizes the human misuse of reason. Although the scene is modeled on the interchange between God and Satan in the Book of Job, it differs significantly in that the Lord gives an explicit reason for allowing the Tempter to function. "Man errs as long as he will," He says, but He adds that Mephistopheles's value is in prodding humanity into action. The introductory scene thus suggests that Mephistopheles will function as an agent of salvation rather than damnation. The Devil's subsequent exchanges with Faust, in Mephistopheles's mind predicated on his own superior knowledge and comprehension, gradually make one realize that the man in significant respects knows more than does the Devil. Mephistopheles, for example, can understand Faust's desire for Margaret only in sexual terms. His witty cynicism seems more and more inadequate to the actual situation. By the end of

Part I, Faust's suffering has enlarged him; but from the beginning, his capacity for sympathy marks his potential superiority to the Devil.

The *Walpurgis Night* section, with the *Walpurgis Night's Dream*, marks a stage in Faust's education and an extreme moment in the play's dramatic structure. Goethe here allows himself to indulge in unrestrained fantasy—grotesque, obscene, comic, with an explosion of satiric energy in the dream. The shifting tone and reference of these passages embody ways in which the diabolic might be thought to operate in human terms. While Margaret suffers the consequences of her sin, Faust experiences the ambiguous freedom of the imagination, always at the edge of horror.

The pattern of Faust's moral development in Part I prepares the reader for a nontragic denouement to the drama as a whole. In Part II, which he worked on for some thirty years, completing it only the year before his death, Goethe moves from the individual to the social. Faust marries Helen of Troy, who gives birth to Euphorion, symbol of new humanity. He turns soldier to save a kingdom; he reclaims land from the sea; finally he rests contented in a vision of happy community generated by the industry of humankind. Mephistopheles thinks this his moment of victory: now Faust has declared himself satisfied. But since his satisfaction depends still on aspiration, on a dream of the future, the Angels rescue him at last and take him to Heaven.

One cannot read *Faust* with twentieth-century expectations of what a play should be like. This is above all *poetic* drama, to be read with pleasure in the richness of its language, the fertility and daring of its imagination. Although its cast of characters natural and supernatural and its sequence of supernaturally generated events are far from "realistic," it addresses problems still very much with us. How can individual ambition and desire be reconciled with responsibility to others? Does a powerful imagination—an artist's, say, or a scientist's—justify its possessor in ignoring social obligations? Goethe investigates such perplexing issues in symbolic terms, drawing his readers into personal involvement by playing on their emotions even as he questions the proper functions and limitations of commitment to desire—that form of emotional energy that leads to the greatest human achievements, but involves the constant danger of debilitating narcissism.

E. Ludwig, *Goethe, The History of a Man, 1749–1832* (1928), is a solid biography. Also useful are V. Lange, ed., *Goethe: A Collection of Critical Essays* (1960); and the essays contained in the critical edition of W. Arndt and C. Hamlin, eds., *Faust* (1976). See also H. Hatfield, *Goethe: A Critical Introduction* (1963), M. Bidney, *Blake and Goethe* (1988); and specifically for *Faust*, L. Dieckmann, *Goethe's Faust: A Critical Reading* (1972). A study relating Goethe's play to other versions of the Faust legend is A. Hoelzel, *The Paradoxical Quest: A Study of Faustian Vicissitudes* (1988). A varied group of essays appears in Reinhold Grimm and Jost Hermand, eds., *Our Faust? Roots and Ramifications of a Modern German Myth* (1987).

PRONOUNCING GLOSSARY

The following list uses common English syllables and stress accents to provide rough equivalents of selected words whose pronunciation may be unfamiliar to the general reader.

Altmayer: *ahlt'-maier*

Auerbach: *aw'-er-bahk*

Elend: *ay'-lend*

encheirisis naturae: *en-kai-ray'-sis nah-tu'-rai*

Euphorion: *oy-foh'-ree-on*

Faust: *fowst*

Goethe: *gur'te*

Leipzig: *laip'-zig*

Proktophantasmist: *prohk-toh-fan-tas'-*   Wagner: *vahg'-ner*
   mist   Walpurgis: *vahl-poor'-gis*
Schierke: *sheer'ke*   Werther: *vayr'-ter*
Sturm und Drang: *shturm unt drahng*   Zenien: *tsay'-nee-en*
Te Deum: *tay day'-um*

Faust[1]

Prologue in Heaven[2]

[*The* LORD, *the* HEAVENLY HOSTS. *Later,* MEPHISTOPHELES.[3] *The three*
ARCHANGELS *step forward.*]
RAPHAEL: The sun intones, in ancient tourney
  With brother spheres, a rival air;
  And his predestinated journey,
  He closes with a thundrous blare.
  His sight, as none can comprehend it,   5
  Gives strength to angels; the array
  Of works, unfathomably splendid,
  Is glorious as on the first day.
GABRIEL: Unfathomably swiftly speeded,
  Earth's pomp revolves in whirling flight,   10
  As Eden's brightness is succeeded
  By deep and dread-inspiring night;
  In mighty torrents foams the ocean
  Against the rocks with roaring song—
  In ever-speeding spheric motion,   15
  Both rock and sea are swept along.
MICHAEL: And rival tempests roar and ravage
  From sea to land, from land to sea,
  And, raging, form a chain of savage,
  Deeply destructive energy.   20
  There flames a flashing devastation
  To clear the thunder's crashing way;
  Yet, Lord, thy herald's admiration
  Is for the mildness of thy day.
THE THREE: The sight, as none can comprehend it,   25
  Gives strength to angels; thy array
  Of works, unfathomably splendid
  Is glorious as on the first day.
MEPHISTOPHELES: Since you, oh Lord, have once again drawn near,
  And ask how we have been, and are so genial,   30
  And since you used to like to see me here,
  You see me, too, as if I were a menial.

---

1. Translated by Walter Kaufman.   **2.** The scene is patterned on Job 1:6–12 and 2:1–6.   **3.** The
origin of the name remains debatable. It may come from Hebrew, Persian, or Greek, with such meanings as "destroyer-liar," "no friend of Faust," and "no friend of light."

I cannot speak as nobly as your staff,
Though by this circle here I shall be spurned:
My pathos would be sure to make you laugh,   35
Were laughing not a habit you've unlearned.
Of suns and worlds I know nothing to say;
I only see how men live in dismay.
The small god of the world will never change his ways
And is as whimsical — as on the first of days.   40
His life might be a bit more fun,
Had you not given him that spark of heaven's sun;
He calls it reason and employs it, resolute
To be more brutish than is any brute.
He seems to me, if you don't mind, Your Grace,   45
Like a cicada of the long-legged race,
That always flies, and, flying, springs,
And in the grass the same old ditty sings;
If only it were grass he could repose in!
There is no trash he will not poke his nose in.   50
THE LORD: Can you not speak but to abuse?
Do you come only to accuse?
Does nothing on the earth seem to you right?
MEPHISTOPHELES: No, Lord. I find it still a rather sorry sight.
Man moves me to compassion, so wretched is his plight.   55
I have no wish to cause him further woe.
THE LORD: Do you know Faust?
MEPHISTOPHELES: The doctor?[4]
THE LORD: Aye, my servant.
MEPHISTOPHELES: Lo!
He serves you[5] most peculiarly, I think.
Not earthly are the poor fool's meat and drink.
His spirit's ferment drives him far,   60
And he half knows how foolish is his quest:
From heaven he demands the fairest star,
And from the earth all joys that he thinks best;
And all that's near and all that's far
Cannot soothe the upheaval in his breast.   65
THE LORD: Though now he serves me but confusedly,
I shall soon lead him where the vapor clears.
The gardener knows, however small the tree,
That bloom and fruit adorn its later years.
MEPHISTOPHELES: What will you bet? You'll lose him yet to me,   70
If you will graciously connive
That I may lead him carefully.
THE LORD: As long as he may be alive,
So long you shall not be prevented.
Man errs as long as he will strive.   75

4. Of philosophy.   5. In the German text, Mephistopheles shifts from *du* to *ihr*, indicating his lack
of respect for God.

MEPHISTOPHELES: Be thanked for that; I've never been contented
  To waste my time upon the dead.
  I far prefer full cheeks, a youthful curly-head.
  When corpses come, I have just left the house—
  I feel as does the cat about the mouse.   80
THE LORD: Enough—I grant that you may try to clasp him,
  Withdraw this spirit from his primal source
  And lead him down, if you can grasp him,
  Upon your own abysmal course—
  And stand abashed when you have to attest: 85
  A good man in his darkling aspiration
  Remembers the right road throughout his quest.
MEPHISTOPHELES: Enough—he will soon reach his station;
  About my bet I have no hesitation,
  And when I win, concede your stake   90
  And let me triumph with a swelling breast:
  Dust he shall eat, and that with zest,
  As my relation does, the famous snake.
THE LORD: Appear quite free on that day, too;
  I never hated those who were like you: 95
  Of all the spirits that negate,
  The knavish jester gives me least to do.
  For man's activity can easily abate,
  He soon prefers uninterrupted rest;
  To give him this companion hence seems best   100
  Who roils and must as Devil help create.
  But you, God's rightful sons, give voice
  To all the beauty in which you rejoice;
  And that which ever works and lives and grows
  Enfold you with fair bonds that love has wrought,   105
  And what in wavering apparition flows
  That fortify with everlasting thought.
    [*The heavens close, the* ARCHANGELS *disperse.*]
MEPHISTOPHELES: [*Alone.*] I like to see the Old Man now and then
  And try to be not too uncivil.
  It's charming in a noble squire when   110
  He speaks humanely with the very Devil.

The First Part of the Tragedy

NIGHT

[*In a high-vaulted, narrow Gothic den,* FAUST, *restless in his armchair
at the desk.*]
FAUST: I have, alas, studied philosophy,
  Jurisprudence and medicine, too,
  And, worst of all, theology
  With keen endeavor, through and through—

And here I am, for all my lore, 5
The wretched fool I was before.
Called Master of Arts, and Doctor to boot,
For ten years almost I confute
And up and down, wherever it goes,
I drag my students by the nose — 10
And see that for all our science and art
We can know nothing. It burns my heart.
Of course, I am smarter than all the shysters,
The doctors, and teachers, and scribes, and Christers;
No scruple nor doubt could make me ill, 15
I am not afraid of the Devil or hell —
But therefore I also lack all delight,
Do not fancy that I know anything right,
Do not fancy that I could teach or assert
What would better mankind or what might convert. 20
I also have neither money nor treasures,
Nor worldly honors or earthly pleasures;
No dog would want to live longer this way!
Hence I have yielded to magic to see
Whether the spirit's mouth and might 25
Would bring some mysteries to light,
That I need not with work and woe
Go on to say what I don't know;
That I might see what secret force
Hides in the world and rules its course. 30
Envisage the creative blazes
Instead of rummaging in phrases.

Full lunar light, that you might stare
The last time now on my despair!
How often I've been waking here 35
At my old desk till you appeared,
And over papers, notes, and books
I caught, my gloomy friend, your looks.
Oh, that up on a mountain height
I could walk in your lovely light 40
And float with spirits round caves and trees,
Weave in your twilight through the leas,
Cast dusty knowledge overboard,
And bathe in dew until restored.

Still this old dungeon, still a mole! 45
Cursed be this moldy walled-in hole
Where heaven's lovely light must pass,
And lose its luster, through stained glass.
Confined with books, and every tome
Is gnawed by worms, covered with dust, 50
And on the walls, up to the dome,
A smoky paper, spots of rust;

Enclosed by tubes and jars that breed
More dust, by instruments and soot,
Ancestral furniture to boot—   55
That is your world! A world indeed!

And need you ask why in your breast
Your cramped heart throbs so anxiously?
Life's every stirring is oppressed
By an unfathomed agony?   60
Instead of living nature which
God made man for with holy breath,
Must[6] stifles you, and every niche
Holds skulls and skeletons and death.

Flee! Out into the open land!   65
And this book full of mystery,
Written in Nostradamus'[7] hand—
Is it not ample company?
Stars' orbits you will know; and bold,
You learn what nature has to teach;   70
Your soul is freed, and you behold
The spirits' words, the spirits' speech.
Though dry reflection might expound
These holy symbols, it is dreary:
You float, oh spirits, all around;   75
Respond to me, if you can hear me.
    [*He opens the book and sees the symbol of the macrocosm.*[8]]
What jubilation bursts out of this sight
Into my senses—now I feel it flowing,
Youthful, a sacred fountain of delight,
Through every nerve, my veins are glowing.   80
Was it a god that made these symbols be
That soothe my feverish unrest,
Filling with joy my anxious breast,
And with mysterious potency
Make nature's hidden powers around me, manifest?   85

Am I a god? Light grows this page—
In these pure lines my eye can see
Creative nature spread in front of me.
But now I grasp the meaning of the sage:
"The realm of spirits is not far away;   90
Your mind is closed, your heart is dead.
Rise, student, bathe without dismay
In heaven's dawn your mortal head."
    [*He contemplates the symbol.*]
All weaves itself into the whole,

6. Mustiness, mold.   7. Latin name of the French astrologer and physician Michel de Notredame
(1503–1566). His collection of rhymed prophecies, *The Centuries*, appeared in 1555.   8. Literally,
"the great world"; the universe as a whole.

Each living in the other's soul. 95
How heaven's powers climb up and descend.
Passing the golden pails from hand to hand!
Bliss-scented, they are winging
Through the sky and earth—their singing
Is ringing through the world. 100

What play! Yet but a play, however vast!
Where, boundless nature, can I hold you fast?
And where you breasts? Wells that sustain
All life—the heaven and the earth are nursed.
The wilted breast craves you in thirst— 105
You well, you still—and I languish in vain?
   [*In disgust, he turns some pages and beholds the symbol of the earth*
   SPIRIT.[9]]
How different is the power of this sign!
You, spirit of the earth, seem close to mine:
I look and feel my powers growing,
As if I'd drunk new wine I'm glowing, 110
I feel a sudden courage, and should dare
To plunge into the world, to bear
All earthly grief, all earthly joy—compare
With gales my strength, face shipwreck without care.
Now there are clouds above— 115
The moon conceals her light—
The lamp dies down.
It steams. Red light rays dash
About my head—a chill
Blows from the vaulting dome 120
And seizes me.
I feel you near me, spirit I implored.
Reveal yourself!
Oh, how my heart is gored
By never felt urges, 125
And my whole body surges—
My heart is yours; yours, too, am I.
You must. You must. Though I should have to die.
   [*He seizes the book and mysteriously pronounces the symbol of the*
   spirit. A reddish flame flashes, and the SPIRIT *appears in the flame.*]
SPIRIT: Who calls me?
FAUST: [*Turning away.*] Vision of fright! 130
SPIRIT: With all your might you drew me near
   You have been sucking at my sphere,
   And now—
FAUST: I cannot bear your sight!
SPIRIT: You have implored me to appear,
   Make known my voice, reveal my face; 135

---

9. The macrocosm represented the ordered, harmonious universe in its totality; this figure seems to be
a symbol for the energy of terrestrial nature—neither good nor bad, merely powerful.

Your soul's entreaty won my grace:
Here I am! What abject fear
Grasps you, oh superman! Where is the soul's impassioned
Call? And where the breast that even now had fashioned
A world to bear and nurse within—that trembled thus,   140
Swollen with joy that it resembled us?
Where are you, Faust, whose voice pierced my domain,
Who surged against me with his might and main?
Could it be you who at my breath's slight shiver
Are to the depths of life aquiver,   145
A miserably writhing worm?
FAUST: Should I, phantom of fire, fly?
It's I, it's Faust; your peer am I!
SPIRIT: In the floods of life and creative storm
To and fro I wave.   150
Weave eternally.
And birth and grave,
An eternal sea,
A changeful strife,
A glowing life: 155
At the roaring loom of the ages I plod
And fashion the life-giving garment of God.
FAUST: You that traverse worlds without end,
Sedulous spirit, I feel close to you.
SPIRIT: Peer of the spirit that you comprehend   160
Not mine! [*Vanishes.*]
FAUST: [*Collapsing.*] Not yours?
Whose then?
I, image of the godhead!
And not even yours!   165
[*A knock.*]
O death! My famulus[1]—I know it well.
My fairest happiness destroyed!
This wealth of visions I enjoyed
The dreary creeper must dispel!
[WAGNER *enters in a dressing gown and night cap, a light in his hand.*
FAUST *turns away in disgust.*]
WAGNER: Forgive! I hear your declamation;   170
Surely, you read a Grecian tragedy?
I'd profit from some work in this vocation,
These days it can be used effectively.
I have been told three times at least
That a comedian could instruct a priest.   175
FAUST: Yes, when the priest is a comedian for all his Te Deum.[2]
As happens more often than one would own.
WAGNER: Ah, when one is confined to one's museum
And sees, the world on holidays alone,

1. Assistant to a medieval scholar.   2. A chant of praise to God.

But from a distance, only on occasion,   180
How can one guide it by persuasion?
FAUST: What you don't feel, you will not grasp by art,
Unless it wells out of your soul
And with sheer pleasure takes control,
Compelling every listener's heart.   185
But sit—and sit, and patch and knead,
Cook a ragout, reheat your hashes,
Blow at the sparks and try to breed
A fire out of piles of ashes!
Children and apes may think it great,   190
If that should titillate your gum,
But from heart to heart you will never create.
If from your heart it does not come.
WAGNER: Yet much depends on the delivery;
I still lack much; don't you agree?   195
FAUST: Oh, let him look for honest gain!
Let him not be a noisy fool!
All that makes sense you can explain
Without the tricks of any school.
If you have anything to say,   200
Why juggle words for a display?
Your glittering rhet'ric, subtly disciplined,
Which for mankind thin paper garlands weaves,
Is as unwholesome as the foggy wind
That blows in autumn through the wilted leaves.   205
WAGNER: Oh God, art is forever
And our life is brief.
I fear that with my critical endeavor
My head and heart may come to grief.
How hard the scholars' means are to array   210
With which one works up to the source;
Before we have traversed but half the course,
We wretched devils pass away.
FAUST: Parchment—is that the sacred fount
From which you drink to still your thirst forever?   215
If your refreshment does not mount.
From your own soul, you gain it never.
WAGNER: Forgive! It does seem so sublime,
Entering into the spirit of the time
To see what wise men, who lived long ago, believed,   220
Till we at last have all the highest aims achieved.
FAUST: Up to the stars—achieved indeed!
My friend, the times that antecede
Our own are books safely protected
By seven seals.[3] What spirit of the time you call,   225
Is but the scholars' spirit, after all,

---

3. Revelation 5:1.

In which times past are now reflected.
In truth, it often is pathetic,
And when one sees it, one would run away:
A garbage pail, perhaps a storage attic,   230
At best a pompous moralistic play
With wonderfully edifying quips,
Most suitable to come from puppets' lips.
WAGNER: And yet the world! Man's heart and spirit! Oh,
That everybody knew part of the same!   235
FAUST: The things that people claim to know!
Who dares to call the child by its true name?
The few that saw something like this and, starry-eyed
But foolishly, with glowing hearts averred
Their feelings and their visions before the common herd   240
Have at all times been burned and crucified.
I beg you, friend, it is deep in the night;
We must break off this interview.
WAGNER: Our conversation was so erudite,
I should have liked to stay awake with you.   245
Yet Easter comes tomorrow; then permit
That I may question you a bit.
Most zealously I've studied matters great and small;
Though I know much, I should like to know all.
    [Exit.]
FAUST: [Alone.] Hope never seems to leave those who affirm,   250
The shallow minds that stick to must and mold—
They dig with greedy hands for gold
And yet are happy if they find a worm.
Dare such a human voice be sounded
Where I was even now surrounded   255
By spirits' might? And yet I thank you just this once,
You, of all creatures the most wretched dunce.
You tore me from despair that had surpassed
My mind and threatened to destroy my sense.
Alas, the apparition was so vast   260
That I felt dwarfed in impotence.

I, image of the godhead, that began
To dream eternal truth was within reach,
Exulting on the heavens' brilliant beach
As if I had stripped off the mortal man;   265
I, more than cherub, whose unbounded might
Seemed even then to flow through nature's veins,
Shared the creative joys of God's domains—
Presumptuous hope for which I pay in pains:
One word of thunder swept me from my height.   270

I may no longer claim to be your peer:
I had the power to attract you here,
But to retain you lacked the might.

In that moment of bliss, alack,
In which I felt so small, so great, 275
You, cruel one, have pushed me back
Into uncertain human fate.
Who teaches me? What should I shun?
Should I give in to that obsession?
Not our sufferings only, the deeds that we have done 280
Inhibit our life's progression.

Whatever noblest things the mind received,
More and more foreign matter spoils the theme;
And when the good of this world is achieved,
What's better seems an idle dream. 285
That gave us our life, the noblest urges
Are petrified in the earth's vulgar surges.

Where fantasy once rose in glorious flight,
Hopeful and bold to capture the sublime,
It is content now with a narrow site, 290
Since joy on joy crashed on the rocks of time.
Deep in the heart there dwells relentless care
And secretly infects us with despair;
Restless, she sways and poisons peace and joy
She always finds new masks she can employ: 295
She may appear as house and home, as child and wife,
As fire, water, poison, knife —
What does not strike, still makes you quail,
And what you never lose, for that you always wail.

I am not like the gods! That was a painful thrust; 300
I'm like the worm that burrows in the dust,
Who, as he makes of dust his meager meal,
Is crushed and buried by a wanderer's heel.
Is it not dust that stares from every rack
And narrows down this vaulting den? 305
This moths' world full of bric-a-brac
In which I live as in a pen?
Here I should find for what I care?
Should I read in a thousand books, maybe,
That men have always suffered everywhere, 310
Though now and then some man lived happily? —
Why, hollow skull, do you grin like a faun?
Save that your brain, like mine, once in dismay
Searched for light day, but foundered in the heavy dawn
And, craving truth, went wretchedly astray. 315
You instruments, of course, can scorn and tease
With rollers, handles, cogs, and wheels:
I found the gate, you were to be the keys;
Although your webs are subtle, you cannot break the seals.
Mysterious in the light of day, 320

Nature, in veils, will not let us perceive her,
And what she is unwilling to betray,
You cannot wrest from her with thumbscrews, wheel, or lever.
You ancient tools that rest upon the rack,
Unused by me, but used once by my sire,[4]   325
You ancient scroll that slowly has turned black
As my lamp on this desk gave off its smoky fire—

Far better had I squandered all of my wretched share
Than groan under this wretched load and thus address it!
What from your fathers you received as heir,   330
Acquire if you would possess it.
What is not used is but a load to bear;
But if today creates it, we can use and bless it.

Yet why does this place over there attract my sight?
Why is that bottle as a magnet to my eyes?   335
Why does the world seem suddenly so bright,
As when in nightly woods one sees the moon arise?
I welcome you, incomparable potion,
Which from your place I fetch now with devotion:
In you I honor human wit and art.   340
You essence from all slumber-bringing flowers,
You extract of all subtly fatal powers,
Bare to your master your enticing heart!
I look upon you, soothed are all my pains,
I seize you now, and all my striving wanes,   345
The spirit's tidal wave now ebbs away.
Slowly I float into the open sea,
The waves beneath me now seem gay and free,
To other shores beckons another day.
A fiery chariot floats on airy pinions   350
Cleaving the ether—tarry and descend!
Uncharted orbits call me, new dominions
Of sheer creation, active without end.
This higher life, joys that no mortal won!
You merit this—but now a worm, despairing?   355
Upon the mild light of the earthly sun
Turn, bold, your back! And with undaunted daring
Tear open the eternal portals
Past which all creatures slink in silent dread.
The time has come to prove by deeds that mortals   360
Have as much dignity as any god,
And not to tremble at that murky cave
Where fantasy condemns itself to dwell
In agony. The passage brave
Whose narrow mouth is lit by all the flames of hell;   365

4. Later we find that Faust's father was a doctor of medicine.

And take this step with cheerful resolution,
Though it involve the risk of utter dissolution.

Now you come down to me, pure crystal vase,
Emerge again out of your ancient case
Of which for many years I did not think.   370
You glistened at my father's joyous feasts
And cheered the solemn-looking guests,
When you were passed around for all to drink.
The many pictures, glistening in the light,
The drinker's duty rhyming to explain them,[5]   375
To scan your depths and in one draught to drain them,
Bring back to mind many a youthful night.
There is no friend now to fulfill this duty,
Nor shall I exercise my wit upon your beauty.
Here is a juice that fast makes drunk and mute;   380
With its brown flood it fills this crystal bowl,
I brewed it and shall drink it whole
And offer this last drink with all my soul
Unto the morning as a festive high salute. [*He puts the bowl to his lips.*]
    [*Chime of bells and choral song.*]
CHOIR OF ANGELS: Christ is arisen.   385
        Hail the meek-spirited
        Whom the ill-merited,
        Creeping, inherited
        Faults held in prison.
FAUST: What deeply humming strokes, what brilliant tone   390
    Draws from my lips the crystal bowl with power?
    Has the time come, deep bells, when you make known
    The Easter holiday's first holy hour?
    Is this already, choirs, the sweet consoling hymn
    That was first sung around his tomb by cherubim,   395
    Confirming the new covenant?
CHOIR OF WOMEN: With myrrh, when bereaved,
        We had adorned him;
        We that believed
        Laid down and mourned him.   400
        Linen we twined
        Round the adored—
        Returning, we cannot find
        Christ, our Lord.
CHOIR OF ANGELS: Christ is arisen.   405
        Blessed be the glorious
        One who victorious
        Over laborious
        Trials has risen.

---

5. Faust here alludes to the drinking of toasts. The maker of a toast often produced impromptu rhymes.

FAUST: Why would you, heaven's tones, compel   410
Me gently to rise from my dust?
Resound where tenderhearted people dwell:
Although I hear the message, I lack all faith or trust;
And faith's favorite child is miracle.
For those far spheres I should not dare to strive,   415
From which these tidings come to me;
And yet these chords, which I have known since infancy:
Call me now, too, back into life.
Once heaven's love rushed at me as a kiss
In the grave silence of the Sabbath day,   420
The rich tones of the bells, it seemed, had much to say,
And every prayer brought impassioned bliss.
An unbelievably sweet yearning
Drove me to roam through wood and lea,
Crying, and as my eyes were burning,   425
I felt a new world grow in me.
This song proclaimed the spring feast's free delight, appealing
To the gay games of youth—they plead:
Now memory entices me with childlike feeling
Back from the last, most solemn deed.   430
Sound on, oh hymns of heaven, sweet and mild!
My tears are flowing; earth, take back your child!

CHOIR OF DISCIPLES: Has the o'ervaulted one
    Burst from his prison,
    The living-exalted one   435
    Gloriously risen,
    Is in this joyous birth
    Zest for creation near—
    Oh, on the breast of earth
    We are to suffer here.   440
    He left his own
    Pining in sadness;
    Alas, we bemoan,
    Master, your gladness.

CHOIR OF ANGELS: Christ is arisen   445
    Out of corruption's womb.
    Leave behind prison,
    Fetters and gloom!
    Those who proceed for him,
    Lovingly bleed for him,   450
    Brotherly feed for him,
    Travel and plead for him,
    And to bliss lead for him,
    For you the Master is near,
    For you he is here.   455

BEFORE THE CITY GATE

[People of all kinds are walking out.]
SOME APPRENTICES: Why do you go that way?
OTHERS: We are going to Hunter's Lodge today.
THE FIRST: But we would rather go to the mill.
AN APPRENTICE: Go to the River Inn, that's my advice.
ANOTHER: I think, the way there isn't nice.   5
THE OTHERS: Where are you going?
A THIRD ONE: Up the hill.
A FOURTH ONE: Burgdorf would be much better. Let's go there with the
   rest:
   The girls there are stunning, their beer is the best,
   And it's first-class, too, for a fight.
A FIFTH ONE: You are indeed a peppy bird,   10
   Twice spanked, you're itching for the third.
   Let's not, the place is really a fright.
SERVANT GIRL: No, no! I'll go back to the town again.
ANOTHER: We'll find him at the poplars, I'm certain it is true.
THE FIRST: What's that to me? Is it not plain,   15
   He'll walk and dance only with you?
   He thinks, you are the only one.
   And why should I care for your fun?
THE OTHER ONE: He will not be alone. He said,
   Today he'd bring the curly-head.   20
STUDENT: Just see those wenches over there!
   Come, brother, let us help the pair.
   A good strong beer, a smarting pipe,
   And a maid, nicely dressed—that is my type!
CITIZEN'S DAUGHTER: Look there and see those handsome blades!   25
   I think it is a crying shame:
   They could have any girl that meets with their acclaim,
   And chase after these silly maids.
SECOND STUDENT: *[To the FIRST.]* Don't go so fast; behind us are two
   more,
   And they are dressed at least as neatly.   30
   I know one girl, she lives next door,
   And she bewitches me completely.
   The way they walk, they seem demure,
   But won't mind company, I'm sure.
THE FIRST: No, brother, I don't like those coy addresses.   35
   Come on, before we lose the wilder prey.
   The hand that wields the broom on Saturday
   Will, comes the Sunday, give the best caresses.
CITIZEN: No, the new mayor is no good, that's what I say.
   Since he's in, he's fresher by the day.   40
   What has he done for our city?
   Things just get worse; it is a pity!

We must obey, he thinks he's clever,
And we pay taxes more than ever.
BEGGAR: [*Sings.*] Good gentlemen and ladies fair, 45
So red of cheek, so rich in dress,
Be pleased to look on my despair,
To see and lighten my distress.
Let me not grind here, vainly waiting!
For only those who give are gay, 50
And when all men are celebrating,
Then I should have my harvest day.
ANOTHER CITIZEN: On Sun- and holidays, there is no better fun,
Than chattering of wars and warlike fray,
When off in Turkey, far away, 55
One people beats the other one.
We stand at the window, drink a wine that is light,
Watch the boats glide down the river, see the foam,
And cheerfully go back at night,
Grateful that we have peace at home. 60
THIRD CITIZEN: Yes, neighbor, that is nicely said.
Let them crack skulls, and wound, and maim,
Let all the world stand on its head;
But here, at home, all should remain the same.
OLD WOMAN: [*To the* CITIZEN'S DAUGHTERS.]
Ah, how dressed up! So pretty and so young! 65
Who would not stop to stare at you?
Don't be puffed up, I'll hold my tongue.
I know your wish, and how to get it, too.
CITIZEN'S DAUGHTER: Come quickly, Agatha! I take good heed
Not to be seen with witches; it's unwise.— 70
Though on St. Andrew's Night[6] she brought indeed
My future lover right before my eyes.
THE OTHER ONE: She showed me mine, but in a crystal ball
With other soldiers, bold and tall;
I have been looking ever since, 75
But so far haven't found my prince.
SOLDIERS: Castles with lofty
Towers and banners,
Maidens with haughty,
Disdainful manners 80
I want to capture.
Fair is the dare,
Splendid the pay.
And we let trumpets
Do our wooing, 85
For our pleasures
And our undoing.

---

6. St. Andrew's Eve, November 29, the traditional time for young girls to consult fortune-tellers about their future lovers or husbands.

Life is all storming,
Life is all splendor,
Maidens and castles   90
Have to surrender.
Fair is the dare,
Splendid the pay.
And then the soldiers
March on away.   95
[FAUST and WAGNER.]
FAUST: Released from the ice are river and creek,
Warmed by the spring's fair quickening eye;
The valley is green with hope and joy;
The hoary winter has grown so weak
He has withdrawn to the rugged mountains.   100
From there he sends, but only in flight,
Impotent showers of icy hail
That streak across the greening vale;
But the sun will not suffer the white;
Everywhere stirs what develops and grows,   105
All he would quicken with color that glows;
Flowers are lacking, blue, yellow, and red,
But he takes dressed-up people instead.
Turn around now and look down
From the heights back to the town.   110
Out of the hollow gloomy gate
Surges and scatters a motley horde.
All seek sunshine. They celebrate
The resurrection of the Lord.
For they themselves are resurrected   115
From lowly houses, musty as stables,
From trades to which they are subjected,
From the pressure of roofs and gables,
From the stifling and narrow alleys,
From the churches' reverent night   120
They have emerged into the light.
Look there! Look, how the crowd now sallies
Gracefully into the gardens and leas,
How on the river, all through the valley,
Frolicsome floating boats one sees,   125
And, overloaded beyond its fill,
This last barge now is swimming away.
From the far pathways of the hill
We can still see how their clothes are gay.
I hear the village uproar rise;   130
Here is the people's paradise,
And great and small shout joyously:
Here I am human, may enjoy humanity.
WAGNER: To take a walk with you, good sir,
Is a great honor and reward,   135

And pondered over nature and every sacred sphere
In his own cranky way, though quite sincere,
With ardent, though with wayward, zeal.   230
And with proficient devotees,
In his black kitchen he would fuse
After unending recipes,
Locked in, the most contrary brews.
They made red lions, a bold wooer came,   235
In tepid baths was mated to a lily;
And then the pair was vexed with a wide-open flame
From one bride chamber to another, willy-nilly.
And when the queen appeared, all pied,
Within the glass after a spell,   240
The medicine was there, and though the patients died,
Nobody questioned: who got well?[9]
And thus we raged fanatically
In these same mountains, in this valley,
With hellish juice worse than the pest.   245
Though thousands died from poison that I myself would give,
Yes, though they perished, I must live
To hear the shameless killers blessed.
WAGNER: I cannot see why you are grieved.
What more can honest people do   250
Than be conscientious and pursue
With diligence the art that they received?
If you respect your father as a youth,
You'll learn from him what you desire;
If as a man you add your share of truth   255
To ancient lore, your son can go still higher.
FAUST: Oh, happy who still hopes to rise
Out of this sea of errors and false views!
What one does *not* know, one could utilize,
And what one knows one cannot use.   260
But let the beauty offered by this hour
Not be destroyed by our spleen!
See how, touched by the sunset's parting power,
The huts are glowing in the green.
The sun moves on, the day has had its round;   265
He hastens on, new life greets his salute.
Oh,[1] that no wings lift me above the ground
To strive and strive in his pursuit!
In the eternal evening light
The quiet world would lie below   270
With every valley tranquil, on fire every height,
The silver stream to golden rivers flow.
Nor could the mountain with its savage guise

9. This confusing sequence evokes a kind of medicine closely allied to magic and inappropriate to the
needs of the ill people seeking help.   1. Alas.

And all its gorges check my godlike ways;
Already ocean with its glistening bays 275
Spreads out before astonished eyes.
At last the god sinks down, I seem forsaken;
But I feel new unrest awaken
And hurry hence to drink his deathless light,
The day before me, and behind me night, 280
The billows under me, and over me the sky.
A lovely dream, while he makes his escape.
The spirit's wings will not change our shape:
Our body grows no wings and cannot fly.
Yet it is innate in our race 285
That our feelings surge in us and long
When over us, lost in the azure space
The lark trills out her glorious song;
When over crags where fir trees quake
In icy winds, the eagle soars, 290
And over plains and over lakes
The crane returns to homeward shores.
WAGNER: I, too, have spells of eccentricity,
But such unrest has never come to me.
One soon grows sick of forest, field, and brook, 295
And I shall never envy birds their wings.
Far greater are the joys the spirit brings—
From page to page, from book to book.
Thus winter nights grow fair and warm the soul;
Yes, blissful life suffuses every limb, 300
And when one opens up an ancient parchment scroll,
The very heavens will descend on him.
FAUST: You are aware of only one unrest;
Oh, never learn to know the other!
Two souls, alas, are dwelling in my breast, 305
And one is striving to forsake its brother.
Unto the world in grossly loving zest,
With clinging tendrils, one adheres;
The other rises forcibly in quest
Of rarefied ancestral spheres. 310
If there be spirits in the air
That hold their sway between the earth and sky,
Descend out of the golden vapors there
And sweep me into iridescent life.
Oh, came a magic cloak into my hands 315
To carry me to distant lands,
I should not trade it for the choicest gown,
Nor for the cloak and garments of the crown.
WAGNER: Do not invoke the well-known throng that flow
Through mists above and spread out in the haze, 320
Concocting danger in a thousand ways
For man wherever he may go.

From the far north the spirits' deadly fangs
Bear down on you with arrow-pointed tongues;
And from the east they come with withering pangs   325
And nourish themselves from your lungs.
The midday sends out of the desert those
Who pile heat upon heat upon your crown,
While evening brings the throng that spells repose—
And then lets you, and fields and meadows, drown.   330
They gladly listen, but are skilled in harm,
Gladly obey, because they like deceit;
As if from heaven sent, they please and charm,
Whispering like angels when they cheat.
But let us go! The air has cooled, the world   335
Turned gray, mists are unfurled.
When evening comes one values home,
Why do you stand amazed? What holds your eyes?
What in the twilight merits such surprise?
FAUST: See that black dog through grain and stubble roam?   340
WAGNER: I noticed him way back, but cared not in the least.
FAUST: Look well! For what would *you* take this strange beast?
WAGNER: Why, for a poodle fretting doggedly
   As it pursues the tracks left by its master.
FAUST: It spirals all around us, as you see,   345
   And it approaches, fast and faster.
   And if I do not err, a fiery eddy
   Whirls after it and marks the trail.
WAGNER: I see the poodle, as I said already;
   As for the rest, your eyesight seems to fail.   350
FAUST: It seems to me that he winds magic snares
   Around our feet, a bond of future dangers.
WAGNER: He jumps around, unsure, and our presence scares
   The dog who seeks his master, and finds instead two strangers.
FAUST: The spiral narrows, he is near!   355
WAGNER: You see, a dog and not a ghost is here.
   He growls, lies on his belly, thus he waits,
   He wags his tail: all canine traits.
FAUST: Come here and walk along with us!
WAGNER: He's poodlishly ridiculous.   360
   You stand and rest, and he waits, too;
   You speak to him, and he would climb on you;
   Lose something, he will bring it back again,
   Jump in the lake to get your cane.
FAUST: You seem quite right, I find, for all his skill,   365
   No trace of any spirit: all is drill.
WAGNER: By dogs that are expertly trained
   The wisest man is entertained.
   He quite deserves your favor: it is prudent
   To cultivate the students' noble student.   370
   [*They pass through the City Gate.*]

STUDY

FAUST: [*Entering with the poodle.*] The fields and meadows I have fled
    As night enshrouds them and the lakes;
    With apprehensive, holy dread
    The better soul in us awakes.
    Wild passions have succumbed to sleep,   5
    All vehement exertions bow;
    The love of man stirs in us deep,
    The love of God is stirring now.

Be quiet, poodle! Stop running around!
Why do you snuffle at the sill like that?   10
Lie down behind the stove — not on the ground:
Take my best cushion for a mat.
As you amused us on our way
With running and jumping and did your best,
Let me look after you and say: 15
Be quiet, please, and be my guest.

    When in our narrow den
    The friendly lamp glows on the shelf,
    Then light pervades our breast again
    And fills the heart that knows itself.   20
    Reason again begins to speak,
    Hope blooms again with ancient force,
    One longs for life and one would seek
    Its rivers and, alas, its source.

Stop snarling poodle! For the sacred strain   25
To which my soul is now submitting
Beastly sounds are hardly fitting.
We are accustomed to see *men* disdain
What they don't grasp;
When it gives trouble, they profane   30
Even the beautiful and the good.
Do dogs, too, snarl at what's not understood?

    Even now, however, though I tried my best,
    Contentment flows no longer through my breast.
    Why does the river rest so soon, and dry up, and   35
    Leave us to languish in the sand?
    How well I know frustration!
    This want, however, we can overwhelm:
    We turn to the supernatural realm,
    We long for the light of revelation   40
    Which is nowhere more magnificent
    Than in our New Testament.
    I would for once like to determine —
    Because I am sincerely perplexed —

How the sacred original text[2]   45
Could be translated into my beloved German.

[*He opens a tome and begins.*]
It says: "In the beginning was the Word."[3]
Already I am stopped. It seems absurd.
The Word does not deserve the highest prize,
I must translate it otherwise   50
If I am well inspired and not blind.
It says: In the beginning was the Mind.
Ponder that first line, wait and see,
Lest you should write too hastily.
Is mind the all-creating source?   55
It ought to say: In the beginning there was Force.
Yet something warns me as I grasp the pen,
That my translation must be changed again.
The spirit helps me. Now it is exact.
I write: In the beginning was the Act.   60

If I am to share my room with you,
Poodle, stop moaning so!
And stop your bellow,
For such a noisy, whiny fellow
I do not like to have around.   65
One of us, black hound,
Will have to give ground.
With reluctance I change my mind:
The door is open, you are not confined.
But what must I see!   70
Can that happen naturally?
Is it a shadow? Am I open-eyed?
How grows my poodle long and wide!
He reaches up like rising fog—
This is no longer the shape of a dog!   75
Oh, what a specter I brought home!
A hippopotamus of foam,
With fiery eyes; how his teeth shine!
You are as good as mine:
For such a semi-hellish brow   80
The Key of Solomon[4] will do.

SPIRITS: [*In the corridor.*] One has been caught inside.
Do not follow him! Abide!
As a fox in a snare,
Hell's old lynx is caught in there.   85
But give heed!
Float up high, float down low,
To and fro,

---

2. That is, the Greek.   3. John 1:1.   4. The *Clavicula Salomonis*, a standard work used by magicians for conjuring; in many medieval legends, Solomon was noted as a great magician.

And he tries, and he is freed.
Can you avail him?   90
Then do not fail him!
For you must not forget,
We are in his debt.
FAUST: Countering the beast, I might well
First use the fourfold spell: 95

Salamander shall broil,
Undene shall grieve,
Sylphe shall leave,
Kobold[5] shall toil.

Whoever ignores   100
The elements' cores,
Their energy
And quality,
Cannot command
In the spirits' land.   105

Disappear flashing,
Salamander!
Flow together, splashing,
Undene!
Glow in meteoric beauty,   110
Sylphe!
Do your domestic duty,
Incubus! Incubus!
Step forward and finish thus.

None of the four   115
Is this beast's core.
It lies quite calmly there and beams;
I have not hurt it yet, it seems.
Now listen well
To a stronger spell.   120

If you should be
Hell's progeny,
Then see this symbol
Before which tremble
The cohorts of Hell!   125

Already it bristles and starts to swell.

Spirit of shame,
Can you read the name
Of the Uncreated,
Defying expression,   130

---

5. A spirit of the earth. The *salamander* was a spirit of the fire. An undine (*undene*) was a water nymph.
A sylph (*sylphe*) was a spirit of the air.

With whom the heavens are sated,
Who was pierced in transgression?

Behind the stove it swells
As an elephant under my spells;
It fills the whole room and quakes,   135
It would turn into mist and fleet.
Stop now before the ceiling breaks!
Lie down at your master's feet!

You see, I do not threaten in vain:
With holy flames I cause you pain.   140
Do not require
The threefold glowing fire![6]
Do not require
My art in its full measure!

MEPHISTOPHELES: [*Steps forward from behind the stove, dressed as a traveling scholar, while the mist clears away.*]
   Why all the noise? Good sir, what is your pleasure?   145
FAUST: Then this was our poodle's core!
   Simply a traveling scholar? The *casus*[7] makes me laugh.
MEPHISTOPHELES: Profound respects to you and to your lore:
   You made me sweat with all your chaff.
FAUST: What is your name?
MEPHISTOPHELES: This question seems minute   150
   For one who thinks the word so beggarly,
   Who holds what seems in disrepute,
   And craves only reality.[8]
FAUST: Your real being no less than your fame
   Is often shown, sirs, by your name,   155
   Which is not hard to analyze
   When one calls you the Liar, Destroyer, God of Flies.[9]
   Enough, who are you then?
MEPHISTOPHELES: Part of that force which would
   Do evil evermore, and yet creates the good.
FAUST: What is it that this puzzle indicates?   160
MEPHISTOPHELES: I am the spirit that negates.
   And rightly so, for all that comes to be
   Deserves to perish wretchedly;
   'Twere better nothing would begin.
   Thus everything that your terms, sin,   165
   Destruction, evil represent—
   That is my proper element.
FAUST: You call yourself a part, yet whole make your debut?
MEPHISTOPHELES: The modest truth I speak to you.

---

6. Perhaps the Trinity or a triangle with divergent rays.   7. Occurrence.   8. Mephistopheles refers to Faust's substitution of *Act* for *Word* in the passage from John (see line 60).   9. An almost literal translation of the name of the Philistine deity Beelzebub.

While man, this tiny world of fools, is droll   170
Enough to think himself a whole,
I am part of the part that once was everything,
Part of the darkness which gave birth to light,
That haughty light which envies mother night
Her ancient rank and place and would be king—   175
Yet it does not succeed: however it contend,
It sticks to bodies in the end.
It streams from bodies, it lends bodies beauty,
A body won't let it progress;
So it will not take long, I guess,   180
And with the bodies it will perish, too.
FAUST: I understand your noble duty:
Too weak for great destruction, you
Attempt it on a minor scale.
MEPHISTOPHELES: And I admit it is of slight avail.   185
What stands opposed to our Nought,
The some, your wretched world—for aught
That I have so far undertaken,
It stands unruffled and unshaken:
With billows, fires, storms, commotion,   190
Calm, after all, remain both land and ocean.
And that accursed lot, the brood of beasts and men,
One cannot hurt them anyhow.
How many have I buried now!
Yet always fresh new blood will circulate again.   195
Thus it goes on—I could rage in despair!
From water, earth, and even air,
A thousand seeds have ever grown
In warmth and cold and drought and mire!
If I had not reserved myself the fire,   200
I should have nothing of my own.
FAUST: And thus, I see, you would resist
The ever-live creative power
By clenching your cold devil's fist
Resentfully—in vain you glower.   205
Try something new and unrelated,
Oh you peculiar son of chaos!
MEPHISTOPHELES: Perchance your reasoning might sway us—
The next few times we may debate it.
But for the present, may I go?   210
FAUST: I cannot see why you inquire.
Now that we met, you ought to know
That you may call as you desire.
Here is the window, here the door,
A chimney there, if that's preferred.   215
MEPHISTOPHELES: I cannot leave you that way, I deplore:
By a small obstacle I am deterred:
The witch's foot on your threshold, see—

FAUST: The pentagram[1] distresses you?
  Then, son of hell, explain to me: 220
  How could you enter here without ado?
  And how was such a spirit cheated?
MEPHISTOPHELES: Behold it well: It is not quite completed;
  One angle—that which points outside—
  Is open just a little bit.   225
FAUST: That was indeed a lucky hit.
  I caught you and you must abide.
  How wonderful, and yet how queer!
MEPHISTOPHELES: The poodle never noticed, when he first jumped in here,
  But now it is a different case;   230
  The Devil cannot leave this place.
FAUST: The window's there. Are you in awe?
MEPHISTOPHELES: The devils and the demons have a law:
  Where they slipped in, they always must withdraw.
  The first time we are free, the second time constrained. 235
FAUST: For hell, too, laws have been ordained?
  Superb! Then one should surely make a pact,
  And one of you might enter my employ.
MEPHISTOPHELES: What we would promise you, you would enjoy,
  And none of it we would subtract.   240
  But that we should not hurry so,
  And we shall talk about it soon;
  For now I ask the single boon
  That you permit me now to go.
FAUST: For just a moment stay with me   245
  And let me have some happy news.
MEPHISTOPHELES: Not now. I'll come back presently,
  Then you may ask me what you choose.
FAUST: You were not caught by my device
  When you were snared like this tonight.   250
  Who holds the Devil, hold him tight!
  He can't expect to catch him twice.
MEPHISTOPHELES: If you prefer it, I shall stay
  With you, and I shall not depart,
  Upon condition that I may   255
  Amuse you with some samples of my art.
FAUST: Go right ahead, you are quite free—
  Provided it is nice to see.
MEPHISTOPHELES: Right in this hour you will obtain
  More for your senses than you gain   260
  In a whole year's monotony.
  What tender spirits now will sing,
  The lovely pictures that they bring
  Are not mere magic for the eye:
  They will delight your sense of smell,   265

1. A magic five-pointed star designed to keep away evil spirits.

Be pleasing to your taste as well,
Excite your touch, and give you joy.
No preparation needs my art,
We are together, let us start.
SPIRITS: Vanish, you darkling   270
       Arches above him.
    Friendlier beaming,
    Sky should be gleaming
    Down upon us.
    Ah, that the darkling   275
    Clouds had departed!
    Stars now are sparkling,
    More tenderhearted
    Suns shine on us.
    Spirits aerial,   280
    Fair and ethereal,
    Wavering and bending,
    Sail by like swallows.
    Yearning unending
    Sees them and follows,   285
    Garments are flowing,
    Ribbons are blowing,
    Covering the glowing
    Land and the bower
    Where, in the hedges,   290
    Thinking and dreaming,
    Lovers make pledges.
    Bower on bower.
    Tendrils are streaming;
    Heavy grapes shower   295
    Their sweet excesses
    Into the presses;
    In streams are flowing
    Wines that are glowing,
    Foam, effervescent,   300
    Through iridescent
    Gems; they are storming
    Down from the mountains;
    Lakes they are forming,
    Beautiful fountains   305
    Where hills are ending,
    Birds are descending,
    Drink and fly onward,
    Fly ever sunward,
    Fly from the highlands   310
    Toward the ocean
    Where brilliant islands
    Sway in soft motion.
    Jubilant choirs

Soothe all desires,   315
And are entrancing
Those who are dancing
Like whirling satyrs,
But the throng scatters.
Some now are scaling   320
Over the mountains,
Others are sailing
Toward the fountains,
Others are soaring,
All life adoring,   325
All crave the far-off
Love-spending star of
Rapturous bliss.
MEPHISTOPHELES: He sleeps. I thank you, airy, tender throng.
You made him slumber with your song.   330
A splendid concert. I appreciate this.
You are not yet the man to hold the Devil fast.
Go, dazzle him with dream shapes, sweet and vast,
Plunge him into an ocean of untruth.
But now, to break the threshold's spell at last,   335
I have to get a rat's sharp tooth.
I need no conjuring today,
One's rustling over there and will come right away.
The lord of rats, the lord of mice,
Of flies and frogs, bedbugs and lice,   340
Bids you to dare now to appear
To gnaw upon this threshold here,
Where he is dabbing it with oil.
Ah, there you come. Begin your toil.
The point that stopped me like a magic hedge   345
Is way up front, right on the edge.
Just one more bite, and that will do.
Now, Faustus, sleep and dream, till I come back to you.
FAUST: [*Awakening.*] Betrayed again? Fooled by a scheme?
Should spirits' wealth so suddenly decay   350
That I behold the Devil in a dream,
And that a poodle jumps away?

STUDY

[FAUST, MEPHISTOPHELES.]
FAUST: A knock? Come in! Who comes to plague me now?
MEPHISTOPHELES: It's I.
FAUST: Come in!
MEPHISTOPHELES: You have to say it thrice.
FAUST: Come in, then.
MEPHISTOPHELES: Now you're nice.
We should get along well, I vow.

To chase your spleen away, allow 5
That I appear a noble squire:[2]
Look at my red and gold attire,
A little cloak of silk brocade,
The rooster's feather in my hat,
And the long, nicely pointed blade— 10
And now it is my counsel that
You, too, should be like this arrayed;
Then you would feel released and free,
And you would find what life can be.
FAUST: I shall not cease to feel in all attires, 15
The pains of our narrow earthly day.
I am too old to be content to play,
Too young to be without desire.
What wonders could the world reveal?
You must renounce! You ought to yield! 20
That is the never-ending drone
Which we must, our life long, hear,
Which, hoarsely, all our hours intone
And grind into our weary ears.
Frightened I waken to the dismal dawn, 25
Wish I had tears to drown the sun
And check the day that soon will scorn
My every wish—fulfill not one.
If I but think of any pleasure,
Bright critic day is sure to chide it, 30
And if my heart creates itself a treasure,
A thousand mocking masks deride it.
When night descends at last, I shall recline
But anxiously upon my bed;
Though all is still, no rest is mine 35
As dreams enmesh my mind in dread.
The god that dwells within my heart
Can stir my depths, I cannot hide—
Rules all my powers with relentless art,
But cannot move the world outside; 40
And thus existence is for me a weight,
Death is desirable, and life I hate.
MEPHISTOPHELES: And yet when death approaches, the welcome is not
  great.
FAUST: Oh, blessed whom, as victory advances,
  He lends the blood-drenched laurel's grace, 45
Who, after wildly whirling dances,
Receives him in a girl's embrace!
Oh, that before the lofty spirit's power
I might have fallen to the ground, unsouled!

---

2. In the popular plays based on the Faust legend, the Devil often appeared as a monk when the
play catered to a Protestant audience and as a noble squire when the audience was predominantly
Catholic.

MEPHISTOPHELES: And yet someone, in that same nightly hour   50
    Refused to drain a certain bowl.
FAUST: You seem to eavesdrop quite proficiently.
MEPHISTOPHELES: Omniscient I am not, but there is much I see.
FAUST: As in that terrifying reeling
    I heard the sweet familiar chimes   55
    That duped the traces of my childhood feeling
    With echoes of more joyous times,
    I now curse all that would enamor
    The human soul with lures and lies,
    Enticing it with flattering glamour   60
    To live on in this cave of sighs.
    Cursed above all our high esteem,
    The spirit's smug self-confidence,
    Cursed be illusion, fraud, and dream
    That flatter our guileless sense!   65
    Cursed be the pleasing make-believe
    Of fame and long posthumous life!
    Cursed be possessions that deceive,
    As slave and plough, and child and wife!
    Cursed, too, be Mammon[3] when with treasures   70
    He spurs us on to daring feats,
    Or lures us into slothful pleasures
    With sumptuous cushions and smooth sheets!
    A curse on wine that mocks our thirst!
    A curse on love's last consummations!   75
    A curse on hope! Faith, too, be cursed!
    And cursed above all else be patience!
CHOIR OF SPIRITS: [*Invisible.*] Alas!
    You have shattered
    The beautiful world   80
    With brazen fist;
    It falls, it is scattered —
    By a demigod destroyed.
    We are trailing
    The ruins into the void   85
    And wailing
    Over beauty undone
    And ended.
    Earth's mighty son,
    More splendid   90
    Rebuild it, you that are strong,
    Build it again within!
    And begin
    A new life, a new way,
    Lucid and gay,   95

3. The Aramaic word for "riches," used in the New Testament of the Bible. Medieval writers interpreted the word as a proper noun, the name of the Devil, as representing covetousness or avarice.

And play
New songs.
MEPHISTOPHELES: These are the small
Ones of my thralls.
Hear how precociously they plead 100
For pleasure and deed!
To worldly strife
From your lonely life
Which dries up sap and sense,
They would lure you hence. 105

Stop playing with your melancholy
That, like a vulture, ravages your breast;
The worst of company still cures this folly,
For you are human with the rest.
Yet that is surely not to say 110
That you should join the herd you hate.
I'm not one of the great,
But if you want to make your way
Through the world with me united,
I should surely be delighted 115
To be yours, as of now,
Your companion, if you allow;
And if you like the way I behave,
I shall be your servant, or your slave.
FAUST: And in return, what do you hope to take? 120
MEPHISTOPHELES: There's so much time — so why insist?
FAUST: No, no! The Devil is an egoist
And would not just for heaven's sake
Turn into a philanthropist.
Make your conditions very clear; 125
Where such a servant lives, danger is near.
MEPHISTOPHELES: *Here* you shall be the master, I be bond,
And at your nod I'll work incessantly;
But when we meet again *beyond,*
Then you shall do the same for me. 130
FAUST: Of the beyond I have no thought;
When you reduce this world to nought,
The other one may have its turn.
My joys come from this earth, and there,
That sun has burnt on my despair: 135
Once I have left those, I don't care:
What happens is of no concern.
I do not even wish to hear
Whether beyond they hate and love,
And whether in that other sphere 140
One realm's below and one above.
MEPHISTOPHELES: So minded, dare it cheerfully.
Commit yourself and you shall see

My arts with joy. I'll give you more
Than any man has seen before.   145
FAUST: What would you, wretched Devil, offer?
Was ever a man's spirit in its noble striving
Grasped by your like, devilish scoffer?
But have you food that is not satisfying,
Red gold that rolls off without rest,   150
Quicksilver-like, over your skin—
A game in which no man can win—
A girl who, lying at my breast,
Ogles already to entice my neighbor,
And honor—that perhaps seems best—   155
Though like a comet it will turn to vapor?
Show me fruit that, before we pluck them, rot,
And trees whose foliage every day makes new!
MEPHISTOPHELES: Such a commission scares me not,
With such things I can wait on you.   160
But, worthy friend, the time comes when we would
Recline in peace and feast on something good.
FAUST: If ever I recline, calmed, on a bed of sloth,
You may destroy me then and there.
If ever flattering you should wile me   165
That in myself I find delight,
If with enjoyment you beguile me,
Then break on me, eternal night!
This bet I offer.
MEPHISTOPHELES: I accept it.
FAUST: Right.
If to the moment I should say: 170
Abide, you are so fair—
Put me in fetters on that day,
I *wish* to perish then, I swear.
Then let the death bell ever toll,
Your service done, you shall be free,   175
The clock may stop, the hand may fall,
As time comes to an end for me.
MEPHISTOPHELES: Consider it, for we shall not forget it.
FAUST: That is a right you need not waive.
I did not boast, and I shall not regret it.   180
As I grow stagnant I shall be a slave,
Whether or not to anyone indebted.
MEPHISTOPHELES: At the doctor's banquet[4] tonight I shall do
My duties as a servant without fail.
But for life's sake, or death's—just one detail: 185
Could you give me a line or two?
FAUST: You pedant need it black on white?
Are man and a man's word indeed new to your sight?

---

4. The dinner given by a successful candidate for a Ph.D. degree.

Is not my spoken word sufficient warrant
When it commits my life eternally?   190
Does not the world rush on in every torrent,
And a mere promise should hold me?
Yet this illusion our heart inherits,
And who would want to shirk his debt?
Blessed who counts loyalty among his merits.   195
No sacrifice will he regret.
And yet a parchment, signed and sealed, is an abhorrent
Specter that haunts us, and it makes us fret.
The word dies when we seize the pen,
And wax and leather lord it then.   200
What, evil spirit, do you ask?
Paper or parchment, stone or brass?
Should I use chisel, style, or quill?
It is completely up to you.
MEPHISTOPHELES: Why get so hot and overdo   205
Your rhetoric? Why must you shrill?
Use any sheet, it is the same;
And with a drop of blood you sign your name.
FAUST: If you are sure you like this game,
Let it be done to humor you.   210
MEPHISTOPHELES: Blood is a very special juice.
FAUST: You need not fear that someday I retract.
That all my striving I unloose
Is the whole purpose of the pact.
Oh, I was puffed up all too boldly,   215
At your rank only is my place.
The lofty spirit spurned me coldly,
And nature hides from me her face.
Torn is the subtle thread of thought,
I loathe the knowledge I once sought.   220
In sensuality's abysmal land
Let our passions drink their fill!
In magic veils, not pierced by skill,
Let every wonder be at hand!
Plunge into time's whirl that dazes my sense,   225
Into the torrent of events!
And let enjoyment, distress,
Annoyance and success
Succeed each other as best they can;
For restless activity proves a man.   230
MEPHISTOPHELES: You are not bound by goal or measure.
If you would nibble everything
Or snatch up something on the wing,
You're welcome to what gives you pleasure.
But help yourself and don't be coy!   235
FAUST: Do you not hear, I have no thought of joy!
The reeling whirl I seek, the most painful excess,

Enamored hate and quickening distress.
Cured from the craving to know all, my mind
Shall not henceforth be closed to any pain,   240
And what is portioned out to all mankind,
I shall enjoy deep in my self, contain
Within my spirit summit and abyss,
Pile on my breast their agony and bliss,
And thus let my own self grow into theirs, unfettered,   245
Till as they are, at last I, too, am shattered.

MEPHISTOPHELES: Believe me who for many a thousand year
Has chewed this cud and never rested,
That from the cradle to the bier
The ancient leaven cannot be digested.   250
Trust one like me, this whole array
Is for a God—there's no contender:
He dwells in his eternal splendor,
To darkness we had to surrender,
And you need night as well as day.   255

FAUST: And yet it is my will.

MEPHISTOPHELES: It does sound bold.
But I'm afraid, though you are clever,
Time is too brief, though art's forever.
Perhaps you're willing to be told.
Why don't you find yourself a poet,   260
And let the gentleman ransack his dreams:
And when he finds a noble trait, let him bestow it
Upon your worthy head in reams and reams:
The lion's daring,
The swiftness of the hind,   265
The northerner's forbearing
And the Italian's fiery mind,
Let him resolve the mystery
How craft can be combined with magnanimity,
Or how a passion-crazed young man   270
Might fall in love after a plan.
If there were such a man, I'd like to meet him,
As Mr. Microcosm I would greet him.

FAUST: Alas, what am I, if I can
Not reach for mankind's crown which merely mocks   275
Our senses' craving like a star?

MEPHISTOPHELES: You're in the end—just what you are!
Put wigs on with a million locks
And put your foot on ell-high socks,
You still remain just what you are.   280

FAUST: I feel, I gathered up and piled up high
In vain the treasures of the human mind:
When I sit down at last, I cannot find
New strength within—it is all dry.

My stature has not grown a whit,   285
No closer to the Infinite.
MEPHISTOPHELES: Well, my good sir, to put it crudely,
You see matters just as they lie;
We have to look at them more shrewdly,
Or all life's pleasures pass us by.   290
Your hands and feet—indeed that's trite—
And head and seat are yours alone;
Yet all in which I find delight,
Should they be less my own?
Suppose I buy myself six steeds: 295
I buy their strength; while I recline
I dash along at whirlwind speeds,
For their two dozen legs are mine.
Come on! Let your reflections rest
And plunge into the world with zest!   300
I say, the man that speculates
Is like a beast that in the sand,
Led by an evil spirit, round and round gyrates,
And all about lies gorgeous pasture land.
FAUST: How shall we set about it?
MEPHISTOPHELES: Simply leave.   305
What torture room is this? What site of grief?
Is this the noble life of prudence—
You bore yourself and bore your students?
Oh, let your neighbor, Mr. Paunch, live so!
Why work hard threshing straw, when it annoys?   310
The best that you could ever know
You may not tell the little boys.
Right now I hear one in the aisle.
FAUST: I simply cannot face the lad.
MEPHISTOPHELES: The poor chap waited quite a while,   315
I do not want him to leave sad.
Give me your cap and gown. Not bad! [*He dresses himself up.*]
This mask ought to look exquisite!
Now you can leave things to my wit.
Some fifteen minutes should be all I need;   320
Meanwhile get ready for our trip, and speed!
[*Exit* FAUST.]
MEPHISTOPHELES: [*In* FAUST*'s long robe.*]
Have but contempt for reason and for science,
Man's noblest force spurn with defiance,
Subscribe to magic and illusion,
The Lord of Lies aids your confusion,   325
And, pact or no, I hold you tight.—
The spirit which he has received from fate
Sweeps ever onward with unbridled might,
Its hasty striving is so great

It leaps over the earth's delights.   330
Through life I'll drag him at a rate,
Through shallow triviality,
That he shall writhe and suffocate;
And his insatiability,
With greedy lips, shall see the choicest plate   335
And ask in vain for all that he would cherish—
And were he not the Devil's mate
And had not signed, he still must perish.
  [A STUDENT enters.]
STUDENT: I have arrived quite recently
  And come, full of humility,   340
  To meet that giant intellect
  Whom all refer to with respect.
MEPHISTOPHELES: This is a charming pleasantry.
  A man as others are, you see.—
  Have you already called elsewhere?   345
STUDENT: I pray you, take me in your care.
  I am, believe me, quite sincere,
  Have some odd cash and lots of cheer;
  My mother scarcely let me go,
  But there is much I hope to know.   350
MEPHISTOPHELES: This is just the place for you to stay.
STUDENT: To be frank, I should like to run away.
  I cannot say I like these walls,
  These gloomy rooms and somber halls.
  It seems so narrow, and I see   355
  No patch of green, no single tree;
  And in the auditorium
  My hearing, sight, and thought grow numb.
MEPHISTOPHELES: That is a question of mere habit.
  The child, offered the mother's breast,   360
  Will not in the beginning grab it;
  But soon it clings to it with zest.
  And thus at wisdom's copious breasts
  You'll drink each day with greater zest.
STUDENT: I'll hang around her neck, enraptured;   365
  But tell me first: how is she captured?
MEPHISTOPHELES: Before we get into my views—
  What Department do you choose?
STUDENT: I should like to be erudite,
  And from the earth to heaven's height   370
  Know every law and every action:
  Nature and science is what I need.
MEPHISTOPHELES: That is the way; you just proceed
  And scrupulously shun distraction.
STUDENT: Body and soul, I am a devotee;   375
  Though, naturally, everybody prays

For some free time and liberty
On pleasant summer holidays.
MEPHISTOPHELES: Use well your time, so swiftly it runs on!
Be orderly, and time is won!   380
My friend, I shall be pedagogic,
And say you ought to start with Logic.
For thus your mind is trained and braced,
In Spanish boots it will be laced,
That on the road of thought maybe   385
It henceforth creep more thoughtfully,
And does not crisscross here and there,
Will-o'-the-wisping through the air.
Days will be spent to let you know
That what you once did at one blow,   390
Like eating and drinking so easy and free,
Can only be done with One, Two, Three.
Yet the web of thought has no such creases
And is more like a weaver's masterpieces:
One step, a thousand threads arise,   395
Hither and thither shoots each shuttle,
The threads flow on, unseen and subtle,
Each blow effects a thousand ties.
The philosopher comes with analysis
And proves it had to be like this: 400
The first was so, the second so,
And hence the third and fourth was so,
And were not the first and the second here,
Then the third and fourth could never appear.
That is what all the students believe,   405
But they have never learned to weave.
Who would study and describe the living, starts
By driving the spirit out of the parts:
In the palm of his hand he holds all the sections,
Lacks nothing, except the spirit's connections.   410
Encheirisis naturae[5] the chemists baptize it,
Mock themselves and don't realize it.
STUDENT: I did not quite get everything.
MEPHISTOPHELES: That will improve with studying:
You will reduce things by and by   415
And also learn to classify.
STUDENT: I feel so dazed by all you said
As if a mill went around in my head.
MEPHISTOPHELES: Then, without further circumvention,
Give metaphysics your attention.   420
There seek profoundly to attain
What does not fit the human brain;

---

5. The natural process by which substances are united into a living organism—a name for an action no one understands.

Whether you do or do not understand,
An impressive word is always at hand.
But now during your first half-year,   425
Keep above all our order here.
Five hours a day, you understand,
And when the bell peals, be on hand.
Before you come, you must prepare,
Read every paragraph with care,   430
Lest you, forbid, should overlook
That all he says is in the book.
But write down everything, engrossed
As if you took dictation from the Holy Ghost.
STUDENT: Don't say that twice—I understood: 435
I see how useful it's to write,
For what we possess black on white
We can take home and keep for good.
MEPHISTOPHELES: But choose a field of concentration!
STUDENT: I have no hankering for jurisprudence.   440
MEPHISTOPHELES: For that I cannot blame the students,
I know this science is a blight.
The laws and statutes of a nation
Are an inherited disease,
From generation unto generation   445
And place to place they drag on by degrees.
Wisdom becomes nonsense; kindness, oppression:
To be a grandson is a curse.
The right that is innate in us
Is not discussed by the profession.   450
STUDENT: My scorn is heightened by your speech.
Happy the man that you would teach!
I almost think theology would pay.
MEPHISTOPHELES: I should not wish to lead you astray.
When it comes to this discipline,   455
The way is hard to find, wrong roads abound,
And lots of hidden poison lies around
Which one can scarcely tell from medicine.
Here, too, it would be best you heard
One only and staked all upon your master's word.   460
Yes, stick to words at any rate;
There never was a surer gate
Into the temple, Certainty.
STUDENT: Yet some idea there must be.
MEPHISTOPHELES: All right. But do not plague yourself too anxiously;   465
For just where no ideas are
The proper word is never far.
With words a dispute can be won,
With words a system can be spun,
In words one can believe unshaken,   470

And from a word no tittle can be taken.
STUDENT: Forgive, I hold you up with many questions,
But there is one more thing I'd like to see.
Regarding medicine, maybe,
You have some powerful suggestions?   475
Three years go by so very fast,
And, God, the field is all too vast.
If but a little hint is shown,
One can attempt to find one's way.
MEPHISTOPHELES: [Aside.] I'm sick of this pedantic tone.   480
The Devil now again I'll play.
[Aloud.] The spirit of medicine is easy to know:
Through the macro-and microcosm you breeze,
And in the end you let it go
As God may please.   485
In vain you roam about to study science,
For each learns only what he can;
Who places on the moment his reliance,
He is the proper man.
You are quite handsome, have good sense,   490
And no doubt, you have courage, too,
And if you have self-confidence,
Then others will confide in you.
And give the women special care;
Their everlasting sighs and groans   495
In thousand tones
Are cured at one point everywhere.
And if you seem halfway discreet,
They will be lying at your feet.
First your degree inspires trust,   500
As if your art had scarcely any peers;
Right at the start, remove her clothes and touch her bust,
Things for which others wait for years and years.
Learn well the little pulse to squeeze,
And with a knowing, fiery glance you seize   505
Her freely round her slender waist
To see how tightly she is laced.
STUDENT: That looks much better, sir. For one sees how and where.
MEPHISTOPHELES: Gray, my dear friend, is every theory,
And green alone life's golden tree.   510
STUDENT: All this seems like a dream, I swear.
Could I impose on you sometime again
And drink more words of wisdom then?
MEPHISTOPHELES: What I can give you, you shall get.
STUDENT: Alas, I cannot go quite yet: 515
My album I must give to you;
Please, sir, show me this favor, too.
MEPHISTOPHELES: All right. [He writes and returns it.]

STUDENT: [*Reads.*] Eritis sicut Deus, scientes bonum et malum.[6] [*Closes
the book reverently and takes his leave.*]
MEPHISTOPHELES: Follow the ancient text and my relation, the snake;   520
Your very likeness to God will yet make you quiver and quake.
[FAUST *enters.*]
FAUST: Where are we heading now?
MEPHISTOPHELES: Wherever you may please.
We'll see the small world, then the larger one.
You will reap profit and have fun
As you sweep through this course with ease.   525
FAUST: With my long beard I hardly may
Live in this free and easy way.
The whole endeavor seems so futile;
I always felt the world was strange and brutal.
With others, I feel small and harassed,   530
And I shall always be embarrassed.
MEPHISTOPHELES: Good friend, you will become less sensitive:
Self-confidence will teach you how to live.
FAUST: How shall we get away from here?
Where are your carriage, groom and steed?   535
MEPHISTOPHELES: I rather travel through the air:
We spread this cloak—that's all we need.
But on this somewhat daring flight,
Be sure to keep your luggage light.
A little fiery air, which I plan to prepare,   540
Will raise us swiftly off the earth;
Without ballast we'll go up fast—
Congratulations, friend, on your rebirth!

AUERBACH'S KELLER IN LEIPZIG

[*Jolly fellows' drinking bout.*]
FROSCH: Will no one drink and no one laugh?
I'll teach you not to look so wry.
Today you look like sodden chaff
And usually blaze to the sky
BRANDER: It's all your fault; you make me sick: 5
No joke, and not a single dirty trick.
FROSCH: [*Pours a glass of wine over* BRANDER's *head.*]
There you have both.
BRANDER: You filthy pig!
FROSCH: You said I shouldn't be a prig.
SIEBEL: Let those who fight, stop or get out!
With all your lungs sing chorus, swill, and shout!   10
Come! Holla-ho!
ALTMAYER: Now this is where I quit.
Get me some cotton or my ears will split.

6. A slight alteration of the serpent's words to Eve in Genesis: "Ye shall be as God, knowing good and
evil" (Latin).

SIEBEL: When the vault echoes and the place
  Is quaking, then you can enjoy a bass.
FROSCH: Quite right! Throw out who fusses because he is lampooned! 15
  A! tara lara da!
ALTMAYER: A! tara lara da!
FROSCH: The throats seem to be tuned.
  [*Sings.*] Dear Holy Roman Empire,   1 1
  What holds you still together? 20
BRANDER: A nasty song! It reeks of politics!
  A wretched song! Thank God in daily prayer,
  That the old Empire isn't your affair!
  At least I think it is much to be grateful for
  That I'm not Emperor nor Chancellor. 25
  And yet we, too, need someone to respect—
  I say, a Pope let us elect.
  You know the part that elevates
  And thereby proves the man who rates.
FROSCH: [*Sings.*] Oh, Dame Nightingale, arise! 30
  Bring my sweet love ten thousand sighs!
SIEBEL: No sighs for your sweet love! I will not have such mush.
FROSCH: A sigh and kiss for her! You cannot make me blush.
  [*Sings*] Ope the latch in silent night!
  Ope the latch, your love invite! 35
  Shut the latch, there is the dawn!
SIEBEL: Go, sing and sing and sing, pay compliments and fawn!
  The time will come when I shall laugh:
  She led me by the nose, and you are the next calf.
  Her lover should be some mischievous gnome! 40
  He'd meet her at a crossroads and make light,
  And an old billy goat that's racing home
  From Blocksberg could still bleat to her "Good night!"
  A decent lad of real flesh and blood
  Is far too good to be her stud. 45
  I'll stand no sighs, you silly ass,
  But throw rocks through her window glass.
BRANDER: [*Pounding on the table.*]
  Look here! Look here! Listen to me!
  My friends, confess I know what's right;
  There are lovers here, and you'll agree 50
  That it's only civility
  That I should try to honor them tonight.
  Watch out! This song's the latest fashion.
  And join in the refrain with passion!
  [*Sings.*] A cellar once contained a rat 55
    That couldn't have been uncouther,
    Lived on grease and butter and grew fat—
  Just like old Doctor Luther.[7]

---

7. Martin Luther (1483–1546), German leader of the Protestant reformation, hence an object of distaste for Catholics.

The cook put poison in his food,
Then he felt cramped and just as stewed,   60
As if love gnawed his vitals.
CHORUS: [*Jubilant.*] As if love gnawed his vitals.
BRANDER: He dashed around, he dashed outdoors,
Sought puddles and swilled rain,
He clawed and scratched up walls and floors,   65
But his frenzy was in vain;
He jumped up in a frightful huff,
But soon the poor beast had enough,
As if love gnawed his vitals.
CHORUS: As if love gnawed his vitals.   70
BRANDER: At last he rushed in open day
Into the kitchen, crazed with fear,
Dropped near the stove and writhed and lay,
And puffed out his career.
The poisoner only laughed: I hope   75
He's at the end now of his rope,
As if love gnawed his vitals.
CHORUS: As if love gnawed his vitals.
SIEBEL: How pleased these stupid chaps are! That's,
I think, indeed a proper art   80
To put out poison for poor rats.
BRANDER: I see, you'd like to take their part.
ALTMAYER: Potbelly with his shiny top!
His ill luck makes him mild and tame.
He sees the bloated rat go flop—   85
And sees himself: they look the same.
    [FAUST *and* MEPHISTOPHELES *enter.*]
MEPHISTOPHELES: Above all else, it seems to me,
You need some jolly company
To see life can be fun—to say the least:
The people here make every day a feast.   90
With little wit and boisterous noise,
They dance and circle in their narrow trails
Like kittens playing with their tails.
When hangovers don't vex these boys,
And while their credit's holding out,   95
They have no cares and drink and shout.
BRANDER: Those two are travelers, I swear.
I tell it right off by the way they stare.
They have been here at most an hour.
FROSCH: No doubt about it. Leipzig is a flower,   100
It is a little Paris and educates its people.
SIEBEL: What may they be? Who knows the truth?
FROSCH: Leave it to me! A drink that interposes—
And I'll pull like a baby tooth
The worms they hide, out of these fellows' noses.   105
They seem to be of noble ancestry,

For they look proud and act disdainfully.
BRANDER: They are mere quacks and born in squalor.
ALTMAYER: Maybe.
FROSCH: Watch out! We shall commence.
MEPHISTOPHELES: [*To* FAUST.] The Devil people never sense,   110
  Though he may hold them by the collar.
FAUST: Good evening, gentlemen.
SIEBEL: Thank you, to you the same.
  [*Softly, looking at* MEPHISTOPHELES *from the side.*]
  Look at his foot. Why is it lame?[8]
MEPHISTOPHELES: We'll join you, if you grant the liberty.
  The drinks they have are poor, their wine not very mellow,   115
  So we'll enjoy your company.
ALTMAYER: You seem a most fastidious fellow.
FROSCH: Did you leave Rippach rather late and walk?
  And did you first have dinner with Master Jackass there?
MEPHISTOPHELES: Tonight we had no time to spare.   120
  Last time, however, we had quite a talk.
  He had a lot to say of his relations
  And asked us to send each his warmest salutations. [*He bows to* FROSCH.]
ALTMAYER: [*Softly.*] You got it! He's all right.
SIEBEL: A pretty repartee!
FROSCH: I'll get him yet. Just wait and see.   125
MEPHISTOPHELES: Just now we heard, if I'm not wrong,
  Some voices singing without fault.
  Indeed this seems a place for song;
  No doubt, it echoes from the vault.
FROSCH: Are you perchance a virtuoso?   130
MEPHISTOPHELES: Oh no, the will is great, the power only so-so.
ALTMAYER: Give us a song!
MEPHISTOPHELES: As many as you please.
SIEBEL: But let us have a brand-new strain!
MEPHISTOPHELES: We have just recently returned from Spain,
  The beauteous land of wine and melodies.   135
  [*Sings.*] A king lived long ago
  Who had a giant flea —
FROSCH: Hear, hear! A flea! That's what I call a jest.
  A flea's a mighty pretty guest.
MEPHISTOPHELES: [*Sings.*] A king lived long ago   140
  Who had a giant flea,
  He loved him just as though
  He were his son and heir.
  He sent his tailor a note
  And offered the tailor riches   145
  If he would measure a coat
  And also take measure for breeches.
BRANDER: Be sure to tell the tailor, if he twinkles,

---

8. By tradition, the Devil had a cloven foot, split like a sheep's hoof.

That he must take fastidious measure;
He'll lose his head, not just the treasure,   150
If in the breeches there are wrinkles.
MEPHISTOPHELES: He was in silk arrayed,
    In velvet he was dressed,
    Had ribbons and brocade,
    A cross upon his chest   155
    A fancy star, great fame—
    A minister, in short;
    And all his kin became
    Lords at the royal court.
    The other lords grew lean   160
    And suffered with their wives,
    The royal maid and the queen
    Were all but eaten alive,
    But weren't allowed to swat them
    And could not even scratch,   165
    While we can swat and blot them
    And kill the ones we catch.
CHORUS: [*Jubilant.*] While we can swat and blot them
    And kill the ones we catch.
FROSCH: Bravo! Bravo! That was a treat!   170
SIEBEL: That is the end all fleas should meet.
BRANDER: Point your fingers and catch 'em fine!
ALTMAYER: Long live our freedom! And long live wine!
MEPHISTOPHELES: When freedom is the toast, my own voice I should
    add,
    Were your forsaken wines only not quite so bad.[9]   175
SIEBEL: You better mind your language, lad.
MEPHISTOPHELES: I only fear the landlord might protest,
    Else I should give each honored guest
    From our cellar a good glass.
SIEBEL: Let's go! The landlord is an ass.   180
FROSCH: If you provide good drinks, you shall be eulogized;
    But let your samples be good-sized.
    When I'm to judge, I'm telling him,
    I want my snout full to the brim.
ALTMAYER: [*Softly.*] They're from the Rhineland, I presume.   185
MEPHISTOPHELES: Bring me a gimlet.
BRANDER: What could that be for?
    You couldn't have the casks in the next room?
ALTMAYER: The landlord keeps his tools right there behind the door.
MEPHISTOPHELES: [*Takes the gimlet. To* FROSCH.]
    What would you like? Something that's cool?
FROSCH: What do you mean? You got a lot of booze?   190
MEPHISTOPHELES: I let each have what he may choose.

9. Cursed.

ALTMAYER: [*To* FROSCH.] Oho! You lick your chops and start to drool.
FROSCH: If it is up to me, I'll have a Rhenish brand:
  There's nothing that competes with our fatherland.
MEPHISTOPHELES: [*Boring a hole near the edge of the table where* FROSCH
  sits.] Now let us have some wax to make a cork that sticks.   195
ALTMAYER: Oh, is it merely parlor tricks?
MEPHISTOPHELES: [*To* BRANDER.] And you?
BRANDER: I want a good champagne—
  Heady; I do not like it plain.
  [MEPHISTOPHELES *bores; meanwhile someone else has made the wax*
  stoppers and plugged the holes.]
BRANDER: Not all that's foreign can be banned,
  For what is far is often fine.   200
  A Frenchman is a thing no German man can stand,
  And yet we like to drink their wine.
SIEBEL: [*As* MEPHISTOPHELES *approaches his place.*]
  I must confess, I think the dry tastes bad,
  The sweet alone is exquisite.
MEPHISTOPHELES: [*Boring.*] Tokay[1] will flow for you, my lad.   205
ALTMAYER: I think, you might as well admit,
  Good gentlemen, that these are simply jests.
MEPHISTOPHELES: Tut, tut! With such distinguished guests
  That would be quite a lot to dare.
  So don't be modest, and declare   210
  What kind of wine you would prefer.
ALTMAYER: I like them all, so I don't care.
  [*After all the holes have been bored and plugged.*]
MEPHISTOPHELES: [*With strange gestures.*] The grape the vine adorns,
  The billy goat sports horns;
  The wine is juicy, vines are wood,   215
  The wooden table gives wine as good,
  Profound insight! Now you perceive
  A miracle; only believe!
  Now pull the stoppers and have fun!
ALL: [*As they pull out the stoppers and the wine each asked for flows into*
  his glass.] A gorgeous well for everyone!   220
MEPHISTOPHELES: Be very careful lest it overrun!
  [*They drink several times.*]
ALL: [*Sing.*] We feel gigantically well,
  Just like five hundred sows.
MEPHISTOPHELES: Look there how well men are when they are free.
FAUST: I should like to get out of here.   225
MEPHISTOPHELES: First watch how their bestiality
  Will in full splendor soon appear.
SIEBEL: [*Drinks carelessly and spills his wine on the floor where it turns*
  into a flame.] Help! Fire! Help! Hell blew a vent!

---

1. A sweet Hungarian wine.

MEPHISTOPHELES: [*Conjuring the flame.*] Be quiet, friendly element!
   [*To the fellow.*] For this time it was only a drop of purgatory.   230
SIEBEL: You'll pay for it, and you can save your story!
   What do you think we are, my friend?
FROSCH: Don't dare do that a second time, you hear!
ALTMAYER: Just let him leave in silence; that is what I say, gents!
SIEBEL: You have the brazen impudence   235
   To do your hocus-pocus here?
MEPHISTOPHELES: Be still, old barrel!
SIEBEL: Broomstick, you!
   Will you insult us? Mind your prose!
BRANDER: Just wait and see, there will be blows.
ALTMAYER: [*Pulls a stopper out of the table and fire leaps at him.*]
   I burn! I burn!
SIEBEL: It's magic, as I said.   240
   He is an outlaw. Strike him dead!
   [*They draw their knives and advance on* MEPHISTOPHELES.]
MEPHISTOPHELES: [*With solemn gestures.*]
     False images prepare
     Mirages in the air.
     Be here and there!
   [*They stand amazed and stare at each other.*]
ALTMAYER: Where am I? What a gorgeous land!   245
FROSCH: And vineyards! Am I mad?
SIEBEL: And grapes right by my hand!
BRANDER: See in the leaves that purple shape?
   I never saw that big a grape!
   [*Grabs* SIEBEL's *nose. They all do it to each other and raise their knives.*]
MEPHISTOPHELES: [*As above.*] Fall from their eyes, illusion's band!
   Remember how the Devil joked.   250
   [*He disappears with* FAUST, *the revelers separate.*]
SIEBEL: What's that?
ALTMAYER: Hah?
FROSCH: Your nose I stroked?
BRANDER: [*To* SIEBEL.] And yours is in my hand!
ALTMAYER: The shock is more than I can bear.
   I think I'll faint. Get me a chair!
FROSCH: What was all this? Who understands?   255
SIEBEL: Where is the scoundrel? I'm so sore,
   If I could only get my hands—
ALTMAYER: I saw him whiz right through the cellar door,
   Riding a flying barrel. Zounds,
   The fright weighs on me like a thousand pounds.   260
   [*Turning toward the table.*] Do you suppose the wine still flows?
SIEBEL: That was a fraud! You're asinine!
FROSCH: I surely thought that I drank wine.
BRANDER: But what about the grapes, I say.
ALTMAYER: Who says there are no miracles today!   265

WITCH'S KITCHEN

[*On a low stove, a large caldron stands over the fire. In the steam that rises from it, one can see several shapes. A longtailed* FEMALE MONKEY *sits near the caldron, skims it, and sees to it that it does not overflow. The* MALE MONKEY *with the little ones sits next to her and warms himself. Walls and ceiling are decorated with the queerest implements of witchcraft.* FAUST *and* MEPHISTOPHELES *enter.*]

FAUST: How I detest this crazy sorcery!
 I should get well, you promise me,
 In this mad frenzy of a mess?
 Do I need the advice of hag fakirs?
 And should this quackish sordidness   5
 Reduce my age by thirty years?
 I'm lost if that's all you could find.
 My hope is drowned in sudden qualm.
 Has neither nature nor some noble mind
 Invented or contrived a wholesome balm?   10
MEPHISTOPHELES: My friend, that was nice oratory!
 Indeed, to make you young there is one way that's apter;
 But, I regret, that is another story
 And forms quite an amazing chapter.
FAUST: I want to know it.
MEPHISTOPHELES: All right, you need no sorcery 15
 And no physician and no dough.
 Just go into the fields and see
 What fun it is to dig and hoe;
 Live simply and keep all your thoughts
 On a few simple objects glued;   20
 Restrict yourself and eat the plainest food;
 Live with the beasts, a beast: it is no thievery
 To dress the fields you work, with your own dung.
 That is the surest remedy:
 At eighty, you would still be young.   25
FAUST: I am not used to that and can't, I am afraid,
 Start now to work with hoe and spade.
 For me a narrow life like that's too small.
MEPHISTOPHELES: We need the witch then after all.
FAUST: Why just the hag with all her grime!   30
 Could you not brew it—with *your* head!
MEPHISTOPHELES: A splendid way to waste my time!
 A thousand bridges I could build instead.[2]
 Science is not enough, nor art;
 In this work patience plays a part.   35
 A quiet spirit plods and plods at length;
 Nothing but time can give the brew its strength.
 With all the things that go into it,

---

2. According to folk legend, the Devil built bridges at the request of human beings. As a reward, he caught either the first or the thirteenth soul to cross each new bridge.

It's sickening just to *see* them do it.
The Devil taught them, true enough 40
But he himself can't make the stuff.
[*He sees the* ANIMALS.]
Just see how delicate they look!
This is the maid, and that the cook.
[*To the* ANIMALS.] It seems the lady isn't home?
ANIMALS: She went to roam 45
Away from home,
Right through the chimney in the dome.
MEPHISTOPHELES: And how long will she walk the street?
ANIMALS: As long as we warm our feet.
MEPHISTOPHELES: [*To* FAUST.] How do you like this dainty pair? 50
FAUST: They are inane beyond comparison.
MEPHISTOPHELES: A conversation like this one
Is just the sort of thing for which I care.
[*To the* ANIMALS.] Now tell me, you accursed group,
Why do you stir that steaming mess? 55
ANIMALS: We cook a watery beggars' soup.
MEPHISTOPHELES: You should do a brisk business.
MALE MONKEY: [*Approaches* MEPHISTOPHELES *and fawns.*]
Oh please throw the dice
And lose, and be nice
And let me get wealthy! 60
We are in the ditch,
And if I were rich,
Then I might be healthy.
MEPHISTOPHELES: How happy every monkey thinks he'd be,
If he could play the lottery. 65
[*Meanwhile the monkey youngsters have been playing with a large
ball, and now they roll it forward.*]
MALE MONKEY: The world and ball
Both rise and fall
And roll and wallow;
It sounds like glass,
It bursts, alas, 70
The inside's hollow.
Here it is light,
There still more bright,
Life's mine to swallow!
Dear son, I say, 75
Please keep away!
You'll die first.
It's made of clay
It will burst.
MEPHISTOPHELES: The sieve there, chief—? 80
MALE MONKEY: [*Gets it down.*] If you were a thief,
I'd be wise to you.
[*He runs to the* FEMALE MONKEY *and lets her see through it.*]

Look through, be brief!
You know the thief,
But may not say *who?*   85
MEPHISTOPHELES: [*Approaching the fire.*] And here this pot?
BOTH BIG MONKEYS: The half-witted sot!
Does not know the pot,
Does not know the kettle!
MEPHISTOPHELES: You impolite beast!   90
MALE MONKEY: Take this brush at least
And sit down and settle!
[*He makes* MEPHISTOPHELES *sit down.*]
FAUST: [*Who has been standing before a mirror all this time, now stepping
close to it, now back.*] What blissful image is revealed
To me behind this magic glass!
Lend me your swiftest pinions, love, that I might pass   95
From here to her transfigured field!
When I don't stay right on this spot, but, pining,
Dare to step forward and go near
Mists cloud her shape and let it disappear.
The fairest image of a woman!   100
Indeed, could woman be so fair?
Or is this body which I see reclining
Heaven's quintessence from another sphere?
Is so much beauty found on earth?
MEPHISTOPHELES: Well, if a god works hard for six whole days, my
friend,   105
And then says bravo in the end,
It ought to have a little worth.
For now, stare to your heart's content!
I could track down for you just such a sweet—
What bliss it would be to get her consent,   110
To marry her and be replete.
[FAUST *gazes into the mirror all the time.* MEPHISTOPHELES, *stretch-
ing in the armchair and playing with the brush, goes on speaking.*]
I sit here like the king upon his throne:
The scepter I hold here, I lack the crown alone.
ANIMALS: [*Who have so far moved around in quaint confusion, bring a
crown to* MEPHISTOPHELES, *clamoring loudly.*] Oh, please be so good.
With sweat and with blood   115
This crown here to lime!
[*They handle the crown clumsily and break it into two pieces with
which they jump around.*]
It's done, let it be!
We chatter and see,
We listen and rhyme—
FAUST: [*At the mirror.*] Alas, I think I'll lose my wits.   120
MEPHISTOPHELES: [*Pointing toward the* ANIMALS.]
I fear that my head, too, begins to reel.
ANIMALS: And if we score hits

And everything fits,
It's thoughts that we feel.
FAUST: [As above.] My heart and soul are catching fire.   125
Please let us go away from here!
MEPHISTOPHELES: [In the same position as above.]
The one thing one has to admire
Is that their poetry is quite sincere.
[The caldron which the FEMALE MONKEY has neglected begins to run
over, and a huge flame blazes up through the chimney. The WITCH
scoots down through the flame with a dreadful clamor.]
WITCH: Ow! Ow! Ow! Ow!
You damned old beast! You cursed old sow!   130
You leave the kettle and singe the frau.
You cursed old beast! [Sees FAUST and MEPHISTOPHELES.]
What goes on here?
Why are you here?
Who are you two?   135
Who sneaked inside?
Come, fiery tide!
Their bones be fried!
[She plunges the skimming spoon into the caldron and spatters
flames at FAUST, MEPHISTOPHELES, and the ANIMALS. The ANIMALS
whine.]
MEPHISTOPHELES: [Reversing the brush he holds in his hand, and striking
into the glasses and pots.]
In two! In two!
There lies the brew.   140
There lies the glass.
A joke, my lass,
The beat, you ass,
For melodies from you.
[As the WITCH retreats in wrath and horror.]
You know me now? You skeleton! You shrew!   145
You know your master and your lord?
What holds me? I could strike at you
And shatter you and your foul monkey horde.
Does not the scarlet coat reveal His Grace?
Do you not know the rooster's feather, ma'am?   150
Did I perchance conceal my face?
Or must I tell you who I am?
WITCH: Forgive the uncouth greeting, though
You have no cloven feet, you know.
And your two ravens, where are they?   155
MEPHISTOPHELES: For just this once you may get by,
For it has been some time, I don't deny,
Since I have come your way,
And culture which licks out at every stew
Extends now to the Devil, too: 160
Gone is the Nordic phantom that former ages saw;

You see no horns, no tail or claw.
And as regards the foot with which I can't dispense,
That does not look the least bit suave;
Like other young men nowadays, I hence   165
Prefer to pad my calves.
WITCH: [*Dancing.*] I'll lose my wits, I'll lose my brain
Since Squire Satan has come back again.
MEPHISTOPHELES: That name is out, hag! Is that plain?
WITCH: But why? It never gave you pain!   170
MEPHISTOPHELES: It's dated, called a fable; men are clever,
But they are just as badly off as ever:
The Evil One is gone, the evil ones remain.
You call me baron, hag, and you look out:
I am a cavalier with cavalierly charms,   175
And my nobility don't dare to doubt!
Look here and you will see my coat of arms!
  [*He makes an indecent gesture.*]
WITCH: [*Laughs immoderately.*] Ha! Ha! That is your manner, sir!
You are a jester as you always were.
MEPHISTOPHELES: [*To* FAUST.] My friend, mark this, but don't repeat it: 180
This is the way a witch likes to be treated.
WITCH: Now tell me why you came in here.
MEPHISTOPHELES: A good glass of the famous juice, my dear!
But I must have the oldest kind:
Its strength increases with each year.   185
WITCH: I got a bottle on this shelf
From which I like to nip myself;
By now it doesn't even stink.
I'll give you some, it has the power.
[*Softly.*] But if, quite unprepared, this man should have a drink, 190
He could, as you know well, not live another hour.
MEPHISTOPHELES: He is a friend of mine, and he will take it well
The best you have is not too good for him.
Now draw your circle, say your spell,
And fill a bumper to the brim.   195
  [WITCH *draws a circle with curious gestures and puts quaint objects
  into it, while the glasses begin to tinkle, the caldrons begin to resound
  and they make music. In the end, she gets a big book and puts the*
  MONKEYS *into the circle, and they serve her as a desk and have to
  hold a torch for her. She motions* FAUST *to step up.*]
FAUST: [*To* MEPHISTOPHELES.] No, tell me why these crazy antics?
The mad ado, the gestures that are frantic,
The most insipid cheat—this stuff
I've known and hated long enough.
MEPHISTOPHELES: Relax! It's fun—a little play;   200
Don't be so serious, so sedate!
Such hocus-pocus is a doctor's way,
Of making sure the juice will operate.
  [*He makes* FAUST *step into the circle.*]

WITCH: [*Begins to recite from the book with great emphasis.*]
    This you must know!
    From one make ten,   205
    And two let go,
    Take three again,
    Then you'll be rich.
    The four you fix.
    From five and six,   210
    Thus says the witch,
    Make seven and eight,
    That does the trick;
    And nine is one,
    And ten is none.   215
    That is the witch's arithmetic.
FAUST: It seems to me the old hag runs a fever.
MEPHISTOPHELES: You'll hear much more before we leave her.
  I know, it sounds like that for many pages.
  I lost much time on this accursed affliction   220
  Because a perfect contradiction
  Intrigues not only fools but also sages.
  This art is old and new, forsooth:
  It was the custom in all ages
  To spread illusion and not truth   225
  With Three in One and One in Three.[3]
  They teach it twittering like birds;
  With fools there is no intervening.
  Men usually believe, if only they hear words,
  That there must also be some sort of meaning.   230
WITCH: [*Continues.*] The lofty prize
    Of science lies
    Concealed today as ever.
    Who has no thought,
    To him it's brought   235
    To own without endeavor.
FAUST: What nonsense does she put before us?
  My head aches from her stupidness.
  It seems as if I heard a chorus
  Of many thousand fools, no less.   240
MEPHISTOPHELES: Excellent sybil, that is quite enough!
  Now pour the drink—just put the stuff
  Into this bowl here. Fill it, sybil, pour;
  My friend is safe from any injuries:
  He has a number of degrees   245
  And has had many drinks before.
    [WITCH *pours the drink into a bowl with many ceremonies; as* FAUST
    puts it to his lips, a small flame spurts up.]

3. The Christian doctrine of the Trinity.

MEPHISTOPHELES: What is the matter? Hold it level!
Drink fast and it will warm you up.
You are familiar with the Devil,
And shudder at a fiery cup?   250
[*The* WITCH *breaks the circle.* FAUST *steps out.*]
MEPHISTOPHELES: Come on! Let's go! You must not rest.
WITCH: And may this gulp give great delight!
MEPHISTOPHELES: [*To the* WITCH.] If there is anything that you request,
Just let me know the next Walpurgis Night.[4]
WITCH: Here is a song; just sing it now and then,   255
And you will feel a queer effect indeed.
MEPHISTOPHELES: [*To* FAUST.] Come quickly now before you tire,
And let me lead while you perspire
So that the force can work out through your skin.
I'll teach you later on to value noble leisure,   260
And soon you will perceive the most delightful pleasure,
As Cupid starts to stir and dance like jumping jinn.[5]
FAUST: One last look at the mirror where I stood!
So beauteous was that woman's form!
MEPHISTOPHELES: No! No! The paragon of womanhood   265
You shall soon see alive and warm.
[*Softly.*] You'll soon find with this potion's aid,
Helen of Troy in every maid.

STREET

[FAUST. MARGARET *passing by.*]
FAUST: Fair lady, may I be so free
To offer my arm and company?
MARGARET: I'm neither a lady nor am I fair,
And can go home without your care.
[*She frees herself and exits.*]
FAUST: By heaven, this young girl is fair!   5
Her like I don't know anywhere.
She is so virtuous and pure,
But somewhat pert and not demure.
The glow of her cheeks and her lips so red
I shall not forget until I am dead.   10
Her downcast eyes, shy and yet smart,
Are stamped forever on my heart;
Her curtness and her brevity
Was sheer enchanting ecstasy!
[MEPHISTOPHELES *enters.*]
FAUST: Get me that girl, and don't ask why!   15
MEPHISTOPHELES: Which one?

---

4. The eve of May Day (May 1), when witches are supposed to assemble on the Brocken, a peak in the Hartz Mountains, which are in central Germany.   5. A supernatural being that can take human or animal form.

FAUST: She only just went by.
MEPHISTOPHELES: That one! She saw her priest just now,
  And he pronounced her free of sin.
  I stood right there and listened in.
  She's so completely blemishless   20
  That there was nothing to confess.
  Over her I don't have any power.
FAUST: She is well past her fourteenth year.
MEPHISTOPHELES: Look at the gay Lothario[6] here!
  He would like to have every flower,   25
  And thinks each prize or pretty trick
  Just waits around for him to pick;
  But sometimes that just doesn't go.
FAUST: My Very Reverend Holy Joe,
  Leave me in peace with law and right!   30
  I tell you, if you don't comply,
  And this sweet young blood doesn't lie
  Between my arms this very night,
  At midnight we'll have parted ways.
MEPHISTOPHELES: Think of the limits of my might.   35
  I need at least some fourteen days
  To find a handy evening.
FAUST: If I had peace for seven hours,
  I should not need the Devil's powers
  To seduce such a little thing.   40
MEPHISTOPHELES: You speak just like a Frenchman. Wait
  I beg you, and don't be annoyed:
  What have you got when it's enjoyed?
  The fun is not nearly so great
  As when you bit by bit imbibe it,   45
  And first resort to playful folly
  To knead and to prepare your dolly,
  The way some Gallic tales describe it.
FAUST: I've appetite without all that.
MEPHISTOPHELES: Now without jokes or tit-for-tat: 50
  I tell you, with this fair young child
  We simply can't be fast or wild.
  We'd waste our time storming and running;
  We have to have recourse to cunning.
FAUST: Get something from the angel's nest!   55
  Or lead me to her place of rest!
  Get me a kerchief from her breast,
  A garter from my darling's knee.
MEPHISTOPHELES: Just so you see, it touches me
  And I would soothe your agony,   60
  Let us not linger here and thus delay:
  I'll take you to her room today.

6. The seducer in Nicholas Rowe's play *The Fair Penitent* (1703); hence, figuratively, any seducer. The
German reads *Hans Liederlich*, meaning a profligate, since *liederlich* means "careless" or "dissolute."

FAUST: And shall I see her? Have her?
MEPHISTOPHELES: No.
To one of her neighbors she has to go.
But meanwhile you may at your leisure   65
Relish the hopes of future pleasure,
Till you are sated with her atmosphere.
FAUST: Can we go now?
MEPHISTOPHELES: It's early yet, I fear.
FAUST: Get me a present for the dear!
    [Exit.]
MEPHISTOPHELES: A present right away? Good! He will be a hit.   70
There's many a nice place I know
With treasures buried long ago;
I better look around a bit.
    [Exit.]

EVENING

[A small neat room.]
MARGARET: [Braiding and binding her hair.]
I should give much if I could say
Who was that gentleman today.
He looked quite gallant, certainly,
And is of noble family;
That much even his forehead told—   5
How else could he have been so bold?
    [Exit. Enter MEPHISTOPHELES, FAUST.]
MEPHISTOPHELES: Come in, but very quietly!
FAUST: [After a short silence.] I beg you, leave and let me be!
MEPHISTOPHELES: [Sniffing around.] She's neater than a lot of girls I see.
    [Exit.]
FAUST: [Looking up and around.] Sweet light of dusk, guest from above 10
That fills this shrine, be welcome you!
Seize now my heart, sweet agony of love
That languishes and feeds on hope's clear dew!
What sense of calm embraces me,
Of order and complete content!   15
What bounty in this poverty!
And in this prison, ah, what ravishment!
    [He throws himself into the leather armchair by the bed.]
Welcome me now, as former ages rested
Within your open arms in grief and joy!
How often was this fathers' throne contested   20
By eager children, prized by girl and boy!
And here, perhaps, her full cheeks flushed with bliss,
My darling, grateful for a Christmas toy,
Pressed on her grandsire's withered hand a kiss.
I feel your spirit, lovely maid,   25
Of ordered bounty breathing here

Which, motherly, comes daily to your aid
To teach you how a rug is best on tables laid
And how the sand should on the floor appear.[7]
Oh godlike hand, to you it's given   30
To make a cottage, a kingdom of heaven.
And here!
    [*He lifts a bed curtain.*]
                What raptured shudder makes me stir?
How I should love to be immured
Where in light dreams nature matured
The angel that's innate in her,   35
Here lay the child, developed slowly,
Her tender breast with warm life fraught,
And here, through weaving pure and holy,
The image of the gods was wrought.

And you! Alas, what brought you here?   40
I feel so deeply moved, so queer!
What do you seek? Why is your heart so sore?
Poor Faust! I do not know you any more.

Do magic smells surround me here?
Immediate pleasure was my bent,   45
But now—in dreams of love I'm all but spent.
Are we mere puppets of the atmosphere?

If she returned this instant from her call,
How for your mean transgression you would pay!
The haughty lad would be so small,   50
Lie at her feet and melt away.
MEPHISTOPHELES: [*Entering.*] Let's go! I see her in the lane!
FAUST: Away! I'll never come again.
MEPHISTOPHELES: Here is a fairly decent case,
    I picked it up some other place.   55
    Just leave it in the chest up there.
    She'll go out of her mind, I swear;
    For I put things in it, good sir,
    To win a better one than her.
    But child is child and play is play.   60
FAUST: I don't know—should I?
MEPHISTOPHELES: Why delay?
    You do not hope to save your jewel?
    Or I'll give your lust this advice:
    Don't waste fair daytime like this twice,
    Nor my exertions: it is cruel.   65
    It is not simple greed, I hope!
    I scratch my head, I fret and mope—
    [*He puts the case into the chest and locks it again.*]

---

7. Floors were sprinkled with sand after cleaning.

Away! Let's go!—
It's just to make the child fulfill
Your heart's desire and your will;   70
And you stand and frown
As if you had to lecture in cap and gown—
As if in gray there stood in front of you
Physics and Metaphysics, too.
Away!   75
    [*Exeunt.*]
MARGARET: [*With a lamp.*] It seems so close, so sultry now,
    [*She opens the window.*]
And yet outside it's not so warm.
I feel so strange, I don't know how—
I wish my mother would come home.
A shudder grips my body, I feel chilly—   80
How fearful I am and how silly!
    [*She begins to sing as she undresses.*]
        In Thule[8] there was a king,
        Faithful unto the grave,
        To whom his mistress, dying,
        A golden goblet gave.   85

        Nothing he held more dear.
        At every meal he used it;
        His eyes would fill with tears
        As often as he mused it.

        And when he came to dying,   90
        The towns in his realm he told.
        Naught to his heir denying,
        Except the goblet of gold.

        He dined at evenfall
        With all his chivalry   95
        In the ancestral hall
        In the castle by the sea.

        The old man rose at last
        And drank life's sunset glow.
        And the sacred goblet he cast   100
        Into the flood below.

        He saw it plunging, drinking.
        And sinking into the sea;
        His eyes were also sinking,
        And nevermore drank he.   105
    [*She opens the chest to put away her clothes and sees the case.*]
How did this lovely case get in my chest?

---

8. The fabled *ultima Thule* of Latin literature—those distant lands just beyond the reach of every explorer. Goethe wrote the ballad in 1774; it was published and set to music in 1782 and later inspired the slow movement of Mendelssohn's *Italian Symphony.*

I locked it after I got dressed.
It certainly seems strange. And what might be in there?
It might be a security
Left for a loan in Mother's care.   110
There is a ribbon with a key;
I think I'll open it and see.
What is that? God in heaven! There—
I never saw such fine array!
These jewels! Why a lord's lady could wear   115
These on the highest holiday.
How would this necklace look on me?
Who owns all this? It is so fine.
    [*She adorns herself and steps before the mirror.*]
If those earrings were only mine!
One looks quite different right away.   120
What good is beauty, even youth?
All that may be quite good and fair,
But does it get you anywhere?
Their praise is half pity, you can be sure.
For gold contend,   125
On gold depend
All things. Woe to us poor!

PROMENADE

[FAUST *walking up and down, lost in thought.* MEPHISTOPHELES
    enters.]
MEPHISTOPHELES: By the pangs of despised love! By the elements of hell
    I wish I knew something worse to curse by it as well!
FAUST: What ails you? Steady now, keep level!
    I never saw a face like yours today.
MEPHISTOPHELES: I'd wish the Devil took me straightaway,   5
    If I myself were not a devil.
FAUST: Has something in your head gone bad?
    It sure becomes you raving like one mad.
MEPHISTOPHELES: Just think, the jewels got for Margaret—
    A dirty priest took the whole set.   10
    The mother gets to see the stuff
    And starts to shudder, sure enough:
    She has a nose to smell things out—
    In prayerbooks she keeps her snout—
    A whiff of anything makes plain   15
    Whether it's holy or profane.
    She sniffed the jewelry like a rat
    And knew no blessings came with that.
    My child, she cried, ill-gotten wealth
    Will soil your soul and spoil your health.   20
    We'll give it to the Mother of the Lord
    And later get a heavenly reward.

Poor Margaret went into a pout;
She thought: a gift horse![9] and, no doubt,
Who[1] brought it here so carefully 25
Could not be godless, certainly.
The mother called a priest at once,
He saw the gems and was no dunce;
He drooled and then said: Without question,
Your instinct is quite genuine, • 30
Who overcomes himself will win.
The Church has a superb digestion,
Whole countries she has gobbled up,
But never is too full to sup;
The Church alone has the good health 35
For stomaching ill-gotten wealth.
FAUST: Why, everybody does: a Jew
And any king can do it, too.
MEPHISTOPHELES: So he picked up a clasp, necklace, and rings,
Like toadstools or some worthless things, 40
And did not thank them more nor less
Than as if it were nuts or some such mess,
And he promised them plenty after they died—
And they were duly edified.
FAUST: And Gretchen?[2]
MEPHISTOPHELES: She, of course, feels blue, 45
She sits and doesn't know what to do,
Thinks day and night of every gem—
Still more of him who furnished them.
FAUST: My darling's grief distresses me.
Go, get her some new jewelry. 50
The first one was a trifling loss.
MEPHISTOPHELES: Oh sure, it's child's play for you, boss.
FAUST: Just fix it all to suit my will;
Try on the neighbor, too, your skill.
Don't, Devil, act like sluggish paste! 55
Get some new jewels and make haste!
MEPHISTOPHELES: Yes, gracious lord, it is a pleasure.
[FAUST exits.]
MEPHISTOPHELES: A fool in love just doesn't care
And, just to sweeten darling's leisure,
He'd make sun, moon, and stars into thin air. 60
[Exit.]

THE NEIGHBOR'S HOUSE

MARTHA: [Alone.] May God forgive my husband! He
Was certainly not good to me.
He went into the world to roam

---

9. Like the wooden horse in which Greek soldiers entered Troy to capture it; an emblem of treachery. 1. Whoever. 2. Diminutive of the German *Margarete*. She is given this name through much of the play.

And left me on the straw at home.
God knows that I have never crossed him,   5
And loved him dearly; yet I lost him.
[*She cries.*] Perhaps—the thought kills me—he died!—
If it were only certified!
   [MARGARET *enters.*]
MARGARET: Dame Martha!
MARTHA: Gretchen, what could it be?
MARGARET: My legs feel faint, though not with pain: 10
I found another case, again
Right in my press,[3] of ebony,
With things more precious all around
Than was the first case that I found.
MARTHA: You must not show them to your mother,   15
She'd tell the priest as with the other.
MARGARET: Oh look at it! Oh see! Please do!
MARTHA: [*Adorns her.*] You lucky, lucky creature, you!
MARGARET: Unfortunately, it's not meet
To wear them in the church or street.   20
MARTHA: Just come here often to see me,
Put on the jewels secretly,
Walk up and down an hour before the mirror here,
And we shall have a good time, dear.
Then chances come, perhaps a holiday,   25
When we can bit by bit, gem after gem display,
A necklace first, than a pearl in your ear;
Your mother—we can fool her, or she may never hear.
MARGARET: Who brought the cases and has not appeared?
It certainly seems very weird.   30
   [*A knock.*]
Oh God, my mother—is it her?
MARTHA: [*Peeping through the curtain.*] It is a stranger—come in, sir!
   [MEPHISTOPHELES *enters.*]
MEPHISTOPHELES: I'll come right in and be so free,
If the ladies will grant me the liberty.
   [*Steps back respectfully as he sees* MARGARET.]
To Martha Schwerdtlein I wished to speak.   35
MARTHA: It's I. What does your honor seek?
MEPHISTOPHELES: [*Softly to her.*] I know you now, that satisfies me,
You have very elegant company;
Forgive my intrusion; I shall come back soon—
If you don't mind, this afternoon.   40
MARTHA: [*Loud.*] Oh goodness gracious! Did you hear?
He thinks you are a lady, dear!
MARGARET: I'm nothing but a poor young maid;
You are much too kind, I am afraid;

---

3. A type of cupboard in which pressed linens were stored.

The gems and jewels are not my own.   45
MEPHISTOPHELES: It is not the jewelry alone!
Your noble eyes—indeed, it is your whole way!
How glad I am that I may stay!
MARTHA: What is your errand? Please, good sir—
MEPHISTOPHELES: I wish I had better news for her!   50
And don't get cross with your poor guest:
Your husband is dead and sends his best.
MARTHA: Is dead? The faithful heart! Oh dear!
My husband is dead! I shall faint right here.
MARGARET: Oh my dear woman! Don't despair!   55
MEPHISTOPHELES: Let me relate the sad affair.
MARGARET: I should sooner never be a bride:
The grief would kill me if he died.
MEPHISTOPHELES: Joy needs woe, woe requires joy.
MARTHA: Tell me of the end of my sweet boy.   60
MEPHISTOPHELES: In Padua, in Italy,
He is buried in St. Anthony
In ground that has been duly blessed
For such cool, everlasting rest.
MARTHA: Surely, there is something more you bring.   65
MEPHISTOPHELES: One solemn and sincere request:
For his poor soul they should three hundred masses sing.
That's all, my purse is empty, though not of course my breast.
MARTHA: What? Not a gem? No work of art?
I am sure, deep in his bag the poorest wanderer   70
Keeps some remembrance that gives pleasure,
And sooner starves than yields this treasure.
MEPHISTOPHELES: Madam, don't doubt it breaks my heart.
And you may rest assured, he was no squanderer.
He knew his errors well, and he repented,   75
Though his ill fortune was the thing he most lamented.
MARGARET: That men are so unfortunate and poor!
I'll say some Requiems, and for his soul I'll pray.
MEPHISTOPHELES: You would deserve a marriage right away,
For you are charming, I am sure.   80
MARGARET: Oh no! I must wait to be wed.
MEPHISTOPHELES: If not a husband, have a lover instead.
It is one of heaven's greatest charms
To hold such a sweetheart in one's arms.
MARGARET: That is not the custom around here.   85
MEPHISTOPHELES: Custom or not, it's done, my dear.
MARTHA: Please tell me more!
MEPHISTOPHELES: I stood beside the bed he died on;
It was superior to manure,
Of rotted straw, and yet he died a Christian, pure,
And found that there was more on his unsettled score.   90
"I'm hateful," he cried; "wicked was my life,

As I forsook my trade and also left my wife.
To think of it now makes me die.
If only she forgave me even so!"
MARTHA: [*Weeping.*] The darling! I forgave him long ago.   95
MEPHISTOPHELES: "And yet, God knows, she was far worse than I."
MARTHA: He lied—alas, lied at the brink of death!
MEPHISTOPHELES: Surely, he made up things with dying breath,
　　If ever I saw death before.
　　"To pass the time, I could not look around," he said;   100
　　"First she got children, then they needed bread—
　　When I say bread, I mean much more—
　　And she never gave peace for me to eat my share."
MARTHA: Did he forget my love, my faithfulness and care
　　And how I slaved both day and night?   105
MEPHISTOPHELES: Oh no, he thought of that with all his might;
　　He said: "When we left Malta for another trip,
　　I prayed for wife and children fervently,
　　So heaven showed good grace to me.
　　And our boat soon caught a Turkish ship   110
　　That had the mighty sultan's gold on it.
　　Then fortitude got its reward,
　　And I myself was given, as was fit,
　　My share of the great sultan's hoard."
MARTHA: Oh how? Oh where? Might it be buried now?   115
MEPHISTOPHELES: The winds have scattered it, and who knows how?
　　A pretty girl in Naples, sweet and slim,
　　Cared for him when he was without a friend
　　And did so many deeds of love for him
　　That he could feel it till his blessed end.   120
MARTHA: The rogue! He robbed children and wife!
　　No misery, no lack of bread
　　Could keep him from his shameful life!
MEPHISTOPHELES: You see! For that he now is dead.
　　If I were in your place, I'd pause   125
　　To mourn him for a year, as meet,
　　And meanwhile I would try to find another sweet.
MARTHA: Oh God, the way my first one was
　　I'll hardly find another to be mine!
　　How could there be a little fool that's fonder?   130
　　Only he liked so very much to wander,
　　And foreign women, and foreign wine,
　　And that damned shooting of the dice.
MEPHISTOPHELES: Well, well! It could have been quite nice,
　　Had he been willing to ignore   135
　　As many faults in you, or more.
　　On such terms, I myself would woo
　　And willingly change rings with you.
MARTHA: The gentleman is pleased to jest.
MEPHISTOPHELES: [*Aside.*] I better get away from here;   140

She'd keep the Devil to his word, I fear.
[*To* GRETCHEN.] And how is your heart? Still at rest?
MARGARET: What do you mean, good sir?
MEPHISTOPHELES: [*Aside.*]   You good, innocent child!
[*Aloud.*] Good-by, fair ladies!
MARGARET: Good-by.
MARTHA: Oh, not so fast and wild!   145
I'd like to have it certified
That my sweetheart was buried, and when and where he died.
I always hate to see things done obliquely
And want to read his death in our weekly.
MEPHISTOPHELES: Yes, lady, what is testified by two   150
Is everywhere known to be true;
And I happen to have a splendid mate
Whom I'll take along to the magistrate.
I'll bring him here.
MARTHA: Indeed, please do!
MEPHISTOPHELES: And will this maiden be here, too?   155
A gallant lad! Has traveled much with me
And shows young ladies all courtesy.
MARGARET: I would have to blush before him, poor thing.[4]
MEPHISTOPHELES: Not even before a king!
MARTHA: Behind the house, in my garden, then,   160
Tonight we shall expect the gentlemen.

STREET

[FAUST. MEPHISTOPHELES.]
FAUST: How is it? Well? Can it be soon?
MEPHISTOPHELES: Oh bravo! Now you are on fire?
Soon Gretchen will still your desire.
At Martha's you may see her later this afternoon:
That woman seems expressly made   5
To ply the pimps' and gypsies' trade.
FAUST: Oh good!
MEPHISTOPHELES: But something's wanted from us, too.
FAUST: One good turn makes another due.
MEPHISTOPHELES: We merely have to go and testify   10
That the remains of her dear husband lie
In Padua where Anthony once sat.
FAUST: Now we shall have to go there. Now that was smart of you!
MEPHISTOPHELES: Sancta simplicitas![5] Who ever thought of that?
Just testify, and hang whether it's true!   15
FAUST: If you know nothing better, this plan has fallen through.
MEPHISTOPHELES: Oh, holy man! You are no less!
Is this the first time in your life that you
Have testified what is not true?
Of God and all the world, and every single part,   20

---

4. Referring to herself, not to Faust.   5. Holy simplicity (Latin).

Of man and all that stirs inside his head and heart
You gave your definitions with power and finesse.
With brazen cheek and haughty breath.
And if you stop to think, I guess,
You know as much of that, you must confess,   25
As you know now of Mr. Schwerdtlein's death.
FAUST: You are and you remain a sophist and a liar.
MEPHISTOPHELES: Yes, if one's knowledge were not just a little higher.
Tomorrow, won't you, pure as air,
Deceive poor Gretchen and declare   30
Your soul's profoundest love, and swear?
FAUST: With all my heart.
MEPHISTOPHELES: Good and fair!
Then faithfulness and love eternal
And the super-almighty urge supernal—
Will that come from your heart as well?   35
FAUST: Leave off! It will.—When, lost in feeling,
For this urge, for this surge
I seek a name, find none, and, reeling
All through the world with all my senses gasping,
At all the noblest words I'm grasping   40
And call this blaze in which I flame,
Infinite, eternal eternally—
Is that a game or devilish jugglery?
MEPHISTOPHELES: I am still right.
FAUST: Listen to me,
I beg of you, and don't wear out my lung: 45
Whoever would be right and only has a tongue,
Always will be.
Come on! I'm sick of prating, spare your voice,
For you are right because I have no choice.

GARDEN

[MARGARET on FAUST's arm, MARTHA with MEPHISTOPHELES, walking
up and down.]
MARGARET: I feel it well, good sir, you're only kind to me:
You condescend—and you abash.
It is the traveler's courtesy
To put up graciously with trash.
I know too well, my poor talk never can   5
Give pleasure to a traveled gentleman.
FAUST: One glance from you, one word gives far more pleasure
Than all the wisdom of this world. [He kisses her hand.]
MARGARET: Don't incommode yourself! How could you kiss it? You?
It is so ugly, is so rough.   10
But all the things that I have had to do!
For Mother I can't do enough.
[They pass.]

MARTHA: And you, sir, travel all the time, you say?

MEPHISTOPHELES: Alas, our trade and duty keeps us going!
Though when one leaves the tears may well be flowing, 15
One never is allowed to stay.

MARTHA: While it may do in younger years
To sweep around the world, feel free and suave,
There is the time when old age nears,
And then to creep alone, a bachelor, to one's grave. 20
That's something everybody fears.

MEPHISTOPHELES: With dread I see it far away.

MARTHA: Then, my dear sir, consider while you may.
[They pass.]

MARGARET: Yes, out of sight is out of mind.
You are polite, you can't deny, 25
And often you have friends and find
That they are cleverer than I.

FAUST: Oh dearest, trust me, what's called clever on this earth
Is often vain and rash rather than clever.

MARGARET: What?

FAUST: Oh, that the innocent and simple never 30
Appreciate themselves and their own worth!
That meekness and humility, supreme
Among the gifts of loving, lavish nature—

MARGARET: If you should think of me one moment only,
I shall have time enough to think of you and dream. 35

FAUST: Are you so often lonely?

MARGARET: Yes; while our household is quite small,
You see, I have to do it all.
We have no maid, so I must cook, and sweep, and knit.
And sew, and run early and late; 40
And mother is in all of it
So accurate!
Not that it's necessary; our need is not so great.
We could afford much more than many another:
My father left a tidy sum to mother, 45
A house and garden near the city gate.
But now my days are rather plain:
A soldier is my brother,
My little sister dead.
Sore was, while she was living, the troubled life I led; 50
But I would gladly go through all of it again:
She was so dear to me.

FAUST: An angel, if like you.

MARGARET: I brought her up, and she adored me, too.
She was born only after father's death;
Mother seemed near her dying breath, 55
As stricken as she then would lie,
Though she got well again quite slowly, by and by.
She was so sickly and so slight,

She could not nurse the little mite;
So I would tend her all alone,   60
With milk and water; she became my own.
Upon my arms and in my lap
She first grew friendly, tumbled, and grew up.
FAUST: You must have felt the purest happiness.
MARGARET: But also many hours of distress.   65
The baby's cradle stood at night
Beside my bed, and if she stirred I'd wake,
I slept so light.
Now I would have to feed her, now I'd take
Her into my bed, now I'd rise   70
And dandling pace the room to calm the baby's cries.
And I would wash before the sun would rise,
Fret in the market and over the kitchen flame,
Tomorrow as today, always the same.
One's spirits, sir, are not always the best,   75
But one can relish meals and relish rest.
[They pass.]
MARTHA: Poor woman has indeed a wretched fate:
A bachelor is not easy to convert.
MEPHISTOPHELES: For one like you the job is not too great;
You might convince me if you are alert.   80
MARTHA: Be frank, dear sir, so far you have not found?
Has not your heart in some way yet been bound?
MEPHISTOPHELES: A hearth one owns and a good wife, we're told,
Are worth as much as pearls and gold.
MARTHA: I mean, have you not ever had a passion?   85
MEPHISTOPHELES: I always was received in the most friendly fashion.
MARTHA: Would say: weren't you ever in earnest in your breast?
MEPHISTOPHELES: With women one should never presume to speak in
jest.
MARTHA: Oh, you don't understand.
MEPHISTOPHELES: I'm sorry I'm so blind!
But I do understand—that you are very kind.   90
[They pass.]
FAUST: Oh little angel, you did recognize
Me as I came into the garden?
MARGARET: Did you not notice? I cast down my eyes.
FAUST: My liberty you're then prepared to pardon?
What insolence presumed to say   95
As you left church the other day?
MARGARET: I was upset, I did not know such daring
And no one could have spoken ill of me.
I thought that something in my bearing
Must have seemed shameless and unmaidenly.   100
He seemed to have the sudden feeling
That this wench could be had without much dealing.
Let me confess, I didn't know that there

Were other feelings stirring in me, and they grew;
But I was angry with myself, I swear, 105
That I could not get angrier with you.
FAUST: Sweet darling!
MARGARET: Let me do this! [*She plucks a daisy and pulls out the
petals one by one.*]
FAUST: A nosegay? Or what shall it be?
MARGARET:
No, it is just a game.
FAUST: What?
MARGARET: Go, you will laugh at me. [*She pulls out pet-
als and murmurs.*]
FAUST: What do you murmur?
MARGARET: [*Half aloud.*] He loves me—loves me not.
FAUST: You gentle countenance of heaven! 110
MARGARET: [*Continues.*] Loves me—not—loves me—not—
[*Tearing out the last leaf, in utter joy.*]
He loves me.
FAUST: Yes, my child. Let this sweet flower's word
Be as a god's word to you. He loves you.
Do you know what this means? He loves you. [*He takes both her hands.*]
MARGARET: My skin creeps. 115
FAUST: Oh, shudder not! But let this glance,
And let this clasp of hands tell you
What is unspeakable:
To yield oneself entirely and feel
A rapture which must be eternal. 120
Eternal! For its end would be despair.
No, no end! No end!
[MARGARET *clasps his hands, frees herself, and runs away. He stands
for a moment, lost in thought; then he follows her.*]
MARTHA: [*Entering.*] The night draws near.
MEPHISTOPHELES: Yes, and we want to go.
MARTHA: I should ask you to tarry even so,
But this place simply is too bad: 125
It is as if nobody had
Work or labor
Except to spy all day long on his neighbor,
And one gets talked about, whatever life one leads.
And our couple?
MEPHISTOPHELES: Up that path I heard them whirr— 130
Frolicking butterflies.
MARTHA: He is taking to her.
MEPHISTOPHELES: And she to him. That's how the world proceeds.

A GARDEN BOWER

[MARGARET *leaps into it, hides behind the door, puts the tip of one
finger to her lips, and peeks through the crack.*]

MARGARET: He comes.
FAUST: [*Entering.*]   Oh rogue, you're teasing me.
  Now I see. [*He kisses her.*]
MARGARET: [*Seizing him and returning the kiss.*]
  Dearest man! I love you from my heart.
      [MEPHISTOPHELES *knocks.*]
FAUST: [*Stamping his foot.*]
  Who's there?
MEPHISTOPHELES:
          A friend.
FAUST: A beast!
MEPHISTOPHELES: The time has come to part.
MARTHA: [*Entering.*]
  Yes, it is late, good sir.
FAUST: May I not take you home?   5
MARGARET: My mother would—Farewell!
FAUST: Must I leave then?
  Farewell.
MARTHA: Adieu.
MARGARET: Come soon again!
      [FAUST *and* MEPHISTOPHELES *exeunt.*]
MARGARET: Dear God, the things he thought and said!
  How much goes on in a man's head!
  Abashed, I merely acquiesce   10
  And cannot answer, except Yes!
  I am a poor, dumb child and cannot see
  What such a man could find in me.
      [*Exit.*]

WOOD AND CAVE

FAUST: [*Alone.*] Exalted spirit, all you gave me, all
  That I have asked. And it was not in vain
  That amid flames you turned your face toward me.
  You gave me royal nature as my own dominion,
  Strength to experience her, enjoy her. Not   5
  The cold amazement of a visit only
  You granted me, but let me penetrate
  Into her heart as into a close friend's.
  You lead the hosts of all that is alive
  Before my eyes, teach me to know my brothers   10
  In quiet bushes and in air and water.
  And when the storm roars in the wood and creaks,
  The giant fir tree, falling, hits and smashes
  The neighbor branches and the neighbor trunks,
  And from its hollow thud the mountain thunders,   15
  Then you lead me to this safe cave and show
  Me to myself, and all the most profound
  And secret wonders of my breast are opened.

And when before my eyes the pure moon rises
And passes soothingly, there float to me 20
From rocky cliffs and out of dewy bushes
The silver shapes of a forgotten age,
And soften meditation's somber joy.
Alas, that man is granted nothing perfect
I now experience. With this happiness 25
Which brings me close and closer to the gods,
You gave me the companion whom I can
Forego no more, though with cold impudence
He makes me small in my own eyes and changes
Your gifts to nothing with a few words' breath. 30
He kindles in my breast a savage fire
And keeps me thirsting after that fair image.
Thus I reel from desire to enjoyment,
And in enjoyment languish for desire.
MEPHISTOPHELES: [*Enters.*] Have you not led this life quite long enough? 35
How can it keep amusing you?
It may be well for once to try such stuff
But then one turns to something new.
FAUST: I wish that you had more to do
And would not come to pester me. 40
MEPHISTOPHELES: All right. I gladly say adieu —
You should not say that seriously.
A chap like you, unpleasant, mad, and cross,
Would hardly be a serious loss.
All day long one can work and slave away. 45
And what he likes and what might cause dismay,
It simply isn't possible to say.
FAUST: That is indeed the proper tone!
He wants my thanks for being such a pest.
MEPHISTOPHELES: If I had left you wretch alone, 50
Would you then live with greater zest?
Was it not I that helped you to disown,
And partly cured, your feverish unrest
Yes, but[6] for me, the earthly zone
Would long be minus one poor guest. 55
And now, why must you sit like an old owl
In caves and rocky clefts, and scowl?
From soggy moss and dripping stones you lap your food
Just like a toad, and sit and brood.
A fair, sweet way to pass the time! 60
Still steeped in your doctoral slime!
FAUST: How this sojourn in the wilderness
Renews my vital force, you cannot guess.
And if you apprehended this,

6. Were it not.

You would be Devil enough, to envy me my bliss.   65
MEPHISTOPHELES: A supernatural delight!
To lie on mountains in the dew and night,
Embracing earth and sky in raptured reeling,
To swell into a god—in one's own feeling—
To probe earth's marrow with vague divination,   70
Sense in your breast the whole work of creation,
With haughty strength enjoy, I know not what,
Then overflow into all things with love so hot,
Gone is all earthly inhibition,
And then the noble intuition— [*With a gesture.*]   75
Of—need I say of what emission?
FAUST: Shame!
MEPHISTOPHELES:
          That does not meet with your acclaim;
You have the right to cry indignant: shame!
One may not tell chaste ears what, beyond doubt,
The chastest heart could never do without.   80
And, once for all, I don't grudge you the pleasure
Of little self-deceptions at your leisure;
But it can't last indefinitely.
Already you are spent again,
And soon you will be rent again,   85
By madness and anxiety.
Enough of that. Your darling is distraught,
Sits inside, glum and in despair,
She can't put you out of her mind and thought
And loves you more than she can bear.   90
At first your raging love was past control,
As brooks that overflow when filled with melted snow;
You poured it out into her soul,
But now your little brook is low.
Instead of posing in the wood,   95
It seems to me it might be good
If for her love our noble lord
Gave the poor monkey some reward.
Time seems to her intolerably long;
She stands at her window and sees the clouds in the sky   100
Drift over the city wall and go by.
Were I a little bird! thus goes her song
For days and half the night long.
Once she may be cheerful, most of the time sad,
Once she has spent her tears,   105
Then she is calm, it appears,
And always loves you like mad.
FAUST: Serpent! Snake!
MEPHISTOPHELES: [*Aside.*] If only I catch the rake!
FAUST: Damnable fiend! Get yourself hence,   110
And do not name the beautiful maid!

Let not the lust for her sweet limbs invade
And ravish once again my frenzied sense!
MEPHISTOPHELES: What do you mean? She thinks you've run away:
And it is half-true, I must say.   115
FAUST: I am near her, however far I be,
She'll never be forgotten and ignored;
Indeed, I am consumed with jealousy
That her lips touch the body of the Lord.[7]
MEPHISTOPHELES: I'm jealous of my friend when she exposes   120
The pair of twins that feed among the roses.[8]
FAUST: Begone, pander!
MEPHISTOPHELES: Fine! Your wrath amuses me.
The God who fashioned man and maid
Was quick to recognize the noblest trade,   125
And procured opportunity.
Go on! It is a woeful pain!
You're to embrace your love again,
Not sink into the tomb.
FAUST: What are the joys of heaven in her arms?   130
Let me embrace her, feel her charms—
Do I not always sense her doom?
Am I not fugitive? without a home?
Inhuman, without aim or rest,
As, like the cataract, from rock to rock I foam,   135
Raging with passion, toward the abyss?
And nearby, she—with childlike blunt desires
Inside her cottage on the Alpine leas,
And everything that she requires
Was in her own small world at ease.   140
And I, whom the gods hate and mock,
Was not satisfied
That I seized the rock
And smashed the mountainside.
Her—her peace I had to undermine.   145
You, hell, desired this sacrifice upon your shrine.
Help, Devil, shorten this time of dread.
What must be done, come let it be.
Let then her fate come shattering on my head,
And let her perish now with me.   150
MEPHISTOPHELES: How now it boils again and how you shout.
Go in and comfort her, you dunce.
Where such a little head sees no way out,
He thinks the end must come at once.
Long live who holds out undeterred!   155
At other times you have the Devil's airs.
In all the world there's nothing more absurd
Than is a Devil who despairs.

7. When the bread of Communion miraculously turns to the body of Christ.   8. Compare Song of
Solomon 4:5: "Thy two breasts are like two young roes that are twins, which feed among the lilies."

GRETCHEN'S ROOM

GRETCHEN: [*At the spinning wheel, alone.*]
My peace is gone,
My heart is sore;
I find it never
And nevermore.

Where him I not have   5
There is my grave.
This world is all
Turned into gall.

And my poor head
Is quite insane,   10
And my poor mind
Is rent with pain.

My peace is gone,
My heart is sore;
I find it never   15
And nevermore.

For him only I look
From my window seat,
For him only I go
Out into the street.   20

His lofty gait,
His noble guise,
The smile of his mouth,
The force of his eyes,

And his words' flow—   25
Enchanting bliss—
The touch of his hand,
And, oh, his kiss.

My peace is gone,
My heart is sore;   30
I find it never
And nevermore.

My bosom surges
For him alone,
Oh that I could clasp him   35
And hold him so,

And kiss him
To my heart's content,
Till in his kisses
I were spent.   40

MARTHA'S GARDEN

[MARGARET. FAUST.]

MARGARET: Promise me, Heinrich.[9]

FAUST: Whatever I can.

MARGARET: How is it with your religion, please admit—
You certainly are a very good man,
But I believe you don't think much of it.

FAUST: Leave that, my child. I love you, do not fear   5
And would give all for those whom I hold dear,
Would not rob anyone of church or creed.

MARGARET: That is not enough, it is faith we need.

FAUST: Do we?

MARGARET: Oh that I had some influence!
You don't respect the holy sacraments.   10

FAUST: I do respect them.

MARGARET: But without desire.
The mass and confession you do not require.
Do you believe in God?

FAUST: My darling who may say
I believe in God?
Ask priests and sages, their reply   15
Looks like sneers that mock and prod
The one who asked the question.

MARGARET: Then you deny him there?

FAUST: Do not mistake me, you who are so fair.
Him—who may name?
And who proclaim: 20
I believe in him?
Who may feel,
Who dare reveal
In words: I believe him not?
The All-Embracing,   25
The All-Sustaining,
Does he not embrace and sustain
You, me, himself?
Does not the heaven vault above?
Is the earth not firmly based down here?   30
And do not, friendly,
Eternal stars rise?
Do we not look into each other's eyes,
And all in you is surging
To your head and heart,   35
And weaves in timeless mystery,
Unseeable, yet seen, around you?
Then let it fill your heart entirely,
And when your rapture in this feeling is complete,

9. Faust. In the legend, Faust's name was generally Johann (John). Goethe changed it to Heinrich (Henry).

Call it then as you will, 40
Call it bliss! heart! love! God!
I do not have a name
For this. Feeling is all;
Names are but sound and smoke
Befogging heaven's blazes. 45
MARGARET: Those are very fair and noble phrases;
The priest says something, too, like what you spoke—
Only his words are not quite so—
FAUST: Wherever you go,
All hearts under the heavenly day 50
Say it, each in its own way;
Why not I in mine?
MARGARET: When one listens to you, one might incline
To let it pass—but I can't agree,
For you have no Christianity. 55
FAUST: Dear child!
MARGARET:　　　It has long been a grief to me
To see you in such company.
FAUST: Why?
MARGARET: The man that goes around with you
Seems hateful to me through and through: 60
In all my life there's not a thing
That gave my heart as sharp a sting
As his repulsive eyes.
FAUST: Sweet doll, don't fear him anywise.
MARGARET: His presence makes me feel quite ill. 65
I bear all other men good will;
But just as to see you I languish,
This man fills me with secret anguish;
He seems a knave one should not trust.
May God forgive me if I am unjust. 70
FAUST: There must be queer birds, too, you know.
MARGARET: But why live with them even so?
Whenever he comes in,
He always wears a mocking grin
And looks half threatening: 75
One sees, he has no sympathy for anything;
It is written on his very face
That he thinks love is a disgrace.
In your arm I feel good and free,
Warm and abandoned as can be; 80
Alas, my heart and feelings are choked when he comes, too.
FAUST: Oh, you foreboding angel, you.
MARGARET: It makes my heart so sore
That, when he only comes our way,
I feel I do not love you any more; 85
And where he is, I cannot pray.
It eats into my heart. Oh you,

Dear Heinrich, must feel that way, too.
FAUST: That is just your antipathy.
MARGARET: I must go.
FAUST: Will there never be 90
At your sweet bosom one hour of rest
When soul touches on soul and breast on breast?
MARGARET: Had I my own room when I sleep,
I should not bolt the door tonight;
But Mother's slumber is not deep, 95
And if she found us thus—oh fright,
Right then and there I should drop dead.
FAUST: My angel, if that's what you dread,
Here is a bottle. Merely shake
Three drops into her cup, 100
And she won't easily wake up.
MARGARET: What should I not do for your sake?
It will not harm her if one tries it?
FAUST: Dear, if it would, would I advise it?
MARGARET: When I but look at you, I thrill, 105
I don't know why, my dear, to do your will;
I have already done so much for you
That hardly anything seems left to do.
[*Exit. Enter* MEPHISTOPHELES.]
MEPHISTOPHELES: The monkey! Is she gone?
FAUST: You spied?
MEPHISTOPHELES: Are you surprised?
I listened and I understood 110
Our learned doctor just was catechized.
I hope that it may do you good.
The girls are quite concerned to be apprised
If one is pious and obeys tradition.
If yes, they trust they can rely on his submission. 115
FAUST: You monster will not see nor own
That this sweet soul, in loyalty,
Full of her own creed
Which alone,
She trusts, can bring salvation, lives in agony 120
To think her lover lost, however she may plead.
MEPHISTOPHELES: You supersensual, sensual wooer,
A maiden leads you by the nose.
FAUST: You freak of filth and fire! Evildoer!
MEPHISTOPHELES: And what a knowledge of physiognomy she shows. 125
She feels, she knows not what, whenever I'm about;
She finds a hidden meaning in my eyes:
I am a demon, beyond doubt,
Perhaps the Devil, that is her surmise.
Well, tonight—?
FAUST: What's that to you? 130
MEPHISTOPHELES: I have my pleasure in it, too.

AT THE WELL

[GRETCHEN *and* LIESCHEN *with jugs.*]

LIESCHEN: Of Barbara you haven't heard?

GRETCHEN: I rarely see people—no, not a word.

LIESCHEN: Well, Sibyl just told me in front of the school:
That girl has at last been made a fool.
That comes from having airs.

GRETCHEN: How so?

LIESCHEN: It stinks!   5
She is feeding two when she eats and drinks.

GRETCHEN: Oh!

LIESCHEN: At last she has got what was coming to her.
She stuck to that fellow like a burr.
That was some prancing,   10
In the village, and dancing,
She was always the first in line;
And he flirted with her over pastries and wine;
And she thought that she looked divine—
But had no honor, no thought of her name,   15
And took his presents without any shame.
The way they slobbered and carried on;
But now the little flower is gone.

GRETCHEN: Poor thing!

LIESCHEN: That you don't say!
When girls like us would be spinning away,   20
And mother kept us at home every night,
She was with her lover in sweet delight
On the bench by the door, in dark alleys they were,
And the time was never too long for her.
Now let her crouch and let her bend down   25
And do penance in a sinner's gown!

GRETCHEN: He will surely take her to be his wife.

LIESCHEN: He would be a fool! A handsome boy
Will elsewhere find more air and joy.
He's already gone.

GRETCHEN: That is not fair!   30

LIESCHEN: And if she gets him, let her beware:
Her veil the boys will throw to the floor,
And we shall strew chaff in front of her door.[1]

[*Exit.*]

GRETCHEN: [*Going home.*] How I once used to scold along
When some poor woman had done wrong.   35
How for another person's shame
I found not words enough of blame.
How black it seemed—I made it blacker still,
And yet not black enough to suit my will.

---

1. In Germany this treatment was reserved for young women who had sexual relations before marriage.

I blessed myself, would boast and grin —   40
And now myself am caught in sin.
Yet — everything that brought me here,
God, was so good, oh, was so dear.

CITY WALL

[*In a niche in the wall, an image of the Mater Dolorosa.*[2] *Ewers with
flowers in front of it.*]

GRETCHEN: [*Puts fresh flowers into the ewers.*]
    Incline,
    Mother of pain,
    Your face in grace to my despair.

    A sword in your heart,
    With pain rent apart,   5
    Up to your son's dread death you stare.

    On the Father your eyes,
    You send up sighs
    For your and your son's despair.

    Who knows   10
    My woes —
    Despair in every bone!

    How my heart is full of anguish,
    How I tremble, how I languish,
    Know but you, and you alone.   15

    Wherever I may go,
    What woe, what woe, what woe
    Is in my bosom aching!

    Scarcely alone am I,
    I cry, I cry, I cry;   20
    My heart in me is breaking.

    The pots in front of my window
    I watered with tears as the dew,
    When early in the morning
    I broke these flowers for you.   25

    When bright into my room
    The sun his first rays shed,
    I sat in utter gloom
    Already on my bed.

    Help! Rescue me from shame and death!   30
    Incline,
    Mother of pain,
    Your face in grace to my despair.

2. Sorrowful mother (Latin, literal trans.); that is, the Virgin Mary.

NIGHT

[*Street in front of* GRETCHEN'S *door.*]
VALENTINE: [*Soldier,* GRETCHEN'*s brother.*]
  When I would sit at a drinking bout
  Where all had much to brag about,
  And many fellows raised their voice
  To praise the maidens of their choice,
  Glass after glass was drained with toasting,   5
  I listened smugly to their boasting,
  My elbow propped up on the table,
  And sneered at fable after fable.
  I'd stroke my beard and smile and say,
  Holding my bumper in my hand: 10
  Each may be nice in her own way,
  But is there one in the whole land
  Like sister Gretchen to outdo her,
  Hear, hear! Clink! Clink! it went around;
  And some would cry: It's true, yes sir,   15
  There is no other girl like her!
  The braggarts sat without a sound.
  And *now*—I could tear out my hair
  And dash my brain out in despair!
  His nose turned up, a scamp can face me,   20
  With taunts and sneers he can disgrace me;
  And I should I sit, like one in debt,
  Each chance remark should make me sweat!
  I'd like to grab them all and maul them,
  But liars I could never call them.   25

  What's coming there? What sneaks in view?
  If I mistake not, there are two.
  If it is he, I'll spare him not,
  He shall not living leave this spot.
    [FAUST *and* MEPHISTOPHELES *enter.*]
FAUST: How from the window of that sacristy   30
  The light of the eternal lamp is glimmering,
  And weak and weaker sideward shimmering,
  As night engulfs it like the sea.
  My heart feels like this nightly street.
MEPHISTOPHELES: And I feel like a cat in heat,   35
  That creeps around a fire escape
  Pressing against the wall its shape.
  I feel quite virtuous, I confess,
  A little thievish lust, a little rammishness.
  Thus I feel spooking through each vein   40
  The wonderful Walpurgis Night.
  In two days it will come again,
  And waking then is pure delight.

FAUST: And will the treasure that gleams over there
 Rise in the meantime up into the air?   45
MEPHISTOPHELES: Quite soon you may enjoy the pleasure
 Of taking from the pot the treasure.
 The other day I took a squint
 And saw fine lion dollars in't.
FAUST: Not any jewelry, not a ring   50
 To adorn my beloved girl?
MEPHISTOPHELES: I did see something like a string,
 Or something like it, made of pearl.
FAUST: Oh, that is fine, for it's unpleasant
 To visit her without a present.   55
MEPHISTOPHELES: It should not cause you such distress
 When you have gratis such success.
 Now that the sky gleams with its starry throng,
 Prepare to hear a work of art:
 I shall sing her a moral song   60
 To take no chance we fool her heart.
 [*Sings to the cither.*[3]]
  It's scarcely day,
  Oh, Katie, say,
  Why do you stay
  Before your lover's door?   65
  Leave now, leave now!
  For in you'll go
  A maid, I know,
  Come out a maid no more.

  You ought to shun   70
  That kind of fun;
  Once it is done,
  Good night, you poor, poor thing.
  For your own sake
  You should not make   75
  Love to a rake
  Unless you have the ring.[4]
VALENTINE: [*Comes forward.*] Whom would you lure? God's element!
 Rat-catching piper! Oh, perdition!
 The Devil take your instrument!   80
 The Devil then take the musician!
MEPHISTOPHELES: The cither is all smashed. It is beyond repair.
VALENTINE: Now let's try splitting skulls. Beware!
MEPHISTOPHELES: [*To* FAUST.] Don't withdraw, doctor! Quick, don't
 tarry!
 Stick close to me, I'll lead the way.   85

---

3. Or zither, a stringed instrument.   4. Lines 63–78 are adapted by Goethe from Shakespeare's *Hamlet* IV.5.

Unsheathe your toothpick, don't delay;
Thrust out at him, and I shall parry.
VALENTINE: Then parry that!
MEPHISTOPHELES: Of course.
VALENTINE: And that.
MEPHISTOPHELES: All right.
VALENTINE: I think the Devil must be in this fight.
    What could that be? My hand is getting lame.   90
MEPHISTOPHELES: [To FAUST.] Thrust home!
VALENTINE: [Falls.] Oh God!
MEPHISTOPHELES: The rogue is tame.
    Now hurry hence, for we must disappear:
    A murderous clamor rises instantly,
    And while the police does not trouble me,   95
    The blood ban is a thing I fear.
MARTHA: [At a window.] Come out! Come out!
GRETCHEN: [At a window.] Quick! Bring a light.
MARTHA: [As above.] They swear and scuffle, yell and fight.
PEOPLE: There is one dead already, see.   100
MARTHA: [Coming out.] The murderers—where did they run?
GRETCHEN: [Coming out.] Who lies there?
PEOPLE: Your own mother's son.
GRETCHEN: Almighty God! What misery!
VALENTINE: I'm dying. That is quickly said,
    And still more quickly done.   105
    Why do you women wail in dread?
    Come here, listen to me.
        [All gather around him.]
    My Gretchen, you are still quite green,
    Not nearly smart enough or keen,
    You do not do things right.   110
    In confidence, I should say more:
    Since after all you are a whore,
    Be one with all your might.
GRETCHEN: My brother! God! What frightful shame!
VALENTINE: Leave the Lord God out of this game.   115
    What has been done, alas, is done,
    And as it must, it now will run.
    You started secretly with one,
    Soon more will come to join the fun,
    And once a dozen lays you down,   120
You might as well invite the town.

    When shame is born and first appears,
    It is an underhand delight,
    And one drags the veil of night
    Over her head and ears;   125
    One is tempted to put her away.
    But as she grows, she gets more bold,

Walks naked even in the day,
Though hardly fairer to behold.
The more repulsive grows her sight, 130
The more she seeks day's brilliant light.

The time I even now discern
When honest citizens will turn,
Harlot, away from you and freeze
As from a corpse that breeds disease. 135
Your heart will flinch, your heart will falter
When they will look you in the face.
You'll wear no gold, you'll wear no lace,
Nor in the church come near the altar.
You will no longer show your skill 140
At dances, donning bow and frill,
But in dark corners on the side
With beggars and cripples you'll seek to hide;
And even if God should at last forgive,
Be cursed as long as you may live! 145
MARTHA: Ask God to show your own soul grace.
Don't make it with blasphemies still more base.
VALENTINE: That I could lay my hands on you,
You shriveled, pimping bugaboo,
Then, I hope, I might truly win 150
Forgiveness for my every sin.
GRETCHEN: My brother! This is agony!
VALENTINE: I tell you, do not bawl at me.
When you threw honor overboard,
You pierced my heart more than the sword. 155
Now I shall cross death's sleeping span
To God, a soldier and an honest man.
[Dies.]

CATHEDRAL

[Service, Organ, and Singing. GRETCHEN among many people. EVIL
SPIRIT behind GRETCHEN.]
EVIL SPIRIT: How different you felt, Gretchen,
When in innocence
You came before this altar;
And from the well-worn little book
You prattled prayers, 5
Half childish games,
Half God in your heart!
Gretchen!
Where are your thoughts?
And in your heart 10
What misdeed?
Do you pray for your mother's soul that went
Because of you from sleep to lasting, lasting pain?

Upon your threshold, whose blood?
And underneath your heart,   15
Does it not stir and swell,
Frightened and frightening you
With its foreboding presence?
GRETCHEN: Oh! Oh!
That I were rid of all the thoughts   20
Which waver in me to and fro
Against me!
CHOIR: Dies irae, dies illa
     Solvet saeclum in favilla.[5]
[*Sound of the organ.*]
EVIL SPIRIT: Wrath grips you.   25
The great trumpet sounds.
The graves are quaking.
And your heart,
Resurrected
From ashen calm   30
To flaming tortures,
Flares up.
GRETCHEN: Would I were far!
I feel as if the organ had
Taken my breath,   35
As if the song
Dissolved my heart!
CHOIR: Judex ergo cum sedebit,
     Quidquid latet adparebit,
     Nil inultum remanebit.[6]   40
GRETCHEN: I feel so close.
The stony pillars
Imprison me.
The vault above
Presses on me.—Air!   45
EVIL SPIRIT: Hide yourself. Sin and shame
Do not stay hidden.
Air? Light?
Woe unto you!
CHOIR: Quid sum miser tunc dicturus?   50
     Quem patronum rogaturus?
     Cum vix justus sit securus.[7]
EVIL SPIRIT: The transfigured turn
Their countenance from you.
To hold out their hands to you   55
Makes the pure shudder.
Woe!

---

5. Day of wrath, that day that dissolves the world into ashes (Latin). This is a famous 13th-century hymn by Thomas Celano.   6. When the judge shall be seated, what is hidden shall appear, nothing shall remain unavenged (Latin).   7. What shall I say in my wretchedness? To whom shall I appeal when scarcely the righteous man is safe? (Latin).

CHOIR: *Quid sum miser tunc dicturus?*
GRETCHEN: Neighbor! Your smelling salts! [*She faints.*]

WALPURGIS NIGHT

[*Harz Mountains. Region of Schierke and Elend.* FAUST *and* MEPHI-
STOPHELES.]
MEPHISTOPHELES: How would you like a broomstick now to fly?
I wish I had a billy goat that's tough.
For on this road we still have to climb high.
FAUST: As long as I feel fresh, and while my legs are spry,
This knotted staff seems good enough.   5
Why should we shun each stumbling block?
To creep first through the valleys' lovely maze,
And then to scale this wall of rock
From which the torrent foams in silver haze—
There is the zest that spices our ways.   10
Around the birches weaves the spring,
Even the fir tree feels its spell:
Should it not stir in our limbs as well?
MEPHISTOPHELES: Of all that I don't feel a thing.
In me the winter is still brisk,   15
I wish my path were graced with frost and snow.
How wretchedly the moon's imperfect disk
Arises now with its red, tardy glow,
And is so dim that one could bump one's head
At every step against a rock or tree!   20
Let's use a will-o'-the-wisp[8] instead!
I see one there that burns quite merrily.
Hello there! Would you come and join us, friend?
Why blaze away to no good end?
Please be so kind and show us up the hill!   25
WILL-O'-THE-WISP: I hope my deep respect will help me force
My generally flighty will;
For zigzag is the rule in our course.
MEPHISTOPHELES: Hear! Hear! It's man you like to imitate!
Now, in the Devil's name, go straight—   30
Or I shall blow your flickering life span out.
WILL-O'-THE-WISP: You are the master of the house, no doubt,
And I shall try to serve you nicely.
But don't forget, the mountain is magic-mad today,
And if Will-o'-the-wisp must guide you on your way,   35
You must not take things too precisely.
FAUST, MEPHISTOPHELES, *and* WILL-O'-THE-WISP: [*In alternating song.*]
In the sphere of dream and spell
We have entered now indeed.
Have some pride and guide us well

---

8. *Ignis fatuus,* a wavering light formed by marsh gas. In German folklore it was thought to lead travelers
to their destruction.

That we get ahead with speed   40
In the vast deserted spaces!

See the trees behind the trees,
See how swiftly they change places,
And the cliffs that bow with ease,
Craggy noses, long and short,   45
How they snore and how they snort!

Through the stones and through the leas
Tumble brooks of every sort.
Is it splash or melodies?
Is it love that wails and prays,   50
Voices of those heavenly days?
What we hope and what we love!
Echoes and dim memories
Of forgotten times come back.

Oo-hoo! Shoo-hoo! Thus they squawk,   55
Screech owl, plover, and the hawk;
Did they all stay up above?
Are those salamanders crawling?
Bellies bloated, long legs sprawling!
And the roots, as serpents, coil   60
From the rocks through sandy soil,
With their eerie bonds would scare us,
Block our path and then ensnare us;
Hungry as a starving leech,
Their strong polyp's tendrils reach   65
For the wanderer. And in swarms
Mice of myriad hues and forms
Storm through moss and heath and lea.
And a host of fireflies
Throng about and improvise   70
The most maddening company.

Tell me: do we now stand still,
Or do we go up the hill?
Everything now seems to mill,
Rocks and trees and faces blend,   75
Will-o'-the-wisps grow and extend
And inflate themselves at will.
MEPHISTOPHELES: Grip my coat and hold on tight!
Here is such a central height
Where one sees, and it amazes,   80
In the mountain, Mammon's blazes.[9]
FAUST: How queer glimmers a dawnlike sheen
Faintly beneath this precipice,

---

9. Mammon is imagined as leading a group of fallen angels in digging out gold and gems from the
ground of Hell, presumably for Satan's palace, as described in Milton's *Paradise Lost* I.678ff.

And plays into the dark ravine
Of the near bottomless abyss.   85
Here mists arise, there vapors spread,
And here it gleams deep in the mountain,
Then creeps along, a tender thread,
And gushes up, a glistening fountain.

Here it is winding in a tangle,   90
With myriad veins the gorges blaze,
And here in this congested angle
A single stream shines through the haze.
There sparks are flying at our right,
As plentiful as golden sand.   95
But look! In its entire height
The rock becomes a firebrand.
MEPHISTOPHELES: Sir Mammon never spares the light
To hold the feast in proper fashion.
How lucky that you saw this sight!   100
I hear the guests approach in wanton passion.
FAUST: The tempests lash the air and rave,
And with gigantic blows they hit my shoulders.
MEPHISTOPHELES: You have to clutch the ribs of those big hoary boulders,
Or they will hurtle you to that abysmal grave.   105
A fog blinds the night with its hood.
Do you hear the crashes in the wood?
Frightened, the owls are scattered.
Hear how the pillars
Of ever green castles are shattered.   110
Quaking and breaking of branches!
The trunks' overpowering groaning!
The roots' creaking and moaning!
In a frightfully tangled fall
They crash over each other, one and all,   115
And through the ruin-covered abysses
The frenzied air howls and hisses.
Do you hear voices up high?
In the distance and nearby?
The whole mountain is afire   120
With a furious magic choir.
WITCHES' CHORUS: The witches ride to Blocksberg's top,
The stubble is yellow, and green the crop.
They gather on the mountainside,
Sir Urian[1] comes to preside.   125
We are riding over crag and brink,
The witches fart, the billy goats stink.
VOICE: Old Baubo[2] comes alone right now,
She is riding on a mother sow.

1. A name for the Devil.   2. In Greek mythology, the nurse of Demeter, noted for her obscenity and bestiality.

A hundred fires in a row, my friend!
They dance, they chat, they cook, they drink, they court;
Now you just tell me where there's better sport!   225
FAUST: When you will introduce us at this revel,
    Will you appear a sorcerer or devil?
MEPHISTOPHELES: I generally travel, without showing my station,
    But on a gala day one shows one's decoration.
    I have no garter[3] I could show,   230
    But here the cloven foot is honored, as you know.
    Do you perceive that snail? It comes, though it seems stiff;
    For with its eager, groping face
    It knows me with a single whiff.
    Though I'd conceal myself, they'd know me in this place.   235
    Come on! From flame to flame we'll make our tour,
    I am the go-between, and you the wooer.
        [To some who sit around dying embers.]
    Old gentlemen, why tarry outside? Enter!
    I'd praise you if I found you in the center,
    Engulfed by youthful waves and foam;   240
    You are alone enough when you are home.
GENERAL: Who ever thought nations were true,
    Though you have served them with your hands and tongue;
    For people will, as women do,
    Reserve their greatest favors for the young.   245
STATESMAN: Now they are far from what is sage;
    The old ones should be kept in awe;
    For, truly, when our word was law,
    Then was indeed the golden age.
PARVENU: We, too, had surely ample wits,   250
    And often did things that we shouldn't;
    But now things are reversed and go to bits,
    Just when we changed our mind and wished they wouldn't.
AUTHOR: Today, who even looks at any book
    That makes some sense and is mature?   255
    And our younger generation—look,
    You never saw one that was so cocksure.
MEPHISTOPHELES: [Who suddenly appears very old.]
    I think the Judgment Day must soon draw nigh,
    For this is the last time I can attend this shrine;
    And as my little cask runs dry,   260
    The world is certain to decline.
HUCKSTER-WITCH: Please, gentlemen, don't pass like that!
    Don't miss this opportunity!
    Look at my goods attentively:
    There is a lot to marvel at.   265
    And my shop has a special charm—
    You will not find its peer on earth:

---

3. That is, he has no decoration of nobility, such as the Order of the Garter.

All that I sell has once done harm
To man and world and what has worth.
There is no dagger here which has not gored;   270
No golden cup from which, to end a youthful life,
A fatal poison was not poured;
No gems that did not help to win another's wife;
No sword but broke the peace with sly attack,
By stabbing, for example, a rival in the back.   275
MEPHISTOPHELES: Dear cousin, that's no good in times like these!
What's done is done; what's done is trite.
You better switch to novelties,
For novelties alone excite.
FAUST: I must not lose my head, I swear;   280
For this is what I call a fair.
MEPHISTOPHELES: This eddy whirls to get above,
And you are shoved, though you may think you shove.
FAUST: And who is that?
MEPHISTOPHELES: That little madam?
That's Lilith.[4]
FAUST: Lilith?
MEPHISTOPHELES: The first wife of Adam.   285
Watch out and shun her captivating tresses:
She likes to use her never-equaled hair
To lure a youth into her luscious lair,
And he won't lightly leave her lewd caresses.
FAUST: There two sit, one is young, one old;   290
They certainly have jumped and trolled!
MEPHISTOPHELES: They did not come here for a rest.
There is another dance. Come, let us do our best.
FAUST: [Dancing with the young one.]
A pretty dream once came to me
In which I saw an apple tree;   295
Two pretty apples gleamed on it,
They lured me, and I climbed a bit.
THE FAIR ONE: You find the little apples nice
Since first they grew in Paradise.
And I am happy telling you   300
That they grow in my garden, too.
MEPHISTOPHELES: [With the old one.]
A wanton dream once came to me
In which I saw a cloven tree.
It had the most tremendous hole;
Though it was big, it pleased my soul.   305
THE OLD ONE: I greet you with profound delight,
My gentle, cloven-footed knight!

---

4. According to rabbinical legend, Adam's first wife; the *female* mentioned in Genesis 1:27: "So God created man in his own image, in the image of God created he him; male and female created he them." After Eve was created, Lilith became a ghost who seduced men and inflicted evil on children.

Provide the proper grafting-twig,
If you don't mind the hole so big.
PROKTOPHANTASMIST:[5] Damnable folk! How dare you make such fuss!   310
Have we not often proved to you
That tales of walking ghosts cannot be true?
And now you dance just like the rest of us!
THE FAIR ONE: [*Dancing.*] What does he want at our fair?
FAUST: [*Dancing.*] Oh, he! You find him everywhere.   315
What others dance, he must assess;
No step has really occurred, unless
His chatter has been duly said.
And what annoys him most, is when we get ahead.
If you would turn in circles, in endless repetition,   320
As he does all the time in his old mill,
Perhaps he would not take it ill,
Especially if you would first get his permission.
PROKTOPHANTASMIST: You still are there! Oh no! That's without precedent.
Please go! Have we not brought enlightenment?   325
By our rules these devils are not daunted;
We are so smart, but Tegel[6] is still haunted.
To sweep illusion out, my energies were spent,
But things never get clean; that's without precedent.
THE FAIR ONE: Why don't you stop annoying us and quit!   330
PROKTOPHANTASMIST: I tell you spirits to your face,
The spirit's despotism's a disgrace:
My spirit can't make rules for it.
     [*The dancing goes on.*]
Today there's nothing I can do;
But traveling is always fun,   335
And I still hope, before my final step is done,
I'll ban the devils, and the poets, too.
MEPHISTOPHELES: He'll sit down in a puddle and unbend:
That is how his condition is improved;
For when the leeches prosper on his fat rear end,[7]   340
The spirits and his spirit are removed.
     [*To* FAUST, *who has left the dance.*]
Why did you let that pretty woman go
Who sang so nicely while you danced?
FAUST: She sang, and suddenly there pranced
Out of her mouth a little mouse, all red.   345
MEPHISTOPHELES: That is a trifle and no cause for dread!
Who cares? At least it was not gray.
Why bother on this glorious lovers' day?
FAUST: Then I saw—

---

5. A German coinage meaning "Rump-ghostler." The figure caricatures Friedrich Nicolai (1733–1811), who opposed modern movements in German thought and literature and had parodied Goethe's *The Sorrows of Young Werther* (1774).   6. A town near Berlin, where ghosts had been reported.   7. Nicolai claimed that he had been bothered by ghosts but had repelled them by applying leeches to his rump.

MEPHISTOPHELES: What?
FAUST: Mephisto, do you see
That pale, beautiful child, alone there on the heather?   350
She moves slowly but steadily,
She seems to walk with her feet chained together.
I must confess that she, forbid,
Looks much as my good Gretchen did.
MEPHISTOPHELES: That does nobody good; leave it alone!   355
It is a magic image, a lifeless apparition.
Encounters are fraught with perdition;
Its icy stare turns human blood to stone
In truth, it almost petrifies;
You know the story of Medusa's[8] eyes.   360
FAUST: Those are the eyes of one that's dead I see,
No loving hand closed them to rest.
That is the breast that Gretchen offered me,
And that is the sweet body I possessed.
MEPHISTOPHELES: That is just sorcery; you're easily deceived!   365
All think she is their sweetheart and are grieved.
FAUST: What rapture! Oh, what agony!
I cannot leave her, cannot flee.
How strange, a narrow ruby band should deck,
The sole adornment, her sweet neck,   370
No wider than a knife's thin blade.
MEPHISTOPHELES: I see it, too; it is quite so.
Her head under her arm she can parade,
Since Perseus lopped it off, you know. —
Illusion holds you captive still.   375
Come, let us climb that little hill,
The Prater's[9] not so full of glee;
And if they're not bewitching me,
There is a theatre I see.
What will it be?
SERVIBILIS: They'll resume instantly.   380
We'll have the seventh play, a brand-new hit;
We do not think, so many are exacting.
An amateur has written it,
And amateurs do all the acting.
Forgive, good sirs, if now I leave you;   385
It amateurs me to draw up the curtain.
MEPHISTOPHELES: When it's on Blocksberg I perceive you,
I'm glad; for that's where you belong for certain.

---

8. The Gorgon with hair of serpents whose glance turned people to stone.   9. A famous park in Vienna.

WALPURGIS NIGHT'S DREAM
OR THE GOLDEN WEDDING OF OBERON AND TITANIA

Intermezzo[1]

STAGE MANAGER: This time we can keep quite still,
 Mieding's[2] progeny;
 Misty vale and hoary hill,
 That's our scenery.

HERALD: To make a golden wedding day   5
 Takes fifty years to the letter;
 But when their quarrels pass away,
 That gold I like much better.

OBERON: If you spirits can be seen,
 Show yourselves tonight;   10
 Fairy king and fairy queen
 Now will reunite.

PUCK: Puck is coming, turns about,
 And drags his feet to dance;
 Hundreds come behind and shout   15
 And join with him and prance.

ARIEL:[3] Ariel stirs up a song,
 A heavenly pure air;
 Many gargoyles come along,
 And many who are fair.   20

OBERON: You would get along, dear couple?
 Learn from us the art;
 If you want to keep love supple,
 You only have to part.

TITANIA: He is sulky, sullen she,   25
 Grab them, upon my soul;
 Take her to the Southern Sea,
 And him up to the pole.

ORCHESTRA TUTTI: [*Fortissimo.*] Snout of Fly, Mosquito Nose,
 With family additions,   30
 Frog O'Leaves and Crick't O'Grass,
 Those are the musicians.

SOLO: Now the bagpipe's joining in,
 A soap bubble it blows;
 Hear the snicker-snacking din   35
 Come through his blunted nose.

SPIRIT IN PROCESS OF FORMATION: Spider feet, belly of toad,
 And little wings, he'll grow 'em;
 There is no animal like that,
 But it's a little poem.   40

A LITTLE COUPLE: Mighty leaps and nimble feet,
 Through honey scent up high;

---

1. Brief interlude. Oberon and Titania are the king and queen of the fairies. 2. Johann Martin
Mieding (died 1782), a master carpenter and scene builder in the Weimar theater. 3. A helpful
sprite, unlike Puck, who is a mischievous spirit.

While you bounce enough, my sweet,
Still you cannot fly.
INQUISITIVE TRAVELER: Is that not mummery right there?   45
Can that be what I see?
Oberon who is so fair
Amid this company!
ORTHODOX: No claws or tail or satyr's fleece!
And yet you cannot cavil: 50
Just like the gods of ancient Greece,
He, too, must be a devil.
NORDIC ARTIST: What I do in the local clime,
Are sketches of this tourney;
But I prepare, while it is time,   55
For my Italian journey.
PURIST: Bad luck brought me to these regions:
They could not be much louder;
And in the bawdy witches' legions
Two only have used powder.   60
YOUNG WITCH: White powder, just like dresses, serves
Old hags who are out of luck;
I want to show my luscious curves,
Ride naked on my buck.
MATRON: Our manners, dear, are far too neat   65
To argue and to scold;
I only hope that young and sweet,
Just as you are, you mold.
CONDUCTOR: Snout of Fly, Mosquito Nose,
Leave off the naked sweet;   70
Frog O'Leaves and Crick't O'Grass
Get back into the beat!
WEATHERCOCK: [*To one side.*] The most exquisite company!
Each girl should be a bride;
The bachelors, grooms; for one can see   75
How well they are allied.
WEATHERCOCK: [*To the other side.*] The earth should open up and gape
To swallow this young revel,
Or I will make a swift escape
To hell to see the Devil.   80
XENIEN:[4] We appear as insects here,
Each with a little stinger,
That we may fittingly revere
Satan, our sire and singer.
HENNINGS:[5] Look at their thronging legions play,   85
Naïve, with little art;
The next thing they will dare to say
Is that they're good at heart.

4. Literally, polemical verses written by Goethe and Friedrich von Schiller (1739–1805). The characters here are versions of Goethe himself.   5. August Adolf von Hennings (1746–1826), publisher of a journal called *Genius of the Age* that had attacked Schiller.

MUSAGET:[6] To dwell among the witches' folk
   Seems quite a lot of fun;   90
   They are the ones I should invoke,
   Not Muses, as I've done.
CI-DEVANT GENIUS OF THE AGE:[7]
   Choose your friends well and you will zoom,
   Join in and do not pass us!
   Blocksberg has almost as much room   95
   As Germany's Parnassus.[8]
INQUISITIVE TRAVELER: Say, who is that haughty man
   Who walks as if he sits?
   He sniffs and snuffles as best he can:
   "He smells out Jesuits."   100
CRANE: I like to fish where it is clear,
   Also in muddy brew;
   That's why the pious man is here
   To mix with devils, too.
CHILD OF THE WORLD: The pious need no fancy prop,   105
   All vehicles seem sound:
   Even up here on Blocksberg's top
   Conventicles abound.
DANCERS: It seems, another choir succeeds,
   I hear the drums resuming.   110
   "That dull sound comes out of the reeds,
   It is the bitterns' booming."
BALLET MASTER: How each picks up his legs and toddles,
   And comes by hook or crook!
   The stooped one jumps, the plump one waddles: 115
   They don't know how they look!
FIDDLER: They hate each other, wretched rabble,
   And each would kill the choir;
   They're harmonized by bagpipe babble,
   As beasts by Orpheus' lyre.[9]   120
DOGMATIST: I am undaunted and resist
   Both skeptic and critique;
   The Devil simply must exist,
   Else *what* would he be? Speak!
IDEALIST: Imagination is in me   125
   Today far too despotic;
   If I am everything I see,
   Then I must be idiotic.
REALIST: The spirits' element is vexing,
   I wish it weren't there;   130
   I never saw what's so perplexing,
   It drives me to despair.

---

6. The title of a collection of Hennings's poetry.   7. That is, "Former Genius of the Age"; probably alludes to the journal's change of title in 1800 to *Genius of the 19th Century*.   8. A mountain sacred to Apollo and the muses; hence figuratively the locale of poetic excellence.   9. In Greek mythology, Orpheus's music was said to have the power to quiet wild animals.

SUPERNATURALIST: I am delighted by this whir,
    And glad that they persist;
    For from the devils I infer,   135
    Good spirits, too, exist.
SKEPTIC: They follow little flames about,
    And think they're near the treasure;
    Devil alliterates with doubt
    So I am here with pleasure.   140
CONDUCTOR: Snout of Fly, Mosquito Nose,
    Damnable amateurs!
    Frog O'Leaves and Crick't O'Grass
    You are musicians, sirs!
ADEPTS: Sansouci,[1] that is the name   145
    Of our whole caboodle;
    Walking meets with ill acclaim,
    So we move on our noodle.
NE'ER-DO-WELLS: We used to be good hangers-on
    And sponged good wine and meat;   150
    We danced till our shoes were gone,
    And now walk on bare feet.
WILL-O'-THE-WISPS: We come out of the swamps where we
    Were born without a penny;
    But now we join the revelry,   155
    As elegant as any.
SHOOTING STAR: I shot down from starry height
    With brilliant, fiery charm;
    But I lie in the grass tonight:
    Who'll proffer me his arm?   160
MASSIVE MOB: All around, give way! Give way!
    Trample down the grass!
    Spirits come, and sometimes they
    Form a heavy mass.
PUCK: Please don't walk like elephants,   165
    And do not be so rough;
    Let no one be as plump as Puck,
    For he is plump enough.
ARIEL: If nature gave with lavish grace,
    Or Spirit, wings and will,   170
    Follow in my airy trace
    Up to the roses' hill!
ORCHESTRA: [*Pianissimo.*] Floating clouds and wreaths of fog
    Dawn has quickly banished;
    Breeze in leaves, wind in the bog,   175
    And everything has vanished.

---

1. Without care or unhappiness (French).

DISMAL DAY

[*Field.* FAUST. MEPHISTOPHELES.]

FAUST: In misery! Despairing! Long lost wretchedly on the earth, and now imprisoned! As a felon locked up in a dungeon with horrible torments, the fair ill-fated creature! It's come to that! To that!— Treacherous, despicable Spirit—and that you have kept from me!—Keep standing there, stand! Roll your devilish eyes wrathfully   5 in your face! Stand and defy me with your intolerable presence! Imprisoned! In irreparable misery! Handed over to evil spirits and judging, unfeeling mankind! And meanwhile you soothe me with insipid diversions; hide her growing grief from me, and let her perish helplessly!   10

MEPHISTOPHELES: She's not the first one.

FAUST: Dog! Abominable monster!—Change him, oh infinite spirit! Change back this worm into his dogshape, as he used to amuse himself in the night when he trotted along before me, rolled in front of the feet of the harmless wanderer and, when he stumbled, clung   15 to his shoulders. Change him again to his favorite form that he may crawl on his belly in the sand before me and I may trample on him with my feet, the caitiff!—Not the first one!—Grief! Grief! past what a human soul can grasp, that more than one creature has sunk into the depth of this misery, that the first one did not enough for   20 the guilt of all the others, writhing in the agony of death before the eyes of the everforgiving one! The misery of this one woman surges through my heart and marrow, and you grin imperturbed over the fate of thousands!

MEPHISTOPHELES: Now we're once again at our wit's end where your   25 human minds snap. Why do you seek fellowship with us if you can't go through with it? You would fly, but get dizzy? Did we impose on you, or you on us?

FAUST: Don't bare your greedy teeth at me like that! It sickens me!— Great, magnificent spirit that deigned to appear to me, that know   30 my heart and soul—why forge me to this monster who gorges himself on harm, and on corruption—feasts.

MEPHISTOPHELES: Have you finished?

FAUST: Save her! or woe unto you! The most hideous curse upon you for millenniums!   35

MEPHISTOPHELES: I cannot loosen the avenger's bonds, nor open his bolts.—Save her!—Who was it that plunged her into ruin? I or you? [FAUST *looks around furiously.*] Are you reaching for thunder? Well that it was not given to you wretched mortals! Shattering those who answer innocently, is the tyrant's way of easing his embarrassment.   40

FAUST: Take me there! She shall be freed!

MEPHISTOPHELES: And the dangers you risk? Know that blood-guilt from your hand still lies on the town. Over the slain man's site avenging spirits hover, waiting for the returning murderer.

FAUST: That, too, from you? A world's murder and death upon you,   45 monster! Guide me to her, I say, and free her!

MEPHISTOPHELES: I shall guide you; hear what I can do. Do I have all
the power in the heaven and on the earth? I shall make the jailer's
senses foggy, and you may get the keys and lead her out with
human hands. I shall stand guard, magic horses shall be prepared,   50
and I shall carry you away. That I can do.
FAUST: Up and away!

NIGHT, OPEN FIELD

[FAUST and MEPHISTOPHELES, *storming along on black horses.*]
FAUST: What are they weaving around the Ravenstone?
MEPHISTOPHELES: I do not know what they do and brew.
FAUST: Floating to, floating fro, bowing and bending.
MEPHISTOPHELES: A witches' guild.
FAUST: They strew and dedicate.   5
MEPHISTOPHELES: Go by! Go by!

DUNGEON

FAUST: [*With a bunch of keys and a lamp before a small iron gate.*]
A long unwonted shudder grips,
Mankind's entire grief grips me.
She's here, behind this wall that drips,
And all her crime was a fond fantasy.
You hesitate to go in?   5
You dread to see her again?
On! Your wavering waves on death's decree. [*He seizes the lock.*]
[*Song from within.*]
GRETCHEN: My mother, the whore,
Who has murdered me—
My father, the rogue,   10
Who has eaten me—
My little sister alone
Picked up every bone,
In a cool place she put them away;
Into a fair bird I now have grown;   15
Fly away, fly away!
FAUST: [*Unlocking.*] She does not dream how her lover at the door
Hears the clanking chains and the rustling straw. [*Enters.*]
MARGARET: [*Hiding on her pallet.*] Oh! Oh! They come. Death's bitter-
ness!
FAUST: [*Softly.*] Still! Still! I come to set you free.   20
MARGARET: [*Groveling toward his feet.*] If you are human, pity my distress.
FAUST: You'll awaken the guards. Speak quietly.
[*He seizes the chains to unlock them.*]
MARGARET: [*On her knees.*] Who, hangman, could give
You over me this might?
You come for me in the middle of the night.   25
Have pity on me, let me live!
Is it not time when the morning chimes have rung?

[*She gets up.*]
I am still so young, so very young.
And must already die.
I was beautiful, too, and that was why.   30
Near was the friend, now he is away.
Torn lies the wreath, the flowers decay.
Do not grip me so brutally. What shall I do?
Spare me. What have I done to you?
Let me not in vain implore.   35
After all, I have never seen you before.

FAUST: After such grief, can I live any more?

MARGARET: Now I am entirely in your might.
Only let me nurse the baby again.
I fondled it all through the night;   40
They took it from me to give me pain,
And now they say I put it away.
And I shall never again be gay.
They sing songs about me. The people are wicked.
An ancient fairy tale ends that way,   45
Who made them pick it?

FAUST: [*Casts himself down.*] One loving you lies at your feet
To end your bondage. Listen, sweet!

MARGARET: [*Casts herself down beside him.*]
Ah, let us kneel, send to the saints our prayers!
See, underneath these stairs,   50
Underneath the sill
There seethes hell.
The Devil
Makes a thundering noise
With his angry revel.   55

FAUST: [*Loud.*] Gretchen! Gretchen!

MARGARET: [*Attentively.*] That was my lover's voice!
[*She jumps up. The chains drop off.*]
Where is he? I heard him call. I am free.
No one shall hinder me.
To his neck I shall fly,   60
On his bosom lie.
He called Gretchen. He stood on the sill.
Amid the wailing and howling of hell,
Through the angry and devilish jeers
The sweet and loving tone touched my ears.   65

FAUST: It is I.

MARGARET: It is you. Oh, do say it again. [*She seizes him.*]
It is he. It is he. Where, then, is all my pain?
Where the fear of the dungeon? the chain?
It is you. Come to save me.   70
I am saved!
Now I see the road again, too,
Where, for the first time, I laid eyes on you—

And the garden and the gate
Where I and Martha stand and wait.   75
FAUST: [*Striving away.*] Come on! Come on!
MARGARET: O Stay!
Because I am so happy where you are staying. [*Caresses him.*]
FAUST: Do not delay.
If you keep on delaying,   80
We shall have to pay dearly therefor.
MARGARET: What? You cannot kiss any more?
My friend, you were not gone longer than this —
And forgot how to kiss?
Why, at your neck, do I feel such dread,   85
When once from your eyes and from what you said
A whole heaven surged down to fill me,
And you would kiss me as if you wanted to kill me?
Kiss me!
Else I'll kiss you. [*She embraces him.*]   90
Oh, grief! Your lips are cold,
Are mute.
Where
Is your loving air?
Who took it from me? [*She turns away from him.*]   95
FAUST: Come, follow me, dearest, and be bold!
I shall caress you a thousandfold;
Only follow me! That is all I plead.
MARGARET: [*Turning toward him.*] And is it you? Is it you indeed?
FAUST: It is I. Come along!   100
MARGARET: You take off the chain,
And take me into your lap again.
How is it that you do not shrink from me? —
Do you know at all, my friend, whom you make free?
FAUST: Come! Come! Soon dawns the light of day.   105
MARGARET: I've put my mother away,
I've drowned my child, don't you see?
Was it not given to you and to me?
You, too — it is you! Could it merely seem?
Give me your hand! It is no dream.   110
Your dear hand! — But alas, it is wet.
Wipe it off! There is yet
Blood on this one.
Oh God! What have you done!
Sheathe your sword;   115
I am begging you.
FAUST: Let the past be forever past — oh Lord,
You will kill me, too.
MARGARET: Oh no, you must outlive us!
I'll describe the graves you should give us.   120
Care for them and sorrow
Tomorrow:

Give the best place to my mother,
And next to her lay my brother;
Me, a little aside,   125
Only don't make the space too wide!
And the little one at my right breast.
Nobody else will lie by my side. —
Oh, to lie with you and to hide
In your arms, what happiness!   130
Now it is more than I can do;
I feel, I must force myself on you,
And you, it seems, push back my caress;
And yet it is you, and look so pure, so devout.

FAUST: If you feel, it is I, come out!   135
MARGARET: Out where?
FAUST: Into the open.
MARGARET: If the grave is there,
    If death awaits us, then come!
    From here to the bed of eternal rest,   140
    And not a step beyond—no!
    You are leaving now? Oh, Heinrich, that I could go!
FAUST: You can! If only you would! Open stands the door.
MARGARET: I may not go; for me there is no hope any more.
    What good to flee? They lie in wait for me.   145
    To have to go begging is misery,
    And to have a bad conscience, too.
    It is misery to stray far and forsaken,
    And, anyhow, I would be taken.
FAUST: I shall stay with you.   150
MARGARET: Quick! Quick! I pray.
    Save your poor child.
    On! Follow the way
    Along the brook,
    Over the bridge,
    Into the wood,   155
    To the left where the planks stick
    Out of the pond.
    Seize it—oh, quick!
    It wants to rise,   160
    It is still struggling.
    Save! Save!
FAUST: Can you not see,
    It takes *one* step, and you are free.
MARGARET: If only we were past the hill!   165
    My mother sits there on a stone,
    My scalp is creeping with dread!
    My mother sits there on a stone
    And wags and wags her head;
    She becks not, she nods not, her head is heavy and sore, 170

She has slept so long, she awakes no more.
She slept that we might embrace.
Those were the days of grace.
FAUST: In vain is my pleading, in vain what I say;
What can I do but bear you away?   175
MARGARET: Leave me! No, I shall suffer no force!
Do not grip me so murderously!
After all, I did everything else you asked.
FAUST: The day dawns. Dearest! Dearest!
MARGARET: Day. Yes, day is coming. The last day breaks;   180
It was to be my wedding day.
Tell no one that you have already been with Gretchen.
My veil! Oh pain!
It just happened that way.
We shall meet again,   185
But not dance that day.
The crowd is pushing, no word is spoken.
The alleys below
And the streets overflow.
The bell is tolling, the wand is broken.   190
How they tie and grab me, now one delivers
Me to the block and gives the sign,
And for every neck quivers
The blade that quivers for mine.
Mute lies the world as a grave.   195
FAUST: That I had never been born!
MEPHISTOPHELES: [*Appears outside.*] Up! Or you are lost.
Prating and waiting and pointless wavering.
My horses are quavering,
Over the sky creeps the dawn.   200
MARGARET: What did the darkness spawn?
He! He! Send him away!
What does he want in this holy place?
He wants me!
FAUST: You shall live.
MARGARET: Judgment of God! I give   205
Myself to you.
MEPHISTOPHELES: [*To* FAUST.]
Come! Come! I shall abandon you with her.
MARGARET: Thine I am, father. Save me!
You angels, hosts of heaven, stir,
Encamp about me, be my guard.   210
Heinrich! I quail at thee.
MEPHISTOPHELES: She is judged.
VOICE: [*From above.*]   Is saved.
MEPHISTOPHELES: [*To* FAUST.]   Hither to me! [*Disappears with*
FAUST.]
VOICE: [*From within, fading away.*] Heinrich! Heinrich!

WILLIAM BLAKE

1757–1827

Few works so ostentatiously "simple" as William Blake's *Songs of Innocence and of Experience* (1794) can ever have aroused such critical perplexity. Employing uncomplicated vocabulary and, often, variants of traditional ballad structure; describing the experience usually of naive subjects; supplying no obvious intellectual substance, these short lyrics have long fascinated and baffled their readers.

With no formal education, Blake, son of a London hosier, was at the age of fourteen apprenticed to the engraver James Basire. He developed both as painter and as engraver, partly influenced by the painter Henry Fuseli and the sculptor John Flaxman, both his friends, but remaining always highly individual in style and technique. An acknowledged mystic, he saw visions from the age of four: trees filled with Angels, God looking at him through the window. His highly personal view of a world penetrated by the divine helped to form both his visual and verbal art. In 1800, Blake moved from London to Felpham, where the poet William Hayley was his patron. He returned to London in 1803 and remained there for the rest of his life, married but childless, engaged in writing, printing, and engraving.

Blake felt a close relation between the visual and the verbal; he illustrated the works of many poets, notably Milton and Dante. His first book, *Poetical Sketches* (1783), was conventionally published, but he produced all his subsequent books himself, combining pictorial engravings with lettering, striking off only a few copies of each work by hand. Gradually, in increasingly long poems, he developed an elaborate private mythology, with important figures appearing in one work after another. His major mythic poems include *The Marriage of Heaven and Hell* (1793), *America* (1793), *The Book of Los* (1795), *Milton* (1804), *Jerusalem* (1804), and *The Four Zoas* (which he never completed).

As his short poem *Mock On, Mock On, Voltaire, Rousseau* testifies, Blake was bitterly opposed to what he thought the destructive and repressive rationalism of the eighteenth century. Voltaire and Rousseau might have been surprised to find themselves thus associated; they belong together, in Blake's view, because both implicitly oppose not only orthodox Christianity but the more private variety of revealed religion so vital to Blake himself. Although, like his contemporaries, Blake idealizes imagination and emotion and believes in the sacredness of the individual, he entirely avoids the "egotistical sublime," neither speaking directly of himself in his poetry, as Wordsworth did, nor, like Goethe, creating self-absorbed characters. In his short lyrics he adopts many different voices; the difficulties of interpretation stem partly from this fact. He insistently deals with metaphysical questions about our place in the universe and with social questions about the nature of human responsibility.

In *Songs of Innocence*, the speaker is often a child: asking questions of a lamb, meditating on his own blackness, describing the experience of a chimney sweep. Ostensibly these children in their innocence feel no anger or bitterness at the realities of the world in which they find themselves. The "little black boy" assures himself of a future when the "little English boy" will resemble him and love him; the child addressing the lamb evokes a realm of pure delight; the chimney sweep comforts himself with conventional morality and with a companion's dream. When an adult observer watches children, as in *Holy Thursday*, he too sees a benign arrangement, in which children are "flowers of London town," supervised by "agèd men, wise guardians of the poor." In the *Introduction* to the volume, the adult speaker receives empowering advice from a child, who instructs him to write. Everything is for the best in this best of all possible worlds.

But not quite. Disturbing undertones reverberate through even the most "innocent" of these songs. Innocence is, after all, by definition a state automatically lost through experience and never possible to regain. If the children evoked by the text still possess their innocence, the adult reader does not. *The Little Black Boy* suggests the kind of ambiguity evoked by the conjunction between innocent speaker and experienced reader. The poem opens with a situation that the speaker does not entirely understand—but one likely to be painfully familiar to the reader. "White as an angel is the English child: / But I am black as if bereaved of light": the child's similes indicate how completely he has incorporated the value judgments of his society, in which white suggests everything good and black means deficiency and deprivation. In this context, the mother's teaching, a comforting myth, becomes comprehensible as a way of dealing with her child's bewilderment and anxiety about his difference. At the end of the poem, the boy extends his mother's story into a prophetic vision in which black means protective power ("I'll shade him from the heat till he can bear / To lean in joy upon our father's knee"), and difference disappears into likeness, hostility into love. The vision evokes an ideal situation located in an imagined afterlife; it has only an antithetical connection to present actuality. Its emphatic divergence from real social conditions creates the subterranean disturbance characteristic of Blake's lyrics, the disturbance that calls attention to the serious social criticism implicit even in lyrics that may appear sweet to the point of blandness.

For all Blake's dislike of the earlier eighteenth century, he shares with his forebears one important assumption: his poetry, too, instructs as well as pleases. The innocent chimney sweep evokes parental death and betrayal, horrifying working conditions (soot and nakedness, darkness and shaved heads), and compensatory dreams. He never complains, but when he ends with the tag, "So if all do their duty, they need not fear harm," it generates moral shock. The discrepancy between the child's purity and his brutal exploitation indicts the society that allows such things. Innocence may be its own protection, these poems suggest, but that fact does not obviate social guilt.

If the *Songs of Innocence*, for all their atmosphere of brightness, cheer, and peace, convey outrage at the ways that social institutions harm those they should protect, the *Songs of Experience* more directly evoke a world worn, constricted, burdened with misery created by human beings. Now a new version of *The Chimney Sweeper* openly states what the earlier poem suggested:

> "And because I am happy, & dance & sing,
> They think they have done me no injury,
> And are gone to praise God & his Priest & King,
> Who make up a heaven of our misery."

The child understands the protective self-blinding of adults.

London in its sixteen lines sums up many of the collection's implications. Like most of the *Songs of Experience*, *London* presents an adult speaker, a wanderer through the city, who finds wherever he goes, in every face, "Marks of weakness, marks of woe." The city is the repository of suffering: men and infants and chimney sweepers cry; soldiers sigh; harlots curse. All are victims of corrupt institutions: blackening Church, bloody palace. Marriage and death interpenetrate; the curses of illness and corruption pass through the generations. The speaker reports only what he sees and hears, without commentary. He evokes a society in dreadful decay, and he conveys his despairing rage at a situation he cannot remedy.

Blake's lyrics, in their mixture of the visionary and the observational, strike notes far different from those of satire. Like the visionary observations of Swift and Voltaire, though, they insist on the connection between literature and life. Literature has transformative capacity, but it works with the raw material of actual experience. And its visions have the power to insist on the necessity of change.

Blake has provided material for an enormous outpouring of critical work. Particularly useful for the student are the collections of critical essays, N. Frye, ed., *Blake* (1966), and H. Adams, ed., *Critical Essays on William Blake* (1991). Valuable longer studies include M. Schorer, *William Blake: The Politics of Vision* (1946); H. Adams, *William Blake: A Reading of the Shorter Poems* (1963); E. D. Hirsch, *Innocence and Experience* (1969); D. G. Gilham, *William Blake* (1973); and S. Gardner, *Blake's Innocence and Experience Retraced* (1986). H. Bloom, ed., *William Blake* (1985), provides a useful compendium of mostly recent criticism; N. Hilton, ed., *Essential Articles for the Study of William Blake* (1986), is more wide ranging. A valuable recent general study is E. Larrissy, *William Blake* (1985).

Songs of Innocence and of Experience

SHEWING THE TWO CONTRARY STATES OF THE HUMAN SOUL

Songs of Innocence[1]

Introduction

Piping down the valleys wild
Piping songs of pleasant glee
On a cloud I saw a child,
And he laughing said to me,

"Pipe a song about a Lamb";   5
So I piped with merry chear;
"Piper pipe that song again"—
So I piped, he wept to hear.

"Drop thy pipe thy happy pipe
Sing thy songs of happy chear";   10
So I sung the same again
While he wept with joy to hear.

"Piper sit thee down and write
In a book that all may read"—
So he vanished from my sight.   15
And I plucked a hollow reed,

And I made a rural pen,
And I stained the water clear,
And I wrote my happy songs
Every child may joy to hear.   20

---

1. The text for all of Blake's works is edited by David V. Erdman and Harold Bloom. *Songs of Innocence* (1789) was later combined with *Songs of Experience* (1794), and the poems were etched and accompanied by Blake's illustrations, the process accomplished by copper engravings stamped on paper, then colored by hand.

The Lamb

Little Lamb, who made thee?
Dost thou know who made thee?
Gave thee life & bid thee feed,
By the stream & o'er the mead;
Gave thee clothing of delight,   5
Softest clothing wooly bright;
Gave thee such a tender voice,
Making all the vales rejoice!
Little Lamb who made thee?
Dost thou know who made thee?   10

Little Lamb I'll tell thee,
Little Lamb I'll tell thee!
He is callèd by thy name,
For he calls himself a Lamb:
He is meek & he is mild,   15
He became a little child:
I a child & thou a lamb,
We are callèd by his name.[1]
Little Lamb God bless thee.
Little Lamb God bless thee.   20

The Little Black Boy

My mother bore me in the southern wild,
And I am black, but O! my soul is white;
White as an angel is the English child:
But I am black as if bereaved of light.

My mother taught me underneath a tree,   5
And sitting down before the heat of day,
She took me on her lap and kissèd me,
And pointing to the east, began to say:

"Look on the rising sun: there God does live,
And gives his light, and gives his heat away;   10
And flowers and trees and beasts and men receive
Comfort in morning, joy in the noon day.

"And we are put on earth a little space,
That we may learn to bear the beams of love,
And these black bodies and this sun-burnt face   15
Is but a cloud, and like a shady grove.

"For when our souls have learned the heat to bear,
The cloud will vanish; we shall hear his voice,
Saying: 'Come out from the grove, my love & care,
And round my golden tent like lambs rejoice.'"   20

---

1. Christians use the name of Christ to designate themselves.

Thus did my mother say, and kissèd me;
And thus I say to little English boy:
When I from black and he from white cloud free,
And round the tent of God like lambs we joy,

I'll shade him from the heat till he can bear   25
To lean in joy upon our father's knee;
And then I'll stand and stroke his silver hair,
And be like him, and he will then love me.

Holy Thursday[1]

'Twas on a Holy Thursday, their innocent faces clean,
The children walking two & two, in red & blue & green,[2]
Grey headed beadles[3] walked before with wands as white as snow,
Till into the high dome of Paul's they like Thames' waters flow.

O what a multitude they seemed, these flowers of London town!   5
Seated in companies they sit with radiance all their own.
The hum of multitudes was there, but multitudes of lambs,
Thousands of little boys & girls raising their innocent hands.

Now like a mighty wind they raise to heaven the voice of song,
Or like harmonious thunderings the seats of heaven among.   10
Beneath them sit the agèd men, wise guardians[4] of the poor;
Then cherish pity, lest you drive an angel from your door.[5]

The Chimney Sweeper

When my mother died I was very young,
And my father sold me[1] while yet my tongue
Could scarcely cry " 'weep![2] 'weep! 'weep! 'weep!"
So your chimneys I sweep & in soot I sleep.

There's little Tom Dacre, who cried when his head   5
That curled like a lamb's back, was shaved, so I said,
"Hush, Tom! never mind it, for when your head's bare,
You know that the soot cannot spoil your white hair."

And so he was quiet, & that very night,
As Tom was a-sleeping he had such a sight!   10
That thousands of sweepers, Dick, Joe, Ned, & Jack,
Were all of them locked up in coffins of black;

And by came an Angel who had a bright key,
And he opened the coffins & set them all free;

1. Ascension Day, forty days after Easter, when children from charity schools were marched to St. Paul's
Cathedral.   2. Each school had its own distinctive uniform.   3. Ushers and minor functionaries,
whose job was to maintain order.   4. The governors of the charity schools.   5. See Hebrews 13:2:
"Be not forgetful to entertain strangers: for thereby some have entertained angels unawares."   1. It
was common practice in Blake's day for fathers to sell, or indenture, their children to become chimney
sweeps. The average age at which such children began working was six or seven; they were generally
employed for seven years, until they were too big to ascend the chimneys.   2. The child's lisping
effort to say "sweep," as he walks the streets looking for work.

Then down a green plain, leaping, laughing they run,   15
And wash in a river and shine in the Sun;

Then naked[3] & white, all their bags left behind,
They rise upon clouds, and sport in the wind.
And the Angel told Tom, if he'd be a good boy,
He'd have God for his father & never want joy.   20

And so Tom awoke; and we rose in the dark
And got with our bags & our brushes to work.
Tho' the morning was cold, Tom was happy & warm;
So if all do their duty, they need not fear harm.

Songs of Experience
Introduction

Hear the voice of the Bard!
Who Present, Past, & Future sees;
Whose ears have heard
The Holy Word
That walked among the ancient trees;[1]   5

Calling the lapsèd Soul
And weeping in the evening dew;[2]
That might control
The starry pole,
And fallen, fallen light renew!   10

"O Earth, O Earth, return!
Arise from out the dewy grass;
Night is worn,
And the morn
Rises from the slumberous mass.   15

"Turn away no more;
Why wilt thou turn away?
The starry floor
The watery shore
Is given thee till the break of day."   20

Earth's Answer

Earth raised up her head,
From the darkness dread & drear.
Her light fled:
Stony dread!
And her locks covered with grey despair.   5

---

3. They climbed up the chimneys naked.   1. Genesis 3:8: "And [Adam and Eve] heard the voice of
the Lord God walking in the garden in the cool of the day."   2. Blake's ambiguous use of pronouns
makes for interpretative difficulties. It would seem that *The Holy Word* (Jehovah, a name for God in
the Old Testament of the Bible) calls *the lapsèd Soul*, and weeps—not the Bard.

"Prisoned on watery shore
Starry Jealousy does keep my den,
Cold and hoar
Weeping o'er
I hear the Father[1] of the ancient men.   10

"Selfish father of men,
Cruel, jealous, selfish fear!
Can delight
Chained in night
The virgins of youth and morning bear?   15

"Does spring hide its joy
When buds and blossoms grow?
Does the sower
Sow by night,
Or the plowman in darkness plow?   20

"Break this heavy chain
That does freeze my bones around;
Selfish! vain!
Eternal bane!
That free Love with bondage bound."   25

The Tyger

Tyger! Tyger! burning bright
In the forests of the night,
What immortal hand or eye
Could frame thy fearful symmetry?

In what distant deeps or skies   5
Burnt the fire of thine eyes?
On what wings dare he aspire?
What the hand dare seize the fire?

And what shoulder, & what art,
Could twist the sinews of thy heart?   10
And when thy heart began to beat,
What dread hand? & what dread feet?

What the hammer? what the chain?
In what furnace was thy brain?
What the anvil? what dread grasp   15
Dare its deadly terrors clasp?

When the stars threw down their spears,
And watered heaven with their tears,
Did he smile his work to see?
Did he who made the Lamb make thee?   20

---

1. In Blake's later prophetic works, one of the four Zoas, representing the four chief faculties of
humankind, is Urizen. In general, he stands for the orthodox conception of the Divine Creator, sometimes Jehovah in the Old Testament, often the God conceived by Newton and Locke—in all instances
a tyrant associated with excessive rationalism, sexual repression, and the opponent of the imagination
and creativity. This may be "the Holy Word" in *Introduction* (see p. 2269, line 4).

Tyger! Tyger! burning bright
In the forests of the night,
What immortal hand or eye
Dare frame thy fearful symmetry?

The Sick Rose

O Rose, thou art sick.
The invisible worm
That flies in the night
In the howling storm

Has found out thy bed   5
Of crimson joy,
And his dark secret love
Does thy life destroy.

London

I wander thro' each chartered[1] street,
Near where the chartered Thames does flow,
And mark in every face I meet
Marks of weakness, marks of woe.

In every cry of every Man,   5
In every Infant's cry of fear,
In every voice, in every ban,
The mind-forged manacles I hear:

How the Chimney-sweeper's cry
Every blackening Church appalls;[2]   10
And the hapless Soldier's sigh
Runs in blood down Palace walls.

But most thro' midnight streets I hear
How the youthful Harlot's curse
Blasts the new-born Infant's tear,[3]   15
And blights with plagues the Marriage hearse.

The Chimney Sweeper

A little black thing among the snow
Crying "'weep, 'weep," in notes of woe!
"Where are thy father & mother? say?"
"They are both gone up to the church to pray.

"Because I was happy upon the heath,   5
And smiled among the winter's snow;

1. Literally, hired. Blake implies that the streets and the river are controlled by commercial interests.
2. Literally, "makes white," punning also on *appall* (to dismay) and *pall* (the cloth covering a corpse or bier). 3. The harlot infects the parents with venereal disease, and thus the infant is inflicted with neonatal blindness.

They clothèd me in the clothes of death,
And taught me to sing the notes of woe.

"And because I am happy, & dance & sing,
They think they have done me no injury,   10
And are gone to praise God & his Priest & King,
Who make up a heaven of our misery."

Mock On, Mock On, Voltaire, Rousseau

Mock on, Mock on, Voltaire, Rousseau;
Mock on, Mock on, 'tis all in vain.
You throw the sand against the wind,
And the wind blows it back again.

And every sand becomes a Gem   5
Reflected in the beams divine;
Blown back, they blind the mocking Eye,
But still in Israel's paths they shine.

The Atoms of Democritus[1]
And Newton's Particles of light[2]   10
Are sands upon the Red sea shore,
Where Israel's tents do shine so bright.

And Did Those Feet

And did those feet[1] in ancient time
Walk upon England's mountains green?
And was the holy Lamb of God
On England's pleasant pastures seen?

And did the Countenance Divine   5
Shine forth upon our clouded hills?
And was Jerusalem builded here,
Among those dark Satanic Mills?[2]

Bring me my Bow of burning gold:
Bring me my Arrows of desire: 10
Bring me my Spear: O clouds unfold!
Bring me my Chariot of fire!

I will not cease from Mental Fight,
Nor shall my Sword sleep in my hand,
Till we have built Jerusalem   15
In England's green & pleasant Land.

---

1. Greek philosopher (460?–362? B.C.), who advanced a theory that all things are merely patterns of atoms.   2. Sir Isaac Newton's (1642–1727) corpuscular theory of light. For Blake, both men were condemned as materialists.   1. A reference to an ancient legend that Jesus came to England with Joseph of Arimathea.   2. Possibly industrial England, but "mills" also meant for Blake 18th-century arid, mechanistic philosophy.

WILLIAM WORDSWORTH
1770–1850

William Wordsworth both proclaimed and embodied the *newness* of the Romantic movement. In his preface to the second edition of *Lyrical Ballads* (1800), a collection of poems by him and his friend Samuel Taylor Coleridge, he announced the advent of a poetic revolution. Like other revolutionaries, Wordsworth and Coleridge created their identities by rebelling against and travestying their predecessors. Now no longer would poets write in "dead" forms; now they had discovered a "new" direction, "new" subject matter; now poetry could at last serve as an important form of human communication. Reading Wordsworth's poems with the excitement of that revolution long past, we can still feel the power of his desire to communicate. The human heart is his subject; he writes, in particular, of growth and of memory and of the perplexities inherent in the human condition.

Born at Cockermouth, Cumberland, to the family of an attorney, Wordsworth attended St. John's College, Cambridge, from 1787 to 1791. The next year, early in the French Revolution, he spent in France, where he met Annette Vallon and had a daughter by her. In 1795, Wordsworth met Coleridge; two years later, Wordsworth and his sister, Dorothy, moved to Alfoxden, near Coleridge's home in Nether Stowey, in the county of Somerset. There the two men conceived the idea of collaboration; in 1798, the first edition of their *Lyrical Ballads* appeared, anonymously. The next year, Wordsworth and his sister settled in the Lake District of northwest England. In 1802, the poet married Mary Hutchinson, with whom he had five children. He received the sinecure of stamp distributor in 1813 and in 1843 succeeded Robert Southey as England's poet laureate, having long since abandoned the political radicalism of his youth.

Wordsworth wrote little prose, except for the famous preface of 1800 and another preface in 1815; his accomplishment was almost entirely poetic. His early work employed conventional eighteenth-century techniques, but *Lyrical Ballads* marked a new direction: an effort to employ simple language and to reveal the high significance of simple themes, the transcendent importance of the everyday. Between 1798 and 1805, he composed his nineteenth-century version of an epic, *The Prelude*, an account of the development of a poet's mind—his own. His subsequent work included odes, sonnets, and many poems written to mark specific occasions.

It would be difficult to overestimate the extent of Wordsworth's historical and poetic importance. In *The Prelude*, not published until 1850, he not only made powerful poetry out of his own experience but also specified a way of valuing experience:

> There are in our existence spots of time,
> That with distinct pre-eminence retain
> A renovating virtue, whence, depressed
> By false opinion and contentious thought,
> Or aught of heavier or more deadly weight,
> In trivial occupations, and the round
> Of ordinary intercourse, our minds
> Are nourished and invisibly repaired;
> A virtue, by which pleasure is enhanced,
> That penetrates, enables us to mount
> When high, more high, and lifts us up when fallen.

To take seriously the moment, this passage suggests, enables us to resist the dulling force of everyday life ("trivial occupations") and provides the means of personal salvation.

Wordsworth often uses religious language (a religious reference is hinted in the idea of being lifted up when fallen) to insist on the importance of his doctrine. He inaugurated an attempt—lasting far into the century—to establish and sustain a secular religion to substitute for Christian faith. The attempt was, even for Wordsworth, only intermittently successful. *The Prelude* records experiences of persuasive visionary intensity, as when the poet speaks of seeing a shepherd in the distance:

> Or him have I descried in distant sky,
> A solitary object and sublime,
> Above all height! like an aerial cross
> Stationed alone upon a spiry rock
> Of the Chartreuse, for worship.

But such "spots of time" exist in isolation; it is difficult to maintain a saving faith on their basis.

The two long poems printed here treat the problem of discovering and sustaining faith. *Lines Composed a Few Miles Above Tintern Abbey*, first published in *Lyrical Ballads*, and *Ode on Intimations of Immortality*, published in 1807 but written between 1802 and 1806, share a preoccupation with loss and with the saving power of memory. Both speak of personal experience, although the ode, a more formal poem, also generalizes to a hypothetical "we." Both insist that nature—the external world experienced through the senses and the containing pattern assumed beyond that world—offers the possibility of wisdom to combat the pain inherent in human growth.

But it would be a mistake to assume that the poems exist to promulgate a doctrine of natural salvation, although some readers have considered their "pantheism" (the belief that God pervades every part of His created universe) their most important aspect. Both poems evoke an intellectual and emotional process, not a conclusion; they sketch dramas of human development.

In *Tintern Abbey*, the speaker conveys his relief at returning to a sylvan scene that has been important to him in memory. His recollections of this natural beauty, he says, have helped sustain him in the confusion and weariness of city life; he thinks they may also have encouraged him toward goodness and serenity. But this second suggestion, that memories of nature have a moral effect, is only hypothetical, qualified in the text by such words and phrases as "I trust" and "perhaps." Indeed, the poem's next section opens with explicit statement that this may "Be but a vain belief." True or false, though, the belief comforts the speaker, who then recalls his more direct relation with nature in the past, when "The sounding cataract / Haunted me like a passion." He hopes, but cannot quite be sure, that his present awareness of "the still, sad music of humanity" and of the great "presence" that infuses nature compensates for what he has sacrificed in losing the immediacy of youthful experience.

The last section of *Tintern Abbey* emphasizes still more that the speaker is struggling with depression over his sense of loss; he observes that the presence of his "dearest Friend," his sister, would protect his "genial spirits" from decay even without his faith in what he has learned. That sister now becomes the focus for his thoughts about nature; he imagines her growth as like his own, but perfected, and her power of memory as able to contain not only the beauties of the landscape but his presence as part of that landscape. The poem thus resolves itself with emphasis on a human relationship, between the man and his sister, as well as on the importance of nature. Its emotional power derives partly from its evocation of the *need* to believe in nature as a form of salvation and of the process of development through which that need manifests itself.

At about the same time that he wrote the *Ode on Intimations of Immortality,* Wordsworth composed his sonnet *The World Is Too Much with Us*:

> . . . we lay waste our powers
> Little we see in Nature that is ours;
> . . . we are out of tune.

Despite the rhapsodic tone that dominates the ode, it too reveals itself as a hard-won act of faith, an effort to combat the view of the present world conveyed in the sonnet.

The ode opens with insistence on loss: "The things which I have seen I now can see no more." The speaker feels grief; he tries to deny it, because it seems at odds with the harmony and joy of the natural world. Yet the effort fails: even natural beauty speaks to him of what he no longer possesses. Stanzas V through VIII emphasize the association of infancy with natural communion and the inevitable deprivation attending growth. In stanza IX, the speaker attempts to value what still remains to him: it's all he has, he's grateful for it. In the concluding stanzas, however, he arrives at a new revelation: now nature acquires value not as a form of unmixed ecstasy, but in connection with the experience of human suffering:

> Though nothing can bring back the hour
> Of splendour in the grass, of glory in the flower;
> We will grieve not, rather find
> Strength in what remains behind; . . .
> In the soothing thoughts that spring
> Out of human suffering . . .

It is "the human heart by which we live" that finally enables the poet to experience the wonder of a flower, now become the source of "Thoughts that do often lie too deep for tears."

The view that the processes of maturing involve giving up a kind of wisdom accessible only to children belongs particularly to the Romantic period, but most people at least occasionally feel that in growing up they have left behind something they would rather keep. Wordsworth's poetic expression of the effort to come to terms with such feelings may remind his readers of barely noticed aspects of their own experience.

G. M. Harper, *Wordsworth* (1916–1929), remains the standard biography. A more recent biographical study is S. C. Gill, *William Wordsworth* (1989). Other important works (critical in emphasis) include R. D. Havens, *The Mind of a Poet* (1950); G. Hartman, *Wordsworth's Poetry* (1964); and J. H. Alexander, *Reading Wordsworth* (1987). A useful collection of critical essays is G. Gilpin, ed., *Critical Essays on William Wordsworth* (1990).

Lines Composed a Few Miles Above Tintern Abbey

On Revisiting the Banks of the Wye During a Tour, July 13, 1798

Five years have past; five summers, with the length
Of five long winters! and again I hear
These waters, rolling from their mountain-springs
With a soft inland murmur.—Once again

Do I behold these steep and lofty cliffs,   5
That on a wild secluded scene impress
Thoughts of more deep seclusion; and connect
The landscape with the quiet of the sky.
The day is come when I again repose
Here, under this dark sycamore, and view   10
These plots of cottage-ground, these orchard-tufts,
Which at this season, with their unripe fruits,
Are clad in one green hue, and lose themselves
'Mid groves and copses. Once again I see
These hedge-rows, hardly hedge-rows, little lines   15
Of sportive wood run wild: these pastoral farms,
Green to the very door; and wreaths of smoke
Sent up, in silence, from among the trees!
With some uncertain notice, as might seem
Of vagrant dwellers in the houseless woods,   20
Or of some Hermit's cave, where by his fire
The Hermit sits alone.

          These beauteous forms,
Through a long absence, have not been to me
As is a landscape to a blind man's eye:
But oft, in lonely rooms, and 'mid the din   25
Of towns and cities, I have owed to them,
In hours of weariness, sensations sweet,
Felt in the blood, and felt along the heart;
And passing even into my purer mind,
With tranquil restoration: — feelings too   30
Of unremembered pleasure: such, perhaps,
As have no slight or trivial influence
On that best portion of a good man's life,
His little, nameless, unremembered, acts
Of kindness and of love. Nor less, I trust,   35
To them I may have owed another gift,
Of aspect more sublime; that blessèd mood,
In which the burthen of the mystery,
In which the heavy and the weary weight
Of all this unintelligible world,   40
Is lightened: — that serene and blessèd mood,
In which the affections gently lead us on, —
Until, the breath of this corporeal frame
And even the motion of our human blood
Almost suspended, we are laid asleep   45
In body, and become a living soul:
While with an eye made quiet by the power
Of harmony, and the deep power of joy,
We see into the life of things.

          If this
Be but a vain belief, yet, oh! how oft —   50
In darkness and amid the many shapes
Of joyless daylight; when the fretful stir
Unprofitable, and the fever of the world,
Have hung upon the beatings of my heart —

How oft, in spirit, have I turned to thee,   55
O sylvan Wye! thou wanderer thro' the woods,
How often has my spirit turned to thee!

And now, with gleams of half-extinguished thought,
With many recognitions dim and faint,
And somewhat of a sad perplexity,   60
The picture of the mind revives again:
While here I stand, not only with the sense
Of present pleasure, but with pleasing thoughts
That in this moment there is life and food
For future years. And so I dare to hope,   65
Though changed, no doubt, from what I was when first
I came among these hills; when like a roe
I bounded o'er the mountains, by the sides
Of the deep rivers, and the lonely streams,
Wherever nature led: more like a man   70
Flying from something that he dreads, than one
Who sought the thing he loved. For nature then
(The coarser pleasures of my boyish days,
And their glad animal movements all gone by)
To me was all in all.—I cannot paint   75
What then I was. The sounding cataract
Haunted me like a passion: the tall rock,
The mountain, and the deep and gloomy wood,
Their colours and their forms, were then to me
An appetite; a feeling and a love,   80
That had no need of a remoter charm,
By thought supplied, nor any interest
Unborrowed from the eye.—That time is past,
And all its aching joys are now no more,
And all its dizzy raptures. Not for this   85
Faint I, nor mourn nor murmur; other gifts
Have followed; for such loss, I would believe,
Abundant recompense. For I have learned
To look on nature, not as in the hour
Of thoughtless youth; but hearing oftentimes   90
The still, sad music of humanity,
Nor harsh nor grating, though of ample power
To chasten and subdue. And I have felt
A presence that disturbs me with the joy
Of elevated thoughts; a sense sublime   95
Of something far more deeply interfused,
Whose dwelling is the light of setting suns,
And the round ocean and the living air,
And the blue sky, and in the mind of man:
A motion and a spirit, that impels   100
All thinking things, all objects of all thought,
And rolls through all things. Therefore am I still
A lover of the meadows and the woods,
And mountains; and of all that we behold
From this green earth; of all the mighty world   105
Of eye, and ear,—both what they half create,
And what perceive; well pleased to recognise

In nature and the language of the sense,
The anchor of my purest thoughts, the nurse,
The guide, the guardian of my heart, and soul   110
Of all my moral being.

                          Nor perchance,
If I were not thus taught, should I the more
Suffer my genial[1] spirits to decay:
For thou art with me here upon the banks
Of this fair river; thou my dearest Friend,   115
My dear, dear Friend; and in thy voice I catch
The language of my former heart, and read
My former pleasures in the shooting lights
Of thy wild eyes. Oh! yet a little while
May I behold in thee what I was once,   120
My dear, dear Sister! and this prayer I make,
Knowing that Nature never did betray
The heart that loved her; 'tis her privilege,
Through all the years of this our life, to lead
From joy to joy: for she can so inform   125
The mind that is within us, so impress
With quietness and beauty, and so feed
With lofty thoughts, that neither evil tongues,
Rash judgments, nor the sneers of selfish men,
Nor greetings where no kindness is, nor all   130
The dreary intercourse of daily life,
   Shall e'er prevail against us, or disturb
Our cheerful faith, that all which we behold
Is full of blessings. Therefore let the moon
Shine on thee in thy solitary walk;   135
And let the misty mountain-winds be free
To blow against thee: and, in after years,
When these wild ecstasies shall be matured
Into a sober pleasure; when thy mind
Shall be a mansion for all lovely forms,   140
Thy memory be as a dwelling-place
For all sweet sounds and harmonies; oh! then,
If solitude, or fear, or pain, or grief
Should be thy portion, with what healing thoughts
Of tender joy wilt thou remember me,   145
And these my exhortations! Nor, perchance—
If I should be where I no more can hear
Thy voice, nor catch from thy wild eyes these gleams
Of past existence—wilt thou then forget
That on the banks of this delightful stream   150
We stood together; and that I, so long
A worshipper of Nature, hither came
Unwearied in that service; rather say
With warmer love—oh! with far deeper zeal
Of holier love. Nor wilt thou then forget   155
That after many wanderings, many years
Of absence, these steep woods and lofty cliffs,

---

1. Generative, creative.

And this green pastoral landscape, were to me
More dear, both for themselves and for thy sake!

Ode on Intimations of Immortality

From Recollections of Early Childhood

The Child is father of the Man;
And I could wish my days to be
Bound each to each by natural piety.

I

There was a time when meadow, grove, and stream,
The earth, and every common sight,
      To me did seem
      Apparelled in celestial light,
The glory and the freshness of a dream.   5
It is not now as it hath been of yore;—
      Turn wheresoe'er I may,
      By night or day,
The things which I have seen I now can see no more.

II

      The Rainbow comes and goes,   10
      And lovely is the Rose;
      The Moon doth with delight
Look round her when the heavens are bare,
      Waters on a starry night
      Are beautiful and fair;   15
      The sunshine is a glorious birth;
      But yet I know, where'er I go,
That there hath past away a glory from the earth.

III

Now, while the birds thus sing a joyous song,
      And while the young lambs bound   20
      As to the tabor's sound,
To me alone there came a thought of grief:
A timely utterance gave that thought relief,
      And I again am strong:
The cataracts blow their trumpets from the steep;   25
No more shall grief of mine the season wrong;
I hear the Echoes through the mountains throng,
The Winds come to me from the fields of sleep,
      And all the earth is gay;
      Land and sea   30
Give themselves up to jollity,
      And with the heart of May
Doth every Beast keep holiday;—
      Thou Child of Joy,

Shout round me, let me hear thy shouts, thou happy   35
   Shepherd-boy!

IV

Ye blessèd Creatures, I have heard the call
   Ye to each other make; I see
The heavens laugh with you in your jubilee;
     My heart is at your festival,   40
     My head hath its coronal,
The fulness of your bliss, I feel—I feel it all.
     Oh evil day! if I were sullen
     While Earth herself is adorning,
       This sweet May-morning,   45
     And the Children are culling
       On every side,
     In a thousand valleys far and wide,
     Fresh flowers; while the sun shines warm,
And the Babe leaps up on his Mother's arm:—   50
     I hear, I hear, with joy I hear!
   —But there's a Tree, of many, one,
A single Field which I have looked upon,
Both of them speak of something that is gone:
       The Pansy at my feet   55
       Doth the same tale repeat:
Whither is fled the visionary gleam?
Where is it now, the glory and the dream?

V

Our birth is but a sleep and a forgetting:
The Soul that rises with us, our life's Star,   60
     Hath had elsewhere its setting,
       And cometh from afar:
     Not in entire forgetfulness,
     And not in utter nakedness,
But trailing clouds of glory do we come   65
     From God, who is our home:
Heaven lies about us in our infancy!
Shades of the prison-house begin to close
     Upon the growing Boy,
But He beholds the light, and whence it flows,   70
     He sees it in his joy;
The Youth, who daily farther from the east
     Must travel, still is Nature's Priest,
     And by the vision splendid
     Is on his way attended;   75
At length the Man perceives it die away,
And fade into the light of common day.

VI

Earth fills her lap with pleasures of her own;
Yearnings she hath in her own natural kind,
And, even with something of a Mother's mind,   80

And no unworthy aim,
The homely Nurse doth all she can
To make her Foster-child, her Inmate, Man,
Forget the glories he hath known,
And that imperial palace whence he came.   85

VII

Behold the Child among his new-born blisses,
A six years' Darling of a pigmy size!
See, where 'mid work of his own hand he lies,
Fretted by sallies of his mother's kisses,
With light upon him from his father's eyes!   90
See, at his feet, some little plan or chart,
Some fragment from his dream of human life,
Shaped by himself with newly-learnèd art;
   A wedding or a festival,
   A mourning or a funeral;   95
   And this hath now his heart,
   And unto this he frames his song:
   Then will he fit his tongue
To dialogues of business, love, or strife;
   But it will not be long   100
   Ere this be thrown aside,
   And with new joy and pride
The little Actor cons another part;
Filling from time to time his "humorous stage"
With all the Persons, down to palsied Age,   105
That Life brings with her in her equipage;
   As if his whole vocation
   Were endless imitation.

VIII

Thou, whose exterior semblance doth belie
   Thy Soul's immensity;   110
Thou best Philosopher, who yet dost keep
Thy heritage, thou Eye among the blind,
That, deaf and silent, read'st the eternal deep,
Haunted for ever by the eternal mind, —
   Mighty Prophet! Seer blest!   115
   On whom those truths do rest,
Which we are toiling all our lives to find,
In darkness lost, the darkness of the grave;
Thou, over whom thy Immortality
Broods like the Day, a Master o'er a Slave,   120
A Presence which is not to be put by;
   [To whom the grave
Is but a lonely bed without the sense or sight
   Of day or the warm light,
A place of thought where we in waiting lie;][1]   125

---

1. The lines within brackets were included in the *Ode* in the 1807 and 1815 editions of Wordsworth's poems but were omitted in the 1820 and subsequent editions, as a result of Coleridge's severe censure of them.

Thou little Child, yet glorious in the might
Of heaven-born freedom on thy being's height,
Why with such earnest pains dost thou provoke
The years to bring the inevitable yoke,
Thus blindly with thy blessedness at strife?   130
Full soon thy Soul shall have her earthly freight,
And custom lie upon thee with a weight,
Heavy as frost, and deep almost as life!

IX

    O joy! that in our embers
    Is something that doth live,   135
    That nature yet remembers
    What was so fugitive!
The thought of our past years in me doth breed
Perpetual benediction: not indeed
For that which is most worthy to be blest;   140
Delight and liberty, the simple creed
Of Childhood, whether busy or at rest,
With new-fledged hope still fluttering in his breast—
    Not for these I raise
    The song of thanks and praise;   145
    But for those obstinate questionings
    Of sense and outward things,
    Fallings from us, vanishings;
    Blank misgivings of a Creature
Moving about in worlds not realized,   150
High instincts before which our mortal Nature
Did tremble like a guilty Thing surprised:
    But for those first affections,
    Those shadowy recollections,
    Which, be they what they may,   155
Are yet the fountain-light of all our day,
Are yet a master-light of all our seeing;
    Uphold us, cherish, and have power to make
Our noisy years seem moments in the being
Of the eternal Silence: truths that wake,   160
    To perish never;
Which neither listlessness, nor mad endeavour,
    Nor Man nor Boy,
Nor all that is at enmity with joy,
Can utterly abolish or destroy!   165
    Hence in a season of calm weather
    Though inland far we be,
Our Souls have sight of that immortal sea
    Which brought us hither,
    Can in a moment travel thither,   170
And see the Children sport upon the shore,
And hear the mighty waters rolling evermore.

X

Then sing, ye Birds, sing, sing a joyous song!
    And let the young Lambs bound

As to the tabor's sound!   175
We in thought will join your throng,
   Ye that pipe and ye that play,
   Ye that through your hearts to-day
   Feel the gladness of the May!
What though the radiance which was once so bright   180
Be now for ever taken from my sight,
   Though nothing can bring back the hour
Of splendour in the grass, of glory in the flower;
   We will grieve not, rather find
   Strength in what remains behind;   185
   In the primal sympathy
   Which having been must ever be;
   In the soothing thoughts that spring
   Out of human suffering;
   In the faith that looks through death,   190
In years that bring the philosophic mind.

                               XI

And O, ye Fountains, Meadows, Hills, and Groves,
Forebode not any severing of our loves!
Yet in my heart of hearts I feel your might;
I only have relinquished one delight   195
To live beneath your more habitual sway.
I love the Brooks which down their channels fret,
Even more than when I tripped lightly as they;
The innocent brightness of a new-born Day
      Is lovely yet;   200
The Clouds that gather round the setting sun
Do take a sober colouring from an eye
That hath kept watch o'er man's mortality;
Another race hath been, and other palms are won.
Thanks to the human heart by which we live,   205
Thanks to its tenderness, its joys, and fears,
To me the meanest flower that blows can give
Thoughts that do often lie too deep for tears.

Composed upon Westminster Bridge, September 3, 1802

Earth has not anything to show more fair:
Dull would he be of soul who could pass by
A sight so touching in its majesty;
This City now doth, like a garment, wear
The beauty of the morning; silent, bare,   5
Ships, towers, domes, theatres, and temples lie
Open unto the fields, and to the sky;
All bright and glittering in the smokeless air.
Never did sun more beautifully steep
In his first splendour, valley, rock, or hill;   10

Ne'er saw I, never felt, a calm so deep!
The river glideth at his own sweet will:
Dear God! the very houses seem asleep;
And all that mighty heart is lying still!

The World Is Too Much with Us

The world is too much with us; late and soon,
Getting and spending, we lay waste our powers:
Little we see in Nature that is ours;
We have given our hearts away, a sordid boon![1]
This Sea that bares her bosom to the moon,   5
The winds that will be howling at all hours,
And are up-gathered now like sleeping flowers;
For this, for everything, we are out of tune;
It moves us not. — Great God! I'd rather be
A Pagan suckled in a creed outworn;   10
So might I, standing on this pleasant lea,
Have glimpses that would make me less forlorn;
Have sight of Proteus[2] rising from the sea;
Or hear old Triton[3] blow his wreathèd horn.

1. Gift. *Sordid:* refers to the act of giving the heart away.   2. An old man of the sea who, in the *Odyssey*, could assume a variety of shapes.   3. A sea deity, usually represented as blowing on a conch shell.

ALEXANDER SERGEYEVICH PUSHKIN
1799–1837

In his best-known story, *The Queen of Spades*, Alexander Pushkin combines familiar elements of Romantic fiction—the penniless young woman; the ambitious, passionate young man; the decayed beauty; the ghost—in a tale with intense ironic overtones, a tale later a favorite of the great Russian novelist Fyodor Dostoevsky. Pushkin's own life story sounds like a Romantic novel. Born into an aristocratic Russian family, neglected by his parents, he early began an extensive amatory and poetic career, publishing his first poem at the age of fifteen and becoming notorious about the same time for his many erotic involvements. At eighteen he graduated from a distinguished boarding school and accepted appointment in the Foreign Service; six years later, the various instances of his defiance of authority resulted in expulsion from the service and confinement, under police surveillance, on a paternal estate. After the assassination of Tsar Alexander I and the abortive military uprising that followed (an uprising involving several of Pushkin's friends, five of whom were subsequently hanged), Pushkin—by then a well-known poet— was befriended (1826) by the new tsar Nicholas. He moved back to Moscow, then to Petersburg, leading a moneyed and relatively carefree life. In 1831, however, he married a nineteen-year-old woman, whose apparently flirtatious behavior embittered his subsequent life. He died after a duel with his wife's putative lover.

Producing short lyrics, narrative poems, a great novel in verse (*Eugene Onegin*), lyrical drama (notably *Boris Gudonov*), versified folk tales, and prose fiction, Pushkin established himself as one of Russia's greatest writers. His interest in his nation's past, his tendency to challenge authority, his fascination with the character and situation of strong individuals: such obsessive concerns link his work with that of his Romantic contemporaries elsewhere in Europe. Goethe, Byron, and early nineteenth-century French novelists had marked influence on him. He retained also, however, the kind of clarity, discipline, and ironic distance more often associated with the literature of the preceding century.

The treatment of love and sexuality in *The Queen of Spades* exemplifies the complexity of Pushkin's approach. First of all we hear the story of the "Muscovite Venus," the beautiful young gambler who pays her debts by learning the secret of three infallible cards. Then we encounter a young woman suffering in her dependent position and longing for a "deliverer." Hermann, the immediate object of Lisaveta's dreams, has his own sexual fantasies: a young man himself, he imagines becoming the lover of the eighty-seven-year-old countess. At this point, if not before, the reader begins to realize that something's wrong here: this is not the kind of romantic tale we're used to. Describing Hermann's first glimpse of Lisaveta, Pushkin writes, "Hermann saw a small, fresh face and a pair of dark eyes. That moment decided his fate." A Romantic cliché—except that the young man sees Lisaveta not as an object of devotion but as a means to an end. He sends her a love letter, copied word for word from a German novel. His rapidly developing passion focuses on financial, not erotic, gain.

Lisaveta's character remains somewhat more ambiguous. The narrator invokes sympathy for her plight, at the mercy of a tyrannical employer who makes endless irrational demands and who never pays her. Her situation prohibits her from enjoying the kinds of amorous gratification other young women can expect. We can understand, therefore, why her dreams should concentrate specifically on a deliverer. Like Hermann, although far less unscrupulous, she may indulge in intrigues as a means to an end—in her case, not money but liberty.

The Queen of Spades contains no completely attractive characters. If Lisaveta's victimization arouses compassion, her lack of moral force or determination may also provoke irritation. Hermann's will to succeed, on the other hand, makes him a potential protagonist, but his obsession with money and his mean-spirited expediency alienate most readers. The countess, old and approaching death, uses the power of her money and rank with utter disregard for the needs or feelings of others. Even such a minor figure as the countess's grandson, Tomsky, playing with Lisaveta's feelings, going through his ritualized flirtation with Princess Polina, seems thoroughly contaminated by the values of the world he inhabits.

Indeed, those values provide the central subject of this tale. Pushkin employs conventions of the kind of ghost story common in folk tales to convey serious criticism of a social structure corrupted by universal concentration on money. Gambling provides not only the chief male activity but also the central metaphor of the story. Everyone is out for what he or she can get. The countess, whose days at the card table are past, uses her money to buy subservience; Lisaveta is willing to risk her reputation, maybe even her chastity, for the possibility of escaping servitude; Hermann frightens someone to death in an effort to make his fortune; Tomsky plays elaborate social games of advance and retreat, trying to get his princess. The queen of spades is a conventional symbol of death; the kind of death most important in Pushkin's story is not literal—not the countess's demise—but figurative: it is the spiritual death suffered by the other characters, over whose world the countess/queen of spades metaphorically presides.

The "Conclusion" of *The Queen of Spades*, a deadpan summary of the characters' future careers, epitomizes the story's central concerns. Hermann's madness dramatizes the financial obsession he has displayed from the beginning; Lisaveta's marriage, to an anonymous "very agreeable young man" with a good position "somewhere," emphasizes the degree to which she has always wished for marriage as rescue, not as attachment to a particular beloved other. In her married state, Lisaveta, ironically, "is bringing up a poor relative," recapitulating the structure of exploitation from which she herself suffered. Tomsky, relatively unimportant to the plot line, supplies the subject for the story's concluding sentence: his promotion and his "good" marriage remind us that everyone in the society here described seeks personal advantage at all costs. Hermann has simply paid the cost in the most dramatic way.

Henri Troyat, *Pushkin* (1971), is an excellent biography. For biography and criticism, the student might also consult Walter Arndt, *Pushkin Threefold: Narrative, Lyric, Polemic and Ribald Verse* (1972); John Bayley, *Pushkin: A Comparative Commentary* (1971); P. Debreczeny, *The Other Pushkin: A Study of Alexander Pushkin's Prose* (1983); John Oliver Killens, *Great Black Russian* (1989); and D. M. Bethea, ed., *Pushkin Today* (1993), an ambitious collection of essays. A useful biography is Stephanie Sandler, *Distant Pleasures* (1989).

PRONOUNCING GLOSSARY

The following list uses common English syllables and stress accents to provide rough equivalents of selected words whose pronunciation may be unfamiliar to the general reader.

Chekalinsky: *che-kah-leen'-skee*

Eletskaya: *ye-lyet'-skah-yuh*

Fedotovna: *fye-daw'-tuv-nah*

Ilyitch: *il-yeech'*

Lisaveta Ivanovna: *lyee-zah-vye'-tah ee-vah'-nuv-nuh*

Richelieu: *ree'-she-lyeuh*

St-Germain: *sanh-zher-manh'*

The Queen of Spades[1]

CHAPTER ONE

> And on rainy days
> They gathered
> Often;
> Their stakes—God help them!—
> Wavered from fifty
> To a hundred,
> And they won
> And marked up their winnings
> With chalk.
> Thus on rainy days
> Were they
> Busy.[2]

There was a card party one day in the rooms of Narumov, an officer of the Horse Guards. The long winter evening slipped by unnoticed; it was

---

1. Translated by Gillon R. Aitken.   2. Like most of the chapter epigraphs, this was presumably written by Pushkin himself.

five o'clock in the morning before the assembly sat down to supper. Those who had won ate with a big appetite; the others sat distractedly before their empty plates. But champagne was brought in, the conversation became more lively, and everyone took a part in it.

"And how did you get on, Surin?" asked the host.

"As usual, I lost. I must confess, I have no luck: I never vary my stake, never get heated, never lose my head, and yet I always lose!"

"And weren't you tempted even once to back[3] on a series . . . ? Your strength of mind astonishes me."

"What about Hermann then," said one of the guests, pointing at the young Engineer.[4] "He's never held a card in his hand, never doubled a single stake in his life, and yet he sits up until five in the morning watching us play."

"The game fascinates me," said Hermann, "but I am not in the position to sacrifice the essentials of life in the hope of acquiring the luxuries."

"Hermann's a German: he's cautious—that's all," Tomsky observed. "But if there's one person I can't understand, it's my grandmother, the Countess Anna Fedotovna."

"How? Why?" the guests inquired noisily.

"I can't understand why it is," Tomsky continued, "that my grandmother doesn't gamble."

"But what's so astonishing about an old lady of eighty not gambling?" asked Narumov.

"Then you don't know . . . ?"

"No, indeed; I know nothing."

"Oh well, listen then:

"You must know that about sixty years ago my grandmother went to Paris, where she made something of a hit. People used to chase after her to catch a glimpse of *la vénus moscovite*; Richelieu[5] paid court to her, and my grandmother vouches that he almost shot himself on account of her cruelty. At that time ladies used to play faro.[6] On one occasion at the Court, my grandmother lost a very great deal of money on credit to the Duke of Orleans. Returning home, she removed the patches[7] from her face, took off her hooped petticoat, announced her loss to my grandfather and ordered him to pay back the money. My late grandfather, as far as I can remember, was a sort of lackey to my grandmother. He feared her like fire; on hearing of such a disgraceful loss, however, he completely lost his temper; he produced his accounts, showed her that she had spent half a million francs in six months, pointed out that neither their Moscow nor their Saratov estates were in Paris, and refused point-blank to pay the debt. My grandmother gave him a box on the ear and went off to sleep on her own as an indication of her displeasure. In the hope that this domestic infliction would have had some effect on him, she sent for her husband the next day; she found him unshakeable. For the first time in her life she

3. Bet.   4. A member of the Corps of Engineers, concerned with fortifications.   5. Louis-Francois-Arnand De Vignerod Du Plessis, Duc de Richelieu (1696–1788), French aristocrat renowned throughout the 18th century for both his military and his sexual exploits. *La vénus moscovite*: the Venus of Moscow (French). Venus was the goddess of love.   6. A card game much used for gambling. 7. That is, beauty patches, artificial "beauty marks" made of black silk or court plaster and worn on the face or neck.

approached him with argument and explanation, thinking that she could bring him to reason by pointing out that there are debts and debts, that there is a big difference between a Prince and a coachmaker. But my grandfather remained adamant, and flatly refused to discuss the subject any further. My grandmother did not know what to do. A little while before, she had become acquainted with a very remarkable man. You have heard of Count St-Germain,[8] about whom so many marvellous stories are related. You know that he held himself out to be the Wandering Jew, and the inventor of the elixir of life, the philosopher's stone and so forth. Some ridiculed him as a charlatan and in his memoirs Casanova declares that he was a spy. However, St-Germain, in spite of the mystery which surrounded him, was a person of venerable appearance and much in demand in society. My grandmother is still quite infatuated with him and becomes quite angry if anyone speaks of him with disrespect. My grandmother knew that he had large sums of money at his disposal. She decided to have recourse to him, and wrote asking him to visit her without delay. The eccentric old man at once called on her and found her in a state of terrible grief. She depicted her husband's barbarity in the blackest light, and ended by saying that she pinned all her hopes on his friendship and kindness.

"St-Germain reflected. 'I could let you have this sum,' he said, 'but I know that you would not be at peace while in my debt, and I have no wish to bring fresh troubles upon your head. There is another solution—you can win back the money.'

" 'But, my dear Count,' my grandmother replied, 'I tell you—we have no money at all.'

" 'In this case money is not essential,' St-Germain replied. 'Be good enough to hear me out.'

"And at this point he revealed to her the secret for which any one of us here would give a very great deal . . ."

The young gamblers listened with still great attention. Tomsky lit his pipe, drew on it and continued:

"That same evening my grandmother went to Versailles, *au jeu de la Reine.*[9] The Duke of Orleans kept the bank; inventing some small tale, my grandmother lightly excused herself for not having brought her debt, and began to play against him. She chose three cards and played them one after the other: all three won and my grandmother recouped herself completely."

"Pure luck!" said one of the guests.

"A fairy-tale," observed Hermann.

"Perhaps the cards were marked!" said a third.

"I don't think so," Tomsky replied gravely.

"What!" cried Narumov. "You have a grandmother who can guess three cards in succession, and you haven't yet contrived to learn her secret."

"No, not much hope of that!" replied Tomsky. "She had four sons, including my father; all four were desperate gamblers, and yet she did not

8. Celebrated adventurer (ca. 1710–1784?) who frequented the French, German, and Russian courts.
9. To the queen's game (French).

reveal her secret to a single one of them, although it would have been a good thing if she had told them—told me, even. But this is what I heard from my uncle, Count Ivan Ilyitch, and he gave me his word for its truth. The late Chaplitsky—the same who died a pauper after squandering millions—in his youth once lost nearly 300,000 roubles—to Zoritch, if I remember rightly. He was in despair. My grandmother, who was most strict in her attitude towards the extravagances of young men, for some reason took pity on Chaplitsky. She told him the three cards on condition that he played them in order; and at the same time she exacted his solemn promise that he would never play again as long as he lived. Chaplitsky appeared before his victor; they sat down to play. On the first card Chaplitsky staked 50,000 roubles and won straight off; he doubled his stake, redoubled—and won back more than he had lost. . . .

"But it's time to go to bed; it's already a quarter to six."

Indeed, the day was already beginning to break. The young men drained their glasses and dispersed.

CHAPTER TWO

> "Il paraît que monsieur est décidément
> pour les suivantes."
> "Que voulez-vous, madame? Elles sont
> plus fraîches."
> FASHIONABLE CONVERSATION

The old Countess ***[1] was seated before the looking-glass in her dressing-room. Three lady's maids stood by her. One held a jar of rouge, another a box of hairpins, and the third a tall bonnet with flame-coloured ribbons. The Countess no longer had the slightest pretensions to beauty, which had long since faded from her face, but she still preserved all the habits of her youth, paid strict regard to the fashions of the seventies, and devoted to her dress the same time and attention as she had done sixty years before. At an embroidery frame by the window sat a young lady, her ward.

"Good morning, grand'maman!" said a young officer as he entered the room. "Bonjour, mademoiselle Lise. Grand'maman,[2] I have a request to make of you."

"What is it, Paul?"

"I want you to let me introduce one of my friends to you, and to allow me to bring him to the ball on Friday."

"Bring him straight to the ball and introduce him to me there. Were you at ***'s yesterday?"

"Of course. It was very gay; we danced until five in the morning. How charming Eletskaya was!"

"But, my dear, what's charming about her? Isn't she like her grand-

---

1. Asterisks in this selection are the author's and are intended to suggest that the proper name of an actual person has been omitted. The epigram can be translated as: "It appears that the gentleman is decidedly in favor of servant girls." "What would you have me do, Madam? They are fresher [than upper-class women]" (French). 2. Russian aristocrats often spoke French. Lisaveta is here called by the French name Lise, and Pavel, Paul.

mother, the Princess Darya Petrovna . . . ? By the way, I dare say she's grown very old now, the Princess Darya Petrovna?"

"What do you mean, 'grown old'?" asked Tomsky thoughtlessly. "She's been dead for seven years."

The young lady raised her head and made a sign to the young man. He remembered then that the death of any of her contemporaries was kept secret from the old Countess, and he bit his lip. But the Countess heard the news, previously unknown to her, with the greatest indifference.

"Dead!" she said. "And I didn't know it. We were maids of honour together, and when we were presented, the Empress . . ."

And for the hundredth time the Countess related the anecdote to her grandson.

"Come, Paul," she said when she had finished her story, "help me to stand up. Lisanka, where's my snuff-box?"

And with her three maids the Countess went behind a screen to complete her dress. Tomsky was left alone with the young lady.

"Whom do you wish to introduce?" Lisaveta Ivanovna asked softly.

"Narumov. Do you know him?"

"No. Is he a soldier or a civilian?"

"A soldier."

"An Engineer?"

"No, he's in the Cavalry. What made you think he was an Engineer?"

The young lady smiled but made no reply.

"Paul!" cried the Countess from behind the screen. "Bring along a new novel with you some time, will you, only please not one of those modern ones."

"What do you mean, grand'maman?"

"I mean not the sort of novel in which the hero strangles either of his parents or in which someone is drowned.[3] I have a great horror of drowned people."

"Such novels don't exist nowadays. Wouldn't you like a Russian one?"

"Are there such things? Send me one, my dear, please send me one."

"Will you excuse me now, grand'maman, I'm in a hurry. Good-bye, Lisaveta Ivanovna. What made you think that Narumov was in the Engineers?"

And Tomsky left the dressing-room.

Lisaveta Ivanovna was left on her own; she put aside her work and began to look out of the window. Presently a young officer appeared from behind the corner house on the other side of the street. A flush spread over her cheeks; she took up her work again and lowered her head over the frame. At this moment, the Countess returned, fully dressed.

"Order the carriage, Lisanka," she said, "and we'll go for a drive."

Lisanka got up from behind her frame and began to put away her work.

"What's the matter with you, my child? Are you deaf?" shouted the Countess. "Order the carriage this minute."

---

3. Novels of the sort the countess does not wish to read were typical of the then current decadent movement in French literature.

"I'll do so at once," the young lady replied softly and hastened into the ante-room.

A servant entered the room and handed the Countess some books from the Prince Pavel Alexandrovitch.

"Good, thank him," said the Countess. "Lisanka, Lisanka, where are you running to?"

"To get dressed."

"Plenty of time for that, my dear. Sit down. Open the first volume and read to me."

The young lady took up the book and read a few lines.

"Louder!" said the Countess. "What's the matter with you, my child? Have you lost your voice, or what . . . ? Wait . . . move that footstool up to me . . . nearer . . . that's right!"

Lisaveta Ivanovna read a further two pages. The Countess yawned.

"Put the book down," she said; "what rubbish! Have it returned to Prince Pavel with my thanks. . . . But where is the carriage?"

"The carriage is ready," said Lisaveta Ivanovna, looking out into the street.

"Then why aren't you dressed?" asked the Countess. "I'm always having to wait for you—it's intolerable, my dear!"

Lisa ran up to her room. Not two minutes elapsed before the Countess began to ring with all her might. The three lady's maids came running in through one door and the valet through another.

"Why don't you come when you're called?" the Countess asked them. "Tell Lisaveta Ivanovna that I'm waiting for her."

Lisaveta Ivanovna entered the room wearing her hat and cloak.

"At last, my child!" said the Countess. "But what clothes you're wearing . . . ! Whom are you hoping to catch? What's the weather like? It seems windy."

"There's not a breath of wind, your Ladyship," replied the valet.

"You never know what you're talking about! Open that small window. There; as I thought: windy and bitterly cold. Unharness the horses. Lisaveta, we're not going out—there was no need to dress up like that."

"And this is my life," thought Lisaveta Ivanovna.

And indeed Lisaveta Ivanovna was a most unfortunate creature. As Dante says: "You shall learn the salt taste of another's bread, and the hard path up and down his stairs";[4] and who better to know the bitterness of dependence than the poor ward of a well-born old lady? The Countess *** was far from being wicked, but she had the capriciousness of a woman who has been spoiled by the world, and the miserliness and cold-hearted egotism of all old people who have done with loving and whose thoughts lie with the past. She took part in all the vanities of the *haut-monde*;[5] she dragged herself to balls, where she sat in a corner, rouged and dressed in old-fashioned style, like some misshapen but essential ornament of the ball-room; on arrival, the guests would approach her with low bows, as if in accordance with an established rite, but after that, they would pay no further attention to her. She received the whole town

4. *Paradiso* 17.59.   5. High society (French).

at her house, and although no longer able to recognise the faces of her guests, she observed the strictest etiquette. Her numerous servants, grown fat and grey in her hall and servants' room, did exactly as they pleased, vying with one another in stealing from the dying old lady. Lisaveta Ivanovna was the household martyr. She poured out the tea, and was reprimanded for putting in too much sugar; she read novels aloud, and was held guilty of all the faults of the authors; she accompanied the Countess on her walks, and was made responsible for the state of the weather and the pavement. There was a salary attached to her position, but it was never paid; meanwhile, it was demanded of her to be dressed like everybody else—that is, like the very few who could afford to dress well. In society she played the most pitiable role. Everybody knew her, but nobody took any notice of her; at balls she danced only when there was a partner short, and ladies only took her arm when they needed to go to the dressing-room to make some adjustment to their dress. She was proud and felt her position keenly, and looked around her in impatient expectation of a deliverer; but the young men, calculating in their flightiness, did not honour her with their attention, despite the fact that Lisaveta Ivanovna was a hundred times prettier than the cold, arrogant but more eligible young ladies on whom they danced attendance. Many a time did she creep softly away from the bright but wearisome drawing-room to go and cry in her own poor room, where stood a papered screen, a chest of drawers, a small looking-glass and a painted bedstead, and where a tallow candle burned dimly in its copper candle-stick.

One day—two days after the evening described at the beginning of this story, and about a week previous to the events just recorded—Lisaveta Ivanovna was sitting at her embroidery frame by the window, when, happening to glance out into the street, she saw a young Engineer, standing motionless with his eyes fixed upon her window. She lowered her head and continued with her work; five minutes later she looked out again— the young officer was still standing in the same place. Not being in the habit of flirting with passing officers, she ceased to look out of the window, and sewed for about two hours without raising her head. Dinner was announced. She got up and began to put away her frame, and, glancing casually out into the street, she saw the officer again. She was considerably puzzled by this. After dinner, she approached the window with a feeling of some disquiet, but the officer was no longer outside, and she thought no more of him.

Two days later, while preparing to enter the carriage with the Countess, she saw him again. He was standing just by the front-door, his face concealed by a beaver collar; his dark eyes shone from beneath his cap. Without knowing why, Lisaveta Ivanovna felt afraid, and an unaccountable trembling came over her as she sat down in the carriage.

On her return home, she hastened to the window—the officer was standing in the same place as before, his eyes fixed upon her; she drew back, tormented by curiosity and agitated by a feeling that was quite new to her.

Since then, not a day had passed without the young man appearing at the customary hour beneath the windows of their house. A sort of mute acquaintance grew up between them. At work in her seat, she used to feel him approaching, and would raise her head to look at him—for longer and longer each day. The young man seemed to be grateful to her for this: she saw, with the sharp eye of youth, how a sudden flush would spread across his pale cheeks on each occasion that their glances met. After a week she smiled at him. . . .

When Tomsky asked leave of the Countess to introduce one of his friends to her; the poor girl's heart beat fast. But on learning that Narumov was in the Horse Guards, and not in the Engineers, she was sorry that, by an indiscreet question, she had betrayed her secret to the light-hearted Tomsky.

Hermann was the son of a Russianised German, from whom he had inherited a small amount of money. Being firmly convinced of the necessity of ensuring his independence, Hermann did not draw on the income that this yielded, but lived on his pay, forbidding himself the slightest extravagance. Moreover, he was secretive and ambitious, and his companions rarely had occasion to laugh at his excessive thrift. He had strong passions and a fiery imagination, but his tenacity of spirit saved him from the usual errors of youth. Thus, for example, although at heart a gambler, he never took a card in his hand, for he reckoned that his position did not allow him (as he put it) "to sacrifice the essentials of life in the hope of acquiring the luxuries"—and meanwhile, he would sit up at the card table for whole nights at a time, and follow the different turns of the game with feverish anxiety.

The story of the three cards had made a strong impression on his imagination, and he could think of nothing else all night.

"What if the old Countess should reveal her secret to me?" he thought the following evening as he wandered through the streets of Petersburg. "What if she should tell me the names of those three winning cards? Why not try my luck . . . ? Become introduced to her, try to win her favour, perhaps become her lover . . . ? But all that demands time, and she's eighty-seven; she might die in a week, in two days . . . ! And the story itself . . . ? Can one really believe it . . . ? No! Economy, moderation and industry; these are my three winning cards, these will treble my capital, increase it sevenfold, and earn for me ease and independence!"

Reasoning thus, he found himself in one of the principal streets of Petersburg, before a house of old-fashioned architecture. The street was crowded with vehicles; one after another, carriages rolled up to the lighted entrance. From them there emerged, now the shapely little foot of some beautiful young woman, now a rattling jack-boot, now the striped stocking and elegant shoe of a diplomat. Furs and capes flitted past the majestic hall-porter. Hermann stopped.

"Whose house is this?" he asked the watchman at the corner.

"The Countess ***'s," the watchman replied.

Hermann started. His imagination was again fired by the amazing story of the three cards. He began to walk around near the house, thinking of its owner and her mysterious faculty. It was late when he returned to his humble rooms; for a long time he could not sleep; and when at last he did drop off, cards, a green table,[6] heaps of banknotes and piles of golden coins appeared to him in his dreams. He played one card after the other, doubled his stake decisively, won unceasingly, and raked in the golden coins and stuffed his pockets with the banknotes. Waking up late, he sighed at the loss of his imaginary fortune, again went out to wander about the town and again found himself outside the house of the Countess ***. Some unknown power seemed to have attracted him to it. He stopped and began to look at the windows. At one he saw a head with long black hair, probably bent down over a book or a piece of work. The head was raised. Hermann saw a small, fresh face and a pair of dark eyes. That moment decided his fate.

CHAPTER THREE

Vous m'écrivez, mon ange, des lettres de
quatre pages plus vite que je ne puis
les lire.[7]

CORRESPONDENCE

Scarcely had Lisaveta Ivanovna taken off her hat and cloak when the Countess sent for her and again ordered her to have the horses harnessed. They went out to take their seats in the carriage. At the same moment as the old lady was being helped through the carriage doors by two footmen, Lisaveta Ivanovna saw her Engineer standing close by the wheel; he seized her hand; before she could recover from her fright, the young man had disappeared—leaving a letter in her hand. She hid it in her glove and throughout the whole of the drive neither heard nor saw a thing. As was her custom when riding in her carriage, the Countess kept up a ceaseless flow of questions: "Who was it who met us just now? What's this bridge called? What's written on that signboard?" This time Lisaveta Ivanovna's answers were so vague and inappropriate that the Countess became angry.

"What's the matter with you, my child? Are you in a trance or something? Don't you hear me or understand what I'm saying . . . ? Heaven be thanked that I'm still sane enough to speak clearly."

Lisaveta Ivanovna did not listen to her. On returning home, she ran up to her room and drew the letter out of her glove; it was unsealed. Lisaveta Ivanovna read it through. The letter contained a confession of love; it was tender, respectful and taken word for word from a German novel. But Lisaveta Ivanovna had no knowledge of German and was most pleased by it.

Nevertheless, the letter made her feel extremely uneasy. For the first time in her life she was entering into a secret and confidential relationship with a young man. His audacity shocked her. She reproached herself for her imprudent behaviour, and did not know what to do. Should she stop sitting at the window and by a show of indifference cool off the young man's desire for further acquaintance? Should she send the letter back to him? Or answer it with cold-hearted finality? There was nobody to whom

---

6. Tables on which gambling took place were typically covered with green baize.   7. My angel, you write me four-page-long letters faster than I can read them (French).

she could turn for advice: she had no friend or preceptress. Lisaveta Ivanovna resolved to answer the letter.

She sat down at her small writing-table, took a pen and some paper, and lost herself in thought. Several times she began her letter—and then tore it up; her manner of expression seemed to her to be either too condescending or too heartless. At last she succeeded in writing a few lines that satisfied her:

> I am sure that your intentions are honourable, and that you did not wish to offend me by your rash behaviour, but our acquaintance must not begin in this way. I return your letter to you and hope that in the future I shall have no cause to complain of undeserved disrespect.

The next day, as soon as she saw Hermann approach, Lisaveta Ivanovna rose from behind her frame, went into the ante-room, opened a small window, and threw her letter into the street, trusting to the agility of the young officer to pick it up. Hermann ran forward, took hold of the letter and went into a confectioner's shop. Breaking the seal of the envelope, he found his own letter and Lisaveta Ivanovna's answer. It was as he had expected, and he returned home, deeply preoccupied with his intrigue.

Three days afterwards, a bright-eyed young girl brought Lisaveta Ivanovna a letter from a milliner's shop. Lisaveta Ivanovna opened it uneasily, envisaging a demand for money, but she suddenly recognised Hermann's handwriting.

"You have made a mistake, my dear," she said; "this letter is not for me."

"Oh, but it is!" the girl answered cheekily and without concealing a sly smile. "Read it."

Lisaveta Ivanovna ran her eyes over the note. Hermann demanded a meeting.

"It cannot be," said Lisaveta Ivanovna, frightened at the haste of his demand and the way in which it was made: "this is certainly not for me."

And she tore the letter up into tiny pieces.

"If the letter wasn't for you, why did you tear it up?" asked the girl. "I would have returned it to the person who sent it."

"Please, my dear," Lisaveta Ivanovna said, flushing at the remark, "don't bring me any more letters in the future. And tell the person who sent you that he should be ashamed of . . ."

But Hermann was not put off. By some means or other, he sent a letter to Lisaveta Ivanovna every day. The letters were no longer translated from the German. Hermann wrote them inspired by passion, and used a language true to his character; these letters were the expression of his obsessive desires and the disorder of his unfettered imagination. Lisaveta Ivanovna no longer thought of returning them to him: she revelled in them, began to answer them, and with each day, her replies became longer and more tender. Finally, she threw out of the window the following letter:

> This evening there is a ball at the *** Embassy. The Countess will be there. We will stay until about two o'clock. Here is your chance to see me alone. As soon as the Countess has left the house, the servants will probably go to their quarters—with the exception of the hall-porter, who normally goes out to his

closet anyway. Come at half-past eleven. Walk straight upstairs. If you meet anybody in the ante-room, ask whether the Countess is at home. You will be told 'No'—and there will be nothing you can do but go away. But it is unlikely that you will meet anybody. The lady's maids sit by themselves, all in the one room. On leaving the hall, turn to the left and walk straight on until you come to the Countess' bedroom. In the bedroom, behind a screen, you will see two small doors: the one on the right leads into the study, which the Countess never goes into; the one on the left leads into a corridor and thence to a narrow winding staircase: this staircase leads to my bedroom.

Hermann quivered like a tiger as he awaited the appointed hour. He was already outside the Countess' house at ten o'clock. The weather was terrible; the wind howled, and a wet snow fell in large flakes upon the deserted streets, where the lamps shone dimly. Occasionally a passing cab-driver leaned forward over his scrawny nag, on the look-out for a late passenger. Feeling neither wind nor snow, Hermann waited, dressed only in his frock-coat. At last the Countess' carriage was brought round. Hermann saw two footmen carry out in their arms the bent old lady, wrapped in a sable fur, and immediately following her, the figure of Lisaveta Ivanovna, clad in a light cloak, and with her head adorned with fresh flowers. The doors were slammed and the carriage rolled heavily away along the soft snow. The hall-porter closed the front door. The windows became dark. Hermann began to walk about near the deserted house; he went up to a lamp and looked at his watch; it was twenty minutes past eleven. He remained beneath the lamp; his eyes fixed upon the hands of his watch, waiting for the remaining minutes to pass. At exactly half-past eleven, Hermann ascended the steps of the Countess' house and reached the brightly-lit porch. The hall-porter was not there. Hermann ran up the stairs, opened the door into the ante-room and saw a servant asleep by the lamp in a soiled antique armchair. With a light, firm tread Hermann stepped past him. The drawing-room and reception-room were in darkness, but the lamp in the ante-room sent through a feeble light. Hermann passed through into the bedroom. Before an icon-case, filled with old-fashioned images,[8] glowed a gold sanctuary lamp. Faded brocade armchairs and dull gilt divans with soft cushions were ranged in sad symmetry around the room, the walls of which were hung with Chinese silk. Two portraits, painted in Paris by Madame Lebrun,[9] were hung from one of the walls. One of these featured a plump, red-faced man of about forty, in a light-green uniform and with a star pinned to his breast; the other—a beautiful young woman with an aquiline nose and powdered hair, brushed back at the temples and adorned with a rose. In the corners of the room stood porcelain shepherdesses, table clocks from the workshop of the celebrated Leroy, little boxes, roulettes,[1] fans and the various lady's playthings which had been popular at the end of the last century, when the Montgolfiers' balloon and Mesmer's magnetism[2] were invented. Hermann went behind

---

8. That is, religious images.   9. Marie Anne Elizabeth Vigée-Lebrun (1755–1842), French portrait painter, particularly of the aristocracy and royalty.   1. Little balls; or possibly portable devices for playing the gambling game of roulette. Julien Leroy (1686–1759), famous French clockmaker. 2. Franz Anton Mesmer (1734–1815) argued that a person can transmit personal force to others in the form of "animal magnetism." Joseph-Michel (1740–1810) and Jacques-Etienne (1745–1799) Montgolfier, French brothers, helped to develop the hot-air balloon and conducted the first untethered flights.

the screen, where stood a small iron bedstead; on the right was the door leading to the study; on the left the one which led to the corridor. Hermann opened the latter, and saw the narrow, winding staircase which led to the poor ward's room. . . . But he turned back and stepped into the dark study.

The time passed slowly. Everything was quiet. The clock in the drawing-room struck twelve; one by one the clocks in all the other rooms sounded the same hour, and then all was quiet again. Hermann stood leaning against the cold stove. He was calm; his heart beat evenly, like that of a man who has decided upon some dangerous but necessary action. One o'clock sounded; two o'clock; he heard the distant rattle of the carriage. He was seized by an involuntary agitation. The carriage drew near and stopped. He heard the sound of the carriage-steps being let down. The house suddenly came alive. Servants ran here and there, voices echoed through the house and the rooms were lit. Three old maid-servants hastened into the bedroom, followed by the Countess, who, tired to death, lowered herself into a Voltairean armchair.[3] Hermann peeped through a crack. Lisaveta Ivanovna went past him. Hermann heard her hurried steps as she went up the narrow staircase. In his heart there echoed something like the voice of conscience, but it grew silent, and his heart once more turned to stone.

The Countess began to undress before the looking-glass. Her rose-bedecked cap was unfastened; her powdered wig was removed from her grey, closely-cropped hair. Pins fell in showers around her. Her yellow dress, embroidered with silver, fell at her swollen feet. Hermann witnessed all the loathsome mysteries of her dress; at last the Countess stood in her dressing-gown and night-cap; in this attire, more suitable to her age, she seemed less hideous and revolting.

Like most old people, the Countess suffered from insomnia. Having undressed, she sat down by the window in the Voltairean armchair and dismissed her maidservants. The candles were carried out; once again the room was lit by a single sanctuary lamp. Looking quite yellow, the Countess sat rocking to and fro in her chair, her flabby lips moving. Her dim eyes reflected a complete absence of thought and, looking at her, one would have thought that the awful old woman's rocking came not of her own volition, but by the action of some hidden galvanism.

Suddenly, an indescribable change came over her death-like face. Her lips ceased to move, her eyes came to life: before the Countess stood an unknown man.

"Don't be alarmed, for God's sake, don't be alarmed," he said in a clear, low voice. "I have no intention of harming you; I have come to beseech a favour of you."

The old woman looked at him in silence, as if she had not heard him. Hermann imagined that she was deaf, and bending right down over her ear, he repeated what he had said. The old woman kept silent as before.

"You can ensure the happiness of my life," Hermann continued, "and it will cost you nothing: I know that you can guess three cards in succession. . . ."

3. A large armchair with a high back.

Hermann stopped. The Countess appeared to understand what was demanded of her; she seemed to be seeking words for her reply.

"It was a joke," she said at last. "I swear to you, it was a joke."

"There's no joking about it," Hermann retorted angrily. "Remember Chaplitsky whom you helped to win."

The Countess was visibly disconcerted, and her features expressed strong emotion; but she quickly resumed her former impassivity.

"Can you name these three winning cards?" Hermann continued.

The Countess was silent. Hermann went on:

"For whom do you keep your secret? For your grandsons? They are rich and they can do without it; they don't know the value of money. Your three cards will not help a spendthrift. He who cannot keep his paternal inheritance will die in want, even if he has the devil at his side. I am not a spendthrift; I know the value of money. Your three cards will not be lost on me. Come . . . . !"

He stopped and awaited her answer with trepidation. The Countess was silent. Hermann fell upon his knees.

"If your heart has ever known the feeling of love," he said, "if you remember its ecstasies, if you ever smiled at the wailing of your new-born son, if ever any human feeling has run through your breast, I entreat you by the feelings of a wife, a lover, a mother, by everything that is sacred in life, not to deny my request! Reveal your secret to me! What is it to you . . . ? Perhaps it is bound up with some dreadful sin, with the loss of eternal bliss, with some contract made with the devil . . . Consider: you are old; you have not long to live—I am prepared to take your sins on my own soul. Only reveal to me your secret. Realise that the happiness of a man is in your hands, that not only I, but my children, my grandchildren, my great-grandchildren will bless your memory and will revere it as something sacred. . . ."

The old woman answered not a word.

Hermann stood up.

"You old witch!" he said, clenching his teeth. "I'll force you to answer. . . ."

With these words he drew a pistol from his pocket. At the sight of the pistol, the Countess, for the second time, exhibited signs of strong emotion. She shook her head and raising her hand as though to shield herself from the shot, she rolled over on her back and remained motionless.

"Stop this childish behaviour now," Hermann said, taking her hand. "I ask you for the last time: will you name your three cards or won't you?"

The Countess made no reply. Hermann saw that she was dead.

CHAPTER FOUR

7 Mai 18**
Homme sans moeurs et sans religion![4]
CORRESPONDENCE

Still in her ball dress, Lisaveta Ivanovna sat in her room, lost in thought. On her arrival home, she had quickly dismissed the sleepy maid who had

---

4. A man without morals and without religion! (French).

reluctantly offered her services, had said that she would undress herself, and with a tremulous heart had gone up to her room, expecting to find Hermann there and yet hoping not to find him. Her first glance assured her of his absence and she thanked her fate for the obstacle that had prevented their meeting. She sat down, without undressing, and began to recall all the circumstances which had lured her so far in so short a time. It was not three weeks since she had first seen the young man from the window—and yet she was already in correspondence with him, and already he had managed to persuade her to grant him a nocturnal meeting! She knew his name only because some of his letters had been signed; she had never spoken to him, nor heard his voice, nor heard anything about him . . . until that very evening. Strange thing! That very evening, Tomsky, vexed with the Princess Polina *** for not flirting with him as she usually did, had wished to revenge himself by a show of indifference: he had therefore summoned Lisaveta Ivanovna and together they had danced an endless mazurka. All the time they were dancing, he had teased her about her partiality to officers of the Engineers, had assured her that he knew far more than she would have supposed possible, and indeed, some of his jests were so successfully aimed that on several occasions Lisaveta Ivanovna had thought that her secret was known to him.

"From whom have you discovered all this?" she asked, laughing.

"From a friend of the person whom you know so well," Tomsky answered; "from a most remarkable man!"

"Who is this remarkable man?"

"He is called Hermann."

Lisaveta made no reply, but her hands and feet turned quite numb.

"This Hermann," Tomsky continued, "is a truly romantic figure: he has the profile of a Napoleon, and the soul of a Mephistopheles. I should think that he has at least three crimes on his conscience. . . . How pale you have turned. . . . !"

"I have a headache. . . . What did this Hermann—or whatever his name is—tell you?"

"Hermann is most displeased with his friend: he says that he would act quite differently in his place . . . I even think that Hermann himself has designs on you; at any rate he listens to the exclamations of his enamoured friend with anything but indifference."

"But where has he seen me?"

"At church, perhaps; on a walk—God only knows! Perhaps in your room, whilst you were asleep: he's quite capable of it . . ."

Three ladies approaching him with the question: *"oublie ou regret?"*[5] interrupted the conversation which had become so agonisingly interesting to Lisaveta Ivanovna.

The lady chosen by Tomsky was the Princess Polina *** herself. She succeeded in clearing up the misunderstanding between them during the many turns and movements of the dance, after which he conducted her to her chair. Tomsky returned to his own place. He no longer had any

5. The ladies cut in, offering the man a choice: *oublie* (forgetting) or *regret*. He does not know which lady is which. He chooses correctly the one with whom he wants to dance.

thoughts for Hermann or Lisaveta Ivanovna, who desperately wanted to renew her interrupted conversation; but the mazurka came to an end and shortly afterwards the old Countess left.

Tomsky's words were nothing but ball-room chatter, but they made a deep impression upon the mind of the young dreamer. The portrait, sketched by Tomsky, resembled the image she herself had formed of Hermann, and thanks to the latest romantic novels, Hermann's quite commonplace face took on attributes that both frightened and captivated her imagination. Now she sat, her uncovered arms crossed, her head, still adorned with flowers, bent over her bare shoulders. . . . Suddenly the door opened, and Hermann entered. She shuddered.

"Where have you been?" she asked in a frightened whisper.

"In the old Countess' bedroom," Hermann answered: "I have just left it. The Countess is dead."

"Good God! What are you saying?"

"And it seems," Hermann continued, "that I am the cause of her death."

Lisaveta Ivanovna looked at him, and the words of Tomsky echoed in her mind: "he has at least three crimes on his conscience"! Hermann sat down beside her on the window sill and told her everything.

Lisaveta Ivanovna listened to him with horror. So those passionate letters, those ardent demands, the whole impertinent and obstinate pursuit— all that was not love! Money—that was what his soul craved for! It was not she who could satisfy his desire and make him happy! The poor ward had been nothing but the unknowing assistant of a brigand, of the murderer of her aged benefactress! . . . She wept bitterly, in an agony of belated repentance. Hermann looked at her in silence; his heart was also tormented; but neither the tears of the poor girl nor the astounding charm of her grief disturbed his hardened soul. He felt no remorse at the thought of the dead old lady. He felt dismay for only one thing: the irretrievable loss of the secret upon which he had relied for enrichment.

"You are a monster!" Lisaveta Ivanovna said at last.

"I did not wish for her death," Hermann answered. "My pistol wasn't loaded."

They were silent.

The day began to break. Lisaveta Ivanovna extinguished the flickering candle. A pale light lit up her room. She wiped her tear-stained eyes and raised them to Hermann: he sat by the window, his arms folded and with a grim frown on his face. In this position he bore an astonishing resemblance to a portrait of Napoleon. Even Lisaveta Ivanovna was struck by the likeness.

"How am I going to get you out of the house?" Lisaveta Ivanovna said at last. "I had thought of leading you along the secret staircase, but that would mean going past the Countess' bedroom, and I am afraid."

"Tell me how to find this secret staircase; I'll go on my own."

Lisaveta Ivanovna stood up, took a key from her chest of drawers, handed it to Hermann, and gave him detailed instructions. Hermann pressed her cold, unresponsive hand, kissed her bowed head and left.

He descended the winding staircase and once more entered the Countess' bedroom. The dead old lady sat as if turned to stone; her face expressed a deep calm. Hermann stopped before her and gazed at her for a long time, as if wishing to assure himself of the dreadful truth; finally, he went into the study, felt for the door behind the silk wall hangings, and, agitated by strange feelings, he began to descend the dark staircase.

"Along this very staircase," he thought, "perhaps at this same hour sixty years ago, in an embroidered coat, his hair dressed à *l'oiseau royal*,[6] his three-cornered hat pressed to his heart, there may have crept into this very bedroom a young and happy man now long since turned to dust in his grave—and to-day the aged heart of his mistress ceased to beat."

At the bottom of the staircase Hermann found a door, which he opened with the key Lisaveta Ivanovna had given him, and he found himself in a corridor which led into the street.

CHAPTER FIVE

That evening there appeared before me
the figure of the late Baroness von V**.
She was all in white and she said to me:
"How are you, Mr. Councillor!"
                                        SWEDENBORG[7]

Three days after the fateful night, at nine o'clock in the morning, Hermann set out for the *** monastery, where a funeral service for the dead Countess was going to be held. Although unrepentant, he could not altogether silence the voice of conscience, which kept on repeating: "You are the murderer of the old woman!" Having little true religious belief, he was extremely superstitious. He believed that the dead Countess could exercise a harmful influence on his life, and he had therefore resolved to be present at the funeral, in order to ask her forgiveness.

The church was full. Hermann could scarcely make his way through the crowd of people. The coffin stood on a rich catafalque beneath a velvet canopy. Within it lay the dead woman, her arms folded upon her chest, and dressed in a white satin robe, with a lace cap on her head. Around her stood the members of her household: servants in black coats, with armorial ribbons upon their shoulders and candles in their hands; the relatives—children, grandchildren, great-grandchildren—in deep mourning. Nobody cried; tears would have been *une affectation*. The Countess was so old that her death could have surprised nobody, and her relatives had long considered her as having outlived herself. A young bishop pronounced the funeral sermon. In simple, moving words, he described the peaceful end of the righteous woman, who for many years had been in quiet and touching preparation for a Christian end. "The angel of death found her," the speaker said, "waiting for the midnight bridegroom, vigilant in godly meditation." The service was completed with sad decorum. The relatives were the first to take leave of the body. Then the numerous guests went up to pay final homage to her who had so long participated in their frivolous amusements. They were followed by all the members of the

6. In the style of the royal bird (French, literal trans.); an antiquated and elaborate hairstyle.
7. Emmanuel Swedenborg (1688–1772), Swedish theologian, believed that he had several experiences of divine revelation, some involving appearances to him of the dead.

Countess' household, the last of whom was an old housekeeper of the same age as the Countess. She was supported by two young girls who led her up to the coffin. She had not the strength to bow down to the ground—and merely shed a few tears as she kissed the cold hand of her mistress. After that, Hermann decided to approach the coffin. He knelt down and for several minutes lay on the cold floor, which was strewn with fir branches; at last he got up, as pale as the dead woman herself; he went up the steps of the catafalque and bent his head over the body of the Countess. . . . At that very moment it seemed to him that the dead woman gave him a mocking glance, and winked at him. Hermann, hurriedly stepping back, missed his footing, and crashed on his back against the ground. He was helped to his feet. At the same moment, Lisaveta Ivanovna was carried out in a faint to the porch of the church. These events disturbed the solemnity of the gloomy ceremony for a few moments. A subdued murmur rose among the congregation, and a tall, thin chamberlain, a near relative of the dead woman, whispered in the ear of an Englishman standing by him that the young officer was the Countess' illegitimate son, to which the Englishman replied coldly: "Oh?"

For the whole of that day Hermann was exceedingly troubled. He went to a secluded inn for dinner and, contrary to his usual custom and in the hope of silencing his inward agitation, he drank heavily. But the wine fired his imagination still more. Returning home, he threw himself on to his bed without undressing, and fell into a heavy sleep.

It was already night when he awoke: the moon lit up his room. He glanced at his watch; it was a quarter to three. He found he could not go back to sleep; he sat down on his bed and thought about the funeral of the old Countess.

At that moment somebody in the street glanced in at his window, and immediately went away again. Hermann paid no attention to the incident. A minute or so later, he heard the door into the front room being opened. Hermann imagined that it was his orderly, drunk as usual, returning from some nocturnal outing. But he heard unfamiliar footsteps and the soft shuffling of slippers. The door opened: a woman in a white dress entered. Hermann mistook her for his old wet-nurse and wondered what could have brought her out at that time of the night. But the woman in white glided across the room and suddenly appeared before him—and Hermann recognised the Countess!

"I have come to you against my will," she said in a firm voice, "but I have been ordered to fulfill your request. Three, seven, ace, played in that order, will win for you, but only on condition that you play not more than one card in twenty-four hours, and that you never play again for the rest of your life. I'll forgive you my death if you marry my ward, Lisaveta Ivanovna. . . ."

With these words, she turned round quietly, walked towards the door and disappeared, her slippers shuffling. Herman heard the door in the hall bang, and again saw somebody look in at him through the window.

For a long time Hermann could not collect his senses. He went out into the next room. His orderly was lying asleep on the floor; Hermann could scarcely wake him. The orderly was, as usual, drunk, and it was impossible to get any sense out of him. The door into the hall was locked. Hermann returned to his room, lit a candle, and recorded the details of his vision.

CHAPTER SIX

"Attendez!"[8]
"How dare you say to me: 'Attendez'?"
"Your Excellency, I said: 'Attendez, sir'!"

Two fixed ideas can no more exist in one mind than, in the physical sense, two bodies can occupy one and the same place. "Three, seven, ace" soon eclipsed from Hermann's mind the form of the dead old lady. "Three, seven, ace" never left his thoughts, were constantly on his lips. At the sight of a young girl, he would say: "How shapely she is! Just like the three of hearts." When asked the time, he would reply: "About seven." Every pot-bellied man he saw reminded him of an ace. "Three, seven, ace," assuming all possible shapes, persecuted him in his sleep: the three bloomed before him in the shape of some luxuriant flower, the seven took on the appearance of a Gothic gateway, the ace—of an enormous spider. To the exclusion of all others, one thought alone occupied his mind—making use of the secret which had cost him so much. He began to think of retirement and of travel. He wanted to try his luck in the public gaming-houses of Paris. Chance spared him the trouble.

There was in Moscow a society of rich gamblers, presided over by the celebrated Chekalinsky, a man whose whole life had been spent at the card-table, and who had amassed millions long ago, accepting his winnings in the form of promissory notes and paying his losses with ready money. His long experience had earned him the confidence of his companions, and his open house, his famous cook and his friendliness and gaiety had won him great public respect. He arrived in Petersburg. The younger generation flocked to his house, forgetting balls for cards, and preferring the enticements of faro to the fascinations of courtship. Narumov took Hermann to meet him.

They passed through a succession of magnificent rooms, full of polite and attentive waiters. Several generals and privy councillors were playing whist; young men, sprawled out on brocade divans, were eating ices and smoking their pipes. In the drawing-room, seated at the head of a long table, around which were crowded about twenty players, the host kept bank. He was a most respectable-looking man of about sixty; his head was covered with silvery grey hair, and his full, fresh face expressed good nature; his eyes, enlivened by a perpetual smile, shone brightly. Narumov introduced Hermann to him. Chekalinsky shook his hand warmly, requested him not to stand on ceremony, and went on dealing.

The game lasted a long time. More than thirty cards lay on the table. Chekalinsky paused after each round in order to give the players time to arrange their cards, wrote down their losses, listened politely to their demands, and more politely still allowed them to retract any stake acciden-

---

8. Wait! (French). Attendants at the gaming table called *Attendez* to indicate the end of the period to place bets.

tally left on the table. At last the game finished. Chekalinsky shuffled the cards and prepared to deal again.

"Allow me to place a stake," Hermann said, stretching out his hand from behind a fat gentleman who was punting[9] there.

Chekalinsky smiled and nodded silently, as a sign of his consent. Narumov laughingly congratulated Hermann on forswearing a longstanding principle and wished him a lucky beginning.

"I've staked," Hermann said, as he chalked up the amount, which was very considerable, on the back of his card.

"How much is it?" asked the banker, screwing up his eyes. "Forgive me, but I can't make it out."

"47,000 roubles," Hermann replied.

At these words every head in the room turned, and all eyes were fixed on Hermann.

"He's gone out of his mind!" Narumov thought.

"Allow me to observe to you," Chekalinsky said with his invariable smile, "that your stake is extremely high: nobody here has ever put more than 275 roubles on any single card."

"What of it?" retorted Hermann. "Do you take me or not?"

Chekalinsky, bowing, humbly accepted the stake.

"However, I would like to say," he said, "that, being judged worthy of the confidence of my friends, I can only bank against ready money. For my own part, of course, I am sure that your word is enough, but for the sake of the order of the game and of the accounts, I must ask you to place your money on the card."

Hermann drew a banknote from his pocket and handed it to Chekalinsky who, giving it a cursory glance, put it on Hermann's card.

He began to deal. On the right a nine turned up, on the left a three.[1]

"The three wins," said Hermann, showing his card.

A murmur arose among the players. Chekalinsky frowned, but instantly the smile returned to his face.

"Do you wish to take the money now?" he asked Hermann.

"If you would be so kind."

Chekalinsky drew a number of banknotes from his pocket and settled up immediately. Hermann took up his money and left the table. Narumov was too astounded even to think. Hermann drank a glass of lemonade and went home.

The next evening he again appeared at Chekalinsky's. The host was dealing. Hermann walked up to the table; the players already there immediately gave way to him. Chekalinsky bowed graciously.

Hermann waited for the next deal, took a card and placed on it his 47,000 roubles together with the winnings of the previous evening.

Chekalinsky began to deal. A knave turned up on the right, a seven on the left.

Hermann showed his seven.

There was a general cry of surprise, and Chekalinsky was clearly discon-

9. Betting against the dealer.   1. Bets in faro are made on the positions of cards. A player selects a card and places it facedown in front of him or her; if the card turns up on the dealer's left, the player wins; if on the right, the dealer wins.

certed. He counted out 94,000 roubles and handed them to Hermann, who pocketed them coolly and immediately withdrew.

The following evening Hermann again appeared at the table. Everyone was expecting him; the generals and privy councillors abandoned their whist in order to watch such unusual play. The young officers jumped up from their divans; all the waiters gathered in the drawing-room. Hermann was surrounded by a crowd of people. The other players held back their cards, impatient to see how Hermann would get on. Hermann stood at the table and prepared to play alone against the pale but still smiling Chekalinsky. Each unsealed a pack of cards. Chekalinsky shuffled. Hermann drew and placed his card, covering it with a heap of banknotes. It was like a duel. A deep silence reigned all around.

His hands shaking, Chekalinsky began to deal. On the right lay a queen, on the left an ace.

"The ace wins," said Hermann and showed his card.

"Your queen has lost," Chekalinsky said kindly.

Hermann started: indeed, instead of an ace, before him lay the queen of spades. He could not believe his eyes, could not understand how he could have slipped up.

At that moment it seemed to him that the queen of spades winked at him and smiled. He was struck by an unusual likeness . . .

"The old woman!" he shouted in terror.

Chekalinsky gathered up his winnings. Hermann stood motionless. When he left the table, people began to converse noisily.

"Famously punted!" the players said.

Chekalinsky shuffled the cards afresh; play went on as usual.

CONCLUSION

Hermann went mad. He is now installed in Room 17 at the Obukhov Hospital; he answers no questions, but merely mutters with unusual rapidity: "Three, seven, ace! Three, seven, queen!"

Lisaveta Ivanovna has married a very agreeable young man, who has a good position in the service somewhere; he is the son of the former steward of the old Countess. Lisaveta Ivanovna is bringing up a poor relative.

Tomsky has been promoted to the rank of Captain, and is going to marry Princess Polina.

WALT WHITMAN
1819–1892

As insistently as Rousseau, but with a far richer sense of the nature and the importance of his social context, Walt Whitman in his poetry makes himself the center of the universe. He brings to his emphatic self-presentation a detailed, partly ironic, partly celebratory sense of what it means to be an American; his poetry suggests something of what life in the United States must have felt like in the middle of the nineteenth century.

Thomas, *The Lunar Light of Whitman's Poetry* (1987); and J. E. Miller, *Leaves of Grass: America's Lyric-Epic of Self and Democracy* (1992).

From Song of Myself[1]

1

I celebrate myself, and sing myself,
And what I assume you shall assume,
For every atom belonging to me as good belongs to you.

I loafe and invite my soul,
I lean and loafe at my ease observing a spear of summer grass.   5

My tongue, every atom of my blood, formed from this soil, this air,
Born here of parents born here from parents the same, and their parents
     the same,
I, now thirty-seven years old in perfect health begin,
Hoping to cease not till death.

Creeds and schools in abeyance,   10
Retiring back a while sufficed at what they are, but never forgotten,
I harbor for good or bad, I permit to speak at every hazard,
Nature without check with original energy.

                    *   *   *

4

Trippers and askers surround me,
People I meet, the effect upon me of my early life or the ward and city I
     live in, or the nation,
The latest dates, discoveries, inventions, societies, authors old and new,
My dinner, dress, associates, looks, compliments, dues,
The real or fancied indifference of some man or woman I love,   5
The sickness of one of my folks or of myself, or ill-doing or loss or lack
     of money, or depressions or exaltations,
Battles, the horrors of fratricidal war, the fever of doubtful news, the
     fitful events;
These come to me days and nights and go from me again,
But they are not the Me myself.

Apart from the pulling and hauling stands what I am,   10
Stands amused, complacent, compassionating, idle, unitary,
Looks down, is erect, or bends an arm on an impalpable certain rest,
Looking with side-curved head curious what will come next,
Both in and out of the game and watching and wondering at it.

Backward I see in my own days where I sweated through fog with
     linguists and contenders,
I have no mockings or arguments, I witness and wait.   15

                    *   *   *

1. First published in 1855. This text is from the 1891–92 edition of *Leaves of Grass*, the so-called Deathbed Edition.

7

Has any one supposed it lucky to be born?
I hasten to inform him or her it is just as lucky to die, and I know it.

I pass death with the dying and birth with the new-washed babe, and am
    not contained between my hat and boots,
And peruse manifold objects, no two alike and every one good,
The earth good and the stars good, and their adjuncts all good. 5

I am not an earth nor an adjunct of an earth,
I am the mate and companion of people, all just as immortal and
    fathomless as myself,
(They do not know how immortal, but I know.)

Every kind for itself and its own, for me mine male and female,
For me those that have been boys and that love women, 10
For me the man that is proud and feels how it stings to be slighted,
For me the sweet-heart and the old maid, for me mothers and the
    mothers of mothers,
For me lips that have smiled, eyes that have shed tears,
For me children and the begetters of children.

Undrape! you are not guilty to me, nor stale nor discarded, 15
I see through the broadcloth and gingham whether or no,
And am around, tenacious, acquisitive, tireless, and cannot be shaken
    away.

*   *   *

16

I am of old and young, of the foolish as much as the wise,
Regardless of others, ever regardful of others,
Maternal as well as paternal, a child as well as a man,
Stuffed with the stuff that is coarse and stuffed with the stuff that is fine,
One of the Nation of many nations, the smallest the same and the
    largest the same, 5
A Southerner soon as a Northerner, a planter nonchalant and hospitable
    down by the Oconee[2] I live,
A Yankee bound my own was ready for trade, my joints the limberest
    joints on earth and the sternest joints on earth,
A Kentuckian walking the vale of the Elkhorn in my deer-skin leggings,
    a Louisianian or Georgian,
A boatman over lakes or bays or along coasts, a Hoosier, Badger,
    Buckeye;
At home on Kanadian snow-shoes or up in the bush, or with fishermen
    off Newfoundland, 10
At home in the fleet of ice-boats, sailing with the rest and tacking,
At home on the hills of Vermont or in the woods of Maine, or the
    Texan ranch,
Comrade of Californians, comrade of free North-Westerners, (loving
    their big proportions,)
Comrade of raftsmen and coalmen, comrade of all who shake hands
    and welcome to drink and meat,
A learner with the simplest, a teacher of the thoughtfullest, 15

2. River in Georgia.

A novice beginning yet experient of myriads of seasons,
Of every hue and caste am I, of every rank and religion,
A farmer, mechanic, artist, gentleman, sailor, quaker,
Prisoner, fancy-man, rowdy, lawyer, physician, priest.

I resist any thing better than my own diversity,   20
Breathe the air but leave plenty after me,
And am not stuck up, and am in my place.

(The moth and the fish-eggs are in their place,
The bright suns I see and the dark suns I cannot see are in their place,
The palpable is in its place and the impalpable is in its place.)   25

*   *   *

21

I am the poet of the Body and I am the poet of the Soul,
The pleasures of heaven are with me and the pains of hell are with me,
The first I graft and increase upon myself, the latter I translate into a
    new tongue.

I am the poet of the woman the same as the man,
And I say it is as great to be a woman as to be a man,   5
And I say there is nothing greater than the mother of men.

I chant the chant of dilation or pride,
We have had ducking and deprecating about enough,
I show that size is only development.

Have you outstript the rest? are you the President?   10
It is a trifle, they will more than arrive there every one, and still pass on.

I am he that walks with the tender and growing night,
I call to the earth and sea half-held by the night.

Press close bare-bosomed night—press close magnetic nourishing night!
Night of south winds—night of the large few stars!   15
Still nodding night—mad naked summer night.

Smile O voluptuous cool-breathed earth!
Earth of the slumbering and liquid trees!
Earth of departed sunset—earth of the mountains misty-topt!
Earth of the vitreous pour of the full moon just tinged with blue!   20
Earth of shine and dark mottling the tide of the river!
Earth of the limpid gray of clouds brighter and clearer for my sake!
Far-swooping elbowed earth—rich apple-blossomed earth!
Smile, for your lover comes.

Prodigal, you have given me love—therefore I to you give love!   25
O unspeakable passionate love.

*   *   *

24

Walt Whitman, a kosmos, of Manhattan the son,
Turbulent, fleshy, sensual, eating, drinking and breeding,
No sentimentalist, no stander above men and women or apart from
    them,
No more modest than immodest.

Unscrew the locks from the doors!   5
Unscrew the doors themselves from their jambs!

Whoever degrades another degrades me,
And whatever is done or said returns at last to me.

Through me the afflatus surging and surging, through me the current
    and index.

I speak the pass-word primeval, I give the sign of democracy,   10
By God! I will accept nothing which all cannot have their counterpart
    of on the same terms.

*   *   *

32

I think I could turn and live with animals, they are so placid and self-con-
    tained,
I stand and look at them long and long.

They do not sweat and whine about their condition,
They do not lie awake in the dark and weep for their sins,
They do not make me sick discussing their duty to God,   5
Not one is dissatisfied, not one is demented with the mania of owning
    things,
Not one kneels to another, nor to his kind that lived thousands of years
    ago,
Not one is respectable or unhappy over the whole earth.

So they show their relations to me and I accept them,
They bring me tokens of myself, they evince them plainly in their
    possession.   10

I wonder where they get those tokens,
Did I pass that way huge times ago and negligently drop them?

Myself moving forward then and now and forever,
Gathering and showing more always and with velocity,
Infinite and omnigenous,[3] and the like of these among them,   15
Not too exclusive toward the reachers of my remembrancers,
Picking out here one that I love, and now go with him on brotherly
    terms.

A gigantic beauty of a stallion, fresh and responsive to my caresses,
Head high in the forehead, wide between the ears,
Limbs glossy and supple, tail dusting the ground,   20
Eyes full of sparkling wickedness, ears finely cut, flexibly moving.

His nostrils dilate as my heels embrace him,
His well-built limbs tremble with pleasure as we race around and return.

I but use you a minute, then I resign you, stallion,
Why do I need your paces when I myself out-gallop them?   25
Even as I stand or sit passing faster than you.

*   *   *

3. Belonging to all races.

46

I know I have the best of time and space, and was never measured and
    never will be measured.

I tramp a perpetual journey, (come listen all!)
My signs are a rain-proof coat, good shoes, and a staff cut from the
    woods,
No friend of mine takes his ease in my chair,
I have no chair, no church, no philosophy,   5
I lead no man to a dinner-table, library, exchange,
But each man and each woman of you I lead upon a knoll,
My left hand hooking you round the waist,
My right hand pointing to landscapes of continents and the public road.

Not I, not any one else can travel that road for you,   10
You must travel it for yourself.

It is not far, it is within reach,
Perhaps you have been on it since you were born and did not know,
Perhaps it is everywhere on water and on land.

Shoulder your duds dear son, and I will mine, and let us hasten forth,   15
Wonderful cities and free nations we shall fetch as we go.

✻   ✻   ✻

51

The past and present wilt—I have filled them, emptied them,
And proceed to fill my next fold of the future.

Listener up there! what have you to confide to me?
Look in my face while I snuff the sidle of evening,[4]
(Talk honestly, no one else hears you, and I stay only a minute longer.) 5

Do I contradict myself?
Very well then I contradict myself,
(I am large, I contain multitudes.)

I concentrate toward them that are nigh, I wait on the door-slab.

Who has done his day's work? who will soonest be through with his
    supper?   10
Who wishes to walk with me?

Will you speak before I am gone? will you prove already too late?

52

The spotted hawk swoops by and accuses me, he complains of my gab
    and my loitering.

I too am not a bit tamed, I too am untranslatable,
I sound my barbaric yawp over the roofs of the world.

The last scud of day holds back for me,
It flings my likeness after the rest and true as any on the shadowed
    wilds,   5
It coaxes me to the vapor and the dusk.

---

4. That is, smell the fragrance of the slowly descending evening.

I depart as air, I shake my white locks at the runaway sun,
I effuse my flesh in eddies, and drift it in lacy jags.

I bequeath myself to the dirt to grow from the grass I love,
If you want me again look for me under your boot-soles. 10

You will hardly know who I am or what I mean,
But I shall be good health to you nevertheless,
And filter and fibre your blood.

Failing to fetch me at first keep encouraged,
Missing me one place search another, 15
I stop somewhere waiting for you.

EMILY DICKINSON
1830–1886

Emily Dickinson forces her readers to acknowledge the startling aspects of ordinary life. "Ordinary life" includes the mysterious actuality of death, but it also includes birds and woods and oceans, arguments between people, the weight of depression. In small facts and large, Dickinson perceives enormous meaning.

The poet's life, like her verse, was somewhat mysterious. Born to a prosperous and prominent Amherst, Massachusetts, family (her father, a lawyer, was also treasurer of Amherst College), Dickinson attended Amherst Academy and later, for a year, the Mount Holyoke Female Seminary. Thereafter, however, she remained almost entirely in her father's house, leading the life of a recluse. She had close family attachments and a few close friendships, pursued mainly through correspondence. The most important of these relationships, from a literary point of view, was with the Boston writer and critic Thomas Wentworth Higginson, who eventually published her poems. She had begun writing verse in the late 1850s; in 1862, after seeing an essay of Higginson's in the *Atlantic Monthly*, Dickinson wrote him to ask his opinion of her poems, about 300 of them in existence by this time. The correspondence thus begun continued to the end of Dickinson's life; Higginson also visited her in Amherst.

At Dickinson's death, 1,775 poems survived; only 7 had been published, anonymously. With the help of another friend, Mabel Todd Loomis, Higginson selected poems for a volume, published in 1890, which proved extremely popular. Further selections continued to appear, but not until 1955 did Dickinson's entire body of work reach print.

By 1843, the English poet Elizabeth Barrett Browning had written in verse an exhortation to social reform (*The Cry of the Children*); in 1857, she published a long poem, *Aurora Leigh*, commenting on the oppressed situation of women. Christina Rossetti, born the same year as Dickinson and like her unmarried, in poems like *Goblin Market* (1862) found indirect ways to meditate on female predicaments. Dickinson, on the other hand, seems only peripherally aware of social facts. She alludes to church services, locomotives, female costume; very occasionally (for example, "My Life had stood—a Loaded Gun—") she refers to the way a woman's life is defined in relation to a man's. More centrally, she finds brilliant and provocative formulations of the emotional import of universal phenomena. We may feel already that death amounts to an incomprehensible and indigestible fact, but we are unlikely to have imagined conversations within a tomb or a personified version of death as carriage driver. By using such images, Dickinson disarmingly suggests a kind of playful innocence. Only gradually does one realize that the naive, childlike perception, devoid of obviously ominous suggestion, conceals a complex, disturbing sense of human self-deception and reluctance to face the truth of experience.

Truth is an important word in Dickinson's poetry. "Tell all the Truth but tell it slant," she advises, pointing out that "The Truth must dazzle gradually / Or every man be blind—." She tells of a man who preaches about " 'Truth' until it proclaimed him a Liar—": truth remains an absolute, both challenging and judging us all. In one of her most haunting poems, she claims the identity of Beauty and Truth (an identity tellingly asserted in Keats's *Ode on a Grecian Urn*) through the fiction of two dead people discussing their profound commitments:

> I died for Beauty—but was scarce
> Adjusted in the Tomb
> When One who died for Truth, was lain
> In an adjoining Room—

Her neighbor asks her why she "failed"; when she explains, he says that beauty and truth "are One":

> And so, as Kinsmen, met a Night—
> We talked between the Rooms—
> Until the Moss had reached our lips—
> And covered up—our names—

Until the last two lines, about the moss, the poem appears to evoke a rather cozy vision of death: neighbors amiably conversing from one room to another, as though at a slumber party ("met a Night"), two "Kinsmen" dedicated to noble abstractions and comforted by the companionship of their dedication. Only the word *failed* (meaning "died") disturbs the comfortable atmosphere, by suggesting a view of death as defeat.

The Keats poem that ends by asserting the identity of truth and beauty implies the permanence of both, as embodied in the work of art, the Grecian urn that stimulates the poet's reflections. Dickinson's poem concludes with troubling suggestions of impermanence. Talk of beauty and truth may reassure the talkers, but death necessarily implies forgetfulness: the dead forget and are forgotten, their very identities ("names") lost, their capacity for communication eliminated. Death *is* defeat; the high Romanticism of Keats's ode, on which this poem implicitly comments, blurs that fact. Despite Dickinson's fanciful images and allegories, her poems insist on their own kind of uncompromising realism. They speak of the universal human effort to imagine experience in reassuring terms, but they do not suggest that reality offers much in the way of reassurance: only brief experiences of natural beauty; and even those challenge human constructions. "I started Early—Took my dog—" a poem about visiting the sea begins; but it ends with the sea encountering "the Solid Town— / No One He seemed to know—" and withdrawing.

Dickinson's eccentric punctuation, with dashes as the chief mark of emphasis and interruption, emphasizes the movements of consciousness in her lyrics. In their early publication, the poems were typically given conventional punctuation; only in 1955 did the body of work appear as Dickinson wrote it. The highly personal mode of punctuation emphasizes the fact that this verse contains also a personal and demanding vision.

Emily Dickinson: An Interpretive Biography (1955), by T. H. Johnson, Dickinson's editor, is indispensable. Useful critical sources include C. Blake, ed., *The Recognition of Emily Dickinson* (1964), a collection of criticism since 1890; Albert Gelpi, *Emily Dickinson: The Mind of the Poet* (1966); S. Juhasz, ed., *Feminist Critics Read Emily Dickinson* (1983), a collection with a specifically feminist orientation; and J. Dobson, *Dickinson and the Strategies of Reticence* (1989). Other critical studies are K. Stocks, *Emily Dickinson and the Modern Consciousness* (1988), and M. N. Smith, *Rowing in Eden: Rereading Emily Dickinson* (1992).

216

Safe in their Alabaster Chambers—
Untouched by Morning
And untouched by Noon—
Sleep the meek members of the Resurrection—
Rafter of satin,   5
And Roof of stone.

Light laughs the breeze
In her Castle above them—
Babbles the Bee in a stolid Ear,
Pipe the Sweet Birds in ignorant cadence—   10
Ah, what sagacity perished here!

258

There's a certain Slant of light,
Winter Afternoons—
That oppresses, like the Heft
Of Cathedral Tunes—

Heavenly Hurt, it gives us—   5
We can find no scar,
But internal difference,
Where the Meanings, are—

None may teach it—Any—
'Tis the Seal Despair—   10
An imperial affliction
Sent us of the Air—

When it comes, the Landscape listens—
Shadows—hold their breath—
When it goes, 'tis like the Distance   15
On the look of Death—

303

The Soul selects her own Society—
Then—shuts the Door—
To her divine Majority—
Present no more—

Unmoved—she notes the Chariots—pausing   5
At her low Gate—
Unmoved—an Emperor be kneeling
Upon her Mat—

I've known her—from an ample nation—
Choose One—   10
Then—close the Valves of her attention—
Like Stone—

328

A Bird came down the Walk—
He did not know I saw—
He bit an Angleworm in halves
And ate the fellow, raw,

And then he drank a Dew   5
From a convenient Grass—
And then hopped sidewise to the Wall
To let a Beetle pass—

He glanced with rapid eyes
That hurried all around—   10
They looked like frightened Beads, I thought—
He stirred his Velvet Head

Like one in danger, Cautious,
I offered him a Crumb
And he unrolled his feathers   15
And rowed him softer home—

Than Oars divide the Ocean,
Too silver for a seam—
Or Butterflies, off Banks of Noon
Leap, plashless as they swim.   20

341

After great pain, a formal feeling comes—
The Nerves sit ceremonious, like Tombs—
The stiff Heart questions was it He, that bore,
And Yesterday, or Centuries before?

The Feet, mechanical, go round—   5
Of Ground, or Air, or Ought[1]—
A Wooden way
Regardless grown,
A Quartz contentment, like a stone—

This is the Hour of Lead—   10
Remembered, if outlived,

1. Zero

As Freezing persons, recollect the Snow—
First—Chill—then Stupor—then the letting go—

435

Much Madness is divinest Sense—
To a discerning Eye—
Much Sense—the starkest Madness—
'Tis the Majority
In this, as All, prevail—   5
Assent—and you are sane—
Demur—you're straightway dangerous—
And handled with a Chain—

449

I died for Beauty—but was scarce
Adjusted in the Tomb
When One who died for Truth, was lain
In an adjoining Room—

He questioned softly "Why I failed"?   5
"For Beauty", I replied—
"And I—for Truth—Themself are One—
We Brethren, are", He said—

And so, as Kinsmen, met a Night—
We talked between the Rooms—   10
Until the Moss had reached our lips—
And covered up—our names—

465

I heard a Fly buzz—when I died—
The Stillness in the Room
Was like the Stillness in the Air—
Between the Heaves of Storm—

The Eyes around—had wrung them dry—   5
And Breaths were gathering firm
For that last Onset—when the King
Be witnessed—in the Room—

I willed my Keepsakes—Signed away
What portion of me be   10
Assignable—and then it was
There interposed a Fly—

With Blue—uncertain stumbling Buzz—
Between the light—and me—
And then the Windows failed—and then   15
I could not see to see—

519

'Twas warm—at first—like Us—
Until there crept upon
A Chill—like frost upon a Glass—
Till all the scene—be gone.

The Forehead copied Stone—   5
The Fingers grew too cold
To ache—and like a Skater's Brook—
The busy eyes—congealed—

It straightened—that was all—
It crowded Cold to Cold   10
It multiplied indifference—
As[1] Pride were all it could—

And even when with Cords—
'Twas lowered, like a Weight—
It made no Signal, nor demurred,   15
But dropped like Adamant.

585

I like to see it lap the Miles—
And lick the Valleys up—
And stop to feed itself at Tanks—
And then—prodigious step

Around a Pile of Mountains—   5
And supercilious peer
In Shanties—by the sides of Roads—
And then a Quarry pare

To fit its Ribs
And crawl between   10
Complaining all the while
In horrid—hooting stanza—
Then chase itself down Hill—

And neigh like Boanerges[2]—
Then—punctual as a Star   15
Stop—docile and omnipotent
At its own stable door—

632

The Brain—is wider than the Sky—
For—put them side by side—
The one the other will contain
With ease—and You—beside—

1. As if.   2. "Sons of thunder," name given by Jesus to the brothers and disciples James and John, presumably because they were thunderous preachers.

The Brain is deeper than the sea—
For—hold them—Blue to Blue—
The one the other will absorb—
As Sponges—Buckets—do—

The Brain is just the weight of God—
For—Heft them—Pound for Pound—
And they will differ—if they do—
As Syllable from Sound—

657

I dwell in Possibility—
A fairer House than Prose—
More numerous of Windows—
Superior—for Doors—

Of Chambers as the Cedars—
Impregnable of Eye—
And for an Everlasting Roof
The Gambrels[1] of the Sky—

Of Visitors—the fairest—
For Occupation—This—
The spreading wide my narrow Hands
To gather Paradise—

712

Because I could not stop for Death—
He kindly stopped for me—
The Carriage held but just Ourselves—
And Immortality.

We slowly drove—He knew no haste
And I had put away
My labor and my leisure too,
For His Civility—

We passed the School, where Children strove
At Recess—in the Ring—
We passed the Fields of Gazing Grain—
We passed the Setting Sun—

Or rather—He passed Us—
The Dews drew quivering and chill—
For only Gossamer, my Gown—
My Tippet—only Tulle[2]—

We paused before a House that seemed
A Swelling of the Ground—

---

1. Slopes, as in the large, arched roofs often seen on barns. 2. Fine, silken netting. *Tippet:* a scarf.

The Roof was scarcely visible—
The Cornice—in the Ground—　　　　　　　　20

Since then—'tis Centuries—and yet
Feels shorter than the Day
I first surmised the Horses' Heads
Were toward Eternity—

754

My Life had stood—a Loaded Gun—
In Corners—till a Day
The Owner passed—identified—
And carried Me away—

And now We roam in Sovereign Woods—　　　　5
And now We hunt the Doe—
And every time I speak for Him—
The Mountains straight reply—

And do I smile, such cordial light
Upon the Valley glow—　　　　　　　　　　10
It is as a Vesuvian face[1]
Had let its pleasure through—

And when at Night—Our good Day done—
I guard My Master's Head—
'Tis better than the Eider-Duck's　　　　　　15
Deep Pillow—to have shared—

To foe of His—I'm deadly foe—
None stir the second time—
On whom I lay a Yellow Eye—
Or an emphatic Thumb—　　　　　　　　　20

Though I than He—may longer live
He longer must—than I—
For I have but the power to kill,
Without—the power to die—

1084

At Half past Three, a single Bird
Unto a silent Sky
Propounded but a single term
Of cautious melody.

At Half past Four, Experiment　　　　　　　5
Had subjugated test
And lo, Her silver Principle
Supplanted all the rest.

At Half past Seven, Element
Nor Implement, be seen—　　　　　　　　10

---

1. A face glowing with light like that from an erupting volcano.

And Place was where the Presence was
Circumference between.

1129

Tell all the Truth but tell it slant—
Success in Circuit lies
Too bright for our infirm Delight
The Truth's superb surprise

As Lightning to the Children eased   5
With explanation kind
The Truth must dazzle gradually
Or every man be blind—

1207

He preached upon "Breadth" till it argued him narrow—
The Broad are too broad to define
And of "Truth" until it proclaimed him a Liar—
The Truth never flaunted a Sign—

Simplicity fled from his counterfeit presence   5
As Gold the Pyrites[1] would shun—
What confusion would cover the innocent Jesus
To meet so enabled[2] a Man!

1564

Pass to thy Rendezvous of Light,
Pangless except for us—
Who slowly ford the Mystery
Which thou hast leaped across!

1593

There came a Wind like a Bugle—
It quivered through the Grass
And a Green Chill upon the Heat
So ominous did pass
We barred the Windows and the Doors   5
As from an Emerald Ghost—
The Doom's electric Moccasin[3]
That very instant passed—
On a strange Mob of panting Trees
And Fences fled away   10
And Rivers where the Houses ran

1. Iron bisulphide, sometimes called fool's gold.   2. Competent.   3. That is, water moccasin, a poisonous snake.

Those looked that lived—that Day—
The Bell within the steeple wild
The flying tidings told—
How much can come   15
And much can go,
And yet abide the World!

comparatively limited area, spread widely and permeated almost all fields of human thought and endeavor. It raised enormous hopes for the future betterment of our condition on earth, especially when Darwin's evolutionary theories fortified the earlier, vaguer faith in unlimited progress. "Liberty," "science," "progress," and "evolution" are the concepts that define the mental atmosphere of the nineteenth century in Europe.

But tendencies hostile to these were by no means absent. Feudal or Catholic conservatism succeeded, especially in Austria-Hungary, in Russia, and in much of southern Europe, in preserving old regimes, and the philosophies of a conservative and religious society were reformulated in modern terms. At the same time, in England the very assumptions of the new industrial middle-class society were powerfully attacked by writers such as Carlyle and Ruskin who recommended a return to medieval forms of social cooperation and handicraft. The industrial civilization of the nineteenth century was also opposed by the fierce individualism of many artists and thinkers who were unhappy in the ugly, commercial, and "Philistine" society of the age. The writings of Nietzsche, toward the end of the century, and the whole movement of "art for art's sake," which asserted the independence of the artist from society, are the most obvious symptoms of this revolt. The free-enterprise system and the liberalism of the ruling middle classes also early clashed with the rising proletariat; diverse forms of socialism developed, preaching a new collectivism with the stress on equality. Socialism could have Christian or romantic motivations, or it could become "scientific" and revolutionary, as Marx's brand of socialism (a certain stage of which he called "communism") claimed to be.

While up through the eighteenth century religion was, at least in name, a major force in European civilization, in the nineteenth century there was a marked decrease in its influence on both intellectual leaders and ordinary people. Local, intense revivals of religious consciousness, such as the Oxford movement in England, did occur, and the traditional religious institutions were preserved everywhere, but the impact of science on religion was such that many tenets of the old faiths crumbled or were severely weakened. The discoveries of astronomy, geology, evolutionary biology, and archaeology as well as biblical criticism forced, almost everywhere, a restatement of the old creeds. Religion, especially in the Protestant countries, was frequently confined to an inner feeling of religiosity or to a system of morality that preserved the ancient Christian virtues. In Germany during the early nineteenth century, Hegel and his predecessors and followers tried to interpret the world in spiritual terms, outside the bounds of traditional religion. There were many attempts even late in the century to restate this view, but the methods and discoveries of science seemed to invalidate it, and various formulas that took science as their base in building new lay religions of hope in humanity gained popularity. French positivism, English utilitarianism, the evolutionism of Herbert Spencer are some of the best-known examples. Meanwhile, for the first time in history, at least in Europe, profoundly pessimistic and atheistic philosophies arose, of which Schopenhauer's was the most subtle, while extreme materialism was the most widespread. Thus the whole gamut of views of the universe was represented during the century in new and impressive formulations.

The plastic arts did not show a similar vitality. For a long time, in most countries, painting and architecture floundered in a sterile eclecticism—in a bewildering variety of historical masquerades in which the neo-Gothic style was replaced by the neo-Renaissance and that by the neo-Baroque and other decorative revivals of past forms. Only in France, painting (with the impressionists) found a new style that was genuinely original. In music the highly Romantic art of Richard Wagner attracted the most attention. Wagner's concept of the *Gesamtkunstwerk*—the "total work" combining music, drama, poetry, and spectacle—influenced Symbolist writers and encouraged the tendency to break down distinctions between genres. Otherwise, the individual national schools either continued in their tradition, like

Italian opera (Verdi) or founded an idiom of their own, often based on a revival of folklore, as in Russia (Tchaikovsky), Poland (Chopin), Bohemia (Dvořák), and Norway (Grieg).

But literature was the most representative and the most widely influential art of nineteenth-century Europe. It found new forms and methods and expressed the social and intellectual situation of the time most fully and memorably. It was this literature, moreover, that served as a model for many non-Western writers seeking to modernize their own literary traditions on the basis of European masterworks. Nowadays, the cultural assumptions of such literary emulation are criticized by some, and many writers seek to rediscover an earlier, precolonial tradition. The literature of nineteenth-century Europe continues nonetheless to be read and admired in its own right.

REALISM AND NATURALISM

After the great wave of the international Romantic movement had spent its force in the fourth decade of the nineteenth century, European literature moved in the direction of what is usually called *realism*. Realism was not a coherent general movement that established itself unchallenged for a long period of time, as classicism had succeeded in doing during the eighteenth century. Exceptions and reservations there were, but still in retrospect the nineteenth century appears as the period of the great realistic writers: Flaubert in France, Dostoevsky and Tolstoy in Russia, Charles Dickens in England, Henry James in America, Ibsen in Norway.

What is meant by *realism*? The term, in literary use (there is a much older philosophical use), apparently dates back to the Germans at the turn of the century—to Friedrich Schiller and August and Friedrich Schlegel. It cropped up in France as early as 1826 but became a commonly accepted literary and artistic slogan only in the 1850s. When Gustave Courbet's paintings were rejected by the Paris World's Fair of 1855, the artist exhibited them separately as "realist" art and wrote a preface to the exhibit catalog that became an unofficial manifesto for realist art. In the following year, a review called *Réalisme* began publication, and in 1857 a novelist and critic, Champfleury (the pseudonym of Jules-François-Félix Husson), published a volume of critical articles with the title *Le Réalisme*. Since then the word has been bandied about, discussed, analyzed, and abused as all slogans are. It is frequently confused with naturalism, an ancient philosophical term for materialism, epicureanism, or any secularism. As a specifically literary term, it crystallized only in France. In French, as in English, naturalist means, of course, simply student of nature, and the analogy between the writer and the naturalist, specifically the botanist and zoologist, was ready at hand. Émile Zola, in the preface to a new edition of his early novel *Thérèse Raquin* (1866), proclaimed the naturalist creed most boldly. His book, he claims, is "an analytical labor on two living bodies like that of a surgeon on corpses." He proudly counts himself among the group of "naturalist writers."

The program of the groups of writers and critics who used these terms can be easily summarized. The realists wanted a truthful representation in literature of reality—that is, of contemporary life and manners. They thought of their method as inductive, observational, and hence "objective." The personality of the author was to be suppressed or was at least to recede into the background, since reality was to be seen "as it is." The naturalistic program, as formulated by Zola, was substantially the same, except that Zola put greater stress on the analogies to science, considering the procedure of the novelist as identical with that of the experimenting scientist. He also more definitely and exclusively embraced the philosophy of scientific materialism, with its deterministic implications and its stress on heredity and environment, while the older realists were not always so clear in drawing the philosophical consequences. These French theories were anticipated, paralleled, or imitated all over the world of Western literature. In

Germany, the movement called Young Germany, with which Heine was associated, had propounded a substantially anti-Romantic realistic program as early as the 1830s, but versions of the French theories definitely triumphed there only in the 1880s. In Russia, as early as the 1840s, the most prominent critic of the time, Vissarion Belinsky, praised the "natural" school of Russian fiction, which described contemporary Russia with fidelity. Italy also, from the late 1870s on, produced an analogous movement, which called itself verismo. The English-speaking countries were the last to adopt the critical programs and slogans of the Continent: George Moore and George Gissing brought the French theories to England in the late 1880s, and in the United States William Dean Howells began his campaign for realism in 1886, when he became editor of Harper's Magazine. Realistic and naturalistic theories of literature have since been widely accepted, either as the basis of literary production or as a standard against which later generations rebel. The once officially promoted doctrine in Russia is called "Socialist Realism," a combination of factual observation and implied socialist message; the novel in the United States is usually considered naturalistic and judged by the standards of nature and truth. Yet twentieth-century novelists in Europe and America have also pushed realism to an extreme in the "literature of fact," in documentary novels, and (rebelling against traditional realism's coherent arrangement of reality) in often-bewildering attempts to describe experience objectively as a series of undifferentiated perceptions given no apparent interpretation by the narrator.

The slogans "realism" and "naturalism" were thus new to the nineteenth century and served as effective formulas directed against the Romantic creed. Truth, contemporaneity, and objectivity were the obvious counterparts of Romantic imagination, of Romantic historicism and its glorification of the past, and of Romantic subjectivity, the exaltation of the ego and the individual. But, of course, the emphasis on truth and objectivity was not really new: these qualities had been demanded by many older, classical theories of imitation, and in the eighteenth century there were great writers such as Denis Diderot who wanted a literal "imitation of life" even on the stage.

The practice of realism, it could be argued, is very old indeed. There are realistic scenes in the Iliad and Odyssey, and there is plenty of realism in ancient comedy and satire, in medieval stories (fabliaux) like some of Chaucer's and Boccaccio's, in many Elizabethan plays, in the Spanish rogue novels, in the English eighteenth-century novel beginning with Daniel Defoe, and so on almost ad infinitum. But while it would be easy to find in early literature anticipations of almost every single element of modern realism, still the systematic description of contemporary society, with a serious purpose, often even with a tragic tone as well, and with sympathy for heroes drawn from the middle and lower classes, was a real innovation of the nineteenth century.

It is usually rash to explain a literary movement in social and political terms. But the new realistic art surely had something to do with the triumph of the middle classes in France after the July revolution in 1830, and in England after the passage of the Reform Bill in 1832, and with the increasing influence of the middle classes in almost every country. Russia is somewhat of an exception as no large middle class could develop there during the nineteenth century. An absolute feudal regime continued in power and the special character of most of Russian literature must be the result of this distinction, but even in Russia there emerged an "intelligentsia" (the term comes from Russia) that was open to Western ideas and was highly critical of the czarist regime and its official "ideology."

But while much nineteenth-century literature reflects the triumph of the middle classes, it would be an error to think of the great realistic writers as spokespeople or mouthpieces of the society they described. Honoré de Balzac was politically a

Catholic monarchist who applauded the Bourbon restoration after the fall of Napoléon, but he had an extraordinary imaginative insight into the processes leading to the victory of the middle classes. Flaubert despised the middle-class society of the Third Empire with an intense hatred and the pride of a self-conscious artist. Dickens became increasingly critical of the middle classes and the assumptions of industrial civilization. Dostoevsky, though he took part in a conspiracy against the Russian government early in his life and spent ten years in exile in Siberia, became the propounder of an extremely conservative nationalistic and religious creed that was definitely directed against the revolutionary forces in Russia. Tolstoy, himself a count and a landowner, was violent in his criticism of the czarist regime, especially later in his life, but he cannot be described as friendly to the middle classes, to the aims of the democratic movements in Western Europe, or to the science of the time. Ibsen's political attitude was that of a proud individualist who condemns the "compact majority" and its tyranny. Possibly all art is critical of its society, but in the nineteenth century this criticism became much more explicit, as social and political issues became much more urgent or, at least, were regarded as more urgent by those writing about or within them. To a far greater degree than in earlier centuries, writers felt their isolation from society, viewed the structure and problems of the prevailing order as debatable and reformable, and in spite of all demands for objectivity became, in many cases, social propagandists and reformers in their own right.

The program of realism, while defensible enough as a reaction against Romanticism, raises critical questions that were not answered theoretically by its defenders. What is meant by "truth" of representation? Photographic copying? This seems the implication of many famous pronouncements: "A novel is a mirror walking along the road," said Stendhal (the pseudonym of Marie-Henri Beyle) as early as 1830. But such statements can hardly be taken literally. All art must select and represent; it cannot be and has never been a simple transcript of reality. What such analogies are intended to convey is rather a claim for an all-inclusiveness of subject matter, a protest against the exclusion of themes that before were considered "low," "sordid," or "trivial" (like the puddles along the road the mirror walks). Chekhov formulated this protest with the usual parallel between the scientist and the writer: "To a chemist nothing on earth is unclean. A writer must be as objective as a chemist; he must abandon the subjective line: he must know that dung heaps play a very respectable part in a landscape, and that evil passions are as inherent in life as good ones." Thus the "truth" of realistic art includes the sordid, the low, the disgusting, and the evil; and the implication is that the subject is treated objectively, without interference and falsification by the artist's personality and his own desires.

But in practice, while realistic art succeeded in expanding the themes of art, it could not fulfill the demand for total objectivity. Works of art are written by human beings and inevitably express their personalities and their points of view. As Joseph Conrad admitted, "even the most artful of writers will give himself (and his morality) away in about every third sentence." Objectivity, in the sense that Zola had in mind when he proposed a scientific method in the writing of novels and conceived of the novelist as a sociologist collecting human documents, is impossible in practice. When it has been attempted, it has led only to bad art, to dullness and the display of inert materials, to the confusion between the art of the novel and reporting, "documentation." The demand for "objectivity" can be understood only as a demand for a specific method of narration, in which the author does not interfere explicitly, in his or her own name, and as a rejection of personal themes of introspection and reverie.

The realistic program, while it has made innumerable new subjects available to art, also implies a narrowing of its themes and methods—a condemnation of the fantastic, the historical, the remote, the idealized, the "unsullied," the idyllic. Realism professes to present us with a "slice of life." But one should recognize that it is an artistic method and convention like any other. Romantic art could, without offending its readers, use coincidences, improbabilities, and even impossibilities that were not, theoretically at least, tolerated in realistic art. Ibsen, for instance, avoided many older conventions of the stage: asides, soliloquies, eavesdropping, sudden unmotivated appearances of new characters, and so on; but his dramas have their own marked conventions, which seem today almost as "unnatural" as those of the Romantics. Realistic theories of literature cannot be upheld in their literal sense; objective and impersonal truth is unobtainable, at least in art, since all art is a "making," a creating of a world of symbols that differs radically from the world that we call reality. The value of realism lies in its negation of the conventions of Romanticism, its expansion of the themes of art, and its new demonstration (never forgotten by artists) that literature has to deal also with its time and society and has, at its best, an insight into reality (not only social reality) that is not necessarily identical with that of science. Many of the great writers make us "realize" the world of their time, evoke an imaginative picture of it that seems truer and will last longer than that of historians and sociologists. But this achievement is due to their imagination and their art, or craft, two requisites that realistic theory tended to forget or minimize.

When we observe the actual practice of the great realistic writers of the nineteenth century, we notice a sharp contradiction between theory and practice, and an independent evolution of the art of the novel that is obscured for us if we pay too much attention to the theories and slogans of the time, even those that the authors themselves propounded. Flaubert, the high priest of a cult of "art for art's sake," the most consistent advocate of absolute objectivity, was actually, at least in a good half of his work, a writer of Romantic fantasies of blood and gold, flesh and jewels. There is some truth in his saying that Madame Bovary is himself, for in the drab story of a provincial adulteress he castigated his own Romanticism and Romantic dreams.

So too with Dostoevsky. Although some of his settings resemble those of the "crime novel," he is actually a writer of high tragedy, of a drama of ideas in which ordinary reality is transformed into a symbol of the spiritual world. His technique is closely associated with Balzac's (it is significant that his first publication was a translation of Balzac's *Eugénie Grandet*) and thus with many devices of the sensational melodramatic novel of French Romanticism. Tolstoy's art is more concretely real than that of any of the other great masters mentioned, yet he is, at the same time, the most personal and even literally autobiographical author in the history of the novel—a writer, besides, who knows nothing of detachment toward social and religious problems but frankly preaches his own very personal religion. And if we turn to Ibsen, we find essentially the same situation. Ibsen began as a writer of historical and fantastic dramas and slowly returned to a style that is fundamentally symbolist. All his later plays are organized by symbols, from the duck of *The Wild Duck* (1884) to the white horses in *Rosmersholm* (1886), the burned manuscript in *Hedda Gabler* (1890), and the tower in *The Master Builder* (1892). Even Zola, the propounder of the most scientific theory, was in practice a novelist who used the most extreme devices of melodrama and Symbolism. In *Germinal* (1885), his novel of mining, the mine is the central symbol, alive as an animal, heaving, breathing. It would be an odd reader who could find literal truth in the final catastrophe of the cave-in or even in such "naturalistic" scenes as a dance where the beer oozes from the nostrils of the drinkers.

One could assert, in short, that all the great realists were at bottom Romanticists, but it is probably wiser to conclude that they were simply artists who created worlds of imagination and knew (at least instinctively) that in art one can say something about reality only through symbols. The attempts at documentary art, at mere reporting and transcribing, are today forgotten.

SYMBOLISM

The later nineteenth century cannot, however, be considered simply an age of realism and naturalism. Poetry addressed in its own way the same questions of truth and reality. By the middle of the century, it was embarked on an exploration of language that would influence all forms of twentieth-century literature. Where prose fiction and drama faced outward, aiming to mirror the real world, poetry turned its attention to the mirror itself: the instrument that reflects and represents reality. Preserving the Romantic notion of the poet as seer or visionary, emphasizing a heightened self-consciousness and an inquiry into the techniques of poetic language, the innovators of nineteenth-century poetry explored both the concept of creativity and philosophic questions of human identity. They examined the perceiving subject's awareness of his or her perceptions and illustrated this awareness in allusive poetry that played with multiple and shifting perspectives and in sensuous evocations of a reality that remained ultimately beyond apprehension. Traditional verse forms exploded in the drive to find new ways of depicting experience, and the new forms heralded not only modern free verse, prose poems, and spatial poetry but also the innovative language of novelists such as James Joyce, William Faulkner, Alain Robbe-Grillet and Marguerite Duras.

The evolution was gradual until the middle of the century. Some poets continued to practice a substantially Romantic art: Tennyson, for instance, and Victor Hugo. In England, the Pre-Raphaelite movement—painters and writers such as J. E. Millais (1829–1896), W. H. Hunt (1827–1910), and D. G. Rossetti (1828–1882)—drew their inspiration from the sensuous detail of Italian medieval art in opposition to the honored Renaissance painter Raphael (1483–1520); they upheld a Romantic, escapist, and antirealist program. In France, a large and diverse group of Parnassian poets stemming from Leconte de Lisle (1818–1894) retained Romantic themes while focusing on a precise and delicate use of detail. The most important writer of this period is Charles Baudelaire (1821–1867), whose poetry and writings on art deeply influenced the course of European poetry. Baudelaire's major collection of poems, *The Flowers of Evil*, was published in the same year that Flaubert was brought to trial for *Madame Bovary* (1857). He inspired a poetic movement that would later be called Symbolism, and he remains today the French poet most widely read outside France.

Symbolism as *symbolic representation* is a philosophical concept, and the use of symbols is not restricted to the nineteenth and twentieth centuries. Using one thing to suggest another, or an image to suggest an idea, is as old as art and language. The Neolithic paintings in the caves at Lascaux, France, are symbolic pictures of the hunt. Medieval Christian literature used a shared set of symbols to signify religious concepts through earthly images: the rose symbolized love, the dove the Holy Spirit, and the serpent Satan. As a literary movement, however, Symbolism is a nineteenth-century French phenomenon with affinities to the visionary writings of eighteenth-century German Romanticism, to the Parnassian cult of artistic form and "art for art's sake," and to the poetic theories of Edgar Allan Poe. Symbolist poetry tries to manipulate language in an almost magical way to evoke hidden meanings behind the appearances of this world. A symbol in this sense is an image or cluster of images created to suggest another plane of reality that cannot be expressed in more direct and rational terms. Each poem transforms reality in its own manner, leading the reader to its own version of truth. The aim is to touch a primitive level of being where, for example, in Baudelaire's poem *Correspondences*, the five senses fuse: colors have taste, sights have physical texture, sounds have odors, and so on. (This fusion is called *synesthesia*.) Symbolist poetry may lead to abstract or visionary conclusions, but it is firmly based in images as realistic as a rotting carcass, logs falling on the pavement, and a mangy cat trying to find a comfortable spot in rainy weather (Baudelaire's *A Carcass, Song of Autumn I*, and *Spleen LXXVIII*). It is not, therefore, an escape from natural reality so much as a transformation of it, the creation of a new world reassembled in the mind from pieces of the old.

After Symbolic allusion, the second great theme of Symbolist poetry is language: language as a means of communication, and language as the necessary but flawed tool of poetic creation. Like Flaubert seeking *le mot juste* (the exact word), Symbolist poets are haunted by the difficulty of writing: Baudelaire described his exhausted brain as a graveyard, and Stéphane Mallarmé felt paralyzed by "the empty paper whose whiteness defends it." The difficulty for the Symbolists is that their ideal poetic language must be distilled out of ordinary language through a totally controlled arrangement of all possible levels of form. Sound patterns, image clusters, and intertwined systems of logical and psychological associations act to create a complex architecture of inner reference. It is the relationship of words that counts, not just their dictionary definitions; the artist is, in a sense, a technician. The extraordinary self-consciousness of the Symbolist poet soon became an accepted element of the poem itself. Some poems focused on difficulties of communication (a characteristic Romantic theme); others, like Baudelaire's *Windows*, asserted joy in using language to imagine other existences and to sense, in return, their own reality. The Symbolists' acute awareness of the possibilities and limitations of language has influenced both philosophers of language and literary theorists in the twentieth century.

Symbolist writers frequently compared their poetry to music, whose characteristics they tried to reproduce; Paul Verlaine, a contemporary of Mallarmé and Rimbaud, is especially known for the musicality of his verse. Both poetry and music they felt to be "pure" arts, in which line and harmony (including calculated dissonance) meant more than separate notes or the definitions of individual words. They saw analogies, too, between their art and painting, where distinctive new methods of depicting reality were being developed in the same period. Symbolist poetry and impressionist art both represented moves away from the conventional realistic representation of reality and, in the poetic as in the art world, they both outraged the average citizen by their apparent betrayal of common sense.

Baudelaire's two most important successors were very different figures: an English teacher, Stéphane Mallarmé (1842–1898) and the adolescent prodigy Arthur Rimbaud (1854–1891). In a short and violent literary career between the ages of fifteen and twenty, Rimbaud attempted to become a seer or *voyant* through hallucinatory writing expressing the "disorder of all the senses." The visionary image sequences of his first major poem (a symbolic voyage titled *The Drunken Boat*), the agonized and mocking autobiographical prose of *A Season in Hell*, and finally the transfigured scenes from real life called *Illuminations* together represent stages in this endeavor to discover—or create—a state of natural innocence and harmony. Rimbaud's rebellion against home and authority, his experiments with drugs and alcohol, his love affair with the poet Paul Verlaine, and his search for a transfigured condition *au-delà* (beyond) all provide themes for this poetic quest. For a while, Rimbaud believed that he could manipulate language to create the vision of an ideal world: "I have strung ropes from steeple to steeple; garlands from window to window; golden chains from star to star, and I dance" (*Sentences*). His *Illuminations* offer a series of transformations that leave only traces of their varied points of departure: bridges in London, plowed fields, a park statue, dawn. They parade illusions and free association, and they cut short logical sequences to develop an almost musical organization of themes and images. Ultimately, Rimbaud became disenchanted with the efficacy of his magical or "alchemical" art, and he abruptly stopped writing. He left for Africa, where he spent the last eighteen years of his life trying to make a living. A good deal of Rimbaud's legend comes from this extraordinary example of a great poet who simply did not find what he sought in literature and, therefore, ceased to write. Rimbaud's work and the integrity of his spiritual commitment had enormous influence on later writers, especially the surrealists.

Stéphane Mallarmé, conversely, was a quiet and somewhat scholarly poet who spent his life in a search for absolute poetry *in language*. Mallarmé loved words and distrusted the sloppiness of everyday speech. (He wrote a somewhat eccentric treatise called *English Words* for the French school system.) He envisaged a special poetic language that would be built out of the precisely planned interaction of ordinary words, in poems that would "give a purer sense to the words of the crowd." Mallarmé's long poem *Dice Thrown*, with its startling arrangement of different type sizes and words scattered to create patterns on the page, heralded concrete poetry and other modern attempts to use the silence of blank space as part of poetry. Toward the end of his life, he considered everything he produced to be a fragment of an ultimate Work that he feared he would never be able to write: a massively interrelated composition of pure poetry whose function would be to assert the dignity of human imagination in the face of universal nothingness. The creative process itself is the central topic of Mallarmé's poetry, whether in the earlier autobiographical poems or in later impersonal scenes from which the narrator is excluded. Mallarmé uses Symbolist tactics, too, in preferring allusion and suggestion to direct speech, or—a specifically Mallarméan theme—potentiality and absence to a fixed and limited reality. Material objects like a bracelet, a fan, a lace curtain, or a mandolin are described so as to evoke other elements in another realm of being. A carved angel's wing gilded by the sun evokes a harp; the "harp" exists only in the imagination, however, and its implied music is doubly unreal because the source is merely suggested, not represented. This music is even more ambiguous than Keats's "melodies . . . unheard," for it is a musical *silence*. Mallarmé points rather than names; he suggests possibilities by keeping several levels of meaning alive at the same time, and he complicates his syntax and even misleads the reader to prolong the pleasure of discovery.

It is paradoxical that none of these poets—Baudelaire, Mallarmé, Rimbaud, or Verlaine—was a member of the Symbolist movement. Symbolist doctrine as such dates to a manifesto issued in 1886 by a minor poet, Jean Moréas (Joannes Papadiamantopoulous, 1856–1910). In many ways the movement is a systematization and popularization of ideas gleaned from Baudelaire, Rimbaud, Mallarmé, and Verlaine; especially influential were Verlaine's essays in 1884 describing Rimbaud, Mallarmé, and Tristan Corbière (1845–1875) as outcast or "accursed poets." A number of young poets (often called "decadents") were attracted to Symbolist ideas, and their publication and literary reviews flourished around the turn of the century. Symbolism as a movement, however, had less impact than the major poets from whom it sprang, and it was the example of these earlier poets that especially influenced writers such as W. B. Yeats, T. S. Eliot, Marcel Proust, Rainer Maria Rilke, Wallace Stevens, Rabindranath Tagore, and others around the world for whom Symbolist poetry became the model for contemporary poetry and poetics.

A NOTE ON FRENCH POETRY

English poetry receives its rhythm from the accent or stress in words, and the most common English line is iambic pentameter ("Whatever is begotten, born, and dies"). In contrast, the rhythm of French poetry is based on *quantity*—on the number and pattern of syllables in a line. The most common French line is the twelve-syllable or "alexandrine" verse, usually divided into balanced segments of six or four syllables. Baudelaire's *Correspondances* (given in French on page 1187) is a sonnet written in alexandrines that displays many of the conventions of French poetry.

Syllables are divided to reflect the sound of the line when read aloud; thus every syllable should begin with a consonant whenever possible. ("Na / tu / re . . . con / fu / ses / pa / roles.") In traditional French poetry, the unaccented or mute *e* counts as a syllable and is pronounced when it occurs before a sounded consonant (but not otherwise): thus "Com / *me* / les / prai / ries" (line 10) sound the mute *e* but "La / Na / tu / *re est* / un / tem / *ple où* /" (line 1) does not. The subtle use of the mute *e* provides rich sonorous effects that are only evident in reading aloud.

French rhymes are categorized as rich, sufficient, or weak, and also as masculine or feminine. Weak rhymes have only one accented vowel in common: prair*ies* / infin*ies* (the *ee* sound). Sufficient rhymes have two elements in common: en*fants* / triom*phants*. A rich rhyme has three or more elements in common: pi*liers* / fami*liers* (*i*, *e*, and the diphthong *ier*). A variety of rhymes is desirable. Feminine rhymes end in the sound of a mute *e*: *paroles* / *symboles* or *rose* / *chose*. All other rhymes are masculine. After the sixteenth century most poets alternated masculine and feminine rhymes. In *Correspondances*, Baudelaire uses the Petrarchan sonnet form (two quatrains, two tercets) with a rhyme scheme alternating masculine and feminine rhymes as follows: *mffm fmmf mfm fmm*. The intricacy of these and other poetic effects makes clear why later poets revered Baudelaire as a master of classical form as well as a visionary.

FURTHER READING

E. Auerbach, *Mimesis: The Representation of Reality in Western Literature* (1953), is a wide-ranging book (from Homer to Proust), with chapters on nineteenth-century realism. G. J. Becker, ed., *Documents of Modern Literary Realism* (1973), surveys the development of modern realism and offers documents and essays from 1835 to 1955. H. Levin, *The Gates of Horn: A Study of Five French Realists* (1963), contains much on realism in general, including Stendhal, Balzac, Flaubert, Zola, and Proust. Linda Nochlin, *Realism* (1971), discusses realism in the visual arts. Marcel Raymond, *From Baudelaire to Surrealism* (1933), is a fundamental study of the evolution of the new poetry. Naomi Schor, *Breaking the Chain: Women, Theory, and French Realist Fiction* (1985), discusses the realist fiction of Flaubert, Zola, Balzac, and others in terms of feminist and psychoanalytic theory. Also helpful is R. Wellek, "The Concept of Realism in Literary Scholarship," in *Concepts of Criticism* (1963). Nicholas Boyle and Martin Swales, eds., *Realism in European Literature: Essays in Honour of J. P. Stern* (1986), is a varied and useful collection that includes a discussion of realism related to modernism and language consciousness. Elise Boulding, *The Underside of History: A View of Women through Time* (1992,), arranged by periods and sociological categories, contains much pertinent information about the role of women that is omitted from traditional histories. John Rignall, *Realist Fiction and the Strolling Spectator* (1992), indebted to Nietzsche and Walter Benjamin, analyzes realism's distanced point of view in eight nineteenth-century and three twentieth-century novelists. Martin Anderson, *The Limits of Realism: Chinese Fiction in the Revolutionary Period* (1990), uses contemporary theoretical perspectives to analyze the development of Chinese realist fiction in the 1920s and 1930s as a new mode based on but different from European predecessors. Laurence M. Porter, *The Crisis of French Symbolism* (1990), offers a good discussion of Symbolist aims and practice from a contemporary theoretical perspective. An influential and still valuable presentation is found in *The Symbolist Movement in Literature* (1980, orig. 1899), by the English Symbolist Arthur Symons.

PRONOUNCING GLOSSARY

The following list uses common English syllables and stress accents to provide rough equivalents of selected words whose pronunciation may be unfamiliar to the general reader.

Balzac: *ball-zak'*

Baudelaire: *boh-d'lair'*

Champfleury: *shom-fler-ee'*

Chekhov: *chek'-off*

Chopin: *sho-panh*

Corbière: *core-bee-air'*

Courbet: *coor-bay'*

Dostoevsky: *dos-toy-eff'-skee*

Dvořák: *dvor'-zhak*

fabliaux: *fah-blee-oh'*

Gesamtkunstwerk: *ge-zamt-koonst'-varck*

Grieg: *greeg*

Mallarmé: *mall-are-may'*

Nietzsche: *neech'-uh*

Réalisme: *ray-al-eezm'*

Rimbaud: *ram-boh'*

Schlegel: *shlay'-gel*

Stendahl: *ston-dall'*

Tchaikovsky: *chai-kof'-skee*

Wagner: *vag'-ner*

Zola: *soh-lah'*

TEXTS	CONTEXTS
1857 Charles Baudelaire, *The Flowers of Evil* • Gustave Flaubert, *Madame Bovary*	
	1859 Charles Darwin, *Origin of Species*
	1861 Serfs emancipated in Russia
	1861–1865 Civil War in the United States
1864 Fyodor Dostoevsky, *Notes from Underground*	
1866 Dostoevsky, *Crime and Punishment*	
1866 Emile Zola's preface to his novel *Thérèse Raquin* argues for a "naturalist" style analogous to methods in experimental science	
1869 Leo Tolstoy, *War and Peace*	1869 Suez Canal completed
	1870 Ernest Renan's *Life of Jesus* offers a historical approach to the New Testament
1871 George Eliot (Mary Ann Evans), *Middlemarch*	
	1874 Claude Monet's painting *Impression: Rising Sun* launches Impressionism as a style
	1876 Invention of the telephone
1877 Gustave Flaubert, *A Simple Heart*	
	1884–1885 Berlin Conference agrees on procedures for European acquisition of African territory; by 1914, all Africa except Ethiopia and Liberia succumbs to European rule

TEXTS	CONTEXTS
1886 Arthur Rimbaud's *Illumina-tions* • Tolstoy, **The Death of Iván Ilyich**	1886 Friedrich Nietzsche's *Beyond Good and Evil* proclaims a "life force," a "will to power," and a "super-man" who embodies these qualities
	1887 Eiffel Tower built for the 1889 Paris World's Fair • Gottlieb Daim-ler's internal combustion engine for the automobile
1890 Henrik Ibsen, **Hedda Gabler** • **Poems** of Emily Dickinson (1830–1886) published posthumously	
	1894 X-rays discovered
	1894–1906 In the Dreyfus Affair, anti-Semitic sentiment polarizes France
	1898 Radium discovered by Marie and Pierre Curie • Spanish-American War breaks out
1904 Anton Chekhov, **The Cherry Orchard** performed	

GUSTAVE FLAUBERT

1821–1880

Gustave Flaubert is rightly considered the exemplary realist novelist. He displays the objectivity, the detachment from his characters demanded by the theory, and is a great virtuoso of the art of composition and of style while giving a clear picture of the society of his time. It is likewise a picture in which we can see much of ourselves.

Flaubert was born in Rouen, Normandy, on December 12, 1821, to the chief surgeon of the Hôtel Dieu. He was extremely precocious; by the age of sixteen he was writing stories in the Romantic taste, which were published only after his death. In 1840 he went to Paris to study law (he had received his baccalaureate from the local *lycée*), but he failed in his examinations and in 1843 suffered a sudden nervous breakdown that kept him at home. In 1846 he moved to Croisset, just outside of Rouen on the Seine, where he made his home for the rest of his life, devoting himself to writing. The same year, in Paris, Flaubert met Louise Colet, a minor poet and lady about town, who became his mistress. In 1849–51 he visited the Levant, traveling extensively in Greece, Syria, and Egypt. After his return he settled down to the writing of *Madame Bovary*, which took him five full years and which was a great popular success. The remainder of his life was uneventful. He made occasional trips to Paris, and one trip, in 1860, to Tunisia to see the ruins of Carthage in preparation for the writing of his novel *Salammbô*. Three more novels followed: *The Sentimental Education* (1869), *The Temptation of St. Anthony* (1874), and the unfinished *Bouvard and Pecuchet* (1881), as well as *Three Tales* (1877), consisting of *A Simple Heart, The Legend of St. Julian the Hospitaler*, and *Herodias*. Flaubert died at Croisset on May 8, 1880.

Flaubert's novel *Madame Bovary* (1856) is deservedly considered the showpiece of French realism. It would be impossible to find a novel, certainly before Flaubert, in which humble persons in a humble setting (the story concerns the adulteries and final suicide of the wife of a simple country doctor) are treated with such seriousness, restraint, verisimilitude, and imaginative clarity. There is nothing of Balzac's lurid melodrama, high-pitched tone, and passionate eloquence in Flaubert's masterpiece. At first sight, *Madame Bovary* is the prosaic description of a prosaic life, set in its daily surroundings, the French province of Normandy about the middle of the nineteenth century. Everything is told soberly, objectively. The author hides his feelings completely behind his personages. All the light falls on Emma Bovary, as we follow the story of her romantic dreams, disillusionment, despair. Every scene is superbly realized, with an extraordinary accuracy of observation, and details, which at times are based on scientific information. The topography of the two villages, the interior of the houses, great scenes—such as those of the ball, the cattle show, the operation of clubfoot, the opera in Rouen, the arsenic poisoning—imprint themselves vividly on our memory. Early readers were puzzled by Flaubert's attitude toward Emma Bovary, so accustomed were they to the usual commentary of an author, approving or condemning every action of his characters. But today, when we know the early unpublished writings of Flaubert and his revealing correspondence, there cannot be any doubt about the tone of the book. Behind all the detachment there is a victory of art over temperament, a self-imposed discipline and restraint. It is, in part, the result of a theory of the objectivity, the complete impersonality of art. According to this view, the artist has to disappear behind his or her creation as God does behind His. Future ages should hardly believe that the artist lived.

If we listen more carefully, however, we become aware of the author's savage satiric attitude toward the romantic illusions of poor Emma, his hatred for the complacent freethinking apothecary Homais, his contempt for the stupid husband and the callous, weak lovers. The pity of it all comes through only because the author lets the facts speak for themselves.

The story of the composition of *Madame Bovary*, which we know from Flaubert's letters, is one of self-inflicted martyrdom, of an artist perversely clinging to an uncongenial and even repulsive subject because he believes that the subject itself is of no importance and that the artist should, by his art, purge himself of personal indulgences and preferences. It is also the story of a struggle for style, for the "right word" (*mot juste*), for which Flaubert worked with the suppressed fury of a galley slave.

A Simple Heart, a late story published in the collection *Three Tales*, is clearly related to *Madame Bovary*. It has the same setting of the Norman countryside, the same houses and farms, some of the same kind of people. And it has the same theme of disillusionment. Félicité is anticipated in *Madame Bovary* by the figure of Catherine Leroux, who at the great agricultural show receives a silver medal, worth twenty-five francs, for fifty-four years of service at one farm. The little old woman, with the "monastic rigidity" of her face, the dumbness and calm of her animal look, has to be almost pushed by the audience to receive her prize. When she walks away with the medal, she is heard muttering, "I'll give it to our *curé* up home, to say some masses for me."

A Simple Heart, like *Madame Bovary*, treats the life of a humble person with complete objectivity, with vivid concrete imagination, clear in every detail. We see and smell the interiors of the houses and farms and can visualize the scenes of almost Dutch simplicity. But the story is also connected with the two other stories in the collection, *The Legend of St. Julian the Hospitaler* and *Hérodias*. Like these it is a saint's legend: like a saint, Félicité undergoes a Calvary of suffering—the betrayal of her lover, the death of the little girl Virginie, the loss of her nephew, the loss of the parrot. Like a saint, too, she meets savage beasts (a bull in the fields), is lashed by a whip on the road, tends the running ulcer of a dying old man, and finally sees a beatific vision, during the Corpus Christi procession, in which the Holy Ghost and the parrot fuse into one.

But one would miss the implications of Flaubert's sophisticated art if one thought of the story merely as a realistic picture of a servant girl's plight or even as a traditional saint's legend in modern times. It is no doubt a combination of these two apparently very different types: we can see a social purpose in the picture of the poor oppressed woman, her devotion to a selfish mistress, her frustration, resignation, and final dying happiness; and we can sense the author's restraint as a device of simplicity to make the tone of the tale approach that of a legend. But such a reading would not capture all the undertones of Flaubert's style. There are disturbing elements in the story, which show that a simple interpretation is insufficient. We have glimpses, for instance, of Flaubert's predilection for the exotic and strange, for the deliberately decorative mosaic: the exotic pictures that constitute "the whole of [Félicité's] literary education," the curious color combinations of the scene at Virginie's deathbed (the spots of red of the candles, the white mist, the yellow face, the blue lips), and the gorgeous Corpus Christi wayside altar—all these clash with the otherwise sober and gray tone of the narrative. More disturbing, there is an undertone of satire and contemptuous mockery of this humble world. In a letter to a correspondent (Madame Roger de Genettes; June 19, 1876) Flaubert denied that "there is anything ironical as you suppose," and went on to declare that "on the contrary, it is very serious and very sad. I want to excite pity, I want to make sensitive souls weep, as I am one of them myself." But surely this professed intention is hard to reconcile with the passages about the parrot, who is shown as grotesque and absurd, an icon of the Holy Ghost (traditionally represented as a dove) but also a moth-eaten relic with a broken wing and stuffing protruding from its stomach. There is "something of the parrot" in the church window's image of the Holy Ghost, a likeness that is confirmed by the highly colored religious print that gives the dove purple wings and an emerald body. Some readers would find not only satire but blasphemy in the description of Félicité swerving toward the parrot from time to time as she says her prayers or glimpsing, on her deathbed, "an opening in the heavens, and a gigantic parrot hovering above her head." Yet there is also imaginative power in this grotesque deathbed vision. The parrot is not absurd in itself but only when seen from an external perspective that measures spiritual insight by traditional religious iconography. Viewed from a different angle, this subversive distortion is part of a creative process by which Félicité re-creates the world around her in the image of her own intense feelings. She enters passionately into the priest's stories of sacred history, trying to understand the various images of divinity in terms of her own experience. After learning that God is "not merely a bird, but a flame as well, and a breath of other times," she interprets these images through her own narration: "It may be His light, she thought, which flits at night about the edge of the marshes, His breathing which drives on the clouds, His voice which gives harmony to the bells." Flaubert insists on Félicité's capacity for reimagining the world: she *becomes* Virginie during the latter's first communion, and she expects to see Victor's house on the map, "so stunted was her mind!" A logic of personal need governs her imaginings; by linking the religious print to the parrot, Félicité both "consecrates" her beloved Loulou and makes the Holy Ghost "more vivid to her eye and more intelligible." Seeking intelligibility (to *know* God, in the tradition of the mystics), she decides that the bird who expresses God's meaning must be one who can speak: therefore, a parrot. If the gigantic parrot of the conclusion seems to mock traditional religious imagery, which it clearly does, it also presides over a world of will and imagination that Félicité—a secular saint—has made her own.

Victor Brombert, *The Novels of Flaubert* (1966), is still a good general work. Jonathan Culler, *Flaubert: The Uses of Uncertainty* (1974), is a clear and carefully argued study that emphasizes the modernity of Flaubert's style. Aimée Israel-Pelletier, *Flaubert's Straight and Suspect Saints: The Unity of Trois Contes* (1991), contains a valuable chapter on *A Simple Heart* and also a bibliography.

PRONOUNCING GLOSSARY

The following list uses common English syllables and stress accents to provide rough equivalents of selected words whose pronunciation may be unfamiliar to the general reader.

Aubain: *oh-banh'*

Félicité: *fay-lee-see-tay'*

Flaubert: *floh-bair'*

Pont l'Evêque: *pohnh lay-veck'*

Virginie: *veer-zheen-ee'*

A Simple Heart[1]

I

Madame Aubain's servant Félicité was the envy of the ladies of Pont-l'Évêque[2] for half a century.

She received a hundred francs a year. For that she was cook and general servant, and did the sewing, washing, and ironing; she could bridle a horse, fatten poultry, and churn butter—and she remained faithful to her mistress, unamiable as the latter was.

Mme. Aubain had married a gay bachelor without money who died at the beginning of 1809, leaving her with two small children and a quantity of debts. She then sold all her property except the farms of Toucques and Geffosses, which brought in five thousand francs a year at most, and left her house in Saint-Melaine for a less expensive one that had belonged to her family and was situated behind the market.

This house had a slate roof and stood between an alley and a lane that went down to the river. There was an unevenness in the levels of the rooms which made you stumble. A narrow hall divided the kitchen from the "parlour" where Mme. Aubain spent her day, sitting in a wicker easy chair by the window. Against the panels, which were painted white, was a row of eight mahogany chairs. On an old piano under the barometer a heap of wooden and cardboard boxes rose like a pyramid. A stuffed arm-chair stood on either side of the Louis-Quinze chimney-piece, which was in yellow marble with a clock in the middle of it modelled like a temple of Vesta.[3] The whole room was a little musty, as the floor was lower than the garden.

The first floor began with "Madame's" room: very large, with a pale-flowered wall-paper and a portrait of "Monsieur" as a dandy of the period. It led to a smaller room, where there were two children's cots without mattresses. Next came the drawing-room, which was always shut up and full of furniture covered with sheets. Then there was a corridor leading to a study. The shelves of a large bookcase were respectably lined with books and papers, and its three wings surrounded a broad writing-table in dark-wood. The two panels at the end of the room were covered with pen-drawings, water-colour landscapes, and engravings by Audran,[4] all relics of better days and vanished splendour. Félicité's room on the top floor got its light from a dormer-window, which looked over the meadows.

She rose at daybreak to be in time for Mass, and worked till evening without stopping. Then, when dinner was over, the plates and dishes in order, and the door shut fast, she thrust the log under the ashes and went to sleep in front of the hearth with her rosary in her hand. Félicité was the stubbornest of all bargainers; and as for cleanness, the polish on her sauce-pans was the despair of other servants. Thrifty in all things, she ate slowly, gathering off the table in her fingers the crumbs of her loaf—a twelve-pound loaf expressly baked for her, which lasted for three weeks.

1. Translated by Arthur MacDowall.   2. A village in Normandy on the Toucques River, twenty-five miles from Caen.   3. Temple of the Roman goddess of the hearth; it was round and enclosed by columns.   4. Gérard Audran (1640–1703) made engravings of many paintings by Poussin, Mignard, and others.

At all times of year she wore a print handkerchief fastened with a pin behind, a bonnet that covered her hair, grey stockings, a red skirt, and a bibbed apron—such as hospital nurses wear—over her jacket.

Her face was thin and her voice sharp. At twenty-five she looked like forty. From fifty onwards she seemed of no particular age; and with her silence, straight figure, and precise movements she was like a woman made of wood, and going by clockwork.

II

She had had her love-story like another.

Her father, a mason, had been killed by falling off some scaffolding. Then her mother died, her sisters scattered, and a farmer took her in and employed her, while she was still quite little, to herd the cows at pasture. She shivered in rags and would lie flat on the ground to drink water from the ponds; she was beaten for nothing, and finally turned out for the theft of thirty sous which she did not steal. She went to another farm, where she became dairy-maid; and as she was liked by her employers her companions were jealous of her.

One evening in August (she was then eighteen) they took her to the assembly at Colleville. She was dazed and stupefied in an instant by the noise of the fiddlers, the lights in the trees, the gay medley of dresses, the lace, the gold crosses, and the throng of people jigging all together. While she kept shyly apart a young man with a well-to-do air, who was leaning on the shaft of a cart and smoking his pipe, came up to ask her to dance. He treated her to cider, coffee, and cake, and bought her a silk handkerchief; and then, imagining she had guessed his meaning, offered to see her home. At the edge of a field of oats he pushed her roughly down. She was frightened and began to cry out; and he went off.

One evening later she was on the Beaumont road. A big haywagon was moving slowly along; she wanted to get in front of it, and as she brushed past the wheels she recognized Theodore. He greeted her quite calmly, saying she must excuse it all because it was "the fault of the drink." She could not think of any answer and wanted to run away.

He began at once to talk about the harvest and the worthies of the commune, for his father had left Colleville for the farm at Les Écots, so that now he and she were neighbours. "Ah!" she said. He added that they thought of settling him in life. Well, he was in no hurry; he was waiting for a wife to his fancy. She dropped her head; and then he asked her if she thought of marrying. She answered with a smile that it was mean to make fun of her.

"But I am not, I swear!"—and he passed his left hand round her waist. She walked in the support of his embrace; their steps grew slower. The wind was soft, the stars glittered, the huge wagon-load of hay swayed in front of them, and dust rose from the dragging steps of the four horses. Then, without a word of command, they turned to the right. He clasped her once more in his arms, and she disappeared into the shadow.

The week after Theodore secured some assignations with her.

They met at the end of farmyards, behind a wall, or under a solitary tree. She was not innocent as young ladies are—she had learned knowledge from the animals—but her reason and the instinct of her honour would not let her fall. Her resistance exasperated Theodore's passion; so much so that to satisfy it—or perhaps quite artlessly—he made her an offer of marriage. She was in doubt whether to trust him, but he swore great oaths of fidelity.

Soon he confessed to something troublesome; the year before his parents had bought him a substitute for the army, but any day he might be taken again, and the idea of serving was a terror to him. Félicité took this cowardice of his as a sign of affection, and it redoubled hers. She stole away at night to see him, and when she reached their meeting-place Theodore racked her with his anxieties and urgings.

At last he declared that he would go himself to the prefecture for information, and would tell her the result on the following Sunday, between eleven and midnight.

When the moment came she sped towards her lover. Instead of him she found one of his friends.

He told her that she would not see Theodore any more. To ensure himself against conscription he had married an old woman, Madame Lehoussais, of Toucques, who was very rich.

There was an uncontrollable burst of grief. She threw herself on the ground, screamed, called to the God of mercy, and moaned by herself in the fields till daylight came. Then she came back to the farm and announced that she was going to leave; and at the end of the month she received her wages, tied all her small belongings with a handkerchief, and went to Pont-l'Évêque.

In front of the inn there she made inquiries of a woman in a widow's cap, who, as it happened, was just looking for a cook. The girl did not know much, but her willingness seemed so great and her demands so small that Mme. Aubain ended by saying:

"Very well, then, I will take you."

A quarter of an hour afterwards Félicité was installed in her house.

She lived there at first in a tremble, as it were, at "the style of the house" and the memory of "Monsieur" floating over it all. Paul and Virginie, the first aged seven and the other hardly four, seemed to her beings of a precious substance; she carried them on her back like a horse; it was a sorrow to her that Mme. Aubain would not let her kiss them every minute. And yet she was happy there. Her grief had melted in the pleasantness of things all round.

Every Thursday regular visitors came in for a game of boston, and Félicité got the cards and foot-warmers ready beforehand. They arrived punctually at eight and left before the stroke of eleven.

On Monday mornings the dealer who lodged in the covered passage spread out all his old iron on the ground. Then a hum of voices began to fill the town, mingled with the neighing of horses, bleating of lambs, grunting of pigs, and the sharp rattle of carts along the street. About noon, when the market was at its height, you might see a tall, hook-nosed old countryman with his cap pushed back making his appearance at the door.

It was Robelin, the farmer of Geffosses. A little later came Liébard, the farmer from Toucques—short, red, and corpulent—in a grey jacket and gaiters shod with spurs.

Both had poultry or cheese to offer their landlord. Félicité was invariably a match for their cunning, and they went away filled with respect for her.

At vague intervals Mme. Aubain had a visit from the Marquis de Gremanville, one of her uncles, who had ruined himself by debauchery and now lived at Falaise on his last remaining morsel of land. He invariably came at the luncheon hour, with a dreadful poodle whose paws left all the furniture in a mess. In spite of efforts to show his breeding, which he carried to the point of raising his hat every time he mentioned "my late father," habit was too strong for him; he poured himself out glass after glass and fired off improper remarks. Félicité edged him politely out of the house—"You have had enough, Monsieur de Gremanville! Another time!"—and she shut the door on him.

She opened it with pleasure to M. Bourais, who had been a lawyer. His baldness, his white stock, frilled shirt, and roomy brown coat, his way of rounding the arm as he took snuff—his whole person, in fact, created that disturbance of mind which overtakes us at the sight of extraordinary men.

As he looked after the property of "Madame" he remained shut up with her for hours in "Monsieur's" study, though all the time he was afraid of compromising himself. He respected the magistracy immensely, and had some pretensions to Latin.

To combine instruction and amusement he gave the children a geography book made up of a series of prints. They represented scenes in different parts of the world: cannibals with feathers on their heads, a monkey carrying off a young lady, Bedouins in the desert, the harpooning of a whale, and so on. Paul explained these engravings to Félicité; and that, in fact, was the whole of her literary education. The children's education was undertaken by Guyot, a poor creature employed at the town hall, who was famous for his beautiful hand and sharpened his penknife on his boots.

When the weather was bright the household set off early for a day at Geffosses Farm.

Its courtyard is on a slope, with the farmhouse in the middle, and the sea looks like a grey streak in the distance.

Félicité brought slices of cold meat out of her basket, and they breakfasted in a room adjoining the dairy. It was the only surviving fragment of a country house which was now no more. The wallpaper hung in tatters, and quivered in the draughts. Mme. Aubain sat with bowed head, overcome by her memories; the children became afraid to speak. "Why don't you play, then?" she would say, and off they went.

Paul climbed into the barn, caught birds, played at ducks and drakes over the pond, or hammered with his stick on the big casks which boomed like drums. Virginie fed the rabbits or dashed off to pick cornflowers, her quick legs showing their embroidered little drawers.

One autumn evening they went home by the fields. The moon was in its first quarter, lighting part of the sky; and mist floated like a scarf over the windings of the Toucques. Cattle, lying out in the middle of the grass, looked quietly at the four people as they passed. In the third meadow some of them got up and made a half-circle in front of the walkers. "There's nothing to be afraid of," said Félicité, as she stroked the nearest on the back with a kind of crooning song; he wheeled round and the others did the same. But when they crossed the next pasture there was a formidable bellow. It was a bull, hidden by the mist. Mme. Aubain was about to run. "No! no! don't go so fast!" They mended their pace, however, and heard a loud breathing behind them which came nearer. His hoofs thudded on the meadow grass like hammers; why, he was galloping now! Félicité turned round, and tore up clods of earth with both hands and threw them in his eyes. He lowered his muzzle, waved his horns, and quivered with fury, bellowing terribly. Mme. Aubain, now at the end of the pasture with her two little ones, was looking wildly for a place to get over the high bank. Félicité was retreating, still with her face to the bull, keeping up a shower of clods which blinded him, and crying all the time, "Be quick! be quick!"

Mme. Aubain went down into the ditch, pushed Virginie first and then Paul, fell several times as she tried to climb the bank, and managed it at last by dint of courage.

The bull had driven Félicité to bay against a rail-fence; his slaver was streaming into her face; another second, and he would have gored her. She had just time to slip between two of the rails, and the big animal stopped short in amazement.

This adventure was talked of at Pont-l'Évêque for many a year. Félicité did not pride herself on it in the least, not having the barest suspicion that she had done anything heroic.

Virginie was the sole object of her thoughts, for the child developed a nervous complaint as a result of her fright, and M. Poupart, the doctor, advised sea-bathing at Trouville.[5] It was not a frequented place then. Mme. Aubain collected information, consulted Bourais, and made preparations as though for a long journey.

Her luggage started a day in advance, in Liébard's cart. The next day he brought round two horses, one of which had a lady's saddle with a velvet back to it, while a cloak was rolled up to make a kind of seat on the crupper of the other. Mme. Aubain rode on that, behind the farmer. Félicité took charge of Virginie, and Paul mounted M. Lechaptois' donkey, lent on condition that great care was taken of it.

The road was so bad that its five miles took two hours. The horses sank in the mud up to their pasterns, and their haunches jerked abruptly in the effort to get out; or else they stumbled in the ruts, and at other moments had to jump. In some places Liébard's mare came suddenly to a halt. He waited patiently until she went on again, talking about the people who had properties along the road, and adding moral reflections to their history. So it was that as they were in the middle of Toucques, and passed under some windows bowered with nasturtiums, he shrugged his shoulders and said: "There's a Mme. Lehoussais lives there; instead of taking a young man she . . ." Félicité did not hear the rest; the horses were trotting and the donkey galloping. They all turned down a bypath; a gate swung open

5. A town on the English Channel, now a popular resort, some five miles from Pont-l'Évêque.

and two boys appeared; and the party dismounted in front of a manure-heap at the very threshold of the farmhouse door.

When Mme. Liébard saw her mistress she gave lavish signs of joy. She served her a luncheon with a sirloin of beef, tripe, black-pudding, a fricasse of chicken, sparkling cider, a fruit tart, and brandied plums; seasoning it all with compliments to Madame, who seemed in better health; Mademoiselle, who was "splendid" now; and Monsieur Paul, who had "filled out" wonderfully. Nor did she forget their deceased grandparents, whom the Liébards had known, as they had been in the service of the family for several generations. The farm, like them, had the stamp of antiquity. The beams on the ceiling were worm-eaten, the walls blackened with smoke, and the window-panes grey with dust. There was an oak dresser laden with every sort of useful article—jugs, plates, pewter bowls, wolf-traps, and sheep-shears; and a huge syringe made the children laugh. There was not a tree in the three courtyards without mushrooms growing at the bottom of it or a tuft of mistletoe on its boughs. Several of them had been thrown down by the wind. They had taken root again at the middle; and all were bending under their wealth of apples. The thatched roofs, like brown velvet and of varying thickness, withstood the heaviest squalls. The cart-shed, however, was falling into ruin. Mme. Aubain said she would see about it, and ordered the animals to be saddled again.

It was another half-hour before they reached Trouville. The little caravan dismounted to pass Écores—it was an overhanging cliff with boats below it—and three minutes later they were at the end of the quay and entered the courtyard of the Golden Lamb, kept by good Mme. David.

From the first days of their stay Virginie began to feel less weak, thanks to the change of air and the effect of the sea-baths. These, for want of a bathing-dress, she took in her chemise; and her nurse dressed her afterwards in a coastguard's cabin which was used by the bathers.

In the afternoons they took the donkey and went off beyond the Black Rocks, in the direction of Hennequeville. The path climbed at first through ground with dells in it like the green sward of a park, and then reached a plateau where grass fields and arable lay side by side. Hollies rose stiffly out of the briary tangle at the edge of the road; and here and there a great withered tree made zigzags in the blue air with its branches.

They nearly always rested in a meadow, with Deauville on their left, Havre on their right, and the open sea in front. It glittered in the sunshine, smooth as a mirror and so quiet that its murmur was scarcely to be heard; sparrows chirped in hiding and the immense sky arched over it all. Mme. Aubain sat doing her needlework; Virginie plaited rushes by her side; Félicité pulled up lavender, and Paul was bored and anxious to start home.

Other days they crossed the Toucques in a boat and looked for shells. When the tide went out sea-urchins, starfish, and jelly-fish were left exposed; and the children ran in pursuit of the foam-flakes which scudded in the wind. The sleepy waves broke on the sand and unrolled all along the beach; it stretched away out of sight, bounded on the land-side by the dunes which parted it from the Marsh, a wide meadow shaped like an arena. As they came home that way, Trouville, on the hill-slope in the background, grew bigger at every step, and its miscellaneous throng of houses seemed to break into a gay disorder.

On days when it was too hot they did not leave their room. From the dazzling brilliance outside light fell in streaks between the laths of the blinds. There were no sounds in the village; and on the pavement below not a soul. This silence round them deepened the quietness of things. In the distance, where men were caulking, there was a tap of hammers as they plugged the hulls, and a sluggish breeze wafted up the smell of tar.

The chief amusement was the return of the fishing-boats. They began to tack as soon as they had passed the buoys. The sails came down on two of the three masts; and they drew on with the foresail swelling like a balloon, gliding through the splash of the waves, and when they had reached the middle of the harbour suddenly dropped anchor. Then the boats drew up against the quay. The sailors threw quivering fish over the side; a row of carts was waiting, and women in cotton bonnets darted out to take the baskets and give their men a kiss.

One of them came up to Félicité one day, and she entered the lodgings a little later in a state of delight. She had found a sister again—and then Nastasie Barette, "wife of Leroux," appeared, holding an infant at her breast and another child with her right hand, while on her left was a little cabin boy with his hands on his hips and a cap over his ear.

After a quarter of an hour Mme. Aubain sent them off; but they were always to be found hanging about the kitchen, or encountered in the course of a walk. The husband never appeared.

Félicité was seized with affection for them. She bought them a blanket, some shirts, and a stove; it was clear that they were making a good thing out of her. Mme. Aubain was annoyed by this weakness of hers, and she did not like the liberties taken by the nephew, who said "thee" and "thou"[6] to Paul. So as Virginie was coughing and the fine weather gone, she returned to Pont-l'Évêque.

There M. Bourais enlightened her on the choice of a boys' school. The one at Caen was reputed to be the best, and Paul was sent to it. He said his good-byes bravely, content enough at going to live in a house where he would have companions.

Mme. Aubain resigned herself to her son's absence as a thing that had to be. Virginie thought about it less and less. Félicité missed the noise he made. But she found an occupation to distract her; from Christmas onward she took the little girl to catechism every day.

III

After making a genuflexion at the door she walked up between the double rows of chairs under the lofty nave, opened Mme. Aubain's pew, sat down, and began to look about her. The choir stalls were filled with the boys on the right and the girls on the left, and the curé stood by the lectern. On a painted window in the apse the Holy Ghost looked down upon the Virgin. Another window showed her on her knees before the

---

6. That is, used the familiar *tu* and *toi* rather than the more respectful *vous*.

child Jesus, and a group carved in wood behind the altar-shrine represented St. Michael overthrowing the dragon.

The priest began with a sketch of sacred history. The Garden, the Flood, the Tower of Babel, cities in flames, dying nations, and overturned idols passed like a dream before her eyes; and the dizzying vision left her with reverence for the Most High and fear of his wrath. Then she wept at the story of the Passion. Why had they crucified Him, when He loved the children, fed the multitudes, healed the blind, and had willed, in His meekness, to be born among the poor, on the dung-heap of a stable? The sowings, harvests, wine-presses, all the familiar things that the Gospel speaks of, were a part of her life. They had been made holy by God's passing; and she loved the lambs more tenderly for her love of the Lamb, and the doves because of the Holy Ghost.

She found it hard to imagine Him in person, for He was not merely a bird, but a flame as well, and a breath at other times. It may be His light, she thought, which flits at night about the edge of the marshes, His breathing which drives on the clouds, His voice which gives harmony to the bells; and she would sit rapt in adoration, enjoying the cool walls and the quiet of the church.

Of doctrines she understood nothing—did not even try to understand. The curé discoursed, the children repeated their lesson, and finally she went to sleep, waking up with a start when their wooden shoes clattered on the flagstones as they went away.

It was thus that Félicité, whose religious education had been neglected in her youth, learned the catechism by dint of hearing it; and from that time she copied all Virginie's observances, fasting as she did and confessing with her. On Corpus Christi Day[7] they made a festal altar together.

The first communion loomed distractingly ahead. She fussed over the shoes, the rosary, the book and gloves; and how she trembled as she helped Virginie's mother to dress her!

All through the mass she was racked with anxiety. She could not see one side of the choir because of M. Bourais but straight in front of her was the flock of maidens, with white crowns above their hanging veils, making the impression of a field of snow; and she knew her dear child at a distance by her dainty neck and thoughtful air. The bell tinkled. The heads bowed, and there was silence. As the organ pealed, singers and congregation took up the "Agnus Dei"[8]; then the procession of the boys began, and after them the girls rose. Step by step, with their hands joined in prayer, they went towards the lighted altar, knelt on the first step, received the sacrament in turn, and came back in the same order to their places. When Virginie's turn came Félicité leaned forward to see her; and with the imaginativeness of deep and tender feeling it seemed to her that she actually was the child; Virginie's face became hers, she was dressed in her clothes, it was her heart beating in her breast. As the moment came to open her mouth she closed her eyes and nearly fainted.

7. Feast day commemorating the founding of the Sacrament of the Eucharist (Corpus Christi is Latin for body of Christ).　　8. "Lamb of God" (Latin)—that is, Jesus; a part of the Roman Catholic Mass.

She appeared early in the sacristy next morning for Monsieur the curé to give her the communion. She took it with devotion, but it did not give her the same exquisite delight.

Mme. Aubain wanted to make her daughter into an accomplished person; and as Guyot could not teach her music or English she decided to place her in the Ursuline Convent at Honfleur[9] as a boarder. The child made no objection. Félicité sighed and thought that Madame lacked feeling. Then she reflected that her mistress might be right; matters of this kind were beyond her.

So one day an old spring-van drew up at the door, and out of it stepped a nun to fetch the young lady. Félicité hoisted the luggage on to the top, admonished the driver, and put six pots of preserves, a dozen pears, and a bunch of violets under the seat.

At the last moment Virginie broke into a fit of sobbing; she threw her arms round her mother, who kissed her on the forehead, saying over and over "Come be brave! be brave!" The step was raised, and the carriage drove off.

Then Mme. Aubain's strength gave way; and in the evening all her friends—the Lormeau family, Mme. Lechaptois, the Rochefeuille ladies, M. de Houppeville, and Bourais—came in to console her.

To be without her daughter was very painful for her at first. But she heard from Virginie three times a week, wrote to her on the other days, walked in the garden, and so filled up the empty hours.

From sheer habit Félicité went into Virginie's room in the mornings and gazed at the walls. It was boredom to her not to have to comb the child's hair now, lace up her boots, tuck her into bed—and not to see her charming face perpetually and hold her hand when they went out together. In this idle condition she tried making lace. But her fingers were too heavy and broke the threads; she could not attend to anything, she had lost her sleep, and was, in her own words, "destroyed."

To "divert herself" she asked leave to have visits from her nephew Victor.

He arrived on Sundays after mass, rosy-cheeked, bare-chested, with the scent of the country he had walked through still about him. She laid her table promptly and they had lunch, sitting opposite each other. She ate as little as possible herself to save expense, but stuffed him with food so generous that at last he went to sleep. At the first stroke of vespers she woke him up, brushed his trousers, fastened his tie, and went to church, leaning on his arm with maternal pride.

Victor was always instructed by his parents to get something out of her—a packet of moist sugar, it might be, a cake of soap, spirits, or even money at times. He brought his things for her to mend and she took over the task, only too glad to have a reason for making him come back.

In August his father took him off on a coasting voyage. It was holiday time, and she was consoled by the arrival of the children. Paul, however, was getting selfish, and Virginie was too old to be called "thou" any longer; this put a constraint and barrier between them.

9. At the mouth of the Seine River, twelve miles from Pont-l'Évêque.

Victor went to Morlaix, Dunkirk, and Brighton[1] in succession and made Félicité a present on his return from each voyage. It was a box made of shells the first time, a coffee cup the next, and on the third occasion a large gingerbread man. Victor was growing handsome. He was well made, had a hint of a moustache, good honest eyes, and a small leather hat pushed backwards like a pilot's. He entertained her by telling stories embroidered with nautical terms.

On a Monday, July 14, 1819 (she never forgot the date), he told her that he had signed on for the big voyage and next night but one he would take the Honfleur boat and join his schooner, which was to weigh anchor from Havre before long. Perhaps he would be gone two years.

The prospect of this long absence threw Félicité into deep distress; one more good-bye she must have, and on the Wednesday evening, when Madame's dinner was finished, she put on her clogs and made short work of the twelve miles between Pont-l'Évêque and Honfleur.

When she arrived in front of the Calvary she took the turn to the right instead of the left, got lost in the timber-yards, and retraced her steps; some people to whom she spoke advised her to be quick. She went all round the harbour basin, full of ships, and knocked against hawsers; then the ground fell away, lights flashed across each other, and she thought her wits had left her, for she saw horses up in the sky.

Others were neighing by the quay-side, frightened at the sea. They were lifted by a tackle and deposited in a boat, where passengers jostled each other among cider casks, cheese baskets, and sacks of grain; fowls could be heard clucking, the captain swore; and a cabin-boy stood leaning over the bows, indifferent to it all. Félicité, who had not recognized him, called "Victor!" and he raised his head; all at once, as she was darting forwards, the gangway was drawn back.

The Honfleur packet, women singing as they hauled it, passed out of harbour. Its framework creaked and the heavy waves whipped its bows. The canvas had swung round, no one could be seen on board now; and on the moon-silvered sea the boat made a black speck which paled gradually, dipped, and vanished.

As Félicité passed by the Calvary she had a wish to commend to God what she cherished most, and she stood there praying a long time with her face bathed in tears and her eyes towards the clouds. The town was asleep, coastguards were walking to and fro; and water poured without cessation through the holes in the sluice, with the noise of a torrent. The clocks struck two.

The convent parlour would not be open before day. If Félicité were late Madame would most certainly be annoyed; and in spite of her desire to kiss the other child she turned home. The maids at the inn were waking up as she came in to Pont-l'Évêque.

So the poor slip of a boy was going to toss for months and months at sea! She had not been frightened by his previous voyages. From England or Brittany you came back safe enough; but America, the colonies, the islands—these were lost in a dim region at the other end of the world.

---

1. In England, across the channel. Morlaix and Dunkirk are in Brittany and Flanders, respectively.

Félicité's thoughts from that moment ran entirely on her nephew. On sunny days she was harassed by the idea of thirst; when there was a storm she was afraid of the lightning on his account. As she listened to the wind growling in the chimney or carrying off the slates she pictured him lashed by that same tempest, at the top of a shattered mast, with his body thrown backwards under a sheet of foam; or else (with a reminiscence of the illustrated geography) he was being eaten by savages, captured in a wood by monkeys, or dying on a desert shore. And never did she mention her anxieties.

Mme. Aubain had anxieties of her own, about her daughter. The good sisters found her an affectionate but delicate child. The slightest emotion unnerved her. She had to give up the piano.

Her mother stipulated for regular letters from the convent. She lost patience one morning when the postman did not come, and walked to and fro in the parlour from her armchair to the window. It was really amazing; not a word for four days!

To console Mme. Aubain by her own example Félicité remarked:

"As for me, Madame, it's six months since I heard . . ."

"From whom, pray?"

"Why . . . from my nephew," the servant answered gently.

"Oh! your nephew!" And Mme. Aubain resumed her walk with a shrug of the shoulders, as much as to say: "I was not thinking of him! And what is more, it's absurd! A scamp of a cabin-boy—what does he matter? . . . whereas my daughter . . . why, just think!"

Félicité, though she had been brought up on harshness, felt indignant with Madame—and then forgot. It seemed the simplest thing in the world to her to lose one's head over the little girl. For her the two children were equally important; a bond in her heart made them one, and their destinies must be the same.

She heard from the chemist that Victor's ship had arrived at Havana. He had read this piece of news in a gazette.

Cigars—they made her imagine Havana as a place where no one does anything but smoke, and there was Victor moving among the negroes in a cloud of tobacco. Could you, she wondered, "in case you needed," return by land? What was the distance from Pont-l'Évêque? She questioned M. Bourais to find out.

He reached for his atlas and began explaining the longitudes; Félicité's consternation provoked a fine pedantic smile. Finally, he marked with his pencil a black, imperceptible point in the indentations of an oval spot, and said as he did so, "Here it is." She bent over the map; the maze of coloured lines wearied her eyes without conveying anything; and on an invitation from Bourais to tell him her difficulty she begged him to show her the house where Victor was living. Bourais threw up his arms, sneezed, and laughed immensely: a simplicity like hers was a positive joy. And Félicité did not understand the reason; how could she when she expected, bvery likely to see the actual image of her nephew—so stunted was her mind!

A fortnight afterwards Liébard came into the kitchen at market-time as usual and handed her a letter from her brother-in-law. As neither of them could read she took it to her mistress.

Mme. Aubain, who was counting the stitches in her knitting, put the work down by her side, broke the seal of the letter, started, and said in a low voice, with a look of meaning:

"It is bad news . . . that they have to tell you. Your nephew . . ."

He was dead. The letter said no more.

Félicité fell on to a chair, leaning her head against the wainscot; and she closed her eyelids, which suddenly flushed pink. Then with bent forehead, hands hanging, and fixed eyes, she said at intervals:

"Poor little lad! poor little lad!"

Liébard watched her and heaved sighs. Mme. Aubain trembled a little.

She suggested that Félicité should go to see her sister at Trouville. Félicité answered by a gesture that she had no need.

There was a silence. The worthy Liébard thought it was time for them to withdraw.

Then Félicité said:

"They don't care, not they!"

Her head dropped again; and she took up mechanically, from time to time, the long needles on her work-table.

Women passed in the yard with a barrow of dripping linen.

As she saw them through the window-panes, she remembered her washing; she had put it to soak the day before, to-day she must wring it out; and she left the room.

Her plank and tub were at the edge of the Toucques. She threw a pile of linen on the bank, rolled up her sleeves, and taking her wooden beater dealt lusty blows whose sound carried to the neighbouring gardens. The meadows were empty, the river stirred in the wind; and down below long grasses wavered, like the hair of corpses floating in the water. She kept her grief down and was very brave until the evening; but once in her room she surrendered to it utterly, lying stretched on the mattress with her face in the pillow and her hands clenched against her temples.

Much later she heard, from the captain himself, the circumstances of Victor's end. They had bled him too much at the hospital for yellow fever. Four doctors held him at once. He had died instantly, and the chief had said:

"Bah! there goes another!"

His parents had always been brutal to him. She preferred not to see them again; and they made no advances, either because they forgot her or from the callousness of the wretchedly poor.

Virginie began to grow weaker.

Tightness in her chest, coughing, continual fever, and veinings on her cheek-bones betrayed some deep-seated complaint. M. Poupart had advised a stay in Provence.[2] Mme. Aubain determined on it, would have brought her daughter home at once but for the climate of Pont-l'Évêque.

She made an arrangement with a job-master, and he drove her to the convent every Tuesday. There is a terrace in the garden, with a view over the Seine. Virginie took walks there over the fallen vine-leaves, on her

2. In southern France.

mother's arm. A shaft of sunlight through the clouds made her blink sometimes, as she gazed at the sails in the distance and the whole horizon from
the castle of Tancarville to the lighthouses at Havre. Afterwards they rested
in the arbour. Her mother had secured a little cask of excellent Malaga;[3]
and Virginie, laughing at the idea of getting tipsy, drank a thimble-full of
it, no more.

Her strength came back visibly. The autumn glided gently away. Félicité reassured Mme. Aubain. But one evening, when she had been out on
a commission in the neighbourhood, she found M. Poupart's gig at the
door. He was in the hall, and Mme. Aubain was tying her bonnet.

"Give me my foot-warmer, purse, gloves. Quicker, come!"

Virginie had inflammation of the lungs; perhaps it was hopeless.

"Not yet!" said the doctor, and they both got into the carriage under
whirling flakes of snow. Night was coming on and it was very cold.

Félicité rushed into the church to light a taper. Then she ran after the
gig, came up with it in an hour, and jumped lightly in behind. As she
hung on by the fringes a thought came into her mind: "The courtyard has
not been shut up; supposing burglars got in!" And she jumped down.

At dawn next day she presented herself at the doctor's. He had come in
and started for the country again. Then she waited in the inn, thinking
that a letter would come by some hand or other. Finally, when it was
twilight, she took the Lisieux coach.

The convent was at the end of a steep lane. When she was about halfway up it she heard strange sounds—a death-bell tolling. "It is for someone
else," thought Félicité, and she pulled the knocker violently.

After some minutes there was a sound of trailing slippers, the door
opened ajar, and a nun appeared.

The good sister, with an air of compunction, said that "she had just
passed away." On the instant the bell of St. Leonard's tolled twice as fast.

Félicité went up to the second floor.

From the doorway she saw Virginie stretched on her back, with her
hands joined, her mouth open, and head thrown back under a black crucifix that leaned towards her, between curtains that hung stiffly, less pale
than was her face. Mme. Aubain, at the foot of the bed which she clasped
with her arms, was choking with sobs of agony. The mother superior stood
on the right. Three candlesticks on the chest of drawers made spots of red,
and the mist came whitely through the windows. Nuns came and took
Mme. Aubain away.

For two nights Félicité never left the dead child. She repeated the same
prayers, sprinkled holy water over the sheets, came and sat down again,
and watched her. At the end of the first vigil she noticed that the face had
grown yellow, the lips turned blue, the nose was sharper, and the eyes
sunk in. She kissed them several times, and would not have been
immensely surprised if Virginie had opened them again; to minds like
hers the supernatural is quite simple. She made the girl's toilette, wrapped
her in her shroud, lifted her down into her bier, put a garland on her
head, and spread out her hair. It was fair, and extraordinarily long for her

---

3. A sweet wine.

age. Félicité cut off a big lock and slipped half of it into her bosom, determined that she should never part with it.

The body was brought back to Pont-l'Évêque, as Mme. Aubain intended; she followed the hearse in a closed carriage.

It took another three-quarters of an hour after the mass to reach the cemetery. Paul walked in front, sobbing. M. Bourais was behind, and then came the chief residents, the women shrouded in black mantles, and Félicité. She thought of her nephew; and because she had not been able to pay these honours to him her grief was doubled, as though the one were being buried with the other.

Mme. Aubain's despair was boundless. It was against God that she first rebelled, thinking it unjust of Him to have taken her daughter from her—she had never done evil and her conscience was so clear! Ah, no!—she ought to have taken Virginie off to the south. Other doctors would have saved her. She accused herself now, wanted to join her child, and broke into cries of distress in the middle of her dreams. One dream haunted her above all. Her husband, dressed as a sailor, was returning from a long voyage, and shedding tears he told her that he had been ordered to take Virginie away. Then they consulted how to hide her somewhere.

She came in once from the garden quite upset. A moment ago—and she pointed out the place—the father and daughter had appeared to her, standing side by side, and they did nothing, but they looked at her.

For several months after this she stayed inertly in her room. Félicité lectured her gently; she must live for her son's sake, and for the other, in remembrance of "her."

"Her?" answered Mme. Aubain, as though she were just waking up. "Ah, yes! . . . yes! . . . You do not forget her!" This was an allusion to the cemetery, where she was strictly forbidden to go.

Félicité went there every day.

Precisely at four she skirted the houses, climbed the hill, opened the gate, and came to Virginie's grave. It was a little column of pink marble with a stone underneath and a garden plot enclosed by chains. The beds were hidden under a coverlet of flowers. She watered their leaves, freshened the gravel, and knelt down to break up the earth better. When Mme. Aubain was able to come there she felt a relief and a sort of consolation.

Then years slipped away, one like another, and their only episodes were the great festivals as they recurred—Easter, the Assumption, All Saints' Day. Household occurrences marked dates that were referred to afterwards. In 1825, for instance, two glaziers white-washed the hall; in 1827 a piece of the roof fell into the courtyard and nearly killed a man. In the summer of 1828 it was Madame's turn to offer the consecrated bread; Bourais, about this time, mysteriously absented himself; and one by one the old acquaintances passed away: Guyot, Liébard, Mme. Lechaptois, Robelin, and Uncle Gremanville, who had been paralysed for a long time.

One night the driver of the mail-coach announced the Revolution of July[4] in Pont-l'Évêque. A new sub-prefect was appointed a few days later— Baron de Larsonnière, who had been consul in America, and brought with

----

4. In 1830 the Bourbons were driven out, and Louis-Philippe became king of France.

him, besides his wife, a sister-in-law and three young ladies, already growing up. They were to be seen about on their lawn, in loose blouses, and
they had a negro and a parrot. They paid a call on Mme. Aubain which
she did not fail to return. The moment they were seen in the distance
Félicité ran to let her mistress know. But only one thing could really move
her feelings—the letters from her son.

He was swallowed up in a tavern life and could follow no career. She
paid his debts, he made new ones; and the sighs that Mme. Aubain uttered
as she sat knitting by the window reached Félicité at her spinning-wheel
in the kitchen.

They took walks together along the espaliered wall, always talking of
Virginie and wondering if such and such a thing would have pleased her
and what, on some occasion, she would have been likely to say.

All her small belongings filled a cupboard in the two-bedded room.
Mme. Aubain inspected them as seldom as she could. One summer day
she made up her mind to it—and some moths flew out of the wardrobe.

Virginie's dresses were in a row underneath a shelf, on which there
were three dolls, some hoops, a set of toy pots and pans, and the basin
that she used. They took out her petticoats as well, and the stockings and
handkerchiefs, and laid them out on the two beds before folding them up
again. The sunshine lit up these poor things, bringing out their stains and
the creases made by the body's movements. The air was warm and blue,
a blackbird warbled, life seemed bathed in a deep sweetness. They found
a little plush hat with thick, chestnut-coloured pile; but it was eaten all
over by moth. Félicité begged it for her own. Their eyes met fixedly and
filled with tears; at last the mistress opened her arms, the servant threw
herself into them, and they embraced each other, satisfying their grief in
a kiss that made them equal.

It was the first time in their lives, Mme. Aubain's nature not being
expansive. Félicité was as grateful as though she had received a favour;
and cherished her mistress from that moment with the devotion of an
animal and a religious worship.

The kindness of her heart unfolded.

When she heard the drums of a marching regiment in the street she
posted herself at the door with a pitcher of cider and asked the soldiers to
drink. She nursed cholera patients and protected the Polish refugees;[5] one
of these even declared that he wished to marry her. They quarrelled, however; for when she came back from the Angelus one morning she found
that he had got into her kitchen and made himself a vinegar salad which
he was quietly eating.

After the Poles came father Colmiche, an old man who was supposed
to have committed atrocities in '93.[6] He lived by the side of the river in
the ruins of a pigsty. The little boys watched him through the cracks in
the wall, and threw pebbles at him which fell on the pallet where he lay
constantly shaken by a catarrh; his hair was very long, his eyes inflamed,
and there was a tumour on his arm bigger than his head. She got him

5. After the Polish uprising against Russia in 1831 was suppressed, many Poles came to France.   6. In
1793 the Reign of Terror during the French Revolution began.

She bought him, and hung him up instead of the Comte d'Artois, so that she could see them both together in one glance. They were linked in her thoughts; and the parrot was consecrated by his association with the Holy Ghost, which became more vivid to her eye and more intelligible. The Father could not have chosen to express Himself through a dove, for such creatures cannot speak; it must have been one of Loulou's ancestors, surely. And though Félicité looked at the picture while she said her prayers she swerved a little from time to time towards the parrot.

She wanted to join the Ladies of the Virgin, but Mme. Aubain dissuaded her.

And then a great event loomed up before them—Paul's marriage.

He had been a solicitor's clerk to begin with, and then tried business, the Customs, the Inland Revenue, and made efforts, even, to get into the Rivers and Forests. By an inspiration from heaven he had suddenly, at thirty-six, discovered his real line—the Registrar's Office. And there he showed such marked capacity that an inspector had offered him his daughter's hand and promised him his influence.

So Paul, grown serious, brought the lady to see his mother.

She sniffed at the ways of Pont-l'Évêque, gave herself great airs, and wounded Félicité's feelings. Mme. Aubain was relieved at her departure.

The week after came news of M. Bourais' death in an inn in Lower Brittany. The rumour of suicide was confirmed, and doubts arose as to his honesty. Mme. Aubain studied his accounts, and soon found out the whole tale of his misdoings—embezzled arrears, secret sales of wood, forged receipts, etc. Besides that he had an illegitimate child, and "relations with a person at Dozulé."

These shameful facts distressed her greatly. In March 1853 she was seized with a pain in the chest; her tongue seemed to be covered with film, and leeches did not ease the difficult breathing. On the ninth evening of her illness she died, just at seventy-two.

She passed as being younger, owing to the bands of brown hair which framed her pale, pock-marked face. There were few friends to regret her, for she had a stiffness of manner which kept people at a distance.

But Félicité mourned for her as one seldom mourns for a master. It upset her ideas and seemed contrary to the order of things, impossible and monstrous, that Madame should die before her.

Ten days afterwards, which was the time it took to hurry there from Besançon,[8] the heirs arrived. The daughter-in-law ransacked the drawers, chose some furniture, and sold the rest; and then they went back to their registering.

Madame's armchair, her small round table, her foot-warmer, and the eight chairs were gone! Yellow patches in the middle of the panels showed where the engravings had hung. They had carried off the two little beds and the mattresses, and all Virginie's belongings had disappeared from the cupboard. Félicité went from floor to floor dazed with sorrow.

The next day there was a notice on the door, and the apothecary shouted in her ear that the house was for sale.

8. In eastern France, near the Swiss border.

She tottered, and was obliged to sit down. What distressed her most of all was to give up her room, so suitable as it was for poor Loulou. She enveloped him with a look of anguish when she was imploring the Holy Ghost, and formed the idolatrous habit of kneeling in front of the parrot to say her prayers. Sometimes the sun shone in at the attic window and caught his glass eye, and a great luminous ray shot out of it and put her in an ecstasy.

She had a pension of three hundred and eighty francs a year which her mistress had left her. The garden gave her a supply of vegetables. As for clothes, she had enough to last her to the end of her days, and she economized in candles by going to bed at dusk.

She hardly ever went out, as she did not like passing the dealer's shop, where some of the old furniture was exposed for sale. Since her fit of giddiness she dragged one leg; and as her strength was failing Mère Simon, whose grocery business had collapsed, came every morning to split the wood and pump water for her.

Her eyes grew feeble. The shutters ceased to be thrown open. Years and years passed, and the house was neither let nor sold.

Félicité never asked for repairs because she was afraid of being sent away. The boards on the roof rotted; her bolster was wet for a whole winter. After Easter she spat blood.

Then Mère Simon called in a doctor. Félicité wanted to know what was the matter with her. But she was too deaf to hear, and the only word which reached her was "pneumonia." It was a word she knew, and she answered softly "Ah! like Madame," thinking it natural that she should follow her mistress.

The time for the festal shrines was coming near. The first one was always at the bottom of the hill, the second in front of the post-office, and the third towards the middle of the street. There was some rivalry in the matter of this one, and the women of the parish ended by choosing Mme. Aubain's courtyard.

The hard breathing and fever increased. Félicité was vexed at doing nothing for the altar. If only she could at least have put something there! Then she thought of the parrot. The neighbours objected that it would not be decent. But the priest gave her permission, which so intensely delighted her that she begged him to accept Loulou, her sole possession, when she died.

From Tuesday to Saturday, the eve of the festival, she coughed more often. By the evening her face had shrivelled, her lips stuck to her gums, and she had vomitings; and at twilight next morning, feeling herself very low, she sent for a priest.

Three kindly women were round her during the extreme unction. Then she announced that she must speak to Fabu. He arrived in his Sunday clothes, by no means at his ease in the funereal atmosphere.

"Forgive me," she said, with an effort to stretch out her arm; "I thought it was you who had killed him."

What did she mean by such stories? She suspected him of murder — a man like him! He waxed indignant, and was on the point of making a row.

"There," said the women, "she is no longer in her senses, you can see it well enough!"

Félicité spoke to shadows of her own from time to time. The women went away, and Mère Simon had breakfast. A little later she took Loulou and brought him close to Félicité with the words:

"Come, now, say good-bye to him!"

Loulou was not a corpse, but the worms devoured him; one of his wings was broken, and the tow was coming out of his stomach. But she was blind now; she kissed him on the forehead and kept him close against her cheek. Mère Simon took him back from her to put him on the altar.

v

Summer scents came up from the meadows; flies buzzed; the sun made the river glitter and heated the slates. Mère Simon came back into the room and fell softly asleep.

She woke at the noise of bells; the people were coming out from vespers. Félicité's delirium subsided. She thought of the procession and saw it as if she had been there.

All the school children, the church-singers, and the firemen walked on the pavement, while in the middle of the road the verger armed with his hallebard and the beadle with a large cross advanced in front. Then came the schoolmaster, with an eye on the boys, and the sister, anxious about her little girls; three of the daintiest, with angelic curls, scattered rose-petals in the air; the deacon controlled the band with outstretched arms; and two censer-bearers turned back at every step towards the Holy Sacrament, which was borne by Monsieur the curé, wearing his beautiful chasuble, under a canopy of dark-red velvet held by four churchwardens. A crowd of people pressed behind, between the white cloths covering the house walls, and they reached the bottom of the hill.

A cold sweat moistened Félicité's temples. Mère Simon sponged her with a piece of linen, saying to herself that one day she would have to go that way.

The hum of the crowd increased, was very loud for an instant and then went further away.

A fusillade shook the window-panes. It was the postilions saluting the monstrance. Félicité rolled her eyes and said as audibly as she could: "Does he look well?" The parrot was weighing on her mind.

Her agony began. A death-rattle that grew more and more convulsed made her sides heave. Bubbles of froth came at the corners of her mouth and her whole body trembled.

Soon the booming of the ophicleides,[9] the high voices of the children, and the deep voices of the men were distinguishable. At intervals all was silent, and the tread of feet, deadened by the flowers they walked on, sounded like a flock pattering on grass.

The clergy appeared in the courtyard. Mère Simon clambered on to a chair to reach the attic window, and so looked down straight upon the shrine. Green garlands hung over the altar, which was decked with a

---

9. An old large brass-wind instrument now replaced by the tuba.

flounce of English lace. In the middle was a small frame with relics in it; there were two orange-trees at the corners, and all along stood silver candlesticks and china vases, with sunflowers, lilies, peonies, foxgloves, and tufts of hortensia. This heap of blazing colour slanted from the level of the altar to the carpet which went on over the pavement; and some rare objects caught the eye. There was a silver-gilt sugar-basin with a crown of violets; pendants of Alençon stone glittered on the moss, and two Chinese screens displayed their landscapes. Loulou was hidden under roses, and showed nothing but his blue forehead, like a plaque of lapis lazuli.

The churchwardens, singers, and children took their places round the three sides of the court. The priest went slowly up the steps, and placed his great, radiant golden sun[1] upon the lace. Everyone knelt down. There was a deep silence; and the censers glided to and fro on the full swing of their chains.

An azure vapour rose up into Félicité's room. Her nostrils met it; she inhaled it sensuously, mystically; and then closed her eyes. Her lips smiled. The beats of her heart lessened one by one, vaguer each time and softer, as a fountain sinks, an echo disappears; and when she sighed her last breath she thought she saw an opening in the heavens, and a gigantic parrot hovering above her head.

---

1. The monstrance containing the consecrated Host.

FYODOR DOSTOEVSKY
1821–1881

Fyodor Dostoevsky has been a central figure in the formation of the modern sensibility. His works are fundamental to the Western tradition of the novel and a strong influence on modern literature in China and Japan. Dostoevsky formulated in fictional terms, in dramatic and even sensational scenes, some of the central predicaments of our time: the choices between God and atheism, good and evil, freedom and tyranny; the recognition of the limits and even of the fall of humanity against the belief in progress, revolution, and utopia. Most important, he captured unforgettably the enormous contradictions of which our common human nature is capable and by which it is torn.

Fyodor Mikhailovich Dostoevsky was born in Moscow on October 30, 1821. His father was a staff doctor at the Hospital for the Poor. Later he acquired an estate and serfs. In 1839 he was killed by one of his peasants in a quarrel. Dostoevsky was sent to the Military Engineering Academy in St. Petersburg, from which he graduated in 1843. He became a civil servant, a draftsman in the St. Petersburg Engineering Corps, but resigned soon because he feared that he would be transferred to the provinces when his writing was discovered. His first novel, Poor People (1846), proved a great success with the critics; his second, The Double (1846), which followed immediately, was a failure.

Subsequently, Dostoevsky became involved in the Petrashevsky circle, a secret society of antigovernment and socialist tendencies. He was arrested on April 23, 1849, and condemned to be shot. On December 22 he was led to public execution, but he was reprieved at the last moment and sent to penal servitude in Siberia (near Omsk), where he worked for four years in a stockade, wearing fetters, completely cut off from communications with Russia. On his release in February 1854, he was assigned as a common soldier to Semipalatinsk, a small town near the Mongolian frontier. There he received several promotions (eventually becoming an ensign); his rank of nobility, forfeited by his sentence, was restored; and he married the widow of a customs official. In July 1859, Dostoevsky was permitted to return to Russia, and finally, in December 1859, to St. Petersburg—after ten years of his life had been spent in Siberia.

In the last year of his exile, Dostoevsky had resumed writing, and in 1861, shortly after his return, he founded a review, *Time* (*Vremya*). This was suppressed in 1863, though Dostoevsky had changed his political opinions and was now strongly nationalistic and conservative in outlook. He made his first trip to France and England in 1862, and traveled in Europe again in 1863 and 1865, to follow a young woman friend, Apollinaria Suslova, and to indulge in gambling. After his wife's death in 1864, and another unsuccessful journalistic venture, *The Epoch* (*Epokha*, 1864–65), Dostoevsky was for a time almost crushed by gambling debts, emotional entanglements, and frequent epileptic seizures. He barely managed to return from Germany in 1865. In the winter of 1866 he wrote *Crime and Punishment* and, before he had finished it, dictated a shorter novel, *The Gambler*, to meet a deadline. He married his secretary, Anna Grigoryevna Snitkina, early in 1867 and left Russia with her to avoid his creditors. For years they wandered over Germany, Italy, and Switzerland, frequently in abject poverty. Their first child died. In 1871, when the initial chapters of *The Possessed* proved a popular success, Dostoevsky returned to St. Petersburg. He became the editor of a weekly, *The Citizen* (*Grazhdanin*), for a short time and then published a periodical written by himself, *The Diary of a Writer* (1876–81), which won great acclaim. His last novel, *The Brothers Karamazov* (1880), was an immense success, and honors and some prosperity came to him at last. At a Pushkin anniversary celebrated in Moscow in 1880 he gave the main speech. But soon after his return to St. Petersburg he died, on January 28, 1881, not yet sixty years old.

Dostoevsky, like every great writer, can be approached in different ways and read on different levels. We can try to understand him as a religious philosopher, a political commentator, a psychologist, and a novelist, and if we know much about his fascinating and varied life, we might also interpret his works as biographical.

The biographical interpretation is the one that has been pushed furthest. The lurid crimes of Dostoevsky's characters (such as the rape of a young girl) have been ascribed to him, and all his novels have been studied as if they constituted a great personal confession. Dostoevsky certainly did draw from his experiences in his books, as every writer does: he several times described the feelings of a man facing a firing squad as he himself faced it on December 22, 1849, only to be reprieved at the last moment. His writings also reflect his years in Siberia: four years working in a loghouse, in chains, as he describes it in an oddly impersonal book, *Memoirs from the House of the Dead* (1862), and six more years as a common soldier on the borders of Mongolia, in a small, remote provincial town. Similarly, he used the experience of his disease (epilepsy), ascribing great spiritual significance to the ecstatic rapture preceding the actual seizure. He assigned his disease to both his most angelic "good" man, the "Idiot," Prince Myshkin, and his most diabolical, inhuman figure, the cold-blooded unsexed murderer of the old Karamazov, the flunky Smerdyakov. Dostoevsky also used something of his experiences in Germany, where in the 1860s he succumbed to a passion for gambling, which he overcame only much later, during his second marriage. The short novel *The Gambler* (1866) gives an especially vivid account of this life and its moods.

There are other autobiographical elements in Dostoevsky's works, but it seems a gross misunderstanding of his methods and the procedures of art in general to conclude from his writings (as Thomas Mann has done) that he was a "saint and criminal" in one. Dostoevsky, after all, was an extremely hard worker who wrote and rewrote some twenty volumes. He was a novelist who employed the methods of the French sensational novel; he was constantly on the lookout for the most striking occurrences—the most shocking crimes and the most horrible disasters and scandals—because only in such fictional situations could he exalt his characters to their highest pitch, bringing out the clash of ideas and temperaments, revealing the deepest layers of their souls. But these fictions cannot be taken as literal transcriptions of reality and actual experience.

Whole books have been written to explain Dostoevsky's religious philosophy and conception of human nature. The Russian philosopher Berdyayev concludes his excellent study by saying, "So great is the value of Dostoevsky that to have produced him is by itself sufficient justification for the existence of the Russian people in the world." But there is no need for such extravagance. Dostoevsky's philosophy of religion is rather a personal version of extreme mystical Christianity, and assumes flesh and blood only in the context of the novels. Reduced to the bare bones of abstract propositions, it amounts to saying that humanity is fallen but is free to choose between evil and Christ. And choosing Christ means taking on oneself the burden of humanity in love and pity, since "everybody is guilty for all and before all." Hence in Dostoevsky there is tremendous stress on personal freedom of choice, and his affirmation of the worth of every individual is combined, paradoxically, with an equal insistence on the substantial identity of all human beings, their equality before God, the bond of love that unites them.

Dostoevsky also develops a philosophy of history, with practical political implications, based on this point of view. According to him, the West is in complete decay; only Russia has preserved Christianity in its original form. The West is either Catholic (and Catholicism is condemned by Dostoevsky as an attempt to force salvation by magic and authority) or bourgeois, and hence materialistic and fallen away from Christ, or socialist, and socialism is to Dostoevsky identical with atheism, as it dreams of a utopia in which human beings would not be free to choose even at the expense of suffering. Dostoevsky—who himself had belonged to a revolutionary group and come into contact with Russian revolutionaries abroad—had an extraordinary insight into the mentality of the Russian underground. In The Possessed (1871–72) he gives a lurid satiric picture of these would-be saviors of Russia and humankind. But while he was afraid of the revolution, Dostoevsky himself hoped and prophesied that Russia would save Europe from the dangers of communism, as Russia alone was the uncorrupted Christian land. Put in terms of political propositions (as Dostoevsky himself preaches them in his journal, The Diary of a Writer, 1876–81), what he propounds is a conservative Russian nationalism with messianic hopes for Russian Christianity.

When translated into abstractions, Dostoevsky's psychology is as unimpressive as his political theory. It is merely a derivative of theories propounded by German writers about the unconscious, the role of dreams, the ambivalence of human feelings. What makes it electric in the novels is his ability to dramatize it in scenes of sudden revelation, in characters who in today's terminology would be called split personalities, in people twisted by isolation, lust, humiliation, and resentment. The dreams of Raskolnikov may be interpreted according to Freudian psychology, but to the reader without any knowledge of science they are comprehensible in their place in the novel and function as warnings and anticipations.

Dostoevsky was first of all an artist—a novelist who succeeded in using his ideas (many old and venerable, many new and fantastic) and psychological insights for the writing of stories of absorbing interest. As an artist, Dostoevsky treated the novel like a drama, constructing it in large, vivid scenes that end with a scandal or a crime or some act of violence, filling it with unforgettable "stagelike" figures torn

by great passions and swayed by great ideas. Then he set this world in an environment of St. Petersburg slums or of towns, monasteries, and country houses, all so
vividly realized that we forget how the setting, the figures, and the ideas blend
together into one cosmos of the imagination only remotely and obliquely related
to any reality of nineteenth-century Russia. We take part in a great drama of pride
and humility, good and evil, in a huge allegory of humanity's search for God and
itself. We understand and share in this world because it is not merely Russia in
the nineteenth century, where people could hardly have talked and behaved as
Dostoevsky's people do, but a myth of humanity, universalized as all art is.

   Notes from Underground (1864) precedes the four great novels: Crime and Punishment (1866), The Idiot (1868), The Possessed, and The Brothers Karamazov
(1880). The Notes can be viewed as a prologue, an important introduction to the
cycle of the four great novels, an anticipation of the mature Dostoevsky's method
and thought. Though it cannot compare in dramatic power and scope with these,
the story has its own peculiar and original artistry. It is made up of two parts, at
first glance seemingly independent: the monologue of the Underground man and
the confession that he makes about himself, called Apropos of Wet Snow. The
monologue, though it includes no action, is dramatic—a long address to an imaginary hostile reader, whom the Underground man ridicules, defies, jeers at, but
also flatters. The confession is an autobiographical reminiscence of the Underground man. It describes events that occurred long before the delivery of the
monologue, but it functions as a confirmation in concrete terms of the self-portrait
drawn in the monologue and as an explanation of the isolation of the hero.

   The narrative of the confession is a comic variation on the old theme of the
rescue of a fallen woman from vice, a seesaw series of humiliations permitting
Dostoevsky to display all the cruelty of his probing psychology. The hero, out of
spite and craving for human company, forces himself into the company of former
schoolfellows and is shamefully humiliated by them. He reasserts his ego (as he
cannot revenge himself on them) in the company of a humble prostitute by
impressing her with florid and moving speeches, which he knows to be insincere,
about her horrible future. Ironically, he converts her, but when she comes to him
and surprises him in a degrading scene with his servant, he humiliates her again.
When, even then, she understands and forgives and thus shows her moral superiority, he crowns his spite by deliberately misunderstanding her and forcing money
on her. She is the moral victor and the Underground man returns to his hideout
to jeer at humanity. It is hard not to feel that we are shown a tortured and twisted
soul almost too despicable to elicit our compassion.

   Still it would be a complete misunderstanding of Dostoevsky's story to take the
philosophy expounded jeeringly in the long monologue of the first part merely as
the irrational railings of a sick personality. The Underground man, though abject
and spiteful, represents not only a specific Russian type of the time—the intellectual divorced from the soil and his nation—but also modern humanity, even
Everyman, and strangely enough, even the author, who through the mouth of this
despicable character, as through a mask, expresses his boldest and most intimate
convictions. In spite of all the exaggerated pathos, wild paradox, and jeering irony
used by the speaker, his self-criticism and his criticism of society and history must
be taken seriously and interpreted patiently if we are to extract the meaning
accepted by Dostoevsky.

   The Underground man is also the hyperconscious man who examines himself
as if in a mirror, and sees himself with pitiless candor. His very self-consciousness
cripples his will and poisons his feelings. He cannot escape from his ego; he knows
that he has acted badly toward the woman but at the same time he cannot help
acting as he does. He knows that he is alone, that there is no bridge from him to
humanity, that the world is hostile to him, and that he is humiliated by everyone

he meets. But though he resents the humiliation, he cannot help courting it, provoking it, and even enjoying it in his perverse manner. He understands (and knows from his own experience) that something within us all enjoys evil and destruction.

His self-criticism widens, then, into a criticism of the assumptions of modern civilization, of nineteenth-century optimism about human nature and progress, of utilitarianism, and of all kinds of utopias. It is possible to identify specific allusions to a contemporary novel by a radical socialist and revolutionary, Chernyshevsky, titled *What Shall We Do?* (1863), but we do not need to know the exact target of Dostoevsky's satire to recognize what he attacks: the view that human nature is good, that we generally seek our enlightened self-interest, that science propounds immutable truths, and that a paradise on earth will be just around the corner once society is reformed along scientific lines. In a series of vivid symbols these assumptions are represented, parodied, exposed. Science says that "twice two makes four" but the Underground man laughs that "twice two makes five is sometimes a very charming thing too." Science means to him (and to Dostoevsky) the victory of the doctrine of fatality, of iron necessity, of determinism, and thus finally of death. Humanity would become an "organ stop," a "piano key," if deterministic science were valid.

Equally disastrous are the implications of the social philosophy of liberalism and of socialism (which Dostoevsky considers its necessary consequence). In this view, we need only follow our enlightened self-interest, need only be rational, and we will become noble and good and the earth will be a place of prosperity and peace. But the Underground man knows that this conception of human nature is entirely false. What if humankind does not follow, and never will follow, its own enlightened self-interest, is consciously and purposely irrational, even bloodthirsty and evil? History seems to the Underground man to speak a clear language: "civilization has made mankind if not more bloodthirsty, at least more vilely, more loathsomely bloodthirsty." Humanity wills the irrational and evil because it does not want to become an organ stop, a piano key, because it wants to be left with the freedom to choose between good and evil. This freedom of choice, even at the expense of chaos and destruction, is what makes us human.

Actually, we love something other than our own well-being and happiness, love even suffering and pain, because we are human and not animals inhabiting some great organized rational "ant heap." The ant heap, the hen house, the block of tenements, and finally the Crystal Palace (then the newest wonder of architecture, a great hall of iron and glass erected for the Universal Exhibition in London) are the images used by the Underground man to represent his hated utopia. The heroine of *What Shall We Do?* had dreamed of a building, made of cast iron and glass and placed in the middle of a beautiful garden where there would be eternal spring and summer, eternal joy. Dostoevsky had recognized there the utopian dream of Charles Fourier, the French socialist whom he had admired in his youth and whose ideals he had come to hate with a fierce revulsion. But we must realize that the Underground man, and Dostoevsky, despise this "ant heap," this perfectly organized society of automatons, in the name of something higher, in the name of freedom. Dostoevsky does not believe that humanity can achieve freedom and happiness at the same time; happiness can be bought only at the expense of freedom, and all utopian schemes seem to him devices to lure us into the yoke of slavery. This freedom is, of course, not political freedom but freedom of choice, indeterminism, even caprice and willfulness, in the paradoxical formulation of the Underground man.

There are hints at a positive solution only in the one chapter (Part I, Chapter X) that was mutilated by the censor. A letter by Dostoevsky to his brother about the "swine of a censor who let through the passages where I jeered at everything and blasphemed ostensibly" refers to the fact that he "suppressed everything where I drew the conclusion that faith in Christ is needed." In Part I, Chapter XI, of the present text (and Dostoevsky never restored the suppressed passages) the Underground man says merely, "I am lying because I know myself that it is not underground that is better, but something different, quite different, for which I am thirsting, but which I cannot find!" This "something . . . quite different" all the other writings of Dostoevsky show to be the voluntary following of the Christian savior even at the expense of suffering and pain.

In a paradoxical form, through the mouth of one of his vilest characters, Dostoevsky reveals in the story his view of humanity and history—of the evil in human nature and of the blood and tragedy in history—and his criticism of the optimistic, utilitarian, utopian, progressive view of humanity that was spreading to Russia from the West during the nineteenth century and that found its most devoted adherents in the Russian revolutionaries. Preoccupied with criticism, Dostoevsky does not here suggest any positive remedy. But if we understand the Notes we can understand how Raskolnikov, the murderer out of intellect in Crime and Punishment, can find salvation at last, and how Dmitri, the guilty-guiltless parricide of The Brothers Karamazov, can sing his hymn to joy in the Siberian mines. We can even understand the legend of the Grand Inquisitor told by Ivan Karamazov, in which we meet the same criticism of a utopia (this time that of Catholicism) and the same exaltation of human freedom even at the price of suffering.

Monroe C. Beardsley, "Dostoevsky's Metaphor of the 'Underground,'" Journal of the History of Ideas, 3 (June 1942): 265–90, is a subtle interpretation of the central metaphor of the Notes. Joseph Frank, "Nihilism and Notes from Underground," Sewanee Review, 69 (1961), interprets the Notes in the context of the history of the times. Robert L. Jackson, The Underground Man in Russian Literature (1981), traces the impact of the Notes on Russian literature. Konstantin Mochulsky, Dostoevsky: Life and Work (1967), is the best general work translated from Russian, the work of an emigré in Paris. René Wellek, ed., Dostoevsky: A Collection of Critical Essays (1962), contains an essay by the editor on the history of Dostoevsky criticism. Alba della Fazia Amoia, Feodor Dostoevsky (1993), is a general introduction to Dostoevsky's work, aimed at a student audience. Joseph Frank, Dostoevsky (1976–1986), is an impressive though still unfinished biographical study in three volumes. Frank's Through the Russian Prism (1990) includes review essays that examine various approaches to Dostoevsky. Louis Breger, Dostoevsky: The Author as Psychoanalyst (1989), takes a psychoanalytic approach in analyzing levels of meaning in Dostoevsky's work as a new sensibility that anticipates the modern novel; he includes a chapter on Notes. Malcolm V. Jones, Dostoyevsky after Bakhtin: Readings in Dostoyevsky's Fantastic Realism (1990), examines Dostoevsky's "higher realism" in various perspectives and includes a chapter on Notes.

PRONOUNCING GLOSSARY

The following list uses common English syllables and stress accents to provide rough equivalents of selected words whose pronunciation may be unfamiliar to the general reader.

Anton Antonych: *ahn-tawn' ahn-taw'-nich*

Apollon: *ah-pah-lawn'*

Ferfichkin: *fehr-feech'-keen*

Fyodor Dostoevsky: *fyo'dor dos-toy-eff'-skee*

Karamazov: *kuh-rah-mah'-zuf*

Kolya: *kawl'-yuh*

Podkharzhevsky: *put-khar-zhef'-skee*

Simonov: *see-muh-nuf*

Trudolyubov: *troo-dah-lyoo'-buf*

Zverkov: *zvyehr-kof'*

From Notes from Underground[1]

I

Underground[2]

I

I am a sick man. . . .[3] I am a spiteful man. I am a most unpleasant man. I think my liver is diseased. Then again, I don't know a thing about my illness; I'm not even sure what hurts. I'm not being treated and never have been, though I respect both medicine and doctors. Besides, I'm extremely superstitious—well at least enough to respect medicine. (I'm sufficiently educated not to be superstitious; but I am, anyway.) No, gentlemen, it's out of spite that I don't wish to be treated. Now then, that's something you probably won't understand. Well, I do. Of course, I won't really be able to explain to you precisely who will be hurt by my spite in this case; I know perfectly well that I can't possibly "get even" with doctors by refusing their treatment; I know better than anyone that all this is going to hurt me alone, and no one else. Even so, if I refuse to be treated, it's out of spite. My liver hurts? Good, let it hurt even more!

I've been living this way for some time—about twenty years. I'm forty now. I used to be in the civil service. But no more. I was a nasty official. I was rude and took pleasure in it. After all, since I didn't accept bribes, at least I had to reward myself in some way. (That's a poor joke, but I won't cross it out. I wrote it thinking that it would be very witty; but now, having realized that I merely wanted to show off disgracefully, I'll make a point of not crossing it out!) When petitioners used to approach my desk for information, I'd gnash my teeth and feel unending pleasure if I succeeded in causing someone distress. I almost always succeeded. For the most part they were all timid people: naturally, since they were petitioners. But among the dandies there was a certain officer whom I particularly couldn't bear. He simply refused to be humble, and he clanged his saber in a loathsome manner. I waged war with him over that saber for about a year and a half. At last I prevailed. He stopped clanging. All this, however, happened a long time ago, during my youth. But do you know, gentlemen, what the main component of my spite really was? Why, the whole point, the most disgusting thing, was the fact that I was shamefully aware at every moment, even at the moment of my greatest bitterness, that not only was I not a spiteful man, I was not even an embittered one, and that I was merely scaring sparrows to no effect and consoling myself by doing so. I was foaming at the mouth—but just bring me some trinket to play with, just serve me a nice cup of tea with sugar, and I'd probably have calmed

---

1. Translated by Michael Katz.   2. Both the author of these notes and the Notes themselves are fictitious, of course. Nevertheless, people like the author of these notes not only may, but actually must exist in our society, considering the general circumstances under which our society was formed. I wanted to bring before the public with more prominence than usual one of the characters of the recent past. He's a representative of the current generation. In the excerpt entitled "Underground" this person introduces himself and his views, and, as it were, wants to explain the reasons why he appeared and why he had to appear in our midst. The following excerpt ["Apropos of Wet Snow"] contains the actual "notes" of this person about several events in his life [Author's note].   3. The ellipses are the author's and do not indicate omissions from this text.

down. My heart might even have been touched, although I'd probably have gnashed my teeth out of shame and then suffered from insomnia for several months afterward. That's just my usual way.

I was lying about myself just now when I said that I was a nasty official. I lied out of spite. I was merely having some fun at the expense of both the petitioners and that officer, but I could never really become spiteful. At all times I was aware of a great many elements in me that were just the opposite of that. I felt how they swarmed inside me, these contradictory elements. I knew that they had been swarming inside me my whole life and were begging to be let out; but I wouldn't let them out, I wouldn't, I deliberately wouldn't let them out. They tormented me to the point of shame; they drove me to convulsions and—and finally I got fed up with them, oh how fed up! Perhaps it seems to you, gentlemen, that I'm repenting about something, that I'm asking your forgiveness for something? I'm sure that's how it seems to you. . . . But really, I can assure you, I don't care if that's how it seems. . . .

Not only couldn't I become spiteful, I couldn't become anything at all: neither spiteful nor good, neither a scoundrel nor an honest man, neither a hero nor an insect. Now I live out my days in my corner, taunting myself with the spiteful and entirely useless consolation that an intelligent man cannot seriously become anything and that only a fool can become something. Yes, sir, an intelligent man in the nineteenth century must be, is morally obliged to be, principally a characterless creature; a man possessing character, a man of action, is fundamentally a limited creature. That's my conviction at the age of forty. I'm forty now; and, after all, forty is an entire lifetime; why it's extreme old age. It's rude to live past forty, it's indecent, immoral! Who lives more than forty years? Answer sincerely, honestly. I'll tell you who: only fools and rascals. I'll tell those old men that right to their faces, all those venerable old men, all those silver-haired and sweet-smelling old men! I'll say it to the whole world right to its face! I have a right to say it because I myself will live to sixty. I'll make it to seventy! Even to eighty! . . . Wait! Let me catch my breath. . . .

You probably think, gentlemen, that I want to amuse you. You're wrong about that, too. I'm not at all the cheerful fellow I seem to be, or that I may seem to be; however, if you're irritated by all this talk (and I can already sense that you are irritated), and if you decide to ask me just who I really am, then I'll tell you: I'm a collegiate assessor. I worked in order to have something to eat (but only for that reason); and last year, when a distant relative of mine left me six thousand rubles in his will, I retired immediately and settled down in this corner. I used to live in this corner before, but now I've settled down in it. My room is nasty, squalid, on the outskirts of town. My servant is an old peasant woman, spiteful out of stupidity; besides, she has a foul smell. I'm told that the Petersburg climate is becoming bad for my health, and that it's very expensive to live in Petersburg with my meager resources. I know all that; I know it better than all those wise and experienced advisers and admonishers. But I shall remain in Petersburg; I shall not leave Petersburg! I shall not leave here because . . . Oh, what difference does it really make whether I leave Petersburg or not?

Now, then, what can a decent man talk about with the greatest pleasure?

Answer: about himself.

Well, then, I too will talk about myself.

II

Now I would like to tell you, gentlemen, whether or not you want to hear it, why it is that I couldn't even become an insect. I'll tell you solemnly that I wished to become an insect many times. But not even that wish was granted. I swear to you, gentlemen, that being overly conscious is a disease, a genuine, full-fledged disease. Ordinary human consciousness would be more than sufficient for everyday human needs—that is, even half or a quarter of the amount of consciousness that's available to a cultured man in our unfortunate nineteenth century, especially to one who has the particular misfortune of living in St. Petersburg, the most abstract and premeditated city in the whole world.[4] (Cities can be either premeditated or unpremeditated.) It would have been entirely sufficient, for example, to have the consciousness with which all so-called spontaneous people and men of action are endowed. I'll bet that you think I'm writing all this to show off, to make fun of these men of action, that I'm clanging my saber just like that officer did to show off in bad taste. But, gentlemen, who could possibly be proud of his illnesses and want to show them off?

But what am I saying? Everyone does that; people do take pride in their illnesses, and I, perhaps, more than anyone else. Let's not argue; my objection is absurd. Nevertheless, I remain firmly convinced that not only is being overly conscious a disease, but so is being conscious at all. I insist on it. But let's leave that alone for a moment. Tell me this: why was it, as if on purpose, at the very moment, indeed, at the precise moment that I was most capable of becoming conscious of the subtleties of everything that was "beautiful and sublime,"[5] as we used to say at one time, that I didn't become conscious, and instead did such unseemly things, things that . . . well, in short, probably everyone does, but it seemed as if they occurred to me deliberately at the precise moment when I was most conscious that they shouldn't be done at all? The more conscious I was of what was good, of everything "beautiful and sublime," the more deeply I sank into the morass and the more capable I was of becoming entirely bogged down in it. But the main thing is that all this didn't seem to be occurring accidentally; rather, it was as if it all had to be so. It was as if this were my most normal condition, not an illness or an affliction at all, so that finally I even lost the desire to struggle against it. It ended when I almost came to believe (perhaps I really did believe) that this might really have been my normal condition. But at first, in the beginning, what agonies I suffered during that struggle! I didn't believe that others were experiencing the same thing; therefore, I kept it a secret about myself all my life.

---

4. Petersburg was conceived as an imposing city; plans called for regular streets, broad avenues, and spacious squares.   5. This phrase originated in Edmund Burke's (1729–1797) *Philosophical Inquiry into the Origin of Our Ideas of the Sublime and Beautiful* (1756) and was repeated in Immanuel Kant's (1724–1804) *Observations on the Feeling of the Beautiful and the Sublime* (1756). It became a cliché in the writings of Russian critics during the 1830s.

I was ashamed (perhaps I still am even now); I reached the point where I felt some secret, abnormal, despicable little pleasure in returning home to my little corner on some disgusting Petersburg night, acutely aware that once again I'd committed some revolting act that day, that what had been done could not be undone, and I used to gnaw and gnaw at myself inwardly, secretly, nagging away, consuming myself until finally the bitterness turned into some kind of shameful, accursed sweetness and at last into genuine, earnest pleasure! Yes, into pleasure, real pleasure! I absolutely mean that. . . . That's why I first began to speak out, because I want to know for certain whether other people share this same pleasure. Let me explain: the pleasure resulted precisely from the overly acute consciousness of one's own humiliation; from the feeling that one had reached the limit; that it was disgusting, but couldn't be otherwise; you had no other choice—you could never become a different person; and that even if there were still time and faith enough for you to change into something else, most likely you wouldn't even want to change, and if you did, you wouldn't have done anything, perhaps because there really was nothing for you to change into. But the main thing and the final point is that all of this was taking place according to normal and fundamental laws of overly acute consciousness and of the inertia which results directly from these laws; consequently, not only couldn't one change, one simply couldn't do anything at all. Hence it follows, for example, as a result of this overly acute consciousness, that one is absolutely right in being a scoundrel, as if this were some consolation to the scoundrel. But enough of this. . . . Oh, my, I've gone on rather a long time, but have I really explained anything? How can I explain this pleasure? But I will explain it! I shall see it through to the end! That's why I've taken up my pen. . . .

For example, I'm terribly proud. I'm as mistrustful and as sensitive as a hunchback or a dwarf; but, in truth, I've experienced some moments when, if someone had slapped my face, I might even have been grateful for it. I'm being serious. I probably would have been able to derive a peculiar sort of pleasure from it—the pleasure of despair, naturally, but the most intense pleasures occur in despair, especially when you're very acutely aware of the hopelessness of your own predicament. As for a slap in the face—why, here the consciousness of being beaten to a pulp would overwhelm you. The main thing is, no matter how I try, it still turns out that I'm always the first to be blamed for everything and, what's even worse, I'm always the innocent victim, so to speak, according to the laws of nature. Therefore, in the first place, I'm guilty inasmuch as I'm smarter than everyone around me. (I've always considered myself smarter than everyone around me, and sometimes, believe me, I've been ashamed of it. At the least, all my life I've looked away and never could look people straight in the eye.) Finally, I'm to blame because even if there were any magnanimity in me, it would only have caused more suffering as a result of my being aware of its utter uselessness. After all, I probably wouldn't have been able to make use of that magnanimity: neither to forgive, as the offender, perhaps, had slapped me in accordance with the laws of nature, and there's no way to forgive the laws of nature; nor to forget, because even if there were any laws of nature, it's offensive nonetheless. Finally, even if I wanted to be entirely unmagnanimous, and had wanted to take revenge on the offender, I couldn't be revenged on anyone for anything because, most likely, I would never have decided to do anything, even if I could have. Why not? I'd like to say a few words about that separately.

Summary   In chapters III and IV, the Underground Man discusses the difficulty, for an overly conscious person, of having simple feelings (such as the desire for pure vengeance); he describes his vain search for a "primary cause" on which to base any action or belief, his refusal to be governed by "the laws of nature, the conclusions of natural science and mathematics," and his insistence on self–assertion and individual will despite logic and "natural law."

VII

But these are all golden dreams. Oh, tell me who was first to announce, first to proclaim that man does nasty things simply because he doesn't know his own true interest; and that if he were to be enlightened, if his eyes were to be opened to his true, normal interests, he would stop doing nasty things at once and would immediately become good and noble, because, being so enlightened and understanding his real advantage, he would realize that his own advantage really did lie in the good; and that it's well known that there's not a single man capable of acting knowingly against his own interest; consequently, he would, so to speak, begin to do good out of necessity. Oh, the child! Oh, the pure, innocent babe! Well, in the first place, when was it during all these millennia, that man has ever acted only in his own self interest? What does one do with the millions of facts bearing witness to the one fact that people knowingly, that is, possessing full knowledge of their own true interests, have relegated them to the background and have rushed down a different path, that of risk and chance, compelled by no one and nothing, but merely as if they didn't want to follow the beaten track, and so they stubbornly, willfully forged another way, a difficult and absurd one, searching for it almost in the darkness? Why, then, this means that stubbornness and willfulness were really more pleasing to them than any kind of advantage. . . . Advantage! What is advantage? Will you take it upon yourself to define with absolute precision what constitutes man's advantage? And what if it turns out that man's advantage sometimes not only may, but even must in certain circumstances, consist precisely in his desiring something harmful to himself instead of something advantageous? And if this is so, if this can ever occur, then the whole theory falls to pieces. What do you think, can such a thing happen? You're laughing; laugh, gentlemen, but answer me: have man's advantages ever been calculated with absolute certainty? Aren't there some which don't fit, can't be made to fit into any classification? Why, as far as I know, you gentlemen have derived your list of human advantages from averages of statistical data and from scientific-economic formulas. But your advantages are prosperity, wealth, freedom, peace, and so on and so forth; so that a man who, for example, expressly and knowingly acts in opposition to this whole list, would be, in you opinion, and in mine, too, of course, either an obscurantist or a complete madman, wouldn't he? But now here's what's astonishing: why is it that when all these statisticians, sages, and lovers of humanity enumerate man's advantages, they invariably leave one out? They don't even take it into consideration in the form in which it should be considered, although the entire calculation depends upon it. There would be no great harm in considering it, this advantage, and adding it to the list. But the whole point is that this particular advantage doesn't fit into any classification and can't be found on any list. I have a friend, for instance. . . . But gentlemen! Why, he's your friend, too! In fact, he's everyone's friend! When he's preparing to do something, this gentleman straight away explains to you eloquently and clearly just how he must act according to the laws of nature and truth. And that's not all: with excitement and passion he'll tell you all about genuine, normal human interests; with scorn he'll reproach the shortsighted fools who understand neither their own advantage nor the real meaning of virtue; and then— exactly a quarter of an hour later, without any sudden outside cause, but precisely because of something internal that's stronger than all his interests—he does a complete about-face; that is, he does something which clearly contradicts what he's been saying: it goes against the laws of reason and his own advantage, in a word, against everything. . . . I warn you that my friend is a collective personage; therefore it's rather difficult to blame only him. That's just it, gentlemen; in fact, isn't there something dearer to every man than his own best advantage, or (so as not to violate the rules of logic) isn't there one more advantageous advantage (exactly the one omitted, the one we mentioned before), which is more important and more advantageous than all others and, on behalf of which, a man will, if necessary, go against all laws, that is, against reason, honor, peace, and prosperity—in a word, against all those splendid and useful things, merely in order to attain this fundamental, most advantageous advantage which is dearer to him than everything else?

"Well, it's advantage all the same," you say, interrupting me. Be so kind as to allow me to explain further; besides, the point is not my pun, but the fact that this advantage is remarkable precisely because it destroys all our classifications and constantly demolishes all systems devised by lovers of humanity for the happiness of mankind. In a word, it interferes with everything. But, before I name this advantage, I want to compromise myself personally; therefore I boldly declare that all these splendid systems, all these theories to explain to mankind its real, normal interests so that, by necessarily striving to achieve them, it would immediately become good and noble—are, for the time being, in my opinion, nothing more than logical exercises! Yes, sir, logical exercises! Why, even to maintain a theory of mankind's regeneration through a system of its own advantages, why, in my opinion, that's almost the same as . . . well, claiming, for instance, following Buckle,[6] that man has become kinder as a result of civilization; consequently, he's becoming less bloodthirsty and less inclined to war. Why, logically it all even seems to follow. But man is so partial to systems and abstract conclusions that he's ready to distort the truth intentionally,

---

6. In his *History of Civilization in England* (1857–61), Henry Thomas Buckle (1821–1862) argued that the development of civilization necessarily leads to the cessation of war. Russia had recently been involved in fierce fighting in the Crimea (1853–56).

ready to deny everything that he himself has ever seen and heard, merely in order to justify his own logic. That's why I take this example, because it's such a glaring one. Just look around: rivers of blood are being spilt, and in the most cheerful way, as if it were champagne. Take this entire nineteenth century of ours during which even Buckle lived. Take Napoleon—both the great and the present one.[7] Take North America—that eternal union.[8] Take, finally, that ridiculous Schleswig-Holstein[9]. . . . What is it that civilization makes kinder in us? Civilization merely promotes a wider variety of sensations in man and . . . absolutely nothing else. And through the development of this variety man may even reach the point where he takes pleasure in spilling blood. Why, that's even happened to him already. Haven't you noticed that the most refined bloodshedders are almost always the most civilized gentlemen to whom all these Attila the Huns and Stenka Razins[1] are scarcely fit to hold a candle; and if they're not as conspicuous as Attila and Stenka Razin, it's precisely because they're too common and have become too familiar to us. At least if man hasn't become more bloodthirsty as a result of civilization, surely he's become bloodthirsty in a nastier, more repulsive way than before. Previously man saw justice in bloodshed and exterminated whomever he wished with a clear conscience; whereas now, though we consider bloodshed to be abominable, we nevertheless engage in this abomination even more than before. Which is worse? Decide for yourselves. They say that Cleopatra (forgive an example from Roman history) loved to stick gold pins into the breasts of her slave girls and take pleasure in their screams and writhing. You'll say that this took place, relatively speaking, in barbaric times; that these are barbaric times too, because (also comparatively speaking), gold pins are used even now; that even now, although man has learned on occasion to see more clearly than in barbaric times, *he's still far from having learned* how to act in accordance with the dictates of reason and science. Nevertheless, you're still absolutely convinced that he will learn how to do so, as soon as he gets rid of some bad, old habits and as soon as common sense and science have completely re-educated human nature and have turned it in the proper direction. You're convinced that then man will voluntarily stop committing blunders, and that he will, so to speak, never willingly set his own will in opposition to his own normal interests. More than that: then, you say, science itself will teach man (though, in my opinion, that's already a luxury) that in fact he possesses neither a will nor any whim of his own, that he never did, and that he himself is nothing more than a kind of piano key or an organ stop;[2] that, moreover, there still exist laws of nature, so that everything he's done has been not in accordance with his own desire, but in and of itself, according to the laws of nature. Consequently, we need only discover

7. The French emperors Napoléon I (1769–1821) and his nephew Napoléon III (1808–1873), both of whom engaged in numerous wars, though on vastly different scales.   8. The United States was in the middle of its Civil War (1861–65).   9. The German duchies of Schleswig and Holstein, held by Denmark since 1773, were reunited with Prussia after a brief war in 1864.   1. Cossack leader (died 1671) who organized a peasant rebellion in Russia. Attila (406?–453 A.D.), king of the Huns, who conducted devastating wars against the Roman emperors.   2. A reference to the last discourse of the French philosopher Denis Diderot (1713–1784) in the *Conversation of D'Alembert and Diderot* (1769).

these laws of nature, and man will no longer have to answer for his own actions and will find it extremely easy to live. All human actions, it goes without saying, will then be tabulated according to these laws, mathematically, like tables of logarithms up to 108,000, and will be entered on a schedule; or even better, certain edifying works will be published, like our contemporary encyclopedic dictionaries, in which everything will be accurately calculated and specified so that there'll be no more actions or adventures left on earth.

At that time, it's still you speaking, new economic relations will be established, all ready-made, also calculated with mathematical precision, so that all possible questions will disappear in a single instant, simply because all possible answers will have been provided. Then the crystal palace[3] will be built. And then . . . Well, in a word, those will be our halcyon days. Of course, there's no way to guarantee (now this is me talking) that it won't be, for instance, terribly boring then (because there won't be anything left to do, once everything has been calculated according to tables); on the other hand, everything will be extremely rational. Of course, what don't people think up out of boredom! Why, even gold pins get stuck into other people out of boredom, but that wouldn't matter. What's really bad (this is me talking again) is that for all I know, people might even be grateful for those gold pins. For man is stupid, phenomenally stupid. That is, although he's not really stupid at all, he's really so ungrateful that it's hard to find another being quite like him. Why, I, for example, wouldn't be surprised in the least, if, suddenly, for no reason at all, in the midst of this future, universal rationalism, some gentleman with an offensive, rather, a retrograde and derisive expression on his face were to stand up, put his hands on his hips, and declare to us all: "How about it, gentlemen, what if we knock over all this rationalism with one swift kick for the sole purpose of sending all these logarithms to hell, so that once again we can live according to our own stupid will!" But that wouldn't matter either; what's so annoying is that he would undoubtedly find some followers; such is the way man is made. And all because of the most foolish reason, which, it seems, is hardly worth mentioning: namely, that man, always and everywhere, whoever he is, has preferred to act as he wished, and not at all as reason and advantage have dictated; one might even desire something opposed to one's own advantage, and sometimes (this is now my idea) one *positively must do so*. One's very own free, unfettered desire, one's own whim, no matter how wild, one's own fantasy, even though sometimes roused to the point of madness—all this constitutes precisely that previously omitted, most advantageous advantage which isn't included under any classification and because of which all systems and theories are constantly smashed to smithereens. Where did these sages ever get the idea that man needs any normal, virtuous desire? How did they ever imagine that man needs any kind of rational, advantageous desire? Man needs only one thing—his own *independent* desire, whatever that independence

---

3. An allusion to the crystal palace described in Vera Pavlovna's fourth dream in Chernyshevsky's *What Is to Be Done?* as well as to the actual building designed by Sir Joseph Paxton, erected for the Great Exhibition in London in 1851 and at that time admired as the newest wonder of architecture; Dostoevsky described it in *Winter Notes on Summer Impressions* (1863).

might cost and wherever it might lead. And as far as desire goes, the devil
only knows. . . .

VIII

"Ha, ha, ha! But in reality even this desire, if I may say so, doesn't exist!"
you interrupt me with a laugh. "Why science has already managed to
dissect man so now we know that desire and so-called free choice are
nothing more than . . ."

"Wait, gentlemen, I myself wanted to begin like that. I must confess
that even I got frightened. I was just about to declare that the devil only
knows what desire depends on and perhaps we should be grateful for that,
but then I remembered about science and I . . . stopped short. But now
you've gone and brought it up. Well, after all, what if someday they really
do discover the formula for all our desires and whims, that is, the thing
that governs them, precise laws that produce them, how exactly they're
applied, where they lead in each and every case, and so on and so forth,
that is, the genuine mathematical formula—why, then all at once man
might stop desiring, yes, indeed, he probably would. Who would want to
desire according to some table? And that's not all: he would immediately
be transformed from a person into an organ stop or something of that sort;
because what is man without desire, without will, and without wishes if
not a stop in an organ pipe? What do you think? Let's consider the probabilities—can this really happen or not?"

"Hmmm . . .," you decide, "our desires are mistaken for the most part
because of an erroneous view of our own advantage. Consequently, we
sometimes desire pure rubbish because, in our own stupidity, we consider
it the easiest way to achieve some previously assumed advantage. Well,
and when all this has been analyzed, calculated on paper (that's entirely
possible, since it's repugnant and senseless to assume in advance that man
will never come to understand the laws of nature) then, of course, all so-
called desires will no longer exist. For if someday desires are completely
reconciled with reason, we'll follow reason instead of desire simply
because it would be impossible, for example, while retaining one's reason,
to *desire* rubbish, and thus knowingly oppose one's reason, and desire
something harmful to oneself. . . . And, since all desires and reasons can
really be tabulated, since someday the laws of our so-called free choice are
sure to be discovered, then, all joking aside, it may be possible to establish
something like a table, so that we could actually desire according to it. If,
for example, someday they calculate and demonstrate to me that I made
a rude gesture because I couldn't possibly refrain from it, that I had to
make precisely that gesture, well, in that case, what sort of *free choice*
would there be, especially if I'm a learned man and have completed a
course of study somewhere? Why, then I'd be able to calculate in advance
my entire life for the next thirty years; in a word, if such a table were to be
drawn up, there'd be nothing left for us to do; we'd simply have to accept
it. In general, we should be repeating endlessly to ourselves that at such a
time and in such circumstances nature certainly won't ask our opinion;
that we must accept it as is, and not as we fantasize it, and that if we really

aspire to prepare a table, a schedule, and, well . . . well, even a laboratory
test tube, there's nothing to be done—one must even accept the test tube!
If not, it'll be accepted even without you. . . .

"Yes, but that's just where I hit a snag! Gentlemen, you'll excuse me for
all this philosophizing; it's a result of my forty years in the underground!
Allow me to fantasize. Don't you see: reason is a fine thing, gentlemen,
there's no doubt about it, but it's only reason, and it satisfies only man's
rational faculty, whereas desire is a manifestation of all life, that is, of all
human life, which includes both reason, as well as all of life's itches and
scratches. And although in this manifestation life often turns out to be
fairly worthless, it's life all the same, and not merely the extraction of
square roots. Why, take me, for instance; I quite naturally want to live in
order to satisfy all my faculties of life, not merely my rational faculty, that
is, some one-twentieth of all my faculties. What does reason know? Reason
knows only what it's managed to learn. (Some things it may never learn;
while this offers no comfort, why not admit it openly?) But human nature
acts as a whole, with all that it contains, consciously and unconsciously;
and although it may tell lies, it's still alive. I suspect, gentlemen, that
you're looking at me with compassion; you repeat that an enlightened and
cultured man, in a word, man as he will be in the future, cannot knowingly desire something disadvantageous to himself, and that this is pure
mathematics. I agree with you: it really is mathematics. But I repeat for
the one-hundredth time, there is one case, only one, when a man may
intentionally, consciously desire even something harmful to himself,
something stupid, even very stupid, namely: in order *to have the right* to
desire something even very stupid and not be bound by an obligation to
desire only what's smart. After all, this very stupid thing, one's own whim,
gentlemen, may in fact be the most advantageous thing on earth for people
like me, especially in certain cases. In particular, it may be more advantageous than any other advantage, even in a case where it causes obvious
harm and contradicts the most sensible conclusions of reason about advantage—because in any case it preserves for us what's most important and
precious, that is, our personality and our individuality. There are some
people who maintain that in fact this is more precious to man than anything else; of course, desire can, if it so chooses, coincide with reason,
especially if it doesn't abuse this option, and chooses to coincide in moderation; this is useful and sometimes even commendable. But very often,
even most of the time, desire absolutely and stubbornly disagrees with
reason and . . . and . . . and, do you know, sometimes this is also useful
and even very commendable? Let's assume, gentlemen, that man isn't
stupid. (And really, this can't possibly be said about him at all, if only
because if he's stupid, then who on earth is smart?) But even if he's not
stupid, he is, nevertheless, monstrously ungrateful. Phenomenally ungrateful. I even believe that the best definition of man is this: a creature who
walks on two legs and is ungrateful. But that's still not all; that's still not
his main defect. His main defect is his perpetual misbehavior, perpetual
from the time of the Great Flood to the Schleswig-Holstein period of
human destiny. Misbehavior, and consequently, imprudence; for it's long
been known that imprudence results from nothing else but misbehavior.

Just cast a glance at the history of mankind; well, what do you see? Is it majestic? Well, perhaps it's majestic; why, the Colossus of Rhodes,[4] for example—that alone is worth something! Not without reason did Mr Anaevsky[5] report that some people consider it to be the product of human hands, while others maintain that it was created by nature itself. Is it colorful? Well, perhaps it's also colorful; just consider the dress uniforms, both military and civilian, of all nations at all times—why, that alone is worth something, and if you include everyday uniforms, it'll make your eyes bulge; not one historian will be able to sort it all out. Is it monotonous? Well, perhaps it's monotonous, too: men fight and fight; now they're fighting; they fought first and they fought last—you'll agree that it's really much too monotonous. In short, anything can be said about world history, anything that might occur to the most disordered imagination. There's only one thing that can't possibly be said about it—that it's rational. You'll choke on the word. Yet here's just the sort of thing you'll encounter all the time: why, in life you're constantly running up against people who are so well-behaved and so rational, such wise men and lovers of humanity who set themselves the lifelong goal of behaving as morally and rationally as possible, so to speak, to be a beacon for their nearest and dearest, simply in order to prove that it's really possible to live one's life in a moral and rational way. And so what? It's a well-known fact that many of these lovers of humanity, sooner or later, by the end of their lives, have betrayed themselves: they've pulled off some caper, sometimes even quite an indecent one. Now I ask you: what can one expect from man as a creature endowed with such strange qualities? Why, shower him with all sorts of earthly blessings, submerge him in happiness over his head so that only little bubbles appear on the surface of this happiness, as if on water, give him such economic prosperity that he'll have absolutely nothing left to do except sleep, eat gingerbread, and worry about the continuation of world history—even then, out of pure ingratitude, sheer perversity, he'll commit some repulsive act. He'll even risk losing his gingerbread, and will intentionally desire the most wicked rubbish, the most uneconomical absurdity, simply in order to inject his own pernicious fantastic element into all this positive rationality. He wants to hold onto those most fantastic dreams, his own indecent stupidity solely for the purpose of assuring himself (as if it were necessary) that men are still men and not piano keys, and that even if the laws of nature play upon them with their own hands, they're still threatened by being overplayed until they won't possibly desire anything more than a schedule. But that's not all: even if man really turned out to be a piano key, even if this could be demonstrated to him by natural science and pure mathematics, even then he still won't become reasonable; he'll intentionally do something to the contrary, simply out of ingratitude, merely to have his own way. If he lacks the means, he'll cause destruction and chaos, he'll devise all kinds of suffering and have his own way! He'll leash a curse upon the world; and, since man alone can do so (it's his privilege and the thing that most distinguishes him from other

---

4. A large bronze statue of the sun god, Helios, built between 292 and 280 B.C. in the harbor of Rhodes (an island in the Aegean Sea) and considered one of the Seven Wonders of the Ancient World.   5. A. E. Anaevsky was a critic whose articles were frequently ridiculed in literary polemics of the period.

animals), perhaps only through this curse will he achieve his goal, that is, become really convinced that he's a man and not a piano key! If you say that one can also calculate all this according to a table, this chaos and darkness, these curses, so that the mere possibility of calculating it all in advance would stop everything and that reason alone would prevail—in that case man would go insane deliberately in order not to have reason, but to have his own way! I believe this, I vouch for it, because, after all, the whole of man's work seems to consist only in proving to himself constantly that he's a man and not an organ stop! Even if he has to lose his own skin, he'll prove it; even if he has to become a troglodyte, he'll prove it. And after that, how can one not sin, how can one not praise the fact that all this hasn't yet come to pass and that desire still depends on the devil knows what . . . ?"

You'll shout at me (if you still choose to favor me with your shouts) that no one's really depriving me of my will; that they're merely attempting to arrange things so that my will, by its own free choice, will coincide with my normal interests, with the laws of nature, and with arithmetic.

"But gentlemen, what sort of free choice will there be when it comes down to tables and arithmetic, when all that's left is two times two makes four? Two times two makes four even without my will. Is that what you call free choice?"

IX

Gentlemen, I'm joking of course, and I myself know that it's not a very good joke; but, after all, you can't take everything as a joke. Perhaps I'm gnashing my teeth while I joke. I'm tormented by questions, gentlemen; answer them for me. Now, for example, you want to cure man of his old habits and improve his will according to the demands of science and common sense. But how do you know not only whether it's possible, but even if it's *necessary* to remake him in this way? Why do you conclude that human desire *must* undoubtedly be improved? In short, how do you know that such improvement will really be to man's advantage? And, to be perfectly frank, why are you so *absolutely* convinced that not to oppose man's real, normal advantage guaranteed by the conclusions of reason and arithmetic is really always to man's advantage and constitutes a law for all humanity? After all, this is still only an assumption of yours. Let's suppose that it's a law of logic, but perhaps not a law of humanity. Perhaps, gentlemen, you're wondering if I'm insane? Allow me to explain. I agree that man is primarily a creative animal, destined to strive consciously toward a goal and to engage in the art of engineering, that, is, externally and incessantly building new roads for himself *wherever they lead*. But sometimes he may want to swerve aside precisely because he's *compelled* to build these roads, and perhaps also because, no matter how stupid the spontaneous man of action may generally be, nevertheless it sometimes occurs to him that the road, as it turns out, almost always leads *somewhere or other*, and that the main thing isn't so much where it goes, but the fact that it' does, and that the well-behaved child, disregarding the art of engineering, shouldn't yield to pernicious idleness which, as is well known, constitutes the mother of all vices. Man loves to create and build roads; that's indisputable. But why is he also so passionately fond of destruction and chaos? Now, then, tell me. But I myself want to say a few words about this separately. Perhaps the reason that he's so fond of destruction and chaos (after all, it's indisputable that he sometimes really loves it, and that's a fact) is that he himself has an instinctive fear of achieving his goal and completing the project under construction? How do you know if perhaps he loves his building only from afar, but not from close up; perhaps he only likes building it, but not living in it, leaving it afterward *aux animaux domestiques*,[6] such as ants or sheep, or so on and so forth. Now ants have altogether different tastes. They have one astonishing structure of a similar type, forever indestructible—the anthill.

The worthy ants began with the anthill, and most likely, they will end with the anthill, which does great credit to their perseverance and steadfastness. But man is a frivolous and unseemly creature and perhaps, like a chess player, he loves only the process of achieving his goal, and not the goal itself. And, who knows (one can't vouch for it), perhaps the only goal on earth toward which mankind is striving consists merely in this incessant process of achieving or to put it another way, in life itself, and not particularly in the goal which, of course, must always be none other than two times two makes four, that is, a formula; after all, two times two makes four is no longer life, gentlemen, but the beginning of death. At least man has always been somewhat afraid of this two times two makes four, and I'm afraid of it now, too. Let's suppose that the only thing man does is search for this two times two makes four; he sails across oceans, sacrifices his own life in the quest; but to seek it out and find it—really and truly, he's very frightened. After all, he feels that as soon as he finds it, there'll be nothing left to search for. Workers, after finishing work, at least receive their wages, go off to a tavern, and then wind up at a police station—now that's a full week's occupation. But where will man go? At any rate a certain awkwardness can be observed each time he approaches the achievement of similar goals. He loves the process, but he's not so fond of the achievement, and that, of course is terribly amusing. In short, man is made in a comical way; obviously there's some sort of catch in all this. But two times two makes four is an insufferable thing, nevertheless. Two times two makes four—why, in my opinion, it's mere insolence. Two times two makes four stands there brazenly with its hands on its hips, blocking your path and spitting at you. I agree that two times two makes four is a splendid thing; but if we're going to lavish praise, then two times two makes five is sometimes also a very charming little thing.

And why are you so firmly, so triumphantly convinced that only the normal and positive—in short, only well-being is advantageous to man? Doesn't reason ever make mistakes about advantage? After all, perhaps man likes something other than well-being? Perhaps he loves suffering just as much? Perhaps suffering is just as advantageous to him as well-being? Man sometimes loves suffering terribly, to the point of passion, and that's a fact. There's no reason to study world history on this point; if indeed you're a man and have lived at all, just ask yourself. As far as my own personal opinion is concerned, to love only well-being is somehow even indecent. Whether good or bad, it's sometimes also very pleasant to demolish something. After all, I'm not standing up for suffering here, nor for well-being, either. I'm standing up for . . . my own whim and for its being guaranteed to me whenever necessary. For instance, suffering is not permitted in vaudevilles,[7] that I know. It's also inconceivable in the crystal palace; suffering is doubt and negation. What sort of crystal palace would it be if any doubt were allowed? Yet, I'm convinced that man will never renounce real suffering, that is, destruction and chaos. After all, suffering is the sole cause of consciousness. Although I stated earlier that in my opinion consciousness is man's greatest misfortune, still I know that man loves it and would not exchange it for any other sort of satisfaction. Consciousness, for example, is infinitely higher than two times two. Of course, after two times two, there's nothing left, not merely nothing to do, but nothing to learn. Then the only thing possible will be to plug up your five senses and plunge into contemplation. Well, even if you reach the same result with consciousness, that is, having nothing left to do, at least you'll be able to flog yourself from time to time, and that will liven things up a bit. Although it may be reactionary, it's still better than nothing.

x^8

You believe in the crystal palace, eternally indestructible, that is, one at which you can never stick out your tongue furtively nor make a rude gesture, even with your fist hidden away. Well, perhaps I'm so afraid of this building precisely because it's made of crystal and it's eternally indestructible, and because it won't be possible to stick one's tongue out even furtively.

Don't you see: if it were a chicken coop instead of a palace, and if it should rain, then perhaps I could crawl into it so as not to get drenched; but I would still not mistake a chicken coop for a palace out of gratitude, just because it sheltered me from the rain. You're laughing, you're even saying that in this case there's no difference between a chicken coop and a mansion. Yes, I reply, if the only reason for living is to keep from getting drenched.

But what if I've taken it into my head that this is not the only reason for living, and, that if one is to live at all, one might as well live in a mansion? Such is my wish, my desire. You'll expunge it from me only when you've changed my desires. Well, then, change them, tempt me with something else, give me some other ideal. In the meantime, I still won't mistake a chicken coop for a palace. But let's say that the crystal palace is a hoax, that according to the laws of nature it shouldn't exist, and that I've invented it only out of my own stupidity, as a result of certain antiquated, irrational habits of my generation. But what do I care if it doesn't exist? What differ-

---

7. A dramatic genre, popular on the Russian stage, consisting of scenes from contemporary life acted with a satirical twist, often in racy dialogue.   8. This chapter was badly mutilated by the censor, as Dostoevsky makes clear in the letter to his brother Mikhail, dated March 26, 1864 (see the headnote).

ence does it make if it exists only in my own desires, or, to be more precise, if it exists as long as my desires exist? Perhaps you're laughing again? Laugh, if you wish; I'll resist all your laughter and I still won't say I'm satiated if I'm really hungry; I know all the same that I won't accept a compromise, an infinitely recurring zero, just because it exists according to the laws of nature and it *really* does exist. I won't accept as the crown of my desires a large building with tenements for poor tenants to be rented for a thousand years and, just in case, with the name of the dentist Wagenheim on the sign. Destroy my desires, eradicate my ideals, show me something better and I'll follow you. You may say, perhaps, that it's not worth getting involved; but, in that case, I'll say the same thing in reply. We're having a serious discussion; if you don't grant me your attention, I won't grovel for it. I still have my underground.

And, as long as I'm still alive and feel desire—may my arm wither away before it contributes even one little brick to that building! Never mind that I myself have just rejected the crystal palace for the sole reason that it won't be possible to tease it by sticking out one's tongue at it. I didn't say that because I'm so fond of sticking out my tongue. Perhaps the only reason I got angry is that among all your buildings there's still not a single one where you don't feel compelled to stick out your tongue. On the contrary, I'd let my tongue be cut off out of sheer gratitude, if only things could be so arranged that I'd no longer want to stick it out. What do I care if things can't be so arranged and if I must settle for some tenements? Why was I made with such desires? Can it be that I was made this way only in order to reach the conclusion that my entire way of being is merely a fraud? Can this be the whole purpose? I don't believe it.

By the way, do you know what? I'm convinced that we underground men should be kept in check. Although capable of sitting around quietly in the underground for some forty years, once he emerges into the light of day and bursts into speech, he talks on and on and on. . . .

XI

The final result, gentlemen, is that it's better to do nothing! Conscious inertia is better! And so, long live the underground! Even though I said that I envy the normal man to the point of exasperation, I still wouldn't want to be him under the circumstances in which I see him (although I still won't keep from envying him. No, no, in any case the underground is more advantageous!) At least there one can . . . Hey, but I'm lying once again! I'm lying because I know myself as surely as two times two, that it isn't really the underground that's better, but something different, altogether different, something that I long for, but I'll never be able to find! To hell with the underground! Why, here's what would be better: if I myself were to believe even a fraction of everything I've written. I swear to you, gentlemen, that I don't believe one word, not one little word of all that I've scribbled. That is, I do believe it, perhaps, but at the very same time, I don't know why, I feel and suspect that I'm lying like a trooper.

"Then why did you write all this?" you ask me.

II

Apropos of Wet Snow

When from the darkness of delusion
I saved your fallen soul
With ardent words of conviction,
And, full of profound torment,
Wringing your hands, you cursed
The vice that had ensnared you;
When, punishing by recollection
Your forgetful conscience,
You told me the tale
Of all that had happened before,
And, suddenly, covering your face,
Full of shame and horror,
You tearfully resolved,
Indignant, shaken . . .
Etc., etc., etc.
                    From the poetry of N. A. Nekrasov[1]

I

At that time I was only twenty-four years old. Even then my life was gloomy, disordered, and solitary to the point of savagery. I didn't associate with anyone; I even avoided talking, and I retreated further and further into my corner. At work in the office I even tried not to look at anyone; I was aware not only that my colleagues considered me eccentric, but that they always seemed to regard me with a kind of loathing. Sometimes I wondered why it was that no one else thinks that others regard him with loathing. One of our office-workers had a repulsive pock-marked face which even appeared somewhat villainous. It seemed to me that with such a disreputable face I'd never have dared look at anyone. Another man had a uniform so worn that there was a foul smell emanating from him. Yet, neither of these two gentlemen was embarrassed—neither because of his clothes, nor his face, nor in any moral way. Neither one imagined that other people regarded him with loathing; and if either had so imagined, it wouldn't have mattered at all, as long as their supervisor chose not to view him that way. It's perfectly clear to me now, because of my unlimited vanity and the great demands I accordingly made on myself, that I frequently regarded myself with a furious dissatisfaction verging on loathing; as a result, I intentionally ascribed my own view to everyone else. For example, I despised my own face; I considered it hideous, and I even suspected that there was something repulsive in its expression. Therefore, every time I arrived at work, I took pains to behave as independently as possible, so that I couldn't be suspected of any malice, and I tried to assume as noble an expression as possible. "It may not be a handsome face," I thought, "but let it be noble, expressive, and above all, extremely *intelligent*." But I was agonizingly certain that my face couldn't possibly

---

1. Nikolay A. Nekrasov (1821–1878) was a famous Russian poet and editor of radical sympathies. The poem quoted dates from 1845, and is without title. It ends with the lines, "And enter my house bold and free / To become its full mistress!"

express all these virtues. Worst of all, I considered it positively stupid. I'd have been reconciled if it had looked intelligent. In fact, I'd even have agreed to have it appear repulsive, on the condition that at the same time people would find my face terribly intelligent.

Of course, I hated all my fellow office-workers from the first to the last and despised every one of them; yet, at the same time it was as if I were afraid of them. Sometimes it happened that I would even regard them as superior to me. At this time these changes would suddenly occur: first I would despise them, then I would regard them as superior to me. A cultured and decent man cannot be vain without making unlimited demands on himself and without hating himself, at times to the point of contempt. But, whether hating them or regarding them as superior, I almost always lowered my eyes when meeting anyone. I even conducted experiments: could I endure someone's gaze? I'd always be the first to lower my eyes. This infuriated me to the point of madness. I slavishly worshipped the conventional in everything external. I embraced the common practice and feared any eccentricity with all my soul. But how could I sustain it? I was morbidly refined, as befits any cultured man of our time. All others resembled one another as sheep in a flock. Perhaps I was the only one in the whole office who constantly thought of himself as a coward and a slave; and I thought so precisely because I was so cultured. But not only did I think so, it actually was so: I was a coward and a slave. I say this without any embarrassment. Every decent man of our time is and must be a coward and a slave. This is his normal condition. I'm deeply convinced of it. This is how he's made and what he's meant to be. And not only at the present time, as the result of some accidental circumstance, but in general at all times, a decent man must be a coward and a slave. This is a law of nature for all decent men on earth. If one of them should happen to be brave about something or other, we shouldn't be comforted or distracted: he'll still lose his nerve about something else. That's the single and eternal way out. Only asses and their mongrels are brave, and even then, only until they come up against a wall. It's not worthwhile paying them any attention because they really don't mean anything at all.

There was one more circumstance tormenting me at that time: no one was like me, and I wasn't like anyone else. "I'm alone," I mused, "and they are *everyone*"; and I sank deep into thought.

From all this it's clear that I was still just a boy.

The exact opposite would also occur. Sometimes I would find it repulsive to go to the office: it reached the point where I would often return home from work ill. Then suddenly, for no good reason at all, a flash of skepticism and indifference would set in (everything came to me in flashes); I would laugh at my own intolerance and fastidiousness, and reproach myself for my *romanticism*. Sometimes I didn't even want to talk to anyone; at other times it reached a point where I not only started talking, but I even thought about striking up a friendship with others. All my fastidiousness would suddenly disappear for no good reason at all. Who knows? Perhaps I never really had any, and it was all affected, borrowed from books. I still haven't answered this question, even up to now. And once I really did become friends with others; I began to visit their houses, play préférance,[2] drink vodka, talk about promotions. . . . But allow me to digress.

We Russians, generally speaking, have never had any of those stupid, transcendent German romantics, or even worse, French romantics, on whom nothing produces any effect whatever: the earth might tremble beneath them, all of France might perish on the barricades, but they remain the same, not even changing for decency's sake; they go on singing their transcendent songs, so to speak, to their dying day, because they're such fools. We here on Russian soil have no fools. It's a well-know fact; that's precisely what distinguishes us from foreigners. Consequently, transcendent natures cannot be found among us in their pure form. That's the result of our "positive" publicists and critics of that period, who hunted for the Kostanzhonglo and the Uncle Pyotr Ivanoviches,[3] foolishly mistaking them for our ideal and slandering our own romantics, considering them to be the same kind of transcendents as one finds in Germany or France. On the contrary, the characteristics of our romantics are absolutely and directly opposed to the transcendent Europeans; not one of those European standards can apply here. (Allow me to use the word "romantic"— it's an old-fashioned little word, well-respected and deserving, familiar to everyone.) The characteristics of our romantics are to understand everything, *to see everything, often to see it much more clearly than our most positive minds*; not to be reconciled with anyone or anything, but, at the same time, not to balk at anything; to circumvent everything, to yield on every point, to treat everyone diplomatically; never to lose sight of some useful, practical goal (an apartment at government expense, a nice pension, a decoration) —to keep an eye on that goal through all his excesses and his volumes of lyrical verse, and, at the same time, to preserve intact the "beautiful and sublime" to the end of their lives; and, incidentally, to preserve themselves as well, wrapped up in cotton like precious jewelry, if only, for example, for the sake of that same "beautiful and sublime." Our romantic has a very broad nature and is the biggest rogue of all, I can assure you of that . . . even by my own experience. Of course, all this is true if the romantic is smart. But what am I saying? A romantic is always smart; I merely wanted to observe that although we've had some romantic fools, they really don't count at all, simply because while still in their prime they would degenerate completely into Germans, and, in order to preserve their precious jewels more comfortably, they'd settle over there, either in Weimar or in the Black Forest. For instance, I genuinely despised my official position and refrained from throwing it over merely out of necessity, because I myself sat there working and received good money for doing it. And, as a result, please note, I still refrained from throwing it over. Our romantic would sooner lose his mind (which, by the way, very rarely occurs) than give it up, if he didn't have another job in mind; nor is he ever kicked out, unless he's hauled off to the insane asylum

2. A card game for three players.   3. A character in Ivan Goncharov's novel *A Common Story* (1847); a high bureaucrat, a factory owner who teaches lessons of sobriety and good sense to the romantic hero, Alexander Aduyev. Konstanzhonglo is the ideal efficient landowner in the second part of Nikolai Gogol's novel *Dead Souls* (1852).

as the "King of Spain,"[4] and only if he's gone completely mad. Then again, it's really only the weaklings and towheads who go mad in our country. An enormous number of romantics later rise to significant rank. What extraordinary versatility! And what a capacity for the most contradictory sensations! I used to be consoled by these thoughts back then, and still am even nowadays. That's why there are so many "broad natures" among us, people who never lose their ideals, no matter how low they fall; even though they never lift a finger for the sake of their ideals, even though they're outrageous villains and thieves, nevertheless they respect their original ideals to the point of tears and are extremely honest men at heart. Yes, only among us Russians can the most outrageous scoundrel be absolutely, even sublimely honest at heart, while at the same time never ceasing to be a scoundrel. I repeat, nearly always do our romantics turn out to be very efficient rascals (I use the word "rascal" affectionately); they suddenly manifest such a sense of reality and positive knowledge that their astonished superiors and the general public can only click their tongues at them in amazement.

Their versatility is really astounding; God only knows what it will turn into, how it will develop under subsequent conditions, and what it holds for us in the future. The material is not all that bad! I'm not saying this out of some ridiculous patriotism or jingoism. However, I'm sure that once again you think I'm joking. But who knows? Perhaps it's quite the contrary, that is, you're convinced that this is what I really think. In any case, gentlemen, I'll consider that both of these opinions constitute an honor and a particular pleasure. And do forgive me for this digression.

Naturally, I didn't sustain any friendships with my colleagues, and soon I severed all relations after quarreling with them; and, because of my youthful inexperience at the same time, I even stopped greeting them, as if I'd cut them off entirely. That, however, happened to me only once. On the whole, I was always alone.

At home I spent most of my time reading. I tried to stifle all that was constantly seething within me with external sensations. And of all external sensations available, only reading was possible for me. Of course, reading helped a great deal—it agitated, delighted, and tormented me. But at times it was terribly boring. I still longed to be active; and suddenly I sank into dark, subterranean, loathsome depravity—more precisely, petty vice. My nasty little passions were sharp and painful as a result of my constant, morbid irritability. I experienced hysterical fits accompanied by tears and convulsions. Besides reading, I had nowhere else to go—that is, there was nothing to respect in my surroundings, nothing to attract me. In addition, I was overwhelmed by depression; I possessed a hysterical craving for contradictions and contrasts; and, as a result, I plunged into depravity. I haven't said all this to justify myself. . . . But, no, I'm lying. I did want to justify myself. It's for myself, gentlemen, that I include this little observation. I don't want to lie. I've given my word.

I indulged in depravity all alone, at night, furtively, timidly, sordidly,

---

4. An allusion to the hero of Gogol's short story *Diary of a Madman* (1835). Poprishchin, a low-ranking civil servant, sees his aspirations crushed by the enormous bureaucracy. He ends by going insane and imagining himself to be king of Spain.

with a feeling of shame that never left me even in my most loathsome moments and drove me at such times to the point of profanity. Even then I was carrying around the underground in my soul. I was terribly afraid of being seen, met, recognized. I visited all sorts of dismal places.

Once, passing by some wretched little tavern late at night, I saw through a lighted window some gentlemen fighting with billiard cues; one of them was thrown out the window. At some other time I would have been disgusted; but just then I was overcome by such a mood that I envied the gentleman who'd been tossed out; I envied him so much that I even walked into the tavern and entered the billiard room. "Perhaps," I thought, "I'll get into a fight, and they'll throw me out the window, too."

I wasn't drunk, but what could I do—after all, depression can drive a man to this kind of hysteria. But nothing came of it. It turned out that I was incapable of being tossed out the window; I left without getting into a fight.

As soon as I set foot inside, some officer put me in my place.

I was standing next to the billiard table inadvertently blocking his way as he wanted to get by; he took hold of me by the shoulders and without a word of warning or explanation, moved me from where I was standing to another place, and he went past as if he hadn't even noticed me. I could have forgiven even a beating, but I could never forgive his moving me out of the way and entirely failing to notice me.

The devil knows what I would have given for a genuine, ordinary quarrel, a decent one, a more *literary* one, so to speak. But I'd been treated as if I were a fly. The officer was about six feet tall, while I'm small and scrawny. The quarrel, however, was in my hands; all I had to do was protest, and of course they would've thrown me out the window. But I reconsidered and preferred . . . to withdraw resentfully.

I left the tavern confused and upset and went straight home; the next night I continued my petty vice more timidly, more furtively, more gloomily than before, as if I had tears in my eyes—but I continued nonetheless. Don't conclude, however, that I retreated from that officer as a result of any cowardice; I've never been a coward at heart, although I've constantly acted like one in deed, but—wait before you laugh—I can explain this. I can explain anything, you may rest assured.

Oh, if only this officer had been the kind who'd have agreed to fight a duel! But no, he was precisely one of those types (alas, long gone) who preferred to act with their billiard cues or, like Gogol's Lieutenant Pirogov,[5] by appealing to the authorities. They didn't fight duels; in any case, they'd have considered fighting a duel with someone like me, a lowly civilian, to be indecent. In general, they considered duels to be somehow inconceivable, free-thinking, French, while they themselves, especially if they happened to be six feet tall, offended other people rather frequently.

In this case I retreated not out of any cowardice, but because of my unlimited vanity. I wasn't afraid of his height, nor did I think I'd receive a

---

5. One of two main characters in Gogol's short story *Nevsky Prospect* (1835). A shallow and self-satisfied officer, he mistakes the wife of a German artisan for a woman of easy virtue and receives a sound thrashing. He decides to lodge an official complaint, but after consuming a cream-filled pastry, thinks better of it.

painful beating and get thrown out the window. In fact, I'd have had sufficient physical courage; it was moral fortitude I lacked. I was afraid that
everyone present—from the insolent billiard marker to the foul-smelling,
pimply little clerks with greasy collars who used to hang about—wouldn't
understand and would laugh when I started to protest and speak to them
in literary Russian. Because, to this very day, it's still impossible for us to
speak about a point of honor, that is, not about honor itself, but a point of
honor (*point d'honneur*), except in literary language. One can't even refer
to a "point of honor" in everyday language. I was fully convinced (a sense
of reality, in spite of all my romanticism!) that they would all simply split
their sides laughing, and that the officer, instead of giving me a simple
beating, that is, an inoffensive one, would certainly apply his knee to my
back and drive me around the billiard table; only then perhaps would he
have the mercy to throw me out the window. Naturally, this wretched
story of mine couldn't possibly end with this alone. Afterward I used to
meet this officer frequently on the street and I observed him very carefully.
I don't know whether he ever recognized me. Probably not; I reached that
conclusion from various observations. As for me, I stared at him with malice and hatred, and continued to do so for several years! My malice
increased and became stronger over time. At first I began to make discreet
inquiries about him. This was difficult for me to do, since I had so few
acquaintances. But once, as I was following him at a distance as though
tied to him, someone called to him on the street: that's how I learned his
name. Another time I followed him back to his own apartment and for a
ten-kopeck piece learned from the doorman where and how he lived, on
what floor, with whom, etc.—in a word, all that could be learned from a
doorman. One morning, although I never engaged in literary activities, it
suddenly occurred to me to draft a description of this officer as a kind of
exposé, a caricature, in the form of a tale. I wrote it with great pleasure. I
exposed him; I even slandered him. At first I altered his name only slightly,
so that it could be easily recognized; but then, upon careful reflection, I
changed it. Then I sent the tale off to *Notes of the Fatherland*.[6] But such
exposés were no longer in fashion, and they didn't publish my tale. I was
very annoyed by that. At times I simply choked on my spite. Finally, I
resolved to challenge my opponent to a duel. I composed a beautiful,
charming letter to him, imploring him to apologize to me; in case he
refused, I hinted rather strongly at a duel. The letter was composed in such
a way that if that officer had possessed even the smallest understanding of
the "beautiful and sublime," he would have come running, thrown his
arms around me, and offered his friendship. That would have been splendid! We would have led such a wonderful life! Such a life! He would have
shielded me with his rank; I would have ennobled him with my culture,
and, well, with my ideas. Who knows what might have come of it! Imagine
it, two years had already passed since he'd insulted me; my challenge was
the most ridiculous anachronism, in spite of all the cleverness of my letter
in explaining and disguising that fact. But, thank God (to this day I thank
the Almighty with tears in my eyes), I didn't send that letter. A shiver runs

---

6. A radical literary and political journal published in Petersburg from 1839 to 1867.

up and down my spine when I think what might have happened if I had. Then suddenly . . . suddenly, I got my revenge in the simplest manner, a stroke of genius! A brilliant idea suddenly occurred to me. Sometimes on holidays I used to stroll along Nevsky Prospect at about four o'clock in the afternoon, usually on the sunny side. That is, I didn't really stroll; rather, I experienced innumerable torments, humiliations, and bilious attacks. But that's undoubtedly just what I needed. I darted in and out like a fish among the strollers, constantly stepping aside before generals, cavalry officers, hussars, and young ladies. At those moments I used to experience painful spasms in my heart and a burning sensation in my back merely at the thought of my dismal apparel as well as the wretchedness and vulgarity of my darting little figure. This was sheer torture, uninterrupted and unbearable humiliation at the thought, which soon became an incessant and immediate sensation, that I was a fly in the eyes of society, a disgusting, obscene fly—smarter than the rest, more cultured, even nobler—all that goes without saying, but a fly, nonetheless, who incessantly steps aside, insulted and injured by everyone. For what reason did I inflict this torment on myself? Why did I stroll along Nevsky Prospect? I don't know. But something simply *drew* me there at every opportunity.

Then I began to experience surges of that pleasure about which I've already spoken in the first chapter. After the incident with the officer I was drawn there even more strongly; I used to encounter him along Nevsky most often, and it was there that I could admire him. He would also go there, mostly on holidays. He, too, would give way before generals and individuals of superior rank; he, too, would spin like a top among them. But he would simply trample people like me, or even those slightly superior; he would walk directly toward them, as if there were empty space ahead of him; and under no circumstance would he ever step aside. I revelled in my malice as I observed him, and . . . bitterly stepped aside before him every time. I was tortured by the fact that even on the street I found it impossible to stand on an equal footing with him. "Why is it you're always first to step aside?" I badgered myself in insane hysteria, at times waking up at three in the morning. "Why always you and not he? After all, there's no law about it; it isn't written down anywhere. Let it be equal, as it usually is when people of breeding meet: he steps aside halfway and you halfway, and you pass by showing each other mutual respect." But that was never the case, and I continued to step aside, while he didn't even notice that I was yielding to him. Then a most astounding idea suddenly dawned on me. "What if," I thought, "what if I were to meet him and . . . not step aside? Deliberately not step aside, even if it meant bumping into him: how would that be?" This bold idea gradually took such a hold that it afforded me no peace. I dreamt about it incessantly, horribly, and even went to Nevsky more frequently so that I could imagine more clearly how I would do it. I was in ecstasy. The scheme was becoming more and more possible and even probable to me. "Of course, I wouldn't really collide with him," I thought, already feeling more generous toward him in my joy, "but I simply won't turn aside. I'll bump into him, not very painfully, but just so, shoulder to shoulder, as much as decency allows. I'll bump into him the same amount as he bumps into me." At last I made up my mind completely. But the preparations took a very long time. First, in order to look as presentable as possible during the execution of my scheme, I had to worry about my clothes. "In any case, what if, for example, it should occasion a public scandal? (And the public there was superflu:[7] a countess, Princess D., and the entire literary world.) It was essential to be well-dressed; that inspires respect and in a certain sense will place us immediately on an equal footing in the eyes of high society." With that goal in mind I requested my salary in advance, and I purchased a pair of black gloves and a decent hat at Churkin's store. Black gloves seemed to me more dignified, more *bon ton*[8] than the lemon-colored ones I'd considered at first. "That would be too glaring, as if the person wanted to be noticed"; so I didn't buy the lemon-colored ones. I'd already procured a fine shirt with white bone cufflinks; but my overcoat constituted a major obstacle. In and of itself it was not too bad at all; it kept me warm; but it was quilted and had a raccoon collar, the epitome of bad taste. At all costs I had to replace the collar with a beaver one, just like on an officer's coat. For this purpose I began to frequent the Shopping Arcade; and, after several attempts, I turned up some cheap German beaver. Although these German beavers wear out very quickly and soon begin to look shabby, at first, when they're brand new, they look very fine indeed; after all, I only needed it for a single occasion. I asked the price: it was still expensive. After considerable reflection I resolved to sell my raccoon collar. I decided to request a loan for the remaining amount—a rather significant sum for me—from Anton Antonych Setochkin, my office chief, a modest man, but a serious and solid one, who never lent money to anyone, but to whom, upon entering the civil service, I'd once been specially recommended by an important person who'd secured the position for me. I suffered terribly. It seemed monstrous and shameful to ask Anton Antonych for money. I didn't sleep for two or three nights in a row; in general I wasn't getting much sleep those days, and I always had a fever. I would have either a vague sinking feeling in my heart, or else my heart would suddenly begin to thump, thump, thump! . . . At first Anton Antonych was surprised, then he frowned, thought it over, and finally gave me the loan, after securing from me a note authorizing him to deduct the sum from my salary two weeks later. In this way everything was finally ready; the splendid beaver reigned in place of the mangy raccoon, and I gradually began to get down to business. It was impossible to set about it all at once, in a foolhardy way; one had to proceed in this matter very carefully, step by step. But I confess that after many attempts I was ready to despair: we didn't bump into each other, no matter what! No matter how I prepared, no matter how determined I was—it seems that we're just about to bump, when I look up—and once again I've stepped aside while he's gone by without even noticing me. I even used to pray as I approached him that God would grant me determination. One time I'd fully resolved to do it, but the result was that I merely stumbled and fell at his feet because, at the very last moment, only a few inches away from him, I lost my nerve. He stepped over me very calmly, and I bounced to one side like a rubber ball. That night I lay ill with a fever once again and was delirious. Then, everything suddenly ended in the best possible way. The night before I decided once and for all not to go through with my pernicious scheme and to give it all up without success; with that in mind I went to Nevsky Prospect for one last time simply in order to see how I'd abandon the whole thing. Suddenly, three paces away from my enemy, I made up my mind unexpectedly; I closed my eyes and—we bumped into each other forcefully, shoulder to shoulder! I didn't yield an inch and walked by him on a completely equal footing! He didn't even turn around to look at me and pretended that he hadn't even noticed; but he was merely pretending, I'm convinced of that. To this very day I'm convinced of that! Naturally, I got the worst of it; he was stronger, but that wasn't the point. The point was that I'd achieved my goal, I'd maintained my dignity, I hadn't yielded one step, and I'd publicly placed myself on an equal social footing with him. I returned home feeling completely avenged for everything. I was ecstatic. I rejoiced and sang Italian arias. Of course, I won't describe what happened to me three days later; if you've read the first part entitled "Underground," you can guess for yourself. The officer was later transferred somewhere else; I haven't seen him for some fourteen years. I wonder what he's doing nowadays, that dear friend of mine! Whom is he trampling underfoot?

Summary In chapter II, the Underground Man examines his daydreams of being rich, famous, a hero and saint; he describes his everyday life and goes to visit his former schoolmate Simonov.

III

I found two more of my former schoolmates there with him. Apparently they were discussing some important matter. None of them paid any attention to me when I entered, which was strange since I hadn't seen them for several years. Evidently they considered me some sort of ordinary house fly. They hadn't even treated me like that when we were in school together, although they'd all hated me. Of course, I understood that they must despise me now for my failure in the service and for the fact that I'd sunk so low, was badly dressed, and so on, which, in their eyes, constituted proof of my ineptitude and insignificance. But I still hadn't expected such a degree of contempt. Simonov was even surprised by my visits. All this disconcerted me; I sat down in some distress and began to listen to what they were saying.

The discussion was serious, even heated, and concerned a farewell dinner which these gentlemen wanted to organize jointly as early as the following day for their friend Zverkov, an army officer who was heading for a distant province. Monsieur Zverkov had also been my schoolmate all along. I'd begun to hate him especially in the upper grades. In the lower grades he was merely an attractive, lively lad whom everyone liked. However, I'd hated him in the lower grades, too, precisely because he was such an attractive, lively lad. He was perpetually a poor student and had gotten

"Tomorrow at five o'clock at the Hôtel de Paris. Don't make any mistakes."

"What about the money?" Ferfichkin started to say in an undertone to Simonov while nodding at me, but he broke off because Simonov looked embarrassed.

"That'll do," Trudolyubov said getting up. "If he really wants to come so much, let him."

"But this is our own circle of friends," Ferfichkin grumbled, also picking up his hat. "It's not an official gathering. Perhaps we really don't want you at all. . . ."

They left. Ferfichkin didn't even say goodbye to me as he went out; Trudolyubov barely nodded without looking at me. Simonov, with whom I was left alone, was irritated and perplexed, and he regarded me in a strange way. He neither sat down nor invited me to.

"Hmmm . . . yes . . . , so, tomorrow. Will you contribute your share of the money now? I'm asking just to know for sure," he muttered in embarrassment.

I flared up; but in doing so, I remembered that I'd owed Simonov fifteen rubles for a very long time, which debt, moreover, I'd forgotten, but had also never repaid.

"You must agree, Simonov, that I couldn't have known when I came here . . . oh, what a nuisance, but I've forgotten. . . ."

He broke off and began to pace around the room in even greater irritation. As he paced, he began to walk on his heels and stomp more loudly.

"I'm not detaining you, am I?" I asked after a few moments of silence.

"Oh, no!" he replied with a start. "That is, in fact, yes. You see, I still have to stop by at . . . It's not very far from here . . . ," he added in an apologetic way with some embarrassment.

"Oh, good heavens! Why didn't you say so?" I exclaimed, seizing my cap; moreover I did so with a surprisingly familiar air, coming from God knows where.

"But it's really not far . . . only a few steps away . . . ," Simonov repeated, accompanying me into the hallway with a bustling air which didn't suit him well at all. "So, then, tomorrow at five o'clock sharp!" he shouted to me on the stairs. He was very pleased that I was leaving. However, I was furious.

"What possessed me, what on earth possessed me to interfere?" I gnashed my teeth as I walked along the street. "And for such a scoundrel, a pig like Zverkov! Naturally, I shouldn't go. Of course, to hell with them. Am I bound to go, or what? Tomorrow I'll inform Simonov by post. . . ."

But the real reason I was so furious was that I was sure I'd go. I'd go on purpose. The more tactless, the more indecent it was for me to go, the more certain I'd be to do it.

There was even a definite impediment to my going: I didn't have any money. All I had was nine rubles. But of those, I had to hand over seven the next day to my servant Apollon for his monthly wages; he lived in and received seven rubles for his meals.

Considering Apollon's character it was impossible not to pay him. But more about that rascal, that plague of mine, later.

In any case, I knew that I wouldn't pay him his wages and that I'd definitely go.

That night I had the most hideous dreams. No wonder: all evening I was burdened with recollections of my years of penal servitude at school and I couldn't get rid of them. I'd been sent off to that school by distant relatives on whom I was dependent and about whom I've heard nothing since. They dispatched me, a lonely boy, crushed by their reproaches, already introspective, taciturn, and regarding everything around him savagely. My schoolmates received me with spiteful and pitiless jibes because I wasn't like any of them. But I couldn't tolerate their jibes; I couldn't possibly get along with them as easily as they got along with each other. I hated them all at once and took refuge from everyone in fearful, wounded and excessive pride. Their crudeness irritated me. Cynically they mocked my face and my awkward build; yet, what stupid faces they all had! Facial expressions at our school somehow degenerated and became particularly stupid. Many attractive lads had come to us, but in a few years they too were repulsive to look at. When I was only sixteen I wondered about them gloomily; even then I was astounded by the pettiness of their thoughts and the stupidity of their studies, games and conversations. They failed to understand essential things and took no interest in important, weighty subjects, so that I couldn't help considering them beneath me. It wasn't my wounded vanity that drove me to it; and, for God's sake, don't repeat any of those nauseating and hackneyed clichés, such as, "I was merely a dreamer, whereas they already understood life." They didn't understand a thing, not one thing about life, and I swear, that's what annoyed me most about them. On the contrary, they accepted the most obvious, glaring reality in a fantastically stupid way, and even then they'd begun to worship nothing but success. Everything that was just, but oppressed and humiliated, they ridiculed hard-heartedly and shamelessly. They mistook rank for intelligence; at the age of sixteen they were already talking about occupying comfortable little niches. Of course, much of this was due to their stupidity and the poor examples that had constantly surrounded them in their childhood and youth. They were monstrously depraved. Naturally, even this was more superficial, more affected cynicism; of course, their youth and a certain freshness shone through their depravity; but even this freshness was unattractive and manifested itself in a kind of rakishness. I hated them terribly, although, perhaps, I was even worse than they were. They returned the feeling and didn't conceal their loathing for me. But I no longer wanted their affection; on the contrary, I constantly longed for their humiliation. In order to avoid their jibes, I began to study as hard as I could on purpose and made my way to the top of the class. That impressed them. In addition, they all began to realize that I'd read certain books which they could never read and that I understood certain things (not included in our special course) about which they'd never even heard. They regarded this with savagery and sarcasm, but they submitted morally, all the more since even the teachers paid me some attention on this account. Their jibes ceased, but their hostility remained, and relations between us became cold and strained. In the end I myself couldn't stand it: as the years went by, my need for people, for friends, increased. I made several attempts to get closer to some of them; but these attempts always turned out to be unnatural and ended of their own accord. Once I even had a friend of sorts. But I was already a despot at heart; I wanted to exercise unlimited power over his soul; I wanted to instill in him contempt for his surroundings; and I demanded from him a disdainful and definitive break with those surroundings. I frightened him with my passionate friendship, and I reduced him to tears and convulsions. He was a naive and giving soul, but as soon as he'd surrendered himself to me totally, I began to despise him and reject him immediately—as if I only needed to achieve a victory over him, merely to subjugate him. But I was unable to conquer them all; my one friend was not at all like them, but rather a rare exception. The first thing I did upon leaving school was abandon the special job in the civil service for which I'd been trained, in order to sever all ties, break with my past, cover it over with dust. . . . The devil only knows why, after all that, I'd dragged myself over to see this Simonov! . . .

Early the next morning I roused myself from bed, jumped up in anxiety, just as if everything was about to start happening all at once. But I believed that some radical change in my life was imminent and was sure to occur that very day. Perhaps because I wasn't used to it, but all my life, at any external event, albeit a trivial one, it always seemed that some sort of radical change would occur. I went off to work as usual, but returned home two hours earlier in order to prepare. The most important thing, I thought, was not to arrive there first, or else they'd all think I was too eager. But there were thousands of most important things, and they all reduced me to the point of impotence. I polished my boots once again with my own hands. Apollon wouldn't polish them twice in one day for anything in the world; he considered it indecent. So I polished them myself, after stealing the brushes from the hallway so that he wouldn't notice and then despise me for it afterward. Next I carefully examined my clothes and found that everything was old, shabby, and worn out. I'd become too slovenly. My uniform was in better shape, but I couldn't go to dinner in a uniform. Worst of all, there was an enormous yellow stain on the knee of my trousers. I had an inkling that the spot alone would rob me of nine-tenths of my dignity. I also knew that it was unseemly for me to think that. "But this isn't the time for thinking. Reality is now looming," I thought, and my heart sank. I also knew perfectly well at that time, that I monstrously exaggerating all these facts. But what could be done? I was no longer able to control myself, and was shaking with fever. In despair I imagined how haughtily and coldly that "scoundrel" Zverkov would greet me; with what dull and totally relentless contempt that dullard Trudolyubov would regard me; how nastily and impudently that insect Ferfichkin would giggle at me in order to win Zverkov's approval; how well Simonov would understand all this and how he'd despise me for my wretched vanity and cowardice; and worst of all, how petty all this would be, not *literary*, but commonplace. Of course, it would have been better not to go at all. But that was no longer possible; once I began to feel drawn to something, I plunged right in, head first. I'd have reproached myself for the rest of my life: "So, you retreated, you retreated before reality, you retreated!" On the contrary, I desperately wanted to prove to all this "rabble" that I really wasn't the coward I imagined myself to be. But that's not all: in the strongest paroxysm of cowardly fever I dreamt of gaining the upper hand, of conquering them, of carrying them away, compelling them to love me— if only "for the nobility of my thought and my indisputable wit." They would abandon Zverkov; he'd sit by in silence and embarassment, and I'd crush him. Afterward, perhaps, I'd be reconciled with Zverkov and drink to our *friendship*, but what was most spiteful and insulting for me was that I knew even then, I knew completely and for sure, that I didn't need any of this at all; that in fact I really didn't want to crush them, conquer them, or attract them, and that if I could have ever achieved all that, I'd be the first to say that it wasn't worth a damn. Oh, how I prayed to God that this day would pass quickly! With inexpressible anxiety I approached the window, opened the transom,[2] and peered out into the murky mist of the thickly falling wet snow. . . .

At last my worthless old wall clock sputtered out five o'clock. I grabbed my hat, and, trying not to look at Apollon—who'd been waiting since early morning to receive his wages, but didn't want to be the first one to mention it out of pride—I slipped out the door past him and intentionally hired a smart cab with my last half-ruble in order to arrive at the Hôtel de Paris in style.

Summary　In chapters IV and V, the Underground Man quarrels with the others at Zverkov's farewell party; intoxicated, he insults Zverkov and challenges Ferfichkin to a duel. The others leave for a brothel; he borrows money to go there too but arrives late. A young girl is brought to him.

VI

Somewhere behind a partition a clock was wheezing as if under some strong pressure, as though someone were strangling it. After this unnaturally prolonged wheezing there followed a thin, nasty, somehow unexpectedly hurried chime, as if someone had suddenly leapt forward. It struck two. I recovered, although I really hadn't been asleep, only lying there half-conscious.

It was almost totally dark in the narrow, cramped, low-ceilinged room, which was crammed with an enormous wardrobe and cluttered with cartons, rags, and all sorts of old clothes. The candle burning on the table at one end of the room flickered faintly from time to time, and almost went out completely. In a few moments total darkness would set in.

It didn't take long for me to come to my senses; all at once, without any effort, everything returned to me, as though it had been lying in ambush ready to pounce on me again. Even in my unconscious state some point had constantly remained in my memory, never to be forgotten, around which my sleepy visions had gloomily revolved. But it was a strange thing: everything that had happened to me that day now seemed, upon awaken-

---

2. A small hinged pane in the window of a Russian house, used for ventilation especially during the winter when the main part of the window is sealed.

ing, to have occurred in the distant past, as if I'd long since left it all behind.

My mind was in a daze. It was as though something were hanging over me, provoking, agitating, and disturbing me. Misery and bile were welling inside me, seeking an outlet. Suddenly I noticed beside me two wide-open eyes, examining me curiously and persistently. The gaze was coldly detached, sullen, as if belonging to a total stranger. I found it oppressive.

A dismal thought was conceived in my brain and spread throughout my whole body like a nasty sensation, such as one feels upon entering a damp, mouldy underground cellar. It was somehow unnatural that only now these two eyes had decided to examine me. I also recalled that during the course of the last two hours I hadn't said one word to this creature, and that I had considered it quite unnecessary; that had even given me pleasure for some reason. Now I'd suddenly realized starkly how absurd, how revolting as a spider, was the idea of debauchery, which, without love, crudely and shamelessly begins precisely at the point where genuine love is consummated. We looked at each other in this way for some time, but she didn't lower her gaze before mine, nor did she alter her stare, so that finally, for some reason, I felt very uneasy.

"What's your name?" I asked abruptly, to put an end to it quickly.

"Liza," she replied, almost in a whisper, but somehow in a very unfriendly way; and she turned her eyes away.

I remained silent.

"The weather today . . . snow . . . foul!" I observed, almost to myself, drearily placing one arm behind my head and staring at the ceiling.

She didn't answer. The whole thing was obscene.

"Are you from around here?" I asked her a moment later, almost angrily, turning my head slightly toward her.

"No."

"Where are you from?"

"Riga," she answered unwillingly.

"German?"

"No, Russian."

"Have you been here long?"

"Where?"

"In this house."

"Two weeks." She spoke more and more curtly. The candle had gone out completely; I could no longer see her face.

"Are your mother and father still living?"

"Yes . . . no . . . they are."

"Where are they?"

"There . . . in Riga."

"Who are they?"

"Just . . ."

"Just what? What do they do?"

"Tradespeople."

"Have you always lived with them?"

"Yes."

"How old are you?"

"Twenty."

"Why did you leave them?"

"Just because . . ."

That "just because" meant: leave me alone, it makes me sick. We fell silent.

Only God knows why, but I didn't leave. I too started to feel sick and more depressed. Images of the previous day began to come to mind all on their own, without my willing it, in a disordered way. I suddenly recalled a scene that I'd witnessed on the street that morning as I was anxiously hurrying to work. "Today some people were carrying a coffin and nearly dropped it," I suddenly said aloud, having no desire whatever to begin a conversation, but just so, almost accidentally.

"A coffin?"

"Yes, in the Haymarket; they were carrying it up from an underground cellar."

"From a cellar?"

"Not a cellar, but from a basement . . . well, you know . . . from downstairs . . . from a house of ill repute . . . There was such filth all around. . . . Eggshells, garbage . . . it smelled foul . . . it was disgusting."

Silence.

"A nasty day to be buried!" I began again to break the silence.

"Why nasty?"

"Snow, slush . . ." (I yawned.)

"It doesn't matter," she said suddenly after a brief silence.

"No, it's foul. . . ." (I yawned again.) "The grave diggers must have been cursing because they were getting wet out there in the snow. And there must have been water in the grave."

"Why water in the grave?" she asked with some curiosity, but she spoke even more rudely and curtly than before. Something suddenly began to goad me on.

"Naturally, water on the bottom, six inches or so. You can't ever dig a dry grave at Volkovo cemetery."

"Why not?"

"What do you mean, why not? The place is waterlogged. It's all swamp. So they bury them right in the water. I've seen it myself . . . many times. . . ."

(I'd never seen it, and I'd never been to Volkovo cemetery, but I'd heard about it from other people.)

"Doesn't it matter to you if you die?"

"Why should I die?" she replied, as though defending herself.

"Well, someday you'll die; you'll die just like that woman did this morning. She was a . . . she was also a young girl . . . she died of consumption."

"The wench should have died in the hospital. . . ." (She knows all about it, I thought, and she even said "wench" instead of "girl.")

"She owed money to her madam," I retorted, more and more goaded on by the argument. "She worked right up to the end, even though she had consumption. The cabbies standing around were chatting with the soldiers, telling them all about it. Her former acquaintances, most likely. They were all laughing. They were planning to drink to her memory at the tavern." (I invented a great deal of this.)

Silence, deep silence. She didn't even stir.

"Do you think it would be better to die in a hospital?"

"Isn't it just the same? . . . Besides, why should I die?" she added irritably.

"If not now, then later?"

"Well, then later . . ."

"That's what you think! Now you're young and pretty and fresh—that's your value. But after a year of this life, you won't be like that any more; you'll fade."

"In a year?"

"In any case, after a year your price will be lower," I continued, gloating. "You'll move out of here into a worse place, into some other house. And a year later, into a third, each worse and worse, and seven years from now you'll end up in a cellar on the Haymarket. Even that won't be so bad. The real trouble will come when you get some disease, let's say a weakness in the chest . . . or you catch cold or something. In this kind of life it's no laughing matter to get sick. It takes hold of you and may never let go. And so, you die."

"Well, then, I'll die," she answered now quite angrily and stirred quickly.

"That'll be a pity."

"For what?"

"A pity to lose a life."

Silence.

"Did you have a sweetheart? Huh?"

"What's it to you?"

"Oh, I'm not interrogating you. What do I care? Why are you angry? Of course, you may have had your own troubles. What's it to me? Just the same, I'm sorry."

"For whom?"

"I'm sorry for you."

"No need . . . ," she whispered barely audibly and stirred once again.

That provoked me at once. What! I was being so gentle with her, while she . . .

"Well, and what do you think? Are you on the right path then?"

"I don't think anything."

"That's just the trouble—you don't think. Wake up, while there's still time. And there is time. You're still young and pretty; you could fall in love, get married, be happy.[3] . . ."

"Not all married women are happy," she snapped in her former, rude manner.

"Not all, of course, but it's still better than this. A lot better. You can even live without happiness as long as there's love. Even in sorrow life can be good; it's good to be alive, no matter how you live. But what's there besides . . . stench? Phew!"

---

3. A popular theme treated by Gogol, Chernyshevsky, and Nekrasov, among others. Typically, an innocent and idealistic young man attempts to rehabilitate a prostitute or "fallen woman."

I turned away in disgust; I was no longer coldly philosophizing. I began to feel what I was saying and grew excited. I'd been longing to expound these cherished *little ideas* that I'd been nurturing in my corner. Something had suddenly caught fire in me, some kind of goal had "manifested itself" before me.

"Pay no attention to the fact that I'm here. I'm no model for you. I may be even worse than you are. Moreover, I was drunk when I came here." I hastened nonetheless to justify myself. "Besides, a man is no example to a woman. It's a different thing altogether; even though I degrade and defile myself, I'm still no one's slave; if I want to leave, I just get up and go. I shake it all off and I'm a different man. But you must realize right from the start that you're a slave. Yes, a slave! You give away everything, all your freedom. Later, if you want to break this chain, you won't be able to; it'll bind you ever more tightly. That's the kind of evil chain it is. I know. I won't say anything else; you might not even understand me. But tell me this, aren't you already in debt to your madam? There, you see!" I added, even though she hadn't answered, but had merely remained silent; but she was listening with all her might. "There's your chain! You'll never buy yourself out. That's the way it's done. It's just like selling your soul to the devil. . . .

"And besides . . . I may be just as unfortunate, how do you know, and I may be wallowing in mud on purpose, also out of misery. After all, people drink out of misery. Well, I came here out of misery. Now, tell me, what's so good about this place? Here you and I were . . . intimate . . . just a little while ago, and all that time we didn't say one word to each other; afterward you began to examine me like a wild creature, and I did the same. Is that the way people love? Is that how one person is supposed to encounter another? It's a disgrace, that's what it is!"

"Yes!" she agreed with me sharply and hastily. The haste of her answer surprised even me. It meant that perhaps the very same idea was flitting through her head while she'd been examining me earlier. It meant that she too was capable of some thought. . . . "Devil take it; this is odd, this *kinship*," I thought, almost rubbing my hands together. "Surely I can handle such a young soul."

It was the sport that attracted me most of all.

She turned her face closer to mine, and in the darkness it seemed that she propped her head up on her arm. Perhaps she was examining me. I felt sorry that I couldn't see her eyes. I heard her breathing deeply.

"Why did you come here?" I began with some authority.

"Just so . . ."

"But think how nice it would be living in your father's house! There you'd be warm and free; you'd have a nest of your own."

"And what if it's worse than that?"

"I must establish the right tone," flashed through my mind. "I won't get far with sentimentality."

However, that merely flashed through my mind. I swear that she really did interest me. Besides, I was somewhat exhausted and provoked. After all, artifice goes along so easily with feeling.

"Who can say?" I hastened to reply. "All sorts of things can happen.

Why, I was sure that someone had wronged you and was more to blame than you are. After all, I know nothing of your life story, but a girl like you doesn't wind up in this sort of place on her own accord. . . ."

"What kind of a girl am I?" she whispered hardly audibly; but I heard it.

"What the hell! Now I'm flattering her. That's disgusting! But, perhaps it's a good thing. . . ." She remained silent.

"You see, Liza, I'll tell you about myself. If I'd had a family when I was growing up, I wouldn't be the person I am now. I think about this often. After all, no matter how bad it is in your own family—it's still your own father and mother, and not enemies or strangers. Even if they show you their love only once a year, you still know that you're at home. I grew up without a family; that must be why I turned out the way I did—so unfeeling."

I waited again.

"She might not understand," I thought. "Besides, it's absurd—all this moralizing."

"If I were a father and had a daughter, I think that I'd have loved her more than my sons, really," I began indirectly, talking about something else in order to distract her. I confess that I was blushing.

"Why's that?"

Ah, so she's listening!

"Just because. I don't know why, Liza. You see, I knew a father who was a stern, strict man, but he would kneel before his daughter and kiss her hands and feet; he couldn't get enough of her, really. She'd go dancing at a party, and he'd stand in one spot for five hours, never taking his eyes off her. He was crazy about her; I can understand that. At night she'd be tired and fall asleep, but he'd wake up, go in to kiss her, and make the sign of the cross over her while she slept. He used to wear a dirty old jacket and was stingy with everyone else, but would spend his last kopeck on her, buying her expensive presents; it afforded him great joy if she liked his presents. A father always loves his daughters more than their mother does. Some girls have a very nice time living at home. I think that I wouldn't even have let my daughter get married."

"Why not?" she asked with a barely perceptible smile.

"I'd be jealous, so help me God. Why, how could she kiss someone else? How could she love a stranger more than her own father? It's even painful to think about it. Of course, it's all nonsense; naturally, everyone finally comes to his senses. But I think that before I'd let her marry, I'd have tortured myself with worry. I'd have found fault with all her suitors. Nevertheless, I'd have ended up by allowing her to marry whomever she loved. After all, the one she loves always seems the worst of all to the father. That's how it is. That causes a lot of trouble in many families."

"Some are glad to sell their daughters, rather than let them marry honorably," she said suddenly.

Aha, so that's it!

"That happens, Liza, in those wretched families where there's neither God nor love," I retorted heatedly. "And where there's no love, there's also no good sense. There are such families, it's true, but I'm not talking about them. Obviously, from the way you talk, you didn't see much kindness in your own family. You must be very unfortunate. Hmm . . . But all this results primarily from poverty."

"And is it any better among the gentry? Honest folk live decently even in poverty."

"Hmmm . . . Yes. Perhaps. There's something else, Liza. Man only likes to count his troubles; he doesn't calculate his happiness. If he figured as he should, he'd see that everyone gets his share. So, let's say that all goes well in a particular family; it enjoys God's blessing, the husband turns out to be a good man, he loves you, cherishes you, and never leaves you. Life is good in that family. Sometimes, even though there's a measure of sorrow, life's still good. Where isn't there sorrow? If you choose to get married, *you'll find out for yourself*. Consider even the first years of a marriage to the one you love: what happiness, what pure bliss there can be sometimes! Almost without exception. At first even quarrels with your husband turn out well. For some women, the more they love their husbands, the more they pick fights with them. It's true; I once knew a woman like that. 'That's how it is,' she'd say. 'I love you very much and I'm tormenting you out of love, so that you'll feel it.' Did you know that one can torment a person intentionally out of love? It's mostly women who do that. Then she thinks to herself, 'I'll love him so much afterward, I'll be so affectionate, it's no sin to torment him a little now.' At home everyone would rejoice over you, and it would be so pleasant, cheerful, serene, and honorable. . . . Some other women are very jealous. If her husband goes away, I knew one like that, she can't stand it; she jumps up at night and goes off on the sly to see. Is he there? Is he in that house? Is he with that one? Now that's bad. Even she herself knows that it's bad; her heart sinks and she suffers because she really loves him. It's all out of love. And how nice it is to make up after a quarrel, to admit one's guilt or forgive him! How nice it is for both of them, how good they both feel at once, just as if they'd met again, married again, and begun their love all over again. No one, no one at all has to know what goes on between a husband and wife, if they love each other. However their quarrel ends, they should never call in either one of their mothers to act as judge or to hear complaints about the other one. They must act as their own judges. Love is God's mystery and should be hidden from other people's eyes, no matter what happens. This makes it holier, much better. They respect each other more, and a great deal is based on this respect. And, if there's been love, if they got married out of love, why should love disappear? Can't it be sustained? It rarely happens that it can't be sustained. If the husband turns out to be a kind and honest man, how can the love disappear? The first phase of married love will pass, that's true, but it's followed by an even better kind of love. Souls are joined together and all their concerns are managed in common; there'll be no secrets from one another. When children arrive, each and every stage, even a very difficult one, will seem happy, as long as there's both love and courage. Even work is cheerful; even when you deny yourself bread for your children's sake, you're still happy. After all, they'll love you for it afterward; you're really saving for your own future. Your children will grow up, and you'll feel that you're a model for them, a support. Even after you die, they'll carry your thoughts and feelings all during their life. They'll take on your image and likeness, since they received it from you. Consequently, it's a great obligation. How can a mother and father keep from growing closer? They say it's difficult to raise children. Who says that? It's heavenly joy! Do you love little children, Liza? I love them dearly. You know—a rosy little boy, suckling at your breast; what husband's heart could turn against his wife seeing her sitting there holding his child? The chubby, rosy little baby sprawls and snuggles; his little hands and feet are plump; his little nails are clean and tiny, so tiny it's even funny to see them; his little eyes look as if he already understood everything. As he suckles, he tugs at your breast playfully with his little hand. When the father approaches, the child lets go of the breast, bends way back, looks at his father, and laughs—as if God only knows how funny it is—and then takes to suckling again. Afterward, when he starts cutting teeth, he'll sometimes bite his mother's breast; looking at her sideways his little eyes seem to say, 'See, I bit you!' Isn't this pure bliss—the three of them, husband, wife, and child, all together? You can forgive a great deal for such moments. No, Liza, I think you must first learn how to live by yourself, and only afterward blame others."

"It's by means of images," I thought to myself, "just such images that I can get to you," although I was speaking with considerable feeling, I swear it; and all at once I blushed. "And what if she suddenly bursts out laughing—where will I hide then?" That thought drove me into a rage. By the end of my speech I'd really become excited, and now my pride was suffering somehow. The silence lasted for a while. I even considered shaking her.

"Somehow you . . ." she began suddenly and then stopped.

But I understood everything already: something was trembling in her voice now, not shrill, rude or unyielding as before, but something soft and timid, so timid that I suddenly was rather ashamed to watch her and felt guilty.

"What?" I asked with tender curiosity.

"Well, you . . ."

"What?"

"You somehow . . . it sounds just like a book," she said, and once again something which was noticeably sarcastic was suddenly heard in her voice.

Her remark wounded me dreadfully. That's not what I'd expected.

Yet, I didn't understand that she was intentionally disguising her feelings with sarcasm; that was usually the last resort of people who are timid and chaste of heart, whose souls have been coarsely and impudently invaded; and who, until the last moment, refuse to yield out of pride and are afraid to express their own feelings to you. I should've guessed it from the timidity with which on several occasions she tried to be sarcastic, until she finally managed to express it. But I hadn't guessed, and a malicious impulse took hold of me.

"Just you wait," I thought.

VII

"That's enough, Liza. What do books have to do with it, when this disgusts me as an outsider? And not only as an outsider. All this has awakened in my heart . . . Can it be, can it really be that you don't find it repulsive here? No, clearly habit means a great deal. The devil only knows what habit can do to a person. But do you seriously think that you'll never grow old, that you'll always be pretty, and that they'll keep you on here forever and ever? I'm not even talking about the filth. . . . Besides, I want to say this about your present life: even though you're still young, good-looking, nice, with soul and feelings, do you know, that when I came to a little while ago, I was immediately disgusted to be here with you! Why, a man has to be drunk to wind up here. But if you were in a different place, living as nice people do, I might not only chase after you, I might actually fall in love with you. I'd rejoice at a look from you, let alone a word; I'd wait for you at the gate and kneel down before you; I'd think of you as my betrothed and even consider that an honor. I wouldn't dare have any impure thoughts about you. But here, I know that I need only whistle, and you, whether you want to or not, will come to me, and that I don't have to do your bidding, whereas you have to do mine. The lowliest peasant may hire himself out as a laborer, but he doesn't make a complete slave of himself; he knows that it's only for a limited term. But what's your term? Just think about it. What are you giving up here? What are you enslaving? Why, you're enslaving your soul, something you don't really own, together with your body! You're giving away your love to be defiled by any drunkard! Love! After all, that's all there is! It's a precious jewel, a maiden's treasure, that's what it is! Why, to earn that love a man might be ready to offer up his own soul, to face death. But what's your love worth now? You've been bought, all of you; and why should anyone strive for your love, when you offer everything even without it? Why, there's no greater insult for a girl, don't you understand? Now, I've heard that they console you foolish girls, they allow you to see your own lovers here. But that's merely child's play, deception, making fun of you, while you believe it. And do you really think he loves you, that lover of yours? I don't believe it. How can he, if he knows that you can be called away from him at any moment? He'd have to be depraved after all that. Does he possess even one drop of respect for you? What do you have in common with him? He's laughing at you and stealing from you at the same time—so much for his love. It's not too bad, as long as he doesn't beat you. But perhaps he does. Go on, ask him, if you have such a lover, whether he'll ever marry you. Why, he'll burst out laughing right in your face, if he doesn't spit at you or smack you. He himself may be worth no more than a few lousy kopecks. And for what, do you think, did you ruin your whole life here? For the coffee they give you to drink, or for the plentiful supply of food? Why do you think they feed you so well? Another girl, an honest one, would choke on every bite, because she'd know why she was being fed so well. You're in debt here, you'll be in debt, and will remain so until the end, until such time comes as the customers begin to spurn you. And that time will come very soon; don't count on your youth. Why, here youth flies by like a stagecoach. They'll kick you out. And they'll not merely kick you out, but for a long time before that they'll pester you, reproach you, and abuse you—as if you hadn't ruined your health for the madam, hadn't given up your youth and your soul for her in vain, but rather, as if you'd ruined her, ravaged her, and robbed her. And don't expect any support. Your friends will also attack you to curry her favor, because they're all in bondage here and have long since lost both conscience and pity. They've become despicable, and there's nothing on earth more despicable, more repulsive, or more insulting than their abuse. You'll lose everything here, everything, without exception—your health, youth, beauty, and hope— and at the age of twenty-two you'll look as if you were thirty-five, and even that won't be too awful if you're not ill. Thank God for that. Why, you probably think that you're not even working, that it's all play! But there's no harder work or more onerous task than this one in the whole world and there never has been. I'd think that one's heart alone would be worn out by crying. Yet you dare not utter one word, not one syllable; when they drive you out, you leave as if you were the guilty one. You'll move to another place, then to a third, then somewhere else, and finally you'll wind up in the Haymarket. And there they'll start beating you for no good reason at all; it's a local custom; the clients there don't know how to be nice without beating you. You don't think it's so disgusting there? Maybe you should go and have a look sometime, and see it with your own eyes. Once, at New Year's, I saw a woman in a doorway. Her own kind had pushed her outside as a joke, to freeze her for a little while because she was wailing too much; they shut the door behind her. At nine o'clock in the morning she was already dead drunk, dishevelled, half-naked, and all beaten up. Her face was powdered, but her eyes were bruised; blood was streaming from her nose and mouth; a certain cabby had just fixed her up. She was sitting on a stone step, holding a piece of salted fish in her hand; she was howling, wailing something about her 'fate,' and slapping the fish against the stone step. Cabbies and drunken soldiers had gathered around the steps and were taunting her. Don't you think you'll wind up the same way? I wouldn't want to believe it myself, but how do you know, perhaps eight or ten years ago this same girl, the one with the salted fish, arrived here from somewhere or other, all fresh like a little cherub, inno-cent, and pure; she knew no evil and blushed at every word. Perhaps she was just like you—proud, easily offended, unlike all the rest; she looked like a queen and knew that total happiness awaited the man who would love her and whom she would also love. Do you see how it all ended? What if at the very moment she was slapping the fish against that filthy step, dead drunk and dishevelled, what if, even at that very moment she'd recalled her earlier, chaste years in her father's house when she was still going to school, and when her neighbor's son used to wait for her along the path and assure her that he'd love her all his life and devote himself entirely to her, and when they vowed to love one another forever and get married as soon as they grew up! No, Liza, you'd be lucky, very lucky, if you died quickly from consumption somewhere in a corner, in a cellar, like that other girl. In a hospital, you say? All right—they'll take you off, but what if the madam still requires your services? Consumption is quite a disease—it's not like dying from a fever. A person continues to hope right up until the last minute and declares that he's in good health. He consoles himself. Now that's useful for your madam. Don't worry, that's the way it is. You've sold your soul; besides, you owe her money—that means you don't dare say a thing. And while you're dying, they'll all abandon you, turn away from you—because there's nothing left to get from you. They'll even reproach you for taking up space for no good reason and for taking so long to die. You won't even be able to ask for something to drink, without their hurling abuse at you: 'When will you croak, you old bitch? You keep on moaning and don't let us get any sleep—and you drive our customers away.' That's for sure; I've overheard such words myself. And as you're breathing your last, they'll shove you into the filthiest corner of the cellar—into darkness and dampness; lying there alone, what will you think about then? After you die, some stranger will lay you out hurriedly, grumbling all the while, impatiently—no one will bless you, no one will sigh over you; they'll merely want to get rid of you as quickly as possible. They'll buy you a wooden trough and carry you out as they did that poor woman I saw today; then they'll go off to a tavern and drink to your memory. There'll be slush, filth, and wet snow in your grave—why bother for the likes of you? 'Let her down, Vanyukha; after all, it's her fate to go down with her legs up, that's the sort of girl she was. Pull up on that rope, you rascal!' 'It's okay like that.' 'How's it okay? See, it's lying on its side. Was she a human being or not? Oh, never mind, cover it up.' They won't want to spend much time arguing over you. They'll cover your coffin quickly with wet, blue clay and then go off to the tavern. . . . That'll be the end of your memory on earth; for other women, children will visit their graves, fathers, husbands—but for you—no tears, no sighs; no remembrances. No one, absolutely no one in the whole world, will ever come to visit you; your name will disappear from the face of the earth, just as if you'd never been born and had never existed. Mud and filth, no matter how you pound on the lid of your coffin at night when other corpses arise: 'Let me out, kind people, let me live on earth for a little while! I lived, but I didn't really see life; my life went down the drain; they drank it away in a tavern at the Haymarket; let me out, kind people, let me live in the world once again!' "

I was so carried away by my own pathos that I began to feel a lump forming in my throat, and . . . I suddenly stopped, rose up in fright, and, leaning over apprehensively, I began to listen carefully as my own heart pounded. There was cause for dismay.

For a while I felt that I'd turned her soul inside out and had broken her heart; the more I became convinced of this, the more I strived to reach my goal as quickly and forcefully as possible. It was the sport, the sport that attracted me; but it wasn't only the sport. . . .

I knew that I was speaking clumsily, artificially, even bookishly; in short, I didn't know how to speak except "like a book." But that didn't bother me, for I knew, I had a premonition, that I would be understood and that this bookishness itself might even help things along. But now, having achieved this effect, I suddenly lost all my nerve. No, never, never before had I witnessed such despair! She was lying there, her face pressed deep into a pillow she was clutching with her hands. Her heart was bursting. Her young body was shuddering as if she were having convulsions. Suppressed sobs shook her breast, tore her apart, and suddenly burst forth in cries and moans. Then she pressed her face even deeper into the pillow: she didn't want anyone, not one living soul, to hear her anguish and her tears. She bit the pillow; she bit her hand until it bled (I noticed that afterward); or else, thrusting her fingers into her dishevelled hair, she became rigid with the strain, holding her breath and clenching her teeth. I was about to say something, to ask her to calm down; but I felt that I didn't dare. Suddenly, all in a kind of chill, almost in a panic, I groped hurriedly to get out of there as quickly as possible. It was dark: no matter how I tried, I couldn't end it quickly. Suddenly I felt a box of matches and a candlestick with a whole unused candle. As soon as the room was lit up, Liza started suddenly, sat up, and looked at me almost senselessly, with a distorted face and a half-crazy smile. I sat down next to her and took her hands; she came to and threw herself at me, wanting to embrace me, yet not daring to. Then she quietly lowered her head before me.

"Liza, my friend, I shouldn't have . . . you must forgive me," I began, but she squeezed my hands so tightly in her fingers that I realized I was saying the wrong thing and stopped.

"Here's my address, Liza. Come to see me."

"I will," she whispered resolutely, still not lifting her head.

"I'm going now, good-bye . . . until we meet again."

I stood up; she did, too, and suddenly blushed all over, shuddered, seized a shawl lying on a chair, threw it over her shoulders, and wrapped herself up to her chin. After doing this, she smiled again somewhat painfully, blushed, and looked at me strangely. I felt awful. I hastened to leave, to get away.

"Wait," she said suddenly as we were standing in the hallway near the door, and she stopped me by putting her hand on my overcoat. She quickly put the candle down and ran off; obviously she'd remembered something or wanted to show me something. As she left she was blushing all over, her eyes were gleaming, and a smile had appeared on her lips— what on earth did it all mean? I waited against my own will; she returned a moment later with a glance that seemed to beg forgiveness for something. All in all it was no longer the same face or the same glance as before—sullen, distrustful, obstinate. Now her glance was imploring, soft, and, at the same time, trusting, affectionate, and timid. That's how children look at people whom they love very much, or when they're asking for something. Her eyes were light hazel, lovely, full of life, as capable of expressing love as brooding hatred.

Without any explanation, as if I were some kind of higher being who was supposed to know everything, she held a piece of paper out toward me. At that moment her whole face was shining with a most naive, almost childlike triumph. I unfolded the paper. It was a letter to her from some medical student containing a high-flown, flowery, but very respectful declaration of love. I don't remember the exact words now, but I can well recall the genuine emotion that can't be feigned shining through that high style. When I'd finished reading the letter, I met her ardent, curious, and childishly impatient gaze. She'd fixed her eyes on my face and was waiting eagerly to see what I'd say. In a few words, hurriedly, but with some joy and pride, she explained that she'd once been at a dance somewhere, in a private house, at the home of some "very, very good people, *family people*, where they *knew nothing*, nothing at all," because she'd arrived at this place only recently and was just . . . well, she hadn't quite decided whether she'd stay here and she'd certainly leave as soon as she'd paid off her debt. . . . Well, and this student was there; he danced with her all evening and talked to her. It turned out he was from Riga; he'd known her as a child, they'd played together, but that had been a long time ago; he was acquainted with her parents—but he knew nothing, absolutely nothing *about this place* and he didn't even suspect it! And so, the very next day, after the dance, (only some three days ago), he'd sent her this letter through the friend with whom she'd gone to the party . . . and . . . well, that's the whole story."

She lowered her sparkling eyes somewhat bashfully after she finished speaking.

The poor little thing, she'd saved this student's letter as a treasure and had run to fetch this one treasure of hers, not wanting me to leave without knowing that she too was the object of sincere, honest love, and that some-one exists who had spoken to her respectfully. Probably that letter was fated to lie in her box without results. But that didn't matter; I'm sure that she'll guard it as a treasure her whole life, as her pride and vindication; and now, at a moment like this, she remembered it and brought it out to exult naively before me, to raise herself in my eyes, so that I could see it for myself and could also think well of her. I didn't say a thing; I shook her hand and left. I really wanted to get away. . . . I walked all the way home in spite of the fact that wet snow was still falling in large flakes. I was exhausted, oppressed, and perplexed. But the truth was already glim-mering behind that perplexity. The ugly truth!

Summary   In chapter VIII, the Underground Man, back at home, worries that Liza will visit him and see his poverty; alternately humiliated and enraged, he quarrels with his valet, Apollon. Liza arrives.

IX

And enter my house bold and free,
To become its full mistress!
From the same poem.[4]

I stood before her, crushed, humiliated, abominably ashamed; I think I was smiling as I tried with all my might to wrap myself up in my tattered, quilted dressing gown— exactly as I'd imagined this scene the other day during a fit of depression. Apollon, after standing over us for a few min-utes, left, but that didn't make things any easier for me. Worst of all was

4. See n. 1, p. 2386.

that she suddenly became embarrassed too, more than I'd ever expected. At the sight of me, of course.

"Sit down," I said mechanically and moved a chair up to the table for her, while I sat on the sofa. She immediately and obediently sat down, staring at me wide-eyed, and, obviously, expecting something from me at once. This naive expectation infuriated me, but I restrained myself.

She should have tried not to notice anything, as if everything were just as it should be, but she . . . And I vaguely felt that she'd have to pay dearly for everything.

"You've found me in an awkward situation, Liza," I began, stammering and realizing that this was precisely the wrong way to begin.

"No, no, don't imagine anything!" I cried, seeing that she'd suddenly blushed. "I'm not ashamed of my poverty. . . . On the contrary, I regard it with pride. I'm poor, but noble. . . . One can be poor and noble," I muttered. "But . . . would you like some tea?"

"No . . . ," she started to say.

"Wait!"

I jumped up and ran to Apollon. I had to get away somehow.

"Apollon," I whispered in feverish haste, tossing down the seven rubles which had been in my fist the whole time, "here are your wages. There, you see, I've given them to you. But now you must rescue me: bring us some tea and a dozen rusks from the tavern at once. If you don't go, you'll make me a very miserable man. You have no idea who this woman is. . . . This means—everything! You may think she's . . . But you've no idea at all who this woman really is!"

Apollon, who'd already sat down to work and had put his glasses on again, at first glanced sideways in silence at the money without abandoning his needle; then, paying no attention to me and making no reply, he continued to fuss with the needle he was still trying to thread. I waited there for about three minutes standing before him with my arms folded *à la Napoleon.*[5] My temples were soaked in sweat. I was pale, I felt that myself. But, thank God, he must have taken pity just looking at me. After finishing with the thread, he stood up slowly from his place, slowly pushed back his chair, slowly took off his glasses, slowly counted the money and finally, after inquiring over his shoulder whether he should get a whole pot, slowly walked out of the room. As I was returning to Liza, it occurred to me: shouldn't I run away just as I was, in my shabby dressing gown, no matter where, and let come what may.

I sat down again. She looked at me uneasily. We sat in silence for several minutes.

"I'll kill him." I shouted suddenly, striking the table so hard with my fist that ink splashed out of the inkwell.

"Oh, what are you saying?" she exclaimed, startled.

"I'll kill him, I'll kill him!" I shrieked, striking the table in an absolute frenzy, but understanding full well at the same time how stupid it was to be in such a frenzy.

5. In the style of Napoleon.

"You don't understand, Liza, what this executioner is doing to me. He's my executioner. . . . He's just gone out for some rusks; he . . ."

And suddenly I burst into tears. It was a nervous attack. I felt so ashamed amidst my sobs, but I couldn't help it. She got frightened.

"What's the matter? What's wrong with you?" she cried, fussing around me.

"Water, give me some water, over there!" I muttered in a faint voice, realizing full well, however, that I could've done both without the water and without the faint voice. But I was *putting on an act*, as it's called, in order to maintain decorum, although my nervous attack was genuine.

She gave me some water while looking at me like a lost soul. At that very moment Apollon brought in the tea. It suddenly seemed that this ordinary and prosaic tea was horribly inappropriate and trivial after everything that had happened, and I blushed. Liza stared at Apollon with considerable alarm. He left without looking at us.

"Liza, do you despise me?" I asked, looking her straight in the eye, trembling with impatience to find out what she thought.

She was embarrassed and didn't know what to say.

"Have some tea," I said angrily. I was angry at myself, but she was the one who'd have to pay, naturally. A terrible anger against her suddenly welled up in my heart; I think I could've killed her. To take revenge I swore inwardly not to say one more word to her during the rest of her visit. "She's the cause of it all," I thought.

Our silence continued for about five minutes. The tea stood on the table; we didn't touch it. It reached the point of my not wanting to drink on purpose, to make it even more difficult for her; it would be awkward for her to begin alone. Several times she glanced at me in sad perplexity. I stubbornly remained silent. I was the main sufferer, of course, because I was fully aware of the despicable meanness of my own spiteful stupidity; yet, at the same time, I couldn't restrain myself.

"I want to . . . get away from . . . that place . . . once and for all," she began just to break the silence somehow; but, poor girl, that was just the thing she shouldn't have said at that moment, stupid enough as it was to such a person as me, stupid as I was. My own heart even ached with pity for her tactlessness and unnecessary straightforwardness. But something hideous immediately suppressed all my pity; it provoked me even further. Let the whole world go to hell. Another five minutes passed.

"Have I disturbed you?" she began timidly, barely audibly, and started to get up.

But as soon as I saw this first glimpse of injured dignity, I began to shake with rage and immediately exploded.

"Why did you come here? Tell me why, please," I began, gasping and neglecting the logical order of my words. I wanted to say it all at once, without pausing for breath; I didn't even worry about how to begin.

"Why did you come here? Answer me! Answer!" I cried, hardly aware of what I was saying. "I'll tell you, my dear woman, why you came here. You came here because I spoke some *words of pity* to you that time. Now you've softened, and want to hear more 'words of pity.' Well, you should know that I was laughing at you then. And I'm laughing at you now. Why are you trembling? Yes, I was laughing at you! I'd been insulted, just prior to that, at dinner, by those men who arrived just before me that evening. I came intending to thrash one of them, the officer; but I didn't succeed; I couldn't find him; I had to avenge my insult on someone, to get my own back; you turned up and I took my anger out at you, and I laughed at you. I'd been humiliated, and I wanted to humiliate someone else; I'd been treated like a rag, and I wanted to exert some power. . . . That's what it was; you thought that I'd come there on purpose to save you, right? Is that what you thought? Is that it?"

I knew that she might get confused and might not grasp all the details, but I also knew that she'd understand the essence of it very well. That's just what happened. She turned white as a sheet; she wanted to say something. Her lips were painfully twisted, but she collapsed onto a chair just as if she'd been struck down with an ax. Subsequently she listened to me with her mouth gaping, her eyes wide open, shaking with awful fear. It was the cynicism, the cynicism of my words that crushed her. . . .

"To save you!" I continued, jumping up from my chair and rushing up and down the room in front of her, "to save you from what? Why, I may be even worse than you are. When I recited that sermon to you, why didn't you throw it back in my face? You should have said to me, 'Why did you come here? To preach morality or what?' Power, it was the power I needed then, I craved the sport, I wanted to reduce you to tears, humiliation, hysteria—that's what I needed then! But I couldn't have endured it myself, because I'm such a wretch. I got scared. The devil only knows why I foolishly gave you my address. Afterward, even before I got home, I cursed you like nothing on earth on account of that address. I hated you already because I'd lied to you then, because it was all playing with words, dreaming in my own mind. But, do you know what I really want now? For you to get lost, that's what! I need some peace. Why, I'd sell the whole world for a kopeck if people would only stop bothering me. Should the world go to hell, or should I go without my tea? I say, let the world go to hell as long as I can always have my tea. Did you know that or not? And I know perfectly well that I'm a scoundrel, a bastard, an egotist, and a sluggard. I've been shaking from fear for the last three days wondering whether you'd ever come. Do you know what disturbed me most of all these last three days? The fact that I'd appeared to you then as such a hero, and that now you'd suddenly see me in this torn dressing gown, dilapidated and revolting. I said before that I wasn't ashamed of my poverty; well, you should know that I am ashamed, I'm ashamed of it more than anything, more afraid of it than anything, more than if I were a thief, because I'm so vain; it's as if the skin's been stripped away from my body so that even wafts of air cause pain. By now surely even you've guessed that I'll never forgive you for having come upon me in this dressing gown as I was attacking Apollon like a vicious dog. Your saviour, your former hero, behaving like a mangy, shaggy mongrel, attacking his own lackey, while that lackey stood there laughing at me! Nor will I ever forgive you for those tears which, like an embarrassed old woman, I couldn't hold back before you. And I'll never forgive you for all that I'm confessing now. Yes—you, you alone must pay for everything because you turned up like this, because I'm a scoundrel, because I'm the nastiest, most ridiculous, pettiest, stupidest, most envious worm of all those living on earth who're no better than me in any way, but who, the devil knows why, never get embarrassed, while all my life I have to endure insults from every louse—that's my fate. What do I care that you don't understand any of this? What do I care, what do I care about you and whether or not you perish there? Why, don't you realize how much I'll hate you now after having said all this with your being here listening to me? After all, a man can only talk like this once in his whole life, and then only in hysteria! . . . . What more do you want? Why, after all this, are you still hanging around here tormenting me? Why don't you leave?"

But at this point a very strange thing suddenly occurred.

I'd become so accustomed to inventing and imagining everything according to books, and picturing everything on earth to myself just as I'd conceived of it in my dreams, that at first I couldn't even comprehend the meaning of this strange occurrence. But here's what happened: Liza, insulted and crushed by me, understood much more than I'd imagined. She understood out of all this what a woman always understands first of all, if she sincerely loves—namely, that I myself was unhappy.

The frightened and insulted expression on her face was replaced at first by grieved amazement. When I began to call myself a scoundrel and a bastard, and my tears had begun to flow (I'd pronounced this whole tirade in tears), her whole face was convulsed by a spasm. She wanted to get up and stop me; when I'd finished, she paid no attention to my shouting, "Why are you here? Why don't you leave?" She only noticed that it must have been very painful for me to utter all this. Besides, she was so defenseless, the poor girl. She considered herself immeasurably beneath me. How could she get angry or take offense? Suddenly she jumped up from the chair with a kind of uncontrollable impulse, and yearning toward me, but being too timid and not daring to stir from her place, she extended her arms in my direction. . . . At this moment my heart leapt inside me, too. Then suddenly she threw herself at me, put her arms around my neck, and burst into tears. I, too, couldn't restrain myself and sobbed as I'd never done before.

"They won't let me . . . I can't be . . . good!"[6] I barely managed to say; then I went over to the sofa, fell upon it face down, and sobbed in genuine hysterics for a quarter of an hour. She knelt down, embraced me, and remained motionless in that position.

But the trouble was that my hysterics had to end sometime. And so (after all, I'm writing the whole loathsome truth), lying there on the sofa and pressing my face firmly into that nasty leather cushion of mine, I began to sense gradually, distantly, involuntarily, but irresistibly, that it would be awkward for me to raise my head and look Liza straight in the eye. What was I ashamed of? I don't know, but I was ashamed. It also occurred to my overwrought brain that now our roles were completely reversed; now she was the heroine, and I was the same sort of humiliated

---

6. This epithet *dobryi* ("good") must be read in combination with that in the second sentence of the work, where the hero describes himself as *zloi*—not only "spiteful" but also "evil."

and oppressed creature she'd been in front of me that evening — only four days ago. . . . And all this came to me during those few minutes as I lay face down on the sofa!

My God! Was it possible that I envied her?

I don't know; to this very day I still can't decide. But then, of course, I was even less able to understand it. After all, I couldn't live without exercising power and tyrannizing over another person. . . . But . . . but, then, you really can't explain a thing by reason; consequently, it's useless to try.

However, I regained control of myself and raised my head; I had to sooner or later. . . . And so, I'm convinced to this day that it was precisely because I felt too ashamed to look at her, that another feeling was suddenly kindled and burst into flame in my heart — the feeling of domination and possession. My eyes gleamed with passion; I pressed her hands tightly. How I hated her and felt drawn to her simultaneously! One feeling intensified the other. It was almost like revenge! . . . At first there was a look of something resembling bewilderment, or even fear, on her face, but only for a brief moment. She embraced me warmly and rapturously.

X

A quarter of an hour later I was rushing back and forth across the room in furious impatience, constantly approaching the screen to peer at Liza through the crack. She was sitting on the floor, her head leaning against the bed, and she must have been crying. But she didn't leave, and that's what irritated me. By this time she knew absolutely everything. I'd insulted her once and for all, but . . . there's nothing more to be said. She guessed that my outburst of passion was merely revenge, a new humiliation for her, and that to my former, almost aimless, hatred there was added now a *personal, envious* hatred of her. . . . However, I don't think that she understood all this explicitly; on the other hand, she fully understood that I was a despicable man, and, most important, that I was incapable of loving her.

I know that I'll be told this is incredible — that it's impossible to be as spiteful and stupid as I am; you may even add that it was impossible not to return, or at least to appreciate, this love. But why is this so incredible? In the first place, I could no longer love because, I repeat, for me love meant tyrannizing and demonstrating my moral superiority. All my life I could never even conceive of any other kind of love, and I've now reached the point that I sometimes think that love consists precisely in a voluntary gift by the beloved person of the right to tyrannize over him. Even in my underground dreams I couldn't conceive of love in any way other than a struggle. It always began with hatred and ended with moral subjugation; afterward, I could never imagine what to do with the subjugated object. And what's so incredible about that, since I'd previously managed to corrupt myself morally; I'd already become unaccustomed to "real life," and only a short while ago had taken it into my head to reproach her and shame her for having come to hear "words of pity" from me. But I never could've guessed that she'd come not to hear words of pity at all, but to love me, because it's in that kind of love that a woman finds her resurrection, all her salvation from whatever kind of ruin, and her rebirth, as it can't appear in any other form. However, I didn't hate her so much as I rushed around the room and peered through the crack behind the screen. I merely found it unbearably painful that she was still there. I wanted her to disappear. I longed for "peace and quiet"; I wanted to remain alone in my underground. "Real life" oppressed me—so unfamiliar was it—that I even found it hard to breathe.

But several minutes passed, and she still didn't stir, as if she were oblivious. I was shameless enough to tap gently on the screen to remind her. . . . She started suddenly, jumped up, and hurried to find her shawl, hat, and coat, as if she wanted to escape from me. . . . Two minutes later she slowly emerged from behind the screen and looked at me sadly. I smiled spitefully; it was forced, however, for *appearance's sake only*; and I turned away from her look.

"Good-bye," she said, going toward the door.

Suddenly I ran up to her, grabbed her hand, opened it, put something in . . . and closed it again. Then I turned away at once and bolted to the other corner, so that at least I wouldn't be able to see. . . .

I was just about to lie—to write that I'd done all this accidentally, without knowing what I was doing, in complete confusion, out of foolishness. But I don't want to lie; therefore I'll say straight out, that I opened her hand and placed something in it . . . out of spite. It occurred to me to do this while I was rushing back and forth across the room and she was sitting there behind the screen. But here's what I can say for sure: although I did this cruel thing deliberately, it was not from my heart, but from my stupid head. This cruelty of mine was so artificial, cerebral, intentionally invented, *bookish*, that I couldn't stand it myself even for one minute—at first I bolted to the corner so as not to see, and then, out of shame and in despair, I rushed out after Liza. I opened the door into the hallway and listened. "Liza! Liza!" I called down the stairs, but timidly, in a soft voice.

There was no answer; I thought I could hear her footsteps at the bottom of the stairs.

"Liza!" I cried more loudly.

No answer. But at that moment I heard down below the sound of the tight outer glass door opening heavily with a creak and then closing again tightly. The sound rose up the stairs.

She'd gone. I returned to my room deep in thought. I felt horribly oppressed.

I stood by the table near the chair where she'd been sitting and stared senselessly into space. A minute or so passed, then I suddenly started: right before me on the chair I saw . . . in a word, I saw the crumpled blue five-ruble note, the very one I'd thrust into her hand a few moments before. It was the same one; it couldn't be any other; I had none other in my apartment. So she'd managed to toss it down on the table when I'd bolted to the other corner.

So what? I might have expected her to do that. Might have expected it? No. I was such an egotist, in fact, I so lacked respect for other people, that I couldn't even conceive that she'd ever do that. I couldn't stand it. A moment later, like a madman, I hurried to get dressed. I threw on whatever I happened to find, and rushed headlong after her. She couldn't have gone more than two hundred paces when I ran out on the street.

It was quiet; it was snowing heavily, and the snow was falling almost perpendicularly, blanketing the sidewalk and the deserted street. There were no passers-by; no sound could be heard. The street lights were flickering dismally and vainly. I ran about two hundred paces to the crossroads and stopped.

"Where did she go? And why am I running after her? Why? To fall down before her, sob with remorse, kiss her feet, and beg her forgiveness! That's just what I wanted. My heart was being torn apart; never, never will I recall that moment with indifference. But—why?" I wondered. "Won't I grow to hate her, perhaps as soon as tomorrow, precisely because I'm kissing her feet today? Will I ever be able to make her happy? Haven't I found out once again today, for the hundredth time, what I'm really worth? Won't I torment her?"

I stood in the snow, peering into the murky mist, and thought about all this.

"And wouldn't it be better, wouldn't it," I fantasized once I was home again, stifling the stabbing pain in my heart with such fantasies, "wouldn't it be better if she were to carry away the insult with her forever? Such an insult—after all, is purification; it's the most caustic and painful form of consciousness. Tomorrow I would have defiled her soul and wearied her heart. But now that insult will never die within her; no matter how abominable the filth that awaits her, that insult will elevate and purify her . . . by hatred . . . hmm . . . perhaps by forgiveness as well. But will that make it any easier for her?"

And now, in fact, I'll pose an idle question of my own. Which is better: cheap happiness or sublime suffering? Well, come on, which is better?

These were my thoughts as I sat home that evening, barely alive with the anguish in my soul. I'd never before endured so much suffering and remorse; but could there exist even the slightest doubt that when I went rushing out of my apartment, I'd turn back again after going only halfway? I never met Liza afterward, and I never heard anything more about her. I'll also add that for a long time I remained satisfied with my theory about the use of insults and hatred, in spite of the fact that I myself almost fell ill from anguish at the time.

Even now, after so many years, all this comes back to me as *very unpleasant*. A great deal that comes back to me now is very unpleasant, but . . . perhaps I should end these *Notes* here? I think that I made a mistake in beginning to write them. At least, I was ashamed all the time I was writing this *tale*: consequently, it's not really literature, but corrective punishment. After all, to tell you long stories about how, for example, I ruined my life through moral decay in my corner, by the lack of appropriate surroundings, by isolation from any living beings, and by futile malice in the underground—so help me God, that's not very interesting. A novel needs a hero, whereas here all the traits of an anti-hero have been assembled *deliberately*; but the most important thing is that all this produces an extremely unpleasant impression because we've all become estranged from life, we're all cripples, every one of us, more or less. We've become so estranged that at times we feel some kind of revulsion for genuine "real life," and therefore we can't bear to be reminded of it. Why, we've reached a point where we almost regard "real life" as hard work, as a job, and we've all agreed in private that it's really better in books. And why do we sometimes fuss, indulge in whims, and make demands? We don't know ourselves. It'd be even worse if all our whimsical desires were fulfilled. Go on, try it. Give us, for example, a little more independence; untie the hands of any one of us, broaden our sphere of activity, relax the controls, and . . . I can assure you, we'll immediately ask to have the controls reinstated. I know that you may get angry at me for saying this, you may shout and stamp your feet: "Speak for yourself," you'll say, "and for your own miseries in the underground, but don't you dare say 'all of us.'" If you'll allow me, gentlemen; after all, I'm not trying to justify myself by saying all of us. What concerns me in particular, is that in my life I've only taken to an extreme that which you haven't even dared to take halfway; what's more, you've mistaken your cowardice for good sense; and, in so deceiving yourself, you've consoled yourself. So, in fact, I may even be "more alive" than you are. Just take a closer look! Why, we don't even know where this "real life" lives nowadays, what it really is, and what it's called. Leave us alone without books and we'll get confused and lose our way at once—we won't know what to join, what to hold on to, what to love or what to hate, what to respect or what to despise. We're even oppressed by being men—men with real bodies and blood of our very own. We're ashamed of it; we consider it a disgrace and we strive to become some kind of impossible "general-human-beings." We're stillborn; for some time now we haven't been conceived by living fathers; we like it more and more. We're developing a taste for it. Soon we'll conceive of a way to be born from ideas. But enough; I don't want to write any more "from Underground. . . ."

However, the "notes" of this paradoxalist don't end here. He couldn't resist and kept on writing. But it also seems to us that we might as well stop here.

CHARLES BAUDELAIRE
1821–1867

Few writers have had such impact on succeeding generations as Charles Baudelaire, called both the "first modern poet" and the "father of modern criticism." Nor is his reputation confined to the West, for Baudelaire is the most widely read French poet around the globe. Yet for a long time Baudelaire's literary image was dominated by his reputation as a scandalous writer whose blatant eroticism and open fascination with evil outraged all right-thinking people. Both he and Flaubert were brought to trial in 1857 for "offenses against public and religious morals"— Flaubert for *Madame Bovary* and Baudelaire for his just-published book of poetry

Les Fleurs de Mal (The flowers of evil). Some of this reputation is justified; the poet did intend to shock, and he displayed in painfully vivid scenes his own spiritual and sensual torment. Haunted by a religiously framed vision of human nature as fallen and corrupt, he lucidly analyzed his own weaknesses as well as the hypocrisy and sins he found in society. Lust, hatred, laziness, a disabling self-awareness that ironized all emotions, a horror of death and decay, and finally an apathy that swallowed up all other vices—all contrasted bitterly with the poet's dreams of a lost Eden, an ideal harmony of being. Perfection existed only in the distance: in scenes of erotic love, faraway voyages, or artistic beauty created often out of ugliness and crude reality. Baudelaire's ability to present realistic detail inside larger symbolic horizons, his constant use of imagery and suggestion, his consummate craftsmanship and the intense musicality of his verse made him a precursor of Symbolism and, in the words of T. S. Eliot, "the greatest exemplar in *modern* poetry in any language."

Baudelaire was born in Paris on April 9, 1821. His father died when he was six, and his widowed mother married Captain (later General) Jacques Aupick a year later. In 1832 the family moved to Lyons, and young Charles was placed in boarding school; in 1836, Aupick and his family were reassigned to Paris. Throughout his life Baudelaire remained greatly attached to his mother and detested his disciplinarian stepfather. He was a rebellious and difficult youth whose unconventional behavior and extravagant lifestyle continued to worry his family, especially after he turned twenty-one and received his father's inheritance. In 1844, they obtained a court order to supervise his finances, and from then on the poet subsisted on allowances paid by a notary.

In contrast to the Romantics with their love of nature and pastoral scenes, Baudelaire was a city poet fascinated by the variety and excitement of modern urban life. Living in Paris, he collaborated with other writers, published poems, translations, and criticism in different journals, and in 1842 began a lifelong liaison with Jeanne Duval, the "black Venus" of many poems. When he read Edgar Allan Poe for the first time, he was struck by the similarity of their ideas: by Poe's dedication to beauty, his fascination with bizarre images and death, and above all by his emphasis on craftsmanship and perfectly controlled art. Baudelaire's translations of Poe, collected in five volumes published from 1856 to 1865, were immensely popular and introduced the American writer to a broad European audience.

Public scandal greeted the appearance in 1857 of Baudelaire's major work, *The Flowers of Evil*. French authorities, already annoyed at Flaubert's acquittal, seized the book immediately. Less than two months later, the poet and his publisher were condemned to pay a fine and to delete six poems. A second edition with more poems appeared in 1861, and new lyrics were added to later printings. By now the poet was also well known as a critic. He championed the modern art of his time, interpreting and upholding the spirit of modernity in the art criticism of his 1845, 1846, and 1859 *Salons*, in remarkable studies of the painters Eugène Delacroix and Constantin Guys, and in a spirited defense of the German composer Richard Wagner. Baudelaire started publishing prose poetry at the beginning of the 1860s, experimenting with a form that was almost unknown in France and in which he hoped to achieve "the miracle of a poetic prose, musical without rhythm or rhyme, able . . . to adapt itself to the soul's lyric movements, to the undulations of reverie, to the sudden starts of consciousness." A slim book of twenty prose poems appeared in 1862; the complete *Prose Poems* (also called *Paris Spleen*) would contain fifty poems in all. Baudelaire's health was precarious during these years. In 1862, he had what was apparently a minor stroke, which he called a "warning" and described with characteristically vivid imagery: "I felt pass over me a draft of wind from imbecility's wing." Four years later, in Belgium, he was stricken with aphasia and hemiplegia; unable to speak, he was brought back to Paris where he died on August 31, 1867.

His audience was never far from Baudelaire's mind. He wished to shock, to startle, to make the reader rethink cherished ideas and values. In the prefatory poem to *The Flowers of Evil*, *To the Reader*, Baudelaire ends a catalogue of human vices by insisting that both he and the reader are caught in a common guilt: "You—hypocrite Reader—my double—my brother!" The poet's insistent theme of *ennui* (pathological boredom or apathy) occurs here at the beginning of the book: it is the melancholy inertia that keeps human beings from acting either for good or for evil, placing them outside the realm of choice much as Dante relegated to Limbo those who were unwilling to take a moral stand. (In Catholic theology, such spiritual inertia is termed *acedia*.) This *spleen*, as it is also called (from the part of the body governing a splenetic or bilious humor), appears throughout *The Flowers of Evil* as an insidious, debilitating force. In *To the Reader* Baudelaire argues that the Devil's most terrifying weapon against humankind is not the litany of sins so colorfully described, but rather his ability to diminish the possibility of action: to evaporate—like a chemist in a laboratory—the precious metal of human will.

The Voyage, placed by Baudelaire at the end of the collection, describes the opposite of inertia: an active search for goals always out of reach. A long poem written in eight sections and intended, according to the poet, to upset current faith in human progress, *The Voyage* describes "progress" as a series of temporary advances that end in disappointment and disgust. These smaller achievements— discovering new lands, inventing new luxuries, gaining fame and fortune, seeking ecstasy in sadism and sensuality—are all bound to deceive because they are merely symbols of a larger unending voyage: the quest for the infinite. Since human beings contain an "inner [spiritual] infinite" they cannot be satisfied with any limits and must constantly travel toward the unknown and the new. The last line, "In the depths of the Unknown, we'll discover the New!" became a famous rallying cry for generations who sought new insights by exploring such unmapped frontiers.

Baudelaire alternates between acid melancholy and glimpses of happiness. Not all voyages are unhappy; one of his rare contented and even tender poems is the lyrical *Invitation to the Voyage*, a lover's invitation to an exotic land of peace, beauty, and sensuous harmony. The voyage is imaginary, of course, implying two forms of escape from reality: an escape out of real time into a primeval accord of the senses, and an escape into another artistic vision—the glowing interiors painted by such Dutch masters as Jan Vermeer. A similar but more cynical voyage of escape occurs in *Her Hair*. Here the poet, abandoning himself to passion, buries his face in the dark tide of his mistress's hair as if to submerge himself in the dark ocean of dream. This escape is available only on a temporary basis, however; the woman remains his "oasis" only so long as he adorns her hair with jewels. In both these poems, and in Baudelaire's poetry in general, we must admit that women do not exist as separate personalities but rather as foils for poetic inspiration: conventional images of beauty, coldness, vision, or vice given one or another form. Similarly, the woman in *The Carcass* exists only as an appropriate listener in a poem that mocks Petrarchan ideals of feminine beauty. Nor are men better treated; they appear not as individuals but generically, in groups, or they are addressed as brothers (or doubles) of the poet himself. Baudelaire's poetry is governed by a strong subjective impulse, no matter how much he reaches into the world for the raw material of his complex imaginative universe.

Baudelaire was convinced that "every good poet has always been a realist," and he himself was a master of realistic details used for effects that go beyond conventional or photographic realism. The rhythmic thump of firewood being delivered is repeated throughout Song of Autumn I, where it coordinates ascending images of death. Maggots swarm over a dead body in "The Carcass," and yet there is a strange beauty in this evocation of a buzzing, vibrating new life superimposed on the now-blurred outlines of a decaying animal carcass. The poem's ostensible theme is familiar—carpe diem, "seize the day" or "think of the future and love me now," since only a poet can preserve beauty—but one has only to compare Yeats's poem, When You Are Old, to recognize the harshness of this address to the beloved. The mixture of tones is more subtle in the Spleen poems, celebrated for their evocation of gray misery. Here Baudelaire inserts mundane items like mangy cats, decks of cards, old-fashioned clothes, uncorked perfume bottles, and noisy rainspouts. Such down-to-earth details give substance to concurrent mythical or allegorical scenes. A chill revelation of mortality emerges from the sequence of thoroughly practical references to water in Spleen LXXVIII, beginning with the rain and fog in the city and including a cat twisting and turning uncomfortably on clammy tiles, the whine of a rainspout, the wheeze of wet wood and a damp clock pendulum, and finally a deck of cards left by an old woman who died of dropsy. If the sequence is interesting as a tour de force of linked images, it also serves cumulatively to evoke an atmosphere of lethargy and decay climaxing in a tiny, altogether unrealistic final scene in which two face cards talk sinisterly of their past loves.

Similar themes are to be found in the prose poems published as Little Poems in Prose or Paris Spleen and generally seen as the first important example of the prose poem although Baudelaire did not actually originate the genre. He was keenly aware, however, of the need for poetic prose to also find its own way to be musical "without rhyme." Stanzas become paragraphs; rhythm is created through variations in sentence length, syntax, and sound patterns, and also through the juxtaposition of scenes and tones. Rhythm is undeniably present, however changed: it is audible in the triple cadence ending Windows (helping him "to live, to feel that I am, and what I am") or in the contrasting dialogue leading up to the soul's explosion at the end of Anywhere out of the World.

The realism that is often buried in the lyrics of The Flowers of Evil appears on the surface in the prose poems. Baudelaire recasts The Voyage's unending search for new experiences as an imaginary dialogue in Anywhere out of the World, and ponders his solitude and the nature of creative genius in Windows. In Windows, after having deduced the life story of an old woman seen across the roofs, he ends by saying that her story is only a "legend"—or, at least, that he does not care whether it is true so long as it provides a point of departure for his own imagination. Correspondingly, the poet relishes crowds because, moving among so many people, he is able to imagine himself in their place: "to be himself or someone else, as he chooses." In each case the artist is visibly alone, experiencing either the melancholy of spleen or the joy of an artistic imagination that creates and populates its own world. In verse or in prose, the alternation between dream and reality continues.

Baudelaire is a complex and ironic poet, an inheritor of that Romantic irony that wishes to embrace all the opposites of human existence: good and evil, love and hate, self and other, dream and reality. His is a universe of relationships, of echoes and correspondences. His best-known poem, in fact, is the sonnet Correspondences. This poem describes a vision of the mystic unity of all nature, which is demonstrated by the reciprocity of our five senses (synesthesia). Nature, says the poet, is a system of perpetual analogies in which one thing always corresponds to another—physical objects to each other (colonnades in a temple, for example, to trees in the forest), spiritual reality to physical reality, and the five senses (taste, smell, touch, sight, and hearing) among themselves—to produce such combinations as "bitter green," a "soft look," or "a harsh sound." Human beings are not usually aware of the "universal analogy"—the forest of the first stanza watches us without our knowing it—but it is the role of the poet to act as seer and guide, urging us toward a state of awareness where both mind and senses fuse in another dimension. *Correspondences* is no vaguely intuitive poem, however. Even though it describes a state of ecstatic awareness, it works through the stages of a logical argument. The thesis is set out in the first stanza, explained in the second, and illustrated with cumulative examples in the third and fourth. Baudelaire's yearning for mystic harmony does not make him neglect either a base in reality or a rigorous application of intellect. His fusion of idealist vision, realistic detail, and artistic discipline made him the most influential poet of the nineteenth century, and the first poet of the modern age.

The selections printed here, from a range of Baudelaire's most influential lyric and prose poems, are translated by different modern poets. While remaining faithful to the original text, each translation necessarily stresses different aspects (for example, images, meter and rhyme, word order, tone, a particular set of associations when more than one is possible) to create a genuine English poem. The footnotes occasionally point out elements that are especially significant in the French text.

Lois Boe Hyslop, *Charles Baudelaire Revisited* (1992), is a useful introductory survey. Enid Starkie, *Baudelaire* (1953), is the fullest biography in English. Henri Peyre, ed., *Baudelaire: A Collection of Critical Essays* (1962), contains eleven essays on *The Flowers of Evil*, with selections by major writers including Proust. Harold Bloom, ed., *Charles Baudelaire* (1987), presents ten contemporary critics on Baudelaire's themes, literary and artistic criticism, selected texts, and relation to Poe. Patricia Clements, *Baudelaire and the English Tradition* (1985), is a penetrating analysis of Baudelaire's influence on English literature from Swinburne to T. S. Eliot; it includes comparisons and contrasts with late symbolist tradition. Margery A. Evans, *Baudelaire and Intertextuality: Poetry at the Crossroads* (1993), analyzes the literary conventions manipulated in the prose poems. Rosemary Lloyd's *Selected Letters of Charles Baudelaire: The Conquest of Solitude* (1986) contains a range of personal and literary letters. Laurence M. Porter, *The Crisis of French Symbolism* (1990), has a interesting chapter on Baudelaire's relation to his imagined audience. F. W. Leakey, *Baudelaire, Les Fleurs du Mal* (1992), is a short guide to the poet's major work.

PRONOUNCING GLOSSARY

The following list uses common English syllables and stress accents to provide rough equivalents of selected words whose pronunciation may be unfamiliar to the general reader.

Baudelaire: *boh-d'lair'*

ennui: *on-wee'*

Pylades: *pill'-ah-deez*

THE FLOWERS OF EVIL

To the Reader[1]

Infatuation, sadism, lust, avarice
possess our souls and drain the body's force;
we spoonfeed our adorable remorse,
like whores or beggars nourishing their lice.

Our sins are mulish, our confessions lies;   5
we play to the grandstand with our promises,
we pray for tears to wash our filthiness,
importantly pissing hogwash through our styes.

The devil, watching by our sickbeds, hissed
old smut and folk-songs to our soul, until   10
the soft and precious metal of our will
boiled off in vapor for this scientist.

Each day his flattery[2] makes us eat a toad,
and each step forward is a step to hell,
unmoved, though previous corpses and their smell   15
asphyxiate our progress on this road.

Like the poor lush who cannot satisfy,
we try to force our sex with counterfeits,
die drooling on the deliquescent tits,
mouthing the rotten orange we suck dry.   20

Gangs of demons are boozing in our brain—
ranked, swarming, like a million warrior-ants,[3]
they drown and choke the cistern of our wants;
each time we breathe, we tear our lungs with pain.

If poison, arson, sex, narcotics, knives   25
have not yet ruined us and stitched their quick,
loud patterns on the canvas of our lives,
it is because our souls are still too sick.[4]

Among the vermin, jackals, panthers, lice,
gorillas and tarantulas that suck   30
and snatch and scratch and defecate and fuck
in the disorderly circus of our vice,

there's one more ugly and abortive birth.
It makes no gestures, never beats its breast,
yet it would murder for a moment's rest,[5]   35
and willingly annihilate the earth.

It's BOREDOM. Tears have glued its eyes together.
You know it well, my Reader. This obscene
beast chain-smokes yawning for the guillotine—
you—hypocrite Reader—my double—my brother!   40

---

1. Translated by Robert Lowell. The translation pays primary attention to the insistent rhythm of the
original poetic language and keeps the *abba* rhyme scheme.   2. The Devil is literally described as a
puppet master controlling our strings.   3. Literally, intestinal worms.   4. Literally, not bold enough.
5. Literally, swallow the world in a yawn.

Correspondences[1]

Nature is a temple whose living colonnades
Breathe forth a mystic speech in fitful sighs;
Man wanders among symbols in those glades
Where all things watch him with familiar eyes.

Like dwindling echoes gathered far away   5
Into a deep and thronging unison
Huge as the night or as the light of day,
All scents and sounds and colors meet as one.

Perfumes there are as sweet as the oboe's sound,
Green as the prairies, fresh as a child's caress,[2]   10
—And there are others, rich, corrupt, profound[3]

And of an infinite pervasiveness,
Like myrrh, or musk, or amber,[4] that excite
The ecstasies of sense, the soul's delight.

Correspondances

La Nature est un temple où de vivants piliers
Laissent parfois sortir de confuses paroles;
L'homme y passe à travers des forêts de symboles
Qui l'observent avec des regards familiers.

Comme de longs échos qui de loin se confondent   5
Dans une ténébreuse et profonde unité,
Vaste comme la nuit et comme la clarté,
Les parfums, les couleurs et les sons se répondent.

Il est des parfums frais comme des chairs d'enfants,
Doux comme les hautbois, verts comme les prairies,   10
—Et d'autres, corrompus, riches et triomphants,

Ayant l'expansion des choses infinies,
Comme l'ambre, le musc, le benjoin et l'encens,
Qui chantent les transports de l'esprit et des sens.

Her Hair[1]

O fleece, that down the neck waves to the nape!
O curls! O perfume nonchalant and rare!
O ecstacy! To fill this alcove[2] shape
With memories that in these tresses sleep,
I would shake them like pennons in the air!   5

1. Translated by Richard Wilbur. The translation keeps the intricate melody of the sonnet's original rhyme scheme.   2. Literally, flesh.   3. Literally, triumphant.   4. Or ambergris, a substance secreted by whales. Ambergris and musk (a secretion of the male musk deer) are used in making perfume.   1. Translated by Doreen Bell. The translation emulates the French original's challenging *abaab* rhyme pattern.   2. Bedroom.

Languorous Asia, burning Africa,
And a far world, defunct almost, absent,
Within your aromatic forest stay!
As other souls on music drift away,
Mine, o my love! still floats upon your scent.   10

I shall go there where, full of sap, both tree
And man swoon in the heat of southern climes;
Strong tresses, be the swell that carries me!
I dream upon your sea of ebony
Of dazzling sails, of oarsmen, masts and flames: 15

A sun-drenched and reverberating port,
Where I imbibe color and sound and scent;
Where vessels, gliding through the gold and moire,
Open their vast arms as they leave the shore
To clasp the pure and shimmering firmament.   20

I'll plunge my head, enamored of its pleasure,
In this black ocean where the other hides;
My subtle spirit then will know a measure
Of fertile idleness and fragrant leisure,
Lulled by the infinite rhythm of its tides!   25

Pavilion, of blue-shadowed tresses spun,
You give me back the azure from afar;
And where the twisted locks are fringed with down
Lurk mingled odors I grow drunk upon
Of oil of coconut, of musk and tar.   30

A long time! always! my hand in your hair
Will sow the stars of sapphire, pearl, ruby,
That you be never deaf to my desire,
My oasis and gourd whence I aspire
To drink deep of the wine of memory![3]   35

A Carcass[1]

Remember, my love, the item you saw
    That beautiful morning in June:
By a bend in the path a carcass reclined
    On a bed sown with pebbles and stones;

Her legs were spread out like a lecherous whore,   5
    Sweating out poisonous fumes,
Who opened in slick invitational style
    Her stinking and festering womb.

The sun on this rottenness focused its rays
    To cook the cadaver till done,   10
And render to Nature a hundredfold gift
    Of all she'd united in one.

---

3. The last two lines are a question: "Are you not...?"   1. Translated by James McGowan with special attention to imagery. The alternation of long and short lines in English emulates the French meter's rhythmic swing between twelve-syllable and eight-syllable lines in an *abab* rhyme scheme.

And the sky cast an eye on this marvelous meat
  As over the flowers in bloom.
The stench was so wretched that there on the grass   15
  You nearly collapsed in a swoon.

The flies buzzed and droned on these bowels of filth
  Where an army of maggots arose,
Which flowed like a liquid and thickening stream
  On the animate rags of her clothes.[2]   20

And it rose and it fell, and pulsed like a wave,
  Rushing and bubbling with health.
One could say that this carcass, blown with vague breath,
  Lived in increasing itself.

And this whole teeming world made a musical sound   25
  Like babbling brooks and the breeze,
Or the grain that a man with a winnowing-fan
  Turns with a rhythmical ease.

The shapes wore away as if only a dream
  Like a sketch that is left on the page   30
Which the artist forgot and can only complete
  On the canvas, with memory's aid.

From back in the rocks, a pitiful bitch
  Eyed us with angry distaste,
Awaiting the moment to snatch from the bones   35
  The morsel she'd dropped in her haste.

—And you, in your turn, will be rotten as this:
  Horrible, filthy, undone,
Oh sun of my nature and star of my eyes,
  My passion, my angel[3] in one!   40

Yes, such will you be, oh regent of grace,
  After the rites have been read,
Under the weeds, under blossoming grass
  As you molder with bones of the dead.

Ah then, oh my beauty, explain to the worms   45
  Who cherish your body so fine,
That I am the keeper for corpses of love
  Of the form, and the essence divine![4]

Invitation to the Voyage[1]

My child, my sister, dream
How sweet all things would seem
Were we in that kind land to live together,

---

2. By extension. The torn flesh is described as "living rags."   3. Series of conventional Petrarchan images that idealize the beloved.   4. "Any form created by man is immortal. For form is independent of matter. . ." from Baudelaire's journal *My Heart Laid Bare*, LXXX.   1. Translated by Richard Wilbur. The translation maintains both the rhyme scheme and the rocking motion of the original meter, which follows an unusual pattern of two five-syllable lines followed by one seven-syllable line, and a seven-syllable couplet as refrain.

And there love slow and long,
There love and die among
Those scenes that image you, that sumptuous weather.
Drowned suns that glimmer there
Through cloud-disheveled air
Move me with such a mystery as appears
Within those other skies
Of your treacherous eyes
When I behold them shining through their tears.

There, there is nothing else but grace and measure,
Richness, quietness, and pleasure.

Furniture that wears
The lustre of the years
Softly would glow within our glowing chamber,
Flowers of rarest bloom
Proffering their perfume
Mixed with the vague fragrances of amber;
Gold ceilings would there be,
Mirrors deep as the sea,
The walls all in an Eastern splendor hung—
Nothing but should address
The soul's loneliness,
Speaking her sweet and secret native tongue.

There, there is nothing else but grace and measure,
Richness, quietness, and pleasure.

See, sheltered from the swells
There in the still canals
Those drowsy ships that dream of sailing forth;
It is to satisfy
Your least desire, they ply
Hither through all the waters of the earth.
The sun at close of day
Clothes the fields of hay,
Then the canals, at last the town entire
In hyacinth and gold:
Slowly the land is rolled
Sleepward under a sea of gentle fire.

There, there is nothing else but grace and measure,
Richness, quietness, and pleasure.

Song of Autumn I[1]

Soon we shall plunge into the chilly fogs;
Farewell, swift light! our summers are too short!
I hear already the mournful fall of logs
Re-echoing from the pavement of the court.

---

1. Translated by C. F. MacIntyre to follow the original rhyme pattern.

All of winter will gather in my soul: 5
Hate, anger, horror, chills, the hard forced work;
And, like the sun in his hell by the north pole,
My heart will be only a red and frozen block.

I shudder, hearing every log that falls;
No scaffold could be built with hollower sounds. 10
My spirit is like a tower whose crumbling walls
The tireless battering-ram brings to the ground.

It seems to me, lulled by monotonous shocks,
As if they were hastily nailing a coffin today.
For whom? — Yesterday was summer. Now autumn knocks. 15
That mysterious sound is like someone's going away.

Spleen LXXVIII[1]

Old Pluvius,[2] month of rains, in peevish mood
Pours from his urn chill winter's sodden gloom
On corpses fading in the near graveyard,
On foggy suburbs pours life's tedium.

My cat seeks out a litter on the stones, 5
Her mangy body turning without rest.
An ancient poet's soul in monotones
Whines in the rain-spouts like a chilblained ghost.

A great bell mourns, a wet log wrapped in smoke
Sings in falsetto to the wheezing clock, 10
While from a rankly perfumed deck of cards
(A dropsical old crone's fatal bequest)
The Queen of Spades, the dapper Jack of Hearts
Speak darkly of dead loves, how they were lost.

Spleen LXXIX[1]

I have more memories than if I had lived a thousand years.

Even a bureau crammed with souvenirs,
Old bills, love letters, photographs, receipts,
Court depositions, locks of hair in plaits,
Hides fewer secrets than my brain could yield. 5
It's like a tomb, a corpse-filled Potter's Field,[2]
A pyramid where the dead lie down by scores.

1. Translated by Kenneth O. Hanson, with emphasis on the imagery. The French original uses identical *abab* rhymes in the two quatrains and shifts to *ccd, eed* in the tercets.   2. Pluvius is literally "the rainy time" (Latin), a period extending from January 20 to February 18 as the fifth month of the French Revolutionary calendar.   1. Translated by Anthony Hecht. The translation follows the original rhymed couplets except for one technical impossibility: Baudelaire's repetition (in a poem about monotony) of an identical rhyme for eight lines (lines 11–18, the sound of long *a*).   2. A general term describing the common cemetery for those buried at public expense.

I am a graveyard that the moon abhors:
Like guilty qualms, the worms burrow and nest
Thickly in bodies that I loved the best. 10
I'm a stale boudoir where old-fashioned clothes
Lie scattered among wilted fern and rose,
Where only the Boucher girls[3] in pale pastels
Can breathe the uncorked scents and faded smells.

Nothing can equal those days for endlessness 15
When in the winter's blizzardy caress
Indifference expanding to Ennui[4]
Takes on the feel of Immortality.
O living matter, henceforth you're no more
Than a cold stone encompassed by vague fear 20
And by the desert, and the mist and sun;
An ancient Sphinx ignored by everyone,
Left off the map, whose bitter irony
Is to sing as the sun sets in that dry sea.[5]

PARIS SPLEEN[1]

Anywhere out of the World[2]

Life is a hospital where every patient is obsessed by the desire of changing beds. One would like to suffer opposite the stove, another is sure he would get well beside the window.

It always seems to me that I should be happy anywhere but where I am, and this question of moving is one that I am eternally discussing with my soul.

"Tell me, my soul, poor chilly soul, how would you like to live in Lisbon? It must be warm there, and you would be as blissful as a lizard in the sun. It is a city by the sea; they say that it is built of marble, and that its inhabitants have such a horror of the vegetable kingdom that they tear up all the trees. You see it is a country after my own heart; a country entirely made of mineral and light, and with liquid to reflect them."

My soul does not reply.

"Since you are so fond of being motionless and watching the pageantry of movement, would you like to live in the beatific land of Holland? Perhaps you could enjoy yourself in that country which you have so long admired in paintings on museum walls. What do you say to Rotterdam,[3] you who love forests of masts, and ships that are moored on the doorsteps of houses?"

3. François Boucher (1703–1770), court painter for Louis XV of France, drew many pictures of young women clothed and nude.   4. Melancholy, paralyzing boredom.   5. Baudelaire combines two references to ancient Egypt, the sphinx and the legendary statue of Memnon at Thebes, which was supposed to sing at sunset.   1. Translated by Louise Varèse.   2. The title (given in English by Baudelaire) is based on a line from Thomas Hood's poem *Bridge of Sighs*: "Anywhere, anywhere—out of the world." Baudelaire probably found the reference in Poe's *Poetic Principle*.   3. Large Dutch seaport.

My soul remains silent.

"Perhaps you would like Batavia[4] better? There, moreover, we should find the wit of Europe wedded to the beauty of the tropics."

Not a word. Can my soul be dead?

"Have you sunk into so deep a stupor that you are happy only in your unhappiness? If that is the case, let us fly to countries that are the counterfeits of Death. I know just the place for us, poor soul. We will pack up our trunks for Torneo.[5] We will go still farther, to the farthest end of the Baltic Sea; still farther from life if possible; we will settle at the Pole. There the sun only obliquely grazes the earth, and the slow alternations of daylight and night abolish variety and increase that other half of nothingness, monotony. There we can take deep baths of darkness, while sometimes for our entertainment, the Aurora Borealis will shoot up its rose-red sheafs like the reflections of the fireworks of hell!"

At last my soul explodes! "Anywhere! Just so it is out of the world!"

4. Former name of Djakarta, capital of the Dutch East Indies and now the capital city of Indonesia.
5. A city in Finland.

LEO TOLSTOY

1828–1910

Count Leo Tolstoy excited the interest of Europe mainly as a public figure: a count owning large estates who decided to give up his wealth and live like a simple Russian peasant—to dress in a blouse, to eat peasant food, and even to plow the fields and make shoes with his own hands. By the time of his death he had become the leader of a religious cult, the propounder of a new religion. It was, in substance, a highly simplified primitive Christianity that he reduced to a few moral commands (such as, "Do not resist evil") and from which he drew, with radical consistency, a complete condemnation of modern civilization: the state, courts and law, war, patriotism, marriage, modern art and literature, science and medicine. In debating this Christian anarchism people have tended to forget that Tolstoy established his command of the public ear as a novelist, or they have exaggerated the contrast between the early worldly novelist and the later prophet who repudiated all his early, great novelistic work: War and Peace, the enormous epic of the 1812 invasion of Russia, and Anna Karenina, the story of an adulterous love, superbly realized in accurately imagined detail.

Tolstoy was born at Yásnaya Polyána, his mother's estate near Tula (about 130 miles south of Moscow), on August 28, 1828. His father was a retired lieutenant colonel; one of his ancestors, the first count, had served Peter the Great as an ambassador. His mother's father was a Russian general-in-chief. Tolstoy lost both parents early in his life and was brought up by aunts. He went to the University of Kazan between 1844 and 1847, drifted along aimlessly for a few years more, and in 1851 became a cadet in the Caucasus. As an artillery officer he saw action in the wars with the mountain tribes and again, in 1854–55, during the Crimean War against the French and English. Tolstoy had written fictional reminiscences of his childhood while he was in the Caucasus, and during the Crimean War he wrote war stories, which established his literary reputation. For some years he lived on his estate, where he founded and himself taught an extremely "progressive" school for peasant children. He made two trips to western Europe, in 1857 and in 1860–61. In 1862 he married the daughter of a physician, Sonya Bers, with whom he had thirteen children.

In the first years of his married life, between 1863 and 1869, he wrote his enormous novel *War and Peace*. The book made him famous in Russia but was not translated into English until long afterward. Superficially, *War and Peace* is an historical novel about the Napoléonic invasion of Russia in 1812, a huge swarming epic of a nation's resistance to the foreigner. Tolstoy himself interprets history in general as a struggle of anonymous collective forces that are moved by unknown irrational impulses, waves of communal feeling. Heroes, great men and women, are actually not heroes but merely insignificant puppets; the best general is the one who does nothing to prevent the unknown course of Providence. But *War and Peace* is not only an impressive and vivid panorama of historical events but also the profound story—centered in two main characters, Pierre Bezukhov and Prince Andrey Bolkonsky—of a search for meaning in life. Andrey finds meaning in love and forgiveness of his enemies. Pierre, at the end of a long groping struggle, an education by suffering, finds it in an acceptance of ordinary existence, its duties and pleasures, the family, the continuity of the race.

Tolstoy's next long novel, *Anna Karenina* (1875–77), resumes this second thread of *War and Peace*. It is a novel of contemporary manners, a narrative of adultery and suicide. But this vivid story, told with incomparable concrete imagination, is counterpointed and framed by a second story, that of Levin, another seeker after the meaning of life, a figure who represents the author as Pierre did in the earlier book; the work ends with a promise of salvation, with the ideal of a life in which we should "remember God." Thus *Anna Karenina* also anticipates the approaching crisis in Tolstoy's life. When it came, with the sudden revulsion he describes in *A Confession* (1879), he condemned his earlier books and spent the next years in writing pamphlets and tracts expounding his religion.

Only slowly did Tolstoy return to the writing of fiction, now regarded entirely as a means of presenting his creed. The earlier novels seemed to him unclear in their message, overdetailed in their method. Hence Tolstoy tried to simplify his art; he wrote plays with a thesis, stories that are like fables or parables, and one long, rather inferior novel, *The Resurrection* (1899), his most savage satire on Russian and modern institutions.

In 1901 Tolstoy was excommunicated. A disagreement with his wife about the nature of the good life and about financial matters sharpened into a conflict over his last will, which finally led to a complete break: he left home in the company of a doctor friend. He caught cold on the train journey south and died in the house of the stationmaster of Astápovo, on November 20, 1910.

If we look back on Tolstoy's work as a whole, we must recognize its continuity. From the very beginning he was a Rousseauist. As early as 1851, when he was in the Caucasus, his diary announced his intention of founding a new, simplified religion. Even as a young man on his estate he had lived quite simply, like a peasant, except for occasional sprees and debauches. He had been horrified by war from the very beginning, though he admired the heroism of the individual soldier and had remnants of patriotic feeling. All his books concern the same theme, the good life, and they all say that the good life lies outside of civilization, near to the soil, in simplicity and humility, in love of one's neighbor. Power, the lust for power, luxury, are always evil.

Tolstoy's roots as a novelist are part of another, older realistic tradition. He read and knew the English writers of the eighteenth century—and also William Makepeace Thackeray and Anthony Trollope—though he did not care for the recent French writers (he was strong in his disapproval of Gustave Flaubert) except for

The Death of Iván Ilyich[1]

I

During an interval in the Melvínski trial in the large building of the Law Courts the members and public prosecutor met in Iván Egórovich Shébek's private room, where the conversation turned on the celebrated Krasóvski case. Fëdor Vasílievich warmly maintained that it was not subject to their jurisdiction, Iván Egórovich maintained the contrary, while Peter Ivánovich, not having entered into the discussion at the start, took no part in it but looked through the *Gazette* which had just been handed in.

"Gentlemen," he said, "Iván Ilyich has died!"

"You don't say!"

"Here read it yourself," replied Peter Ivánovich, handing Fëdor Vasílievich the paper still damp from the press. Surrounded by a black border were the words: "Praskóvya Fëdorovna Goloviná, with profound sorrow, informs relatives and friends of the demise of her beloved husband Iván Ilyich Golovín, Member of the Court of Justice, which occurred on February the 4th of this year 1882. The funeral will take place on Friday at one o'clock in the afternoon."

Iván Ilyich had been a colleague of the gentlemen present and was liked by them all. He had been ill for some weeks with an illness said to be incurable. His post had been kept open for him, but there had been conjectures that in case of his death Alexéev might receive his appointment, and that either Vínnikov or Shtábel would succeed Alexéev. So on receiving the news of Iván Ilyich's death the first thought of each of the gentlemen in that private room was of the changes and promotions it might occasion among themselves or their acquaintances.

"I shall be sure to get Shtábel's place or Vínnikov's," thought Fëdor Vasílievich. "I was promised that long ago, and the promotion means an extra eight hundred rubles a year for me besides the allowance."

"Now I must apply for my brother-in-law's transfer from Kalúga," thought Peter Ivánovich. "My wife will be very glad, and then she won't be able to say that I never do anything for her relations."

"I thought he would never leave his bed again," said Peter Ivánovich aloud. "It's very sad."

"But what really was the matter with him?"

"The doctors couldn't say—at least they could, but each of them said something different. When last I saw him I thought he was getting better."

"And I haven't been to see him since the holidays. I always meant to go."

"Had he any property?"

"I think his wife had a little—but something quite trifling."

"We shall have to go to see her, but they live so terribly far away."

"Far away from you, you mean. Everything's far away from your place."

"You see, he never can forgive my living on the other side of the river," said Peter Ivánovich, smiling at Shébek. Then, still talking of the distances

---

1. Translated by Louise Maude and Aylmer Maude.

between different parts of the city, they returned to the Court.
Besides considerations as to the possible transfers and promotions likely
to result from Iván Ilyich's death, the mere fact of the death of a near
acquaintance aroused, as usual, in all who heard of it the complacent
feeling that, "it is he who is dead and not I."

Each one thought or felt, "Well, he's dead but I'm alive!" But the more
intimate of Iván Ilyich's acquaintances, his so-called friends, could not
help thinking also that they would now have to fulfil the very tiresome
demands of propriety by attending the funeral service and paying a visit of
condolence to the widow.

Fëdor Vasílievich and Peter Ivánovich had been his nearest acquaintances. Peter Ivánovich had studied law with Iván Ilyich and had considered himself to be under obligations to him.

Having told his wife at dinner-time of Iván Ilyich's death, and of his
conjecture that it might be possible to get her brother transferred to their
circuit, Peter Ivánovich sacrificed his usual nap, put on his evening
clothes, and drove to Iván Ilyich's house.

At the entrance stood a carriage and two cabs. Leaning against the wall
in the hall downstairs near the cloak-stand was a coffin-lid covered with
cloth of gold, ornamented with gold cord and tassels, that had been polished up with metal powder. Two ladies in black were taking off their fur
cloaks. Peter Ivánovich recognized one of them as Iván Ilyich's sister, but
the other was a stranger to him. His colleague Schwartz was just coming
downstairs, but on seeing Peter Ivánovich enter he stopped and winked at
him, as if to say: "Iván Ilyich has made a mess of things—not like you and
me."

Schwartz's face with his Piccadilly whiskers, and his slim figure in evening dress, had as usual an air of elegant solemnity which contrasted with
the playfulness of his character and had a special piquancy here, or so it
seemed to Peter Ivánovich.

Peter Ivánovich allowed the ladies to precede him and slowly followed
them upstairs. Schwartz did not come down but remained where he was,
and Peter Ivánovich understood that he wanted to arrange where they
should play bridge that evening. The ladies went upstairs to the widow's
room, and Schwartz with seriously compressed lips but a playful look in
his eyes, indicated by a twist of his eyebrows the room to the right where
the body lay.

Peter Ivánovich, like everyone else on such occasions, entered feeling
uncertain what he would have to do. All he knew was that at such times
it is always safe to cross oneself. But he was not quite sure whether one
should make obeisances while doing so. He therefore adopted a middle
course. On entering the room he began crossing himself and made a slight
movement resembling a bow. At the same time, as far as the motion of his
head and arm allowed, he surveyed the room. Two young men—apparently nephews, one of whom was a high-school pupil—were leaving the
room, crossing themselves as they did so. An old woman was standing
motionless, and a lady with strangely arched eyebrows was saying something to her in a whisper. A vigorous, resolute Church Reader, in a frock-
coat, was reading something in a loud voice with an expression that pre-

cluded any contradiction. The butler's assistant, Gerásim, stepping lightly in front of Peter Ivánovich, was strewing something on the floor. Noticing this, Peter Ivánovich was immediately aware of a faint odour of a decomposing body.

The last time he had called on Iván Ilyich, Peter Ivánovich had seen Gerásim in the study. Iván Ilyich had been particularly fond of him and he was performing the duty of a sick nurse.

Peter Ivánovich continued to make the sign of the cross slightly inclining his head in an intermediate direction between the coffin, the Reader, and the icons on the table in a corner of the room. Afterwards, when it seemed to him that this movement of his arm in crossing himself had gone on too long, he stopped and began to look at the corpse.

The dead man lay, as dead men always lie, in a specially heavy way, his rigid limbs sunk in the soft cushions of the coffin, with the head forever bowed on the pillow. His yellow waxen brow with bald patches over his sunken temples was thrust up in the way peculiar to the dead, the protruding nose seeming to press on the upper lip. He was much changed and had grown even thinner since Peter Ivánovich had last seen him, but, as is always the case with the dead, his face was handsomer and above all more dignified than when he was alive. The expression on the face said that what was necessary had been accomplished, and accomplished rightly. Besides this there was in that expression a reproach and a warning to the living. This warning seemed to Peter Ivánovich out of place, or at least not applicable to him. He felt a certain discomfort and so he hurriedly crossed himself once more and turned and went out of the door—too hurriedly and too regardless of propriety, as he himself was aware.

Schwartz was waiting for him in the adjoining room with legs spread wide apart and both hands toying with his top-hat behind his back. The mere sight of that playful, well-groomed, and elegant figure refreshed Peter Ivánovich. He felt that Schwartz was above all these happenings and could not surrender to any depressing influences. His very look said that this incident of a church service for Iván Ilyich could not be a sufficient reason for infringing the order of the session—in other words, that it would certainly not prevent his unwrapping a new pack of cards and shuffling them that evening while a footman placed four fresh candles on the table: in fact, that there was no reason for supposing that this incident would hinder their spending the evening agreeably. Indeed he said this in a whisper as Peter Ivánovich passed him, proposing that they should meet for a game at Fëdor Vasílievich's. But apparently Peter Ivánovich was not destined to play bridge that evening. Praskóvya Fëdorovna (a short, fat woman who despite all efforts to the contrary had continued to broaden steadily from her shoulders downwards and who had the same extraordinary arched eyebrows as the lady who had been standing by the coffin), dressed all in black, her head covered with lace, came out of her own room with some other ladies, conducted them to the room where the dead body lay, and said: "The service will begin immediately. Please go in."

Schwartz, making an indefinite bow, stood still, evidently neither accepting nor declining this invitation. Praskóvya Fëdorovna recognizing Peter Ivánovich, sighed, went close up to him, took his hand, and said: "I know you were a true friend to Iván Ilyich . . ." and looked at him awaiting some suitable response. And Peter Ivánovich knew that, just as it had been the right thing to cross himself in that room, so what he had to do here was to press her hand, sigh, and say, "Believe me . . ." So he did all this and as he did it felt that the desired result had been achieved: that both he and she were touched.

"Come with me. I want to speak to you before it begins," said the widow. "Give me your arm."

Peter Ivánovich gave her his arm and they went to the inner rooms, passing Schwartz who winked at Peter Ivánovich compassionately.

"That does for our bridge! Don't object if we find another player. Perhaps you can cut in when you do escape," said his playful look.

Peter Ivánovich sighed still more deeply and despondently, and Praskóvya Fëdorovna pressed his arm gratefully. When they reached the drawing-room, upholstered in pink cretonne and lighted by a dim lamp, they sat down at the table—she on a sofa and Peter Ivánovich on a low hassock, the springs of which yielded spasmodically under his weight. Praskóvya Fëdorovna had been on the point of warning him to take another seat, but felt that such a warning was out of keeping with her present condition and so changed her mind. As he sat down on the hassock Peter Ivánovich recalled how Iván Ilyich had arranged this room and had consulted him regarding this pink cretonne with green leaves. The whole room was full of furniture and knick-knacks, and on her way to the sofa the lace of the widow's black shawl caught on the carved edge of the table. Peter Ivánovich rose to detach it, and the springs of the hassock, relieved of his weight, rose also and gave him a push. The widow began detaching her shawl herself, and Peter Ivánovich again sat down, suppressing the rebellious springs of the hassock under him. But the widow had not quite freed herself and Peter Ivánovich got up again, and again the hassock rebelled and even creaked. When this was all over she took out a clean cambric handkerchief and began to weep. The episode with the shawl and the struggle with the hassock had cooled Peter Ivánovich's emotions and he sat there with a sullen look on his face. This awkward situation was interrupted by Sokolóv, Iván Ilyich's butler, who came to report that the plot in the cemetery that Praskóvya Fëdorovna had chosen would cost two hundred rubles. She stopped weeping and, looking at Peter Ivánovich with the air of a victim, remarked in French that it was very hard for her. Peter Ivánovich made a silent gesture signifying his full conviction that it must indeed be so.

"Please smoke," she said in a magnanimous yet crushed voice, and turned to discuss with Sokolóv the price of the plot for the grave.

Peter Ivánovich while lighting his cigarette heard her inquiring very circumstantially into the prices of different plots in the cemetery and finally decide which she would take. When that was done she gave instructions about engaging the choir. Sokolóv then left the room.

"I look after everything myself," she told Peter Ivánovich, shifting the albums that lay on the table; and noticing that the table was endangered by his cigarette-ash, she immediately passed him an ashtray, saying as she did so: "I consider it an affectation to say that my grief prevents my attending to practical affairs. On the contrary, if anything can—I won't say console me, but—distract me, it is seeing to everything concerning him." She again took out her handkerchief as if preparing to cry, but suddenly, as if mastering her feeling, she shook herself and began to speak calmly. "But there is something I want to talk to you about."

Peter Ivánovich bowed, keeping control of the springs of the hassock, which immediately began quivering under him.

"He suffered terribly the last few days."

"Did he?" said Peter Ivánovich.

"Oh, terribly! He screamed unceasingly, not for minutes but for hours. For the last three days he screamed incessantly. It was unendurable. I cannot understand how I bore it; you could hear him three rooms off. Oh, what I have suffered!"

"Is it possible that he was conscious all that time?" asked Peter Ivánovich.

"Yes," she whispered. "To the last moment. He took leave of us a quarter of an hour before he died, and asked us to take Vásya away."

The thought of the sufferings of this man he had known so intimately, first as a merry little boy, then as a school-mate, and later as a grown-up colleague, suddenly struck Peter Ivánovich with horror, despite an unpleasant consciousness of his own and this woman's dissimulation. He again saw that brow, and that nose pressing down on the lip, and felt afraid for himself.

"Three days of frightful suffering and then death! Why, that might suddenly, at any time, happen to me," he thought, and for a moment felt terrified. But—he did not himself know how—the customary reflection at once occurred to him that this had happened to Iván Ilyich and not to him, and that it should not and could not happen to him, and that to think that it could would be yielding to depression which he ought not to do, as Schwartz's expression plainly showed. After which reflection Peter Ivánovich felt reassured, and began to ask with interest about the details of Iván Ilyich's death, as though death was an accident natural to Iván Ilyich but certainly not to himself.

After many details of the really dreadful physical sufferings Iván Ilyich had endured (which details he learnt only from the effect those sufferings had produced on Praskóvya Fëdorovna's nerves) the widow apparently found it necessary to get to business.

"Oh, Peter Ivánovich, how hard it is! How terribly, terribly hard!" and she again began to weep.

Peter Ivánovich sighed and waited for her to finish blowing her nose. When she had done so he said, "Believe me . . ." and she again began talking and brought out what was evidently her chief concern with him— namely, to question him as to how she could obtain a grant of money from the government on the occasion of her husband's death. She made it appear that she was asking Peter Ivánovich's advice about her pension, but he soon saw that she already knew about that to the minutest detail, more even than he did himself. She knew how much could be got out of the government in consequence of her husband's death, but wanted to find out whether she could possibly extract something more. Peter Ivánovich tried to think of some means of doing so, but after reflecting for a while and, out of propriety, condemning the government for its niggardliness, he said he thought that nothing more could be got. Then she sighed and evidently began to devise means of getting rid of her visitor. Noticing this, he put out his cigarette, rose, pressed her hand, and went out into the anteroom.

In the dining-room where the clock stood that Iván Ilyich had liked so much and had bought at an antique shop, Peter Ivánovich met a priest and a few acquaintances who had come to attend the service, and he recognized Iván Ilyich's daughter, a handsome young woman. She was in black and her slim figure appeared slimmer than ever. She had a gloomy, determined, almost angry expression, and bowed to Peter Ivánovich as though he were in some way to blame. Behind her, with the same offended look, stood a wealthy young man, an examining magistrate, whom Peter Ivánovich also knew and who was her fiancé, as he had heard. He bowed mournfully to them and was about to pass into the death-chamber, when from under the stairs appeared the figure of Iván Ilyich's schoolboy son, who was extremely like this father. He seemed a little Iván Ilyich, such as Peter Ivánovich remembered when they studied law together. His tear-stained eyes had in them the look that is seen in the eyes of boys of thirteen or fourteen who are not pure-minded.

When he saw Peter Ivánovich he scowled morosely and shamefacedly. Peter Ivánovich nodded to him and entered the death-chamber. The service began: candles, groans, incense, tears, and sobs. Peter Ivánovich stood looking gloomily down at his feet. He did not look once at the dead man, did not yield to any depressing influence, and was one of the first to leave the room. There was no one in the anteroom, but Gerásim darted out of the dead man's room, rummaged with his strong hands among the fur coats to find Peter Ivánovich's and helped him on with it.

"Well, friend Gerásim," said Peter Ivánovich, so as to say something. "It's a sad affair, isn't it?"

"It's God's will. We shall all come to it some day," said Gerásim, displaying his teeth—the even, white teeth of a healthy peasant—and, like a man in the thick of urgent work, he briskly opened the front door, called the coachman, helped Peter Ivánovich into the sledge, and sprang back to the porch as if in readiness for what he had to do next.

Peter Ivánovich found the fresh air particularly pleasant after the smell of incense, the dead body, and carbolic acid.

"Where to, sir?" asked the coachman.

"It's not too late even now. . . . I'll call round on Fëdor Vasílievich."

He accordingly drove there and found them just finishing the first rubber, so that it was quite convenient for him to cut in.

II

Iván Ilyich's life had been most simple and most ordinary and therefore most terrible.

He had been a member of the Court of Justice, and died at the age of forty-five. His father had been an official who after serving in various ministries and departments in Petersburg had made the sort of career which brings men to positions from which by reason of their long service they cannot be dismissed, though they are obviously unfit to hold any responsible position, and for whom therefore posts are specially created, which though fictitious, carry salaries of from six to ten thousand rubles that are not fictitious, and in receipt of which they live on to a great age.

Such was the Privy Councillor and superfluous member of various superfluous institutions, Ilya Efímovich Golovín.

He had three sons, of whom Iván Ilyich was the second. The eldest son was following in his father's footsteps only in another department, and was already approaching that stage in the service at which a similar sinecure would be reached. The third son was a failure. He had ruined his prospects in a number of positions and was now serving in the railway department. His father and brothers, and still more their wives, not merely disliked meeting him, but avoided remembering his existence unless compelled to do so. His sister had married Baron Greff, a Petersburg official of her father's type. Iván Ilyich was *le phénix de la famille*[2] as people said. He was neither as cold and formal as his elder brother nor as wild as the younger, but was a happy mean between them—an intelligent, polished, lively and agreeable man. He had studied with his younger brother at the School of Law, but the latter had failed to complete the course and was expelled when he was in the fifth class. Iván Ilyich finished the course well. Even when he was at the School of Law he was just what he remained for the rest of his life: a capable, cheerful, good-natured, and sociable man, though strict in the fulfilment of what he considered to be his duty: and he considered his duty to be what was so considered by those in authority. Neither as a boy nor as a man was he a toady, but from early youth was by nature attracted to people of high station as a fly is drawn to the light, assimilating their ways and views of life and establishing friendly relations with them. All the enthusiasms of childhood and youth passed without leaving much trace on him; he succumbed to sensuality, to vanity, and latterly among the highest classes to liberalism, but always within limits which his instinct unfailingly indicated to him as correct.

At school he had done things which had formerly seemed to him very horrid and made him feel disgusted with himself when he did them; but when later on he saw that such actions were done by people of good position and that they did not regard them as wrong, he was able not exactly to regard them as right, but to forget about them entirely or not be at all troubled at remembering them.

Having graduated from the School of Law and qualified for the tenth rank of the civil service, and having received money from his father for his equipment, Iván Ilyich ordered himself clothes at Scharmer's, the fashionable tailor, hung a medallion inscribed *respice finem*[3] on his watchchain, took leave of his professor and the prince who was patron of the school, had a farewell dinner with his comrades at Donon's first-class restaurant, and with his new and fashionable portmanteau, linen, clothes,

---

2. The phoenix of the family (French). The word *phoenix* is used here to mean "rare bird," "prodigy."
3. Regard the end (a Latin motto).

shaving and other toilet appliances, and a travelling rug, all purchased at the best shops, he set off for one of the provinces where, through his father's influence, he had been attached to the governor as an official for special service.

In the province Iván Ilyich soon arranged as easy and agreeable a position for himself as he had at the School of Law. He performed his official tasks, made his career, and at the same time amused himself pleasantly and decorously. Occasionally he paid official visits to country districts, where he behaved with dignity both to his superiors and inferiors, and performed the duties entrusted to him, which related chiefly to the sectarians,[4] with an exactness and incorruptible honesty of which he could not but feel proud.

In official matters, despite his youth and taste for frivolous gaiety, he was exceedingly reserved, punctilious, and even severe; but in society he was often amusing and witty, and always good-natured, correct in his manner, and *bon enfant*, as the governor and his wife—with whom he was like one of the family—used to say of him.

In the province he had an affair with a lady who made advances to the elegant young lawyer, and there was also a milliner; and there were carousals with aides-de-camp who visited the district, and after-supper visits to a certain outlying street of doubtful reputation; and there was too some obsequiousness to his chief and even to his chief's wife, but all this was done with such a tone of good breeding that no hard names could be applied to it. It all came under the heading of the French saying: *"Il faut que jeunesse se passe."*[5] It was all done with clean hands, in clean linen, with French phrases, and above all among people of the best society and consequently with the approval of people of rank.

So Iván Ilyich served for five years and then came a change in his official life. The new and reformed judicial institutions were introduced, and new men were needed. Iván Ilyich became such a new man. He was offered the post of Examining Magistrate, and he accepted it though the post was in another province and obliged him to give up the connexions he had formed and to make new ones. His friends met to give him a sendoff; they had a group-photograph taken and presented him with a silver cigarette-case, and he set off to his new post.

As examining magistrate Iván Ilyich was just as *comme il faut* and decorous a man, inspiring general respect and capable of separating his official duties from his private life, as he had been when acting as an official on special service. His duties now as examining magistrate were far more interesting and attractive than before. In his former position it had been pleasant to wear an undress uniform made by Scharmer, and to pass through the crowd of petitioners and officials who were timorously awaiting an audience with the governor, and who envied him as with free and easy gait he went straight into his chief's private room to have a cup of tea and a cigarette with him. But not many people had then been directly dependent on him—only police officials and the sectarians when he went

---

4. The Old Believers, a large group of Russians (about twenty-five million in 1900), members of a sect that originated in a break with the Orthodox Church in the 17th century; they were subject to many legal restrictions.   5. Youth must have its fling [Translator's note].

on special missions—and he liked to treat them politely, almost as comrades, as if he were letting them feel that he who had the power to crush them was treating them in this simple, friendly way. There were then but few such people. But now, as an examining magistrate, Iván Ilyich felt that everyone without exception, even the most important and self-satisfied, was in his power, and that he need only write a few words on a sheet of paper with a certain heading, and this or that important, self-satisfied person would be brought before him in the role of an accused person or a witness, and if he did not choose to allow him to sit down, would have to stand before him and answer his questions. Iván Ilyich never abused his power; he tried on the contrary to soften its expression, but the consciousness of it and of the possibility of softening its effect, supplied the chief interest and attraction of his office. In his work itself, especially in his examinations, he very soon acquired a method of eliminating all considerations irrelevant to the legal aspect of the case, and reducing even the most complicated case to a form in which it would be presented on paper only in its externals, completely excluding his personal opinion of the matter, while above all observing every prescribed formality. The work was new and Iván Ilyich was one of the first men to apply the new Code of 1864.[6]

On taking up the post of examining magistrate in a new town, he made new acquaintances and connexions, placed himself on a new footing, and assumed a somewhat different tone. He took up an attitude of rather dignified aloofness towards the provincial authorities, but picked out the best circle of legal gentlemen and wealthy gentry living in the town and assumed a tone of slight dissatisfaction with the government, of moderate liberalism, and of enlightened citizenship. At the same time, without at all altering the elegance of his toilet, he ceased shaving his chin and allowed his beard to grow as it pleased.

Iván Ilyich settled down very pleasantly in this new town. The society there, which inclined towards opposition to the governor, was friendly, his salary was larger, and he began to play *vint* [a form of bridge], which he found added not a little to the pleasure of life, for he had a capacity for cards, played good-humouredly, and calculated rapidly and astutely, so that he usually won.

After living there for two years he met his future wife, Praskóvya Fëdorovna Míkhel, who was the most attractive, clever, and brilliant girl of the set in which he moved, and among other amusements and relaxations from his labours as examining magistrate, Iván Ilyich established light and playful relations with her.

While he had been an official on special service he had been accustomed to dance, but now as an examining magistrate it was exceptional for him to do so. If he danced now, he did it as if to show that though he served under the reformed order of things, and had reached the fifth official rank, yet when it came to dancing he could do it better than most

6. The emancipation of the serfs in 1861 was followed by a thorough all-round reform of judicial proceedings [Translator's note].

people. So at the end of an evening he sometimes danced with Praskóvya Fëdorovna, and it was chiefly during these dances that he captivated her. She fell in love with him. Iván Ilyich had at first no definite intention of marrying, but when the girl fell in love with him he said to himself: "Really, why shouldn't I marry?"

Praskóvya Fëdorovna came of a good family, was not bad looking, and had some little property. Iván Ilyich might have aspired to a more brilliant match, but even this was good. He had his salary, and she, he hoped, would have an equal income. She was well connected, and was a sweet, pretty, and thoroughly correct young woman. To say that Iván Ilyich married because he fell in love with Praskóvya Fëdorovna and found that she sympathized with his views of life would be as incorrect as to say that he married because his social circle approved of the match. He was swayed by both these considerations: the marriage gave him personal satisfaction, and at the same time it was considered the right thing by the most highly placed of his associates.

So Iván Ilyich got married.

The preparations for marriage and the beginning of married life, with its conjugal caresses, the new furniture, new crockery, and new linen, were very pleasant until his wife became pregnant—so that Iván Ilyich had begun to think that marriage would not impair the easy, agreeable, gay, and always decorous character of his life, approved of by society and regarded by himself as natural, but would even improve it. But from the first months of his wife's pregnancy, something new, unpleasant, depressing, and unseemly, and from which there was no way of escape, unexpectedly showed itself.

His wife, without any reason—de gaieté de coeur[7] as Iván Ilyich expressed it to himself—began to disturb the pleasure and propriety of their life. She began to be jealous without any cause, expected him to devote his whole attention to her, found fault with everything, and made coarse and ill-mannered scenes.

At first Iván Ilyich hoped to escape from the unpleasantness of this state of affairs by the same easy and decorous relation to life that had served him heretofore: he tried to ignore his wife's disagreeable moods, continued to live in his usual easy and pleasant way, invited friends to his house for a game of cards, and also tried going out to his club or spending his evenings with friends. But one day his wife began upbraiding him so vigorously, using such coarse words, and continued to abuse him every time he did not fulfil her demands, so resolutely and with such evident determination not to give way till he submitted—that is, till he stayed at home and was bored just as she was—that he became alarmed. He now realized that matrimony—at any rate with Praskóvya Fëdorovna—was not always conducive to the pleasures and amenities of life, but on the contrary often infringed both comfort and propriety, and that he must therefore entrench himself against such infringement. And Iván Ilyich began to seek for means of doing so. His official duties were the one thing that imposed

7. From sheer animal spirits (French).

upon Praskóvya Fëdorovna, and by means of his official work and the duties attached to it he began struggling with his wife to secure his own independence.

With the birth of their child, the attempts to feed it and the various failures in doing so, and with the real and imaginary illnesses of mother and child, in which Iván Ilyich's sympathy was demanded but about which he understood nothing, the need of securing for himself an existence outside his family life became still more imperative.

As his wife grew more irritable and exacting and Iván Ilyich transferred the centre of gravity of his life more and more to his official work, so did he grow to like his work better and became more ambitious than before.

Very soon, within a year of his wedding, Iván Ilyich had realized that marriage, though it may add some comforts to life, is in fact a very intricate and difficult affair towards which in order to perform one's duty, that is, to lead a decorous life approved of by society, one must adopt a definite attitude just as towards one's official duties.

And Iván Ilyich evolved such an attitude towards married life. He only required of it those conveniences—dinner at home, housewife, and bed— which it could give him, and above all that propriety of external forms required by public opinion. For the rest he looked for light-hearted pleasure and propriety, and was very thankful when he found them, but if he met with antagonism and querulousness he at once retired into his separate fenced-off world of official duties, where he found satisfaction.

Iván Ilyich was esteemed a good official, and after three years was made Assistant Public Prosecutor. His new duties, their importance, the possibility of indicting and imprisoning anyone he chose, the publicity his speeches received, and the success he had in all these things, made his work still more attractive.

More children came. His wife became more and more querulous and ill-tempered, but the attitude Iván Ilyich had adopted towards his home life rendered him almost impervious to her grumbling.

After seven years' service in that town he was transferred to another province as Public Prosecutor. They moved, but were short of money and his wife did not like the place they moved to. Though the salary was higher the cost of living was greater, besides which two of their children died and family life became still more unpleasant for him.

Praskóvya Fëdorovna blamed her husband for every inconvenience they encountered in their new home. Most of the conversations between husband and wife, especially as to the children's education, led to topics which recalled former disputes, and those disputes were apt to flare up again at any moment. There remained only those rare periods of amorousness which still came to them at times but did not last long. These were islets at which they anchored for a while and then again set out upon that ocean of veiled hostility which showed itself in their aloofness from one another. This aloofness might have grieved Iván Ilyich had he considered that it ought not to exist, but he now regarded the position as normal, and even made it the goal at which he aimed in family life. His aim was to free himself more and more from those unpleasantnesses and to give them a semblance of harmlessness and propriety. He attained this by spending less and less time with his family, and when obliged to be at home he tried to safeguard his position by the presence of outsiders. The chief thing however was that he had his official duties. The whole interest of his life now centered in the official world and that interest absorbed him. The consciousness of his power, being able to ruin anybody he wished to ruin, the importance, even the external dignity of his entry into court, or meetings with his subordinates, his success with superiors and inferiors, and above all his masterly handling of cases, of which he was conscious—all this gave him pleasure and filled his life, together with chats with his colleagues, dinners, and bridge. So that on the whole Iván Ilyich's life continued to flow as he considered it should do—pleasantly and properly.

So things continued for another seven years. His eldest daughter was already sixteen, another child had died, and only one son was left, a schoolboy and a subject of dissensions. Iván Ilyich wanted to put him in the School of Law, but to spite him Praskóvya Fëdorovna entered him at the High School. The daughter had been educated at home and had turned out well: the boy did not learn badly either.

III

So Iván Ilyich lived for seventeen years after his marriage. He was already a Public Prosecutor of long standing, and had declined several proposed transfers while awaiting a more desirable post, when an unanticipated and unpleasant occurrence quite upset the peaceful course of his life. He was expecting to be offered the post of presiding judge in a University town, but Hoppe somehow came to the front and obtained the appointment instead. Iván Ilyich became irritable, reproached Hoppe, and quarrelled both with him and with his immediate superiors—who became colder to him and again passed him over when other appointments were made.

This was in 1880, the hardest year of Iván Ilyich's life. It was then that it became evident on the one hand that his salary was insufficient for them to live on, and on the other that he had been forgotten, and not only this, but that what was for him the greatest and most cruel injustice appeared to others a quite ordinary occurrence. Even his father did not consider it his duty to help him. Iván Ilyich felt himself abandoned by everyone, and that they regarded his position with a salary of 3,500 rubles as quite normal and even fortunate. He alone knew that with the consciousness of the injustices done him, with his wife's incessant nagging, and with the debts he had contracted by living beyond his means his position was far from normal.

In order to save money that summer he obtained leave of absence and went with his wife to live in the country at her brother's place.

In the country, without his work, he experienced *ennui* for the first time in his life, and not only *ennui* but intolerable depression, and he decided that it was impossible to go on living like that, and that it was necessary to take energetic measures.

Having passed a sleepless night pacing up and down the veranda, he decided to go to Petersburg and bestir himself, in order to punish those who had failed to appreciate him and to get transferred to another ministry.

Next day, despite many protests from his wife and her brother, he started for Petersburg with the sole object of obtaining a post with a salary of five thousand rubles a year. He was no longer bent on any particular department, or tendency, or kind of activity. All he now wanted was an appointment to another post with a salary of five thousand rubles, either in the administration, in the banks, with the railways, in one of the Empress Márya's Institutions,[8] or even in the customs—but it had to carry with it a salary of five thousand rubles and be in a ministry other than that in which they had failed to appreciate him.

And this quest of Iván Ilyich's was crowned with remarkable and unexpected success. At Kursk an acquaintance of his, F. I. Ilyín, got into the first-class carriage, sat down beside Iván Ilyich, and told him of a telegram just received by the governor of Kursk announcing that a change was about to take place in the ministry: Peter Ivánovich was to be superseded by Iván Semënovich.

The proposed change, apart from its significance for Russia, had a special significance for Iván Ilyich, because by bringing forward a new man, Peter Petróvich, and consequently his friend Zachár Ivánovich, it was highly favourable for Iván Ilyich, since Zachár Ivánovich was a friend and colleague of his.

In Moscow his news was confirmed, and on reaching Petersburg Iván Ilyich found Zachár Ivánovich and received a definite promise of an appointment in his former department of Justice.

A week later he telegraphed to his wife: "Zachár in Miller's place. I shall receive appointment on presentation of report."

Thanks to this change of personnel, Iván Ilyich had unexpectedly obtained an appointment in his former ministry which placed him two stages above his former colleagues besides giving him five thousand rubles salary and three thousand five hundred rubles for expenses connected with his removal. All his ill humour towards his former enemies and the whole department vanished, and Iván Ilyich was completely happy.

He returned to the country more cheerful and contented than he had been for a long time. Praskóvya Fëdorovna also cheered up and a truce was arranged between them. Iván Ilyich told of how he had been fêted by everybody in Petersburg, how all those who had been his enemies were put to shame and now fawned on him, how envious they were of his appointment, and how much everybody in Petersburg had liked him.

Praskóvya Fëdorovna listened to all this and appeared to believe it. She did not contradict anything, but only made plans for their life in the town to which they were going. Iván Ilyich saw with delight that these plans were his plans, that he and his wife agreed, and that, after a stumble, his life was regaining its due and natural character of pleasant lightheartedness and decorum.

Iván Ilyich had come back for a short time only, for he had to take up

---

8. Reference to the charitable organization founded by the Empress Márya, wife of Paul I, late in the 18th century.

his new duties on the 10th of September. Moreover, he needed time to
settle into the new place, to move all his belongings from the province,
and to buy and order many additional things: in a word, to make such
arrangements as he had resolved on, which were almost exactly what
Praskóvya Fëdorovna too had decided on.

Now that everything had happened so fortunately, and that he and his
wife were at one in their aims and moreover saw so little of one another
they got on together better than they had done since the first years of
marriage. Iván Ilyich had thought of taking his family away with him at
once, but the insistence of his wife's brother and her sister-in-law, who
had suddenly become particularly amiable and friendly to him and his
family, induced him to depart alone.

So he departed, and the cheerful state of mind induced by his success
and by the harmony between his wife and himself, the one intensifying
the other, did not leave him. He found a delightful house, just the thing
both he and his wife had dreamt of. Spacious, lofty reception rooms in the
old style, a convenient and dignified study, rooms for his wife and daughter, a study for his son—it might have been specially built for them. Iván
Ilyich himself superintended the arrangements, chose the wallpapers, supplemented the furniture (preferably with antiques which he considered
particularly *comme il faut*), and supervised the upholstering. Everything
progressed and progressed and approached the ideal he had set himself:
even when things were only half completed they exceeded his expectations. He saw what a refined and elegant character, free from vulgarity, it
would all have when it was ready. On falling asleep he pictured to himself
how the reception-room would look. Looking at the yet unfinished drawing-room he could see the fireplace, the screen, the what-not, the little
chairs dotted here and there, the dishes and plates on the walls, and the
bronzes, as they would be when everything was in place. He was pleased
by the thought of how his wife and daughter, who shared his taste in this
matter, would be impressed by it. They were certainly not expecting as
much. He had been particularly successful in finding, and buying
cheaply, antiques which gave a particularly aristocratic character to the
whole place. But in his letters he intentionally understated everything in
order to be able to surprise them. All this so absorbed him that his new
duties—though he liked his official work—interested him less than he had
expected. Sometimes he even had moments of absent-mindedness during
the Court Sessions, and would consider whether he should have straight
or curved cornices for his curtains. He was so interested in it all that he
often did things himself, rearranging the furniture, or rehanging the curtains. Once when mounting a step-ladder to show the upholsterer, who
did not understand, how he wanted the hangings draped, he made a false
step and slipped, but being a strong and agile man he clung on and only
knocked his side against the knob of the window frame. The bruised place
was painful but the pain soon passed, and he felt particularly bright and
well just then. He wrote: "I feel fifteen years younger." He thought he
would have everything ready by September, but it dragged on till mid-
October. But the result was charming not only in his eyes but to everyone
who saw it.

In reality it was just what is usually seen in the houses of people of moderate means who want to appear rich, and therefore succeed only in resembling others like themselves: there were damasks, dark wood, plants, rugs, and dull and polished bronzes—all the things people of a certain class have in order to resemble other people of that class. His house was so like the others that it would never have been noticed, but to him it all seemed to be quite exceptional. He was very happy when he met his family at the station and brought them to the newly furnished house all lit up, where a footman in a white tie opened the door into the hall decorated with plants, and when they went on into the drawing room and the study uttering exclamations of delight. He conducted them everywhere, drank in their praises eagerly, and beamed with pleasure. At tea that evening, when Praskóvya Fëdorovna among other things asked him about his fall, he laughed, and showed them how he had gone flying and had frightened the upholsterer.

"It's a good thing I'm a bit of an athlete. Another man might have been killed, but I merely knocked myself, just here; it hurts when it's touched, but it's passing off already—it's only a bruise."

So they began living in their new home—in which, as always happens, when they got thoroughly settled in they found they were just one room short—and with the increased income, which as always was just a little (some five hundred rubles) too little, but it was all very nice.

Things went particularly well at first, before everything was finally arranged and while something had still to be done: this thing bought, that thing ordered, another thing moved, and something else adjusted. Though there were some disputes between husband and wife, they were both so well satisfied and had so much to do that it all passed off without any serious quarrels. When nothing was left to arrange it became rather dull and something seemed to be lacking, but they were then making acquaintances, forming habits, and life was growing fuller.

Iván Ilyich spent his mornings at the law court and came home to dinner, and at first he was generally in a good humour, though he occasionally became irritable just on account of his house. (Every spot on the tablecloth or the upholstery, and every broken window-blind string, irritated him. He had devoted so much trouble to arranging it all that every disturbance of it distressed him.) But on the whole his life ran its course as he believed life should do: easily, pleasantly, and decorously.

He got up at nine, drank his coffee, read the paper, and then put on his undress uniform and went to the law courts. There the harness in which he worked had already been stretched to fit him and he donned it without a hitch: petitioners, inquiries at the chancery, the chancery itself, and the sittings public and administrative. In all this the thing was to exclude everything fresh and vital, which always disturbs the regular course of official business, and to admit only official relations with people, and then only on official grounds. A man would come, for instance, wanting some information. Iván Ilyich, as one in whose sphere the matter did not lie, would have nothing to do with him: but if the man had some business with him in his official capacity, something that could be expressed on officially stamped paper, he would do everything, positively everything he could within the limits of such relations, and in doing so would maintain the semblance of friendly human relations, that is, would observe the courtesies of life. As soon as the official relations ended, so did everything else. Iván Ilyich possessed this capacity to separate his real life from the official side of affairs and not mix the two, in the highest degree, and by long practice and natural aptitude had brought it to such a pitch that sometimes, in the manner of a virtuoso, he would even allow himself to let the human and official relations mingle. He let himself do this just because he felt that he could at any time he chose resume the strictly official attitude again and drop the human relation. And he did it all easily, pleasantly, correctly, and even artistically. In the intervals between the sessions he smoked, drank tea, chatted a little about politics, a little about general topics, a little about cards, but most of all about official appointments. Tired, but with the feelings of a virtuoso—one of the first violins who has played his part in an orchestra with precision—he would return home to find that his wife and daughter had been out paying calls, or had a visitor, and that his son had been to school, had done his homework with his tutor, and was duly learning what is taught at High Schools. Everything was as it should be. After dinner, if they had no visitors, Iván Ilyich sometimes read a book that was being much discussed at the time, and in the evening settled down to work, that is, read official papers, compared the depositions of witnesses, and noted paragraphs of the Code applying to them. This was neither dull nor amusing. It was dull when he might have been playing bridge, but if no bridge was available it was at any rate better than doing nothing or sitting with his wife. Iván Ilyich's chief pleasure was giving little dinners to which he invited men and women of good social position, and just as his drawing-room resembled all other drawing-rooms so did his enjoyable little parties resemble all other such parties.

Once they even gave a dance. Iván Ilyich enjoyed it and everything went off well, except that it led to a violent quarrel with his wife about the cakes and sweets. Praskóvya Fëdorovna had made her own plans, but Iván Ilyich insisted on getting everything from an expensive confectioner and ordered too many cakes, and the quarrel occurred because some of those cakes were left over and the confectioner's bill came to forty-five rubles. It was a great and disagreeable quarrel. Praskóvya Fëdorovna called him "a fool and an imbecile," and he clutched at his head and made angry allusions to divorce.

But the dance itself had been enjoyable. The best people were there, and Iván Ilyich had danced with Princess Trúfonova, a sister of the distinguished founder of the Society "Bear my Burden."

The pleasures connected with his work were pleasures of ambition; his social pleasures were those of vanity; but Iván Ilyich's greatest pleasure was playing bridge. He acknowledged that whatever disagreeable incident happened in his life, the pleasure that beamed like a ray of light above everything else was to sit down to bridge with good players, not noisy partners, and of course to four-handed bridge (with five players it was annoying to have to stand out, though one pretended not to mind), to play a clever and serious game (when the cards allowed it) and then to have supper and drink a glass of wine. After a game of bridge, especially if he had won a little (to win a large sum was unpleasant), Iván Ilyich went to bed in specially good humour.

So they lived. They formed a circle of acquaintances among the best people and were visited by people of importance and by young folk. In their views as to their acquaintances, husband, wife, and daughter were entirely agreed, and tacitly and unanimously kept at arm's length and shook off the various shabby friends and relations who, with much show of affection, gushed into the drawing-room with its Japanese plates on the walls. Soon these shabby friends ceased to obtrude themselves and only the best people remained in the Golovíns' set.

Young men made up to Lisa, and Petríshchev, an examining magistrate and Dmítri Ivánovich Petríschchev's son and sole heir, began to be so attentive to her that Iván Ilyich had already spoken to Praskóvya Fëdorovna about it, and considered whether they should not arrange a party for them, or get up some private theatricals.

So they lived, and all went well, without change, and life flowed pleasantly.

IV

They were all in good health. It could not be called ill health if Iván Ilyich sometimes said that he had a queer taste in his mouth and felt some discomfort in his left side.

But this discomfort increased and, though not exactly painful, grew into a sense of pressure in his side accompanied by ill humour. And his irritability became worse and worse and began to mar the agreeable, easy, and correct life that had established itself in the Golovín family. Quarrels between husband and wife became more and more frequent, and soon the ease and amenity disappeared and even the decorum was barely maintained. Scenes again became frequent, and very few of those islets remained on which husband and wife could meet without an explosion. Praskóvya Fëdorovna now had good reason to say that her husband's temper was trying. With characteristic exaggeration she said he had always had a dreadful temper, and that it had needed all her good nature to put up with it for twenty years. It was true that now the quarrels were started by him. His bursts of temper always came just before dinner, often just as he began to eat his soup. Sometimes he noticed that a plate or dish was chipped, or the food was not right, or his son put his elbow on the table, or his daughter's hair was not done as he liked it, and for all this he blamed Praskóvya Fëdorovna. At first she retorted and said disagreeable things to him, but once or twice he fell into such a rage at the beginning of dinner that she realized it was due to some physical derangement brought on by taking food, and so she restrained herself and did not answer, but only hurried to get the dinner over. She regarded this self-restraint as highly praiseworthy. Having come to the conclusion that her husband had a dreadful temper and made her life miserable, she began to feel sorry for herself, and the more she pitied herself the more she hated her husband. She began to wish he would die; yet she did not want him to die because then his salary would cease. And this irritated her against him still more. She considered herself dreadfully unhappy just because not even his death could save her, and though she concealed her exasperation, that hidden exasperation of hers increased his irritation also.

After one scene in which Iván Ilyich had been particularly unfair and after which he had said in explanation that he certainly was irritable but that it was due to his not being well, she said that if he was ill it should be attended to, and insisted on his going to see a celebrated doctor.

He went. Everything took place as he had expected and as it always does. There was the usual waiting and the important air assumed by the doctor, with which he was so familiar (resembling that which he himself assumed in court), and the sounding and listening, and the questions which called for answers that were foregone conclusions and were evidently unnecessary, and the look of importance which implied that "if only you put yourself in our hands we will arrange everything—we know indubitably how it has to be done, always in the same way for everybody alike." It was all just as it was in the law courts. The doctor put on just the same air towards him as he himself put on towards an accused person.

The doctor said that so-and-so indicated that there was so-and-so inside the patient, but if the investigation of so-and-so did not confirm this, then he must assume that and that. If he assumed that and that, then . . . and so on. To Iván Ilyich only one question was important: was his case serious or not? But the doctor ignored that inappropriate question. From his point of view it was not the one under consideration, the real question was to decide between a floating kidney, chronic catarrh, or appendicitis. It was not a question of Iván Ilyich's life or death, but one between a floating kidney and appendicitis. And that question the doctor solved brilliantly, as it seemed to Iván Ilyich, in favour of the appendix, with the reservation that should an examination of the urine give fresh indications the matter would be reconsidered. All this was just what Iván Ilyich had himself brilliantly accomplished a thousand times in dealing with men on trial. The doctor summed up just as brilliantly, looking over his spectacles triumphantly and even gaily at the accused. From the doctor's summing up Iván Ilyich concluded that things were bad, but that for the doctor, and perhaps for everybody else, it was a matter of indifference, though for him it was bad. And this conclusion struck him painfully, arousing in him a great feeling of pity for himself and of bitterness towards the doctor's indifference to a matter of such importance.

He said nothing of this, but rose, placed the doctor's fee on the table, and remarked with a sigh: "We sick people probably often put inappropriate questions. But tell me, in general, is this complaint dangerous or not? . . ."

The doctor looked at him sternly over his spectacles with one eye, as if to say: "Prisoner, if you will not keep to the questions put to you, I shall be obliged to have you removed from the court."

"I have already told you what I consider necessary and proper. The analysis may show something more." And the doctor bowed.

Iván Ilyich went out slowly, seated himself disconsolately in his sledge, and drove home. All the way home he was going over what the doctor had said, trying to translate those complicated, obscure, scientific phrases into plain language and find in them an answer to the question: "Is my condition bad? Is it very bad? Or is there as yet nothing much wrong?" And it seemed to him that the meaning of what the doctor had said was it was very bad. Everything in the streets seemed depressing. The cabmen, the houses, the passers-by, and the shops, were dismal. His ache, this dull gnawing ache that never ceased for a moment, seemed to have acquired a new and more serious significance from the doctor's dubious remarks. Iván Ilyich now watched it with a new and oppressive feeling.

He reached home and began to tell his wife about it. She listened, but in the middle of his account his daughter came in with her hat on, ready to go out with her mother. She sat down reluctantly to listen to this tedious story, but could not stand it long, and her mother too did not hear him to the end.

"Well, I am very glad," she said. "Mind now to take your medicine regularly. Give me the prescription and I'll send Gerásim to the chemist's." And she went to get ready to go out.

While she was in the room Iván Ilyich had hardly taken time to breathe, but he sighed deeply when she left it.

"Well," he thought, "perhaps it isn't so bad after all."

He began taking his medicine and following the doctor's directions, which had been altered after the examination of the urine. But then it happened that there was a contradiction between the indications drawn from the examination of the urine and the symptoms that showed themselves. It turned out that what was happening differed from what the doctor had told him, and that he had either forgotten, or blundered, or hidden something from him. He could not, however, be blamed for that, and Iván Ilyich still obeyed his orders implicitly and at first derived some comfort from doing so.

From the time of his visit to the doctor, Iván Ilyich's chief occupation was the exact fulfilment of the doctor's instructions regarding hygiene and the taking of medicine, and the observation of his pain and his excretions. His chief interests came to be people's ailments and people's health. When sickness, deaths, or recoveries were mentioned in his presence, especially when the illness resembled his own, he listened with agitation which he tried to hide, asked questions, and applied what he heard to his own case.

The pain did not grow less, but Iván Ilyich made efforts to force himself to think that he was better. And he could do this so long as nothing agitated him. But as soon as he had any unpleasantness with his wife, any lack of success in his official work, or held bad cards at bridge, he was at once acutely sensible of his disease. He had formerly borne such mischances, hoping soon to adjust what was wrong, to master it and attain success, or make a grand slam. But now every mischance upset him and plunged him into despair. He would say to himself. "There now, just as I was beginning to get better and the medicine had begun to take effect, comes this accursed misfortune, or unpleasantness . . ." And he was furious with the mishap, or with the people who were causing the unpleasantness and killing him, for he felt that this fury was killing him but could not restrain it. One would have thought that it should have been clear to him that this exasperation with circumstances and people aggravated his illness, and that he ought therefore to ignore unpleasant occurrences. But he drew the very opposite conclusion: he said that he needed peace, and he watched for everything that might disturb it and became irritable at the slightest infringement of it. His condition was rendered worse by the fact that he read medical books and consulted doctors. The progress of his disease was so gradual that he could deceive himself when comparing one day with another—the difference was so slight. But when he consulted the doctors it seemed to him that he was getting worse, and even very rapidly. Yet despite this he was continually consulting them.

That month he went to see another celebrity, who told him almost the same as the first had done but put his questions rather differently, and the interview with this celebrity only increased Iván Ilyich's doubts and fears. A friend of a friend of his, a very good doctor, diagnosed his illness again quite differently from the others, and though he predicted recovery, his questions and suppositions bewildered Iván Ilyich still more and increased his doubts. A homeopathist diagnosed the disease in yet another way, and prescribed medicine which Iván Ilyich took secretly for a week. But after a week, not feeling any improvement and having lost confidence both in the former doctor's treatment and in this one's, he became still more despondent. One day a lady acquaintance mentioned a cure effected by a wonder-working icon. Iván Ilyich caught himself listening attentively and beginning to believe that it had occurred. This incident alarmed him. "Has my mind really weakened to such an extent?" he asked himself. "Nonsense! It's all rubbish. I mustn't give way to nervous fears but having chosen a doctor must keep strictly to his treatment. That is what I will do. Now it's all settled. I won't think about it, but will follow the treatment seriously till summer, and then we shall see. From now there must be no more of this wavering!" This was easy to say but impossible to carry out. The pain in his side oppressed him and seemed to grow worse and more incessant, while the taste in his mouth grew stranger and stranger. It seemed to him that his breath had a disgusting smell, and he was conscious of a loss of appetite and strength. There was no deceiving himself: something terrible, new, and more important than anything before in his life, was taking place within him of which he alone was aware. Those about him did not understand or would not understand it, but thought everything in the world was going on as usual. That tormented Iván Ilyich more than anything. He saw that his household, especially his wife and daughter who were in a perfect whirl of visiting, did not understand anything of it and were annoyed that he was so depressed and so exacting, as if he were to blame for it. Though they tried to disguise it he saw that he was an obstacle in their path, and that his wife had adopted a definite line in regard to his illness and kept to it regardless of anything he said or did. Her attitude was this: "You know," she would say to her friends, "Iván Ilyich can't do as other people do, and keep to the treatment prescribed for him. One day he'll take his drops and keep strictly to his diet and go to bed in good time, but the next day unless I watch him he'll suddenly forget his medicine, eat sturgeon—which is forbidden—and sit up playing cards till one o'clock in the morning."

"Oh, come, when was that?" Iván Ilyich would ask in vexation. "Only once at Peter Ivánovich's."

"And yesterday with Shébek."

"Well, even if I hadn't stayed up, this pain would have kept me awake."

"Be that as it may you'll never get well like that, but will always make us wretched."

Praskóvya Fédorovna's attitude to Iván Ilyich's illness, as she expressed it both to others and to him, was that it was his own fault and was another of the annoyances he caused her. Iván Ilyich felt that this opinion escaped her involuntarily—but that did not make it easier for him.

At the law courts too, Iván Ilyich noticed, or thought he noticed, a strange attitude towards himself. It sometimes seemed to him that people were watching him inquisitively as a man whose place might soon be vacant. Then again, his friends would suddenly begin to chaff him in a friendly way about his low spirits, as if the awful, horrible, and unheard-of thing that was going on within him, incessantly gnawing at him and irresistibly drawing him away, was a very agreeable subject for jests. Schwartz in particular irritated him by his jocularity, vivacity, and savoir-faire, which reminded him of what he himself had been ten years ago.

Friends came to make up a set and they sat down to cards. They dealt, bending the new cards to soften them, and he sorted the diamonds in his hand and found he had seven. His partner said "No trumps" and supported him with two diamonds. What more could be wished for? It ought to be jolly and lively. They would make a grand slam. But suddenly Iván Ilyich was conscious of that gnawing pain, that taste in his mouth, and it seemed ridiculous that in such circumstances he should be pleased to make a grand slam.

He looked at his partner Mikháil Mikháylovich, who rapped the table with his strong hand and instead of snatching up the tricks pushed the cards courteously and indulgently towards Iván Ilyich that he might have the pleasure of gathering them up without the trouble of stretching out his hand for them. "Does he think I am too weak to stretch out my arm?" thought Iván Ilyich, and forgetting what he was doing he over-trumped his partner, missing the grand slam by three tricks. And what was most awful of all was that he saw how upset Mikháil Mikháylovich was about it but did not himself care. And it was dreadful to realize why he did not care.

They all saw that he was suffering, and said: "We can stop if you are tired. Take a rest." Lie down? No, he was not at all tired, and he finished the rubber. All were gloomy and silent. Iván Ilyich felt that he had diffused this gloom over them and could not dispel it. They had supper and went away, and Iván Ilyich was left alone with the consciousness that his life was poisoned and was poisoning the lives of others, and that this poison did not weaken but penetrated more and more deeply into his whole being.

With this consciousness, and with physical pain besides the terror, he must go to bed, often to lie awake the greater part of the night. Next morning he had to get up again, dress, go to the law courts, speak, and write; or if he did not go out, spend at home those twenty-four hours a day each of which was a torture. And he had to live thus all alone on the brink of an abyss, with no one who understood or pitied him.

V

So one month passed and then another. Just before the New Year his brother-in-law came to town and stayed at their house. Iván Ilyich was at the law courts and Praskóvya Fëdorovna had gone shopping. When Iván Ilyich came home and entered his study he found his brother-in-law there—a healthy, florid man—unpacking his portmanteau himself. He raised his head on hearing Iván Ilyich's footsteps and looked up at him for a moment without a word. That stare told Iván everything. His brother-in-law opened his mouth to utter an exclamation of surprise but checked himself, and that action confirmed it all.

"I have changed, eh?"

"Yes, there is a change."

And after that, try as he would to get his brother-in-law to return to the subject of his looks, the latter would say nothing about it. Praskóvya Fëdorovna came home and her brother went out to her. Iván Ilyich locked the door and began to examine himself in the glass, first full face, then in profile. He took up a portrait of himself taken with his wife, and compared it with what he saw in the glass. The change in him was immense. Then he bared his arms to the elbow, looked at them, drew the sleeves down again, sat down on an ottoman, and grew blacker than night.

"No, no, this won't do!" he said to himself, and jumped up, went to the table, took up some law papers and began to read them, but could not continue. He unlocked the door and went into the reception-room. The door leading to the drawing-room was shut. He approached it on tiptoe and listened.

"No, you are exaggerating!" Praskóvya Fëdorovna was saying.

"Exaggerating! Don't you see it? Why, he's a dead man! Look at his eyes—there's no light in them. But what is it that is wrong with him?"

"No one knows. Nikoláevich [that was another doctor] said something, but I don't know what. And Leshchetítsky [this was the celebrated specialist] said quite the contrary. . ."

Iván Ilyich walked away, went to his own room, lay down and began musing: "The kidney, a floating kidney." He recalled all the doctors had told him of how it detached itself and swayed about. And by an effort of imagination he tried to catch that kidney and arrest it and support it. So little was needed for this, it seemed to him. "No, I'll go to see Peter Ivánovich again." [That was the friend whose friend was a doctor.] He rang, ordered the carriage, and got ready to go.

"Where are you going, Jean?" asked his wife, with a specially sad and exceptionally kind look.

This exceptionally kind look irritated him. He looked morosely at her.

"I must go to see Peter Ivánovich."

He went to see Peter Ivánovich, and together they went to see his friend, the doctor. He was in, and Iván Ilyich had a long talk with him. Reviewing the anatomical and physiological details of what in the doctor's opinion was going on inside him, he understood it all.

There was something, a small thing, in the vermiform appendix. It might all come right. Only stimulate the energy of one organ and check the activity of another, then absorption would take place and everything would come right. He got home rather late for dinner, ate his dinner, and conversed cheerfully, but could not for a long time bring himself to go back to work in his room. At last, however, he went to his study and did what was necessary, but the consciousness that he had put something aside—an important, intimate matter which he would revert to when his work was done—never left him. When he had finished his work he remembered that this intimate matter was the thought of his vermiform appendix. But he did not give himself up to it, and went to the drawing-room for tea. There were callers there, including the examining magistrate who was a desirable match for his daughter, and they were conversing, playing the piano, and singing. Iván Ilyich, as Praskóvya Fëdorovna remarked, spent that evening more cheerfully than usual, but he never for a moment forgot that he had postponed the important matter of the appendix. At eleven o'clock he said good-night and went to his bedroom. Since his illness he had slept alone in a small room next to his study. He undressed and took up a novel by Zola,[9] but instead of reading it he fell into thought, and in his imagination that desired improvement in the vermiform appendix occurred. There was the absorption and evacuation and the reestablishment of normal activity. "Yes, that's it!" he said to himself. "One need only assist nature, that's all." He remembered his medicine, rose, took it, and lay down on his back watching for the beneficent action of the medicine and for it to lessen the pain. "I need only take it regularly and avoid all injurious influences. I am already feeling better, much better." He began touching his side: it was not painful to the touch. "There, I really don't feel it. It's much better already." He put out the light and turned on his side. . . . "The appendix is getting better, absorption is occurring." Suddenly he felt the old, familiar, dull, gnawing pain, stubborn and serious. There was the same familiar loathsome taste in his mouth. His heart sank and he felt dazed. "My God! My God!" he muttered. "Again, again! And it will never cease." And suddenly the matter presented itself in a quite different aspect. "Vermiform appendix! Kidney!" he said to himself. "It's not a question of appendix or kidney, but of life and . . . death. Yes, life was there and now it is going, going and I cannot stop it. Yes. Why deceive myself? Isn't it obvious to everyone but me that I'm dying, and that it's only a question of weeks, days . . . it may happen this moment. There was light and now there is darkness. I was here and now I'm going there! Where?" A chill came over him, his breathing ceased, and he felt only the throbbing of his heart.

"When I am not, what will there be? There will be nothing. Then

---

9. Émile Zola (1840–1902), French novelist, author of the *Rougon-Macquart* novels (*Nana, Germinal,* and so on). Tolstoy condemned Zola for his naturalistic theories and considered his novels crude and gross.

arms on the arms of his oak chair; bending over as usual to a colleague and drawing his papers nearer he would interchange whispers with him, and then suddenly raising his eyes and sitting erect would pronounce certain words and open the proceedings. But suddenly in the midst of those proceedings the pain in his side, regardless of the stage the proceedings had reached, would begin its own gnawing work. Iván Ilyich would turn his attention to it and try to drive the thought of it away, but without success. It would come and stand before him and look at him, and he would be petrified and the light would die out of his eyes, and he would again begin asking himself whether It alone was true. And his colleagues and subordinates would see with surprise and distress that he, the brilliant and subtle judge, was becoming confused and making mistakes. He would shake himself, try to pull himself together, manage somehow to bring the sitting to a close, and return home with the sorrowful consciousness that his judicial labours could not as formerly hide from him what he wanted them to hide, and could not deliver him from It. And what was worst of all was that It drew his attention to itself not in order to make him take some action but only that he should look at It, look it straight in the face: look at it without doing anything, suffer inexpressibly.

And to save himself from this condition Iván Ilyich looked for consolations—new screens—and new screens were found and for a while seemed to save him, but then they immediately fell to pieces or rather became transparent, as It penetrated them and nothing could veil It.

In these latter days he would go into the drawing-room he had arranged—that drawing-room where he had fallen and for the sake of which (how bitterly ridiculous it seemed) he had sacrificed his life—for he knew that his illness originated with that knock. He would enter and see that something had scratched the polished table. He would look for the cause of this and find that it was the bronze ornamentation of an album, that had got bent. He would take up the expensive album which he had lovingly arranged, and feel vexed with his daughter and her friends for their untidiness—for the album was torn here and there and some of the photographs turned upside down. He would put it carefully in order and bend the ornamentation back into position. Then it would occur to him to place all those things in another corner of the room, near the plants. He would call the footman, but his daughter or wife would contradict him, and he would dispute and grow angry. But that was all right, for then he did not think about It. It was invisible.

But then, when he was moving something himself, his wife would say: "Let the servants do it. You will hurt yourself again." And suddenly It would flash through the screen and he would see it. It was just a flash, and he hoped it would disappear, but he would involuntarily pay attention to his side. "It sits there as before, gnawing just the same!" And he could no longer forget It, but could distinctly see it looking at him from behind the flowers. "What is it all for?"

"It really is so! I lost my life over that curtain as I might have done when storming a fort. Is that possible? How terrible and how stupid. It can't be true! It can't, but it is."

He would go to his study, lie down, and again be alone with *It*: face to face with *It*. And nothing could be done with *It* except to look at it and shudder.

VII

How it happened it is impossible to say because it came about step by step, unnoticed, but in the third month of Iván Ilyich's illness, his wife, his daughter, his son, his acquaintances, the doctors, the servants, and above all he himself, were aware that the whole interest he had for other people was whether he would soon vacate his place, and at last release the living from the discomfort caused by his presence and be himself released from his sufferings.

He slept less and less. He was given opium and hypodermic injections of morphine, but this did not relieve him. The dull depression he experienced in a somnolent condition at first gave him a little relief, but only as something new; afterwards it became as distressing as the pain itself or even more so.

Special foods were prepared for him by the doctors' orders, but all those foods became increasingly distasteful and disgusting to him.

For his excretions also special arrangements had to be made, and this was a torment to him every time—a torment from the uncleanliness, the unseemliness, and the smell, and from knowing that another person had to take part in it.

But just through this most unpleasant matter, Iván Ilyich obtained comfort. Gerásim, the butler's young assistant, always came in to carry the things out. Gerásim was a clean, fresh peasant lad, grown stout on town food and always cheerful and bright. At first the sight of him, in his clean Russian peasant costume, engaged on that disgusting task embarrassed Iván Ilyich.

Once when he got up from the commode too weak to draw up his trousers, he dropped into a soft armchair and looked with horror at his bare, enfeebled thighs with the muscles so sharply marked on them.

Gerásim with a firm light tread, his heavy boots emitting a pleasant smell of tar and fresh winter air, came in wearing a clean Hessian apron, the sleeves of his print shirt tucked up over his strong bare young arms; and refraining from looking at his sick master out of consideration for his feelings, and restraining the joy of life that beamed from his face, he went up to the commode.

"Gerásim!" said Iván Ilyich in a weak voice.

Gerásim started, evidently afraid he might have committed some blunder, and with a rapid movement turned his fresh, kind, simple young face which just showed the first downy sign of a beard.

"Yes, sir?"

"That must be very unpleasant for you. You must forgive me. I am helpless."

"Oh, why, sir," and Gerásim's eyes beamed and he showed his glistening white teeth, "what's a little trouble? It's a case of illness with you, sir."

And his deft strong hands did their accustomed task, and he went out of the room stepping lightly. Five minutes later he as lightly returned.

Iván Ilyich was still sitting in the same position in the armchair. "Gerásim," he said when the latter had replaced the freshly-washed utensil. "Please come here and help me." Gerásim went up to him. "Lift me up. It is hard for me to get up, and I have sent Dmítri away."

Gerásim went up to him, grasped his master with his strong arms deftly but gently, in the same way that he stepped—lifted him, supported him with one hand, and with the other drew up his trousers and would have set him down again, but Iván Ilyich asked to be led to the sofa. Gerásim, without an effort and without apparent pressure, led him, almost lifting him, to the sofa and placed him on it.

"Thank you. How easily and well you do it all!"

Gerásim smiled again and turned to leave the room. But Iván Ilyich felt his presence such a comfort that he did not want to let him go.

"One thing more, please move up that chair. No, the other one—under my feet. It is easier for me when my feet are raised."

Gerásim brought the chair, set it down gently in place, and raised Iván Ilyich's legs on to it. It seemed to Iván Ilyich that he felt better while Gerásim was holding up his legs.

"It's better when my legs are higher," he said. "Place that cushion under them."

Gerásim did so. He again lifted the legs and placed them, and again Iván Ilyich felt better while Gerásim held his legs. When he set them down Iván Ilyich fancied he felt worse.

"Gerásim," he said. "Are you busy now?"

"Not at all, sir," said Gerásim, who had learnt from the townsfolk how to speak to gentlefolk.

"What have you still to do?"

"What have I to do? I've done everything except chopping the logs for to-morrow."

"Then hold my legs up a bit higher, can you?"

"Of course I can. Why not?" And Gerásim raised his master's legs higher and Iván Ilyich thought that in that position he did not feel any pain at all.

"And how about the logs?"

"Don't trouble about that, sir. There's plenty of time."

Iván Ilyich told Gerásim to sit down and hold his legs, and began to talk to him. And strange to say it seemed to him that he felt better while Gerásim held his legs up.

After that Iván Ilyich would sometimes call Gerásim and get him to hold his legs on his shoulders, and he liked talking to him. Gerásim did it all easily, willingly, simply, and with a good nature that touched Iván Ilyich. Health, strength, and vitality in other people were offensive to him, but Gerásim's strength and vitality did not mortify but soothed him.

What tormented Iván Ilyich most was the deception, the lie, which for some reason they all accepted, that he was not dying but was simply ill, and that he only need keep quiet and undergo a treatment and then something very good would result. He however knew that do what they would nothing would come of it, only still more agonizing suffering and death. This deception tortured him—their not wishing to admit what they all knew and what he knew, but wanting to lie to him concerning his terrible condition, and wishing and forcing him to participate in that lie. Those lies—lies enacted over him on the eve of his death and destined to degrade this awful, solemn act to the level of their visitings, their curtains, their sturgeon for dinner—were a terrible agony for Iván Ilyich. And strangely enough, many times when they were going through their antics over him he had been within a hairbreadth of calling out to them: "Stop lying! You know and I know that I am dying. Then at least stop lying about it!" But he had never had the spirit to do it. The awful, terrible act of his dying was, he could see, reduced by those about him to the level of a casual, unpleasant, and almost indecorous incident (as if someone entered a drawing-room diffusing an unpleasant odour) and this was done by that very decorum which he had served all his life long. He saw that no one felt for him, because no one even wished to grasp his position. Only Gerásim recognized and pitied him. And so Iván Ilyich felt at ease only with him. He felt comforted when Gerásim supported his legs (sometimes all night long) and refused to go to bed, saying: "Don't you worry, Iván Ilyich. I'll get sleep enough later on," or when he suddenly became familiar and exclaimed: "If you weren't sick it would be another matter, but as it is, why should I grudge a little trouble?" Gerásim alone did not lie; everything showed that he alone understood the facts of the case and did not consider it necessary to disguise them, but simply felt sorry for his emaciated and enfeebled master. Once when Iván Ilyich was sending him away he even said straight out: "We shall all of us die, so why should I grudge a little trouble?"—expressing the fact that he did not think his work burdensome, because he was doing it for a dying man and hoped someone would do the same for him when his time came.

Apart from this lying, or because of it, what most tormented Iván Ilyich was that no one pitied him as he wished to be pitied. At certain moments after prolonged suffering he wished most of all (though he would have been ashamed to confess it) for someone to pity him as a sick child is pitied. He longed to be petted and comforted. He knew he was an important functionary, that he had a beard turning grey, and that therefore what he longed for was impossible, but still he longed for it. And in Gerásim's attitude towards him there was something akin to what he wished for, and so that attitude comforted him. Iván Ilyich wanted to weep, wanted to be petted and cried over, and then his colleague Shébek would come, and instead of weeping and being petted, Iván Ilyich would assume a serious, severe, and profound air, and by force of habit would express his opinion on a decision of the Court of Appeal and would stubbornly insist on that view. This falsity around him and within him did more than anything else to poison his last days.

VIII

It was morning. He knew it was morning because Gerásim had gone, and Peter the footman had come and put out the candles, drawn back one of the curtains, and begun quietly to tidy up. Whether it was morning or evening, Friday or Sunday, made no difference, it was all just the same:

the gnawing, unmitigated, agonizing pain, never ceasing for an instant, the consciousness of life inexorably waning but not yet extinguished, the approach of that ever dreaded and hateful Death which was the only reality, and always the same falsity. What were days, weeks, hours, in such a case?

"Will you have some tea, sir?"

"He wants things to be regular, and wishes the gentlefolk to drink tea in the morning," thought Iván Ilyich, and only said "No."

"Wouldn't you like to move onto the sofa, sir?"

"He wants to tidy up the room, and I'm in the way. I am uncleanliness and disorder," he thought, and said only:

"No, leave me alone."

The man went on bustling about. Iván Ilyich stretched out his hand. Peter came up, ready to help.

"What is it, sir?"

"My watch."

Peter took the watch which was close at hand and gave it to his master. "Half-past eight. Are they up?"

"No sir, except Vladímir Ivánich" (the son) "who has gone to school. Praskóvya Fëdorovna ordered me to wake her if you asked for her. Shall I do so?"

"No, there's no need to." "Perhaps I'd better have some tea," he thought, and added aloud: "Yes, bring me some tea."

Peter went to the door, but Iván Ilyich dreaded being left alone. "How can I keep him here? Oh yes, my medicine." "Peter, give me my medicine." "Why not? Perhaps it may still do me some good." He took a spoonful and swallowed it. "No, it won't help. It's all tomfoolery, all deception," he decided as soon as he became aware of the familiar, sickly, hopeless taste. "No, I can't believe in it any longer. But the pain, why this pain? If it would only cease just for a moment!" And he moaned. Peter turned towards him. "It's all right. Go and fetch me some tea."

Peter went out. Left alone Iván Ilyich groaned not so much with pain, terrible though that was, as from mental anguish. Always and forever the same, always these endless days and nights. If only it would come quicker! If only *what* would come quicker? Death, darkness? . . . No, no! Anything rather than death!

When Peter returned with the tea on a tray, Iván Ilyich stared at him for a time in perplexity, not realizing who and what he was. Peter was disconcerted by that look and his embarrassment brought Iván Ilyich to himself.

"Oh, tea! All right, put it down. Only help me to wash and put on a clean shirt."

And Iván Ilyich began to wash. With pauses for rest, he washed his hands and then his face, cleaned his teeth, brushed his hair, and looked in the glass. He was terrified by what he saw, especially by the limp way in which his hair clung to his pallid forehead.

While his shirt was being changed he knew that he would be still more frightened at the sight of his body, so he avoided looking at it. Finally he was ready. He drew on a dressing-gown, wrapped himself in a plaid, and sat down in the armchair to take his tea. For a moment he felt refreshed, but as soon as he began to drink the tea he was again aware of the same taste, and the pain also returned. He finished it with an effort, and then lay down stretching out his legs, and dismissed Peter.

Always the same. Now a spark of hope flashes up, then a sea of despair rages, and always pain; always pain, always despair, and always the same. When alone he had a dreadful and distressing desire to call someone, but he knew beforehand that with others present it would be still worse. "Another dose of morphine—to lose consciousness. I will tell him, the doctor, that he must think of something else. It's impossible, impossible, to go on like this."

An hour and another pass like that. But now there is a ring at the door bell. Perhaps it's the doctor? It is. He comes in fresh, hearty, plump, and cheerful, with that look on his face that seems to say: "There now, you're in a panic about something, but we'll arrange it all for you directly!" The doctor knows this expression is out of place here, but he has put it on once for all and can't take it off—like a man who has put on a frock-coat in the morning to pay a round of calls.

The doctor rubs his hands vigorously and reassuringly.

"Brr! How cold it is! There's such a sharp frost; just let me warm myself!" he says, as if it were only a matter of waiting till he was warm, and then he would put everything right.

"Well now, how are you?"

Iván Ilyich feels that the doctor would like to say: "Well, how are our affairs?" but that even he feels that this would not do, and says instead: "What sort of a night have you had?"

Iván Ilyich looks at him as much as to say: "Are you really never ashamed of lying?" But the doctor does not wish to understand this question, and Iván Ilyich says: "Just as terrible as ever. The pain never leaves me and never subsides. If only something . . ."

"Yes, you sick people are always like that. . . . There, now I think I'm warm enough. Even Praskóvya Fëdorovna, who is so particular, could find no fault with my temperature. Well, now I can say good-morning," and the doctor presses his patient's hand.

Then, dropping his former playfulness, he begins with a most serious face to examine the patient, feeling his pulse and taking his temperature, and then begins the sounding and auscultation.

Iván Ilyich knows quite well and definitely that all this is nonsense and pure deception, but when the doctor, getting down on his knee, leans over him, putting his ear first higher then lower, and performs various gymnastic movements over him with a significant expression on his face, Iván Ilyich submits to it all as he used to submit to the speeches of the lawyers, though he knew very well that they were all lying and why they were lying.

The doctor, kneeling on the sofa, is still sounding him when Praskóvya Fëdorovna's silk dress rustles at the door and she is heard scolding Peter for not having let her know of the doctor's arrival.

She comes in, kisses her husband, and at once proceeds to prove that she has been up a long time already, and only owing to a misunderstanding failed to be there when the doctor arrived.

Iván Ilyich looks at her, scans her all over, sets against her the whiteness and plumpness and cleanness of her hands and neck, the gloss of her
hair, and the sparkle of her vivacious eyes. He hates her with his whole
soul. And the thrill of hatred he feels for her makes him suffer from her
touch.

Her attitude towards him and his disease is still the same. Just as the
doctor had adopted a certain relation to his patient which he could not
abandon, so had she formed one towards him—that he was not doing
something he ought to do and was himself to blame, and that she
reproached him lovingly for this—and she could not now change that
attitude.

"You see he doesn't listen to me and doesn't take his medicine at the
proper time. And above all he lies in a position that is no doubt bad for
him—with his legs up."

She described how he made Gerásim hold his legs up.

The doctor smiled with a contemptuous affability that said: "What's to
be done? These sick people do have foolish fancies of that kind, but we
must forgive them."

When the examination was over the doctor looked at his watch, and
then Praskóvya Fëdorovna announced to Iván Ilyich that it was of course
as he pleased, but she had sent to-day for a celebrated specialist who would
examine him and have a consultation with Michael Danílovich (their regular doctor).

"Please don't raise any objections. I am doing this for my own sake,"
she said ironically, letting it be felt that she was doing it all for his sake
and only said this to leave him no right to refuse. He remained silent,
knitting his brows. He felt that he was so surrounded and involved in a
mesh of falsity that it was hard to unravel anything.

Everything she did for him was entirely for her own sake, and she told
him she was doing for herself what she actually was doing for herself, as if
that was so incredible that he must understand the opposite.

At half-past eleven the celebrated specialist arrived. Again the sounding
began and the significant conversations in his presence and in other
rooms, about the kidneys and the appendix, and the questions and
answers, with such an air of importance that again, instead of the real
question of life and death which now alone confronted him, the question
arose of the kidney and the appendix which were not behaving as they
ought to and would now be attacked by Michael Danílovich and the specialist and forced to amend their ways.

The celebrated specialist took leave of him with a serious though not
hopeless look, and in reply to the timid question in Iván Ilyich, with eyes
glistening with fear and hope, put to him as to whether there was a chance
of recovery, said that he could not vouch for it but there was a possibility.
The look of hope with which Iván Ilyich watched the doctor out was so
pathetic that Praskóvya Fëdorovna, seeing it, even wept as she left the
room to hand the doctor his fee.

The gleam of hope kindled by the doctor's encouragement did not last
long. The same room, the same pictures, curtains, wallpaper, medicine
bottles, were all there, and the same aching suffering body, and Iván Ilyich

began to moan. They gave him a subcutaneous injection and he sank into oblivion.

It was twilight when he came to. They brought him his dinner and he swallowed some beef tea with difficulty, and then everything was the same again and night was coming on.

After dinner, at seven o'clock, Praskóvya Fëdorovna came into the room in evening dress, her full bosom pushed up by her corset, and with traces of powder on her face. She had reminded him in the morning that they were going to the theatre. Sarah Bernhardt[2] was visiting the town and they had a box, which he had insisted on their taking. Now he had forgotten about it and her toilet offended him, but he concealed his vexation when he remembered that he had himself insisted on their securing a box and going because it would be an instructive and aesthetic pleasure for the children.

Praskóvya Fëdorovna came in, self-satisfied but yet with a rather guilty air. She sat down and asked how he was, but, as he saw, only for the sake of asking and not in order to learn about it, knowing that there was nothing to learn—and then went on to what she really wanted to say: that she would not on any account have gone but that the box had been taken and Helen and their daughter were going, as well as Petríshchev (the examining magistrate, their daughter's fiancé) and that it was out of the question to let them go alone; but that she would have much preferred to sit with him for a while; and he must be sure to follow the doctor's orders while she was away.

"Oh, and Fëdor Petróvich" (the fiancé) "would like to come in. May he? And Lisa?"

"All right."

Their daughter came in in full evening dress, her fresh young flesh exposed (making a show of that very flesh which in his own case caused so much suffering), strong, healthy, evidently in love, and impatient with illness, suffering, and death, because they interfered with her happiness.

Fëdor Petróvich came in too, in evening dress, his hair curled à la Capoul, a tight stiff collar round his long sinewy neck, an enormous white shirt-front and narrow black trousers tightly stretched over his strong thighs. He had one white glove tightly drawn on, and was holding his opera hat in his hand.

Following him the schoolboy crept in unnoticed, in a new uniform, poor little fellow, and wearing gloves. Terribly dark shadows showed under his eyes, the meaning of which Iván Ilyich knew well.

His son had always seemed pathetic to him, and now it was dreadful to see the boy's frightened look of pity. It seemed to Iván Ilyich that Vásya was the only one besides Gerásim who understood and pitied him.

They all sat down and again asked how he was. A silence followed. Lisa asked her mother about the opera-glasses, and there was an altercation between mother and daughter as to who had taken them and where they had been put. This occasioned some unpleasantness.

Fëdor Petróvich inquired of Iván Ilyich whether he had ever seen Sarah

---

2. Stage name of Rosine Bernard (1844–1923), famed for romantic and tragic roles.

Bernhardt. Iván Ilyich did not at first catch the question, but then replied: "No, have you seen her before?"

"Yes, in *Adrienne Lecouvreur.*"[3]

Praskóvya Fëdorovna mentioned some rôles in which Sarah Bernhardt was particularly good. Her daughter disagreed. Conversation sprang up as to the elegance and realism of her acting—the sort of conversation that is always repeated and is always the same.

In the midst of the conversation Fëdor Petróvich glanced at Iván Ilyich and became silent. The others also looked at him and grew silent. Iván Ilyich was staring with glittering eyes straight before him, evidently indignant with them. This had to be rectified, but it was impossible to do so. The silence had to be broken, but for a time no one dared to break it and they all became afraid that the conventional deception would suddenly become obvious and the truth become plain to all. Lisa was the first to pluck up courage and break that silence, but by trying to hide what everybody was feeling, she betrayed it.

"Well, if we are going it's time to start," she said, looking at her watch, a present from her father, and with a faint and significant smile at Fëdor Petróvich relating to something known only to them. She got up with a rustle of her dress.

They all rose, said good-night, and went away.

When they had gone it seemed to Iván Ilyich that he felt better; the falsity had gone with them. But the pain remained—that same pain and that same fear that made everything monotonously alike, nothing harder and nothing easier. Everything was worse.

Again minute followed minute and hour followed hour. Everything remained the same and there was no cessation. And the inevitable end of it all became more and more terrible.

"Yes, send Gerásim here," he replied to a question Peter asked.

IX

His wife returned late at night. She came in on tiptoe, but he heard her, opened his eyes, and made haste to close them again. She wished to send Gerásim away and to sit with him herself, but he opened his eyes and said: "No, go away."

"Are you in great pain?"

"Always the same."

"Take some opium."

He agreed and took some. She went away.

Till about three in the morning he was in a state of stupefied misery. It seemed to him that he and his pain were being thrust into a narrow, deep black sack, but though they were pushed further and further in they could not be pushed to the bottom. And this, terrible enough in itself, was accompanied by suffering. He was frightened yet wanted to fall through the sack, he struggled but yet co-operated. And suddenly he broke

3. A play (1849) by the French dramatist Eugène Scribe (1791–1861), in which the heroine was a famous actress of the 18th century. Tolstoy considered Scribe, who wrote over four hundred plays, a shoddy, commercial playwright.

through, fell, and regained consciousness. Gerásim was sitting at the foot of the bed dozing quietly and patiently, while he himself lay with his emaciated stockinged legs resting on Gerásim's shoulders; the same shaded candle was there and the same unceasing pain.

"Go away, Gerásim," he whispered.

"It's all right, sir. I'll stay a while."

"No. Go away."

He removed his legs from Gerásim's shoulders, turned sideways onto his arm, and felt sorry for himself. He only waited till Gerásim had gone into the next room and then restrained himself no longer but wept like a child. He wept on account of his helplessness, his terrible loneliness, the cruelty of man, the cruelty of God, and the absence of God.

"Why hast Thou done all this? Why hast Thou brought me here? Why, dost Thou torment me so terribly?"

He did not expect an answer and yet wept because there was no answer and could be none. The pain again grew more acute, but he did not stir and did not call. He said to himself: "Go on! Strike me! But what is it for? What have I done to Thee? What is it for?"

Then he grew quiet and not only ceased weeping but even held his breath and became all attention. It was as though he were listening not to an audible voice but to a voice of his soul, to the current of thoughts arising within him.

"What is it you want?" was the first clear conception capable of expression in words, that he heard.

"What do you want? What do you want?" he repeated to himself.

"What do I want? To live and not to suffer," he answered.

And again he listened with such concentrated attention that even his pain did not distract him.

"To live? How?" asked his inner voice.

"Why, to live as I used to—well and pleasantly."

"As you lived before, well and pleasantly?" the voice repeated.

And in imagination he began to recall the moments of his pleasant life. But strange to say none of those best moments of his pleasant life now seemed at all what they had then seemed—none of them except the first recollections of childhood. There, in childhood, there had been something really pleasant with which it would be possible to live if it could return. But the child who had experienced that happiness existed no longer, it was like a reminiscence of somebody else.

As soon as the period began which had produced the present Iván Ilyich, all that had then seemed joys now melted before his sight and turned into something trivial and often nasty.

And the further he departed from childhood and the nearer he came to the present the more worthless and doubtful were the joys. This began with the School of Law. A little that was really good was still found there— there was light-heartedness, friendship, and hope. But in the upper classes there had already been fewer of such good moments. Then during the first years of his official career, when he was in the service of the Governor, some pleasant moments again occurred: they were the memories of love for a woman. Then all became confused and there was still less of what

was good; later on again there was still less that was good, and the further
he went the less there was. His marriage, a mere accident, then the disenchantment that followed it, his wife's bad breath and the sensuality and
hypocrisy: then that deadly official life and those preoccupations about
money, a year of it, and two, and ten, and twenty, and always the same
thing. And the longer it lasted the more deadly it became. "It is as if I had
been going downhill while I imagined I was going up. And that is really
what it was. I was going up in public opinion, but to the same extent life
was ebbing away from me. And now it is all done and there is only death."

"Then what does it mean? Why? It can't be that life is so senseless and
horrible. But if it really has been so horrible and senseless, why must I die
and die in agony? There is something wrong!"

"Maybe I did not live as I ought to have done," it suddenly occurred to
him. "But how could that be, when I did everything properly?" he replied,
and immediately dismissed from his mind this, the sole solution of all the
riddles of life and death, as something quite impossible.

"Then what do you want now? To live? Live how? Live as you lived in
the law courts when the usher proclaimed 'The judge is coming!' The
judge is coming, the judge!" he repeated to himself. "Here he is, the
judge. But I am not guilty!" he exclaimed angrily. "What is it for?" And
he ceased crying, but turning his face to the wall continued to ponder on
the same question: Why, and for what purpose, is there all this horror?
But however much he pondered he found no answer. And whenever the
thought occurred to him, as it often did, that it all resulted from his not
having lived as he ought to have done, he at once recalled the correctness
of his whole life, and dismissed so strange an idea.

X

Another fortnight passed. Iván Ilyich now no longer left his sofa. He
would not lie in bed but lay on the sofa, facing the wall nearly all the
time. He suffered ever the same unceasing agonies and in his loneliness
pondered always on the same insoluble question: "What is this? Can it be
that it is Death?" And the inner voice answered: "Yes, it is Death."

"Why these sufferings?" And the voice answered, "For no reason—they
just are so." Beyond and besides this there was nothing.

From the very beginning of his illness, ever since he had first been to
see the doctor, Iván Ilyich's life had been divided between two contrary
and alternating moods: now it was despair and the expectation of this
uncomprehended and terrible death, and now hope and an intently interested observation of the functioning of his organs. Now before his eyes
there was only a kidney or an intestine that temporarily evaded its duty,
and now only that incomprehensible and dreadful death from which it
was impossible to escape.

These two states of mind had alternated from the very beginning of his
illness, but the further it progressed the more doubtful and fantastic
became the conception of the kidney, and the more real the sense of
impending death.

He had but to call to mind what he had been three months before and what he was now, to call to mind with what regularity he had been going downhill, for every possibility of hope to be shattered.

Latterly during that loneliness in which he found himself as he lay facing the back of the sofa, a loneliness in the midst of a populous town and surrounded by numerous acquaintances and relations but that yet could not have been more complete anywhere—either at the bottom of the sea or under the earth—during that terrible loneliness Iván Ilyich had lived only in memories of the past. Pictures of his past rose before him one after another. They always began with what was nearest in time and then went back to what was most remote—to his childhood—and rested there. If he thought of the stewed prunes that had been offered him that day, his mind went back to the raw shrivelled French plums of his childhood, their peculiar flavour and the flow of saliva when he sucked their stones, and along with the memory of that taste came a whole series of memories of those days: his nurse, his brother, and their toys. "No, I mustn't think of that. . . . It is too painful," Iván Ilyich said to himself, and brought himself back to the present—to the button on the back of the sofa and the creases in its morocco. "Morocco is expensive, but it does not wear well: there had been a quarrel about it. It was a different kind of quarrel and a different kind of morocco that time when we tore father's portfolio and were punished, and mamma brought us some tarts. . . ." And again his thoughts dwelt on his childhood, and again it was painful and he tried to banish them and fix his mind on something else.

Then again together with that chain of memories another series passed through his mind—of how his illness had progressed and grown worse. There also the further back he looked the more life there had been. There had been more of what was good in life and more of life itself. The two merged together. "Just as the pain went on getting worse and worse, so my life grew worse and worse," he thought. "There is one bright spot there at the back, at the beginning of life, and afterwards all becomes blacker and blacker and proceeds more and more rapidly—in inverse ratio to the square of the distance from death," thought Iván Ilyich. And the example of a stone falling downwards with increasing velocity entered his mind. Life, a series of increasing sufferings, flies further and further towards its end—the most terrible suffering. "I am flying. . . ." He shuddered, shifted himself, and tried to resist, but was already aware that resistance was impossible, and again with eyes weary of gazing but unable to cease seeing what was before them, he stared at the back of the sofa and waited—awaiting that dreadful fall and shock and destruction.

"Resistance is impossible!" he said to himself. "If I could only understand what it is all for! But that too is impossible. An explanation would be possible if it could be said that I have not lived as I ought to. But it is impossible to say that," and he remembered all the legality, correctitude, and propriety of his life. "That at any rate can certainly not be admitted," he thought, and his lips smiled ironically as if someone could see that smile and be taken in by it. "There is no explanation! Agony, death. . . . What for?"

XI

Another two weeks went by in this way and during that fortnight an event occurred that Iván Ilyich and his wife had desired. Petríshchev formally proposed. It happened in the evening. The next day Praskóvya Fëdorovna came into her husband's room considering how best to inform him of it, but that very night there had been a fresh change for the worse in his condition. She found him still lying on the sofa but in a different position. He lay on his back, groaning and staring fixedly straight in front of him.

She began to remind him of his medicines, but he turned his eyes towards her with such a look that she did not finish what she was saying; so great an animosity, to her in particular, did that look express.

"For Christ's sake let me die in peace!" he said.

She would have gone away, but just then their daughter came in and went up to say good morning. He looked at her as he had done at his wife, and in reply to her inquiry about his health said dryly that he would soon free them all of himself. They were both silent and after sitting with him for a while went away.

"Is it our fault?" Lisa said to her mother. "It's as if we were to blame! I am sorry for papa, but why should we be tortured?"

The doctor came at his usual time. Iván Ilyich answered "Yes" and "No," never taking his angry eyes from him, and at last said: "You know you can do nothing for me, so leave me alone."

"We can ease your sufferings."

"You can't even do that. Let me be."

The doctor went into the drawing-room and told Praskóvya Fëdorovna that the case was very serious and that the only resource left was opium to allay her husband's sufferings, which must be terrible.

It was true, as the doctor said, that Iván Ilyich's physical sufferings were terrible, but worse than the physical sufferings were his mental sufferings which were his chief torture.

His mental sufferings were due to the fact that that night, as he looked at Gerásim's sleepy, good-natured face with its prominent cheek-bones, the question suddenly occurred to him: "What if my whole life has really been wrong?"

It occurred to him that what had appeared perfectly impossible before, namely that he had not spent his life as he should have done, might after all be true. It occurred to him that his scarcely perceptible attempts to struggle against what was considered good by the most highly placed people, those scarcely noticeable impulses which he had immediately suppressed, might have been the real thing, and all the rest false. And his professional duties and the whole arrangement of his life and of his family, and all his social and official interests, might all have been false. He tried to defend all those things to himself and suddenly felt the weakness of what he was defending. There was nothing to defend.

"But if that is so," he said to himself, "and I am leaving this life with the consciousness that I have lost all that was given me and it is impossible to rectify it—what then?"

He lay on his back and began to pass his life in review in quite a new way. In the morning when he saw first his footman, then his wife, then his daughter, and then the doctor, their every word and movement confirmed to him the awful truth that had been revealed to him during the night. In them he saw himself—all that for which he had lived—and saw clearly that it was not real at all, but a terrible and huge deception which had hidden both life and death. This consciousness intensified his physical suffering tenfold. He groaned and tossed about, and pulled at his clothing which choked and stifled him. And he hated them on that account.

He was given a large dose of opium and became unconscious, but at noon his sufferings began again. He drove everybody away and tossed from side to side.

His wife came to him and said:

"Jean, my dear, do this for me. It can't do any harm and often helps. Healthy people often do it."

He opened his eyes wide.

"What? Take communion? Why? It's unnecessary! However . . ."

She began to cry.

"Yes, do, my dear. I'll send for our priest. He is such a nice man."

"All right. Very well," he muttered.

When the priest came and heard his confession, Iván Ilyich was softened and seemed to feel a relief from his doubts and consequently from his sufferings, and for a moment there came a ray of hope. He again began to think of the vermiform appendix and the possibility of correcting it. He received the sacrament with tears in his eyes.

When they laid him down again afterwards he felt a moment's ease, and the hope that he might live awoke in him again. He began to think of the operation that had been suggested to him. "To live! I want to live!" he said to himself.

His wife came in to congratulate him after his communion, and when uttering the usual conventional words she added:

"You feel better, don't you?"

Without looking at her he said "Yes."

Her dress, her figure, the expression of her face, the tone of her voice, all revealed the same thing. "This is wrong, it is not as it should be. All you have lived for and still live for is falsehood and deception, hiding life and death from you." And as soon as he admitted that thought, his hatred and his agonizing physical suffering again sprang up, and with that suffering a consciousness of the unavoidable, approaching end. And to this was added a new sensation of grinding shooting pain and a feeling of suffocation.

The expression of his face when he uttered that "yes" was dreadful. Having uttered it, he looked her straight in the eyes, turned on his face with a rapidity extraordinary in his weak state and shouted:

"Go away! Go away and leave me alone!"

XII

From that moment the screaming began that continued for three days, and was so terrible that one could not hear it through two closed doors without horror. At the moment he answered his wife he realized that he was lost, that there was no return, that the end had come, the very end, and his doubts were still unsolved and remained doubts.

"Oh! Oh! Oh!" he cried in various intonations. He had begun by screaming "I won't!" and continued screaming on the letter "o."

For three whole days, during which time did not exist for him, he struggled in that black sack into which he was being thrust by an invisible, resistless force. He struggled as a man condemned to death struggles in the hands of the executioner, knowing that he cannot save himself. And every moment he felt that despite all his efforts he was drawing nearer and nearer to what terrified him. He felt that his agony was due to his being thrust into that black hole and still more to his not being able to get right into it. He was hindered from getting into it by his conviction that his life had been a good one. That very justification of his life held him fast and prevented his moving forward, and it caused him most torment of all.

Suddenly some force struck him in the chest and side, making it still harder to breathe, and he fell through the hole and there at the bottom was a light. What had happened to him was like the sensation one sometimes experiences in a railway carriage when one thinks one is going backwards while one is really going forwards and suddenly becomes aware of the real direction.

"Yes, it was all not the right thing," he said to himself, "but that's no matter. It can be done. But what is the right thing?" he asked himself, and suddenly grew quiet.

This occurred at the end of the third day, two hours before his death. Just then his schoolboy son had crept softly in and gone up to the bedside. The dying man was still screaming desperately and waving his arms. His hand fell on the boy's head, and the boy caught it, pressed it to his lips, and began to cry.

At that very moment Iván Ilyich fell through and caught sight of the light, and it was revealed to him that though his life had not been what it should have been, this could still be rectified. He asked himself, "What is the right thing?" and grew still, listening. Then he felt that someone was kissing his hand. He opened his eyes, looked at his son, and felt sorry for him. His wife came up to him and he glanced at her. She was gazing at him open-mouthed, with undried tears on her nose and cheek and a despairing look on her face. He felt sorry for her too.

"Yes, I am making them wretched," he thought. "They are sorry, but it will be better for them when I die." He wished to say this but had not the strength to utter it. "Besides, why speak? I must act," he thought. With a look at his wife he indicated his son and said: "Take him away . . . sorry for him . . . sorry for you too. . . ." He tried to add, "forgive me," but said "forgo" and waved his hand, knowing that He whose understanding mattered would understand.

And suddenly it grew clear to him that what had been oppressing him and would not leave him was all dropping away at once from two sides, from ten sides, and from all sides. He was sorry for them, he must act so as not to hurt them: release them and free himself from these sufferings. "How good and how simple!" he thought. "And the pain?" he asked himself. "What has become of it? Where are you, pain?"

He turned his attention to it.

"Yes, here it is. Well, what of it? Let the pain be."

"And death . . . where is it?"

He sought his former accustomed fear of death and did not find it. "Where is it? What death?" There was no fear because there was no death. In place of death there was light.

"So that's what it is!" he suddenly exclaimed aloud. "What joy!"

To him all this happened in a single instant, and the meaning of that instant did not change. For those present his agony continued for another two hours. Something rattled in his throat, his emaciated body twitched, then the gasping and rattle became less and less frequent.

"It is finished!" said someone near him.

He heard these words and repeated them in his soul.

"Death is finished," he said to himself. "It is no more!"

He drew in a breath, stopped in the midst of a sigh, stretched out, and died.

HENRIK IBSEN

1828–1906

Henrik Ibsen was the foremost playwright of his time—treating social themes and ideas and often satirizing the nineteenth-century bourgeoisie—and not only in Norway, his native land. His plays may be viewed historically as the culmination point of the *bourgeois* drama that has flourished fitfully, in France and Germany particularly, since the eighteenth century, when Diderot advocated and wrote plays about the middle classes, their "conditions" and problems. But they may also be seen as the fountainhead of much twentieth-century drama; in the West the plays of George Bernard Shaw and John Galsworthy, who discuss social problems, and of Maurice Maeterlinck and Anton Chekhov, who learned from the later "symbolist" Ibsen. Ibsen's drama of domestic and political crisis was also immensely popular in China and influenced a generation of modern playwrights.

Ibsen was born at Skien, in Norway, on March 20, 1828. His family had sunk into poverty and finally complete bankruptcy. In 1844, at the age of sixteen, he was sent to Grimstad, another small coastal town, as an apothecary's apprentice. There he lived in almost complete isolation and cut himself off from his family, except for his sister Hedvig. In 1850 he managed to get to Oslo (then Christiana) and to enroll at the university. But he never passed his examinations and in the following year left for Bergen, where he had acquired the position of playwright and assistant stage manager at the newly founded Norwegian Theater. Ibsen supplied the small theater with several historical and romantic plays. In 1857 he was appointed artistic director at the Mollergate Theater in Christiana, and a year later he married Susannah Thoresen. *Love's Comedy* (1862) was his first major success on the stage. Ibsen was then deeply affected by Scandinavianism, the movement for solidarity of the northern nations, and when in 1864 Norway refused to do anything to support Denmark in its war with Prussia and Austria over Schleswig-Holstein, he was so disgusted with his country that he left it for what he thought would be permanent exile. He lived in Rome, in Dresden, in Munich, and in smaller summer resorts, and during this time wrote all his later plays.

After a long period of incubation and experimentation with romantic and historical themes, Ibsen wrote a series of "problem" plays, beginning with *The Pillars of Society* (1877), which in their time created a furor by their fearless criticism of the nineteenth-century social scene: the subjection of women, hypocrisy, hereditary disease, seamy politics, and corrupt journalism. He wrote these plays using naturalistic modes of presentation: ordinary colloquial speech, a simple setting in a drawing room or study, a natural way of introducing or dismissing characters. Ibsen had learned from the "well-made" Parisian play (typified by those of Eugène Scribe) how to confine his action to one climactic situation and how gradually to uncover the past by retrogressive exposition. But he went far beyond it in technical skill and intellectual honesty.

The success of Ibsen's problem plays was international. But we must not forget that he was a Norwegian, the first writer of his small nation (its population at that time was less than two million) to win a reputation outside of Norway. Ibsen more than anyone else widened the scope of world literature beyond the confines of the "great" modern nations, which had entered its community roughly in this order: Italy, Spain, France, England, Germany, Russia. Since the time of Ibsen, other small nations have begun to play their part in the concert of world literature. Paradoxically, however, Ibsen rejected his own land. He had dreamed of becoming a great national poet. Instead, the plays he wrote during his voluntary exile depicted Norwegian society as consisting largely of a stuffy, provincial middle class, redeemed by a few upright, even fiery, individuals of initiative and courage. Only in 1891, when he was sixty-three, did Ibsen return to Christiana for good. He was then famous and widely honored, but lived a very retired life. In 1900 he suffered a stroke that made him a complete invalid for the last years of his life. He died on May 23, 1906, in Christiana.

Ibsen could hardly have survived his time if he had been merely a painter of society, a dialectician of social issues, and a magnificent technician of the theater. True, many of his discussions are now dated. We smile at some of what happens in *A Doll's House* (1879) and *Ghosts* (1881). His stagecraft is not unusual, even on Broadway. But Ibsen stays with us because he has more to offer—because he was an artist who managed to create, at his best, works of poetry that, under their mask of sardonic humor, express his dream of humanity reborn by intelligence and self-sacrifice.

Hedda Gabler (1890) surprised and puzzled the large audience all over Europe that Ibsen had won in the 1880s. The play shows nothing of Ibsen's reforming zeal: no general theme emerges that could be used in spreading progressive ideas such as the emancipation of women dramatized in *A Doll's House* (1879), nor is the play an example of Ibsen's peculiar technique of retrospective revelation exhibited in *Rosmersholm* (1886). At first glance it seems mainly a study of a complex, exceptional, and even unique woman. Henry James, reviewing the first English performance, saw it as the picture of "a state of nerves as well as of soul, a state of temper, of health, of chagrin, of despair." Undoubtedly, Hedda is the central figure of the play, but she is no conventional heroine. She behaves atrociously to everyone with whom she comes in contact, and her moral sense is thoroughly defective: she is perverse, egotistical, sadistic, callous, even evil and demonic, truly a *femme fatale*. Still, this impression, while not mistaken, ignores another side of her personality and her situation. The play is, after all, a tragedy (though there are comic touches), and we are to feel pity and terror. Hedda is not simply evil and perverse. We must imagine her as distinguished, well bred, proud, beautiful, and even grand in her defiance of her surroundings and in the final gesture of her suicide. Not for nothing have great actresses excelled in this role. We must pity her as a tortured, tormented creature caught in a web of circumstance, as a victim, in spite of her desperate struggles to dominate and control the fate of those around her.

We are carefully prepared to understand her heritage. She is General Gabler's daughter. Ibsen tells us himself (in a letter to Count Moritz Prozor, dated December 4, 1890) that "I intended to indicate thereby that as a personality she is to be regarded rather as her father's daughter than as her husband's wife." She has inherited an aristocratic view of life. Her father's portrait hangs in her apartment. His pistols tell of the code of honor and the ready escape they offer in a self-inflicted death. Hedda lives in Ibsen's Norway, a stuffy, provincial, middle-class society, and is acutely, even morbidly afraid of scandal. She has, to her own regret, rejected the advances of Eilert, theatrically threatening him with her father's pistol. She envies Thea for the boldness with which she deserted her husband to follow Eilert. She admires Eilert for his escapades, which she romanticizes with the recurrent metaphor of his returning with "vine-leaves in his hair." But she cannot break out of the narrow confines of her society. She is not an emancipated woman.

When she is almost thirty, in reduced circumstances, she accepts a suitable husband, George Tesman. The marriage of convenience turns out to be a ghastly error for which she cannot forgive herself: Tesman is an amiable bore absorbed in his research into the "Domestic Industries of Brabant During the Middle Ages." His expectations of a professorship in his home town turn out to be uncertain. He has gone into debt, even to his guileless old aunt, in renting an expensive house, and, supreme humiliation for her, Hedda is pregnant by him. The dream of luxury, of becoming a hostess, of keeping thoroughbred horses, is shattered the very first day after their return from the prolonged honeymoon, which for Tesman was also a trip to rummage around in archives. Hedda is deeply stirred by the return of Eilert, her first suitor. She seems vaguely to think of a new relationship, at least, by spoiling his friendship with Thea. She plays with the attentions of Judge Brack. But everything quickly comes to nought: she is trapped in her marriage, unable and unwilling to become unfaithful to her husband; she is deeply disappointed by Eilert's ugly death, saying, "Oh, why does everything I touch become mean and ludicrous? It's like a curse!" She fears the scandal that will follow when her role in Eilert's suicide is discovered and she is called before the police; she can avoid it only by coming under the power of Judge Brack, who is prepared to blackmail her with his knowledge of the circumstances. Her plot to destroy Thea and Eilert's brainchild is frustrated by Thea's having preserved notes and drafts, which Thea eagerly starts to reconstruct with the help of Tesman. Still, while Hedda is in a terrible impasse, her suicide remains a shock, an abrupt, even absurd deed, eliciting the final line from the commonsensical Judge Brack: "But, good God! People don't do such things!" But we must assume that Hedda had pondered suicide long before: the pistol she gave to Eilert implies an unspoken suicide pact. He bungled it; she does it the right way, dying in beauty, shot in the temple and not in the abdomen.

The play is not, however, simply a character study, though Hedda is an extraordinarily complex, contradictory, subtle woman whose portrait, at least on the stage, could not be easily paralleled before Ibsen. It is also an extremely effective, swiftly moving play of action, deftly plotted in its clashes and climaxes. At the end of Act I Hedda seems to have won. The Tesmans, husband and aunt, are put in their place. Thea is lured into making confidences. The scene in Act II in which Hedda appeals to Eilert's pride in his independence and induces him to join in Judge Brack's party is a superb display of Hedda's power and skill. Act II ends with Eilert going off and the two women left alone in their tense though suppressed antagonism. Act III ends with Hedda alone, burning the precious manuscript about the "forces that will shape our civilization and the direction in which that civilization may develop," an obvious contrast to Tesman's research into an irrelevant past. (Ibsen himself always believed in progress, in a utopia he called "the Third Realm.")

The action is compressed into about thirty-six hours and located in a house where only the moving of furniture (the piano into the back room) or the change of light or costumes indicates the passing of time. Tesman is something of a fool. He is totally unaware of Hedda's inner turmoil, he obtusely misunderstands allusions to her pregnancy, he comically encourages the advances of Judge Brack, he complacently settles down to the task of assembling the fragments of Eilert's manuscript, recognizing that "putting other people's papers into order is rather my specialty." Though he seems amiably domestic in his love for his aunts, proud of having won Hedda, ambitious to provide an elegant home for her, his behavior is by no means above reproach. He envies and fears Eilert, gloats over his bad reputation, surreptitiously brings home the lost manuscript, conceals its recovery from Thea; when Hedda tells of its being burned, he is at first shocked, reacting comically with the legal phrase about "appropriating lost property," but is then easily persuaded to accept it when Hedda tells him that she did it for his sake and is completely won over when she reveals her pregnancy. After Eilert's death he feels, however, some guilt and tries to make up by helping in the reconstruction of the manuscript, now that his rival no longer threatens his career. Tesman is given strong speech mannerisms: the frequent use of "what?"—which Hedda, commenting at the end on the progress of the work on the manuscript, imitates sarcastically—and the use of "fancy that." His last inappropriate words, "She's shot herself! Shot herself in the head! Fancy that!" lend a grotesque touch to the tragic end. Aunt Juliana belongs with him: she is a fussy, kindly person, proud of her nephew, awed by his new wife, eager to help with the expected baby, but also easily consoled after the death of her sister: "There's always some poor invalid who needs care and attention."

The other pair, Eilert Loevborg and Thea Elvsted, are sharply contrasted. Thea had the courage to leave her husband; she is devoted to Eilert and seems to have cured him of his addiction to drink but fears that he cannot resist a new temptation. Eilert tells Hedda unkindly that Thea is "silly," and there is some truth to that, inasmuch as she is so easily taken in by Hedda. Her quick settling down to work on the manuscript after Eilert's death suggests some obtuseness, though we must, presumably, excuse it as a theatrical foreshortening.

Judge Brack is a "man of the world," a sensualist who hardly conceals his desire to make Hedda his mistress, by blackmail if necessary, and is dismayed when she escapes his clutches: in his facile philosophy "people usually learn to accept the inevitable."

Eilert, we must assume, is some kind of genius. His book, we have to take on trust, is an important work. We are told that he had squandered an inheritance, had engaged in orgies, and had regaled Hedda with tales of his exploits before she chased him with her pistol. When he comes back to town, ostensibly reformed, dressed conventionally, he immediately starts courting Hedda again. Stung by her contempt for his abstinence, he rushes off to Brack's party, which degenerates into a disgraceful brawl in a brothel. His relapse and the loss of the manuscript destroy his self-esteem and hope for any future. He accepts Hedda's pistol but dies an ignominious, ugly death. We see Eilert mainly reflected in Hedda's imagination as a figure of pagan freedom who, she thinks, has done something noble, beautiful, and courageous in "rising from the feast of life so early." She dies in beauty as she wanted Eilert to die.

This aesthetic suicide must seem to us a supremely futile gesture of revolt. Ibsen always admired the great rebels, the fighters for freedom, but *Hedda Gabler* will appear almost a parodic version of his persistent theme: the individual against society, defying it and escaping it in death.

J. W. McFarlane, ed., *Discussions of Henrik Ibsen* (1962), contains Henry James's "On the Occasion of 'Hedda Gabler.'" John Northam, *Ibsen: A Critical Study* (1973), has a chapter on *Hedda Gabler*, as do Bernard Shaw, *The Quintes-*

sence of Ibsenism (1913), and Hermann J. Weigand, *The Modern Ibsen* (1925). Rolf Fjelde, ed., *Ibsen: A Collection of Critical Essays* (1965), has a good essay on *Hedda Gabler*. For more general comment, see Yvonne Shafter, *Henrik Ibsen: Life, Work, and Criticism* (1985). *Ibsen's Heroines* (1985), by Ibsen's friend Lou Andreas-Salomé, has an interesting chapter on Hedda Gabler as an empty soul reaching for greatness. Frederick J. Marker and Lise-Lone Marker, *Ibsen's Lively Art: A Performance Study of the Major Plays* (1989), use descriptions of the various performances of *Hedda Gabler* to examine differing interpretations of the main characters.

PRONOUNCING GLOSSARY

The following list uses common English syllables and stress accents to provide rough equivalents of selected words whose pronunciation may be unfamiliar to the general reader.

Eilert Loevborg: *ai'-lert leuhv'-borg*

fjord: *fyoord*

Rosmersholm: *ross'-merss-holm*

Thea Elvsted: *tay'-ah aelf'-sted*

Hedda Gabler[1]

CHARACTERS

GEORGE TESMAN, *research graduate in cultural history*	MRS. ELVSTED
	JUDGE BRACK
HEDDA, *his wife*	EILERT LOEVBORG
MISS JULIANA TESMAN, *his aunt*	BERTHA, *a maid*

The action takes place in TESMAN's *villa in the fashionable quarter of town.*

Act I

SCENE—*A large drawing room, handsomely and tastefully furnished; decorated in dark colors. In the rear wall is a broad open doorway, with curtains drawn back to either side. It leads to a smaller room, decorated in the same style as the drawing room. In the right-hand wall of the drawing room, a folding door leads out to the hall. The opposite wall, on the left, contains french windows, also with curtains drawn back on either side. Through the glass we can see part of a verandah, and trees in autumn colors. Downstage stands an oval table, covered by a cloth and surrounded by chairs. Downstage right, against the wall, is a broad stove tiled with dark porcelain; in front of it stand a high-backed armchair, a cushioned footrest, and two footstools. Upstage right, in an alcove, is a corner sofa, with a small, round table. Downstage left, a little away from the wall, is another sofa. Upstage of the french windows, a piano. On either side of the open doorway in the rear wall stand what-nots holding ornaments of terra cotta and majolica. Against the rear wall of the smaller room can be seen a sofa, a table, and a couple of chairs. Above this sofa hangs the*

1. Translated by Michael Meyer.

*portrait of a handsome old man in general's uniform. Above the table a
lamp hangs from the ceiling, with a shade of opalescent, milky glass. All
round the drawing room bunches of flowers stand in vases and glasses.
More bunches lie on the tables. The floors of both rooms are covered
with thick carpets. Morning light. The sun shines in through the french
windows.*

*MISS JULIANA TESMAN, wearing a hat and carrying a parasol, enters from
the hall, followed by BERTHA, who is carrying a bunch of flowers wrapped
in paper. MISS TESMAN is about sixty-five, of pleasant and kindly appearance. She is neatly but simply dressed in grey outdoor clothes. BERTHA,
the maid, is rather simple and rustic-looking. She is getting on in years.*

MISS TESMAN: [*Stops just inside the door, listens, and says in a hushed
voice.*] No, bless my soul! They're not up yet.

BERTHA: [*Also in hushed tones.*] What did I tell you, miss? The boat didn't
get in till midnight. And when they did turn up—Jesus, miss, you
should have seen all the things Madam made me unpack before she'd
go to bed!

MISS TESMAN: Ah, well. Let them have a good lie in. But let's have some
nice fresh air waiting for them when they do come down. [*Goes to the
french windows and throws them wide open.*]

BERTHA: [*Bewildered at the table, the bunch of flowers in her hand.*] I'm
blessed if there's a square inch left to put anything. I'll have to let it lie
here, miss. [*Puts it on the piano.*]

MISS TESMAN: Well, Bertha dear, so now you have a new mistress. Heaven
knows it nearly broke my heart to have to part with you.

BERTHA: [*Snivels.*] What about me, Miss Juju? How do you suppose I felt?
After all the happy years I've spent with you and Miss Rena?

MISS TESMAN: We must accept it bravely, Bertha. It was the only way.
George needs you to take care of him. He could never manage without
you. You've looked after him ever since he was a tiny boy.

BERTHA: Oh, but Miss Juju, I can't help thinking about Miss Rena, lying
there all helpless, poor dear. And that new girl! She'll never learn the
proper way to handle an invalid.

MISS TESMAN: Oh, I'll manage to train her. I'll do most of the work myself,
you know. You needn't worry about my poor sister, Bertha dear.

BERTHA: But Miss Juju, there's another thing. I'm frightened Madam may
not find me suitable.

MISS TESMAN: Oh, nonsense, Bertha. There may be one or two little things
to begin with——

BERTHA: She's a real lady. Wants everything just so.

MISS TESMAN: But of course she does! General Gabler's daughter! Think
of what she was accustomed to when the General was alive. You
remember how we used to see her out riding with her father? In that
long black skirt? With the feather in her hat?

BERTHA: Oh, yes, miss. As if I could forget! But, Lord! I never dreamed I'd
live to see a match between her and Master Georgie.

MISS TESMAN: Neither did I. By the way, Bertha, from now on you must
stop calling him Master Georgie. You must say: Dr. Tesman.

BERTHA: Yes, Madam said something about that too. Last night—the moment they'd set foot inside the door. Is it true, then, miss?

MISS TESMAN: Indeed it is. Just imagine, Bertha, some foreigners have made him a doctor. It happened while they were away. I had no idea till he told me when they got off the boat.

BERTHA: Well, I suppose there's no limit to what he won't become. He's that clever. I never thought he'd go in for hospital work, though.

MISS TESMAN: No, he's not that kind of doctor. [*Nods impressively.*] In any case, you may soon have to address him by an even grander title.

BERTHA: You don't say! What might that be, miss?

MISS TESMAN: [*Smiles.*] Ah! If you only knew! [*Moved.*] Dear God, if only poor dear Joachim could rise out of his grave and see what his little son has grown into! [*Looks round.*] But Bertha, why have you done this? Taken the chintz covers off all the furniture!

BERTHA: Madam said I was to. Can't stand chintz covers on chairs, she said.

MISS TESMAN: But surely they're not going to use this room as a parlor?

BERTHA: So I gathered, miss. From what Madam said. He didn't say anything. The Doctor.

[GEORGE TESMAN *comes into the rear room, from the right, humming, with an open, empty travelling bag in his hand. He is about thirty-three, of medium height and youthful appearance, rather plump, with an open, round, contented face, and fair hair and beard. He wears spectacles, and is dressed in comfortable, indoor clothes.*]

MISS TESMAN: Good morning! Good morning, George!

TESMAN: [*In open doorway.*] Auntie Juju! Dear Auntie Juju! [*Comes forward and shakes her hand.*] You've come all the way out here! And so early! What?

MISS TESMAN: Well, I had to make sure you'd settled in comfortably.

TESMAN: But you can't have had a proper night's sleep.

MISS TESMAN: Oh, never mind that.

TESMAN: We were so sorry we couldn't give you a lift. But you saw how it was—Hedda had so much luggage—and she insisted on having it all with her.

MISS TESMAN: Yes, I've never seen so much luggage.

BERTHA: [*To* TESMAN.] Shall I go and ask Madam if there's anything I can lend her a hand with?

TESMAN: Er—thank you, Bertha; no, you needn't bother. She says if she wants you for anything she'll ring.

BERTHA: [*Over to right.*] Oh. Very good.

TESMAN: Oh, Bertha—take this bag, will you?

BERTHA: [*Takes it.*] I'll put it in the attic. [*Goes out into the hall.*]

TESMAN: Just fancy, Auntie Juju, I filled that whole bag with notes for my book. You know, it's really incredible what I've managed to find rooting through those archives. By Jove! Wonderful old things no one even knew existed—

MISS TESMAN: I'm sure you didn't waste a single moment of your honeymoon, George dear.

TESMAN: No, I think I can truthfully claim that. But, Auntie Juju, do take your hat off. Here. Let me untie it for you. What?

MISS TESMAN: [*As he does so.*] Oh dear, oh dear! It's just as if you were still living at home with us.

TESMAN: [*Turns the hat in his hand and looks at it.*] I say! What a splendid new hat!

MISS TESMAN: I bought it for Hedda's sake.

TESMAN: For Hedda's sake? What?

MISS TESMAN: So that Hedda needn't be ashamed of me, in case we ever go for a walk together.

TESMAN: [*Pats her cheek.*] You still think of everything, don't you, Auntie Juju? [*Puts the hat down on a chair by the table.*] Come on, let's sit down here on the sofa. And have a little chat while we wait for Hedda.

[*They sit. She puts her parasol in the corner of the sofa.*]

MISS TESMAN: [*Clasps both his hands and looks at him.*] Oh, George, it's so wonderful to have you back, and be able to see you with my own eyes again! Poor dear Joachim's own son!

TESMAN: What about me! It's wonderful for me to see you again, Auntie Juju. You've been a mother to me. And a father, too.

MISS TESMAN: You'll always keep a soft spot in your heart for your old aunties, won't you, George dear?

TESMAN: I suppose Auntie Rena's no better? What?

MISS TESMAN: Alas, no. I'm afraid she'll never get better, poor dear. She's lying there just as she has for all these years. Please God I may be allowed to keep her for a little longer. If I lost her I don't know what I'd do. Especially now I haven't you to look after.

TESMAN: [*Pats her on the back.*] There, there, there!

MISS TESMAN: [*With a sudden change of mood.*] Oh but George, fancy you being a married man! And to think it's you who've won Hedda Gabler! The beautiful Hedda Gabler! Fancy! She was always so surrounded by admirers.

TESMAN: [*Hums a little and smiles contentedly.*] Yes, I suppose there are quite a few people in this town who wouldn't mind being in my shoes. What?

MISS TESMAN: And what a honeymoon! Five months! Nearly six.

TESMAN: Well, I've done a lot of work, you know. All those archives to go through. And I've had to read lots of books.

MISS TESMAN: Yes, dear, of course. [*Lowers her voice confidentially.*] But tell me, George — haven't you any — any extra little piece of news to give me?

TESMAN: You mean, arising out of the honeymoon?

MISS TESMAN: Yes.

TESMAN: No, I don't think there's anything I didn't tell you in my letters. My doctorate, of course — but I told you about that last night, didn't I?

MISS TESMAN: Yes, yes, I didn't mean that kind of thing. I was just wondering — are you — are you expecting——?

TESMAN: Expecting what?

MISS TESMAN: Oh, come on George, I'm your old aunt!

TESMAN: Well actually — yes, I am expecting something.

MISS TESMAN: I knew it!

TESMAN: You'll be happy to hear that before very long I expect to become a professor.

MISS TESMAN: Professor?

TESMAN: I think I may say that the matter has been decided. But, Auntie Juju, you know about this.

MISS TESMAN: [*Gives a little laugh.*] Yes, of course. I'd forgotten. [*Changes her tone.*] But we were talking about your honeymoon. It must have cost a dreadful amount of money, George?

TESMAN: Oh well, you know, that big research grant I got helped a good deal.

MISS TESMAN: But how on earth did you manage to make it do for two?

TESMAN: Well, to tell the truth it was a bit tricky. What?

MISS TESMAN: Especially when one's traveling with a lady. A little bird tells me that makes things very much more expensive.

TESMAN: Well, yes, of course it does make things a little more expensive. But Hedda has to do things in style, Auntie Juju. I mean, she has to. Anything less grand wouldn't have suited her.

MISS TESMAN: No, no, I suppose not. A honeymoon abroad seems to be the vogue nowadays. But tell me, have you had time to look round the house?

TESMAN: You bet. I've been up since the crack of dawn.

MISS TESMAN: Well, what do you think of it?

TESMAN: Splendid. Absolutely splendid. I'm only wondering what we're going to do with those two empty rooms between that little one and Hedda's bedroom.

MISS TESMAN: [*Laughs slyly.*] Ah, George dear, I'm sure you'll manage to find some use for them—in time.

TESMAN: Yes, of course, Auntie Juju, how stupid of me. You're thinking of my books. What?

MISS TESMAN: Yes, yes, dear boy. I was thinking of your books.

TESMAN: You know, I'm so happy for Hedda's sake that we've managed to get this house. Before we became engaged she often used to say this was the only house in town she felt she could really bear to live in. It used to belong to Mrs. Falk—you know, the Prime Minister's widow.

MISS TESMAN: Fancy that! And what a stroke of luck it happened to come into the market. Just as you'd left on your honeymoon.

TESMAN: Yes, Auntie Juju, we've certainly had all the luck with us. What?

MISS TESMAN: But, George dear, the expense! It's going to make a dreadful hole in your pocket, all this.

TESMAN: [*A little downcast.*] Yes, I—I suppose it will, won't it?

MISS TESMAN: Oh, George, really!

TESMAN: How much do you think it'll cost? Roughly, I mean? What?

MISS TESMAN: I can't possibly say till I see the bills.

TESMAN: Well, luckily Judge Brack's managed to get it on very favorable terms. He wrote and told Hedda so.

MISS TESMAN: Don't you worry, George dear. Anyway I've stood security for all the furniture and carpets.

TESMAN: Security? But dear, sweet Auntie Juju, how could you possibly stand security?

MISS TESMAN: I've arranged a mortgage on our annuity.

TESMAN: [*Jumps up.*] What? On your annuity? And—Auntie Rena's?

MISS TESMAN: Yes. Well, I couldn't think of any other way.

TESMAN: [*Stands in front of her.*] Auntie Juju, have you gone completely out of your mind? That annuity's all you and Auntie Rena have.

MISS TESMAN: All right, there's no need to get so excited about it. It's a pure formality, you know. Judge Brack told me so. He was so kind as to arrange it all for me. A pure formality; those were his very words.

TESMAN: I dare say. All the same—

MISS TESMAN: Anyway, you'll have a salary of your own now. And, good heavens, even if we did have to fork out a little—tighten our belts for a week or two—why, we'd be happy to do so for your sake.

TESMAN: Oh, Auntie Juju! Will you never stop sacrificing yourself for me?

MISS TESMAN: [*Gets up and puts her hands on his shoulders.*] What else have I to live for but to smooth your road a little, my dear boy? You've never had any mother or father to turn to. And now at last we've achieved our goal. I won't deny we've had our little difficulties now and then. But now, thank the good Lord, George dear, all your worries are past.

TESMAN: Yes, it's wonderful really how everything's gone just right for me.

MISS TESMAN: Yes! And the enemies who tried to bar your way have been struck down. They have been made to bite the dust. The man who was your most dangerous rival has had the mightiest fall. And now he's lying there in the pit he dug for himself, poor misguided creature.

TESMAN: Have you heard any news of Eilert? Since I went away?

MISS TESMAN: Only that he's said to have published a new book.

TESMAN: What! Eilert Loevborg? You mean—just recently? What?

MISS TESMAN: So they say. I don't imagine it can be of any value, do you? When your new book comes out, that'll be another story. What's it going to be about?

TESMAN: The domestic industries of Brabant[2] in the Middle Ages.

MISS TESMAN: Oh, George! The things you know about!

TESMAN: Mind you, it may be some time before I actually get down to writing it. I've made these very extensive notes, and I've got to file and index them first.

MISS TESMAN: Ah, yes! Making notes; filing and indexing; you've always been wonderful at that. Poor dear Joachim was just the same.

TESMAN: I'm looking forward so much to getting down to that. Especially now I've a home of my own to work in.

MISS TESMAN: And above all, now that you have the girl you set your heart on, George dear.

TESMAN: [*Embraces her.*] Oh, yes, Auntie Juju, yes! Hedda's the loveliest thing of all! [*Looks towards the doorway.*] I think I hear her coming. What?

---

2. In the Middle Ages, a duchy located in parts of what are now Belgium and the Netherlands.

[HEDDA *enters the rear room from the left, and comes into the draw-*
ing room. She is a woman of twenty-nine. Distinguished, aristocratic
face and figure. Her complexion is pale and opalescent. Her eyes are
steel-grey, with an expression of cold, calm serenity. Her hair is of a
handsome auburn color, but is not especially abundant. She is
dressed in an elegant, somewhat loose-fitting morning gown.]

MISS TESMAN: [*Goes to greet her.*] Good morning, Hedda dear! Good
morning!

HEDDA: [*Holds out her hand.*] Good morning, dear Miss Tesman. What
an early hour to call. So kind of you.

MISS TESMAN: [*Seems somewhat embarrassed.*] And has the young bride
slept well in her new home?

HEDDA: Oh—thank you, yes. Passably well.

TESMAN: [*Laughs.*] Passably. I say, Hedda, that's good! When I jumped out
of bed, you were sleeping like a top.

HEDDA: Yes. Fortunately. One has to accustom oneself to anything new,
Miss Tesman. It takes time. [*Looks left.*] Oh, that maid's left the french
windows open. This room's flooded with sun.

MISS TESMAN: [*Goes towards the windows.*] Oh—let me close them.

HEDDA: No, no, don't do that. Tesman dear, draw the curtains. This light's
blinding me.

TESMAN: [*At the windows.*] Yes, yes, dear. There, Hedda, now you've got
shade and fresh air.

HEDDA: This room needs fresh air. All these flowers—But my dear Miss
Tesman, won't you take a seat?

MISS TESMAN: No, really not, thank you. I just wanted to make sure you
have everything you need. I must see about getting back home. My poor
dear sister will be waiting for me.

TESMAN: Be sure to give her my love, won't you? Tell her I'll run over and
see her later today.

MISS TESMAN: Oh yes, I'll tell her that. Oh, George——[*Fumbles in*
the pocket of her skirt.] I almost forgot. I've brought something for
you.

TESMAN: What's that, Auntie Juju? What?

MISS TESMAN: [*Pulls out a flat package wrapped in newspaper and gives it*
to him.] Open and see, dear boy.

TESMAN: [*Opens the package.*] Good heavens! Auntie Juju, you've kept
them! Hedda, this is really very touching. What?

HEDDA: [*By the what-nots, on the right.*] What is it, Tesman?

TESMAN: My old shoes! My slippers, Hedda!

HEDDA: Oh, them. I remember you kept talking about them on our honeymoon.

TESMAN: Yes, I missed them dreadfully. [*Goes over to her.*] Here, Hedda,
take a look.

HEDDA: [*Goes away towards the stove.*] Thanks, I won't bother.

TESMAN: [*Follows her.*] Fancy, Hedda, Auntie Rena's embroidered them
for me. Despite her being so ill. Oh, you can't imagine what memories
they have for me.

HEDDA: [*By the table.*] Not for me.

MISS TESMAN: No, Hedda's right there, George.

TESMAN: Yes, but I thought since she's one of the family now——

HEDDA: [*Interrupts.*] Tesman, we really can't go on keeping this maid.

MISS TESMAN: Not keep Bertha?

TESMAN: What makes you say that, dear? What?

HEDDA: [*Points.*] Look at that! She's left her old hat lying on the chair.

TESMAN: [*Appalled, drops his slippers on the floor.*] But, Hedda——!

HEDDA: Suppose someone came in and saw it?

TESMAN: But Hedda—that's Auntie Juju's hat.

HEDDA: Oh?

MISS TESMAN: [*Picks up the hat.*] Indeed it's mine. And it doesn't happen
to be old, Hedda dear.

HEDDA: I didn't look at it very closely, Miss Tesman.

MISS TESMAN: [*Tying on the hat.*] As a matter of fact, it's the first time I've
worn it. As the good Lord is my witness.

TESMAN: It's very pretty, too. Really smart.

MISS TESMAN: Oh, I'm afraid it's nothing much really. [*Looks round.*] My
parasol? Ah, here it is. [*Takes it.*] This is mine, too. [*Murmurs.*] Not
Bertha's.

TESMAN: A new hat and a new parasol! I say, Hedda, fancy that!

HEDDA: Very pretty and charming.

TESMAN: Yes, isn't it? What? But Auntie Juju, take a good look at Hedda
before you go. Isn't she pretty and charming?

MISS TESMAN: Dear boy, there's nothing new in that. Hedda's been a
beauty ever since the day she was born. [*Nods and goes right.*]

TESMAN: [*Follows her.*] Yes, but have you noticed how strong and healthy
she's looking? And how she's filled out since we went away?

MISS TESMAN: [*Stops and turns.*] Filled out?

HEDDA: [*Walks across the room.*] Oh, can't we forget it?

TESMAN: Yes, Auntie Juju—you can't see it so clearly with that dress on.
But I've good reason to know——

HEDDA: [*By the french windows, impatiently.*] You haven't good reason to
know anything.

TESMAN: It must have been the mountain air up there in the Tyrol——

HEDDA: [*Curtly, interrupts him.*] I'm exactly the same as when I went
away.

TESMAN: You keep on saying so. But you're not. I'm right, aren't I, Auntie
Juju?

MISS TESMAN: [*Has folded her hands and is gazing at her.*] She's beautiful—beautiful. Hedda is beautiful. [*Goes over to* HEDDA, *takes her head
between her hands, draws it down and kisses her hair.*] God bless and
keep you, Hedda Tesman. For George's sake.

HEDDA: [*Frees herself politely.*] Oh—let me go, please.

MISS TESMAN: [*Quietly, emotionally.*] I shall come see you both every day.

TESMAN: Yes, Auntie Juju, please do. What?

MISS TESMAN: Good-bye! Good-bye!

[*She goes out into the hall.* TESMAN *follows her. The door remains
open.* TESMAN *is heard sending his love to* AUNT RENA *and thanking*
MISS TESMAN *for his slippers. Meanwhile* HEDDA *walks up and down*

the room raising her arms and clenching her fists as though in desperation. Then she throws aside the curtains from the french windows
and stands there, looking out. A few moments later, TESMAN returns
and closes the door behind him.]

TESMAN: [Picks up his slippers from the floor.] What are you looking at,
Hedda?

HEDDA: [Calm and controlled again.] Only the leaves. They're so golden.
And withered.

TESMAN: [Wraps up the slippers and lays them on the table.] Well, we're
in September now.

HEDDA: [Restless again.] Yes. We're already into September.

TESMAN: Auntie Juju was behaving rather oddly, I thought, didn't you?
Almost as though she was in church or something. I wonder what came
over her. Any idea?

HEDDA: I hardly know her. Does she often act like that?

TESMAN: Not to the extent she did today.

HEDDA: [Goes away from the french windows.] Do you think she was hurt
by what I said about the hat?

TESMAN: Oh, I don't think so. A little at first, perhaps—

HEDDA: But what a thing to do, throw her hat down in someone's drawing
room. People don't do such things.

TESMAN: I'm sure Auntie Juju doesn't do it very often.

HEDDA: Oh well, I'll make it up with her.

TESMAN: Oh Hedda, would you?

HEDDA: When you see them this afternoon invite her to come out here
this evening.

TESMAN: You bet I will! I say, there's another thing which would please
her enormously.

HEDDA: Oh?

TESMAN: If you could bring yourself to call her Auntie Juju. For my sake,
Hedda? What?

HEDDA: Oh no, really Tesman, you mustn't ask me to do that. I've told you
so once before. I'll try to call her Aunt Juliana. That's as far as I'll go.

TESMAN: [After a moment.] I say, Hedda, is anything wrong? What?

HEDDA: I'm just looking at my old piano. It doesn't really go with all this.

TESMAN: As soon as I start getting my salary we'll see about changing it.

HEDDA: No, no, don't let's change it. I don't want to part with it. We can
move it into that little room and get another one to put in here.

TESMAN: [A little downcast.] Yes, we—might do that.

HEDDA: [Picks up the bunch of flowers from the piano.] These flowers
weren't here when we arrived last night.

TESMAN: I expect Auntie Juju brought them.

HEDDA: Here's a card. [Takes it out and reads.] "Will come back later
today." Guess who it's from?

TESMAN: No idea. Who? What?

HEDDA: It says: "Mrs. Elvsted."

TESMAN: No, really? Mrs. Elvsted! She used to be Miss Rysing, didn't she?

HEDDA: Yes. She was the one with that irritating hair she was always showing off. I hear she used to be an old flame of yours.

TESMAN: [*Laughs.*] That didn't last long. Anyway, that was before I got to know you, Hedda. By Jove, fancy her being in town!

HEDDA: Strange she should call. I only knew her at school.

TESMAN: Yes, I haven't seen her for—oh, heaven knows how long. I don't know how she manages to stick it out up there in the north. What?

HEDDA: [*Thinks for a moment, then says suddenly.*] Tell me, Tesman, doesn't he live somewhere up in those parts? You know—Eilert Loevborg?

TESMAN: Yes, that's right. So he does.

[BERTHA *enters from the hall.*]

BERTHA: She's here again, madam. The lady who came and left the flowers. [*Points.*] The ones you're holding.

HEDDA: Oh, is she? Well, show her in.

[BERTHA *opens the door for* MRS. ELVSTED *and goes out.* MRS. ELVSTED *is a delicately built woman with gentle, attractive features. Her eyes are light blue, large, and somewhat prominent, with a frightened, questioning expression. Her hair is extremely fair, almost flaxen, and is exceptionally wavy and abundant. She is two or three years younger than* HEDDA: *She is wearing a dark visiting dress, in good taste but not quite in the latest fashion.*]

HEDDA: [*Goes cordially to greet her.*] Dear Mrs. Elvsted, good morning. How delightful to see you again after all this time.

MRS. ELVSTED: [*Nervously, trying to control herself.*] Yes, it's many years since we met.

TESMAN: And since *we* met. What?

HEDDA: Thank you for your lovely flowers.

MRS. ELVSTED: Oh, please—I wanted to come yesterday afternoon. But they told me you were away—

TESMAN: You've only just arrived in town, then? What?

MRS. ELVSTED: I got here yesterday, around midday. Oh, I became almost desperate when I heard you weren't here.

HEDDA: Desperate? Why?

TESMAN: My dear Mrs. Rysing—Elvsted—

HEDDA: There's nothing wrong, I hope?

MRS. ELVSTED: Yes, there is. And I don't know anyone else here whom I can turn to.

HEDDA: [*Puts the flowers down on the table.*] Come and sit with me on the sofa—

MRS. ELVSTED: Oh, I feel too restless to sit down.

HEDDA: You must. Come along, now.

[*She pulls* MRS. ELVSTED *down on to the sofa and sits beside her.*]

TESMAN: Well? Tell us, Mrs.—er—

HEDDA: Has something happened at home?

MRS. ELVSTED: Yes—that is, yes and no. Oh, I do hope you won't misunderstand me—

HEDDA: Then you'd better tell us the whole story, Mrs. Elvsted.

TESMAN: That's why you've come. What?

MRS. ELVSTED: Yes—yes, it is. Well, then—in case you don't already know—Eilert Loevborg is in town.

HEDDA: Loevborg here?

TESMAN: Eilert back in town? By Jove, Hedda, did you hear that?

HEDDA: Yes, of course I heard.

MRS. ELVSTED: He's been here a week. A whole week! In this city. Alone. With all those dreadful people —

HEDDA: But my dear Mrs. Elvsted, what concern is he of yours?

MRS. ELVSTED: [Gives her a frightened look and says quickly.] He's been tutoring the children.

HEDDA: Your children?

MRS. ELVSTED: My husband's. I have none.

HEDDA: Oh, you mean your stepchildren.

MRS. ELVSTED: Yes.

TESMAN: [Gropingly.] But was he sufficiently — I don't know how to put it — sufficiently regular in his habits to be suited to such a post? What?

MRS. ELVSTED: For the past two to three years he has been living irreproachably.

TESMAN: You don't say! By Jove, Hedda, hear that?

HEDDA: I hear.

MRS. ELVSTED: Quite irreproachably, I assure you. In every respect. All the same — in this big city — with money in his pockets — I'm so dreadfully frightened something may happen to him.

TESMAN: But why didn't he stay up there with you and your husband?

MRS. ELVSTED: Once his book had come out, he became restless.

TESMAN: Oh, yes — Auntie Juju said he's brought out a new book.

MRS. ELVSTED: Yes, a big new book about the history of civilization. A kind of general survey. It came out a fortnight ago. Everyone's been buying it and reading it — it's created a tremendous stir —

TESMAN: Has it really? It must be something he's dug up, then.

MRS. ELVSTED: You mean from the old days?

TESMAN: Yes.

MRS. ELVSTED: No, he's written it all since he came to live with us.

TESMAN: Well, that's splendid news, Hedda. Fancy that!

MRS. ELVSTED: Oh, yes! If only he can go on like this!

HEDDA: Have you met him since you came here?

MRS. ELVSTED: No, not yet, I had such dreadful difficulty finding his address. But this morning I managed to track him down at last.

HEDDA: [Looks searchingly at her.] I must say I find it a little strange that your husband — hm —

MRS. ELVSTED: [Starts nervously.] My husband! What do you mean?

HEDDA: That he should send you all the way here on an errand of this kind. I'm surprised he didn't come himself to keep an eye on his friend.

MRS. ELVSTED: Oh, no, no — my husband hasn't the time. Besides, I — er — wanted to do some shopping here.

HEDDA: [With a slight smile.] Ah. Well, that's different.

MRS. ELVSTED: [Gets up quickly, restlessly.] Please, Mr. Tesman, I beg you — be kind to Eilert Loevborg if he comes here. I'm sure he will. I mean, you used to be such good friends in the old days. And you're both studying the same subject, as far as I can understand. You're in the same field, aren't you?

TESMAN: Well, we used to be, anyway.

MRS. ELVSTED: Yes—so I beg you earnestly, do please, please, keep an eye on him. Oh, Mr. Tesman, do promise me you will.

TESMAN: I shall be only too happy to do so, Mrs. Rysing.

HEDDA: Elvsted.

TESMAN: I'll do everything for Eilert that lies in my power. You can rely on that.

MRS. ELVSTED: Oh, how good and kind you are! [*Presses his hands.*] Thank you, thank you, thank you. [*Frightened.*] My husband's so fond of him, you see.

HEDDA: [*Gets up.*] You'd better send him a note, Tesman. He may not come to you of his own accord.

TESMAN: Yes, that'd probably be the best plan, Hedda. What?

HEDDA: The sooner the better. Why not do it now?

MRS. ELVSTED: [*Pleadingly.*] Oh yes, if only you would!

TESMAN: I'll do it this very moment. Do you have his address, Mrs.—er—Elvsted?

MRS. ELVSTED: Yes. [*Takes a small piece of paper from her pocket and gives it to him.*]

TESMAN: Good, good. Right, well I'll go inside and—— [*Looks round.*] Where are my slippers? Oh yes, here. [*Picks up the package and is about to go.*]

HEDDA: Try to sound friendly. Make it a nice long letter.

TESMAN: Right, I will.

MRS. ELVSTED: Please don't say anything about my having seen you.

TESMAN: Good heavens no, of course not. What? [*Goes out through the rear room to the right.*]

HEDDA: [*Goes over to* MRS. ELVSTED, *smiles, and says softly.*] Well! Now we've killed two birds with one stone.

MRS. ELVSTED: What do you mean?

HEDDA: Didn't you realize I wanted to get him out of the room?

MRS. ELVSTED: So that he could write the letter?

HEDDA: And so that I could talk to you alone.

MRS. ELVSTED: [*Confused.*] About this?

HEDDA: Yes, about this.

MRS. ELVSTED: [*In alarm.*] But there's nothing more to tell, Mrs. Tesman. Really there isn't.

HEDDA: Oh, yes there is. There's a lot more. I can see that. Come along, let's sit down and have a little chat.

[*She pushes* MRS. ELVSTED *down into the armchair by the stove and seats herself on one of the footstools.*]

MRS. ELVSTED: [*Looks anxiously at her watch.*] Really, Mrs. Tesman, I think I ought to be going now.

HEDDA: There's no hurry. Well? How are things at home?

MRS. ELVSTED: I'd rather not speak about that.

HEDDA: But my dear, you can tell me. Good heavens, we were at school together.

MRS. ELVSTED: Yes, but you were a year senior to me. Oh, I used to be terribly frightened of you in those days.

HEDDA: Frightened of me?

MRS. ELVSTED: Yes, terribly frightened. Whenever you met me on the staircase you used to pull my hair.

HEDDA: No, did I?

MRS. ELVSTED: Yes. And once you said you'd burn it all off.

HEDDA: Oh, that was only in fun.

MRS. ELVSTED: Yes, but I was so silly in those days. And then afterwards— I mean, we've drifted so far apart. Our backgrounds were so different.

HEDDA: Well, now we must try to drift together again. Now listen. When we were at school we used to call each other by our Christian names——

MRS. ELVSTED: No, I'm sure you're mistaken.

HEDDA: I'm sure I'm not. I remember it quite clearly. Let's tell each other our secrets, as we used to in the old days. [*Moves closer on her footstool.*] There, now. [*Kisses her on the cheek.*] You must call me Hedda.

MRS. ELVSTED: [*Squeezes her hands and pats them.*] Oh, you're so kind. I'm not used to people being so nice to me.

HEDDA: Now, now, now. And I shall call you Tora, the way I used to.

MRS. ELVSTED: My name is Thea.

HEDDA: Yes, of course. Of course. I meant Thea. [*Looks at her sympathetically.*] So you're not used to kindness, Thea? In your own home?

MRS. ELVSTED: Oh, if only I had a home! But I haven't. I've never had one.

HEDDA: [*Looks at her for a moment.*] I thought that was it.

MRS. ELVSTED: [*Stares blankly and helplessly.*] Yes—yes—yes.

HEDDA: I can't remember exactly now, but didn't you first go to Mr. Elvsted as a housekeeper?

MRS. ELVSTED: Governess, actually. But his wife—at the time, I mean— she was an invalid, and had to spend most of her time in bed. So I had to look after the house too.

HEDDA: But in the end, you became mistress of the house.

MRS. ELVSTED: [*Sadly.*] Yes, I did.

HEDDA: Let me see. Roughly how long ago was that?

MRS. ELVSTED: When I got married, you mean?

HEDDA: Yes.

MRS. ELVSTED: About five years.

HEDDA: Yes; it must be about that.

MRS. ELVSTED: Oh, those five years! Especially that last two or three. Oh, Mrs. Tesman, if you only knew——

HEDDA: [*Slaps her hand gently.*] Mrs. Tesman? Oh, Thea!

MRS. ELVSTED: I'm sorry, I'll try to remember. Yes—if you had any idea——

HEDDA: [*Casually.*] Eilert Loevborg's been up there too, for about three years, hasn't he?

MRS. ELVSTED: [*Looks at her uncertainly.*] Eilert Loevborg? Yes, he has.

HEDDA: Did you know him before? When you were here?

MRS. ELVSTED: No, not really. That is—I knew him by name, of course.

HEDDA: But up there, he used to visit you?

MRS. ELVSTED: Yes, he used to come and see us every day. To give the children lessons. I found I couldn't do that as well as manage the house.

HEDDA: I'm sure you couldn't. And your husband——? I suppose being a magistrate he has to be away from home a good deal?

MRS. ELVSTED: Yes. You see, Mrs.——you see, Hedda, he has to cover the whole district.

HEDDA: [Leans against the arm of MRS. ELVSTED's chair.] Poor, pretty little Thea! Now you must tell me the whole story. From beginning to end.

MRS. ELVSTED: Well—what do you want to know?

HEDDA: What kind of a man is your husband, Thea? I mean, as a person. Is he kind to you?

MRS. ELVSTED: [Evasively.] I'm sure he does his best to be.

HEDDA: I only wonder if he isn't too old for you. There's more than twenty years between you, isn't there?

MRS. ELVSTED: [Irritably.] Yes, there's that too. Oh, there are so many things. We're different in every way. We've nothing in common. Nothing whatever.

HEDDA: But he loves you, surely? In his own way?

MRS. ELVSTED: Oh, I don't know. I think he just finds me useful. And then I don't cost much to keep. I'm cheap.

HEDDA: Now you're being stupid.

MRS. ELVSTED: [Shakes her head.] It can't be any different. With him. He doesn't love anyone except himself. And perhaps the children—a little.

HEDDA: He must be fond of Eilert Loevborg, Thea.

MRS. ELVSTED: [Looks at her.] Eilert Loevborg? What makes you think that?

HEDDA: Well, if he sends you all the way down here to look for him——
[Smiles almost imperceptibly.] Besides, you said so yourself to Tesman.

MRS. ELVSTED: [With a nervous twitch.] Did I? Oh yes, I suppose I did.
[Impulsively, but keeping her voice low.] Well, I might as well tell you the whole story. It's bound to come out sooner or later.

HEDDA: But my dear Thea——?

MRS. ELVSTED: My husband had no idea I was coming here.

HEDDA: What? Your husband didn't know?

MRS. ELVSTED: No, of course not. As a matter of fact, he wasn't even there. He was away at the assizes. Oh, I couldn't stand it any longer, Hedda! I just couldn't. I'd be so dreadfully lonely up there now.

HEDDA: Go on.

MRS. ELVSTED: So I packed a few things. Secretly. And went.

HEDDA: Without telling anyone?

MRS. ELVSTED: Yes. I caught the train and came straight here.

HEDDA: But my dear Thea! How brave of you!

MRS. ELVSTED: [Gets up and walks across the room.] Well, what else could I do?

HEDDA: But what do you suppose your husband will say when you get back?

MRS. ELVSTED: [By the table, looks at her.] Back there? To him?

HEDDA: Yes. Surely——?

MRS. ELVSTED: I shall never go back to him.

HEDDA: [Gets up and goes closer.] You mean you've left your home for good?

MRS. ELVSTED: Yes. I didn't see what else I could do.

HEDDA: But to do it so openly!

MRS. ELVSTED: Oh, it's no use trying to keep a thing like that secret.

HEDDA: But what do you suppose people will say?

MRS. ELVSTED: They can say what they like. [Sits sadly, wearily on the sofa.] I had to do it.

HEDDA: [After a short silence.] What do you intend to do now? How are you going to live?

MRS. ELVSTED: I don't know. I only know that I must live wherever Eilert Loevborg is. If I am to go on living.

HEDDA: [Moves a chair from the table, sits on it near MRS. ELVSTED and strokes her hands.] Tell me, Thea, how did this—friendship between you and Eilert Loevborg begin?

MRS. ELVSTED: Oh, it came about gradually. I developed a kind of—power over him.

HEDDA: Oh?

MRS. ELVSTED: He gave up his old habits. Not because I asked him to. I'd never have dared to do that. I suppose he just noticed I didn't like that kind of thing. So he gave it up.

HEDDA: [Hides a smile.] So you've made a new man of him. Clever little Thea!

MRS. ELVSTED: Yes—anyway, he says I have. And he's made a—sort of—real person of me. Taught me to think—and to understand all kinds of things.

HEDDA: Did he give you lessons too?

MRS. ELVSTED: Not exactly lessons. But he talked to me. About—oh, you've no idea—so many things! And then he let me work with him. Oh, it was wonderful. I was so happy to be allowed to help him.

HEDDA: Did he allow you to help him!

MRS. ELVSTED: Yes. Whenever he wrote anything we always—did it together.

HEDDA: Like good pals?

MRS. ELVSTED: [Eagerly.] Pals! Yes—why, Hedda, that's exactly the word he used! Oh, I ought to feel so happy. But I can't. I don't know if it will last.

HEDDA: You don't seem very sure of him.

MRS. ELVSTED: [Sadly.] Something stands between Eilert Loevberg and me. The shadow of another woman.

HEDDA: Who can that be?

MRS. ELVSTED: I don't know. Someone he used to be friendly with in—in the old days. Someone he's never been able to forget.

HEDDA: What has he told you about her?

MRS. ELVSTED: Oh, he only mentioned her once, casually.

HEDDA: Well! What did he say?

MRS. ELVSTED: He said when he left her she tried to shoot him with a pistol.

HEDDA: [Cold, controlled.] What nonsense. People don't do such things. The kind of people we know.

MRS. ELVSTED: No, I think it must have been that red-haired singer he used to——

HEDDA: Ah yes, very probably.

MRS. ELVSTED: I remember they used to say she always carried a loaded pistol.

HEDDA: Well then, it must be her.

MRS. ELVSTED: But Hedda, I hear she's come back, and is living here. Oh, I'm so desperate——!

HEDDA: [Glances toward the rear room.] Ssh! Tesman's coming. [Gets up and whispers.] Thea, we mustn't breathe a word about this to anyone.

MRS. ELVSTED: [Jumps up.] Oh, no, no! Please don't!

[GEORGE TESMAN appears from the right in the rear room with a letter in his hand, and comes into the drawing room.]

TESMAN: Well, here's my little epistle all signed and sealed.

HEDDA: Good. I think Mrs. Elvsted wants to go now. Wait a moment—I'll see you as far as the garden gate.

TESMAN: Er—Hedda, do you think Bertha could deal with this?

HEDDA: [Takes the letter.] I'll give her instructions.

[BERTHA enters from the hall.]

BERTHA: Judge Brack is here and asks if he may pay his respects to Madam and the Doctor.

HEDDA: Yes, ask him to be so good as to come in. And—wait a moment— drop this letter in the post box.

BERTHA: [Takes the letter.] Very good, madam.

[She opens the door for JUDGE BRACK, and goes out. JUDGE BRACK is forty-five; rather short, but well-built, and elastic in his movements. He has a roundish face with an aristocratic profile. His hair, cut short, is still almost black, and is carefully barbered. Eyes lively and humorous. Thick eyebrows. His moustache is also thick, and is trimmed square at the ends. He is wearing outdoor clothes which are elegant but a little too youthful for him. He has a monocle in one eye; now and then he lets it drop.]

BRACK: [Hat in hand, bows.] May one presume to call so early?

HEDDA: One may presume.

TESMAN: [Shakes his hand.] You're welcome here any time. Judge Brack— Mrs. Rysing.

[HEDDA sighs.]

BRACK: [Bows.] Ah—charmed——

HEDDA: [Looks at him and laughs.] What fun to be able to see you by daylight for once, Judge.

BRACK: Do I look—different?

HEDDA: Yes. A little younger, I think.

BRACK: Obliged.

TESMAN: Well, what do you think of Hedda? What? Doesn't she look well? Hasn't she filled out——?

HEDDA: Oh, do stop it. You ought to be thanking Judge Brack for all the inconvenience he's put himself to——

BRACK: Nonsense, it was a pleasure——

HEDDA: You're a loyal friend. But my other friend is pining to get away. Au revoir, Judge. I won't be a minute.

[*Mutual salutations.* MRS. ELVSTED *and* HEDDA *go out through the hall.*]

BRACK: Well, is your wife satisfied with everything?

TESMAN: Yes, we can't thank you enough. That is—we may have to shift one or two things around, she tells me. And we're short of one or two little items we'll have to purchase.

BRACK: Oh? Really?

TESMAN: But you musn't worry your head about that. Hedda says she'll get what's needed. I say, why don't we sit down? What?

BRACK: Thanks, just for a moment. [*Sits at the table.*] There's something I'd like to talk to you about, my dear Tesman.

TESMAN: Oh? Ah yes, of course. [*Sits.*] After the feast comes the reckoning. What?

BRACK: Oh, never mind about the financial side—there's no hurry about that. Though I could wish we'd arranged things a little less palatially.

TESMAN: Good heavens, that'd never have done. Think of Hedda, my dear chap. You know her. I couldn't possibly ask her to live like a suburban housewife.

BRACK: No, no—that's just the problem.

TESMAN: Anyway, it can't be long now before my nomination[3] comes through.

BRACK: Well, you know, these things often take time.

TESMAN: Have you heard any more news? What?

BRACK: Nothing definite. [*Changing the subject.*] Oh, by the way, I have one piece of news for you.

TESMAN: What?

BRACK: Your old friend Eilert Loevborg is back in town.

TESMAN: I know that already.

BRACK: Oh? How did you hear that?

TESMAN: She told me. That lady who went out with Hedda.

BRACK: I see. What was her name? I didn't catch it.

TESMAN: Mrs. Elvsted.

BRACK: Oh, the magistrate's wife. Yes, Loevborg's been living up near them, hasn't he?

TESMAN: I'm delighted to hear he's become a decent human being again.

BRACK: Yes, so they say.

TESMAN: I gather he's published a new book, too. What?

BRACK: Indeed he has.

TESMAN: I hear it's created rather a stir.

BRACK: Quite an unusual stir.

TESMAN: I say, isn't that splendid news! He's such a gifted chap—and I was afraid he'd gone to the dogs for good.

BRACK: Most people thought he had.

---

3. For the professorship. Professors at European universities were less numerous and more socially prominent than their contemporary American counterparts.

TESMAN: But I can't think what he'll do now. How on earth will he manage to make ends meet? What?

[*As he speaks his last words,* HEDDA *enters from the hall.*]

HEDDA: [*To* BRACK, *laughs slightly scornfully.*] Tesman is always worrying about making ends meet.

TESMAN: We were talking about poor Eilert Loevborg, Hedda dear.

HEDDA: [*Gives him a quick look.*] Oh, were you? [*Sits in the armchair by the stove and asks casually.*] Is he in trouble?

TESMAN: Well, he must have run through his inheritance long ago by now. And he can't write a new book every year. What? So I'm wondering what's going to become of him.

BRACK: I may be able to enlighten you there.

TESMAN: Oh?

BRACK: You mustn't forget he has relatives who wield a good deal of influence.

TESMAN: Relatives? Oh, they've quite washed their hands of him, I'm afraid.

BRACK: They used to regard him as the hope of the family.

TESMAN: Used to, yes. But he's put an end to that.

HEDDA: Who knows? [*With a little smile.*] I hear the Elvsteds have made a new man of him.

BRACK: And then this book he's just published——

TESMAN: Well, let's hope they find something for him. I've just written him a note. Oh, by the way, Hedda, I asked him to come over and see us this evening.

BRACK: But my dear chap, you're coming to me this evening. My bachelor party.[4] You promised me last night when I met you at the boat.

HEDDA: Had you forgotten, Tesman?

TESMAN: Good heavens, yes, I'd quite forgotten.

BRACK: Anyway, you can be quite sure he won't turn up here.

TESMAN: Why do you think that? What?

BRACK: [*A little unwillingly, gets up and rests his hands on the back of his chair.*] My dear Tesman—and you, too, Mrs. Tesman—there's something I feel you ought to know.

TESMAN: Concerning Eilert?

BRACK: Concerning him and you.

TESMAN: Well, my dear Judge, tell us, please!

BRACK: You must be prepared for your nomination not to come through quite as quickly as you hope and expect.

TESMAN: [*Jumps up uneasily.*] Is anything wrong? What?

BRACK: There's a possibility that the appointment may be decided by competition——

TESMAN: Competition! By Jove, Hedda, fancy that!

HEDDA: [*Leans further back in her chair.*] Ah! How interesting!

TESMAN: But who else——? I say, you don't mean——?

BRACK: Exactly. By competition with Eilert Loevborg.

TESMAN: [*Clasps his hands in alarm.*] No, no, but this is inconceivable! It's absolutely impossible! What?

---

4. A party for men only, whether single or married.

BRACK: Hm. We may find it'll happen, all the same.

TESMAN: No, but—Judge Brack, they couldn't be so inconsiderate toward me! [*Waves his arms.*] I mean, by Jove, I—I'm a married man! It was on the strength of this that Hedda and I *got* married! We ran up some pretty hefty debts. And borrowed money from Auntie Juju! I mean, good heavens, they practically promised me the appointment. What?

BRACK: Well, well, I'm sure you'll get it. But you'll have to go through a competition.

HEDDA: [*Motionless in her armchair.*] How exciting, Tesman. It'll be a kind of duel, by Jove.

TESMAN: My dear Hedda, how can you take it so lightly?

HEDDA: [*As before.*] I'm not. I can't wait to see who's going to win.

BRACK: In any case, Mrs. Tesman, it's best you should know how things stand. I mean before you commit yourself to these little items I hear you're threatening to purchase.

HEDDA: I can't allow this to alter my plans.

BRACK: Indeed? Well, that's your business. Good-bye. [*To* TESMAN.] I'll come and collect you on the way home from my afternoon walk.

TESMAN: Oh, yes, yes. I'm sorry, I'm all upside down just now.

HEDDA: [*Lying in her chair, holds out her hand.*] Good-bye, Judge. See you this afternoon.

BRACK: Thank you. Good-bye, good-bye.

TESMAN: [*Sees him to the door.*] Good-bye, my dear Judge. You will excuse me, won't you?

[JUDGE BRACK *goes out through the hall.*]

TESMAN: [*Pacing up and down.*] Oh, Hedda! One oughtn't to go plunging off on wild adventures. What?

HEDDA: [*Looks at him and smiles.*] Like you're doing?

TESMAN: Yes. I mean, there's no denying it, it was a pretty big adventure to go off and get married and set up house merely on expectation.

HEDDA: Perhaps you're right.

TESMAN: Well, anyway, we have our home, Hedda. By Jove, yes. The home we dreamed of. And set our hearts on. What?

HEDDA: [*Gets up slowly, wearily.*] You agreed that we should enter society. And keep open house. That was the bargain.

TESMAN: Yes. Good heavens, I was looking forward to it all so much. To seeing you play hostess to a select circle! By Jove! What? Ah, well, for the time being we shall have to make do with each other's company, Hedda. Perhaps have Auntie Juju in now and then. Oh dear, this wasn't at all what you had in mind——

HEDDA: I won't be able to have a liveried footman.[5] For a start.

TESMAN: Oh no, we couldn't possibly afford a footman.

HEDDA: And that thoroughbred horse you promised me——

TESMAN: [*Fearfully.*] Thoroughbred horse!

HEDDA: I mustn't even think of that now.

TESMAN: Heaven forbid!

5. A uniformed servant.

HEDDA: [*Walks across the room.*] Ah, well. I still have one thing left to amuse myself with.

TESMAN: [*Joyfully.*] Thank goodness for that. What's that, Hedda? What?

HEDDA: [*In the open doorway, looks at him with concealed scorn.*] My pistols, George darling.

TESMAN: [*Alarmed.*] Pistols!

HEDDA: [*Her eyes cold.*] General Gabler's pistols.

[*She goes into the rear room and disappears.*]

TESMAN: [*Runs to the doorway and calls after her.*] For heaven's sake, Hedda dear, don't touch those things. They're dangerous. Hedda— please—for my sake! What?

Act II

SCENE— *The same as in Act I except that the piano has been removed and an elegant little writing table, with a bookcase, stands in its place. By the sofa on the left a smaller table has been placed. Most of the flowers have been removed.* MRS. ELVSTED's *bouquet stands on the larger table, downstage. It is afternoon.*

HEDDA, *dressed to receive callers, is alone in the room. She is standing by the open french windows, loading a revolver. The pair to it is lying in an open pistol case on the writing table.*

HEDDA: [*Looks down into the garden and calls.*] Good afternoon, Judge.

BRACK: [*In the distance, below.*] Afternoon, Mrs. Tesman.

HEDDA: [*Raises the pistol and takes aim.*] I'm going to shoot you, Judge Brack.

BRACK: [*Shouts from below.*] No no, no! Don't aim that thing at me!

HEDDA: This'll teach you to enter houses by the back door. [*Fires.*]

BRACK: [*Below.*] Have you gone completely out of your mind?

HEDDA: Oh dear! Did I hit you?

BRACK: [*Still outside.*] Stop playing these silly tricks.

HEDDA: All right, Judge. Come along in.

[JUDGE BRACK, *dressed for a bachelor party, enters through the french windows. He has a light overcoat on his arm.*]

BRACK: For God's sake! Haven't you stopped fooling around with those things yet? What are you trying to hit?

HEDDA: Oh, I was just shooting at the sky.

BRACK: [*Takes the pistol gently from her hand.*] By your leave, ma'am. [*Looks at it.*] Ah, yes—I know this old friend well. [*Looks around.*] Where's the case? Oh, yes. [*Puts the pistol in the case and closes it.*] That's enough of that little game for today.

HEDDA: Well, what on earth *am* I to do?

BRACK: You haven't had any visitors?

HEDDA: [*Closes the french windows.*] Not one. I suppose the best people are all still in the country.

BRACK: Your husband isn't home yet?

HEDDA: [*Locks the pistol case away in a drawer of the writing table.*] No. The moment he'd finished eating he ran off to his aunties. He wasn't expecting you so early.

BRACK: Ah, why didn't I think of that? How stupid of me.

HEDDA: [*Turns her head and looks at him.*] Why stupid?

BRACK: I'd have come a little sooner.

HEDDA: [*Walks across the room.*] There'd have been no one to receive you. I've been in my room since lunch, dressing.

BRACK: You haven't a tiny crack in the door through which we might have negotiated?

HEDDA: You forgot to arrange one.

BRACK: Another stupidity.

HEDDA: Well, we'll have to sit down here. And wait. Tesman won't be back for some time.

BRACK: Sad. Well, I'll be patient.

[HEDDA *sits on the corner of the sofa.* BRACK *puts his coat over the back of the nearest chair and seats himself, keeping his hat in his hand. Short pause. They look at each other.*]

HEDDA: Well?

BRACK: [*In the same tone of voice.*] Well?

HEDDA: I asked first.

BRACK: [*Leans forward slightly.*] Yes, well, now we can enjoy a nice, cosy little chat—Mrs. Hedda.

HEDDA: [*Leans further back in her chair.*] It seems such ages since we had a talk. I don't count last night or this morning.

BRACK: You mean: à deux?[6]

HEDDA: Mm—yes. That's roughly what I meant.

BRACK: I've been longing so much for you to come home.

HEDDA: So have I.

BRACK: You? Really, Mrs. Hedda? And I thought you were having such a wonderful honeymoon.

HEDDA: Oh, yes. Wonderful!

BRACK: But your husband wrote such ecstatic letters.

HEDDA: He! Oh, yes! He thinks life has nothing better to offer than rooting around in libraries and copying old pieces of parchment, or whatever it is he does.

BRACK: [*A little maliciously.*] Well, that *is* his life. Most of it, anyway.

HEDDA: Yes, I know. Well, it's all right for him. But for me! Oh no, my dear Judge. I've been bored to death.

BRACK: [*Sympathetically.*] Do you mean that? Seriously?

HEDDA: Yes. Can you imagine? Six whole months without ever meeting a single person who was one of us, and to whom I could talk about the kind of things we talk about.

BRACK: Yes, I can understand. I'd miss that, too.

HEDDA: That wasn't the worst, though.

BRACK: What was?

6. Just the two of us.

HEDDA: Having to spend every minute of one's life with—with the same person.

BRACK: [*Nods.*] Yes. What a thought! Morning; noon; and——

HEDDA: [*Coldly.*] As I said: every minute of one's life.

BRACK: I stand corrected. But dear Tesman is such a clever fellow, I should have thought one ought to be able——

HEDDA: Tesman is only interested in one thing, my dear Judge. His special subject.

BRACK: True.

HEDDA: And people who are only interested in one thing don't make the most amusing company. Not for long, anyway.

BRACK: Not even when they happen to be the person one loves?

HEDDA: Oh, don't use that sickly, stupid word.

BRACK: [*Starts.*] But, Mrs. Hedda——!

HEDDA: [*Half laughing, half annoyed.*] You just try it, Judge. Listening to the history of civilization morning, noon and——

BRACK: [*Corrects her.*] Every minute of one's life.

HEDDA: All right. Oh, and those domestic industries of Brabant in the Middle Ages! That really is beyond the limit.

BRACK: [*Looks at her searchingly.*] But, tell me—if you feel like this why on earth did you—? Ha——

HEDDA: Why on earth did I marry George Tesman?

BRACK: If you like to put it that way.

HEDDA: Do you think it so very strange?

BRACK: Yes—and no, Mrs. Hedda.

HEDDA: I'd danced myself tired, Judge. I felt my time was up——[*Gives a slight shudder.*] No, I mustn't say that. Or even think it.

BRACK: You've no rational cause to think it.

HEDDA: Oh—cause, cause——[*Looks searchingly at him.*] After all, George Tesman—well, I mean, he's a very respectable man.

BRACK: Very respectable, sound as a rock. No denying that.

HEDDA: And there's nothing exactly ridiculous about him. Is there?

BRACK: Ridiculous? No-no, I wouldn't say that.

HEDDA: Mm. He's very clever at collecting material and all that, isn't he? I mean, he may go quite far in time.

BRACK: [*Looks at her a little uncertainly.*] I thought you believed, like everyone else, that he would become a very prominent man.

HEDDA: [*Looks tired.*] Yes, I did. And when he came and begged me on his bended knees to be allowed to love and to cherish me, I didn't see why I shouldn't let him.

BRACK: No, well—if one looks at it like that——

HEDDA: It was more than my other admirers were prepared to do, Judge dear.

BRACK: [*Laughs.*] Well, I can't answer for the others. As far as I myself am concerned, you know I've always had a considerable respect for the institution of marriage. As an institution.

HEDDA: [*Lightly.*] Oh, I've never entertained any hopes of you.

BRACK: All I want is to have a circle of friends whom I can trust, whom I can help with advice or—or by any other means, and into whose houses I may come and go as a—trusted friend.

HEDDA: Of the husband?

BRACK: [*Bows.*] Preferably, to be frank, of the wife. And of the husband too, of course. Yes, you know, this kind of—triangle is a delightful arrangement for all parties concerned.

HEDDA: Yes, I often longed for a third person while I was away. Oh, those hours we spent alone in railway compartments——

BRACK: Fortunately your honeymoon is now over.

HEDDA: [*Shakes her head.*] There's a long way still to go. I've only reached a stop on the line.

BRACK: Why not jump out and stretch your legs a little, Mrs. Hedda?

HEDDA: I'm not the jumping sort.

BRACK: Aren't you?

HEDDA: No. There's always someone around who——

BRACK: [*Laughs.*] Who looks at one's legs?

HEDDA: Yes. Exactly.

BRACK: Well, but surely——

HEDDA: [*With a gesture of rejection.*] I don't like it. I'd rather stay where I am. Sitting in the compartment. *À deux.*

BRACK: But suppose a third person were to step into the compartment?

HEDDA: That would be different.

BRACK: A trusted friend—someone who understood——

HEDDA: And was lively and amusing——

BRACK: And interested in—more subjects than one——

HEDDA: [*Sighs audibly.*] Yes, that'd be a relief.

BRACK: [*Hears the front door open and shut.*] The triangle is completed.

HEDDA: [*Half under breath.*] And the train goes on.

[GEORGE TESMAN, *in grey walking dress with a soft felt hat, enters from the hall. He has a number of paper-covered books under his arm and in his pockets.*]

TESMAN: [*Goes over to the table by the corner sofa.*] Phew! It's too hot to be lugging all this around. [*Puts the books down.*] I'm positively sweating, Hedda. Why, hullo, hullo! You here already, Judge? What? Bertha didn't tell me.

BRACK: [*Gets up.*] I came in through the garden.

HEDDA: What are all those books you've got there?

TESMAN: [*Stands glancing through them.*] Oh, some new publications dealing with my special subject. I had to buy them.

HEDDA: Your special subject?

BRACK: His special subject, Mrs. Tesman.

[BRACK *and* HEDDA *exchange a smile.*]

HEDDA: Haven't you collected enough material on your special subject?

TESMAN: My dear Hedda, one can never have too much. One must keep abreast of what other people are writing.

HEDDA: Yes. Of course.

TESMAN: [*Rooting among the books.*] Look—I bought a copy of Eilert Loevborg's new book, too. [*Holds it out to her.*] Perhaps you'd like to have a look at it, Hedda? What?

HEDDA: No, thank you. Er—yes, perhaps I will, later.

TESMAN: I glanced through it on my way home.

BRACK: What's your opinion—as a specialist on the subject?

TESMAN: I'm amazed how sound and balanced it is. He never used to write like that. [*Gathers his books together.*] Well, I must get down to these at once. I can hardly wait to cut the pages.[7] Oh, I've got to change, too. [*To* BRACK.] We don't have to be off just yet, do we? What?

BRACK: Heavens, no. We've plenty of time yet.

TESMAN: Good, I needn't hurry, then. [*Goes with his books, but stops and turns in the doorway.*] Oh, by the way, Hedda, Auntie Juju won't be coming to see you this evening.

HEDDA: Won't she? Oh—the hat, I suppose.

TESMAN: Good heavens, no. How could you think such a thing of Auntie Juju? Fancy——! No, Auntie Rena's very ill.

HEDDA: She always is.

TESMAN: Yes, but today she's been taken really bad.

HEDDA: Oh, then it's quite understandable that the other one should want to stay with her. Well, I shall have to swallow my disappointment.

TESMAN: You can't imagine how happy Auntie Juju was in spite of everything. At your looking so well after the honeymoon!

HEDDA: [*Half beneath her breath, as she rises.*] Oh, these everlasting aunts!

TESMAN: What?

HEDDA: [*Goes over to the french windows.*] Nothing.

TESMAN: Oh. All right. [*Goes into the rear room and out of sight.*]

BRACK: What was that about the hat?

HEDDA: Oh, something that happened with Miss Tesman this morning. She'd put her hat down on a chair. [*Looks at him and smiles.*] And I pretended to think it was the servant's.

BRACK: [*Shakes his head.*] But my dear Mrs. Hedda, how could you do such a thing? To that poor old lady?

HEDDA: [*Nervously, walking across the room.*] Sometimes a mood like that hits me. And I can't stop myself. [*Throws herself down in the armchair by the stove.*] Oh, I don't know how to explain it.

BRACK: [*Behind her chair.*] You're not really happy. That's the answer.

HEDDA: [*Stares ahead of her.*] Why on earth should I be happy? Can you give me a reason?

BRACK: Yes. For one thing you've got the home you always wanted.

HEDDA: [*Looks at him.*] You really believe that story?

BRACK: You mean it isn't true?

HEDDA: Oh, yes, it's partly true.

BRACK: Well?

HEDDA: It's true I got Tesman to see me home from parties last summer——

BRACK: It was a pity my home lay in another direction.

HEDDA: Yes. Your interests lay in another direction, too.

---

7. Books used to be sold with the pages folded but uncut as they came from the printing press; the owner had to cut the pages to read the book.

BRACK: [*Laughs.*] That's naughty of you, Mrs. Hedda. But to return to you and Tesman——

HEDDA: Well, we walked past this house one evening. And poor Tesman was fidgeting in his boots trying to find something to talk about. I felt sorry for the great scholar——

BRACK: [*Smiles incredulously.*] Did you? Hm.

HEDDA: Yes, honestly I did. Well, to help him out of his misery, I happened to say quite frivolously how much I'd love to live in this house.

BRACK: Was that all?

HEDDA: That evening, yes.

BRACK: But—afterwards?

HEDDA: Yes. My little frivolity had its consequences, my dear Judge.

BRACK: Our little frivolities do. Much too often, unfortunately.

HEDDA: Thank you. Well, it was our mutual admiration for the late Prime Minister's house that brought George Tesman and me together on common ground. So we got engaged, and we got married, and we went on our honeymoon, and—Ah well, Judge, I've—made my bed and I must lie in it, I was about to say.

BRACK: How utterly fantastic! And you didn't really care in the least about the house?

HEDDA: God knows I didn't.

BRACK: Yes, but now that we've furnished it so beautifully for you?

HEDDA: Ugh—all the rooms smell of lavender and dried roses. But perhaps Auntie Juju brought that in.

BRACK: [*Laughs.*] More likely the Prime Minister's widow, rest her soul.

HEDDA: Yes, it's got the odor of death about it. It reminds me of the flowers one has worn at a ball—the morning after. [*Clasps her hands behind her neck, leans back in the chair and looks up at him.*] Oh, my dear Judge, you've no idea how hideously bored I'm going to be out here.

BRACK: Couldn't you find some kind of occupation, Mrs. Hedda? Like your husband?

HEDDA: Occupation? That'd interest me?

BRACK: Well—preferably.

HEDDA: God knows what. I've often thought——[*Breaks off.*] No, that wouldn't work either.

BRACK: Who knows? Tell me about it.

HEDDA: I was thinking—if I could persuade Tesman to go into politics, for example.

BRACK: [*Laughs.*] Tesman! No, honestly, I don't think he's quite cut out to be a politician.

HEDDA: Perhaps not. But if I could persuade him to have a go at it?

BRACK: What satisfaction would that give you? If he turned out to be no good? Why do you want to make him do that?

HEDDA: Because I'm bored. [*After a moment.*] You feel there's absolutely no possibility of Tesman becoming Prime Minister, then?

BRACK: Well, you know, Mrs. Hedda, for one thing he'd have to be pretty well off before he could become that.

HEDDA: [*Gets up impatiently.*] There you are! [*Walks across the room.*] It's this wretched poverty that makes life so hateful. And ludicrous. Well, it is!

BRACK: I don't think that's the real cause.

HEDDA: What is, then?

BRACK: Nothing really exciting has ever happened to you.

HEDDA: Nothing serious, you mean?

BRACK: Call it that if you like. But now perhaps it may.

HEDDA: [*Tosses her head.*] Oh, you're thinking of this competition for that wretched professorship? That's Tesman's affair. I'm not going to waste my time worrying about that.

BRACK: Very well, let's forget about that then. But suppose you were to find yourself faced with what people call—to use the conventional phrase—the most solemn of human responsibilities? [*Smiles.*] A new responsibility, little Mrs. Hedda.

HEDDA: [*Angrily.*] Be quiet! Nothing like that's going to happen.

BRACK: [*Warily.*] We'll talk about it again in a year's time. If not earlier.

HEDDA: [*Curtly.*] I've no leanings in that direction, Judge. I don't want any—responsibilities.

BRACK: But surely you must feel some inclination to make use of that— natural talent which every woman—

HEDDA: [*Over by the french windows.*] Oh, be quiet, I say! I often think there's only one thing for which I have any natural talent.

BRACK: [*Goes closer.*] And what is that, if I may be so bold as to ask?

HEDDA: [*Stands looking out.*] For boring myself to death. Now you know. [*Turns, looks toward the rear room and laughs.*] Talking of boring, here comes the Professor.

BRACK: [*Quietly, warningly.*] Now, now, now, Mrs. Hedda!

[GEORGE TESMAN, *in evening dress, with gloves and hat in his hand, enters through the rear room from the right.*]

TESMAN: Hedda, hasn't any message come from Eilert? What?

HEDDA: No.

TESMAN: Ah, then we'll have him here presently. You wait and see.

BRACK: You really think he'll come?

TESMAN: Yes, I'm almost sure he will. What you were saying about him this morning is just gossip.

BRACK: Oh?

TESMAN: Yes. Auntie Juju said she didn't believe he'd ever dare to stand in my way again. Fancy that!

BRACK: Then everything in the garden's lovely.

TESMAN: [*Puts his hat, with his gloves in it, on a chair, right.*] Yes, but you really must let me wait for him as long as possible.

BRACK: We've plenty of time. No one'll be turning up at my place before seven or half past.

TESMAN: Ah, then we can keep Hedda company a little longer. And see if he turns up. What?

HEDDA: [*Picks up* BRACK's *coat and hat and carries them over to the corner sofa.*] And if the worst comes to the worst, Mr. Loevborg can sit here and talk to me.

BRACK: [*Offering to take his things from her.*] No, please. What do you mean by "if the worst comes to the worst"?

HEDDA: If he doesn't want to go with you and Tesman.

TESMAN: [*Looks doubtfully at her.*] I say, Hedda, do you think it'll be all right for him to stay here with you? What? Remember Auntie Juju isn't coming.

HEDDA: Yes, but Mrs. Elvsted is. The three of us can have a cup of tea together.

TESMAN: Ah, that'll be all right then.

BRACK: [*Smiles.*] It's probably the safest solution as far as he's concerned.

HEDDA: Why?

BRACK: My dear Mrs. Tesman, you always say of my little bachelor parties that they should be attended only by men of the strongest principles.

HEDDA: But Mr. Loevborg is a man of principle now. You know what they say about a reformed sinner——

[BERTHA *enters from the hall.*]

BERTHA: Madam, there's a gentleman here who wants to see you——

HEDDA: Ask him to come in.

TESMAN: [*Quietly.*] I'm sure it's him. By Jove. Fancy that!

[EILERT LOEVBORG *enters from the hall. He is slim and lean, of the same age as* TESMAN, *but looks older and somewhat haggard. His hair and beard are of a blackish-brown; his face is long and pale, but with a couple of reddish patches on his cheekbones. He is dressed in an elegant and fairly new black suit, and carries black gloves and a top hat in his hand. He stops just inside the door and bows abruptly. He seems somewhat embarrassed.*]

TESMAN: [*Goes over and shakes his hand.*] My dear Eilert! How grand to see you again after all these years!

EILERT LOEVBORG: [*Speaks softly.*] It was good of you to write, George. [*Goes nearer to* HEDDA.] May I shake hands with you, too, Mrs. Tesman?

HEDDA: [*Accepts his hand.*] Delighted to see you, Mr. Loevborg. [*With a gesture.*] I don't know if you two gentlemen——

LOEVBORG: [*Bows slightly.*] Judge Brack, I believe.

BRACK: [*Also with a slight bow.*] Correct. We—met some years ago——

TESMAN: [*Puts his hands on* LOEVBORG's *shoulders.*] Now you're to treat this house just as though it were your own home, Eilert. Isn't that right, Hedda? I hear you've decided to settle here again? What?

LOEVBORG: Yes, I have.

TESMAN: Quite understandable. Oh, by the bye—I've just bought your new book. Though to tell the truth I haven't found time to read it yet.

LOEVBORG: You needn't bother.

TESMAN: Oh? Why?

LOEVBORG: There's nothing much in it.

TESMAN: By Jove, fancy hearing that from you!

BRACK: But everyone's praising it.

LOEVBORG: That was exactly what I wanted to happen. So I only wrote what I knew everyone would agree with.

BRACK: Very sensible.

TESMAN: Yes, but my dear Eilert——

LOEVBORG: I want to try to re-establish myself. To begin again—from the beginning.

TESMAN: [*A little embarrassed.*] Yes, I—er—suppose you do. What?

LOEVBORG: [*Smiles, puts down his hat and takes a package wrapped in paper from his coat pocket.*] But when this gets published—George Tesman—read it. This is my real book. The one in which I have spoken with my own voice.

TESMAN: Oh, really? What's it about?

LOEVBORG: It's the sequel.

TESMAN: Sequel? To what?

LOEVBORG: To the other book.

TESMAN: The one that's just come out?

LOEVBORG: Yes.

TESMAN: But my dear Eilert, that covers the subject right up to the present day.

LOEVBORG: It does. But this is about the future.

TESMAN: The future! But, I say, we don't know anything about that.

LOEVBORG: No. But there are one or two things that need to be said about it. [*Opens the package.*] Here, have a look.

TESMAN: Surely that's not your handwriting?

LOEVBORG: I dictated it. [*Turns the pages.*] It's in two parts. The first deals with the forces that will shape our civilization. [*Turns further on towards the end.*] And the second indicates the direction in which that civilization may develop.

TESMAN: Amazing! I'd never think of writing about anything like that.

HEDDA: [*By the french windows, drumming on the pane.*] No. You wouldn't.

LOEVBORG: [*Puts the pages back into their cover and lays the package on the table.*] I brought it because I thought I might possibly read you a few pages this evening.

TESMAN: I say, what a kind idea! Oh, but this evening——? [*Glances at BRACK.*] I'm not quite sure whether——

LOEVBORG: Well, some other time, then. There's no hurry.

BRACK: The truth is, Mr. Loevborg, I'm giving a little dinner this evening. In Tesman's honor, you know.

LOEVBORG: [*Looks round for his hat.*] Oh—then I mustn't——

BRACK: No, wait a minute. Won't you do me the honor of joining us?

LOEVBORG: [*Curtly, with decision.*] No I can't. Thank you so much.

BRACK: Oh, nonsense. Do—please. There'll only be a few of us. And I can promise you we shall have some good sport, as Mrs. Hed—as Mrs. Tesman puts it.

LOEVBORG: I've no doubt. Nevertheless——

BRACK: You could bring your manuscript along and read it to Tesman at my place. I could lend you a room.

TESMAN: By Jove, Eilert, that's an idea. What?

HEDDA: [*Interposes.*] But Tesman, Mr. Loevborg doesn't want to go. I'm sure Mr. Loevborg would much rather sit here and have supper with me.

LOEVBORG: [*Looks at her.*] With you, Mrs. Tesman?

HEDDA: And Mrs. Elvsted.

LOEVBORG: Oh. [*Casually.*] I ran into her this afternoon.

HEDDA: Did you? Well, she's coming here this evening. So you really must stay, Mr. Loevborg. Otherwise she'll have no one to see her home.

LOEVBORG: That's true. Well—thank you, Mrs. Tesman, I'll stay then.

HEDDA: I'll just tell the servant.

    [*She goes to the door which leads into the hall, and rings.* BERTHA *enters.* HEDDA *talks softly to her and points towards the rear room.* BERTHA *nods and goes out.*]

TESMAN: [*To* LOEVBORG, *as* HEDDA *does this.*] I say, Eilert. This new subject of yours—the—er—future—is that the one you're going to lecture about?

LOEVBORG: Yes.

TESMAN: They told me down at the bookshop that you're going to hold a series of lectures here during the autumn.

LOEVBORG: Yes, I am, I—hope you don't mind, Tesman.

TESMAN: Good heavens, no! But——?

LOEVBORG: I can quite understand it might queer your pitch a little.

TESMAN: [*Dejectedly.*] Oh well, I can't expect you to put them off for my sake.

LOEVBORG: I'll wait till your appointment's been announced.

TESMAN: You'll wait! But—but—aren't you going to compete with me for the post? What?

LOEVBORG: No. I only want to defeat you in the eyes of the world.

TESMAN: Good heavens! Then Auntie Juju was right after all! Oh, I knew it, I knew it! Hear that, Hedda? Fancy! Eilert *doesn't* want to stand in our way.

HEDDA: [*Curtly.*] Our? Leave me out of it, please.

    [*She goes towards the rear room, where* BERTHA *is setting a tray with decanters and glasses on the table.* HEDDA *nods approval, and comes back into the drawing room.* BERTHA *goes out.*]

TESMAN: [*While this is happening.*] Judge Brack, what do you think about all this? What?

BRACK: Oh, I think honor and victory can be very splendid things——

TESMAN: Of course they can. Still——

HEDDA: [*Looks at* TESMAN *with a cold smile.*] You look as if you'd been hit by a thunderbolt.

TESMAN: Yes, I feel rather like it.

BRACK: There was a black cloud looming up, Mrs. Tesman. But it seems to have passed over.

HEDDA: [*Points toward the rear room.*] Well, gentlemen, won't you go in and take a glass of cold punch?

BRACK: [*Glances at his watch.*] A stirrup cup?[8] Yes, why not?

TESMAN: An admirable suggestion, Hedda. Admirable! Oh, I feel so relieved!

HEDDA: Won't you have one, too, Mr. Loevborg?

---

8. A drink before parting. (Originally, it was taken by riders on horseback just before setting forth.)

LOEVBORG: No, thank you. I'd rather not.

BRACK: Great heavens, man, cold punch isn't poison. Take my word for it.

LOEVBORG: Not for everyone, perhaps.

HEDDA: I'll keep Mr. Loevborg company while you drink.

TESMAN: Yes, Hedda dear, would you?

[*He and* BRACK *go into the rear room, sit down, drink punch, smoke cigarettes and talk cheerfully during the following scene.* EILERT LOEVBORG *remains standing by the stove.* HEDDA *goes to the writing table.*]

HEDDA [*Raising her voice slightly.*] I've some photographs I'd like to show you, if you'd care to see them. Tesman and I visited the Tyrol on our way home.

[*She comes back with an album, places it on the table by the sofa and sits in the upstage corner of the sofa.* EILERT LOEVBORG *comes toward her, stops and looks at her. Then he takes a chair and sits down on her left, with his back toward the rear room.*]

HEDDA: [*Opens the album.*] You see these mountains, Mr. Loevborg? That's the Ortler group. Tesman has written the name underneath. You see: "The Ortler Group near Meran."[9]

LOEVBORG: [*Has not taken his eyes from her; says softly, slowly.*] Hedda— Gabler!

HEDDA: [*Gives him a quick glance.*] Ssh!

LOEVBORG: [*Repeats softly.*] Hedda Gabler!

HEDDA: [*Looks at the album.*] Yes, that used to be my name. When we first knew each other.

LOEVBORG: And from now on—for the rest of my life—I must teach myself never to say: Hedda Gabler.

HEDDA: [*Still turning the pages.*] Yes, you must. You'd better start getting into practice. The sooner the better.

LOEVBORG: [*Bitterly.*] Hedda Gabler married? And to George Tesman?

HEDDA: Yes. Well—that's life.

LOEVBORG: Oh, Hedda, Hedda! How could you throw yourself away like that?

HEDDA: [*Looks sharply at him.*] Stop it.

LOEVBORG: What do you mean?

[TESMAN *comes in and goes toward the sofa.*]

HEDDA: [*Hears him coming and says casually.*] And this, Mr. Loevborg, is the view from the Ampezzo valley. Look at those mountains. [*Glances affectionately up at* TESMAN.] What did you say those curious mountains were called, dear?

TESMAN: Let me have a look. Oh, those are the Dolomites.

HEDDA: Of course. Those are the Dolomites, Mr. Loevborg.

TESMAN: Hedda, I just wanted to ask you, can't we bring some punch in here? A glass for you, anyway. What?

HEDDA: Thank you, yes. And a biscuit[1] or two, perhaps.

---

9. Or Merano, a city in the Austrian Tyrol, since 1918 in Italy. The scenic features mentioned here and later are tourist attractions. The Ortler Group and the Dolomites are ranges of the Alps. The Ampezzo Valley lies beyond the Dolomites to the east. The Brenner Pass is a major route through the Alps to Austria.   1. Cookie.

TESMAN: You wouldn't like a cigarette?

HEDDA: No.

TESMAN: Right.

[*He goes into the rear room and over to the right.* BRACK *is sitting there, glancing occasionally at* HEDDA *and* LOEVBORG.]

LOEVBORG: [*Softly, as before.*] Answer me, Hedda. How could you do it?

HEDDA: [*Apparently absorbed in the album.*] If you go on calling me Hedda I won't talk to you any more.

LOEVBORG: Mayn't I even when we're alone?

HEDDA: No. You can think it. But you mustn't say it.

LOEVBORG: Oh, I see. Because you love George Tesman.

HEDDA: [*Glances at him and smiles.*] Love? Don't be funny.

LOEVBORG: You don't love him?

HEDDA: I don't intend to be unfaithful to him. That's not what I want.

LOEVBORG: Hedda—just tell me one thing—

HEDDA: Ssh!

[TESMAN *enters from the rear room, carrying a tray.*]

TESMAN: Here we are! Here come the goodies! [*Puts the tray down on the table.*]

HEDDA: Why didn't you ask the servant to bring it in?

TESMAN: [*Fills the glasses.*] I like waiting on you, Hedda.

HEDDA: But you've filled both glasses. Mr. Loevborg doesn't want to drink.

TESMAN: Yes, but Mrs. Elvsted'll be here soon.

HEDDA: Oh yes, that's true. Mrs. Elvsted—

TESMAN: Had you forgotten her? What?

HEDDA: We're so absorbed with these photographs. [*Shows him one.*] You remember this little village?

TESMAN: Oh, that one down by the Brenner Pass. We spent a night there—

HEDDA: Yes, and met all those amusing people.

TESMAN: Oh yes, it was there, wasn't it? By Jove, if only we could have had you with us, Eilert! Ah, well. [*Goes back into the other room and sits down with* BRACK.]

LOEVBORG: Tell me one thing, Hedda.

HEDDA: Yes?

LOEVBORG: Didn't you love me either? Not—just a little?

HEDDA: Well now, I wonder? No, I think we were just good pals—Really good pals who could tell each other anything. [*Smiles.*] You certainly poured your heart out to me.

LOEVBORG: You begged me to.

HEDDA: Looking back on it, there was something beautiful and fascinating—and brave—about the way we told each other everything. That secret friendship no one else knew about.

LOEVBORG: Yes, Hedda, yes! Do you remember? How I used to come up to your father's house in the afternoon—and the General sat by the window and read his newspapers—with his back toward us—

HEDDA: And we sat on the sofa in the corner—

LOEVBORG: Always reading the same illustrated magazine—

HEDDA: We hadn't any photograph album.

LOEVBORG: Yes, Hedda. I regarded you as a kind of confessor. Told you things about myself which no one else knew about—then. Those days and nights of drinking and— Oh, Hedda, what power did you have to make me confess such things?

HEDDA: Power? You think I had some power over you?

LOEVBORG: Yes—I don't know how else to explain it. And all those— oblique questions you asked me——

HEDDA: You knew what they meant.

LOEVBORG: But that you could sit there and ask me such questions! So unashamedly——

HEDDA: I thought you said they were oblique.

LOEVBORG: Yes, but you asked them so unashamedly. That you could question me about—about that kind of thing!

HEDDA: You answered willingly enough.

LOEVBORG: Yes—that's what I can't understand—looking back on it. But tell me, Hedda—what you felt for me—wasn't that—love? When you asked me those questions and made me confess my sins to you, wasn't it because you wanted to wash me clean?

HEDDA: No, not exactly.

LOEVBORG: Why did you do it, then?

HEDDA: Do you find it so incredible that a young girl, given the chance to do so without anyone knowing, should want to be allowed a glimpse into a forbidden world of whose existence she is supposed to be ignorant?

LOEVBORG: So that was it?

HEDDA: One reason. One reason—I think.

LOEVBORG: You didn't love me, then. You just wanted—knowledge. But if that was so, why did you break it off?

HEDDA: That was your fault.

LOEVBORG: It was you who put an end to it.

HEDDA: Yes, when I realized that our friendship was threatening to develop into something—something else. Shame on you, Eilert Loevborg! How could you abuse the trust of your dearest friend?

LOEVBORG: [Clenches his fists.] Oh, why didn't you do it? Why didn't you shoot me dead? As you threatened to?

HEDDA: I was afraid. Of the scandal.

LOEVBORG: Yes, Hedda. You're a coward at heart.

HEDDA: A dreadful coward. [Changes her tone.] Luckily for you. Well, now you've found consolation with the Elvsteds.

LOEVBORG: I know what Thea's been telling you.

HEDDA: I dare say you told her about us.

LOEVBORG: Not a word. She's too silly to understand that kind of thing.

HEDDA: Silly?

LOEVBORG: She's silly about that kind of thing.

HEDDA: And I am a coward. [Leans closer to him, without looking him in the eyes, and says quietly.] But let me tell you something. Something you don't know.

LOEVBORG: [*Tensely.*] Yes?

HEDDA: My failure to shoot you wasn't my worst act of cowardice that evening.

LOEVBORG: [*Looks at her for a moment, realizes her meaning and whispers passionately.*] Oh, Hedda! Hedda Gabler! Now I see what was behind those questions. Yes! It wasn't knowledge you wanted! It was life!

HEDDA: [*Flashes a look at him and says quietly.*] Take care! Don't you delude yourself!

[*It has begun to grow dark.* BERTHA, *from outside, opens the door leading into the hall.*]

HEDDA: [*Closes the album with a snap and cries, smiling.*] Ah, at last! Come in, Thea dear!

[MRS. ELVSTED *enters from the hall, in evening dress. The door is closed behind her.*]

HEDDA: [*On the sofa, stretches out her arms toward her.*] Thea darling, I thought you were never coming!

[MRS. ELVSTED *makes a slight bow to the gentlemen in the rear room as she passes the open doorway, and they to her. Then she goes to the table and holds out her hand to* HEDDA. EILERT LOEVBORG *has risen from his chair. He and* MRS. ELVSTED *nod silently to each other.*]

MRS. ELVSTED: Perhaps I ought to go in and say a few words to your husband?

HEDDA: Oh, there's no need. They're happy by themselves. They'll be going soon.

MRS. ELVSTED: Going?

HEDDA: Yes, they're off on a spree this evening.

MRS. ELVSTED: [*Quickly, to* LOEVBORG.] You're not going with them?

LOEVBORG: No.

HEDDA: Mr. Loevborg is staying here with us.

MRS. ELVSTED: [*Takes a chair and is about to sit down beside him.*] Oh, how nice it is to be here!

HEDDA: No, Thea darling, not there. Come over here and sit beside me. I want to be in the middle.

MRS. ELVSTED: Yes, just as you wish.

[*She goes right of the table and sits on the sofa, on* HEDDA's *right.* LOEVBORG *sits down again in his chair.*]

LOEVBORG: [*After a short pause, to* HEDDA.] Isn't she lovely to look at?

HEDDA: [*Strokes her hair gently.*] Only to look at?

LOEVBORG: Yes. We're just good pals. We trust each other implicitly. We can talk to each other quite unashamedly.

HEDDA: No need to be oblique?

MRS. ELVSTED: [*Nestles close to* HEDDA *and says quietly.*] Oh, Hedda I'm so happy. Imagine — he says I've inspired him!

HEDDA: [*Looks at her with a smile.*] Dear Thea! Does he really?

LOEVBORG: She has the courage of her convictions, Mrs. Tesman.

MRS. ELVSTED: I? Courage?

LOEVBORG: Absolute courage. Where friendship is concerned.

HEDDA: Yes. Courage. Yes. If only one had that——

LOEVBORG: Yes?

HEDDA: One might be able to live. In spite of everything. [*Changes her tone suddenly.*] Well, Thea darling, now you're going to drink a nice glass of cold punch.

MRS. ELVSTED: No, thank you. I never drink anything like that.

HEDDA: Oh. You, Mr. Loevborg?

LOEVBORG: Thank you, I don't either.

MRS. ELVSTED: No, he doesn't, either.

HEDDA: [*Looks into his eyes.*] But if I want you to?

LOEVBORG: That doesn't make any difference.

HEDDA: [*Laughs.*] Have I no power over you at all? Poor me!

LOEVBORG: Not where this is concerned.

HEDDA: Seriously, I think you should. For your own sake.

MRS. ELVSTED: Hedda!

LOEVBORG: Why?

HEDDA: Or perhaps I should say for other people's sake.

LOEVBORG: What do you mean?

HEDDA: People might think you didn't feel absolutely and unashamedly sure of yourself. In your heart of hearts.

MRS. ELVSTED: [*Quietly.*] Oh, Hedda, no!

LOEVBORG: People can think what they like. For the present.

MRS. ELVSTED: [*Happily.*] Yes, that's true.

HEDDA: I saw it so clearly in Judge Brack a few minutes ago.

LOEVBORG: Oh. What did you see?

HEDDA: He smiled so scornfully when he saw you were afraid to go in there and drink with them.

LOEVBORG: Afraid! I wanted to stay here and talk to you.

MRS. ELVSTED: That was only natural, Hedda.

HEDDA: But the Judge wasn't to know that. I saw him wink at Tesman when you showed you didn't dare to join their wretched little party.

LOEVBORG: Didn't dare! Are you saying I didn't dare?

HEDDA: I'm not saying so. But that was what Judge Brack thought.

LOEVBORG: Well, let him.

HEDDA: You're not going, then?

LOEVBORG: I'm staying here with you and Thea.

MRS. ELVSTED: Yes, Hedda, of course he is.

HEDDA: [*Smiles, and nods approvingly to* LOEVBORG.] Firm as a rock! A man of principle! That's how a man should be! [*Turns to* MRS. ELVSTED *and strokes her cheek.*] Didn't I tell you so this morning when you came here in such a panic——

LOEVBORG: [*Starts.*] Panic?

MRS. ELVSTED: [*Frightened.*] Hedda! But—Hedda!

HEDDA: Well, now you can see for yourself. There's no earthly need for you to get scared to death just because——[*Stops.*] Well! Let's all three cheer up and enjoy ourselves.

LOEVBORG: Mrs. Tesman, would you mind explaining to me what this is all about?

MRS. ELVSTED: Oh, my God, my God, Hedda, what are you saying? What are you doing?

HEDDA: Keep calm. That horrid Judge has his eye on you.

LOEVBORG: Scared to death, were you? For my sake?

MRS. ELVSTED: [*Quietly, trembling.*] Oh, Hedda! You've made me so unhappy!

LOEVBORG: [*Looks coldly at her for a moment. His face is distorted.*] So that was how much you trusted me.

MRS. ELVSTED: Eilert dear, please listen to me——

LOEVBORG: [*Takes one of the glasses of punch, raises it and says quietly, hoarsely.*] Skoal, Thea! [*Empties the glass, puts it down and picks up one of the others.*]

MRS. ELVSTED: [*Quietly.*] Hedda, Hedda! Why did you want this to happen?

HEDDA: I—want it? Are you mad?

LOEVBORG: Skoal to you too, Mrs. Tesman. Thanks for telling me the truth. Here's to the truth! [*Empties his glass and refills it.*]

HEDDA: [*Puts her hand on his arm.*] Steady. That's enough for now. Don't forget the party.

MRS. ELVSTED: No, no, no!

HEDDA: Ssh! They're looking at you.

LOEVBORG: [*Puts down his glass.*] Thea, tell me the truth——

MRS. ELVSTED: Yes!

LOEVBORG: Did your husband know you were following me?

MRS. ELVSTED: Oh, Hedda!

LOEVBORG: Did you and he have an agreement that you should come here and keep an eye on me? Perhaps he gave you the idea? After all, he's a magistrate.[2] I suppose he needed me back in his office. Or did he miss my companionship at the card table?

MRS. ELVSTED: [*Quietly, sobbing.*] Eilert, Eilert!

LOEVBORG: [*Seizes a glass and is about to fill it.*] Let's drink to him, too.

HEDDA: No more now. Remember you're going to read your book to Tesman.

LOEVBORG: [*Calm again, puts down his glass.*] That was silly of me, Thea. To take it like that, I mean. Don't be angry with me, my dear. You'll see—yes, and they'll see, too—that though I fell, I—I have raised myself up again. With your help, Thea.

MRS. ELVSTED: [*Happily.*] Oh, thank God!

[BRACK *has meanwhile glanced at his watch. He and* TESMAN *get up and come into the drawing room.*]

BRACK: [*Takes his hat and overcoat.*] Well, Mrs. Tesman. It's time for us to go.

HEDDA: Yes, I suppose it must be.

LOEVBORG: [*Gets up.*] Time for me too, Judge.

MRS. ELVSTED: [*Quietly, pleadingly.*] Eilert, please don't!

HEDDA: [*Pinches her arm.*] They can hear you.

MRS. ELVSTED: [*Gives a little cry.*] Oh!

LOEVBORG: [*To* BRACK.] You were kind enough to ask me to join you.

BRACK: Are you coming?

LOEVBORG: If I may.

---

2. Also translated "sheriff." A civil official with duties associated with the courts.

BRACK: Delighted.

LOEVBORG: [*Puts the paper package in his pocket and says to* TESMAN.] I'd like to show you one or two things before I send it off to the printer.

TESMAN: I say, that'll be fun. Fancy——! Oh, but Hedda, how'll Mrs. Elvsted get home? What?

HEDDA: Oh, we'll manage somehow.

LOEVBORG: [*Glances over toward the ladies.*] Mrs. Elvsted? I shall come back and collect her, naturally. [*Goes closer.*] About ten o'clock, Mrs. Tesman? Will that suit you?

HEDDA: Yes. That'll suit me admirably.

TESMAN: Good, that's settled. But you mustn't expect me back so early, Hedda.

HEDDA: Stay as long as you c—as long as you like, dear.

MRS. ELVSTED: [*Trying to hide her anxiety.*] Well then, Mr. Loevborg, I'll wait here till you come.

LOEVBORG: [*His hat in his hand.*] Pray do, Mrs. Elvsted.

BRACK: Well, gentlemen, now the party begins. I trust that, in the words of a certain fair lady, we shall enjoy good sport.

HEDDA: What a pity the fair lady can't be there, invisible.

BRACK: Why invisible?

HEDDA: So as to be able to hear some of your uncensored witticisms, your honor.

BRACK: [*Laughs.*] Oh, I shouldn't advise the fair lady to do that.

TESMAN: [*Laughs too.*] I say, Hedda, that's good. By Jove! Fancy that!

BRACK: Well, good night, ladies, good night!

LOEVBORG: [*Bows farewell.*] About ten o'clock, then.

[BRACK, LOEVBORG *and* TESMAN *go out through the hall. As they do so* BERTHA *enters from the rear room with a lighted lamp. She puts it on the drawing-room table, then goes out the way she came.*]

MRS. ELVSTED: [*Has got up and is walking uneasily to and fro.*] Oh Hedda, Hedda! How is all this going to end?

HEDDA: At ten o'clock, then. He'll be here. I can see him. With a crown of vine-leaves in his hair.[3] Burning and unashamed!

MRS. ELVSTED: Oh, I do hope so!

HEDDA: Can't you see? Then he'll be himself again! He'll be a free man for the rest of his days!

MRS. ELVSTED: Please God you're right.

HEDDA: That's how he'll come! [*Gets up and goes closer.*] You can doubt him as much as you like. I believe in him! Now we'll see which of us——

MRS. ELVSTED: You're after something, Hedda.

HEDDA: Yes, I am. For once in my life I want to have the power to shape a man's destiny.

MRS. ELVSTED: Haven't you that power already?

HEDDA: No, I haven't. I've never had it.

MRS. ELVSTED: What about your husband?

HEDDA: Him! Oh, if you could only understand how poor I am. And you're

---

3. Like Bacchus, the Greek god of wine, and his followers.

She goes to the writing table, takes a small hand mirror from it and arranges her hair. Then she goes to the door leading into the hall and presses the bell. After a few moments, BERTHA *enters.*]

BERTHA: Did you want anything, madam?

HEDDA: Yes, put some more wood on the fire. I'm freezing.

BERTHA: Bless you, I'll soon have this room warmed up. [*She rakes the embers together and puts a fresh piece of wood on them. Suddenly she stops and listens.*] There's someone at the front door, madam.

HEDDA: Well, go and open it. I'll see to the fire.

BERTHA: It'll burn up in a moment.

[*She goes out through the hall.* HEDDA *kneels on the footstool and puts more wood in the stove. After a few seconds,* GEORGE TESMAN *enters from the hall. He looks tired, and rather worried. He tiptoes toward the open doorway and is about to slip through the curtains.*]

HEDDA: [*At the stove, without looking up.*] Good morning.

TESMAN: [*Turns.*] Hedda! [*Comes nearer.*] Good heavens, are you up already? What?

HEDDA: Yes, I got up very early this morning.

TESMAN: I was sure you'd still be sleeping. Fancy that!

HEDDA: Don't talk so loud. Mrs. Elvsted's asleep in my room.

TESMAN: Mrs. Elvsted? Has she stayed the night here?

HEDDA: Yes. No one came to escort her home.

TESMAN: Oh. No, I suppose not.

HEDDA: [*Closes the door of the stove and gets up.*] Well. Was it fun?

TESMAN: Have you been anxious about me? What?

HEDDA: Not in the least. I asked if you'd had fun.

TESMAN: Oh yes, rather! Well, I thought, for once in a while—The first part was the best; when Eilert read his book to me. We arrived over an hour too early—what about that, eh? By Jove! Brack had a lot of things to see to, so Eilert read to me.

HEDDA: [*Sits at the right-hand side of the table.*] Well? Tell me about it.

TESMAN: [*Sits on a footstool by the stove.*] Honestly, Hedda, you've no idea what a book that's going to be. It's really one of the most remarkable things that's ever been written. By Jove!

HEDDA: Oh, never mind about the book—

TESMAN: I'm going to make a confession to you, Hedda. When he'd finished reading a sort of beastly feeling came over me.

HEDDA: Beastly feeling?

TESMAN: I found myself envying Eilert for being able to write like that. Imagine that, Hedda!

HEDDA: Yes. I can imagine.

TESMAN: What a tragedy that with all those gifts he should be so incorrigible.

HEDDA: You mean he's less afraid of life than most men?

TESMAN: Good heavens, no. He just doesn't know the meaning of the word moderation.

HEDDA: What happened afterwards?

TESMAN: Well, looking back on it I suppose you might almost call it an orgy, Hedda.

HEDDA: Had he vine-leaves in his hair?

TESMAN: Vine-leaves? No, I didn't see any of them. He made a long, rambling oration in honor of the woman who'd inspired him to write this book. Yes, those were the words he used.

HEDDA: Did he name her?

TESMAN: No. But I suppose it must be Mrs. Elvsted. You wait and see!

HEDDA: Where did you leave him?

TESMAN: On the way home. We left in a bunch—the last of us, that is— and Brack came with us to get a little fresh air. Well, then, you see, we agreed we ought to see Eilert home. He'd had a drop too much.

HEDDA: You don't say?

TESMAN: But now comes the funny part, Hedda. Or I should really say the tragic part. Oh, I'm almost ashamed to tell you. For Eilert's sake, I mean——

HEDDA: Why, what happened?

TESMAN: Well, you see, as we were walking toward town I happened to drop behind for a minute. Only for a minute—er—you understand——

HEDDA: Yes, yes——?

TESMAN: Well then, when I ran on to catch them up, what do you think I found by the roadside. What?

HEDDA: How on earth should I know?

TESMAN: You mustn't tell anyone, Hedda. What? Promise me that—for Eilert's sake. [*Takes a package wrapped in paper from his coat pocket.*] Just fancy! I found this.

HEDDA: Isn't this the one he brought here yesterday?

TESMAN: Yes! The whole of that precious, irreplaceable manuscript! And he went and lost it! Didn't even notice! What about that? By Jove! Tragic.

HEDDA: But why didn't you give it back to him?

TESMAN: I didn't dare to, in the state he was in.

HEDDA: Didn't you tell any of the others?

TESMAN: Good heavens, no. I didn't want to do that. For Eilert's sake, you understand.

HEDDA: Then no one else knows you have his manuscript?

TESMAN: No. And no one must be allowed to know.

HEDDA: Didn't it come up in the conversation later?

TESMAN: I didn't get a chance to talk to him any more. As soon as we got into the outskirts of town, he and one or two of the others gave us the slip. Disappeared, by Jove!

HEDDA: Oh? I suppose they took him home.

TESMAN: Yes, I imagine that was the idea. Brack left us, too.

HEDDA: And what have you been up to since then?

TESMAN: Well, I and one or two of the others—awfully jolly chaps, they were—went back to where one of them lived, and had a cup of morning coffee. Morning-after coffee—what? Ah, well. I'll just lie down for a bit and give Eilert time to sleep it off, poor chap, then I'll run over and give this back to him.

HEDDA: [*Holds out her hand for the package.*] No, don't do that. Not just yet. Let me read it first.

TESMAN: Oh no, really, Hedda dear, honestly, I daren't do that.

HEDDA: Daren't?

TESMAN: No—imagine how desperate he'll be when he wakes up and finds his manuscript's missing. He hasn't any copy, you see. He told me so himself.

HEDDA: Can't a thing like that be rewritten?

TESMAN: Oh no, not possibly, I shouldn't think. I mean, the inspiration, you know——

HEDDA: Oh, yes. I'd forgotten that. [*Casually.*] By the way, there's a letter for you.

TESMAN: Is there? Fancy that!

HEDDA: [*Holds it out to him.*] It came early this morning.

TESMAN: I say, it's from Auntie Juju! What on earth can it be? [*Puts the package on the other footstool, opens the letter, reads it and jumps up.*] Oh, Hedda! She says poor Auntie Rena's dying.

HEDDA: Well, we've been expecting that.

TESMAN: She says if I want to see her I must go quickly. I'll run over at once.

HEDDA: [*Hides a smile.*] Run?

TESMAN: Hedda dear, I suppose you wouldn't like to come with me? What about that, eh?

HEDDA: [*Gets up and says wearily and with repulsion.*] No, no, don't ask me to do anything like that. I can't bear illness or death. I loathe anything ugly.

TESMAN: Yes, yes. Of course. [*In a dither.*] My hat? My overcoat? Oh yes, in the hall. I do hope I won't get there too late, Hedda? What?

HEDDA: You'll be all right if you run.

[BERTHA *enters from the hall.*]

BERTHA: Judge Brack's outside and wants to know if he can come in.

TESMAN: At this hour? No, I can't possibly receive him now.

HEDDA: I can. [*To* BERTHA.] Ask his honor to come in.

[BERTHA *goes.*]

HEDDA: [*Whispers quickly.*] The manuscript, Tesman. [*She snatches it from the footstool.*]

TESMAN: Yes, give it to me.

HEDDA: No, I'll look after it for now.

[*She goes over to the writing table and puts it in the bookcase.* TESMAN *stands dithering, unable to get his gloves on.* JUDGE BRACK *enters from the hall.*]

HEDDA: [*Nods to him.*] Well, you're an early bird.

BRACK: Yes, aren't I? [*To* TESMAN.] Are you up and about, too?

TESMAN: Yes, I've got to go and see my aunts. Poor Auntie Rena's dying.

BRACK: Oh dear, is she? Then you mustn't let me detain you. At so tragic a——

TESMAN: Yes, I really must run. Good-bye! Good-bye! [*Runs out through the hall.*]

HEDDA: [*Goes nearer.*] You seem to have had excellent sport last night—Judge.

BRACK: Indeed yes, Mrs. Hedda. I haven't even had time to take my clothes off.

HEDDA: *You* haven't either?

BRACK: As you see. What's Tesman told you about last night's escapades?

HEDDA: Oh, only some boring story about having gone and drunk coffee somewhere.

BRACK: Yes, I've heard about that coffee party. Eilert Loevborg wasn't with them, I gather?

HEDDA: No, they took him home first.

BRACK: Did Tesman go with him?

HEDDA: No, one or two of the others, he said.

BRACK: [*Smiles.*] George Tesman is a credulous man, Mrs. Hedda.

HEDDA: God knows. But—has something happened?

BRACK: Well, yes, I'm afraid it has.

HEDDA: I see. Sit down and tell me.

[*She sits on the left of the table,* BRACK *at the long side of it, near her.*]

HEDDA: Well?

BRACK: I had a special reason for keeping track of my guests last night. Or perhaps I should say some of my guests.

HEDDA: Including Eilert Loevborg?

BRACK: I must confess—yes.

HEDDA: You're beginning to make me curious.

BRACK: Do you know where he and some of my other guests spent the latter half of last night, Mrs. Hedda?

HEDDA: Tell me. If it won't shock me.

BRACK: Oh, I don't think it'll shock you. They found themselves participating in an exceedingly animated *soirée.*[4]

HEDDA: Of a sporting character?

BRACK: Of a highly sporting character.

HEDDA: Tell me more.

BRACK: Loevborg had received an invitation in advance—as had the others. I knew all about that. But he had refused. As you know, he's become a new man.

HEDDA: Up at the Elvsteds', yes. But he went?

BRACK: Well, you see, Mrs. Hedda, last night at my house, unhappily, the spirit moved him.

HEDDA: Yes, I hear he became inspired.

BRACK: Somewhat violently inspired. And as a result, I suppose, his thoughts strayed. We men, alas, don't always stick to our principles as firmly as we should.

HEDDA: I'm sure you're an exception, Judge Brack. But go on about Loevborg.

BRACK: Well, to cut a long story short, he ended up in the establishment of a certain Mademoiselle Danielle.

HEDDA: Mademoiselle Danielle?

4. Evening party.

BRACK: She was holding the *soirée*. For a selected circle of friends and admirers.

HEDDA: Has she got red hair?

BRACK: She has.

HEDDA: A singer of some kind?

BRACK: Yes—among other accomplishments. She's also a celebrated huntress—of men, Mrs. Hedda. I'm sure you've heard about her. Eilert Loevborg used to be one of her most ardent patrons. In his salad days.[5]

HEDDA: And how did all this end?

BRACK: Not entirely amicably, from all accounts. Mademoiselle Danielle began by receiving him with the utmost tenderness and ended by resorting to her fists.

HEDDA: Against Loevborg?

BRACK: Yes. He accused her, or her friends, of having robbed him. He claimed his pocketbook had been stolen. Among other things. In short, he seems to have made a bloodthirsty scene.

HEDDA: And what did this lead to?

BRACK: It led to a general free-for-all, in which both sexes participated. Fortunately, in the end the police arrived.

HEDDA: The police too?

BRACK: Yes. I'm afraid it may turn out to be rather an expensive joke for Master Eilert. Crazy fool!

HEDDA: Oh?

BRACK: Apparently he put up a very violent resistance. Hit one of the constables on the ear and tore his uniform. He had to accompany them to the police station.

HEDDA: Where did you learn all this?

BRACK: From the police.

HEDDA: [*To herself.*] So that's what happened. He didn't have a crown of vine-leaves in his hair.

BRACK: Vine-leaves, Mrs. Hedda?

HEDDA: [*In her normal voice again.*] But, tell me, Judge, why do you take such a close interest in Eilert Loevborg?

BRACK: For one thing it'll hardly be a matter of complete indifference to me if it's revealed in court that he came there straight from my house.

HEDDA: Will it come to court?

BRACK: Of course. Well, I don't regard that as particularly serious. Still, I thought it my duty, as a friend of the family, to give you and your husband a full account of his nocturnal adventures.

HEDDA: Why?

BRACK: Because I've a shrewd suspicion that he's hoping to use you as a kind of screen.

HEDDA: What makes you think that?

BRACK: Oh, for heaven's sake, Mrs. Hedda, we're not blind. You wait and see. This Mrs. Elvsted won't be going back to her husband just yet.

HEDDA: Well, if there were anything between those two there are plenty of other places where they could meet.

5. Indiscreet youth.

when it comes into the world. I want to see people respect and honor
you again. And the joy! The joy! I want to share it with you!

LOEVBORG: Thea—our book will never come into the world.

HEDDA: Ah!

MRS. ELVSTED: Not——?

LOEVBORG: It cannot. Ever.

MRS. ELVSTED: Eilert—what have you done with the manuscript? Where
is it?

LOEVBORG: Oh Thea, please don't ask me that!

MRS. ELVSTED: Yes, yes—I must know. I've a right to know. Now!

LOEVBORG: The manuscript. I've torn it up.

MRS. ELVSTED: [*Screams.*] No, no!

HEDDA: [*Involuntarily.*] But that's not——!

LOEVBORG: [*Looks at her.*] Not true, you think?

HEDDA: [*Controls herself.*] Why—yes, of course it is, if you say so. It just
sounded so incredible——

LOEVBORG: It's true, nevertheless.

MRS. ELVSTED: Oh, my God, my God, Hedda—he's destroyed his own
book!

LOEVBORG: I have destroyed my life. Why not my life's work, too?

MRS. ELVSTED: And you—did this last night?

LOEVBORG: Yes, Thea. I tore it into a thousand pieces. And scattered them
out across the fjord.[6] It's good, clean, salt water. Let it carry them away;
let them drift in the current and the wind. And in a little while, they
will sink. Deeper and deeper. As I shall, Thea.

MRS. ELVSTED: Do you know, Eilert—this book—all my life I shall feel as
though you'd killed a little child?

LOEVBORG: You're right. It is like killing a child.

MRS. ELVSTED: But how could you? It was my child, too!

HEDDA: [*Almost inaudibly.*] Oh—the child——!

MRS. ELVSTED: [*Breathes heavily.*] It's all over, then. Well—I'll go now,
Hedda.

HEDDA: You're not leaving town?

MRS. ELVSTED: I don't know what I'm going to do. I can't see anything
except—darkness.

[*She goes out through the hall.*]

HEDDA: [*Waits a moment.*] Aren't you going to escort her home, Mr.
Loevborg?

LOEVBORG: I? Through the streets? Do you want me to let people see her
with me?

HEDDA: Of course I don't know what else may have happened last night.
But is it so utterly beyond redress?

LOEVBORG: It isn't just last night. It'll go on happening. I know it. But the
curse of it is, I don't want to live that kind of life. I don't want to start
all that again. She's broken my courage. I can't spit in the eyes of the
world any longer.

HEDDA: [*As though to herself.*] That pretty little fool's been trying to shape

6. Inlet of the sea.

a man's destiny. [*Looks at him.*] But how could you be so heartless toward her?

LOEVBORG: Don't call me heartless!

HEDDA: To go and destroy the one thing that's made her life worth living? You don't call that heartless?

LOEVBORG: Do you want to know the truth, Hedda?

HEDDA: The truth?

LOEVBORG: Promise me first—give me your word—that you'll never let Thea know about this.

HEDDA: I give you my word.

LOEVBORG: Good. Well; what I told her just now was a lie.

HEDDA: About the manuscript?

LOEVBORG: Yes. I didn't tear it up. Or throw it in the fjord.

HEDDA: You didn't? But where is it, then?

LOEVBORG: I destroyed it, all the same. I destroyed it, Hedda!

HEDDA: I don't understand.

LOEVBORG: Thea said that what I had done was like killing a child.

HEDDA: Yes. That's what she said.

LOEVBORG: But to kill a child isn't the worst thing a father can do to it.

HEDDA: What could be worse than that?

LOEVBORG: Hedda—suppose a man came home one morning, after a night of debauchery, and said to the mother of his child: "Look here. I've been wandering round all night. I've been to—such-and-such a place and such-and-such a place. And I had our child with me. I took him to—these places. And I've lost him. Just—lost him. God knows where he is or whose hands he's fallen into."

HEDDA: I see. But when all's said and done, this was only a book——

LOEVBORG: Thea's heart and soul were in that book. It was her whole life.

HEDDA: Yes. I understand.

LOEVBORG: Well, then you must also understand that she and I cannot possibly ever see each other again.

HEDDA: Where will you go?

LOEVBORG: Nowhere. I just want to put an end to it all. As soon as possible.

HEDDA: [*Takes a step toward him.*] Eilert Loevborg, listen to me. Do it— beautifully!

LOEVBORG: Beautifully? [*Smiles.*] With a crown of vine-leaves in my hair? The way you used to dream of me—in the old days?

HEDDA: No. I don't believe in that crown any longer. But—do it beauti- fully, all the same. Just this once. Good-bye. You must go now. And don't come back.

LOEVBORG: Adieu, madam. Give my love to George Tesman. [*Turns to go.*]

HEDDA: Wait. I want to give you a souvenir to take with you.

[*She goes over to the writing table, opens the drawer and the pistol- case, and comes back to* LOEVBORG *with one of the pistols.*]

LOEVBORG: [*Looks at her.*] This? Is this the souvenir?

HEDDA: [*Nods slowly.*] You recognize it? You looked down its barrel once.

LOEVBORG: You should have used it then.

HEDDA: Here! Use it now!

LOEVBORG: [*Puts the pistol in his breast pocket.*] Thank you.
HEDDA: Do it beautifully, Eilert Loevborg. Only promise me that!
LOEVBORG: Good-bye, Hedda Gabler.
[*He goes out through the hall.* HEDDA *stands by the door for a moment, listening. Then she goes over to the writing table, takes out the package containing the manuscript, glances inside it, pulls some of the pages half out and looks at them. Then she takes it to the armchair by the stove and sits down with the package in her lap. After a moment, she opens the door of the stove; then she opens the packet.*]
HEDDA: [*Throws one of the pages into the stove and whispers to herself.*] I'm burning your child, Thea! You with your beautiful wavy hair! [*She throws a few more pages into the stove.*] The child Eilert Loevborg gave you. [*Throws the rest of the manuscript in.*] I'm burning it! I'm burning your child!

Act IV

SCENE— *The same. It is evening. The drawing room is in darkness. The small room is illuminated by the hanging lamp over the table. The curtains are drawn across the french windows.* HEDDA, *dressed in black, is walking up and down in the darkened room. Then she goes into the small room and crosses to the left. A few chords are heard from the piano. She comes back into the drawing room.*

BERTHA *comes through the small room from the right with a lighted lamp, which she places on the table in front of the corner sofa in the drawing room. Her eyes are red with crying, and she has black ribbons on her cap. She goes quietly out, right.* HEDDA *goes over to the french windows, draws the curtains slightly to one side and looks out into the darkness.*

A few moments later, MISS TESMAN *enters from the hall. She is dressed in mourning, with a black hat and veil.* HEDDA *goes to meet her and holds out her hand.*

MISS TESMAN: Well, Hedda, here I am in the weeds of sorrow. My poor sister has ended her struggles at last.
HEDDA: I've already heard. Tesman sent me a card.
MISS TESMAN: Yes, he promised me he would. But I thought, no, I must go and break the news of death to Hedda myself—here, in the house of life.
HEDDA: It's very kind of you.
MISS TESMAN: Ah, Rena shouldn't have chosen a time like this to pass away. This is no moment for Hedda's house to be a place of mourning.
HEDDA: [*Changing the subject.*] She died peacefully, Miss Tesman?
MISS TESMAN: Oh, it was quite beautiful! The end came so calmly. And she was so happy at being able to see George once again. And say good-bye to him. Hasn't he come home yet?
HEDDA: No. He wrote that I mustn't expect him too soon. But please sit down.

MISS TESMAN: No, thank you, Hedda dear—bless you. I'd like to. But I've so little time. I must dress her and lay her out as well as I can. She shall go to her grave looking really beautiful.

HEDDA: Can't I help with anything?

MISS TESMAN: Why, you mustn't think of such a thing! Hedda Tesman mustn't let her hands be soiled by contact with death. Or her thoughts. Not at this time.

HEDDA: One can't always control one's thoughts.

MISS TESMAN: [*Continues.*] Ah, well, that's life. Now we must start to sew poor Rena's shroud. There'll be sewing to be done in this house too before long, I shouldn't wonder. But not for a shroud, praise God.

[GEORGE TESMAN *enters from the hall.*]

HEDDA: You've come at last! Thank heavens!

TESMAN: Are you here, Auntie Juju? With Hedda? Fancy that!

MISS TESMAN: I was just on the point of leaving, dear boy. Well, have you done everything you promised me?

TESMAN: No, I'm afraid I forgot half of it. I'll have to run over again tomorrow. My head's in a complete whirl today. I can't collect my thoughts.

MISS TESMAN: But George dear, you mustn't take it like this.

TESMAN: Oh? Well—er—how should I?

MISS TESMAN: You must be happy in your grief. Happy for what's happened. As I am.

TESMAN: Oh, yes, yes. You're thinking of Aunt Rena.

HEDDA: It'll be lonely for you now, Miss Tesman.

MISS TESMAN: For the first few days, yes. But it won't last long, I hope. Poor dear Rena's little room isn't going to stay empty.

TESMAN: Oh? Whom are you going to move in there? What?

MISS TESMAN: Oh, there's always some poor invalid who needs care and attention.

HEDDA: Do you really want another cross like that to bear?

MISS TESMAN: Cross! God forgive you, child. It's been no cross for me.

HEDDA: But now—if a complete stranger comes to live with you——?

MISS TESMAN: Oh, one soon makes friends with invalids. And I need so much to have someone to live for. Like you, my dear. Well, I expect there'll soon be work in this house too for an old aunt, praise God!

HEDDA: Oh—please!

TESMAN: By Jove, yes! What a splendid time the three of us could have together if——

HEDDA: If?

TESMAN: [*Uneasily.*] Oh, never mind. It'll all work out. Let's hope so—what?

MISS TESMAN: Yes, yes. Well, I'm sure you two would like to be alone. [*Smiles.*] Perhaps Hedda may have something to tell you, George. Good-bye. I must go home to Rena. [*Turns to the door.*] Dear God, how strange! Now Rena is with me and with poor dear Joachim.

TESMAN: Fancy that. Yes, Auntie Juju! What?

[MISS TESMAN *goes out through the hall.*]

HEDDA: [*Follows* TESMAN *coldly and searchingly with her eyes.*] I really believe this death distresses you more than it does her.

TESMAN: Oh, it isn't just Auntie Rena. It's Eilert I'm so worried about.

HEDDA: [*Quickly.*] Is there any news of him?

TESMAN: I ran over to see him this afternoon. I wanted to tell him his manuscript was in safe hands.

HEDDA: Oh? You didn't find him?

TESMAN: No. He wasn't at home. But later I met Mrs. Elvsted and she told me he'd been here early this morning.

HEDDA: Yes, just after you'd left.

TESMAN: It seems he said he'd torn the manuscript up. What?

HEDDA: Yes, he claimed to have done so.

TESMAN: You told him we had it, of course?

HEDDA: No. [*Quickly.*] Did you tell Mrs. Elvsted?

TESMAN: No, I didn't like to. But you ought to have told him. Think if he should go home and do something desperate! Give me the manuscript, Hedda. I'll run over to him with it right away. Where did you put it?

HEDDA: [*Cold and motionless, leaning against the armchair.*] I haven't got it any longer.

TESMAN: Haven't got it? What on earth do you mean?

HEDDA: I've burned it.

TESMAN: [*Starts, terrified.*] Burned it! Burned Eilert's manuscript!

HEDDA: Don't shout. The servant will hear you.

TESMAN: Burned it! But in heaven's name——! Oh, no, no, no! This is impossible!

HEDDA: Well, it's true.

TESMAN: But Hedda, do you realize what you've done? That's appropriating lost property! It's against the law! By Jove! You ask Judge Brack and see if I'm not right.

HEDDA: You'd be well advised not to talk about it to Judge Brack or anyone else.

TESMAN: But how could you go and do such a dreadful thing? What on earth put the idea into your head? What came over you? Answer me! What?

HEDDA: [*Represses an almost imperceptible smile.*] I did it for your sake, George.

TESMAN: For my sake?

HEDDA: When you came home this morning and described how he'd read his book to you——

TESMAN: Yes, yes?

HEDDA: You admitted you were jealous of him.

TESMAN: But, good heavens, I didn't mean it literally!

HEDDA: No matter. I couldn't bear the thought that anyone else should push you into the background.

TESMAN: [*Torn between doubt and joy.*] Hedda—is this true? But—but—but I never realized you loved me like that! Fancy——

HEDDA: Well, I suppose you'd better know. I'm going to have—— [*Breaks off and says violently.*] No, no—you'd better ask your Auntie Juju. She'll tell you.

TESMAN: Hedda! I think I understand what you mean. [*Clasps his hands.*] Good heavens, can it really be true! What?

HEDDA: Don't shout. The servant will hear you.

TESMAN: [*Laughing with joy.*] The servant! I say, that's good! The servant! Why, that's Bertha! I'll run out and tell her at once!

HEDDA: [*Clenches her hands in despair.*] Oh, it's destroying me, all this— it's destroying me!

TESMAN: I say, Hedda, what's up? What?

HEDDA: [*Cold, controlled.*] Oh, it's all so—absurd—George.

TESMAN: Absurd? That I'm so happy? But surely——? Ah, well—perhaps I won't say anything to Bertha.

HEDDA: No, do. She might as well know too.

TESMAN: No, no, I won't tell her yet. But Auntie Juju—I must let her know! And you—you called me George! For the first time! Fancy that! Oh, it'll make Auntie Juju so happy, all this! So very happy!

HEDDA: Will she be happy when she hears I've burned Eilert Loevborg's manuscript—for your sake?

TESMAN: No, I'd forgotten about that. Of course no one must be allowed to know about the manuscript. But that you're burning with love for me, Hedda, I must certainly let Auntie Juju know that. I say, I wonder if young wives often feel like that toward their husbands? What?

HEDDA: You might ask Auntie Juju about that too.

TESMAN: I will, as soon as I get the chance. [*Looks uneasy and thoughtful again.*] But I say, you know, that manuscript. Dreadful business. Poor Eilert!

[MRS. ELVSTED, *dressed as on her first visit, with hat and overcoat, enters from the hall.*]

MRS. ELVSTED: [*Greets them hastily and tremulously.*] Oh, Hedda dear, do please forgive me for coming here again.

HEDDA: Why, Thea, what's happened?

TESMAN: Is it anything to do with Eilert Loevborg? What?

MRS. ELVSTED: Yes—I'm so dreadfully afraid he may have met with an accident.

HEDDA: [*Grips her arm.*] You think so?

TESMAN: But, good heavens, Mrs. Elvsted, what makes you think that?

MRS. ELVSTED: I heard them talking about him at the boarding-house, as I went in. Oh, there are the most terrible rumors being spread about him in town today.

TESMAN: Fancy. Yes, I heard about them too. But I can testify that he went straight home to bed. Fancy that!

HEDDA: Well—what did they say in the boarding-house?

MRS. ELVSTED: Oh, I couldn't find out anything. Either they didn't know, or else—— They stopped talking when they saw me. And I didn't dare to ask.

TESMAN: [*Fidgets uneasily.*] We must hope—we must hope you misheard them, Mrs. Elvsted.

MRS. ELVSTED: No, no, I'm sure it was he they were talking about. I heard them say something about a hospital——

TESMAN: Hospital!

HEDDA: Oh no, surely that's impossible!

MRS. ELVSTED: Oh, I became so afraid. So I went up to his rooms and asked to see him.

HEDDA: Do you think that was wise, Thea?

MRS. ELVSTED: Well, what else could I do? I couldn't bear the uncertainty any longer.

TESMAN: But you didn't manage to find him either? What?

MRS. ELVSTED: No. And they had no idea where he was. They said he hadn't been home since yesterday afternoon.

TESMAN: Since yesterday? Fancy that!

MRS. ELVSTED: I'm sure he must have met with an accident.

TESMAN: Hedda, I wonder if I ought to go into town and make one or two enquiries?

HEDDA: No, no, don't you get mixed up in this.

[JUDGE BRACK *enters from the hall, hat in hand.* BERTHA, *who has opened the door for him, closes it. He looks serious and greets them silently.*]

TESMAN: Hullo, my dear Judge. Fancy seeing you!

BRACK: I had to come and talk to you.

TESMAN: I can see Auntie Juju's told you the news.

BRACK: Yes, I've heard about that too.

TESMAN: Tragic, isn't it?

BRACK: Well, my dear chap, that depends on how you look at it.

TESMAN: [*Looks uncertainly at him.*] Has something else happened?

BRACK: Yes.

HEDDA: Another tragedy?

BRACK: That also depends on how you look at it, Mrs. Tesman.

MRS. ELVSTED: Oh, it's something to do with Eilert Loevborg!

BRACK: [*Looks at her for a moment.*] How did you guess? Perhaps you've heard already——?

MRS. ELVSTED: [*Confused.*] No, no, not at all—I——

TESMAN: For heaven's sake, tell us!

BRACK: [*Shrugs his shoulders.*] Well, I'm afraid they've taken him to the hospital. He's dying.

MRS. ELVSTED: [*Screams.*] Oh God, God!

TESMAN: The hospital! Dying!

HEDDA: [*Involuntarily.*] So quickly!

MRS. ELVSTED: [*Weeping.*] Oh, Hedda! And we parted enemies!

HEDDA: [*Whispers.*] Thea—Thea!

MRS. ELVSTED: [*Ignoring her.*] I must see him! I must see him before he dies!

BRACK: It's no use, Mrs. Elvsted. No one's allowed to see him now.

MRS. ELVSTED: But what's happened to him? You must tell me!

TESMAN: He hasn't tried to do anything to himself? What?

HEDDA: Yes, he has. I'm sure of it.

TESMAN: Hedda, how can you——?

BRACK: [*Who has not taken his eyes from her.*] I'm afraid you've guessed correctly, Mrs. Tesman.

MRS. ELVSTED: How dreadful!

TESMAN: Attempted suicide! Fancy that!

HEDDA: Shot himself!

BRACK: Right again, Mrs. Tesman.

MRS. ELVSTED: [*Tries to compose herself.*] When did this happen, Judge Brack?

BRACK: This afternoon. Between three and four.

TESMAN: But, good heavens—where? What?

BRACK: [*A little hesitantly.*] Where? Why, my dear chap, in his rooms of course.

MRS. ELVSTED: No, that's impossible. I was there soon after six.

BRACK: Well, it must have been somewhere else, then. I don't know exactly. I only know that they found him. He'd shot himself—through the breast.

MRS. ELVSTED: Oh, how horrible! That he should end like that!

HEDDA: [*To* BRACK.] Through the breast, you said?

BRACK: That is what I said.

HEDDA: Not through the head?

BRACK: Through the breast, Mrs. Tesman.

HEDDA: The breast. Yes; yes. That's good, too.

BRACK: Why, Mrs. Tesman?

HEDDA: Oh—no, I didn't mean anything.

TESMAN: And the wound's dangerous you say? What?

BRACK: Mortal. He's probably already dead.

MRS. ELVSTED: Yes, yes—I feel it! It's all over. All over. Oh Hedda——!

TESMAN: But, tell me, how did you manage to learn all this?

BRACK: [*Curtly.*] From the police. I spoke to one of them.

HEDDA: [*Loudly, clearly.*] At last! Oh, thank God!

TESMAN: [*Appalled.*] For God's sake, Hedda, what are you saying?

HEDDA: I am saying there's beauty in what he has done.

BRACK: Mm—Mrs. Tesman——

TESMAN: Beauty! Oh, but I say!

MRS. ELVSTED: Hedda, how can you talk of beauty in connection with a thing like this?

HEDDA: Eilert Loevborg has settled his account with life. He's had the courage to do what—what he had to do.

MRS. ELVSTED: No, that's not why it happened. He did it because he was mad.

TESMAN: He did it because he was desperate.

HEDDA: You're wrong! I know!

MRS. ELVSTED: He must have been mad. The same as when he tore up the manuscript.

BRACK: [*Starts.*] Manuscript? Did he tear it up?

MRS. ELVSTED: Yes. Last night.

TESMAN: [*Whispers.*] Oh, Hedda, we shall never be able to escape from this.

BRACK: Hm. Strange.

TESMAN: [*Wanders round the room.*] To think of Eilert dying like that. And not leaving behind him the thing that would have made his name endure.

MRS. ELVSTED: If only it could be pieced together again!

TESMAN: Yes, fancy! If only it could! I'd give anything——

MRS. ELVSTED: Perhaps it can, Mr. Tesman.

TESMAN: What do you mean?

MRS. ELVSTED: [*Searches in the pocket of her dress.*] Look! I kept the notes he dictated it from.

HEDDA: [*Takes a step nearer.*] Ah!

TESMAN: You kept them, Mrs. Elvsted! What?

MRS. ELVSTED: Yes, here they are. I brought them with me when I left home. They've been in my pocket ever since.

TESMAN: Let me have a look.

MRS. ELVSTED: [*Hands him a wad of small sheets of paper.*] They're in a terrible muddle. All mixed up.

TESMAN: I say, just fancy if we can sort them out! Perhaps if we work on them together——?

MRS. ELVSTED: Oh, yes! Let's try, anyway!

TESMAN: We'll manage it. We must! I shall dedicate my life to this.

HEDDA: *You*, George? Your life?

TESMAN: Yes—well, all the time I can spare. My book'll have to wait. Hedda, you do understand? What? I owe it to Eilert's memory.

HEDDA: Perhaps.

TESMAN: Well, my dear Mrs. Elvsted, you and I'll have to pool our brains. No use crying over spilt milk, what? We must try to approach this matter calmly.

MRS. ELVSTED: Yes, yes, Mr. Tesman. I'll do my best.

TESMAN: Well, come over here and let's start looking at these notes right away. Where shall we sit? Here? No, the other room. You'll excuse us, won't you, Judge? Come along with me, Mrs. Elvsted.

MRS. ELVSTED: Oh, God! If only we can manage to do it!

[TESMAN *and* MRS. ELVSTED *go into the rear room. He takes off his hat and overcoat. They sit at the table beneath the hanging lamp and absorb themselves in the notes.* HEDDA *walks across to the stove and sits in the armchair. After a moment,* BRACK *goes over to her.*]

HEDDA: [*Half aloud.*] Oh, Judge! This act of Eilert Loevborg's—doesn't it give one a sense of release!

BRACK: Release, Mrs. Hedda? Well, it's a release for him, of course——

HEDDA: Oh, I don't mean him—I mean me! The release of knowing that someone can do something really brave! Something beautiful!

BRACK: [*Smiles.*] Hm—my dear Mrs. Hedda——

HEDDA: Oh, I know what you're going to say. You're a bourgeois at heart too, just like—ah, well!

BRACK: [*Looks at her.*] Eilert Loevborg has meant more to you than you're willing to admit to yourself. Or am I wrong?

HEDDA: I'm not answering questions like that from you. I only know that Eilert Loevborg has had the courage to live according to his own principles. And now, at last, he's done something big! Something beautiful! To have the courage and the will to rise from the feast of life so early!

BRACK: It distresses me deeply, Mrs. Hedda, but I'm afraid I must rob you of that charming illusion.

HEDDA: Illusion?

BRACK: You wouldn't have been allowed to keep it for long, anyway.

HEDDA: What do you mean?

BRACK: He didn't shoot himself on purpose.

HEDDA: Not on purpose?

BRACK: No. It didn't happen quite the way I told you.

HEDDA: Have you been hiding something? What is it?

BRACK: In order to spare poor Mrs. Elvsted's feelings, I permitted myself one or two small—equivocations.

HEDDA: What?

BRACK: To begin with, he is already dead.

HEDDA: He died at the hospital?

BRACK: Yes. Without regaining consciousness.

HEDDA: What else haven't you told us?

BRACK: The incident didn't take place at his lodgings.

HEDDA: Well, that's utterly unimportant.

BRACK: Not utterly. The fact is, you see, that Eilert Loevborg was found shot in Mademoiselle Danielle's boudoir.

HEDDA: [Almost jumps up, but instead sinks back in her chair.] That's impossible. He can't have been there today.

BRACK: He was there this afternoon. He went to ask for something he claimed they'd taken from him. Talked some crazy nonsense about a child which had got lost——

HEDDA: Oh! So that was the reason!

BRACK: I thought at first he might have been referring to his manuscript. But I hear he destroyed that himself. So he must have meant his pocket-book—I suppose.

HEDDA: Yes, I suppose so. So they found him there?

BRACK: Yes; there. With a discharged pistol in his breast pocket. The shot had wounded him mortally.

HEDDA: Yes. In the breast.

BRACK: No. In the—hm—stomach. The—lower part——

HEDDA: [Looks at him with an expression of repulsion.] That too! Oh, why does everything I touch become mean and ludicrous? It's like a curse!

BRACK: There's something else, Mrs. Hedda. It's rather disagreeable, too.

HEDDA: What?

BRACK: The pistol he had on him——

HEDDA: Yes? What about it?

BRACK: He must have stolen it.

HEDDA: [Jumps up.] Stolen it! That isn't true! He didn't!

BRACK: It's the only explanation. He must have stolen it. Ssh!

[TESMAN and MRS. ELVSTED have got up from the table in the rear room and come into the drawing room.]

TESMAN: [*His hands full of papers.*] Hedda, I can't see properly under that lamp. Think!

HEDDA: I am thinking.

TESMAN: Do you think we could possibly use your writing table for a little? What?

HEDDA: Yes, of course. [*Quickly.*] No, wait! Let me tidy it up first.

TESMAN: Oh, don't you trouble about that. There's plenty of room.

HEDDA: No, no, let me tidy it up first, I say. I'll take this in and put them on the piano. Here.

[*She pulls an object, covered with sheets of music, out from under the bookcase, puts some more sheets on top and carries it all into the rear room and away to the left.* TESMAN *puts his papers on the writing table and moves the lamp over from the corner table. He and* MRS. ELVSTED *sit down and begin working again.* HEDDA *comes back.*]

HEDDA: [*Behind* MRS. ELVSTED*'s chair, ruffles her hair gently.*] Well, my pretty Thea! And how is work progressing on Eilert Loevborg's memorial?

MRS. ELVSTED: [*Looks up at her, dejectedly.*] Oh, it's going to be terribly difficult to get these into any order.

TESMAN: We've got to do it. We must! After all, putting other people's papers into order is rather my specialty, what?

[HEDDA *goes over to the stove and sits on one of the footstools.* BRACK *stands over her, leaning against the armchair.*]

HEDDA: [*Whispers.*] What was that you were saying about the pistol?

BRACK: [*Softly.*] I said he must have stolen it.

HEDDA: Why do you think that?

BRACK: Because any other explanation is unthinkable, Mrs. Hedda, or ought to be.

HEDDA: I see.

BRACK: [*Looks at her for a moment.*] Eilert Loevborg was here this morning. Wasn't he?

HEDDA: Yes.

BRACK: Were you alone with him?

HEDDA: For a few moments.

BRACK: You didn't leave the room while he was here?

HEDDA: No.

BRACK: Think again. Are you sure you didn't go out for a moment?

HEDDA: Oh—yes, I might have gone into the hall. Just for a few seconds.

BRACK: And where was your pistol-case during this time?

HEDDA: I'd locked it in that—

BRACK: Er—Mrs. Hedda?

HEDDA: It was lying over there on my writing table.

BRACK: Have you looked to see if both the pistols are still there?

HEDDA: No.

BRACK: You needn't bother. I saw the pistol Loevborg had when they found him. I recognized it at once. From yesterday. And other occasions.

HEDDA: Have you got it?

BRACK: No. The police have it.

HEDDA: What will the police do with this pistol?
BRACK: Try to trace the owner.
HEDDA: Do you think they'll succeed?
BRACK: [Leans down and whispers.] No, Hedda Gabler. Not as long as I hold my tongue.
HEDDA: [Looks nervously at him.] And if you don't?
BRACK: [Shrugs his shoulders.] You could always say he'd stolen it.
HEDDA: I'd rather die!
BRACK: [Smiles.] People say that. They never do it.
HEDDA: [Not replying.] And suppose the pistol wasn't stolen? And they trace the owner? What then?
BRACK: There'll be a scandal, Hedda.
HEDDA: A scandal!
BRACK: Yes, a scandal. The thing you're so frightened of. You'll have to appear in court. Together with Mademoiselle Danielle. She'll have to explain how it all happened. Was it an accident, or was it—homicide? Was he about to take the pistol from his pocket to threaten her? And did it go off? Or did she snatch the pistol from his hand, shoot him and then put it back in his pocket? She might quite easily have done it. She's a resourceful lady, is Mademoiselle Danielle.
HEDDA: But I had nothing to do with this repulsive business.
BRACK: No. But you'll have to answer one question. Why did you give Eilert Loevborg this pistol? And what conclusions will people draw when it is proved you did give it to him?
HEDDA: [Bows her head.] That's true. I hadn't thought of that.
BRACK: Well, luckily there's no danger as long as I hold my tongue.
HEDDA: [Looks up at him.] In other words, I'm in your power, Judge. From now on, you've got your hold over me.
BRACK: [Whispers, more slowly.] Hedda, my dearest—believe me—I will not abuse my position.
HEDDA: Nevertheless, I'm in your power. Dependent on your will, and your demands. Not free. Still not free! [Rises passionately.] No. I couldn't bear that. No.
BRACK: [Looks half-derisively at her.] Most people resign themselves to the inevitable, sooner or later.
HEDDA: [Returns his gaze.] Possibly they do.
[She goes across to the writing table.]
HEDDA: [Represses an involuntary smile and says in TESMAN's voice.] Well, George. Think you'll be able to manage? What?
TESMAN: Heaven knows, dear. This is going to take months and months.
HEDDA: [In the same tone as before.] Fancy that, by Jove! [Runs her hands gently through MRS. ELVSTED's hair.] Doesn't it feel strange, Thea? Here you are working away with Tesman just the way you used to work with Eilert Loevborg.
MRS. ELVSTED: Oh—if only I can inspire your husband too!
HEDDA: Oh, it'll come. In time.
TESMAN: Yes—do you know, Hedda, I really think I'm beginning to feel a bit—well—that way. But you go back and talk to Judge Brack.
HEDDA: Can't I be of use to you two in any way?

TESMAN: No, none at all. [*Turns his head.*] You'll have to keep Hedda company from now on, Judge, and see she doesn't get bored. If you don't mind.

BRACK. [*Glances at* HEDDA.] It'll be a pleasure.

HEDDA: Thank you. But I'm tired this evening. I think I'll lie down on the sofa in there for a little while.

TESMAN: Yes, dear—do. What?

[HEDDA *goes into the rear room and draws the curtain behind her. Short pause. Suddenly she begins to play a frenzied dance melody on the piano.*]

MRS. ELVSTED: [*Starts up from her chair.*] Oh, what's that?

TESMAN: [*Runs to the doorway.*] Hedda dear, please! Don't play dance music tonight! Think of Auntie Rena. And Eilert.

HEDDA: [*Puts her head out through the curtains.*] And Auntie Juju. And all the rest of them. From now on I'll be quiet. [*Closes the curtains behind her.*]

TESMAN: [*At the writing table.*] It distresses her to watch us doing this. I say, Mrs. Elvsted, I've an idea. Why don't you move in with Auntie Juju? I'll run over each evening, and we can sit and work there. What?

MRS. ELVSTED: Yes, that might be the best plan.

HEDDA: [*From the rear room.*] I can hear what you're saying, Tesman. But how shall I spend the evenings out here?

TESMAN: [*Looking through his papers.*] Oh, I'm sure Judge Brack'll be kind enough to come over and keep you company. You won't mind my not being here, Judge?

BRACK: [*In the armchair, calls gaily.*] I'll be delighted, Mrs. Tesman. I'll be here every evening. We'll have great fun together, you and I.

HEDDA: [*Loud and clear.*] Yes, that'll suit you, won't it, Judge? The only cock on the dunghill——!

[*A shot is heard from the rear room.* TESMAN, MRS. ELVSTED *and* JUDGE BRACK *start from their chairs.*]

TESMAN: Oh, she's playing with those pistols again.

[*He pulls the curtains aside and runs in.* MRS. ELVSTED *follows him.* HEDDA *is lying dead on the sofa. Confusion and shouting.* BERTHA *enters in alarm from the right.*]

TESMAN: [*Screams to* BRACK.] She's shot herself! Shot herself in the head! By Jove! Fancy that!

BRACK: [*Half paralyzed in the armchair.*] But, good God! People don't do such things!

ANTON CHEKHOV

1860–1904

In plays and stories Anton Chekhov depicts Russia around the turn of the twentieth century with great pity, gentleness, and kindness of heart. More important, with a deep humanity that has outlasted all the problems of his time, he dramatizes universal and almost timeless feelings rather than ideas that date and pass. He differs sharply from the two giants of Russian literature, Dostoevsky and Tolstoy. For one thing, his work is of smaller scope. With the exception of an immature, forgotten novel and a travel book, he wrote only short stories and plays. He belongs, furthermore, to a very different moral and spiritual atmosphere. Chekhov had studied medicine and practiced it for a time. He shared the scientific outlook of his age and had too skeptical a mind to believe in Christianity or in any metaphysical system. He confessed that an intelligent believer was a puzzle to him. His attitude toward his materials and characters is detached, "objective," and his letters to friends insist that a good writer must present both physical details and a character's state of mind without overt interpretation or judgment. He is thus much more in the stream of Western realism than either Tolstoy or Dostoevsky, and the delicate, precise realism of his short stories has served as a model for later writers in Europe, China, and the United States. But extended reading of Chekhov does convey an impression of his view of life. There is implied in his stories a philosophy of kindness and humanity, a love of beauty, a sense of the unexplainable mystery of life, a sense, especially, of the individual's utter loneliness in this universe and among other people. Chekhov's pessimism has nothing of the defiance of the universe or the horror at it which we meet in other writers with similar attitudes; it is somehow merely sad, often pathetic, and yet also comforting and comfortable.

The Russia depicted in Chekhov's stories and plays is of a later period than that presented by Tolstoy and Dostoevsky. It seems to be nearing its end; there is a sense of decadence and frustration which heralds the approach of catastrophe. The aristocracy still keeps up a beautiful front but is losing its fight without much resistance, resignedly. Officialdom is stupid and venal. The Church is backward and narrow minded. The intelligentsia are hopelessly ineffectual, futile, lost in the provinces or absorbed in their egos. The peasants live subject to the lowest degradations of poverty and drink, apparently rather aggravated than improved since the much-heralded emancipation of the serfs in 1861. There seems no hope for society except in a gradual spread of enlightenment, good sense, and hygiene, for Chekhov is skeptical of the revolution and revolutionaries as well as of Tolstoy's followers.

Anton Pavlovich Chekhov was born on January 17, 1860, at Taganrog, a small town on the Sea of Azov. His father was a grocer and haberdasher; his grandfather, a serf who had bought his freedom. Chekhov's father went bankrupt in 1876, and the family moved to Moscow, leaving Anton to finish school in his home town. After his graduation in 1879, he followed his family to Moscow, where he studied medicine. To earn additional money for his family and himself, he started to write humorous sketches and stories for magazines. In 1884 he became a doctor and published his first collection of stories, *Tales of Melpomene*. In the same year he had his first hemorrhage. All the rest of his life he struggled against tuberculosis. His first play, *Ivanov*, was performed in 1887. Three years later, he undertook an arduous journey through Siberia to the island of Sakhalin (north of Japan) and back by boat through the Suez Canal. He saw there the Russian penal settlements and wrote a moving account of his trip in *Sakhalin Island* (1892). In 1898 his play *The Sea Gull* was a great success at the Moscow Art Theater. The next year he moved to Yalta, in the Crimea, and in 1901 married the actress Olga Knipper. He died on July 2, 1904, at Badenweiler in the Black Forest.

The plays of Chekhov seem to go furthest in the direction of naturalism, the depiction of a "slice of life," on stage. Compared with Ibsen's plays they seem plotless; they could be described as a succession of little scenes, composed like a mosaic or like the dots or strokes in an impressionist painting. The characters rarely engage in the usual dialogue; they speak often in little soliloquies, hardly justified by the situation; and they often do not listen to the words of their ostensible partners. They seem alone even in a crowd. Human communication seems difficult and even impossible. There is no clear message, no zeal for social reform; life seems to flow quietly, even sluggishly, until interrupted by some desperate outbreak or even a pistol shot.

Chekhov's last play, *The Cherry Orchard* (composed in 1903, first performed at the Moscow Art Theater on January 17, 1904) differs, however, from this pattern in several respects. It has a strongly articulated central theme—the loss of the orchard—and it has a composition that roughly follows the traditional scheme of a well-made play. Arrival and departure from the very same room, the nursery, frame the two other acts: the outdoor idyll of Act II and the dance in Act III. Act III is the turning point of the action: Lopahin appears and announces, somewhat shamefacedly, that he has bought the estate. The orchard was lost from the very beginning—there is no real struggle to prevent its sale—but still the news of Lopahin's purchase is a surprise as he had no intention of buying it but did so only when during the auction sale a rival seemed to have a chance of acquiring it. A leading action runs its course, and many—one may even argue too many—subplots crisscross each other: the shy and awkward love affair of the student Trofimov and the daughter Anya; the love triangle among the three dependents, Yepihodov (the unlucky clerk), Dunyasha (the chambermaid), and Yasha (the conceited and insolent footman). Varya, the practical stepdaughter, has her troubles with Lopahin, and Simeonov-Pishchik is beset by the same financial problems as the owners of the orchard and is rescued by the discovery of some white clay on his estate. The German governess Charlotta drifts around alluding to her obscure origins and past. There are undeveloped references to events preceding the action on stage—the lover in Paris, the drowned boy Grisha—but there is no revelation of the past as in Ibsen, no mystery, no intrigue.

While the events on the stage follow each other naturally, though hardly always in a logical, causal order, a symbolic device is used conspicuously: in Act II after a pause, "suddenly a distant sound is heard, coming from the sky as it were, the sound of a snapping string, mournfully dying away." It occurs again at the very end of the play followed by "the strokes of the ax against a tree far away in the orchard." An attempt is made to explain this sound at its first occurrence as a bucket's fall in a faraway pit or as the cries of a heron or an owl, but the effect is weird and even supernatural; it establishes an ominous mood. Even the orchard carries more than its obvious meaning: it is white, drowned in blossoms when the party arrives in the spring; it is bare and desolate in the autumn when the axes are heard cutting it down. "The old bark on the trees gleams faintly, and the cherry trees seem to be dreaming of things that happened a hundred, two hundred years ago and to be tormented by painful visions," declaims Trofimov, defining his feeling for the orchard as a symbol of repression and serfdom. For Lubov Ranevskaya it is an image of her lost innocence and of the happier past, while Lopahin sees it only as an investment. It seems to draw together the meaning of the play.

But what is this meaning? Can we even decide whether it is a tragedy or a comedy? It has been commonly seen as the tragedy of the downfall of the Russian aristocracy (or more correctly, the landed gentry) victimized by the newly rich, upstart peasantry. One could see the play as depicting the defeat of a group of feckless people at the hand of a ruthless "developer" who destroys nature and natural beauty for profit. Or one can see it as prophesying, through the mouth of the student Trofimov, the approaching end of feudal Russia and the coming happier future. Soviet interpretations and performances lean that way.

Surely none of these interpretations can withstand inspection in the light of the actual play. They all run counter to Chekhov's professed intentions. He called the play a comedy. In a letter of September 15, 1903, he declared expressly that the play "has not turned out as drama but as comedy, in places even a farce" and a few days later (September 21, 1903) he wrote that "the whole play is gay and frivolous." Chekhov did not like the staging of the play at the Moscow Art Theater and complained of its tearful tone and its slow pace. He objected that "they obstinately call my play a drama in playbill and newspaper advertisements" while he had called it a comedy (April 10, 1904).

No doubt, there are many comical and even farcical characters and scenes in the play. Charlotta with her nut-eating dog, her card tricks, her ventriloquism, her disappearing acts, is a clownish figure. Gayev, the landowner, though "suave and elegant," is a boor, obsessed by his passion for billiards, constantly popping candy into his mouth, telling the waiters in a restaurant about the "decadents" in Paris. Yepihodov, the clerk, carries a revolver and, threatening suicide, asks foolishly whether you have read Buckle (the English historian) and complains of his ill-luck: a spider on his chest, a cockroach in his drink. Simeonov-Pishchik empties a whole bottle of pills, eats half a bucket of pickles, quotes Nietzsche supposedly recommending the forging of banknotes, and, fat as he is, puffs and prances at the dance ordering the "cavaliers à genoux." Even the serious characters are put into ludicrous predicaments: Trofimov falls down the stairs; Lopahin, coming to announce the purchase of the estate, is almost hit with a stick by Varya (and was hit in the original version). Lopahin, teasing his intended Varya, "moos like a cow." The ball, the hunting for the galoshes, and the champagne drinking by Yasha in the last act have all a touch of absurdity. The grand speeches, Gayev's addresses to the bookcase and to nature or Trofimov's about "mankind going forward" and "All Russia is our orchard," are undercut by the contrast between words and character: Gayev is callous and shallow; the "perpetual student," Trofimov never did a stitch of work. He is properly ridiculed and insulted by Lubov for his scant beard and his silly professions of being "above love." One can sympathize with Chekhov's irritation at the pervading gloom imposed by the Moscow production.

Still we cannot, in spite of the author, completely dismiss the genuine pathos of the central situation and of the central figure, Lubov Ranevskaya. Whatever one may say about her recklessness in financial matters and her guilt in relation to her lover in France, we must feel her deep attachment to the house and the orchard, to the past and her lost innocence, clearly and unhumorously expressed in the first act on her arrival, again and again at the impending sale of the estate, and finally at the parting from her house: "Oh, my orchard—my dear, sweet, beautiful orchard! . . . My life, my youth, my happiness—Good-bye!" That Gayev, before the final parting, seems to have overcome the sense of loss and even looks forward to his job in the bank and that Lubov acknowledges that her "nerves are better" and that "she sleeps well" testifies to the indestructible spirit of brother and sister, but cannot minimize the sense of loss, the pathos of parting, the nostalgia for happier times. Nor is the conception of Lopahin simple. Chekhov emphasized, in a letter to Konstantin Stanislavsky who was to play the part, that "Lopahin is a decent person in the full sense of the word, and his bearing must be that of a completely dignified and intelligent man." He is not, he says, a profiteering peasant (kulachok, October 30, 1903). He admires Lubov and thinks of her with gratitude. He senses the beauty of the poppies in his fields. Even the scene of the abortive encounter with Varya at the end has its quiet pathos in spite of all its awkwardness and the comic touches such as the reference to the broken thermometer. Firs, the eighty-seven-year-old valet, may be grotesque in his deafness and his nostalgia for the good old days of serfdom, but the very last scene when we see him abandoned in the locked-up house surely ends the play on a note of desolation and even despair.

Chekhov, we must conclude, achieved a highly original and even paradoxical blend of comedy and tragedy, or rather of farce and pathos. The play presents a social picture firmly set in a specific historical time—the dissolution of the landed gentry, the rise of the peasant, the encroachment of the city—but it does not propound an obvious social thesis. Chekhov, in his tolerance and tenderness, in his distrust of ideologies and heroics, extends his sympathy to all his characters (with the exception of the crudely ambitious valet Yasha). The glow of his humanity, untrammeled by time and place, keeps *The Cherry Orchard* alive in quite different social and political conditions, as it has the universalizing power of great art.

Donald Rayfield, *The Cherry Orchard: Catastrophe and Comedy* (1994), presents an extended discussion of the play; good chapters are also found in Beverly Hahn, *Chekhov: A Study of the Major Stories and Plays* (1977), Harvey Pitcher, *The Chekhov Play: A New Interpretation* (1973), and Richard Pearce, *Chekhov: A Study of the Four Major Plays* (1983). Francis Fergusson compares Ibsen and Chekhov in "*Ghosts* and *The Cherry Orchard*," in *The Idea of the Theatre* (1949). There is helpful critical analysis in R. L. Jackson, ed., *Chekhov: A Collection of Critical Essays* (1967) and *Reading Chekhov's Text* (1993), in D. Rayfield, *Chekhov: The Evolution of His Art* (1975), and in René Wellek and N. D. Wellek, eds. *Chekhov: New Perspectives* (1984); the latter includes a sketch of Chekhov criticism in England and America. J. L. Styan discusses *The Cherry Orchard* from a different perspective in *Chekhov in Performance: A Commentary on the Major Plays* (1971), and Nicholas Worrall, *File on Chekhov* (1986), offers an introductory survey with useful cited passages and suggestions for further study.

PRONOUNCING GLOSSARY

The following list uses common English syllables and stress accents to provide rough equivalents of selected words whose pronunciation may be unfamiliar to the general reader.

Anton Chekhov: *ahn-tawn' che'-khuf*

Charlotta Ivanovna: *shar-law'-tuh ee-vah'-nuv-nuh*

Firs: *feers*

Leonid Andreyevich Gayev: *lay-ah-neet' ahn-dray'-uh-veech gah'-yef*

Lubov Andreyevna Ranevskaya: *lyu-bawf' ahn-dray'-uv-nuh rah-nyef'-skah-yuh*

Pyotr Sergeyevich Trofimov: *pyaw'-tr sehr-gay'-eh-veech trah-fee'-muf*

Semyon Yepihodov: *seem-yawn' ye-pee-khaw'-duf*

Simeonov-Pishchik: *see-may-awn'-uf peesh'-cheek*

Yermolay Alexeyevich Lopahin: *yehr-mah-lai' ah-lex-ay'-eh-veech lah-pah'-kheen*

The Cherry Orchard[1]

CHARACTERS

LUBOV ANDREYEVNA RANEVSKAYA, *a landowner*

ANYA, *her seventeen-year-old daughter*

VARYA, *her adopted daughter, twenty-four years old*

LEONID ANDREYEVICH GAYEV, Mme. *Ranevskaya's brother*

CHARLOTTA IVANOVNA, *a governess*

SEMYON YEPIHODOV, *a clerk*

DUNYASHA, *a maid*

FIRS, *a manservant, aged eighty-seven*

YASHA, *a young valet*

A TRAMP

STATIONMASTER

1. Translated by Avrahm Yarmolinsky.

YERMOLAY ALEXEYEVICH LOPAHIN, *a*   POST OFFICE CLERK
  merchant   GUESTS
PYOTR SERGEYEVICH TROFIMOV, *a*   SERVANTS
  student
SIMEONOV-PISHCHIK, *a landowner*

The action takes place on MME. RANEVSKAYA'*s estate.*

Act I

A room that is still called the nursery. One of the doors leads into ANYA'*s room. Dawn, the sun will soon rise. It is May, the cherry trees are in blossom, but it is cold in the orchard; there is a morning frost. The windows are shut. Enter* DUNYASHA *with a candle, and* LOPAHIN *with a book in his hand.*

LOPAHIN: The train is in, thank God. What time is it?
DUNYASHA: Nearly two. [*Puts out the candle.*] It's light already.
LOPAHIN: How late is the train, anyway? Two hours at least. [*Yawns and stretches.*] I'm a fine one! What a fool I've made of myself! I came here on purpose to meet them at the station, and then I went and overslept. I fell asleep in my chair. How annoying! You might have waked me . . .
DUNYASHA: I thought you'd left. [*Listens.*] I think they're coming!
LOPAHIN: [*Listens.*] No, they've got to get the luggage, and one thing and another . . . [*Pause.*] Lubov Andreyevna spent five years abroad, I don't know what she's like now. . . . She's a fine person—lighthearted, simple. I remember when I was a boy of fifteen, my poor father—he had a shop here in the village then—punched me in the face with his fist and made my nose bleed. We'd come into the yard, I don't know what for, and he'd had a drop too much. Lubov Andreyevna, I remember her as if it were yesterday—she was still young and so slim—led me to the washbasin, in this very room . . . in the nursery. "Don't cry, little peasant," she said, "it'll heal in time for your wedding . . ." [*Pause.*] Little peasant . . . my father was a peasant, it's true, and here I am in a white waistcoat and yellow shoes. A pig in a pastry shop, you might say. It's true I'm rich. I've got a lot of money. . . . But when you look at it closely, I'm a peasant through and through. [*Pages the book.*] Here I've been reading this book and I didn't understand a word of it. . . . I was reading it and fell asleep . . . [*Pause.*]
DUNYASHA: And the dogs were awake all night, they feel that their masters are coming.
LOPAHIN: Dunyasha, why are you so—
DUNYASHA: My hands are trembling. I'm going to faint.
LOPAHIN: You're too soft, Dunyasha. You dress like a lady, and look at the way you do your hair. That's not right. One should remember one's place.
    [*Enter* YEPIHODOV *with a bouquet; he wears a jacket and highly polished boots that squeak badly. He drops the bouquet as he comes in.*]
YEPIHODOV: [*Picking up the bouquet.*] Here, the gardener sent these, said

you're to put them in the dining room. [*Hands the bouquet to* DUN-YASHA.]

LOPAHIN: And bring me some kvass.[2]

DUNYASHA: Yes, sir. [*Exits.*]

YEPIHODOV: There's a frost this morning—three degrees below—and yet the cherries are all in blossom. I cannot approve of our climate. [*Sighs.*] I cannot. Our climate does not activate properly. And, Yermolay Alexeyevich, allow me to make a further remark. The other day I bought myself a pair of boots, and I make bold to assure you, they squeak so that it is really intolerable. What should I grease them with?

LOPAHIN: Oh, get out! I'm fed up with you.

YEPIHODOV: Every day I meet with misfortune. And I don't complain, I've got used to it, I even smile.

[DUNYASHA *enters, hands* LOPAHIN *the kvass.*]

YEPIHODOV: I am leaving. [*Stumbles against a chair, which falls over.*] There! [*Triumphantly, as it were.*] There again, you see what sort of circumstance, pardon the expression. . . . It is absolutely phenomenal! [*Exits.*]

DUNYASHA: You know, Yermolay Alexeyevich, I must tell you, Yepihodov has proposed to me.

LOPAHIN: Ah!

DUNYASHA: I simply don't know . . . he's a quiet man, but sometimes when he starts talking, you can't make out what he means. He speaks nicely— and it's touching—but you can't understand it. I sort of like him though, and he is crazy about me. He's an unlucky man . . . every day something happens to him. They tease him about it here . . . they call him, Two-and-Twenty Troubles.

LOPAHIN: [*Listening.*] There! I think they're coming.

DUNYASHA: They *are* coming! What's the matter with me? I feel cold all over.

LOPAHIN: They really are coming. Let's go and meet them. Will she recognize me? We haven't seen each other for five years.

DUNYASHA: [*In a flutter.*] I'm going to faint this minute. . . . Oh, I'm going to faint!

[*Two carriages are heard driving up to the house.* LOPAHIN *and* DUN-YASHA *go out quickly. The stage is left empty. There is a noise in the adjoining rooms.* FIRS, *who had driven to the station to meet* LUBOV ANDREYEVNA RANEVSKAYA, *crosses the stage hurriedly, leaning on a stick. He is wearing an old-fashioned livery and a tall hat. He mutters to himself indistinctly. The hubbub offstage increases. A* VOICE: "Come, let's go this way." *Enter* LUBOV ANDREYEVNA, ANYA, *and* CHARLOTTA IVANOVNA *with a pet dog on a leash, all in traveling dresses;* VARYA, *wearing a coat and kerchief;* GAYEV, SIMEONOV-PISHCHIK, LOPAHIN, DUNYASHA *with a bag and an umbrella, servants with luggage. All walk across the room.*]

ANYA: Let's go this way. Do you remember what room this is, Mamma?

MME. RANEVSKAYA: [*Joyfully, through her tears.*] The nursery!

---

2. Russian beer, made from rye or barley.

VARYA: How cold it is! My hands are numb. [*To* MME. RANEVSKAYA.] Your rooms are just the same as they were, Mamma, the white one and the violet.

MME. RANEVSKAYA: The nursery! My darling, lovely room! I slept here when I was a child . . . [*Cries.*] And here I am, like a child again! [*Kisses her brother and* VARYA, *and then her brother again.*] Varya's just the same as ever, like a nun. And I recognized Dunyasha. [*Kisses* DUN-YASHA.]

GAYEV: The train was two hours late. What do you think of that? What a way to manage things!

CHARLOTTA: [*To* PISHCHIK.] My dog eats nuts, too.

PISHCHIK: [*In amazement.*] You don't say!

[*All go out, except* ANYA *and* DUNYASHA.]

DUNYASHA: We've been waiting for you for hours. [*Takes* ANYA's *hat and coat.*]

ANYA: I didn't sleep on the train for four nights and now I'm frozen . . .

DUNYASHA: It was Lent when you left; there was snow and frost, and now . . . My darling! [*Laughs and kisses her.*] I have been waiting for you, my sweet, my darling! But I must tell you something . . . I can't put it off another minute . . .

ANYA: [*Listlessly.*] What now?

DUNYASHA: The clerk, Yepihodov, proposed to me, just after Easter.

ANYA: There you are, at it again . . . [*Straightening her hair.*] I've lost all my hairpins . . . [*She is staggering with exhaustion.*]

DUNYASHA: Really, I don't know what to think. He loves me—he loves me so!

ANYA: [*Looking toward the door of her room, tenderly.*] My own room, my windows, just as though I'd never been away. I'm home! Tomorrow morning I'll get up and run into the orchard. Oh, if I could only get some sleep. I didn't close my eyes during the whole journey—I was so anxious.

DUNYASHA: Pyotr Sergeyevich came the day before yesterday.

ANYA: [*Joyfully.*] Petya!

DUNYASHA: He's asleep in the bathhouse. He has settled there. He said he was afraid of being in the way. [*Looks at her watch.*] I should wake him, but Miss Varya told me not to. "Don't you wake him," she said.

[*Enter* VARYA *with a bunch of keys at her belt.*]

VARYA: Dunyasha, coffee, and be quick. . . . Mamma's asking for coffee.

DUNYASHA: In a minute. [*Exits.*]

VARYA: Well, thank God, you've come. You're home again. [*Fondling* ANYA.] My darling is here again. My pretty one is back.

ANYA: Oh, what I've been through!

VARYA: I can imagine.

ANYA: When we left, it was Holy Week, it was cold then, and all the way Charlotta chattered and did her tricks. Why did you have to saddle me with Charlotta?

VARYA: You couldn't have travelled all alone, darling—at seventeen!

ANYA: We got to Paris, it was cold there, snowing. My French is dreadful.

Mamma lived on the fifth floor; I went up there, and found all kinds of Frenchmen, ladies, an old priest with a book. The place was full of tobacco smoke, and so bleak. Suddenly I felt sorry for Mamma, so sorry, I took her head in my arms and hugged her and couldn't let go of her. Afterward Mamma kept fondling me and crying . . .

VARYA: [*Through tears.*] Don't speak of it . . . don't.

ANYA: She had already sold her villa at Mentone, she had nothing left, nothing. I hadn't a kopeck left either, we had only just enough to get home. And Mamma wouldn't understand! When we had dinner at the stations, she always ordered the most expensive dishes, and tipped the waiters a whole ruble. Charlotta, too. And Yasha kept ordering, too—it was simply awful. You know Yasha's Mamma's footman now, we brought him here with us.

VARYA: Yes, I've seen the blackguard.

ANYA: Well, tell me—have you paid the interest?

VARYA: How could we?

ANYA: Good heavens, good heavens!

VARYA: In August the estate will be put up for sale.

ANYA: My God!

LOPAHIN: [*Peeps in at the door and bleats*]. Meh-h-h. [*Disappears.*]

VARYA: [*Through tears.*] What I couldn't do to him! [*Shakes her fist threateningly.*]

ANYA: [*Embracing* VARYA, *gently.*] Varya, has he proposed to you? [VARYA *shakes her head.*] But he loves you. Why don't you come to an understanding? What are you waiting for?

VARYA: Oh, I don't think anything will ever come of it. He's too busy, he has no time for me . . . pays no attention to me. I've washed my hands of him—I can't bear the sight of him. They all talk about our getting married, they all congratulate me—and all the time there's really nothing to it—it's all like a dream. [*In another tone.*] You have a new brooch—like a bee.

ANYA: [*Sadly.*] Mamma bought it. [*She goes into her own room and speaks gaily like a child.*] And you know, in Paris I went up in a balloon.

VARYA: My darling's home, my pretty one is back! [DUNYASHA *returns with the coffeepot and prepares coffee.* VARYA *stands at the door of* ANYA's *room.*] All day long, darling, as I go about the house, I keep dreaming. If only we could marry you off to a rich man, I should feel at ease. Then I would go into a convent, and afterward to Kiev, to Moscow . . . I would spend my life going from one holy place to another . . . I'd go on and on. . . . What a blessing that would be!

ANYA: The birds are singing in the orchard. What time is it?

VARYA: It must be after two. Time you were asleep, darling. [*Goes into* ANYA's *room.*] What a blessing that would be!

[YASHA *enters with a plaid and a traveling bag, crosses the stage.*]

YASHA: [*Finically.*] May I pass this way, please?

DUNYASHA: A person could hardly recognize you, Yasha. Your stay abroad has certainly done wonders for you.

YASHA: Hm-m . . . and who are you?

DUNYASHA: When you went away I was that high—[*Indicating with her hand.*] I'm Dunyasha—Fyodor Kozoyedev's daughter. Don't you remember?

YASHA: Hm! What a peach!

[*He looks round and embraces her. She cries out and drops a saucer.* YASHA *leaves quickly.*]

VARYA: [*In the doorway, in a tone of annoyance.*] What's going on here?

DUNYASHA: [*Through tears.*] I've broken a saucer.

VARYA: Well, that's good luck.

ANYA: [*Coming out of her room.*] We ought to warn Mamma that Petya's here.

VARYA: I left orders not to wake him.

ANYA: [*Musingly.*] Six years ago father died. A month later brother Grisha was drowned in the river. . . . Such a pretty little boy he was—only seven. It was more than Mamma could bear, so she went away, went away without looking back . . . [*Shudders.*] How well I understand her, if she only knew! [*Pause.*] And Petya Trofimov was Grisha's tutor, he may remind her of it all . . .

[*Enter* FIRS, *wearing a jacket and a white waistcoat. He goes up to the coffeepot.*]

FIRS: [*Anxiously.*] The mistress will have her coffee here. [*Puts on white gloves.*] Is the coffee ready? [*Sternly, to* DUNYASHA.] Here, you! And where's the cream?

DUNYASHA: Oh, my God! [*Exits quickly.*]

FIRS: [*Fussing over the coffeepot.*] Hah! the addlehead! [*Mutters to himself.*] Home from Paris. And the old master used to go to Paris too . . . by carriage. [*Laughs.*]

VARYA: What is it, Firs?

FIRS: What is your pleasure, Miss? [*Joyfully.*] My mistress has come home, and I've seen her at last! Now I can die. [*Weeps with joy.*]

[*Enter* MME. RANEVSKAYA, GAYEV, *and* SIMEONOV-PISHCHIK: *The latter is wearing a tight-waisted, pleated coat of fine cloth, and full trousers.* GAYEV, *as he comes in, goes through the motions of a billiard player with his arms and body.*]

MME. RANEVSKAYA: Let's see, how does it go? Yellow ball in the corner! Bank shot in the side pocket!

GAYEV: I'll tip it in the corner! There was a time, Sister, when you and I used to sleep in this very room and now I'm fifty-one, strange as it may seem.

LOPAHIN: Yes, time flies.

GAYEV: Who?

LOPAHIN: I say, time flies.

GAYEV: It smells of patchouli here.

ANYA: I'm going to bed. Good night, Mamma. [*Kisses her mother.*]

MME. RANEVSKAYA: My darling child! [*Kisses her hands.*] Are you happy to be home? I can't come to my senses.

ANYA: Good night, Uncle.

GAYEV: [*Kissing her face and hands.*] God bless you, how like your mother you are! [*To his sister.*] At her age, Luba, you were just like her.

[ANYA *shakes hands with* LOPAHIN *and* PISHCHIK, *then goes out, shutting the door behind her.*]

MME. RANEVSKAYA: She's very tired.

PISHCHIK: Well, it was a long journey.

VARYA: [*To* LOPAHIN *and* PISHCHIK.] How about it, gentlemen? It's past two o'clock—isn't it time for you to go?

MME. RANEVSKAYA: [*Laughs.*] You're just the same as ever, Varya. [*Draws her close and kisses her.*] I'll have my coffee and then we'll all go. [FIRS *puts a small cushion under her feet.*] Thank you, my dear. I've got used to coffee. I drink it day and night. Thanks, my dear old man. [*Kisses him.*]

VARYA: I'd better see if all the luggage has been brought in. [*Exits.*]

MME. RANEVSKAYA: Can it really be I sitting here? [*Laughs.*] I feel like dancing, waving my arms about. [*Covers her face with her hands.*] But maybe I am dreaming! God knows I love my country, I love it tenderly; I couldn't look out of the window in the train, I kept crying so. [*Through tears.*] But I must have my coffee. Thank you, Firs, thank you, dear old man. I'm so happy that you're still alive.

FIRS: Day before yesterday.

GAYEV: He's hard of hearing.

LOPAHIN: I must go soon, I'm leaving for Kharkov about five o'clock. How annoying! I'd like to have a good look at you, talk to you. . . . You're just as splendid as ever.

PISHCHIK: [*Breathing heavily.*] She's even better-looking. . . . Dressed in the latest Paris fashion. . . . Perish my carriage and all its four wheels. . . .

LOPAHIN: Your brother, Leonid Andreyevich, says I'm a vulgarian and an exploiter. But it's all the same to me—let him talk. I only want you to trust me as you used to. I want you to look at me with your touching, wonderful eyes, as you used to. Dear God! My father was a serf of your father's and grandfather's, but you, you yourself, did so much for me once . . . so much . . . that I've forgotten all about that; I love you as though you were my sister—even more.

MME. RANEVSKAYA: I can't sit still, I simply can't. [*Jumps up and walks about in violent agitation.*] This joy is too much for me. . . . . Laugh at me, I'm silly! My own darling bookcase! My darling table! [*Kisses it.*]

GAYEV: While you were away, nurse died.

MME. RANEVSKAYA: [*Sits down and takes her coffee.*] Yes, God rest her soul; they wrote me about it.

GAYEV: And Anastasy is dead. Petrushka Kossoy has left me and has gone into town to work for the police inspector. [*Takes a box of sweets out of his pocket and begins to suck one.*]

PISHCHIK: My daughter Dashenka sends her regards.

LOPAHIN: I'd like to tell you something very pleasant—cheering. [*Glancing at his watch.*] I am leaving directly. There isn't much time to talk. But I will put it in a few words. As you know, your cherry orchard is to be sold to pay your debts. The sale is to be on the twenty-second of August; but don't you worry, my dear, you may sleep in peace; there is a way out. Here is my plan. Give me your attention! Your estate is only fifteen miles from the town; the railway runs close by it; and if the

ANTON CHEKHOV

cherry orchard and the land along the riverbank were cut up into lots and these leased for summer cottages, you would have an income of at least 25,000 rubles a year out of it.

GAYEV: Excuse me. . . . What nonsense.

MME. RANEVSKAYA: I don't quite understand you, Yermolay Alexeyevich.

LOPAHIN: You will get an annual rent of at least ten rubles per acre, and if you advertise at once, I'll give you any guarantee you like that you won't have a square foot of ground left by autumn, all the lots will be snapped up. In short, congratulations, you're saved. The location is splendid— by that deep river. . . . Only, of course, the ground must be cleared . . . all the old buildings, for instance, must be torn down, and this house, too, which is useless, and, of course, the old cherry orchard must be cut down.

MME. RANEVSKAYA: Cut down? My dear, forgive me, but you don't know what you're talking about. If there's one thing that's interesting— indeed, remarkable—in the whole province, it's precisely our cherry orchard.

LOPAHIN: The only remarkable thing about this orchard is that it's a very large one. There's a crop of cherries every other year, and you can't do anything with them; no one buys them.

GAYEV: This orchard is even mentioned in the encyclopedia.

LOPAHIN: [Glancing at his watch.] If we can't think of a way out, if we don't come to a decision, on the twenty-second of August the cherry orchard and the whole estate will be sold at auction. Make up your minds! There's no other way out—I swear. None, none.

FIRS: In the old days, forty or fifty years ago, the cherries were dried, soaked, pickled, and made into jam, and we used to—

GAYEV: Keep still, Firs.

FIRS: And the dried cherries would be shipped by the cartload. It meant a lot of money! And in those days the dried cherries were soft and juicy, sweet, fragrant. . . . They knew the way to do it, then.

MME. RANEVSKAYA: And why don't they do it that way now?

FIRS: They've forgotten. Nobody remembers it.

PISHCHIK: [To MME. RANEVSKAYA.] What's doing in Paris? Eh? Did you eat frogs there?

MME. RANEVSKAYA: I ate crocodiles.

PISHCHIK: Just imagine!

LOPAHIN: There used to be only landowners and peasants in the country, but now these summer people have appeared on the scene. . . . All the towns, even the small ones, are surrounded by these summer cottages; and in another twenty years, no doubt, the summer population will have grown enormously. Now the summer resident only drinks tea on his porch, but maybe he'll take to working his acre, too, and then your cherry orchard will be a rich, happy, luxuriant place.

GAYEV: [Indignantly.] Poppycock!

[Enter VARYA and YASHA.]

VARYA: There are two telegrams for you, Mamma dear. [Picks a key from the bunch at her belt and noisily opens an old-fashioned bookcase.] Here they are.

MME. RANEVSKAYA: They're from Paris. [*Tears them up without reading them.*] I'm through with Paris.

GAYEV: Do you know, Luba, how old this bookcase is? Last week I pulled out the bottom drawer and there I found the date burnt in it. It was made exactly a hundred years ago. Think of that! We could celebrate its centenary. True, it's an inanimate object, but nevertheless, a bookcase . . .

PISHCHIK: [*Amazed.*] A hundred years! Just imagine!

GAYEV: Yes. [*Tapping it.*] That's something. . . . Dear, honored bookcase, hail to you who for more than a century have served the glorious ideals of goodness and justice! Your silent summons to fruitful toil has never weakened in all those hundred years [*through tears*], sustaining, through successive generations of our family, courage and faith in a better future, and fostering in us ideals of goodness and social consciousness. . . . [*Pauses.*]

LOPAHIN: Yes . . .

MME. RANEVSKAYA: You haven't changed a bit, Leonid.

GAYEV: [*Somewhat embarrassed.*] I'll play it off the red in the corner! Tip it in the side pocket!

LOPAHIN: [*Looking at his watch.*] Well, it's time for me to go . . .

YASHA: [*Handing pillbox to* MME. RANEVSKAYA.] Perhaps you'll take your pills now.

PISHCHIK: One shouldn't take medicines, dearest lady, they do neither harm nor good. . . . Give them here, my valued friend. [*Takes the pillbox, pours the pills into his palm, blows on them, puts them in his mouth, and washes them down with some kvass.*] There!

MME. RANEVSKAYA: [*Frightened.*] You must be mad!

PISHCHIK: I've taken all the pills.

LOPAHIN: What a glutton!

[*All laugh.*]

FIRS: The gentleman visited us in Easter week, ate half a bucket of pickles, he did . . . [*Mumbles.*]

MME. RANEVSKAYA: What's he saying?

VARYA: He's been mumbling like that for the last three years—we're used to it.

YASHA: His declining years!

[CHARLOTTA IVANOVNA, *very thin, tightly laced, dressed in white, a lorgnette at her waist, crosses the stage.*]

LOPAHIN: Forgive me, Charlotta Ivanovna, I've not had time to greet you. [*Tries to kiss her hand.*]

CHARLOTTA: [*Pulling away her hand.*] If I let you kiss my hand, you'll be wanting to kiss my elbow next, and then my shoulder.

LOPAHIN: I've no luck today. [*All laugh.*] Charlotta Ivanovna, show us a trick.

MME. RANEVSKAYA: Yes, Charlotta, do a trick for us.

CHARLOTTA: I don't see the need. I want to sleep. [*Exits.*]

LOPAHIN: In three weeks we'll meet again. [*Kisses* MME. RANEVSKAYA'*s hand.*] Good-bye till then. Time's up. [*To* GAYEV.] Bye-bye. [*Kisses* PISHCHIK.] Bye-bye. [*Shakes hands with* VARYA, *then with* FIRS *and* YASHA.] I hate to leave. [*To* MME. RANEVSKAYA.] If you make up your mind about the cottages, let me know; I'll get you a loan of 50,000 rubles.[3] Think it over seriously.

VARYA: [*Crossly.*] Will you never go!

LOPAHIN: I'm going, I'm going. [*Exits.*]

GAYEV: The vulgarian. But, excuse me . . . Varya's going to marry him, he's Varya's fiancé.

VARYA: You talk too much, Uncle.

MME. RANEVSKAYA: Well, Varya, it would make me happy. He's a good man.

PISHCHIK: Yes, one must admit, he's a most estimable man. And my Dashenka . . . she too says that . . . she says . . . lots of things. [*Snores; but wakes up at once.*] All the same, my valued friend, could you oblige me . . . with a loan of 240 rubles? I must pay the interest on the mortgage tomorrow.

VARYA: [*Alarmed.*] We can't, we can't!

MME. RANEVSKAYA: I really haven't any money.

PISHCHIK: It'll turn up. [*Laughs.*] I never lose hope, I thought everything was lost, that I was done for, when lo and behold, the railway ran through my land . . . and I was paid for it. . . . And something else will turn up again, if not today, then tomorrow . . . Dashenka will win two hundred thousand . . . she's got a lottery ticket.

MME. RANEVSKAYA: I've had my coffee, now let's go to bed.

FIRS: [*Brushes off* GAYEV; *admonishingly.*] You've got the wrong trousers on again. What am I to do with you?

VARYA: [*Softly.*] Anya's asleep. [*Gently opens the window.*] The sun's up now, it's not a bit cold. Look, Mamma dear, what wonderful trees. And heavens, what air! The starlings are singing!

GAYEV: [*Opens the other window.*] The orchard is all white. You've not forgotten it? Luba? That's the long alley that runs straight, straight as an arrow; how it shines on moonlight nights, do you remember? You've not forgotten?

MME. RANEVSKAYA: [*Looking out of the window into the orchard.*] Oh, my childhood, my innocent childhood. I used to sleep in this nursery—I used to look out into the orchard, happiness waked with me every morning, the orchard was just the same then . . . nothing has changed. [*Laughs with joy.*] All, all white! Oh, my orchard! After the dark, rainy autumn and the cold winter, you are young again, and full of happiness, the heavenly angels have not left you. . . . If I could free my chest and my shoulders from this rock that weighs on me, if I could only forget the past!

GAYEV: Yes, and the orchard will be sold to pay our debts, strange as it may seem.

MME. RANEVSKAYA: Look! There is our poor mother walking in the orchard . . . all in white . . . [*Laughs with joy.*] It is she!

GAYEV: Where?

3. The basic unit of currency. One ruble is equal to one hundred kopecks.

VARYA: What are you saying, Mamma dear!

MME. RANEVSKAYA: There's no one there, I just imagined it. To the right, where the path turns toward the arbor, there's a little white tree, leaning over, that looks like a woman . . .

[TROFIMOV *enters, wearing a shabby student's uniform and spectacles.*]

MME. RANEVSKAYA: What an amazing orchard! White masses of blossom, the blue sky . . .

TROFIMOV: Lubov Andreyevna! [*She looks round at him.*] I just want to pay my respects to you, then I'll leave at once. [*Kisses her hand ardently.*] I was told to wait until morning, but I hadn't the patience . . .

[MME. RANEVSKAYA *looks at him, perplexed.*]

VARYA: [*Through tears.*] This is Petya Trofimov.

TROFIMOV: Petya Trofimov, formerly your Grisha's tutor. . . . Can I have changed so much?

[MME. RANEVSKAYA *embraces him and weeps quietly.*]

GAYEV: [*Embarrassed.*] Don't, don't, Luba.

VARYA: [*Crying.*] I told you, Petya, to wait until tomorrow.

MME. RANEVSKAYA: My Grisha . . . my little boy . . . Grisha . . . my son.

VARYA: What can one do, Mamma dear, it's God's will.

TROFIMOV: [*Softly, through tears.*] There . . . there.

MME. RANEVSKAYA: [*Weeping quietly.*] My little boy was lost . . . drowned. Why? Why, my friend? [*More quietly.*] Anya's asleep in there, and here I am talking so loudly . . . making all this noise. . . . But tell me, Petya, why do you look so badly? Why have you aged so?

TROFIMOV: A mangy master, a peasant woman in the train called me.

MME. RANEVSKAYA: You were just a boy then, a dear little student, and now your hair's thin—and you're wearing glasses! Is it possible you're still a student? [*Goes toward the door.*]

TROFIMOV: I suppose I'm a perpetual student.

MME. RANEVSKAYA: [*Kisses her brother, then* VARYA.] Now, go to bed. . . . You have aged, too, Leonid.

PISHCHIK: [*Follows her.*] So now we turn in. Oh, my gout! I'm staying the night here . . . Lubov Andreyevna, my angel, tomorrow morning . . . I do need 240 rubles.

GAYEV: He keeps at it.

PISHCHIK: I'll pay it back, dear . . . it's a trifling sum.

MME. RANEVSKAYA: All right, Leonid will give it to you. Give it to him, Leonid.

GAYEV: Me give it to him! That's a good one!

MME. RANEVSKAYA: It can't be helped. Give it to him! He needs it. He'll pay it back.

[MME. RANEVSKAYA, TROFIMOV, PISHCHIK, *and* FIRS *go out;* GAYEV, VARYA, *and* YASHA *remain.*]

GAYEV: Sister hasn't got out of the habit of throwing money around. [*To* YASHA.] Go away, my good fellow, you smell of the barnyard.

YASHA: [*With a grin.*] And you, Leonid Andreyevich, are just the same as ever.

GAYEV: Who? [*To* VARYA.] What did he say?

VARYA: [*To* YASHA.] Your mother's come from the village; she's been sitting in the servants' room since yesterday, waiting to see you.

YASHA: Botheration!

VARYA: You should be ashamed of yourself!

YASHA: She's all I needed! She could have come tomorrow. [*Exits.*]

VARYA: Mamma is just the same as ever; she hasn't changed a bit. If she had her own way, she'd keep nothing for herself.

GAYEV: Yes . . . [*Pauses.*] If a great many remedies are offered for some disease, it means it is incurable; I keep thinking and racking my brains; I have many remedies, ever so many, and that really means none. It would be fine if we came in for a legacy; it would be fine if we married off our Anya to a very rich man; or we might go to Yaroslavl and try our luck with our aunt, the Countess. She's very rich, you know . . .

VARYA: [*Weeping.*] If only God would help us!

GAYEV: Stop bawling. Aunt's very rich, but she doesn't like us. In the first place, Sister married a lawyer who was no nobleman . . . [ANYA *appears in the doorway.*] She married beneath her, and it can't be said that her behavior has been very exemplary. She's good, kind, sweet, and I love her, but no matter what extenuating circumstances you may adduce, there's no denying that she has no morals. You sense it in her least gesture.

VARYA: [*In a whisper.*] Anya's in the doorway.

GAYEV: Who? [*Pauses.*] It's queer, something got into my right eye—my eyes are going back on me. . . . And on Thursday, when I was in the circuit court—

[*Enter* ANYA.]

VARYA: Why aren't you asleep, Anya?

ANYA: I can't get to sleep, I just can't.

GAYEV: My little pet! [*Kisses* ANYA's *face and hands.*] My child! [*Weeps.*] You are not my niece, you're my angel! You're everything to me. Believe me, believe—

ANYA: I believe you, Uncle. Everyone loves you and respects you . . . but, Uncle dear, you must keep still. . . . You must. What were you saying just now about my mother? Your own sister? What made you say that?

GAYEV: Yes, yes . . . [*Covers his face with her hand.*] Really, that was awful! Good God! Heaven help me! Just now I made a speech to the bookcase . . . so stupid! And only after I was through, I saw how stupid it was.

VARYA: It's true, Uncle dear, you ought to keep still. Just don't talk, that's all.

ANYA: If you could only keep still, it would make things easier for you, too.

GAYEV: I'll keep still. [*Kisses* ANYA's *and* VARYA's *hands.*] I will. But now about business. On Thursday I was in court; well, there were a number of us there, and we began talking of one thing and another, and this and that, and do you know, I believe it will be possible to raise a loan on a promissory note to pay the interest at the bank.

VARYA: If only God would help us!

GAYEV: On Tuesday I'll go and see about it again. [*To* VARYA.] Stop bawling. [To ANYA.] Your mamma will talk to Lopahin, and he, of course, will not refuse her . . . and as soon as you're rested, you'll go to Yaroslavl to the Countess, your great-aunt. So we'll be working in three directions at once, and the thing is in the bag. We'll pay the interest—I'm sure of it. [*Puts a candy in his mouth.*] I swear on my honor, I swear by anything you like, the estate shan't be sold. [*Excitedly.*] I swear by my own happiness! Here's my hand on it, you can call me a swindler and a scoundrel if I let it come to an auction! I swear by my whole being.

ANYA: [*Relieved and quite happy again.*] How good you are, Uncle, and how clever! [*Embraces him.*] Now I'm at peace, quite at peace, I'm happy.

[*Enter* FIRS.]

FIRS: [*Reproachfully.*] Leonid Andreyevich, have you no fear of God? When are you going to bed?

GAYEV: Directly, directly. Go away, Firs, I'll . . . yes, I will undress myself. Now, children, 'nightie-'nightie. We'll consider details tomorrow, but now go to sleep. [*Kisses* ANYA *and* VARYA.] I am a man of the eighties; they have nothing good to say of that period nowadays. Nevertheless, in the course of my life, I have suffered not a little for my convictions. It's not for nothing that the peasant loves me; one should know the peasant; one should know from which—

ANYA: There you go again, Uncle.

VARYA: Uncle dear, be quiet.

FIRS: [*Angrily.*] Leonid Andreyevich!

GAYEV: I'm coming, I'm coming! Go to bed! Double bank shot in the side pocket! Here goes a clean shot . . .

[*Exits,* FIRS *hobbling after him.*]

ANYA: I am at peace now. I don't want to go to Yaroslavl—I don't like my great-aunt, but still, I am at peace, thanks to Uncle. [*Sits down.*]

VARYA: We must get some sleep. I'm going now. While you were away, something unpleasant happened. In the old servants' quarters, there are only the old people as you know; Yefim, Polya, Yevstigney, and Karp, too. They began letting all sorts of rascals in to spend the night. . . . I didn't say anything. Then I heard they'd been spreading a report that I gave them nothing but dried peas to eat—out of stinginess, you know . . . and it was all Yevstigney's doing. . . . All right, I thought, if that's how it is, I thought, just wait. I sent for Yevstigney . . . [*Yawns.*] He comes. . . . "How's this, Yevstigney?" I say, "You fool . . ." [*Looking at* ANYA.] Anichka! [*Pauses.*] She's asleep. [*Puts her arm around* ANYA.] Come to your little bed. . . . Come . . . [*Leads her.*] My darling has fallen asleep. . . . Come.

[*They go out. Far away beyond the orchard, a shepherd is piping.*

TROFIMOV *crosses the stage and, seeing* VARYA *and* ANYA, *stands still.*]

VARYA: Sh! She's asleep . . . asleep. . . . Come, darling.

ANYA: [*Softly, half-asleep.*] I'm so tired. Those bells . . . Uncle . . . dear. . . . Mamma and Uncle . . .

VARYA: Come, my precious, come along. [*They go into* ANYA'*s room.*]
TROFIMOV: [*With emotion.*] My sunshine, my spring!

Act II

A meadow. An old, long-abandoned, lopsided little chapel; near it a well, large slabs, which had apparently once served as tombstones, and an old bench. In the background the road to the Gayev estate. To one side poplars loom darkly, where the cherry orchard begins. In the distance a row of telegraph poles, and far off, on the horizon, the faint outline of a large city which is seen only in fine, clear weather. The sun will soon be setting. CHARLOTTA, YASHA, *and* DUNYASHA *are seated on the bench.* YEPIHODOV *stands near and plays a guitar. All are pensive.* CHARLOTTA *wears an old peaked cap. She has taken a gun from her shoulder and is straightening the buckle on the strap.*

CHARLOTTA: [*Musingly.*] I haven't a real passport, I don't know how old I am, and I always feel that I am very young. When I was a little girl, my father and mother used to go from fair to fair and give performances, very good ones. And I used to do the *salto mortale,*[4] and all sorts of other tricks. And when papa and mamma died, a German lady adopted me and began to educate me. Very good. I grew up and became a governess. But where I come from and who am I, I don't know. . . . Who were my parents? Perhaps they weren't even married. . . . I don't know . . . [*Takes a cucumber out of her pocket and eats it.*] I don't know a thing. [*Pause.*] One wants so much to talk, and there isn't anyone to talk to. . . . I haven't anybody.
YEPIHODOV: [*Plays the guitar and sings.*] "What care I for the jarring world? What's friend or foe to me? . . ." How agreeable it is to play the mandolin.
DUNYASHA: That's a guitar, not a mandolin. [*Looks in a hand mirror and powders her face.*]
YEPIHODOV: To a madman in love it's a mandolin. [*Sings.*] "Would that the heart were warmed by the fire of mutual love!"
[YASHA *joins in.*]
CHARLOTTA: How abominably these people sing. Pfui! Like jackals!
DUNYASHA: [*To* YASHA.] How wonderful it must be though to have stayed abroad!
YASHA: Ah, yes, of course, I cannot but agree with you there. [*Yawns and lights a cigar.*]
YEPIHODOV: Naturally. Abroad, everything has long since achieved full perfection.
YASHA: That goes without saying.
YEPIHODOV: I'm a cultivated man, I read all kinds of remarkable books. And yet I can never make out what direction I should take, what is it that I want, properly speaking. Should I live, or should I shoot myself,

4. Somersault (Italian).

properly speaking? Nevertheless, I always carry a revolver about me. . . .
Here it is . . . [*Shows revolver.*]

CHARLOTTA: I've finished. I'm going. [*Puts the gun over her shoulder.*] You
are a very clever man, Yepihodov, and a very terrible one; women must
be crazy about you. Br-r-r! [*Starts to go.*] These clever men are all so
stupid; there's no one for me to talk to . . . always alone, alone, I haven't
a soul . . . and who I am, and why I am, nobody knows. [*Exits unhur-
riedly.*]

YEPIHODOV: Properly speaking and letting other subjects alone, I must say
regarding myself, among other things, that fate treats me mercilessly,
like a storm treats a small boat. If I am mistaken, let us say, why then do
I wake up this morning, and there on my chest is a spider of enormous
dimensions . . . like this . . . [*Indicates with both hands.*] Again, I take
up a pitcher of kvass to have a drink, and in it there is something
unseemly to the highest degree, something like a cockroach. [*Pause.*]
Have you read Buckle?[5] [*Pause.*] I wish to have a word with you, Avdotya Fyodorovna, if I may trouble you.

DUNYASHA: Well, go ahead.

YEPIHODOV: I wish to speak with you alone. [*Sighs.*]

DUNYASHA: [*Embarassed.*] Very well. Only first bring me my little cape.
You'll find it near the wardrobe. It's rather damp here.

YEPIHODOV: Certainly, ma'am; I will fetch it, ma'am. Now I know what to
do with my revolver. [*Takes the guitar and goes off playing it.*]

YASHA: Two-and-Twenty Troubles! An awful fool, between you and me.
[*Yawns.*]

DUNYASHA: I hope to God he doesn't shoot himself! [*Pause.*] I've become
so nervous, I'm always fretting. I was still a little girl when I was taken
into the big house, I am quite unused to the simple life now, and my
hands are white, as white as a lady's. I've become so soft, so delicate, so
refined, I'm afraid of everything. It's so terrifying; and if you deceive
me, Yasha, I don't know what will happen to my nerves. [YASHA *kisses
her.*]

YASHA: You're a peach! Of course, a girl should never forget herself; and
what I dislike more than anything is when a girl don't behave properly.

DUNYASHA: I've fallen passionately in love with you; you're educated—you
have something to say about everything. [*Pause.*]

YASHA: [*Yawns.*] Yes, ma'am. Now the way I look at it, if a girl loves someone, it means she is immoral. [*Pause.*] It's agreeable smoking a cigar in
the fresh air. [*Listens.*] Someone's coming this way. . . . It's our madam
and the others. [DUNYASHA *embraces him impulsively.*] You go home,
as though you'd been to the river to bathe; go to the little path, or else
they'll run into you and suspect me of having arranged to meet you
here. I can't stand that sort of thing.

DUNYASHA: [*Coughing softly.*] Your cigar's made my head ache.

[*Exits.* YASHA *remains standing near the chapel. Enter* MME. RANEV-
SKAYA, GAYEV, *and* LOPAHIN.]

---

5. Henry Thomas Buckle (1821–1862) wrote a *History of Civilization in England* (1857–61), which was
considered daringly materialistic and free thinking.

LOPAHIN: You must make up your mind once and for all—there's no time to lose. It's quite a simple question, you know. Do you agree to lease your land for summer cottages or not? Answer in one word, yes or no; only one word!

MME. RANEVSKAYA: Who's been smoking such abominable cigars here? [*Sits down.*]

GAYEV: Now that the railway line is so near, it's made things very convenient. [*Sits down.*] Here we've been able to have lunch in town. Yellow ball in the side pocket! I feel like going into the house and playing just one game.

MME. RANEVSKAYA: You can do that later.

LOPAHIN: Only one word! [*Imploringly.*] Do give me an answer!

GAYEV: [*Yawning.*] Who?

MME. RANEVSKAYA: [*Looks into her purse.*] Yesterday I had a lot of money and now my purse is almost empty. My poor Varya tries to economize by feeding us just milk soup; in the kitchen the old people get nothing but dried peas to eat, while I squander money thoughtlessly. [*Drops the purse, scattering gold pieces.*] You see, there they go . . . [*Shows vexation.*]

YASHA: Allow me—I'll pick them up. [*Picks up the money.*]

MME. RANEVSKAYA: Be so kind. Yasha. And why did I go to lunch in town? That nasty restaurant, with its music and the tablecloth smelling of soap. . . . Why drink so much, Leonid? Why eat so much? Why talk so much? Today again you talked a lot, and all so inappropriately about the seventies, about the decadents.[6] And to whom? Talking to waiters about decadents!

LOPAHIN: Yes.

GAYEV: [*Waving his hand.*] I'm incorrigible; that's obvious.[*Irritably, to* YASHA.] Why do you keep dancing about in front of me?

YASHA: [*Laughs.*] I can't hear your voice without laughing—

GAYEV: Either he or I—

MME. RANEVSKAYA: Go away, Yasha; run along.

YASHA: [*Handing* MME. RANEVSKAYA *her purse.*] I'm going at once. [*Hardly able to suppress his laughter.*] This minute. [*Exits.*]

LOPAHIN: That rich man, Deriganov, wants to buy your estate. They say he's coming to the auction himself.

MME. RANEVSKAYA: Where did you hear that?

LOPAHIN: That's what they are saying in town.

GAYEV: Our aunt in Yaroslavl has promised to help, but when she will send the money, and how much, no one knows.

LOPAHIN: How much will she send? A hundred thousand? Two hundred?

MME. RANEVSKAYA: Oh, well, ten or fifteen thousand; and we'll have to be grateful for that.

LOPAHIN: Forgive me, but such frivolous people as you are, so queer and unbusinesslike—I never met in my life. One tells you in plain language that your estate is up for sale, and you don't seem to take it in.

---

6. A group of French poets of the 1880s (Mallarmé is today the most famous) were labeled "decadents" by their enemies and sometimes adopted the name themselves, proud of their refinement and sensitivity.

MME. RANEVSKAYA: What are we to do? Tell us what to do.

LOPAHIN: I do tell you, every day; every day I say the same thing! You must lease the cherry orchard and the land for summer cottages, you must do it and as soon as possible—right away. The auction is close at hand. Please understand! Once you've decided to have the cottages, you can raise as much money as you like, and you're saved.

MME. RANEVSKAYA: Cottages—summer people—forgive me, but it's all so vulgar.

GAYEV: I agree with you absolutely.

LOPAHIN: I shall either burst into tears or scream or faint! I can't stand it! You've worn me out! [To GAYEV.] You're an old woman!

GAYEV: Who?

LOPAHIN: An old woman! [Gets up to go.]

MME. RANEVSKAYA: [Alarmed.] No, don't go! Please stay, I beg you, my dear. Perhaps we shall think of something.

LOPAHIN: What is there to think of?

MME. RANEVSKAYA: Don't go, I beg you. With you here it's more cheerful anyway. [Pause.] I keep expecting something to happen, it's as though the house were going to crash about our ears.

GAYEV: [In deep thought.] Bank shot in the corner. . . . Three cushions in the side pocket. . . .

MME. RANEVSKAYA: We have been great sinners . . .

LOPAHIN: What sins could you have committed?

GAYEV: [Putting a candy in his mouth.] They say I've eaten up my fortune in candy! [Laughs.]

MME. RANEVSKAYA: Oh, my sins! I've squandered money away recklessly, like a lunatic, and I married a man who made nothing but debts. My husband drank himself to death on champagne, he was a terrific drinker. And then, to my sorrow, I fell in love with another man, and I lived with him. And just then—that was my first punishment—a blow on the head: my little boy was drowned here in the river. And I went abroad, went away forever . . . never to come back, never to see this river again . . . I closed my eyes and ran, out of my mind. . . . But he followed me, pitiless, brutal. I bought a villa near Mentone, because he fell ill there; and for three years, day and night, I knew no peace, no rest. The sick man wore me out, he sucked my soul dry. Then last year, when the villa was sold to pay my debts, I went to Paris, and there he robbed me, abandoned me, took up with another woman; I tried to poison myself—it was stupid, so shameful—and then suddenly I felt drawn back to Russia, back, to my own country, to my little girl. [Wipes her tears away.] Lord, Lord! Be merciful, forgive me my sins—don't punish me anymore! [Takes a telegram out of her pocket.] This came today from Paris—he begs me to forgive him, implores me to go back . . . [Tears up the telegram.] Do I hear music? [Listens.]

GAYEV: That's our famous Jewish band, you remember? Four violins, a flute, and a double bass.

MME. RANEVSKAYA: Does it still exist? We ought to send for them some evening and have a party.

LOPAHIN: [Listens.] I don't hear anything. [Hums softly.] "The Germans for a fee will Frenchify a Russian."[7] [*Laughs.*] I saw a play at the theater yesterday—awfully funny.

MME. RANEVSKAYA: There was probably nothing funny about it. You shouldn't go to see plays, you should look at yourselves more often. How drab your lives are—how full of unnecessary talk.

LOPAHIN: That's true; come to think of it, we do live like fools. [*Pause.*] My pop was a peasant, an idiot; he understood nothing, never taught me anything, all he did was beat me when he was drunk, and always with a stick. Fundamentally, I'm just the same kind of blockhead and idiot. I was never taught anything—I have a terrible handwriting. I write so that I feel ashamed before people, like a pig.

MME. RANEVSKAYA: You should get married, my friend.

LOPAHIN: Yes . . . that's true.

MME. RANEVSKAYA: To our Varya, she's a good girl.

LOPAHIN: Yes.

MME. RANEVSKAYA: She's a girl who comes of simple people, she works all day long; and above all, she loves you. Besides, you've liked her for a long time now.

LOPAHIN: Well, I've nothing against it. She's a good girl. [*Pause.*]

GAYEV: I've been offered a place in the bank—6,000 a year. Have you heard?

MME. RANEVSKAYA: You're not up to it. Stay where you are.

[FIRS *enters, carrying an overcoat.*]

FIRS: [*To* GAYEV.] Please put this on, sir, it's damp.

GAYEV: [*Putting it on.*] I'm fed up with you, brother.

FIRS: Never mind. This morning you drove off without saying a word. [*Looks him over.*]

MME. RANEVSKAYA: How you've aged, Firs.

FIRS: I beg your pardon?

LOPAHIN: The lady says you've aged.

FIRS: I've lived a long time; they were arranging my wedding and your papa wasn't born yet. [*Laughs.*] When freedom came[8] I was already head footman. I wouldn't consent to be set free then; I stayed on with the master . . . [*Pause.*] I remember they were all very happy, but why they were happy, they didn't know themselves.

LOPAHIN: It was fine in the old days! At least there was flogging!

FIRS: [*Not hearing.*] Of course. The peasants kept to the masters, the masters kept to the peasants; but now they've all gone their own ways, and there's no making out anything.

GAYEV: Be quiet, Firs. I must go to town tomorrow. They've promised to introduce me to a general who might let us have a loan.

LOPAHIN: Nothing will come of that. You won't even be able to pay the interest, you can be certain of that.

MME. RANEVSKAYA: He's raving, there isn't any general.

[*Enter* TROFIMOV, ANYA, *and* VARYA.]

GAYEV: Here come our young people.

---

7. Satirical reference to Russian efforts, from the time of Peter the Great (1672–1725), to imitate Western Europe and particularly Parisian culture.　8. Czar (or Tsar) Alexander II (ruled 1855–81) emancipated the serfs in 1861.

ANYA: There's Mamma, on the bench.

MME. RANEVSKAYA: [*Tenderly.*] Come here, come along, my darlings. [*Embraces* ANYA *and* VARYA.] If you only knew how I love you both! Sit beside me—there, like that. [*All sit down.*]

LOPAHIN: Our perpetual student is always with the young ladies.

TROFIMOV: That's not any of your business.

LOPAHIN: He'll soon be fifty, and he's still a student!

TROFIMOV: Stop your silly jokes.

LOPAHIN: What are you so cross about, you queer bird?

TROFIMOV: Oh, leave me alone.

LOPAHIN: [*Laughs.*] Allow me to ask you, what do you think of me?

TROFIMOV: What I think of you, Yermolay Alexeyevich, is this: you are a rich man who will soon be a millionaire. Well, just as a beast of prey, which devours everything that comes in its way, is necessary for the process of metabolism to go on, so you, too, are necessary. [*All laugh.*]

VARYA: Better tell us something about the planets, Petya.

MME. RANEVSKAYA: No, let's go on with yesterday's conversation.

TROFIMOV: What was it about?

GAYEV: About man's pride.

TROFIMOV: Yesterday we talked a long time, but we came to no conclusion. There is something mystical about man's pride in your sense of the word. Perhaps you're right, from your own point of view. But if you reason simply, without going into subtleties, then what call is there for pride? Is there any sense in it, if man is so poor a thing physiologically, and if, in the great majority of cases, he is coarse, stupid, profoundly unhappy? We should stop admiring ourselves. We should work, and that's all.

GAYEV: You die, anyway.

TROFIMOV: Who knows? And what does it mean—to die? Perhaps man has a hundred senses, and at his death only the five we know perish, while the other ninety-five remain alive.

MME. RANEVSKAYA: How clever you are, Petya!

LOPAHIN: [*Ironically.*] Awfully clever!

TROFIMOV: Mankind goes forward, developing its powers. Everything that is now unattainable for it will one day come within man's reach and be clear to him; only we must work, helping with all our might those who seek the truth. Here among us in Russia only the very few work as yet. The great majority of the intelligentsia, as far as I can see, seek nothing, do nothing, are totally unfit for work of any kind. They call themselves the intelligentsia, yet they are uncivil to their servants, treat the peasants like animals, are poor students, never read anything serious, do absolutely nothing at all, only talk about science, and have little appreciation of the arts. They are all solemn, have grim faces, they all philosophize and talk of weighty matters. And meanwhile the vast majority of us, ninety-nine out of a hundred, live like savages. At the least provocation—a punch in the jaw, and curses. They eat disgustingly, sleep in filth and stuffiness, bedbugs everywhere, stench and damp and moral slovenliness. And obviously, the only purpose of all our fine talk is to hoodwink ourselves and others. Show me where the public nurseries are that we've heard so much about, and the libraries. We read about them in novels, but in reality they don't exist, there is nothing but dirt, vulgarity, and Asiatic backwardness. I don't like very solemn faces, I'm afraid of them, I'm afraid of serious conversations. We'd do better to keep quiet for a while.

LOPAHIN: Do you know, I get up at five o'clock in the morning, and I work from morning till night; and I'm always handling money, my own and other people's, and I see what people around me are really like. You've only to start doing anything to see how few honest, decent people there are. Sometimes when I lie awake at night, I think: "Oh, Lord, thou hast given us immense forests, boundless fields, the widest horizons, and living in their midst, we ourselves ought really to be giants."

MME. RANEVSKAYA: Now you want giants! They're only good in fairy tales; otherwise they're frightening.

[YEPIHODOV *crosses the stage at the rear, playing the guitar.*]

MME. RANEVSKAYA: [*Pensively.*] There goes Yepihodov.

GAYEV: Ladies and gentlemen, the sun has set.

TROFIMOV: Yes.

GAYEV: [*In a low voice, declaiming as it were.*] Oh, Nature, wondrous Nature, you shine with eternal radiance, beautiful and indifferent! You, whom we call our mother, unite within yourself life and death! You animate and destroy!

VARYA: [*Pleadingly.*] Uncle dear!

ANYA: Uncle, again!

TROFIMOV: You'd better bank the yellow ball in the side pocket.

GAYEV: I'm silent, I'm silent . . .

[*All sit plunged in thought. Stillness reigns. Only* FIRS's *muttering is audible. Suddenly a distant sound is heard, coming from the sky as it were, the sound of a snapping string, mournfully dying away.*]

MME. RANEVSKAYA: What was that?

LOPAHIN: I don't know. Somewhere far away, in the pits, a bucket's broken loose; but somewhere very far away.

GAYEV: Or it might be some sort of bird, perhaps a heron.

TROFIMOV: Or an owl . . .

MME. RANEVSKAYA: [*Shudders.*] It's weird, somehow. [*Pause.*]

FIRS: Before the calamity the same thing happened—the owl screeched, and the samovar hummed all the time.

GAYEV: Before what calamity?

FIRS: Before the Freedom. [*Pause.*]

MME. RANEVSKAYA: Come, my friends, let's be going. It's getting dark. [*To* ANYA.] You have tears in your eyes. What is it, my little one? [*Embraces her.*]

ANYA: I don't know, Mamma; it's nothing.

TROFIMOV: Somebody's coming.

[*A* TRAMP *appears, wearing a shabby white cap and an overcoat. He is slightly drunk.*]

TRAMP: Allow me to inquire, will this short cut take me to the station?

GAYEV: It will. Just follow that road.

TRAMP: My heartfelt thanks. [*Coughing.*] The weather is glorious.

"Les cavaliers à genoux et remerciez vos dames!"[4] FIRS, *wearing a dress coat, brings in soda water on a tray.* PISHCHIK *and* TROFIMOV *enter the drawing room.*

PISHCHIK: I have high blood pressure; I've already had two strokes. Dancing's hard work for me; but as they say, "If you run with the pack, you can bark or not, but at least wag your tail." Still, I'm as strong as a horse. My late lamented father, who would have his joke, God rest his soul, used to say, talking about our origin, that the ancient line of the Simeonov-Pishchiks was descended from the very horse that Caligula had made a senator.[5] [*Sits down.*] But the trouble is, I have no money. A hungry dog believes in nothing but meat. [*Snores, and wakes up at once.*] It's the same with me—I can think of nothing but money.

TROFIMOV: You know, there *is* something equine about your figure.

PISHCHIK: Well, a horse is a fine animal—one can sell a horse.

[*Sound of billiards being played in an adjoining room.* VARYA *appears in the archway.*]

TROFIMOV: [*Teasing her.*] Madam Lopahina! Madam Lopahina!

VARYA: [*Angrily.*] Mangy master!

TROFIMOV: Yes, I am a mangy master and I'm proud of it.

VARYA: [*Reflecting bitterly.*] Here we've hired musicians, and what shall we pay them with? [*Exits.*]

TROFIMOV: [*To* PISHCHIK.] If the energy you have spent during your lifetime looking for money to pay interest had gone into something else, in the end you could have turned the world upside down.

PISHCHIK: Nietzsche,[6] the philosopher, the greatest, most famous of men, that colossal intellect, says in his works that it is permissible to forge banknotes.

TROFIMOV: Have you read Nietzsche?

PISHCHIK: Well . . . Dashenka told me. . . . And now I've got to the point where forging banknotes is the only way out for me. . . . The day after tomorrow I have to pay 310 rubles—I already have 130 . . . [*Feels in his pockets. In alarm.*] The money's gone! I've lost my money! [*Through tears.*] Where's my money? [*Joyfully.*] Here it is! Inside the lining . . . I'm all in a sweat . . .

[*Enter* MME. RANEVSKAYA *and* CHARLOTTA.]

MME. RANEVSKAYA: [*Hums the "Lezginka."*[7]] Why isn't Leonid back yet? What is he doing in town? [*To* DUNYASHA.] Dunyasha, offer the musicians tea.

TROFIMOV: The auction hasn't taken place, most likely.

MME. RANEVSKAYA: It's the wrong time to have the band, and the wrong time to give a dance. Well, never mind. [*Sits down and hums softly.*]

CHARLOTTA. [*Hands* PISHCHIK *a pack of cards.*] Here is a pack of cards. Think of any card you like.

---

4. Gentlemen, on your knees and thank your ladies! (French).   5. The mad emperor Caligula (12–41 A.D.) brought his favorite horse into the Roman senate to make it a senator.   6. Friedrich W. Nietzsche (1844–1900), German philosopher.   7. The music that in the Caucasus mountains accompanies a courtship dance in which the man dances with abandon around the woman, who moves with grace and ease.

PISHCHIK: I've thought of one.

CHARLOTTA: Shuffle the pack now. That's right. Give it here, my dear Mr. Pishchik. *Eins, zwei, drei!*[8] Now look for it—it's in your side pocket.

PISHCHIK: [*Taking the card out of his pocket.*] The eight of spades! Perfectly right! Just imagine!

CHARLOTTA: [*Holding the pack of cards in her hands. To* TROFIMOV.] Quickly, name the top card.

TROFIMOV: Well, let's see—the queen of spades.

CHARLOTTA: Right! [*To* PISHCHIK.] Now name the top card.

PISHCHIK: The ace of hearts.

CHARLOTTA: Right! [*Claps her hands and the pack of cards disappears.*] Ah, what lovely weather it is today! [*A mysterious feminine* VOICE, *which seems to come from under the floor, answers her:* "Oh, yes, it's magnificent weather, madam."] You are my best ideal. [VOICE: "And I find you pleasing too, madam."]

STATIONMASTER.[*Applauding.*] The lady ventriloquist, bravo!

PISHCHIK: [*Amazed.*] Just imagine! Enchanting Charlotta Ivanovna, I'm simply in love with you.

CHARLOTTA: In love? [*Shrugs her shoulders.*] Are you capable of love? *Guter Mensch, aber schlechter Musikant!*[9]

TROFIMOV: [*Claps* PISHCHIK *on the shoulder.*] You old horse, you!

CHARLOTTA: Attention please! One more trick! [*Takes a plaid*[1] *from a chair.*] Here is a very good plaid; I want to sell it. [*Shaking it out.*] Does anyone want to buy it?

PISHCHIK: [*In amazement.*] Just imagine!

CHARLOTTA: *Eins, zwei, drei!* [*Raises the plaid quickly, behind it stands* ANYA. *She curtsies, runs to her mother, embraces her, and runs back into the ballroom, amid general enthusiasm.*]

MME. RANEVSKAYA: [*Applauds.*] Bravo! Bravo!

CHARLOTTA: Now again! *Eins, zwei, drei!* [*Lifts the plaid; behind it stands* VARYA, *bowing.*]

PISHCHIK: [*In amazement.*] Just imagine!

[CHARLOTTA *throws the plaid at* PISHCHIK, *curtsies, and runs into the ballroom.*]

PISHCHIK: [*Running after her.*] The rascal! What a woman, what a woman! [*Exits.*]

MME. RANEVSKAYA: And Leonid still isn't here. What is he doing in town so long? I don't understand. It must be all over by now. Either the estate has been sold, or the auction hasn't taken place. Why keep us in suspense so long?

VARYA: [*Trying to console her.*] Uncle's bought it, I feel sure of that.

TROFIMOV: [*Mockingly.*] Oh, yes!

VARYA: Great-aunt sent him an authorization to buy it in her name, and to transfer the debt. She's doing it for Anya's sake. And I'm sure that God will help us, and Uncle will buy it.

8. One, two, three (German). 9. "A good man, but a bad musician" (German), usually quoted in the plural: "*Gute Leute, schlechte Musikanten.*" It comes from *Das Buch le Grand* (1826) by the German poet Heinrich Heine (1799–1856). Here it suggests that Pishchik may be a good man but a bad lover. 1. A small plaid blanket, or lap robe.

MME. RANEVSKAYA: Great-aunt sent fifteen thousand to buy the estate in her name, she doesn't trust us, but that's not even enough to pay the interest. [*Covers her face with her hands.*] Today my fate will be decided, my fate—

TROFIMOV: [*Teasing* VARYA.] Madam Lopahina!

VARYA: [*Angrily.*] Perpetual student! Twice already you've been expelled from the university.

MME. RANEVSKAYA: Why are you so cross, Varya? He's teasing you about Lopahin. Well, what of it? If you want to marry Lopahin, go ahead. He's a good man, and interesting; if you don't want to, don't. Nobody's compelling you, my pet!

VARYA: Frankly, Mamma dear, I take this thing seriously; he's a good man and I like him.

MME. RANEVSKAYA: All right then, marry him. I don't know what you're waiting for.

VARYA: But, Mamma, I can't propose to him myself. For the last two years, everyone's been talking to me about him—talking. But he either keeps silent, or else cracks jokes. I understand; he's growing rich, he's absorbed in business—he has no time for me. If I had money, even a little, say, 100 rubles, I'd throw everything up and go far away—I'd go into a nunnery.

TROFIMOV: What a blessing . . .

VARYA: A student ought to be intelligent. [*Softly, with tears in her voice.*] How homely you've grown, Petya! How old you look! [*To* MME. RANEVSKAYA, *with dry eyes.*] But I can't live without work, Mamma dear; I must keep busy every minute.

[*Enter* YASHA.]

YASHA: [*Hardly restraining his laughter.*] Yepihodov has broken a billiard cue! [*Exits.*]

VARYA: Why is Yepihodov here? Who allowed him to play billiards? I don't understand these people! [*Exits.*]

MME. RANEVSKAYA: Don't tease her, Petya. She's unhappy enough with that.

TROFIMOV: She bustles so—and meddles in other people's business. All summer long she's given Anya and me no peace. She's afraid of a love affair between us. What business is it of hers? Besides, I've given no grounds for it, and I'm far from such vulgarity. We are above love.

MME. RANEVSKAYA: And I suppose I'm beneath love? [*Anxiously.*] What can be keeping Leonid? If I only knew whether the estate has been sold or not. Such a calamity seems so incredible to me that I don't know what to think—I feel lost. . . . I could scream. . . . I could do something stupid. . . . Save me, Petya, tell me something, talk to me!

TROFIMOV: Whether the estate is sold today or not, isn't it all one? That's all done with long ago—there's no turning back, the path is overgrown. Calm yourself, my dear. You mustn't deceive yourself. For once in your life you must face the truth.

MME. RANEVSKAYA: What truth? You can see the truth, you can tell it from falsehood, but I seem to have lost my eyesight, I see nothing. You settle every great problem so boldly, but tell me, my dear boy, isn't it because you're young, because you don't yet know what one of your problems means in terms of suffering? You look ahead fearlessly, but isn't it because you don't see and don't expect anything dreadful, because life is still hidden from your young eyes? You're bolder, more honest, more profound than we are, but think hard, show just a bit of magnanimity, spare me. After all, I was born here, my father and mother lived here, and my grandfather; I love this house. Without the cherry orchard, my life has no meaning for me, and if it really must be sold, then sell me with the orchard. [*Embraces* TROFIMOV, *kisses him on the forehead.*] My son was drowned here. [*Weeps.*] Pity me, you good, kind fellow!

TROFIMOV: You know, I feel for you with all my heart.

MME. RANEVSKAYA: But that should have been said differently, so differently! [*Takes out her handkerchief—a telegram falls on the floor.*] My heart is so heavy today—you can't imagine! The noise here upsets me— my inmost being trembles at every sound—I'm shaking all over. But I can't go into my own room; I'm afraid to be alone. Don't condemn me, Petya. . . . I love you as though you were one of us, I would gladly let you marry Anya—I swear I would—only, my dear boy, you must study—you must take your degree—you do nothing, you let yourself be tossed by Fate from place to place—it's so strange. It's true, isn't it? And you should do something about your beard, to make it grow somehow! [*Laughs.*] You're so funny!

TROFIMOV: [*Picks up the telegram.*] I've no wish to be a dandy.

MME. RANEVSKAYA: That's a telegram from Paris. I get one every day. One yesterday and one today. That savage is ill again—he's in trouble again. He begs forgiveness, implores me to go to him, and really I ought to go to Paris to be near him. Your face is stern, Petya; but what is there to do, my dear boy? What am I to do? He's ill, he's alone and unhappy, and who is to look after him, who is to keep him from doing the wrong thing, who is to give him his medicine on time? And why hide it or keep still about it—I love him! That's clear. I love him, love him! He's a millstone round my neck, he'll drag me to the bottom, but I love that stone, I can't live without it. [*Presses* TROFIMOV's *hand.*] Don't think badly of me. Petya, and don't say anything, don't say . . .

TROFIMOV: [*Through tears.*] Forgive me my frankness in heaven's name; but, you know, he robbed you!

MME. RANEVSKAYA: No, no, no, you mustn't say such things! [*Covers her ears.*]

TROFIMOV: But he's a scoundrel! You're the only one who doesn't know it. He's a petty scoundrel—a nonentity!

MME. RANEVSKAYA: [*Controlling her anger.*] You are twenty-six or twenty-seven years old, but you're still a schoolboy.

TROFIMOV: That may be.

MME. RANEVSKAYA: You should be a man at your age. You should understand people who love—and ought to be in love yourself. You ought to fall in love! [*Angrily.*] Yes, yes! And it's not purity in you, it's prudishness, you're simply a queer fish, a comical freak!

TROFIMOV: [*Horrified.*] What is she saying?

MME. RANEVSKAYA: "I am above love!" You're not above love, but simple, as our Firs says, you're an addlehead. At your age not to have a mistress!

TROFIMOV: [*Horrified.*] This is frightful! What is she saying! [*Goes rapidly into the ballroom, clutching his head.*] It's frightful—I can't stand it, I won't stay! [*Exits, but returns at once.*] All is over between us! [*Exits into anteroom.*]

MME. RANEVSKAYA: [*Shouts after him.*] Petya! Wait! You absurd fellow, I was joking. Petya!

[*Sound of somebody running quickly downstairs and suddenly falling down with a crash.* ANYA *and* VARYA *scream. Sound of laughter a moment later.*]

MME. RANEVSKAYA: What's happened?

[ANYA *runs in.*]

ANYA: [*Laughing.*] Petya's fallen downstairs! [*Runs out.*]

MME. RANEVSKAYA: What a queer bird that Petya is!

[STATIONMASTER, *standing in the middle of the ballroom, recites Alexey Tolstoy's "Magdalene,"*[2] *to which all listen, but after a few lines, the sound of a waltz is heard from the anteroom and the reading breaks off. All dance.* TROFIMOV, ANYA, VARYA *and* MME. RANEVSKAYA *enter from the anteroom.*]

MME. RANEVSKAYA: Petya, you pure soul, please forgive me. . . . Let's dance.

[*Dances with* PETYA, ANYA *and* VARYA *dance.* FIRS *enters, puts his stick down by the side door.* YASHA *enters from the drawing room and watches the dancers.*]

YASHA: Well, Grandfather?

FIRS: I'm not feeling well. In the old days it was generals, barons, and admirals that were dancing at our balls, and now we have to send for the Post Office Clerk and the Stationmaster, and even they aren't too glad to come. I feel kind of shaky. The old master that's gone, their grandfather, dosed everyone with sealing wax, whatever ailed 'em. I've been taking sealing wax every day for twenty years or more. Perhaps that's what's kept me alive.

YASHA: I'm fed up with you, Grandpop. [*Yawns.*] It's time you croaked.

FIRS: Oh, you addlehead! [*Mumbles.*]

[TROFIMOV *and* MME. RANEVSKAYA *dance from the ballroom into the drawing room.*]

MME. RANEVSKAYA: Merci. I'll sit down a while. [*Sits down.*] I'm tired.

[*Enter* ANYA.]

ANYA: [*Excitedly.*] There was a man in the kitchen just now who said the cherry orchard was sold today.

MME. RANEVSKAYA: Sold to whom?

ANYA: He didn't say. He's gone. [*Dances off with* TROFIMOV.]

YASHA: It was some old man gabbing, a stranger.

FIRS: And Leonid Andreyevich isn't back yet, he hasn't come. And he's

---

2. Called *The Sinning Woman* in Russian, it begins: "A bustling crowd with happy laughter, / with twanging lutes and clashing cymbals / with flowers and foliage all around / the colonnaded portico." Alexey Tolstoy (1817–1875), popular in his time as a dramatist and poet, was a distant relative of Leo Tolstoy.

wearing his lightweight between-season overcoat; like enough, he'll catch cold. Ah, when they're young they're green.

MME. RANEVSKAYA: This is killing me. Go, Yasha, find out to whom it has been sold.

YASHA: But the old man left long ago. [*Laughs.*]

MME RANEVSKAYA: What are you laughing at? What are you pleased about?

YASHA: That Yepihodov is such a funny one. A funny fellow, Two-and-Twenty Troubles!

MME. RANEVSKAYA: Firs, if the estate is sold, where will you go?

FIRS: I'll go where you tell me.

MME. RANEVSKAYA: Why do you look like that? Are you ill? You ought to go to bed.

FIRS: Yes! [*With a snigger.*] Me go to bed, and who's to hand things round? Who's to see to things? I'm the only one in the whole house.

YASHA: [*To* MME. RANEVSKAYA.] Lubov Andreyevna, allow me to ask a favor of you, be so kind! If you go back to Paris, take me with you, I beg you. It's positively impossible for me to stay here. [*Looking around; sotto voce.*] What's the use of talking? You see for yourself, it's an uncivilized country, the people have no morals, and then the boredom! The food in the kitchen's revolting, and besides there's this Firs wanders about mumbling all sorts of inappropriate words. Take me with you, be so kind!

[*Enter* PISHCHIK.]

PISHCHIK: May I have the pleasure of a waltz with you, charming lady? [MME. RANEVSKAYA *accepts.*] All the same, enchanting lady, you must let me have 180 rubles. . . . You must let me have [*dancing*] just one hundred and eighty rubles. [*They pass into the ballroom.*]

YASHA: [*Hums softly.*] "Oh, wilt thou understand the tumult in my soul?"

[*In the ballroom a figure in a gray top hat and checked trousers is jumping about and waving its arms; shouts:* "Bravo, Charlotta Ivanovna!"]

DUNYASHA: [*Stopping to powder her face; to* FIRS.] The young miss has ordered me to dance. There are so many gentlemen and not enough ladies. But dancing makes me dizzy, my heart begins to beat fast, Firs Nikolayevich. The Post Office Clerk said something to me just now that quite took my breath away.

[*Music stops.*]

FIRS: What did he say?

DUNYASHA: "You're like a flower," he said.

YASHA: [*Yawns.*] What ignorance. [*Exits.*]

DUNYASHA: "Like a flower!" I'm such a delicate girl. I simply adore pretty speeches.

FIRS: You'll come to a bad end.

[*Enter* YEPIHODOV.]

YEPIHODOV: [*To* DUNYASHA.] You have no wish to see me, Avdotya Fyodorovna . . . as though I was some sort of insect. [*Sighs.*] Ah, life!

DUNYASHA: What is it you want?

YEPIHODOV: Indubitably you may be right. [*Sighs.*] But of course, if one looks at it from the point of view, if I may be allowed to say so, and apologizing for my frankness, you have completely reduced me to a state of mind. I know my fate. Every day some calamity befalls me, and I grew used to it long ago, so that I look upon my fate with a smile. You gave me your word, and though I —

DUNYASHA: Let's talk about it later, please. But just now leave me alone, I am daydreaming. [*Plays with a fan.*]

YEPIHODOV: A misfortune befalls me every day; and if I may be allowed to say so, I merely smile, I even laugh.

    [*Enter* VARYA.]

VARYA: [*To* YEPIHODOV.] Are you still here? What an impertinent fellow you are really! Run along, Dunyasha. [*To* YEPIHODOV.] Either you're playing billiards and breaking a cue, or you're wandering about the drawing room as though you were a guest.

YEPIHODOV: You cannot, permit me to remark, penalize me.

VARYA: I'm not penalizing you; I'm just telling you. You merely wander from place to place, and don't do your work. We keep you as a clerk, but heaven knows what for.

YEPIHODOV: [*Offended.*] Whether I work or whether I walk, whether I eat or whether I play billiards, is a matter to be discussed only by persons of understanding and of mature years.

VARYA: [*Enraged.*] You dare say that to me—you dare? You mean to say I've no understanding? Get out of here at once! This minute!

YEPIHODOV: [*Scared.*] I beg you to express yourself delicately.

VARYA: [*Beside herself.*] Clear out this minute! Out with you!

    [YEPIHODOV goes toward the door, VARYA *following.*]

VARYA: Two-and-Twenty Troubles! Get out—don't let me set eyes on you again!

    [*Exit* YEPIHODOV: *His voice is heard behind the door:* "I shall lodge a complaint against you!"]

VARYA: Oh, you're coming back? [*She seizes the stick left near door by* FIRS.] Well, come then . . . come . . . I'll show you. . . . Ah, you're coming? You're coming? . . . Come . . . [*Swings the stick just as* LOPAHIN *enters.*]

LOPAHIN: Thank you kindly.

VARYA: [*Angrily and mockingly.*] I'm sorry.

LOPAHIN: It's nothing. Thank you kindly for your charming reception.

VARYA: Don't mention it. [*Walks away, looks back and asks softly.*] I didn't hurt you, did I?

LOPAHIN: Oh, no, not at all. I shall have a large bump, though.

    [*Voices from the ballroom:* "Lopahin is here! Lopahin!" *Enter* PISH-CHIK.]

PISHCHIK: My eyes do see, my ears do hear! [*Kisses* LOPAHIN.] You smell of cognac, my dear friend. And we've been celebrating here, too.

    [*Enter* MME. RANEVSKAYA.]

MME. RANEVSKAYA: Is that you, Yermolay Alexeyevich? What kept you so long? Where's Leonid?

LOPAHIN: Leonid Andreyevich arrived with me. He's coming.

MME. RANEVSKAYA: Well, what happened? Did the sale take place? Speak!

LOPAHIN: [*Embarrassed, fearful of revealing his joy.*] The sale was over at four o'clock. We missed the train—had to wait till half-past nine. [*Sighing heavily.*] Ugh. I'm a little dizzy.

[*Enter* GAYEV: *In his right hand he holds parcels, with his left he is wiping away his tears.*]

MME. RANEVSKAYA: Well, Leonid? What news? [*Impatiently, through tears.*] Be quick, for God's sake!

GAYEV: [*Not answering, simply waves his hand. Weeping, to* FIRS.] Here, take these; anchovies, Kerch herrings . . . I haven't eaten all day. What I've been through! [*The click of billiard balls comes through the open door of the billiard room and* YASHA's *voice is heard:* "Seven and eighteen!" GAYEV's *expression changes, he no longer weeps.*] I'm terribly tired. Firs, help me change. [*Exits, followed by* FIRS.]

PISHCHIK: How about the sale? Tell us what happened.

MME. RANEVSKAYA: Is the cherry orchard sold?

LOPAHIN: Sold.

MME. RANEVSKAYA: Who bought it?

LOPAHIN: I bought it.

[*Pause,* MME. RANEVSKAYA *is overcome. She would fall to the floor, were it not for the chair and table near which she stands.* VARYA *takes the keys from her belt, flings them on the floor in the middle of the drawing room and goes out.*]

LOPAHIN: I bought it. Wait a bit, ladies and gentlemen, please, my head is swimming, I can't talk. [*Laughs.*] We got to the auction and Deriganov was there already. Leonid Andreyevich had only 15,000 and straight off Deriganov bid 30,000 over and above the mortgage. I saw how the land lay, got into the fight, bid 40,000. He bid 45,000. I bid fifty-five. He kept adding five thousands, I ten. Well . . . it came to an end. I bid ninety above the mortgage and the estate was knocked down to me. Now the cherry orchard's mine! Mine! [*Laughs uproariously.*] Lord! God in Heaven! The cherry orchard's mine! Tell me that I'm drunk—out of my mind—that it's all a dream. [*Stamps his feet.*] Don't laugh at me! If my father and my grandfather could rise from their graves and see all that has happened—how their Yermolay, who used to be flogged, their half-literate Yermolay, who used to run about barefoot in winter, how that very Yermolay has bought the most magnificent estate in the world. I bought the estate where my father and grandfather were slaves, where they weren't even allowed to enter the kitchen. I am asleep—it's only a dream—I only imagine it. . . . It's the fruit of your imagination, wrapped in the darkness of the unknown! [*Picks up the keys, smiling genially.*] She threw down the keys, wants to show she's no longer mistress here. [*Jingles keys.*] Well, no matter. [*The band is warming up.*] Hey, musicians! Strike up! I want to hear you! Come, everybody, and see how Yermolay Lopahin will lay the ax to the cherry orchard and how the trees will fall to the ground. We will build summer cottages there, and our grandsons and great grandsons will see a new life here. Music! Strike up!

[*The band starts to play.* MME RANEVSKAYA *has sunk into a chair and is weeping bitterly.*]

LOPAHIN: [*Reproachfully.*] Why, why didn't you listen to me? My dear friend, my poor friend, you can't bring it back now. [*Tearfully.*] Oh, if only this were over quickly! Oh, if only our wretched, disordered life were changed!

PISHCHIK: [*Takes him by the arm; sotto voce.*] She's crying. Let's go into the ballroom. Let her be alone. Come. [*Takes his arm and leads him into the ballroom.*]

LOPAHIN: What's the matter? Musicians, play so I can hear you! Let me have things the way I want them.[*Ironically.*] Here comes the new master, the owner of the cherry orchard. [*Accidentally he trips over a little table, almost upsetting the candelabra.*] I can pay for everything. [*Exits with* PISHCHIK.]

[MME. RANEVSKAYA, *alone, sits huddled up, weeping bitterly. Music plays softly. Enter* ANYA *and* TROFIMOV *quickly.* ANYA *goes to her mother and falls on her knees before her.* TROFIMOV *stands in the doorway.*]

ANYA: Mamma, Mamma, you're crying! Dear, kind, good Mamma, my precious, I love you, I bless you! The cherry orchard is sold, it's gone, that's true, quite true. But don't cry, Mamma, life is still before you, you still have your kind, pure heart. Let us go, let us go away from here, darling. We will plant a new orchard, even more luxuriant than this one. You will see it, you will understand, and like the sun at evening, joy—deep, tranquil joy—will sink into your soul, and you will smile, Mamma. Come, darling, let us go.

Act IV

Scene as in Act I. No window curtains or pictures, only a little furniture, piled up in a corner, as if for sale. A sense of emptiness. Near the outer door and at the back, suitcases, bundles, etc., are piled up. A door open on the left and the voices of VARYA *and* ANYA *are heard.* LOPAHIN *stands waiting.* YASHA *holds a tray with glasses full of champagne.* YEPIHODOV *in the anteroom is tying up a box. Behind the scene a hum of voices: peasants have come to say good-bye. Voice of* GAYEV: *"Thanks, brothers, thank you."*

YASHA: The country folk have come to say good-bye. In my opinion, Yermolay Alexeyevich, they are kindly souls, but there's nothing in their heads.

[*The hum dies away. Enter* MME. RANEVSKAYA *and* GAYEV: *She is not crying, but is pale, her face twitches and she cannot speak.*]

GAYEV: You gave them your purse, Luba. That won't do! That won't do!

MME. RANEVSKAYA: I couldn't help it! I couldn't! [*They go out.*]

LOPAHIN: [*Calls after them.*] Please, I beg you, have a glass at parting. I didn't think of bringing any champagne from town and at the station I could find only one bottle. Please, won't you? [*Pause.*] What's the matter, ladies and gentlemen, don't you want any? [*Moves away from the door.*] If I'd known, I wouldn't have bought it. Well, then I won't drink any, either. [YASHA *carefully sets the tray down on a chair.*] At least you have a glass, Yasha.

YASHA: Here's to the travelers! And good luck to those that stay! [*Drinks.*] This champagne isn't the real stuff, I can assure you.

LOPAHIN: Eight rubles a bottle. [*Pause.*] It's devilishly cold here.

YASHA: They didn't light the stoves today—it wasn't worth it, since we're leaving. [*Laughs.*]

LOPAHIN: Why are you laughing?

YASHA: It's just that I'm pleased.

LOPAHIN: It's October, yet it's as still and sunny as though it were summer. Good weather for building. [*Looks at his watch, and speaks off.*] Bear in mind, ladies and gentlemen, the train goes in forty-seven minutes, so you ought to start for the station in twenty minutes. Better hurry up!

[*Enter* TROFIMOV, *wearing an overcoat.*]

TROFIMOV: I think it's time to start. The carriages are at the door. The devil only knows what's become of my rubbers; they've disappeared. [*Calling off.*] Anya! My rubbers are gone. I can't find them.

LOPAHIN: I've got to go to Kharkov. I'll take the same train you do. I'll spend the winter in Kharkov. I've been hanging round here with you, till I'm worn out with loafing. I can't live without work—I don't know what to do with my hands, they dangle as if they didn't belong to me.

TROFIMOV: Well, we'll soon be gone, then you can go on with your useful labors again.

LOPAHIN: Have a glass.

TROFIMOV: No, I won't.

LOPAHIN: So you're going to Moscow now?

TROFIMOV: Yes, I'll see them into town, and tomorrow I'll go on to Moscow.

LOPAHIN: Well, I'll wager the professors aren't giving any lectures, they're waiting for you to come.

TROFIMOV: That's none of your business.

LOPAHIN: Just how many years have you been at the university?

TROFIMOV: Can't you think of something new? Your joke's stale and flat. [*Looking for his rubbers.*] We'll probably never see each other again, so allow me to give you a piece of advice at parting: don't wave your hands about! Get out of the habit. And another thing: building bungalows, figuring that summer residents will eventually become small farmers, figuring like that is just another form of waving your hands about. . . . Never mind, I love you anyway; you have fine, delicate fingers, like an artist; you have a fine delicate soul.

LOPAHIN: [*Embracing him.*] Good-bye, my dear fellow. Thank you for everything. Let me give you some money for the journey, if you need it.

TROFIMOV: What for? I don't need it.

LOPAHIN: But you haven't any.

TROFIMOV: Yes, I have, thank you. I got some money for a translation— here it is in my pocket. [*Anxiously.*] But where are my rubbers?

VARYA: [*From the next room.*] Here! Take the nasty things. [*Flings a pair of rubbers onto the stage.*]

TROFIMOV: What are you so cross about, Varya? Hm . . . and these are not my rubbers.

LOPAHIN: I sowed three thousand acres of poppies in the spring, and now I've made 40,000 on them, clear profit; and when my poppies were in bloom, what a picture it was! So, as I say, I made 40,000; and I am offering you a loan because I can afford it. Why turn up your nose at it? I am a peasant—I speak bluntly.

TROFIMOV: Your father was a peasant, mine was a druggist—that proves absolutely nothing whatever. [LOPAHIN *takes out his wallet.*] Don't, put that away! If you were to offer me two hundred thousand, I wouldn't take it. I'm a free man. And everything that all of you, rich and poor alike, value so highly and hold so dear hasn't the slightest power over me. It's like so much fluff floating in the air. I can get on without you, I can pass you by, I'm strong and proud. Mankind is moving toward the highest truth, toward the highest happiness possible on earth, and I am in the front ranks.

LOPAHIN: Will you get there?

TROFIMOV: I will. [*Pause.*] I will get there, or I will show others the way to get there.

[*The sound of axes chopping down trees is heard in the distance.*]

LOPAHIN: Well, good-bye, my dear fellow. It's time to leave. We turn up our noses at one another, but life goes on just the same. When I'm working hard, without resting, my mind is easier, and it seems to me that I, too, know why I exist. But how many people are there in Russia, brother, who exist nobody knows why? Well, it doesn't matter. That's not what makes the wheels go round. They say Leonid Andreyevich has taken a position in the bank, 6,000 rubles a year. Only, of course, he won't stick to it, he's too lazy. . . .

ANYA: [*In the doorway.*] Mamma begs you not to start cutting down the cherry trees until she's gone.

TROFIMOV: Really, you should have more tact! [*Exits.*]

LOPAHIN: Right away—right away! Those men . . . [*Exits.*]

ANYA: Has Firs been taken to the hospital?

YASHA: I told them this morning. They must have taken him.

ANYA: [*To* YEPIHODOV, *who crosses the room.*] Yepihodov, please find out if Firs has been taken to the hospital.

YASHA: [*Offended.*] I told Yegor this morning. Why ask a dozen times?

YEPIHODOV: The aged Firs, in my definitive opinion, is beyond mending. It's time he was gathered to his fathers. And I can only envy him. [*Puts a suitcase down on a hat box and crushes it.*] There now, of course, I knew it! [*Exits.*]

YASHA: [*Mockingly.*] Two-and-Twenty Troubles!

VARYA: [*Through the door.*] Has Firs been taken to the hospital?

ANYA: Yes.

VARYA: Then why wasn't the note for the doctor taken too?

ANYA: Oh! Then someone must take it to him. [*Exits.*]

VARYA: [*From adjoining room.*] Where's Yasha? Tell him his mother's come and wants to say good-bye.

YASHA: [*Waves his hand.*] She tries my patience.

[DUNYASHA *has been occupied with the luggage. Seeing* YASHA *alone, she goes up to him.*]

DUNYASHA: You might just give me one little look, Yasha. You're going away. . . . You're leaving me . . . [*Weeps and throws herself on his neck.*]

YASHA: What's there to cry about? [*Drinks champagne.*] In six days I shall be in Paris again. Tomorrow we get into an express train and off we go, that's the last you'll see of us. . . . I can scarcely believe it. *Vive la France!*[3] It don't suit me here, I just can't live here. That's all there is to it. I'm fed up with the ignorance here, I've had enough of it. [*Drinks champagne.*] What's there to cry about? Behave yourself properly, and you'll have no cause to cry.

DUNYASHA: [*Powders her face, looking in pocket mirror.*] Do send me a letter from Paris. You know I loved you, Yasha, how I loved you! I'm a delicate creature, Yasha.

YASHA: Somebody's coming! [*Busies himself with the luggage; hums softly.*]

[*Enter* MME. RANEVSKAYA, GAYEV, ANYA, *and* CHARLOTTA.]

GAYEV: We ought to be leaving. We haven't much time. [*Looks at* YASHA.] Who smells of herring?

MME. RANEVSKAYA: In about ten minutes we should be getting into the carriages. [*Looks around the room.*] Good-bye, dear old home, good-bye, grandfather. Winter will pass, spring will come, you will no longer be here, they will have torn you down. How much these walls have seen! [*Kisses* ANYA *warmly.*] My treasure, how radiant you look! Your eyes are sparkling like diamonds. Are you glad? Very?

ANYA: [*Gaily.*] Very glad. A new life is beginning, Mamma.

GAYEV: Well, really, everything is all right now. Before the cherry orchard was sold, we all fretted and suffered; but afterward, when the question was settled finally and irrevocably, we all calmed down, and even felt quite cheerful. I'm a bank employee now, a financier. The yellow ball in the side pocket! And anyhow, you are looking better, Luba, there's no doubt of that.

MME. RANEVSKAYA: Yes, my nerves are better, that's true. [*She is handed her hat and coat.*] I sleep well. Carry out my things, Yasha. It's time. [*To* ANYA.] We shall soon see each other again, my little girl. I'm going to Paris, I'll live there on the money your great-aunt sent us to buy the estate with—long live Auntie! But that money won't last long.

ANYA: You'll come back soon, soon, Mamma, won't you? Meanwhile I'll study. I'll pass my high school examination, and then I'll go to work and help you. We'll read all kinds of books together, Mamma, won't we? [*Kisses her mother's hands.*] We'll read in the autumn evenings, we'll read lots of books, and a new wonderful world will open up before us. [*Falls into a revery.*] Mamma, do come back.

3. Long live France! (French).

MME. RANEVSKAYA: I will come back, my precious.
[*Embraces her daughter. Enter* LOPAHIN *and* CHARLOTTA, *who is humming softly.*]
GAYEV: Charlotta's happy: she's singing.
CHARLOTTA: [*Picks up a bundle and holds it like a baby in swaddling clothes.*] Bye, baby, bye. [*A baby is heard crying:* "Wah! Wah!"] Hush, hush, my pet, my little one. ["Wah! Wah!"] I'm so sorry for you! [*Throws the bundle down.*] You will find me a position, won't you? I can't go on like this.
LOPAHIN: We'll find one for you, Charlotta Ivanovna, don't worry.
GAYEV: Everyone's leaving us. Varya's going away. We've suddenly become of no use.
CHARLOTTA: There's no place for me to live in town, I must go away. [*Hums.*]
   [*Enter* PISHCHIK.]
LOPAHIN: There's nature's masterpiece!
PISHCHIK: [*Gasping.*] Oh . . . let me get my breath . . . I'm in agony. . . . Esteemed friends . . . Give me a drink of water. . . .
GAYEV: Wants some money, I suppose. No, thank you . . . I'll keep out of harm's way. [*Exits.*]
PISHCHIK: It's a long while since I've been to see you, most charming lady. [*To* LOPAHIN.] So you are here . . . glad to see you, you intellectual giant . . . There . . . [*Gives* LOPAHIN *money.*] Here's 400 rubles, and I still owe you 840.
LOPAHIN: [*Shrugging his shoulders in bewilderment.*] I must be dreaming. . . . Where did you get it?
PISHCHIK: Wait a minute . . . it's hot. . . . A most extraordinary event! Some Englishmen came to my place and found some sort of white clay on my land . . . [*To* MME. RANEVSKAYA.] And 400 for you . . . most lovely . . . most wonderful . . . [*Hands her the money.*] The rest later. [*Drinks water.*] A young man in the train was telling me just now that a great philosopher recommends jumping off roofs. "Jump!" says he; "that's the long and the short of it!" [*In amazement.*] Just imagine! Some more water!
LOPAHIN: What Englishmen?
PISHCHIK: I leased them the tract with the clay on it for twenty-four years. . . . And now, forgive me, I can't stay. . . . I must be dashing on. . . . I'm going over to Znoikov . . . to Kardamanov . . . I owe them all money . . . [*Drinks water.*] Good-bye, everybody . . . I'll look in on Thursday . . .
MME. RANEVSKAYA: We're just moving into town; and tomorrow I go abroad.
PISHCHIK: [*Upset.*] What? Why into town? That's why the furniture is like that . . . and the suitcases. . . . Well, never mind! [*Through tears.*] Never mind . . . men of colossal intellect, these Englishmen. . . . Never mind . . . Be happy. God will come to your help. . . . Never mind . . . everything in this world comes to an end. [*Kisses* MME. RANEVSKAYA'*s hand.*] If the rumor reaches you that it's all up with me, remember this old . . . horse, and say: "Once there lived a certain . . . Simeonov-Pishchik . . . the kingdom of Heaven be his. . . ." Glorious weather! . . . Yes . . . [*Exits,*

in great confusion, but at once returns and says in the doorway.] My daughter Dashenka sends her regards. [*Exits.*]

MME. RANEVSKAYA: Now we can go. I leave with two cares weighing on me. The first is poor old Firs. [*Glancing at her watch.*] We still have about five minutes.

ANYA: Mamma, Firs has already been taken to the hospital. Yasha sent him there this morning.

MME. RANEVSKAYA: My other worry is Varya. She's used to getting up early and working; and now, with no work to do, she is like a fish out of water. She has grown thin and pale, and keeps crying, poor soul. [*Pause.*] You know this very well, Yermolay Alexeyevich; I dreamed of seeing her married to you, and it looked as though that's how it would be. [*Whispers to* ANYA, *who nods to* CHARLOTTA *and both go out.*] She loves you. You find her attractive. I don't know, I don't know why it is you seem to avoid each other; I can't understand it.

LOPAHIN: To tell you the truth, I don't understand it myself. It's all a puzzle. If there's still time, I'm ready now, at once. Let's settle it straight off, and have done with it! Without you, I feel I'll never be able to propose.

MME. RANEVSKAYA: That's splendid. After all, it will only take a minute. I'll call her once. . . .

LOPAHIN: And luckily, here's champagne, too. [*Looks at the glasses.*] Empty! Somebody's drunk it all. [*Yasha coughs.*] That's what you might call guzzling . . .

MME. RANEVSKAYA: [*Animatedly.*] Excellent! We'll go and leave you alone. Yasha, *allez!*[4] I'll call her. [*At the door.*] Varya, leave everything and come here. Come! [*Exits with* YASHA.]

LOPAHIN: [*Looking at his watch.*] Yes . . . [*Pause behind the door, smothered laughter and whispering; at last, enter* VARYA.]

VARYA: [*Looking over the luggage in leisurely fashion.*] Strange, I can't find it . . .

LOPAHIN: What are you looking for?

VARYA: Packed it myself, and I don't remember . . . [*Pause.*]

LOPAHIN: Where are you going now, Varya?

VARYA: I? To the Ragulins'. I've arranged to take charge there—as housekeeper, if you like.

LOPAHIN: At Yashnevo? About fifty miles from here. [*Pause.*] Well, life in this house is ended!

VARYA: [*Examining luggage.*] Where is it? Perhaps I put it in the chest. Yes, life in this house is ended. . . . There will be no more of it.

LOPAHIN: And I'm just off to Kharkov—by this next train. I've a lot to do there. I'm leaving Yepihodov here . . . I've taken him on.

VARYA: Oh!

LOPAHIN: Last year at this time, it was snowing, if you remember, but now it's sunny and there's no wind. It's cold, though. . . . It must be three below.

4. Go on! (French).

VARYA: I didn't look. [*Pause.*] And besides, our thermometer's broken. [*Pause.* VOICE *from the yard:* "Yermolay Alexeyevich!"]

LOPAHIN: [*As if he had been waiting for the call.*] This minute! [*Exits quickly.*]

[VARYA *sits on the floor and sobs quietly, her head on a bundle of clothes. Enter* MME. RANEVSKAYA *cautiously.*]

MME. RANEVSKAYA: Well? [*Pause.*] We must be going.

VARYA: [*Wiping her eyes.*] Yes, it's time, Mamma dear. I'll be able to get to the Ragulins' today, if only we don't miss the train.

MME. RANEVSKAYA: [*At the door.*] Anya, put your things on.

[*Enter* ANYA, GAYEV, CHARLOTTA. GAYEV *wears a heavy overcoat with a hood. Enter servants and coachmen.* YEPIHODOV *bustles about the luggage.*]

MME. RANEVSKAYA: Now we can start on our journey.

ANYA: [*Joyfully.*] On our journey!

GAYEV: My friends, my dear, cherished friends, leaving this house forever, can I be silent? Can I, at leave-taking, refrain from giving utterance to those emotions that now fill my being?

ANYA: [*Imploringly.*] Uncle!

VARYA: Uncle, Uncle dear, don't.

GAYEV: [*Forlornly.*] I'll bank the yellow in the side pocket . . . I'll be silent . . .

[*Enter* TROFIMOV, *then* LOPAHIN.]

TROFIMOV: Well, ladies and gentlemen, it's time to leave.

LOPAHIN: Yepihodov, my coat.

MME. RANEVSKAYA: I'll sit down just a minute. It seems as though I'd never before seen what the walls of this house were like, the ceilings, and now I look at them hungrily, with such tender affection.

GAYEV: I remember when I was six years old sitting on that window sill on Whitsunday,[5] watching my father going to church.

MME. RANEVSKAYA: Has everything been taken?

LOPAHIN: I think so. [*Putting on his overcoat.*] Yepihodov, see that everything's in order.

YEPIHODOV: [*In a husky voice.*] You needn't worry, Yermolay Alexeyevich.

LOPAHIN: What's the matter with your voice?

YEPIHODOV: I just had a drink of water. I must have swallowed something.

YASHA: [*Contemptuously.*] What ignorance!

MME. RANEVSKAYA: When we're gone, not a soul will be left here.

LOPAHIN: Until the spring.

[VARYA *pulls an umbrella out of a bundle, as though about to hit someone with it.* LOPAHIN *pretends to be frightened.*]

VARYA: Come, come, I had no such idea!

TROFIMOV: Ladies and gentlemen, let's get into the carriages—it's time. The train will be in directly.

VARYA: Petya, there they are, your rubbers, by that trunk. [*Tearfully.*] And what dirty old things, they are!

5. Or Pentecost, a Christian festival occurring on the seventh Sunday after Easter.

TROFIMOV: [*Puts on rubbers.*] Let's go, ladies and gentlemen.

GAYEV: [*Greatly upset, afraid of breaking down.*] The train . . . the station.
. . . Three cushions in the side pocket, I'll bank this one in the corner . . .

MME. RANEVSKAYA: Let's go.

LOPAHIN: Are we all here? No one in there? [*Locks the side door on the left.*] There are some things stored here, better lock up. Let us go!

ANYA: Good-bye, old house! Good-bye, old life!

TROFIMOV: Hail to you, new life!

[*Exits with* ANYA: VARYA *looks round the room and goes out slowly.* YASHA *and* CHARLOTTA *with her dog go out.*]

LOPAHIN: And so, until the spring. Go along, friends . . . Bye-bye! [*Exits.*]

[MME. RANEVSKAYA *and* GAYEV *remain alone. As though they had been waiting for this, they throw themselves on each other's necks, and break into subdued, restrained sobs, afraid of being overheard.*]

GAYEV: [*In despair.*] My sister! My sister!

MME. RANEVSKAYA: Oh, my orchard—my dear, sweet, beautiful orchard! My life, my youth, my happiness—good-bye! Good-bye!

[*Voice of* ANYA, *gay and summoning:* "Mamma!" *Voice of* TROFIMOV, *gay and excited:* "Halloo!"]

MME. RANEVSKAYA: One last look at the walls, at the windows. . . . Our poor mother loved to walk about this room . . .

GAYEV: My sister, my sister!

[*Voice of* ANYA: "Mamma!" *Voice Of* TROFIMOV: "Halloo!"]

MME. RANEVSKAYA: We're coming.

[*They go out. The stage is empty. The sound of doors being locked, of carriages driving away. Then silence. In the stillness is heard the muffled sound of the ax striking a tree, a mournful, lonely sound.*

Footsteps are heard. FIRS *appears in the doorway on the right. He is dressed as usual in a jacket and white waistcoat and wears slippers. He is ill.*]

FIRS: [*Goes to the door, tries the handle.*] Locked! They've gone . . . [*Sits down on the sofa.*] They've forgotten me. . . . Never mind . . . I'll sit here a bit . . . I'll wager Leonid Andreyevich hasn't put his fur coat on, he's gone off in his light overcoat . . . [*Sighs anxiously.*] I didn't keep an eye on him. . . . Ah, when they're young, they're green . . . [*Mumbles something indistinguishable.*] Life has gone by as if I had never lived. [*Lies down.*] I'll lie down a while. . . There's no strength left in you, old fellow; nothing is left, nothing. Ah, you addlehead!

[*Lies motionless. A distant sound is heard coming from the sky, as it were, the sound of a snapping string mournfully dying away. All is still again, and nothing is heard but the strokes of the ax against a tree far away in the orchard.*]

Part VI

THE TWENTIETH
CENTURY:
SELF AND OTHER IN
GLOBAL CONTEXT

GREENLAND
(Den.)

ALASKA
(U.S.)

C A N A D A

ICELAND
(Den.)

GREAT
BRITAIN

IRELAND

ENGLAND

ATLANTIC
OCEAN

UNITED
STATES

MEXICO

Hawaiian Islands
(U.S.)

BR.
HONDURAS

CUBA

Bermuda
(Br.)

Bahamas (Br.)

HAITI

DOMINICAN REPUBLIC

Puerto Rico (U.S.)

Guadeloupe (Fr.)

Martinique (Fr.)

JAMAICA

Grenada
(Br.)

Barbados (Br.)

Trinidad (Br.)

GUATEMALA
EL SALVADOR
HONDURAS
NICARAGUA
COSTA RICA

PANAMA

VENEZUELA

BR. GUIANA
DUTCH GUIANA
FR. GUIANA

COLOMBIA

Galapagos Is.

ECUADOR

Marquesas Is.

French Polynesia

Tahiti

PERU

BOLIVIA

B R A Z I L

PARAGUAY

CHILE

ARGENTINA

URUGUAY

Falkland Is.
(Br.)

P A C I F I C

O C E A N

Azores
(Port.)

PORTUGAL

SPAIN

Madeira
(Port.)

MOROCCO

Canary Is.
(Sp.)

RIO DE ORO

Cape Verde Is.
(Port.)

FRENCH

SENEGAL

GAMBIA
PORT. GUINEA
SIERRA LEONE
LIBERIA

IVORY COAST
GOLD COAST
TOGOLAND
NIGERIA
CAMEROONS
SP. GUINEA
FR. CONGO

Ascension
(Br.)

St. Helena
(Br.)

GE
SOUTH

A T L A N T I

O C E A N

Tristan da Cunha
(Br.)

FRAN

The World
ca. 1913

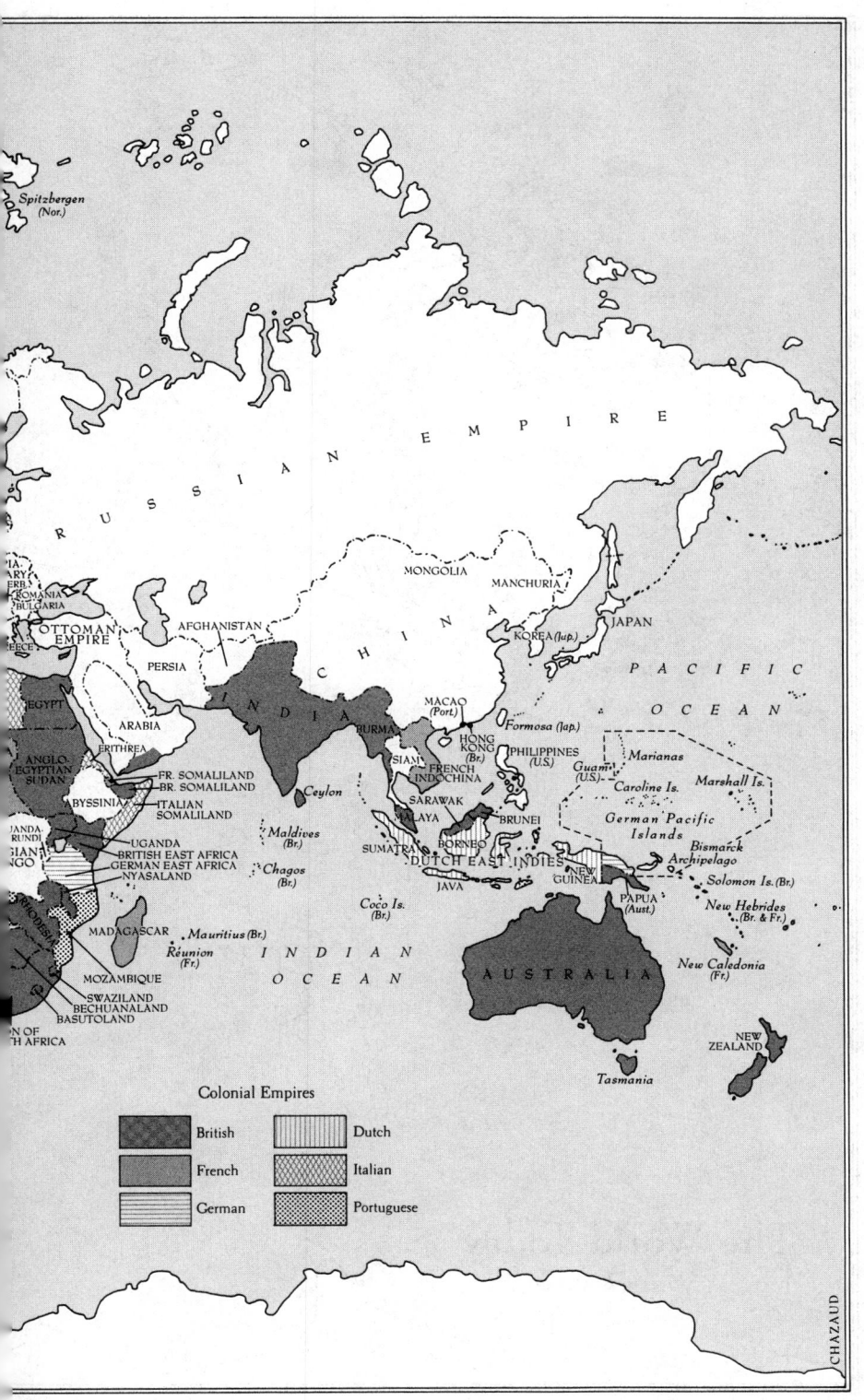

Spitzbergen
(Nor.)

R U S S I A N   E M P I R E

MONGOLIA   MANCHURIA

IA
ARY
ERB
BULGARIA

OTTOMAN
EMPIRE
EECE

AFGHANISTAN

PERSIA

C H I N A

KOREA (Jap.)   JAPAN

EGYPT

ARABIA

ERITREA

FR. SOMALILAND
BR. SOMALILAND
ITALIAN
SOMALILAND

ABYSSINIA

I N D I A

BURMA

SIAM

FRENCH
INDOCHINA

MACAO
(Port.)

Formosa (Jap.)

HONG
KONG
(Br.)

PHILIPPINES
(U.S.)

P A C I F I C

O C E A N

Marianas

Guam
(U.S.)

Caroline Is.

Marshall Is.

ANGLO-
EGYPTIAN
SUDAN

Ceylon

SARAWAK

MALAYA

BRUNEI

BORNEO

SUMATRA

German Pacific
Islands

Bismarck
Archipelago

)ANDA-
RUNDI
GIAN
GO

UGANDA
BRITISH EAST AFRICA
GERMAN EAST AFRICA
NYASALAND

Maldives
(Br.)

Chagos
(Br.)

DUTCH EAST INDIES

JAVA

NEW
GUINEA

Solomon Is. (Br.)

New Hebrides
(Br. & Fr.)

Coco Is.
(Br.)

PAPUA
(Aust.)

ODES

MADAGASCAR

Mauritius (Br.)

Réunion
(Fr.)

I N D I A N

O C E A N

A U S T R A L I A

New Caledonia
(Fr.)

MOZAMBIQUE

SWAZILAND
BECHUANALAND
BASUTOLAND

N OF
H AFRICA

NEW
ZEALAND

Tasmania

Colonial Empires

British		Dutch	
French		Italian	
German		Portuguese	

CHAZAUD

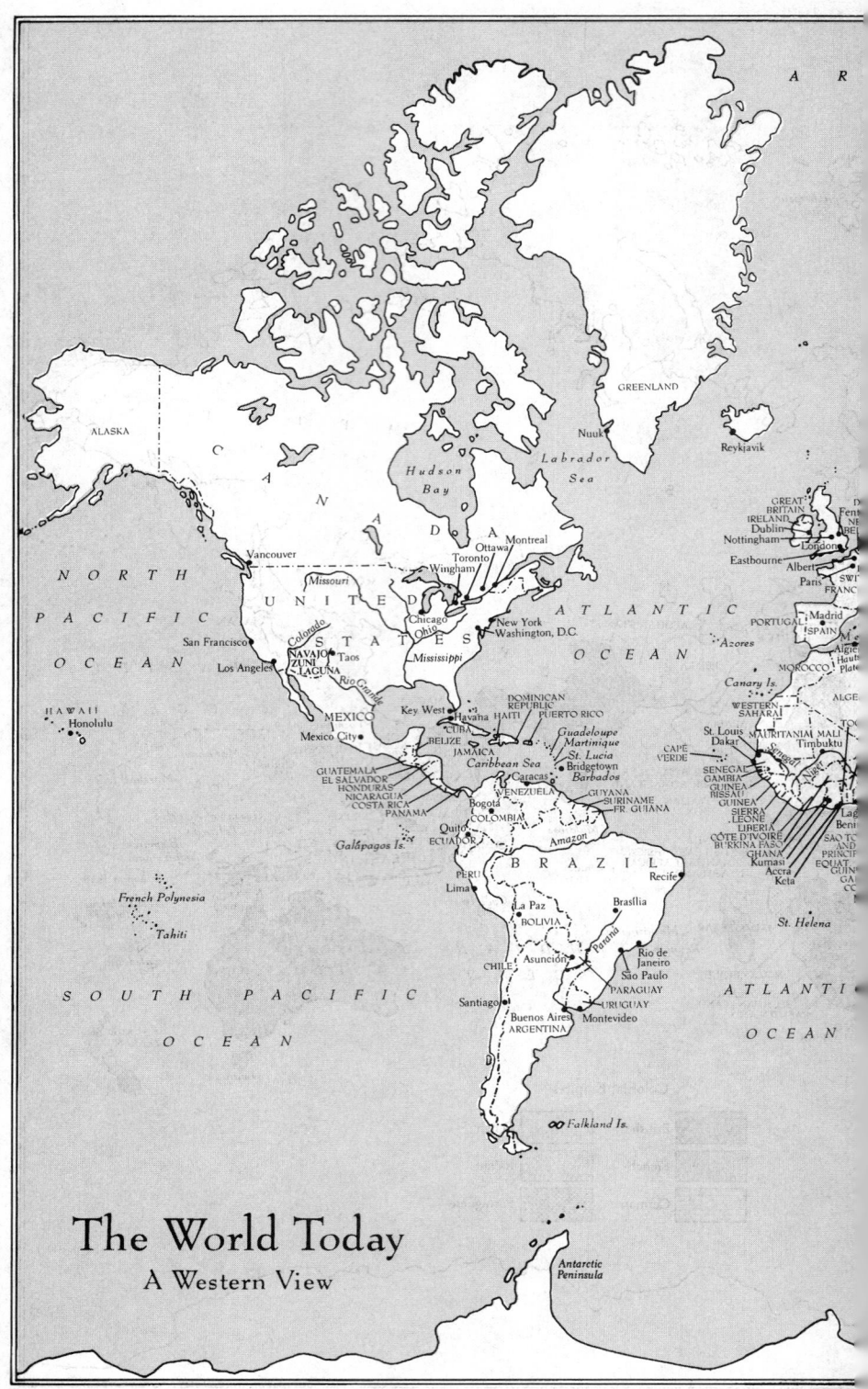

The World Today

A Western View

ARCTIC OCEAN

Spitzbergen

Neva
St. Petersburg
(Leningrad/Petrograd)
Moscow • Talnovo

BELARUS
UKRAINE
MOL.
GEORGIA
Black Sea
Istanbul/
Byzantium
TURKEY
SYRIA
LEB.
ISR.
Cairo
EGYPT
JORD.
Damascus
IRAQ
Baghdad
KUWAIT
QATAR
BAHRAIN
SAUDI
ARABIA
Medina
Mecca
Riyadh
U.A.E.
Muscat
Sanaa
YEMEN
OMAN
Djibouti
SUDAN
ERITREA
ETHIOPIA
SOMALIA
Mogadishu
UGANDA
KENYA
Mombasa
BURUNDI
TANZANIA
MADAGASCAR
Limpopo
SWAZILAND
Johannesburg
Durban
LESOTHO

Neva
Voronezh
Don
KAZAKHSTAN
ARM.
AZER.
Baku
TURKM.
TAJIK.
AFGHAN.
IRAN
Tehran
PAKISTAN
Jumna
NEPAL
Himalayas
TIBET

R U S S I A

Ob
Yenisey
Lena
Lake Baikal

S I B E R I A

Bering Sea

Aleutian Islands

MONGOLIA

XINJIANG

KYRGYZ.
UZBEK.

C H I N A

Yellow
Yangtse

N. KOREA
S. KOREA

JAPAN

Iwo Jima

Taiwan

INDIA
MYANMAR
(BURMA)
BANGLADESH
THAILAND
LAOS
VIETNAM
CAMBODIA
BRUNEI
MALAYSIA
PHILIPPINES

MICRONESIA

Caroline Is.

MARSHALL
ISLANDS

KIRIBATI

TUVALU

Arabian
Sea

Bay of
Bengal

SRI LANKA

I N D I A N

O C E A N

INDONESIA

PAPUA
NEW GUINEA

SOLOMON
ISLANDS

Samoa Is.
WESTERN
SAMOA
VANUATU
FIJI
TONGA

New Caledonia

AUSTRALIA

NEW
ZEALAND

Tasmania

CHAZAUD.

The World Today
An Eastern View

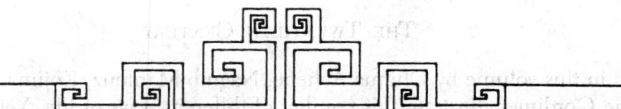

The Twentieth Century

Modern consciousness in the twentieth century is remarkable. Not because it is "modern" (every period is modern in its own eyes), but because it is for the first time beginning to be truly global. No beckoning frontier, no large area of the globe remains unvisited and mysterious for future explorers to map. Breathtaking advances in technology, transformations of modern states, the rapid spread of international corporations, cultural exchanges occurring rapidly and inevitably as communication and transportation networks link all sections of the world—all have created an era in which the essential reality is interconnectedness rather than isolation. Not that this simplifies matters. Connections bring their own problems, and they are not always welcome. Connections inevitably change the system, disrupt tradition, and confront people with many more choices than they were aware of previously. In many ways, this is the story of the twentieth century as it draws to a close.

These days the terms *modern* and *modernization* reappear everywhere as a key to change. They can be used as a weapon to bring about "progress," or rejected in favor of "tradition," or defined differently according to context and situation. In the West (understood as Europe and America), modernization has meant industrial progress, an openness to uncertainty in definitions of the world, and a desire to transcend narrowly nationalist politics. Elsewhere, modernization has been equated with "Westernization" (especially in technology, industry, democratic systems, and mass culture) and has been supported or rejected with that understanding.

Modernization has also arrived at different speeds in different parts of the world, growing gradually in Europe out of previous centuries, but coming far more rapidly to non-Western countries, often as a forced change brought about by colonialist politics and economic necessity. Little pockets of Western prosperity around the world—colonial enclaves in China, Africa, India, and South America—drove home the difference between colonizing and colonized societies, and the wealthy Western countries made a tempting model for regions beset by poverty, disease, and social unrest. Political leaders soon equated progress with Westernization, and many sought prosperity by transforming their societies into the closest possible imitation of Europe. Western success, they felt (and were told), was the result not merely of industrialization but also of a whole set of distinctive values and institutions—the concepts of individualism and democracy, attention to literacy and general education, private ownership and a thriving middle class, religious freedom, scientific method, public institutions, and (sometimes) the emancipation of women.

Colonial governments considered it their duty to disseminate these values by setting up school systems where European languages were used instead of local ones, and Western literature and philosophy were taught instead of indigenous culture. As a result, twentieth-century Westernization in many countries not only promised advances in literacy and standard of living but seemed to require the suppression of indigenous traditions, including centuries of literature (much of it oral) as well as languages, philosophy, religion, and models of community life.

Works in this volume by Chinua Achebe, Naguib Mahfouz, Kojima Nobuo, and Nadine Gordimer illustrate this conflict of different ways of life. Yet these same works also demonstrate another fact of global existence: that the clash of opposites is also a set of inextricably intermingled experiences, pointing to a fuller understanding of cultural (and multicultural) identity.

Modernism is not the same as modernization. Twentieth-century modernism is a literary and artistic movement with roots in Europe, and modernist works—translated and republished in great numbers—were exported around the globe along with the general expansion of Western culture. Many non-Western writers and intellectuals saw modernist style as the latest image of a progressive Western culture and a technique embodying an "advanced" way of thought. They borrowed artistic forms that were a gradual outgrowth of experimentation and literary evolution in Europe and America and used them as instant models in a new pattern of global crisscrossing that has overlaid narrower lines of literary evolution. In some instances, the militantly new aura of modernist works was prized as a way of rejecting traditional authority, an oblique means of transforming local perceptions. Although a reaction has since set in owing to shifts in economic and political power and to a greater acceptance of cultural difference, Western concepts of modernism continue to influence modern literature and literary theory the world over.

THE EUROPEAN ORIGINS OF TWENTIETH-CENTURY MODERNISM

Western modernity evolved out of, and in contrast to, a specific historical situation. This situation differed in other parts of the world, especially in feudal societies without industry, middle class, or a popular press and where artistic tradition supported highly stylized works with mythological subjects. Change followed different lines, therefore, according to whether the immediate past was feudal or democratic and whether the audience favored exquisite craftsmanship or, as in the West, versions of realism. In conservative societies such as China, Japan, and India, the foreign examples that helped usher in modern literature were likely to come from the same European realism against which Western modernism reacted. By the end of the twentieth century, however, Western modernist techniques could be found in literature around the world, usually blended with perspectives drawn from Realism.

In Europe, the idea of modernity was already a source of public debate and widespread anxiety as the Industrial Revolution transformed social, economic, and political life faster, it seemed, than such changes could peacefully be absorbed. Some saw it as a time of decadence and the loss of stable values. Others saw it, more optimistically, as an era in which a progressive Europe would lead the rest of the world to its own pinnacle of achievement (a point of view shared only briefly by the colonized countries). In science, philosophy, social theory, and the arts, the nineteenth century prepared both the evolution and the rebellion of the twentieth.

Scientific Rationalism

By the end of the nineteenth century, unprecedented developments in science had encouraged Westerners to believe that they would soon master all the secrets of the universe. The Enlightenment notion of the world as a machine—something whose parts could be named and seen to function—came back into favor. Discoveries in different fields seemed to make the universe more rational and hence predictable. In chemistry, there was John Dalton's (1766–1844) atomic theory and Dimitri Mendeleyev's (1834–1907) periodic table of elements; in physics, James Maxwell's (1831–1879) field theory unifying the study of electricity, magnetism, and light. The further development of Newtonian ideas made it possible to study the fixed stars, and spectral analysis showed the essential homogeneity of the universe. Technological applications suggested that these discoveries would serve humanity, not master it. Thermodynamics explained the processes of energy transformation, and locomotives and steamships promised rapid transportation throughout the world. Daguerreotype photography (developed by Louis Daguerre [1787–1851]) provided a documentary record. Finally, the history of living nature itself became an object of study when Charles Darwin (1809–1882) examined the evolution of species according to material evidence, without reference to divine laws or purpose.

The enthusiasm for scientific discovery was not confined to scientists. Auguste Comte (1798–1857), a French philosopher known as the founder of "positivism," held that scientific method constituted a total world view in which everything would ultimately be explained, including human society. Comte proposed a science of humanity that would analyze and define the laws governing human society (the first sociology). It became evident, however, that the results of scientific method depended on the objectivity of the scientist's point of view. Count Gobineau (1816–1882) proposed a "scientific" description of society in which there were three races (white, black, and yellow) with innate qualities and in which the white race (predictably, for this white Frenchman) was the superior category. Gobineau's writings laid the groundwork for much "scientific" racism later on, until he himself became a subject of analysis for scientists interested in explaining the history of race prejudice.

In literature, the historian and critic Hippolyte Taine (1828–1893) proposed a science of culture in which each literary work could be categorized as the combined product of its "race, milieu, and time." The novelist Emile Zola offered as scientific justification for his series on the degeneracy of the Rougon-Macquart family an *Introduction to the Study of Experimental Medicine* by Dr. Claude Bernard (1813–1878). Nowadays, it is easier to recognize the preexisting bias that flaws these large explanatory systems and to be cautious of claims of "scientific truth," especially in descriptions of human nature. The enormous wealth created by technology and scientific method, however, offered a powerful incentive for other regions of the world to imitate the Western example.

Western social theorists shared with the philosopher Comte the vision of creating a perfect society by understanding social "laws." Utopian socialists like the French Charles Fourier (1772–1837) and the Comte de Saint-Simon (1760–1825) and the Welsh industrialist Robert Owen (1771–1858) proposed various methods for organizing society and planning its economy. The English philosopher and economist John Stuart Mill (1806–1873) preached the dignity of man, the rights of women, and the possibility of happiness for all. By far the most important and influential theorist was the German Karl Marx (1819–1883), whose *Communist Manifesto* (1848) and *Capital* (1867) proposed a scientific theory of world history driven by broad economic forces. According to Marx, the most basic material needs—food, shelter, and the social relationships enabling group survival—provide an economic foundation from which all other aspects of human culture are derived. His description of modern workers as alienated cogs in the industrial economic machine, no longer owning their own labor, expressed for many the antihuman aspect of modern technological progress. Like his contemporaries, he believed in the power of rational systems to find answers for social ills; he described the division of modern industrial society into the two competing forces of capital and labor (the proletariat) and proposed the theory of dialectical materialism to explain the processes of history.

Reactions to Rationalism

The debate about scientific rationalism was inevitably a debate about knowledge and human values. In the nineteenth century, one of the strongest opponents of positivism and its belief in rational solutions was the German philosopher Friedrich Nietzsche (1844–1900). Nietzsche focused on the individual, not society, and admired only the *Übermensch*, the superhuman being who refused to be bound by the prevailing social paradigms of nationalism, Christianity, faith in science, loyalty to the state, or bourgeois civilized comfort. Nietzsche's distinction between Dionysian (instinctual) and Apollonian (intellectual) forces in human beings, his insistence on the individual's complete freedom (and responsibility) in a world that lacks transcendental law ("God is dead"), and his attack on the unimaginative mediocrity of mass society in the modern industrial world have made him a powerful influence in twentieth-century Western thought.

The shape and intensity of this debate in Europe were dictated for many years by a historical event that turned the younger generations against everything inherited from the recent past: the Great War (World War I, 1914–18). In spite of the confident rationalism of the political leaders of "Papa's Europe" (a term of resentment used by many to describe an authoritarian, patriarchal society that claimed to have all the answers), World War I had for the first time involved the whole continent of Europe and the United States in battle (reaching, with Turkey, into Asia Minor) and was the first "total war" in which modern weapons spared no one, including civilians. Clearly, something was wrong. An entire generation was lost in the trenches, and the survivors emerged resolved to reexamine the bases of certainty, the structures of knowledge, the systems of belief, and the repositories of authority in a society that had allowed such a war to occur. Their reaction would also be reflected in literature, not only in subject matter but—for many—in a new use of language, in new ways of representing our knowledge of the world, and, most especially, new hesitations about subscribing to any single mode of understanding it. They drew on areas beyond the intellect, interrogating modes of human consciousness and feeling in an intellectual attempt to go beyond the self-imposed limitations of previous rationalism.

Several thinkers were particularly important in formulating alternatives to the narrow rationalism of positivist philosophy. The French philosopher Henri Bergson (1859–1941) attacked scientific rationality as artificial and unreal because it froze everything in conceptual space; it ignored the whole dimension of life as it is actually experienced. For Bergson, reality was a fluid, living force (*élan vital*) that could only be apprehended by consciousness. Instead of quantitative and logical inquiry, he proposed intuiting the "immediate data of consciousness" as an alternate, nonscientific means of knowledge. Authors were not slow to perceive the implications of his prescription for representing reality. Marcel Proust, for example, searching to discover his identity through layers of "lost time and recollected experience," reflects a twentieth-century, Bergsonian change in the way literary style expresses reality. Bergson himself received the Nobel Prize in literature in 1927, both for the creative imagination shown in his own work and for his literary influence.

Sigmund Freud (1856–1939), the founder of psychoanalysis, was another influential figure. Freud's study of subconscious motives and instinctual drives revealed a level of activity that had been largely ignored outside of literature and was not considered a productive subject for continued "rational" inquiry. His essays and case studies argued that dreams and manias contain their own networks of meaning and that human beings cannot properly be understood without taking into consideration the irrational as well as the rational level of their existence. All are caught up, he suggested, in the process of mediating the same sexual drives and civilizational repressions that caused neurosis in his own patients.

Many of Freud's theories are questioned today (his assumption that every woman considers herself an incomplete man, for example). Some of his psychoanalytic categories seem too rigid. The mythic images he used to convey some of his basic concepts, like the Oedipus complex, were drawn from a heavily patriarchal Western mythology and are, therefore, less persuasive to societies—like India, for example—whose mythology contains strong matriarchal images. Freud's chief importance lies in his brilliant and even poetic attempts to clarify patterns of human thought and emotion. He focused attention on the way everyday "rational" behavior is shaped by unconscious impulses and hidden motivations and on the way human beings actually create (and modify) their images of self through engaging in dialogue with others. It is probably impossible for any poet, novelist, or playwright after Freud to write without taking into consideration the psychological undercurrents of human behavior—whether or not the author has read him.

Literature, however, is also a matter of words and not just themes and patterns of consciousness. Different concepts of language have colored literary expression at different times, and twentieth-century literature is no exception. Innovations in literary style during the early part of the century show the influence of psychoanalysis and of Symbolist poetics. Their syntax and imagery emulate Freudian free association, the complex inner patterns favored by nineteenth-century Symbolist poetry and the artistic effects of Impressionist or Cubist painting. Later works reflect a change in linguistic theory itself. Nineteenth-century positivism had assumed that language was an accurate tool for direct reference to reality (a view parodied in "The sun is called a sun because it *looks* like a sun"). In contrast, the Swiss linguist Ferdinand de Saussure (1857–1913) and the Austrian philosopher Ludwig Wittgenstein (1889–1951) emphasized that language is tied to society and usage: descriptions are not "accurate," for they can never grasp absolute reality or give "real" names. All that language can do, as they see it, is to create socially agreed-upon labels. Language may even be described as a "game" played with words: a crucial game, however, since it shapes our vision of reality. Modernist literature shows how words reshape the world we think we know.

In this perspective, both literature and linguistic systems manipulate combinations of *pieces* (words) and *rules* (grammar, syntax, and other conventions). At its most extreme, this theory rejects communication and views all language as an endless networking of associations. "Reality," instead of becoming more accessible, ultimately disappears inside language itself.

Yet these are not the only conclusions to be drawn from game theory. If a work by Jorge Luis Borges persuades us that language determines how we see the world as well as our own place in it, then we will look for that shaping use of language, and become better readers. The shifting perspectives recognized by game theory have been adopted in modern advertising. Television commercials fragment and reconstruct reality, racing through sets of highly associative words and images to persuade you that the sponsor "speaks your language" and can deliver what you really want. Literary criticism has learned to recognize hitherto unseen structures and systems of reference embedded in the written text or alive in oral performance. Nor are new techniques of reading restricted to contemporary texts, for the idea of inexhaustible word play has also illuminated traditional literary masterworks, proving that they can bear reading and rereading by different generations and even different cultures. Such works are not exhausted by a single audience because they interact with the world on many different planes, making accessible many systems of meaning.

Concurrent developments in the physical and social sciences also integrated shifting perspectives and theories of play. Psychology, anthropology, and physics stressed relationships as they redefined current concepts of human nature and the material world. Gestalt psychology (*Gestalt* is German for "form") after 1912 suggested that the meaning of individual phenomena was found in organized wholes rather than in analysis of separate pieces. It was the overall "shape of things" that mattered. In structural anthropology, Claude Lévi-Strauss (born 1908) described human society as a system of worldviews or "codes" that could be compared from culture to culture.

Lévi-Strauss's "structural method" appealed to literary critics as a way to illuminate simultaneously a work's inner structural relationship and its relationships to the individual and culture that produced it. Other structures were proposed by Jungian psychology—based on the work of Carl Gustav Jung (1875–1961)—which claimed that humanity shares a "collective unconscious," a buried level of universal experience tapped by myth, religion, and art. Accordingly, the common experience of our species is revealed in archetypes (master patterns) like the figures of the hero, seer, or Great Mother, the image of the quest, or the process of death and rebirth.

When the "hard" sciences of physics and mathematics turned their attention to the role played by the receiver, their results shocked the general public and intrigued writers and artists. Albert Einstein's theory of relativity (1905) abandoned the concepts of absolute motion and the absolute difference of space and time and, working from pure mathematical logic, proposed that reality should be understood as a four-dimensional continuum (called space-time) that literally could not be expressed either in words or in the old three-dimensional models of Newtonian physics. Since *relativity* implied "relativism" in the popular mind, Einstein's discovery (despite his own religious beliefs) was widely thought to pull the ground out from under any certainty—scientific or religious—about the physical world. Even more disturbing, Werner Heisenberg's "uncertainty principle" (1927) proclaimed that scientific measurement (in this case, the measurement of electrons) was always a matter of statistical approximation, a "probability function" and not an exact description. Ironically, what was scientifically an increasingly *accurate* perception of the nature of things often seemed just the opposite to the general public. People could no longer refer to "self-evident truths" in nature, or go "back to basics," when scientists had just shown that the "basic" world was not what it seemed. Many writers, however, and Proust among the earliest, welcomed what they saw as a richer view of experience and scientific confirmation that reality could be represented in a shifting and fluid perspective.

The modern philosophy that coincides with the rise of Modernism is similarly an inquiry into the reliability of appearances. Not that such an inquiry is new, or even Western: the world's major religions and philosophies have all had something to say about the nature of reality, whether it be the details of daily life or dimensions that exceed ordinary measurement. Still, ever since Plato, Western philosophers have struggled systematically to understand the relationship between appearance and reality. In the twentieth century, such issues are the central concern of the philosophy known as phenomenology (phenomena are literally *things as they appear*) and its off-shoot, existentialism. Both approaches investigate the role of perception in establishing reality. The phenomenology proposed by Edmund Husserl (1859–1938) described all consciousness as consciousness *of* something *by* someone and concluded that every object of study should be imagined in "brackets"—not as a thing in itself but as part of a relationship between perceiver and perceived.

The ethical implications of this view were taken up by the philosophers Martin Heidegger (1889–1976) and Jean-Paul Sartre (1905–1980), who questioned the meaning of existence in a world without preexisting truths, values, or moral laws. Existentialism's popular appeal in the 1940s and 1950s was undoubtedly enhanced by the fact that it was a philosophic attempt to recover clear vision—and a basis for action—in a perplexed and apparently meaningless world. The notion of philosophical absurdity corresponded to a very real confusion caused by the radical historical changes taking place in the first half of the century. By 1950, there had been two world wars, the second of which was truly global, and a sweeping realignment of geopolitical forces that saw the flourishing of Marxism and the establishment of major Communist states. Almost all the old monarchies had been overthrown and colonial empires were being dismantled as the emerging nations of Africa and Asia struggled for independence and self-definition. The wielders of authority became the enormous buck-passing bureaucracies of the modern state, multinational corporations, international governmental organizations, and ethnic alliances. Progress in transportation and telecommunications created but also shrank the global community. The rise of the modern industrial state set up new political, cultural, and economic tensions, the most important of which was a widening gulf between the West and "less developed" countries.

These changes in historical conditions had visible repercussions on modern literature and art. Cultural parochialism—the belief that there is only one correct view of the world (one's own)—was much harder to maintain when people traveled widely and experienced different ways of life. Racial and ethnic stereotypes were challenged, and traditional ideas of identity and social class broken down. Romantic heroism and aristocratic "rank" seemed irrelevant to soldiers who died anonymously in the trenches of World War I or civilians killed at a distance by bombing raids in both wars. The appropriate symbol for modern, impersonal warfare was the Tomb of the Unknown Soldier, first erected in Paris, after World War I, to honor the nameless soldiers who had died defending their country. In literature it was the "common man," not the Romantic hero, whose plight was portrayed. The conventional roles of the sexes also came under examination. Western women achieved civil rights they had been denied for centuries: the right to vote (1920 in the United States), the right to have bank accounts and to own and control their own property, the right to be educated equally with men, and the right to enter professions not previously open to them. When women held many jobs previously thought to be masculine ("Rosie the Riveter" was the subject of a famous American poster in World War II), it was no longer possible to pretend that they were incapable of work outside the home. Indeed, it was clear not only that women were quite capable but that they enjoyed taking responsibility in a variety of careers. Later in the century, the image of the emancipated Western woman would be presented as a shocking and even heretical example in traditional Mideastern and African societies; in contrast, the modern Communist Chinese state insisted on women's equality in the workplace. International organizations began to discuss, and women writers to describe, the situation of women in different countries.

A Century of Isms

The literary and artistic movements of the twentieth century are part of this evolution; they were shaped by it and helped shape it for others. Many flourished in Europe and America and were exported to other parts of the globe where they flourished or failed according to their relevance for local conditions. The twentieth century has been called by some a "century of isms," or of "vanguardism," reflecting the fact that so many different groups have tried to find an appropriate artistic response to contemporary history. European Expressionism, Dadaism, Surrealism, and Futurism—each worth exploring—are all different ways of expressing the "reality" of the world. Some appear very unreal at first glance, but all reveal an inner (presumably more important) truth than can be shown by documentary detail alone. Thus Expressionists refused the direct representation of reality, or even impressions of it (as in Impressionism), in favor of expressing an inner vision, emotion, or spiritual reality. *The Scream*, a painting by the Norwegian Edvard Munch (1863–1944), evokes a whole realm of spiritual agony. Expressionist writers bring out an underlying psychological distress that "objective" descriptions fail to capture, by letting emotion dictate the structure of their works, emphasizing rhythm, disrupted narrative line and broken syntax, and distorted imagery.

Futurism loudly proclaimed its enthusiasm for the dynamic new machine age. F. T. Marinetti (1876–1944) wrote in the first Futurist Manifesto (1908) that "a roaring motor car which seems to run on machine-gun fire is more beautiful than the Winged Victory of Samothrace" (a famous Greek statue). The Futurists' experiments in typography, in free association, in rapid shifts and breaks of syntax; their manipulation of sounds and word placement for special effects; their harshness and stark vision; and above all their eagerness to depict the new age were widely imitated.

Dada-Surrealism is the best known of the European "isms" and the only one to have followers today. Dada began in Zurich in 1916 as a movement of absolute revolt against Papa's Europe, and the word *dada* is a nonsense word that represents the disgust the Dadaists felt for the traditional middle-class values (patriotism, religion, morality, and rationalism) that they blamed for World War I. Dada set out to subvert authority and break all the rules (including those of art), hoping to liberate the creative imagination. Surrealists aimed especially to bring about a fuller awareness of human experience, including both conscious and unconscious states. In France, the Surrealist Manifestoes of 1924 and 1930 proclaimed that Surrealism was a means of expressing "the actual functioning of thought," "the total recuperation of our psychic force by a means that is nothing else than the dizzying descent into ourselves." André Breton, the Surrealist leader, had been a medical intern in a psychiatric clinic during World War I and was interested in Freud's theories of the unconscious. The Surrealists experimented with various means to liberate the unconscious imagination and reach a sublime state they called "the marvelous." Dream writing, automatic writing (writing rapidly and continuously whatever comes to mind), riddling games, interruption and collage, and chiefly the creation of startling images opened the mind to new possibilities. Surrealist language is structured to arouse the free play of the mind, and its antirational and open-ended style foreshadows the emphasis, in later "post-modernist" literature, on word play and radical language games.

Known for its intensity, playfulness, and openness to change, Surrealism has proved to be the most influential and enduring of all these movements, with adherents around the globe. Its impudent rejection of authority and rational thought inspired rebellious writers everywhere, especially in countries where the government linked correct thinking to realistic art. Surrealist influence has also spread beyond art and literature to advertising, fashion, and MTV, and the term *surrealist* has become a convenient word for unconventional or fantastic works that have no real connection with the movement.

Modernism is the accepted general term for the change in attitudes and artistic strategy that occurred in Europe and America at the beginning of the century. In its broadest sense, it embraces all the separate movements just described. Taken more narrowly, Modernism refers to a group of Anglo-American writers (many associated with the Imagists, 1908–17) who favored clear, precise images and "common speech" and who thought of the work primarily as an art object produced by consummate craft. James Joyce, Ezra Pound, T. S. Eliot, William Faulkner, and Virginia Woolf are examples of Anglo-American modernism and of the larger modernism, too. European modernists used language in an exploratory way, redefining the world of art much as the philosophers and scientists had redefined the world of their own disciplines. They disassembled in order to reconstruct, playing with shifting and contradictory appearances to suggest the shifting and uncertain nature of reality (Luigi Pirandello). They broke up the logically developing plot typical of the nineteenth-century novel and offered instead unexpected connections or sudden changes of perspective (Virginia Woolf). They used interior monologues and free association to express the rhythm of consciousness (Joyce, Woolf). They made much greater use of image clusters, thematic associations, and "musical" patterning to supply the basic structures of both fiction and poetry (Marcel Proust, Eliot). They drew attention to style instead of trying to make it invisible or "transparent" (Eliot, Bertolt Brecht). They blended fantasy with reality while representing real historical or psychological dilemmas (Franz Kafka). They raised age-old questions of human identity in terms of contemporary philosophy and psychology (Proust). And they explored ancient and non-Western literatures in search of universal themes and fresh modes of expression (Eliot). Whether their style was elaborate or spare, wordy or elliptical, abstract or concrete, modernist works displayed a highly self-conscious use of language, aiming not only to transform the way we see the world but also to change the way we understand language. This aspect of modernism gave it cultural as well as artistic impact, and young writers in other countries frequently adopted modernist techniques as a way to transform their own society's vision. Yet modernists in the early twentieth century are still close to nineteenth-century thought in one important respect. Their enterprise assumed, through all its fragmentation, a profoundly rich and unified core to human experience. Modernist experiments with perspective and language were carried on inside still-traditional concepts of individual psychological depth and of the art work as a coherent aesthetic whole. The combination of discontinuous, experimental style with a continuing belief in the wholeness of the human personality and of the art work carries with it the stamp of what we call the modernist (as opposed to the "postmodernist") tradition.

MODERNISM EXPANDS AND EVOLVES

The influence of Modernism, or other isms, on non-Western literary developments of the twentieth century has proved more varied. The smaller movements inside Western modernism lost their separate status when exported, becoming merely part of the whole mosaic of twentieth-century Western culture. This mosaic in turn meshed with local priorities such as an emerging national consciousness, religious tradition, or cultural customs, and the entire picture changed in the process. In some cases, Western literary models were adapted to represent the views of a particular national, religious, or ethnic group. In others, exposure to the West inspired a rediscovery of national literary traditions. In yet others, new ideologies of Western origin—social, political, religious, philosophical—had a much greater pollinating effect than any literary movement. While it is impossible to describe the full range of traditions included in this anthology, a few examples will indicate how modernism and modernity were refracted in twentieth-century non-Western civilizations.

Countries like Japan that attempted to reinvent themselves as equals of the materially advanced and economically powerful Western nations undertook a tortuous process of cultural absorption and transformation. Technology transfer and economic integration proved inseparable from institutional change and cultural diffusion. As the Japanese of the late nineteenth century learned the practical aspects of Western civilization—bookkeeping, smelting, cotton spinning, ship-building, principles of the joint-stock corporation—their curiosity about the world and their traditional receptivity to foreign ways soon transfigured the fabric of Japanese life.

For intellectuals, including writers, the real issue was not whether modernism offered a superior refraction of reality, although they would take advantage of modernist style when it suited them. More fundamental questions came to the fore. Cultural identity is a theme to which writers return again and again. Natsume Sōseki, perhaps the most introspective of Japan's modern novelists, frames the same question and concludes that each wave of Westernization hitting Japan is "like sitting at a dinner table and having one dish after another set before us and then taken away so quickly that, far from getting a good taste of each one, we can't even enjoy a clear look at what is being served. A nation, a people, that incurs a civilization like this can only feel a sense of emptiness, a dissatisfaction and anxiety." Yet it was a Western concept, individualism, that Japanese writers saw as the possible salvation. Part and parcel of Japan's modernization was its discovery of the emphasis that Western societies place on human beings as autonomous individual selves. For much of Japanese history, people in this conservative, group-oriented society were thought of as members of a unit (a clan, a fief, a class) who fitted somewhere quite precisely on a Confucian grid of relationships (between ruler and subject, father and son, husband and wife, elder brother and younger, friend and friend). The mesh of these two networks was the source of one's identity: an unproblematic part of a larger whole.

Modern Japanese novels describe a society mutating so fast that one generation after another must confront the confusion of new freedoms, new relationships, new dynamics, new challenges. In the early years of the century, language itself seemed unstable. Writers felt increasingly dissatisfied with the written medium at their disposal. It had become too florid, or baroque, too removed from everyday speech and, at the same time, both too restrictive and too playful to express the dilemmas of the new age. There was even talk of jettisoning Japanese in favor of English. In the end, through a convoluted process of language reform, literary style was streamlined into a more flexible and colloquial vehicle, producing literature that in its various aspects was the expression of a deeply felt need to grapple with the complexities of contemporary Japanese reality. For the last century, Japanese writers have struggled to assert the authenticity of the individual personality at the same time that they delineated the consequences of the liberation of the self: guilt, betrayal, loneliness, and alienation. Their modernism has as much in common with the realism of Ibsen and Chekhov as it does with the innovative strategies of Proust or Pirandello. Relying on the conceit of an accurate, detailed description of an external reality, combined with psychological appraisal of motivation, they offered their readers a valuable literary compass for situating the bewilderment of identity, self-interest, and "belonging" in a convulsive age of cultural ambiguity.

In twentieth-century China, on the other hand, modernization ended a feudal system that had controlled social and artistic expression for more than two thousand years. The Revolution of 1911 was only the first of many conflicts—revolutions, civil war, or differing programs of social reform, each harshly administered—reflecting the intellectual and political ferment as China emerged from the old Confucian order into the People's Republic of China. (The philosopher Confucius lived between 551 and 479 B.C.) Unchanging, however, was the social importance attributed to writing, which was expected to embody and preserve the core of Chinese cultural identity. This privileged position for literature, visibly different from the Western norm that distinguishes between artistic dedication and social responsibility, could be quite uncomfortable when the ruling powers (as earlier in Russia) enforced political guidelines for writers. The famous speech by Mao Zedong (1893–1976) at the Yan'an Forum on Literature and Art in 1942 warned Chinese writers to think positively and eliminate personal introspection from their work: it was the nation, not the individual, that should be the focus of their attention. The traditional Confucian concept of the ethical artist (like many other Confucian concepts) survives in modern China, although adapted to new circumstances and a greatly changed political scene.

Western readers are generally surprised to find that the Chinese government for thousands of years required literary examinations for any government post. Confucius had proposed an influential model of moral development and related social responsibility, and in 136 B.C., during the Han Dynasty of emperors, Confucianism was proclaimed the state doctrine. The Four Books of Confucian writings were prescribed subjects for the imperial civil service examinations from 1414 until the examinations themselves were abolished in 1905. Confucian principles defined the forms of education and the (mainly literary) examinations, governed the writing of history, prescribed social and family relationships, and extended the rules of family obedience to include obedience to the emperor as head of the "family" state. The literature favored by Confucianists was a subtly disciplined poetry (not fiction, which was thought trivial), and it was written in a refined and elegant classical Chinese whose mastery required years of study.

At the turn of the century, Chinese intellectuals who had traveled abroad began to adapt literary models encountered in Japan, Europe, and America. The most striking change in this first wave of literary modernization had political as well as literary importance: use of the vernacular (popular speech) in both poetry and prose, and depiction of social problems. Lu Xun's Diary of a Madman (1918) introduced the use of vernacular prose, and the modernist rhythms of its broken, hallucinated narrative gave a cannibalistic picture of Confucian social order. Poetry in the 1920s was not only written in the vernacular but also rejected classical prosody, which had been used for thousands of years; instead, it experimented with free verse, and echoed such foreign writers as Wordsworth, Whitman, Goethe, and Tagore. Playwrights who had read Ibsen and Chekhov dramatized contemporary social problems and the clash of opposed ideas against a realistic background. Yet this modern literature was not imitatively "Western" but rather an attempt by a new generation of writers to find different and perhaps fuller ways of expressing Chinese cultural experience. Their actions were never without political implications, both in this original opening up of traditional forms to a variety of different models and in the later turn away from Western examples toward a Marxist literature and political structure that seemed more congenial to China's group-oriented society.

With the formation of a League of Left-Wing Writers in 1930, Mao's proclamations at the Yan'an Forum, and the establishment of the Communist People's Republic of China under his control in 1949, a new conservatism in literature and art returned. Modernism in the Western sense of a liberal, experimental, and individually focused art was thought bourgeois, dilettantish, and antisocial—and was very dangerous to attempt. During the Cultural Revolution, writers and intellectuals who did not actively support socialist realism (the realistic depiction of the Communist state as a workers' paradise and of individuals as representative class figures) were imprisoned and persecuted. Very little was actually published, because little met the approval of the censors. Yet the People's Republic does not represent all Chinese literature, and writers in the Republic of China on Taiwan (some of whom had fled the mainland) followed their own path, writing a variety of prose fiction and founding a "Modernist School" in 1956 that sought a modern Chinese poetry "transplanted" from Europe rather than "inherited" from classical tradition. On the mainland, it was not until 1979 that writers felt free publicly to explore personal themes and use modernist forms. The risk of social disapproval has not disappeared: the campaign against "Spiritual Pollution" in 1983, the expulsion from the party of the prominent writer Liu Binyan in 1987, and the tight control over the translation and publication of minority literatures show otherwise. Yet contemporary Chinese writers are once more part of a worldwide community of artists as they strive to develop a literature that is both characteristically modern and characteristically Chinese.

The situation of modern India is quite different, linguistically and literarily. European trade had been active in India for almost two centuries before British political rule dominated the continent in 1800. Independence from Britain came only in 1947, and by then Western culture and technology had permeated the subcontinent. The civil service and educational system were British, and genera-tions of Indians—the future lawyers, teachers, writers, businesspeople, and govern-ment officials—had gone to Europe for university training. English was and remains the common language, the language used in government, although India itself is a mosaic of two hundred regional languages among which are Tamil, Gujarati, Oriya, Hindi, Bengali, Urdu, Kannada, and Sindhi. Some indigenous languages have no written form, and oral literature remains an important element in a society where a large part of the population is still illiterate. Indian works written in English, or translated into English (Indo-Anglian literature), can be read across regional linguistic barriers, and they have consequently come to represent Indian literature to the world outside India. Tagore, for example, who revolution-ized Bengali literature, is more widely known abroad for his works in English.

The long-standing political and linguistic link with Europe had foreseeable liter-ary results. Indian intellectuals were educated in the same Western heritage as Europeans, reading in recent literature Wordsworth, Baudelaire, Goethe, and Ibsen; and second, that Western literary forms—tragic drama, the short story, the realistic novel, and personal lyrics, together with the use of the vernacular—edged out the classical Indian traditions of epic, devotional poetry, and oral literature. Realistic novels analyzed Indian social problems, including caste barriers, the posi-tion of women, religious strife, and national identity. Personal and autobiographi-cal perspectives, psychological explorations, and depictions of modern society replaced a more impersonal focus on mythological or devotional subjects. Tradi-tional prosody gave way to experiments with new forms, including free verse. Writ-ten literature flourished, offering a wide range of perspectives as it adapted European genres to local topics and settings. The performance-oriented Indian aesthetic tradition, in contrast, moved into the background.

The might and prestige of the British Empire had another, obliquely demoraliz-ing effect on Indian cultural consciousness. The Empire's conviction that Western literature far outshone Indian tradition encouraged a general belief in the superior-ity of Western ways and a neglect if not outright suppression of indigenous litera-ture and languages. According to Lord Macaulay (1800–1859) in the previous century, a shelf of European masterworks was worth the whole of Indian art and literature: this attitude informed the education provided in British schools. Reac-tions, literary as well as political, were inevitable. Premchand (1880–1936), who established the realistic short story in Indian literature, used that form to describe the misery of peasant life under British bureaucracy; the bureaucracy responded by burning his first collection in 1909. Postcolonial writers (those writing after Indian independence) commonly attacked British colonial arrogance and, as part of rejecting capitalist colonialism, turned to Marxism for a vision of social structure that would correspond to the traditionally group-oriented nature of Indian society. Many authors wrote about the difficult position of women in public and private life, and the strain on interpersonal and family relationships, caused by conflicting social paradigms. Others returned to traditional religious themes and imagery in a modern landscape. One of the major self-imposed tasks of postcolonial literature has been to break free of European perspectives, to rediscover Indian traditions in art and literature, and finally to explore the implications of "Indianness" and also cultural ambiguity in a nation with so many competing cultures.

Whether it is a question of "Indianness" versus "Westernness" or of the multi-cultural identity that is now a global fact of life, Indian literature provides some of the most striking examples. The language of this literature is a hotly debated issue, as it is for African writers. Some critics assert that a truly Indian literature must be written in one of the ethnic languages and that indigenous experience cannot be accurately expressed in the colonizer's tongue. Despite the current government's encouragement of literary and linguistic pluralism, however, most of modern India's regional literature has not reached a wide audience because it is not available in translation—either into European or into other Indian languages. Who is to represent India, and to whom? The purist point of view rejects, perhaps rightly, the notion that Indian culture can be represented as a whole; yet it also denies the authenticity of Indian writers who choose to write in English. Some of these writers are major artists who ponder the question of "Indianness" in their own terms, whether as an assertion of traditional values or in the somber analysis of unfulfilled personal identities. Perhaps the most poignant example of intertwined literary cultures is Salman Rushdie, born a Muslim in 1947 in Bombay, India, who now lives in hiding in England because the modernist style, secular irony, and clashing cultural perspectives of his satiric novel *The Satanic Verses* (1988) caused conservative Muslim clerics to order his death for heresy. Throughout the twentieth century, in one form or another, questions of cultural identity and the challenge of a mixed heritage have been part of Indian literary tradition.

In the varied panorama of Middle Eastern countries, modernism and modernization have been linked as two categories of change brought by Western political and economic influence. It is the change of revolution, not evolution, and of a strong (though disputed) push to transform society rapidly in all aspects. The introduction of new generic forms like the novel and the modern short story, and the evolution, or modernization, of the older forms like poetry and drama, meant that Middle Eastern writers ceased to find their themes and forms principally within their own cultural tradition and attempted to internalize and naturalize an imported tradition. Initially, they seemed more drawn by content than form, or, rather, the structural looseness of modern Western poetry made it hard for Middle Eastern poets to see it as poetry at all. They were used to more highly codified forms of poetry, and for a long time they wrote politically engaged poems using traditional rhyme and meter. The link between modernist themes and modernist forms is so strong, however, that few poets now attempt to distinguish between them.

Writers sought an audience within the new middle class, for traditional aristocratic patronage had disappeared. Languages were transformed, sometimes acquiring a new alphabet; literary language became freer, more personal and colloquial; prose fiction, depicting everyday life and social issues, asserted itself in a tradition that had favored poetry and craftsmanship. In some ways, these changes are like those that took place in the West—the development of a new literary language, the recasting of the tradition's myths, the replacement of poetry with prose, the discovery of new heroes and antiheroes—but others are special to the non-Western world in its encounter with Western modernity: for example, the wrenching dislocations experienced by the first generations to be educated in the new learning. To accept Western modernity with its emphasis on the secular world, and its preference for the new, was to engage in a radical transformation of society and, with it, the near annihilation of traditional culture. Such a transformation has been the subject of a series of novels and short stories by the Egyptian writer Naguib Mahfouz (born 1911).

The encounter with European literature divided Middle Eastern intellectuals and writers into two camps: those who believed that the only hope of their respective communities lay in the wholehearted appropriation of Western culture and those who vehemently opposed it. Many in the former group began with the expectation that some essential elements of their native tradition could be maintained, but there were also many who were willing to jettison centuries of accumulated artistic tradition. According to an enthusiastic Turkish formula, citizens should "belong to the Turkish nation, the Moslem religion and European civilization." Modernism flourished in Turkey, where prose writers like Tawfiq al-Hakim

(1898–1989) recast traditional subjects in modern form and where vers libre, poetic realism, and surrealism found their way into an increasingly diverse poetry after World War II. The underlying tension is reaffirmed, however, by events in Iran (ancient Persia). Postwar Iranian poetry, inspired by European models, developed both a hermetic, Symbolist-inspired style and a poetry of social action. After the Islamic Revolution of 1979 brought religious traditionalists once more to power, however, the freedom to write in Western modes dwindled sharply and most modernist writers fled the country.

The most striking example of Westernization in the Mideast is surely the transformation of Turkey from a feudal society ruled by a sultan to a modern, thoroughly Westernized state. Kemal Ataturk, president of the Turkish Republic (1923–38), led the Turks into a radical secularization and separation from the past by changing the basis of the Turkish alphabet from Arabic to Latin. His stated intention was to return Turkey to its pre-Islamic roots, but the effect was that within a generation the Turks lost access to the literary tradition of the preceding six centuries and to the Arabic and Persian literature on which it had been nourished. (The same sort of deracination by alphabet reform occurred in the Islamic Republics of the USSR.) A more moderate response, and one that more nearly characterizes the approach of Mideast modernist poets and writers, was that of al-Hakim, who felt that Middle Eastern writers should both appropriate Western classical mythology and recast their own in modern forms. The aesthetic battle has largely been won, and by the modernizers, although current shifts in political climate may still bring about change (as in Iran).

It is not possible to discuss modern literature in the Middle East without mentioning Israel, whose political and cultural identity differs sharply from its neighbors'. Israel's past was biblical, not Koranic. Moreover, the first generation of Israeli poets and writers were not only influenced by European literature but had often grown up in that tradition themselves. Yet Israel's poets and writers have faced many of the same dilemmas as other Middle Eastern authors. In language, they have sought to create a new, colloquial idiom to replace the formal, elitist idiom they had inherited: Hebrew had not been used as a colloquial idiom for millennia. In literature, they undertook to give modern form to their inherited tradition. They shared with their Middle Eastern counterparts a commitment to use writing as a means of engaging in the discussion the central political questions of the time. Some of the most interesting writing in contemporary Israel is produced by writers of a mixed Israeli-Arab heritage who, like their peers in other regions, explore the richness and difficulty of multicultural identity in the modern world.

Modern African literature is probably better known to Western readers than writing from any other part of the globe, for a variety of reasons. The fact that many works were originally written in English, French, and Portuguese made them accessible to a wider audience. The African slave diaspora, which linked ethnic groups in Africa, the United States, and the Caribbean, created a far-flung audience with shared concerns. The colonial education system, which meant that many Europeans taught in African schools and many Africans went to European universities, generated a continuing cultural exchange. Finally, the fascination of European artists and intellectuals at the beginning of the century with the "otherness" of black African art and civilization became part of the European intellectual and artistic tradition. Many connections exist, but also an unmistakable separation. Black African writers' sense of a distinct, non-European, racially defined identity, a division partly imposed by European colonialism and partly by their own urge to define black culture, permeates the development of modern literature on this continent of mixed African, Arabic, and European heritage. No one can ignore the impact of race on African thought and literature, and the South African writer Nadine Gordimer is keenly aware of her own ambiguously privileged white perspective when she analyzes the shifting overtones of everyday relationships between black and white in a changing Africa.

The importance of "négritude," or consciousness of black identity, can hardly be overestimated. Coined by the Caribbean Aimé Césaire (born 1913) in his *Notebook of a Return to the Native Land* (1939), prefigured by earlier Harlem Renaissance writings about black cultural identity, affirmed and illustrated by Léopold Sédar Senghor (born 1906) in a widely influential anthology of 1948, the term is an amalgam of ideas derived from the passionate discussions of black intellectuals gathered in Paris during the 1920s and 1930s. Interpreted differently by different thinkers—as an absolute genetic inheritance or as an oppositional movement linked to specific historical circumstances—négritude provided a counterconcept to colonialist images of Western ethnic and cultural superiority. It crystallized the opposition and offered a positive definition of blackness around which art, literature, and philosophy could rally.

Négritude is most usefully understood as a powerful concept and a reference point rather than as absolute reality. After centuries of intermingled traditions, it is difficult for any society to wrest apart fused layers of cultural identity. (This fact many Indian authors have recognized about their own postcolonial condition, as have Chinese authors after attempting to root out Confucianism.) Senghor himself has frequently described the two voices, African and French, that resonate in his poetry, and while his experience may be the best known, it is not unique. Birago Diop, Wole Soyinka, Césaire, Chinua Achebe, Derek Walcott, and Kamau Brathwaite also express, in different ways, the interweaving of European and black African or Caribbean identities.

One of the more pressing issues for black African writers has been the use of language. This is not a debate over style, or the language of European modernism with its ruptures, broken images, and stream of consciousness. Such stylistic concerns have less significance here than other social, quasi-existential, themes of personal and cultural identity. The immediate issue is whether to write in the European languages they have learned from childhood—which are now associated with colonialism—or, by translating earlier texts, writing in an African language, or emphasizing performance, to recreate an indigenous artistic tradition. Senghor echoes this tradition when he composes poetry on African themes that is intended to be chanted before a group and accompanied by musical instruments. Some authors follow the example of the Kenyan Ngugi wa Thiongo (born 1938), who chooses now to write in Gikuyu after having made a reputation as a novelist in English; others, like Diop (1906–1992) and Wole Soyinka (born 1934), join to their own work in French and English the translation and adaptation of folk tales; still others, like Chinua Achebe, write about African topics in a European language permeated by their own indigenous references and turns of speech. To the extent that this twentieth-century literature is chiefly a *written* literature, exploiting the genres of novel, drama, short story, essay and lyric poetry, the question of language is already compromised by a link with European culture. African tradition (like that of India) emphasized oral and performance-oriented art. Modern African literature, like that of other postcolonial societies, incorporates the dynamism and internal tensions of an evolving society in which indigenous traditions, the colonial heritage, and an ongoing intellectual and artistic ferment coexist as parts of a common history.

In the West, modernism was transformed after midcentury, partly in the normal course of literary evolution and partly under the pressure of changing historical circumstances. With the passage of time, the modernist world no longer seemed "modern" (hence the invention of the term *postmodern*). Writers in the 1960s considered their predecessors in the earlier half century—Proust, Eliot, Woolf, and Mann—part of a relatively concentrated "high Modernism" that emphasized formal innovation but preserved roots in conservative mainstream thought. Nor did the focus on European tradition go unchallenged, as other regions reasserted their own cultural aims. Seen from a non-Western perspective, the modernist search for profound reality no longer appeared revolutionary: instead, it was the latest development of a Western tradition reaching back to Homer and the Bible. Seeking a common image of essential human nature seemed utopian in a world where more than six thousand languages were spoken and where (by 1994) the United Nations had 184 member nations.

Other political and economic changes have had their effect. The first half of the century was marked by two world wars that enlisted forces around the globe in two large alliances, and the Cold War that succeeded World War II also cast global conflict in terms of two superpowers, the United States and the U.S.S.R. This relatively monolithic opposition was not to endure. The breakup of colonial empires (and of the U.S.S.R. in 1991), the creation of many new nations eager to assert their identity, and the emergence of new centers of trade (Japan, the oil-producing Middle Eastern countries acting together as OPEC) distributed power throughout a more diverse system. Nor were nations necessarily the holders of power, for the second half of the century saw the rise of multinational corporations whose chief loyalty was to business, and of transnational religious movements (like Islamic fundamentalism) that fought to assume authority in formerly secular states. The United Nations provided a forum in which global issues were publicly discussed, and television spread the images around the world. The developing countries of Africa, Asia, and Latin America, possessing many of the world's resources but few industries or corporate structures, called on the former colonial states to share their wealth and expertise. International agencies coordinated aid in the face of environmental catastrophes, epidemics, and famine; crime organizations also operated internationally; and the image of shared global problems moved into the foreground. Thousands of people migrated from poorer countries to seek jobs in wealthier regions, bringing different cultural groups in contact at the same time that they changed local economies. A host of smaller wars, sometimes driven by religious or ethnic allegiances that led to genocide or "ethnic cleansing," forced millions from their homes, and in 1994 the United Nations reported that 1 out of every 114 people in the world had been displaced by military conflict. Individuals were no longer so tied to their native countries; for some, their countries had disappeared in new political arrangements and for others, their simultaneous ties to more than one country created a new dimension of bicultural, hybrid, or "migrant" identity. Mass culture, radio, and television stretched to every part of the globe, often effacing local traditions as they introduced people to a broader horizon. With the disappearance of an old world order, the political picture became at once more fragmented and more interconnected, a situation that is reflected in contemporary literature and art.

Postmodernism

The term *postmodernism* has been proposed to suggest this change, defining an attitude that derives from modernist thought but turns away from it in several important ways. Even if the term is still debated (and more widely accepted by critics than by writers), to contrast modernism with postmodernism can illuminate many of the themes and strategies present in contemporary literature. Where modernism tries to reveal a core of profound experience through innovative form, postmodernism is suspicious of claims of "profundity," which it associates with hidden value judgments (calling something "profound" implies that the speaker finds it specially true and valuable). Consequently, postmodernist writers who avoid the search for "profundity" tend to avoid images of depth and prefer to describe inconclusive surface images. Similar contrasts between modernism and postmodernism (sometimes called *poststructuralism*) are drawn between principles of *construction* and *deconstruction*, *center*, and *dissemination* or more generally between the concept of an organic whole dependent on a central motivating principle and a web of shifting relationships depicted without a frame or center. Throughout, the postmodernist notion is that modernism's emphasis on meaningful aesthetic form anchored in a central vision suggests an image of human experience that is too finished, too symmetrical — that a human reality which is basically "jagged" (Ezra Pound's term) needs to be represented in all its incompleteness and rough edges. Postmodernist art, although it rejects the concept of "art" or "aesthetic" completion, has its own recognizable style, one that favors visual and verbal strategies that undermine all forms of certainty.

This shift of artistic sensibility takes to its logical conclusion the modernist's use of fragmentation and discontinuity. Both modernist and postmodernist thinkers are indebted to the evolution of scientific thought in the twentieth century and most of all to its emphasis on randomness and shifting perceptions. The physicist Werner Heisenberg's uncertainty principle (mentioned earlier) stresses the *approximate* nature of any description of reality as well as the fact that the observer's position relative to what is observed changes from moment to moment. The mathematician Kurt Gödel describes the ultimate incompleteness (and, therefore, lack of authority) of all logical systems. A similar emphasis on shifting patterns of perception appears in the later development of Freudian psychoanalysis with the concepts of transference and countertransference. Here, attention is displaced from subconscious and instinctual drives to the concept of dialogue and exchange. Therapists no longer "cure" patients of specific psychoses, but engage them in a process of self-definition through interaction with others. Finally, semiotics, literally a science of *signs*, studies the "gamelike" construction of meaning and is undoubtedly the purest expression of postmodern consciousness.

The *literature* called postmodernist displays an impersonal, coolly decentered, or self-reflexive style with frequent gaps and endless ramifications. It stresses shifts and the play of surfaces, rather than asserting any specific version of reality; it avoids commitment. Postmodernist *theory* covers more than one style of literary expression and is in fact a philosophy of knowledge. In contrast to the dominant Kantian tradition, this philosophy emphasizes relationships but not coherence, particulars but not universality, instability rather than system, internal contradictions rather than harmony, and, throughout, constant change. It expresses what the poet W. H. Auden called an "age of anxiety," analyzing that age and its preoccupation with questions of identity. Postmodernist theory is fascinated by claims of cultural specificity (specificity implies difference) and also by the simultaneous occurrence of more than one cultural perspective; it studies the relationship of interwoven traditions, and it undertakes to unfold layers of complicity and contradiction in any text, no matter how reputedly "pure."

Postmodernist critics suggest that contemporary works not only are different but that they should be read differently from earlier ones. The modernist author guides and controls the reader's response while the postmodernist author creates an "open" work with alternate meanings, so that the reader, by decoding, shares in "writing" a new text. The line is not always easy to draw, however: Luigi Pirandello, Marcel Proust, Bertolt Brecht, and particularly Franz Kafka and James Joyce are modernist writers who have also been called precursors of postmodernism.

Readers will find that there are certain easily identified strategies at work in this literature, strategies whose general aim is to avoid creating any sense of completeness or central reference point. Just as there is no unified authorial perspective, so individual characters do not develop psychologically as they would be expected to in a nineteenth-century realistic work. There is no plot, and the narrative line is not patterned by a beginning, middle, and end; overall, there is no sense of action developing toward a logical conclusion. The ambiguity of appearances is heightened by putting history and fantasy on the same level (Borges). Style can be allusive, disrupted, contradictory, and confusing, as if to disorient a reader who might wish to extract a single authorized meaning.

All these strategies actually serve to engage readers in a new and challenging way. They refuse to provide a coherent interpretation of reality, and offer instead a collection of ambiguously related fragments, strangely emphasized silences, and merely *potential* themes. The burden, in fact, is placed squarely and openly on the reader to construct a meaning. Similar challenges are evident in Brecht's "alienation technique," which, by refusing to let spectators lose themselves in dramatic illusion, forces them to interpret events in a wider (in this case political) context. These forms are built on a calculated refusal of easy coherence, an apparently nihilistic "antiform," which in fact requires a great deal of artistic patterning to be convincing. Some of these texts have been called "antiliterature" for their refusal to provide the aesthetic completion suggested by the term *literature*. Incompleteness and a delight in ambiguity do not exclude strong impressions of moral or cultural judgment. Borges, often considered the originator of postmodernism in his labyrinthine, self-reflexive style, includes a subtle contrast of cultural and national prejudices in The Garden of Forking Paths. And a truly random work, however, would be nothing more than a collection of unrelated words (like Tzara's Dada poem, created from newspaper clippings shaken in a paper bag). To impress the reader with the fact that the world does *not* correspond to neatly packaged artistic representations, the authors of "incomplete" literature—with complete logic—devise new artistic forms to focus our attention on the artificiality of any "total" perspective.

There are also contemporary authors who draw primarily on other traditions. Writers like Kojima Nobuo and Naguib Mahfouz rely on the style of the realistic novel as they lament the difficulty of preserving individual dignity and cultural values in a world of rapidly interpenetrating societies. Nadine Gordimer describes, with similar realism, the human cost of living in a racially torn community. Extending twentieth-century attempts to recapture and preserve ethnic traditions (such as that represented by the Navaho "Night Chant"), many writers choose to recreate or adapt American Indian legends.

Faith in a common version of reality has faded in the literature of the second half of the century, where it more and more appears that we will rediscover human nature only by juxtaposing many diverse and fluid images. The realistic representation of issues involving women and their position in society—or of gender relationships themselves—emerges with particular force in this part of the century. "Masculine" and "feminine" behavior—defined, as anthropologists have shown, so differently in different societies—is more likely to be a topic for analysis and not just a preexisting role into which characters must fit. Feminist critics have also taken a new look at canonical texts, asking, for example, what it means when heroic protagonists are almost always men and when women (unless they die, or subside into obscurity at the end of the drama) are supporting characters in a masculine narrative. Without diminishing the picture of social reality in earlier twentieth-century literature, it is still possible to say that recent years have brought an unprecedented recognition of different ethnic, sexual, and cultural identities, both as political facts and as the subject matter of literature. This recognition has transformed our understanding of "Western" world literature, as regional and ethnic identities (for example, African-American, Yiddish, Chicano, Québecois, and native American literatures) represent their traditional self-images and values. What was once a simpler model of the Western heritage has turned out, on examination, to be much more heterogeneous and much more interesting.

What does this mean for the concept of masterpiece? Each of the major civilizations has works that it considers, and other traditions consider, to be of enduring value and more than local interest. A masterpiece, in brief, speaks not only to its own time and time-bound audience, but to future generations and other cultures. It lasts; it travels well.

Some critics locate this strength in a work's aesthetic character and power of reference: the scope and complexity of its external and internal relations, and the compound impression of interactivating thought, shape, feel, and sound that it imposes on—and awakens in—the mind. In this more technical perspective, a "masterpiece" continues to be relevant because it constitutes a coherent structure of reference and representation that is neither easily exhausted nor tied to a single context. Other critics locate a work's strength in its ability to inform us about ourselves and our fellow human beings, about the terror and wonder of the universe we live in, the miseries it is possible to suffer, the grandeurs it is possible to attain: all this through an imaginative sharing of experience that is qualitatively different from historical or anthropological perspectives. In this definition, a masterpiece remains a masterpiece as long as it provides mature insight into the condition, the plight, the art of being human.

Each of these emphases is valid, but incomplete. Works in this anthology possess inexhaustibly challenging structures of dynamic reference that bring to imaginative life a variety of intellectual and moral concerns of lasting importance. As recent revisionary readings of many canonical masterworks show (for example, the Greek dramatists, or Shakespeare), works having both these dimensions continue to respond to the most diverse and often confrontational approaches. The major works of twentieth-century literature will encounter similar tests in a hundred years.

The intricate meeting of cultures, lively interaction of ethnic, sexual, or racial identities, and inquiries into the nature of art and language have combined to create a global literature that in its insistent teasing-out of contradictory layers of reality corresponds to the diversity of our new geopolitical age with its philosophy of openness and change.

FURTHER READING

Monique Chefdor, Ricardo Quinones, Albert Wachtel, eds., *Modernism: Challenges and Perspectives* (1986), offers valuable essays on international modernism. David Hayman, *Re-Forming the Narrative: Toward a Mechanics of Modernist Fiction* (1987), proposes five tactics that distinguish modernist narrative from earlier fiction. Harry Levin, "What Was Modernism?" (1962, rep. in *Refractions*, 1966), is a survey of modernist writers as humanists and inheritors of the Enlightenment. H. H. Arnason, *History of Modern Art: Painting, Sculpture, Architecture* (1977, illustrated), follows the evolution of the arts in the West from the nineteenth century to the 1960s. Matei Calinescu, *Five Faces of Modernity* (1987), is an informative collection of essays on the aesthetics of modernism, avant-garde, decadence, and kitsch. Peter Nicholls, *Modernisms* (1995), offers an informative and analytic overview of twentieth-century modernisms. Morton P. Levitt, *Modernist Survivors: The Contemporary Novel in England, the United States, France, and Latin America* (1987), analyzes the impact of literary modernism and the continuity of humanist values. James F. Knapp, *Literary Modernism and the Transformation of Work* (1988), examines work-related themes in English and American modernist literature and modernism's contradictory attitudes toward a changing economic order. Harry R. Garvin, ed., *Romanticism, Modernism, Postmodernism* (1980), is a collection of essays that attempts to define changing views of the artistic imagination.

Marjorie Perloff, *The Poetics of Indeterminacy* (1981), has significance beyond its primary focus on contemporary English and American poetry stemming from the French tradition. See also Perloff, ed., *Postmodern Genres* (1989), for a collection of essays on postmodernism in art and literature. Ihab and Sally Hassan, eds., *Essays in Innovation/Renovation: New Perspectives on the Humanities* (1983), explores change in contemporary Western culture. Susan Rubin Suleiman, *Subversive Intent: Gender, Politics, and the Avant-garde* (1990), analyzes the cultural implications of avant-garde artistic practices. Nancy K. Miller, ed., *The Poetics of Gender* (1986), presents essays on various aspects of feminist criticism. Elise Boulding, *The Underside of History: A View of Women through Time* (1992), complements traditional histories by drawing attention to the position and contributions of women. Frederick Buell, *National Culture and the New Global System* (1994), analyzes literary examples in a discussion of twentieth-century cultural globalization that moves beyond the concept of "three worlds." Sarah Lawall, ed., *Reading World Literature: Theory, History, Practice* (1994), includes a theoretical introduction to the subject of world literature and twelve essays on specific topics. Janheinz Jahn, *Muntu: African Culture and the Western World*, trans. Marjorie Grene (1990, orig. 1961), is an influential discussion of the interface of two cultures. J. M. Roberts, *History of the World* (1993), is an up-to-date history of world events in a contemporary perspective.

TEXTS	CONTEXTS
1893 Rabindranath Tagore, **Punish-ment**	
1895 Higuchi Ichiyō, *Child's Play*	
ca. 1897–1902 Washington Matthews conducts studies of the Navajo **Night Chant**	1899–1902 Boer War in South Africa 1900 Boxer uprisings in China protest European presence • Max Planck proposes quantum theory, the first step in the discovery of the atom
1902 Joseph Conrad, *Heart of Darkness*	
1903 Henry James, *The Ambassadors*	1903 Wright brothers invent the powered airplane
1905 Sigmund Freud, *Dora (Fragment of an Analysis of a Case of Hysteria)* • F. T. Marinetti, *Futurist Manifesto*	1905 Modern labor movement begins with foundation of International Workers of the World (IWW) • Partition of Bengal based on Hindu and Muslim populations
1907 August Strindberg, *The Ghost Sonata*	1907 Japanese immigration to the United States prohibited
1908 Gertrude Stein, *Three Lives*	
	1909 Commercial manufacture of plastic begins
	1910 China abolishes slavery • Mexican Revolution (1910–11) • NAACP founded in United States • Post-Impressionist Exhibition in London
	1911 Revolution establishes Chinese Republic after 267 years of Manchu rule
1912 Rabindranath Tagore, *Gitanjali*	1912–1913 Balkan wars
1913 Marcel Proust, **Swann's Way**, first volume of *Remembrance of Things Past* (1913–27) • Thomas Mann, *Death in Venice* • D. H. Lawrence, *Sons and Lovers*	
	1914–1918 World War I involves Europe, Turkey, and the United States

TEXTS	CONTEXTS
	1915 Albert Einstein formulates general theory of relativity • First transcontinental phone call, in America
1916 Franz Kafka, *The Metamorphosis* • James Joyce, *A Portrait of the Artist as a Young Man*	
1917 T. S. Eliot, *Prufrock and Other Observations*	1917 Russian Revolution overthrows Romanov Dynasty
1918 Lu Xun, *Diary of a Madman*, the first story in Chinese vernacular	1918 Women over 30 given vote in Great Britain
	1918–1920 Global influenza epidemic kills millions
	1919 League of Nations formed (U.S. Senate rejects membership, 1920)
1920 Edith Wharton, *The Age of Innocence*	1920 Mahatma Gandhi leads India's struggle for independence from Britain
1921 Luigi Pirandello, *Six Characters in Search of an Author*	1921–1929 Harlem Renaissance, black literary and artistic movement
1921–1924 Knud Rasmussen documents Inuit culture and collects Inuit Songs during the Fifth Thule Expedition	
1922 T. S. Eliot, *The Waste Land* • Paris publication of James Joyce, *Ulysses* (imported copies burned in U.S. Post Office) • Rainer Maria Rilke, *Sonnets to Orpheus*	1922 Turkey becomes a republic • Irish Free State established • USSR formed • Discovery of Egyptian pharaoh Tutankhamen's tomb
1923 Rainer Maria Rilke, *Duino Elegies*	1923 Earthquakes destroy centers of Tokyo and Yokohama
1924 Thomas Mann, *The Magic Mountain* • André Breton, *First Surrealist Manifesto* • Premchand, *The Road to Salvation*	1924 Insecticides first used
1925 *Geriguigatugo* and other tales narrated by Úke Iwágu Úo published in Italian and Bororo	

TEXTS	CONTEXTS
1926 Franz Kafka, *The Castle*	
1927 Virginia Woolf, *To the Lighthouse*	
1928 William Butler Yeats, *The Tower*	1928 Sixty-five states sign Kellogg-Briand antiwar pact in Paris • First Five Year Plan in USSR • Penicillin discovered • First scheduled television broadcasts
1929 William Faulkner, *The Sound and the Fury*	1929 Stock market crash heralds beginning of world economic crisis; Great Depression lasts until 1937
1932 Zuni Ritual Poetry published by anthropologist Ruth L. Bunzel	
1933 Federico García Lorca, *Blood Wedding*	1933 Adolf Hitler given dictatorial powers in Germany • Nazis build first concentration camps
	1934 Stalin begins purges of Communist Party
1935–1947 Kawabata Yasunari, *Snow Country*	
1936 Premchand, *The Cow* • Leo Frobenius, *History of African Civilizations*	
1937 Wallace Stevens, *The Man with the Blue Guitar*	
1939 Aimé Césaire, *Notebook of a Return to the Native Land*	1939 Germany invades Poland and all Europe is drawn into World War II
1940 Richard Wright, *Native Son*	
1941 Bertolt Brecht, **Mother Courage and Her Children**	1941 United States and Japan enter World War II
1942 Albert Camus, *The Stranger*	
1943 T. S. Eliot, *Four Quartets*	
1944 Jorge Luis Borges, **The Garden of Forking Paths** • Ralph Ellison, *King of the Bingo Game*	

TEXTS	CONTEXTS
1945 Leopold Sedar Senghor, *Chants d'ombre*	1945 World War II ends with dropping of atomic bombs on Hiroshima and Nagasaki • United Nations, Arab League founded
	1946 Churchill's "Iron Curtain" speech marks beginning of Cold War • Pan-African Federation formed
1947 Birago Diop, *Tales of Amadou Koumba*	1947 Religious massacres accompany partition of India and Pakistan into independent states • Transistor invented
1948 Ezra Pound, *Pisan Cantos*	1948 Creation of Jewish state in Palestine
	1949 Communist People's Republic of China established • Apartheid instituted in South Africa
	1950–1953 Korean War involves North and South Korea, the United Nations, and China
1952 Ralph Ellison, *Invisible Man*	1952 Revolution in Egypt, which becomes a republic in 1953 • First hydrogen bomb
	1953 Discovery of DNA structure launches modern genetic science
1954 Kojima Nobuo, **The American School**	
1955 Alain Robbe-Grillet, *The Voyeur*	
1956 Tanizaki Jun'ichiro, *The Key*	1956 First Congress of Black Writers meets in Paris
1956–1957 Naguib Mahfouz, *The Cairo Trilogy*	
1957 Samuel Beckett, *Endgame* • Albert Camus, *Exile and the Kingdom*, which includes *The Guest*	
1958 Chinua Achebe, **Things Fall Apart**	1958 European Common Market established • Algerian War of Independence (1958–62)

THE NIGHT CHANT

Navajo ceremonialism, like Iroquois law and Maya architecture, ranks among the glories of native American achievement. Esteemed for its therapeutic values and duly respected by Western medicine, it has proved a magnet for students of religion and an inexhaustible field for research in the arts and various sciences. Directed primarily toward healing and the restoration of harmony between individuals and the environment, the ceremonies of Mountainway, Beautyway, Enemyway, and Blessingway, to name only a few of the better known, create a spiritual universe of song, prayer, drama, and graphic art, rooted in an oral literature of epic proportions. With its induction of new initiates, its unique all-night sing, and its lofty portrayal of deities, the famous Nightway occupies a place of honor among these "ways," or "chants," and some observers have regarded Nightway as the most important of them all.

Literally rendered "night-way chant," the name is almost always abbreviated to "nightway" in Navajo usage but was called *Night Chant* by its preeminent translator, Washington Matthews (whose Night Chant studies were conducted mainly during the 1890s). It was Matthews who translated the phrase "walk in beauty," often reiterated by poets and occasionally used as a salutation by speakers of English outside the Navajo community.

The shared quest for *beauty*—a broad term that includes "perfection," "normality," "success," and "well-being"—as exemplified by the Night Chant and other ceremonials, is reflected in the remarkable vitality of the Navajo nation and its culture. The Navajo reservation, located in northern Arizona and adjacent New Mexico, is the largest in the contiguous United States; it is the most populous and has the greatest number of native speakers. Farming, sheep ranching, weaving, and silversmithing have long been important industries in the Navajo homeland. The staging of the ceremonials has also been a noteworthy, if small, element in the economy. Ceremonialism, at least in theory, provides a livelihood for the specialist, or chanter, who must organize dancers, singers, and other helpers, whose services are paid for by a sponsor, or host.

Although the chant is attended by a large audience of relatives, friends, and visitors, its power is aimed primarily at a single person, usually called "the patient" in anthropological writings. Each of the Navajo ceremonials is said to be effective against a particular group of disorders; in the case of the Night Chant, paralytic stroke and ailments of the head. So narrow a view of its virtues, however, is belied by the wide interest it evokes and by the constant demand for performances. In the late twentieth century, its practitioners are being called on throughout the winter, with as many as half a dozen Night Chants in progress at any given moment, and bookings for a chant must be made two years in advance. Abbreviated versions may be ordered on shorter notice. Evidently, the chant in its full form is not an emergency therapy; among its more obvious benefits are the prestige it brings to the host who sponsors it and the opportunities it provides for cultural reaffirmation, socializing, and general spiritual revival.

Performed only in fall or winter, the nine-day Night Chant falls into two four-day parts, followed by a climactic ninth-night reprise, the night of nights, in which the long-awaited spirit of thunder is summoned. At this point the ceremony breaks free in a torrent of song continuing unabated until dawn. In part 1 the emphasis is on rites that exorcise evil influences and invoke the distant gods. Part 2 is distinguished by spacious and intricate sand paintings, made of dry pigments sprinkled on the earth. The paintings depict the gods and enable the patient to merge with their divine invulnerability. Through it all, the ceremonial leader, or chanter,

directs the included song recitals and intones the prescribed prayers. The two
selections printed here are the prayer to thunder that begins the final night and
the last of the Finishing Songs that bring it to a close.

A text of the Night Chant may be read in John Bierhorst, *Four Masterworks of
American Indian Literature* (1974). The selections printed here are from Washington Matthews, *The Night Chant: A Navaho Ceremony* (1902). For survey articles
on ceremonialism and other Navajo topics, see Alfonso Ortiz, ed., *Southwest*, vol.
10 of *Handbook of North American Indians* (1983). James C. Faris, *The Nightway:
A History and a History of Documentation of a Navajo Ceremonial* (1990), brings
Night Chant scholarship up to date.

From The Night Chant[1]

Prayer to Thunder[2]

＊   ＊   ＊

In Tsegíhi,[3]
In the house made of the dawn,
In the house made of the evening twilight,
In the house made of the dark cloud,
In the house made of the he-rain,   5
In the house made of the dark mist,
In the house made of the she-rain,[4]
In the house made of pollen,[5]
In the house made of grasshoppers,
Where the dark mist curtains the doorway,   10
The path to which is on the rainbow,
Where the zigzag lightning stands high on top,
Where the he-rain stands high on top,
Oh, male divinity![6]
With your moccasins of dark cloud, come to us.   15
With your leggings of dark cloud, come to us.
With your shirt of dark cloud, come to us.
With your headdress of dark cloud, come to us.
With your mind enveloped in dark cloud, come to us.
With the dark thunder above you, come to us soaring.   20
With the shapen cloud at your feet, come to us soaring.
With the far darkness made of the dark cloud
    over your head, come to us soaring.
With the far darkness made of the he-rain
    over your head, come to us soaring.
With the far darkness made of the dark mist
    over your head, come to us soaring.
With the far darkness made of the she-rain
    over your head, come to us soaring.   25
With the zigzag lightning flung out on high
    over your head, come to us soaring.

---

1. Both selections translated by Washington Matthews.   2. In performance each line of the prayer is
first recited by the chanter, then repeated by the patient.   3. Pronounced *tsay-gee'-hee*, a distant canyon and site of the *house made of dawn* (line 2), a prehistoric ruin, regarded as the home of deities.
4. Rain without thunder. *He-rain:* rain with thunder.   5. Emblem of peace, of happiness, of prosperity [Translator's note].   6. Thunder, regarded as a bird.

With the rainbow hanging high over your head,
　　come to us soaring.
With the far darkness made of the dark cloud on
　　the ends of your wings, come to us soaring.
With the far darkness made of the he-rain on
　　the ends of your wings, come to us soaring.
With the far darkness made of the dark mist on
　　the ends of your wings, come to us soaring.　　　　　　　　　30
With the far darkness made of the she-rain on
　　the ends of your wings, come to us soaring.
With the zigzag lightning flung out on high on
　　the ends of your wings, come to us soaring.
With the rainbow hanging high on the ends of
　　your wings, come to us soaring.
With the near darkness made of the dark cloud, of
　　the he-rain, of the dark mist, and of the
　　she-rain, come to us.
With the darkness on the earth, come to us.　　　　　　　　　35
With these I wish the foam floating on the flowing
　　water over the roots of the great corn.
I have made your sacrifice.
I have prepared a smoke[7] for you.
My feet restore for me.
My limbs restore for me.　　　　　　　　　　　　　　　　　40
My body restore for me.
My mind restore for me.
My voice restore for me.
Today, take out your spell for me.
Today, take away your spell for me.　　　　　　　　　　　　45
Away from me you have taken it.
Far off from me it is taken.
Far off you have done it.
Happily I recover.
Happily my interior becomes cool.　　　　　　　　　　　　50
Happily my eyes regain their power.
Happily my head becomes cool.
Happily my limbs regain their power.
Happily I hear again.
Happily for me *the spell*[8] is taken off.　　　　　　　　　　55
Happily may I walk.
Impervious to pain, may I walk.
Feeling light within, may I walk.
With lively feelings, may I walk.
Happily abundant dark clouds I desire.　　　　　　　　　　60
Happily abundant dark mists I desire.
Happily abundant passing showers I desire.
Happily an abundance of vegetation I desire.
Happily an abundance of pollen I desire.
Happily abundant dew I desire.　　　　　　　　　　　　　65
Happily may fair white corn, to the ends of the
　　earth, come with you.

---

7. Painted reed filled with native tobacco, offered as a sacrifice.　　8. Words added by the translator.

Happily may fair yellow corn, to the ends of the
   earth, come with you.
Happily may fair blue corn, to the ends of the
   earth, come with you.
Happily may fair corn of all kinds, to the ends
   of the earth, come with you.
Happily may fair plants of all kinds, to the ends
   of the earth, come with you.   70
Happily may fair goods of all kinds, to the ends
   of the earth, come with you.
Happily may fair jewels of all kinds, to the ends
   of the earth, come with you.
With these before you, happily may they come
   with you.
With these behind you, happily may they come
   with you.
With these below you, happily may they come
   with you.   75
With these above you, happily may they come
   with you.
With these all around you, happily may they
   come with you.
Thus happily you accomplish your tasks.
Happily the old men will regard you.
Happily the old women will regard you.   80
Happily the young men will regard you.
Happily the young women will regard you.
Happily the boys will regard you.
Happily the girls will regard you.
Happily the children will regard you.   85
Happily the chiefs will regard you.
Happily, as they scatter in different directions,
   they will regard you.
Happily, as they approach their homes, they will
   regard you.
Happily may their roads home be on the trail of pollen.
Happily may they all get back.   90
In beauty I walk.
With beauty before me, I walk.
With beauty behind me, I walk.
With beauty below me, I walk.
With beauty above me, I walk.   95
With beauty all around me, I walk.
It is finished in beauty,
It is finished in beauty,
It is finished in beauty,
It is finished in beauty.   100

Finishing Song

   From the pond in the white valley—
   The young man doubts it—
   He takes up his sacrifice,

With that he now heals.
With that your kindred thank you now.   5

From the pools in the green meadow[9] —
The young woman doubts it—
He takes up his sacrifice,[1]
With that he now heals.
With that your kindred thank you now.   10

9. A contrast of landscapes, of the beginning and end of a stream. It rises in a green valley in the mountains and flows down to the lower plains, where it spreads into a single sheet of water. As the dry season approaches, it shrinks, leaving a white saline efflorescence called alkali. The male is associated with the sterile, unattractive alkali flat in the first stanza, while the female is named with the pleasant mountain meadow in the second stanza [adapted from Translator's note]. 1. The deity accepts the sacrificial offering (see n. 7, p. 2616) and effects the healing that benefits the patient and his kindred — though young men and young women, with the irreverence of youth, may doubt the truth of the ceremony.

RABINDRANATH TAGORE

1861–1941

The preeminent figure in the history of modern literature in Bengali (the language of the state of West Bengal in eastern India, and of the neighboring nation of Bangladesh), poet and novelist Rabindranath Tagore has deeply influenced writers in the other Indian languages as well. Winner of the Nobel prize for literature in 1913, Tagore is also perhaps the Indian writer whose name is likely to be familiar to most readers in the West. No less a poet than W. B. Yeats was responsible for Tagore's fame in European and American literary circles, but Tagore did not wear well in translation. He was mistakenly perceived as a mystical poet, Western tastes in poetry changed rather rapidly, and, in spite of the many translations of his poetry and fiction that appeared in English and other European languages after 1913, few outside of Bengal have been aware of Tagore's achievement as a writer or of his substantial contributions to the history of ideas in the modern age.

Tagore was born in Calcutta, the capital of British India in the nineteenth century, into an illustrious Hindu family. The Tagores were pioneers of the Bengal Renaissance, a movement led by Bengali intellectuals who were in many ways shaped by English education, which had been introduced in Bengal by the British government, but who at the same time reacted with profound ambivalence to colonial rule and the imposition of Western cultural norms on Indians. Through their writings, and through the institutions they founded, the leaders of the Renaissance sought to refashion Indian society to meet the challenges of the modern world, but to do so without losing its moorings in the highest values and ideals of traditional Indian culture. Tagore's father, Debendranath Tagore, was among the first leaders of the Brahmo Samaj, a major Hindu social reform organization that was founded on just such a blend of Western and Indian ideas.

Each of Debendranath Tagore's fourteen children (including his daughter, Swarnakumari) made significant contributions to Bengali literature and culture. None of them, however, equaled Rabindranath, the youngest, in breadth and importance of achievement. In the course of a life that spanned the period during which India emerged from colonial domination to independent nationhood, Tagore wrote poems, novels, short stories, plays, and essays, transforming extant Bengali literary forms and creating new ones. *Gitanjali* (Song offering), an anthology of lyric poems that the poet himself translated from the Bengali into English, brought him international recognition in the form of the Nobel prize. Tagore's own translations of the *Gitanjali* poems, and Yeats's praise of them in his preface to the first edition of the anthology, contributed to the misleading stereotyping of the poems as a combination of romantic lyricism and vague Eastern mysticism. The truth is that the *Gitanjali* poems reflect only one facet of Tagore's poetic sensibility, and that not accurately. On the one hand, he drew on earlier lyric traditions in Sanskrit and Bengali with great sensitivity; on the other, he nearly single-handedly brought the Bengali language and Bengali poetry into the domain of the modern. Tagore continued to write poetry to the end of his life, experimenting with language and with a variety of poetic forms, combining a spare, direct style with vivid yet deeply suggestive images in ways that are difficult to convey in translation. In addition to the lyric poems in *Gitanjali* and other collections (these are not true songs), Tagore composed and set to music nearly two thousand songs, which continue to dominate the Bengali song repertoire in the twentieth century. Included in these songs are the national anthems of India and Bangladesh.

Among Tagore's lasting contributions are Shantiniketan and Viswabharati, the school and the international university he founded near Calcutta as alternatives to colonial education and as arenas and training grounds for international cooperation. He used the international attention he gained as a result of the Nobel Prize to travel widely in Europe, Asia, and America, speaking out against the evils of colonialism, wars based on narrow nationalism, and abuses of human rights all over the world. When Mahatma Gandhi led the Indian people in their nonviolent (and ultimately successful) struggle for freedom from British colonial rule in the period between the two world wars, Tagore stood by Gandhi and his movement but pointed out the dangers of focusing on exclusively nationalistic goals, arguing instead for a new world order based on transnational values and ideals. A true "renaissance" figure, Tagore left no aspect of human experience untouched in his life and writings. The universalistic humanism that informs all his writings makes him one of the towering figures of the twentieth century.

Although the Bengali language had a rich tradition of medieval lyric and narrative poetry, Bengali prose fiction emerged in the late nineteenth century as a result of the impact of English education and Western literary forms. The novels of Tagore's elder contemporary Bankim Chandra Chatterjee (1838–1894) were mainly historical romances modeled on the novels of Sir Walter Scott, though Chatterjee also used the novel as a vehicle for social critique and nationalist propaganda. Concern about social issues, especially the need for the emancipation of Bengali women from oppressive cultural practices, dominates Tagore's major novels, beginning with *Cokher bali* (Speck in the eye) and *Nastanir* (The broken nest), published serially in 1901. Here, as well as in his more than one hundred short stories, his preoccupation with the emotional and psychological lives of his characters and his passionate championship of the integrity of the individual strike a new note in Bengali literature.

Tagore's short stories are the first major examples of the genre in any Indian language. Between 1891 and 1895 forty-four of his stories appeared in Bengali periodicals, the majority of them in the monthly journal *Sadhana* (Endeavor), edited by members of the Tagore family. The rest were written in the 1920s. *Punishment* (*Sasti*, 1893) belongs to the earlier stories, which were inspired by Tagore's experience of rural Bengal during the decade he spent there as manager of the family estates in Shelidah. Shelidah is in what was formerly the British province of East Bengal, which became East Pakistan following the partition of India in 1947 and is now the independent nation of Bangladesh. The characters in Tagore's major fiction tend to be drawn from the Bengali middle class, which he knew well; but a number of these early stories are about the peasants and villagers with whom he came in contact during the Shelidah years. Here the great Padma River and the agricultural landscape of eastern Bengal become the focus of the love of nature and the lyrical, romantic sensibility that are characteristic of all the writer's works.

The stories of this period are by no means idyllic pictures of village life. In *Punishment*, Tagore's sensitive portrayal of the complex relationships among the members of the low-caste Rui family and between them and the upper-class rural society that exploits them suggests both realism and a sense of tragedy. The transactions among Chandara, the proud and beautiful young woman; her husband, the farm-laborer Chidam; and landlord Ramlochan Chakravarti, "pillar of the village," reveal Tagore's intimate understanding both of the ways in which economic, social, and patriarchal oppression are intrinsically linked and of the ability of the oppressed to resist even the most powerful forms of oppression. However, as in his other stories and novels, his real interest in *Punishment* is in delineating the psychological ramifications of social and familial relationships. Chandara is a typical Tagore protagonist, representing the power and dignity of the human will in the face of societal degradation. And yet Tagore's world is a tragic one, populated by individuals who, trapped in what he called the "dreary desert sand of dead habit," are ultimately unable to transcend the tyranny of institutions.

Two recent histories of Bengali literature, Dushan Zbavitel, *Bengali Literature* (1976), and Asit Kumar Bandhyopadhyay, *Modern Bengali Literature* (1986), provide information about the context of Tagore's achievement. Humayun Kabir, *The Bengali Novel* (1968), discusses Tagore with reference to the development of the Bengali novel. William Radice, *Rabindranath Tagore: Selected Short Stories* (1991), offers faithful, readable translations of thirty of Tagore's early short stories, including some of his best known ones. For a comparison of Tagore's short stories with those of later Bengali writers on the themes of oppression and resistance, see Kalpana Bardhan, ed. and trans., *Of Women, Outcastes, Peasants, and Rebels* (1990). Krishna Kripalani, *Rabindranath Tagore* (1962), is the authoritative Tagore biography, and Amiya Chakravarty, ed., *A Tagore Reader* (1961), remains the best introduction to the full range of Tagore's writing.

PRONOUNCING GLOSSARY

The following list uses common English syllables and stress accents to provide rough equivalents of selected words whose pronunciation may be unfamiliar to the general reader.

Baṛobau: *baroh'-bau*

Chandara: *chuhn'-duh-rah*

Chidam Rui: *chee'-duhm roo'-yee*

Dukhiram Rui: *doo-khee'-rahm roo'-yee*

Kashi Majumdar: *kah'-shee muh'-joom-dahr*

koel: *koh'-yuhl*

Rabindranath Tagore: *ruh-beend'-run-naht tuh-gohr'*

Ram: *rahm*

Ramlochan Chakravarti: *rahm'-loh-chuhn chuhk'-ruh-vuhr-tee*

Ṭhākur: *thah'-koor*

zamindar: *zuh-meen'-dahr*

Punishment[1]

I

When the brothers Dukhiram Rui and Chidam Rui went out in the
morning with their heavy farm-knives, to work in the fields, their wives
would quarrel and shout. But the people near by were as used to the
uproar as they were to other customary, natural sounds. When they heard
the shrill screams of the women, they would say, "They're at it again"—
that is, what was happening was only to be expected: it was not a violation
of Nature's rules. When the sun rises at dawn, no one asks why; and whenever the two wives in this *kuri*-caste[2] household let fly at each other, no
one was at all curious to investigate the cause.

Of course this wrangling and disturbance affected the husbands more
than the neighbours, but they did not count it a major nuisance. It was as
if they were riding together along life's road in a cart whose rattling, clattering, unsprung wheels were inseparable from the journey. Indeed, days
when there was no noise, when everything was uncannily silent, carried a
greater threat of unpredictable doom.

The day on which our story begins was like this. When the brothers
returned home at dusk, exhausted by their work, they found the house
eerily quiet. Outside, too, it was extremely sultry. There had been a sharp
shower in the afternoon, and clouds were still massing. There was not a
breath of wind. Weeds and scrub round the house had shot up after the
rain: the heavy scent of damp vegetation, from these and from the waterlogged jute-fields, formed a solid wall all around. Frogs croaked from the
milkman's pond behind the house, and the buzz of crickets filled the
leaden sky.

Not far off the swollen Padma[3] looked flat and sinister under the mounting clouds. It had flooded most of the grain-fields, and had come close to
the houses. Here and there, roots of mango and jackfruit trees on the
slipping bank stuck up out of the water, like helpless hands clawing at the
air for a last fingerhold.

That day, Dukhiram and Chidam had been working near the zamindar's office. On a sandbank opposite, paddy[4] had ripened. The paddy
needed to be cut before the sandbank was washed away, but the village
people were busy either in their own fields or in cutting jute: so a messenger came from the office and forcibly engaged the two brothers. As the
office roof was leaking in places, they also had to mend that and make
some new wickerwork panels: it had taken them all day. They couldn't
come home for lunch; they just had a snack from the office. At times they
were soaked by the rain; they were not paid normal labourers' wages;
indeed, they were paid mainly in insults and sneers.

When the two brothers returned at dusk, wading through mud and
water, they found the younger wife, Chandara, stretched on the ground
with her sari[5] spread out. Like the sky, she had wept buckets in the after-

---

1. Translated by William Radice.   2. In Bengal, a low caste originally of bird catchers, but by the
19th century, general laborers.   3. A major river in what is now Bangladesh.   4. The rice crop.
Zamindar: landlord.   5. A long strip of cloth draped around the body, Indian women's traditional
clothing.

noon, but had now given way to sultry exhaustion. The elder wife, Radha, sat on the verandah sullenly: her eighteen-month son had been crying, but when the brothers came in they saw him lying naked in a corner of the yard, asleep.

Dukhiram, famished, said gruffly, "Give me my food."

Like a spark on a sack of gunpowder, the elder wife exploded, shrieking out, "Where is there food? Did you give me anything to cook? Must I earn money myself to buy it?"

After a whole day of toil and humiliation, to return—raging with hunger—to a dark, joyless, foodless house, to be met by Radha's sarcasm, especially her final jibe, was suddenly unendurable. "What?" he roared, like a furious tiger, and then, without thinking, plunged his knife into her head. Radha collapsed into her sister-in-law's lap, and in minutes she was dead.

"What have you done?" screamed Chandara, her clothes soaked with blood. Chidam pressed his hand over her mouth. Dukhiram, throwing aside the knife, fell to his knees with his head in his hands, stunned. The little boy woke up and started to wail in terror.

Outside there was complete quiet. The herd-boys were returning with the cattle. Those who had been cutting paddy on the far sandbanks were crossing back in groups in a small boat—with a couple of bundles of paddy on their heads as payment. Everyone was heading for home.

Ramlochan Chakravarti, pillar of the village, had been to the post office with a letter, and was now back in his house, placidly smoking. Suddenly he remembered that his sub-tenant Dukhiram was very behind with his rent: he had promised to pay some today. Deciding that the brothers must be home by now, he threw his chadar[6] over his shoulders, took his umbrella, and stepped out.

As he entered the Ruis' house, he felt uneasy. There was no lamp alight. On the dark verandah, the dim shapes of three or four people could be seen. In a corner of the verandah there were fitful, muffled sobs: the little boy was trying to cry for his mother, but was stopped each time by Chidam.

"Dukhi," said Ramlochan nervously, "are you there?"

Dukhiram had been sitting like a statue for a long time; now, on hearing his name, he burst into tears like a helpless child.

Chidam quickly came down from the verandah into the yard, to meet Ramlochan. "Have the women been quarelling again?" Ramlochan asked. "I heard them yelling all day."

Chidam, all this time, had been unable to think what to do. Various impossible stories occurred to him. All he had decided was that later that night he would move the body somewhere. He had never expected Ramlochan to come. He could think of no swift reply. "Yes," he stumbled, "today they were quarrelling terribly."

"But why is Dukhi crying so?" asked Ramlochan, stepping towards the verandah.

6. In Bengal, a sheet of cloth draped around the shoulders, usually worn by men but sometimes by women.

Seeing no way out now, Chidam blurted, "In their quarrel, Choṭobau struck at Baṛobau's[7] head with a farm-knife."

When immediate danger threatens, it is hard to think of other dangers. Chidam's only thought was to escape from the terrible truth—he forgot that a lie can be even more terrible. A reply to Ramlochan's question had come instantly to mind, and he had blurted it out.

"Good grief," said Ramlochan in horror. "What are you saying? Is she dead?"

"She's dead," said Chidam, clasping Ramlochan's feet.

Ramlochan was trapped. "Rām, Rām,"[8] he thought, "what a mess I've got into this evening. What if I have to be a witness in court?" Chidam was still clinging to his feet, saying, "Ṭhākur,[9] how can I save my wife?"

Ramlochan was the village's chief source of advice on legal matters. Reflecting further he said, "I think I know a way. Run to the police station: say that your brother Dukhi returned in the evening wanting his food, and because it wasn't ready he struck his wife on the head with his knife. I'm sure that if you say that, she'll get off."

Chidam felt a sickening dryness in his throat. He stood up and said, "Ṭhākur, if I lose my wife I can get another, but if my brother is hanged, how can I replace him?" In laying the blame on his wife, he had not seen it that way. He had spoken without thought; now, imperceptibly, logic and awareness were returning to his mind.

Ramlochan appreciated his logic. "Then say what actually happened," he said. "You can't protect yourself on all sides."

He had soon, after leaving, spread it round the village that Chandara Rui had, in a quarrel with her sister-in-law, split her head open with a farm-knife. Police charged into the village like a river in flood. Both the guilty and the innocent were equally afraid.

II

Chidam decided he would have to stick to the path he had chalked out for himself. The story he had given to Ramlochan Chakravarti had gone all round the village; who knew what would happen if another story was circulated? But he realized that if he kept to the story he would have to wrap it in five more stories if his wife was to be saved.

Chidam asked Chandara to take the blame on to herself. She was dumbfounded. He reassured her: "Don't worry—if you do what I tell you, you'll be quite safe." But whatever his words, his throat was dry and his face was pale.

Chandara was not more than seventeen or eighteen. She was buxom, well-rounded, compact and sturdy—so trim in her movements that in walking, turning, bending or climbing there was no awkwardness at all. She was like a brand-new boat: neat and shapely, gliding with ease, not a loose joint anywhere. Everything amused and intrigued her; she loved to

---

7. "Elder Daughter-in-Law"; members of a family address each other by kinship terms. Choṭobau: "Younger Daughter-in-Law."   8. God's name, repeated to express great emotion.   9. "Master" or "lord," term of address for gods and upper-class (Brahmin) men. Tagore is an anglicized form of Ṭhākur.

gossip; her bright, restless, deep black eyes missed nothing as she walked to the *ghāṭ*,[1] pitcher on her hip, parting her veil slightly with her finger.

The elder wife had been her exact opposite: unkempt, sloppy and slovenly. She was utterly disorganized in her dress, housework, and the care of her child. She never had any proper work in hand, yet never seemed to have time for anything. The younger wife usually refrained from comment, for at the mildest barb Radha would rage and stamp and let fly at her, disturbing everyone around.

Each wife was matched by her husband to an extraordinary degree. Dukhiram was a huge man—his bones were immense, his nose was squat, in his eyes and expression he seemed not to understand the world very well, yet he never questioned it either. He was innocent yet fearsome: a rare combination of power and helplessness. Chidam, however, seemed to have been carefully carved from shiny black rock. There was not an inch of excess fat on him, not a wrinkle or dimple anywhere. Each limb was a perfect blend of strength and finesse. Whether jumping from a riverbank, or punting a boat, or climbing up bamboo-shoots for sticks, he showed complete dexterity, effortless grace. His long black hair was combed with oil back from his brow and down to his shoulders—he took great care over his dress and appearance. Although he was not unresponsive to the beauty of other women in the village, and was keen to make himself charming in their eyes, his real love was for his young wife. They quarrelled sometimes, but there was mutual respect too: neither could defeat the other. There was a further reason why the bond between them was firm: Chidam felt that a wife as nimble and sharp as Chandara could not be wholly trusted, and Chandara felt that all eyes were on her husband—that if she didn't bind him tightly to her she might one day lose him.

A little before the events in this story, however, they had a major row. Chandara had noticed that when her husband's work took him away for two days or more, he brought no extra earnings. Finding this ominous, she also began to overstep the mark. She would hang around by the *ghāṭ*, or wander about talking rather too much about Kashi Majumdar's middle son.

Something now seemed to poison Chidam's life. He could not settle his attention on his work. One day his sister-in-law rounded on him: she shook her finger and said in the name of her dead father, "That girl runs before the storm. How can I restrain her? Who knows what ruin she will bring?"

Chandara came out of the next room and said sweetly, "What's the matter, *Didi*?"[2] and a fierce quarrel broke out between them.

Chidam glared at his wife and said, "If I ever hear that you've been to the *ghāṭ* on your own, I'll break every bone in your body."

"The bones will mend again," said Chandara, starting to leave. Chidam sprang at her, grabbed her by the hair, dragged her back to the room and locked her in.

---

1. Steps leading down to a pond or river; meeting place, especially for women, who go there to get water or to wash clothes.   2. "Elder Sister," respectful form of address for Bengali women.

When he returned from work that evening he found that the room was empty. Chandara had fled three villages away, to her maternal uncle's house. With great difficulty Chidam persuaded her to return, but he had to surrender to her. It was as hard to restrain his wife as to hold a handful of mercury; she always slipped through his fingers. He did not have to use force any more, but there was no peace in the house. Ever-fearful love for his elusive young wife wracked him with intense pain. He even once or twice wondered if it would be better if she were dead: at least he would get some peace then. Human beings can hate each other more than death. It was at this time that the crisis hit the house.

When her husband asked her to admit to the murder, Chandara stared at him, stunned; her black eyes burnt him like fire. Then she shrank back, as if to escape his devilish clutches. She turned her heart and soul away from him. "You've nothing to fear," said Chidam. He taught her repeatedly what she should say to the police and the magistrate. Chandara paid no attention—sat like a wooden statue whenever he spoke.

Dukhiram relied on Chidam for everything. When he told him to lay the blame on Chandara, Dukhiram said, "But what will happen to her?" "I'll save her," said Chidam. His burly brother was content with that.

III

This was what he instructed his wife to say: "The elder wife was about to attack me with the vegetable-slicer. I picked up a farm-knife to stop her, and it somehow cut into her." This was all Ramlochan's invention. He had generously supplied Chidam with the proofs and embroidery that the story would require.

The police came to investigate. The villagers were sure now that Chandara had murdered her sister-in-law, and all the witnesses confirmed this. When the police questioned Chandara, she said, "Yes, I killed her."

"Why did you kill her?"

"I couldn't stand her any more."

"Was there a brawl between you?"

"No."

"Did she attack you first?"

"No."

"Did she ill-treat you?"

"No."

Everyone was amazed at these replies, and Chidam was completely thrown off balance. "She's not telling the truth," he said. "The elder wife first—"

The inspector silenced him sharply. He continued according to the rules of cross-examination and repeatedly received the same reply: Chandara would not accept that she had been attacked in any way by her sister-in-law. Such an obstinate girl was never seen! She seemed absolutely bent on going to the gallows; nothing would stop her. Such fierce, passionate pride! In her thoughts, Chandara was saying to her husband, "I shall give my youth to the gallows instead of to you. My final ties in this life will be with them."

Chandara was arrested, and left her home for ever, by the paths she knew so well, past the festival carriage, the market-place, the *ghāṭ*, the Majumdars' house, the post office, the school—an ordinary, harmless, flirtatious, fun-loving village wife; leaving a shameful impression on all the people she knew. A bevy of boys followed her, and the women of the village, her friends and companions—some of them peering through their veils, some from their doorsteps, some from behind trees—watched the police leading her away and shuddered with embarrassment, fear and contempt.

To the Deputy Magistrate, Chandara again confessed her guilt, claiming no ill-treatment from her sister-in-law at the time of the murder. But when Chidam was called to the witness-box he broke down completely, weeping, clasping his hands and saying, "I swear to you, sir, my wife is innocent." The magistrate sternly told him to control himself, and began to question him. Bit by bit the true story came out.

The magistrate did not believe him, because the chief, most trustworthy, most educated witness—Ramlochan Chakravarti—said: "I appeared on the scene a little after the murder. Chidam confessed everything to me and clung to my feet saying, 'Tell me how I can save my wife.' I did not say anything one way or the other. Then Chidam said, 'If I say that my elder brother killed his wife in a fit of fury because his food wasn't ready, then she'll get off.' I said, 'Be careful, you rogue: don't say a single false word in court—there's no worse offence than that.' " Ramlochan had previously prepared lots of stories that would save Chandara, but when he found that she herself was bending her neck to receive the noose, he decided, "Why take the risk of giving false evidence now? I'd better say what little I know." So Ramlochan said what he knew—or rather said a little more than he knew.

The Deputy Magistrate committed the case to a sessions trial.[3] Meanwhile in fields, houses, markets and bazaars, the sad or happy affairs of the world carried on; and just as in previous years, torrential monsoon rains fell on to the new rice-crop.

Police, defendant and witnesses were all in court. In the civil court opposite hordes of people were waiting for their cases. A Calcutta lawyer had come on a suit about the sharing of a pond behind a kitchen; the plaintiff had thirty-nine witnesses. Hundreds of people were anxiously waiting for hair-splitting judgements, certain that nothing, at present, was more important. Chidam stared out of the window at the constant throng, and it seemed like a dream. A *koel*-bird[4] was hooting from a huge banyan tree in the compound: no courts or cases in *his* world!

Chandara said to the judge, "Sir, how many times must I go on saying the same thing?"

The judge explained, "Do you know the penalty for the crime you have confessed?"

"No," said Chandara.

"It is death by the hanging."

---

3. A trial that is settled through a special court *sessions* in one continuous sitting.   4. Common Indian songbird.

"Then please give it to me, sir," said Chandara. "Do what you like—I can't take any more."

When her husband was called to the court, she turned away. "Look at the witness," said the judge, "and say who he is."

"He is my husband," said Chandara, covering her face with her hands.

"Does he not love you?"

"He loves me greatly."

"Do you not love him?"

"I love him greatly."

When Chidam was questioned, he said, "I killed her."

"Why?"

"I wanted my food and my sister-in-law didn't give it to me."

When Dukhiram came to give evidence, he fainted. When he had come round again, he answered, "Sir, I killed her."

"Why?"

"I wanted a meal and she didn't give it to me."

After extensive cross-examination of various other witnesses, the judge concluded that the brothers had confessed to the crime in order to save the younger wife from the shame of the noose. But Chandara had, from the police investigation right through to the sessions trial, said the same thing repeatedly—she had not budged an inch from her story. Two barristers did their utmost to save her from the death-sentence, but in the end were defeated by her.

Who, on that auspicious night when, at a very young age, a dusky, diminutive, round-faced girl had left her childhood dolls in her father's house and come to her in-laws' house, could have imagined these events? Her father, on his deathbed, had happily reflected that at least he had made proper arrangements for his daughter's future.

In gaol,[5] just before the hanging, a kindly Civil Surgeon asked Chandara, "Do you want to see anyone?"

"I'd like to see my mother," she replied.

"Your husband wants to see you," said the doctor. "Shall I call him?"

"To hell with him,"[6] said Chandara.

5. Jail. 6. "Death to him" (literal trans.); an expression usually uttered in jest.

LUIGI PIRANDELLO
1867–1936

"Who am I?" and "What is real?" are the persistent and even agonized questions that underlie Luigi Pirandello's novels, short stories, and plays. The term *Pirandellismo* or "Pirandellism"—coined from the author's name—suggests that there are as many truths as there are points of view. Here are already the basic issues of later existential philosophy as seen in writers like Jean-Paul Sartre and Albert Camus: the difficulty of achieving a sense of identity, the impossibility of authentic communication between people, and the overlapping frontiers of appearance and reality. These dilemmas are dramatic crises in self-knowledge and as such are particularly suited for demonstration in the theater. Indeed, Pirandello is best known as an innovative dramatist who revolutionized European stage techniques to break down comfortable illusions of compartmentalized, stable reality. Instead of the late nineteenth-century's "well-made play"—with its neatly constructed plot that packaged real life into a conventional beginning, middle, and end, and its consistent characters remaining safely inaccessible on the other side of the foot-lights—he offers unpredictable plots and characters whose ambiguity puts into question the solidity of identities assumed in everyday life. It is not easy to know the truth, he suggests, or to make oneself known behind the face or "naked mask" that each of us wears in society. Pirandello's theater readily displays its nature as dramatic illusion: plays exist within plays until one is not sure where the "real" play begins or ends, and characters question their own reality and that of the audience. In their manipulation of ambiguous appearances and tragicomic effects, these plays foreshadow the absurdist theater of Samuel Beckett, Eugène Ionesco, and Harold Pinter, the cosmic irony of Antonin Artaud's "theater of cruelty," and the emphasis on spectacle and illusion in works by Jean Genet. Above all, they insist that the most "real" life is that which changes from moment to moment, exhibiting a fluidity that renders difficult and perhaps impossible any single formu-lation of either character or situation. This fluidity is a cause of existential anguish because it implies perpetual loss; readers may wish to contrast Pirandello's cosmos of uncertain boundaries with the sense of continuity throughout different dimen-sions of existence that informs Wole Soyinka's Death and the King's Horseman.

Pirandello was born in Girgenti (now Agrigento), Sicily, on June 28, 1867. His father was a sulfur merchant who intended his son to go into business like himself, but Pirandello preferred language and literature. After studying in Palermo and the University of Rome, he traveled to the University of Bonn in 1888 where he received a doctorate in romance philology in 1891 with a thesis on the dialect of his hometown. In 1894, Pirandello made an arranged marriage with the daughter of a rich sulfur merchant. They lived for ten years in Rome, where he wrote poetry and short stories, until the collapse of the sulfur mines destroyed the fortunes of both families, and he was suddenly forced to earn a living. To add to his misfor-tunes, his wife became insane with a jealous paranoia that lasted until her death in 1918. The author himself died on December 1, 1936.

Pirandello's early work shows a number of different influences. His poetry was indebted to nineteenth-century Italian predecessors like Giosuè Carducci (1835–1907), and in 1896 he translated Goethe's Roman Elegies. Soon, however, he turned to short stories or novelle under the influence of a narrative style called verismo (realism) exemplified in the work of the Sicilian writer Giovanni Verga (1840–1922). Pirandello wrote hundreds of stories of all lengths and—in his clar-ity, realism, and psychological acuteness (often including a taste for the gro-tesque)—is recognized as an Italian master of the story much as was Guy de Maupassant in France. Collections include the 1894 Love Without Love and an anthology in 1922 entitled A Year's Worth of Stories.

In such stories, and in his early novels, Pirandello begins to develop his charac-teristic themes: the questioning of appearance and reality, and problems of iden-tity. In The Outcast (1901), an irate husband drives his innocent wife out of the house only to take her back when—without his knowing it—the supposed adultery has actually occurred. The hero of Pirandello's best-known novel, The Late Mattia Pascal, tries to create a fresh identity for himself and leave behind the old Mattia Pascal. When things become too difficult he returns to his "late" self and begins to write his life story, an early example of the tendency in Pirandello's works to comment on their own composition. The protagonists in these and other works are visibly commonplace, middle-class citizens, neither heroic nor villainous, but prototypes of the twentieth-century "antihero" who remains aggressively average while taking the center of the stage.

The questions of identity that obsessed Pirandello (he speaks of them as reflecting the "pangs of my spirit") are explored on social, psychological, and metaphysical levels. He was acquainted with the experimental psychology of his day, and learned from works such as Alfred Binet's *Personality Alterations* (1892) about the existence of a subconscious personality beneath our everyday awareness (a theme Pirandello shares with Proust and Freud). Successive layers of personality, conflicts among the various parts, and the simultaneous existence of multiple perspectives shape an identity that is never fixed but always fluid and changing. This identity escapes the grasp of onlookers and subject alike, and expresses a basic incongruity in human existence that challenges the most earnest attempts to create a unified self. The protagonist of a later novel, *One, None, and a Hundred Thousand* (1925–26) finds that what "he" is depends on the viewpoint of a great number of people. Such incongruity can be tragic or comic—or both at once—according to one's attitude, a topic that Pirandello explored in a 1908 essay, *On Humor*, and that is echoed in the double-edged humor of his plays. The "Pirandellian" themes of ambiguous identity, lack of communication, and deceptive appearance reappear in all the genres, however, reaching a particular intensity in his first dramatic success, *It Is So [If You Think So]* (1917), and in the play included here, *Six Characters in Search of an Author*.

Six Characters in Search of an Author and Henry IV established Pirandello's stature as a major dramatist. He directed his own company (the Teatro d'Arte di Roma) from 1924 to 1928 and received the Nobel Prize for Literature in 1934. His later plays, featuring fantastic and grotesque elements, did not achieve the wide popularity of their predecessors. In 1936, he published a collection of forty-three plays as *Naked Masks*, a title conceived in 1918 after Luigi Chiarelli's "grotesque theater." Pirandello's characters are "naked" and vulnerable inside the social roles or masks they put on to survive: Henry IV, trapped for life inside a pretense of insanity, or the Father in *Six Characters*, forced to play out a demeaning role in which, he insists, only part of his true nature is revealed. The term *naked mask* also suggests Pirandello's superb manipulation of theatrical ambiguity—the confusion between the actor and the character portrayed—that ultimately prolongs the confusion of appearance and reality, which is one of his chief themes. Pirandello is famous in twentieth-century theater for his use of the play within a play, a technique of embedded dramatic episodes that maintain a life of their own while serving as foil to the overall or governing plot. Dividing lines are sometimes hard to draw when stage dialogue can be taken as referring to either context—a situation that allows for double meanings at the same time that it reiterates the impossibility of real communication.

Six Characters in Search of an Author combines all these elements in an extraordinarily self-reflexive style. At the very beginning, the Stage Hand's interrupted hammering suggests that the audience has chanced on a rehearsal—of still another play by Pirandello—instead of coming to a finished performance; concurrently, Pirandello's stage dialogue pokes fun at his own reputation for obscurity. Just as the Actors are apparently set to rehearse *The Rules of the Game*, six unexpected persons come down the aisle seeking the Producer: they are Characters out of an unwritten novel who demand to be given dramatic existence. The play *Six Characters* is continually in the process of being composed: composed as the interwoven double plot we see on stage, written down in shorthand by the Prompter for the Actors to reproduce, and potentially composed as the Characters' inner drama finally achieves its rightful existence as a work of art. The conflicts between the different levels of the play finally prevent the completion of any but the first work, but it has created a convincing dramatic illusion in the meantime that incorporates the psychological drama of the "six characters" as well as a discussion of the relationship of life and art.

The initial absurdity of the play appears when the six admittedly fictional characters arrive with their claim to be "truer and more real" than the "real" characters they confront. (Of course, to the audience all the actors on stage are equally unreal.) Their greater "truth" is the truth of art with its profound but formally fixed glimpses into human nature. Each Character represents, specifically and in depth, a particular identity created by the author, who later suggested that the Characters should wear masks to distinguish them from the Actors. These masks are not the conventional masks of ancient Greek drama or the Japanese nō theater, nor do they function as the ceremonial masks representing spirits in African ritual, masks that temporarily invest the wearer with the spirit's identity and authority. Instead, they are a theatrical device, a symbol and visual reminder of each character's unchanging essence. The Six Characters are incapable of developing outside their roles and are condemned, in their search for existence, painfully to reenact their essential selves.

Conversely, the fictional characters have a more stable personality than "real" people who are still "nobody," incomplete, open to change and misinterpretation. Characters are "somebody" because their nature has been decided once and for all. Yet there is a further complication to this contrast between real and fictional characters: the Characters have real anxieties in that they want to play their own roles and are disturbed at the prospect of having Actors represent them incorrectly. All human beings, suggests Pirandello, whether fictional or real, are subject to misunderstanding. We even misunderstand ourselves when we think we are the same person in all situations. "We always have the illusion of being the same person for everybody," says the Father, "but it's not true!" When he explains himself as a very human philosopher driven by the Demon of Experiment, his self-image is quite different from the picture held by his vengeful Stepdaughter or the passive Mother who blames him for her expulsion from the house. The Stepdaughter, in turn, appears to love an innocent little sister because she reminds her of an earlier self. It is an entanglement of motives and deceit of mutual understanding that goes beyond the tabloid level of a sordid family scandal and claims a broader scope. Pirandello, in fact, does not intend merely to describe a particular setting or situation; that is the concern of what he calls "historical writers." He belongs to the opposite category of "philosophical writers" whose characters and situations embody "a particular sense of life and acquire from it a universal value."

Six Characters in Search of an Author underwent an interesting evolution to become the play that we see today. First performed in Rome in 1921, where its unsettling plot and characters already scandalized a traditionalist audience, it was reshaped in more radical theatrical form after the remarkable performance produced by Georges Pitoëff in Paris in 1923. Pirandello, who came to Paris somewhat wary of Pitoëff's innovations (he brought on the Characters in a green-lit stage elevator), was soon convinced that the Russian director's stagecraft suggested changes that would enhance the original text. Pitoëff had used his knowledge of technical effects to accentuate the interrelationships of appearance and reality: he extended the stage with several steps leading down into the auditorium (a break in the conventional stage's "fourth wall" that Pirandello was quick to exploit); he underscored the play within a play with rehearsal effects, showing the Stage Hand hammering and the Director arranging suitable props and lighting; he emphasized the division between Characters and Actors by separating groups on stage and dressing the Characters (all except the Little Girl) in black. Pirandello welcomed and expanded on many of these changes. To distinguish even further the Characters from the Actors, he proposed stylized masks as well as black clothes for the former and light-colored summery clothing for the latter. To bring out Madame

Pace's grotesque fictionality, he changed her costume from a sober black gown to a garish red silk dress and carrot-colored wool wig. Most striking, however, is the dramatist's development of Pitoëff's steps into a real bridge between the world of the stage and the auditorium, a strategy that allows his Actors (and Characters) to come and go in the "real world" of the audience. Pirandello's revised ending to *Six Characters in Search of an Author* makes a final break with theatrical illusion: with the other characters immobilized on stage, the Stepdaughter races down the steps, through the auditorium, and out into the foyer from which the audience can still hear her distraught laughter.

Pirandello does not hold his audience by uttering grand philosophical truths. There is constant suspense and a process of discovery in *Six Characters*, from the moment that the rehearsal with its complaining Actors and Manager is interrupted and the initial hints of melodrama and family scandal catch our attention in the Stepdaughter's and Mother's complaints. It is a story that could be found in the most sensational papers: an adulterous wife thrust out of her home and supporting herself and her children after her lover's death by sewing, the daughter's turn to prostitution to support the family, the Father's unknowing attempt to seduce his Stepdaughter (interpreted by the latter as the continuation of an old and perverse impulse), and the final drowning and suicide of the two youngest children. Pirandello plays with the sensational aspect of his story by focusing the play on the characters' repeated attempts to portray the seduction scene; Actors and Manager perceive the salable quality of such "human-interest" events and are eager to let the story unfold. The Stepdaughter's protective fondness for her doomed baby sister and her enigmatic reproach to the little Boy ("instead of killing myself, I'd have killed one of those two") hint at the inner plot that is revealed only as the action continues. The interplay of illusion and reality persists to the very end, when the Actors argue about whether the Boy is dead or not, the Producer is terrified as the lights change eerily around the surviving Characters, and the Stepdaughter breaks away from the ending tableau to escape into the audience.

The translation by John Linstrum has been selected on the one hand for its accuracy to the Italian text and its fluent use of contemporary English idiom and on the other for its quality as a performance-oriented script, staged in London in 1979. Readers are encouraged to test the continued liveliness of Pirandello's dialogue by rehearsing their own selection of scenes—or perhaps by relocating them in a contemporary setting. According to director Robert Brustein, whose 1988 production of *Six Characters in Search of an Author* set the action in New York and replaced Madame Pace with a pimp, "Pirandello both encourages and stimulates a pluralism in theater because there can be dozens, hundreds, thousands of productions of *Six Characters*, and every one of them is going to be different."

A good biography and general introduction is found in Susan Bassnett-McGuire, *Pirandello* (1984). Walter Starkie, *Luigi Pirandello, 1867–1936* (1965), a general study against the background of twentieth-century Italian literature, treats novels, stories, plays, and themes. Glauco Cambon, ed., *Pirandello: A Collection of Critical Essays* (1967), emphasizes the plays. Richard Sogliuzzo, *Luigi Pirandello, Director* (1982), deals with Pirandello's dramatic theories and practices; it contains a discussion of *Six Characters*. John Louis DiGaetani, ed., *A Companion to Pirandello Studies* (1991), is an excellent collection of twenty-seven essays and four appendices on diverse aspects of Pirandello's thought and work; many essays take up *Six Characters*.

PRONOUNCING GLOSSARY

The following list uses common English syllables and stress accents to provide rough equivalents of selected words whose pronunciation may be unfamiliar to the general reader.

commedia dell'arte: *com-may'-dee-ah del ar'-tay*
Luigi Pirandello: *loo-ee'-jee pee-ran-del'-oh*
Pace: *pah'-chay*
Pitoëff: *pee'-toh-eff*

Six Characters in Search of an Author[1]

A Comedy in the Making

THE CHARACTERS   THE COMPANY

FATHER   THE PRODUCER
MOTHER   THE STAGE STAFF
STEPDAUGHTER   THE ACTORS
SON
BOY
LITTLE GIRL
MADAME PACE

Act One

When the audience enters, the curtain is already up and the stage is just as it would be during the day. There is no set; it is empty, in almost total darkness. This is so that from the beginning the audience will have the feeling of being present, not at a performance of a properly rehearsed play, but at a performance of a play that happens spontaneously. Two small sets of steps, one on the right and one on the left, lead up to the stage from the auditorium. On the stage, the top is off the PROMPTER's box and is lying next to it. Downstage, there is a small table and a chair with arms for the PRODUCER: it is turned with its back to the audience.

Also downstage there are two small tables, one a little bigger than the other, and several chairs, ready for the rehearsal if needed. There are more chairs scattered on both left and right for the ACTORS: to one side at the back and nearly hidden is a piano.

When the houselights go down the STAGE HAND comes on through the back door. He is in blue overalls and carries a tool bag. He brings some pieces of wood on, comes to the front, kneels down and starts to nail them together.

The STAGE MANAGER rushes on from the wings.

STAGE MANAGER: Hey! What are you doing?
STAGE HAND: What do you think I'm doing? I'm banging nails in.

---

1. Translated by John Linstrum. In the Italian editions, Pirandello notes that he did not divide the play into formal acts or scenes. The translator has marked the divisions for clarity, however, according to the stage directions.

STAGE MANAGER: Now? [*He looks at his watch.*] It's half-past ten already. The Producer will be here in a moment to rehearse.

STAGE HAND: I've got to do my work some time, you know.

STAGE MANAGER: Right—but not now.

STAGE HAND: When?

STAGE MANAGER: When the rehearsal's finished. Come on, get all this out of the way and let me set for the second act of *The Rules of the Game.*[2]

[*The* STAGE HAND *picks up his tools and wood and goes off, grumbling and muttering. The* ACTORS *of the company come in through the door, men and women, first one then another, then two together and so on: there will be nine or ten, enough for the parts for the rehearsal of a play by Pirandello, The Rules of the Game, today's rehearsal. They come in, say their "Good-mornings" to the* STAGE MANAGER *and each other. Some go off to the dressing-rooms; others, among them the* PROMPTER *with the text rolled up under his arm, scatter about the stage waiting for the* PRODUCER *to start the rehearsal. Meanwhile, sitting or standing in groups, they chat together; some smoke, one complains about his part, another one loudly reads something from "The Stage." It would be as well if the* ACTORS *and* ACTRESSES *were dressed in colourful clothes, and this first scene should be improvised naturally and vivaciously. After a while somebody might sit down at the piano and play a song; the younger* ACTORS *and* ACTRESSES *start dancing.*]

STAGE MANAGER: [*Clapping his hands to call their attention.*] Come on, everybody! Quiet please. The Producer's here.

[*The piano and the dancing both stop. The* ACTORS *turn to look out into the theatre and through the door at the back comes the* PRODUCER; *he walks down the gangway between the seats and, calling "Good-morning" to the* ACTORS, *climbs up one of the sets of stairs onto the stage. The* SECRETARY *gives him the post, a few magazines, a script. The* ACTORS *move to one side of the stage.*]

PRODUCER: Any letters?

SECRETARY: No. That's all the post there is. [*Giving him the script.*]

PRODUCER: Put it in the office. [*Then looking round and turning to the* STAGE MANAGER.] I can't see a thing here. Let's have some lights please.

STAGE MANAGER: Right. [*Calling.*] Workers please!

[*In a few seconds the side of the stage where the* ACTORS *are standing is brilliantly lit with white light. The* PROMPTER *has gone into his box and spread out his script.*]

PRODUCER: Good. [*Clapping hands.*] Well then, let's get started. Anybody missing?

STAGE MANAGER: [*Heavily ironic.*] Our leading lady.

PRODUCER: Not again! [*Looking at his watch.*] We're ten minutes late already. Send her a note to come and see me. It might teach her to be on time for rehearsals. [*Almost before he has finished, the* LEADING ACTRESS'*s voice is heard from the auditorium.*]

---

2. *Il giuoco delle parti*, written in 1918. The hero, Leone Gala, pretends to ignore his wife Silia's infidelity until the end, when he takes revenge by tricking her lover Guido Venanzi into taking his place in a fatal duel she had engineered to get rid of her husband.

LEADING ACTRESS: Morning everybody. Sorry I'm late. [*She is very expensively dressed and is carrying a lap-dog. She comes down the aisle and goes up on to the stage.*]

PRODUCER: You're determined to keep us waiting, aren't you?

LEADING ACTRESS: I'm sorry. I just couldn't find a taxi anywhere. But you haven't started yet and I'm not on at the opening anyhow. [*Calling the* STAGE MANAGER, *she gives him the dog.*]. Put him in my dressing-room for me will you?

PRODUCER: And she's even brought her lap-dog with her! As if we haven't enough lap-dogs here already. [*Clapping his hands and turning to the* PROMPTER.] Right then, the second act of *The Rules of the Game.* [*Sits in his arm-chair.*] Quiet please! Who's on?

[*The* ACTORS *clear from the front of the stage and sit to one side, except for three who are ready to start the scene—and the* LEADING ACTRESS. *She has ignored the* PRODUCER *and is sitting at one of the little tables.*]

PRODUCER: Are you in this scene, then?

LEADING ACTRESS: No—I've just told you.

PRODUCER: [*Annoyed.*] Then get off, for God's sake. [*The* LEADING ACTRESS *goes and sits with the others. To the* PROMPTER.] Come on then, let's get going.

PROMPTER: [*Reading his script.*] "The house of Leone Gala. A peculiar room, both dining-room and study."

PRODUCER: [*To the* STAGE MANAGER.] We'll use the red set.

STAGE MANAGER: [*Making a note.*] The red set—right.

PROMPTER: [*Still reading.*] "The table is laid and there is a desk with books and papers. Bookcases full of books and china cabinets full of valuable china. An exit at the back leads to Leone's bedroom. An exit to the left leads to the kitchen. The main entrance is on the right."

PRODUCER: Right. Listen carefully everybody: there, the main entrance, there, the kitchen. [*To the* LEADING ACTOR *who plays Socrates.*[3]] Your entrances and exits will be from there [*To the* STAGE MANAGER.] We'll have the French windows there and put the curtains on them.

STAGE MANAGER: [*Making a note.*] Right.

PROMPTER: [*Reading.*] "Scene One. Leone Gala, Guido Venanzi, and Filippo, who is called Socrates." [*To* PRODUCER.] Have I to read the directions as well?

PRODUCER: Yes, you have! I've told you a hundred times.

PROMPTER: [*Reading.*] "When the curtain rises, Leone Gala, in a cook's hat and apron, is beating an egg in a dish with a little wooden spoon. Filippo is beating another and he is dressed as a cook too. Guido Venanzi is sitting listening."

LEADING ACTOR: Look, do I really have to wear a cook's hat?

PRODUCER: [*Annoyed by the question.*] I expect so! That's what it says in the script. [*Pointing to the script.*]

LEADING ACTOR: If you ask me it's ridiculous.

PRODUCER: [*Leaping to his feet furiously.*] Ridiculous? It's ridiculous, is it?

---

3. Nickname given to Gala's servant, Philip, in *The Rules of the Game*, the play they are rehearsing.

What do you expect me to do if nobody writes good plays any more[4] and we're reduced to putting on plays by Pirandello? And if you can understand them you must be very clever. He writes them on purpose so nobody enjoys them, neither actors nor critics nor audience. [*The* ACTORS *laugh. Then crosses to* LEADING ACTOR *and shouts at him.*] A cook's hat and you beat eggs. But don't run away with the idea that that's all you are doing—beating eggs. You must be joking! You have to be symbolic of the shells of the eggs you are beating. [*The* ACTORS *laugh again and start making ironical comments to each other.*] Be quiet! Listen carefully while I explain. [*Turns back to* LEADING ACTOR.] Yes, the shells, because they are symbolic of the empty form of reason, without its content, blind instinct! You are reason and your wife is instinct: you are playing a game where you have been given parts and in which you are not just yourself but the puppet of yourself.[5] Do you see?

LEADING ACTOR: [*Spreading his hands.*] Me? No.

PRODUCER: [*Going back to his chair.*] Neither do I! Come on, let's get going; you wait till you see the end! You haven't seen anything yet! [*Confidentially.*] By the way, I should turn almost to face the audience if I were you, about three-quarters face. Well, what with the obscure dialogue and the audience not being able to hear you properly in any case, the whole lot'll go to hell. [*Clapping hands again.*] Come on. Let's get going!

PROMPTER: Excuse me, can I put the top back on the prompt-box? There's a bit of a draught.

PRODUCER: Yes, yes, of course. Get on with it.

[*The* STAGE DOORKEEPER, *in a braided cap, has come into the auditorium, and he comes all the way down the aisle to the stage to tell the* PRODUCER *the* SIX CHARACTERS *have come, who, having come in after him, look about them a little puzzled and dismayed. Every effort must be made to create the effect that the* SIX CHARACTERS *are very different from the* ACTORS *of the company. The placings of the two groups, indicated in the directions, once the* CHARACTERS *are on the stage, will help this: so will using different coloured lights. But the most effective idea is to use masks for the* CHARACTERS, *masks specially made of a material that will not go limp with perspiration and light enough not to worry the actors who wear them: they should be made so that the eyes, the nose and the mouth are all free. This is the way to bring out the deep significance of the play. The* CHARACTERS *should not appear as ghosts, but as created realities, timeless creations of the imagination, and so more real and consistent than the changeable realities of the* ACTORS. *The masks are designed to give the impression of figures constructed by art, each one fixed forever in its own fundamental emotion; that is,* Remorse *for the* FATHER, Revenge *for the* STEPDAUGHTER, Scorn *for the* SON, Sorrow *for the* MOTHER. *Her mask should have wax tears in the corners of*

---

4. The producer refers to the realistic, tightly constructed plays (often French) that were internationally popular in the late 19th century and a staple of Italian theaters at the beginning of the 20th.   5. Leone Gala is a rationalist and an aesthete—the opposite of his impulsive, passionate wife, Silia. By masking his feelings and constantly playing the role of gourmet cook, he chooses his own role and thus becomes his own "puppet."

the eyes and down the cheeks like the sculptured or painted weeping Madonna in a church. Her dress should be of a plain material, in stiff folds, looking almost as if it were carved and not of an ordinary material you can buy in a shop and have made up by a dressmaker.

The FATHER is about fifty: his reddish hair is thinning at the temples, but he is not bald: he has a full moustache that almost covers his young-looking mouth, which often opens in an uncertain and empty smile. He is pale, with a high forehead: he has blue oval eyes, clear and sharp: he is dressed in light trousers and a dark jacket: his voice is sometimes rich, at other times harsh and loud.

The MOTHER appears crushed by an intolerable weight of shame and humiliation. She is wearing a thick black veil and is dressed simply in black; when she raises her veil she shows a face like wax, but not suffering, with her eyes turned down humbly.

The STEPDAUGHTER, who is eighteen years old, is defiant, even insolent. She is very beautiful, dressed in mourning as well, but with striking elegance. She is scornful of the timid, suffering, dejected air of her YOUNG BROTHER, a grubby little boy of fourteen, also dressed in black; she is full of a warm tenderness, on the other hand, for the LITTLE SISTER, a girl of about four, dressed in white with a black silk sash round her waist.

The SON is twenty-two, tall, almost frozen in an air of scorn for the FATHER and indifference to the MOTHER: he is wearing a mauve overcoat and a long green scarf round his neck.]

DOORMAN: Excuse me, sir.

PRODUCER: [Angrily.] What the hell is it now?

DOORMAN: There are some people here—they say they want to see you, sir.

[The PRODUCER and the ACTORS are astonished and turn to look out into the auditorium.]

PRODUCER: But I'm rehearsing! You know perfectly well that no-one's allowed in during rehearsals. [Turning to face out front.] Who are you? What do you want?

FATHER: [Coming forward, followed by the others, to the foot of one of the sets of steps.] We're looking for an author.

PRODUCER: [Angry and astonished.] An author? Which author?

FATHER: Any author will do, sir.

PRODUCER: But there isn't an author here because we're not rehearsing a new play.

STEPDAUGHTER: [Excitedly as she rushes up the steps.] That's better still, better still! We can be your new play.

ACTORS: [Lively comments and laughter from the ACTORS.] Oh, listen to that, etc.

FATHER: [Going up on the stage after the STEPDAUGHTER.] Maybe, but if there isn't an author here . . . [To the PRODUCER.] Unless you'd like to be . . .

[Hand in hand, the MOTHER and the LITTLE GIRL, followed by the LITTLE BOY, go up on the stage and wait. The SON stays sullenly behind.]

PRODUCER: Is this some kind of joke?

FATHER: Now, how can you think that? On the contrary, we are bringing you a story of anguish.

STEPDAUGHTER: We might make your fortune for you!

PRODUCER: Do me a favour, will you? Go away. We haven't time to waste on idiots.

FATHER: [*Hurt but answering gently.*] You know very well, as a man of the theatre, that life is full of all sorts of odd things which have no need at all to pretend to be real because they are actually true.

PRODUCER: What the devil are you talking about?

FATHER: What I'm saying is that you really must be mad to do things the opposite way round: to create situations that obviously aren't true and try to make them seem to be really happening. But then I suppose that sort of madness is the only reason for your profession.

[*The* ACTORS *are indignant.*]

PRODUCER: [*Getting up and glaring at him.*] Oh, yes? So ours is a profession of madmen, is it?

FATHER: Well, if you try to make something look true when it obviously isn't, especially if you're not forced to do it, but do it for a game . . . Isn't it your job to give life on the stage to imaginary people?

PRODUCER: [*Quickly answering him and speaking for the* ACTORS *who are growing more indignant.*] I should like you to know, sir, that the actor's profession is one of great distinction. Even if nowadays the new writers only give us dull plays to act and puppets to present instead of men, I'd have you know that it is our boast that we have given life, here on this stage, to immortal works.

[*The* ACTORS, *satisfied, agree with and applaud the* PRODUCER.]

FATHER: [*Cutting in and following hard on his argument.*] There! You see? Good! You've given life! You've created living beings with more genuine life than people have who breathe and wear clothes! Less real, perhaps, but nearer the truth. We are both saying the same thing.

[*The* ACTORS *look at each other, astonished.*]

PRODUCER: But just a moment! You said before . . .

FATHER: I'm sorry, but I said that before, about acting for fun, because you shouted at us and said you'd no time to waste on idiots, but you must know better than anyone that Nature uses human imagination to lift her work of creation to even higher levels.

PRODUCER: All right then: but where does all this get us?

FATHER: Nowhere. I want to try to show that one can be thrust into life in many ways, in many forms: as a tree or a stone, as water or a butterfly— or as a woman. It might even be as a character in a play.

PRODUCER: [*Ironic, pretending to be annoyed.*] And you, and these other people here, were thrust into life, as you put it, as characters in a play?

FATHER: Exactly! And alive, as you can see.

[*The* PRODUCER *and the* ACTORS *burst into laughter as if at a joke.*]

FATHER: I'm sorry you laugh like that, because we carry in us, as I said before, a story of terrible anguish as you can guess from this woman dressed in black.

[*Saying this, he offers his hand to the* MOTHER *and helps her up the last steps and, holding her still by the hand, leads her with a sense of tragic solemnity across the stage which is suddenly lit by a fantastic light.*

The LITTLE GIRL *and the* BOY *follow the* MOTHER: *then the* SON *comes up and stands to one side in the background: then the* STEP-DAUGHTER *follows and leans against the proscenium arch: the* ACTORS *are astonished at first, but then, full of admiration for the "entrance," they burst into applause—just as if it were a performance specially for them.*]

PRODUCER: [*At first astonished and then indignant.*] My God! Be quiet all of you. [*Turns to the* CHARACTERS.] And you lot get out! Clear off! [*Turns to the* STAGE MANAGER.] Jesus! Get them out of here.

STAGE MANAGER: [*Comes forward but stops short as if held back by something strange.*] Go on out! Get out!

FATHER: [*To* PRODUCER.] Oh no, please, you see, we . . .

PRODUCER: [*Shouting.*] We came here to work, you know.

LEADING ACTOR: We really can't be messed about like this.

FATHER: [*Resolutely, coming forward.*] I'm astonished! Why don't you believe me? Perhaps you are not used to seeing the characters created by an author spring into life up here on the stage face to face with each other. Perhaps it's because we're not in a script? [*He points to the* PROMPTER*'s box.*]

STEPDAUGHTER: [*Coming down to the* PRODUCER, *smiling and persuasive.*] Believe me, sir, we really are six of the most fascinating characters. But we've been neglected.

FATHER: Yes, that's right, we've been neglected. In the sense that the author who created us, living in his mind, wouldn't or couldn't make us live in a written play for the world of art.[6] And that really is a crime sir, because whoever has the luck to be born a character can laugh even at death. Because a character will never die! A man will die, a writer, the instrument of creation: but what he has created will never die! And to be able to live for ever you don't need to have extraordinary gifts or be able to do miracles. Who was Sancho Panza? Who was Prospero?[7] But they will live for ever because—living seeds—they had the luck to find a fruitful soil, an imagination which knew how to grow them and feed them, so that they will live for ever.

PRODUCER: This is all very well! But what do you want here?

FATHER: We want to live, sir.

PRODUCER: [*Ironically.*] For ever!

FATHER: No, no: only for a few moments—in you.

AN ACTOR: Listen to that!

LEADING ACTRESS: They want to live in us!

YOUNG ACTOR: [*Pointing to the* STEPDAUGHTER.] I don't mind . . . so long as I get her.

---

6. In the 1925 preface to *Six Characters*, Pirandello explains that these characters came to him first as characters for a novel that he later abandoned. Haunted by their half-realized personalities, he decided to use the situation in a play.   7. The magician and exiled duke of Milan in Shakespeare's *The Tempest*. Sancho Panza was Don Quixote's servant in Cervantes's novel *Don Quixote* (1605–15).

FATHER: Listen, listen: the play is all ready to be put together and if you and your actors would like to, we can work it out now between us.

PRODUCER: [*Annoyed.*] But what exactly do you want to do? We don't make up plays like that here! We present comedies and tragedies here.

FATHER: That's right, we know that of course. That's why we've come.

PRODUCER: And where's the script?

FATHER: It's in us, sir. [*The* ACTORS *laugh.*] The play is in us: we are the play and we are impatient to show it to you: the passion inside us is driving us on.

STEPDAUGHTER: [*Scornfully, with the tantalising charm of deliberate impudence.*] My passion, if only you knew! My passion for him! [*She points at the* FATHER *and suggests that she is going to embrace him: but stops and bursts into a screeching laugh.*]

FATHER: [*With sudden anger.*] You keep out of this for the moment! And stop laughing like that!

STEPDAUGHTER: Really? Then with your permission, ladies and gentlemen; even though it's only two months since I became an orphan, just watch how I can sing and dance.

[*The* ACTORS, *especially the younger, seem strangely attracted to her while she sings and dances and they edge closer and reach out their hands to catch hold of her.*[8] *She eludes them, and when the* ACTORS *applaud her and the* PRODUCER *speaks sharply to her she stays still quite removed from them all.*]

FIRST ACTOR: Very good! etc.

PRODUCER: [*Angrily.*] Be quiet! Do you think this is a nightclub? [*Turns to* FATHER *and asks with some concern.*] Is she a bit mad?

FATHER: Mad? Oh no—it's worse than that.

STEPDAUGHTER: [*Suddenly running to the* PRODUCER.] Yes. It's worse, much worse! Listen please! Let's put this play on at once, because you'll see that at a particular point I—when this darling little girl here—[*Taking the* LITTLE GIRL *by the hand from next to the* MOTHER *and crossing with her to the* PRODUCER.] Isn't she pretty? [*Takes her in her arms.*] Darling! Darling! [*Puts her down again and adds, moved very deeply but almost without wanting to.*] Well, this lovely little girl here, when God suddenly takes her from this poor Mother: and this little idiot here [*Turning to the* LITTLE BOY *and seizing him roughly by the sleeve.*] does the most stupid thing, like the half-wit he is,—then you will see me run away! Yes, you'll see me rush away! But not yet, not yet! Because, after all the intimate things there have been between him and me [*In the direction of the* FATHER, *with a horrible vulgar wink.*] I can't stay with them any longer, to watch the insult to this mother through that supercilious cretin over there. [*Pointing to the* SON.] Look at him! Look at him! Condescending, stand-offish, because he's the legitimate son, him! Full of contempt for me, for the boy and for the little girl: because we are bastards. Do you understand? Bastards. [*Running to the* MOTHER

---

8. Pirandello uses a contemporary popular song, "Chu-Chin-Chow" from the Ziegfeld Follies of 1917, for the Stepdaughter to display her talents.

and embracing her.] And this poor mother—she—who is the mother of all of us—he doesn't want to recognise her as his own mother—and he looks down on her, he does, as if she were only the mother of the three of us who are bastards—the traitor. [*She says all this quickly, with great excitement, and after having raised her voice on the word "bastards" she speaks quietly, half-spitting the word "traitor."*]

MOTHER: [*With deep anguish to the* PRODUCER.] Sir, in the name of these two little ones, I beg you . . . [*Feels herself grow faint and sways.*] Oh, my God.

FATHER: [*Rushing to support her with almost all the* ACTORS *bewildered and concerned.*] Get a chair someone . . . quick, get a chair for this poor widow.

[*One of the* ACTORS *offers a chair: the others press urgently around. The* MOTHER, *seated now, tries to stop the* FATHER *lifting her veil.*]

ACTORS: Is it real? Has she really fainted? etc.

FATHER: Look at her, everybody, look at her.

MOTHER: No, for God's sake, stop it.

FATHER: Let them look?

MOTHER: [*Lifting her hands and covering her face, desperately.*] Oh, please, I beg you, stop him from doing what he is trying to do; it's hateful.

PRODUCER: [*Overwhelmed, astounded.*] It's no use, I don't understand this any more. [*To the* FATHER.] Is this woman your wife?

FATHER: [*At once.*] That's right, she is my wife.

PRODUCER: How is she a widow, then, if you're still alive?

[*The* ACTORS *are bewildered too and find relief in a loud laugh.*]

FATHER: [*Wounded, with rising resentment.*] Don't laugh! Please don't laugh like that! That's just the point, that's her own drama. You see, she had another man. Another man who ought to be here.

MOTHER: No, no! [*Crying out.*]

STEPDAUGHTER: Luckily for him he died. Two months ago, as I told you: we are in mourning for him, as you can see.

FATHER: Yes, he's dead: but that's not the reason he isn't here. He isn't here because—well just look at her, please, and you'll understand at once—hers is not a passionate drama of the love of two men, because she was incapable of love, she could feel nothing—except, perhaps a little gratitude (but not to me, to him). She's not a woman; she's a mother. And her drama—and, believe me, it's a powerful one—her drama is focused completely on these four children of the two men she had.

MOTHER: I had them? How dare you say that I had them, as if I wanted them myself? It was him, sir! He forced the other man on me. He made me go away with him!

STEPDAUGHTER: [*Leaping up, indignantly.*] It isn't true!

MOTHER: [*Bewildered.*] How isn't it true?

STEPDAUGHTER: It isn't true, it just isn't true.

MOTHER: What do you know about it?

STEPDAUGHTER: It isn't true. [*To the* PRODUCER.] Don't believe it! Do you know why she said that? She said it because of him, over there. [*Pointing to the* SON.] She tortures herself, she exhausts herself with worry and all because of the indifference of that son of hers. She wants to make him believe that she abandoned him when he was two years old because the Father made her do it.

MOTHER: [*Passionately.*] He did! He made me! God's my witness. [*To the* PRODUCER.] Ask him if it isn't true. [*Pointing to the* FATHER.] Make him tell our son it's true. [*Turning to the* STEPDAUGHTER.] You don't know anything about it.

STEPDAUGHTER: I know that when my father was alive you were always happy and contented. You can't deny it.

MOTHER: No, I can't deny it.

STEPDAUGHTER: He was always full of love and care for you. [*Turning to the* LITTLE BOY *with anger.*] Isn't it true? Admit it. Why don't you say something, you little idiot?

MOTHER: Leave the poor boy alone! Why do you want to make me appear ungrateful? You're my daughter. I don't in the least want to offend your father's memory. I've already told him that it wasn't my fault or even to please myself that I left his house and my son.

FATHER: It's quite true. It was my fault.

LEADING ACTOR: [*To other actors.*] Look at this. What a show!

LEADING ACTRESS: And we're the audience.

YOUNG ACTOR: For a change.

PRODUCER: [*Beginning to be very interested.*] Let's listen to them! Quiet! Listen!

[*He goes down the steps into the auditorium and stands there as if to get an idea of what the scene will look like from the audience's viewpoint.*]

SON: [*Without moving, coldly, quietly, ironically.*] Yes, listen to his little scrap of philosophy. He's going to tell you all about the Daemon of Experiment.

FATHER: You're a cynical idiot, and I've told you so a hundred times. [*To the* PRODUCER *who is now in the stalls.*] He sneers at me because of this expression I've found to defend myself.

SON: Words, words.

FATHER: Yes words, words! When we're faced by something we don't understand, by a sense of evil that seems as if it's going to swallow us, don't we all find comfort in a word that tells us nothing but that calms us?

STEPDAUGHTER: And dulls your sense of remorse, too. That more than anything.

FATHER: Remorse? No, that's not true. It'd take more than words to dull the sense of remorse in me.

STEPDAUGHTER: It's taken a little money too, just a little money. The money that he was going to offer as payment, gentlemen.

[*The* ACTORS *are horrified.*]

SON: [*Contemptuously to his stepsister.*] That's a filthy trick.

STEPDAUGHTER: A filthy trick? There it was in a pale blue envelope on the little mahogany table in the room behind the shop at Madame Pace's.

You know Madame Pace, don't you? One of those Madames who sell "Robes et Manteaux" so that they can attract poor girls like me from decent families into their workroom.[9]

SON: And she's bought the right to tyrannise over the whole lot of us with that money—with what he was going to pay her: and luckily—now listen carefully—he had no reason to pay it to her.

STEPDAUGHTER: But it was close!

MOTHER: [*Rising up angrily.*] Shame on you, daughter! Shame!

STEPDAUGHTER: Shame? Not shame, revenge! I'm desperate, desperate to live that scene! The room . . . over here the showcase of coats, there the divan, there the mirror, and the screen, and over there in front of the window, that little mahogany table with the pale blue envelope and the money in it. I can see it all quite clearly. I could pick it up! But you should turn your faces away, gentlemen: because I'm nearly naked! I'm not blushing any longer—I leave that to him. [*Pointing at the* FATHER.] But I tell you he was very pale, very pale then. [*To the* PRODUCER.] Believe me.

PRODUCER: I don't understand any more.

FATHER: I'm not surprised when you're attacked like that! Why don't you put your foot down and let me have my say before you believe all these horrible slanders she's so viciously telling about me.

STEPDAUGHTER: We don't want to hear any of your long winded fairy-stories.

FATHER: I'm not going to tell any fairy-stories! I want to explain things to him.

STEPDAUGHTER: I'm sure you do. Oh, yes! In your own special way.

[*The* PRODUCER *comes back up on stage to take control.*]

FATHER: But isn't that the cause of all the trouble? Words! We all have a world of things inside ourselves and each one of us has his own private world. How can we understand each other if the words I use have the sense and the value that I expect them to have, but whoever is listening to me inevitably thinks that those same words have a different sense and value, because of the private world he has inside himself too. We think we understand each other: but we never do. Look! All my pity, all my compassion for this woman [*Pointing to the* MOTHER.] she sees as ferocious cruelty.

MOTHER: But he turned me out of the house!

FATHER: There, do you hear? I turned her out! She really believed that I had turned her out.

MOTHER: You know how to talk. I don't . . . But believe me, sir, [*Turning to the* PRODUCER.] after he married me . . . I can't think why! I was a poor, simple woman.

FATHER: But that was the reason! I married you for your simplicity, that's what I loved in you, believing—[*He stops because she is making gestures of contradiction. Then, seeing the impossibility of making her understand, he throws his arms wide in a gesture of desperation and*

9. The implication is that Madame Pace (Italian for "peace") runs a call-girl operation under the guise of selling fashionable "dresses and coats."

turns back to the PRODUCER.] No, do you see? She says no! It's terrifying, sir, believe me, terrifying, her deafness, her mental deafness. [*He taps his forehead.*] Affection for her children, oh yes. But deaf, mentally deaf, deaf, sir, to the point of desperation.

STEPDAUGHTER: Yes, but make him tell you what good all his cleverness has brought us.

FATHER: If only we could see in advance all the harm that can come from the good we think we are doing.

> [*The* LEADING ACTRESS, *who has been growing angry watching the* LEADING ACTOR *flirting with the* STEPDAUGHTER, *comes forward and snaps at the* PRODUCER.]

LEADING ACTRESS: Excuse me, are we going to go on with our rehearsal?

PRODUCER: Yes, of course. But I want to listen to this first.

YOUNG ACTOR: It's such a new idea.

YOUNG ACTRESS: It's fascinating.

LEADING ACTRESS: For those who are interested. [*She looks meaningfully at the* LEADING ACTOR.]

PRODUCER: [*To the* FATHER.] Look here, you must explain yourself more clearly. [*He sits down.*]

FATHER: Listen then. You see, there was a rather poor fellow working for me as my assistant and secretary, very loyal: he understood her in everything. [*Pointing to the* MOTHER.] But without a hint of deceit, you must believe that: he was good and simple, like her: neither of them was capable even of thinking anything wrong, let alone doing it.

STEPDAUGHTER: So instead he thought of it for them and did it too!

FATHER: It's not true! What I did was for their good—oh yes and mine too, I admit it! The time had come when I couldn't say a word to either of them without there immediately flashing between them a sympathetic look: each one caught the other's eye for advice, about how to take what I had said, how not to make me angry. Well, that was enough, as I'm sure you'll understand, to put me in a bad temper all the time, in a state of intolerable exasperation.

PRODUCER: Then why didn't you sack this secretary of yours?

FATHER: Right! In the end I did sack him! But then I had to watch this poor woman wandering about in the house on her own, forlorn, like a stray animal you take in out of pity.

MOTHER: It's quite true.

FATHER: [*Suddenly, turning to her, as if to stop her.*] And what about the boy? Is that true as well?

MOTHER: But first he tore my son from me, sir.

FATHER: But not out of cruelty! It was so that he could grow up healthy and strong, in touch with the earth.

STEPDAUGHTER: [*Pointing to the* SON *jeeringly.*] And look at the result!

FATHER: [*Quickly.*] And is it my fault, too, that he's grown up like this? I took him to a nurse in the country, a peasant, because his mother didn't seem strong enough to me, although she is from a humble family herself. In fact that was what made me marry her. Perhaps it was superstitious of me; but what was I to do? I've always had this dreadful longing for a kind of sound moral healthiness.

[*The* STEPDAUGHTER *breaks out again into noisy laughter.*]
Make her stop that! It's unbearable.

PRODUCER: Stop it will you? Let me listen, for God's sake.

[*When the* PRODUCER *has spoken to her, she resumes her previous position . . . absorbed and distant, a half-smile on her lips. The* PRODUCER *comes down into the auditorium again to see how it looks from there.*]

FATHER: I couldn't bear the sight of this woman near me. [*Pointing to the* MOTHER.] Not so much because of the annoyance she caused me, you see, or even the feeling of being stifled, being suffocated that I got from her, as for the sorrow, the painful sorrow that I felt for her.

MOTHER: And he sent me away.

FATHER: With everything you needed, to the other man, to set her free from me.

MOTHER: And to set yourself free!

FATHER: Oh, yes, I admit it. And what terrible things came out of it. But I did it for the best, and more for her than for me: I swear it! [*Folds his arms: then turns suddenly to the* MOTHER.] I never lost sight of you did I? Until that fellow, without my knowing it, suddenly took you off to another town one day. He was idiotically suspicious of my interest in them, a genuine interest, I assure you, without any ulterior motive at all. I watched the new little family growing up round her with unbelievable tenderness, she'll confirm that. [*He points to the* STEPDAUGHTER.]

STEPDAUGHTER: Oh yes, I can indeed. I was a pretty little girl, you know, with plaits down to my shoulders and my little frilly knickers showing under my dress—so pretty—he used to watch me coming out of school. He came to see how I was maturing.

FATHER: That's shameful! It's monstrous.

STEPDAUGHTER: No it isn't! Why do you say it is?

FATHER: It's monstrous! Monstrous. [*He turns excitedly to the* PRODUCER *and goes on in explanation.*] After she'd gone away [*Pointing to the* MOTHER.], my house seemed empty. She'd been like a weight on my spirit but she'd filled the house with her presence. Alone in the empty rooms I wandered about like a lost soul. This boy here, [*Indicating the* SON.] growing up away from home—whenever he came back to the home—I don't know—but he didn't seem to be mine any more. We needed the mother between us, to link us together, and so he grew up by himself, apart, with no connection to me either through intellect or love. And then—it must seem odd, but it's true—first I was curious about and then strongly attracted to the little family that had come about because of what I'd done. And the thought of them began to fill all the emptiness that I felt around me. I needed, I really needed to believe that she was happy, wrapped up in the simple cares of her life, · lucky because she was better off away from the complicated torments of a soul like mine. And to prove it, I used to watch that child coming out of school.

STEPDAUGHTER: Listen to him! He used to follow me along the street; he used to smile at me and when we came near the house he'd wave his hand—like this! I watched him, wide-eyed, puzzled. I didn't know who he was. I told my mother about him and she knew at once who it must be. [MOTHER *nods agreement.*] At first, she didn't let me go to school again, at any rate for a few days. But when I did go back, I saw him standing near the door again—looking ridiculous—with a brown paper bag in his hand. He came close and petted me: then he opened the bag and took out a beautiful straw hat with a hoop of rosebuds round it—for me!

PRODUCER: All this is off the point, you know.

SON: [*Contemptuously.*] Yes . . . literature, literature.

FATHER: What do you mean, literature? This is real life: real passions.

PRODUCER: That may be! But you can't put it on the stage just like that.

FATHER: That's right you can't. Because all this is only leading up to the main action. I'm not suggesting that this part should be put on the stage. In any case, you can see for yourself, [*Pointing at the* STEPDAUGHTER.] she isn't a pretty little girl any longer with plaits down to her shoulders.

STEPDAUGHTER: —and with frilly knickers showing under her frock.

FATHER: The drama begins now: and it's new and complex.

STEPDAUGHTER: [*Coming forward, fierce and brooding.*] As soon as my father died . . .

FATHER: [*Quickly, not giving her time to speak.*] They were so miserable. They came back here, but I didn't know about it because of the Mother's stubbornness. [*Pointing to the* MOTHER.] She can't really write you know; but she could have got her daughter to write, or the boy, or tell me that they needed help.

MOTHER: But tell me, sir, how could I have known how he felt?

FATHER: And hasn't that always been your fault? You've never known anything about how I felt.

MOTHER: After all the years away from him and after all that had happened.

FATHER: And was it my fault if that fellow took you so far away? [*Turning back to the* PRODUCER.] Suddenly, overnight, I tell you, he'd found a job away from here without my knowing anything about it. I couldn't possibly trace them; and then, naturally I suppose, my interest in them grew less over the years. The drama broke out, unexpected and violent, when they came back: when I was driven in misery by the needs of my flesh, still alive with desire . . . and it is misery, you know, unspeakable misery for the man who lives alone and who detests sordid, casual affairs; not old enough to do without women, but not young enough to be able to go and look for one without shame! Misery? Is that what I called it. It's horrible, it's revolting, because there isn't a woman who will give her love to him any more. And when he realises this, he should do without . . . It's easy to say though. Each of us, face to face with other men, is clothed with some sort of dignity, but we know only too well all the unspeakable things that go on in the heart. We surrender, we give in to temptation: but afterwards we rise up out of it very quickly, in a desperate hurry to rebuild our dignity, whole and firm as if it were a gravestone that would cover every sign and memory of our shame, and hide it from even our own eyes. Everyone's like that, only some of us haven't the courage to talk about it.

STEPDAUGHTER: But they've all got the courage to do it!

FATHER: Yes! But only in secret! That's why it takes more courage to talk about it! Because if a man does talk about it—what happens then?—everybody says he's a cynic. And it's simply not true; he's just like everybody else; only better perhaps, because he's not afraid to use his intelligence to point out the blushing shame of human bestiality, that man, the beast, shuts his eyes to, trying to pretend it doesn't exist. And what about woman—what is she like? She looks at you invitingly, teasingly. You take her in your arms. But as soon as she feels your arms round her she closes her eyes. It's the sign of her mission, the sign by which she says to a man, "Blind yourself—I'm blind!"

STEPDAUGHTER: And when she doesn't close her eyes any more? What then? When she doesn't feel the need to hide from herself any more, to shut her eyes and hide her own shame. When she can see instead, dispassionately and dry-eyed this blushing shame of a man who has blinded himself, who is without love. What then? Oh, then what disgust, what utter disgust she feels for all these intellectual complications, for all this philosophy that points to the bestiality of man and then tries to defend him, to excuse him ... I can't listen to him, sir. Because when a man says he needs to "simplify" life like this—reducing it to bestiality—and throws away every human scrap of innocent desire, genuine feeling, idealism, duty, modesty, shame, then there's nothing more contemptible and nauseating than his remorse—crocodile tears!

PRODUCER: Let's get to the point, let's get to the point. This is all chat.

FATHER: Right then! But a fact is like a sack—it won't stand up if it's empty. To make it stand up, first you have to put in it all the reasons and feelings that caused it in the first place. I couldn't possibly have known that when that fellow died they'd come back here, that they were desperately poor and that the Mother had gone out to work as a dressmaker, nor that she'd gone to work for Madame Pace, of all people.

STEPDAUGHTER: She's a very high-class dressmaker—you must understand that. She apparently has only high-class customers, but she has arranged things carefully so that these high-class customers in fact serve her—they give her a respectable front ... without spoiling things for the other ladies at the shop who are not quite so high-class at all.

MOTHER: Believe me, sir, the idea never entered my head that the old hag gave me work because she had an eye on my daughter ...

STEPDAUGHTER: Poor Mummy! Do you know what that woman would do when I took back the work that my mother had been doing? She would point out how the dress had been ruined by giving it to my mother to sew: she bargained, she grumbled. So, you see, I paid for it, while this poor woman here thought she was sacrificing herself for me and these two children, sewing dresses all night for Madame Pace.

[The ACTORS *make gestures and noises of disgust.*]

PRODUCER: [*Quickly.*] And there one day, you met ...

STEPDAUGHTER: [*Pointing at the* FATHER.] Yes, him. Oh, he was an old customer of hers! What a scene that's going to be, superb!

FATHER: With her, the mother, arriving—

STEPDAUGHTER: [*Quickly, viciously.*]—Almost in time!

FATHER: [*Crying out.*]—No, just in time, just in time! Because, luckily, I found out who she was in time. And I took them all back to my house, sir. Can you imagine the situation now, for the two of us living in the same house? She, just as you see her here: and I, not able to look her in the face.

STEPDAUGHTER: It's so absurd! Do you think it's possible for me, sir, after what happened at Madame Pace's, to pretend that I'm a modest little miss, well brought up and virtuous just so that I can fit in with his damned pretensions to a "sound moral healthiness"?

FATHER: This is the real drama for me; the belief that we all, you see, think of ourselves as one single person: but it's not true: each of us is several different people, and all these people live inside us. With one person we seem like this and with another we seem very different. But we always have the illusion of being the same person for everybody and of always being the same person in everything we do. But it's not true! It's not true! We find this out for ourselves very clearly when by some terrible chance we're suddenly stopped in the middle of doing something and we're left dangling there, suspended. We realise then, that every part of us was not involved in what we'd been doing and that it would be a dreadful injustice of other people to judge us only by this one action as we dangle there, hanging in chains, fixed for all eternity, as if the whole of one's personality were summed up in that single, interrupted action. Now do you understand this girl's treachery? She accidentally found me somewhere I shouldn't have been, doing something I shouldn't have been doing! She discovered a part of me that shouldn't have existed for her: and now she wants to fix on me a reality that I should never have had to assume for her: it came from a single brief and shameful moment in my life. This is what hurts me most of all. And you'll see that the play will make a tremendous impact from this idea of mine. But then, there's the position of the others. His . . . [*Pointing to the* SON.]

SON: [*Shrugging his shoulders scornfully.*] Leave me out of it. I don't come into this.

FATHER: Why don't you come into this?

SON: I don't come into it and I don't want to come into it, because you know perfectly well that I wasn't intended to be mixed up with you lot.

STEPDAUGHTER: We're vulgar, common people, you see! He's a fine gentleman. But you've probably noticed that every now and then I look at him contemptuously, and when I do, he lowers his eyes—he knows the harm he's done me.

SON: [*Not looking at her.*] I have?

STEPDAUGHTER: Yes, you. It's your fault, dearie, that I went on the streets! Your fault! [*Movement of horror from the* ACTORS.] Did you or didn't you, with your attitude, deny us—I won't say the intimacy of your home—but that simple hospitality that makes guests feel comfortable? We were intruders who had come to invade the country of your "legitimacy"! [*Turning to the* PRODUCER.] I'd like you to have seen some of the little scenes that went on between him and me, sir. He says that I tyrannised over everyone. But don't you see? It was because of the way he treated us. He called it "vile" that I should insist on the right we had to move into his house with my mother—and she's his mother too. And I went into the house as its mistress.

SON: [*Slowly coming forward.*] They're really enjoying themselves, aren't they, sir? It's easy when they all gang up against me. But try to imagine what happened: one fine day, there is a son sitting quietly at home and he sees arrive as bold as brass, a young woman like this, who cheekily asks for his father, and heaven knows what business she has with him. Then he sees her come back with the same brazen look in her eye accompanied by that little girl there: and he sees her treat his father— without knowing why—in a most ambiguous and insolent way—asking him for money in a tone that leads one to suppose he really ought to give it, because he is obliged to do so.

FATHER: But I was obliged to do so: I owed it to your mother.

SON: And how was I to know that? When had I ever seen her before? When had I ever heard her mentioned? Then one day I see her come in with her [*Pointing at the* STEPDAUGHTER.], that boy and that little girl: they say to me, "Oh, didn't you know? This is your mother, too." Little by little I began to understand, mostly from her attitude. [*Points to* STEPDAUGHTER.] Why they'd come to live in the house so suddenly. I can't and I won't say what I feel, and what I think. I wouldn't even like to confess it to myself. So I can't take any active part in this. Believe me, sir, I am a character who has not been fully developed dramatically, and I feel uncomfortable, most uncomfortable, in their company. So please leave me out of it.

FATHER: What! But it's precisely because you feel like this . . .

SON: [*Violently exasperated.*] How do you know what I feel?

FATHER: All right! I admit it! But isn't that a situation in itself? This withdrawing of yourself, it's cruel to me and to your mother: when she came back to the house, seeing you almost for the first time, not recognising you, but knowing that you're her own son . . . [*Turning to point out the* MOTHER *to the* PRODUCER.] There, look at her: she's weeping.

STEPDAUGHTER: [*Angrily, stamping her foot.*] Like the fool she is!

FATHER: [*Quickly pointing at the* STEPDAUGHTER *to the* PRODUCER.] She can't stand that young man, you know. [*Turning and referring to the* SON.] He says that he doesn't come into it, but he's really the pivot of the action! Look here at this little boy, who clings to his mother all the time, frightened, humiliated. And it's because of him over there! Perhaps this little boy's problem is the worst of all: he feels an outsider, more than the others do; he feels so mortified, so humiliated just being in the house,—because it's charity, you see. [*Quietly.*] He's like his father: timid; he doesn't say anything . . .

PRODUCER: It's not a good idea at all, using him: you don't know what a nuisance children are on the stage.

FATHER: He won't need to be on the stage for long. Nor will the little girl—she's the first to go.

PRODUCER: That's good! Yes. I tell you all this interests me—it interests me very much. I'm sure we've the material here for a good play.

STEPDAUGHTER: [*Trying to push herself in.*] With a character like me you have!

FATHER: [*Driving her off, wanting to hear what the* PRODUCER *has decided.*] You stay out of it!

PRODUCER: [*Going on, ignoring the interruption.*] It's new, yes.

FATHER: Oh, it's absolutely new!

PRODUCER: You've got a nerve, though, haven't you, coming here and throwing it at me like this?

FATHER: I'm sure you understand. Born as we are for the *stage* . . .

PRODUCER: Are you amateur actors?

FATHER: No! I say we are born for the stage because . . .

PRODUCER: Come on now! You're an old hand at this, at acting!

FATHER: No I'm not. I only act, as everyone does, the part in life that he's chosen for himself, or that others have chosen for him. And you can see that sometimes my own passion gets a bit out of hand, a bit theatrical, as it does with all of us.

PRODUCER: Maybe, maybe . . . But you do see, don't you, that without an author . . . I could give you someone's address . . .

FATHER: Oh no! Look here! You do it.

PRODUCER: Me? What are you talking about?

FATHER: Yes, you. Why not?

PRODUCER: Because I've never written anything!

FATHER: Well, why not start now, if you don't mind my suggesting it? There's nothing to it. Everybody's doing it. And your job is even easier, because we're here, all of us, alive before you.

PRODUCER: That's not enough.

FATHER: Why isn't it enough? When you've seen us live our drama . . .

PRODUCER: Perhaps so. But we'll still need someone to write it.

FATHER: Only to write it down, perhaps, while it happens in front of him— live—scene by scene. It'll be enough to sketch it out simply first and then run through it.

PRODUCER: [*Coming back up, tempted by the idea.*] Do you know I'm almost tempted . . . just for fun . . . it might work.

FATHER: Of course it will. You'll see what wonderful scenes will come right out of it! I could tell you what they will be!

PRODUCER: You tempt me . . . you tempt me! We'll give it a chance. Come with me to the office. [*Turning to the* ACTORS.] Take a break: but don't go far away. Be back in a quarter of an hour or twenty minutes. [*To the* FATHER.] Let's see, let's try it out. Something extraordinary might come out of this.

FATHER: Of course it will! Don't you think it'd be better if the others came too? [*Indicating the other* CHARACTERS.]

PRODUCER: Yes, come on, come on. [*Going, then turning to speak to the* ACTORS.] Don't forget: don't be late: back in a quarter of an hour.

[*The* PRODUCER *and the* SIX CHARACTERS *cross the stage and go. The* ACTORS *look at each other in astonishment.*]

LEADING ACTOR: Is he serious? What's he going to do?

YOUNG ACTOR: I think he's gone round the bend.

ANOTHER ACTOR: Does he expect to make up a play in five minutes?

YOUNG ACTOR: Yes, like the old actors in the commedia dell'arte![1]

LEADING ACTRESS: Well if he thinks I'm going to appear in that sort of nonsense . . .

YOUNG ACTOR: Nor me!

FOURTH ACTOR: I should like to know who they are.

THIRD ACTOR: Who do you think? They're probably escaped lunatics—or crooks.

YOUNG ACTOR: And is he taking them seriously?

YOUNG ACTRESS: It's vanity. The vanity of seeing himself as an author.

LEADING ACTOR: I've never heard of such a thing! If the theatre, ladies and gentlemen, is reduced to this . . .

FIFTH ACTOR: I'm enjoying it!

THIRD ACTOR: Really! We shall have to wait and see what happens next I suppose.

[*Talking, they leave the stage. Some go out through the back door, some to the dressing-rooms.*

The curtain stays up.

The interval lasts twenty minutes.]

Act Two

The theatre warning-bell sounds to call the audience back. From the dressing-rooms, the door at the back and even from the auditorium, the ACTORS, *the* STAGE MANAGER, *the* STAGE HANDS, *the* PROMPTER, *the* PROPERTY MAN *and the* PRODUCER, *accompanied by the* SIX CHARACTERS *all come back on to the stage.*

The house lights go out and the stage lights come on again.

PRODUCER: Come on, everybody! Are we all here? Quiet now! Listen! Let's get started! Stage manager?

STAGE MANAGER: Yes, I'm here.

PRODUCER: Give me that little parlour setting, will you? A couple of plain flats and a door flat will do. Hurry up with it!

[*The* STAGE MANAGER *runs off to order someone to do this immediately and at the same time the* PRODUCER *is making arrangements with the* PROPERTY MAN, *the* PROMPTER, *and the* ACTORS: *the two flats and the door flat are painted in pink and gold stripes.*]

PRODUCER: [*To* PROPERTY MAN.] Go see if we have a sofa in stock.

PROPERTY MAN: Yes, there's that green one.

STEPDAUGHTER: No, no, not a green one! It was yellow, yellow velvet with flowers on it: it was enormous! And so comfortable!

PROPERTY MAN: We haven't got one like that.

PRODUCER: It doesn't matter! Give me whatever there is.

STEPDAUGHTER: What do you mean, it doesn't matter? It was Mme. Pace's famous sofa.

---

1. A form of popular theater beginning in 16th-century Italy; the actors improvised dialogue according to basic comic or dramatic plots and in response to the audience's reaction.

PRODUCER: It's only for a rehearsal! Please, don't interfere. [*To the* STAGE MANAGER.] Oh, and see if there's a shop window, will you—preferably a long, low one.

STEPDAUGHTER: And a little table, a little mahogany table for the blue envelope.

STAGE MANAGER: [*To the* PRODUCER.] There's that little gold one.

PRODUCER: That'll do—bring it.

FATHER: A mirror!

STEPDAUGHTER: And a screen! A screen, please, or I won't be able to manage, will I?

STAGE MANAGER: All right. We've lots of big screens, don't you worry.

PRODUCER: [*To* STEPDAUGHTER.] Then don't you want some coat-hangers and some clothes racks?

STEPDAUGHTER: Yes, lots of them, lots of them.

PRODUCER: [*To the* STAGE MANAGER]. See how many there are and have them brought up.

STAGE MANAGER: Right, I'll see to it.

[*The* STAGE MANAGER *goes off to do it: and while the* PRODUCER *is talking to the* PROMPTER, *the* CHARACTERS *and the* ACTORS, *the* STAGE MANAGER *is telling the* SCENE SHIFTERS *where to step up the furniture they have brought.*]

PRODUCER: [*To the* PROMPTER.] Now you, go sit down, will you? Look, this is an outline of the play, act by act. [*He hands him several sheets of paper.*] But you'll need to be on your toes.

PROMPTER: Shorthand?

PRODUCER: [*Pleasantly surprised.*] Oh, good! You know shorthand?

PROMPTER: I don't know much about prompting, but I do know about shorthand.

PRODUCER: Thank God for that anyway! [*He turns to a* STAGE HAND.] Go fetch me some paper from my office—lots of it—as much as you can find!

[*The* STAGE HAND *goes running off and then comes back shortly with a bundle of paper that he gives to the* PROMPTER.]

PRODUCER: [*Crossing to the* PROMPTER.] Follow the scenes, one after another, as they are played and try to get the lines down . . . at least the most important ones. [*Then turning to the* ACTORS.] Get out of the way everybody! Here, go over to the prompt side [*Pointing to stage left.*] and pay attention.

LEADING ACTRESS: But, excuse me, we . . .

PRODUCER: [*Anticipating her.*] You won't be expected to improvise, don't worry!

LEADING ACTOR: Then what are we expected to do?

PRODUCER: Nothing! Just go over there, listen and watch. You'll all be given your parts later written out. Right now we're going to rehearse, as well as we can. And they will be doing the rehearsal. [*He points to the* CHARACTERS.]

FATHER: [*Rather bewildered, as if he had fallen from the clouds into the middle of the confusion on the stage.*] We are? Excuse me, but what do you mean, a rehearsal?

PRODUCER: I mean a rehearsal—a rehearsal for the benefit of the actors. [*Pointing to the* ACTORS.]

FATHER: But if we are the characters . . .

PRODUCER: That's right, you're "the characters": but characters don't act here, my dear chap. It's actors who act here. The characters are there in the script—[*Pointing to the* PROMPTER.] that's when there is a script.

FATHER: That's the point! Since there isn't one and you have the luck to have the characters alive in front of you. . .

PRODUCER: Great! You want to do everything yourselves, do you? To act your own play, to produce your own play!

FATHER: Well yes, just as we are.

PRODUCER: That would be an experience for us, I can tell you!

LEADING ACTOR: And what about us? What would we be doing then?

PRODUCER: Don't tell me you think you know how to act! Don't make me laugh! [*The* ACTORS *in fact laugh.*] There you are, you see, you've made them laugh. [*Then remembering.*] But let's get back to the point! We need to cast the play. Well, that's easy: it almost casts itself. [*To the* SECOND ACTRESS.] You, the mother. [*To the* FATHER.] You'll need to give her a name.

FATHER: Amalia.

PRODUCER: But that's the real name of your wife isn't it? We can't use her real name.

FATHER: But why not? That is her name . . . But perhaps if this lady is to play the part . . . [*Indicating the* ACTRESS *vaguely with a wave of his hand.*] I don't know what to say . . . I'm already starting to . . . how can I explain it . . . to sound false, my own words sound like someone else's.

PRODUCER: Now don't worry yourself about it, don't worry about it at all. We'll work out the right tone of voice. As for the name, if you want it to be Amalia, then Amalia it shall be: or we can find another. For the moment we'll refer to the characters like this: [*To the* YOUNG ACTOR, *the juvenile lead.*] you are The Son. [*To the* LEADING ACTRESS.] You, of course, are The Stepdaughter.

STEPDAUGHTER: [*Excitedly.*] What did you say? That woman is me? [*Bursts into laughter.*]

PRODUCER: [*Angrily.*] What are you laughing at?

LEADING ACTRESS: [*Indignantly.*] Nobody has ever dared to laugh at me before! Either you treat me with respect or I'm walking out! [*Starting to go.*]

STEPDAUGHTER: I'm sorry. I wasn't really laughing at you.

PRODUCER: [*To the* STEPDAUGHTER.] You should feel proud to be played by . . .

LEADING ACTRESS: [*Quickly, scornfully.*] . . . that woman!

STEPDAUGHTER: But I wasn't thinking about her, honestly. I was thinking about me: I can't see myself in you at all . . . you're not a bit like me!

FATHER: Yes, that's right: you see, our meaning . . .

PRODUCER: What are you talking about, "our meaning"? Do you think you have exclusive rights to what you represent? Do you think it can only exist inside you? Not a bit of it!

FATHER: What? Don't we even have our own meaning?

PRODUCER: Not a bit of it! Whatever you mean is only material here, to which the actors give form and body, voice and gesture, and who, through their art, have given expression to much better material than what you have to offer: yours is really very trivial and if it stands up on the stage, the credit, believe me, will all be due to my actors.

FATHER: I don't dare to contradict you. But you for your part, must believe me—it doesn't seem trivial to us. We are suffering terribly now, with these bodies, these faces . . .

PRODUCER: [*Interrupting impatiently.*] Yes, well, the make-up will change that, make-up will change that, at least as far as the faces are concerned.

FATHER: Yes, but the voices, the gestures . . .

PRODUCER: That's enough! You can't come on the stage here as yourselves. It is our actors who will represent you here: and let that be the end of it!

FATHER: I understand that. But now I think I see why our author who saw us alive as we are here now, didn't want to put us on the stage. I don't want to offend your actors. God forbid that I should! But I think that if I saw myself represented . . . by I don't know whom . . .

LEADING ACTOR: [*Rising majestically and coming forward, followed by a laughing group of* YOUNG ACTRESSES.] By me, if you don't object.

FATHER: [*Respectfully, smoothly.*] I shall be honoured, sir. [*He bows.*] But I think, that no matter how hard this gentleman works with all his will and all his art to identify himself with me . . . [*He stops, confused.*]

LEADING ACTOR: Yes, go on.

FATHER: Well, I was saying the performance he will give, even if he is made up to look like me . . . I mean with the difference in our appearance . . . [*All the* ACTORS *laugh.*] it will be difficult for it to be a performance of me as I really am. It will be more like—well, not just because of his figure—it will be more an interpretation of what I am, what he believes me to be, and not how I know myself to be. And it seems to me that this should be taken into account by those who are going to comment on us.

PRODUCER: So you are already worrying about what the critics will say, are you? And I'm still waiting to get this thing started! The critics can say what they like: and we'll worry about putting on the play. If we can! [*Stepping out of the group and looking around.*] Come on, come on! Is the scene set for us yet? [*To the* ACTORS *and* CHARACTERS.] Out of the way! Let's have a look at it. [*Climbing down off the stage.*] Don't let's waste any more time. [*To the* STEPDAUGHTER.] Does it look all right to you?

SON: What! That? I don't recognise it at all.

PRODUCER: Good God! Did you expect us to reconstruct the room at the back of Mme. Pace's shop here on the stage? [*To the* FATHER.] Did you say the room had flowered wallpaper?

FATHER: White, yes.

PRODUCER: Well it's not white: it's striped. That sort of thing doesn't matter at all! As for the furniture, it looks to me as if we have nearly everything we need. Move that little table a bit further downstage. [*A* STAGE HAND *does it. To the* PROPERTY MAN.] Go and fetch an envelope, pale blue if

you can find one, and give it to that gentleman there. [*Pointing to the*
FATHER.]

STAGE HAND: An envelope for letters?

PRODUCER: } Yes, an envelope for letters!
FATHER:

STAGE HAND: Right. [*He goes off.*]

PRODUCER: Now then, come on! The first scene is the young lady's. [*The*
LEADING ACTRESS *comes to the centre.*] No, no, not yet. I said the young
lady's. [*He points to the* STEPDAUGHTER.] You stay there and watch.

STEPDAUGHTER: [*Adding quickly.*] . . . how I bring it to life.

LEADING ACTRESS: [*Resenting this.*] I shall know how to bring it to life,
don't you worry, when I am allowed to.

PRODUCER: [*His head in his hands.*] Ladies, please, no more arguments!
Now then. The first scene is between the young lady and Mme. Pace.
Oh! [*Worried, turning round and looking out into the auditorium.*]
Where is Mme. Pace?

FATHER: She isn't here with us.

PRODUCER: So what do we do now?

FATHER: But she is real. She's real too!

PRODUCER: All right. So where is she?

FATHER: May I deal with this? [*Turns to the* ACTRESSES.] Would each of
you ladies be kind enough to lend me a hat, a coat, a scarf or something?

ACTRESSES: [*Some are surprised or amused.*] What? My scarf? A coat?
What's he want my hat for? What are you wanting to do with them?
[*All the* ACTRESSES *are laughing.*]

FATHER: Oh, nothing much, just hang them up here on the racks for a
minute or two. Perhaps someone would be kind enough to lend me a
coat?

ACTORS: Just a coat? Come on, more! The man must be mad.

AN ACTRESS: What for? Only my coat?

FATHER: Yes, to hang up here, just for a moment. I'm very grateful to you.
Do you mind?

ACTRESSES: [*Taking off various hats, coats, scarves, laughing and going to
hang them on the racks.*] Why not? Here you are. I really think it's
crazy. Is it to dress the set?

FATHER: Yes, exactly. It's to dress the set.

PRODUCER: Would you mind telling me what you are doing?

FATHER: Yes, of course: perhaps, if we dress the set better, she will be
drawn by the articles of her trade and, who knows, she may even come
to join us . . . [*He invites them to watch the door at the back of the set.*]
Look! Look!

[*The door at the back opens and* MME. PACE *takes a few steps downstage: she is a gross old harridan wearing a ludicrous carroty-coloured
wig with a single red rose stuck in at one side, Spanish fashion: gar-
ishly made-up: in a vulgar but stylish red silk dress, holding an
ostrich-feather fan in one hand and a cigarette between two fingers
in the other. At the sight of this apparition, the* ACTORS *and the* PRO-
DUCER *immediately jump off the stage with cries of fear, leaping*

down into the auditorium and up the aisles. The STEPDAUGHTER, *however, runs across to* MME. PACE, *and greets her respectfully, as if she were the mistress.*]

STEPDAUGHTER: [*Running across to her.*] Here she is! Here she is!

FATHER: [*Smiling broadly.*] It's her! What did I tell you? Here she is!

PRODUCER: [*Recovering from his shock, indignantly.*] What sort of trick is this?

LEADING ACTOR: [*Almost at the same time as the others.*] What the hell is happening?

JUVENILE LEAD: Where on earth did they get that extra from?

YOUNG ACTRESS: They were keeping her hidden!

LEADING ACTRESS: It's a game, a conjuring trick!

FATHER: Wait a minute! Why do you want to spoil a miracle by being factual. Can't you see this is a miracle of reality, that is born, brought to life, lured here, reproduced, just for the sake of this scene, with more right to be alive here than you have? Perhaps it has more truth than you have yourselves. Which actress can improve on Mme. Pace there? Well? That is the real Mme. Pace. You must admit that the actress who plays her will be less true than she is herself—and there she is in person! Look! My daughter recognised her straight away and went to meet her. Now watch—just watch this scene.

[*Hesitantly, the* PRODUCER *and the* ACTORS *move back to their original places on the stage.*

But the scene between the STEPDAUGHTER *and* MME. PACE *had already begun while the* ACTORS *were protesting and the* FATHER *explaining: it is being played under their breaths, very quietly, very naturally, in a way that is obviously impossible on stage. So when the* ACTORS' *attention is recalled by the* FATHER *they turn and see that* MME. PACE *has just put her hand under the* STEPDAUGHTER's *chin to make her lift her head up: they also hear her speak in a way that is unintelligible to them. They watch and listen hard for a few moments, then they start to make fun of them.*]

PRODUCER: Well?

LEADING ACTOR: What's she saying?

LEADING ACTRESS: Can't hear a thing!

JUVENILE LEAD: Louder! Speak up!

STEPDAUGHTER: [*Leaving* MME. PACE *who has an astonishing smile on her face, and coming down to the* ACTORS.] Louder? What do you mean, "Louder"? What we're talking about you can't talk about loudly. I could shout about it a moment ago to embarrass him [*Pointing to the* FATHER.] to shame him and to get my own back on him! But it's a different matter for Mme. Pace. It would mean prison for her.

PRODUCER: What the hell are you on about? Here in the theatre you have to make yourself heard! Don't you see that? We can't hear you even from here, and we're on the stage with you! Imagine what it would be like with an audience out front! You need to make the scene go! And after all, you would speak normally to each other when you're alone, and you will be, because we shan't be here anyway. I mean we're only here because it's a rehearsal. So just imagine that there you are in the room at the back of the shop, and there's no one to hear you.

[*The* STEPDAUGHTER, *with a knowing smile, wags her finger and her head rather elegantly, as if to say no.*]

PRODUCER: Why not?

STEPDAUGHTER: [*Mysteriously, whispering loudly.*] Because there is someone who will hear if she speaks normally. [*Pointing to* MME. PACE.]

PRODUCER: [*Anxiously.*] You're not going to make someone else appear are you?

[*The* ACTORS *get ready to dive off the stage again.*]

FATHER: No, no. She means me. I ought to be over there, waiting behind the door: and Mme. Pace knows I'm there, so excuse me will you: I'll go there now so that I shall be ready for my entrance.

[*He goes towards the back of the stage.*]

PRODUCER: [*Stopping him.*] No, no wait a minute! You must remember the stage conventions! Before you can go on to that part . . .

STEPDAUGHTER: [*Interrupts him.*] Oh yes, let's get on with that part. Now! Now! I'm dying to do that scene. If he wants to go through it now, I'm ready!

PRODUCER: [*Shouting.*] But before that we must have, clearly stated, the scene between you and her. [*Pointing to* MME. PACE.] Do you see?

STEPDAUGHTER: Oh God! She's only told me what you already know, that my mother's needlework is badly done again, the dress is spoilt and that I shall have to be patient if I want her to go on helping us out of our mess.

MME. PACE: [*Coming forward, with a great air of importance.*] Ah, yes, sir, for that I do not wish to make a profit, to make advantage.

PRODUCER: [*Half frightened.*] What? Does she really speak like that?

[*All the* ACTORS *burst out laughing.*]

STEPDAUGHTER: [*Laughing too.*] Yes, she speaks like that, half in Spanish, in the silliest way imaginable!

MME. PACE: Ah it is not good manners that you laugh at me when I make myself to speak, as I can, English, señor.

PRODUCER: No, no, you're right! Speak like that, please speak like that, madam. It'll be marvelous. Couldn't be better! It'll add a little touch of comedy to a rather crude situation. Speak like that! It'll be great!

STEPDAUGHTER: Great! Why not? When you hear a proposition made in that sort of accent, it'll almost seem like a joke, won't it? Perhaps you'll want to laugh when you hear that there's an "old señor"[2] who wants to "amuse himself with me" — isn't that right, Madame?

MME. PACE: Not so old . . . but not quite young, no? But if he is not to your taste . . . he is, how you say, discreet!

[*The* MOTHER *leaps up, to the astonishment and dismay of the* ACTORS *who had not been paying any attention to her, so that when she shouts out they are startled and then smilingly restrain her: however she has already snatched off* MME. PACE's *wig and flung it on the floor.*]

---

2. Old gentleman.

MOTHER: You witch! Witch! Murderess! Oh, my daughter!

STEPDAUGHTER: [*Running across and taking hold of the* MOTHER.] No! No! Mother! Please!

FATHER: [*Running across to her as well.*] Calm yourself, calm yourself! Come and sit down.

MOTHER: Get her away from here!

STEPDAUGHTER: [*To the* PRODUCER *who has also crossed to her.*] My mother can't bear to be in the same place with her.

FATHER: [*Also speaking quietly to the* PRODUCER.] They can't possibly be in the same place! That's why she wasn't with us when we first came, do you see! If they meet, everything's given away from the very beginning.

PRODUCER: It's not important, that's not important! This is only a first run-through at the moment! It's all useful stuff, even if it is confused. I'll sort it all out later. [*Turning to the* MOTHER *and taking her to sit down on her chair.*] Come on, my dear, take it easy; take it easy: come and sit down again.

STEPDAUGHTER: Go on, Mme. Pace.

MME. PACE: [*Offended.*] Oh no, thank-you! I no longer do nothing here with your mother present.

STEPDAUGHTER: Get on with it, bring in this "old señor" who wants to "amuse himself with me"! [*Turning majestically to the others.*] You see, this next scene has got to be played out—we must do it now. [*To* MME. PACE.] Oh, you can go!

MME. PACE: Ah, I go, I go—I go! Most probably! I go!

[*She leaves banging her wig back into place, glaring furiously at the* ACTORS *who applaud her exit, laughing loudly.*]

STEPDAUGHTER: [*To the* FATHER.] Now you come on! No, you don't need to go off again! Come back! Pretend you've just come in! Look, I'm standing here with my eyes on the ground, modestly—well, come on, speak up! Use that special sort of voice, like somebody who has just come in. "Good afternoon, my dear."

PRODUCER: [*Off the stage by now.*] Look here, who's the director here, you or me? [*To the* FATHER *who looks uncertain and bewildered.*] Go on, do as she says: go upstage—no, no don't bother to make an entrance. Then come down stage again.

[*The* FATHER *does as he is told, half mesmerised. He is very pale but already involved in the reality of his re-created life, smiles as he draws near the back of the stage, almost as if he genuinely is not aware of the drama that is about to sweep over him. The* ACTORS *are immediately intent on the scene that is beginning now.*]

The Scene

FATHER: [*Coming forward with a new note in his voice.*] Good afternoon, my dear.

STEPDAUGHTER: [*Her head down trying to hide her fright.*] Good afternoon.

FATHER: [*Studying her a little under the brim of her hat which partly hides her face from him and seeing that she is very young, he exclaims to himself a little complacently and a little guardedly because of the danger of being compromised in a risky adventure.*] Ah . . . but . . . tell me, this won't be the first time, will it? The first time you've been here?

STEPDAUGHTER: No, sir.

FATHER: You've been here before? [*And after the* STEPDAUGHTER *has nodded an answer.*] More than once? [*He waits for her reply: tries again to look at her under the brim of her hat: smiles: then says.*] Well then . . . it shouldn't be too . . . May I take off your hat?

STEPDAUGHTER: [*Quickly, to stop him, unable to conceal her shudder of fear and disgust.*] No, don't! I'll do it!

[*She takes it off unsteadily.*

The MOTHER *watches the scene intently with the* SON *and the two smaller children who cling close to her all the time: they make a group on one side of the stage opposite the* ACTORS: *She follows the words and actions of the* FATHER *and the* STEPDAUGHTER *in this scene with a variety of expressions on her face—sadness, dismay, anxiety, horror: sometimes she turns her face away and sobs.*]

MOTHER: Oh God! Oh God!

FATHER: [*He stops as if turned to stone by the sobbing: then he goes on in the same tone of voice.*] Here, give it to me. I'll hang it up for you. [*He takes the hat in his hand.*] But such a pretty, dear little head like yours should have a much smarter hat than this! Would you like to help me choose one, then, from these hats of Madame's hanging up here? Would you?

YOUNG ACTRESS: [*Interrupting.*] Be careful! Those are our hats!

PRODUCER: [*Quickly and angrily.*] For God's sake, shut up! Don't try to be funny! We're rehearsing! [*Turns back to the* STEPDAUGHTER.] Please go on, will you, from where you were interrupted.

STEPDAUGHTER: [*Going on.*] No, thank you, sir.

FATHER: Oh, don't say no to me please! Say you'll have one—to please me. Isn't this a pretty one—look! And then it will please Madame too, you know. She's put them out here on purpose, of course.

STEPDAUGHTER: No, look, I could never wear it.

FATHER: Are you thinking of what they would say at home when you went in wearing a new hat? Goodness me! Don't you know what to do? Shall I tell you what to say at home?

STEPDAUGHTER: [*Furiously, nearly exploding.*] That's not why! I couldn't wear it because . . . as you can see: you should have noticed it before. [*Indicating her black dress.*]

FATHER: You're in mourning! Oh, forgive me. You're right, I see that now. Please forgive me. Believe me, I'm really very sorry.

STEPDAUGHTER: [*Gathering all her strength and making herself overcome her contempt and revulsion.*] That's enough. Don't go on, that's enough. I ought to be thanking you and not letting you blame yourself and get upset. Don't think any more about what I told you, please. And I should do the same. [*Forcing herself to smile and adding.*] I should try to forget that I'm dressed like this.

PRODUCER: [*Interrupting, turning to the* PROMPTER *in the box and jumping up on the stage again*]. Hold it, hold it! Don't put that last line

down, leave it out. [*Turning to the* FATHER *and the* STEPDAUGHTER.] It's
going well! It's going well! [*Then to the* FATHER *alone.*] Then we'll put
in there the bit that we talked about. [*To the* ACTORS.] That scene with
the hats is good, isn't it?

STEPDAUGHTER: But the best bit is coming now! Why can't we get on with
it?

PRODUCER: Just be patient, wait a minute. [*Turning and moving across to
the* ACTORS.] Of course, it'll all have to be made a lot more light-hearted.

LEADING ACTOR: We shall have to play it a lot quicker, I think.

LEADING ACTRESS: Of course: there's nothing particularly difficult in it.
[*To the* LEADING ACTOR.] Shall we run through it now?

LEADING ACTOR: Yes right . . . Shall we take it from my entrance? [*He goes
to his position behind the door upstage.*]

PRODUCER: [*To the* LEADING ACTRESS.] Now then, listen, imagine the
scene between you and Mme. Pace is finished. I'll write it up myself
properly later on. You ought to be over here I think—[*She goes the
opposite way.*] Where are you going now?

LEADING ACTRESS: Just a minute, I want to get my hat—[*She crosses to
take her hat from the stand.*]

PRODUCER: Right, good, ready now? You are standing here with your head
down.

STEPDAUGHTER: [*Very amused.*] But she's not dressed in black!

LEADING ACTRESS: Oh, but I shall be, and I'll look a lot better than you
do, darling.

PRODUCER: [*To the* STEPDAUGHTER.] Shut up, will you! Go over there and
watch! You might learn something! [*Clapping his hands.*] Right! Come
on! Quiet please! Take it from his entrance.

[*He climbs off stage so that he can see better. The door opens at the
back of the set and the* LEADING ACTOR *enters with the lively, knowing
air of an ageing roué.*[3] *The playing of the following scene by the*
ACTORS *must seem from the very beginning to be something quite
different from the earlier scene, but without having the faintest air of
parody in it.*

Naturally the STEPDAUGHTER *and the* FATHER *unable to see themselves in the* LEADING ACTOR *and* LEADING ACTRESS, *hearing their
words said by them, express their reactions in different ways, by gestures, or smiles or obvious protests so that we are aware of their suffering, their astonishment, their disbelief.*

The PROMPTER's *voice is heard clearly between every line in the
scene, telling the* ACTORS *what to say next.*]

LEADING ACTOR: Good afternoon, my dear.

FATHER: [*Immediately, unable to restrain himself.*] Oh, no!

[*The* STEPDAUGHTER, *watching the* LEADING ACTOR *enter this way,
bursts into laughter.*]

PRODUCER: [*Furious.*] Shut up, for God's sake! And don't you dare laugh
like that! We're never going to get anywhere at this rate.

STEPDAUGHTER: [*Coming to the front.*] I'm sorry, I can't help it! The lady

3. Dissipated lover.

stands exactly where you told her to stand and she never moved. But if it were me and I heard someone say good afternoon to me in that way and with a voice like that I should burst out laughing—so I did.

FATHER: [*Coming down a little too.*] Yes, she's right, the whole manner, the voice . . .

PRODUCER: To hell with the manner and the voice! Get out of the way, will you, and let me watch the rehearsal!

LEADING ACTOR: [*Coming down stage.*] If I have to play an old man who has come to a knocking shop—

PRODUCER: Take no notice, ignore them. Go on please! It's going well, it's going well! [*He waits for the* ACTOR *to begin again.*] Right, again!

LEADING ACTOR: Good afternoon, my dear.

LEADING ACTRESS: Good afternoon.

LEADING ACTOR: [*Copying the gestures of the* FATHER, *looking under the brim of the hat, but expressing distinctly the two emotions, first, complacent satisfaction and then anxiety.*] Ah! But tell me . . . this won't be the first time I hope.

FATHER: [*Instinctively correcting him.*] Not "I hope"—"will it," "will it."

PRODUCER: Say "will it"—and it's a question.

LEADING ACTOR: [*Glaring at the* PROMPTER.] I distinctly heard him say "I hope."

PRODUCER: So what? It's all the same, "I hope" or "isn't it." It doesn't make any difference. Carry on, carry on. But perhaps it should still be a little bit lighter; I'll show you—watch me! [*He climbs up on the stage again, and going back to the entrance, he does it himself.*] Good afternoon, my dear.

LEADING ACTRESS: Good afternoon.

PRODUCER: Ah, tell me . . . [*He turns to the* LEADING ACTOR *to make sure that he has seen the way he has demonstrated of looking under the brim of the hat.*] You see—surprise . . . anxiety and self-satisfaction. [*Then, starting again, he turns to the* LEADING ACTRESS.] This won't be the first time, will it? The first time you've been here? [*Again turns to the* LEADING ACTOR *questioningly.*] Right? [*To the* LEADING ACTRESS.] And then she says, "No, sir." [*Again to* LEADING ACTOR.] See what I mean? More subtlety. [*And he climbs off the stage.*]

LEADING ACTRESS: No, sir.

LEADING ACTOR: You've been here before? More than once?

PRODUCER: No, no, no! Wait for it, wait for it. Let her answer first. "You've been here before?"

[*The* LEADING ACTRESS *lifts her head a little, her eyes closed in pain and disgust, and when the* PRODUCER *says "Now" she nods her head twice.*]

STEPDAUGHTER: [*Involuntarily.*] Oh, my God! [*And she immediately claps her hand over her mouth to stifle her laughter.*]

PRODUCER: What now?

STEPDAUGHTER: [*Quickly.*] Nothing, nothing!

PRODUCER: [*To* LEADING ACTOR.] Come on, then, now it's you.

LEADING ACTOR: More than once? Well then, it shouldn't be too . . . May I take off your hat?

[*The* LEADING ACTOR *says this last line in such a way and adds to it such a gesture that the* STEPDAUGHTER, *even with her hand over her mouth trying to stop herself laughing, can't prevent a noisy burst of laughter.*]

LEADING ACTRESS: [*Indignantly turning.*] I'm not staying any longer to be laughed at by that woman!

LEADING ACTOR: Nor am I! That's the end—no more!

PRODUCER: [*To* STEPDAUGHTER, *shouting.*] Once and for all, will you shut up! Shut up!

STEPDAUGHTER: Yes, I'm sorry . . . I'm sorry.

PRODUCER: You're an ill-mannered little bitch! That's what you are! And you've gone too far this time!

FATHER: [*Trying to interrupt.*] Yes, you're right, she went too far, but please forgive her . . .

PRODUCER: [*Jumping on the stage.*] Why should I forgive her? Her behaviour is intolerable!

FATHER: Yes, it is, but the scene made such a peculiar impact on us . . .

PRODUCER: Peculiar? What do you mean peculiar? Why peculiar?

FATHER: I'm full of admiration for your actors, for this gentleman [*To the* LEADING ACTOR.] and this lady. [*To the* LEADING ACTRESS.] But, you see, well . . . they're not us!

PRODUCER: Right! They're not! They're actors!

FATHER: That's just the point—they're actors. And they are acting our parts very well, both of them. But that's what's different. However much they want to be the same as us, they're not.

PRODUCER: But why aren't they? What is it now?

FATHER: It's something to do with . . . being themselves, I suppose, not being us.

PRODUCER: Well we can't do anything about that! I've told you already. You can't play the parts yourselves.

FATHER: Yes, I know, I know . . .

PRODUCER: Right then. That's enough of that. [*Turning back to the* ACTORS.] We'll rehearse this later on our own, as we usually do. It's always a bad idea to have rehearsals with authors there! They're never satisfied. [*Turns back to the* FATHER *and the* STEPDAUGHTER.] Come on, let's get on with it; and let's see if it's possible to do it without laughing.

STEPDAUGHTER: I won't laugh any more, I won't really. My best bit's coming up now, you wait and see!

PRODUCER: Right: when you say "Don't think any more about what I told you, please. And I should do the same." [*Turning to the* FATHER.] Then you come in immediately with the line "I understand, ah yes, I understand" and then you ask . . .

STEPDAUGHTER: [*Interrupting.*] Ask what? What does he ask?

PRODUCER: Why you're in mourning.

STEPDAUGHTER: No! No! That's not right! Look: when I said that I should try not to think abut the way I was dressed, do you know what he said? "Well then, let's take it off, we'll take it off at once, shall we, your little black dress."

PRODUCER: That's great! That'll be wonderful! That'll bring the house down!

STEPDAUGHTER: But it's the truth!

PRODUCER: The truth! Do me a favour will you? This is the theatre you know! Truth's all very well up to a point but . . .

STEPDAUGHTER: What do you want to do then?

PRODUCER: You'll see! You'll see! Leave it all to me.

STEPDAUGHTER: No. No I won't. I know what you want to do! Out of my feeling of revulsion, out of all the vile and sordid reasons why I am what I am, you want to make a sugary little sentimental romance. You want him to ask me why I'm in mourning and you want me to reply with the tears running down my face that it is only two months since my father died. No. No. I won't have it! He must say to me what he really did say. "Well then, let's take it off, we'll take it off at once, shall we, your little black dress." And I, with my heart still grieving for my father's death only two months before, I went behind there, do you see? Behind that screen and with my fingers trembling with shame and loathing I took off the dress, unfastened my bra . . .

PRODUCER: [*His head in his hands.*] For God's sake! What are you saying!

STEPDAUGHTER: [*Shouting excitedly.*] The truth! I'm telling you the truth!

PRODUCER: All right then, Now listen to me. I'm not denying it's the truth. Right. And believe me I understand your horror, but you must see that we can't really put a scene like that on the stage.

STEPDAUGHTER: You can't? Then thanks very much. I'm not stopping here.

PRODUCER: No, listen . . .

STEPDAUGHTER: No, I'm going. I'm not stopping. The pair of you have worked it all out together, haven't you, what to put in the scene. Well, thank you very much! I understand everything now! He wants to get to the scene where he can talk about his spiritual torments but I want to show you my drama! Mine!

PRODUCER: [*Shaking with anger.*] Now we're getting to the real truth of it, aren't we? Your drama—yours! But it's not only yours, you know. It's drama for the other people as well! For him [*Pointing to the* FATHER.] and for your mother! You can't have one character coming on like you're doing, trampling over the others, taking over the play. Everything needs to be balanced and in harmony so that we can show what has to be shown! I know perfectly well that we've all got a life inside us and that we all want to parade it in front of other people. But that's the difficulty, how to present only the bits that are necessary in relation to the other characters: and in the small amount we show, to hint at all the rest of the inner life of the character! I agree, it would be so much simpler, if each character, in a soliloquy or in a lecture could pour out to the audience what's bubbling away inside him. But that's not the way we work. [*In an indulgent, placating tone.*] You must restrain yourself, you see. And believe me, it's in your own interests: because you could so easily make a bad impression, with all this uncontrollable anger, this disgust and exasperation. That seems a bit odd, if you don't mind my saying so, when you've admitted that you'd been with other men at Mme. Pace's and more than once.

STEPDAUGHTER: I suppose that's true. But you know, all the other men were all him as far as I was concerned.

PRODUCER: [*Not understanding.*] Uum—? What? What are you talking about?

STEPDAUGHTER: If someone falls into evil ways, isn't the responsibility for all the evil which follows to be laid at the door of the person who caused the first mistake? And in my case, it's him, from before I was even born. Look at him: see if it isn't true.

PRODUCER: Right then! What about the weight of remorse he's carrying? Isn't that important? Then, give him the chance to show it to us.

STEPDAUGHTER: But how? How on earth can he show all his long-suffering remorse, all his moral torments as he calls them, if you don't let him show his horror when he finds me in his arms one fine day, after he had asked me to take my dress off, a black dress for my father who had just died: and he finds that I'm the child he used to go and watch as she came out of school, me, a woman now, and a woman he could buy. [*She says these last words in a voice trembling with emotion.*]

[*The* MOTHER, *hearing her say this, is overcome and at first gives way to stifled sobs: but then she bursts out into uncontrollable crying. Everyone is deeply moved. There is a long pause.*]

STEPDAUGHTER: [*As soon as the* MOTHER *has quietened herself she goes on, firmly and thoughtfully.*] At the moment we are here on our own and the public doesn't know about us. But tomorrow you will present us and our story in whatever way you choose, I suppose. But wouldn't you like to see the real drama? Wouldn't you like to see it explode into life, as it really did?

PRODUCER: Of course, nothing I'd like better, then I can use as much of it as possible.

STEPDAUGHTER: Then persuade my mother to leave.

MOTHER: [*Rising and her quiet weeping changing to a loud cry.*] No! No! Don't let her! Don't let her do it!

PRODUCER: But they're only doing it for me to watch—only for me, do you see?

MOTHER: I can't bear it, I can't bear it!

PRODUCER: But if it's already happened, I can't see what's the objection.

MOTHER: No! It's happening now, as well: it's happening all the time. I'm not acting my suffering! Can't you understand that? I'm alive and here now but I can never forget that terrible moment of agony, that repeats itself endlessly and vividly in my mind. And these two little children here, you've never heard them speak have you? That's because they don't speak any more, not now. They just cling to me all the time: they help to keep my grief alive, but they don't really exist for themselves any more, not for themselves. And she [*indicating the* STEPDAUGHTER] . . . she has gone away, left me completely, she's lost to me, lost . . . you see her here for one reason only: to keep perpetually before me, always real, the anguish and the torment I've suffered on her account.

FATHER: The eternal moment, as I told you, sir. She is here [*indicating the* STEPDAUGHTER] to keep me too in that moment, trapped for all eternity, chained and suspended in that one fleeting shameful moment

of my life. She can't give up her role and you cannot rescue me from
it.

PRODUCER: But I'm not saying that we won't present that bit. Not at all! It
will be the climax of the first act, when she [*he points to the* MOTHER]
surprises you.

FATHER: That's right, because that is the moment when I am sentenced:
all our suffering should reach a climax in her cry. [*Again indicating the*
MOTHER.]

STEPDAUGHTER: I can still hear it ringing in my ears! It was that cry that
sent me mad! You can have me played just as you like: it doesn't matter!
Dressed, too, if you want, so long as I can have at least an arm—only
an arm—bare, because, you see, as I was standing like this [*she moves
across to the* FATHER *and leans her head on his chest*] with my head
like this and my arms round his neck, I saw a vein, here in my arm,
throbbing: and then it was almost as if that throbbing vein filled me
with a shivering fear, and I shut my eyes tightly like this, like this and
buried my head in his chest. [*Turning to the* MOTHER.] Scream,
Mummy, scream. [*She buries her head in the* FATHER's *chest, and with
her shoulders raised as if to try not to hear the scream, she speaks with
a voice tense with suffering.*] Scream, as you screamed then!

MOTHER: [*Coming forward to pull them apart.*] No! She's my daughter!
My daughter! [*Tearing her from him.*] You brute, you animal, she's my
daughter! Can't you see she's my daughter?

PRODUCER: [*Retreating as far as the footlights while the* ACTORS *are full of
dismay.*] Marvellous! Yes, that's great! And then curtain, curtain!

FATHER: [*Running downstage to him, excitedly.*] That's it, that's it!
Because it really was like that!

PRODUCER: [*Full of admiration and enthusiasm.*] Yes, yes, that's got to be
the curtain line! Curtain! Curtain!

[*At the repeated calls of the* PRODUCER, *the* STAGE MANAGER *lowers
the curtain, leaving on the apron in front, the* PRODUCER *and the*
FATHER.]

PRODUCER: [*Looking up to heaven with his arms raised.*] The idiots! I
didn't mean now! The bloody idiots—dropping it in on us like that! [*To
the* FATHER, *and lifting up a corner of the curtain.*] That's marvellous!
Really marvellous! A terrific effect! We'll end the act like that! It's the
best tag line I've heard for ages. What a First Act ending! I couldn't
have done better if I'd written it myself!

[*They go through the curtain together.*]

Act Three

When the curtain goes up we see that the STAGE MANAGER and STAGE
HANDS *have struck the first scene and have set another, a small garden
fountain.*

From one side of the stage the ACTORS *come on and from the other the*
CHARACTERS. *The* PRODUCER *is standing in the middle of the stage with
his hand over his mouth, thinking.*

PRODUCER: [*After a short pause, shrugging his shoulders.*] Well, then: let's get on to the second act! Leave it all to me, and everything will work out properly.

STEPDAUGHTER: This is where we go to live at his house [*pointing to the* FATHER] in spite of the objections of him over there. [*Pointing to the* SON.]

PRODUCER: [*Getting impatient.*] All right, all right! But leave it all to me, will you?

STEPDAUGHTER: Provided that you make it clear that he objected!

MOTHER: [*From the corner, shaking her head.*] That doesn't matter. The worse it was for us, the more he suffered from remorse.

PRODUCER: [*Impatiently.*] I know, I know! I'll take it all into account. Don't worry!

MOTHER: [*Pleading.*] To set my mind at rest, sir, please do make sure it's clear that I tried all I could—

STEPDAUGHTER: [*Interrupting her scornfully and going on.*] —to pacify me, to persuade me that this despicable creature wasn't worth making trouble about! [*To the* PRODUCER.] Go on, set her mind at rest, because it's true, she tried very hard. I'm having a whale of a time now! You can see, can't you, that the meeker she was and the more she tried to worm her way into his heart, the more lofty and distant he became! How's that for a dramatic situation!

PRODUCER: Do you think that we can actually begin the Second Act?

STEPDAUGHTER: I won't say another word! But you'll see that it won't be possible to play everything in the garden, like you want to do.

PRODUCER: Why not?

STEPDAUGHTER: [*Pointing to the* SON.] Because to start with, he stays shut up in his room in the house all the time! And then all the scenes for this poor little devil of a boy happen in the house. I've told you once.

PRODUCER: Yes, I know that! But on the other hand we can't put up a notice to tell the audience where the scene is taking place, or change the set three or four times in each Act.

LEADING ACTOR: That's what they used to do in the good old days.

PRODUCER: Yes, when the audience was about as bright as that little girl over there!

LEADING ACTRESS: And it makes it easier to create an illusion.

FATHER: [*Leaping up.*] An illusion? For pity's sake don't talk about illusions! Don't use that word, it's especially hurtful to us!

PRODUCER: [*Astonished.*] And why, for God's sake?

FATHER: It's so hurtful, so cruel! You ought to have realised that!

PRODUCER: What else should we call it? That's what we do here—create an illusion for the audience . . .

LEADING ACTOR: With our performance . . .

PRODUCER: A perfect illusion of reality!

FATHER: Yes, I know that, I understand. But on the other hand, perhaps you don't understand us yet. I'm sorry! But you see, for you and for your actors what goes on here on the stage is, quite rightly, well, it's only a game.

LEADING ACTRESS: [*Interrupting indignantly.*] A game! How dare you!
We're not children! What happens here is serious!

FATHER: I'm not saying that it isn't serious. And I mean, really, not just a
game but an art, that tries, as you've just said, to create the perfect
illusion of reality.

PRODUCER: That's right!

FATHER: Now try to imagine that we, as you see us here, [*he indicates
himself and the other* CHARACTERS] that we have no other reality outside
this illusion.

PRODUCER: [*Astonished and looking at the* ACTORS *with the same sense of
bewilderment as they feel themselves.*] What the hell are you talking
about now?

FATHER: [*After a short pause as he looks at them, with a faint smile.*] Isn't
it obvious? What other reality is there for us? What for you is an illusion
you create, for us is our only reality. [*Brief pause. He moves towards the*
PRODUCER *and goes on.*] But it's not only true for us, it's true for others
as well, you know. Just think about it. [*He looks intently into the* PRO-
DUCER'*s eyes.*] Do you really know who you are? [*He stands pointing at
the* PRODUCER.]

PRODUCER: [*A little disturbed but with a half smile.*] What? Who I am? I
am me!

FATHER: What if I told you that that wasn't true: what if I told you that you
were me?

PRODUCER: I would tell you that you were mad!

[*The* ACTORS *laugh.*]

FATHER: That's right, laugh! Because everything here is a game! [*To the*
PRODUCER.] And yet you object when I say that it is only for a game that
the gentleman there [*pointing to the* LEADING ACTOR] who is "himself"
has to be "me," who, on the contrary, am "myself." You see, I've caught
you in a trap.

[*The* ACTORS *start to laugh.*]

PRODUCER: Not again! We've heard all about this a little while ago.

FATHER: No, no. I didn't really want to talk about this. I'd like you to forget
about your game. [*Looking at the* LEADING ACTRESS *as if to anticipate
what she will say.*] I'm sorry—your artistry! Your art!—that you usually
pursue here with your actors; and I am going to ask you again in all
seriousness, who are you?

PRODUCER: [*Turning with a mixture of amazement and annoyance, to the*
ACTORS.] Of all the bloody nerve! A fellow who claims he is only a
character comes and asks me who I am!

FATHER: [*With dignity but without annoyance.*] A character, my dear sir,
can always ask a man who he is, because a character really has a life of
his own, a life full of his own specific qualities, and because of these
he is always "someone." While a man—I'm not speaking about you
personally, of course, but man in general—well, he can be an absolute
"nobody."

PRODUCER: All right, all right! Well, since you've asked me, I'm the Director, the Producer—I'm in charge! Do you understand?

FATHER: [*Half smiling, but gently and politely.*] I'm only asking to try to

find out if you really see yourself now in the same way that you saw
yourself, for instance, once upon a time in the past, with all the illusions
you had then, with everything inside and outside yourself as it seemed
then—and not only seemed, but really was! Well then, look back on
those illusions, those ideas that you don't have any more, on all those
things that no longer seem the same to you. Don't you feel that not only
this stage is falling away from under your feet but so is the earth itself,
and that all these realities of today are going to seem tomorrow as if they
had been an illusion?

PRODUCER: So? What does that prove?

FATHER: Oh, nothing much. I only want to make you see that if we [*pointing to himself and the other* CHARACTERS] have no other reality outside
our own illusion, perhaps you ought to distrust your own sense of reality:
because whatever is a reality today, whatever you touch and believe in
and that seems real for you today, is going to be—like the reality of
yesterday—an illusion tomorrow.

PRODUCER: [*Deciding to make fun of him.*] Very good! So now you're
saying that you as well as this play you're going to show me here, are
more real than I am?

FATHER: [*Very seriously.*] There's no doubt about that at all.

PRODUCER: Is that so?

FATHER: I thought you'd realised that from the beginning.

PRODUCER: More real than I am?

FATHER: If your reality can change between today and tomorrow—

PRODUCER: But everybody knows that it can change, don't they? It's always
changing! Just like everybody else's!

FATHER: [*Crying out.*] But ours doesn't change! Do you see? That's the
difference! Ours doesn't change, it can't change, it can never be different, never, because it is already determined, like this, for ever, that's
what's so terrible! We are an eternal reality. That should make you
shudder to come near us.

PRODUCER: [*Jumping up, suddenly struck by an idea, and standing directly
in front of the* FATHER.] Then I should like to know when anyone saw
a character step out of his part and make a speech like you've done,
proposing things, explaining things. Tell me when, will you? I've never
seen it before.

FATHER: You've never seen it because an author usually hides all the difficulties of creating. When the characters are alive, really alive and standing in front of their author, he has only to follow their words, the actions
that they suggest to him: and he must want them to be what they want
to be: and it's his bad luck if he doesn't do what they want! When a
character is born he immediately assumes such an independence even
of his own author that everyone can imagine him in scores of situations
that his author hadn't even thought of putting him in, and he sometimes acquires a meaning that his author never dreamed of giving him.

PRODUCER: Of course I know all that.

FATHER: Well, then. Why are you surprised by us? Imagine what a disaster
it is for a character to be born in the imagination of an author who then
refuses to give him life in a written script. Tell me if a character, left

like this, suspended, created but without a final life, isn't right to do what we are doing now, here in front of you. We spent such a long time, such a very long time, believe me, urging our author, persuading him, first me, then her, [*pointing to the* STEPDAUGHTER] then this poor Mother . . .

STEPDAUGHTER: [*Coming down the stage as if in a dream.*] It's true, I would go, would go and tempt him, time after time, in his gloomy study just as it was growing dark, when he was sitting quietly in an armchair not even bothering to switch a light on but leaving the shadows to fill the room: the shadows were swarming with us, we had come to tempt him. [*As if she could see herself there in the study and is annoyed by the presence of the* ACTORS.] Go away will you! Leave us alone! Mother there, with that son of hers—me with the little girl—that poor little kid always on his own—and then me with him [*pointing to the* FATHER] and then at last, just me, on my own, all on my own, in the shadows. [*She turns quickly as if she wants to cling on to the vision she has of herself, in the shadows.*] Ah, what scenes, what scenes we suggested to him! What a life I could have had! I tempted him more than the others!

FATHER: Oh yes, you did! And it was probably all your fault that he did nothing about it! You were so insistent, you made too many demands.

STEPDAUGHTER: But he wanted me to be like that! [*She comes closer to the* PRODUCER *to speak to him in confidence.*] I think it's more likely that he felt discouraged about the theatre and even despised it because the public only wants to see . . .

PRODUCER: Let's go on, for God's sake, let's go on. Come to the point will you?

STEPDAUGHTER: I'm sorry, but if you ask me, we've got too much happening already, just with our entry into his house. [*Pointing to the* FATHER.] You said that we couldn't put up a notice or change the set every five minutes.

PRODUCER: Right! Of course we can't! We must combine things, group them together in one continuous flowing action: not the way you've been wanting, first of all seeing your little brother come home from school and wander about the house like a lost soul, hiding behind the doors and brooding on some plan or other that would—what did you say it would do?

STEPDAUGHTER: Wither him . . . shrivel him up completely.

PRODUCER: That's good! That's a good expression. And then you "can see it there in his eyes, getting stronger all the time"—isn't that what you said?

STEPDAUGHTER: Yes, that's right. Look at him! [*Pointing to him as he stands next to his* MOTHER.]

PRODUCER: Yes, great! And then, at the same time, you want to show the little girl playing in the garden, all innocence. One in the house and the other in the garden—we can't do it, don't you see that?

STEPDAUGHTER: Yes, playing in the sun, so happy! It's the only pleasure I have left, her happiness, her delight in playing in the garden: away from the misery, the squalor of that sordid flat where all four of us slept and where she slept with me—with me! Just think of it! My vile, contaminated body close to hers, with her little arms wrapped tightly round my neck, so lovingly, so innocently. In the garden, wherever she saw me, she would run and take my hand. She never wanted to show me the big flowers, she would run about looking for the "little weeny" ones, so that she could show them to me; she was so happy, so thrilled! [*As she says this, tortured by the memory, she breaks out into a long desperate cry, dropping her head on her arms that rest on a little table. Everybody is very affected by her. The* PRODUCER *comes to her almost paternally and speaks to her in a soothing voice.*]

PRODUCER: We'll have the garden scene, we'll have it, don't worry: and you'll see, you'll be very pleased with what we do! We'll play all the scenes in the garden! [*He calls out to a* STAGE HAND *by name.*] Hey . . . , let down a few bits of tree, will you? A couple of cypresses will do, in front of the fountain. [*Someone drops in the two cypresses and a* STAGE HAND *secures them with a couple of braces and weights.*]

PRODUCER: [*To the* STEPDAUGHTER.] That'll do for now, won't it? It'll just give us an idea. [*Calling out to a* STAGE HAND *by name again.*] Hey, . . . give me something for the sky will you?

STAGE HAND: What's that?

PRODUCER: Something for the sky! A small cloth to come in behind the fountain. [*A white cloth is dropped from the flies.*] Not white! I asked for a sky! Never mind: leave it! I'll do something with it. [*Calling out.*] Hey lights! Kill everything will you? Give me a bit of moonlight—the blues in the batten and a blue spot on the cloth . . . [*They do.*] That's it! That'll do! [*Now on the scene there is the light he asked for, a mysterious blue light that makes the* ACTORS *speak and move as if in the garden in the evening under a moon. To the* STEPDAUGHTER.] Look here now: the little boy can come out here in the garden and hide among the trees instead of hiding behind the doors in the house. But it's going to be difficult to find a little girl to play the scene with you where she shows you the flowers. [*Turning to the* LITTLE BOY.] Come on, come on, son, come across here. Let's see what it'll look like. [*But the* BOY *doesn't move.*] Come on will you, come on. [*Then he pulls him forward and tries to make him hold his head up, but every time it falls down again on his chest.*] There's something very odd about this lad . . . What's wrong with him? My God, he'll have to say something sometime! [*He comes over to him again, puts his hand on his shoulder and pushes him between the trees.*] Come a bit nearer: let's have a look. Can you hide a bit more? That's it. Now pop your head out and look round. [*He moves away to look at the effect and as the* BOY *does what he has been told to do, the* ACTORS *watch impressed and a little disturbed.*] Ahh, that's good, very good . . . [*He turns to the* STEPDAUGHTER.] How about having the little girl, surprised to see him there, run across. Wouldn't that make him say something?

STEPDAUGHTER: [*Getting up.*] It's no use hoping he'll speak, not as long as that creature's there. [*Pointing to the* SON.] You'll have to get him out of the way first.

SON: [*Moving determinedly to one of the sets of steps leading off the stage.*] With pleasure! I'll go now! Nothing will please me better!

PRODUCER: [*Stopping him immediately.*] Hey, no! Where are you going? Hang on!

[*The* MOTHER *gets up, anxious at the idea that he is really going and instinctively raising her arms as if to hold him back, but without moving from where she is.*]

SON: [*At the footlights, to the* PRODUCER *who is restraining him there.*] There's no reason why I should be here! Let me go will you? Let me go!

PRODUCER: What do you mean there's no reason for you to be here?

STEPDAUGHTER: [*Calmly, ironically.*] Don't bother to stop him. He won't go!

FATHER: You have to play that terrible scene in the garden with your mother.

SON: [*Quickly, angry and determined.*] I'm not going to play anything! I've said that all along! [*To the* PRODUCER.] Let me go will you?

STEPDAUGHTER: [*Crossing to the* PRODUCER.] It's all right. Let him go. [*She moves the* PRODUCER'*s hand from the* SON. *Then she turns to the* SON *and says.*] Well, go on then! Off you go!

[*The* SON *stays near the steps but as if pulled by some strange force he is quite unable to go down them: then to the astonishment and even the dismay of the* ACTORS, *he moves along the front of the stage towards the other set of steps down into the auditorium: but having got there, he again stays near and doesn't actually go down them. The* STEPDAUGHTER *who has watched him scornfully but very intently, bursts into laughter.*]

STEPDAUGHTER: He can't, you see? He can't! He's got to stay here! He must. He's chained to us for ever! No, I'm the one who goes, when what must happen does happen, and I run away, because I hate him, because I can't bear the sight of him any longer. Do you think it's possible for him to run away? He has to stay here with that wonderful father of his and his mother there. She doesn't think she has any other son but him. [*She turns to the* MOTHER.] Come on, come on, Mummy, come on! [*Turning back to the* PRODUCER *to point her out to him.*] Look, she's going to try to stop him . . . [*To the* MOTHER, *half compelling her, as if by some magic power.*] Come on, come on. [*Then to the* PRODUCER *again.*] Imagine how she must feel at showing her affection for him in front of your actors! But her longing to be near him is so strong that—look! She's going to go through that scene with him again! [*The* MOTHER *has now actually come close to the* SON *as the* STEPDAUGHTER *says the last line: she gestures to show that she agrees to go on.*]

SON: [*Quickly.*] But I'm not! I'm not! If I can't get away then I suppose I shall have to stay here; but I repeat that I will not have any part in it.

FATHER: [*To the* PRODUCER, *excitedly.*] You must make him!

SON: Nobody's going to make me do anything!

FATHER: I'll make you!

STEPDAUGHTER: Wait! Just a minute! Before that, the little girl has to go to the fountain. [*She turns to take the* LITTLE GIRL, *drops on her knees in front of her and takes her face between her hands.*] My poor little darling, those beautiful eyes, they look so bewildered. You're wondering where you are, aren't you? Well, we're on a stage, my darling! What's a stage? Well, it's a place where you pretend to be serious. They put on plays here. And now we're going to put on a play. Seriously! Oh, yes! Even you . . . [*She hugs her tightly and rocks her gently for a moment.*] Oh, my little one, my little darling, what a terrible play it is for you! What horrible things have been planned for you! The garden, the fountain . . . Oh, yes, it's only a pretend fountain, that's right. That's part of the game, my pretty darling: everything is pretends here. Perhaps you'll like a pretends fountain better than a real one: you can play here then. But it's only a game for the others; not for you, I'm afraid, it's real for you, my darling, and your game is in a real fountain, a big beautiful green fountain with bamboos casting shadows, looking at your own reflection, with lots of baby ducks paddling about, shattering the reflections. You want to stroke one! [*With a scream that electrifies and terrifies everybody.*] No, Rosetta, no! Your mummy isn't watching you, she's over there with that selfish bastard! Oh, God, I feel as if all the devils in hell were tearing me apart inside . . . And you . . . [*Leaving the* LITTLE GIRL *and turning to the* LITTLE BOY *in the usual way.*] What are you doing here, hanging about like a beggar? It'll be your fault too, if that little girl drowns; you're always like this, as if I wasn't paying the price for getting all of you into this house. [*Shaking his arm to make him take his hand out of his pocket.*] What have you got there? What are you hiding? Take it out, take your hand out! [*She drags his hand out of his pocket and to everyone's horror he is holding a revolver. She looks at him for a moment, almost with satisfaction: then she says, grimly.*] Where on earth did you get that? [*The* BOY, *looking frightened, with his eyes wide and empty, doesn't answer.*] You idiot, if I'd been you, instead of killing myself, I'd have killed one of those two: either or both, the father and the son. [*She pushes him toward the cypress trees where he then stands watching: then she takes the* LITTLE GIRL *and helps her to climb in to the fountain, making her lie so that she is hidden: after that she kneels down and puts her head and arms on the rim of the fountain.*]

PRODUCER: That's good! It's good! [*Turning to the* STEPDAUGHTER.] And at the same time . . .

SON: [*Scornfully.*] What do you mean, at the same time? There was nothing at the same time! There wasn't any scene between her and me. [*Pointing to the* MOTHER.] She'll tell you the same thing herself, she'll tell you what happened.

[*The* SECOND ACTRESS *and the* JUVENILE LEAD *have left the group of* ACTORS *and have come to stand nearer the* MOTHER *and the* SON *as if to study them so as to play their parts.*]

MOTHER: Yes, it's true. I'd gone to his room . . .

SON: Room, do you hear? Not the garden!

PRODUCER: It's not important! We've got to reorganize the events anyway. I've told you that already.

SON: [*Glaring at the* JUVENILE LEAD *and the* SECOND ACTRESS.] What do you want?

JUVENILE LEAD: Nothing. I'm just watching.

SON: [*Turning to the* SECOND ACTRESS.] You as well! Getting ready to play her part are you? [*Pointing to the* MOTHER.]

PRODUCER: That's it. And I think you should be grateful—they're paying you a lot of attention.

SON: Oh, yes, thank you! But haven't you realised yet that you'll never be able to do this play? There's nothing of us inside you and you actors are only looking at us from the outside. Do you think we could go on living with a mirror held up in front of us that didn't only freeze our reflection for ever, but froze us in a reflection that laughed back at us with an expression that we didn't even recognise as our own?

FATHER: That's right! That's right!

PRODUCER: [*To* JUVENILE LEAD *and* SECOND ACTRESS.] Okay. Go back to the others.

SON: It's quite useless. I'm not prepared to do anything.

PRODUCER: Oh, shut up, will you, and let me listen to your mother. [*To the* MOTHER.] Well, you'd gone to his room, you said.

MOTHER: Yes, to his room. I couldn't bear it any longer. I wanted to empty my heart to him, tell him about all the agony that was crushing me. But as soon as he saw me come in . . .

SON: Nothing happened. I got away! I wasn't going to get involved. I never have been involved. Do you understand?

MOTHER: It's true! That's right!

PRODUCER: But we must make up the scene between you, then. It's vital!

MOTHER: I'm ready to do it! If only I had the chance to talk to him for a moment, to pour out all my troubles to him.

FATHER: [*Going to the* SON *and speaking violently.*] You'll do it! For your Mother! For your Mother!

SON: [*More than ever determined.*] I'm doing nothing!

FATHER: [*Taking hold of his coat collar and shaking him.*] For God's sake, do as I tell you! Do as I tell you! Do you hear what she's saying? Haven't you any feelings for her?

SON: [*Taking hold of his* FATHER.] No I haven't! I haven't! Let that be the end of it!

[*There is a general uproar. The* MOTHER *frightened out of her wits, tries to get between them and separate them.*]

MOTHER: Please stop it! Please!

FATHER: [*Hanging on.*] Do as I tell you! Do as I tell you!

SON: [*Wrestling with him and finally throwing him to the ground near the steps. Everyone is horrified.*] What's come over you? Why are you so frantic? Do you want to parade our disgrace in front of everybody? Well, I'm having nothing to do with it! Nothing! And I'm doing what our author wanted as well—he never wanted to put us on the stage.

PRODUCER: Then why the hell did you come here?

SON: [*Pointing to the* FATHER.] He wanted to, I didn't.

PRODUCER: But you're here now, aren't you?

SON: He was the one who wanted to come and he dragged all of us here with him and agreed with you in there about what to put in the play: and that meant not only what had really happened, as if that wasn't bad enough, but what hadn't happened as well.

PRODUCER: All right, then, you tell me what happened. You tell me! Did you rush out of your room without saying anything?

SON: [*After a moment's hesitation.*] Without saying anything. I didn't want to make a scene.

PRODUCER: [*Needling him.*] What then? What did you do then?

SON: [*He is now the centre of everyone's agonised attention and he crosses the stage.*] Nothing . . . I went across the garden . . . [*He breaks off gloomy and absorbed.*]

PRODUCER: [*Urging him to say more, impressed by his reluctance to speak.*] Well? What then? You crossed the garden?

SON: [*Exasperated, putting his face into the crook of his arm.*] Why do you want me to talk about it? It's horrible! [*The* MOTHER *is trembling with stifled sobs and looking towards the fountain.*]

PRODUCER: [*Quietly, seeing where she is looking and turning to the* SON *with growing apprehension.*] The little girl?

SON: [*Looking straight in front, out to the audience.*] There, in the fountain . . .

FATHER: [*On the floor still, pointing with pity at the* MOTHER.] She was trailing after him!

PRODUCER: [*To the* SON, *anxiously.*] What did you do then?

SON: [*Still looking out front and speaking slowly.*] I dashed across. I was going to jump in and pull her out . . . But something else caught my eye: I saw something behind the tree that made my blood run cold: the little boy, he was standing there with a mad look in his eyes: he was standing looking into the fountain at his little sister, floating there, drowned.

[*The* STEPDAUGHTER *is still bent at the fountain hiding the* LITTLE GIRL, *and she sobs pathetically, her sobs sounding like an echo. There is a pause.*]

SON: [*Continued.*] I made a move towards him: but then . . .

[*From behind the trees where the* LITTLE BOY *is standing there is the sound of a shot.*]

MOTHER: [*With a terrible cry she runs along with the* SON *and all the* ACTORS *in the midst of a great general confusion.*] My son! My son! [*And then from out of the confusion and crying her voice comes out.*] Help! Help me!

PRODUCER: [*Amidst the shouting he tries to clear a space whilst the* LITTLE BOY *is carried by his feet and shoulders behind the white skycloth.*] Is he wounded? Really wounded?

[*Everybody except the* PRODUCER *and the* FATHER *who is still on the floor by the steps, has gone behind the skycloth and stays there talking anxiously. Then independently the* ACTORS *start to come back into view.*]

LEADING ACTRESS: [*Coming from the right, very upset.*] He's dead! The poor boy! He's dead! What a terrible thing!

LEADING ACTOR: [*Coming back from the left and smiling.*] What do you mean, dead? It's all make-believe. It's a sham! He's not dead. Don't you believe it!

OTHER ACTORS FROM THE RIGHT: Make-believe? It's real! Real! He's dead!

OTHER ACTORS FROM THE LEFT: No, he isn't. He's pretending! It's all make-believe.

FATHER: [*Running off and shouting at them as he goes.*] What do you mean, make-believe? It's real! It's real, ladies and gentlemen! It's reality! [*And with desperation on his face he too goes behind the skycloth.*]

PRODUCER: [*Not caring any more.*] Make-believe?! Reality?! Oh, go to hell the lot of you! Lights! Lights! Lights!

[*At once all the stage and auditorium is flooded with light. The PRO-DUCER heaves a sigh of relief as if he has been relieved of a terrible weight and they all look at each other in distress and with uncertainty.*]

PRODUCER: God! I've never known anything like this! And we've lost a whole day's work! [*He looks at the clock.*] Get off with you, all of you! We can't do anything now! It's too late to start a rehearsal. [*When the ACTORS have gone, he calls out.*] Hey, lights! Kill everything! [*As soon as he has said this, all the lights go out completely and leave him in the pitch dark.*] For God's sake!! You might have left the workers![4] I can't see where I'm going!

[*Suddenly, behind the skycloth, as if because of a bad connection, a green light comes up to throw on the cloth a huge sharp shadow of the CHARACTERS, but without the LITTLE BOY and the LITTLE GIRL. The PRODUCER, seeing this, jumps off the stage, terrified. At the same time the flood of light on them is switched off and the stage is again bathed in the same blue light as before. Slowly the SON comes on from the right, followed by the MOTHER with her arms raised towards him. Then from the left, the FATHER enters.*

They come together in the middle of the stage and stand there as if transfixed. Finally from the left the STEPDAUGHTER comes on and moves towards the steps at the front: on the top step she pauses for a moment to look back at the other three and then bursts out in a raucous laugh, dashes down the steps and turns to look at the three figures still on the stage. Then she runs out of the auditorium and we can still hear her manic laughter out into the foyer and beyond. After a pause the curtain falls slowly.]

4. Working lights.

MARCEL PROUST
1871–1922

Proust's influence in twentieth-century letters is unequaled by that of any other writer. His massive novel sequence, *Remembrance of Things Past* (*À la recherche du temps perdu*), broke from nineteenth-century tradition to provide the example of a new kind of characterization and narrative line, a monumentally complex and precisely coordinated aesthetic structure, and a concept of the individual's cumulatively created profound identity—much of it buried in the experience of our senses—that has influenced writers everywhere modern Western literature is known. All of these innovations refer to an exploration of time in terms that parallel the influential work of Proust's contemporary, the philosopher Henri Bergson, with its emphasis on experience as duration, or *lived* time (rather than the artificial measurements of clock or calendar), and the importance of intuitive knowledge. Proust's plot refuses the immediate sense of direction given by traditional nineteenth-century novels: it acquires purpose gradually, through the relationship of different themes, and its collective intent appears only at the end when Marcel's suddenly catalyzed memory grasps the relationship of all parts. Characters are not sketched in fully from the beginning but are revealed piece by piece, evolving inside the different perspectives of individual chapters; even the protagonist is not fully outlined before the end. Proust's novel is a monumental construction coordinated down to its smallest parts not by the development of traditional novel form but by a new structural vision; it suggested the availability of intuitive or nonrational elements as organizational principles in an example that continues to be a reference point for twentieth-century writers.

Marcel Proust was born on July 10, 1871, the older of two sons in a wealthy middle-class Parisian family. His father was a well-known doctor and professor of medicine, a Catholic from a small town outside Paris. His mother, a sensitive, scrupulous, and highly educated woman to whom Marcel was devoted, came from an urban Jewish family. Proust fell ill with severe asthma when he was nine and thereafter spent his childhood holidays at a seaside resort in Normandy that became the fictional model for Balbec. In spite of his illness, which limited what he could do, he graduated with honors from the Lycée Condorcet in Paris in 1889 and did a year's military service at Orléans (the fictional Doncières). As a student, Proust had met many young writers and composers, and he began to frequent the salons of the wealthy bourgeoisie and the aristocracy of the Faubourg Saint-Germain (an elegant area of Paris), from which he drew much of the material for his portraits of society. He wrote for Symbolist magazines such as *Le Banquet* and *La Revue blanche* and published a collection of essays, poems, and stories in an elegant book, *Pleasures and Days* (1896), with drawings by Madeleine Lemaire and music by Reynaldo Hahn. In 1899 (with his mother's help since he knew no English), he began to translate the English moralist and art critic, John Ruskin.

Proust is known as the author of one work: the enormous, seven-volume exploration of time and consciousness called *Remembrance of Things Past*. As early as 1895, he had begun work on a shorter novel that traced the same themes and autobiographical awareness, but *Jean Santeuil* (published posthumously in 1952) never found a coherent structure for its numerous episodes and Proust abandoned it in 1899. Many episodes from the unfinished manuscript reflected Proust's interest in current events, and especially the Dreyfus Affair (1894–1906) that was dividing France around issues of military honor, anti-Semitism, and national security. Themes, ideas, and some episodes from the earlier novel were absorbed into *Remembrance of Things Past*, and it is striking that the major difference (aside from length) between the two works is simply the extremely sophisticated and subtle structure that Proust devised for the later one.

Proust's health started seriously to decline in 1902, and to make matters worse, he lost both parents by 1905. The following year, his asthma worsening, he moved into a cork-lined, fumigated room at 102 Boulevard Haussmann in Paris, where he stayed until forced to move in 1919. From 1907 to 1914, he spent summers in the seacoast town of Cabourg (another source of material for the fictional Balbec), but when in Paris emerged rarely from his apartment and then only late at night for dinners with friends. In 1909 he conceived the structure of his novel as a whole and wrote its first and last chapters together. A first draft was finished by September 1912, but Proust had difficulty finding a publisher and finally published the first volume at his own expense in 1913. Though *Swann's Way* (*Du côté de chez Swann*) was a success, World War I delayed publication of subsequent volumes, and Proust began the painstaking revision and enlargement of the whole manu-

social roles and habits of mind through the interaction of different types of speech. When Charles and the Princesse de Guermantes meet in a bourgeois salon, their manner of speaking to each other creates a small "in-group" dialogue of the aristocracy and sets them off from everyone else. The flexibility of Proust's style, representing thought and habits of speech rather than following a superimposed common code, makes him an example of verbal and visionary innovation that is paralleled by other writers of the same period, such as James Joyce and Virginia Woolf, and is enormously influential on later writers of the "new novel" tradition.

The selection printed here, *Overture*, is the first chapter of *Swann's Way*, the first full volume of Proust's novel. "Swann's way" is one of the two directions in which Marcel's family used to take walks from their home in Combray, toward Tansonville, home of Charles Swann, and is associated with various scenes and anecdotes of love and private life. The longer walk toward the estate of the Guermantes (*The Guermantes' Way*), a fictional family of the highest aristocracy appearing frequently in the novel, evokes an aura of high society and French history, a more public sphere. Fictional people and places mingle throughout with the real; names that are not annotated are Proust's inventions. The narrator of *Overture* is Marcel as an old man, and the French verb tense used in his recollections (here and throughout all but the final volume) is appropriately the imperfect, a tense of uncompleted action ("I used to . . . I would ask myself").

As the chapter title suggests, *Overture* introduces the work's themes and methods rather like the overture of an opera. All but one of the main characters appear or are mentioned, and the patterns of future encounters are set. Marcel, waiting anxiously for his beloved mother's response to a note sent down to her during dinner, suffers the same agony of separation as does Swann in his love for the promiscuous Odette, or the older Marcel himself for Albertine. The strange world of half-sleep, half-waking with which the novel begins prefigures later awakenings of memory. Long passages of intricate introspection, and sudden shifts of time and space, introduce us to the style and point of view of the rest of the book. The narrator shares the painful anxiety of little Marcel's desperate wait for his mother's bedtime kiss; for though his observations and judgments are tempered with mature wisdom, he is only at the beginning of his progress to full consciousness. The remembrance of things past is a key to further discovery but not an end in itself.

Overture ends with Proust's most famous image, summing up for many readers the world, the style, and the process of discovery of the Proustian vision. Nibbling at a madeleine (a small, rich cookie-like pastry) that he has dipped in lime-blossom tea, Marcel suddenly has an overwhelming feeling of happiness. He soon associates this tantalizing, puzzling phenomenon with the memory of earlier times when he sipped tea with his Aunt Leonie. He realizes that there is something valuable about such passive, spontaneous, and sensuous memory, quite different from the abstract operations of reason. Although the Marcel of "Combray" does not yet know it, he will pursue the elusive significance of this moment of happiness until, in *Time Regained*, he can as a complete artist bring it to the surface and link past and present time in a fuller and richer identity.

Roger Shattuck, *Proust* (1974), is a general study including advice on "how to read" Proust; it is still useful although it predates the revised translation used here. An excellent general study is Germaine Brée, *Marcel Proust and Deliverance from Time* (1969), translated by R. J. Richards and A. D. Truitt. Terence Kilmartin, *A Reader's Guide to Remembrance of Things Past* (1984), is a handbook guide to Proust's characters, to persons referred to in the text, to places, and to themes, all keyed to the revised translation by the translator. René Girard, *Proust: A Collection of Critical Essays* (1962); Harold Bloom, ed., *Marcel Proust's Remembrance of Things Past* (1987); and Barbara J. Bucknall, ed., *Critical Essays on Marcel Proust* (1987), are also recommended.

PRONOUNCING GLOSSARY

The following list uses common English syllables and stress accents to provide rough equivalents of selected words whose pronunciation may be unfamiliar to the general reader.

Bathilde: *bah-teeld'*	Maubant: *moh-bawnh'*
Chartres: *shar'-tr*	Maulévrier: *moh-lay'-vree-ay'*
Charlus: *shar-lews'*	Proust: *proost*
Combray: *cohm-bray'*	Quai d'Orléans: *kay dor-lay-onh*
Corot: *core-oh'*	Saint-Cloud: *sanh–cloo'*
Duc: *dewk*	Saint-Loup: *sanh–loo'*
Faubourg Saint-Germain; *foh-boor'*	Sévigné: *say-veen-yay'*
sanh zhair–manh'	Vinteuil: *van-teuh'-ee*
George Sand: *zhorzh sond*	

Remembrance of Things Past[1]

Swann's Way. Overture[2]

For a long time I used to go to bed early. Sometimes, when I had put out my candle, my eyes would close so quickly that I had not even time to say to myself: "I'm falling asleep." And half an hour later the thought that it was time to go to sleep would awaken me; I would make as if to put away the book which I imagined was still in my hands, and to blow out the light; I had gone on thinking, while I was asleep, about what I had just been reading, but these thoughts had taken a rather peculiar turn; it seemed to me that I myself was the immediate subject of my book: a church, a quartet, the rivalry between François I and Charles V.[3] This impression would persist for some moments after I awoke; it did not offend my reason, but lay like scales upon my eyes and prevented them from registering the fact that the candle was no longer burning. Then it would begin to seem unintelligible, as the thoughts of a former existence must be to a reincarnate spirit; the subject of my book would separate itself from me, leaving me free to apply myself to it or not; and at the same time my sight would return and I would be astonished to find myself in a state of darkness, pleasant and restful enough for my eyes, but even more, perhaps, for my mind, to which it appeared incomprehensible, without a cause, something dark indeed.

I would ask myself what time it could be; I could hear the whistling of trains, which, now nearer and now farther off, punctuating the distance like the note of a bird in a forest, showed me in perspective the deserted countryside through which a traveller is hurrying towards the nearby sta-

---

1. Translated by C. K. Scott Moncrieff and Terence Kilmartin.   2. The opening section of Combray, the first volume of *Swann's Way*.   3. Francis I (1496–1567), king of France, and Charles V (1500–1558), Holy Roman emperor and king of Spain, fought four wars over the empire's expansion in Europe.

tion; and the path he is taking will be engraved in his memory by the excitement induced by strange surroundings, by unaccustomed activities, by the conversation he has had and the farewells exchanged beneath an unfamiliar lamp, still echoing in his ears amid the silence of the night, by the imminent joy of going home.

I would lay my cheeks gently against the comfortable cheeks of my pillow, as plump and blooming as the cheeks of babyhood. I would strike a match to look at my watch. Nearly midnight. The hour when an invalid, who has been obliged to set out on a journey and to sleep in a strange hotel, awakened by a sudden spasm, sees with glad relief a streak of daylight showing under his door. Thank God, it is morning! The servants will be about in a minute: he can ring, and someone will come to look after him. The thought of being assuaged gives him strength to endure his pain. He is certain he heard footsteps: they come nearer, and then die away. The ray of light beneath his door is extinguished. It is midnight; someone has just turned down the gas; the last servant has gone to bed, and he must lie all night in agony with no one to bring him relief.

I would fall asleep again, and thereafter would reawaken for short snatches only, just long enough to hear the regular creaking of the wainscot,[4] or to open my eyes to stare at the shifting kaleidoscope of the darkness, to savour, in a momentary glimmer of consciousness, the sleep which lay heavy upon the furniture, the room, the whole of which I formed but an insignificant part and whose insensibility I should very soon return to share. Or else while sleeping I had drifted back to an earlier stage in my life, now for ever outgrown, and had come under the thrall of one of my childish terrors, such as that old terror of my great-uncle's pulling my curls which was effectually dispelled on the day—the dawn of a new era to me—when they were finally cropped from my head. I had forgotten that event during my sleep, but I remembered it again immediately I had succeeded in waking myself up to escape my great-uncle's fingers, and as a measure of precaution I would bury the whole of my head in the pillow before returning to the world of dreams.

Sometimes, too, as Eve was created from a rib of Adam, a woman would be born during my sleep from some strain in the position of my thighs. Conceived from the pleasure I was on the point of consummating, she it was, I imagined, who offered me that pleasure. My body, conscious that its own warmth was permeating hers, would strive to become one with her, and I would awake. The rest of humanity seemed very remote in comparison with this woman whose company I had left but a moment ago; my cheek was still warm from her kiss, my body ached beneath the weight of hers. If, as would sometimes happen, she had the features of some woman whom I had known in waking hours, I would abandon myself altogether to the sole quest of her, like people who set out on a journey to see with their eyes some city of their desire, and imagine that one can taste in reality what has charmed one's fancy. And then, gradually, the memory of her would dissolve and vanish, until I had forgotten the girl of my dream.

---

4. The wooden paneling of the walls.

When a man is asleep, he has in a circle round him the chain of the hours, the sequence of the years, the order of the heavenly host. Instinctively, when he awakes, he looks to these, and in an instant reads off his own position on the earth's surface and the time that has elapsed during his slumbers; but this ordered procession is apt to grow confused, and to break its ranks. Suppose that, towards morning, after a night of insomnia, sleep descends upon him while he is reading, in quite a different position from that in which he normally goes to sleep, he has only to lift his arm to arrest the sun and turn it back in its course,[5] and, at the moment of waking, he will have no idea of the time, but will conclude that he has just gone to bed. Or suppose that he dozes off in some even more abnormal and divergent position, sitting in an armchair, for instance, after dinner: then the world will go hurtling out of orbit, the magic chair will carry him at full speed through time and space, and when he opens his eyes again he will imagine that he went to sleep months earlier in another place. But for me it was enough if, in my own bed, my sleep was so heavy as completely to relax my consciousness; for then I lost all sense of the place in which I had gone to sleep, and when I awoke in the middle of the night, not knowing where I was, I could not even be sure at first who I was; I had only the most rudimentary sense of existence, such as may lurk and flicker in the depths of an animal's consciousness; I was more destitute than the cave-dweller; but then the memory—not yet of the place in which I was, but of various other places where I had lived and might now very possibly be—would come like a rope let down from heaven to draw me up out of the abyss of not-being, from which I could never have escaped by myself: in a flash I would traverse centuries of civilisation, and out of a blurred glimpse of oil-lamps, then of shirts with turned-down collars, would gradually piece together the original components of my ego.

Perhaps the immobility of the things that surround us is forced upon them by our conviction that they are themselves and not anything else, by the immobility of our conception of them. For it always happened that when I awoke like this, and my mind struggled in an unsuccessful attempt to discover where I was, everything revolved around me through the darkness: things, places, years. My body, still too heavy with sleep to move, would endeavour to construe from the pattern of its tiredness the position of its various limbs, in order to deduce therefrom the direction of the wall, the location of the furniture, to piece together and give a name to the house in which it lay. Its memory, the composite memory of its ribs, its knees, its shoulder-blades, offered it a whole series of rooms in which it had at one time or another slept, while the unseen walls, shifting and adapting themselves to the shape of each successive room that it remembered, whirled round it in the dark. And even before my brain, lingering in cogitation over when things had happened and what they had looked like, had reassembled the circumstances sufficiently to identify the room, it, my body, would recall from each room in succession the style of the bed, the position of the doors, the angle at which the daylight came in at

---

5. If his uplifted arm prevents him from seeing the sunlight, he will think it is still night.

the windows, whether there was a passage outside, what I had had in my
mind when I went to sleep and found there when I awoke. The stiffened
side on which I lay would, for instance, in trying to fix its position, imagine
itself to be lying face to the wall in a big bed with a canopy; and at once I
would say to myself, "Why, I must have fallen asleep before Mamma came
to say good night," for I was in the country at my grandfather's, who died
years ago; and my body, the side upon which I was lying, faithful guardians
of a past which my mind should never have forgotten, brought back before
my eyes the glimmering flame of the night-light in its urn-shaped bowl of
Bohemian glass that hung by chains from the ceiling, and the chimney-
piece of Siena marble[6] in my bedroom at Combray, in my grandparents'
house, in those far distant days which at this moment I imagined to be in
the present without being able to picture them exactly, and which would
become plainer in a little while when I was properly awake.

Then the memory of a new position would spring up, and the wall
would slide away in another direction; I was in my room in Mme de Saint-
Loup's[7] house in the country; good heavens, it must be ten o'clock, they
will have finished dinner! I must have overslept myself in the little nap
which I always take when I come in from my walk with Mme de Saint-
Loup, before dressing for the evening. For many years have now elapsed
since the Combray days when, coming in from the longest and latest
walks, I would still be in time to see the reflection of the sunset glowing
in the panes of my bedroom window. It is a very different kind of life that
one leads at Tansonville, at Mme de Saint-Loup's, and a different kind of
pleasure that I derive from taking walks only in the evenings, from visiting
by moonlight the roads on which I used to play as a child in the sunshine;
while the bedroom in which I shall presently fall asleep instead of dressing
for dinner I can see from the distance as we return from our walk, with its
lamp shining through the window, a solitary beacon in the night.

These shifting and confused gusts of memory never lasted for more than
a few seconds; it often happened that, in my brief spell of uncertainty as
to where I was, I did not distinguish the various suppositions of which it
was composed any more than, when we watch a horse running, we isolate
the successive positions of its body as they appear upon a bioscope.[8] But I
had seen first one and then another of the rooms in which I had slept
during my life, and in the end I would revisit them all in the long course
of my waking dream: rooms in winter, where on going to bed I would at
once bury my head in a nest woven out of the most diverse materials—
the corner of my pillow, the top of my blankets, a piece of a shawl, the
edge of my bed, and a copy of a children's paper—which I had contrived
to cement together, bird-fashion, by dint of continuous pressure; rooms
where, in freezing weather, I would enjoy the satisfaction of being shut in
from the outer world (like the sea-swallow which builds at the end of a
dark tunnel and is kept warm by the surrounding earth), and where, the
fire keeping in all night, I would sleep wrapped up, as it were, in a great

6. From central Italy, mottled and reddish in color. *Bohemian glass:* likely to have been ornately
engraved. Bohemia (now part of the Czech Republic) was a major center of the glass industry.
7. Charles Swann's daughter, Gilberte, who has married Robert de Saint-Loup, a nephew of the Guermantes.   8. An early moving-picture machine that showed photographs in rapid succession.

cloak of snug and smoky air, shot with the glow of the logs intermittently breaking out again in flame, a sort of alcove without walls, a cave of warmth dug out of the heart of the room itself, a zone of heat whose boundaries were constantly shifting and altering in temperature as gusts of air traversed them to strike freshly upon my face, from the corners of the room or from parts near the window or far from the fireplace which had therefore remained cold;—or rooms in summer, where I would delight to feel myself a part of the warm night, where the moonlight striking upon the half-opened shutters would throw down to the foot of my bed its enchanted ladder, where I would fall asleep, as it might be in the open air, like a titmouse which the breeze gently rocks at the tip of a sunbeam;—or sometimes the Louis XVI room,[9] so cheerful that I never felt too miserable in it, even on my first night, and in which the slender columns that lightly supported its ceiling drew so gracefully apart to reveal and frame the site of the bed;—sometimes, again, the little room with the high ceiling, hollowed in the form of a pyramid out of two separate storeys, and partly walled with mahogany, in which from the first moment, mentally poisoned by the unfamiliar scent of vetiver,[1] I was convinced of the hostility of the violet curtains and of the insolent indifference of a clock that chattered on at the top of its voice as though I were not there; in which a strange and pitiless rectangular cheval-glass, standing across one corner of the room, carved out for itself a site I had not looked to find tenanted in the soft plenitude of my normal field of vision;[2] in which my mind, striving for hours on end to break away from its moorings, to stretch upwards so as to take on the exact shape of the room and to reach to the topmost height of its gigantic funnel, had endured many a painful night as I lay stretched out in bed, my eyes staring upwards, my ears straining, my nostrils flaring, my heart beating; until habit had changed the colour of the curtains, silenced the clock, brought an expression of pity to the cruel, slanting face of the glass, disguised or even completely dispelled the scent of vetiver, and appreciably reduced the apparent loftiness of the ceiling. Habit! that skilful but slow-moving arranger who begins by letting our minds suffer for weeks on end in temporary quarters, but whom our minds are none the less only too happy to discover at last, for without it, reduced to their own devices, they would be powerless to make any room seem habitable.

Certainly I was now well awake; my body had veered round for the last time and the good angel of certainty had made all the surrounding objects stand still, had set me down under my bedclothes, in my bedroom, and had fixed, approximately in their right places in the uncertain light, my chest of drawers, my writing-table, my fireplace, the window overlooking the street, and both the doors. But for all that I now knew that I was not in any of the houses of which the ignorance of the waking moment had, in a flash, if not presented me with a distinct picture, at least persuaded me of the possible presence, my memory had been set in motion; as a rule

9. Furnished in late-18th-century style, named for the French monarch of the time and marked by great elegance. The room is that in which Marcel visits Robert de Saint-Loup in *Guermantes' Way*. 1. The aromatic root of a tropical grass packaged as a moth repellent.   2. The narrator's room at the fictional seaside resort of Balbec, a setting in *Within a Budding Grove*.

I did not attempt to go to sleep again at once, but used to spend the greater part of the night recalling our life in the old days at Combray with my great-aunt, at Balbec, Paris, Doncières, Venice, and the rest; remembering again all the places and people I had known, what I had actually seen of them, and what others had told me.

At Combray, as every afternoon ended, long before the time when I should have to go to bed and lie there, unsleeping, far from my mother and grandmother, my bedroom became the fixed point on which my melancholy and anxious thoughts were centred. Someone had indeed had the happy idea of giving me, to distract me on evenings when I seemed abnormally wretched, a magic lantern,[3] which used to be set on top of my lamp while we waited for dinner-time to come; and, after the fashion of the master-builders and glass-painters of gothic days, it substituted for the opaqueness of my walls an impalpable iridescence, supernatural phenomena of many colours, in which legends were depicted as on a shifting and transitory window. But my sorrows were only increased thereby, because this mere change of lighting was enough to destroy the familiar impression I had of my room, thanks to which, save for the torture of going to bed, it had become quite endurable. Now I no longer recognised it, and felt uneasy in it, as in a room in some hotel or chalet, in a place where I had just arrived by train for the first time.

Riding at a jerky trot, Golo,[4] filled with an infamous design, issued from the little triangular forest which dyed dark-green the slope of a convenient hill, and advanced fitfully towards the castle of poor Geneviève de Brabant. This castle was cut off short by a curved line which was in fact the circumference of one of the transparent ovals in the slides which were pushed into position through a slot in the lantern. It was only the wing of a castle, and in front of it stretched a moor on which Geneviève stood lost in contemplation, wearing a blue girdle.[5] The castle and the moor were yellow, but I could tell their colour without waiting to see them, for before the slides made their appearance the old-gold sonorous name of Brabant had given me an unmistakable clue. Golo stopped for a moment and listened sadly to the accompanying patter read aloud by my great-aunt,[6] which he seemed perfectly to understand, for he modified his attitude with a docility not devoid of a degree of majesty, so as to conform to the indications given in the text; then he rode away at the same jerky trot. And nothing could arrest his slow progress. If the lantern were moved I could still distinguish Golo's horse advancing across the window-curtains, swelling out with their curves and diving into their folds. The body of Golo himself, being of the same supernatural substance as his steed's, overcame every material obstacle—everything that seemed to bar his way—by taking it as an ossature[7] and embodying it in himself: even the door-handle, for instance, over which, adapting itself at once, would float irresistibly his red cloak or his pale face, which never lost its nobility or its melancholy, never betrayed the least concern at this transvertebration.

3. A kind of slide projector.   4. Villain of a 5th-century legend. He falsely accuses Geneviève de Brabant of adultery. Brabant was a principality in what is now Belgium.   5. Belt.   6. Marcel's great-aunt is reading the story to him as they wait for dinner.   7. Skeleton.

And, indeed, I found plenty of charm in these bright projections, which seemed to emanate from a Merovingian[8] past and shed around me the reflections of such ancient history. But I cannot express the discomfort I felt at this intrusion of mystery and beauty into a room which I had succeeded in filling with my own personality until I thought no more of it than of myself. The anaesthetic effect of habit being destroyed, I would begin to think—and to feel—such melancholy things. The door-handle of my room, which was different to me from all the other door-handles in the world, inasmuch as it seemed to open of its own accord and without my having to turn it, so unconscious had its manipulation become—lo and behold, it was now an astral body[9] for Golo. And as soon as the dinner-bell rang I would hurry down to the dining-room, where the big hanging lamp, ignorant of Golo and Bluebeard[1] but well acquainted with my family and the dish of stewed beef, shed the same light as on every other evening; and I would fall into the arms of my mother, whom the misfortunes of Geneviève de Brabant had made all the dearer to me, just as the crimes of Golo had driven me to a more than ordinarily scrupulous examination of my own conscience.

But after dinner, alas, I was soon obliged to leave Mamma, who stayed talking with the others, in the garden if it was fine, or in the little parlour where everyone took shelter when it was wet. Everyone except my grandmother, who held that "It's a pity to shut oneself indoors in the country," and used to have endless arguments with my father on the very wettest days, because he would send me up to my room with a book instead of letting me stay out of doors. "That is not the way to make him strong and active," she would say sadly, "especially this little man, who needs all the strength and will-power that he can get." My father would shrug his shoulders and study the barometer, for he took an interest in meteorology, while my mother, keeping very quiet so as not to disturb him, looked at him with tender respect, but not too hard, not wishing to penetrate the mysteries of his superior mind. But my grandmother, in all weathers, even when the rain was coming down in torrents and Françoise had rushed the precious wicker armchairs indoors so that they should not get soaked, was to be seen pacing the deserted rain-lashed garden, pushing back her disordered grey locks so that her forehead might be freer to absorb the health-giving draughts of wind and rain. She would say, "At last one can breathe!" and would trot up and down the sodden paths—too straight and symmetrical for her liking, owing to the want of any feeling for nature in the new gardener, whom my father had been asking all morning if the weather were going to improve—her keen, jerky little step regulated by the various effects wrought upon her soul by the intoxication of the storm, the power of hygiene, the stupidity of my upbringing and the symmetry of gardens, rather than by any anxiety (for that was quite unknown to her) to save her plum-coloured skirt from the mudstains beneath which it would gradually disappear to a height that was the constant bane and despair of her maid.

8. The first dynasty of French kings (A.D. 500–751).   9. Spiritual counterpart of the physical body. According to the doctrine of Theosophy (a spiritualist movement originating in 1875), the astral body survives the death of the physical body.   1. The legendary wife murderer, presumably depicted on another set of slides.

When these walks of my grandmother's took place after dinner there was one thing which never failed to bring her back to the house: this was if (at one of those points when her circular itinerary brought her back, moth-like, in sight of the lamp in the little parlour where the liqueurs were set out on the card-table) my great-aunt called out to her: "Bathilde! Come in and stop your husband drinking brandy!" For, simply to tease her (she had brought so different a type of mind into my father's family that everyone made fun of her), my great-aunt used to make my grandfather, who was forbidden liqueurs, take just a few drops. My poor grandmother would come in and beg and implore her husband not to taste the brandy; and he would get angry and gulp it down all the same, and she would go out again sad and discouraged, but still smiling, for she was so humble of heart and so gentle that her tenderness for others and her disregard for herself and her own troubles blended in a smile which, unlike those seen on the majority of human faces, bore no trace of irony save for herself, while for all of us kisses seemed to spring from her eyes, which could not look upon those she loved without seeming to bestow upon them passionate caresses. This torture inflicted on her by my great-aunt, the sight of my grandmother's vain entreaties, of her feeble attempts, doomed in advance, to remove the liqueur-glass from my grandfather's hands—all these were things of the sort to which, in later years, one can grow so accustomed as to smile at them and to take the persecutor's side resolutely and cheerfully enough to persuade oneself that it is not really persecution; but in those days they filled me with such horror that I longed to strike my great-aunt. And yet, as soon as I heard her "Bathilde! Come in and stop your husband drinking brandy," in my cowardice I became at once a man, and did what all we grown men do when face to face with suffering and injustice: I preferred not to see them; I ran up to the top of the house to cry by myself in a little room beside the schoolroom and beneath the roof, which smelt of orris-root[2] and was scented also by a wild currant-bush which had climbed up between the stones of the outer wall and thrust a flowering branch in through the half-opened window. Intended for a more special and a baser use, this room, from which, in the daytime, I could see as far as the keep[3] of Roussainville-le-Pin, was for a long time my place of refuge, doubtless because it was the only room whose door I was allowed to lock, whenever my occupation was such as required an inviolable solitude: reading or day-dreaming, secret tears or sensual gratification. Alas! I little knew that my own lack of will-power, my delicate health, and the consequent uncertainty as to my future, weighed far more heavily on my grandmother's mind than any little dietary indiscretion by her husband in the course of those endless perambulations, afternoon and evening, during which we used to see her handsome face passing to and fro, half raised towards the sky, its brown and wrinkled cheeks, which with age had acquired almost the purple hue of tilled fields in autumn, covered, if she were "going out," by a half-lifted veil, while upon them either the cold or some sad reflection invariably left the drying traces of an involuntary tear.

---

2. A powder then used as a deodorizer for rooms.   3. The best-fortified tower of a medieval castle. *Baser use:* as a toilet.

My sole consolation when I went upstairs for the night was that Mamma would come in and kiss me after I was in bed. But this good night lasted for so short a time, she went down again so soon, that the moment in which I heard her climb the stairs, and then caught the sound of her garden dress of blue muslin, from which hung little tassels of plaited straw, rustling along the double-doored corridor, was for me a moment of the utmost pain; for it heralded the moment which was bound to follow it, when she would have left me and gone downstairs again. So much so that I reached the point of hoping that this good night which I loved so much would come as late as possible, so as to prolong the time of respite during which Mamma would not yet have appeared. Sometimes when, after kissing me, she opened the door to go, I longed to call her back, to say to her "Kiss me just once more," but I knew that then she would at once look displeased, for the concession which she made to my wretchedness and agitation in coming up to give me this kiss of peace always annoyed my father, who thought such rituals absurd, and she would have liked to try to induce me to outgrow the need, the habit, of having her there at all, let alone get into the habit of asking her for an additional kiss when she was already crossing the threshold. And to see her look displeased destroyed all the calm and serenity she had brought me a moment before, when she had bent her loving face down over my bed, and held it out to me like a host[4] for an act of peace-giving communion in which my lips might imbibe her real presence and with it the power to sleep. But those evenings on which Mamma stayed so short a time in my room were sweet indeed compared to those on which we had guests to dinner, and therefore she did not come at all. Our "guests" were usually limited to M. Swann, who, apart from a few passing strangers, was almost the only person who ever came to the house at Combray, sometimes to a neighbourly dinner (but less frequently since his unfortunate marriage, as my family did not care to receive his wife) and sometimes after dinner, uninvited. On those evenings when, as we sat in front of the house round the iron table beneath the big chestnut-tree, we heard, from the far end of the garden, not the shrill and assertive alarm bell which assailed and deafened with its ferruginous,[5] interminable, frozen sound any member of the household who set it off on entering "without ringing," but the double tinkle, timid, oval, golden, of the visitors' bell, everyone would at once exclaim "A visitor! Who in the world can it be?" but they knew quite well that it could only be M. Swann. My great-aunt, speaking in a loud voice to set an example, in a tone which she endeavoured to make sound natural, would tell the others not to whisper so; that nothing could be more offensive to a stranger coming in, who would be led to think that people were saying things about him which he was not meant to hear; and then my grandmother, always happy to find an excuse for an additional turn in the garden, would be sent out to reconnoitre, and would take the opportunity to remove surreptitiously, as she passed, the stakes of a rose-tree or two, so as to make the roses look a little more natural, as a mother might run her

4. Communion wafer.   5. Iron-like.

hand through her boy's hair after the barber has smoothed it down, to make it look naturally wavy.

We would all wait there in suspense for the report which my grandmother would bring back from the enemy lines, as though there might be a choice between a large number of possible assailants, and then, soon after, my grandfather would say: "I can hear Swann's voice." And indeed one could tell him only by his voice, for it was difficult to make out his face with its arched nose and green eyes, under a high forehead fringed with fair, almost red hair, done in the Bressant style,[6] because in the garden we used as little light as possible, so as not to attract mosquitoes; and I would slip away unobtrusively to order the liqueurs to be brought out, for my grandmother made a great point, thinking it "nicer," of their not being allowed to seem anything out of the ordinary, which we kept for visitors only. Although a far younger man, M. Swann was very much attached to my grandfather, who had been an intimate friend of Swann's father, an excellent but eccentric man the ardour of whose feelings and the current of whose thoughts would often be checked or diverted by the most trifling thing. Several times in the course of a year I would hear my grandfather tell at table the story, which never varied, of the behaviour of M. Swann the elder upon the death of his wife, by whose bedside he had watched day and night. My grandfather, who had not seen him for a long time, hastened to join him at the Swanns' family property on the outskirts of Combray, and managed to entice him for a moment, weeping profusely, out of the death-chamber, so that he should not be present when the body was laid in its coffin. They took a turn or two in the park, where there was a little sunshine. Suddenly M. Swann seized my grandfather by the arm and cried, "Ah, my dear old friend, how fortunate we are to be walking here together on such a charming day! Don't you see how pretty they are, all these trees, my hawthorns, and my new pond, on which you have never congratulated me? You look as solemn as the grave. Don't you feel this little breeze? Ah! whatever you may say, it's good to be alive all the same, my dear Amédée!" And then, abruptly, the memory of his dead wife returned to him, and probably thinking it too complicated to inquire into how, at such a time, he could have allowed himself to be carried away by an impulse of happiness, he confined himself to a gesture which he habitually employed whenever any perplexing question came into his mind: that is, he passed his hand across his forehead, rubbed his eyes, and wiped his glasses. And yet he never got over the loss of his wife, but used to say to my grandfather, during the two years by which he survived her, "It's a funny thing, now; I very often think of my poor wife, but I cannot think of her for long at a time." "Often, but a little at a time, like poor old Swann," became one of my grandfather's favourite sayings, which he would apply to all manner of things. I should have assumed that this father of Swann's had been a monster if my grandfather, whom I regarded as a better judge than myself, and whose word was my law and often led me in the long run to pardon offences which I should have been inclined to

6. Close-cropped, like a crew cut; named after a French actor.

condemn, had not gone on to exclaim, "But, after all, he had a heart of gold."

For many years, during the course of which—especially before his marriage—M. Swann the younger came often to see them at Combray, my great-aunt and my grandparents never suspected that he had entirely ceased to live in the society which his family had frequented, and that, under the sort of incognito which the name of Swann gave him among us, they were harbouring—with the complete innocence of a family of respectable innkeepers who have in their midst some celebrated highwayman without knowing it—one of the most distinguished members of the Jockey Club, a particular friend of the Comte de Paris and of the Prince of Wales, and one of the men most sought after in the aristocratic world of the Faubourg Saint-Germain.[7]

Our utter ignorance of the brilliant social life which Swann led was, of course, due in part to his own reserve and discretion, but also to the fact that middle-class people in those days took what was almost a Hindu view of society, which they held to consist of sharply defined castes, so that everyone at his birth found himself called to that station in life which his parents already occupied, and from which nothing, save the accident of an exceptional career or of a "good" marriage, could extract you and translate you to a superior caste. M. Swann the elder had been a stockbroker; and so "young Swann" found himself immured for life in a caste whose members' fortunes, as in a category of tax-payers, varied between such and such limits of income. One knew the people with whom his father had associated, and so one knew his own associates, the people with whom he was "in a position to mix." If he knew other people besides, those were youthful acquaintances on whom the old friends of his family, like my relatives, shut their eyes all the more good-naturedly because Swann himself, after he was left an orphan, still came most faithfully to see us; but we would have been ready to wager that the people outside our acquaintance whom Swann knew were of the sort to whom he would not have dared to raise his hat if he had met them while he was walking with us. Had it been absolutely essential to apply to Swann a social coefficient peculiar to himself, as distinct from all the other sons of other stockbrokers in his father's position, his coefficient would have been rather lower than theirs, because, being very simple in his habits, and having always had a craze for "antiques" and pictures, he now lived and amassed his collections in an old house which my grandmother longed to visit but which was situated on the Quai d'Orléans,[8] a neighbourhood in which my great-aunt thought it most degrading to be quartered. "Are you really a connoisseur, now?" she would say to him: "I ask for your own sake, as you are likely to have fakes palmed off on you by the dealers," for she did not, in fact, endow him with any critical faculty, and had no great opinion of the

7. A fashionable area of Paris on the left bank of the Seine; many of the French aristocracy lived there. *Jockey Club:* an exclusive men's club devoted not only to horseracing but to other diversions (such as the opera). The Comte de Paris (1838–1894) was heir apparent to the French throne, in the unlikely event that the monarchy were reinstated. The Prince of Wales became in 1901 King Edward VII of England. The implication is that Swann's social connections were not merely of the highest but of an idle and somewhat hedonistic sort.   8. A beautiful though less fashionable section in the heart of Paris, along the Seine.

so harmoniously in the sound of his voice as if it were no more than a transparent envelope, that each time we see the face or hear the voice it is these notions which we recognise and to which we listen. And so, no doubt, from the Swann they had constructed for themselves my family had left out, in their ignorance, a whole host of details of his life in the world of fashion, details which caused other people, when they met him, to see all the graces enthroned in his face and stopping at the line of his aquiline nose as at a natural frontier; but they had contrived also to put into this face divested of all glamour, vacant and roomy as an untenanted house, to plant in the depths of these undervalued eyes, a lingering residuum, vague but not unpleasing—half-memory and half-oblivion—of idle hours spent together after our weekly dinners, round the card-table or in the garden, during our companionable country life. Our friend's corporeal envelope had been so well lined with this residuum, as well as various earlier memories of his parents, that their own special Swann had become to my family a complete and living creature; so that even now I have the feeling of leaving someone I know for another quite different person when, going back in memory, I pass from the Swann whom I knew later and more intimately to this early Swann—this early Swann in whom I can distinguish the charming mistakes of my youth, and who in fact is less like his successor than he is like the other people I knew at that time, as though one's life were a picture gallery in which all the portraits of any one period had a marked family likeness, a similar tonality—this early Swann abounding in leisure, fragrant with the scent of the great chestnut-tree, of baskets of raspberries and of a sprig of tarragon.

And yet one day, when my grandmother had gone to ask some favour of a lady whom she had known at the Sacré Cœur[9] (and with whom, because of our notions of caste, she had not cared to keep up any degree of intimacy in spite of several common interests), the Marquise de Ville-parisis, of the famous house of Bouillon, this lady had said to her:

"I believe you know M. Swann very well; he's a great friend of my nephews, the des Laumes."[1]

My grandmother had returned from the call full of praise for the house, which overlooked some gardens, and in which Mme de Villeparisis had advised her to rent a flat, and also for a repairing tailor and his daughter who kept a little shop in the courtyard, into which she had gone to ask them to put a stitch in her skirt, which she had torn on the staircase. My grandmother had found these people perfectly charming: the girl, she said, was a jewel, and the tailor the best and most distinguished man she had ever seen. For in her eyes distinction was a thing wholly independent of social position. She was in ecstasies over some answer the tailor had made to her, saying to Mamma:

"Sévigné[2] would not have put it better!" and, by way of contrast, of a nephew of Mme de Villeparisis whom she had met at the house:

---

9. A convent school in Paris, attended by daughters of the aristocracy and the wealthy bourgeoisie.   1. A fictional family. The Marquise de Villeparisis was a member of the Guermantes family. Proust enhances the apparent reality of the Guermantes by relating them to the historical house of Bouillon, a famous aristocratic family tracing its descent from the Middle Ages.   2. The Marquise de Sévigné (1626–1696), known for the lively style of her letters.

"My dear, he is so common!"

Now, the effect of the remark about Swann had been, not to raise him in my great-aunt's estimation, but to lower Mme de Villeparisis. It appeared that the deference which, on my grandmother's authority, we owed to Mme de Villeparisis imposed on her the reciprocal obligation to do nothing that would render her less worthy of our regard, and that she had failed in this duty by becoming aware of Swann's existence and in allowing members of her family to associate with him. "What! She knows Swann? A person who, you always made out, was related to Marshal Mac-Mahon!"[3] This view of Swann's social position which prevailed in my family seemed to be confirmed later on by his marriage with a woman of the worst type, almost a prostitute, whom, to do him justice, he never attempted to introduce to us—for he continued to come to our house alone, though more and more seldom—but from whom they felt they could establish, on the assumption that he had found her there, the circle, unknown to them, in which he ordinarily moved.

But on one occasion my grandfather read in a newspaper that M. Swann was one of the most regular attendants at the Sunday luncheons given by the Duc de X——, whose father and uncle had been among our most prominent statesmen in the reign of Louis-Philippe.[4] Now my grandfather was curious to learn all the smallest details which might help him to take a mental share in the private lives of men like Molé, the Duc Pasquier, or the Duc de Broglie.[5] He was delighted to find that Swann associated with people who had known them. My great-aunt, on the other hand, interpreted this piece of news in a sense discreditable to Swann; for anyone who chose his associates outside the caste in which he had been born and bred, outside his "proper station," automatically lowered himself in her eyes. It seemed to her that such a one abdicated all claim to enjoy the fruits of the splendid connections with people of good position which prudent parents cultivate and store up for their children's benefit, and she had actually ceased to "see" the son of a lawyer of our acquaintance because he had married a "Highness" and had thereby stepped down—in her eyes—from the respectable position of a lawyer's son to that of those adventurers, upstart footmen or stable-boys mostly, to whom, we are told, queens have sometimes shown their favours. She objected, therefore, to my grandfather's plan of questioning Swann, when next he came to dine with us, about these people whose friendship with him we had discovered. At the same time my grandmother's two sisters, elderly spinsters who shared her nobility of character but lacked her intelligence, declared that they could not conceive what pleasure their brother-in-law could find in talking about such trifles. They were ladies of lofty aspirations, who for that reason were incapable of taking the least interest in what might be termed gossip, even if it had some historical import, or, generally speaking, in anything that was not directly associated with some aesthetic or virtuous

---

3. Marshal of France (1808–1893), elected president of the French Republic in 1873.   4. King of France from 1830 to 1848, father of the Comte de Paris.   5. Duc Achille Charles Leonce Victor de Broglie (1785–1870) had a busy public career that ended in 1851. Comte Louis Mathieu Molé (1781–1855) held various cabinet positions before becoming premier of France in 1836. Duc Etienne Denis de Pasquier (1767–1862) also held important public positions up to 1837. All were active during the reign of Louis Philippe.

object. So complete was their negation of interest in anything which seemed directly or indirectly connected with worldly matters that their sense of hearing—having finally come to realise its temporary futility when the tone of the conversation at the dinner-table became frivolous or merely mundane without the two old ladies' being able to guide it back to topics dear to themselves—would put its receptive organs into abeyance to the point of actually becoming atrophied. So that if my grandfather wished to attract the attention of the two sisters, he had to resort to some such physical stimuli as alienists adopt in dealing with their distracted patients: to wit, repeated taps on a glass with the blade of a knife, accompanied by a sharp word and a compelling glance, violent methods which these psychiatrists are apt to bring with them into their everyday life among the sane, either from force of professional habit or because they think the whole world a trifle mad.

Their interest grew, however, when, the day before Swann was to dine with us, and when he had made them a special present of a case of Asti, my great-aunt, who had in her hand a copy of the *Figaro* in which to the name of a picture then on view in a Corot exhibition were added the words, "from the collection of M. Charles Swann," asked: "Did you see that Swann is 'mentioned' in the *Figaro*?"[6]

"But I've always told you," said my grandmother, "that he had a great deal of taste."

"You would, of course," retorted my great-aunt, "say anything just to seem different from *us.*" For, knowing that my grandmother never agreed with her, and not being quite confident that it was her own opinion which the rest of us invariably endorsed, she wished to extort from us a wholesale condemnation of my grandmother's views, against which she hoped to force us into solidarity with her own. But we sat silent. My grandmother's sisters having expressed a desire to mention to Swann this reference to him in the *Figaro*, my great-aunt dissuaded them. Whenever she saw in others an advantage, however trivial, which she herself lacked, she would persuade herself that it was no advantage at all, but a drawback, and would pity so as not to have to envy them.

"I don't think that would please him at all; I know very well that I should hate to see my name printed like that, as large as life, in the paper, and I shouldn't feel at all flattered if anyone spoke to me about it."

She did not, however, put any very great pressure upon my grandmother's sisters, for they, in their horror of vulgarity, had brought to such a fine art the concealment of a personal allusion in a wealth of ingenious circumlocution, that it would often pass unnoticed even by the person to whom it was addressed. As for my mother, her only thought was of trying to induce my father to speak to Swann, not about his wife but about his daughter, whom he worshipped, and for whose sake it was understood that he had ultimately made his unfortunate marriage.

"You need only say a word; just ask him how she is. It must be so very hard for him."

---

6. Leading Parisian newspaper. *Asti:* an Italian white wine. Jean Corot (1796–1875) was a French landscape painter, very popular at the time.

My father, however, was annoyed: "No, no; you have the most absurd ideas. It would be utterly ridiculous."

But the only one of us in whom the prospect of Swann's arrival gave rise to an unhappy foreboding was myself. This was because on the evenings when there were visitors, or just M. Swann, in the house, Mamma did not come up to my room. I dined before the others, and afterwards came and sat at table until eight o'clock, when it was understood that I must go upstairs; that frail and precious kiss which Mamma used normally to bestow on me when I was in bed and just going to sleep had to be transported from the dining-room to my bedroom where I must keep it inviolate all the time that it took me to undress, without letting its sweet charm be broken, without letting its volatile essence diffuse itself and evaporate; and it was precisely on those very evenings when I needed to receive it with special care that I was obliged to take it, to snatch it brusquely and in public, without even having the time or the equanimity to bring to what I was doing the single-minded attention of lunatics who compel themselves to exclude all other thoughts from their minds while they are shutting a door, so that when the sickness of uncertainty sweeps over them again they can triumphantly oppose it with the recollection of the precise moment when they shut the door.

We were all in the garden when the double tinkle of the visitors' bell sounded shyly. Everyone knew that it must be Swann, and yet they looked at one another inquiringly and sent my grandmother to reconnoitre.

"See that you thank him intelligibly for the wine," my grandfather warned his two sisters-in-law. "You know how good it is, and the case is huge."

"Now, don't start whispering!" said my great-aunt. "How would you like to come into a house and find everyone muttering to themselves?"

"Ah! There's M. Swann," cried my father. "Let's ask him if he thinks it will be fine to-morrow."

My mother fancied that a word from her would wipe out all the distress which my family had contrived to cause Swann since his marriage. She found an opportunity to draw him aside for a moment. But I followed her: I could not bring myself to let her out of my sight while I felt that in a few minutes I should have to leave her in the dining-room and go up to my bed without the consoling thought, as on ordinary evenings, that she would come up later to kiss me.

"Now, M. Swann," she said, "do tell me about your daughter. I'm sure she already has a taste for beautiful things, like her papa."

"Come along and sit down here with us all on the verandah," said my grandfather, coming up to him. My mother had to abandon her quest, but managed to extract from the restriction itself a further delicate thought, like good poets whom the tyranny of rhyme forces into the discovery of their finest lines.

"We can talk about her again when we are by ourselves," she said, or rather whispered to Swann. "Only a mother is capable of understanding these things. I'm sure that hers would agree with me."

And so we all sat down round the iron table. I should have liked not to think of the hours of anguish which I should have to spend that evening alone in my room, without being able to go to sleep: I tried to convince myself that they were of no importance since I should have forgotten them next morning, and to fix my mind on thoughts of the future which would carry me, as on a bridge, across the terrifying abyss that yawned at my feet. But my mind, strained by this foreboding, distended like the look which I shot at my mother, would not allow any extraneous impression to enter. Thoughts did indeed enter it, but only on the condition that they left behind them every element of beauty, or even of humour, by which I might have been distracted or beguiled. As a surgical patient, thanks to a local anaesthetic, can look on fully conscious while an operation is being performed upon him and yet feel nothing, I could repeat to myself some favourite lines, or watch my grandfather's efforts to talk to Swann about the Duc d' Audiffret-Pasquier,[7] without being able to kindle any emotion from the one or amusement from the other. Hardly had my grandfather begun to question Swann about that orator when one of my grandmother's sisters, in whose ears the question echoed like a solemn but untimely silence which her natural politeness bade her interrupt, addressed the other with:

"Just fancy, Flora, I met a young Swedish governess today who told me some most interesting things about the co-operative movement in Scandinavia. We really must have her to dine here one evening."

"To be sure!" said her sister Flora, "but I haven't wasted my time either. I met such a clever old gentleman at M. Vinteuil's who knows Maubant[8] quite well, and Maubant has told him every little thing about how he gets up his parts. It's the most interesting thing I ever heard. He's a neighbour of M. Vinteuil's, and I never knew; and he is so nice besides."

"M. Vinteuil is not the only one who has nice neighbours," cried my aunt Céline in a voice that was loud because of shyness and forced because of premeditation, darting, as she spoke, what she called a "significant glance" at Swann. And my aunt Flora, who realised that this veiled utterance was Céline's way of thanking Swann for the Asti, looked at him also with a blend of congratulation and irony, either because she simply wished to underline her sister's little witticism, or because she envied Swann his having inspired it, or because she imagined that he was embarrassed, and could not help having a little fun at his expense.

"I think it would be worth while," Flora went on, "to have this old gentleman to dinner. When you get him going on Maubant or Mme Materna[9] he will talk for hours on end."

"That must be delightful," sighed my grandfather, in whose mind nature had unfortunately forgotten to include any capacity whatsoever for becoming passionately interested in the Swedish co-operative movement or in the methods employed by Maubant to get up his parts, just as it had forgotten to endow my grandmother's two sisters with a grain of that precious salt which one has oneself to "add to taste" in order to extract any savour from a narrative of the private life of Molé or of the Comte de Paris.

7. A fictitious nobleman. 8. Actor at the Comédie Française, the French national theater. M. Vinteuil is a fictitious composer and neighbor of the family. 9. Austrian soprano, who took part in the premiere of Wagner's *Ring* cycle at Bayreuth in 1876.

"By the way," said Swann to my grandfather, "what I was going to tell you has more to do than you might think with what you were asking me just now, for in some respects there has been very little change. I came across a passage in Saint-Simon[1] this morning which would have amused you. It's in the volume which covers his mission to Spain; not one of the best, little more in fact than a journal, but at least a wonderfully well written journal, which fairly distinguishes it from the tedious journals we feel bound to read morning and evening."

"I don't agree with you: there are some days when I find reading the papers very pleasant indeed," my aunt Flora broke in, to show Swann that she had read the note about his Corot in the *Figaro*.

"Yes," aunt Céline went one better, "when they write about things or people in whom we are interested."

"I don't deny it," answered Swann in some bewilderment. "The fault I find with our journalism is that it forces us to take an interest in some fresh triviality or other every day, whereas only three or four books in a lifetime give us anything that is of real importance. Suppose that, every morning, when we tore the wrapper off our paper with fevered hands, a transmutation were to take place, and we were to find inside it—oh! I don't know; shall we say Pascal's *Pensées*?"[2] He articulated the title with an ironic emphasis so as not to appear pedantic. "And then, in the gilt and tooled volumes which we open once in ten years," he went on, showing that contempt for worldly matters which some men of the world like to affect, "we should read that the Queen of the Hellenes had arrived at Cannes, or that the Princesse de Léon had given a fancy dress ball. In that way we should arrive at a happy medium." But at once regretting that he had allowed himself to speak of serious matters even in jest, he added ironically: "What a fine conversation we're having! I can't think why we climb to these lofty heights," and then, turning to my grandfather: "Well, Saint-Simon tells how Maulévrier had had the audacity to try to shake hands with his sons.[3] You remember how he says of Maulévrier, 'Never did I find in that coarse bottle anything but ill-humour, boorishness, and folly.' "

"Coarse or not, I know bottles in which there is something very different," said Flora briskly, feeling bound to thank Swann as well as her sister, since the present of Asti had been addressed to them both. Céline laughed.

Swann was puzzled, but went on: " 'I cannot say whether it was ignorance or cozenage,' writes Saint-Simon. 'He tried to give his hand to my children. I noticed it in time to prevent him.' "

My grandfather was already in ecstasies over "ignorance or cozenage," but Mlle Céline—the name of Saint-Simon, a "man of letters," having arrested the complete paralysis of her auditory faculties—was indignant:

1. The memoirs of the Duc de Saint-Simon (1675–1755) describe court life and intrigue during the reigns of Louis XIV and Louis XV. He was sent to Spain in 1721 to arrange the marriage of Louis XV and the daughter of the king of Spain. 2. The "Thoughts" of the French mathematician and religious philosopher Blaise Pascal (1623–1662) are comments on the human condition and one of the triumphant works of French classicism. 3. Maulévrier was the French ambassador to Spain. Saint-Simon considered him of inferior birth, and refused to let his own children shake Maulévrier's hand (*Memoirs*, vol. XXXIX).

"What! You admire that? Well, that's a fine thing, I must say! But what's it supposed to mean? Isn't one man as good as the next? What difference can it make whether he's a duke or a groom so long as he's intelligent and kind? He had a fine way of bringing up his children, your Saint-Simon, if he didn't teach them to shake hands with all decent folk. Really and truly, it's abominable. And you dare to quote it!"

And my grandfather, utterly depressed, realising how futile it would be, against this opposition, to attempt to get Swann to tell him the stories which would have amused him, murmured to my mother: "Just tell me again that line of yours which always comforts me so much on these occasions. Oh, yes: 'What virtues, Lord, Thou makest us abhor!'[4] How good that is!"

I never took my eyes off my mother. I knew that when they were at table I should not be permitted to stay there for the whole of dinner-time, and that Mamma, for fear of annoying my father, would not allow me to kiss her several times in public, as I would have done in my room. And so I promised myself that in the dining-room, as they began to eat and drink and as I felt the hour approach, I would put beforehand into this kiss, which was bound to be so brief and furtive, everything that my own efforts could muster, would carefully choose in advance the exact spot on her cheek where I would imprint it, and would so prepare my thoughts as to be able, thanks to these mental preliminaries, to consecrate the whole of the minute Mamma would grant me to the sensation of her cheek against my lips, as a painter who can have his subject for short sittings only prepares his palette, and from what he remembers and from rough notes does in advance everything which he possibly can do in the sitter's absence. But to-night, before the dinner-bell had sounded, my grandfather said with unconscious cruelty: "The little man looks tired; he'd better go up to bed. Besides, we're dining late to-night."

And my father, who was less scrupulous than my grandmother or my mother in observing the letter of a treaty, went on: "Yes; run along; off to bed."

I would have kissed Mamma then and there, but at that moment the dinner-bell rang.

"No, no, leave your mother alone. You've said good night to one another, that's enough. These exhibitions are absurd. Go on upstairs."

And so I must set forth without viaticum;[5] must climb each step of the staircase "against my heart," as the saying is, climbing in opposition to my heart's desire, which was to return to my mother, since she had not, by kissing me, given my heart leave to accompany me forth. That hateful staircase, up which I always went so sadly, gave out a smell of varnish which had, as it were, absorbed and crystallised the special quality of sorrow that I felt each evening, and made it perhaps even crueller to my sensibility because, when it assumed this olfactory guise, my intellect was powerless to resist it. When we have gone to sleep with a raging toothache and are conscious of it only as of a little girl whom we attempt, time after

---

4. From *Pompey's Death* (line 1072), a tragedy by the French dramatist Pierre Corneille (1606–1684).
5. The communion wafer and wine given to the dying in Catholic rites.

time, to pull out of the water, or a line of Molière[6] which we repeat incessantly to ourselves, it is a great relief to wake up, so that our intelligence
can disentangle the idea of toothache from any artificial semblance of
heroism or rhythmic cadence. It was the converse of this relief which I
felt when my anguish at having to go up to my room invaded my consciousness in a manner infinitely more rapid, instantaneous almost, a manner at once insidious and brutal, through the inhalation—far more
poisonous than moral penetration—of the smell of varnish peculiar to that
staircase.

Once in my room I had to stop every loophole, to close the shutters, to
dig my own grave as I turned down the bedclothes, to wrap myself in the
shroud of my nightshirt. But before burying myself in the iron bed which
had been placed there because, on summer nights, I was too hot among
the rep curtains of the four-poster,[7] I was stirred to revolt, and attempted
the desperate stratagem of a condemned prisoner. I wrote to my mother
begging her to come upstairs for an important reason which I could not
put in writing. My fear was that Françoise, my aunt's cook who used to be
put in charge of me when I was at Combray, might refuse to take my note.
I had a suspicion that, in her eyes, to carry a message to my mother when
there was a guest would appear as flatly inconceivable as for the doorkeeper of a theatre to hand a letter to an actor upon the stage. On the
subject of things which might or might not be done she possessed a code
at once imperious, abundant, subtle, and uncompromising on points
themselves imperceptible or irrelevant, which gave it a resemblance to
those ancient laws which combine such cruel ordinances as the massacre
of infants at the breast with prohibitions of exaggerated refinement against
"seething the kid in his mother's milk," or "eating of the sinew which is
upon the hollow of the thigh."[8] This code, judging by the sudden obstinacy which she would put into her refusal to carry out certain of our
instructions, seemed to have provided for social complexities and refine-
ments of etiquette which nothing in Françoise's background or in her
career as a servant in a village household could have put into her head;
and we were obliged to assume that there was latent in her some past
existence in the ancient history of France, noble and little understood, as
in those manufacturing towns where old mansions still testify to their former courtly days, and chemical workers toil among delicately sculptured
scenes from Le Miracle de Théophile or Les quatre fils Aymon.[9]

In this particular instance, the article of her code which made it highly
improbable that—barring an outbreak of fire—Françoise would go down
and disturb Mamma in the presence of M. Swann for so unimportant a
person as myself was one embodying the respect she showed not only for
the family (as for the dead, for the clergy, or for royalty), but also for the
stranger within our gates; a respect which I should perhaps have found
touching in a book, but which never failed to irritate me on her lips,
because of the solemn and sentimental tones in which she would express

6. French dramatist (1622–1673).   7. Bed with corner pillars to support a canopy and curtains. Rep:
a heavy, ribbed fabric.   8. Refers to the strict dietary laws of Deuteronomy 14:21 and Genesis 32:32.
9. "The four sons of Aymon" (French), heroic knights who together rode the magic horse Bayard.
Théophile was saved from damnation by the Virgin Mary after having signed a pact with the Devil.

it, and which irritated me more than usual this evening when the sacred character with which she invested the dinner-party might have the effect of making her decline to disturb its ceremonial. But to give myself a chance of success I had no hesitation in lying, telling her that it was not in the least myself who had wanted to write to Mamma, but Mamma who, on saying good night to me, had begged me not to forget to send her an answer about something she had asked me to look for, and that she would certainly be very angry if this note were not taken to her. I think that Françoise disbelieved me, for, like those primitive men whose senses were so much keener than our own, she could immediately detect, from signs imperceptible to the rest of us, the truth or falsehood of anything that we might wish to conceal from her. She studied the envelope for five minutes as though an examination of the paper itself and the look of my handwriting could enlighten her as to the nature of the contents, or tell her to which article of her code she ought to refer the matter. Then she went out with an air of resignation which seemed to imply: "It's hard lines on parents having a child like that."

A moment later she returned to say that they were still at the ice stage and that it was impossible for the butler to deliver the note at once, in front of everybody; but that when the finger-bowls were put round he would find a way of slipping it into Mamma's hand. At once my anxiety subsided; it was now no longer (as it had been a moment ago) until tomorrow that I had lost my mother, since my little note—though it would annoy her, no doubt, and doubly so because this stratagem would make me ridiculous in Swann's eyes—would at least admit me, invisible and enraptured, into the same room as herself, would whisper about me into her ear; since that forbidden and unfriendly dining-room, where but a moment ago the ice itself—with burned nuts in it—and the finger-bowls seemed to me to be concealing pleasures that were baleful and of a mortal sadness because Mamma was tasting of them while I was far away, had opened its doors to me and, like a ripe fruit which bursts through its skin, was going to pour out into my intoxicated heart the sweetness of Mamma's attention while she was reading what I had written. Now I was no longer separated from her; the barriers were down; an exquisite thread united us. Besides, that was not all: for surely Mamma would come.

As for the agony through which I had just passed, I imagined that Swann would have laughed heartily at it if he had read my letter and had guessed its purpose; whereas, on the contrary, as I was to learn in due course, a similar anguish[1] had been the bane of his life for many years, and no one perhaps could have understood my feelings at that moment so well as he; to him, the anguish that comes from knowing that the creature one adores is in some place of enjoyment where oneself is not and cannot follow—to him that anguish came through love, to which it is in a sense predestined, by which it will be seized upon and exploited; but when, as had befallen me, it possesses one's soul before love has yet entered into one's life, then it must drift, awaiting love's coming, vague and free, without precise attachment, at the disposal of one sentiment to-

---

1. That is, his unhappy love for Odette de Crécy, described in *Swann in Love*.

day, of another to-morrow, of filial piety or affection for a friend. And the joy with which I first bound myself apprentice, when Françoise returned to tell me that my letter would be delivered, Swann, too, had known well—that false joy which a friend or relative of the woman we love can give us, when, on his arrival at the house or theatre where she is to be found, for some ball or party or "first-night" at which he is to meet her, he sees us wandering outside, desperately awaiting some opportunity of communicating with her. He recognises us, greets us familiarly, and asks what we are doing there. And when we invent a story of having some urgent message to give to his relative or friend, he assures us that nothing could be simpler, takes us in at the door, and promises to send her down to us in five minutes. How we love him—as at that moment I loved Françoise—the good-natured intermediary who by a single word has made supportable, human, almost propitious the inconceivable, infernal scene of gaiety in the thick of which we had been imagining swarms of enemies, perverse and seductive, beguiling away from us, even making laugh at us, the woman we love! If we are to judge of them by him—this relative who has accosted us and who is himself an initiate in those cruel mysteries— then the other guests cannot be so very demoniacal. Those inaccessible and excruciating hours during which she was about to taste of unknown pleasures—suddenly, through an unexpected breach, we have broken into them; suddenly we can picture to ourselves, we possess, we intervene upon, we have almost created, one of the moments the succession of which would have composed those hours, a moment as real as all the rest, if not actually more important to us because our mistress is more intensely a part of it: namely, the moment in which he goes to tell her that we are waiting below. And doubtless the other moments of the party would not have been so very different from this one, would be no more exquisite, no more calculated to make us suffer, since this kind friend has assured us that "Of course, she will be delighted to come down! It will be far more amusing for her to talk to you than to be bored up there." Alas! Swann had learned by experience that the good intentions of a third party are powerless to influence a woman who is annoyed to find herself pursued even into a ballroom by a man she does not love. Too often, the kind friend comes down again alone.

My mother did not appear, but without the slightest consideration for my self-respect (which depended upon her keeping up the fiction that she had asked me to let her know the result of my search for something or other) told Françoise to tell me, in so many words: "There is no answer"— words I have so often, since then, heard the hall-porters in grand hotels and the flunkeys in gambling-clubs and the like repeat to some poor girl who replies in bewilderment: "What! he said nothing? It's not possible. You did give him my letter, didn't you? Very well, I shall wait a little longer." And, just as she invariably protests that she does not need the extra gas which the porter offers to light for her, and sits on there, hearing nothing further except an occasional remark on the weather which the porter exchanges with a bell-hop whom he will send off suddenly, when he notices the time, to put some customer's wine on the ice, so, having declined Françoise's offer to make me some tea or to stay beside me, I let her go off again to the pantry, and lay down and shut my eyes, trying not to hear the voices of my family who were drinking their coffee in the garden.

But after a few seconds I realised that, by writing that note to Mamma, by approaching—at the risk of making her angry—so near to her that I felt I could reach out and grasp the moment in which I should see her again, I had cut myself off from the possibility of going to sleep until I actually had seen her, and my heart began to beat more and more painfully as I increased my agitation by ordering myself to keep calm and to acquiesce in my ill-fortune. Then, suddenly, my anxiety subsided, a feeling of intense happiness coursed through me, as when a strong medicine begins to take effect and one's pain vanishes: I had formed a resolution to abandon all attempts to go to sleep without seeing Mamma, had made up my mind to kiss her at all costs, even though this meant the certainty of being in disgrace with her for long afterwards—when she herself came up to bed. The calm which succeeded my anguish filled me with an extraordinary exhilaration, no less than my sense of expectation, my thirst for and my fear of danger. Noiselessly I opened the window and sat down on the foot of my bed. I hardly dared to move in case they should hear me from below. Outside, things too seemed frozen, rapt in a mute intentness not to disturb the moonlight which, duplicating each of them and throwing it back by the extension in front of it of a shadow denser and more concrete than its substance, had made the whole landscape at once thinner and larger, like a map which, after being folded up, is spread out upon the ground. What had to move—a leaf of the chestnut-tree, for instance— moved. But its minute quivering, total, self-contained, finished down to its minutest gradation and its last delicate tremor, did not impinge upon the rest of the scene, did not merge with it, remained circumscribed. Exposed upon this surface of silence which absorbed nothing of them, the most distant sounds, those which must have come from gardens at the far end of the town, could be distinguished with such exact "finish" that the impression they gave of coming from a distance seemed due only to their "pianissimo" execution, like those movements on muted strings so well performed by the orchestra of the Conservatoire[2] that, even though one does not miss a single note, one thinks nonetheless that they are being played somewhere outside, a long way from the concert hall, so that all the old subscribers—my grandmother's sisters too, when Swann had given them his seats—used to strain their ears as if they had caught the distant approach of an army on the march, which had not yet rounded the corner of the Rue de Trévise.[3]

I was well aware that I had placed myself in a position than which none could be counted upon to involve me in graver consequences at my parents' hands; consequences far graver, indeed, than a stranger would have imagined, and such as (he would have thought) could follow only some really shameful misdemeanour. But in the upbringing which they had given me faults were not classified in the same order as in that of other children, and I had been taught to place at the head of the list (doubtless

2. The national music conservatory in Paris.   3. A street in Combray.

because there was no other class of faults from which I needed to be more carefully protected) those in which I can now distinguish the common feature that one succumbs to them by yielding to a nervous impulse. But such a phrase had never been uttered in my hearing; no one had yet accounted for my temptations in a way which might have led me to believe that there was some excuse for my giving in to them, or that I was actually incapable of holding out against them. Yet I could easily recognise this class of transgressions by the anguish of mind which preceded as well as by the rigour of the punishment which followed them; and I knew that what I had just done was in the same category as certain other sins for which I had been severely punished, though infinitely more serious than they. When I went out to meet my mother on her way up to bed, and when she saw that I had stayed up in order to say good night to her again in the passage, I should not be allowed to stay in the house a day longer, I should be packed off to school[4] next morning; so much was certain. Very well: had I been obliged, the next moment, to hurl myself out of the window, I should still have preferred such a fate. For what I wanted now was Mamma, to say good night to her. I had gone too far along the road which led to the fulfilment of this desire to be able to retrace my steps.

I could hear my parents' footsteps as they accompanied Swann to the gate, and when the clanging of the bell assured me that he had really gone, I crept to the window. Mamma was asking my father if he had thought the lobster good, and whether M. Swann had had a second helping of the coffee-and-pistachio ice. "I thought it rather so-so," she was saying. "Next time we shall have to try another flavour."

"I can't tell you," said my great-aunt, "what a change I find in Swann. He is quite antiquated!" She had grown so accustomed to seeing Swann always in the same stage of adolescence that it was a shock to her to find him suddenly less young than the age she still attributed to him. And the others too were beginning to remark in Swann that abnormal, excessive, shameful and deserved senescence of bachelors, of all those for whom it seems that the great day which knows no morrow must be longer than for other men, since for them it is void of promise, and from its dawn the moments steadily accumulate without any subsequent partition[5] among offspring.

"I fancy he has a lot of trouble with that wretched wife of his, who lives with a certain Monsieur de Charlus,[6] as all Combray knows. It's the talk of the town."

My mother observed that, in spite of this, he had looked much less unhappy of late. "And he doesn't nearly so often do that trick of his, so like his father, of wiping his eyes and drawing his hand across his forehead. I think myself that in his heart of hearts he no longer loves that woman."

"Why, of course he doesn't," answered my grandfather. "He wrote me a letter about it, ages ago, to which I took care to pay no attention, but it left no doubt as to his feelings, or at any rate his love, for his wife. Hullo! you two; you never thanked him for the Asti," he went on, turning to his sisters-in-law.

---

4. That is, boarding school.   5. Sharing, as under a will.   6. Brother of the Duc de Guermantes.

"What! we never thanked him? I think, between you and me, that I put it to him quite neatly," replied my aunt Flora.

"Yes, you managed it very well; I admired you for it," said my aunt Céline. "But you did it very prettily, too."

"Yes; I was rather proud of my remark about 'nice neighbours.' "

"What! Do you call that thanking him?" shouted my grandfather. "I heard that all right, but devil take me if I guessed it was meant for Swann. You may be quite sure he never noticed it."

"Come, come; Swann isn't a fool. I'm sure he understood. You didn't expect me to tell him the number of bottles, or to guess what he paid for them."

My father and mother were left alone and sat down for a moment; then my father said: "Well, shall we go up to bed?"

"As you wish, dear, though I don't feel at all sleepy. I don't know why; it can't be the coffee-ice—it wasn't strong enough to keep me awake like this. But I see a light in the servants' hall: poor Françoise has been sitting up for me, so I'll get her to unhook me while you go and undress."

My mother opened the latticed door which led from the hall to the staircase. Presently I heard her coming upstairs to close her window. I went quietly into the passage; my heart was beating so violently that I could hardly move, but at least it was throbbing no longer with anxiety, but with terror and joy. I saw in the well of the stair a light coming upwards, from Mamma's candle. Then I saw Mamma herself and I threw myself upon her. For an instant she looked at me in astonishment, not realising what could have happened. Then her face assumed an expression of anger. She said not a single word to me; and indeed I used to go for days on end without being spoken to, for far more venial offences than this. A single word from Mamma would have been an admission that further intercourse with me was within the bounds of possibility, and that might perhaps have appeared to me more terrible still, as indicating that, with such a punishment as was in store for me, mere silence and black looks would have been puerile. A word from her then would have implied the false calm with which one addresses a servant to whom one has just decided to give notice; the kiss one bestows on a son who is being packed off to enlist, which would have been denied him if it had merely been a matter of being angry with him for a few days. But she heard my father coming from the dressing-room, where he had gone to take off his clothes, and, to avoid the "scene" which he would make if he saw me, she said to me in a voice half-stifled with anger: "Off you go at once. Do you want your father to see you waiting there like an idiot?"

But I implored her again: "Come and say good night to me," terrified as I saw the light from my father's candle already creeping up the wall, but also making use of his approach as a means of blackmail, in the hope that my mother, not wishing him to find me there, as find me he must if she continued to refuse me, would give in and say: "Go back to your room. I will come."

Too late: my father was upon us. Instinctively I murmured, though no one heard me, "I'm done for!"

I was not, however. My father used constantly to refuse to let me do things which were quite clearly allowed by the more liberal charters granted me by my mother and grandmother, because he paid no heed to "principles," and because for him there was no such thing as the "rule of law."[7] For some quite irrelevant reason, or for no reason at all, he would at the last moment prevent me from taking some particular walk, one so regular, so hallowed, that to deprive me of it was a clear breach of faith; or again, as he had done this evening, long before the appointed hour he would snap out: "Run along up to bed now; no excuses!" But at the same time, because he was devoid of principles (in my grandmother's sense), he could not, strictly speaking, be called intransigent. He looked at me for a moment with an air of surprise and annoyance, and then when Mamma had told him, not without some embarrassment, what had happened, said to her: "Go along with him, then. You said just now that you didn't feel very sleepy, so stay in his room for a little. I don't need anything."

"But, my dear," my mother answered timidly, "whether or not I feel sleepy is not the point; we mustn't let the child get into the habit . . . ."

"There's no question of getting into a habit," said my father, with a shrug of the shoulders; "you can see quite well that the child is unhappy. After all, we aren't jailers. You'll end by making him ill, and a lot of good that will do. There are two beds in his room; tell Françoise to make up the big one for you, and stay with him for the rest of the night. Anyhow, I'm off to bed; I'm not so nervy as you. Good night."

It was impossible for me to thank my father; he would have been exasperated by what he called mawkishness. I stood there, not daring to move; he was still in front of us, a tall figure in his white nightshirt, crowned with the pink and violet cashmere scarf which he used to wrap around his head since he had begun to suffer from neuralgia, standing like Abraham in the engraving after Benozzo Gozzoli[8] which M. Swann had given me, telling Sarah that she must tear herself away from Isaac. Many years have passed since that night. The wall of the staircase up which I had watched the light of his candle gradually climb was long ago demolished. And in myself, too, many things have perished which I imagined would last for ever, and new ones have arisen, giving birth to new sorrows and new joys which in those days I could not have foreseen, just as now the old are hard to understand. It is a long time, too, since my father has been able to say to Mamma: "Go along with the child." Never again will such moments be possible for me. But of late I have been increasingly able to catch, if I listen attentively, the sound of the sobs which I had the strength to control in my father's presence, and which broke out only when I found myself alone with Mamma. In reality their echo has never ceased; and it is only because life is now growing more and more quiet round about me that I hear them anew, like those convent bells which are so effectively drowned during the day by the noises of the street that one would suppose them to have stopped, until they ring out again through the silent evening air.

---

7. Reference to the *ius gentium*, the "law of nations" or natural law supposed to govern international and public relations. Marcel sees the relationship between himself and his mother and grandmother as a social contract; his father is the unpredictable tyrant.   8. Florentine painter (1420–1497) whose frescoes at Pisa contain scenes from the life of the biblical patriarch Abraham.

Mamma spent that night in my room: when I had just committed a sin so deadly that I expected to be banished from the household, my parents gave me a far greater concession than I could ever have won as the reward of a good deed. Even at the moment when it manifested itself in this crowning mercy, my father's behaviour towards me still retained that arbitrary and unwarranted quality which was so characteristic of him and which arose from the fact that his actions were generally dictated by chance expediencies rather than based on any formal plan. And perhaps even what I called his severity, when he sent me off to bed, deserved that title less than my mother's or my grandmother's attitude, for his nature, which in some respects differed more than theirs from my own, had probably prevented him from realising until then how wretched I was every evening, something which my mother and grandmother knew well; but they loved me enough to be unwilling to spare me that suffering, which they hoped to teach me to overcome, so as to reduce my nervous sensibility and to strengthen my will. Whereas my father, whose affection for me was of another kind, would not, I suspect, have had the same courage, for as soon as he had grasped the fact that I was unhappy he had said to my mother: "Go and comfort him."

Mamma stayed that night in my room, and it seemed that she did not wish to mar by recrimination those hours which were so different from anything that I had had a right to expect, for when Françoise (who guessed that something extraordinary must have happened when she saw Mamma sitting by my side, holding my hand and letting me cry unchided) said to her: "But, Madame, what is young master crying for?" she replied: "Why, Françoise, he doesn't know himself: it's his nerves. Make up the big bed for me quickly and then go off to your own." And thus for the first time my unhappiness was regarded no longer as a punishable offence but as an involuntary ailment which had been officially recognised, a nervous condition for which I was in no way responsible: I had the consolation of no longer having to mingle apprehensive scruples with the bitterness of my tears; I could weep henceforth without sin. I felt no small degree of pride, either, in Françoise's presence at this return to humane conditions which, not an hour after Mamma had refused to come up to my room and had sent the snubbing message that I was to go to sleep, raised me to the dignity of a grown-up person, brought me of a sudden to a sort of puberty of sorrow, a manumission of tears. I ought to have been happy; I was not. It struck me that my mother had just made a first concession which must have been painful to her, that it was a first abdication on her part from the ideal she had formed for me, and that for the first time she who was so brave had to confess herself beaten. It struck me that if I had just won a victory it was over her, that I had succeeded, as sickness or sorrow or age might have succeeded, in relaxing her will, in undermining her judgment; a black date in the calendar. And if I had dared now, I should have said to Mamma: "No, I don't want you to, you mustn't sleep here." But I was conscious of the practical wisdom, of what would nowadays be called the realism, with which she tempered the ardent idealism of my grandmother's nature, and I knew that now the mischief was done she would prefer to let me enjoy the soothing pleasure of her company, and not to disturb my father again. Certainly my mother's beautiful face seemed to shine again with youth that evening, as she sat gently holding my hands and trying to check my tears; but this was just what I felt should not have been; her anger would have saddened me less than this new gentleness, unknown to my childhood experience; I felt that I had with an impious and secret finger traced a first wrinkle upon her soul and brought out a first white hair on her head. This thought redoubled my sobs, and then I saw that Mamma, who had never allowed herself to indulge in any undue emotion with me, was suddenly overcome by my tears and had to struggle to keep back her own. When she realised that I had noticed this, she said to me with a smile: "Why, my little buttercup, my little canary-boy, he's going to make Mamma as silly as himself if this goes on. Look, since you can't sleep, and Mamma can't either, we mustn't go on in this stupid way; we must do something; I'll get one of your books." But I had none there. "Would you like me to get out the books now that your grand-mother is going to give you for your birthday? Just think it over first, and don't be disappointed if there's nothing new for you then."

I was only too delighted, and Mamma went to fetch a parcel of books of which I could not distinguish, through the paper in which they were wrapped, any more than their short, wide format but which, even at this first glimpse, brief and obscure as it was, bade fair to eclipse already the paintbox of New Year's Day and the silkworms of the year before. The books were *La Mare au Diable, François le Champi, La Petite Fadette* and *Les Maîtres Sonneurs*.[9] My grandmother, as I learned afterwards, had at first chosen Musset's poems, a volume of Rousseau, and *Indiana*; for while she considered light reading as unwholesome as sweets and cakes, she did not reflect that the strong breath of genius might have upon the mind even of a child an influence at once more dangerous and less invigorating than that of fresh air and sea breezes upon his body. But when my father had almost called her an imbecile on learning the names of the books she proposed to give me,[1] she had journeyed back by herself to Jouy-le-Vicomte to the bookseller's, so that there should be no danger of my not having my present in time (it was a boiling hot day, and she had come home so unwell that the doctor had warned my mother not to allow her to tire herself so), and had fallen back upon the four pastoral novels of George Sand.

"My dear," she had said to Mamma, "I could not bring myself to give the child anything that was not well written."

The truth was that she could never permit herself to buy anything from which no intellectual profit was to be derived, above all the profit which fine things afford us by teaching us to seek our pleasures elsewhere than in the barren satisfaction of worldly wealth. Even when she had to make someone a present of the kind called "useful," when she had to give an armchair or some table-silver or a walking-stick, she would choose

9. Novels of idealized country life by the French woman writer George Sand (1806–1876). The titles can be translated as *The Devil's Pool, François the Foundling Discovered in the Fields, Little Fadette,* and *The Master Bellringers.*   1. The works of Alfred de Musset (1810–1857) and Jean-Jacques Rousseau (1712–1778), often romantic and sometimes confessional, and some works by Sand (*Indiana* was a novel of free love), would be thought unsuitable reading for a young child.

"antiques," as though their long desuetude had effaced from them any semblance of utility and fitted them rather to instruct us in the lives of the men of other days than to serve the common requirements of our own. She would have liked me to have in my room photographs of ancient buildings or of beautiful places. But at the moment of buying them, and for all that the subject of the picture had an aesthetic value, she would find that vulgarity and utility had too prominent a part in them, through the mechanical nature of their reproduction by photography. She attempted by a subterfuge, if not to eliminate altogether this commercial banality, at least to minimise it, to supplant it to a certain extent with what was art still, to introduce, as it were, several "thicknesses" of art: instead of photographs of Chartres Cathedral, of the Fountains of Saint-Cloud, or of Vesuvius, she would inquire of Swann whether some great painter had not depicted them, and preferred to give me photographs of "Chartres Cathedral" after Corot, of the "Fountains of Saint-Cloud" after Hubert Robert, and of "Vesuvius" after Turner,[2] which were a stage higher in the scale of art. But although the photographer had been prevented from reproducing directly these masterpieces or beauties of nature, and had there been replaced by a great artist, he resumed his odious position when it came to reproducing the artist's interpretation. Accordingly, having to reckon again with vulgarity, my grandmother would endeavour to postpone the moment of contact still further. She would ask Swann if the picture had not been engraved, preferring, when possible, old engravings with some interest of association apart from themselves, such, for example, as show us a masterpiece in a state in which we can no longer see it to-day (like Morghen's print of Leonardo's "Last Supper" before its deface-ment).[3] It must be admitted that the results of this method of interpreting the art of making presents were not always happy. The idea which I formed of Venice, from a drawing by Titian[4] which is supposed to have the lagoon in the background, was certainly far less accurate than what I should have derived from ordinary photographs. We could no longer keep count in the family (when my great-aunt wanted to draw up an indictment of my grandmother) of all the armchairs she had presented to married couples, young and old, which on a first attempt to sit down upon them had at once collapsed beneath the weight of their recipients. But my grandmother would have thought it sordid to concern herself too closely with the solidity of any piece of furniture in which could still be discerned a flourish, a smile, a brave conceit of the past. And even what in such pieces answered a material need, since it did so in a manner to which we are no longer accustomed, charmed her like those old forms of speech in which we can still see traces of a metaphor whose fine point has been worn away by the rough usage of our modern tongue. As it happened, the pastoral novels of George Sand which she was giving me for my birthday were regular lumber-rooms full of expressions that have fallen out of use

2. The Cathedral of Chartres, painted in 1830 by Corot. The fountains in the old park at Saint-Cloud, outside Paris, painted by Hubert Robert (1733–1809). Vesuvius, the famous volcano near Naples, painted by J. M. W. Turner (1775–1851).   3. Leonardo da Vinci's *Last Supper* was the subject of a famous engraving by Morghen, a late-18th-century engraver. The paints in the original fresco had deteri-orated rapidly, and a major restoration took place in the 19th century.   4. Venetian painter (1477–1576).

and become quaint and picturesque, and are now only to be found in country dialects. And my grandmother had bought them in preference to other books, as she would more readily have taken a house with a gothic dovecot or some other such piece of antiquity as will exert a benign influence on the mind by giving it a hankering for impossible journeys through the realms of time.

Mamma sat down by my bed; she had chosen *François le Champi*, whose reddish cover and incomprehensible title[5] gave it, for me, a distinct personality and a mysterious attraction. I had not then read any real novels. I had heard it said that George Sand was a typical novelist. This predisposed me to imagine that *François le Champi* contained something inexpressibly delicious. The narrative devices designed to arouse curiosity or melt to pity, certain modes of expression which disturb or sadden the reader, and which, with a little experience, he may recognise as common to a great many novels, seemed to me—for whom a new book was not one of a number of similar objects but, as it were, a unique person, absolutely self-contained—simply an intoxicating distillation of the peculiar essence of *François le Champi*. Beneath the everyday incidents, the ordinary objects and common words, I sensed a strange and individual tone of voice. The plot began to unfold: to me it seemed all the more obscure because in those days, when I read, I used often to daydream about something quite different for page after page. And the gaps which this habit left in my knowledge of the story were widened by the fact that when it was Mamma who was reading to me aloud she left all the love-scenes out. And so all the odd changes which take place in the relations between the miller's wife and the boy, changes which only the gradual dawning of love can explain, seemed to me steeped in a mystery the key to which (I readily believed) lay in that strange and mellifluous name of *Champi*, which invested the boy who bore it, I had no idea why, with its own vivid, ruddy, charming colour. If my mother was not a faithful reader, she was none the less an admirable one, when reading a work in which she found the note of true feeling, in the respectful simplicity of her interpretation and the beauty and sweetness of her voice. Even in ordinary life, when it was not works of art but men and women whom she was moved to pity or admire, it was touching to observe with what deference she would banish from her voice, her gestures, from her whole conversation, now the note of gaiety which might have distressed some mother who had once lost a child, now the recollection of an event or anniversary which might have reminded some old gentleman of the burden of his years, now the household topic which might have bored some young man of letters. And so, when she read aloud the prose of George Sand, prose which is everywhere redolent of that generosity and moral distinction which Mamma had learned from my grandmother to place above all other qualities in life, and which I was not to teach her until much later to refrain from placing above all other qualities in literature too, taking pains to banish from her voice any pettiness or affectation which might have choked that powerful stream of language, she supplied all the natural tenderness, all the lavish sweetness

---

5. *Champi* is an old French word the child Marcel would not have known.

which they demanded to sentences which seemed to have been composed for her voice and which were all, so to speak, within the compass of her sensibility. She found, to tackle them in the required tone, the warmth of feeling which pre-existed and dictated them, but which is not to be found in the words themselves, and by this means she smoothed away, as she read, any harshness or discordance in the tenses of verbs, endowing the imperfect and the preterite[6] with all the sweetness to be found in generosity, all the melancholy to be found in love, guiding the sentence that was drawing to a close towards the one that was about to begin, now hastening, now slackening the pace of the syllables so as to bring them, despite their differences of quantity, into a uniform rhythm, and breathing into this quite ordinary prose a kind of emotional life and continuity.

My aching heart was soothed; I let myself be borne upon the current of this gentle night on which I had my mother by my side. I knew that such a night could not be repeated; that the strongest desire I had in the world, namely, to keep my mother in my room through the sad hours of darkness, ran too much counter to general requirements and to the wishes of others for such a concession as had been granted me this evening to be anything but a rare and artificial exception. To-morrow night my anguish would return and Mamma would not stay by my side. But when my anguish was assuaged, I could no longer understand it; besides, to-morrow was still a long way off; I told myself that I should still have time to take preventive action, although that time could bring me no access of power since these things were in no way dependent upon the exercise of my will, and seemed not quite inevitable only because they were still separated from me by this short interval.

And so it was that, for a long time afterwards, when I lay awake at night and revived old memories of Combray, I saw no more of it than this sort of luminous panel, sharply defined against a vague and shadowy background, like the panels which the glow of a Bengal light[7] or a searchlight beam will cut out and illuminate in a building the other parts of which remain plunged in darkness: broad enough at its base, the little parlour, the dining-room, the opening of the dark path from which M. Swann, the unwitting author of my sufferings, would emerge, the hall through which I would journey to the first step of that staircase, so painful to climb, which constituted, all by itself, the slender cone of this irregular pyramid; and, at the summit, my bedroom, with the little passage through whose glazed[8] door Mamma would enter; in a word, seen always at the same evening hour, isolated from all its possible surroundings, detached and solitary against the dark background, the bare minimum of scenery necessary (like the decor one sees prescribed on the title-page of an old play, for its performance in the provinces) to the drama of my undressing; as though all Combray had consisted of but two floors joined by a slender staircase, and as though there had been no time there but seven o'clock at night. I must own[9] that I could have assured any questioner that Combray did include

6. The imperfect is the tense of continued and incomplete action in the past, whereas the preterite describes a single completed action.   7. Fireworks.   8. That is, with glass panes.   9. Admit.

other scenes and did exist at other hours than these. But since the facts which I should then have recalled would have been prompted only by voluntary memory, the memory of the intellect, and since the pictures which that kind of memory shows us preserve nothing of the past itself, I should never have had any wish to ponder over this residue of Combray. To me it was in reality all dead.

Permanently dead? Very possibly.

There is a large element of chance in these matters, and a second chance occurrence, that of our own death, often prevents us from awaiting for any length of time the favours of the first.

I feel that there is much to be said for the Celtic belief that the souls of those whom we have lost are held captive in some inferior being, in an animal, in a plant, in some inanimate object, and thus effectively lost to us until the day (which to many never comes) when we happen to pass by the tree or to obtain possession of the object which forms their prison.[1] Then they start and tremble, they call us by our name, and as soon as we have recognised their voice the spell is broken. Delivered by us, they have overcome death and return to share our life.

And so it is with our own past. It is a labour in vain to attempt to recapture it: all the efforts of our intellect must prove futile. The past is hidden somewhere outside the realm, beyond the reach of intellect, in some material object (in the sensation which that material object will give us) of which we have no inkling. And it depends on chance whether or not we come upon this object before we ourselves must die.

Many years had elapsed during which nothing of Combray, save what was comprised in the theatre and the drama of my going to bed there, had any existence for me, when one day in winter, on my return home, my mother, seeing that I was cold, offered me some tea, a thing I did not ordinarily take. I declined at first, and then, for no particular reason, changed my mind. She sent for one of those squat, plump little cakes called "petites madeleines," which look as though they had been moulded in the fluted valve of a scallop shell. And soon, mechanically, dispirited after a dreary day with the prospect of a depressing morrow, I raised to my lips a spoonful of the tea in which I had soaked a morsel of the cake. No sooner had the warm liquid mixed with the crumbs touched my palate than a shudder ran through me and I stopped, intent upon the extraordinary thing that was happening to me. An exquisite pleasure had invaded my senses, something isolated, detached, with no suggestion of its origin. And at once the vicissitudes of life had become indifferent to me, its disasters innocuous, its brevity illusory—this new sensation having had on me the effect which love has of filling me with a precious essence; or rather this essence was not in me, it *was* me. I had ceased now to feel mediocre, contingent, mortal. Whence could it have come to me, this all-powerful joy? I sensed that it was connected with the taste of the tea and the cake, but that it infinitely transcended those savours, could not, indeed, be of the same nature. Whence did it come? What did it mean? How could I seize and apprehend it?

1. A belief attributed to Druids, the priests of the ancient Celtic peoples.

I drink a second mouthful, in which I find nothing more than in the first, then a third, which gives me rather less than the second. It is time to stop; the potion is losing its magic. It is plain that the truth I am seeking lies not in the cup but in myself. The drink has called it into being, but does not know it, and can only repeat indefinitely, with a progressive diminution of strength, the same message which I cannot interpret, though I hope at least to be able to call it forth again and to find it there presently, intact and at my disposal, for my final enlightenment. I put down the cup and examine my own mind. It alone can discover the truth. But how? What an abyss of uncertainty, whenever the mind feels overtaken by itself; when it, the seeker, is at the same time the dark region through which it must go seeking and where all its equipment will avail it nothing. Seek? More than that: create. It is face to face with something which does not yet exist, to which it alone can give reality and substance, which it alone can bring into the light of day.

And I begin again to ask myself what it could have been, this unremembered state which brought with it no logical proof, but the indisputable evidence, of its felicity, its reality, and in whose presence other states of consciousness melted and vanished. I decide to attempt to make it reappear. I retrace my thoughts to the moment at which I drank the first spoonful of tea. I rediscover the same state, illuminated by no fresh light. I ask my mind to make one further effort, to bring back once more the fleeting sensation. And so that nothing may interrupt it in its course I shut out every obstacle, every extraneous idea, I stop my ears and inhibit all attention against the sounds from the next room. And then, feeling that my mind is tiring itself without having any success to report, I compel it for a change to enjoy the distraction which I have just denied it, to think of other things, to rest and refresh itself before making a final effort. And then for the second time I clear an empty space in front of it; I place in position before my mind's eye the still recent taste of that first mouthful, and I feel something start within me, something that leaves its resting-place and attempts to rise, something that has been embedded like an anchor at a great depth; I do not know yet what it is, but I can feel it mounting slowly; I can measure the resistance, I can hear the echo of great spaces traversed.

Undoubtedly what is thus palpitating in the depths of my being must be the image, the visual memory which, being linked to that taste, is trying to follow it into my conscious mind. But its struggles are too far off, too confused and chaotic; scarcely can I perceive the neutral glow into which the elusive whirling medley of stirred-up colours is fused, and I cannot distinguish its form, cannot invite it, as the one possible interpreter, to translate for me the evidence of its contemporary, its inseparable paramour, the taste, cannot ask it to inform me what special circumstance is in question, from what period in my past life.

Will it ultimately reach the clear surface of my consciousness, this memory, this old, dead moment which the magnetism of an identical moment has travelled so far to importune, to disturb, to raise up out of the very depths of my being? I cannot tell. Now I feel nothing; it has stopped, has perhaps sunk back into its darkness, from which who can say whether it will ever rise again? Ten times over I must essay the task, must lean down over the abyss. And each time the cowardice that deters us from every difficult task, every important enterprise, has urged me to leave the thing alone, to drink my tea and to think merely of the worries of to-day and my hopes for to-morrow, which can be brooded over painlessly.

And suddenly the memory revealed itself. The taste was that of the little piece of madeleine which on Sunday mornings at Combray (because on those mornings I did not go out before mass), when I went to say good morning to her in her bedroom, my aunt Léonie used to give me, dipping it first in her own cup of tea or tisane. The sight of the little madeleine had recalled nothing to my mind before I tasted it; perhaps because I had so often seen such things in the meantime, without tasting them, on the trays in pastry-cooks' windows, that their image had dissociated itself from those Combray days to take its place among others more recent; perhaps because of those memories, so long abandoned and put out of mind, nothing now survived, everything was scattered; the shapes of things, including that of the little scallop-shell of pastry, so richly sensual under its severe, religious folds, were either obliterated or had been so long dormant as to have lost the power of expansion which would have allowed them to resume their place in my consciousness. But when from a long-distant past nothing subsists, after the people are dead, after the things are broken and scattered, taste and smell alone, more fragile but more enduring, more unsubstantial, more persistent, more faithful, remain poised a long time, like souls, remembering, waiting, hoping, amid the ruins of all the rest; and bear unflinchingly, in the tiny and almost impalpable drop of their essence, the vast structure of recollection.

And as soon as I had recognised the taste of the piece of madeleine[2] soaked in her decoction of lime-blossom which my aunt used to give me (although I did not yet know and must long postpone the discovery of why this memory made me so happy) immediately the old grey house upon the street, where her room was, rose up like a stage set to attach itself to the little pavilion opening on to the garden which had been built out behind it for my parents (the isolated segment which until that moment had been all that I could see); and with the house the town, from morning to night and in all weathers, the Square where I used to be sent before lunch, the streets along which I used to run errands, the country roads we took when it was fine. And as in the game wherein the Japanese amuse themselves by filling a porcelain bowl with water and steeping in it little pieces of paper which until then are without character or form, but, the moment they become wet, stretch and twist and take on colour and distinctive shape, become flowers or houses or people, solid and recognisable, so in that moment all the flowers in our garden and in M. Swann's park, and the water-lilies on the Vivonne[3] and the good folk of the village and their little dwellings and the parish church and the whole of Combray and its surroundings, taking shape and solidity, sprang into being, town and gardens alike, from my cup of tea.

---

2. A small, rich cookie-like pastry.   3. The local river.

RAINER MARIA RILKE
1875–1926

Rainer Maria Rilke's search for the "great mysteries" of the universe combines his own intensely personal awareness with a range of broad questions that are ordinarily called religious. Whether his gaze is turned toward the objects and creatures of earth, which he describes with extraordinary clarity and affection, or toward a higher intuited realm whose enigma remains to be deciphered, he seeks throughout a comprehensive vision of cosmic unity. Rilke absorbs what he sees around him—objects, people, gestures—until they become part of his consciousness and are ready to emerge in the words of a poem. "Looking is such a wonderful thing, about which we as yet know so little," he wrote his wife, Clara; "we are turned completely outward, but just when we are most outward, things seem to happen inside us." The poet's role, he says, is to observe with a fresh sensitivity "this fleeting world, which in some strange way / keeps calling to us," and to bear witness, through language, to the transfiguration of its materiality in human emotions. Rilke writes at a transitional moment in modern European letters: inheritor of the Symbolists in his allusive imagery and intuitions of cosmic order, and modernist in the "thing-centered" concreteness of individual descriptions, he also foreshadows existentialism as he struggles to comprehend the self's relation to the universe. The best-known and most influential German poet of the twentieth century, Rilke has been read and translated outside Europe in countries as far apart as the United States and Japan. He speaks to a variety of cultures and audiences in spite of the fact that he was perhaps the least socially oriented poet of his time.

Born in Prague on December 4, 1875, to German-speaking parents who separated when he was nine, Rilke had an unhappy childhood that included being dressed as a girl when he was young (thus his mother compensated for the earlier loss of a baby daughter) and being sent to military academies, where he was lonely and miserable, from 1886 to 1891. Illness caused his departure from the second academy and, after a year in business school, he worked in his uncle's law firm and studied at the University of Prague. Rilke hoped to persuade his family that he should devote himself to a literary career rather than business or law, and energetically wrote poetry (*Sacrifice to the Lares*, 1895, *Crowned by Dream*, 1896), plays, stories, and reviews. Moving to Munich in 1897, he met and fell in love with a fascinating and cultured older woman, Lou Andreas-Salomé, who would be a constant influence on him throughout his life. He accompanied Andreas-Salomé and her husband to Russia in 1899, where he met Leo Tolstoy and the painter Leonid Pasternak and—fascinated with Russian mysticism and the Russian landscape—wrote most of the poems later published as *The Book of Hours: The Book of Monastic Life* (1905) as well as a Romantic verse tale that became extremely popular, *The Tale of Love and Death of Cornet Christoph Rilke* (1906). After a second trip to Russia, Rilke spent some time at an artists' colony called Worpswede where he met his future wife, the sculptor Clara Westhoff. They were married in March 1901 and settled in a cottage near the colony where Rilke wrote the second part of *The Book of Hours: The Book of Pilgrimage*. He and Clara separated in the following year, and Rilke moved to Paris where he embarked on a study of the French sculptor Auguste Rodin (1903).

Unhappy in Paris, where he felt lonely and isolated, he fled to Italy in 1903 to write the last section of *The Book of Hours: The Book of Poverty and Death*. Nonetheless, he had found in Paris a new kind of literary and artistic inspiration. He read French writers and especially Baudelaire, whose minutely realistic but

existence. Nor is there any place to escape from the lesson, once it is recognized; instead, "You must change your life."

Ultimately, Rilke is celebrating the power of human creativity to refashion the world in its own image. The poet observes reality and creates from it a new form, a new being. For the poet, however, it is a process of making the visible angelically "invisible," and a bridge between two worlds; he "delivers" things by absorbing them into his imagination's inner dimension, asking, as at the end of the ninth *Elegy*, "Earth, isn't this what you want: to arise within us, / *invisible?*" Rilke's poetic journey, from the *New Poems* to the *Elegies* and the *Sonnets to Orpheus*, was an inward journey that created a bridge between two worlds, preserving the most intense moments of human experience by subjecting them to the transfiguring perspective of art.

J. F. Hendry, *The Sacred Threshold: A Life of Rainer Maria Rilke* (1983), and Patricia Pollock Brodsky, *Rainer Maria Rilke* (1988), are brief and readable biographies with numerous citations from Rilke's letters and work. Heinz F. Peters, *Rainer Maria Rilke: Masks and the Man* (1977), is a biographical and thematic study of Rilke's work and influence. Donald Prater, *A Ringing Glass: The Life of Rainer Maria Rilke* (1986), is an excellent account of the poet's life and the conditions in which his work developed and includes extensive quotations from many unpublished letters. *Rainer Maria Rilke, Aspects of His Mind and Poetry*, edited by William Rose and G. Craig Houston (1970), contains an excellent essay by C. M. Bowra on the *New Poems*.

PRONOUNCING GLOSSARY

The following list uses common English syllables and stress accents to provide rough equivalents of selected words whose pronunciation may be unfamiliar to the general reader.

Dinggedichte: *ding'-ge-dikh-tuh*

Duino: *doo-ee'-noh*

Muzot: *moo-zoh'*

FROM NEW POEMS[1]

Archaic Torso of Apollo[2]

We cannot know his legendary head[3]
with eyes like ripening fruit. And yet his torso
is still suffused with brilliance from inside,
like a lamp, in which his gaze, now turned to low,

gleams in all its power. Otherwise   5
the curved breast could not dazzle you so, nor could

1. All selections translated by Stephen Mitchell.   2. The first poem in the second volume of Rilke's *New Poems* (1908), which were dedicated "to my good friend, Auguste Rodin" (the French sculptor, 1840–1917, whose secretary Rilke was for a brief period and on whom he wrote two monographs, in 1903 and 1907). The poem itself was inspired by an ancient Greek statue discovered at Miletus (a Greek colony on the coast of Asia Minor) that was called simply the *Torso of a Youth from Miletus*; since the god Apollo was an ideal of youthful male beauty, his name was often associated with such statues.   3. In a torso, the head and limbs are missing.

a smile run through the placid hips and thighs
to that dark center where procreation flared.

Otherwise this stone would seem defaced
beneath the translucent cascade of the shoulders   10
and would not glisten like a wild beast's fur:

would not, from all the borders of itself,
burst like a star: for here there is no place
that does not see you. You must change your life.

Archaïscher Torso Apollos

Wir kannten nicht sein unerhörtes Haupt,
darin die Augenäpfel reiften. Aber
sein Torso glüht noch wie ein Kandelaber,
in dem sein Schauen, nur zurückgeschraubt,

sich hält und glänzt. Sonst könnte nicht der Bug   5
der Brust dich blenden, und im leisen Drehen
der Lenden könnte nicht ein Lächeln gehen
zu jener Mitte, die die Zeugung trug.

Sonst stünde dieser Stein entstellt und kurz
unter der Schultern durchsichtigem Sturz   10
und flimmerte nicht so wie Raubtierfelle;

und bräche nicht aus allen seinen Rändern
aus wie ein Stern: denn da ist keine Stelle,
die dich nicht sieht. Du mußt dein Leben ändern.

The Panther

In the Jardin des Plantes, Paris[1]

His vision, from the constantly passing bars,
has grown so weary that it cannot hold
anything else. It seems to him there are
a thousand bars; and behind the bars, no world.

As he paces in cramped circles, over and over,   5
the movement of his powerful soft strides
is like a ritual dance around a center
in which a mighty will stands paralyzed.

Only at times, the curtain of the pupils
lifts, quietly—. An image enters in,   10
rushes down through the tensed, arrested muscles,
plunges into the heart and is gone.

---

1. The *Jardin des Plantes* is a zoo in Paris. Rilke also admired, at Rodin's studio, the plaster cast of an ancient statue of a panther.

The Swan

This laboring through what is still undone,
as though, legs bound, we hobbled along the way,
is like the awkward walking of the swan.

And dying—to let go, no longer feel
the solid ground we stand on every day—   5
is like his anxious letting himself fall

into the water, which receives him gently
and which, as though with reverence and joy,
draws back past him in streams on either side;
while, infinitely silent and aware,   10
in his full majesty and ever more
indifferent, he condescends to glide.

Spanish Dancer[1]

As on all its sides a kitchen-match darts white
flickering tongues before it bursts into flame:
with the audience around her, quickened, hot,
her dance begins to flicker in the dark room.

And all at once it is completely fire.   5

One upward glance and she ignites her hair
and, whirling faster and faster, fans her dress
into passionate flames, till it becomes a furnace
from which, like startled rattlesnakes, the long
naked arms uncoil, aroused and clicking.[2]   10

And then: as if the fire were too tight
around her body, she takes and flings it out
haughtily, with an imperious gesture,
and watches: it lies raging on the floor,
still blazing up, and the flames refuse to die—,   15
Till, moving with total confidence and a sweet
exultant smile, she looks up finally
and stamps it out with powerful small feet.

Duino Elegies

The First Elegy

Who, if I cried out, would hear me among the angels'[1]
hierarchies? and even if one of them pressed me

1. A traditional Spanish dance, the *flamenco* (from *flamear*, to flame).   2. The dancer accompanies
herself with the rhythmic clicking of castanets (worn on the fingers).   1. "The 'angel' of the Elegies
has nothing to do with the angel of the Christian heaven. . . . The angel of the Elegies is that being
which stands for the idea of recognizing a higher order of reality in invisibility" [Rilke: Letter to his
Polish translator Witold Hulewicz, November 13, 1925].

suddenly against his heart: I would be consumed
in that overwhelming existence. For beauty is nothing
but the beginning of terror, which we still are just able to endure,   5
and we are so awed because it serenely disdains
to annihilate us. Every angel is terrifying.
     And so I hold myself back and swallow the call-note
of my dark sobbing. Ah, whom can we ever turn to
in our need? Not angels, not humans,   10
and already the knowing animals are aware
that we are not really at home in
our interpreted[2] world. Perhaps there remains for us
some tree on a hillside, which every day we can take
into our vision; there remains for us yesterday's street   15
and the loyalty of a habit so much at ease
when it stayed with us that it moved in and never left.
     Oh and night: there is night, when a wind full of infinite space
gnaws at our faces. Whom would it not remain for—that longed-after,
mildly disillusioning presence, which the solitary heart   20
so painfully meets. Is it any less difficult for lovers?
But they keep on using each other to hide their own fate.
     Don't you know yet? Fling the emptiness out of your arms
into the spaces we breathe; perhaps the birds
will feel the expanded air with more passionate flying.   25

Yes—the springtimes needed you. Often a star
was waiting for you to notice it. A wave rolled toward you
out of the distant past, or as you walked
under an open window, a violin
yielded itself to your hearing. All this was mission.   30
But could you accomplish it? Weren't you always
distracted by expectation, as if every event
announced a beloved? (Where can you find a place
to keep her, with all the huge strange thoughts inside you
going and coming and often staying all night.)   35
But when you feel longing, sing of women in love;
for their famous passion is still not immortal. Sing
of women abandoned and desolate (you envy them, almost)
who could love so much more purely than those who were gratified.
Begin again and again the never-attainable praising;   40
remember: the hero lives on; even his downfall was
merely a pretext for achieving his final birth.
But Nature, spent and exhausted, takes lovers back
into herself, as if there were not enough strength
to create them a second time. Have you imagined   45
Gaspara Stampa[3] intensely enough so that any girl
deserted by her beloved might be inspired
by that fierce example of soaring, objectless love
and might say to herself, "Perhaps I can be like her"?
Shouldn't this most ancient of sufferings finally grow   50
more fruitful for us? Isn't it time that we lovingly

---

2. Unlike animals, who live in unconscious harmony with earth, human beings interpret or conceptual-
ize whatever they see.   3. An Italian poet (1523–1554) who wrote a series of two hundred sonnets
recording her unhappy love for Count Collalto, who abandoned her.

freed ourselves from the beloved and, quivering, endured:[4]
as the arrow endures the bowstring's tension, so that
gathered in the snap of release it can be more than
itself. For there is no place where we can remain.   55

Voices. Voices. Listen, my heart, as only
saints have listened: until the gigantic call lifted them
off the ground; yet they kept on, impossibly,
kneeling and didn't notice at all:
so complete was their listening. Not that you could endure   60
God's voice—far from it. But listen to the voice of the wind
and the ceaseless message that forms itself out of silence.
It is murmuring toward you now from those who died young.
Didn't their fate, whenever you stepped into a church
in Naples or Rome, quietly come to address you?   65
Or high up, some eulogy entrusted you with a mission,
as, last year, on the plaque in Santa Maria Formosa.[5]
What they want of me is that I gently remove the appearance
of injustice about their death—which at times
slightly hinders their souls from proceeding onward.   70

Of course, it is strange to inhabit the earth no longer,
to give up customs one barely had time to learn,
not to see roses and other promising Things
in terms of a human future; no longer to be
what one was in infinitely anxious hands; to leave   75
even one's own first name behind, forgetting it
as easily as a child abandons a broken toy.
Strange to no longer desire one's desires. Strange
to see meanings that clung together once, floating away
in every direction. And being dead is hard work   80
and full of retrieval before one can gradually feel
a trace of eternity.—Though the living are wrong to believe
in the too-sharp distinctions which they themselves have created.
Angels (they say) don't know whether it is the living
they are moving among, or the dead. The eternal torrent   85
whirls all ages along in it, through both realms
forever, and their voices are drowned out in its thunderous roar.

In the end, those who were carried off early no longer need us:
they are weaned from earth's sorrows and joys, as gently as children
outgrow the soft breasts of their mothers. But we, who do need   90
such great mysteries, we for whom grief is so often
the source of our spirit's growth—: could we exist without *them*?
Is the legend meaningless that tells how, in the lament for Linus,[6]
the daring first notes of song pierced through the barren numbness;
and then in the startled space which a youth as lovely as a god   95

4. Reference to a passage from the *Portuguese Letters* (a 17th-century French epistolary novel supposedly written by a Portuguese nun) in which the heroine, Marianna Alcoforado, writes that her love no longer depends on its being reciprocated by the man who has clearly abandoned her.   5. A church in Venice (which Rilke visited in 1911) where a plaque commemorating the death of a Hermann Wilhelm in 1593 reads, in part, "I have not perished but live to myself in cold marble" (*non perii at gelido in marmore vivo mihi*).   6. The Linus song (Homer's *Iliad* XVIII.570) is a dirge for a man who died young and whose death is associated with the passing of summer; those paralyzed by his loss were revived only by the perfect music of the song of mourning (attributed to Apollo or Orpheus).

had suddenly left forever, the Void felt for the first time
that harmony which now enraptures and comforts and helps us?

The Ninth Elegy

Why, if this interval of being can be spent serenely
in the form of a laurel,[1] slightly darker than all
other green, with tiny waves on the edges
of every leaf (like the smile of a breeze) — : why then
have to be human — and, escaping from fate,   5
keep longing for fate? . . .[2]

                Oh *not* because happiness *exists*,
that too-hasty profit snatched from approaching loss.
Not out of curiosity, not as practice for the heart, which
would exist in the laurel too. . . .   10

But because *truly* being here is so much; because everything here
apparently needs us, this fleeting world, which in some strange way
keeps calling to us. Us, the most fleeting of all.
Once for each thing. Just once; no more. And we too,
just once. And never again. But to have been   15
this once, completely, even if only once:
to have been at one with the earth, seems beyond undoing.

And so we keep pressing on, trying to achieve it,
trying to hold it firmly in our simple hands,
in our overcrowded gaze, in our speechless heart.   20
Trying to become it. — Whom can we give it to? We would
hold on to it all, forever . . . Ah, but what can we take along
into that other realm? Not the art of looking,
which is learned so slowly, and nothing that happened here. Nothing.
The sufferings, then. And, above all, the heaviness,   25
and the long experience of love, — just what is wholly
unsayable. But later, among the stars,
what good is it — *they* are *better* as they are: unsayable.
For when the traveler returns from the mountain-slopes into the valley,
he brings, not a handful of earth, unsayable to others, but instead 30
some word he has gained, some pure word, the yellow and blue
gentian. Perhaps we are *here* in order to say: house,
bridge, fountain, gate, pitcher, fruit-tree, window —
at most: column, tower. . . . But to *say* them, you must understand,
oh to say them *more* intensely than the Things themselves   35
ever dreamed of existing. Isn't the secret intent
of this taciturn earth, when it forces lovers together,
that inside their boundless emotion all things may shudder with joy?
Threshold: what it means for two lovers
to be wearing down, imperceptibly, the ancient threshold of
    their door —   40
they too, after the many who came before them
and before those to come. . . . , lightly.

---

1. The nymph Daphne, escaping from the pursuit of her would-be lover Apollo, was changed by that
god into a laurel tree (Ovid's *Metamorphoses* I.548ff.).   2. Here and elsewhere in the elegies, Rilke's
ellipsis marks indicate a pause, not an omission.

Here is the time for the *sayable, here* is its homeland.
Speak and bear witness. More than ever
the Things that we might experience are vanishing, for   45
what crowds them out and replaces them is an imageless act.
An act under a shell, which easily cracks open as soon as
the business inside outgrows it and seeks new limits.
Between the hammers our heart
endures, just as the tongue does   50
between the teeth and, despite that,
still is able to praise.

Praise this world to the angel, not the unsayable one,
you can't impress *him* with glorious emotion; in the universe
where he feels more powerfully, you are a novice. So show him   55
something simple which, formed over generations,
lives as our own, near our hand and within our gaze.
Tell him of Things. He will stand astonished; as *you* stood
by the rope-maker in Rome or the potter along the Nile.
Show him how happy a Thing can be, how innocent and ours,   60
how even lamenting grief purely decides to take form,
serves as a Thing, or dies into a Thing—, and blissfully
escapes far beyond the violin.—And these Things,
which live by perishing, know you are praising them; transient,
they look to us for deliverance: us, the most transient of all.   65
They want us to change them, utterly, in our invisible heart,
within—oh endlessly—within us! Whoever we may be at last.

Earth, isn't this what you want: to arise within us,
invisible? Isn't it your dream
to be wholly invisible someday?—O Earth: invisible!   70
What, if not transformation, is your urgent command?
Earth, my dearest, I will. Oh believe me, you no longer
need your springtimes to win me over—one of them,
ah, even one, is already too much for my blood.
Unspeakably I have belonged to you, from the first.   75
You were always right, and your holiest inspiration
is our intimate companion, Death.

Look, I am living. On what? Neither childhood nor future
grows any smaller. . . . Superabundant being
wells up in my heart.   80

LU XUN

1881–1936

No country in the world has had so long, continuous, and essentially autonomous
a culture as China. For the past century Chinese intellectuals have struggled to
free themselves from the oppressive weight of their past and to discover a Chinese
cultural identity independent of the traditional civilization. This has, in fact, been
a central concern throughout modern Chinese literature. The rapid importation

of Western fiction, drama, and poetry in the early twentieth century provided a set of literary models quite distinct from those of the Chinese tradition. Rather than finding in the Western models new possibilities of art, however, many Chinese writers sought in them instruments by which to change the culture or a medium by which to analyze the problems posed by China's cultural legacy. Western writers have often had similar aims, but the marginal status of the writer in European civilization has been a helpful counterweight to such grand purposes. By contrast, the centrality of the writer and intellectual has proved to be one of the tenacious assumptions of traditional Chinese culture, and it is ironic that this assumption stands behind the continuing hope of modern Chinese writers to free China of the weight of its traditional civilization.

Modern China has produced many talented writers, on whom critical opinion is divided. There is, however, almost universal agreement on one authentic genius among them: Lu Xun (also romanized Lu Hsün), the pen name of Zhou Shuren. Few writers of fiction have gained so much fame for such a small oeuvre. His reputation rests entirely on twenty-five stories published between 1918 and 1926, gathered into two collections: *Cheering from the Sidelines* and *Wondering Where to Turn*. In addition to this fiction he published a collection of prose poems, *Wild Grasses*, and a large number of literary and political essays. His small body of stories gives a ruthlessly bleak portrayal of an entire culture that has failed. Whether the culture had indeed failed is less important than the powerful representation he gives of it and the way in which his representations touched a deep chord of response in Chinese readers. Lu was a controlled ironist and a craftsman whose narrative skill far exceeded that of most of his contemporaries; yet underneath his mastery the reader senses the depth of his anger at traditional culture.

Lu was well prepared to engage traditional culture on its own terms. Born into a Shaoxing family of Confucian scholar-officials, he had a traditional education and became a classical scholar of considerable erudition and a writer of poetry in the classical language. Sometimes he displays this learning in his fiction, but there it is always undercut by irony. He grew up at a time when the traditional education system, based on the Confucian classics, was being supplanted by a modern one; and after the early death of his father in 1896, Lu, like so many young Chinese intellectuals of the period, went abroad to study—first at Tokyo and then in 1904 at Sendai, a remote Japanese university where he studied medicine. Because it was successfully modernizing a traditional culture, Japan attracted many young Chinese intellectuals. At the time, the Russians and Japanese were at war in the former Chinese territory of Manchuria. In a famous anecdote describing his moment of decision to become a writer, Lu tells of seeing a slide of a Chinese prisoner about to be decapitated as a Russian spy. What shocked the young medical student was the apathetic crowd of Chinese onlookers, gathered around to watch the execution. At that moment he decided that it was their dulled spirits rather than their bodies that were in need of healing.

Returning to Tokyo, Lu founded a journal in which he published literary essays and set to work translating Western works of fiction. In 1909 financial difficulties drove him back to China, where he worked as a teacher in Hangzhou. When the Republican revolution came in 1911, he joined the ministry of education, moving north to Peking, where he also taught at various universities. The Republican government was soon at the mercy of the powerful armies competing for regional power, and during this period, perhaps for self-protection, Lu devoted himself to traditional scholarship. One might have expected the revolutionary writer of narrative to write the first history of Chinese fiction, as Lu did; but he also produced an erudite and painstaking textual study of the third-century writer Xi Kang that is still used.

On May 4, 1919, a massive student strike forced the Chinese government not to sign the Versailles Peace Treaty, which would have given Japan effective control over the Chinese province of Shandong. The date gave its name to the May Fourth Movement, a group of young intellectuals who advocated the use of vernacular Chinese in all writing and a repudiation of classical Chinese literature.* Though Lu himself kept out of the May Fourth Movement, it was during this period (1918–26) that he wrote all but one of his short stories. During the last decade of his life, he became a political activist and put his satirical talents at the service of the left, becoming one of the favorite writers of the Communist leader Mao Zedong.

Diary of a Madman, Lu's earliest story, takes its title from a work of the Russian novelist Gogol. On one level, it is a parable of the way in which Chinese society devours its members, told under the guise of the discovery of a continuing history of literal cannibalism. But the diarist who makes the "discovery" is indeed, as the title tells us, a madman, and his paranoid raving compels the reader to take the point of view of "sane" society, all the while uncomfortably recognizing that the diarist's claims are true in a figurative sense.

Lu's literary anger at Chinese culture was far from a new phenomenon in Chinese fiction. Traditional novels such as The Travels of Lao Can had often ruthlessly satirized the falseness and corruption of the social order. But in traditional Chinese satirical fiction, as in most premodern satire worldwide, the capacity to make moral judgments presumed a secure sense of what was right (whether or not such a sense agreed with conventional morality). In Lu's satire, however, the very capacity to judge evil is itself corrupted by that evil, a circularity perfectly embodied in the figure of a cannibalistic society that feeds on itself.

Diary of a Madman opens with a preface in mannered classical Chinese, giving an account of the discovery of the diary. Such ironic use of classical Chinese to suggest a falsely polite world of social appearances was quite common in traditional Chinese fiction; but its presence usually suggested the alternative possibility of immediate, direct, and genuine language, a language of the heart set against a language of society. The diary that follows the preface is indeed immediate, direct, and genuine, but it is also deluded and twisted. The diarist becomes increasingly convinced that everyone around him wants to eat him; from this growing circle of cannibals observed in the present, the diarist then turns to examine old texts, only to discover that the entire history of the culture has been one of secret cannibalism. Beneath society's false politeness, represented by the voice in the preface, he detects a violent bestiality lurking, a hunger to assimilate others, to "eat men."

As the diary progresses, it becomes increasingly clear that the diarist, who sees himself as the potential victim, is no less the mirror of the society he describes, assimilating everyone around him into his own fixed view of the world. His reading of ancient texts to discover evidence of cannibalism is a parody of traditional Confucian scholarship, the distorting discovery of "secret meanings" that only serve to confirm beliefs already held. His is a world entirely closed in on itself, one that survives by feeding on itself and its young, a voracity that gives Lu his famous last line, "Save the children . . ."

Leo Ou-fan Lee, Voices from the Iron House: A Study of Lu Xun (1987), is an excellent introduction to Lu Xun's work, placing it in the context of his life and

---

*Written Chinese ranges between two extremes: the "classical" language, which is essentially that of the fourth to third centuries B.C., and the "vernacular," which attempts to represent the spoken language. Poetry and essays tended to be in classical Chinese, while traditional fiction tended to use the vernacular (although there was also fiction in the classical language). In the modern period, poetry and essays also came to be written in vernacular Chinese. Traditional drama used a mixed style; modern drama, the vernacular.

Chinese cultural history, and Lee, *Lu Xun and His Legacy* (1985), is a collection of scholarly articles treating Lu's literary work, his politics, and his influence. William A. Lyell, *Lu Hsün's Vision of Reality* (1976), is also useful.

PRONOUNCING GLOSSARY

The following list uses common English syllables to provide rough equivalents of selected words whose pronunciation may be unfamiliar to the general reader.

Lu Xun: *loo shoon*   Xu Xilin: *shoo shee-lin*

Luosi: *lwoh-suh*   Zhao: *jao*

Mao Zedong: *mao dzuh-doong*   Zhou Shuren: *joe shoo-ren*

Shaoxing: *shao-shing*

Diary of a Madman[1]

There was once a pair of male siblings whose actual names I beg your indulgence to withhold. Suffice it to say that we three were boon companions during our school years. Subsequently, circumstances contrived to rend us asunder so that we were gradually bereft of knowledge regarding each other's activities.

Not too long ago, however, I chanced to hear that one of them had been hard afflicted with a dread disease. I obtained this intelligence at a time when I happened to be returning to my native haunts and, hence, made so bold as to detour somewhat from my normal course in order to visit them. I encountered but one of the siblings. He apprised me that it had been his younger brother who had suffered the dire illness. By now, however, he had long since become sound and fit again; in fact he had already repaired to other parts to await a substantive official appointment.[2]

The elder brother apologized for having needlessly put me to the inconvenience of this visitation, and concluding his disquisition with a hearty smile, showed me two volumes of diaries which, he assured me, would reveal the nature of his brother's disorder during those fearful days.

As to the lapsus calami[3] *that occur in the course of the diaries, I have altered not a word. Nonetheless, I have changed all the names, despite the fact that their publication would be of no great consequence since they are all humble villagers unknown to the world at large.*

Recorded this 2nd day in the 7th year of the Republic.[4]

---

1. Translated by and with notes adapted from William A. Lyell.   2. When there were too many officials for the number of offices to be filled, a man might well be appointed to an office that already had an incumbent. The new appointee would proceed to his post and wait until said office was vacated. Sometimes there would be a number of such appointees waiting their turns.   3. "The fall of the reed [writing instrument]" (literal trans.); hence, lapses in writing.   4. The Qing Dynasty was overthrown and the Republic of China was established in 1911; thus it is April 2, 1918. The introduction is written in classical Chinese, whereas the diary entries that follow are all in the colloquial language.

1

Moonlight's really nice tonight. Haven't seen it in over thirty years. Seeing it today, I feel like a new man. I know now that I've been completely out of things for the last three decades or more. But I've still got to be *very* careful. Otherwise, how do you explain those dirty looks the Zhao family's dog gave me?

I've got good reason for my fears.

2

No moonlight at all tonight—something's not quite right. When I made my way out the front gate this morning—ever so carefully—there was something funny about the way the Venerable Old Zhao looked at me: seemed as though he was afraid of me and yet, at the same time, looked as though he had it in for me. There were seven or eight other people who had their heads together whispering about me. They were afraid I'd see them too! All up and down the street people acted the same way. The meanest looking one of all spread his lips out wide and actually *smiled* at me! A shiver ran from the top of my head clear down to the tips of my toes, for I realized that meant they already had their henchmen well deployed, and were ready to strike.

But I wasn't going to let that intimidate *me*. I kept right on walking. There was a group of children up ahead and they were talking about me too. The expressions in their eyes were just like the Venerable Old Zhao's, and their faces were iron gray. I wondered what grudge the children had against me that they were acting this way too. I couldn't contain myself any longer and shouted, "Tell me, tell me!" But they just ran away.

Let's see now, what grudge can there be between me and the Venerable Old Zhao, or the people on the street for that matter? The only thing I can think of is that twenty years ago I trampled the account books kept by Mr. Antiquity, and he was hopping mad about it too. Though the Venerable Old Zhao doesn't know him, he must have gotten wind of it somehow. Probably decided to right the injustice I had done Mr. Antiquity by getting all those people on the street to gang up on me. But the children? Back then they hadn't even come into the world yet. Why should they have given me those funny looks today? Seemed as though they were afraid of me and yet, at the same time, looked as though they would like to do me some harm. That really frightens me. Bewilders me. Hurts me.

I have it! Their fathers and mothers have *taught* them to be like that!

3

I can never get to sleep at night. You really have to study something before you can understand it.

Take all those people: some have worn the cangue on the district magistrate's order, some have had their faces slapped by the gentry, some have had their wives ravished by *yamen*[5] clerks, some have had their dads and

5. Local government offices. The petty clerks who worked in them were notorious for relying on their proximity to power to bully and abuse the common people. *Cangue:* a split board, hinged at one end and locked at the other; holes were cut out to accommodate the prisoner's neck and wrists.

moms dunned to death by creditors; and yet, right at the time when all those terrible things were taking place, the expressions on their faces were never as frightened, or as savage, as the ones they wore yesterday.

Strangest of all was that woman on the street. She slapped her son and said: "Damn it all, you've got me so riled up I could take a good bite right out of your hide!" She was talking to him, but she was looking at me! I tried, but couldn't conceal a shudder of fright. That's when that ghastly crew of people, with their green faces and protruding fangs, began to roar with laughter. Old Fifth Chen[6] ran up, took me firmly in tow, and dragged me away.

When we got back, the people at home all pretended not to know me. The expressions in their eyes were just like all the others too. After he got me into the study, Old Fifth Chen bolted the door from the outside—just the way you would pen up a chicken or a duck! That made figuring out what was at the bottom of it all harder than ever.

A few days back one of our tenant farmers came in from Wolf Cub Village to report a famine. Told my elder brother the villagers had all ganged up on a "bad" man and beaten him to death. Even gouged out his heart and liver. Fried them up and ate them to bolster their own courage! When I tried to horn in on the conversation, Elder Brother and the tenant farmer both gave me sinister looks. I realized for the first time today that the expression in their eyes was just the same as what I saw in those people on the street.

As I think of it now, a shiver's running from the top of my head clear down to the tips of my toes.

If they're capable of eating people, then who's to say they won't eat *me*?

Don't you see? That woman's words about "taking a good bite," and the laughter of that ghastly crew with their green faces and protruding fangs, and the words of our tenant farmer a few days back—it's perfectly clear to me now that all that talk and all that laughter were really a set of secret signals. Those words were poison! That laughter, a knife! Their teeth are bared and waiting—white and razor sharp! Those people are cannibals!

As I see it myself, though I'm not what you'd call an evil man, still, ever since I trampled the Antiquity family's account books, it's hard to say *what* they'll do. They seem to have something in mind, but I can't begin to guess what. What's more, as soon as they turn against someone, they'll *say* he's evil anyway. I can still remember how it was when Elder Brother was teaching me composition.[7] No matter how good a man was, if I could find a few things wrong with him he would approvingly underline my words; on the other hand, if I made a few allowances for a bad man, he'd say I was "an extraordinary student, an absolute genius." When all is said and done, how can I possibly guess what people like *that* have in mind, especially when they're getting ready for a cannibals' feast?

You have to *really* go into something before you can understand it. I seemed to remember, though not too clearly, that from ancient times on

---

6. People were often referred to by their hierarchical position within their extended family.   7. That is, to compose essays in the classical style.

people have often been eaten, and so I started leafing through a history book to look it up. There were no dates in this history, but scrawled this way and that across every page were the words BENEVOLENCE, RIGHTEOUS- NESS, and MORALITY. Since I couldn't get to sleep anyway, I read that history very carefully for most of the night, and finally I began to make out what was written *between* the lines; the whole volume was filled with a single phrase: EAT PEOPLE!

The words written in the history book, the things the tenant farmer said—all of it began to stare at me with hideous eyes, began to snarl and growl at me from behind bared teeth!

Why sure, *I'm* a person too, and they want to eat *me!*

4

In the morning I sat in the study for a while, calm and collected. Old Fifth Chen brought in some food—vegetables and a steamed fish. The fish's eyes were white and hard. Its mouth was wide open, just like the mouths of those people who wanted to eat human flesh. After I'd taken a few bites, the meat felt so smooth and slippery in my mouth that I couldn't tell whether it was fish or human flesh. I vomited.

"Old Fifth," I said, "tell Elder Brother that it's absolutely stifling in here and that I'd like to take a walk in the garden." He left without answering, but sure enough, after a while the door opened. I didn't even budge—just sat there waiting to see what they'd do to me. I *knew* that they wouldn't be willing to set me loose.

Just as I expected! Elder Brother came in with an old man in tow and walked slowly toward me. There was a savage glint in the old man's eyes. He was afraid I'd see it and kept his head tilted toward the floor while stealing sidewise glances at me over the temples of his glasses. "You seem to be fine today," said Elder Brother.

"You bet!" I replied.

"I've asked Dr. He to come and examine your pulse today."

"He's welcome!" I said. But don't think for one moment that I didn't know the old geezer was an executioner in disguise! Taking my pulse was nothing but a ruse; he wanted to feel my flesh and decide if I was fat enough to butcher yet. He'd probably even get a share of the meat for his troubles. I wasn't a *bit* afraid. Even though I don't eat human flesh, I still have a lot more courage than those who do. I thrust both hands out to see how the old buzzard would make his move. Sitting down, he closed his eyes and felt my pulse[8] for a good long while. Then he froze. Just sat there without moving a muscle for another good long while. Finally he opened his spooky eyes and said: "Don't let your thoughts run away with you. Just convalesce in peace and quiet for a few days and you'll be all right."

Don't let my thoughts run away with me? Convalesce in peace and quiet? If I convalesce till I'm good and fat, they get more to eat, but what do *I* get out of it? How can I possibly be *all right?* What a bunch! All they think about is eating human flesh, and then they go sneaking around,

___

8. In Chinese medicine the pulse is taken at both wrists.

thinking up every which way they can to camouflage their real intentions. They were comical enough to crack *anybody* up. I couldn't hold it in any longer and let out a good loud laugh. Now *that* really felt good. I knew in my heart of hearts that my laughter was *packed* with courage and righteousness. And do you know what? They were so completely subdued by it that the old man and my elder brother both went pale!

But the more *courage* I had, the more that made them want to eat me so that they could get a little of it for free. The old man walked out. Before he had taken many steps, he lowered his head and told Elder Brother, "To be eaten as soon as possible!" He nodded understandingly. So, Elder Brother, you're in it too! Although that discovery seemed unforeseen, it really wasn't, either. My own elder brother had thrown in with the very people who wanted to eat me!

My elder brother is a cannibal!

I'm brother to a cannibal.

Even though I'm to be the victim of cannibalism, I'm *brother* to a cannibal all the same!

5

During the past few days I've taken a step back in my thinking. Supposing that old man wasn't an executioner in disguise but really was a doctor—well, he'd still be a cannibal just the same. In *Medicinal ... something or other* by Li Shizhen,[9] the grandfather of the doctor's trade, it says quite clearly that human flesh can be eaten, so how can that old man say that *he's* not a cannibal too?

And as for my own elder brother, I'm not being the least bit unfair to him. When he was explaining the classics to me, he said with his very own tongue that it was all right to *exchange children and eat them*. And then there was another time when he happened to start in on an evil man and said that not only should the man be killed, but his *flesh should be eaten* and *his skin used as a sleeping mat*[1] as well.

When our tenant farmer came in from Wolf Cub Village a few days back and talked about eating a man's heart and liver, Elder Brother didn't seem to see anything out of the way in that either—just kept nodding his head. You can tell from that alone that his present way of thinking is every bit as malicious as it was when I was a child. If it's all right to exchange *children* and eat them, then *anyone* can be exchanged, anyone can be eaten. Back then I just took what he said as explanation of the classics and let it go at that, but now I realize that while he was explaining, the grease of human flesh was smeared all over his lips, and what's more, his mind was filled with plans for further cannibalism.

---

9. Lived from 1518 to 1593. *Taxonomy of Medicinal Herbs*, a gigantic work, was the most important pharmacopoeia in traditional China.　1. Both italicized expressions are from the *Zuozhuan* (Zuo commentary to the *Spring and Summer Annals*, a historical work that dates from the 3rd century B.C.). In 448 B.C., an officer who was exhorting his own side not to surrender is recorded as having said, "When the army of Chu besieged the capital of Song [in 603 B.C.], the people exchanged their children and ate them, and used the bones for fuel; and still they would not submit to a covenant at the foot of their walls. For us who have sustained no great loss, to do so is to cast our state away" (translated by James Legge, 5.817). It is also recorded that in 551 B.C. an officer boasting of his own prowess before his ruler pointed to two men whom his ruler considered brave and said, "As to those two, they are like beasts, whose flesh I will eat, and then sleep upon their skins" (Legge 5.492).

6

Pitch black out. Can't tell if it's day or night. The Zhao family's dog has started barking again.

Savage as a lion, timid as a rabbit, crafty as a fox . . .

7

I'm on to the way they operate. They'll never be willing to come straight out and kill me. Besides, they wouldn't dare. They'd be afraid of all the bad luck it might bring down on them if they did. And so, they've gotten everyone into cahoots with them and have set traps all over the place so that I'll do *myself* in. When I think back on the looks of those men and women on the streets a few days ago, coupled with the things my elder brother's been up to recently, I can figure out eight or nine tenths of it. From their point of view, the best thing of all would be for me to take off my belt, fasten it around a beam, and hang myself. They wouldn't be guilty of murder, and yet they'd still get everything they're after. Why, they'd be so beside themselves with joy, they'd sob with laughter. Or if they couldn't get me to do that, maybe they could torment me until I died of fright and worry. Even though I'd come out a bit leaner that way, they'd still nod their heads in approval.

Their kind only know how to eat dead meat. I remember reading in a book somewhere about something called the *hai-yi-na*.[2] Its general appearance is said to be hideous, and the expression in its eyes particularly ugly and malicious. Often eats carrion, too. Even chews the bones to a pulp and swallows them down. Just thinking about it's enough to frighten a man.

The *hai-yi-na* is kin to the wolf. The wolf's a relative of the dog, and just a few days ago the Zhao family dog gave me a funny look. It's easy to see that he's in on it too. How did that old man expect to fool *me* by staring at the floor?

My elder brother's the most pathetic of the whole lot. Since he's a human being too, how can he manage to be so totally without qualms, and what's more, even gang up with them to eat me? Could it be that he's been used to this sort of thing all along and sees nothing wrong with it? Or could it be that he's lost all conscience and just goes ahead and does it even though he knows it's wrong?

If I'm going to curse cannibals, I'll have to start with him. And if I'm going to *convert* cannibals, I'll have to start with him too.

8

Actually, by now even they should long since have understood the truth of this . . .

Someone came in. Couldn't have been more than twenty or so. I wasn't able to make out what he looked like too clearly, but he was all smiles. He

---

2. Three Chinese characters are used here for phonetic value only; that is, *hai yi na* is a transliteration into Chinese of the English word *hyena*.

nodded at me. His smile didn't look like the real thing either. And so I asked him, "Is this business of eating people right?"

He just kept right on smiling and said, "Except perhaps in a famine year, how could anyone get eaten?" I knew right off that he was one of them—one of those monsters who devour people!

At that point my own courage increased a hundredfold and I asked him, "Is it right?"

"Why are you talking about this kind of thing anyway? You really know how to . . . uh . . . how to pull a fellow's leg. Nice weather we're having."

"The weather *is* nice. There's a nice moon out, too, but I *still* want to know if it's right."

He seemed quite put out with me and began to mumble, "It's not—"

"Not right? Then how come they're still eating people?"

"No one's eating anyone."

"No one's *eating* anyone? They're eating people in Wolf Cub Village this very minute. And it's written in all the books, too, written in bright red blood!"

His expression changed and his face went gray like a slab of iron. His eyes started out from their sockets as he said, "Maybe they are, but it's always been that way, it's—"

"Just because it's always been that way, does that make it *right?*"

"I'm not going to discuss such things with you. If you insist on talking about that, then *you're* the one who's in the wrong!"

I leaped from my chair, opened my eyes, and looked around—but the fellow was nowhere to be seen. He was far younger than my elder brother, and yet he was actually one of them. It must be because his mom and dad taught him to be that way. And he's probably already passed it on to his own son. No wonder that even the children give me murderous looks.

9

They want to eat others and at the same time they're afraid that other people are going to eat them. That's why they're always watching each other with such suspicious looks in their eyes.

But all they'd have to do is give up that way of thinking, and then they could travel about, work, eat, and sleep in perfect security. Think how happy they'd feel! It's only a threshold, a pass. But what do they do instead? What is it that these fathers, sons, brothers, husbands, wives, friends, teachers, students, enemies, and even people who don't know each other *really* do? Why they all join together to hold each other back, and talk each other out of it!

That's it! They'd rather *die* than take that one little step.

10

I went to see Elder Brother bright and early. He was standing in the courtyard looking at the sky. I went up behind him so as to cut him off from the door back into the house. In the calmest and friendliest of tones, I said, "Elder Brother, there's something I'd like to tell you."

"Go right ahead." He immediately turned and nodded his head.

"It's only a few words, really, but it's hard to get them out. Elder Brother, way back in the beginning, it's probably the case that primitive peoples *all* ate some human flesh. But later on, because their ways of thinking changed, some gave up the practice and tried their level best to improve themselves; they kept on changing until they became human beings, *real* human beings. But the others didn't; they just kept right on with their cannibalism and stayed at that primitive level.

"You have the same sort of thing with evolution[3] in the animal world. Some reptiles, for instance, changed into fish, and then they evolved into birds, then into apes, and then into human beings. But the others didn't want to improve themselves and just kept right on being reptiles down to this very day.

"Think how ashamed those primitive men who have remained cannibals must feel when they stand before *real* human beings. They must feel even more ashamed than reptiles do when confronted with their brethren who have evolved into apes.

"There's an old story from ancient times about Yi Ya boiling his son and serving him up to Jie Zhou.[4] But if the truth be known, people have *always* practiced cannibalism, all the way from the time when Pan Gu separated heaven and earth down to Yi Ya's son, down to Xu Xilin,[5] and on down to the man they killed in Wolf Cub Village. And just last year when they executed a criminal in town, there was even someone with T.B. who dunked a steamed bread roll in his blood and then licked it off.

"When they decided to eat me, by yourself, of course, you couldn't do much to prevent it, but why did you have to go and *join* them? Cannibals are capable of anything! If they're capable of eating me, then they're capable of eating *you* too! Even within their own group, they think nothing of devouring each other. And yet all they'd have to do is turn back— *change*—and then everything would be fine. Even though people may say, 'It's always been like this,' we can still do our best to improve. And we can start today!

"You're going to tell me it can't be done! Elder Brother, I think you're very likely to say that. When that tenant wanted to reduce his rent the day before yesterday, wasn't it you who said it couldn't be done?"

At first he just stood there with a cold smile, but then his eyes took on a murderous gleam. (I had exposed their innermost secrets.) His whole face had gone pale. Some people were standing outside the front gate. The Venerable Old Zhao and his dog were among them. Stealthily peering this way and that, they began to crowd through the open gate. Some I couldn't

---

3. Charles Darwin's (1809–1892) theory of evolution was immensely important to Chinese intellectuals during Lu's lifetime and the common coin of much discourse.   4. An early philosophical text, *Guan Zi*, reports that the famous cook Yi Ya boiled his son and served him to his ruler, Duke Huan of Qi (685–643 B.C.), because the meat of a human infant was one of the few delicacies the duke had never tasted. Ji and Zhou were the last evil rulers of the Sang (1776–1122 B.C.) and Zhou (1122–221 B.C.) dynasties. The madman has mixed up some facts here.   5. From Lu's hometown, Shaoxing (1873–1907). After studies in Japan, he returned to China and served as head of the Anhui Police Academy. When a high Qing official, En Ming, participated in a graduation ceremony at the academy, Xu assassinated him, hoping that this would touch off the revolution. After the assassination, he and some of his students at the academy occupied the police armory and managed, for a while, to hold off En Ming's troops. When Xu was finally captured, En Ming's personal body guards dug out his heart and liver and ate them. Pan Gu (literally, "Coiled-up Antiquity") was born out of an egg. As he stood up he separated heaven and earth. The world as we know it was formed from his body.

make out too well—their faces seemed covered with cloth. Some looked the same as ever—smiling green faces with protruding fangs. I could tell at a glance that they all belonged to the same gang, that they were all cannibals. But at the same time I also realized that they didn't all think the same way. Some thought *it's always been like this* and that they really should eat human flesh. Others knew they shouldn't but went right on doing it anyway, always on the lookout for fear someone might give them away. And since that's exactly what I had just done, I knew they must be furious. But they were all *smiling* at me—cold little smiles!

At this point Elder Brother suddenly took on an ugly look and barked, "Get out of here! All of you! What's so funny about a madman?"

Now I'm on to *another* of their tricks: not only are they unwilling to change, but they're already setting me up for their next cannibalistic feast by labeling me a "madman." That way, they'll be able to eat me without getting into the slightest trouble. Some people will even be grateful to them. Wasn't that the very trick used in the case that the tenant reported? Everybody ganged up on a "bad" man and ate him. It's the same old thing.

Old Fifth Chen came in and made straight for me, looking mad as could be. But he wasn't going to shut *me* up! I was going to tell that bunch of cannibals off, and no two ways about it!

"You can change! You can change from the bottom of your hearts! You ought to know that in the future they're not going to allow cannibalism in the world anymore. If you don't change, you're going to devour each other anyway. And even if a lot of you *are* left, a real human being's going to come along and eradicate the lot of you, just like a hunter getting rid of wolves—or reptiles!"

Old Fifth Chen chased them all out. I don't know where Elder Brother disappeared to. Old Fifth talked me into going back to my room.

It was pitch black inside. The beams and rafters started trembling overhead. They shook for a bit, and then they started getting bigger and bigger. They piled themselves up into a great heap on top of my body!

The weight was incredibly heavy and I couldn't even budge—they were trying to kill me! But I knew their weight was an illusion, and I struggled out from under them, my body bathed in sweat. I was still going to have my say. "Change this minute! Change from the bottom of your hearts! You ought to know that in the future they're not going to allow cannibals in the world anymore . . . ."

11

The sun doesn't come out. The door doesn't open. It's two meals a day.

I picked up my chopsticks and that got me thinking about Elder Brother. I realized that the reason for my younger sister's death lay entirely with him. I can see her now—such a lovable and helpless little thing, only five at the time. Mother couldn't stop crying, but *he* urged her to stop, probably because he'd eaten sister's flesh himself and hearing mother cry over her like that shamed him! But if he's still capable of feeling shame, then maybe . . .

Younger Sister was eaten by Elder Brother. I have no way of knowing whether Mother knew about it or not.

I think she *did* know, but while she was crying she didn't say anything about it. She probably thought it was all right, too. I can remember once when I was four or five, I was sitting out in the courtyard taking in a cool breeze when Elder Brother told me that when parents are ill, a son, in order to be counted as a really good person, should slice off a piece of his own flesh, boil it, and let them eat it.[6] At the time Mother didn't come out and say there was anything wrong with that. But if it was all right to eat one piece, then there certainly wouldn't be anything wrong with her eating the whole body. And yet when I think back to the way she cried and cried that day, it's enough to break my heart. It's all strange—very, very strange.

12

Can't think about it anymore. I just realized today that I too have muddled around for a good many years in a place where they've been continually eating people for four thousand years. Younger Sister happened to die at just the time when Elder Brother was in charge of the house. Who's to say he didn't slip some of her meat into the food we ate?

Who's to say I didn't eat a few pieces of my younger sister's flesh without knowing it? And now it's my turn . . .

Although I wasn't aware of it in the beginning, now that I *know* I'm someone with four thousand years' experience of cannibalism behind me, how hard it is to look real human beings in the eye!

13

Maybe there are some children around who still haven't eaten human flesh.

Save the children . . .

April 1918

6. In traditional literature, stories about such gruesome acts of filial piety were not unusual.

VIRGINIA WOOLF
1882–1941

An experimental novelist who developed an extraordinary poetic style for prose fiction, Virginia Woolf is known for her precise evocations of states of mind—the sensuous as well as rational perceptions that make up human consciousness. It is through this recording of moments of awareness that she joins Proust and Joyce in the move away from the linear development and objective descriptions of the nineteenth-century novel and works toward a different way of structuring both her protagonists' personal awareness and the relationships of different parts of the text. Blocks of time are juxtaposed in the memory or in different points of view; incomplete perspectives play off one another to create a larger pattern; alternating modes of narration remind the reader that a poetic (or fictional) creation is involved. Adapting the "stream of consciousness" technique inside a narrative style that ranges from precise, mundane details to lyric elaboration, and keenly aware of the way perception is further shaped by cultural habits, Woolf shows the creative imagination to be as necessary in our lives as it is in the creation of artistic texts.

She was born Adeline Virginia Stephen on January 25, 1882, one of the four children of the eminent Victorian editor and historian Leslie Stephen and his wife, Julia. The family actively pursued intellectual and artistic interests, and Julia was admired and sketched by some of the most famous Pre-Raphaelite artists. Following the customs of the day, only the sons, Adrian and Thoby, were given formal and university education; Virginia and her sister, Vanessa (later the painter Vanessa Bell), were instructed at home by their parents, and depended for further education on their father's immense library. Virginia bitterly resented this unequal treatment and the systematic discouragement of women's intellectual development that it implied. Throughout her own work, themes of society's different attitudes toward men and women play a strong role, especially in the essay collection *A Room of One's Own* (1929)—which contains the famous anecdote of her having been warned off the grass and forbidden entrance to a university library because she was a woman—and *Three Guineas* (1938). *A Room of One's Own* examines the history of literature written by women and contains also an impassioned plea that women writers be given conditions equal to those available for men: specifically, the privacy of a room in which to write and economic independence. (At the time Woolf wrote, it was very unusual for women to have any money of their own or to be able to devote themselves to a career with the same freedom as men.) After her mother's death in 1895, Woolf was expected to take over the supervision of the family household, which she did until her father's death in 1904. Of fragile physical health after an attack of whooping cough when she was six, she suffered in addition a nervous breakdown after the death of each parent.

Woolf moved to central London with her sister and brother Adrian after their father's death, and took a house in the Bloomsbury district (where the British Museum is located). They soon became the focus of what was later called the Bloomsbury Group, a gathering of writers, artists, and intellectuals impatient with conservative Edwardian society and eager to explore new modes of thought. Members of the group included the novelist E. M. Forster, the historian Lytton Strachey, the economist John Maynard Keynes, and the art critics Clive Bell (who married Vanessa) and Roger Fry (who introduced the group to postimpressionist painters such as Édouard Manet and Paul Cézanne). Woolf was not yet writing fiction, but contributed reviews to the *Times Literary Supplement*, taught literature and composition at Morley College (an institution with a volunteer faculty that provided educational opportunities for workers), and worked for the adult suffrage movement and a feminist group. In 1912 she married Leonard Woolf, who encouraged her to write and with whom she founded the Hogarth Press in 1917. The press became one of the most respected of the small literary presses and published works by such major authors as T. S. Eliot, Katherine Mansfield, Lytton Strachey, E. M. Forster, Maxim Gorky, and John Middleton Murry as well as Woolf's own novels and translations of Freud. Over the next two decades she produced her best-known fiction while coping with frequent bouts of physical and mental illness. Already depressed during World War II and exhausted after the completion of her last novel, *Between the Acts* (1941), she sensed the approach of a serious attack of insanity and the confinement it would entail: in such situations, she was obliged to "rest" and forbidden to read or write. In March 1941, she drowned herself in a river close to her Sussex home.

As a writer, Woolf is best known for her poetic evocations of the way we think and feel. Like Proust and Joyce, she is superbly capable of evoking all the concrete, sensuous details of everyday experience; like them, she explores the structures of consciousness. What she really deplored was the microscopic, documentary realism that contemporaries like Arnold Bennett and John Galsworthy drew from the nineteenth-century masters. The contemporary realists' pretense of scientific objectivity was false, she felt, since they refused to take into account the fact that there are no neutral observers—that "reality" is reported differently by different people. Worse, their goal of scientific objectivity often resulted in a mere chronological accumulation of details, the "appalling narrative business of . . . getting from lunch to dinner." Woolf preferred a more subjective and, she hoped, a more accurate account of the real. Her focus was not so much the object under observation as the way the observer perceived it: "Let us record the atoms as they fall upon the mind in the order in which they fall, let us trace the pattern, however disconnected and incoherent in appearance, which each sight or incident scores upon the consciousness."

Woolf's writing has been compared with postimpressionist art in the way that it emphasizes the abstract arrangement of perspectives to suggest additional networks of meaning. After two relatively traditional novels, she began to develop a more flexible approach that openly manipulated fictional structure. The continuously developing plot gave way to an organization by juxtaposed points of view; the experience of "real" or chronological time was displaced (although not completely) by a mind ranging ambiguously among its memories; and an intricate pattern of symbolic themes connected otherwise unrelated characters in the same story. All these techniques made new demands on the reader's ability to synthesize and re-create a whole picture. In *Jacob's Room* (1922), a picture of the hero must be assembled from a series of partial points of view. In *The Waves* (1931), the multiple perspective of different characters soliloquizing on their relationship to the dead Percival is broken by ten interludes that together construct an additional, interacting perspective when they describe the passage of a single day from dawn to dusk. The same novel may expand or telescope the sense of time: *Mrs. Dalloway* (1925) focuses apparently on Clarissa Dalloway's preparations for a party that evening but at the same time calls up—at different times, and according to different contexts—her whole life from childhood to her present age of fifty. Problems of identity are a constant concern in these shifting perspectives, and Woolf often portrays the search of unfulfilled personalities for whatever will complete them. Her work is studded with moments of heightened awareness (comparable to Joyce's epiphanies) in which a character suddenly *sees into* a person or situation. With Woolf, this moment is less a matter of mystical insight (as it is with Joyce) than a creation of the mind using all its faculties.

No one can read Woolf without being struck by the importance she gives to the creative imagination. Her major characters display a sensitivity beyond rational logic, and her narrative style celebrates the aesthetic impulse to coordinate many dimensions inside one harmoniously significant whole. Human beings are not complete, Woolf suggests, without exercising their intuitive and imaginative faculties. Like other modernist writers, she is fascinated by the creative process and often makes reference to it in her work. Whether describing the struggles of a painter in *To the Lighthouse* (1927) or of a writer in *An Unwritten Novel*, she simultaneously illustrates the exploratory and creative work of the human imagination. Not all this work is visible in the finished painting or novel: observing, sifting, coordinating, projecting different interpretations and relationships, the mind performs an enormous labor of coordinating consciousness that cannot be captured entirely in any fixed form.

In *An Unwritten Novel*, Woolf humorously describes the embryonic stages of composition by taking the reader through the tentative beginnings of a novel that might have been. The story moves back and forth between two sides of imagination and reality, both contributing to the potential novel, as the narrator mentally tests out possible versions based on her observation of a particular person in the railway carriage. On the one hand, she records the actual words and gestures of her fellow passengers on the train: on the other, she projects their imagined life into a completely fictional creation as she perceives, empathizes, and shapes what she sees to fit her own preconceptions. The process of composition appears in all its experiments, false starts, and corrections for tone and consistency: the narrator must find the appropriate imagined crime for Minnie's repressed air, supply ferns instead of rhododendrons to fit a given scene, and add or subtract characters to round out the story. Nor does Woolf ignore the narrator's own character as a motivating force. Although the narrator prides herself on starting from a solid base of concrete observation, her artist's joy in the pure exercise of creativity quickly leads to elaboration for its own sake (the broken eggshell that becomes a map, blocks of marble, and Spanish silver and gold: her delighted transformation of James Moggridge into a clinically functioning organism as her x-ray vision penetrates "the spine tough as whalebone, straight as oaktree; the ribs radiating branches; the flesh taut tarpaulin; the red hollows; the suck and regurgitation of the heart; while from above meat falls in brown cubes and beer gushes to be churned to blood again"). Like Baudelaire in *The Windows*, she triumphantly asserts the value of creativity over mere factual evidence. When her first tale has comically been disproved and she is left "bare as a bone," it is not long before instinct takes over and she starts spinning stories anew. In this richly textured story, which combines the dimensions of objective reality and self-deception with a passionate statement of the liberating power of art, Woolf pokes gentle fun at herself and at the whole tradition of the novel as a mirror of reality. The essayist's critical and self-analytic perspective gives way at the end, however, to a lyric reaffirmation of the artist's obsession with the fascinating, "adorable world" of colorful sights and mysterious figures, all waiting to be created.

Phyllis Rose, *Woman of Letters: A Life of Virginia Woolf* (1978), is a valuable biography; Edward Bishop, *Virginia Woolf* (1991), is a recent brief introduction. A useful and readable overview of the texts is provided by Avrom Fleishman, *Virginia Woolf: A Critical Reading* (1975). Two valuable collections of essays of Woolf's writing and her position in the modernist/postmodernist tradition are Patricia Clements and Isobel Grundy, eds., *Virginia Woolf: New Critical Essays* (1983), and Margaret Homans, ed., *Virginia Woolf: A Collection of Critical Essays* (1993). Dean R. Baldwin, *Virginia Woolf: A Study of the Short Fiction* (1989), offers a brief discussion, six essays by other critics, and two essays by Woolf on modern fiction. Jane Marcus, *New Feminist Essays on Virginia Woolf* (1981), includes representative feminist critiques of Virginia Woolf as writer and social thinker. Patricia Ondek Laurence situates Woolf in *The Reading of Silence: Virginia Woolf in the English Tradition* (1991); comparative studies include Richard Pearce, *The Politics of Narration: James Joyce, William Faulkner, and Virginia Woolf* (1991), and Bette London, *The Appropriated Voice: Narrative Authority in Conrad, Forster, and Woolf* (1990).

An Unwritten Novel

Such an expression of unhappiness was enough by itself to make one's eyes slide above the paper's edge to the poor woman's face—insignificant without that look, almost a symbol of human destiny with it. Life's what you see in people's eyes; life's what they learn, and, having learnt it, never, though they seek to hide it, cease to be aware of—what? That life's like that, it seems. Five faces opposite—five mature faces—and the knowledge in each face. Strange though, how people want to conceal it! Marks of reticence are on all those faces: lips shut, eyes shaded, each one of the five doing something to hide or stultify his knowledge. One smokes; another reads; a third checks entries in a pocket book; a fourth stares at the map of the line framed opposite; and the fifth—the terrible thing about the fifth is that she does nothing at all. She looks at life. Ah, but my poor, unfortunate woman, do play the game—do, for all our sakes, conceal it!

As if she heard me, she looked up, shifted slightly in her seat and sighed. She seemed to apologize and at the same time to say to me, "If only you knew!" Then she looked at life again. "But I do know," I answered silently, glancing at the Times[1] for manners' sake. "I know the whole business. 'Peace between Germany and the Allied Powers was yesterday officially ushered in at Paris—Signor Nitti, the Italian Prime Minister—a passenger train at Doncaster was in collision with a goods train . . .' We all know— the Times knows—but we pretend we don't." My eyes had once more crept over the paper's rim. She shuddered, twitched her arm queerly to the middle of her back and shook her head. Again I dipped into my great reservoir of life. "Take what you like," I continued, "births, deaths, marriages, Court Circular,[2] the habits of birds, Leonardo da Vinci, the Sandhills murder, high wages and the cost of living—oh, take what you like," I repeated, "it's all in the Times!" Again with infinite weariness she moved her head from side to side until, like a top exhausted with spinning, it settled on her neck.

The Times was no protection against such sorrow as hers. But other human beings forbade intercourse. The best thing to do against life was to fold the paper so that it made a perfect square, crisp, thick, impervious even to life. This done, I glanced up quickly, armed with a shield of my own. She pierced through my shield; she gazed into my eyes as if searching any sediment of courage at the depths of them and damping it to clay. Her twitch alone denied all hope, discounted all illusion.

So we rattled through Surrey and across the border into Sussex.[3] But with my eyes upon life I did not see that the other travellers had left, one by one, till, save for the man who read, we were alone together. Here was Three Bridges station. We drew slowly down the platform and stopped. Was he going to leave us? I prayed both ways—I prayed last that he might stay. At that instant he roused himself, crumpled his paper contemptuously, like a thing done with, burst open the door, and left us alone.

The unhappy woman, leaning a little forward, palely and colourlessly addressed me—talked of stations and holidays, of brothers at Eastbourne,[4] and the time of year, which was, I forget now, early or late. But at last looking from the window and seeing, I knew, only life, she breathed, "Staying away—that's the drawback of it—" Ah, now we approached the catastrophe.[5] "My sister-in-law"—the bitterness of her tone was like lemon

---

1. Major London newspaper, reputed to cover everything from international and royal news to a variety of local topics.   2. Royal news.   3. The train is passing through the southeastern English countryside, headed away from London.   4. A seaside resort.   5. In the literary sense: a dénouement or crucial revelation.

on cold steel, and speaking, not to me, but to herself, she muttered, "Nonsense, she would say—that's what they all say," and while she spoke she fidgeted as though the skin on her back were as a plucked fowl's in a poulterer's shop-window.

"Oh, that cow!" she broke off nervously, as though the great wooden cow in the meadow had shocked her and saved her from some indiscretion. Then she shuddered, and then she made the awkward angular movement that I had seen before, as if, after the spasm, some spot between the shoulders burnt or itched. Then again she looked the most unhappy woman in the world, and I once more reproached her, though not with the same conviction, for if there were a reason, and if I knew the reason, the stigma was removed from life.

"Sisters-in-law," I said—

Her lips pursed as if to spit venom at the word; pursed they remained. All she did was to take her glove and rub hard at a spot on the windowpane. She rubbed as if she would rub something out for ever—some stain, some indelible contamination. Indeed, the spot remained for all her rubbing, and back she sank with the shudder and the clutch of the arm I had come to expect. Something impelled me to take my glove and rub my window. There, too, was a little speck on the glass. For all my rubbing it remained. And then the spasm went through me; I crooked my arm and plucked at the middle of my back. My skin, too, felt like the damp chicken's skin in the poulterer's shop-window; one spot between the shoulders itched and irritated, felt clammy, felt raw. Could I reach it? Surreptitiously I tried. She saw me. A smile of infinite irony, infinite sorrow, flitted and faded from her face. But she had communicated, shared her secret, passed her poison; she would speak no more. Leaning back in my corner, shielding my eyes from her eyes, seeing only the slopes and hollows, greys and purples, of the winter's landscape, I read her message, deciphered her secret, reading it beneath her gaze.

Hilda's the sister-in-law. Hilda? Hilda? Hilda Marsh—Hilda the blooming, the full bosomed, the matronly. Hilda stands at the door as the cab draws up, holding a coin. "Poor Minnie, more of a grasshopper than ever—old cloak she had last year. Well, well, with two children these days one can't do more. No, Minnie, I've got it; here you are, cabby—none of your ways with me. Come in, Minnie. Oh, I could carry *you*, let alone your basket!" So they go into the dining-room. "Aunt Minnie, children."

Slowly the knives and forks sink from the upright. Down they get (Bob and Barbara), hold out hands stiffly; back again to their chairs, staring between the resumed mouthfuls. [But this we'll skip; ornaments, curtains, trefoil china plate, yellow oblongs of cheese, white squares of biscuit—skip, oh, but wait! Halfway through luncheon one of those shivers; Bob stares at her, spoon in mouth. "Get on with your pudding, Bob"; but Hilda disapproves. "Why *should* she twitch?" Skip, skip, till we reach the landing on the upper floor; stairs brass-bound; linoleum worn; oh, yes! little bedroom looking out over the roofs of Eastbourne—zigzagging roofs like the spines of caterpillars, this way, that way, striped red and yellow, with blueblack slating.] Now, Minnie, the door's shut; Hilda heavily descends to the basement; you unstrap the straps of your basket, lay on the bed a meagre nightgown, stand side by side furred felt slippers. The looking-glass—no, you avoid the looking-glass. Some methodical disposition of hat-pins. Perhaps the shell box has something in it? You shake it; it's the pearl stud there was last year—that's all. And then the sniff, the sigh, the sitting by the window. Three o'clock on a December afternoon; the rain drizzling! one light low in the skylight of a drapery emporium; another high in a servant's bedroom—this one goes out. That gives her nothing to look at. A moment's blankness—then, what are you thinking? (Let me peep across at her opposite; she's asleep or pretending it; so what would she think about sitting at the window at three o'clock in the afternoon? Health, money, bills, her God?) Yes, sitting on the very edge of the chair looking over the roofs of Eastbourne, Minnie Marsh prays to God. That's all very well; and she may rub the pane too, as though to see God better; but what God does she see? Who's the God of Minnie Marsh, the God of the back streets of Eastbourne, the God of three o'clock in the afternoon? I, too, see roofs, I see sky; but, oh, dear—this seeing of Gods! More like President Kruger than Prince Albert[6]—that's the best I can do for him; and I see him on a chair, in a black frock-coat, not so very high up either; I can manage a cloud or two for him to sit on; and then his hand trailing in the cloud holds a rod, a truncheon is it?—black, thick, thorned—a brutal old bully—Minnie's God! Did he send the itch and the patch and the twitch? Is that why she prays? What she rubs on the window is the stain of sin. Oh, she committed some crime!

I have my choice of crimes. The woods flit and fly—in summer there are bluebells; in the opening there, when spring comes, primroses. A parting, was it, twenty years ago? Vows broken? Not Minnie's! . . . She was faithful. How she nursed her mother! All her savings on the tombstone— wreaths under glass—daffodils in jars. But I'm off the track. A crime. . . . They would say she kept her sorrow, suppressed her secret—her sex, they'd say—the scientific people. But what flummery to saddle *her* with sex! No—more like this. Passing down the streets of Croydon twenty years ago, the violet loops of ribbon in the draper's window spangled in the electric light catch her eye. She lingers—past six. Still by running she can reach home. She pushes through the glass wing door. It's sale-time. Shallow trays brim with ribbons. She pauses, pulls this, fingers that with the raised roses on it—no need to choose, no need to buy, and each tray with its surprises. "We don't shut till seven," and then it *is* seven. She runs, she rushes, home she reaches, but too late. Neighbours—the doctor—baby brother—the kettle—scalded—hospital—dead—or only the shock of it, the blame? Ah, but the detail matters nothing! It's what she carries with her; the spot, the crime, the thing to expiate, always there between her shoulders. "Yes," she seems to nod to me, "it's the thing I did."

Whether you did, or what you did, I don't mind; it's not the thing I want. The draper's window looped with violet—that'll do; a little cheap perhaps, a little commonplace—since one has a choice of crimes, but

---

6. Husband of the British Queen Victoria; he was a popular figure known for political moderation (1819–1861). Paul Kruger (1825–1904), Transvaal statesman strongly opposed to British influence in South Africa, president of the Boer Republic for twenty years. Contemporary pictures show him in formal frock coat with a severe, bearded face.

then so many (let me peep across again—still sleeping, or pretending sleep! white, worn, the mouth closed—a touch of obstinacy, more than one would think—no hint of sex)—so many crimes aren't your crime; your crime was cheap, only the retribution solemn; for now the church door opens, the hard wooden pew receives her; on the brown tiles she kneels; every day, winter, summer, dusk, dawn (here she's at it) prays. All her sins fall, fall, for ever fall. The spot receives them. It's raised, it's red, it's burning. Next she twitches. Small boys point. "Bob at lunch today"—But elderly women are the worst.

Indeed now you can't sit praying any longer. Kruger's sunk beneath the clouds—washed over as with a painter's brush of liquid grey, to which he adds a tinge of black—even the tip of the truncheon gone now. That's what always happens! Just as you've seen him, felt him, someone interrupts. It's Hilda now.

How you hate her! She'll even lock the bathroom door overnight, too, though it's only cold water you want, and sometimes when the night's been bad it seems as if washing helped. And John at breakfast—the children—meals are worst, and sometimes there are friends—ferns don't altogether hide 'em—they guess, too; so out you go along the front, where the waves are grey, and the papers blow, and the glass shelters green and draughty, and the chairs cost tuppence[7]—too much—for there must be preachers along the sands. Ah, that's a nigger—that's a funny man—that's a man with parakeets—poor little creatures! Is there no one here who thinks of God?—just up there, over the pier, with his rod—but no—there's nothing but grey in the sky or if it's blue the white clouds hide him, and the music—it's military music—and what are they fishing for? Do they catch them? How the children stare! Well, then home a back way—"Home a back way!" The words have meaning; might have been spoken by the old man with whiskers—no, no, he didn't really speak; but everything has meaning—placards leaning against doorways—names above shop-windows—red fruit in baskets—women's heads in the hairdresser's—all say "Minnie Marsh!" But here's a jerk. "Eggs are cheaper!"[8] That's what always happens! I was heading her over the waterfall, straight for madness, when, like a flock of dream sheep, she turns t'other way and runs between my fingers. Eggs are cheaper. Tethered to the shores of the world, none of the crimes, sorrows, rhapsodies, or insanities for poor Minnie Marsh; never late for luncheon; never caught in a storm without a mackintosh; never utterly unconscious of the cheapness of eggs. So she reaches home—scrapes her boots.

Have I read you right? But the human face—the human face at the top of the fullest sheet of print holds more, withholds more. Now, eyes open, she looks out; and in the human eye—how d'you define it?—there's a break—a division—so that when you've grasped the stem the butterfly's off—the moth that hangs in the evening over the yellow flower—move, raise your hand, off, high, away. I won't raise my hand. Hang still, then, quiver, life, soul, spirit, whatever you are of Minnie Marsh—I, too, on my

7. Chairs were available for rent along the waterfront.   8. The narrator's silent imaginings are interrupted and brought down to earth when Minnie Marsh, preparing to eat her snack of hard-boiled egg, comments out loud that "Eggs are cheaper."

flower—the hawk over the down—alone, or what were the worth of life? To rise; hang still in the evening, in the midday; hang still over the down. The flicker of a hand—off, up! then poised again. Alone, unseen; seeing all so still down there, all so lovely. None seeing, none caring. The eyes of others our prisons; their thoughts our cages. Air above, air below. And the moon and immortality. . . . Oh, but I drop to the turf! Are you down too, you in the corner, what's your name—woman—Minnie Marsh; some such name as that? There she is, tight to her blossom; opening her hand-bag, from which she takes a hollow shell—an egg—who was saying that eggs were cheaper? You or I? Oh, it was you who said it on the way home, you remember, when the old gentleman, suddenly opening his umbrella—or sneezing was it? Anyhow, Kruger went, and you came "home a back way," and scraped your boots. Yes. And now you lay across your knees a pocket-handkerchief into which drop little angular fragments of eggshell—fragments of a map—a puzzle. I wish I could piece them together! If you would only sit still. She's moved her knees—the map's in bits again. Down the slopes of the Andes the white blocks of marble go bounding and hurtling, crushing to death a whole troop of Spanish mule-teers, with their convoy—Drake's booty, gold and silver.[9] But to return—

To what, to where? She opened the door, and, putting her umbrella in the stand—that goes without saying: so, too, the whiff of beef from the basement; dot, dot, dot. But what I cannot thus eliminate, what I must, head down, eyes shut, with the courage of a battalion and the blindness of a bull, charge and disperse are, indubitably, the figures behind the ferns, commercial travellers. There, I've hidden them all this time in the hope that somehow they'd disappear, or better still emerge, as indeed they must, if the story's to go on gathering richness and rotundity, destiny and tragedy, as stories should, rolling along with it two, if not three, commercial travel-lers and a whole grove of aspidistra. "The fronds of the aspidistra only partly concealed the commercial traveller[1]—" Rhododendrons would conceal him utterly, and into the bargain give me my fling of red and white, for which I starve and strive; but rhododendrons in Eastbourne—in December—on the Marshes' table—no, no, I dare not;[2] it's all a matter of crusts and cruets, frills and ferns. Perhaps there'll be a moment later by the sea. Moreover, I feel, pleasantly pricking through the green fretwork and over the glacis of cut glass, a desire to peer and peep at the man opposite—one's as much as I can manage. James Moggridge is it, whom the Marshes call Jimmy? [Minnie, you must promise not to twitch till I've got this straight.] James Moggridge travels in—shall we say buttons?[3]—but the time's not come for bringing them in—the big and the little on the long cards, some peacock-eyed, others dull gold; cairngorms[4] some, and others coral sprays—but I say the time's not come. He travels, and on Thursdays, his Eastbourne day, takes his meals with the Marshes. His red

9. The yellow and white fragments of egg inspire another series of images. Sir Francis Drake (1540?–1596) was an English explorer and sea captain who captured Spanish ships returning from South America laden with gold and silver stolen from the Indians. The Indians are imagined as rolling blocks of marble down the Andes mountains to crush the invaders.   1. Traveling salesman.   2. Aspidistra (a long-leaved, common house plant) is more appropriate for the imagined story's middle-class setting than rhododendron, which would not fit the season or context.   3. The commercial traveler given the name James Moggridge is imagined as selling buttons; there follows a brief description of his merchan-dise on its display cards.   4. A yellow quartz.

face, his little steady eyes—by no means altogether commonplace—his enormous appetite (that's safe; he won't look at Minnie till the bread's swamped the gravy dry), napkin tucked diamond-wise—but this is primitive, and, whatever it may do the reader, don't take me in. Let's dodge to the Moggridge household, set that in motion. Well, the family boots are mended on Sundays by James himself. He reads *Truth*.[5] But his passion? Roses—and his wife a retired hospital nurse—interesting—for God's sake let me have one woman with a name I like! But no; she's of the unborn children of the mind, illicit, none the less loved, like my rhododendrons. How many die in every novel that's written—the best, the dearest, while Moggridge lives. It's life's fault. Here's Minnie eating her egg at the moment opposite and at t'other end of the line—are we past Lewes?[6]— there must be Jimmy—or what's her twitch for?

There must be Moggridge—life's fault. Life imposes her laws; life blocks the way; life's behind the fern; life's the tyrant; oh, but not the bully! No, for I assure you I come willingly; I come wooed by Heaven knows what compulsion across ferns and cruets, table splashed and bottles smeared. I come irresistibly to lodge myself somewhere on the firm flesh, in the robust spine, wherever I can penetrate or find foothold on the person, in the soul, of Moggridge the man. The enormous stability of the fabric; the spine tough as whalebone, straight as oaktree; the ribs radiating branches; the flesh taut tarpaulin; the red hollows; the suck and regurgitation of the heart; while from above meat falls in brown cubes and beer gushes to be churned to blood again—and so we reach the eyes. Behind the aspidistra they see something: black, white, dismal; now the plate again; behind the aspidistra they see an elderly woman; "Marsh's sister. Hilda's more my sort"; the tablecloth now. "Marsh would know what's wrong with Morrises . . ." talk that over; cheese has come; the plate again; turn it round—the enormous fingers; now the woman opposite. "Marsh's sister—not a bit like Marsh; wretched, elderly female. . . . You should feed your hens. . . . God's truth, what's set her twitching? Not what *I* said? Dear, dear, dear! these elderly women. Dear, dear!"

[Yes, Minnie; I know you've twitched, but one moment—James Moggridge.]

"Dear, dear, dear!" How beautiful the sound is! like the knock of a mallet on seasoned timber, like the throb of the heart of an ancient whaler when the seas press thick and the green is clouded. "Dear, dear!" what a passing bell for the souls of the fretful to soothe them and solace them, lap them in linen, saying, "So long. Good luck to you!" and then, "What's your pleasure?" for though Moggridge would pluck his rose for her, that's done, that's over. Now what's the next thing? "Madam, you'll miss your train," for they don't linger.

That's the man's way; that's the sound that reverberates; that's St. Paul's,[7] and the motor-omnibuses. But we're brushing the crumbs off. Oh, Moggridge, you won't stay? You must be off? Are you driving through Eastbourne this afternoon in one of those little carriages? Are you the man who's walled up in green cardboard boxes, and sometimes sits so solemn staring like a sphinx; and always there's a look of the sepulchral, something of the undertaker, the coffin, and the dusk about horse and driver? Do tell me—but the doors slammed. We shall never meet again. Moggridge, farewell!

Yes, yes, I'm coming. Right up to the top of the house. One moment I'll linger. How the mud goes round in the mind—what a swirl these monsters leave, the waters rocking, the weeds waving and green here, black there, striking to the sand, till by degrees the atoms reassemble, the deposit sifts itself, and again through the eyes one sees clear and still, and there comes to the lips some prayer for the departed, some obsequy for the souls of those one nods to, the people one never meets again.

James Moggridge is dead now, gone for ever. Well, Minnie—"I can face it no longer." If she said that—(Let me look at her. She is brushing the eggshell into deep declivities). She said it certainly, leaning against the wall of the bedroom, and plucking at the little balls which edge the claret-coloured curtain. But when the self speaks to the self, who is speaking?—the entombed soul, the spirit driven in, in, in to the central catacomb; the self that took the veil[8] and left the world—a coward perhaps, yet somehow beautiful, as it flits with its lantern restlessly up and down the dark corridors. "I can bear it no longer," her spirit says. "That man at lunch—Hilda—the children." Oh, heavens, her sob! It's the spirit wailing its destiny, the spirit driven hither, thither, lodging on the diminishing carpets—meagre footholds—shrunken shreds of all the vanishing universe—love, life, faith, husband, children, I know not what splendours and pageantries glimpsed in girlhood. "Not for me—not for me."

But then—the muffins, the bald elderly dog? Bead mats I should fancy and the consolation of underlinen. If Minnie Marsh were run over and taken to hospital, nurses and doctors themselves would exclaim.[9] . . . There's the vista and the vision—there's the distance—the blue blot at the end of the avenue, while, after all, the tea is rich, the muffin hot, and the dog—"Benny, to your basket, sir, and see what mother's brought you!" So, taking the glove with the worn thumb, defying once more the encroaching demon of what's called going in holes, you renew the fortifications, threading the grey wool, running it in and out.

Running it in and out, across and over, spinning a web through which God himself—hush, don't think of God! How firm the stitches are! You must be proud of your darning. Let nothing disturb her. Let the light fall gently, and the clouds show an inner vest of the first green leaf. Let the sparrow perch on the twig and shake the raindrop hanging to the twig's elbow. . . . Why look up? Was it a sound, a thought? Oh, heavens! Back again to the thing you did, the plate glass with the violet loops? But Hilda will come. Ignominies, humiliations, oh! Close the breach.

Having mended her glove, Minnie Marsh lays it in the drawer. She shuts the drawer with decision. I catch sight of her face in the glass. Lips are pursed. Chin held high. Next she laces her shoes. Then she touches

8. Became a nun.   9. The hospital attendants are to exclaim at the neatness of Minnie Marsh's underwear. Immaculate and well-kept clothing—both inside and out—was one of the signs of a proper lady.

her throat. What's your brooch? Mistletoe or merrythought?[1] And what is happening? Unless I'm much mistaken, the pulse's quickened, the moment's coming, the threads are racing, Niagara's ahead. Here's the crisis! Heaven be with you! Down she goes. Courage, courage! Face it, be it! For God's sake don't wait on the mat now! There's the door! I'm on your side. Speak! Comfort her, confound her soul![2]

"Oh, I beg your pardon! Yes, this is Eastbourne. I'll reach it down for you. Let me try the handle." [But Minnie, though we keep up pretences, I've read you right—I'm with you now.]

"That's all your luggage?"

"Much obliged, I'm sure."

(But why do you look about you? Hilda won't come to the station, nor John; and Moggridge is driving at the far side of Eastbourne.)

"I'll wait by my bag, ma'am, that's safest. He said he'd meet me. . . . Oh, there he is! That's my son."

So they walk off together.

Well, but I'm confounded. . . . Surely, Minnie, you know better! A strange young man. . . . Stop! I'll tell him—Minnie!—Miss Marsh!—I don't know though. There's something queer in her cloak as it blows. Oh, but it's untrue, it's indecent. . . . Look how he bends as they reach the gateway. She finds her ticket. What's the joke? Off they go, down the road, side by side. . . . Well, my world's done for! What do I stand on? What do I know? That's not Minnie. There never was Moggridge. Who am I? Life's bare as bone.

And yet the last look of them—he stepping from the kerb and she following him round the edge of the big building brims me with wonder—floods me anew. Mysterious figures! Mother and son. Who are you? Why do you walk down the street? Where tonight will you sleep, and then, tomorrow? Oh, how it whirls and surges—floats me afresh! I start after them. People drive this way and that. The white light splutters and pours. Plate-glass windows. Carnations; chrysanthemums. Ivy in dark gardens. Milk carts at the door. Wherever I go, mysterious figures, I see you, turning the corner, mothers and sons; you, you, you. I hasten, I follow. This, I fancy, must be the sea. Grey is the landscape; dim as ashes; the water murmurs and moves. If I fall on my knees, if I go through the ritual, the ancient antics, it's you, unknown figures, you I adore; if I open my arms, it's you I embrace, you I draw to me—adorable world!

1. Wishbone.   2. The narrator imagines a major confrontation between the poor spinster Minnie Marsh and Hilda.

FRANZ KAFKA
1883–1924

The predicament of Franz Kafka's writing is, for many, the predicament of modern civilization. Nowhere is the anxiety and alienation of twentieth-century society more visible than in his stories of individuals struggling to prevail against a vast, meaningless, and apparently hostile system. Identifying that system as bureaucracy, family, religion, language, or the invisible network of social habit is less important than recognizing the protagonists' bewilderment at being placed in impossible situations. Kafka's heroes are driven to find answers in an unresponsive world, and they are required to act according to incomprehensible rules administered by an inaccessible authority; small wonder that they fluctuate between fear, hope, anger, resignation, and despair. Kafka's fictional world has long fascinated contemporary writers, who find in it an extraordinary blend of prosaic realism and nightmarish, infinitely interpretable symbolism. Whether evoking the multilayered bureaucracy of the modern state, the sense of guilt felt by those facing the accusations of authority, or the vulnerability of characters who cannot make themselves understood, Kafka's descriptions are believable because of their scrupulous attention to detail: the flea on a fur collar, the dust under an unmade bed, the creases and yellowing of an old newspaper, or the helplessness of a beetle turned upside down. The sheer *ordinariness* of these details grounds the entire narrative, giving the reader a continuing expectation of reality even when events escape all logic and the situation is at its most hallucinatory. This paradoxical combination has appealed to a range of contemporary writers—each quite different from the other—who have read and absorbed Kafka's lesson: Samuel Beckett, Harold Pinter, Alain Robbe-Grillet, Gabriel García Márquez.

Kafka was born into cultural alienation: Jewish (though not truly part of the Jewish community) in Catholic Czechoslovakia, son of a German-speaking shopkeeper when German was the language of the imposed Austro-Hungarian government, and drawn to literature when his father—a domineering, self-made man—pushed him toward success in business. Nor was he happier at home. Resenting his father's overbearing nature and feeling deprived of maternal love, he nonetheless lived with his parents for most of his life and complained in long letters about his coldness and inability to love (despite numerous liaisons). Kafka took a degree in law to qualify himself for a position in a large accident-insurance corporation, where he worked until illness forced his retirement in 1922. By the time of his death from tuberculosis two years later, he had published a number of short stories and two novellas (*The Metamorphosis*, 1915; *In the Penal Colony*, 1919), but left behind him the manuscripts of three near-complete novels that—considering himself a failure—he asked to have burned. Instead, Kafka's executor Max Brod published the novels (*The Trial*, 1925; *The Castle*, 1926; *Amerika*, 1927) and a biography celebrating the genius of his tormented, guilt-ridden friend.

In spite of the indubitable fact that Franz Kafka became a respected senior executive handling claims, litigations, public relations, and his institute's annual reports, and was one of the few top German executives retained when Czechoslovakia finally gained independence in 1918, his image in the modern imagination is derived from the portraits of inner anguish given in his fiction, diaries, and letters. This "Kafka" is a tormented and sensitive soul, guiltily resentful of his job in a giant bureaucracy, unable to free himself from his family or to cope with the demands of love, physically feeble, and constantly beset by feelings of inferiority and doom in an existence whose laws he can never quite understand. "Before the Law," a parable published in Kafka's lifetime and included in *The Trial*, recounts the archetypal setting of the "Kafka" character: a countryman waits and waits throughout his lifetime for permission to enter a crucial Gate, where the doorkeeper (the first of many) repeatedly refuses him entrance. He tries everything from good behavior to bribes without success. Finally, as the now-aged countryman dies in frustration, he is told that the gate existed only for him, and that it is now being closed. For the countryman (as for Vladimir and Estragon in Beckett's *Waiting for Godot*, and indeed for much modern literature), there is no response.

The Law that governs our existence is all-powerful but irrational; at least it is not to be understood by its human suppliants, a lesson that Kafka could have derived equally well from his readings in the Danish philosopher Søren Kierkegaard, in Friedrich Nietzsche, or in the Jewish Talmud.

The combination of down-to-earth, matter-of-fact setting and unreal or nightmarish events is the hallmark of Kafka's style. His characters speak prosaically and react in a commonsense way when such a response (given the situation) is utterly grotesque. A young businessman is changed overnight into a giant beetle (*The Metamorphosis*) or charged with undefined crimes and finally executed (*The Trial*); a would-be land surveyor is unable to communicate with the castle that employs him and keeps sending incomprehensible messages (*The Castle*); a visitor to a penal colony observes a gigantic machine whose function is to execute condemned criminals by inscribing their sentence deeper and deeper into their flesh (*In the Penal Colony*). The term *surrealist* is often attached to this blend of everyday reality and dream configuration, with its implication of psychic undercurrents and cosmic significance stirring beneath the most ordinary-seeming existence. Kafka, however, had no connection with the Surrealists, whose vision of a miraculous level of existence hidden behind everyday life is the obverse of his heroes' vain attempts to maintain control over the impossible and the absurd.

Kafka's stories are not allegories, although many readers have been tempted to find in them an underlying message. A political reading sees them as indictments of faceless bureaucracy controlling individual lives in the modern totalitarian state. The sense of being found guilty by an entire society recalls the traditional theme of the Wandering Jew, and predicts for many the Holocaust of World War II (in fact, Kafka's three sisters died in concentration camps). His heroes' self-conscious quest to fit into some meaningful structure, their ceaseless attempts to do the right thing when there is no rational way of knowing what that is, is the very picture of absurdity and alienation that existentialist philosophers and writers examined during and after World War II. The assumption that there is a Law, and the presence of protagonists who die in search for purity (*The Hunger Artist*) or in a humble admission of guilt (*The Trial*) allow the stories to be taken as religious metaphors. Kafka's desperately lucid analysis of the way his parents' influence shaped an impressionable child into an unhappy adult (*Letter to My Father*) articulates emotional tangles and parent-child rivalry with an openness and detail that recalls decades of psychoanalytical criticism following Freud. The picture of a sick society where individual rights and sensitivity no longer count and unreasoning torment is visited on the ignorant has been read as an indictment of disintegrating modern culture. Yet no one allegorical interpretation is finally possible, for all these potential meanings overlap as they expand toward social, familial, political, philosophical, and religious dimensions and constitute the richly allusive texture of separate tales by a master storyteller.

The Metamorphosis, Kafka's longest complete work published in his lifetime, is first of all a consummate narrative: the question "What happens next?" never disappears from the moment that Gregor Samsa wakes up to find himself transformed. "It was no dream," no nightmarish fantasy in which Gregor temporarily identified himself with other downtrodden vermin of society. Instead, this grotesque transformation is permanent, a single unshakable fact that renders almost comic his family's calculations and attempts to adjust. "The terror of art," said Kafka in a conversation about *The Metamorphosis*, is that "the dream reveals the reality." This artistic dream, become Gregor's reality, sheds light on the intolerable nature of his former daily existence. The other side of his job is its mechanical rigidity, personal rivalries, and threatening suspicion of any deviation from the norm. Gregor himself is part of this world, as he shows when he fawns on the manager and tries to manipulate him by criticizing their boss.

More disturbing is the transformation that takes place in Gregor's family, where the expected love and support turns into shamed acceptance and animal resentment now that Gregor has let the family down. Mother and sister are ineffectual, and their sympathy is slowly replaced by disgust. Gregor's father quickly reassumes his position of authority and beats the beetle back into his room: first with the businesslike newspaper and manager's cane, and later with a barrage of apples from the family table. Just before his death Gregor has become an "it" whose death is warmly wished by the whole family—and perhaps they are right, in one of Kafka's ironies. The beetle's death brings not remorse but a new lease on life to his family. Weak and passive when Gregor took care of them, they regain strength and vitality under the pressure of earning a living. Mother, father, and sister celebrate Gregor's death with a holiday trip out of town, into the sunshine and open air, where they make plans for the future.

Gregor Samsa may be a pathetic figure but he is not a tragic one. In his passiveness and unvoiced resentment, his willingness to exist at a surface level of adjustment to job and family, he has become an accomplice in his own fate. His descent into animal consciousness is not a true pilgrimage to inner awareness, even though it involves letting go the trappings of civilization. Rather, it is an obscuring of consciousness that is perfectly represented when he is swept out onto the dustheap at the end. From that point on, it is the family's story, continuing a career that has meant death for Gregor and joyous survival for his family, but in which both are reduced to existence on an animal level.

Anthony Thorlby, *Kafka: A Study* (1972), is a brief general introduction. Heinz Politzer, *Franz Kafka: Parable and Paradox* (1966), presents an interesting, readable study of symbolic relationships. Ernest Pawel, *The Nightmare of Reason: A Life of Franz Kafka* (1984), is an excellent contemporary biography with penetrating descriptions of his family and friends. Max Brod, *Franz Kafka: A Biography* (1960), is an early, admiring biography by a close friend and Kafka's executor. Ronald Gray, ed., *Kafka: A Collection of Critical Essays* (1962), is a useful early collection of essays on different works. Harold Bloom, ed., *Franz Kafka's The Metamorphosis* (1988), collects essays on spiritual, metaphorical, formal, social, and psychoanalytic aspects of *The Metamorphosis*. Jack Murray analyzes the sense of space in *The Landscapes of Alienation: Ideological Subversion in Kafka, Celine, and Onetti* (1991). Kurt Fickert, *End of a Mission: Kafka's Search for Truth in His Last Stories* (1993), interprets the stories as metaphors for an autobiographical quest to resolve personal problems.

The Metamorphosis[1]

I

When Gregor Samsa woke up one morning from unsettling dreams, he found himself changed in his bed into a monstrous vermin. He was lying on his back as hard as armor plate, and when he lifted his head a little, he saw his vaulted brown belly, sectioned by arch-shaped ribs, to whose dome the cover, about to slide off completely, could barely cling. His many legs, pitifully thin compared with the size of the rest of him, were waving helplessly before his eyes.

"What's happened to me?" he thought. It was no dream. His room, a

1. Translated by Stanley Corngold.

regular human room, only a little on the small side, lay quiet between the four familiar walls. Over the table, on which an unpacked line of fabric samples was all spread out—Samsa was a traveling salesman—hung the picture which he had recently cut out of a glossy magazine and lodged in a pretty gilt frame. It showed a lady done up in a fur hat and a fur boa, sitting upright and raising up against the viewer a heavy fur muff in which her whole forearm had disappeared.

Gregor's eyes then turned to the window, and the overcast weather—he could hear raindrops hitting against the metal window ledge—completely depressed him. "How about going back to sleep for a few minutes and forgetting all this nonsense," he thought, but that was completely impracticable, since he was used to sleeping on his right side and in his present state could not get into that position. No matter how hard he threw himself onto his right side, he always rocked onto his back again. He must have tried it a hundred times, closing his eyes so as not to have to see his squirming legs, and stopped only when he began to feel a slight, dull pain in his side, which he had never felt before.

"Oh God," he thought, "what a grueling job I've picked. Day in, day out—on the road. The upset of doing business is much worse than the actual business in the home office, and besides, I've got the torture of traveling, worrying about changing trains, eating miserable food at all hours, constantly seeing new faces, no relationships that last or get more intimate. To the devil with it all!" He felt a slight itching up on top of his belly; shoved himself slowly on his back closer to the bedpost, so as to be able to lift his head better; found the itchy spot, studded with small white dots which he had no idea what to make of; and wanted to touch the spot with one of his legs but immediately pulled it back, for the contact sent a cold shiver through him.

He slid back again into his original position. "This getting up so early," he thought, "makes anyone a complete idiot. Human beings have to have their sleep. Other traveling salesmen live like harem women. For instance, when I go back to the hotel before lunch to write up the business I've done, these gentlemen are just having breakfast. That's all I'd have to try with my boss; I'd be fired on the spot. Anyway, who knows if that wouldn't be a very good thing for me. If I didn't hold back for my parents' sake, I would have quit long ago, I would have marched up to the boss and spoken my piece from the bottom of my heart. He would have fallen off the desk! It is funny, too, the way he sits on the desk and talks down from the heights to the employees, especially when they have to come right up close on account of the boss's being hard of hearing. Well, I haven't given up hope completely; once I've gotten the money together to pay off my parents' debt to him—that will probably take another five or six years—I'm going to do it without fail. Then I'm going to make the big break. But for the time being I'd better get up, since my train leaves at five."

And he looked over at the alarm clock, which was ticking on the chest of drawers. "God Almighty!" he thought. It was six-thirty, the hands were quietly moving forward, it was actually past the half-hour, it was already nearly a quarter to. Could it be that the alarm hadn't gone off? You could see from the bed that it was set correctly for four o'clock; it certainly had gone off, too. Yes, but was it possible to sleep quietly through a ringing that made the furniture shake? Well, he certainly hadn't slept quietly, but probably all the more soundly for that. But what should he do now? The next train left at seven o'clock; to make it, he would have to hurry like a madman, and the line of samples wasn't packed yet, and he himself didn't feel especially fresh and ready to march around. And even if he did make the train, he could not avoid getting it from the boss, because the messenger boy had been waiting at the five-o'clock train and would have long ago reported his not showing up. He was a tool of the boss, without brains or backbone. What if he were to say he was sick? But that would be extremely embarrassing and suspicious because during his five years with the firm Gregor had not been sick even once. The boss would be sure to come with the health-insurance doctor, blame his parents for their lazy son, and cut off all excuses by quoting the health-insurance doctor, for whom the world consisted of people who were completely healthy but afraid to work. And, besides, in this case would he be so very wrong? In fact, Gregor felt fine, with the exception of his drowsiness, which was really unnecessary after sleeping so late, and he even had a ravenous appetite.

Just as he was thinking all this over at top speed, without being able to decide to get out of bed—the alarm clock had just struck a quarter to seven—he heard a cautious knocking at the door next to the head of his bed. "Gregor," someone called—it was his mother—"it's a quarter to seven. Didn't you want to catch the train?" What a soft voice! Gregor was shocked to hear his own voice answering, unmistakably his own voice, true, but in which, as if from below, an insistent distressed chirping intruded, which left the clarity of his words intact only for a moment really, before so badly garbling them as they carried that no one could be sure if he had heard right. Gregor had wanted to answer in detail and to explain everything, but, given the circumstances, confined himself to saying, "Yes, yes, thanks, Mother, I'm just getting up." The wooden door must have prevented the change in Gregor's voice from being noticed outside, because his mother was satisfied with this explanation and shuffled off. But their little exchange had made the rest of the family aware that, contrary to expectations, Gregor was still in the house, and already his father was knocking on one of the side doors, feebly but with this fist. "Gregor, Gregor," he called, "what's going on?" And after a little while he called again in a deeper, warning voice, "Gregor! Gregor!" At the other side door, however, his sister moaned gently, "Gregor? Is something the matter with you? Do you want anything?" Toward both sides Gregor answered: "I'm all ready," and made an effort, by meticulous pronunciation and by inserting long pauses between individual words, to eliminate everything from his voice that might betray him. His father went back to his breakfast, but his sister whispered, "Gregor, open up, I'm pleading with you." But Gregor had absolutely no intention of opening the door and complimented himself instead on the precaution he had adopted from his business trips, of locking all the doors during the night even at home.

First of all he wanted to get up quietly, without any excitement; get dressed; and the main thing, have breakfast, and only then think about what to do next, for he saw clearly that in bed he would never think things through to a rational conclusion. He remembered how even in the past he had often felt some kind of slight pain, possibly caused by lying in an uncomfortable position, which, when he got up, turned out to be purely imaginary, and he was eager to see how today's fantasy would gradually fade away. That the change in his voice was nothing more than the first sign of a bad cold, an occupational ailment of the traveling salesman, he had no doubt in the least.

It was very easy to throw off the cover; all he had to do was puff himself up a little, and it fell off by itself. But after this, things got difficult, especially since he was so unusually broad. He would have needed hands and arms to lift himself up, but instead of that he had only his numerous little legs, which were in every different kind of perpetual motion and which, besides, he could not control. If he wanted to bend one, the first thing that happened was that it stretched itself out; and if he finally succeeded in getting this leg to do what he wanted, all the others in the meantime, as if set free, began to work in the most intensely painful agitation. "Just don't stay in bed being useless," Gregor said to himself.

First he tried to get out of bed with the lower part of his body, but this lower part—which by the way he had not seen yet and which he could not form a clear picture of—proved too difficult to budge; it was taking so long; and when finally, almost out of his mind, he lunged forward with all his force, without caring, he had picked the wrong direction and slammed himself violently against the lower bedpost, and the searing pain he felt taught him that exactly the lower part of his body was, for the moment anyway, the most sensitive.

He therefore tried to get the upper part of his body out of bed first and warily turned his head toward the edge of the bed. This worked easily, and in spite of its width and weight, the mass of his body finally followed, slowly, the movement of his head. But when at last he stuck his head over the edge of the bed into the air, he got too scared to continue any further, since if he finally let himself fall in this position, it would be a miracle if he didn't injure his head. And just now he had better not for the life of him lose consciousness; he would rather stay in bed.

But when, once again, after the same exertion, he lay in his original position, sighing, and again watched his little legs struggling, if possible more fiercely, with each other and saw no way of bringing peace and order into this mindless motion, he again told himself that it was impossible for him to stay in bed and that the most rational thing was to make any sacrifice for even the smallest hope of freeing himself from the bed. But at the same time he did not forget to remind himself occasionally that thinking things over calmly—indeed, as calmly as possible—was much better than jumping to desperate decisions. At such moments he fixed his eyes as sharply as possible on the window, but unfortunately there was little confidence and cheer to be gotten from the view of the morning fog, which shrouded even the other side of the narrow street. "Seven o'clock already," he said to himself as the alarm clock struck again, "seven o'clock already and still such a fog." And for a little while he lay quietly, breathing shallowly, as if expecting, perhaps, from the complete silence the return of things to the way they really and naturally were.

But then he said to himself, "Before it strikes a quarter past seven, I must be completely out of bed without fail. Anyway, by that time someone from the firm will be here to find out where I am, since the office opens before seven." And now he started rocking the complete length of his body out of the bed with a smooth rhythm. If he let himself topple out of bed in this way, his head, which on falling he planned to lift up sharply, would presumably remain unharmed. His back seemed to be hard; nothing was likely to happen to it when it fell onto the carpet. His biggest misgiving came from his concern about the loud crash that was bound to occur and would probably create, if not terror, at least anxiety behind all the doors. But that would have to be risked.

When Gregor's body already projected halfway out of bed—the new method was more of a game than a struggle, he only had to keep on rocking and jerking himself along—he thought how simple everything would be if he could get some help. Two strong persons—he thought of his father and the maid—would have been completely sufficient; they would only have had to shove their arms under his arched back, in this way scoop him off the bed, bend down with their burden, and then just be careful and patient while he managed to swing himself down onto the floor, where his little legs would hopefully acquire some purpose. Well, leaving out the fact that the doors were locked, should he really call for help? In spite of all his miseries, he could not repress a smile at this thought.

He was already so far along that when he rocked more strongly he could hardly keep his balance, and very soon he would have to commit himself, because in five minutes it would be a quarter past seven—when the doorbell rang. "It's someone from the firm," he said to himself and almost froze, while his little legs only danced more quickly. For a moment everything remained quiet. "They're not going to answer," Gregor said to himself, captivated by some senseless hope. But then, of course, the maid went to the door as usual with her firm stride and opened up. Gregor only had to hear the visitor's first word of greeting to know who it was—the office manager himself. Why was only Gregor condemned to work for a firm where at the slightest omission they immediately suspected the worst? Were all employees louts without exception, wasn't there a single loyal, dedicated worker among them who, when he had not fully utilized a few hours of the morning for the firm, was driven half-mad by pangs of conscience and was actually unable to get out of bed? Really, wouldn't it have been enough to send one of the apprentices to find out—if this prying were absolutely necessary—did the manager himself have to come, and did the whole innocent family have to be shown in this way that the investigation of this suspicious affair could be entrusted only to the intellect of the manager? And more as a result of the excitement produced in Gregor by these thoughts than as a result of any real decision, he swung himself out of bed with all his might. There was a loud thump, but it was not a real crash. The fall was broken a little by the carpet, and Gregor's back was more elastic than he had thought, which explained the not very noticeable muffled sound. Only he had not held his head carefully enough and hit it; he turned it and rubbed it on the carpet in anger and pain.

"Something fell in there," said the manager in the room on the left. Gregor tried to imagine whether something like what had happened to him today could one day happen even to the manager; you really had to grant the possibility. But, as if in rude reply to this question, the manager took a few decisive steps in the next room and made his patent leather boots creak. From the room on the right his sister whispered, to inform Gregor, "Gregor, the manager is here." "I know," Gregor said to himself; but he did not dare raise his voice enough for his sister to hear.

"Gregor," his father now said from the room on the left, "the manager has come and wants to be informed why you didn't catch the early train. We don't know what we should say to him. Besides, he wants to speak to you personally. So please open the door. He will certainly be so kind as to excuse the disorder of the room." "Good morning, Mr. Samsa," the manager called in a friendly voice. "There's something the matter with him," his mother said to the manager while his father was still at the door, talking. "Believe me, sir, there's something the matter with him. Otherwise how would Gregor have missed a train? That boy has nothing on his mind but the business. It's almost begun to rile me that he never goes out nights. He's been back in the city for eight days now, but every night he's been home. He sits there with us at the table, quietly reading the paper or studying timetables. It's already a distraction for him when he's busy working with his fretsaw. For instance, in the span of two or three evenings he carved a little frame. You'll be amazed how pretty it is; it's hanging inside his room. You'll see it right away when Gregor opens the door. You know, I'm glad that you've come, sir. We would never have gotten Gregor to open the door by ourselves; he's so stubborn. And there's certainly something wrong with him, even though he said this morning there wasn't." "I'm coming right away," said Gregor slowly and deliberately, not moving in order not to miss a word of the conversation. "I haven't any other explanation myself," said the manager. "I hope it's nothing serious. On the other hand, I must say that we businessmen—fortunately or unfortunately, whichever you prefer—very often simply have to overcome a slight indisposition for business reasons." "So can the manager come in now?" asked his father, impatient, and knocked on the door again. "No," said Gregor. In the room on the left there was an embarrassing silence; in the room on the right his sister began to sob.

Why didn't his sister go in to the others? She had probably just got out of bed and not even started to get dressed. Then what was she crying about? Because he didn't get up and didn't let the manager in, because he was in danger of losing his job, and because then the boss would start hounding his parents about the old debts? For the time being, certainly, her worries were unnecessary. Gregor was still here and hadn't the slightest intention of letting the family down. True, at the moment he was lying on the carpet, and no one knowing his condition could seriously have expected him to let the manager in. But just because of this slight discourtesy, for which an appropriate excuse would easily be found later on, Gregor could not simply be dismissed. And to Gregor it seemed much more sensible to leave him alone now than to bother him with crying and persuasion. But it was just the uncertainty that was tormenting the others and excused their behavior.

"Mr. Samsa," the manager now called, raising his voice, "what's the matter? You barricade yourself in your room, answer only 'yes' and 'no,' cause your parents serious, unnecessary worry, and you neglect—I mention this only in passing—your duties to the firm in a really shocking manner. I am speaking here in the name of your parents and of your employer and ask you in all seriousness for an immediate, clear explanation. I'm amazed, amazed. I thought I knew you to be a quiet, reasonable person, and now you suddenly seem to want to start strutting about, flaunting strange whims. The head of the firm did suggest to me this morning a possible explanation for your tardiness—it concerned the cash payments recently entrusted to you—but really, I practically gave my word of honor that this explanation could not be right. But now, seeing your incomprehensible obstinacy, I am about to lose even the slightest desire to stick up for you in any way at all. And your job is not the most secure. Originally I intended to tell you all this in private, but since you make me waste my time here for nothing, I don't see why your parents shouldn't hear too. Your performance of late has been very unsatisfactory; I know it is not the best season for doing business, we all recognize that; but a season for not doing any business, there is no such thing, Mr. Samsa, such a thing cannot be tolerated."

"But sir," cried Gregor, beside himself, in his excitement forgetting everything else, "I'm just opening up, in a minute. A slight indisposition, a dizzy spell, prevented me from getting up. I'm still in bed. But I already feel fine again. I'm just getting out of bed. Just be patient for a minute! I'm not as well as I thought yet. But really I'm fine. How something like this could just take a person by surprise! Only last night I was fine, my parents can tell you, or wait, last night I already had a slight premonition. They must have been able to tell by looking at me. Why didn't I report it to the office! But you always think that you'll get over a sickness without staying home. Sir! Spare my parents! There's no basis for any of the accusations that you're making against me now; no one has ever said a word to me about them. Perhaps you haven't seen the last orders I sent in. Anyway, I'm still going on the road with the eight o'clock train; these few hours of rest have done me good. Don't let me keep you, sir. I'll be at the office myself right away, and be so kind as to tell them this, and give my respects to the head of the firm."

And while Gregor hastily blurted all this out, hardly knowing what he was saying, he had easily approached the chest of drawers, probably as a result of the practice he had already gotten in bed, and now he tried to raise himself up against it. He actually intended to open the door, actually present himself and speak to the manager; he was eager to find out what the others, who were now so anxious to see him, would say at the sight of him. If they were shocked, then Gregor had no further responsibility and could be calm. But if they took everything calmly, then he, too, had no reason to get excited and could, if he hurried, actually be at the station by eight o'clock. At first he slid off the polished chest of drawers a few times,

was unable to work, but that's exactly the right time to remember his past accomplishments and to consider that later on, when the obstacle has been removed, he's bound to work all the harder and more efficiently. I'm under so many obligations to the head of the firm, as you know very well. Besides, I also have my parents and my sister to worry about. I'm in a tight spot, but I'll also work my way out again. Don't make things harder for me than they already are. Stick up for me in the office, please. Traveling salesmen aren't well liked there, I know. People think they make a fortune leading the gay life. No one has any particular reason to rectify this prejudice. But you, sir, you have a better perspective on things than the rest of the office, an even better perspective, just between the two of us, than the head of the firm himself, who in his capacity as owner easily lets his judgment be swayed against an employee. And you also know very well that the traveling salesman, who is out of the office practically the whole year round, can so easily become the victim of gossip, coincidences, and unfounded accusations, against which he's completely unable to defend himself, since in most cases he knows nothing at all about them except when he returns exhausted from a trip, and back home gets to suffer on his own person the grim consequences, which can no longer be traced back to their causes. Sir, don't go away without a word to tell me you think I'm at least partly right!"

But at Gregor's first words the manager had already turned away and with curled lips looked back at Gregor only over his twitching shoulder. And during Gregor's speech he did not stand still for a minute but, without letting Gregor out of his sight, backed toward the door, yet very gradually, as if there were some secret prohibition against leaving the room. He was already in the foyer, and from the sudden movement with which he took his last step from the living room, one might have thought he had just burned the sole of his foot. In the foyer, however, he stretched his right hand far out toward the staircase, as if nothing less than an unearthly deliverance were awaiting him there.

Gregor realized that he must on no account let the manager go away in this mood if his position in the firm were not to be jeopardized in the extreme. His parents did not understand this too well; in the course of the years they had formed the conviction that Gregor was set for life in this firm; and furthermore, they were so preoccupied with their immediate troubles that they had lost all consideration for the future. But Gregor had this forethought. The manager must be detained, calmed down, convinced, and finally won over; Gregor's and the family's future depended on it! If only his sister had been there! She was perceptive; she had already begun to cry when Gregor was still lying calmly on his back. And certainly the manager, this ladies' man, would have listened to her; she would have shut the front door and in the foyer talked him out of his scare. But his sister was not there, Gregor had to handle the situation himself. And without stopping to realize that he had no idea what his new faculties of movement were, and without stopping to realize either that his speech had possibly—indeed, probably—not been understood again, he let go of the wing of the door; he shoved himself through the opening, intending to go to the manager, who was already on the landing, ridiculously holding onto the banisters with both hands; but groping for support, Gregor immediately fell down with a little cry onto his numerous little legs. This had hardly happened when for the first time that morning he had a feeling of physical well-being; his little legs were on firm ground; they obeyed him completely, as he noted to his joy; they even strained to carry him away wherever he wanted to go; and he already believed that final recovery from all his sufferings was imminent. But at that very moment, as he lay on the floor rocking with repressed motion, not far from his mother and just opposite her, she, who had seemed so completely self-absorbed, all at once jumped up, her arms stretched wide, her fingers spread, and cried, "Help, for God's sake, help!" held her head bent as if to see Gregor better, but inconsistently darted madly backward instead; had forgotten that the table laden with the breakfast dishes stood behind her; sat down on it hastily, as if her thoughts were elsewhere, when she reached it; and did not seem to notice at all that near her the big coffeepot had been knocked over and coffee was pouring in a steady stream onto the rug.

"Mother, Mother," said Gregor softly and looked up at her. For a minute the manager had completely slipped his mind; on the other hand at the sight of the spilling coffee he could not resist snapping his jaws several times in the air. At this his mother screamed once more, fled from the table, and fell into the arms of his father, who came rushing up to her. But Gregor had no time now for his parents; the manager was already on the stairs; with his chin on the banister, he was taking a last look back. Gregor was off to a running start, to be as sure as possible of catching up with him; the manager must have suspected something like this, for he leaped down several steps and disappeared; but still he shouted "Agh," and the sound carried through the whole staircase. Unfortunately the manager's flight now seemed to confuse his father completely, who had been relatively calm until now, for instead of running after the manager himself, or at least not hindering Gregor in his pursuit, he seized in his right hand the manager's cane, which had been left behind on a chair with his hat and overcoat, picked up in his left hand a heavy newspaper from the table, and stamping his feet, started brandishing the cane and the newspaper to drive Gregor back into his room. No plea of Gregor's helped, no plea was even understood; however humbly he might turn his head, his father merely stamped his feet more forcefully. Across the room his mother had thrown open a window in spite of the cool weather, and leaning out, she buried her face, far outside the window, in her hands. Between the alley and the staircase a strong draft was created, the window curtains blew in, the newspapers on the table rustled, single sheets fluttered across the floor. Pitilessly his father came on, hissing like a wild man. Now Gregor had not had any practice at all walking in reverse, it was really very slow going. If Gregor had only been allowed to turn around, he could have gotten into his room right away, but he was afraid to make his father impatient by this time-consuming gyration, and at any minute the cane in his father's hand threatened to come down on his back or his head with a deadly blow. Finally, however, Gregor had no choice, for he noticed with horror that in reverse he could not even keep going in one direction; and so, incessantly throwing uneasy side-glances at his father, he began to turn around as quickly as possible, in reality turning only very slowly. Perhaps his father realized his good intentions, for he did not interfere with him; instead, he even now and then directed the maneuver from afar with the tip of his cane. If only his father did not keep making this intolerable hissing sound! It made Gregor lose his head completely. He had almost finished the turn when—his mind continually on this hissing—he made a mistake and even started turning back around to his original position. But when he had at last successfully managed to get his head in front of the opened door, it turned out that his body was too broad to get through as it was. Of course in his father's present state of mind it did not even remotely occur to him to open the other wing of the door in order to give Gregor enough room to pass through. He had only the fixed idea that Gregor must return to his room as quickly as possible. He would never have allowed the complicated preliminaries Gregor needed to go through in order to stand up on one end and perhaps in this way fit through the door. Instead he drove Gregor on, as if there were no obstacle, with exceptional loudness; the voice behind Gregor did not sound like that of only a single father; now this was really no joke any more, and Gregor forced himself—come what may—into the doorway. One side of his body rose up, he lay lop-sided in the opening, one of his flanks was scraped raw, ugly blotches marred the white door, soon he got stuck and could not have budged any more by himself, his little legs on one side dangled tremblingly in midair, those on the other were painfully crushed against the floor—when from behind his father gave him a hard shove, which was truly his salvation, and bleeding profusely, he flew far into his room. The door was slammed shut with the cane, then at last everything was quiet.

II

It was already dusk when Gregor awoke from his deep, comalike sleep. Even if he had not been disturbed, he would certainly not have woken up much later, for he felt that he had rested and slept long enough, but it seemed to him that a hurried step and a cautious shutting of the door leading to the foyer had awakened him. The light of the electric street-lamps lay in pallid streaks on the ceiling and on the upper parts of the furniture, but underneath, where Gregor was, it was dark. Groping clumsily with his antennae, which he was only now beginning to appreciate, he slowly dragged himself toward the door to see what had been happening there. His left side felt like one single long, unpleasantly tautening scar, and he actually had to limp on his two rows of legs. Besides, one little leg had been seriously injured in the course of the morning's events—it was almost a miracle that only one had been injured—and dragged along lifelessly.

Only after he got to the door did he notice what had really attracted him—the smell of something to eat. For there stood a bowl filled with fresh milk, in which small slices of white bread were floating. He could almost have laughed for joy, since he was even hungrier than he had been in the morning, and he immediately dipped his head into the milk, almost to over his eyes. But he soon drew it back again in disappointment; not only because he had difficulty eating on account of the soreness in his left side—and he could eat only if his whole panting body cooperated—but because he didn't like the milk at all, although it used to be his favorite drink, and that was certainly why his sister had put it in the room; in fact, he turned away from the bowl almost with repulsion and crawled back to the middle of the room.

In the living room, as Gregor saw through the crack in the door, the gas had been lit, but while at this hour of the day his father was in the habit of reading the afternoon newspaper in a loud voice to his mother and sometimes to his sister too, now there wasn't a sound. Well, perhaps this custom of reading aloud, which his sister was always telling him and writing him about, had recently been discontinued altogether. But in all the other rooms too it was just as still, although the apartment certainly was not empty. "What a quiet life the family has been leading," Gregor said to himself, and while he stared rigidly in front of him into the darkness, he felt very proud that he had been able to provide such a life in so nice an apartment for his parents and his sister. But what now if all the peace, the comfort, the contentment were to come to a horrible end? In order not to get involved in such thoughts, Gregor decided to keep moving, and he crawled up and down the room.

During the long evening first one of the side doors and then the other was opened a small crack and quickly shut again; someone had probably had the urge to come in and then had had second thoughts. Gregor now settled into position right by the living-room door, determined somehow to get the hesitating visitor to come in, or at least to find out who it might be; but the door was not opened again, and Gregor waited in vain. In the morning, when the doors had been locked, everyone had wanted to come in; now that he had opened one of the doors and the others had evidently been opened during the day, no one came in, and now the keys were even inserted on the outside.

It was late at night when the light finally went out in the living room, and now it was easy for Gregor to tell that his parents and his sister had stayed up so long, since, as he could distinctly hear, all three were now retiring on tiptoe. Certainly no one would come in to Gregor until the morning; and so he had ample time to consider undisturbed how best to rearrange his life. But the empty high-ceilinged room in which he was forced to lie flat on the floor made him nervous, without his being able to tell why—since it was, after all, the room in which he had lived for the past five years—and turning half unconsciously and not without a slight feeling of shame, he scuttled under the couch where, although his back was a little crushed and he could not raise his head any more, he immediately felt very comfortable and was only sorry that his body was too wide to go completely under the couch.

There he stayed the whole night, which he spent partly in a sleepy trance, from which hunger pangs kept waking him with a start, partly in worries and vague hopes, all of which, however, led to the conclusion that for the time being he would have to lie low and, by being patient and showing his family every possible consideration, help them bear the inconvenience which he simply had to cause them in his present condition.

Early in the morning—it was still almost night—Gregor had the opportunity of testing the strength of the resolutions he had just made, for his
sister, almost fully dressed, opened the door from the foyer and looked in
eagerly. She did not see him right away, but when she caught sight of him
under the couch—God, he had to be somewhere, he couldn't just fly
away—she became so frightened that she lost control of herself and
slammed the door shut again. But, as if she felt sorry for her behavior, she
immediately opened the door again and came in on tiptoe, as if she were
visiting someone seriously ill or perhaps even a stranger. Gregor had
pushed his head forward just to the edge of the couch and was watching
her. Would she notice that he had left the milk standing, and not because
he hadn't been hungry, and would she bring in a dish of something he'd
like better? If she were not going to do it of her own free will, he would
rather starve than call it to her attention, although, really, he felt an enormous urge to shoot out from under the couch, throw himself at his sister's
feet, and beg her for something good to eat. But his sister noticed at once,
to her astonishment, that the bowl was still full, only a little milk was
spilled around it; she picked it up immediately—not with her bare hands,
of course, but with a rag—and carried it out. Gregor was extremely curious
to know what she would bring him instead, and he racked his brains on
the subject. But he would never have been able to guess what his sister,
in the goodness of her heart, actually did. To find out his likes and dislikes,
she brought him a wide assortment of things, all spread out on an old
newspaper: old, half-rotten vegetables; bones left over from the evening
meal, caked with congealed white sauce; some raisins and almonds; a
piece of cheese, which two days before Gregor had declared inedible; a
plain slice of bread, a slice of bread and butter, and one with butter and
salt. In addition to all this she put down some water in the bowl apparently
permanently earmarked for Gregor's use. And out of a sense of delicacy,
since she knew that Gregor would not eat in front of her, she left hurriedly
and even turned the key, just so that Gregor should know that he might
make himself as comfortable as he wanted. Gregor's legs began whirring
now that he was going to eat. Besides, his bruises must have completely
healed, since he no longer felt any handicap, and marveling at this he
thought how, over a month ago, he had cut his finger very slightly with a
knife and how this wound was still hurting him only the day before yesterday. "Have I become less sensitive?" he thought, already sucking greedily
at the cheese, which had immediately and forcibly attracted him ahead of
all the other dishes. One right after the other, and with eyes streaming
with tears of contentment, he devoured the cheese, the vegetables, and
the sauce; the fresh foods, on the other hand, he did not care for; he
couldn't even stand their smell and even dragged the things he wanted to
eat a bit farther away. He had finished with everything long since and was
just lying lazily at the same spot when his sister slowly turned the key as a
sign for him to withdraw. That immediately startled him, although he was
almost asleep, and he scuttled under the couch again. But it took great
self-control for him to stay under the couch even for the short time his
sister was in the room, since his body had become a little bloated from the
heavy meal, and in his cramped position he could hardly breathe. In

between slight attacks of suffocation he watched with bulging eyes as his unsuspecting sister took a broom and swept up, not only his leavings, but even the foods which Gregor had left completely untouched—as if they too were no longer usable—and dumping everything hastily into a pail, which she covered with a wooden lid, she carried everything out. She had hardly turned her back when Gregor came out from under the couch, stretching and puffing himself up.

This, then, was the way Gregor was fed each day, once in the morning, when his parents and the maid were still asleep, and a second time in the afternoon after everyone had had dinner, for then his parents took a short nap again, and the maid could be sent out by his sister on some errand. Certainly they did not want him to starve either, but perhaps they would not have been able to stand knowing any more about his meals than from hearsay, or perhaps his sister wanted to spare them even what was possibly only a minor torment, for really, they were suffering enough as it was.

Gregor could not find out what excuses had been made to get rid of the doctor and the locksmith on that first morning, for since the others could not understand what he said, it did not occur to any of them, not even to his sister, that he could understand what they said, and so he had to be satisfied, when his sister was in the room, with only occasionally hearing her sighs and appeals to the saints. It was only later, when she had begun to get used to everything—there could never, of course, be any question of a complete adjustment—that Gregor sometimes caught a remark which was meant to be friendly or could be interpreted as such. "Oh, he liked what he had today," she would say when Gregor had tucked away a good helping, and in the opposite case, which gradually occurred more and more frequently, she used to say, almost sadly, "He's left everything again."

But if Gregor could not get any news directly, he overheard a great deal from the neighboring rooms, and as soon as he heard voices, he would immediately run to the door concerned and press his whole body against it. Especially in the early days, there was no conversation that was not somehow about him, if only implicitly. For two whole days there were family consultations at every mealtime about how they should cope; this was also the topic of discussion between meals, for at least two members of the family were always at home, since no one probably wanted to stay home alone and it was impossible to leave the apartment completely empty. Besides, on the very first day the maid—it was not completely clear what and how much she knew of what had happened—had begged his mother on bended knees to dismiss her immediately; and when she said goodbye a quarter of an hour later, she thanked them in tears for the dismissal, as if for the greatest favor that had ever been done to her in this house, and made a solemn vow, without anyone asking her for it, not to give anything away to anyone.

Now his sister, working with her mother, had to do the cooking too; of course that did not cause her much trouble, since they hardly ate anything. Gregor was always hearing one of them pleading in vain with one of the others to eat and getting no answer except, "Thanks, I've had enough," or something similar. They did not seem to drink anything either. His sister often asked her father if he wanted any beer and gladly offered to go out for it herself; and when he did not answer, she said, in order to remove any hesitation on his part, that she could also send the janitor's wife to get it, but then his father finally answered with a definite "No," and that was the end of that.

In the course of the very first day his father explained the family's financial situation and prospects to both the mother and the sister. From time to time he got up from the table to get some kind of receipt or notebook out of the little strongbox he had rescued from the collapse of his business five years before. Gregor heard him open the complicated lock and secure it again after taking out what he had been looking for. These explanations by his father were to some extent the first pleasant news Gregor had heard since his imprisonment. He had always believed that his father had not been able to save a penny from the business, at least his father had never told him anything to the contrary, and Gregor, for his part, had never asked him any questions. In those days Gregor's sole concern had been to do everything in his power to make the family forget as quickly as possible the business disaster which had plunged everyone into a state of total despair. And so he had begun to work with special ardor and had risen almost overnight from stock clerk to traveling salesman, which of course had opened up very different money-making possibilities, and in no time his successes on the job were transformed, by means of commissions, into hard cash that could be plunked down on the table at home in front of his astonished and delighted family. Those had been wonderful times, and they had never returned, at least not with the same glory, although later on Gregor earned enough money to meet the expenses of the entire family and actually did so. They had just gotten used to it, the family as well as Gregor, the money was received with thanks and given with pleasure, but no special feeling of warmth went with it any more. Only his sister had remained close to Gregor, and it was his secret plan that she who, unlike him, loved music and could play the violin movingly, should be sent next year to the Conservatory, regardless of the great expense involved, which could surely be made up for in some other way. Often during Gregor's short stays in the city, the Conservatory would come up in his conversations with his sister, but always merely as a beautiful dream which was not supposed to come true, and his parents were not happy to hear even these innocent allusions; but Gregor had very concrete ideas on the subject and he intended solemnly to announce his plan on Christmas Eve.

Thoughts like these, completely useless in his present state, went through his head as he stood glued to the door, listening. Sometimes out of general exhaustion he could not listen any more and let his head bump carelessly against the door, but immediately pulled it back again, for even the slight noise he made by doing this had been heard in the next room and made them all lapse into silence. "What's he carrying on about in there now?" said his father after a while, obviously turning toward the door, and only then would the interrupted conversation gradually be resumed.

Gregor now learned in a thorough way—for his father was in the habit of often repeating himself in his explanations, partly because he himself had not dealt with these matters for a long time, partly, too, because his mother did not understand everything the first time around—that in spite of all their misfortunes a bit of capital, a very little bit, certainly, was still intact from the old days, which in the meantime had increased a little through the untouched interest. But besides that, the money Gregor had brought home every month—he had kept only a few dollars for himself— had never been completely used up and had accumulated into a tidy principal. Behind his door Gregor nodded emphatically, delighted at this unexpected foresight and thrift. Of course he actually could have paid off more of his father's debt to the boss with this extra money, and the day on which he could have gotten rid of his job would have been much closer, but now things were undoubtedly better the way his father had arranged them.

Now this money was by no means enough to let the family live off the interest; the principal was perhaps enough to support the family for one year, or at the most two, but that was all there was. So it was just a sum that really should not be touched and that had to be put away for a rainy day; but the money to live on would have to be earned. Now his father was still healthy, certainly, but he was an old man who had not worked for the past five years and who in any case could not be expected to undertake too much; during these five years, which were the first vacation of his hard-working yet unsuccessful life, he had gained a lot of weight and as a result had become fairly sluggish. And was his old mother now supposed to go out and earn money, when she suffered from asthma, when a walk through the apartment was already an ordeal for her, and when she spent every other day lying on the sofa under the open window, gasping for breath? And was his sister now supposed to work—who for all her seventeen years was still a child and whom it would be such a pity to deprive of the life she had led until now, which had consisted of wearing pretty clothes, sleeping late, helping in the house, enjoying a few modest amusements, and above all playing the violin? At first, whenever the conversation turned to the necessity of earning money, Gregor would let go of the door and throw himself down on the cool leather sofa which stood beside it, for he felt hot with shame and grief.

Often he lay there the whole long night through, not sleeping a wink and only scrabbling on the leather for hours on end. Or, not balking at the huge effort of pushing an armchair to the window, he would crawl up to the window sill and, propped up in the chair, lean against the window, evidently in some sort of remembrance of the feeling of freedom he used to have from looking out the window. For, in fact, from day to day he saw things even a short distance away less and less distinctly; the hospital opposite, which he used to curse because he saw so much of it, was now completely beyond his range of vision, and if he had not been positive that he was living in Charlotte Street—a quiet but still very much a city street— he might have believed that he was looking out of his window into a desert where the gray sky and the gray earth were indistinguishably fused. It took his observant sister only twice to notice that his armchair was standing by the window for her to push the chair back to the same place by the window each time she had finished cleaning the room, and from then on she even left the inside casement of the window open.

If Gregor had only been able to speak to his sister and thank her for everything she had to do for him, he could have accepted her services more easily; as it was, they caused him pain. Of course his sister tried to ease the embarrassment of the whole situation as much as possible, and as time went on, she naturally managed it better and better, but in time Gregor, too, saw things much more clearly. Even the way she came in was terrible for him. Hardly had she entered the room than she would run straight to the window without taking time to close the door—though she was usually so careful to spare everyone the sight of Gregor's room—then tear open the casements with eager hands, almost as if she were suffocating, and remain for a little while at the window even in the coldest weather, breathing deeply. With this racing and crashing she frightened Gregor twice a day; the whole time he cowered under the couch, and yet he knew very well that she would certainly have spared him this if only she had found it possible to stand being in a room with him with the window closed.

One time—it must have been a month since Gregor's metamorphosis, and there was certainly no particular reason any more for his sister to be astonished at Gregor's appearance—she came a little earlier than usual and caught Gregor still looking out the window, immobile and so in an excellent position to be terrifying. It would not have surprised Gregor if she had not come in, because his position prevented her from immediately opening the window, but not only did she not come in, she even sprang back and locked the door; a stranger might easily have thought that Gregor had been lying in wait for her, wanting to bite her. Of course Gregor immediately hid under the couch, but he had to wait until noon before his sister came again, and she seemed much more uneasy than usual. He realized from this that the sight of him was still repulsive to her and was bound to remain repulsive to her in the future, and that she probably had to overcome a lot of resistance not to run away at the sight of even the small part of his body that jutted out from under the couch. So, to spare her even this sight, one day he carried the sheet on his back to the couch—the job took four hours—and arranged it in such a way that he was now completely covered up and his sister could not see him even when she stooped. If she had considered this sheet unnecessary, then of course she could have removed it, for it was clear enough that it could not be for his own pleasure that Gregor shut himself off altogether, but she left the sheet the way it was, and Gregor thought that he had even caught a grateful look when one time he cautiously lifted the sheet a little with his head in order to see how his sister was taking the new arrangement.

During the first two weeks, his parents could not bring themselves to come in to him, and often he heard them say how much they appreciated his sister's work, whereas until now they had frequently been annoyed with her because she had struck them as being a little useless. But now both of them, his father and his mother, often waited outside Gregor's room while his sister straightened it up, and as soon as she came out she had to tell them in great detail how the room looked, what Gregor had eaten, how he had behaved this time, and whether he had perhaps shown a little improvement. His mother, incidentally, began relatively soon to want to visit Gregor, but his father and his sister at first held her back with reasonable arguments to which Gregor listened very attentively and of which he whole-heartedly approved. But later she had to be restrained by force, and then when she cried out, "Let me go to Gregor, he is my unfortunate boy! Don't you understand that I have to go to him?" Gregor thought that it might be a good idea after all if his mother did come in, not every day of course, but perhaps once a week; she could still do everything much better than his sister, who, for all her courage, was still only a child and in the final analysis had perhaps taken on such a difficult assignment only out of childish flightiness.

Gregor's desire to see his mother was soon fulfilled. During the day Gregor did not want to show himself at the window, if only out of consideration for his parents, but he couldn't crawl very far on his few square yards of floor space, either; he could hardly put up with just lying still even at night; eating soon stopped giving him the slightest pleasure, so, as a distraction, he adopted the habit of crawling crisscross over the walls and the ceiling. He especially liked hanging from the ceiling; it was completely different from lying on the floor; one could breathe more freely; a faint swinging sensation went through the body; and in the almost happy absent-mindedness which Gregor felt up there, it could happen to his own surprise that he let go and plopped onto the floor. But now, of course, he had much better control of his body than before and did not hurt himself even from such a big drop. His sister immediately noticed the new entertainment Gregor had discovered for himself—after all, he left behind traces of his sticky substance wherever he crawled—and so she got it into her head to make it possible for Gregor to crawl on an altogether wider scale by taking out the furniture which stood in his way—mainly the chest of drawers and the desk. But she was not able to do this by herself; she did not dare ask her father for help; the maid would certainly not have helped her, for although this girl, who was about sixteen, was bravely sticking it out after the previous cook had left, she had asked for the favor of locking herself in the kitchen at all times and of only opening the door on special request. So there was nothing left for his sister to do except to get her mother one day when her father was out. And his mother did come, with exclamations of excited joy, but she grew silent at the door of Gregor's room. First his sister looked to see, of course, that everything in the room was in order; only then did she let her mother come in. Hurrying as fast as he could, Gregor had pulled the sheet down lower still and pleated it more tightly—it really looked just like a sheet accidentally thrown over the couch. This time Gregor also refrained from spying from under the sheet; he renounced seeing his mother for the time being and was simply happy that she had come after all. "Come on, you can't see him," his sister said, evidently leading her mother in by the hand. Now Gregor could hear the two frail women moving the old chest of drawers—heavy for anyone— from its place and his sister insisting on doing the harder part of the job herself, ignoring the warnings of her mother, who was afraid that she would overexert herself. It went on for a long time. After struggling for a good quarter of an hour, his mother said that they had better leave the chest where it was, because, in the first place, it was too heavy, they would not finish before his father came, and with the chest in the middle of the room, Gregor would be completely barricaded; and, in the second place, it was not at all certain that they were doing Gregor a favor by removing his furniture. To her the opposite seemed to be the case; the sight of the bare wall was heart-breaking; and why shouldn't Gregor also have the same feeling, since he had been used to his furniture for so long and would feel abandoned in the empty room. "And doesn't it look," his mother concluded very softly—in fact she had been almost whispering the whole time, as if she wanted to avoid letting Gregor, whose exact where-abouts she did not know, hear even the sound of her voice, for she was convinced that he did not understand the words—"and doesn't it look as if by removing his furniture we were showing him that we have given up all hope of his getting better and are leaving him to his own devices without any consideration? I think the best thing would be to try to keep the room exactly the way it was before, so that when Gregor comes back to us again, he'll find everything unchanged and can forget all the more easily what's happened in the meantime."

When he heard his mother's words, Gregor realized that the monotony of family life, combined with the fact that not a soul had addressed a word directly to him, must have addled his brain in the course of the past two months, for he could not explain to himself in any other way how in all seriousness he could have been anxious to have his room cleared out. Had he really wanted to have his warm room, comfortably fitted with furniture that had always been in the family, changed into a cave, in which, of course, he would be able to crawl around unhampered in all directions but at the cost of simultaneously, rapidly, and totally forgetting his human past? Even now he had been on the verge of forgetting, and only his mother's voice, which he had not heard for so long, had shaken him up. Nothing should be removed; everything had to stay; he could not do without the beneficial influence of the furniture on his state of mind; and if the furniture prevented him from carrying on this senseless crawling around, then that was no loss but rather a great advantage.

But his sister unfortunately had a different opinion; she had become accustomed, certainly not entirely without justification, to adopt with her parents the role of the particularly well-qualified expert whenever Gregor's affairs were being discussed; and so her mother's advice was now sufficient reason for her to insist, not only on the removal of the chest of drawers and the desk, which was all she had been planning at first, but also on the removal of all the furniture with the exception of the indispensable couch. Of course it was not only childish defiance and the self-confidence she had recently acquired so unexpectedly and at such a cost that led her to make this demand; she had in fact noticed that Gregor needed plenty of room to crawl around in; and on the other hand, as best she could tell, he never used the furniture at all. Perhaps, however, the romantic enthusiasm of girls her age, which seeks to indulge itself at every opportunity, played a part, by tempting her to make Gregor's situation even more terrifying in order that she might do even more for him. Into a room in which Gregor ruled the bare walls all alone, no human being beside Grete was ever likely to set foot.

And so she did not let herself be swerved from her decision by her mother, who, besides, from the sheer anxiety of being in Gregor's room, seemed unsure of herself, soon grew silent, and helped her daughter as best she could to get the chest of drawers out of the room. Well, in a pinch Gregor could do without the chest, but the desk had to stay. And hardly had the women left the room with the chest, squeezing against it and groaning, than Gregor stuck his head out from under the couch to see how he could feel his way into the situation as considerately as possible. But unfortunately it had to be his mother who came back first, while in the next room Grete was clasping the chest and rocking it back and forth by herself, without of course budging it from the spot. His mother, how-ever, was not used to the sight of Gregor, he could have made her ill, and so Gregor, frightened, scuttled in reverse to the far end of the couch but could not stop the sheet from shifting a little at the front. That was enough to put his mother on the alert. She stopped, stood still for a moment, and then went back to Grete.

Although Gregor told himself over and over again that nothing special was happening, only a few pieces of furniture were being moved, he soon had to admit that this coming and going of the women, their little calls to each other, the scraping of the furniture along the floor had the effect on him of a great turmoil swelling on all sides, and as much as he tucked in his head and his legs and shrank until his belly touched the floor, he was forced to admit that he would not be able to stand it much longer. They were clearing out his room; depriving him of everything that he loved; they had already carried away the chest of drawers, in which he kept the fretsaw and other tools; were now budging the desk firmly embedded in the floor, the desk he had done his homework on when he was a student at business college, in high school, yes, even in public school—now he really had no more time to examine the good intentions of the two women, whose existence, besides, he had almost forgotten, for they were so exhausted that they were working in silence, and one could hear only the heavy shuffling of their feet.

And so he broke out—the women were just leaning against the desk in the next room to catch their breath for a minute—changed his course four times, he really didn't know what to salvage first, then he saw hanging conspicuously on the wall, which was otherwise bare already, the picture of the lady all dressed in furs, hurriedly crawled up on it and pressed himself against the glass, which gave a good surface to stick to and soothed his hot belly. At least no one would take away this picture, while Gregor completely covered it up. He turned his head toward the living-room door to watch the women when they returned.

They had not given themselves much of a rest and were already coming back; Grete had put her arm around her mother and was practically car-rying her. "So what should we take now?" said Grete and looked around. At that her eyes met Gregor's as he clung to the wall. Probably only because of her mother's presence she kept her self-control, bent her head down to her mother to keep her from looking around, and said, though in a quavering and thoughtless voice: "Come, we'd better go back into the living room for a minute." Grete's intent was clear to Gregor, she wanted to bring his mother into safety and then chase him down from the wall. Well, just let her try! He squatted on his picture and would not give it up. He would rather fly in Grete's face.

But Grete's words had now made her mother really anxious; she stepped to one side, caught sight of the gigantic brown blotch on the flowered wallpaper, and before it really dawned on her that what she saw was Gregor, cried in a hoarse, bawling voice: "Oh, God, Oh, God!"; and as if giving up completely, she fell with outstretched arms across the couch and did not stir. "You, Gregor!" cried his sister with raised fist and piercing eyes. These were the first words she had addressed directly to him since his metamorphosis. She ran into the next room to get some kind of spirits to revive her mother; Gregor wanted to help too—there was time to rescue the picture—but he was stuck to the glass and had to tear himself loose by force; then he too ran into the next room, as if he could give his sister some sort of advice, as in the old days; but then had to stand behind her doing nothing while she rummaged among various little bottles; moreover, when she turned around she was startled, a bottle fell on the floor and broke, a splinter of glass wounded Gregor in the face, some kind of corrosive medicine flowed around him; now without waiting any longer, Grete grabbed as many little bottles as she could carry and ran with them inside to her mother; she slammed the door behind her with her foot. Now Gregor was cut off from his mother, who was perhaps near death through his fault; he could not dare open the door if he did not want to chase away his sister, who had to stay with his mother; now there was nothing for him to do except wait; and tormented by self-reproaches and worry, he began to crawl, crawled over everything, walls, furniture and ceiling, and finally in desperation, as the whole room was beginning to spin, fell down onto the middle of the big table.

A short time passed; Gregor lay there prostrate; all around, things were quiet, perhaps that was a good sign. Then the doorbell rang. The maid, of course, was locked up in her kitchen and so Grete had to answer the door. His father had come home. "What's happened?" were his first words; Grete's appearance must have told him everything. Grete answered in a muffled voice, her face was obviously pressed against her father's chest; "Mother fainted, but she's better now. Gregor's broken out." "I knew it," his father said. "I kept telling you, but you women don't want to listen." It was clear to Gregor that his father had put the worst interpretation on Grete's all-too-brief announcement and assumed that Gregor was guilty of some outrage. Therefore Gregor now had to try to calm his father down, since he had neither the time nor the ability to enlighten him. And so he fled to the door of his room and pressed himself against it for his father to see, as soon as he came into the foyer, that Gregor had the best intentions of returning to his room immediately and that it was not necessary to drive him back; if only the door were opened for him, he would disappear at once.

But his father was in no mood to notice such subtleties; "Ah!" he cried as he entered, in a tone that sounded as if he were at once furious and glad. Gregor turned his head away from the door and lifted it toward his father. He had not really imagined his father looking like this, as he stood in front of him now; admittedly Gregor had been too absorbed recently in his newfangled crawling to bother as much as before about events in the rest of the house and should really have been prepared to find some changes. And yet, and yet—was this still his father? Was this the same man who in the old days used to lie wearily buried in bed when Gregor left on a business trip; who greeted him on his return in the evening, sitting in his bathrobe in the armchair, who actually had difficulty getting to his feet but as a sign of joy only lifted up his arms; and who, on the rare occasions when the whole family went out for a walk, on a few Sundays in June and on the major holidays, used to shuffle along with great effort between Gregor and his mother, who were slow walkers themselves, always a little more slowly than they, wrapped in his old overcoat, always carefully planting down his crutch-handled cane, and, when he wanted to say something, nearly always stood still and assembled his escort around him? Now, however, he was holding himself very erect, dressed in a tight-fitting blue uniform with gold buttons, the kind worn by messengers at banking concerns; above the high stiff collar of the jacket his heavy chin protruded; under his bushy eyebrows his black eyes darted bright, piercing glances; his usually rumpled white hair was combed flat, with a scrupulously exact, gleaming part. He threw his cap—which was adorned with a gold monogram, probably that of a bank—in an arc across the entire room onto the couch, and with the tails of his long uniform jacket slapped back, his hands in his pants pockets, went for Gregor with a sullen look on his face. He probably did not know himself what he had in mind; still he lifted his feet unusually high off the floor, and Gregor staggered at the gigantic size of the soles of his boots. But he did not linger over this, he had known right from the first day of his new life that his father considered only the strictest treatment called for in dealing with him. And so he ran ahead of his father, stopped when his father stood still, and scooted ahead again when his father made even the slightest movement. In this way they made more than one tour of the room, without anything decisive happening; in fact the whole movement did not even have the appearance of a chase because of its slow tempo. So Gregor kept to the floor for the time being, especially since he was afraid that his father might interpret a flight onto the walls or the ceiling as a piece of particular nastiness. Of course Gregor had to admit that he would not be able to keep up even this running for long, for whenever his father took one step, Gregor had to execute countless movements. He was already beginning to feel winded, just as in the old days he had not had very reliable lungs. As he now staggered around, hardly keeping his eyes open in order to gather all his strength for the running; in his obtuseness not thinking of any escape other than by running; and having almost forgotten that the walls were at his disposal, though here of course they were blocked up with elaborately carved furniture full of notches and points—at that moment a lightly flung object hit the floor right near him and rolled in front of him. It was an apple; a second one came flying right after it; Gregor stopped dead with fear; fur-

ther running was useless, for his father was determined to bombard him.
He had filled his pockets from the fruit bowl on the buffet and was now
pitching one apple after another, for the time being without taking good
aim. These little red apples rolled around on the floor as if electrified,
clicking into each other. One apple, thrown weakly, grazed Gregor's back
and slid off harmlessly. But the very next one that came flying after it
literally forced its way into Gregor's back; Gregor tried to drag himself
away, as if the startling, unbelievable pain might disappear with a change
of place; but he felt nailed to the spot and stretched out his body in a
complete confusion of all his senses. With his last glance he saw the door
of his room burst open, as his mother rushed out ahead of his screaming
sister, in her chemise, for his sister had partly undressed her while she was
unconscious in order to let her breathe more freely; saw his mother run
up to his father and on the way her unfastened petticoats slide to the floor
one by one; and saw as, stumbling over the skirts, she forced herself onto
his father, and embracing him, in complete union with him—but now
Gregor's sight went dim—her hands clasping his father's neck, begged for
Gregor's life.

III

Gregor's serious wound, from which he suffered for over a month—the
apple remained imbedded in his flesh as a visible souvenir since no one
dared to remove it—seemed to have reminded even his father that Gregor
was a member of the family, in spite of his present pathetic and repulsive
shape, who could not be treated as an enemy; that, on the contrary, it was
the commandment of family duty to swallow their disgust and endure
him, endure him and nothing more.

And now, although Gregor had lost some of his mobility probably for
good because of his wound, and although for the time being he needed
long, long minutes to get across his room, like an old war veteran—crawling above ground was out of the question—for this deterioration of his
situation he was granted compensation which in his view was entirely
satisfactory: every day around dusk the living-room door—which he was
in the habit of watching closely for an hour or two beforehand—was
opened, so that, lying in the darkness of his room, invisible from the living
room, he could see the whole family sitting at the table under the lamp
and could listen to their conversation, as it were with general permission;
and so it was completely different from before.

Of course these were no longer the animated conversations of the old
days, which Gregor used to remember with a certain nostalgia in small
hotel rooms when he'd had to throw himself wearily into the damp bedding. Now things were mostly very quiet. Soon after supper his father
would fall asleep in his armchair; his mother and sister would caution
each other to be quiet; his mother, bent low under the light, sewed delicate lingerie for a clothing store; his sister, who had taken a job as a sales-
girl, was learning shorthand and French in the evenings in order to attain
a better position some time in the future. Sometimes his father woke up,
and as if he had absolutely no idea that he had been asleep, said to his

mother, "Look how long you're sewing again today!" and went right back to sleep, while mother and sister smiled wearily at each other. With a kind of perverse obstinacy his father refused to take off his official uniform even in the house; and while his robe hung uselessly on the clothes hook, his father dozed, completely dressed, in his chair, as if he were always ready for duty and were waiting even here for the voice of his superior. As a result his uniform, which had not been new to start with, began to get dirty in spite of all the mother's and sister's care, and Gregor would often stare all evening long at this garment, covered with stains and gleaming with its constantly polished gold buttons, in which the old man slept most uncomfortably and yet peacefully.

As soon as the clock struck ten, his mother tried to awaken his father with soft encouraging words and then persuade him to go to bed, for this was no place to sleep properly, and his father badly needed his sleep, since he had to be at work at six o'clock. But with the obstinacy that had possessed him ever since he had become a messenger, he always insisted on staying at the table a little longer, although he invariably fell asleep and then could be persuaded only with the greatest effort to exchange his armchair for bed. However much mother and sister might pounce on him with little admonitions, he would slowly shake his head for a quarter of an hour at a time, keeping his eyes closed, and would not get up. Gregor's mother plucked him by the sleeves, whispered blandishments into his ear, his sister dropped her homework in order to help her mother, but all this was of no use. He only sank deeper into his armchair. Not until the women lifted him up under his arms did he open his eyes, look alternately at mother and sister, and usually say, "What a life. So this is the peace of my old age." And leaning on the two women, he would get up laboriously, as if he were the greatest weight on himself, and let the women lead him to the door, where, shrugging them off, he would proceed independently, while Gregor's mother threw down her sewing and his sister her pen as quickly as possible so as to run after his father and be of further assistance.

Who in this overworked and exhausted family had time to worry about Gregor any more than was absolutely necessary? The household was stinted more and more; now the maid was let go after all; a gigantic bony cleaning woman with white hair fluttering about her head came mornings and evenings to do the heaviest work; his mother took care of everything else, along with all her sewing. It even happened that various pieces of family jewelry, which in the old days his mother and sister had been overjoyed to wear at parties and celebrations, were sold, as Gregor found out one evening from the general discussion of the prices they had fetched. But the biggest complaint was always that they could not give up the apartment, which was much too big for their present needs, since no one could figure out how Gregor was supposed to be moved. But Gregor understood easily that it was not only consideration for him which prevented their moving, for he could easily have been transported in a suitable crate with a few air holes; what mainly prevented the family from moving was their complete hopelessness and the thought that they had been struck by a misfortune as none of their relatives and acquaintances had ever been hit. What the world demands of poor people they did to the utmost of their ability; his father brought breakfast for the minor officials at the bank, his mother sacrificed herself to the underwear of strangers, his sister ran back and forth behind the counter at the request of the customers; but for anything more than this they did not have the strength. And the wound in Gregor's back began to hurt anew when mother and sister, after getting his father to bed, now came back, dropped their work, pulled their chairs close to each other and sat cheek to cheek; when his mother, pointing to Gregor's room, said, "Close that door, Grete"; and when Gregor was back in darkness, while in the other room the women mingled their tears or stared dry-eyed at the table.

Gregor spent the days and nights almost entirely without sleep. Sometimes he thought that the next time the door opened he would take charge of the family's affairs again, just as he had done in the old days; after this long while there again appeared in his thoughts the boss and the manager, the salesmen and the trainees, the handyman who was so dense, two or three friends from other firms, a chambermaid in a provincial hotel—a happy fleeting memory—a cashier in a millinery store, whom he had courted earnestly but too slowly—they all appeared, intermingled with strangers or people he had already forgotten; but instead of helping him and his family, they were all inaccessible, and he was glad when they faded away. At other times he was in no mood to worry about his family, he was completely filled with rage at his miserable treatment, and although he could not imagine anything that would pique his appetite, he still made plans for getting into the pantry to take what was coming to him, even if he wasn't hungry. No longer considering what she could do to give Gregor a special treat, his sister, before running to business every morning and afternoon, hurriedly shoved any old food into Gregor's room with her foot; and in the evening, regardless of whether the food had only been toyed with or—the most usual case—had been left completely untouched, she swept it out with a swish of the broom. The cleaning up of Gregor's room, which she now always did in the evenings, could not be done more hastily. Streaks of dirt ran along the walls, fluffs of dust and filth lay here and there on the floor. At first, whenever his sister came in, Gregor would place himself in those corners which were particularly offending, meaning by his position in a sense to reproach her. But he could probably have stayed there for weeks without his sister's showing any improvement; she must have seen the dirt as clearly as he did, but she had just decided to leave it. At the same time she made sure—with an irritableness that was completely new to her and which had in fact infected the whole family—that the cleaning of Gregor's room remain her province. One time his mother had submitted Gregor's room to a major housecleaning, which she managed only after employing a couple of pails of water—all this dampness, of course, irritated Gregor too and he lay prostrate, sour and immobile, on the couch—but his mother's punishment was not long in coming. For hardly had his sister noticed the difference in Gregor's room that evening than, deeply insulted, she ran into the living room and, in spite of her mother's imploringly uplifted hands, burst out in a fit of crying, which his parents—his father had naturally been startled out of his armchair—at first watched in helpless amazement; until they too got going; turning to the right, his father blamed his mother for not letting his sister clean Gregor's room; but turning to the left, he screamed at his sister that she would never again be allowed to clean Gregor's room; while his mother tried to drag his father, who was out of his mind with excitement, into the bedroom; his sister, shaken with sobs, hammered the table with her small fists; and Gregor hissed loudly with rage because it did not occur to any of them to close the door and spare him such a scene and a row.

But even if his sister, exhausted from her work at the store, had gotten fed up with taking care of Gregor as she used to, it was not necessary at all for his mother to take her place and still Gregor did not have to be neglected. For now the cleaning woman was there. This old widow, who thanks to her strong bony frame had probably survived the worst in a long life, was not really repelled by Gregor. Without being in the least inquisitive, she had once accidentally opened the door of Gregor's room, and at the sight of Gregor—who, completely taken by surprise, began to race back and forth although no one was chasing him—she had remained standing, with her hands folded on her stomach, marveling. From that time on she never failed to open the door a crack every morning and every evening and peek in hurriedly at Gregor. In the beginning she also used to call him over to her with words she probably considered friendly, like, "Come over here for a minute, you old dung beetle!" or "Look at that old dung beetle!" To forms of address like these Gregor would not respond but remained immobile where he was, as if the door had not been opened. If only they had given this cleaning woman orders to clean up his room every day, instead of letting her disturb him uselessly whenever the mood took her. Once, early in the morning—heavy rain, perhaps already a sign of approaching spring, was beating on the window panes—Gregor was so exasperated when the cleaning woman started in again with her phrases that he turned on her, of course slowly and decrepitly, as if to attack. But the cleaning woman, instead of getting frightened, simply lifted up high a chair near the door, and as she stood there with her mouth wide open, her intention was clearly to shut her mouth only when the chair in her hand came crashing down on Gregor's back. "So, is that all there is?" she asked when Gregor turned around again, and she quietly put the chair back in the corner.

Gregor now hardly ate anything anymore. Only when he accidentally passed the food laid out for him would he take a bite into his mouth just for fun, hold it in for hours, and then mostly spit it out again. At first he thought that his grief at the state of his room kept him off food, but it was the very changes in his room to which he quickly became adjusted. His family had gotten into the habit of putting in this room things for which they could not find any other place, and now there were plenty of these, since one of the rooms in the apartment had been rented to three boarders. These serious gentlemen—all three had long beards, as Gregor was able to register once through a crack in the door—were obsessed with neatness, not only in their room, but since they had, after all, moved in here, throughout the entire household and especially in the kitchen. They could not stand useless, let alone dirty junk. Besides, they had brought along most of their own household goods. For this reason many things had become superfluous, and though they certainly weren't salable, on the other hand they could not just be thrown out. All these things migrated into Gregor's room. Likewise the ash can and the garbage can from the kitchen. Whatever was not being used at the moment was just flung into Gregor's room by the cleaning woman, who was always in a big hurry; fortunately Gregor generally saw only the object involved and the hand that held it. Maybe the cleaning woman intended to reclaim the things as soon as she had a chance or else to throw out everything together in one fell swoop, but in fact they would have remained lying wherever they had been thrown in the first place if Gregor had not squeezed through the junk and set it in motion, at first from necessity, because otherwise there would have been no room to crawl in, but later with growing pleasure, although after such excursions, tired to death and sad, he did not budge again for hours.

Since the roomers sometimes also had their supper at home in the common living room, the living-room door remained closed on certain evenings, but Gregor found it very easy to give up the open door, for on many evenings when it was opened he had not taken advantage of it, but instead, without the family's noticing, had lain in the darkest corner of his room. But once the cleaning woman had left the living-room door slightly open, and it also remained opened a little when the roomers came in in the evening and the lamp was lit. They sat down at the head of the table where in the old days his father, his mother, and Gregor had eaten, unfolded their napkins, and picked up their knives and forks. At once his mother appeared in the doorway with a platter of meat, and just behind her came his sister with a platter piled high with potatoes. A thick vapor steamed up from the food. The roomers bent over the platters set in front of them as if to examine them before eating, and in fact the one who sat in the middle, and who seemed to be regarded by the other two as an authority, cut into a piece of meat while it was still on the platter, evidently to find out whether it was tender enough or whether it should perhaps be sent back to the kitchen. He was satisfied, and mother and sister, who had been watching anxiously, sighed with relief and began to smile.

The family itself ate in the kitchen. Nevertheless, before going into the kitchen, his father came into this room and, bowing once, cap in hand, made a turn around the table. The roomers rose as one man and mumbled something into their beards. When they were alone again, they ate in almost complete silence. It seemed strange to Gregor that among all the different noises of eating he kept picking up the sound of their chewing teeth, as if this were a sign to Gregor that you needed teeth to eat with and that even with the best make of toothless jaws you couldn't do a thing. "I'm hungry enough," Gregor said to himself, full of grief, "but not for these things. Look how these roomers are gorging themselves, and I'm dying!"

On this same evening—Gregor could not remember having heard the violin during the whole time—the sound of violin playing came from the kitchen. The roomers had already finished their evening meal, the one in the middle had taken out a newspaper, given each of the two others a page, and now, leaning back, they read and smoked. When the violin began to play, they became attentive, got up, and went on tiptoe to the door leading to the foyer, where they stood in a huddle. They must have been heard in the kitchen, for his father called, "Perhaps the playing bothers you, gentlemen? It can be stopped right away." "On the contrary," said the middle roomer. "Wouldn't the young lady like to come in to us and play in here where it's much roomier and more comfortable?" "Oh, certainly," called Gregor's father, as if he were the violinist. The boarders went back into the room and waited. Soon Gregor's father came in with the music stand, his mother with the sheet music, and his sister with the violin. Calmly his sister got everything ready for playing; his parents— who had never rented out rooms before and therefore behaved toward the roomers with excessive politeness—did not even dare sit down on their own chairs; his father leaned against the door, his right hand inserted between two buttons of his uniform coat, which he kept closed; but his mother was offered a chair by one of the roomers, and since she left the chair where the roomer just happened to put it, she sat in a corner to one side.

His sister began to play. Father and mother, from either side, attentively followed the movements of her hands. Attracted by the playing, Gregor had dared to come out a little further and already had his head in the living room. It hardly surprised him that lately he was showing so little consideration for the others; once such consideration had been his greatest pride. And yet he would never have had better reason to keep hidden; for now, because of the dust which lay all over his room and blew around at the slightest movement, he too was completely covered with dust; he dragged around with him on his back and along his sides fluff and hairs and scraps of food; his indifference to everything was much too deep for him to have gotten on his back and scrubbed himself clean against the carpet, as once he had done several times a day. And in spite of his state, he was not ashamed to inch out a little farther on the immaculate living-room floor.

Admittedly no one paid any attention to him. The family was completely absorbed by the violin-playing; the roomers, on the other hand, who at first had stationed themselves, hands in pockets, much too close behind his sister's music stand, so that they could all have followed the score, which certainly must have upset his sister, soon withdrew to the window, talking to each other in an undertone, their heads lowered, where they remained, anxiously watched by his father. It now seemed only too obvious that they were disappointed in their expectation of hearing beautiful or entertaining violin-playing, had had enough of the whole performance, and continued to let their peace be disturbed only out of politeness. Especially the way they all blew the cigar smoke out of their nose and mouth toward the ceiling suggested great nervousness. And yet his sister was playing so beautifully. Her face was inclined to one side, sadly and probingly her eyes followed the lines of music. Gregor crawled forward a little farther, holding his head close to the floor, so that it might be possible to catch her eye. Was he an animal, that music could move him so? He felt as if the way to the unknown nourishment he longed for were coming to light. He was determined to force himself on until he reached his sister, to pluck at her skirt, and to let her know in this way that she should bring her violin into his room, for no one here appreciated her playing the way he would appreciate it. He would never again let her out of his room—at least not for as long as he lived; for once, his nightmarish looks would be of use to him; he would be at all the doors of his room at the same time and hiss and spit at the aggressors; his sister, however, should not be forced to stay with him, but would do so of her own free will; she should sit next to him on the couch, bending her ear down to him, and then he would confide to her that he had had the firm intention of sending her to the Conservatory, and that, if the catastrophe had not intervened, he would have announced this to everyone last Christmas— certainly Christmas had come and gone?—without taking notice of any objections. After this declaration his sister would burst into tears of emotion, and Gregor would raise himself up to her shoulder and kiss her on the neck which, ever since she started going out to work, she kept bare, without a ribbon or collar.

"Mr. Samsa!" the middle roomer called to Gregor's father and without wasting another word pointed his index finger at Gregor, who was slowly moving forward. The violin stopped, the middle roomer smiled first at his friends, shaking his head, and then looked at Gregor again. Rather than driving Gregor out, his father seemed to consider it more urgent to start by soothing the roomers although they were not at all upset, and Gregor seemed to be entertaining them more than the violin-playing. He rushed over to them and tried with outstretched arms to drive them into their room and at the same time with his body to block their view of Gregor. Now they actually did get a little angry—it was not clear whether because of his father's behavior or because of their dawning realization of having had without knowing it such a next door neighbor as Gregor. They demanded explanations from his father; in their turn they raised their arms, plucked excitedly at their beards, and, dragging their feet, backed off toward their room. In the meantime his sister had overcome the abstracted mood into which she had fallen after her playing had been so suddenly interrupted; and all at once, after holding violin and bow for a while in her slackly hanging hands and continuing to follow the score as if she were still playing, she pulled herself together, laid the instrument on the lap of her mother—who was still sitting in her chair, fighting for breath, her lungs violently heaving—and ran into the next room, which the roomers, under pressure from her father, were nearing more quickly than before. One could see the covers and bolsters on the beds, obeying his sister's practiced hands, fly up and arrange themselves. Before the boarders had reached the room, she had finished turning down the beds and had slipped out. Her father seemed once again to be gripped by his perverse obstinacy to such a degree that he completely forgot any respect still due his tenants. He drove them on and kept on driving until, already at the bedroom door, the middle boarder stamped his foot thunderingly and thus brought him to a standstill. "I herewith declare," he said, raising his hand and casting his eyes around for Gregor's mother and sister too, "that in view of the disgusting conditions prevailing in this apartment and

"And now?" Gregor asked himself, looking around in the darkness. He soon made the discovery that he could no longer move at all. It did not surprise him; rather, it seemed unnatural that until now he had actually been able to propel himself on these thin little legs. Otherwise he felt relatively comfortable. He had pains, of course, throughout his whole body, but it seemed to him that they were gradually getting fainter and fainter and would finally go away altogether. The rotten apple in his back and the inflamed area around it, which were completely covered with fluffy dust, already hardly bothered him. He thought back on his family with deep emotion and love. His conviction that he would have to disappear was, if possible, even firmer than his sister's. He remained in this state of empty and peaceful reflection until the tower clock struck three in the morning. He still saw that outside the window everything was beginning to grow light. Then, without his consent, his head sank down to the floor, and from his nostrils streamed his last weak breath.

When early in the morning the cleaning woman came—in sheer energy and impatience she would slam all the doors so hard although she had often been asked not to, that once she had arrived, quiet sleep was no longer possible anywhere in the apartment—she did not at first find anything out of the ordinary on paying Gregor her usual short visit. She thought that he was deliberately lying motionless, pretending that his feelings were hurt; she credited him with unlimited intelligence. Because she happened to be holding the long broom, she tried from the doorway to tickle Gregor with it. When this too produced no results, she became annoyed and jabbed Gregor a little, and only when she had shoved him without any resistance to another spot did she begin to take notice. When she quickly became aware of the true state of things, she opened her eyes wide, whistled softly, but did not dawdle; instead, she tore open the door of the bedroom and shouted at the top of her voice into the darkness: "Come and have a look, it's croaked; it's lying there, dead as a doornail!"

The couple Mr. and Mrs. Samsa sat up in their marriage bed and had a struggle overcoming their shock at the cleaning woman before they could finally grasp her message. But then Mr. and Mrs. Samsa hastily scrambled out of bed, each on his side, Mr. Samsa threw the blanket around his shoulders, Mrs. Samsa came out in nothing but her nightgown; dressed this way, they entered Gregor's room. In the meantime the door of the living room had also opened, where Grete had been sleeping since the roomers had moved in; she was fully dressed, as if she had not been asleep at all; and her pale face seemed to confirm this. "Dead?" said Mrs. Samsa and looked inquiringly at the cleaning woman, although she could scrutinize everything for herself and could recognize the truth even without scrutiny. "I'll say," said the cleaning woman, and to prove it she pushed Gregor's corpse with her broom a good distance sideways. Mrs. Samsa made a movement as if to hold the broom back but did not do it. "Well," said Mr. Samsa, "now we can thank God!" He crossed himself, and the three women followed his example. Grete, who never took her eyes off the corpse, said, "Just look how thin he was. Of course he didn't eat anything for such a long time. The food came out again just the way it went in." As a matter of fact, Gregor's body was completely flat and dry;

this was obvious now for the first time, really, since the body was no longer raised up by his little legs and nothing else distracted the eye.

"Come in with us for a little while, Grete," said Mrs. Samsa with a melancholy smile, and Grete, not without looking back at the corpse, followed her parents into their bedroom. The cleaning woman shut the door and opened the window wide. Although it was early in the morning, there was already some mildness mixed in with the fresh air. After all, it was already the end of March.

The three boarders came out of their room and looked around in astonishment for their breakfast; they had been forgotten. "Where's breakfast?" the middle roomer grumpily asked the cleaning woman. But she put her finger to her lips and then hastily and silently beckoned the boarders to follow her into Gregor's room. They came willingly and then stood, their hands in the pockets of their somewhat shabby jackets, in the now already very bright room, surrounding Gregor's corpse.

At that point the bedroom door opened, and Mr. Samsa appeared in his uniform, his wife on one arm, his daughter on the other. They all looked as if they had been crying; from time to time Grete pressed her face against her father's sleeve.

"Leave my house immediately," said Mr. Samsa and pointed to the door, without letting go of the women. "What do you mean by that?" said the middle roomer, somewhat nonplussed, and smiled with a sugary smile. The two others held their hands behind their back and incessantly rubbed them together, as if in joyful anticipation of a big argument, which could only turn out in their favor. "I mean just what I say," answered Mr. Samsa and with his two companions marched in a straight line toward the roomer. At first the roomer stood still and looked at the floor, as if the thoughts inside his head were fitting themselves together in a new order. "So, we'll go, then," he said and looked up at Mr. Samsa as if, suddenly overcome by a fit of humility, he were asking for further permission even for this decision. Mr. Samsa merely nodded briefly several times, his eyes wide open. Thereupon the roomer actually went immediately into the foyer, taking long strides; his two friends had already been listening for a while, their hands completely still, and now they went hopping right after him, as if afraid that Mr. Samsa might get into the foyer ahead of them and interrupt the contact with their leader. In the foyer all three took their hats from the coatrack, pulled their canes from the umbrella stand, bowed silently, and left the apartment. In a suspicious mood which proved completely unfounded, Mr. Samsa led the two women out onto the landing; leaning over the banister, they watched the three roomers slowly but steadily going down the long flight of stairs, disappearing on each landing at a particular turn of the stairway and a few moments later emerging again; the farther down they got, the more the Samsa family's interest in them wore off, and when a butcher's boy with a carrier on his head came climbing up the stairs with a proud bearing, toward them and then up on past them, Mr. Samsa and the women quickly left the banister and all went back, as if relieved, into their apartment.

They decided to spend this day resting and going for a walk; they not only deserved a break in their work, they absolutely needed one. And so they sat down at the table and wrote three letters of excuse, Mr. Samsa to the management of the bank, Mrs. Samsa to her employer, and Grete to the store owner. While they were writing, the cleaning woman came in to say that she was going, since her morning's work was done. The three letter writers at first simply nodded without looking up, but as the cleaning woman still kept lingering, they looked up, annoyed. "Well?" asked Mr. Samsa. The cleaning woman stood smiling in the doorway, as if she had somegreat good news to announce to the family but would do so only if she were thoroughly questioned. The little ostrich feather which stood almost upright on her hat and which had irritated Mr. Samsa the whole time she had been with them swayed lightly in all directions. "What do you want?" asked Mrs. Samsa, who inspired the most respect in the cleaning woman. "Well," the cleaning woman answered, and for good-natured laughter could not immediately go on, "look, you don't have to worry about getting rid of the stuff next door. It's already been taken care of." Mrs. Samsa and Grete bent down over their letters, as if to continue writing; Mr. Samsa, who noticed that the cleaning woman was now about to start describing everything in detail, stopped her with a firmly outstretched hand. But since she was not going to be permitted to tell her story, she remembered that she was in a great hurry, cried, obviously insulted, "So long, everyone," whirled around wildly, and left the apartment with a terrible slamming of doors.

"We'll fire her tonight," said Mr. Samsa, but did not get an answer from either his wife or his daughter, for the cleaning woman seemed to have ruined their barely regained peace of mind. They got up, went to the window, and stayed there, holding each other tight. Mr. Samsa turned around in his chair toward them and watched them quietly for a while. Then he called, "Come on now, come over here. Stop brooding over the past. And have a little consideration for me, too." The women obeyed him at once, hurried over to him, fondled him, and quickly finished their letters.

Then all three of them left the apartment together, something they had not done in months, and took the trolley into the open country on the outskirts of the city. The car, in which they were the only passengers, was completely filled with warm sunshine. Leaning back comfortably in their seats, they discussed their prospects for the time to come, and it seemed on closer examination that these weren't bad at all, for all three positions—about which they had never really asked one another in any detail—were exceedingly advantageous and especially promising for the future. The greatest immediate improvement in their situation would come easily, of course, from a change in apartments; they would now take a smaller and cheaper apartment, but one better situated and in every way simpler to manage than the old one, which Gregor had picked for them. While they were talking in this vein, it occurred almost simultaneously to Mr. and Mrs. Samsa, as they watched their daughter getting livelier and livelier, that lately, in spite of all the troubles which had turned her cheeks pale, she had blossomed into a good-looking, shapely girl. Growing quieter and communicating almost unconsciously through glances, they thought that it would soon be time, too, to find her a good husband. And it was like a confirmation of their new dreams and good intentions when at the end of the ride their daughter got up first and stretched her young body.

T. S. ELIOT
1888–1965

In poetry and in literary criticism, Thomas Stearns Eliot has a unique position as a writer who not only expressed but helped to define modernist taste and style. He rejected the narrative, moralizing, and frequently "noble" style of late Victorian poetry, employing instead precisely focused and often startling images and an elliptical, allusive, and ironic voice that had enormous influence on modern American poetry. His early essays on literature and literary history helped bring about not only a new appreciation of seventeenth-century "metaphysical" poetry but also a different understanding of the text, no longer seen as the inspired overflow of spontaneous emotion but as a carefully made aesthetic object. Yet much of Eliot's immediate impact was not merely formal but spiritual or philosophical. The search for meaning that pervades his work created a famous picture of the barrenness of modern culture in *The Waste Land* (1922), which juxtaposed images of past nobility and present decay, civilizations near and far, and biblical, mythical, and Buddhist allusions to evoke the dilemma of a composite, anxious, and infinitely vulnerable modern soul. Readers in different countries who know nothing of Eliot's other works are often familiar with *The Waste Land* as a literary-historical landmark representing the cultural crisis in European society after World War I. In many ways, Eliot's combination of spiritual insight and technical innovation carries on the tradition of the Symbolist poet who was both visionary artist and consummate craftsman.

Two countries, England and the United States, claim Eliot as part of their national literature. Born September 26, 1888, to a prosperous and educated family in St. Louis, Eliot went to Harvard University for his undergraduate and graduate education and moved to England only in 1915, where he became a British citizen in 1927. While at Harvard, Eliot was influenced by the anti-Romantic humanist Irving Babbitt and the philosopher and aesthetician George Santayana. He later wrote a doctoral dissertation on the philosophy of F. H. Bradley, whose examination of private consciousness *(Appearance and Reality)* appears in Eliot's own later essays and poems. Eliot also found literary examples that would be important for him in future years: the poetry of Dante and John Donne, and the Elizabethan and Jacobean dramatists. In 1908 he read Arthur Symons's *The Symbolist Movement in Literature* and became acquainted with the French Symbolist poets whose richly allusive images—as well as highly self-conscious, ironic, and craftsmanlike technique—he would adopt for his own. Eliot began writing poetry while in college, and published his first major poem, *The Love Song of J. Alfred Prufrock*, in Chicago's *Poetry* magazine in 1915. When he moved to England, however, he began a many-sided career as poet, reviewer, essayist, editor, and later playwright. By the time he received the Nobel Prize for literature in 1948, Eliot was recognized as one of the most influential twentieth-century writers in English.

Eliot's first poems, in 1915, already displayed the evocative yet startling images, abrupt shifts in focus, and combination of human sympathy and ironic wit that would attract and puzzle his readers. The *Preludes* linked the "notion of some infinitely gentle / Infinitely suffering thing" with a harsh fatalism in which "The worlds revolve like ancient women / Gathering fuel in vacant lots." Prufrock's dramatic monologue openly tried to startle readers by asking them to imagine the evening spread out "like a patient etherised upon a table" and by changing focus abruptly between imaginary landscapes, metaphysical questions, drawing-room chatter, literary and biblical allusions, and tones of high seriousness set against the most banal and even sing-song speech. "I grow old . . . I grow old. . . . / I shall wear the bottoms of my trousers rolled." The individual stanzas of *Prufrock* are individual scenes, each with its own coherence (for example, the third stanza's yellow fog as a cat). Together, they compose a symbolic landscape sketched in the narrator's mind as a combination of factual observation and subjective feelings: the delicately stated eroticism of the arm "downed with light brown hair," and the frustrated aggression in "I should have been a pair of ragged claws / Scuttling across the floors of silent seas." In its discontinuity, precise yet evocative imagery, mixture of romantic and everyday reference, formal and conversational speech, and in the complex and ironic self-consciousness of its most unheroic hero, *The Love Song of J. Alfred Prufrock* already displays many of the modernist traits typical of Eliot's entire work. Also typical is the theme of spiritual void and of a disoriented protagonist who—at least at this point—does not know how to cope with a crisis that is as much that of modern Western culture as it is his own personal tragedy.

Once established in London, Eliot married, taught briefly before taking a job in the foreign department of Lloyd's Bank (1917–25), and in 1925 joined the publishing firm of Faber & Faber. He wrote a number of essays and book reviews that were published in *The Sacred Wood* (1920) and *Homage to Dryden* (1924) and enjoyed a great deal of influence as assistant editor of the *Egoist* (1917–19) and founding editor of the quarterly *Criterion* from 1922 until it folded in 1939. Eliot helped shape changing literary tastes as much by his essays and literary criticism as by his poetry. Influenced himself by T. E. Hulme's proposal that the time had come for a classical literature of "hard, dry wit" after Romantic vagueness and religiosity and following Imagism's goal of clear, precise physical images phrased in everyday language, he outlined his own definitions of literature and literary history and contributed to a theoretical approach later known as the *New Criticism*. In his essay *Tradition and the Individual Talent* (1919), Eliot proclaimed that there existed a special level of great works—"masterpieces"—that formed among themselves an "ideal order" of quality even though, as individual works, they expressed the characteristic sensibility of their age. The best poets were aware of fitting into the cumulative "mind of Europe" (for Eliot, the humanistic tradition of Homer, Dante, and Shakespeare) and thus of being to some extent depersonalized in their works. Eliot's "impersonal theory of poetry" emphasizes the medium in which a writer works, rather than his or her inner state; craft and control rather than the Romantic ideal of a spontaneous overflow of private emotion. In a famous passage that compares the creative mind to the untouched catalyst of a chemistry experiment, he insists that the writer makes the art object out of language and the experience of any number of people. "The poet's mind is in fact a receptacle for seizing and storing up numberless feelings, phrases, images, which remain there until all the particles which can unite to form a new compound are present together." Poetry can and should express the whole being—intellectual and emotional, conscious and unconscious. In a review of Herbert Grierson's edition of the seventeenth-century Metaphysical poets (1921), Eliot praised the complex mixture of intellect and passion that characterized John Donne and the other Metaphysicals (and that characterized Eliot himself) and criticized the tendency of English literature after the seventeenth century to separate the language of analysis from that of feeling. His criticism of this "dissociation of sensibility" implied a change in literary tastes: from Milton to Donne, from Tennyson to Gerard Manley Hopkins, from Romanticism to classicism, from simplicity to complexity.

The great poetic example of this change came with *The Waste Land* in 1922. Eliot dedicated the poem to Ezra Pound, who had helped him revise the first draft, with a quotation from Dante praising the "better craftsman." Quotations from, or allusions to, a wide range of sources, including Shakespeare, Dante, Charles Baudelaire, Richard Wagner, Ovid, St. Augustine, Buddhist sermons, folk songs, and the anthropologists Jessie Weston and James Frazer, punctuate this lengthy poem, to which Eliot actually added explanatory notes when it was first published in book form. *The Waste Land* describes modern society in a time of cultural and spiritual crisis and sets off the fragmentation of modern experience against references (some in foreign languages) to a more stable cultural heritage. The ancient Greek prophet Tiresias is juxtaposed with the contemporary charlatan Madame Sosostris; celebrated lovers like Antony and Cleopatra with a house-agent's clerk who mechanically seduces an uninterested typist at the end of her day; the religious vision of St. Augustine and Buddhist sermons with a sterile world of rock and dry sand where "one can neither stand nor lie nor sit." The modern wasteland could be redeemed if it learned to answer (or perhaps, to ask) the right questions: a situation Eliot symbolized by oblique references to the legend of a knight passing an evening of trial in a Chapel Perilous, and healing a Fisher King by asking the right questions about the Holy Grail and its lance. The series of references (many from literary masterworks) that Eliot integrated into his poem were so many "fragments I have shored against my ruins," pieces of a puzzle whose resolution would bring "shantih," or the peace that passes understanding, but that is still out of reach as the poem's final lines in a foreign language suggest.

The most influential technical innovation in *The Waste Land* was the deliberate use of fragmentation and discontinuity. Eliot pointedly refused to supply any transitional passages or narrative thread and expected the reader to construct a pattern whose implications would make sense as a whole. This was a direct attack on linear habits of reading, which are here broken up with sudden introductions of a different scene or unexplained literary references, shifts in perspective, interpolation of a foreign language, changes from elegant description to barroom gossip, from Elizabethan to modern scenes, from formal to colloquial language. Eliot's rupture of traditional expectations served several functions. It contributed to the general picture of cultural disintegration that the poem expressed, it allowed him to exploit the Symbolist or allusive powers of language inasmuch as they now carried the burden of meaning, and finally—by drawing attention to its own technique—it exemplified modernist "self-reflexive" or self-conscious style. It is impossible to read a triple shift such as "I remember / Those are pearls that were his eyes. / 'Are you alive, or not? Is there nothing in your head?' "—moving from the narrator's meditative recall to a quotation from Shakespeare and the woman's blunt attack—without noticing the abrupt changes in style and tone. Eliot's "heap of broken images" and "fragments shored against my ruins" also took the shape of fragments of thought and speech, and as such embodied a new tradition of literary language.

The spiritual search of *Prufrock, Gerontion* (1919), and *The Waste Land* entered a new phase for Eliot in 1927, when he became a member of the Anglican Church. *Ash Wednesday* (1930) and a verse play on the death of the English St. Thomas à Becket (*Murder in the Cathedral,* 1935) display the same distress over the human condition but now within a framework of hope for those who have accepted religious discipline. Eliot began writing plays to reach a larger audience, of which the best known are *The Family Reunion* (1939), which recasts the Orestes story from Greek tragedy, and *The Cocktail Party* (1949), a drawing room comedy that also explored its characters' search for salvation. He is still best known for his poetry, however, and his last major work in that genre is the *Four Quartets,* begun in 1934 and published in its entirety in 1943.

Bernard Bergonzi, *T. S. Eliot* (1972), and Tony Sharpe, *T. S. Eliot: A Literary Life* (1991), are brief and readable introductions to the life and works. Martin Scofield, *T. S. Eliot; The Poems* (1988), offers a concise, balanced discussion of the evolution of Eliot's poetry. *The Waste Land* is discussed in Jay Martin, ed., *Twentieth-Century Interpretations of The Waste Land* (1968); Lois A. Cuddy and David H. Hirsch, eds., *Critical Essays on T. S. Eliot's The Waste Land* (1991); and as part of John Mayer, *T. S. Eliot's Silent Voices* (1989), which analyzes themes of awareness and self-consciousness in the early poetry. *Little Gidding* is examined in Steve Ellis, *The English Eliot: Design, Language, and Landscape in Four Quartets* (1991), and John Paul Riquelme, *Harmony of Dissonances: T. S. Eliot, Romanticism, and Imagination* (1991), which links Eliot's response to Romanticism with postmodern views. Useful general collections are Linda Wagner, ed., *T. S. Eliot: A Collection of Criticism* (1974), and Ronald Bush, ed., *T. S. Eliot: The Modernist in History* (1991).

The Love Song of J. Alfred Prufrock

> *S'io credesse che mia risposta fosse*
> *A persona che mai tornasse al mondo,*
> *Questa fiamma staria senza piu scosse.*
> *Ma perciocche giammai di questo fondo*
> *Non torno vivo alcun, s'i'odo il vero,*
> *Senza tema d'infamia ti rispondo.*[1]

Let us go then, you and I,
When the evening is spread out against the sky
Like a patient etherised upon a table;
Let us go, through certain half-deserted streets,
The muttering retreats   5
Of restless nights in one-night cheap hotels
And sawdust restaurants with oyster-shells:
Streets that follow like a tedious argument
Of insidious intent
To lead you to an overwhelming question . . .   10
Oh, do not ask, "What is it?"
Let us go and make our visit.

In the room the women come and go
Talking of Michelangelo.[2]

The yellow fog that rubs its back upon the window-panes, 15
The yellow smoke that rubs its muzzle on the window-panes
Licked its tongue into the corners of the evening,
Lingered upon the pools that stand in drains,
Let fall upon its back the soot that falls from chimneys,
Slipped by the terrace, made a sudden leap,   20
And seeing that it was a soft October night,
Curled once about the house, and fell asleep.

---

1. From Dante's *Inferno* 27.61–66, where the false counselor Guido da Montefeltro, enveloped in flame, explains that he would never reveal his past if he thought the traveler could report it: "If I thought that my reply would be to one who would ever return to the world, this flame would stay without further movement. But since none has ever returned alive from this depth, if what I hear is true, I answer you without fear of infamy."   2. Michelangelo Buonarroti (1475–1564), famous Italian Renaissance sculptor, painter, architect, and poet; here, merely a topic of fashionable conversation.

And indeed there will be time[3]
For the yellow smoke that slides along the street,
Rubbing its back upon the window-panes;   25
There will be time, there will be time
To prepare a face to meet the faces that you meet;
There will be time to murder and create,
And time for all the works and days of hands[4]
That lift and drop a question on your plate;   30
Time for you and time for me,
And time yet for a hundred indecisions,
And for a hundred visions and revisions,
Before the taking of a toast and tea.

   In the room the women come and go   35
Talking of Michelangelo.

   And indeed there will be time
To wonder, "Do I dare?" and, "Do I dare?"
Time to turn back and descend the stair,
With a bald spot in the middle of my hair—   40
(They will say: "How his hair is growing thin!")
My morning coat, my collar mounting firmly to the chin,
My necktie rich and modest, but asserted by a simple pin—
(They will say: "But how his arms and legs are thin!")
Do I dare   45
Disturb the universe?
In a minute there is time
For decisions and revisions which a minute will reverse.

   For I have known them all already, known them all—
Have known the evenings, mornings, afternoons,   50
I have measured out my life with coffee spoons;
I know the voices dying with a dying fall[5]
Beneath the music from a farther room.
   So how should I presume?

   And I have known the eyes already, known them all— 55
The eyes that fix you in a formulated phrase,
And when I am formulated, sprawling on a pin,
When I am pinned and wriggling on the wall,
Then how should I begin
To spit out all the butt-ends of my days and ways?   60
   And how should I presume?

   And I have known the arms already, known them all—
Arms that are braceleted and white and bare
(But in the lamplight, downed with light brown hair!)
Is it perfume from a dress   65
That makes me so digress?
Arms that lie along a table, or wrap about a shawl.
   And should I then presume?
   And how should I begin?

---

3. Echo of a love poem by Andrew Marvell (1621–1678), *To His Coy Mistress:* "Had we but world enough and time."   **4.** An implied contrast with the more productive agricultural labor of hands in the *Works and Days* of the Greek poet Hesiod (8th century B.C.).   **5.** Recalls Duke Orsino's description of a musical phrase in Shakespeare's *Twelfth Night* (1.1.4): "It has a dying fall."

. . .

Shall I say, I have gone at dusk through narrow streets   70
And watched the smoke that rises from the pipes
Of lonely men in shirt-sleeves, leaning out of windows? . . .

I should have been a pair of ragged claws
Scuttling across the floors of silent seas.

. . .

And the afternoon, the evening, sleeps so peacefully!   75
Smoothed by long fingers,
Asleep . . . tired . . . or it malingers,
Stretched on the floor, here beside you and me.
Should I, after tea and cakes and ices,
Have the strength to force the moment to its crisis?   80
But though I have wept and fasted, wept and prayed,
Though I have seen my head (grown slightly bald) brought in upon a
    platter,
I am no prophet[6]—and here's no great matter;
I have seen the moment of my greatness flicker,
And I have seen the eternal Footman hold my coat, and snicker,   85
And in short, I was afraid.

And would it have been worth it, after all,
After the cups, the marmalade, the tea,
Among the porcelain, among some talk of you and me,
Would it have been worth while,   90
To have bitten off the matter with a smile,
To have squeezed the universe into a ball
To roll it toward some overwhelming question,[7]
To say: "I am Lazarus, come from the dead,[8]
Come back to tell you all, I shall tell you all"—   95
If one, settling a pillow by her head,
    Should say: "That is not what I meant at all.
    That is not it, at all."

And would it have been worth it, after all,
Would it have been worth while,   100
After the sunsets and the dooryards and the sprinkled streets,
After the novels, after the teacups, after the skirts that trail along the
    floor—
And this, and so much more?—
It is impossible to say just what I mean!
But as if a magic lantern[9] threw the nerves in patterns on a screen: 105
Would it have been worth while
If one, settling a pillow or throwing off a shawl,
And turning toward the window, should say:
    "That is not it at all,
    That is not what I meant, at all."   110

---

6. Salome obtained the head of the prophet John the Baptist on a platter as a reward for dancing before the tetrarch Herod (Matthew 14:3–11).   7. Another echo of *To His Coy Mistress*, when the lover suggests rolling "all our strength and all / our sweetness up into one ball" to send against the "iron gates of life."   8. The story of Lazarus, raised from the dead, is told in John 11:1–44.   9. A slide projector.

. . .

No! I am not Prince Hamlet, nor was meant to be;
Am an attendant lord, one that will do
To swell a progress,[1] start a scene or two,
Advise the prince; no doubt, an easy tool,
Deferential, glad to be of use,   115
Politic, cautious, and meticulous;
Full of high sentence, but a bit obtuse;
At times, indeed, almost ridiculous—
Almost, at times, the Fool.

I grow old . . . I grow old . . .   120
I shall wear the bottoms of my trousers rolled.

Shall I part my hair behind? Do I dare to eat a peach?
I shall wear white flannel trousers, and walk upon the beach.
I have heard the mermaids singing, each to each.

I do not think that they will sing to me.   125

I have seen them riding seaward on the waves
Combing the white hair of the waves blown back
When the wind blows the water white and black.

We have lingered in the chambers of the sea
By sea-girls wreathed with seaweed red and brown   130
Till human voices wake us, and we drown.

The Waste Land[1]

"Nam Sibyllam quidem Cumis ego ipse oculis meis vidi in ampulla
pendere, et cum illi pueri dicerent: Σίβυλλα τί θέλεισ; respondebat
illa: ἀποθανεῖν θέλω."[2]

For Ezra Pound
il miglior fabbro.[3]

I. THE BURIAL OF THE DEAD[4]

April is the cruellest month, breeding
Lilacs out of the dead land, mixing
Memory and desire, stirring
Dull roots with spring rain.
Winter kept us warm, covering   5
Earth in forgetful snow, feeding

1. A procession of attendants accompanying a king or nobleman across the stage, as in Elizabethan drama.   1. Eliot provided footnotes for *The Waste Land* when it was first published in book form; these notes are included here. A general note at the beginning referred readers to the religious symbolism described in Jessie L. Weston's study of the Grail legend, *From Ritual to Romance* (1920), and to fertility myths and vegetation ceremonies (especially those involving Adonis, Attis, and Osiris) as described in the *The Golden Bough* (1890–1918) by the anthropologist Sir James Frazer.   2. Lines from Petronius's *Satyricon* (ca. A.D. 60) describing the Sibyl, a prophetess shriveled with age and suspended in a bottle. "For indeed I myself have seen with my own eyes the Sibyl at Cumae, hanging in a bottle, and when those boys would say to her: 'Sibyl, what do you want?' she would reply: 'I want to die.'"   3. The dedication to Ezra Pound, who suggested cuts and changes in the first manuscript of *The Waste Land*, borrows words used by Guido Guinizelli to describe his predecessor, the Provençal poet Arnaut Daniel, in Dante's *Purgatorio* (26.117): he is "the better craftsman."   4. From the burial service of the Anglican Church.

A little life with dried tubers.
Summer surprised us, coming over the Starnbergersee[5]
With a shower of rain; we stopped in the colonnade,
And went on in sunlight, into the Hofgarten,[6]   10
And drank coffee, and talked for an hour.
Bin gar keine Russin, stamm' aus Litauen, echt deutsch.[7]
And when we were children, staying at the archduke's,
My cousin's, he took me out on a sled,
And I was frightened. He said, Marie,   15
Marie, hold on tight. And down we went.
In the mountains, there you feel free.
I read, much of the night, and go south in the winter.

What are the roots that clutch, what branches grow
Out of this stony rubbish? Son of man,[8]   20
You cannot say, or guess, for you know only
A heap of broken images, where the sun beats,
And the dead tree gives no shelter, the cricket no relief,[9]
And the dry stone no sound of water. Only
There is shadow under this red rock,   25
(Come in under the shadow of this red rock),
And I will show you something different from either
Your shadow at morning striding behind you
Or your shadow at evening rising to meet you;
I will show you fear in a handful of dust.   30
                    Frisch weht der Wind
                    Der Heimat zu
                    Mein Irisch Kind,
                    Wo weilest du?[1]
"You gave me hyacinths first a year ago;   35
"They called me the hyacinth girl."
—Yet when we came back, late, from the Hyacinth garden,
Your arms full, and your hair wet, I could not
Speak, and my eyes failed, I was neither
Living nor dead, and I knew nothing,   40
Looking into the heart of light, the silence.
Oed' und leer das Meer.[2]

Madame Sosostris, famous clairvoyante,[3]
Had a bad cold, nevertheless
Is known to be the wisest woman in Europe,   45
With a wicked pack of cards.[4] Here, said she,

---

5. A lake near Munich. Lines 8–16 recall *My Past*, the memoirs of Countess Marie Larisch.   6. A public park.   7. "I am certainly no Russian, I come from Lithuania and am pure German." German settlers in Lithuania considered themselves superior to the Slavic natives.   8. "Cf. Ezekiel II,i" [Eliot's note]. The passage reads "Son of man, stand upon thy feet, and I will speak unto thee."   9. "Cf. Ecclesiastes XII,v" [Eliot's note]. "Also when they shall be afraid of that which is high, and fears shall be in the way . . . the grasshopper shall be a burden, and desire shall fail."   1. "V. *Tristan und Isolde*, I, verses 5–8" [Eliot's note]. A sailor in Richard Wagner's opera sings "The wind blows fresh / Towards the homeland / My Irish child / Where are you waiting?"   2. "Id. III, verse 24" [Eliot's note]. "Barren and empty is the sea" is the erroneous report the dying Tristan hears as he waits for Isolde's ship in the third act of Wagner's opera.   3. A fortune-teller with an assumed Egyptian name, possibly suggested by a similar figure in a novel by Aldous Huxley (*Crome Yellow*, 1921).   4. "I am not familiar with the exact constitution of the Tarot pack of cards, from which I have obviously departed to suit my own convenience. The Hanged Man, a member of the traditional pack, fits my purpose in two ways: because he is associated in my mind with the Hanged God of Frazer, and because I associate him with the hooded figure in the passage of the disciples to Emmaus in Part V. The Phoenician Sailor and the Merchant appear later; also the 'crowds of people,' and Death by Water is executed in Part IV. The

Is your card, the drowned Phoenician Sailor,
(Those are pearls that were his eyes.⁵ Look!)
Here is Belladonna, the Lady of the Rocks,
The lady of situations.   50
Here is the man with three staves, and here the Wheel,
And here is the one-eyed merchant, and this card,
Which is blank, is something he carries on his back,
Which I am forbidden to see. I do not find
The Hanged Man. Fear death by water.   55
I see crowds of people, walking round in a ring.
Thank you. If you see dear Mrs. Equitone,
Tell her I bring the horoscope myself:
One must be so careful these days.

    Unreal City,⁶   60
Under the brown fog of a winter dawn,
A crowd flowed over London Bridge, so many,
I had not thought death had undone so many.⁷
Sighs, short and infrequent, were exhaled,⁸
And each man fixed his eyes before his feet.   65
Flowed up the hill and down King William Street,
To where Saint Mary Woolnoth kept the hours
With a dead sound on the final stroke of nine.⁹
There I saw one I knew, and stopped him, crying: "Stetson!
"You who were with me in the ships at Mylae!¹   70
"That corpse you planted last year in your garden,
"Has it begun to sprout? Will it bloom this year?
"Or has the sudden frost disturbed its bed?
"Oh keep the Dog far hence, that's friend to men,²

Man with Three Staves (an authentic member of the Tarot pack) I associate, quite arbitrarily, with the Fisher King himself" [Eliot's note]. Tarot cards are used for telling fortunes; the four suits (cup, lance, sword, and dish) are life symbols related to the Grail legend and, as Eliot suggests, various figures on the cards are associated with different characters and situations in *The Waste Land*. For example: the "drowned Phoenician Sailor" recurs in the merchant from Smyrna (III) and Phlebas the Phoenician (IV); Belladonna (a poison, hallucinogen, medicine, and cosmetic; in Italian, "beautiful lady"; also an echo of Leonardo da Vinci's painting of the Virgin, *Madonna of the Rocks*) heralds the neurotic society woman amid her jewels and perfumes (II); the Wheel is the wheel of fortune; the Hanged Man becomes the sacrificed fertility god whose death ensures resurrection and new life for his people.   5. A line from Ariel's song in Shakespeare's *The Tempest* (1.2.398), which describes the transformation of a drowned man.   6. "Cf. Baudelaire: 'Fourmillante cité, cité pleine de rêves, / Où le spectre en plein jour raccroche le passant' " [Eliot's note]. "Swarming city, city full of dreams, / Where the specter in broad daylight accosts the passerby"; a description of Paris from "The Seven Old Men" in *The Flowers of Evil* (1857).   7. "Cf. *Inferno* III, 55–57: 'si lunga tratta / di gente, ch'io non avrei mai creduto / che morte tanta n'avesse disfatta' " [Eliot's note]. "So long a train / of people, that I would never have believed / death had undone so many"; not only is Dante amazed at the number of people who have died but he is also describing a crowd of people who were neither good nor bad—nonentities denied even the entrance to Hell.   8. "Cf. *Inferno* IV, 25–27: 'Quivi, secondo che per ascoltare, / non avea pianto, ma' che di sospiri, / che l'aura eterna facevan tremare' " [Eliot's note]. "Here, so far as I could tell by listening, there was no weeping but so many sighs that they caused the everlasting air to tremble"; the first circle of Hell, or Limbo, contained the souls of virtuous people who lived before Christ or had not been baptized.   9. "A phenomenon which I have often noticed" [Eliot's note]. The church is in the financial district of London, where King William Street is also located.   1. An "average" modern name (with business associations) linked to the ancient battle of Mylae (260 B.C.), where Rome was victorious over its commercial rival, Carthage.   2. "Cf. the Dirge in Webster's *White Devil*" [Eliot's note]. The dirge, or song of lamentation, sung by Cornelia in John Webster's play (1625), asks to "keep the wolf far thence, that's foe to men," so that the wolf's nails may not dig up the bodies of her murdered relatives. Eliot's reversal of dog for wolf, and friend for foe, domesticates the grotesque scene; it may also foreshadow rebirth since (according to Weston's book), the rise of the Dog Star Sirius announced the flooding of the Nile and the consequent return of fertility to Egyptian soil.

"Or with his nails he'll dig it up again!   75
"You! hypocrite lecteur! — mon semblable, — mon frère!"[3]

II. A GAME OF CHESS[4]

   The Chair she sat in, like a burnished throne,[5]
Glowed on the marble, where the glass
Held up by standards wrought with fruited vines
From which a golden Cupidon peeped out   80
(Another hid his eyes behind his wing)
Doubled the flames of sevenbranched candelabra
Reflecting light upon the table as
The glitter of her jewels rose to meet it,
From satin cases poured in rich profusion.   85
In vials of ivory and coloured glass
Unstoppered, lurked her strange synthetic perfumes,
Unguent, powdered, or liquid — troubled, confused
And drowned the sense in odours; stirred by the air
That freshened from the window, these ascended   90
In fattening the prolonged candle-flames,
Flung their smoke into the laquearia,[6]
Stirring the pattern on the coffered ceiling.
Huge sea-wood fed with copper
Burned green and orange, framed by the coloured stone,   95
In which sad light a carvèd dolphin swam.
Above the antique mantel was displayed
As though a window gave upon the sylvan scene[7]
The change of Philomel,[8] by the barbarous king
So rudely forced; yet there the nightingale[9]   100
Filled all the desert with inviolable voice
And still she cried, and still the world pursues,
"Jug Jug"[1] to dirty ears.
And other withered stumps of time
Were told upon the walls; staring forms   105
Leaned out, leaning, hushing the room enclosed.
Footsteps shuffled on the stair.
Under the firelight, under the brush, her hair
Spread out in fiery points
Glowed into words, then would be savagely still.   110

---

3. "V. Baudelaire, Preface to *Fleurs du Mal*" [Eliot's note]. Baudelaire's poem preface, titled "To the
Reader," ended "Hypocritical reader! — my likeness! — my brother!" The poet challenges the reader to
recognize that both are caught up in the worst sin of all — the moral wasteland of *ennui* ("boredom") as
lack of will, the refusal to care one way or the other.   4. Reference to a play, *A Game of Chess* (1627)
by Thomas Middleton (1580–1627); see n. 4, p. 2794. Part II juxtaposes two scenes of modern sterility:
an initial setting of wealthy boredom, neurosis, and lack of communication, and a pub scene where
similar concerns of appearance, sexual attraction, and thwarted childbirth are brought out more visibly,
and in more vulgar language.   5. "Cf. *Antony and Cleopatra*, II, ii, l. 190" [Eliot's note]. A paler
version of Cleopatra's splendor as she met her future lover Antony: "The barge she sat in, like a burnished throne, / Burned on the water."   6. "Laquearia. V. *Aeneid*, I, 726: dependent lychni laquearibus
aureis incensi, et noctem flammis funalia vincunt" [Eliot's note]. "Glowing lamps hang from the gold-
paneled ceiling, and the torches conquer night with their flames"; the banquet setting of another classical love scene, where Dido is inspired with a fatal passion for Aeneas.   7. "Sylvan scene. V. Milton,
Paradise Lost, IV, 140" [Eliot's note]. Eden as first seen by Satan.   8. "V. Ovid, *Metamorphoses*, VI,
Philomela" [Eliot's note]. Philomela was raped by her brother-in-law, King Tereus, who cut out her
tongue so that she could not tell her sister, Procne. Later Procne is changed into a swallow, and Philomela into a nightingale, to save them from the king's rage after they have revenged themselves by killing
his son.   9. "Cf. Part III, l. 204" [Eliot's note].   1. Represents the nightingale's song in Elizabethan poetry.

"My nerves are bad to-night. Yes, bad. Stay with me.
Speak to me. Why do you never speak. Speak.
What are you thinking of? What thinking? What?
I never know what you are thinking. Think."

I think we are in rats' alley[2]   115
Where the dead men lost their bones.

"What is that noise?"
       The wind under the door.[3]
"What is that noise now? What is the wind doing?"
       Nothing again nothing.   120
          "Do
"You know nothing? Do you see nothing? Do you remember
"Nothing?"

   I remember
Those are pearls that were his eyes.   125
"Are you alive, or not? Is there nothing in your head?"
             But
O O O O that Shakespeherian Rag—
It's so elegant
So intelligent   130
"What shall I do now? What shall I do?"
"I shall rush out as I am, and walk the street
"With my hair down, so. What shall we do to-morrow?
"What shall we ever do?"
       The hot water at ten.   135
And if it rains, a closed car at four.
And we shall play a game of chess,[4]
Pressing lidless eyes and waiting for a knock upon the door.

 When Lil's husband got demobbed,[5] I said—
I didn't mince my words, I said to her myself,   140
HURRY UP PLEASE ITS TIME[6]
Now Albert's coming back, make yourself a bit smart.
He'll want to know what you done with that money he gave you
To get yourself some teeth. He did, I was there.
You have them all out, Lil, and get a nice set,   145
He said, I swear, I can't bear to look at you.
And no more can't I, I said, and think of poor Albert,
He's been in the army four years, he wants a good time,
And if you don't give it him, there's others will, I said.
Oh is there, she said. Something o' that, I said.   150
Then I'll know who to thank, she said, and give me a straight look.
HURRY UP PLEASE ITS TIME
If you don't like it you can get on with it, I said.
Others can pick and choose if you can't.
But if Albert makes off, it won't be for lack of telling. 155
You ought to be ashamed, I said, to look so antique.

---

2. "Cf. Part III, 1. 195" [Eliot's note]. 3. "Cf. Webster: 'Is the wind in that door still?'" [Eliot's note]. From *The Devil's Law Case* (1623), 3.2.162, with the implied meaning "is there still breath in him?" 4. "Cf. the game of chess in Middleton's *Women Beware Women*" [Eliot's note]. In this scene, a woman is seduced in a series of strategic steps that parallel the moves of a chess game occupying her mother-in-law at the same time. 5. Demobilized, discharged from the army. 6. The British bartender's warning that the pub is about to close.

(And her only thirty-one.)
I can't help it, she said, pulling a long face,
It's them pills I took, to bring it off, she said.
(She's had five already, and nearly died of young George.)   160
The chemist[7] said it would be all right, but I've never been the same.
You are a proper fool, I said.
Well, if Albert won't leave you alone, there it is, I said,
What you get married for if you don't want children?
HURRY UP PLEASE ITS TIME   165
Well, that Sunday Albert was home, they had a hot gammon,[8]
And they asked me in to dinner, to get the beauty of it hot—
HURRY UP PLEASE ITS TIME
HURRY UP PLEASE ITS TIME
Goonight Bill. Goonight Lou. Goonight May. Goonight.   170
Ta ta. Goonight. Goonight.
Good night, ladies, good night, sweet ladies, good night, good night.[9]

III. THE FIRE SERMON[1]

The river's tent is broken: the last fingers of leaf
Clutch and sink into the wet bank. The wind
Crosses the brown land, unheard. The nymphs are departed.   175
Sweet Thames, run softly, till I end my song.[2]
The river bears no empty bottles, sandwich papers,
Silk handkerchiefs, cardboard boxes, cigarette ends
Or other testimony of summer nights. The nymphs are departed.
And their friends, the loitering heirs of city directors;   180
Departed, have left no addresses.
By the waters of Leman[3] I sat down and wept . . .
Sweet Thames, run softly till I end my song,
Sweet Thames, run softly, for I speak not loud or long.
But at my back in a cold blast I hear[4]   185
The rattle of the bones, and chuckle spread from ear to ear.

A rat crept softly through the vegetation
Dragging its slimy belly on the bank
While I was fishing in the dull canal
On a winter evening round behind the gashouse   190
Musing upon the king my brother's wreck
And on the king my father's death before him.[5]
White bodies naked on the low damp ground
And bones cast in a little low dry garret,
Rattled by the rat's foot only, year to year.   195

---

7. The druggist, who gave her pills to cause a miscarriage.   8. Ham.   9. The popular song for a
party's end ("Good Night, Ladies") shifts into Ophelia's last words in *Hamlet* (4.5.72) as she goes off to
drown herself.   1. Reference to the Buddha's Fire Sermon (see n. 1, p. 2799) in which he denounced
the fiery lusts and passions of earthly experience. "All things are on fire . . . with the fire of passion . . .
of hatred . . . of infatuation." Part III describes the degeneration of even these passions in the sterile
decadence of the modern Waste Land.   2. "V. Spenser, *Prothalamion*" [Eliot's note]. The line is the
refrain of a marriage song by the Elizabethan poet Edmund Spenser (1552?–1599) and evokes a river
of unpolluted pastoral beauty.   3. Lake Geneva (where Eliot wrote much of *The Waste Land*). A
leman is a mistress or lover. In Psalm 137:1, the exiled Hebrews sit by the rivers of Babylon and weep
for their lost homeland.   4. Distorted echo of Andrew Marvell's (1621–1678) poem *To His Coy Mistress:* "But at my back I always hear / Time's wingèd chariot hurrying near."   5. "Cf. *The Tempest*
I.ii" [Eliot's note]. Ferdinand, the king's son, believing his father drowned and mourning his death,
hears in the air a song containing the line that Eliot quotes earlier at lines 48 and 126.

But at my back from time to time I hear[6]
The sound of horns and motors, which shall bring[7]
Sweeney to Mrs. Porter in the spring.
O the moon shone bright on Mrs. Porter[8]
And on her daughter   200
They wash their feet in soda water
Et O ces voix d'enfants, chantant dans la coupole![9]

Twit twit twit
Jug jug jug jug jug jug
So rudely forc'd.   205
Tereu[1]

    Unreal City
Under the brown fog of a winter noon
Mr. Eugenides, the Smyrna merchant
Unshaven, with a pocket full of currants   210
C.i.f. London: documents at sight,[2]
Asked me in demotic French
To luncheon at the Cannon Street Hotel
Followed by a weekend at the Metropole.[3]

    At the violet hour, when the eyes and back   215
Turn upward from the desk, when the human engine waits
Like a taxi throbbing waiting,
I Tiresias,[4] though blind, throbbing between two lives,
Old man with wrinkled female breasts, can see
At the violet hour, the evening hour that strives   220
Homeward, and brings the sailor home from sea,[5]
The typist home at teatime, clears her breakfast, lights
Her stove, and lays out food in tins.
Out of the window perilously spread
Her drying combinations touched by the sun's last rays,   225

---

6. "Cf. Marvell, 'To His Coy Mistress' " [Eliot's note].   7. "Cf. Day, *Parliament of Bees:* 'When of
the sudden, listening, you shall hear, / A noise of horns and hunting, which shall bring / Actaeon to
Diana in the spring, / Where all shall see her naked skin.' " [Eliot's note]. The young hunter Actaeon
was changed into a stag, hunted down, and killed when he came upon the goddess Diana bathing.
Sweeney is in no such danger from his visit to Mrs. Porter.   8. "I do not know the origin of the ballad
from which these lines are taken: it was reported to me from Sydney, Australia" [Eliot's note]. A song
popular among Allied troops during World War I. One version continues lines 199–201 as follows: "And
so they oughter / To keep them clean."   9. "V. Verlaine, *Parsifal*" [Eliot's note]. "And O these children's voices, singing in the dome!"; the last lines of a sonnet by Paul Verlaine (1844–1896), which
ambiguously celebrates the Grail hero's chaste restraint. In Richard Wagner's opera, Parsifal's feet are
washed to purify him before entering the presence of the Grail.   1. Tereus, who raped Philomela (see
line 99); also the nightingale's song.   2. "The currants were quoted at a price 'carriage and insurance
free to London'; and the Bill of Lading etc. were to be handed to the buyer upon payment of the sight
draft" [Eliot's note].   3. Smyrna is an ancient Phoenician seaport, and early Smyrna merchants spread
the Eastern fertility cults. In contrast, their descendant Mr. Eugenides ("Well-born") invites the poet to
lunch in a large commercial hotel and a weekend at a seaside resort in Brighton.   4. "Tiresias,
although a mere spectator and not indeed a 'character,' is yet the most important personage in the
poem, uniting all the rest. Just as the one-eyed merchant, seller of currants, melts into the Phoenician
Sailor, and the latter is not wholly distinct from Ferdinand Prince of Naples, so all the women are one
woman, and the two sexes meet in Tiresias. What Tiresias *sees*, in fact, is the substance of the poem.
The whole passage from Ovid is one of great anthropological interest" [Eliot's note]. The passage then
quoted from Ovid's *Metamorphoses* (3.320–38) describes how Tiresias spent seven years of his life as a
woman and thus experienced love from the point of view of both sexes. Blinded by Juno, he was
recompensed by Jove with the gift of prophecy.   5. "This may or may not appear as exact as Sappho's
lines, but I had in mind the 'longshore' or 'dory' fisherman, who returns at nightfall" [Eliot's note]. The
Greek poet Sappho's poem describes how the evening star brings home those whom dawn has sent
abroad; there is also an echo of Robert Louis Stevenson's (1850–1894) *Requiem*, 1.221: "Home is the
sailor, home from the sea."

On the divan are piled (at night her bed)
Stockings, slippers, camisoles, and stays.
I Tiresias, old man with wrinkled dugs
Perceived the scene, and foretold the rest—
I too awaited the expected guest.   230
He, the young man carbuncular, arrives,
A small house agent's clerk, with one bold stare,
One of the low on whom assurance sits
As a silk hat on a Bradford[6] millionaire.
The time is now propitious, as he guesses,   235
The meal is ended, she is bored and tired,
Endeavours to engage her in caresses
Which still are unreproved, if undesired.
Flushed and decided, he assaults at once;
Exploring hands encounter no defence;   240
His vanity requires no response,
And makes a welcome of indifference.
(And I Tiresias have foresuffered all
Enacted on this same divan or bed;
I who have sat by Thebes below the wall   245
And walked among the lowest of the dead.)[7]
Bestows one final patronising kiss,
And gropes his way, finding the stairs unlit . . .

     She turns and looks a moment in the glass,
Hardly aware of her departed lover;   250
Her brain allows one half-formed thought to pass:
"Well now that's done: and I'm glad it's over."
When lovely woman stoops to folly and[8]
Paces about her room again, alone,
She smoothes her hair with automatic hand,   255
And puts a record on the gramophone.

"This music crept by me upon the waters"[9]
And along the Strand, up Queen Victoria Street.
O City city,[1] I can sometimes hear
Beside a public bar in Lower Thames Street,   260
The pleasant whining of a mandoline
And a clatter and a chatter from within
Where fishmen lounge at noon: where the walls
Of Magnus Martyr hold[2]
Inexplicable splendour of Ionian white and gold.   265

---

6. A manufacturing town in Yorkshire, which prospered greatly during World War I.   7. Tiresias
prophesied in the marketplace at Thebes for many years before dying and continuing to prophesy in
Hades.   8. "V. Goldsmith, the song in *The Vicar of Wakefield*" [Eliot's note]. "When lovely woman
stoops to folly / And finds too late that men betray / What charm can soothe her melancholy, / What
art can wash her guilt away?" Oliver Goldsmith (ca. 1730–1774), *The Vicar of Wakefield* (1766).
9. "V. *The Tempest*, as above" [Eliot's note, referring to line 191]. Spoken by Ferdinand as he hears
Ariel sing of his father's transformation by the sea, his eyes turning to pearls, his bones to coral, and
everything else he formerly was into "something rich and strange."   1. A double invocation: the city
of London and the City as London's central financial district (see lines 60 and 207). See also lines 375–
6, the great cities of Western civilization.   2. "The interior of St. Magnus Martyr is to my mind one
of the finest among Wren's interiors. See *The Proposed Demolition of Nineteen City Churches*: (P. S.
King & Son, Ltd)" [Eliot's note]. The architect was Christopher Wren (1632–1723), and the church is
located just below London Bridge on Lower Thames Street.

The river sweats[3]
Oil and tar
The barges drift
With the turning tide
Red sails   270
Wide
To leeward, swing on the heavy spar.
The barges wash
Drifting logs
Down Greenwich reach   275
Past the Isle of Dogs.[4]
     Weialala leia
     Wallala leialala

Elizabeth and Leicester[5]
Beating oars   280
The stern was formed
A gilded shell
Red and gold
The brisk swell
Rippled both shores   285
Southwest wind
Carried down stream
The peal of bells
White towers
     Weialala leia   290
     Wallala leialala

"Trams and dusty trees.
Highbury bore me. Richmond and Kew
Undid me.[6] By Richmond I raised my knees
Supine on the floor of a narrow canoe."   295

"My feet are at Moorgate,[7] and my heart
Under my feet. After the event
He wept. He promised 'a new start.'
I made no comment. What should I resent?"

"On Margate Sands.[8]   300
I can connect
Nothing with nothing.
The broken fingernails of dirty hands.
My people humble people who expect

---

3. "The Song of the (three) Thames-daughters begins here. From line 292 to 306 inclusive they speak
in turn. V. *Götterdämmerung* III.i: the Rhine-daughters" [Eliot's note]. In Wagner's opera *The Twilight
of the Gods* (1876), the three Rhine-maidens mourn the loss of their gold, which gave the river its
sparkling beauty; lines 177–8 here echo the Rhine-maidens' refrain.   4. A peninsula opposite Greenwich on the Thames.   5. "V. Froude, *Elizabeth*, vol. I, ch. iv, letter of De Quadra to Philip of Spain:
'In the afternoon we were in a barge, watching the games on the river. (The queen) was alone with
Lord Robert and myself on the poop, when they began to talk nonsense, and went so far that Lord
Robert at last said, as I was on the spot there was no reason why they should not be married if the
queen pleased" [Eliot's note]. Sir Robert Dudley (1532–1588) was the earl of Leicester, a favorite of
Queen Elizabeth who at one point hoped to marry her.   6. "Cf. *Purgatorio*, V, 133: 'Ricordati di
me, che son la Pia, / Siena mi fe', disfecemi Maremma' " [Eliot's note]. La Pia, in Purgatory, recalls
her seduction: "Remember me, who am La Pia. / Siena made me, Maremma undid me." Eliot's parody
substitutes Highbury (a London suburb) and Richmond and Kew, popular excursion points on the
Thames.   7. A London slum.   8. A seaside resort on the Thames.

Nothing."   305
    la la
To Carthage then I came[9]
Burning burning burning burning[1]
O Lord Thou pluckest me out[2]
O Lord Thou pluckest   310

burning

IV. DEATH BY WATER

Phlebas the Phoenician, a fortnight dead,
Forgot the cry of gulls, and the deep sea swell
And the profit and loss.
          A current under sea   315
Picked his bones in whispers. As he rose and fell
He passed the stages of his age and youth
Entering the whirlpool.
          Gentile or Jew
O you who turn the wheel and look to windward,   320
Consider Phlebas, who was once handsome and tall as you.

V. WHAT THE THUNDER SAID[3]

After the torchlight red on sweaty faces
After the frosty silence in the gardens
After the agony in stony places
The shouting and the crying   325
Prison and palace and reverberation
Of thunder of spring over distant mountains
He who was living is now dead[4]
We who were living are now dying
With a little patience   330

    Here is no water but only rock
Rock and no water and the sandy road
The road winding above among the mountains
Which are mountains of rock without water
If there were water we should stop and drink   335
Amongst the rock one cannot stop or think
Sweat is dry and feet are in the sand

---

9. "V. St. Augustine's *Confessions:* 'to Carthage then I came, where a cauldron of unholy loves sang all about mine ears' " [Eliot's note]. The youthful Augustine is described. Carthage is also the scene of Dido's faithful love for Aeneas, referred to in line 92.   1. "The complete text of the Buddha's Fire Sermon (which corresponds in importance to the Sermon on the Mount) from which these words are taken, will be found translated in the late Henry Clarke Warren's *Buddhism in Translation* (Harvard Oriental Studies). Mr. Warren was one of the great pioneers of Buddhist studies in the Occident" [Eliot's note]. The Sermon on the Mount is in Matthew 5–7.   2. "From St. Augustine's *Confessions* again. The collocation of these two representatives of eastern and western asceticism, as the culmination of this part of the poem is not an accident" [Eliot's note]. See also Zechariah 3:2, where the high priest Joshua is described as a "brand plucked out of the fire."   3. "In the first part of Part V three themes are employed: the journey to Emmaus, the approach to the Chapel Perilous (see Miss Weston's book) and the present decay of eastern Europe" [Eliot's note]. On their journey to Emmaus (Luke 24:13–34), Jesus' disciples were joined by a stranger who later revealed himself to be the crucified and resurrected Christ. The Thunder of the title is a divine voice in the Hindu *Upanishads* (see n. 2, p. 2801). 4. Allusions to stages in Christ's Passion: the betrayal, prayer in the garden of Gethsemane, imprisonment, trial, crucifixion, and burial. Despair reigns, for this is death before the Resurrection.

If there were only water amongst the rock
'Dead mountain mouth of carious teeth that cannot spit
Here one can neither stand nor lie nor sit   340
There is not even silence in the mountains
But dry sterile thunder without rain
There is not even solitude in the mountains
But red sullen faces sneer and snarl
From doors of mudcracked houses   345
                    If there were water
   And no rock
   If there were rock
   And also water
   And water   350
   A spring
   A pool among the rock
   If there were the sound of water only
   Not the cicada[5]
   And dry grass singing   355
   But sound of water over a rock
   Where the hermit-thrush[6] sings in the pine trees
   Drip drop drip drop drop drop drop
But there is no water

Who is the third who walks always beside you?   360
When I count, there are only you and I together[7]
But when I look ahead up the white road
There is always another one walking beside you
Gliding wrapt in a brown mantle, hooded
I do not know whether a man or a woman   365
—But who is that on the other side of you?

   What is that sound high in the air[8]
Murmur of maternal lamentation
Who are those hooded hordes swarming
Over endless plains, stumbling in cracked earth   370
Ringed by the flat horizon only
What is the city over the mountains
Cracks and reforms and bursts in the violet air
Falling towers
Jerusalem Athens Alexandria   375
Vienna London
Unreal

   A woman drew her long black hair out tight
And fiddled whisper music on those strings
And bats with baby faces in the violet light   380
Whistled, and beat their wings

5. Grasshopper or cricket; see line 23.   6. "The hermit-thrush which I have heard in Quebec Province. . . . Its 'water-dripping song' is justly celebrated" [Eliot's note].   7. "The following lines were
stimulated by the account of one of the Antarctic expeditions (I forget which, but I think one of Shack-
leton's): it was related that the party of explorers, at the extremity of their strength, had the constant
delusion that there was *one more member* than could actually be counted" [Eliot's note]. See also n. 3,
p. 2799.   8. Eliot's note to lines 367–77 refers to Hermann Hesse's *Blick ins Chaos* (Glimpse into
chaos), and a passage that reads, translated, "Already half of Europe, already at least half of Eastern
Europe is on the way to Chaos, drives drunk in holy madness on the edge of the abyss and sings at the
same time, sings drunk and hymn-like, as Dimitri Karamazov sang [in Dostoevsky's *The Brothers Karamazov*]. The offended bourgeois laughs at the songs; the saint and the seer hear them with tears."

And crawled head downward down a blackened wall
And upside down in air were towers
Tolling reminiscent bells, that kept the hours
And voices singing out of empty cisterns and exhausted wells. 385

   In this decayed hole among the mountains
In the faint moonlight, the grass is singing
Over the tumbled graves, about the chapel
There is the empty chapel, only the wind's home.
It has no windows, and the door swings, 390
Dry bones can harm no one.
Only a cock stood on the rooftree
Co co rico co co rico[9]
In a flash of lightning. Then a damp gust
Bringing rain 395

   Ganga was sunken, and the limp leaves
Waited for rain, while the black clouds
Gathered far distant, over Himavant.[1]
The jungle crouched, humped in silence.
Then spoke the thunder 400
DA
Datta: what have we given?[2]
My friend, blood shaking my heart
The awful daring of a moment's surrender
Which an age of prudence can never retract 405
By this, and this only, we have existed
Which is not to be found in our obituaries
Or in memories draped by the beneficent spider[3]
Or under seals broken by the lean solicitor
In our empty rooms 410
DA
Dayadhvam:[4] I have heard the key
Turn in the door once and turn once only
We think of the key, each in his prison
Thinking of the key, each confirms a prison 415
Only at nightfall, aethereal rumours
Revive for a moment a broken Coriolanus[5]

9. European version of the cock's crow: cock-a-doodle-doo. The cock crowed in Matthew 26:34, 74, after Peter had denied Jesus three times.   1. A mountain in the Himalayas. *Ganga*: the river Ganges in India.   2. " 'Datta, dayadhvam, damyata' (Give, sympathise, control). The fable of the meaning of the Thunder is found in the *Brihadaranyaka*—Upanishad 5,1" [Eliot's note]. In the fable, the word DA, spoken by the supreme being Prajapati, is interpreted as *Datta* (to give alms), *Dayadhvam* (to sympathize or have compassion), and *Damyata* (to have self-control) by gods, human beings, and demons respectively. The conclusion is that when the thunder booms DA DA DA, Prajapati is commanding that all three virtues be practiced simultaneously.   3. "Cf. Webster, *The White Devil*, V, vi: '... they'll remarry / Ere the worm pierce your winding-sheet, ere the spider / Make a thin curtain for your epitaphs" [Eliot's note].   4. Eliot's note on the command to "sympathize" or reach outside the self cites two descriptions of helpless isolation. The first comes from Dante's *Inferno* 33:46: as Ugolino, imprisoned in a tower with his children to die of starvation, says "And I heard below the door of the horrible tower being locked up"). The second is a modern description by the English philosopher F. H. Bradley (1846–1924) of the inevitably self-enclosed or private nature of consciousness: "My external sensations are no less private to myself than are my thoughts or my feelings. In either case my experience falls within my own circle, a circle closed on the outside; and, with all its elements alike, every sphere is opaque to the others which surround it. ... In brief, regarded as an existence which appears in a soul, the whole world for each is peculiar and private to that soul" (*Appearance and Reality*).   5. A proud Roman patrician who was exiled and led an army against his homeland. In Shakespeare's play, both his grandeur and his downfall come from a desire to be ruled only by himself.

DA
Damyata: The boat responded
Gaily, to the hand expert with sail and oar   420
The sea was calm, your heart would have responded
Gaily, when invited, beating obedient
To controlling hands
                    I sat upon the shore
Fishing,[6] with the arid plain behind me   425
Shall I at least set my lands in order?
London Bridge is falling down falling down falling down
Poi s'ascose nel foco che gli affina[7]
Quando fiam uti chelidon[8]—O swallow swallow
Le Prince d'Aquitaine à la tour abolie[9]   430
These fragments I have shored against my ruins
Why then Ile fit you. Hieronymo's mad againe.[1]
Datta. Dayadhvam. Damyata.
          Shantih   shantih   shantih[2]

6. "V. Weston: *From Ritual to Romance;* chapter on the Fisher King" [Eliot's note].   7. Eliot's note quotes a passage in the *Purgatorio* in which Arnaut Daniel (see n. 3, p. 2790) asks Dante to remember his pain. The line cited here, "then he hid himself in the fire which refines them" (*Purgatorio* 26.148), shows Daniel departing in fire which—in Purgatory—exists as a purifying rather than a destructive element.   8. "V. *Pervigilium Veneris.* Cf. Philomela in Parts II and III [Eliot's note]. "When shall I be as a swallow?" A line from the *Vigil of Venus,* an anonymous late Latin poem, that asks for the gift of song; here associated with Philomela as a swallow, not the nightingale of lines 99–103 and 203–6. 9. "V. Gerard de Nerval, Sonnet *El Desdichado*" [Eliot's note]. The Spanish title means "The Disinherited One," and the sonnet is a monologue describing the speaker as a melancholy, ill-starred dreamer: "the Prince of Aquitaine in his ruined tower." Another line recalls the scene at the end of *Love Song of J. Alfred Prufrock* (p. 2790): "I dreamed in the grotto where sirens swim."   1. "V. Kyd's *Spanish Tragedy*" [Eliot's note]. Thomas Kyd's revenge play (1594) is subtitled "Hieronymo's Mad Againe." The protagonist "fits" his son's murderers into appropriate roles in a court entertainment so that they may all be killed.   2. "Shantih. Repeated as here, a formal ending to an Upanishad. 'The Peace which passeth understanding' is our equivalent to this word' " [Eliot's note]. The *Upanishads* comment on the sacred Hindu scriptures, the *Vedas.*

ANNA AKHMATOVA
1889–1966

The voice of Anna Akhmatova is intensely personal, whether she speaks as lover, wife, and mother or as a national poet commemorating the mute agony of millions. From the subjective love lyrics of her earliest work to the communal mourning of *Requiem* and the many-layered drama of *Poem without a Hero,* she expresses universal themes in terms of individual experience, and historical events through the filter of basic emotions like fear, love, hope, and pain. Akhmatova is one of the great Russian poets of the twentieth century, but she retains a broad sense of European culture, both past and present, and fills her later works with references to Western music, literature, and art that give a startling breadth and scope to her very personalized poetry. Too cosmopolitan and too independent to be tolerated by the authorities, Akhmatova was viciously attacked and her books suppressed (1922–40) because they did not fit the government-approved model of literature: they were too "individualistic" and were not "socially useful." Although she was rehabilitated in the 1960s and achieved recognized status as national poet, Akhmatova was read in secret for a long time, chiefly for the perfection of her early love lyrics. After the death of Joseph Stalin in 1953, however, her collected poems—including poems of the war years and unknown texts written during the periods of enforced silence—brought the full range of her work to public attention.

She was born Anna Andreevna Gorenko on June 11, 1889, in a suburb of the Black Sea port of Odessa and in a traditional society that she described as "Dostoevsky's Russia." Her father was a maritime engineer and her mother an independent woman of populist sympathies who belonged to an early revolutionary group called People's Will. The poet took the pen name of Akhmatova (accented on the second syllable) from her maternal great-grandmother, who was of Tatar descent. Her family soon moved to Tsarskoe Selo ("the Czar's Village"), a small town outside St. Petersburg that had been for centuries the summer palace of the czars, and also—perhaps more important for Akhmatova—a place where the great Romantic poet Alexandr Pushkin wrote his youthful works. She attended the local school at Tsarskoe Selo, but completed her degree in Kiev; in 1907, she briefly studied law at the Kiev College for Women before moving to St. Petersburg to study literature.

In Tsarskoe Selo, Akhmatova met Nikolai Gumilyov, whom she would marry in April 1910. After their marriage, the couple visited Paris during the spring of 1910 and 1911, meeting many writers and artists, including Amedeo Modigliani, who sketched Akhmatova several times and with whom she recalled wandering around Paris and reading aloud the poetry of Paul Verlaine. It was a time of change in the arts, and when the couple returned to St. Petersburg Gumilyov helped organize a Poets' Guild that became the core of a new small literary movement, Acmeism, which rejected the romantic, quasi-religious aims of Russian Symbolism, and (like Imagism) valued clarity and concreteness, and a closeness to things of this earth. The Symbolist–Acmeist debate went on inside a lively literary and social life, while the three main figures of Acmeism—Akhmatova, Gumilyov, and Osip Mandelstam—gained a reputation as important poets.

Akhmatova's first collection of poems, *Evening*, was published in the spring of 1912; it is an intensely personal collection of lyrics in which the poet describes evening as a time of awakening to love—and grief. There is a new clarity and directness to these traditionally romantic subjects, however, as for the first time in Russian poetry a woman in love expresses and analyzes her own emotions. In October of the same year, her son, Lev Gumilyov, was born; it was his arrest and imprisonment in 1935 that inspired the first poems of the cycle that would become *Requiem*. Lev was ultimately imprisoned for a total of fourteen years as the government sought a way to punish his mother, who would not or could not write according to the approved Socialist Realist style praising the government. Even after she had become a national poet known for her patriotic poetry during World War II, Akhmatova was still criticized by the Stalinist régime as a reactionary "half-harlot, half-nun" who wrote subjective love lyrics without social significance: the love poetry of *Evening*, *Rosary* (1914), and *The White Flock* (1917, published a month before the start of the Russian Revolution).

The White Flock was published during World War I, the destruction of which so shocked Akhmatova that she wrote, "This untimely death is so terrible / I cannot look at God's world." Yet more bloodshed was to follow in the civil war following the Revolution of 1917. Akhmatova refused to flee abroad, as many Russians were doing. Her marriage with Gumilyov was breaking up, and they divorced in 1918; she remarried an Assyriologist, Vladimir Shileiko, who did not approve of his wife's writing poetry and burned some of her poems (she divorced him in 1928). Akhmatova's political difficulties began in 1922. Although she and Gumilyov were divorced, his arrest and execution for counterrevolutionary activities in 1921 put her own status into question. After 1922 and the publication of *Anno Domini*, she was no longer allowed to publish, and was forced into the unwilling withdrawal from public activity that Russians call "internal emigration." Officially forgotten, she was not forgotten in fact; in the schools, her poems were copied out by hand and circulated among students who would never hear her name mentioned in a literature class.

Depending on a meager and irregular pension, Akhmatova prepared essays on the life and works of Pushkin, and wrote poems that that would not appear until much later. Stalin's "Great Purge" of 1935–38 sent millions of people to prison camps, and made the 1930s a time of terror and uncertainty for everyone. It is this fear and misery that is expressed in *Requiem*, as the poet blends personal references to her own life with an awareness of the common plight. The art critic Nikolai Punin, with whom she lived from 1926 to 1940, was arrested briefly in 1935; Osip Mandelstam, her great friend, was exiled to Voronezh in May 1934, and then sent to a prison camp in 1938 where he died the same year; her son, Lev, was arrested briefly in 1935 and then again in 1938, remaining imprisoned until 1941 when he was allowed to enroll in military service. Composing *Requiem* itself was a risky act carried out over several years, and Akhmatova and her friend Lidia Chukovskaya memorized the stanzas to preserve the poem in the absence of written copy. Akhmatova wrote of Mandelstam (but perhaps of them all), that "in the room of the poet in disgrace / Fear and the Muse keep watch by turns / And the night comes on / That knows no dawn." A temporary lifting of the ban against her works in 1940 did not last; although she was allowed to publish a new collection, *From Six Books*, the edition was recalled by officials after six months.

It was in 1940 that Akhmatova became interested in larger musical forms and began thinking in terms of cycles of poems instead of her accustomed separate lyrics. She envisaged a larger framework for the core poems of *Requiem* in this year, and wrote the "Dedication" and two epilogues. She also began work on the *Poem without a Hero*, a long and complex verse narrative in three parts that sums up many of her earlier themes: love, death, creativity, the unity of European culture, and the suffering of her people. During World War II the poet was allowed a partial return to public life, addressing women on the radio during the siege of Leningrad (St. Petersburg) in 1941, and writing patriotic lyrics such as the famous *Courage* (published in *Pravda* in 1942) which rallied the Russian people to defend their homeland (and national language) from enslavement. In spite of her patriotic activities, she was subject to vicious official attacks after the war. Stalin's Minister of Culture, Andrei Zhdanov, in a famous Report of 1946 proclaimed the doctrine of Socialist Realism as the official style, and attacked Akhmatova's "individualistic" writing as the "poetry of an overwrought upper-class lady who frantically races back and forth between boudoir and chapel." Akhmatova was immediately expelled from the Writer's Union, which meant that she was not officially recognized as a professional writer (and hence could not earn her living in that career).

Unable once more to publish her work, she supported herself between 1946 and 1958 by translating poetry from a number of foreign languages. Her son had been arrested again in 1949, and hoping to obtain his release, she wrote the kind of adulatory poetry in praise of Stalin that the regime required. The attempt was unsuccessful, and her son remained in prison until 1956. The Stalinist cycle, *In Praise of Peace* (1950), contains such clumsy imitations of socialist-realist poetry that it has been considered a parody: "Where a tank rumbled, there is now a peaceful tractor." Akhmatova later directed that it be omitted from her collected works.

During the slow thaw that followed Stalin's death in 1953, Akhmatova was rehabilitated. Gradually her poems were allowed back into print; an edition of selected poems with added texts was published in 1958, and in the same year she was even elected to an honorary position on the executive council of the Writer's Union. In 1965 a larger collection appeared, *The Flight of Time*, which contained a new series called *The Seventh Book* as well as part of the still-unfinished *Poem without a Hero.* She took an interest in the young writers who flocked to her and supported those who—like Josif Brodsky—were accused by the new order of being a "parasite on the state." Akhmatova's work was already recognized internationally: Robert Frost visited her on his trip to the Soviet Union in 1962, *Requiem* was first published "without her consent" in Munich in 1963 (not until 1987 was the full text published in the Soviet Union), and in 1964 she traveled to Italy to receive the Taormina poetry prize. She was surrounded by admirers when she visited England in 1965 to receive an honorary degree from Oxford University. Her death in 1966 signaled the end of an era in modern Russian poetry, for she was the last of the famous "quartet" that also included Mandelstam, Tsvetaeva, and Pasternak.

Requiem is a lyrical cycle, a series of poems written on a common theme, but it is also a short epic narrative. The story it tells is acutely personal, even autobiographical, but like an epic it also transcends personal significance and describes (as in *The Song of Roland*) a moment in the history of a nation. Akhmatova, who had seen her husband and son arrested and her friends die in prison camps, was only one of millions who had suffered similar losses in the purges of the 1930s. The "Preface," "Dedication," and two epilogues to *Requiem* constitute a framework examining this image of a common fate, while the core of numbered poems develops a more subjective picture, and the stages of an individual drama. In the inner poems, Akhmatova blends her separate personal losses—husband, son, and friends—to create a single focus, the figure of a mother grieving for her condemned son. In the frame, the poet identifies herself with the crowd of women with whom she waited for seventeen months outside the Leningrad prison—women who, in turn, represent bereaved women throughout the Soviet Union. The "I" of the speaker throughout remains anonymous, in spite of the fact that she describes her personal emotions in the central poems; her identity is that of a sorrowing mother, and she is distinguished from her fellow-suffers only by the poetic gift which makes her the "exhausted mouth, / Through which a hundred million scream." *Requiem* is at once a public and a private poem, a picture of individual grief simultaneously linked to a national disaster, and a vision of community suffering that extends past even national disaster into medieval Russian history and Greek mythology. The martyrdom of the Soviet people is consistently pictured in religious terms, from the recurrent mention of crosses and crucifixion to the culminating image of maternal suffering in Mary, the mother of Christ.

The "Dedication" and "Prologue" establish the context for the poem as a whole: the mass arrests in the 1930s after the assassination on December 1, 1934, of Sergei Kirov, the top Communist Party official in Leningrad. The women waiting outside the Kresty ("Crosses") prison of Leningrad arrive at dawn in the coldest of weather, waiting for news of their loved ones, hoping to be allowed to pass them a parcel or a letter, and fearing the sentence of death or exile to the prison camps of frozen Siberia. Instead of living a natural life where "for someone the sunset luxuriates," these women and the prisoners are forced into a suspended existence of separation and uncertainty in which all values are inverted and the city itself has become only the setting for its prisons. It is a situation before which the great forces of nature bow in silent horror.

With the numbered poems, Akhmatova recounts the growing anguish of a bereaved mother as her son is arrested and sentenced to death. The speaker describes her husband's arrest at dawn, in the midst of the family. Her son was arrested later, and in the rest of the poem she relives her numbed incomprehension as she struggles against the increasing likelihood that he will be condemned to death. Recalling her own carefree adolescence in contrast to her current situation as she weeps outside the prison walls, or pleads with Stalin to relent, the mother has a premonition of his fate that pushes her into the temporary relief of insanity and forgetting, and to a desire for her own arrest and death. After sentence is passed, the traumatized mother can speak of his execution only in oblique terms that are at once universal and potentially consoling: by shifting the image of death onto the plane of the Crucifixion and God's will. It is a tragedy that cannot be comprehended or looked at directly just as, she suggests, at the Crucifixion "No one glanced and no one would have dared" to look at the grieving Mary. In the two epilogues, the grieving speaker returns from religious transcendence to earth and current history. Here she takes on a newly composite identity, seeing herself not as an isolated sufferer but as reciprocally identified with the women whose fate she has shared. It is their memory she perpetuates by writing Requiem and it is in their memory that she herself lives on. No longer the victim of purely personal tragedy, she has become a bronze statue commemorating a community of suffering, a figure shaped by circumstances into a monument of public and private grief.

Sam Driver, Anna Akhmatova (1972), is an excellent introduction to Akhmatova's work and its historical context that stresses the years up to 1922. Amanda Haight, Anna Akhmatova: A Poetic Pilgrimage (1976), and Susan Amert, In a Shattered Mirror: The Later Poetry of Anna Akhmatova (1992), are perceptive booklength studies. Ronald Hingley, Nightingale Fever: Russian Poets in Revolution (1981), discusses Akhmatova, Pasternak, Tsvetaeva, and Mandelstam in the context of Russian literary history and Soviet politics up to the early years of World War II. Wendy Rosslyn, ed., The Speech of Unknown Eyes: Akhmatova's Readers on Her Poetry (1990), collects a range of different responses. Sharon Leiter, Akhmatova's Petersburg (1983), examines the image of St. Petersburg as a focus for spiritual and historical themes in Akhmatova's poetry. Editor Roberta Reeder's introduction to the poet's life and works prefaces Judith Hemschemeyer's translations in the bilingual The Complete Poems of Anna Akhmatova (1990). Anna Akhmatova, My Half Century: Selected Prose, ed. Ronald Meyer (1992), includes autobiographical material, correspondence, short pieces on other writers, and an essay on Akhmatova's prose.

Requiem[1]

1935–1940

No, not under the vault of alien skies,[2]
And not under the shelter of alien wings—
I was with my people then,
There, where my people, unfortunately, were.

1961

Instead of a Preface

In the terrible years of the Yezhov terror,[3] I spent seventeen months in the prison lines of Leningrad. Once, someone "recognized" me. Then a woman with bluish lips standing behind me, who, of course, had never heard me called by name before, woke up from the stupor to which everyone had succumbed and whispered in my ear (everyone spoke in whispers there):

---

1. Translated by Judith Hemschemeyer.   2. A phrase borrowed from *Message to Siberia* by the Russian poet Pushkin (1799–1837).   3. In 1937–38, mass arrests were carried out by the secret police, headed by Nikolai Yezhov.

"Can you describe this?"
And I answered: "Yes, I can."
Then something that looked like a smile passed over what had once been her face.

April 1, 1957
Leningrad[4]

Dedication

Mountains bow down to this grief,
Mighty rivers cease to flow,
But the prison gates hold firm,
And behind them are the "prisoners' burrows"
And mortal woe.   5
For someone a fresh breeze blows,
For someone the sunset luxuriates—
We[5] wouldn't know, we are those who everywhere
Hear only the rasp of the hateful key
And the soldiers' heavy tread.   10
We rose as if for an early service,
Trudged through the savaged capital
And met there, more lifeless than the dead;
The sun is lower and the Neva[6] mistier,
But hope keeps singing from afar.   15
The verdict . . . And her tears gush forth,
Already she is cut off from the rest,
As if they painfully wrenched life from her heart,
As if they brutally knocked her flat,
But she goes on . . . Staggering . . . Alone . . .   20
Where now are my chance friends
Of those two diabolical years?
What do they imagine is in Siberia's storms,[7]
What appears to them dimly in the circle of the moon?
I am sending my farewell greeting to them.   25

March 1940

Prologue

That was when the ones who smiled
Were the dead, glad to be at rest.
And like a useless appendage, Leningrad
Swung from its prisons.
And when, senseless from torment,   5
Regiments of convicts marched,
And the short songs of farewell
Were sung by locomotive whistles.
The stars of death stood above us
And innocent Russia writhed   10

---

4. The prose preface was written after her son had been released from prison and it was possible to think of editing the poem for publication.   5. The women waiting in line before the prison gates.
6. The large river that flows through St. Petersburg.   7. Victims of the purges who were not executed were condemned to prison camps in Siberia. Their wives were allowed to accompany them into exile, although they had to live in towns at a distance from the camps.

Under bloody boots
And under the tires of the Black Marias.[8]

I

They led you away at dawn,
I followed you, like a mourner,
In the dark front room the children were crying,[9]
By the icon shelf the candle was dying.
On your lips was the icon's chill.[1]   5
The deathly sweat on your brow . . . Unforgettable! —
I will be like the wives of the Streltsy,
Howling under the Kremlin towers.[2]

1935

II

Quietly flows the quiet Don,[3]
Yellow moon slips into a home.

He slips in with cap askew,
He sees a shadow, yellow moon.

This woman is ill,   5
This woman is alone,

Husband in the grave,[4] son in prison,
Say a prayer for me.

III

No, it is not I, it is somebody else who is suffering.
I would not have been able to bear what happened,
Let them shroud it in black,
And let them carry off the lanterns . . .
                                                    Night.   5

1940

IV

You should have been shown, you mocker,
Minion of all your friends,
Gay little sinner of Tsarskoye Selo,[5]
What would happen in your life —
How three-hundredth in line, with a parcel,   5
You would stand by the Kresty prison,

8. Police cars for conveying those arrested.   9. Akhmatova's third husband, the art historian Nikolai Punin, was arrested at dawn while the children (his daughter and her cousin) cried.   1. The icon—a small religious painting—was set on a shelf before which a candle was kept lit. Punin had kissed the icon before being taken away.   2. *The Streltsy*, elite troops organized by Ivan the Terrible around 1550, rebelled and were executed by Peter the Great in 1698. Pleading in vain, their wives and mothers saw the men killed under the towers of the Kremlin.   3. The great Russian river, often celebrated in folk songs. This poem is modeled on a simple, rhythmic short folk song known as a *chastuska*.
4. Akhmatova's first husband, the poet Nikolai Gumilyov, was shot in 1921.   5. Akhmatova recalls her early, carefree, and privileged life in Tsarskoe Selo outside St. Petersburg.

Your tempestuous tears
Burning through the New Year's ice.
Over there the prison poplar bends,
And there's no sound—and over there how many   10
Innocent lives are ending now . . .

V

For seventeen months I've been crying out,
Calling you home.
I flung myself at the hangman's feet,[6]
You are my son and my horror.
Everything is confused forever,   5
And it's not clear to me
Who is a beast now, who is a man,
And how long before the execution.
And there are only dusty flowers,
And the chinking of the censer, and tracks   10
From somewhere to nowhere.
And staring me straight in the eyes,
And threatening impending death,
Is an enormous star.[7]

1939

VI

The light weeks will take flight,
I won't comprehend what happened.
Just as the white nights[8]
Stared at you, dear son, in prison

So they are staring again,   5
With the burning eyes of a hawk,
Talking about your lofty cross,
And about death.

1939

VII

THE SENTENCE

And the stone word fell
On my still-living breast.
Never mind, I was ready.
I will manage somehow.

Today I have so much to do: 5
I must kill memory once and for all,

---

6. Stalin. Akhmatova wrote a letter to him pleading for the release of her son.   7. The star, the censer and foliage, and the confusion between beast and man recall apocalyptic passages in the Book of Revelation (8:5, 7, 10–11 and 9:7–10).   8. In St. Petersburg, because it is so far north, the nights around the summer solstice are never totally dark.

I must turn my soul to stone,
I must learn to live again —

Unless . . . Summer's ardent rustling
Is like a festival outside my window.   10
For a long time I've foreseen this
Brilliant day, deserted house.

June 22, 1939[9]
Fountain House

VIII

TO DEATH

You will come in any case — so why not now?
I am waiting for you — I can't stand much more.
I've put out the light and opened the door
For you, so simple and miraculous.
So come in any form you please,   5
Burst in as a gas shell
Or, like a gangster, steal in with a length of pipe,
Or poison me with typhus fumes.
Or be that fairy tale you've dreamed up,[1]
So sickeningly familiar to everyone —   10
In which I glimpse the top of a pale blue cap[2]
And the house attendant white with fear.
Now it doesn't matter anymore. The Yenisey[3] swirls,
The North Star shines.
And the final horror dims   15
The blue luster of beloved eyes.

August 19, 1939
Fountain House

IX

Now madness half shadows
My soul with its wing,
And makes it drunk with fiery wine
And beckons toward the black ravine.

And I've finally realized   5
That I must give in,
Overhearing myself
Raving as if it were somebody else.

And it does not allow me to take
Anything of mine with me   10
(No matter how I plead with it,
No matter how I supplicate):

9. The date that her son was sentenced to labor camp.   1. A denunciation to the police for imaginary crimes, common during the purges as people hastened to protect themselves by accusing their neighbor. 2. The NKVD (secret police) wore blue caps.   3. A river in Siberia along which there were many prison camps.

Not the terrible eyes of my son—
Suffering turned to stone,
Not the day of the terror,   15
Not the hour I met with him in prison,

Not the sweet coolness of his hands,
Not the trembling shadow of the lindens,
Not the far-off, fragile sound—
Of the final words of consolation.   20

May 4, 1940
Fountain House

X

CRUCIFIXION

"Do not weep for Me, Mother,
I am in the grave."

1

A choir of angels sang the praises of that momentous hour,
And the heavens dissolved in fire.
To his Father He said: "Why hast Thou forsaken me!"[4]
And to his Mother: "Oh, do not weep for Me. . ."[5]

1940
Fountain House

2

Mary Magdalene beat her breast and sobbed,
The beloved disciple[6] turned to stone,
But where the silent Mother stood, there
No one glanced and no one would have dared.

1943
Tashkent

Epilogue I

I learned how faces fall,
How terror darts from under eyelids,
How suffering traces lines
Of stiff cuneiform on cheeks,
How locks of ashen-blonde or black   5
Turn silver suddenly,
Smiles fade on submissive lips
And fear trembles in a dry laugh.
And I pray not for myself alone,

---

4. Jesus' last words from the Cross (Matthew 27:46).   5. These words and the epigraph refer to a line from the Russian Orthodox prayer sung at services on Easter Saturday: "Weep not for Me, Mother, when you look upon the grave." Jesus is comforting Mary with the promise of his resurrection.
6. The apostle John.

But for all those who stood there with me 10
In cruel cold, and in July's heat,
At that blind, red wall.

Epilogue II

Once more the day of remembrance[7] draws near.
I see, I hear, I feel you:

The one they almost had to drag at the end,
And the one who tramps her native land no more,

And the one who, tossing her beautiful head, 5
Said: "Coming here's like coming home."

I'd like to name them all by name,
But the list has been confiscated and is nowhere to be found.[8]

I have woven a wide mantle for them
From their meager, overheard words. 10

I will remember them always and everywhere,
I will never forget them no matter what comes.

And if they gag my exhausted mouth
Through which a hundred million scream,

Then may the people remember me 15
On the eve of my remembrance day.

And if ever in this country
They decide to erect a monument to me,

I consent to that honor
Under these conditions—that it stand 20

Neither by the sea, where I was born:
My last tie with the sea is broken,

Nor in the tsar's garden near the cherished pine stump,[9]
Where an inconsolable shade[1] looks for me,

But here, where I stood for three hundred hours, 25
And where they never unbolted the doors for me.

This, lest in blissful death
I forget the rumbling of the Black Marias,

Forget how that detested door slammed shut
And an old woman howled like a wounded animal. 30

And may the melting snow stream like tears
From my motionless lids of bronze,

And a prison dove coo in the distance,
And the ships of the Neva sail calmly on.

March 1940

7. In the Russian Orthodox Church, a memorial service is held on the anniversary of a death. 8. The lists of prisoners were taken away and lost. 9. The gardens and park surrounding the summer palace in Tsarskoe Selo. Akhmatova writes elsewhere of the stump of a favorite tree in the gardens and of the poet Pushkin whom she describes as walking in the park. 1. A ghost, probably the restless spirit of Akhmatova's executed husband Gumilyov, who courted her in Tsarskoe Selo.

BERTOLT BRECHT
1898–1956

Bertolt Brecht is a dominant figure in modern drama not only as the author of half a dozen plays which rank as modern classics but as the first master of a powerful new concept of theater. He was dissatisfied with the traditional notion, derived from Aristotle's *Poetics*, that drama should draw its spectators into identification with and sympathy for the characters, and with the realist aesthetic of naturalness and psychological credibility. Brecht saw only harm in such uncritical submission to illusions created on stage. Like Pirandello, he believed that the modern stage should break open the closed world established as a dramatic convention by writers such as Ibsen and Chekhov, whose audiences were to look at the action from a distance, as if it were a slice of real life going on behind an invisible "fourth wall." Unlike Pirandello, however, Brecht did not stress the anguish of individuals in society and the difficulty of knowing who we are; his focus was the community at large, and social responsibility. For Brecht, a political activist, the modern audience must not be allowed to indulge in passive emotional identification at a safe distance, or in the subjective whirlpool of existential identity crises. His characters are to be seen as members of society, and his audience must be educated and moved to action. The movement called "epic theater," which was born in the 1920s, suited his needs well, and through his plays, theoretical writings, and dramatic productions he developed its basic ideas into one of the most powerful theatrical styles of the century.

Eugen Berthold Brecht was born in the medieval town of Augsburg, Bavaria, on February 10, 1898. His father was a respected town citizen, director of a paper mill, and a Catholic. His mother, the daughter of a civil servant from the Black Forest, was a Protestant who raised young Berthold in her own faith. (The spelling *Bertolt* was adopted later.) Brecht attended local schools until 1917, when he enrolled in Munich University to study natural science and medicine. He continued his studies while acting as drama critic for an Augsburg newspaper and writing his own plays: *Drums in the Night* (1918) won the Kleist Prize in 1922. In 1918, Brecht was mobilized for a year as an orderly in a military hospital, and he pursued medical studies at Munich until 1921. In 1929 he married Helene Weigel, an actress who worked closely with him and for whom he wrote many leading roles. Together, they would direct and make famous the theater group founded for them in 1949 in East Berlin: the Berliner Ensemble.

Moving to Berlin, Brecht worked briefly with the directors Max Reinhardt and Erwin Piscator but was chiefly interested in his own writing. In this pre-Marxist period he is especially concerned with the plight of the individual "common man," pushed around by social and economic forces beyond his control until he loses both identity and humanity. In *A Man's a Man* (1924–25), the timid dock worker Galy Gay is transformed by fright and persuasion into another person, the ferociously successful soldier Jeriah Jip. When Jip turns up at the end of the play, he is given Gay's former papers and forced to assume Gay's old identity. The play teaches that human personalities can be broken down and reassembled like a machine; the only weapon against such mindless manipulation is awareness, an awareness that enables people to understand and control their destiny.

Most of Brecht's plays are didactic, either openly or by implication. After he became a fervent Marxist in the mid-1920s, he considered it even more his moral and artistic duty to encourage the audience to remedy social ills. *The Threepenny Opera* (1928), a ballad opera written with composer Kurt Weill (1900–50) and modeled on John Gay's *The Beggar's Opera* (1728), satirizes capitalist society from the point of view of outcasts and romantic thieves. Brecht also wrote a number of "lesson" plays intended to set forth Communist doctrine and to instruct the workers of Germany in the meaning of social revolution. The lesson was particularly harsh in *The Measures Taken* (1930), which describes the necessary execution of a young party member who has broken discipline and helped the local poor, thus postponing the revolution. Such drama, however doctrinally pure, was not likely to win adherents to the cause, and the lesson plays were condemned as unattractive and "intellectualist" by the Communist press in Berlin and Moscow.

Brecht's unorthodoxy, his pacifism, his enthusiasm for Marx, and his desire to create an activist popular theater that would embody a Marxist view of art all put him at odds with the rising power of Hitler's National Socialism. He fled Germany for Denmark in 1933, before the Nazis could include him in their purge of left-wing intellectuals; in 1935, he was deprived of his German citizenship. Brecht was to flee several more times as the Nazi invasions expanded throughout Europe: in 1939 he went to Sweden, in 1940 to Finland, and in 1941 to the United States, where he joined a colony of German expatriates in Santa Monica, California, working for the film industry. This was the period of some of his greatest plays: *The Life of Galileo* (1938–39), which attacks society for suppressing Galileo's discovery that the earth revolves around the sun, but also condemns the scientist for not insisting openly on the truth; *Mother Courage and Her Children* (1939), included here; *The Good Woman of Setzuan* (1938–40), which shows how an instinctively good and generous person can only survive in this world by putting on a mask of hardness and calculation; and *The Caucasian Chalk Circle* (1944–45), which adapts the legendary choice of Solomon between two mothers who claim the same infant and decides in favor of the servant girl—who cared for the child—over the wealthy mother (the implied comparison is between those who do the work of society and those who merely profit from their possessions). In America, Brecht arranged for the translation of his work into English, and *Galileo*, with Charles Laughton in the title role, was produced in 1947. In the same year, he was questioned by the House Un-American Activities Committee as part of a wide-ranging inquiry into possible Communist activity in the entertainment business. No charges were brought, but he left for Europe the day after being brought before the committee.

After leaving the United States, Brecht worked for a year in Zurich before going to Berlin with his wife, Helene Weigel, to stage *Mother Courage*. The East Berlin government offered the couple positions as directors of their own troupe, the Berliner Ensemble, and Brecht—who had just finished a theoretical work on the theater, *A Little Organon for the Theater* (1949)—turned his attention to the professional role of director. Although the East Berliners subsidized Brecht's work and advertised the artist's presence among them as a tribute to their own political system, they also obliged him to defend some of his plays against charges of political unorthodoxy and indeed to revise them. After 1934, the prevailing Communist Party view had upheld a style called "socialist realism," whose goal was to offer simple messages and to foster identification with revolutionary heroes. Brecht's mind was too keen and questioning, too attracted by irony and paradox, for him to provide the simplistic drama desired or to have a comfortable relation with authority, either of the right or of the left. After settling in East Berlin, he wrote no major new plays but only minor propaganda pieces and adaptations of classical works such as Molière's *Don Juan* and Shakespeare's *Coriolanus*. As an additional measure of protection, he took out Austrian citizenship through his wife's nationality. Brecht died in Berlin on August 14, 1956.

The "epic theater" for which Brecht is known derives its name from a famous essay, *On Epic and Dramatic Poetry*, by Goethe and Schiller, who in 1797 described *dramatic* poetry as pulling the audience into emotional identification, in contrast to *epic* poetry, which by being distanced in the time, place, and nature of the action could be absorbed in calm contemplation. The idea of an epic theater is a paradox: how can a play engage an audience that is still held at a distance? Brecht's solution was to employ many "alienation effects" that were genuinely dramatic, but that prevented total identification with the characters and forced spectators to think critically about what was taking place. These alienation effects have since become standard production techniques in the modern theater. In spite of Brecht's intentions and frequent revisions, however, the characters and situations of his plays remain emotionally engrossing, especially in his best-known works, such as *Mother Courage and Her Children.*

Brecht's concept of an epic theater touches on all aspects of the form: dramatic structure, stage setting, music, and the actor's performance. The structure is to be open, episodic, and broken by dramatic or musical interludes. It is a "chronicle" that recounts events in an epic or distanced perspective. Episodes may also be performed independently as self-contained dramatic parables, instead of being organically tied to a centrally developing plot. Skits appear between scenes: in *A Man's a Man*, there is a fantastic interlude in which an elephant is accused of having murdered its mother. Sometimes a narrator comments on the action (as in *The Three-Penny Opera* and *A Man's a Man*). The alienation effects are also heightened by setting most of the plays in far-away lands (China in *The Good Woman of Setzuan*, India in *A Man's a Man*, England in *The Three-Penny Opera*, the Soviet Union in *The Caucasian Chalk Circle*, Chicago in *Saint Joan of the Stockyards* and *The Resistible Rise of Arturo Ui*) or distant times (the seventeenth century in *Mother Courage*, Renaissance Italy in *Galileo*, or an imagined ghostly afterlife in *The Trial of Lucullus*).

Stagecraft and performance further support Brecht's concept of a critical, intellectualized theater. Events on stage are announced beforehand by signs, or are accompanied by projected films and images during the action itself. Place names are printed on signs and suspended over the actors, and footlights and stage machinery are openly displayed. Songs that interrupt the dramatic action are addressed directly to the audience, and are often heralded by a sign Brecht called a "musical emblem: in *Mother Courage*, 'a trumpet, a drum, a flag, and electric globes that lit up.' " In addition, Brecht described a special kind of acting: actors should "demonstrate" their parts instead of being submerged in them. At rehearsals, Brecht often asked actors to speak their parts in the third person instead of the first. Masks were occasionally used for wicked people or soldiers' faces were chalked white to suggest a stylized fear. Such constant artificiality introduced into all aspects of the performance makes it difficult for the audience to identify completely and unself-consciously with the characters on stage.

Audiences may react emotionally to Brecht's plays and characters, but their reactions are never simple. Brecht's characters are complex and inhabit complex situations. Galileo is both a dedicated scientist who sacrifices his reputation for honesty so as to complete his work, and a weak sensualist who fails to realize how his recantation will affect others' pursuit of scientific knowledge. In *The Good Woman of Setzuan*, the overgenerous Shen Te can survive only by periodically adopting the mask of a harshly practical "cousin," Shui Ta. Mother Courage is both a tragic mother figure and a small-time profiteer who loses her children as she battens on war. Brecht's work teems with such paradoxes at all levels. He is a cynic who deflates religious zeal, militant patriotism, and heroic example as delusions that lead the masses on to futile sacrifice; yet he is also a preacher who makes prominent use of traditional biblical language and imagery, and themes of individual sacrifice.

Mother Courage, written shortly after Brecht turned forty, combines all these elements. The play is set in Germany, in the middle years of the Thirty Years' War (1618–48), a conflict involving all of Europe and believed at the time of Brecht's writing to have destroyed half the German population. But senseless violence, religious intolerance, artificial patriotism, and cynical opportunism were equally apparent in seventeenth-century Germany and in the Nazi state, and the setting gave Brecht what he needed to write a strongly pacifist play in 1939, the year in which World War II was to begin.

Mother Courage evoked the sympathy of early audiences for her tragic inability to prevent her children's death. Such was not Brecht's intention, and he rewrote several sections of the play to bring out her avarice and blindness, and her belief that she can use the war and profit from others' misery without endangering her own family. To Brecht, the tragedy of her life lay in her failure to relate the general fate of society to that of her own family. In trying to manipulate the system for her personal advantage, she denies the personal rights of others: she calls to others to enlist but not to her own children, and she would rather sell shirts to the officers than use them to bind a peasant's wounds. Yet the war that Mother Courage sees as a good provider ends by killing her three children, and even sooner because of their virtues (Eilif's martial zeal, Swiss Cheese's honesty, Kattrin's pity). Mother Courage is ruined, all the more so since she has learned nothing from the war and does not protest it. Instead, her bitter "Song of the Great Capitulation" presents compromise as inevitable, and at the end of the play she is chasing after a new regiment to continue her peddler's career.

Each of the twelve parable-like scenes of *Mother Courage* presents a particular aspect or lesson of the war. Setting and props encourage the audience to see the action as a "demonstration" by drawing attention to the way the play is put on. Signs or titles are projected onto a screen to announce what is about to happen; a revolving stage and projected backgrounds suggest the wagon's travels in a highly stylized way; a group of musicians sits in full view beside the stage to accompany the songs; realistic but sketchy three-dimensional structures represent buildings. The main piece of stage furniture is Mother Courage's canteen wagon, whose increasingly dilapidated appearance reveals her fall from prosperity into lonely poverty. In the first scene, the whole family appears with the wagon: at the end, Mother Courage pulls it alone.

Brecht hoped that *Mother Courage and Her Children* would show its audiences "that in wartime the big profits are not made by little people. That war, which is a continuation of business by other means, makes the human virtues fatal even to their possessors. That no sacrifice is too great for the struggle against war." This last point is demonstrated by Kattrin's death, for she is the only one of Mother Courage's family whose virtue is not perverted by the war, and whose death is meant to provide a moral example. Drumming frantically to awaken the endangered city of Halle, she sacrifices her life to save the city's threatened children. Religious and secular themes join at this point as they do so often in the course of the play, for Kattrin acts immediately after hearing the peasant family bemoan their helplessness and pray to God for miraculous aid. It is action like hers, not passive prayer, that Brecht hopes to evoke with his epic theater. Both the play itself and its self-conscious, "alienated" staging try to move the audience toward a clearer understanding of the societal forces that condition their destinies — and to a responsible choice of their own roles.

Martin Esslin, *Brecht, The Man and His Work* (1974), provides a basic biography and overview. John Willett, ed. and trans., *Brecht on Theatre: The Development of an Aesthetic* (1964), contains Brecht's own essays and lectures on his theater. Other views of Brecht are found in Peter Demetz, ed., *Brecht: A Collection of Critical Essays* (1962), and Siegfried Mews, ed., *Critical Essays on Bertolt Brecht*

(1989). Ronald Hayman, *Brecht: A Biography* (1983), offers a detailed view of Brecht's life. Eric Bentley, *The Brecht Commentaries 1943–1986* (1987), offers lively essays on the major plays, on Brecht's stagecraft, and on his place in modern culture by a friend and sometime colleague. The essays in Walter Benjamin, *Understanding Brecht* (1983), provide important insights into Brecht's work and modern thought by a close friend and major intellectual figure.

PRONOUNCING GLOSSARY

The following list uses common English syllables and stress accents to provide rough equivalents of selected words whose pronunciation may be unfamiliar to the general reader.

Eilif: *ai'-lif*

Fichtelgebirge: *fikh-tel-ge-beer'-guh*

Fierling: *feer'-ling*

Mother Courage and Her Children[1]

A Chronicle of the Thirty Years' War[2]

CHARACTERS

MOTHER COURAGE	THE OLD COLONEL
KATTRIN, her mute daughter	A CLERK
EILIF, her elder son	A YOUNG SOLDIER
SWISS CHEESE, her younger son	AN OLDER SOLDIER
THE RECRUITER	A PEASANT
THE SERGEANT	THE PEASANT'S WIFE
THE COOK	THE YOUNG MAN
THE GENERAL	THE OLD WOMAN
THE CHAPLAIN	ANOTHER PEASANT
THE ORDNANCE OFFICER	THE PEASANT WOMAN
YVETTE POTTIER	A YOUNG PEASANT
THE MAN WITH THE PATCH OVER HIS	THE LIEUTENANT
EYE	SOLDIERS
THE OTHER SERGEANT	A VOICE

---

1. Translated by Ralph Manheim.   2. Actually a series of wars fought in central Europe from 1618 to 1648. At the time *Mother Courage* opens, in 1624, a Swedish army has been fighting in Poland for three years. After winning the coastal province of Livonia (now in Latvia and Estonia), it invades Germany in 1630 under the command of King Gustavus Adolphus. The king, however, fails to relieve the siege of Magdeburg by the imperial general Johan Tserclaes, count of Tilly, and the Protestant bishopric is burned to the ground. Gustavus Adolphus later defeats Tilly in two major battles, but in 1632 both are killed, and two years later the Swedish force is destroyed by the Imperial Army. The ensuing peace is brief, for in 1635 a new Swedish army, joined by troops from Catholic France, renews the fighting. This last phase of the war has just begun at the end of *Mother Courage*, and lasting peace will come only twelve years later. (Brecht is true to history as he knew it; only recently have historians disputed the traditional belief that the war devastated Germany and halved its population.)

1

Spring 1624. General Oxenstjerna recruits troops in Dalarna for the
Polish campaign. The canteen woman, Anna Fierling, known as Mother
Courage, loses a son.[3]

Highway near a city.

A SERGEANT *and a* RECRUITER *stand shivering.*

THE RECRUITER: How can anybody get a company together in a place like
this? Sergeant, sometimes I feel like committing suicide. The general
wants me to recruit four platoons by the twelfth, and the people around
here are so depraved I can't sleep at night. I finally get hold of a man, I
close my eyes and pretend not to see that he's chicken-breasted and he's
got varicose veins, I get him good and drunk and he signs up. While
I'm paying for the drinks, he steps out, I follow him to the door because
I smell a rat: Sure enough, he's gone, like a fart out of a goose. A man's
word doesn't mean a thing, there's no honor, no loyalty. This place has
undermined my faith in humanity, sergeant.

THE SERGEANT: It's easy to see these people have gone too long without a
war. How can you have morality without a war, I ask you? Peace is a
mess, it takes a war to put things in order. In peacetime the human race
goes to the dogs. Man and beast are treated like so much dirt. Everybody
eats what they like, a big piece of cheese on white bread, with a slice of
meat on top of the cheese. Nobody knows how many young men or
good horses there are in that town up ahead, they've never been
counted. I've been in places where they hadn't had a war in as much as
seventy years, the people had no names, they didn't even know who
they were. It takes a war before you get decent lists and records; then
your boots are done up in bales and your grain in sacks, man and beast
are properly counted and marched away, because people realize that
without order they can't have a war.

THE RECRUITER: How right you are!

THE SERGEANT: Like all good things, a war is hard to get started. But once
it takes root, it's vigorous; then people are as scared of peace as dice
players are of laying off, because they'll have to reckon up their losses.
But at first they're scared of war. It's the novelty.

THE RECRUITER: Say, there comes a wagon. Two women and two young
fellows. Keep the old woman busy, sergeant. If this is another flop, you
won't catch me standing out in this April wind any more.

[*A Jew's harp is heard. Drawn by two young men, a covered wagon*[4]
approaches. In the wagon sit MOTHER COURAGE *and her mute daughter* KATTRIN.]

MOTHER COURAGE: Good morning, sergeant.

SERGEANT: [*Barring the way.*] Good morning, friends. Who are you?

---

3. The heading for this and each new scene is projected on a screen on stage; it situates the action and
tells what will happen. General Oxenstjerna was one of the Swedish generals. Dalarna is a rural province
in central Sweden. A *canteen woman* sells provisions to soldiers.   4. "A cross between a military vehicle and a general store" [Brecht's note]. *Jew's harp:* a small, twangy instrument held against the teeth,
associated with folk music.

MOTHER COURAGE: Business people. [*Sings.*]
    Hey, Captains, make the drum stop drumming
    And let your soldiers take a seat.
    Here's Mother Courage, with boots she's coming
    To help along their aching feet.
    How can they march off to the slaughter
    With baggage, cannon, lice and fleas
    Across the rocks and through the water
    Unless their boots are in one piece?
        The spring is come. Christian, revive![5]
        The snowdrifts melt. The dead lie dead.
        And if by chance you're still alive
        It's time to rise and shake a leg.

    O Captains, don't expect to send them
    To death with nothing in their crops.
    First you must let Mother Courage mend them
    In mind and body with her schnapps.[6]
    On empty bellies it's distressing
    To stand up under shot and shell.
    But once they're full, you have my blessing
    To lead them to the jaws of hell.
        The spring is come. Christian, revive!
        The snowdrifts melt, the dead lie dead.
        And if by chance you're still alive
        It's time to rise and shake a leg.
THE SERGEANT: Halt, you scum. Where do you belong?
THE ELDER SON: Second Finnish Regiment.
THE SERGEANT: Where are your papers?
MOTHER COURAGE: Papers?
THE YOUNGER SON: But she's Mother Courage!
THE SERGEANT: Never heard of her. Why Courage?
MOTHER COURAGE: They call me Courage, sergeant, because when I saw
    ruin staring me in the face I drove out of Riga through cannon fire with
    fifty loaves of bread in my wagon. They were getting moldy, it was high
    time, I had no choice.
THE SERGEANT: No wisecracks. Where are your papers?
MOTHER COURAGE: [*Fishing a pile of papers out of a tin box and climbing
    down.*] Here are my papers, sergeant. There's a whole missal, picked it
    up in Alt-Ötting to wrap cucumbers in, and a map of Moravia,[7] God
    knows if I'll ever get there, if I don't it's total loss. And this here certifies
    that my horse hasn't got hoof-and-mouth disease, too bad, he croaked
    on us, he cost fifteen guilders,[8] but not out of my pocket, glory be. Is
    that enough paper?

---

5. The phrase in German parodies religious announcements of Easter and Christ's resurrection.
6. Liquor, especially gin. (The original says *wein*, "wine.")   7. Part of the Czech Republic. *Missal*: prayer book. *Alt-Ötting*: a place of pilgrimage fifty miles east of Munich in the south German kingdom of Bavaria.   8. The basic unit of Dutch money, also called a *florin*. When Brecht was writing, one guilder was worth about twenty-five cents.

THE SERGEANT: Are you trying to pull my leg? I'll teach you to get smart. You know you need a license.

MOTHER COURAGE: You mind your manners and don't go telling my innocent children that I'd go anywhere near your leg, it's indecent. I want no truck with you. My license in the Second Regiment is my honest face, and if you can't read it, that's not my fault. I'm not letting anybody put his seal on it.

THE RECRUITER: Sergeant, I detect a spirit of insubordination in this woman. In our camp we need respect for authority.

MOTHER COURAGE: Wouldn't sausage be better?

THE SERGEANT: Name.

MOTHER COURAGE: Anna Fierling.

THE SERGEANT: Then you're all Fierlings.

MOTHER COURAGE: What do you mean? Fierling is my name. Not theirs.

THE SERGEANT: Aren't they all your children?

MOTHER COURAGE: That they are, but why should they all have the same name? [*Pointing at the elder son.*] This one, for instance. His name is Eilif Nojocki. How come? Because his father always claimed to be called Kojocki or Mojocki. The boy remembers him well, except the one he remembers was somebody else, a Frenchman with a goatee. But aside from that, he inherited his father's intelligence, that man could strip the pants off a peasant's ass without his knowing it. So, you see, we've each got our own name.

THE SERGEANT: Each different, you mean?

MOTHER COURAGE: Don't act so innocent.

THE SERGEANT: I suppose that one's a Chinaman? [*Indicating the younger son.*]

MOTHER COURAGE: Wrong. He's Swiss.

THE SERGEANT: After the Frenchman?

MOTHER COURAGE: What Frenchman? I never heard of any Frenchman. Don't get everything balled up or we'll be here all day. He's Swiss, but his name is Fejos, the name has nothing to do with his father. He had an entirely different name, he was an engineer, built fortifications, but he drank.

[SWISS CHEESE *nods, beaming; the mute* KATTRIN *is also tickled.*]

THE SERGEANT: Then how can his name be Fejos?

MOTHER COURAGE: I wouldn't want to offend you, but you haven't got much imagination. Naturally his name is Fejos because when he came I was with a Hungarian, it was all the same to him, he was dying of kidney trouble though he never touched a drop, a very decent man. The boy takes after him.

THE SERGEANT: But you said he wasn't his father?

MOTHER COURAGE: He takes after him all the same. I call him Swiss Cheese, how come, because he's good at pulling the wagon. [*Pointing at her daughter.*] Her name is Kattrin Haupt, she's half German.

THE SERGEANT: A fine family, I must say.

MOTHER COURAGE: Yes, I've been all over the world with my wagon.

THE SERGEANT: It's all being taken down. [*He takes it down.*] You're from Bamberg, Bavaria. What brings you here?

MOTHER COURAGE: I couldn't wait for the war to kindly come to Bamberg.

THE RECRUITER: You wagon pullers ought to be called Jacob Ox and Esau[9] Ox. Do you ever get out of harness?

EILIF: Mother, can I clout him one on the kisser? I'd like to.

MOTHER COURAGE: And I forbid you. You stay put. And now, gentlemen, wouldn't you need a nice pistol, or a belt buckle, yours is all worn out, sergeant.

THE SERGEANT: I need something else. I'm not blind. Those young fellows are built like tree trunks, big broad chests, sturdy legs. Why aren't they in the army? That's what I'd like to know.

MOTHER COURAGE: [Quickly.] Nothing doing, sergeant. My children aren't cut out for soldiers.

THE RECRUITER: Why not? There's profit in it, and glory. Peddling shoes is woman's work. [To EILIF.] Step up; let's feel if you've got muscles or if you're a sissy.

MOTHER COURAGE: He's a sissy. Give him a mean look and he'll fall flat on his face.

THE RECRUITER: And kill a calf if it happens to be standing in the way. [Tries to lead him away.]

MOTHER COURAGE: Leave him alone. He's not for you.

THE RECRUITER: He insulted me. He referred to my face as a kisser. Him and me will now step out in the field and discuss this thing as man to man.

EILIF: Don't worry, mother. I'll take care of him.

MOTHER COURAGE: You stay put. You no-good! I know you, always fighting. He's got a knife in his boot, he's a knifer.

THE RECRUITER: I'll pull it out of him like a milk tooth. Come on, boy.

MOTHER COURAGE: Sergeant, I'll report you to the colonel. He'll throw you in the lock-up. The lieutenant is courting my daughter.

THE SERGEANT: No rough stuff, brother. [To MOTHER COURAGE.] What have you got against the army? Wasn't his father a soldier? Didn't he die fair and square? You said so yourself.

MOTHER COURAGE: He's only a child. You want to lead him off to slaughter, I know you. You'll get five guilders for him.

THE RECRUITER: He'll get a beautiful cap and top boots.

EILIF: Not from you.

MOTHER COURAGE: Oh, won't you come fishing with me? said the fisherman to the worm. [To SWISS CHEESE.] Run and yell that they're trying to steal your brother. [She pulls a knife.] Just try to steal him. I'll cut you down, you dogs. I'll teach you to put him in your war! We do an honest business in ham and shirts, we're peaceful folk.

THE SERGEANT: I can see by the knife how peaceful you are. You ought to be ashamed of yourself, put that knife away, you bitch. A minute ago you admitted you lived off war, how else would you live, on what? How can you have a war without soldiers?

MOTHER COURAGE: It doesn't have to be my children.

THE SERGEANT: I see. You'd like the war to eat the core and spit out the

---

9. Biblical twin brothers (Genesis 26:22–26).

apple. You want your brood to batten on war, tax-free. The war can look out for itself, is that it? You call yourself Courage, eh? And you're afraid of the war that feeds you. Your sons aren't afraid of it, I can see that.

EILIF: I'm not afraid of any war.

THE SERGEANT: Why should you be? Look at me: Has the soldier's life disagreed with me? I was seventeen when I joined up.

MOTHER COURAGE: You're not seventy yet.

THE SERGEANT: I can wait.

MOTHER COURAGE: Sure. Under ground.

THE SERGEANT: Are you trying to insult me? Telling me I'm going to die?

MOTHER COURAGE: But suppose it's the truth? I can see the mark on you. You look like a corpse on leave.

SWISS CHEESE: She's got second sight. Everybody says so. She can tell the future.

THE RECRUITER: Then tell the sergeant his future. It might amuse him.

THE SERGEANT: I don't believe in that stuff.

MOTHER COURAGE: Give me your helmet. [*He gives it to her.*]

THE SERGEANT: It doesn't mean any more than taking a shit in the grass. But go ahead for the laugh.

MOTHER COURAGE: [*Takes a sheet of parchment and tears it in two.*] Eilif, Swiss Cheese, Kattrin: That's how we'd all be torn apart if we got mixed up too deep in the war. [*To the* SERGEANT.] Seeing it's you, I'll do it for nothing. I make a black cross on this piece. Black is death.

SWISS CHEESE: She leaves the other one blank. Get it?

MOTHER COURAGE: Now I fold them, and now I shake them up together. Same as we're all mixed up together from the cradle to the grave. And now you draw, and you'll know the answer.

[*The* SERGEANT *hesitates.*]

THE RECRUITER: [*To* EILIF.] I don't take everybody, I'm known to be picky and choosey, but you've got spirit, I like that.

THE SERGEANT: [*Fishing in the helmet.*] Damn foolishness! Hocus-pocus!

SWISS CHEESE: He's pulled a black cross. He's through.

THE RECRUITER: Don't let them scare you, there's not enough bullets for everybody.

THE SERGEANT: [*Hoarsely.*] You've fouled me up.

MOTHER COURAGE: You fouled yourself up the day you joined the army. And now we'll be going, there isn't a war every day, I've got to take advantage.

THE SERGEANT: Hell and damnation! Don't try to hornswoggle me. We're taking your bastard to be a soldier.

EILIF: I'd like to be a soldier, mother.

MOTHER COURAGE: You shut your trap, you Finnish devil.

EILIF: Swiss Cheese wants to be a soldier too.

MOTHER COURAGE: That's news to me. I'd better let you draw too, all three of you. [*She goes to the rear to mark crosses on slips of parchment.*]

THE RECRUITER: [*To* EILIF.] It's been said to our discredit that a lot of religion goes on in the Swedish camp, but that's slander to blacken our reputation. Hymn singing only on Sunday, one verse! And only if you've got a voice.

MOTHER COURAGE: [*Comes back with the slips in the* SERGEANT'S *helmet.*] Want to sneak away from their mother, the devils, and run off to war like calves to a salt lick. But we'll draw lots on it, then they'll see that the world is no vale of smiles[1] with a "Come along, son, we're short on generals." Sergeant, I'm very much afraid they won't come through the war. They've got terrible characters, all three of them. [*She holds out the helmet to* EILIF.] There. Pick a slip. [*He picks one and unfolds it. She snatches it away from him.*] There you have it. A cross! Oh, unhappy mother that I am, Oh, mother of sorrows. Has he got to die? Doomed to perish in the springtime of his life? If he joins the army, he'll bite the dust, that's sure. He's too brave, just like his father. If he's not smart, he'll go the way of all flesh, the slip proves it. [*She roars at him.*] Are you going to be smart?

EILIF: Why not?

MOTHER COURAGE: The smart thing to do is to stay with your mother, and if they make fun of you and call you a sissy, just laugh.

THE RECRUITER: If you're shitting in your pants, we'll take your brother.

MOTHER COURAGE: I told you to laugh. Laugh! And now you pick, Swiss Cheese. I'm not so worried about you, you're honest. [*He picks a slip.*] Oh! Why, have you got that strange look? It's got to be blank. There can't be a cross on it. No, I can't lose you. [*She takes the slip.*] A cross? Him too? Maybe it's because he's so stupid. Oh, Swiss Cheese, you'll die too, unless you're very honest the whole time, the way I've taught you since you were a baby, always bringing back the change when I sent you to buy bread. That's the only way you can save yourself. Look sergeant, isn't that a black cross?

THE SERGEANT: It's a cross all right. I don't see how I could have pulled one. I always stay in the rear. [*To the* RECRUITER.] It's on the up and up. Her own get it too.

SWISS CHEESE: I get it too. But I can take a hint.

MOTHER COURAGE: [*To* KATTRIN.] Now you're the only one I'm sure of, you're a cross[2] yourself because you've got a good heart. [*She holds up the helmet to* KATTRIN *in the wagon, but she herself takes out the slip.*] It's driving me to despair. It can't be right, maybe I mixed them wrong. Don't be too good-natured, Kattrin, don't, there's a cross on your path too. Always keep very quiet, that ought to be easy seeing you're dumb. Well, now you know. Be careful, all of you, you'll need to be. And now we'll climb up and drive on. [*She returns the* SERGEANT's *helmet and climbs up into the wagon.*]

THE RECRUITER: [*To the* SERGEANT.] Do something!

THE SERGEANT: I'm not feeling so good.

THE RECRUITER: Maybe you caught cold when you took your helmet off in the wind. Tell her you want to buy something. Keep her busy. [*Aloud.*] You could at least take a look at that buckle, sergeant. After all, selling things is these good people's living. Hey, you, the sergeant wants to buy that belt buckle.

---

1. Parodying the traditional description of this world as a "vale of tears."   2. That is, a heavy burden.

MOTHER COURAGE: Half a guilder. A buckle like that is worth two guilders. [*She climbs down.*]

THE SERGEANT: It's not new. This wind! I can't examine it here. Let's go where it's quiet. [*He goes behind the wagon with the buckle.*]

MOTHER COURAGE: I haven't noticed wind.

THE SERGEANT: Maybe it is worth half a guilder. It's silver.

MOTHER COURAGE: [*Joins him behind the wagon.*] Six solid ounces.

THE RECRUITER: [*To* EILIF.] And then we'll have a drink, just you and me. I've got your enlistment bonus right here. Come on.

[EILIF *stands undecided.*]

MOTHER COURAGE: All right. Half a guilder.

THE SERGEANT: I don't get it. I always stay in the rear. There's no safer place for a sergeant. You can send the men up forward to win glory. You've spoiled my dinner. It won't go down, I know it, not a bite.

MOTHER COURAGE: Don't take it to heart. Don't let it spoil your appetite. Just keep behind the lines. Here, take a drink of schnapps, man. [*She hands him the bottle.*]

THE RECRUITER: [*Has taken* EILIF*'s arm and is pulling him away toward the rear.*] A bonus of ten guilders, and you'll be a brave man and you'll fight for the king, and the women will tear each other's hair out over you. And you can clout me one on the kisser for insulting you. [*Both go out.*]

[*Mute* KATTRIN *jumps down from the wagon and emits raucous sounds.*]

MOTHER COURAGE: Just a minute, Kattrin. Just a minute. The sergeant's paying up. [*Bites the half guilder.*] I'm always suspicious of money. I'm a burnt child, sergeant. But your coin is good. And now we'll be going. Where's Eilif?

SWISS CHEESE: He's gone with the recruiter.

MOTHER COURAGE: [*Stands motionless, then.*] You simple soul. [*To* KATTRIN.] I know. You can't talk, you couldn't help it.

THE SERGEANT: You could do with a drink yourself, mother. That's the way it goes. Soldiering isn't the worst thing in the world. You want to live off the war, but you want to keep you and yours out of it. Is that it?

MOTHER COURAGE: Now you'll have to pull with your brother, Kattrin.

[*Brother and sister harness themselves to the wagon and start pulling.* MOTHER COURAGE *walks beside them. The wagon rolls off.*]

THE SERGEANT: [*Looking after them.*]
        If you want the war to work for you
        You've got to give the war its due.

2

In 1625 and 1626 Mother Courage crosses Poland in the train[3] of the Swedish armies. Outside the fortress of Wallhof[4] she meets her son again.—A capon is successfully sold, the brave son's fortunes are at their zenith.

3. That is, with the supplies and baggage at the end of the line of march.   4. Fictional city.

The general's tent.

Beside it the kitchen. The thunder of cannon. The cook is arguing with MOTHER COURAGE, *who is trying to sell him a capon.*

THE COOK: Sixty hellers[5] for that pathetic bird?

MOTHER COURAGE: Pathetic bird? You mean this plump beauty? Are you trying to tell me that a general who's the biggest eater for miles around—God help you if you haven't got anything for his dinner— can't afford a measly sixty hellers?

THE COOK: I can get a dozen like it for ten hellers right around the corner.

MOTHER COURAGE: What, you'll find a capon like this right around the corner? With a siege on and everybody so starved you can see right through them. Maybe you'll scare up a rat, maybe, I say, 'cause they've all been eaten, I've seen five men chasing a starved rat for hours. Fifty hellers for a giant capon in the middle of a siege.

THE COOK: We're not besieged; they are. We're the besiegers, can't you get that through your head?

MOTHER COURAGE: But we haven't got anything to eat either, in fact we've got less than the people in the city. They've hauled it all inside. I hear their life is one big orgy. And look at us. I've been around to the peasants, they haven't got a thing.

THE COOK: They've got plenty. They hide it.

MOTHER COURAGE: [*Triumphantly.*] Oh, no! They're ruined, that's what they are. They're starving. I've seen them. They're so hungry they're digging up roots. They lick their fingers when they've eaten a boiled strap. That's the situation. And here I've got a capon and I'm supposed to let it go for forty hellers.

THE COOK: Thirty, not forty. Thirty, I said.

MOTHER COURAGE: It's no common capon. They tell me this bird was so talented that he wouldn't eat unless they played music, he had his own favorite march. He could add and subtract, that's how intelligent he was. And you're trying to tell me forty hellers is too much. The general will bite your head off if there's nothing to eat.

THE COOK: You know what I'm going to do? [*He takes a piece of beef and sets his knife to it.*] Here I've got a piece of beef. I'll roast it. Think it over. This is your last chance.

MOTHER COURAGE: Roast and be damned. It's a year old.

THE COOK: A day old. That ox was running around only yesterday afternoon, I saw him with my own eyes.

MOTHER COURAGE: Then he must have stunk on the hoof.

THE COOK: I'll cook it five hours if I have to. We'll see if it's still tough. [*He cuts it.*]

MOTHER COURAGE: Use plenty of pepper, maybe the general won't notice the stink.

[*The* GENERAL, *the* CHAPLAIN, *and* EILIF *enter the tent.*]

THE GENERAL: [*Slapping* EILIF *on the back.*] All right, son, into your general's tent you go, you'll sit at my right hand. You've done a heroic deed

5. A small coin formerly used in Austria and Germany.

and you're a pious trooper, because this is a war of religion and what you did was done for God, that's what counts with me. I'll reward you with a gold bracelet when I take the city. We come here to save their souls and what do those filthy, shameless peasants do? They drive their cattle away. And they stuff their priests with meat, front and back. But you taught them a lesson. Here's a tankard of red wine for you. [*He pours.*] We'll down it on one gulp. [*They do so.*] None for the chaplain, he's got his religion. What would you like for dinner, sweetheart?

EILIF: A scrap of meat. Why not?

THE GENERAL: Cook! Meat!

THE COOK: And now he brings company when there's nothing to eat.

[*Wanting to listen,* MOTHER COURAGE *makes him stop talking.*]

EILIF: Cutting down peasants whets the appetite.

MOTHER COURAGE: God, it's my Eilif.

THE COOK: Who?

MOTHER COURAGE: My eldest. I haven't seen hide nor hair of him in two years, he was stolen from me on the highway. He must be in good if the general invites him to dinner, and what have you got to offer? Nothing. Did you hear what the general's guest wants for dinner? Meat! Take my advice, snap up this capon. The price is one guilder.

THE GENERAL: [*Has sat down with* EILIF. *Bellows.*] Food, Lamb, you lousy, no-good cook, or I'll kill you.

THE COOK: All right, hand it over. This is extortion.

MOTHER COURAGE: I thought it was a pathetic bird.

THE COOK: Pathetic is the word. Hand it over. Fifty hellers! It's highway robbery.

MOTHER COURAGE: One guilder, I say. For my eldest son, the general's honored guest, I spare no expense.

THE COOK: [*Gives her the money.*] Then pluck it at least while I make the fire.

MOTHER COURAGE: [*Sits down to pluck the capon.*] Won't he be glad to see me! He's my brave, intelligent son. I've got a stupid one too, but he's honest. The girl's a total loss. But at least she doesn't talk, that's something.

THE GENERAL: Take another drink, son, it's my best Falerno,[6] I've only got another barrel or two at the most, but it's worth it to see that there's still some true faith in my army. The good shepherd here just looks on, all he knows how to do is preach. Can he do anything? No. And now, Eilif my son, tell us all about it, how cleverly you hoodwinked those peasants and captured those twenty head of cattle. I hope they'll be here soon.

EILIF: Tomorrow. Maybe the day after.

MOTHER COURAGE: Isn't my Eilif considerate, not bringing those oxen in until tomorrow, or you wouldn't have even said hello to my capon.

EILIF: Well, it was like this: I heard the peasants were secretly—mostly at night—rounding up the oxen they'd hidden in a certain forest. The city people had arranged to come and get them. I let them round the oxen up, I figured they'd find them easier than I would. I made my men

6. A famous wine made from grapes grown in Falerno in Italy.

ravenous for meat, put them on short rations for two days until their mouths watered if they even heard a word beginning with *me* . . . like measles.

THE GENERAL: That was clever of you.

EILIF: Maybe. The rest was a pushover. Except the peasants had clubs and there were three times more of them and they fell on us like bloody murder. Four of them drove me into a clump of bushes, they knocked my sword out of my hand and yelled: Surrender! Now what'll I do, I says to myself, they'll make hash out of me.

THE GENERAL: What did you do?

EILIF: I laughed.

THE GENERAL: You laughed?

EILIF: I laughed. Which led to a conversation. The first thing you know, I'm bargaining. Twenty guilders is too much for that ox, I say, how about fifteen? Like I'm meaning to pay. They're flummoxed, they scratch their heads. Quick, I reach for my sword and mow them down. Necessity knows no law. See what I mean?

THE GENERAL: What do you say to that, shepherd?

CHAPLAIN: Strictly speaking, that maxim is not in the Bible. But our Lord was able to turn five loaves into five hundred.[7] So there was no question of poverty; he could tell people to love their neighbors because their bellies were full. Nowadays it's different.

THE GENERAL: [*Laughs.*] Very different. All right, you Pharisee, take a swig. [*To* EILIF.] You mowed them down, splendid, so my fine troops could have a decent bite to eat. Doesn't the Good Book say: "Whatsoever thou doest for the least of my brethren, thou doest for me"?[8] And what have you done for them? You've got them a good chunk of beef for their dinner. They're not used to moldy crusts; in the old days they had a helmetful of white bread and wine before they went out to fight for God.

EILIF: Yes, I reached for my sword and I mowed them down.

THE GENERAL: You're a young Caesar. You deserve to see the king.

EILIF: I have, in the distance. He shines like a light. He's my ideal.

THE GENERAL: You're a something like him already, Eilif. I know the worth of a brave soldier like you. When I find one, I treat him like my own son. [*He leads him to the map.*] Take a look at the situation, Eilif; we've still got a long way to go.

MOTHER COURAGE: [*Who has been listening starts plucking her capon furiously.*] He must be a rotten general.

THE COOK: Eats like a pig, but why rotten?

MOTHER COURAGE: Because he needs brave soldiers, that's why. If he planned his campaigns right, what would he need brave soldiers for? The run-of-the-mill would do. Take it from me, whenever you find a lot of virtues, it shows that something's wrong.

THE COOK: I'd say it proves that something is all right.

MOTHER COURAGE: No, that something's wrong. See, when a general or a

---

7. Episode in the Gospels when Jesus fed five thousand people with five loaves and two fishes (Matthew 15:33ff.).   8. Spoken by Jesus in the Gospels (Matthew 25:40ff.). *Pharisee*: religious hypocrite, quibbler on religious doctrine.

king is real stupid and leads his men up shit creek, his troops need courage, that's a virtue. If he's stingy and doesn't hire enough soldiers, they've all got to be Herculeses. And if he's a slob and lets everything go to pot, they've got to be as sly as serpents or they're done for. And if he's always expecting too much of them, they need an extra dose of loyalty. A country that's run right, or a good king or a good general, doesn't need any of these virtues. You don't need virtues in a decent country, the people can all be perfectly ordinary, medium-bright, and cowards too for my money.

THE GENERAL: I bet your father was a soldier.

EILIF: A great soldier, I'm told. My mother warned me about it. Makes me think of a song.

THE GENERAL: Sing it! [*Bellowing.*] Where's that food!

EILIF: It is called: The Song of the Old Wife and the Soldier. [*He sings, doing a war dance with his saber.*]

>A gun or a pike they can kill who they like
>And the torrent will swallow a wader
>You had better think twice before battling with ice
>Said the old wife to the soldier.
>Cocking his rifle he leapt to his feet
>Laughing for joy as he heard the drum beat
>The wars cannot hurt me, he told her.
>He shouldered his gun and he picked up his knife
>To see the wide world. That's the soldier's life.
>Those were the words of the soldier.
>
>Ah, Deep will they lie who wise counsel defy
>Learn wisdom from those that are older
>Oh, don't venture too high or you'll fall from the sky
>Said the old wife to the soldier.
>But the young soldier with knife and with gun
>Only laughed a cold laugh and stepped into the run.
>The water can't hurt me, he told her.
>And when the moon on the rooftop shines white
>We'll be coming back. You can pray for that night.
>Those were the words of the soldier.

MOTHER COURAGE: [*In the kitchen, continues the song, beating a pot with a spoon.*]

>Like the smoke you'll be gone and no warmth linger on
>And your deeds only leave me the colder!
>Oh, see the smoke race. Oh, dear God keep him safe!
>That's what she said of the soldier.

EILIF: What's that?

MOTHER COURAGE: [*Goes on singing.*]

>And the young soldier with knife and with gun
>Was swept from his feet till he sank in the run
>And the torrent swallowed the waders.
>Cold shone the moon on the rooftop white
>But the soldier was carried away with the ice

And what was it she heard from the soldier?
Like the smoke he was gone and no warmth lingered on
And his deeds only left her the colder.
Ah, deep will they lie who wise counsel defy!
That's what she said to the soldier.

THE GENERAL: What do they think they're doing in my kitchen?

EILIF: [Has gone into the kitchen. He embraces his mother.] Mother! It's you! Where are the others?

MOTHER COURAGE: [In his arms.] Snug as a bug in a rug. Swiss Cheese is paymaster of the Second Regiment; at least he won't be fighting, I couldn't keep him out altogether.

EILIF: And how about your feet?

MOTHER COURAGE: Well, it's hard getting my shoes on in the morning.

THE GENERAL: [Has joined them.] Ah, so you're his mother. I hope you've got more sons for me like this fellow here.

EILIF: Am I lucky! There you're sitting in the kitchen hearing your son being praised.

MOTHER COURAGE: I heard it all right! [She gives him a slap in the face.]

EILIF: [Holding his cheek.] For capturing the oxen?

MOTHER COURAGE: No. For not surrendering when the four of them were threatening to make hash out of you! Didn't I teach you to take care of yourself? You Finnish devil!

[The GENERAL and the CHAPLAIN laugh.]

3

Three years later Mother Courage and parts of a Finnish[9] regiment are taken prisoner. She is able to save her daughter and her wagon, but her honest son dies.

Army camp.

Afternoon. On a pole the regimental flag. MOTHER COURAGE has stretched a clothesline between her wagon, on which all sorts of merchandise is hung in display, and a large cannon. She and KATTRIN are folding washing and piling it on the cannon. At the same time she is negotiating with an ORDNANCE OFFICER[1] over a sack of bullets. SWISS CHEESE, now in the uniform of a paymaster, is looking on. A pretty woman, YVETTE POTTIER, is sitting with a glass of brandy in front of her, sewing a gaudy-colored hat. She is in her stocking feet, her red high-heeled shoes are on the ground beside her.

THE ORDNANCE OFFICER: I'll let you have these bullets for two guilders. It's cheap, I need the money, because the colonel's been drinking with the officers for two days and we're out of liquor.

MOTHER COURAGE: That's ammunition for the troops. If it's found here, I'll be court-martialed. You punks sell their bullets and the men have nothing to shoot at the enemy.

---

9. Finland was under Swedish rule at this time.   1. Officer in charge of weapons, particularly explosives.

THE ORDNANCE OFFICER: Don't be hard-hearted, you scratch my back, I'll scratch yours.

MOTHER COURAGE: I'm not taking any army property. Not at that price.

THE ORDNANCE OFFICER: You can sell it for five guilders, maybe eight, to the ordnance officer of the Fourth before the day is out, if you're quiet about it and give him a receipt for twelve. He hasn't an ounce of ammunition left.

MOTHER COURAGE: Why don't you do it yourself?

THE ORDNANCE OFFICER: Because I don't trust him, he's a friend of mine.

MOTHER COURAGE: [*Takes the sack.*] Hand it over. [*To* KATTRIN.] Take it back there and pay him one and a half guilders. [*In response to the* ORDNANCE OFFICER'*s protest.*] One and a half guilders, I say. [KATTRIN *drags the sack behind the wagon, the* ORDNANCE OFFICER *follows her.* MOTHER COURAGE *to* SWISS CHEESE.] Here's your underdrawers, take good care of them, this is October, might be coming on fall, I don't say it will be, because I've learned that nothing is sure to happen the way we think, not even the seasons. But whatever happens, your regimental funds have to be in order. Are your funds in order?

SWISS CHEESE: Yes, mother.

MOTHER COURAGE: Never forget that they made you paymaster because you're honest and not brave like your brother, and especially because you're too simple-minded to get the idea of making off with the money. That's a comfort to me. And don't go mislaying your drawers.

SWISS CHEESE: No, mother. I'll put them under my mattress. [*Starts to go.*]

ORDNANCE OFFICER: I'll go with you, paymaster.

MOTHER COURAGE: Just don't teach him any of your tricks.   °

    [*Without saying good-bye the* ORDNANCE OFFICER *goes out with* SWISS CHEESE.]

YVETTE: [*Waves her hand after the* ORDNANCE OFFICER.] You might say good-bye, officer.

MOTHER COURAGE: [*To* YVETTE.] I don't like to see those two together. He's not the right kind of company for my Swiss Cheese. But the war's getting along pretty well. More countries are joining in all the time, it can go on for another four, five years, easy. With a little planning ahead, I can do good business if I'm careful. Don't you know you shouldn't drink in the morning with your sickness?

YVETTE: Who says I'm sick, it's slander.

MOTHER COURAGE: Everybody says so.

YVETTE: Because they're all liars. Mother Courage, I'm desperate. They all keep out of my way like I'm a rotten fish on account of those lies. What's the good of fixing my hat? [*She throws it down.*] That's why I drink in the morning, I never used to, I'm getting crow's-feet, but it doesn't matter now. In the Second Finnish Regiment they all know me. I should have stayed home when my first love walked out on me. Pride isn't for the likes of us. If we can't put up with shit, we're through.

MOTHER COURAGE: Just don't start in on your Pieter and how it all happened in front of my innocent daughter.

YVETTE: She's just the one to hear it, it'll harden her against love.

MOTHER COURAGE: Nothing can harden them.

YVETTE: Then I'll talk about it because it makes me feel better. It begins
with my growing up in fair Flanders, because if I hadn't I'd never have
laid eyes on him and I wouldn't be here in Poland now, because he was
an army cook, blond, a Dutchman, but skinny. Kattrin, watch out for
the skinny ones, but I didn't know that then, and another thing I didn't
know is that he had another girl even then, and they all called him Pete
the Pipe, because he didn't even take his pipe out of his mouth when
he was doing it, that's all it meant to him. [*She sings the* Song of Frater-
nization.]

When I was only sixteen
The foe came into our land.
He laid aside his saber
And with a smile he took my hand.
After the May parade
The May light starts to fade.
The regiment dressed by the right[2]
Then drums were beaten, that's the drill.[3]
The foe took us behind the hill
And fraternized all night.

There were so many foes came
And mine worked in the mess.[4]
I loathed him in the daytime.
At night I loved him none the less.
After the May parade
The May light starts to fade.
The regiment dressed by the right
Then drums were beaten, that's the drill.
The foe took us behind the hill
And fraternized all night.

The love which came upon me
Was wished on me by fate.
My friends could never grasp why
I found it hard to share their hate.
The fields were wet with dew
When sorrow first I knew.
The regiment dressed by the right
Then drums were beaten, that's the drill.
And then the foe, my lover still
Went marching from our sight.

Well, I followed him, but I never found him. That was five years ago.
[*She goes behind the wagon with an unsteady gait.*]
MOTHER COURAGE: You've left your hat.
YVETTE: Anybody that wants it can have it.
MOTHER COURAGE: Let that be a lesson to you, Kattrin. Have no truck with
soldiers. It's love that makes the world go round, so you'd better watch

2. That is, each man aligned himself with the man on his right to form straight ranks for the parade.
3. That's the usual thing.   4. The kitchen.

out. Even with a civilian it's no picnic. He says he'd kiss the ground you put your little feet on, talking of feet, did you wash yours yesterday, and then you're his slave. Be glad you're dumb, that way you'll never contradict yourself or want to bite your tongue off because you've told the truth, it's a gift of God to be dumb. Here comes the general's cook, I wonder what he wants.

[*The* COOK *and the* CHAPLAIN *enter.*]

THE CHAPLAIN: I've got a message for you from your son Eilif. The cook here thought he'd come along, he's taken a shine to you.

THE COOK: I only came to get a breath of air.

MOTHER COURAGE: You can always do that here if you behave, and if you don't, I can handle you. Well, what does he want? I've got no money to spare.

THE CHAPLAIN: Actually he wanted me to see his brother, the paymaster.

MOTHER COURAGE: He's not here any more, or anywhere else either. He's not his brother's paymaster. I don't want him leading him into temptation and being smart at his expense [*Gives him money from the bag slung around her waist.*] Give him this, it's a sin, he's speculating on mother love and he ought to be ashamed.

THE COOK: He won't do it much longer, then he'll be marching off with his regiment, maybe to his death, you never can tell. Better make it a little more, you'll be sorry later. You women are hard-hearted, but afterwards you're sorry. A drop of brandy wouldn't have cost much when it was wanted, but it wasn't given, and later, for all you know, he'll be lying in the cold ground and you can't dig him up again.

THE CHAPLAIN: Don't be sentimental, cook. There's nothing wrong with dying in battle, it's a blessing, and I'll tell you why. This is a war of religion. Not a common war, but a war for the faith, and therefore pleasing to God.

THE COOK: That's a fact. In a way you could call it a war, because of the extortion and killing and looting, not to mention a bit of rape, but it's a war of religion, which makes it different from all other wars, that's obvious. But it makes a man thirsty all the same, you've got to admit that.

THE CHAPLAIN: [*To* MOTHER COURAGE, *pointing at the cook.*] I tried to discourage him, but he says you've turned his head, he sees you in his dreams.

THE COOK: [*Lights a short-stemmed pipe.*] All I want is a glass of brandy from your fair hand, nothing more sinful. I'm already so shocked by the jokes the chaplain's been telling me, I bet I'm still red in the face.

MOTHER COURAGE: And him a clergyman! I'd better give you fellows something to drink or you'll be making me immoral propositions just to pass the time.

THE CHAPLAIN: This is temptation, said the deacon, and succumbed to it. [*Turning toward* KATTRIN *as he leaves.*] And who is this delightful young lady?

MOTHER COURAGE: She's not delightful, she's a respectable young lady.

[*The* CHAPLAIN *and the* COOK *go behind the wagon with* MOTHER COURAGE. KATTRIN *looks after them, then she walks away from the washing and approaches the hat. She picks it up, sits down and puts on the red shoes. From the rear* MOTHER COURAGE *is heard talking politics with the chaplain and the cook.*]

MOTHER COURAGE: The Poles here in Poland shouldn't have butted in. All right, our king marched his army into their country. But instead of keeping the peace, the Poles start butting into their own affairs and attack the king while he's marching quietly through the landscape. That was a breach of the peace and the blood is on their head.

THE CHAPLAIN: Our king had only one thing in mind; freedom. The emperor had everybody under his yoke, the Poles as much as the Germans; the king had to set them free.

THE COOK: I see it this way, your brandy's first-rate, I can see why I liked your face, but we were talking about the king. This freedom he was trying to introduce into Germany cost him a fortune, he had to levy a salt tax in Sweden, which, as I said, cost the poor people a fortune. Then he had to put the Germans in jail and break them on the rack because they liked being the emperor's slaves. Oh yes, the king made short shrift of anybody that didn't want to be free. In the beginning he only wanted to protect Poland against wicked people, especially the emperor, but the more he ate the more he wanted, and pretty soon he was protecting all of Germany.[5] But the Germans didn't take it lying down and the king got nothing but trouble for all his kindness and expense, which he naturally had to defray from taxes, which made for bad blood, but that didn't discourage him. He had one thing in his favor, the word of God, which was lucky, because otherwise people would have said he was doing it all for himself and what he hoped to get out of it. As it was, he always had a clear conscience and that was all he really cared about.

MOTHER COURAGE: It's easy to see you're not a Swede, or you wouldn't talk like that about the Hero-King.

THE CHAPLAIN: You're eating his bread, aren't you?

THE COOK: I don't eat his bread, I bake it.

MOTHER COURAGE: He can't be defeated because his men believe in him. [*Earnestly.*] When you listen to the big wheels talk, they're making war for reasons of piety, in the name of everything that's fine and noble. But when you take another look, you see that they're not so dumb; they're making war for profit. If they weren't, the small fry like me wouldn't have anything to do with it.[6]

THE COOK: That's a fact.

THE CHAPLAIN: And it wouldn't hurt you as a Dutchman to take a look at that flag up there before you express opinions in Poland.

MOTHER COURAGE: We're all good Protestants here! Prosit![7]

[KATTRIN *has started strutting about with* YVETTE'S *hat on, imitating* YVETTE'S *gait. Suddenly cannon fire and shots are heard. Drums.* MOTHER COURAGE, *the* COOK, *and the* CHAPLAIN *run out from behind the wagon, the two men still with glasses in hand. The* ORDNANCE

---

5. Allusion to Hitler's expansion of German territory allegedly to protect German-speaking peoples, first in Bohemia (now part of the Czech Republic) and then, in 1938, through the annexation of Austria. 6. The German expression can also be translated, "Wouldn't be doing the same thing." 7. A common drinking toast (literally, "May it do good," Latin).

OFFICER *and a* SOLDIER *rush up to the cannon and try to push it away.*]

MOTHER COURAGE: What's going on? Let me get my washing first, you lugs. [*She tries to rescue her washing.*]

THE ORDNANCE OFFICER: The Catholics. They're attacking. I don't know as we'll get away. [*To the* SOLDIER.] Get rid of the gun! [*Runs off.*]

THE COOK: Christ, I've got to find the general. Courage, I'll be back for a little chat in a day or two. [*Rushes out.*]

MOTHER COURAGE: Stop, you've forgotten your pipe.

THE COOK: [*From the distance.*] Keep it for me! I'll need it.

MOTHER COURAGE: Just when we were making a little money!

THE CHAPLAIN: Well, I guess I'll be going too. It might be dangerous though, with the enemy so close. Blessed are the peaceful[8] is the best motto in wartime. If only I had a cloak to cover up with.

MOTHER COURAGE: I'm not lending any cloaks, not on your life. I've had bitter experience in that line.

THE CHAPLAIN: But my religion puts me in special danger.

MOTHER COURAGE: [*Bringing him a cloak.*] It's against my better conscience. And now run along.

THE CHAPLAIN: Thank you kindly, you've got a good heart. But maybe I'd better sit here a while. The enemy might get suspicious if they see me running.

MOTHER COURAGE: [*To the* SOLDIER.] Leave it lay, you fool, you won't get paid extra. I'll take care of it for you, you'd only get killed.

THE SOLDIER: [*Running away.*] I tried. You're my witness.

MOTHER COURAGE: I'll swear it on the Bible. [*Sees her daughter with the hat.*] What are you doing with that floozy hat? Take it off, have you gone out of your mind? Now of all times, with the enemy on top of us? [*She tears the hat off* KATTRIN's *head.*] You want them to find you and make a whore out of you? And those shoes! Take them off, you woman of Babylon![9] [*She tries to pull them off.*] Jesus Christ, chaplain, make her take those shoes off! I'll be right back. [*She runs to the wagon.*]

YVETTE: [*Enters, powdering her face.*] What's this I hear? The Catholics are coming? Where is my hat? Who's been stamping on it? I can't be seen like this if the Catholics are coming. What'll they think of me? I haven't even got a mirror. [*To the* CHAPLAIN.] How do I look? Too much powder?

THE CHAPLAIN: Just right.

YVETTE: And where are my red shoes? [*She doesn't see them because* KATTRIN *hides her feet under her skirt.*] I left them here. I've got to get back to my tent. In my bare feet. It's disgraceful! [*Goes out.*]

[SWISS CHEESE *runs in carrying a small box.*]

MOTHER COURAGE: [*Comes out with her hands full of ashes. To* KATTRIN.] Ashes. [*To* SWISS CHEESE.] What you got there?

SWISS CHEESE: The regimental funds.

---

8. A parody of Jesus' Sermon on the Mount: "Blessed are the peacemakers, for they shall be called the children of God" (Matthew 5:9). 9. Sinful woman. The ancient Asian city of Babylon is a biblical locus for sin and decadence: "Babylon the great, the mother of harlots and abominations of the earth" (Revelation 17:5).

MOTHER COURAGE: Throw it away! No more paymastering for you.

SWISS CHEESE: I'm responsible for it. [*He goes rear.*]

MOTHER COURAGE: [*To the* CHAPLAIN.] Take your clergyman's coat off, chaplain, or they'll recognize you, cloak or no cloak. [*She rubs* KAT-TRIN'*s face with ashes.*] Hold still! There. With a little dirt you'll be safe. What a mess! The sentries were drunk. Hide your light under a bushel,[1] as the Good Book says. When a soldier, especially a Catholic, sees a clean face, she's a whore before she knows it. Nobody feeds them for weeks. When they finally loot some provisions, the next thing they want is women. That'll do it. Let me look at you. Not bad. Like you'd been wallowing in a pigsty. Stop shaking. You're safe now. [*To* SWISS CHEESE.] What did you do with the cashbox?

SWISS CHEESE: I thought I'd put it in the wagon.

MOTHER COURAGE: [*Horrified.*] What! In my wagon? Of all the sinful stupidity! If my back is turned for half a second! They'll hang us all!

SWISS CHEESE: Then I'll put it somewhere else, or I'll run away with it.

MOTHER COURAGE: You'll stay right here. It's too late.

THE CHAPLAIN: [*Still changing, comes forward.*] Heavens, the flag!

MOTHER COURAGE: [*Takes down the regimental flag.*] Bozhe moi![2] I'm so used to it I don't see it. Twenty-five years I've had it.

[*The cannon fire grows louder.*]

[*Morning, three days later. The cannon is gone.* MOTHER COURAGE, KATTRIN, *the* CHAPLAIN, *and* SWISS CHEESE *are sitting dejectedly over a meal.*]

SWISS CHEESE: This is the third day I've been sitting here doing nothing; the sergeant has always been easy on me, but now he must be starting to wonder: where can Swiss Cheese be with the cashbox?

MOTHER COURAGE: Be glad they haven't tracked you down.

THE CHAPLAIN: What about me? I can't hold a service here either. The Good Book says: "Whosoever hath a full heart, his tongue runneth over."[3] Heaven help me if mine runneth over.

MOTHER COURAGE: That's the way it is. Look what I've got on my hands: one with a religion and one with a cashbox. I don't know which is worse.

THE CHAPLAIN: Tell yourself that we're in the hands of God.

MOTHER COURAGE: I don't think we're that bad off, but all the same I can't sleep at night. If it weren't for you, Swiss Cheese, it'd be easier. I think I've put myself in the clear. I told them I was against the antichrist;[4] he's a Swede with horns, I told them, and I'd noticed the left horn was kind of worn down. I interrupted the questioning to ask where I could buy holy candles cheap. I knew what to say because Swiss Cheese's father was a Catholic and he used to make jokes about it. They didn't really believe me, but their regiment had no provisioner, so they looked

---

1. Also parodies the Sermon on the Mount: "Neither do men light a candle, and put it under a bushel [basket], but on a candlestick; and it giveth light unto all that are in the house" (Matthew 5:15). 2. My God! (Polish and Russian expression). 3. From Matthew 12:34: "For out of the abundance of the heart the mouth speaketh" (Jesus to the Pharisees). The biblical proverb means that one's words reflect the good or evil in one's heart. 4. Figure of evil, whose appearance on earth is supposed to foreshadow the end of the world and the coming of the Last Judgment.

the other way. Maybe we stand to gain. We're prisoners, but so are lice on a dog.

THE CHAPLAIN: This milk is good. Though there's not much of it or of anything else. Maybe we'll have to cut down on our Swedish appetites. But such is the lot of the vanquished.

MOTHER COURAGE: Who's vanquished? Victory and defeat don't always mean the same thing to the big wheels up top and the small fry underneath. Not by a long shot. In some cases defeat is a blessing to the small fry. Honor's lost, but nothing else. One time in Livonia[5] our general got such a shellacking from the enemy that in the confusion I laid hands on a beautiful white horse from the baggage train. That horse pulled my wagon for seven months, until we had a victory and they checked up. On the whole, you can say that victory and defeat cost us plain people plenty. The best thing for us is when politics gets bogged down. [To SWISS CHEESE.] Eat!

SWISS CHEESE: I've lost my appetite. How's the sergeant going to pay the men?

MOTHER COURAGE: Troops never get paid when they're running away.

SWISS CHEESE: But they've got it coming to them. If they're not paid, they don't need to run. Not a step.

MOTHER COURAGE: Swiss Cheese, you're too conscientious, it almost frightens me. I brought you up to be honest, because you're not bright, but somewhere it's got to stop. And now me and the chaplain are going to buy a Catholic flag and some meat. Nobody can buy meat like the chaplain, he goes into a trance and heads straight for the best piece, I guess it makes his mouth water and that shows him the way. At least they let me carry on my business. Nobody cares about a shopkeeper's religion, all they want to know is the price. Protestant pants are as warm as any other kind.

THE CHAPLAIN: Like the friar[6] said when somebody told him the Lutherans were going to stand the whole country on its head. They'll always need beggars, he says. [MOTHER COURAGE *disappears into the wagon.*] But she's worried about that cashbox. They've taken no notice of us so far, they think we're all part of the wagon, but how long can that go on?

SWISS CHEESE: I can take it away.

THE CHAPLAIN: That would be almost more dangerous. What if somebody sees you? They've got spies. Yesterday morning, just as I'm relieving myself, one of them jumps out of the ditch. I was so scared I almost let out a prayer. That would have given me away. I suppose they think they can tell a Protestant by the smell of his shit. He was a little runt with a patch over one eye.

MOTHER COURAGE: [*Climbing down from the wagon with a basket.*] Look what I've found. You shameless slut! [*She holds up the red shoes triumphantly.*] Yvette's red shoes! She's swiped them in cold blood. It's your fault. Who told her she was a delightful young lady? [*She puts them into the basket.*] I'm giving them back. Stealing Yvette's shoes! She ruins herself for money, that I can understand. But you'd like to do it free of charge, for pleasure. I've told you, you'll have to wait for peace. No soldiers! Just wait for peace with your worldly ways.

THE CHAPLAIN: She doesn't seem very worldly to me.

MOTHER COURAGE: Too worldly for me. In Dalarna she was like a stone, which is all they've got around there. The people used to say: We don't see the cripple. That's the way I like it. That way she's safe. [*To* SWISS CHEESE.] You leave that box where it is, hear? And keep an eye on your sister, she needs it. The two of you will be the death of me. I'd sooner take care of a bag of fleas. [*She goes off with the* CHAPLAIN. KATTRIN *starts clearing away the dishes.*]

SWISS CHEESE: Won't be many more days when I can sit in the sun in my shirtsleeves. [KATTRIN *points to a tree.*] Yes, the leaves are all yellow. [KATTRIN *asks him, by means of gestures, whether he wants a drink.*] Not now. I'm thinking. [*Pause.*] She says she can't sleep. I'd better get the cashbox out of here, I've found a hiding place. All right, get me a drink. [KATTRIN *goes behind the wagon.*] I'll hide it in the rabbit hole down by the river until I can take it away. Maybe late tonight, I'll go get it and take it to the regiment. I wonder how far they've run in three days? Won't the sergeant be surprised! Well, Swiss Cheese, this is a pleasant disappointment, that's what he'll say. I trust you with the regimental cashbox and you bring it back.

[*As* KATTRIN *comes out from behind the wagon with a glass of brandy, she comes face to face with two men. One is a* SERGEANT. *The other removes his hat and swings it through the air in a ceremonious greeting. He has a patch over one eye.*]

THE MAN WITH THE PATCH: Good morning, my dear. Have you by any chance seen a man from the headquarters of the Second Finnish Regiment?

[*Scared out of her wits,* KATTRIN *runs front, spilling the brandy. The two exchange looks and withdraw after seeing* SWISS CHEESE *sitting there.*]

SWISS CHEESE: [*Starting up from his thoughts.*] You've spilled half of it. What's the fuss about? Poke yourself in the eye? I don't understand you. I'm getting out of here, I've made up my mind, it's best. [*He stands up. She does everything she can think of to call his attention to the danger. He only evades her.*] I wish I could understand you. Poor thing, I know you're trying to tell me something, you just can't say it. Don't worry about spilling the brandy, I'll be drinking plenty more. What's one glass? [*He takes the cashbox out of the wagon and hides it under his jacket.*] I'll be right back. Let me go, you're making me angry. I know you mean well. If only you could talk.

[*When she tries to hold him back, he kisses her and tears himself away. He goes out. She is desperate, she races back and forth, uttering short inarticulate sounds. The* CHAPLAIN *and* MOTHER COURAGE *come back.* KATTRIN *gesticulates wildly at her mother.*]

MOTHER COURAGE: What's the matter? You're all upset. Has somebody hurt you? Where's Swiss Cheese? Tell it to me in order, Kattrin. Your mother understands you. What, the no-good's taken the cashbox? I'll hit him over the head with it, the sneak. Take your time, don't talk nonsense, use your hands, I don't like it when you howl like a dog, what will the chaplain think? It gives him the creeps. A one-eyed man?

THE CHAPLAIN: The one-eyed man is a spy. Did they arrest Swiss Cheese? [KATTRIN *shakes her head and shrugs her shoulders.*] We're done for.

MOTHER COURAGE: [*Takes a Catholic flag out of her basket. The* CHAPLAIN *fastens it to the flagpole.*] Hoist the new flag!

THE CHAPLAIN: [*Bitterly.*] All good Catholics here.

[*Voices are heard from the rear. The two men bring in* SWISS CHEESE.]

SWISS CHEESE: Let me go, I haven't done anything. Stop twisting my shoulder, I'm innocent.

THE SERGEANT: He belongs here. You know each other.

MOTHER COURAGE: What makes you think that?

SWISS CHEESE: I don't know them. I don't even know who they are. I had a meal here, it cost me ten hellers. Maybe you saw me sitting here, it was too salty.

THE SERGEANT: Who are you anyway?

MOTHER COURAGE: We're respectable people. And it's true. He had a meal here. He said it was too salty.

THE SERGEANT: Are you trying to tell me you don't know each other?

MOTHER COURAGE: Why should I know him? I don't know everybody. I don't ask people what their name is or if they're heathens; if they pay, they're not heathens. Are you a heathen?

SWISS CHEESE: Of course not.

THE CHAPLAIN: He ate his meal and he behaved himself. He didn't open his mouth except when he was eating. Then you have to.

THE SERGEANT: And who are you?

MOTHER COURAGE: He's only my bartender. You gentlemen must be thirsty, I'll get you a drink of brandy, you must be hot and tired.

THE SERGEANT: We don't drink on duty. [*To* SWISS CHEESE.] You were carrying something. You must have hidden it by the river. You had something under your jacket when you left here.

MOTHER COURAGE: Was it really him?

SWISS CHEESE: I think you must have seen somebody else. I saw a man running with something under his jacket. You've got the wrong man.

MOTHER COURAGE: That's what I think too, it's a misunderstanding. These things happen. I'm a good judge of people. I'm Mother Courage, you've heard of me, everybody knows me. Take it from me, this man has an honest face.

THE SERGEANT: We're looking for the cashbox of the Second Finnish Regiment. We know what the man in charge of it looks like. We've been after him for two days. You're him.

SWISS CHEESE: I'm not.

THE SERGEANT: Hand it over. If you don't you're a goner, you know that. Where is it?

MOTHER COURAGE: [*With urgency.*] He'd hand it over, wouldn't he, knowing he was a goner if he didn't? I've got it, he'd say, take it, you're stronger. He's not that stupid. Speak up, you stupid idiot, the sergeant's giving you a chance.

SWISS CHEESE: But I haven't got it.

THE SERGEANT: In that case come along. We'll get it out of you.

[*They lead him away.*]

MOTHER COURAGE: [*Shouts after them.*] He'd tell you. He's not that stupid. And don't twist his shoulder off! [*Runs after them.*]

[*The same evening. The* CHAPLAIN *and mute* KATTRIN *are washing dishes and scouring knives.*]

THE CHAPLAIN: That boy's in trouble. There are cases like that in the Bible. Take the Passion of our Lord and Savior. There's an old song about it. [*He sings the* Song of the Hours.]

In the first hour Jesus mild
Who had prayed since even
Was betrayed and led before
Pontius[7] the heathen.

Pilate found him innocent
Free from fault and error.
Therefore, having washed his hands
Sent him to King Herod.

In the third hour he was scourged
Stripped and clad in scarlet
And a plaited crown of thorns
Set upon his forehead.

On the Son of Man they spat
Mocked him and made merry.
Then the cross of death was brought
Given him to carry.

At the sixth hour with two thieves
To the cross they nailed him
And the people and the thieves
Mocked him and reviled him.

This is Jesus King of Jews
Cried they in derision
Till the sun withdrew its light
From that awful vision.

At the ninth hour Jesus wailed
Why hast thou me forsaken?
Soldiers brought him vinegar
Which he left untaken.

Then he yielded up the ghost
And the earth was shaken.

7. Roman judge before whom Jesus was arraigned by the Scribes (Matthew 27:1–24).

Rended was the temple's veil[8]
And the saints were wakened.

Soldiers broke the two thieves' legs
As the night descended
Thrust a spear in Jesus' side
When his life had ended.

Still they mocked, as from his wound
Flowed the blood and water
Thus blasphemed the Son of Man
With their cruel laughter.

MOTHER COURAGE: [*Enters in a state of agitation.*] His life's at stake. But they say the sergeant will listen to reason. Only it mustn't come out that he's our Swiss Cheese, or they'll say we've been giving him aid and comfort. All they want is money. But where will we get the money? Hasn't Yvette been here? I met her just now, she's latched onto a colonel, he's thinking of buying her a provisioner's business.

THE CHAPLAIN: Are you really thinking of selling?

MOTHER COURAGE: How else can I get the money for the sergeant?

THE CHAPLAIN: But what will you live on?

MOTHER COURAGE: That's the hitch.

[YVETTE POTTIER *comes in with a doddering* COLONEL.]

YVETTE: [*Embracing* MOTHER COURAGE.] My dear Mother Courage. Here we are again! [*Whispering.*] He's willing. [*Aloud.*] This is my dear friend who advises me on business matters. I just chanced to hear that you wish to sell your wagon, due to circumstances. I might be interested.

MOTHER COURAGE: Mortgage it, not sell it, let's not be hasty. It's not so easy to buy a wagon like this in wartime.

YVETTE: [*Disappointed.*] Only mortgage it? I thought you wanted to sell it. In that case, I don't know if I'm interested. [*To the* COLONEL.] What do you think?

THE COLONEL: Just as you say, my dear.

MOTHER COURAGE: It's only being mortgaged.

YVETTE: I thought you needed money.

MOTHER COURAGE: [*Firmly.*] I need the money, but I'd rather run myself ragged looking for an offer than sell now. The wagon is our livelihood. It's an opportunity for you, Yvette, God knows when you'll find another like it and have such a good friend to advise you. See what I mean?

YVETTE: My friend thinks I should snap it up, but I don't know. If it's only being mortgaged . . . Don't you agree that we ought to buy?

THE COLONEL: Yes, my dear.

MOTHER COURAGE: Then you'll have to look for something that's for sale, maybe you'll find something if you take your time and your friend goes around with you. Maybe in a week or two you'll find the right thing.

YVETTE: Then we'll go looking, I love to go looking for things, and I love

---

8. Matthew reports that at the moment of Jesus' death, the veil, or curtain, in the temple that set off the sanctuary was torn from top to bottom; the earth shook, and the dead rose from their graves (Matthew 27:51–53).

to go around with you, Poldi, it's a real pleasure. Even if it takes two weeks. When would you pay the money back if you get it?

MOTHER COURAGE: I can pay it back in two weeks, maybe one.

YVETTE: I can't make up my mind, Poldi, chéri,[9] tell me what to do. [*She takes the* COLONEL *aside.*] I know she's got to sell, that's definite. The lieutenant, you know who I mean, the blond one, he'd be glad to lend me the money. He's mad about me, he says I remind him of somebody. What do you think?

THE COLONEL: Keep away from that lieutenant. He's no good. He'll take advantage. Haven't I told you I'd buy you something, pussykins?

YVETTE: I can't accept it from you. But then if you think the lieutenant might take advantage . . . Poldi, I'll accept it from you.

THE COLONEL: I hope so.

YVETTE: Your advice is to take it?

THE COLONEL: That's my advice.

YVETTE: [*Goes back to* MOTHER COURAGE.] My friend advises me to do it. Write me out a receipt, say the wagon belongs to me complete with stock and furnishings when the two weeks are up. We'll take the inventory right now, then I'll bring you the two hundred guilders. [*To the* COLONEL.] You go back to camp, I'll join you in a little while, I've got to take inventory, I don't want anything missing from my wagon. [*She kisses him. He leaves. She climbs up in the wagon.*] I don't see very many boots.

MOTHER COURAGE: Yvette. This is no time to inspect your wagon if it is yours. You promised to see the sergeant about my Swiss Cheese, you've got to hurry. They say he's to be court-martialed in an hour.

YVETTE: Just let me count the shirts.

MOTHER COURAGE: [*Pulls her down by the skirt.*] You hyena, it's Swiss Cheese, his life's at stake. And don't tell anybody where the offer comes from, in heaven's name say it's your gentleman friend, or we'll all get it, they'll say we helped him.

YVETTE: I've arranged to meet One-Eye in the woods, he must be there already.

THE CHAPLAIN: And there's no need to start out with the whole two hundred, offer a hundred and fifty, that's plenty.

MOTHER COURAGE: Is it your money? You just keep out of this. Don't worry, you'll get your bread and soup. Go on now and don't haggle. It's his life. [*She gives* YVETTE *a push to start her on her way.*]

THE CHAPLAIN: I didn't mean to butt in, but what are we going to live on? You've got an unemployable daughter on your hands.

MOTHER COURAGE: You muddlehead, I'm counting on the regimental cashbox. They'll allow for his expenses, won't they?

THE CHAPLAIN: But will she handle it right?

MOTHER COURAGE: It's in her own interest. If I spend her two hundred, she gets the wagon. She's mighty keen on it, how long can she expect to hold on to her colonel? Kattrin, you scour the knives, use pumice. And you, don't stand around like Jesus on the Mount of Olives,[1] bestir

9. Darling. Poldi is her pet name for Leopold.   1. The ridge of hills outside Jerusalem where Jesus waited after the Last Supper to be captured and taken before the high priest.

yourself, wash those glasses, we're expecting at least fifty for dinner, and then it'll be the same old story: "Oh my feet, I'm not used to running around, I don't run around in the pulpit." I think they'll set him free. Thank God they're open to bribery. They're not wolves, they're human and out for money. Bribe-taking in humans is the same as mercy in God. It's our only hope. As long as people take bribes, you'll have mild sentences and even the innocent will get off once in a while.

YVETTE: [*Comes in panting.*] They want two hundred. And we've got to be quick. Or it'll be out of their hands. I'd better take One-Eye to see my colonel right away. He confessed that he'd had the cashbox, they put the thumb screws on him. But he threw it in the river when he saw they were after him. The box is gone. Should I run and get the money from my colonel?

MOTHER COURAGE: The box is gone? How will I get my two hundred back?

YVETTE: Ah, so you thought you could take it out of the cashbox? You thought you'd put one over on me. Forget it. If you want to save Swiss Cheese, you'll just have to pay, or maybe you'd like me to drop the whole thing and let you keep your wagon?

MOTHER COURAGE: This is something I hadn't reckoned with. But don't rush me, you'll get the wagon, I know it's down the drain, I've had it for seventeen years. Just let me think a second, it's all so sudden. What'll I do, I can't give them two hundred, I guess you should have bargained. If I haven't got a few guilders to fall back on, I'll be at the mercy of the first Tom, Dick, or Harry. Say I'll give them a hundred and twenty, I'll lose my wagon anyway.

YVETTE: They won't go along. One-Eye's in a hurry, he's so keyed-up he keeps looking behind him. Hadn't I better give them the whole two hundred?

MOTHER COURAGE: [*In despair.*] I can't do it. Thirty years I've worked. She's twenty-five and no husband. I've got her to keep too. Don't needle me, I know what I'm doing. Say a hundred and twenty or nothing doing.

YVETTE: It's up to you. [*Goes out quickly.*]

[MOTHER COURAGE *looks neither at the* CHAPLAIN *nor at her daughter. She sits down to help* KATTRIN *scour the knives.*]

MOTHER COURAGE: Don't break the glasses. They're not ours any more. Watch what you're doing, you'll cut yourself. Swiss Cheese will be back, I'll pay two hundred if I have to. You'll have your brother. With eighty guilders we can buy a peddler's pack and start all over. Worse things have happened.

THE CHAPLAIN: The Lord will provide.

MOTHER COURAGE: Rub them dry. [*They scour the knives in silence. Suddenly* KATTRIN *runs sobbing behind the wagon.*]

YVETTE: [*Comes running.*] They won't go along. I warned you. One-Eye wanted to run out on me, he said it was no use. He said we'd hear the drums any minute, meaning he'd been sentenced. I offered a hundred and fifty. He didn't even bother to shrug his shoulders. When I begged and pleaded, he promised to wait till I'd spoken to you again.

MOTHER COURAGE: Say I'll give him the two hundred. Run. [YVETTE *runs off. They sit in silence. The* CHAPLAIN *has stopped washing the glasses.*]

Maybe I bargained too long. [*Drums are heard in the distance. The* CHAPLAIN *stands up and goes to the rear.* MOTHER COURAGE *remains seated. It grows dark. The drums stop. It grows light again.* MOTHER COURAGE *has not moved.*]

YVETTE: [*Enters, very pale.*] Now you've done it with your haggling and wanting to keep your wagon. Eleven bullets he got, that's all. I don't know why I bother with you any more, you don't deserve it. But I've picked up a little information. They don't believe the cashbox is really in the river. They suspect it's here and they think you were connected with him. They're going to bring him here, they think maybe you'll give yourself away when you see him. I'm warning you: You don't know him, or you're all dead ducks. I may as well tell you, they're right behind me. Should I keep Kattrin out of the way? [MOTHER COURAGE *shakes her head.*] Does she know? Maybe she didn't hear the drums or maybe she didn't understand.

MOTHER COURAGE: She knows. Get her.

[YVETTE *brings* KATTRIN, *who goes to her mother and stands beside her.* MOTHER COURAGE *takes her by the hand. Two* SOLDIERS *come in with a stretcher on which something is lying under a sheet. The* SERGEANT *walks beside them. They set the stretcher down.*]

THE SERGEANT: We've got a man here and we don't know his name. We need it for the records. He had a meal with you. Take a look, see if you know him. [*He removes the sheet.*] Do you know him? [MOTHER COURAGE *shakes her head.*] What? You'd never seen him before he came here for a meal? [MOTHER COURAGE shakes her head.] Pick him up. Throw him on the dump. Nobody knows him.

[*They carry him away.*]

4

Mother Courage sings the *Song of the Great Capitulation.*

Outside an officer's tent.

MOTHER COURAGE *is waiting. A* CLERK *looks out of the tent.*

THE CLERK: I know you. You had a Protestant paymaster at your place, he was hiding. I wouldn't put in any complaints if I were you.

MOTHER COURAGE: I'm putting in a complaint. I'm innocent. If I take this lying down, it'll look as if I had a guilty conscience. First they ripped up my whole wagon with their sabers, then they wanted me to pay a fine of five talers[2] for no reason at all.

THE CLERK: I'm advising you for your own good: Keep your trap shut. We haven't got many provisioners and we'll let you keep on with your business, especially if you've got a guilty conscience and pay a fine now and then.

MOTHER COURAGE: I'm putting in a complaint.

THE CLERK: Have it your way. But you'll have to wait till the captain can see you. [*Disappears into the tent.*]

2. German silver coins.

A YOUNG SOLDIER: [*Enters in a rage.*] Bouque la Madonne![3] Where's that stinking captain? He embezzled my reward and now he's drinking it up with his whores. I'm going to get him!

AN OLDER SOLDIER: [*Comes running after him.*] Shut up. They'll put you in the stocks!

THE YOUNG SOLDIER: Come on out, you crook! I'll make chops out of you. Embezzling my reward! Who jumps in the river? Not another man in the whole squad, only me. And I can't even buy myself a beer. I won't stand for it. Come on out and let me cut you to pieces!

THE OLDER SOLDIER: Holy Mary! He'll ruin himself.

MOTHER COURAGE: They didn't give him a reward?

THE YOUNG SOLDIER: Let me go. I'll run you through too, the more the merrier.

THE OLDER SOLDIER: He saved the colonel's horse and they didn't give him a reward. He's young, he hasn't been around long.

MOTHER COURAGE: Let him go, he's not a dog, you don't have to tie him up. Wanting a reward is perfectly reasonable. Why else would he distinguish himself?

THE YOUNG SOLDIER: And him drinking in there! You're all a lot of yellow-bellies. I distinguished myself and I want my reward.

MOTHER COURAGE: Young man, don't shout at me. I've got my own worries and besides, go easy on your voice, you may need it. You'll be hoarse when the captain comes out, you won't be able to say boo and he won't be able to put you in the stocks till you're blue in the face. People that yell like that don't last long, maybe half an hour, then they're so exhausted you have to sing them to sleep.

THE YOUNG SOLDIER: I'm not exhausted and who wants to sleep? I'm hungry. They make our bread out of acorns and hemp seed, and they skimp on that. He's whoring away my reward and I'm hungry. I'll murder him.

MOTHER COURAGE: I see. You're hungry. Last year your general made you cut across the fields to trample down the grain. I could have sold a pair of boots for ten guilders if anybody'd had ten guilders and if I'd had any boots. He thought he'd be someplace else this year, but now he's still here and everybody's starving. I can see that you might be good and mad.

THE YOUNG SOLDIER: He can't do this to me, save your breath, I won't put up with injustice.

MOTHER COURAGE: You're right, but for how long? How long won't you put up with injustice? An hour? Two hours? You see, you never thought of that, though it's very important, because it's miserable in the stocks when it suddenly dawns on you that you *can* put up with injustice.

THE YOUNG SOLDIER: I don't know why I listen to you. Bouque la Madonne! Where's the captain?

MOTHER COURAGE: You listen to me because I'm not telling you anything new. You know your temper has gone up in smoke, it was a short temper and you need a long one, but that's a hard thing to come by.

3. Screw the Virgin! (French).

THE YOUNG SOLDIER: Are you trying to say I've no right to claim my reward?

MOTHER COURAGE: Not at all. I'm only saying your temper isn't long enough, it won't get you anywhere. Too bad. If you had a long temper, I'd even egg you on. Chop the bastard up, that's what I'd say, but suppose you don't chop him up, because your tail's drooping and you know it. I'm left standing there like a fool and the captain takes it out on me.

THE OLDER SOLDIER: You're right. He's only blowing off steam.

THE YOUNG SOLDIER: We'll see about that. I'll cut him to pieces. [*He draws his sword.*] When he comes, I'll cut him to pieces.

THE CLERK: [*Looks out.*] The captain will be here in a moment. Sit down. [*The* YOUNG SOLDIER *sits down.*]

MOTHER COURAGE: There he sits. What did I tell you? Sitting, aren't you? Oh, they know us like a book, they know how to handle us. Sit down! And down we sit. You can't start a riot sitting down. Better not stand up again, you won't be able to stand the way you were standing before. Don't be embarrassed on my account, I'm no better, not a bit of it. We were full of piss and vinegar, but they've bought it off. Look at me. No back talk, it's bad for business. Let me tell you about the great capitulation. [*She sings the* Song of the Great Capitulation.][4]
When I was young, no more than a spring chicken
I too thought that I was really quite the cheese
(No common peddler's daughter, not I with my looks and my talent
    and striving for higher things!)
One little hair in the soup would make me sicken
And at me no man would dare to sneeze.
(It's all or nothing, no second best for me. I've got what it takes, the
    rules are for somebody else!)
But a chickadee
Sang wait and see!
    And you go marching with the show
    In step, however fast or slow
    And rattle off your little song:
    It won't be long.
    And then the whole thing slides.
    You think God provides—
    But you've got it wrong.

And before one single year had wasted
I had learned to swallow down the bitter brew
(Two kids on my hands and the price of bread and who do they take
    me for anyway!)
Man, the double-edged shellacking that I tasted
On my ass and knees I was when they were through.
(You've got to get along with people, one good turn deserves another,
    no use trying to ram your head through the wall!)
And the chickadee

---

4. Mother Courage punctuates the story of her own gradual disillusionment with proverbs and common sayings that represent a folk wisdom of successful adjustment.

Sang wait and see!
And she goes marching with the show
In step, however fast or slow
And rattles off her little song:
It won't be long.
And then the whole thing slides
You think God provides—
But you've got it wrong.

I've seen many fired by high ambition
No star's big or high enough to reach out for.
(It's ability that counts, where there's a will there's a way, one way or
    another, we'll swing it!)
Then while moving mountains they get a suspicion
That to wear a straw hat is too big a chore.
(No use being too big for your britches!)
And the chickadee
Sings wait and see!
And they go marching with the show
In step, however fast or slow
And rattle off their little song:
It won't be long.
And then the whole thing slides!
You think God provides—
But you've got it wrong!

MOTHER COURAGE: [*To the* YOUNG SOLDIER.] So here's what I think: Stay
here with your sword if your anger's big enough, I know you have good
reason, but if it's a short quick anger, better make tracks!

THE YOUNG SOLDIER: Kiss my ass! [*He staggers off, the* OLDER SOLDIER *after
him.*]

THE CLERK: [*Sticking his head out.*] The captain is here. You can put in
your complaint now.

MOTHER COURAGE: I've changed my mind. No complaint. [*She goes out.*]

5

Two years have passed. The war has spread far and wide. With scarcely
a pause Mother Courage's little wagon rolls through Poland, Moravia,
Bavaria, Italy, and back again to Bavaria in 1631. Tilly's victory at Magdeburg[5] costs Mother Courage four officers' shirts.

MOTHER COURAGE's *wagon has stopped in a devastated village.*

Thin military music is heard from the distance. Two SOLDIERS *at the
bar are being waited on by* KATTRIN *and* MOTHER COURAGE: *One of them
is wearing a lady's fur coat over his shoulders.*

MOTHER COURAGE: What's that? You can't pay? No money, no schnapps.
Plenty of victory marches for the Lord but no pay for the men.

THE SOLDIER: I want my schnapps. I came too late for the looting. The

5. City eighty miles west of Berlin, besieged by the Imperial Army in 1630.

general skunked us: permission to loot the city for exactly one hour.
Says he's not a monster; the mayor must have paid him.
THE CHAPLAIN: [*Staggers in.*] There's still some wounded in the house.
The peasant and his family. Help me, somebody, I need linen.
    [*The* SECOND SOLDIER *goes out with him.* KATTRIN *gets very excited
    and tries to persuade her mother to hand out linen.*]
MOTHER COURAGE: I haven't got any. The regiment's bought up all my
    bandages. You think I'm going to rip up my officers' shirts for the likes
    of them?
THE CHAPLAIN: [*Calling back.*] I need linen, I tell you.
MOTHER COURAGE: [*Sitting down on the wagon steps to keep* KATTRIN *out.*]
    Nothing doing. They don't pay, they got nothing to pay with.
THE CHAPLAIN: [*Bending over a* WOMAN *whom he has carried out.*] Why
    did you stay here in all that gunfire?
THE PEASANT WOMAN: [*Feebly.*] Farm.
MOTHER COURAGE: You won't catch them leaving their property. And I'm
    expected to foot the bill. I won't do it.
THE FIRST SOLDIER: They're Protestants. Why do they have to be Protes-
    tants?
MOTHER COURAGE: Religion is the least of their worries. They've lost their
    farm.
THE SECOND SOLDIER: They're no Protestants. They're Catholics like us.
THE FIRST SOLDIER: How do we know who we're shooting at?
A PEASANT: [*Whom the* CHAPLAIN *brings in.*] They got my arm.
THE CHAPLAIN: Where's the linen?
    [*All look at* MOTHER COURAGE, *who does not move.*]
MOTHER COURAGE: I can't give you a thing. What with all my taxes, duties,
    fees and bribes! [*Making guttural sounds,* KATTRIN *picks up a board and
    threatens her mother with it.*] Are you crazy? Put that board down, you
    slut, or I'll smack you. I'm not giving anything, you can't make me. I've
    got to think of myself. [*The* CHAPLAIN *picks her up from the step and
    puts her down on the ground. Then he fishes out some shirts and tears
    them into strips.*]
    My shirts! Half a guilder apiece! I'm ruined!
    [*The anguished cry of a baby is heard from the house.*]
THE PEASANT: The baby's still in there!
    [KATTRIN *runs in.*]
THE CHAPLAIN: [*To the* WOMAN.] Don't move. They're bringing him out.
MOTHER COURAGE: Get her out of there. The roof'll cave in.
THE CHAPLAIN: I'm not going in there again.
MOTHER COURAGE: [*Torn.*] Don't run hog-wild with my expensive linen.
    [KATTRIN *emerges from the ruins carrying an infant.*]
MOTHER COURAGE: Oh, so you've found another baby to carry around with
    you? Give that baby back to its mother this minute, or it'll take me all
    day to get it away from you. Do you hear me? [*To the* SECOND SOLDIER.]
    Don't stand there gaping, go back and tell them to stop that music, I
    can see right here that they've won a victory. Your victory's costing me
    a pretty penny.
    [KATTRIN *rocks the baby in her arms, humming a lullaby.*]

MOTHER COURAGE: There she sits, happy in all this misery; give it back this minute, the mother's coming to. [*She pounces on the* FIRST SOLDIER *who has been helping himself to the drinks and is now making off with the bottle.*] Pshagreff![6] Beast! Haven't you had enough victories for today? Pay up.

FIRST SOLDIER: I'm broke.

MOTHER COURAGE: [*Tears the fur coat off him.*] Then leave the coat here, it's stolen anyway.

THE CHAPLAIN: There's still somebody in there.

6

Outside Ingolstadt[7] in Bavaria Mother Courage attends the funeral of Tilly, the imperial field marshal. Conversations about heroes and the longevity of the war. The chaplain deplores the waste of his talents. Mute Kattrin gets the red shoes. 1632.

Inside MOTHER COURAGE*'s tent.*

A bar open to the rear. Rain. In the distance drum rolls and funeral music. The CHAPLAIN *and the regimental* CLERK *are playing a board game.* MOTHER COURAGE *and her daughter are taking inventory.*

THE CHAPLAIN: The procession's starting.

MOTHER COURAGE: It's a shame about the general—socks: twenty-two pairs—I hear he was killed by accident. On account of the fog in the fields. He's up front encouraging the troops. "Fight to the death, boys," he sings out. Then he rides back, but he gets lost in the fog and rides back forward. Before you know it he's in the middle of the battle and stops a bullet—lanterns: we're down to four. [*A whistle from the rear. She goes to the bar.*] You men ought to be ashamed, running out on your late general's funeral! [*She pours drinks.*]

THE CLERK: They shouldn't have been paid before the funeral. Now they're getting drunk instead.

THE CHAPLAIN: [*To the* CLERK.] Shouldn't you be at the funeral?

THE CLERK: In this rain?

MOTHER COURAGE: With you it's different, the rain might spoil your uniform. It seems they wanted to ring the bells, naturally, but it turned out the churches had all been shot to pieces by his orders, so the poor general won't hear any bells when they lower him into his grave. They're going to fire a three-gun salute instead, so it won't be too dull— seventeen sword belts.

CRIES: [*From the bar.*] Hey! Brandy!

MOTHER COURAGE: Money first! No, you can't come into my tent with your muddy boots! You can drink outside, rain or no rain. [*To the* CLERK.] I'm only letting officers in. It seems the general had been having his troubles. Mutiny in the Second Regiment because he hadn't paid them. It's a war of religion, he says, should they profit by their faith?

---

6. Son of a bitch! (Polish).   7. City forty miles north of Munich.

[*Funeral march. All look to the rear.*]

THE CHAPLAIN: Now they're marching past the body.

MOTHER COURAGE: I feel sorry when a general or an emperor passes away like this, maybe he thought he'd do something big, that posterity would still be talking about and maybe put up a statue in his honor, conquer the world, for instance, that's a nice ambition for a general, he doesn't know any better. So he knocks himself out, and then the common people come and spoil it all, because what do they care about greatness, all they care about is a mug of beer and maybe a little company. The most beautiful plans have been wrecked by the smallness of the people that are supposed to carry them out. Even an emperor can't do anything by himself, he needs the support of his soldiers and his people. Am I right?

THE CHAPLAIN: [*Laughing.*] Courage, you're right, except about the soldiers. They do their best. With those fellows out there, for instance, drinking their brandy in the rain. I'll undertake to carry on one war after another for a hundred years, two at once if I have to, and I'm not a general by trade.

MOTHER COURAGE: Then you don't think the war might stop?

THE CHAPLAIN: Because the general's dead? Don't be childish. They grow by the dozen, there'll always be plenty of heroes.

MOTHER COURAGE: Look here, I'm not asking you for the hell of it. I've been wondering whether to lay in supplies while they're cheap, but if the war stops, I can throw them out the window.

THE CHAPLAIN: I understand. You want a serious answer. There have always been people who say: "The war will be over some day." I say there's no guarantee the war will ever be over. Naturally a brief intermission is conceivable. Maybe the war needs a breather, a war can even break its neck, so to speak. There's always a chance of that, nothing is perfect here below. Maybe there never will be a perfect war, one that lives up to all our expectations. Suddenly, for some unforeseen reason, a war can bog down, you can't think of everything. Some little oversight and your war's in trouble. And then you've got to pull it out of the mud. But the kings and emperors, not to mention the pope, will always come to its help in adversity. On the whole, I'd say this war has very little to worry about, it'll live to a ripe old age.

A SOLDIER: [*Sings at the bar.*]

> A drink, and don't be slow!
> A soldier's got to go
> And fight for his religion.

> Make it double, this is a holiday.

MOTHER COURAGE: If I could only be sure . . .

THE CHAPLAIN: Figure it out for yourself. What's to stop the war?

THE SOLDIER: [*Sings.*]

> Your breasts, girl, don't be slow!
> A soldier's got to go
> And ride away to Pilsen.[8]

8. City in Bohemia, near the German border.

THE CLERK: [*Suddenly.*] But why can't we have peace? I'm from Bohemia,
I'd like to go home when the time comes.
THE CHAPLAIN: Oh, you'd like to go home? Ah, peace! What becomes of
the hole when the cheese has been eaten?
THE SOLDIER: [*Sings.*]
> Play cards, friends, don't be slow!
> A soldier's got to go
> No matter if it's Sunday.
>
> A prayer, priest, don't be slow!
> A soldier's got to go
> And die for king and country.

THE CLERK: In the long run nobody can live without peace.
THE CHAPLAIN: The way I see it, war gives you plenty of peace. It has its
peaceful moments. War meets every need, including the peaceful ones,
everything's taken care of, or your war couldn't hold its own. In a war
you can shit the same as in the dead of peace, you can stop for a beer
between battles, and even on the march you can always lie down on
your elbows and take a little nap by the roadside. You can't play cards
when you're fighting; but then you can't when you're plowing in the
dead of peace either, but after a victory the sky's the limit. Maybe you've
had a leg shot off, at first you raise a howl; you make a big thing of it.
But then you calm down or they give you schnapps, and in the end
you're hopping around again and the war's no worse off than before.
And what's to prevent you from multiplying in the thick of the slaughter, behind a barn or someplace, in the long run how can they stop you,
and then the war has your progeny to help it along. Take it from me,
the war will always find an answer. Why would it have to stop?
[KATTRIN *has stopped working and is staring at the* CHAPLAIN.]
MOTHER COURAGE: Then I'll buy the merchandise. You've convinced me.
[KATTRIN *suddenly throws down a basket full of bottles and runs out.*]
Kattrin! [*Laughs.*] My goodness, the poor thing's been hoping for peace.
I promised her she'd get a husband when peace comes. [*She runs after
her.*]
THE CLERK: [*Getting up.*] I win, you've been too busy talking. Pay up.
MOTHER COURAGE: [*Comes back with* KATTRIN.] Be reasonable, the war'll
go on a little longer and we'll make a little more money, then peace
will be even better. Run along to town now, it won't take you ten minutes, and get the stuff from the Golden Lion, only the expensive things,
we'll pick up the rest in the wagon later, it's all arranged, the regimental
clerk here will go with you. They've almost all gone to the general's
funeral, nothing can happen to you. Look sharp, don't let them take
anything away from you, think of your dowry.
[KATTRIN *puts a kerchief over her head and goes with the clerk.*]
THE CHAPLAIN: Is it all right letting her go with the clerk?
MOTHER COURAGE: Who'd want to ruin her? She's not pretty enough.
THE CHAPLAIN: I've come to admire the way you handle your business and
pull through every time. I can see why they call you Mother Courage.
MOTHER COURAGE: Poor people need courage. Why? Because they're

sunk. In their situation it takes gumption just to get up in the morning. Or to plow a field in the middle of a war. They even show courage by bringing children into the world, because look at the prospects. The way they butcher and execute each other, think of the courage they need to look each other in the face. And putting up with an emperor and a pope takes a whale of a lot of courage, because those two are the death of the poor. [*She sits down, takes a small pipe from her pocket and smokes.*] You could be making some kindling.

THE CHAPLAIN: [*Reluctantly takes his jacket off and prepares to chop.*] Chopping wood isn't really my trade, you know, I'm a shepherd of souls.

MOTHER COURAGE: Sure. But I have no soul and I need firewood.

THE CHAPLAIN: What's that pipe?

MOTHER COURAGE: Just a pipe.

THE CHAPLAIN: No, it's not "just a pipe," it's a very particular pipe.

MOTHER COURAGE: Really?

THE CHAPLAIN: It's the cook's pipe from the Oxenstjerna regiment.

MOTHER COURAGE: If you know it all, why the mealy-mouthed questions?

THE CHAPLAIN: I didn't know if *you* knew. You could have been rummaging through your belongings and laid hands on some pipe and picked it up without thinking.

MOTHER COURAGE: Yes. Maybe that's how it was.

THE CHAPLAIN: Except it wasn't. You knew who that pipe belongs to.

MOTHER COURAGE: What of it?

THE CHAPLAIN: Courage, I'm warning you. It's my duty. I doubt if you ever lay eyes on the man again, but that's no calamity, in fact you're lucky. If you ask me, he wasn't steady. Not at all.

MOTHER COURAGE: What makes you say that? He was a nice man.

THE CHAPLAIN: Oh, you think he was nice? I differ. Far be it from me to wish him any harm, but I can't say he was nice. I'd say he was a scheming Don Juan.[9] If you don't believe me, take a look at his pipe. You'll have to admit that it shows up his character.

MOTHER COURAGE: I don't see anything. It's beat up.

THE CHAPLAIN: It's half bitten through. A violent man. That is the pipe of a ruthless, violent man, you must see that if you've still got an ounce of good sense.

MOTHER COURAGE: Don't wreck my chopping block.

THE CHAPLAIN: I've told you I wasn't trained to chop wood. I studied theology. My gifts and abilities are being wasted on muscular effort. The talents that God gave me are lying fallow. That's a sin. You've never heard me preach. With one sermon I can whip a regiment into such a state that they take the enemy for a flock of sheep. Then men care no more about their lives than they would about a smelly old sock that they're ready to throw away in hopes of final victory. God has made me eloquent. You'll swoon when you hear me preach.

MOTHER COURAGE: I don't want to swoon. What good would that do me?

THE CHAPLAIN: Courage, I've often wondered if maybe you didn't conceal

9. Philanderer.

a warm heart under that hard-bitten talk of yours. You too are human, you need warmth.

MOTHER COURAGE: The best way to keep this tent warm is with plenty of firewood.

THE CHAPLAIN: Don't try to put me off. Seriously, Courage, I sometimes wonder if we couldn't make our relationship a little closer. I mean, seeing that the whirlwind of war has whirled us so strangely together.

MOTHER COURAGE: Seems to me it's close enough. I cook your meals and you do chores, such as chopping wood, for instance.

THE CHAPLAIN: [Goes toward her.] You know what I mean by "closer"; it has nothing to do with meals and chopping wood and such mundane needs. Don't harden your heart, let it speak.

MOTHER COURAGE: Don't come at me with that ax. That's too close a relationship.

THE CHAPLAIN: Don't turn it to ridicule. I'm serious. I've given it careful thought.

MOTHER COURAGE: Chaplain, don't be silly. I like you, I don't want to have to scold you. My aim in life is to get through, me and my children and my wagon. I don't think of it as mine and besides I'm not in the mood for private affairs. Right now I'm taking a big risk, buying up merchandise with the general dead and everybody talking peace. What'll you do if I'm ruined? See? You don't know. Chop that wood, then we'll be warm in the evening, which is a good thing in times like these. Now what? [She stands up.]

[Enter KATTRIN out of breath, with a wound across her forehead and over one eye. She is carrying all sort of things, packages, leather goods, a drum, etc.]

MOTHER COURAGE: What's this? Assaulted? On the way back? She was assaulted on the way back. Must have been that soldier that got drunk here! I shouldn't have let you go! Throw the stuff down! It's not bad, only a flesh wound. I'll bandage it, it'll heal in a week. They're worse than wild beasts. [She bandages the wound.]

THE CHAPLAIN: I can't find fault with them. At home they never raped anybody. I blame the people that start wars, they're the ones that dredge up man's lowest instincts.

MOTHER COURAGE: Didn't the clerk bring you back? That's because you're respectable, they don't give a damn. It's not a deep wound, it won't leave a mark. There, all bandaged. Don't fret, I've got something for you. I've been keeping it for you on the sly, it'll be a surprise. [She fishes YVETTE's red shoes out of a sack.] See? You've always wanted them. Now you've got them. Put them on quick before I regret it. It won't leave a mark, though I wouldn't mind if it did. The girls that attract them get the worst of it. They drag them around till there's nothing left of them. If you don't appeal to them, they won't harm you. I've seen girls with pretty faces, a few years later they'd have given a wolf the creeps. They can't step behind a bush without fearing the worst. It's like trees. The straight tall ones get chopped down for ridgepoles, the crooked ones enjoy life. In other words, it's a lucky break. The shoes are still in good condition, I've kept them nicely polished.

[KATTRIN *leaves the shoes where they are and crawls into the wagon.*]
THE CHAPLAIN: I hope she won't be disfigured.
MOTHER COURAGE: There'll be a scar. She can stop waiting for peace.
THE CHAPLAIN: She didn't let them take anything.
MOTHER COURAGE: Maybe I shouldn't have drummed it into her. If I only
knew what went on in her head. One night she stayed out, the only
time in all these years. Afterwards she traipsed around as usual, except
she worked harder. I never could find out what happened. I racked my
brains for quite some time. [*She picks up the articles brought by* KAT-
TRIN *and sorts them angrily.*] That's war for you! A fine way to make a
living!
   [*Cannon salutes are heard.*]
THE CHAPLAIN: Now they're burying the general. This is a historic
moment.
MOTHER COURAGE: To me it's a historic moment when they hit my daughter over the eye. She's a wreck, she'll never get a husband now, and
she's so crazy about children. It's the war that made her dumb too, a
soldier stuffed something in her mouth when she was little. I'll never
see Swiss Cheese again and where Eilif is, God knows. God damn the
war.

7

Mother Courage at the height of her business career.

Highway.

The CHAPLAIN, MOTHER COURAGE, *and her daughter* KATTRIN *are pulling the wagon. New wares are hanging on it.* MOTHER COURAGE *is wearing
a necklace of silver talers.*

MOTHER COURAGE: Stop running down the war. I won't have it. I know it
destroys the weak, but the weak haven't a chance in peacetime either.
And war is a better provider. [*Sings.*]
           If you're not strong enough to take it
           The victory will find you dead.
           A war is only what you make it.
           It's business, not with cheese but lead.
And what good is it staying in one place? The stay-at-homes are the first
to get it. [*Sings.*]
           Some people think they'd like to ride out
           The war, leave danger to the brave
           And dig themselves a cozy hideout—
           They'll dig themselves an early grave.
           I've seen them running from the thunder
           To find a refuge from the war
           But once they're resting six feet under
           They wonder what they hurried for.
   [*They plod on.*]

8

In the same year Gustavus Adolphus, King of Sweden, is killed at the battle of Lützen.[1] Peace threatens to ruin Mother Courage's business. Her brave son performs one heroic deed too many and dies an ignominious death.

A camp.

A summer morning. An OLD WOMAN *and her* SON *are standing by the wagon. The son is carrying a large sack of bedding.*

MOTHER COURAGE'S VOICE: [*From the wagon.*] Does it have to be at this unearthly hour?

THE YOUNG MAN: We've walked all night, twenty miles, and we've got to go back today.

MOTHER COURAGE'S VOICE: What can I do with bedding? The people haven't any houses.

THE YOUNG MAN: Wait till you've seen it.

THE OLD WOMAN: She won't take it either. Come on.

THE YOUNG MAN: They'll sell the roof from over our heads for taxes. Maybe she'll give us three guilders if you throw in the cross. [*Bells start ringing.*] Listen, mother!

VOICES: [*From the rear.*] Peace! The king of Sweden is dead!

MOTHER COURAGE: [*Sticks her head out of the wagon. She has not yet done her hair.*] Why are the bells ringing in the middle of the week?

THE CHAPLAIN: [*Crawls out from under the wagon.*] What are they shouting?

MOTHER COURAGE: Don't tell me peace has broken out when I've just taken in more supplies.

THE CHAPLAIN: [*Shouting toward the rear.*] Is it true? Peace?

VOICE: Three weeks ago, they say. But we just found out.

THE CHAPLAIN: [*To* MOTHER COURAGE.] What else would they ring the bells for?

VOICE: There's a whole crowd of Lutherans, they've driven their carts into town. They brought the news.

THE YOUNG MAN: Mother, it's peace. What's the matter?

[*The* OLD WOMAN *has collapsed.*]

MOTHER COURAGE: [*Going back into the wagon.*] Heavenly saints! Kattrin, peace! Put your black dress on! We're going to church. We owe it to Swiss Cheese. Can it be true?

THE YOUNG MAN: The people here say the same thing. They've made peace. Can you get up? [*The* OLD WOMAN *stands up, still stunned.*] I'll get the saddle shop started again. I promise. Everything will be all right. Father will get his bed back. Can you walk? [*To the* CHAPLAIN.] She fainted. It was the news. She thought peace would never come again. Father said it would. We'll go straight home. [*Both go out.*]

MOTHER COURAGE'S VOICE: Give her some brandy.

---

1. Town a few miles from the great Protestant city of Leipzig.

THE CHAPLAIN: They're gone.

MOTHER COURAGE'S VOICE: What's going on in camp?

THE CHAPLAIN: A big crowd. I'll go see. Shouldn't I put on my clericals?

MOTHER COURAGE'S VOICE: Better make sure before you step out in your antichrist costume. I'm glad to see peace, even if I'm ruined. At least I've brought two of my children through the war. Now I'll see my Eilif again.

THE CHAPLAIN: Look who's coming down the road. If it isn't the general's cook!

THE COOK: [*Rather bedraggled, carrying a bundle.*] Can I believe my eyes? The chaplain!

THE CHAPLAIN: Courage! A visitor!

[MOTHER COURAGE *climbs down.*]

THE COOK: Didn't I promise to come over for a little chat as soon as I had time? I've never forgotten your brandy, Mrs. Fierling.

MOTHER COURAGE: Mercy, the general's cook! After all these years! Where's Eilif, my eldest?

THE COOK: Isn't he here yet? He left ahead of me, he was coming to see you too.

THE CHAPLAIN: I'll put on my clericals, wait for me. [*Goes out behind the wagon.*]

MOTHER COURAGE: Then he'll be here any minute. [*Calls into the wagon.*] Kattrin, Eilif's coming! Bring the cook a glass of brandy! [KATTRIN *does not appear.*] Put a lock of hair over it, and forget it! Mr. Lamb is no stranger. [*Gets the brandy herself.*] She won't come out. Peace doesn't mean a thing to her, it's come too late. They hit her over the eye, there's hardly any mark, but she thinks people are staring at her.

THE COOK: Ech, war! [*He and* MOTHER COURAGE *sit down.*]

MOTHER COURAGE: Cook, you find me in trouble. I'm ruined.

THE COOK: What? Say, that's a shame.

MOTHER COURAGE: Peace has done me in. Only the other day I stocked up. The chaplain's advice. And now they'll all demobilize and leave me sitting on my merchandise.

THE COOK: How could you listen to the chaplain? If I'd had time, I'd have warned you against him, but the Catholics came too soon. He's a fly-by-night. So now he's the boss here?

MOTHER COURAGE: He washed my dishes and helped me pull the wagon.

THE COOK: Him? Pulling? I guess he's told you a few of his jokes too, I wouldn't put it past him, he has an unsavory attitude toward women, I tried to reform him, it was hopeless. He's not steady.

MOTHER COURAGE: Are you steady?

THE COOK: If nothing else, I'm steady. Prosit!

MOTHER COURAGE: Steady is no good. I've only lived with one steady man, thank the Lord. I never had to work so hard, he sold the children's blankets when spring came, and he thought my harmonica was unchristian. In my opinion you're not doing yourself any good by admitting you're steady.

THE COOK: You've still got your old bite, but I respect you for it.

MOTHER COURAGE: Don't tell me you've been dreaming about my old bite.

THE COOK: Well, here we sit, with the bells of peace and your world-famous brandy, that hasn't its equal.

MOTHER COURAGE: The bells of peace don't strike my fancy right now. I don't see them paying the men, they're behindhand already. Where does that leave me with my famous brandy? Have you been paid?

THE COOK: [*Hesitantly.*] Not really. That's why we demobilized ourselves. Under the circumstances, I says to myself, why should I stay on? I'll go see my friends in the meantime. So here we are.

MOTHER COURAGE: You mean you're out of funds?

THE COOK: If only they'd stop those damn bells! I'd be glad to go into some kind of business. I'm sick of being a cook. They give me roots and shoe leather to work with, and then they throw the hot soup in my face. A cook's got a dog's life these days. I'd rather be in combat, but now we've got peace. [*The* CHAPLAIN *appears in his original dress.*] We'll discuss it later.

THE CHAPLAIN: It's still in good condition. There were only a few moths in it.

THE COOK: I don't see why you bother. They won't take you back. Who are you going to inspire now to be an honest soldier and earn his pay at the risk of his life? Besides, I've got a bone to pick with you. Advising this lady to buy useless merchandise on the ground that the war would last forever.

THE CHAPLAIN: [*Heatedly.*] And why, I'd like to know, is it any of your business?

THE COOK: Because it's unscrupulous. How can you meddle in other people's business and give unsolicited advice?

THE CHAPLAIN: Who's meddling? [*To* MOTHER COURAGE.] I didn't know you were accountable to this gentleman, I didn't know you were so intimate with him.

MOTHER COURAGE: Don't get excited, the cook is only giving his private opinion. And you can't deny that your war was a dud.

THE CHAPLAIN: Courage, don't blaspheme against peace. You're a battlefield hyena.

MOTHER COURAGE: What am I?

THE COOK: If you insult this lady, you'll hear from me.

THE CHAPLAIN: I'm not talking to you. Your intentions are too obvious. [*To* MOTHER COURAGE.] But when I see you picking up peace with thumb and forefinger like a snotty handkerchief, it revolts my humanity; you don't want peace, you want war, because you profit by it, but don't forget the old saying: "He hath need of a long spoon that eateth with the devil."

MOTHER COURAGE: I've no use for war and war hasn't much use for me. Anyway, I'm not letting anybody call me a hyena, you and me are through.

THE CHAPLAIN: How can you complain about peace when it's such a relief to everybody else? On account of the old rags in your wagon?

MOTHER COURAGE: My merchandise isn't old rags, it's what I live off, and so did you.

THE CHAPLAIN: Off war, you mean. Aha!

THE COOK: [*To the* CHAPLAIN.] You're a grown man, you ought to know there's no sense in giving advice. [*To* MOTHER COURAGE.] The best thing you can do now is to sell off certain articles quick, before the prices hit the floor. Dress yourself and get started, there's no time to lose.

MOTHER COURAGE: That's very sensible advice. I think I'll do it.

THE CHAPLAIN: Because the cook says so!

MOTHER COURAGE: Why didn't *you* say so? He's right, I'd better run over to the market. [*She goes into the wagon.*]

THE COOK: My round, chaplain. No presence of mind. Here's what you should have said: me give you advice? All I ever did was talk politics! Don't try to take me on. Cockfighting is undignified in a clergyman.

THE CHAPLAIN: If you don't shut up, I'll murder you, undignified or not.

THE COOK: [*Taking off his shoe and unwinding the wrappings from his feet.*] If the war hadn't made a godless bum out of you, you could easily come by a parsonage now that peace is here. They won't need cooks, there's nothing to cook, but people still do a lot of believing, that hasn't changed.

THE CHAPLAIN: See here, Mr. Lamb. Don't try to squeeze me out. Being a bum has made me a better man. I couldn't preach to them any more.

[YVETTE POTTIER *enters, elaborately dressed in black, with a cane. She is much older and fatter and heavily powdered. Behind her a servant.*]

YVETTE: Hello there! Is this the residence of Mother Courage?

THE CHAPLAIN: Right you are. With whom have we the pleasure?

YVETTE: The Countess Starhemberg, my good people. Where is Mother Courage?

THE CHAPLAIN: [*Calls into the wagon.*] Countess Starhemberg wishes to speak to you!

MOTHER COURAGE: I'm coming.

YVETTE: It's Yvette!

MOTHER COURAGE'S VOICE: My goodness! It's Yvette!

YVETTE: Just dropped in to see how you're doing. [*The* COOK *has turned around in horror.*] Pieter!

THE COOK: Yvette!

YVETTE: Blow me down! How did you get here?

THE COOK: In a cart.

THE CHAPLAIN: Oh, you know each other? Intimately?

YVETTE: I should think so. [*She looks the* COOK *over.*] Fat!

THE COOK: You're not exactly willowy yourself.

YVETTE: All the same I'm glad I ran into you, you bum. Now I can tell you what I think of you.

THE CHAPLAIN: Go right ahead, spare no details, but wait until Courage comes out.

MOTHER COURAGE: [*Comes out with all sorts of merchandise.*] Yvette! [*They embrace.*] But what are you in mourning for?

YVETTE: Isn't it becoming? My husband the colonel died a few years ago.

MOTHER COURAGE: The old geezer that almost bought my wagon?

YVETTE: His elder brother.

MOTHER COURAGE: You must be pretty well fixed. It's nice to find some-body that's made a good thing out of the war.

YVETTE: Oh well, it's been up and down and back up again.

MOTHER COURAGE: Let's not say anything bad about colonels. They make money by the bushel.

THE CHAPLAIN: If I were you, I'd put my shoes back on again. [*To* YVETTE.] Countess Starhemberg, you promised to tell us what you think of this gentleman.

THE COOK: Don't make a scene here.

MOTHER COURAGE: He's a friend of mine, Yvette.

YVETTE: He's Pete the Pipe, that's who he is.

THE COOK: Forget the nicknames, my name is Lamb.

MOTHER COURAGE: [*Laughs.*] Pete the Pipe! That drove the women crazy! Say, I've saved your pipe.

THE CHAPLAIN: And smoked it.

YVETTE: It's lucky I'm here to warn you. He's the worst rotter that ever infested the coast of Flanders. He ruined more girls than he's got fingers.

THE COOK: That was a long time ago. I've changed.

YVETTE: Stand up when a lady draws you into a conversation! How I loved this man! And all the while he was seeing a little bandy-legged brunette, ruined her, too, naturally.

THE COOK: Seems to me I started you off on a prosperous career.

YVETTE: Shut up, you depressing wreck! Watch your step with him, his kind are dangerous even when they've gone to seed.

MOTHER COURAGE: [*To* YVETTE.] Come along, I've got to sell my stuff before the prices drop. Maybe you can help me, with your army connections. [*Calls into the wagon.*] Kattrin, forget about church, I'm running over to the market. When Eilif comes, give him a drink. [*Goes out with* YVETTE.]

YVETTE: [*In leaving.*] To think that such a man could lead me astray! I can thank my lucky stars that I was able to rise in the world after that. I've put a spoke in your wheel, Pete the Pipe, and they'll give me credit for it in heaven when my time comes.

THE CHAPLAIN: Our conversation seems to illustrate the old adage: The mills of God grind slowly.[2] What do you think of my jokes now?

THE COOK: I'm just unlucky. I'll come clean: I was hoping for a hot meal. I'm starving. And now they're talking about me, and she'll get the wrong idea. I think I'll beat it before she comes back.

THE CHAPLAIN: I think so too.

THE COOK: Chaplain, I'm fed up on peace already. Men are sinners from the cradle, fire and sword are their natural lot. I wish I were cooking for the general again. God knows where he is, I'd roast a fine fat capon, with mustard sauce and a few carrots.

THE CHAPLAIN: Red cabbage. Red cabbage with capon.

THE COOK: That's right, but he wanted carrots.

THE CHAPLAIN: He was ignorant.

THE COOK: That didn't prevent you from gorging yourself.

---

2. From a saying by Friedrich von Logan (1605–1655), as translated by Longfellow: "Though the mills of God grind slowly, / Yet they grind exceeding small."

THE CHAPLAIN: With repugnance.

THE COOK: Anyway you'll have to admit those were good times.

THE CHAPLAIN: I might admit that.

THE COOK: Now you've called her a hyena, your good times here are over. What are you staring at?

THE CHAPLAIN: Eilif? [EILIF *enters, followed by* SOLDIERS *with pikes. His hands are fettered. He is deathly pale.*] What's wrong?

EILIF: Where's mother?

THE CHAPLAIN: Gone to town.

EILIF: I heard she was here. They let me come and see her.

THE COOK: [*To the* SOLDIERS.] Where are you taking him?

A SOLDIER: No good place.

THE CHAPLAIN: What has he done?

THE SOLDIER: Broke into a farm. The peasant's wife is dead.

THE CHAPLAIN: How could you do such a thing?

EILIF: It's what I've been doing all along.

THE COOK: But in peacetime!

EILIF: Shut your trap. Can I sit down till she comes?

THE SOLDIER: We haven't time.

THE CHAPLAIN: During the war they honored him for it, he sat at the general's right hand. Then it was bravery. Couldn't we speak to the officer?

THE SOLDIER: No use. What's brave about taking a peasant's cattle?

THE COOK: It was stupid.

EILIF: If I'd been stupid, I'd have starved, wise guy.

THE COOK: And for being smart your head comes off.

THE CHAPLAIN: Let's get Kattrin at least.

EILIF: Leave her be. Get me a drink of schnapps.

THE SOLDIER: No time. Let's go!

THE CHAPLAIN: And what should we tell your mother?

EILIF: Tell her it wasn't any different, tell her it was the same. Or don't tell her anything.

[*The* SOLDIERS *drive him away.*]

THE CHAPLAIN: I'll go with you on your hard journey.

EILIF: I don't need any sky pilot.

THE CHAPLAIN: You don't know yet. [*He follows him.*]

THE COOK: [*Calls after them.*] I'll have to tell her, she'll want to see him.

THE CHAPLAIN: Better not tell her anything. Or say he was here and he'll come again, maybe tomorrow. I'll break it to her when I get back. [*Hurries out.*]

[*The* COOK *looks after them, shaking his head, then he walks anxiously about. Finally he approaches the wagon.*]

THE COOK: Hey! Come on out! I can see why you'd hide from peace. I wish I could do it myself. I'm the general's cook, remember? Wouldn't you have a bite to eat, to do me till your mother gets back? A slice of ham or just a piece of bread while I'm waiting. [*He looks in.*] She's buried her head in a blanket.

[*The sound of gunfire in the rear.*]

MOTHER COURAGE: [*Runs in. She is out of breath and still has her merchandise.*] Cook, the peace is over, the war started up again three days ago. I hadn't sold my stuff yet when I found out. Heaven be praised! They're shooting each other up in town, the Catholics and Lutherans. We've got to get out of here. Kattrin, start packing. What have *you* got such a long face about? What's wrong?

THE COOK: Nothing.

MOTHER COURAGE: Something's wrong, I can tell by your expression.

THE COOK: Maybe it's the war starting up again. Now I probably won't get anything hot to eat before tomorrow night.

MOTHER COURAGE: That's a lie, cook.

THE COOK: Eilif was here. He couldn't stay.

MOTHER COURAGE: He was here? Then we'll see him on the march. I'm going with our troops this time. How does he look?

THE COOK: The same.

MOTHER COURAGE: He'll never change. The war couldn't take him away from me. He's smart. Could you help me pack? [*She starts packing.*] Did he tell you anything? Is he in good with the general? Did he say anything about his heroic deeds?

THE COOK: [*Gloomily.*] They say he's been at one of them again.

MOTHER COURAGE: Tell me later, we've got to be going. [KATTRIN *emerges.*] Kattrin, peace is over. We're moving. [*To the* COOK.] What's the matter with you?

THE COOK: I'm going to enlist.

MOTHER COURAGE: I've got a suggestion. Why don't . . . ? Where's the chaplain?

THE COOK: Gone to town with Eilif.

MOTHER COURAGE: Then come a little way with me, Lamb. I need help.

THE COOK: That incident with Yvette . . .

MOTHER COURAGE: It hasn't lowered you in my estimation. Far from it. Where there's smoke there's fire. Coming?

THE COOK: I won't say no.

MOTHER COURAGE: The Twelfth Regiment has shoved off. Take the shaft. Here's a chunk of bread. We'll have to circle around to meet the Lutherans. Maybe I'll see Eilif tonight. He's my favorite. It's been a short peace. And we're on the move again. [*She sings, while the* COOK *and* KATTRIN *harness themselves to the wagon.*]

> From Ulm to Metz, from Metz to Pilsen[3]
> Courage is right there in the van.
> The war both in and out of season
> With shot and shell will feed its man.
> But lead alone is not sufficient
> The war needs soldiers to subsist!
> Its diet elseways is deficient.
> The war is hungry! So enlist!

---

3. Ulm is about eighty miles west of Munich. Metz, in the province of Lorraine (ceded to France at the end of the Thirty Years' War), is about two hundred miles west of Ulm. To travel from Metz to Pilsen one must cross the whole of Germany.

9

The great war of religion has been going on for sixteen years. Germany has lost more than half its population. Those whom the slaughter has spared have been laid low by epidemics. Once-flourishing countrysides are ravaged by famine. Wolves prowl through the charred ruins of the cities. In the fall of 1634 we find Mother Courage in Germany, in the Fichtelgebirge[4] at some distance from the road followed by the Swedish armies. Winter comes early and is exceptionally severe. Business is bad, begging is the only resort. The cook receives a letter from Utrecht[5] and is dismissed.

Outside a half-demolished presbytery.

Gray morning in early winter. Gusts of wind. MOTHER COURAGE *and the* COOK *in shabby sheepskins by the wagon.*

THE COOK: No light. Nobody's up yet.

MOTHER COURAGE: But it's a priest. He'll have to crawl out of bed to ring the bells. Then he'll get himself a nice bowl of hot soup.

THE COOK: Go on, you saw the village, everything's been burned to a crisp.

MOTHER COURAGE: But somebody's here, I heard a dog bark.

THE COOK: If the priest's got anything, he won't give it away.

MOTHER COURAGE: Maybe if we sing . . .

THE COOK: I've had it up to here. [*Suddenly.*] I got a letter from Utrecht. My mother's died of cholera and the tavern belongs to me. Here's the letter if you don't believe me. It's no business of yours what my aunt says about my evil ways, but never mind, read it.

MOTHER COURAGE:[6] [*Reads the letter.*] Lamb, I'm sick of roaming around, myself. I feel like a butcher's dog that pulls the meat cart but doesn't get any for himself. I've nothing left to sell and the people have no money to pay for it. In Saxony a man in rags tried to foist a cord of books on me for two eggs, and in Württemberg they'd have let their plow go for a little bag of salt. What's the good of plowing? Nothing grows but brambles. In Pomerania[7] they say the villagers have eaten up all the babies, and that nuns have been caught at highway robbery.

THE COOK: It's the end of the world.

MOTHER COURAGE: Sometimes I have visions of myself driving through hell, selling sulfur and brimstone, or through heaven peddling refreshments to the roaming souls. If me and the children I've got left could find a place where there's no shooting, I wouldn't mind a few years of peace and quiet.

THE COOK: We could open up the tavern again. Think it over, Anna. I made up my mind last night; with or without you, I'm going back to Utrecht. In fact I'm leaving today.

MOTHER COURAGE: I'll have to talk to Kattrin. It's kind of sudden, and I

---

4. A range of mountains in Germany near the Bohemian border.   5. City in the south of Holland.
6. In this scene, Mother Courage and the Cook for the first time use *du*, the familiar form of *you* in German. (The familiar form is used between lovers, close friends and family, and young people; the formal *Sie* is used otherwise.)   7. Saxony, Württemberg, and Pomerania are German principalities.

don't like to make decisions in the cold with nothing in my stomach. Kattrin! [KATTRIN *climbs out of the wagon.*] Kattrin, I've got something to tell you. The cook and me are thinking of going to Utrecht. They've left him a tavern there. You'd be living in one place, you'd meet people. A lot of men would be glad to get a nice, well-behaved girl, looks aren't everything. I'm all for it. I get along fine with the cook. I've got to hand it to him: He's got a head for business. We'd eat regular meals, wouldn't that be nice? And you'd have your own bed, wouldn't you like that? It's no life on the road, year in year out. You'll go to rack and ruin. You're crawling with lice already. We've got to decide, you see, we could go north with the Swedes, they must be over there. [*She points to the left.*] I think we'll do it, Kattrin.

THE COOK: Anna, could I have a word with you alone?

MOTHER COURAGE: Get back in the wagon, Kattrin.

[KATTRIN *climbs back in.*]

THE COOK: I interrupted you because I see there's been a misunderstanding, I thought it was too obvious to need saying. But if it isn't, I'll just have to say it. You can't take her, it's out of the question. Is that plain enough for you?

[KATTRIN *sticks her head out of the wagon and listens.*]

MOTHER COURAGE: You want me to leave Kattrin?

THE COOK: Look at it this way. There's no room in the tavern. It's not one of those places with three taprooms. If the two of us put our shoulder to the wheel, we can make a living, but not three, it can't be done. Kattrin can keep the wagon.

MOTHER COURAGE: I'd been thinking she could find a husband in Utrecht.

THE COOK: Don't make me laugh! How's she going to find a husband? At her age? And dumb! And with that scar!

MOTHER COURAGE: Not so loud.

THE COOK: Shout or whisper, the truth's the truth. And that's another reason why I can't have her in the tavern. The customers won't want a sight like that staring them in the face. Can you blame them?

MOTHER COURAGE: Shut up. Not so loud, I say.

THE COOK: There's a light in the presbytery. Let's sing.

MOTHER COURAGE: How could she pull the wagon by herself? She's afraid of the war. She couldn't stand it. The dreams she must have! I hear her groaning at night. Especially after battles. What she sees in her dreams, God knows. It's pity that makes her suffer so. The other day the wagon hit a hedgehog, I found it hidden in her blanket.

THE COOK: The tavern's too small. [*He calls.*] Worthy gentleman and members of the household! We shall now sing the Song of Solomon, Julius Caesar, and other great men, whose greatness didn't help them any. Just to show you that we're God-fearing people ourselves, which makes it hard for us, especially in the winter. [*They sing.*]

> You saw the wise King Solomon[8]
> You know what came of him.
> To him all hidden things were plain.

---

8. Biblical ruler celebrated for his wisdom.

He cursed the hour gave birth to him[9]
And saw that everything was vain.
How great and wise was Solomon!
Now think about his case. Alas
A useful lesson can be won.
It's wisdom that had brought him to that pass!
How happy is the man with none!

Our beautiful song proves that virtues are dangerous things, better steer clear of them, enjoy life, eat a good breakfast, a bowl of hot soup, for instance. Take me, I haven't got any soup and wish I had, I'm a soldier, but what has my bravery in all those battles got me, nothing, I'm starving, I'd be better off if I'd stayed home like a yellowbelly. And I'll tell you why.

You saw the daring Caesar[1] next
You know what he became.
They deified him in his life
But then they killed him just the same.
And as they raised the fatal knife
How loud he cried: "You too, my son!"
Now think about his case. Alas
A useful lesson can be won.
It's daring that had brought him to that pass!
How happy is the man with none!

[*In an undertone.*] They're not even looking out. Worthy gentleman and members of the household! Maybe you'll say, all right, if bravery won't keep body and soul together, try honesty. That may fill your belly or at least get you a drop to drink. Let's look into it.

You've heard of honest Socrates[2]
Who never told a lie.
They weren't so grateful as you'd think
Instead they sentenced him to die
And handed him the poisoned drink.
How honest was the people's noble son!
Now think about his case. Alas
A useful lesson can be won.
His honesty had brought him to that pass.
How happy is the man with none!

Yes, they tell us to be charitable and to share what we have, but what if we haven't got anything? Maybe philanthropists have a rough time of it too, it stands to reason, they need a little something for themselves. Yes, charity is a rare virtue, because it doesn't pay.

St. Martin couldn't bear to see
His fellows in distress.
He saw a poor man in the snow.

9. The cook confuses Solomon with the biblical Job, who curses the day he was born (Job 3:1).
1. Roman general and dictator (100–44 B.C.), assassinated by a republican clique—that included his young friend Brutus—when suspected of imperial ambitions.   2. Greek philosopher, condemned to death in 399 B.C. for teaching the young to question accepted beliefs.

"Take half my cloak!"[3] He did, and lo!
They both of them froze none the less.
He thought his heavenly reward was won.
Now think about his case. Alas
A useful lesson can be won.
Unselfishness had brought him to that pass.
How happy is the man with none!

That's our situation. We're God-fearing folk, we stick together, we don't steal, we don't murder, we don't set fire to anything! You could say that we set an example which bears out the song, we sink lower and lower, we seldom see any soup, but if we were different, if we were thieves and murderers, maybe our bellies would be full. Because virtue isn't rewarded, only wickedness, the world needn't be like this, but it is.

And here you see God-fearing folk
Observing God's ten laws.
So far He hasn't taken heed.
You people sitting warm indoors
Help to relieve our bitter need!
Our virtue can be counted on.
Now think about our case. Alas
A useful lesson can be won.
The fear of God has brought us to this pass.
How happy is the man with none!

VOICE: [*From above.*] Hey, down there! Come on up! We've got some good thick soup.

MOTHER COURAGE: Lamb, I couldn't get anything down. I know what you say makes sense, but is it your last word? We've always been good friends.

THE COOK: My last word. Think it over.

MOTHER COURAGE: I don't need to think it over. I won't leave her.

THE COOK: It wouldn't be wise, but there's nothing I can do. I'm not inhuman, but it's a small tavern. We'd better go in now, or there won't be anything left, we'll have been singing in the cold for nothing.

MOTHER COURAGE: I'll get Kattrin.

THE COOK: Better bring it down for her. They'll get a fright if the three of us barge in. [*They go out.*]

[KATTRIN *climbs out of the wagon. She is carrying a bundle. She looks around to make sure the others are gone. Then she spreads out an old pair of the cook's trousers and a skirt belonging to her mother side by side on a wheel of the wagon so they can easily be seen. She is about to leave with her bundle when* MOTHER COURAGE *comes out of the house.*]

MOTHER COURAGE: [*With a dish of soup.*] Kattrin! Stop! Kattrin! Where do you think you're going with that bundle? Have you taken leave of your wits? [*She examines the bundle.*] She's packed her things. Were you listening? I've told him it's no go with Utrecht and his lousy tavern,

3. As a young soldier in the Roman army, Martin (330–397) divided his military cloak with a beggar. He dreamed of Christ that night and was baptized thereafter, later becoming bishop of Tours.

what would we do there? A tavern's no place for you and me. The war still has a thing or two up its sleeve for us. [*She sees the trousers and skirt.*] You're stupid. Suppose I'd seen that and you'd been gone? [KAT-TRIN *tries to leave,* MOTHER COURAGE *holds her back.*] And don't go thinking I've given him the gate on your account. It's the wagon. I won't part with the wagon, I'm used to it, it's not you, it's the wagon. We'll go in the other direction, we'll put the cook's stuff out here where he'll find it, the fool. [*She climbs up and throws down a few odds and ends, to join the trousers.*] There. Now we're shut of him, you won't see me taking anyone else into the business. From now on it's you and me. This winter will go by like all the rest. Harness up, it looks like snow.

[*They harness themselves to the wagon, turn it around and pull it away. When the* COOK *comes out he sees his things and stands dumbfounded.*]

10

Throughout 1635 Mother Courage and her daughter Kattrin pull the wagon over the roads of central Germany in the wake of the increasingly bedraggled armies.

Highway.

MOTHER COURAGE *and* KATTRIN *are pulling the wagon. They come to a peasant's house. A voice is heard singing from within.*

THE VOICE:
> The rose bush in our garden
> Rejoiced our hearts in spring
> It bore such lovely flowers.
> We planted it last season
> Before the April showers.
> A garden is a blessèd thing
> It bore such lovely flowers.
>
> When winter comes a-stalking
> And gales great snow storms bring
> They trouble us but little.
> We've lately finished caulking
> The roof with moss and wattle.
> A sheltering roof's a blessèd thing
> When winter comes a-stalking.

[MOTHER COURAGE *and* KATTRIN *have stopped to listen. Then they move on.*]

11

January 1636. The imperial troops threaten the Protestant city of Halle.[4] The stone speaks. Mother Courage loses her daughter and goes on alone. The end of the war is not in sight.

---

4. Twenty miles northwest of Leipzig.

The wagon, much the worse for wear, is standing beside a peasant house with an enormous thatch roof. The house is built against the side of a stony hill. Night.

A LIEUTENANT *and three* SOLDIERS *in heavy armor step out of the woods.*

THE LIEUTENANT: I don't want any noise. If anybody yells, run him through with your pikes.

FIRST SOLDIER: But we need a guide. We'll have to knock if we want them to come out.

THE LIEUTENANT: Knocking sounds natural. It could be a cow bumping against the barn wall.

[*The* SOLDIERS *knock on the door. A* PEASANT WOMAN *opens. They hold their hands over her mouth. Two* SOLDIERS *go in.*]

A MAN'S VOICE: [*Inside.*] Who's there?

[*The* SOLDIERS *bring out a* PEASANT *and his* SON.]

THE LIEUTENANT: [*Points to the wagon, in which* KATTRIN *has appeared.*] There's another one. [*A* SOLDIER *pulls her out.*] Anybody else live here?

THE PEASANT COUPLE: This is our son.—That's a dumb girl.—Her mother's gone into the town on business—Buying up people's belongings, they're selling cheap because they're getting out.—They're provisioners.

THE LIEUTENANT: I'm warning you to keep quiet, one squawk and you'll get a pike over the head. All right. I need somebody who can show us the path to the city. [*Points to the* YOUNG PEASANT.] You. Come here!

THE YOUNG PEASANT: I don't know no path.

THE SECOND SOLDIER: [*Grinning.*] He don't know no path.

THE YOUNG PEASANT: I'm not helping the Catholics.

THE LIEUTENANT: [*To the* SECOND SOLDIER.] Give him a feel of your pike!

THE YOUNG PEASANT: [*Forced down on his knees and threatened with the pike.*] You can kill me. I won't do it.

THE FIRST SOLDIER: I know what'll make him think twice. [*He goes over to the barn.*] Two cows and an ox. Get this: If you don't help us, I'll cut them down.

THE YOUNG PEASANT: Not the animals!

THE PEASANT WOMAN: [*In tears.*] Captain, spare our animals or we'll starve.

THE LIEUTENANT: If he insists on being stubborn, they're done for.

THE FIRST SOLDIER: I'll start with the ox.

THE YOUNG PEASANT: [*To the* OLD MAN.] Do I have to? [*The* OLD WOMAN *nods.*] I'll do it.

THE PEASANT WOMAN: And thank you kindly for your forbearance, Captain, for ever and ever, amen.

[*The* PEASANT *stops her from giving further thanks.*]

THE FIRST SOLDIER: Didn't I tell you? With them it's the animals that come first.

[*Led by the* YOUNG PEASANT, *the* LIEUTENANT *and the* SOLDIERS *continue on their way.*]

THE PEASANT: I wish I knew what they're up to. Nothing good.

THE PEASANT WOMAN: Maybe they're only scouts.—What are you doing?

THE PEASANT: [*Putting a ladder against the roof and climbing up.*] See if they're alone. [*On the roof.*] Men moving in the woods. All the way to the quarry. Armor in the clearing. And a cannon. It's more than a regiment. God have mercy on the city and everybody in it.

THE PEASANT WOMAN: See any light in the city?

THE PEASANT: No. They're all asleep. [*He climbs down.*] If they get in, they'll kill everybody.

THE PEASANT WOMAN: The sentry will see them in time.

THE PEASANT: They must have killed the sentry in the tower on the hill, or he'd have blown his horn.

THE PEASANT WOMAN: If there were more of us . . .

THE PEASANT: All by ourselves up here with a cripple . . .

THE PEASANT WOMAN: We can't do a thing. Do you think . . .

THE PEASANT: Not a thing.

THE PEASANT WOMAN: We couldn't get down there in the dark.

THE PEASANT: The whole hillside is full of them. We can't even give a signal.

THE PEASANT WOMAN: They'd kill us.

THE PEASANT: No, we can't do a thing.

THE PEASANT WOMAN: [*To* KATTRIN.] Pray, poor thing, pray! We can't stop the bloodshed. If you can't talk, at least you can pray. He'll hear you if nobody else does. I'll help you. [*All kneel,* KATTRIN *behind the* PEASANTS.] Our Father which art in heaven, hear our prayer. Don't let the town perish with everybody in it, all asleep and unsuspecting. Wake them, make them get up and climb the walls and see the enemy coming through the night with cannon and pikes, through the fields and down the hillside. [*Back to* KATTRIN.] Protect our mother and don't let the watchman sleep, wake him before it's too late. And succor our brother-in-law, he's in there with his four children, let them not perish, they're innocent and don't know a thing. [*To* KATTRIN, *who groans.*] The littlest is less than two, the oldest is seven. [*Horrified,* KATTRIN *stands up.*] Our Father, hear us, for Thou alone canst help, we'll all be killed, we're weak, we haven't any pikes or anything, we are powerless and in Thine hands, we and our animals and the whole farm, and the city too, it's in Thine hands, and the enemy is under the walls with great might.

[KATTRIN *has crept unnoticed to the wagon, taken something out of it, put it under her apron and climbed up the ladder to the roof of the barn.*]

THE PEASANT WOMAN: Think upon the children in peril, especially the babes in arms and the old people that can't help themselves and all God's creatures.

THE PEASANT: And forgive us our trespasses as we forgive them that trespass against us. Amen.

[KATTRIN, *sitting on the roof, starts beating the drum that she has taken out from under her apron.*]

THE PEASANT WOMAN: Jesus! What's she doing?

THE PEASANT: She's gone crazy.

THE PEASANT WOMAN: Get her down, quick!

[*The* PEASANT *runs toward the ladder, but* KATTRIN *pulls it up on the roof.*]

THE PEASANT WOMAN: She'll be the death of us all.

THE PEASANT: Stop that, you cripple!

THE PEASANT WOMAN: She'll have the Catholics down on us.

THE PEASANT: [*Looking around for stones.*] I'll throw rocks at you.

THE PEASANT WOMAN: Have you no pity? Have you no heart? We're dead if they find out it's us! They'll run us through!

[KATTRIN *stares in the direction of the city, and goes on drumming.*]

THE PEASANT WOMAN: [*To the* PEASANT.] I told you not to let those tramps stop here. What do they care if the soldiers drive our last animals away?

THE LIEUTENANT: [*Rushes in with his* SOLDIERS *and the* YOUNG PEASANT.] I'll cut you to pieces!

THE PEASANT WOMAN: We're innocent, captain. We couldn't help it. She sneaked up there. We don't know her.

THE LIEUTENANT: Where's the ladder?

THE PEASANT: Up top.

THE LIEUTENANT: [*To* KATTRIN.] Throw down that drum. It's an order!

[KATTRIN *goes on drumming.*]

THE LIEUTENANT: You're all in this together! This'll be the end of you!

THE PEASANT: They've felled some pine trees in the woods over there. We could get one and knock her down . . .

THE FIRST SOLDIER: [*To the* LIEUTENANT.] Request permission to make a suggestion. [*He whispers something in the* LIEUTENANT'*s ear. He nods.*] Listen. We've got a friendly proposition. Come down, we'll take you into town with us. Show us your mother and we won't touch a hair of her head.

[KATTRIN *goes on drumming.*]

THE LIEUTENANT: [*Pushes him roughly aside.*] She doesn't trust you. No wonder with your mug. [*He calls up.*] If I give you my word? I'm an officer, you can trust my word of honor.

[*She drums still louder.*]

THE LIEUTENANT: Nothing is sacred to her.

THE YOUNG PEASANT: It's not just her mother, lieutenant!

THE FIRST SOLDIER: We can't let this go on. They'll hear it in the city.

THE LIEUTENANT: We'll have to make some kind of noise that's louder than the drums. What could we make noise with?

THE FIRST SOLDIER: But we're not supposed to make noise.

THE LIEUTENANT: An innocent noise, stupid. A peaceable noise.

THE PEASANT: I could chop wood.

THE LIEUTENANT: That's it, chop! [*The* PEASANT *gets an ax and chops at a log.*] Harder! Harder! You're chopping for your life.

[*Listening,* KATTRIN *has been drumming more softly. Now she looks anxiously around and goes on drumming as before.*]

THE LIEUTENANT: [*To the* PEASANT.] Not loud enough. [*To the* FIRST SOLDIER.] You chop too.

THE PEASANT: There's only one ax. [*Stops chopping.*]

THE LIEUTENANT: We'll have to set the house on fire. Smoke her out.

THE PEASANT: That won't do any good, Captain. If the city people see fire up here, they'll know what's afoot.

[*Still drumming,* KATTRIN *has been listening again. Now she laughs.*]

THE LIEUTENANT: Look, she's laughing at us. I'll shoot her down, regardless. Get the musket!

[*Two* SOLDIERS *run out.* KATTRIN *goes on drumming.*]

THE PEASANT WOMAN: I've got it, captain. That's their wagon over there. If we start smashing it up, she'll stop. The wagon's all they've got.

THE LIEUTENANT: [*To the* YOUNG PEASANT.] Smash away. [*To* KATTRIN.] We'll smash your wagon if you don't stop.

[*The* YOUNG PEASANT *strikes a few feeble blows at the wagon.*]

THE PEASANT WOMAN: Stop it, you beast!

[KATTRIN *stares despairingly at the wagon and emits pitiful sounds. But she goes on drumming.*]

THE LIEUTENANT: Where are those stinkers with the musket?

THE FIRST SOLDIER: They haven't heard anything in the city yet, or we'd hear their guns.

THE LIEUTENANT: [*To* KATTRIN.] They don't hear you. And now we're going to shoot you down. For the last time: Drop that drum!

THE YOUNG PEASANT: [*Suddenly throws the plank away.*] Keep on drumming! Or they'll all be killed! Keep on drumming, keep on drumming . . .

[*The* SOLDIER *throws him down and hits him with his pike.* KATTRIN *starts crying, but goes on drumming.*]

THE PEASANT WOMAN: Don't hit him in the back! My God, you're killing him.

[*The* SOLDIERS *run in with the musket.*]

THE SECOND SOLDIER: The colonel's foaming at the mouth. We'll be court-martialed.

THE LIEUTENANT: Set it up! Set it up! [*To* KATTRIN, *while the musket is being set up on its stand.*] For the last time: Stop that drumming! [KATTRIN *in tears drums as loud as she can.*] Fire!

[*The* SOLDIERS *fire,* KATTRIN *is hit. She beats the drum for a few times more and then slowly collapses.*]

THE LIEUTENANT: Now we'll have some quiet.

[*But* KATTRIN's *last drumbeats are answered by the city's cannon. A confused hubbub of alarm bells and cannon is heard in the distance.*]

THE FIRST SOLDIER: She's done it.

12

Night, toward morning. The fifes and drums of troops marching away.

Outside the wagon MOTHER COURAGE *sits huddled over her daughter. The* PEASANT COUPLE *are standing beside them.*

THE PEASANT: [*Hostile.*] You'll have to be going, woman. There's only one more regiment to come. You can't go alone.[5]

MOTHER COURAGE: Maybe I can get her to sleep. [*She sings.*]
            Lullaby baby
            What stirs in the hay?

---

5. That is, for protection and customers, Mother Courage must travel with the army.

> The neighbor brats whimper
> Mine are happy and gay.
> They go in tatters
> And you in silk down
> Cut from an angel's
> Best party gown.
>
> They've nothing to munch on
> And you will have pie
> Just tell your mother
> In case it's too dry.
> Lullaby baby
> What stirs in the hay?
> That one lies in Poland
> The other—who can say?

Now she's asleep. You shouldn't have told her about your brother-in-law's children.

THE PEASANT: Maybe it wouldn't have happened if you hadn't gone to town to swindle people.

MOTHER COURAGE: I'm glad she's sleeping now.

THE PEASANT WOMAN: She's not sleeping, you'll have to face it, she's dead.

THE PEASANT: And it's time you got started. There are wolves around here, and what's worse, marauders.

MOTHER COURAGE: Yes. [*She goes to the wagon and takes out a sheet of canvas to cover the body with.*]

THE PEASANT WOMAN: Haven't you anybody else? Somebody you can go to?

MOTHER COURAGE: Yes, there's one of them left. Eilif.

THE PEASANT: [*While* MOTHER COURAGE *covers the body.*] Go find him. We'll attend to this one, give her a decent burial. Set your mind at rest.

MOTHER COURAGE: Here's money for your expenses. [*She gives the* PEASANT *money.*]

[*The* PEASANT *and his* SON *shake hands with her and carry* KATTRIN *away.*]

THE PEASANT WOMAN: [*On the way out.*] Hurry up!

MOTHER COURAGE: [*Harnesses herself to the wagon.*] I hope I can pull the wagon alone. I'll manage, there isn't much in it. I've got to get back in business.

[*Another regiment marches by with fifes and drums in the rear.*]

MOTHER COURAGE: Hey, take me with you! [*She starts to pull.*]

[*Singing is heard in the rear.*]

> With all the killing and recruiting
> The war will worry on a while.
> In ninety years they'll still be shooting.
> It's hardest on the rank-and-file.
> Our food is swill, our pants all patches
> The higher-ups steal half our pay
> And still we dream of God-sent riches.
> Tomorrow is another day!

The spring is come! Christian, revive!
The snowdrifts melt, the dead lie dead!
And if by chance you're still alive
It's time to rise and shake a leg.

JORGE LUIS BORGES
1899–1986

Although other modernist writers are known for their formal innovations, it is the Argentinian Jorge Luis Borges who represents, above all, the gamelike or playful aspect of literary creation. The "real world" is only one of the possible realities in Borges's multiple universe, which treats history, fantasy, and science fiction as having equal claim on our attention: since they all can be imagined, they all are perhaps equally real. His is a world of pure thought, where abstract fictional games are played out when an initial situation or concept is pushed to its elegantly logical extreme. If everything is possible, there is no need for the artificial constraints imposed by conventional artistic attempts to represent reality: no need for psychological consistency, for a realistic setting, or for a story that unfolds in ordinary time and space. The voice telling the story becomes lost inside the setting it creates, just as a drawing by Saul Steinberg or Maurits Escher depicts a pen drawing the rest of the landscape in which it appears. Not unexpectedly, this thorough immersion in the play of subjective imagination appealed to writers like the French "new novelists," who were experimenting with shifting perspectives and a refusal of "objective" reality. For a long time, Borges's European reputation outstripped his prestige in his native land.

Borges was born in Buenos Aires, Argentina, on August 24, 1899, to a prosperous family whose ancestors were distinguished in Argentinian history. The family moved early to a large house whose library and garden were to form an essential part of his literary imagination. His paternal grandmother being English, the young Borges knew English as soon as Spanish and was educated by an English tutor until he was nine. Traveling in Europe, the family was caught in Geneva at the outbreak of World War I; Borges attended secondary school in Switzerland and throughout the war, at which time he learned French and German. After the war they moved to Spain, where he associated with a group of young experimental poets known as the Ultraists. When Borges returned home in 1921, he founded his own group of Argentinian Ultraists (their mural-review, *Prisma*, was printed on sign paper and plastered on walls); became close friends with the philosopher Macedonio Fernandez, whose dedication to pure thought and linguistic intricacies greatly influenced his own attitudes; and contributed regularly to the avant-garde review *Martin Fierro*, at that time associated with an apolitical "art for art's sake" attitude quite at odds with that of the Boedo group of politically committed writers. Although devoted to pure art, Borges consistently opposed the military dictatorship of Juan Perón and made his political views plain in speeches and nonliterary writings even if they were not included in his fiction. His attitude did not go unnoticed: in 1946, the Perón regime removed him from the librarian's post that he had held since 1938 and offered him a job as a chicken inspector.

During the 1930s, Borges turned to short narrative pieces and in 1935 published a collection of sketches titled *Universal History of Infamy*. His more mature stories—brief, metaphysical fictions whose density and elegance at times approach poetry—came as an experiment after a head injury and operation in 1938. *The Garden of Forking Paths* (1941), his first major collection, introduced him to a wider public as an intellectual and idealist writer, whose short stories subordinated familiar techniques of character, scene, plot, and narrative voice to a central idea, which was often a philosophical concept. This concept was not used as a lesson or dogma, but as the starting point of fantastic elaborations to entertain readers within the game of literature.

Borges's imaginative world is an immense labyrinth, a "garden of forking paths" in which images of mazes and infinite mirroring, cyclical repetition and recall, illustrate the effort of an elusive narrative voice to understand its own significance and that of the world. In *Borges and I*, he comments on the parallel existence of two Borgeses: the one who exists in his work (the one his readers know) and the living, fleshly identity felt by the man who sets pen to paper. "Little by little, I am giving over everything to him . . . I do not know which one of us has written this page." Borges has written on the idea (derived from the British philosophers David Hume and George Berkeley) of the individual self as a cluster of different perceptions, and he further elaborates this notion in his fictional proliferation of identities and alternate realities. Disdaining the "psychological fakery" of realistic novels (the "draggy novel of characters"), he prefers writing that is openly artful, concerned with technique for its own sake, and invents its own multidimensional reality.

Stories in *The Garden of Forking Paths*, *Fictions* (1944), and *The Aleph* (1949) develop these themes in a variety of styles. Borges is fond of detective stories (and has written a number of them) in which the search for an elusive explanation, given carefully planted clues, matters more than how recognizable the characters may be. In *Death and the Compass*, a mysterious murderer leaves tantalizing traces that refer to points of the compass and lead the detective into a fatal trap that closes on him at a fourth compass point symbolized by the architectural lozenges of the house where he dies. The author composes an art of puzzles and discovery, a grand code that treats our universe as a giant library where meaning is locked away in endless hexagonal galleries (*The Library of Babel*), as an enormous lottery whose results are all the events of our lives (*The Lottery in Babylon*), as a series of dreams within dreams (*The Circular Ruins*), or as a small iridescent sphere containing all of the points in space (*The Aleph*). In *Pierre Menard, Author of the Quixote*, the narrator is a scholarly reviewer of a certain fictitious Menard, whose masterwork has been to rewrite *Don Quixote* as if it were created today: not revise it, or yet transcribe it, but actually *reinvent* it word for word. He has succeeded; the two texts are "verbally identical" although Menard's modern version is "more ambiguous" than Cervantes's and thus "infinitely richer."

The imaginary universe of *Tlön, Uqbar, Orbis Tertius* exemplifies the mixture of fact and fiction with which Borges invites us to speculate on the solidity of our own world. The narrator is engaged in tracking down mysterious references to a country called Tlön, whose language, science, and literature are exactly opposite (and perhaps related to) our own. For example, the Tlönians use verbs or adjectives instead of nouns, since they have no concept of objects in space, and their science consists of an association of ideas in which the most astounding theory becomes the truth. In a postscript, the narrator reveals that the encyclopedia has turned out to be an immense scholarly hoax, yet also mentions that strange and unearthly objects—recognizably from Tlön—have recently been found.

The intricate, riddling, mazelike ambiguity of Borges's stories earned him international reputation and influence, to the point that a "style like Borges" has become a recognized term. In Argentina, he was given the prestigious post of Director of the National Library after the fall of Perón in 1955 and in 1961 he shared the International Publishers' Prize with Samuel Beckett. Always near-sighted, he grew increasingly blind in the mid-1950s and he was forced to dictate his work. Nonetheless, he continued to travel, teach, and lecture in the company of his wife, Else Astete Milan, whom he married in 1967. Borges lived until his death in his beloved Buenos Aires, the city he celebrated in his first volume of poetry.

The Garden of Forking Paths begins as a simple spy story purporting to reveal the hidden truth about a German bombing raid during World War I. Borges alludes to documented facts: the geographic setting of the town of Albert and the Ancre River; a famous Chinese novel as Ts'ui Pên's proposed model; the History of the World War (1914–1918) published by B. H. Liddell Hart in 1934. Official history is undermined on the first page, however, both by the newly discovered confession of Dr. Yu Tsun and by his editor's suspiciously defensive footnote. Ultimately, Yu Tsun will learn from his ancestor's novel that history is a labyrinth of alternate possibilities (much like the "alternate worlds" of science fiction).

Borges executes his detective story with the traditional carefully planted clues. We know from the beginning that Yu Tsun—even though arrested—has success-fully outwitted his rival Captain Richard Madden; that his problem was to convey the name of a bombing target to his chief in Berlin; that he went to the telephone book to locate someone capable of transmitting his message; and that he had one bullet in his revolver. The cut-off phone call, the chase at the railroad station, and Madden's hasty arrival at Dr. Albert's house provide the excitement and pressure expected in a straightforward detective plot. Quite different spatial and temporal horizons open up halfway through, however. Coincidences—those chance rela-tionships that might well have happened differently—introduce the idea of forking paths or alternate possible routes for history. Both Yu Tsun and Richard Madden are aliens trying to prove their worth inside their respective bureaucracies; the road to Stephen Albert's house turns mazelike always to the left; the only suitable name in the phone book—the man Yu Tsun must kill—is a Sinologist who has recon-structed the labyrinthine text written long ago by Yu Tsun's ancestor. This text, Ts'ui Pên's The Garden of Forking Paths, describes the universe as an infinite series of alternate versions of experience. In different versions of the story (taking place at different times), Albert and Yu Tsun are enemies—or friends—or not even there. The war and Richard Madden appear diminished (although no less real) in such a kaleidoscopic perspective, for they exist in only one of many possi-ble dimensions. Yet Madden hurries up the walk, and current reality returns to demand Albert's death. It may seem as though the vision of other worlds in which Albert continues to exist (or is Yu Tsun's enemy) would soften the murderer's remorse for his deed. Instead, it makes more poignant the narrator's realization that in this dimension no other way could be found.

George R. McMurray, Jorge Luis Borges (1980), and Martin S. Stabb, Borges Revisited (1991), are general introductions to the man and his work. Jaime Alaz-raki, ed., Critical Essays on Jorge Luis Borges (1987), assembles articles and reviews (including the 1970 Autobiographical Essay), four comparative essays, and a gen-eral introduction that offer valuable perspectives on Borges's writing as well as his impact on American writers and critics. Edna Aizenberg, ed., Borges and His Successors: the Borgesian Impact on Literature and the Arts (1990), is a wide-rang-ing collection of essays describing Borges as the precursor of postmodern fiction and criticism. Anna Maria Barrenechea, Borges The Labyrinth Maker (1965), dis-cusses Borges's intricate style while Daniel Balderston, Out of Context: Historical Reference and the Representation of Reality in Borges (1993), focuses on the texts' manipulation of fictional and historical reality. Fernando Sorrentino, Seven Con-versations with Jorge Luis Borges (1981), is a series of informal, widely ranging interviews from 1972, with a prefaced list of the topics of each conversation.

PRONOUNCING GLOSSARY

The following list uses common English syllables and stress accents to provide rough equivalents of selected words whose pronunciation may be unfamiliar to the general reader.

Borges: *bore'-hess*   Ts'ui Pên: *tsoo-ay pun*

Hsi P'êng: *shee pung*   Yu Tsun: *yew tsoo-en*

Hung Lu Meng: *hoong low mung*

The Garden of Forking Paths[1]

On page 22 of Liddell Hart's *History of World War I* you will read that an attack against the Serre-Montauban line by thirteen British divisions (supported by 1,400 artillery pieces), planned for the 24th of July, 1916, had to be postponed until the morning of the 29th. The torrential rains, Captain Liddell Hart comments, caused this delay, an insignificant one, to be sure.

The following statement, dictated, reread and signed by Dr. Yu Tsun, former professor of English at the *Hochschule* at Tsingtao,[2] throws an unsuspected light over the whole affair. The first two pages of the document are missing.

"... and I hung up the receiver. Immediately afterwards, I recognized the voice that had answered in German. It was that of Captain Richard Madden. Madden's presence in Viktor Runeberg's apartment meant the end of our anxieties and—but this seemed, *or should have seemed*, very secondary to me—also the end of our lives. It meant that Runeberg had been arrested or murdered.[3] Before the sun set on that day, I would encounter the same fate. Madden was implacable. Or rather, he was obliged to be so. An Irishman at the service of England, a man accused of laxity and perhaps of treason, how could he fail to seize and be thankful for such a miraculous opportunity: the discovery, capture, maybe even the death of two agents of the German Reich?[4] I went up to my room; absurdly I locked the door and threw myself on my back on the narrow iron cot. Through the window I saw the familiar roofs and the cloud-shaded six o'clock sun. It seemed incredible to me that that day without premonitions or symbols should be the one of my inexorable death. In spite of my dead father, in spite of having been a child in a symmetrical garden of Hai Feng, was I—now—going to die? Then I reflected that everything happens to a man precisely, precisely *now*. Centuries of centuries and only in the present do things happen; countless men in the air, on the face of the earth and the sea, and all that really is happening is happening to me ... The almost intolerable recollection of Madden's horselike face banished these wanderings. In the midst of my hatred and terror (it means nothing to me now to speak of terror, now that I have mocked Richard Madden,

1. Translated by Donald A. Yates.   2. Or Ch'ing-tao; a major port in east China, part of territory leased to (and developed by) Germany in 1898. *Hochschule:* university (German).   3. "A hypothesis both hateful and odd. The Prussian spy Hans Rabener, alias Viktor Runeberg, attacked with drawn automatic the bearer of the warrant for his arrest, Captain Richard Madden. The latter, in self-defense, inflicted the wound which brought about Runeberg's death [Editor's note]." This entire note is by Borges as "Editor."   4. Empire (German).

now that my throat yearns for the noose) it occurred to me that that tumultuous and doubtless happy warrior did not suspect that I possessed the Secret. The name of the exact location of the new British artillery park on the River Ancre. A bird streaked across the gray sky and blindly I translated it into an airplane and that airplane into many (against the French sky) annihilating the artillery station with vertical bombs. If only my mouth, before a bullet shattered it, could cry out that secret name so it could be heard in Germany . . . My human voice was very weak. How might I make it carry to the ear of the Chief? To the ear of that sick and hateful man who knew nothing of Runeberg and me save that we were in Staffordshire[5] and who was waiting in vain for our report in his arid office in Berlin, endlessly examining newspapers . . . I said out loud: *I must flee.* I sat up noiselessly, in a useless perfection of silence, as if Madden were already lying in wait for me. Something—perhaps the mere vain ostentation of proving my resources were nil—made me look through my pockets. I found what I knew I would find. The American watch, the nickel chain and the square coin, the key ring with the incriminating useless keys to Runeberg's apartment, the notebook, a letter which I resolved to destroy immediately (and which I did not destroy), a crown, two shillings and a few pence, the red and blue pencil, the handkerchief, the revolver with one bullet. Absurdly, I took it in my hand and weighed it in order to inspire courage within myself. Vaguely I thought that a pistol report can be heard at a great distance. In ten minutes my plan was perfected. The telephone book listed the name of the only person capable of transmitting the message; he lived in a suburb of Fenton,[6] less than a half hour's train ride away.

I am a cowardly man. I say it now, now that I have carried to its end a plan whose perilous nature no one can deny. I know its execution was terrible. I didn't do it for Germany, no. I care nothing for a barbarous country which imposed upon me the abjection of being a spy. Besides, I know of a man from England—a modest man—who for me is no less great than Goethe.[7] I talked with him for scarcely an hour, but during that hour he was Goethe . . . I did it because I sensed that the Chief somehow feared people of my race—for the innumerable ancestors who merge within me. I wanted to prove to him that a yellow man could save his armies. Besides, I had to flee from Captain Madden. His hands and his voice could call at my door at any moment. I dressed silently, bade farewell to myself in the mirror, went downstairs, scrutinized the peaceful street and went out. The station was not far from my home, but I judged it wise to take a cab. I argued that in this way I ran less risk of being recognized; the fact is that in the deserted street I felt myself visible and vulnerable, infinitely so. I remember that I told the cab driver to stop a short distance before the main entrance. I got out with voluntary, almost painful slowness; I was going to the village of Ashgrove but I bought a ticket for a more distant station. The train left within a very few minutes, at eight-fifty. I hurried; the next one would leave at nine-thirty. There was

---

5. County in west central England.   6. In Lincolnshire, a county in east England.   7. Johann Wolfgang von Goethe (1749–1832), German poet, novelist, and dramatist, author of *Faust;* often taken as representing the peak of German cultural achievement.

hardly a soul on the platform. I went through the coaches; I remember a few farmers, a woman dressed in mourning, a young boy who was reading with fervor the *Annals* of Tacitus,[8] a wounded and happy soldier. The coaches jerked forward at last. A man whom I recognized ran in vain to the end of the platform. It was Captain Richard Madden. Shattered, trembling, I shrank into the far corner of the seat, away from the dreaded window.

From this broken state I passed into an almost abject felicity. I told myself that the duel had already begun and that I had won the first encounter by frustrating, even if for forty minutes, even if by a stroke of fate, the attack of my adversary. I argued that this slightest of victories foreshadowed a total victory. I argued (no less fallaciously) that my cowardly felicity proved that I was a man capable of carrying out the adventure successfully. From this weakness I took strength that did not abandon me. I foresee that man will resign himself each day to more atrocious undertakings; soon there will be no one but warriors and brigands; I give them this counsel: *The author of an atrocious undertaking ought to imagine that he has already accomplished it, ought to impose upon himself a future as irrevocable as the past.* Thus I proceeded as my eyes of a man already dead registered the elapsing of that day, which was perhaps the last, and the diffusion of the night. The train ran gently along, amid ash trees. It stopped, almost in the middle of the fields. No one announced the name of the station. "Ashgrove?" I asked a few lads on the platform. "Ashgrove," they replied. I got off.

A lamp enlightened the platform but the faces of the boys were in shadow. One questioned me, "Are you going to Dr. Stephen Albert's house?" Without waiting for my answer, another said, "The house is a long way from here, but you won't get lost if you take this road to the left and at every crossroads turn again to your left." I tossed them a coin (my last), descended a few stone steps and started down the solitary road. It went downhill, slowly. It was of elemental earth; overhead the branches were tangled; the low, full moon seemed to accompany me.

For an instant, I thought that Richard Madden in some way had penetrated my desperate plan. Very quickly, I understood that that was impossible. The instructions to turn always to the left reminded me that such was the common procedure for discovering the central point of certain labyrinths. I have some understanding of labyrinths: not for nothing am I the great grandson of that Ts'ui Pên who was governor of Yunnan and who renounced worldly power in order to write a novel that might be even more populous than the *Hung Lu Meng*[9] and to construct a labyrinth in which all men would become lost. Thirteen years he dedicated to these heterogeneous tasks, but the hand of a stranger murdered him—and his novel was incoherent and no one found the labyrinth. Beneath English trees I meditated on that lost maze: I imagined it inviolate and perfect at

---

8. Cornelius Tacitus (55–117), Roman historian whose *Annals* give a vivid picture of the decadence and corruption of the Roman Empire under Tiberius, Claudius, and Nero. 9. *The Dream of the Red Chamber* (1791) by Ts'ao Hsüeh-ch'in; the most famous Chinese novel, a love story and panorama of Chinese family life involving more than 430 separate characters. (Also called *The Story of the Stone*; see above, p. 1770.)

the secret crest of a mountain; I imagined it erased by rice fields or beneath the water; I imagined it infinite, no longer composed of octagonal kiosks and returning paths, but of rivers and provinces and kingdoms . . . I thought of a labyrinth of labyrinths, of one sinuous spreading labyrinth that would encompass the past and the future and in some way involve the stars. Absorbed in these illusory images, I forgot my destiny of one pursued. I felt myself to be, for an unknown period of time, an abstract perceiver of the world. The vague, living countryside, the moon, the remains of the day worked on me, as well as the slope of the road which eliminated any possibility of weariness. The afternoon was intimate, infinite. The road descended and forked among the now confused meadows. A high-pitched, almost syllabic music approached and receded in the shifting of the wind, dimmed by leaves and distance. I thought that a man can be an enemy of other men, of the moments of other men, but not of a country: not of fireflies, words, gardens, streams of water, sunsets. Thus I arrived before a tall, rusty gate. Between the iron bars I made out a poplar grove and a pavilion. I understood suddenly two things, the first trivial, the second almost unbelievable: the music came from the pavilion, and the music was Chinese. For precisely that reason I had openly accepted it without paying it any heed. I do not remember whether there was a bell or whether I knocked with my hand. The sparkling of the music continued.

From the rear of the house within a lantern approached: a lantern that the trees sometimes striped and sometimes eclipsed, a paper lantern that had the form of a drum and the color of the moon. A tall man bore it. I didn't see his face for the light blinded me. He opened the door and said slowly, in my own language: "I see that the pious Hsi P'êng persists in correcting my solitude. You no doubt wish to see the garden?"

I recognized the name of one of our consuls and I replied, disconcerted, "The garden?"

"The garden of forking paths."

Something stirred in my memory and I uttered with incomprehensible certainty, "The garden of my ancestor Ts'ui Pên."

"Your ancestor? Your illustrious ancestor? Come in."

The damp path zigzagged like those of my childhood. We came to a library of Eastern and Western books. I recognized bound in yellow silk several volumes of the Lost Encyclopedia, edited by the Third Emperor of the Luminous Dynasty but never printed.[1] The record on the phonograph revolved next to a bronze phoenix. I also recall a *famille rose*[2] vase and another, many centuries older, of that shade of blue which our craftsmen copied from the potters of Persia . . .

Stephen Albert observed me with a smile. He was, as I have said, very tall, sharp-featured, with gray eyes and a gray beard. He told me that he had been a missionary in Tientsin "before aspiring to become a Sinologist."

---

1. The Yung-lo emperor of the Ming ("bright") Dynasty commissioned a massive encyclopedia between 1403 and 1408. A single copy of the 11,095 manuscript volumes was made in the mid-1500s; the original was later destroyed and only 370 volumes of the copy remain today.   2. Pink family (French); refers to a Chinese decorative enamel ranging in color from an opaque pink to purplish rose. *Famille rose* pottery was at its best during the reign of Yung Chên (1723–1735).

We sat down—I on a long, low divan, he with his back to the window and a tall circular clock. I calculated that my pursuer, Richard Madden, could not arrive for at least an hour. My irrevocable determination could wait.

"An astounding fate, that of Ts'ui Pên," Stephen Albert said. "Governor of his native province, learned in astronomy, in astrology and in the tireless interpretation of the canonical books, chess player, famous poet and calligrapher—he abandoned all this in order to compose a book and a maze. He renounced the pleasures of both tyranny and justice, of his populous couch, of his banquets and even of erudition—all to close himself up for thirteen years in the Pavilion of the Limpid Solitude. When he died, his heirs found nothing save chaotic manuscripts. His family, as you may be aware, wished to condemn them to the fire; but his executor—a Taoist or Buddhist monk—insisted on their publication."

"We descendants of Ts'ui Pên," I replied, "continue to curse that monk. Their publication was senseless. The book is an indeterminate heap of contradictory drafts. I examined it once: in the third chapter the hero dies, in the fourth he is alive. As for the other undertaking of Ts'ui Pên, his labyrinth . . ."

"Here is Ts'ui Pên's labyrinth," he said, indicating a tall lacquered desk.

"An ivory labyrinth!" I exclaimed. "A minimum labyrinth."

"A labyrinth of symbols," he corrected. "An invisible labyrinth of time. To me, a barbarous Englishman, has been entrusted the revelation of this diaphanous mystery. After more than a hundred years, the details are irretrievable; but it is not hard to conjecture what happened. Ts'ui Pên must have said once: *I am withdrawing to write a book.* And another time: *I am withdrawing to construct a labyrinth.* Every one imagined two works; to no one did it occur that the book and the maze were one and the same thing. The Pavilion of the Limpid Solitude stood in the center of a garden that was perhaps intricate; that circumstance could have suggested to the heirs a physical labyrinth. Ts'ui Pên died; no one in the vast territories that were his came upon the labyrinth; the confusion of the novel suggested to me that *it* was the maze. Two circumstances gave me the correct solution of the problem. One: the curious legend that Ts'ui Pên had planned to create a labyrinth which would be strictly infinite. The other: a fragment of a letter I discovered."

Albert rose. He turned his back on me for a moment; he opened a drawer of the black and gold desk. He faced me and in his hands he held a sheet of paper that had once been crimson, but was now pink and tenuous and cross-sectioned. The fame of Ts'ui Pên as a calligrapher had been justly won. I read, uncomprehendingly and with fervor, these words written with a minute brush by a man of my blood: *I leave to the various futures (not to all) my garden of forking paths.* Wordlessly, I returned the sheet. Albert continued:

"Before unearthing this letter, I had questioned myself about the ways in which a book can be infinite. I could think of nothing other than a cyclic volume, a circular one. A book whose last page was identical with the first, a book which had the possibility of continuing indefinitely. I remembered too that night which is at the middle of the Thousand and

One Nights when Scheherazade[3] (through a magical oversight of the copyist) begins to relate word for word the story of the Thousand and One Nights, establishing the risk of coming once again to the night when she must repeat it, and thus on to infinity. I imagined as well a Platonic, hereditary work, transmitted from father to son, in which each new individual adds a chapter or corrects with pious care the pages of his elders. These conjectures diverted me; but none seemed to correspond, not even remotely, to the contradictory chapters of Ts'ui Pên. In the midst of this perplexity, I received from Oxford the manuscript you have examined. I lingered, naturally, on the sentence: *I leave to the various futures (not to all) my garden of forking paths.* Almost instantly, I understood: 'The garden of forking paths' was the chaotic novel; the phrase 'the various futures (not to all)' suggested to me the forking in time, not in space. A broad rereading of the work confirmed the theory. In all fictional works, each time a man is confronted with several alternatives, he chooses one and eliminates the others; in the fiction of Ts'ui Pên, he chooses—simultaneously—all of them. He creates, in this way, diverse futures, diverse times which themselves also proliferate and fork. Here, then, is the explanation of the novel's contradictions. Fang, let us say, has a secret; a stranger calls at his door; Fang resolves to kill him. Naturally, there are several possible outcomes: Fang can kill the intruder, the intruder can kill Fang, they both can escape, they both can die, and so forth. In the work of Ts'ui Pên, all possible outcomes occur; each one is the point of departure for other forkings. Sometimes, the paths of this labyrinth converge: for example, you arrive at this house, but in one of the possible pasts you are my enemy, in another, my friend. If you will resign yourself to my incurable pronunciation, we shall read a few pages."

His face, within the vivid circle of the lamplight, was unquestionably that of an old man, but with something unalterable about it, even immortal. He read with slow precision two versions of the same epic chapter. In the first, an army marches to a battle across a lonely mountain; the horror of the rocks and shadows makes the men undervalue their lives and they gain an easy victory. In the second, the same army traverses a palace where a great festival is taking place; the resplendent battle seems to them a continuation of the celebration and they win the victory. I listened with proper veneration to these ancient narratives, perhaps less admirable in themselves than the fact that they had been created by my blood and were being restored to me by a man of a remote empire, in the course of a desperate adventure, on a Western isle. I remember the last words, repeated in each version like a secret commandment: *Thus fought the heroes, tranquil their admirable hearts, violent their swords, resigned to kill and to die.*

From that moment on, I felt about me and within my dark body an invisible, intangible swarming. Not the swarming of the divergent, parallel and finally coalescent armies, but a more inaccessible, more intimate agitation that they in some manner prefigured. Stephen Albert continued:

3. The narrator of the collection also known as the *Arabian Nights*, a thousand and one tales supposedly told by Scheherazade to her husband, Shahrayar, king of Samarkand, to postpone her execution (see p. 923).

"I don't believe that your illustrious ancestor played idly with these variations. I don't consider it credible that he would sacrifice thirteen years to the infinite execution of a rhetorical experiment. In your country, the novel is a subsidiary form of literature; in Ts'ui Pên's time it was a despicable form. Ts'ui Pên was a brilliant novelist, but he was also a man of letters who doubtless did not consider himself a mere novelist. The testimony of his contemporaries proclaims—and his life fully confirms—his metaphysical and mystical interests. Philosophic controversy usurps a good part of the novel. I know that of all problems, none disturbed him so greatly nor worked upon him so much as the abysmal problem of time. Now then, the latter is the only problem that does not figure in the pages of the *Garden*. He does not even use the word that signifies *time*. How do you explain this voluntary omission?"

I proposed several solutions—all unsatisfactory. We discussed them. Finally, Stephen Albert said to me:

"In a riddle whose answer is chess, what is the only prohibited word?"

I thought a moment and replied, "The word *chess*."

"Precisely," said Albert. "*The Garden of Forking Paths* is an enormous riddle, or parable, whose theme is time; this recondite cause prohibits its mention. To omit a word always, to resort to inept metaphors and obvious periphrases, is perhaps the most emphatic way of stressing it. That is the tortuous method preferred, in each of the meanderings of his indefatigable novel, by the oblique Ts'ui Pên. I have compared hundreds of manuscripts, I have corrected the errors that the negligence of the copyists has introduced, I have guessed the plan of this chaos, I have re-established—I believe I have re-established—the primordial organization, I have translated the entire work: it is clear to me that not once does he employ the word 'time.' The explanation is obvious: *The Garden of Forking Paths* is an incomplete, but not false, image of the universe as Ts'ui Pên conceived it. In contrast to Newton and Schopenhauer,[4] your ancestor did not believe in a uniform, absolute time. He believed in an infinite series of times, in a growing, dizzying net of divergent, convergent and parallel times. This network of times which approached one another, forked, broke off, or were unaware of one another for centuries, embraces *all* possibilities of time. We do not exist in the majority of these times; in some you exist, and not I; in others I, and not you; in others, both of us. In the present one, which a favorable fate has granted me, you have arrived at my house; in another, while crossing the garden, you found me dead; in still another, I utter these same words, but I am a mistake, a ghost."

"In every one," I pronounced, not without a tremble to my voice, "I am grateful to you and revere you for your re-creation of the garden of Ts'ui Pên."

"Not in all," he murmured with a smile. "Time forks perpetually toward innumerable futures. In one of them I am your enemy."

Once again I felt the swarming sensation of which I have spoken. It

---

4. German philosopher (1788–1860), whose concept of will proceeded from a concept of the self as enduring through time. In *Seven Conversations with Jorge Luis Borges*, Borges also comments on Schopenhauer's interest in the "oneiric [dreamlike] essence of life." Isaac Newton (1642–1727), English mathematician and philosopher best known for his formulation of laws of gravitation and motion.

seemed to me that the humid garden that surrounded the house was infinitely saturated with invisible persons. Those persons were Albert and I, secret, busy and multiform in other dimensions of time. I raised my eyes and the tenuous nightmare dissolved. In the yellow and black garden there was only one man; but this man was as strong as a statue . . . this man was approaching along the path and he was Captain Richard Madden.

"The future already exists," I replied, "but I am your friend. Could I see the letter again?"

Albert rose. Standing tall, he opened the drawer of the tall desk; for the moment his back was to me. I had readied the revolver. I fired with extreme caution. Albert fell uncomplainingly, immediately. I swear his death was instantaneous—a lightning stroke.

The rest is unreal, insignificant. Madden broke in, arrested me. I have been condemned to the gallows. I have won out abominably; I have communicated to Berlin the secret name of the city they must attack. They bombed it yesterday; I read it in the same papers that offered to England the mystery of the learned Sinologist Stephen Albert who was murdered by a stranger, one Yu Tsun. The Chief had deciphered this mystery. He knew my problem was to indicate (through the uproar of the war) the city called Albert, and that I had found no other means to do so than to kill a man of that name. He does not know (no one can know) my innumerable contrition and weariness.

For Victoria Ocampo

NAGUIB MAHFOUZ
born 1911

The foremost novelist writing in Arabic traces his roots to the civilization of the ancient Egyptians, seven thousand years ago. Past and present combine for Naguib Mahfouz as he interrogates the destiny of his people and their often-traumatic adjustment to modern industrial society. Without Mahfouz, it is said, the turbulent history of twentieth-century Egypt would never be known. His fictional families and frustrated middle-class clerks have documented the successive stages of Egyptian social and political life from the time the country cast off foreign rule and became a "postcolonial" society. Time, in fact, is the real protagonist of his novels: the time in which individuals live and die, governments come and go, and social values are transformed—time, ultimately, as the conqueror that reduces human endeavor to nothing and forces attention on spiritual truth. Mahfouz's novels and short stories have millions of readers throughout the Arab world, and a growing audience in the West, because they deal with basic human issues in a realistic social context. Generations of Arabs have read his works or seen them adapted to film and television, and his characters have become household words. Mahfouz the craftsman has also wrought a change in Arabic prose, synthesizing traditional literary style and modern speech to create a new literary language understood by Arabs everywhere.

Readers of his best-known works, however, will find many similarities with the nineteenth-century realist novel in Europe. Mahfouz has been called the "Balzac of Egypt"—a comparison to the great French novelist and panoramic chronicler of society Honoré de Balzac (1799–1850)—and he is well acquainted with the works of Gustave Flaubert, Leo Tolstoy, and other nineteenth-century novelists. Traditional Arabic literature has many forms of narrative, but the novel is not one of them, and contemporary writers like Mahfouz have adapted the Western form to their own needs. Their readers will find familiar nineteenth-century strategies such as a chronological plot, unified characters, the inclusion of documentary information and realistic details, a panoramic view of society including a strong moral and humanistic perspective, and—typically if not necessarily—a picture of urban middle-class life. Among twentieth-century authors Mahfouz might be compared with Alexander Solzhenitsyn for his realist style and analysis of national identity. The Egyptian author employs allegory much more than do traditionally realist authors, however, and his most recent work has made use of fragmented and absurdist techniques as well as a variety of classical Arabic forms. He continues to be preoccupied with individual experience inside what he calls the "tragedies of society," although his focus is not restricted to the individualized existentialism of Jean-Paul Sartre or Albert Camus and embraces a complex of social relationships. Like the nineteenth-century novelists he follows, Mahfouz believes in the social function of art and the concomitant responsibility of the writer. His books have been censored and banned in many Arab countries, and he was blacklisted for several years for supporting Egypt's 1979 peace treaty with Israel.

Naguib Mahfouz was born in Cairo on December 11, 1911, the youngest of seven children in the family of a civil servant. The family moved from their home in the old Jamaliya district to the suburbs of Cairo when the boy was young. He attended government schools and entered the University of Cairo in 1930, graduating in 1934 with a degree in philosophy. These were not quiet years: Egypt, officially under Turkish rule, had been occupied by the British since 1883 and was declared a British protectorate at the start of World War I in 1914. Mahfouz grew up in the midst of an ongoing struggle for national independence that culminated in a violent uprising against the British in 1919, and the negotiation of a constitutional monarchy in 1923. The consistent focus on Egyptian cultural identity that permeates his work may well have its roots in this early turbulent period. The difficulty of disentangling cultural traditions, however, is indicated by the fact that Mahfouz's first published book was a 1932 translation of an English work on ancient Egypt.

While at the university, Mahfouz made friends with the socialist and Darwinian thinker Salama Musa and began to write articles for Musa's journal Al-Majalla al-Jadida (The Modern Magazine). In 1938, he published his first collection of stories, Whispers of Madness, and in 1939 the first of three historical novels set in ancient Egypt. He planned at that time to write a set of forty books on the model of the historical romance written by the British novelist Sir Walter Scott (1771–1832). These first novels already included modern references, and few missed the criticism of King Farouk in Radubis (1943) or the analogy in The Struggle for Thebes (1944) between the ancient Egyptian battle to expel Hyksos usurpers and twentieth-century rebellions against foreign rule. In 1945 Mahfouz shifted decisively to the realistic novel and a portrayal of modern society. He focused on the social and spiritual dilemmas of the middle class in Cairo, documenting in vivid detail the life of an urban society that represented modern Egypt.

The major work of this period, and Mahfouz's masterwork in many eyes, is The Cairo Trilogy (1956–57), three volumes depicting the experience of three generations of a Cairo family between 1918 and 1944. Into this story, whose main protagonist Mahfouz has called Time, is woven a social history of Egypt after

World War I. Mahfouz's achievement was recognized in the State Prize for literature in 1956, but he himself temporarily ceased to write after finishing the *Trilogy*
in 1952. In that year, an officers' coup headed by Gamal Abdel-Nasser overthrew
the monarchy and instituted a republic that promised democratic reforms, and
there was a change in the panorama of Egyptian society that Mahfouz described.
Although the author was at first optimistic about the new order, he soon recognized that not much had changed for the general populace. When he started
publishing again in 1959, his works included much open criticism of the Nasser
régime.

Although he had become the best-known writer in the Arab world, his works
read by millions, Mahfouz like other Arab authors could not make a living from
his books. Copyright protection was minimal, and without copyright protection
even best-selling authors received only small sums for their books. Until he began
writing for motion pictures in the 1960s, he supported himself and his family
through various positions in governmental ministries and as a contributing editor
for the leading newspaper, *Al-Ahram*. Attached to the Ministry of Culture in 1954,
he adapted novels for film and television and later became director-general of the
governmental Cinema Organization. (Cinema, radio, and television are national-
ized industries in Egypt.) After his retirement from the civil service in 1971, Mahfouz continued to publish articles and short stories in *Al-Ahram*, where most of his
novels have appeared in serialized form before being issued as paperbacks. When
he received the Nobel Prize in 1988, at the age of seventy-seven, he was still
publishing a weekly column, "Point of View," in *Al-Ahram*.

Three years after *The Cairo Trilogy* brought him international praise, Mahfouz
shocked many readers with a new book, *Children of Gebelawi*. Serialized in *Al-
Ahram*, *Children of Gebelawi* is on the surface another description of a patriarchal
family evolving in modern times. The story of the patriarch Gebelawi and his
disobedient or ambitious children, however, is also an allegory of religious history.
Its personification of God, Adam, and the prophets—among whom science is
included as the youngest and most destructive son—and its simultaneous portrayal
of the prophets as primarily social reformers rather than religious figures, scandalized orthodox believers. The book was banned throughout the Arab world except
in Lebanon, and the Jordan League of Writers attacked Mahfouz as a "delinquent
man" whose novels were "plagued with sex and drugs." *Children of Gebelawi*
remains unpublished in Egypt to this day.

Mahfouz took up writing short stories again in the early 1960s after concentrating on novels for two decades. His second collection, *God's World* (1963), combined social realism and metaphysical speculation. He also began to move away
from an "objective," realistic style toward one that emphasized subjective or existential awareness. The perceptions of individual characters govern works such as
The Thief and the Dogs (1962), the story of a released prisoner who—seeking
revenge on his unfaithful wife and the man who betrayed him—is trapped by
police dogs and shot; and *Miramar* (1967), in which different points of view
describe the disappointed love of a young servant girl, her determination to shape
her own career, and the death of a lodger. Mahfouz did not abandon social commentary in his new mode. Individual characters represent particular classes or
even (with *Miramar's* servant girl) Egypt itself, and the film made from *Miramar*
attracted large audiences for its sharp criticism of the dominant political party,
the Arab Socialist Union. In *Mirrors* (1972), brief accounts of fifty-four different
characters "mirror" various aspects of contemporary Egyptian society.

Mahfouz's approach changed again in the late 1960s; social commentary in the
novels became even more direct, while individual stories grew more fragmented
and even absurdist in style. Egypt's defeat by Israel in the June 1967 war had a
shattering effect on the nation's self-confidence, and Mahfouz responded to what

he saw as the country's spiritual dilemma. Stories written between October and December 1967 and collected in *Under the Bus Shelter* repeatedly show contradictory and incomprehensible events happening to perplexed and frustrated people. An almost cinematic style emerged, emphasizing dialogue over interpretation; some pieces in later collections resemble one-act plays. In the title story of *Under the Bus Shelter*, people waiting for a bus observe beatings, a car crash with several deaths, a couple making love on a corpse, dancing, the rapid construction of a monumental grave in which both corpses and lovers are buried, inaudible speeches, a man who may possibly be the director of the film (if it *is* a film) but may also be a thug, a decapitation, and finally "a group of official-looking men wandering around" whose appearance frightens off the others—until the puzzled observers are shot by a previously apathetic policeman when they ask questions. Several novels in the 1970s and 1980s reveal a similar bleak perspective in a more didactic style; *There Only Remains One Hour* (1982), for example, portrays current events as a sequence of failed efforts to achieve peace and prosperity.

Mahfouz's style continues to evolve in new directions. His most recent work has adapted classical Arabic narrative forms such as the *maqama* (elaborate rhymed trickster tales) or folk narratives like the *Arabian Nights* into imaginative sequences such as *The Nights of "The Thousand and One Nights"* or *The Epic of the Riff-Raff*. While these latest works have disconcerted adherents of his earlier, realistic style, they are an integral part of the Egyptian writer's attempt to find new ways to express Arabic culture and to comment from a broader, often prophetic perspective on the contemporary scene. That Mahfouz is impelled by a sense of moral purpose is evident throughout his works, and perhaps no more so than in his Nobel Prize acceptance speech in 1988. Speaking first for Arabic letters but also as a representative of the Third World, he addressed the leaders of a Western civilization that has allowed science and technology to outweigh basic human values. "The developed world and the third world are but one family. Each human being bears responsibility towards it by the degree of what he has obtained of knowledge, wisdom, and civilization. . . . in the name of the third world: Be not spectators to our miseries." The "able ones, the civilized ones," he added, perhaps ironically, must be guided by the collective needs of humanity.

Zaabalawi, a story included in *God's World*, contains many of Mahfouz's predominant themes. Written two years after *Children of Gebelawi*, it echoes the earlier work's religious symbolism in the mysterious character of Zaabalawi himself. It is also a social document: the narrator's quest for Zaabalawi brings him before various representatives of modern Egyptian society inside a realistically described Cairo. *Zaabalawi*, therefore, takes on the character of a social and metaphysical allegory. Its terminally ill narrator seeks to be cured in a quest that implies not only physical healing but also religious salvation. He has already exhausted the resources of medical science and, in desperation, he decides to seek out a holy man whose name he recalls from childhood tales.

In the initial stage of his search, the protagonist is coldly received by a lawyer and a district officer, former acquaintances of Zaabalawi who have become worldly, materialistic, and highly successful. Moreover, these bureaucrats who depend on reason, technology, and businesslike efficiency can do no more than send him to old addresses or draw him city maps. Zaabalawi is still alive, they say, but he is unpredictable and hard to find now that he no longer inhabits his old home—a now-dilapidated mansion in front of which an old bookseller sells used books on mysticism and theology. In contrast, the calligrapher and composer to whom the narrator next turns welcome him as a person. Indeed, the composer reproves him for thinking only of his errand and overlooking the value of getting to know another human being. The relationship among art, human sympathy, and spiritual values is made clear, for Zaabalawi is close to both artists and has provided inspiration for their best works. In the last scene at the Negma Bar, Mahfouz fuses the realistic description of a hardened drinker with a dream-vision of another, peaceful world. At this stage of the quest, the narrator is not even allowed to state his errand but must place himself on a level with his drunken host before being allowed to speak. When he does sink into oblivion (in stages that suggest a mystic stripping-away of rational faculties), he is rewarded in his dreams by a glimpse of Paradise and wakes to find that Zaabalawi has been beside him as he slept. *Zaabalawi* ends as it began—"I have to find Zaabalawi"—but the seeker is now more confident, and the route more clearly marked.

Roger M. A. Allen, *The Arabic Novel: An Historical and Critical Introduction* (1982), is an authoritative introduction that situates Mahfouz in the context of modern Arabic literature and includes a bibliography of works in Arabic and Western languages. Sasson Somekh, *"Za'balawi"*—Author, Theme and Technique" in *Journal of Arabic Literature* 1 (1970), 24–35, examines the story as a "double-layered" structure governed by references to Sufi mysticism. Michael Beard and Adnan Haydar, eds., *Naguib Mahfouz* (1993), assemble eleven original essays on themes, individual works, and cultural contexts in Mahfouz's work. Trevor le Gassick, ed., *Critical Perspectives on Naguib Mahfouz* (1991), reprints articles on Mahfouz's work up to the 1970s. Rasheed El-Enany, ed., *Naguib Mahfouz: The Pursuit of Meaning* (1993), is an excellent study that includes biography, analyses of novels, short stories, and plays and a guide for further reading. Mona Mikhail, *Studies in the Short Fiction of Mahfouz and Idris* (1992), an introductory work, juxtaposes themes in Hemingway, Idris, Mahfouz, and Camus.

PRONOUNCING GLOSSARY

The following list uses common English syllables and stress accents to provide rough equivalents of selected words whose pronunciation may be unfamiliar to the general reader.

Hassanein: *hassan-ayn'*

Naguib Mahfouz: *nah-geeb' mah-fooz'*

Qamar: *ka'-mar*

Umm al-Ghulam: *oom' al-ghol-am'*

Wanas al-Damanhouri: *wah'-nahs' al-daman-hoo'-ree*

Zaabalawi: *zah-bah-lah'-wee*

Zaabalawi[1]

Finally I became convinced that I had to find Sheikh[2] Zaabalawi. The first time I had heard of his name had been in a song:

> Oh what's become of the world, Zaabalawi?
> They've turned it upside down and taken away its taste.

It had been a popular song in my childhood, and one day it had occurred to me to demand of my father, in the way children have of asking endless questions:

"Who is Zaabalawi?"

He had looked at me hesitantly as though doubting my ability to understand the answer. However, he had replied, "May his blessing descend

---

1. Translated by Denys Johnson-Davies.   2. A title of respect (originally "old man"), often indicating rulership.

upon you, he's a true saint of God, a remover of worries and troubles. Were it not for him I would have died miserably—"

In the years that followed, I heard my father many a time sing the praises of this good saint and speak of the miracles he performed. The days passed and brought with them many illnesses, for each one of which I was able, without too much trouble and at a cost I could afford, to find a cure, until I became afflicted with that illness for which no one possesses a remedy. When I had tried everything in vain and was overcome by despair, I remembered by chance what I had heard in my childhood: Why, I asked myself, should I not seek out Sheikh Zaabalawi? I recollected my father saying that he had made his acquaintance in Khan Gaafar[3] at the house of Sheikh Qamar, one of those sheikhs who practiced law in the religious courts, and so I took myself off to his house. Wishing to make sure that he was still living there, I made inquiries of a vendor of beans whom I found in the lower part of the house.

"Sheikh Qamar!" he said, looking at me in amazement. "He left the quarter ages ago. They say he's now living in Garden City and has his office in al-Azhar Square."[4]

I looked up the office address in the telephone book and immediately set off to the Chamber of Commerce Building, where it was located. On asking to see Sheikh Qamar, I was ushered into a room just as a beautiful woman with a most intoxicating perfume was leaving it. The man received me with a smile and motioned me toward a fine leather-upholstered chair. Despite the thick soles of my shoes, my feet were conscious of the lushness of the costly carpet. The man wore a lounge suit and was smoking a cigar; his manner of sitting was that of someone well satisfied both with himself and with his worldly possessions. The look of warm welcome he gave me left no doubt in my mind that he thought me a prospective client, and I felt acutely embarrassed at encroaching upon his valuable time.

"Welcome!" he said, prompting me to speak.

"I am the son of your old friend Sheikh Ali al-Tatawi," I answered so as to put an end to my equivocal position.

A certain languor was apparent in the glance he cast at me; the languor was not total in that he had not as yet lost all hope in me.

"God rest his soul," he said. "He was a fine man."

The very pain that had driven me to go there now prevailed upon me to stay.

"He told me," I continued, "of a devout saint named Zaabalawi whom he met at Your Honor's. I am in need of him, sir, if he be still in the land of the living."

The languor became firmly entrenched in his eyes, and it would have come as no surprise if he had shown the door to both me and my father's memory.

"That," he said in the tone of one who has made up his mind to terminate the conversation, "was a very long time ago and I scarcely recall him now."

3. Gaafar Market, an area of shops.   4. An area of Cairo close to the famous mosque and university of al-Azhar.

Rising to my feet so as to put his mind at rest regarding my intention of going, I asked, "Was he really a saint?"

"We used to regard him as a man of miracles."

"And where could I find him today?" I asked, making another move toward the door.

"To the best of my knowledge he was living in the Birgawi Residence in al-Azhar," and he applied himself to some papers on his desk with a resolute movement that indicated he would not open his mouth again. I bowed my head in thanks, apologized several times for disturbing him, and left the office, my head so buzzing with embarrassment that I was oblivious to all sounds around me.

I went to the Birgawi Residence, which was situated in a thickly populated quarter. I found that time had so eaten at the building that nothing was left of it save an antiquated façade and a courtyard that, despite being supposedly in the charge of a caretaker, was being used as a rubbish dump. A small, insignificant fellow, a mere prologue to a man, was using the covered entrance as a place for the sale of old books on theology and mysticism.

When I asked him about Zaabalawi, he peered at me through narrow, inflamed eyes and said in amazement, "Zaabalawi! Good heavens, what a time ago that was! Certainly he used to live in this house when it was habitable. Many were the times he would sit with me talking of bygone days, and I would be blessed by his holy presence. Where, though, is Zaabalawi today?"

He shrugged his shoulders sorrowfully and soon left me, to attend to an approaching customer. I proceeded to make inquiries of many shopkeepers in the district. While I found that a large number of them had never even heard of Zaabalawi, some, though recalling nostalgically the pleasant times they had spent with him, were ignorant of his present whereabouts, while others openly made fun of him, labeled him a charlatan, and advised me to put myself in the hands of a doctor—as though I had not already done so. I therefore had no alternative but to return disconsolately home.

With the passing of days like motes in the air, my pains grew so severe that I was sure I would not be able to hold out much longer. Once again I fell to wondering about Zaabalawi and clutching at the hope his venerable name stirred within me. Then it occurred to me to seek the help of the local sheikh of the district; in fact, I was surprised I had not thought of this to begin with. His office was in the nature of a small shop, except that it contained a desk and a telephone, and I found him sitting at his desk, wearing a jacket over his striped galabeya.[5] As he did not interrupt his conversation with a man sitting beside him, I stood waiting till the man had gone. The sheikh then looked up at me coldly. I told myself that I should win him over by the usual methods, and it was not long before I had him cheerfully inviting me to sit down.

"I'm in need of Sheikh Zaabalawi," I answered his inquiry as to the purpose of my visit.

5. The traditional Arabic robe, over which this modernized district officer wears a European jacket.

He gazed at me with the same astonishment as that shown by those I had previously encountered.

"At least," he said, giving me a smile that revealed his gold teeth, "he is still alive. The devil of it is, though, he has no fixed abode. You might well bump into him as you go out of here, on the other hand you might spend days and months in fruitless searching."

"Even you can't find him!"

"Even I! He's a baffling man, but I thank the Lord that he's still alive!"

He gazed at me intently, and murmured, "It seems your condition is serious."

"Very."

"May God come to your aid! But why don't you go about it systematically?" He spread out a sheet of paper on the desk and drew on it with unexpected speed and skill until he had made a full plan of the district, showing all the various quarters, lanes, alleyways, and squares. He looked at it admiringly and said, "These are dwelling-houses, here is the Quarter of the Perfumers, here the Quarter of the Coppersmiths, the Mouski,[6] the police and fire stations. The drawing is your best guide. Look carefully in the cafés, the places where the dervishes perform their rites, the mosques and prayer-rooms, and the Green Gate,[7] for he may well be concealed among the beggars and be indistinguishable from them. Actually, I myself haven't seen him for years, having been somewhat preoccupied with the cares of the world, and was only brought back by your inquiry to those most exquisite times of my youth."

I gazed at the map in bewilderment. The telephone rang, and he took up the receiver.

"Take it," he told me, generously. "We're at your service."

Folding up the map, I left and wandered off through the quarter, from square to street to alleyway, making inquiries of everyone I felt was familiar with the place. At last the owner of a small establishment for ironing clothes told me, "Go to the calligrapher[8] Hassanein in Umm al-Ghulam—they were friends."

I went to Umm al-Ghulam,[9] where I found old Hassanein working in a deep, narrow shop full of signboards and jars of color. A strange smell, a mixture of glue and perfume, permeated its every corner. Old Hassanein was squatting on a sheepskin rug in front of a board propped against the wall; in the middle of it he had inscribed the word "Allah"[1] in silver lettering. He was engrossed in embellishing the letters with prodigious care. I stood behind him, fearful of disturbing him or breaking the inspiration that flowed to his masterly hand. When my concern at not interrupting him had lasted some time, he suddenly inquired with unaffected gentleness, "Yes?"

Realizing that he was aware of my presence, I introduced myself. "I've been told that Sheikh Zaabalawi is your friend; I'm looking for him," I said.

6. The central bazaar.   7. A medieval gate in Cairo.   8. One who does calligraphy. The art of decorative lettering (literally "beautiful writing") is respected as a fine art in Arabic and Asian culture.   9. A street in Cairo.   1. The Arabic word for "God."

His hand came to a stop. He scrutinized me in astonishment. "Zaabalawi! God be praised!" he said with a sigh.

"He *is* a friend of yours, isn't he?" I asked eagerly.

"He was, once upon a time. A real man of mystery: he'd visit you so often that people would imagine he was your nearest and dearest, then would disappear as though he'd never existed. Yet saints are not to be blamed."

The spark of hope went out with the suddenness of a lamp snuffed by a power-cut.

"He was so constantly with me," said the man, "that I felt him to be a part of everything I drew. But where is he today?"

"Perhaps he is still alive?"

"He's alive, without a doubt. . . . He had impeccable taste, and it was due to him that I made my most beautiful drawings."

"God knows," I said, in a voice almost stifled by the dead ashes of hope, "how dire my need for him is, and no one knows better than you[2] of the ailments in respect of which he is sought."

"Yes, yes. May God restore you to health. He is, in truth, as is said of him, a man, and more. . . ."

Smiling broadly, he added, "And his face possesses an unforgettable beauty. But where is he?"

Reluctantly I rose to my feet, shook hands, and left. I continued wandering eastward and westward through the quarter, inquiring about Zaabalawi from everyone who, by reason of age or experience, I felt might be likely to help me. Eventually I was informed by a vendor of lupine[3] that he had met him a short while ago at the house of Sheikh Gad, the well-known composer. I went to the musician's house in Tabakshiyya,[4] where I found him in a room tastefully furnished in the old style, its walls redolent with history. He was seated on a divan, his famous lute beside him, concealing within itself the most beautiful melodies of our age, while somewhere from within the house came the sound of pestle and mortar and the clamor of children. I immediately greeted him and introduced myself, and was put at my ease by the unaffected way in which he received me. He did not ask, either in words or gesture, what had brought me, and I did not feel that he even harbored any such curiosity. Amazed at his understanding and kindness, which boded well, I said, "O Sheikh Gad, I am an admirer of yours, having long been enchanted by the renderings of your songs."

"Thank you," he said with a smile.

"Please excuse my disturbing you," I continued timidly, "but I was told that Zaabalawi was your friend, and I am in urgent need of him."

"Zaabalawi!" he said, frowning in concentration. "You need him? God be with you, for who knows, O Zaabalawi, where you are."

"Doesn't he visit you?" I asked eagerly.

"He visited me some time ago. He might well come right now; on the other hand I mightn't see him till death!"

---

2. One of the calligrapher's major tasks is to write religious documents and prayers to Allah.
3. Beans.   4. A quarter named for the straw trays made and sold there.

I gave an audible sigh and asked, "What made him like that?"

The musician took up his lute. "Such are saints or they would not be saints," he said, laughing.

"Do those who need him suffer as I do?"

"Such suffering is part of the cure!"

He took up the plectrum and began plucking soft strains from the strings. Lost in thought, I followed his movements. Then, as though addressing myself, I said, "So my visit has been in vain."

He smiled, laying his cheek against the side of the lute. "God forgive you," he said, "for saying such a thing of a visit that has caused me to know you and you me!"

I was much embarrassed and said apologetically, "Please forgive me; my feelings of defeat made me forget my manners."

"Do not give in to defeat. This extraordinary man brings fatigue to all who seek him. It was easy enough with him in the old days when his place of abode was known. Today, though, the world has changed, and after having enjoyed a position attained only by potentates, he is now pursued by the police on a charge of false pretenses. It is therefore no longer an easy matter to reach him, but have patience and be sure that you will do so."

He raised his head from the lute and skillfully fingered the opening bars of a melody. Then he sang:

> I make lavish mention, even though I blame myself, of those I love,
> For the stories of the beloved are my wine.[5]

With a heart that was weary and listless, I followed the beauty of the melody and the singing.

"I composed the music to this poem in a single night," he told me when he had finished. "I remember that it was the eve of the Lesser Bairam.[6] Zaabalawi was my guest for the whole of that night, and the poem was of his choosing. He would sit for a while just where you are, then would get up and play with my children as though he were one of them. Whenever I was overcome by weariness or my inspiration failed me, he would punch me playfully in the chest and joke with me, and I would bubble over with melodies, and thus I continued working till I finished the most beautiful piece I have ever composed."

"Does he know anything about music?"

"He is the epitome of things musical. He has an extremely beautiful speaking voice, and you have only to hear him to want to burst into song and to be inspired to creativity. . . ."

"How was it that he cured those diseases before which men are powerless?"

"That is his secret. Maybe you will learn it when you meet him."

But when would that meeting occur? We relapsed into silence, and the hubbub of children once more filled the room.

Again the sheikh began to sing. He went on repeating the words "and I have a memory of her" in different and beautiful variations until the very

---

5. Words from a poem by the medieval mystic poet Ibn al-Farid.   6. A major Islamic holiday, celebrated for three days to end the month's fasting during Ramadan.

walls danced in ecstasy. I expressed my wholehearted admiration, and he gave me a smile of thanks. I then got up and asked permission to leave, and he accompanied me to the front door. As I shook him by the hand, he said, "I hear that nowadays he frequents the house of Hagg Wanas al-Damanhouri. Do you know him?"

I shook my head, though a modicum of renewed hope crept into my heart.

"He is a man of private means," the sheikh told me, "who from time to time visits Cairo, putting up at some hotel or other. Every evening, though, he spends at the Negma Bar in Alfi Street."

I waited for nightfall and went to the Negma Bar. I asked a waiter about Hagg Wanas, and he pointed to a corner that was semisecluded because of its position behind a large pillar with mirrors on all four sides. There I saw a man seated alone at a table with two bottles in front of him, one empty, the other two-thirds empty. There were no snacks or food to be seen, and I was sure that I was in the presence of a hardened drinker. He was wearing a loosely flowing silk galabeya and a carefully wound turban; his legs were stretched out toward the base of the pillar, and as he gazed into the mirror in rapt contentment, the sides of his face, rounded and handsome despite the fact that he was approaching old age, were flushed with wine. I approached quietly till I stood but a few feet away from him. He did not turn toward me or give any indication that he was aware of my presence.

"Good evening, Mr. Wanas," I greeted him cordially.

He turned toward me abruptly, as though my voice had roused him from slumber, and glared at me in disapproval. I was about to explain what had brought me to him when he interrupted in an almost imperative tone of voice that was none the less not devoid of an extraordinary gentleness, "First, please sit down, and, second, please get drunk!"

I opened my mouth to make my excuses but, stopping up his ears with his fingers, he said, "Not a word till you do what I say."

I realized I was in the presence of a capricious drunkard and told myself that I should at least humor him a bit. "Would you permit me to ask one question?" I said with a smile, sitting down.

Without removing his hands from his ears he indicated the bottle. "When engaged in a drinking bout like this, I do not allow any conversation between myself and another unless, like me, he is drunk, otherwise all propriety is lost and mutual comprehension is rendered impossible."

I made a sign indicating that I did not drink.

"That's your lookout," he said offhandedly. "And that's my condition!"

He filled me a glass, which I meekly took and drank. No sooner had the wine settled in my stomach than it seemed to ignite. I waited patiently till I had grown used to its ferocity, and said, "It's very strong, and I think the time has come for me to ask you about—"

Once again, however, he put his fingers in his ears. "I shan't listen to you until you're drunk!"

He filled up my glass for the second time. I glanced at it in trepidation; then, overcoming my inherent objection, I drank it down at a gulp. No sooner had the wine come to rest inside me than I lost all willpower. With the third glass, I lost my memory, and with the fourth the future vanished. The world turned round about me and I forgot why I had gone there. The man leaned toward me attentively, but I saw him—saw everything—as a mere meaningless series of colored planes. I don't know how long it was before my head sank down onto the arm of the chair and I plunged into deep sleep. During it, I had a beautiful dream the like of which I had never experienced. I dreamed that I was in an immense garden surrounded on all sides by luxuriant trees, and the sky was nothing but stars seen between the entwined branches, all enfolded in an atmosphere like that of sunset or a sky overcast with cloud. I was lying on a small hummock of jasmine petals, more of which fell upon me like rain, while the lucent spray of a fountain unceasingly sprinkled the crown of my head and my temples. I was in a state of deep contentedness, of ecstatic serenity. An orchestra of warbling and cooing played in my ear. There was an extraordinary sense of harmony between me and my inner self, and between the two of us and the world, everything being in its rightful place, without discord or distortion. In the whole world there was no single reason for speech or movement, for the universe moved in a rapture of ecstasy. This lasted but a short while. When I opened my eyes, consciousness struck at me like a policeman's fist and I saw Wanas al-Damanhouri regarding me with concern. Only a few drowsy customers were left in the bar.

"You have slept deeply," said my companion. "You were obviously hungry for sleep."

I rested my heavy head in the palms of my hands. When I took them away in astonishment and looked down at them, I found that they glistened with drops of water.

"My head's wet," I protested.

"Yes, my friend tried to rouse you," he answered quietly.

"Somebody saw me in this state?"

"Don't worry, he is a good man. Have you not heard of Sheikh Zaabalawi?"

"Zaabalawi!" I exclaimed, jumping to my feet.

"Yes," he answered in surprise. "What's wrong?"

"Where is he?"

"I don't know where he is now. He was here and then he left."

I was about to run off in pursuit but found I was more exhausted than I had imagined. Collapsed over the table, I cried out in despair, "My sole reason for coming to you was to meet him! Help me to catch up with him or send someone after him."

The man called a vendor of prawns and asked him to seek out the sheikh and bring him back. Then he turned to me. "I didn't realize you were afflicted. I'm very sorry. . . ."

"You wouldn't let me speak," I said irritably.

"What a pity! He was sitting on this chair beside you the whole time. He was playing with a string of jasmine petals he had around his neck, a gift from one of his admirers, then, taking pity on you, he began to sprinkle some water on your head to bring you around."

"Does he meet you here every night?" I asked, my eyes not leaving the doorway through which the vendor of prawns had left.

"He was with me tonight, last night and the night before that, but before that I hadn't seen him for a month."

"Perhaps he will come tomorrow," I answered with a sigh.

"Perhaps."

"I am willing to give him any money he wants."

Wanas answered sympathetically, "The strange thing is that he is not open to such temptations, yet he will cure you if you meet him."

"Without charge?"

"Merely on sensing that you love him."

The vendor of prawns returned, having failed in his mission.

I recovered some of my energy and left the bar, albeit unsteadily. At every street corner I called out "Zaabalawi!" in the vague hope that I would be rewarded with an answering shout. The street boys turned contemptuous eyes on me till I sought refuge in the first available taxi.

The following evening I stayed up with Wanas al-Damanhouri till dawn, but the sheikh did not put in an appearance. Wanas informed me that he would be going away to the country and would not be returning to Cairo until he had sold the cotton crop.

I must wait, I told myself; I must train myself to be patient. Let me content myself with having made certain of the existence of Zaabalawi, and even of his affection for me, which encourages me to think that he will be prepared to cure me if a meeting takes place between us.

Sometimes, however, the long delay wearied me. I would become beset by despair and would try to persuade myself to dismiss him from my mind completely. How many weary people in this life know him not or regard him as a mere myth! Why, then, should I torture myself about him in this way?

No sooner, however, did my pains force themselves upon me than I would again begin to think about him, asking myself when I would be fortunate enough to meet him. The fact that I ceased to have any news of Wanas and was told he had gone to live abroad did not deflect me from my purpose; the truth of the matter was that I had become fully convinced that I had to find Zaabalawi.

Yes, I have to find Zaabalawi.

KOJIMA NOBUO

born 1915

Kojima Nobuo, a deft satirist, belongs to the generation of writers in Japan who came of age during World War II. Their experiences in war, disastrous defeat, and humiliating occupation inevitably made them connoisseurs of absurdity. Together in particular with Yasuoka Shōtarō (born 1920), Kojima uses irony and ridicule to articulate the postwar pathology of the Japanese antihero: the befuddled ordinary man uprooted by failure, crushed by society, oppressed by go-getters, and so paralyzed by the flux all around him that he surrenders those few privileges still given the Confucian-based head of the household. Now even home denies refuge to the timid and profoundly ineffectual Japanese male. This may surprise American readers. Nowhere in the fiction of Kojima will we recognize the dynamos who built the world's most successful postwar economy (unless, of course, we are seeing them with their masks off, neuroses exposed in the empty hours away from their devotions to the Company).

Kojima was born near the town of Gifu in central Japan, the son of a carpenter who made Buddhist altars. An avid reader from childhood, he explored as a student a range of world literature, including British, American, and Russian writers. He would later aver that Gogol, the nineteenth-century Russian satirist, was a particularly important influence; one can also detect the impact of Kafka and Dostoevsky. In 1941 Kojima graduated with a degree in English literature from the prestigious University of Tokyo. His senior thesis, *Thackeray as a Humorist*, foretold his own future as a satirical writer. Throughout his career, he has combined the work of a novelist with teaching, translation, and writing literary criticism. During his tenure as a professor of English literature at Meiji University in Tokyo, he has published a number of scholarly volumes, including literary biography, and translated a baker's half-dozen of American writers (William Saroyan, Sherwood Anderson, Dorothy Parker, Nathaniel Hawthorne, Robert Penn Warren, Irwin Shaw, and Bernard Malamud).

Without doubt, though, it was Kojima's wartime and immediate postwar experiences that most shaped his fiction. Both periods seemed to demonstrate the randomness and futility of life. No sooner had he mastered the English language as a university student and begun to earn his living teaching English after graduating than he found his country and himself at war with virtually every English-speaking nation. In basic training for the army he was promptly ordered to forget the enemy's hateful tongue. He was also taunted—for being a university graduate, for wearing eyeglasses. Army officers made him drink more liquor than he could hold. He was sent to Manchuria, where scouting missions took on the color of childhood games of hide-and-seek. "When we went out on punitive expeditions," he would later write, "I always felt a great sense of futility. Of course, it would be futile to be killed in battle, but it was truly miserable to be scrambling around looking for an enemy. Whenever we went out looking for them, it was always after they had already run away."[*]

Then orders were reversed, and in 1944 Kojima was assigned to an intelligence unit in Peking, where he was to use his English after all. Here he spent his days intercepting radio communications of the U.S. Air Force and relaying the information to headquarters. On a slow day, or a particularly creative one, by Kojima's own admission, half the "decoded messages" were the products of sheer invention, the author's first fiction. It may even be said that English saved his life. His former battalion, sent to the Philippines not long after he was posted to Peking, was annihilated by General MacArthur's forces in the battle of Leyte at the end of 1944. As the war hurtled to conclusion, his final linguistic duty was to teach his commanding officers to say "I am not a war criminal" and "Would you care for a drink?"

Not surprisingly, then, English figures in Kojima's early fiction. From his intelligence post in China he returned to a homeland completely devastated. More than three million Japanese had died during the war, almost one million of them civilians. Air raids and two atomic bombs had destroyed all but one of Japan's major cities. Over 30 percent of the Japanese people had lost their homes. Food shortages brought black marketeering and near starvation. Once prosperous families were reduced to trading heirlooms for basic necessities. The yen plummeted to barely a hundredth of its prewar value. Industry hardly existed. Perhaps most shocking of all: five hundred thousand former enemy troops, mostly American, now occupied

[*]Van C. Gessel, *The Sting of Life: Four Contemporary Japanese Novelists* (1989) 15.

the country. The Allied Occupation of Japan lasted from 1945 to 1952, first to maintain order and establish a new Japanese government and then to oversee extensive political, social, and economic reforms that would purge Japan of "irresponsible militarism" and refashion the country into an American-style democracy. The commanding presence of General MacArthur—whom some viewed as a latter-day *shogun* in the long tradition of Japan's military dictators, whose victories tolerated the continued existence of a figurehead emperor—seemed, like his many soldiers, to be everywhere, and so did their language.

Kojima might have been expected to benefit from this situation. But as his satiric masterpiece *The American School* (1954) makes patently clear, he views those who use the victors' language as carpetbaggers, or opportunists. The antagonist of the story, Yamada, an unctuous teacher of English dying for approval in defeated, shame-ridden Japan, tries to turn an excursion with his fellow teachers to a model school on one of the new American military bases into a demonstration that he alone, by virtue of his English fluency, is worthy of American respect. But as is often the case with people who must have the approval of others in order to respect themselves, Yamada is pathetic and dangerous because he stands for nothing except catering to those in power. For his foil he chooses Isa, the protagonist, a meek, inadequate colleague who is already quite beleaguered even before Yamada proposes a "demonstration" in front of the Americans. It is Isa's misfortune to despise the very language that he teaches, or to despise the uses to which it is now put by his compatriots. When they speak English, those who don't mind toadying enter a twilight zone of colonialism and opportunity. Their obsequious actions are made painless and unreal by the distancing that a foreign language automatically furnishes. They cease, in short, in Isa's eyes, to be Japanese. Yet, of course, they can never be American. Neither fish nor fowl, they let English transport them to an unreal world of license where they humiliate themselves without feeling any shame.

For its relentless, ironic evocation of the insidious shattering of a principled world and for its implied commentary on both Japan's postwar confusion and its historical tendency, at certain watersheds, to let others set its standards (China in the seventh century, the West in the nineteenth, and the United States in the third quarter of the twentieth), *The American School* won Kojima the Akutagawa Prize, one of his country's highest literary honors. With this work, Kojima consolidated his position as a chronicler of the helpless lot of postwar Japanese intellectuals. From his debut story in 1952, *The Rifle*, the portrait of a soldier who sells his soul to the army, to his most famous novel, *A Close Family* (1965), a record of the exact opposite, and his more recent success, *Reasons for Parting* (1982), an immense novel hailed as a landmark in modern Japanese fiction, he has continued to bear witness to what he sees as the slow but discernible disintegration of humanity.

Kojima's novels and the bulk of his short fiction remain untranslated. *Stars*, however, from the same year as *The American School*, is included in Van C. Gessel and Tomone Matsumoto, eds., *The Shōwa Anthology: Modern Japanese Short Stories* (1985), a good source for modern and contemporary Japanese short fiction. Howard Hibbett, ed., *Contemporary Japanese Literature: An Anthology of Fiction, Film, and Other Writing Since 1945* (1977), and Yukiko Tanaka and Elizabeth Hanson, eds., *This Kind of Woman: Ten Stories by Japanese Women Writers, 1960–1976* (1982), also are good sources for modern Japanese literature. Works in English by members of Kojima's loose-knit coterie in the 1950s include Van C. Gessel's translation, *Stained Glass Elegies: Stories by Shūsaku Endō* (1984); Kären Wigen Lewis's translation of Yasuoka Shōtarō, *A View by the Sea* (1984); and Kathryn Sparling's translation of Shimao Toshio, *"The Sting of Death" and Other Stories* (1985). Also highly recommended are E. Dale Saunders's translation of Abe Kōbō, *The Woman in the Dunes* (1964), and John Nathan's translation of Ōe

Kenzaburō, *A Personal Matter* (1968). For a critical study of Kojima, Yasuoka, Shimao, and Endō, see Van C. Gessel, *The Sting of Life: Four Contemporary Japanese Novelists* (1989).

PRONOUNCING GLOSSARY

The following list uses common English syllables to provide rough equivalents of selected words whose pronunciation may be unfamiliar to the general reader.

Gifu: *gee-foo*

Michiko: *mee-chee-koh*

Jizo: *jee-zoh*

Shibamoto: *shee-bah-moh-toh*

Kojima Nobuo: *koh-jee-mah noh-boo-oh*

Yasuoka Shōtarō: *yah-soo-oh-kah shoh-tah-roh*

Meiji: *may-jee*

The American School[1]

It was past eight-thirty and still the official had not appeared. The teachers had been told to assemble by this hour for their excursion to the American school, and most of them had come twenty minutes or so early. Having made their way to the Prefectural Office[2] through the morning throngs of commuters, all thirty of them were now left sitting here and there on the deserted stairs and around the gravel drive. There was one woman among them. She had apparently gone to some trouble to dress for the occasion; but her high heels, hat, and new plaid suit only made her look more sad and shabby.

As soon as they were all present, the teachers went en masse to the Office of Education on the second floor, only to be driven back down to this place which had not even been mentioned at the organization meeting a week ago. Right after the roll call the chairman of that meeting, an administrator from the Office of Education, had read off a list of instructions. The first was to assemble promptly at the appointed time. The second was to dress impeccably. The latter had created a stir which did not die down until the promulgation of the third point, that they must maintain a solemn silence at all times. Finally, they were to pack a lunch, for they would have to march to and from the school, a total distance of some eight miles; and even teachers had learned to feel proper hunger pangs in the three years since the War.

An American jeep ploughed through the gravel of the driveway, rounded the sharp curve, and came to a stop in front of the prefectural building. A teacher who had been sitting just inside the door jumped to his feet and moved away.

There was one man who had all the while been standing straight as a ramrod. The best-dressed and healthiest-looking of the group, he was conspicuous in an almost disconcerting way. At the previous week's meeting he had repeatedly raised his hand with questions for the chairman, a

1. Translated by William F. Sibley.   2. A state-level government office.

man by the name of Shibamoto. "Are we only supposed to observe?" he had inquired at one juncture. "What do you mean?" Shibamoto asked. "I was just wondering," he said, "if we might not give them a demonstration of our oral method." With a slight swagger that accentuated his heavy judo wrestler's build, the official reiterated loudly that the purpose of the excursion was to observe. He added that the Office of Education had gone to considerable lengths to secure permission for the visit. The man, whose name was Yamada, had at last given up this line of questioning.

He seized the floor once again in the commotion that followed the remarks on proper dress. "Quite right, sir," he said. "We must all present a neat appearance, whatever the cost. Any sloppiness would reflect on the profession. Worst of all, it would raise serious doubts about our competence to teach English. They despise us as a defeated people to begin with, and when they see the clothes we wear—I know, because I interpreted for the inspectors when they came to our school—they just look the other way. Not to mention the toilets . . ." His speech was interrupted at this point, and by now everyone was staring at him, with particular attention to his feet. There was scarcely another pair of leather shoes in sight. Undaunted, he resumed as soon as the mutters died down. They should avoid speaking Japanese in front of their hosts, he insisted, in order to display to the fullest extent their command of English. This was greeted by more general muttering, and a shrill outcry from the man sitting next to him: "What nonsense!" Yamada turned to face the heckler. But before he could launch into a longwinded defense of his proposal, Shibamoto called for order with the request that both Mr. Yamada and Mr. Isa refrain from intemperate language.

Isa had once been pressed into service at election time as interpreter for the Occupation inspection team (all elections were to be conducted impartially under the watchful eyes of the authorities). He was taken by jeep from one small village to the next, and was expected to keep his American counterpart informed of what was going on. Still only about thirty years old, he had never had a single conversation in English; occasional attempts at practical application of the language in the classroom had left him tingling with embarrassment; and when word came that the Americans would soon be visiting his school he had feigned illness, lying in bed for several days with an icebag pressed against his forehead, where there was not the slightest trace of fever. Only fear of unknown reprisals at the hands of the Occupation officials had deterred him from a similar stratagem at the time of the elections.

The moment he was packed into the jeep with a Negro soldier, he had turned to the fellow and said, in English: "I am truly very sorry to have kept you waiting." This was met with silence, and when he repeated the words three times over, the soldier only stared at him coldly and uncomprehendingly. The phrase he had prepared several days ago and practiced constantly since was clearly too formal and correct. From then on he limited himself to two words, "stop" and "go." For those five hours he felt as if he were being boiled alive, though outwardly he appeared to be merely loafing on the job. And in either case, the result was that he was of no use to anyone.

As soon as they approached the first polling-place, he fled. He tried to reason with himself, before sneaking off to hide, that it would go still worse with him than if he had refused to come in the first place. But the prospect of being addressed in that unfamiliar language in front of a crowd made his knees quake. By the time the Negro noticed his absence and came back to find him, he was long gone.

Isa was not by nature so craven; indeed, as the jeep drove into the village he had felt a strong impulse to do violence to his keeper. But after they slowed down, it seemed easier to escape, and so he jumped off the rear and made for the wooded slope above the road. On discovering that his passenger had fled, the soldier went after him, partly out of fear at being left alone in these dark hills. Deep in the woods Isa saw the man coming. He called out to him in Japanese: "You'll have to speak our language. Speak Japanese or else! What would you do if someone really said that to you?" As the face of his adversary drew near, a neatly trimmed beard, features strained in an effort to make out the indistinct words, it gave a feeling of loneliness. The beard contributed an incongruously civilized air, and as the face moved still closer it seemed almost to show some understanding of the stream of Japanese that issued forth from behind the trees. Isa babbled on as fast as he could. When the Negro at last realized that the words were not in his language, he threw up his hands and shrugged his shoulders. Seated behind the wheel again, he looked even lonelier than before, as if unaccountably intimidated by this creature who spoke scarcely a word of normal English, and who would lapse without warning into Japanese gibberish. He ceased to pay any attention at all to Isa, and proceeded as though chauffeuring an honored guest around the countryside. A pointless errand on the whole; but at least, it occurred to him, the man might be of some service in helping him deal with hostile natives.

Each time an American jeep drove up, Isa drifted a little away from the prefectural building. Yamada's foolish suggestions at the organization meeting were still fresh in his mind, especially the proposal of a demonstration class, which had aroused in him an instant panic that persisted to this moment. Well, he would simply keep a close watch on Yamada and shut him up if necessary. He had, however, already yielded on one point: he was wearing a pair of black leather civilian shoes. They were an odd match with his khaki uniform, but he had wanted at least to spare himself the embarrassment of army boots. Likewise, having set out with his lunch box in an old army bag, along the way he had taken the box out, folded up the incriminating bag, and stuck it under his arm.

Yamada continued to stand alone surveying the scene expectantly. Whenever a jeep pulled up he would bustle over to explain the situation. "We represent the English teachers of this prefecture," he would begin stiffly. "We are very devoted to the English language. We work very hard to teach the English. We are now utilizing the latest methods of instruction, just like you have in your country."

"If you work so goddam hard, what are you hanging around for at this hour?" one driver replied, reaching down with a look of extreme boredom to hand him a cigarette.

"I do not smoke," said Yamada.

"Are you the chief?"

"Our leader is an official of this prefecture. He is very late for our appointment. Government officials are lazy people. But you must not think that all Japanese are like that."

The soldier, who was black, threw up his hands in disgust. "I am truly very sorry to have kept you waiting," he said, and drove off.

Yamada did not know what to make of this parting remark. The American had perhaps been mocking Japanese officials. He looked at his watch again and muttered to himself. What would their hosts think if they arrived late at the school? Something must be done. He called out to those of his colleagues who were sprawled within earshot, "Will some of you come up to the Education Office with me? If we don't do something we'll be late. They have our names on file at the school. We'll be disgraced. 'What can you expect from a defeated people?' they'll say."

Yamada noticed that Isa, who was sitting only a few feet away, kept his back turned as though preoccupied with some important business. He went over to investigate and found him with his lunch box open on his lap. Isa had been up since three, riding his bicycle to the nearest station, then taking a combination of streetcars and trains until he reached this distant city. He was hungry; rather, he thought he ought to be hungry by now.

Yamada stood for a moment in silent amazement. "This is not time to be eating," he said. "Come with me to the Education Office. If the officials there won't cooperate, we'll speak to the Occupation personnel."

The bare mention of the local Occupation force was enough to upset Isa. He had already noticed the bearded Negro in one of the jeeps, and had seen Yamada accost him. Indeed, it was one reason for beginning his lunch now. This was a high-risk area where he might be addressed in English at any moment. A mouthful of food would, he sensed, offer some defense against any demand that might be made of him. And so he did not answer Yamada, and regretted having challenged him at last week's meeting, thus attracting his attention. Isa had decided not to speak a word in any language today, for if he began by conversing in Japanese he would surely end by having to speak English. The best strategy was a tight-lipped silence that would lead people to believe he was indisposed. Then no one, neither official nor colleague, would think it strange if, when his turn came to talk at the school, he had nothing to say. Without looking up from his lunch he waved his chopsticks in the air by way of a reply.

"What kind of answer is that?" Yamada put his question in both languages and waited for an answer. Isa pretended not to hear. Yamada was given to venting his wrath in English. "Oh, for shame!" he exclaimed, stalking off towards the overdressed instructress, Michiko, who capitulated on the spot and followed him up the stairs.

On their way into the office they bumped into the tardy official. Shibamoto was wearing his Sunday best, which consisted of a long overcoat and a soft felt hat. As he led them out of the building, he blew a whistle to assemble the others. Yamada protested that the whistle would sound a shrill note of unreconstructed militarism; furthermore, for the same reason, they should not march in a solid phalanx.[3] Shibamoto granted his point and ordered the group to fall out. When the command was given to reassemble in loose ranks, Yamada placed himself like a staff adjutant at Shibamoto's side. The rest of the teachers straggled behind in a long procession, with Isa bringing up the rear.

Shibamoto made a brief announcement: "We received notification that the time for our visit had been changed. Sorry for the inconvenience. They were very pleased with the first group. Try to keep up the good record. Ready?"

It was about four miles to the American school down an asphalt road that ran straight as the crow flies from the outskirts of the city. Strung out like a chain gang, the teachers set out with Shibamoto and Yamada in the lead. Isa, at the other end, made no effort to move up. He found himself walking beside the woman, and this was somehow reassuring. Within ten minutes they had reached the asphalt road. There was an uninterrupted flow of traffic traveling to and fro among the various installations of the large base that stretched out for miles around the school. A sigh rippled through the group at the sight of this long black ribbon which was clearly not made for walking.

Isa watched with secret admiration as Michiko took a pair of sneakers from her cloth bundle and put them on. What foresight! The men around him were all wearing long overcoats, with a sprinkling of army issue such as he himself had on. The poverty revealed in their bulky clothing showed up starkly against the hard pavement. "I don't want you in rows, but do move closer together," Shibamoto cautioned. "You mustn't look so straggly—there are Occupation personnel all around you." Cars and jeeps were in fact flying by, thick and fast, though there was not another pedestrian to be seen anywhere on the forbidding road.

The presence of a single woman in their midst was enough to mitigate the ragged, faintly subversive spectacle created by the twenty-nine men. Before five minutes had gone by, a car coming from the opposite direction pulled up beside Michiko. A soldier stuck his head out the window and spoke to her. "What are you people doing here?" he asked, echoing the question put to them several times in front of the prefectural building. Michiko stated the purpose of their excursion in clear, correct English. "You're an English teacher, are you? Well, you're pretty damn good, I'd say." The soldier thrust some cans of cheese in her hands and drove off.

It was not until Michiko laughed out loud and tugged at his sleeve that Isa turned to face her. With eyes studiously averted from the exchange with the soldier, he had begun to reconsider his choice of companion. Walking beside the woman, he was easy prey for any number of foreign soldiers. He felt the weight of the can that Michiko had stuffed into his pocket while he was staring at the rice paddies below the road. Living in an era when true goodwill was translated into gifts of food, he was naturally

3. Soldiers marching in rank and file.

pleased and flattered, and especially so for having failed to notice that she had received two cans from the soldier and had to give one away to keep the other. What if he was a little more vulnerable being next to her, he had only to look the other way when the enemy approached, and there were these unexpected benefits.

It had occurred to Michiko as they started down the asphalt road that she had forgotten something. In her rush this morning to change after sending off her son, her only child by the husband she had lost in the War (he too had been a teacher), it must have slipped her mind. She poked around in the cloth bundle and her suspicions were confirmed. Luckily the missing article was one that could be borrowed in a pinch; and at the moment the two cans of cheese plopped into her hands, she had picked Isa as her most likely benefactor.

Tranquilly and with unexpected warmth, the winter sun shone down upon the black surface until the glare began to affect one's eyes. Cars continued to pass by in both directions, and then a jeep drove up, this time from behind, and slowed down almost to the pace of the procession. Two soldiers, one white, one black, leaned out to look the group over. Yamada turned around and waited until the jeep drew up beside him. "Haro[4] boys! What are you doing?" he hailed them.

With a look of mild surprise one of the soldiers asked in return: "Only one woman?" Having verified with their own eyes, without listening to Yamada's reply, that the woman they had passed was the only one, they stopped the jeep in the middle of the road and waited. As Michiko approached they called out to her: "Ojosan![5] Ojosan!" They asked where she was going and told her to get in. Her quick response was livelier than when she spoke in Japanese, her face more expressive, even distinctly feminine. "I'm on a group excursion," she said. "I really can't go ahead by myself."

The soldiers exchanged an approving glance as they inspected the proper Japanese lady from top to bottom. They tore the wrapper from two bars of chocolate and, with a parting nod full of regret, tossed them down to Michiko. She broke one of the bars into pieces and passed them out to a few people around her, this time omitting Isa. Afterward the teachers who had dropped back toward her at this point showed no disposition to move up again.

They had not been marching in close ranks from the outset, and by now the group had split into two separate platoons: Shibamoto, Yamada, and their followers in the lead, Michiko and her attendants in the rear, with a gap of over a hundred yards in between.

It came to Isa by slow degrees that his shoes hurt. Each step brought new pains. He began to regret having worn these ill-fitting genuine leather shoes; and when he reflected that he had put them on to please Yamada, to speak the foreign tongue in the right style—simply to hold down his job—his regrets gave way to anger. The pain grew more and more acute. He struggled to keep up with Michiko, but even this was too much for

---

4. "Hello." The soldier is making fun of the inability of Japanese to discriminate between the sounds *l* and *r* in the English language.   5. A term of address for a young lady, similar to our "Miss."

him. He now noticed with a twinge of envy how smooth and easy her stride had become since she abandoned her high heels for sneakers. No one else, either in his platoon or the group up front, showed signs of suffering from the same problem. He himself had never paid much attention to shoes until this moment. The offending pair, on loan from a colleague, had seemed just right when he first tried them on. A tiny discrepancy was enough, it appeared, to cause a great deal of pain. Isa became suspicious of the colleague who had lent him the shoes. For all he knew, the man could be in league with Yamada.

There was no telling how much farther they had to go, for the view ahead was blocked by a rise in the road. When Isa looked back to see how much ground they had covered he was distressed to find the prefectural building looming still quite large behind them.

About fifteen feet ahead, Michiko stood looking over her shoulder in his direction. "Is something wrong?" she asked when at last he caught up with her. At his mumbled reply apropos of shoes her face took on a look of utmost gravity. Having set out in new shoes herself, she had more than an inkling of what she would have endured but for the sneakers. "That will never do. We still have a long way to go. Maybe you should hitch a ride—why don't you stop one of these jeeps?"

Isa's pain yielded to astonishment and terror. What she suggested would not have occurred to him in his wildest dreams. "If it ever came to that!" he muttered as he stumbled forward in an effort to keep up, putting as much weight as possible on his toes to relieve the pinch on his insteps. He hoped to set her mind at ease and avoid further suggestions of drastic remedies, but he soon realized that his awkward gait only made matters worse.

Michiko slackened her pace and walked silently at Isa's side as if to subdue his pain by force of her own calm will. Until now she had found him a tedious companion, thoroughly wrapped up in himself for no apparent reason. But as soon as she began to share in his suffering, faint memories stirred within her of the love, long forgotten, that a woman can also share with a man. She did not, however, lose sight of her objective. She meant to have from him that homely article left behind in her haste. What love she felt for him was bound up with her hopes of getting it, and seemed to emanate like hunger pangs from somewhere near the pit of her empty stomach. While more cars whizzed by she spoke to him again in a soothing tone, as if to stroke his heaving back. "You really ought to get yourself a lift," she said. "Shall I ask for you?"

"No! No thank you! Never mind! I'd sooner go barefoot."

"Now really, I don't see why . . ."

Isa felt like biting his tongue for breaking his vow of silence. Yet had he kept quiet Michiko would no doubt have hailed a jeep immediately, and at her fluent English they would have picked him up without further ado. Then where would he be? No matter how dire his need, the very thought of riding next to a foreigner again made him sick. He remembered all too vividly his day of torture with the black soldier. He had felt as though at any moment he could murder the man, and if it had gone on for another day he surely would have done so, unless, of course, he had first found a way to escape.

The tender feelings which Michiko had summoned up from deep within her subsided in the face of Isa's stubborn refusal. The sweat now trickling down her body served as a nagging reminder of her impure motives. Very well, she thought, she would get what she was after anyway. And even that didn't really matter so much; she could if necessary do without. Resolved to not so much as look back at him, she forged ahead toward Yamada's platoon. The others followed in her wake, leaving Isa far behind.

Up front, Yamada and Shibamoto were trading boasts. Shibamoto, by his own account, had been one of a handful of judo experts in the prefecture before the War disrupted things—a fifth-degree black belt, no less. And contrary to malicious postwar propaganda, devotees of the martial arts were not all war criminals. One had only to consider himself, holder of a prominent post in the administrative section of the prefectural Education Office. Moreover, he taught judo not only to the local police, but to the Occupation personnel themselves, and had in fact got the job through his American supervisor.

Yamada's ears perked up at the mention of Occupation personnel. He was intensely interested in every kind of contact with the Americans, though so far his own had been restricted to interpreting. He had a consuming ambition to study abroad, to which end he schemed and fretted the livelong day.

Eager to establish his credentials with such a well-connected man, Yamada explained that he had conducted any number of demonstration classes at his school; that although they were supposedly professional teachers of English, few of his colleagues made a good showing ... Yes, said Shibamoto, he had heard about all that. From a leather briefcase the likes of which were seldom seen in these times, Yamada removed a mimeographed schedule of a typical demonstration class, which he happened to have brought along.

"Rook heah, see for yourself," he said, breaking momentarily into English. "I hope sometime soon to hold a teaching seminar here in the city—with the backing of the administrative section, of course. And we would certainly welcome cooperation from the Americans." He handed Shibamoto his card. His name and titles appeared in Japanese script on one side, Roman on the other. "I might not look it now, but I hold a second-degree black belt in fencing," he volunteered.

"Is that so? I suppose you've had some experience in your day," said Shibamoto.

"You bet I have!" Yamada slashed the air with an imaginary sword. "This might not be the time to mention it, but when I was in OTS[6] I got to whet my blade a bit, if you know what I mean."

"It must be hard, cutting off heads."

6. Officers' Training School.

"Not really. It takes a good arm, a sharp sword, and practice, of course. That's all."

"How many did you polish off?"

"Let's see . . ." Yamada paused and looked around. "About twenty, I guess. Half of them must've been POWs."

"Any Yanks?"

"Naturally."

"How did they compare with the Chinese?"

"Well, there's quite a difference in how they take it. When you come right down to it, they show their lack of what you might call Oriental philosophy."

"You're lucky they never caught up with you."

". . . I was only following orders."

Yamada was suddenly aware of the dangerous turn in the conversation. What had he been saying? He fell silent. Noticing that Shibamoto had removed his overcoat, he hastily took off his own and stuck it under his arm. He looked over his shoulder at the disorderly procession and his taut, swarthy features collapsed into a disdainful grimace.

"What do you think of this mess?" he said to Shibamoto. "If the War were still on and this were a real march. . . ! But what can you expect from a bunch of high school teachers?"

Yamada fixed Isa hawklike in a distant gaze. In this perspective the laggard could not fail to arouse contempt and indignation. While Yamada stood at the side of the road the group straggled by in little clumps, their pace so listless that he wanted to ask with the Americans what business they had on this highway. He made up his mind to stay where he was and wait for Isa to come along. Over the past week he had not forgotten Isa's vague but unmistakable hostility. As he waited, the word "insubordinate" popped into his head. It seemed to furnish a key to understanding this queer fellow. With his own tales of martial valor still ringing in his ears, Yamada became again the company commander he had been until three years before. But for all the brutal self-assurance restored to him in this transformation, he did not bark out a reprimand to Isa, preferring to take him by surprise.

Michiko passed by first. "His shoes pinch," she explained, pointing back at Isa.

"His shoes pinch? Ridiculous!" This went beyond simple insubordination. To dawdle over such an infantile triviality was inexcusable. At this rate he was likely to start whining about his bladder or a sore throat and fall still farther behind. Well, what was the matter with his shoes? Yamada stared at the black blobs of Isa's feet scraping across the asphalt in the distance. He waited till the dusty shoes had shuffled up diffidently under his nose before he spoke. "Are those your shoes?" he snapped, in English.

Isa had not noticed Yamada at the side of the road. His eyes were wide open with the effort of bearing the pain, but he could not see a thing.

"It's your fault this group is in such a shambles. It only takes one straggler like you to throw everyone out of step."

Michiko came back and repeated to Yamada her suggestion that Isa ask for a ride.

"From the Americans?" Yamada's shoulders fell as he studied Isa's feet. Ignoring Michiko, he lashed out again at Isa: "That is out of the question. Mistah Isa, have you no pride? Maybe for ap-pen-di-ci-tis. But for *shoes?*"

Several other teachers had wandered back to see what was holding things up and stood looking over Yamada's shoulder. "He'd do better to go barefoot," one of them said. This solution had occurred to Isa any number of times since the pain began. But each time he had rejected it for fear of being spotted by the Americans, who were sure to question him about his bare feet and force him to ride in a jeep.

Yamada changed his tone. "Try to keep moving, at least. You've got everyone stopped in their tracks wondering what to do about you—Oh, Mr. Shibamoto. What do you think, sir?"

When Yamada failed to return to the front rank, Shibamoto had planted himself at the roadside like a stone Jizo.[7] Once the leaders dropped out, the rest of the procession ground to a halt.

"If this keeps up we'll be late, sir. We'll be disgraced. The main thing is to make sure the Americans don't see him. Oh, for shame!"

"What seems to be the trouble here?" Shibamoto had not yet grasped the cause of Yamada's excitement. When the problem was put to him he proposed that Isa go ahead and remove his shoes. Yamada and a few others would walk along on either side and shield him from the passers-by.

Shibamoto's proposal was duly adopted and Isa was promptly relieved of his suffering. It even struck him that this pavement could have been made for bare feet, which were not, after all, without some resemblance to the rubber tires of a car.

Michiko brooded over the man who was once more walking beside her, though likely soon to lag behind again. Isa seemed as unresponsive as ever, and she made no attempt to speak to him. But his stubborn streak had begun to remind her of her late husband. Surrounded by Yamada and the others, he strode along unshod and full of purpose, a shy but spirited little man in the jaws of adversity. That is what her husband had been when he went off to war.

Her thoughts drifted back to that day when she had struggled to keep up with the column of soldiers bound for the front as they marched the five miles from their base to the station. They had not paused once along the way, pushing ahead at an unrelenting pace that did not allow for last-minute farewells. Her husband marched with clenched teeth and scarcely cast a glance in her direction. The only time he turned his head to face her, he made a curt gesture with his hand as if to drive her away. There had of course been others besides herself, among them aged mothers calling out their son's names as they stumbled after the swift procession.

Michiko had understood her husband's embarrassment then. The feelings of the barefoot man next to her now were no doubt of the same kind. Perhaps she would speak to him once they were at the school. She was suddenly aware again of the high heels pressing through the cloth against

---

7. A stone statue of the guardian deity of children.

her hands like hard little buds about to flower. Yes, after she had changed her shoes at the school she would have a word with him.

Isa showed no sign of faltering, indeed he fairly loped along, with none of the strain that was beginning to tell on the others. He was, however, still shy of foreign eyes, though his fears were very different from Yamada's, and he walked somewhat stooped over. He hurried ahead driven by the desire to reach his destination at the earliest possible moment, and in the happy expectation of freedom from any further need to propel himself. He was too absorbed in the delicate task of simultaneously staying out of sight and rushing forward to reflect that he would still have to move about at the school, and then make the trek back to the city.

Taking but small comfort in Isa's return to the fold and the restoration of some semblance of order, Yamada dwelt on the disgust which the man's every action stirred up in him. He decided the time had come to broach to Shibamoto the subject that had been in the back of his mind all day. "You know, sir," he began, "we really ought to give a demonstration class while we're there. It's a rare opportunity to show them what we can do, and maybe we can get them to evaluate and rank us while we're at it."

Shibamoto was busy surveying the buildings of the American school, which had come into view as soon as they passed the crest in the road. He gave Yamada a doubtful look and did not reply. When Yamada pressed the point by suggesting that he himself could make the request, Shibamoto wearily repeated that their hosts might find the exercise troublesome.

"I don't see why it should be any trouble. It will be our show—a demonstration of what English teachers in this country are capable of. Afterwards we'll let them give us a few pointers, that's all. As a judo expert I'm sure you can see the wisdom of our taking the offensive, so to speak."

This was a thrust that Shibamoto could not parry. He would have to let the man have his way. He had never met such a cocky instructor, he thought, as Yamada announced once again that he would take the bull by the horns.

Isa did not miss a word of this exchange. When he saw Shibamoto weaken, his thoughts turned instinctively to escape. Slipping easily through the loose cordon they had strung around him, he sidled off to the edge of the road and unbuttoned his fly. Yamada was still preoccupied and failed to notice this dereliction; the others were too tired to bother with him.

Just then Michiko was accosted by another jeep. She broke into a cold sweat as she ascertained that the melancholy black face looking down at her wanted to know about Isa, who stood relieving himself up the road. But her fears were set to rest when she heard the soldier ask, "What's with the bare feet?" She explained, and the jeep rumbled off in Isa's direction.

Isa wheeled around in alarm, and at one glance recognized his old adversary. He backed away, stunned by the accuracy of his presentiment that he would see the man again today. When he reached the shoulder of the road he turned and leaped into the field below. Here he was far less protected than he had been on that wooded slope. The soldier was beckoning to him with a miniature package of cigarettes. The next moment Yamada was yelling at him. "He's only trying to do you a favor. What's the matter with you!" Joining forces, the soldier and Yamada clambered into the field. Together they dragged Isa back up to the road and bundled him into the jeep. The vehicle bearing the solitary captive soon vanished in a cloud of sand, and raucous laughter swept through the ranks.

Above the road ahead some crows flocked and veered off to one side as if to clear a path for the car passing far below. Or perhaps they were preparing to scavenge around the American school. Michiko watched this scene and savored a certain relief, accompanied by a quiet, private laugh, at the removal of the burden that Isa had become for her. She no longer imagined that she could understand his excessive timidity, unless, she speculated, he had done something awful during the War.

Isa sat hunched up in the back of the jeep. He quickly averted his eyes from the driver's seat and peered out at the dwindling faces of his colleagues. Although their features were already blurred, he could clearly see that they were laughing. Yet, for all their scorn, their company was far preferable to the predicament that now filled him with despair. The general laughter left little doubt that Yamada would succeed in squeezing out of him some sort of performance in English. As far as he was concerned, it was now all but inevitable; that is, it seemed quite within the realm of possibility, which was for Isa tantamount to inevitability.

On their first encounter the Negro had mistaken Isa's cowed silence for sullen contempt, with overtones of a personal animus against himself. Afterwards he had Isa's credentials checked through the Education Office, without bothering to state the cause of his curiosity; and when the record showed no reason for the man's refusal to speak English, he felt that his suspicions had been confirmed. This unlooked-for second meeting was a stroke of luck: he would have a little revenge for that business in the woods.

The jeep screeched to a halt and Isa found a pistol pointing into his face. Then came the command: "Speak English, man. Let's hear it again. 'I am truly very sorry to have kept you waiting.'"

Isa trembled all over and stammered out the phrase as dictated. Below the trim moustache the mouth of his captor opened in a loud guffaw. The pistol was only a toy, he said. Humming a jazz tune, he started up the engine and drove on.

At the American school the soldier bade Isa a friendly farewell as he climbed out of the jeep. "Maybe we'll meet again," he said, with some appreciation, it appeared, of the karma[8] that had already brought them together twice. Isa felt weak inside at the mere suggestion.

As soon as the jeep was out of sight Isa, still barefoot, ran toward the fence enclosing the school playground. After a few moments' rest he put on his shoes and crouched down to look around. The children at recess on the playground, boys and girls mixed together, ranged from the early grades through junior high school. Even now, in midwinter, they were scampering about in a colorful assortment of light clothes, a sweater here,

---

8. Fate in the Buddhist religion; the outcome of one's actions in previous existences, since Buddhism holds that we are endlessly reborn unless we achieve enlightenment and thus escape the cycle of death and rebirth.

a blouse and jumper there. Isa retreated into the shadow of one of the buildings to continue his inspection from a less public vantage point.

Along with a sense of relative security, he experienced an overwhelming mental fatigue. He closed his eyes for fear of fainting and felt the tears well up behind his eyelids. At first he could not tell what had brought on his tears, but he knew it was a joy so intense as to be close to sorrow. With his eyes still closed he slowly discerned the source of his bliss in a murmuring of soft voices, sweet and clear as a mountain stream. They seemed to come from another world, perhaps in part because the words made little sense to him.

Isa opened his eyes and saw a cluster of young girls, twelve or thirteen years old, chatting with each other about fifty feet from where he was hiding. He concluded that he and his colleagues were members of a pathetic race which had no place here.

Listening to these mellifluous English voices, he could not account for the fear and horror which the language had always inspired in him. At the same time his own inner voice whispered: It is foolish for Japanese to speak this language like foreigners. If they do, it makes them foreigners, too. And that is a real disgrace.

He pictured clearly to himself the outlandish gestures that Yamada affected when he spoke English. There was no dignity in talking just like a foreigner. But it was equally demeaning to speak a foreign tongue like a Japanese. This was the fate that awaited him today, he knew, if he were called upon to talk at the school. The few times that he had begun his class with a halting goodo-moaning-ebury-body he had afterward flushed crimson and felt himself at the bottom of some dark ravine. No! That was not for him. He would sooner make himself over into a whole new man.

Enrapt with the schoolgirls' merry fugue, Isa did not hear the jeep return. The soldier got out, whistling another tune. Some distance from where Isa remained hidden, he stood leaning over the fence and searched out his son. Having been on urgent business to the barracks that adjoined the school, only after it was finished did he remember Isa's feet. The boy, who looked to be of junior-high-school age, came running to his father, and a few moments later disappeared into the school.

Presently a beautiful tall lady of a type one often sees in American movies appeared before Isa's eyes. With the black boy in tow, she advanced swiftly and purposefully toward the fence. Isa stole off into the shade of a nearby grove, lest she find him crouching there and take him for a thief. He shut his eyes and mentally blocked his ears, to no avail; he could distinctly hear her footsteps and the sound of her voice calling out as she came closer and closer. Although he suspected that her call was meant for him, and had in any case resigned himself by now to being caught, he still did not respond. He kept his head down and his eyes closed until he felt a touch on his shoulders and heard the word ". . . shoes?" At this he stood up and bowed.

When he opened his eyes and saw the lady standing right beside him, he was all but blinded by the look of abundance on her face: features that spoke of an ample diet, material well-being, and pride of race. She was for all that only human, and a fellow schoolteacher as well. So he tried to tell himself, but he could not quite believe it. Next to her—she stood at least a head taller than he—Isa felt weak around the knees, and in reply to her questions he only nodded and bowed. In the end, like a timid servant with his mistress, he allowed himself to be led off toward the school.

Isa caught enough of the cascade of soothing words that poured from her lips like melting snow to realize that he had that meddlesome Negro to thank for his new predicament. "I only want to do something about those feet," the lady said. "I'm not going to poison you." He wanted to say thank you—that much he could manage. But once he had opened his mouth she would expect him to keep up a steady conversation. He had better just play dumb and follow her like a dog.

Isa sank back into despondency when he thought of the interrogation to which, as a solitary Japanese among a horde of foreigners, and an English teacher of sorts, he was sure to be subjected. He was too busy brooding to notice the gaggle of students that trailed behind him as he limped along, until a few sharp words from the lady sent them shouting and laughing back to the playground.

She kept smiling at him and making what sounded like friendly remarks, which required him to play deaf as well as dumb. But he had begun to receive contradictory signals from his conscience. To atone for the appearance of incivility he had given so far, he was tempted to fall down and kiss the lady's feet, or at least the ground beneath them. Caught between these conflicting impulses, Isa took it into his head to carry her books for her. He moved abruptly to her side and, without a word, tried to wrest the heavy books from her arms. He had the appropriate phrase on the tip of his tongue but was too embarrassed to say it. Perplexed by this dumbshow, the lady clutched the books to her breast. When he continued to tug at the books, bowing and grinning abjectly, she eventually guessed his intention and thanked him; but she would not surrender her burden.

It was enough for Isa that she had recognized his gesture. Hereafter, however incompetent he might appear at the school, he would not be considered a barbaric ingrate. As they approached the building, he felt something like the relief of a condemned criminal who had made one last plea for forgiveness from his fellow men.

Since the nurse was not to be found in the dispensary, the schoolmistress led Isa to her own office, where she shut the door firmly and turned the key. Once again Isa had a sinking feeling, such as the toy pistol had produced in him a while ago. "Sit down," said the lady, whose name, he gathered from the sign on the door, was Emily. "We lock the door so we can smoke," she explained. "Even the men do. It sets a bad example for the students, you see."

It took Isa some time to decipher this statement. From the moment he entered the room he kept his eyes glued to the floor and let his ears tune out her speech, which he dimly imagined to be a reproach for his earlier rudeness. In any case the words seemed to have nothing to do with his feet, and it was not until he raised his head, afraid of appearing very rude indeed, that he saw the smoke and half grasped their meaning. Still standing in silence, he traced the upward spiral of smoke with his eyes, the better to extricate himself from Miss Emily's gaze.

Out of the clear blue sky came the order: "Take off your shoes!" Or so he interpreted her sharp utterance. But no sooner was he down to his army socks than she burst out laughing and murmured something about coffee. Then he thought he heard her say, though it made little sense to him, that he should "help himself." When Isa, thoroughly confused, began to pull up his socks, in a single violent motion Miss Emily lunged at him and stripped them off. She gaped at his exposed feet, at first with simple curiosity, then with a look of distress on detecting the raw wound where the skin had been scraped away. "Dear me," she exclaimed, putting out her cigarette.

It was by no means easy for Isa to make such a spectacle of himself in front of a foreign lady, here in this secret room. But so long as he was not obliged to speak, he was resigned to suffering these minor indignities. Nevertheless, he was desperately eager to return to the group, to become again only one among many.

After drinking a cup of coffee by herself, Miss Emily went out into the corridor, locking the door behind her. As she left, Isa understood her to say that she was going to consult with the nurse, which was encouraging— but why had she locked the door? Only then did he finish puzzling out her remark upon entering the room, to the effect that they mustn't let the students see them smoke. Yet that was only part of it, he knew. She was also worried about his wandering around the school on the loose, or still worse, escaping again, like a wounded animal that runs away when one is only trying to help it. As soon as Isa reached this point in his train of thought he felt an irresistible impulse to flee that very moment. He immediately opened the window, jumped out, and started to run.

After a few steps he felt the ground against his bare feet and remembered his shoes. He could not just leave them there, they did not belong to him. As he was hoisting himself back up through the window, the door opened across the room and he found himself face to face with Miss Emily.

While Isa was still lurking behind the trim modern buildings of the American school, Yamada wasted no time in approaching Michiko. In the past he had seen her from a distance conversing with foreigners in a free and easy manner. Since the beginning of today's excursion, when he dragged her off to the Education Office, he had been scheming for a chance to examine her English at first hand. It was not uncommon for members of his profession to test each other's mettle on some trivial pretext, like samurai picking quarrels simply to show off their prowess. Yamada was a past master at this sort of thing. And when he came up against colleagues whose English was better than his own, especially if they were women, he would try to defeat them on other grounds, to browbeat them if need be with the brute strength of his manly will. But in the end he often lost anyway.

Yamada had bided his time while Isa was tagging along beside Michiko, with what seemed to be warm encouragement on her part. Now that that nuisance had been removed, he could proceed with his interrogation. He unleashed a barrage of questions in English that left her scarcely a moment to catch her breath. What schools had she gone to, where did she graduate, had she taken special lessons in conversation, how many American friends did she have????

At first, even Michiko, with her considerable abilities, could not bring herself to reply in kind to her countryman's tirade in a foreign language. She answered only haltingly, and half in Japanese. But when Yamada showed no sign of relenting, she saw what he was up to, and resented his contempt for her sex.

And what, if she might inquire, was the big attraction of English for him? Would he like to try a demonstration class with her sometime? Wasn't it curious that he pronounced certain words with a kind of Boston accent, others in a sort of Southern drawl, which was a little like mixing Kyushu speech with the slow country dialect of Aomori?[9]

Yamada was staggered by the woman's counterattack, delivered in rapid-fire, thoroughly natural English. It was not so much her fluency as the substance of her remarks that defeated him. She was more than a match for him, he conceded; he would have to find some other weakness. In his experience, when dealing with women, food and clothing were the best bet.

"That's a fine outfit you're wearing," he said, lapsing back into Japanese. "Did you get it before the War?"

"Yes," she answered softly. "That is, the material comes from a robe that belonged to my husband. He was killed in the War."

"I'm sorry to hear that. It must be hard for you." Yamada peered shrewdly into Michiko's face as he added: "If you need rice, I can get it fairly cheap."

"That's very kind of you," she said. "May I have your card?"

"And if you'd like a little piecework to do at home, perhaps I could find you something."

"I would certainly appreciate it. Men really are much better at arranging these things, aren't they!"

The procession had at last come to a halt in front of the gate to the school compound. As soon as Yamada noticed the guard looking over their credentials, he burst in with the information that one of their number had preceded them by jeep. Turning back to Michiko, he then announced in English: "I imagine that he is still barefoot, and has concealed himself somewhere behind the school."

"What makes you think that?" asked Michiko.

"Elementary," said Yamada. "The man does not know the language." Lowering his voice, but still speaking English, he suggested that the time had come for her to change her shoes.

Michiko did not need prompting; it had been on her mind all day long. Yet Yamada's sharpness surprised her. He must have been watching her closely since the march began. From now on, she in turn would have to keep an eye on him. Maybe he had Isa pegged, too, she thought. But

---

9. The northern-most prefecture on the main island of Japan, where speech patterns tend toward the terse; according to one theory, this is because of cold temperatures. Kyushu is a southern island where temperatures are warm and speech habits are more easy-going.

was it possible that the poor fellow was still slinking around behind some building? She searched the corners of the compound as their final destination came into full view.

At the center of a large tract of land traversed by neat rows of houses stood the long-awaited school, an almost solid wall of glass on the side facing south. The fields that once occupied the site had been leveled away without a trace. An American observer would not have found the compound remarkable, much less luxurious. But the solid houses planted sparsely over the landscape, the spacious bedrooms illuminated by lamps even in broad daylight, the young Japanese maids attending to the needs of American babies—all of this was clearly revealed at a glance, and impressed the weary visitors as a vignette of some heavenly dwelling place.

Michiko reflected that her command of a foreign language and her general level of education might set her far above most of the residents; nevertheless, it was she who had walked four miles for the privilege of visiting their school, she who had reveled secretly in the pathetic expectation of showing off her high-heeled shoes. Surrounded by this verdant park, she now saw herself as too small and destitute even to set foot in such a place.

"What's the point of our sitting in on their classes?" she overheard a colleague complain to Shibamoto. He was the one, she recalled, who had been so quick to urge Isa to go barefoot. "What can we hope to learn from classes held in a place like this? The only lesson we'll leave with is the one we've learned just getting here: we lost! These magnificent buildings that we're only allowed to peek at—they were built with our taxes. Doesn't it make you want to cry?"

Michiko turned away, ashamed that she had perhaps been noticed before with her hands pressed sorrowfully over her eyes. She felt equally awkward in her present pose, and so she moved a few steps apart from the group, bent over and, though it scarcely mattered anymore, put on her high heels. The first thing she saw as she raised her head again was Isa, shoes still dangling down from one hand, coming toward her across the playground—and standing motionless in the background, the beautiful figure of an American schoolmistress. Michiko wanted to change back into sneakers.

The long march on an empty stomach had reduced some of the group to sullen anger, others to a numb exhaustion. Their leader rose up to his full height, and with a few heaves of his broad shoulders began to harangue them. "You mustn't forget that you're here by special invitation. We in the administrative section worked hard to get it for you, and if anyone misbehaves we are the ones who'll be blamed—You there, what do you think you're doing?" As he spoke, Shibamoto's roving gaze was arrested by a man sitting on the ground with his back to the group. It was Isa. Shibamoto resumed in the same hectoring tone: "I must ask you not to sit down right in front of the school. You look like a beggar. When did you get back?"

"You see, sir, that's what I meant," Yamada interjected. "We have to put our best foot forward, bargain from strength. Otherwise we might as well not have come in the first place. Leave it to me."

Shibamoto cut him off with a vague "We'll see," and quickly moved on to the next item on the agenda. He took a sheaf of printed questionnaires from his briefcase and passed them out to the teachers. As they studied the form he explained that they were to use it to record in detail their impressions of the school; afterwards it would be collected and put on file for future reference.

"What can we possibly write down? What would it prove, anyway?" cried Michiko in a shrill voice. She was visibly overwrought.

"Never mind," Yamada interrupted again. "You can just put down what I have. I intend to comment very critically on the instructional objectives of this school, the aptitude of their teachers, and so forth. I'll show it around when I'm done, and everyone can use it as a model. You needn't worry about that. Instead you might give some thought to . . ."

"No, no, you've missed the point," said Michiko impatiently.

"Well, then, what is the problem?"

Michiko fell silent. There was no use trying to explain to the likes of Yamada. And Isa—what a timid little soul! But he did seem to have a way with women. She would have to get to the bottom of this business with the schoolmistress. For the moment Yamada and Isa were confused in her troubled thoughts.

Just then the iron gate in front of the school opened and a thirtyish, bespectacled man stood before them with a welcoming smile. He introduced himself to the group as Mr. Williams, the Principal. At his appearance the teachers ceased their idle chatter and prepared to begin their visit. Yamada barged through the gate ahead of the others, who hesitated and deferred to one another before following him in. Isa came last, dragging his feet, as the gate swung shut behind them.

Hardly any doubt remained in Isa's mind about Yamada's devious plan, which he had sniffed out from its inception, to face off with him in a demonstration class before the day was over. He was determined to silence Yamada on this subject and prevent the encounter at any cost. But so far no suitable defense had suggested itself, and he approached the potentially fateful classrooms with ever more halting steps.

The group advanced in double file so as not to interfere with the students passing to and fro. Yamada had already attached himself to Mr. Williams. After the Principal's every utterance he would raise his hand as if to call for attention, turn to the person behind him, and communicate his version of the remark. This would be relayed in some form or other from one teacher to the next until it reached the end of the line: a procedure arrived at spontaneously, whether as a throwback to the rigid military chain of command or by simple analogy with a bucket brigade. It took some time for the message to be transmitted to Michiko and Isa in the rear, and in the interval all but the most provocative implications were filtered out.

Mr. Williams's opening remarks, that is, Yamada's rendering of them, went as follows: "Since the school was to be built with Japanese funds, we had little choice but to go along with the specifications given to us by some Japanese architects. The results, as you can see for yourselves, were less than satisfactory. To begin with, the budget was barely twenty percent of what would be considered normal back in the States. In our country we place great emphasis on bright and cheerful surroundings, and this school certainly does not meet those standards. We have twenty students in a class here, which is three too many. The ideal is seven-*teen*. Now I understand that in your country there are seven-*ty* in a class. Imagine! Classes that size are really out of the question. They necessitate regimentation, and this inevitably leads to militarism."

Here Yamada's voice trailed off into silence as Mr. Williams's expression took on a sudden severity, accompanied by a pudgy finger pointed at Yamada's forehead. When Yamada resumed interpreting, he spoke at first in tremulous tones.

The subject had changed to salaries, which, Mr. Williams assured them, were paid by the American government. The lowest salary level at the school, the one for beginning instructresses, was still about ten times the average wage of Japanese teachers, according to the figures he had heard. This was, it was true, a bit more than they would receive in comparable jobs at home; but things were a good deal more expensive in such a remote country; and if the discrepancy seemed excessive, it should be borne in mind that the standard of living which American teachers had to maintain was, after all, extremely high, so it was only natural that the basic salary be of a different order.

The only part of this speech to reach Isa's ear was the startling information, passed down the line with a collective sigh, that the teachers at this school got ten times as much money as they did. This so amazed Michiko that as she repeated it to Isa she had to lean on him to keep her balance. "We should have listened to our colleague there," she commented. "We should have just turned around and gone home."

"Right. That's so," said Isa.

"Did that woman do something about your feet?"

"Right. She did."

"What did you talk about?"

"Nothing."

"Look at those two over there—how disgusting!" Michiko muttered censoriously.

Isa looked in the direction she had indicated and focused on two students who stood holding hands in a corner of the corridor, their eyes closed in mutual infatuation. Miss Emily came up behind the couple and tapped them both gently on the back, not so much to chastise them, it appeared, as to alert them to the presence of visitors. Afterward she turned toward Michiko and smiled.

"It looks like paradise from the outside," said Michiko, "but there's no telling what goes on between these walls."

"Right. That's so."

Michiko did not know what to make of Isa's laconic responses. She looked at his frightened, rabbitlike eyes and recalled what Yamada had said about him. Then he broke his silence.

"Why must I go through this humiliating ordeal?"

"What ordeal? You mean having to go barefoot before?"

"No. I mean having to look at all this beauty."

"Beauty? From a certain point of view, I suppose."

"I'll tell you why. Simply because I'm a so-called English teacher."

"Oh? You don't like speaking English?"

"I d-d-detest it!"

Michiko was not surprised. There were a lot of men like that, the opposite type from Yamada, and Isa must be one of them.

Although the teachers had been told that they should each choose a class to visit and go their separate ways, they preferred to stick together. In the end Shibamoto divided them arbitrarily into three subgroups and dispatched them to different classrooms, with the veiled threat of force that was always present in his judo master's bearing. These smaller units soon congealed so that each proceeded as one, like flocks of peasants being herded around the capital.

Michiko hovered next to Isa. She could hardly forget the small favor she had yet to beg of him, after dwelling on it the length of that asphalt road. Moreover, it was reassuring to have him by her side—here, where almost anything might happen, and now, while she felt so despicably drab in the shadow of the foreign lady. Isa seemed to her the perfect companion for the occasion.

Meanwhile, Isa stayed as close as possible to Yamada, watching his every move, and fervently wishing that he might fall down some stairs and break his neck. He was even prepared, should the opportunity arise, to give him a little nudge. Failing that, in his present position he could at least intervene without delay if Yamada broached the subject of a demonstration class. And as one of his entourage, Isa was spared the necessity of pronouncing a single word of English, for Yamada had appropriated the role of spokesman for their party.

Isa and Michiko followed hard on Yamada's heels as together they entered the designated room, where they found a drawing class in session. Yamada soon retired to the supply closet to note down his observations. When he had finished he faced Michiko and whispered slyly: "Take a good look. With all their money and their fancy buildings, the children can't draw worth a damn."

There was a meek chorus of agreement from several colleagues who stood nearby, hanging on Yamada's every word. Michiko herself shared his opinion of the drawings, but she did not wish to be associated in any way with these people. They were the mean and cunning sort of Japanese; she and Isa were different, Michiko told herself, looking to Isa for confirmation. She caught him stooping over his shoes again: a new pair of sneakers which, she quickly deduced, must have come from that schoolmistress. They were much too big for him and he was trying to compensate by lacing them up tight. The moment Isa's eyes met hers, he blushed and turned the other way.

Michiko proposed that they have a closer look at the work now in progress. As they moved into the classroom and studied the drawings, they found themselves submerged in a waterless sea teeming with fish of various colors, shapes, and sizes. They were all unique, each one the product of a collaborative effort by a small group. Over by the window a few junior-high-school students of both sexes were sketching the thatched-roof cottages which appeared in the distance, beyond the confines of the American compound. They began to steal glances at the visitors over their shoulders, then one of the boys pointed at Shibamoto with his right hand while with his left he indicated a drawing of a seadevil. On closer inspection of other drawings, it was discovered that Yamada had been turned into a shark, Isa into a flying fish, suggested, perhaps, by his emaciated figure, and Michiko a goldfish. In the same fashion the whole party emerged within the next few moments as a school of highly distinctive fish.

As soon as they were back in the corridor, Yamada said to Shibamoto: "What kind of school are they running here, allowing such insulting behavior—and even toward a lady! I think we should submit a written protest. How about the rest of you? And you, Mrs. . . . ?"

"I didn't really mind it so much," said Michiko. "In fact, we sort of asked for it, with our down-and-out attitude."

"Down-and-out? I'm talking about a serious failing in their instructional objectives, a complete lack of discipline. That art teacher ought to be severely reprimanded. But why should I waste my breath! If you don't mind being turned into a goldfish, that's your business."

Not a glint of amusement alleviated Yamada's peevish expression as he finished berating Michiko and began to make further notations in his little book. "What did they do with you?" he asked Isa, looking up from his book. "Oh yes. It was a flying fish, and quite a masterpiece, too. They must have got the idea from the way you were flitting around in your bare feet."

Isa was at the moment too intent on his malevolent wishes to hear.

Isa stood at the door of the classroom in his borrowed sneakers and listened to the lady whose initials they bore teach English. Michiko had gone inside with the others, this time without trying to coax him into coming along. After a while the group filed back into the corridor one by one and clustered together to exchange comments in a half-whisper.

"You might almost say that our English is better than theirs," Yamada observed to Michiko in Japanese. "Weren't you amazed at all the mistakes in their grammar?"

"But the teacher is pretty, isn't she?"

"Hmm. It's like hiring a movie star to teach at a ridiculous salary."

"You were right about *him*—he really does hate English," said Michiko, switching languages as she again changed the subject.

"I know all that. I am also aware that he harbors some marice toward me."

Michiko acknowledged to herself that in referring to Isa as "him" and making her remark in English she had stilled the pangs of guilt which she would normally have felt in this betrayal of trust. And that, she reflected, was no doubt one reason for Isa's hatred of the foreign language: when you spoke it you stopped being yourself. It was too easy to be carried away by the titillation of the words, words not exactly your own. She knew she ought to get away from Yamada, the sooner the better.

When Michiko was back at Isa's side again she startled herself by blurting out, "If you hate speaking English so much, you must hate me too."
"It's different with women," said Isa.
"Women make good mimics. Is that what you mean?"
Maybe that *was* what he had meant, Isa could not be sure.
Without warning Michiko leaned over and whispered something in his ear. She had reverted to Japanese, to Isa's relief, but he could still make out only the general drift.
"You mean even you . . . ?" Isa blushed a deeper hue than Michiko, though she had brought the matter up.
"Have I embarrassed you again?" she asked.
It was perhaps in part the extraordinary scene now unfolding before their eyes that had driven her to divulge such a delicate matter, and so impetuously. They were now in the gymnasium, where, in preparation for tomorrow's basketball game with a neighboring school, a rally was being conducted by a spirited cheering section. A trio of girls in uniform, sixteen or seventeen years old, stood in front of the others calling out the names of the players with mounting fervor. When the shouting had risen to a high pitch of frenzied excitement, like a line of chorus girls they all began to lift up their skirts while the cheerleaders launched into cartwheels and somersaults.
"It's all set for the demonstration class this afternoon—you and me," said Yamada, who had appeared out of nowhere and taken Isa by surprise.
"I-I-I don't know what you're talking about. I have nothing to do with it."
"Well, you know now. Shibamoto decided on the two of us. I'll meet you after lunch, as soon as the hour for visiting classes is over. And don't try to run away. Shibamoto would not be pleased." Thrusting his jaw out toward Michiko, he added in an insinuating tone: "I'm sure you can get some coaching from her."
Yamada had in fact not the slightest desire to stand in front of a class next to Isa. The man was sure to bring disgrace on the whole profession. But in the middle of the rally he had caught sight of Michiko whispering in Isa's ear, then watched as Isa blushed and nodded in agreement. At that moment he had declared war.
Yamada went directly to the Principal and made his proposal with the same lunatic zeal he had shown to Shibamoto. Shibamoto stood by, wondering anxiously how the Principal would react to this bizarre request, which sounded less like a bid for a classroom demonstration than a demand for satisfaction by a man whose honor had been challenged. Yet, whether because like Shibamoto he saw no way out, or because he was soon to return to America and hoped it might yield a piece of Japanese bravado to regale his friends with, the Principal had accepted the proposal on the spot.
Yamada took leave of Isa and Michiko with a few curt instructions as to where they were to eat their lunch: on some benches in the schoolyard, about three hundred feet outside the gate—and nowhere else.
With quivering lips Isa stared vacantly after Yamada as he retreated across the gymnasium.

"Isa-san.[1] I'll take your place this afternoon," said Michiko.
"It's too late for that," Isa replied. "Either I knock him out, or I quit my job . . . or else I go ahead with the class and just stand there without saying a word."

Isa made as if to run after Yamada, but the sores on his feet seemed to be acting up again, and he had barely managed to limp forward a few steps when Michiko seized him by the hand and held him back.

"Wait a minute," she said. "Please don't forget the little favor I asked you a moment ago. If you'll let me have them now, I'll wash them right away."

Isa's immediate response was a blank look and an incessant blinking of his rabbit-eyes.

"You know, what we talked about before," Michiko prompted.

Isa finally understood what she wanted. All right, she could have them. But only after he had finished with them. Even at this juncture, on the brink of coming to blows with Yamada, he could not ignore his other concern, one from which he was never altogether free.

With sudden resolution Isa removed from his satchel a small bundle wrapped in newspaper and thrust it toward Michiko, all the while keeping his eyes on Yamada's vanishing figure. Michiko reached out in some confusion to take the coveted article from him—hardly ten seconds had passed since he had at last seemed to grasp her wish. But like an overeager relay runner, Isa had moved too soon, and he was off before the bundle was safely in her hands. Uneasy about the transaction to begin with, Michiko now blushed furiously, fumbled, and in the end lost her balance. Her high heels slid out from under her, and with a piercing shriek that filled the corridor she toppled over onto the floor. The bundle lay open where she had hurled it aside in her fall, revealing a pair of black chopsticks.

It remained a secret shared by Isa and Michiko alone that she had fallen while clutching at this homely artifact of their native land. As soon as Mr. Williams arrived on the scene, he loudly ordered the Japanese who had gathered around to disperse, whereupon up and down the corridor foreigners came rushing out of every other door. The Principal drove off this new crowd, leaving only a few women to help Michiko to the dispensary.[2]

Afterward, as he questioned Shibamoto' about the accident, Mr. Williams kept adjusting his glasses in an irritable gesture that suggested he found it all very regrettable. What had Michiko and Isa been up to? he wanted to know. Yamada, having rejoined them, interpreted stiffly for Shibamoto to the effect that the man with the limp had been struggling to catch up with yours truly to request that he be allowed to substitute for his colleague in today's demonstration class; meanwhile, the lady, who cherished similar aspirations, had been strenuously attempting to dissuade her colleague from his determined course when she slipped and fell. "It all proceeded from their pedagogical dedication," Yamada concluded on Shibamoto's behalf, "and their devotion to the English language."

"Ah yes. The old kamikaze spirit," said the Principal.

---

1. *San* is a title attached to names, corresponding to our Mr., Miss, Mrs., etc.   2. An office in a school, hospital, or other institution where medicines and medical aid are dispensed.

The heavy irony was lost on Yamada, who took the remark as a compliment, and presented it as such to his superior. Shibamoto fluttered his eyelashes in silent modesty.

Seeing that his sally had been deflected by misinterpretation, Mr. Williams pushed back his glasses again and turned on them with his sternest expression. "From now on, there are two things which I must strictly forbid," he announced. "The first is for any Japanese instructor to conduct a class here, to engage in any attempts to do so, or in any way to involve himself in the educational process at this school. Secondly, in the future high heels will not be permitted on these premises. If there are any violations, we will have to terminate all further visits."

After spitting out these injunctions with an air of finality, the Principal strode rapidly down the corridor to the door of the dispensary. He showed no inclination to enter, merely surveying the situation from outside.

A long pause ensued during which Yamada neglected to translate Mr. Williams's last pronouncement. When he was summoned back to reality by a poke in the ribs from Shibamoto, he spun around and fled toward the exit, without so much as a word of explanation. Then, with Shibamoto in the lead, the rest of the group hurried after, as though suddenly reminded of some vital errand. Only Isa was left behind, alone once again.

NADINE GORDIMER
born 1923

In the introduction to her *Selected Stories* (1983), Nadine Gordimer observes that "a writer is selected by his subject—his subject being the *consciousness* of his own era." The emphasis is Gordimer's, her way of insisting that the writer's vision is bounded by time and place, thus fundamentally conditioned by historical context. Gordimer's observation reflects a universal truth of literary creation, but it has a more immediate bearing on her own situation in her native South Africa, until recently under the apartheid system. It speaks to the public aspect of literature as testimony, and illuminates her conception of the social responsibility of the writer, a responsibility that, in her case, derives its force from the steady moral consciousness she has brought to her vocation in the racially divided society created by apartheid. Gordimer's work is a response to the institutional racism that was for decades the distinguishing feature of the political, economic, and social life of her country; it is an expression of her refusal to accommodate herself to the system, despite her status as a member of the dominant white minority. She has summed up the active sense of commitment that informs her writings in a terse remark in *The Essential Gesture* (1988): "The tension between standing apart and being fully involved—that is what makes a writer. That is where we begin."

But although Gordimer has acknowledged the moral imperative of imaginative expression in her circumstances, she has had to contend with two major problems in her development as a writer. The first has to do with the limitations imposed on her personal experience by the racial divide in her society. For if her moral consciousness sets her apart from the majority of her white compatriots, her very status seems to preclude her from a direct grasp of the experience of the nonwhite population, whose depressed condition provides the framework of her fictional universe. She has had, therefore, to risk an inadequate representation of this population in her depiction of their lives. She has also had to consider the weight of conviction her own work could assume for the disadvantaged majority of her country, even as she took on their cause, a problem she has examined with clarity in her essay *Where Do Whites Fit In?* Nonetheless, her imaginative entry into these other domains of life in South Africa has been nothing less than authoritative, carried by the powerful flow of her sympathy and facilitated by her keen observations and precise formulations.

The second problem arises from the inevitable tensions between high moral purpose and the muddy complexities of actual human lives. Gordimer's reflection in essay after essay on the pressures exerted on her art by the lived situation that forms the background to her work provides evidence, beyond her fiction, of her acute consciousness of this problem. The sensitiveness of her portrayals and the technical scruple she displays bear witness to her attention to the pitfalls of a political moralism that reduces the human condition to the single dimension of an ideological viewpoint, however generous or well meaning. Thus, even as the focus of her work remains the world of apartheid, this world takes shape as a social and moral universe within which the drama of human existence is played out. The political and social reference endows with solidity and heightened meaning such perennial themes as love and sexuality, the need for heroic sacrifice, and ultimately, the consciousness of mortality. These and other themes are developed within the symbolic framework of the South African landscape itself, which is evoked as a force in human life. Gordimer has shaped her perceptions into a personal statement that is sustained by a formal organization expressive of a mature vision of the world. While the fictional works proceed from a deep moral impulse, they also represent a mode of negotiation between the apparently conflicting demands of aesthetics and politics. It is Gordimer's constant attention to this tension that confers on her fictional works an integrity all their own.

Gordimer was born in 1923, in Springs, a small town near Johannesburg, in the Transvaal, the principal gold mining region of South Africa. She was the younger of two sisters born to a Jewish jeweler who had emigrated as a child from Lithuania and an Englishwoman. Though the family was associated with the liberal tradition of English-speaking South Africans, little in Gordimer's background suggests the radical direction her work was to take, for her early life was spent in the comfortable environment of the white minority in South Africa, the setting from which many of her novels move out to connect with events and situations in the world beyond. She has indicated that, although her formal education was by no means spotty, she was an indifferent student, describing herself as a "bolter" who in her early teens preferred the open spaces of the South African veld or the corridors of the local library to the classrooms at the Convent of Our Lady of Mercy. Her early passion for reading can be attributed to her secluded childhood, from which literature provided the most agreeable diversion, taking her out of the mundane reality of her provincial town not only into the world of children's books but also into the agitated world of adult experience. She has cited Maupassant, Chekov, Maugham, and Lawrence among the early stimulators of her imagination. Writing seems to have come to her naturally. Her first published work, a short story titled *The Quest for Seen Gold*, appeared in the children's section of the Johannesburg *Sunday Express* when she was only fourteen. She entered the University of the Witwatersrand in Johannesburg in 1945, but found it stifling and left after only a year. She thereafter devoted herself entirely to writing, producing at this stage of her career a series of short stories published in local journals, later collected as *Face to Face* (1949). Her second collection, *The Soft Voice of the Serpent*, was published in England in 1952 and quickly established her international reputation as an accomplished short story writer.

When Gordimer turned to a more extended form with her first novel, *The Lying Days* (1953), she drew on her own experience in Springs to portray the restless emotional state of Helen, her adolescent heroine, as she seeks an anchor in the world. The first-person narrative records Helen's growing disaffection toward the complacent and narrow-minded white community and her emerging dissidence, provoked in part by political developments in South Africa immediately following World War II, when the first measures were being taken by the Afrikaner government to disenfranchise Africans and the Africans themselves were displaying early resistance. Gordimer's novel registers the impact of these developments, but they remain subordinated to its primary psychological concern, in which the influence of Virginia Woolf is discernible. Still, the narrative retains a strong connection with realism in its incidental depiction of the harsh social realities of South Africa. This aspect of the work relates in particular to the situation of the Africans, who hover on the margins of the heroine's consciousness but whose plight and struggle are the prime factors in the awakening of her social awareness. Recognizable here already is what was to become an increasing preoccupation with the relationship between private experience and public events.

Gordimer confronts the problem of race relations more directly in her second novel, *A World of Strangers* (1958), which dwells on the obstacles apartheid presents to normal self-expression. The frustrating attempts of a group of black and white intellectuals and artists to establish human relations across racial lines are narrated by a young Englishman, Toby Hood, an outsider whose detached attitude to the problems of life in an atmosphere of political repression seems intended as an indictment of the shallow liberalism of many of her white compatriots. *Occasion for Loving* (1963) brings a further complication to the racial theme in its story of an uneasy love affair between a black artist and a married white woman. Here, Gordimer employs a female narrator who shares the social conventions of the white minority but is progressively drawn into the drama of the main characters. Her involvement affords a vantage point for exposing the complacency and hypocrisy of the white middle class.

Gordimer's first three novels show her evolving a personal style in which rhetorical eloquence serves a tough intelligence. In their different ways, these novels are innovative, but they appear as tentative moves toward the involved narrative strategies of her subsequent work, beginning with *The Late Bourgeois World* (1966). The overtly political plot of this novella is constructed around its protagonist's recollections of her relations with her previous husband, a white revolutionary who turns out to have betrayed his African friends and whose death is announced at the beginning of the story. The retrospective nature of her reflections, fit into a single day, sets the tone for a meditation on the possibilities of human solidarity in the face of adverse social forces. The ironic title conveys the work's critique of traditional liberalism as a response to the authoritarian posture of the apartheid regime. A certain utopianism haunts the radicalism that emerges at the end of the novella, but it is dissipated by the change of setting for Gordimer's next novel, *A Guest of Honour* (1971). Within the broad sweep of its action, which is centered on a newly independent African country, the novel explores through the psychology and fortunes of its characters, white and black, the ambiguities of political options as they flow from the personal dispositions of actors on the public stage.

The Conservationist (1974) is a parable of South Africa that offers an interpretation of the country's racial divide in cultural terms, opposing the confident materialism of its protagonist, Mehring, a white industrialist, to the mythical imagination of the Africans who work the farm he has acquired on the outskirts of Johannesburg. The novel's powerful evocation of the South African landscape establishes the symbolic context for a development in which the submerged consciousness of the Africans is reasserted over the white man's domineering and insensitive attitude to the world. The element of parable is also felt in the reversal of situations projected by Gordimer in *July's People* (1981), whose contrived plot involves a white family driven by an uprising to seek refuge with their African servant in his village. The family's painful adjustments to its displacement affords a view into the antagonisms by which South African society is riven and suggests at the same time the prospects for their resolution.

Gordimer's struggle to express formally her thematic concerns is amply demonstrated in *Burger's Daughter* (1979), a novel about the intersection between private experience and public events. Its action progresses through the long argument Rosa Burger conducts with herself on the competing claims of the ordinary life around her and pious affection for her father, a martyr of the antiapartheid movement. Gordimer's subtle delineation of Burger's mind alternates with a meticulous reconstruction of her character's social background. The density of the prose imparts to Burger's introspection a note of high seriousness: "But the change from life to death—what had all the certainties I had from my father to do with that?" Burger is finally granted the insight that these certainties—"Justice, equality, the brotherhood of man, human dignity"—are not mere abstract concepts but terms denoting universal values without whose active manifestation in the public realm private life itself may well be compromised. The procession of female characters in Gordimer's novels is given a remarkable turn in *A Sport of Nature* (1987), in the figure of Hillela, a white girl whose disrupted childhood in South Africa leads her to the personal odyssey she undertakes across Africa as she seeks to establish a total relationship, sensual and emotional, with the continent of her birth. Gordimer's latest novel, *My Son's Story* (1990), reassembles the themes of her previous work in its double perspective on the ordeals of Sonny, a "coloured" schoolteacher turned political activist whose extramarital affair with a white woman devoted to the liberal cause provokes a crisis in his family, a crisis that Gordimer places in the wider context of public experience and political commitment.

Though Gordimer is best known for her novels, she is widely acknowledged as one of the greatest contemporary practitioners of the genre of the short story. *Oral History*, from *A Soldier's Embrace* (1980) demonstrates her skilled handling of the form. The parallel between the intrusion of Christianity into the lives of the backwoods Africans (*seek, and ye shall find*) and their historical burden of colonial domination (*seek and destroy*) provides the historical and cultural background for the story's focus on the psychology of the informer. The village chief, alienated from his people by his ambiguous situation as the despised representative of a foreign power, is in the grip of a moral confusion. The wholeness of Gordimer's depiction of his community, fashioned from carefully positioned details, lends its full weight to the irony of the title, with its suggestion of the discrepancy between the status of the chief as the trusted repository of tradition and his act of betrayal, which appears less as a sign of loyalty to the colonial government than as his response to his solitude.

The story's tragic outcome is not merely a realistic report on the methods of colonial repression; it is also a measure of Gordimer's sympathy for its victims. Her identification finds symbolic expression in the numerous references to the mopane tree, whose various roles and changing features become integral to the development and meaning of the story. As the "blood and rust" of its vegetation during the spring foreshadows the calamity to come, so the mopane tree at the end of the story represents the clan's stubborn resilience. The tree thus functions as the symbolic center of the story, its suggestion of the continuity of the clan expanding the narrative scope beyond its immediate theme of the informer, to touch on that of the bond between individual and community. Thus the story does not merely record a tragic incident in modern African experience but captures a dramatic moment in the turns and paradoxes of African history.

The high esteem in which Gordimer is held stems in part from her principled stand against apartheid; no other creative writer has informed the international perception of South Africa as fully and effectively as she has done. This esteem also stems from the recognition of her accomplishment as a writer, for her work does not merely reflect events and situations in the real world but also achieves a formal distinction that is the product of a deeply considered aesthetics. The fine balance she maintains between the factual and the imaginative puts her in the company of the great political writers of our time, such as Milan Kundera and Gabriel García Márquez, while the convergence in her work of moral earnestness and technical range recalls Conrad. Her status as one of the major writers of the century has been confirmed by the many prizes and honors that have come her way, culminating in the award of the Nobel Prize for literature in 1991.

Robert F. Haugh, Nadine Gordimer: The Meticulous Vision (1974), is a valuable early study. Stephen Clingman, The Novels of Nadine Gordimer: History from the Inside (1986), and Andrew Vogel Ettin, Betrayals of the Body Politic: The Literary Commitments of Nadine Gordimer (1993), offer comprehensive assessments of Gordimer's fiction, while Dominic Head, Nadine Gordimer (1994), focuses on the relationship between Gordimer's political themes and her formal preoccupations. Rowland Smith, ed., Critical Essays on Nadine Gordimer (1990), contains chapters by various writers on individual works and aspects of her work. The Essential Gesture: Writing, Politics and Places (1988) is an important collection of Gordimer's essays; its value is enhanced by the excellent introduction and commentaries on the items by the editor, Stephen Clingman. Nancy Topping Bazin and Marilyn Dallman Seymour, eds., Conversations with Nadine Gordimer (1990), bring together Gordimer's interviews, dating back to 1958, thus providing a historical perspective on the evolution of her ideas in relation to her work.

PRONOUNCING GLOSSARY

The following list uses common English syllables to provide rough equivalents of selected words whose pronunciation may be unfamiliar to the general reader.

assegai: *ah-see-guy*

Empangeni: *em-pang-gay-nee*

mopane: *mo-pah-nay*

Oral History

There's always been one house like a white man's house in the village of Dilolo.[1] Built of brick with a roof that bounced signals from the sun. You could see it through the mopane[2] trees as you did the flash of paraffin tins the women carried on their heads, bringing water from the river. The rest of the village was built of river mud, grey, shaped by the hollows of hands, with reed thatch and poles of mopane from which the leaves had been ripped like fish-scales.

---

1. From the context, a village in Zimbabwe, formerly Southern Rhodesia, where the war of independence (ca. 1966–80) was based on guerrilla tactics.   2. A shrublike tree.

It was the chief's house. Some chiefs have a car as well but this was not an important chief, the clan is too small for that, and he had the usual stipend from the government.[3] If they had given him a car he would have had no use for it. There is no road: the army patrol Land Rovers come upon the people's cattle, startled as buck, in the mopane scrub. The village has been there a long time. The chief's grandfather was the clan's grandfathers' chief, and his name is the same as that of the chief who waved his warriors to down assegais[4] and took the first bible from a Scottish Mission Board white man.[5] *Seek and ye shall find*, the missionaries said.

The villagers in those parts don't look up, any more, when the sting-shaped army planes fly over twice a day. Only fish-eagles are disturbed, take off, screaming, keen swerving heads lifting into their invaded domain of sky. The men who have been away to work on the mines can read, but there are no newspapers. The people hear over the radio the government's count of how many army trucks have been blown up, how many white soldiers are going to be buried with *full military honours*—something that is apparently white people's way with their dead.

The chief had a radio, and he could read. He read to the headmen the letter from the government saying that anyone hiding or giving food and water to those who were fighting against the government's army would be put in prison. He read another letter from the government saying that to protect the village from these men who went over the border[6] and came back with guns to kill people and burn huts, anybody who walked in the bush after dark would be shot. Some of the young men who, going courting or drinking to the next village, might have been in danger, were no longer at home in their fathers' care, anyway. The young go away: once it was to the mines, now—the radio said—it was over the border to learn how to fight. Sons walked out of the clearing of mud huts; past the chief's house; past the children playing with the models of police patrol Land Rovers made out of twisted wire. The children called out, Where are you going? The young men didn't answer and they hadn't come back.

There was a church of mopane and mud with a mopane flagpole to fly a white flag when somebody died; the funeral service was more or less the same protestant one the missionaries brought from Scotland and it was combined with older rituals to entrust the newly-dead to the ancestors. Ululating[7] women with whitened faces sent them on their way to the missionaries' last judgment. The children were baptized with names chosen by portent in consultation between the mother and an old man who read immutable fate in the fall of small bones cast like dice from a horn cup. On all occasions and most Saturday nights there was a beer-drink, which the chief attended. An upright chair from his house was brought out for him although everyone else squatted comfortably on the sand, and he was offered the first taste from an old decorated gourd dipper (other people

---

3. Under the British system of "indirect rule," African chiefs were paid a small salary for their services to the colonial government.   4. A short spear perfected by Chaka, the Zulu conqueror, for use in close combat.   5. Christian missionary activity became intense in the 1880s and 1890s in southern Africa.   6. Most likely a reference to Zambia, a neighboring country that provided a safe haven for the freedom fighters.   7. Wailing.

drank from baked-bean or pilchard tins[8])—it is the way of people of the village.

It is also the way of the tribe to which the clan belongs and the subcontinent to which the tribe belongs, from Matadi in the west to Mombasa in the east, from Entebbe in the north to Empangeni[9] in the south, that everyone is welcome at a beer-drink. No traveller or passer-by, poling down the river in his pirogue,[1] leaving the snake-skin trail of his bicycle wheels through the sand, betraying his approach—if the dogs are sleeping by the cooking fires and the children have left their home-made highways—only by the brittle fragmentation of the dead leaves as he comes unseen through miles of mopane, is a presence to be questioned. Everyone for a long way round on both sides of the border near Dilolo has a black skin, speaks the same language and shares the custom of hospitality. Before the government started to shoot people at night to stop more young men leaving when no one was awake to ask, "Where are you going?" people thought nothing of walking ten miles from one village to another for a beer-drink.

But unfamiliar faces have become unusual. If the firelight caught such a face, it backed into darkness. No one remarked the face. Not even the smallest child who never took its eyes off it, crouching down among the knees of men with soft, little boy's lips held in wonderingly over teeth as if an invisible grown-up hand were clamped there. The young girls giggled and flirted from the background, as usual. The older men didn't ask for news of relatives or friends outside the village. The chief seemed not to see one face or faces in distinction from any other. His eyes came to rest instead on some of the older men. He gazed and they felt it.

Coming out of the back door of his brick house with its polished concrete steps, early in the morning, he hailed one of them. The man was passing with his hobbling cows and steadily bleating goats; stopped, with the turn of one who will continue on his way in a moment almost without breaking step. But the summons was for him. The chief wore a frayed collarless shirt and old trousers, like the man, but he was never barefoot. In the hand with a big steel watch on the wrist, he carried his thick-framed spectacles, and drew down his nose between the fingers of the other hand; he had the authoritative body of a man who still has his sexual powers but his eyes flickered against the light of the sun and secreted flecks of matter like cold cream at the corners. After the greetings usual between a chief and one of his headmen together with whom, from the retreat in the mopane forest where they lay together in the same age-group recovering from circumcision,[2] he had long ago emerged a man, the chief said, "When is your son coming back?"

"I have no news."

"Did he sign for the mines?"[3]

"No."

8. Tins that originally contained canned fish; they were recycled for drinking.   9. A royal village in Zululand. Matadi is a port in Zaire on the Atlantic Ocean. Mombasa is a coastal town in Kenya, on the Indian Ocean. Entebbe is the principal city in Uganda.   1. Canoe.   2. The central element in the rites of initiation.   3. That is, become a migrant worker in the gold mines in the Republic of South Africa.

"He's gone to the tobacco farms?"

"He didn't tell us."

"Gone away to find work and doesn't tell his mother? What sort of child is that? Didn't you teach him?"

The goats were tongue-ing three hunchback bushes that were all that was left of a hedge round the chief's house. The man took out a round tin dented with child's tooth-marks and taking care not to spill any snuff, dosed himself. He gestured at the beasts, for permission: "They're eating up your house . . ." He made a move towards the necessity to drive them on.

"There is nothing left there to eat." The chief ignored his hedge, planted by his oldest wife who had been to school at the mission up the river. He stood among the goats as if he would ask more questions. Then he turned and went back to his yard, dismissing himself. The other man watched. It seemed he might call after; but instead drove his animals with the familiar cries, this time unnecessarily loud and frequent.

Often an army patrol Land Rover came to the village. No one could predict when this would be because it was not possible to count the days in between and be sure that so many would elapse before it returned, as could be done in the case of a tax-collector or cattle-dipping officer.[4] But it could be heard minutes away, crashing through the mopane like a frightened animal, and dust hung marking the direction from which it was coming. The children ran to tell. The women went from hut to hut. One of the chief's wives would enjoy the importance of bearing the news: "The government is coming to see you." He would be out of his house when the Land Rover stopped and a black soldier (murmuring towards the chief the required respectful greeting in their own language) jumped out and opened the door for the white soldier. The white soldier had learned the names of all the local chiefs. He gave greetings with white men's brusqueness: "Everything all right?" And the chief repeated to him: "Everything is all right." "No one been bothering you in this village?" "No one is troubling us." But the white soldier signalled to his black men and they went through every hut busy as wives when they are cleaning, turning over bedding, thrusting gun-butts into the pile of ash and rubbish where the chickens searched, even looking in, their eyes dazzled by darkness, to the hut where one of the old women who had gone crazy had to be kept most of the time. The white soldier stood beside the Land Rover waiting for them. He told the chief of things that were happening not far from the village; not far at all. The road that passed five kilometres away had been blown up. "Someone plants land-mines in the road and as soon as we repair it they put them there again. Those people come from across the river[5] and they pass this way. They wreck our vehicles and kill people."

The heads gathered round weaved as if at the sight of bodies laid there horrifyingly before them.

"They will kill you, too—burn your huts, all of you—if you let them stay with you."

---

4. The veterinary officer who supervised the forced wading of cattle into a shallow pool of water mixed with disinfectant, to rid them of ticks and other parasites.   5. The Zambesi.

A woman turned her face away: "Aïe-aïe-aïe-aïe."

His forefinger half-circled his audience. "I'm telling you. You'll see what they do."

The chief's latest wife, taken only the year before and of the age-group of his elder grandchildren, had not come out to listen to the white man. But she heard from others what he had said, and fiercely smoothing her legs with grease, demanded of the chief, "Why does he want us to die, that white man!"

Her husband, who had just been a passionately shuddering lover, became at once one of the important old with whom she did not count and could not argue. "You talk about things you don't know. Don't speak for the sake of making a noise."

To punish him, she picked up the strong, young girl's baby she had borne him and went out of the room where she slept with him on the big bed that had come down the river by barge, before the army's machine guns were pointing at the other bank.

He appeared at his mother's hut. There, the middle-aged man on whom the villagers depended, to whom the government looked when it wanted taxes paid and culling orders[6] carried out, became a son—the ageless category, no matter from which age-group to another he passed in the progression of her life and his. The old woman was at her toilet.[7] The great weight of her body settled around her where she sat on a reed mat outside the door. He pushed a stool under himself. Set out was a small mirror with a pink plastic frame and stand, in which he caught sight of his face, screwed up. A large black comb; a little carved box inlaid with red lucky beans she had always had, he used to beg to be allowed to play with it fifty years ago. He waited, not so much out of respect as in the bond of indifference to all outside their mutual contact that reasserts itself when lions and their kin lie against one another.

She cocked a glance, swinging the empty loops of her stretched earlobes. He did not say what he had come for.

She had chosen a tiny bone spoon from the box and was poking with trembling care up each round hole of distended nostril. She cleaned the crust of dried snot and dust from her delicate instrument and flicked the dirt in the direction away from him.

She said: "Do you know where your sons are?"

"Yes, I know where my sons are. You have seen three of them here today. Two are in school at the mission. The baby—he's with the mother." A slight smile, to which the old woman did not respond. Her preferences among the sons had no connection with sexual pride.

"Good. You can be glad of all that. But don't ask other people about theirs."

As often when people who share the same blood share the same thought, for a moment mother and son looked exactly alike, he old-womanish, she mannish.

6. A regulation designed to control the cattle population. 7. That is, cleaning herself.

"If the ones we know are missing, there are not always empty places," he said.

She stirred consideringly in her bulk. Leaned back to regard him: "It used to be that all children were our own children. All sons our sons. *Old-fashion*, these people here"—the hard English word rolled out of their language like a pebble, and came to rest where aimed, at his feet.

It was spring: the mopane leaves turn, drying up and dying, spattering the sand with blood and rust—a battlefield, it must have looked, from the patrol planes. In August there is no rain to come for two months yet. Nothing grows but the flies hatch. The heat rises daily and the nights hold it, without a stir, till morning. On these nights the radio voice carried so clearly it could be heard from the chief's house all through the village. Many were being captured in the bush and killed by the army—*seek and destroy* was what the white men said now—and many in the army were being set upon in the bush or blown up in their trucks and buried with full military honours. This was expected to continue until October because the men in the bush knew that it was their last chance before the rains came and chained their feet in mud.

On these hot nights when people cannot sleep anyway, beer-drinks last until very late. People drink more; the women know this, and brew more. There is a fire but no one sits close round it.

Without a moon the dark is thick with heat; when the moon is full the dark shimmers thinly in a hot mirage off the river. Black faces are blue, there are watermarks along noses and biceps. The chief sat on his chair and wore shoes and socks in spite of the heat; those drinking nearest him could smell the suffering of his feet. The planes of jaw and lips he noticed in moonlight molten over them, moonlight pouring moths broken from white cases on the mopane and mosquitoes rising from the river, pouring glory like the light in the religious pictures people got at the mission—he had seen those faces about lately in the audacity of day, as well. An ox had been killed and there was the scent of meat sizzling in the village (just look at the behaviour of the dogs, they knew) although there was no marriage or other festival that called for someone to slaughter one of his beasts. When the chief allowed himself, at least, to meet the eyes of a stranger, the whites that had been showing at an oblique angle disappeared and he took rather than saw the full gaze of the seeing eye: the pupils with their defiance, their belief, their claim, hold, on him. He let it happen only once. For the rest, he saw their arrogant lifted jaws to each other and warrior smiles to the girls, as they drank. The children were drawn to them, fighting one another silently for places close up. Towards midnight—his watch had its own glowing galaxy—he left his chair and did not come back from the shadows where men went to urinate. Often at beer-drinks the chief would go home while others were still drinking.

He went to his brick house whose roof shone almost bright as day. He did not go to the room where his new wife and sixth son would be sleeping in the big bed, but simply took from the kitchen, where it was kept when not in use, a bicycle belonging to one of his hangers-on, relative or retainer. He wheeled it away from the huts in the clearing, his village and grandfather's village that disappeared so quickly behind him in the mopane, and began to ride through the sand. He was not afraid he would meet a patrol and be shot; alone at night in the sand forest, the forested desert he had known before and would know beyond his span of life, he didn't believe in the power of a roving band of government men to end that life. The going was heavy but he had mastered when young the art of riding on this, the only terrain he knew, and the ability came back. In an hour he arrived at the army post, called out who he was to the sentry with a machine gun, and had to wait, like a beggar rather than a chief, to be allowed to approach and be searched. There were black soldiers on duty but they woke the white man. It was the one who knew his name, his clan, his village, the way these modern white men were taught. He seemed to know at once why the chief had come; frowning in concentration to grasp details, his mouth was open in a smile and the point of his tongue curled touching at back teeth the way a man will verify facts one by one on his fingers. "How many?"

"Six or ten or—but sometimes it's only, say, three or one . . . I don't know. One is here, he's gone; they come again."

"They take food, they sleep, and off. Yes. They make the people give them what they want, that's it, eh? And you know who it is who hides them—who shows them where to sleep—of course you know."

The chief sat on one of the chairs in that place, the army's place, and the white soldier was standing. "Who is it—" the chief was having difficulty in saying what he wanted in English, he had the feeling it was not coming out as he had meant nor being understood as he had expected. "I can't know who is it"—a hand moved restlessly, he held a breath and released it—"in the village there's many, plenty people. If it's this one or this one—" He stopped, shaking his head with a reminder to the white man of his authority, which the white soldier was quick to placate. "Of course. Never mind. They frighten the people; the people can't say no. They kill people who say no, eh; cut their ears off, you know that? Tear away their lips. Don't you see the pictures in the papers?"

"We never saw it. I heard the government say on the radio."

"They're still drinking . . . How long—an hour ago?"

The white soldier checked with a look the other men, whose stance had changed to that of bodies ready to break into movement: grab weapons, run, fling themselves at the Land Rovers guarded in the dark outside. He picked up the telephone receiver but blocked the mouth-piece as if it were someone about to make an objection. "Chief, I'll be with you in a moment. —Take him to the duty room and make coffee. Just wait—" he leaned his full reach towards a drawer in a cabinet on the left of the desk and, scrabbling to get it open, took out a half-full bottle of brandy. Behind the chief's back he gestured the bottle towards the chief, and a black soldier jumped obediently to take it.

The chief went to a cousin's house in a village the other side of the army post later that night. He said he had been to a beer-drink and could not ride home because of the white men's curfew.

The white soldier had instructed that he should not be in his own vil-

lage when the arrests were made so that he could not be connected with
these and would not be in danger of having his ears cut off for taking heed
of what the government wanted of him, or having his lips mutilated for
what he had told.

His cousin gave him blankets. He slept in a hut with her father. The
deaf old man was aware neither that he had come nor was leaving so early
that last night's moon, the size of the bicycle's reflector, was still shiny in
the sky. The bicycle rode up on spring-hares without disturbing them, in
the forest; there was a stink of jackal-fouling still sharp on the dew. Smoke
already marked his village; early cooking fires were lit. Then he saw that
the smoke, the black particles spindling at his face, were not from cooking
fires. Instead of going faster as he pumped his feet against the weight of
sand the bicycle seemed to slow along with his mind, to find in each
revolution of its wheels the countersurge: to stop; not go on. But there was
no way not to reach what he found. The planes only children bothered to
look up at any longer had come in the night and dropped something
terrible and alive that no one could have read or heard about enough to
be sufficiently afraid of. He saw first a bloody kaross,[8] a dog caught on the
roots of an upturned tree. The earth under the village seemed to have
burst open and flung away what it carried: the huts, pots, gourds, blankets,
the tin trunks, alarm-clocks, curtain-booth photographs, bicycles, radios
and shoes brought back from the mines, the bright cloths young wives
wound on their heads, the pretty pictures of white lambs and pink children
at the knees of the golden-haired Christ the Scottish Mission Board first
brought long ago—all five generations of the clan's life that had been
chronicled by each succeeding generation in episodes told to the next.
The huts had staved in like broken anthills. Within earth walls baked
and streaked by fire the thatch and roof-poles were ash. He bellowed and
stumbled from hut to hut, nothing answered frenzy, not even a chicken
rose from under his feet. The walls of his house still stood. It was gutted
and the roof had buckled. A black stiff creature lay roasted on its chain in
the yard. In one of the huts he saw a human shape transformed the same
way, a thing of stiff tar daubed on a recognizable framework. It was the
hut where the mad woman lived; when those who had survived fled, they
had forgotten her.

The chief's mother and his youngest wife were not among them. But
the baby boy lived, and will grow up in the care of the older wives. No
one can say what it was the white soldier said over the telephone to his
commanding officer, and if the commanding officer had told him what
was going to be done, or whether the white soldier knew, as a matter of
procedure laid down in his military training for this kind of war, what
would be done. The chief hanged himself in the mopane. The police or
the army (much the same these days, people confuse them) found the
bicycle beneath his dangling shoes. So the family hanger-on still rides it;
it would have been lost if it had been safe in the kitchen when the raid

---

8. A cloak made of animal skin.

came. No one knows where the chief found a rope, in the ruins of his village.

The people are beginning to go back. The dead are properly buried in ancestral places in the mopane forest. The women are to be seen carrying tins and grain panniers of mud[9] up from the river. In talkative bands they squat and smear, raising the huts again. They bring sheaves of reeds exceeding their own height, balanced like the cross-stroke of a majuscular[1] T on their heads. The men's voices sound through the mopane as they choose and fell trees for the roof supports.

A white flag on a mopane pole hangs outside the house whose white walls, built like a white man's, stand from before this time.

9. For rebuilding homes. *Panniers:* large baskets, usually slung over the backs of animals.   1. Capital.

CHINUA ACHEBE

born 1930

The best-known African writer today is the Nigerian Chinua Achebe, whose first novel, *Things Fall Apart*, exploded the colonialist image of Africans as childlike people living in a primitive society. Achebe's novels, stories, poetry, and essays have made him a respected and prophetic figure in Africa. In Western countries, where he has traveled, taught, and lectured widely, he is admired as a major writer who has given an entirely new direction to the English-language novel. Achebe has created not only the African postcolonial novel with its new themes and characters, but also a complex narrative point of view that questions cultural images — including its own — with a subtle irony and compassion born from bicultural experience. His vantage point is different from that of Doris Lessing or Albert Camus, two authors whose work is also concerned with African experience: Achebe writes, as he says, "from the inside." For him as for many other writers in this volume, literature is important because it liberates the human imagination; it "begins as an adventure in self-discovery and ends in wisdom and human conscience."

Chinua Achebe was born in the town of Ogidi, an Igbo-speaking town of Eastern Nigeria, on November 16, 1930. He was the fifth of six children in the family of Isaiah Okafor Achebe, a teacher for the Church Missionary Society, and his wife, Janet. Achebe's parents christened him Albert after Prince Albert, husband of Queen Victoria. When he entered the university the author rejected his British name in favor of his indigenous name Chinua, which abbreviates Chinualumogu, or "My spirit come fight for me." Achebe's novels offer a picture of Igbo society with its fierce egalitarianism and "town meeting" debates. Two cultures co-existed in Ogidi: on the one hand, African social customs and traditional religion, and on the other, British colonial authority and Christianity. Instead of being torn between the two, Achebe found himself curious about both ways of life and fascinated with the dual perspective that came from living "at the crossroads of cultures."

He attended Church schools in Ogidi where instruction was carried out in English after the first two years. Achebe read the various books in his father's library, most of them primers or Church related, but he also listened eagerly to his mother and sister when they told traditional Igbo stories. Entering a prestigious government college (secondary school) in Umuahia, he immediately took advantage of its well-stocked library. Achebe later commented on the crucial importance of books in creating writers and committed readers, noting that private secondary schools had few if any books and that almost all the first generation of Nigerian writers—including himself and Wole Soyinka (born 1934)—had gone to a government college.

After graduating in 1948, Achebe entered University College, Ibadan, on a scholarship to study medicine. In the following year he changed to a program in liberal arts that combined English, history, and religious studies. Research in the last two fields deepened his knowledge of Nigerian history and culture; the assigned literary texts, however, brought into sharp focus the distorted image of African culture offered by British colonial literature. Reading Joyce Cary's *Mister Johnson* (1939), a novel recommended for its depiction of life in Nigeria, he was shocked to find Nigerians described as violent savages with passionate instincts and simple minds: "and so I thought if this was famous, then perhaps someone ought to try and look at this from the inside." He began writing while at the university, contributing articles and sketches to several campus papers, and publishing four stories in the *University Herald*, a magazine whose editor he became in his third year.

Upon receiving his B.A. in 1953, Achebe joined the Nigerian Broadcasting Service, working in the Talks Section and traveling to London in 1956 to attend the British Broadcasting Corporation Staff School. Promotions came quickly; he was named head of the Talks Section in 1957, controller of the Eastern Region Stations in 1959, and in 1961 director of External Services in charge of the Voice of Nigeria. The radio position was more than a merely administrative post, for Achebe and his colleagues were working to create a sense of shared national identity through broadcasting national news and information about Nigerian culture. Ever since the end of World War II, Nigeria had been torn by intellectual and political rivalries that overlaid the common struggle for independence (achieved in 1960). The three major ethnolinguistic groups—Yoruba, Hausa-Fulani, and Igbo (once spelled Ibo)—were increasingly locked in economic and political rivalry at the same time they were fighting to erase the vestiges of British colonial rule. These problems eventually boiled over in the Nigerian Civil War (1967–1970). The persistence of political corruption is depicted in *A Man of the People* (1966) and *Anthills of the Savannah* (1987).

Achebe is convinced of the writer's social responsibility, and he draws frequent contrasts between the European "art for art's sake" tradition and an African belief in the indivisibility of art and society. His favorite example is the Owerri Igbo custom of *mbari*, a communal art project in which villagers selected by the priest of the earth goddess Ala live in a forest clearing for a year or more, working under the direction of master artists to prepare a temple of images in the goddess's honor. This creative communal enterprise and its culminating festival are diametrically opposed, he says, to the European custom of secluding art objects in museums or private collections. Instead, *mbari* celebrates art as a cultural process, affirming that "art belongs to all and is a 'function' of society." Achebe's own practice as novelist, poet, essayist, founder and editor of two journals, lecturer, and active representative of African letters exemplifies this commitment to the community.

His first novel, *Things Fall Apart* (1958), was a conscious attempt to counteract the distortions of Cary's *Mister Johnson* by describing the richness and complexity of traditional African society before the colonial and missionary invasion. It was important, Achebe said, to "teach my readers that their past—with all its imperfections—was not one long night of savagery from which the first Europeans acting on God's behalf delivered them." The novel was recognized immediately as an extraordinary work of literature in English. It also became the first classic work of modern African fiction, translated into nine languages, and Achebe became for many readers and writers the teacher of a whole generation. In 1959 he received the Margaret Wrong Memorial prize, and in 1960—after the publication of a sequel, *No Longer at Ease*—he received the Nigerian National Trophy for literature. His later novels continue to examine the individual and cultural dilemmas of Nigerian society, although their background varies from the traditional religious society of *Arrow of God* (1964) to thinly disguised accounts of contemporary political strife.

Achebe's reputation as the "father of the African novel in English" does not depend solely on his accounts of Nigerian society. In contrast with writers such as Ngugi wa Thiong'o (born 1938), who insist that the contemporary African writer has a moral obligation to write in one of the tribal languages, Achebe maintains his right to compose in the English he has used since his school days. His literary language is an English skillfully blended with Igbo vocabulary, proverbs, images, and speech patterns to create a new voice embodying the linguistic pluralism of modern African experience. By including standard English, Igbo, and pidgin in different contexts, Achebe demonstrates the existence of a diverse society that is otherwise concealed behind language barriers—a culture, he suggests, that escaped colonial officials who wrote about African character without ever understanding the language. He also thereby acknowledges that his primary African audience is composed of younger, schooled readers who are relatively fluent in English.

It is hard to overestimate the influence of Nigerian politics on Achebe's life after 1966. In January, a military coup d'état led by young Igbo officers overthrew the government; six months later, a second coup led by non-Igbo officers took power. Ethnic rivalries intensified: thousands of Igbos were killed and driven out of the north. Achebe and his family fled the capital of Lagos when soldiers were sent to find him, and the novelist became a senior research fellow at the University of Nigeria, Nsukka (in Eastern Nigeria). In May 1967 the eastern region, mainly populated by Igbo-speakers, seceded as the new nation of Biafra. From then on until the defeat of Biafra in January 1970, a bloody civil war was waged with high civilian casualties and widespread starvation. Achebe traveled in Europe, North America, and Africa to win support for Biafra, proclaiming that "no government, black or white, has the right to stigmatize and destroy groups of its own citizens without undermining the basis of its own existence." A group of his poems about the war won the Commonwealth Poetry Prize in 1972, the same year that he published a volume of short stories, *Girls at War*, and left Nigeria to take up a three-year position at the University of Massachusetts at Amherst. Returning to Nsukka as professor of literature in 1976, Achebe continued to participate in his country's political life. He published an attack on the corrupt leadership in *The Trouble with Nigeria* (1983) and—drawing on circumstances surrounding a fifth military coup in 1985—produced his fifth novel, *Anthills of the Savannah*, in 1987. Although it reiterates Achebe's familiar indictment of ruthless politicians, alienated intellectuals, and those who accept dictatorship as a route to reform, this novel offers hope for the future through a return to the people and a symbolic child born at the end: a girl child with a boy's name, "May the Path Never Close." Badly hurt in a car accident the year after *Anthills* was published, Achebe slowly recovered and returned to his writing. He currently teaches at Bard College.

A predominant theme in Achebe's novels and essays is the notion of balance or interdependence: balance between earth and sky, individual and community, man and woman, or different perspectives on the same situation. Igbo thought is fundamentally dualistic, the novelist explains: "Wherever Something stands, Something Else will stand beside it. Nothing is absolute." Extremes carry the seeds of destruction. Indeed, destruction follows in Achebe's novels whenever balance is disturbed: when Okonkwo in *Things Fall Apart* represses any signs of "female" softness; when the priest Ezeulu in *Arrow of God* is imprisoned and refuses to authorize the feast of the New Yam, without which his people cannot plant their crops; and when, in later books, the lust for power and possessions blinds Nigerian leaders to the needs of the people.

The fundamental image of this balance is contained in the Igbo concept of *chi*, which recurs throughout Achebe's work. *Chi* is a personal deity, a fragment of the supreme being unique for each individual. A person's *chi*, says Achebe, may be visualized "as his other identity in spirit-land—his *spirit being* complementing his terrestrial *human being*." It is both all-powerful and subject to persuasion: "When a man says yes his *chi* says yes also" but at the same time "a man does not challenge his *chi* to a wrestling match." *Chi* is simultaneously destiny and an internal commitment that cannot be denied, a religious concept and also a picture of psychic harmony. Both aspects are linked throughout Achebe's novels, beginning with *Things Fall Apart*. In killing Ikemefuna, whom he loves and who calls him father, Okonkwo sins not only against the earth goddess, protector of family relations, but also against his inmost feelings and thus against his *chi*. If Okonkwo's destiny (*chi*) is marked by bad luck, one reason may be that—driven by fear of resembling his father—he struggles to repress part of his personality (*chi*), with predictably ill results. In the final assessment, no one can fully explain *chi*: it is mysteriously uncertain, the element of fate over which we have no real control.

Things Fall Apart is both Okonkwo's tragedy and that of his society. The title (taken from William Butler Yeats's *The Second Coming*) introduces a narrative in which a complex and dignified traditional society disintegrates before foreign invaders who assault its political, economic, and religious institutions. The setting is eastern Nigeria around the turn of the century in the clan of Umuofia, which is composed of nine interrelated villages. One of these villages, Iguedo, is the home of the protagonist Okonkwo, an ambitious and powerful man who is driven by the memory of his father's failure and weakness.

During the first two-thirds of the book, Achebe paints the picture of a rich and coherent society, establishing an image of traditional African culture into which the final chapters' missionaries, court messengers, and district commissioner intrude as alien and disruptive elements. In sharp contrast to the simplified vision of African life given by European novelists Joyce Cary, Joseph Conrad, or Graham Greene, he explores the complex feelings and interpersonal relationships of diverse villagers seen as men, women, parents, children, friends, neighbors, or priests of the local deities. The intricate patterns of Umuofia's economic and social customs also emerge, belying European images of African "primitive" simplicity. No one who has read about Obierika's intricate marriage negotiations, the etiquette of *kola* hospitality, the religious "week of peace," Ezeudu's elaborate funeral rites, the domestic arbitration conducted by the *egwugwu* court, the female kinship customs linking families and villages, or indeed Umuofia's entire set of taboos and punishments, will find this a simple society. The title system itself, which plays such a large part in the novel, is an ingenious social strategy for redistributing wealth throughout the community. The four honorific ozo titles (*Ozo, Idemili, Omalo,* and *Erulu*), through which a man enters the spiritual community of his ancestors and achieves increasing levels of prestige, are acquired in festivities during which the candidate divests himself of excess material wealth. There is a dignity and purpose to this society despite inner tensions that—as Achebe shows—create pain as well as vulnerability to attack from outside. The moderate Obierika disapproves of killing Ikemefuna and begins to question the practice of throwing away twins; one of the first converts to Christianity is a woman who gave birth to several sets of twins, all of whom were exposed (left in the wild) at birth. The general subordination of women is another source of tensions which have taken longer to surface. Whatever its cultural differences from European society, however, this is a highly organized and complex society that offers a great deal of continuity and coherence to its members.

Igbo names, like names throughout black Africa, consist of whole phrases or sentences. Some names are dictated by circumstance (referring to the day of birth, for example) and some (the "given" name selected by the child's father, for example) reflect the family situation or a child's expected destiny. Adults may earn additional titles of honor. Achebe uses the connotations of personal names to reinforce important themes in *Things Fall Apart*. Okonkwo's father's character as a lazy, artistic, and improvident man is suggested by the name Unoka, signifying "the home is supreme." Okonkwo's son Nwoye, who has inherited his grandfather's peace-loving nature and artistic qualities, is named after the second day of the Igbo week (*Oye*); unlike Okonkwo, Nwoye lacks a prefix specifying adulthood or even gender, for Nwa means "child." Ikemefuna, who is condemned to death by the Oracle and will be killed by his adoptive father, is named "My strength should not be dissipated." Although all names have significance, only those with some relevance to the story will be annotated in this edition.

Okonkwo's character and career suggest epic dimensions. He is on the one hand a hero of enormous energy and determination, "one of the greatest men in Umuofia" as his friend Obierika says, but his particular mode of greatness also causes his downfall. Like Achilles in Homer's *Iliad*, Okonkwo clings to traditionally respected values of pride and warlike aggression, and he will die to preserve those values. His unwillingness to change sets him apart from the community and eventually isolates him from the clan with its emphasis on group decisions. Okonkwo is a passionate man who counts on physical strength, hard work, and courage to make his way. Humiliated by his father's laziness, shameful death, and lack of title, compelled early to support the entire family, he struggles desperately to root out any sign of inherited "feminine" weakness in himself or his son Nwoye. By cultivating strength and valor, he finds a way to surpass his father and become one of the village leaders. Okonkwo is not without tender feelings: he loves his wife Ekwefi; his daughter, Ezinma; and the youth Ikemefuna who is given to him to foster. When he cuts down Ikemefuna so as not to appear weak, he is shattered for days thereafter. Nonetheless, his obsession with fierce masculinity, and his open disrespect for "womanly" qualities of gentleness, compassion and peace, separate him not only from other members of his clan such as the more balanced Obierika but also from the earth goddess herself. This imbalance leads to disaster.

C. L. Innes, *Chinua Achebe* (1990), is a comprehensive study of Achebe's work through 1988; it emphasizes his literary techniques and Africanization of the novel. Simon Gikandi, *Reading Chinua Achebe: Language and Ideology in Fiction* (1991), is also recommended. Robert M. Wren, *Achebe's World: The Historical and Cultural Context of the Novels of Chinua Achebe* (1980), provides historical background and cultural context for Achebe's novels and includes glossary and bibliography. Studies of *Things Fall Apart* include Kate Turkington, *Chinua Achebe: Things Fall Apart* (1977), a concise introductory study, and the multiple perspectives in Bernth Lindfors, ed., *Approaches to Teaching Achebe's Things Fall Apart* (1991). C. L. Innes and Bernth Lindfors, eds., *Critical Perspectives on Chinua Achebe*, (1978), collect twenty-one essays on Achebe's work (almost exclusively the novels) through 1973. G. D. Killam, *The Writings of Chinua Achebe* (1977), is a commentary on Achebe's work through the mid-1970s, concentrating on the first four novels.

PRONOUNCING GLOSSARY

The following list uses common English syllables and stress accents to provide rough equivalents of selected words whose pronunciation may be unfamiliar to the general reader. Most of the names in *Things Fall Apart* are pronounced basically as they would be in English (for example, Okonkwo as *oh-kon'-kwo*), except that Igbo (like other African languages and Chinese) is a tonal language and also uses high or low tones for individual syllables.

Chielo: *chee-e'-loh*

Chinua Achebe: *chin'-oo-ah ah-chay'-be*

egwugwu: *e'-gwoo-gwoo*

Erulu: *air-oo'-loo*

Ezeani: *ez-ah'-nee*

Ezeugo: *e-zoo'-goh*

Idemili: *ee-de'-mee-lee*

Igbo: *ee'-boh*

Ikemefuna: *ee-kay-may'-foo-na*

mbari: *mbah'-ree*

Ndulue: *n'-doo-le*

Nwakibie: *nwa'-kee-byeh'*

Nwayieke: *nwah-ye'-ke*

Umuofia: *oo'-moo-off'-yah*

Things Fall Apart

Turning and turning in the widening gyre
The falcon cannot hear the falconer;
Things fall apart; the centre cannot hold;
Mere anarchy is loosed upon the world . . .
 —W. B. Yeats, "The Second Coming"

Part One

1

Okonkwo[1] was well known throughout the nine villages and even beyond. His fame rested on solid personal achievements. As a young man of eighteen he had brought honor to his village by throwing Amalinze the Cat. Amalinze was the great wrestler who for seven years was unbeaten, from Umuofia to Mbaino.[2] He was called the Cat because his back would never touch the earth. It was this man that Okonkwo threw in a fight which the old men agreed was one of the fiercest since the founder of their town engaged a spirit of the wild for seven days and seven nights.

The drums beat and the flutes sang and the spectators held their breath. Amalinze was a wily craftsman, but Okonkwo was as slippery as a fish in water. Every nerve and every muscle stood out on their arms, on their backs and their thighs, and one almost heard them stretching to breaking point. In the end Okonkwo threw the Cat.

That was many years ago, twenty years or more, and during this time Okonkwo's fame had grown like a bush-fire in the harmattan.[3] He was tall

---

1. "Four Settlements." Umuofia means "Man [*oko*] Born on Nkwo Day"; the name also suggests stubborn male pride.   2. Literally, "Children of the Forest" but *ofia*, "forest," also means "bush" or land untouched by European influence.   3. A dusty wind from the Sahara.

and huge, and his bushy eyebrows and wide nose gave him a very severe look. He breathed heavily, and it was said that, when he slept, his wives and children in their houses could hear him breathe. When he walked, his heels hardly touched the ground and he seemed to walk on springs, as if he was going to pounce on somebody. And he did pounce on people quite often. He had a slight stammer and whenever he was angry and could not get his words out quickly enough, he would use his fists. He had no patience with unsuccessful men. He had had no patience with his father.

Unoka,[4] for that was his father's name, had died ten years ago. In his day he was lazy and improvident and was quite incapable of thinking about tomorrow. If any money came his way, and it seldom did, he immediately bought gourds of palm-wine, called round his neighbors and made merry. He always said that whenever he saw a dead man's mouth he saw the folly of not eating what one had in one's lifetime. Unoka was, of course, a debtor, and he owed every neighbor some money, from a few cowries[5] to quite substantial amounts.

He was tall but very thin and had a slight stoop. He wore a haggard and mournful look except when he was drinking or playing on his flute. He was very good on his flute, and his happiest moments were the two or three moons after the harvest when the village musicians brought down their instruments, hung above the fireplace. Unoka would play with them, his face beaming with blessedness and peace. Sometimes another village would ask Unoka's band and their dancing egwugwu[6] to come and stay with them and teach them their tunes. They would go to such hosts for as long as three or four markets,[7] making music and feasting. Unoka loved the good fare and the good fellowship, and he loved this season of the year, when the rains had stopped and the sun rose every morning with dazzling beauty. And it was not too hot either, because the cold and dry harmattan wind was blowing down from the north. Some years the harmattan was very severe and a dense haze hung on the atmosphere. Old men and children would then sit round log fires, warming their bodies. Unoka loved it all, and he loved the first kites[8] that returned with the dry season, and the children who sang songs of welcome to them. He would remember his own childhood, how he had often wandered around looking for a kite sailing leisurely against the blue sky. As soon as he found one he would sing with his whole being, welcoming it back from its long, long journey, and asking it if it had brought home any lengths of cloth.

That was years ago, when he was young. Unoka, the grown-up, was a failure. He was poor and his wife and children had barely enough to eat. People laughed at him because he was a loafer, and they swore never to lend him any more money because he never paid back. But Unoka was such a man that he always succeeded in borrowing more, and piling up his debts.

4. "Home Is Supreme."   5. Glossy half-inch-long tan-and-white shells, collected in strings and used as money. A bag of twenty-four thousand cowries weighed about sixty pounds and, at the time of the story, was worth approximately one British pound.   6. Here, masked performers as part of musical entertainment.   7. Counting one important market day a week, roughly two English weeks. The Igbo week has four days: Eke, Oye, Afo, and Nkwo. Eke is a rest day and the main market day; Afo, a half day on the farm; and Oye and Nkwo, full work days.   8. A kind of hawk.

One day a neighbor called Okoye[9] came in to see him. He was reclining on a mud bed in his hut playing on the flute. He immediately rose and shook hands with Okoye, who then unrolled the goatskin which he carried under his arm, and sat down. Unoka went into an inner room and soon returned with a small wooden disc containing a kola nut, some alligator pepper and a lump of white chalk.[1]

"I have kola," he announced when he sat down, and passed the disc over to his guest.

"Thank you. He who brings kola brings life. But I think you ought to break it," replied Okoye, passing back the disc.

"No, it is for you, I think," and they argued like this for a few moments before Unoka accepted the honor of breaking the kola. Okoye, meanwhile, took the lump of chalk, drew some lines on the floor, and then painted his big toe.[2]

As he broke the kola, Unoka prayed to their ancestors for life and health, and for protection against their enemies. When they had eaten they talked about many things: about the heavy rains which were drowning the yams, about the next ancestral feast and about the impending war with the village of Mbaino. Unoka was never happy when it came to wars. He was in fact a coward and could not bear the sight of blood. And so he changed the subject and talked about music, and his face beamed. He could hear in his mind's ear the blood-stirring and intricate rhythms of the *ekwe* and the *udu* and the *ogene*,[3] and he could hear his own flute weaving in and out of them, decorating them with a colorful and plaintive tune. The total effect was gay and brisk, but if one picked out the flute as it went up and down and then broke up into short snatches, one saw that there was sorrow and grief there.

Okoye was also a musician. He played on the *ogene*. But he was not a failure like Unoka. He had a large barn full of yams and he had three wives. And now he was going to take the Idemili title,[4] the third highest in the land. It was a very expensive ceremony and he was gathering all his resources together. That was in fact the reason why he had come to see Unoka. He cleared his throat and began:

"Thank you for the kola. You may have heard of the title I intend to take shortly."

Having spoken plainly so far, Okoye said the next half a dozen sentences in proverbs. Among the Ibo the art of conversation is regarded very highly, and proverbs are the palm-oil with which words are eaten. Okoye was a great talker and he spoke for a long time, skirting round the subject and then hitting it finally. In short, he was asking Unoka to return the two

---

9. "Man Born on Oye Day"; a generic "Everyman" name.   1. Signifies coolness and peace and is offered in rituals of hospitality so that the guest may draw his personal emblem on the floor. *Kola nut:* a bitter, caffeine-rich nut that is broken and eaten ceremonially; it indicates life or vitality. *Alligator pepper:* black pepper, known as the "pepper for kola" to distinguish it from cooking pepper, or chilies. 2. If the guest has taken the first title, he marks his big toe. Higher titles require different facial markings.   3. A bell-shaped gong made from two pieces of sheet iron. *Ekwe:* a wooden drum, about three feet long; it produces high and low tones (as does the Igbo language). *Udu:* a clay pot with a hole to one side of the neck opening; various resonant tones are produced when the hole is struck with one hand while the other hand covers or uncovers the top.   4. A title of honor named after the river god Idemili, to whom the python is sacred. *Barn:* not a building, but a walled enclosure for the yam stacks (frames on which individual yams are tied, shaded with palm leaves, and exposed to circulating air).

hundred cowries he had borrowed from him more than two years before. As soon as Unoka understood what his friend was driving at, he burst out laughing. He laughed loud and long and his voice rang out clear as the *ogene*, and tears stood in his eyes. His visitor was amazed, and sat speechless. At the end, Unoka was able to give an answer between fresh outbursts of mirth.

"Look at that wall," he said, pointing at the far wall of his hut, which was rubbed with red earth so that it shone. "Look at those lines of chalk;" and Okoye saw groups of short perpendicular lines drawn in chalk. There were five groups, and the smallest group had ten lines. Unoka had a sense of the dramatic and so he allowed a pause, in which he took a pinch of snuff and sneezed noisily, and then he continued: "Each group there represents a debt to someone, and each stroke is one hundred cowries. You see, I owe that man a thousand cowries. But he has not come to wake me up in the morning for it. I shall pay you, but not today. Our elders say that the sun will shine on those who stand before it shines on those who kneel under them. I shall pay my big debts first." And he took another pinch of snuff, as if that was paying the big debts first. Okoye rolled his goatskin and departed.

When Unoka died he had taken no title at all and he was heavily in debt. Any wonder then that his son Okonkwo was ashamed of him? Fortunately, among these people a man was judged according to his worth and not according to the worth of his father. Okonkwo was clearly cut out for great things. He was still young but he had won fame as the greatest wrestler in the nine villages. He was a wealthy farmer and had two barns full of yams, and had just married his third wife. To crown it all he had taken two titles and had shown incredible prowess in two inter-tribal wars. And so although Okonkwo was still young, he was already one of the greatest men of his time. Age was respected among his people, but achievement was revered. As the elders said, if a child washed his hands he could eat with kings. Okonkwo had clearly washed his hands and so he ate with kings and elders. And that was how he came to look after the doomed lad who was sacrificed to the village of Umuofia by their neighbors to avoid war and bloodshed. The ill-fated lad was called Ikemefuna.[5]

2

Okonkwo had just blown out the palm-oil lamp and stretched himself on his bamboo bed when he heard the *ogene* of the town crier piercing the still night air. *Gome, gome, gome, gome,* boomed the hollow metal. Then the crier gave his message, and at the end of it beat his instrument again. And this was the message. Every man of Umuofia was asked to gather at the market place tomorrow morning. Okonkwo wondered what was amiss, for he knew certainly that something was amiss. He had discerned a clear overtone of tragedy in the crier's voice, and even now he could still hear it as it grew dimmer and dimmer in the distance.

The night was very quiet. It was always quiet except on moonlight nights. Darkness held a vague terror for these people, even the bravest

5. "My strength should not be dissipated."

among them. Children were warned not to whistle at night for fear of evil spirits. Dangerous animals became even more sinister and uncanny in the dark. A snake was never called by its name at night, because it would hear. It was called a string. And so on this particular night as the crier's voice was gradually swallowed up in the distance, silence returned to the world, a vibrant silence made more intense by the universal trill of a million million forest insects.

On a moonlight night it would be different. The happy voices of children playing in open fields would then be heard. And perhaps those not so young would be playing in pairs in less open places, and old men and women would remember their youth. As the Ibo say: "When the moon is shining the cripple becomes hungry for a walk."

But this particular night was dark and silent. And in all the nine villages of Umuofia a town crier with his *ogene* asked every man to be present tomorrow morning. Okonkwo on his bamboo bed tried to figure out the nature of the emergency—war with a neighboring clan? That seemed the most likely reason, and he was not afraid of war. He was a man of action, a man of war. Unlike his father he could stand the look of blood. In Umuofia's latest war he was the first to bring home a human head. That was his fifth head; and he was not an old man yet. On great occasions such as the funeral of a village celebrity he drank his palm-wine from his first human head.

In the morning the market place was full. There must have been about ten thousand men there, all talking in low voices. At last Ogbuefi Ezeugo stood up in the midst of them and bellowed four times, "*Umuofia kwenu*,"[6] and on each occasion he faced a different direction and seemed to push the air with a clenched fist. And ten thousand men answered "*Yaa!*" each time. Then there was perfect silence. Ogbuefi Ezeugo was a powerful orator and was always chosen to speak on such occasions. He moved his hand over his white head and stroked his white beard. He then adjusted his cloth, which was passed under his right armpit and tied above his left shoulder.

"*Umuofia kwenu*," he bellowed a fifth time, and the crowd yelled in answer. And then suddenly like one possessed he shot out his left hand and pointed in the direction of Mbaino, and said through gleaming white teeth firmly clenched: "Those sons of wild animals have dared to murder a daughter of Umuofia." He threw his head down and gnashed his teeth, and allowed a murmur of suppressed anger to sweep the crowd. When he began again, the anger on his face was gone and in its place a sort of smile hovered, more terrible and more sinister than the anger. And in a clear unemotional voice he told Umuofia how their daughter had gone to market at Mbaino and had been killed. That woman, said Ezeugo, was the wife of Ogbuefi Udo,[7] and he pointed to a man who sat near him with a bowed head. The crowd then shouted with anger and thirst for blood.

Many others spoke, and at the end it was decided to follow the normal

---

6. "United Umuofia!" An orator's call on the audience to respond as a group. *Ogbuefi*: "Cow Killer" (literal trans.); indicates someone who has taken a high title (for example, the Idemili title) for which the celebration ceremony requires the slaughter of a cow. *Ezeugo*: a name denoting a priest or high initiate, someone who wears the eagle feather.   7. "Peace."

course of action. An ultimatum was immediately dispatched to Mbaino asking them to choose between war on the one hand, and on the other the offer of a young man and a virgin as compensation.

Umuofia was feared by all its neighbors. It was powerful in war and in magic, and its priests and medicine men were feared in all the surrounding country. Its most potent war-medicine was as old as the clan itself. Nobody knew how old. But on one point there was general agreement—the active principle in that medicine had been an old woman with one leg. In fact, the medicine itself was called *agadi-nwayi*, or old woman. It had its shrine in the center of Umuofia, in a cleared spot. And if anybody was so foolhardy as to pass by the shrine after dusk he was sure to see the old woman hopping about.

And so the neighboring clans who naturally knew of these things feared Umuofia, and would not go to war against it without first trying a peaceful settlement. And in fairness to Umuofia it should be recorded that it never went to war unless its case was clear and just and was accepted as such by its Oracle—the Oracle of the Hills and the Caves. And there were indeed occasions when the Oracle had forbidden Umuofia to wage a war. If the clan had disobeyed the Oracle they would surely have been beaten, because their dreaded *agadi-nwayi* would never fight what the Ibo call *a fight of blame*.

But the war that now threatened was a just war. Even the enemy clan knew that. And so when Okonkwo of Umuofia arrived at Mbaino as the proud and imperious emissary of war, he was treated with great honor and respect, and two days later he returned home with a lad of fifteen and a young virgin. The lad's name was Ikemefuna, whose sad story is still told in Umuofia unto this day.

The elders, or *ndichie*, met to hear a report of Okonkwo's mission. At the end they decided, as everybody knew they would, that the girl should go to Ogbuefi Udo to replace his murdered wife. As for the boy, he belonged to the clan as a whole, and there was no hurry to decide his fate. Okonkwo was, therefore, asked on behalf of the clan to look after him in the interim. And so for three years Ikemefuna lived in Okonkwo's household.

Okonkwo ruled his household with a heavy hand. His wives, especially the youngest, lived in perpetual fear of his fiery temper, and so did his little children. Perhaps down in his heart Okonkwo was not a cruel man. But his whole life was dominated by fear, the fear of failure and of weakness. It was deeper and more intimate than the fear of evil and capricious gods and of magic, the fear of the forest, and of the forces of nature, malevolent, red in tooth and claw. Okonkwo's fear was greater than these. It was not external but lay deep within himself. It was the fear of himself, lest he should be found to resemble his father. Even as a little boy he had resented his father's failure and weakness, and even now he still remembered how he had suffered when a playmate had told him that his father was *agbala*. That was how Okonkwo first came to know that *agbala* was not only another name for a woman, it could also mean a man who had taken no title. And so Okonkwo was ruled by one passion—to hate everything that his father Unoka had loved. One of those things was gentleness and another was idleness.

During the planting season Okonkwo worked daily on his farms from cock-crow until the chickens went to roost. He was a very strong man and rarely felt fatigue. But his wives and young children were not as strong, and so they suffered. But they dared not complain openly. Okonkwo's first son, Nwoye,[8] was then twelve years old but was already causing his father great anxiety for his incipient laziness. At any rate, that was how it looked to his father, and he sought to correct him by constant nagging and beating. And so Nwoye was developing into a sad-faced youth.

Okonkwo's prosperity was visible in his household. He had a large compound enclosed by a thick wall of red earth. His own hut, or *obi*, stood immediately behind the only gate in the red walls. Each of his three wives had her own hut, which together formed a half moon behind the *obi*. The barn was built against one end of the red walls, and long stacks of yam stood out prosperously in it. At the opposite end of the compound was a shed for the goats, and each wife built a small attachment to her hut for the hens. Near the barn was a small house, the "medicine house" or shrine where Okonkwo kept the wooden symbols of his personal god and of his ancestral spirits. He worshiped them with sacrifices of kola nut, food and palm-wine, and offered prayers to them on behalf of himself, his three wives and eight children.

So when the daughter of Umuofia was killed in Mbaino, Ikemefuna came into Okonkwo's household. When Okonkwo brought him home that day he called his most senior wife and handed him over to her.

"He belongs to the clan," he told her. "So look after him."

"Is he staying long with us?" she asked.

"Do what you are told, woman," Okonkwo thundered, and stammered. "When did you become one of the *ndichie* of Umuofia?"

And so Nwoye's mother took Ikemefuna to her hut and asked no more questions.

As for the boy himself, he was terribly afraid. He could not understand what was happening to him or what he had done. How could he know that his father had taken a hand in killing a daughter of Umuofia? All he knew was that a few men had arrived at their house, conversing with his father in low tones, and at the end he had been taken out and handed over to a stranger. His mother had wept bitterly, but he had been too surprised to weep. And so the stranger had brought him, and a girl, a long, long way from home, through lonely forest paths. He did not know who the girl was, and he never saw her again.

3

Okonkwo did not have the start in life which many young men usually had. He did not inherit a barn from his father. There was no barn to inherit. The story was told in Umuofia, of how his father, Unoka, had

8. "Child Born on Oye Day."

gone to consult the Oracle of the Hills and the Caves to find out why he always had a miserable harvest.

The Oracle was called Agbala,[9] and people came from far and near to consult it. They came when misfortune dogged their steps or when they had a dispute with their neighbors. They came to discover what the future held for them or to consult the spirits of their departed fathers.

The way into the shrine was a round hole at the side of a hill, just a little bigger than the round opening into a henhouse. Worshipers and those who came to seek knowledge from the god crawled on their belly through the hole and found themselves in a dark, endless space in the presence of Agbala. No one had ever beheld Agbala, except his priestess. But no one who had ever crawled into his awful shrine had come out without the fear of his power. His priestess stood by the sacred fire which she built in the heart of the cave and proclaimed the will of the god. The fire did not burn with a flame. The glowing logs only served to light up vaguely the dark figure of the priestess.

Sometimes a man came to consult the spirit of his dead father or relative. It was said that when such a spirit appeared, the man saw it vaguely in the darkness, but never heard its voice. Some people even said that they had heard the spirits flying and flapping their wings against the roof of the cave.

Many years ago when Okonkwo was still a boy his father, Unoka, had gone to consult Agbala. The priestess in those days was a woman called Chika.[1] She was full of the power of her god, and she was greatly feared. Unoka stood before her and began his story.

"Every year," he said sadly, "before I put any crop in the earth, I sacrifice a cock to Ani, the owner of all land. It is the law of our fathers. I also kill a cock at the shrine of Ifejioku, the god of yams. I clear the bush and set fire to it when it is dry. I sow the yams when the first rain has fallen, and stake them when the young tendrils appear. I weed—"

"Hold your peace!" screamed the priestess, her voice terrible as it echoed through the dark void. "You have offended neither the gods nor your fathers. And when a man is at peace with his gods and his ancestors, his harvest will be good or bad according to the strength of his arm. You, Unoka, are known in all the clan for the weakness of your machete and your hoe. When your neighbors go out with their ax to cut down virgin forests, you sow your yams on exhausted farms that take no labor to clear. They cross seven rivers to make their farms; you stay at home and offer sacrifices to a reluctant soil. Go home and work like a man."

Unoka was an ill-fated man. He had a bad *chi* or personal god, and evil fortune followed him to the grave, or rather to his death, for he had no grave. He died of the swelling which was an abomination to the earth goddess. When a man was afflicted with swelling in the stomach and the limbs he was not allowed to die in the house. He was carried to the Evil Forest and left there to die. There was the story of a very stubborn man who staggered back to his house and had to be carried again to the forest and tied to a tree. The sickness was an abomination to the earth, and so

---

9. The Oracle is masculine, but his priestess, or Voice, is feminine.   1. "Sky Is Supreme."

the victim could not be buried in her bowels. He died and rotted away above the earth, and was not given the first or the second burial. Such was Unoka's fate. When they carried him away, he took with him his flute.

With a father like Unoka, Okonkwo did not have the start in life which many young men had. He neither inherited a barn nor a title, nor even a young wife. But in spite of these disadvantages, he had begun even in his father's lifetime to lay the foundations of a prosperous future. It was slow and painful. But he threw himself into it like one possessed. And indeed he was possessed by the fear of his father's contemptible life and shameful death.

There was a wealthy man in Okonkwo's village who had three huge barns, nine wives and thirty children. His name was Nwakibie[2] and he had taken the highest but one title which a man could take in the clan. It was for this man that Okonkwo worked to earn his first seed yams.

He took a pot of palm-wine and a cock to Nwakibie. Two elderly neighbors were sent for, and Nwakibie's two grown-up sons were also present in his *obi*. He presented a kola nut and an alligator pepper, which were passed round for all to see and then returned to him. He broke the nut saying: "We shall all live. We pray for life, children, a good harvest and happiness. You will have what is good for you and I will have what is good for me. Let the kite perch and let the eagle perch too. If one says no to the other, let his wing break."

After the kola nut had been eaten Okonkwo brought his palm-wine from the corner of the hut where it had been placed and stood it in the center of the group. He addressed Nwakibie, calling him "Our father."

"*Nna ayi*," he said. "I have brought you this little kola. As our people say, a man who pays respect to the great paves the way for his own greatness. I have come to pay you my respects and also to ask a favor. But let us drink the wine first."

Everybody thanked Okonkwo and the neighbors brought out their drinking horns from the goatskin bags they carried. Nwakibie brought down his own horn, which was fastened to the rafters. The younger of his sons, who was also the youngest man in the group, moved to the center, raised the pot on his left knee and began to pour out the wine. The first cup went to Okonkwo, who must taste his wine before anyone else.[3] Then the group drank, beginning with the eldest man. When everyone had drunk two or three horns, Nwakibie sent for his wives. Some of them were not at home and only four came in.

"Is Anasi not in?" he asked them. They said she was coming. Anasi was the first[4] wife and the others could not drink before her, and so they stood waiting.

Anasi was a middle-aged woman, tall and strongly built. There was authority in her bearing and she looked every inch the ruler of the women-folk in a large and prosperous family. She wore the anklet of her husband's titles, which the first wife alone could wear.

---

2. "The Child Surpasses His Neighbors."   3. A ceremonial gesture; one who gives wine tastes it first to show that it is not poisoned.   4. "First" or "favorite" wife—not always the same.

She walked up to her husband and accepted the horn from him. She then went down on one knee, drank a little and handed back the horn. She rose, called him by his name and went back to her hut. The other wives drank in the same way, in their proper order, and went away.

The men then continued their drinking and talking. Ogbuefi Idigo was talking about the palm-wine tapper, Obiako, who suddenly gave up his trade.

"There must be something behind it," he said, wiping the foam of wine from his mustache with the back of his left hand. "There must be a reason for it. A toad does not run in the daytime for nothing."

"Some people say the Oracle warned him that he would fall off a palm tree and kill himself," said Akukalia.

"Obiako has always been a strange one," said Nwakibie. "I have heard that many years ago, when his father had not been dead very long, he had gone to consult the Oracle. The Oracle said to him, 'Your dead father wants you to sacrifice a goat to him.' Do you know what he told the Oracle? He said, 'Ask my dead father if he ever had a fowl when he was alive.'" Everybody laughed heartily except Okonkwo, who laughed uneasily because, as the saying goes, an old woman is always uneasy when dry bones are mentioned in a proverb. Okonkwo remembered his own father.

At last the young man who was pouring out the wine held up half a horn of the thick, white dregs and said, "What we are eating is finished." "We have seen it," the others replied. "Who will drink the dregs?" he asked. "Whoever has a job in hand," said Idigo, looking at Nwakibie's elder son Igwelo with a malicious twinkle in his eye.

Everyone agreed that Igwelo should drink the dregs. He accepted the half-full horn from his brother and drank it. As Idigo had said, Igwelo had a job in hand because he had married his first wife a month or two before. The thick dregs of palm-wine were supposed to be good for men who were going in to their wives.

After the wine had been drunk Okonkwo laid his difficulties before Nwakibie.

"I have come to you for help," he said. "Perhaps you can already guess what it is. I have cleared a farm but have no yams to sow. I know what it is to ask a man to trust another with his yams, especially these days when young men are afraid of hard work. I am not afraid of work. The lizard that jumped from the high iroko tree to the ground said he would praise himself if no one else did. I began to fend for myself at an age when most people still suck at their mothers' breasts. If you give me some yam seeds I shall not fail you."

Nwakibie cleared his throat. "It pleases me to see a young man like you these days when our youth has gone so soft. Many young men have come to me to ask for yams but I have refused because I knew they would just dump them in the earth and leave them to be choked by weeds. When I say no to them they think I am hard-hearted. But it is not so. Eneke the bird[5] says that since men have learned to shoot without missing, he has

---

5. Proverbial.

learned to fly without perching. I have learned to be stingy with my yams. But I can trust you. I know it as I look at you. As our fathers said, you can tell a ripe corn by its look. I shall give you twice four hundred yams. Go ahead and prepare your farm."

Okonkwo thanked him again and again and went home feeling happy. He knew that Nwakibie would not refuse him, but he had not expected he would be so generous. He had not hoped to get more than four hundred seeds. He would now have to make a bigger farm. He hoped to get another four hundred yams from one of his father's friends at Isiuzo.[6]

Sharecropping was a very slow way of building up a barn of one's own. After all the toil one only got a third of the harvest. But for a young man whose father had no yams, there was no other way. And what made it worse in Okonkwo's case was that he had to support his mother and two sisters from his meager harvest. And supporting his mother also meant supporting his father. She could not be expected to cook and eat while her husband starved. And so at a very early age when he was striving desperately to build a barn through sharecropping Okonkwo was also fending for his father's house. It was like pouring grains of corn into a bag full of holes. His mother and sisters worked hard enough, but they grew women's crops, like coco-yams, beans and cassava. Yam, the king of crops, was a man's crop.[7]

The year that Okonkwo took eight hundred seed-yams from Nwakibie was the worst year in living memory. Nothing happened at its proper time; it was either too early or too late. It seemed as if the world had gone mad. The first rains were late, and, when they came, lasted only a brief moment. The blazing sun returned, more fierce than it had ever been known, and scorched all the green that had appeared with the rains. The earth burned like hot coals and roasted all the yams that had been sown. Like all good farmers, Okonkwo had begun to sow with the first rains. He had sown four hundred seeds when the rains dried up and the heat returned. He watched the sky all day for signs of rain clouds and lay awake all night. In the morning he went back to his farm and saw the withering tendrils. He had tried to protect them from the smoldering earth by making rings of thick sisal leaves around them. But by the end of the day the sisal rings were burned dry and gray. He changed them every day, and prayed that the rain might fall in the night. But the drought continued for eight market weeks and the yams were killed.

Some farmers had not planted their yams yet. They were the lazy easygoing ones who always put off clearing their farms as long as they could. This year they were the wise ones. They sympathized with their neighbors with much shaking of the head, but inwardly they were happy for what they took to be their own foresight.

Okonkwo planted what was left of his seed-yams when the rains finally returned. He had one consolation. The yams he had sown before the

6. "Head of the Road," a small town.   7. Yams, a staple food in Western Africa, were a sacred crop generally cultivated only by men and eaten either roasted or boiled. Coco-yams (a brown root also called taro) and cassava (or manioc, which is fermented to remove natural arsenic) were low-status root vegetables, prepared for eating by boiling and pounding.

drought were his own, the harvest of the previous year. He still had the eight hundred from Nwakibie and the four hundred from his father's friend. So he would make a fresh start.

But the year had gone mad. Rain fell as it had never fallen before. For days and nights together it poured down in violent torrents, and washed away the yam heaps. Trees were uprooted and deep gorges appeared everywhere. Then the rain became less violent. But it went from day to day without a pause. The spell of sunshine which always came in the middle of the wet season did not appear. The yams put on luxuriant green leaves, but every farmer knew that without sunshine the tubers would not grow.

That year the harvest was sad, like a funeral, and many farmers wept as they dug up the miserable and rotting yams. One man tied his cloth to a tree branch and hanged himself.

Okonkwo remembered that tragic year with a cold shiver throughout the rest of his life. It always surprised him when he thought of it later that he did not sink under the load of despair. He knew that he was a fierce fighter, but that year had been enough to break the heart of a lion.

"Since I survived that year," he always said, "I shall survive anything." He put it down to his inflexible will.

His father, Unoka, who was then an ailing man, had said to him during that terrible harvest month: "Do not despair. I know you will not despair. You have a manly and a proud heart. A proud heart can survive a general failure because such a failure does not prick its pride. It is more difficult and more bitter when a man fails *alone*."

Unoka was like that in his last days. His love of talk had grown with age and sickness. It tried Okonkwo's patience beyond words.

4

"Looking at a king's mouth," said an old man, "one would think he never sucked at his mother's breast." He was talking about Okonkwo, who had risen so suddenly from great poverty and misfortune to be one of the lords of the clan. The old man bore no ill will towards Okonkwo. Indeed he respected him for his industry and success. But he was struck, as most people were, by Okonkwo's brusqueness in dealing with less successful men. Only a week ago a man had contradicted him at a kindred meeting which they held to discuss the next ancestral feast. Without looking at the man Okonkwo had said: "This meeting is for men." The man who had contradicted him had no titles. That was why he had called him a woman. Okonkwo knew how to kill a man's spirit.

Everybody at the kindred meeting took sides with Osugo[8] when Okonkwo called him a woman. The oldest man present said sternly that those whose palm-kernels were cracked for them by a benevolent spirit should not forget to be humble. Okonkwo said he was sorry for what he had said, and the meeting continued.

But it was really not true that Okonkwo's palm-kernels had been cracked for him by a benevolent spirit. He had cracked them himself. Anyone who knew his grim struggle against poverty and misfortune could

8. "Low-Status [*osu*] Person."

not say he had been lucky. If ever a man deserved his success, that man was Okonkwo. An an early age he had achieved fame as the greatest wrestler in all the land. That was not luck. At the most one could say that his *chi* or personal god was good. But the Ibo people have a proverb that when a man says yes his *chi* says yes also. Okonkwo said yes very strongly; so his *chi* agreed. And not only his *chi* but his clan too, because it judged a man by the work of his hands. That was why Okonkwo had been chosen by the nine villages to carry a message of war to their enemies unless they agreed to give up a young man and a virgin to atone for the murder of Udo's wife. And such was the deep fear that their enemies had for Umuofia that they treated Okonkwo like a king and brought him a virgin who was given to Udo as wife, and the lad Ikemefuna.

The elders of the clan had decided that Ikemefuna should be in Okonkwo's care for a while. But no one thought it would be as long as three years. They seemed to forget all about him as soon as they had taken the decision.

At first Ikemefuna was very much afraid. Once or twice he tried to run away, but he did not know where to begin. He thought of his mother and his three-year-old sister and wept bitterly. Nwoye's mother was very kind to him and treated him as one of her own children. But all he said was: "When shall I go home?" When Okonkwo heard that he would not eat any food he came into the hut with a big stick in his hand and stood over him while he swallowed his yams, trembling. A few moments later he went behind the hut and began to vomit painfully. Nwoye's mother went to him and placed her hands on his chest and on his back. He was ill for three market weeks, and when he recovered he seemed to have overcome his great fear and sadness.

He was by nature a very lively boy and he gradually became popular in Okonkwo's household, especially with the children. Okonkwo's son, Nwoye, who was two years younger, became quite inseparable from him because he seemed to know everything. He could fashion out flutes from bamboo stems and even from the elephant grass. He knew the names of all the birds and could set clever traps for the little bush rodents. And he knew which trees made the strongest bows.

Even Okonkwo himself became very fond of the boy—inwardly of course. Okonkwo never showed any emotion openly, unless it be the emotion of anger. To show affection was a sign of weakness; the only thing worth demonstrating was strength. He therefore treated Ikemefuna as he treated everybody else—with a heavy hand. But there was no doubt that he liked the boy. Sometimes when he went to big village meetings or communal ancestral feasts he allowed Ikemefuna to accompany him, like a son, carrying his stool and his goatskin bag. And, indeed, Ikemefuna called him father.

Ikemefuna came to Umuofia at the end of the carefree season between harvest and planting. In fact he recovered from his illness only a few days before the Week of Peace began. And that was also the year Okonkwo broke the peace, and was punished, as was the custom, by Ezeani, the priest of the earth goddess.

Okonkwo was provoked to justifiable anger by his youngest wife, who went to plait her hair at her friend's house and did not return early enough to cook the afternoon meal. Okonkwo did not know at first that she was not at home. After waiting in vain for her dish he went to her hut to see what she was doing. There was nobody in the hut and the fireplace was cold.

"Where is Ojiugo?" he asked his second wife, who came out of her hut to draw water from a gigantic pot in the shade of a small tree in the middle of the compound.

"She has gone to plait her hair."

Okonkwo bit his lips as anger welled up within him.

"Where are her children? Did she take them?" he asked with unusual coolness and restraint.

"They are here," answered his first wife, Nwoye's mother. Okonkwo bent down and looked into her hut. Ojiugo's children were eating with the children of his first wife.

"Did she ask you to feed them before she went?"

"Yes," lied Nwoye's mother, trying to minimize Ojiugo's thoughtlessness.

Okonkwo knew she was not speaking the truth. He walked back to his *obi* to await Ojiugo's return. And when she returned he beat her very heavily. In his anger he had forgotten that it was the Week of Peace. His first two wives ran out in great alarm pleading with him that it was the sacred week. But Okonkwo was not the man to stop beating somebody half-way through, not even for fear of a goddess.

Okonkwo's neighbors heard his wife crying and sent their voices over the compound walls to ask what was the matter. Some of them came over to see for themselves. It was unheard of to beat somebody during the sacred week.

Before it was dusk Ezeani, who was the priest of the earth goddess, Ani, called on Okonkwo in his *obi*. Okonkwo brought out kola nut and placed it before the priest.

"Take away your kola nut. I shall not eat in the house of a man who has no respect for our gods and ancestors."

Okonkwo tried to explain to him what his wife had done, but Ezeani seemed to pay no attention. He held a short staff in his hand which he brought down on the floor to emphasize his points.

"Listen to me," he said when Okonkwo had spoken. "You are not a stranger in Umuofia. You know as well as I do that our forefathers ordained that before we plant any crops in the earth we should observe a week in which a man does not say a harsh word to his neighbor. We live in peace with our fellows to honor our great goddess of the earth without whose blessing our crops will not grow. You have committed a great evil." He brought down his staff heavily on the floor. "Your wife was at fault, but even if you came into your *obi* and found her lover on top of her, you would still have committed a great evil to beat her." His staff came down again. "The evil you have done can ruin the whole clan. The earth goddess whom you have insulted may refuse to give us her increase, and we shall all perish." His tone now changed from anger to command. "You will bring to the shrine of Ani tomorrow one she-goat, one hen, a length of cloth and a hundred cowries." He rose and left the hut.

Okonkwo did as the priest said. He also took with him a pot of palm-wine. Inwardly, he was repentant. But he was not the man to go about telling his neighbors that he was in error. And so people said he had no respect for the gods of the clan. His enemies said his good fortune had gone to his head. They called him the little bird *nza* who so far forgot himself after a heavy meal that he challenged his *chi*.[9]

No work was done during the Week of Peace. People called on their neighbors and drank palm-wine. This year they talked of nothing else but the *nso-ani*[1] which Okonkwo had committed. It was the first time for many years that a man had broken the sacred peace. Even the oldest men could only remember one or two other occasions somewhere in the dim past.

Ogbuefi Ezeudu, who was the oldest man in the village, was telling two other men who came to visit him that the punishment for breaking the Peace of Ani had become very mild in their clan.

"It has not always been so," he said. "My father told me that he had been told that in the past a man who broke the peace was dragged on the ground through the village until he died. But after a while this custom was stopped because it spoiled the peace which it was meant to preserve."

"Somebody told me yesterday," said one of the younger men, "that in some clans it is an abomination for a man to die during the Week of Peace."

"It is indeed true," said Ogbuefi Ezeudu. "They have that custom in Obodoani.[2] If a man dies at this time he is not buried but cast into the Evil Forest. It is a bad custom which these people observe because they lack understanding. They throw away large numbers of men and women without burial. And what is the result? Their clan is full of the evil spirits of these unburied dead, hungry to do harm to the living."

After the Week of Peace every man and his family began to clear the bush to make new farms. The cut bush was left to dry and fire was then set to it. As the smoke rose into the sky kites appeared from different directions and hovered over the burning field in silent valediction. The rainy season was approaching when they would go away until the dry season returned.

Okonkwo spent the next few days preparing his seed-yams. He looked at each yam carefully to see whether it was good for sowing. Sometimes he decided that a yam was too big to be sown as one seed and he split it deftly along its length with his sharp knife. His eldest son, Nwoye, and Ikemefuna helped him by fetching the yams in long baskets from the barn and in counting the prepared seeds in groups of four hundred. Sometimes Okonkwo gave them a few yams each to prepare. But he always found fault with their effort, and he said so with much threatening.

"Do you think you are cutting up yams for cooking?" he asked Nwoye. "If you split another yam of this size, I shall break your jaw. You think you

9. Personal god. *Nza*: "the one that talks back" (literal trans.); a small aggressive bird. In the story, it is easily defeated (alternatively, caught by a hawk) when it becomes foolish enough to challenge its personal god.   1. Sin, abomination against the earth goddess Ani.   2. "The Town of the Land" (literal trans); that is, Anytown, Nigeria.

are still a child. I began to own a farm at your age. And you," he said to Ikemefuna, "do you not grow yams where you come from?"

Inwardly Okonkwo knew that the boys were still too young to understand fully the difficult art of preparing seed-yams. But he thought that one could not begin too early. Yam stood for manliness, and he who could feed his family on yams from one harvest to another was a very great man indeed. Okonkwo wanted his son to be a great farmer and a great man. He would stamp out the disquieting signs of laziness which he thought he already saw in him.

"I will not have a son who cannot hold up his head in the gathering of the clan. I would sooner strangle him with my own hands. And if you stand staring at me like that," he swore, "Amadiora³ will break your head for you!"

Some days later, when the land had been moistened by two or three heavy rains, Okonkwo and his family went to the farm with baskets of seed-yams, their hoes and machetes, and the planting began. They made single mounds of earth in straight lines all over the field and sowed the yams in them.

Yam, the king of crops, was a very exacting king. For three or four moons it demanded hard work and constant attention from cock-crow till the chickens went back to roost. The young tendrils were protected from earth-heat with rings of sisal leaves. As the rains became heavier the women planted maize, melons and beans between the yam mounds. The yams were then staked, first with little sticks and later with tall and big tree branches. The women weeded the farm three times at definite periods in the life of the yams, neither early nor late.

And now the rains had really come, so heavy and persistent that even the village rain-maker no longer claimed to be able to intervene. He could not stop the rain now, just as he would not attempt to start it in the heart of the dry season, without serious danger to his own health. The personal dynamism required to counter the forces of these extremes of weather would be far too great for the human frame.

And so nature was not interfered with in the middle of the rainy season. Sometimes it poured down in such thick sheets of water that earth and sky seemed merged in one gray wetness. It was then uncertain whether the low rumbling of Amadiora's thunder came from above or below. At such times, in each of the countless thatched huts of Umuofia, children sat around their mother's cooking fire telling stories, or with their father in his *obi* warming themselves from a log fire, roasting and eating maize. It was a brief resting period between the exacting and arduous planting season and the equally exacting but light-hearted month of harvests.

Ikemefuna had begun to feel like a member of Okonkwo's family. He still thought about his mother and his three-year-old sister, and he had moments of sadness and depression. But he and Nwoye had become so deeply attached to each other that such moments became less frequent and less poignant. Ikemefuna had an endless stock of folk tales. Even those

---

3. God of thunder and lightning.

which Nwoye knew already were told with a new freshness and the local flavor of a different clan. Nwoye remembered this period very vividly till the end of his life. He even remembered how he had laughed when Ikemefuna told him that the proper name for a corn cob with only a few scattered grains was *eze-agadi-nwayi*, or the teeth of an old woman. Nwoye's mind had gone immediately to Nwayieke,[4] who lived near the udala tree. She had about three teeth and was always smoking her pipe.

Gradually the rains became lighter and less frequent, and earth and sky once again became separate. The rain fell in thin, slanting showers through sunshine and quiet breeze. Children no longer stayed indoors but ran about singing:

> The rain is falling, the sun is shining,
> Alone Nnadi[5] is cooking and eating.

Nwoye always wondered who Nnadi was and why he should live all by himself, cooking and eating. In the end he decided that Nnadi must live in that land of Ikemefuna's favorite story where the ant holds his court in splendor and the sands dance forever.

5

The Feast of the New Yam was approaching and Umuofia was in a festival mood. It was an occasion for giving thanks to Ani, the earth goddess and the source of all fertility. Ani played a greater part in the life of the people than any other deity. She was the ultimate judge of morality and conduct. And what was more, she was in close communion with the departed fathers of the clan whose bodies had been committed to earth.

The Feast of the New Yam was held every year before the harvest began, to honor the earth goddess and the ancestral spirits of the clan. New yams could not be eaten until some had first been offered to these powers. Men and women, young and old, looked forward to the New Yam Festival because it began the season of plenty—the new year. On the last night before the festival, yams of the old year were all disposed of by those who still had them. The new year must begin with tasty, fresh yams and not the shriveled and fibrous crops of the previous year. All cooking pots, calabashes and wooden bowls were thoroughly washed, especially the wooden mortar in which yam was pounded. Yam foo-foo[6] and vegetable soup was the chief food in the celebration. So much of it was cooked that, no matter how heavily the family ate or how many friends and relatives they invited from neighboring villages, there was always a large quantity of food left over at the end of the day. The story was always told of a wealthy man who set before his guests a mound of foo-foo so high that those who sat on one side could not see what was happening on the other, and it was not until late in the evening that one of them saw for the first time his in-law who had arrived during the course of the meal and had fallen to on the opposite

---

4. "Woman Born on Eke Day." *Udala*: the African star apple tree.   5. "Father Is There" or "Father Exists."   6. A mashed, edible base that is shaped into balls with the fingers and then indented for cupping and eating soup.

side. It was only then that they exchanged greetings and shook hands over what was left of the food.

The New Yam Festival was thus an occasion for joy throughout Umuofia. And every man whose arm was strong, as the Ibo people say, was expected to invite large numbers of guests from far and wide. Okonkwo always asked his wives' relations, and since he now had three wives his guests would make a fairly big crowd.

But somehow Okonkwo could never become as enthusiastic over feasts as most people. He was a good eater and he could drink one or two fairly big gourds of palm-wine. But he was always uncomfortable sitting around for days waiting for a feast or getting over it. He would be very much happier working on his farm.

The festival was now only three days away. Okonkwo's wives had scrubbed the walls and the huts with red earth until they reflected light. They had then drawn patterns on them in white, yellow and dark green. They then set about painting themselves with cam wood and drawing beautiful black patterns on their stomachs and on their backs. The children were also decorated, especially their hair, which was shaved in beautiful patterns. The three women talked excitedly about the relations who had been invited, and the children reveled in the thought of being spoiled by these visitors from the motherland. Ikemefuna was equally excited. The New Yam Festival seemed to him to be a much bigger event here than in his own village, a place which was already becoming remote and vague in his imagination.

And then the storm burst. Okonkwo, who had been walking about aimlessly in his compound in suppressed anger, suddenly found an outlet.

"Who killed this banana tree?" he asked.

A hush fell on the compound immediately.

"Who killed this tree? Or are you all deaf and dumb?"

As a matter of fact the tree was very much alive. Okonkwo's second wife had merely cut a few leaves off it to wrap some food, and she said so. Without further argument Okonkwo gave her a sound beating and left her and her only daughter weeping. Neither of the other wives dared to interfere beyond an occasional and tentative, "It is enough, Okonkwo," pleaded from a reasonable distance.

His anger thus satisfied, Okonkwo decided to go out hunting. He had an old rusty gun made by a clever blacksmith who had come to live in Umuofia long ago. But although Okonkwo was a great man whose prowess was universally acknowledged, he was not a hunter. In fact he had not killed a rat with his gun. And so when he called Ikemefuna to fetch his gun, the wife who had just been beaten murmured something about guns that never shot. Unfortunately for her, Okonkwo heard it and ran madly into his room for the loaded gun, ran out again and aimed at her as she clambered over the dwarf wall of the barn. He pressed the trigger and there was a loud report accompanied by the wail of his wives and children. He threw down the gun and jumped into the barn, and there lay the woman, very much shaken and frightened but quite unhurt. He heaved a heavy sigh and went away with the gun.

In spite of this incident the New Yam Festival was celebrated with great joy in Okonkwo's household. Early that morning as he offered a sacrifice of new yam and palm-oil to his ancestors he asked them to protect him, his children and their mothers in the new year.

As the day wore on his in-laws arrived from three surrounding villages, and each party brought with them a huge pot of palm-wine. And there was eating and drinking till night, when Okonkwo's in-laws began to leave for their homes.

The second day of the new year was the day of the great wrestling match between Okonkwo's village and their neighbors. It was difficult to say which the people enjoyed more—the feasting and fellowship of the first day or the wrestling contest of the second. But there was one woman who had no doubt whatever in her mind. She was Okonkwo's second wife, Ekwefi, whom he nearly shot. There was no festival in all the seasons of the year which gave her as much pleasure as the wrestling match. Many years ago when she was the village beauty Okonkwo had won her heart by throwing the Cat in the greatest contest within living memory. She did not marry him then because he was too poor to pay her bride-price. But a few years later she ran away from her husband and came to live with Okonkwo. All this happened many years ago. Now Ekwefi[7] was a woman of forty-five who had suffered a great deal in her time. But her love of wrestling contests was still as strong as it was thirty years ago.

It was not yet noon on the second day of the New Yam Festival. Ekwefi and her only daughter, Ezinma,[8] sat near the fireplace waiting for the water in the pot to boil. The fowl Ekwefi had just killed was in the wooden mortar. The water began to boil, and in one deft movement she lifted the pot from the fire and poured the boiling water over the fowl. She put back the empty pot on the circular pad in the corner, and looked at her palms, which were black with soot. Ezinma was always surprised that her mother could lift a pot from the fire with her bare hands.

"Ekwefi," she said, "is it true that when people are grown up, fire does not burn them?" Ezinma, unlike most children, called her mother by her name.

"Yes," replied Ekwefi, too busy to argue. Her daughter was only ten years old but she was wiser than her years.

"But Nwoye's mother dropped her pot of hot soup the other day and it broke on the floor."

Ekwefi turned the hen over in the mortar and began to pluck the feathers.

"Ekwefi," said Ezinma, who had joined in plucking the feathers, "my eyelid is twitching."

"It means you are going to cry," said her mother.

"No," Ezinma said, "it is this eyelid, the top one."

"That means you will see something."

"What will I see?" she asked.

"How can I know?" Ekwefi wanted her to work it out herself.

"Oho," said Ezinma at last. "I know what it is—the wrestling match."

---

7. An abbreviation of "Do you have a cow?"; the cow being a symbol of wealth. Okonkwo would presumably have repaid Ekwefi's bride-price to her first husband.   8. "True Beauty" or goodness.

At last the hen was plucked clean. Ekwefi tried to pull out the horny beak but it was too hard. She turned round on her low stool and put the beak in the fire for a few moments. She pulled again and it came off.

"Ekwefi!" a voice called from one of the other huts. It was Nwoye's mother, Okonkwo's first wife.

"Is that me?" Ekwefi called back. That was the way people answered calls from outside. They never answered yes for fear it might be an evil spirit calling.

"Will you give Ezinma some fire to bring to me?" Her own children and Ikemefuna had gone to the stream.

Ekwefi put a few live coals into a piece of broken pot and Ezinma carried it across the clean swept compound to Nwoye's mother.

"Thank you, Nma," she said. She was peeling new yams, and in a basket beside her were green vegetables and beans.

"Let me make the fire for you," Ezinma offered.

"Thank you, Ezigbo," she said. She often called her Ezigbo, which means "the good one."

Ezinma went outside and brought some sticks from a huge bundle of firewood. She broke them into little pieces across the sole of her foot and began to build a fire, blowing it with her breath.

"You will blow your eyes out," said Nwoye's mother, looking up from the yams she was peeling. "Use the fan." She stood up and pulled out the fan which was fastened into one of the rafters. As soon as she got up, the troublesome nanny goat, which had been dutifully eating yam peelings, dug her teeth into the real thing, scooped out two mouthfuls and fled from the hut to chew the cud in the goats' shed. Nwoye's mother swore at her and settled down again to her peeling. Ezinma's fire was now sending up thick clouds of smoke. She went on fanning it until it burst into flames. Nwoye's mother thanked her and she went back to her mother's hut.

Just then the distant beating of drums began to reach them. It came from the direction of the ilo, the village playground. Every village had its own ilo which was as old as the village itself and where all the great ceremonies and dances took place. The drums beat the unmistakable wrestling dance—quick, light and gay, and it came floating on the wind.

Okonkwo cleared his throat and moved his feet to the beat of the drums. It filled him with fire as it had always done from his youth. He trembled with the desire to conquer and subdue. It was like the desire for a woman.

"We shall be late for the wrestling," said Ezinma to her mother.

"They will not begin until the sun goes down."

"But they are beating the drums."

"Yes. The drums begin at noon but the wrestling waits until the sun begins to sink. Go and see if your father has brought out yams for the afternoon."

"He has. Nwoye's mother is already cooking."

"Go and bring our own, then. We must cook quickly or we shall be late for the wrestling."

Ezinma ran in the direction of the barn and brought back two yams from the dwarf wall.

Ekwefi peeled the yams quickly. The troublesome nanny goat sniffed about, eating the peelings. She cut the yams into small pieces and began to prepare a pottage, using some of the chicken.

At that moment they heard someone crying just outside their compound. It was very much like Obiageli,[9] Nwoye's sister.

"Is that not Obiageli weeping?" Ekwefi called across the yard to Nwoye's mother.

"Yes," she replied. "She must have broken her waterpot."

The weeping was now quite close and soon the children filed in, carrying on their heads various sizes of pots suitable to their years. Ikemefuna came first with the biggest pot, closely followed by Nwoye and his two younger brothers. Obiageli brought up the rear, her face streaming with tears. In her hand was the cloth pad on which the pot should have rested on her head.

"What happened?" her mother asked, and Obiageli told her mournful story. Her mother consoled her and promised to buy her another pot.

Nwoye's younger brothers were about to tell their mother the true story of the accident when Ikemefuna looked at them sternly and they held their peace. The fact was that Obiageli had been making inyanga[1] with her pot. She had balanced it on her head, folded her arms in front of her and began to sway her waist like a grown-up young lady. When the pot fell down and broke she burst out laughing. She only began to weep when they got near the iroko tree outside their compound.

The drums were still beating, persistent and unchanging. Their sound was no longer a separate thing from the living village. It was like the pulsation of its heart. It throbbed in the air, in the sunshine, and even in the trees, and filled the village with excitement.

Ekwefi ladled her husband's share of the pottage into a bowl and covered it. Ezinma took it to him in his obi.

Okonkwo was sitting on a goatskin already eating his first wife's meal. Obiageli, who had brought it from her mother's hut, sat on the floor waiting for him to finish. Ezinma placed her mother's dish before him and sat with Obiageli.

"Sit like a woman!" Okonkwo shouted at her. Ezinma brought her two legs together and stretched them in front of her.

"Father, will you go to see the wrestling?" Ezinma asked after a suitable interval.

"Yes," he answered. "Will you go?"

"Yes." And after a pause she said: "Can I bring your chair for you?"

"No, that is a boy's job." Okonkwo was specially fond of Ezinma. She looked very much like her mother, who was once the village beauty. But his fondness only showed on very rare occasions.

"Obiageli broke her pot today," Ezinma said.

"Yes, she has told me about it," Okonkwo said between mouthfuls.

"Father," said Obiageli, "people should not talk when they are eating or pepper may go down the wrong way."

9. "Born to Eat" (born into prosperity).   1. Showing off.

"That is very true. Do you hear that, Ezinma? You are older than Obia-geli but she has more sense."

He uncovered his second wife's dish and began to eat from it. Obiageli took the first dish and returned to her mother's hut. And then Nkechi came in, bringing the third dish. Nkechi was the daughter of Okonkwo's third wife.

In the distance the drums continued to beat.

6

The whole village turned out on the *ilo*, men, women and children. They stood round in a huge circle leaving the center of the playground free. The elders and grandees of the village sat on their own stools brought there by their young sons or slaves. Okonkwo was among them. All others stood except those who came early enough to secure places on the few stands which had been built by placing smooth logs on forked pillars.

The wrestlers were not there yet and the drummers held the field. They too sat just in front of the huge circle of spectators, facing the elders. Behind them was the big and ancient silk-cotton tree which was sacred. Spirits of good children lived in that tree waiting to be born. On ordinary days young women who desired children came to sit under its shade.

There were seven drums and they were arranged according to their sizes in a long wooden basket. Three men beat them with sticks, working feverishly from one drum to another. They were possessed by the spirit of the drums.

The young men who kept order on these occasions dashed about, con-sulting among themselves and with the leaders of the two wrestling teams, who were still outside the circle, behind the crowd. Once in a while two young men carrying palm fronds ran round the circle and kept the crowd back by beating the ground in front of them or, if they were stubborn, their legs and feet.

At last the two teams danced into the circle and the crowd roared and clapped. The drums rose to a frenzy. The people surged forward. The young men who kept order flew around, waving their palm fronds. Old men nodded to the beat of the drums and remembered the days when they wrestled to its intoxicating rhythm.

The contest began with boys of fifteen or sixteen. There were only three such boys in each team. They were not the real wrestlers; they merely set the scene. Within a short time the first two bouts were over. But the third created a big sensation even among the elders who did not usually show their excitement so openly. It was as quick as the other two, perhaps even quicker. But very few people had ever seen that kind of wrestling before. As soon as the two boys closed in, one of them did something which no one could describe because it had been as quick as a flash. And the other boy was flat on his back. The crowd roared and clapped and for a while drowned the frenzied drums. Okonkwo sprang to his feet and quickly sat down again. Three young men from the victorious boy's team ran forward, carried him shoulder high and danced through the cheering crowd. Everybody soon knew who the boy was. His name was Maduka, the son of Obierika.[2]

The drummers stopped for a brief rest before the real matches. Their bodies shone with sweat, and they took up fans and began to fan themselves. They also drank water from small pots and ate kola nuts. They became ordinary human beings again, talking and laughing among themselves and with others who stood near them. The air, which had been stretched taut with excitement, relaxed again. It was as if water had been poured on the tightened skin of a drum. Many people looked around, perhaps for the first time, and saw those who stood or sat next to them.

"I did not know it was you," Ekwefi said to the woman who had stood shoulder to shoulder with her since the beginning of the matches.

"I do not blame you," said the woman. "I have never seen such a large crowd of people. Is it true that Okonkwo nearly killed you with his gun?"

"It is true indeed, my dear friend. I cannot yet find a mouth with which to tell the story."

"Your *chi* is very much awake, my friend. And how is my daughter, Ezinma?"

"She has been very well for some time now. Perhaps she has come to stay."

"I think she has. How old is she now?"

"She is about ten years old."

"I think she will stay. They usually stay if they do not die before the age of six."

"I pray she stays," said Ekwefi with a heavy sigh.

The woman with whom she talked was called Chielo.[3] She was the priestess of Agbala, the Oracle of the Hills and the Caves. In ordinary life Chielo was a widow with two children. She was very friendly with Ekwefi and they shared a common shed in the market. She was particularly fond of Ekwefi's only daughter, Ezinma, whom she called "my daughter." Quite often she bought beancakes and gave Ekwefi some to take home to Ezinma. Anyone seeing Chielo in ordinary life would hardly believe she was the same person who prophesied when the spirit of Agbala was upon her.

The drummers took up their sticks and the air shivered and grew tense like a tightened bow.

The two teams were ranged facing each other across the clear space. A young man from one team danced across the center to the other side and pointed at whomever he wanted to fight. They danced back to the center together and then closed in.

There were twelve men on each side and the challenge went from one side to the other. Two judges walked around the wrestlers and when they thought they were equally matched, stopped them. Five matches ended in this way. But the really exciting moments were when a man was thrown. The huge voice of the crowd then rose to the sky and in every direction. It was even heard in the surrounding villages.

2. "The Heart Eats [enjoys] more."   3. "Chi Who Plants."

The last match was between the leaders of the teams. They were among the best wrestlers in all the nine villages. The crowd wondered who would throw the other this year. Some said Okafo was the better man; others said he was not the equal of Ikezue.[4] Last year neither of them had thrown the other even though the judges had allowed the contest to go on longer than was the custom. They had the same style and one saw the other's plans beforehand. It might happen again this year.

Dusk was already approaching when their contest began. The drums went mad and the crowds also. They surged forward as the two young men danced into the circle. The palm fronds were helpless in keeping them back.

Ikezue held out his right hand. Okafo seized it, and they closed in. It was a fierce contest. Ikezue strove to dig in his right heel behind Okafo so as to pitch him backwards in the clever *ege* style. But the one knew what the other was thinking. The crowd had surrounded and swallowed up the drummers, whose frantic rhythm was no longer a mere disembodied sound but the very heartbeat of the people.

The wrestlers were now almost still in each other's grip. The muscles on their arms and their thighs and on their backs stood out and twitched. It looked like an equal match. The two judges were already moving forward to separate them when Ikezue, now desperate, went down quickly on one knee in an attempt to fling his man backwards over his head. It was a sad miscalculation. Quick as the lightning of Amadiora, Okafo raised his right leg and swung it over his rival's head. The crowd burst into a thunderous roar. Okafo was swept off his feet by his supporters and carried home shoulder high. They sang his praise and the young women clapped their hands:

> Who will wrestle for our village?
> Okafo will wrestle for our village.
> Has he thrown a hundred men?
> He has thrown four hundred men.
> Has he thrown a hundred Cats?
> He has thrown four hundred Cats.
> Then send him word to fight for us.

7

For three years Ikemefuna lived in Okonkwo's household and the elders of Umuofia seemed to have forgotten about him. He grew rapidly like a yam tendril in the rainy season, and was full of the sap of life. He had become wholly absorbed into his new family. He was like an elder brother to Nwoye, and from the very first seemed to have kindled a new fire in the younger boy. He made him feel grown-up; and they no longer spent the evenings in mother's hut while she cooked, but now sat with Okonkwo in his *obi*, or watched him as he tapped his palm tree for the evening wine. Nothing pleased Nwoye now more than to be sent for by his mother or another of his father's wives to do one of those difficult and masculine tasks in the home, like splitting wood, or pounding food. On receiving

---

4. "Strength Is Complete" (a boastful name).

such a message through a younger brother or sister, Nwoye would feign annoyance and grumble aloud about women and their troubles.

Okonkwo was inwardly pleased at his son's development, and he knew it was due to Ikemefuna. He wanted Nwoye to grow into a tough young man capable of ruling his father's household when he was dead and gone to join the ancestors. He wanted him to be a prosperous man, having enough in his barn to feed the ancestors with regular sacrifices. And so he was always happy when he heard him grumbling about women. That showed that in time he would be able to control his women-folk. No matter how prosperous a man was, if he was unable to rule his women and his children (and especially his women) he was not really a man. He was like the man in the song who had ten and one wives and not enough soup for his foo-foo.

So Okonkwo encouraged the boys to sit with him in his *obi*, and he told them stories of the land—masculine stories of violence and bloodshed. Nwoye knew that it was right to be masculine and to be violent, but somehow he still preferred the stories that his mother used to tell, and which she no doubt still told to her younger children—stories of the tortoise and his wily ways, and of the bird *eneke-nti-oba*[5] who challenged the whole world to a wrestling contest and was finally thrown by the cat. He remembered the story she often told of the quarrel between Earth and Sky long ago, and how Sky withheld rain for seven years, until crops withered and the dead could not be buried because the hoes broke on the stony Earth. At last Vulture was sent to plead with Sky, and to soften his heart with a song of the suffering of the sons of men. Whenever Nwoye's mother sang this song he felt carried away to the distant scene in the sky where Vulture, Earth's emissary, sang for mercy. At last Sky was moved to pity, and he gave to Vulture rain wrapped in leaves of coco-yam. But as he flew home his long talon pierced the leaves and the rain fell as it had never fallen before. And so heavily did it rain on Vulture that he did not return to deliver his message but flew to a distant land, from where he had espied a fire. And when he got there he found it was a man making a sacrifice. He warmed himself in the fire and ate the entrails.

That was the kind of story that Nwoye loved. But he now knew that they were for foolish women and children, and he knew that his father wanted him to be a man. And so he feigned that he no longer cared for women's stories. And when he did this he saw that his father was pleased, and no longer rebuked him or beat him. So Nwoye and Ikemefuna would listen to Okonkwo's stories about tribal wars, or how, years ago, he had stalked his victim, overpowered him and obtained his first human head. And as he told them of the past they sat in darkness or the dim glow of logs, waiting for the women to finish their cooking. When they finished, each brought her bowl of foo-foo and bowl of soup to her husband. An oil lamp was lit and Okonkwo tasted from each bowl, and then passed two shares to Nwoye and Ikemefuna.

In this way the moons and the seasons passed. And then the locusts

---

5. "The swallow with the ear of a crocodile [who is deaf]"(literal trans.); a bird who proverbially flies without perching.

came. It had not happened for many a long year. The elders said locusts came once in a generation, reappeared every year for seven years and then disappeared for another lifetime. They went back to their caves in a distant land, where they were guarded by a race of stunted men. And then after another lifetime these men opened the caves again and the locusts came to Umuofia.

They came in the cold harmattan season after the harvests had been gathered, and ate up all the wild grass in the fields.

Okonkwo and the two boys were working on the red outer walls of the compound. This was one of the lighter tasks of the after-harvest season. A new cover of thick palm branches and palm leaves was set on the walls to protect them from the next rainy season. Okonkwo worked on the outside of the wall and the boys worked from within. There were little holes from one side to the other in the upper levels of the wall, and through these Okonkwo passed the rope, or *tie-tie*,[6] to the boys and they passed it round the wooden stays and then back to him; and in this way the cover was strengthened on the wall.

The women had gone to the bush to collect firewood, and the little children to visit their playmates in the neighboring compounds. The harmattan was in the air and seemed to distill a hazy feeling of sleep on the world. Okonkwo and the boys worked in complete silence, which was only broken when a new palm frond was lifted on to the wall or when a busy hen moved dry leaves about in her ceaseless search for food.

And then quite suddenly a shadow fell on the world, and the sun seemed hidden behind a thick cloud. Okonkwo looked up from his work and wondered if it was going to rain at such an unlikely time of the year. But almost immediately a shout of joy broke out in all directions, and Umuofia, which had dozed in the noon-day haze, broke into life and activity.

"Locusts are descending," was joyfully chanted everywhere, and men, women and children left their work or their play and ran into the open to see the unfamiliar sight. The locusts had not come for many, many years, and only the old people had seen them before.

At first, a fairly small swarm came. They were the harbingers sent to survey the land. And then appeared on the horizon a slowly moving mass like a boundless sheet of black cloud drifting towards Umuofia. Soon it covered half the sky, and the solid mass was now broken by tiny eyes of light like shining star dust. It was a tremendous sight, full of power and beauty.

Everyone was now about, talking excitedly and praying that the locusts should camp in Umuofia for the night. For although locusts had not visited Umuofia for many years, everybody knew by instinct that they were very good to eat. And at last the locusts did descend. They settled on every tree and on every blade of grass; they settled on the roofs and covered the bare ground. Mighty tree branches broke away under them, and the whole country became the brown-earth color of the vast, hungry swarm.

Many people went out with baskets trying to catch them, but the elders

6. A creeper used as a rope to lash sections in building (pidgin English from "to tie").

counseled patience till nightfall. And they were right. The locusts settled in the bushes for the night and their wings became wet with dew. Then all Umuofia turned out in spite of the cold harmattan, and everyone filled his bags and pots with locusts. The next morning they were roasted in clay pots and then spread in the sun until they became dry and brittle. And for many days this rare food was eaten with solid palm-oil.

Okonkwo sat in his *obi* crunching happily with Ikemefuna and Nwoye, and drinking palm-wine copiously, when Ogbuefi Ezeudu came in. Ezeudu was the oldest man in this quarter of Umuofia. He had been a great and fearless warrior in his time, and was now accorded great respect in all the clan. He refused to join in the meal, and asked Okonkwo to have a word with him outside. And so they walked out together, the old man supporting himself with his stick. When they were out of earshot, he said to Okonkwo:

"That boy calls you father. Do not bear a hand in his death." Okonkwo was surprised, and was about to say something when the old man continued:

"Yes, Umuofia has decided to kill him. The Oracle of the Hills and the Caves has pronounced it. They will take him outside Umuofia as is the custom, and kill him there. But I want you to have nothing to do with it. He calls you his father."

The next day a group of elders from all the nine villages of Umuofia came to Okonkwo's house early in the morning, and before they began to speak in low tones Nwoye and Ikemefuna were sent out. They did not stay very long, but when they went away Okonkwo sat still for a very long time supporting his chin in his palms. Later in the day he called Ikemefuna and told him that he was to be taken home the next day. Nwoye overheard it and burst into tears, whereupon his father beat him heavily. As for Ikemefuna, he was at a loss. His own home had gradually become very faint and distant. He still missed his mother and his sister and would be very glad to see them. But somehow he knew he was not going to see them. He remembered once when men had talked in low tones with his father; and it seemed now as if it was happening all over again.

Later, Nwoye went to his mother's hut and told her that Ikemefuna was going home. She immediately dropped her pestle with which she was grinding pepper, folded her arms across her breast and sighed, "Poor child."

The next day, the men returned with a pot of wine. They were all fully dressed as if they were going to a big clan meeting or to pay a visit to a neighboring village. They passed their cloths under the right arm-pit, and hung their goatskin bags and sheathed machetes over their left shoulders. Okonkwo got ready quickly and the party set out with Ikemefuna carrying the pot of wine. A deathly silence descended on Okonkwo's compound. Even the very little children seemed to know. Throughout that day Nwoye sat in his mother's hut and tears stood in his eyes.

At the beginning of their journey the men of Umuofia talked and laughed about the locusts, about their women, and about some effeminate men who had refused to come with them. But as they drew near to the outskirts of Umuofia silence fell upon them too.

The sun rose slowly to the center of the sky, and the dry, sandy footway began to throw up the heat that lay buried in it. Some birds chirruped in the forests around. The men trod dry leaves on the sand. All else was silent. Then from the distance came the faint beating of the *ekwe*. It rose and faded with the wind—a peaceful dance from a distant clan.

"It is an *ozo* dance,"[7] the men said among themselves. But no one was sure where it was coming from. Some said Ezimili, others Abame or Aninta. They argued for a short while and fell into silence again, and the elusive dance rose and fell with the wind. Somewhere a man was taking one of the titles of his clan, with music and dancing and a great feast.

The footway had now become a narrow line in the heart of the forest. The short trees and sparse undergrowth which surrounded the men's village began to give way to giant trees and climbers which perhaps had stood from the beginning of things, untouched by the ax and the bush-fire. The sun breaking through their leaves and branches threw a pattern of light and shade on the sandy footway.

Ikemefuna heard a whisper close behind him and turned round sharply. The man who had whispered now called out aloud, urging the others to hurry up.

"We still have a long way to go," he said. Then he and another man went before Ikemefuna and set a faster pace.

Thus the men of Umuofia pursued their way, armed with sheathed machetes, and Ikemefuna, carrying a pot of palm-wine on his head, walked in their midst. Although he had felt uneasy at first, he was not afraid now. Okonkwo walked behind him. He could hardly imagine that Okonkwo was not his real father. He had never been fond of his real father, and at the end of three years he had become very distant indeed. But his mother and his three-year-old sister . . . of course she would not be three now, but six. Would he recognize her now? She must have grown quite big. How his mother would weep for joy, and thank Okonkwo for having looked after him so well and for bringing him back. She would want to hear everything that had happened to him in all these years. Could he remember them all? He would tell her about Nwoye and his mother, and about the locusts. . . . Then quite suddenly a thought came upon him. His mother might be dead. He tried in vain to force the thought out of his mind. Then he tried to settle the matter the way he used to settle such matters when he was a little boy. He still remembered the song:

> *Eze elina, elina!*
> Sala
> *Eze ilikwa ya*
> *Ikwaba akwa oligholi*
> *Ebe Danda nechi eze*
> *Ebe Uzuzu nete egwu*
> Sala[8]

---

7. Part of the *ozo* rituals, the spiritual ceremonies that accompanied the taking of titles.   8. "King don't eat, don't eat / Sala / King if you eat it / You will weep for the abomination / Where Danda installs a king / Where Uzuzu dances / Sala." *Sala*: meaningless refrain. *Danda*: the ant. *Uzuzu*: sand. Ikemefuna reassures himself by singing his favorite song about the country where the "sands dance forever" (see p. 2952).

He sang it in his mind, and walked to its beat. If the song ended on his right foot, his mother was alive. If it ended on his left, she was dead. No, not dead, but ill. It ended on the right. She was alive and well. He sang the song again, and it ended on the left. But the second time did not count. The first voice gets to Chukwu, or God's house. That was a favorite saying of children. Ikemefuna felt like a child once more. It must be the thought of going home to his mother.

One of the men behind him cleared his throat. Ikemefuna looked back, and the man growled at him to go on and not stand looking back. The way he said it sent cold fear down Ikemefuna's back. His hands trembled vaguely on the black pot he carried. Why had Okonkwo withdrawn to the rear? Ikemefuna felt his legs melting under him. And he was afraid to look back.

As the man who had cleared his throat drew up and raised his machete, Okonkwo looked away. He heard the blow. The pot fell and broke in the sand. He heard Ikemefuna cry, "My father, they have killed me!" as he ran towards him. Dazed with fear, Okonkwo drew his machete and cut him down. He was afraid of being thought weak.

As soon as his father walked in, that night, Nwoye knew that Ikemefuna had been killed, and something seemed to give way inside him, like the snapping of a tightened bow. He did not cry. He just hung limp. He had had the same kind of feeling not long ago, during the last harvest season. Every child loved the harvest season. Those who were big enough to carry even a few yams in a tiny basket went with grown-ups to the farm. And if they could not help in digging up the yams, they could gather firewood together for roasting the ones that would be eaten there on the farm. This roasted yam soaked in red palm-oil and eaten in the open farm was sweeter than any meal at home. It was after such a day at the farm during the last harvest that Nwoye had felt for the first time a snapping inside him like the one he now felt. They were returning home with baskets of yams from a distant farm across the stream when they heard the voice of an infant crying in the thick forest. A sudden hush had fallen on the women, who had been talking, and they had quickened their steps. Nwoye had heard that twins were put in earthenware pots and thrown away in the forest, but he had never yet come across them. A vague chill had descended on him and his head had seemed to swell, like a solitary walker at night who passes an evil spirit on the way. Then something had given way inside him. It descended on him again, this feeling, when his father walked in, that night after killing Ikemefuna.

8

Okonkwo did not taste any food for two days after the death of Ikemefuna. He drank palm-wine from morning till night, and his eyes were red and fierce like the eyes of a rat when it was caught by the tail and dashed against the floor. He called his son, Nwoye, to sit with him in his *obi*. But the boy was afraid of him and slipped out of the hut as soon as he noticed him dozing.

He did not sleep at night. He tried not to think about Ikemefuna, but the more he tried the more he thought about him. Once he got up from bed and walked about his compound. But he was so weak that his legs could hardly carry him. He felt like a drunken giant walking with the limbs of a mosquito. Now and then a cold shiver descended on his head and spread down his body.

On the third day he asked his second wife, Ekwefi, to roast plantains for him. She prepared it the way he liked—with slices of oil-bean and fish.

"You have not eaten for two days," said his daughter Ezinma when she brought the food to him. "So you must finish this." She sat down and stretched her legs in front of her. Okonkwo ate the food absent-mindedly. 'She should have been a boy,' he thought as he looked at his ten-year-old daughter. He passed her a piece of fish.

"Go and bring me some cold water," he said. Ezinma rushed out of the hut, chewing the fish, and soon returned with a bowl of cool water from the earthen pot in her mother's hut.

Okonkwo took the bowl from her and gulped the water down. He ate a few more pieces of plantain and pushed the dish aside.

"Bring me my bag," he asked, and Ezinma brought his goatskin bag from the far end of the hut. He searched in it for his snuff-bottle. It was a deep bag and took almost the whole length of his arm. It contained other things apart from his snuff-bottle. There was a drinking horn in it, and also a drinking gourd, and they knocked against each other as he searched. When he brought out the snuff-bottle he tapped it a few times against his knee-cap before taking out some snuff on the palm of his left hand. Then he remembered that he had not taken out his snuff-spoon. He searched his bag again and brought out a small, flat, ivory spoon, with which he carried the brown snuff to his nostrils.

Ezinma took the dish in one hand and the empty water bowl in the other and went back to her mother's hut. "She should have been a boy," Okonkwo said to himself again. His mind went back to Ikemefuna and he shivered. If only he could find some work to do he would be able to forget. But it was the season of rest between the harvest and the next planting season. The only work that men did at this time was covering the walls of their compound with new palm fronds. And Okonkwo had already done that. He had finished it on the very day the locusts came, when he had worked on one side of the wall and Ikemefuna and Nwoye on the other.

"When did you become a shivering old woman," Okonkwo asked himself, "you, who are known in all the nine villages for your valor in war? How can a man who has killed five men in battle fall to pieces because he has added a boy to their number? Okonkwo, you have become a woman indeed."

He sprang to his feet, hung his goatskin bag on his shoulder and went to visit his friend, Obierika.

Obierika was sitting outside under the shade of an orange tree making thatches from leaves of the raffia-palm. He exchanged greetings with Okonkwo and led the way into his *obi*.

"I was coming over to see you as soon as I finished that thatch," he said, rubbing off the grains of sand that clung to his thighs.

"Is it well?" Okonkwo asked.

"Yes," replied Obierika. "My daughter's suitor is coming today and I hope we will clinch the matter of the bride-price. I want you to be there."

Just then Obierika's son, Maduka, came into the *obi* from outside, greeted Okonkwo and turned towards the compound.

"Come and shake hands with me," Okonkwo said to the lad. "Your wrestling the other day gave me much happiness." The boy smiled, shook hands with Okonkwo and went into the compound.

"He will do great things," Okonkwo said. "If I had a son like him I should be happy. I am worried about Nwoye. A bowl of pounded yams can throw him in a wrestling match. His two younger brothers are more promising. But I can tell you, Obierika, that my children do not resemble me. Where are the young suckers that will grow when the old banana tree dies? If Ezinma had been a boy I would have been happier. She has the right spirit."

"You worry yourself for nothing," said Obierika. "The children are still very young."

"Nwoye is old enough to impregnate a woman. At his age I was already fending for myself. No, my friend, he is not too young. A chick that will grow into a cock can be spotted the very day it hatches. I have done my best to make Nwoye grow into a man, but there is too much of his mother in him."

"Too much of his grandfather," Obierika thought, but he did not say it. The same thought also came to Okonkwo's mind. But he had long learned how to lay that ghost. Whenever the thought of his father's weakness and failure troubled him he expelled it by thinking about his own strength and success. And so he did now. His mind went to his latest show of manliness.

"I cannot understand why you refused to come with us to kill that boy," he asked Obierika.

"Because I did not want to," Obierika replied sharply. "I had something better to do."

"You sound as if you question the authority and the decision of the Oracle, who said he should die."

"I do not. Why should I? But the Oracle did not ask me to carry out its decision."

"But someone had to do it. If we were all afraid of blood, it would not be done. And what do you think the Oracle would do then?"

"You know very well, Okonkwo, that I am not afraid of blood; and if anyone tells you that I am, he is telling a lie. And let me tell you one thing, my friend. If I were you I would have stayed at home. What you have done will not please the Earth. It is the kind of action for which the goddess wipes out whole families."

"The Earth cannot punish me for obeying her messenger," Okonkwo said. "A child's fingers are not scalded by a piece of hot yam which its mother puts into its palm."

"That is true," Obierika agreed. "But if the Oracle said that my son should be killed I would neither dispute it nor be the one to do it."

They would have gone on arguing had Ofoedu[9] not come in just then.

9. "The Ancestors Are Our Guide."

It was clear from his twinkling eyes that he had important news. But it would be impolite to rush him. Obierika offered him a lobe of the kola nut he had broken with Okonkwo. Ofoedu ate slowly and talked about the locusts. When he finished his kola nut he said:

"The things that happen these days are very strange."

"What has happened?" asked Okonkwo.

"Do you know Ogbuefi Ndulue?"[1] Ofoedu asked.

"Ogbuefi Ndulue of Ire village," Okonkwo and Obierika said together.

"He died this morning," said Ofoedu.

"That is not strange. He was the oldest man in Ire," said Obierika.

"You are right," Ofoedu agreed. "But you ought to ask why the drum has not beaten to tell Umuofia of his death."

"Why?" asked Obierika and Okonkwo together.

"That is the strange part of it. You know his first wife who walks with a stick?"

"Yes. She is called Ozoemena."[2]

"That is so," said Ofoedu. "Ozoemena was, as you know, too old to attend Ndulue during his illness. His younger wives did that. When he died this morning, one of these women went to Ozoemena's hut and told her. She rose from her mat, took her stick and walked over to the *obi*. She knelt on her knees and hands at the threshold and called her husband, who was laid on a mat. 'Ogbuefi Ndulue,' she called, three times, and went back to her hut. When the youngest wife went to call her again to be present at the washing of the body, she found her lying on the mat, dead."

"That is very strange, indeed," said Okonkwo. "They will put off Ndulue's funeral until his wife has been buried."[3]

"That is why the drum has not been beaten to tell Umuofia."

"It was always said that Ndulue and Ozoemena had one mind," said Obierika. "I remember when I was a young boy there was a song about them. He could not do anything without telling her."

"I did not know that," said Okonkwo. "I thought he was a strong man in his youth."

"He was indeed," said Ofoedu.

Okonkwo shook his head doubtfully.

"He led Umuofia to war in those days," said Obierika.

Okonkwo was beginning to feel like his old self again. All that he required was something to occupy his mind. If he had killed Ikemefuna during the busy planting season or harvesting it would not have been so bad; his mind would have been centered on his work. Okonkwo was not a man of thought but of action. But in absence of work, talking was the next best.

Soon after Ofoedu left, Okonkwo took up his goatskin bag to go.

"I must go home to tap my palm trees for the afternoon," he said.

"Who taps your tall trees for you?" asked Obierika.

"Umezulike," replied Okonkwo.

---

1. "Life Has Arrived."   2. "Another Bad Thing Will Not Happen."   3. A wife dying shortly after her husband was sometimes considered guilty of his death, so the village preserves appearances by burying Ozoemena before announcing Ogbuefi Ndulue's death.

"Sometimes I wish I had not taken the *ozo* title," said Obierika. "It wounds my heart to see these young men killing palm trees in the name of tapping."

"It is so indeed," Okonkwo agreed. "But the law of the land must be obeyed."

"I don't know how we got that law," said Obierika. "In many other clans a man of title is not forbidden to climb the palm tree. Here we say he cannot climb the tall tree but he can tap the short ones standing on the ground. It is like Dimaragana, who would not lend his knife for cutting up dogmeat because the dog was taboo to him, but offered to use his teeth."

"I think it is good that our clan holds the *ozo* title in high esteem," said Okonkwo. "In those other clans you speak of, *ozo* is so low that every beggar takes it."

"I was only speaking in jest," said Obierika. "In Abame and Aninta the title is worth less than two cowries. Every man wears the thread of title on his ankle, and does not lose it even if he steals."

"They have indeed soiled the name of *ozo*," said Okonkwo as he rose to go.

"It will not be very long now before my in-laws come," said Obierika.

"I shall return very soon," said Okonkwo, looking at the position of the sun.

There were seven men in Obierika's hut when Okonkwo returned. The suitor was a young man of about twenty-five, and with him were his father and uncle. On Obierika's side were his two elder brothers and Maduka, his sixteen-year-old son.

"Ask Akueke's mother to send us some kola nuts," said Obierika to his son. Maduka vanished into the compound like lightning. The conversation at once centered on him, and everybody agreed that he was as sharp as a razor.

"I sometimes think he is too sharp," said Obierika, somewhat indulgently. "He hardly ever walks. He is always in a hurry. If you are sending him on an errand he flies away before he has heard half of the message."

"You were very much like that yourself," said his eldest brother. "As our people say, 'When mother-cow is chewing grass its young ones watch its mouth.' Maduka has been watching your mouth."

As he was speaking the boy returned, followed by Akueke,[4] his half-sister, carrying a wooden dish with three kola nuts and alligator pepper. She gave the dish to her father's eldest brother and then shook hands, very shyly, with her suitor and his relatives. She was about sixteen and just ripe for marriage. Her suitor and his relatives surveyed her young body with expert eyes as if to assure themselves that she was beautiful and ripe.

She wore a coiffure which was done up into a crest in the middle of the head. Cam wood was rubbed lightly into her skin, and all over her body

---

4. "Wealth of Eke" (a divinity). Similar names built on *ako* ("wealth") connote riches and are associated with the idea of women as a form of exchangeable material wealth.

were black patterns drawn with *uli*.[5] She wore a black necklace which hung down in three coils just above her full, succulent breasts. On her arms were red and yellow bangles, and on her waist four or five rows of *jigida*, or waist beads.

When she had shaken hands, or rather held out her hand to be shaken, she returned to her mother's hut to help with the cooking.

"Remove your *jigida* first," her mother warned as she moved near the fireplace to bring the pestle resting against the wall. "Every day I tell you that *jigida* and fire are not friends. But you will never hear. You grew your ears for decoration, not for hearing. One of these days your *jigida* will catch fire on your waist, and then you will know."

Akueke moved to the other end of the hut and began to remove the waist-beads. It had to be done slowly and carefully, taking each string separately, else it would break and the thousand tiny rings would have to be strung together again. She rubbed each string downwards with her palms until it passed the buttocks and slipped down to the floor around her feet.

The men in the *obi* had already begun to drink the palm-wine which Akueke's suitor had brought. It was a very good wine and powerful, for in spite of the palm fruit hung across the mouth of the pot to restrain the lively liquor, white foam rose and spilled over.

"That wine is the work of a good tapper," said Okonkwo.

The young suitor, whose name was Ibe, smiled broadly and said to his father: "Do you hear that?" He then said to the others: "He will never admit that I am a good tapper."

"He tapped three of my best palm trees to death," said his father, Ukegbu.

"That was about five years ago," said Ibe, who had begun to pour out the wine, "before I learned how to tap." He filled the first horn and gave to his father. Then he poured out for the others. Okonkwo brought out his big horn from the goatskin bag, blew into it to remove any dust that might be there, and gave it to Ibe to fill.

As the men drank, they talked about everything except the thing for which they had gathered. It was only after the pot had been emptied that the suitor's father cleared his voice and announced the object of their visit.

Obierika then presented to him a small bundle of short broomsticks. Ukegbu counted them.

"They are thirty?" he asked.

Obierika nodded in agreement.

"We are at last getting somewhere," Ukegbu said, and then turning to his brother and his son he said: "Let us go out and whisper together." The three rose and went outside. When they returned Ukegbu handed the bundle of sticks back to Obierika. He counted them; instead of thirty there were now only fifteen. He passed them over to his eldest brother, Machi, who also counted them and said:

"We had not thought to go below thirty. But as the dog said, 'If I fall

5. A liquid made from crushed seeds, which caused the skin to pucker temporarily. It was used to create black tattoolike decorations. *Cam wood*: a shrub. The powdered red heartwood of the shrub was used as a cosmetic dye.

down for you and you fall down for me, it is play.' Marriage should be a play and not a fight; so we are falling down again." He then added ten sticks to the fifteen and gave the bundle to Ukegbu.

In this way Akuke's bride-price was finally settled at twenty bags of cowries. It was already dusk when the two parties came to this agreement.

"Go and tell Akueke's mother that we have finished," Obierika said to his son, Maduka. Almost immediately the women came in with a big bowl of foo-foo. Obierika's second wife followed with a pot of soup, and Maduka brought in a pot of palm-wine.

As the men ate and drank palm-wine they talked about the customs of their neighbors.

"It was only this morning," said Obierika, "that Okonkwo and I were talking about Abame and Aninta, where titled men climb trees and pound foo-foo for their wives."

"All their customs are upside-down. They do not decide bride-price as we do, with sticks. They haggle and bargain as if they were buying a goat or a cow in the market."

"That is very bad," said Obierika's eldest brother. "But what is good in one place is bad in another place. In Umunso they do not bargain at all, not even with broomsticks. The suitor just goes on bringing bags of cowries until his in-laws tell him to stop. It is a bad custom because it always leads to a quarrel."

"The world is large," said Okonkwo. "I have even heard that in some tribes a man's children belong to his wife and her family."

"That cannot be," said Machi. "You might as well say that the woman lies on top of the man when they are making the children."

"It is like the story of white men who, they say, are white like this piece of chalk," said Obierika. He held up a piece of chalk, which every man kept in his *obi* and with which his guests drew lines on the floor before they ate kola nuts. "And these white men, they say, have no toes."[6]

"And have you never seen them?" asked Machi.

"Have you?" asked Obierika.

"One of them passes here frequently," said Machi. "His name is Amadi."

Those who knew Amadi laughed. He was a leper, and the polite name for leprosy was "the white skin."

9

For the first time in three nights, Okonkwo slept. He woke up once in the middle of the night and his mind went back to the past three days without making him feel uneasy. He began to wonder why he had felt uneasy at all. It was like a man wondering in broad daylight why a dream had appeared so terrible to him at night. He stretched himself and scratched his thigh were a mosquito had bitten him as he slept. Another one was wailing near his right ear. He slapped the ear and hoped he had killed it. Why do they always go for one's ears? When he was a child his mother had told him a story about it. But it was as silly as all women's

6. They wear shoes.

stories. Mosquito, she had said, had asked Ear to marry him, whereupon Ear fell on the floor in uncontrollable laughter. "How much longer do you think you will live?" she asked. "You are already a skeleton." Mosquito went away humiliated, and any time he passed her way he told Ear that he was still alive.

Okonkwo turned on his side and went back to sleep. He was roused in the morning by someone banging on his door.

"Who is that?" he growled. He knew it must be Ekwefi. Of his three wives Ekwefi was the only one who would have the audacity to bang on his door.

"Ezinma is dying," came her voice, and all the tragedy and sorrow of her life were packed in those words.

Okonkwo sprang from his bed, pushed back the bolt on his door and ran into Ekwefi's hut.

Ezinma lay shivering on a mat beside a huge fire that her mother had kept burning all night.

"It is iba,"[7] said Okonkwo as he took his machete and went into the bush to collect the leaves and grasses and barks of trees that went into making the medicine for iba.

Ekwefi knelt beside the sick child, occasionally feeling with her palm the wet, burning forehead.

Ezinma was an only child and the center of her mother's world. Very often it was Ezinma who decided what food her mother should prepare. Ekwefi even gave her such delicacies as eggs, which children were rarely allowed to eat because such food tempted them to steal. One day as Ezinma was eating an egg Okonkwo had come in unexpectedly from his hut. He was greatly shocked and swore to beat Ekwefi if she dared to give the child eggs again. But it was impossible to refuse Ezinma anything. After her father's rebuke she developed an even keener appetite for eggs. And she enjoyed above all the secrecy in which she now ate them. Her mother always took her into their bedroom and shut the door.

Ezinma did not call her mother Nne like all children. She called her by her name, Ekwefi, as her father and other grown-up people did. The relationship between them was not only that of mother and child. There was something in it like the companionship of equals, which was strengthened by such little conspiracies as eating eggs in the bedroom.

Ekwefi had suffered a good deal in her life. She had borne ten children and nine of them had died in infancy, usually before the age of three. As she buried one child after another her sorrow gave way to despair and then to grim resignation. The birth of her children, which should be a woman's crowning glory, became for Ekwefi mere physical agony devoid of promise. The naming ceremony after seven market weeks became an empty ritual. Her deepening despair found expression in the names she gave her children. One of them was a pathetic cry, Onwumbiko—"Death, I implore you." But Death took no notice; Onwumbiko died in his fifteenth month. The next child was a girl, Ozoemena—"May it not happen again." She died in her eleventh month, and two others after her. Ekwefi then

---

7. A fever accompanied by jaundice, probably caused by malaria.

became defiant and called her next child Onwuma—"Death may please himself." And he did.

After the death of Ekwefi's second child, Okonkwo had gone to a medicine man, who was also a diviner of the Afa Oracle,[8] to inquire what was amiss. This man told him that the child was an *ogbanje*, one of those wicked children who, when they died, entered their mothers' wombs to be born again.

"When your wife becomes pregnant again," he said, "let her not sleep in her hut. Let her go and stay with her people. In that way she will elude her wicked tormentor and break its evil cycle of birth and death."

Ekwefi did as she was asked. As soon as she became pregnant she went to live with her old mother in another village. It was there that her third child was born and circumcised on the eighth day. She did not return to Okonkwo's compound until three days before the naming ceremony. The child was called Onwumbiko.

Onwumbiko was not given proper burial when he died. Okonkwo had called on another medicine man who was famous in the clan for his great knowledge about *ogbanje* children. His name was Okagbue Uyanwa. Okagbue was a very striking figure, tall, with a full beard and a bald head. He was light in complexion and his eyes were red and fiery. He always gnashed his teeth as he listened to those who came to consult him. He asked Okonkwo a few questions about the dead child. All the neighbors and relations who had come to mourn gathered round them.

"On what market-day was it born?" he asked.

"*Oye*," replied Okonkwo.

"And it died this morning?"

Okonkwo said yes, and only then realized for the first time that the child had died on the same market-day as it had been born. The neighbors and relations also saw the coincidence and said among themselves that it was very significant.

"Where do you sleep with your wife, in your *obi* or in her own hut?" asked the medicine man.

"In her hut."

"In future call her into your *obi*."

The medicine man then ordered that there should be no mourning for the dead child. He brought out a sharp razor from the goatskin bag slung from his left shoulder and began to mutilate the child. Then he took it away to bury in the Evil Forest, holding it by the ankle and dragging it on the ground behind him. After such treatment it would think twice before coming again, unless it was one of the stubborn ones who returned, carrying the stamp of their mutilation—a missing finger or perhaps a dark line where the medicine man's razor had cut them.

By the time Onwumbiko died Ekwefi had become a very bitter woman. Her husband's first wife had already had three sons, all strong and healthy. When she had borne her third son in succession, Okonkwo had gathered a goat for her, as was the custom. Ekwefi had nothing but good wishes for her. But she had grown so bitter about her own *chi* that she could not

8. One communicates with the clients' ancestors by reading patterns made by objects (for example, seeds, teeth, shells) thrown on a flat surface.

rejoice with others over their good fortune. And so, on the day that Nwoye's mother celebrated the birth of her three sons with feasting and music, Ekwefi was the only person in the happy company who went about with a cloud on her brow. Her husband's wife took this for malevolence, as husbands' wives were wont to. How could she know that Ekwefi's bitterness did not flow outwards to others but inwards into her own soul; that she did not blame others for their good fortune but her own evil *chi* who denied her any?

At last Ezinma was born, and although ailing she seemed determined to live. At first Ekwefi accepted her, as she had accepted others—with listless resignation. But when she lived on to her fourth, fifth and sixth years, love returned once more to her mother, and, with love, anxiety. She determined to nurse her child to health, and she put all her being into it. She was rewarded by occasional spells of health during which Ezinma bubbled with energy like fresh palm-wine. At such times she seemed beyond danger. But all of a sudden she would go down again. Everybody knew she was an *ogbanje*. These sudden bouts of sickness and health were typical of her kind. But she had lived so long that perhaps she had decided to stay. Some of them did become tired of their evil rounds of birth and death, or took pity on their mothers, and stayed. Ekwefi believed deep inside her that Ezinma had come to stay. She believed because it was that faith alone that gave her own life any kind of meaning. And this faith had been strengthened when a year or so ago a medicine man had dug up Ezinma's *iyi-uwa*. Everyone knew then that she would live because her bond with the world of *ogbanje* had been broken. Ekwefi was reassured. But such was her anxiety for her daughter that she could not rid herself completely of her fear. And although she believed that the *iyi-uwa* which had been dug up was genuine, she could not ignore the fact that some really evil children sometimes misled people into digging up a specious one.

But Ezinma's *iyi-uwa* had looked real enough. It was a smooth pebble wrapped in a dirty rag. The man who dug it up was the same Okagbue who was famous in all the clan for his knowledge in these matters. Ezinma had not wanted to cooperate with him at first. But that was only to be expected. No *ogbanje* would yield her secrets easily, and most of them never did because they died too young—before they could be asked questions.

"Where did you bury your *iyi-uwa?*" Okagbue had asked Ezinma. She was nine then and was just recovering from a serious illness.

"What is *iyi-uwa?*" she asked in return.

"You know what it is. You buried it in the ground somewhere so that you can die and return again to torment your mother."

Ezinma looked at her mother, whose eyes, sad and pleading, were fixed on her.

"Answer the question at once," roared Okonkwo, who stood beside her. All the family were there and some of the neighbors too.

"Leave her to me," the medicine man told Okonkwo in a cool, confident voice. He turned again to Ezinma. "Where did you bury your *iyi-uwa?*"

"Where they bury children," she replied, and the quiet spectators murmured to themselves.

"Come along then and show me the spot," said the medicine man.

The crowd set out with Ezinma leading the way and Okagbue following closely behind her. Okonkwo came next and Ekwefi followed him. When she came to the main road, Ezinma turned left as if she was going to the stream.

"But you said it was where they bury children?" asked the medicine man.

"No," said Ezinma, whose feeling of importance was manifest in her sprightly walk. She sometimes broke into a run and stopped again suddenly. The crowd followed her silently. Women and children returning from the stream with pots of water on their heads wondered what was happening until they saw Okagbue and guessed that it must be something to do with *ogbanje*. And they all knew Ekwefi and her daughter very well.

When she got to the big udala tree Ezinma turned left into the bush, and the crowd followed her. Because of her size she made her way through trees and creepers more quickly then her followers. The bush was alive with the tread of feet on dry leaves and sticks and the moving aside of tree branches. Ezinma went deeper and deeper and the crowd went with her. Then she suddenly turned round and began to walk back to the road. Everybody stood to let her pass and then filed after her.

"If you bring us all this way for nothing I shall beat sense into you," Okonkwo threatened.

"I have told you to let her alone. I know how to deal with them," said Okagbue.

Ezinma led the way back to the road, looked left and right and turned right. And so they arrived home again.

"Where did you bury your *iyi-uwa?*" asked Okagbue when Ezinma finally stopped outside her father's *obi*. Okagbue's voice was unchanged. It was quiet and confident.

"It is near that orange tree," Ezinma said.

"And why did you not say so, you wicked daughter of Akalogoli?" Okonkwo swore furiously. The medicine man ignored him.

"Come and show me the exact spot," he said quietly to Ezinma.

"It is here," she said when they got to the tree.

"Point at the spot with your finger," said Okagbue.

"It is here," said Ezinma touching the ground with her finger. Okonkwo stood by, rumbling like thunder in the rainy season.

"Bring me a hoe," said Okagbue.

When Ekwefi brought the hoe, he had already put aside his goatskin bag and his big cloth and was in his underwear, a long and thin strip of cloth wound round the waist like a belt and then passed between the legs to be fastened to the belt behind. He immediately set to work digging a pit where Ezinma had indicated. The neighbors sat around watching the pit becoming deeper and deeper. The dark top soil soon gave way to the bright red earth with which women scrubbed the floors and walls of huts. Okagbue worked tirelessly and in silence, his back shining with perspiration. Okonkwo stood by the pit. He asked Okagbue to come up and rest while he took a hand. But Okagbue said he was not tired yet.

Ekwefi went into her hut to cook yams. Her husband had brought out more yams than usual because the medicine man had to be fed. Ezinma went with her and helped in preparing the vegetables.

"There is too much green vegetable," she said.

"Don't you see the pot is full of yams?" Ekwefi asked. "And you know how leaves become smaller after cooking."

"Yes," said Ezinma, "that was why the snake-lizard killed his mother."

"Very true," said Ekwefi.

"He gave his mother seven baskets of vegetables to cook and in the end there were only three. And so he killed her," said Ezinma.

"That is not the end of the story."

"Oho," said Ezinma. "I remember now. He brought another seven baskets and cooked them himself. And there were again only three. So he killed himself too."

Outside the *obi* Okagbue and Okonkwo were digging the pit to find where Ezinma had buried her *iyi-uwa*. Neighbors sat around, watching. The pit was now so deep that they no longer saw the digger. They only saw the red earth he threw up mounting higher and higher. Okonkwo's son, Nwoye, stood near the edge of the pit because he wanted to take in all that happened.

Okagbue had again taken over the digging from Okonkwo. He worked, as usual, in silence. The neighbors and Okonkwo's wives were now talking. The children had lost interest and were playing.

Suddenly Okagbue sprang to the surface with the agility of a leopard.

"It is very near now," he said. "I have felt it."

There was immediate excitement and those who were sitting jumped to their feet.

"Call your wife and child," he said to Okonkwo. But Ekwefi and Ezinma had heard the noise and run out to see what it was.

Okagbue went back into the pit, which was now surrounded by spectators. After a few more hoe-fuls of earth he struck the *iyi-uwa*. He raised it carefully with the hoe and threw it to the surface. Some women ran away in fear when it was thrown. But they soon returned and everyone was gazing at the rag from a reasonable distance. Okagbue emerged and without saying a word or even looking at the spectators he went to his goatskin bag, took out two leaves and began to chew them. When he had swallowed them, he took up the rag with his left hand and began to untie it. And then the smooth, shiny pebble fell out. He picked it up.

"Is this yours?" he asked Ezinma.

"Yes," she replied. All the women shouted with joy because Ekwefi's troubles were at last ended.

All this had happened more than a year ago and Ezinma had not been ill since. And then suddenly she had begun to shiver in the night. Ekwefi brought her to the fireplace, spread her mat on the floor and built a fire. But she had got worse and worse. As she knelt by her, feeling with her palm the wet, burning forehead, she prayed a thousand times. Although her husband's wives were saying that it was nothing more than *iba*, she did not hear them.

Okonkwo returned from the bush carrying on his left shoulder a large bundle of grasses and leaves, roots and barks of medicinal trees and shrubs. He went into Ekwefi's hut, put down his load and sat down.

"Get me a pot," he said, "and leave the child alone."

Ekwefi went to bring the pot and Okonkwo selected the best from his bundle, in their due proportions, and cut them up. He put them in the pot and Ekwefi poured in some water.

"Is that enough?" she asked when she had poured in about half of the water in the bowl.

"A little more . . . I said a *little*. Are you deaf?" Okonkwo roared at her.

She set the pot on the fire and Okonkwo took up his machete to return to his *obi*.

"You must watch the pot carefully," he said as he went, "and don't allow it to boil over. If it does its power will be gone." He went away to his hut and Ekwefi began to tend the medicine pot almost as if it was itself a sick child. Her eyes went constantly from Ezinma to the boiling pot and back to Ezinma.

Okonkwo returned when he felt the medicine had cooked long enough. He looked it over and said it was done.

"Bring me a low stool for Ezinma," he said, "and a thick mat."

He took down the pot from the fire and placed it in front of the stool. He then roused Ezinma and placed her on the stool, astride the steaming pot. The thick mat was thrown over both. Ezinma struggled to escape from the choking and overpowering steam, but she was held down. She started to cry.

When the mat was at last removed she was drenched in perspiration. Ekwefi mopped her with a piece of cloth and she lay down on a dry mat and was soon asleep.

10

Large crowds began to gather on the village *ilo* as soon as the edge had worn off the sun's heat and it was no longer painful on the body. Most communal ceremonies took place at that time of the day, so that even when it was said that a ceremony would begin "after the midday meal" everyone understood that it would begin a long time later, when the sun's heat had softened.

It was clear from the way the crowd stood or sat that the ceremony was for men. There were many women, but they looked on from the fringe like outsiders. The titled men and elders sat on their stools waiting for the trials to begin. In front of them was a row of stools on which nobody sat. There were nine of them. Two little groups of people stood at a respectable distance beyond the stools. They faced the elders. There were three men in one group and three men and one woman in the other. The woman was Mgbafo and the three men with her were her brothers. In the other group were her husband, Uzowulu, and his relatives. Mgbafo and her brothers were as still as statues into whose faces the artist has molded defiance. Uzowulu and his relatives, on the other hand, were whispering together. It looked like whispering, but they were really talking at the top of their voices. Everybody in the crowd was talking. It was like the market. From a distance the noise was a deep rumble carried by the wind.

An iron gong sounded, setting up a wave of expectation in the crowd. Everyone looked in the direction of the *egwugwu*[9] house. *Gome, gome, gome* went the gong, and a powerful flute blew a high-pitched blast. Then came the voices of the *egwugwu*, guttural and awesome. The wave struck the women and children and there was a backward stampede. But it was momentary. They were already far enough where they stood and there was room for running away if any of the *egwugwu* should go towards them.

The drum sounded again and the flute blew. The *egwugwu* house was now a pandemonium of quavering voices: *Aru oyim de de de dei!*[1] filled the air as the spirits of the ancestors, just emerged from the earth, greeted themselves in their esoteric language. The *egwugwu* house into which they emerged faced the forest, away from the crowd, who saw only its back with the many-colored patterns and drawings done by specially chosen women at regular intervals. These women never saw the inside of the hut. No woman ever did. They scrubbed and painted the outside walls under the supervision of men. If they imagined what was inside, they kept their imagination to themselves. No woman ever asked questions about the most powerful and the most secret cult in the clan.

Aru oyim de de de dei! flew around the dark, closed hut like tongues of fire. The ancestral spirits of the clan were abroad. The metal gong beat continuously now and the flute, shrill and powerful, floated on the chaos.

And then the *egwugwu* appeared. The women and children sent up a great shout and took to their heels. It was instinctive. A woman fled as soon as an *egwugwu* came in sight. And when, as on that day, nine of the greatest masked spirits in the clan came out together it was a terrifying spectacle. Even Mgbafo took to her heels and had to be restrained by her brothers.

Each of the nine *egwugwu* represented a village of the clan. Their leader was called Evil Forest. Smoke poured out of his head.

The nine villages of Umuofia had grown out of the nine sons of the first father of the clan. Evil Forest represented the village of Umueru, or the children of Eru, who was the eldest of the nine sons.

"Umuofia kwenu!" shouted the leading *egwugwu*, pushing the air with his raffia arms. The elders of the clan replied, "Yaa!"

"Umuofia kwenu!"

"Yaa!"

"Umuofia kwenu!"

"Yaa!"

Evil Forest then thrust the pointed end of his rattling staff into the earth. And it began to shake and rattle, like something agitating with a metallic

---

9. Here the term refers to the village's highest spiritual and judicial authority, prominent men who, after putting on elaborate ceremonial costumes, embody the village's ancestral spirits.   1. "Body of my friend, greetings!"

life. He took the first of the empty stools and the eight other *egwugwu* began to sit in order of seniority after him.

Okonkwo's wives, and perhaps other women as well, might have noticed that the second *egwugwu* had the springy walk of Okonkwo. And they might also have noticed that Okonkwo was not among the titled men and elders who sat behind the row of *egwugwu*. But if they thought these things they kept them within themselves. The *egwugwu* with the springy walk was one of the dead fathers of the clan. He looked terrible with the smoked raffia body, a huge wooden face painted white except for the round hollow eyes and the charred teeth that were as big as a man's fingers. On his head were two powerful horns.

When all the *egwugwu* had sat down and the sound of the many tiny bells and rattles on their bodies had subsided, Evil Forest addressed the two groups of people facing them.

"Uzowulu's body, I salute you," he said. Spirits always addressed humans as "bodies." Uzowulu bent down and touched the earth with his right hand as a sign of submission.

"Our father, my hand has touched the ground," he said.

"Uzowulu's body, do you know me?" asked the spirit.

"How can I know you, father? You are beyond our knowledge."

Evil Forest then turned to the other group and addressed the eldest of the three brothers.

"The body of Odukwe, I greet you," he said, and Odukwe bent down and touched the earth. The hearing then began.

Uzowulu stepped forward and presented his case.

"That woman standing there is my wife, Mgbafo. I married her with my money and my yams. I do not owe my in-laws anything. I owe them no yams. I owe them no coco-yams. One morning three of them came to my house, beat me up and took my wife and children away. This happened in the rainy season. I have waited in vain for my wife to return. At last I went to my in-laws and said to them, 'You have taken back your sister. I did not send her away. You yourselves took her. The law of the clan is that you should return her bride-price.' But my wife's brothers said they had nothing to tell me. So I have brought the matter to the fathers of the clan. My case is finished. I salute you."

"Your words are good," said the leader of the *egwugwu*. "Let us hear Odukwe. His words may also be good."

Odukwe was short and thickset. He stepped forward, saluted the spirits and began his story.

"My in-law has told you that we went to his house, beat him up and took our sister and her children away. All that is true. He told you that he came to take back her bride-price and we refused to give it him. That also is true. My in-law, Uzowulu, is a beast. My sister lived with him for nine years. During those years no single day passed in the sky without his beating the woman. We have tried to settle their quarrels time without number and on each occasion Uzowulu was guilty—"

"It is a lie!" Uzowulu shouted.

"Two years ago," continued Odukwe, "when she was pregnant, he beat her until she miscarried."

"It is a lie. She miscarried after she had gone to sleep with her lover."

"Uzowulu's body, I salute you," said Evil Forest, silencing him. "What kind of lover sleeps with a pregnant woman?" There was a loud murmur of approbation from the crowd. Odukwe continued:

"Last year when my sister was recovering from an illness, he beat her again so that if the neighbors had not gone in to save her she would have been killed. We heard of it, and did as you have been told. The law of Umuofia is that if a woman runs away from her husband her bride-price is returned. But in this case she ran away to save her life. Her two children belong to Uzowulu. We do not dispute it, but they are too young to leave their mother. If, in the other hand, Uzowulu should recover from his madness and come in the proper way to beg his wife to return she will do so on the understanding that if he ever beats her again we shall cut off his genitals for him."

The crowd roared with laughter. Evil Forest rose to his feet and order was immediately restored. A steady cloud of smoke rose from his head. He sat down again and called two witnesses. They were both Uzowulu's neighbors, and they agreed about the beating. Evil Forest then stood up, pulled out his staff and thrust it into the earth again. He ran a few steps in the direction of the women; they all fled in terror, only to return to their places almost immediately. The nine *egwugwu* then went away to consult together in their house. They were silent for a long time. Then the metal gong sounded and the flute was blown. The *egwugwu* had emerged once again from their underground home. They saluted one another and then reappeared on the *ilo*.

"*Umuofia kwenu!*" roared Evil Forest, facing the elders and grandees of the clan.

"*Yaa!*" replied the thunderous crowd; then silence descended from the sky and swallowed the noise.

Evil Forest began to speak and all the while he spoke everyone was silent. The eight other *egwugwu* were as still as statues.

"We have heard both sides of the case," said Evil Forest. "Our duty is not to blame this man or to praise that, but to settle the dispute." He turned to Uzowulu's group and allowed a short pause.

"Uzowulu's body, I salute you," he said.

"Our father, my hand has touched the ground," replied Uzowulu, touching the earth.

"Uzowulu's body, do you know me?"

"How can I know you, father? You are beyond our knowledge," Uzowulu replied.

"I am Evil Forest. I kill a man on the day that his life is sweetest to him."

"That is true," replied Uzowulu.

"Go to your in-laws with a pot of wine and beg your wife to return to you. It is not bravery when a man fights with a woman." He turned to Odukwe, and allowed a brief pause.

"Odukwe's body, I greet you," he said.

"My hand is on the ground," replied Odukwe.

"Do you know me?"

"No man can know you," replied Odukwe.

"I am Evil Forest, I am Dry-meat-that-fills-the-mouth, I am Fire-that-burns-without-faggots. If your in-law brings wine to you, let your sister go with him. I salute you." He pulled his staff from the hard earth and thrust it back.

"*Umuofia kwenu!*" he roared, and the crowd answered.

"I don't know why such a trifle should come before the *egwugwu*," said one elder to another.

"Don't you know what kind of man Uzowulu is? He will not listen to any other decision," replied the other.

As they spoke two other groups of people had replaced the first before the *egwugwu*, and a great land case began.

11

The night was impenetrably dark. The moon had been rising later and later every night until now it was seen only at dawn. And whenever the moon forsook evening and rose at cock-crow the nights were as black as charcoal.

Ezinma and her mother sat on a mat on the floor after their supper of yam foo-foo and bitter-leaf soup. A palm-oil lamp gave out yellowish light. Without it, it would have been impossible to eat; one could not have known where one's mouth was in the darkness of that night. There was an oil lamp in all the four huts on Okonkwo's compound, and each hut seen from the others looked like a soft eye of yellow half-light set in the solid massiveness of night.

The world was silent except for the shrill cry of insects, which was part of the night, and the sound of wooden mortar and pestle as Nwayieke pounded her foo-foo. Nwayieke lived four compounds away, and she was notorious for her late cooking. Every woman in the neighborhood knew the sound of Nwayieke's mortar and pestle. It was also part of the night.

Okonkwo had eaten from his wives' dishes and was now reclining with his back against the wall. He searched his bag and brought out his snuff-bottle. He turned it on to his left palm, but nothing came out. He hit the bottle against his knee to shake up the tobacco. That was always the trouble with Okeke's snuff. It very quickly went damp, and there was too much saltpeter in it. Okonkwo had not bought snuff from him for a long time. Idigo was the man who knew how to grind good snuff. But he had recently fallen ill.

Low voices, broken now and again by singing, reached Okonkwo from his wives' huts as each woman and her children told folk stories. Ekwefi and her daughter, Ezinma, sat on a mat on the floor. It was Ekwefi's turn to tell a story.

"Once upon a time," she began, "all the birds were invited to a feast in the sky. They were very happy and began to prepare themselves for the great day. They painted their bodies with red cam wood and drew beautiful patterns on them with *uli*.

"Tortoise saw all these preparations and soon discovered what it all meant. Nothing that happened in the world of the animals ever escaped his notice; he was full of cunning. As soon as he heard of the great feast in the sky his throat began to itch at the very thought. There was a famine in those days and Tortoise had not eaten a good meal for two moons. His body rattled like a piece of dry stick in his empty shell. So he began to plan how he would go to the sky."

"But he had no wings," said Ezinma.

"Be patient," replied her mother. "That is the story. Tortoise had no wings, but he went to the birds and asked to be allowed to go with them.

" 'We know you too well,' said the birds when they had heard him. 'You are full of cunning and you are ungrateful. If we allow you to come with us you will soon begin your mischief.'

" 'You do not know me,' said Tortoise. 'I am a changed man. I have learned that a man who makes trouble for others is also making it for himself.'

"Tortoise had a sweet tongue, and within a short time all the birds agreed that he was a changed man, and they each gave him a feather, with which he made two wings.

"At last the great day came and Tortoise was the first to arrive at the meeting place. When all the birds had gathered together, they set off in a body. Tortoise was very happy and voluble as he flew among the birds, and he was soon chosen as the man to speak for the party because he was a great orator.

" 'There is one important thing which we must not forget,' he said as they flew on their way. 'When people are invited to a great feast like this, they take new names for the occasion. Our hosts in the sky will expect us to honor this age-old custom.'

"None of the birds had heard of this custom but they knew that Tortoise, in spite of his failings in other directions, was a widely traveled man who knew the customs of different peoples. And so they each took a new name. When they had all taken, Tortoise also took one. He was to be called *All of you*.

"At last the party arrived in the sky and their hosts were very happy to see them. Tortoise stood up in his many-colored plumage and thanked them for their invitation. His speech was so eloquent that all the birds were glad they had brought him, and nodded their heads in approval of all he said. Their hosts took him as the king of the birds, especially as he looked somewhat different from the others.

"After kola nuts had been presented and eaten, the people of the sky set before their guests the most delectable dishes Tortoise had ever seen or dreamed of. The soup was brought out hot from the fire and in the very pot in which it had been cooked. It was full of meat and fish. Tortoise began to sniff aloud. There was pounded yam and also yam pottage cooked with palm-oil and fresh fish. There were also pots of palm-wine. When everything had been set before the guests, one of the people of the sky came forward and tasted a little from each pot. He then invited the birds to eat. But Tortoise jumped to his feet and asked: 'For whom have you prepared this feast?'

" 'For all of you,' replied the man.

"Tortoise turned to the birds and said: 'You remember that my name is *All of you*. The custom here is to serve the spokesman first and the others later. They will serve you when I have eaten.'

"He began to eat and the birds grumbled angrily. The people of the sky thought it must be their custom to leave all the food for their king. And so Tortoise ate the best part of the food and then drank two pots of palm-wine, so that he was full of food and drink and his body filled out in his shell.

"The birds gathered round to eat what was left and to peck at the bones he had thrown all about the floor. Some of them were too angry to eat. They chose to fly home on an empty stomach. But before they left each took back the feather he had lent to Tortoise. And there he stood in his hard shell full of food and wine but without any wings to fly home. He asked the birds to take a message for his wife, but they all refused. In the end Parrot, who had felt more angry than the others, suddenly changed his mind and agreed to take the message.

" 'Tell my wife,' said Tortoise, 'to bring out all the soft things in my house and cover the compound with them so that I can jump down from the sky without very great danger.'

"Parrot promised to deliver the message, and then flew away. But when he reached Tortoise's house he told his wife to bring out all the hard things in the house. And so she brought out her husband's hoes, machetes, spears, guns and even his cannon. Tortoise looked down from the sky and saw his wife bringing things out, but it was too far to see what they were. When all seemed ready he let himself go. He fell and fell and fell until he began to fear that he would never stop falling. And then like the sound of his cannon he crashed on the compound."

"Did he die?" asked Ezinma.

"No," replied Ekwefi. "His shell broke into pieces. But there was a great medicine man in the neighborhood. Tortoise's wife sent for him and he gathered all the bits of shell and stuck them together. That is why Tortoise's shell is not smooth."

"There is no song in the story," Ezinma pointed out.

"No," said Ekwefi. "I shall think of another one with a song. But it is your turn now."

"Once upon a time," Ezinma began, "Tortoise and Cat went to wrestle against Yams—no, that is not the beginning. Once upon a time there was a great famine in the land of animals. Everybody was lean except Cat, who was fat and whose body shone as if oil was rubbed on it . . ."

She broke off because at that very moment a loud and high-pitched voice broke the outer silence of the night. It was Chielo, the priestess of Agbala, prophesying. There was nothing new in that. Once in a while Chielo was possessed by the spirit of her god and she began to prophesy. But tonight she was addressing her prophecy and greetings to Okonkwo, and so everyone in his family listened. The folk stories stopped.

"*Agbala do-o-o-o! Agbala ekeneo-o-o-o-o*,"[2] came the voice like a sharp

---

2. "Agbala wants something! Agbala greets . . ."

knife cutting through the night. *"Okonkwo! Agbala ekene gio-o-o-o! Agbala cholu ifu ada ya Ezinmao-o-o-o!"*[3]

At the mention of Ezinma's name Ekwefi jerked her head sharply like an animal that had sniffed death in the air. Her heart jumped painfully within her.

The priestess had now reached Okonkwo's compound and was talking with him outside his hut. She was saying again and again that Agbala wanted to see his daughter, Ezinma. Okonkwo pleaded with her to come back in the morning because Ezinma was now asleep. But Chielo ignored what he was trying to say and went on shouting that Agbala wanted to see his daughter. Her voice was as clear as metal, and Okonkwo's women and children heard from their huts all that she said. Okonkwo was still pleading that the girl had been ill of late and was asleep. Ekwefi quickly took her to their bedroom and placed her on their high bamboo bed.

The priestess screamed. "Beware, Okonkwo!" she warned. "Beware of exchanging words with Agbala. Does a man speak when a god speaks? Beware!"

She walked through Okonkwo's hut into the circular compound and went straight toward Ekwefi's hut. Okonkwo came after her.

"Ekwefi," she called, "Agbala greets you. Where is my daughter, Ezinma? Agbala wants to see her."

Ekwefi came out from her hut carrying her oil lamp in her left hand. There was a light wind blowing, so she cupped her right hand to shelter the flame. Nwoye's mother, also carrying an oil lamp, emerged from her hut. The children stood in the darkness outside their hut watching the strange event. Okonkwo's youngest wife also came out and joined the others.

"Where does Agbala want to see her?" Ekwefi asked.

"Where else but in his house in the hills and the caves?" replied the priestess.

"I will come with you, too," Ekwefi said firmly.

"Tufia-a!"[4] the priestess cursed, her voice cracking like the angry bark of thunder in the dry season. "How dare you, woman, to go before the mighty Agbala of your own accord? Beware, woman, lest he strike you in his anger. Bring me my daughter."

Ekwefi went into her hut and came out again with Ezinma.

"Come, my daughter," said the priestess. "I shall carry you on my back. A baby on its mother's back does not know that the way is long."

Ezinma began to cry. She was used to Chielo calling her "my daughter." But it was a different Chielo she now saw in the yellow half-light.

"Don't cry, my daughter," said the priestess, "lest Agbala be angry with you."

"Don't cry," said Ekwefi, "she will bring you back very soon. I shall give you some fish to eat." She went into the hut again and brought down the smoke-black basket in which she kept her dried fish and other ingredients

---

3. "Agbala greets you! Agbala wants to see his daughter Ezinma!"   4. A curse in words meaning "spitting" or "clearing out," often accompanied by spitting.

for cooking soup. She broke a piece in two and gave it to Ezinma, who clung to her.

"Don't be afraid," said Ekwefi, stroking her head, which was shaved in places, leaving a regular pattern of hair. They went outside again. The priestess bent down on one knee and Ezinma climbed on her back, her left palm closed on her fish and her eyes gleaming with tears.

"Agbala do-o-o-o! Agbala ekeneo-o-o-o! . . ." Chielo began once again to chant greetings to her god. She turned round sharply and walked through Okonkwo's hut, bending very low at the eaves. Ezinma was crying loudly now, calling on her mother. The two voices disappeared into the thick darkness.

A strange and sudden weakness descended on Ekwefi as she stood gazing in the direction of the voices like a hen whose only chick has been carried away by a kite. Ezinma's voice soon faded away and only Chielo was heard moving farther and farther into the distance.

"Why do you stand there as though she had been kidnapped?" asked Okonkwo as he went back to his hut.

"She will bring her back soon," Nwoye's mother said.

But Ekwefi did not hear these consolations. She stood for a while, and then, all of a sudden, made up her mind. She hurried through Okonkwo's hut and went outside. "Where are you going?" he asked.

"I am following Chielo," she replied and disappeared in the darkness. Okonkwo cleared his throat, and brought out his snuff-bottle from the goatskin bag by his side.

The priestess's voice was already growing faint in the distance. Ekwefi hurried to the main footpath and turned left in the direction of the voice. Her eyes were useless to her in the darkness. But she picked her way easily on the sandy footpath hedged on either side by branches and damp leaves. She began to run, holding her breasts with her hands to stop them flapping noisily against her body. She hit her left foot against an outcropped root, and terror seized her. It was an ill omen. She ran faster. But Chielo's voice was still a long way away. Had she been running too? How could she go so fast with Ezinma on her back? Although the night was cool, Ekwefi was beginning to feel hot from her running. She continually ran into the luxuriant weeds and creepers that walled in the path. Once she tripped up and fell. Only then did she realize, with a start, that Chielo had stopped her chanting. Her heart beat violently and she stood still. Then Chielo's renewed outburst came from only a few paces ahead. But Ekwefi could not see her. She shut her eyes for a while and opened them again in an effort to see. But it was useless. She could not see beyond her nose.

There were no stars in the sky because there was a rain-cloud. Fireflies went about with their tiny green lamps, which only made the darkness more profound. Between Chielo's outbursts the night was alive with the shrill tremor of forest insects woven into the darkness.

"Agbala do-o-o-o! . . . Agbala ekeneo-o-o-o! . . ." Ekwefi trudged behind, neither getting too near nor keeping too far back. She thought they must be going towards the sacred cave. Now that she walked slowly she had time to think. What would she do when they got to the cave? She would not dare to enter. She would wait at the mouth, all alone in that fearful place. She thought of all the terrors of the night. She remembered that night, long ago, when she had seen *Ogbu-agali-odu*, one of those evil essences loosed upon the world by the potent "medicines" which the tribe had made in the distant past against its enemies but had now forgotten how to control. Ekwefi had been returning from the stream with her mother on a dark night like this when they saw its glow as it flew in their direction. They had thrown down their water-pots and lain by the roadside expecting the sinister light to descend on them and kill them. That was the only time Ekwefi ever saw *Ogbu-agali-odu*. But although it had happened so long ago, her blood still ran cold whenever she remembered that night.

The priestess's voice came at longer intervals now, but its vigor was undiminished. The air was cool and damp with dew. Ezinma sneezed. Ekwefi muttered, "Life to you." At the same time the priestess also said, "Life to you, my daughter." Ezinma's voice from the darkness warmed her mother's heart. She trudged slowly along.

And then the priestess screamed. "Somebody is walking behind me!" she said. "Whether you are spirit or man, may Agbala shave your head with a blunt razor! May he twist your neck until you see your heels!"

Elkwefi stood rooted to the spot. One mind said to her: "Woman, go home before Agbala does you harm." But she could not. She stood until Chielo had increased the distance between them and she began to follow again. She had already walked so long that she began to feel a slight numbness in the limbs and in the head. Then it occurred to her that they could not have been heading for the cave. They must have by-passed it long ago; they must be going towards Umuachi, the farthest village in the clan. Chielo's voice now came after long intervals.

It seemed to Ekwefi that the night had become a little lighter. The cloud had lifted and a few stars were out. The moon must be preparing to rise, its sullenness over. When the moon rose late in the night, people said it was refusing food, as a sullen husband refuses his wife's food when they have quarrelled.

"*Agbala do-o-o-o! Umuachi! Agbala ekene unuo-o-o!*" It was just as Ekwefi had thought. The priestess was now saluting the village of Umuachi. It was unbelievable, the distance they had covered. As they emerged into the open village from the narrow forest track the darkness was softened and it became possible to see the vague shape of trees. Ekwefi screwed her eyes up in an effort to see her daughter and the priestess, but whenever she thought she saw their shape it immediately dissolved like a melting lump of darkness. She walked numbly along.

Chielo's voice was now rising continuously, as when she first set out. Ekwefi had a feeling of spacious openness, and she guessed they must be on the village *ilo*, or playground. And she realized too with something like a jerk that Chielo was no longer moving forward. She was, in fact, returning. Ekwefi quickly moved away from her line of retreat. Chielo passed by, and they began to go back the way they had come.

It was a long and weary journey and Ekwefi felt like a sleepwalker most of the way. The moon was definitely rising, and although it had not yet appeared on the sky its light had already melted down the darkness. Ekwefi could now discern the figure of the priestess and her burden. She slowed down her pace so as to increase the distance between them. She was afraid of what might happen if Chielo suddenly turned round and saw her.

She had prayed for the moon to rise. But now she found the half-light of the incipient moon more terrifying than darkness. The world was now peopled with vague, fantastic figures that dissolved under her steady gaze and then formed again in new shapes. At one stage Ekwefi was so afraid that she nearly called out to Chielo for companionship and human sympathy. What she had seen was the shape of a man climbing a palm tree, his head pointing to the earth and his legs skywards. But at that very moment Chielo's voice rose again in her possessed chanting, and Ekwefi recoiled, because there was no humanity there. It was not the same Chielo who sat with her in the market and sometimes bought bean-cakes for Ezinma, whom she called her daughter. It was a different woman—the priestess of Agbala, the Oracle of the Hills and Caves. Ekwefi trudged along between two fears. The sound of her benumbed steps seemed to come from some other person walking behind her. Her arms were folded across her bare breasts. Dew fell heavily and the air was cold. She could no longer think, not even about the terrors of night. She just jogged along in a half-sleep, only waking to full life when Chielo sang.

At last they took a turning and began to head for the caves. From then on, Chielo never ceased in her chanting. She greeted her god in a multitude of names—the owner of the future, the messenger of earth, the god who cut a man down when his life was sweetest to him. Ekwefi was also awakened and her benumbed fears revived.

The moon was now up and she could see Chielo and Ezinma clearly. How a woman could carry a child of that size so easily and for so long was a miracle. But Ekwefi was not thinking about that. Chielo was not a woman that night.

"Agbala do-o-o-o! Agbala ekeneo-o-o-o! Chi negbu madu ubosi ndu ya nato ya uto daluo-o-o! . . ."[5]

Ekwefi could already see the hills looming in the moonlight. They formed a circular ring with a break at one point through which the foot-track led to the center of the circle.

As soon as the priestess stepped into this ring of hills her voice was not only doubled in strength but was thrown back on all sides. It was indeed the shrine of a great god. Ekwefi picked her way carefully and quietly. She was already beginning to doubt the wisdom of her coming. Nothing would happen to Ezinma, she thought. And if anything happened to her could she stop it? She would not dare to enter the underground caves. Her coming was quite useless, she thought.

As these things went through her mind she did not realize how close they were to the cave mouth. And so when the priestess with Ezinma on her back disappeared through a hole hardly big enough to pass a hen, Ekwefi broke into a run as though to stop them. As she stood gazing at the

---

5. "Agbala wants something! Agbala greets . . . God who kills a man on the day his life is so pleasant he gives thanks!"

circular darkness which had swallowed them, tears gushed from her eyes, and she swore within her that if she heard Ezinma cry she would rush into the cave to defend her against all the gods in the world. She would die with her.

Having sworn that oath, she sat down on a stony ledge and waited. Her fear had vanished. She could hear the priestess's voice, all its metal taken out of it by the vast emptiness of the cave. She buried her face in her lap and waited.

She did not know how long she waited. It must have been a very long time. Her back was turned on the footpath that led out of the hills. She must have heard a noise behind her and turned round sharply. A man stood there with a machete in his hand. Ekwefi uttered a scream and sprang to her feet.

"Don't be foolish," said Okonkwo's voice. "I thought you were going into the shrine with Chielo," he mocked.

Ekwefi did not answer. Tears of gratitude filled her eyes. She knew her daughter was safe.

"Go home and sleep," said Okonkwo. "I shall wait here."

"I shall wait too. It is almost dawn. The first cock has crowed."

As they stood there together, Ekwefi's mind went back to the days when they were young. She had married Anene because Okonkwo was too poor then to marry. Two years after her marriage to Anene she could bear it no longer and she ran away to Okonkwo. It had been early in the morning. The moon was shining. She was going to the stream to fetch water. Okonkwo's house was on the way to the stream. She went in and knocked at his door and he came out. Even in those days he was not a man of many words. He just carried her into his bed and in the darkness began to feel around her waist for the loose end of her cloth.

12

On the following morning the entire neighborhood wore a festive air because Okonkwo's friend, Obierika, was celebrating his daughter's *uri*. It was the day on which her suitor (having already paid the greater part of her bride-price) would bring palm-wine not only to her parents and immediate relatives but to the wide and extensive group of kinsmen called *umunna*. Everybody had been invited — men, women and children. But it was really a woman's ceremony and the central figures were the bride and her mother.

As soon as day broke, breakfast was hastily eaten and women and children began to gather at Obierika's compound to help the bride's mother in her difficult but happy task of cooking for a whole village.

Okonkwo's family was astir like any other family in the neighborhood. Nwoye's mother and Okonkwo's youngest wife were ready to set out for Obierika's compound with all their children. Nwoye's mother carried a basket of coco-yams, a cake of salt and smoked fish which she would present to Obierika's wife. Okonkwo's youngest wife, Ojiugo, also had a basket of plantains and coco-yams and a small pot of palm-oil. Their children carried pots of water.

Ekwefi was tired and sleepy from the exhausting experiences of the previous night. It was not very long since they had returned. The priestess, with Ezinma sleeping on her back, had crawled out of the shrine on her belly like a snake. She had not as much as looked at Okonkwo and Ekwefi or shown any surprise at finding them at the mouth of the cave. She looked straight ahead of her and walked back to the village. Okonkwo and his wife followed at a respectful distance. They thought the priestess might be going to her house, but she went to Okonkwo's compound, passed through his *obi* and into Ekwefi's hut and walked into her bedroom. She placed Ezinma carefully on the bed and went away without saying a word to anybody.

Ezinma was still sleeping when everyone else was astir, and Ekwefi asked Nwoye's mother and Ojiugo to explain to Obierika's wife that she would be late. She had got ready her basket of coco-yams and fish, but she must wait for Ezinma to wake.

"You need some sleep yourself," said Nwoye's mother. "You look very tired."

As they spoke Ezinma emerged from the hut, rubbing her eyes and stretching her spare frame. She saw the other children with their water-pots and remembered that they were going to fetch water for Obierika's wife. She went back to the hut and brought her pot.

"Have you slept enough?" asked her mother.

"Yes," she replied, "Let us go."

"Not before you have had your breakfast," said Ekwefi. And she went into her hut to warm the vegetable soup she had cooked last night.

"We shall be going," said Nwoye's mother. "I will tell Obierika's wife that you are coming later." And so they all went to help Obierika's wife — Nwoye's mother with her four children and Ojiugo with her two.

As they trooped through Okonkwo's *obi* he asked: "Who will prepare my afternoon meal?"

"I shall return to do it," said Ojiugo.

Okonkwo was also feeling tired, and sleepy, for although nobody else knew it, he had not slept at all last night. He had felt very anxious but did not show it. When Ekwefi had followed the priestess, he had allowed what he regarded as a reasonable and manly interval to pass and then gone with his machete to the shrine, where he thought they must be. It was only when he had got there that it had occurred to him that the priestess might have chosen to go round the villages first. Okonkwo had returned home and sat waiting. When he thought he had waited long enough he again returned to the shrine. But the Hills and the Caves were as silent as death. It was only on his fourth trip that he had found Ekwefi, and by then he had become gravely worried.

Obierika's compound was as busy as an anthill. Temporary cooking tri-pods were erected on every available space by bringing together three blocks of sun-dried earth and making a fire in their midst. Cooking pots went up and down the tripods, and foo-foo was pounded in a hundred wooden mortars. Some of the women cooked the yams and the cassava, and others prepared vegetable soup. Young men pounded the foo-foo or split firewood. The children made endless trips to the stream.

Three young men helped Obierika to slaughter the two goats with which the soup was made. They were very fat goats, but the fattest of all was tethered to a peg near the wall of the compound. It was as big as a small cow. Obierika had sent one of his relatives all the way to Umuike to buy that goat. It was the one he would present alive to his in-laws.

"The market of Umuike is a wonderful place," said the young man who had been sent by Obierika to buy the giant goat. "There are so many people on it that if you threw up a grain of sand it would not find a way to fall to earth again."

"It is the result of a great medicine," said Obierika. "The people of Umuike wanted their market to grow and swallow up the markets of their neighbors. So they made a powerful medicine. Every market day, before the first cock-crow, this medicine stands on the market ground in the shape of an old woman with a fan. With this magic fan she beckons to the market all the neighboring clans. She beckons in front of her and behind her, to her right and to her left."

"And so everybody comes," said another man, "honest men and thieves. They can steal your cloth from off your waist in that market."

"Yes," said Obierika. "I warned Nwankwo to keep a sharp eye and a sharp ear. There was once a man who went to sell a goat. He led it on a thick rope which he tied round his wrist. But as he walked through the market he realized that people were pointing at him as they do to a madman. He could not understand it until he looked back and saw that what he led at the end of the tether was not a goat but a heavy log of wood."

"Do you think a thief can do that kind of thing single-handed?" asked Nwankwo.

"No," said Obierika. "They use medicine."

When they had cut the goats' throats and collected the blood in a bowl, they held them over an open fire to burn off the hair, and the smell of burning hair blended with the smell of cooking. Then they washed them and cut them up for the women who prepared the soup.

All this anthill activity was going smoothly when a sudden interruption came. It was a cry in the distance: *Oji odu achu ijiji-o-o!* (*The one that uses its tail to drive flies away!*) Every woman immediately abandoned whatever she was doing and rushed out in the direction of the cry.

"We cannot all rush out like that, leaving what we are cooking to burn in the fire," shouted Chielo, the priestess. "Three or four of us should stay behind."

"It is true," said another woman. "We will allow three or four women to stay behind."

Five women stayed behind to look after the cooking-pots, and all the rest rushed away to see the cow that had been let loose. When they saw it they drove it back to its owner, who at once paid the heavy fine which the village imposed on anyone whose cow was let loose on his neighbors' crops. When the women had exacted the penalty they checked among themselves to see if any woman had failed to come out when the cry had been raised.

"Where is Mgbogo?" asked one of them.

"She is ill in bed," said Mgbogo's next-door neighbor. "She has *iba.*"

"The only other person is Udenkwo," said another woman, "and her child is not twenty-eight days yet."

Those women whom Obierika's wife had not asked to help her with the cooking returned to their homes, and the rest went back, in a body, to Obierika's compound.

"Whose cow was it?" asked the women who had been allowed to stay behind.

"It was my husband's," said Ezelagbo. "One of the young children had opened the gate of the cowshed."

Early in the afternoon the first two pots of palm-wine arrived from Obierika's in-laws. They were duly presented to the women, who drank a cup or two each, to help them in their cooking. Some of it also went to the bride and her attendant maidens, who were putting the last delicate touches of razor to her coiffure and cam wood on her smooth skin.

When the heat of the sun began to soften, Obierika's son, Maduka, took a long broom and swept the ground in front of his father's *obi.* And as if they had been waiting for that, Obierika's relatives and friends began to arrive, every man with his goatskin bag hung on one shoulder and a rolled goatskin mat under his arm. Some of them were accompanied by their sons bearing carved wooden stools. Okonkwo was one of them. They sat in a half-circle and began to talk of many things. It would not be long before the suitors came.

Okonkwo brought out his snuff-bottle and offered it to Ogbuefi Ezenwa, who sat next to him. Ezenwa[6] took it, tapped it on his kneecap, rubbed his left palm on his body to dry it before tipping a little snuff into it. His actions were deliberate, and he spoke as he performed them:

"I hope our in-laws will bring many pots of wine. Although they come from a village that is known for being closefisted, they ought to know that Akueke is the bride for a king."

"They dare not bring fewer than thirty pots," said Okonkwo. "I shall tell them my mind if they do."

At that moment Obierika's son, Maduka, led out the giant goat from the inner compound, for his father's relatives to see. They all admired it and said that that was the way things should be done. The goat was then led back to the inner compound.

Very soon after, the in-laws began to arrive. Young men and boys in single file, each carrying a pot of wine, came first. Obierika's relatives counted the pots as they came. Twenty, twenty-five. There was a long break, and the hosts looked at each other as if to say, "I told you." Then more pots came. Thirty, thirty-five, forty, forty-five. The hosts nodded in approval and seemed to say, "Now they are behaving like men." Altogether there were fifty pots of wine. After the pot-bearers came Ibe, the suitor, and the elders of his family. They sat in a half-moon, thus completing a circle with their hosts. The pots of wine stood in their midst. Then the bride, her mother and a half a dozen other women and girls emerged from

6. "King from Childhood" (strong praise).

the inner compound, and went round the circle shaking hands with all. The bride's mother led the way, followed by the bride and the other women. The married women wore their best cloths and the girls wore red and black waist-beads and anklets of brass.

When the women retired, Obierika presented kola nuts to his in-laws. His eldest brother broke the first one. "Life to all of us," he said as he broke it. "And let there be friendship between your family and ours."

The crowd answered: "*Ee-e-e!*"

"We are giving you our daughter today. She will be a good wife to you. She will bear you nine sons like the mother of our town."

"*Ee-e-e!*"

The oldest man in the camp of the visitors replied: "It will be good for you and it will be good for us."

"*Ee-e-e!*"

"This is not the first time my people have come to marry your daughter. My mother was one of you."

"*Ee-e-e!*"

"And this will not be the last, because you understand us and we understand you. You are a great family."

"*Ee-e-e!*"

"Prosperous men and great warriors." He looked in the direction of Okonkwo. "Your daughter will bear us sons like you."

"*Ee-e-e!*"

The kola was eaten and the drinking of palm-wine began. Groups of four or five men sat round with a pot in their midst. As the evening wore on, food was presented to the guests. There were huge bowls of foo-foo and steaming pots of soup. There were also pots of yam pottage. It was a great feast.

As night fell, burning torches were set on wooden tripods and the young men raised a song. The elders sat in a big circle and the singers went round singing each man's praise as they came before him. They had something to say for every man. Some were great farmers, some were orators who spoke for the clan; Okonkwo was the greatest wrestler and warrior alive. When they had gone round the circle they settled down in the center, and girls came from the inner compound to dance. At first the bride was not among them. But when she finally appeared holding a cock in her right hand, a loud cheer rose from the crowd. All the other dancers made way for her. She presented the cock to the musicians and began to dance. Her brass anklets rattled as she danced and her body gleamed with cam wood in the soft yellow light. The musicians with their wood, clay and metal instruments went from song to song. And they were all gay. They sang the latest song in the village:

> If I hold her hand
> She says, "Don't touch!"
> If I hold her foot
> She says, "Don't touch!"
> But when I hold her waist-beads
> She pretends not to know.

The night was already far spent when the guests rose to go, taking their bride home to spend seven market weeks with her suitor's family. They sang songs as they went, and on their way they paid short courtesy visits to prominent men like Okonkwo, before they finally left for their village. Okonkwo made a present of two cocks to them.

13

Go-di-di-go-go-di-go. Di-go-go-di-go. It was the *ekwe* talking to the clan. One of the things every man learned was the language of the hollowed-out wooden instrument. Diim! Diim! Diim! boomed the cannon at intervals.

The first cock had not crowed, and Umuofia was still swallowed up in sleep and silence when the *ekwe* began to talk, and the cannon shattered the silence. Men stirred on their bamboo beds and listened anxiously. Somebody was dead. The cannon seemed to rend the sky. Di-go-go-di-go-di-di-go-go floated in the message-laden night air. The faint and distant wailing of women settled like a sediment of sorrow on the earth. Now and again a full-chested lamentation rose above the wailing whenever a man came into the place of death. He raised his voice once or twice in manly sorrow and then sat down with the other men listening to the endless wailing of the women and the esoteric language of the *ekwe*. Now and again the cannon boomed. The wailing of the women would not be heard beyond the village, but the *ekwe* carried the news to all the nine villages and even beyond. It began by naming the clan: *Umuofia obodo dike,* "the land of the brave." *Umuofia obodo dike! Umuofia obodo dike!* It said this over and over again, and as it dwelt on it, anxiety mounted in every heart that heaved on a bamboo bed that night. Then it went nearer and named the village: *Iguedo[7] of the yellow grinding-stone!"* It was Okonkwo's village. Again and again Iguedo was called and men waited breathlessly in all the nine villages. At last the man was named and people sighed "E-u-u, Ezeudu is dead." A cold shiver ran down Okonkwo's back as he remembered the last time the old man had visited him. "That boy calls you father," he had said. "Bear no hand in his death."

Ezeudu was a great man, and so all the clan was at his funeral. The ancient drums of death beat, guns and cannon were fired, and men dashed about in frenzy, cutting down every tree or animal they saw, jumping over walls and dancing on the roof. It was a warrior's funeral, and from morning till night warriors came and went in their age groups. They all wore smoked raffia skirts and their bodies were painted with chalk and charcoal. Now and again an ancestral spirit or *egwugwu* appeared from the underworld, speaking in a tremulous, unearthly voice and completely covered in raffia. Some of them were very violent, and there had been a mad rush for shelter earlier in the day when one appeared with a sharp machete and was only prevented from doing serious harm by two men who restrained him with the help of a strong rope tied round his waist. Sometimes he

---

7. "The yellow grindstone."

turned round and chased those men, and they ran for their lives. But they always returned to the long rope he trailed behind. He sang, in a terrifying voice, that Ekwensu, or Evil Spirit, had entered his eye.

But the most dreaded of all was yet to come. He was always alone and was shaped like a coffin. A sickly odor hung in the air wherever he went, and flies went with him. Even the greatest medicine men took shelter when he was near. Many years ago another *egwugwu* had dared to stand his ground before him and had been transfixed to the spot for two days. This one had only one hand and it carried a basket full of water.

But some of the *egwugwu* were quite harmless. One of them was so old and infirm that he leaned heavily on a stick. He walked unsteadily to the place where the corpse was laid, gazed at it a while and went away again— to the underworld.

The land of the living was not far removed from the domain of the ancestors. There was coming and going between them, especially at festivals and also when an old man died, because an old man was very close to the ancestors. A man's life from birth to death was a series of transition rites which brought him nearer and nearer to his ancestors.

Ezeudu had been the oldest man in his village, and at his death there were only three men in the whole clan who were older, and four or five others in his own age group. Whenever one of these ancient men appeared in the crowd to dance unsteadily the funeral steps of the tribe, younger men gave way and the tumult subsided.

It was a great funeral, such as befitted a noble warrior. As the evening drew near, the shouting and the firing of guns, the beating of drums and the brandishing and clanging of machetes increased.

Ezeudu had taken three titles in his life. It was a rare achievement. There were only four titles in the clan, and only one or two men in any generation ever achieved the fourth and highest. When they did, they became the lords of the land. Because he had taken titles, Ezeudu was to be buried after dark with only a glowing brand to light the sacred ceremony.

But before this quiet and final rite, the tumult increased tenfold. Drums beat violently and men leaped up and down in frenzy. Guns were fired on all sides and sparks flew out as machetes clanged together in warriors' salutes. The air was full of dust and the smell of gunpowder. It was then that the one-handed spirit came, carrying a basket full of water. People made way for him on all sides and the noise subsided. Even the smell of gunpowder was swallowed in the sickly smell that now filled the air. He danced a few steps to the funeral drums and then went to see the corpse.

"Ezeudu!" he called in his guttural voice. "If you had been poor in your last life I would have asked you to be rich when you come again. But you were rich. If you had been a coward, I would have asked you to bring courage. But you were a fearless warrior. If you had died young, I would have asked you to get life. But you lived long. So I shall ask you to come again the way you came before. If your death was the death of nature, go in peace. But if a man caused it, do not allow him a moment's rest." He danced a few more steps and went away.

The drums and the dancing began again and reached fever-heat. Darkness was around the corner, and the burial was near. Guns fired the last salute and the cannon rent the sky. And then from the center of the delirious fury came a cry of agony and shouts of horror. It was as if a spell had been cast. All was silent. In the center of the crowd a boy lay in a pool of blood. It was the dead man's sixteen-year-old son, who with his brothers and half-brothers had been dancing the traditional farewell to their father. Okonkwo's gun had exploded and a piece of iron had pierced the boy's heart.

The confusion that followed was without parallel in the tradition of Umuofia. Violent deaths were frequent, but nothing like this had ever happened.

The only course open to Okonkwo was to flee from the clan. It was a crime against the earth goddess to kill a clansman, and a man who committed it must flee from the land. The crime was of two kinds, male and female. Okonkwo had committed the female, because it had been inadvertent. He could return to the clan after seven years.

That night he collected his most valuable belongings into head-loads. His wives wept bitterly and their children wept with them without knowing why. Obierika and half a dozen other friends came to help and to console him. They each made nine or ten trips carrying Okonkwo's yams to store in Obierika's barn. And before the cock crowed Okonkwo and his family were fleeing to his motherland. It was a little village called Mbanta,[8] just beyond the borders of Mbaino.

As soon as the day broke, a large crowd of men from Ezeudu's quarter stormed Okonkwo's compound, dressed in garbs of war. They set fire to his houses, demolished his red walls, killed his animals and destroyed his barn. It was the justice of the earth goddess, and they were merely her messengers. They had no hatred in their hearts against Okonkwo. His greatest friend, Obierika, was among them. They were merely cleansing the land which Okonkwo had polluted with the blood of a clansman.

Obierika was a man who thought about things. When the will of the goddess had been done, he sat down in his *obi* and mourned his friend's calamity. Why should a man suffer so grievously for an offense he had committed inadvertently? But although he thought for a long time he found no answer. He was merely led into greater complexities. He remembered his wife's twin children, whom he had thrown away. What crime had they committed? The Earth had decreed that they were an offense on the land and must be destroyed. And if the clan did not exact punishment for an offense against the great goddess, her wrath was loosed on all the land and not just on the offender. As the elders said, if one finger brought oil it soiled the others.

8. "Small Town."

Part Two

14

Okonkwo was well received by his mother's kinsmen in Mbanta. The old man who received him was his mother's younger brother, who was now the eldest surviving member of that family. His name was Uchendu,[9] and it was he who had received Okonkwo's mother twenty and ten years before when she had been brought home from Umuofia to be buried with her people. Okonkwo was only a boy then and Uchendu still remembered him crying the traditional farewell: "Mother, mother, mother is going."

That was many years ago. Today Okonkwo was not bringing his mother home to be buried with her people. He was taking his family of three wives and their children to seek refuge in his motherland. As soon as Uchendu saw him with his sad and weary company he guessed what had happened, and asked no questions. It was not until the following day that Okonkwo told him the full story. The old man listened silently to the end and then said with some relief: "It is a female *ochu*."[1] And he arranged the requisite rites and sacrifices.

Okonkwo was given a plot of ground on which to build his compound, and two or three pieces of land on which to farm during the coming planting season. With the help of his mother's kinsmen he built himself an *obi* and three huts for his wives. He then installed his personal god and the symbols of his departed fathers. Each of Uchendu's five sons contributed three hundred seed-yams to enable their cousin to plant a farm, for as soon as the first rain came farming would begin.

At last the rain came. It was sudden and tremendous. For two or three moons the sun had been gathering strength till it seemed to breathe a breath of fire on the earth. All the grass had long been scorched brown, and the sands felt like live coals to the feet. Evergreen trees wore a dusty coat of brown. The birds were silenced in the forests, and the world lay panting under the live, vibrating heat. And then came the clap of thunder. It was an angry, metallic and thirsty clap, unlike the deep and liquid rumbling of the rainy season. A mighty wind arose and filled the air with dust. Palm trees swayed as the wind combed their leaves into flying crests like strange and fantastic coiffure.

When the rain finally came, it was in large, solid drops of frozen water which the people called "the nuts of the water of heaven." They were hard and painful on the body as they fell, yet young people ran about happily picking up the cold nuts and throwing them into their mouths to melt.

The earth quickly came to life and the birds in the forests fluttered around and chirped merrily. A vague scent of life and green vegetation was diffused in the air. As the rain began to fall more soberly and in smaller liquid drops, children sought for shelter, and all were happy, refreshed and thankful.

Okonkwo and his family worked very hard to plant a new farm. But it was like beginning life anew without the vigor and enthusiasm of youth, like

9. "The Thought Created by Life."   1. Murder, manslaughter.

learning to become left-handed in old age. Work no longer had for him the pleasure it used to have, and when there was no work to do he sat in a silent half-sleep.

His life had been ruled by a great passion—to become one of the lords of the clan. That had been his life-spring. And he had all but achieved it. Then everything had been broken. He had been cast out of his clan like a fish onto a dry, sandy beach, panting. Clearly his personal god or *chi* was not made for great things. A man could not rise beyond the destiny of his *chi*. The saying of the elders was not true—that if a man said yea his *chi* also affirmed. Here was a man whose *chi* said nay despite his own affirmation.

The old man, Uchendu, saw clearly that Okonkwo had yielded to despair and he was greatly troubled. He would speak to him after the *isa-ifi*[2] ceremony.

The youngest of Uchendu's five sons, Amikwu, was marrying a new wife. The bride-price had been paid and all but the last ceremony had been performed. Amikwu and his people had taken palm-wine to the bride's kinsmen about two moons before Okonkwo's arrival in Mbanta. And so it was time for the final ceremony of confession.

The daughters of the family were all there, some of them having come a long way from their homes in distant villages. Uchendu's eldest daughter had come from Obodo, nearly half a day's journey away. The daughters of Uchendu's brothers were also there. It was a full gathering of *umuada*,[3] in the same way as they would meet if a death occurred in the family. There were twenty-two of them.

They sat in a big circle on the ground and the bride sat in the center with a hen in her right hand. Uchendu sat by her, holding the ancestral staff of the family. All the other men stood outside the circle, watching. Their wives watched also. It was evening and the sun was setting.

Uchendu's eldest daughter, Njide, asked the questions.

"Remember that if you do not answer truthfully you will suffer or even die at childbirth," she began. "How many men have lain with you since my brother first expressed the desire to marry you?"

"None," she answered simply.

"Answer truthfully," urged the other women.

"None?" asked Njide.

"None," she answered.

"Swear on this staff of my fathers," said Uchendu.

"I swear," said the bride.

Uchendu took the hen from her, slit its throat with a sharp knife and allowed some of the blood to fall on his ancestral staff.

From that day Amikwu took the young bride to his hut and she became his wife. The daughters of the family did not return to their homes immediately but spent two or three days with their kinsmen.

---

2. A ceremony to ascertain that a wife (here, a promised bride) had been faithful to her husband during a separation.   3. The daughters, who, according to Igbo custom, married outside the clan, perform a special initiation upon returning home for important gatherings.

On the second day Uchendu called together his sons and daughters and his nephew, Okonkwo. The men brought their goatskin mats, with which they sat on the floor, and the women sat on a sisal mat spread on a raised bank of earth. Uchendu pulled gently at his gray beard and gnashed his teeth. Then he began to speak, quietly and deliberately, picking his words with great care:

"It is Okonkwo that I primarily wish to speak to," he began. "But I want all of you to note what I am going to say. I am an old man and you are all children. I know more about the world than any of you. If there is any one among you who thinks he knows more let him speak up." He paused, but no one spoke.

"Why is Okonkwo with us today? This is not his clan. We are only his mother's kinsmen. He does not belong here. He is an exile, condemned for seven years to live in a strange land. And so he is bowed with grief. But there is just one question I would like to ask him. Can you tell me, Okonkwo, why it is that one of the commonest names we give our children is Nneka, or "Mother is Supreme?" We all know that a man is the head of the family and his wives do his bidding. A child belongs to its father and his family and not to its mother and her family. A man belongs to his fatherland and not to his motherland. And yet we say Nneka—'Mother is Supreme.' Why is that?"

There was silence. "I want Okonkwo to answer me," said Uchendu.

"I do not know the answer," Okonkwo replied.

"You do not know the answer? So you see that you are a child. You have many wives and many children—more children than I have. You are a great man in your clan. But you are still a child, *my* child. Listen to me and I shall tell you. But there is one more question I shall ask you. Why is it that when a woman dies she is taken home to be buried with her own kinsmen? She is not buried with her husband's kinsmen. Why is that? Your mother was brought home to me and buried with my people. Why was that?"

Okonkwo shook his head.

"He does not know that either," said Uchendu, "and yet he is full of sorrow because he has come to live in his motherland for a few years." He laughed a mirthless laughter, and turned to his sons and daughters. "What about you? Can you answer my question?"

They all shook their heads.

"Then listen to me," he said and cleared his throat. "It's true that a child belongs to its father. But when a father beats his child, it seeks sympathy in its mother's hut. A man belongs to his fatherland when things are good and life is sweet. But when there is sorrow and bitterness he finds refuge in his motherland. Your mother is there to protect you. She is buried there. And that is why we say that mother is supreme. Is it right that you, Okonkwo, should bring to your mother a heavy face and refuse to be comforted? Be careful or you may displease the dead. Your duty is to comfort your wives and children and take them back to your fatherland after seven years. But if you allow sorrow to weigh you down and kill you, they will all die in exile." He paused for a long while. "These are now your kinsmen." He waved at his sons and daughters. "You think you are the greatest sufferer in the world? Do you know that men are sometimes banished for life? Do you know that men sometimes lose all their yams and even their children? I had six wives once. I have none now except that young girl who knows not her right from her left. Do you know how many children I have buried—children I begot in my youth and strength? Twenty-two. I did not hang myself, and I am still alive. If you think you are the greatest sufferer in the world ask my daughter, Akueni, how many twins she has borne and thrown away. Have you not heard the song they sing when a woman dies?

> For whom is it well, for whom is it well?
> There is no one for whom it is well.

"I have no more to say to you."

15

It was in the second year of Okonkwo's exile that his friend, Obierika, came to visit him. He brought with him two young men, each of them carrying a heavy bag on his head. Okonkwo helped them put down their loads. It was clear that the bags were full of cowries.

Okonkwo was very happy to receive his friend. His wives and children were very happy too, and so were his cousins and their wives when he sent for them and told them who his guest was.

"You must take him to salute our father," said one of the cousins.

"Yes," replied Okonkwo. "We are going directly." But before they went he whispered something to his first wife. She nodded, and soon the children were chasing one of their cocks.

Uchendu had been told by one of his grandchildren that three strangers had come to Okonkwo's house. He was therefore waiting to receive them. He held out his hands to them when they came into his obi, and after they had shaken hands he asked Okonkwo who they were.

"This is Obierika, my great friend. I have already spoken to you about him."

"Yes," said the old man, turning to Obierika. "My son has told me about you, and I am happy you have come to see us. I knew your father, Iweka. He was a great man. He had many friends here and came to see them quite often. Those were good days when a man had friends in distant clans. Your generation does not know that. You stay at home, afraid of your next-door neighbor. Even a man's motherland is strange to him nowadays." He looked at Okonkwo. "I am an old man and I like to talk. That is all I am good for now." He got up painfully, went into an inner room and came back with a kola nut.

"Who are the young men with you?" he asked as he sat down again on his goatskin. Okonkwo told him.

"Ah," he said. "Welcome, my sons." He presented the kola nut to them, and when they had seen it and thanked him, he broke it and they ate.

"Go into that room," he said to Okonkwo, pointing with his finger. "You will find a pot of wine there."

Okonkwo brought the wine and they began to drink. It was a day old, and very strong.

"Yes," said Uchendu after a long silence. "People traveled more in those days. There is not a single clan in these parts that I do not know very well. Aninta, Umuazu, Ikeocha, Elumelu, Abame—I know them all."

"Have you heard," asked Obierika, "that Abame is no more?"

"How is that?" asked Uchendu and Okonkwo together.

"Abame has been wiped out," said Obierika. "It is a strange and terrible story. If I had not seen the few survivors with my own eyes and heard their story with my own ears, I would not have believed. Was it not on an Eke day that they fled into Umuofia?" he asked his two companions, and they nodded their heads.

"Three moons ago," said Obierika, "on an Eke market day a little band of fugitives came into our town. Most of them were sons of our land whose mothers had been buried with us. But there were some too who came because they had friends in our town, and others who could think of nowhere else open to escape. And so they fled into Umuofia with a woeful story." He drank his palm-wine, and Okonkwo filled his horn again. He continued:

"During the last planting season a white man had appeared in their clan."

"An albino," suggested Okonkwo.

"He was not an albino. He was quite different." He sipped his wine. "And he was riding an iron horse.[4] The first people who saw him ran away, but he stood beckoning to them. In the end the fearless ones went near and even touched him. The elders consulted their Oracle and it told them that the strange man would break their clan and spread destruction among them." Obierika again drank a little of his wine. "And so they killed the white man and tied his iron horse to their sacred tree because it looked as if it would run away to call the man's friends. I forgot to tell you another thing which the Oracle said. It said that other white men were on their way. They were locusts, it said, and that first man was their harbinger sent to explore the terrain. And so they killed him."

"What did the white man say before they killed him?" asked Uchendu.

"He said nothing," answered one of Obierika's companions.

"He said something, only they did not understand him," said Obierika. "He seemed to speak through his nose."

"One of the men told me," said Obierika's other companion, "that he repeated over and over again a word that resembled Mbaino. Perhaps he had been going to Mbaino and had lost his way."

"Anyway," resumed Obierika, "they killed him and tied up his iron horse. This was before the planting season began. For a long time nothing happened. The rains had come and yams had been sown. The iron horse was still tied to the sacred silk-cotton tree. And then one morning three white men led by a band of ordinary men like us came to the clan. They saw the iron horse and went away again. Most of the men and women of Abame had gone to their farms. Only a few of them saw these white men

4. Bicycle.

and their followers. For many market weeks nothing else happened. They have a big market in Abame on every other Afo day and, as you know, the whole clan gathers there. That was the day it happened. The three white men and a very large number of other men surrounded the market. They must have used a powerful medicine to make themselves invisible until the market was full. And they began to shoot. Everybody was killed, except the old and the sick who were at home and a handful of men and women whose *chi* were wide awake and brought them out of that market."[5] He paused.

"Their clan is now completely empty. Even the sacred fish in their mysterious lake have fled and the lake has turned the color of blood. A great evil has come upon their land as the Oracle had warned."

There was a long silence. Uchendu ground his teeth together audibly. Then he burst out:

"Never kill a man who says nothing. Those men of Abame were fools. What did they know about the man?" He ground his teeth again and told a story to illustrate his point. "Mother Kite once sent her daughter to bring food. She went, and brought back a duckling. 'You have done very well,' said Mother Kite to her daughter, 'but tell me, what did the mother of this duckling say when you swooped and carried its child away?' 'It said nothing,' replied the young kite. 'It just walked away.' 'You must return the duckling,' said Mother Kite. 'There is something ominous behind the silence.' And so Daughter Kite returned the duckling and took a chick instead. 'What did the mother of this chick do?' asked the old kite. 'It cried and raved and cursed me,' said the young kite. 'Then we can eat the chick,' said her mother. 'There is nothing to fear from someone who shouts.' Those men of Abame were fools."

"They were fools," said Okonkwo after a pause. "They had been warned that danger was ahead. They should have armed themselves with their guns and their machetes even when they went to market."

"They have paid for their foolishness," said Obierika. "But I am greatly afraid. We have heard stories about white men who made the powerful guns and the strong drinks and took slaves away across the seas, but no one thought the stories were true."

"There is no story that is not true," said Uchendu. "The world has no end, and what is good among one people is an abomination with others. We have albinos among us. Do you not think that they came to our clan by mistake, that they have strayed from their way to a land where everybody is like them?"

Okonkwo's first wife soon finished her cooking and set before their guests a big meal of pounded yams and bitter-leaf soup. Okonkwo's son, Nwoye, brought in a pot of sweet wine tapped from the raffia palm.

"You are a big man now," Obierika said to Nwoye. "Your friend Anene asked me to greet you."

"Is he well?" asked Nwoye.

5. Achebe bases his account on a similar incident in 1905 when British troops massacred the town of Ahiara in reprisal for the death of a missionary.

"We are all well," said Obierika.

Ezinma brought them a bowl of water with which to wash their hands. After that they began to eat and to drink the wine.

"When did you set out from home?" asked Okonkwo.

"We had meant to set out from my house before cock-crow," said Obierika. "But Nweke did not appear until it was quite light. Never make an early morning appointment with a man who has just married a new wife." They all laughed.

"Has Nweke married a wife?" asked Okonkwo.

"He has married Okadigbo's second daughter," said Obierika.

"That is very good," said Okonkwo. "I do not blame you for not hearing the cock crow."

When they had eaten, Obierika pointed at the two heavy bags. "That is the money from your yams," he said. "I sold the big ones as soon as you left. Later on I sold some of the seed-yams and gave out others to sharecroppers. I shall do that every year until you return. But I thought you would need the money now and so I brought it. Who knows what may happen tomorrow? Perhaps green men will come to our clan and shoot us."

"God will not permit it," said Okonkwo. "I do not know how to thank you."

"I can tell you," said Obierika. "Kill one of your sons for me."

"That will not be enough," said Okonkwo.

"Then kill yourself," said Obierika.

"Forgive me," said Okonkwo, smiling. "I shall not talk about thanking you any more."

16

When nearly two years later Obierika paid another visit to his friend in exile the circumstances were less happy. The missionaries had come to Umuofia. They had built their church there, won a handful of converts and were already sending evangelists to the surrounding towns and villages. That was a source of great sorrow to the leaders of the clan; but many of them believed that the strange faith and the white man's god would not last. None of his converts was a man whose word was heeded in the assembly of the people. None of them was a man of title. They were mostly the kind of people that were called *efulefu*, worthless, empty men. The imagery of an *efulefu* in the language of the clan was a man who sold his machete and wore the sheath to battle. Chielo, the priestess of Agbala, called the converts the excrement of the clan, and the new faith was a mad dog that had come to eat it up.

What moved Obierika to visit Okonkwo was the sudden appearance of the latter's son, Nwoye, among the missionaries in Umuofia.

"What are you doing here?" Obierika had asked when after many difficulties the missionaries had allowed him to speak to the boy.

"I am one of them," replied Nwoye.

"How is your father?" Obierika asked, not knowing what else to say.

"I don't know. He is not my father," said Nwoye, unhappily.

And so Obierika went to Mbanta to see his friend. And he found that Okonkwo did not wish to speak about Nwoye. It was only from Nwoye's mother that he heard scraps of the story.

The arrival of the missionaries had caused a considerable stir in the village of Mbanta. There were six of them and one was a white man. Every man and woman came out to see the white man. Stories about these strange men had grown since one of them had been killed in Abame and his iron horse tied to the sacred silk-cotton tree. And so everybody came to see the white man. It was the time of the year when everybody was at home. The harvest was over.

When they had all gathered, the white man began to speak to them. He spoke through an interpreter who was an Ibo man, though his dialect was different and harsh to the ears of Mbanta. Many people laughed at his dialect and the way he used words strangely. Instead of saying "myself" he always said "my buttocks."[6] But he was a man of commanding presence and the clansmen listened to him. He said he was one of them, as they could see from his color and his language. The other four black men were also their brothers, although one of them did not speak Ibo. The white man was also their brother because they were all sons of God. And he told them about this new God, the Creator of all the world and all the men and women. He told them that they worshipped false gods, gods of wood and stone. A deep murmur went through the crowd when he said this. He told them that the true God lived on high and that all men when they died went before Him for judgment. Evil men and all the heathen who in their blindness bowed to wood and stone were thrown into a fire that burned like palm-oil. But good men who worshipped the true God lived forever in His happy kingdom. "We have been sent by this great God to ask you to leave your wicked ways and false gods and turn to Him so that you may be saved when you die," he said.

"Your buttocks understand our language," said someone light-heartedly and the crowd laughed.

"What did he say?" the white man asked his interpreter. But before he could answer, another man asked a question: "Where is the white man's horse?" he asked. The Ibo evangelists consulted among themselves and decided that the man probably meant bicycle. They told the white man and he smiled benevolently.

"Tell them," he said, "that I shall bring many iron horses when we have settled down among them. Some of them will even ride the iron horse themselves." This was interpreted to them but very few of them heard. They were talking excitedly among themselves because the white man had said he was going to live among them. They had not thought about that.

At this point an old man said he had a question. "Which is this god of

---

6. The Igbo language has high and low tones so that the same word may have different meanings according to its pronunciation. Here, Achebe is probably referring to a famous pair of near-homonyms: *iké* ("strength") and *ike* ("buttocks").

yours," he asked, "the goddess of the earth, the god of the sky, Amadiora of the thunderbolt, or what?"

The interpreter spoke to the white man and he immediately gave his answer. "All the gods you have named are not gods at all. They are gods of deceit who tell you to kill your fellows and destroy innocent children. There is only one true God and He has the earth, the sky, you and me and all of us."

"If we leave our gods and follow your god," asked another man, "who will protect us from the anger of our neglected gods and ancestors?"

"Your gods are not alive and cannot do you any harm," replied the white man. "They are pieces of wood and stone."

When this was interpreted to the men of Mbanta they broke into derisive laughter. These men must be mad, they said to themselves. How else could they say that Ani and Amadiora were harmless? And Idemili and Ogwugwu too? And some of them began to go away.

Then the missionaries burst into song. It was one of those gay and rollicking tunes of evangelism which had the power of plucking at silent and dusty chords in the heart of an Ibo man. The interpreter explained each verse to the audience, some of whom now stood enthralled. It was a story of brothers who lived in darkness and in fear, ignorant of the love of God. It told of one sheep out on the hills, away from the gates of God and from the tender shepherd's care.

After the singing the interpreter spoke about the Son of God whose name was Jesu Kristi. Okonkwo, who only stayed in the hope that it might come to chasing the men out of the village or whipping them, now said: "You told us with your own mouth that there was only one god. Now you talk about his son. He must have a wife, then." The crowd agreed.

"I did not say He had a wife," said the interpreter, somewhat lamely.

"Your buttocks said he had a son," said the joker. "So he must have a wife and all of them must have buttocks."

The missionary ignored him and went on to talk about the Holy Trinity. At the end of it Okonkwo was fully convinced that the man was mad. He shrugged his shoulders and went away to tap his afternoon palm-wine.

But there was a young lad who had been captivated. His name was Nwoye, Okonkwo's first son. It was not the mad logic of the Trinity that captivated him. He did not understand it. It was the poetry of the new religion, something felt in the marrow. The hymn about brothers who sat in darkness and in fear seemed to answer a vague and persistent question that haunted his young soul—the question of the twins crying in the bush and the question of Ikemefuna who was killed. He felt a relief within as the hymn poured into his parched soul. The words of the hymn were like the drops of frozen rain melting on the dry palate of the panting earth. Nwoye's callow mind was greatly puzzled.

17

The missionaries spent their first four or five nights in the marketplace, and went into the village in the morning to preach the gospel. They asked who the king of the village was, but the villagers told them that there was no king. "We have men of high title and the chief priests and the elders," they said.

It was not very easy getting the men of high title and the elders together after the excitement of the first day. But the missionaries persevered, and in the end they were received by the rulers of Mbanta. They asked for a plot of land to build their church.

Every clan and village had its "evil forest." In it were buried all those who died of the really evil diseases, like leprosy and smallpox. It was also the dumping ground for the potent fetishes of great medicine men when they died. An "evil forest" was, therefore, alive with sinister forces and powers of darkness. It was such a forest that the rulers of Mbanta gave to the missionaries. They did not really want them in their clan, and so they made them that offer which nobody in his right senses would accept.

"They want a piece of land to build their shrine," said Uchendu to his peers when they consulted among themselves. "We shall give them a piece of land." He paused, and there was a murmur of surprise and disagreement. "Let us give them a portion of the Evil Forest. They boast about victory over death. Let us give them a real battlefield in which to show their victory." They laughed and agreed, and sent for the missionaries, whom they had asked to leave them for a while so that they might "whisper together." They offered them as much of the Evil Forest as they cared to take. And to their greatest amazement the missionaries thanked them and burst into song.

"They do not understand," said some of the elders. "But they will understand when they go to their plot of land tomorrow morning." And they dispersed.

The next morning the crazy men actually began to clear a part of the forest and to build their house. The inhabitants of Mbanta expected them all to be dead within four days. The first day passed and the second and third and fourth, and none of them died. Everyone was puzzled. And then it became known that the white man's fetish had unbelievable power. It was said that he wore glasses on his eyes so that he could see and talk to evil spirits. Not long after, he won his first three converts.

Although Nwoye had been attracted to the new faith from the very first day, he kept it secret. He dared not go too near the missionaries for fear of his father. But whenever they came to preach in the open marketplace or the village playground, Nwoye was there. And he was already beginning to know some of the simple stories they told.

"We have now built a church," said Mr. Kiaga, the interpreter, who was now in charge of the infant congregation. The white man had gone back to Umuofia, where he built his headquarters and from where he paid regular visits to Mr. Kiaga's congregation at Mbanta.

"We have now built a church," said Mr. Kiaga, "and we want you all to come in every seventh day to worship the true God."

On the following Sunday, Nwoye passed and repassed the little red-earth and thatch building without summoning enough courage to enter. He heard the voice of singing and although it came from a handful of men it was loud and confident. Their church stood on a circular clearing that looked like the open mouth of the Evil Forest. Was it waiting to snap its teeth together? After passing and re-passing by the church, Nwoye returned home.

It was well known among the people of Mbanta that their gods and ancestors were sometimes long-suffering and would deliberately allow a man to go on defying them. But even in such cases they set their limit at seven market weeks or twenty-eight days. Beyond that limit no man was suffered to go. And so excitement mounted in the village as the seventh week approached since the impudent missionaries built their church in the Evil Forest. The villagers were so certain about the doom that awaited these men that one or two converts thought it wise to suspend their allegiance to the new faith.

At last the day came by which all the missionaries should have died. But they were still alive, building a new red-earth and thatch house for their teacher, Mr. Kiaga. That week they won a handful more converts. And for the first time they had a woman. Her name was Nneka, the wife of Amadi, who was a prosperous farmer. She was very heavy with child.

Nneka had had four previous pregnancies and childbirths. But each time she had borne twins, and they had been immediately thrown away. Her husband and his family were already becoming highly critical of such a woman and were not unduly perturbed when they found she had fled to join the Christians. It was a good riddance.

One morning Okonkwo's cousin, Amikwu, was passing by the church on his way from the neighboring village, when he saw Nwoye among the Christians. He was greatly surprised, and when he got home he went straight to Okonkwo's hut and told him what he had seen. The women began to talk excitedly, but Okonkwo sat unmoved.

It was late afternoon before Nwoye returned. He went into the *obi* and saluted his father, but he did not answer. Nwoye turned round to walk into the inner compound when his father, suddenly overcome with fury, sprang to his feet and gripped him by the neck.

"Where have you been?" he stammered.

Nwoye struggled to free himself from the choking grip.

"Answer me," roared Okonkwo, "before I kill you!" He seized a heavy stick that lay on the dwarf wall and hit him two or three savage blows.

"Answer me!" he roared again. Nwoye stood looking at him and did not say a word. The women were screaming outside, afraid to go in.

"Leave that boy at once!" said a voice in the outer compound. It was Okonkwo's uncle, Uchendu. "Are you mad?"

Okonkwo did not answer. But he left hold of Nwoye, who walked away and never returned.

He went back to the church and told Mr. Kiaga that he had decided to go to Umuofia where the white missionary had set up a school to teach young Christians to read and write.

Mr. Kiaga's joy was very great. "Blessed is he who forsakes his father and his mother for my sake," he intoned. "Those that hear my words are my father and my mother."

Nwoye did not fully understand. But he was happy to leave his father.

He would return later to his mother and his brothers and sisters and convert them to the new faith.

As Okonkwo sat in his hut that night, gazing into a log fire, he thought over the matter. A sudden fury rose within him and he felt a strong desire to take up his machete, go to the church and wipe out the entire vile and miscreant gang. But on further thought he told himself that Nwoye was not worth fighting for. Why, he cried in his heart, should he, Okonkwo, of all people, be cursed with such a son? He saw clearly in it the finger of his personal god or *chi*. For how else could he explain his great misfortune and exile and now his despicable son's behavior? Now that he had time to think of it, his son's crime stood out in its stark enormity. To abandon the gods of one's father and go about with a lot of effeminate men clucking like old hens was the very depth of abomination. Suppose when he died all his male children decided to follow Nwoye's steps and abandon their ancestors? Okonkwo felt a cold shudder run through him at the terrible prospects, like the prospect of annihilation. He saw himself and his fathers crowding round their ancestral shrine waiting in vain for worship and sacrifice and finding nothing but ashes of bygone days, and his children the while praying to the white man's god. If such a thing were ever to happen, he, Okonkwo, would wipe them off the face of the earth.

Okonkwo was popularly called the "Roaring Flame." As he looked into the log fire he recalled the name. He was a flaming fire. How then could he have begotten a son like Nwoye, degenerate and effeminate? Perhaps he was not his son. No! he could not be. His wife had played him false. He would teach her! But Nwoye resembled his grandfather, Unoka, who was Okonkwo's father. He pushed the thought out of his mind. He, Okonkwo, was called a flaming fire. How could he have begotten a woman for a son? At Nwoye's age Okonkwo had already become famous throughout Umuofia for his wrestling and his fearlessness.

He sighed heavily, and as if in sympathy the smoldering log also sighed. And immediately Okonkwo's eyes were opened and he saw the whole matter clearly. Living fire begets cold, impotent ash. He sighed again, deeply.

18

The young church in Mbanta had a few crises early in its life. At first the clan had assumed that it would not survive. But it had gone on living and gradually becoming stronger. The clan was worried, but not overmuch. If a gang of *efulefu* decided to live in the Evil Forest it was their own affair. When one came to think of it, the Evil Forest was a fit home for such undesirable people. It was true they were rescuing twins from the bush, but they never brought them into the village. As far as the villagers were concerned, the twins still remained where they had been thrown away. Surely the earth goddess would not visit the sins of the missionaries on the innocent villagers?

But on one occasion the missionaries had tried to overstep the bounds. Three converts had gone into the village and boasted openly that all the gods were dead and impotent and that they were prepared to defy them by burning all their shrines.

"Go and burn your mothers' genitals," said one of the priests. The men were seized and beaten until they streamed with blood. After that nothing happened for a long time between the church and the clan.

But stories were already gaining ground that the white man had not only brought a religion but also a government. It was said that they had built a place of judgment in Umuofia to protect the followers of their religion. It was even said that they had hanged one man who killed a missionary.

Although such stories were now often told they looked like fairy-tales in Mbanta and did not as yet affect the relationship between the new church and the clan. There was no question of killing a missionary here, for Mr. Kiaga, despite his madness, was quite harmless. As for his converts, no one could kill them without having to flee from the clan, for in spite of their worthlessness they still belonged to the clan. And so nobody gave serious thought to the stories about the white man's government or the consequences of killing the Christians. If they became more troublesome than they already were they would simply be driven out of the clan.

And the little church was at that moment too deeply absorbed in its own troubles to annoy the clan. It all began over the question of admitting outcasts.

These outcasts, or *osu*, seeing that the new religion welcomed twins and such abominations, thought that it was possible that they would also be received. And so one Sunday two of them went into the church. There was an immediate stir; but so great was the work the new religion had done among the converts that they did not immediately leave the church when the outcasts came in. Those who found themselves nearest to them merely moved to another seat. It was a miracle. But it only lasted till the end of the service. The whole church raised a protest and was about to drive these people out, when Mr. Kiaga stopped them and began to explain.

"Before God," he said, "there is no slave or free. We are all children of God and we must receive these our brothers."

"You do not understand," said one of the converts. "What will the heathen say of us when they hear that we receive *osu* into our midst? They will laugh."

"Let them laugh," said Mr. Kiaga. "God will laugh at them on the judgment day. Why do the nations rage and the peoples imagine a vain thing? He that sitteth in the heavens shall laugh. The Lord shall have them in derision."

"You do not understand," the convert maintained. "You are our teacher, and you can teach us the things of the new faith. But this is a matter which we know." And he told him what an *osu* was.

He was a person dedicated to a god, a thing set apart—a taboo for ever, and his children after him. He could neither marry nor be married by the free-born. He was in fact an outcast, living in a special area of the village, close to the Great Shrine. Wherever he went he carried with him the mark of his forbidden caste—long, tangled and dirty hair. A razor was taboo to him. An *osu* could not attend an assembly of the free-born, and they, in turn, could not shelter under his roof. He could not take any of the four titles of the clan, and when he died he was buried by his kind in the Evil Forest. How could such a man be a follower of Christ?

"He needs Christ more than you and I," said Mr. Kiaga.

"Then I shall go back to the clan," said the convert. And he went. Mr. Kiaga stood firm, and it was his firmness that saved the young church. The wavering converts drew inspiration and confidence from his unshakable faith. He ordered the outcasts to shave off their long, tangled hair. At first they were afraid they might die.

"Unless you shave off the mark of your heathen belief I will not admit you into the church," said Mr. Kiaga. "You fear that you will die. Why should that be? How are you different from other men who shave their hair? The same God created you and them. But they have cast you out like lepers. It is against the will of God, who has promised everlasting life to all who believe in His holy name. The heathen say you will die if you do this or that, and you are afraid. They also said I would die if I built my church on this ground. Am I dead? They said I would die if I took care of twins. I am still alive. The heathen speak nothing but falsehood. Only the word of our God is true."

The two outcasts shaved off their hair, and soon they were the strongest adherents of the new faith. And what was more, nearly all the *osu* in Mbanta followed their example. It was in fact one of them who in his zeal brought the church into serious conflict with the clan a year later by killing the sacred python, the emanation of the god of water.

The royal python was the most revered animal in Mbanta and all the surrounding clans. It was addressed as "Our Father," and was allowed to go wherever it chose, even into people's beds. It ate rats in the house and sometimes swallowed hens' eggs. If a clansman killed a royal python accidentally, he made sacrifices of atonement and performed an expensive burial ceremony such as was done for a great man. No punishment was prescribed for a man who killed the python knowingly. Nobody thought that such a thing could ever happen.

Perhaps it never did happen. That was the way the clan at first looked at it. No one had actually seen the man do it. The story had arisen among the Christians themselves.

But, all the same, the rulers and elders of Mbanta assembled to decide on their action. Many of them spoke at great length and in fury. The spirit of wars was upon them. Okonkwo, who had begun to play a part in the affairs of his motherland, said that until the abominable gang was chased out of the village with whips there would be no peace.

But there were many others who saw the situation differently, and it was their counsel that prevailed in the end.

"It is not our custom to fight for our gods," said one of them. "Let us not presume to do so now. If a man kills the sacred python in the secrecy of his hut, the matter lies between him and the god. We did not see it. If we put ourselves between the god and his victim we may receive blows intended for the offender. When a man blasphemes, what do we do? Do we go and stop his mouth? No. We put our fingers into our ears to stop us hearing. That is a wise action."

"Let us not reason like cowards," said Okonkwo. "If a man comes into my hut and defecates on the floor, what do I do? Do I shut my eyes? No! I take a stick and break his head. That is what a man does. These people are daily pouring filth over us, and Okeke says we should pretend not to see." Okonkwo made a sound full of disgust. This was a womanly clan, he thought. Such a thing could never happen in his fatherland, Umuofia.

"Okonkwo has spoken the truth," said another man. "We should do something. But let us ostracize these men. We would then not be held accountable for their abominations."

Everybody in the assembly spoke, and in the end it was decided to ostracize the Christians. Okonkwo ground his teeth in disgust.

That night a bell-man went through the length and breadth of Mbanta proclaiming that the adherents of the new faith were thenceforth excluded from the life and privileges of the clan.

The Christians had grown in number and were now a small community of men, women and children, self-assured and confident. Mr. Brown, the white missionary, paid regular visits to them. "When I think that it is only eighteen months since the Seed was first sown among you," he said, "I marvel at what the Lord hath wrought."

It was Wednesday in Holy Week and Mr. Kiaga had asked the women to bring red earth and white chalk and water to scrub the church for Easter; and the women had formed themselves into three groups for this purpose. They set out early that morning, some of them with their water-pots to the stream, another group with hoes and baskets to the village red-earth pit, and the others to the chalk quarry.

Mr. Kiaga was praying in the church when he heard the women talking excitedly. He rounded off his prayer and went to see what it was all about. The women had come to the church with empty water-pots. They said that some young men had chased them away from the stream with whips. Soon after, the women who had gone for red earth returned with empty baskets. Some of them had been heavily whipped. The chalk women also returned to tell a similar story.

"What does it all mean?" asked Mr. Kiaga, who was greatly perplexed.

"The village has outlawed us," said one of the women. "The bell-man announced it last night. But it is not our custom to debar anyone from the stream or the quarry."

Another woman said, "They want to ruin us. They will not allow us into the markets. They have said so."

Mr. Kiaga was going to send into the village for his men-converts when he saw them coming on their own. Of course they had all heard the bell-man, but they had never in all their lives heard of women being debarred from the stream.

"Come along," they said to the women. "We will go with you to meet those cowards." Some of them had big sticks and some even machetes.

But Mr. Kiaga restrained them. He wanted first to know why they had been outlawed.

"They say that Okoli killed the sacred python," said one man. "It is false," said another. "Okoli told me himself that it was false." Okoli was not there to answer. He had fallen ill on the previous night. Before the day was over he was dead. His death showed that the gods were still able to fight their own battles. The clan saw no reason then for molesting the Christians.

19

The last big rains of the year were falling. It was the time for treading red earth with which to build walls. It was not done earlier because the rains were too heavy and would have washed away the heap of trodden earth; and it could not be done later because harvesting would soon set in, and after that the dry season.

It was going to be Okonkwo's last harvest in Mbanta. The seven wasted and weary years were at last dragging to a close. Although he had prospered in his motherland Okonkwo knew that he would have prospered even more in Umuofia, in the land of his fathers where men were bold and warlike. In these seven years he would have climbed to the utmost heights. And so he regretted every day of his exile. His mother's kinsmen had been very kind to him, and he was grateful. But that did not alter the facts. He had called the first child born to him in exile Nneka—"Mother is Supreme"—out of politeness to his mother's kinsmen. But two years later when a son was born he called him Nwofia—"Begotten in the Wilderness."

As soon as he entered his last year in exile Okonkwo sent money to Obierika to build him two huts in his old compound where he and his family would live until he built more huts and the outside wall of his compound. He could not ask another man to build his own *obi* for him, nor the walls of his compound. Those things a man built for himself or inherited from his father.

As the last heavy rains of the year began to fall, Obierika sent word that the two huts had been built and Okonkwo began to prepare for his return, after the rains. He would have liked to return earlier and build his compound that year before the rains stopped, but in doing so he would have taken something from the full penalty of seven years. And that could not be. So he waited impatiently for the dry season to come.

It came slowly. The rain became lighter and lighter until it fell in slanting showers. Sometimes the sun shone through the rain and a light breeze blew. It was a gay and airy kind of rain. The rainbow began to appear, and sometimes two rainbows, like a mother and her daughter, the one young and beautiful, and the other an old and faint shadow. The rainbow was called the python of the sky.

Okonkwo called his three wives and told them to get things together for a great feast. "I must thank my mother's kinsmen before I go," he said.

Ekwefi still had some cassava left on her farm from the previous year. Neither of the other wives had. It was not that they had been lazy, but that they had many children to feed. It was therefore understood that Ekwefi would provide cassava for the feast. Nwoye's mother and Ojiugo would provide the other things like smoked fish, palm-oil and pepper for the soup. Okonkwo would take care of meat and yams.

Ekwefi rose early on the following morning and went to her farm with her daughter, Ezinma, and Ojiugo's daughter, Obiageli, to harvest cassava tubers. Each of them carried a long cane basket, a machete for cutting down the soft cassava stem, and a little hoe for digging out the tuber. Fortunately, a light rain had fallen during the night and the soil would not be very hard.

"It will not take us long to harvest as much as we like," said Ekwefi.

"But the leaves will be wet," said Ezinma. Her basket was balanced on her head, and her arms folded across her breasts. She felt cold. "I dislike cold water dropping on my back. We should have waited for the sun to rise and dry the leaves."

Obiageli called her "Salt" because she said that she disliked water. "Are you afraid you may dissolve?"

The harvesting was easy, as Ekwefi had said. Ezinma shook every tree violently with a long stick before she bent down to cut the stem and dig out the tuber. Sometimes it was not necessary to dig. They just pulled the stump, and earth rose, roots snapped below, and the tuber was pulled out.

When they had harvested a sizable heap they carried it down in two trips to the stream, where every woman had a shallow well for fermenting her cassava.

"It should be ready in four days or even three," said Obiageli. "They are young tubers."

"They are not all that young," said Ekwefi. "I planted the farm nearly two years ago. It is a poor soil and that is why the tubers are so small."

Okonkwo never did things by halves. When his wife Ekwefi protested that two goats were sufficient for the feast he told her that it was not her affair.

"I am calling a feast because I have the wherewithal. I cannot live on the bank of a river and wash my hands with spittle. My mother's people have been good to me and I must show my gratitude."

And so three goats were slaughtered and a number of fowls. It was like a wedding feast. There was foo-foo and yam pottage, egusi[7] soup and bitter-leaf soup and pots and pots of palm-wine.

All the umunna[8] were invited to the feast, all the descendants of Okolo, who had lived about two hundred years before. The oldest member of this extensive family was Okonkwo's uncle, Uchendu. The kola nut was given him to break, and he prayed to the ancestors. He asked them for health and children. "We do not ask for wealth because he that has health and children will also have wealth. We do not pray to have more money but to have more kinsmen. We are better than animals because we have kinsmen. An animal rubs its itching flank against a tree, a man asks his kinsman to scratch him." He prayed especially for Okonkwo and his family. He then broke the kola nut and threw one of the lobes on the ground for the ancestors.

---

7. Melon seed, which is roasted, ground, and cooked in soup.   8. "Children of the Father" (literal trans.); the clan (male).

As the broken kola nuts were passed round, Okonkwo's wives and children and those who came to help them with the cooking began to bring out the food. His sons brought out the pots of palm-wine. There was so much food and drink that many kinsmen whistled in surprise. When all was laid out, Okonkwo rose to speak.

"I beg you to accept this little kola," he said. "It is not to pay you back for all you did for me in these seven years. A child cannot pay for its mother's milk. I have only called you together because it is good for kinsmen to meet."

Yam pottage was served first because it was lighter than foo-foo and because yam always came first. Then the foo-foo was served. Some kinsmen ate it with egusi soup and others with bitter-leaf soup. The meat was then shared so that every member of the umunna had a portion. Every man rose in order of years and took a share. Even the few kinsmen who had not been able to come had their shares taken out for them in due term.

As the palm-wine was drunk one of the oldest members of the umunna rose to thank Okonkwo:

"If I say that we did not expect such a big feast I will be suggesting that we did not know how open-handed our son, Okonkwo, is. We all know him, and we expected a big feast. But it turned out to be even bigger than we expected. Thank you. May all you took out return again tenfold. It is good in these days when the younger generation consider themselves wiser than their sires to see a man doing things in the grand, old way. A man who calls his kinsmen to a feast does not do so to save them from starving. They all have food in their own homes. When we gather together in the moonlit village ground it is not because of the moon. Every man can see it in his own compound. We come together because it is good for kinsmen to do so. You may ask why I am saying all this. I say it because I fear for the younger generation, for you people." He waved his arm where most of the young men sat. "As for me, I have only a short while to live, and so have Uchendu and Unachukwu and Emefo. But I fear for you young people because you do not understand how strong is the bond of kinship. You do not know what it is to speak with one voice. And what is the result? An abominable religion has settled among you. A man can now leave his father and his brothers. He can curse the gods of his fathers and his ancestors, like a hunter's dog that suddenly goes mad and turns on his master. I fear for you; I fear for the clan." He turned again to Okonkwo and said, "Thank you for calling us together."

Part Three

20

Seven years was a long time to be away from one's clan. A man's place was not always there, waiting for him. As soon as he left, someone else rose and filled it. The clan was like a lizard; if it lost its tail it soon grew another.

Okonkwo knew these things. He knew that he had lost his place among the nine masked spirits who administered justice in the clan. He had lost the chance to lead his warlike clan against the new religion, which, he was told, had gained ground. He had lost the years in which he might have taken the highest titles in the clan. But some of these losses were not irreparable. He was determined that his return should be marked by his people. He would return with a flourish, and regain the seven wasted years.

Even in his first year in exile he had begun to plan for his return. The first thing he would do would be to rebuild his compound on a more magnificent scale. He would build a bigger barn than he had had before and he would build huts for two new wives. Then he would show his wealth by initiating his sons into the *ozo* society. Only the really great men in the clan were able to do this. Okonkwo saw clearly the high esteem in which he would be held, and he saw himself taking the highest title in the land.

As the years of exile passed one by one it seemed to him that his *chi* might now be making amends for the past disaster. His yams grew abundantly, not only in his motherland but also in Umuofia, where his friend gave them out year by year to sharecroppers.

Then the tragedy of his first son had occurred. At first it appeared as if it might prove too great for his spirit. But it was a resilient spirit, and in the end Okonkwo overcame his sorrow. He had five other sons and he would bring them up in the way of the clan.

He sent for the five sons and they came and sat in his *obi*. The youngest of them was four years old.

"You have all seen the great abomination of your brother. Now he is no longer my son or your brother. I will only have a son who is a man, who will hold his head up among my people. If any one of you prefers to be a woman, let him follow Nwoye now while I am alive so that I can curse him. If you turn against me when I am dead I will visit you and break your neck."

Okonkwo was very lucky in his daughters. He never stopped regretting that Ezinma was a girl. Of all his children she alone understood his every mood. A bond of sympathy had grown between them as the years had passed.

Ezinma grew up in her father's exile and became one of the most beautiful girls in Mbanta. She was called Crystal of Beauty, as her mother had been called in her youth. The young ailing girl who had caused her mother so much heartache had been transformed, almost overnight, into a healthy, buoyant maiden. She had, it was true, her moments of depression when she would snap at everybody like an angry dog. These moods descended on her suddenly and for no apparent reason. But they were very rare and short-lived. As long as they lasted, she could bear no other person but her father.

Many young men and prosperous middle-aged men of Mbanta came to marry her. But she refused them all, because her father had called her one evening and said to her: "There are many good and prosperous people here, but I shall be happy if you marry in Umuofia when we return home."

That was all he had said. But Ezinma had seen clearly all the thought and hidden meaning behind the few words. And she had agreed.

"Your half-sister, Obiageli, will not understand me," Okonkwo said. "But you can explain to her."

Although they were almost the same age, Ezinma wielded a strong influence over her half-sister. She explained to her why they should not marry yet, and she agreed also. And so the two of them refused every offer of marriage in Mbanta.

"I wish she were a boy," Okonkwo thought within himself. She understood things so perfectly. Who else among his children could have read his thoughts so well? With two beautiful grown-up daughters his return to Umuofia would attract considerable attention. His future sons-in-law would be men of authority in the clan. The poor and unknown would not dare to come forth.

Umuofia had indeed changed during the seven years Okonkwo had been in exile. The church had come and led many astray. Not only the low-born and the outcast but sometimes a worthy man had joined it. Such a man was Ogbuefi Ugonna,[9] who had taken two titles, and who like a madman had cut the anklet of his titles and cast it away to join the Christians. The white missionary was very proud of him and he was one of the first men in Umuofia to receive the sacrament of Holy Communion, or Holy Feast as it was called in Ibo. Ogbuefi Ugonna had thought of the Feast in terms of eating and drinking, only more holy than the village variety. He had therefore put his drinking-horn into his goatskin bag for the occasion.

But apart from the church, the white men had also brought a government. They had built a court where the District Commissioner judged cases in ignorance. He had court messengers who brought men to him for trial. Many of these messengers came from Umuru on the bank of the Great River, where the white men first came many years before and where they had built the center of their religion and trade and government. These court messengers were greatly hated in Umuofia because they were foreigners and also arrogant and high-handed. They were called *kotma*,[1] and because of their ash-colored shorts they earned the additional name of Ashy-Buttocks. They guarded the prison, which was full of men who had offended against the white man's law. Some of these prisoners had thrown away their twins and some had molested the Christians. They were beaten in the prison by the *kotma* and made to work every morning clearing the government compound and fetching wood for the white Commissioner and the court messengers. Some of these prisoners were men of title who should be above such mean occupation. They were grieved by the indignity and mourned for their neglected farms. As they cut grass in the morning the younger men sang in time with the strokes of their machetes:

---

9. "Father's Honor" (with the eagle feather).   1. Pidgin English for "court messenger."

> *Kotma* of the ash buttocks,
> He is fit to be a slave.
> The white man has no sense,
> He is fit to be a slave.

The court messengers did not like to be called Ashy-Buttocks, and they beat the men. But the song spread in Umuofia.

Okonkwo's head was bowed in sadness as Obierika told him these things.

"Perhaps I have been away too long," Okonkwo said, almost to himself. "But I cannot understand these things you tell me. What is it that has happened to our people? Why have they lost the power to fight?"

"Have you not heard how the white man wiped out Abame?" asked Obierika.

"I have heard," said Okonkwo. "But I have also heard that Abame people were weak and foolish. Why did they not fight back? Had they no guns and machetes? We would be cowards to compare ourselves with the men of Abame. Their fathers had never dared to stand before our ancestors. We must fight these men and drive them from the land."

"It is already too late," said Obierika sadly. "Our own men and our sons have joined the ranks of the stranger. They have joined his religion and they help to uphold his government. If we should try to drive out the white men in Umuofia we should find it easy. There are only two of them. But what of our own people who are following their way and have been given power? They would go to Umuru and bring the soldiers, and we would be like Abame." He paused for a long time and then said: "I told you on my last visit to Mbanta how they hanged Aneto."

"What has happened to that piece of land in dispute?" asked Okonkwo.

"The white man's court has decided that it should belong to Nnama's family, who had given much money to the white man's messengers and interpreter."

"Does the white man understand our custom about land?"

"How can he when he does not even speak our tongue? But he says that our customs are bad; and our own brothers who have taken up his religion also say that our customs are bad. How do you think we can fight when our own brothers have turned against us? The white man is very clever. He came quietly and peaceably with his religion. We were amused at his foolishness and allowed him to stay. Now he has won our brothers, and our clan can no longer act like one. He has put a knife on the things that held us together and we have fallen apart."

"How did they get hold of Aneto to hang him?" asked Okonkwo.

"When he killed Oduche in the fight over the land, he fled to Aninta to escape the wrath of the earth. This was about eight days after the fight, because Oduche had not died immediately from his wounds. It was on the seventh day that he died. But everybody knew that he was going to die and Aneto got his belongings together in readiness to flee. But the Christians had told the white man about the accident, and he sent his *kotma* to catch Aneto. He was imprisoned with all the leaders of his family. In the end Oduche died and Aneto was taken to Umuru and hanged. The other people were released, but even now they have not found the mouth with which to tell of their suffering."

The two men sat in silence for a long while afterwards.

21

There were many men and women in Umuofia who did not feel as strongly as Okonkwo about the new dispensation. The white man had indeed brought a lunatic religion, but he had also built a trading store and for the first time palm-oil and kernel[2] became things of great price, and much money flowed into Umuofia.

And even in the matter of religion there was a growing feeling that there might be something in it after all, something vaguely akin to method in the overwhelming madness.

This growing feeling was due to Mr. Brown, the white missionary, who was very firm in restraining his flock from provoking the wrath of the clan. One member in particular was very difficult to restrain. His name was Enoch and his father was the priest of the snake cult. The story went around that Enoch had killed and eaten the sacred python, and that his father had cursed him.

Mr. Brown preached against such excess of zeal. Everything was possible, he told his energetic flock, but everything was not expedient. And so Mr. Brown came to be respected even by the clan, because he trod softly on its faith. He made friends with some of the great men of the clan and on one of his frequent visits to the neighboring villages he had been presented with a carved elephant tusk, which was a sign of dignity and rank. One of the great men in that village was called Akunna[3] and he had given one of his sons to be taught the white man's knowledge in Mr. Brown's school.

Whenever Mr. Brown went to that village he spent long hours with Akunna in his *obi* talking through an interpreter about religion. Neither of them succeeded in converting the other but they learned more about their different beliefs.

"You say that there is one supreme God who made heaven and earth," said Akunna on one of Mr. Brown's visits. "We also believe in Him and call Him Chukwu. He made all the world and the other gods."

"There are no other gods," said Mr. Brown. "Chukwu is the only God and all others are false. You carve a piece of wood—like that one" (he pointed at the rafters from which Akunna's carved *Ikenga*[4] hung), "and you call it a god. But it is still a piece of wood."

"Yes," said Akunna. "It is indeed a piece of wood. The tree from which it came was made by Chukwu, as indeed all minor gods were. But He

---

2. The red fleshy husk of the palm nut is crushed manually to produce cooking oil, leaving a fibrous residue along with hard kernels. The Europeans bought both the red oil and the kernels, from which they could extract a very fine oil by using machines.   3. "Father's Wealth."   4. A carved wooden figure with the horns of a ram that symbolized the strength of a man's right hand. Every adult male kept an *Ikenga* in his personal shrine.

made them for His messengers so that we could approach Him through them. It is like yourself. You are the head of your church."

"No," protested Mr. Brown. "The head of my church is God Himself."

"I know," said Akunna, "but there must be a head in this world among men. Somebody like yourself must be the head here."

"The head of my church in that sense is in England."

"That is exactly what I am saying. The head of your church is in your country. He has sent you here as his messenger. And you have also appointed your own messengers and servants. Or let me take another example, the District Commissioner. He is sent by your king."

"They have a queen," said the interpreter on his own account.

"Your queen sends her messenger, the District Commissioner. He finds that he cannot do the work alone and so he appoints *kotma* to help him. It is the same with God, or Chukwu. He appoints the smaller gods to help Him because His work is too great for one person."

"You should not think of Him as a person," said Mr. Brown. "It is because you do so that you imagine He must need helpers. And the worst thing about it is that you give all the worship to the false gods you have created."

"That is not so. We make sacrifices to the little gods, but when they fail and there is no one else to turn to we go to Chukwu. It is right to do so. We approach a great man through his servants. But when his servants fail to help us, then we go to the last source of hope. We appear to pay greater attention to the little gods but that is not so. We worry them more because we are afraid to worry their Master. Our fathers knew that Chukwu was the Overlord and that is why many of them gave their children the name Chukwuka—"Chukwu is Supreme.""

"You said one interesting thing," said Mr. Brown. "You are afraid of Chukwu. In my religion Chukwu is a loving Father and need not be feared by those who do His will."

"But we must fear Him when we are not doing His will," said Akunna. "And who is to tell His will? It is too great to be known."

In this way Mr. Brown learned a good deal about the religion of the clan and he came to the conclusion that a frontal attack on it would not succeed. And so he built a school and a little hospital in Umuofia. He went from family to family begging people to send their children to his school. But at first they only sent their slaves or sometimes their lazy children. Mr. Brown begged and argued and prophesied. He said that the leaders of the land in the future would be men and women who had learned to read and write. If Umuofia failed to send her children to the school, strangers would come from other places to rule them. They could already see that happening in the Native Court, where the D.C. was surrounded by strangers who spoke his tongue. Most of these strangers came from the distant town of Umuru on the bank of the Great River where the white man first went.

In the end Mr. Brown's arguments began to have an effect. More people came to learn in his school, and he encouraged them with gifts of singlets[5]

5. Undershirts, T-shirts.

and towels. They were not all young, these people who came to learn. Some of them were thirty years old or more. They worked on their farms in the morning and went to school in the afternoon. And it was not long before the people began to say that the white man's medicine was quick in working. Mr. Brown's school produced quick results. A few months in it were enough to make one a court messenger or even a court clerk. Those who stayed longer became teachers; and from Umuofia laborers went forth into the Lord's vineyard. New churches were established in the surrounding villages and a few schools with them. From the very beginning religion and education went hand in hand.

Mr. Brown's mission grew from strength to strength, and because of its link with the new administration it earned a new social prestige. But Mr. Brown himself was breaking down in health. At first he ignored the warning signs. But in the end he had to leave his flock, sad and broken.

It was in the first rainy season after Okonkwo's return to Umuofia that Mr. Brown left for home. As soon as he had learned of Okonkwo's return five months earlier, the missionary had immediately paid him a visit. He had just sent Okonkwo's son, Nwoye, who was now called Isaac,[6] to the new training college for teachers in Umuru. And he had hoped that Okonkwo would be happy to hear of it. But Okonkwo had driven him away with the threat that if he came into his compound again, he would be carried out of it.

Okonkwo's return to his native land was not as memorable as he had wished. It was true his two beautiful daughters aroused great interest among suitors and marriage negotiations were soon in progress, but, beyond that, Umuofia did not appear to have taken any special notice of the warrior's return. The clan had undergone such profound change during his exile that it was barely recognizable. The new religion and government and the trading stores were very much in the people's eyes and minds. There were still many who saw these new institutions as evil, but even they talked and thought about little else, and certainly not about Okonkwo's return.

And it was the wrong year too. If Okonkwo had immediately initiated his two sons into the *ozo* society as he had planned he would have caused a stir. But the initiation rite was performed once in three years in Umuofia, and he had to wait for nearly two years for the next round of ceremonies.

Okonkwo was deeply grieved. And it was not just a personal grief. He mourned for the clan, which he saw breaking up and falling apart, and he mourned for the warlike men of Umuofia, who had so unaccountably become soft like women.

22

Mr. Brown's successor was the Reverend James Smith, and he was a different kind of man. He condemned openly Mr. Brown's policy of compromise and accommodation. He saw things as black and white. And

6. Son of Abraham, offered to God as a sacrifice (Genesis 22).

black was evil. He saw the world as a battlefield in which the children of light were locked in mortal conflict with the sons of darkness. He spoke in his sermons about sheep and goats and about wheat and tares. He believed in slaying the prophets of Baal.

Mr. Smith was greatly distressed by the ignorance which many of his flock showed even in such things as the Trinity and the Sacraments. It only showed that they were seeds sown on a rocky soil. Mr. Brown had thought of nothing but numbers. He should have known that the kingdom of God did not depend on large crowds. Our Lord Himself stressed the importance of fewness. Narrow is the way and few the number. To fill the Lord's holy temple with an idolatrous crowd clamoring for signs was a folly of everlasting consequence. Our Lord used the whip only once in His life—to drive the crowd away from His church.

Within a few weeks of his arrival in Umuofia Mr. Smith suspended a young woman from the church for pouring new wine into old bottles. This woman had allowed her heathen husband to mutilate her dead child. The child had been declared an *ogbanje*, plaguing its mother by dying and entering her womb to be born again. Four times this child had run its evil round. And so it was mutilated to discourage it from returning.

Mr. Smith was filled with wrath when he heard of this. He disbelieved the story which even some of the most faithful confirmed, the story of really evil children who were not deterred by mutilation, but came back with all the scars. He replied that such stories were spread in the world by the Devil to lead men astray. Those who believed such stories were unworthy of the Lord's table.

There was a saying in Umuofia that as a man danced so the drums were beaten for him. Mr. Smith danced a furious step and so the drums went mad. The over-zealous converts who had smarted under Mr. Brown's restraining hand now flourished in full favor. One of them was Enoch, the son of the snake-priest who was believed to have killed and eaten the sacred python. Enoch's devotion to the new faith had seemed so much greater than Mr. Brown's that the villagers called him the outsider who wept louder than the bereaved.

Enoch was short and slight of build, and always seemed in great haste. His feet were short and broad, and when he stood or walked his heels came together and his feet opened outwards as if they had quarreled and meant to go in different directions. Such was the excessive energy bottled up in Enoch's small body that it was always erupting in quarrels and fights. On Sundays he always imagined that the sermon was preached for the benefit of his enemies. And if he happened to sit near one of them he would occasionally turn to give him a meaningful look, as if to say, "I told you so." It was Enoch who touched off the great conflict between church and clan in Umuofia which had been gathering since Mr. Brown left.

It happened during the annual ceremony which was held in honor of the earth deity. At such times the ancestors of the clan who had been committed to Mother Earth at their death emerged again as *egwugwu* through tiny ant-holes.

One of the greatest crimes a man could commit was to unmask an *egwugwu* in public, or to say or do anything which might reduce its immortal prestige in the eyes of the uninitiated. And this was what Enoch did.

The annual worship of the earth goddess fell on a Sunday, and the masked spirits were abroad. The Christian women who had been to church could not therefore go home. Some of their men had gone out to beg the egwugwu to retire for a short while for the women to pass. They agreed and were already retiring, when Enoch boasted aloud that they would not dare to touch a Christian. Whereupon they all came back and one of them gave Enoch a good stroke of the cane, which was always carried. Enoch fell on him and tore off his mask. The other egwugwu immediately surrounded their desecrated companion, to shield him from the profane gaze of women and children, and led him away. Enoch had killed an ancestral spirit, and Umuofia was thrown into confusion.

That night the Mother of the Spirits walked the length and breadth of the clan, weeping for her murdered son. It was a terrible night. Not even the oldest man in Umuofia had ever heard such a strange and fearful sound, and it was never to be heard again. It seemed as if the very soul of the tribe wept for a great evil that was coming—its own death.

On the next day all the masked egwugwu of Umuofia assembled in the marketplace. They came from all the quarters of the clan and even from the neighboring villages. The dreaded Otakagu came from Imo, and Ekwensu, dangling a white cock, arrived from Uli. It was a terrible gathering. The eerie voices of countless spirits, the bells that clattered behind some of them, and the clash of machetes as they ran forwards and backwards and saluted one another, sent tremors of fear into every heart. For the first time in living memory the sacred bull-roarer was heard in broad daylight.

From the marketplace the furious band made for Enoch's compound. Some of the elders of the clan went with them, wearing heavy protections of charms and amulets. These were men whose arms were strong in ogwu, or medicine. As for the ordinary men and women, they listened from the safety of their huts.

The leaders of the Christians had met together at Mr. Smith's parsonage on the previous night. As they deliberated they could hear the Mother of Spirits wailing for her son. The chilling sound affected Mr. Smith, and for the first time he seemed to be afraid.

"What are they planning to do?" he asked. No one knew, because such a thing had never happened before. Mr. Smith would have sent for the District Commissioner and his court messengers, but they had gone on tour on the previous day.

"One thing is clear," said Mr. Smith. "We cannot offer physical resistance to them. Our strength lies in the Lord." They knelt down together and prayed to God for delivery.

"O Lord, save Thy people," cried Mr. Smith.

"And bless Thine inheritance," replied the men.

They decided that Enoch should be hidden in the parsonage for a day or two. Enoch himself was greatly disappointed when he heard this, for he had hoped that a holy war was imminent; and there were a few other

Christians who thought like him. But wisdom prevailed in the camp of the faithful and many lives were thus saved.

The band of *egwugwu* moved like a furious whirlwind to Enoch's compound and with machete and fire reduced it to a desolate heap. And from there they made for the church, intoxicated with destruction.

Mr. Smith was in his church when he heard the masked spirits coming. He walked quietly to the door which commanded the approach to the church compound, and stood there. But when the first three or four *egwugwu* appeared on the church compound he nearly bolted. He overcame this impulse and instead of running away he went down the two steps that led up to the church and walked towards the approaching spirits.

They surged forward, and a long stretch of the bamboo fence with which the church compound was surrounded gave way before them. Discordant bells clanged, machetes clashed and the air was full of dust and weird sounds. Mr. Smith heard a sound of footsteps behind him. He turned round and saw Okeke, his interpreter. Okeke had not been on the best of terms with his master since he had strongly condemned Enoch's behavior at the meeting of the leaders of the church during the night. Okeke had gone as far as to say that Enoch should not be hidden in the parsonage, because he would only draw the wrath of the clan on the pastor. Mr. Smith had rebuked him in very strong language, and had not sought his advice that morning. But now, as he came up and stood by him confronting the angry spirits, Mr. Smith looked at him and smiled. It was a wan smile, but there was deep gratitude there.

For a brief moment the onrush of the *egwugwu* was checked by the unexpected composure of the two men. But it was only a momentary check, like the tense silence between blasts of thunder. The second onrush was greater than the first. It swallowed up the two men. Then an unmistakable voice rose above the tumult and there was immediate silence. Space was made around the two men, and Ajofia began to speak.

Ajofia was the leading *egwugwu* of Umuofia. He was the head and spokesman of the nine ancestors who administered justice in the clan. His voice was unmistakable and so he was able to bring immediate peace to the agitated spirits. He then addressed Mr. Smith, and as he spoke clouds of smoke rose from his head.

"The body of the white man, I salute you," he said, using the language in which immortals spoke to men.

"The body of the white man, do you know me?" he asked.

Mr. Smith looked at his interpreter, but Okeke, who was a native of distant Umuru, was also at a loss.

Ajofia laughed in his guttural voice. It was like the laugh of rusty metal. "They are strangers," he said, "and they are ignorant. But let that pass." He turned round to his comrades and saluted them, calling them the fathers of Umuofia. He dug his rattling spear into the ground and it shook with metallic life. Then he turned once more to the missionary and his interpreter.

"Tell the white man that we will not do him any harm," he said to the interpreter. "Tell him to go back to his house and leave us alone. We liked his brother who was with us before. He was foolish, but we liked him, and for his sake we shall not harm his brother. But this shrine which he built must be destroyed. We shall no longer allow it in our midst. It has bred untold abominations and we have come to put an end to it." He turned to his comrades. "Fathers of Umuofia, I salute you"; and they replied with one guttural voice. He turned again to the missionary. "You can stay with us if you like our ways. You can worship your own god. It is good that a man should worship the gods and the spirits of his fathers. Go back to your house so that you may not be hurt. Our anger is great but we have held it down so that we can talk to you."

Mr. Smith said to his interpreter: "Tell them to go away from here. This is the house of God and I will not live to see it desecrated."

Okeke interpreted wisely to the spirits and leaders of Umuofia: "The white man says he is happy you have come to him with your grievances, like friends. He will be happy if you leave the matter in his hands."

"We cannot leave the matter in his hands because he does not understand our customs, just as we do not understand his. We say he is foolish because he does not know our ways, and perhaps he says we are foolish because we do not know his. Let him go away."

Mr. Smith stood his ground. But he could not save his church. When the *egwugwu* went away the red-earth church which Mr. Brown had built was a pile of earth and ashes. And for the moment the spirit of the clan was pacified.

23

For the first time in many years Okonkwo had a feeling that was akin to happiness. The times which had altered so unaccountably during his exile seemed to be coming round again. The clan which had turned false on him appeared to be making amends.

He had spoken violently to his clansmen when they had met in the marketplace to decide on their action. And they had listened to him with respect. It was like the good old days again, when a warrior was a warrior. Although they had not agreed to kill the missionary or drive away the Christians, they had agreed to do something substantial. And they had done it. Okonkwo was almost happy again.

For two days after the destruction of the church, nothing happened. Every man in Umuofia went about armed with a gun or a machete. They would not be caught unawares, like the men of Abame.

Then the District Commissioner returned from his tour. Mr. Smith went immediately to him and they had a long discussion. The men of Umuofia did not take any notice of this, and if they did, they thought it was not important. The missionary often went to see his brother white man. There was nothing strange in that.

Three days later the District Commissioner sent his sweet-tongued messenger to the leaders of Umuofia asking them to meet him in his headquarters. That also was not strange. He often asked them to hold such palavers, as he called them. Okonkwo was among the six leaders he invited.

Okonkwo warned the others to be fully armed. "An Umuofia man does not refuse a call," he said. "He may refuse to do what he is asked; he does not refuse to be asked. But the times have changed, and we must be fully prepared."

And so the six men went to see the District Commissioner, armed with their machetes. They did not carry guns, for that would be unseemly. They were led into the courthouse where the District Commissioner sat. He received them politely. They unslung their goatskin bags and their sheathed machetes, put them on the floor, and sat down.

"I have asked you to come," began the Commissioner, "because of what happened during my absence. I have been told a few things but I cannot believe them until I have heard your own side. Let us talk about it like friends and find a way of ensuring that it does not happen again."

Ogbuefi Ekwueme[7] rose to his feet and began to tell the story.

"Wait a minute," said the Commissioner. "I want to bring in my men so that they too can hear your grievances and take warning. Many of them come from distant places and although they speak your tongue they are ignorant of your customs. James! Go and bring in the men." His interpreter left the courtroom and soon returned with twelve men. They sat together with the men of Umuofia, and Ogbuefi Ekwueme began to tell the story of how Enoch murdered an *egwugwu*.

It happened so quickly that the six men did not see it coming. There was only a brief scuffle, too brief even to allow the drawing of a sheathed machete. The six men were handcuffed and led into the guardroom.

"We shall not do you any harm," said the District Commissioner to them later, "if only you agree to cooperate with us. We have brought a peaceful administration to you and your people so that you may be happy. If any man ill-treats you we shall come to your rescue. But we will not allow you to ill-treat others. We have a court of law where we judge cases and administer justice just as it is done in my own country under a great queen. I have brought you here because you joined together to molest others, to burn people's houses and their place of worship. That must not happen in the dominion of our queen, the most powerful ruler in the world. I have decided that you will pay a fine of two hundred bags of cowries. You will be released as soon as you agree to this and undertake to collect that fine from your people. What do you say to that?"

The six men remained sullen and silent and the Commissioner left them for a while. He told the court messengers, when he left the guardroom, to treat the men with respect because they were the leaders of Umuofia. They said, "Yes, sir," and saluted.

As soon as the District Commissioner left, the head messenger, who was also the prisoners' barber, took down his razor and shaved off all the hair on the men's heads. They were still handcuffed, and they just sat and moped.

"Who is the chief among you?" the court messengers asked in jest. "We see that every pauper wears the anklet of title in Umuofia. Does it cost as much as ten cowries?"

The six men ate nothing throughout that day and the next. They were

7. "A Person Who Does What He Says" (a praise name).

not even given any water to drink, and they could not go out to urinate or go into the bush when they were pressed. At night the messengers came in to taunt them and to knock their shaven heads together.

Even when the men were left alone they found no words to speak to one another. It was only on the third day, when they could no longer bear the hunger and the insults, that they began to talk about giving in.

"We should have killed the white man if you had listened to me," Okonkwo snarled.

"We could have been in Umuru now waiting to be hanged," someone said to him.

"Who wants to kill the white man?" asked a messenger who had just rushed in. Nobody spoke.

"You are not satisfied with your crime, but you must kill the white man on top of it." He carried a strong stick, and he hit each man a few blows on the head and back. Okonkwo was choked with hate.

As soon as the six men were locked up, court messengers went into Umuofia to tell the people that their leaders would not be released unless they paid a fine of two hundred and fifty bags of cowries.

"Unless you pay the fine immediately," said their head-man, "we will take your leaders to Umuru before the big white man, and hang them."

This story spread quickly through the villages, and was added to as it went. Some said that the men had already been taken to Umuru and would be hanged on the following day. Some said that their families would also be hanged. Others said that soldiers were already on their way to shoot the people of Umuofia as they had done in Abame.

It was the time of the full moon. But that night the voice of children was not heard. The village *ilo* where they always gathered for a moon-play was empty. The women of Iguedo did not meet in their secret enclosure to learn a new dance to be displayed later to the village. Young men who were always abroad in the moonlight kept to their huts that night. Their manly voices were not heard on the village paths as they went to visit their friends and lovers. Umuofia was like a startled animal with ears erect, sniffing the silent, ominous air and not knowing which way to run.

The silence was broken by the village crier beating his sonorous *ogene*. He called every man in Umuofia, from the Akakanma age group upwards, to a meeting in the marketplace after the morning meal. He went from one end of the village to the other and walked all its breadth. He did not leave out any of the main footpaths.

Okonkwo's compound was like a deserted homestead. It was as if cold water had been poured on it. His family was all there, but everyone spoke in whispers. His daughter Ezinma had broken her twenty-eight-day visit to the family of her future husband, and returned home when she heard that her father had been imprisoned, and was going to be hanged. As soon as she got home she went to Obierika to ask what the men of Umuofia were going to do about it. But Obierika had not been home since morning. His wives thought he had gone to a secret meeting. Ezinma was satisfied that something was being done.

On the morning after the village crier's appeal the men of Umuofia met in the marketplace and decided to collect without delay two hundred and fifty bags of cowries to appease the white man. They did not know that fifty bags would go to the court messengers, who had increased the fine for that purpose.

24

Okonkwo and his fellow prisoners were set free as soon as the fine was paid. The District Commissioner spoke to them again about the great queen, and about peace and good government. But the men did not listen. They just sat and looked at him and at his interpreter. In the end they were given back their bags and sheathed machetes and told to go home. They rose and left the courthouse. They neither spoke to anyone nor among themselves.

The courthouse, like the church, was built a little way outside the village. The footpath that linked them was a very busy one because it also led to the stream, beyond the court. It was open and sandy. Footpaths were open and sandy in the dry season. But when the rains came the bush grew thick on either side and closed in on the path. It was now dry season.

As they made their way to the village the six men met women and children going to the stream with their waterpots. But the men wore such heavy and fearsome looks that the women and children did not say "*nno*" or "welcome" to them, but edged out of the way to let them pass. In the village little groups of men joined them until they became a sizable company. They walked silently. As each of the six men got to his compound, he turned in, taking some of the crowd with him. The village was astir in a silent, suppressed way.

Ezinma had prepared some food for her father as soon as news spread that the six men would be released. She took it to him in his *obi*. He ate absent-mindedly. He had no appetite; he only ate to please her. His male relations and friends had gathered in his *obi*, and Obierika was urging him to eat. Nobody else spoke, but they noticed the long stripes on Okonkwo's back where the warder's whip had cut into his flesh.

The village crier was abroad again in the night. He beat his iron gong and announced that another meeting would be held in the morning. Everyone knew that Umuofia was at last going to speak its mind about the things that were happening.

Okonkwo slept very little that night. The bitterness in his heart was now mixed with a kind of childlike excitement. Before he had gone to bed he had brought down his war dress, which he had not touched since his return from exile. He had shaken out his smoked raffia skirt and examined his tall feather head-gear and his shield. They were all satisfactory, he had thought.

As he lay on his bamboo bed he thought about the treatment he had received in the white man's court, and he swore vengeance. If Umuofia decided on war, all would be well. But if they chose to be cowards he would go out and avenge himself. He thought about wars in the past. The noblest, he thought, was the war against Isike. In those days Okudo[8] was still alive. Okudo sang a war song in a way that no other man could. He was not a fighter, but his voice turned every man into a lion.

"Worthy men are no more," Okonkwo sighed as he remembered those days. "Isike will never forget how we slaughtered them in that war. We killed twelve of their men and they killed only two of ours. Before the end of the fourth market week they were suing for peace. Those were days when men were men."

As he thought of these things he heard the sound of the iron gong in the distance. He listened carefully, and could just hear the crier's voice. But it was very faint. He turned on his bed and his back hurt him. He ground his teeth. The crier was drawing nearer and nearer until he passed by Okonkwo's compound.

"The greatest obstacle in Umuofia," Okonkwo thought bitterly, "is that coward, Egonwanne.[9] His sweet tongue can change fire into cold ash. When he speaks he moves our men to impotence. If they had ignored his womanish wisdom five years ago, we would not have come to this." He ground his teeth. "Tomorrow he will tell them that our fathers never fought a 'war of blame.' If they listen to him I shall leave them and plan my own revenge."

The crier's voice had once more become faint, and the distance had taken the harsh edge off his iron gong. Okonkwo turned from one side to the other and derived a kind of pleasure from the pain his back gave him. "Let Egonwanne talk about a 'war of blame' tomorrow and I shall show him my back and head." He ground his teeth.

The marketplace began to fill as soon as the sun rose. Obierika was waiting in his *obi* when Okonkwo came along and called him. He hung his goat-skin bag and his sheathed machete on his shoulder and went out to join him. Obierika's hut was close to the road and he saw every man who passed to the marketplace. He had exchanged greetings with many who had already passed that morning.

When Okonkwo and Obierika got to the meeting place there were already so many people that if one threw up a grain of sand it would not find its way to the earth again. And many more people were coming from every quarter of the nine villages. It warmed Okonkwo's heart to see such strength of numbers. But he was looking for one man in particular, the man whose tongue he dreaded and despised so much.

"Can you see him?" he asked Obierika.

"Who?"

"Egonwanne," he said, his eyes roving from one corner of the huge marketplace to the other. Most of the men sat on wooden stools they had brought with them.

"No," said Obierika, casting his eyes over the crowd. "Yes, there he is, under the silk-cotton tree. Are you afraid he would convince us not to fight?"

8. "Great Eagle Feather" (a praise name).   9. "Wealth of a Sibling."

"Afraid? I do not care what he does to *you*. I despise him and those who listen to him. I shall fight alone if I choose."

They spoke at the top of their voices because everybody was talking, and it was like the sound of a great market.

"I shall wait till he has spoken," Okonkwo thought. "Then I shall speak."

"But how do you know he will speak against war?" Obierika asked after a while.

"Because I know he is a coward," said Okonkwo. Obierika did not hear the rest of what he said because at that moment somebody touched his shoulder from behind and he turned round to shake hands and exchange greetings with five or six friends. Okonkwo did not turn round even though he knew the voices. He was in no mood to exchange greetings. But one of the men touched him and asked about the people of his compound.

"They are well," he replied without interest.

The first man to speak to Umuofia that morning was Okika, one of the six who had been imprisoned. Okika was a great man and an orator. But he did not have the booming voice which a first speaker must use to establish silence in the assembly of the clan. Onyeka[1] had such a voice; and so he was asked to salute Umuofia before Okika began to speak.

"Umuofia kwenu!" he bellowed, raising his left arm and pushing the air with his open hand.

"Yaa!" roared Umuofia.

"Umuofia kwenu!" he bellowed again, and again and again, facing a new direction each time. And the crowd answered, "Yaa!"

There was immediate silence as though cold water had been poured on a roaring flame.

Okika sprang to his feet and also saluted his clansmen four times. Then he began to speak:

"You all know why we are here, when we ought to be building our barns or mending our huts, when we should be putting our compounds in order. My father used to say to me: 'Whenever you see a toad jumping in broad daylight, then know that something is after its life.' When I saw you all pouring into this meeting from all the quarters of our clan so early in the morning, I knew that something was after our life." He paused for a brief moment and then began again:

"All our gods are weeping. Idemili is weeping, Ogwugwu is weeping, Agbala is weeping, and all the others. Our dead fathers are weeping because of the shameful sacrilege they are suffering and the abomination we have all seen with our eyes." He stopped again to steady his trembling voice.

"This is a great gathering. No clan can boast of greater numbers or greater valor. But are we all here? I ask you: Are all the sons of Umuofia with us here?" A deep murmur swept through the crowd.

"They are not," he said. "They have broken the clan and gone their several ways. We who are here this morning have remained true to our fathers, but our brothers have deserted us and joined a stranger to soil their

---

1. "Who Surpasses [God]?" (a rhetorical question).

fatherland. If we fight the stranger we shall hit our brothers and perhaps shed the blood of a clansman. But we must do it. Our fathers never dreamed of such a thing, they never killed their brothers. But a white man never came to them. So we must do what our fathers would never have done. Eneke the bird was asked why he was always on the wing and he replied: 'Men have learned to shoot without missing their mark and I have learned to fly without perching on a twig.' We must root out this evil. And if our brothers take the side of evil we must root them out too. And we must do it *now*. We must bail this water now that it is only ankle-deep. . . ."

At this point there was a sudden stir in the crowd and every eye was turned in one direction. There was a sharp bend in the road that led from the marketplace to the white man's court, and to the stream beyond it. And so no one had seen the approach of the five court messengers until they had come round the bend, a few paces from the edge of the crowd. Okonkwo was sitting at the edge.

He sprang to his feet as soon as he saw who it was. He confronted the head messenger, trembling with hate, unable to utter a word. The man was fearless and stood his ground, his four men lined up behind him.

In that brief moment the world seemed to stand still, waiting. There was utter silence. The men of Umuofia were merged into the mute backcloth of trees and giant creepers, waiting.

The spell was broken by the head messenger. "Let me pass!" he ordered.

"What do you want here?"

"The white man whose power you know too well has ordered this meeting to stop."

In a flash Okonkwo drew his machete. The messenger crouched to avoid the blow. It was useless. Okonkwo's machete descended twice and the man's head lay beside his uniformed body.

The waiting backcloth jumped into tumultuous life and the meeting was stopped. Okonkwo stood looking at the dead man. He knew that Umuofia would not go to war. He knew because they had let the other messengers escape. They had broken into tumult instead of action. He discerned fright in that tumult. He heard voices asking: "Why did he do it?"

He wiped his machete on the sand and went away.

25

When the District Commissioner arrived at Okonkwo's compound at the head of an armed band of soldiers and court messengers he found a small crowd of men sitting wearily in the *obi*. He commanded them to come outside, and they obeyed without a murmur.

"Which among you is called Okonkwo?" he asked through his interpreter.

"He is not here," replied Obierika.

"Where is he?"

"He is not here!"

The Commissioner became angry and red in the face. He warned the men that unless they produced Okonkwo forthwith he would lock them all up. The men murmured among themselves, and Obierika spoke again.

"We can take you where he is, and perhaps your men will help us."

The Commissioner did not understand what Obierika meant when he said, "Perhaps your men will help us." One of the most infuriating habits of these people was their love of superfluous words, he thought.

Obierika with five or six others led the way. The Commissioner and his men followed, their firearms held at the ready. He had warned Obierika that if he and his men played any monkey tricks they would be shot. And so they went.

There was a small bush behind Okonkwo's compound. The only opening into this bush from the compound was a little round hole in the red-earth wall through which fowls went in and out in their endless search for food. The hole would not let a man through. It was to this bush that Obierika led the Commissioner and his men. They skirted round the compound, keeping close to the wall. The only sound they made was with their feet as they crushed dry leaves.

Then they came to the tree from which Okonkwo's body was dangling, and they stopped dead.

"Perhaps your men can help us bring him down and bury him," said Obierika. "We have sent for strangers from another village to do it for us, but they may be a long time coming."

The District Commissioner changed instantaneously. The resolute administrator in him gave way to the student of primitive customs.

"Why can't you take him down yourselves?" he asked.

"It is against our custom," said one of the men. "It is an abomination for a man to take his own life. It is an offense against the Earth, and a man who commits it will not be buried by his clansmen. His body is evil, and only strangers may touch it. That is why we ask your people to bring him down, because you are strangers."

"Will you bury him like any other man?" asked the Commissioner.

"We cannot bury him. Only strangers can. We shall pay your men to do it. When he has been buried we will then do our duty by him. We shall make sacrifices to cleanse the desecrated land."

Obierika, who had been gazing steadily at his friend's dangling body, turned suddenly to the District Commissioner and said ferociously: "That man was one of the greatest men in Umuofia. You drove him to kill himself; and now he will be buried like a dog. . . ." He could not say any more. His voice trembled and choked his words.

"Shut up!" shouted one of the messengers, quite unnecessarily.

"Take down the body," the Commissioner ordered his chief messenger, "and bring it and all these people to the court."

"Yes, sah," the messenger said, saluting.

The Commissioner went away, taking three or four of the soldiers with him. In the many years in which he had toiled to bring civilization to different parts of Africa he had learned a number of things. One of them was that a District Commissioner must never attend to such undignified details as cutting a hanged man from the tree. Such attention would give the natives a poor opinion of him. In the book which he planned to write he would stress that point. As he walked back to the court he thought about that book. Every day brought him some new material. The story of this man who had killed a messenger and hanged himself would make interesting reading. One could almost write a whole chapter on him. Perhaps not a whole chapter but a reasonable paragraph, at any rate. There was so much else to include, and one must be firm in cutting out details. He had already chosen the title of the book, after much thought: *The Pacification of the Primitive Tribes of the Lower Niger.*

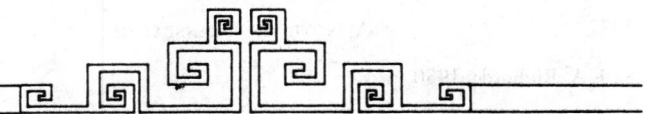

A Note on Translation

Reading literature in translation is a pleasure on which it is fruitless to frown. The purist may insist that we ought always read in the original languages, and we know ideally that this is true. But it is a counsel of perfection, quite impractical even for the purist, since no one in a lifetime can master all the languages whose literatures it would be a joy to explore. Master languages as fast as we may, we shall always have to read to some extent in translation, and this means we must be alert to what we are about: if in reading a work of literature in translation we are not reading the "original," what precisely are we reading? This is a question of great complexity, to which justice cannot be done in a brief note, but the following sketch of some of the considerations may be helpful.

One of the memorable scenes of ancient literature is the meeting of Hector and Andromache in Book VI of Homer's *Iliad*. Hector, leader and mainstay of the armies defending Troy, is implored by his wife Andromache to withdraw within the city walls and carry on the defense from there, where his life will not be constantly at hazard. In Homer's text her opening words to him are these: δαιμόνιε, φθίσει σε τὸ σὸν μένος (daimonie, phthisei se to son menos). How should they be translated into English?

Here is how they have actually been translated into English by capable translators, at various periods, in verse and prose:

1. George Chapman, 1598:

O noblest in desire,
Thy mind, inflamed with others' good, will set thy self on fire.

2. John Dryden, 1693:

Thy dauntless heart (which I foresee too late),
Too daring man, will urge thee to thy fate.

3. Alexander Pope, 1715:

Too daring Prince! . . .
For sure such courage length of life denies,
And thou must fall, thy virtue's sacrifice.

4. William Cowper, 1791:

Thy own great courage will cut short thy days,
My noble Hector. . .

5. Lang, Leaf, and Myers, 1883 (prose):

Dear my lord, this thy hardihood will undo thee. . . .

6. A. T. Murray, 1924 (prose):

Ah, my husband, this prowess of thine will be thy doom. . . .

7. E. V. Rieu, 1950 (prose):

"Hector," she said, "you are possessed. This bravery of yours will be your end."

8. I. A. Richards, 1950 (prose):

"Strange man," she said, "your courage will be your destruction."

9. Richmond Lattimore, 1951:

> Dearest,
> Your own great strength will be your death. . . .

10. Robert Fitzgerald, 1979:

> O my wild one, your bravery will be
> Your own undoing!

11. Robert Fagles, 1990:

> reckless one,
> Your own fiery courage will destroy you!

From these strikingly different renderings of the same six words, certain facts about the nature of translation begin to emerge. We notice, for one thing, that Homer's word μένος (menos) is diversified by the translators into "mind," "dauntless heart," "such courage," "great courage," "hardihood," "prowess," "bravery," "courage," "great strength," "bravery," and "fiery courage." The word has in fact all these possibilities. Used of things, it normally means "force"; of animals, "fierceness" or "brute strength" or (in the case of horses) "mettle"; of men and women, "passion" or "spirit" or even "purpose." Homer's application of it in the present case points our attention equally—whatever particular sense we may imagine Andromache to have uppermost—to Hector's force, strength, fierceness in battle, spirited heart and mind. But since English has no matching term of like inclusiveness, the passage as the translators give it to us reflects this lack and we find one attribute singled out to the exclusion of the rest.

Here then is the first and most crucial fact about any work of literature read in translation. It cannot escape the linguistic characteristics of the language into which it is turned: the grammatical, syntactical, lexical, and phonetic boundaries that constitute collectively the individuality or "genius" of that language. A Greek play or a Russian novel in English will be governed first of all by the resources of the English language, resources that are certain to be in every instance very different, as the efforts with μένος show, from those of the original.

Turning from μένος to δαιμόνιε (daimonie) in Homer's clause, we encounter a second crucial fact about translations. Nobody knows exactly what shade of meaning δαιμόνιε had for Homer. In later writers the word normally suggests divinity, something miraculous, wondrous; but in Homer it appears as a vocative of address for both chieftain and commoner, man and wife. The coloring one gives it must therefore be determined either by the way one thinks a Greek wife of Homer's era might actually address her husband (a subject on which we have no information whatever) or in the way one thinks it suitable for a hero's wife to address her husband in an epic poem, that is to say, a highly stylized and formal work. In general, the translators of our century will be seen to have abandoned formality to stress the intimacy; the wifeliness; and, especially in Lattimore's case, a certain chiding tenderness, in Andromache's appeal: (6) "Ah, my husband," (7) "Hector" (with perhaps a hint, in "you are possessed," of the alarmed distaste with which wives have so often viewed their husbands' bellicose moods), (8) "Strange man," (9) "Dearest," (10) "O my wild one" (mixing an almost motherly admiration with reproach and concern), and (11) "reckless one." On the other hand, the older translators have obviously removed Andromache to an epic or heroic distance from her beloved, whence she sees and kindles to his selfless courage, acknowledging, even in the moment of pleading with him to be otherwise, his moral grandeur and the tragic destiny this too certainly implies: (1) "O noblest in desire, . . . inflamed by others' good"; (2) "Thy dauntless heart (which I foresee too late), / Too daring man"; (3) "Too daring Prince! . . . / And thou must fall, thy virtue's sacrifice"; (4) "My noble Hector." Even the less specific "Dear my lord" of Lang, Leaf, and Myers looks in the same direction because of its echo of the speech of countless Shakespearean men and women who have shared this powerful moral sense: "Dear my lord, make me acquainted with your cause of grief"; "Perseverance, dear my lord, keeps honor bright"; etc.

The fact about translation that emerges from all this is that just as the translated work reflects the individuality of the language it is turned into, so it reflects the individuality of the age in which it is made, and the age will permeate it everywhere like yeast in dough. We think of one kind of permeation when we think of the governing verse forms and attitudes toward verse at a given epoch. In Chapman's time, experiments seeking an "heroic" verse form for English were widespread, and accordingly he tries a "fourteener" couplet (two rhymed lines of seven stresses each) in his *Iliad* and a pentameter couplet in his *Odyssey*. When Dryden and Pope wrote, a closed pentameter couplet had become established as the heroic form par excellence. By Cowper's day, thanks largely to the prestige of *Paradise Lost*, the couplet had gone out of fashion for narrative poetry in favor of blank verse. Our age, inclining to prose and in verse to proselike informalities and relaxations, has, predictably, produced half a dozen excellent prose translations of the *Iliad* but only three in verse (by Fagles, Lattimore, and Fitzgerald), all relying on rhythms that are much of the time closer to the verse of William Carlos Williams and some of the prose of novelists like Faulkner than to the swift firm tread of Homer's Greek. For if it is true that what we translate from a given work is what, wearing the spectacles of our time, we see in it, it is also true that we see in it what we have the power to translate.

Of course, there are other effects of the translator's epoch on a translation besides those exercised by contemporary taste in verse and verse forms. Chapman writes in a great age of poetic metaphor and, therefore, almost instinctively translates his understanding of Homer's verb φθίσει (phthisei, "to cause to wane, consume, waste, pine") into metaphorical terms of flame, presenting his Hector to us as a man of burning generosity who will be consumed by his very ardor. This is a conception rooted in large part in the psychology of the Elizabethans, who had the habit of speaking of the soul as "fire," of one of the four temperaments as "fiery," of even the more material bodily processes, like digestion, as if they were carried on by the heat of fire ("concoction," "decoction"). It is rooted too in that characteristic Renaissance élan so unforgettably expressed in characters such as Tamburlaine and Dr. Faustus, the former of whom exclaims to the stars above:

> . . . I, the chiefest lamp of all the earth,
> First rising in the East with mild aspect,
> But fixèd now in the meridian line,
> Will send up fire to your turning spheres,
> And cause the sun to borrow light of you. . . .

Pope and Dryden, by contrast, write to audiences for whom strong metaphor has become suspect. They therefore reject the fire image (which we must recall is not present in the Greek) in favor of a form of speech more congenial to their age, the *sententia* or aphorism, and give it extra vitality by making it the scene of a miniature drama: in Dryden's case, the hero's dauntless heart "urges" him (in the double sense of physical as well as moral pressure) to his fate; in Pope's, the hero's courage, like a judge, "denies" continuance of life, with the consequence that he "falls"—and here Pope's second line suggests analogy to the sacrificial animal—the victim of his own essential nature, of what he is.

To pose even more graphically the pressures that a translator's period brings, consider the following lines from Hector's reply to Andromache's appeal that he withdraw, first in Chapman's Elizabethan version, then in Lattimore's twentieth-century one:

Chapman, 1598:

> The spirit I did first breathe
> Did never teach me that—much less since the contempt of death
> Was settled in me, and my mind knew what a Worthy was,
> Whose office is to lead in fight and give no danger pass
> Without improvement. In this fire must Hector's trial shine.
> Here must his country, father, friends be in him made divine.

Lattimore, 1951:

> and the spirit will not let me, since I have learned to be valiant
> and to fight always among the foremost ranks of the Trojans,
> winning for my own self great glory, and for my father.

If one may exaggerate to make a necessary point, the world of Henry V and Othello suddenly gives way here to our own, a world whose discomfort with any form of heroic self-assertion is remarkably mirrored in the burial of Homer's key terms (*spirit, valiant, fight, foremost, glory*)—five out of twenty-two words in the original, five out of thirty-six words in the translation—in a cushioning huddle of harmless sounds.

Besides the two factors so far mentioned (language and period) as affecting the character of a translation, there is inevitably a third—the translator, with a particular degree of talent; a personal way of regarding the work to be translated; a special hierarchy of values, moral, aesthetic, metaphysical (which may or may not be summed up in a "worldview"); and a unique style or lack of it. But this influence all readers are likely to bear in mind, and it needs no laboring here. That, for example, two translators of Hamlet, one a Freudian, the other a Jungian, will produce impressively different translations is obvious from the fact that when Freudian and Jungian argue about the play in English they often seem to have different plays in mind.

We can now return to the question from which we started. After all allowances have been made for language, age, and individual translator, is anything of the original left? What, in short, does the reader of translations read? Let it be said at once that in utility prose—prose whose function is mainly referential—the reader who reads a translation reads everything that matters. "Nicht Rauchen," "Défense de Fumer," and "No Smoking," posted in a railway car, make their point, and the differences between them in sound and form have no significance for us in that context. Since the prose of a treatise and of most fiction is preponderantly referential, we rightly feel, when we have paid close attention to Cervantes or Montaigne or Machiavelli or Tolstoy in a good English translation, that we have had roughly the same experience as a native Spaniard, Frenchman, Italian, or Russian. But *roughly* is the correct word; for good prose points iconically *to* itself as well as referentially beyond itself, and everything that it points to in itself in the original (rhythms, sounds, idioms, wordplay, etc.) must alter radically in being translated. The best analogy is to imagine a Van Gogh painting reproduced in the medium of tempera, etching, or engraving: the "picture" remains, but the intricate interanimation of volumes with colorings with brushstrokes has disappeared.

When we move on to poetry, even in its longer narrative and dramatic forms— plays like *Oedipus*, poems like the *Iliad* or the *Divine Comedy*—our situation as

English readers worsens appreciably, as the many unlike versions of Andromache's appeal to Hector make very clear. But, again, only appreciably. True, this is the point at which the fact that a translation is *always* an interpretation explodes irresistibly on our attention; but if it is the best translation of its time, like John Ciardi's translation of the *Divine Comedy* for our time, the result will be not only a sensitive interpretation but also a work with intrinsic interest in its own right—at very best, a true work of art, a new poem. In these longer works, moreover, even if the translation is uninspired, many distinctive structural features—plot, setting, characters, meetings, partings, confrontations, and specific episodes generally—survive virtually unchanged. Hence even in translation it remains both possible and instructive to compare, say, concepts of the heroic or attitudes toward women or uses of religious ritual among civilizations as various as those reflected in the *Iliad*, the *Mahābhārata, Beowulf,* and the epic of *Son-Jara*. It is only when the shorter, primarily lyrical forms of poetry are presented that the reader of translations faces insuperable disadvantage. In these forms, the referential aspect of language has a tendency to disappear into, or, more often, draw its real meaning and accreditation from, the iconic aspect. Let us look for just a moment at a brief poem by Federico García Lorca and its English translation (by Stephen Spender and J. L. Gili):

> ¡Alto pinar!
> Cuatro palomas por el aire van.
>
> Cuatro palomas
> vuelan y tornan.
> Llevan heridas
> sus cuatro sombras.
>
> ¡Bajo pinar!
> Cuatro palomas en la tierra están.

> Above the pine trees:
> Four pigeons go through the air.
>
> Four pigeons
> fly and turn round.
> They carry wounded
> their four shadows.
>
> Below the pine trees:
> Four pigeons lie on the earth.

In this translation the referential sense of the English words follows with remarkable exactness the referential sense of the Spanish words they replace. But the life of Lorca's poem does not lie in that sense. It lies in such matters as the abruptness, like an intake of breath at a sudden revelation, of the two exclamatory lines (1 and 7), which then exhale musically in images of flight and death; or as the echoings of *palomas* in *heridas* and *sombras*, bringing together (as in fact the hunter's gun has done) these unrelated nouns and the unrelated experiences they stand for in a sequence that seems, momentarily, to have all the logic of a tragic action, in which *doves* become *wounds* become *shadows*, or as the external and internal rhyming among the five verbs, as though all motion must (as in fact it must) end with *están*.

Since none of this can be brought over into another tongue (least of all Lorca's rhythms), the translator must decide between leaving a reader to wonder why Lorca is a poet to be bothered about at all and making a new but true poem, whose merit will almost certainly be in inverse ratio to its likeness to the original. Samuel Johnson made such a poem in translating Horace's famous *Diffugere nives*, and so did A. E. Housman. If we juxtapose the last two stanzas of each translation, and the corresponding Latin, we can see at a glance that each has the consistency and inner life of a genuine poem and that neither of them (even if we consider only what is obvious to the eye, the line-lengths) is very close to Horace:

> Cum semel occideris, et de te splendida Minos
>   fecerit arbitria,
> non, Torquate, genus, non te facundia, non te
>   restituet pietas.
>
> Infernis neque enim tenebris Diana pudicum
>   liberat Hippolytum
> nec Lethaea valet Theseus abrumpere caro
>   vincula Pirithoo.

Johnson:

> Not you, Torquatus, boast of Rome,
> When Minos once has fixed your doom,
> Or eloquence, or splendid birth,
> Or virtue, shall restore to earth.
> Hippolytus, unjustly slain,
> Diana calls to life in vain;
> Nor can the might of Theseus rend
> The chains of hell that hold his friend.

Housman:

> When thou descendest once the shades among,
>   The stern assize and equal judgment o'er,
> Not thy long lineage nor thy golden tongue,
>   No, nor thy righteousness, shall friend thee more.
>
> Night holds Hippolytus the pure of stain,
>   Diana steads him nothing, he must stay;
> And Theseus leaves Pirithous in the chain
>   The love of comrades cannot take away.

The truth of the matter is that when the translator of short poems chooses to be literal, most or all of the poetry is lost; and when the translator succeeds in forging a new poetry, most or all of the original author is lost. Since there is no way out of this dilemma, we have always been sparing, in this anthology, in our use of short poems in translation.

In this Expanded Edition in One Volume, we have adjusted our policy to take account of the two great non-Western literatures in which the short lyric or "song" has been the principal and by far most cherished expression of the national genius. During much of its history from earliest times, the Japanese imagination has cheerfully exercised itself, with all the delicacy and grace of an Olympic figure skater, inside a rigorous verse pattern of five lines and thirty-one syllables: the *tanka.* Chinese poetry, while somewhat more liberal to itself in line length, has been equally fertile in the fine art of compression and has only occasionally, even in its earliest, most experimental phase, indulged in verse lines of more than seven characters, often just four, or in poems of more than fifty lines, usually fewer than twenty. What makes the Chinese and Japanese lyric more difficult than most other lyrics to translate satisfactorily into English is that these compressions combine with a flexibility of syntax (Japanese) or a degree of freedom from it (Chinese) not available in our language. They also combine with a poetic sensibility that shrinks from exposition in favor of sequences and juxtapositions of images: images grasped and recorded in, or *as if in*, a moment of pure perception unencumbered by the explanatory linkages, background scenarios, and other forms of contextualization that the Western mind is instinctively driven to establish.

Whole books, almost whole libraries, have been written recently on the contrast of East and West in worldviews and value systems as well as on the need of each for the other if there is ever to be a community of understanding adequate to the realities both face. Put baldly, much too simply, and without the many exceptions and qualifications that rightly spring to mind, it may be said that a central and characteristic Western impulse, from the Greeks on down, has been to see the world around us as something to be *acted on:* weighed, measured, managed, used, even (when economic interests prevail over all others) fouled. Likewise, put oversimply, it may be said that a central and characteristic Eastern counterpart to this over many centuries (witness Taoism, Buddhism, and Hinduism, among others) has been to see that same world as something to be *received:* contemplated, touched, tasted, smelled, heard, and most especially, immersed in until observer and observed are one. To paint a bamboo, a stone, a butterfly, a person—so runs a classical Chinese admonition for painters—you must *become* that bamboo, that stone, that butterfly, that person, then paint from the inside. No one need be ashamed of being poor, says Confucius, putting a similar emphasis on *receiving* experience, "only of not being cultivated in the perception of beauty."

The problem that these differences in linguistic freedom and philosophical outlook pose for the English translator of classical Chinese and Japanese poetry may be glimpsed, even if not fully grasped, by considering for a moment in some detail a typical Japanese *tanka* (*Kokinshu*, 9) and a typical Chinese "song" (*Book of Songs*, 23). In its own language but transliterated in the Latin alphabet of the West, the *tanka* looks like this:

> kasumi tachi
> ko no me mo haru no
> yuki fureba
> hana naki sato mo
> hana zo chirikeru

In a literal word-by-word translation (so far as this is possible in Japanese, since the language uses many particles without English equivalents and without dictionary meaning in modifying and qualifying functions—for example, *no, mo,* and *no* in line 2), the poem looks like this:

> haze rises
> tree-buds swell
> when snow falls
> village(s) without flower(s)
> flower(s) fall(s)

The three best-known English renderings of this *tanka* look like this:

1. Helen Craig McCullough:

> When snow comes in spring—
> fair season of layered haze
> and burgeoning buds—
> flowers fall in villages
> where flowers have yet to bloom.

2. Laurel Rasplica Rodd and Mary Catherine Henkenius:

> When the warm mists veil
> all the buds swell while yet the
> spring snows drift downward
> even in the hibernal
> village crystal blossoms fall.

3. Robert H. Brower and Earl Miner:

> With the spreading mists
> The tree buds swell in early spring
> And wet snow petals fall —
> So even my flowerless country village
> Already lies beneath its fallen flowers.

The reader will notice at once how much the three translators have felt it desirable or necessary to add, alter, rearrange, and explain. In McCullough's version the time of year is affirmed twice, both as "spring" and as "fair season of . . . haze"; the haze is now "layered"; the five coordinate perceptions of the original (haze, swelling buds, a snowfall, villages without flowers, flowers drifting down) have been structured into a single sentence with one main verb and two subordinate clauses spelling out "when" and "where"; and the original poem's climax, in a scene of drifting petallike snowflakes, has been shifted to a bleak scenery of absence: "flowers have yet to bloom." The final stress, in other words, is not on the fulfilled moment in which snow flowers replace the cherry blossoms, but on the cherry blossoms not yet arrived.

Similar additions and explanations occur in Rodd and Henkenius's version. This time the mist is "warm" and "veil[s] all" to clarify its connection with "buds." Though implicit already in "warm" and "burgeoning," spring is invoked again in "spring snows," and the snows are given confirmation in the following line by the insistently Latinate "hibernal," chosen, we may reasonably guess, along with "veil," "all," "swell," "while," "crystal," and "fall" to replace some of the chiming internal rhyme in the Japanese: *ko, no, mo, no, sato, mo, zo.* To leave no *i* undotted, "crystal" is imported to assure us that the falling "blossoms" of line 5 are really snowflakes, and the scene of flowerlessness that in the original (line 4) accounts for a special joy in the "flowering" of the snowflakes (line 5) vanishes without trace.

Brower and Miner's also fills in the causative links between "spreading mists" and swelling buds; makes sure that we do not fail to see the falling snow in flower terms ("wet snow petals"), thus losing, alas, the element of surprise, even magic, in the transformation of snowflakes into flowers that the original poem holds in store in its last two lines; and tells us (somewhat redundantly) that villages are a "country" phenomenon and (somewhat surprisingly) that this one is the speaker's home. In this version, as in the original and Rodd and Henkenius's, the poem closes with the snow scene, but here it is a one-time affair and "already" complete (lines 4 and 5), not a recurrent phenomenon that may appear under certain conditions anywhere at any time.

Some of the differences in these translations arise inevitably from different trade-offs, as in the first version, where the final vision of falling snow blossoms is let go presumably to achieve the lovely lilting echo and rhetorical turn of "flowers fall in villages / where flowers have yet to bloom." Or as in Rodd and Henkenius's version, where preoccupations with internal rhyme have obviously influenced word choices, not always for the better. Or as in all three versions, where different efforts to remind the reader of the wordplay on *haru* (in the Japanese poem both a noun meaning "spring" and a verb meaning "swell") have had dissimilar but perhaps equally indifferent results. Meantime, the immense force compacted into that small word in the original as both noun and verb, season of springtime and principal of growth, cause and effect (and thus in a sense the whole mighty process of earth's renewal, in which an interruption by snow only foretells a greater loveliness to come) fizzles away unfelt. A few differences do seem to arise from insufficient command of the nerves and sinews of English poetry, but most spring from the staggering difficulties of responding in any uniform way to the minimal clues proffered by the original text. The five perceptions—haze, buds, snowfall, flowerless villages, flowers falling—do not as they stand in the Japanese or any literal translation quite compose for readers accustomed to Western poetic traditions an adequate poetic whole. This is plainly seen in the irresistible urge each of the translators has felt to catch up the individual perceptions, as English tends to require, in a tighter overall grammatical and syntactical structure than the original insists on. In this way they provide a clarifying network of principal and subordinate, time when, place where, and cause why. Yet the inevitable result is a disassembling, a spinning out, spelling out, thinning out of what in the Japanese is an as yet unraveled imagistic excitement, creating (or memorializing) in the poet's mind, and then in the mind of the Japanese readers, the original thrill of consciousness when these images, complete with the magical transformation of snow into the longed-for cherry blossoms, first flashed on the inward eye.

What is comforting for us who must read this and other Japanese poems in translation is that each of the versions given here retains in some form or other all or most of the five images intact. What is less comforting is that the simplicity and suddenness, the explosion in the mind, have been diffused and defused.

When we turn to the Chinese song, we find similarly contesting forces at work. In one respect, the Chinese language comes over into English more readily than Japanese, being like English comparatively uninflected and heavily dependent on word order for its meanings. But in other respects, since Chinese like Japanese lacks distinctions of gender, of singular and plural, of *a* and *the*, and in the classical mode in which the poems in this anthology are composed, also of tenses, the pressure of the English translator to rearrange, straighten out, and fill in to "make sense" for his or her readers remains strong.

Let us examine song no. 23 of the *Shijing*. In its own Chinese characters, it looks like this:

野有死麕

野有死麕
白茅

包之。有女懷春。

吉士誘之。野有

林有樸樕。野有死鹿。

白茅純束。

有女如玉。

舒而脫脫兮。無

感我帨兮。無使

尨也吠。

Eleven lines in all, each line having four characters as its norm, the poem seemingly takes shape around an implicit parallel between a doe in the forest, possibly killed by stealth and hidden under long grass or rushes (though on this point as on all others the poem refuses to take us wholly into confidence), and a young girl possibly "ruined" (as she certainly would have been in the post-Confucian society in which the *Shijing* was prized and circulated, though here again the poem keeps its own counsel) by loss of her virginity before marriage.

In its bare bones, with each character given an approximate English equivalent, a translation might look like this:

wild(s)	is	dead	deer
white	grass(es)	wrap/cover	(it).
is	girl	feel	spring.
fine	man	tempt	(her).
woods	is(are)	bush(es),	underbrush.	5
wild(s)	is	dead	deer.
white	grass(es)	bind	bundle.
is	girl	like	jade.
slow	___	slow	slow.
not	move	my	sash.	10
not	cause	dog	bark.

Lines 1 to 4, it seems plain, propose the parallel of slain doe and girl, whatever that parallel may be intended to mean. Lines 5 to 8 restate the parallel, adding that the girl is as beautiful as jade and (apparently) that the doe lies where the "wild" gives way to smaller growth. If we allow ourselves to account for the repetition (here again is a Western mind-set in search of explanatory clues) by supposing that lines 1 to 4 signal at some subliminal level the initiation of the seduction and lines 5 to 8, again subliminally, its progress or possibly its completion, lines 9 to 11 fall easily into place as a miniature drama enacting in direct speech the man's advances and the girl's gradually crumbling resistance. They also imply, it seems, that the seduction takes place not in the forest, as we might have been led to suppose by lines 1 to 8, but in a dwelling with a vigilant guard dog.

Interpreted just far enough to accommodate English syntax, the poem reads as follows:

1. Wai-lim Yip:

> In the wilds, a dead doe.
> White reeds to wrap it.
> A girl, spring-touched.
> A fine man to seduce her.
> In the woods, bushes.   5
> In the wilds, a dead deer.
> White reeds in bundles.
> A girl like jade.
> Slowly. Take it easy.
> Don't feel my sash!   10
> Don't make the dog bark!

Interpreted a stage further in a format some have thought better suited to English poetic traditions, the poem reads:

2. Arthur Waley:

> In the wilds there is a dead doe,
> With white rushes we cover her.
> There was a lady longing for spring,
> A fair knight seduced her.
>
> In the woods there is a clump of oaks,   5
> And in the wilds a dead deer
> With white rushes well bound.
> There was a lady fair as jade.
>
> "Heigh, not so hasty, not so rough.
> "Heigh, do not touch my handkerchief.   10
> "Take care or the dog will bark."

Like the original and the literal translation, this version leaves the relationship between the doe's death and the girl's seduction unspecified and problematic. It holds the doe story in present tenses, assigning the girl story to the past. Still, much has been changed to give the English poem an explanatory scenario. The particular past assigned to the girl story, indeterminate in the Chinese original, is here fixed as the age of knights and ladies; and the seduction itself, which in the Chinese hovers as an eternal possibility within the timeless situation of man and maid ("A fine man *to* seduce her"), is established as completed long ago: "A fair knight seduced her." A teasing oddity in this version is the mysterious "we" who "cover" the slain doe, never to be heard from again.

Take interpretation toward its outer limits and we reach what is perhaps best called a "variation" on this theme:

3. Ezra Pound:

> Lies a dead doe on yonder plain
> whom white grass covers,
> A melancholy maid in spring
> > is luck
> > for   5
> > lovers.
> Where the scrub elm skirts the wood
> be it not in white mat bound,
> As a jewel flawless found
> > dead as a doe is maidenhood.   10
> Hark!
> Unhand my girdle knot.
> > Stay, stay, stay
> > or the dog
> > may   15
> > bark.

Here too the present is pushed back to a past by the language the translator uses: not a specific past, as with the era of knights and ladies, but any past in which contemporary speech still features such (to us) archaic formalisms as "Unhand" or "Hark," and in which the term "maid" still signifies a virgin and in which virginity is prized to an extent that equates its loss with the doe's loss of life. But these evocations of time past are so effectively countered by the obtrusively present tense throughout (lines 1, 2, 4, 7, 8, 10, 11, 12, 13, and 15) that the freewheeling "variation" remains in this important respect closer to the spirit of the original than Waley's translation. On the other hand, it departs from the original and the two other versions by brushing aside the reticence that they carefully preserve as to the precise implications of the girl-deer parallel, choosing instead to place the seduction in the explanatory framework of the oldest story in the world: the way of a man with a maid in the springtime of life.

What both these examples make plain is that the Chinese and Japanese lyric, however contrasting in some ways, have in common at their center a complex of highly charged images generating something very like a magnetic field of potential meanings that cannot be got at in English without bleeding away much of the voltage. In view of this, the best practical advice for those of us who must read these marvelous poems in English translations is to focus intently on these images and ask ourselves what there is in them or in their effect on each other that produces the electricity. To that extent, we can compensate for a part of our losses, learn something positive about the immense explosive powers of imagery, and rest easy in the secure knowledge that translation even in the mode of the short poem brings us (despite losses) closer to the work itself than not reading it at all. "To a thousand cavils," said Samuel Johnson, "one answer is sufficient; the purpose of a writer is to be read, and the criticism which would destroy the power of pleasing must be blown aside." Johnson was defending Pope's Homer for those marks of its own time and place that make it the great interpretation it is, but Johnson's exhilarating common sense applies equally to the problem we are considering here. Literature is to be read, and the criticism that would destroy the reader's power to make some form of contact with much of the world's great writing must indeed be blown aside.

MAYNARD MACK

Sources

Brower, Robert H., and Earl Miner. *Japanese Court Poetry*. Stanford: Stanford University Press, 1961.

The Classic Anthology Defined by Confucius. Tr. Ezra Pound. New Directions, 1954.

Kokinshū: A Collection of Poems Ancient and Modern. Tr. Laurel Rasplica Rodd and Mary Catherine Henkenius. Princeton: Princeton University Press, 1984.

Kokin Wakashū: The First Imperial Anthology of Japanese Poetry. Tr. and ed. Helen Craig McCullough. Stanford: Stanford University Press, 1985.

Legge, James. *The Chinese Classics*. Hong Kong: Hong Kong University Press, 1960.

Waley, Arthur. *170 Chinese Poems*. New York, 1919.

Index